INTERNATIONAL LITERARY MARKET PLACE™

# ILMP
# 2006

*International Literary Market Place*™
39th Edition

**Publisher**
*Thomas H. Hogan*

**Vice President, Content**
*Dick Kaser*

**Director, ITI Reference Group**
*Owen O'Donnell*

**Managing Editor**
*Karen Hallard*

**Associate Editors**
*Kathryn Eaton; Mary-Anne Lutter*


**Tampa Operations:**

**Production Manager, Tampa Editoral**
*Debbie James*

**Project Coordinator, Tampa Editorial**
*Carolyn Victor*

**Associate Project Coordinator, Tampa Editorial**
*Paula Watts*

**Data Entry Clerk, Tampa Editorial**
*Barbara Lauria*

# INTERNATIONAL LITERARY MARKET PLACE™

# ILMP 2006

## The Directory of the
## International Book Publishing Industry

### OVER 180 COUNTRIES COVERED

*Published by*

Information Today, Inc.
143 Old Marlton Pike
Medford, NJ 08055-8750
Phone: (609) 654-6266
Fax: (609) 654-4309
E-mail (Orders): custserv@infotoday.com
Web site: http://www.infotoday.com

ISSN 0074-6827
ISBN 1-57387-218-0
Library of Congress Catalog Card Number 77-70295

Information Today, Inc.
143 Old Marlton Pike
Medford, NJ 08055-8750
Phone:   800-300-9868 (Customer Service)
         800-409-4929 (Editorial)
Fax: 609-654-4309
E-mail (orders): custserv@infotoday.com
Web Site: www.infotoday.com


Printed in the United States of America

US $240

ISBN 1-57387-218-0

24000>

9 781573 872188

# CONTENTS

# Preface

Since 1965, *International Literary Market Place (ILMP)* and its companion *Literary Market Place*, have covered the world of book publishing. These directories provide detailed information on the global book publishing industry. This edition of *ILMP* includes over 16,100 entries in over 180 countries. Publishers account for 10,141 of these entries.

## Organization & Content

The six areas of coverage into which *ILMP* is arranged are as follows: Publishing, Manufacturing, Book Trade Information, Literary Associations & Prizes, Book Trade Calendar and Library Resources. Within most chapters, companies are sorted first by their country, then by key words in the company name. Sorting preference is determined by the entrant.

Pertinent information regarding each country represented - such as capital, language, population, currency, trade and copyright restrictions - can be found at the beginning of that country's listings in the Publishers section. The basic content of company entries includes - but is not limited to - address, telecommunications data, key personnel, a descriptive annotation and assorted statistics.

There are exceptions to this arrangement. International Publishing Services, located within the Publishing chapter, contains U.S. and Canadian companies that do a significant amount of international business and wish to advertise their services to users of *ILMP*. Also, those U.S. and Canadian book manufacturing companies that do 10% or more of their business overseas are included in the appropriate sections within the Manufacturing chapter.

## Compilation

*ILMP* is updated throughout the year via a number of methods. A questionnaire is mailed to every current listing to corroborate and update the information contained on our database. All returned mailers are edited for the next product release. If a reply is not received, public sources are researched to determine the status of the listee.

Information on new listings is gathered using a similar method. *ILMP* editors identify possible new listings through their daily research or as a result of nominations from the organization itself or from third parties. A questionnaire is then sent to gather the essential listing information. Unless we receive information directly from the organization, the new listing will not be included in the *ILMP* database.

Updated information or suggestions for new listings can also be submitted by using the form that follows this preface.

Simply fill in the information requested and send the form to:

> *International Literary Market Place*
> 630 Central Avenue
> New Providence, NJ 07974
> United States of America
> Fax: 908-219-0192

**An updating method using Internet technology is also available for *ILMP* listings:**

You can use the *Literary Market Place* web site to update an *ILMP* listing. **Literarymarketplace.com** allows you the opportunity to provide new information for a listing by clicking on the option to Update or Correct Your Entry. The Feedback option on the home page of the web site can be used to suggest new entries as well.

Once information regarding a suggested new entry or a correction to an existing listing has been submitted, our editors verify the data with the organization to ensure the accuracy of the update.

## Related Services

*International Literary Market Place*, along with its companion publication *Literary Market Place*, is now available through the World Wide Web at **www.literarymarketplace.com**. Designed to give users simple, logical access to the information they require, the site offers the choice of searching for data alphabetically, geographically, by type, or by subject. Continuously updated by Information Today, Inc.'s team of editors, this is a truly enhanced version of the *ILMP* and *LMP* databases, incorporating features that make "must have" information easily available.

Your feedback is important to us. We strongly encourage you to contact us with comments on this 2006 edition of *ILMP*, as well as suggestions and comments for future editions. Our editorial office can be reached by phone at 1-800-409-4929 or 908-286-1090, or by e-mail at khallard@infotoday.com. Most importantly, thanks are due to those entrants who took the time to respond to our questionnaires.

**Return this form to:**
*International Literary Market Place*
Information Today, Inc.
630 Central Avenue
New Providence, NJ 07974, USA
Fax: 908-219-0192

# INTERNATIONAL LITERARY MARKET PLACE™
# EDITORIAL REVISION FORM

Company Name:_____

The company listing is found on page number:_____

☐ Please check here if you are nominating this organization for a new listing in the directory

## General Information

Address:_____

City:_____ State/Province:_____ Postal Code:_____

Phone:_____ Fax:_____

E-mail:_____ Web Site:_____

Brief Description:_____

## Personnel

☐ Addition        ☐ Deletion        ☐ Correction

First Name:_____ Last Name:_____ Title:_____

☐ Addition        ☐ Deletion        ☐ Correction

First Name:_____ Last Name:_____ Title:_____

☐ Addition        ☐ Deletion        ☐ Correction

First Name:_____ Last Name:_____ Title:_____

☐ Addition        ☐ Deletion        ☐ Correction

First Name:_____ Last Name:_____ Title:_____

(continued on back)

## Other Information

Indicate other information to be added to or corrected in this listing; please be as specific as possible, noting erroneous data to be deleted.

_____

_____

_____

_____

_____

_____

_____

## Verification

Data for this listing will not be updated without the following information (*indicates mandatory information)

*Your First Name:_____ *Your Last Name:_____

Organization Name:_____

*Address:_____

*City:_____ *State/Province:_____ *Postal Code:_____

*Phone:_____ E-mail:_____

*Indicate if you are a: ☐ Representative of this Organization  ☐ User of this directory  ☐ Other

If other, please specify:_____

**Thank you for helping Information Today, Inc. maintain the most up-to-date information available.**
**Please return by fax to: 908-219-0192, or visit www.literarymarketplace.com and**
**click on the option to Update or Correct Your Entry under Free Services.**

# Copyright Conventions

**The Universal Copyright Convention** was sponsored by Unesco in 1952. It states that 'Each signatory country extends to foreign works covered by UCC the same protection which such country extends to works of its own nationals published within its own borders.'

**The Berne Convention** is a system of international copyright which is maintained among countries which have become signatories of the International Copyright Union for the Protection of Literary and Artistic Works. This Union plan, which was first agreed upon at Berne, Switzerland, in 1886, has been subject to later revisions.

The basic principle of the agreement is that any work properly copyrighted in its country of origin has protection in every Union country. Any work originating in a non-Union country, if it is simultaneously published in a Union country, has the same standing as it would if it had originated in a Union country. Different countries have different relationships under one or more of the revisions (Berlin, 1908; Rome, 1928; Brussels, 1948; Stockholm, 1968; and Paris, 1971).

**The Florence Agreement**, also known as the 'free flow of book', is a Unesco-sponsored international agreement aimed at easing the flow of books and other scientific, educational and cultural materials, through the elimination or reduction of tariffs and other barriers.

**The Buenos Aires Convention**: In most Latin-American countries, compliance with the copyright law of the country of first publication protects the work in other countries of the Buenos Aires Convention (1910). To secure copy-right, each work must carry a notice to the effect that any use of the book or article will not be permitted without the consent of the copyright owner, and that copyright is reserved in English or any other language; for complete safety it is advised to add 'All rights reserved'. A later revision of the Buenos Aires Convention was made at the Washington Conference (Pan-American Copyright Convention) of 1946 which goes into greater detail than the Buenos Aires Convention.

See the General Information for each country in the Publishers Section for country specific copyright information.

# The ISBN System

## Background

The question of the need and feasibility of an international numbering system for books was first discussed at the third International Conference on Book Market Research and Rationalization in the Book Trade held in November 1966 in Berlin. At this time a number of publishers and book distributors in Europe were considering the use of computers in order processing and inventory control; and it was evident that a prerequisite of an efficient automated system was a unique and simple identification number for a published item.

The system which fulfilled this requirement and which became known as the International Standard Book Number (ISBN) System developed out of the book numbering system introduced into the United Kingdom in 1967.

In a report to the British Publishers Association, Professor F.G. Foster of the London School of Economics stated that there was '...a clear need of the introduction into the book trade of standard numbering...and substantial benefits would accrue to all parties therefrom'. After further study and deliberation, a detailed plan for standard numbering was produced. At the same time, the Technical Committee on Documentation of the International Standards Organization (ISO/TC 46) set up a working party (with the British Standards Institution acting as secretariat) to investigate the possibility of adapting the British system for international use. A meeting was held in London in 1968 with representatives from Denmark, France, Federal Republic of Germany, Eire, the Netherlands, Norway, the United Kingdom, the United States of America and an observer from Unesco. Other countries contributed written suggestions and expressions of interest. A report of the meeting was circulated to all countries belonging to the ISO. Comments on this report and subsequent proposals were considered at meetings held in Berlin and Stockholm in 1969.

As a result of these meetings there emerged ISO Recommendations 2108 which sets out the principles and procedures for international standard book numbering. The purpose of the ISO Recommendations is to coordinate and standardize internationally the use of book numbers so that an International Standard Book Number (ISBN) identifies one title or edition of a title from one specific publisher and is unique to that edition.

The ISBN applies in the main to books - for which the system was originally created - but, by extension, it may be used for any item produced by publishers or collected by libraries.

## How the International Standard Book Number (ISBN) Is Built Up

Every International Standard Book Number (ISBN) consists of ten digits; and whenever it is printed it is preceded by the letters ISBN. (Note: In those countries where the Latin alphabet is not used, an abbreviation in the characters of the local alphabet may be used in addition to the Latin letters ISBN.)

The ten-digit number is divided into four parts of variable length, each part when printed being separated by a hyphen or space. (Note: Experience suggests that the hyphen is preferable to the space.)

The four parts are as follows:

*Part 1. Group Identifier*
This part identifies the national, geographic or other similar grouping of publishers.

*Part 2. Publisher's Prefix*
This part identifies a particular publisher within a group.

*Part 3. Title Identifier*
This part identifies a particular title or edition of a title published by a particular publisher.

*Part 4. Check Digit*
This is a single digit at the end of the ISBN which provides an automatic check on the correctness of the ISBN.

*Group Identifier*
Group identifiers are allocated by the International ISBN Agency and a publisher wishing to participate in the ISBN system must belong to a recognized ISBN group. Groups are determined by national, geographic, language or other pertinent considerations. Experience has shown that groups based on national or geographic consideration are the most satisfactory. The following group identifiers are in use at present:

| | |
|---|---|
| 0 and 1 | Australia, Bermuda, English-speaking Canada, Gibralter, Ireland, Namibia, New Zealand, Puerto Rico, South Africa, Swaziland, UK, USA, Zimbabwe |
| 2 | France, French-speaking Belgium, French-speaking Canada, Luxembourg, French-speaking Switzerland |
| 3 | Austria, Germany, German-speaking Belgium, German-speaking Switzerland |
| 4 | Japan |
| 5 | Kazakhstan (also 9965), Moldova (also 9975), Russia |
| 7 | China (People's Republic of) |
| 80 | Czech Republic, Slovakia |
| 81 | India (also 93) |
| 82 | Norway |
| 83 | Poland |
| 84 | Spain |
| 85 | Brazil |
| 86 | Montenegro, Serbia, Slovenia (also 961) |
| 87 | Denmark |
| 88 | Italy, Italian-speaking Switzerland |
| 89 | Republic of Korea |
| 90 | Netherlands, Flemish-speaking Belgium |
| 91 | Sweden |
| 92 | International Publishers (Unesco, EU); European Community Organizations |
| 93 | India (also 81) |
| 950 | Argentina (also 987) |
| 951 | Finland (also 952) |
| 952 | Finland (also 951) |
| 953 | Croatia |
| 954 | Bulgaria |
| 955 | Sri Lanka |
| 956 | Chile |
| 957 | Taiwan, China (also 986) |
| 958 | Colombia |
| 959 | Cuba |
| 960 | Greece |
| 961 | Slovenia (also 86) |
| 962 | Hong Kong (People's Republic of China) (also 988) |
| 963 | Hungary |
| 964 | Iran |
| 965 | Israel |
| 966 | Ukraine |

| | | | | | |
|---|---|---|---|---|---|
| 967 | Malaysia (also 983) | 9949 | Estonia (also 9985) | 9984 | Latvia |
| 968 | Mexico (also 970) | 9950 | Palestine | 9985 | Estonia (also 9949) |
| 969 | Pakistan | 9951 | Kosova | 9986 | Lithuania (also 9955) |
| 970 | Mexico (also 968) | 9952 | Azerbaijan | 9987 | Tanzania (also 9976) |
| 971 | Philippines | 9953 | Lebanon | 9988 | Ghana (also 9964) |
| 972 | Portugal (also 989) | 9954 | Morocco (also 9981) | 9989 | Macedonia |
| 973 | Romania | 9955 | Lithuania (also 9986) | 99901 | Bahrain |
| 974 | Thailand | 9956 | Cameroon | 99902 | Gabon (reserved) |
| 975 | Turkey | 9957 | Jordan | 99903 | Mauritius (also 99949) |
| 976 | Caribbean Community (CARICOM): Antigua and Barbuda, Bahamas, Barbados, Belize, Bermuda, British Virgin Islands, Cayman Islands, Dominica, Grenada, Guyana, Haiti, Jamaica, Montserrat, St. Kitts and Nevis, St. Lucia, St. Maarten, St. Vincent and the Grenadines, Trinidad and Tobago, Turks and Caicos Islands | 9958 | Bosnia and Herzegovina | 99904 | Netherlands Antilles, Aruba |
| | | 9959 | Libya | 99905 | Bolivia |
| | | 9960 | Saudi Arabia | 99906 | Kuwait |
| | | 9961 | Algeria (also 9947) | 99908 | Malawi |
| | | 9962 | Panama | 99909 | Malta (also 99932) |
| 977 | Egypt | 9963 | Cyprus | 99910 | Sierra Leone |
| 978 | Nigeria | 9964 | Ghana (also 9988) | 99911 | Lesotho |
| 979 | Indonesia | 9965 | Kazakhstan (also 5) | 99912 | Botswana |
| 980 | Venezuela | 9966 | Kenya | 99913 | Andorra (also 99920) |
| 981 | Republic of Singapore (also 9971) | 9967 | Kyrgyz Republic | 99914 | Suriname |
| 982 | South Pacific: Cook Islands, Fiji, Kiribati, Marshall Islands, Micronesia (Federated States of), Nauru, New Caledonia, Niue, Palau, Solomon Islands, Tokelau, Tonga, Tuvalu, Vanuatu, Western Samoa | 9968 | Costa Rica (also 9977) | 99915 | Maldives |
| | | 9970 | Uganda | 99916 | Namibia (also 1) |
| | | 9971 | Republic of Singapore (also 981) | 99917 | Brunei Darussalam |
| 983 | Malaysia (also 967) | 9972 | Peru | 99918 | Faroe Islands |
| 984 | Bangladesh | 9973 | Tunisia | 99919 | Benin |
| 985 | Belarus | 9974 | Uruguay | 99921 | Qatar |
| 986 | Taiwan, China (also 957) | 9975 | Moldova (also 5) | 99922 | Guatemala (also 99939) |
| 987 | Argentina (also 950) | 9976 | Tanzania (also 9987) | 99923 | El Salvador |
| 988 | Hong Kong (People's Republic of China) (also 962) | 9977 | Costa Rica (also 9968) | 99924 | Nicaragua |
| | | 9978 | Ecuador | 99925 | Paraguay |
| 989 | Portugal (also 972) | 9979 | Iceland | 99926 | Honduras |
| 9945 | Dominican Republic (also 99934) | 9980 | Papua New Guinea | 99927 | Albania (also 99943) |
| 9946 | Korea (People's Democratic Republic) | 9981 | Morocco (also 9954) | 99928 | Georgia (also 99940) |
| 9947 | Algeria (also 9961) | 9982 | Zambia | 99929 | Mongolia |
| 9948 | United Arab Emirates | 9983 | Gambia | 99930 | Armenia (also 99941) |

| 99931 | Seychelles |
| 99932 | Malta (also 99909) |
| 99933 | Nepal (also 99946) |
| 99934 | Dominican Republic (also 9945) |
| 99935 | Haiti |
| 99936 | Bhutan |
| 99937 | Macau |
| 99938 | Srpska |
| 99939 | Guatemala (also 99922) |
| 99940 | Georgia (also 99928) |
| 99941 | Armenia (also 99930) |
| 99942 | Sudan |
| 99943 | Albania (also 99927) |
| 99944 | Ethiopia |
| 99946 | Nepal (also 99933) |
| 99947 | Tajikistan |
| 99948 | Eritrea |
| 99949 | Mauritius (also 99903) |
| 99950 | Cambodia |
| 99951 | Democratic Republic of the Congo |
| 99952 | Mali |

*Publisher's Prefix*
The publisher's prefix designates the publisher of a given book. Publishers with a large output of books are assigned a short publisher's prefix; publishers with a small output of books are assigned a longer publisher's prefix.

*Title Identifier*
The title identifier is assigned to a particular title or edition of a title by the publisher from within the range of numbers assigned to him and which will depend upon the length of his publisher's prefix. Title identifiers are normally assigned by the publisher himself. Publishers who assign their own title identifiers may use them to identify titles in the publishing house throughout the planning stages.

*Check Digit*
The 'check digit' is the last digit in an ISBN and is computed as the result of an elaborate calculation on the other nine digits. This calculation is performed almost instana-neously by an electronic computing device, and is a means of detecting incorrectly transcribed numbers. The check digit is calculated on a modulus 11 with

weights 10-2, using X in lieu of 10 where ten would occur as a check digit. This means that each of the first nine digits on the ISBN - i.e. excluding the check digit itself - is multiplied by a number ranging from 10 to 2; and the sum of the products thus obtained, plus the check digit, must be divisible, without remainder, by 11. For example:

|  | Group Identifier | | Publisher's Prefix | |
|---|---|---|---|---|
| ISBN | 0 | 8 | 4 | 3 | 6 |
| Weight | 10 | 9 | 8 | 7 | 6 |
| Products | 0+ | 72+ | 32+ | 21+ | 36+ |

|  | Title Number | | Check Digit | |
|---|---|---|---|---|
| ISBN | 1 | 0 | 7 | 2 | 7 |
| Weight | 5 | 4 | 3 | 2 | |
| Products | 5+ | 0+ | 21+ | 4+ | 7+ |

Total: 198

As 198 can be divided by 11 without remainder 0 8436 1072 is a valid International Standard Book Number.

*The number of digits in each part, and how to recognize them in an ISBN*
The number of digits in each of the identifying parts 1, 2 and 3 is variable, though the total number of digits contained in these parts is always 9. These nine digits together with the check digit bring the total number of digits in an ISBN to ten.

The number of digits in the group identifier will vary according to the likely output of books in a group. Thus, groups with an expected large output will get numbers of one or two digits; and publishers with an expected large output will get numbers of two or three digits.

Exceptionally, a one-digit number may be assigned to a publisher, but it will be appreciated that the assignment of one-digit publisher identifiers greatly reduces the range of possible identifiers in the group. For ease of reading, the four parts of the ISBN are divided by spaces or hyphens. These spaces or hyphens, however, are not retained in a computer which depends upon the special distribution of ranges of numbers for the recognition of the parts.

**Scope of the ISBN**

For the purposes of the ISBN system books and other items to be numbered include:

Printed books and pamphlets

Mixed media publications

Other similar media including educational films/ videos and transparencies

Books on cassettes

Microcomputer software (educational only)

Electronic publications
— machine-readable tapes (designed to produce readable printout)
— CD-ROM etc

Micro-form publications

Braille publications

Atlases & Maps

*Except:*
Ephemeral printed materials such as diaries, calendars, advertising matter and the like

Art prints and art folders without title page and text

Sound recordings

Serial publications

**Principles and procedures to be observed by the publisher numbering his own publications**

A publisher must ensure that a competent person is responsible for the assignment of ISBN and the application of the pertinent regulations. A publisher will be assigned a publisher identifier (publisher's prefix) by the group agency which will determine the range of title identifiers available to him. The number of title identifiers will depend upon the length of the publisher identifier assigned to him. The publisher should ensure that the group agency has as much information as possible about his back lists of books still available; and present and future publication programmes in order that a suitable publisher identifier can be assigned. A publisher is responsible for assigning title identifiers to the individual items he publishes.

A publisher may wish to incorporate an existing non-classifying identification system into his ISBN allocation. This may be arranged provided that such incorporation does not alter the fundantal characteristics of the ISBN system or reduce the amount of numbers available. For example: the publisher must not incorporate digits other than numerals which cause the resulting ISBN to be longer than or shorter than ten digits, nor must the publisher attempt to build in special meanings or hierarchical order to groups of numbers, if by so doing he reduces the amount of available numbers in the range allocated to him.

**Non-participating publishers**

If by choice, or for any other reason, a publisher does not accept responsibility for assigning ISBN to his publications, two alternatives are open to the group agency.

1. The group agency can allocate a block of numbers for miscellaneous publishers and number all titles within that block irrespective of the publisher. In such a case the resulting ISBN will not identify the publisher of a specific title. (It is strongly recommended that this procedure should be reserved for publishers who

only publish an occasional title and who are never likely to be in a position to assume the responsibility for numbering themselves.)

2. The group agency can assume responsibility for assigning a publisher identifier, a block of ISBNs associated with the publisher identifier and a number to each publication as well as informing the publisher before publication of the number assigned. In such a case, if the publisher agrees to do so, the ISBN can be printed in the book. It is expected that such a publisher will eventually assume full responsibility for assigning his own ISBN.

## Application of ISBN

### General

A separate ISBN must be assigned to every different edition of a book; but NOT to an unchanged impression or unchanged reprint of the same book in the same format and by the same publisher. Price changes do not need new ISBN.

### Facsimile reprints

A separate ISBN must be assigned to a facsimile reprint produced by a different publisher.

### Books in different formats

A separate ISBN must be assigned to the different formats in which a particular title is published. For example: a hardback edition and a paperback edition each receives a separate ISBN. On the same principle, a microform edition receives a separate ISBN.

### Looseleaf publications

If a publication appears in looseleaf form, an ISBN is allocated to identify an edition at a given time. Individual issues of additions or replacement sheets will likewise be given an ISBN.

### Multi-volume works

An ISBN must be assigned to the whole set of volumes of a multi-volume work, as well as to each individual volume in the set.

### Back stock

A publisher is required to number his back stock and publish the ISBN in his catalogues. He must also print the ISBN in the first available reprint of an item from his back stock.

### Collaborative publications

A publication issued as a coedition or joint imprint with other publishers is assigned an ISBN by the publisher in charge of distribution. Books sold or distributed by agents According to the principles of the ISBN system, a particular edition published by a particular publisher receives only one ISBN; this ISBN must be retained no matter where or by whom the book is distributed or sold.

A book imported by an exclusive distributor or sole agent from an area not yet in the ISBN system and for which, therefore, no ISBN has been assigned may be assigned an ISBN by the exclusive distributor.

A book imported by an exclusive distributor or sole agent to which a new title-page, bearing the imprint of the exclusive distributor, has been added in place of the title page of the original publisher, is to be given a new ISBN by the exclusive distributor or sole agent. The ISBN of the original publisher is also to be given as a related ISBN.

A book imported by several distributors from an area not yet in the ISBN system and for which, therefore, no ISBN has been assigned may be assigned an ISBN by the group agency responsible for those distributors.

### Publishers with more than one place of publication

A publisher operating in a number of places which are listed together in the imprint of a book will assign only one ISBN to the book. A pub-lisher operating separate and distinct offices or branches in different places may have a publisher identifier for each office or branch. Nevertheless, each book published is to be assigned only one ISBN, the assignment being made by the office or branch responsible for publication.

### Register of ISBNs

Every publisher must keep a register of ISBNs that have been assigned to published and forthcoming books. The register is to be kept in numerical sequence giving ISBN, author, title and edition (where appropriate).

### ISBNs are not to be re-used under any circumstances

An ISBN once allocated must not under any circumstances be re-used. This is of the utmost importance to avoid confusion. It is recognized that, owing to clerical errors, numbers will be incorrectly assigned. If this happens, the number must be deleted from the list of usable numbers and must not be assigned to another title. Every publisher will have sufficient numbers in his range for the loss of these numbers to be insignificant. Publishers should advise the group agency of the numbers thus deleted and of the titles to which they were erroneously assigned.

## Guidelines for ISBN assignment to software

An ISBN is used to identify a specific software product. If there is more than one version (perhaps versions adapted for different machines, carrier media or language version), each version must have a different ISBN. When a software product is updated, revised or otherwise amended and the changes are sufficiently substantial for the product to be called a new edition (and thus probably the subject of a new launch, or marketing push) then a new ISBN must be allocated. A relaunch of an existing product, even in new packaging, where there is no basic difference in the performance of the new and the old product, does NOT justify a new ISBN, and the original ISBN must be used.

When software is accompanied by a manual, useful only as an adjunct to the software, and the software needs the manual before it can be operated, and the two items are always sold as a package, one ISBN must be used to cover both items. When two or more items in a software package (as above) can be used separately, or are sold separately as well as together, then
(i) the package as a whole must have an ISBN
(ii) each item in the package must have its own ISBN.

ISBNs should be allocated to a software product independent of its physical form, eg, if software is only available from a remote database form whence it is downloaded to the customer.

As well as identifying the product itself, an ISBN identifies the publisher or manufacturer; it should not be used to identify a distributor or wholesaler.

## Printing of the ISBN

### General

The ISBN must appear on the item itself. This is essential for the efficient running of the system.

Printing of ISBN on books In the case of books, the ISBN must appear whenever possible:

On the reverse of the title page, or, if this is not possible, on the base of the title page, or, if this too is not possible, at some other conspicuous location in the book.

On the base of the spine.

On the back of the cover in 9-point type or larger.

On the back of the dust jacket, and on the back of any other protective case or wrapper.

The ISBN should always be printed in type large enough to be easily legible (i.e. not smaller than 9 point).

### Printing of ISBN on books in machine readable coding

In the last few years there has been much work done on machine-readable representations of the ISBN. The rapid, worldwide extension of bar code scanning has brought into prominence the agreement reached between the International Article Numbering Association (EAN) and the International ISBN Agency, which allows the ISBN to be translated into an EAN bar code.

All EAN bar codes start with a national identifier **except** those on books and periodicals. The agreement replaces the usual national identifier with a special 'Bookland' identifier represented by the digits 978 for books and 977 for periodicals. The 978 Bookland/EAN prefix is followed by the first nine digits of the ISBN. The check digit of the ISBN is dropped and replaced by a check digit calculated according to the EAN rules.

*Optional 5-digit add-on code*
There is an optional 5-digit add-on code which can be used for additional information. In the publishing industry it can be used for price information which may have the following formats: a) Five-digit bar code indicating the price with human readable numbers above the bar code or b) Five-digit bar code indicating the price with no human readable numbers.

## Administration of the ISBN System

*General*
The administration of the ISBN system is carried on at three levels. These are the international, group and publisher levels.

*International administration*
The international administration of the system is in the hands of the International Standard Book Number Agency which has an Advisory Panel representing the ISO and the publishing and library world. The address of the International Agency is:

International ISBN Agency
Staatsbibliothek zu Berlin
Preussischer Kulturbesitz
10772 Berlin
Germany

The principal functions of the International Agency are:

To supervise the use of the system

To approve the definition and structure of groups

To allocate identifiers to groups

To advise groups on the setting up and functioning of group agencies

To advise group agencies on the allocation of publisher identifiers

To promote the worldwide use of the system

In addition, the International Agency also offers the following services. It will:

Provide a group agency with lists of ISBNs (with computer-generated check digits) for the use of publishers in the group

Provide international registers of publishers, prefixes and publishers' names

Provide from information supplied by group agencies a computer printout of lists of publishers' prefixes, names and locations

Provide from information supplied by group agencies a computer printout of invalid or duplicate ISBNs

*Group administration*
Groups are administered by Group Agencies. Within the group there may be several national agencies, eg. group 0/1 has separate agencies in USA, United Kingdom, Canada, Australia, etc, with the main agency for the whole group in the UK.

The functions of a group agency are:

To manage and administer the affairs of the group

To handle relations with the International ISBN Agency on behalf of all the publishers in the group

To decide, in consultation with trade organizations and publishers, the publisher identifier ranges required

To allocate publishers' prefixes to publishers eligible to join the group and to maintain a register of publishers and their prefixes

To decide, in consultation with trade organizations and publishers, which publishers shall assign numbers to their own titles and which publishers shall have numbers assigned to their titles by the group agency

To provide technical advice and assistance to the publishers and to ensure that standards and approved procedures are observed in the group

To make available a manual of instruction for publishers

To make available computer printouts of ISBNs to publishers numbering their own books with check digits already calculated (Such printouts may be obtained from the International Agency on request)

To validate all ISBNs assigned by publishers numbering their own books and keep a register of them

To inform publishers of any invalid or duplicate ISBNs assigned by them

To assign numbers to all publications from those publishers who do not assign their own ISBNs and advise the publishers concerned of ISBNs assigned upon request

To achieve, thereby, total numbering in the group

To arrange with book listing and bibliographic agencies for the publication of ISBNs with the titles to which they refer

To arrange with publishers for the numbering of their back lists and for the publication of these in appropriate trade lists and bibliographies

To maintain liaison with all elements of the book trade and introduce new publishers to the system

To assist the trade in the use of the ISBN in computer systems

The national agencies are:

*Albania*
Ms. Violeta Viso, Biblioteka Kombetare, Agjensia Kombetare e ISBN, Sheshi "Skenderbe", Tirana

*Algeria*
Mlle. Hayet Gounni, Bibliotheque Nationale d'Algerie, BP 127, Hamma-el Annassers, Alger

*Andorra*
Sr. Pilar Burgues Monserrat, Andorran Standard Book Num-bering Agency, Biblioteca Nacional, Placeta Sant Esteve s/n, Andorra la Vella

*Argentina*
Claudia Rodriguez, Camara Argentina del Libro, Agencia Argentina ISBN, Avenida Belgrano 1580, 1093 Buenos Aires

*Armenia*
Dr. Hovhannes Bekmezyan, National Book Chamber of Armenia, ISBN Agency, G. Kochar St. 21, 375009 Yerevan

*Australia*
Ms. Maria Watt, ISBN Agency, C3, 85 Turner St, Port Melbourne, Vic 3207

*Austria*
Lea Raffl, Hauptverband des Osterreichischen Buchhandels, Grunangergasse 4, 1010 Vienna

*Azerbaijan*
Tatyana Zaytceva, Khazar University, 11, Mehseti St., Baku AZ1096

*Bahrain*
Mr. Jamal Dawood Salman, Directorate of Publication & Press, Ministry of Information, PO Box 253, Manama

*Bangladesh*
Mr. Golam Mostofa, National Library of Bangladesh, Directorate of Archives & Libraries, ISBN Agency, 32, Justice S. M. Morshed Sarani, Sher-e-Bangla Nagar (Agargaon), Dhaka 1207

*Belarus*
Mr. Anatoli I. Voronko, National Book Chamber of Belarus, ISBN Agency, 31a V Khoryzhey Str, 220002 Minsk

*Belgium* (Flemish-speaking)
Mr. Maarten van den Heuvel, Bureau ISBN, Centraal Boekhuis, Postbus 360, 4100 AJ Culemborg

*Belgium* (French-speaking)
Ms. Joelle Aernoudt, AFNIL (Agence Francophone pour la Numerotation Internationale du Livre), 35 rue Gregoire de Tours, 75006 Paris

*Belgium* (German-speaking)
Ms. Anke Lehr, MVB Marketing- und Verlagsservice des Buchhandels GmbH, ISBN-Agentur fur die Bundesrepublik Deutschland, Postfach 10 04 42, 60004 Frankfurt am Main

*Benin*
Adio Nourou Akadiri, Agence Nationale ISBN, Bibliotheque Nationale, BP 401, Porto-Novo

*Bermuda*
Ms. Maryse Plouffe, National Library of Canada, Canadian ISBN Agency, 395 Wellington St, Ottawa, Ontario K1A 0N4

*Bhutan*
Mr. Sonam Kinga, The Centre for Bhutan Studies, ISBN Agency, Post Box 111, Thimphu

*Bolivia*
Sra. Marlene Perez, Camara Boliviana del Libro, Agencia ISBN, Calle Capitan, Ravelo, No. 2116, Casilla 682, La Paz

*Bosnia and Herzegovina*
Mrs. Nevenka Hajdarovic, National and University Library of Bosnia and Herzegovina, ISBN Centre, Zmaja od Bosne 8b, 71000 Sarajevo

*Botswana*
Ms. Sinah Marope, Botswana National Library Service, Private Bag 0036, Gaborone

*Brazil*
Ms. Celia Ribeiro Zaher, Fundacao Biblioteca Nacional Agencia Brasileira do ISBN, Av Rio Branco, n. 219/31 – 1 andar, Centro - Rio de Janeiro – RJ 20040-008

*Brunei Darussalam*
Mr. Haji Abu Bakar Bin Haji Zainal, Pusat Kebangsaan ISBN, Dewan Bahasa Dan Pustaka, Jalan Elizabeth II, Bandar Seri Begawan BB3510, Negara

*Bulgaria*
Ms. Tatjana Dermendzieva, National Library St Cyril and St Methodiuos, National ISBN Agency, Boulevard V Levski 88, 1037 Sofia

*Cambodia*
Thonevath Pou, National Library of Cambodia, ISBN Agency, Street #92 (Christopher Howes), Daun Penh District, Phnom Penh

*Cameroon*
Agence ISBN, Bibliotheque Nationale, Yaounde

*Canada* (English-speaking)
Ms. Maryse Plouffe, National Library of Canada,

Canadian ISBN Agency, 395 Wellington St, Ottawa, Ontario K1A 0N4

*Canada* (French-speaking)
Mme. Lucie Martel, ISBN/BNQ, Bibliotheque nationale du Quebec, 2275, rue Holt, Montreal, Quebec H2G 3H1

*Caribbean Community*
Ms. Maureen Newton, Caribbean Community Secretariat, Documentation Centre, Bank of Guyana Bldg, PO Box 10827, Georgetown, Guyana

*Chile*
Jaime Pizarro Carrasco, Agencia Chilena ISBN, Camara Chilena del Libro AG, Avda Libertador Bernardo O'Higgins 1370, Oficina 502, Santiago de Chile

*China* (People's Republic of)
Mr. Li Lu, China ISBN Agency, China Bar Code Agency, 85 Dongsinan Street, Beijing 100703

*Colombia*
Sra. Sandra Del Mar Sacanamboy Franco, Agencia Colombiana del ISBN, Camara Colombiana del Libro, Calle 35, No. 5 A-05, Bogota D.C.

*Congo* (Democratic Repubic of)
Christophe Cassiau, ISBNAgency, Bibliotheque Nationale du Congo, 10 Bld Colonel Tshatshi, B.P., 5432 Kinshasa-Gombe

*Costa Rica*
Srta. Susan Coronado, Departamento Unidad Tecnica, Biblioteca Nacional, Ave 3 calles 15 y 17, APDO 10008-1000 San Jose

*Croatia*
Ms. Jasenka Zajec, Hrvatski ured za ISBN, Nacionalna i sveucilisna knijzica, Hrvatske bratske zajednice 4, HR-10000 Zagreb

*Cuba*
Sra. Rosa Amelia Lay Portuondo, Camara Cubana del Libro, Agencia Cubana del ISBN, Calle 15 No 602 esq C, Vedado, Ciudad Havana

*Cyprus*
Mr. Antonis Maratheftis, Cyprus Library, Eleftheria Square, 1011 Nicosia

*Czech Republic*
Mr. Antonin Jerabek, Narodni knihovna Ceske republiky, Narodni agentura ISBN v CR, Klementinum 190, 110 01 Prague 1

*Denmark*
Ms. Hanne Ekstrom, Dansk Biblioteks Center, Tempovej 7-11, 2750 Ballerup

*Dominican Republic*
Agencia Domenicana de ISBN, Biblioteca Nacional Pedro Henriquez Urena, Calle Cesar Nicolas Penson No 91, Plaza de la Cultura, Santo Domingo

*Ecuador*
Sr. Patricio Mena, Agencia Ecuatoriana del ISBN, Av Eloy Alfaro N29-61 e Inglaterra, Edif Eloy Alfaro Piso Nº 9, Quito

*Egypt*
Prof. Mohammed Galal Ghandour, National Library and Archives, Corniche El Nil-Boulac, Cairo

*El Salvador*
Sra. Doris Elizabeth Siliezar Orellana, Biblioteca Nacional, Agencia ISBN, Av Monsenor. Oscar A. Romero, y 4a Calle Oriente Nº 124, San Salvador

*Eritrea*
Solomon Drar, ISBN Agency Eritrea, Hdri Publishers, 178 Tegadelti Street, House No. 35, P.O. Box 1081, Asmara

*Estonia*
Ms. Mai Valtna, Estonian ISBN Agency, National Library of Estonia, Tonismagi 2, 15189 Tallinn

*Ethiopia*
Mr. Solomon Mulugeta, ISBN Agency, National Archives and Library of Ethiopia, PO Box 717, Addis Ababa

*European Community Organizations*
Ms. Madeleine Kiss, Office for official publications for the European Community, Authors Service Unit, ISBN Agency, 2, rue Mercier, 2985 Luxembourg, Luxembourg

*Faroe Islands*
Mr. Erhard Jacobsen, Foroya Landsbokasavn, Faroese ISBN office, J.C. Svabosgotu 16, PO Box 61, FR-110 Torshavn

*Finland*
Ms. Maarit Huttunen, Finnish ISBN Agency, Helsinki University Library, National Library of Finland, PO Box 26, (Teollisuuskatu 23), 00014 University of Helsinki

*France*
Ms. Joelle Aernoudt, AFNIL (Agence Francophone pour la Numerotation Internationale du Livre), 35, rue Gregoire de Tours, 75006 Paris

*Gambia*
Mr. Abdou Wally Mbye, The Chief Librarian, Gambia National Library, R.G. Pye Lane, Banjul

*Georgia*
Mrs. Nino Simonishvili, Georgian Parliament I. Chavchavadze National Library, ISBN Centre, 5 Gudiashvili st., 380007 Tbilisi

*Germany*
Ms. Anke Lehr, MVB Marketing- und Verlagsservice des Buchhandels GmbH, ISBN-Agentur fur die Bundesrepublik Deutschland,

Postfach 10 04 42, 60004 Frankfurt am Main

**Ghana**
Mr. Omari Mensah Tenkorang, Ghana Library Board, George Padmore, Research Library on African Affairs, PO Box GP2970, Accra

**Gibraltar**
Mrs. G. Finlayson, The John Mackintosh Hall, Knightsfield Holdings Ltd., 308 Main St, PO Box 939, Gibraltar

**Greece**
Afrodite Papaioannou, National Library of Greece, National Centre of ISBN, Panepistimiou 32, 10679 Athens

**Guatemala**
Sra. Silvia Regina De Leon, Agencia ISBN, Gremial de Editores de Guatemala, Ruta 6, 9-21 zona 4, Edificio Camara de Industria 8vo nivel, Ciudad Guatemala

**Haiti**
Ms. Nadege Constant, Bibliotheque Nationale d'Haiti, 193, Rue du Centre, Port-au-Prince

**Honduras**
Sr. Remo Jose Flores Escobar, Biblioteca Nacional, Agencia ISBN de Honduras, Barrio El Centro, Avda Cervantes, 1 cuadra al Sur Hotel Prado, Tegucigalpa, MDC

**Hong Kong (People's Republic of China)**
Ms. Chow Kam-sheung, Leisure and Cultural Services Department, Books Registration Office, Room 805, 8/F, Lai Chi Kok Government Offices, 19 Lai Wan Rd, Lai Chi Kok, Kowloon

**Hungary**
Ms. Orsolya Szabo, Magyar ISBN Iroda, Orszagos Szechenyi Konyvtar, Budavari Palota F epulet, H-1827 Budapest

**Iceland**
Nanna Bjarnadottir, ISBN Agency Iceland, National and University Library of Iceland, Arngrimsgotu 3, 107 Reykjavik

**India**
Dr. Suresh Chand, Raja Rammohun Roy, National Agency for ISBN, Government of India, Ministry of Human Resource Development, A2/ W4, Curzon Road Barracks, New Delhi 110001

**Indonesia**
Dra. Sauliah Saleh, Directorate of Legal Deposit, National Library of Indonesia, Jl Salemba Raya 28, PO Box 3624, Jakarta 10002

**International Publishers (Unesco, EU)**
Ms. Maha Bulos, UNESCO, Division of Arts and Cultural Enterprise, 1 rue Miollis, 75732 Paris Cedex 15, France

**Iran**
Mr. Vahraz Nowruzpur Deilami, Iran Book House, Iran ISBN Agency, 1178 Enqelab St, 13156 Tehran

**Ireland (Republic of)**
Julian Sowa, ISBN Agency, Midas House, 3rd Floor, 62 Goldsworth Road, Woking GU21 6LQ

**Israel**
Ms. Anna Sela, Israeli ISBN Group Agency, Israeli Center for Libraries, Baruch Hirsh 22, POB 801, Bnei Brak 51108

**Italy**
Paola Seghi, EDISER srl, Via delle Erbe 2, 20121 Milan

**Japan**
Mr. Iwao Sekiguchi, Japan ISBN Agency, c/o Japan Publishers Bldg, 6 Fukuro machi Shinjuku-ku, Tokyo 162-0828

**Jordan**
Mr. Mamoun Tharwat Talhouni, The Department of the National Library, ISBN Agency, PO Box 6070, Amman 11118

**Kazakhstan**
Ms. K. M. Mukhataeva, Book Chamber of Kazakhstan, ISBN Agency, Ulica Puskina 2, Almaty 480016

**Kenya**
Kenya National Library Services, ISBN Agency, PO Box 30573-00100 GPO, Nairobi

**Korea (Democratic People's Republic)**
Mr. Jean Bahng. Korea Science and Encyclopedia Publishing House, ISBN DPR Korea Agency, PO Box 73, Pyongyang

**Korea (Republic of)**
Ms. Ryu, Eun Young, The National Library of Korea, Korea ISBN Agency, 60-1 Banpo-Dong, Seocho-Gu, Seoul 137-702

**Kosova**
Sali Bashota, The National Library of Kosova, Sheshi "Hasan Prishtina," Prishtina, Kosava

**Kuwait**
Mrs. Wafa'a H. Al-Sane, National Library of Kuwait, ISBN Agency, PO Box 26182, 13122 Safat

**Kyrgyz Republic**
Ms. Mambetkazieva Mairam Orozbaevna,. ISBN Agency, National Book Chamber, Sovetskaya 170a, p/b 806, 720000 Bischek

**Latvia**
Ms. Laimdota Pruse, ISBN/ISMN Agency, Anglikaou Street 5, Riga 1816 LV

**Lebanon**
Ms. Rita Akl, Ministry of Culture, ISBN Agency,

Bristol Street, Hamra, Hatab Bldg, 6th Floor, Beirut

**Lesotho**
Ms. Mamothepane Kotele, ISBN Agency, The National University of Lesotho Library, PO Roma 180, Lesotho

**Libya**
Mr. Saleh M. Najim, National Library of Libya, PO Box 9127, Benghazi

**Lithuania**
Ms. Dalia Smoriginiene, Martynas Mazvydas, National Library of Lithuania, Gediminas av.5l, 01504 Vilnius

**Luxembourg**
Mr. Andre-Nicolas Schoup, Bibliotheque nationale Grand-Duche de Luxembourg, 37, bd F-D Roosevelt, L-2450 Luxembourg

**Macau**
Mr. Tang Va Chio, Agencia do ISBN, Biblioteca Central de Macau, Av Conselheiro Ferreira de Almeida, no. 89A-B, Macau

**Macedonia**
Ms. Zlata Talaganova, Narodna i Univerzitetska Biblioteka, "Sv. Kliment Ohridski", ISBN Agencija, Bul. Goce Delcev, 6, 1000 Skopje

**Malawi**
Mr. Stanley S. Gondwe, Malawi National ISBN Agency, National Archives of Malawi, Mkulichi Rd, PO Box 62, Zomba

**Malaysia**
Mr. Zulkefli Abdul Samad, National Library of Malaysia, National Depository Centre, ISBN National Centre, 232 Jalan Tun Razak, 50572 Kuala Lumpur

**Maldives**
Mr. Mohammed Waheed, Ministry of Education, Ghaazee Bldg, Ameeru Ahmed Magu, Male 20-05

**Mali**
Cheick Oumar Sissoko, Direction Nationale des Bibliotheques et la Documentation du Mali, Hamdallaye ACI 2000, Bamako

**Malta**
Mr. Emanuel Debattista, Publishers Enterprises Group (PEG) Ltd, PEG Bldg, UB7 Industrial Estate, San Gwann SGN 09

**Mauritius**
Ms. Sadhna Ramlallah, Editions de l'Ocean Indien, Stanley, Rose Hill

**Mexico**
Jose Gilberto Garduno Fernandez, Agencia ISBN Mexico, Calle Dinamarca 84, 2° piso, Colonia Juarez, Delegacion Cuauhtemoc, 06600 Mexico, DF

*Moldova*
Ms. Valentina Chitoroaga, Chambre Nationale du Livre, Agence ISBN, bd Stefan cel Mare, 180, Office 202, 2004 Chisinau

*Mongolia*
Ms. Tsagaach, Mongolian Book Publishers' Association, Amar Str., Building #1, Room 306, Central Post Box 5, Ulan Bator

*Montenegro*
Jelena Djurovic, Central National Library of Montenegro, "Djurdje Crnojevic," Bul. Crnogorskih junaka 163, Cetinje 81250, Montenegro

*Morocco*
Mme. Meryem Moussaid, Agence Marocaine de l'ISBN, Bibliotheque Generale et Archives, Service du depot legal, Av Ibn Battouta, BP 1003, Rabat

*Namibia*
Johan Loubser, National Library of Namibia, Private Bag 13349, Windhoek

*Nepal*
Mr. Krishna Mani Bhandary, Tribhuvan University, Central Library, ISBN National Agency, Kirtipur, Kathmandu

*Netherlands*
Mr. Maarten van den Heuvel, Centraal Boekhuis, Postbus 360, 4100 AJ Culemborg

*Netherlands Antilles*
Mrs. Navisella Ignacio, Bureau Intellectual Property, Berg Carmelweg 10A, Willenstad-Curacao

*New Zealand*
Ms. Joy Grove, ISBN Agency, National Library of New Zealand, PO Box 1467, Wellington

*Nicaragua*
Sra. Maribel Otero, Agencia Nacional ISBN, Palacio Nacional de la Cultura, Apartado Postal 101, Managua

*Nigeria*
Dr. I. Oketunji, National Bibliographic Control Dept, National Library of Nigeria, Nigerian ISBN Agency, 4 Wesley St, PMB 12626, Lagos

*Norway*
Ms. Ingebjorg Rype, ISBN-kontoret Norge, Katalogseksjonen, Bibliografiske tjenester, Nasjonalbiblioteket, avdeling Oslo, Postboks 2674, Solli, 0203 Oslo

*Pakistan*
Mr. Syed Ghyour Hussain, National Library of Pakistan, Constitution Ave, Islamabad 44000

*Palestine*
Prof. Mohammed S. Dajani, Palestine ISBN Agency, PO Box 4414, Al-Bireh Palestine

*Panama*
Guadalupe G. de Rivera, Agencia Panamena del ISBN, Biblioteca Nacional de Panama, San Francisco, Via Porras, Parque Recreativo y Cultural Omar, Apartado Postal 7906, Zona 9, Panama

*Papua New Guinea*
Mr. Chris Kelly Meti, Bibliographical Services Librarian, Papua New Guinea ISBN Agency, National Library Service, PO Box 734, Waigani, NCD

*Paraguay*
Sr. Francisco Perez Maricevich, Viceministerio de Cultura, Agencia ISBN, Humaita 145, Calle Independencia Nacional y Nuestra Senora, Asuncion

*Peru*
Sra. Alejandrina Garcia Caballero, Biblioteca Nacional del Peru, Av Abancay 4ta Cdra S/N, Lima

*Philippines*
Ms. Leonila DA. Tominez, The National Library of the Philippines, Standard Book Numbering Agency, PO Box 2926, Remita Manila 1000

*Poland*
Ms. Hanna Zawado, National Library, Bibliographic Institute, al Niepodleglosci 213, 02-086 Warsaw

*Portugal*
Ms. Ana Ribeiro, Associacao Portuguesa de Editores e Livreiros, Av Estados Unidos da America, 97-6° Esq, 1700-167 Lisbon

*Qatar*
Mr. Sami Abdel Jawad, National Library, ISBN group agency, PO Box 205, Doha

*Romania*
Ms. Mihaela Laura Stanciu, Biblioteca Nationala a Romaniei, Centrul National de Numerotare Standardizata, (ISBN, ISMN, ISSN, CIP), Str Ion Ghica 4, sector 3, 79708 Bucharest

*Russia*
Valerii Aleksandrovich Siroyenko, Russian Book Chamber, Russian ISBN Agency, Kremlevskaja nab 1/9, 109019 Moscow

*Saudi Arabia*
Mr. Musaed A. Al-Swailem, King Fahd National Library, Book Registration & Numbering Dept, PO Box 7572, Riyadh 11472

*Serbia*
Emilija Brasic, National Library of Serbia, Skerliceva 1, 11000 Belgrade

*Seychelles*
Ms. Pamela Denousse, Ministry of Local Government Sports & Culture, National Library, Victoria, PO Box 45, Mahe

*Sierra Leone*
Sallieu Turay, Sierra Leone Library Board, ISBN Agency, PO Box 326, Freetown

*Singapore (Republic of)*
Ms. Annick Wong, National Library Board, Library Supply Centre, 3 Changi South St 2, Tower B, #03-00, Singapore 486548

*Slovakia*
Ms. Erika Poloncova, Slovak ISBN Group Agency, Slovak National Library, Nam J.C. Hronskeho 1, 03601 Martin

*Slovenia*
Ms. Alenka Kanic, National and University Library, Turjaska 1, p.p. 259, 1000 Ljubljana

*South Africa*
Ms. Magret Kibido, The National Library of South Africa, ISN Agency, PO Box 397, Pretoria 0001

*South Pacific*
Ms. Joan Yee, Regional ISBN Centre, The University of the South Pacific Library, PO Box 1168, Suva, Fiji

*Spain*
Sra. Pilar Gomez Font, Agencia Espanola del ISBN, Calle Santiago Rusinol, 8, 28040 Madrid

*Sri Lanka*
Mr. M.S.U. Amarasiri, National Library and Documentation Services Board, No 14, Independence Ave, Colombo

*Srpska (Repubic of)*
Ms. Biljana Bilbija, National and University Library of Srpska, ISBN Agency, Jevrejska 30, 78000 Banjaluka, Bosnia and Herzegovina

*Sudan*
Mr. Yassin Mohammed Abdalla, National Library, ISBN Agency, PO Box 6279, Khartoum

*Suriname*
Mr. E. Hogenboom, Publishers Association Suriname, Standard Book Numbering Agency, Domineestr 32 boven, PO Box 1841, Paramaribo

*Swaziland*
Ms. A.T. Ndzimandze, University of Swaziland Libraries, Private Bag 4, Kwaluseni

*Sweden*
Ms. Anna Hulten, The Royal Library, Swedish National ISBN Agency, Legal Deposits, Box 5039, 102 41 Stockholm

*Switzerland (French-speaking)*
Ms. Karin Fux, ISBN-Agentur Schweiz, c/o Schweizer Buchhandler- und Verleger-Verband (SBVV), Alderstrasse 40, Postfach, 8034 Zurich

*Switzerland (German-speaking)*
Ms. Stefanie Nubling, ISBN-Agentur Schweiz,

c/o Schweizer Buchhandler- und Verleger-Verband (SBVV), Alderstrasse 40, Postfach, 8034 Zurich

*Switzerland* (Italian-speaking)
Paola Seghi, EDISER srl, Via delle Erbe 2, 20121 Milan, Italy

*Taiwan, China*
Ms. Li-chien Lee, National Central Library, 20 Chung Shan South Rd, Taipei 100

*Tajikistan*
Amirkhan Ahmadkhaov, Cultural Deputy Minister, ISBN Agency, Dushanbe

*Tanzania*
M.S. Mkenga, Tanzania Library Services Board, National Bibliographic Agency, PO Box 9283, Dar es Salaam

*Thailand*
Ms. Chantana Lorvidhaya, National Library of Thailand, Samsen Rd., Bangkok 10300

*Tunisia*
Ms. Ben Sedrine Nabiha, National ISBN Agency, Bibliotheque Nationale, Service de la Documentation et de l'Information, 20 Souk El Attarine, BP 42, 1008 Tunis

*Turkey*
Dr. Mehmet Demir, ISBN Turkiye Ajansy, Kultur ve Turizm Bakanlyoy, Kutuphaneler ve Yayymlar, Genel Mudurlugu, Necatibey Cad 55, 06440 Syhhyye Ankara

*Uganda*
Mr. Martin Okia, Uganda Publishers and Booksellers Association, PO Box 7732, Kampala

*Ukraine*
Ms. Iryna Pogorelovs'ka, Knyzkova Palata Ukrainy, National ISBN Agency, 27, Yuri Gagarin Ave, 02660 Kiev

*United Arab Emirates*
Fawzi Al Jaberi, Ministry of Information and Culture, Copyright Section, ISBN Agency, PO Box 17, Abu Dhabi

*United Kingdom*
Julian Sowa, ISBN Agency, Midas House, 3rd Floor, 62 Goldsworth Road, Woking GU21 6LQ

*United Nations* see *International Publishers*

*United States of America*
Doreen Gravesande, R.R. Bowker Co., LLC, International Standard Book Numbering, United States Agency, 630 Central Ave., New Providence, NJ 07974

*Uruguay*
Julio Castro, Biblioteca Nacional, Seccion Bibliografia Nacional - Agencia ISBN, 18 de julio 1790, 11200 Montevideo

*Venezuela*
Sra. Angela Negrin, Agencia Venezolana del ISBN, Parque Central, Torre Este, piso 3, Caracas 1011

*Zambia*
Dr. H. Mwacalimba, Booksellers & Publishers Association of Zambia, The ISBN Secretariat, c/o University of Zambia Library, PO Box 32379, Lusaka

*Zimbabwe*
Director, National Archives of Zimbabwe, Causeway, Private Bag 7729, Harare

## ISBN and ISSN

In addition to the International Standard Book Number System, a complementary numbering system for serial publications has also been established.

A serial is defined as any publication issued in successive parts, usually bearing numerical or chronological designations and intended to be continued indefinitely.

Serials include periodicals, yearbooks and monographic series.

The International Standard Serial Number system (ISSN) is administered by the ISSN International Centre, whose address is:

ISSN International Centre
20, rue Bachaumont
75002 Paris
France

Publishers of serials should apply to the ISSN International Centre or to their National Serials Data Centre, if there is one, for ISSNs for their serial publications.

Certain publications, such as yearbooks, annuals, monographic series, etc, should be assigned an ISSN for the serial title (which will remain the same for all the parts or individual volumes of the serial) and an ISBN for each individual volume.

Both ISSN and ISBN, when they are assigned, must be given on the publication and clearly identified.

(The preceding information is mainly from the ISBN User's Manual, compiled by the International ISBN Agency, Staatsbibliothek zu Berlin, Preussischer Kulturbesitz, Berlin, Germany.)

# Abbreviations

| | |
|---|---|
| + | Publisher's indication of interest in buying/selling international rights or editions |
| † | Organizations that are international in scope |
| § | Publications that are international in scope |
| — | Organizations with publishing activities |
| ‡ | United nations agencies with publishing activities |
| * | Prizes with no geographical restriction placed upon recipients |
| AB | aktiebolag (=public limited company) |
| AE | anonymous etaireia |
| AG | Aktiengesellschaft (=public limited company) |
| al | aleja |
| Apdo | apartado (=post-box) |
| ApS | anpartsselskab (=private limited company) |
| A/S | (Norwegian) aksjeselskap. (Swedish) aaktieselskab (=limited company) |
| AS | anonim sirketi |
| ASBL | association sans but lucratif (=non-profit-making society) |
| Av | (Spanish) avenida |
| Ave | (English, French) avenue. (Portuguese) avenida |
| Bldg | Building |
| Blvd | (Bulgarian, Romanian) bulevard. (English, French) boulevard |
| BP | boite postale (=post-box) |
| BV | besloten vennootschap (=private limited company) |
| C | compagnia (=company) |
| CA | compania anonima (=public limited company) |
| CEDEX | Courrier d'enterpise a distribution exceptionnelle |
| CFA | Communaute financiere africaine |
| CFP | comptoirs fracais du Pacifique |
| Cia | companhia, compania (=company) |
| Cie | compagnie (=company) |
| Co | (English) company, county. (German) Kompanie |
| c/o | care of |
| CP | (Italian) casetta postale. (Portuguese) caixa postal, (=post-box) |
| CV | commanditaire vennootschap (=limited partnership) |
| Dept | department |
| Dir | Director |
| EE | eterorruthmos etaireia |
| eV | einetragener Verein (=registered society) |
| ext | extension |
| GmbH | Gesellschaft mit beschrankter Haftung (=private limited company) |
| Inc | incorporated |
| ISBN | international standard book number |
| Jl | jalan (=street) |
| KG | Kommanditgesellschatt (=partnership) |
| KK | kabushiki kaisha (=public limited company) |
| Lda | limitida (=limited) |
| Ltd | limited |
| Ltda | limitada (=limited) |
| Man Dir | Managing Director |
| Nachf | Nachfolger(s) (=successor(s)) |
| nam | namesti (=square) |
| NV | naamloze vennootschap (=public limited company) |
| OE | omorruthmos etaireia of oficina (=office) |
| Off | office |
| Oy | osakeyhitio (=limited company) |
| pA | per Adresse (=care of) |
| Pl | (Bulgarian) ploshtad. (English, French) place. (Polish) |

| | |
|---|---|
| plac. | (Russian) ploshchad. (Spanish) plaza |
| PL | postriokero (=post-box) |
| PLC | public limited company |
| PMB | private mail bag |
| PO | Post Office |
| Prof | Professor |
| Pty | proprietary |
| PVBA | personenvennootschap met beperkte aansprakelijkheid (=private limited company) |
| Pvt | private |
| Rd | Road |
| SA | (French) societe anonyyme. (Portuguese) sociedade anonima.(Spanish) sociedad anonima (=public limited company) |
| Sarl | societe a responsabilite limitee (=private limited company) |
| SAS | societa in accomandita semplice (=limited partnership) |
| SCA | sociedad en comandita por acciones (=limited partner ship) |
| S de RL | sociedad de responsabilidad limitada (=private limited company) |
| Sdn Bhd | sendirian berhad (=private limited company) |
| SL | sociedad de responsabilidad limitada (=private limited company) |
| SNC | societa in nome collettivo (=partnership) |
| SpA | societa per azioni (=public limited company) |
| SPRL | societe de personnes a responsabilite (=private limited company) |
| SRL | (Italian) societa a responsabilita limita. (Spanish) sociedad de responsabilida limitada. (=private limited company) |
| St | Saint, street |
| STD | subscriber trunk dialing |
| Str | (Danish) straede. (Dutch) straat. (German) Strasse. (Icelandic) straeti. (Italian) strada. (Romanian) strada (=street) |
| Sq | square |
| Tel | telephone number |
| u | utca (=street) |
| UCC | Universal Copyright Convention |
| ul | (Bulgarian) ulitsa. (Czech) ulice. (Polish) ulica. (Roma nian) ulita. (Russian) ulitsa. (Serbocroatian, Slovak, Slovene) ulica. (=street) |
| UK | United Kingdom |
| USA | United States of America |
| VEB | volkseigener Betrieb (=people's enterprise) |
| VZW | vereniging zonder winstoogmerk (=non-profit-making society) |

A limited company is a corporation owned by shareholders (or stock-holders) who may contribute capital to the company but are not other-wise generally liable for its debts.

A public company may invite anyone to become a shareholder, and its shares (or stock) are usually traded on a stock exchange.

A private, or proprietary, company has a restricted number of share-holders and its shares are not traded on a stock exchange.

The owners of a partnership or proprietorship are generally liable for its debts, but a limited partnership has some owners who only contrib-ute capital and are not otherwise liable for debts.

# Publishing

## Publishers

This section covers book publishers throughout the world, with the exception of U.S. and Canadian publishers, which can be found in the companion publication, *Literary Market Place*. Publishers and their imprints are listed alphabetically within their country of business. General information for each country can be found preceding the entries for that country.

+ following a publisher's name indicates those who are involved in the buying or selling of international rights.

Immediately following this section are indexes that list publishers by type of publication and by subjects.

# Afghanistan

## General Information

*Capital:* Kabul
*Language:* Pushtu and Dari Afghan
*Religion:* Sunni Muslim with approximately 1 million Shiite Muslim
*Population:* 16.1 million
*Bank Hours:* 0800-1200, 1300-1600 Saturday-Wednesday; 0800-1300 Thursday
*Shop Hours:* 0800-about 1800 Saturday-Thursday
*Currency:* 100 puls = 2 krans = 1 afghani
*Copyright:* Florence (see Copyright Conventions, pg xi)

**Book Publishing Institute**
Herat
Founded: 1970 (by cooperation of Government Press and citizens of Herat)
Subjects: Fiction, History, Religion - Other

**Franklin Book Programs Inc**
PO Box 332, Kabul

**Government Press**
Kabul
*Tel:* 26851
Founded: 1870
Under supervision of Ministry of Information & Culture.
Subjects: Ethnicity, History, Regional Interests

**Ministry of Education, Department of Educational Publications**
PO Box 717, Kabul
*Tel:* (0873) 32076 *Fax:* (0873) 15051

**Pushtu Toulana, Afghan Academy**
Alikhan St, Kabul
*Tel:* 20350

# Albania

## General Information

*Capital:* Tirane
*Language:* Albanian
*Religion:* Islamic, Orthodox, Roman Catholic
*Population:* 3.3 million
*Bank Hours:* 0730-2330 Monday-Saturday
*Shop Hours:* 0900-1200 and 1600-2000; one day per week is holiday
*Currency:* 100 qintars = 1 lek
*Export/Import Information:* Importation of books is through State Trading Organization, Nd. Shperndarjes Te (or NST) Librit, Blvd K e Pezes, Tirana. Correspondence should be in English, French, German or Italian. Copies of correspondence to Albanian Legation in Rome. Some import licenses but no strict exchange controls.
*Copyright:* Berne (see Copyright Conventions, pg xi)

**Botimpex Publications Import-Export Agency**
Rr "Naim Frasheri" P 84/ Sh 2/ Ap 37, Tirana
*Tel:* (042) 34023 *Fax:* (042) 26886
*E-mail:* botimpex@albaniaonline.net; botimpex@icc-al.org; ebega@albmail.com
*Web Site:* pages.albaniaonline.net/botimpex/
*Key Personnel*
Dir: Dr Estref Bega *E-mail:* ebega@albmail.com
Founded: 1991
Subjects: Biography, Fiction, History, Literature, Literary Criticism, Essays, Poetry
ISBN Prefix(es): 99927-628; 99927-823
Number of titles published annually: 11 Print

**Fan Noli+**
Bulev, Shqip e Re, Pallati 23/4/8, Tirana
*Tel:* (04) 244 399
Founded: 1991
Subjects: Fiction, Nonfiction (General)
ISBN Prefix(es): 99927-859
Total Titles: 670 Print

**NL SH+**
Rruga Muhamet Gjollesha, Tirana
*Tel:* (042) 34207 *Fax:* (042) 34207
*Key Personnel*
Dir: Hilmi Brace
Subjects: Accounting, Advertising, Aeronautics, Aviation, Agriculture, Americana, Regional, Animals, Pets, Anthropology, Antiques, Archaeology, Architecture & Interior Design, Art, Astronomy, Biblical Studies, Biography, Biological Sciences, Business, Career Development, Chemistry, Chemical Engineering, Child Care & Development, Cookery, Crafts, Games, Hobbies, Developing Countries, Drama, Theater, Earth Sciences, Economics, Education, Electronics, Electrical Engineering, Energy, Engineering (General), English as a Second Language, Finance, Foreign Countries, Gardening, Plants, Geography, Geology, Government, Political Science, History, Humor, Labor, Industrial Relations, Language Arts, Linguistics, Law, Library & Information Sciences, Literature, Literary Criticism, Essays, Management, Marketing, Mathematics, Mechanical Engineering, Medicine, Nursing, Dentistry, Microcomputers, Military Science, Music, Dance, Mysteries, Native American Studies, Nonfiction (General), Philosophy, Photography, Physical Sciences, Physics, Poetry, Psychology, Psychiatry, Public Administration, Publishing & Book Trade Reference, Radio, TV, Science (General), Science Fiction, Fantasy, Securities, Self-Help, Social Sciences, Sociology, Sports, Athletics, Technology, Theology, Veterinary Science, Women's Studies
Total Titles: 9,999 Print
*Branch Office(s)*
Rruga Kavajes, NR 116, Tirana *Tel:* (042) 47129; (042) 47130
Distributed by Zina Bunjaj
Distributor for Klodiana Peci
*Showroom(s):* Tirana *Tel:* (042) 47130

**Shtepia Botuese Enciklopedike** (Encyclopaedia Publishing House)
Rr Muhamet Gjollesha, Tirana
*Tel:* (04) 228064 *Fax:* (04) 228064
*Key Personnel*
General Dir: Arben Xoxa
Founded: 1991
Subjects: Labor, Industrial Relations, Regional Interests

# Algeria

## General Information

*Capital:* Algiers (El Djazair)
*Language:* Arabic. French is the language of business and administration
*Religion:* Islamic
*Population:* 26.7 million
*Bank Hours:* 0900-1500 or 1600 Saturday-Wednesday
*Shop Hours:* 0900-1200, 1500-1900 Monday-Saturday
*Currency:* 100 centimes = 1 Algerian dinar

*Export/Import Information:* Books may be imported or exported only by or with permission of SNED State Monopoly, 3 blvd Zirout Yousef, BP 49, Alger Strasbourg. There are also quota restrictions. Permission to import usually entitles holder to obtain necessary foreign exchange; strict controls are in effect. Documentation formalities are rigidly enforced.
*Copyright:* UCC (see Copyright Conventions, pg xi)

**Chihab**
Formerly SAR DAR-Echihab
10, ave Brahim Gharafa, BEO, 16009 Algiers
*Tel:* (021) 97 54 53; (021) 85 95 01; (021) 85 01 75 *Fax:* (021) 97 64 77; (021) 97 51 91; (021) 85 01 75
*E-mail:* chihab.dz@caramail.com
ISBN Prefix(es): 9961-63
Subsidiaries: Chihab 2000
*Showroom(s):* 11, ave Brahim Gharafa, 16009 Algiers
*Bookshop(s):* Ave de l'independence n 10, Batna

**Enterprise Nationale du Livre (ENAL)+**
23 Nahj al-'Arabi St, Algiers
*Tel:* (021) 737494; (021) 735841 *Fax:* (021) 735841
*Telex:* 53845 Sneda *Cable:* SNEDA ALGER
*Key Personnel*
Dir General: Seghir Benamar
Editorial: Abdel Kader M'Silti; Abdel Krim Saiighi
Founded: 1983 (SNED 1966)
Subjects: Biography, Fiction, History, Nonfiction (General), Philosophy, Poetry, Regional Interests, Religion - Other, Science (General), Social Sciences, Sociology, Sports, Athletics, Travel

**SAR DAR-Echihab**, see Chihab

# Angola

## General Information

*Capital:* Luanda
*Language:* Portuguese (official), several African languages also in common use
*Religion:* Christian (mainly Roman Catholic)
*Population:* 8.9 million
*Currency:* 100 iwei = 1 new kwanza
*Export/Import Information:* No tariff on books and advertising. Very restricted issuance of import licenses. Advertising matter is currently given considerably lower priority. Exchange controls.

**Biblioteca Nacional de Angola** (Angola National Library)
Ave Commandante Jika, Luanda
Mailing Address: CP 2915, Luanda
*Tel:* (02) 322 070 *Fax:* (02) 323 979

# Antigua & Barbuda

## General Information

*Capital:* St John's
*Language:* English (official) and local dialects
*Religion:* Predominantly Angelican; other Protestant sects; some Roman Catholic

*Population:* 64,246
*Currency:* 2.70 East Caribbean dollars = $1 US

**FT Caribbean (BVI) Ltd**
PO Box 1037, Saint John's
*Tel:* 462-3392; 462-3692 *Fax:* 462-3492
*E-mail:* ftcarib@candw.ag
*Key Personnel*
Publisher: Edna Fortescue
Founded: 1978
Specialize in Caribbean economic-business & tourism publications.
ISBN Prefix(es): 976-8033
Total Titles: 1 Print
*Branch Office(s)*
PO Box 675, Saint George's, Grenada, Contact: Yvonne Warren *Tel:* 444-4930 *Fax:* 444-3391 *E-mail:* warrenp@caribsurf.com (Caribbean South)
19 Mercers Rd, London N19 4PH, United Kingdom, Man Editor: Lindsay Maxwell *Tel:* (020) 7281-5746 *Fax:* (020) 7281-7157 *E-mail:* ftcaribbean@btinternet.com (international)

# Argentina

## General Information

*Capital:* Buenos Aires
*Language:* Spanish
*Religion:* Roman Catholic
*Population:* 33 million
*Bank Hours:* 1000-1500 Monday-Friday
*Shop Hours:* 0900-1900 Monday-Saturday
*Currency:* 100 centavos = 1 nuevo peso argentino
*Export/Import Information:* No import licenses required. Import duties are assessed ad valorem. However, no import duties on books or similar material.
*Copyright:* UCC, Berne, Buenos Aires (see Copyright Conventions, pg xi)

**Editorial Abaco de Rodolfo Depalma SRL+**
Tucuman 1429 Piso 4°, 1050 Buenos Aires
*Tel:* (011) 4371-1675 *Fax:* (011) 4371-5802
*E-mail:* info@abacoeditorial.com.ar
*Web Site:* www.abacoeditorial.com.ar
*Key Personnel*
Man Dir & Editorial: Rodolfo Depalma
Production: Susana P Garcia de Gigena
Founded: 1975
Subjects: Economics, History, Journalism, Law, Philosophy, Psychology, Psychiatry, Public Administration, Social Sciences, Sociology
ISBN Prefix(es): 950-569
Number of titles published annually: 20 Print
Total Titles: 150 Print

**Abeledo-Perrot SAE e I+**
Lavalle 1280/1328, 1048 Buenos Aires
*Tel:* (011) 4124-9750 *Fax:* (011) 4371-5156
*E-mail:* editorial@abeledo-perrot.com
*Key Personnel*
Man Dir: Emilio Jose Perrot *E-mail:* eperrot@abeledo-perrot.com
General Manager: Carlos Alberto Pazos *E-mail:* cpazos@abeledo-perrot.com
Founded: 1901
Subjects: Criminology, Law, Philosophy, Public Administration
ISBN Prefix(es): 950-20
Total Titles: 17 CD-ROM

**Editorial Abril SA+**
Moreno 1617, 1093 Buenos Aires
*Tel:* (011) 4331-0112
*Telex:* 22630 Ryela
*Key Personnel*
Man Dir, Editor, Sales & Publicity: Roberto M Ares
Rights & Permissions: Alberto Cervetto
Founded: 1961
Editorial Huemul SA is the division of the company producing secondary & primary school textbooks.
Subjects: Fiction, Nonfiction (General)
ISBN Prefix(es): 950-10
*Parent Company:* Bramihuemul

**Academia Argentina de Letras** (Argentine Academy of Letters)
Sanchez de Bustamante 2663, 1425 Buenos Aires
*Tel:* (011) 4802-3814; (011) 4802-7509; (011) 4802-5161 *Fax:* (011) 4-8028340
*E-mail:* aaldespa@fibertel.com.ar; aaladmin@fibertel.com.ar; aalbibl@fibertel.com.ar
Founded: 1931
Specialize in Literature, Philology & Linguistics.
Subjects: Language Arts, Linguistics, Literature, Literary Criticism, Essays
ISBN Prefix(es): 950-585
Number of titles published annually: 4 Print

**Editorial Acme SA+**
Suipacha 245, 1008 Buenos Aires
*Tel:* (011) 4328-1508; (011) 4328-1662 *Fax:* (011) 4328-9345
*E-mail:* acme@redynet.com.ar
*Key Personnel*
Man Dir: Eduardo I Ederra
Founded: 1928
Subjects: Biography, Fiction, How-to
ISBN Prefix(es): 950-566

**Ada Korn Editora SA+**
Uruguay 651, floor 8 H, 1015 Buenos Aires
*Tel:* (011) 4374-6199 *Fax:* (011) 4374-9699
*E-mail:* adakorn@datamarkets.com.ar
*Key Personnel*
President: Ada Korn
Founded: 1984
Subjects: Drama, Theater, Fiction, Nonfiction (General), Science (General)
ISBN Prefix(es): 950-9540
Number of titles published annually: 3 Print
Total Titles: 50 Print

**Aguilar Altea Taurus Alfaguara SA de Ediciones**
Beazley 3860, 1437 Buenos Aires
*Tel:* (011) 4912-7220 *Fax:* (011) 4912-7440
*E-mail:* info@alfaguara.com.ar
*Web Site:* www.alfaguara.com.ar
*Key Personnel*
President & General Manager: Esteban Fernandez Rosado
Editorial Dir: Juan Martini
Founded: 1946
Subjects: Economics, Literature, Literary Criticism, Essays, Philosophy
ISBN Prefix(es): 950-511
*Parent Company:* Grupo Santillana Argentina

**Libreria Akadia Editorial+**
Paraguay 2078, 1121 Buenos Aires
*Tel:* (011) 4961-8614; (011) 4964-2230 *Fax:* (011) 4961-8614
*E-mail:* akadia@arnet.com.ar
*Key Personnel*
President: Jose Patlallan
Dir: Daniel Patlallan
Founded: 1967
Specialize in medical books.
Membership(s): Argentina Book Association.

Subjects: Health, Nutrition, Medicine, Nursing, Dentistry
ISBN Prefix(es): 950-9020

**Editorial Albatros SACI+**
Torres Las Plazas, J Salguero 2745, Piso 5°, oficina 51, 1425 Buenos Aires
*Tel:* (011) 4807-2030 *Fax:* (011) 4807-2010
*E-mail:* info@edalbatros.com.ar
*Web Site:* www.edalbatros.com.ar
*Key Personnel*
President: Andrea Ines Canevaro
Vice President, Executive: Gustavo Gabriel Canevaro
Founded: 1945
Subjects: Agriculture, Animals, Pets, Astrology, Occult, Economics, Electronics, Electrical Engineering, Environmental Studies, Gardening, Plants, Health, Nutrition, Medicine, Nursing, Dentistry, Social Sciences, Sociology, Sports, Athletics, Veterinary Science
ISBN Prefix(es): 950-24
Distributed by Artemis Distribuciones (Guatemala); Centro Libros Book Shop (Puerto Rico); Daisy Sel S Kuan Lau (Nicaragua); Distribuidora Lewis (Panama); Distribuidora Luongo SA (Argentina); Edaf (Spain); Edaf y Morales SA (Mexico); Editorial La Celba (El Salvador); La Familia Distribuidora de Libros SA (Peru); Gaierna SRL (Argentina); Lectorum Publications (United States); Libreria Amenguai (Dominican Republic); Libreria Lehmann SA (Costa Rica); Libreria Libertad (Chile); Libro Shop (Argentina); Libros Sin Fronteras (United States); Litexsa Venezolana (Venezuela); Mr Books (Ecuador); Multicor SRL (Uruguay); Panamericana Libreria y Papeleria (Colombia)
*Bookshop(s):* Libreria Editorial Albatros SACI, J Salguero 2745, 1425 Buenos Aires

**Alfagrama SRL ediciones**
Bolivar 547, Piso 2A, 1066 Buenos Aires
*Tel:* (011) 4342-2452; (011) 4345-2299
*Fax:* (011) 4345-5411
*E-mail:* libros@alfagrama.com.ar
*Web Site:* www.alfagrama.com.ar
*Key Personnel*
Contact: Alfredo Nunez
Subjects: Disability, Special Needs, Gay & Lesbian, Library & Information Sciences, Publishing & Book Trade Reference, Science (General), Technology, Women's Studies
ISBN Prefix(es): 987-95615

**Alianza Editorial de Argentina SA+**
Av Belgrano 355, Piso 10°, 1092 Buenos Aires
*Tel:* (011) 4342-4426; (011) 4342-9029
*Fax:* (011) 4342-4426; (011) 4342-9025
*E-mail:* gconosur@satlink.com
*Key Personnel*
General Manager: Jorge Laforque
Founded: 1985
Subjects: Anthropology, Fiction, History, Literature, Literary Criticism, Essays, Philosophy, Psychology, Psychiatry, Social Sciences, Sociology
ISBN Prefix(es): 84-206; 950-40
*Parent Company:* Alianza Editorial SA, Juan Ignacio Luca de Tena, 15, 28027 Madrid, Spain
*Showroom(s):* Av Cordoba 2064, 1120 Buenos Aires
*Bookshop(s):* Av Cordoba 2064, 1120 Buenos Aires

**Amorrortu Editores SA+**
Paraguay 1225, Piso 7, 1057 Buenos Aires
*Tel:* (011) 4816-5812; (011) 4816-5869
*Fax:* (011) 4816-3321
*E-mail:* info@amorrortueditores.com
*Web Site:* www.amorrortueditores.com

*Key Personnel*
President: Horacio de Amorrortu
Founded: 1967
Subjects: Anthropology, Economics, Education, Philosophy, Psychology, Psychiatry, Regional Interests, Religion - Other, Social Sciences, Sociology
ISBN Prefix(es): 950-518; 84-610

**Editorial Argentina Plaza y Janes SA**
Lambare 893, 1185 Buenos Aires
*Tel:* (011) 4862-6769; (011) 4862-6785
*Fax:* (011) 4864-4970
*Key Personnel*
Man Dir: Jorge Perez
Sales Dir: Ernesto Pena
Subjects: Fiction, Nonfiction (General)
ISBN Prefix(es): 950-644

**Argentine Bible Society+**
Tucuman 352/58, 1049 Buenos Aires
*Tel:* (011) 4312-5787; (011) 4312-8558
*Fax:* (011) 4312-3400
*E-mail:* socbiblicaarg@biblica.org
*Web Site:* www.biblesociety.org
*Key Personnel*
General Secretary: Marcelo Figuero
General Manager: Juan Terranova
Subjects: Biblical Studies
ISBN Prefix(es): 950-711; 950-99044
*Branch Office(s)*
Centro Regional de las Americas, 1989 NW 88 Court, Miami, FL 33177, United States
Obispo Salguero 141, 5000 Cordoba
Avda Francia 1129, 2000 Rosario

**Asociacion Bautista Argentina de Publicaciones+**
Ave Rivadavia 3464, 1203 Buenos Aires
*Tel:* (011) 4863-8924 *Fax:* (011) 4863-6745
*Key Personnel*
Assistant Manager: Emanuel Benavidez
Founded: 1911
Subjects: Religion - Other
ISBN Prefix(es): 950-841; 950-9074
*Branch Office(s)*
Tucuman 351, 5000 Cordoba
San Martin 1572, 2000 Rosario, Santa Fe

**Asociacion Educacionista Argentina,** see Editorial Stella

**Editorial Astrea de Alfredo y Ricardo Depalma SRL+**
Lavalle 1208, 1048 Buenos Aires
*Tel:* (011) 4382-1880 *Toll Free Tel:* 800-345-278732 *Fax:* (011) 4382-4203
*E-mail:* info@astrea.com.ar
*Web Site:* www.astrea.com.ar
*Key Personnel*
Man Dir: Alfredo Depalma
Sales Dir: Ricardo Depalma
Founded: 1968
Subjects: Economics, Government, Political Science, History, Law, Philosophy, Social Sciences, Sociology
ISBN Prefix(es): 950-508
Number of titles published annually: 65 Print
Total Titles: 1,000 Print
*Bookshop(s):* Libreria Astrea *Tel:* (011) 4382 5115

**Editorial Atlantida SA+**
Azopardo 579, 3 Piso, 1307 Buenos Aires
*Tel:* (011) 4331-4591; (011) 4331-4599
*Fax:* (011) 4331-3341
*E-mail:* info@atlantida.com.ar
*Web Site:* www.atlantida.com.ar
*Telex:* 21163 *Cable:* EDIATLAN
*Key Personnel*
Executive Dir: Alfredo Vercelli

Editorial Dir: Jorge Naveiro
Founded: 1918
Subjects: Fiction, Nonfiction (General)
ISBN Prefix(es): 950-08
*U.S. Office(s):* 31 W 57th St, 6th floor, New York, NY 10019, United States, Contact: Maria Campbell
*Bookshop(s):* Galerias Pacifico, San Martin 760, Local 5215, 1004 Buenos Aires *Tel:* (011) 3116411; Nuevo Centro Shopping, D Quiros 1400, Local 2241, 5000 Cordoba *Tel:* (051) 891440
*Shipping Address:* Rio Cuarto 1907, 1292 Buenos Aires
*Warehouse:* Rio Cuarto 1907, 1292 Buenos Aires

**AZ Editora SA+**
Paraguay 2351, 1121 Buenos Aires
*Tel:* (011) 4961-4036; (011) 4961-4037; (011) 4961-4038; (011) 4961-0088 *Fax:* (011) 4961-0089
*E-mail:* correo@az-editora.com
*Web Site:* www.az-editora.com.ar
*Key Personnel*
President: Dante Omar Villalba
Vice President: Luis Alberto Villone
Technical Dir: Luis Mendez Davila
Founded: 1976
Subjects: Economics, History, Law, Psychology, Psychiatry
ISBN Prefix(es): 950-534

**La Azotea Editorial Fotografica SRL**
Paraguay 1480, 1061 Buenos Aires
*Tel:* (011) 4811-0931 *Fax:* (011) 4811-0931
*E-mail:* azotea@laazotea.com.ar
*Web Site:* www.laazotea.com.ar
ISBN Prefix(es): 950-9536

**Beas Ediciones SRL+**
Inclan 3945, 1258 Buenos Aires
*Tel:* (011) 4923-4030; (011) 4924-5337
*Fax:* (011) 4924-0217
*Key Personnel*
President: Hugo S Beas
Commercial Dir: Jorge Luis Sanchez
Founded: 1992
Subjects: Fiction, Humor, Nonfiction (General), Self-Help
ISBN Prefix(es): 950-834
*Parent Company:* Circulo del Buen Lecetor SRL, Argentina
*Associate Companies:* Circulo del Buen Lector SA de CV, Mexico

**Beatriz Viterbo Editora+**
Espana 1150, 2000 Rosario-Santa Fe
*Tel:* (0341) 4487521 *Fax:* (0341) 4261919
*Key Personnel*
Contact: Adriana Astutti *E-mail:* aastutti@arnet.com.ar; Sandra Contreras
Founded: 1991
Subjects: Drama, Theater, Fiction, Literature, Literary Criticism, Essays, Nonfiction (General), Poetry
ISBN Prefix(es): 950-845; 950-99766
Distributed by Fernando Garcia Cambeiro e Hijos

**Revista Biblica,** *imprint of* Editorial Guadalupe

**Bonum Editorial SACI+**
Av Corrientes 6687, 1427 Buenos Aires
*Tel:* (011) 4554-1414 *Fax:* (011) 4554-1414
*E-mail:* produccion@editorialbonum.com.ar
*Web Site:* www.editorialbonum.com.ar *Cable:* BONUM
*Key Personnel*
Dir Commerce: Martin Gremmelspacher
Founded: 1960
Membership(s): Argentina Book Association, Foreign Trade.

Subjects: Drama, Theater, Education, Literature, Literary Criticism, Essays, Music, Dance, Nonfiction (General), Philosophy, Psychology, Psychiatry, Religion - Catholic, Religion - Other, Securities, Self-Help, Theology
ISBN Prefix(es): 950-507
*Bookshop(s):* Maipu 869, 1006 Buenos Aires
*Fax:* (011) 4314-0888

**Bosco Don Ediciones Argentina**, see Ediciones Don Bosco Argentina

**Ediciones Botella al Mar**
Luis Agote 2280, Piso 7°, 1425 Buenos Aires
*Tel:* (011) 4803-8246
*E-mail:* edicionesbotellaalmar@hotmail.com
ISBN Prefix(es): 950-513

**Editorial Cangallo SACI+**
Av Belgrano 609, 1092 Buenos Aires
*Tel:* (011) 4331-0204; (011) 4331-8848
*Key Personnel*
Man Dir: Norberto del Hoyo
President: Rosa del Valle Cardozo
Founded: 1968
Subjects: Business, Economics, Law
ISBN Prefix(es): 950-543

**Editorial Caymi SACI**
15 de Noviembre de 1889 N° 1149, 1130 Buenos Aires
*Tel:* (011) 4304-2474 *Fax:* (011) 4304-2474
Founded: 1945
Subjects: Animals, Pets, Astrology, Occult, Automotive, Cookery, Gardening, Plants, Medicine, Nursing, Dentistry, Science Fiction, Fantasy, Self-Help, Sports, Athletics
ISBN Prefix(es): 950-501

**Centro Editor de America Latina SA**
Tucuman 1736, 1050 Buenos Aires
*Tel:* (011) 4371-2411 *Cable:* Centroedit
*Key Personnel*
Man Dir: Jose Boris Spivacow
Sales Dir: Aldo Antonio Sangoi
Founded: 1966
Subjects: Art, Biography, Education, History, How-to, Literature, Literary Criticism, Essays, Psychology, Psychiatry, Science (General), Social Sciences, Sociology
ISBN Prefix(es): 950-25

**Cesarini Hermanos+**
Sarmiento 3219/31, C1196 AA1 Buenos Aires
*Tel:* (011) 4861-1152 *Fax:* (011) 4861-1152
*E-mail:* cesarinihnos@movi.com.ar
*Key Personnel*
Associate Manager: Osvaldo Cesarini
Founded: 1940
Membership(s): Argentina Book Association.
Subjects: Environmental Studies, Music, Dance, Nonfiction (General), Technology
ISBN Prefix(es): 950-526

**Cientifica Interamericana SACI, Editorial**
Marcelo T de Alvear 2147, 1122 Buenos Aires
*Tel:* (011) 4822-8883 *Fax:* (011) 4827-0486
*E-mail:* edit@interame.satlink.net
*Key Personnel*
President: Mauricio Modai
ISBN Prefix(es): 950-9428

**Editorial Ciudad Nueva de la Sefoma+**
Lezica 4358, 1202 Buenos Aires
*Tel:* (011) 4981-4885 *Fax:* (011) 4981-4885
*E-mail:* ciudadnueva@ciudadnueva.org.ar
*Web Site:* www.ciudadnueva.org.ar
*Key Personnel*
Manager: Alejandro Frere
Editor: Carlos Mana

Founded: 1964
Subjects: Biography, Education, Religion - Catholic, Securities, Theology
ISBN Prefix(es): 950-586
*Parent Company:* Citta Nuova Editrice (for associate companies), Italy
Distributed by Ciudad Nueva (Chile, Uruguay, Paraguay, Colombia, Mexico)

**Editorial Claretiana+**
Lima 1360, 1138 Buenos Aires
*Tel:* (011) 4305-9597; (011) 4305-9510
*Fax:* (011) 4305-6552
*E-mail:* editorial@editorialclaretiana.com.ar
*Web Site:* www.editorialclaretiana.com.ar *Cable:* EDITORIAL CLARETIANA
*Key Personnel*
Man Dir, Editorial, Rights & Permissions: Gustavo Larrazabal
Manager: Eduardo Righetti
Publicity: Jose Luis Perez
Founded: 1956
Subjects: Religion - Catholic, Theology
ISBN Prefix(es): 950-512

**Editorial Claridad SA+**
Viamonte 1730, Piso 1°, 1055 Buenos Aires
*Tel:* (011) 4371-5546 *Fax:* (011) 4375-1659
*E-mail:* editorial@heliasta.com.ar
*Web Site:* www.heliasta.com.ar *Cable:* CLARIDAD BAIRES
*Key Personnel*
President: Dr Ana Maria Cabanellas
Vice President: Dr Guillermo Cabanellas
Founded: 1922
Subjects: Biography, Government, Political Science, History, Law, Philosophy, Poetry
ISBN Prefix(es): 950-620
Subsidiaries: Editorial Heliasta SRL

**Club de Lectores+**
Solis 282, 1078 Buenos Aires
*Tel:* (011) 4382-2798
*E-mail:* libreriaaccion@uolsinectis.com.ar
*Key Personnel*
Man Dir: Mercedes Fontenla
Sales: Carlos A Alvano
Publicity: Cesar Tomas Fontenla
Founded: 1938
Subjects: History, Philosophy, Psychology, Psychiatry, Religion - Other, Social Sciences, Sociology
ISBN Prefix(es): 950-9034
*Bookshop(s):* Libreria Accion, Av de Mayo 624, 1084 Buenos Aires; Libreria Universitaria Fontis, Av de Mayo 624, 1084 Buenos Aires

**Coleccion Juridica Bco de Datos en Computacion**, *imprint of* Editorial Zeus SRL

**Libreria del Colegio SA+**
Humberto I 531, 1103 Buenos Aires
*Tel:* (011) 4300-5400; (011) 4362-1222
*Fax:* (011) 4362-7364
*E-mail:* edsudame@satlink.com *Cable:* LIBRECOL
*Key Personnel*
Contact: Javier Lopez Llovet
Founded: 1830
Subjects: Education
ISBN Prefix(es): 950-548
*Parent Company:* Editorial Sudamericana SA

**Colmegna Libreria y Editorial**
San Martin 2546, 3000 Sante Fe
*Tel:* (042) 423102; (042) 4557345 *Fax:* (042) 4557345
*Key Personnel*
President: Jose Luis Anessi
Manager: Guillermo Goatherd
Founded: 1889

Subjects: Literature, Literary Criticism, Essays, Poetry
ISBN Prefix(es): 950-535

**Concilium**, *imprint of* Editorial Guadalupe

**Ediciones Corregidor SAICI y E+**
Rodriguez Pena 452, 1020 Buenos Aires
*Tel:* (011) 4374-5000; (011) 4374-4959
*Fax:* (011) 4374-5000
*E-mail:* corregidor@corregidor.com
*Web Site:* www.corregidor.com
*Key Personnel*
Dir: Manuel Pampin *E-mail:* manuel.pampin@corregidor.com
Founded: 1970
Subjects: Drama, Theater, Economics, Literature, Literary Criticism, Essays, Music, Dance, Poetry, Cinema
ISBN Prefix(es): 950-05
Number of titles published annually: 50 Print
Total Titles: 3,000 Print
*Warehouse:* Pasaje Berg 4060, Lanus Oeste, 1826 Buenos Aires

**Cosmopolita SRL**
Piedras 744, 1070 Buenos Aires
*Tel:* (011) 4361-8925; (011) 4361-8049
*Fax:* (011) 4361-8049; (011) 4361-8925
*Key Personnel*
Man Dir: Eva Ruth F de Rapp
Founded: 1940
Subjects: Agriculture
ISBN Prefix(es): 950-9069

**Critica+**
Independencia, 1668 Buenos Aires 1100
*Tel:* (011) 4382-4045; (011) 4382-4043
*Fax:* (011) 4383-3793
*E-mail:* info@grijalbo.com.ar
*Key Personnel*
General Manager: Felipe Munde
*E-mail:* fmunoz@grijalbo.com.ar
Subjects: Fiction, Nonfiction (General)
ISBN Prefix(es): 950-28; 987-9317
*Parent Company:* Grijalbo Mondadori SA

**Studia Croatica**
Matienzo 2530, 1426 Buenos Aires
*Tel:* (011) 4771-4954 *Fax:* (011) 4771-4954
*E-mail:* webmasters@studiacroatica.com
ISBN Prefix(es): 987-95467

**Ediciones de la Flor SRL+**
Gorriti 3695, C1172ACE Buenos Aires
*Tel:* (011) 4963-7950 *Fax:* (011) 4963-5616
*E-mail:* edic-flor@datamarkets.com.ar
*Web Site:* www.edicionesdelaflor.com.ar
*Key Personnel*
Dir: Daniel Divinsky *Tel:* (011) 4963-1460
Man Dir: Ana M Miler *Tel:* (011) 4963-1460
*E-mail:* kukimiler@datamarkets.com.ar
Publicity & Advertising Dir, Rights & Permissions: Daniel Borenstein
Founded: 1967
Subjects: Biography, Drama, Theater, Fiction, History, Humor, Literature, Literary Criticism, Essays, Philosophy, Psychology, Psychiatry, Social Sciences, Sociology
ISBN Prefix(es): 950-515
Number of titles published annually: 30 Print
Total Titles: 700 Print

**Depalma SRL+**
Talcahuano 494, 1013 Buenos Aires
*Tel:* (011) 5382-8806 *Fax:* (011) 5382-8888
*E-mail:* info@depalma.ssdnet.com.ar
*Key Personnel*
Man Dir, Production: Roberto Suardiaz
General Manager: Alberto Evaristo Baron
International Marketing Manager: Nicolas von der Pahlen

Founded: 1944
Subjects: Business, History, Law, Social Sciences, Sociology
ISBN Prefix(es): 950-14
Distributor for Iberiamerican Juridical Books
*Showroom(s):* Lavalle 1302, Buenos Aires

**Diana Argentina SA, Editorial**
Beauchef 559, 1424 Buenos Aires
*Tel:* (011) 4922-5035; (011) 4922-5036
   *Fax:* (011) 4922-5035; (011) 4922-5036
*E-mail:* to_dianaarg@sinectis.com.ar
*Key Personnel*
General Dir: Jorge Baez Arganaraz
Subjects: Accounting, Animals, Pets, Art, Biography, Business, Communications, Computer Science, Economics, Education, Engineering (General), History, Journalism, Language Arts, Linguistics, Literature, Literary Criticism, Essays, Marketing, Medicine, Nursing, Dentistry, Music, Dance, Philosophy, Photography, Religion - Other, Self-Help, Sports, Athletics, Travel
ISBN Prefix(es): 987-96980
*Parent Company:* Casa Amtriz

**Diario la Voz del Interior**
Tte Gral Peron 1628, Piso 2, 1037 Buenos Aires
*Tel:* (011) 4382-2267 *Fax:* (011) 3822508
*E-mail:* info@nueva.com.ar
*Key Personnel*
Dir: Cuesta Carlos Enrique
ISBN Prefix(es): 950-879; 950-884

**Editorial Ruy Diaz SAEIC+**
Elpidio Gonzalez 5562/66, 1407 Buenos Aires
*Tel:* (011) 4567-4918; (011) 4567-2865
   *Fax:* (011) 4567-4918
*E-mail:* editorial@ruydiaz.com.ar
*Web Site:* www.ruydiaz.com.ar *Cable:* EDIRUY
*Key Personnel*
President: Rafael Juan Zucotti
Man Dir: Gustavo H Zuccotti
Founded: 1966
Membership(s): Argentina Book Association.
Subjects: Cookery, Education, Law
ISBN Prefix(es): 950-9023; 987-516
*Branch Office(s)*
Casilla de Correo 46, Suc 6, 1406 Buenos Aires

**Ediciones Don Bosco Argentina+**
Don Bosco 4069, 1206 Buenos Aires
*Tel:* (011) 4981-7314; (011) 4981-1388
   *Fax:* (011) 4958-1506
*E-mail:* e.d.b.sofrasa@interlink.com.ar
*Key Personnel*
Contact: Roque R Cella
Founded: 1941
Membership(s): Camara del Libro.
Subjects: Accounting, Drama, Theater, Education, History, Journalism, Radio, TV, Religion - Catholic
ISBN Prefix(es): 950-514
Distributed by Centro Salesiano de Estudios
Distributor for Edebe
*Bookshop(s):* Don Bosco 4069, 1206 Capital Federal
*Orders to:* Don Bosco 4069, 1206 Capital Federal

**Ediciones del Eclipse+**
Julian Alvarez 843, 1414 Buenos Aires
*Tel:* (011) 4771-3583 *Fax:* (011) 4771-3583
*E-mail:* info@deleclipse.com
*Web Site:* www.deleclipse.com
*Key Personnel*
President: Maria Del Rosario Charquero
Subjects: Literature, Literary Criticism, Essays, Psychology, Psychiatry
ISBN Prefix(es): 987-9011; 950-99530

**Edicial SA+**
Rivadavia 761, 1002 Buenos Aires
*Tel:* (011) 4342-8481; (011) 4342-8482; (011) 4342-8483 *Fax:* (011) 4342-8481
*E-mail:* edicial@edicial.com.ar
*Key Personnel*
President: Juan A Musset
Founded: 1931
Subjects: Communications, Language Arts, Linguistics, Literature, Literary Criticism, Essays, Philosophy, Regional Interests
ISBN Prefix(es): 950-506
*U.S. Office(s):* Distribooks, 8220 N Christiana Ave, Skokie, IL 60076-2911, United States
*Showroom(s):* Palacio del Libro International, Suipacha 1136, 1008 Buenos Aires

**Editorial Kapelusz SA**, see Kapelusz Editora SA

**Editorial Universitaria de Buenos Aires**, see EUDEBA (Editorial Universitaria de Buenos Aires)

**EDIUM**, see Editorial Idearium de la Universidad de Mendoza (EDIUM)

**Emece Editores SA+**
Member of Grupo Planeta
Independencia 1668, 1100 Buenos Aires
*Tel:* (011) 4382-4045; (011) 4382-4043
   *Fax:* (011) 4383-3793
*E-mail:* info@eplaneta.com.ar; pasiusis@planeta.com.ar
*Web Site:* www.emece.com.ar
*Key Personnel*
President: Ing Alfredo del Carril *E-mail:* acarril@emece.com.ar
General Director: Francisco F del Carril *E-mail:* fcarril@emece.com.ar
Administration: Marcos I Fantin
Editorial Director: Bonifacio P del Carril *E-mail:* bcarril@emece.com.ar
Editorial: Eduardo Garcia Belsunce *E-mail:* edicion@emece.com.ar
Sales Dir, Export: Carlos A Bustillo *E-mail:* cbustillo@emece.com.ar
Editorial Dept: Stella Maris Rozas *E-mail:* srozas@emece.com.ar
Founded: 1939
Subjects: Art, Biography, Fiction, History, Literature, Literary Criticism, Essays, Mysteries, Nonfiction (General)
ISBN Prefix(es): 950-04
Number of titles published annually: 120 Print
*Associate Companies:* Emece Editores SA, Mallorca 237 Entlo, 1a, 08008 Barcelona, Spain, Contact: Siprid Kraus *Tel:* (03) 215-1199 *Fax:* (03) 215-4636; Emece Mexicana SA, de CV Vito Alessio Robles 140, Col Florida CP, 01030 Mexico, DF, Mexico, Contact: Iuan Mozo *Tel:* (05) 661-7590 *Fax:* (05) 661-4110 *E-mail:* emece@podernet.com.ar; Emece/Urano SA, av Francisco Bilbao, 2809 Santiago de Chile, Chile, Contact: Ricardo Ulasteliga *Tel:* (02) 341-6731 *Fax:* (02) 225-3896 *E-mail:* emc-uran A entelchile.net; Av Uruguay 1579, Montevideo, Uruguay, Contact: Reinaldo Rodriguez *Tel:* (02) 42-9358 *Fax:* (02) 42-9359 *E-mail:* pero@adinet.com.uy
*U.S. Office(s):* Sanford J Greenburger Associates Inc, 55 Fifth Ave, New York, NY 10003, United States, Contact: Carol Frederick *Tel:* 212-206-5600 *Fax:* 212-463-8718; 212-687-9281

**Errepar SA+**
Parana 725, 1017 Buenos Aires
*Tel:* (011) 4370-2002 *Fax:* (011) 4307-9541
*E-mail:* clientes@errepar.com
*Web Site:* www.errepar.com

*Key Personnel*
Vice President: Dr Francisco Canada
International Rights Contact: Veronica Parada; Irene Acero
Subjects: Astrology, Occult, Cookery, Economics, Education, Religion - Catholic, Religion - Hindu, Religion - Other, Self-Help
ISBN Prefix(es): 950-739; 950-9524; 987-01

**Espasa-Calpe Argentina SA+**
Member of Grupo Planeta
Independencea 1668, 1100 Buenos Aires
*Tel:* (011) 4382-4043; (011) 4382-4045
   *Fax:* (011) 4383-3793
*E-mail:* info@eplaneta.com.ar
*Key Personnel*
Dir General: Guillermo Schavelzon
Founded: 1929
ISBN Prefix(es): 950-852
Subsidiaries: Seix Barral; Destino; Ariel; Deusto; Austral

**Angel Estrada y Cia SA**
Bolivar 462/66, 1066 Buenos Aires
*Tel:* (011) 4344-5500 *Fax:* (011) 4331-6527
*E-mail:* editocom@estrada.com.ar
*Web Site:* www.estrada.com.ar
*Telex:* 17990 Estra
*Key Personnel*
President: Zsolt Arardy
Director: Tomas de Estrada
Publishing Manager: Marcela Iraola
Founded: 1869
Subjects: Education, How-to
ISBN Prefix(es): 950-01

**EUDEBA (Editorial Universitaria de Buenos Aires)+**
Av Rivadavia 1573, C1033AAF Buenos Aires
*Tel:* (011) 4383-8025 *Fax:* (011) 4383-2202
*E-mail:* eudeba@eudeba.com
*Web Site:* www.eudeba.com.ar
*Key Personnel*
President: Alicia Rosalia Wigdorovitz de Camilloni
Manager of Institutional Relations: Martin Unzue *E-mail:* institucionales@eudeba.com.ar
Publishing Manager: Victor Palaces *E-mail:* geditorial@eudeba.com.ar
Commercial Manager: Gustavo Kogan *E-mail:* ventas@eudeba.com.ar
Founded: 1958
Subjects: Accounting, Archaeology, Architecture & Interior Design, Art, Astrology, Occult, Chemistry, Chemical Engineering, Drama, Theater, Economics, Education, Geography, Geology, History, Law, Literature, Literary Criticism, Essays, Mathematics, Medicine, Nursing, Dentistry, Music, Dance, Philosophy, Physics, Psychology, Psychiatry, Science (General), Theology, Veterinary Science
ISBN Prefix(es): 950-23
Number of titles published annually: 150 Print; 5 CD-ROM
*Bookshop(s):* Pasaje El Fundador-Loca, 9 Obispo Trejo, 29 Cordoba, 5000 Codigo

**Ediciones Librerias Fausto+**
Av Corrientes 1316, 1043 Buenos Aires
*Tel:* (011) 4372-4919 *Fax:* (011) 4372-3914
*E-mail:* fausto@fausto.com
*Web Site:* www.fausto.com
*Key Personnel*
President: Rafael Pedro Zorrilla
Manager: Jose Luis Retes
ISBN Prefix(es): 950-653
*Branch Office(s)*
Corrientes 1243, 1715 Santa Fe
Galerias Pacifico, 1311 Santa Fe
*Bookshop(s):* Libreria Fausto

**Fundacion Editorial de Belgrano**
Federico Lacroze 1959, Piso 4º, 1426 Buenos
    Aires
*Tel:* (011) 4772-4014 *Fax:* (011) 4775-8788
*Key Personnel*
President: Avelino J Porto
Subjects: Architecture & Interior Design, Eco-
    nomics, Government, Political Science, Law,
    Literature, Literary Criticism, Essays, Psychol-
    ogy, Psychiatry, Radio, TV, Social Sciences,
    Sociology
ISBN Prefix(es): 950-577; 987-95823

**Ediciones de Arte Gaglianone**
Cnel M Chilavert 1136/1146, 1437 Buenos Aires
*Tel:* (011) 4923-2579; (011) 4923-0150
    *Fax:* (011) 4923-0150; (011) 4923-2579
*E-mail:* ediciones@gaglianone.com.ar
*Key Personnel*
President: Jose Horacio Gaglianone
General Manager: Oscar A Aimar
Editor: Patricio Lopez Tobares
Accounting & Finances: Gustavo Portela
Subjects: Music, Dance
ISBN Prefix(es): 950-720; 950-9004

**Editorial Galerna SRL+**
Lambare 893, 1185 Buenos Aires
*Tel:* (011) 4867-1661 *Fax:* (011) 4862-5031
*E-mail:* gventas@hg.com.ar *Cable:* GALERNA
*Key Personnel*
Dir: Hugo Benjamin Levin; Juan Jose
    D'AAbtibua
Founded: 1967
Afiliados a la Camara Argentina del Libro.
Membership(s): Argentina Book Association.
Subjects: Drama, Theater, History, Humor, Liter-
    ature, Literary Criticism, Essays, Poetry, Social
    Sciences, Sociology, Theology
ISBN Prefix(es): 950-556
Subsidiaries: Librogal SRL
*Bookshop(s):* Gueemes 369, Loc 50, Haedo; Li-
    breria Galerna, Corrientes 1776, Mar del Plata,
    Buenos Aires; Nazarre 3175, Loc 119/20,
    Buenos Aires; Rivadavia 3050, Loc 21, Mar
    del Plata, Buenos Aires; Septimo Rayo, Callao
    729, Buenos Aires; Ramon L Falcon 7115, Loc
    305, Buenos Aires

**Gram Editora**
Cochabamba 1652, 1148 Buenos Aires
*Tel:* (011) 4304-4833; (011) 4305-8397
    *Fax:* (011) 4304-5692
*E-mail:* grameditora@infovia.com.ar
*Web Site:* www.grameditora.com.ar
*Key Personnel*
Dir: Manuel Herrero Montes
Founded: 1925
Subjects: Computer Science, Education, Religion
    - Catholic, Religion - Other
ISBN Prefix(es): 950-530
*Branch Office(s)*
Libreria Marista, Av Callao 226, 1148 Buenos
    Aires *Tel:* (011) 374-3114 *Fax:* (011) 374-3146

**Editorial Guadalupe+**
Mansilla 3865, 1425 Buenos Aires
*Tel:* (011) 4826-8587 *Fax:* (011) 4826-8587
*E-mail:* ventas@editorialguadalupe.com.ar
*Web Site:* www.editorialguadalupe.com.ar
*Key Personnel*
Dir: Lorenzo Goyeneche
Man Dir, Production: Mario V Keiner
Publicity Dir: Osvaldo Lopez
Founded: 1895
Membership(s): Argentina Book Association.
Subjects: Anthropology, Education, History, Lan-
    guage Arts, Linguistics, Literature, Literary
    Criticism, Essays, Music, Dance, Philosophy,
    Psychology, Psychiatry, Religion - Catholic,
    Social Sciences, Sociology, Theology
ISBN Prefix(es): 950-500

Imprints: Revista Biblica; Concilium
*Branch Office(s)*
Libreria Verbo Divino, Velez Sarsfield 76-5000
    Cordoba
*Bookshop(s):* Libreria Guadalupe, Mansilla 3865,
    1425 Buenos Aires; Libreria Verbo Divino,
    Velez Sarsfield 76, 5000 Cordoba

**Editorial Heliasta SRL**
Viamonte 1730 Piso 1, 1055 Buenos Aires
*Tel:* (011) 4371-5546 *Fax:* (011) 4375-1659
*E-mail:* editorial@heliasta.com.ar
*Web Site:* www.heliasta.com.ar
ISBN Prefix(es): 950-9065; 950-885

**Editorial Hemisferio Sur SA+**
Pasteur 743, 1028 Buenos Aires
*Tel:* (011) 49529825 *Fax:* (011) 49528454
*E-mail:* informe@hemisferiosur.com.ar
*Web Site:* www.hemisferiosur.com.ar
*Key Personnel*
President & Man Dir, Licensing: Adolfo Julian
    Pena
Founded: 1966
Subjects: Agriculture, Animals, Pets, Biological
    Sciences, Gardening, Plants, Science (General),
    Veterinary Science, Wine & Spirits
ISBN Prefix(es): 950-504

**Editorial Huemul SA**, see Editorial Abril SA

**Libreria Huemul SA+**
Ave Santa Fe 2237, 1123 Buenos Aires
*Tel:* (011) 4822-1666; (011) 4825-2290
    *Fax:* (011) 822-1666
*Key Personnel*
President & Manager: Antonio Rego
Sales, Publicity, Rights & Permissions: Carlos L
    Sanchez
Founded: 1941
ISBN Prefix(es): 950-571; 84-8201

**Editorial Idearium de la Universidad de
    Mendoza (EDIUM)**
Aristides Villanueva 773, 5500 Mendoza
*Tel:* (0261) 420-2017; (0261) 420-0740
    *Fax:* (0261) 420-1100
*E-mail:* umimen@um.edu.ar
*Web Site:* www.um.edu.ar/um/
*Key Personnel*
Dir: Dr Juan Carlos Menghini
Manager: Jose Miguel Ciarcia
Founded: 1979
Subjects: Architecture & Interior Design, Com-
    puter Science, Economics, Education, Electron-
    ics, Electrical Engineering, Engineering (Gen-
    eral), Environmental Studies, History, Language
    Arts, Linguistics, Law, Mathematics, Medicine,
    Nursing, Dentistry, Philosophy, Physics, Social
    Sciences, Sociology, Technology
ISBN Prefix(es): 950-624
Distributed by Abeledo-Perrot

**INCYTH**, see Instituto Nacional de Ciencia y
    Tecnica Hidrica (INCYTH)

**Inter-Medica+**
Junin 917, Piso 1 A, 1113 Buenos Aires
*Tel:* (011) 4961-9234 *Fax:* (011) 4961-5572
*E-mail:* info@inter-medica.com.ar
*Web Site:* www.inter-medica.com.ar
*Key Personnel*
President: Jorge Modyeievsky
Vice President: Sonia M B de Modyeievsky
General Manager: Tatiana Modyeievsky Baken-
    roth; Eduardo Modyeievsky Bakenroth; Daniel
    Sergio
Founded: 1959
Subjects: Veterinary Science

ISBN Prefix(es): 950-555
*Branch Office(s)*
Editorial Intervet SA, Junin 917-1 A, Capital
    1113

**Juegos & Co SRL+**
Av Corrientes 1312, Piso 8, 1043 Buenos Aires
*Tel:* (011) 4374-7903; (011) 4371-1825
    *Fax:* (011) 4372-3829
*E-mail:* juegosyc@impsat1.com.ar
*Web Site:* www.demente.com
*Key Personnel*
Dir: Jaime Poniachik
Editor: Diego Uribe
Founded: 1980
Membership(s): Argentine Association of Maga-
    zine Publishers.
Subjects: Mathematics
ISBN Prefix(es): 950-765
*Associate Companies:* Zugarto Ediciones, Madrid,
    Spain

**Juris Editorial+**
Moreno 1580, 2000 Rosario
*Tel:* (0341) 4267301; (0341) 4267302 *Fax:* (0341)
    4267301; (0341) 4267302
*E-mail:* editorialjuris@arnet.com.ar
*Web Site:* www.editorialjuris.com
*Key Personnel*
International Contact: Luis Maesano
Founded: 1952
Subjects: Criminology, Law
ISBN Prefix(es): 950-817; 950-99649
Number of titles published annually: 25 Print

**Kapelusz Editora SA**
San Jose 831, 1076 Buenos Aires
*Tel:* (011) 5236-5000 *Fax:* (011) 5236-5050
*E-mail:* editorial@kapelusz.com.ar
*Web Site:* www.kapelusz.com.ar
*Telex:* 18342 Ekasa *Cable:* Kapelusz
*Key Personnel*
President: Tomas Castle
Vice President: Juan Silva Baptist
Dir: Ivan Dario Pineda
Sales Manager: Hernando S Ferreres
Publicity: Carlos O Otero
Founded: 1905
Subjects: Education, Psychology, Psychiatry
ISBN Prefix(es): 950-13
Subsidiaries: Editorial Cincel SA; Editorial
    Kapelusz Colombiana SA; Editorial Kapelusz
    Mexicana SA; Editorial Kapelusz SA; Editorial
    Kapelusz Venezolana SA
*Bookshop(s):* Corrientes 999, Buenos Aires

**Editorial Kier SACIFI+**
Ave Santa Fe 1260, 1059 Buenos Aires
*Tel:* (011) 4811-0507 *Fax:* (011) 4811-3395
*E-mail:* ediciones@kier.com.ar
*Web Site:* www.kier.com.ar
*Key Personnel*
President: Hector Pibernus
Vice President: Alfonso Sergio Pibernus
Man Dir: Osvaldo Pibernus
Sales Dir: Sergio F Pibernus
Founded: 1907
Specialize in medicine.
Subjects: Anthropology, Astrology, Occult,
    Health, Nutrition, Parapsychology, Religion -
    Buddhist, Religion - Hindu, Religion - Islamic,
    Religion - Jewish, Religion - Other, Self-Help
ISBN Prefix(es): 950-17
Number of titles published annually: 40 Print
Total Titles: 800 Print
*Bookshop(s):* Libreria Kier, Ave Santa Fe 1260,
    1059 Buenos Aires

**Laffont Ediciones Electronicas SA**
Av Reg Patricios 929, 1265 Buenos Aires
*Tel:* (011) 4302-8668 *Fax:* (011) 4301-2525
*E-mail:* info@laffont.com.ar
*Web Site:* www.laffont.com.ar

*Key Personnel*
Contact: Dr Julio Laffont
Membership(s): Camara del Libro.
Subjects: Art, Education, Geography, Geology,
    History, Science (General)
ISBN Prefix(es): 987-9220; 987-95410

**Ediciones Larousse Argentina SA**
Valentin Gomez 3530, 1191 Buenos Aires
*Tel:* (011) 4865-9581; (011) 4865-9582; (011)
    4865-9583 *Toll Free Tel:* 800-333-5757
    *Fax:* (011) 4865-9581; (011) 4865-9582; (011)
    4865-9583 *Toll Free Fax:* 800-333-5757
*E-mail:* editorial@aique.com.ar; comercial@
    aique.com.ar
*Web Site:* www.larousse.com.ar
*Telex:* 0121783 *Cable:* Editlarousse
*Key Personnel*
President: Dominique Bertin
ISBN Prefix(es): 950-538

**Latina SA**, see Ediciones Preescolar SA

**La Ley SA Editora e Impresora+**
Tucuman 1471, 1050 Buenos Aires
*Tel:* (011) 4378-4841 *Fax:* (011) 4372-0953
*E-mail:* atcliente1@laley.com.ar
*Web Site:* www.la-ley.com.ar
*Telex:* 17465 Laley
*Key Personnel*
President: Juan C Milberg
Vice President: Enrique J Algorta
General Dir: Enrique J Algorta Gaona
Commercial Manager: Manuel E Schkolnik
Production: Roberto Pedretti
Founded: 1935
Subjects: Economics, History, Law, Philosophy
ISBN Prefix(es): 950-527

**Libres**, *imprint of* Ediciones Macchi

**Librograf Editora+**
Chacabuco 1185/87, 1069 Buenos Aires
*Tel:* (011) 4300-3670; (011) 4300-1466
    *Fax:* (011) 4300-3670
*Key Personnel*
Contact: Adriana Arribas; Eduardo Rosales
Founded: 1968
Subjects: Cookery, Education
ISBN Prefix(es): 950-848; 950-99827

**Ediciones Lidiun**
Patagones 2459, 1282 Buenos Aires
*Tel:* (011) 4942-9002 *Fax:* (011) 4942-9162
*E-mail:* info@ateneo.com
Founded: 1970
Subjects: Animals, Pets, Health, Nutrition, Out-
    door Recreation, Psychology, Psychiatry, Reli-
    gion - Other, Sports, Athletics
ISBN Prefix(es): 950-524

**Lopez Libreros Editores S R L**
Av Cordoba 2370, 1120 Buenos Aires
*Tel:* (011) 4963-9646
*Key Personnel*
Man Dir: Dr Pablo A Lopez; Josefina A Lopez
Founded: 1927
Subjects: Medicine, Nursing, Dentistry
ISBN Prefix(es): 950-505

**Editorial Losada SA+**
Corrientes 1551, 1042 Buenos Aires
*Tel:* (011) 4373-4006; (011) 4375-5001
    *Fax:* (011) 4373-4006; (011) 4375-5001
*E-mail:* administra@editoriallosada.com
*Cable:* EDILOSADA
*Key Personnel*
President: Jose Juan Fernandez Reguera
Vice President: Dr Moretti Luis Angel
Secretary: Mabel Peremarti

Founded: 1938
Membership(s): Camara Argentina del Libro.
Subjects: Biography, Drama, Theater, Education,
    Fiction, History, Law, Philosophy, Poetry, Psy-
    chology, Psychiatry
ISBN Prefix(es): 950-03

**Ediciones LR SA+**
Sarmiento 835, 1041 Buenos Aires
*Tel:* (011) 4326-3725; (011) 4326-3826
*Telex:* 22087 Elerre
*Key Personnel*
President: Bautista L Tello
Founded: 1981
Membership(s): Camara Argentina de Publica-
    ciones.
ISBN Prefix(es): 950-604
*Parent Company:* Libreria Rodriguez SA
*Associate Companies:* LR Distribuidora SA
Distributor for LR Distribuidora SA
*Warehouse:* Boedo 377, 1206 Buenos Aires

**Ediciones Macchi+**
Alsina 1535/37, 1088 Buenos Aires
*Tel:* (011) 4375-1195 *Fax:* (011) 4375-1870;
    (011) 4374-2506
*E-mail:* info@macchi.com.ar
*Web Site:* www.macchi.com
*Key Personnel*
President: Raul Luis Macchi
Founded: 1947
ISBN Prefix(es): 950-537
*Imprints:* Libres
*Bookshop(s):* Ave Cordoba 2015, 1120 Bueno
    Aires *Tel:* (011) 4961-8355

**Macchi Grupo Editors SA**, see Ediciones
    Macchi

**Marymar Ediciones SA+**
Chile 1432, 1098 Buenos Aires
*Tel:* (011) 4381-9083
*Key Personnel*
President: Isay Klasse
Vice President: Saul Chernicoff
Founded: 1960
Also book packager.
Subjects: Architecture & Interior Design, Eco-
    nomics, Education, Environmental Studies,
    Fiction, Film, Video, Government, Political
    Science, History, Library & Information Sci-
    ences, Music, Dance, Philosophy, Psychology,
    Psychiatry, Science (General), Social Sciences,
    Sociology, Technology
ISBN Prefix(es): 950-503

**Editorial Medica Panamericana SA+**
Marcelo T de Alvear 2145, 1122 Buenos Aires
*Tel:* (011) 4821-5520; (011) 4821-0175
    *Fax:* (011) 4821-1214
*E-mail:* info@medicapanamericana.com
*Web Site:* www.medicapanamericana.com.ar
*Key Personnel*
President: Hugo Brik
Founded: 1953
Subjects: Biological Sciences, Medicine, Nursing,
    Dentistry, Psychology, Psychiatry
ISBN Prefix(es): 950-06
*Branch Office(s)*
Carrera 7a A N° 69-19, Santa Fe de Bogota DC,
    Colombia
Alberto Alcocer 24, 28036 Madrid, Spain
Calzada de Tlalpan N°5022, Colonia La Joya,
    14090 Mexico DF, Mexico
Edificio Polar, Torre Oeste, Piso 6, Oficina 6-C,
    Plaza Venezuela, Urbanizacion Los Caobos,
    Parroquia El Recreo, Municipio Libertador,
    Distrito Federal, Venezuela

**Ediciones Medicas SA**
Cerrito 512 Piso 2, 1010 Buenos Aires

*Tel:* (011) 4384-0750 *Fax:* (011) 4384-0750
*E-mail:* emsa@havasmedimedia.com.ar
*Key Personnel*
Dir: Juan Jose Vallory
ISBN Prefix(es): 987-97055; 987-9492

**Ediciones Minotauro SA**
Independencia 1668, 1100 Ciudad Autonoma de
    Bs As
*Tel:* (011) 4382-4043; (011) 4382-4045
    *Fax:* (011) 4383-3793
*E-mail:* sansaldi@eplaneta.com.ar
*Web Site:* www.edicionesminotauro.com
Founded: 1955
Subjects: Fiction, Science Fiction, Fantasy
ISBN Prefix(es): 950-547
Number of titles published annually: 15 Print
Total Titles: 15 Print
*Parent Company:* Grupo Editorial Planeta SAIC
Distributed by Grupo Editorial Planeta
*Warehouse:* Interbook
*Distribution Center:* Interbook

**Instituto Nacional de Ciencia y Tecnica
    Hidrica (INCYTH)**
Empalme Ruta 205 KM 2.5, Lomas de Zamora,
    1832 Buenos Aires
*Tel:* (011) 4295-1503 *Fax:* (011) 4800094
*Key Personnel*
President: Dr Mario Rodolfo de Marco Naon
Subjects: Computer Science, Earth Sciences, Ge-
    ography, Geology, Law, Library & Information
    Sciences, Mathematics, Technology
ISBN Prefix(es): 950-634

**Instituto de Publicaciones Navales+**
Division of Centro Naval - Argentina
Cordoba 354, 1054 Buenos Aires
*Tel:* (011) 4311-0042; (011) 4311-0043
*E-mail:* ipn@web-mail.com.ar; ipn@fibertel.com.
    ar
*Web Site:* www.centronaval.org.ar
*Key Personnel*
President: Carlos Frasch
Manager: Jorge Bergallo
Founded: 1961
Specialize in strategy, naval history, international
    relations & maritime issues.
Membership(s): Argentina Book Association.
Subjects: Biography, Maritime, Military Science,
    Sports, Athletics, International Relations, Nar-
    rative, Nautical Sports, Sailing, Strategics
ISBN Prefix(es): 950-9016; 950-899
Number of titles published annually: 7 Print
Total Titles: 155 Print
Distributed by Tuskets Editores

**Editorial Norte SA+**
Jose Marmol 2131, 1255 Buenos Aires
*Tel:* (011) 4921-1440 *Fax:* (011) 4921-1440
*Key Personnel*
Dir General: Alejandro I Lamarque
Founded: 1961
Specializes in marketing.
Subjects: Education
ISBN Prefix(es): 950-27; 950-598

**Ediciones Nueva Vision SAIC+**
Tucuman 3748, 1189 Buenos Aires
*Tel:* (011) 4863-1461; (011) 4864-5050
    *Fax:* (011) 4863-5980
*E-mail:* ednuevavision@ciudad.com.ar
*Key Personnel*
Man Dir: Haydee P de Giacone
Sales Manager: Anibal Victor Giacone
Founded: 1954
Subjects: Architecture & Interior Design, Art,
    Drama, Theater, Psychology, Psychiatry, Social
    Sciences, Sociology
ISBN Prefix(es): 950-602

**Oikos+**
Rivadavia 1823, Piso 9, 1033 Buenos Aires
*Tel:* (011) 4951-9489; (011) 4951-8129
*E-mail:* postmaster@atlas.edu.ar
*Key Personnel*
President: Mario C Fuschini Mejia
Founded: 1975
Subjects: Earth Sciences, Geography, Geology,
   Social Sciences, Sociology
ISBN Prefix(es): 950-601
*Bookshop(s):* Hipolito Yrigoyen 1970, 1089
   Buenos Aires

**Editorial Paidos SAICF**
Defensa, 599, 1°, 1065 Buenos Aires
*Tel:* (011) 4331-2275 *Fax:* (011) 4343-0954
*E-mail:* direccion@editorialpaidos.com.ar
*Web Site:* www.paidosargentina.com.ar
*Key Personnel*
Man Dir, Rights & Permissions: Maria Gottheil
Founded: 1945
Subjects: Child Care & Development, Commu-
   nications, Education, Environmental Studies,
   Government, Political Science, Philosophy,
   Psychology, Psychiatry, Self-Help, Social Sci-
   ences, Sociology, Women's Studies
ISBN Prefix(es): 950-12
Subsidiaries: Ediciones Paidos Iberica SA (Mex-
   ico & Spain)

**Editora Patria Grande**
Rivadavia 6369, 1406 Buenos Aires
*Tel:* (011) 4631-6446
*Key Personnel*
General Manager, Rights & Permissions: Wash-
   ington Uranga
Editorial: Carlos J Duran
Sales: Elsa S de Fernandez
Production: Carlos D Arnedillo
Publicity: Duilio Lopez
Founded: 1974
Subjects: Poetry, Religion - Other
ISBN Prefix(es): 950-546
*Branch Office(s)*
Casilla de Correo 5, Suc 8, 1408 Buenos Aires
*Bookshop(s):* Libreria Didaje, Jose Cubas 3543,
   Buenos Aires

**Pearson Educacion de Argentina**
Avenida Regimiento Patricios 1959, 1266 Buenos
   Aires
*Tel:* (011) 4309 6100 *Fax:* (011) 4309 6199
*Web Site:* www.pearsoneducacion.net
*Key Personnel*
President - Southern Cone: Juan Carlos Cavin
Manager, Finance & Administration: Ernesto
   Merlo
Manager, Argentinean ELT/School: Diane Repetto
Publisher, Manager Professional/Trade: Guillermo
   Rivas
Publisher, Manager College: Esteban Lo Presti

**Editorial Planeta Argentina SAIC+**
Member of Grupo Planeta
Av Independencia 1668, 1100 Buenos Aires
*Tel:* (011) 4382-4045; (011) 4382-4043
   *Fax:* (011) 4383-3793
*E-mail:* info@eplaneta.com.ar; lpasiusis@planeta.
   com.ar
*Key Personnel*
Executive President: Julio Perez Vega
General Dir: Guillermo Schavelzon
Editorial Manager: Leandro de Sagastizabal
Editorial Manager: Ricardo Sabanes
Founded: 1983
Subjects: Biography, Environmental Studies, Fic-
   tion, Health, Nutrition, History, How-to, Lit-
   erature, Literary Criticism, Essays, Nonfiction
   (General), Parapsychology, Psychology, Psychi-
   atry, Religion - Other

ISBN Prefix(es): 950-742; 950-9216; 950-49
Subsidiaries: Ariel; Destino; Deusto; Espese
   Calpe; Montiuez Rica; Seix Barral; Teures de
   Teay

**Plaza & Janes**, see Editorial Argentina Plaza y
   Janes SA

**Editorial Pleamar**
Pena 3161, Piso 7 B, 1425 Buenos Aires
*Tel:* (011) 485-6597
*Key Personnel*
Man Dir: Andres Alfonso Bravo
Founded: 1965
Subjects: Government, Political Science, Social
   Sciences, Sociology
ISBN Prefix(es): 950-583

**Editorial Plus Ultra SA**
Callao 575, 1022 Buenos Aires
*Tel:* (011) 4374-2973; (011) 4374-5092
   *Fax:* (011) 4374-2973
*E-mail:* plus_ultra@epu.virtual.ar.net *Cable:*
   Plusultra
*Key Personnel*
President: Rafael Roman Picon
Man Dir: Lorenzo Marengo
Editorial: Carlos Alberto Loprete; Jose Isaacson
Sales: Ricardo Errea
Production: Renato Gardoni
Publicity: Lily Sosa de Newton
Founded: 1964
Subjects: Economics, Education, Government, Po-
   litical Science, History, Law, Literature, Liter-
   ary Criticism, Essays, Philosophy, Psychology,
   Psychiatry, Social Sciences, Sociology
ISBN Prefix(es): 950-21

**Editorial Polemos SA+**
Moreno 1785 5° piso, 1093 Buenos Aires
*Tel:* (011) 4383-5291 *Fax:* (011) 4382-4181
*E-mail:* editorial@polemos.com.ar
*Web Site:* www.polemos.com.ar
*Key Personnel*
President: Juan Carlos Stagnaro
Founded: 1990
Subjects: Behavioral Sciences, Medicine, Nurs-
   ing, Dentistry, Psychology, Psychiatry, Science
   (General), Social Sciences, Sociology, Psycho-
   analysis
ISBN Prefix(es): 987-9165; 987-99545

**Biblioteca Popular Judia**
Larrea 744, 1030 Buenos Aires
*Tel:* (011) 4961-4534 *Fax:* (011) 4963-7056
*E-mail:* cjl@mayo.com.ar *Cable:*
   WORLDGRESS BAIRES
*Key Personnel*
Editorial: Roberto Brzostowski; Pedro Olschansky
ISBN Prefix(es): 987-99868
*Parent Company:* Congreso Judio Latinoameri-
   cano

**Ediciones Preescolar SA+**
Argerich 1928, 1416 Buenos Aires
*Tel:* (011) 4581-3182 *Fax:* (011) 4581-3182
*Key Personnel*
Editorial: Juan Carlos Orgueira
Founded: 1971 (1984)
Incorporating Latina SA.
Subjects: Cookery, Education, Health, Nutrition,
   Sports, Athletics
ISBN Prefix(es): 950-9574

**Editorial Quetzal-Domingo Cortizo+**
Barragan 740, 1408 Buenos Aires
*Tel:* (011) 4641-5639
*E-mail:* profika@ciudad.com.ar
Founded: 1952

Subjects: Art, Biography, Drama, Theater, Litera-
   ture, Literary Criticism, Essays, Music, Dance,
   Poetry
ISBN Prefix(es): 950-590; 987-97723

**Ricordi Americana SAEC**
Tte Gral J D Peron 1558, Piso 2°, 1037 Buenos
   Aires
*Tel:* (011) 4371-9841; (011) 4371-9843
   *Fax:* (011) 4372-3459
*E-mail:* ricordi@sminter.com.ar
*Telex:* 1222580 for Ricordi *Cable:*
   Ricordamericana
*Key Personnel*
President, General Manager: Renzo Valcarenghi
Dir & Deputy Manager: Ernesto R Larcade
Marketing: Claudio Firmenich
Founded: 1924
Subjects: Education, Music, Dance
ISBN Prefix(es): 950-22
*Associate Companies:* Ricordi Brasileira S/A, Rua
   Conselheiro Nebias 1136, 01203 Sao Paulo SP,
   Brazil; G e C Ricordi SpA, Italy; G Ricordi &
   Co, Paseo de la Reforma 481-A, 06500 Mexico
   DF, Mexico

**Ediciones La Rocca+**
Talcahuano 467, 1013 Buenos Aires
*Tel:* (011) 4382 8526 *Fax:* (011) 4384 5774
*E-mail:* ed-larocca@sinectis.com
*Key Personnel*
Dir: Alfonso La Rocca
Founded: 1985
Subjects: Law
ISBN Prefix(es): 950-9714; 987-517

**San Pablo+**
Riobamba 230, 1025 Buenos Aires
*Tel:* (011) 5555-2400; (011) 555-2401 *Fax:* (011)
   5555-2425
*E-mail:* sobicain@san-pablo.com.ar
*Web Site:* www.san-pablo.com.ar
*Key Personnel*
Man Dir: P Arcangel Cadenas
Founded: 1931
Subjects: Biblical Studies, Education, Health, Nu-
   trition, Human Relations, Language Arts, Lin-
   guistics, Psychology, Psychiatry, Religion -
   Catholic, Self-Help, Theology
ISBN Prefix(es): 950-861
Distributed by Paulinas (Brazil); San Pablo
   (Brazil)
Distributor for San Pablo (Colombia, Chile,
   Spain)

**Editorial Santiago Rueda**
French 3016, 1425 Buenos Aires
*Tel:* (011) 4825-7337
*E-mail:* esantiruedaediciones@hotmail.com
*Key Personnel*
Man Dir: Enrique S Rueda
Founded: 1940
Subjects: Literature, Literary Criticism, Essays
ISBN Prefix(es): 950-564; 987-98745

**Seix Barral+**
Member of Grupo Planeta
Av da Independencia 1668, 1100 Buenos Aires
*Tel:* (011) 4382-4043; (011) 4382-4045; (011)
   4381-8285 *Fax:* (011) 4383-3793
*E-mail:* editorial@seix-barral.es
*Web Site:* www.seix-barral.es
*Key Personnel*
General Dir: Guillermo Schavelzon
Founded: 1950
Subjects: Literature, Literary Criticism, Essays
ISBN Prefix(es): 950-742; 950-9216; 950-49

**Sigmar**, *imprint of* Editorial Sigmar SACI

**Editorial Sigmar SACI+**
Av Belgrano 1580, 7 Piso, 1089 Buenos Aires
*Tel:* (011) 4381-2844; (011) 4381-2241
   *Fax:* (011) 4383-5633
*E-mail:* editorial@sigmar.com.ar
*Web Site:* www.sigmar.com.ar *Cable:* SIGMAR
*Key Personnel*
President & Man Dir: Robert G Chwat
   *E-mail:* rchwat@sigmar.com.ar
Founded: 1941
Membership(s): Argentina Book Association.
ISBN Prefix(es): 950-11
Number of titles published annually: 100 Print
Total Titles: 1,200 Print
Imprints: Sigmar
Distributor for Albatros (Argentina & Latin
   America)

**Editorial Sopena Argentina SACI e I**
Maza 2138/40, 1240 Buenos Aires
*Tel:* (011) 4912-2383 *Fax:* (011) 4912-2383
*E-mail:* edsopena@elsitio.net
*Key Personnel*
President: Roberto Omar Antonio
Dir: Marta A J Olsen; Leopoldo Costa Urruty
Manager: Hipolito Oscar Dhers
Subjects: Ethnicity, Government, Political Sci-
   ence, Health, Nutrition, History, How-to, Lan-
   guage Arts, Linguistics, Literature, Literary
   Criticism, Essays
ISBN Prefix(es): 950-542

**Editorial Stella**
Viamonte 1984, 1056 Buenos Aires
*Tel:* (011) 4374-0346 *Fax:* (011) 4374-8719
*E-mail:* admin@editorialstella.com.ar
*Web Site:* www.editorialstella.com.ar
Founded: 1941
Membership(s): Asociacion Educacionista Ar-
   gentina.
Subjects: Nonfiction (General)
ISBN Prefix(es): 950-525

**Editorial Sudamericana SA+**
Division of Random House-Mondadori
Humberto 1° 555, C1103ACK Buenos Aires
*Tel:* (011) 4300-5400 *Fax:* (011) 4362-7364
*E-mail:* info@edsudamericana.com.ar
*Web Site:* www.edsudamericana.com.ar *Cable:*
   LIBRECOL
*Key Personnel*
President: Javier Lopez Llovet
Editor: Gloria Lopez Llovet de Rodrigue
Sales Dir: Francisco La Falce
Publicity Dir: Ana Maria Muchnik
Rights & Permissions: Susana Kaluzynski
Founded: 1939
Subjects: Biography, Fiction, History, Literature,
   Literary Criticism, Essays, Nonfiction (Gen-
   eral), Philosophy, Psychology, Psychiatry
ISBN Prefix(es): 950-07; 950-37
*Parent Company:* Editorial Sudamericana
*Associate Companies:* Random House-Mondadori,
   Edificio del Comercio, Momjitas 392, Piso
   11 Of. 1101/1102, Comuna de Santiago,
   Chile *Tel:* (02) 782-8200 *Fax:* (02) 782-8210
   *E-mail:* sudchile@edsudamericana.com.ar;
   Editorial Sudamericana Uraguaya, Concep-
   cionArenal 1769, 11800 Montevideo, Uruguay
   *Tel:* (02) 203 3668 *Fax:* (02) 203 3668
Subsidiaries: Editorial Sudamericana Chilena

**Theoria SRL Distribuidora y Editora+**
Av Rivadavia 1255, Piso 4 407, 1033 Buenos
   Aires
*Tel:* (011) 4381-0131 *Fax:* (011) 4381-0131
*E-mail:* edicionestheoria@ciudad.com.ar
*Key Personnel*
Man Dir: Jorge O Orus
Sales Dir: Jose Luis Menendez
Founded: 1954

Subjects: Anthropology, Biography, Genealogy,
   Government, Political Science, History, Lit-
   erature, Literary Criticism, Essays, Military
   Science, Religion - Catholic
ISBN Prefix(es): 950-99711; 987-9048

**Tipografica Editora Argentina**
Lavalle 1430, Piso 1, 1048 Buenos Aires
*Tel:* (011) 4373-2581 *Fax:* (011) 4775-2521
*E-mail:* bernardosm@sinectis.com.ar
*Key Personnel*
President: Pedro G San Martin
Founded: 1946
Subjects: Anthropology, Archaeology, History,
   Law
ISBN Prefix(es): 950-521

**Instituto Torcuato Di Tella**
Minones 2177, Piso 1, 1428 Buenos Aires
*Tel:* (011) 4783-8680; (011) 4784-0084
   *Fax:* (011) 4783-3061
*E-mail:* postmaster@itdtar.edu.ar
*Web Site:* www.itdt.edu *Cable:* INSTELLA
   BAIRES
*Key Personnel*
President: Guido Di Tella
Founded: 1958
Subjects: Economics, Government, Political Sci-
   ence, History, Social Sciences, Sociology
ISBN Prefix(es): 950-621

**Editorial Troquel SA+**
Pichincha 969, 1219 Buenos Aires
*Tel:* (011) 4308-3638; (011) 4308-3637
   *Fax:* (011) 4941-3110
*E-mail:* info@troquel.com.ar
*Web Site:* www.troquel.com.ar *Cable:*
   TROQUELSA
*Key Personnel*
President: Gustavo Ressia
Founded: 1954
Subjects: Literature, Literary Criticism, Essays,
   Psychology, Psychiatry, Religion - Other, Tech-
   nology
ISBN Prefix(es): 950-16

**Editorial Universidad SRL+**
Rivadavia 1225, 1003 Buenos Aires
*Tel:* (011) 4382-9022; (011) 4382-6850
   *Fax:* (011) 4381-2005
*E-mail:* univers@nat.com.ar
*Web Site:* www.nat.com.ar/universidad
*Key Personnel*
Partner: Raul Caracciolo; Alejandro lo Iacono;
   Rafael del Buono
Founded: 1970
Membership(s): Camara Argentina del Libro.
Subjects: Economics, Law, Social Sciences, Soci-
   ology
ISBN Prefix(es): 950-679; 950-9072
*Branch Office(s)*
Facultad de Derecho, UBA
*Bookshop(s):* Talcahuano 487, 1013 Buenos Aires

**Universidad Nacional de la Patagonia**, see
   Editoria Universitaria de la Patagonia

**Editoria Universitaria de la Patagonia**
Ciudad Universitaria Rm 4, Comodoro Rivadavia,
   9000 Chubut
*Tel:* (02967) 428834; (02967) 424969
*E-mail:* rcesar@unpbib.edu.ar
*Key Personnel*
Dir: Romeo Cesar
Founded: 1993
Subjects: Agriculture, Biological Sciences, Fic-
   tion, Geography, Geology, History, Philosophy
ISBN Prefix(es): 950-763

**Javier Vergara Editor SA+**
Paseo Colon 221, Piso 6, 1399 Buenos Aires

*Tel:* (011) 4343-7510; (011) 4343-7706
   *Fax:* (011) 4334-0173
*E-mail:* ediciones-b-arg@ciudad.com.ar
*Key Personnel*
President: Javier Vergara
Vice President & Rights: Gabriela Cruz de Ver-
   gara
Editorial Dir: Trinidad Vergara
Sales Dir: Ricardo Bianchini
Publicity Manager: Marilen Stengel
Founded: 1975
Subjects: Biography, Business, Fiction, History,
   Music, Dance, Nonfiction (General), Psychol-
   ogy, Psychiatry, Self-Help
ISBN Prefix(es): 950-15
*Branch Office(s)*
Rancagua 549, Casilla Postale 10471, Santiago,
   Chile *Tel:* (02) 2049583 *Fax:* (02) 2096929
Carrera 53 A No 81-24, Bodega Entre Rios, Bo-
   gota, Colombia *Tel:* (01) 2507297 *Fax:* (01)
   2506005
Ctra Boadilla del Monte, KM 5800, Poligono In-
   dustrial Ventorro del Cano, 28925 Alcorcon,
   Madrid, Spain *Tel:* (01) 6332395 *Fax:* (01)
   6332312
Kansas 161, Col Ampliacion Napoles, Delegacion
   Benito Juarez, CP 03840 Mexico, DF, Mexico
   *Tel:* (05) 6829636 *Fax:* (05) 6829511
Edificio Yolanda Local Norte, Calle Madrid con
   Av Trieste, California Sur, Estado Miranda,
   Caracas, Venezuela *Tel:* (02) 228854 *Fax:* (02)
   228854
*Warehouse:* Vieytes 1534, 1275 Buenos Aires

**Manrique Zago Ediciones SRL**
Av San Martin 7210, 1419 Buenos Aires
*Tel:* (011) 4382-8880; (011) 4501-1497; (011)
   4383-2611 *Fax:* (011) 4502-7937
*E-mail:* mzago@lvd.com.ar
*Key Personnel*
Dir: Manrique Zago
Subjects: Art, Ethnicity
ISBN Prefix(es): 950-9517; 987-509

**Victor P de Zavalia SA+**
Alberti 835, 1223 Buenos Aires
*Tel:* (011) 942-1274; (011) 942-3046 *Fax:* (011)
   942-5706
*Key Personnel*
Man Dir: Victor H de Zavalia
Sales Dir: Ricardo L de Zavalia
Founded: 1950
Subjects: Law
ISBN Prefix(es): 950-572

**Editorial Zeus SRL+**
Balcarce 730, Rosario, 2000 Santa Fe
*Tel:* (0341) 449-5585 *Fax:* (0341) 425-4259
*E-mail:* editorialzeus@citynet.net.ar
*Web Site:* www.editorial-zeus.com.ar
*Key Personnel*
President & Editor: Gustavo Luis Caviglia
Founded: 1970
Subjects: Law
ISBN Prefix(es): 950-664
Imprints: Coleccion Juridica Bco de Datos en
   Computacion

# Armenia

## General Information

*Capital:* Yerevan
*Language:* Armenian (officially) and Kurdish
*Religion:* Predominantly Christian (Armenian
   Apostolic Church)
*Population:* 3.4 million
*Bank Hours:* Generally open for short hours be-
   tween 0930-1230 Monday-Friday

*Shop Hours:* Generally 0900-1800 Monday-Friday; often open weekends
*Currency:* 100 kopeks = 1 rubl
*Export/Import Information:* According to Ukrainian quotas and customs duties, companies engaged in trade should register with the Ukraine Ministry of Foreign Economic Relations. Licenses for export and import are also required for trade with Russia.

**Ajstan Publishers+**
Isaakjana 28, 37509 Erevan
*Tel:* (01) 528520
*Key Personnel*
Dir: D M Sarkissian
Editor in Chief: V K Sanbekian
Founded: 1921
Subjects: Agriculture, Government, Political Science, Law, Literature, Literary Criticism, Essays, Military Science, Science (General)
ISBN Prefix(es): 5-540

**Arevik** (Little Sun)+
Terjan Str 91, 375009 Erevan
*Tel:* (02) 524561 *Fax:* (02) 520536
*E-mail:* arevikp@freenet.am; arevick@netsys.am
*Web Site:* www.arevik.am
*Key Personnel*
President: David Hovhannes
Founded: 1986
Membership(s): Armenian Publishers' Association.
Subjects: Chemistry, Chemical Engineering, Crafts, Games, Hobbies, Education, English as a Second Language, Fiction, Gardening, Plants, Geography, Geology, History, Humor, Language Arts, Linguistics, Mathematics, Natural History, Poetry, Science Fiction, Fantasy
ISBN Prefix(es): 5-8077
Number of titles published annually: 28 Print
Total Titles: 2,000 Print

# Australia

## General Information

*Capital:* Canberra
*Language:* English
*Religion:* Predominantly Christian
*Population:* 17.6 million
*Bank Hours:* 1000-1500 Monday-Thursday; 1000-1700 Friday
*Shop Hours:* 0900-1700 Monday-Saturday
*Currency:* 100 cents = 1 Australian dollar
*Export/Import Information:* No tariffs on books. Most books, especially of literary or educational nature, free of sales tax. No import licenses for books; no seditious literature permitted.
*Copyright:* UCC, Berne (see Copyright Conventions, pg xi)

**ABC Books (Australian Broadcasting Corporation)+**
GPO Box 9994, Sydney, NSW 2001
*Tel:* (02) 8333 3959 *Fax:* (02) 8333 3999
*E-mail:* abcbooks@abc.net.au
*Web Site:* abcshop.com.au
*Key Personnel*
General Manager: Grahame Grassby
Publisher: Stuart Neal *E-mail:* neal.stuart@abc.net.au
Subjects: Fiction, Nonfiction (General)
ISBN Prefix(es): 0-7333
Number of titles published annually: 95 Print; 50 Audio
*Parent Company:* ABC Enterprises

*Ultimate Parent Company:* Australian Broadcasting Corporation
Distributed by Allen & Unwin Pty Ltd
*Orders to:* Allen & Unwin Pty Ltd, 83 Alexander St, Crows Nest, NSW 2065, Liz Bray
*Tel:* (02) 8425 0100 *Fax:* (02) 9906 2218
*E-mail:* frontdesk@allen-unwin.net.au

**Aboriginal Studies Press**
Lawson Crescent, Acton, Canberra, ACT 2601
*Tel:* (02) 6246 1183 *Fax:* (02) 6261 4285
*E-mail:* sales@aiatsis.gov.au
*Web Site:* www.aiatsis.gov.au
*Key Personnel*
Principal: Steve Larkin
Dir: Rhonda Black *E-mail:* rhonda.black@aiatsis.gov.au
Deputy Dir: Gabby Lhuede *E-mail:* gabby.lhuede@aiatsis.gov.au
Subjects: Anthropology, Archaeology, Art, Biography, Education, Health, Nutrition, History, Language Arts, Linguistics, Music, Dance, Regional Interests, Social Sciences, Sociology, Women's Studies, Cultural Studies, Native Title/Land Rights
ISBN Prefix(es): 0-85575
Number of titles published annually: 10 Print; 1 CD-ROM
Total Titles: 120 Print; 4 CD-ROM
*Parent Company:* Australian Institute of Aboriginal & Torres Strait Islander Studies, GPO Box 553, Canberra, ACT 2601

**Academic Press**, *imprint of* Elsevier Australia

**Access Press**, *imprint of* Access Press

**Access Press+**
PO Box 132, Northbridge, WA 6865
*Tel:* (08) 9328 9188 *Fax:* (08) 9379 3199
*Key Personnel*
Publicity & Rights & Permission: John Harper-Nelson
Founded: 1978
Standard publishing contract but also specialize in small print runs privately funded.
Subjects: Biography, Genealogy, History, Literature, Literary Criticism, Essays, Nonfiction (General), Poetry
ISBN Prefix(es): 0-949795
Number of titles published annually: 14 Print
Total Titles: 90 Print
*Parent Company:* Reeve Pty Ltd as trustee for Reeve Unit Trust
*Ultimate Parent Company:* Reeve Etc
Imprints: Access Press

**ACER Press+**
347 Camberwell Rd, Camberwell, Victoria 3124
Mailing Address: 19 Prospect Hill Rd, Private Bag 55, Camberwell, Victoria 3124
*Tel:* (03) 9277 5555; (03) 9835 7447 (customer service) *Toll Free Tel:* (800) 338 402 (customer service) *Fax:* (03) 9277 5500; (02) 9835 7499 (customer service)
*E-mail:* sales@acer.edu.au
*Web Site:* www.acer.edu.au
*Key Personnel*
Publishing Manager: Anne Peterson *Tel:* (03) 9835 7461
Founded: 1930
Subjects: Education, Human Relations, Psychology, Psychiatry, Parenting
ISBN Prefix(es): 0-86431; 0-85563

**ACHPER Inc (Australian Council for Health, Physical Education & Recreation)**
214 Port Rd, Hindmarsh, SA 5007
Mailing Address: PO Box 304, Hindmarsh, SA 5007
*Tel:* (08) 8340 3388 *Fax:* (08) 8340 3399

*E-mail:* achper@achper.org.au
*Web Site:* www.achper.org.au
*Key Personnel*
Executive Dir: Jeff Emmel
National President: Dr Colvin
National Vice President: Ms Sheehan
Contact: Felicity Vanderheul
*E-mail:* membership@achper.org.au
Founded: 1955
Specialize in Community Fitness & Movement Sciences, Dance, Health Education, Physical Education, Recreation, Sports.
Subjects: Education, Sports, Athletics
ISBN Prefix(es): 0-909120; 0-9595612; 1-86352
*Branch Office(s)*
73 Wakefield St, 1st floor, Adelaide, SA 5000, Matt Schmidt *E-mail:* info@achpersa.com.au
PO Box 57, Claremont, WA 6010, Denyse Passmore *E-mail:* denyse@achperwa.asn.au
PO Box 84, Croydon, NSW 2132, Julie Percival *E-mail:* achperns@ozemail.com.au
PO Box 789, Jamieson, ACT 2614, Jodie Sindeberry *E-mail:* ihellyer@dynoamite.com.au
C1-117 Canning St, Launceston, Tas 7250, Peter Daniel
GPO BOX 412C, Melbourne, Victoria 3001, Mary Wilson *E-mail:* achvic@unite.com.au
PO Box 8141, Woolloongabba, Qld 4102, Jill Duffield *E-mail:* achqld@ecn.net.au
*Bookshop(s):* Achper Healthy Lifestyles Bookshop, Emma Price *E-mail:* bookshop@achper.org.au

**Acorn Press**, *imprint of* Rainbow Book Agencies Pty Ltd

**ACP Publishing Pty Ltd+**
54-58 Park St, Sydney, NSW 2001
*Tel:* (02) 9282 8000 *Fax:* (02) 9267 4361
*Key Personnel*
Publisher: Richard Walsh
Subjects: Cookery
ISBN Prefix(es): 0-949892; 1-86396; 0-949128; 0-9598059
*Parent Company:* Australian Consolidated Press
Imprints: The Australian Women's Weekly; Home Library
*Branch Office(s)*
Arnoul Media Services Pty Ltd, 45 Ward St, North Adelaide, SA 5006 *Tel:* (08) 8361 9999 *Fax:* (08) 8361 9990
Bowengate Office Park, 2nd floor, Corner Bowen Bridge Rd & Campbell St, Bowen Hills, Qld 4006 *Tel:* (07) 3000 8500 *Fax:* (07) 3000 8555
73 Atherton Rd, Oakleigh, Victoria 3166 *Tel:* (03) 9567 4200 *Fax:* (03) 9563 4554
102-108 Toorak Rd, South Yarra, Victoria 3141 *Tel:* (03) 9823 6333 *Fax:* (03) 9823 6300
Foreign Rep(s): Melanie Franklin (Asia, Europe, The Pacific, US); Christian Hyland (Asia, Europe, The Pacific, US); Michael Sport (Asia, Europe, The Pacific, US)

**Addison Wesley**, *imprint of* Pearson Education Australia

**The Advancement Centre**
9 Brett Ave, Wentworthville, NSW 2145
*Tel:* (02) 9896 2311 *Fax:* (02) 9368 323
Subjects: Education, Psychology, Psychiatry
ISBN Prefix(es): 0-9586212
Distributed by University of NSW

**Aeolian Press**
PO Box 303, Claremont, WA 6010
*Tel:* (08) 9761 2772 *Fax:* (08) 9761 4151
Founded: 1985
Subjects: Art, Poetry, Australian Art, Italian Classic Text & Illustration
ISBN Prefix(es): 1-875306
Distributor for Edizioni Tallone (Australia); Edizioni Valdonega (Australia)

**Aerospace Publications Pty Ltd**
PO Box 1777, Fyshwick, ACT 2609
*Tel:* (02) 6280 0111 *Fax:* (02) 6280 0007
*E-mail:* mail@ausaviation.com.au
*Web Site:* www.ausaviation.com.au
Subjects: Aeronautics, Aviation
ISBN Prefix(es): 0-9587978; 1-875671

**AHB Publications+**
24/14 Lansell Rd, Toorak, Victoria 3142
Subjects: Foreign Countries
Distributor for Random House (Australia)

**AIFS**, see Australian Institute of Family Studies
(AIFS)

**Aletheia Publishing**
18 Willow St, Albany Creek, Qld 4035
*Tel:* (07) 3855 2056
*E-mail:* aletheia@powerup.com.au
*Key Personnel*
Contact: David Holden
Founded: 1992
Subjects: Biblical Studies, History, Religion -
   Protestant, Religion - Other, Theology
ISBN Prefix(es): 0-9587113; 0-9578052
Total Titles: 3 Print

**Allen & Unwin Pty Ltd+**
83 Alexander St, Crows Nest, NSW 2065
Mailing Address: PO Box 8500, St Leonards,
   NSW 1590
*Tel:* (02) 8425 0100 *Fax:* (02) 9906 2218
*E-mail:* frontdesk@allenandunwin.com
*Web Site:* www.allenandunwin.com
*Key Personnel*
Man & Publishing Dir: Patrick Gallagher
Sales & Marketing Dir: Paul Donovan
Rights & Export Manager: Angela Namoi
Head of Publicity: Andrew Hawkins
Finance & Distribution Dir: Peter Eichorn
National Sales Manager: Lou Johnson
Children's Publishing Dir: Rosalind Price
Academic Publisher: Elizabeth Weiss
Academic & Professional Marketing Manager:
   Carolyn Crowther
Founded: 1976
Membership(s): Australian Publishers Associa-
   tion (APA); Publish Australia (PA); Australian
   Multimedia Industry Association (AMIA).
Subjects: Alternative, Art, Asian Studies, Be-
   havioral Sciences, Business, Cookery, Earth
   Sciences, Economics, Education, Ethnicity,
   Fiction, Gay & Lesbian, Government, Politi-
   cal Science, Health, Nutrition, History, Labor,
   Industrial Relations, Literature, Literary Crit-
   icism, Essays, Nonfiction (General), Science
   (General)
ISBN Prefix(es): 1-86448; 1-86508; 1-74114
Number of titles published annually: 250 Print
Subsidiaries: Osborne House
*Branch Office(s)*
406 Albert St, East Melbourne, Victoria
One John St, Kingswood, Adelaide, SA
One Park Rd, Milton, Brisbane 4064
Distributor for Osborne House
*Warehouse:* ADS, PO Box 520, 9 Pioneer Ave,
   Tuggerah, NSW 2259 *Tel:* (02) 43901300
   *Fax:* (02) 43901333
*Orders to:* ADS, PO Box 520, 9 Pioneer Ave,
   Tuggerah, NSW 2259 *Tel:* (02) 43901300
   *Fax:* (02) 43901333

**AMCS**, see Australian Marine Conservation
   Society Inc (AMCS)

**AMPCO**, see Australasian Medical Publishing
   Company Ltd (AMPCO)

**Anchor**, *imprint of* Random House Australia

**Anchor**, *imprint of* Transworld Publishers Pty Ltd

**Robert Andersen & Associates Pty Ltd+**
433 Wellington St, Clifton Hill, Melbourne, Vic-
   toria 3068
*Tel:* (03) 9489 3968 *Fax:* (03) 9482 2416
*E-mail:* 100357.354@compuserve.com
*Key Personnel*
Man Dir: Bob Andersen
Subjects: Education
ISBN Prefix(es): 0-949133

**Anderson**, *imprint of* Random House Australia

**Michelle Anderson Publishing+**
PO Box 6032, Chapel St N, South Yarra, Victoria
   3141
*Tel:* (03) 9826 9028 *Fax:* (03) 9826 8552
*E-mail:* mapubl@bigpond.net.au
*Web Site:* www.michelleandersonpublishing.com
*Key Personnel*
Publisher, Rights & Permissions: Michelle Ander-
   son
Founded: 1965
Membership(s): Australian Publishers Associa-
   tion.
Subjects: Health, Nutrition, Philosophy, Psychol-
   ogy, Psychiatry, Babies & Motherhood, Bush-
   walking, Cycling
ISBN Prefix(es): 0-85572
Number of titles published annually: 15 Print
Total Titles: 70 Print
Distributed by Bookwise International (Australia);
   Deep Books UK (UK); Peter Hyde & Asso-
   ciates (South Africa)
Foreign Rep(s): Choicemaker (Korea); Prava:
   Provida (Russia); Lennart Sane (Sweden)
Foreign Rights: Thomas Schluck (Germany); Su-
   san Schulman (US)
*Warehouse:* Matrae P/L, 568 Geelong Rd, West
   Footscray, Melbourne, Victoria

**Angel Publications**
5 Lithgow St, Goulburn, NSW 2580
*Tel:* (02) 4821 1463
*Key Personnel*
Contact: Steven Shackel *E-mail:* shack@goulburn.
   net.au
Founded: 1982
Subjects: Astrology, Occult, Fiction, Parapsychol-
   ogy, Philosophy, Self-Help
ISBN Prefix(es): 0-9593419

**Ansay Pty Ltd+**
PO Box 90, Leichhardt, NSW 2040
*Tel:* (02) 95602044 *Fax:* (02) 95694585
*Key Personnel*
Man Dir: Philip Lindsay
Editorial, Production & Publicity: H E Lindsay
Sales, Rights & Permissions: P S Lindsay
Founded: 1972
Subjects: Education, Fiction
ISBN Prefix(es): 0-909245
*Parent Company:* A L Lindsay & Co Pty Ltd
Imprints: Dollar Books

**Anzea Publishers Ltd+**
3-5 Richmond Rd, Homebush West, NSW 2140
*Tel:* (02) 7631211 *Fax:* (02) 7643201
*Key Personnel*
Head of Company: Jeffrey Blair
Subjects: Religion - Other
ISBN Prefix(es): 0-85892
Imprints: Lancer; Scripture Union
Divisions: Boronia Book Agencies; Emu Book
   Agencies; Waverley House

**APACE**, see Appropriate Technology
   Development Group (Inc) WA

**APACE Aid Inc**, *imprint of* Appropriate
   Technology Development Group (Inc) WA

**Appropriate Technology Development Group**
   **(Inc) WA**
One Johannah St, North Fremantle, WA 6159
*Tel:* (08) 9336 1262 *Fax:* (08) 9430 5729
*E-mail:* apace@argo.net.au
*Web Site:* www.argo.net.au/apace
*Key Personnel*
President: Richard Cooke
Coordinator: Tony Freeman
Founded: 1983
Not for profit community group - environmental.
Subjects: Alternative, Environmental Studies,
   Technology, Appropriate Technology, Bush
   Regeneration, Revegetation
ISBN Prefix(es): 0-9590309
Number of titles published annually: 5 Print
*Associate Companies:* Apace Aid Inc
Imprints: APACE Aid Inc

**Aquila Press**
Anglican Youthworks, Level 2, St Andrews
   House, 464 Kent St, Sydney South, NSW 1235
Mailing Address: PO Box A287, Sydney South,
   NSW 2000
*Tel:* (02) 8268 3333 *Fax:* (02) 8268 3357
*E-mail:* sales@youthworks.asn.au
*Web Site:* www.youthworks.net.au
*Key Personnel*
Chief Executive Officer: Alan Stewart
Founded: 1994
Subjects: Biblical Studies, Religion - Protestant
ISBN Prefix(es): 1-875861
*Parent Company:* Anglican Press Australia
Imprints: Christian Education Publications

**Arcadia**, *imprint of* Australian Scholarly
   Publishing

**Argyle-Pacific**, *imprint of* Austed Publishing Co

**Edward Arnold (Australia) Pty Ltd+**
12 Strathalbyn St, Kew East, Victoria 3102
Mailing Address: PO Box 885, Kew, Victoria
   3101
*Tel:* (03) 9859 9011 *Fax:* (03) 9859 9141
*Key Personnel*
Man Dir: Malcolm Edwards
General Manager: R Bartlett
Publishing: Anita Ray
Production: Jane Hazell
Marketing: Penny Doust
Tertiary: Louise Cook
Founded: 1966
Acts as agent for Edward Arnold (UK), Taylor &
   Francis & Blackie & Sons (secondary only).
Membership(s): Australian Book Publishers Asso-
   ciation.
Subjects: Accounting, Asian Studies, Behavioral
   Sciences, Career Development, Computer Sci-
   ence, Cookery, Geography, Geology, Govern-
   ment, Political Science, Health, Nutrition, Law,
   Mathematics, Nonfiction (General), Psychology,
   Psychiatry, Technology
ISBN Prefix(es): 0-7131; 0-7267
*Parent Company:* Hodder & Stoughton (Australia)
   Pty Ltd
*Ultimate Parent Company:* Hodder & Stoughton
   Ltd, United Kingdom
*Warehouse:* Hodder & Stoughton Pty Ltd, 10-16
   South St, Rydalmere, NSW 2116
*Orders to:* Hodder & Stoughton (Australia) Pty
   Ltd, PO Box 386, Rydalmere, NSW 2116

**Arrow**, *imprint of* Random House Australia

**Art Gallery of South Australia Bookshop**
North Terrace, Adelaide, SA 5000
*Tel:* (08) 8207 7029 *Fax:* (08) 8207 7069

*E-mail:* agsa.bookshop@saugov.sa.gov.au
*Web Site:* www.artgallery.sa.gov.au
*Key Personnel*
Head of Company: Ron Radford
Bookshop Manager: Letitia Ashworth
   *E-mail:* ashworth.letitia@saugov.sa.gov.au
Subjects: Art
ISBN Prefix(es): 0-7308

**Art Gallery of Western Australia+**
Perth Cultural Centre, 47 James St, Perth, WA
   6000
Mailing Address: Perth Business Centre, PO Box
   8363, Perth, WA 6849
*Tel:* (08) 9492 6600 *Fax:* (08) 9492 6655
*E-mail:* admin@artgallery.wa.gov.au
*Web Site:* www.artgallery.wa.gov.au
*Key Personnel*
Dir: Alan R Dodge
Chief Curator: Gary Dufour
Dir, Strategic & Commercial Programs: Keith
   Lord
Manager Information Services: Joyce Carter
   *Tel:* (08) 9492 6622
Founded: 1895
Exhibition catalogues.
Subjects: Art
ISBN Prefix(es): 0-7309; 0-7244; 0-7307
Total Titles: 22 Print

**Art on the Move**
GPO Box M937, Perth, WA 6000
*Tel:* (08) 9227 7505 *Fax:* (08) 9227 5304
*E-mail:* artmoves@highwayl.com.au
*Key Personnel*
Dir: Paul Thompson
Founded: 1996
Subjects: Architecture & Interior Design, Art,
   Marketing
ISBN Prefix(es): 0-9585326; 0-9578242; 0-
   9581859

**Artemis Publishing**, *imprint of* Rainbow Book
   Agencies Pty Ltd

**Artmoves Inc+**
27 Burwood Ave, Hawthorn East, Victoria 3123
*Tel:* (03) 9882 8116 *Fax:* (03) 9882 8162
*E-mail:* artmoves@bigpond.com
*Key Personnel*
Contact: Helen Vivian
Founded: 1987
Subjects: Art, History, Women's Studies
ISBN Prefix(es): 0-646

**Ashling Books+**
26 Hewlett Court, Florey, ACT 2615
*Tel:* (02) 6259 1027
*Key Personnel*
Man Dir & International Rights: Edward J
   Murtagh
Founded: 1992
Subjects: Fiction, How-to, Poetry, Religion -
   Catholic, Self-Help
ISBN Prefix(es): 0-9585244

**Ashton Egan**, *imprint of* Egan Publishing Pty Ltd

**Ashwood House**, *imprint of* Dellasta Publishing
   Pty Ltd

**Ashwood House Medical**, *imprint of* Dellasta
   Publishing Pty Ltd

**Ausinfo**, see Australian Government Information
   Management Office

**Auslib Press Pty Ltd+**
PO Box 622, Blackwood, SA 5051

*Tel:* (08) 8278 4363 *Fax:* (08) 8278 4000
*E-mail:* info@auslib.com.au
*Web Site:* www.auslib.com.au
*Key Personnel*
Man Dir: Judith Bundy
Editorial & Sales Manager: Dr Alan Bundy
Founded: 1984
Specialize in Library & Information Science Ti-
   tles, Information Literacy Titles, Literary Di-
   rectories, Mailing Labels for Australian & New
   Zealand Libraries.
Subjects: Education, Library & Information Sci-
   ences
ISBN Prefix(es): 1-875145; 0-9589895
Number of titles published annually: 4 Print
Total Titles: 47 Print

**Ausmed Publications Pty Ltd+**
275-277 Mt Alexander Rd, Ascot Vale, Victoria
   3032
*Tel:* (03) 9375 7311 *Fax:* (03) 9375 7299
*E-mail:* ausmed@ausmed.com.au
*Web Site:* www.ausmed.com.au
*Key Personnel*
Head of Company & Dir: Cynthea Wellings
   *E-mail:* cwelling@ausmed.com.au
General Manager: Natalie Angove
   *E-mail:* nangove@ausmed.com.au
Man Editor: Bernadette Keane *E-mail:* bkeane@
   ausmed.com.au
Founded: 1987
Specialize in books & conferences for nurses &
   other workers in related health fields.
Subjects: Behavioral Sciences, Ethnicity, Health,
   Nutrition, Medicine, Nursing, Dentistry, Social
   Sciences, Sociology, Allied Health, Clinical
   Issues
ISBN Prefix(es): 0-9587113; 0-646; 0-9587171;
   0-9577988; 0-9750445; 0-9579876
Total Titles: 24 Print

**Aussie Books**
Unit 6, 30 Lensworth St, Coopers Plains, Qld
   4108
Mailing Address: PO Box 383, Archerfield, Qld
   4108
*Tel:* (07) 3345 4253 *Fax:* (07) 3344 1582
*E-mail:* sildale@yahoo.com
*Web Site:* www.treasureenterprises.com
*Key Personnel*
Dir: David A Cooper
Founded: 1977
Supplier of Detection & Treasure Hunting Equip-
   ment.
Subjects: Earth Sciences, Geography, Geology,
   History
ISBN Prefix(es): 0-947336
*Parent Company:* Sildale Pty Ltd
Distributor for Hesperian Press

**Aussies Afire Publishing**
PO Box 954, Port Macquarie, NSW 2444
*Tel:* (02) 6581 0654 *Fax:* (02) 6581 0745
*Web Site:* www.gracechurchpm.org.au
*Key Personnel*
Head of Company: Kerry Medway
   *E-mail:* kerry@gracechurchpm.org.au
Founded: 1989
Subjects: Humor, Regional Interests, Religion -
   Protestant
ISBN Prefix(es): 0-646
Number of titles published annually: 1 Print
Total Titles: 5 Print

**Austed Publishing Co+**
PO Box 8025, Subiaco East, WA 6008
*Tel:* (08) 9203 6044 *Fax:* (08) 9203 6055
*E-mail:* net@austed.com.au
*Web Site:* www.austed.com.au
*Key Personnel*
Man Dir: W B R Banks

Head of Company: K Chesson *E-mail:* kc@
   austed.com.au
Founded: 1983
Subjects: Accounting, Animals, Pets, Education,
   Fiction, Mathematics
ISBN Prefix(es): 1-86307; 0-9592597
Imprints: Argyle-Pacific; Churchill House

**Australasian Medical Publishing Company Ltd
   (AMPCO)+**
26-32 Pyrmont Bridge Rd, Level 2, Pyrmont,
   NSW 2009
Mailing Address: Locked Bag 3030, Strawberry
   Hills, NSW 2012
*Tel:* (02) 9562 6666 *Fax:* (02) 9562 6699
*E-mail:* medjaust@ampco.com.au
*Web Site:* www.mja.com.au
*Key Personnel*
Chief Executive: Dr Martin Van Der Weyden
Advertising Manager: Peter Butterfield
Media Coordinator: Stephanie Elliott
Founded: 1913
Publisher of *The Medical Journal of Australia* &
   *Medical Directory of Australia.*
Distributor of medical publications.
Membership(s): ABP, commercial & publishing
   arm of the Australian Medical Association.
Subjects: History, Medicine, Nursing, Dentistry
ISBN Prefix(es): 0-85557
*Parent Company:* Australian Medical Association
   Limited

**Australasian Textiles & Fashion Publishers**
19-21 Broadbeach Rd, Jan Juc, Victoria 3228
Mailing Address: PO Box 286, Belmont, Victoria
   3216
*Tel:* (03) 5261 3966 *Fax:* (03) 5261 6950
*Web Site:* www.atfmag.com
*Key Personnel*
Publisher: Rosemary Boston *E-mail:* roseboston@
   atfmag.com
Dir: Stan Boston *E-mail:* sboston@atfmag.com
Managing Editor: James Boston
Associate Editor: Jack Finlay *E-mail:* jfinlay@
   atfmag.com
Subjects: Fashion, Textiles
ISBN Prefix(es): 0-9590875

**Australian Academic Press Pty Ltd+**
32 Jeays St, Bowen Hills, Qld 4006
*Tel:* (07) 3257 1176 *Fax:* (07) 3252 5908
*E-mail:* info@australianacademicpress.com.au
*Web Site:* www.australianacademicpress.com.au
*Key Personnel*
Man Dir: Stephen May
Founded: 1987
Specialize in book production; also acts as book
   packager. Independent publisher for the behav-
   ioral sciences.
Subjects: Behavioral Sciences, Psychology, Psy-
   chiatry
ISBN Prefix(es): 1-875378

**Australian Academy of Science**
Ian Potter House, Gordon St, Canberra, ACT
   2601
Mailing Address: GPO Box 783, Canberra, ACT
   2601
*Tel:* (02) 6247 5777 *Fax:* (02) 6257 4620
*E-mail:* eb@science.org.au; aas@science.org.au
*Web Site:* www.science.org.au
*Key Personnel*
Publications: Maureen Swanage *E-mail:* maureen.
   swanage@science.org.au
Founded: 1956
Subjects: Biological Sciences, Chemistry, Chemi-
   cal Engineering, Environmental Studies, Geog-
   raphy, Geology, Mathematics
ISBN Prefix(es): 0-85847

**Australian Association for the Study of
   Religion**, *imprint of* Rainbow Book Agencies
   Pty Ltd

**Australian Broadcasting Authority**
Darling Park, Level 15, 201 Sussex St, Sydney, NSW 2000
Mailing Address: PO Box Q500, Queen Victoria Bldg, Sydney, NSW 1230
*Tel:* (02) 9344 7700 *Toll Free Tel:* 800 22 6667 (Australia only) *Fax:* (02) 9334 7799
*E-mail:* info@aba.gov.au
*Web Site:* www.aba.gov.au
*Key Personnel*
Chairman: Prof David Flint
Publisher: Anne Hewer
Manager Media & Public Relations: Donald Robertson
Founded: 1992
Subjects: Communications, Broadcasting
ISBN Prefix(es): 0-642
*Branch Office(s)*
Blue Bldg, Benjamin Offices, Chan St, Belconnen, Canberra, ACT 2617 *Tel:* (02) 6256 2800 *Fax:* (02) 6253 3277

**Australian Broadcasting Corporation**, see ABC Books (Australian Broadcasting Corporation)

**Australian Chart Book Pty Ltd**
PO Box 148, Turramurra, NSW 2074
*Tel:* (02) 9489 4786 *Fax:* (02) 9487 2089
*Web Site:* www.austchartbook.com.au
*Key Personnel*
Contact: David Kent *E-mail:* davidkent@austchartbook.com.au
Founded: 1970
ISBN Prefix(es): 0-646

**Australian Council for Education Research**, see ACER Press

**Australian Film Television & Radio School**
Corner Epping & Balaclava Roads, North Ryde, NSW 2113
Mailing Address: PO Box 126, North Ryde, NSW 1670
*Tel:* (02) 9805 6611 *Fax:* (02) 9805 1275
*E-mail:* info_nsw@aftrs.edu.au
*Web Site:* www.aftrs.edu.au
*Key Personnel*
Publisher & Training Officer: Meredith Quinn *E-mail:* meredith.quinn@syd.aftrs.edu.au
Founded: 1973
Subjects: Film, Video, Radio, TV
ISBN Prefix(es): 1-876351
*Branch Office(s)*
5 Trumpeter St, Battery Point, Tas 7004, Representative: Craig Kirkwood *Tel:* (03) 6223 8703 *Fax:* (03) 6224 6143 *E-mail:* info_tas@aftrs.edu.au
Judith Wright Centre of Contemporary Arts, Centre Brunswick & Berwick St, Level 2, PO Box 1480, Fortitude Valley, Qld 4006, Manager: Alex Daw *Tel:* (07) 3257 7646 *Fax:* (07) 3257 7641 *E-mail:* info_qld@aftrs.edu.au
92 Adelaide St, Fremantle, WA 6160, Tom Lubin *Tel:* (08) 9335 1055 *Fax:* (08) 9335 1283 *E-mail:* info_wa@aftrs.edu.au
SAFS Studios, 3 Butler Dr, Hendon, SA 5014, Representative: Ann Walton *Tel:* (08) 8244 0357 *Fax:* (08) 8244 5608 *E-mail:* info_sa@aftrs.edu.au
144 Moray St, 1st floor, PO Box 1008, South Melbourne, Victoria 3205, Manager: Simon Britton *Tel:* (03) 9690 7111 *Fax:* (03) 9690 1283 *E-mail:* info_vic@aftrs.edu.au
Distributed by Allen & Unwin

**Australian Government Information Management Office**
Formerly Ausinfo
Dept of Finance & Administration, John Gorton Bldg, King Edward Terrace, Parkes, ACT 2600
*Tel:* (02) 6215 2222 *Fax:* (02) 6215 1609

*Web Site:* www.agimo.gov.au/information/publishing
*Key Personnel*
Chief Information Officer: Ann Steward
Division Manager: Patrick Callioni
Founded: 1970
ISBN Prefix(es): 0-642; 0-644

**Australian Institute of Criminology**
74 Leichhardt St, Griffith, ACT 2603
Mailing Address: GPO Box 2944, Caberra, ACT 2601
*Tel:* (02) 6260 9200 *Fax:* (02) 6260 9201
*E-mail:* aicpress@aic.gov.au
*Web Site:* www.aic.gov.au
*Key Personnel*
Acting Dir: Dr Toni Makkai *Tel:* (02) 6260 9205 *E-mail:* toni.makkai@aic.gov.au
Executive Officer, Research: Leanne Huddy *Tel:* (02) 6260 9255 *E-mail:* leanne.huddy@aic.gov.au
Founded: 1976
Subjects: Criminology
ISBN Prefix(es): 0-642
*U.S. Office(s):* Criminal Justice Press, PO Box 249, Monsey, NY 10952, United States
*Orders to:* CanPrint Information Services, PO Box 7456, Canberra MC, ACT 2610 *Toll Free Tel:* 300 889 873 *Fax:* (02) 6293 8333 *E-mail:* sales@infoservices.com.au

**Australian Institute of Family Studies (AIFS)**
300 Queen St, Melbourne, Victoria 3000
*Tel:* (03) 9214 7888 *Fax:* (03) 9214 7839
*E-mail:* publications@aifs.org.au
*Web Site:* www.aifs.org.au
*Key Personnel*
Marketing Manager: Catherine Rosenbrock *Tel:* (03) 9214 7804 *E-mail:* cathr@aifs.org.au
Founded: 1980
Undertake research & factors affecting family stability & well-being; Australian government statutory authority.
Subjects: Behavioral Sciences, Criminology, Disability, Special Needs, Economics, Human Relations, Social Sciences, Sociology, Women's Studies
ISBN Prefix(es): 0-642; 1-876513
Number of titles published annually: 3 Print; 1 CD-ROM
Total Titles: 12 Print; 4 CD-ROM

**Australian Marine Conservation Society Inc (AMCS)**
PO Box 3139, Yeronga, Qld 4104
*Tel:* (07) 3848 5235 *Toll Free Tel:* 800 066 299 *Fax:* (07) 3892 5814
*E-mail:* amcs@amcs.org.au
*Web Site:* www.amcs.org.au
*Key Personnel*
Dir: E J Hegerl
National Coordinator: Kate Davey *E-mail:* katedavey@amcs.org.au
Subjects: Biological Sciences, Earth Sciences, Environmental Studies, Geography, Geology, Maritime, Natural History
*Branch Office(s)*
c/o Conservation Council of South Australia, 120 Wakefield St, Adelaide, SA 5000, Contact: John Emmett *Tel:* (08) 8223 5155 *E-mail:* affadavid@hotmail.com
Penneshaw, Kangaroo Island, SA 5222, Contact: John Lavers *Tel:* (08) 8553 1072 *E-mail:* echidna@kin.net.au
PO Box 2415, Fitzroy, Victoria 3065, Contact: Michelle Barret-Dean *E-mail:* amcsmelbourne@hotmail.com.au
PO Box 404, Wynnum, Qld 4178, Contact: Michael Lusis *Tel:* (07) 3822 6824 *E-mail:* lusisfam@bigpond.com.au
2 Delhi St, City West Lotteries House, West Perth, WA 6005, Secretary: Dennis Beros

*Tel:* (08) 9420 7209 *Fax:* (08) 9486 7833
*E-mail:* amcswa@iinet.net.au
Great Oceans Rd, Victoria, Contact: Terry Gunn *Tel:* (03) 5263 1392

**Australian National University Press**, *imprint of* A S Wilson Inc

**Australian Rock Art Research Association+**
3 Buxton St, Elsternwick, Victoria 3185
Mailing Address: PO Box 216, Caulfield South, Victoria 3162
*Tel:* (03) 9523 0549 *Fax:* (03) 9523 0549
*E-mail:* auraweb@hotmail.com
*Web Site:* mc2.vicnet.net.au/home/aura/web/index.html
*Key Personnel*
Dir & International Rights: Robert Bednarik *E-mail:* robertbednarik@hotmail.com
Founded: 1983
Books, Periodicals, Academic Textbooks & Conference Proceedings.
Subjects: Anthropology, Archaeology, Art
ISBN Prefix(es): 0-646
Number of titles published annually: 2 Print
Distributed by ANH Publications (Australia); Piedra Pintada Books (USA)

**Australian Scholarly**, *imprint of* Australian Scholarly Publishing

**Australian Scholarly Publishing+**
PO Box 299, Kew, Victoria 3101
*Tel:* (03) 98175208 *Fax:* (03) 8176431
*E-mail:* aspic@ozemail.com.au
*Key Personnel*
Publisher: Nicholas Walker
Senior Editor: Dr Diane Carlyle
Founded: 1991
Subjects: Environmental Studies, Geography, Geology, Government, Political Science, History, Nonfiction (General), Publishing & Book Trade Reference, Social Sciences, Sociology, Wine & Spirits
ISBN Prefix(es): 1-875606; 1-74097
Imprints: Arcadia; Australian Scholarly
*Distribution Center:* Kirby Book Co, 7 Help St, Suite 704, Chatswood, NSW 2064

**The Australian Women's Weekly**, *imprint of* ACP Publishing Pty Ltd

**Australia's Best Garden Guide Series**, *imprint of* Hyland House Publishing Pty Ltd

**Autonomous Learning Publications & Specialists**, *imprint of* Hawker Brownlow

**Avon**, *imprint of* Random House Australia

**Axiom Publishers & Distributors**
One Union St, Unit 2, Stepney, SA 5069
*Tel:* (08) 83627052 *Fax:* (08) 83629430
*E-mail:* axiompub@camtech.net.au
*Key Personnel*
Contact: John Gallehawk
ISBN Prefix(es): 0-947338; 0-9594164; 1-86476

**Babel Handbooks**, *imprint of* Nimrod Publications

**Babysitters Club**, *imprint of* Scholastic Australia Pty Ltd

**Bahloo Publishers Real-Life Education**, *imprint of* R J Cleary Publishing

**Ballantine**, *imprint of* Random House Australia

**Bandicoot Books**
PO Box 373, Margate, Tas 7054
*Tel:* (03) 6267 2530 *Fax:* (03) 6267 1223
*Web Site:* www.bandicootbooks.com
*Key Personnel*
Contact: Marion Isham *E-mail:* ishams@ozemail.
com.au
Subjects: Animals, Pets, Fiction, Foreign Countries, History, Language Arts, Linguistics, Mysteries, Poetry
ISBN Prefix(es): 0-9586536
Distributed by Roots & Wings Books (US & Canada)

**Bantam Books**, *imprint of* Random House Australia

**Bantam**, *imprint of* Transworld Publishers Pty Ltd

**Bay Books**, *imprint of* Murdoch Books

**Bayda Books**
PO Box 178, East Brunswick, Victoria 3057
*Tel:* (0613) 9387-2799 *Fax:* (0613) 9387-2799
*Web Site:* www.bayda.com.au
*Key Personnel*
Manager: Yuri Tkacz *E-mail:* ytkacz@bigpond.
net.au
Founded: 1976
Specialize in books in Russian & Ukrainian.
Also acts as mail order book supplier & library supplier.
Total Titles: 11 Print; 3 Audio
Distributor for Lastivka Press

**Joycelyn Bayne**
2 Lee St, Fulham Gardens, SA 5024
Mailing Address: PO Box 59, Brooklyn Park, SA 5022
*Tel:* (08) 8356 1748
Subjects: History
ISBN Prefix(es): 0-7316

**BBC Worldwide**, *imprint of* Random House Australia

**Beazer Publishing Company Pty Ltd**
PO Box 150, Paynesville, Victoria 3880
*Tel:* (03) 5156 0556 *Fax:* (03) 5156 0556
*E-mail:* info@beazerpublishing.com
*Web Site:* www.beazerpublishing.com
*Key Personnel*
Contact: Margaret Beazer
Founded: 1994
Subjects: Earth Sciences, Environmental Studies, Law, Science (General)
ISBN Prefix(es): 1-876435
Total Titles: 8 Print; 1 Audio

**BEC Publications**, *imprint of* Hawker Brownlow

**Barbara Beckett Publishing Pty Ltd**
14 Hargrave St, Paddington, NSW 2021
*Tel:* (02) 93312871 *Fax:* (02) 93603106
*Key Personnel*
Publisher: Barbara Beckett
Founded: 1994
Subjects: Art, Cookery
ISBN Prefix(es): 1-875891
*Book Club(s):* Doubleday Australia

**Bellcourt Books**
63 Gray St, Hamilton, Victoria 3300
SAN: 902-4646
*Tel:* (03) 5572 1310 *Fax:* (03) 5572 1310
*E-mail:* bellcourt@ansonic.com.au
*Key Personnel*
Contact: Guy Stephens

Founded: 1983
Independent bookshop.

**Beri Publishing+**
36 Alfred Rd, Burwood, Victoria 3125
*Tel:* (03) 9809 1434 *Fax:* (03) 9809 1434
*E-mail:* beripub@ozemail.com.au
*Key Personnel*
Head of Company: Nola Schlegel
Founded: 1991
Subjects: Education
ISBN Prefix(es): 0-9587113; 0-646; 0-9577233

**Bernal Publishing+**
4 Frank St, Box Hill South, Victoria 3128
*Tel:* (0613) 9808-3775 *Fax:* (0613) 9888-7572
*E-mail:* sales@bernalpublishing.com
*Web Site:* www.bernalpublishing.com
*Key Personnel*
Man Editor: Robert Martin
Founded: 1991
Subjects: Agriculture, Biography, History, Nonfiction (General), Farming (Commercial Chick Sexing)
ISBN Prefix(es): 0-646

**Robert Berthold Photography**
11 Wolfe Rd, North Ryde, NSW 2113
*Tel:* (02) 9887 3986 *Fax:* (02) 9887 3986
*Key Personnel*
Head of Company: Robert Berthold
Subjects: Biological Sciences, Environmental Studies, Maritime, Natural History, Outdoor Recreation, Photography, Physics, Science (General), Sports, Athletics
ISBN Prefix(es): 0-646

**Better Homes & Gardens**, *imprint of* Murdoch Books

**Beyond Bullying Association**, *imprint of* Rainbow Book Agencies Pty Ltd

**Bible Society in Australia National Headquarters+**
30 York Rd, Ingleburn, ACT 2565
Mailing Address: GPO Box 507, Canberra, ACT 2601
*Tel:* (02) 6248 5188 *Fax:* (02) 6288 6168
*E-mail:* customer.service@bible.org.au; bsadm@ bible.com.au
*Web Site:* www.biblesociety.com.au
*Key Personnel*
Marketing Manager: Gregory N Page
*E-mail:* greg.page@bbla.org.au
Founded: 1817
Specialize in Bibles & related publications.
Membership(s): United Bible Societies.
Subjects: Biblical Studies, Religion - Catholic, Religion - Protestant, Theology
ISBN Prefix(es): 0-647
*Branch Office(s)*
5 Byfield St, Macquarie Park, NSW 2113
*Tel:* (02) 9888 6588; 1300 552 537 *Fax:* (02) 9888 7820 *E-mail:* infonsw@bible.com.au
2-6 Albert St, Blackburn, VIC 3130 *Tel:* (03) 9877 9277; (03) 9877 9233 *Fax:* (03) 9877 8399 *E-mail:* infovic@bible.com.au
GPO Box 1228, Brisbane, Qld 4001 *Tel:* (07) 3221 5683; 1300 139 179 *Fax:* (07) 3229 0063 *E-mail:* infoqld@bible.com.au
133 Rundle Mall, Adelaide, SA 5000 *Tel:* (08) 8223 3833 *Fax:* (08) 8223 3286 *E-mail:* infosa@bible.com.au
122 Adelaide Terrace, East Perth, WA 6004 *Tel:* (08) 9221 3488 *Fax:* (08) 9325 4557 *E-mail:* infowa@bible.com.au
PO Box 971, Launceston, TAS 7250 *Tel:* (03) 6331 0248; 1300 139 179 *Fax:* (03) 6331 0249 *E-mail:* infotas@bible.com.au

PO Box 147, Sanderson, NT 0813 *Tel:* (08) 8927 3056 *Fax:* (08) 8927 2794 *E-mail:* infont@ bible.com.au
*Bookshop(s):* 2-6 Albert St, Blackburn, Victoria 3130 *Tel:* (03) 9877 9233 *Fax:* (03) 9877 8399 *E-mail:* shopvic@bible.com.au; 212 Main St, Lilydale, Victoria 3140 *Tel:* (03) 9735 0410 *Fax:* (03) 9735 2013 *E-mail:* shopvic@ bible.com.au; Locked Bag 3, Minto, NSW 2566 *Tel:* 1300 139 179 *Fax:* (02) 9829 4685 *E-mail:* bsdirect@bible.org.au; 95 Bathurst St, Sydney, NSW 2000 *Tel:* (02) 9267 6862 *Fax:* (02) 9267 7415 *E-mail:* shopnsw@ biblesociety.com.au; 133 Rundle Mall, Adelaide, SA 5000 *Tel:* (08) 8223 3936 *Fax:* (08) 8223 3286 *E-mail:* shopsa@bible.com.au

**Bio Concepts Publishing**
Unit 9/783 Kingsford Smith Dr, Eagle Farm, Qld 4009
Mailing Address: PO Box 1492, Eagle Farm, Qld 4009
*Tel:* (07) 3868 0699 *Fax:* (07) 3868 0600
*E-mail:* info@bioconcepts.com.au
*Web Site:* www.bioconcepts.com.au
*Key Personnel*
President: Henry Osiecki
Sales Manager: Mary Waldie
Subjects: Alternative, Health, Nutrition, Self-Help, Sports, Athletics
ISBN Prefix(es): 1-875239; 1-74105

**Birchgrove Books**
18 Louisa Rd, Birchgrove, NSW 2041
*Tel:* (02) 9810 5040 *Fax:* (02) 9810 6040
*E-mail:* 100406.343@compuserve.com
ISBN Prefix(es): 0-646

**Black Dog Books+**
15 Gertrude St, Fitzroy, Victoria 3065
*Tel:* (03) 9419 9406 *Fax:* (03) 9419 1214
*E-mail:* dog@bdb.com.au
*Web Site:* www.bdb.com.au
*Key Personnel*
Contact: Andrew Kelly *E-mail:* andrew@bdb.
com.au
ISBN Prefix(es): 1-876372

**Black Swan**, *imprint of* Random House Australia

**Black Swan**, *imprint of* Transworld Publishers Pty Ltd

**Blackbooks Co-operative for Aborigines Ltd**
11-13 Mansfield St, Glebe, NSW 2037
*Tel:* (0612) 9660 2396 *Fax:* (0612) 9660 1924
*E-mail:* tranby@tranby.com.au
*Web Site:* www.tranby.com.au
*Key Personnel*
Head of Company: Kevin Cook
Founded: 1982
Specialize in Aboriginal & Torres Strait Islands.
*Orders to:* Allbooks Distribution, 16 Darghan St, Glebe, NSW 2037

**Blackstone**, *imprint of* Pascoe Publishing Pty Ltd

**Blackstone Press Pty Ltd**
500 Oxford St, 18th floor, Bondi Junction, NSW 2022
*Tel:* (02) 9389 7677
*E-mail:* c.l.e.@laams.com.au
Subjects: Law
ISBN Prefix(es): 1-875114

**Blackwell Publishing Asia+**
550 Swanston St, Carlton South, Victoria 3053
Mailing Address: PO Box 378, Carlton South, Victoria 3053
*Tel:* (03) 8359 1011 *Fax:* (03) 8359 1120
*E-mail:* info@blackwellpublishingasia.com.au
*Web Site:* www.blacksci.co.uk

*Key Personnel*
Chief Executive, Man Dir: Mark Robertson
Marketing & Operations Dir: Neil Walsh
Publishing & Finance Dir: Jane Watson
Customer Service: Robert Turner
Founded: 1971
Subjects: Computer Science, Earth Sciences, En-
gineering (General), Mathematics, Medicine,
Nursing, Dentistry, Physical Sciences, Physics,
Psychology, Psychiatry, Science (General)
ISBN Prefix(es): 0-86793
*Parent Company:* Blackwell Science Ltd, United
Kingdom
Subsidiaries: Blackwell Science KK
*U.S. Office(s):* Blackwell Publishing Inc, Com-
merce Pl, 350 Main St, Malden, MA 02148,
United States *Tel:* 781-388-8200 *Fax:* 781-388-
8210
Distributor for American Society for Microbiol-
ogy; American Psychiatric Press Inc; Garland
Publishers; Jones & Bartlett; Springer Verlag
(Australia & New Zealand only)
*Warehouse:* 26 Albert St, Brunswick, Victoria
3056

**Horst Blaich Pty Ltd**
24 John St, Bayswater, Victoria 3153
*Tel:* (03) 9720 2658 *Fax:* (03) 9762 4225
ISBN Prefix(es): 1-86347

**Joan Blair**
15 Antrim St, Kiama, NSW 2533
Mailing Address: PO Box 432, Kiama, NSW
2533
*Tel:* (02) 4232 1642
*Key Personnel*
Author & Publisher: Joan Blair
Founded: 1986
Subjects: Human Relations, Self-Help
ISBN Prefix(es): 1-86252
Distributed by ROSE Education & Training (Aus-
tralia)

**Bloomings**, *imprint of* Bloomings Books

**Bloomings Books+**
7 Newry St, Richmond, Victoria 3121
*Tel:* (03) 9427 1234 *Fax:* (03) 9427 9066
*E-mail:* sales@bloomings.com.au
*Web Site:* www.bloomings.com.au
*Key Personnel*
Publisher: Warwick Forge *E-mail:* warwick@
bloomings.com.au
Founded: 1994
Publish, distribute & wholesale horticulture &
natural history books.
Subjects: Gardening, Plants, Natural History
ISBN Prefix(es): 1-876473
Total Titles: 12 Print
Imprints: Bloomings; Rodale; Timber

**Blubber Head Press**
81 Salamanca Pl, 1st floor, Hobart, Tas 7000
Mailing Address: PO Box 475, Sandy Bay, Tas
7006
*Tel:* (03) 6223 8644 *Fax:* (03) 6223 8644
*E-mail:* books@astrolabebooks.com.au
*Web Site:* www.astrolabebooks.com.au
*Key Personnel*
Proprietor: Michael Sprod *E-mail:* michael@
astrolabebooks.com.au
Founded: 1978
Subjects: History, Regional Interests, Travel
ISBN Prefix(es): 0-908528
*Bookshop(s):* Astrolabe Antiquarian Booksellers

**Board of Studies**
117 Clarence St, Sydney, NSW 2000
Mailing Address: GPO Box 5300, Sydney, NSW
2001
*Tel:* (02) 9367 8111 *Fax:* (02) 9367 8484

*E-mail:* customerliason@boardofstudies.nsw.edu.
au
*Web Site:* www.boardofstudies.nsw.edu.au
*Key Personnel*
President: Prof Gordon Stanley *Tel:* (02) 9367
8176
General Manager: Dr John Bennett *Tel:* (02) 9367
8169
Membership(s): NSW Government Dept.
Subjects: Education
ISBN Prefix(es): 0-7305; 0-7310

**Boat Books Group**
31 Albany St, Crows Nest, NSW 2065
*Tel:* (02) 94391133 *Fax:* (02) 94398517
*E-mail:* boatbook@boatbooks-aus.com.au
*Web Site:* www.boatbooks-aust.com.au
*Key Personnel*
Contact: Philip Brook
Founded: 1973
Subjects: Nautical Titles (recreational & profes-
sional)
*Branch Office(s)*
109 Albert St, Brisbane, Qld 4000
*E-mail:* boatbks@bluesky.net.au
214 St Kilda Rd, St Kilda, Victoria 3182
*Tel:* (03) 9626 3444 *Fax:* (03) 9535 3355

**Boinkie Publishers**
PO Box 27, Brighton-Le-Sands, NSW 2216
*Tel:* (02) 9588-7010 *Fax:* (02) 9311-3428
ISBN Prefix(es): 0-9587468

**Bolinda**, *imprint of* Bolinda Publishing Pty Ltd

**Bolinda Audio**, *imprint of* Bolinda Publishing Pty
Ltd

**Bolinda Press**, *imprint of* Bolinda Publishing Pty
Ltd

**Bolinda Publishing Pty Ltd+**
17 Mohr St, Tullamarine, Victoria 3043
*Tel:* (03) 9338 0666 *Fax:* (03) 9335 1903
*Web Site:* www.bolinda.com
*Key Personnel*
Dir: Philip Walshe
Marketing Manager: Rebecca Walshe
Founded: 1985
Specialize in unabridged audio books & large-
print publishing.
Subjects: Disability, Special Needs, Fiction, Non-
fiction (General)
ISBN Prefix(es): 0-947072; 1-86340; 1-74030; 1-
876584; 1-74093; 1-74094
Number of titles published annually: 12 Print;
120 Audio
Imprints: Bolinda; Bolinda Audio; Bolinda Press
*U.S. Office(s):* Bolinda Publishing Inc, Shelton
Pointe, 2 Trap Falls Rd, Suite 113, Shelton,
CT 06484, United States *Tel:* 203-925-7791
*Fax:* 203-925-8943 *E-mail:* usa@bolinda.com
Distributor for Center Point Publishing; Clipper
Audio; Clipper Large Print; Mills & Boon;
Thorndike Press

**Herbert Bolles**
130 Warks Hill Rd, Kurrajong Heights, NSW
2758
*Tel:* (02) 4567 7350 *Fax:* (02) 4567 7350
*E-mail:* bolles@pnc.com.au
ISBN Prefix(es): 0-646

**Boobook Publications**
PO Box 238, Tea Gardens, NSW 2324
*Tel:* (02) 4997 0811 *Fax:* (02) 4997 1089
*Key Personnel*
Head of Company: Ian Hoyle; Sally Hoyle
Founded: 1981

Subjects: Sports, Athletics
ISBN Prefix(es): 0-908121

**Book Agencies of Tasmania+**
5 Cleve Court, Howrah, Tas 7018
Mailing Address: PO Box 327, Rosny Park, Tas
7018
*Tel:* (03) 6247 7405 *Fax:* (03) 6247 1116
*E-mail:* bookagencies@trump.net.au
*Key Personnel*
Manager: Graeme Thurlow
Founded: 1982
Subjects: Regional Interests
Number of titles published annually: 2 Print
Total Titles: 15 Print

**Book Collectors' Society of Australia**
678 Victoria Rd, Unit 150, Ryde, NSW 2112
*Tel:* (02) 9807 5489 *Fax:* (02) 9807 5489
*Key Personnel*
President: Neil Radford
Secretary: Jeff Bidgood *E-mail:* bidgood@
bigpond.net.au
Founded: 1944
ISBN Prefix(es): 0-646; 0-9586761; 0-9587263;
0-9589220
Number of titles published annually: 5 Print

**The Book Company Publishing Pty Ltd**
Austlink Corporate Park, One Minna Close, Bel-
rose, Sydney, NSW 2085
*Tel:* (02) 94863711 *Fax:* (02) 94863722
*E-mail:* sales@thebookcompany.com.au
*Web Site:* www.thebookcompany.com.au
*Key Personnel*
Chief Operating Officer: Andrew G Steele-Smith
*Tel:* (0402) 214 218 *E-mail:* andrewss@
thebookcompany.com.au
Publisher: Glenn Johnstone
Founded: 1986
Specialize in innovative childrens' novelty books
& adult stationery items.
Number of titles published annually: 200 Print

**Book Lures Inc**, *imprint of* Hawker Brownlow

**Bookman Health**
Level 9, Trak Centre, 443-449 Toorak Rd,
Toorak, Victoria 3142
*Tel:* (03) 9521 3250 *Toll Free Tel:* 800 060 555
*Fax:* (03) 9826 1744
*E-mail:* sales@bookman.com.au
*Web Site:* www.bookman.com.au

**Books & Writers**, *imprint of* Wild & Woolley

**Boolarong Press**
35 Hamilton Rd, Moorooka, Qld 4105
*Tel:* (07) 3848 8200 *Fax:* (07) 3848 8077
*E-mail:* mail@boolarongpress.com.au
*Web Site:* www.boolarongpress.com.au
*Key Personnel*
Head of Company: Lester Padman
General Manager, Sales & Publicity: R J Keirnan
Editorial: M Weaver
Production: C L Padman
Founded: 1977
Subjects: Art, Biography, Business, History, Man-
agement, Nonfiction (General)
ISBN Prefix(es): 0-86439; 0-908175; 1-86439
*Parent Company:* Artists Associated Pty Ltd

**Boombana Publications+**
PO Box 118, Mount Nebo, Qld 4520
*Tel:* (07) 3289 8106 *Fax:* (07) 3289 8107
*Web Site:* www.boombanapublications.com
*Key Personnel*
Contact: Jean-Claude Lacherez *E-mail:* j.
lacherez@uq.net.au
Founded: 1992

Subjects: Language Arts, Linguistics, Literature, Literary Criticism, Essays, Nonfiction (General)
ISBN Prefix(es): 0-9586685

**M J Bowen**
18 Ranfurlie Drive, Glen Waverley, Victoria 3150
*Tel:* (03) 9561 3425 *Fax:* (03) 9882 9405
*Key Personnel*
Dir: M J Bowen
ISBN Prefix(es): 0-7316

**Boxtree**, *imprint of* Pan Macmillan Australia Pty Ltd

**David Boyce Publishing & Associates+**
44 Regent St, Redfern, NSW 2016
*Tel:* (02) 6997484
*Key Personnel*
Owner, Publisher & Sales Dir: David Boyce
    *E-mail:* david@boyces.com
Founded: 1975
Specialize in automotive manuals for workshops
    & software.
Subjects: Automotive, Technology
ISBN Prefix(es): 0-909682
Distributor for Robert Bosch

**Louis Braille Audio**
31-51 Commercial Rd, South Yarra, Victoria
    3141
Mailing Address: PO Box 860, Hawthorn, Victoria 3122
*Tel:* (03) 9864 9645 *Fax:* (03) 9864 9646
*E-mail:* lba.sales@visionaustralia.org.au
*Web Site:* www.louisbrailleaudio.com
*Key Personnel*
Managing Dir: Rose Blustein *E-mail:* rose.
    blustein@visionaustralia.org.au
Publishing & Rights Manager: Edwina Kenrick
    *Tel:* (03) 9864 9615 *E-mail:* edwina.kenrick@
    visionaustralia.org.au
Founded: 1993
Subjects: Biography, Fiction, History, Travel
ISBN Prefix(es): 0-7320; 0-86764
Total Titles: 258 Print; 258 Audio
*Parent Company:* Vision Australia Foundation
    Library
*Ultimate Parent Company:* Vision Australia Foundation

**Bridge To Peace Publications+**
149 Dartford Rd, Thornleigh, NSW 2120
*Tel:* (02) 9875 1912
*E-mail:* books@bridgetopeace.com.au; adesso@
    bridgetopeace.com.au
*Web Site:* www.bridgetopeace.com.au
*Key Personnel*
General Manager: Jim Scarano
Founded: 1997
Specialize in internet e-mail orders for all books
    published.
Subjects: Alternative, History, How-to, Human
    Relations, Nonfiction (General), Philosophy,
    Psychology, Psychiatry, Self-Help, Alexander
    Technique, Italian Culture, Yoga, Meditation &
    Personal Development
ISBN Prefix(es): 0-9587094; 0-9577615; 0-
    9581323; 0-9752107
Subsidiaries: Adesso Studio
*Branch Office(s)*
Paul Laccona, 341 Farleigh Terrace, Marietta, GA
    30068, United States

**Bridgeway Publications+**
12 Christina Pl, Belmont, Qld 4153
Mailing Address: GPO Box 2547, Brisbane, Qld
    4001
*Tel:* (07) 3390 4323 *Fax:* (07) 3390 4323
*E-mail:* info@bridgeway.org.au
*Web Site:* www.bridgeway.org.au

*Key Personnel*
Executive Dir: Don Fleming
    *E-mail:* donfleming@bridgeway.org.au
Founded: 1988
Non-profit organization which sends sponsored
    Christian reference materials to churches & institutions in needy countries.
Subjects: Biblical Studies, Religion - Protestant,
    Theology
ISBN Prefix(es): 0-947342
Total Titles: 15 Print
Distributed by AMG Publishers (USA); Copperbelt Christian Publications (Zambia); Horizon
    Publishers (India); Riverside World Inc (USA)
*Shipping Address:* Harvest Products, PO Box 108,
    Upper Gravatt, Qld 4122, Contact: Gordon
    Cowell *Tel:* (07) 3849 1812 *Fax:* (07) 3849
    1820 *E-mail:* harvest@tpgi.com.au
*Warehouse:* Harvest Products, PO Box 108, Upper Gravatt, Qld 4122, Contact: Gordon Cowell *Tel:* (07) 3849 1812 *Fax:* (07) 3849 1820
    *E-mail:* harvest@tpgi.com.au
*Orders to:* Harvest Products, PO Box 108, Upper Gravatt, Qld 4122, Contact: Gordon Cowell *Tel:* (07) 3849 1812 *Fax:* (07) 3849 1820
    *E-mail:* harvest@tpgi.com.au

**E J Brill, Robert Brown & Associates+**
154 Bentinck St, Bathurst, NSW 2795
*Tel:* (063) 318577 *Fax:* (063) 321273
*Key Personnel*
Man Editor: Robert Brown
Subjects: Natural History, Travel
ISBN Prefix(es): 0-949267; 0-909197; 1-86173;
    1-86273
Total Titles: 24 Print

**R A Broadberh**, *imprint of* Universal Press Pty
Ltd

**Broadway Books**, *imprint of* Random House
Australia

**Broadway Dela Corte**, *imprint of* Transworld
Publishers Pty Ltd

**Brookfield Press**
871 Upper Brookfield Rd, Upper Brookfield, Qld
    4069
Mailing Address: PO Box 738, Kenmore, Qld
    4069
*Tel:* (07) 3374 1053 *Fax:* (07) 3374 2059
*Key Personnel*
Dir: Frank Stacey *E-mail:* frank.stacey@csiro.au
Subjects: Earth Sciences, Geography, Geology,
    Physics

**Brooks Waterloo**, *imprint of* John Wiley & Sons
Australia, Ltd

**Bureau of Resource Sciences**
PO Box E11, Kingston, ACT 2604
*Tel:* (02) 6272 4282 *Fax:* (02) 6272 4747
*Key Personnel*
Dir: Ian Lambert *E-mail:* ian@mailpc.brs.gov.au
Subjects: Agriculture, Biological Sciences, Science (General), Veterinary Science
ISBN Prefix(es): 0-642; 0-644

**Butterworths Australia Ltd**
Member of The LexisNexis Group
Tower 2, 475-495 Victoria Ave, Chatswood, NSW
    2067
Mailing Address: Level 9, Locked Bag 2222,
    Chatswood Delivery Centre, Chatswood NSW
    2067
*Tel:* (02) 9422 2189 *Toll Free Tel:* 800 772 772
    *Fax:* (02) 9422 2406
*E-mail:* orders@butterworths.com.au; customer.
    relations@lexisnexis.com.au

*Web Site:* www.butterworths.com.au
*Key Personnel*
CEO & Man Dir: Tony Kinnear
Publishing Dir: James Broadfoot
Finance Dir: Philip Cauwood
Sales & Marketing Dir: Catherine Yeomans
Human Resources Manager: Rachel Sutton
Founded: 1910
A division of Reed International Books Australia
    Pty Ltd (ABN 7000 1002 357).
Subjects: Accounting, Business, Law
ISBN Prefix(es): 0-409
*Parent Company:* Reed Elsevier Australia Pty Ltd
*Ultimate Parent Company:* Reed Elsevier plc, 25
    Victoria St, London SW1H 0EX, United Kingdom
*Associate Companies:* Butterworth & Co (Publishers) Ltd UK; Butterworth Publishers (Pty)
    Ltd, South Africa; Butterworths Canada Ltd;
    Butterworth & Co (Asia) Pte Ltd, India; Butterworths (Ireland) Ltd; Butterworths Asia,
    Singapore; Butterworths of New Zealand Ltd;
    Guiffre Editore SpA, Italy; Editions du Juris-
    Classeur, France; Malayan Law Journal Sdn
    Bhd, Malaysia; Wydawnictwa Prawnicze PWN,
    Poland; Verlag Stampfli, Switzerland; Lexis-
    Nexis USA
*Branch Office(s)*
St George Centre, 60 Marcus Clarke St, Canberra,
    ACT 2600
Adelaide Chambers, 122 Pirie St, Adelaide, SA
    5000
461 Bourke St, Melbourne, Victoria 3000
44 St George's Terrace, Perth, WA 6000
286 Montague Rd, West End, Qld 4101

**Cairns Art Society Inc**
Cominos House, Greenslopes St, Edge Hill, Qld
    4870
Mailing Address: PO Box 992, Cairns, Qld 4870
*Tel:* (07) 4032 1506
*Key Personnel*
President: Mr K Ryan
Founded: 1931
ISBN Prefix(es): 0-7316

**Cambridge University Press**
477 Williamstown Rd, Port Melbourne, Victoria
    3207
Mailing Address: Private Bag 31, Port Melbourne, Victoria 3207
*Tel:* (03) 8671 1400 *Fax:* (03) 9676 9966
*E-mail:* info@cambridge.edu.au;
    customerservice@cambridge.edu.au
*Web Site:* www.cambridge.edu.au
*Key Personnel*
Dir: Kim Harris
Subjects: Education
ISBN Prefix(es): 0-521
*Parent Company:* Cambridge University Press,
    United Kingdom
*U.S. Office(s):* Cambridge University Press, 40 W
    20 St, New York, New York, NY 10011-4211,
    United States
Distributor for Currency Press (Australia);
    Stanford University Press (Australia & New
    Zealand)

**Rod Campbell Books**, *imprint of* Pan Macmillan
Australia Pty Ltd

**Canadian Conference of Catholic Bishops**,
    *imprint of* Rainbow Book Agencies Pty Ltd

**Candlelight Trust T/A Candlelight Farm**
PO Box 1125, Midland Business Centre, WA
    6936
*Tel:* (08) 92944141 *Fax:* (08) 92944141
*Key Personnel*
Editorial Manager: Ross Mars *E-mail:* rossmars@
    yahoo.com
Subjects: Agriculture, Education, Environmental
    Studies, Gardening, Plants

ISBN Prefix(es): 0-9587626
Total Titles: 4 Print

**Jonathon Cape**, *imprint of* Random House
Australia

**Captain Jonas Publications**
Campells Ridge Rd, Sandy Creek, Qld 4740
Mailing Address: Rosslyn Crannog, Mail Service
60, Mackay, Qld 4740
*Tel:* (07) 4956 5022 *Fax:* (07) 4956 2633
*E-mail:* aarfw@ozemail.com.au
*Key Personnel*
Manager: Anthony G Wheeler

**Carter's (Antiques & Collectibles) P/L**
PO Box 7246, Baulkham Hills BC, NSW 2153
*Tel:* (02) 8850 4600 *Fax:* (02) 8850 4100
*E-mail:* info@carters.com.au
*Web Site:* www.carters.com.au
*Key Personnel*
Contact: Trent McVey *E-mail:* trent@carters.com.
au
Founded: 1980
Subjects: Antiques, Collectibles
ISBN Prefix(es): 1-876079
Number of titles published annually: 2 Print
Total Titles: 2 Print
Subsidiaries: Carter's Publications - New Zealand
Ltd

**Casket Publications**
c/o D B Waterson, Macquarie University, NSW
2109
*Tel:* (02) 9805 8878; (02) 9481 9145 *Fax:* (02)
9875 5382
*Key Personnel*
Contact: Prof D B Waterson
Founded: 1992
Self publishing: research tools. Queensland politi-
cal biographical retailers.
Subjects: Biography, History
ISBN Prefix(es): 0-646
Total Titles: 2 Print
*Branch Office(s)*
20 Angophora Place, Pennant Hills, Sydney,
NSW 2120 *Tel:* 9481 9145 *Fax:* 9875 5382

**Cassel PLC**, *imprint of* Hawker Brownlow

**Catchfire Press Inc**
PO Box 2101, Dangar, NSW 2309
*Tel:* (02) 4951 8859
*E-mail:* catchfire@idl.com.au
*Web Site:* www.cust.idl.com.au/catchfire
*Key Personnel*
Convenor: Zenovia Doratis
Treasurer: Jackie Jools

**Catholic Institute of Sydney+**
99 Albert Rd, Strathfield, NSW 2135
*Tel:* (02) 9752 9500 *Fax:* (02) 9746 6022
*E-mail:* cisinfo@cis.catholic.edu.au
*Web Site:* www.cis.catholic.edu.au
*Key Personnel*
President: Rev Dr Gerard Kelly *Tel:* (02) 9752
9510
Subjects: Biblical Studies, History, Philosophy,
Religion - Catholic, Theology
ISBN Prefix(es): 0-908224

**Cavendish Publishing**, *imprint of* Cavendish
Publishing Pty Ltd

**Cavendish Publishing Pty Ltd+**
45 Beach St, Coogee, NSW 2034
*Tel:* (02) 9664 0909 *Fax:* (02) 9664 5420
*E-mail:* info@cavendishpublishing.com
*Web Site:* www.cavendishpublishing.com.au

*Key Personnel*
Chief Executive Officer: Mr Sonny Leong
*Tel:* (020) 7278 8000 *E-mail:* sonnyleong@
cavendishpublishing.com
Specialize in Law & Medicine.
Subjects: Law, Medicine, Nursing, Dentistry
ISBN Prefix(es): 1-85941; 1-876213; 1-876905
Total Titles: 400 Print
*Ultimate Parent Company:* Cavendish Publish-
ing Ltd, The Glass House, Wharton St, London
WC1X 9PX, United Kingdom
Imprints: Cavendish Publishing

**Centenary of Technical Education in
Bairnsdale**
32 Grant St, Bairnsdale, Victoria 3875
*Tel:* (03) 5152-4556
*Key Personnel*
Editorial Manager: Lorna Prendergast
Subjects: History
ISBN Prefix(es): 0-9587113

**Centre for Comparative Literature & Cultural
Studies**
Monash University, Clayton Campus, Clayton,
Victoria 3168
*Tel:* (03) 9905 4000; (03) 9905 3059 *Fax:* (03)
9905 4007
*Web Site:* www.arts.monash.edu/au/cclcs
*Key Personnel*
Editorial Manager: C G Worth *E-mail:* chris.
worth@arts.monash.edu.au
Subjects: Ethnicity, Literature, Literary Criticism,
Essays
ISBN Prefix(es): 0-7326; 0-86746; 0-909835

**Centre for Creative Learning**, *imprint of*
Hawker Brownlow

**Centre Publications+**
PO Box 359, Warwick, Qld 4370
*Tel:* (03) 8700149
*Key Personnel*
Man Dir: Robert Snow
Founded: 1974
Subjects: Education, Health, Nutrition
ISBN Prefix(es): 0-909698
*Associate Companies:* THE Foundation; The
Yoga Education Centre, 226 Moggill Rd,
Taringa, Qld 4068

**Century**, *imprint of* Random House Australia

**Chalkface Press Pty Ltd+**
PO Box 23, Cottesloe, Perth, WA 6011
*Tel:* (08) 9385 1923 *Fax:* (08) 9385 1923
*E-mail:* info@chalkface.net.au; sales@
wooldridges.com.au (orders)
*Web Site:* www.chalkface.net.au
*Key Personnel*
Dir: Bronwyn Mellor; Stephen Mellor
Founded: 1987
Membership(s): Australian Publishers Associa-
tion.
ISBN Prefix(es): 1-875136
Distributed by English & Media Centre (UK)
Distributor for English & Media Centre (UK)
Foreign Rep(s): Gould Media (US)

**Channel 4**, *imprint of* Pan Macmillan Australia
Pty Ltd

**Chapter & Verse**, *imprint of* Wellington Lane
Press Pty Ltd

**Chatto & Windus**, *imprint of* Random House
Australia

**Childerset Pty Ltd+**
16 Tunba Court, Cooroy, Qld 4563
*Tel:* (074) 425510 *Fax:* (074) 425512
*E-mail:* tessgsp@ozemail.com.au
*Key Personnel*
Man Dir: David Ridyard
Founded: 1970
ISBN Prefix(es): 0-909405; 0-949130

**China Books**
234 Swanston St, 2nd Floor, Melbourne, Victoria
3000
*Tel:* (03) 9663 8822 *Fax:* (03) 9663 8821
*E-mail:* info@chinabooks.com.au
*Web Site:* www.chinabooks.com.au
*Key Personnel*
Man Dir: Ian Fox; Tony McGlinchey
Founded: 1989
Book importer, wholesaler & retailer/specialist.
Subjects: Asian Studies, Language Arts, Linguis-
tics, China, Chinese Studies
ISBN Prefix(es): 0-646
*Bookshop(s):* 81 Enmore Rd, Enmore, NSW
2042 *Tel:* (02) 9557 2701 *Fax:* (02) 9661 8727
*E-mail:* chinabooks@hotkey.net.au

**Chingchic Publishers**
83 River Walk Ave, Robina, Qld 4226
*E-mail:* chingchic@winshop.com.au
*Web Site:* www.chingchic.com
*Key Personnel*
Proprietor: Judy Eather
Manager, Author & Historian: Charles E Eather
Founded: 1993
Subjects: Aeronautics, Aviation
ISBN Prefix(es): 0-646; 0-9586746; 0-949756
Total Titles: 2 CD-ROM

**Chiron Media**
PO Box 6069, Mooloolah, Qld 4553
*Tel:* (074) 947311 *Fax:* (074) 947890
*E-mail:* chiron@acslink.net.au
*Key Personnel*
Contact: Helen Penridge
Founded: 1990
Subjects: Animals, Pets, Environmental Studies,
Government, Political Science, Public Adminis-
tration, Veterinary Science
ISBN Prefix(es): 0-9586784
*Parent Company:* Penridge Information Pty Ltd

**CHOICE Magazine+**
57 Carrington Rd, Marrickville, NSW 2204
*Tel:* (02) 9577 3399 *Fax:* (02) 9577 3377
*E-mail:* ausconsumer@choice.com.au
*Web Site:* www.choice.com.au
*Key Personnel*
Publisher: Keren Lavelle
General Manager: Norm Crothers
Founded: 1960
Membership(s): Australian Publishers' Associa-
tion, Publish Australia.
Subjects: Architecture & Interior Design, Au-
tomotive, Health, Nutrition, House & Home,
Self-Help, Travel
ISBN Prefix(es): 0-947277; 0-9591120; 0-
9596536; 1-920705
*Parent Company:* Australian Consumers' Associa-
tion

**Christian Education Publications**, *imprint of*
Aquila Press

**Christian Literature Crusade**
Division of CLC Publications
125 New Rd, West Pennant Hills, NSW 2120
*Tel:* (02) 9875 1330 *Fax:* (02) 9481 8304
*Key Personnel*
Contact: K T Ridley
ISBN Prefix(es): 0-9595552
*U.S. Office(s):* PO Box 1449, Fort Washington,
PA 19034-8449, United States

**Christian Research Association**, *imprint of* Rainbow Book Agencies Pty Ltd

**Church Archivists Press**
PO Box 130, Virginia, Qld 4014
*Tel:* (07) 3865 0466 *Fax:* (07) 3865 0458
*Key Personnel*
Dir: Leo J Ansell *E-mail:* ANSELL@staff.nudgee.com
Founded: 1980 (Known as Church Archives Society Press until 1992)
Subjects: Biography, Computer Science, Genealogy, History, Poetry, Theology
ISBN Prefix(es): 1-876194
Total Titles: 75 Print

**Churchill House**, *imprint of* Austed Publishing Co

**Churchill Livingstone**, *imprint of* Elsevier Australia

**CIS Publishers**
22 Salmon St, Port Melbourne, Victoria 3027
*Tel:* (03) 92467131 *Fax:* (03) 3470175
*E-mail:* samone.underwood@reeducation.com.au
*Key Personnel*
Man Dir: Elio Guarnuccio
Subjects: Education
ISBN Prefix(es): 0-949919; 1-875633; 1-86391; 1-74070

**Classroom Magazine**, *imprint of* Scholastic Australia Pty Ltd

**R J Cleary Publishing+**
PO Box 939, Darlinghurst, NSW 2010
*Tel:* (02) 2643750
*Key Personnel*
Man Dir: R J Cleary
Founded: 1969
Subjects: Film, Video, Regional Interests
ISBN Prefix(es): 0-85567
Imprints: Bahloo Publishers Real-Life Education; Education; Success Education

**Cole Publications**
5 Cooba St, Canterbury, Victoria 3126
*Tel:* (03) 9830 4242 *Fax:* (03) 9830 4242
*Key Personnel*
Head of Company: Merron Cullum
Editorial Manager: Cole Turnley
Founded: 1868
Subjects: Humor
ISBN Prefix(es): 0-909900
*Parent Company:* Alterns Pty Ltd

**Commonwealth Scientific & Industrial Research Organisation**, see CSIRO Publishing (Commonwealth Scientific & Industrial Research Organisation)

**Companion Travel Guide Books+**
19 Kilmorey St, Busby, NSW 2168
*Tel:* (02) 9608-1169 *Fax:* (02) 9608-1169
*E-mail:* 6LEI937764@aol.com
*Key Personnel*
International Rights: G R Leitner
Founded: 1990
Subjects: Travel, Latin America
ISBN Prefix(es): 0-646; 0-9587498
Distributed by Hunter Publishing Inc (USA, Canada, Central America, Caribbean)

**Constitutional Publishing Co Pty Ltd**
622 Hay St, Perth, WA 6000
Mailing Address: GPO Box D152, Perth, WA 6001
*Tel:* (08) 9421 6216 *Fax:* (08) 9221 1572

*Key Personnel*
Customer Service: Roger L Day
ISBN Prefix(es): 0-646

**Cookery Book**
31 Albany St, Crows Nest, NSW 2065
*Tel:* (02) 9439 3144 *Fax:* (02) 9439 3405
*E-mail:* answers@cookerybook.com.au
*Web Site:* www.cookerybook.com.au
*Key Personnel*
Man Dir: John T Ivimey
Founded: 1985
Australia's only exclusive distributor of cookery books for the professional chef & the home cook.
Subjects: Cookery, Wine & Spirits, Culinary Arts
Total Titles: 3,200 Print
*Parent Company:* Ivimey & Associates Pty Ltd
*Branch Office(s)*
9 Axon St, Subiaco, WA 6008, Jennie Ivimey
*Tel:* (08) 9382 2122 *Fax:* (08) 9381 3256

**Coolabah Publishing**
5 Coolabah Close, Tamworth, NSW 2340
*Tel:* (02) 6766 4420 *Fax:* (02) 6766 1058
*E-mail:* narnia@mpx.com.au
*Key Personnel*
International Rights: Patrick O'Connor
Founded: 1991
Subjects: Education, Aboriginal
ISBN Prefix(es): 1-876400

**Corgi**, *imprint of* Random House Australia

**Corgi**, *imprint of* Transworld Publishers Pty Ltd

**Cornford Press**
6 Salisbury Crescent, Launceston, Tas 7250
*Tel:* (03) 6331 9658 *Fax:* (03) 6331 9658
*E-mail:* info@cornfordpress.com
*Web Site:* www.cornfordpress.com
*Key Personnel*
Managing Editor: Tim Thorne
Founded: 1989
Subjects: Biography, Poetry, Travel
ISBN Prefix(es): 0-9577565; 0-9581960
Number of titles published annually: 3 Print
Total Titles: 10 Print
Distributor for CACTI

**Cornucopia Press**
PO Box 27, Subiaco, WA 6008
*Tel:* (08) 9388 1965 *Fax:* (09) 3817341
*E-mail:* cornucop@aoi.com.au
*Key Personnel*
Principal: David Noel
Founded: 1982
Subjects: Agriculture, Gardening, Plants, Trees, Tree Crops, Useful Horticulture
ISBN Prefix(es): 0-9593205; 0-947260
Imprints: R*O*D Books
Subsidiaries: Personal Publishing Press Services
*Showroom(s):* Tree Crops Centre, 208 Nicholson Rd, Subiaco, WA 6008

**Covenanter Press**
159 Bourke St, Dapto, NSW 2530
Mailing Address: PO Box 636, Lithgow, NSW 2790
*Tel:* (02) 4257 9188
*E-mail:* adslsouw@tpg.com.au
*Web Site:* www.covenanterpress.com.au
*Key Personnel*
Sales Manager: Don Burgess *E-mail:* don.burgess@prc.org.au
Founded: 1967
Publisher of Christian books.
Subjects: History, Religion - Protestant, Theology
ISBN Prefix(es): 0-908189
Number of titles published annually: 2 Print

Total Titles: 50 Print
*Parent Company:* Presbyterian Reformed Church of Australia

**Craftsman House**, *imprint of* Fine Art Publishing Pty Ltd

**Crawford House Publishing Pty Ltd+**
PO Box 50, Belair, SA 5052
*Tel:* (08) 8370 0300; (08) 8370 3555 (orders)
*Fax:* (08) 8370 0344; (08) 8370 3566 (orders)
*Web Site:* www.crawfordhouse.com.au
*Key Personnel*
Man Dir: Anthony L Crawford
*E-mail:* tonycraw@bigpond.net.au
Editorial Manager: David H Barrett
*E-mail:* chpdavid@chp.com.au
Secretary: Jennifer Crawford *E-mail:* frontdesk@chp.com.au
Founded: 1989
Subjects: Anthropology, Asian Studies, Biography, Government, Political Science, History, Maritime, Natural History, Science Fiction, Fantasy, Self-Help, Social Sciences, Sociology, Travel, Wine & Spirits
ISBN Prefix(es): 1-86333
Number of titles published annually: 15 Print
Total Titles: 82 Print
Imprints: Pants on Fire
Distributed by University of Hawaii Press

**Creative Learning Consultants**, *imprint of* Hawker Brownlow

**Creative Learning Press**, *imprint of* Hawker Brownlow

**Crista International+**
PO Box 8096, Bundall, Qld 9726
*Tel:* (07) 5537 2956 *Fax:* (07) 5537 2956
*Key Personnel*
Principal: Helen Derrington
Founded: 1994
How-to publishing for consultants & sales professionals.
Subjects: Business, How-to, Marketing, Self-Help
ISBN Prefix(es): 0-9587262

**Critical Thinking Press & Software**, *imprint of* Hawker Brownlow

**Crossroad Distributors Pty Ltd**
9 Euston St, Rydalmere, NSW 2116
*Tel:* (02) 8845 7744 *Fax:* (02) 8845 7755
*E-mail:* custserv@crossroad.com.au
Subjects: Biblical Studies, Child Care & Development, Human Relations, Religion - Protestant, Self-Help, Theology

**Crown Publishing Group**, *imprint of* Random House Australia

**Crystal Publishing+**
6 Park St, Saint Kilda, Victoria 3182
*Tel:* (03) 9525 4549
*E-mail:* minx@alphalink.com.au
*Key Personnel*
President: Beryl K Rohan
Founded: 1980
Specialize in Economics & Sociology.
Subjects: Economics, Government, Political Science, Philosophy, Social Sciences, Sociology
ISBN Prefix(es): 0-9593859

**CSIRO Publishing (Commonwealth Scientific & Industrial Research Organisation)+**
150 Oxford St, Collingwood, Victoria 3066
Mailing Address: PO Box 1139, Collingwood, Victoria 3066
*Tel:* (03) 9662 7500 *Fax:* (03) 9662 7555
*E-mail:* publishing@csiro.au

*Web Site:* www.publish.csiro.au
*Telex:* 30236
*Key Personnel*
General Manager: Paul Reekie *Tel:* (03) 9662 7650
Founded: 1926
Subjects: Agriculture, Biological Sciences, Chemistry, Chemical Engineering, Environmental Studies, Natural History, Physical Sciences, Physics, Science (General), Technology
ISBN Prefix(es): 0-643; 0-52285; 0-52163
Number of titles published annually: 50 Print
Distributed by Antipodes Books & Beyond Ltd (USA & Canada); Eurospan (UK, Europe, Middle East & North Africa); Manaaki Whenua Press (New Zealand); Publishers Marketing Services Pte Ltd (Singapore, Malaysia & Brunei)

**Currency Press Pty Ltd+**
201 Cleveland St, Redfern, NSW 2016
Mailing Address: PO Box 2287, Strawberry Hills, NSW 2012
*Tel:* (02) 9319 5877 *Fax:* (02) 9319 3649
*E-mail:* enquiries@currency.com.au
*Web Site:* www.currency.com.au
*Key Personnel*
Chairman: Nicholas Parsons
Publisher: Victoria Chance
Sales & Marketing Dir: Deborah Franco
    *E-mail:* franco@currency.com.au
Founded: 1971
Specialize in Australian performing arts.
Subjects: Drama, Theater, Film, Video, Music, Dance
ISBN Prefix(es): 0-86819
Number of titles published annually: 30 Print
Total Titles: 450 Print
Distributor for Nick Hern Books (Australia); Oberon Books (Australia)
*Distribution Center:* Antipodes Books & Beyond Ltd, 9707 Fairway Ave, Silver Springs, MD 20910-3001, United States *Tel:* 301-602-9519 *Fax:* 301-565-0160 *E-mail:* antipodes@antipodesbooks.com *Web Site:* www.antipodes.com

**Curriculum Associates Inc**, *imprint of* Hawker Brownlow

**Curriculum Corporation+**
Casselden Pl, Level 5, 2 Lonsdale St, Melbourne, Victoria 3000
Mailing Address: PO Box 177, Carlton South, Victoria 3053
*Tel:* (03) 9207 9600 *Fax:* (03) 9639 1616
*E-mail:* sales@curriculum.edu.au
*Web Site:* www.curriculum.edu.au *Cable:* EDUCATION CANBERRA
*Key Personnel*
Chief Executive Officer: Bruce Wilson
    *E-mail:* bruce.wilson@curriculum.edu.au
Executive Dir: David Francis
Publishing Manager: Esther Grounds
Sales & Marketing Dir: Sandra Hay
    *E-mail:* sandra.hay@curriculum.edu.au
Business Development Manager: Martin Murley
    *E-mail:* martin.murley@curriculum.edu.au
Production Manager: Bernie Handley
    *E-mail:* bernie.handley@curriculum.edu.au
General Manager, Curriculum Operations: Keith Gove *E-mail:* keith.gove@curriculum.edu.au
General Manager, Curriculum Programs: Pamela Macklin *E-mail:* pamela.macklin@curriculum.edu.au
Founded: 1990
Specialize in curriculum & education support material.
Subjects: Education
ISBN Prefix(es): 1-86366

*Parent Company:* Australian Ministers for Education
*Orders to:* PO Box 177, Carlton South, Victoria 3053

**Eleanor Curtain Publishing+**
12 Claremont St, South Yarra, Victoria 3141
*Tel:* (03) 9826 3222 *Fax:* (03) 9826 9699
*E-mail:* enquiries@ecpublishing.com.au
*Web Site:* www.ecpublishing.com/au
*Key Personnel*
Man Dir: Eleanor Curtain *E-mail:* ecurtain@ozemail.com.au
International Rights: Jane Curtain
Subjects: Education, Literature, Literary Criticism, Essays, Poetry
ISBN Prefix(es): 1-875327; 1-876917; 1-876975
Distributed by Horwitz Martin
Distributor for Heinemann US; Stenhouse

**Cygnet Books**, *imprint of* University of Western Australia Press

**Cygnet Young Fiction**, *imprint of* University of Western Australia Press

**D&B Marketing Pty Ltd**
479 St Kilda Rd, Melbourne, NSW 3004
*Tel:* (03) 9828 3333 *Fax:* (03) 9828 3300
*E-mail:* csc.austral@dnb.com.au
*Web Site:* www.dnb.com.au
*Key Personnel*
Public Relations: Chris Gray
Founded: 1887
Subjects: Business, Finance
ISBN Prefix(es): 0-9593441
*Parent Company:* D&B (Australia) Pty Ltd
Divisions: Riddell Publishing

**Dabill Publications**
PO Box 707, Wollongong, NSW 2520
*Tel:* (02) 4228 8836 *Fax:* (02) 4226 9367
*Web Site:* www.dabill.com.au
*Key Personnel*
Author: Tim Cattell *E-mail:* tim@dabill.com.au
Business Manager: Frances Cattell
Founded: 1980
Subjects: Economics, Education, Environmental Studies, Geography, Geology, Social Sciences, Sociology

**Dagraja Press+**
3 Verco St, Hackett, ACT 2602
*Tel:* (02) 6247 0782; (02) 6262 7533
*E-mail:* granorab@ozemail.com.au
*Key Personnel*
Owner: Mr Graeme Barrow
Founded: 1977
Specialize in bushwalking guides & local history.
Subjects: History
ISBN Prefix(es): 0-9587552
Number of titles published annually: 1 Print
Total Titles: 4 Print
Distributed by MacStyle Media

**Dandy Lion Publications**, *imprint of* Hawker Brownlow

**Dangaroo Press+**
GPO Box 1209, Sydney, NSW 2001
*Tel:* (02) 49545938 *Fax:* (02) 49546531
*Key Personnel*
Sales Manager: Allan Rich
Founded: 1978
Subjects: Art, Ethnicity, Literature, Literary Criticism, Essays, Nonfiction (General), Poetry, Social Sciences, Sociology, Women's Studies
ISBN Prefix(es): 1-871049; 1-875523

**D'Artagnan Publishing+**
8 Thinkell Ave, Beaumont, SA 5066
*Tel:* (08) 3493425
*Key Personnel*
Head of Business: Hazel I Barrett
Writer: Elizabeth Whitbread
Founded: 1982
Membership(s): Australian Journalist Association.
Subjects: Animals, Pets, Art, Romance
ISBN Prefix(es): 0-9593142; 1-875201

**D'Assis Books+**
44 Tristania Dr, Marcus Beach, Qld 4573
Mailing Address: PO Box 1189, Noosa Heads, Qld 4567
*Tel:* (07) 5448 2145 *Fax:* (07) 5447 5200
ISBN Prefix(es): 0-646
*Orders to:* Gemcraft, 14 Duffy St, Burwood, Melbourne, Victoria 3125
Warwick Page Eagle Heights Relaxation Retreat, 168 McDonell Rd, Eagle Heights, Mount Harborite, Qld 4271 *Tel:* (075) 545-3903 *Fax:* (075) 545-2426
Bhudens, PO Box 163, West Burleigh, Qld *Tel:* (075) 534 9200 *Fax:* (073) 302 2998

**Deakin University Press+**
Pigdons Rd, Geelong, Victoria 3217
*Tel:* (03) 5227 8144 *Fax:* (03) 5227 2020
*E-mail:* lynnew@deakin.edu.au
*Web Site:* www.deakin.edu.au
*Telex:* 35625
*Key Personnel*
Chief Executive: Ed Brumby
Manager: Marie Kelly
Manager, Sales: David Oswell *E-mail:* doswell@deakin.edu.au
Founded: 1979
Membership(s): Australian Book Publishers Association, National Book Council.
Subjects: Anthropology, Business, Environmental Studies, Mathematics, Medicine, Nursing, Dentistry, Women's Studies
ISBN Prefix(es): 0-949823; 0-86828; 0-7300
Total Titles: 356 Print
*Parent Company:* Learning Resources Services Deakin University

**Del Rey**, *imprint of* Random House Australia

**Dell**, *imprint of* Transworld Publishers Pty Ltd

**Dell Publishing**, *imprint of* Random House Australia

**Dellasta Publishing Pty Ltd+**
PO Box 777, Mount Waverley, Victoria 3149
*Tel:* (03) 9888 9188 *Fax:* (03) 9888 7806
*E-mail:* dellasta@publishaust.net.au
*Key Personnel*
Man Dir: Christian Esterhuyse
Customer Service: Irene Horwood
Founded: 1986
Membership(s): Publish Australia.
Subjects: Education, Environmental Studies, Geography, Geology, Language Arts, Linguistics, Mathematics, Science (General)
ISBN Prefix(es): 0-947138; 1-875627; 1-875640
Imprints: Ashwood House; Ashwood House Medical
Divisions: Ashwood Medical; Ashwood House Medical
Distributor for Green Submarine (UK); Learning Resources Inc (USA); Ver Lag An Der Ruhr (Germany)
*Orders to:* PO Box 777, Mount Waverley, Victoria 3149

**Demonvamp Publications**
24 Kiah St, Glen Waverley, Victoria 3150
*Tel:* (03) 9802 3875

*Key Personnel*
Publisher: W H Brook
ISBN Prefix(es): 1-86252

**Department of Energy (NSW)+**
Level 17, 227 Elizabeth St, Sydney, NSW 2001
Mailing Address: GPO Box 3889, Sydney, NSW 2001
*Tel:* (02) 8281 7777 *Fax:* (02) 8281 7799
*E-mail:* information@deus.nsw.gov.au
*Web Site:* www.doe.nsw.gov.au
*Key Personnel*
Dir General: Brian Steffen
Marketing: Peter Walker
Subjects: Earth Sciences

**Department of Mineral Resources (NSW)**, see Department of Energy (NSW)

**Department of Primary Industries, Queensland**
Primary Industries Bldg, 1st floor, Publishing Services, 80 Ann St, Brisbane, Qld 4000
Mailing Address: GPO Box 46, Brisbane, Qld 4001
*Tel:* (07) 3239 3772 *Fax:* (07) 3239 6509
*E-mail:* books@dpi.qld.gov.au
*Web Site:* www.dpi.qld.gov.au
Subjects: Agriculture, Animals, Pets, Gardening, Plants
ISBN Prefix(es): 0-7242
*Orders to:* DPI Publications, Primary Industries Bldg, Brisbane, Qld 4000

**Desbooks**, *imprint of* Rainbow Book Agencies Pty Ltd

**Desbooks Pty Ltd**
56 Wales St, Thornbury, Victoria 3071
*Tel:* (03) 9484 2465 *Fax:* (03) 9484 3877
*E-mail:* desb@alphalink.com.au
*Key Personnel*
Contact: Hugh McGinlay
Founded: 1981
Subjects: Religion - Other, Theology
ISBN Prefix(es): 0-949824
Imprints: Wisdom Press

**Desert Pea Press**, *imprint of* The Federation Press

**Deva Wings Publications+**
PO Box 322, Daylesford, Victoria 3460
*Tel:* (03) 5348 1414 *Fax:* (03) 5348 1414
*E-mail:* devawings@netconnect.com.au
*Web Site:* www.spacountry.net.au/devawings
*Key Personnel*
Contact: Arjuna Govindamurti
Founded: 1994
Subjects: Human Relations, Nonfiction (General), Psychology, Psychiatry, Self-Help
ISBN Prefix(es): 0-9587202

**Dollar Books**, *imprint of* Ansay Pty Ltd

**Doubleday**, *imprint of* Random House Australia

**Doubleday**, *imprint of* Transworld Publishers Pty Ltd

**Dryden Press**, *imprint of* Elsevier Australia

**Dryden Press**
Imprint of Harcourt Australia Pty Ltd
PO Box 46, Darlinghurst, NSW 2010
*Tel:* (02) 331-4571 *Fax:* (02) 398-9782
*Key Personnel*
Contact: Ian R Stubbin

Subjects: Business, History, Travel
ISBN Prefix(es): 0-909162

**Dubois Publishing**
88 Jin Sha Lane, Mungay Creek, NSW 2440
*Tel:* (02) 6567 1407 *Fax:* (02) 9211 1865
*Key Personnel*
Publisher & Author: Bob Wood *Tel:* (02) 65671407 *E-mail:* bobbydubois@yahoo.com
Distributor: Ron Wood *E-mail:* books@elt.com.an
Subjects: Mathematics
ISBN Prefix(es): 0-7316
Total Titles: 1 Print
Distributed by Melting Pot Press

**Dun & Bradstreet Marketing Pty Ltd**, see D&B Marketing Pty Ltd

**Dynamo House P/L+**
4-10 Yorkshire St, Richmond, Victoria 3121
Mailing Address: PO Box 110, Richmond, Victoria 3121
*Tel:* (03) 9427 0955; (03) 9428 3636 *Fax:* (03) 9429 8036
*E-mail:* info@dynamoh.com.au
*Web Site:* www.dynamoh.com.au
*Key Personnel*
Publisher: Stefan Mager
Founded: 1979
Subjects: Astrology, Occult, Health, Nutrition, Humor, Alternative Therapies & Philosophies, Aromatherapy, Reflexology
ISBN Prefix(es): 0-949266; 1-876100; 0-949383
Subsidiaries: Dynamo Press
Distributed by Aromaland Inc (USA); Asiapac Books (Singapore); Milk & Honey, Inc. (USA)

**EA Books+**
2 Ernest St, Level 4, Crows Nest, NSW 2065
Mailing Address: PO Box 588, Crows Nest, NSW 1585
*Tel:* (02) 9438 1533 *Fax:* (02) 9438 5934
*E-mail:* eabooks@engaust.com.au
*Web Site:* www.engaust.com.au
*Key Personnel*
General Manager: Bruce Roff *E-mail:* broff@engaust.com.au
Editor: Dietrich Georg *E-mail:* dgeorg@engaust.com.au
Editorial: Bob Jackson *E-mail:* bjackson@engaust.com.au; Nathan Menser *E-mail:* nmenser@engaust.com.au; Paul Woolnough *E-mail:* pwoolnough@engaust.com.au
Advertising Manager: Terry Marsden *E-mail:* tmarsden@engaust.com.au
Advertising Sales: Maria Mamone *E-mail:* mmamone@engaust.com.au
Subscriptions: Pam Chenery *E-mail:* jmcgregor@engaugst.com.au
Founded: 1919 (I E Aust, 1976 E A Books)
Subjects: Chemistry, Chemical Engineering, Civil Engineering, Electronics, Electrical Engineering, Mechanical Engineering, Railway Engineering
ISBN Prefix(es): 0-85825
Number of titles published annually: 5 Print
*Parent Company:* Institution of Engineers Australia, 11 National Circuit, Barton, ACT 2600
*Associate Companies:* Chemical Engineering in Australia Magazine; Engineering World Magazine; Engineers Australia Magazine
Imprints: IE Aust Publications

**Ebury Press**, *imprint of* Random House Australia

**Echidna Books**, *imprint of* Heinemann Library

**The Edge of It**, *imprint of* Feakle Press

**Edubook**, *imprint of* Egan Publishing Pty Ltd

**Education**, *imprint of* R J Cleary Publishing

**Educational Advantage+**
29 Meninya St, Moama, NSW 2731
Mailing Address: PO Box 1068, Echuca, Victoria 3564
*Tel:* (03) 5480 9466 *Fax:* (03) 5480 9462
*E-mail:* joe@mathsmate.net
*Web Site:* www.mathsmate.net
*Key Personnel*
Manager: Joanna Tutos
Contact: Joseph B Wright
Founded: 1995
Subjects: Education, Mathematics
ISBN Prefix(es): 1-876081
Total Titles: 46 Print
*Associate Companies:* Learning Cycles USA; Math's Mate USA
Foreign Rep(s): Kathy Frick (US); Trish Kidd (New Zealand)

**Educational Assessment Service Inc**, *imprint of* Hawker Brownlow

**Educational Impressions**, *imprint of* Hawker Brownlow

**Educational Insights**, *imprint of* Hawker Brownlow

**Educational Supplies Pty Ltd (The Dominie Group)**
8 Cross St, Brookvale, NSW 2100
Mailing Address: PO Box 33, Brookvale, NSW 2100
*Tel:* (02) 99050201 *Fax:* (02) 99055209
*Key Personnel*
Man Dir: Ross Martin *E-mail:* ross@educationalsuppliesptyltd.com.au
Founded: 1951
ISBN Prefix(es): 1-86251; 0-909268; 0-949029

**Edwina Publishing+**
20 Willandra Ave, Canterbury, Victoria 3126
*Tel:* (03) 9836 3810 *Fax:* (03) 9830 1356
*Web Site:* www.edwinapublishing.com
*Key Personnel*
President: Christopher J Venn
Author: Susan L Venn
Founded: 1991
Subjects: Art
ISBN Prefix(es): 0-646
Total Titles: 3 Print

**Egan Publishing Pty Ltd+**
8 Waverley St, East Brighton, Victoria 3187
*Tel:* (03) 5923451 *Fax:* (03) 95931026
*Key Personnel*
Head of Company: Cecilia Egan
Founded: 1986
Subjects: Animals, Pets, Cookery, Crafts, Games, Hobbies, Fiction, Gardening, Plants
ISBN Prefix(es): 0-947272; 0-9593542; 0-9581361
Imprints: Edubook; Ashton Egan

**Egmont**, *imprint of* Random House Australia

**Elephas Books Pty Ltd+**
1/18 Mooney St, Bayswater, WA 6053
*Tel:* (08) 9370 1461 *Fax:* (08) 9341 8952
*Key Personnel*
Head of Company: Alan Falkson; Rume Karlson
Founded: 1989
Specialize in How-to & informational titles, also acts as importer & distributor of small press titles through Practical Books subsidiary.
Subjects: How-to, Library & Information Sciences
ISBN Prefix(es): 1-875273
*Parent Company:* The Firs
Imprints: Wilbur

**David Ell Press Pty Ltd+**
PMB 14, Balmain, NSW 2041
*Tel:* (02) 5551634 *Fax:* (02) 5557067
*Key Personnel*
Head of Company: David Ell
Man Editor: Kathryn Lamberton
Founded: 1978
Subjects: Art, Crafts, Games, Hobbies
ISBN Prefix(es): 0-908197
Imprints: Ellsyd Press (paperbacks & children's)
Subsidiaries: Ellsyd Press Pty Ltd; Longueville Publications
*Orders to:* Tower Books, 2 Sydenham Rd, Brookvale, NSW 2100

**Ellsyd Press**, *imprint of* David Ell Press Pty Ltd

**Elsevier Australia+**
30-52 Smidmore St, Marrickville, NSW 2204
Mailing Address: Locked Bag 16, St Peters, NSW 2044
*Tel:* (029) 5178999 *Toll Free Tel:* 1-800 263 951 (within Australia); 0-800 170 165 (to Australia from New Zealand) *Fax:* (029) 5172249 *Toll Free Fax:* 0-800 170 160 (from Australia to New Zealand)
*E-mail:* service@elsevier.com.au
*Web Site:* www.elsevier.com.au
*Key Personnel*
Man Dir: Brian Brennan *Fax:* (02) 95506007 *E-mail:* bbrennan@harcourt.com.au
Financial Controller & Operations Manager: Jim Robinson *Fax:* (02) 95506007 *E-mail:* jrobinson@harcourt.com.au
General Manager College Division: Paul Barry *Fax:* (02) 95506007 *E-mail:* pbarry@harcourt.com.au
TPC General Manager: Dianne Lissner *Fax:* (02) 95506007 *E-mail:* dlissner@harcourt.com.au
General Manager STM Division: Anneke Baeten *Fax:* (02) 95506007 *E-mail:* abaeten@harcourt.com.au
Founded: 1972
Also several divisions: college, medical, psychological testing & professional/trade.
Subjects: Business, Education, Mathematics, Medicine, Nursing, Dentistry, Psychology, Psychiatry, Science (General), Social Sciences, Sociology, Veterinary Science
ISBN Prefix(es): 0-7295
Total Titles: 8,000 Print; 65 CD-ROM
*Parent Company:* Harcourt Inc, 6277 Sea Harbor Dr, Orlando, FL 32887, United States
*Associate Companies:* Harcourt Brace Japan Inc, Ichibancho Central Bldg, 22-1, Ichibancho, Chiyoda-ku, Tokyo 102, Japan; Academic Press Ltd, Harcourt Place, 32 Jamestown Road, London NW1 7BY, United Kingdom; Bailliere Tindall Ltd, Harcourt Place, 32 Jamestown Road, London NW1 7BY, United Kingdom; Harcourt Publishers Ltd, Harcourt Place, 32 Jamestown Road, London NW1 7BY, United Kingdom; Academic Press Inc, 1250 Sixth Ave, San Diego, CA 92101, United States; Harcourt Inc, 6277 Sea Harbor Dr, Orlando, FL 32821, United States; W B Saunders Co, The Curtis Center, Independence Sq, Philadelphia, PA 19106-3399, United States; Holt Rinehart & Winston Inc, 1627 Woodland Ave, Austin, TX 78741, United States; Harcourt College Publishers, 301 Commerce St, Suite 3700, Fort Worth, TX 78741, United States; The Psychological Corporation, 555 Academic Court, San Antonio, TX 78204-0952, United States
Imprints: Academic Press; Churchill Livingstone; Dryden Press; Harcourt Brace; Holt, Rinehart and Winston; Industrial Press; Mayfield Publishing; Morgan Kaufmann; Mosby; The Psychological Corporation; W B Saunders/Bailliere Tindall; Saunders College; Singular Press; Technomic Publishing
*Branch Office(s)*
Level 3, 71 Queens Rd, Melbourne, Victoria 3004

236 Dominion Rd, Mt Eden, Auckland 3, New Zealand
Distributor for Mayfield (Australia & New Zealand); Technomic Publishing (Australia & New Zealand)

**Elton Publications+**
57 Camden St, Wembly Downs, WA 6019
*Tel:* (08) 9 446 1328 *Fax:* (08) 9 445 8229
*E-mail:* elton@iinet.net.au
*Web Site:* www.elton.iinet.net.au
*Key Personnel*
Contact: Richard Lyon
Founded: 1994
Blackline Masters books which are used by teachers; educational, internet, Australia, Aborigines.
Membership(s): Copyright Agency Ltd.
Subjects: History, Culture, Wildlife
ISBN Prefix(es): 0-646; 1-876486
Number of titles published annually: 8 Print; 1 E-Book
Total Titles: 49 Print; 6 E-Book
Distributed by Chalkies n Kids Dominie; Dominie; Holding Educational Aids; Narnia Bookshop; Wooldridges

**Emerald City Books+**
21 Redmyre Rd, Strathfield, NSW 2135
*Tel:* (02) 7641115 *Fax:* (02) 7641115
*E-mail:* emeraldcitybooks@hotmail.com
*Key Personnel*
Dir: Ken Preece
Founded: 1995
Subjects: Biological Sciences, Business, Chemistry, Chemical Engineering, Computer Science, Economics, Mathematics, Physics, Science (General)
ISBN Prefix(es): 1-876133

**Emmaus Productions**, *imprint of* Rainbow Book Agencies Pty Ltd

**Emperor Publishing+**
55 Oxford St, Darlinghurst, NSW 2010
*Tel:* (02) 9261 4055 *Fax:* (02) 9264 9435
*E-mail:* pa@oxfordsquare.com.au
*Key Personnel*
Head of Company & Dir: Phil Birnbaum
Founded: 1989
Subjects: Anthropology, Biography, Foreign Countries, Humor, Nonfiction (General), Photography, Travel
ISBN Prefix(es): 0-7316
Total Titles: 2 Print

**Encyclopaedia Britannica (Australia) Inc**
90 Mount St, Level 1, North Sydney, NSW 2060
*Tel:* (02) 9923 5600 *Fax:* (02) 9929 3758
*E-mail:* sales@britannica.com.au
*Web Site:* www.britannica.com.au
*Telex:* 23044 Enbrit
*Key Personnel*
Man Dir: David Campbell
General Manager, Sales & Marketing: James Buckle
Subjects: Art, Biological Sciences, Geography, Geology, Science (General)
ISBN Prefix(es): 0-909263
*Parent Company:* Encyclopaedia Britannica Inc, Britannica Centre, 310 South Michigan Ave, Chicago, IL 60604, United States
*Associate Companies:* Encyclopaedia Britannica International Ltd UK

**Enrich**, *imprint of* Hawker Brownlow

**Enterprise Publications+**
POB 16, Goodwood, SA 5034
*Tel:* (08) 8261 9528 *Fax:* (08) 8261 9528
Founded: 1972

Membership(s): Fellow of Royal Photographic Society (FRPS).
Subjects: History, Maritime, Natural History, Outdoor Recreation, Photography, Regional Interests
ISBN Prefix(es): 0-85913
Distributed by State Mutual Books (USA)

**Envirobook+**
38 Rose St, Annandale, NSW 2038
*Tel:* (02) 9518 6154 *Fax:* (02) 9518 6156
*E-mail:* trekaway@sia.net.au
*Telex:* 271206
*Key Personnel*
Man Dir: Patrick Thompson
Subjects: Environmental Studies, Natural History, Outdoor Recreation, Aboriginal Children
ISBN Prefix(es): 0-85881
Number of titles published annually: 15 Print
Total Titles: 30 Print

**ERA Picture Books**, *imprint of* Era Publications

**Era Publications+**
220 Grange Rd, Flinders Park, SA 5025
Mailing Address: PO Box 231, Brooklyn Park, SA 5032
*Tel:* (08) 8352 4122 *Fax:* (08) 8234 0023
*E-mail:* admin@erapublications.com; service@erapublications.com
*Web Site:* www.erapublications.com
*Key Personnel*
Chief Executive Officer & Man Dir: Dr Rodney Martin *E-mail:* rod@erapublications.com
Founded: 1971
Primary school educational materials.
Subjects: Education, Nonfiction (General), Primary/Elementary School Literature
ISBN Prefix(es): 1-86374; 1-74120; 0-947212; 0-908507
Total Titles: 250 Print; 1 CD-ROM; 28 Audio
*Parent Company:* R D Martin Pty Ltd
Imprints: ERA Picture Books; Magic Bean
Distributed by Ragged Bears (UK, Picture Books)
Distributor for Gareth Stevens Inc; Moonlight (Australia); Tessloff
Foreign Rep(s): The Choice Maker InterAustralia Co (Korea); Daniel Doglioli (Italy); Martina Oepping (France)

**Escutcheon Press**
37 Cornelian Rd, Pearl Beach, NSW 2256
*Tel:* (02) 4344 2304 *Fax:* (02) 4341 1248
*Key Personnel*
Contact: R E Summers
ISBN Prefix(es): 1-875862; 0-9588066

**Essien**, *imprint of* Hudson Publishing Services Pty Ltd

**Experimental Art Foundation**
Lion Arts Centre, N Terrace & Morphett St, Adelaide, SA 5000
Mailing Address: PO Box 8091, Station Arcade, Adelaide, SA 5000
*Tel:* (08) 8211 7505 *Fax:* (08) 8211 7323
*E-mail:* eaf@eaf.asn.au
*Web Site:* www.eaf.asn.au
*Key Personnel*
Director: Melentie Pandilovski
Administrator: Julie Lawton
Founded: 1974
Subjects: Art, Literature, Literary Criticism, Essays, Philosophy
ISBN Prefix(es): 0-949836; 0-9596729
*Associate Companies:* Otis Rush Magazine & Little Esther Books

**Extraordinary People Press+**
27 Meymott St, Randwick, NSW 2031
*Tel:* (02) 9326 6609 *Fax:* (02) 9399 6587
*E-mail:* info@extraordinarypeoplepress.com

*Web Site:* www.extraordinarypeoplepress.com
*Key Personnel*
Commissions Editor: Katrina Fox
  *E-mail:* katfox@easynet.co.uk
International Rights: K Butler
Founded: 1997
Subjects: Behavioral Sciences, Gay & Lesbian, Health, Nutrition, Human Relations, Nonfiction (General), Psychology, Psychiatry, Self-Help, Social Sciences, Sociology
ISBN Prefix(es): 0-9529482
*Bookshop(s):* Turnaround, Unit 3, Olympia Trading Estate, Cobury Rd, Wood Crear, London N22, United Kingdom


**Fairfield Press**, *imprint of* Rainbow Book Agencies Pty Ltd


**Family Circle**, *imprint of* Murdoch Books


**Family Health Publications+**
PO Box 3100, Nedlands, WA 6009
*Tel:* (08) 9389 8777 *Fax:* (08) 9389 8444
*Web Site:* www.familyhealth.info
*Key Personnel*
President: Allan Borushek *E-mail:* allan@calorieking.com
Founded: 1972
Subjects: Health, Nutrition
ISBN Prefix(es): 0-947091
*U.S. Office(s):* Allan Borushek & Associates Inc, 1760 Monrovia Ave, PO Box 1616, Costa Mesa, CA 92628, United States *Tel:* 949-642-8500 *Fax:* 949-642-8900


**Family Reading Publications**
B100 Ring Rd, Ballarat, Victoria 3350
*Tel:* (03) 5334 3244 *Fax:* (03) 5334 3299
*E-mail:* info@familyreading.com.au
*Web Site:* www.familyreading.com.au
*Key Personnel*
Contact: Colin Handreck *E-mail:* colin.handreck@familyreading.com.au; Ian Ruddick
Founded: 1976
Wholesale distributor - Christian books.
Distributor for Baker Book House; Christian Focus Publications (Australia); J Countryman; Harvest House Publishing; Intervarsity Press (Australia); Thomas Nelson; Tommy Nelson; Word Publishing; Zondervan (Australia)


**Fawcett**, *imprint of* Random House Australia


**Feakle Press**
126 Lennox St, Newtown, NSW 2042
*Tel:* (02) 9557 3248
*Key Personnel*
International Rights: Colleen Burke
Founded: 1992
Subjects: Poetry
ISBN Prefix(es): 0-646
Imprints: The Edge of It; Wildlife in Newtown


**Fearon Teacher Aids**, *imprint of* Hawker Brownlow


**The Federation Press+**
71 John St, Leichhardt, NSW 2040
Mailing Address: PO Box 45, Annandale, NSW 2038
*Tel:* (02) 9552-2200 *Fax:* (02) 9552-1681
*E-mail:* info@federationpress.com.au
*Web Site:* www.federationpress.com.au
*Key Personnel*
Dir: Christopher Holt; Diane Young *E-mail:* d.young@federationpress.com.au
Founded: 1988
Legal & social issues publisher.
Subjects: Business, Environmental Studies, Law, Academic Texts

ISBN Prefix(es): 1-86287
Total Titles: 300 Print
Imprints: Desert Pea Press; Hawkins Press
Distributed by Dunmore Press (New Zealand); Willan Publishing UK (Australiasia)
Distributor for Criminal Justice Press US; Dunmore Press (New Zealand)


**Fernfawn Publications+**
83 Weekes Rd, Moggill, Qld 4070
Mailing Address: PO Box 1010, Kenmore, Qld 4069
*Tel:* (07) 3202 6157 *Fax:* (07) 3202 6157
*Key Personnel*
Head of Company: Jarvis L Finger
Founded: 1992
Subjects: Education, Humor, Law, Management
ISBN Prefix(es): 0-646


**Finch Publishing+**
PO Box 120, Lane Cove, NSW 2066
*Tel:* (02) 9418 6247 *Fax:* (02) 9418 8878
*E-mail:* info@finch.com.au
*Web Site:* www.finch.com.au
*Key Personnel*
Publisher: Rex Finch
Dir: Vicki Finch
Marketing Coordinator: Julian Sheedy
Editor: Sean Doyle
Founded: 1992
Subjects: Child Care & Development, Communications, Education, Human Relations, Nonfiction (General), Psychology, Psychiatry, Self-Help, Social Sciences, Sociology, Women's Studies, Parenting, Relationships, Mens Studies, Social Issues, Children's Health
ISBN Prefix(es): 1-876451
Number of titles published annually: 10 Print
Total Titles: 17 Print
Distributed by Double & Newman Pty Ltd (Territory: Asia); Simon & Schuster (Territory: Australia); Southern Publishers Group (Territory: New Zealand); Pearson Education South (Territory: South Africa); Deep Books (Territory: UK)


**Fine Art Publishing Pty Ltd+**
42 Chandos St, St Leonards, NSW 2065
*Tel:* (02) 99668400 *Fax:* (02) 99660355
*E-mail:* info@gbpub.com.au
*Web Site:* www.gbpub.com.au *Cable:* IMPRINT SYDNEY
*Key Personnel*
Publisher: Sam Ure Smith
Editor: Dinah Dysart; Leon Paroissien
Editorial Manager: Hannah Fink
Founded: 1963
Art & Australia, quarterly journal, company also produces books for other publishers.
Subjects: Art
ISBN Prefix(es): 0-86917; 1-877004
Imprints: Craftsman House
Divisions: Craftsman House (Book Division)


**The Five Mile Press Pty Ltd**
950 Stud Rd, Rowville, Victoria 3178
Mailing Address: PO Box 177, Ferntree Gully, Victoria 3156
*Tel:* (03) 8756 5500 *Fax:* (03) 8756 5588
*E-mail:* publishing@fivemile.com.au
*Web Site:* www.fivemile.com.au
*Key Personnel*
Man Dir: David Horgan
Subjects: Regional Interests
ISBN Prefix(es): 0-86788; 1-875971; 1-86503


**Flactem**
1429A Toorak Rd, Camberwell, Victoria 3124
*Tel:* (03) 9889 6855 *Fax:* (03) 98888948
*Key Personnel*
Contact: Judith Paphazy
ISBN Prefix(es): 0-646

**Flora Publications International Pty Ltd+**
371 Queen St, 8th Floor, Brisbane, Qld 4001
Mailing Address: GPOB 2927, Brisbane, Qld 4001
*Tel:* (07) 3229 6366 *Fax:* (07) 3378 7102
*E-mail:* info@flora.com.au
*Key Personnel*
President & International Rights: Paul Niederer
Founded: 1995
Subjects: Gardening, Plants, Outdoor Recreation, Horticulture
ISBN Prefix(es): 1-876060
*Associate Companies:* Infomedia Publishing Pty Ltd, Brisbane, Qld
Imprints: Infomedia


**Florilegium+**
PO Box 644, Rozelle, NSW 2039
*Tel:* (02) 95558589 *Fax:* (02) 98184409
*E-mail:* florileg@ozemail.com.au
*Key Personnel*
Manager: Gilbert Teague
Founded: 1989
Membership(s): ABPA, NIAA.
Subjects: Gardening, Plants
ISBN Prefix(es): 0-9586498; 1-876314


**Fodor**, *imprint of* Random House Australia


**Forge**, *imprint of* Pan Macmillan Australia Pty Ltd


**Foundation for Critical Thinking**, *imprint of* Hawker Brownlow


**Fraser Publications+**
PO Box 215, Rutherglen, Victoria 3685
*Tel:* (018) 039845 *Fax:* (057) 261775
*E-mail:* fraspub@albury.net.au
*Key Personnel*
Manager: Ian C Fraser
Founded: 1987
Subjects: Health, Nutrition, Medicine, Nursing, Dentistry, Self-Help
ISBN Prefix(es): 0-9588384


**Free Spirit Publishing Inc**, *imprint of* Hawker Brownlow


**Fremantle Arts Centre Press**
25 Quarry St, Fremantle, WA 6160
Mailing Address: PO Box 158, North Fremantle, WA 6159
*Tel:* (08) 9430 6331 *Fax:* (08) 9430 5242
*E-mail:* facp@iinet.net.au
*Web Site:* facp.iinet.net.au
*Key Personnel*
Publisher: Ray Coffey
General Manager: Clive Newman
Founded: 1976
Subjects: Art, Biography, Education, Fiction, History, Literature, Literary Criticism, Essays, Poetry
ISBN Prefix(es): 1-86368; 0-949144; 0-949206; 1-920731
Number of titles published annually: 35 Print
Total Titles: 250 Print
Imprints: Sandcastle Books
Distributed by Penguin Books (NZ) Ltd (New Zealand); Penguin Books Australia Ltd (Australia)
Foreign Rep(s): International Specialized Book Services (North America)
*Distribution Center:* International Specialized Book Service, 5804 NE Hassala St, Portland, OR 97213-3644, United States, Contact: Tamma Greenfield *Tel:* 503-287-3093 *Fax:* 503-280-8832 *E-mail:* orders@isbs.com *Web Site:* www.isbs.com (US distribution only)

**Freshet Press+**
2 Lyttleton Ave, Castlemaine, Victoria 3450
*Tel:* (03) 53483085
*Key Personnel*
International Rights: J Richards
Founded: 1982
Subjects: Gardening, Plants, Literature, Literary Criticism, Essays, Philosophy, Poetry, Psychology, Psychiatry, Religion - Other, Social Sciences, Sociology
ISBN Prefix(es): 0-9593361

**Full Circle Publications Co-Operative**
12 Cornell St, Camberwell, Victoria 3124
*Tel:* (03) 9830 4253
ISBN Prefix(es): 0-9587113
Distributor for Australian Council for Educational Research
*Bookshop(s):* Politics & Prose Bookstore, 5015 Connecticut Ave NW, Washington, DC 20008, United States *Tel:* 202-364-1919

**Galations Group**, *imprint of* Rainbow Book Agencies Pty Ltd

**Galley Press Publishing+**
50 Arthur St, Surry Hills, NSW 2010
*Tel:* (02) 9698 9262 *Fax:* (02) 9360 1968
*E-mail:* isbin@ozemail.com.au
*Key Personnel*
Contact: Tony Markidis
Founded: 1992
Also acts as bookshop & infoserver, stop distribution service.
Subjects: Fiction, Poetry, Sports, Athletics
ISBN Prefix(es): 1-875701
Total Titles: 15 Print
*Associate Companies:* Home Grown Book Distribution Co-op Ltd; Isbin Bookspider

**Gamco Industries Inc**, *imprint of* Hawker Brownlow

**Gangan Publishing+**
PO Box 522, Strawberry Hills, NSW 2012
*Tel:* (02) 9280 2120 *Fax:* (02) 9280 2130
*E-mail:* books@gangan.com
*Web Site:* www.gangan.com
*Key Personnel*
Publisher: Gerald Ganglbauer *Tel:* (0411) 156 309 *E-mail:* gerald@gangan.com
Founded: 1984
Subjects: Fiction, Literature, Literary Criticism, Essays, Poetry, Regional Interests, Contemporary literature from Australia & Austria
ISBN Prefix(es): 1-86336
Imprints: Gangaroo
*Orders to:* Brodtrager & Partner OEG, Rainleiten 62, A-8045 Graz, Austria, Guenter Brodtrager *Tel:* (0316) 670 4090 *Fax:* (0316) 670 4096 *E-mail:* gbrodtrager@greenbrains.com

**Gangaroo**, *imprint of* Gangan Publishing

**Garr Publishing+**
Palm Court, 464 The Entrance Rd, Erina Heights, NSW 2260
*Tel:* (02) 4367 7223 *Fax:* (02) 4367 7762
*E-mail:* garrpublishing@digisurf.net.au
*Web Site:* www.garrpublishing.com.au
*Key Personnel*
Contact: Robert Symington *E-mail:* books@ digisurf.net.au
Founded: 1994
An all Australian Enterprise, whose aim is to introduce, establish & market Australian works to the national & international markets.
Specialize in fiction based on fact (Australian authors).
Subjects: Fiction

Number of titles published annually: 3 Print; 5 CD-ROM; 6 Online; 4 E-Book; 5 Audio
Total Titles: 7 Print; 6 CD-ROM; 8 Online; 6 E-Book; 5 Audio
Subsidiaries: Softmail Computing

**Garradunga Press**
1/33 Jensen St, Manoora, Qld 4870
*Tel:* (0409) 320 619 (mobile) *Fax:* (07) 4032 5918
*E-mail:* bolton@iig.com.au
*Key Personnel*
Contact: Colleen Rowe
Specialize in travel.
Subjects: Travel
ISBN Prefix(es): 0-646

**John Garratt Publishing+**
32 Glenvale Crescent, Private Bag 400, Mulgrave, Victoria 3170
*Tel:* (03) 9545 3111 *Toll Free Tel:* 300 650 878 *Fax:* (03) 9545 3222
*E-mail:* sales@johngarratt.com.au
*Web Site:* www.johngarratt.com.au
*Key Personnel*
Man Dir: Garry Eastman *E-mail:* garryeastman@ johngarratt.com.au
Founded: 1995
Importation & marketing of overseas religious titles.
Membership(s): CBAA.
Subjects: Religion - Other
ISBN Prefix(es): 1-875938; 1-920682; 1-920721
Number of titles published annually: 5 Print
Total Titles: 20 Print
Distributor for Emmas Publications; General Synod of the Anglican Church of Australia
*Book Club(s):* Sophia Booknet

**Anne Geddes**, *imprint of* Hachette Livre Australia

**Germinal Press**
PO Box 345, Toowong, Qld 4066

**Gifted Children Information Centre**, *imprint of* Hawker Brownlow

**Ginninderra Press**
PO Box 53, Charnwood, ACT 2615
*Tel:* (02) 6258 9060 *Fax:* (02) 6258 9069
*Web Site:* www.ginninderrapress.com.au
*Key Personnel*
Publisher: Stephen Matthews *E-mail:* stephenmatthews@ginninderrapress. com.au
Founded: 1996
Subjects: Biography, Disability, Special Needs, Education, Fiction, Health, Nutrition, History, Library & Information Sciences, Music, Dance, Poetry
ISBN Prefix(es): 1-876259; 0-9586825; 1-74027
Number of titles published annually: 40 Print
Total Titles: 200 Print
Imprints: Indigo; Mockingbird

**Global Business Network**, *imprint of* Prospect Media

**Gnostic Editions**
12 Miller Ave, Kew, Victoria 3101
Mailing Address: PO Box 410, Kew, Victoria 3101
*Tel:* (03) 9853 1401 *Fax:* (03) 9853 1481
*E-mail:* mail@gnoticeditions.com
*Key Personnel*
Dir: Ian Watchorn *E-mail:* ian@ianwatchorn.com
Contact: Robyn Lambert
Founded: 1992

Associate companies located in Brazil, Portugal, Spain, Thailand & United Kingdom.
Subjects: Alternative, Anthropology, Archaeology, Astrology, Occult, Human Relations, Mysteries, Parapsychology, Philosophy, Psychology, Psychiatry, Religion - Other, Self-Help, Theology
ISBN Prefix(es): 0-646
Number of titles published annually: 2 Print
Total Titles: 10 Print
*Parent Company:* Nous Editores, Calle Mina Nº 209, Col Tetela del Monte, CP 62130, Cuernavaca Morelos DF, Mexico
*Associate Companies:* Anubis Publishers International (Canada)

**Gould Genealogy**
Unit 4, 247 Milne Rd, Modbury North, SA 5092
Mailing Address: PO Box 675, Modbury, SA 5092
*Tel:* (08) 8396 1110 *Fax:* (08) 8396 1163
*E-mail:* inquiries@gould.com.au
*Web Site:* www.gould.com.au
*Key Personnel*
Contact: Alan Phillips *E-mail:* alan@gould.com. au
Founded: 1976
Subjects: Genealogy, History
ISBN Prefix(es): 0-947284

**Graffiti Publications+**
69 Forest St, Castlemaine, Victoria 3450
Mailing Address: PO Box 2328, Castlemaine, Victoria 3450
*Tel:* (03) 5472 3805
*E-mail:* graffiti@netcon.net.au
*Web Site:* www.graffitipub.com.au
*Key Personnel*
Dir: Larry O'Toole
Founded: 1976
Subjects: Automotive, Crafts, Games, Hobbies
ISBN Prefix(es): 0-949398
Total Titles: 16 Print
Distributed by Celebrity Books (New Zealand); MotorBooks International
Distributor for The Rodder's Journal; Tex Smith Library
Foreign Rep(s): Motorbooks International (North America)

**Grainger Museum**
Information Division, University of Melbourne, Melbourne, Victoria 3010
*Tel:* (03) 8344 5270 *Fax:* (03) 9349 1707
*E-mail:* grainger@unimelb.edu.au
*Web Site:* www.lib.unimelb.edu.au/collections/ grainger
*Telex:* AA 35185
*Key Personnel*
Curator: Rosemary Florrimell
Founded: 1938
Subjects: Music, Dance

**Granrott Press**
The Old Rectory, Lule Rd, Clarendon, SA 5157
*Tel:* (08) 383 6081 *Fax:* (08) 383 6067
*Key Personnel*
Dir: N Hjorth
Founded: 1984
Family business that was founded based on the need to cross boundaries of an autobiographical book with feminine based visual arts.
Subjects: Art, Theology, Women's Studies
ISBN Prefix(es): 0-9590720
Total Titles: 4 Print

**Grass Roots**, *imprint of* Grass Roots Publishing

**Grass Roots Publishing**
PO Box 117, Seymour, Victoria 3661
*Tel:* (03) 5794 7256 *Fax:* (03) 5794 7285

*Key Personnel*
Head of Company: David A Miller
Production: Meg Miller
Founded: 1973
ISBN Prefix(es): 0-9595244; 0-9590152; 0-947065; 0-9580894; 1-876321
Imprints: Grass Roots

**Great Western Press Pty Ltd+**
PO Box 482, Chatswood, NSW 2067
*Tel:* (02) 4124 394 *Fax:* (02) 9144 5566
*Key Personnel*
Man Dir: John Isaacs *E-mail:* jisaacssydney@aol.com
Sales: Anne Isaacs
Rights & Permissions: Robert Elliott
Founded: 1974
Subjects: How-to, Romance, Science (General), Autobiographies, Memoirs
ISBN Prefix(es): 0-86901
Number of titles published annually: 2 Print
Total Titles: 57 Print
*Associate Companies:* Pymble Trading Pty Ltd
Imprints: GWP
*Shipping Address:* ACP Customs Services Pty Ltd, PO Box 148, Rosebery, NSW 2018, Contact: Geoff Dickson *Tel:* (02) 9669 0966 *Fax:* (02) 9669 0999 *E-mail:* acpcustoms@att.net.au
*Warehouse:* Unit 3, 809-821 Botany Rd, Rosebery, NSW 2018, Contact: Peter Reid

**Greater Glider Productions Australia Pty Ltd+**
Book Farm, 8 Rees Lane, Maleny, Qld 4552
*Tel:* (07) 5494 3000 *Fax:* (07) 5494 3284
*Key Personnel*
Publishing Dir: Jill Morris *E-mail:* jillmorris@greaterglider.com.au
Manager: Cheryl Wickes
Founded: 1983
Membership(s): Australian Publishers Association.
Subjects: Education, Health, Nutrition, Natural History, Science (General)
ISBN Prefix(es): 0-947304
Foreign Rep(s): Australia for Kids (Roots & Wings) (US); The Choicemaker (Korea); Portfolio Children's Books (UK)
Foreign Rights: The Choicemaker (Korea); Quarter Marketing (South Africa)
*Bookshop(s):* Peace of Green, Maple St, Maleny 4552
*Book Club(s):* Choice Magazine; Scholastic; Wilderness Society

**Gregory's**, *imprint of* Universal Press Pty Ltd

**Griffin**, *imprint of* Pan Macmillan Australia Pty Ltd

**GWP**, *imprint of* Great Western Press Pty Ltd

**Hachette Livre Australia+**
Level 17, 207 Kent Str, Sydney, NSW 2000
*Tel:* (02) 8248 0800; (02) 4390 1300 (customer service) *Fax:* (02) 8248 0810
*E-mail:* aspub@hachette.com.au (Australian publishing); hsales@alliancedist.com.au; adscs@alliancedist.com.au (customer service)
*Web Site:* www.hachette.com.au
*Key Personnel*
Man Dir: Malcolm Edwards *Tel:* (02) 8248 0802 *E-mail:* malcolm.edwards@hachette.com.au
Sales & Marketing Director: Mary Drum *Tel:* (02) 8248 0854 *E-mail:* mary.drum@hachette.com.au
Australian Publishing Director: Lisa Highton *Tel:* (02) 8248 0818 *E-mail:* lisa.highton@hachette.com.au

Sales & Marketing Dir Hachette Children's Books: Chris Raine *Tel:* (02) 8248 0826 *E-mail:* chris.raine@hachette.com.au
Publishing & Production Director: Fiona Hazard *Tel:* (02) 8248 0806 *E-mail:* fiona.hazard@hachette.com.au
Founded: 1958
Also distributor of group product agents for Piatkus (UK).
Membership(s): Australian Booksellers Association; Australian Publishers Association.
ISBN Prefix(es): 0-7499; 0-340; 0-7472; 0-7553; 0-412; 0-7336; 0-750; 0-719; 1-869
Number of titles published annually: 120 Print
Total Titles: 1,500 Print
*Ultimate Parent Company:* Hachette Livre
Imprints: Anne Geddes; Headline; Help Yourself; Hodder; Hodder & Stoughton; Hodder Arnold; Hodder (Australia); Hodder Moa Beckett; Hodder Mobius; Hodder Religious; MILK; John Murray; NIV; Piatkus; Review; Sceptre; Teach Yourself

**Halbooks Publishing+**
PO Box 224, Coogee, NSW 2034
*Tel:* (02) 9326 4250 *Fax:* (02) 9326 4250
*E-mail:* sean@iotaproductions.com.au
*Key Personnel*
Contact: Alan Halbish
Also acts as print broker & literary agent.
ISBN Prefix(es): 0-9585807; 0-9578908

**Hale & Iremonger Pty Ltd+**
76-82 Chapel St, Marrickville, NSW 2204
Mailing Address: PO Box 205, 2015 Alexandria, NSW
*Tel:* (02) 9560 0470 *Fax:* (02) 9550 0097
*E-mail:* info@haleiremonger.com
*Web Site:* www.haleiremonger.com
*Key Personnel*
Marketing Manager: Matthew Harrigan *E-mail:* matthew@haleiremonger.com
Publisher & General Manager: Sylvia Hale *E-mail:* sylvia@haleiremonger.com
Founded: 1977
Membership(s): Australian Publishers Association, Australian Booksellers Association.
Subjects: Asian Studies, Biography, Business, Career Development, Child Care & Development, Genealogy, Government, Political Science, Health, Nutrition, History, Management, Nonfiction (General), Philosophy, Psychology, Psychiatry, Public Administration, Self-Help, Women's Studies
ISBN Prefix(es): 0-86806; 0-908094; 0-949818
Number of titles published annually: 10 Print
Total Titles: 200 Print
Distributed by Forrester Books 2 (New Zealand); Pacific Island Books (USA); Roundhouse Publishing Group (UK & Western Europe)

**F H Halpern+**
2/75 Gardenvale Rd, Elsternwick, Victoria 3185
*Tel:* (03) 9596 1436 *Fax:* (03) 9596 1436
*Key Personnel*
Contact: F H Halpern
Subjects: History, Travel
ISBN Prefix(es): 0-7223; 0-7316
*Branch Office(s)*
Melbourne

**Kerri Hamer+**
347 Maroubra Rd, Maroubra, NSW 2035
*Tel:* (02) 9349 5170 *Fax:* (02) 9349 5170
*Key Personnel*
Publisher & Author: Kerri Hamer *E-mail:* khamer@oakhill.nsw.edu.au
Subjects: Behavioral Sciences, Communications, Education, How-to, Human Relations, Psychology, Psychiatry, Self-Help, Social Sciences, Sociology
ISBN Prefix(es): 0-646

**Hamish Hamilton**, *imprint of* Penguin Group (Australia)

**Hamlyn Childrens**, *imprint of* Random House Australia

**Geoffrey Hamlyn-Harris**
5 Garden St, Stanthorpe, Qld 4380
*Tel:* (076) 811450 *Fax:* (018) 63662
*Key Personnel*
Proprietor & Author: Geoffrey Hamlyn-Harris
Subjects: Drama, Theater, Fiction, Nonfiction (General), Poetry, Science Fiction, Fantasy
ISBN Prefix(es): 0-9592203
Total Titles: 7 Print; 7 Online; 1 Audio

**Hampden Press+**
PO Box 134, Five Dock, NSW 2046
*Tel:* (02) 9351 9070 *Fax:* (02) 9351 9323
*E-mail:* j.higgs@cchs.usyd.edu.au
*Key Personnel*
Publisher: Saul Kamerman *E-mail:* saulk@bigpond.com
Subjects: Child Care & Development, Medicine, Nursing, Dentistry, Psychology, Psychiatry
ISBN Prefix(es): 1-875648; 0-947115; 0-9587861

**H&H Publishing**
6 Southern Court, Forest Hill, Victoria 3131
*Tel:* (03) 98774428 *Fax:* (03) 98774222
*Key Personnel*
Contact: Malcolm Raymond Harris *E-mail:* malh@melbpc.com.au
Founded: 1981
Subjects: Civil Engineering, Mechanical Engineering
ISBN Prefix(es): 0-646

**Harcourt Brace**, *imprint of* Elsevier Australia

**Harcourt Education Australia+**
Formerly Reed Educational Publishing Australia
Division of Harcourt Education International
22 Salmon St, Port Melbourne, Victoria 3207
Mailing Address: PO Box 460, Port Melbourne, Victoria 3207
*Tel:* (03) 9245 7188 *Toll Free Tel:* 800-810-372 *Fax:* (03) 9245 7333
*E-mail:* customerservice@harcourteducation.com.au
*Web Site:* www.harcourteducation.com.au
*Key Personnel*
Man Dir: David O'Brien
Founded: 1982
Subjects: Art, Chemistry, Chemical Engineering, Environmental Studies, Geography, Geology, Health, Nutrition, History, Mathematics, Physics
Total Titles: 5,000 Print; 50 CD-ROM; 20 Audio
Imprints: Heinemann
Divisions: Heinemann; Heinemann Library; Rigby; Rigby Heinemann

**Hargreen Publishing Co**
430 William St, Melbourne, Victoria 3000
*Tel:* (03) 9329 9714 *Fax:* (03) 9329 5295
*E-mail:* em@execmedia.com.au
*Key Personnel*
Chief Executive: Michael Haratsis, Sr
Editorial & Production: Rick Navarro
Founded: 1972
Specialize in Australian history.
Subjects: Education, History, Nonfiction (General)
ISBN Prefix(es): 0-949905; 0-9596696
*Parent Company:* Scotshouse Corp Pty Ltd

**HarperCollinsPublishers (Australia) Pty Ltd+**
25 Ryde Rd, Pymble, NSW 2073
Mailing Address: PO Box 321, Pymble, NSW 2073
*Tel:* (02) 9952 5000 *Fax:* (02) 9952 5555
*Web Site:* www.harpercollins.com.au

*Key Personnel*
Man Dir: Robert Gorman
Man Dir, Home Entertainment: Lil Velis
Finance Dir: Malcolm Boyd
Publishing Dir: Shona Martyn
Marketing Dir: Jim Demetriou
Publicity Manager: Christine Farmer
Production Manager: Jill Donald
Art Dir: Russell Jeffrey
IT Manager: Richard Beath
Manager, Multimedia & Internet Services: Laura Tricker
Rights Manager: Airlie Lawson
ISBN Prefix(es): 0-7322
*Parent Company:* HarperCollins Publishers Group
*Associate Companies:* Angus & Robertson Publishers; Bartholomew, United Kingdom; Bay Books; Collins Dove; Collins Inc; Fontana, United Kingdom; Scott Foresman; Golden Press, New Zealand; Grafton Books, United Kingdom; HarperCollins; HarperCollins General Books, United Kingdom; HarperCollins Ltd, Hong Kong; HarperCollins Publishers, New Zealand; HarperCollins Publishers Asia Pte Ltd, Singapore; HarperCollins Publishers India (P) Ltd, India; HarperCollins Publishers - Japan, Japan; HarperCollins Publishers (SA) (Pty) Ltd, South Africa; Marshall Pickering, United Kingdom; Thorsons Times Books, United Kingdom; Zondervan
*Distribution Center:* Yarrawa Rd, PO Box 264, Moss Vale NSW 2577 *Tel:* (02) 4860 2900 *Fax:* (02) 4860 2990

**HarperCollinsReligious**
Imprint of HarperCollinsPublishers Australia
25 Ryde St, Pymble, NSW 2073
Mailing Address: PO Box 321, Pymble, NSW 2073
*Tel:* (011) 6222900 *Fax:* (011) 6223553
*E-mail:* fiona.mclennan@harpercollins.com.au
*Web Site:* www.harpercollinsreligious.com.au
*Key Personnel*
Permissions: Annette Renshaw *E-mail:* annette.renshaw@harpercollins.com.au
Rights: Airlie Lawson *E-mail:* airlie.lawson@harpercollins.com.au
Founded: 1962
Subjects: Biblical Studies, Fiction, Nonfiction (General)
ISBN Prefix(es): 0-00; 0-00

**Hartys Creek Press**
PO Box 342, Wauchope, NSW 2446
*Tel:* (02) 6587 1100
*Key Personnel*
Contact: Lois Higgins
Subjects: Art, Environmental Studies, Geography, Geology, Humor, Travel
ISBN Prefix(es): 0-646
Publication(s): *Antartica Alphabetically*; *Australia Alphabetically*; *Log Book of an Antarctic Journey*

**Roland Harvey Studios+**
9 Delta St, Port Melbourne, Victoria 3207
*Tel:* (03) 9836 6655 *Fax:* (03) 9836 6652
*E-mail:* sales@rolandharvey.com.au
*Key Personnel*
Publisher: Roland Harvey
Contact: Dinah Lewis
Founded: 1978
Membership(s): ABPA.
ISBN Prefix(es): 0-949714
Imprints: Periscope Press
*Warehouse:* Unit 1, 13 Downarh St, Braeside, Victoria 3195

**Hat Box Press**
3 Huntingfield Drive, Hoppers Crossing, Victoria 3029
*Tel:* (03) 9749 2510

*Key Personnel*
Contact: Bronwen Hickman *E-mail:* bronwenh@vicnet.net.au
Subjects: Fiction, History, Literature, Literary Criticism, Essays, Short stories by Mary Gaunt
ISBN Prefix(es): 0-9590422
Number of titles published annually: 1 Print

**Hawker Brownlow+**
1123a Nepean Highway, Highett, Victoria 3190
Mailing Address: PO Box 580, Moorabbin, Victoria 3189
*Tel:* (03) 9555 1344 *Toll Free Tel:* 800-334-603 *Fax:* (03) 9553 4538 *Toll Free Fax:* 800-150-445
*E-mail:* orders@hbe.com.au
*Web Site:* www.hbe.com.au
*Key Personnel*
Man Dir: David Brownlow
General Manager: Elaine Brownlow *E-mail:* ebrownlow@hbe.com.au
Founded: 1981
Subjects: Asian Studies, Human Relations, Mathematics, Technology
ISBN Prefix(es): 1-86299; 1-86401; 0-947326; 1-74025; 1-74101
*Parent Company:* Hawker Brownlow Education
Imprints: Autonomous Learning Publications & Specialists; BEC Publications; Book Lures Inc; Cassel PLC; Centre for Creative Learning; Creative Learning Consultants; Creative Learning Press; Critical Thinking Press & Software; Curriculum Associates Inc; Dandy Lion Publications; Educational Assessment Service Inc; Educational Impressions; Educational Insights; Enrich; Fearon Teacher Aids; Foundation for Critical Thinking; Free Spirit Publishing Inc; Gamco Industries Inc; Gifted Children Information Centre; The Learner's Dimensions; The Learning Works; Michael Grinder & Associates; Modern Learning Press; New Horizons for Learning; Ohio Psychology Press; Perfection Learning Corporation; Personal Power Press International Inc; Prufrock Press; Skylight Publishing Inc; Star Teaching; Sterling Publishing Co Inc; Sundance Inc; Teacher Created Materials; Trillium Press; United Educational Services (DDK); Zephyr Press
Subsidiaries: Learner's World

**Hawkins Press**, *imprint of* The Federation Press

**Hayes Publishing Co**
52 Dewar Terrace, Sherwood, Qld 4075
*Tel:* (07) 3379 4137 *Fax:* (07) 3379 4137
*Key Personnel*
Contact: P C Hayes *E-mail:* p.hayes@minmet.uq.edu.au
Subjects: Engineering (General)
ISBN Prefix(es): 0-9589197
Number of titles published annually: 1 Print
Total Titles: 1 Print
*Orders to:* Koala Books of Canada, 14327-95A Ave, Edmonton, AB T5N 0B6, Canada *Tel:* (780) 452 5149

**Hayward Books**, *imprint of* In-Tune Books

**Headline**, *imprint of* Hachette Livre Australia

**Heinemann**, *imprint of* Harcourt Education Australia

**Heinemann First Library**, *imprint of* Heinemann Library

**Heinemann Library**
Division of Harcourt Education
20 Thackray Rd, Port Melbourne, Victoria 3207
*Tel:* (03) 9245 7188 *Fax:* (03) 9245 7265

*E-mail:* int.schools@harcourteducation.com.au
*Web Site:* www.heinemannlibrary.com.au
*Key Personnel*
General Manager: Rod Morahan *Tel:* (03) 9245 7558 *E-mail:* rod.morahan@harcourteducation.com.au
Sales & Marketing Manager: Gail Weston *Tel:* (03) 9245 7559 *E-mail:* gail.weston@harcourteducation.com.au
Non-fiction resources for school libraries.
ISBN Prefix(es): 0-949919; 1-875633; 1-86391; 1-74070
Imprints: Echidna Books; Heinemann First Library; Heinemann Library Australia; Infosearch; Little Nippers; Young Explorer
Distributor for Atlantic Europe; Barrington Stoke; Chrysalis; Evans Brothers; Heinemann Library UK; Heinemann Library US; Raintree; Times Editions (children's list); Zoe Books

**Heinemann Library Australia**, *imprint of* Heinemann Library

**William Heinemann**, *imprint of* Random House Australia

**Help Yourself**, *imprint of* Hachette Livre Australia

**Hema Maps Pty Ltd+**
25 McKechnie Drive, Eight Mile Plains, Qld 4113
Mailing Address: PO Box 4365, Eight Mile Plains, Qld 4113
*Tel:* (07) 3340 0000 *Fax:* (07) 3340 0099
*E-mail:* manager@hemamaps.com.au
*Web Site:* www.hemamaps.com
*Key Personnel*
Man Dir: Henry Boegheim
Founded: 1983
Membership(s): IMTA.
Subjects: Travel
ISBN Prefix(es): 1-875610; 1-875992; 1-86500
Distributed by Brettschneider GmbH (Germany); Cartotheque (France); T B Clarke (Overseas) Pty Ltd; Craenen Cartografie (Belgium); Estate Publications (United Kingdom); Freytag & Berndt u Artaria (Austria); Geocentre (Germany); Gordon & Gotch (PNG) Pty Ltd (Papua New Guinea); Hema Maps NZ Ltd (New Zealand); Inteligentni Turisticke Mapy (Czech Republic); ITMB Publishing Ltd (Canada); Jana Seta (Latvia); Kartbutiken (Sweden); Magellan Buchversand (Germany); Map Co Trading (Singapore); Map House Co Ltd (Tokyo); Map Link Inc (USA); Namdo Net (South Korea); Nilsson & Lamm (Holland); OLF (Switzerland); Scanvik Books (Denmark)
Distributor for AA-New Zealand; AA-UK; Ausmap; Australian Geographic; Berndtson & Berndtson; Boiling Billy; Cartographics; CMA New South Wales; Collins; DOLA; Forestry Maps-NSW; Mapland; Nelles Maps; Periplus; Rand McNally; Sunmap; Tasmap; Universal Maps; Vicmaps; Westprint (all Australia)

**Henry Holt**, *imprint of* Pan Macmillan Australia Pty Ltd

**Heresy Press**, *imprint of* Prospect Media

**Hihorse Publishing Pty Ltd+**
59 Princess St, Williamstown, Victoria 3016
*Tel:* (03) 9397 3084 *Fax:* (03) 9397 3084
*E-mail:* hihorse@c031.aone.net.au
*Key Personnel*
Contact: Patricia Kovac
Founded: 1995
Subjects: Alternative, Astrology, Occult, Parapsychology, Self-Help, Aromatherapy, Meditation, Crystal Healing

ISBN Prefix(es): 0-909223
*Associate Companies:* Gemcraft Pty Ltd, 14 Duffy St, Burwood, Victoria 3125, Afghanistan

**Histec Publications**
c/o B E Lloyd & Associates, 13 Connor St, East Brighton, Victoria 3187
*Tel:* (03) 9592 3787 *Fax:* (03) 9592 2823
*Web Site:* www.histec.com
*Key Personnel*
Dir: Dr Brian E Lloyd *E-mail:* belloyd@projectx. com.au
Founded: 1987
Subjects: Biography, Engineering (General), History, Labor, Industrial Relations, Regional Interests, Social Sciences, Sociology
ISBN Prefix(es): 0-9587705
Number of titles published annually: 2 Print; 1 CD-ROM
Total Titles: 20 Print; 3 CD-ROM
*Parent Company:* B E Lloyd & Associates Histec Nominees Pty Ltd

**Hodder**, *imprint of* Hachette Livre Australia

**Hodder & Stoughton**, *imprint of* Hachette Livre Australia

**Hodder Arnold**, *imprint of* Hachette Livre Australia

**Hodder (Australia)**, *imprint of* Hachette Livre Australia

**Hodder Moa Beckett**, *imprint of* Hachette Livre Australia

**Hodder Mobius**, *imprint of* Hachette Livre Australia

**Hodder Religious**, *imprint of* Hachette Livre Australia

**Holt, Rinehart and Winston**, *imprint of* Elsevier Australia

**Home Library**, *imprint of* ACP Publishing Pty Ltd

**Homestead Books**
29 Lisbeth Ave, Donvale, Victoria 3111
*Tel:* (03) 9873 7202 *Fax:* (03) 9873-0542
*E-mail:* service@theruralstore.com.au
*Web Site:* www.theruralstore.com.au
*Key Personnel*
Proprietor: Jim Lowden *E-mail:* jim@ theruralstore.com.au

**Horan Wall & Walker+**
162 Goulburn St, Darlinghurst NSW 2010
Mailing Address: PO Box 996, Darlinghurst NSW 2010
*Tel:* (02) 8268 8268 *Fax:* (02) 8268 8267
*E-mail:* info@hww.com.au
*Web Site:* www.hww.com.au
*Key Personnel*
Man Dir: Stephen Wall
Founded: 1974
Subjects: Cookery, Crafts, Games, Hobbies, Finance, Real Estate, Travel, Entertainment, Leisure
ISBN Prefix(es): 0-9590027; 0-9599177; 1-875700
*Parent Company:* HWW Pty Ltd
*Associate Companies:* Australian Property Monitors

**Hospitality Books**
7 Regent St, Ryde, NSW 2112
Mailing Address: PO Box 3007, Putney, NSW 2112
*Tel:* (02) 9809 5793 *Fax:* (02) 9809 4884
*Web Site:* www.hospitalitybooks.com.au
*Key Personnel*
Head of Company & Dir: Maureen Puckeridge *E-mail:* sales@hospitalitybooks.com.au
Founded: 1987
Publish "how-to" books on professional bartending, waiting, the Australian Wine Guide & Hospitality Core Units.
Membership(s): Copyright Agency Ltd.
Subjects: How-to, Wine & Spirits, Food & Beverage Service, Hospitality Industry
ISBN Prefix(es): 0-9587113; 0-957703
Total Titles: 4 Print

**Hudson Publishing Services Pty Ltd+**
Division of NS Hudson Publishing Services P/L
9 Panmure St, Newstead, Victoria 3462
*Tel:* (03) 5476 2795 *Fax:* (03) 5476 2744
*E-mail:* travturf@bigpond.com
*Web Site:* www.hudson-publishing.com
*Key Personnel*
Head of Company, Editorial Dir & Manager: Nick Hudson
Founded: 1985
Membership(s): Australian Publishers Association.
Subjects: Literature, Literary Criticism, Essays, Nonfiction (General)
ISBN Prefix(es): 0-949873
Total Titles: 50 Print
Imprints: Essien
Distributed by Jenny Nagle Addenda Publishing Sales & Marketing Services (New Zealand)
*Warehouse:* Peribo P/L, 50 Beaumont Rd, Mount Kuring Gai, NSW 2080 *Tel:* (02) 9457 0011 *Fax:* (02) 9457 0022 (national distributor)
*Orders to:* Peribo P/L, 50 Beaumont Rd, Mount Kuring Gai, NSW 2080 *Tel:* (02) 9457 0011 *Fax:* (02) 9457 0022 (national distributor)

**Hungry Minds Australia**, *imprint of* John Wiley & Sons Australia, Ltd

**Hunter Books**
PO Box 3362, Weston Creek, ACT 2611
Subjects: Fiction
ISBN Prefix(es): 0-646

**Hunter House Publications+**
8 Swan St, Hinton, NSW 2321
*Tel:* (02) 4930 5992 *Fax:* (02) 4930 5993
*E-mail:* wf&mc@hunterlink.net.au
*Key Personnel*
Author & Publisher: Cynthia Hunter
Founded: 1991
Specialize in history research.
Subjects: History
ISBN Prefix(es): 0-646; 1-876388
Number of titles published annually: 1 Print
Total Titles: 5 Print

**Hutchinson**, *imprint of* Random House Australia

**Hyland House Publishing Pty Ltd+**
50 Pin Oak Crescent, Flemington, Victoria 3031
Mailing Address: PO Box 122, Flemington, Victoria 3031
*Tel:* (03) 9376 4461 *Fax:* (03) 9376 4461
*E-mail:* hyland3@netspace.net.au
*Key Personnel*
Man Dir: Michael Schoo
Founded: 1976
Subjects: Animals, Pets, Asian Studies, Gardening, Plants, How-to, Nonfiction (General), Organizational Histories

ISBN Prefix(es): 0-908090; 0-947062; 1-875657; 1-86447
*Associate Companies:* Australian Book Distribution Group
Imprints: Australia's Best Garden Guide Series; Hylanders
*Warehouse:* Australian Book Group, Calway St, Drouin, Victoria 3818 *Tel:* (03) 5625 4290 *Fax:* (03) 5625 4272
*Distribution Center:* Gazelle Book Services, White Cross Mills, Hightown, Lancaster LA1 4XS, United Kingdom, Contact: Trevor Witcher *Tel:* (01524) 68765 *Fax:* (01524) 63232 (UK)
*Orders to:* Australian Book Group, Calway St, Drouin, Victoria 3818 *Tel:* (03) 5625 4290 *Fax:* (03) 5625 4272

**Hylanders**, *imprint of* Hyland House Publishing Pty Ltd

**IAD**, see Institute of Aboriginal Development (IAD Press)

**IE Aust Publications**, *imprint of* EA Books

**Illert Publications+**
2/3 Birch Crescent, East Corrimal, NSW 2518
*Tel:* (02) 4283 3009 *Fax:* (02) 4283 3009
*E-mail:* illert@keira.hotkey.net.au
*Key Personnel*
Editorial Manager: C Illert
Subjects: Anthropology, Asian Studies, Biological Sciences, Computer Science, Education, Environmental Studies, Genealogy, History, Language Arts, Linguistics, Mathematics, Natural History, Physics, Science (General), Technology
ISBN Prefix(es): 0-949357; 0-9597201

**The Images Publishing Group Pty Ltd+**
Images House, 6 Bastow Pl, Mulgrave, Victoria 3170
*Tel:* (03) 9561 5544 *Fax:* (03) 9561 4860
*E-mail:* books@images.com.au
*Web Site:* www.imagespublishinggroup.com
*Key Personnel*
Dir: Alessina Rose Brooks; Paul Alan Latham
Founded: 1983
Subjects: Accounting, Advertising, Architecture & Interior Design, Art, Biography, Civil Engineering, Engineering (General), Fashion
ISBN Prefix(es): 1-875498; 0-9589598; 1-876907; 1-920744
Number of titles published annually: 40 Print
*Parent Company:* Images Australia Pty Ltd
Distributed by ACC UK; ACC US; Antique Collectors' Club (Europe & USA); Bookwise International (Australia); Gingko Bookspan; Nippan IPS (Asia); Anthony Rudkin Associates (Middle East excluding Israel, Malta, Cypress, Turkey & Iran)

**In-Tune Books+**
PO Box 193, Avalon Beach, NSW 2107
*Tel:* (02) 9974 5981 *Fax:* (02) 9974 4552
*Web Site:* www.haywardbooks.com.au
*Key Personnel*
Manager: Malcolm Cohan *E-mail:* mcohan@ ozemail.com.au
Founded: 1984
Subjects: Alternative, Art, Philosophy, Self-Help
ISBN Prefix(es): 0-9577024; 0-9577025; 0-9590439
Imprints: Hayward Books
Distributed by Alternate Books (South Africa); HarperCollins (New Zealand)
*Distribution Center:* WORDS Distributing Co, 7900 Edgewater Dr, Oakland, CA 94621, United States

World Leisure Marketing, Unit 11, Newmarket Court, Newmarket Dr, Derby DE24 8NW, United Kingdom *Tel:* (01332) 573 737 *Fax:* (01332) 573 399

**Indigo**, *imprint of* Ginninderra Press

**Indra Publishing+**
142 Ryans Rd, Eltham North, Victoria 3095
Mailing Address: PO Box 7, Briar Hill, Victoria 3088
*Tel:* (03) 9439 7555 *Fax:* (03) 9439 7555
*Web Site:* www.indra.com.au
*Key Personnel*
Dir: Ian James Fraser *E-mail:* ian@indra.com.au
Founded: 1987
Membership(s): Australian Publisher's Association.
Subjects: Asian Studies, Biography, Disability, Special Needs, Ethnicity, Fiction, Foreign Countries, Literature, Literary Criticism, Essays, Romance, Women's Studies, Asia, Australia, Pacific
ISBN Prefix(es): 0-9587718; 0-9585805; 0-9578735; 1-9207870
Number of titles published annually: 6 Print; 1 Audio
Total Titles: 34 Print; 3 Audio
Distributed by Australian Book Group P/L (Australia); Gazelle Book Services Ltd (Europe); Horizon Books Pte Ltd (Southeast Asia); International Specialized Book Services (USA & Canada)
Foreign Rep(s): ISBS Corp (Canada, US)
Foreign Rights: Alice Gruenfelder Literary Agency (Europe)

**Industrial Press**, *imprint of* Elsevier Australia

**Infomedia**, *imprint of* Flora Publications International Pty Ltd

**Infosearch**, *imprint of* Heinemann Library

**Inner City Books**, *imprint of* Rainbow Book Agencies Pty Ltd

**Instauratio Press**
PO Box 36, Yarra Junction, Victoria 3797
*Tel:* (03) 59666217 *Fax:* (03) 59666447
*E-mail:* catholic@scservnet.com
*Key Personnel*
Head of Company: Andrina McLean
Founded: 1982
Subjects: Religion - Catholic
ISBN Prefix(es): 0-9587113; 0-646
Subsidiaries: St Benedict Book Centre
*Branch Office(s)*
Instauratio Press, Box 1789, Post Falls, ID 83854, United States
Distributor for The Angelus Press (USA); Neumann Books (USA); Tan Books (USA)

**Institute of Aboriginal Development (IAD Press)+**
3 South Terrace, Alice Springs, NT 0871
Mailing Address: PO Box 2531, Alice Springs, NT 0871
*Tel:* (08) 8951 1311 *Fax:* (08) 8952 2527
*E-mail:* ozlit@netspace.net.au
*Web Site:* home.vicnet.au/~ozlit/iadpress.html
*Key Personnel*
Dir: Eileen Shaw
Publisher: Josie Douglas
Founded: 1969 (Aboriginal community controlled, publishing arm of Institute for Aboriginal Development)
Indigenous publishing house producing works by Aboriginal & Torres Strait Islander peoples of Australia.

Membership(s): APA (Australian Publishers Association) & Publish Australia.
Subjects: Anthropology, Art, Biography, Education, History, Language Arts, Linguistics, Literature, Literary Criticism, Essays, Natural History, Nonfiction (General), Regional Interests
ISBN Prefix(es): 0-949659; 1-86465; 1-9596206
Number of titles published annually: 10 Print; 1 E-Book; 1 Audio
Total Titles: 55 Print; 1 CD-ROM; 3 E-Book; 3 Audio
Imprints: Jukurrpa Books
*U.S. Office(s):* ISBS International Specialized Book Services, 5804 NE Massalo St, Portland, OR 97213-3644, United States, Contact: Tamma Greenfield *Tel:* 503-287-3093 *Fax:* 503-280-8882 *E-mail:* tamma@isbs.com

**INT Press+**
386 Mt Alexander Rd, Ascot Vale, Victoria 3032
*Tel:* (03) 9326 2416 *Fax:* (03) 9326 2413
*E-mail:* sales@intpress.com.au
*Web Site:* www.intpress.com.au
*Key Personnel*
International Rights: Luiai Rizzo
Founded: 1981
Subjects: English as a Second Language, Ethnicity
ISBN Prefix(es): 1-86310
*Associate Companies:* INT Press Distribution Pty Ltd
*Bookshop(s):* The LOTE INT Bookshop

**Intext Book Company Pty Ltd**
825 Glenferrie Rd, Hawthorn, Victoria 3122
*Tel:* (03) 9819-4500 *Fax:* (03) 9819-4511
*E-mail:* customerservice@intextbook.com.au
*Web Site:* www.intextbook.com.au
*Key Personnel*
Man Dir: Jillian Taylor *E-mail:* jillian@intextbook.com.au
Founded: 1982
Specialize in foreign languages other than English; distribution & promotion.
Subsidiaries: Language International Bookshop
Distributor for ALC Press (Japan); Alma Edizione (Italy); Bonacci (Italy); Cheng & T sui (USA); Cle International; Duerr Kessler (Germany); Diesterweg (Germany); Difusion (Spain); Duden (Germany); Edelsa (Spain); Ediciones SM (Spain); European School Books (UK); Gallimard (France); Giunti (Italy); Guerra (Italy); Hachette Livre International (France); Hatier/Didier (France); Klett (Germany); Kumon (Japan); Langenscheidt Texts & Dictionaries (Germany); Larousse (France); Menschenkinder (Germany); Nathan (France); Nihongo Journal (Japan); Ravensburger (Germany); Robert (France); SGEL (Spain); Santillana (Spain); Senmon Kyouiku (Japan); Soleil (Canada); The Japan Times (Japan); Vut Caps (Australia)

**Inwardpath Publishers**
76 McArthur Rd, Ivanhoe, Victoria 3079
*Tel:* (03) 9499 3405 *Fax:* (03) 9497 5656
Subjects: Philosophy, Esoteric, New Age
ISBN Prefix(es): 0-9585722
Distributor for Specialist Publications (Australia & Territories)
Foreign Rep(s): Four Corners (England)

**Island Press Co-operative**
29 Park Rd, Woodford, NSW 2778
*Tel:* (02) 4758 6635
*E-mail:* isphaw@hermes.net.au
*Key Personnel*
Man Dir: Philip Hammial
Founded: 1970
Subjects: Poetry
ISBN Prefix(es): 0-909771

Number of titles published annually: 4 Print
Total Titles: 45 Print

**Jabiru Press**
13 Ferdinand Ave, Balwyn North, Victoria 3104
*Tel:* (03) 9609 3535 *Fax:* (03) 9857 9110
*Key Personnel*
Contact: Dick Johnson *E-mail:* djohnson@netspace.net.au
ISBN Prefix(es): 0-908104

**James Nicholas Publishers Pty Ltd**
PO Box 244, Albert Park, Victoria 3206
*Tel:* (03) 9690 5955 (customer service); (03) 9696 5545 (editorial office) *Fax:* (03) 9699 2040
*E-mail:* info@jamesnicholaspublishers.com.au; info@jnponline.com
*Web Site:* www.jamesnicholaspublishers.com.au; www.jnponline.com
*Key Personnel*
Publisher & Editor: Ms Rea Zajda
Founded: 1978
Subjects: Business, Communications, Education, Government, Political Science, Health, Nutrition, Management, Marketing, Medicine, Nursing, Dentistry, Social Sciences, Sociology
ISBN Prefix(es): 1-875408
Total Titles: 10 Print

**Jared Publishing**
PO Box 51, Mitcham, Victoria 3132
*Tel:* (03) 9874 2415
ISBN Prefix(es): 0-9589481

**Jarrah Publications+**
42 Chisholm Circle, Heritage Estate, Armadale, WA 6112
Mailing Address: PO Box 1041, Kelmscott Delivery Centre, Kelmscott, WA 6997
*Tel:* (08) 9495 4569 *Fax:* (08) 9495 4569
*Key Personnel*
Head of Company: W F Vormair
Sales Dir & International Rights: Willy Frank
Author: Jean Vormair
Editor & International Rights: Jan Margaret
Founded: 1987
Partnership specializing in fantasy & contemporary issues.
Subjects: Fiction, Human Relations, Romance, Science Fiction, Fantasy
ISBN Prefix(es): 0-9587113; 0-646
Total Titles: 2 Print

**Jenelle Press**
PO Box 656, Gladesville, NSW 2111
*Tel:* (02) 4281531 *Fax:* (02) 4284144
*Key Personnel*
Head of Company: Mark Robert Mannering
Subjects: Education
ISBN Prefix(es): 1-875734

**Jesuit Publications+**
Unit of Society of Jesus
PO Box 553, Richmond, Victoria 3121
*Tel:* (03) 9427 7311 *Fax:* (03) 9428 4450
*E-mail:* jespub@jespub.jesuit.org.au
*Web Site:* www.jesuitpublications.com.au
*Key Personnel*
Dir: Christopher Gleeson
Publisher: Andrew Hamilton
Business Manager: Mark Dowell *E-mail:* mark@jespub.jesuit.org.au
Marketing: Kirsty Grant
Production: Geraldine Battersby; Irene Hunter
Founded: 1988
Subjects: Poetry, Religion - Catholic, Religion - Protestant, Religion - Other, Theology
ISBN Prefix(es): 0-9586796
Divisions: Aurora Books; Australian Catholics; Eureka Street; Madonna

**Jesuit Publications/Aurora Books**, *imprint of* Rainbow Book Agencies Pty Ltd

**Jika Publishing+**
3 Witney Way, Bundoora, Victoria 3083
*Tel:* (03) 9467 3295 *Fax:* (03) 9467 1770
*E-mail:* jordanca@alphalink.com.au
Subjects: Drama, Theater, Poetry
ISBN Prefix(es): 0-9587113; 0-646

**JL Publications+**
Division of Submariner Publication, P/C
26 Highgate Gue, Ashburton, Victoria 3147
Mailing Address: PO Box 387, Ashburton, Victoria 3147
*Tel:* (03) 98860200 *Fax:* (03) 98860200
*E-mail:* jlpubs@c031.aone.net.au
*Key Personnel*
Contact: John Lippmann
Subjects: Scuba Diving Safety
Total Titles: 12 Print
Distributed by Aqua Quest Publications (New York)

**Michael Joseph**, *imprint of* Penguin Group (Australia)

**Journeys**, *imprint of* Lonely Planet Publications Pty Ltd

**Joval Publications**
PO Box 618, Bacchus Marsh, Victoria 3340
*Tel:* (053) 674593
*Key Personnel*
Contact: John Reid
Founded: 1986
Subjects: History, Photography, Poetry
ISBN Prefix(es): 0-9588112

**Jukurrpa Books**, *imprint of* Institute of Aboriginal Development (IAD Press)

**Kangaroo Press**, *imprint of* Simon & Schuster (Australia) Pty Ltd

**Kangaroo Press+**
Imprint of Simon & Schuster Australia
PO Box 6125, Dural Delivery Centre, NSW 2158
*Tel:* (02) 6541502 *Fax:* (02) 6541338
*Key Personnel*
Publisher: David Rosenberg
Publicity Manager: Priscilla Rosenberg
Founded: 1981
Subjects: Biography, Crafts, Games, Hobbies, Gardening, Plants, History, Natural History, Nonfiction (General), Regional Interests, Sports, Athletics, Transportation, Travel
ISBN Prefix(es): 0-949924; 0-86417
Imprints: Roo Books

**Gregory Kefalas Publishing**
5A Byron St, Campsie, NSW 2194
*Tel:* (02) 9789 6049 *Fax:* (02) 97876181
Subjects: Automotive
ISBN Prefix(es): 0-9586798

**Ken Fin**, *imprint of* Social Club Books

**Killara Press+**
MS 660, Proston, Qld 4613
*Tel:* (07) 5499-7717 *Fax:* (07) 4168-0244
*Key Personnel*
Contact: Sylvia Seiler *E-mail:* seiler@elr.com.au
Founded: 1991
Writing & publishing.
Subjects: Disability, Special Needs, Fiction, Human Relations
ISBN Prefix(es): 0-9585731

**Kingfisher Books+**
Cnr Brixton & Wangara Rds, Cheltenham, Victoria 3192
*Tel:* (03) 9819 9100 *Fax:* (03) 9819 0977
Founded: 1989
Subjects: Maritime
ISBN Prefix(es): 0-9593999

**Kingsclear Books+**
36 Kingsclear Rd, Alexandria, NSW 2015
Mailing Address: PO Box 335, Alexandria, NSW 1435
*Tel:* (02) 95574367 *Fax:* (02) 95572337
*E-mail:* kingsclear@wr.com.au
*Web Site:* www.kingsclearbooks.com.au
*Key Personnel*
Chief Executive Officer & Dir Sales & Production: Catherine Warne
Founded: 1983
Specialize in local history, alternative health, tourism & true crime.
Subjects: Criminology, Health, Nutrition, History, Travel
ISBN Prefix(es): 0-908272
Number of titles published annually: 6 Print
Total Titles: 40 Print
Imprints: Kingsclear Books Pty Ltd
Subsidiaries: Atrand Pty Ltd
Distributed by Envirobooks
*Shipping Address:* Tower Books, 2/19 Rodborough Rd, Frenchs Forest, NSW 2086, Contact: Dale Druckman *Tel:* (02) 9975-5586 *Fax:* (02) 9975-5599
*Warehouse:* Federation Press, 71 John St, Leichhardt, NSW 2040, Contact: John Xenos *Tel:* (09552) 2200

**Kingsclear Books Pty Ltd**, *imprint of* Kingsclear Books

**Knopf Publishing**, *imprint of* Random House Australia

**Kookaburra Technical Publications Pty Ltd**
6 Colvin Court, Glen Waverley, Victoria 3150
*Tel:* (03) 9560 0841 *Fax:* (03) 9545 1121
*Web Site:* www.boundy39.com/hkooka/HkookaFSO.htm
*Key Personnel*
Head of Company: Geoff Pentland
Customer Service: Jenny Martin
Founded: 1963
Specialize in reference books for modelers & historians.
Subjects: Aeronautics, Aviation
ISBN Prefix(es): 0-85880

**Kurlana Publishing**
PO Box 481, North Adelaide, SA 5006
*Tel:* (08) 3886619
Founded: 1988
Subjects: Psychology, Psychiatry
ISBN Prefix(es): 0-9587998

**Lancer**, *imprint of* Anzea Publishers Ltd

**Landarc Publications**
46 McIlwraith St, North Carlton, Victoria 3054
*Tel:* (03) 93801276 *Fax:* (03) 93801276
*E-mail:* carmar@bigpond.com
*Key Personnel*
Manager: Carolyn Pike
Founded: 1981
Subjects: Gardening, Plants
ISBN Prefix(es): 0-9587100; 0-9594220
Total Titles: 3 Print

**Lansdowne Publishing Pty Ltd+**
PO Box 48, Milson's Point, NSW 2061
*Tel:* (02) 9240 9222 *Fax:* (02) 9241 4818

*E-mail:* sales@lanspub.com.au
*Key Personnel*
Chief Executive: Steven Morris
Publisher: Deborah Nixon
Publicity & Office Manager: Valerie Sadlier
  *Tel:* (02) 9240 9201 *E-mail:* valerie@lanspub.com.au
Production Manager: Sally Davies
Subjects: Animals, Pets, Cookery, Gardening, Plants, Health, Nutrition, History, Mythology
ISBN Prefix(es): 1-86302; 0-947116; 0-949708
*Parent Company:* Kirin Publishing Pty Ltd

**Laurel Press+**
850 Huon Rd, Ferntree, Tas 7054
Mailing Address: PO Box 132, Sandy Bay, Tas 7006
*Tel:* (03) 6239 1139 *Fax:* (03) 6239 1139
*Key Personnel*
Head of Company: Chris Bell *E-mail:* chrisjen@southcom.com.au
Founded: 1990
Publisher of on-going large-format fine editions.
Subjects: Natural History, Photography
ISBN Prefix(es): 0-646
Total Titles: 2 Print

**Law Book Co Information Services**, see LBC Information Services

**LBC Information Services+**
Formerly Law Book Co Information Services
50 Waterloo Rd, North Ryde, NSW 2113
*Tel:* (02) 99366444 *Fax:* (02) 98882229
*Telex:* 27995 Asbook *Cable:* Asbook
*Key Personnel*
Publishing Manager: E Costigan; A M O'Neill
National Sales Manager: B Crane
Marketing Manager: C Simmons
Manager, Editorial: Y Stewart
Founded: 1898
Subjects: Accounting, Business, Criminology, Environmental Studies, Finance, Labor, Industrial Relations, Law, Medicine, Nursing, Dentistry, Real Estate
ISBN Prefix(es): 0-455
*Parent Company:* Thomson Corporation Publishing Ltd, United Kingdom
*Ultimate Parent Company:* The Thomson Corp, Suite 2706, Toronto Dominion Bank Tower, Toronto, ON M5K 1A1, Canada
Subsidiaries: Centre for Professional Development; Newsletter Information Services
*Branch Office(s)*
Thomson International Publishing Group, Metro Center, One Station Place, Stamford, CT 06902, United States
*Bookshop(s):* 1/40 Queen St, Brisbane, Qld 4000; 560 Lonsdale St, Melbourne, Victoria 3000; 77 St Georges Terr, 13th Floor, Perth, WA 6000; 4/167 Phillip St, Sydney, NSW 2000

**The Learner's Dimensions**, *imprint of* Hawker Brownlow

**The Learning Works**, *imprint of* Hawker Brownlow

**Sandra Lee Agencies**
58 Scott St, Beaumaris, Victoria 3193
Mailing Address: PO Box 32, Brighton, Victoria 3186
*Tel:* (03) 9592 5235 *Fax:* (03) 9592 7608
*E-mail:* winston@ozonline.com.au
*Key Personnel*
Marketing: Sandra Lewin-Smith
Founded: 1970
Subjects: Cookery
ISBN Prefix(es): 0-7316

**Legal Books**, *imprint of* Prospect Media

**Let's Go**, *imprint of* Pan Macmillan Australia Pty Ltd

**Levanter Publishing & Associates+**
2 Bowlers Ave, Bexley, NSW 2207
*Tel:* (02) 9371 7824
*Key Personnel*
Head of Company: David Ehrlich
Sales Manager: Claudine Auger
Editor: Frank Hariri
Founded: 1991
Subjects: Fiction, Romance
ISBN Prefix(es): 0-646
*Showroom(s):* Flat 5, No 3, Rockley St, Bondi, NSW 2026
*Warehouse:* Flat 5, No 3, Rockley St, Bondi, NSW 2026
*Orders to:* Flat 5, No 3, Rockley St, Bondi, NSW 2026

**Libra Books Pty Ltd**
GPO Box 10, Hobart, Tas 7001
*Tel:* (03) 6230 2656 *Fax:* (03) 6225 0900
*Key Personnel*
Head of Company: Bert Wicks *E-mail:* bwicks@trump.net.au
Founded: 1972
ISBN Prefix(es): 0-909619

**Library of Australian History**
17 Mitchell St, North Sydney, NSW 2060
Mailing Address: PO Box 795, North Sydney, NSW 2059
*Tel:* (02) 9929 5087 *Fax:* (02) 9929 5087
*E-mail:* grdxxx@ozemail.com.au
*Key Personnel*
Editorial Manager: Keith Johnson
Founded: 1977
Subjects: Genealogy, History, Regional Interests, Australian History & Reference, Family History
ISBN Prefix(es): 0-908120; 0-9579524
Subsidiaries: Genealogical Research Directory
*U.S. Office(s):* 130 E Montecito Ave, No 120, Sierra Madre, CA 91024-1924, United States, John Poole *Tel:* 626-792-1339 *E-mail:* grdusa@earthlink.net

**Life Planning Foundation of Australia, Inc**
341 Queen St, Ground floor, Melbourne, Victoria 3000
*Tel:* (03) 9670 4417 *Fax:* (03) 9640 0094
*E-mail:* lifeclub@vicnet.net.au
*Web Site:* www.life.org.au
*Key Personnel*
Executive Dir: John Vial
Founded: 1974
Subjects: Finance, Health, Nutrition, Human Relations, Nonfiction (General), Self-Help
ISBN Prefix(es): 0-9590567

**Lineup**, *imprint of* Troll Books of Australia

**Linking-Up Publishing+**
99 First Ave, Five Dock, NSW 2046
Mailing Address: PO Box W28, Wareemba, NSW 2046
*Tel:* (02) 9712 5576 *Fax:* (02) 9712 1963
*Key Personnel*
Contact: Julian Raimundo
Subjects: Psychology, Psychiatry
ISBN Prefix(es): 0-646
Distributor for Castalia Publishing; Chevron Corp; Taylor Publishing

**Little Hills Press Pty Ltd+**
103 Kurrajong Ave, Unit 12, Mount Druitt, NSW 2770
SAN: 901-7682
*Tel:* (02) 9677 9658 *Fax:* (02) 9677 9152

*E-mail:* lhills@bigpond.net.au; sales@littlehills.com
*Web Site:* www.littlehills.com
*Key Personnel*
Chief Executive & Sales: Charles C Burfitt
Founded: 1981
Membership(s): Australian Booksellers Association.
Subjects: Crafts, Games, Hobbies, Fashion, Nonfiction (General), Travel
ISBN Prefix(es): 0-949773; 1-86315
Total Titles: 59 Print
Imprints: Mount
Distributed by Cimino Publishing (USA); Pelican (USA); Roundhouse Distribution (UK); Ulysses Books (Canada)
Distributor for Bilingual Books Inc; Cato Publishing; Eclipse Press; Facts on Demand; Firefly Books; Frederick Fell Inc; Gambit Publishing; JPM Guides; Laser Publishing; Little Hills Press; Marston House; Pelican Publishing; Penton Overseas; Ulysses Travel Publishers

**Little Nippers**, *imprint of* Heinemann Library

**Little Red Apple Publishing+**
PO Box 67, Thornleigh, NSW 2120
*Tel:* (02) 9430 6867
*E-mail:* littleredapple@hotmail.com
*Key Personnel*
Contact: Rosa Solomon
Founded: 1988
Specialize in novels, plays, Aboriginal myths & legends. Network for author, publisher & artists.
Subjects: Biography, Child Care & Development, Disability, Special Needs, Education, Fiction, History, Human Relations, Humor, Nonfiction (General), Poetry, Religion - Catholic, Religion - Other, Romance, Plays
ISBN Prefix(es): 0-9587113; 1-875329
Number of titles published annually: 10 Print
Total Titles: 26 Print
Distributor for Il Castello; Ripostes
*Distribution Center:* PO Box K152, Haymarket, NSW 1240

**Living Books**, *imprint of* Random House Australia

**Local Consumption Publications**
42 Forbes St, Newtown (Sydney), NSW 2042
*Tel:* (02) 95141960 *Fax:* (02) 95197503
*Key Personnel*
Contact: Stephen Muecke *E-mail:* stephen.muecke@uts.edu.au
ISBN Prefix(es): 0-949793

**Lonely Planet Publications Pty Ltd+**
ABN 36 005 607 983, Locked Bag 1, Footscray, Victoria 3011
*Tel:* (03) 8379 8000 *Fax:* (03) 8379 8111
*E-mail:* talk2us@lonelyplanet.com.au
*Web Site:* www.lonelyplanet.com.au
*Key Personnel*
Dir: Maureen Wheeler; Tony Wheeler
Publisher: Sue Galley; Rob van Dreisum; Susan Keogh; Sally Steward; Paul Smitz
Rights & Permissions: Annalisa Guidici
Production: Graham Imeson
Promotions & Publicity: Anna Bolger
Co-General Manager: Steve Hibbard
Founded: 1973
Phrasebooks, travel literature, walking & diving guides & pictorials.
Subjects: Travel
ISBN Prefix(es): 0-908086; 0-86442; 1-86450; 1-74079; 1-74104
Imprints: Journeys; Pisces
*Branch Office(s)*
Lonely Planet, One rue du Dahomey, 75011 Paris,

France *Tel:* (01) 55 25 33 00 *Fax:* (01) 55 25 33 01 *E-mail:* bip@lonelyplanet.fr
Lonely Planet, 72-82 Rosebery Ave, Clerkenwell, London EC1R 4RW, United Kingdom *Tel:* (020) 7841 9000 *Fax:* (020) 7841 9001 *E-mail:* go@lonelyplanet.co.au
*U.S. Office(s):* Lonely Planet Publications Inc, 150 Linden St, Oakland, CA 94607, United States *Tel:* 510-893-8555 *Fax:* 510-893-8563 *E-mail:* info@lonelyplanet.com

**Lonestone Press**, *imprint of* Oceans Enterprises

**Longman**, *imprint of* Pearson Education Australia

**Lothian Books**, see Thomas C Lothian Pty Ltd

**Thomas C Lothian Pty Ltd+**
Level 5, 132 Albert Rd, South Melbourne, Victoria 3205
*Tel:* (03) 9694 4900 *Fax:* (03) 9645 0705
*E-mail:* books@lothian.com.au
*Web Site:* www.lothian.com.au
*Key Personnel*
Man Dir & Publishing: Peter Lothian *E-mail:* peter_lothian@lothian.com.au
Sales & Marketing Dir: Bruce Hilliard *E-mail:* bruce_hilliard@lothian.com.au
Founded: 1888
Membership(s): Australian Publishers Association.
Subjects: Biography, Business, Health, Nutrition, Nonfiction (General), Self-Help, Sports, Athletics, Australiana
ISBN Prefix(es): 0-85091; 0-7344
Number of titles published annually: 110 Print
Total Titles: 800 Print
Distributed by Forrester Books (New Zealand); Phambili Agencies CC (South Africa); Ragged Bears (Children); Roundhouse Publishing GRP (Adult); Star Bright Books USA; STP/Times Publishing Group (Singapore); Vanwell Publishing (Canada)
Distributor for Barron's; Lothian Publishing Co; North South Books
*Distribution Center:* MDS

**David Lovell Publishing**, *imprint of* Rainbow Book Agencies Pty Ltd

**Lowden Publishing Co**
29 Lisbeth Ave, Donvale, Victoria 3111
*Tel:* (03) 9873 7202 *Fax:* (03) 9873 0542
*E-mail:* service@theruralstore.com.au
*Web Site:* www.theruralstore.com.au
*Key Personnel*
Man Dir: Jim Lowden *E-mail:* jim@theruralstore.com.au
Founded: 1969
Subjects: Biography, History, Religion - Other, Transportation
ISBN Prefix(es): 0-909706
*Associate Companies:* The Rural Store (Agricultural Booksellers)

**Lucasville Press**
Lukis House, 1a Dalzell Rd, Raaf Base, Point Cook, Victoria 3030
*Tel:* (03) 9395 1446
*Key Personnel*
Head of Company: S Campbell-Wright
Founded: 1987
Specialize in Australian history.
Subjects: Biography, Genealogy, History
ISBN Prefix(es): 0-9587113; 0-646

**MacLennan & Petty Pty Ltd+**
152 Bunnerong Rd, Suite 405, Eastgardens, NSW 2036
*Tel:* (02) 9349 5811 *Fax:* (02) 9349 5911
*E-mail:* macpetty@zip.com.au

*Key Personnel*
Man Dir & International Rights Contact: Pamela
  Petty
Special Projects Dir: Rod Mead *E-mail:* rmead@
  maclennanpetty.com.au
Founded: 1988
Specialize in human services.
Subjects: Disability, Special Needs, Education,
  Health, Nutrition, Medicine, Nursing, Dentistry
ISBN Prefix(es): 0-86433
Number of titles published annually: 10 Print
Total Titles: 55 Print
Distributed by APAC Publishers (Southeast Asia);
  F A Davis (United States); Jessica Kingsley
  Publishing Co; Springer Publishing Co (Europe
  & UK)
Distributor for Adis Press (New Zealand); As-
  pen Publishers Inc (US); Brookes Publishing
  Co (United States); F A Davis; Health Press
  (United Kingdom); Health Professions Press
  (United States); Icon Learning Systems (United
  States); Isis Medical Media (United Kingdom);
  J & S Publishing (United States); Love Pub-
  lishing Co; MacLennan & Petty (Australia);
  Merit Publishing (United Kingdom); Paul H
  Brookes; Pavilion Publishers (United King-
  dom); Quay Books (Div of Mark Allen Pub-
  lishing) (United Kingdom); Roeher Institute
  (Canada); Slack Inc (United States); Spring-
  house Publishing (United States); Springhouse
  (United States); Whurr Publishers (United
  Kingdom); York Press (United States)

**Macmillan**, *imprint of* Pan Macmillan Australia
Pty Ltd

**Macmillan Education Australia+**
Level 4, 627 Chapel St, South Yarra, Victoria
  3141
*Tel:* (03) 9825 1025 *Fax:* (03) 9825 1010
*E-mail:* mea@macmillan.com.au
*Web Site:* www.macmillan.com.au
*Key Personnel*
Man Dir: Shane Armstrong *E-mail:* shane.
  armstrong@macmillan.com.au
Sales Dir: Peter Huntley *E-mail:* peter.huntley@
  macmillan.com.au
Marketing Manager: Christine Powers
  *E-mail:* christine.powers@macmillan.com.au
Senior Sales Coordinator: Vicky Cheong
  *E-mail:* vicky.cheong@macmillan.com.au
Founded: 1896
Subjects: Accounting, Behavioral Sciences, Eco-
  nomics, Education, Geography, Geology, Gov-
  ernment, Political Science, History, Manage-
  ment, Mathematics, Physics, Science (General),
  Social Sciences, Sociology
ISBN Prefix(es): 0-7329; 0-7330
*Parent Company:* Macmillan Publishers Australia
  Pty Ltd
*Branch Office(s)*
Level 2, St Martins Tower, 31 Market St, Sydney,
  NSW 2000 *Tel:* (02) 9264 0522 *Fax:* (02) 9264
  0770 *E-mail:* measyd@macmillan.com.au
*Warehouse:* Macmillan Distribution Services Pty
  Ltd, 56 Parkwest Dr, Derrimut, Victoria 3030,
  Man Dir: Andy Palmer *Tel:* (03) 9825 1000
  *Fax:* (03) 9825 3210 *E-mail:* mds@macmillan.
  com.au *Web Site:* www.ozemail.com.au/~mds/;
  www.macmillan.com.au

**Macmillan Publishers Australia Pty Ltd+**
Subsidiary of Macmillan Publishers (UK) Ltd
627 Chapel St, Level 4, South Yarra, Victoria
  3141
*Tel:* (03) 9825 1000 *Fax:* (03) 9825 1015
*Web Site:* www.panmacmillan.com.au
*Key Personnel*
Man Dir: Ross Gibb *E-mail:* ross.gibb@
  macmillan.com.au
Sales/Trade Manager: Laurie Giles
College Sales Manager: Harry Khoury

Customer Service: Younia Jarmam
Founded: 1968
Subjects: Education, Engineering (General), Lit-
  erature, Literary Criticism, Essays, Military
  Science, Psychology, Psychiatry, Science (Gen-
  eral), Social Sciences, Sociology
ISBN Prefix(es): 0-02; 0-08; 0-9585743; 1-
  876832
Subsidiaries: Australian National University Press
*Sales Office(s):* Melbourne
Sydney
*Warehouse:* 2-A Lord St, Botany, NSW 2019

**Macquarie Library**, *imprint of* Pan Macmillan
Australia Pty Ltd

**The Macquarie Library Pty Ltd**
Macquarie University, Sydney, NSW 2109
*Tel:* (02) 9805 9800 *Fax:* (02) 9888 2984
*E-mail:* alison@dict.mq.edu
*Key Personnel*
Publisher: Richard Tardif
Founded: 1980
ISBN Prefix(es): 0-949757; 1-876429
*Parent Company:* Kirin Publishing Pty Ltd
*Orders to:* Gary Allen Pty Ltd, 9 Cooper St,
  Smithfield, Sydney, NSW 2164

**Magabala Books Aboriginal Corporation+**
PO Box 668, Broome, WA 6725
*Tel:* (08) 9192 1991 *Fax:* (08) 9193 5254
*E-mail:* info@magabala.com
*Web Site:* www.magabala.com
*Key Personnel*
Publishing Manager: Bruce Sims
Administration Manager: Jill Walsh
Management Committee Chairperson: Arnhem
  Hunter
Founded: 1987
Specialize in indigenous publishing.
Subjects: Anthropology, Art, Biography, Drama,
  Theater, Fiction, Human Relations, Literature,
  Literary Criticism, Essays, Natural History,
  Nonfiction (General), Philosophy, Religion -
  Other
ISBN Prefix(es): 1-875641; 0-9588101
*Warehouse:* Discount Freight Express, PO Box
  260, Bentley, WA 6102

**Magic Bean**, *imprint of* Era Publications

**Magpie Books**
PO Box 2038, Brighton, Victoria 3186
*Tel:* (0613) 9592 9931 *Fax:* (0613) 9592 2045
*E-mail:* admin01@magpiebooks.com.au
*Web Site:* www.magpiebooks.com.au
Founded: 1980
Publisher of price guides for the second hand
  book trade.
Subjects: Publishing & Book Trade Reference

**Magpie Publications**
PO Box 3427, Weston Creek, ACT 2611
*Tel:* (06) 2509442
*Key Personnel*
Contact: T A Orchard
Specialize in Philately.
Subjects: Philately & Postal History
ISBN Prefix(es): 0-9587862; 1-875579

**Magpies Magazine Pty Ltd**
13 Frome St, Grange, Qld 4051
Mailing Address: PO Box 98, Grange, Qld 4051
*Tel:* (07) 3356 4503 *Fax:* (07) 3356 4649
*E-mail:* james@magpies.net.au
*Web Site:* www.magpies.net.au
*Key Personnel*
Editor: Ray Turton
Founded: 1986
Subjects: Library & Information Sciences
ISBN Prefix(es): 1-875249

**Mammoth UK**, *imprint of* Random House
Australia

**Margaret Hamilton Books Pty Ltd+**
Imprint of Scholastic Australia
76-80 Railway Crescent, Lisarow, NSW 2250
Mailing Address: PO Box 579, Gosford, NSW
  2250
*Tel:* (02) 4328 3555 *Toll Free Tel:* 800-021-233
  *Fax:* (02) 4323 3827 *Toll Free Fax:* 800-789-
  948
*E-mail:* customer_service@scholastic.com.au
*Web Site:* www.scholastic.com.au
*Key Personnel*
Dir: Margaret Hamilton
Sr Editor: Margrete Lamond *Tel:* (02) 9413 8343
Founded: 1988
ISBN Prefix(es): 0-947241; 1-876289
*Ultimate Parent Company:* Scholastic Inc

**Margin Magazines**, *imprint of* Mulini Press

**Marketing Focus**
26 Central Rd, Kalamunda, WA 6076
*Tel:* (08) 92571777 *Fax:* (08) 92571888
*Web Site:* www.marketingfocus.net.au
*Key Personnel*
Head of Company & Man Dir: Barry Ross
  Urquhart *E-mail:* urquhart@marketingfocus.
  net.au
Founded: 1978
Marketing & strategic planning consultant.
Subjects: Business, Marketing
ISBN Prefix(es): 0-9586558

**Marque Publishing Co Pty Ltd**
470 Pacific Highway, Wyoming, NSW
Mailing Address: PO Box 1896, Gosford, NSW
  2250
*Tel:* (02) 4322 4803 *Fax:* (02) 4329 1475
*E-mail:* books@marque.com.au
*Web Site:* www.marque.com.au
*Key Personnel*
Editorial Dir: Ewan Kennedy
Business Manager: Alistair Kennedy
Founded: 1987
Specialize in motoring books.
Subjects: Transportation
ISBN Prefix(es): 0-947079
Distributed by Bookworks Pty Ltd

**Tracy Marsh Publications Pty Ltd+**
1/79 Osmond Terrace, Norwood, SA 5067
*Tel:* (08) 8363 1248 *Fax:* (08) 8363 1352
*E-mail:* tracy@tracymarsh.com
*Web Site:* www.tracymarsh.com
*Key Personnel*
Chief Executive: Tracy Marsh
Co-Editions Manager: Jane Moseley
Founded: 1984
Subjects: Crafts, Games, Hobbies, Travel
ISBN Prefix(es): 1-875899; 0-9590174

**Horwitz Martin Education+**
Horwitz House, 55 Chandos St, St Leonards,
  NSW 2065
Mailing Address: PO Box 5555, St Leonards,
  NSW 2065
*Tel:* (02) 9901 6100 *Fax:* (02) 9901 6166
*Key Personnel*
General Manager: Stephen Wilson
  *E-mail:* stephenw@horwitz.com.au
Founded: 1958
Educational publishing company
Specialize in elementary textbook & literacy ma-
  terials.
Subjects: Education, Literature, Literary Criti-
  cism, Essays, Literacy
ISBN Prefix(es): 0-7253; 0-7252; 0-7255
Number of titles published annually: 120 Print

Total Titles: 500 Print
*Parent Company:* Horwitz Publications Pty Ltd

**Matthias Media**
42 Gardeners Rd, Suite 1, Kingsford, NSW 2032
Mailing Address: PO Box 225, Kingsford, NSW 2032
*Tel:* (02) 3100813; (02) 9663-1478 (overseas)
*Toll Free Tel:* 800 814 360 *Fax:* (02) 9663-3265; (02) 9663-3265
*E-mail:* info@matthiasmedia.com.au
*Web Site:* www.matthiasmedia.com.au
*Key Personnel*
Man Dir & International Rights: Ian Carmichael
Founded: 1988
Subjects: Education, Religion - Protestant, Christianity, Bible, Evangelicalism, Ministry
ISBN Prefix(es): 1-875245
*Parent Company:* St Matthias Press

**Mayfield Publishing**, *imprint of* Elsevier Australia

**Mayne Publishing+**
MS 422, Clifton, Qld 4361
*Tel:* (07) 4697 3228 *Fax:* (07) 4697 3228
*E-mail:* sales@maynepublishing.com.au
*Web Site:* www.maynepublishing.com.au
*Key Personnel*
Contact: C Mayne
Founded: 1995
Subjects: Behavioral Sciences, Cookery, Crafts, Games, Hobbies, Fiction, Government, Political Science, Health, Nutrition, How-to, Self-Help
ISBN Prefix(es): 0-9578142; 0-646

**Yvonne McBurney**
Educational Material Aid, 140L Obley Rd, MS3, Dubbo, NSW 2830
*Tel:* (02) 6887 3608
*Key Personnel*
Dir: Yvonne McBurney
Founded: 1976
Subjects: History, Regional Interests
ISBN Prefix(es): 0-908053
*Warehouse:* 140L Obley Rd MS3, Dubbo, NSW 2830 *Tel:* (068) 873608

**McGraw-Hill Australia Pty Ltd+**
Subsidiary of The McGraw-Hill Companies
82 Waterloo Rd, North Ryde, NSW 2113
Mailing Address: Locked bag 2233, Business Centre, North Ryde, NSW 1670
*Tel:* (02) 9900 1800; (02) 9900 1806 (customer service); (02) 9900 1802 (customer service)
*Fax:* (02) 9878 8280 (customer service)
*E-mail:* cservice_sydney@mcgraw-hill.com.au
*Web Site:* www.mcgraw-hill.com.au
*Key Personnel*
General Manager: Yasminka Nemet
*E-mail:* yasminka_nemet@mcgraw-hill.com
Publishing Manager, Science, Humanities & Vocational Education & Training: Michael Tully
*E-mail:* michael_tully@mcgraw-hill.com
Sponsoring Editor, Business Publishing: Alisa Brackley du Bois
*E-mail:* alisa_brackleydebois@mcgraw-hill.com
Marketing Coordinator, Business: Paula McGuinness *Tel:* (02) 9900 1890 *Fax:* (02) 9878 8881
*E-mail:* cherie_cadongan@mcgraw-hill.com
Marketing Coordinator, Medical: Sam McGown
*Tel:* (02) 9900 1836 *Fax:* (02) 9878 8881
*E-mail:* sam_mcgown@mcgraw-hill.com
Editorial Assistant: Eiko Bron *Tel:* (02) 9900 1905 *Fax:* (02) 9878 8881 *E-mail:* eiko_bron@mcgraw-hill.com
Founded: 1964
Subjects: Accounting, Advertising, Aeronautics, Aviation, Anthropology, Architecture & Interior Design, Art, Automotive, Behavioral Sciences, Biological Sciences, Chemistry, Chemical En-gineering, Child Care & Development, Computer Science, Criminology, Disability, Special Needs, Earth Sciences, Economics, Education, Electronics, Electrical Engineering, Engineering (General), English as a Second Language, Environmental Studies, Film, Video, Geography, Geology, Health, Nutrition, Journalism, Labor, Industrial Relations, Language Arts, Linguistics, Management, Maritime, Marketing, Mathematics, Mechanical Engineering, Medicine, Nursing, Dentistry, Philosophy, Photography, Physical Sciences, Physics, Psychology, Psychiatry, Social Sciences, Sociology, Sports, Athletics
ISBN Prefix(es): 0-07; 0-697; 0-256
*Associate Companies:* McGraw-Hill Book Co NZ Ltd, 56-60 Cawley St, Level 8, Ellerslie, Auckland, New Zealand, Contact: Max Loveridge
*Tel:* (09) 526 6200 *Fax:* (09) 526 6216
Imprints: PressXpress
*Branch Office(s)*
Melbourne Office, 8 Yarra St, Hawthorn, Victoria 3122, PTR State Manager: Nick Dallas
*Tel:* (03) 9819 0511 *Fax:* (03) 9819 0524
Brisbane Office, 588 Boundary St, Spring Hill, Qld 4000, Professional Division State Manager: Brent Pattison *Tel:* (07) 3835 1166 *Fax:* (07) 3831 7119
Distributed by Amacom (American Mangement); Active Path (Wrox); American Education Publishing; Appleton & Lange; ASQ (American Society of Quality); Barnell Loft Ltd; Benziger Publishing Co; Brown & Benchmark; William C Brown; Business Week Books; Certification Press; Charles E Merrill; Citrix Press; Clearway Exam Questions (HSC); Clearway Textbooks; CommerceNet Press; Computing McGraw-Hill; Contemporary Publications/NTC; Corel Press; Custom Publications; Dushkin Publishing Group; J D Edwards; Fine Arts Press; Friends of Ed; Glencoe/McGraw; Harvard Business School Press; International Marine; Irwin Publishers; Richard D Irwin; James Town Publishers/NTC; Keats Publishing/NTC; Learning Triangle Press; London House; MacMillan/McGraw-Hill School; Mayfield Publishing Co; McGraw-Hill Canada; Tata McGraw-Hill India; McGraw-Hill Italy; McGraw-Hill Microsoft Press; McGraw-Hill Singapore; McGraw-Hill UK; McGraw-Hill USA; Metric Schaum; New Holland Publishers; NTC (National Textbook Co); Oracle Press; Osborne; Platts (USA); Possum Press; Prmis; Quicken Press; Quilt Digest Press/NTC; Ragged Mountain Press; Rebol Press; Republic of Texas Press; RSA Press; Sapphire Books; Schaum; Science Research Associates (SRA); Tab Books; Terrific Science Press; Visual Education Corp (School); Webster Publishing; Windcrest; Wordware Publishing; Wright Group/McGraw-Hill; Wrox Press; Xebec/McGraw-Hill
Distributor for Alfred Waller (UK); Amacom - American Management (USA); Barnell Loft Ltd (USA); Benziger Publishing Co (USA); Brown & Benchmark; William C Brown; Clearway Textbooks; Custom Publications ((USA) part of McGraw); Charles E Merrill (USA); Clearway Exam Questions-HSC; Dushkin Publishing Group; Glencoe/McGraw (USA); Harvard Business School Press (USA); International Marine (USA); Irwin Professional PRO (USA); Irwin Publishers (USA); Richard D Irwin (USA); London House (USA); Webster Publishing; MacMillan/McGraw-Hill School (USA); McGraw-Hill Canada (Canada); McGraw-Hill Italy (Italy); McGraw-Hill Singapore (Singapore); Tata McGraw-Hill India (India); McGraw-Hill (UK); McGraw-Hill USA (USA); Metric Schaum (Singapore); Osborne (USA); Possum Press (Australia); Primis; Ragged Mountain Press ((USA) part of McGraw); Republic of Texas Press (USA); Sapphire Books (Australia); Schaum (USA); Science Research Associates SRA (USA); Tab Books (USA); Wordware Publishing (USA); Wrox Press; Windcrest

**J M McGregor Pty Ltd+**
PO Box 40, Double Bay, NSW 2028
*Tel:* (02) 9135 1923
*Key Personnel*
Man Dir: Malcolm McGregor
Founded: 1968
Subjects: Crafts, Games, Hobbies, Education, Photography
ISBN Prefix(es): 0-85921
Subsidiaries: J M McGregor NZ Ltd

**Media East Press**
PO Box 363, Kingsford, NSW 2032
*Tel:* (02) 9349 6683 *Fax:* (02) 9349 6683
*Key Personnel*
Man Dir: Thomas E King
Founded: 1977
Award-winning editorial agency/book publisher specializing in golf venues & travel destinations.
Membership(s): Australian Society of Travel Writers & Australian Society of Authors.
Subjects: Nonfiction (General), Travel
Total Titles: 5 Print
*Parent Company:* Media East Pty Ltd

**Melbourne Institute of Applied Economic & Social Research**
University of Melbourne, 6th floor, Parkville, Victoria 3010
*Tel:* (03) 8344 2100 *Fax:* (03) 8344 2111
*E-mail:* melb-inst@unimelb.edu.au
*Web Site:* www.melbourneinstitute.com
*Key Personnel*
Dir & Prof: Peter Dawkins *Tel:* (03) 8344 7915
*E-mail:* p.dawkins@unimelb.edu.au
Deputy Dir & Associate Prof: David Johnson
*Tel:* (03) 8344 7485 *E-mail:* d.johnson@unimelb.edu.au
Founded: 1963
Specialize in Economic & Social research, publishing working papers, newsletters & reports.
Subjects: Economics, Social Sciences, Sociology
*Orders to:* Blackwell Publishers Journals, 108 Cowley Rd, PO Box 805, Oxford OX4 1FH, United Kingdom *Tel:* (01865) 244083 *Fax:* (01865) 381381 *E-mail:* jnlinfo@blackwellpublishers.co.uk *Web Site:* www.blackwellpublishers.co.uk (Only for Australian Economic Review)

**Melbourne University Press+**
268 Drummond St, Carlton South, Victoria 3053
Mailing Address: PO Box 1167, Carlton, Victoria 3053
*Tel:* (03) 9342 0300 *Fax:* (03) 9342 0399
*E-mail:* mup-info@unimelb.edu.au
*Web Site:* www.mup.unimelb.edu.au
*Key Personnel*
Dir: Louise Adler *E-mail:* adlerl@unimelb.edu.au
General Manager: Ross Wallis *Tel:* (03) 9420305
*E-mail:* rwallis@unimelb.edu.au
Marketing Manager: John Denithorne
*E-mail:* johnad@unimelb.edu.au
Comm Editor (General Nonfiction): Sybil Nolan
Founded: 1922
Subjects: Biography, History, Literature, Literary Criticism, Essays, Natural History, Nonfiction (General), Psychology, Psychiatry, Travel
ISBN Prefix(es): 0-522; 0-734
Number of titles published annually: 50 Print; 2 CD-ROM; 10 E-Book
Total Titles: 600 Print; 3 CD-ROM; 1 E-Book
*Parent Company:* The University of Melbourne
Imprints: Miegunyah Press
*Warehouse:* Palgrave Macmillan, 627 Chapel St, South Yarra, Victoria 3141 *Tel:* (03) 9825 1113 *Fax:* (03) 9825 1010 *E-mail:* customer.

service@macmillan.com.au *Web Site:* www. macmillan.com
*Orders to:* Palgrave Macmillan, 627 Chapel St, South Yarra, Victoria 3141 *Tel:* (03) 9825 1113 *Fax:* (03) 9825 1010 *E-mail:* customer. service@macmillan.com.au *Web Site:* www. macmillan.com

**Melting Pot Press+**
10 Grafton St, Chippendale, NSW 2008
SAN: 901-1005
*Tel:* (02) 9211 1660 *Fax:* (02) 9211 1868
*E-mail:* books@elt.com.au
*Key Personnel*
Dir: Ron Wood *Tel:* (02) 9211 1178; Rita Yip *Tel:* (02) 9212 1882
Founded: 1983
Specialize in distributing & publishing English Language Teaching (ELT) titles.
Subjects: English as a Second Language
ISBN Prefix(es): 0-947103
Total Titles: 3 Print; 3 Audio
Distributor for Academic English Press; Catt Publishing; Dubois Publishing; Migsico-Piscean Productions; Leigh Slater

**Melway Publishing Pty Ltd**
32 Ricketts Rd, Mount Waverley, Victoria 3149
*Tel:* (03) 9585 9888 *Fax:* (03) 9585 9800
*E-mail:* melway@ausway.com
*Web Site:* www.ausway.com
*Key Personnel*
Dir: Murray Godfrey *E-mail:* murray@ausway. com
Founded: 1966
Membership(s): IMTA.
Subjects: Publishing & Book Trade Reference
Total Titles: 2 Print; 2 CD-ROM
*Parent Company:* Ausway Publishing Pty Ltd
*Associate Companies:* Sydway Publishing Pty Ltd, PO Box 693, Coogee, NSW 2034, Contact: Murray Godfrey *Tel:* (03) 9585 9808 *Fax:* (03) 9585 9800 *E-mail:* murray@ausway. com

**Michael Grinder & Associates**, *imprint of* Hawker Brownlow

**Miegunyah Press**, *imprint of* Melbourne University Press

**MILK**, *imprint of* Hachette Livre Australia

**Mimosa Publications Pty Ltd+**
8 Yarra St, Hawthorn, Victoria 3122
*Tel:* (03) 9819 0511 *Fax:* (03) 9819 0524
*E-mail:* info@mimosa.pub.com.au
*Key Personnel*
International Marketing & Publishing Dir: Sue Donovan
Man Dir: John Gilder
Founded: 1980
Subjects: English as a Second Language, Language Arts, Linguistics, Mathematics, Poetry, Science (General), Reading
ISBN Prefix(es): 0-7327
*Parent Company:* Tribune Co
*Associate Companies:* Mimosa Education Inc, 50 South Steele St, Suite 755, Denver, CO 80209, United States
Subsidiaries: Dragon Media P/L
Divisions: Mimosa Shortland

**Minerva**, *imprint of* Random House Australia

**Mission Publications of Australia**
19 Cascade St, Lawson, NSW 2783
*Tel:* (02) 4759 1003 *Fax:* (02) 4759 1101
*E-mail:* missionpublaust@bigpond.com
Founded: 1960

Specialize in Easy English Christian Literature.
Subjects: Religion - Other
ISBN Prefix(es): 0-909448; 1-86288
*Associate Companies:* Aborigines Inland Mission & United Aborigines Mission

**Mockingbird**, *imprint of* Ginninderra Press

**Modern Learning Press**, *imprint of* Hawker Brownlow

**Moon-Ta-Gu Books**
10A East Parade, Leura, NSW 2780
*Tel:* (02) 6336 0317 *Fax:* (02) 6336 1319
*E-mail:* wtba@ozemail.com.au
*Key Personnel*
Contact: Erle Montaigue
Subjects: Health, Nutrition, Self-Help, Martial Arts
ISBN Prefix(es): 0-949132

**Moonlight Publishing**
PO Box 5, Golden Square, Victoria 3555
*Tel:* (03) 5447 8221
*E-mail:* moonlight@impulse.net.au
*Key Personnel*
Manager: Chris Spencer *E-mail:* chris_spencer@ bssc.edu.au
Founded: 1989
Subjects: Music, Dance
ISBN Prefix(es): 1-876187; 0-9586515
Total Titles: 60 Print; 1 Audio
Imprints: Windwood

**Morgan Kaufmann**, *imprint of* Elsevier Australia

**Mosby**, *imprint of* Elsevier Australia

**K & Z Mostafanejad+**
PO Box 118, Geraldton, WA 6531
*Tel:* (08) 9923 3741 *Fax:* (08) 9923 3741
*Key Personnel*
Head of Company: Karola Mostafanejad
Sales Manager: Zaim Mostafanejad
Founded: 1989
Subjects: Mathematics, Science (General), Science Fiction, Fantasy
ISBN Prefix(es): 0-646

**Mostly Unsung+**
PO Box 20, Gardenvale, Victoria 3186
*Tel:* (03) 9555 5401 *Fax:* (03) 9555 5401
*E-mail:* milhis@alphalink.com.au
*Key Personnel*
Head of Company: Neil C Smith
Founded: 1990
Subjects: History, Military Science, Regional Interests
ISBN Prefix(es): 1-876179
Total Titles: 35 Print
*U.S. Office(s):* c/o Anzar Services Inc, PO Box 274, Lexington, VA 24450, United States

**Mount**, *imprint of* Little Hills Press Pty Ltd

**Mountain House Press**
370 Wallace Rd, The Channon, NSW 2480
*Tel:* (02) 6688 6318 *Fax:* (02) 6688 6318
*Key Personnel*
Contact: Margery J Kemp *E-mail:* kkemp@nor. com.au
Subjects: Art, Photography, Poetry
ISBN Prefix(es): 0-9586639

**Mouse House Press**
30 Kinkead St, Evatt, ACT 2617
*Tel:* (02) 93512612 *Fax:* (02) 93512606
*E-mail:* s.juan@edfac.usyd.edu.au

*Key Personnel*
Contact: M L Beggs
Subjects: Behavioral Sciences, Health, Nutrition
ISBN Prefix(es): 1-875397

**Mulavon Press Pty Ltd+**
131 Ryedale Rd, West Ryde, NSW 2114
*Tel:* (02) 9808 3662 *Fax:* (02) 9552 1608
*Key Personnel*
Contact: Rebecca Pinchin
Subjects: Environmental Studies, Natural History, Nonfiction (General), Outdoor Recreation, Australia Flora & Fauna
ISBN Prefix(es): 0-85899

**Mulini Press+**
PO Box 82, Jamison Centre, Canberra, ACT 2614
*Tel:* (02) 6251 2519 *Fax:* (02) 6251 2519
*Key Personnel*
Dir: Victor Crittenden
Founded: 1965
Specialize in early Australian history.
Subjects: Biography, Gardening, Plants, History, Literature, Literary Criticism, Essays, Poetry
ISBN Prefix(es): 0-949910; 0-9598414; 0-9751784
Number of titles published annually: 10 Print
Total Titles: 80 Print
Imprints: Margin Magazines

**Murdoch Books+**
Pier 8/9, 23 Hickson Rd, Millers Point, Sydney, NSW 2000
Mailing Address: GPO Box 1203, Sydney, NSW 2001
*Tel:* (02) 8220 2000 *Fax:* (02) 8220 2020
*Web Site:* www.mm.com.au
*Key Personnel*
International Sales Dir: Mark Newman *E-mail:* markn@mm.com.au
Chief Executive Officer & Publisher: Anne Wilson *E-mail:* annew@mm.com.au
Founded: 1989
General nonfiction illustrated publisher.
Subjects: Domestic & Decorative Arts
ISBN Prefix(es): 0-86411; 0-74045
Total Titles: 800 Print
*Parent Company:* Murdoch Magazines Pty Ltd
Imprints: Bay Books; Better Homes & Gardens; Family Circle
*Warehouse:* Unit 2, 8A Ethel Ave, Brookvale, NSW 2100

**John Murray**, *imprint of* Hachette Livre Australia

**Museum of Victoria**
GPO Box 666E, Melbourne, Victoria 3001
*Tel:* (03) 8341 7777 *Fax:* (03) 8341 7778
*Web Site:* www.museum.vic.gov.au
*Key Personnel*
Productions Manager: Teresa Paterson *E-mail:* tpater@mov.vic.gov.au
Subjects: Education, History

**Narkaling Inc+**
39 Helena St, Midland, WA 6936
Mailing Address: PO Box 1409, Midland, WA 6936
*Tel:* (08) 9274 8022 *Fax:* (08) 9274 8362
*E-mail:* info@narkaling.com.au
*Web Site:* www.narkaling.com.au
*Key Personnel*
Executive Dir: Marion Slany
Administrative Officer: Erika Troy
Founded: 1997
Non-profit organization which provides educational sources to people with reading difficulties: adults, teenagers & children.
Subjects: Fiction, Nonfiction (General)
ISBN Prefix(es): 0-86457

Number of titles published annually: 40 Audio
Total Titles: 300 Audio

**National Association of Forest Industries Ltd**
PO Box E89, Kingston, ACT 2604
*Tel:* (02) 6285 3833 *Fax:* (02) 6285 3855
*E-mail:* enquiries@nafi.com.au
*Web Site:* www.nafi.com.au
ISBN Prefix(es): 1-86346

**National Gallery of Australia+**
Parkes Pl, Canberra, ACT 2601
Mailing Address: GPO Box 1150, Canberra, ACT 2601
*Tel:* (02) 6240 6501; (02) 6240 6502 *Fax:* (06) 6240 6427
*E-mail:* information@nga.gov.au
*Web Site:* www.nga.gov.au
*Telex:* 61500 *Cable:* NGA CANBERRA
*Key Personnel*
Publications Manager: Jane Arms *E-mail:* jane.arms@nga.gov.au
Editorial: Alistair McGhie
Rights & Permissions: Leanne Handreck *E-mail:* copyright@nga.gov.au
Founded: 1982
Subjects: Art
ISBN Prefix(es): 0-642

**National Gallery of Victoria**
180 St Kilda Rd, Melbourne, Victoria 3004
Mailing Address: PO Box 7259, Melbourne, Victoria 8004
*Tel:* (03) 8620 2212 *Fax:* (03) 8620 2535
*E-mail:* enquiries@ngv.vic.gov.au
*Web Site:* www.ngv.vic.gov.au
*Key Personnel*
Dir: Gerard Vaughan
Publications Manager: Philip Jago *E-mail:* philip.jago@ngv.vic.gov.au
Founded: 1861
Specialize in large collections of art for the state of Victoria, Australia.
Subjects: Art, Fashion
ISBN Prefix(es): 0-7241
Number of titles published annually: 10 Print
Total Titles: 75 Print
*Bookshop(s):* The Gallery Shop *Tel:* (03) 8620 2242; (03) 8620 1542 *Fax:* (03) 8620 2580; (03) 8620 1550 *E-mail:* gallery.shop@ngv.vic.gov.au
*Distribution Center:* Woodstocker Books/ACC (USA & Canada)

**National Library of Australia**
Parkes Pl, Canberra, ACT 2600
*Tel:* (02) 6262 1111 *Fax:* (02) 6257 1703
*E-mail:* www@nla.gov.au
*Web Site:* www.nla.gov.au
*Telex:* AA62100
*Key Personnel*
Publications Dir: Dr Paul Hetherington *Tel:* (02) 6262 1474 *E-mail:* phetheri@nla.gov.au
Manager, Publications: Nicola Mackay-Sim *E-mail:* nmackays@nla-gov.au
Editor: Paul Cliff
Founded: 1960
ISBN Prefix(es): 0-642

**Navarine Publishing**
PO Box 1275, Woden, ACT 2606
*Tel:* (02) 62824602
*Key Personnel*
Contact: Graeme Broxam *E-mail:* gjbroxam@bigpond.com.au
Founded: 1992
Membership(s): Roebuck Society.
Subjects: Genealogy, History, Maritime, Nonfiction (General), Regional Interests, Transportation
ISBN Prefix(es): 0-9586561; 0-9751331

Number of titles published annually: 2 Print
Total Titles: 8 Print
*Associate Companies:* The Roebuck Society, PO Box 1275, Woden, ACT 2606
Distributor for Roebuck Society

**New American Library,** *imprint of* Penguin Group (Australia)

**New Creation Publications Ministries & Resource Centre**
936 Ackland Hill Rd, Coromandel Valley, SA 5051
Mailing Address: PO Box 403, Blackwood, SA 5051
*Tel:* (08) 8270 1497; (08) 8270 1861 *Fax:* (08) 8270 4003
*E-mail:* ministry@newcreation.org.au
*Web Site:* www.newcreation.org.au
*Key Personnel*
Dir, Ministry: Martin Bleby
General Manager: John David Skewes *E-mail:* john@newcreation.org.au
Founded: 1974
Christian publishing.
Subjects: Biblical Studies, Fiction, Human Relations, Theology
ISBN Prefix(es): 0-86408; 0-949851
Number of titles published annually: 10 Print
Total Titles: 390 Print
Imprints: Troubadour Press

**New Endeavour Press+**
PO Box 1596, Strawberry Hills, NSW 2012
*Tel:* (02) 3182384 *Fax:* (02) 3103613
*Key Personnel*
Head of Company: Philippe Tanguy
Founded: 1989
Specialize in quality Australian fiction, poetry & art books.
Subjects: Anthropology, Art, Fiction, Humor, Journalism, Language Arts, Linguistics, Poetry
ISBN Prefix(es): 1-875505
*Associate Companies:* New South Wales University Press

**New Era Publications Australia Pty Ltd**
Subsidiary of New Era Publications International
Level 1, 61-65 Wentworth Ave, Surry Hills, NSW 2010
*Tel:* (02) 9211 0692 *Fax:* (02) 9211 0686
*E-mail:* books@newerapublications.com
*Web Site:* www.newerapublications.com
*Key Personnel*
Executive Dir: Gabi Lumsden *Tel:* (02) 9211 0691
Founded: 1969
Also specialize in L Ron Hubbard books.
Subjects: Fiction, Self-Help
ISBN Prefix(es): 0-9586577
Total Titles: 16 Print; 17 Audio
Distributed by Victorian Wholesellers

**New Horizons for Learning,** *imprint of* Hawker Brownlow

**New Music Articles,** see NMA Publications

**Newman Centre Publications**
Cardinal Newman Catechist Centre, One Chetwynd Rd, Merrylands, NSW 2160
*Tel:* (02) 9637 9406 *Fax:* (02) 9637 3351
*Key Personnel*
Contact: Rev B J H Tierney
Founded: 1974
Subjects: Education, Fiction, Philosophy, Religion - Catholic, Catholic Catechism
ISBN Prefix(es): 0-9587535

**Nimaroo Publishers**
PO Box 2046, Wollongong, NSW 2500
*Tel:* (042) 292297
*Key Personnel*
Manager & Publicity: Stephen Standish
Editorial: P Balnaves
Sales: T Balnaves
Production: M Standish
Rights & Permissions: N Standish
Founded: 1978
Subjects: Business, Science (General)
ISBN Prefix(es): 0-9596525
*Branch Office(s)*
11 Airds Rd, Lower Templestone, Victoria 3107

**Nimrod Publications+**
Dept of English, University of Newcastle, Newcastle, NSW 2308
*Tel:* (02) 4957 5562; (02) 4921 5173 *Fax:* (02) 4957 5562
*E-mail:* nimrod@hunterlink.com.au
Founded: 1964
Subjects: Language Arts, Linguistics, Literature, Literary Criticism, Essays, Poetry, Science Fiction, Fantasy
ISBN Prefix(es): 0-909242 (Nimrod & Babel)
Imprints: Babel Handbooks
Subsidiaries: Babel Handbooks

**NIV,** *imprint of* Hachette Livre Australia

**NMA Publications**
PO Box 5034, Burnley, Victoria 3121
*Tel:* (03) 9428 2405
*Web Site:* www.rainerlinz.net/NMA/
*Key Personnel*
Publisher: R G Linz *E-mail:* rlinz@alphalink.com.au
Founded: 1982
Subjects: Literature, Literary Criticism, Essays, Music, Dance
ISBN Prefix(es): 0-9587113; 0-646; 0-9577549
Total Titles: 1 Print
Distributed by Frog Peak Music (USA)

**NSW Agriculture**
161 Kite St, Orange, NSW 2800
Mailing Address: Locked Bag 21, Orange, NSW 2800
*Tel:* (02) 6391 3100 *Fax:* (02) 6391 3336
*E-mail:* nsw.agriculture@agric.nsw.gov.au
*Web Site:* www.agric.nsw.gov.au
*Key Personnel*
Publisher: Geof Murray
*U.S. Office(s):* Florida Science Source Inc, PO Box 927, Lake Alfred, FL 33850-0927, United States

**Ocean Press+**
Hasta 1a Victoria Street Bookshop, 360 Victoria St, North Melbourne, Victoria 3051
Mailing Address: GPO Box 3279, Melbourne, Victoria 3001
*Tel:* (03) 9326 4280 *Fax:* (03) 9329 5040
*E-mail:* edit@oceanpress.com.au; info@oceanbooks.com.au
*Web Site:* www.oceanbooks.com.au
*Key Personnel*
President: David Deutschmann
Founded: 1989
Subjects: Biography, Developing Countries, Environmental Studies, Government, Political Science, History, Social Sciences, Sociology, Women's Studies
ISBN Prefix(es): 1-875284; 1-876175
Total Titles: 60 Print
*U.S. Office(s):* Ocean Press, Old Chelsea Station, PO Box 1186, New York, NY 10113-1186, United States *Tel:* 718-246-4160 *E-mail:* info@oceanbooks.com.au
*Warehouse:* LPC Warehouse, 4029 W George St, Chicago, IL 60641, United States *E-mail:* ftg@lpcgroup.com

*Distribution Center:* LPC Group, 1436 W Randolph St, Chicago, IL 60607, United States
*Orders to:* LPC, 1436 W Randolph St, Chicago, IL 60607, United States
*Returns:* LPC, 4029 W George St, Chicago, IL 60641, United States

**Oceans Enterprises+**
303 Commercial Rd, Yarram, Victoria 3971
*Tel:* (03) 5182 5108 *Fax:* (03) 5182 5823
*Web Site:* www.oceans.com.au
*Key Personnel*
Contact: Peter Stone *E-mail:* peter@oceans.com.au
Founded: 1982
Specialize in marine, military & history publications, commercial & sport scuba diving.
Subjects: History, Maritime, Military Science, Sports, Athletics, Travel
ISBN Prefix(es): 0-9586657
Imprints: Lonestone Press
Subsidiaries: Lonestone Press
Distributed by Gary Allen PL, Sydney

**Anne O'Donovan Pty Ltd+**
171 La Trobe St, Level 1, Melbourne 3000
*Tel:* (03) 9819 5372 *Fax:* (03) 9818 6849
*E-mail:* odonovan@netspace.net.au
*Key Personnel*
Head of Company: Anne O'Donovan
Founded: 1978
Subjects: Cookery, Finance, Health, Nutrition, Music, Dance, Nonfiction (General), Self-Help
ISBN Prefix(es): 1-876026; 0-908476
Distributed by Penguin Books Australia Ltd (Australia)
*Warehouse:* Penguin Books, 487 Maroondah Hwy, Ringwood, Victoria 3134
*Orders to:* Penguin Books, 487 Maroondah Hwy, Ringwood, Victoria 3134

**Off the Shelf Publishing+**
32 Thomas St, Lewisham, NSW 2049
*Tel:* (02) 9560 3058 *Fax:* (02) 9564 0758
*E-mail:* offshelf@ozemail.com.au
*Key Personnel*
Publisher: Gillian Souter
Co-Proprietor: John Souter
Founded: 1991
Specialize in illustrated international craft & leisure books.
Subjects: Crafts, Games, Hobbies, Travel
ISBN Prefix(es): 0-646; 0-9586682; 1-876779
Total Titles: 20 Print
Distributed by Australian Book Group in Australia (Australia)

**Ohio Psychology Press**, *imprint of* Hawker Brownlow

**Oidium Books+**
PO Box 191, Corio, Victoria 3214
*Tel:* (052) 757045
*E-mail:* tecnilab@ozemail.com.au
*Key Personnel*
Contact: Richard Turner
Founded: 1985
Subjects: Health, Nutrition
ISBN Prefix(es): 0-9589510

**Oliver Freeman Editions**, *imprint of* Prospect Media

**Ollif Publishing Co+**
41 Galston Rd, Hornsby, NSW 2077
Mailing Address: PO Box 439, Hornsby, NSW 2077
*Tel:* (02) 9477-3496
*Key Personnel*
President: Lorna Ollif
Founded: 1965

Subjects: Biography, Fiction, History
ISBN Prefix(es): 0-9599183; 0-9577276
Number of titles published annually: 1 Print
Total Titles: 6 Print
Distributed by NSW Military Historical Society

**Omnibus Books+**
52 Fullarton Rd, Norwood, SA 5067
*Tel:* (08) 8363 2333 *Fax:* (08) 8363 1420
*E-mail:* omnibus@scholastic.com.au
*Key Personnel*
Publisher: Dyan Blacklock
General Manager: Dyan Blacklock
Senior Editor: Penny Matthews
Founded: 1980
Subjects: Fiction, Nonfiction (General), Poetry
ISBN Prefix(es): 0-86896; 1-86291; 0-949641
Number of titles published annually: 25 Print
Total Titles: 238 Print
*Parent Company:* Scholastic Australia Ltd, Railway Terrace, Lisarow, Gosford, NSW
*Shipping Address:* Scholastic Australia Ltd, Railway Terrace, Lisarow, Gosford, NSW
*Warehouse:* Scholastic Australia Ltd, Railway Terrace, Lisarow, Gosford, NSW

**On The Stone+**
252 Durham St, Bathurst, NSW 2795
*Tel:* (02) 6334 3442 *Fax:* (02) 6334 3009
*Web Site:* www.onthestone.com.au
*Key Personnel*
Man Dir: Marje Prior *E-mail:* m.prior@onthestone.com
Subjects: Asian Studies, Regional Interests
ISBN Prefix(es): 0-9585719

**Online Information Resources**
42 Waller Crescent, Campbell, ACT 2612
Mailing Address: PO Box 57, Ainslie, ACT 2602
*Tel:* (03) 6257 9177 *Fax:* (03) 6257 9030
*Key Personnel*
Dir: Sherrey Quinn
Subjects: Library & Information Sciences
ISBN Prefix(es): 0-646

**Open Training & Education Network**, see OTEN (Open Training & Education Network)

**Openbook Publishers+**
205 Halifax St, Adelaide, SA 5000
Mailing Address: GPO Box 1368, Adelaide, SA 5001
*Tel:* (08) 8223 5468 *Fax:* (08) 8223 4552
*E-mail:* openbook@peg.apc.org; service@openbook.com.au
*Web Site:* www.openbook.com.au
*Key Personnel*
General Manager: Chris Pfeiffer *E-mail:* chrisp@openbook.com.au
Editorial & Rights & Permission: John Pfitzner *E-mail:* johnp@openbook.com.au
Founded: 1913
Subjects: Education, Religion - Protestant, Religion - Other
ISBN Prefix(es): 0-85910
Number of titles published annually: 20 Print
Total Titles: 200 Print

**Oriental Publications+**
18 Market St, Adelaide, SA 5000
*Tel:* (08) 8212 6055 *Fax:* (08) 8410 0863
*E-mail:* oriental@dove.mtx.net.au
*Key Personnel*
Dir: Tiny Bruzzone
Subjects: Antiques, Art, Asian Studies, Cookery, Language Arts, Linguistics, Religion - Buddhist, Religion - Hindu, Religion - Islamic
ISBN Prefix(es): 0-9587113

**Orin Books**
PO Box 2089, St Kilda, West Victoria 3182

*Tel:* (03) 9534 5680; (03) 9534 4746 *Fax:* (03) 9527 6995
*Key Personnel*
Man Dir: S E Shifrin
Membership(s): Australian Publishers Association.
Subjects: Humor
ISBN Prefix(es): 1-875230; 0-9588190; 0-9588648; 0-9592263

**OTEN (Open Training & Education Network)+**
51 Wentworth Rd, Strathfield, NSW 2135
*Tel:* (02) 9715 8000; (02) 9715 8222 (sales) *Fax:* (02) 9715 8111; (02) 9715 8174 (sales)
*E-mail:* oten.courseinfo@tafensw.edu.au
*Web Site:* www.oten.edu.au
*Key Personnel*
Dir: Greeme Dobbs
Founded: 1994
Specialize in college textbooks & video cassettes.
Membership(s): Australian Publishers Association.
Subjects: Accounting, Aeronautics, Aviation, Agriculture, Automotive, Business, Child Care & Development, Civil Engineering, Computer Science, Disability, Special Needs, Electronics, Electrical Engineering, English as a Second Language, Fashion, Finance, Management, Maritime, Marketing, Microcomputers, Real Estate
*Parent Company:* New South Wales Technical & Further Education Commission

**Outback Books**, *imprint of* Outback Books - CQU Press

**Outback Books - CQU Press**
PO Box 1615, Rockhampton, Qld 4701
*Tel:* (07) 4923 2520 *Fax:* (07) 4923 2525
*E-mail:* cqupress@cqu.edu.au
*Web Site:* www.outbackbooks.com
*Key Personnel*
Dir: Prof David Myers *E-mail:* d.myers@cqu.edu.au
Founded: 1993
Specialize in subjects about country heritage, regional history, South Pacific & Australiana.
Subjects: Biography, History, Nonfiction (General), Regional Interests
ISBN Prefix(es): 1-875998; 1-876780
Imprints: Outback Books; South Pacific Books

**Outdoor Press Pty Ltd+**
PO Box 866, Shepparton, Victoria 3632
*Tel:* (03) 5790 5226 *Fax:* (03) 5790 5393
*Web Site:* www.goldexpeditions.com.au
*Key Personnel*
Manager: Douglas M Stone *Tel:* (0438) 369919 *E-mail:* dougstone@goldexpeditions.com.au
Founded: 1976
Specialize in gold & gemstone guides to Australia.
Subjects: Gold & Gemstones
Total Titles: 4 Print

**Owl Books**, *imprint of* Pan Macmillan Australia Pty Ltd

**Owl Publishing**
22 Rooding St, Brighton, Victoria 3186
*Tel:* (03) 95966064 *Fax:* (03) 95966942
*E-mail:* owlbooks@bigpond.com
*Key Personnel*
Publisher: Helen Nickas
Founded: 1992
Subjects: Ethnicity, Literature, Literary Criticism, Essays, Poetry
ISBN Prefix(es): 0-9586390
Number of titles published annually: 1 Print
Total Titles: 15 Print

**Oxfam Community Aid Abroad**
Affiliate of Oxfam International
156 George St, 1st floor, Fitzroy, Victoria 3065
*Tel:* (03) 9289 9444 *Fax:* (03) 9419 5895
*E-mail:* enquire@caa.org.au
*Web Site:* www.caa.org.au
*Key Personnel*
Publications Coordinator: Sarah Lowe
    *E-mail:* sarahlo@caa.org.au
Specialize in overseas aid & development.
Subjects: Economics, Education, Environmental
    Studies, Foreign Countries, Genealogy, Gov-
    ernment, Political Science, Health, Nutrition,
    Women's Studies
ISBN Prefix(es): 0-9587791; 0-9599636; 0-
    875870
*Associate Companies:* Oxfam Great Britain
Distributed by Oxfam Great Britain


**Jill Oxton Publications Pty Ltd+**
PO Box 283, Park Holme, SA 5043
*Tel:* (08) 2762722 *Fax:* (08) 3743494
*E-mail:* jill@jilloxtonxstitch.com
*Web Site:* www.jilloxtonxstitch.com
*Key Personnel*
Contact: Jill Oxton
Founded: 1989
Publishing cross stitch & beading charted designs.
Subjects: Crafts, Games, Hobbies
ISBN Prefix(es): 0-9587576
Number of titles published annually: 4 Print
Total Titles: 50 Print


**Pacific Publications (Australia) Pty Ltd**
35-51 Mitchell St, McMahons Point, NSW 2060
*Tel:* (02) 9464 3300 *Fax:* (02) 9464 3375
*Web Site:* pacificpubs.com.au
*Key Personnel*
Publisher: Geoff Husey
Founded: 1930
Papua New Guinea Handbook.
Subjects: Agriculture, Regional Interests
ISBN Prefix(es): 0-85807
*Parent Company:* Seven Network Ltd
*Branch Office(s)*
Pacific Publications Brisbane, Centro on James,
    10B, 23 James St, Fortitude Valley, Qld 4006
Pacific Publications Melbourne, 160 Harbour Es-
    planade, Docklands, Victoria
*Orders to:* Robert Brown & Associates, 7 Ather-
    ton St, Buranda, Qld 4102


**Pademelon Press+**
7/3 Packard Ave, Castle Hill, NSW 2154
Mailing Address: PO Box 6500, Baulkham Hills
    BC, NSW 2153
*Tel:* (02) 9634-4655 *Fax:* (02) 9680-4634
*E-mail:* info@pademelonpress.com.au
*Web Site:* www.pademelonpress.com.au
*Key Personnel*
Dir & International Rights: Rodney Kenner
Founded: 1990
Specialize in early childhood teacher resource &
    reference books.
Subjects: Child Care & Development, Education
ISBN Prefix(es): 1-876138
Number of titles published annually: 4 Print
Total Titles: 15 Print
*Parent Company:* Pademelon Press Pty Ltd
Distributed by Gryphon House Inc (USA &
    Canada only)
Distributor for Building Blocks; Child Care Infor-
    mation Exchange; Gryphon House; High/Scope
    Press; National Association for the Educa-
    tion of Young Children; New Horizons; Our
    Kids Press; Redleaf Press; School-Age Notes;
    Teacher's College Press; Teaching Strategies;
    William Publishing Co (all restricted to Aus-
    tralia & New Zealand)
Foreign Rep(s): Gryphon House Inc (Canada, US)


**Charles Paine Pty Ltd**
204 Clarence St, Sydney, NSW 2000
*Tel:* (02) 9890 1388 *Fax:* (02) 9890 1915
ISBN Prefix(es): 0-909687


**Palm Beach Press**
40 Ocean Rd, Palm Beach, NSW 2108
*Tel:* (02) 6646 1622 *Fax:* (02) 9946 1515
*Key Personnel*
Contact: Nat Young *E-mail:* nato@hor.com.au
Founded: 1976
Subjects: Surfing
ISBN Prefix(es): 0-9591816


**Palms Press**
87 Newport Rd, Dora Creek, NSW 2264
*Tel:* (02) 4973 1236
*Key Personnel*
Contact: H K Garland
Subjects: Environmental Studies, History, How-to,
    Humor, Public Administration
ISBN Prefix(es): 0-9593041


**Pan**, *imprint of* Pan Macmillan Australia Pty Ltd


**Pan Macmillan Australia Pty Ltd+**
Level 18, St Martins Tower, 31 Market St, Syd-
    ney, NSW 2000
*Tel:* (02) 9285 9100 *Fax:* (02) 9285 9100
*E-mail:* pansyd@macmillan.com.au;
    panpublicity@macmillan.com.au (publicity)
*Web Site:* www.panmacmillan.com.au
*Key Personnel*
Publishing Dir: James Fraser *E-mail:* james.
    fraser@macmillan.com.au
Sales Dir, Melbourne Office: Peter Phillips
    *Tel:* (03) 9825 1000 *Fax:* (03) 9825 1015
    *E-mail:* peter.phillips@macmillan.com.au
Product Department Manager, Melbourne Office:
    Andrew Farrell *Tel:* (03) 9825 1000 *Fax:* (03)
    9825 1015 *E-mail:* andrew.farrell@macmillan.
    com.au
Founded: 1983
Submissions must include a short cover letter (1
    or 2 pages), along with a detailed chapter out-
    line for nonfiction or a synopsis of the plot for
    fiction. See web site for additional submission
    information. No children's picture books, short
    story collections or poetry.
Subjects: Biography, Fiction, Health, Nutrition,
    Humor, Literature, Literary Criticism, Essays,
    Nonfiction (General), Self-Help, Travel
ISBN Prefix(es): 0-330; 0-7329
*Parent Company:* Macmillan Ltd, United King-
    dom
Imprints: Boxtree; Rod Campbell Books; Chan-
    nel 4; Forge; Griffin; Henry Holt; Let's Go;
    Macmillan; Macquarie Library; Owl Books;
    Pan; Pancake; Papermac; Picador; Priddy &
    Bicknell; Sidgwick & Jackson; St Martins;
    Sun; Tor Books
*Branch Office(s)*
Level 4, 627 Chapel St, South Yarra, Victo-
    ria 3141 *Tel:* (03) 9825 1000 *Fax:* (03) 9825
    1015 *E-mail:* panmel@macmillan.com.au *Web
    Site:* www.panmacmillan.com.au
*Warehouse:* Macmillan Distribution Services Pty
    Ltd, 56 Parkwest Dr, Derrimut, Victoria 3030,
    Man Dir: Andy Palmer *Tel:* (03) 9825 1000
    *Fax:* (03) 9825 3210 *E-mail:* mds@macmillan.
    com.au *Web Site:* www.ozemail.com.au/~mds;
    www.macmillan.com.au


**Pancake**, *imprint of* Pan Macmillan Australia Pty
Ltd


**Pandani Press**
17 Derwentwater Ave, Sand Bay, Tas 7005
*Tel:* (03) 6225 1956
*E-mail:* pandani@iprimus.com.au


*Key Personnel*
Head of Company: Sue Backhouse
Subjects: Art, Natural History
ISBN Prefix(es): 0-9587113; 0-85901
Total Titles: 1 Print


**Panorama Books**, *imprint of* St George Books


**Pantheon**, *imprint of* Random House Australia


**Pants on Fire**, *imprint of* Crawford House
Publishing Pty Ltd


**Papermac**, *imprint of* Pan Macmillan Australia
Pty Ltd


**Papyrus Publishing**
c/o Post Office, Scarsdale, Victoria 3351
*Tel:* (03) 5342 2394 *Fax:* (03) 5342 2423
*E-mail:* editor@papyrus.com.au
*Web Site:* www.papyrus.com.au
*Key Personnel*
Contact: Herbert Stein
Founded: 1991
Subjects: Ethnicity, Fiction, Literature, Literary
    Criticism, Essays, Poetry
ISBN Prefix(es): 1-875934


**Parabel Place+**
67 Exeter Rd, North Croydon, Victoria 3136
*Tel:* (03) 9727 1894 *Fax:* (03) 9727 1857
*Key Personnel*
Head of Company: Brigitte Lambert
Founded: 1991
Membership(s): Society of Women Writers (Vic-
    toria Branch) Australia.
Subjects: Cookery, Women's Studies
ISBN Prefix(es): 0-9586591


**Pascal Press+**
PO Box 250, Glebe, NSW 2037
*Tel:* (02) 8585 4044 *Fax:* (02) 8585 4001
*E-mail:* contact@pascalprcss.com.au; info@
    pascalpress.com.au
*Web Site:* www.pascalpress.com.au
*Key Personnel*
Man Dir: Matthew B Sandblom *Tel:* (0612)
    8585 4024 *Fax:* (0612) 8585 4024
    *E-mail:* matthew@pascalpress.com.au
Primary Publisher: Katy Pike *Tel:* (0612) 9518
    6777 *Fax:* (0612) 9518 6888
Founded: 1989
Specialize in school publishing.
Membership(s): Australian Publishers Associa-
    tion.
Subjects: Education
ISBN Prefix(es): 1-74020; 1-74125; 1-875312; 1-
    875777; 1-877085; 1-920728
Total Titles: 1,000 Print; 16 CD-ROM; 50 Online;
    50 E-Book; 20 Audio
*Parent Company:* S D & M Software Pty Ltd
Subsidiaries: Blake Education Pty Ltd; Video Ed-
    ucation Australia
Distributed by Nelson Thomes (United Kingdom);
    Sundance (United States)
Distributor for Wild Daisies (New Zealand)
*Shipping Address:* TLD Distribution, 15-23
    Hellen Ave, Moorebank, NSW 2170, Contact:
    Chris Stasis *Tel:* (0612) 8585 4044 *Fax:* (0612)
    8585 4001


**Pascoe Publishing Pty Ltd+**
PO Box 42, Apollo Bay, Victoria 3233
*Tel:* (03) 5237 9227 *Fax:* (03) 5237 6559
*Web Site:* www.bruce-pascoe.pho-online.net
*Key Personnel*
Dir: Bruce Pascoe *E-mail:* pascoe@vicnet.net.au
Dir & International Rights: Lyn Harwood
Founded: 1983

Subjects: Fiction, History, Literature, Literary Criticism, Essays, Social Sciences, Sociology, Australian Literary Fiction
ISBN Prefix(es): 0-947087; 0-9592104
Number of titles published annually: 4 Print
Total Titles: 110 Print
Imprints: Blackstone; Seaglass
Subsidiaries: Koori Tours

**Kevin J Passey+**
3/156 Clive Steele Ave, Monash, ACT 2904
Mailing Address: PO Box 971, Albury, NSW 2640
*Tel:* (02) 62914932 *Fax:* (060) 412 950
*E-mail:* lk7@primus.com.au
*Key Personnel*
Head of Company: Kevin J Passey
Founded: 1986
Also acts as a script writer.
Membership(s): Australian Institute of History & Arts; Australian Writers Guild, History-Bushranging.
Subjects: History, Regional Interests
ISBN Prefix(es): 0-9588470

**Pavillion**, *imprint of* Random House Australia

**PCE Press**
35 Amelia St, Fortitude Valley, Qld 4006
Mailing Address: PO Box 1508, Fortitude Valley, Qld 4006
*Tel:* (07) 3252 1114 *Fax:* (07) 3852 1564
*E-mail:* pcq@gil.com.au
*Web Site:* www.pcq.org.au
*Key Personnel*
Dir: Rev J C Nicol *E-mail:* director@pcq.org.au
Publications Department of the Presbyterian Church of Queensland.
Subjects: Religion - Protestant
ISBN Prefix(es): 1-86269

**Pearson Education Australia+**
Unit 4, Level 2, 14 Aquatic Drive, Frenchs Forest, NSW 2086
Mailing Address: LMB 507, Frenchs Forest, NSW 1640
*Tel:* (02) 9454 2200 *Fax:* (02) 9453 0089
*E-mail:* firstname.lastname@pearsoned.com.au
*Web Site:* www.pearson.com.au
*Key Personnel*
Man Dir: Pat Evans
Financial Controller: Ted Impey
General Manager, Humanities & Sciences: David Barnett
General Manager, Professional & Vocational Education: Gillian May
General Manager, Business & Economics: Michael Page
General Manager, Computer, Trade & Reference: Paul Summers
Educational publishers.
Subjects: Accounting, Anthropology, Behavioral Sciences, Biological Sciences, Business, Child Care & Development, Communications, Computer Science, Criminology, Economics, Education, Engineering (General), Fiction, Government, Political Science, Health, Nutrition, History, Journalism, Labor, Industrial Relations, Language Arts, Linguistics, Law, Library & Information Sciences, Management, Mathematics, Medicine, Nursing, Dentistry, Science (General), Social Sciences, Sociology
ISBN Prefix(es): 1-74091; 1-74103
Number of titles published annually: 500 Print
*Parent Company:* Pearson Plc
Imprints: Prentice Hall; Addison Wesley; Longman
*Branch Office(s)*
Suite B, Level 2, 57 Coronation Drive, Milton, Qld 4000 *Tel:* (07) 3236 5901 *Fax:* (07) 3236 5907 (Queensland & Northern Territory)

95 Coventry St, South Melbourne, Victoria 3205 (Victoria & Tasmania)
PO Box 353, Mitcham S/C, Torrens Park 5062 (South Australia)
177 Great Eastern Hwy, Belmont 6104 *Tel:* (08) 9477 1539 *Fax:* (08) 9466 1547 (Western Australia)

**Penguin**, *imprint of* Penguin Group (Australia)

**Penguin Group (Australia)+**
250 Camberwell Rd, Camberwell, Victoria 3124
Mailing Address: PO Box 701, Hawthorn, Victoria 3122
*Tel:* (03) 9811 2400 *Fax:* (03) 9811 2620
*Web Site:* www.penguin.com.au
*Key Personnel*
Chief Executive Officer: P Field
Publishing Dir: Robert Sessions *Tel:* (03) 9811 2468 *Fax:* (03) 9811 2621 *E-mail:* robert.sessions@au.penguingroup.com
Sales Dir: P Blake
Rights Manager: Peg McColl
Founded: 1946
Subjects: Biography, Cookery, Fiction, Humor, Literature, Literary Criticism, Essays, Nonfiction (General), Science Fiction, Fantasy, Self-Help, Travel
ISBN Prefix(es): 0-14; 0-670; 1-872031; 0-86914
*Parent Company:* Pearson Australia Group Pty Ltd
*Ultimate Parent Company:* Pearson plc (London)
*Associate Companies:* Pearson Education; Penguin Books Canada Ltd, 7050 B Bramalea Rd, Unit 52, Mississauga, ON L5S 1S9, Canada *E-mail:* info@penguin.ca *Web Site:* www.penguin.ca; Penguin Books India Pvt Ltd, 11 Community Centre, Panchsheel Park, New Delhi 110017, India *E-mail:* admin@penguin-india.com *Web Site:* www.penguinbooksindia.com; Penguin Books New Zealand, Private Bag 102902, North Shore Mail Centre, Auckland 10, New Zealand *Web Site:* www.penguin.co.nz; Penguin Books (South Africa) (Pty) Ltd, PO Box 9, Parklands 2121, South Africa; Penguin Putnam Inc, 375 Hudson St, New York, NY 10014-3657, United States *Tel:* 212-366-2000 *Fax:* 212-366-2666 *E-mail:* online@penguin.com *Web Site:* www.penguinputnam.com
Imprints: Hamish Hamilton; Michael Joseph; New American Library; Penguin; Puffin; Signet; Viking; Frederick Warne
Divisions: Penguin Adult, Penguin Children
*Distribution Center:* 30 Centre Rd, Scoresby, Victoria

**Perfection Learning Corporation**, *imprint of* Hawker Brownlow

**Peribo Pty Ltd**
58 Beaumont Rd, Mount Kuring-gai, NSW 2080
*Tel:* (02) 9457-0011 *Fax:* (02) 9457-0022
*E-mail:* peribo@bigpond.com
*Key Personnel*
Chairman: Edward Coffey
Founded: 1981
ISBN Prefix(es): 1-86322

**Periscope Press**, *imprint of* Roland Harvey Studios

**Personal Power Press International Inc**, *imprint of* Hawker Brownlow

**Peter Pan Publications+**
PO Box 342, Moorooka, Qld 4105
*Tel:* (07) 3848 0350 *Fax:* (07) 3848 4945
*E-mail:* paramountbooks@optusnet.com.au
*Web Site:* www.peterpan.ziby.net

*Key Personnel*
Man Dir: Donald Jefferies
Founded: 1982
Also distributors.
Subjects: Regional Interests, Religion - Other
ISBN Prefix(es): 0-9596931
Number of titles published annually: 1 Online; 1 E-Book
Total Titles: 5 Print; 1 Online
*Parent Company:* Donald Jefferies (Q) Pty Ltd
Subsidiaries: Paramount Books

**Phoenix Education Pty Ltd+**
102 Charles St, Putney, NSW 2112
Mailing Address: PO Box 3141, Putney, NSW 2112
*Tel:* (02) 9809 3579; (03) 9699 8377 *Fax:* (02) 9808 1430; (03) 9699 9242
*E-mail:* service@phoenixeduc.com
*Web Site:* www.phoenixeduc.com
*Key Personnel*
Dir: Barney Rivers
Founded: 1991
Subjects: Language Arts, Linguistics, Mathematics
ISBN Prefix(es): 1-876580
Number of titles published annually: 20 Print
Total Titles: 200 Print

**Piatkus**, *imprint of* Hachette Livre Australia

**Picador**, *imprint of* Pan Macmillan Australia Pty Ltd

**Pimlico**, *imprint of* Random House Australia

**Pinchgut Press**
6 Oaks Ave, Cremorne, NSW 2090
*Tel:* (02) 9908-2402 *Fax:* (02) 9960-4689
*Key Personnel*
Chief Executive & Dir: Marjorie Pizer
Art Dir: Judy Lane
Founded: 1947
Small independent publisher.
Subjects: Poetry, Self-Help
ISBN Prefix(es): 0-9598913; 0-949625
Total Titles: 17 Print

**Pinevale Publications+**
PO Box 822, Mareeba, Qld 4880
*Tel:* (07) 93-3169
*Key Personnel*
Publisher & Editor: Glenville Pike
Founded: 1981
Subjects: Biography, History, Travel
ISBN Prefix(es): 0-9593783; 1-875375
Number of titles published annually: 2 Print
Total Titles: 23 Print
*Distribution Center:* 45 Pike Rd, Emerald Creek, Mareeba, Qld *Tel:* (07) 933169
*Orders to:* 45 Pike Rd, Emerald Creek, Mareeba, Qld *Tel:* (07) 933169

**Pioneer Design Studio Pty Ltd+**
31 North Rd, Lilydale, Victoria 3140
*Tel:* (03) 735 5505
*Key Personnel*
Head of Company: Derrick I Stone
Sales Manager: Carolyn R Stone
Subjects: Environmental Studies, Gardening, Plants, History
ISBN Prefix(es): 0-909674

**Pisces**, *imprint of* Lonely Planet Publications Pty Ltd

**Plantagenet Press+**
PO Box 934, Fremantle, WA 6159
*Tel:* (09) 4304466 *Fax:* (09) 4305217
*E-mail:* rogergarwood@compuserve.com
*Key Personnel*
Dir: Trish Ainslie

Founded: 1989
Also acts as distributor.
Subjects: Fiction, History, Humor, Journalism,
  Nonfiction (General)
ISBN Prefix(es): 1-875968
*Book Club(s):* Lucky Book Club

**Playbox Theatre Co+**
113 Sturt St, Southbank, Victoria 3006
*Tel:* (03) 9685 5100 *Fax:* (03) 9685 5112
*E-mail:* playbox@netspace.net.au
*Web Site:* www.playbox.com.au
*Key Personnel*
General Manager: Jill Smith
Development, presentation & promotion of new
  Australian plays & playwrights.
Subjects: Drama, Theater
ISBN Prefix(es): 0-7326
Number of titles published annually: 12 Print
Distributed by Currency Press
Distributor for Currency Press

**Playlab Press**
7 Pender St, The Gap, Qld 4061
*Tel:* 3236 1396 *Fax:* 3236 1026
*E-mail:* cluster@thehub.com.au
*Key Personnel*
Project Officer: Louise Terry
Founded: 1972
Subjects: Drama, Theater, History, Humor, Litera-
  ture, Literary Criticism, Essays, Music, Dance,
  Women's Studies, Australian, Youth, Comedy
ISBN Prefix(es): 0-908156

**Jurriaan Plesman**
54 Beach Rd, Bondi Beach, NSW 2026
*Tel:* (02) 9130 6247 *Fax:* (02) 9130 6202
*E-mail:* jurplesman@hotmail.com
Subjects: Behavioral Sciences, Criminology,
  Health, Nutrition, How-to, Medicine, Nursing,
  Dentistry, Psychology, Psychiatry, Self-Help,
  Social Sciences, Sociology
ISBN Prefix(es): 1-86252

**Plum Press+**
PO Box 419, Toowong, Qld 4066
*Tel:* (07) 3870 2964 *Fax:* (07) 3870 2860
*E-mail:* tom@justasktom.com
*Web Site:* www.justasktom.com
*Key Personnel*
Head of Company: Neil Flanagan *E-mail:* neilfl@
  squirrel.com.au
Founded: 1989
Subjects: Management
ISBN Prefix(es): 0-9587113

**Pluto Press Australia Pty Ltd+**
PO Box 617, North Melbourne, Victoria 2038
*Tel:* (02) 9692 5111; (03) 9328 3811 *Fax:* (02)
  9692 5192; (03) 9329 9939
*E-mail:* pluto@plutoaustralia.com
*Web Site:* www.plutoaustralia.com
*Key Personnel*
Man Dir: Sean Kidney
Founded: 1984
Subjects: Environmental Studies, Government,
  Political Science, History, Labor, Industrial Re-
  lations, Social Sciences, Sociology, Women's
  Studies
ISBN Prefix(es): 0-949138; 1-86403
*Parent Company:* Social Change Media
*Associate Companies:* Social Change On-Line
Divisions: University of NSW Press
*Orders to:* University of NSW Press, 45 Beach
  St, Coogee 2031 *Tel:* (02) 9664 0999 *Fax:* (02)
  9664 5420

**The Polding Press+**
322 Lonsdale St, Melbourne, Victoria 3000
*Tel:* (03) 9639 0844 *Fax:* (03) 9639 0879
*E-mail:* manager@catholicbookshop.com.au

*Web Site:* www.catholicbookshop.com.au
Founded: 1968
Subjects: Biography, History, Religion - Other
ISBN Prefix(es): 0-85884
*Bookshop(s):* Central Catholic Library Bookshop,
  322 Lonsdale St, Melbourne, Victoria 3000
  *Tel:* (03) 9639 0844

**Power Publications+**
Power Institute, Mills Bldg, A26, University of
  Sydney, Sydney, NSW 2006
*Tel:* (02) 9351 6904 *Fax:* (02) 9351 7323
*E-mail:* power.publications@arts.usyd.edu.au
*Web Site:* www.power.arts.usyd.edu.au/institute
*Key Personnel*
Dir: Prof Roger Benjamin
Managing Editor: Victoria Dawson
Founded: 1987
Subjects: Art, Film, Video
ISBN Prefix(es): 0-909952

**Prentice Hall**, *imprint of* Pearson Education
Australia

**Press for Success+**
One Ensign Lane, East Perth, WA 6004
Mailing Address: PO Box 8142, Perth Business
  Center, WA 6849
*Tel:* (08) 9221 6166 *Fax:* (08) 9221 6166
*E-mail:* press4@press4success.com.au
*Web Site:* www.press4success.com.au
*Key Personnel*
Dir: Jill Yelland
Founded: 1993
Membership(s): International Type Designers As-
  sociation A Type 1.
Subjects: Architecture & Interior Design, Art,
  Business, How-to
ISBN Prefix(es): 0-646; 0-9577374
*Parent Company:* Yelland & Associates Pty Ltd
*Associate Companies:* Yelland INK

**PressXpress**, *imprint of* McGraw-Hill Australia
Pty Ltd

**Price Publishing+**
Unit 2, 40 Benelong Rd, Cremorne, NSW 2090
*Tel:* (02) 9904 9811
*E-mail:* pricesys@localnet.com.au
Founded: 1994
Subjects: Education, Microcomputers, Learning &
  Training
ISBN Prefix(es): 0-646

**Priddy & Bicknell**, *imprint of* Pan Macmillan
Australia Pty Ltd

**Priestley Consulting+**
12 Trinidad St, Kawana Island, Qld 4575
*Tel:* (07) 4937179 *Fax:* (07) 54458288
*E-mail:* adpriestley@ozemail.com.au
*Key Personnel*
Contact: Andrew Priestly *E-mail:* adpriestly@
  ozemail.com.au
Subjects: Advertising, Child Care & Develop-
  ment, Education, Marketing, Self-Help, Social
  Sciences, Sociology
ISBN Prefix(es): 0-9587298

**Primary English Teaching Association**
PO Box 3106, Marrickville, NSW 2204
*Tel:* (02) 9565 1277 *Fax:* (02) 9565 1070
*E-mail:* info@peta.edu.au
*Web Site:* www.peta.edu.au
*Key Personnel*
Executive Dir: Peter O'Brien
Founded: 1972
ISBN Prefix(es): 0-909955; 1-875622

**Private Equity Media**
PO Box 324, Five Dock, NSW 2046
*Tel:* (02) 9713 7608 *Fax:* (02) 9713 1004
*E-mail:* info@privateequitymedia.com.au
*Web Site:* www.privateequitymedia.com.au
*Key Personnel*
Editor & Publisher: Victor Bivell
  *E-mail:* vbivell@vcjournal.com.au
Founded: 1992
Subjects: Anthropology, Ethnicity, Foreign Coun-
  tries, History, Literature, Literary Criticism,
  Essays, Regional Interests, Social Sciences, So-
  ciology, Macedonians of Greece, Human Rights
ISBN Prefix(es): 0-9586789
Total Titles: 6 Print

**Prospect**, *imprint of* Prospect Media

**Prospect Media+**
475-495 Victoria Ave, Tower 2, Chatswood, NSW
  2067
*Tel:* (02) 9422 2222 *Fax:* (02) 9422 2444
*Web Site:* www.lexisnexis.com.au
*Key Personnel*
Man Dir & Publisher: Oliver Freeman
Finance Manager: Vicky Mahadeva
Managing Editor: Jenny Berich
Senior Editor: Carolyn Stott
Marketing Manager: Matthew Langman
Sales Manager: Sue Howard
Founded: 1987
Membership(s): Australian Publishers Associa-
  tion; Publish Australia.
Subjects: Accounting, Business, Computer Sci-
  ence, Environmental Studies, Finance, Law
ISBN Prefix(es): 1-86316; 0-947309; 0-949553
Total Titles: 40 Print
*Parent Company:* Lexis Nexis Australia
Imprints: Global Business Network; Heresy Press;
  Legal Books; Prospect; Oliver Freeman Edi-
  tions
Subsidiaries: Australian Business Network Pty
  Ltd
Divisions: Legal Books; Legal Publications;
  Prospect
*Bookshop(s):* Legal Publications, 121 William St,
  Melbourne, Victoria 3000
*Book Club(s):* ABN Bookclub
*Shipping Address:* Mezzanine Level, G10 Bldg,
  60-70 Elizabeth St, Sydney, NSW 2000
*Orders to:* Mezzanine Level, G10 Bldg, 60-70
  Elizabeth St, Sydney, NSW 2000

**Protestant Publications**
7 Park St, Peakhurst, NSW 2210
*Tel:* (02) 9868 4591 *Fax:* (02) 9868 7953
*Key Personnel*
Contact: D Shelton
Founded: 1945
Subjects: History, Religion - Catholic, Religion -
  Protestant
ISBN Prefix(es): 0-949926

**Prufrock Press**, *imprint of* Hawker Brownlow

**The Psychological Corporation**, *imprint of*
Elsevier Australia

**Puffin**, *imprint of* Penguin Group (Australia)

**Quakers Hill Press+**
6 Caper Pl, Quakers Hill, NSW 2763
*Tel:* (02) 9626 6112 *Fax:* (02) 9626 9846
*E-mail:* dayp@mpx.com.au
*Key Personnel*
Publisher: Peter Day
Founded: 1993
Subjects: Biography, Fiction, History, Mathemat-
  ics, Nonfiction (General), Philosophy
ISBN Prefix(es): 1-876192

**Queen Victoria Museum & Art Gallery
Publications**
Division of Launceston City Council
2 Wellington St, Launceston, Tas 7250
*Tel:* (03) 6323 3777 *Fax:* (03) 6323 3776
*E-mail:* library@qvmag.tas.gov.au
*Web Site:* www.qvmag.tas.gov.au
*Key Personnel*
Editor: Mr Chris B Tassell *E-mail:* chris.tassell@
qvmag.tas.gov.au
Publications Coordinator: Kaye Dimmack
*E-mail:* kaye.dimmack@qvmag.tas.gov.au
Founded: 1891
Operated as a department of Launceston City
Council.
Subjects: Anthropology, Archaeology, Art, Bio-
logical Sciences, Earth Sciences, History, Natu-
ral History, Physical Sciences
ISBN Prefix(es): 0-7246
Number of titles published annually: 1 Print
Total Titles: 27 Print

**Queensland Art Gallery**
Melbourne St, South Brisbane, Qld 4101
Mailing Address: PO Box 3686, South Brisbane,
Qld 4101
*Tel:* (07) 3840 7333; (07) 3840 7303 *Fax:* (07)
3844 8865; (07) 3840 7350
*E-mail:* gallery@qag.qld.gov.au
*Web Site:* www.qag.qld.gov.au
*Key Personnel*
Manager Gallery Shop: Linda Mehan
*E-mail:* linda.mehan@qag.qld.gov.au
Gallery Dir: Doug Hall
Senior Editor: Ian Were *E-mail:* ian.were@qag.
qld.gov.au
Subjects: Art, Asian Studies
Number of titles published annually: 6 Print
Total Titles: 15 Print
Distributed by James Bennett Pty Ltd; DAP;
IDEA; Thames & Hudson Australia Pty Ltd;
Timezone 8; Worldwide Books; YBP Library
Services
*Orders to:* Gallery Shop, South Brisbane, Qld,
Contact: Peter Beiers *Tel:* (07) 38 40 713 2
*Fax:* (07) 38 40 714 9 *E-mail:* peter.beiers@
qag.qld.gov.au *Web Site:* www.gallerystore.com.
au

**R & R Publications Pty Ltd+**
12 Edward St, Brunswick, Victoria 3056
Mailing Address: PO Box 254, Carlton North,
Victoria 3054
*Tel:* (03) 9381 2199 *Toll Free Tel:* 800 063 296
*Fax:* (03) 9381 2689
*Key Personnel*
Publisher & International Rights: Richard Carroll
*E-mail:* richardc@bigpond.net.au
Founded: 1989
Book packagers; Specializes in cooking, drinking
& lifestyles.
Subjects: Cookery, Crafts, Games, Hobbies, Gar-
dening, Plants, Health, Nutrition, How-to,
Sports, Athletics, Wine & Spirits, Lifestyle
ISBN Prefix(es): 1-875655; 1-74022
Number of titles published annually: 60 Print
Total Titles: 140 Print; 4 CD-ROM

**R*O*D Books**, *imprint of* Cornucopia Press

**Radiating Books**
6 Sapphire Crescent, Coffs Harbour, NSW 2450
*Tel:* (066) 536 280 *Fax:* (066) 514 970
*Key Personnel*
Head of Company: Helen Seccombe
Membership(s): OMCE (Organization for Man-
agement of Cultural Endeavour).
ISBN Prefix(es): 0-646

**Rainbow Book Agencies Pty Ltd+**
303 Arthur St, Fairfield, Victoria 3078

*Tel:* (03) 9481 6611 *Fax:* (03) 9481 2371
*E-mail:* rba@rainbowbooks.com.au; custserv@
rainbowbooks.com.au; despatch@
rainbowbooks.com.au (warehouse)
*Web Site:* www.rainbowbooks.com.au
*Key Personnel*
Dir: Rob Humphrys *E-mail:* rob.humphrys@
rainbowbooks.com.au
Founded: 1985
National distribution to the religious & mind,
body & spirit trade in Australia.
Subjects: Religion - Other
ISBN Prefix(es): 1-875138
Imprints: Acorn Press; Artemis Publishing; Aus-
tralian Association for the Study of Religion;
Beyond Bullying Association; Canadian Con-
ference of Catholic Bishops; Christian Research
Association (CRA); Desbooks; Emmaus Pro-
ductions; Fairfield Press; Galations Group;
Inner City Books; Jesuit Publications/Aurora
Books; David Lovell Publishing; Templegate
Publishers; Word of Life Distributors Pty Ltd
Distributed by Ateliers Et Presses de Taize; Aus-
tralian Thelogical Forum (Australia); Carpe
Diem Books (South Africa); Cluster Publica-
tions (South Africa); Columba Publications
(Ireland); Comsoda Communications (Aus-
tralia); Darton Longman & Todd (UK); Do-
minican Publications (Ireland); Eclipse Mu-
sic; Emmanuel Community (Australia); Em-
maus Productions (Australia); Gujarat Sahitya
Prakash (India); Joshua Press (Canada); David
Lovell Publishing (Australia); Maryknoll Pro-
ductions (USA); Medical Mission Sisters
(USA); Leigh Newton; Oregan Catholic Press
(USA); Paraclete Press (USA); Pastoral Press
(USA); Pauline Books & Media (UK); Random
House NY (religious titles only); Redemptorist
Publications; Regina Press-Malhame; Resources
for Christian Living (USA); Editions du Signe
(France); Spectrum Publications; Templeton
Foundation Press (USA); Tanya Wittwer &
Leigh Newton
Distributor for Ateliers et Presses de Taize; INTJ
Books; Liguori Publication/Triumph Books;
Liturgy Training Publications; Merciful Love
Music (UK); Orbis Books; Our Sunday Vis-
itor; Paulist Press; Resource Publications; St
Anthony Messenger Press/Franciscan Commu-
nications; St Valdimir's Seminary Press (SVS
Press); World Library Publications

**Raincloud Productions**
6 Castlereagh Crescent, Macquarie, ACT 2614
*Tel:* (02) 6251 1765
*Key Personnel*
Head of Company: Craig Dent
Founded: 1989
Subjects: Photography, Poetry
ISBN Prefix(es): 0-7316
*Orders to:* PO Box 451, Albury, NSW 2640

**Rainforest Publishing+**
8 Napier St, Paddington, NSW 2021
*Tel:* (02) 93313004 *Fax:* (02) 93805729
*E-mail:* rod.ritchie@sfine.arts.sa.edu.au
*Key Personnel*
Head of Company: Rod Ritchie
Founded: 1985
Subjects: Environmental Studies, History
ISBN Prefix(es): 0-947134
Distributed by Tower Books

**Rams Skull Press**
12 Fairyland Rd, Kuranda, Qld 4881
*Tel:* (07) 4093 7474 *Fax:* (07) 4051 4484
*E-mail:* ramskull@tpg.com.au
*Key Personnel*
Publisher: Ron Edwards
Founded: 1950
Subjects: Alternative, Cookery, Crafts, Games,
Hobbies, Folklore

Number of titles published annually: 20 Print
Total Titles: 130 Print

**Random House**, *imprint of* Random House
Australia

**Random House Australia+**
Subsidiary of Bertelsmann AG
20 Alfred St, Milson's Point, NSW 2061
*Tel:* (02) 8923 9863 *Fax:* (02) 9753 3944
*E-mail:* randomhouse@randomhouse.com.au
*Key Personnel*
Man Dir: Margaret Seale
Head of Publishing, Random House: Jane Palfrey-
man
Sales & Marketing Dir: Carol Davidson
Deputy Man Dir: Margaret Seale
Publisher, Bantam Doubleday: Fiona Henderson
Children's Publisher: Linsay Knight
Illustrated - Managing Editor: Jude McGee
Head of Publicity: Karen Reid
Rights & Permission: Nerrilee Weir
Business Man: Andrew Leake
Production Man: Lisa Hanrahan
Agencies: Andersen Press; Everyman's Library;
TSR; Pavillion; Robinson; Virgin; World Book
International, BBC.
Membership(s): APA Australia.
Subjects: Fiction, Nonfiction (General)
ISBN Prefix(es): 0-09; 1-74051; 0-7352; 0-7593
*Associate Companies:* Random House NZ,
18 Poland Road, Glenfield, Auckland, New
Zealand *Tel:* (09) 444 7197 *Fax:* (09) 444
7524; Random House South Africa, Endulini,
East Wing, 5A Jubilee Road, Parktown 2193,
South Africa *Tel:* (011) 484 3538 *Fax:* (011)
484 6180; Random House UK, 20 Vauxhall
Bridge Rd, London SWIV 2SA, United King-
dom *Tel:* (020) 8840 8400 *Fax:* (020) 8840
8408; Random House, Inc, 201 E 50th St, New
York, NY 10022, United States *Tel:* (212) 940-
7478 *Fax:* (212) 572-6045
Imprints: Anchor; Anderson; Arrow; Avon; Bal-
lantine; Bantam Books; BBC Worldwide; Black
Swan; Broadway Books; Jonathon Cape; Cen-
tury; Chatto & Windus; Corgi; Crown Pub-
lishing Group; Del Rey; Dell Publishing;
Doubleday; Ebury Press; Egmont; Fawcett;
Fodor; Hamlyn Childrens; William Heinemann;
Hutchinson; Knopf Publishing; Living Books;
Mammoth UK; Minerva; Pantheon; Pavillion;
Pimlico; Random House; Ravette; Red Fox;
Rider; Robinson; Running Press; Secker &
Warburg; Sesame Street; Vermillion; Vintage;
Virgin
*Shipping Address:* 16 Dalmore Dr, Scoresby, Vic-
toria 3179 *Tel:* (03) 9753 4511 *Fax:* (03) 9753
3944
*Warehouse:* 16 Dalmore Dr, Scoresby, Victoria
3179
*Orders to:* 16 Dalmore Dr, Scoresby, Victoria
3179 *Tel:* (03) 97534511 *Fax:* (03) 94533944

**Rankin Publishers**
PO Box 500, Sumner Park, Qld 4074
*Tel:* (07) 3376 9115 *Fax:* (07) 3376 9360
*E-mail:* info@rankin.com.au
*Web Site:* www.rankin.com.au
*Key Personnel*
Proprietor & International Rights: Robert Rankin
Founded: 1980
Subjects: Outdoor Recreation, Photography,
Physics, Science (General), Australiana
ISBN Prefix(es): 0-9592418

**Ravette**, *imprint of* Random House Australia

**Rawlhouse Publishing**
PO Box 145, West Perth, WA 6005
*Tel:* (08) 9321 8951 *Fax:* (08) 9481 1914
*E-mail:* info@rawlhouse.com
*Web Site:* www.rawlinsons.com

*Key Personnel*
Dir & Editor: I A Baillie
Founded: 1983
Construction cost reference books.
ISBN Prefix(es): 0-9587406; 0-9587853
Total Titles: 2 Print

**RD Press**, *imprint of* Reader's Digest (Australia)
Pty Ltd

**Reader's Digest (Australia) Pty Ltd+**
26-32 Waterloo St, Surry Hills, Sydney, NSW
2010
*Tel:* (02) 96906935 *Fax:* (02) 96906390
*Cable:* READIGEST SYDNEY
*Key Personnel*
Man Dir: William Toohey
Editorial, Condensed Books: Joshua Shrubb
Editorial, General Books: Margaret Fraser
Publisher, Catalog & Trade Books: Robert Sarsfield
Founded: 1946
Subjects: Education
ISBN Prefix(es): 0-86438; 0-909486; 0-949819;
0-86449; 0-9577023; 1-876691
*Parent Company:* The Reader's Digest Association Inc, PO Box 235, Pleasantville, NY 10570, United States
Imprints: RD Press; Reader's Digest Condensed Books
*Book Club(s):* Reader's Digest Condensed Books
*Orders to:* Hodder Headline Australia, PO Box 386, Rydalmere, NSW 2116

**Reader's Digest Condensed Books**, *imprint of*
Reader's Digest (Australia) Pty Ltd

**Ready-Ed Publications+**
11/17 Foley St, Balcatta, WA 6021
*Tel:* (08) 9349 6111 *Fax:* (08) 9349 7222
*E-mail:* info@readyed.com.au
*Web Site:* www.readyed.com.au
*Key Personnel*
International Rights: Tim Lowson *E-mail:* tim@
readyed.com.au
Founded: 1984
Subjects: Education
ISBN Prefix(es): 1-83697; 1-875268

**The Real Estate Institute of Australia+**
16 Thesiger Court, Deakin, ACT 2600
Mailing Address: PO Box 234, Deakin, West
ACT 2600
*Tel:* (02) 6282 4277 *Fax:* (02) 6285 2444
*E-mail:* reia@reiaustralia.com.au
*Web Site:* www.reiaustralia.com.au
*Key Personnel*
Chief Executive Officer: Bryan Stevens
*E-mail:* bryan.stevens@reiaustralia.com.au
Public Affairs Manager: Alison Verhoeven
*E-mail:* alison.verhoeven@reiaustralia.com.au
Research Manager: David Wesney *E-mail:* david.
wesney@reiaustralia.com.au
Finance Manager: Trevor Smith *E-mail:* trevor.
smith@reiaustralia.com.au
Publisher: Sandra Green
Subjects: Accounting, Advertising, Business, Finance, Management, Marketing, Real Estate,
Self-Help
ISBN Prefix(es): 0-909784
Imprints: REIA; RIAL
Distributor for Dearborn Trade (Australia & New
Zealand)

**Red Fox**, *imprint of* Random House Australia

**Reed Educational Publishing Australia**, *see*
Harcourt Education Australia

**Reed for Kids**
17 Redwood Drive, Dingly, Victoria 3172
*Tel:* (03) 5516111 *Fax:* (03) 95517490
*Key Personnel*
Man Dir: Robert Ungar
ISBN Prefix(es): 0-86801; 0-947192; 0-908505;
0-7323

**Regency Publishing+**
Division of Regency Institute TAFE
Days Rd, Regency Park, SA 5010
*Tel:* (08) 8348 4599 *Toll Free Tel:* 800 649 898
(ext 4599) *Fax:* (08) 8348 4400
*E-mail:* regencypublishing@regency.tafe.sa.edu.au
*Web Site:* www.regencypublishing.com.au; www.
tafe.sa.edu.au/institutes/regency/regency-
publishing/main.htm
*Key Personnel*
Manager: Mimma Trimboli *E-mail:* mimma.
trimboli@regency.tafe.sa.edu.au
Educational textbooks specifically related to the
vocational training sector.
Subjects: Cookery, Engineering (General), Health,
Nutrition, Wine & Spirits, Cosmetology, Food
Processing, Hairdressing, Hospitality Operations & Management, Recreation, Sport &
Tourism
ISBN Prefix(es): 1-86418
Total Titles: 120 Print; 2 CD-ROM

**REIA**, *imprint of* The Real Estate Institute of
Australia

**Review**, *imprint of* Hachette Livre Australia

**RIAL**, *imprint of* The Real Estate Institute of
Australia

**RIC Publications Pty Ltd+**
4 Bendsten Pl, Balcatta, WA 6021
*Tel:* (09) 9240 9888 *Fax:* (09) 9240 1513
*E-mail:* mail@ricgroup.com.au
*Web Site:* www.ricgroup.com.au
*Key Personnel*
Man Dir: Peter Woods *E-mail:* peter@ricgroup.
com.au
Founded: 1986
Subjects: Education
ISBN Prefix(es): 1-86311; 1-74126
Number of titles published annually: 90 Print
Total Titles: 800 Print
Subsidiaries: Prim Ed Publishing PM Ltd
*Branch Office(s)*
Prim-Ed Publishing Ltd, Bosheen New Ross,
County Wexford, Ireland
Prim Ed Publishing (UK) Ltd, 5A Kelsey Close,
Attleborough Field, Nuneaton CVII 6RS,
United Kingdom

**Rider**, *imprint of* Random House Australia

**RLCP**, *imprint of* University of New South Wales
Press Ltd

**RMIT Press**, *imprint of* RMIT Publishing

**RMIT Publishing+**
Level 3, 449 Swanston St, Melbourne, Victoria
3000
Mailing Address: PO Box 12058, A'Beckett St,
Melbourne, Victoria 8006
*Tel:* (03) 9925 8100 *Fax:* (03) 9925 8134
*E-mail:* info@rmitpublishing.com.au
*Web Site:* www.rmitpublishing.com.au
*Key Personnel*
Training Liaison Officer: Judy Benson
Membership(s): Australian Publishers Association
National Book Council; also acts as distributor.
Subjects: Accounting, Business, Child Care &
Development, Engineering (General), Fash-

ion, Language Arts, Linguistics, Management,
Travel
ISBN Prefix(es): 0-7241; 0-7306
Imprints: RMIT Press; TAFE Publications

**Tom Roberts (Pat Roberts)+**
241 West Beach Rd, Richmond, SA 5033
*Tel:* (08) 8143 7578
*Key Personnel*
Owner & Dir: Pat Roberts
Founded: 1971
Specialize in Equestrian Control.
Subjects: Animals, Pets, Family History, Horse
Training & Educating, War, World War II Diaries
ISBN Prefix(es): 0-9599413
Total Titles: 6 Print
*Branch Office(s)*
Western International Inc, 1875 Oddie Blvd,
Sparks, NV 89431-6238, United States
*Tel:* 775-359-4400 *Fax:* 775-359-4439
Distributed by Rom Kerrigan; Western International Inc (USA)
*Orders to:* Western International Inc, 1875 Oddie
Blvd, Sparks, NV 89431-6238, United States
*Tel:* 775-359-4400 *Fax:* 775-359-4439

**Robinson**, *imprint of* Random House Australia

**Robinson's**, *imprint of* Universal Press Pty Ltd

**Rodale**, *imprint of* Bloomings Books

**Roo Books**, *imprint of* Kangaroo Press

**Royal Society of New South Wales**
University of Sydney, Darlington Campus, 121
Darlington Rd, Sydney, NSW 2006
Mailing Address: University of Sydney, Bldg
H47, Sydney, NSW 2006
*Tel:* (02)9036 5282 *Fax:* (02) 9036 5309
*E-mail:* info@nsw.royalsoc.org.au
*Web Site:* nsw.royalsoc.org.au
Founded: 1821
Subjects: Chemistry, Chemical Engineering, Environmental Studies, Geography, Geology, Mathematics, Medicine, Nursing, Dentistry, Physics,
Science (General)
ISBN Prefix(es): 0-9598274

**Royal Society of Victoria Inc**
9 Victoria St, Melbourne, Victoria 3000
*Tel:* (03) 9663 5259 *Fax:* (03) 9663 2301
*E-mail:* sciencevictoria@org.au; rsvinc@vicnet.
net.au
*Web Site:* www.sciencevictoria.org.au
*Key Personnel*
Executive Officer: Camilla van Megen
Founded: 1854
Learned scientific organization.
Subjects: Science (General)
Number of titles published annually: 1 Print

**Rumsby Scientific Publishing**
PO Box Q355, QVB, Sydney, NSW 2000
*Tel:* (02) 98076184 *Fax:* (02) 98076184
*Web Site:* www.angelfire.com/biz/rumsby
Subjects: Mathematics
ISBN Prefix(es): 0-646; 0-7316

**Running Press**, *imprint of* Random House
Australia

**Ruskin Rowe Press+**
28 Ruskin Rowe, Avalon Beach, NSW 2107
*Tel:* (02) 9918-8810 *Fax:* (02) 9918-8884
*Key Personnel*
Author & International Rights: Dr Jan Roberts
Founded: 1996

Subjects: Architecture & Interior Design, Art, Biography, Education, History, Nonfiction (General), Regional Interests, Women's Studies
ISBN Prefix(es): 0-9587095

**St Clair Press+**
PO Box 287, Rozelle, NSW 2039
*Tel:* (02) 9818 1942 *Fax:* (02) 9418 1923
*E-mail:* stclair@australis.net.au
*Web Site:* www.stclairpress.com.au
*Key Personnel*
Dir: Bruce Watson
Subjects: Education
ISBN Prefix(es): 0-949898
Total Titles: 63 Print
Distributor for Broadview Press (Restrictions in Australia); Carcanet (Australia); Seren (Australia); University of Hull (Australia); University of Wales (Australia)

**St George Books**
125 St George's Terrace, Perth, WA 6000
*Tel:* (08) 9482 9051 *Fax:* (08) 9482 9043
*Key Personnel*
Publications Manager: Simon Waight *Tel:* (08) 9482 9043 *E-mail:* simon.waight@wanews. com.au
Founded: 1980
Subjects: Nonfiction (General), Regional Interests
ISBN Prefix(es): 0-86778; 0-949864; 0-909699
Total Titles: 40 Print; 1 CD-ROM
*Parent Company:* West Australian Newspapers Holdings Ltd
Imprints: Panorama Books; WA Newspaper
Distributor for Orin Books (Western Australia)

**St Joseph Publications+**
Provincial House, 34 Liverpool Rd, Croydon, NSW 2132
*Tel:* (02) 99297344 *Fax:* (02) 91303678; (02) 99297994
*E-mail:* sosjelt@internet-australia.com
*Key Personnel*
Contact: Sister Marie Levey; Sister Bernadette O'Sullivan
Founded: 1981
Subjects: Education, History, Music, Dance, Religion - Catholic
ISBN Prefix(es): 1-875933; 0-9592316; 0-9579976
Total Titles: 30 Print
*Showroom(s):* Mary MacKillof Place, 7 Mount St, North Sydney, NSW 2060

**St Martins**, *imprint of* Pan Macmillan Australia Pty Ltd

**St Pauls Publications+**
60-70 Broughton Rd, Strathfield, NSW 2135
Mailing Address: PO Box 906, Strathfield, NSW 2135
*Tel:* (02) 9746 2288 *Fax:* (02) 9746 1140
*E-mail:* publications@stpauls.com.au; info@ stpauls.com.au; sales@stpauls.com.au
*Web Site:* www.stpauls.com.au
*Key Personnel*
Head of Company: Bruno Colombari
Founded: 1953
Membership(s): Christian Bookselling Association of Australia (CBAA).
Subjects: Biblical Studies, Biography, Education, Human Relations, Nonfiction (General), Religion - Catholic, Social Sciences, Sociology, Theology
ISBN Prefix(es): 0-949080; 0-909986; 1-875570; 1-876295
Distributed by Alba House (US); Editions Mediaspaul (Canada); St Pauls Distribution (Ireland); St Pauls Publishing (United Kingdom)

**Saltwater Publications**
8 Wattle Ave, Mount Martha, Victoria 3934
Mailing Address: PO Box 160, Mount Martha, Victoria 3934
*Tel:* (03) 5974 1959 *Fax:* (03) 5974 1959
*Key Personnel*
Contact: Richard Hawkins
Founded: 1983
Subjects: Maritime, Outdoor Recreation, Boating guides
ISBN Prefix(es): 0-9592578

**Sandcastle Books**, *imprint of* Fremantle Arts Centre Press

**W B Saunders/Bailliere Tindall**, *imprint of* Elsevier Australia

**Saunders College**, *imprint of* Elsevier Australia

**Sceptre**, *imprint of* Hachette Livre Australia

**Scholastic Australia Pty Ltd**
76-80 Railway Crescent, Lisarow, NSW 2250
Mailing Address: PO Box 579, Gosford, NSW 2250
*Tel:* (02) 4328 3555 *Toll Free Tel:* 800-021-233 *Fax:* (02) 4323 3827 *Toll Free Fax:* 800-789-948
*E-mail:* customerservice@scholastic.com.au
*Web Site:* www.scholastic.com.au
*Key Personnel*
Man Dir: Ken A Jolly
Publishing, Rights & Permissions: David Harris
Corporate Communications Manager: Leanie Sweeney
Founded: 1968
Subjects: Education
ISBN Prefix(es): 0-86896; 1-86388; 1-86504; 0-9689600
*Parent Company:* Scholastic Inc, 557 Broadway, New York, NY 10012-3999, United States
*Associate Companies:* Margaret Hamilton Books; Omnibus Books, 335 Linley Rd, Malvern, SA *Tel:* (08) 8363 2333 *Fax:* (08) 8363 1420
Imprints: Classroom Magazine; Babysitters Club
*Branch Office(s)*
1091 Toorak Rd, Hartwell, Victoria 3124
2/350 Lytton Rd, Morningside, Qld 4170
52 Fullarton Rd, Norwood 5067
*Book Club(s):* Arrow; Lucky; Star; Teachers Bookshelf; Wombat
*Shipping Address:* Railway Crescent, Lisarow, via Gosford, NSW 2250

**Science Press+**
Unit 16, 102 Edinburgh Rd, Marrickville, NSW 2204
*Tel:* (02) 9516 1122 *Fax:* (02) 9550 1915
*Key Personnel*
Man Dir: William Boden
General Manager: Robert Koo
Marketing Manager: Barry Brown
Founded: 1945
Subjects: Education
ISBN Prefix(es): 0-85583

**Scripture Union**, *imprint of* Anzea Publishers Ltd

**Scroll Publishers**
PO Box 112, Oxenford, Qld 4210
*Tel:* (07) 5573 0835 *Fax:* (07) 5529 9155
Subjects: Alternative
ISBN Prefix(es): 0-646

**Seaglass**, *imprint of* Pascoe Publishing Pty Ltd

**Seanachas Press**
PO Box 169, Maroubra, NSW 2035
*Tel:* (02) 6299 5434
*Key Personnel*
Contact: Peter Gibson
Founded: 1993
Subjects: Genealogy, History, Family History
ISBN Prefix(es): 0-9586638

**Secker & Warburg**, *imprint of* Random House Australia

**See Australia Guides P/L+**
Valley Farm Bound, Healesville, Victoria 3777
*Tel:* (03) 5962 5723 *Fax:* (03) 5962 4718
*E-mail:* sag@minopher.net.au
*Key Personnel*
Dir: Greg Dunnett
Founded: 1990
Subjects: Travel
ISBN Prefix(es): 0-9586439

**Sesame Street**, *imprint of* Random House Australia

**The Sheringa Book Committee**
Lake Hamilton Station, PMB 73, Port Lincoln, SA 5607
*Tel:* (086) 878750
*Key Personnel*
Head of Company: William Nosworthy
Subjects: History
ISBN Prefix(es): 0-7316

**Sidgwick & Jackson**, *imprint of* Pan Macmillan Australia Pty Ltd

**Signet**, *imprint of* Penguin Group (Australia)

**Simon & Schuster Australia**, *imprint of* Simon & Schuster (Australia) Pty Ltd

**Simon & Schuster (Australia) Pty Ltd+**
Division of Simon & Schuster Inc
PO Box 507, East Roseville, NSW 2069
*Tel:* (02) 9415 9900 *Fax:* (02) 9417 3188 (customer service); (02) 9417 4292 (editorial); (02) 9417 1087 (publicity)
*E-mail:* cservice@simonandschuster.com.au; rights.dept@simonandschuster.com.au
*Web Site:* www.simonsays.com; www. simonandschuster.com.au
*Key Personnel*
Man Dir: Jon Attenborough
Founded: 1987
Subjects: Alternative, Animals, Pets, Anthropology, Child Care & Development, Cookery, Crafts, Games, Hobbies, Health, Nutrition, History, House & Home, How-to, Management, Natural History, Nonfiction (General), Outdoor Recreation, Self-Help
ISBN Prefix(es): 0-7318; 0-86417 (Kangaroo Press)
Number of titles published annually: 70 Print
Total Titles: 700 Print
*Ultimate Parent Company:* Viacom Inc, 1515 Broadway, New York, NY 10036, United States
*Associate Companies:* Simon & Schuster UK Ltd, Africa House, 64-78 Kingsway, London WC2B 6AH, United Kingdom *Tel:* (020) 7316 1900 *Fax:* (020) 7316 0032
Imprints: Kangaroo Press; Simon & Schuster Australia
Distributed by The Search Press (craft only - UK & Europe)
Distributor for AA Publishing; Australian Women's Weekly; Duncan Baird; Kyle Cathie; Finch Publishing; Gaia Books; Jenman Group; National Geographic; Ten Speed Press

**Single X Publications+**
PO Box 227, Glenside, SA 5065
*Tel:* (08) 8127 0827
*Key Personnel*
Editor & Author: Michael X Savvas
    *E-mail:* msavvas@usa.net
Founded: 1994
Subjects: Biography, Self-Help, Sports, Athletics,
    Travel, Motivational
ISBN Prefix(es): 0-9577777

**Singular Press**, *imprint of* Elsevier Australia

**Skills Publishing**
PO Box 514, Hazelbrook, NSW 2779
*Tel:* (02) 4759 2844 *Fax:* (02) 4759 3721
*E-mail:* aww@skillspublish.com.au
*Web Site:* www.skillspublish.com.au
*Key Personnel*
Publisher: Art Burrows
Man Dir: Steven Burrows
Founded: 1985
Publisher of books & magazines in woodworking,
    metalworking, home construction & renovation.
Subjects: Crafts, Games, Hobbies, House &
    Home, How-to
ISBN Prefix(es): 0-646

**Skylight Publishing Inc**, *imprint of* Hawker
    Brownlow

**Slouch Hat Publications+**
PO Box 174, Rosebud, Victoria 3939
*Tel:* (03) 5986-6437 *Fax:* (03) 5986-6312
*E-mail:* slouchat@surf.net.au
*Web Site:* www.slouch-hat.com.au
*Key Personnel*
Contact: Ron Austin
Founded: 1989
Subjects: History, Military Science
ISBN Prefix(es): 0-9585296; 0-9579752

**Social Club Books**
6-10 Keele St, Collingwood, Victoria 3066
Mailing Address: PO Box 2937, Fitzroy, Mel-
    bourne, Victoria 3065
*Tel:* (03) 9473 5555 *Fax:* (03) 9417 5574
*E-mail:* info@scb.com.au
*Web Site:* www.scb.com.au
*Key Personnel*
Man Dir: Ken Finlayson *E-mail:* kenf@scb.com.
    au
Founded: 1983
Subjects: Astrology, Occult, Cookery, Gardening,
    Plants
Imprints: Ken Fin

**Social Science Press+**
Imprint of Thomson Learning
102 Dodds St, Southbank, Victoria 3006
*Tel:* 800-654-831 *Fax:* 800-641-823
*E-mail:* newtext@thomsonlearning.com.au
*Web Site:* www.thomsonlearning.com.au/higher/
    index.asp
Founded: 1980
Subjects: Education
ISBN Prefix(es): 0-949218; 1-876033

**Somerset Publications**
PO Box 8, Samford, Qld 4520
*Tel:* (07) 3425 1857 *Fax:* (07) 3425 1857
*E-mail:* info@crabbetarabian.com;
    crabbetarabian@hotkey.net.au
*Web Site:* www.crabbetarabian.com; www.hotkey.
    net.au/~crabbetarabian
*Key Personnel*
Editor: Joan Flynn; Coralie Gordon
Founded: 1987
Specialize in books & magazines on Arabian
    horses.
Subjects: Arabian Horses

ISBN Prefix(es): 0-947256
*Parent Company:* Limbale Pty Ltd
Distributed by J A Allen & Co; Alexander
    Heriot; Silver Monarch POB (USA)
Distributor for J A Allen & Co (UK); Alexander
    Heriot (UK); Borden Publishing (USA); Gor-
    don & Gotch

**South Australian Government-Department of
    Education, Training & Employment**
The Education Centre, 31 Flinders St, Adelaide,
    SA 5001
Mailing Address: GPO Box 1152, Adelaide, SA
    5001
*Tel:* (08) 8226 1527
*E-mail:* www.decscustomrs@saugov.sa.gov.au
*Key Personnel*
Managing Editor: Pamela Ball
Founded: 1974
Membership(s): Australian Publishers Associa-
    tion.
Subjects: Education
ISBN Prefix(es): 0-7243; 7-308
*Bookshop(s):* The Shop, The Orphanage Teach-
    ers Centre, 181 Coodwood Rd, Millswood, SA
    5034
*Orders to:* Curriculum Resources Australia, PO
    Box 33, Campbelltown, SA 5074 *Tel:* (08)
    8373 6077 *Fax:* (08) 8234 5086

**South Head Press**
1102 Windsong, 212 Marine Parade, Labrador,
    Qld 4215
Mailing Address: PO Box 59, Southport, Qld
    4215
*Tel:* (07) 5526 4670
*Key Personnel*
Head of Company: John Millett
    *E-mail:* johnmarion@telstra.com
Founded: 1964
Subjects: Poetry
ISBN Prefix(es): 0-909185; 0-901760

**South Pacific Books**, *imprint of* Outback Books -
    CQU Press

**Southern Cross PR & Press Services**
Arakoon, Via Tenterfield, NSW 2372
*Tel:* (02) 6737 5436 *Fax:* (02) 6737 5436
*Key Personnel*
Contact: Joan Starr
ISBN Prefix(es): 0-9588021

**Spacevision Publishing+**
12 Fry's Track, Newborough, Victoria 3825
*Tel:* (03) 5127 2398
*Key Personnel*
Head of Company: A E Allison
Founded: 1994
Subjects: Mysteries
ISBN Prefix(es): 0-646

**Spaniel Books+**
PO Box 167, Paddington, NSW 2021
*Tel:* (02) 9360 9985 *Fax:* (02) 9331 4653
*E-mail:* spanielbooks@hotmail.com
*Key Personnel*
Contact: Michael Giffin
Founded: 1995
Subjects: Literature, Literary Criticism, Essays,
    Theology
ISBN Prefix(es): 0-9579568

**Specialist Publications**
1-5 Edwin St, Mortlake, NSW 2137
*Tel:* (02) 9736 2191 *Fax:* (02) 9736 2663
*Key Personnel*
Contact: John Brooks *E-mail:* john@specialist.
    com.au
ISBN Prefix(es): 0-9588973; 1-86434

**Spectrum Publications+**
PO Box 75, Richmond, Victoria 3121
*Tel:* (03) 9415 9750 *Fax:* (03) 9419 0783
*E-mail:* spectrum@spectrumpublications.com.au
*Web Site:* www.spectrumpublications.com.au
*Key Personnel*
Man Dir: Peter Henry Rohr
Sales Manager: Maria Peters
Founded: 1974
Membership(s): Australian Publishers Associa-
    tion.
Subjects: Biography, Education, Gay & Lesbian,
    History, Music, Dance, Nonfiction (General),
    Psychology, Psychiatry, Religion - Buddhist,
    Religion - Catholic, Religion - Hindu, Religion
    - Islamic, Religion - Jewish, Religion - Protes-
    tant, Religion - Other, Self-Help, Theology,
    Australiana, Grief, Inspirational
ISBN Prefix(es): 0-86786; 0-909837
Number of titles published annually: 10 Print
Total Titles: 70 Print

**Spellbound Promotions**
7 Market St, Woolgoolga, NSW 2456
*Tel:* (066) 542133 *Fax:* (066) 541258
*E-mail:* Jodiadv@oncs.com.au
*Key Personnel*
Manager: Ron Blackmore
Founded: 1987
Publishing, Promotion, Typesetting, Editing &
    Cover Design
Privately owned company.
ISBN Prefix(es): 1-876005
Total Titles: 3 Print; 3 Audio
Distributed by Crown Publishing (Taiwan)
Foreign Rep(s): Crown Publishing (Taiwan)

**Spinifex Press+**
504 Queensberry St, North Melbourne, Victoria
    3051
Mailing Address: PO Box 212, North Melbourne,
    Victoria 3051
*Tel:* (03) 9329-6088 *Fax:* (03) 9329-9238
*E-mail:* women@spinifexpress.com.au
*Web Site:* www.spinifexpress.com.au
*Key Personnel*
Dir: Susan Hawthorne *E-mail:* hawsu@
    spinifexpress.com.qu; Renate Klein
Founded: 1991
Specialize in feminist publishing.
Membership(s): APA
Subjects: Alternative, Art, Asian Studies, Astrol-
    ogy, Occult, Astronomy, Developing Countries,
    Disability, Special Needs, Economics, Educa-
    tion, Environmental Studies, Fiction, Gay &
    Lesbian, Health, Nutrition, Literature, Literary
    Criticism, Essays, Nonfiction (General), Poetry,
    Social Sciences, Sociology, Technology, Travel,
    Women's Studies, Feminism
ISBN Prefix(es): 1-875559; 1-876756
Number of titles published annually: 10 Print
Total Titles: 150 Print
Foreign Rights: Arts & Licensing International
    Inc (China, Hong Kong, Malaysia, Taiwan);
    Best Literary & Rights Agency (Korea); Bestun
    Korea Literary Agency (Korea); BookCos-
    mos (Korea); The Harris/Elon Agency (Is-
    rael); Imprima Korea Agency (Korea); Inter-
    national Editors' Co (Argentina, Spain); Iris
    Agency (Greece); Vanessa Kling & Michele
    Kanonidis (France); Literarische Agentur
    (Germany); Natoli, Stefan & Oliva (Italy);
    Pikarski Literary Agency (Israel); Read n'
    Right Agency (Greece); Tuttle Mori Agency
    (Japan); Eric Yang Agency (Korea); Tatjana
    Zoldnere (Latvia)
*Distribution Center:* Macmillan Distribution Ser-
    vices, 627 Chapel St, Level 4, South Yarra,
    Victoria 3141 *Toll Free Tel:* 300 135 113 *Toll
    Free Fax:* 300 135 103 *E-mail:* customer.
    service@macmillan.com.au (Australia)

Addenda, PO Box 78-224, GrayLynn, Auckland, New Zealand *Tel:* (09) 8367471 *Fax:* (09)
8367401 *E-mail:* addenda@addenda.co.nz
A Star Distributor, One Tannery Rd, No 04-01,
Cencon 1 347719 *Tel:* 6746 3165 *Fax:* 6745
6729 *E-mail:* astargp@mbox3.singnet.com.sg
Fernwood Books Ltd, PO Box 1981, Peterborough, ON K9J 7X7, Canada *Tel:* 705-743-
8990 *Fax:* 705-743-8353 *E-mail:* lgray@
broadviewpress.com (Canada - trade & academic orders)
Gazelle, Falcon House, Queen Sq, Lancaster
LA1 1RN, United Kingdom *E-mail:* sales@
gazellebooks.co.uk
Independent Publishers Group, Order Department, 814 N Franklin St, Chicago, IL 60610,
United States *Tel:* 312-337-0747 *Fax:* 312-337-
5985 *E-mail:* frontdesk@ipgbook.com *Web
Site:* www.ipgbook.com
Missing Link, Westerstr 114-116, 28199 Bremen,
Germany *Tel:* (0421) 50 43 48 *Fax:* (0421) 50
43 16 *E-mail:* info@missing-link.de (Europe
(bookshops only))

**Standards Association of Australia**
PO Box 458, North Sydney, NSW 2060
*Tel:* (02) 99634231 *Fax:* (02) 9746 8450
*Telex:* AA26514
*Key Personnel*
Chief Executive: Ross Wraight
Founded: 1922
Subjects: Chemistry, Chemical Engineering, Civil
Engineering, Communications, Electronics,
Electrical Engineering, Engineering (General),
Mechanical Engineering, Technology
ISBN Prefix(es): 0-7262

**Star Teaching**, *imprint of* Hawker Brownlow

**State Library of NSW Press+**
Macquarie St, Sydney, NSW 2000
*Tel:* (02) 92731568 *Fax:* (02) 92731259
*E-mail:* helene@ilanet.slnsw.gov.au
*Web Site:* www.sl.nsw.gov.au
*Key Personnel*
Manager: Judith Kelly *E-mail:* jkelly@ilanet.
slnsw.gov.au
Founded: 1988
Membership(s): Australian Publishers Associa-
tion.
Subjects: Art, Biography, Ethnicity, Genealogy,
History, Literature, Literary Criticism, Essays,
Natural History, Nonfiction (General), Social
Sciences, Sociology, Women's Studies
ISBN Prefix(es): 0-7305; 0-7310
*Parent Company:* Library Council of NSW
Distributed by Peribo Pty Ltd (Australia/NZ/
PNG)

**State Library of Victoria**
328 Swanston St, Melbourne, Victoria 3000
*Tel:* (03) 8664 7002 *Fax:* (03) 9639 4737
*Web Site:* www.slv.vic.gov.au
*Key Personnel*
Publisher: Rob Blackmore
ISBN Prefix(es): 0-9585959; 0-9750153

**State Publishing Unit of State Print SA+**
282 Richmond Rd, Netley, SA 5037
Mailing Address: PO Box 210, Plympton, SA
5038
*Tel:* (08) 9226 4677 *Fax:* (08) 9226 4726
*Key Personnel*
General Manager: Tony Fitzsimmons
Founded: 1986
Also acts as Agents.
Subjects: History, Regional Interests
ISBN Prefix(es): 0-7243

**Sterling Publishing Co Inc**, *imprint of* Hawker
Brownlow

**Ian Stewart Marine Publications**
8 Pollard Way, Wambro, WA 6169
Mailing Address: PO Box 5154, Rockingham
Beach, WA 6168
*Tel:* (08) 9593 1331 *Fax:* (08) 9593 1331
*Key Personnel*
Dir: Ian Graham Stewart
Founded: 1992
Subjects: Maritime, Shipping
ISBN Prefix(es): 0-646
Total Titles: 2 Print
Distributed by Anthony Cooke (UK & Europe);
Cordillera Press (Canada & US)
Distributor for Carmania Press

**Stirling Press**
43 Alexander Rd, Padbury, WA 6025
*Tel:* (08) 9401 6598
*E-mail:* stirl@ozemail.com.au
Subjects: Business, Health, Nutrition, Self-Help
ISBN Prefix(es): 0-949142
*Showroom(s):* 100 King William Rd, Hyde Park,
SA 5034

**Strucmech Publishing**
1A Southey St, Sandringham, Victoria 3191
*Tel:* (03) 95989245 *Fax:* (03) 95989245
*Key Personnel*
Author & Manager: Alan K Hosking
Founded: 1984
Subjects: Civil Engineering, Applied structural
design
ISBN Prefix(es): 0-9586580

**Success Education**, *imprint of* R J Cleary
Publishing

**Summer Institute of Linguistics, Australian
Aborigines Branch**
60 Vanderlin Dr, Berrimah, NT 5788
*Tel:* (08) 8922 5700 *Fax:* (08) 8922 5717
*E-mail:* sildarwin@taunet.net.au
Founded: 1961
Subjects: Anthropology, Education, Language
Arts, Linguistics, Australian Aboriginal & Tor-
res Strait Islander Languages
ISBN Prefix(es): 0-86892
*Parent Company:* Summer Institute of Linguistics,
Attn: Academic Publications, 7500 W Camp
Wisdom Rd, Dallas, TX 75326, United States

**Sun**, *imprint of* Pan Macmillan Australia Pty Ltd

**Sundance Inc**, *imprint of* Hawker Brownlow

**Systex**
2 Ayres Rd, Saint Ives, NSW 2075
*Tel:* (02) 9944 2668
*Key Personnel*
Head of Company: Peter Burke
ISBN Prefix(es): 0-646

**T & A**, *imprint of* Turton & Armstrong Pty Ltd
Publishers

**Tabletop Press+**
2 Lambell Close, Palmerston, ACT 2913
*Tel:* (06) 6242 0995 *Fax:* (06) 6242 0674
*Key Personnel*
Head of Company: Klaus Hueneke
Founded: 1985
Also acts as distributor.
Subjects: Geography, Geology, History, Photogra-
phy, Regional Interests
ISBN Prefix(es): 0-9590841; 0-9587049
Distributed by Evirobook; Tower Books

**TAFE Publications**, *imprint of* RMIT Publishing

**Tamarind Publications**
PO Box 624, Warner's Bay, NSW 2282
*Tel:* (02) 467934 *Fax:* (02) 659515
*E-mail:* sigi@hunterlink.net.au
*Key Personnel*
Principal: Pauline Clare Egan
Founded: 1996
Subjects: Philosophy, Poetry, Religion - Buddhist
ISBN Prefix(es): 0-9586836
Number of titles published annually: 1 Print
Total Titles: 2 Print

**Teach Yourself**, *imprint of* Hachette Livre
Australia

**Teacher Created Materials**, *imprint of* Hawker
Brownlow

**Technomic Publishing**, *imprint of* Elsevier
Australia

**Templegate Publishers**, *imprint of* Rainbow
Book Agencies Pty Ltd

**Terania Rainforest Publishing**
Terania Creek Rd, The Channon, NSW 2480
*Tel:* (02) 6688 6204 *Fax:* (02) 6688 6227
*E-mail:* terania@nrg.com.au
*Key Personnel*
Contact: Nan J Nicholson
Founded: 1985
Subjects: Environmental Studies, Gardening,
Plants, Natural History, Botany, Rainforest
ISBN Prefix(es): 0-9589436
Total Titles: 5 Print
Distributed by Frith & Frith (Australia); Tower
Books (Australia)

**Tertiary Press+**
12-50 Norton Rd, Croydon, Victoria 3136
*Tel:* (03) 9726 1505 *Fax:* (03) 9726 1706
*E-mail:* tertiarypress@swin.edu.au
*Web Site:* www.tertiarypress.com.au
*Key Personnel*
Manager: Cathy Grundy *Tel:* (03) 9726 1674
*E-mail:* cgrundy@swin.edu.au
Founded: 1995
Subjects: Accounting, Business, Child Care &
Development, Computer Science, Economics,
Human Relations, Management, Marketing,
Microcomputers, Technology
ISBN Prefix(es): 1-875794; 1-875886; 0-86458
Number of titles published annually: 35 Print; 2
CD-ROM; 1 Audio
Total Titles: 200 Print
*Parent Company:* Swinburne University of Tech-
nology
Foreign Rep(s): Educational Books Ltd (New
Zealand)

**Text**, *imprint of* The Text Publishing Company
Pty Ltd

**The Text Publishing Company Pty Ltd+**
171 Latrobe St, Melbourne, Victoria 3000
*Tel:* (03) 9272 4700 *Fax:* (03) 9926 4854
*E-mail:* books@textmedia.com.au
*Web Site:* www.textpublishing.com.au
*Key Personnel*
Publisher: Michael Heyward *Tel:* (03) 9272 4716
Publicist: Emily Booth
Founded: 1990
Subjects: Biography, Fiction, History, Humor, Lit-
erature, Literary Criticism, Essays, Nonfiction
(General), Political Science
ISBN Prefix(es): 1-875847; 1-876485; 1-877008;
1-86372
Number of titles published annually: 40 Print
Total Titles: 105 Print

*Associate Companies:* The Text Media Group Pty Ltd
Imprints: Text
Distributed by Archetype Book Agents; Penguin Books Australia
Foreign Rights: Agencia Litterari BMSR (Brazil); Antonella Antonelli Agencia (Italy); Agencia Litteraria Carmen Balcells (Portugal, Spain); Bardon-Chinese Media Agency (China, Taiwan); Eliane Benisti Agency (France); Paul & Peter Fritz (Germany); Caroline van Gelderen (Netherlands); Graal Ltd (Poland); International Copyright Agency (Romania); Katai & Bolza (Hungary); Korea Copyright Centre (Korea); Leonhardt & Hoier (Scandinavia); Lutyens & Rubinstein (UK); Tuttle-Mori Agency (Japan); Andrew Nurnberg Associates (Baltic States); Witherspoon Associates Inc (US)
*Warehouse:* Peguin Books Australia, 30 Centre Rd, Scoresby, Victoria 3179 *Tel:* (03) 9811 2555 *Fax:* (03) 9811 8309
*Orders to:* Peguin Books Australia, 30 Centre Rd, Scoresby, Victoria 3179 *Tel:* (03) 9811 2555 *Fax:* (03) 9811 8309

**Thames & Hudson (Australia) Pty Ltd**
Portside Business Park, 11 Central Blvd, Fishermans Bend, Victoria 3207
*Tel:* (03) 9646 7788 *Fax:* (03) 9646 8790
*E-mail:* enquiries@thaust.com.au
*Web Site:* www.thaust.com.au
*Key Personnel*
Man Dir: Peter Shaw
Customer Service Manager: Elizabeth Ioannidis
Founded: 1968 (Wholly owned subsidiary of Thames & Hudson UK)
Distribute books for Thames & Hudson UK & other publishers.
Subjects: Archaeology, Architecture & Interior Design, Art, Fashion, Foreign Countries, History, Literature, Literary Criticism, Essays, Music, Dance, Natural History, Photography, Travel
ISBN Prefix(es): 0-500
Subsidiaries: Thames & Hudson
Distributor for AA Gallery of New South Wales; AA Gallery of Queensland; AA Gallery of South Australia; Abrams (Australia); Boothe-Clibborn Editions; British Museum Press (Australia); Craftsman House (Australia); Flammarion (Australia); Lawrence King (Australia); MOMA (Australia); National Gallery of Australia (Australia); Rizzoli/Universe; RotoVision; SCALO (Australia); SKIRA (Australia); Tate Gallery (Australia); Vision On

**The Jacaranda Press**, *imprint of* John Wiley & Sons Australia, Ltd

**Thornbill Press**
4 Thornbill Crescent, Coromandel Valley, SA 5051
*Tel:* (08) 82705172
*Key Personnel*
Head of Company: Graeme Webster
Subjects: Law, Literature, Literary Criticism, Essays
ISBN Prefix(es): 0-9586973
*Parent Company:* Thornbill Professional Services Pty Ltd (ACN 050 019 915)

**Caroline Thornton+**
18 Doonan Rd, Nedlands, WA 6009
*Tel:* (08) 9386 1555 *Fax:* (08) 9389 5162
Founded: 1988
Subjects: History
ISBN Prefix(es): 0-7316

**Thorpe-Bowker+**
Division of R R Bowker LLC

85 Turner St, Bldg C3, Port Melbourne, Victoria 3207
*Tel:* (03) 8645 0300 *Fax:* (03) 8645 0333
*E-mail:* yoursay@thorpe.com.au
*Web Site:* www.thorpe.com.au
*Key Personnel*
General Manager: Richard Siegersma *Tel:* (03) 8645 0374 *E-mail:* richards@thorpe.com.au
Founded: 1921
Bibliographic & library reference publisher.
Membership(s): ABA, APA, ALIA.
Subjects: Business, Library & Information Sciences, Publishing & Book Trade Reference
ISBN Prefix(es): 0-909532; 1-875589; 1-86452
Distributor for Bowker; R R Bowker; Whitaker

**Three Sisters Publications Pty Ltd**
PO Box 104, Winmalee, NSW 2777
*Tel:* (047) 588138
*Key Personnel*
Principal Officer: Margaret Baker
Founded: 1983
Subjects: Archaeology, Biological Sciences, Gardening, Plants, Geography, Geology, History, Natural History
ISBN Prefix(es): 0-9590203

**Threshold Publishing**
PO Box 60, Croydon, Victoria 3136
*Tel:* (03) 9724 9067 *Fax:* (03) 9724 9067
*E-mail:* threshol@alphalink.com.au
*Key Personnel*
Manager: Adrian Anderson *E-mail:* adrian@alphalink.com.au
Founded: 1992
ISBN Prefix(es): 0-646

**Timber**, *imprint of* Bloomings Books

**Time Life Australia Pty Ltd**
Level 10, 77 Pacific Hwy, North Sydney, NSW 2060
Mailing Address: PO Box 3814, Sydney, NSW 2001
*Tel:* (02) 1300 364 437 *Toll Free Tel:* 300 364 437 *Fax:* (02) 9957 2773
*E-mail:* tlservice@timelife.com
*Web Site:* www.timelife.com.au
*Key Personnel*
Man Dir: Bonita L Boezeman
Founded: 1961
Subjects: Books, Music, Videos & Direct Marketing
ISBN Prefix(es): 0-8094
*Parent Company:* Time Warner Inc
Subsidiaries: Record Clubs of Australia
*Branch Office(s)*
Time Life Inc, 5 Ottho Heldringstr, 1066 AZ Amsterdam, Netherlands *Tel:* (020) 48 74 293 *Web Site:* www.timelife.nl
*U.S. Office(s):* Time Life, PO Box 85060, Richmond, VA 32285-5060, United States *Tel:* 804-261-1300 *Web Site:* www.timelife.com
Distributed by Collins New Zealand; Hodder Headline Australia
*Book Club(s):* The Softback Preview

**Tirian Publications**
116 Queens Cliff Rd, Queenscliff, NSW 2096
*Tel:* (02) 9908 1196 *Fax:* (02) 9907 1196
*E-mail:* Tirian@bigpond.com; infoweb@tirian.com
*Web Site:* www.users.bigpond.com/tirian
Subjects: Education
ISBN Prefix(es): 0-9586056

**Tom Publications+**
153 McDonald St, Yoodanna, WA 6060
*Tel:* (08) 9444 4570
*Key Personnel*
Contact: Radmila Mijatovic

Membership(s): WA Writers.
Subjects: Ethnicity, Fiction, Nonfiction (General), Poetry, Romance, Migrants
ISBN Prefix(es): 0-9594810; 1-875715

**Tomorrow Publications+**
33 Mitchell St, Merewether, NSW 2291
Mailing Address: PO Box 313, Merewether, NSW 2291
*Tel:* (02) 4961 2115
*E-mail:* tomorrowtrading@hotmail.com
*Key Personnel*
Contact: Paula Morrow
Subjects: Alternative, Fiction, Health, Nutrition, How-to, Science Fiction, Fantasy, Self-Help
ISBN Prefix(es): 0-646

**Tor Books**, *imprint of* Pan Macmillan Australia Pty Ltd

**Tower Books**
17 Rodborough Rd, Unit 2, French's Forest, NSW 2086
*Tel:* (02) 9975 5566 *Fax:* (02) 9975 5599
*E-mail:* info@towerbooks.com.au
*Web Site:* www.towerbooks.com.au
*Key Personnel*
Contact: Dale Druckman

**Transpareon Press+**
PO Box 4, Hornsby, NSW 2077
*Tel:* (02) 99874570 *Fax:* (02) 99874570
*Key Personnel*
Dir: Frances Wheelhouse
Founded: 1970
Membership(s): Australian Book Publishers Association.
Subjects: Agriculture, Anthropology, Biography, History, Regional Interests, Science (General), Women's Studies, Australian History, Biographies, Medicine
ISBN Prefix(es): 0-908021

**Transworld Publishers Pty Ltd+**
20 Alfred St S, Milsons Point, NSW 2061
*Tel:* (02) 9954 9966 *Fax:* (02) 9954 4562
*Key Personnel*
Man Dir & Chief Executive Officer: Geoff Rumpf
Deputy Man Officer Finance & Operations: Greg Little
Publisher: Shona Martyn
National Sales Manager: Chris Raine
Head Publicity & Promotions: Maggie Hamilton
Founded: 1980
Subjects: Fiction, Health, Nutrition, Humor, Nonfiction (General), Romance, Science Fiction, Fantasy, Self-Help
ISBN Prefix(es): 0-552; 0-86824; 0-7338; 0-86451; 0-947189; 1-86359
*Parent Company:* Random House Australia
*Associate Companies:* Transworld Publishers, United Kingdom; Bantam Doubleday Dell Inc, 1540 Broadway, New York, NY 19936, United States
Imprints: Bantam; Corgi; Doubleday; Dell; Anchor; Broadway Dela Corte; Black Swan
*U.S. Office(s):* Bantam Doubleday Dell, 1540 Broadway, New York, NY 10036, United States
Distributed by Transworld Publishers (New Zealand)
Distributor for Avon; Potentials Unlimited; Ravette; Running Press; Workman
*Book Club(s):* Doubleday Book & Music Clubs

**Travelog**, *imprint of* Universal Press Pty Ltd

**Trillium Press**, *imprint of* Hawker Brownlow

**Troll Books of Australia+**
20 Barcoo St, East Roseville, NSW 2069

*Tel:* (02) 9417 2699 *Fax:* (02) 9417 1599
*E-mail:* webmaster@troll.com
*Web Site:* www.troll.com
*Key Personnel*
Chief Executive: Terry T Hughes
Founded: 1997
Subjects: Fiction, Nonfiction (General), Science (General), Activity, Teacher Resources with Specialist Materials on early reading & reading recovery
ISBN Prefix(es): 1-875675
*Parent Company:* Troll Communications LLC, 100 Corporate Dr, Mahwah, NJ 07430, United States
Imprints: Lineup; Watermill
*Branch Office(s)*
Auckland, New Zealand

**Tropicana Press+**
7 Sheoak Pl, Alfords Point, NSW 2234
Mailing Address: PO Box 385, Padstow, NSW 2211
*Tel:* (02) 9543 7728
*Key Personnel*
Contact: R B Shaw *E-mail:* rsshaw@netspace.net.au
Subjects: Fiction
ISBN Prefix(es): 0-9581418

**Troubadour Press**, *imprint of* New Creation Publications Ministries & Resource Centre

**Troubadour Press**
Imprint of New Creation Publications Ministries & Resource Center
PO Box 403, Blackwood, SA 5051
*Tel:* (08) 8270 1861 *Fax:* (08) 8270 4003
*E-mail:* newcreat@camtech.net.au
*Key Personnel*
Head of Company: Geoffrey Bingham
ISBN Prefix(es): 1-875653

**Turton & Armstrong Pty Ltd Publishers+**
21 Lister St, Wahroonga, NSW 2076
*Tel:* (02) 9489 6719 *Fax:* (02) 9489 6719
*E-mail:* turtarm@attglobal.net
*Key Personnel*
Dir: Paul T Armstrong
Founded: 1977
Nonfiction book publisher.
Subjects: Aeronautics, Aviation, Automotive, Biography, Crafts, Games, Hobbies, History, Maritime, Music, Dance, Nonfiction (General), Transportation, Special Interest & Motor Racing
ISBN Prefix(es): 0-908031
Number of titles published annually: 6 Print
Total Titles: 40 Print
Imprints: T & A
Distributed by Bookworks Pty Ltd
*Orders to:* Bookworks PLC, 56 Bonds Rd, Punchbowl, NSW 2196 *Tel:* (02) 9740 6766 *E-mail:* sales@bookworks.com.au

**UBD**, *imprint of* Universal Press Pty Ltd

**Unichurch Publishing**
Level 9, 222 Pit St, Sydney, NSW 2000
Mailing Address: PO Box A2178, Sydney South, NSW 1235
*Tel:* (02) 8267 4308 *Fax:* (02) 9267 4716
*E-mail:* insights@nsw.uca.org.au
*Web Site:* www.nsw.uca.org.au/cu/publishing.htm
*Key Personnel*
Unit Manager, Editor: Marjorie Lewis-Jones
ISBN Prefix(es): 0-908525

**United Educational Services (DDK)**, *imprint of* Hawker Brownlow

**Uniting Church Press**, *imprint of* Uniting Education

**Uniting Education**
PO Box 1245, Collingwood, Victoria 3066
*Tel:* (03) 9416 4262 *Fax:* (03) 9416 4264
*E-mail:* contact@unitinged.org.au
*Web Site:* www.unitinged.org.au
*Key Personnel*
Dir: John Emmett *E-mail:* john@unitinged.org.au
Books Manager: Hugh McGinlay
Founded: 1914
Specialize in Christian Education Resources.
Subjects: Education, Human Relations, Religion - Protestant, Theology
ISBN Prefix(es): 0-85819; 1-86407
Imprints: Uniting Church Press
Distributed by National Christian Education Council (UK)
*Orders to:* Rainbow Books, 303 Arthur St, Fairfield, Victoria 3068 *Tel:* (03) 9481 6611 *Fax:* (03) 9481 2371 *E-mail:* rainbowb@axs.com.au

**Unity Press**
4 Young St, Suite 367, Neutral Bay, NSW 2089
*Tel:* (02) 95186718 *Fax:* (02) 9736-2663
*E-mail:* hingley@telpacific.com.au
*Key Personnel*
Dir: Nevill Drury; Anna Voigt
Subjects: Anthropology, Art, Astrology, Occult, Health, Nutrition, Music, Dance, Mysteries, Parapsychology, Philosophy, Poetry, Psychology, Psychiatry, Religion - Buddhist, Religion - Other, Self-Help, Women's Studies
ISBN Prefix(es): 0-9589759
*Parent Company:* Voigt Drury Publishing Pty Ltd

**Universal Press Pty Ltd+**
One Waterloo Rd, Macquarie Park, NSW 2113
*Tel:* (02) 857 3700 *Toll Free Tel:* 800 021 987 *Fax:* (02) 888 9074 *Toll Free Fax:* 800 636 197
*E-mail:* unipress@unipress.com.au
*Key Personnel*
Sales & Marketing Manager: Kim Mouret
Founded: 1950
Large range of D I Y Service, repair car manuals for popular imported & Australian produced vehicles; also list of automotive technical vehicles & automotive technical publications for trade education.
Subjects: Automotive, Travel, Automotive Publications, Maps, Street Directories & Guides
ISBN Prefix(es): 0-85566; 0-7319; 0-949164; 1-86939; 1-86949
Imprints: R A Broadberh; Gregory's; Robinson's; Travelog; UBD
Distributor for Berlitz; Fielding Worldwide; Geographer's A-Z; Michelin; National Geographic Society (maps only); Rand McNally; Replogle Globes

**University of New South Wales Press Ltd+**
Cliffbrook Campus, 45 Beach St, Coogee, NSW 2034
Mailing Address: University of New South Wales, Sydney, NSW 2052
*Tel:* (02) 9664 0900 *Fax:* (02) 9664 5420
*E-mail:* info.press@unsw.edu.au
*Web Site:* www.unswpress.com.au
*Key Personnel*
Man Dir: Dr Robin Derricourt *E-mail:* r.derricourt@unsw.edu.au
Publishing Manager: John Elliot *E-mail:* john.elliot@unsw.edu.au
Marketing Manager: Nella Softerboek *E-mail:* nella.s@unsw.edu.au
Founded: 1962
Membership(s): Australian Publishers Association.
Subjects: Architecture & Interior Design, Biography, Biological Sciences, Child Care & Devel-

opment, Earth Sciences, Engineering (General), Environmental Studies, Gardening, Plants, Government, Political Science, History, Natural History, Nonfiction (General), Public Administration, Science (General), Social Sciences, Sociology, Technology, Women's Studies
ISBN Prefix(es): 0-86840; 0-947205
Number of titles published annually: 60 Print
Total Titles: 350 Print
Imprints: UNSW Press; RLCP
*Sales Office(s):* University & Reference Publishers Services UNIREPS, University of New South Wales, Sydney, NSW 2052
Distributed by Addenda Ltd; Apac Publishers Services Pte Ltd; Eurospan (UK); United Publishers Services Ltd; University & Reference Publishers Services UNIREPS; University of British Columbia Press; University of Washington Press
Distributor for Aboriginal Studies Press; Auckland University Press; Broadview; Brookings Institution Press; Canterbury University Press; Cavendish Publishing; CSIRO Publishing; Currency Press; Edinburgh University Press; C Hurst & Co; Indiana University Press; McGill-Queen's University Press; Pandanus Books; Craig Potton Publishing; Reaktion Books; Rivers Oram (Pandora); Rosenberg Publishing; Signal Books; Singapore University Press; University of Otago Press; University of Wales Press; University of Washington Press
*Bookshop(s):* UNSW Bookshop, Sydney, NSW 2052
*Warehouse:* UNSW Press, Govett St, Randwick, NSW 2031

**University of Newcastle**
Callaghan Campus, University Drive, Callaghan, NSW 2308
*Tel:* (02) 4921 8865
*Web Site:* www.newcastle.edu.au
ISBN Prefix(es): 0-7259; 1-920701

**University of Queensland Press+**
Unit of The University of Queensland
Staff House Rd, St Lucia, Qld 4067
Mailing Address: PO Box 6042, Brisbane, Qld 4067
*Tel:* (07) 3365 2127; (07) 3377 7244; (07) 3365 2440 (sales) *Fax:* (07) 3365 7579
*E-mail:* uqp@uqp.uq.edu.au
*Web Site:* www.uqp.uq.edu.au
*Key Personnel*
General Manager: Greg Bain
Managing Editor: Madonna Duffy *E-mail:* editor@uqp.uq.edu.au
Rights Manager: Dinah Johnson *Tel:* (07) 3365 7244 *E-mail:* dinah@uqp.uq.edu.au
Founded: 1948
Publisher of quality literary works of fiction & nonfiction
Also specialize in Black Australian writings, Aboriginal studies & social & political issues, reference books.
Subjects: Biography, Fiction, History, Literature, Literary Criticism, Essays, Nonfiction (General), Poetry, Sports, Athletics, Travel
ISBN Prefix(es): 0-7022
Number of titles published annually: 60 Print
Imprints: UQP
*Branch Office(s)*
International Specialized Book Services Inc, 5804 NE Hassalo St, Portland, OR, 97213-3640, United States *Tel:* 503-287-3093 *Fax:* 503-380-8832
Distributed by Penguin Books Australia Ltd
Foreign Rep(s): Literary Agent (France); Lora Fountain (France, Italy, Belgium & Germany)
Foreign Rights: Inter Australia Company (Korea)

**University of Western Australia Press+**
35 Stirling Highway, Crawley, WA 6009
*Tel:* (08) 9380 3670 *Fax:* (08) 9380 1027

*E-mail:* uwap@cyllene.uwa.edu.au
*Web Site:* www.uwapress.uwa.edu.au
*Key Personnel*
Dir: Dr Jenny Gregory *E-mail:* jag@cyllene.uwa.edu.au
Marketing Manager: Anastasia Stachewicz *E-mail:* ana@cyllene.uwa.edu.au
Sales Manager: J Brown *E-mail:* jbrown@cyllene.uwa.edu.au
Founded: 1954
Subjects: Biography, Fiction, History, Literature, Literary Criticism, Essays, Natural History, Nonfiction (General), Regional Interests, Science Fiction, Fantasy, Social Sciences, Sociology, Women's Studies
ISBN Prefix(es): 1-875560; 1-876268; 1-920694
Number of titles published annually: 30 Print
Imprints: Cygnet Books; Cygnet Young Fiction
*U.S. Office(s):* ISBS, 5824 NE Hassalo St, Portland, OR 97213-3644, United States *Tel:* 503-287-3093 *Fax:* 503-280-8832 *E-mail:* orders@isbn.com *Web Site:* www.isbs.com
Distributed by Addenda Ltd; Eurospan; ISBS Inc; United Publishing Services (UPS) (Japan)
Distributor for Centre for Studies in WA History, University of Western Australia; Westerly Centre, University of Western Australia

**UNSW Press**, *imprint of* University of New South Wales Press Ltd

**UQP**, *imprint of* University of Queensland Press

**The Useful Publishing Co+**
2/795 Beaufort St, Mount Lawley, Perth, WA 6050
*Tel:* (08) 9370 4577 *Fax:* (08) 9370 2540
*Key Personnel*
Contact: Murray Davey
Founded: 1992
Subjects: Career Development, Finance, Nonfiction (General)
ISBN Prefix(es): 1-875693
*Associate Companies:* Davey Business Accountants Pty Ltd

**VCTA Publishing+**
Imprint of Macmillan Education Australia
Level 1, 102 Victoria Rd, Carlton, Victoria 3053
*Tel:* (03) 94199622 *Fax:* (03) 94191205
*E-mail:* vcta@vcta.asn.au
*Web Site:* www.vcta.asn.au
*Key Personnel*
Dir: Robert Taylor
Publishing Manager: Susan Watson
Production Editor: Maree Keating
Founded: 1953
Subjects: Accounting, Business, Career Development, Communications, Economics, Finance, Law, Regional Interests
ISBN Prefix(es): 0-86859; 0-909715

**Veritas Press**
PO Box 1653, Bundaberg, Qld 4670
*Fax:* (071) 529256
*E-mail:* copytype@interworx.com.au
*Key Personnel*
President & Author: J West
General Manager & Editor: Rob Giles
Founded: 1987
Subjects: Anthropology, Archaeology, Astrology, Occult, Health, Nutrition, Medicine, Nursing, Dentistry, Poetry, Science (General), Expose books in Science & Medicine
ISBN Prefix(es): 0-9588131
Subsidiaries: Whale Books
Distributed by Lilly Books (USA); Veritas Publishing (Australia); Whales Books (UK)
Distributor for Random House (Australia)

**Vermillion**, *imprint of* Random House Australia

**Victorian Arts Centre Trust**
100 St Kilda Rd, Melbourne, Victoria 3004
Mailing Address: PO Box 7585, Melbourne, Victoria 8004
*Tel:* (03) 9281 8560 *Fax:* (03) 9281 8530
*Web Site:* www.artscentre.net.au
*Telex:* Vicart AA 39141
*Key Personnel*
Chief Executive Officer: Tim Jacobs
ISBN Prefix(es): 0-646; 0-7241

**Viking**, *imprint of* Penguin Group (Australia)

**Villamonta Publishing Services Inc+**
2 Downes Pl, Geelong, Victoria 3220
*Tel:* (03) 5229 2029 *Fax:* (03) 5222 5399
*E-mail:* villapub@ozemail.com.au
*Key Personnel*
Executive Officer: Charles Lucas
Founded: 1993
Subjects: Disability, Special Needs, Law
ISBN Prefix(es): 0-9587635; 1-876493
Total Titles: 14 Print

**Vintage**, *imprint of* Random House Australia

**Virgin**, *imprint of* Random House Australia

**Vista Publications+**
PO Box 76, St Kilda, Victoria 3182
*Tel:* (03) 9534 8881 *Fax:* (03) 9534 9711
*E-mail:* vistaof@mbox.com.au
*Key Personnel*
Editorial Dir: Christine Mitchell
International Rights: Eva Fabian
Founded: 1996
Publishing nonfiction books (small company).
Membership(s): Victorian Writers' Centre.
Subjects: Biography, Education, Environmental Studies, Government, Political Science, Health, Nutrition, History, How-to, Nonfiction (General), Poetry, Social Sciences, Sociology, Community Development, Peace
ISBN Prefix(es): 0-9586496; 0-9592816; 1-876370
Total Titles: 18 Print

**Vital**, *imprint of* Vital Publications

**Vital Publications**
PO Box 101, North Essendon, Melbourne, Victoria 3041
*Tel:* (03) 9379-1219 *Fax:* (03) 9379-0015
*E-mail:* vitalpubs@churchesofchrist.org.au; aceditor@ozemail.com.au
*Key Personnel*
Marketing Representative: Don Smith
Contact: Nigel Pegram
Religious publications.
Subjects: Biblical Studies, Education, Religion - Other
ISBN Prefix(es): 0-909116; 1-875915
Number of titles published annually: 3 Print
*Parent Company:* National Council Churches of Christ
Imprints: Vital

**WA Newspaper**, *imprint of* St George Books

**Wakefield Crime Classics**, *imprint of* Wakefield Press Pty Ltd

**Wakefield Press Pty Ltd+**
Wakefield Press Distribution, One The Parade West, Kent Town, SA 5067
Mailing Address: PO Box 2266, Kent Town, SA 5071
*Tel:* (08) 8362 8800 *Fax:* (08) 8362 7592
*E-mail:* info@wakefieldpress.com.au

*Web Site:* www.wakefieldpress.com.au
*Key Personnel*
Dir: Michael Bollen; Stephanie Johnston
*E-mail:* stephanie@wakefieldpress.com.au
Founded: 1989
Subjects: Art, Biography, Cookery, Fiction, History, Literature, Literary Criticism, Essays, Mysteries, Travel
ISBN Prefix(es): 1-86254; 0-949268
Number of titles published annually: 30 Print
Total Titles: 600 Print
Imprints: Wakefield Crime Classics
Distributor for AATE Interface Series (Australia); Akashic Books (USA); Allison & Busby (UK); Arsenal Pulp Press (Canada); Avocado Press (New Zealand); Bookends Books (Australia); Bookhappy Books (USA); Calypso Press (Australia); City of Adelaide (Australia); Conway's Collectables (Australia); Council Oak Books (USA); Cybersell Online (Australia); Davam Place (Australia); Delafon Press (Australia); Department of Environment (Australia); Department of Transport (Australia); DFK Management (Australia); Dilettante Press (USA); E&E Productions (Australia); ECW Press (Canada); Ellipsis (UK); Encounter Books (USA); Girl Press Books (USA); David R Godine (USA); Headpress (UK); The Gerald & Mark Hoberman Collection (UK & USA); Kensington West Productions (UK); Key Porter Books (Canada); Lythrum Press (Australia); Macleay Press (Australia); Tracy Marsh (Australia); Metro Publications (UK); Mosaic Press (Canada); Prospect Books (UK); Rakennusteito (Finland); RDR Books (USA); RDV Books (USA); Santa Monica Press (USA); Scout Outdoor Centre (Australia); Select Books (USA); Serif (UK); Splash Publishing (Australia); State Records of South Australia; Still Life Cards (Australia); Suhas (Australia); surfBrains.com Books (New Zealand); Tomahawk Press (UK); Uglytown (USA); Voice (Australia); Wakefield Press (Australia); Welcome Rain Publishers (USA); Whereabouts Press (USA)
Foreign Rep(s): Airlift Book Company (UK, Europe); Independent Publishers Group (North America)
Foreign Rights: Eliane Benisti (France); Peng Cheng (China); Fritz Agency (Germany); Mirah Hong (Korea); Gundhild Lenz-Mulligan (UK, Scandinavia); Daniela Micura (Italy); Maru de Monserrat (Spain); Michele Rubin (North America); Flavio Sala (Brazil)
*Orders to:* Wakefield Press Distribution, One The Parade West, Kent Town, SA 5067, Contact: John Inverarity *Tel:* (08) 8362 8800 *Fax:* (08) 8362 7592 *E-mail:* warehouse@wakefieldpress.com.au

**Frederick Warne**, *imprint of* Penguin Group (Australia)

**The Watermark Press+**
3-A Llewellyn St, Balmain, NSW 2041
*Tel:* (02) 9818 5677 *Fax:* (02) 9818 5581
*E-mail:* books@nsw.bigpond.net.au
*Key Personnel*
Head of Company: Simon Blackall
Founded: 1983
Subjects: Animals, Pets, Architecture & Interior Design, Cookery, Crafts, Games, Hobbies, Gardening, Plants, Humor, Military Science, Nonfiction (General), Travel, Wine & Spirits
ISBN Prefix(es): 0-949284

**Watermill**, *imprint of* Troll Books of Australia

**Franklin Watts Australia**
31/56 O'Riordan St, Alexandria, NSW 2015
*Tel:* (02) 8338 8800 *Fax:* (02) 8338 8881
*E-mail:* info@wattspub.com.au
*Web Site:* www.wattspub.com.au

*Key Personnel*
General Manager: Tony Watts
ISBN Prefix(es): 0-86415
*Parent Company:* Watts Publishing Group Ltd, 96 Leonard St, London EC2A 4XD, United Kingdom
*Ultimate Parent Company:* Scholastic Library Publishing
*Associate Companies:* Children's Press; Grolier Educational Inc; Grolier Electronic Publishing Inc; Orchard, United Kingdom; Orchard Books, United Kingdom; Franklin Watts, United Kingdom
Divisions: Grolier Educational Australia

**Weather Press+**
PO Box 107, Boronia, Victoria 3155
*Tel:* (03) 9762 1647
*Key Personnel*
International Rights: Philip Johns
Subjects: Fiction

**WebsterWorld Pty Ltd**
36-38 Wattle Rd, Brookvale, NSW 2100
*Tel:* (02) 9939 5505 *Fax:* (02) 9939 8355
*E-mail:* webpub@websterpublishing.com
*Web Site:* www.websterpublishing.com; www.websterworld.com; www.websterselearning.com
Founded: 1985
ISBN Prefix(es): 1-86398; 0-947302

**Wellington Lane Press Pty Ltd+**
120 Wycombe Rd, Neutral Bay, NSW 2089
*Tel:* (02) 99040962 *Fax:* (02) 99040962
*Key Personnel*
Publisher: Carol Dettmann *E-mail:* dettmann@bigpond.net.au
Founded: 1976
Subjects: Art, Photography, Regional Interests
ISBN Prefix(es): 0-908022; 0-947322
Imprints: Chapter & Verse

**Wellness Australia+**
Box 519, Subiaco, WA 6904
*Tel:* (08) 9387 6134 *Fax:* (08) 9383 7323
*E-mail:* info@workteams.com
*Key Personnel*
Head of Company & Dir: Grant Donovan *E-mail:* grant@workteams.com
Founded: 1988
Subjects: Health, Nutrition, Management, Psychology, Psychiatry
ISBN Prefix(es): 1-875139
Subsidiaries: Workplace Global Network

**Wilbur**, *imprint of* Elephas Books Pty Ltd

**Wild & Woolley+**
17 Military Rd, Watsons Bay, NSW 2030
Mailing Address: PO Box W76, Watsons Bay, NSW 2030
*Tel:* (02) 9337 6844 *Fax:* (02) 9337 6822
*E-mail:* pwoolley@fastbooks.com.au
*Web Site:* www.wildandwoolley.com.au
*Key Personnel*
President & Man Dir: Pat Woolley
Founded: 1974
Australian authors only. Books & Writers imprint for self publishers. Wild & Woolley imprint general trade publishing.
Membership(s): APA.
ISBN Prefix(es): 0-909331; 1-74018
Imprints: Books & Writers
Divisions: Fast Books In Print
Foreign Rights: Pat Woolley (Worldwide)

**Wild Publications Pty Ltd**
389 Malvern Rd, South Yarra, Victoria 3141
Mailing Address: PO Box 415, Prahran, Victoria 3181
*Tel:* (03) 9826-8482 *Fax:* (03) 9826-3787

*E-mail:* management@wild.com.au
*Web Site:* www.wild.com.au
*Key Personnel*
Dir: Chris Baxter
Founded: 1981
Publisher of *Wild Magazine* & *Rock Magazine*
Specialize in rockclimbing & hiking magazines & guidebooks to Australia.
Subjects: Sports, Athletics, Canoeing, Caving, Cross-Country Skiing, Hiking, Rock Climbing
*Parent Company:* Hamilton Foulser Pty Ltd; Wild Holdings Pty Ltd
Distributed by Macstyle (Australia)

**Wildlife in Newtown**, *imprint of* Feakle Press

**Wildscape Australia**
Division of Thunderhead Publishing
6 Ardmore Park, Kuranda, Qld 4872
*Tel:* (07) 4093 7171 *Fax:* (07) 4093 8897
*Key Personnel*
Manager: Debbie Jarver
Contact: Peter Jarver *E-mail:* jarver@ozemail.com.au
Founded: 1979
Specialize in books of photographs taken by Peter Jarver.
Subjects: Photography of landscapes, skyscapes, Top End, Central Australia & Queensland
ISBN Prefix(es): 0-9589067; 1-876500
Total Titles: 5 Print

**Wileman Publications+**
Chidon Court, One Cronin Ave, Main Beach, Qld 4217
*Tel:* (07) 312770
*E-mail:* wileman@onthenet.com.au
*Key Personnel*
International Rights: Bud Wileman
Subjects: Art, Behavioral Sciences, Criminology, Education, English as a Second Language, How-to, Human Relations, Language Arts, Linguistics, Law, Parapsychology, Psychology, Psychiatry, Self-Help, Social Sciences, Sociology
ISBN Prefix(es): 0-949026
Distributed by Barnes & Noble (North America)

**John Wiley & Sons**, *imprint of* John Wiley & Sons Australia, Ltd

**John Wiley & Sons Australia, Ltd+**
33 Park Rd, 3rd Floor, Milton, Qld 4064
Mailing Address: PO Box 1226, Milton, Qld 4064
*Tel:* (07) 3859 9755 *Fax:* (07) 3859 9715
*E-mail:* brisbane@johnwiley.com.au
*Web Site:* www.johnwiley.com.au
*Key Personnel*
Man Dir: Peter C Donoughue
Dir Finance & Administration: Andrew Betts
General Manager, School: Peter Van Noorden
General Manager, Higher Education: Lucy Russell
General Manager, Distribution: Jim Dwyer
Manager, Contracts & Licensing: Julie Barnett
Information Services: Heather Linaker
Founded: 1954
Membership(s): Australian Publishers Association.
Subjects: Education, Nonfiction (General)
ISBN Prefix(es): 0-395; 0-471; 0-393; 1-740; 1-876; 0-7314; 0-7016
*Parent Company:* John Wiley & Sons Inc, 111 River St, Hoboken, NJ 07030, United States
*Associate Companies:* John Wiley & Sons Canada Ltd, Canada; John Wiley & Sons (Asia) Pte Ltd, Singapore, Singapore; John Wiley & Sons Ltd, United Kingdom
Imprints: The Jacaranda Press; Wrightbooks; John Wiley & Sons; Hungry Minds Australia; Brooks Waterloo

*Branch Office(s)*
Level 3, 2 Railway Parade, Camberwell 3124
*Tel:* (03) 9811-1333 *Fax:* (03) 9811-1344
*E-mail:* melbourne@johnwiley.com.au
Suite 4A, 113 Wicks Rd, North Ryde, NSW 2113 *Tel:* (02) 9856-0200 *Fax:* (02) 9805 1597
*E-mail:* sydney@johnwiley.com.au
Distributor for Houghton Mifflin; W W Norton
*Warehouse:* Australian Center, 33 Windorah St, Stafford 4053 *Tel:* 3354-8455 *Fax:* 3352-7109
*Distribution Center:* Australian Distribution Centre

**A S Wilson Inc+**
PO Box 296, Jannali, NSW 2226
*Tel:* (02) 9528 8977
*Key Personnel*
President: Charles M Iossi
Agent, McMahon Publishers: Brian McMahon
Founded: 1994 (Acquired from Maxwell MacMillan Australia Pty Ltd)
High School study guides, trade & tertiary titles.
ISBN Prefix(es): 0-02; 0-08
Total Titles: 60 Print
*Parent Company:* c/o Ennis Cavuoto & Co, 7 Main St, Glen Rock, NJ 07632, United States
Imprints: Australian National University Press
*Shipping Address:* Elsevier Science, Locked Bag 16, Marricksville, NSW 2204 *Tel:* (02) 517 8999 *Fax:* (02) 517 2249

**Windhorse Books+**
PO Box 574, Newtown, NSW 2042
*Tel:* (02) 9519 8826 *Fax:* (02) 9519 8826
*E-mail:* books@windhorse.com.au
*Web Site:* www.windhorse.com.au
*Key Personnel*
Contact: Dh Ratnajyoti
Founded: 1994
Specialize in Buddhism & Meditation.
Subjects: Asian Studies, Human Relations, Poetry, Psychology, Psychiatry, Religion - Buddhist, Self-Help, Women's Studies
ISBN Prefix(es): 1-920815
Distributor for Aloka Publications (United Kingdom); ClearPoint Press (USA); Dharma Publishing (United States); Gorum Publications (Australia); Pali Text Society (United Kingdom); Edition Rabten (Switzerland); Rangjung Yeshe Publications (Hong Kong); Siddhi Publications (Canada); Weatherlight Press (United Kingdom); Wildmind (USA); Windhorse Publications (United Kingdom); Zhyisil Chokyi Ghatsal Publications (New Zealand)

**Windward Publications+**
RMB 206 Woodhill Mountain Rd, Via Berry, NSW 2535
*Tel:* (02) 4464 1977 *Fax:* (02) 4464 1906
*E-mail:* sales@windward.com.au
*Web Site:* www.windward.com.au
*Key Personnel*
Contact: David Colfelt *E-mail:* dc@windward.com.au
Founded: 1984
Subjects: Maritime, Travel, Great Barrier Reef, Whitsunday Islands
ISBN Prefix(es): 0-9590830; 0-9586989

**Windwood**, *imprint of* Moonlight Publishing

**Winetitles**
Imprint of Wine Publishers Pty Ltd
97 Carrington St, Adelaide, SA 5000
Mailing Address: PO Box 6015, Halifax St, SA 5000
*Tel:* (08) 8233 4799 *Fax:* (08) 8233 4790
*E-mail:* admin@winetitles.com.au
*Web Site:* www.winetitles.com.au

*Key Personnel*
Publisher: Paul Clancy *E-mail:* pclancy@
winetitles.com.au
Dir: Fran Clancy *E-mail:* fclancy@winetitles.com.
au
Publish two magazines: *Australian Viticulture &*
*The Australian & New Zealand Wine Industry*
*Journal.* Also annual wine industry directory,
books on viticulture & oenology & an annual
wine industry yearbook. Designs & builds web-
sites for wineries.
Subjects: Agriculture, Wine & Spirits, Wine &
Viticulture Industries
ISBN Prefix(es): 1-875130
Number of titles published annually: 5 Print
Total Titles: 25 Print; 1 CD-ROM

**Wisdom Press,** *imprint of* Desbooks Pty Ltd

**Wizard Books Pty Ltd+**
PO Box 304, Ballarat, Victoria 3353
*Tel:* (03) 5332 3435 *Fax:* (03) 5331 1488
*E-mail:* admin@wizardbooks.com.au
*Web Site:* www.wizardbooks.com.au
*Key Personnel*
Dir & International Rights: Richard McRoberts
Dir: Valerie McRoberts
Founded: 1991
Membership(s): Australian Publishers Association
(APA).
Subjects: Drama, Theater, Education, Literature,
Literary Criticism, Essays, Science (General)
ISBN Prefix(es): 1-875739; 1-876367
Distributed by Claire Publications (UK); EPB
(Singapore)

**Women's Health Advisory Service+**
PO Box 689, Camden, NSW 2570
*Tel:* (02) 4655 8855; (02) 4655 4666 *Fax:* (02)
4655 8699
*Web Site:* www.whas.com.au
*Key Personnel*
Head of Company: Jacqui Comley
Author: Sandra Cabot *E-mail:* sandracabot@
whas.com.au
Founded: 1990
Subjects: Health, Nutrition, Women's Studies,
Weight Loss
ISBN Prefix(es): 0-646
Total Titles: 10 Print
*Associate Companies:* Health Direction Pty Ltd;
SCB International
*U.S. Office(s):* SCB International Inc *Tel:* 602-
860-4299
Distributed by Ten Speed Press

**Woodlands Publications**
9 Bryant St, Tighes Hill, NSW 2297
*Tel:* (02) 4969 3961 *Fax:* (02) 4962 3162
*E-mail:* woodlands@whopres.com.au
*Web Site:* www.woodlandspublications.com
*Key Personnel*
Contact: A N Bendeich
Founded: 1982
Subjects: Business, Career Development, Commu-
nications, Education, Finance, Travel
ISBN Prefix(es): 1-875457; 0-9593057

**Word of Life Distributors Pty Ltd,** *imprint of*
Rainbow Book Agencies Pty Ltd

**Workaway Guides**
PO Box 206, Tugun, Qld 4224
*Tel:* (04) 1621 4257
*E-mail:* workaway@bigpond.com
*Web Site:* www.users.bigpond.com/workaway
*Key Personnel*
Contact: Karen Halliday

**Worsley Press+**
37 Latrobe St, Mentone, Victoria 3194

*Tel:* (03) 9583-0788 *Fax:* (03) 9583-0788
*E-mail:* info@worsleypress.com
*Web Site:* www.worsleypress.com
*Key Personnel*
Owner, Publisher & International Rights: Geoff
Heard *E-mail:* gheard@worsleypress.com
Founded: 1991
Specialize in books on publication production.
Subjects: Business, How-to, Publishing & Book
Trade Reference
ISBN Prefix(es): 1-875750
Number of titles published annually: 3 Print
Total Titles: 10 Print
Distributed by Eyelevel Books (UK); Florida
Academic Press (North America)

**Wrightbooks,** *imprint of* John Wiley & Sons
Australia, Ltd

**Wrightbooks Pty Ltd+**
Imprint of John Wiley & Sons Australia Ltd
PO Box 270, Elsternwick, Victoria 3185
*Tel:* (03) 9532 7082 *Toll Free Tel:* 800 777 474
*Fax:* (03) 9532 7082 *Toll Free Fax:* 800 802
258
*E-mail:* custservice@johnwiley.com.au
*Web Site:* www.wrightbooks.com.au
*Key Personnel*
Man Dir: Geoff Wright
Publisher: Lesley A Beaumont
Founded: 1988
Membership(s): ABPA.
Subjects: Business, Career Development, Finance,
Management, Real Estate, Self-Help
ISBN Prefix(es): 0-947351; 1-875857; 1-876627
Total Titles: 90 Print

**Yanagang Publishing**
41 Beaufort Rd, Croydon, Victoria 3136
*Tel:* (03) 9870-3052 *Fax:* (03) 9876-1853
*E-mail:* gallerywithoutwalls@hotmail.com
*Key Personnel*
Contact: Dindy Vaughan
Subjects: Art, Environmental Studies, Music,
Dance, Poetry
ISBN Prefix(es): 0-9588046; 0-9577974; 0-
9577975
Number of titles published annually: 2 Print
*Orders to:* PO Box 668, Ringwood, Qld 3134

**Young Explorer,** *imprint of* Heinemann Library

**Zephyr Press,** *imprint of* Hawker Brownlow

**Zoe Publishing Pty Ltd+**
PO Box 77, Tugun, Qld 4224
*Tel:* (07) 5534 1522 *Fax:* (07) 5534 1502
*E-mail:* zoemkt@onthenet.com.au
*Key Personnel*
Contact: Tim McClymont
Founded: 1995
Subjects: Child Care & Development, Health, Nu-
trition, Parenting & Mother & Child Health
Guide
ISBN Prefix(es): 0-9586581

# Austria

## General Information

*Capital:* Vienna
*Language:* German, small Croat & Slovene
speaking minorities
*Religion:* Predominantly Roman Catholic, some
Protestant and Muslim
*Population:* 8.1 million

*Bank Hours:* 0800-1230, 1330-1500 Monday-
Wednesday, Friday; 0800-1230, 1300-1730
Thursday
*Shop Hours:* 0800-1800 Monday-Friday; 0800-
1200 or 1300 Saturday
*Currency:* 100 Eurocents = 1 Euro; 13.7603
schillings = 1 Euro
*Export/Import Information:* Import licenses not
required for books. No exchange controls. 10%
VAT on books.
*Copyright:* UCC, Berne, Florence (see Copyright
Conventions, pg xi)

**Aarachne Verlag+**
Vergengasse 6, RH 14, 1220 Vienna
*Tel:* (01) 2855353 *Fax:* (01) 2855353
*E-mail:* spinne@aarachne.at
*Web Site:* www.aarachne.at
*Key Personnel*
Manager: Ernst Petz
Marketing: Astrid Rossbacher
Founded: 1992
Subjects: Drama, Theater, Ethnicity, Fiction, Hu-
man Relations, Journalism, Literature, Literary
Criticism, Essays, Mysteries, Science Fiction,
Fantasy
ISBN Prefix(es): 3-85255

**Abakus Verlag GmbH+**
Pezoltgasse 50, 5020 Salzburg
*Tel:* (0662) 632076 *Fax:* (0662) 8044137
Founded: 1979
Subjects: Environmental Studies, Language Arts,
Linguistics, Mathematics
ISBN Prefix(es): 3-7044

**Aeneas Verlagsgesellschaft GmbH+**
Hauptstr 38, 2340 Moedling
*Tel:* (02236) 25422
*Key Personnel*
Manager: Johanna Theurer; Hermann Theurer
Founded: 1989
ISBN Prefix(es): 3-85065

**Agens-Werk, Geyer & Reisser, Druck und**
**Verlagsgesellschaft mbH**
Arbeitergasse 1-7, 1051 Vienna
*Tel:* (01) 5445641-46 *Fax:* (01) 5445641-46
*E-mail:* prepress@agens-werk.at
*Key Personnel*
Man Dir: Friedrich Geyer
ISBN Prefix(es): 3-7033; 3-85202

**Akademische Druck-u Verlagsanstalt Dr Paul**
**Struzl GmbH+**
Auersperggasse 12, 8010 Graz
Mailing Address: Postfach 598, 8011 Graz
*Tel:* (0316) 3644 *Fax:* (0316) 3644-24
*E-mail:* info@adeva.com
*Web Site:* www.adeva.com *Cable:* ADEVA GRAZ
*Key Personnel*
General Manager: Dr Hubert C Konrad
*Tel:* (0316) 936 44-50 *E-mail:* konrad@adeva.
com
Editor: Dr Christine Brandstaetter *Tel:* (0316)
36 44-34 *E-mail:* bradstaetter@adeva.com;
Gerhard Lechner *Tel:* (0316) 36 44-45
*E-mail:* lechner@adeva.com
Founded: 1949
Specializes in Facsimile.
Subjects: Anthropology, Archaeology, Art, Bi-
ography, Language Arts, Linguistics, Military
Science, Music, Dance, Regional Interests
ISBN Prefix(es): 3-201; 3-900144
Number of titles published annually: 10 Print
Total Titles: 2,000 Print
Subsidiaries: Codices Selecti

**Alekto Verlag GmbH+**
St Veiter Ring 22, 9020 Klagenfurt

Mailing Address: Postfach 502, 9020 Klagenfurt
*Tel:* (0463) 591180 *Fax:* (0463) 593217
*E-mail:* bali@bali.co.at
*Key Personnel*
Man Dir: Stefan Zefferer *E-mail:* stefan.zefferer@
bali.co.at
Manager & Marketing Dir: Harry Haberl
*E-mail:* harry.haberl@bali.co.at
Founded: 1986
Specialize in Austrian Literature.
Subjects: History, Poetry, Politics
ISBN Prefix(es): 3-900743; 3-902202
Total Titles: 200 Print; 5 CD-ROM; 5 E-Book
Foreign Rep(s): VG Dr Glas

**Amalthea-Verlag**
Subsidiary of Buchverlage Langen-Mueller/Her-
big
Am Heumarkt 19, 1030 Vienna
*Tel:* (01) 712 35 60 *Fax:* (01) 713 89 95
*E-mail:* amalthea.verlag@amalthea.at
*Web Site:* www.amalthea.at
*Key Personnel*
Greschf: Dr Herbert Fleissner
International Rights: Dorothea Esthermann
Founded: 1917
Membership(s): Buchverlage Ullstein Langen
Mueller/Herbig, Germany.
Subjects: Art, Fiction, Music, Dance
ISBN Prefix(es): 3-85002
*Associate Companies:* Ullstein Langen Mueller

**Andreas und Andreas Verlagsbuchhandel+**
Hans-Seebachstr 10, 5023 Salzburg
*Tel:* (0662) 6575-0 *Fax:* (0662) 6575-5 *Cable:*
ANDREASVERLAG SALZBURG
*Key Personnel*
Publisher: Ingrid Andreas; Wolf-Dietrich Andreas
Dir: Franz Pemwieser
Founded: 1956
Subjects: Fiction
ISBN Prefix(es): 3-85012
*Branch Office(s)*
Andreas und Andreas Verlagsbuchhandel
Zweigniederlassing, 8228 Freilassingy, Ger-
many
Andreas und Andreas Verlagsanstal, 9490 Vaduz,
Liechtenstein
Oskar Andreas Nachfolger Herzog & Co, Reise-
und Versandbuchhande, Parhamerpl 9, 1170
Vienna

**Annette Betz**, *imprint of* Verlag Carl Ueberreuter
GmbH

**Verlag Der Apfel+**
Schottenfeldgasse 65, 1070 Vienna
*Tel:* (01) 52 661 52 *Fax:* (01) 52 287 18
*Key Personnel*
Man Dir: Thomas C Cubasch
Founded: 1984
Subjects: Art, History, Literature, Literary Criti-
cism, Essays, Music, Dance, Arts Restoration
& Conservation, Musicology
ISBN Prefix(es): 3-85450
Number of titles published annually: 20 Print
Total Titles: 80 Print

**Astor-Verlag, Willibald Schlager+**
Rosentalgasse 5/1/5, 1140 Vienna
*Tel:* (01) 9144281 *Fax:* (01) 9144281
*Key Personnel*
Owner: Willi Schlager *E-mail:* willi.schlager@
chello.at
Founded: 1975
Subjects: Biography, Fiction, Humor, Literature,
Literary Criticism, Essays, Regional Interests
ISBN Prefix(es): 3-900277

**Autorensolidaritat - Verlag der
Interessengemeinschaft osterreichischer
Autorinnen und Autoren**
Literaturhaus, Seidengasse 13, 1070 Vienna
*Tel:* (01) 526 20 44-13 *Fax:* (01) 526 20 44-55
*E-mail:* ig@literaturhaus.at
*Key Personnel*
President: Milo Dor
Man Dir: Gerhard Ruiss
Founded: 1982
Subjects: Publishing & Book Trade Reference
ISBN Prefix(es): 3-419

**Verlag Alexander Bernhardt**
Vomperberg, 6134 Vomp/Tirol
*Tel:* (05242) 62131-0 *Fax:* (05242) 72801
*Key Personnel*
Contact: Siegfried Bernhardt
Founded: 1945
Subjects: Philosophy
ISBN Prefix(es): 3-87860
*Associate Companies:* Verlag der Stiftung
Gralsbotschaft GmbH, Lenzhalde 15, 70192
Stuttgart, Germany *E-mail:* info@gral.de *Web
Site:* www.gral.de
*U.S. Office(s):* Grail Foundation of America,
2081 Partridge Lane, Binghamton, NY 13903,
United States, Richard H Gehl
Grail Movement of America, 7204 Lucern Court,
Charlotte, NC 28277, United States, Emanuel
O'Biorah
*Orders to:* Verlag der Stiftung Gralsbotschaft
GmbH, Schuckerstr 8, 71254 Ditzingen, Ger-
many

**Bethania Verlag+**
Theresiengasse 33, 1180 Vienna
*Tel:* (01) 6672216
*Key Personnel*
Contact: Helene Mirtl
Founded: 1982
Subjects: Biological Sciences, Chemistry, Chemi-
cal Engineering, Philosophy, Physical Sciences,
Science (General)
ISBN Prefix(es): 3-900085

**Annette Betz Verlag im Verlag Carl
Ueberreuter+**
Alser Str 24, 1091 Vienna
Mailing Address: Postfach 306, 1091 Vienna
*Tel:* (01) 40 444-172 *Fax:* (01) 40 444-5
*Web Site:* www.annettebetz.com; www.
ueberreuter.at
*Telex:* 114802 *Cable:* UEBER A
*Key Personnel*
Man Dir: Dr Fritz Panzer; Dr Richard Starkel
Editorial: Irmgard Harrer
Contact: Dr Susanne Czeitschner *Tel:* (01) 40
444-165 *E-mail:* czeitschner@ueberreuter.at
Founded: 1962
ISBN Prefix(es): 3-219
*Parent Company:* Verlag Carl Ueberreuter
*Shipping Address:* Dr Franz Hain Ver-
lagsauscieferung, Dr Otto-Neurath-Gasse 5,
1220 Vienna *Tel:* (01) 2826565 *Fax:* (01)
2825282
*Warehouse:* Dr Franz Hain Verlagsauscieferung,
Dr Otto-Neurath-Gasse 5, 1220 Vienna

**Bibliothek der Provinz**, see Richard Pils
Publication PN°1

**Der Baum Wolfgang Biedermann Verlag+**
Apollogasse 14, 1070 Vienna
*Tel:* (01) 526 2720
*Key Personnel*
President & Publisher: Wolfgang Bedermann
Subjects: Literature, Literary Criticism, Essays
ISBN Prefix(es): 3-901133

**Boehlau Verlag GmbH & Co KG+**
Sachsenplatz 4-6, 1201 Vienna
Mailing Address: Postfach 87, 1201 Vienna
*Tel:* (01) 330 24 27 *Fax:* (01) 330 24 32
*E-mail:* boehlau@boehlau.at
*Web Site:* www.boehlau.at
*Telex:* 114506 Spriw A
*Key Personnel*
Man Dir: Dr Peter Rauch *E-mail:* peter.rauch@
boehlau.at
Editorial: Dr Eva Reinhold-Weisz *E-mail:* eva.
reinholdweisz@boehlau.at
Press: Elisabeth Dechant *E-mail:* elisabeth.
dechant@boehlau.at
Production: Ulrike Dietmayer *E-mail:* ulrike.
dietmayer@boehlau.at
Marketing Sales: Roland Tomrle *E-mail:* roland.
tomrle@boehlau.at
Founded: 1947
Subjects: Art, Government, Political Science, His-
tory, Language Arts, Linguistics, Law, Science
(General), Social Sciences, Sociology, Women's
Studies
ISBN Prefix(es): 3-205
*Associate Companies:* Boehlau-Verlag GmbH &
Cie, Cologne, Germany
*Orders to:* Springer Verlagsauslieferung, Postfach
8, 1201 Vienna *Tel:* (01) 3302415

**Bohmann Druck und Verlag GmbH & Co KG**
Leberstr 122, 1110 Vienna
*Tel:* (01) 74095 114 *Fax:* (01) 74095 111
*E-mail:* g.huber.zv@bohmann.at
*Web Site:* www.bohmann.co.at
*Key Personnel*
President Supervisory Board: Dr Rudolf Bohmann
Manager: Dr Gabriele Ambros
Founded: 1936
Subjects: Automotive, Business, Computer Sci-
ence, Environmental Studies, Transportation,
Travel
ISBN Prefix(es): 3-901983

**Braintrust Marketing Services Ges mbH
Verlag**
Schopenhauerstr 36, 1180 Vienna
*Tel:* (01) 40416-0 *Fax:* (01) 40416-33
*E-mail:* braintrust@magnet.at
*Web Site:* www.braintrust.at
*Key Personnel*
Man Dir: Thomas Stern *E-mail:* stern@braintrust.
at
Dir: Christian Seifert *E-mail:* seifert@braintrust.at
Founded: 1989
Subjects: Career Development, Education, Man-
agement
ISBN Prefix(es): 3-901116

**Christian Brandstaetter Verlagsgesellschaft
mbH+**
Schwarzenbergstr 5, 1015 Vienna
*Tel:* (01) 512 15 43 *Fax:* (01) 512 15 43-231
*E-mail:* cbv@oebv.co.at
*Web Site:* www.brandstaetter-verlag.at
*Key Personnel*
Publisher: Dr Christian Brandstaetter
Manager: Mag Walter Amon; Dr Robert Sedlacek
Founded: 1982
Subjects: Architecture & Interior Design, Art, Bi-
ography, Photography, Regional Interests
ISBN Prefix(es): 3-85447; 3-206; 3-85498
Total Titles: 236 Print
*Parent Company:* Oesterreichischer Bundesverlag
GmbH

**BSE Verlag Dr Bernhard Schuttengruber+**
Klosterwiegasse 52, 8010 Graz
*Tel:* (0316) 839600; (0316) 283170
Founded: 1984
Subjects: History, Poetry
ISBN Prefix(es): 3-900542

**Buchkultur Verlags GmbH Zeitschrift fuer Literatur & Kunst**
Huetteldorferstr 26, 1150 Vienna
*Tel:* (01) 7863380 *Fax:* (01) 7863380-10
*E-mail:* office@buchkultur.net
*Web Site:* www.buchkultur.net
*Key Personnel*
Geschf: Michael Schnepf
Founded: 1989
Subjects: Communications, Journalism, Literature, Literary Criticism, Essays, Publishing & Book Trade Reference, Regional Interests
ISBN Prefix(es): 3-901052
*Branch Office(s)*
Birkenstr 7, 85774 Unterfoehring, Germany
*Fax:* (089) 958216-92

**Fachverlag fur Burgerinformation, Eigenvelag+**
Grabenstr 117, 8010 Graz
*Tel:* (0316) 686727 *Fax:* (0316) 6867274
*E-mail:* fachverlag@sime.com
*Key Personnel*
Manager: Alfred Steingruber
Founded: 1986
Subjects: Public Administration
ISBN Prefix(es): 3-85363

**Camera Austria+**
Lendkai 1, 8020 Graz
*Tel:* (0316) 81 55 50-0 *Fax:* (0316) 81 55 50-9
*E-mail:* office@camera-austria.at
*Web Site:* www.camera-austria.at
*Key Personnel*
Publisher: Manfred Willmann
Editor: Christine Frisinghelli; Maren Luebbke
Founded: 1980
Subjects: Art, Photography
ISBN Prefix(es): 3-900508; 3-9501098

**Carinthia Verlag**
Voelkermarkter Ring 25, 9020 Klagenfurt
*Tel:* (0463) 50 12 20-220 *Fax:* (0463) 50 12 20-214
*Web Site:* www.verlag.carinthia.com
*Key Personnel*
Dir: Karin Waldner *Tel:* (0463) 50 12 20-210
  *E-mail:* karin.waldner@carinthia.com
Founded: 1893
Subjects: Archaeology, Art, Cookery, History, Religion - Other
ISBN Prefix(es): 3-85378; 3-900184
Number of titles published annually: 20 Print
Total Titles: 120 Print

**CEEBA Publications Antenne d'Autriche+**
2340 Saint Gabriel, Moedling
*Tel:* (02236) 803115 *Fax:* (02236) 8033
*E-mail:* svd@steyler.at
*Web Site:* www.ceeba.at
*Key Personnel*
Man Dir, Editorial: Dr Hermann Hochegger
  *E-mail:* hochegger@steyler.at
Founded: 1965
Specialize in paperback, rituals. Also a study center for traditional culture of Black Africa & Haiti.
Subjects: Agriculture, Anthropology, Art, Ethnicity, Health, Nutrition, History, Language Arts, Linguistics, Literature, Literary Criticism, Essays, Psychology, Psychiatry, Religion - Other, Social Sciences, Sociology
ISBN Prefix(es): 3-902011
Number of titles published annually: 4 Print
Total Titles: 2 Print
*Parent Company:* CEEBA, Bandundu, Kongo
Foreign Rep(s): Antenne d'Antride

**Compass-Verlag GmbH**
Matznergasse 17, 1141 Vienna
Mailing Address: Postfach 160, 1141 Vienna
*Tel:* (01) 981 16-113; (01) 981 16-114 *Fax:* (01) 981 16-118; (01) 981 16-108
*E-mail:* hfu@compass.at; ssc@compass.at; office@compass.at
*Web Site:* www.compass.at; www.cmd.at
*Key Personnel*
Man Dir: Werner Futter; Horst Dolezal
Sales Dir: Michael Bayer *E-mail:* mba@compass.al
Founded: 1867
Specialize in Internet databases.
Membership(s): OeAVV, EAVV.
Subjects: Business, Economics, Finance
ISBN Prefix(es): 3-85041
Number of titles published annually: 4 Print; 2 CD-ROM
Total Titles: 4 Print
Subsidiaries: Comp Almanach Kft

**Cura Verlag GmbH**
Beatrixgasse 32, 1037 Vienna
Mailing Address: Postfach 49, Vienna
*Tel:* (01) 7136480 *Fax:* (01) 7126258; (01) 7126219
*Key Personnel*
Man Dir: Brigitte Podoschek
Publicity Manager: Eva M Plattner
Subjects: Education, Regional Interests, Religion - Other
ISBN Prefix(es): 3-7027

**Czernin Verlag Ltd+**
Kupkagasse 4, 1080 Vienna
*Tel:* (01) 403 35 63 *Fax:* (01) 403 35 63-15
*E-mail:* office@czernin-verlag.com
*Web Site:* www.czernin-verlag.com
*Key Personnel*
Publisher: Hubertus Czernin *E-mail:* hoz@czernin-verlag.com
Production: Klaus Gadermaier
  *E-mail:* gadermaier@czernin-verlag.com
Marketing & Press: Benedikt Foeger
  *E-mail:* foeger@czernin-verlag.com
Founded: 1999
Subjects: Cookery, Film, Video, History, Law, Literature, Literary Criticism, Essays, Poetry
ISBN Prefix(es): 3-7076
Number of titles published annually: 15 Print
Total Titles: 120 Print

**DachsVerlag GmbH+**
Praterstra 25/92, 1020 Vienna
*Tel:* (01) 285 22 05-0 *Fax:* (01) 285 22 05-15
*E-mail:* office@dachs.at
*Web Site:* www.dachs.at
*Key Personnel*
Man Dir: Dr Hubert Hladej *E-mail:* hladej.sen@dachs.at
Founded: 1921
Subjects: Art, Education, Ethnicity, Literature, Literary Criticism, Essays, Music, Dance, Psychology, Psychiatry, Social Sciences, Sociology
ISBN Prefix(es): 3-900763; 3-85191

**Danubia Werbung und Verlagsservice**
Viehmarktgasse 4, 1030 Vienna
*Tel:* (01) 792666 *Fax:* (01) 792666443
*Key Personnel*
Man Dir: N Schnabl
Publicity Dir: Dr P Wasservogel
Founded: 1952
Subjects: Art, Fiction, Science (General)
ISBN Prefix(es): 3-7006; 3-85044

**dbv-Druck Beratungs-und Verlags GmbH Verlag fur die Technische Universitaet Graz+**
Geidorfguertel 20, 8010 Graz
*Tel:* (0316) 38 30 33 *Fax:* (0316) 38 30 43
*E-mail:* office@dbv.at
*Web Site:* www.dbv.at

*Key Personnel*
Man Dir: Gerhard E Erker
Founded: 1976
ISBN Prefix(es): 3-7041

**Denkmayr GmbH Druck & Verlag+**
Reslweg 3, 4020 Linz
Mailing Address: Postfach 14, 4020 Linz
*Tel:* (0732) 654511 *Fax:* (0732) 65451117
*E-mail:* denkmayr.linz@magnet.at
*Key Personnel*
Contact: Ernst Denkmayr
International Rights: Regina Noebauer
Founded: 1989
Subjects: Poetry, Regional Interests, Self-Help
ISBN Prefix(es): 3-901838; 3-901123

**Verlag Harald Denzel, Auto- und Freizeitfuehrer+**
Maximilianstr 9, 6020 Innsbruck
*Tel:* (0512) 586880 *Fax:* (0512) 586880
*E-mail:* denzel-verlag@web.de
*Web Site:* members.telering.at/denzel-verlag
*Key Personnel*
Contact: Harald Denzel
Founded: 1952
Subjects: Geography, Geology, Outdoor Recreation, Travel, Illustrated Guide Books
ISBN Prefix(es): 3-85047

**Deuticke im Paul Zsolnay Verlag+**
Prinz-Eugen-Str 30, 1040 Vienna
*Tel:* (01) 505 76 61-0 *Fax:* (01) 505 76 61-10
*E-mail:* info@deuticke.at
*Web Site:* www.deuticke.at
*Key Personnel*
Program Manager: Dr Martina Schmidt *Tel:* (01) 505 76 61-25 *E-mail:* schmidt@zsolnay.at
Marketing & Sales: Michaela Puchberger *Tel:* (01) 505 76 61-24 *E-mail:* puchberger@zsolnay.at
Press & Public Relations: Friederike Rumschoettel *Tel:* (01) 505 76 61-28 *E-mail:* rumschoettel@zsolnay.at
Founded: 1878
Specialize in psychology.
Subjects: Literature, Literary Criticism, Essays, Mysteries, Nonfiction (General), Regional Interests
ISBN Prefix(es): 3-7005; 3-552
Total Titles: 629 Print
*Orders to:* Verlegerdienst Muenchen, Gutenbergstr 1, 82205 Gilching, Germany *Fax:* (081) 05 388-210

**Development News Ltd**
Pragerstr 92, Stg 4, Vienna
*Tel:* (0222) 3880324 *Toll Free Tel:* (0222) 3880324
*Key Personnel*
Man Dir & Publisher: Dr Yemi D Ogunyemi
Editorial Manager: Simon Adewale Ebine
Publications Manager: Willy Bruckner
Publicity Executive: Pius Eyitayo Ogunyemi
Sales Executive: T A Ogunyemi
Founded: 1983
Also promotes Nigerian/African literatures through seminars, lectures, symposia, conferences, book presentations & writing workshops.
Subjects: Agriculture, Animals, Pets, Anthropology, Child Care & Development, Communications, Developing Countries, Education, English as a Second Language, Ethnicity, Fiction, Government, Political Science, History, Journalism, Literature, Literary Criticism, Essays, Nonfiction (General), Poetry, Regional Interests, Religion - Other, Social Sciences, Sociology, Women's Studies
ISBN Prefix(es): 978-2843
*U.S. Office(s):* Diaspora Press of America, 91 Ames St, Box C340, Boston, MA 02124-3033, United States

**Diotima Presse+**
Bachgasse 22, 3200 Obergrafendorf
*Tel:* (043) 2747-8528 *Fax:* (043) 2747-8528
*E-mail:* buecher4web@diotimapresse.com
*Web Site:* www.diotimapresse.com
Founded: 2000
Handcrafted books with mainly original illustrations.
Subjects: Philosophy, Poetry
Number of titles published annually: 6 Print
Total Titles: 23 Print

**Ludwig Doblinger (Bernhard Herzmansky) Musikverlag KG**
Dorotheergasse 10, 1010 Vienna
*Tel:* (01) 515 03-0 *Fax:* (01) 515 03-51
*E-mail:* music@doblinger.at
*Web Site:* www.doblinger.at
*Key Personnel*
Man Dir: Helmuth Pany
Sales Manager: Peter Pany *E-mail:* peter.pany@doblinger.at
Rights & Licensing: Christine Prindl
Advertising Manager: Dr Christian Heindl
    *E-mail:* christian.heindl@doblinger.at
Founded: 1876
Specializes in music-notes & books.
Subjects: Music, Dance
ISBN Prefix(es): 3-900695; 3-900035
Distributor for Musikwissenschaftlicher Verlag Wien (MWV)
*Bookshop(s):* Musikhaus Doblinger, Vienna

**Doecker Verlag GmbH & Co KG+**
Hintzerstr 11/3, 1030 Vienna
Mailing Address: Postfach 91, 1030 Vienna
*Tel:* (01) 7159200 *Fax:* (01) 715920076
*E-mail:* doecker@ping.at
*Key Personnel*
Man Dir, Production & Rights & Permissions: Ulrike Doecker
Editorial: Peter Horn
Sales, Publicity: Petra Hartlieb
Founded: 1980
Subjects: Archaeology, Biography, Education, Fiction, Film, Video, History, Journalism, Labor, Industrial Relations, Outdoor Recreation, Women's Studies
ISBN Prefix(es): 3-85115

**Literature Verlag Droschl+**
Alberstr 18, 8010 Graz
*Tel:* (0316) 32-64-04 *Fax:* (0316) 32-40-71
*E-mail:* droschl@droschl.com; literaturverlag@droschl.com
*Web Site:* www.droschl.com
*Key Personnel*
Contact: Dr Rainer Gotz *E-mail:* rainer@droschl.com
Founded: 1978
Publishing honor for contemporary European literature
Books & Audio CD's.
Subjects: Art, Drama, Theater, Literature, Literary Criticism, Essays, Poetry
ISBN Prefix(es): 3-85420
Number of titles published annually: 18 Print
Total Titles: 300 Print; 5 Audio
Imprints: Edition Neue Text

**Edition Neue Text**, *imprint of* Literature Verlag Droschl

**Edition S der OSD+**
Rennweg 16, 1037 Vienna
*Tel:* (01) 61077-315 *Fax:* (01) 61077-419
*E-mail:* office@verlagoesterreich.at
*Telex:* 131 805 *Cable:* OESTAATSDRUCK WIEN
*Key Personnel*
Man Dir: Dr Manfred A Schmid

Founded: 1985
Subjects: Criminology, Fiction, Film, Video, History, Human Relations, Literature, Literary Criticism, Essays, Maritime, Parapsychology
ISBN Prefix(es): 3-7046; 3-85201
*Parent Company:* Oesterreichische Staatsdruckerei

**Ennsthaler GesmbH & Co KG+**
Stadtplatz 26, 4400 Steyr
*Tel:* (07252) 52053-10 *Fax:* (07252) 52053-16
*E-mail:* buero@ennsthaler.at
*Web Site:* www.ennsthaler.at
Founded: 1880
Subjects: Cookery, Health, Nutrition, History, Medicine, Nursing, Dentistry, Poetry, Regional Interests, Religion - Catholic, Theology
ISBN Prefix(es): 3-85068

**Edition Ergo Sum+**
Berggasse 31, 2391 Kaltenleutgeben
*Tel:* (02238) 77078 *Fax:* (02238) 77076
*E-mail:* apverlag@magnet.at
*Key Personnel*
Owner: Anna Pichler
Owner & International Rights: Heinz Lasta
Founded: 1989
Subjects: Environmental Studies, Fiction, Nonfiction (General), Philosophy, Poetry
ISBN Prefix(es): 3-901087; 3-902008
Distributed by Dessauer; EDIS

**Evangelischer Presseverband in Osterreich**
Ungargasse 9, 1030 Vienna
*Tel:* (01) 712 54 61 *Fax:* (01) 712 54 75
*E-mail:* epv@evang.at
*Key Personnel*
Man Dir: Paul Weiland
Founded: 1925
ISBN Prefix(es): 3-85073
*Warehouse:* Ungargasse 12, 1030 Vienna

**Fassbaender Verlag**
Lichtgasse 10, 1150 Vienna
*Tel:* (01) 8923546 *Fax:* (01) 8923546-22
*E-mail:* mail@fassbaender.com
*Web Site:* www.fassbaender.com
*Key Personnel*
Executive: Ernst Becvar *Tel:* (01) 8923546-12
    *E-mail:* becvar-senior@inode.at
Founded: 1987
Specialize in Literature, Literary Criticism.
Subjects: History, Language Arts, Linguistics, Science (General)
ISBN Prefix(es): 3-900538; 3-900338
Number of titles published annually: 5 Print
Total Titles: 70 Print

**Ferdinand Berger und Sohne**
Wienerstr 80, 3580 Horn
*Tel:* (02982) 4161-332 *Fax:* (02982) 4161-382
*E-mail:* druckerei.office@berger.at
*Web Site:* www.berger.at
*Telex:* 78613 *Cable:* BERGER HORN
*Key Personnel*
Man Dir: Peter Berger *E-mail:* peter.jun@berger.at
Founded: 1868
Subjects: Anthropology, Archaeology, Art, Natural History
ISBN Prefix(es): 3-85028
*Branch Office(s)*
Pulverturmasse 3, 1090 Vienna *Tel:* (01) 313 35-0 *Fax:* (01) 313 35-19

**Folio Verlagsgesellschaft mbH+**
Gruengasse 9, 1050 Vienna
*Tel:* (01) 5813708-0 *Fax:* (01) 5813708-20
*E-mail:* office@folioverlag.com; folio@thing.at; folio@dialogon.at
*Web Site:* www.folioverlag.com/books.php
Founded: 1992

ISBN Prefix(es): 3-85256
Number of titles published annually: 30 Print
Total Titles: 130 Print
*Branch Office(s)*
Mitterweg 16a, 39100 Bozen, Italy *Tel:* (0471) 971323 *Fax:* (0471) 971603

**Fremdenverkehrs Aktiengesellschaft+**
Schwarzstr 15, Postfach 6, 5024 Salzburg
*Tel:* (0662) 88861011 *Fax:* (0662) 8886202
*Telex:* 633588 *Cable:* BERGLANDBUCH SALZBURG
*Key Personnel*
Man Dir: Alfred Schulz
Founded: 1929
Subjects: Fiction, History, Regional Interests, Science (General)
ISBN Prefix(es): 3-7023
*Orders to:* Morawa & Co, Hackingerstr 52, A-1140

**Freytag-Berndt und Artaria, Kartographische Anstalt+**
Brunner-Str 69, 1231 Vienna
*Tel:* (01) 869 90 90-83 *Fax:* (01) 869 90 90-61
*E-mail:* office@freytagberndt.at
*Telex:* 133526
*Key Personnel*
Chairman: Bernd Mahr
Man Dir: Christian Halbwachs
Sales Manager: Wolfgang Kaiser
Founded: 1770
Subjects: Geography, Geology
ISBN Prefix(es): 3-85084; 3-7079
*Bookshop(s):* Wilhelm-Greil Str 15, 6020 Innsbruck; Kohlmarkt 9, 1010 Vienna; Schottenfeldgasse 62, Postfach 169, 1070 Vienna

**Georg Fromme und Co**
Arbeitergasse 1-7, 1051 Vienna
*Tel:* (01) 5445641 *Fax:* (01) 544564166
*Telex:* 111969
*Key Personnel*
Man Dir: Friedrich Geyer
Founded: 1748
Subjects: Science (General)
ISBN Prefix(es): 3-85086

**Edition Dr Heinrich Fuchs**
Thimiggasse 82, 1180 Vienna
*Tel:* (01) 4792381 *Fax:* (01) 4792381
*E-mail:* edition.h.fuchs@aon.at
Subjects: Art
ISBN Prefix(es): 3-85390

**Gangan Verlag+**
Rainleiten 62, 8045 Graz
*Tel:* (0316) 670 4090 *Fax:* (0316) 670 4096
*Web Site:* www.gangan.com
*Key Personnel*
Publisher: Gerald Ganglbauer *E-mail:* gerald@gangan.com
Distributor: Guenter Brodtrager
    *E-mail:* gbrodtrager@greenbrains.com
Editor: Rudi Krausmann
Founded: 1985
Subjects: Literature, Literary Criticism, Essays
ISBN Prefix(es): 3-900530
Number of titles published annually: 2 E-Book
Total Titles: 24 Print; 12 E-Book
Imprints: GanGAROO (The OZlit Collection)
Subsidiaries: Gangan Books Australia
*Branch Office(s)*
15 Naranja Way, Portola Valley, CA 94028, United States, Contact: Janet Wells

**GanGAROO**, *imprint of* Gangan Verlag

**Gerold & Co**
Rathausstr 5, 1010 Vienna
*Tel:* (01) 532 0102 *Fax:* (01) 532 01 02-15; (01) 532 01 02-22

*E-mail:* office@gerold.at
*Web Site:* www.gerold.at
*Telex:* 847136157 Gerol; 76157 *Cable:*
  Geroldbuch Vienna
*Key Personnel*
Man Dir: Hans Neusser
Subjects: Language Arts, Linguistics, Philosophy
ISBN Prefix(es): 3-900190

**Verlag fuer Geschichte und Politik**
Neulinggasse 26/12, 1030 Vienna
*Tel:* (01) 712 62 58 *Fax:* (01) 712 62 58 19
*E-mail:* office@oldenbourg.at
*Key Personnel*
Man Dir: Dr Erika Ruedegger
Sales Dir: Gerda Adler
Publicity & Advertising: Dr Ursula Huber
  *E-mail:* ursula.huber@oldenbourg.co.at
Founded: 1947
Subjects: Economics, Government, Political Sci-
  ence, History, Social Sciences, Sociology
ISBN Prefix(es): 3-7028
*Associate Companies:* Verlag Oldenbourg

**Verlag Lynkeus/H Hakel Gesellschaft+**
Traisengasse 17/28, 1200 Vienna
*Tel:* (01) 7342294
*Key Personnel*
Man Dir: Emmerich Kolovic
Founded: 1988
Subjects: Biography, Fiction, Humor, Literature,
  Literary Criticism, Essays, Poetry
ISBN Prefix(es): 3-900924

**Globus Buchvertrieb**
Seilerstatte 22/1, 1010 Vienna
*Tel:* (01) 513 96 92 0 *Fax:* (01) 513 96 92 9
*Key Personnel*
General Manager: Hans Jauker; H Zaslawski
Founded: 1945
Firms are also general representatives & distribu-
  tors.
Subjects: Government, Political Science
ISBN Prefix(es): 3-85364

**Alois Goschl & Co**
Trummelhofgasse 12, 1190 Vienna
*Tel:* (01) 321180 *Fax:* (01) 651899
*Key Personnel*
Proprietor: Hiltraud Lechner
Founded: 1949
Subjects: Health, Nutrition, Psychology, Psychia-
  try, Veterinary Science
ISBN Prefix(es): 3-85096

**Edition Graphischer Zirkel**
Langegasse 14/44, 1080 Vienna
*Tel:* (01) 0277346615
Subjects: Art, Fiction, Literature, Literary Criti-
  cism, Essays, Poetry, Travel
ISBN Prefix(es): 3-900308

**Graz Stadtmuseum**
Sackstr 18, 8010 Graz
*Tel:* (0316) 822580-0 *Fax:* (0316) 822580-6
*Key Personnel*
Dir: Dr Guenther Dienes
Subjects: Art, History, Regional Interests
ISBN Prefix(es): 3-900764
Total Titles: 275 Print

**Guthmann & Peterson Liber Libri, Edition+**
Elsslergasse 17, 1130 Vienna
*Tel:* (01) 877 04 26 *Fax:* (01) 876 40 04
*E-mail:* verlag@guthmann-peterson.de
*Web Site:* www.guthmann-peterson.de
*Key Personnel*
Man Dir: W Peterson
Founded: 1988
Subjects: Developing Countries, Government, Po-
  litical Science, Literature, Literary Criticism,

Essays, Science (General), Social Sciences, So-
  ciology
ISBN Prefix(es): 3-900782; 3-85306; 3-85481
Divisions: Edition Garamond

**Hand-Presse**
Hottingergasse 41, 6020 Innsbruck
*Tel:* (0512) 87975
*Key Personnel*
Owner: Hans Augustin
ISBN Prefix(es): 3-900862

**Haymon-Verlag GesmbH+**
Kochstr 10, 6020 Innsbruck
*Tel:* (0512) 576300 *Fax:* (0512) 576300-14
*E-mail:* office@haymonverlag.at
*Web Site:* www.haymonverlag.at
*Key Personnel*
Man Dir & Rights & Permissions: Dr
  Michael Forcher *E-mail:* michael.forcher@
  haymonverlag.at
Sales & International Rights: Valerie Besl
  *Tel:* (0512) 567300-16 *E-mail:* valerie.besl@
  haymonverlag.at
Sales: Gerhard Roedlach *Tel:* (0512) 576300-11
  *E-mail:* gerhard.roedlach@haymonverlag.at
Production: Dr Benno Peter *Tel:* (0512) 576300-
  15 *E-mail:* bennopeter@haymonverlag.at
Founded: 1982
Subjects: Architecture & Interior Design, Art, Bi-
  ography, Cookery, Criminology, Fiction, His-
  tory, Literature, Literary Criticism, Essays,
  Mysteries, Philosophy, Social Sciences, Soci-
  ology
ISBN Prefix(es): 3-85218
Number of titles published annually: 25 Print
Total Titles: 350 Print

**Helbling Verlagsgesellschaft mbH**
Kaplanstr 9, 6063 Rum/Innsbruck
Mailing Address: Postfach 12, 6063 Rum/Inns-
  bruck
*Tel:* (0512) 262333-0 *Fax:* (0512) 262333-111
*E-mail:* office@helbling.co.at
*Web Site:* www.helbling.com
*Key Personnel*
President: Markus Spielmann
International Rights: Klaus Mayerl *E-mail:* k.
  mayerl@helbling.co.at
Founded: 1946
Specialize in choral music books.
Subjects: Education, English as a Second Lan-
  guage, Music, Dance, Choral Music
ISBN Prefix(es): 3-85061; 3-900590

**Verlag Herder & Co**, see Verlag Kerle im Verlag
  Herder & Co

**Hermagoras/Mohorjeva+**
Viktringer ring 26, 9020 Klagenfurt, Celovec
*Tel:* (0463) 56515 21 *Fax:* (0463) 514189
*E-mail:* office@mohorjeva.at
*Web Site:* www.mohorjeva.at
*Telex:* 422801
*Key Personnel*
Man Dir: Dr Anton Koren
Sales & Publicity: Karl Boehm; Janko Ferk
Editorial & Production: Franz Kattnig
Founded: 1851
Specializes in books in Slovenian & German.
ISBN Prefix(es): 3-85013; 3-900119
*Parent Company:* Mohorjeva Druzba/Hermagoras
  Gesellschaft
Subsidiaries: Korotan Import-Export GmbH

**Herold Business Data AG+**
Guntramsdorfer Str 105, 2340 Moedling
*Tel:* (02236) 401-0 *Fax:* (02236) 401-8
*E-mail:* kundendienst@herold.at
*Web Site:* www.herold.co.at
*Telex:* 114336 herol a

*Key Personnel*
Manager: Yon M Martinsen
Founded: 1918
Subjects: Marketing
ISBN Prefix(es): 3-85110

**Herold Druck-und Verlagsgesellschaft mbH+**
Spiegelgasse 3, 1014 Vienna
*Tel:* (01) 512350331 *Fax:* (01) 795 94-115
*Telex:* 111760 Wspro
*Key Personnel*
Man Dir: Franz Hoermann; Leopold Kurz
Founded: 1893
Subjects: Art, History, Religion - Catholic
ISBN Prefix(es): 3-7008; 3-9500004; 3-901628

**Johannes Heyn GmbH & Co KG**
Kramergasse 2-4, 9020 Klagenfurt
*Tel:* (0463) 54 2 49 *Fax:* (0463) 54 2 49-41
*E-mail:* buch@heyn.at
*Web Site:* www.heyn.at
*Telex:* 042401; 422401 *Cable:* Heyn Klagenfurt
*Key Personnel*
Editor: Bernhard Koessler
Founded: 1868
Subjects: Art, Biography, Fiction, History, How-
  to, Music, Dance, Poetry, Science (General)
ISBN Prefix(es): 3-85366; 3-7084
*Bookshop(s):* Buchhandlung Johannes Heyn

**Edition E Hilger**
Dorotheergasse 5, 1010 Vienna
*Tel:* (01) 512 53 15-0 *Fax:* (01) 513 91 26
*E-mail:* hilger@hilger.at
*Key Personnel*
Man Dir & Production: Ernst Hilger
Sales & Publicity: Monica Zimmermann
Founded: 1973
Subjects: Art
ISBN Prefix(es): 3-900318

**Verlag Hoelder-Pichler-Tempsky+**
Frankgasse 4, 1090 Vienna
*Tel:* (01) 401 36-139 *Fax:* (01) 401 36-128
*E-mail:* hpt@hpt.co.at
*Key Personnel*
Man Dir: Gustav Gloeckler
Founded: 1690
Subjects: Mathematics, Philosophy, Physics
ISBN Prefix(es): 3-7004; 3-209
Subsidiaries: hpt Verlagsges mbH & Co KG
*Warehouse:* Jochen-Rindt-Str 11, Postfach 107,
  1232 Vienna

**Dr Verena Hofstaetter**
Steinfeldgasse 5, 1190 Vienna
*Tel:* (01) 370 33 02 *Fax:* (01) 370 59 34
*E-mail:* verlag@vh-communications.at
Subjects: Communications, Film, Video, Market-
  ing, Social Sciences, Sociology
ISBN Prefix(es): 3-900936

**Hollinek Bruder & Co mbH**
  **Gesellschaftsdruckerei &**
  **Verlagsbuchhandring+**
Luisenstr 20, 3002 Purkersdorf
*Tel:* (02231) 67365 *Fax:* (02231) 67365
*E-mail:* hollinek@via.at
*Key Personnel*
Man Dir: R Hollinek
Founded: 1872
Subjects: Law
ISBN Prefix(es): 3-85119

**IAEA - International Atomic Energy Agency**
Division of Conference & Document Services,
  PO Box 100, 1400 Vienna
*Tel:* (01) 2600-0; (01) 2600-22530 *Fax:* (01)
  2600-7
*E-mail:* official.mail@iaea.org
*Web Site:* www.iaea.org/worldatom/Books

*Telex:* 112645 ATOM A
*Key Personnel*
Dir General: Dr Mohamed ElBaradei
Head, Publishing Section: Manfred F Boemeke
  *E-mail:* m.f.boemeke@iaea.org
Founded: 1957
Serves as the worlds central intergovernmental
  forum for scientific & technical cooperation in
  the nuclear field.
International Organization.
Subjects: Agriculture, Biological Sciences, Chem-
  istry, Chemical Engineering, Energy, Environ-
  mental Studies, Geography, Geology, Health,
  Nutrition, Law, Physical Sciences, Physics,
  Technology, Veterinary Science, Nuclear Sci-
  ence
ISBN Prefix(es): 92-0
Number of titles published annually: 40 Print; 5
  CD-ROM
Total Titles: 2,000 Print; 3 CD-ROM

**Ibera VerlagsgesmbH+**
Hegelgasse 15, 1010 Vienna
*Tel:* (01) 513 19 72 *Fax:* (01) 513 19 72-28
*E-mail:* presse@ibera.at
*Web Site:* www.ibera.at
*Key Personnel*
Manager: Brigitte Strobele *E-mail:* strobele@
  ibera.at
Press: Simon Hoeller *E-mail:* hoeller@ibera.at
Sales: Matthias Strobele *E-mail:* sales@ibera.at
Subjects: Nonfiction (General)
ISBN Prefix(es): 3-900436; 3-85052
Distributed by Herold Verlagsauslieferung GmbH
  (Germany); Mohr-Morawa

**IG Autorinnen Autoren** (Austrian Author's
  Association)
im Literaturhaus, Seidengasse 13, 1070 Vienna
*Tel:* (01) 526 20 44-13 *Fax:* (01) 526 20 44-55
*E-mail:* ig@literaturhaus.at
*Web Site:* www.literaturhaus.at/lh/ig
*Key Personnel*
President: Milo Dor
Vice President: Peter Turrini; Anna Mitgutsch
Man Dir: Gerhard Ruiss *Tel:* (01) 526 20 44-35
Founded: 1971
Subjects: Publishing & Book Trade Reference
ISBN Prefix(es): 3-900419

**IIASA**, see International Institute for Applied
  Systems Analysis (IIASA)

**Innverlag + Gatt+**
Hunoldstr 12, 6020 Innsbruck
*Tel:* (0512) 34 53 31 *Fax:* (0512) 34 12 90
*E-mail:* innverlag@tirol.com; info@innverlag.at
*Web Site:* www.innverlag.at *Cable:* INNVERLAG
  INNSBRUCK
*Key Personnel*
Production: Klaus Hagleitner
Sales: Manfred Hagleitner
Founded: 1947
Subjects: History, Public Administration, Sports,
  Athletics
ISBN Prefix(es): 3-85123
*Bookshop(s):* Kommissions-Reise & Versandbuch-
  handlung, Innsbruck

**Interessengemeinschaft oesterreichischer
  Autorinnen und Autoren**, see IG Autorinnen
  Autoren

**International Atomic Energy Agency**, see IAEA
  - International Atomic Energy Agency

**International Institute for Applied Systems
  Analysis (IIASA)**
Schlossplatz 1, 2361 Laxenburg
*Tel:* (02236) 807 433 *Fax:* (02236) 71313
*E-mail:* info@iiasa.ac.at; publications@iiasa.ac.at

*Web Site:* www.iiasa.ac.at
Founded: 1972
Subjects: Computer Science, Energy, Environmen-
  tal Studies, Management, Mathematics, Science
  (General)
ISBN Prefix(es): 3-7045

**Verlag Jungbrunnen - Wiener
  Spielzeugschachtel GesellschaftmbH+**
Rauhensteingasse 5, 1010 Vienna
*Tel:* (01) 512-1299 *Fax:* (01) 512-1299-75
*E-mail:* office@jungbrunnen.co.at
*Key Personnel*
Man Dir, Editorial: Hildegard Gaertner
Rights & Permissions: Christina Krajicek
Founded: 1923
Subjects: Developing Countries, Fiction, Human
  Relations
ISBN Prefix(es): 3-7026

**Junius Verlags- und Vertriebs GmbH**
Brunnengasse 3, 1160 Vienna
*Tel:* (01) 4921272
*Key Personnel*
President & Publisher: Mat Dillinger
ISBN Prefix(es): 3-900370

**Jupiter Verlagsgesellschaft mbH**
Robertgasse 2, 1020 Vienna
*Tel:* (01) 21422940 *Fax:* (01) 2160720
*Telex:* 111563
*Key Personnel*
Manager: Dr Hans Georg Zeiner
ISBN Prefix(es): 3-900063

**Juridica Verlag GmbH**
Kohlmarkt 16, 1010 Vienna
*Tel:* (01) 533 37 47-0 *Fax:* (01) 533 37 47-196
*E-mail:* juridica@manz.at
*Web Site:* www.juridica.at
*Key Personnel*
Manager: Grete Grill; Werner Sopper
ISBN Prefix(es): 3-85131

**Kaerntner Druck- und Verlags-GmbH**
Viktringer Ring 28, 9010 Klagenfurt
*Tel:* (0463) 5866 *Fax:* (0463) 5866-321
*E-mail:* info@kaerntner-druckerei.at
*Web Site:* www.kaerntner-druckerei.at
*Telex:* 422415
*Key Personnel*
Contact: Wolbert Ebner *Tel:* (0463) 5855-261
  *Fax:* (0463) 5866-111 *E-mail:* wolbert.ebner@
  kaerntner-druckerei.at
Founded: 1949
ISBN Prefix(es): 3-85391
*Bookshop(s):* Kaerntner Buchhandlung, Neuer
  Platz 11, 9020 Klagenfurt; Universitaetsstr 90,
  9020 Klagenfurt; 8-Mai-Platz 3, 9500 Villach;
  Joh-Offner-Str 11, 9400 Wolfsberg

**Karolinger Verlag GmbH & Co KG+**
Kutschkergasse 12, 1180 Vienna
*Tel:* (01) 4092279 *Fax:* (01) 4092279
*Key Personnel*
Man Dir, Sales: Jean-Jacques Langendorf
Editorial: Dr Peter Weiss
Publicity: Cornelia Langendorf
Rights & Permissions: Hans Hofinger
Founded: 1980
Subjects: Fiction, Government, Political Science,
  History, Literature, Literary Criticism, Essays
ISBN Prefix(es): 3-85418
Number of titles published annually: 6 Print
Total Titles: 82 Print
Distributed by Brockhaus Commission

**Verlag Kerle im Verlag Herder & Co+**
Wollzeile 33, 1010 Vienna
*Tel:* (01) 5121413-60 *Fax:* (01) 5121413-65

*E-mail:* vertriebsbuero@herder.at *Cable:*
  HERDERBUCH VIENNA
*Key Personnel*
Man Dir: Prof Erich M Wolf
Editorial: Dr Evelyn Kapaun
Sales: Susanne Pratscher
Advertising, Rights: Helga Thiele
Founded: 1886
ISBN Prefix(es): 3-210; 3-85303
*Associate Companies:* Verlag Herder GmbH &
  Co KG, Germany; Herder Editrice e Libreria,
  Italy; Editorial Herder SA, Spain; Herder AG,
  Switzerland
Subsidiaries: Herder Kiado
*Bookshop(s):* Herder & Co, Wollzeile 33, 1010
  Vienna
*Warehouse:* Herder, Viktor Kaplanstr 9, 2201
  Gerasdorf

**Johann Kliment KG Musikverlag**
Kolingasse 15, 1090 Vienna
*Tel:* (01) 317 51 47 *Fax:* (01) 310 08 27
*E-mail:* office@kliment.at
*Web Site:* www.kliment.at
Founded: 1928
ISBN Prefix(es): 3-85139
*Bookshop(s):* Neuer Markt 8, 39210 Zwettl

**Horst Knapp Finanznachrichten**
Lisztstr 10, 1037 Vienna
Mailing Address: PO Box 97, 1037 Vienna
*Tel:* (01) 7154460-0 *Fax:* (01) 7154460-22
*Key Personnel*
Owner: Horst Knapp
Subjects: Business, Economics, Finance, Govern-
  ment, Political Science
ISBN Prefix(es): 3-900068

**Edition Koenigstein+**
Anzengrubergasse 50, 3400 Klosterneuburg
*Tel:* (02243) 26046 *Fax:* (02243) 26046
*E-mail:* edition.koenigstein@aon.at
*Web Site:* members.aon.at/edition_koenigstein
*Key Personnel*
Master of Arts: Georg Koenigstein
Contact: Christine Koenigstein
Founded: 1987
Specialize in fine editions & poetry.
Subjects: Art, Poetry
ISBN Prefix(es): 3-901495
Number of titles published annually: 5 Print
Total Titles: 49 Print

**Verlag A F Koska**
Esterhazygasse 35, 1060 Vienna
*Tel:* (0222) 5874344
*Key Personnel*
Manager: Prof Alfred F Koska
ISBN Prefix(es): 3-85334

**Kremayr & Scheriau Verlag+**
Wahringerstr 76, 1090 Vienna
*Tel:* (01) 713 8770-10 *Fax:* (01)713 8770-20
*E-mail:* m.scheriau@kremayr-scheriau.at
*Key Personnel*
Man Dir: Dr Maria Seifert *Tel:* (01) 713 8770-12
  *Fax:* (01) 713 8770-20 *E-mail:* maria.seifert@
  bertelsmann.de
Founded: 1950
Subjects: Art, History, Music, Dance, Nonfiction
  (General)
ISBN Prefix(es): 3-218
*Parent Company:* Bertelsmann AG, Germany
*Bookshop(s):* Buchhandlung uend Zeitschriften-
  vertrieb Kremayr und Scheriau, Niederhofstr
  37, 1121 Vienna
*Book Club(s):* Buchgemeinschaft Donauland Kre-
  mayr & Scheriau
*Orders to:* Dr Otto-Neurath-Gasse 5, 1220 Vienna

**Kuemmerly und Frey Verlags GmbH**
Nikolsdorfergasse 8, 1050 Vienna

*Tel:* (01) 545 14 45 *Fax:* (01) 545 10 80-83
*E-mail:* kuemmerly-frey@xpoint.at
Subjects: Travel
ISBN Prefix(es): 3-900382
*Associate Companies:* J Fink-Kuemmerly und
Frey Verlag GmbH, Germany; Kuemmerly und
Frey, Switzerland (Geographischer Verlag)

**Verlag Lafite+**
Hegelgasse 13, 1010 Vienna
*Tel:* (01) 5126869 *Fax:* (01) 51268699
*E-mail:* redaktion@musikzeit.at
*Key Personnel*
Contact: Prof Dr Diederichs-Lafite
Founded: 1962
Specialize in music.
Publisher of the *Austrian Music Magazine.*
Subjects: Journalism, Music, Dance
ISBN Prefix(es): 3-85151
*Associate Companies:* Internationale Schonberg
Gesellschaft, Vienna

**Landesverlag**, *imprint of* Niederosterreichisches
Pressehaus Druck- und Verlagsgesellschaft
mbH

**Langenscheidt-Verlag GmbH**
Sulzengasse 2, 1232 Vienna
*Tel:* (01) 6887133 *Fax:* (01) 68014140
*Telex:* 131912
Membership(s): Langenscheidt Group, Germany.
ISBN Prefix(es): 3-208
*Parent Company:* Langenscheidt KG, Germany

**Gerda Leber Buch-Kunst-und Musikverlag
   Proscenium Edition+**
Wallnerstr 4, 1010 Vienna
*Tel:* (01) 5332858; (01) 6390025
*Key Personnel*
Contact: Dr Gerda Leber-Hageneau
Founded: 1965
Subjects: Drama, Theater, Music, Dance
ISBN Prefix(es): 3-900217; 3-900297

**Leopold Stocker Verlag+**
Hofgasse 5, 8011 Graz
Mailing Address: Postfach 189, 8011 Graz
*Tel:* (0316) 82 16 36 *Fax:* (0316) 83 56 12
*E-mail:* stocker-verlag@stocker-verlag.com
*Web Site:* www.stocker-verlag.com *Cable:*
   STOCKERVERLAG GRAZ
*Key Personnel*
Publisher: Wolfgang Dvorak-Stocker
Founded: 1917
Subjects: Agriculture, Cookery, Gardening, Plants,
Government, Political Science, History, Mili-
tary Science, Wine & Spirits
ISBN Prefix(es): 3-7020
*Associate Companies:* Buecherquelle Buchhand-
lungs GmbH

**Leykam Buchverlagsges mbH**
Stempfergasse 3, 8010 Graz
*Tel:* (0316) 8076-531 *Fax:* (0316) 8076-539
*E-mail:* verlag@leykam.com
*Web Site:* www.leykam.com; www.leykamverlag.
   at
*Telex:* 032209 *Cable:* LEYKAM GRAZ
*Key Personnel*
Man Dir: Klaus Brunner *Tel:* (0316) 2800-204
   *E-mail:* klaus.brunner@leykam.com
Founded: 1585
Subjects: Art, Fiction
ISBN Prefix(es): 3-7011

**Linde Verlag Wien GmbH+**
Scheydgasse 24, 1211 Vienna
*Tel:* (01) 24630-0 *Fax:* (01) 24630-23
*E-mail:* office@lindeverlag.at; presse@
   lindeverlag.at
*Web Site:* www.linde-verlag.at

*Key Personnel*
Manager: Dr Oskar Mennel *Tel:* (01) 24630-10
   *E-mail:* oskar.mennel@lindeverlag.at
Editor: Dr Eleonore Breitegger *Tel:* (01)
   278 05 26-21 *Fax:* (01) 278 05 26-51
   *E-mail:* redaktion@lindeverlag.at
Public Relations: Christine Reisinger *Tel:* (01)
   278 05 26-30 *Fax:* (01) 278 05 26-53
   *E-mail:* presse@lindeverlag.at
Sales: Sabine Purger *Tel:* (01) 278 05 26-83
   *Fax:* (01) 278 05 26-53 *E-mail:* sabine.
   purger@lindeverlag.at
Advertising: Gertraud Reznicek *Tel:* (01) 278 05
   26-62 *Fax:* (01) 278 05 26-53 *E-mail:* gertraud.
   reznicek@lindeverlag.at
Founded: 1925
Subjects: Accounting, Business, Communications,
Economics, How-to, Labor, Industrial Rela-
tions, Law, Management, Marketing
ISBN Prefix(es): 3-85122; 3-7073
Number of titles published annually: 120 Print; 3
CD-ROM
Total Titles: 300 Print; 20 CD-ROM

**Literas Universitaetsverlag**
Fischerstrand 9, 1220 Vienna
*Tel:* (01) 269 22 07 *Fax:* (01) 269 22 07
*Telex:* 116529 Icpfa
Founded: 1981
Subjects: Psychology, Psychiatry
ISBN Prefix(es): 3-85429
*Associate Companies:* Facultas Verlag

**Loecker Verlag+**
Annagasse 5, 1015 Vienna
*Tel:* (01) 512 02 82 *Fax:* (01) 512 02 82-22
*E-mail:* lverlag@loecker.at
*Web Site:* www.loecker.at
*Key Personnel*
General Manager: Erhard Loecker
Rights & Permissions: Dr Alexander Lellek
Founded: 1974
Subjects: Architecture & Interior Design, Art,
History, Literature, Literary Criticism, Essays,
Photography
ISBN Prefix(es): 3-85409
*Bookshop(s):* Antiquariat Loecker un Woegen-
stein, Annagasse 5, 1010 Vienna; Loecker
GmbH, Gluckgasse 3, 1010 Vienna

**LOG-Internationale Zeitschrift fuer Literatur+**
Donaustadtstr 30/16, 1220 Vienna
*Tel:* (01) 2313433 *Fax:* (01) 2313433
*Key Personnel*
Publisher: Leo Detela; Prof Wolfgang Mayer
   Koenig
Founded: 1978
Subjects: Art, Drama, Theater, Language Arts,
Linguistics, Literature, Literary Criticism, Es-
says, Poetry
ISBN Prefix(es): 3-900647
*Orders to:* Eigenauslieferung

**Mangold Kinderbucher+**
Saint Peter Hauptstr 28, 8042 Graz-St Peter
*Tel:* (0316) 475613 *Fax:* (0316) 475613
   *Cable:* MANGOLDVERLAG
*Key Personnel*
Man Dir: Bernhard Lernpeiss
Founded: 1977
ISBN Prefix(es): 3-900301; 3-901282

**MANZ'sche Verlags- und
   Universitaetsbuchhandlung GMBH**
Kohlmarkt 16, 1010 Vienna
*Tel:* (01) 531 61-161 *Fax:* (01) 531 61-181
*E-mail:* verlag@manz.at
*Web Site:* www.manz.at
*Telex:* 75310631
*Key Personnel*
Management: Dr Kristin Hanusch-Linser; Lucas
   Schneider-Manns-Au

Founded: 1849
Specialize in law books in Europe.
Subjects: Economics, Law
ISBN Prefix(es): 3-214; 3-7067
Distributor for Amt der Europaeischen Gemein-
schaften; Auslieferung fuer Oesterreich
*Bookshop(s):* Kohlmarkt 16, Postfach 163, 1014
Vienna; FRIC, Technische Fachbuchhandlung,
Wiedner Hauptstr 13, 1040 Vienna
*Warehouse:* Siebenbrunnengasse 21, 1050 Vienna
*Orders to:* Siebenbrunnengasse 21, 1050 Vienna

**Wilhelm Maudrich KG+**
Lazarettgasse 1, 1096 Vienna
*Tel:* (01) 4024712 *Fax:* (01) 4085080
*E-mail:* medbook@maudrich.com
*Web Site:* www.maudrich.com
*Telex:* 135177 *Cable:* MAUDRICH VERLAG
   VIENNA
*Key Personnel*
Man Dir: Dr Heinz Pinker; Prof Gerhard Grois
Founded: 1929
Subjects: Medicine, Nursing, Dentistry, Psychol-
ogy, Psychiatry
ISBN Prefix(es): 3-85175
Distributed by Stein und Co (Germany); Verlag
Hans Huber (Switzerland)
Distributor for Point Verlag (Austria, Germany &
Switzerland)
*Bookshop(s):* Spitalgasse 21a, 1096 Vienna
   *Tel:* (01) 4024712 *Fax:* (01) 4085080

**Medien & Recht+**
Danhausergasse 6, 1040 Vienna
*Tel:* (01) 5052766 *Fax:* (01) 5052766-15
*E-mail:* verlag@medien-recht.ccom
*Web Site:* www.medien-recht.com
*Key Personnel*
University Prof: Dr Heinz Wittmann *E-mail:* h.
   wittmann@medien-recht.com
Founded: 1985
Subjects: Communications, Computer Science,
Journalism, Law
ISBN Prefix(es): 3-900741
*Parent Company:* Medien & Recht Verlags GmbH

**Merbod Verlag+**
Herrengasse 2, 2700 Wiener Neustadt
Mailing Address: Postfach 201, 2700 Wiener
Neustadt
*Tel:* (02622) 81724 *Fax:* (02622) 817244
*Key Personnel*
Contact: Peter Zumpf
Founded: 1989
Specializes in: Local listings & authors.
Subjects: Fiction, History, Humor, Literature, Lit-
erary Criticism, Essays, Nonfiction (General),
Poetry
ISBN Prefix(es): 3-900844
Total Titles: 45 Print

**Metrica Fachverlag u Versandbuchhandlung
   Ing Bartak+**
Neugebaeudestr 18-12-8, 1110 Vienna
*Tel:* (01) 769 51 60 *Fax:* (01) 769 51 60
*Key Personnel*
Publisher: Ing Werner H Bartak
Founded: 1978
Subjects: Energy, Engineering (General), Technol-
ogy
ISBN Prefix(es): 3-900368; 3-900329

**Milena Verlag+**
Lange Gasse 51/10, 1080 Vienna
*Tel:* (01) 402 59 90 *Fax:* (01) 408 88 58
*E-mail:* frauenverlag@milena-verlag.at
*Key Personnel*
Contact: Karin Ballauff; Martina Kopf
Founded: 1980
Subjects: Biography, Fiction, Gay & Lesbian,
History, Library & Information Sciences, Lit-

erature, Literary Criticism, Essays, Nonfiction (General), Philosophy, Social Sciences, Sociology, Women's Studies
ISBN Prefix(es): 3-900399; 3-85286
Total Titles: 160 Print
*Orders to:* Mohr Z-G, Sulzengasse 2, 1230 Vienna *Tel:* (01) 68014-231 *Fax:* (01) 68014-140 *E-mail:* momo@mohr-morawa.co.at

**Thomas Mlakar Verlag**
Michlbauerweg 1, 8755 Saint Peter ob Judenburg
*Tel:* (03579) 2258 *Fax:* (03579) 2258
*E-mail:* mlakar-media@gmx.at
Founded: 1970
Subjects: Fashion, History, Literature, Literary Criticism, Essays, Natural History
ISBN Prefix(es): 3-900289

**Modulverlag+**
Mahlerstr 3, 1010 Vienna
*Tel:* (01) 5129892 *Fax:* (01) 5129893
*Key Personnel*
Contact: Dr Berthold Schwanzer
Founded: 1973
Specialize in architecture-marketing research.
Subjects: Architecture & Interior Design, Art, Marketing
ISBN Prefix(es): 3-900507
Distributor for Visual Reference Publications Inc (USA for Austria, retail books)

**Moedling,** *imprint of* Verlag St Gabriel

**Verlag Monte Verita+**
Hahngasse 15, 1090 Vienna
*Tel:* (01) 5487080 *Fax:* (01) 5487081
*Web Site:* www.anares.org
*Key Personnel*
Publisher: Peter Stipkovics
Founded: 1982
Subjects: History, Literature, Literary Criticism, Essays, Philosophy
ISBN Prefix(es): 3-900434

**Otto Mueller Verlag**
Ernst-Thunstr 11, 5020 Salzburg
Mailing Address: Postfach 167, 5021 Salzburg
*Tel:* (0662) 881974-0 *Fax:* (0662) 872387
*E-mail:* onb@onb.ac.at *Cable:* MULLER VERLAG
*Key Personnel*
Man Dir, Sales & Publicity: Arno Kleibel
Founded: 1937
Subjects: History, Literature, Literary Criticism, Essays, Poetry, Psychology, Psychiatry, Religion - Other, Theology
ISBN Prefix(es): 3-7013

**Mueller-Speiser Wissenschaftlicher Verlag**
Mitterweg 6, 5081 Anif/Salzburg
*Tel:* (06246) 73166 *Fax:* (06246) 73166
*E-mail:* verlag@mueller-speiser.at
*Web Site:* www.mueller-speiser.at
*Key Personnel*
Contact: Ursula Mueller-Speiser
Founded: 1989
Subjects: Drama, Theater, Music, Dance, Philosophy, Religion - Other, Theology, General Religion & Musicscience/Musicethnology
ISBN Prefix(es): 3-85145
Total Titles: 78 Print

**Paul Neff Verlag KG+**
Hackingerstr 52, 1140 Vienna
*Tel:* (01) 94061115 *Fax:* (01) 947641288 *Cable:* Neffverlag
*Key Personnel*
Man Dir: Dagmar Stecher-Konsalik
Founded: 1829
Subjects: Art, Biography, Fiction, Music, Dance

ISBN Prefix(es): 3-7014
*Parent Company:* Hestia-Verlag GmbH, Germany

**Verlag Neues Leben**
Thueringerberg 77, 6721 Thueringerberg
*Tel:* (05550) 3979 *Fax:* (05550) 3979
*Key Personnel*
Man Dir: Dr Rudolf Ingrisch
Founded: 1946
Subjects: Biography, Drama, Theater, Economics, Medicine, Nursing, Dentistry
ISBN Prefix(es): 3-85335

**Edition Neues Marchen+**
Kloster, 8413 St Georgen a d Stiefing
*Tel:* (03184) 2417 *Fax:* (03183) 7400
*Key Personnel*
Owner: Folke Tegetthoff
Founded: 1990
Subjects: Poetry
ISBN Prefix(es): 3-85325

**Neufeld-Verlag und Galerie**
Schillerstr 7, 6890 Lustenau
*Tel:* (05577) 46 57
*Telex:* 59162 *Cable:* Neufeld
*Key Personnel*
Man Dir: K G Loepfe
Editorial, Rights & Permissions: Ivo Loepfe
Founded: 1962
ISBN Prefix(es): 3-900651
*Parent Company:* Loepfe KG
*Branch Office(s)*
Nordstr 227, 8037 Zurich, Switzerland

**Wolfgang Neugebauer Verlag GmbH**
Kalvarienguertel 62, 8020 Graz
*Tel:* (05522) 747 70 *Fax:* (05522) 747 70
*E-mail:* wnverlag@utanet.at
*Key Personnel*
Man Dir: Wolfgang Neugebauer
Founded: 1975
Subjects: History, Language Arts, Linguistics, Literature, Literary Criticism, Essays, Theology
ISBN Prefix(es): 3-85376
Total Titles: 100 Print
*Bookshop(s):* Buchhandlung Bayer, Inh W Neugebauer Verlag GmbH, Kreuzgasse 6, 6800 Feldkirch *E-mail:* bayer.buch@utanet.at
*Orders to:* Kreuzgasse 6, 6800 Feldkirch

**Dr Waltraud Neuwirth Selbstverlag** (Dr Waltraud Neuwirth Self Publishing House)
Barawitzkagasse 27/1/4/31, 1190 Vienna
*Tel:* (01) 3207323 *Fax:* (01) 3200225
*E-mail:* waltraud.neuwith@eunet.at
Founded: 1976
ISBN Prefix(es): 3-900282

**Niederosterreichisches Pressehaus Druck- und Verlagsgesellschaft mbH+**
Gutenbergstr 12, 3100 Saint Poelten
*Tel:* (02742) 802-1412 *Fax:* (02742) 802-1431
*E-mail:* verlag@np-buch.at
*Web Site:* www.np-buch.at
*Telex:* 015512
*Key Personnel*
Man Dir: Herwig Bitsche *Tel:* (02742) 802-1410 *E-mail:* h.bitsche@np-buch.at
Publicity: Johanna Stromberger *E-mail:* j.stromberger@np-buch.at
Marketing: Roswitha Wonka
Founded: 1889
Subjects: Biography, Cookery, Health, Nutrition, History, Human Relations, Humor, Nonfiction (General), Outdoor Recreation, Travel, Wine & Spirits
ISBN Prefix(es): 3-85214; 3-85326; 3-85236
Number of titles published annually: 40 Print
Total Titles: 200 Print
Imprints: Landesverlag; NP Buchverlag

*Orders to:* Mohr Morawa, Buchvertrieb GmbH, Sulzengasse 2, 1232 Vienna *Tel:* (01) 680 14-0 *Fax:* (01) 688 71-30 *E-mail:* momo@mohr-morawa.co.at

**NOI - Verlag**
Morresstr 13, 9020 Klagenfurt, Oostenrijk
*Tel:* (0463) 224722 *Fax:* (0463) 224744
*E-mail:* office@noisapil.com
*Key Personnel*
Owner: Dr Dietfried Schoenemann
Subjects: Education, Environmental Studies, Ethnicity, Health, Nutrition, History, Social Sciences, Sociology
ISBN Prefix(es): 3-900453

**NP Buchverlag,** *imprint of* Niederosterreichisches Pressehaus Druck- und Verlagsgesellschaft mbH

**Obelisk-Verlag+**
Falkstr 1, 6020 Innsbruck
*Tel:* (0512) 58 07 33 *Fax:* (0512) 58 07 33 13
*E-mail:* obelisk-verlag@utanet.at
*Web Site:* www.obelisk-verlag.at
*Key Personnel*
Proprietor: Helga Buchroithner
Founded: 1946
ISBN Prefix(es): 3-85197

**OEAW,** see Verlag der Oesterreichischen Akademie der Wissenschaften (OEAW)

**oebv & hpt Verlagsgesellschaft mbH & Co KG+**
Frankgasse 4, 1090 Vienna
*Tel:* (01) 40136-0 *Fax:* (01) 40136-185
*E-mail:* office@oebvhpt.at
*Web Site:* www.oebvhpt.at
*Key Personnel*
Contact: Werner Brunner
International Rights: Hubert W Krenn
Marketing Manager: Herwig Arlt *Tel:* (01) 400 90-91 *Fax:* (01) 400 90-40 *E-mail:* vertrieb@oebvhpt.at
Advertising: Martina Moosleitner *Tel:* (01) 400 90-11 *Fax:* (01) 400 90-40 *E-mail:* werbung@oebvhpt.at
Founded: 1985
Subjects: Education, Mysteries, Nonfiction (General), Romance
ISBN Prefix(es): 3-85128
Divisions: Neuer Breitschopf Verlag; Ed Boesskraut & Bernardi; Kurz & Bundigi, hpt Extra
*Orders to:* Mohr-Morawa, Sulzeng 2, 1230 Vienna *Tel:* (01) 684614-0

**Verlag Oesterreich GmbH+**
Kandlgasse 21, 1070 Vienna
*Tel:* (01) 61077-0 *Fax:* (01) 61077-419
*E-mail:* office@verlagoesterreich.at
*Web Site:* www.verlagoesterreich.at
*Key Personnel*
Manager: Dr Norbert Gugerbauer *Tel:* (01) 610771401 *Fax:* (01) 610771419 *E-mail:* gugerbauer@jusline.com
Membership(s): Haupt Verband des Osterr Buchhandels & Deutscher Borsevrerein Frankfurt.
ISBN Prefix(es): 3-7046
Number of titles published annually: 60 Print
Total Titles: 2,500 Print; 20 CD-ROM; 1 Online; 1 E-Book
*Bookshop(s):* Jurbooks, Wollzeile 16, 1010 Vienna, Contact: Velislava Vlaykova *Tel:* (01) 5124885 *Fax:* (01) 5120663 *E-mail:* buchhandlung@verlagoesterreich.at

**Oesterreichische Staatsdruckerei** (Austrian State Printing Office)
Kandlgasse 21, 1070 Vienna
*Tel:* (01) 61077-0 *Fax:* (01) 61077-419

*E-mail:* office@verlagoesterreich.at
*Key Personnel*
Dir: Aribert Schwarzmann
ISBN Prefix(es): 3-7046; 3-85201

**Oesterreichische Verlagsanstalt GmbH**
Arbeitergasse 1-7, 1051 Vienna
*Tel:* (01) 5445641-46 *Fax:* (01) 5445641-46
*E-mail:* prepress@agens-werk.at
*Key Personnel*
Man Dir: Friedrich Geyer
ISBN Prefix(es): 3-7033; 3-85202

**Verlag der Oesterreichischen Akademie der Wissenschaften (OEAW)** (Austrian Academy of Sciences Press)+
Postgasse 7, 1010 Vienna
Mailing Address: Postfach 471, 1010 Vienna
*Tel:* (01) 512 9050; (01) 51581-3401 *Fax:* (01) 51581-3400
*E-mail:* verlag@oeaw.ac.at
*Web Site:* verlag.oeaw.ac.at
*Key Personnel*
Manager: Mag Herwig Stoeger *Tel:* (01) 51581-3405 *E-mail:* herwig.stoeger@oeaw.ac.at
Founded: 1973
Subjects: Archaeology, Asian Studies, Biography, Biological Sciences, History, Language Arts, Linguistics, Law, Physical Sciences, Science (General), Social Sciences, Sociology
ISBN Prefix(es): 3-7001
Number of titles published annually: 80 Print; 3 Audio
Total Titles: 20 Audio
Distributed by Rinson Books (Japan); University of Washington Press (USA)

**Verlag des Oesterreichischen Gewerkschaftsbundes GmbH**
Altmannsdorfer Str 154-156, 1231 Vienna
*Tel:* (01) 662 32 96 *Fax:* (01) 662 32 96-63 85
*E-mail:* office@oegbverlag.at
*Web Site:* www.verlag-oegb.co.at
*Telex:* 1311326
*Key Personnel*
Man Dir: Friedrich Loew
Editor-in-Chief: Fritz Fadler
Founded: 1947
Subjects: Career Development, Government, Political Science, History, Labor, Industrial Relations, Law
ISBN Prefix(es): 3-7035
Subsidiaries: Elbemuhl GmbH; EDV Gmbh; Printex GmbH; Pichler GmbH
*Book Club(s):* Buechergilde Gutenberg

**Oesterreichischer Agrarverlag, Druck- und Verlags- GmbH+**
Achauer Str 49A, 2335 Leopoldsdorf bei Wien
*Tel:* (02235) 404-440 *Fax:* (02235) 404-459
*E-mail:* buch@agrarverlag.at
*Web Site:* www.agrarverlag.at
*Telex:* 14030 *Cable:* AGRARVERLAG
*Key Personnel*
Man Dir: Dr Wolfgang Brandstetter
Founded: 1945
Subjects: Agriculture, Environmental Studies, Fiction
ISBN Prefix(es): 3-7040
Subsidiaries: Hugo H Hitschmann Verlag
*Warehouse:* Hennersdorfer Str 32/6, 2333 Leopoldsdorf
*Orders to:* Ing H Fischer/AV Buchhandlung, Linzerstr 32, 1141 Vienna *Fax:* (01) 951501-289

**Oesterreichischer Bundesverlag Gmbh**
Schwarzenbergstr 5, 1015 Vienna
*Tel:* (01) 5262091-0 *Fax:* (01) 526209111
*E-mail:* oebz@oebv.co.at
*Web Site:* www.oebv.at

*Telex:* 79246
*Key Personnel*
Contact: Dr Othmar Spachinger
International Rights: Wilbirg Stoger
Founded: 1772
Subjects: Biological Sciences, Career Development, Chemistry, Chemical Engineering, Education, English as a Second Language, History, Language Arts, Linguistics, Music, Dance, Nonfiction (General), Philosophy, Sports, Athletics
ISBN Prefix(es): 3-215

**Oesterreichischer Gewerbeverlag GmbH**
Herrengasse 10, 1014 Vienna
Mailing Address: Postfach 182, 1014 Vienna
*Tel:* (01) 535 9404 *Fax:* (01) 5330768030
*E-mail:* gewerbeverlag@tbxa.telecom.at
*Key Personnel*
Man Dir, Sales & Publicity: Franz Scharetzer
Editorial, Rights & Permissions: Dr Josef Peter Ortner
Production: Heinz Stuiber
Founded: 1945
Subjects: Career Development, English as a Second Language
ISBN Prefix(es): 3-85207
*Parent Company:* Oesterreichischer Bundesverlag GmbH

**Oesterreichischer Jagd -und Fischerei-Verlag**
Wickenburggasse 3, 1080 Vienna
*Tel:* (01) 405 16 36-39 *Fax:* (01) 405 16 36-36
*E-mail:* verlag@jagd.at
*Web Site:* www.jagd.at
*Key Personnel*
Publisher: Dr Peter Lebersorger
ISBN Prefix(es): 3-85208

**Oesterreichischer Kunst und Kulturverlag+**
Freundgasse 11, 1040 Vienna
*Tel:* (01) 587 85 51 *Fax:* (01) 587 85 52
*E-mail:* office@kunstundkulturverlag.at
*Key Personnel*
Contact: Dr Michael Martischnig
Founded: 1981
Subjects: Antiques, Architecture & Interior Design, Communications, Engineering (General), History, Nonfiction (General), Regional Interests, Social Sciences, Sociology
ISBN Prefix(es): 3-85437
Total Titles: 350 Print; 3 CD-ROM; 3 Audio

**Oesterreichisches Katholisches Bibelwerk**
Stiftsplatz 8, 3400 Klosterneuburg
Mailing Address: Postfach 48, 3400 Klosterneuburg
*Tel:* (02243) 2938 *Fax:* (02243) 2939
*Telex:* (61) 3222523
*Key Personnel*
Man Dir, Editorial, Rights & Permissions: Dr Norbert Hoeslinger
Sales: Elisabeth Csencsics
Publicity: Erika Pruckmoser
Founded: 1966
Membership(s): AMB & WCBFA (World Catholic Federation for the Biblical Apostolate).
Subjects: Religion - Other
ISBN Prefix(es): 3-85396
*Bookshop(s):* Singerstr 7, 1010 Vienna

**Verlag Oldenbourg+**
Neulinggasse 26/12, 1030 Vienna
*Tel:* (01) 712 62 58 *Fax:* (01) 712 62 58-19
*E-mail:* office@oldenbourg.at
*Key Personnel*
Sales Dir: Gerda Adler
Publicity & Advertising: Dr Ursula Huber
  *E-mail:* ursula.huber@oldenbourg.co.at

Mag: Veronika Weidenholzer *E-mail:* veronika.weidenholzer@oldenbourg.co.at
Founded: 1957
Subjects: Engineering (General), History, Philosophy, Science (General), Social Sciences, Sociology
ISBN Prefix(es): 3-7029
*Parent Company:* R Oldenbourg Verlag GmbH, Germany
*Associate Companies:* Verlag fuer Geschichte und Politik

**Verlag Orac im Verlag Kremayr & Scheriau+**
Waehringer Str 76/8, 1090 Vienna
*Tel:* (01) 713 87 70 *Fax:* (01) 713 87 70-20
*E-mail:* office@kremayr-scheriau.at
*Web Site:* www.kremayr-scheriau.at
*Key Personnel*
Publisher: Prof Leo Mazakarini
Program Development: Dr Michal Scheriau
Production: Claudia Rinne
Press & Public Relations: Astrid Lefenda
Founded: 1946
Subjects: Cookery, Economics, Environmental Studies, Government, Political Science, Health, Nutrition, Management, Nonfiction (General)
ISBN Prefix(es): 3-7015; 3-85368
*Parent Company:* Kremayr & Scheriau
*Orders to:* Dr Otto Neurath-Gasse 5, 1220 Vienna, Contact: Dr Franz Hain *Tel:* (01) 282 65 65 *Fax:* (01) 282 52 82 *E-mail:* office@hain.at

**Verlag des Osterr Kneippbundes GmbH+**
Kunigundenweg 10, 8700 Leoben
*Tel:* (03842) 21682; (03842) 21718; (03842) 24094 *Fax:* (03842) 2171832
*E-mail:* office@kneippverlag.com
*Web Site:* www.kneippverlag.com
*Key Personnel*
Manager: Waltraud Ruth
Founded: 1985
Specializing in health & medicine.
Subjects: Alternative, Child Care & Development, Cookery, Health, Nutrition, Medicine, Nursing, Dentistry, Outdoor Recreation, Philosophy, Psychology, Psychiatry, Sports, Athletics
ISBN Prefix(es): 3-900696; 3-901794; 3-902191
Distributed by B&M Medien Service (Switzerland); Knoe (Germany); Morawa (Austria); Weltbild
Distributor for Kneipp-Verlag Bad Woerishofen

**Osterreichischer Wirtschaftsverlag Druck-und Verlagsgesellschaft mbH**
Nikolsdorfer Gasse 7-11, 1051 Vienna
*Tel:* (01) 546 64-0 *Fax:* (01) 546 64-215
*E-mail:* office@oewv.at
*Key Personnel*
Man Dir: Robert Graf
ISBN Prefix(es): 3-85212

**Passagen Verlag GmbH+**
Walfischgasse 15-14, 1010 Vienna
*Tel:* (01) 513 77 61 *Fax:* (01) 512 63 27
*E-mail:* office@passagen.at
*Web Site:* www.passagen.at
*Key Personnel*
Publisher: Dr Peter Engelmann
  *E-mail:* engelmann@passagen.at
Founded: 1987
Subjects: Architecture & Interior Design, Art, Economics, Government, Political Science, Literature, Literary Criticism, Essays, Philosophy, Theology
ISBN Prefix(es): 3-900767; 3-85165
Total Titles: 600 Print
*Orders to:* Bugrim Verlagsauslieferung, Saalburgstr 3, 12099 Berlin, Germany, Contact: Herr Lindemann *Tel:* (030) 6068457 *Fax:* (030) 6063476 *E-mail:* bugrim@t-online.de *Web Site:* www.bugrim.de

**E Perlinger Naturprodukte Handelsgesellschaft mbH+**
Itter 300, 6300 Woergl
*Tel:* (05332) 524 40 *Fax:* (05332) 516 79
*E-mail:* engelberts.naturprodukte@tirol.com
*Telex:* 051205 Teltaz *Cable:* Perlinger Verlag
   Woergl
*Key Personnel*
Man Dir: Engelbert Perlinger
Founded: 1977
Subjects: Astrology, Occult, Ethnicity, Medicine,
   Nursing, Dentistry
ISBN Prefix(es): 3-85399

**Verlag Sankt Peter**
Erzabtei St Peter, 5010 Salzburg
Mailing Address: Postfach 113, 5010 Salzburg
*Tel:* (0662) 842166-82 *Fax:* (0662) 842166-80
*E-mail:* verlag-st.peter@magnet.at
*Web Site:* www.stift-stpeter.at
*Telex:* 063094
*Key Personnel*
Man Dir: Dr R Rinnerthaler
   *E-mail:* rinnerthaler@hotmail.com
Founded: 1946
Subjects: Art, Regional Interests, Religion - Other
ISBN Prefix(es): 3-900173

**Pichler Verlag GmbH & Co KG**
Imprint of Styria Pichler Verlag GmbH & Co KG
Lobkowitzplatz 1, 1010 Vienna
*Tel:* (01) 203 28 28-0 *Fax:* (01) 203 28 28-6875
*E-mail:* office@styriapichler.at
*Web Site:* www.styriapichler.at
*Key Personnel*
Dir: Michael Hlatky *Tel:* (01) 2032828-6870
   *E-mail:* michael.hlatky@pichlerverlag.at
Public Relations: Dr Barbara Brunner *Tel:* (01)
   624673955 *E-mail:* barbara.brunner@utanet.at
Founded: 1793
ISBN Prefix(es): 3-85431
*Bookshop(s):* Wipplingerstr 37, 1010 Vienna; Fa-
   voritenstr 42, 1040 Vienna

**Richard Pils Publication PN°1+**
Grosswolfgers 29, 3970 Weitra
*Tel:* (0043) 2856 3794 *Fax:* (0043) 2856 3792
*E-mail:* verlag@bibliothekderprovinz.at
*Web Site:* www.bibliothekderprovinz.at
*Key Personnel*
Contact: Richard Pils
Founded: 1989
Subjects: Art, Cookery, Drama, Theater, Fiction,
   Literature, Literary Criticism, Essays, Photogra-
   phy, Poetry
ISBN Prefix(es): 3-900878; 3-85252
Number of titles published annually: 50 Print
Total Titles: 700 Print

**Pinguin-Verlag, Pawlowski GmbH+**
Lindenbuehelweg 2, 6020 Innsbruck
*Tel:* (0512) 281183-0 *Fax:* (0512) 293243 *Cable:*
   PINGUINVERLAG INNSBRUCK
*Key Personnel*
Man Dir: Hella Pawlowski; Olaf Pawlowski
Founded: 1945
Subjects: Art, Astrology, Occult, Cookery, For-
   eign Countries, Geography, Geology, Nonfic-
   tion (General), Physical Sciences, Travel
ISBN Prefix(es): 3-7016
Distributor for Readers Digest; Verlag Frankfurt

**Georg Prachner KG+**
Kaerntner Str 30, 1010 Vienna
*Tel:* (01) 512 85 49-0 *Fax:* (01) 512-01-58
*Key Personnel*
Man Dir: O G Prachner
Founded: 1931
Subjects: Agriculture, Art, Fiction, History
ISBN Prefix(es): 3-85367
Divisions: Prachner GmbH, Verlag und Grosshan-
   del

**Progress-Verlag Dr Micolini's Witwe**
Glacisstr 57, 8010 Graz
*Tel:* (0316) 829508 *Fax:* (0316) 829508
   *Cable:* Micolini Graz
Founded: 1934
ISBN Prefix(es): 3-85237

**Promedia Verlagsges mbH+**
Wickenburggasse 5/12, 1080 Vienna
*Tel:* (01) 405 27 02 *Fax:* (01) 405 71 59 22
*E-mail:* promedia@mediashop.at
*Web Site:* www.mediashop.at
*Key Personnel*
Contact: Hannes Hofbauer
Founded: 1982
Subjects: Anthropology, Architecture & Interior
   Design, Biography, Developing Countries, For-
   eign Countries, Government, Political Science,
   History, Nonfiction (General), Travel, Women's
   Studies
ISBN Prefix(es): 3-900478; 3-85371
Number of titles published annually: 20 Print
Total Titles: 200 Print
*Distribution Center:* Mohr Morawa Buchvertrieb
   Ges mbH, Sulzeng 2, 1230 Vienna *Tel:* (01) 68
   0 14-5 *Fax:* (01) 68 0 14-140
Prolit Verlagsauslieferung, Siemensstr 16, 35463
   Fernwald, Germany *Tel:* (0641) 94393-23
   *Fax:* (0641) 94393-29
Scheidegger & Co bei AVA, Centralweg 16, 8910
   Affoltern, Switzerland *Tel:* (01) 762 42 10
   *Fax:* (061) 272 94 76 *E-mail:* buchundinfo@
   ava.ch

**Prugg Verlag**
Haydngasse 10, 7000 Eisenstadt
*Tel:* (02682) 2114
ISBN Prefix(es): 3-85238

**Verlag Anton Pustet+**
Bergstr 12, 5020 Salzburg
*Tel:* (0662) 87 35 07-55 *Fax:* (0662) 87 35 07-79
*E-mail:* buch@verlag-anton-pustet.at
*Web Site:* www.verlag-anton-pustet.at
*Key Personnel*
Rights & Permissions: M A Mona Muery-Leitner
   *Tel:* (0662) 87 35 07-54
Contact: Dr Roman Hoellbacher *Tel:* (0662) 87
   35 07-53
Founded: 1598
Subjects: Architecture & Interior Design, Art,
   Cookery, History, Philosophy, Psychology, Psy-
   chiatry, Theology, Travel
ISBN Prefix(es): 3-7025
Total Titles: 90 Print

**Reinhold Schmidt Verlag**
Kastanienweg 9, 2362 Biedermannsdorf
*Tel:* (02236) 72469 *Fax:* (02236) 73784
*Key Personnel*
Editor-in-Chief: Herbert Schwestka
ISBN Prefix(es): 3-900124

**Resch Verlag+**
Maria-Eich-Str 77, 82166 Graefelfing
*Tel:* (089) 8 54 65-0 *Fax:* (089) 8 54 65-11
*E-mail:* info@resch-verlag.com
*Web Site:* www.resch-verlag.com
*Key Personnel*
Publisher: Dr Ingo Resch
Contact: Prof P Andreas Resch, PhD; Mag Priska
   Kapferer
Founded: 1974
Subjects: Parapsychology, Physics, Science (Gen-
   eral), Theology, Ethics
ISBN Prefix(es): 3-85382

**Residenz Verlag GmbH+**
Gaisbergstr 6, 5025 Salzburg
*Tel:* (0662) 641986-0 *Fax:* (0662) 643548
*E-mail:* info@residenzverlag.at

*Web Site:* www.residenzverlag.at
*Key Personnel*
Man Dir: Hernig Bitsche *E-mail:* h.bitsche@np-
   buch.at
Sales Manager: Roswitha Wonka
Foreign Rights & Permissions: Ingrid Fuehrer
   *E-mail:* ingrid.fuehrer@oebv.co.at
Editorial: Dr Astrid Graf *E-mail:* astrid.graf@
   oebv.co.at
Founded: 1956
Subjects: Art, Drama, Theater, Film, Video, Mu-
   sic, Dance, Poetry, Contemporary Literature
ISBN Prefix(es): 3-7017
Number of titles published annually: 25 Print
Total Titles: 350 Print
*Parent Company:* Niederoesterreichisches Presse-
   haus, Saint Poelten

**Rhombus Verlag**
Schottenfeldgasse 65, 1070 Vienna
*Tel:* (01) 526 61 52 *Fax:* (01) 522 87 18
*Key Personnel*
Man Dir: Thomas C Cubasch
Subjects: Literature, Literary Criticism, Essays,
   Avant Garde & Experimental Literature
ISBN Prefix(es): 3-85394
Number of titles published annually: 1 Print
Total Titles: 20 Print

**Ritter Druck und Verlags KEG+**
Hagenstr 3, 9020 Klagenfurt
*Tel:* (0463) 42631 *Fax:* (0463) 42631-77
*E-mail:* office@ritterbooks.com
*Web Site:* www.ritterbooks.com
*Key Personnel*
Contact: Karin Ritter
Founded: 1980
Subjects: Architecture & Interior Design, Art,
   Literature, Literary Criticism, Essays, Music,
   Dance, Art Theory, Exhibition
ISBN Prefix(es): 3-85415

**Verlag Roeschnar+**
Beethovenstr 4, 9065 Pfaffendorf
*Tel:* (0463) 740513 *Fax:* (0463) 740817
*E-mail:* roesch@eunet.at
*Web Site:* members.eunet.at/roesch
*Key Personnel*
Publishing Manager: Renate Peball
Founded: 1876
Subjects: Poetry
ISBN Prefix(es): 3-900735; 3-85277

**Roetzer Druck GmbH & Co KG**
Bundesstr 50, 7000 Eisenstadt
*Tel:* (02682) 2473 *Fax:* (02682) 65008
*E-mail:* roetzeredition@wellcom.at
*Key Personnel*
Man Dir: Rainer Roetzer
Founded: 1969
Subjects: Physics
ISBN Prefix(es): 3-85253

**Verlag St Gabriel+**
Gabrielerstr 171, 2340 Moedling
*Tel:* (02236) 803-225 *Fax:* (02236) 24483
*E-mail:* zeitschriften.stgabriel@steyler.at@steyler.
   at
*Web Site:* www.steyler.at
*Key Personnel*
Man: Elisabeth Birklhuber *Tel:* (02236) 803163
   *E-mail:* ltg.verlag@steyler.at
Contact: Gerd Milcke *E-mail:* bur.verlag@steyler.
   at
Founded: 1901
Subjects: Religion - Catholic, Theology
ISBN Prefix(es): 3-85264
Number of titles published annually: 8 Print
Total Titles: 40 Print
*Parent Company:* Missionshaus Sankt Gabriel

*Ultimate Parent Company:* Gesellschaft des Got-
tlichen Wortes, Provinz Osterreich
Imprints: Moedling
Distributed by Rex-Verlag; Steyler Verlag
*Bookshop(s):* Missions Buch Handlung St
Gabriel, Contact: Mr Queder *Tel:* (02236)
47834 *Fax:* (02236) 803273; Stephansplatz
6, 1010 Vienna *Tel:* (01) 5122105 *Fax:* (01)
5122105
*Distribution Center:* Verlagsauslieferungen,
1220 Vienna, Contact: Ms Korecky *Tel:* (01)
282656524 *Fax:* (01) 2825282 *E-mail:* office@
hain.at

**Verlag der Salzburger Druckerei**
Bergstr 12, 5020 Salzburg
*Tel:* (0662) 873507-56 *Fax:* (0662) 873507-62
*E-mail:* verlag@salzburger-druckerei.at
ISBN Prefix(es): 3-85338

**Salzburger Kulturvereinigung**
Waagplatz 1a Trakl-Haus, 5010 Salzburg
Mailing Address: Postfach 42, 5010 Salzburg
*Tel:* (0662) 845346 *Fax:* (0662) 842665
*E-mail:* kulturvereinigung@salzburg.co.at
*Web Site:* www.salzburg.com/kulturvereinigung
*Key Personnel*
Manager: Dr Heinz Klier
Classic concerts with orchestras.
Subjects: Music, Dance
ISBN Prefix(es): 3-85259

**Salzburger Nachrichten Verlagsgesellschaft
mbH & Co KG**
Karolingerstr 40, 5020 Salzburg
*Tel:* (0662) 8373-0; (0662) 8373-210 *Fax:* (0662)
8373-210
*E-mail:* anzeigen@salzburg.com
*Web Site:* www.salzburg.com
*Telex:* 633383
*Key Personnel*
Publisher & Man Dir: Dr Maximillian Dasch
Man Dir: Ramon Torra
Editor-in-Chief: Ronald Barazon
Subjects: Architecture & Interior Design, Drama,
Theater, History, Music, Dance, Regional Inter-
ests
ISBN Prefix(es): 3-85304

**Verlag fuer Sammler+**
St Peter Hauptstr 35e, 8042 Graz
*Tel:* (0316) 47 22 30 *Fax:* (0316) 67 39 87
*E-mail:* ssu@literaturhaus.at
*Web Site:* www.literaturhaus.at/buch/
verlagsportraits/sammler.html
*Key Personnel*
Owner: Uta Gratzl
Founded: 1968
Subjects: Art, History, Natural History, Social
Sciences, Sociology
ISBN Prefix(es): 3-85365
*Showroom(s):* Koeroesistr 17/4, 8010 Graz

**Sankt Hermagoras Bruderschaft,** see
Hermagoras/Mohorjeva

**Paul Sappl, Schulbuch- und Lehrmittelverlag**
Eichelwang 15, 6330 Kufstein
*Tel:* (05372) 64300 *Fax:* (05372) 64300-17
*Telex:* 5119115
Founded: 1953
ISBN Prefix(es): 3-85263
*Branch Office(s)*
Stolberggasse 31-33, 1050 Vienna

**Dr A Schendl GmbH und Co KG**
Geblergasse 95, 1170 Vienna
*Tel:* (01) 484 17 85-0 *Fax:* (01) 484 17 85-15
*E-mail:* info@schendl.at
*Web Site:* www.schendl.at

*Key Personnel*
Dir: Martin Oegg
Founded: 1965
Also acts as packager, warehouse, promoter.
Subjects: Economics, Ethnicity, Geography, Ge-
ology, History, Literature, Literary Criticism,
Essays, Music, Dance, Natural History
ISBN Prefix(es): 3-85268

**Schlager Verlag,** see Astor-Verlag, Willibald
Schlager

**Andreas Schnider Verlags-Atelier**
Peterstalerstr 127, 8042 Graz-St Peter
*Tel:* (0316) 471302 *Fax:* (0316) 4713024
*E-mail:* bookstore@net.burger.at
*Key Personnel*
Owner: Andreas Schnider
Founded: 1989
Subjects: Archaeology, Architecture & Interior
Design, Art, Computer Science, Education,
Electronics, Electrical Engineering, Fiction,
Government, Political Science, History, Law,
Literature, Literary Criticism, Essays, Photog-
raphy, Poetry, Psychology, Psychiatry, Religion
- Catholic, Religion - Other, Theology, Veteri-
nary Science
ISBN Prefix(es): 3-900993; 0-902020
*Branch Office(s)*
Attila Mudrok, Vak u 6, H-2500 Grztergom
*U.S. Office(s):* Roy Mittelman, 607 West End
Ave, New York, NY 10024, United States
*Tel:* 212-769-3323 *Fax:* 212-769-2325

**Verlag Anton Schroll & Co+**
Spengergasse 37, 1051 Vienna
*Tel:* (01) 5445641-46 *Fax:* (01) 544564166
*E-mail:* prepress@agens-werk.at *Cable:*
Schrollverlag Vienna
*Key Personnel*
Man Dir: Friedrich Geyer
Founded: 1884
Subjects: Art, History, Travel
ISBN Prefix(es): 3-7031
*Branch Office(s)*
Anton Schroll & Co GmbH, Germany

**Schubert & Franzke Gesellschaft mbH**
Kranzbichlerstr 57, 3100 Saint Poelten
*Tel:* (02742) 78 501-0 *Fax:* (02742) 78 501-15
*E-mail:* office@schubert-franzke.com
*Web Site:* www.map2web.cc/schubert-franzke
*Key Personnel*
Manager: Josef Scheibenreif *E-mail:* j.
scheibenreif@schubert-franzke.com
Sales & Marketing: Peter Labas *E-mail:* p.labas@
schubert-franzke.com
ISBN Prefix(es): 3-7056; 3-900938

**Verlagsbuero Karl Schwarzer**
Ziegelofengasse 27/1/2, 1050 Vienna
*Tel:* (01) 548 31 15-0 *Fax:* (01) 548 31 15-39
*E-mail:* verlagsbuero@schwarzer.at
*Web Site:* www.schwarzer.at
ISBN Prefix(es): 3-900392

**Verlag Josef Otto Slezak+**
Wiedner Hauptstr 40-42, 1040 Vienna
*Tel:* (01) 587 02 59 *Fax:* (01) 587 02 59
*E-mail:* verlag.slezak@aon.at
*Web Site:* www.byronny.at/index.html
*Key Personnel*
Sales Manager: Ilse Slezak
Contact: Josef Otto Slezak
Founded: 1960
Specialize in railway books.
Membership(s): Oesterreichische Verkehrswis-
senschaftliche Gesellschaft.
Subjects: Foreign Countries, History, Transporta-
tion
ISBN Prefix(es): 3-85416; 3-900134

Number of titles published annually: 4 Print
Total Titles: 50 Print
Distributed by Minirex (Switzerland)

**SN-Verlag,** see Salzburger Nachrichten
Verlagsgesellschaft mbH & Co KG

**Springer-Verlag Wien+**
Sachsenplatz 4-6, 1200 Vienna
Mailing Address: PO Box 89, 1201 Vienna
*Tel:* (01) 3302415 *Fax:* (01) 3302426
*E-mail:* books@springer.at (orders); journals@
springer.at (orders)
*Web Site:* www.springer.at
*Key Personnel*
Dir, Ed, Art, Cultural Studies: Rudolf Siegle
*E-mail:* siegle@springer.at
Founded: 1924
Subjects: Anthropology, Architecture & Interior
Design, Art, Biological Sciences, Business,
Chemistry, Chemical Engineering, Civil Engi-
neering, Communications, Computer Science,
Economics, Education, Electronics, Electrical
Engineering, Engineering (General), Environ-
mental Studies, Law, Mathematics, Mechani-
cal Engineering, Medicine, Nursing, Dentistry,
Philosophy, Physics, Psychology, Psychiatry,
Science (General), Technology
ISBN Prefix(es): 3-211
*Associate Companies:* Springer-Verlag New York
Inc, 175 Fifth Ave, New York, NY 10010,
United States
Distributor for Birkhaaeuser; Boehlau; L Mueller;
Springer; Steinkopff
*Bookshop(s):* Minerva Wissenschaftliche Buch-
handlung GmbH, Sachsenplatz 4-6, 1200 Vi-
enna

**J Steinbrener OHG+**
Im Eichbuchl 1, 4780 Scharding
*Tel:* (07712) 2038 *Fax:* (07712) 2038-20
*E-mail:* steinbrener@aon.at
Founded: 1855
Subjects: Religion - Other
ISBN Prefix(es): 3-85296
*Associate Companies:* J Steinbrener OHG
Zweigneiderlassung Neuhaus, Wagnerstr 21,
Neuhaus, Germany

**Dr Paul Struzl GmbH,** see Akademische
Druck-u Verlagsanstalt Dr Paul Struzl GmbH

**Studien Verlag Gmbh+**
Amraser Str 118, 6020 Innsbruck
*Tel:* (0512) 395045 *Fax:* (0512) 395045-15
*E-mail:* order@studienverlag.at
*Web Site:* www.studienverlag.at
*Key Personnel*
Contact: Martin Kofler
Founded: 1984
Publishing company for scientific books.
Subjects: Communications, Education, History,
Journalism, Language Arts, Linguistics, Litera-
ture, Literary Criticism, Essays, Music, Dance,
Philosophy, Science (General), Women's Stud-
ies
ISBN Prefix(es): 3-901160; 3-7065
Number of titles published annually: 80 Print
Total Titles: 1,000 Print

**Verlag Styria+**
Imprint of Styria Pichler Verlag GmbH & Co KG
Schoenaugasse 64, 8010 Graz
*Tel:* (0316) 8063 7601 *Fax:* (0316) 8063 7004
*E-mail:* office@styriapichler.at
*Web Site:* www.verlagstyria.com *Cable:*
STYRIAVERLAG GRAZ
*Key Personnel*
Man Dir: Dietmar Sternad *Tel:* (0316) 8063 7001
*E-mail:* dietmar.sternad@styriapichler.at

Sales: Isabella Scheuringer *E-mail:* isabella. scheuringer@styriapichler.at
Founded: 1869
Subjects: Biography, Education, History, Journalism, Philosophy, Religion - Other
ISBN Prefix(es): 3-222; 3-7012
Number of titles published annually: 70 Print
*Associate Companies:* Verlag Corinthion, Volkermarkter Ring 25, 9020 Ulapenfurt
*Branch Office(s)*
Verlag Styria Koeen, Rodenberg 18, Kuerten-Bechen
*Bookshop(s):* Buchhandlung Styria, Albrechtgasse 5, 8010 Graz; Buchhandlung und Antiquariat Moser, Herrengasse 23, 8010 Graz

**Suedwind - Buchwelt GmbH**
Baumgasse 79, 1034 Vienna
*Tel:* (01) 798 83 49 *Fax:* (01) 798 83 75
*E-mail:* versand@suedwind.at
*Web Site:* www.suedwind.at
*Key Personnel*
Contact: Barbara Hosp
Founded: 1984
Subjects: Government, Political Science, Nonfiction (General)
ISBN Prefix(es): 3-900592
Total Titles: 25 Print

**Edition Tau u Tau Type Druck Verlags-und Handels GmbH+**
Biriczweg 1, Postfach 19, 7202 Bad Sauerbrunn
*Tel:* (02625) 32000 *Fax:* (02625) 320003
*Key Personnel*
Publisher: Erich Greistorfer
Production Dir: Peter Feigl
Contact: Klaus Kopinitsch
Founded: 1988
Subjects: Biography, Nonfiction (General), Religion - Other
ISBN Prefix(es): 3-900977; 3-901997

**Thanhaeuser Edition**
Wallseerstr 6, 4100 Ottensheim
Mailing Address: Postfach 9, 4100 Ottensheim
*Tel:* (07234) 83800 *Fax:* (07234) 83800
*E-mail:* thanhaeuser@bibliotheca-selecta.de
*Key Personnel*
Contact: Christian Thanhaeuser; Irmgard Thanhaeuser
Founded: 1989
Subjects: Poetry
ISBN Prefix(es): 3-900986
Total Titles: 40 Print

**Edition Thurnhof KEG**
Wiener Str 2, 3580 Horn
*Tel:* (02982) 629-54 *Fax:* (02982) 3333
*E-mail:* edition@thurnhof.at
*Web Site:* www.thurnhof.at
*Key Personnel*
Publisher: Toni Kurz *E-mail:* toni.kurz@eunet.at
Founded: 1983
Subjects: Art, Poetry
ISBN Prefix(es): 3-900678
Divisions: Galerie-Thurnhof
*Branch Office(s)*
Druckerei & Atelier, 3580 Muehlfeld 43

**Trauner Verlag**
Koeglstr 14, 4021 Linz
*Tel:* (0732) 77 82 41-212 *Fax:* (0732) 77 82 41-400
*E-mail:* office@trauner.at
*Web Site:* www.trauner.at
*Key Personnel*
Man Dir: Rudolf Trauner
Founded: 1946
Subjects: Cookery, Medicine, Nursing, Dentistry, Science (General)
ISBN Prefix(es): 3-85320

**Edition Tusch+**
Heigerleinstr 36-40, 1160 Vienna
*Tel:* (01) 485 40 01 *Fax:* (01) 485 40 01-15
*E-mail:* citypost@cpz.at
*Telex:* 116262 Tusch *Cable:* EDITUSCH VIENNA
*Key Personnel*
Man Dir: Anton Tusch
Editorial: Wolfgang Prager
Founded: 1972
Subjects: Architecture & Interior Design, Art, Ethnicity
ISBN Prefix(es): 3-85063

**Tyrolia Verlagsanstalt GmbH**
Exlgasse 20, 6020 Innsbruck
*Tel:* (0512) 2233-510 *Fax:* (0512) 2233-512
*E-mail:* pgh@tyrolia.at
*Web Site:* www.tyrolia.at
*Telex:* 053620 *Cable:* TYROLIA VERLAG INNSBRUCK
*Key Personnel*
Dir: Dr Schiemer
Founded: 1888
Subjects: Nonfiction (General), Religion - Other, Travel
ISBN Prefix(es): 3-7022
*Bookshop(s):* Tyrolia, Exlgasse 20, Postfach 220, 6020 Innsbruck

**Verlag Carl Ueberreuter**, see Annette Betz Verlag im Verlag Carl Ueberreuter

**Verlag Carl Ueberreuter GmbH+**
Alser Str 24, 1091 Vienna
Mailing Address: Postfach 306, 1091 Vienna
*Tel:* (01) 40 444-172 *Fax:* (01) 40 444-5
*E-mail:* office-v@ueberreutes.at
*Web Site:* www.ueberreuter.de
*Key Personnel*
Holding: Ing Michael Salzer
Editorial: Britta Groiss; Irmgard Harrer; Gudula Jungeblodt; Dr Alfred Schierer; Thomas Zauner
Production: Maria Schuster
Publicity: Iris Seidenstricker
Sales: Petra Thomsen
Rights & Permissions: Dr Sibylle Goeller *Tel:* (01) 40444173 *E-mail:* goeller@ ueberreuter.at
Man Dir: Dr Fritz Panzer
Contact: Monika Reisenbauer *Tel:* (01) 40444-171 *E-mail:* reisenbauer@ueberreuter.at
Founded: 1548
Subjects: Animals, Pets, Art, Astrology, Occult, Biography, Economics, Fiction, Government, Political Science, Health, Nutrition, History, Music, Dance, Nonfiction (General), Science (General), Science Fiction, Fantasy
ISBN Prefix(es): 3-220
Number of titles published annually: 140 Print
Total Titles: 800 Print
Imprints: Annette Betz
Subsidiaries: Annette Betz Verlag
Foreign Rights: A R T Dialog (Czech Republic); ACER; Akcali; Ball & Co; Bettiua & Julia Nibbe; China Consult (China, Taiwan); Ashley Grayson (US); Hercules (China, Taiwan); Imprima Korea (Korea); Iris; Liu Media (China); Onon L J Pren (Japan); Margit Schaleck; Shing-Shang (Taiwan); Tuttle Mori (Japan)
*Shipping Address:* BTG Spedition & Logistik GmbH, Neudorfstr 114, 2353 Guntramsdorf
*Warehouse:* BTG Spedition & Logistik GmbH, Neudorfstr 114, 2353 Guntramsdorf

**Universal Edition AG**
Karlsplatz 6, 1010 Vienna
*Tel:* (01) 337 23-0 *Fax:* (01) 337 23-400
*E-mail:* office@universaledition.com
*Web Site:* www.universaledition.com *Cable:* MUSIKEDITION VIENNA

*Key Personnel*
Man Dir: Johann Juranek; Marion von Hartlieb
Sales, Marketing & Public Relations: Ferdinand Walcher *E-mail:* walcher@universaledition.com
Founded: 1901
Subjects: Music, Dance
ISBN Prefix(es): 3-7024
Subsidiaries: Urtext Edition-Musikverlag GmbH KG (jointly owned with B Schott's Soehne, Germany)

**Urban und Schwarzenberg GmbH**
Frankgasse 4, 1090 Vienna
*Tel:* (01) 4052731-0 *Fax:* (01) 405272441
*Key Personnel*
Manager: Gunter Royer
Founded: 1866
Subjects: Medicine, Nursing, Dentistry, Physics, Psychology, Psychiatry
ISBN Prefix(es): 3-85327
*Parent Company:* Williams & Wilkins Ltd, 428 East Preston St, Baltimore, MD 21202, United States
*Associate Companies:* Urban und Schwarzenberg GmbH, Verlag fuer Medizin, Germany

**Edition Va Bene+**
Max-Kahrer-G 32, 3400 Klosterneuburg
Mailing Address: Reichsratsstr 17, 1010 Vienna
*Tel:* (02243) 22 159; (0664) 1616356 (mobile) *Fax:* (02243) 22 159
*E-mail:* edition@vabene.at
*Web Site:* www.vabene.at
*Key Personnel*
Owner: Dr Walter Weiss
Founded: 1991
Subjects: Anthropology, Asian Studies, Communications, Developing Countries, Ethnicity, Foreign Countries, Health, Nutrition, Literature, Literary Criticism, Essays, Philosophy, Physical Sciences, Poetry, Religion - Catholic, Romance, Science (General), Theology, Travel
ISBN Prefix(es): 3-85167
Total Titles: 160 Print
*Warehouse:* Dr Franz Hain, Dr Otto Neurath-Gasse 5, 1220 Vienna *Tel:* (01) 28265650 *Fax:* (01) 2825282

**Verband der Wissenschaftlichen Gesellschaften Oesterreichs (VWGOe)**
Lindengasse 37, 1070 Vienna
*Tel:* (01) 932166; (01) 934756 *Fax:* (01) 5262054
*Key Personnel*
Man Dir: Dr Rainer Zitta
Founded: 1954
Subjects: Archaeology, Business, Education, History, Mathematics, Music, Dance, Philosophy, Physical Sciences
ISBN Prefix(es): 3-85369

**Verein Gruppe Wespennest**, *imprint of* Wespennest - Zeitschrift fuer brauchbare Texte und Bilder

**Verlag Veritas Mediengesellschaft mbH+**
Hafenstr 1-3, 4020 Linz
*Tel:* (0732) 776451-250 *Fax:* (0732) 776451-239
*E-mail:* veritas@veritas.at
*Web Site:* www.veritas.at
*Key Personnel*
Man Dir: Christl Manfred
Chief Editor: M Griessner *Tel:* (0732) 776451732 *E-mail:* mgriessner@veritas.co.at
Sales & Publicity: Meraner Manfred
Founded: 1945
Subjects: Cookery, Education, Health, Nutrition, Outdoor Recreation, Regional Interests
ISBN Prefix(es): 3-85329; 3-7058; 3-85214
Total Titles: 450 Print; 5 CD-ROM; 20 Audio
*Parent Company:* Cornelsen, Germany

Subsidiaries: Ehrenwirth Verlag; Salzburger Jugend-Verlag
*Bookshop(s):* Buchhandlung Veritas, Harrachstr 5, 4020 Linz
*Warehouse:* Wertpraesent, Boschstr 31, 4600 Weis
*Tel:* (7242) 696-0

**Vorarlberger Verlagsanstalt Aktiengesellschaft**
Schwefel 81, 6850 Dornbirn
*Tel:* (05572) 24 6 97-0 *Fax:* (05572) 24 6 97-78
*E-mail:* office@vva.at
*Web Site:* www.vva.at
*Key Personnel*
Contact: Karl-Heinz Milz *E-mail:* kh.milz@vva.at; Marlene Sutter
Founded: 1920
Subjects: Geography, Geology, History, Regional Interests
ISBN Prefix(es): 3-85430

**VWGOe,** see Verband der Wissenschaftlichen Gesellschaften Oesterreichs (VWGOe)

**Universitaetsverlag Wagner GmbH**
Andreas-Hoferstr 13, 6010 Innsbruck
Mailing Address: Postfach 165, 6010 Innsbruck
*Tel:* (0512) 597721 *Fax:* (0512) 582209
*E-mail:* mail@uvw.at
  *Cable:* UNIVERSITAETSVERLAG WAGNER INNSBRUCK
*Key Personnel*
Man Dir: Gottfried Grasl
Contact: Dr Blaas Mercedes *E-mail:* mercedes.blaas@uvw.at
Founded: 1554
Subjects: Archaeology, Automotive, Geography, Geology, History, Language Arts, Linguistics, Science (General)
ISBN Prefix(es): 3-7030

**Verlag Mag Wanzenbock+**
Landstrasser Hauptstr 88/6, 1030 Vienna
*Tel:* (01) 7148542 *Fax:* (01) 7135814
*Key Personnel*
Dir: Hans Wanzenbock *E-mail:* johann.wanzenboeck@chello.at
Founded: 1990
Subjects: English as a Second Language
ISBN Prefix(es): 3-901682
Number of titles published annually: 2 Print
Total Titles: 1 Print
*Orders to:* Oebz, Iz Noe Sued Str 1, OBJ 34, 2355 Wiener Neudorf, Contact: Mrs Prinz
*Tel:* (02263) 63535 *Fax:* (02263) 63535243

**Weilburg Verlag**
Fleschgasse 34, 1130 Vienna
*Tel:* (02622) 29538 *Fax:* (02622) 2953822
*Key Personnel*
Owner & Man Dir: Helmut Dresel
Sales: Selbst Liefert
Subjects: Art, Poetry
ISBN Prefix(es): 3-900100; 3-85246

**Dr Otfried Weise Verlag Tabula Smaragdina+**
Anton-Langer-Gasse 46/2/5, 1130 Vienna
*Tel:* (01) 804 2974 *Fax:* (01) 961 8287
*E-mail:* tabula@smaragdina.at
*Web Site:* smaragdina.at
*Key Personnel*
Man Dir: Otfried Weise
Founded: 1991
Subjects: Astrology, Occult, Health, Nutrition, Nonfiction (General)
ISBN Prefix(es): 3-9802471; 3-931138

**Herbert Weishaupt Verlag+**
Hauptplatz 27, 8342 Gnas
*Tel:* (03151) 8487 *Fax:* (03151) 84874
*E-mail:* verlag@weishaupt.at
*Web Site:* www.weishaupt.at

*Key Personnel*
Contact: Herbert Weishaupt; Annemarie Weishaupt
Founded: 1980
Subjects: Aeronautics, Aviation, Maritime, Military Science, Natural History, Nonfiction (General), Regional Interests, Travel
ISBN Prefix(es): 3-7059; 3-900310
Number of titles published annually: 35 Print; 1 CD-ROM; 1 Audio
Total Titles: 320 Print

**Verlag Welsermuehl+**
Maria-Theresiastr 41, 4600 Wels
*Tel:* (07242) 231-0 *Fax:* (07242) 23118
*Telex:* 25586 *Cable:* WELSERMUHLDRUCK WELS
*Key Personnel*
Dir: Karl Pramendorfer
Founded: 1928
ISBN Prefix(es): 3-85339
*Branch Office(s)*
Kufsteinerstr 8, 81679 Munich, Germany

**Verlag Galerie Welz Salzburg**
Sigmund-Haffner Gasse 16, 5020 Salzburg
*Tel:* (0662) 841771; (0662) 840990 *Fax:* (0662) 84177120
*E-mail:* office@galerie-welz.at
*Web Site:* www.galerie-welz.at
*Key Personnel*
Publisher: Franz Eder
Sales: Hannes Lueftenegger
Subjects: Art
ISBN Prefix(es): 3-85349

**Wespennest - Zeitschrift fuer brauchbare Texte und Bilder+**
Rembrandtstr 31/4, 1020 Vienna
*Tel:* (01) 332 66 91 *Fax:* (01) 333 29 70
*E-mail:* office@wespennest.at
*Web Site:* www.wespennest.at
*Key Personnel*
Managing Editor: Walter Famler
Contact: Friederike Schwabel
Founded: 1969
Literary essayistic cultural magazine, quarterly publication.
Subjects: Literature, Literary Criticism, Essays
ISBN Prefix(es): 3-85458
Imprints: Verein Gruppe Wespennest
Distributed by Deutsche Verlagsanstalt

**Wiener Dom-Verlag GmbH**
Spiegelgasse 3/D, 1014 Vienna
Mailing Address: Postfach 152, 1014 Vienna
*Tel:* (01) 5123503 *Fax:* (01) 5123503-30
*Web Site:* www.buchwirtschaft.at
*Telex:* 111760
*Key Personnel*
Man Dir: Franz Pollhammer
  *E-mail:* pollhammer@domverlag.at
Founded: 1946
Subjects: Religion - Catholic
ISBN Prefix(es): 3-85351
Divisions: Kunsthandlung
*Bookshop(s):* Rathausplatz 10, 3390 Melk; Bahnstr 1, 2130 Mistelbach; Stephansplatz 5, 1010 Vienna; Favoritenstr 115, 1100 Vienna; Domgasse 3, 2700 Wiener Neustadt

**Wienerland Zeitung & Verlag**
Pammessergasse 13, 2103 Langenzersdorf
Mailing Address: Postfach 33, 2103 Langenzersdorf
*Tel:* (02244) 3536 *Fax:* (02244) 3536-4
*E-mail:* wienerland@asn.or.at
*Telex:* 75211689 avw a
*Key Personnel*
Contact: Peterka Fritz
Founded: 1973

Subjects: Travel
ISBN Prefix(es): 3-900451

**Wieser Verlag+**
Ebentaler Str 34b, 9020 Klagenfurt/Celovec
*Tel:* (0463) 37036 *Fax:* (0463) 37635
*E-mail:* office@wieser-verlag.com
*Web Site:* www.wieser-verlag.com
*Key Personnel*
Publisher: Lojze Wieser
Founded: 1987
Subjects: Biography, Drama, Theater, Fiction, Government, Political Science, Literature, Literary Criticism, Essays, Poetry
ISBN Prefix(es): 3-85129

**Verlag Wilhelm Braumuller Universitats-Verlagsbuchhandlung GmbH**
Servitengasse 5, 1092 Vienna
*Tel:* (01) 319 11 59 *Fax:* (01) 310 28 05
*E-mail:* office@braumueller.at
*Web Site:* www.braumueller.at
ISBN Prefix(es): 3-7003

**Kunstverlag Wolfrum**
Augustinerstr 10, 1010 Vienna
*Tel:* (01) 512 53 98-0 *Fax:* (01) 512 53 98-57
*E-mail:* your-welcome@wolfrum.at
*Web Site:* www.wolfrum.at/html/wolfrum.htm
*Telex:* 75311081 Wolb *Cable:* WITWOLF VIENNA
*Key Personnel*
Man Dir: Monika Engel
Founded: 1919
Subjects: Art
ISBN Prefix(es): 3-900178

**WUV/Facultas Universitaetsverlag**
Mountain Lane 5, 1090 Vienna
*Tel:* (01) 310 53 56 *Fax:* (01) 319 70 50
*E-mail:* verlag@facultas.at
*Web Site:* www.wuv-verlag.at
*Telex:* 116529 Icpfa
*Key Personnel*
Manager: Thomas Stauffer *E-mail:* stauffer@facultas.at
Marketing: Christine Bernert *E-mail:* bernert@facultas.at
Publisher: Dr Michael Huter *E-mail:* huter@facultas.at
Editor: Dr Sigrid Neulinger *E-mail:* neulinger@facultas.at
Founded: 1962
Subjects: Art, Behavioral Sciences, Communications, History, Language Arts, Linguistics, Law, Medicine, Nursing, Dentistry, Nonfiction (General), Philosophy, Psychology, Psychiatry, Science (General), Social Sciences, Sociology, Women's Studies, Specialize in scientific literature
ISBN Prefix(es): 3-85076; 3-85114
*Associate Companies:* Facultas Universitaetsverlag

**WUV/Service Fachverlag+**
Berggasse 5, 1090 Vienna
*Tel:* (01) 310 53 56 *Fax:* (01) 319 70 50
*E-mail:* verlag@facultas.at
*Web Site:* www.wuv-verlag.at/WUV
*Telex:* 135720 hwusv
*Key Personnel*
Publishing Dir: Dr Christin Draexler
Founded: 1981
Subjects: Accounting, Business, Career Development, Economics, Finance, Law, Management, Marketing
ISBN Prefix(es): 3-85428
*Bookshop(s):* Universitat Buchhandlung, Doblinger Hauptstr 7A/12, 1190 Vienna
*Orders to:* Augasse 2-6, 1090 Vienna
  *Tel:* (01) 317 91 62 *Fax:* (01) 317 91 62-45
  *E-mail:* wuv-buchhandlung@facultas.at

**Zirkular - Verlag der Dokumentationsstelle fuer neuere oesterreichische Literatur**
Silk Lane 13, 1070 Vienna
*Tel:* (01) 526 20 44-0 *Fax:* (01) 526 20 44-30
*E-mail:* info@literaturhaus.at
*Web Site:* www.literaturhaus.at
*Key Personnel*
Founder: Dr Heinz Lunzer *Tel:* (01) 526 20 44-17
  *E-mail:* hl@literaturhaus.at
President: Dr Uwe Baur
Founded: 1979
Subjects: Biography, Literature, Literary Criticism, Essays
ISBN Prefix(es): 3-900467

**Paul Zsolnay Verlag GmbH+**
Prinz-Eugenstr 30, 1040 Vienna
Mailing Address: Postfach 142, 1040 Vienna
*Tel:* (01) 50576610 *Fax:* (01) 505766110
*E-mail:* info@zsolnay.at
*Web Site:* www.zsolnay.at *Cable:* ZSOLNAYVERLAG WIEN
*Key Personnel*
Man Dir: Stephan Joss; Michael Krueger
Rights & Permissions: Annette Lechner
Sales Manager: Felicitas Feilhauer
Editorial Dir: Herbert Ohrlinger
Production: Stefanie Schelleis
Contact: Bettina Woergoetter *Tel:* (01) 5057661-14
Founded: 1923
Subjects: Biography, Fiction, History, Nonfiction (General), Poetry
ISBN Prefix(es): 3-552; 3-223; 3-85190
Number of titles published annually: 40 Print
Total Titles: 500 Print
*Parent Company:* Carl Hanser GmbH & Co, Vilshofenerstr 10, 81679 Munich, Germany
*Orders to:* Dr Franz Hain, Dr Otto-Neurath-Gasse 5, 1220 Vienna *Tel:* (01) 2826565 *Fax:* (01) 2825282
Verlegerdienst Muenchen, Gutenbergstr 1, 82205 Gilching, Germany, Contact: Evelyne Weindl *Tel:* (08105) 388-122 *Fax:* (08105) 388-100 *E-mail:* weindl@verlegerdienst.de

# Azerbaijan

## General Information

*Capital:* Baku
*Language:* Azerbaijani
*Religion:* Predominantly Muslim (Shiite and Sunni); also Christian (mainly Russian Orthodox & Armenian Apostolic)
*Population:* 7.5 million
*Bank Hours:* Generally open for short hours between 0930-1230 Monday-Friday
*Shop Hours:* Generally 0900-1800 Monday-Friday; often open weekends
*Currency:* 1 kopeks = 1 rubl
*Export/Import Information:* According to Ukrainian quotas & customs duties, companies engaged in trade should register with the Ukraine Ministry of Foreign Economic Relations. Licenses for export & import are also required for trade with Russia.
*Copyright:* UCC (see Copyright Conventions, pg xi)

**Azernesr**
Gusi Gadzieva 4, 370005 Baku
*Tel:* (012) 925015
*Key Personnel*
Dir: A Mustafazade
Editor-in-Chief: A Guseinzade
Founded: 1924

Subjects: Agriculture, Fiction, Government, Political Science, Science (General), Technology
ISBN Prefix(es): 5-552

**Sada, Literaturno-Izdatel'skij Centr+**
Ul Bol'saja Krepostnaja, 28, 370004 Baku
*Tel:* (012) 927564 *Fax:* (012) 929843
*Key Personnel*
Contact: Guliev Tarlan
Subjects: Accounting, Asian Studies, Astrology, Occult, Business, Child Care & Development, Disability, Special Needs, Drama, Theater, Earth Sciences, Economics, Education, English as a Second Language, Finance, History, Humor, Language Arts, Linguistics, Management, Marketing, Music, Dance, Mysteries, Natural History
ISBN Prefix(es): 5-86874
*Parent Company:* National Peace Fund

# Bahrain

## General Information

*Capital:* Manama
*Language:* Arabic (English also widely spoken)
*Religion:* Muslims of the Shiite & Sunni sects
*Population:* 551,000
*Bank Hours:* 0730-1200 Saturday-Wednesday; 0730-1100 Thursday
*Currency:* 1000 Fils = 1 Bahrain dinar
*Export/Import Information:* Generally books dutied at 10%, most schoolbooks free of duty; none on advertising matter. No import license required but no obscene literature permitted & for books (not for advertising) a Chamber of Commerce certificate is mandatory. No exchange controls.

**Arab Communicators**
PO Box 551, Manama
*Tel:* (0973) 254 258 *Fax:* (0973) 531 837
*Key Personnel*
Publisher & Editor-in-Chief: Ahmed A Fakhri
Publisher: Hamed A Abul
Founded: 1981
*Parent Company:* ArabConsult
Subsidiaries: Arabvision; Arabad

**Al Hilal Publications**
Government Ave, Manama
Mailing Address: PO Box 224, Manama
*Tel:* 231122
*Telex:* 8981 Hilal
*Key Personnel*
Contact: Mr Silveira Haydn
*Bookshop(s):* Al Hilal Bookshop

# Bangladesh

## General Information

*Capital:* Dhaka
*Language:* Bengali (English widely used commercially)
*Religion:* Predominately Muslim with some Hindu
*Population:* 129.2 million
*Bank Hours:* 0900-330 Saturday-Wednesday; 0900-1100 Thursday
*Shop Hours:* 1000-2030 Saturday-Thursday
*Currency:* 100 pisha = 1 taka (Tk)

*Export/Import Information:* No tariff on books and advertising matter. Import licenses required for all imports.
*Copyright:* UCC (see Copyright Conventions, pg xi)

**Academic Publishers+**
2/7 Nawab-Habibullah Rd, Dhaka 1000
*Tel:* (02) 507355; (02) 507366 *Fax:* (02) 863060
*Key Personnel*
Joint Man Dir: Habibur Rahman
Founded: 1982
Subjects: Social Sciences, Sociology
ISBN Prefix(es): 984-08

**Adeyle Brothers & Co**
60 Patuatuly, Dhaka 1100
*Tel:* (02) 233508
ISBN Prefix(es): 984-402

**Ankur Prakashani+**
38/4 Bangla Bazar, Dhaka 1100
*Tel:* (02) 250132 *Fax:* (02) 9567730
*E-mail:* ankur@bangla.net
Founded: 1986
Also acts as a library supplier & importer of reference books.
Subjects: Anthropology, Asian Studies, Economics, Education, Fiction, Government, Political Science, Literature, Literary Criticism, Essays, Nonfiction (General)
ISBN Prefix(es): 984-464; 984-8010
Distributor for Narosa (India); Prints India
*Orders to:* 40/1 Purana Paltan, Dhaka 1000

**Bangladesh Government Press, Ministry of Establishment, Government of the Peoples Republic of Bangladesh**
Tejgaon, Dhaka 1209
*Tel:* (02) 606 316 *Fax:* (02) 8113095
*E-mail:* adab@bdonline.com
ISBN Prefix(es): 984-01

**Bangladesh Publishers+**
45 Patuatuli Rd, Dhaka 1100
*Tel:* (02) 233135
*Key Personnel*
Dir: Maya Rani Ghosal
Founded: 1952
Membership(s): Book Sellers & Publication Association of Bangladesh, Pranab Math (a philanthropic organization that helps in free education). Also acts as distributor of books & periodicals of both local & foreign countries.
Subjects: Accounting, Drama, Theater, Economics, Physics, Public Administration, Religion - Hindu
ISBN Prefix(es): 984-8012
*Associate Companies:* Ratan & Sons
*Bookshop(s):* 38/19/B Banglabazar, 2nd floor, Dhaka 1100

**Boighar**
110-286 Bipani Bitan, Chittagong
*Tel:* (031) 252745
ISBN Prefix(es): 984-423

**Chalantika Boighar**
14 Banglabazar, 1st floor, Dhaka 1100
*Tel:* (02) 257345 *Fax:* (02) 7115691
ISBN Prefix(es): 984-8019

**Gatidhara+**
38/2-ka Banglabazar, Dhaka 1100
*Tel:* (02) 7392077 (press); (02) 7113117 (res); (02) 7115630 (res); (02) 7117515 (showroom); (02) 7118273 (showroom) *Fax:* (02) 9134617; (02) 9566456
*E-mail:* akter@aitlbd.net; gatidara@bdonline.com

*Key Personnel*
Publisher & Chief Executive: Sikder Abul Bashar
Founded: 1988
Also acts as distributor & exporter.
Membership(s): Publishers Association; Publishers Guild.
Subjects: Behavioral Sciences, Child Care & Development, Drama, Theater, Education, Fiction, Health, Nutrition, Humor, Literature, Literary Criticism, Essays, Poetry, Religion - Islamic
ISBN Prefix(es): 984-461
Subsidiaries: Gatidhara Computers
*Bookshop(s):* 38/2 Banglabazar, Dhaka 1100
*Book Club(s):* National Book Center; National Library
*Warehouse:* Kumarpatty Rd, Jhalakati 8400
*Orders to:* 38/4 Banglabazar, Dhaka 1100

**Gono Prakashani, Gono Shasthya Kendra+**
14/E Dhanmondhi R/A, Dhaka 1205
*Tel:* (02) 500406; (02) 839366 *Fax:* (02) 863567; (02) 833182
*E-mail:* gk.mail@drik.bgd.toolnet.org *Cable:* GRAM GORO, DHAKA
*Key Personnel*
Man Dir: Mr Shafiq Khan
Editor: Mr Bazlur Rahim
Chairman & President Editorial Board: Dr Zafrullah Chowdhury
Founded: 1978
Subjects: Child Care & Development, Health, Nutrition, Medicine, Nursing, Dentistry, Self-Help, Social Sciences, Sociology
ISBN Prefix(es): 984-431
*Parent Company:* Gonoshasthaya Kendra Trust
*Associate Companies:* Gonoshasthaya Pharmaceutical, Ltd; Gonoshasthaya Antibiotic Ltd
Subsidiaries: Gono Mudran (printing company)
Distributed by Baulman Prakason (Kolkata, India)
*Showroom(s):* Gono Prakashani Aziz Cooperative Market Shahbagh, Dhaka
*Bookshop(s):* Gono Prakashani Aziz Cooperative Market Shahbagh, Dhaka
*Shipping Address:* Gono Prakashani Po Mirzanaga, Nayarhat, 1344 Dhaka
*Warehouse:* Gono Prakashani Po Mirzanagar, Nayarhat, Dhaka 1344
*Orders to:* Gono Prakashani Po Mirzanagar, Nayarhat, Dhaka 1344

**Mullick Bros**
3/1 Bangla Bazar, Dhaka 1100
*Tel:* (02) 280728
Subjects: Education
ISBN Prefix(es): 984-411; 984-8272

**Agamee Prakashani+**
36 Banglabazar, Dhaka 1100
*Tel:* (02) 711-1332; (02) 711-0021 *Fax:* (02) 9562018; (02) 7123945
*E-mail:* agamee@bdonline.com
*Web Site:* www.agameeprakashani-bd.com *Cable:* AGAMEE
*Key Personnel*
Chief Executive Officer: Osman Gani *Tel:* (02) 189219024 *Fax:* (02) 9340856 *E-mail:* bfdr@bdonline.com
Founded: 1986
Membership(s): Bangladesh Publishers & Book Sellers Association; Dhaka Chamber of Commerce & Industry; FBCCI; Bangladesh Publishers Council.
Subjects: Fiction, Government, Political Science, Journalism, Literature, Literary Criticism, Essays, Music, Dance, Philosophy, Poetry, Science (General), Social Sciences, Sociology, Women's Studies
ISBN Prefix(es): 984-401
Number of titles published annually: 70 Print
Total Titles: 802 Print
Distributed by Phuthipatra (Kalkata)

Distributor for Muktadhara (USA)
*Book Club(s):* Bangladesh Book Club (Bangladesh)

**The University Press Ltd+**
Red Crescent Bldg, 114 Motijheel C/A, Dhaka 1000
Mailing Address: GPO Box 2611, Dhaka 1000
*Tel:* (02) 861208; (02) 255789 *Fax:* (02) 8332112
*E-mail:* upl@bangla.net; upl@bttb.net.bd
*Telex:* 642460 bhlbj *Cable:* DUNIPRESS
*Key Personnel*
Man Dir & Publisher: Mr Mohiuddin Ahmed
Senior Manager Editorial: Badiuddin Nazir
Sales Manager: M A Halim
Production Executive: Abdar Rahman
Founded: 1975
Specializes in publishing, selling & importing.
Subjects: Agriculture, Anthropology, Archaeology, Architecture & Interior Design, Art, Biography, Economics, Education, Environmental Studies, Finance, Geography, Geology, Government, Political Science, History, Management, Military Science, Public Administration, Publishing & Book Trade Reference, Religion - Islamic, Technology, Travel, Women's Studies
ISBN Prefix(es): 984-05
Number of titles published annually: 70 Print
Total Titles: 500 Print
*Branch Office(s)*
146 Dampara, Chittagong & 86 K D Ghose Rd, Khulna
Distributed by Intermediate Technology (UK); Manohar Publishers & Distributors (New Delhi, India); Oxford University Press (Pakistan); Paragon Enterprise (India); ZED Books (UK)
Distributor for Intermediate Technology (UK); Manohar Publishers & Distributors (India); Oxford University Press (UK, Pakistan & India); ZED Books (UK)
*Distribution Center:* Government New Market, Gulshan, Banani, Hotel Sonargaon, Zia International Airport, Dhaka

# Barbados

## General Information

*Capital:* Bridgetown
*Language:* English
*Religion:* Anglican
*Population:* 263,000
*Bank Hours:* 0800-1500 Monday-Thursday; 0800-1750 Friday
*Shop Hours:* 0800-1600 Monday-Friday; 0800-1200 Saturday
*Currency:* 100 cents = 1 Barbados dollar
*Export/Import Information:* No tariff on books. Import license covering exchange required; no obscene literature permitted.
*Copyright:* Berne, UCC (see Copyright Conventions, pg xi)

**Business Tutors**
124 Chancery Lane, Christ Church
*Tel:* (246) 428-5664 *Fax:* (246) 429-4854
*E-mail:* pchad@caribsurf.com
Subjects: Astrology, Occult, Business, Disability, Special Needs, Management, Microcomputers, Self-Help
ISBN Prefix(es): 976-8084
Subsidiaries: P & R Chad Ltd

**Carib Research & Publications Inc**
PO Box 556, Bridgetown
*Tel:* 438-0580
*Key Personnel*
Chief Executive: Dr Farley Brathwaite
Founded: 1986

Also acts as agent for Antilles Publications.
Subjects: Regional Interests
ISBN Prefix(es): 976-8051
*Associate Companies:* Antilles Publications

# Belarus

## General Information

*Capital:* Minsk
*Language:* Belarussian
*Religion:* Predominantly Christian (mostly Roman Catholic & Eastern Orthodox)
*Population:* 10.4 million
*Bank Hours:* Generally open for short hours between 0930-1230 Monday-Friday
*Shop Hours:* Generally 0900-1800 Monday-Friday; often open weekends
*Currency:* 100 kopeks = 1 rubl
*Export/Import Information:* According to Ukrainian quotas & customs duties, companies engaged in trade should register with the Ukraine Ministry of Foreign Economic Relations. Licenses for export & import are also required for trade with Russia.
*Copyright:* UCC (see Copyright Conventions, pg xi)

**Belarus Vydavectva**
Prospect Maserova, 11, 220600 Minsk
*Tel:* (017) 2 238742 *Fax:* (017) 2 238731
*Key Personnel*
Dir: V L Dubovsky
Editor-in-Chief: L N Teterina
Founded: 1921
Subjects: Art, Economics, Government, Political Science, Medicine, Nursing, Dentistry, Music, Dance
ISBN Prefix(es): 5-338; 985-01

**Belaruskaya Encyklapedyya** (Byelossian Encyclopaedia)
vul Akademichnaya, 15A, 220072 Minsk
*Tel:* 2840600; 2841767 *Fax:* 2840983
*Key Personnel*
Editor-in-Chief: Genadz P Pashkou
Founded: 1967
Subjects: Agriculture, Archaeology, Architecture & Interior Design, Art, Biography, Biological Sciences, Cookery, Crafts, Games, Hobbies, Drama, Theater, Education, Fiction, Finance, Health, Nutrition, History, House & Home, Language Arts, Linguistics, Law, Literature, Literary Criticism, Essays, Mathematics, Medicine, Nursing, Dentistry, Natural History, Parapsychology, Photography, Physics, Poetry, Religion - Other, Science (General), Sports, Athletics
ISBN Prefix(es): 5-85700; 985-11

**Interdigest Publishing House+**
vul Zaharava 24, k 20, 220005 Minsk
Mailing Address: 24 Zakharov Ave, Off 20, 172, 220005 Minsk
*Tel:* (017) 2133073 *Fax:* (017) 843778
*Key Personnel*
President: Anatoli Kudrjavtsev
Vice President: Vladimir Sivchik
Founded: 1991
Subjects: Animals, Pets, Automotive, Biography, Career Development, Child Care & Development, Criminology, Fiction, Health, Nutrition, Music, Dance, Nonfiction (General), Women's Studies
ISBN Prefix(es): 985-10
Total Titles: 25,000 Print
*Associate Companies:* Digest & Kolm, Kaliningrad, Russian Federation; TOO Echo, Smolensk, Russian Federation

Distributed by TOO Echo (Smolensk, Russia)
Distributor for TOO Echo (Smolensk, Russia)
*Showroom(s):* 34, Skaryna Ave, Off 25, 220005 Minsk
*Bookshop(s):* 124, Partizanski Prospect, Minsk
*Shipping Address:* 3, Ingenernaja, Minsk
*Warehouse:* 3, Ingenernaja, Minsk

**Kavaler Publishers+**
7 Ignatenko St, 220035 Minsk
*Tel:* (0172) 2506485; (0172) 548198 *Fax:* (0172) 238041
*E-mail:* Kavaler@inbox.ru
*Key Personnel*
Dir & Publisher: Constantine Khotyanovsky
Deputy Dir: Svetlana Morozova
Founded: 1991
All editions are prize winners of the annual national contests *Art of the Book.*
Membership(s): Belarusian Association of Book Publishers & Book Distributors; Belarusian Union of Artists.
Subjects: Advertising, Business, English as a Second Language, Fiction, History, Nonfiction (General), Poetry, Wine & Spirits, German as a Second Language
ISBN Prefix(es): 985-6427
Number of titles published annually: 8 Print
Total Titles: 70 Print
*Book Club(s):* Minsk Book Exhibition-Sale Club Belakk

**Izdatelstvo Mastatskaya Litaratura**
Maserava prospect 11, 220600 Minsk
*Tel:* (017) 2235809; (017) 2238664
*Key Personnel*
Dir: S A Andreyuk
Editor-in-Chief: N S Kusenkov
Founded: 1972
Subjects: Fiction, Literature, Literary Criticism, Essays
ISBN Prefix(es): 5-340; 985-02

**Narodnaya Asveta+**
prasp Malerava 11, 220600 Minsk
*Tel:* 2236131 *Fax:* 2236184
*E-mail:* ngpna@asveta.belpak.minsk.by
*Key Personnel*
Dir: I Laptenok
Founded: 1951
Subjects: Biological Sciences, Economics, Environmental Studies, Geography, Geology, History, Mathematics
ISBN Prefix(es): 5-341; 985-03; 985-12

# Belgium

## General Information

*Capital:* Brussels
*Language:* Dutch in the north, French in the south. Brussels is officially bilingual. German in eastern Belgium
*Religion:* Predominantly Roman Catholic, some Protestant
*Population:* 10.2 million
*Bank Hours:* Main towns: 0900-1200/1300 & 1400-1530/1600: Monday-Friday
*Shop Hours:* 0900-1900 with variations
*Currency:* 100 Eurocents = 1 Euro; 40.3399 Belgian francs = 1 Euro
*Export/Import Information:* Member of the European Economic Community. No import license required, just Model A form of notice declaration of payment. No exchange controls. 6% VAT on books.
*Copyright:* UCC, Berne, Florence (see Copyright Conventions, pg xi)

**Abimo+**
Beukenlaan 8, 9250 Waasmunster
*Tel:* (052) 462407 *Fax:* (052) 461962
*E-mail:* info@abimo-uitgeverij.com
*Web Site:* www.abimo-uitgeverij.com
*Key Personnel*
Publisher: K David *E-mail:* k.david@ planetinternet.be
Founded: 1993
Membership(s): Vlaamse Uitgevers Vereniging.
Subjects: Drama, Theater, Earth Sciences, Education, Foreign Countries, Specialize in Geography
ISBN Prefix(es): 90-75905; 90-801767; 90-5932

**Academia-Bruylant+**
Subsidiary of Bruylant
Grand'Place 29, 1348 Louvain-la-Neuve
*Tel:* (010) 45 23 95 *Fax:* (010) 45 44 80
*E-mail:* academia.bruylant@skynet.be
*Web Site:* www.academia-bruylant.be
*Key Personnel*
President: Jean Vandeveld
Founded: 1987
Membership(s): ADEB.
Subjects: Accounting, Anthropology, Journalism, Law, Physical Sciences, Religion - Islamic, Social Sciences, Sociology
ISBN Prefix(es): 2-87209
Total Titles: 500 Print

**Academia Press+**
Eekhout 2, 9000 Ghent
*Tel:* (09) 233 80 88 *Fax:* (09) 233 14 09
*E-mail:* info@academiapress.be
*Web Site:* www.academiapress.be
*Key Personnel*
International Rights: Peter Laroy
Founded: 1989
Scientific Publishers.
Subjects: Business, Economics, Journalism, Psychology, Psychiatry, Science (General), Social Sciences, Sociology
ISBN Prefix(es): 90-382
*Parent Company:* J Story-Scientia Scientia bvba, Van Duyseplein 8, 9000 Ghent

**Uitgeverij Acco**
Brusselstr 153, 3000 Leuven
*Tel:* (016) 62 80 41 *Fax:* (016) 62 80 01
*E-mail:* uitgeverij@acco.be
*Web Site:* www.acco.be
*Key Personnel*
Dir: Herman Peeters *Tel:* (016) 62 80 10
    *E-mail:* herman.peeters@acco.be
Founded: 1960
Subjects: Criminology, Economics, Education, History, Language Arts, Linguistics, Law, Mathematics, Medicine, Nursing, Dentistry, Philosophy, Psychology, Psychiatry, Religion - Other, Science (General), Social Sciences, Sociology
ISBN Prefix(es): 90-334
Imprints: De Horstink
Subsidiaries: Acco; Broadcast Book Services (UK & Ireland)
*Orders to:* Tiensestr 134-136, 3000 Leuven

**Actualquarto+**
Allee des Bouleaux, 20, 6280 Gerpinnes
*Tel:* (071) 21 61 53 *Fax:* (071) 21 77 13
*Key Personnel*
Man Dir & Sales, Rights & Permission: Michel Paunet
Editorial: Jean Delahaut
Founded: 1970
Subjects: Education

**Centre Aequatoria**
Stationsstraat 48, 3360 Lovenjoel
*Tel:* (016) 46 44 84

*E-mail:* info@abbol.com
*Web Site:* www.aequatoria.be; www.abbol.com
*Key Personnel*
Dir: Honore Vinck *E-mail:* vinck.aequatoria@ skynet.be
Documentaliste: Guillaume Essalo
Founded: 1980
Promotes research on Central African humanities preference for Central African authors.
Subjects: Anthropology, Biography, Ethnicity, History, Language Arts, Linguistics, Regional Interests, Social Sciences, Sociology
*Branch Office(s)*
BP 276, Mbandaka, Congo
*U.S. Office(s):* The Missionaries of the S Heart (Aequatoria), 305 S Lake St, PO Box 270, Aurora, IL 60507, United States *Fax:* 630-892-3071 *E-mail:* mscusafin@ibm.net (only for payments of subscriptions to Annales Aequatoria)
Distributed by Editions St Paul (Zaire)

**Alamire vzw, Music Publishers+**
Division of Musica VZW
Toekomstlaan 5B, 3910 Neerpelt
*Tel:* (011) 610 510 *Fax:* (011) 610 511
*E-mail:* info@alamire.com
*Web Site:* www.alamire.com
*Key Personnel*
Dir: Herman Baeten *E-mail:* herman.baeten@ alamire.com
Marketing: Annelies Van Boxel *E-mail:* annelies. vanboxel@alamire.com
Founded: 1978
Specialize in early music facsimiles.
Subjects: Library & Information Sciences, Music, Dance
ISBN Prefix(es): 90-6853

**Altina+**
Dirk Lippens Vredestraat 34, 8400 Ostende
*Tel:* (059) 80-16-51 *Fax:* (059) 51-27-17
*Key Personnel*
President & International Rights: Dirk Lippens *Tel:* (059) 703324
Author: Christiane Beerlandt *Tel:* (059) 70 3324
Administration: Davina Doom *Tel:* (059) 80 1651
Founded: 1996
Publish works of Belgian author Christiane Beerlandt
Audio.
Subjects: Alternative, Astrology, Occult, Health, Nutrition, Music, Dance, Nonfiction (General), Philosophy, Psychology, Psychiatry, Self-Help, Philosophy of Joyful Life, Original Fairy Tales, Psychological Causes for Disease, Self Knowledge & realization, Physical Immortality, Health & Nutrition
ISBN Prefix(es): 90-75849
Number of titles published annually: 10 Print; 1 Audio
Total Titles: 25 Print; 3 Audio

**Amnesty International VZW**
Kerkstraat 156, 2060 Antwerp
*Tel:* (03) 271 16 16 *Fax:* (03) 235 78 12
*E-mail:* amnesty@aivl.be
*Web Site:* www.aivl.be
*Telex:* 32079
*Key Personnel*
Dir: Jane Brocatus *E-mail:* janb@aivl.be
Contact: Katrien Scholiers *E-mail:* promotie@ aivl.be
ISBN Prefix(es): 90-70895

**Artel SC**
2 Place Baudouin-ler, 5004 Namur, Bouge
*Tel:* (081) 21 37 00 *Fax:* (081) 21 23 72
*E-mail:* erasme@skynet.be
*Key Personnel*
General Manager: Joseph Ponet
Editorial Dir: Francoise Dury

Subjects: Biological Sciences, Environmental Studies, Government, Political Science, History, Mathematics, Religion - Catholic, Social Sciences, Sociology, Theology
ISBN Prefix(es): 2-87374
*Parent Company:* Editions Erasme SA
Divisions: Ciaco editeur
Distributed by GM Diffusion (Switzerland); Liber-T (Canada); Presses de Belgique
Distributor for Bit-IIo; Feuilles famILales

**Artis-Historia+**
One rue Carli, 1140 Brussels
*Tel:* (02) 2409200 *Fax:* (02) 2480818
*E-mail:* info@artis-historia.be
*Web Site:* www.artis-historia.be
*Key Personnel*
Chief Executive, Editing & Marketing Dir: Christian Kremer
Founded: 1948 (Companies merged to form Artis-Historia in 1976)
Subjects: Art, Cookery, Crafts, Games, Hobbies, Geography, Geology, History, Music, Dance, Natural History, Travel
ISBN Prefix(es): 2-87391; 90-5657; 90-940163
Total Titles: 180 Print
*Parent Company:* Vicindo
*Ultimate Parent Company:* Belgian Post Group
Divisions: Artoria

**Assimil NV**
Rue du Congres 13, 1000 Brussels
*Tel:* (02) 5114502 *Fax:* (02) 5129138
*E-mail:* contact@assimil.be
*Web Site:* www.assimil.be
*Key Personnel*
Dir: S Peters
Editorial: E Defraene; R Deblomme
Founded: 1939
Membership(s): VBVB-VUNB; CBL-ADEB.
Subjects: Language Arts, Linguistics, Language Study Method
ISBN Prefix(es): 90-70077; 90-74996

**Aurelia Books PVBA**
Museumlaan 17, 9831 Sint-Martens Latem
*Tel:* (091) 82 55 82 *Fax:* (091) 82 72 47
*Key Personnel*
Dir: A d'Oosterlynck
Sales & Publicity: L Bullaert
Founded: 1972
Subjects: Medicine, Nursing, Dentistry, Regional Interests, Religion - Other
ISBN Prefix(es): 90-70827

**Maison d'Editions Baha'ies ASBL**
rue du Trone, 205, 1050 Brussels
*Tel:* (02) 647 07 49 *Fax:* (02) 646 21 77
*E-mail:* meb@swing.be
*Web Site:* www.adeb.irisnet.be
*Key Personnel*
Dir: Louis Henuzet
Founded: 1970
Membership(s): Association of Belgian Publishers.
Subjects: Biography, History, Law, Philosophy, Religion - Other
ISBN Prefix(es): 2-87203

**Bakermat NV**
Wollemarkt 18, 2800 Mechelen
*Tel:* (015) 42 05 08 *Fax:* (015) 42 05 73
*E-mail:* info@bakermat.com
*Web Site:* www.bakermat.com
*Key Personnel*
General Dir: Jos Baekens
Founded: 1991
ISBN Prefix(es): 90-5461; 90-5924

**Barbianx de Garve**
Formerly Uitgeverij De Garve

Groene Poortdreef 27, 8200 Brugge
*Tel:* (050) 380707 *Fax:* (050) 388099
*E-mail:* info@degarve.be
*Web Site:* www.varin.be/degarve
*Key Personnel*
Dir: G Barbiaux
Founded: 1909
Subjects: Biography, Government, Political Science, Language Arts, Linguistics, Law, Mathematics, Music, Dance, Physics, Social Sciences, Sociology
ISBN Prefix(es): 90-5148; 90-940078; 90-940082
*Parent Company:* Drukkerij PVBA G Barbiaux

**Bartleby & Co+**
15, Rue des Pretres, 1000 Brussels
*Tel:* (02) 538 10 51
*E-mail:* bartleby@skynet.be
*Key Personnel*
President: Thorsten Baensch
Founded: 1996
Specialize in artist books & limited edition prints.
Subjects: Art, Literature, Literary Criticism, Essays
ISBN Prefix(es): 2-930279
Number of titles published annually: 3 Print
Total Titles: 15 Print

**Bibliotheque des Signes**, *imprint of* Editions Delta SA

**Editions Gerard Blanchart & Cie SA+**
Ave Ernest Masoin, 15, 1090 Brussels
*Tel:* (02) 4783706 *Fax:* (02) 4786429
*Key Personnel*
President: Charles Blanchart *E-mail:* charles.blanchart@chello.be
Production, Rights & Permissions: Therese Chantrenne
Founded: 1958
Specialize in railways & animals.
Subjects: Animals, Pets, Art, Biblical Studies, Photography, Religion - Catholic, Religion - Protestant, Religion - Other, Transportation
ISBN Prefix(es): 2-87202; 90-74760
Total Titles: 13 Print

**Editions Blanco SA+**
61/17 Ch des Deux-Maisons, 1200 Brussels
*Tel:* (02) 7720320 *Fax:* (02) 7706429
*Key Personnel*
Administrator & General Dir: Guy Leblanc
Founded: 1987
ISBN Prefix(es): 2-87297; 90-73106

**Blitz**, *imprint of* De Schaar/Geknipt Papier

**De Boeck et Larcier SA+**
Fond Jean-Paques, 4, 1348 Louvain-la-Neuve
*Tel:* (010) 48 2500 *Fax:* (010) 48 2519
*E-mail:* acces+cde@deboeck.be
*Web Site:* www.larcier.be/larcier.html
*Key Personnel*
Man Dir: Goerges Hoyos
Editor: Olivier Cruysmans *Tel:* (010) 48 26 19 *Fax:* (010) 48 26 50 *E-mail:* olivier.cruysmans@larcier.be
Editor, School Books: Francoise Goethals
Editor, University Books: Michel Jezierski
Assistant Editor: Anne Eloy *Tel:* (010) 48 26 20 *Fax:* (010) 48 26 50 *E-mail:* anne.eloy@larcier.be; Patricia Keunings *Tel:* (010) 48 26 13 *Fax:* (010) 48 26 50 *E-mail:* patricia.keunings@larcier.be
Founded: 1918
Subjects: Education, English as a Second Language, Language Arts, Linguistics, Literature, Literary Criticism, Essays
ISBN Prefix(es): 2-8011
*Parent Company:* Groupe de Boeck SA

*Associate Companies:* Acces+ SPRL; De Boeck & Larcier SA
Distributed by Editions Belin (France); G M Diffusion (Suisse); Litec (France); Editions du Renouveau Pedagogique (Canada)
*Showroom(s):* Rue des Minimes 39, 1000 Brussels *Tel:* (02) 548 07 11 *Fax:* (02) 513 90 09
*Orders to:* Acces Plus SPRL, Fond Jean-Paques 4, 1348 Louvain-La-Neuve

**Bourdeaux-Capelle SA**
359 rue St-Jacques, 5500 Dinant
*Tel:* (082) 222283; (082) 222277 *Fax:* (082) 226378
*Key Personnel*
Dir: Michel Bourdeaux
Founded: 1913
Subjects: Language Arts, Linguistics

**Brepols**, *imprint of* Brepols Publishers NV

**Brepols Publishers NV+**
Begijnhof 67, 2300 Turnhout
*Tel:* (014) 448020 *Fax:* (014) 428919
*E-mail:* info@brepols.net
*Web Site:* www.brepols.net
*Key Personnel*
Chairman: J L de Cartier de Marchienne
General Manager: Paul De Jongh *Tel:* (014) 44-80-21 *E-mail:* paul.dejongh@brepols.net
Commercial Manager: Hans Deraeve *Tel:* (014) 44-80-22 *E-mail:* hans.deraeve@brepols.net
Publishing Manager: Johan Van der Beke *Tel:* 212-737-0518 *Fax:* 212-288-7044 *E-mail:* johan.van.der.beke@brepols.net; Chris Vanden Borre *Tel:* (014) 44-80-27 *E-mail:* chris.vandenborre@brepols.net; Roland Demeulenaere *Tel:* (050) 368822 *Fax:* (050) 371457 *E-mail:* roland.demeulenaere@brepols.net; Simon Forde *Tel:* (020) 7284-4359, (014) 44-80-25 *Fax:* (020) 7267-8764 *E-mail:* simon.forde@brepols.net; Luc Jocque *Tel:* (050) 368820 *Fax:* (050) 371457 *E-mail:* luc.jocque@brepols.net; Christophe Lebbe *Tel:* (014) 44-80-26 *E-mail:* christophe.lebbe@brepols.net; Roel Vander Plaetse *Tel:* (050) 368821 *Fax:* (050) 371457 *E-mail:* roel.vander.plaetse@brepols.net
Production Manager: Jean Verstraete *Tel:* (014) 44-80-28 *E-mail:* jean.verstraete@brepols.net
Marketing Manager: Patrick Daemen *Tel:* (014) 44-80-31 *E-mail:* patrick.daemen@brepols.net
Administration & IT Manager: Wim Borgers *Tel:* (014) 44-80-39 *E-mail:* wim.borgers@brepols.net
Customer Care Manager: Ann Duchene *Tel:* (014) 44-80-34 *E-mail:* ann.duchene@brepols.net
Founded: 1796
International academic publishers.
Subjects: Archaeology, Architecture & Interior Design, Art, Asian Studies, Biblical Studies, History, Language Arts, Linguistics, Literature, Literary Criticism, Essays, Native American Studies, Philosophy, Religion - Other
ISBN Prefix(es): 2-503; 90-5622; 2-85006; 90-72100
Number of titles published annually: 240 Print; 5 CD-ROM; 5 Online
Total Titles: 5,000 Print
*Parent Company:* Brepols Group NV
Imprints: Brepols; Corpus Christianorum; Harvey Miller
Warehouse: Tieblokken 67, Gate C, 2300 Turnhout
*Distribution Center:* David Brown Book Distribution (USA)
Marston Book Services (UK)
Sogedin (France)

**Vanden Broele NV+**
Lieven Bauwensstr 33, 8200 Brugge
*Tel:* (050) 456 177 *Fax:* (050) 456 199

*E-mail:* graphic.group@vandenbroele.be
*Web Site:* www.vandenbroele.be
*Key Personnel*
Dir: E de Jonghe
Founded: 1957
Subjects: Government, Political Science, Law, Public Administration, Social Sciences, Sociology
ISBN Prefix(es): 90-5753; 90-6267; 90-5946

**Etablissements Emile Bruylant SA+**
rue de la Regence 67, 1000 Brussels
*Tel:* (02) 512 98 45 *Fax:* (02) 511 72 02
*E-mail:* info@bruylant.be
*Web Site:* www.bruylant.be
*Key Personnel*
President & Dir: Jean Vandeveld *Tel:* (02) 512 98 42 *Fax:* (02) 511 94 77 *E-mail:* jean@bruylant.be
Founded: 1838
Publisher & bookseller of law books & law periodicals.
Subjects: Government, Political Science, Law
ISBN Prefix(es): 2-8027
Number of titles published annually: 90 Print
Total Titles: 1,600 Print
*Associate Companies:* Academia-Bruylant, Grand-Place, 29, 1348 Louvain-la-Neuve *Tel:* (010) 45 23 95 *Fax:* (010) 45 44 80 *Web Site:* www.academia-bruylant.be
Distributed by Arts, Lettres et Techniques; Dokumente Verlag; Dott A Giuffre Editore; Um Fieldgen Buchandlung; Grande Librairie Specialise Fendri Ali; LGDJ - Montchrestien; Librairie Ernster; Librairie Le Point; Libraria Ferin; Licosa - Libreria Commissionaria Sansoni; Marcial Pons; Martinus Nijhoff; Miura Shoten Booksellers Ltd; La Nuova Italia Bibliografica; Promoculture; Sochepress; Editions Zoe
Distributor for Editorial Aranzadi; BECK'sche Verlag; Matthew Bender & Co Inc; Butterworths; Cambridge University Press; Cujas; Dalloz Sirey; Editions Legislatives et Administratives; Forum Europeen de la Communication (FEC); A Giuffre Editore; GLN Joly Editions; Helbing & Lichtenhan; Carl Heymanns Verlag; Juris-Classeur; Kluwer Law & Taxation; Kluwer Law International; LGDJ - Montchrestien; Litec; Lloyd's of London; MANZ'sche Verlag; Martinus Nijhoff; Nomos Verlag; Nouvelles Editions Fiduciaires; Pedone; Oxford University Press; Sakkoulas; Staempfli; Sweet & Maxwell; Themis; West Publishing Co; Wiley Law

**Campinia Media VZW+**
Kleinhoefstr 4, 2440 Geel
*Tel:* (014) 59 09 59 *Fax:* (014) 59 03 44
*E-mail:* info@campiniamedia.be
*Web Site:* www.campiniamedia.be
*Key Personnel*
Dir: Erik Borgmans *E-mail:* erik.borgmans@campiniamedia.be
Contact: Eveline Loos
Founded: 1983
Subjects: Agriculture, Behavioral Sciences, Biological Sciences, Computer Science, Language Arts, Linguistics, Physics, Science (General), Social Sciences, Sociology
ISBN Prefix(es): 90-356

**Caramel**, *imprint of* Caramel, Uitgeverij

**Caramel, Uitgeverij+**
Pagodenlaan 7, 1020 Brussels
*Tel:* (02) 2452427 *Fax:* (02) 2558493
*E-mail:* caramel@skynet.be
*Key Personnel*
Contact: Yvan Meyers *E-mail:* yvan.meyers@caramel.de

International Rights: Dirk Mennes *Tel:* (02) 263 2046 *E-mail:* production@caramel.de
Founded: 1993
Also acts as packager.
Subjects: Crafts, Games, Hobbies, Fiction
ISBN Prefix(es): 90-5562; 90-5828
Number of titles published annually: 250 Print
Imprints: Caramel

**Carmelitana VZW+**
Burgstr 92, 9000 Ghent
*Tel:* (09) 225.48.36 *Fax:* (09) 224.06.01
*E-mail:* boekhandel@carmelitana.be
*Web Site:* www.carmelitana.be
*Key Personnel*
President: Jos Rymen
Editor: F Lodewijckx
Founded: 1941
Subjects: Religion - Other
ISBN Prefix(es): 90-70092; 90-76671

**Carto BVBA**
Pagodenlaan 241, 1020 Brussels
*Tel:* (02) 2680345 *Fax:* (02) 2680345 *Cable:* Cartopress
*Key Personnel*
Man Dir: Michiel Plaizier
Founded: 1950
Subjects: Education, Geography, Geology, History, Travel
ISBN Prefix(es): 90-74437
Subsidiaries: Carpress, International Press Agency; Cremers Cartographic Institute; Cremers (Schoollandkaarten) PVBA; European Cartographic Institute

**Cartoeristiek (Federatie van Belgische Autobus- en Autocarondernemers) (BAAV)+**
Motestraat 41, 8800 Roeselare
*Tel:* (051) 226060 *Fax:* (051) 229273
*Key Personnel*
Contact: Luc Glorieux
Secretary: Mrs Riet Espeel *E-mail:* riet.espeel@busworld.org
Subjects: Travel
ISBN Prefix(es): 90-71408

**Editions Casterman SA+**
rue Royale, 132-boite 2, 1000 Brussels
*Tel:* (02) 209 83 00 *Fax:* (02) 209 83 01
*E-mail:* info@casterman.com
*Web Site:* www.casterman.com
*Key Personnel*
Man Dir: Frederic Morel
General Manager: Louis Delas
Dir, Production: Moline France
International Dir: Willy Insipidity
Marketing: Simon Casterman
International Rights Manager: Fabiana Angelini
Founded: 1780
ISBN Prefix(es): 2-203; 2-542
*Parent Company:* Editions Flammarion
*Ultimate Parent Company:* RCS Group

**Casterman NV+**
Subsidiary of Editions Casterman SA
Ganzeweidestr 303, 1130 Brussels
*Tel:* (02) 2409320 *Fax:* (02) 2163598
*Key Personnel*
General Manager: Pierre Rummens
ISBN Prefix(es): 90-303

**Ced-Samsom Wolters Kluwer Belgie**
Formerly Wolters Kluwer Belgie
Kouterveld 14, 1831 Diegem
*Tel:* (02) 7231111 *Fax:* (02) 7231288
*Key Personnel*
Man Dir: Daniel Lefebvre
Founded: 1964

Subjects: Accounting, Business, Economics, Labor, Industrial Relations, Law, Social Sciences, Sociology
ISBN Prefix(es): 90-5334; 90-5754; 90-940109
*Parent Company:* Wolters Kluwer Belgium NV
*Ultimate Parent Company:* Wolters Kluwer NV

**Editions du CEFAL+**
Affiliate of UDC Consortium
Blvd Frere-Orban 31, 4000 Liege
*Tel:* (04) 254 25 20 *Fax:* (04) 254 24 40
*E-mail:* cefal.celes@skynet.be
*Web Site:* www.cefal.com
*Key Personnel*
Dir: Jacques Burlet
Founded: 1993
Membership(s): French Editor UDC Consortium; Editions de l'Universite de Liege.
Subjects: Library & Information Sciences, Specialize in Para-Literary - school books
ISBN Prefix(es): 2-87130
Number of titles published annually: 30 Print
Total Titles: 80 Print
Distributor for Editions de l'Universite de Liege (Belgium)
*Distribution Center:* Alterdis, 5, rue du Marechal Leclerc, 28600 Luisant, France
Edipresse, 945 ave Beaumont, Nontical, Canada

**Centrale d'Impression et d'Achats en Cooperative**, see CIACO

**Centre de Recherches Culturelles Africanistes**, see Centre Aequatoria

**Centre International de Recherches 'Primitifs Flamands' ASBL+**
One parc du Cinquantenaire, 1040 Brussels
*Tel:* (02) 7396866 *Fax:* (02) 7320105
*Key Personnel*
President & Rights & Permissions: H Pauwels
Scientific Editor & Sales: H Mund
 *E-mail:* helene.mund@kikirpa.be; C Stroo
 *E-mail:* cyriel.stroo@kikirpa.be
Founded: 1950
Specialize in Flemish Painting XV Century.
Subjects: Art
ISBN Prefix(es): 2-87033

**Centre National Infor-Jeunes (CNIJ)** (Centre of Information for Youth)
2, impasse des Capucins bte 8, 5000 Namur
*Tel:* (081) 22 08 72 *Fax:* (081) 22 82 64
*Key Personnel*
Dir: Georges Vallee
Membership(s): ERYICA (European Youth Information & Counselling Agency).
ISBN Prefix(es): 2-8091

**Editions de la Chambre de Commerce et d'Industrie SA (ECCI)+**
Palais de Congres, Esplanade de l'Europe, 2, 4020 Liege
*Tel:* (04) 344-50-88 *Fax:* (04) 343-05-53
*E-mail:* lvenanzi@ecci.be
*Web Site:* www.ecci.be
Founded: 1998
Subjects: Accounting, Business, Law
ISBN Prefix(es): 2-930287; 90-76924
Number of titles published annually: 15 Print
Total Titles: 50 Print
*Distribution Center:* Patrimoine, Rue du Noyer, 7030 Brussels
Soficom, 15, rue du Docteur Lancereaux, 75008 Paris, France *Tel:* (01) 42 56 45 71 *Fax:* (01) 42 56 45 72 *E-mail:* soficom@soficom-diffusion.com
UNIVERS, Senc, 845, rue Marie-Victorin, Saint-Nicolas (Levis), QC G7A 3S8, Canada *Tel:* 418-831-7474 *Fax:* 418-831-4021 *E-mail:* d.univers@videotron.ca

**Editions Chanlis**
52 rue de Lennery, 5650 Walcourt
*Tel:* (071) 326394
*Telex:* 51832 ManoDLB
*Key Personnel*
Man Dir: Pierre Magain
Sales: M Nowak
Founded: 1968
Subjects: Antiques, Archaeology, Art, Crafts, Games, Hobbies, History, Military Science
ISBN Prefix(es): 2-87039

**Chantecler**, *imprint of* Zuid-Nederlandse Uitgeverij NV/Central Uitgeverij

**Editions Chantecler+**
Vluchtenburgstr 7, 2630 Aartselaar
*Tel:* (03) 8 70 44 00 *Fax:* (03) 8 77 21 15
*Telex:* 31739 Zuidb
*Key Personnel*
Man Dir: Jan Vande Velden
Editorial: Bart Clinckemalie
Production: Eric Feyten
Rights & Permissions: Wilfried Wuyts
Founded: 1947
Subjects: Fiction, Nonfiction (General)
ISBN Prefix(es): 2-8034; 90-243; 90-447
*Parent Company:* Zuidnederlandse Uitgeverij NV
Imprints: Pre-Ecole

**La Charte Editions juridiques**
rue Guimard 19/2, 1040 Brussels
*Tel:* (02) 512 29 49 *Fax:* (02) 512 26 93
*E-mail:* info@lacharte.be
*Web Site:* www.lacharte.be
*Key Personnel*
Dir Editor-Legal: Rik Carton
Dir Editor-Educational: Jean-Paul Steevens
Founded: 1948
Subjects: Government, Political Science, Language Arts, Linguistics, Law, Social Sciences, Sociology
ISBN Prefix(es): 2-87403

**CIACO+**
Chez Erasme 2, pl Baudoin-ler, 5004 Bouge-Namur
*Tel:* (018) 213700 *Fax:* (018) 212372
*Key Personnel*
Dir: Gerard Lambert
Founded: 1983
ISBN Prefix(es): 2-87085
Subsidiaries: Artel SC

**CIEFR (Centre International d'Etudes de la Formation Religieuse)**, see Editions Lumen Vitae ASBL

**Uitgeverij Clavis+**
Vooruitzichtstr 42, 3500 Hasselt
*Tel:* (011) 28 68 68 *Fax:* (011) 28 68 69
*E-mail:* info@clavis.be
*Web Site:* www.clavis.be
*Key Personnel*
Man Dir, Editorial: Philippe Werck
Licensing Manager: Sigrid Werck
Rights & Permissions: Tina Troonbeeckx
Production: Lisette Aerts
Promotion: Tanja Appellants *E-mail:* tanja@clavis.be
Financial Dir: Jos Rens
Editorial: Mark Lens; Hilde Vanmechelen
Founded: 1981
Subjects: Fiction, Nonfiction (General)
ISBN Prefix(es): 90-6822; 90-5933; 90-77106; 90-448; 90-77060
Total Titles: 560 Print
Imprints: Mozaiek
*Bookshop(s):* Poespas, Kapelstr 38, 3500 Hasselt

**CNIJ**, see Centre National Infor-Jeunes (CNIJ)

**Coach & Bus Federation**, see Cartoeristiek (Federatie van Belgische Autobus- en Autocaronderemers) (BAAV)

**Coalition of the Flemish North South Movement**, see Koepel van de Vlaamse Noord - Zuidbeweging 11.11.11

**Editions Complexe+**
24, Rue de Bosnie, 1060 Brussels
*Tel:* (02) 538 88 46 *Fax:* (02) 538 88 42
*E-mail:* complexe@editionscomplexe.com
*Web Site:* www.editionscomplexe.com
*Telex:* 64507 Patica
*Key Personnel*
Man Dir, Publicity: Danielle Vincken
Man Dir, Editorial: Andre Versaille
Founded: 1971
Subjects: History, Literature, Literary Criticism, Essays, Science (General)
ISBN Prefix(es): 2-87027; 2-8048
*Associate Companies:* Nouvelle Diffusion SPRL DPI

**Concraid-Editions SA+**
Parc de la Sablonniere bte 707, 7000 Mons
*Tel:* (065) 34-72-34 *Fax:* (065) 34-72-34
*Key Personnel*
General Dir: E Preud'homme
Founded: 1983
Specialize in finance, stockmarket & health.
Membership(s): ADEB.
ISBN Prefix(es): 2-87189

**Conservart SA+**
Chee Alsemberg 975, 1180 Brussels
*Tel:* (02) 3322538 *Fax:* (02) 3322840
*E-mail:* conservart@skynet.be
*Key Personnel*
General Dir: Jean-Claude Echement
Subjects: Architecture & Interior Design, Art, Chemistry, Chemical Engineering, Literature, Literary Criticism, Essays, Photography
ISBN Prefix(es): 2-930022

**Uitgeverij Contact NV**
Capucienenlaan 49, 9300 Aalst
*Tel:* (03) 4572024 *Fax:* (03) 4581327
*Key Personnel*
Dir: A J H Binneweg
Founded: 1946
Subjects: Art, Crafts, Games, Hobbies, Education, Literature, Literary Criticism, Essays, Sports, Athletics
ISBN Prefix(es): 90-73185

**Corpus Christianorum**, *imprint of* Brepols Publishers NV

**Creadif**
67 Rue de la Regence, 1000 Brussels
*Tel:* (02) 512 98 45 *Fax:* (02) 511 72 02
*Key Personnel*
Dir: Jean Vandeveld
Founded: 1974
Publisher of law books.
Subjects: Business, Economics, Ethnicity, Geography, Geology, History, Law, Travel
ISBN Prefix(es): 2-8022

**Cremers (Schoollandkaarten) PVBA**
Pagodenlaan 241, 1020 Brussels
*Tel:* (02) 2680345 *Fax:* (02) 2680345 *Cable:* Cartopress
*Key Personnel*
Dir: Michiel Plazier
Founded: 1950
Subjects: Ethnicity, Geography, Geology, History, Travel

ISBN Prefix(es): 90-74437
*Parent Company:* Carto BVBA

**Le Cri Editions+**
One Rue Victor Greyson, 1050 Brussels
*Tel:* (02) 6466533 *Fax:* (02) 6466607
*E-mail:* lecri@skynet.be
*Key Personnel*
Dir: Lutz Christian
Founded: 1981
Subjects: Biography, History, Literature, Literary Criticism, Essays
ISBN Prefix(es): 2-87106

**Cultura**
Hoenderstr 22, 9230 Wetteren
*Tel:* (032) 093691595 *Fax:* (032) 093695925
*E-mail:* info@cultura-net.com
*Web Site:* www.cultura-net.com; www.cultura.be
*Key Personnel*
President: Rene De Meester, Sr
Vice President: Jan De Meester, Jr
Specialize in numismatic publications.
ISBN Prefix(es): 90-74623

**Le Daily-Bul**
rue Daily Bul 29, 7100 La Louviere
*Tel:* (064) 222973 *Fax:* (064) 222973
*Key Personnel*
Man Dir: Andre Balthazar
Founded: 1957
Subjects: Art, Literature, Literary Criticism, Essays, Poetry
ISBN Prefix(es): 2-930136

**Daphne Diffusion SA**
Poortakkerstr, 29, 9051 Ghent
*Tel:* (09) 221 45 91 *Fax:* (09) 220 16 12
*E-mail:* info@daphne.be
*Telex:* 11659
*Key Personnel*
General Manager: Francois Dubrulle
Administrator & Sales Manager: Pierre Dubrulle
Subjects: Travel
ISBN Prefix(es): 2-504

**Davidsfonds Uitgeverij NV+**
Blijde-Inkomststr 79-81, 3000 Leuven
*Tel:* (016) 310600 *Fax:* (016) 310608
*E-mail:* informatie@davidsfonds.be
*Web Site:* www.davidsfonds.be
*Key Personnel*
Dir: Rudi Teirlinck
Subjects: Art, Fiction, History
ISBN Prefix(es): 90-6152; 90-6565
Number of titles published annually: 110 Print
Distributor for NBCC (Netherlands)
*Bookshop(s):* Blijde-Inkomststr 79-81, 3000 Leuven
*Warehouse:* Distributiecentrum AGORA, De Vunt 5, 3220 Holsbeek

**Editions De Boeck-Larcier SA+**
rue des Minimes 39, 1000 Brussels
*Tel:* (02) 548 07 11 *Fax:* (02) 513 90 09
*Web Site:* www.deboeck.be
*Key Personnel*
President: Christian De Boeck *E-mail:* christian.deboeck@deboeck.be
Dir: Georges Hoyos *E-mail:* georges.hoyos@deboeck.be
University Publications: Michel Jezierski *E-mail:* michel.jezierski@deboeck.be
Educational Publishing: Francoise Goethals *E-mail:* francoise.goethals@deboeck.be
Press Officer: Nora Jezierski-Ramakers *E-mail:* nora.jezierski@deboeck.be
Law: Patricia Wilhelm
R/D: Genevieve Dieu
Founded: 1883

Subjects: Accounting, Anthropology, Art, Behavioral Sciences, Biological Sciences, Business, Chemistry, Chemical Engineering, Communications, Economics, Education, English as a Second Language, Environmental Studies, Finance, Geography, Geology, Government, Political Science, Health, Nutrition, Human Relations, Language Arts, Linguistics, Law, Management, Marketing, Mathematics, Medicine, Nursing, Dentistry, Philosophy, Physical Sciences, Psychology, Psychiatry, Science (General), Social Sciences, Sociology
ISBN Prefix(es): 2-8041
*Parent Company:* Groupe De Boeck SA
*Associate Companies:* Acces Plus SPRL
Divisions: De Boeck Universite; De Boeck-Wesmael, Larcier; Dessain; Duculot; Didacta
*Showroom(s):* Acces Plus SPRL, Fond Jean-Paques 4, 1348 Louvain-la-Neuve *Tel:* (010) 482500 *Fax:* (010) 482519
*Bookshop(s):* Acces Plus SPRL, Fond Jean-Paques 4, 1348 Louvain-la-Neuve *Tel:* (010) 482500 *Fax:* (010) 482519
*Shipping Address:* Acces Plus SPRL, Fond Jean-Paques 4, 1348 Louvain-la-Neuve *Tel:* (010) 482500 *Fax:* (010) 482519
*Warehouse:* Acces Plus SPRL, Fond Jean-Paques 4, 1348 Louvain-la-Neuve *Tel:* (010) 482500 *Fax:* (010) 482519
*Orders to:* Acces Plus SPRL, Fond Jean-Paques 4, 1348 Louvain-la-Neuve *Tel:* (010) 482500 *Fax:* (010) 482519 *E-mail:* acces+cde@deboeck.be

**DEF (De Blauwe Vogel) NV/SA+**
Jan Carlierstraat, 1, Bus, 3800 Sint-Truiden
*Tel:* (011) 685751-2 *Fax:* (011) 67-21-70
*Telex:* 39810
*Key Personnel*
Contact: Willy-Paul Carlier
Founded: 1929
Subjects: Travel
ISBN Prefix(es): 90-72432
*Parent Company:* G O Bluebird

**Editions Claude Dejaie+**
1154 chaussee de Dinant, 5100 Namur-Wepian
*Tel:* (081) 460748
*Key Personnel*
Dir: M Claude M Dejaie
Founded: 1972
Subjects: Art, Literature, Literary Criticism, Essays, Philosophy
ISBN Prefix(es): 2-87157

**Editions Delta SA** (Delta Publications)+
416, ave Louise, 1050 Brussels
*Tel:* (02) 217 55 55 *Fax:* (02) 217 93 93
*E-mail:* editions.delta@skynet.be
*Key Personnel*
Man Dir: Georges-Francis Seingry
Founded: 1976
Specialize in European public affairs & art books.
Subjects: Art, Biography, Public Administration
ISBN Prefix(es): 2-8029
Number of titles published annually: 8 Print
*Parent Company:* Euro-references
Imprints: Bibliotheque des Signes
Distributed by Bernan (USA); Cedar Media House; LGDJ-Montchrestien
Foreign Rep(s): Bernan; Cedar Media; LGDJ Montchretien

**Deltas,** *imprint of* Zuid-Nederlandse Uitgeverij NV/Central Uitgeverij

**Dessain - Departement de De Boeck & Larcier SA+**
rue Des Minimes, 39, 1000 Brussels
*Tel:* (02) 548 07 11 *Fax:* (02) 513 90 09
*E-mail:* adeb@adeb.be

*Web Site:* www.adeb.irisnet.be
*Key Personnel*
President: Christian De Boeck
 *E-mail:* christiandeboeck@deboeck.be
Dir: Georges Hoyos *E-mail:* georges.hoyos@deboeck.be
Editor, Scholarly Books: Francoise Goethals
Founded: 1719
Subjects: Education, Geography, Geology, Mathematics, Natural History, Physics, Religion - Catholic, Science (General)
ISBN Prefix(es): 2-8041; 2-502
*Parent Company:* Groupe De Boeck SA
*Associate Companies:* De Boeck & Larcier SA - Acces Plus Sprl
*Warehouse:* Acces Plus SPRL, Fond Jean-Paques 4, 1348 Louvain-la-Neuve *Tel:* (010) 482500 *Fax:* (010) 482519
*Orders to:* Acces Plus SPRL, Fond Jean-Paques 4, 1348 Louvain *Tel:* (010) 482500 *Fax:* (010) 482519

**Dexia Bank+**
Activites culturelles, RC 1/0, Blvd Pacheco 44, 1000 Brussels
*Tel:* (02) 222 54 89 *Fax:* (02) 222 57 52
*E-mail:* cultureline@dexia.be
*Web Site:* www.dexia.be/culture
*Key Personnel*
Contact: Renaud Gahide
Founded: 1860
Subjects: Art, Genealogy, Geography, Geology, History, Music, Dance, Photography
ISBN Prefix(es): 90-5066; 2-87193
Number of titles published annually: 10 Print
Total Titles: 90 Print; 8 E-Book
Distributed by Exhibitions International

**Diligentia-Uitgeverij**
Schrijnwerkerstr 11, 9240 Zele
*Tel:* (052) 44 45 11 *Fax:* (052) 44 45 22
*E-mail:* diligentia.book@planetinternet.be
*Key Personnel*
Contact: C Van den broeck
Founded: 1908
ISBN Prefix(es): 90-70978

**Documenta CV**
21, Rue des Drappiers, 1050 Brussels
*Tel:* (02) 5102313 *Fax:* (02) 5102497
*Key Personnel*
President: Philippe de Buck van Overstraeten
Manager: Christian Franzen
Founded: 1986
Subjects: Business, Economics, Electronics, Electrical Engineering, Management, Technology
ISBN Prefix(es): 2-930096; 90-75062
Distributed by Academia
Distributor for Academia; Mim

**Duculot,** see De Boeck et Larcier SA

**Editions Dupuis SA+**
Rue Destree 52, 6001 Marcinelle
*Tel:* (071) 600 500 *Fax:* (071) 600 599
*E-mail:* info@dupuis.com
*Web Site:* www.dupuis.com
*Key Personnel*
Dir General: Jean Deneumostier
Editorial Dir: Philippe Vandooren
Sales Dir: Philippe Buck
Finance: Stephane Desmet
Rights & Permissions: Jean-Philippe Doutrelugne
Dir Audiovisual & Development: Leon Perahia
Founded: 1898
Subjects: Humor
ISBN Prefix(es): 2-8001; 90-314; 90-6574
*Parent Company:* Groupe Jean Dupuis SA
*Associate Companies:* Editions Dupuis France SA; Mediatoon SA

**Easy Computing NV**
Bourdon 100, 1180 Brussels
*Tel:* (02) 346 52 52 *Fax:* (02) 346 01 20
*E-mail:* info@easycomputing.com
*Web Site:* www.easycomputing.com
*Key Personnel*
Contact: F Wiener *Tel:* (02) 3401521
 *E-mail:* fwiener@easycomputing.com
Founded: 1989
Subjects: Computer Science, Electronics, Electrical Engineering, Microcomputers
ISBN Prefix(es): 90-5167; 90-456; 2-87208
Total Titles: 100 Print; 70 CD-ROM
Subsidiaries: Easy Computing bv
Distributor for Micro Application

**ECCI,** see Editions de la Chambre de Commerce et d'Industrie SA (ECCI)

**Ecobooks**
Heerbaan 132, 1840 Steenhuffel
*Tel:* (052) 37 11 38 *Fax:* (052) 37 11 51
*E-mail:* ecobooks@ping.be
*Key Personnel*
Contact: Mevr M Muylaert
International Rights: Hugo Vanderstadt
Subjects: Ecology, Sustainability
ISBN Prefix(es): 90-75855

**Ediblanchart sprl+**
Ave Ernest Masoin, 15, 1090 Brussels
*Tel:* (02) 4783706 *Fax:* (02) 4786429
*Key Personnel*
President & Administrator: Charles Blanchart
 *E-mail:* charles.blanchart@chello.be
Founded: 1962
Subjects: Animals, Pets, Transportation, Railways, Flowers
ISBN Prefix(es): 2-87202
Number of titles published annually: 2 Print
Total Titles: 11 Print

**Editest, SPRL+**
16 rue de Chambery, 1040 Brussels
*Tel:* (02) 6476284 *Fax:* (02) 7325629
*Key Personnel*
Dir: B Evrard
Specialize in psychological tests.
Subjects: Psychology, Psychiatry
ISBN Prefix(es): 2-8000

**Uitgeverij de Eenhoorn+**
Vlasstraat 17, 8710 Wielsbeke
*Tel:* (056) 60 54 60 *Fax:* (056) 61 69 81
*E-mail:* info@eenhoorn.be
*Web Site:* www.eenhoorn.be
*Key Personnel*
Man Dir & International Rights: Bart Desmyter
 *E-mail:* bart.desmyter@eenhoorn.be
Founded: 1990
Subjects: Fiction
ISBN Prefix(es): 90-73913; 90-5838
Number of titles published annually: 50 Print
Imprints: Medaillon

**EMPC,** see Editions Medicales et Paramedicales de Charleroi (EMPC)

**Editions les Eperonniers**
62B rue St Catherine, 1370 Jodoigne
*Tel:* (010) 813614 *Fax:* (010) 815386
*Key Personnel*
President: Lysiane D'Haeyere-Antoine
Subjects: Literature, Literary Criticism, Essays, Philosophy, Science (General)
ISBN Prefix(es): 2-87132; 2-87015; 2-87159

**EPO Publishers, Printers, Booksellers+**
Lange Pastoorstr 25-27, 2600 Berchem-Antwerp
*Tel:* (03) 2396874 *Fax:* (03) 2184604
*E-mail:* publishers@epo.be
*Web Site:* www.epo.be

*Key Personnel*
Man Dir: Jos Hennes
Publisher: Hugo Franssen
Sales: Kris Van Kersschaever
Founded: 1978
Subjects: Anthropology, Biography, Communications, Developing Countries, Fiction, History, Journalism, Literature, Literary Criticism, Essays, Nonfiction (General), Psychology, Psychiatry, Social Sciences, Sociology
ISBN Prefix(es): 90-6445; 2-87262
*Branch Office(s)*
Chaussee de Haecht L55, 1030 Brussels
  *Tel:* (02) 215 6651 *Fax:* (02) 215 6604
  *E-mail:* editions@epo.be
Distributed by De Geus (The Netherlands)
Distributor for Coutinho (The Netherlands); De Geus (The Netherlands)
*Bookshop(s):* Groene Waterman, Wolstr 7, 2000 Antwerp; Librairie Internationale, Ave LeMonnier 171, 1000 Brussels
*Book Club(s):* Komma's en Punten

**Esco BVBA**
Venusstraat 31, 2000 Antwerp
*Tel:* (03) 2223800 *Fax:* (03) 2223838
*Key Personnel*
Contact: Jan Fremeijer
ISBN Prefix(es): 90-6415

**Editions Espace de Libertes**, *imprint of* Espace de Libertes

**Espace de Libertes+**
av Arnaud Fraiteur, ULB, Bd du Triomphe, Campus de la Plane, CP 236, 1050 Brussels
*Tel:* (02) 6276860 *Fax:* (02) 6266861
*Key Personnel*
Collections Dir: Patrice Dartevelle
  *E-mail:* espace@cal.ulb.ac.be
Founded: 1979
Membership(s): A D E B.
Subjects: Biography, Government, Political Science, History, Philosophy, Religion - Other, Social Sciences, Sociology
ISBN Prefix(es): 2-930001
Imprints: Editions Espace de Libertes

**EVO**, see Les Editions Vie ouvriere ASBL

**Facet NV+**
Willem Linnigstr 13, 2060 Antwerp
*Tel:* (03) 227 40 28 *Fax:* (03) 227 37 92
*E-mail:* facet@village.uunet.be
*Web Site:* www.mijnweb.nu/be021988
*Key Personnel*
Publisher: Walter A P Soethoudt
Founded: 1986
Specialize in children's books.
ISBN Prefix(es): 90-5016

**Garant Publishers Ltd**
Somersstr 13-15, 2018 Antwerp
*Tel:* (03) 231 29 00 *Fax:* (03) 233 26 59
*E-mail:* uitgeverij@garant.be
*Web Site:* www.garant.be
*Key Personnel*
Dir: Huug Van Gompel *E-mail:* huug. vangompel@garant.be
Publisher: Liesbeth Driesen
Promotion: Werner Peeters
Founded: 1990
Subjects: Economics, Education, Social Sciences, Sociology
ISBN Prefix(es): 90-441
Number of titles published annually: 120 Print
Total Titles: 1,500 Print
*Associate Companies:* Maklu Publishers
Distributed by Central Books; Coronet Books

**Uitgevery Gelbis NV+**
Cockerillaai 30, 2000 Antwerp
*Tel:* (03) 2410202 *Fax:* (03) 2410200
*E-mail:* gelbis.boeken@lequana.com
*Key Personnel*
Contact: Leo van der Linden
Founded: 1982
Subjects: Automotive, Travel
ISBN Prefix(es): 90-71288
Divisions: GelbiStudio; Gelbis Boekhandel

**Geocart Uitg Cartogr AG Claus BVBA+**
Breedstr 94, 9100 Sint-Niklaas
*Tel:* (03) 760 14 60 *Fax:* (03) 760 15 28
*E-mail:* site@geocart.be
*Web Site:* www.geocart.be
*Key Personnel*
Algemene Dir: Egide Van Eyck
Founded: 1972
Specialize in cartography.
ISBN Prefix(es): 90-6736
Subsidiaries: Girault Gilbert, BVBA
Divisions: Geocart Information System
*Warehouse:* Libricart, Breedstr 94, 9100 Sint-Niklaas

**Georeto-Geogidsen**
Rozenstr 11, 3723 Kortessem
*Tel:* (011) 37 52 54 *Fax:* (011) 37 52 54
*E-mail:* georeto@pandora.be
*Web Site:* www.geogidsen.be
*Key Personnel*
Contact: P Diriken
Founded: 1991
Subjects: Geography, Geology, History, Outdoor Recreation
Number of titles published annually: 4 Print
Total Titles: 45 Print

**Girault Gilbert bvba+**
50, Rue de l'Association, 1000 Brussels
*Tel:* (02) 2171430; (02) 2175880 *Fax:* (02) 2173375
*Key Personnel*
President: Egide Van Eyck
Founded: 1928 (Reconstituted: 1956)
ISBN Prefix(es): 2-87273
*Warehouse:* Libricart, Breedstr 94, 9100 Sint-Niklaas

**Glenat Benelux SA+**
131 rue Saint-Lambert, 1200 Brussels
*Tel:* (02) 7612640 *Fax:* (02) 7612645
*E-mail:* glenat@glenat.be
*Web Site:* www.glenat.com
*Key Personnel*
Dir, Editor & International Rights: Paul Herman
Administrative Delegate: Dominique Leblan
Founded: 1985
Subjects: Antiques, Art, Automotive, Crafts, Games, Hobbies, Humor, Regional Interests, Wine & Spirits, Comics
ISBN Prefix(es): 2-87176; 90-6969
Subsidiaries: Glenat France
Distributor for Vent D'Ouest
*Bookshop(s):* Slumberland, 20 rue des sables, 1000 Brussels; Slumberland, 131 rue Saint-Lambert, 1200 Brussels; Slumberland, 3 Louvain-la-Neuve

**Globe**, *imprint of* Infotex Scoop NV

**Globe**, *imprint of* Roularta Books NV

**Graton Editeur NV+**
Av du Perou, 1000 Brussels
*Tel:* (02) 6756 666 *Fax:* (02) 6756 363
*E-mail:* graton.sa@skynet.be
*Key Personnel*
Executive: Ph Graton
Founded: 1981

Subjects: Film, Video, Journalism, Photography, Sports, Athletics, Motorracing, Comic Strips
ISBN Prefix(es): 90-70816; 2-87098
Divisions: Kurz & Bundigi, hpt Extra
Distributed by Diffulivre (Switzerland); Dupuis (Belgium); Hachette (France); Mediavision (USA); Seven Island (Germany)

**Groeninghe NV**
Lange Steenstr 2, 8500 Kortrijk
*Tel:* (056) 22 40 77 *Fax:* (056) 22 82 86
*Web Site:* www.groeninghe.com
*Key Personnel*
General Dir: Robert Timperman
Founded: 1924
Subjects: Archaeology, Art, History
ISBN Prefix(es): 90-71868
*Parent Company:* Groeninghe Printers
*Associate Companies:* Groeninghe Bookbinders
*Showroom(s):* Budastr 64, 8500 Kortrijk

**Den Gulden Engel**, *imprint of* Uitgeverij Houtekiet

**Hadewijch**, *imprint of* Uitgeverij Houtekiet

**Imprimerie Hayez SPRL**
Rue Fernand Brunfaut 19, 1080 Brussels
*Tel:* (02) 413 02 00 *Fax:* (02) 411 23 78
*E-mail:* com@hayez.be
*Web Site:* www.hayez.be
*Telex:* 63467 Hayez
*Key Personnel*
Man Dir: Frederic Hayez *E-mail:* fh@hayez.be; Maximilien Hayez *E-mail:* mh@hayez.be
Founded: 1780
Subjects: History, Medicine, Nursing, Dentistry, Philosophy, Poetry, Religion - Other, Science (General), Sports, Athletics
ISBN Prefix(es): 2-87126

**Heideland-Orbis NV**
Santvoortbeekln 21-23, 2100 Deurne
*Tel:* (03) 3600211 *Fax:* (03) 3600212
*Telex:* 3600212 *Cable:* 33649
*Key Personnel*
Dir: C van Baelen
Editorial Manager: R Fransen
Production: H Leduc
Founded: 1969
ISBN Prefix(es): 90-291

**Uitgeverij Helios NV**
Kapelsestr 222, 2080 Kapellen
*Tel:* (03) 6645320
*Telex:* 32242 Anvers Dnb
*Key Personnel*
Man Dir: J Pelckmans
Founded: 1976
ISBN Prefix(es): 90-333
*Associate Companies:* Uitgeverij De Nederlandsche Boekhandel

**Helyode Editions (SA-ADN)+**
Coccinelle Edition, Chaussee d'Alsemberg, 1180 Brussels
*Tel:* (02) 3444934 *Fax:* (02) 3475534
*Key Personnel*
General Dir: Patrice le Hodey
Dir: Marie Vernofstede
Founded: 1991
Specialize in cartoons.
Subjects: Fiction, History, Humor
ISBN Prefix(es): 2-87353; 90-5415
Subsidiaries: Memoire D'Europe

**Van Hemeldonck NV+**
Van Hemeldonckstr, 5, 2350 Vosselaar
*Tel:* (014) 611034 *Fax:* (014) 620288
*E-mail:* booksell@innet.be

*Key Personnel*
President: Johan Van Hemeldonck
Vice President: Georges Aerts
Founded: 1932
Specialize in large prints.
ISBN Prefix(es): 90-5274
*Associate Companies:* Grootdruk-Uitgevery Eindhoven BV, Netherlands

**Editions Hemma+**
106, rue de Chevron, 4987 Chevron
*Tel:* (086) 43 01 01 *Fax:* (086) 43 36 40
*Web Site:* www.hemma.be
*Key Personnel*
Dir: Albert Hemmerlin
Founded: 1952
Subjects: Crafts, Games, Hobbies, Fiction, Mysteries, Science Fiction, Fantasy
ISBN Prefix(es): 2-8006; 90-380
Subsidiaries: Editions Diffusion Hemma; Hemma Verlag GmbH; Hemma Joven SA
Distributed by Dar Almoufid (Lebanon); Diffusion Transat SA (Switzerland); Impato (Switzerland); Les Presses D-Or (Canada) Inc (Canada); Messageries du Livre (Luxembourg); Socadis Inc (Canada)

**De Horstink**, *imprint of* Uitgeverij Acco

**Uitgeverij Houtekiet**
Subsidiary of Veen, Bosch & Keuning Uitgevers NV
Vrijheidstraat 33, 2000 Antwerp
*Tel:* (03) 2381296 *Fax:* (03) 2388041
*E-mail:* info@houtekiet.be
*Web Site:* www.boekenwereld.com
*Telex:* 43272beka
*Key Personnel*
Dir: Marij Bertram
Publisher: Leo de Haes
Marketing & Sales: Hendrik de Leeuw
Publicity: Melanie Elst *E-mail:* melanie.elst@houtekiet.com
Sales: Thea Bon; Ingrid Kee; Petra Wildvank
ISBN Prefix(es): 90-5067; 90-5240; 90-70876
Imprints: Hadewijch; Den Gulden Engel

**Huis Van Het Boek**
Hof ter Schrieklaan 17, 2600 Berchem, Antwerp
*Tel:* (03) 230 89 23 *Fax:* (03) 281 22 40
*E-mail:* info@boek.be
*Web Site:* www.boek.be
*Key Personnel*
Dir: Dorian Van Der Brempt *E-mail:* dorian.van.der.brempt@vbvb.be
Founded: 1929
Professional organization for booksellers, distributors & editors.
Subjects: Literature, Literary Criticism, Essays, Publishing & Book Trade Reference
ISBN Prefix(es): 90-72103; 90-77165; 90-940004

**IMPS SA+**
85 rue du Cerf, 1332 Genval
*Tel:* (02) 6520220 *Fax:* (02) 6520160
*Key Personnel*
Dir General: Hendrik Coysman
Founded: 1984
Licensor of the Smurfs.
ISBN Prefix(es): 2-87345

**Infoboek NV**
Lil 51, 2450 Meerhout
*Tel:* (014) 369292 *Fax:* (014) 369293
*E-mail:* info@infoboek.be
*Web Site:* www.infoboek.com
*Key Personnel*
Dir: W Verhaert
Founded: 1971
Subjects: Crafts, Games, Hobbies, Education, Language Arts, Linguistics, Literature, Literary

Criticism, Essays, Music, Dance, Philosophy, Religion - Other, Sports, Athletics
ISBN Prefix(es): 90-5535

**Infotex NV**
Forelstr 22, 9000 Ghent
*Tel:* (09) 265 64 23 *Fax:* (09) 225 84 06
*Telex:* 11228
*Key Personnel*
Man Dir: J van Haverbeke
ISBN Prefix(es): 90-6334
*Bookshop(s):* Boekhandel Het Volk

**Infotex Scoop NV+**
Subsidiary of VUM Group
Forelstr 22, 9000 Ghent
*Tel:* (09) 2056430 *Fax:* (09) 2056449
*E-mail:* scoop@infotex.be
*Key Personnel*
Delegate Dir: Johan De Koning
Editor: Leen Van Troys *E-mail:* leen.vantroys@infotex.be
Founded: 1991
Subjects: Biography, Business, Career Development, Economics, Government, Political Science, History, Journalism, Literature, Literary Criticism, Essays, Management, Marketing, Travel
ISBN Prefix(es): 90-5312; 90-900261; 90-940062
Number of titles published annually: 30 Print; 1 CD-ROM
Imprints: Globe

**Institut Royal des Relations Internationales**
(Royal Institute for International Relations)
Rue de Namur 69, 1000 Brussels
*Tel:* (02) 2234114 *Fax:* (02) 2234116
*E-mail:* info@irri-kiib.be
*Web Site:* www.irri-kiib.be
*Key Personnel*
President: Vte E Davignon
Dir General: Claude Misson
Founded: 1947
Research institute.
Subjects: Developing Countries, Economics, Foreign Countries, Government, Political Science, Law
ISBN Prefix(es): 2-9600353
Number of titles published annually: 5 Print
Total Titles: 2 Print

**International Institute of Catechetics & Pastoral Studies**, see Editions Lumen Vitae ASBL

**International Peace Information Service**, see IPIS vzw (International Peace Information Service)

**Intersentia Uitgevers NV**
Churchilllaan 108, 2900 Schoten-Antwerp
*Tel:* (03) 680 15 50 *Fax:* (03) 658 71 21
*E-mail:* mail@intersentia.be
*Web Site:* www.intersentia.com
*Key Personnel*
Publisher, Law: Kris Moeremans *E-mail:* k.moeremans@intersentia.be
Founded: 1996
Academic publishing house specializing in Belgian, Dutch, European & international law & economics.
Subjects: Accounting, Finance, Law, Human Rights, European Law
ISBN Prefix(es): 90-5095
Number of titles published annually: 70 Print; 3 CD-ROM
Total Titles: 420 Print; 2 Online
Distributed by Aditya Books (India); James Bennett Pty Ltd (Australia); Gaunt Inc (North America); Hart Publishing (UK); Mare Nostrum (France, Italy, Spain & Portugal); Ver-

lag Oesterreich (Austria & Czech Republic); Schulthess Verlag (Germany & Switzerland)
Distributor for Hart Publishing

**Invader**, *imprint of* Zuid-Nederlandse Uitgeverij NV/Central Uitgeverij

**IPIS vzw (International Peace Information Service)+**
98a Italielei, 2000 Antwerp
*Tel:* (03) 225 00 22; (03) 225 21 96 *Fax:* (03) 231 0151
*E-mail:* info@ipisresearch.be
*Web Site:* www.ipisresearch.be
*Key Personnel*
Dir: Johan Peleman *E-mail:* johan@ipisresearch.be
Research: An Yrankx *E-mail:* an@ipisresearch.be
Founded: 1981
Specialize in world security & human rights, conflict areas, arms trade & international relations.
Membership(s): NGO.
Subjects: Developing Countries, Foreign Countries, Government, Political Science, Military Science, Nonfiction (General)
ISBN Prefix(es): 90-70316; 90-71247

**IRRI-KIIB**, see Institut Royal des Relations Internationales

**Uitgeverij J van In+**
Nijverheidsstr 92/5, 2160 Wommelgem
*Tel:* (03) 4805511 *Fax:* (03) 4807664
*Key Personnel*
Man Dir & Rights & Permissions: Dr Laurent Woestenburg
Editorial: Ludo Camps
Production: Danielle Brabants
Publicity: Fred Caluwe
Founded: 1833
Firm is part of Educational Book Publishing division of VNU BV, Netherlands.
Subjects: Education, Language Arts, Linguistics, Law
ISBN Prefix(es): 90-306
Subsidiaries: J Van In Editions
Divisions:

**Die Keure+**
Oude Gentweg 108, 8000 Brugge
*Tel:* (050) 47 12 72 *Fax:* (050) 34 37 68
*E-mail:* info@diekeure.be
*Web Site:* www.diekeure.be
*Key Personnel*
Dir: Jean Paul Steevens
Founded: 1948
Subjects: Education
ISBN Prefix(es): 90-6200; 90-5751; 90-5958

**King Baudouin Foundation**
Rue Brederodestr 21, 1000 Brussels
*Tel:* (02) 511 18 40 *Fax:* (02) 511 52 21
*E-mail:* proj@kbs-frb.be
*Web Site:* www.kbs-frb.be
*Key Personnel*
Man Dir: Luc Tayart de Borms
Improve living conditions for the population taking economic, social, scientific & cultural factors into account.
Subjects: Agriculture, Architecture & Interior Design, Economics, Labor, Industrial Relations, Social Sciences, Sociology
ISBN Prefix(es): 90-5130; 2-87212

**Kluwer Editions**
Avenue Louise 326, 1050 Brussells
*Tel:* (0800) 16 868 *Fax:* (02) 300 30 03
*E-mail:* info@editionskluwer.be
*Web Site:* www.editionskluwer.be
*Telex:* 33649
*Key Personnel*
Dir: B Houdmont

Manager: B Houdmont; G VanPeel
Publisher: A Knops; D Lefebvre; D Vanhove
Logistic Manager: A Geladi
Founded: 1977
Subjects: Economics, Law
ISBN Prefix(es): 90-6321; 90-5583; 90-6716; 90-5928; 90-5062; 90-5938; 90-465; 2-87377
*Parent Company:* Wolters Kluwer Belgie NV
*Ultimate Parent Company:* Wolters Kluwer NV, Apollolaan 153, Amsterdam, Netherlands
Imprints: E Story-Scientia; Service

**KnackBibliotheek/Radio 1**, *imprint of* Roularta Books NV

**Koepel van de Vlaamse Noord - Zuidbeweging 11.11.11** (Coalition of the Flemish North South Movement)+
Vlasfabriekstraat 11, 1060 Brussels
*Tel:* (02) 536-11-13 *Fax:* (02) 536-19-10
*E-mail:* info@11.be
*Web Site:* www.11.be
*Key Personnel*
Education Coordinator: Bart Demedts *Tel:* (02) 536-11-14 *Fax:* (02) 536-19-02 *E-mail:* bart.demedts@11.be
Founded: 1966
Specialize in Third World affairs.
Subjects: Anthropology, Child Care & Development, Cookery, Developing Countries, Economics, Geography, Geology, Government, Political Science, Health, Nutrition, Journalism, Labor, Industrial Relations, Literature, Literary Criticism, Essays, Travel
ISBN Prefix(es): 90-71665
Distributed by Jan Van Arkel (Netherlands); Van Haelewyck-Uitgeverij (Belgium)
Distributor for Kit (Netherlands); Jan Mets (Netherlands); Novib (Netherlands)
*Orders to:* Eric Vander Borght *Tel:* (02) 536 1122 *E-mail:* eric.vanderborght@ncos.ngonet.be

**Koninklijke Vlaamse Academie van Belgie voor Wetenschappen en Kunsten**
(Dutch-Speaking Royal Belgian Academy of Sciences, Letters & Fine Arts)
Paleis der Academien, Hertogsstr 1, 1000 Brussels
*Tel:* (02) 550 23 23 *Fax:* (02) 550 23 25
*E-mail:* info@kvab.be
*Web Site:* www.kvab.be
*Key Personnel*
Permanent Secretary: Niceas Schamp *E-mail:* niceas.schamp@kvab.be
Publications: Gilbert Reynders *Tel:* (02) 550 23 32 *E-mail:* gilbert.reynders@kvab.be
Founded: 1938
Membership(s): International Academic Association.
Subjects: Art, Music, Dance, Philosophy, Science (General)
ISBN Prefix(es): 90-6569
*Orders to:* Brepols Publishers IGP, Begynhof 67, 2300 Turnhout *Tel:* (014) 448 020 *Fax:* (014) 428 919 *E-mail:* info@brepols.com *Web Site:* www.brepols.net/publishers

**De Krijger+**
Dorpsstraat, 144, 9420 Erpe-Mere
*Tel:* (053) 808449 *Fax:* (053) 808453
*E-mail:* de.krijger@primemedia.be
*Key Personnel*
Owner: Vammabost Koem
Founded: 1987
Subjects: Military Science
ISBN Prefix(es): 90-72547; 90-5868
Number of titles published annually: 15 Print
Total Titles: 68 Print

**Editions Labor**
Quai du Commerce 29, 1000 Brussels

*Tel:* (02) 250-06-70 *Fax:* (02) 217-71-97
*E-mail:* labor@labor.be
*Web Site:* www.labor.be
*Telex:* 25532 Labor
*Key Personnel*
President: Th Vanderworst
Assistant Dir: Fabienne Herc *E-mail:* herc@labor.be
General Services: Jean-Pierre Van Mullem *E-mail:* vanmullen@labor.be
Founded: 1927
Subjects: Biography, Economics, Education, History, Philosophy, Poetry, Psychology, Psychiatry, Science (General), Social Sciences, Sociology
ISBN Prefix(es): 2-8040

**Uitgeverij Lannoo NV+**
Kasteelstr 97, 8700 Tielt
*Tel:* (051) 42 42 11 *Fax:* (051) 40 11 52
*E-mail:* lannoo@lannoo.be
*Web Site:* www.lannoo.com
*Key Personnel*
President: Matthias Lannoo
Man Dir: Luc Demeester
Editorial Dir: Lieven Sercu
Founded: 1909
Subjects: Architecture & Interior Design, Art, Biography, Cookery, Economics, Gardening, Plants, Government, Political Science, Health, Nutrition, History, House & Home, Management, Nonfiction (General), Photography, Poetry, Religion - Catholic, Self-Help, Travel, Greeting Cards & Staty
ISBN Prefix(es): 90-209
*Associate Companies:* Bakermat NV, Mechelen; Distrimedia NV, Tielt; Touring Lanno NV, Brussels
Subsidiaries: ASDU International; Lannoo Campus; Editions Racine; Uitgeverij Terra Lannoo
Divisions: Lannoo Publishers; Lannoo Graphics
Distributed by Terra (Netherlands); Vilo (France & Canada)
Distributor for Academic Service (Netherlands); ANWB (Netherlands); Apress (Germany); Averbode (Belgium); Bakermat Uitgevers (Belgium); Beta Plus (Belgium); D-Publications (Belgium); Lonely Planet (UK); Microsoft Press (Ireland); Editions Moulinsart (Belgium); Nieuwezilds (Netherlands); O'Reilly (UK); Racine (Belgium); Sdu (Netherlands); Terra (Netherlands); Touring Lannoo (Belgium); Wiley (UK)
*Warehouse:* DistriMedia nv, Meulebeeksesteenweg 20, 8700 Tielt

**Lansman Editeur** (Lansman Publisher)+
65, rue Royale, 7141 Carnieres-Morlanwelz
*Tel:* (064) 23-78-40 *Fax:* (064) 44-31-02; (064) 23-78-49
*E-mail:* info@lansman.org
*Web Site:* www.lansman.org
*Key Personnel*
Dir: Emile Lansman
Press, Bookshop: Caroline Cullus
Founded: 1989
Specialize in theatre in French language (plays & research books).
Subjects: Art, Drama, Theater, Education, Literature, Literary Criticism, Essays
ISBN Prefix(es): 2-87282
Number of titles published annually: 35 Print
Total Titles: 450 Print
Distributor for Le bruit des Autres (outside France); Cahiers de Theatre Jeu (Europe); Solitaires Intempestifs (outside France)
*Distribution Center:* Casteilla SA, 10 rue Leon Foucault, 78180 Montigny-le-Bretonneux, France *Tel:* (01) 30 14 19 30 *Fax:* (01) 34 60 31 32 *E-mail:* casteilla@wanadoo.fr

Diffusion Dimedia Inc, 539, Blvd Lebeau, Saint-Laurent, QC H4N 1S2, Canada *Tel:* 514-336-3941 *Fax:* 514-331-3916 *E-mail:* general@dimedia.qc.ca

**Larcier-Department of De Boeck & Larcier SA**
Rue des Minimes 39, 1000 Brussels
Mailing Address: Fond Jean-Pacques 4, 1348 Louvain-la-Neuve
*E-mail:* deboeck.larcier@deboeck.be
*Web Site:* www.larcier.be
*Key Personnel*
Chairman of the Board: Christian de Boeck *Tel:* (010) 10-48 26 21 *Fax:* (010) 10-48 26 50 *E-mail:* christian.deboeck@deboeck.be
Man Dir: Bernard Houdmont
Dir: Georges Hoyos *Tel:* (010) 10-48 26 04 *Fax:* (010) 10-48 26 50 *E-mail:* georges.hoyos@deboeck.be
Group Editorial Dir: Yann Delalande
Founded: 1839
Subjects: Law
ISBN Prefix(es): 2-8044
*Parent Company:* Groupe De Boeck SA
*Associate Companies:* De Boeck & Larcier SA-Acces Plus SPRL
Distributed by LITEC (France only)
*Orders to:* Acces Plus SPRL, Fond Jean-Paques 4, 1348 Louvain-La-Neuve

**Claude Lefrancq Editeur+**
chaussee d'Alsemberg, 1180 Brussels
*Tel:* (02) 344-49-34 *Fax:* (02) 347-55-34
*E-mail:* claude.lefrancq@skynet.be
*Key Personnel*
Chairman & Man Dir: R Demartin
Editor: Claude Lefrancq
Founded: 1995
Subjects: Anthropology, Biography, Film, Video, Humor, Literature, Literary Criticism, Essays, Mysteries, Romance
ISBN Prefix(es): 2-87153; 90-71987; 90-75388

**Editions Lessius ASBL+**
Division of South Belgian Area of the Company of Jesus
Blvd Saint-Michel, 24, 1040 Brussels
*Tel:* (02) 739 34 90 *Fax:* (02) 739 34 91
*E-mail:* info@editions-lessius.be
*Web Site:* www.adeb.irisnet.be/annuaire/lessius.htm
*Key Personnel*
Dir: Daniel Dideberg *Tel:* (02) 739 34 92 *E-mail:* d.dideberg@iet.be
Dir of Collection: Rene Lafontaine; Benoit Malvaux; Jacques Scheuer; Jean-Pierre Sonnet
Communication Manager: Nathalie Dubois *Tel:* (02) 739 34 93 *E-mail:* nath.dubois@skynet.be
Founded: 1997
Specialize in exegetic Biblical commentaries; essays (language, philosophy, theology, psychology, art, law); meditation & pray; biography; & meeting between religions.
Subjects: Art, Biblical Studies, Biography, Language Arts, Linguistics, Law, Literature, Literary Criticism, Essays, Philosophy, Religion - Catholic, Religion - Hindu, Religion - Jewish, Social Sciences, Sociology, Theology
ISBN Prefix(es): 2-87299
Number of titles published annually: 12 Print
Total Titles: 120 Print
Distributed by Editions du Cerf

**Leuven University Press+**
Blijde-Inkomststr 5, 3000 Leuven
*Tel:* (016) 32 53 45 *Fax:* (016) 32 53 52
*E-mail:* info@upers.kuleuven.be
*Web Site:* www.lup.be; www.kuleuven.be/upers/
*Key Personnel*
President: Dirk Van den Auweele

Dir: Hilde Lens-Gielis *E-mail:* hilde.gielis@upers.
kuleuven.be
Publisher: Beatrice Van Eeghem *E-mail:* beatrice.
vaneeghem@upers.kuleuven.be
Public Relations & Marketing: Ineke Deckers
*E-mail:* ineke.deckers@upers.kuleuven.be; Pa-
tricia Di Costanzo *E-mail:* patricia.dicostanzo@
upers.kuleuven.be
Accounting: Regine Vanswijgenhoven
*E-mail:* regine.vanswijgenhoven@upers.
kuleuven.be
Founded: 1971
Membership(s): International Association of
Scholarly Publishers.
Subjects: Agriculture, Archaeology, Biological
Sciences, Criminology, Economics, Education,
Environmental Studies, Geography, Geology,
Government, Political Science, History, Lan-
guage Arts, Linguistics, Law, Literature, Liter-
ary Criticism, Essays, Mathematics, Medicine,
Nursing, Dentistry, Music, Dance, Philosophy,
Physical Sciences, Physics, Psychology, Psy-
chiatry, Science (General), Social Sciences,
Sociology, Theology
ISBN Prefix(es): 90-6186; 90-5867
Number of titles published annually: 100 Print; 1
Audio
Total Titles: 1,400 Print; 5 CD-ROM; 3 Audio
*Distribution Center:* Coronet Books, 311
Bainbridge St, Philadelphia 19147, United
States *Tel:* 215-925-2762 *Fax:* 215-925-1912
(www.coronetbooks.com)
*Orders to:* Coronet Books, 311 Bainbridge
St, Philadelphia 19147, United States
*Tel:* 212-925-2762 *Fax:* 212-925-1912
(www.coronetbooks.com)

**Liberica**, *imprint of* Zuid-Nederlandse Uitgeverij
NV/Central Uitgeverij

**Ligue pour la lecture de la Bible+**
Subsidiary of Scripture Union
Ave Giele, 23, 1090 Brussels
*Tel:* (02) 427-92-77 *Fax:* (02) 428-82-06
*E-mail:* llb_ibb@freegates.be
*Key Personnel*
Man Dir: J Makkink
Founded: 1955
Subjects: Religion - Other
ISBN Prefix(es): 2-87001
Number of titles published annually: 3 Print
Distributed by Lique pour la Lecture de la Bible
France; Lique pour la Lecture de la Bible Que-
bec, Canada; Maison de la Bible Suisse
Distributor for Ligue pour la Lecture de la Bible
France; Ligue pour la Lecture de la Bible Su-
isse

**Editeurs de Litterature Biblique+**
Chaussee de Tubize, 479, 1420 Braine-l'Alleud
*Tel:* (02) 384-54-02; (02) 384-52-12 *Fax:* (02)
384-98-66
*E-mail:* elbpub@elbeurope.org
*Web Site:* www.elbeurope.org
*Key Personnel*
Dir: Joel Rousseau
Founded: 1959
Subjects: Crafts, Games, Hobbies, Education,
Music, Dance, Philosophy, Religion - Other,
Sports, Athletics
ISBN Prefix(es): 2-8045
*U.S. Office(s):* Biblical Publications, 22 W 569
Winthrop, Glen Ellyn, IL 60139, United States

**Uitgeverij Loempia+**
Mechelsesteenweg, 123, 2018 Antwerp
*Tel:* (03) 2184292
*Key Personnel*
Man Dir: Jef Meert
Founded: 1983
ISBN Prefix(es): 90-6771

**Les Editions du Lombard SA+**
Subsidiary of Sofidar
7 av Paul-Henri-Spaak, 1060 Brussels
*Tel:* (02) 5266811 *Fax:* (02) 5204405
*E-mail:* info@lombard.be
*Web Site:* www.lelombard.com
*Telex:* 23097 *Cable:* LOMBARBEL BRUSSELS
*Key Personnel*
General Manager: Francois Pernot
Editorial Manager: Yves Sente
Public Relations: Anne-Marie De Coster
*E-mail:* annemarie.decoster@lelombard.be
Licensing, Rights, Press: Jean-Philippe Buyss-
chaert *E-mail:* jeanphilippe.buysschaert@
edlbm.be
Rights & Permissions: Sophie Castille
Founded: 1946
Subjects: Fiction, History, Humor, Science Fic-
tion, Fantasy
ISBN Prefix(es): 2-8036; 2-87389
Subsidiaries: Citel & Dargaud; Dargaud Benelux;
Dargaud Marina; Dargaud Suisse
*Branch Office(s)*
15-27 rue Moussorgski, 75018 Paris, France
*Tel:* (01) 53 26 32 32 *Fax:* (01) 53 26 32 40
*Orders to:* MDS, ZI de la Gaudree, 91417 Cedex,
Dourdan, France *Tel:* (01) 60818700 *Fax:* (01)
64593063

**La Longue Vue+**
Division of RVJ Editions
Dreve Pittoresque 92, 1640 Rhode Saint-Genese
*Tel:* (02) 358 23 93 *Fax:* (02) 358 17 37
*E-mail:* longuevue@skynet.be
*Key Personnel*
Dir, Editions: Charles de Trazegnies *Tel:* (02) 358
23 93
Founded: 1984
Specialize in Belgian literature & translation; also
acts as a translation agency.
Subjects: Biblical Studies, Fiction, Literature, Lit-
erary Criticism, Essays, Philosophy, Poetry
ISBN Prefix(es): 2-87121
Total Titles: 100 Print
Distributed by Nord-Sud Diffusion (Belgium);
Casteilla-Chiron (France)

**Editions Lumen Vitae ASBL+**
Division of CIEFR Centre Lumen Vitae
184-186 rue Washington, 1050 Brussels
*Tel:* (02) 3490399; (02) 3490370 *Fax:* (02)
3490385
*E-mail:* international@lumenvitae.be
*Web Site:* www.catho.be/lumen
*Key Personnel*
Publishing Dir: Henri Derroitte
Secretary & International Rights: Gabriella Tihon-
Gyorffy *E-mail:* gabriella.tihon@lumenvitae.be
Founded: 1935
Subjects: Biblical Studies, Education, Religion -
Catholic, Theology
ISBN Prefix(es): 2-87324
Number of titles published annually: 25 Print
Total Titles: 100 Print
Distributed by Cerf (France & Switzerland); No-
valis (Canada & USA)

**Maklu+**
Somersstraat 13-15, 2018 Antwerp 1
*Tel:* (03) 231-29-00 *Fax:* (03) 233-26-59
*E-mail:* info@maklu.be
*Web Site:* www.maklu.be
*Key Personnel*
Dir: Bert Boerwinkel; Huug Van Gompel
*E-mail:* huug.vangompel@maklu.be
Publisher: Stephan Svacina
Promotion: Werner Peeters
Founded: 1972
Also acts as wholesaler (Dutch books).
Specialize in law books & dictionaries.

Subjects: Economics, Government, Political Sci-
ence, Law, Management, Social Sciences, Soci-
ology
ISBN Prefix(es): 90-6215
Number of titles published annually: 80 Print
Total Titles: 800 Print
*Associate Companies:* Garant Publishers Ltd
Subsidiaries: Maklu bv
Distributed by Bayliss (London); Gaunt & Sons
(USA); Juridik & Samhaelle (Sweden); Nomos
Verlag (Germany); Schulthess Verlag (Switzer-
land)

**Manteau**, *imprint of* Standaard Uitgeverij

**Marabout+**
Ave de l'Energie, 30, 4432 Alleur
*Tel:* (04) 246 3863; (04) 146 3815 *Fax:* (04) 246
3635
*Key Personnel*
President: Jacques Firmin
Dir: Jean Arache
Financial Dir: Andre Palmans
Foreign Rights: Michele Boschis
Founded: 1949
Subjects: Animals, Pets, Astrology, Occult, Be-
havioral Sciences, Career Development, Child
Care & Development, Computer Science,
Cookery, Crafts, Games, Hobbies, English as
a Second Language, Gardening, Plants, Geneal-
ogy, Health, Nutrition, History, Human Rela-
tions, Humor, Medicine, Nursing, Dentistry,
Self-Help
ISBN Prefix(es): 2-501
*Parent Company:* Hachette
Distributed by Diffulivre Suisse; Hachette
Canada; Hachette Livre France; Tous Pays

**Mardaga, Pierre, Editeur**
Hayen 11, 4140 Sprimont
*Tel:* (04) 3684242 *Fax:* (04) 3684240
*Key Personnel*
Dir & Rights & Permissions: Pierre Mardaga
Founded: 1938
1600 titles on catalogue.
Subjects: Architecture & Interior Design, Edu-
cation, Human Relations, Language Arts, Lin-
guistics, Music, Dance, Philosophy, Psychol-
ogy, Psychiatry
ISBN Prefix(es): 2-87009; 2-8047
Number of titles published annually: 45 Print

**Medaillon**, *imprint of* Uitgeverij de Eenhoorn

**Editions Medicales et Paramedicales de
Charleroi (EMPC)**
rue Saint-Charles, 9, 6061 Montignies-sur-Sambre
*Tel:* (071) 324689 *Fax:* (071) 324689
*Key Personnel*
General Dir: Chantal Zanella
ISBN Prefix(es): 2-87133

**Editions Memor**
Rue Gustave Biot 23-25, 1050 Brussels
*Tel:* (02) 644-04-43 *Fax:* (02) 644-04-43
*Key Personnel*
Dir: John F Ellyton *E-mail:* john.ellyton@skynet.
be
Founded: 1995
Specialize in general Collection Couleurs
Teenagers, Transparences Adults.
Subjects: Fiction, Literature, Literary Criticism,
Essays
ISBN Prefix(es): 2-930133; 2-915394
Number of titles published annually: 8 Print
Total Titles: 3 Print
Foreign Rep(s): Alterdis (France)

**Mercatorfonds NV+**
Meir 85, 2000 Antwerp
*Tel:* (03) 2027260 *Fax:* (03) 2311319

E-mail: artbooks@mercatorfonds.be
Web Site: www.mercatorfonds.be
Key Personnel
Publisher: Jan Martens E-mail: jm@
  mercatorfonds.be
Founded: 1965
Publisher of fine art books & illustrated historical
  studies.
Subjects: Architecture & Interior Design, Art,
  History
ISBN Prefix(es): 90-6153
Number of titles published annually: 10 Print

**Michelin Editions des Voyages**
33 quai de Willebroek, 1000 Brussels
Tel: (02) 274 45 03 Fax: (02) 274 43 62
E-mail: kontakt@viamichelin.com
Web Site: www.viamichelin.com Cable:
  PNEUMICLIN
Key Personnel
Dir: Robert Van Keerberghen E-mail: robert-
  vankeerberghen@be.michelin.com
Founded: 1913
Subjects: Travel, Tourist Guides
Parent Company: Michelin Editions Des Voyages
Ultimate Parent Company: Manufacture Francaise
  Des Pneumatiques Michelin
U.S. Office(s): Michelin Travel Publications &
  Michelin Tire Corporation, One Parkway S,
  Greenville, SC 29615, United States

**Harvey Miller**, imprint of Brepols Publishers NV

**Mozaiek**, imprint of Uitgeverij Clavis

**Nauwelaerts Edition SA+**
Eglise St Sulpice 19, 1320 Beauvechain
Tel: (010) 86 67 37 Fax: (010) 86 16 55
Key Personnel
Man Dir: Stephane Rouget
Founded: 1934
Subjects: Economics, History, Literature, Literary
  Criticism, Essays, Medicine, Nursing, Den-
  tistry, Philosophy, Psychology, Psychiatry, So-
  cial Sciences, Sociology, Theology
ISBN Prefix(es): 2-8038
Associate Companies: Vander Publishing

**Nouvelle Diffusion SPRL DPI**, see Editions
  Complexe

**Les Nouvelles Editions Marabout SA**, see
  Marabout

**Petraco-Pandora NV+**
Indiestr 21, 2000 Antwerp
Tel: (03) 2338770 Fax: (03) 2333399
Founded: 1988
Subjects: Art, Catalogues, Monographs, Catalogue
  Raisonne
ISBN Prefix(es): 90-5325
Number of titles published annually: 30 Print
Total Titles: 180 Print

**Paradox Express - Manuscripten**, imprint of
  Paradox Pers vzw

**Paradox Pers vzw+**
Leopoldstraat 55/1, 2000 Antwerp
Tel: (03) 2318873 Fax: (03) 2386605
E-mail: paradox@glo.be; paradoxpers@belgacom.
  be
Key Personnel
Dir: Dirk Claus
Founded: 1960
Subjects: Fiction, Philosophy, Poetry
ISBN Prefix(es): 90-72533
Number of titles published annually: 10 Print
Imprints: Paradox Express - Manuscripten
Distributed by EPO (Belgium)

**Parasol NV+**
Mechelse Steenweg 434, 2650 Edegem
Tel: (03) 460 1880 Fax: (03) 460 1881
E-mail: info@parasol.be
Web Site: www.parasol.be
Key Personnel
Man Dir: Wilfried Wuyts Fax: (03) 460 1888
  E-mail: ww@parasol.be
Founded: 1994
Specialize in children's books ; publish in Dutch
  & French.
ISBN Prefix(es): 90-5593; 90-5888
Number of titles published annually: 60 Print
Total Titles: 300 Print

**Parsifal BVBA**
Gulden Vlieslaan 67, 8000 Brugge
Tel: (050) 339516 Fax: (050) 333386
E-mail: info@parsifal.be
Web Site: www.parsifal.be
Key Personnel
Chief Executive, Rights & Permissions: Christian
  Vandekerkhove
Production: Erna Droesbeke
Founded: 1974
Subjects: Astrology, Occult, Parapsychology, Phi-
  losophy
ISBN Prefix(es): 90-6458; 2-87259
Associate Companies: Editions Verrycken
Branch Office(s)
Steenhouwersvest, 2000 Antwerp Tel: (03)
  2316039
Bookshop(s): Librairie Verrycken, Weigstr 30,
  2000 Antwerp (jointly owned with Editions
  Verrycsen); Occult Bookshop, Hoogstr 68, B-
  2000 Antwerp

**La Part de L'Oeil+**
Rue du Midi, 144, 1000 Brussels
Tel: (02) 514 18 41 Fax: (02) 514 18 41
E-mail: lapartdeloeil@brunette.brucity.be
Key Personnel
Contact: Lucien Massaert
International Rights Contact: Karine Barbareau
Founded: 1985
La Part de L'Oeil is a theoretical arts review pub-
  lished in French.
Subjects: Art, Language Arts, Linguistics, Liter-
  ature, Literary Criticism, Essays, Philosophy,
  Poetry, Psychology, Psychiatry
ISBN Prefix(es): 2-930174
Number of titles published annually: 4 Print
Total Titles: 32 Print
Distributed by La Federation Diffusion (France,
  Quebec & Switzerland); UD-Union Distribution
  (France, Quebec & Switzerland)
Foreign Rep(s): Karine Barbareau

**Uitgeverij Peeters Leuven (Belgie)** (Peeters
  Publishers & Booksellers)+
Bondgenotenlaan 153, 3000 Leuven
Tel: (016) 23 51 70 Fax: (016) 22 85 00
E-mail: peeters@peeters-leuven.be
Web Site: www.peeters-leuven.be
Key Personnel
Dir: Mr P Peeters
Founded: 1857
Publish books & journals in English, French, Ger-
  man & Dutch. Publish original research as well
  as bibliographic data, reviews & reference ma-
  terial.
Subjects: Archaeology, Art, Asian Studies, Bib-
  lical Studies, History, Language Arts, Linguis-
  tics, Literature, Literary Criticism, Essays, Phi-
  losophy, Religion - Other, Theology, Classical
  Studies, Ethics, History of Art, Medieval Stud-
  ies, Oriental Studies
ISBN Prefix(es): 2-87723; 90-6831; 90-429; 2-
  8017
Number of titles published annually: 150 Print; 2
  CD-ROM; 50 Online
Total Titles: 3,500 Print; 50 Online

Subsidiaries: Peeters
Distribution Center: Book Representation &
  Distribution Ltd, 244a London Rd, Hadleigh-
  Essex SS7 2DE, United Kingdom Tel: (17) 02-
  552912 Fax: (17) 02-556095 E-mail: sales@
  bookreps.com
The David Brown Book Co, PO Box 511,
  Oakville, CT 06679, United States, Contact:
  I Stevens E-mail: david.brown.bk.co@snet.net
  Web Site: www.davidbrownbookco.com
VRIN, 6 Place de la Sodonne, 75005 Paris,
  France Tel: (01) 43540347 Fax: (01) 43544818
  E-mail: contact@vrin.fr

**Pelckmans NV, De Nederlandsche Boekhandel+**
Kapelsestraat 222, 2950 Kapellen
Tel: (03) 660 27 00 Fax: (03) 660 27 01
E-mail: uitgeverij@pelckmans.be
Web Site: www.pelckmans.be
Key Personnel
General Director: Jan en Rudi Pelckmans
Founded: 1892
Subjects: Geography, Geology, History, Language
  Arts, Linguistics, Literature, Literary Criticism,
  Essays, Mathematics, Philosophy, Religion -
  Catholic
ISBN Prefix(es): 90-289

**Uitgeverij Pelckmans NV**
Kapelsestr 222, 2950 Kapellen
Tel: (03) 6602700 Fax: (03) 66022701
E-mail: uitgeverij@pelckmans.be
Web Site: www.pelckmans.be
Telex: 32242 Anvers Dnb
Key Personnel
Man Dir: J Pelckmans; R Pelckmans
Founded: 1892
Subjects: History, Philosophy, Religion - Other,
  Social Sciences, Sociology
ISBN Prefix(es): 90-289
Associate Companies: Uitgeverij Helios; Uitgev-
  erij Patmos
Bookshop(s): Sint Jacobsmarkt 7, 2000 Antwerp

**Poeziecentrum+**
Vrydagmarkt 36, 9000 Ghent
Tel: (09) 225 22 25 Fax: (09) 225 90 54
E-mail: info@poeziecentrum.be
Web Site: www.poeziecentrum.be
Key Personnel
Man Dir: Willy Tibergien
Founded: 1980
Subjects: Poetry
ISBN Prefix(es): 90-5655; 90-70968
Number of titles published annually: 10 Print

**Le Pole Nord ASBL**
Rue du Nord, 66, 1000 Brussels
Tel: (02) 2184576 Fax: (02) 2184576
E-mail: pole.nord@skynet.be
Key Personnel
President: Anny Frenay
Secretary: Charlotte Goetz
Founded: 1983
Also acts as Scientific Research Association.
Subjects: History, French Revolution, Jean-Paul
  Marat
ISBN Prefix(es): 2-930040
Distributed by Pole Nord Asbl

**Pre-Ecole**, imprint of Editions Chantecler

**Preschool**, imprint of Zuid-Nederlandse
  Uitgeverij NV/Central Uitgeverij

**Presses agronomiques de Gembloux ASBL+**
2, Passage des Deportes, 5030 Gembloux
Tel: (081) 62 22 42 Fax: (081) 62 22 42
E-mail: pressesagro@fsagx.ac.be
Web Site: www.bib.fsagx.ac.be/presses/

*Key Personnel*
Dir: Mr B Pochet
Founded: 1964
Specialize also in chemistry & the food industry.
Subjects: Agriculture, Biological Sciences, Environmental Studies, Mathematics, Technology
ISBN Prefix(es): 2-87016
Number of titles published annually: 3 Print
Total Titles: 30 Print
Foreign Rep(s): Lavoisier (Canada, France)

**Presses Universitaires de Bruxelles asbl**
Campus Solbosch, bâtiment V (2e étage), Ave
  Paul Heger, 42, 1000 Brussels
Mailing Address: CP 149, 1000 Brussels
*Tel:* (02) 641 79 62 *Fax:* (02) 647 79 62
*Key Personnel*
President: Thierry Lambrecht
Sales: Henri De Smet
Founded: 1958
Subjects: Architecture & Interior Design, Economics, Engineering (General), Medicine, Nursing, Dentistry, Philosophy, Science (General)
ISBN Prefix(es): 2-500

**Presses Universitaires de Liege**
Domaine Universi du Sart-Tilman, Batiment 87,
  bte 27, 4000 Liege
*Tel:* (041) 562218
Founded: 1969
Subjects: Government, Political Science, Law, Medicine, Nursing, Dentistry, Social Sciences, Sociology
ISBN Prefix(es): 2-87014
*Branch Office(s)*
7, Place du 20-Aout Bat A1, 04000 Leige
  *Tel:* (041) 420080

**Presses Universitaires de Namur ASBL**
Rempart de la Vierge 13, 5000 Namur
*Tel:* (081) 72 48 84 *Fax:* (081) 72 49 12
*E-mail:* pun@fundp.ac.be
*Web Site:* www.pun.be
*Key Personnel*
Dir: Rene Robaye
Editor: Myriam Despineux *Tel:* (081) 72 48 86
  *E-mail:* myriam.despineux@fundp.ac.be
Public Relations: Stephanie Herfurth *Tel:* (081)
  72 48 85 *E-mail:* stephanie.herfurth@fundp.ac.
  be
Founded: 1977
Membership(s): ADEB (Association des Editeurs Belges).
ISBN Prefix(es): 2-87037
Number of titles published annually: 15 Print

**Prodim SPRL+**
184, Blvd General Jacques, 1050 Brussels
*Tel:* (02) 640 59 70 *Fax:* (02) 640 59 91
*E-mail:* prodim.books@prodim.be
*Web Site:* www.prodim.be
*Key Personnel*
President: Mdme Nile Patrick
Founded: 1968
Physiotherapy.
Membership(s): ADEB.
Subjects: Medicine, Nursing, Dentistry
ISBN Prefix(es): 2-87017
Subsidiaries: de Visscher
Distributor for Jibena (Belgium); Similia (Belgium)
Foreign Rep(s): Nile Patrick

**Production et Diffusion de Medias SPRL**, see
  Prodim SPRL

**Henri Proost & Co, Pvba**
Everdongenlaan 23, 2300 Turnhout
*Tel:* (014) 40 08 11 *Fax:* (014) 42 87 94
*Web Site:* www.proost.be

*Telex:* 33185
*Key Personnel*
Man Dir: Herman Peeters *E-mail:* herman.
  peeters@proost.be
Sales Dir: Jan Jacobs
Subjects: Cookery, Gardening, Plants, History, Religion - Other, Travel
ISBN Prefix(es): 90-6150
Subsidiaries: Bedford Editions Ltd; Salamander Books Ltd

**Publications des Facultes Universitaires Saint Louis+**
Blvd du Jardin Botanique 43, 1000 Brussels
*Tel:* (02) 211 78 94 *Fax:* (02) 211 79 97
*Web Site:* www.fusl.ac.be
*Key Personnel*
Man Dir: Francois Ost
Sales & Publicity: Marie-Francoise Thoua
  *E-mail:* thoua@fusl.ac.be
Founded: 1973
Subjects: Economics, History, Law, Philosophy, Psychology, Psychiatry, Social Sciences, Sociology, Theology
ISBN Prefix(es): 2-8028

**Andre De Rache Editeur**
18 rue de Transinne, 6890 Redu
*Tel:* (061) 656091 *Fax:* (061) 656091
*Key Personnel*
Man Dir: Andre de Rache
Founded: 1954
Subjects: Art, Biography, Poetry
ISBN Prefix(es): 2-8015

**Editions Racine+**
Rue du Chatelain 49, 1050 Brussels
*Tel:* (02) 646 44 44 *Fax:* (02) 646 55 70
*E-mail:* info@racine.be
*Web Site:* www.racine.be
*Key Personnel*
Dir: Emmanuel Brutsaert
Founded: 1993
Specialize also in nature.
Subjects: Architecture & Interior Design, Art, History, Nonfiction (General)
ISBN Prefix(es): 2-87386
Total Titles: 160 Print
*Parent Company:* Lannoo
*Ultimate Parent Company:* Lannoo
Distributed by Lannoo (Belgium); Vilo (France); Altera Diffusion (Begium)

**Rainbow Grafics Intl - Baronian Books SC+**
63 rue de la Vallee, 1050 Brussels
*Tel:* (02) 649 53 91 *Fax:* (02) 649 27 57
*Key Personnel*
Man Dir: Mdme Anne Lous Baronian
Editorial Dir: Jehn Baptiste Lous Baronian
Specialize in international co-production.

**Reader's Digest SA**
Paapsemlaan 20, 1070 Brussels
*Tel:* (02) 5268111 *Fax:* (02) 5268112
*E-mail:* service@readersdigest.be
*Web Site:* www.rd.com
*Telex:* 21876
*Key Personnel*
Man Dir: J H Beauduin
Founded: 1947
Subjects: Education, Geography, Geology, History, Sports, Athletics, Travel
ISBN Prefix(es): 90-70818; 2-87101

**La Renaissance du Livre+**
14/1 Rue de Paris, 7500 Tournai
*Tel:* (069) 89 15 55 *Fax:* (069) 89 15 50
*Web Site:* www.larenaissancedulivre.com
Founded: 1923
Subjects: Art, History
ISBN Prefix(es): 2-8041; 2-87148; 2-8046

Distributed by Exhibitions International (Dutch-speaking Belgium & Netherlands); Vivendi Universal Publishing (French-speaking Belgium & Grand Duchy)

**Roularta Books NV+**
Meiboomlaan 33, 8800 Roeselare
*Tel:* (051) 266967 *Fax:* (051) 266680
*E-mail:* info@roularta.be
*Web Site:* www.roulartabooks.be
*Key Personnel*
President: Jan Ingelbeen
Business Manager: Lieve Claeys
Founded: 1988
Subjects: Architecture & Interior Design, Art, Business, Economics, Gardening, Plants, Literature, Literary Criticism, Essays, Management, Marketing, Nonfiction (General), Sports, Athletics, Travel
ISBN Prefix(es): 90-5466; 90-72411; 90-940073
Imprints: Globe; KnackBibliotheek/Radio 1

**Scaillet, SA+**
Rue de Marchienne 203, 6110 Montigny-le-Tilleul
*Tel:* (071) 516335 *Fax:* (071) 511795
*Key Personnel*
Administrative Delegate: Andre Scaillet
Founded: 1984
Also acts as a printing office.
Subjects: History
ISBN Prefix(es): 2-930002

**Schaar**, *imprint of* De Schaar/Geknipt Papier

**De Schaar/Geknipt Papier+**
Penitentenstr 24, 9000 Ghent
*Tel:* (09) 225 5414 *Fax:* (09) 225 9724
*E-mail:* geknipt@skynet.be
*Key Personnel*
International Rights: Carla Wauben
Contact: Paul D'Haene
Founded: 1989
Subjects: Comics
ISBN Prefix(es): 90-5775; 90-73619
Imprints: Blitz; Schaar; Scissors

**Paul Schiltz**
3 Place Rotenberg, 4700 Eupen
*Tel:* (087) 553271
*Key Personnel*
Man Dir: Paul Schiltz
Founded: 1963
Subjects: Medicine, Nursing, Dentistry
ISBN Prefix(es): 2-87058

**Schott Freres SA (Editeurs de Musique)**
26-28 Rue Ravenstein, 1000 Brussels
*Tel:* (02) 5132742 *Fax:* (02) 5133049
*E-mail:* eric.junne@skynet.be
*Web Site:* www.classicalscores.com
*Key Personnel*
Man Dir: Jean-Jacques Junne
Founded: 1823
Subjects: Music, Dance
*Associate Companies:* Schott Freres Sarl, France

**Scissors**, *imprint of* De Schaar/Geknipt Papier

**Service**, *imprint of* Kluwer Editions

**Uitgeverij De Sikkel NV+**
Nijverheidsstr 8, 2390 Oostmalle
*Tel:* (03) 312 86 30 *Fax:* (03) 311 77 39
*E-mail:* informatie@deboeck.be
*Web Site:* www.desikkel.be
*Key Personnel*
Man Dir: Bart Hye *Tel:* (03) 3128643
  *E-mail:* bhye@desikkel.be

Contact: Bieke Berhaers *E-mail:* bberhaers@
desikkel.be; Patrick Vandevelde *Tel:* (03)
3128644 *E-mail:* pvandevelde@desikkel.be
Founded: 1919
Membership(s): Flemish Publishers Association.
Subjects: Education, English as a Second Lan-
guage
ISBN Prefix(es): 90-260
*Parent Company:* De Pioen, Oostmalle
Distributor for Dijkstra (Groningen); Ediciones
SM (Madrid); Panta Rhei; Spruyt; Ver-
pleegkundig fonds (Leiden); Von Mantgem en
de Does; UBS (Oegstgeest); De Vey-Mestdagh
(Middelburg); Westermann Lernspiel (Braun-
schweig)
*Bookshop(s):* De Pioen, Oostmalle

**Snoeck-Ducaju en Zoon NV**
Begijnhoflaan 464, 9000 Ghent
*Tel:* (09) 267.04.11 *Fax:* (09) 267.04.60
*E-mail:* sdz@sdz.be
*Web Site:* www.sdz.be
*Telex:* 12765
*Key Personnel*
Algemene Dir: S Snoeck
Founded: 1782
Subjects: Literature, Literary Criticism, Essays
ISBN Prefix(es): 90-70481; 90-5349

**Sonneville Press (Uitgeverij) VTW**
Karel De Stoutelaan 142, 8000 Brugge
*Tel:* (050) 321112
*Key Personnel*
Dir: J Sonneville
Founded: 1987
Subjects: Art, Education, Ethnicity, Geography,
Geology, Government, Political Science, His-
tory, Language Arts, Linguistics, Law, Litera-
ture, Literary Criticism, Essays, Music, Dance,
Philosophy, Religion - Other, Social Sciences,
Sociology, Sports, Athletics, Travel
ISBN Prefix(es): 90-5149

**Stafeto**, *imprint of* Vlaamse Esperantobond VZW

**Standaard Uitgeverij+**
Belgielei 147a, 2018 Antwerp
*Tel:* (03) 285 72 00 *Fax:* (03) 285 72 99
*E-mail:* info@standaarduitgeverij.be
*Web Site:* www.standaarduitgeverij.be
*Key Personnel*
Man Dir: Eric Willems
Editorial Dir: Johan de Koning; Diane Devriendt
Publisher: Wim Verheije
Editorial Dir: Jacques Germonprez
Founded: 1906
Subjects: Biography, Fiction, Humor, Poetry
ISBN Prefix(es): 90-02
*Parent Company:* PCM Algemene Boeken bv,
Nieuwekade 1, 3511 RV Utrecht, Netherlands
Imprints: Manteau
*Warehouse:* Libridis-Bulkmagazijn Temse,
Schoenstr 6, 9140 Temse
*Orders to:* Libridis-Bulkmagazijn Temse, Schoen-
str 6, 9140 Temse

**Stichting Kunstboek bvba+**
Legeweg 165, 8020 Oostkamp
*Tel:* (050) 461910 *Fax:* (050) 461918
*Key Personnel*
Contact: Jaak van Damme; Karel Puype
Founded: 1992
Subjects: Architecture & Interior Design, Art,
Crafts, Games, Hobbies, Gardening, Plants,
History, Music, Dance
ISBN Prefix(es): 90-74377; 90-5856

**Stichting Ons Erfdeel VZW**
Murissonstr 260, 8930 Rekkem
*Tel:* (056) 41 12 01 *Fax:* (056) 41 47 07
*E-mail:* info@onserfdeel.be

*Web Site:* www.onserfdeel.be
*Key Personnel*
Man Dir & Chief Editor: Luc Devoldere
Head, Administration: Bernard Viaene
*E-mail:* adm@onserfdeel.be
Founded: 1970
Specialize in promoting cultural cooperation
among all speakers of the Dutch language &
increase awareness of Flemish & Dutch culture
abroad. Publish & distribute a range of peri-
odicals & other publications, both in Dutch &
other languages.
Subjects: Art, Ethnicity, Language Arts, Linguis-
tics, Literature, Literary Criticism, Essays, Re-
gional Interests
ISBN Prefix(es): 90-70831; 90-75862
*Branch Office(s)*
Rijvoortshoef 265, 4941 VJ Raamsdonksveer,
Netherlands *Tel:* (0162) 513425 *Fax:* (0162)
519227

**E Story-Scientia**, *imprint of* Kluwer Editions

**Editions Techniques et Scientifiques SPRL**
37 rue Borrens, 1050 Brussels
*Tel:* (02) 6401040 *Fax:* (02) 6400739
*Key Personnel*
Man Dir: A Louis
Founded: 1919
Subjects: Ethnicity, Geography, Geology, History,
Law, Mathematics, Science (General), Technol-
ogy, Travel
ISBN Prefix(es): 2-87004

**Toneelfonds J Janssens BVBA+**
Te Boelaerlei 107, 2140 Borgerhout-Antwerp
*Tel:* (03) 366 44 00 *Fax:* (03) 366 45 01
*E-mail:* info@toneelfonds.be
*Web Site:* www.toneelfonds.be
*Key Personnel*
Dir: Jessica Janssens *E-mail:* jessica.janssens@
toneelfonds.be
Founded: 1880
Publisher of plays & brochures. Also acts as liter-
ary agent for playwrights.
Subjects: Drama, Theater
ISBN Prefix(es): 90-385
Number of titles published annually: 100 Print

**Toulon Uitgeverij**
Sportstr 35, 8400 Oostende
*Tel:* (059) 800927
*Key Personnel*
Dir: P A Toulon
Subjects: Education
ISBN Prefix(es): 90-70270

**UCL**, see Presses Universitaires de Louvain-UCL

**UGA Editions (Uitgeverij)**
Stijn Streuvelslaan 73, 8501 Courtrai
*Tel:* (056) 36 32 00 *Fax:* (056) 35 60 96
*E-mail:* publ@uga.be
*Web Site:* www.uga.be *Cable:* UGA
*Key Personnel*
Dir: L Deschildre
Editorial, Sales: Patrick van Assche *E-mail:* pva@
uga.be
Founded: 1948
Also acts as packager.
Subjects: History, Language Arts, Linguistics,
Law, Public Administration, Social Sciences,
Sociology
ISBN Prefix(es): 90-6768
*Branch Office(s)*
CAD, rue Guimard, 19 - Boite 2, 1040 Brussels
*Tel:* (02) 512 09 75 *Fax:* (02) 512 26 93

**Uitgeverij Averbode NV** (Averbode Publishers)+
Abdijstraat 1, 3271 Averbode
*Tel:* (013) 780 184 *Fax:* (013) 780 183

*E-mail:* educational@verbode.be
*Web Site:* www.averbode.com
*Key Personnel*
Business Unit Manager: Patrick Hermans
*E-mail:* patrick.hermans@verbode.be
Rights & License Assistant: Ann Vanoppen
Founded: 1993
Subjects: Education, Religion - Catholic, Educa-
tional youth magazines, teacher support materi-
als
ISBN Prefix(es): 90-317
Number of titles published annually: 40 Print
Total Titles: 250 Print

**Uitgeverij De Garve**, see Barbianx de Garve

**Unistad Verspreiding CV+**
Jan Moorkensstr 46, 2600 Berchem
*Tel:* (03) 2307725 *Fax:* (03) 2307725
*Key Personnel*
Dir: Rob Claes
Editorial: Bennie Callebaut
Founded: 1984
Subjects: Religion - Other
ISBN Prefix(es): 90-70276; 90-6721
*Parent Company:* Citta Nuova Editrice, Italy

**Universitaire Pers Leuven**, see Leuven
University Press

**Presses Universitaires de Louvain-UCL**
Place de l'Universite Catholique de Louvain, 1,
1348 Louvain-la-Neuve
*Tel:* (010) 47 21 11 *Fax:* (010) 47 25 31
*Web Site:* www.ucl.ac.be
*Telex:* UCL AC 59516
*Key Personnel*
Dir: Jacqueline Tulkens
Membership(s): ADEB.
Subjects: Science (General)
ISBN Prefix(es): 2-87200; 90-06; 2-930344

**Editions de l'Universite de Bruxelles+**
Ave Paul Heger, 26, 1000 Brussels
*Tel:* (02) 650 37 97 *Fax:* (02) 650 37 94
*Web Site:* www.editions-universite-bruxelles.be
Founded: 1972
Subjects: Economics, Government, Political Sci-
ence, History, Law, Mathematics, Medicine,
Nursing, Dentistry, Philosophy, Social Sciences,
Sociology
ISBN Prefix(es): 2-8004
Number of titles published annually: 20 Print
Total Titles: 260 Print
Distributed by Somabec (Canada)

**Vaillant - Carmanne, Imprimerie**
20 Zevenputtenstr, 3690 Zutendaal
*Tel:* (011) 612452 *Fax:* (011) 612451
*Key Personnel*
Man Dir: G Dengis
Founded: 1838
Subjects: Education, Government, Political Sci-
ence, History, Law, Medicine, Nursing, Den-
tistry, Religion - Other, Science (General)
ISBN Prefix(es): 2-87021

**Marc Van de Wiele bvba+**
Jakobinessenstr 5, 8000 Brugge
*Tel:* (050) 333805 *Fax:* (050) 346457
*Key Personnel*
Contact: M van de Wiele
Founded: 1979
Subjects: Art, History
ISBN Prefix(es): 90-6966; 90-76297
*Bookshop(s):* Antiquariaat Marc Van de Wiele, St
Salvator Keru Hof 7, 8000 Brugge; Zeewindstr
4, 8300 Knouue-Heist

**Vander Editions, SA**
321 Ave des Volontaires, 1150 Brussels

*Tel:* (02) 7629804 *Fax:* (02) 7620662
*Key Personnel*
Man Dir: Willy Vandermeulen
Editorial Dir: Stephane Rouget
Founded: 1880
Subjects: Economics, Government, Political Science, Law, Psychology, Psychiatry, Science (General), Social Sciences, Sociology
ISBN Prefix(es): 2-8008
*Associate Companies:* Nauwelaerts Edition SA

**VBVB**, see Huis Van Het Boek

**Les Editions Vie ouvriere ASBL**
rue Anderlecht 4, 1000 Brussels
*Tel:* (02) 5125090 *Fax:* (02) 5145231
*Key Personnel*
Chief Executive: Andre Samain
Founded: 1958
Subjects: Economics, History, Photography, Psychology, Psychiatry, Religion - Other, Social Sciences, Sociology
ISBN Prefix(es): 2-87003

**Vita+**
Speelstraat 14, 9750 Zingem
*Tel:* (091) 3842114 *Fax:* (09) 3842114
*Key Personnel*
Contact: Eric De Preester
Founded: 1964
Subjects: Alternative, Crafts, Games, Hobbies, Health, Nutrition, Literature, Literary Criticism, Essays, Philosophy, Poetry, Theology
ISBN Prefix(es): 90-73323
Number of titles published annually: 3 Print
Total Titles: 22 Print

**Vlaamse Esperantobond VZW+**
Frankrijklei 140, 2000 Antwerp
*Tel:* (03) 2343400 *Fax:* (03) 2335433
*E-mail:* esperanto@agoranet.be
*Key Personnel*
General Dir: Paul Peeraerts *E-mail:* pp@fel. agoranet.be
Founded: 1979
Subjects: Education, Fiction, Language Arts, Linguistics, Poetry
ISBN Prefix(es): 90-71205; 90-77066
Total Titles: 10 Print
Imprints: Stafeto
*U.S. Office(s):* Esperanto League of North America, PO Box 1129, El Cerrito, CA 94530-1129, United States

**C De Vries Brouwers BVBA**
Haantjeslei 80, 2018 Antwerp
*Tel:* (03) 2374180 *Fax:* (03) 2377001
*Key Personnel*
Dir: I de Vries
Founded: 1946
Subjects: History
ISBN Prefix(es): 90-6174; 90-5927

**VUB Brussels University Press+**
Waversesteenweg 1077, 1160 Brussels
*Tel:* (02) 629 35 90 *Fax:* (02) 629 26 94
*E-mail:* vubpress@vub.ac.be
*Web Site:* www.vubpress.org
*Key Personnel*
General Manager: Kris Van Scharen
    *E-mail:* kvschare@vub.ac.be
Founded: 1987
Specialize in scientific publications.
Subjects: Communications, Environmental Studies, Government, Political Science, History, Philosophy, Science (General), Social Sciences, Sociology, Women's Studies
ISBN Prefix(es): 90-5487
Number of titles published annually: 30 Print
Total Titles: 400 Print

**Wereldwijd Mediahuis VzW+**
Hoogstr 139, 1000 Brussels
*Tel:* (02) 3-2162935 *Fax:* (02) 3-2377757
*E-mail:* wereldwijd@wereldwijd.ngonet.be
*Key Personnel*
Dir: Agnes Van Speybroeck
Founded: 1970
Membership(s): VBVB.
Subjects: Developing Countries
ISBN Prefix(es): 90-76421

**Editions Luce Wilquin+**
rue d'Atrive 48, 4280 Avin
*Tel:* (019) 69 98 13 *Fax:* (019) 69 98 13
*E-mail:* wilquin.bouquin@skynet.be
*Web Site:* www.wilquin.com
Founded: 1992
Subjects: Art, Fiction, History, Literature, Literary Criticism, Essays, Romance
ISBN Prefix(es): 2-88161; 2-88253
Number of titles published annually: 20 Print
Total Titles: 170 Print

**Wolters Kluwer Belgie**, see Ced-Samsom Wolters Kluwer Belgie

**Wolters Plantyn Educatieve Uitgevers**
Santvoortbeeklaan 21-25, 2600 Deurne
*Tel:* (03) 360 03 37 *Fax:* (03) 360 03 30
*E-mail:* klantendienst@woltersplantyn.be
*Web Site:* www.woltersplantyn.be
Founded: 1959
Educational publishers.
Subjects: Computer Science, Economics, Education, Language Arts, Linguistics, Mathematics, Physics, Psychology, Psychiatry, Science (General)
ISBN Prefix(es): 90-309; 90-301
*Parent Company:* Wolters Kluwer Belgie NV
*Ultimate Parent Company:* Wolters Kluwer NV, Netherlands
*Orders to:* Zeutestr 5, 2800 Mechelen

**Zuid En Noord VZW**
Hanebergstraat 75, 3581 Beringen
*Tel:* (011) 34 4991
*Web Site:* www.boekenwereld.com
*Key Personnel*
Algemene Directie: Edith Oeyen *E-mail:* edith. oeyen@telenet.be
Subjects: Biography, Literature, Literary Criticism, Essays, Poetry, Romance
ISBN Prefix(es): 90-72087; 90-5684

**Zuid-Nederlandse Uitgeverij NV/Central Uitgeverij+**
Vluchtenburgstr 7, 2630 Aartselaar
*Tel:* (03) 8774400 *Fax:* (03) 8772115
*Telex:* 31739 Zuidb
*Key Personnel*
Man Dir: Jan Vande Velden
Publisher: Bart Clinckemalie
Production: Eric Feyten
Sales Dir: Wilfried Wuyts
Founded: 1946
Subjects: Animals, Pets, Child Care & Development, Crafts, Games, Hobbies, English as a Second Language, Gardening, Plants, Humor
ISBN Prefix(es): 2-8034; 90-243; 90-447
Imprints: Chantecler; Deltas; Invader; Liberica; Preschool
Subsidiaries: Editions Chantecler; Centrale Uitgeverij; Invader Ltd; Liberica

# Benin

## General Information

*Capital:* Porto-Novo
*Language:* French
*Religion:* About 15% Christian (mostly Roman Catholic), 13% Islamic, remainder traditional beliefs
*Population:* 4.5 million
*Bank Hours:* 0800-1000, 1500-1600 Monday-Friday
*Shop Hours:* 0800-1300, 1500-1900 Monday-Saturday. Larger ones close Monday, some open for a few hours Sunday morning
*Currency:* 100 centimes = CFA franc
*Export/Import Information:* Import license required but issued automatically for imports from EEC countries. Exchange controls for non-franc zone.
*Copyright:* Berne (see Copyright Conventions, pg xi)

**Les Editions du Flamboyant**
Immeuble EYEBIYI, Carre 236, BP 08-271, Cotonou
*Tel:* 310220 *Fax:* 312079
*E-mail:* IPEC@leland.bj
*Key Personnel*
Contact: Oscar de Souza
Founded: 1997
ISBN Prefix(es): 2-909130; 99919-41

**Logos de l'Office**, *imprint of* Office National d'Edition de Presse et d'Imprimerie (ONEPI)

**Office National d'Edition de Presse et d'Imprimerie (ONEPI)**
PO Box 1210, Cotonou
*Tel:* 300299; 301152 *Fax:* 303463
*Key Personnel*
Administrator: Innocent Adjaho
Founded: 1975
Imprints: Logos de l'Office

**ONEPI**, see Office National d'Edition de Presse et d'Imprimerie (ONEPI)

# Bermuda

## General Information

*Capital:* Hamilton
*Language:* English & some Portuguese
*Religion:* Predominantly Anglican
*Population:* 60,213
*Bank Hours:* 0930-1500 Monday-Thursday; 0930-1500, 1630-1800 Friday
*Shop Hours:* 0900-1700 Monday-Saturday
*Currency:* 100 cents = 1 Bermuda dollar. US currency circulates
*Export/Import Information:* No tariff on books and advertising matter. No import license. Exchange controls on imports valued over $100.
*Copyright:* Berne (see Copyright Conventions, pg xi)

**The Bermudian Publishing Co**
PO Box HM283, Hamilton HM AX
*Tel:* 295-0695 *Fax:* 295-8616
*E-mail:* info@thebermudian.com
*Web Site:* www.thebermudian.com *Cable:* BERPUBLISH
*Key Personnel*
Publisher: Tina Stevenson
Founded: 1930

Publish magazines.
Subjects: Business, Fiction, Social Sciences, Sociology, Sports, Athletics, Specializes in Bermuda
ISBN Prefix(es): 976-8143
*Warehouse:* Addendum Lane, Pitts Bay Rd, Pembroke

# Bolivia

## General Information

*Capital:* Sucre
*Religion:* Predominantly Roman Catholic
*Population:* 7.3 million
*Bank Hours:* 0900-1200, 1400-1630 Monday-Friday
*Shop Hours:* 0900-1200, 1400-1800 Monday-Friday; 0900-1200 Saturday
*Currency:* 100 centavos = 1 Boliviano
*Export/Import Information:* Member of the Latin American Free Trade Association. No tariffs on books, except for 10% luxury bindings. No import licenses, except for textbooks, but no pornography allowed. No advertising that includes imitation money, stamps, etc, allowed. No exchange controls.
*Copyright:* UCC, Berne, Buenos Aires (see Copyright Conventions, pg xi)

**Los Amigos del Libro Ediciones+**
Member of Distripress
Calle Heroinas, No E-0311, esquina Espana, Cochabamba
Mailing Address: Apdo Aereo 450, Cochabamba
*Tel:* (04) 254114 *Fax:* (04) 251140
*Web Site:* www.librosbolivia.com
*Key Personnel*
President & Man Dir: Werner Guttentag
   *E-mail:* gutten@amigol.bo.net
Sales Dir: Ingrid Guttentag *E-mail:* gutten@amigol.bo.net
Foreign Sales Manager: Eva Guttentag
Production: Norma de Rivero; Rita Arze
Founded: 1945
Member of Distripress.
Subjects: Regional Interests, All aspects of Bolivia
ISBN Prefix(es): 84-8370; 99905-45
Number of titles published annually: 1,250 Print
Total Titles: 600 Print
*Parent Company:* Los Amigos del Libro, Cochabamba
Subsidiaries: Bio Bibliografia Boliviana
*Branch Office(s)*
La Paz
Santa Cruz
Distributed by Fondo de Cultura Economica (Argentina & Chile)
Distributor for Time; Newsweek; Fondo de Cultura Economica; Serres
*Bookshop(s):* Libreria los Amigos del Libro, Casilla 450 Avenida Ayacucho, S-0156 Cochabamba

**Editorial Don Bosco**
Av 16 de Julio 1899, Casilla de Correo 4458, La Paz
*Tel:* (02) 357755; (02) 371149 *Fax:* (02) 362822 *Cable:* EDEBE-LA PAZ
*Key Personnel*
Dir: Gramaglia Magliano; R P Giorgio
Subjects: Chemistry, Chemical Engineering, History, Literature, Literary Criticism, Essays, Mathematics, Philosophy, Physics, Religion - Catholic, Science (General)

**Gisbert y Cia SA**
Comercio 1270, La Paz

Mailing Address: Casilla Postal 195, La Paz
*Tel:* (02) 20 26 26 *Fax:* (02) 20 29 11
*E-mail:* libgis@ceibo.entelnet.bo *Cable:* GISBERCIA
*Key Personnel*
President: Javier Gisbert
Manager: Antonio Schulczewski; Maria del Carmen Schulczewski
Founded: 1907
Subjects: History, Law
Number of titles published annually: 2 Print
Distributor for Pearson Education

**Universidad Autonoma Tomas Frias, Div de Extension Universitaria**
Casilla 36, Av Civica y Serrudo, Potosi
*Tel:* (062) 2-73-28; (062) 2-73-00 *Fax:* (062) 2-66-63; (062) 2-31-96
*E-mail:* rector@rect.nrp.edu.bo
*Web Site:* www.unam.mx/udal/afiliacion/Bolivia/frias.htm
Subjects: History, Literature, Literary Criticism, Essays

**Universidad Mayor de San Andres, Editorial Universitaria**
Avda Villazon 1995, Casilla 4787, La Paz
*Tel:* (02) 359491
*Key Personnel*
Contact: David Barrientos Zapata

# Bosnia and Herzegovina

## General Information

*Capital:* Sarajevo
*Language:* Bosnian, Servian, Croatian
*Religion:* Predominantly Sunni Muslim, also Serbian Orthodox and Roman Catholic
*Population:* 4.4 million
*Currency:* 100 convertible pfenniga = 1 convertible marka (KM)
*Copyright:* UCC, Berne (see Copyright Conventions, pg xi)

**Bemust** (Bemust Printing House, Publishing & Trade Company)
Put Famosa 38, 71000 Sarajevo
*Tel:* (033) 414-050; (061) 173780 *Fax:* (033) 414-050
*E-mail:* bemust@bih.net.ba
Subjects: Education, Geography, Geology, History, Law, Philosophy, Poetry, Regional Interests, Religion - Islamic, Technology
ISBN Prefix(es): 9958-725

**IP Oslobodenje**
Dzemala Bijedica 185, 71000 Sarajevo
*Tel:* (033) 276900; (033) 468054
*E-mail:* info@oslobodjenje.com.ba
*Web Site:* www.oslobodjenje.com.ba
*Telex:* 41148; 41136
*Key Personnel*
Dir: Ivica Lovric
ISBN Prefix(es): 86-319; 9958-719; 99938-678

**Veselin Maslesa**
Obla Kulina bana 4, 71000 Sarajevo
*Tel:* (033) 667735; (033) 667736 *Fax:* (033) 668351; (033) 667738
*E-mail:* sapublishing@bihart.com
*Telex:* 41154 Yu Vesmas *Cable:* Vesmas Maslesa
*Key Personnel*
Man Dir, Editorial, Rights & Permissions: Alija Velic

Founded: 1950
Subjects: Fiction, Government, Political Science, Philosophy, Science (General)
ISBN Prefix(es): 86-21
*Branch Office(s)*
Zagreb, Croatia
Skopje, The Former Yugoslav Republic of Macedonia
Belgrade, Serbia and Montenegro

**Sarajevo Publishing**, see Veselin Maslesa

**Svjetlost**
Muhameda Kantardzica 3, 71000 Sarajevo
*Tel:* (033) 442634; (033) 200066 *Fax:* (033) 443435
*E-mail:* ipsvjet@bih.net.ba
*Telex:* 41326 Yu Ikpres *Cable:* Svjetlost Sarajevo
*Key Personnel*
Man Dir: Abdulah Jesenkovic
Sales Dir: Rizvanbegovic Enver
Editorial: Miodrag Bogicvic
Subjects: Business, Science (General)
ISBN Prefix(es): 86-81903; 9958-9701
*Branch Office(s)*
Subiceva 65, Zagreb, Croatia
Obilicev venac 10, Belgrade, Serbia and Montenegro

# Botswana

## General Information

*Capital:* Gaborone
*Language:* English (official) & Setswana (national)
*Religion:* Traditional African
*Population:* 1.3 million
*Bank Hours:* 0830-1300 Monday-Friday; 0830-1100 Saturday
*Shop Hours:* 0800-1300, 1400-1700 or 1800 Monday-Saturday
*Currency:* 100 thebe = 1 pula
*Export/Import Information:* No import license required; no obscene literature. Exchange controls.

**The Botswana Society**
Uni-Span Bldg, Lot 54, International Commerce Park, Kgale View, Gaborone
Mailing Address: PO Box 71, Gaborone
*Tel:* 3919673 *Fax:* 3919745
*E-mail:* botsoc@botsnet.bw
*Web Site:* www.botswanasociety.com
*Key Personnel*
Editor: Dr Ian Taylor
Executive Secretary: Trevor Burnett
Founded: 1968
Subjects: Archaeology, Art, Earth Sciences, Environmental Studies, Government, Political Science, History, Language Arts, Linguistics, Law, Music, Dance, Natural History, Regional Interests
ISBN Prefix(es): 99912-60

**Heinemann Education Botswana**
PO Box 10103, Village Post Office, Gaborone
*Tel:* 372305 *Fax:* 371832
*Key Personnel*
Man Dir: Lesedi Seitei
ISBN Prefix(es): 99912-63
*Parent Company:* Heinemann Publishers Ltd, Oxford, United Kingdom
*Ultimate Parent Company:* Reed Elsevier plc, 25 Victoria St, London SW1H 0EX, United Kingdom

**Maskew Miller Longman**
PO Box 1083, Gaborone
*Tel:* 322969 *Fax:* 322682
*E-mail:* longman@info.bw
*Key Personnel*
Man Dir: Joe Chalashika
Sales & Marketing Manager: Carlson Moilwa
Publishing Manager: Michelle Aarons
Subjects: English as a Second Language, Fiction,
Geography, Geology, History, Language Arts,
Linguistics, Literature, Literary Criticism, Es-
says, Poetry, Travel
ISBN Prefix(es): 99912-66; 99912-73
*Parent Company:* Pearson Education
*Ultimate Parent Company:* Pearson Plc, United
Kingdom

**Morula Press, Business School of Botswana**
PO Box 402492, Gaborone
*Tel:* (0267) 353499 *Fax:* (0267) 304809
*Key Personnel*
Contact: Mr A Briscoe
Founded: 1994
Subjects: Business, Law
ISBN Prefix(es): 99912-902; 99912-909; 99912-
912; 99912-952; 99912-968; 99912-969;
99912-991; 99912-992

**National Library Service**
Private Bag 0036, Gaborone
*Tel:* 352288; 352397 *Fax:* 301149
*E-mail:* vmaje@gov.bw
ISBN Prefix(es): 99912-0

**Sygma Publishing**
PO Box 753, Gaborone
*Tel:* 351371 *Fax:* 372531
*E-mail:* sygma@info.bw
*Key Personnel*
International Rights: Mary-Anne Lovera

# Brazil

## General Information

*Capital:* Brasilia
*Language:* Portuguese
*Religion:* Predominantly Roman Catholic
*Population:* 157 million
*Bank Hours:* Generally 1000-1500 Monday-
Friday
*Shop Hours:* 0900-1700 Monday-Friday (many
open much later); 0900-1400 Saturday
*Currency:* 100 centavos = 1 real
*Export/Import Information:* Member of the Latin
American Free Trade Association. No tariffs
on books & advertising, but luxury bindings &
children's picture books are duted. Import li-
censes & deposits required; exchange controls
operate.
*Copyright:* UCC, Berne, Buenos Aires, Florence
(see Copyright Conventions, pg xi)

**A & A & A Edicoes e Promocoes
Internacionais Ltda+**
R Jose Lemos, 82, 25725-020 Petropolis-RJ
*Tel:* (024) 221-3359 *Fax:* (024) 221-2740
*E-mail:* aaaipe@compuland.com.br
*Key Personnel*
President: Gianvittore Calvi
General Dir: Lucilla Martinez
Founded: 1977
Membership(s): National Syndication of Book
Publishers.
Subjects: Child Care & Development, Cookery,
Education, Library & Information Sciences,
Public Administration, Science Fiction, Fantasy
ISBN Prefix(es): 85-7210

Subsidiaries: IPE Amarelo Criacao Multimidia
Ltda
*Branch Office(s)*
Gian Calvi & Asun Balzola & Assn, Calle de
Clara del Rey, 39 Ofic 708, 28002 Madrid,
Spain
*Showroom(s):* Livraria Amais, Rua Real
Grandeza, 314 Botafogo

**A Laser**, *imprint of* Centro de Estudos
Juridicosdo Para (CEJUP)

**Abril SA**
Av Otaviaro Alves de Lima, 4400, 02909-900 Sao
Paulo-SP
*Tel:* (011) 877-1319 *Fax:* (011) 877-1437
*Web Site:* abril.com.br
*Telex:* 21-34716
*Key Personnel*
Contact: Sir Roberto Civita
Founded: 1983
Subjects: Cookery, Science (General)
ISBN Prefix(es): 85-86476
*Parent Company:* Editora Abril SA Sao Paulo
*Associate Companies:* Time-Life Inc, Alexandria,
VA, United States

**Action Editora Ltda+**
Avenida das Americas, 3333 sala 817, 22631-003
Rio de Janeiro-RJ
*Tel:* (021) 3325-7229 *Fax:* (021) 3325-7229
*E-mail:* action@plugue.com.br
*Web Site:* www.editora.com.br
*Key Personnel*
Dir: Carlos Lorch
Business Manager: Raimundo Carlos Bezerra
Founded: 1986
Specialize in military history, natural history, avi-
ation.
Membership(s): SNEL (Sindicato Nacional de
Editores de Livros).
Subjects: Aeronautics, Aviation, History, Military
Science, Sports, Athletics
ISBN Prefix(es): 85-85654
Number of titles published annually: 8 Print
Total Titles: 60 Print
Distributed by Howell Press (USA)

**Addison Wesley**, *imprint of* Pearson Education
Do Brasil

**Affonso & Reichmann Editores Associados+**
Rua do Ouvidor 161/1302, 20040-030 Rio de
Janeiro
*Tel:* (021) 507-1270 *Fax:* (021) 507-1270
*E-mail:* correio@ra.inf.br
*Key Personnel*
Dir: Renato Reichmann *E-mail:* rrre@lb.com
Contact: Aluisia Affonso *E-mail:* aaff@ar.inf
Subjects: STM
ISBN Prefix(es): 85-87148
Number of titles published annually: 18 Print

**Agalma Psicanalise Editora Ltda+**
Av Anita Garibaldi, 1815, Centro Medico Em-
presarial, Bloco 'B' Saia 401, 40170-130
Salvador-Bahia
*Tel:* (071) 332-8776 *Fax:* (071) 245-7883
*E-mail:* pedidos@agalma.com.br
*Web Site:* www.agalma.com.br
*Key Personnel*
Contact: Marcus Do Rio Teixeira
Founded: 1991
Membership(s): National Syndicate of Book Pub-
lishers of Brazil (SNEL).
Subjects: Anthropology, Child Care & Develop-
ment, Nonfiction (General), Philosophy, Psy-
chology, Psychiatry, Romance
ISBN Prefix(es): 85-85458
Distributor for Editions De L'Association Freudi-
enne

**AGIR S/A Editora+**
Rua dos Invalidos, 198 - Centro, 20231-020 Rio
de Janeiro-RJ
*Tel:* (021) 221-6424 *Fax:* (021) 252-0410
*E-mail:* info@agireditora.com.br
*Web Site:* www.visualnet.com.br/cmaya/cm-ft-01.
htm *Cable:* AGIRSA
*Key Personnel*
President: Jose de Paula Machado
Editorial: Regina Lemos
Founded: 1944
Subjects: Architecture & Interior Design, Art, Bi-
ography, Communications, Cookery, Drama,
Theater, Education, Fiction, History, Literature,
Literary Criticism, Essays, Philosophy, Social
Sciences, Sociology
ISBN Prefix(es): 85-220; 85-85076
Distributor for Armand Collin; Ed Nathan; Ed
Seuil; HarperCollins; Random House
*Bookshop(s):* Livraria Agir, Rua Mexico, 98-B,
20031-141
*Book Club(s):* Circulo do Livro

**Editora Agora Ltda+**
Rua Itapicuru 613 7º Andar, 05006-000 Perdizes-
SP
*Tel:* (011) 38723322 *Fax:* (011) 38727476
*E-mail:* agora@editoraagora.com.br
*Web Site:* www.gruposummus.com.br/agora
*Key Personnel*
Editor: Edith M Elek
Founded: 1979
Subjects: Astrology, Occult, Health, Nutrition,
Psychology, Psychiatry, Self-Help
ISBN Prefix(es): 85-7183

**Aide Editora e Comercio de Livros Ltda**
Rua Bela, 740, Sao Cristovao, 20930-380 Rio de
Janeiro-RJ
*Tel:* (021) 2589-9926 *Fax:* (021) 2589-9926
*E-mail:* aideeditora@radnet.com.br
*Web Site:* www.radnet.com.br/aideeditora
*Key Personnel*
President: Ruy de Castro
Editor: Joao Virgilio de Castro *Tel:* (0371)
5724958
Founded: 1976
Membership(s): SNEL.
Subjects: Law
ISBN Prefix(es): 85-321
Total Titles: 5 Print

**Livraria Alema Ltda Brasileitura+**
Rua Sete de Setembro, 1760-Centro, 89010-202
Blumenau
*Tel:* (047) 3260499 *Fax:* (0473) 3263062
*E-mail:* alemaeko@nutecnet.com.br
*Key Personnel*
Executive: Juergen Konig
Founded: 1989
ISBN Prefix(es): 85-85415; 85-7324
Subsidiaries: Editora EKO/Disbribuidora Alema

**Editora Alfa Omega Ltda+**
Rua Lisboa, 489, 05413-000 Sao Paulo-SP
*Tel:* (011) 3062-6400; (011) 3062-6690
*Fax:* (011) 3083-0746
*E-mail:* alfaomega@alfaomega.com.br
*Web Site:* www.alfaomega.com.br
*Telex:* 011 22888 XPSPBR
*Key Personnel*
Editorial Dir: Fernando Celso De C Mangarielo
Founded: 1973
Subjects: Anthropology, Behavioral Sciences, Bi-
ography, Economics, History, Law, Manage-
ment, Philosophy, Social Sciences, Sociology
ISBN Prefix(es): 85-295
Divisions: Alfa Omega Data; Distribuidora Alfa
Omega e Disque Livros; Estudio Alfa Omega

**Livraria Francisco Alves Editora SA+**
Rua Urguaiana, 94-13 andar-Centro, 20050-091
  Rio de Janeiro-RJ
*Tel:* (021) 221-3198 *Fax:* (021) 242-3438
Founded: 1854
Membership(s): Sindicato Nacional de Editores de
  Livros.
Subjects: Astrology, Occult, Criminology, Fiction,
  Literature, Literary Criticism, Essays, Non-
  fiction (General), Science (General), Science
  Fiction, Fantasy
ISBN Prefix(es): 85-265
*Warehouse:* Rua Luis de Camoes 100, Rio de
  Janeiro-RJ

**Antenna Edicoes Tecnicas Ltda+**
Ave Marechal Floriano, 151-1°-Andar, 20080-005
  Rio de Janeiro-RJ
*Tel:* (021) 2223-2442 *Fax:* (021) 2263-8840
*E-mail:* antenna@anep.com.br
*Web Site:* www.anep.com.br
*Key Personnel*
Man Dir: Maria Beatriz Affonso Penna
Publicity: Sergio Porto
Founded: 1926
Subjects: Computer Science, Electronics, Electri-
  cal Engineering, Microcomputers, Technology
ISBN Prefix(es): 85-7036
Number of titles published annually: 5 Print
Total Titles: 60 Print
*Bookshop(s):* Lojas do Livro Electronico, Ave
  Mal Floriano 151, 20080-005 Rio de Janeiro-
  RJ
*Book Club(s):* SNEL-Sind Nac Editors Livros,
  Ave Rio Branco 37, 20090-003 Rio de Janeiro-
  RJ *Tel:* (021) 2233-6481 *Fax:* (021) 2253-8502
  *E-mail:* snel@snel.org.br

**Editora Antroposofica Ltda+**
Rua da Fraternidade, 174, 04738-020 Sao Paulo-
  SP
*Tel:* (011) 5687-9714; (011) 5686-4550
  *Fax:* (011) 2479714
*E-mail:* editora@antroposofica.com.br
*Web Site:* www.sab.org.br/edit; www.
  antroposofica.com.br
*Key Personnel*
General Manager & International Rights: Jacira S
  Cardoso *E-mail:* jacira.c@zaz.com.br
Founded: 1981
Specializes in therapy & anthroposophy.
Membership(s): Brazilian House of Books.
Subjects: Agriculture, Child Care & Develop-
  ment, Cookery, Disability, Special Needs, Eco-
  nomics, Education, Health, Nutrition, Medicine,
  Nursing, Dentistry, Philosophy, Psychology,
  Psychiatry, Anthroposophy, Therapy
ISBN Prefix(es): 85-7122
Number of titles published annually: 15 Print
Total Titles: 140 Print
*Parent Company:* Livraria Antroposofica
*Ultimate Parent Company:* Sociedade Antro-
  posofica no Brasil

**Ao Livro Tecnico Industria e Comercio Ltda+**
Rua Sa Freire, 40, Sao Cristovao, 20930-430 Rio
  de Janeiro-RJ
*Tel:* (021) 580-6230; (021) 580-1168 *Fax:* (021)
  580-9955
*E-mail:* contatos@editoraaolivrotecnico.com.br
*Web Site:* www.editoraaolivrotecnico.com.br
  *Cable:* LITECNICO
*Key Personnel*
Man Dir: Reynaldo Max Paul Bluhm
Editorial, Production, Sales, Rights & Permis-
  sions, Publicity: Gisela Bluhm
Founded: 1933
Membership(s): IPA.
Subjects: Education, Language Arts, Linguistics,
  Sports, Athletics
ISBN Prefix(es): 85-215

*Associate Companies:* Sociedade Distribuidora de
  Livros Ltda (Sodilivro)
Subsidiaries: DISAL (Distribuidores Associados
  de Livros Ltda); SODILIVRO (Sociedade Distribuidora de Livros Ltda)

**Editora Aquariana Ltda+**
R Pamplona, 935-Cj 11, 01405-001 Sao Paulo-SP
*Tel:* (011) 288 7139 *Fax:* (011) 283 0476
*E-mail:* aquariana@ground.com.br
*Key Personnel*
Executive Director: Jose Carlos Rolo Venancio
  *E-mail:* jcvenancio@ground.com.br
Founded: 1988
Membership(s): the Brazilian Association of Pub-
  lishers.
Subjects: Alternative, Environmental Studies,
  Management, Marketing, Self-Help, Occult,
  Health & New Science
ISBN Prefix(es): 85-7217
*Parent Company:* Editora Ground Ltda
*Associate Companies:* Editora Ground Ltda, R
  Lacedomonia, 68, Sao Paulo-SP, Contact:
  Jose Carlos Venancio *Tel:* (011) 5031 1500
  *Fax:* (011) 5031 3462 *E-mail:* editora@ground.
  com.br

**M J Bezerra de Araujo Editora Ltda**
Rua Haddoc Lobo, 72, Sala 507 e-508, 20260-
  132 Rio de Janeiro-RJ
*Tel:* (021) 5024435 *Fax:* (021) 5024435
*Key Personnel*
Dir & President: Maria Jose Bezerra de Araujo
ISBN Prefix(es): 85-85767
*Branch Office(s)*
Alameda Santos 734, Apt 02, Jardim Paulista,
  01418-100 Sao Paulo-SP
*Warehouse:* Rua Haddock Lobo 17B, Estacio, RJ,
  Bradesco AG 2013-3, 9958-9 Conta

**Arquivo Nacional**
Rua Azeredo Coutinho, 77-3° Andar, Centro,
  20230-170 Rio de Janeiro-RJ
*Tel:* (021) 232-6938 *Fax:* (021) 224-4525
*E-mail:* arqnacdg@rio.com.br
ISBN Prefix(es): 85-7009

**Ars Poetica Editora Ltda+**
Av Irai, 79, Cj 114-B, 04082-001 Sao Paulo-SP
*Tel:* (011) 2405598 *Fax:* (011) 5312648
*Key Personnel*
Contact: Ubiratan Ramos-Mascarenhas
Founded: 1991
Subjects: Anthropology, Archaeology, Biography,
  Language Arts, Linguistics, Poetry, Psychol-
  ogy, Psychiatry, Religion - Protestant, Sports,
  Athletics, Theology
ISBN Prefix(es): 85-85470

**Artes e Oficios Editora Ltda+**
Rua Henrique Dias, 201, 90035-100 Porto Alegre
*Tel:* (051) 311 0832; (051) 311 5442 *Fax:* (051)
  311 0832
*E-mail:* artesofi@pro.via-rs.com.br
*Key Personnel*
Contact: Sergio Boeck-Ludtke
Founded: 1991
Subjects: Biography, Fiction, Human Relations,
  Humor, Journalism, Psychology, Psychiatry,
  Romance, Travel
ISBN Prefix(es): 85-7421; 85-87239
*Branch Office(s)*
Rua Eudoro Berlink, 988 Auxiliadora, 90450-160
  Porto Alegre *Tel:* (051) 3317387 *Fax:* (051)
  3317387

**Editora Artes Medicas Ltda+**
R Dr Cesario Motta Jr, 63, 01221-020 Sao Paulo-
  SP
*Tel:* (011) 221-9033 *Fax:* (011) 223-6635
*E-mail:* artesmedicas@artesmedicas.com.br

*Web Site:* www.artesmedicas.com.br *Cable:*
  LEAM
*Key Personnel*
Man Dir: Henrique Hecht
Editorial, Production: M Hecht
Sales: C dos Santos
Publicity: J Hecht
Founded: 1964
Subjects: Medicine, Nursing, Dentistry
ISBN Prefix(es): 85-7404

**ARTMED Editora+**
Av Jeronimo de Ornelas 670, 90040-340 Porto
  Alegre-RS
*Tel:* (051) 33303444 *Fax:* (051) 3302378
*E-mail:* artmed@artmed.com.br
*Web Site:* www.artmed.com.br
*Key Personnel*
President: Henrique L Kiperman
Vice President: Celso Kiperman
International Rights Manager & Permissions: An-
  gelo I Castrogiovanni *E-mail:* angelo@artmed.
  com.br
Founded: 1973
Membership(s): Brazilian Book Association; Pub-
  lishers Club of Southern Rio Grande.
Subjects: Architecture & Interior Design, Behav-
  ioral Sciences, Biological Sciences, Child Care
  & Development, Civil Engineering, Computer
  Science, Economics, Education, Health, Nutri-
  tion, Management, Marketing, Medicine, Nurs-
  ing, Dentistry, Psychology, Psychiatry, Science
  (General), Sports, Athletics, Technology, Vet-
  erinary Science
ISBN Prefix(es): 85-7307
Number of titles published annually: 90 Print; 3
  CD-ROM
Total Titles: 893 Print; 11 CD-ROM
*Associate Companies:* Bookman Companhia Edi-
  tora Ltda, Patio Revista Pedagogica
*Branch Office(s)*
Av Reboucas, 1073, 05414-020 Sao Paulo-SP
  *Tel:* (011) 3062 3757 *Fax:* (011) 3062 2487
*Bookshop(s):* Rua General Vitorino 277, 90020
  Porto Alegre-RS, Dir: Celso Kiperman
  *Tel:* (051) 32251579
*Warehouse:* Artomed Aeditora Ltda, Rua Ernesto
  Alves 150, Porto Alegre-RS 90000-000
  *Tel:* (051) 32251579
*Distribution Center:* Artomed Aeditora Ltda, Rua
  Ernesto Alves 150, Porto Alegre-RS 90000-000
  *Tel:* (051) 32251579

**Associacao Arvore da Vida**
Rua Tuiuti, 1372, Tatuape, 03081-000 Sao Paulo-
  SP
*Tel:* (011) 2185399 *Fax:* (011) 2181401
*E-mail:* editora@eavida.com.br
*Key Personnel*
Dir: Ildeu R Dos Santos
Contact: Andre Dong
Founded: 1981
Membership(s): Camara Brasileira de Livros.
Subjects: Biblical Studies
ISBN Prefix(es): 85-7304
Divisions: Jornal Arvore Da Vida
*Book Club(s):* Sindicato Nacional de Editores
  (SNEL)

**Associacao Palas Athena do Brasil+**
Rua Serra de Paracaina, 240, 01522-020
  Cambuci-Sao Paulo SP
*Tel:* (011) 3209-6288 *Fax:* (011) 3277-8137
*E-mail:* grafica@palasathena.org; editora@
  palasathena.org
*Web Site:* www.palasathena.org
*Key Personnel*
Contact: Basilio Pawlowicz
Founded: 1972
Subjects: Anthropology, Philosophy, Psychology,
  Psychiatry, Religion - Other

ISBN Prefix(es): 85-7242
*Orders to:* R Jose Bento 384, 01523-030 Sao
Paulo-SP

**Editora Atheneu Ltda+**
Rua Jesuino Pascoal, 30, 01224-050 Sao Paulo-
SP
*Tel:* (011) 220-9186 *Fax:* (011) 221-3389
*E-mail:* atheneau@nutecnet.com.br
*Web Site:* www.atheneu.com.br *Cable:* ZIGADAG
*Key Personnel*
Man Dir & Editorial Dir: Paulo Rezinski
Sales Dir: Alexandre Massa
Production Dir: Prado Orimar
Founded: 1928
Subjects: Medicine, Nursing, Dentistry, Psychol-
ogy, Psychiatry
ISBN Prefix(es): 85-7379
Subsidiaries: Editora Atheneu Cultura
*Branch Office(s)*
Rua Domingos Vieira 319 Conj 1.104,
Santa Efigenia, Belo Horizonte 30150-240
*E-mail:* atheneu@u-net.com.br

**Editora Atica SA**
Rua Barao de Iguape 110, 01507-900 Sao Paulo-
SP
*Tel:* (011) 278 93 22 *Fax:* (011) 279 2185
*Telex:* 32969 Edat *Cable:* BOMLIVRO
*Key Personnel*
Edit Dir: Sr Renato Jose Laporta Filho Pimazzoni
*E-mail:* rpimazzoni@atica.com.br
Publicity Dir: Vera Elena Hoexter Esau
Contact: Nelson Dos Reis
Founded: 1965
Subjects: Literature, Literary Criticism, Essays,
Regional Interests
ISBN Prefix(es): 85-08
*Branch Office(s)*
Rua Barao de Uba 173, Praca da Bandeira, 20260
Rio de Janeiro-RJ

**Editora Atlas SA+**
Rue Conselheiro Nebias, 1384, Campos Elisios,
01203-904 Sao Paulo-SP
*Tel:* (011) 3357-9144
*E-mail:* edatlas@editora-atlas.com.br
*Web Site:* www.edatlas.com.br; www.atlasnet.com.
br *Cable:* ATLASEDITA
*Key Personnel*
Vice President: Luiz Herrmann, Jr
Editorial & Marketing Dir: A B Brandao
Production: S Gerencer
Founded: 1944
Subjects: Accounting, Business, Economics, Fi-
nance, Law, Management, Marketing
ISBN Prefix(es): 85-224
*Branch Office(s)*
Amazonas
Brazilia
Bahia
Ceara
Goias
Minas Gerais
Parana
Pernambuco
Rio Grande do Sul
Santa Catarina
*Bookshop(s):* Livraria Atlas Ltda, Rua Pedroso
Alvarenga, 1285 - Itaim, 04531-012 Sao Paulo
*Tel:* (011) 881-8799

**Berkeley Brasil Editora Ltda+**
AV Raimundo Pereira De Magalhaes, 3305, 3
Andar, 05145-200 Sao Paulo-SP
*Tel:* (011) 839-5525 *Fax:* (011) 261-1342
*E-mail:* berkeley@siciliano.com.br
*Key Personnel*
President: Osvaldo Siciliano, Jr
Executive Vice President: Ricardo Reinprecht
Founded: 1986
Specialize in computer & business books.

Subjects: Business, Computer Science, Microcomputers, Technology
ISBN Prefix(es): 85-7251

**Bertrand Brasil**, *imprint of* Editora Bertrand
Brasil Ltda

**Editora Bertrand Brasil Ltda+**
Subsidiary of Distribuidora Record de Servicos de
Imprensa SA
Rua Argentina, 171, Sao Cristoras, 20921-380
Rio de Janeiro-RJ
Mailing Address: CP 884, 20001-970 Rio de
Janeiro-RJ
*Tel:* (021) 2585 2000 *Fax:* (021) 2585 2085
*E-mail:* record@record.com.br
*Web Site:* www.record.com.br
*Key Personnel*
President: Sergio Abreu Da Cruz Machado
*E-mail:* smachado@record.com.br
Rights & Permissions: Rosemary Alves
*E-mail:* rosemary@bertrandbrasil.com.br
Founded: 1951 (as Difusao Editorial SA
(DIFEL))
Subjects: Anthropology, Astrology, Occult, Be-
havioral Sciences, Biography, Cookery, Drama,
Theater, Education, Fiction, Geography, Geol-
ogy, Government, Political Science, Literature,
Literary Criticism, Essays, Nonfiction (Gen-
eral), Poetry, Religion - Buddhist, Religion -
Hindu, Religion - Jewish, Romance, Self-Help,
Women's Studies
ISBN Prefix(es): 85-286
Number of titles published annually: 80 Print
Total Titles: 1,000 Print
Imprints: Bertrand Brasil; Difel
*Branch Office(s)*
R do Paraiso 139, 7° andar, 04103-000 Sao
Paulo-SP *Tel:* (011) 3171-1540 *Fax:* (011)
3285-0251

**Editora Betania S/C+**
Rua Padre Pinto, 2435 Venda Nova, 31510-000
Belo Horizonte-MG
*Tel:* (031) 3451-1122 *Fax:* (031) 3451-1638
*E-mail:* betanhdv@prover.com.br
*Web Site:* www.editorabetania.com.br
*Key Personnel*
Dir: Luiz Dirceu dos Arjos *E-mail:* director@
editorabetania.com.br
Founded: 1967
Subjects: Religion - Other
Imprints: Temos Grafica Propria

**Bloch Editores SA**
Rua do Russell, 766-10° Andar, 22210-010 Rio
de Janeiro-RJ
*Tel:* (021) 555-4167 *Fax:* (021) 555-4069
*E-mail:* blocheditores@ieg.com.br
*Key Personnel*
Publicity: Expedito Jose Chaves Grossi
Contact: Anna Maria de Oliveira Rennhack
ISBN Prefix(es): 85-258

**Editora Edgard Blucher Ltda**
Rua Pedroso Alvarenga 1245, 04531-012 Sao
Paulo-SP
*Tel:* (011) 852-5366 *Fax:* (011) 852 2707
*E-mail:* eblucher@uol.com.br *Cable:*
BLUCHERLIVRO
*Key Personnel*
Man Dir: Edgard Blucher
Founded: 1966
Subjects: Biological Sciences, Earth Sciences,
Electronics, Electrical Engineering, Engineering
(General), Management, Mathematics, Physics,
Science (General), Technology
ISBN Prefix(es): 85-212

**Editora Brasil-America (EBAL) SA+**
Rua General Almerio de Moura 302/320, 20921-
060 Rio de Janeiro-RJ
*Tel:* (021) 5800303 *Fax:* (021) 5801637
*Key Personnel*
Man Dir: Luba Aizen
Editorial: Naumim Aizen
Dir: Paulo Adolfo Aizen
Production: Fernando Albagli
Founded: 1945
Subjects: Film, Video, Children & Young Peo-
ple's Books
ISBN Prefix(es): 85-272

**Editora do Brasil SA+**
Rua Conselheiro Nebias, 887, 01203-001 Sao
Paulo-SP
*Tel:* (011) 222 0211 *Fax:* (011) 222 5583
*E-mail:* edbrasil@uol.com.br *Cable:*
EDITABRAS
*Key Personnel*
President: Dr Carlos Costa
Superintendent: Luis Roberto Netto
Founded: 1943
Subjects: Education, History, Psychology, Psychi-
atry, Social Sciences, Sociology
ISBN Prefix(es): 85-10
*Branch Office(s)*
Rua do Resende 89, 20231 Rio de Janeiro-RJ
*Tel:* (021) 224-8123

**Instituto Brasileiro de Informacao em Ciencia
e Tecnologia**
SAS Qd 5, Lote 6, Bloco H - 5° andar, 70070-
914 Brasilia-DF
*Tel:* (061) 217-6360; (061) 217-6350 *Fax:* (061)
226-2677
*E-mail:* webmaster@ibict.br
*Web Site:* www.ibict.br
*Telex:* (061) 2481
ISBN Prefix(es): 85-7013

**Editora Brasiliense SA+**
Rua Airi, 22, Tatuape, 03310-010 Sao Paulo-SP
*Tel:* (011) 6198-1488 *Fax:* (011) 6198-1488
*E-mail:* brasilienseedit@uol.com.br
*Web Site:* www.editorabrasiliense.com.br
*Cable:* EDIBRASA
*Key Personnel*
Man Dir & Editor: Teresa B Lima; Yolanda Prado
Production: Celia Rogalsky
Founded: 1943
Subjects: Education, Literature, Literary Criti-
cism, Essays, Social Sciences, Sociology
ISBN Prefix(es): 85-11; 85-206
*Bookshop(s):* Livraria Brasiliense Editora SA,
Rua Emilia Marengo, 216-Tatuape, 03336-
000 Sao Paulo-SP *Tel:* (011) 6675-0188
*Fax:* (011) 6675-0188 *E-mail:* brasiliensedit@
editorabrasiliense.com.br

**Brasilivros Editora e Distribuidora Ltda**
Rua Conselheiro Ramalho, 701, Matriz Loja 22,
01325-001 Sao Paolo
*Tel:* (011) 3284-8155; (011) 3371-5140
*Fax:* (011) 3371-5166 *Toll Free Fax:* 800 555-
546 *Fax on Demand:* (800) 555-546
*E-mail:* vendas@brasilivros.com.br
*Web Site:* www.brasilivros.com.br
*Key Personnel*
Executive: Juarez Cordeiro de Oliveira

**Brinque Book Editora de Livros Ltda+**
Av Dr Guilherme Dumot Villares, 2352 1 andar,
05640-004 Sao Paulo-SP
*Tel:* (011) 8428142 *Fax:* (011) 8432235
*E-mail:* brinquebook@infantil.net
*Key Personnel*
President: Suzana Taves de Sanson
Founded: 1990
Specialize in children's literature.

Membership(s): SNEL, FNLIJ & CBL.
Subjects: Cookery, Music, Dance
ISBN Prefix(es): 85-7412

**Cadence Publicacoes Internacionais Ltda+**
Rua Visconde Inhauma 134, Sala 1532, 20091-
000 Rio de Janeiro-RJ
*Tel:* (021) 2637885 *Fax:* (021) 2830812
*E-mail:* cadence@mtecnet.com.br
*Key Personnel*
Associate Manager: Reinaldo C Palmeira
Executive Secretary: Geni Celia Miranda
Founded: 1980
Subjects: Science (General), Technology
*Parent Company:* Cadence

**Callis Editora Ltda+**
Rua Afonso Bras 203, 04511-010 Sao Paulo-SP
*Tel:* (011) 3842-2066 *Fax:* (011) 3849-5882
*E-mail:* editorial@callis.com.br; callis@callis.
com.br
*Web Site:* www.callis.com.br
*Key Personnel*
President: Miriam Gabbai
Founded: 1987
Subjects: Art, Computer Science, Cookery, Mi-
crocomputers, Military Science, Nonfiction
(General)
ISBN Prefix(es): 85-85642; 85-7416

**Camara Dos Deputados Coordenacao De
Publicacoes** (Chamber of Deputies,
Coordination of Publications)
Division of Chamber of Deputies
Praca dos Tres Poderes, 70160-900 Brasilia-DF
*Tel:* (061) 216-0000 *Fax:* (061) 318-2190
*E-mail:* publicacoes.cedi@camara.gov.br
*Web Site:* www.camara.gov.br
*Key Personnel*
Coordination of Publications Dir: Nelda Raulino
Librarian: Andrea Perna *Tel:* (061) 318-6864
*E-mail:* andrea.perna@camara.gov.br
Founded: 1971
Produces & distributes Chamber of Deputies
printed publications. Created primarily to sat-
isfy the printing needs of Chamber of Deputies,
today has contributed to disseminate Brazilian
legislative information around the country &
the world.
Subjects: Government, Political Science, Public
Administration
ISBN Prefix(es): 85-7365
Number of titles published annually: 60 Print
Total Titles: 781 Print

**Editora Caminho Suave Ltda**
rua Fagundes 157, 01508-030 Sao Paulo-SP
*Tel:* (011) 2733377 *Fax:* (011) 2783537
*Key Personnel*
Contact: Branca Alves de Lima
ISBN Prefix(es): 85-85473

**Instituto Campineiro de Ensino Agricola Ltda**
Rua Romoaldo Andreazzi, 425, Jd do Trevo,
13036-100 Campinas-SP
*Tel:* (019) 3272-2280 *Fax:* (019) 3272-6004
*E-mail:* icea@icea.com.br
*Web Site:* www.icea.com.br
*Key Personnel*
Contact: Gervasio de Souza Cavalcanti
Founded: 1955
Subjects: Agriculture
ISBN Prefix(es): 85-7121

**Editora Campus Ltda+**
Rua Sete de Setembro, 111, 16 Andar, 20050-002
Centro Rio de Janeiro RJ
*Tel:* (021) 3970-9300 *Fax:* (021) 2507-1991
*E-mail:* info@elsevier.com.br
*Web Site:* www.campus.com.br

*Key Personnel*
Publishing Manager: Ricardo Redisch
*E-mail:* ricardo@campus.com.br
Production Dir: Daniel Sant'Anna
Rights & Permissions: Emilia Fernandez
Founded: 1976
Subjects: Art, Civil Engineering, Communica-
tions, Computer Science, Economics, Elec-
tronics, Electrical Engineering, Engineering
(General), Environmental Studies, Government,
Political Science, Health, Nutrition, History,
Microcomputers, Nonfiction (General), Physics,
Psychology, Psychiatry, Science (General), So-
cial Sciences, Sociology, Travel
ISBN Prefix(es): 85-7001; 85-352
Number of titles published annually: 190 Print
*Parent Company:* Elsevier Science
*Ultimate Parent Company:* Reed Elsevier plc
*Branch Office(s)*
Rua da Consolacao 348/10, Andar-Conj 102, Sao
Paulo-SP 01302-000 *Fax:* (011) 259 9944

**Alzira Chagas Carpigiani+**
Av Gethsemani, 85, 05625-090 Sao Paulo
Mailing Address: Caixa Postal 3702, Cep 01060-
970, Sao Paulo SP
*Tel:* (011) 849-0189 *Fax:* (011) 227-3384
*E-mail:* kerredit@uol.com.br
*Key Personnel*
Executive: Alzira Chagas Carpigiani
Founded: 1997
Subjects: Literature, Literary Criticism, Essays,
Religion - Protestant, Romance
Subsidiaries: Kerr Editorial Ltda
Divisions: Rua Maua 960-Casa 10

**CEJUP**, see Centro de Estudos Juridicosdo Para
(CEJUP)

**Centro de Estudos Juridicosdo Para (CEJUP)+**
Travessa Rui Barbosa 726, 66053-260 Belem-PA
*Tel:* (091) 225-0355 *Fax:* (091) 241-3184
*E-mail:* cejup@expert.com.br
*Key Personnel*
Contact: Gengis Freire de Souza
Founded: 1979
Membership(s): Associacao Nacional de Livrarias
(ANL) & Sindicato Nacional de Livrarias
(SNL).
Subjects: Biological Sciences, Criminology,
Drama, Theater, Education, Fiction, Law, Sci-
ence Fiction, Fantasy, Social Sciences, Sociol-
ogy
ISBN Prefix(es): 85-338
Imprints: A Laser; Off Set
*Branch Office(s)*
Av Rio Branco, 37 Sala 601, 20040-004 Rio de
Janeiro-RJ
*Bookshop(s):* Assis de Vasconcelos, N 498, CEP
66017-070 Belem PA

**Centro Editor de Psicologia Aplicada Ltda**, see
CEPA - Centro Editor de Psicologia Aplicada
Ltda

**CEPA - Centro Editor de Psicologia Aplicada
Ltda**
Rua Senador Dantas 118, GR 901 a 920, 20031-
201 Rio de Janeiro-RJ
*Tel:* (021) 2220-6545 *Fax:* (021) 2262-2717
*E-mail:* psicocepa@psicocepa.com.br
*Web Site:* www.psicocepa.com.br *Cable:*
EDICEPA
*Key Personnel*
Man Dir: Antonio Rodrigues, Jr
Founded: 1952
Subjects: Psychology, Psychiatry
ISBN Prefix(es): 85-7043

**Cia Editora Nacional**
Rua Joli 294, 03016-020 Sao Paulo-SP

*Tel:* (011) 66926985 *Fax:* (011) 66926985
*E-mail:* nacional@uol.com.br *Cable:* EDITORA
*Key Personnel*
Man Dir, Rights & Permissions: Jorge Antonio
Miguel Yunes
Editorial: Paulo Marti
Founded: 1925
Subjects: Business, Education, Fiction, History,
Philosophy, Psychology, Psychiatry, Science
(General), Social Sciences, Sociology, Technol-
ogy
ISBN Prefix(es): 85-04
*Branch Office(s)*
Aracatuba
Bauru
Belem
Belo Horizonte
Edificio Venancio VI - DS bloco 0 - lojas 13 e
17, Brasilia
Campo Grande
Caruaru
Cuiaba
Curitiba
Fortaleza
Goiania
Manaus
Natal
Porto Alegre
Presidente Prudente
Recife
Ribeirao Preto
Ave Lobo Junior 1011, Bairro Penha, Rio de
Janeiro
Sa Luis
Salvador
Sao Jose do Rio Preto
Teresina
Vila Velho

**Editora Cidade Nova+**
Rua Jose Ernesto Tozzi, 198, 06730-000 Vargem
Grande Paulista-SP
*Tel:* (011) 4158-2252 *Fax:* (011) 4158-2252
*E-mail:* editora@cidadenova.org.br
*Web Site:* www.cidadenova.org.br
*Key Personnel*
President Dir: Ekkehard Andreas Schneider
Man Dir: Olavo de Freitas
Publisher & Editor: Klaus Brueschke
Founded: 1960
Subjects: Biblical Studies, Religion - Catholic,
Social Sciences, Sociology, Theology
ISBN Prefix(es): 85-7112; 85-89736
*Parent Company:* Citta Nuova Editrice, Italy
*Branch Office(s)*
Rua Arthur da Silva Bernardes, 769, Loja 34,
80320-300 Curitiba-PR
Av Assis Brasil, 115, Sala 308, 50020-036
Recife-PE
*U.S. Office(s):* City New Press, 206 Skillman
Ave, Brooklyn, NY 11211, United States
Living City, PO Box 837, New York, NY, United
States
*Showroom(s):* Av Arthur da Silva Bernardes
769, Loja 34, 80320-300 Curitiba-PR; Av As-
sis Brasil, 115, Sala 308, 50010-036 Recife-
PE; Rua Domingos de Moraes, 348 Loja 46,
04009-000 Sao Paulo-SP

**Editora Civilizacao Brasileira**, *imprint of*
Distribuidora Record de Servicos de Imprensa
SA

**Codice Comercio Distriduicao e Casa Editorial
Ltda+**
Rua Simoes Pinto, 120, 04356-100 Sao Paulo-SP
*Tel:* (011) 5031-8033
*E-mail:* codice@codicenet.com.br
*Key Personnel*
Contact: Eduardo Augusto-Serverino
Founded: 1991

**Comissao Nacional de Energia Nuclear
(CNEN)**
Rua General Severiano, 90 Terreo, Botafogo,
22294-900 Rio de Janeiro-RJ
*Tel:* (021) 2295-9596 *Fax:* (021) 2295-8696
*E-mail:* macedo@cnen.gov.br
*Web Site:* www.cnen.gov.br
*Key Personnel*
President: Odair Dias Goncalves
	*E-mail:* presidencia@cnen.gov.br
Founded: 1970
Acts as the Brazilian national center for the In-
	ternational Nuclear Information System (INIS)
	& for the Energy Technology Data Exchange
	(ETDE).
Subjects: Energy, Engineering (General), Environ-
	mental Studies, Nuclear Energy
ISBN Prefix(es): 85-344

**Editora Companhia das Letras/Editora
Schwarcz Ltda+**
Rua Bandeira Paulista, 702, cj 72, 04532-002 Sao
	Paulo-SP
*Tel:* (011) 3707-3500 *Fax:* (011) 3707-3501
*E-mail:* editora@companhiadasletras.com.br
*Web Site:* www.companhiadasletras.com.br
*Key Personnel*
Editor: Luiz Schwarcz
Foreign Rights Manager: Ruth Lanna
	*E-mail:* ruth.lanna@companhiadasletras.com.br
Founded: 1986
Subjects: Anthropology, Biblical Studies, Biog-
	raphy, Cookery, Fiction, History, Humor, Lit-
	erature, Literary Criticism, Essays, Philosophy,
	Photography, Poetry
ISBN Prefix(es): 85-7164; 85-85095; 85-85466
Number of titles published annually: 150 Print
Distributed by Jorge Zahar (Rio de Janeiro)
Distributor for Jorge Zahar (Sao Paulo)
Foreign Rights: Carmen Balcells for Rubem Fon-
	seca (Europe); Melanie Jackson for Rubem
	Fonseca & Patricia Melo (US); Ray-Guede
	Mertin (Europe); Anne Marie Vallat for Mil-
	ton Hatoum (Spain)

**Companhia Editora Naciona**, see Cia Editora
Nacional

**Concordia Editora Ltda**
Av Sao Pedro, 633, Bairro Sao Geraldo, 90230-
	120 Porto Alegre-RS
*Tel:* (051) 3342 2699 *Fax:* (051) 3342 2699
*E-mail:* pedido@editoraconcordia.com.br;
	editora@editoraconcordia.com.br
*Web Site:* www.editoraconcordia.com.br
	*Cable:* CONCORDIA
*Key Personnel*
Man Dir: Martinho Krebs
Sales & Publicity: Walter Eidam
Founded: 1923
Subjects: Music, Dance, Religion - Other, Theol-
	ogy
*Parent Company:* Igreja Evangelica Luterana do
	Brasil
*Branch Office(s)*
Ave Getulio Vargas 4388, Sao Leopoldo-RS

**Conquista, Empresa de Publicacoes Ltda**
Av 28 de Setembro, 174, V Isabel, 20551-031
	Rio de Janeiro-RJ
*Tel:* (021) 228-6752 *Fax:* (021) 228-5709
*Key Personnel*
Dir: Nilde Hersen Aragao da Fonseca; Leonardo
	Hersen da Costa
Sales Dir: Antonio da Silva Aragao da Fonseca
Founded: 1951
Subjects: Art, Cookery, Literature, Literary Criti-
	cism, Essays
ISBN Prefix(es): 85-7066
*Bookshop(s):* Livraria Conquista

**Consultor Assessoria de Planejamento Ltda**
Rua General Gurjao, 479, 20931-040 Rio de
	Janeiro-RJ
*Tel:* (021) 5893030 *Fax:* (021) 580-2163
*Key Personnel*
Contact: Sra Andreia Niskier Chelman; Selmado
	Amaral
Founded: 1988
Subjects: Education, Literature, Literary Criti-
	cism, Essays
ISBN Prefix(es): 85-85206; 85-7434

**Editora Contexto (Editora Pinsky Ltda)+**
Rua Acopiara 199, 05083-110 Sao Paulo-SP
*Tel:* (011) 3832-5838 *Fax:* (011) 3832-1043
*E-mail:* contexto@editoracontexto.com.br
*Web Site:* www.editoracontexto.com.br
*Key Personnel*
Executive: Jaime Pinsky *E-mail:* pinsky@
	editoracontexto.com.br
Founded: 1987
Membership(s): Camara Brasileina do Livro.
Subjects: Economics, Education, Health, Nutri-
	tion, History
ISBN Prefix(es): 85-7244; 85-85134
Number of titles published annually: 30 Print
Total Titles: 20 Print

**Editora Crescer Ltda+**
Rua Do Ouro 104, Conj 501-Serra, 30220-000
	Belo Horizonte-MG
*Tel:* (031) 221-9335 *Fax:* (031) 3227-0729
*E-mail:* crescer@crescer.com.br
*Web Site:* www.crescer.com.br
*Key Personnel*
Executive: Clara Feldman
Founded: 1983
Subjects: Human Relations, Self-Help
ISBN Prefix(es): 85-85615

**Editora Cultura Medica Ltda+**
Rua Sao Francisco Xavier, 111 - Tijuca, 20550-
	010 Rio de Janeiro-RJ
*Tel:* (021) 2567-3888 *Fax:* (021) 2569-5443
*E-mail:* atendimento@culturamedica.com.br
*Web Site:* www.culturamedica.com.br
*Key Personnel*
Man Dir: Ezequiel Feldman
Founded: 1966
Subjects: Medicine, Nursing, Dentistry,
	Biomedicine
ISBN Prefix(es): 85-7006
*Orders to:* Rua Lucio de Mendonca, 37, Apt 401,
	20470-040 Rio de Janeiro-RJ

**Difel**, *imprint of* Editora Bertrand Brasil Ltda

**Editorial Dimensao Ltda+**
Rua Santo Cristo, 201, 20220-301 Rio de Janeiro-
	RJ
*Tel:* (021) 233-2764 *Fax:* (021) 233-2570
*E-mail:* memoria@ig.com.br
*Key Personnel*
Contact: Gilberto Gusmao Andrade
Founded: 1985
Membership(s): the Brazilian House of Books.
Subjects: Law, Psychology, Psychiatry
ISBN Prefix(es): 85-86163

**Editora e Distribuidora Irradiacao Cultural
Ltda**
Rua Visconde de Santa Isabel 46-Fundos, 20560-
	120 Rio de Janeiro-RJ
*Tel:* (021) 5773522 *Fax:* (021) 5771249
*E-mail:* irradcult@ax.apc.org
*Key Personnel*
Dir, President: Stelio De Andrade Soares
Founded: 1980
ISBN Prefix(es): 85-85677

**Livraria Duas Cidades Ltda**
Rua Bento Freitas 158, 01220-000 Sao Paulo-SP
*Tel:* (011) 220 5134 *Fax:* (011) 220-5813
*E-mail:* livraria@duascidades.com.br
*Web Site:* www.duascidades.com.br
*Key Personnel*
Man Dir: Jose Petronillo de Santa Cruz
Sales Dir: Mitsuro Nagata
Publicity Dir: Mara Valles
Founded: 1956
Subjects: Literature, Literary Criticism, Essays,
	Philosophy, Psychology, Psychiatry, Religion -
	Other, Social Sciences, Sociology
ISBN Prefix(es): 85-235
*Branch Office(s)*
Ave Rio Branco 9, Sala 116, Centro, 20090 Rio
	de Janeiro-RJ

**Dumara Distribuidora de Publicacoes Ltda+**
Rua Barata Ribeiro 17 - SI 202, 22011-000 Rio
	de Janeiro-RJ
*Tel:* (021) 5646869 *Fax:* (021) 2750294
*E-mail:* relume@re-dumara.com.br
*Key Personnel*
Contact: Alberto Jak Schprejer; Ari Roitman
Founded: 1989
Subjects: Anthropology, Drama, Theater, Fiction,
	Social Sciences, Sociology
ISBN Prefix(es): 85-7316

**E P U Editora Pedagogica e Universitaria Ltd**
Rua Joaquim Floriano, 72-6 andar Conjuntos 65/
	68, 04534-000 Sao Paulo-SP
*Tel:* (011) 3168-6077 *Fax:* (011) 3078-5803
*E-mail:* epu@epu.com.br
*Web Site:* www.epu.com.br
*Key Personnel*
Executive: Wolfgang Knapp *E-mail:* knapp@epu.
	com.br
Founded: 1952
Subjects: Education, Medicine, Nursing, Den-
	tistry, Philosophy, Psychology, Psychiatry
ISBN Prefix(es): 85-12

**EBAL**, see Editora Brasil-America (EBAL) SA

**Edicon Editora e Consultorial Ltda**
Rua Herculano de Freitas, 181, Cerqueira Cesar,
	01308-020 Sao Paulo-SP
*Tel:* (011) 3255-1002 *Fax:* (011) 3255-9822
*E-mail:* edicon@edicon.com.br
*Web Site:* www.edicon.com.br
*Key Personnel*
Executive: Valentina Ljubschenko
Founded: 1981
Subjects: Antiques, Art, Astrology, Occult,
	Drama, Theater, Earth Sciences, Education,
	Gay & Lesbian, Mathematics, Philosophy,
	Physics, Poetry, Romance, Science Fiction,
	Fantasy
ISBN Prefix(es): 85-290

**Edipro-Edicoes Profissionais Ltda+**
Rua 1 de Agosto, 2-51, 17010-011 Bauru
*Tel:* (014) 232-3753 *Fax:* (014) 232-4684
*E-mail:* edipro@vol.com.br
*Key Personnel*
Contact: Jair Lot-Viera
Subjects: Law
ISBN Prefix(es): 85-7283

**Companhia Editora Forense+**
Av Erasmo Braga, 227 B e 299, Centro, 20020-
	000 Rio de Janeiro-RJ
*Tel:* (021) 2533-5537 *Fax:* (021) 2533-5537
*E-mail:* forense@forense.com.br
*Web Site:* www.forense.com.br
*Key Personnel*
President: Regina Bilac Pinto
Vice President: Francisco Bilac Pinto
Founded: 1904

Subjects: Biography, Cookery, Criminology, Education, Health, Nutrition, History, Law, Music, Dance, Nonfiction (General), Philosophy, Psychology, Psychiatry, Religion - Buddhist, Romance, Self-Help, Social Sciences, Sociology, Sports, Athletics, Travel, Women's Studies
ISBN Prefix(es): 85-309
Number of titles published annually: 360 Print
Imprints: Editora Gryphus
Subsidiaries: Companhia Forense de Artes Graficas (printing plant)
*Branch Office(s)*
Rua Guajajaras, 337 Lj 3, Barro Preto-MG, 30180-100 Belo Horizonte *Tel:* (031) 222-2184
Rua Senador Feijo, 137, Centro-SP, 01006-001 Sao Paulo *Tel:* (011) 3105-0111

**Editora 34**, see 34 Literatura S/C Ltda

**EDUSC - Editora da Universidade do Sagrado Coracao** (Sacred Heart University Press)+
Rua Irma Arminda, 10-50, 17011-160 Bauru-SP
*Tel:* (014) 3235-7111 *Fax:* (014) 3235-7219
*E-mail:* edusc@usc.br
*Web Site:* www.edusc.com.br
*Key Personnel*
President: Sr Jacinta Turolo Garcia
Publisher: Dr Luiz Eugenio Vescio
   *E-mail:* lpelegrin@usc.br
Founded: 1996
Subjects: Biological Sciences, Child Care & Development, Education, Health, Nutrition, History, Journalism, Law, Literature, Literary Criticism, Essays, Philosophy, Psychology, Psychiatry, Religion - Catholic, Science (General), Social Sciences, Sociology, Brazilian originals
Number of titles published annually: 80 Print
*Distribution Center:* Rio de Janeiro
Sao Paulo

**EFE Tres D-Pub Juridicas Ltda**
Rua Torres Galvao, 35, 1 andar, 59032-160 Natal RN
*Tel:* (084) 2233394 *Fax:* (084) 2232263
*E-mail:* f3dsat@truenetrn.com.br
*Key Personnel*
Contact: Manoel Digesio de Costa

**Editora Elevacao+**
Affiliate of Brazilian Book Chamber
Av Rudge, 938, Bom Retiro, 01134-000 Sao Paulo-SP
*Tel:* (011) 3358-6868; (011) 3358-6875; (011) 3358-6869 *Fax:* (011) 3331-5803
*E-mail:* info@elevacao.com.br
*Web Site:* www.elevacao.com.br
*Key Personnel*
Contact: Marcus Alexandre Pineze
   *E-mail:* mpineze@uol.com.br
Founded: 1998
Subjects: Biblical Studies, Biography, Business, Communications, Education, Health, Nutrition, Human Relations, Parapsychology, Philosophy, Poetry, Religion - Other, Romance, Self-Help, Sports, Athletics, Theology
Number of titles published annually: 84 Print; 2 Audio
Total Titles: 35 Print; 2 Audio
Distributed by Distribooks Inc

**Emporio de Promocoes Artistica Cultural e Editora Ltda+**
Rua Ceara 184, 01243-010 Sao Paulo-SP
*Tel:* (011) 8262992 *Fax:* (011) 661135
*Key Personnel*
Contact: Luiz Bueno D'Horta
Founded: 1989
Membership(s): CBL.
ISBN Prefix(es): 85-85431

**Empresa Brasileira de Pesquisa Agropecuaria** (Embrapa Publishing House)+
Parque Estacao Biologica-PqEB S/N, Edificio Sede, Plano Piloto, 70770-901 Brasilia DF
*Tel:* (061) 348-4113 *Fax:* (061) 347-1041
*E-mail:* webmaster@sct.embrapa.br
*Web Site:* www.embrapa.br
*Key Personnel*
President & Dir: Clayton Campanhola
   *E-mail:* presid@sede.embrapa.br
Subjects: Agriculture, Biological Sciences, Earth Sciences, Economics, Journalism, Social Sciences, Sociology, Technology, Veterinary Science
ISBN Prefix(es): 85-7383

**Escrituras Editora e Distribuidora de Livros Ltda+**
Rua Maestro Callia, 123, Vila Mariana, 04012-100 Sao Paulo-SP
*Tel:* (011) 5082-4190 *Fax:* (011) 5082-4190
*E-mail:* escrituras@escrituras.com.br
*Web Site:* www.escrituras.com.br
*Key Personnel*
Executive Editor: Raimundo Nonato Rocha Gadelha
ISBN Prefix(es): 85-86303

**Editora Expressao e Cultura-Exped Ltda**
Est dos Bandeirantes, 1700, 22710-113 Rio de Janeiro-RJ
*Tel:* (021) 444 06 00 *Fax:* (021) 440700
*E-mail:* exped@embratel.net.br
*Telex:* 33280
*Key Personnel*
Publisher: Gilberto Huber
Dir & Editor: Ferdinando Bastos de Souza
Editorial Manager: Paulo Schvinger
Founded: 1967
Subjects: Education, Literature, Literary Criticism, Essays
ISBN Prefix(es): 85-208
*Parent Company:* Grupo Gilberto Huber
*Associate Companies:* Ebid-Editora Paginas Amarelas SA
*Orders to:* CP 20030, Rio de Janeiro-RJ

**FAE**, see Fundacao de Assistencia ao Estudante

**Editora FCO Ltda+**
Av Amazonas, nº 115-Sala 1310, 30180-000 Belo Horizonte-MG
*Tel:* (031) 2131288 *Fax:* (031) 2243825
*E-mail:* editorafco@ig.com.br
*Key Personnel*
Contact: Sr Lucio Fernando Borges
Founded: 1994
Subjects: Civil Engineering, Education, Engineering (General), Management

**FEI**, *imprint of* Editora Gaia Ltda

**Livraria Martins Fontes Editora Ltda+**
Rua Conselheiro Ramalho 330, 01325-000 Sao Paulo-SP
*Tel:* (011) 3241-3677 *Fax:* (0800) 11-3619
*E-mail:* info@martinsfontes.com.br
*Web Site:* www.martinsfontes.com.br *Cable:* CABOGRAMA
*Key Personnel*
Contact: Waldir Martins Fontes
Founded: 1960
Subjects: Art, Education, English as a Second Language, History, Law, Nonfiction (General), Philosophy, Psychology, Psychiatry, Social Sciences, Sociology
ISBN Prefix(es): 85-336

**Editora Forense Universitaria Ltda+**
Rua Sa Freire, 25, 20930-430 Rio de Janeiro-RJ
*Tel:* (011) 580-0776 *Fax:* (011) 589-2084

*E-mail:* foruniv@unisys.com.br
*Key Personnel*
Dir: Regina Bilac Pinto
Founded: 1973
Membership(s): National Book Publishers of Rio de Janeiro, Brasil.
Subjects: Economics, Government, Political Science, Language Arts, Linguistics, Law, Philosophy, Psychology, Psychiatry, Social Sciences, Sociology
ISBN Prefix(es): 85-218
*Bookshop(s):* Livraria Forense Universitaria Lg Sao Francisco, Lg Sao Francisco, 20, 01005-010 Sao Paulo-SP, Paulo Abrantes *Tel:* (011) 31040396
*Warehouse:* Rua Sa Freire, 25, 20930-430 Rio De Janeiro-RJ

**Formato Editorial ltda+**
Av Marques de Sao Vicente, 1697-Barra Funda, 01139-904 San Paulo-SP
*Tel:* (011) 3613-3000 *Fax:* (011) 3611-3308
*E-mail:* falecom@formatoeditorial.com.br
*Web Site:* www.formatoeditorial.com.br
*Key Personnel*
Dir: Jose de Alencar Mayrink *E-mail:* alencar@formatoeditorial.com.br; Claudia Pereira-Rezende *Tel:* (031) 4211777 *E-mail:* claudia@graficaformato.com.br
Editor: Sonia Marta Junqueira *Tel:* (031) 4218544 *E-mail:* soniajunqueira@formatoeditorial.com.br
Founded: 1986
Membership(s): Camara Brasileira do Livro & Fundacao Nacional do Livro Infantil e Juvenil.
Subjects: Education, Literature, Literary Criticism, Essays
ISBN Prefix(es): 85-7208
Number of titles published annually: 35 Print
Total Titles: 268 Print

**Livraria Freitas Bastos Editora SA+**
Avenida Londre, 381 Bonsucesso, 21041-030 Rio de Janeiro-RJ
*Tel:* (021) 290-9949 *Fax:* (021) 290-9949
*E-mail:* fbastos@netfly.com.br; freitasbastos@freitasbastos.com.br *Cable:* ETIEL
*Key Personnel*
President: Isaac Delgado Abulafia *E-mail:* isaac@netfly.com.br
Founded: 1917
Membership(s): the Association of Brazilian Publishers.
Subjects: Accounting, Law
ISBN Prefix(es): 85-353

**Editora FTD SA**
Rua Manoel Dutra, 225, Bairro Bela Vista, 01328-010 Sao Paulo-SP
*Tel:* (011) 3284-8500 *Fax:* (011) 3283-5011
*E-mail:* ftd@dial&ta.br
*Web Site:* www.ftd.com.br
*Key Personnel*
Man Dir: Joao Tissi
Contact: Romeu Rossi
Founded: 1897
ISBN Prefix(es): 85-322
*Branch Office(s)*
Rua Agenor Meira 4/67, Bauro, Sao Paulo-SP
Rua Lavras 235, Carmo Sion, Belo Horizonte-MG
Ave Goias 1146, Goiania-GO
Ave Tiradentes 963, Maringa
Rua Andre Cavalcanti 78, Rio de Janeiro-GB
Ave Joana Angelica 963, Salvador-BA
Rua Mal Deodoro 887, Curitiba-PR
Ave do Imperador 1203, Fortaleza-CE
Ave Rio Branco 185, Londrina-PR
Rua Martins Junior 39, Recife-PE
Rua Prof Baltazar 12, Vitoria-ES

**Fundacao Cultural Avatar**
R Pereira Nunes, 141 - Inga, 24210-430 Niteroi-RJ
*Tel:* (021) 621-0217 *Fax:* (021) 2621-0217
*E-mail:* fcavatar@nitnet.com.br
*Web Site:* www.nitnet.com.br/~fcavatar
*Key Personnel*
President: Prof Tania Goncalves de Araujo
Dir, Administration & Financial: Dr Jayme Treiger
Dir, Culture: Prof Ruth Machado Barbosa
Subjects: Asian Studies, Astrology, Occult, Biography, Education, Philosophy, Psychology, Psychiatry, Religion - Other
ISBN Prefix(es): 85-7104

**Fundacao de Assistencia ao Estudante**
SAS Quadra 1- BI/A Sl 806, 70729-000 Brasilia-DF
*Tel:* (061) 223-9329 *Fax:* (061) 226-6270
*Key Personnel*
Man Dir: Rubens Jose de Castro Albuquerque
Editorial Dir: Luiz Pasquale Filho
Sales Dir: Avari de Campos
Production Manager: Maria Aparecida de Oliveira
Publicity Manager: Geni Hirata
Rights & Permissions: Jose Ribeiro de Castro Neto
Founded: 1967
276 bookshops throughout Brazil.
ISBN Prefix(es): 85-222

**Fundacao Instituto Brasileiro de Geografia e Estatistica (IBGE - CDDI/DECOP)** (Brazilian Institute of National Statistics & Geography)
Rua General Canabarro, 706/174-Maracana, 20271-201 Rio de Janeiro
*Tel:* (021) 569-2043 *Fax:* (021) 234-6189
*E-mail:* marisa@ibge.gov.br
*Web Site:* www.ibge.gov.br
*Telex:* (021) 2139128
*Key Personnel*
President: Sergio Besserman Vianna *Fax:* (021) 220-5943
Senior Technician: Raul Aloysio Telles Ribeiro *Tel:* (021) 569-2043 *E-mail:* raultri@ibge.gov.br
Founded: 1936
Subjects: Economics, Geography, Geology, Mathematics
ISBN Prefix(es): 85-240
*Bookshop(s):* Av Franklin Roosevet, 146 lj.A, 20021 Castelo-RJ
*Orders to:* IBGE - CDDI/DECOP/DICOM, Rua General Canabarro 666, Bloco B - 2/Andar, 20271-200 Rio de Janerio-RJ, Contact: Carlos Lessa *Tel:* (021) 569-2043 *Fax:* (021) 234-8480 *E-mail:* atandicddi@ibge.gov.br

**Fundacao Joaquim Nabuco-Editora Massangana+**
Av Dezessete de Agosto, 2187, Casa Forte, 52061-540 Recife-PE
*Tel:* (081) 3441-5500 *Fax:* (081) 3441-5600
*E-mail:* editora@fundaj.gov.br
*Web Site:* www.fundaj.gov.br
*Telex:* 081 1180
*Key Personnel*
Dir General: Leonardo Dantas Silva
Founded: 1978
Subjects: Anthropology, Economics, Education, History, Social Sciences, Sociology
ISBN Prefix(es): 85-7019

**Fundacao Sao Paulo, EDUC+**
Rua Ministro Godoi, 1213, 05015-001 Sao Paulo-SP
*Tel:* (011) 3873-3359 *Fax:* (011) 38733359
*E-mail:* educsp@puc001.pucsp.ansp.br
*Key Personnel*
Dir: Maria do Carmo Guedes
Vice Dir: Maria Eliza Mazzilli Pereira

Founded: 1984
Membership(s): CBL, ABEU, ABEC.
Subjects: Anthropology, Biological Sciences, Communications, Disability, Special Needs, Economics, Education, English as a Second Language, Geography, Geology, Government, Political Science, History, Humor, Language Arts, Linguistics, Law, Literature, Literary Criticism, Essays, Mathematics, Medicine, Nursing, Dentistry, Music, Dance, Philosophy, Psychology, Psychiatry, Social Sciences, Sociology, Theology
ISBN Prefix(es): 85-283
Total Titles: 230 Print; 1 Audio
*Parent Company:* Pontificia Universidade Catolica de Sao Paulo
*Ultimate Parent Company:* Funda cao Cultural Sao Paulo
*Bookshop(s):* Espaco EDUC, Rua Monte Alegre, 984 *Tel:* (011) 36708297 *Fax:* (011) 38733359
*Orders to:* Livraria Cultura, Avenida Paulista, 2073, Conj Nacional Cerqueira Cesar, 01310-300 Sao Paulo-SP, Contact: Ana Regina *Tel:* (011) 2854033 *Fax:* (011) 2854457 *E-mail:* livro@livcultura.com.br

**Editora Gaia Ltda+**
Rua Pirapitingui, 111, 01508-020 Sao Paulo-SP
*Tel:* (011) 2777999 *Fax:* (011) 2778141
*E-mail:* gaia@dialdata.com.br
*Key Personnel*
Prof: Carlos Alberto Pereira de Oliveira
Founded: 1989
Subjects: Cookery, Environmental Studies, Health, Nutrition, Self-Help
ISBN Prefix(es): 85-85351
*Parent Company:* Global Editora E Distribuidora Ltda
*Associate Companies:* Editora Ground Ltda
Imprints: FEI

**Editora Gente Livraria e Editora Ltda+**
Rua Pedro Soares de Almeida 114, 05029-030 Sao Paulo-SP
*Tel:* (011) 3675 2505 *Fax:* (011) 3675 0430
*E-mail:* gentedit@mandic.com.br
*Key Personnel*
Editor: Rosely Boschini
Founded: 1976
Subjects: Philosophy, Psychology, Psychiatry
ISBN Prefix(es): 85-7312

**Global Editora e Distribuidora Ltda+**
Rua Pirapitingui, 111, Liberdade, 01508-020 Sao Paulo-SP
*Tel:* (011) 2777999 *Fax:* (011) 2778141
*E-mail:* global@dialdata.com.br
*Key Personnel*
Man Dir, Sales: Luis Alves, Jr
Editorial, Production, Rights & Permissions: Jose Venancio
Founded: 1973
Subjects: Anthropology, Biography, Education, Fashion, Health, Nutrition, History, Music, Dance, Poetry, Romance, Social Sciences, Sociology
ISBN Prefix(es): 85-260
*Associate Companies:* Editora Ground Ltda; Editora Gaia Ltda
Imprints: Parma; Prol; Sao Paulo Editora
Subsidiaries: Centro Editorial Latino Americano Ltda

**Editora Globo SA+**
Av Jaguare, 1485, 05346-902 Sao Paulo-SP
*Tel:* (011) 3767-7886 *Fax:* (011) 3767-7870
*E-mail:* wcarelli@edglobo.com.br
*Web Site:* www.editoraglobo.com.br
*Telex:* 81574
*Key Personnel*
General Dir: Ricardo Alberto Fischer
Editorial Dir: Flavio Barros Pinto

Sales Dir: Fernando Alberto Costa
Founded: 1954
Subjects: Biography, Business, Cookery, Drama, Theater, Economics, Education, Environmental Studies, Fiction, History, How-to, Humor, Journalism, Language Arts, Linguistics, Law, Literature, Literary Criticism, Essays, Medicine, Nursing, Dentistry, Music, Dance, Mysteries, Poetry, Science (General), Self-Help, Sports, Athletics, Travel
ISBN Prefix(es): 85-250; 85-217
*Branch Office(s)*
Rua Itapiru, 1209, 20251 Rio de Janeiro
*Warehouse:* Alameda Tocantins, 679 Alphaville Barueri, Sao Paulo

**Edicoes Graal Ltda+**
Rua Hermenegildo de Barros, 31-A-Gloria, 20241-040 Rio de Janeiro-RJ
*Tel:* (011) 2236522 *Fax:* (011) 2236290
*E-mail:* producao@pazeterra.com.br
*Key Personnel*
Man Dir, Editorial & Publicity Dir & Rights & Permissions: Fernando Gasparian
Sales & Production Dir: Marcus F Gasparian
Founded: 1977
Subjects: Economics, Education, History, Medicine, Nursing, Dentistry, Philosophy, Psychology, Psychiatry, Social Sciences, Sociology
ISBN Prefix(es): 85-7038
*Associate Companies:* Editora Paz e Terra

**Ordem do Graal na Terra**
CP 128, 06801-970 Embu-SP
*Tel:* (011) 4781-0006 *Fax:* (011) 4781-0006 (ext 217)
*E-mail:* graal@graal.org.br
*Web Site:* www.graal.org.br
*Key Personnel*
President: Harald Schuler
Distribution Mgr: Paulo Nobre *Tel:* (011) 4781 1671 *Fax:* (011) 4781 1671 *E-mail:* nobrebooks@graal.org.br
Founded: 1947
Subjects: Philosophy, Religion - Other, Self-Help, New-Age, Spiritualism
ISBN Prefix(es): 85-7279
Number of titles published annually: 3 Print
Total Titles: 55 Print
*U.S. Office(s):* Nobre Books Distributor, 5117 Black Diamond Court, Raleigh, NC 27604, United States *Tel:* 919-212-6211 *E-mail:* nobrebooks@graal.org.br
*Bookshop(s):* Av Sao Luiz, 192-lj14, Sao Paulo, SP 01046-000 *Tel:* (011) 259-7646
*Shipping Address:* Biblio Distribution, 15200 NBN Way, Blue Ridge Summit, PA 17214, United States
*Warehouse:* Biblio Distribution, 15200 NBN Way, Blue Ridge Summit, PA 17214, United States
*Distribution Center:* Biblio Distribution, 15200 NBN Way, Blue Ridge Summit, PA 17214, United States
*Orders to:* Biblio Distribution, 15200 NBN Way, Blue Ridge Summit, PA 17214, United States
*Returns:* Biblio Distribution, 15200 NBN Way, Blue Ridge Summit, PA 17214, United States

**Editora e Grafica Carisio Ltda, Minas Editora+**
CP 221, Rua Wenceslau, 276-Centro, 38440-000 Araguari-MG
*Tel:* (034) 2413557 *Fax:* (034) 2413310
*Key Personnel*
Contact: Publio Carisio de Paula
Founded: 1984
Subjects: Fiction, Religion - Other, Self-Help
ISBN Prefix(es): 85-86030

**Grafica Editora Primor Ltda+**
Rua Presidente Dutra 2611, 21535-500 Rio de Janeiro
*Tel:* (021) 4744966

*Key Personnel*
Man Dir: Sergio Jacques Waissman; Simao
    Waissman
Sales & Publicity: Miguel Paixao
Production: Paulo Duante
Founded: 1969
Subjects: Art, Education
ISBN Prefix(es): 85-7024
*Parent Company:* Editora Primor Ltda

**Editora Ground Ltda+**
Rua Lacedemonia, 68, 04634-020 Sao Paulo-SP
*Tel:* (011) 5031-1500 *Fax:* (011) 5031-3462
*E-mail:* editora@ground.com.br; vendas@ground.
    com.br; marketing@ground.com.br
*Web Site:* www.ground.com.br
*Key Personnel*
Executive & Publisher: Jose Carlos Rolo Venan-
    cio *E-mail:* jcvenancio@ground.com.br
Founded: 1973
Subjects: Asian Studies, Astrology, Occult, Envi-
    ronmental Studies, Health, Nutrition, Philoso-
    phy
ISBN Prefix(es): 85-7187
*Associate Companies:* Editora Aquariana
    Ltda, Rua Lacedemonia, 68, Sao Paulo
    *E-mail:* aquariana@ground.com.br

**Editora Gryphus**, *imprint of* Companhia Editora
    Forense

**Editora Guanabara Koogan SA+**
Travessa do Ouvidor 11, 1° AO 8° Andares,
    20040-040 Rio de Janeiro-RJ
*Tel:* (021) 3970-9450 *Fax:* (021) 2252-2732
*E-mail:* gbk@editoraguanabara.com.br
*Web Site:* www.editoraguanabara.com.br
*Key Personnel*
Dir: Joao Pedro Lorch; Mauro Koogan Lorch
Rights & Permissions: Christina Noren
Founded: 1930
Subjects: Biological Sciences, Environmental
    Studies, Medicine, Nursing, Dentistry, Veteri-
    nary Science
ISBN Prefix(es): 85-277; 85-226

**Enio Matheus Guazzelli e Cia Ltd**, see Livraria
    Pioneira Editora/Enio Matheus Guazzelli e Cia
    Ltd

**Editora Harbra Ltda+**
Rua Joaquim Tavora, 779, Vila Mariana, 04015-
    001 Sao Paulo-SP
*Tel:* (011) 5084-2403; (011) 5084-2482; (011)
    5571-1122; (011) 5549-2244; (011) 5571-0276
    *Fax:* (011) 5575-6876; (011) 5571-9777
*E-mail:* editorial@harbra.com.br
*Web Site:* www.harbra.com.br
*Key Personnel*
Dir: Julio Esteban Emod-Eghy *Tel:* (011)
    50842482 *E-mail:* emod@harbra.com.br
Founded: 1986
Subjects: Behavioral Sciences, Biography, Bio-
    logical Sciences, Computer Science, Earth Sci-
    ences, Management, Physical Sciences, Science
    (General), Self-Help, Social Sciences, Sociol-
    ogy
ISBN Prefix(es): 85-294
Total Titles: 250 Print; 1 CD-ROM; 1 Audio
*Branch Office(s)*
Rua 70, No 687 Qd 127 Lt 05, 74055-120 Goia-
    nia *Tel:* (062) 212-9875; (062) 225-8632
    *Fax:* (062) 212-9874
Rua do Riachuelo 453, Loja 7, 50050-400 Re-
    cife *Tel:* (081) 3221-0700; (081) 3222-2808
    *Fax:* (081) 3221-3655
Rua Conde de Bomfim 944-A (Tijuca), 20520-
    000 Rio de Janeiro *Tel:* (021) 572-4668; (021)
    238-4670 *Fax:* (021) 572-8576

Rua Guajajaras 1148, 30180-100 Belo Horizonte
    *Fax:* (031) 3275-4016
Distributor for editora Edgard Blucher; editora
    Universidade de Brasilia

**Hemus Editora Ltda+**
Rua da Gloria 312, 01510-000 Sao Paulo-SP
*Tel:* (011) 55219058 *Fax:* (011) 55219058
*Telex:* 32005 Edil *Cable:* HETEC
*Key Personnel*
President: Rachel Behar
Man Dir: Maxim Behar
Founded: 1965
Subjects: Archaeology, Architecture & Interior
    Design, Astrology, Occult, Career Develop-
    ment, Civil Engineering, Electronics, Electrical
    Engineering, Law, Philosophy
ISBN Prefix(es): 85-289

**Horus Editora Ltda+**
Rua dos Ingleses, 222 cj 121, 01329-902 Sao
    Paulo-SP
*Tel:* (011) 288-7681 *Fax:* (011) 288-7681
*E-mail:* horus@horuseditora.com.br
*Web Site:* www.horuseditora.com.br
*Key Personnel*
President: Juan Ferre' Serrano
Manager: Roberto Ferre' Serrano
Founded: 1977
Also acts as distributor.
Subjects: Astrology, Occult, Music, Dance, Psy-
    chology, Psychiatry, Religion - Buddhist, Re-
    ligion - Catholic, Religion - Hindu, Religion
    - Islamic, Religion - Jewish, Religion - Other,
    Theology
ISBN Prefix(es): 85-86204

**Livro Ibero-Americano Ltda**
Hermenegildo de Barros, 40-Gloria, 20241-040
    Rio de Janeiro-RJ
*Tel:* (021) 2221 2026 *Fax:* (021) 2252 8814
    *Cable:* NEBRIJA
*Key Personnel*
Man Dir: Sir Joao Francisco J Gomes
Founded: 1946
Subjects: Agriculture, Art, Electronics, Electri-
    cal Engineering, History, Language Arts, Lin-
    guistics, Philosophy, Photography, Psychology,
    Psychiatry, Religion - Other
ISBN Prefix(es): 85-7032
*Branch Office(s)*
Rua Conselheiro Crispiniano 29 - 1 pav, Sao
    Paulo-SP

**IBGE - CDDI/DECOP**, see Fundacao Instituto
    Brasileiro de Geografia e Estatistica (IBGE -
    CDDI/DECOP)

**IBICT**, see Instituto Brasileiro de Informacao em
    Ciencia e Tecnologia

**IBRASA (Instituicao Brasileira de Difusao
    Cultural Ltda)+**
Rua Treze De Maio, 365/367, 01327-000 Sao
    Paulo-SP
*Tel:* (011) 3107 41 00 *Fax:* (011) 3107 35 13
*E-mail:* editora.ibrasa@uol.com.br
*Web Site:* www.ibrasa.com.br
*Key Personnel*
Man Dir: Jorge Leite
Founded: 1958
Subjects: Economics, Education, Government, Po-
    litical Science, Health, Nutrition, History, Lit-
    erature, Literary Criticism, Essays, Medicine,
    Nursing, Dentistry, Parapsychology, Philoso-
    phy, Psychology, Psychiatry, Science (General),
    Social Sciences, Sociology, Sports, Athletics,
    Physical education
ISBN Prefix(es): 85-348

*Bookshop(s):* IBREX - Distribuidora de Livros e
    Material de Escritorio Ltda
*Orders to:* IBREX Ltda, Rua Treze de Maio 361,
    01327-000 Sao Paulo-SP

**Icone Editora Ltda+**
Rua das Palmeiras, 213, 01226-010 Sao Paulo-SP
*Tel:* (011) 36663095; (021) 826-9510 *Fax:* (011)
    36663095
*Key Personnel*
President: Luiz Carlos Fanelli
Vice President: Tatiana Fanelli
Founded: 1985
Membership(s): Brazilian House of Books; Na-
    tional Syndication of Books; Brazilian Asso-
    ciation of Books & Collections; also acts as
    distributor.
Subjects: Agriculture, Astrology, Occult, Biogra-
    phy, Crafts, Games, Hobbies, Law, Medicine,
    Nursing, Dentistry, Science (General), Sports,
    Athletics, Technology
ISBN Prefix(es): 85-274; 85-85503

**Iglu Editora Ltda**
Rua Duilio 386, Lapa, 05043-020 Sao Paulo-SP
*Tel:* (011) 3873-0227 *Fax:* (011) 3873-0227
*E-mail:* iglueditiora@ig.com.br
*Key Personnel*
Contact: Julio Igliori Netto
Founded: 1987
Subjects: Economics, Education, Health, Nutri-
    tion, Law
ISBN Prefix(es): 85-7494

**Iluminuras - Projetos e Producoes Editoriais
    Ltda+**
Rua Oscar Freire 1233, 01426-001 Sao Paulo-SP
*Tel:* (011) 3068-9433; (011) 8678583 *Fax:* (011)
    3082-5317
*E-mail:* iluminuras@ilumunuras.com.br
*Key Personnel*
Contact: Beatriz Costa; Sir Samuel Leon
Founded: 1987
ISBN Prefix(es): 85-85219

**Imago Editora Ltda+**
Rua da Quintanda, n° 52/8° andar, Centro, 20011-
    030 Rio de Janeiro-RJ
*Tel:* (021) 2242-0627 *Fax:* (021) 2224-8359
*E-mail:* imago@imagoeditora.com.br
*Web Site:* www.imagoeditora.com.br
*Key Personnel*
President: Jayme Salomao
Executive Dir: Eduardo Salomao
Founded: 1967
Membership(s): SNEL, CBL.
Subjects: Biblical Studies, Biography, Drama,
    Theater, Fiction, Film, Video, Health, Nutrition,
    History, How-to, Language Arts, Linguistics,
    Literature, Literary Criticism, Essays, Myster-
    ies, Nonfiction (General), Philosophy, Psychol-
    ogy, Psychiatry, Religion - Other, Romance,
    Science Fiction, Fantasy, Self-Help
ISBN Prefix(es): 85-312

**Editora Index Ltda+**
Av Rio Branco, 45 - S1 1707, Centro, 20090-003
    Rio de Janeiro-RJ
*Tel:* (021) 516 2336 *Fax:* (021) 253 3507
*E-mail:* editoraindex@ax.ibase.org.br
*Key Personnel*
President: Jose Paulo M Soares; Christina Ferrao
Founded: 1982
Membership(s): Chealsea Arts Club (London).
Subjects: Art, Environmental Studies, History
ISBN Prefix(es): 85-7083
*Associate Companies:* Editora Libris
*Warehouse:* Rua Sacadura Cabral 81 gr 804, Rio
    de Janeiro 20221

**Instituicao Brasileira de Difusao Cultural Ltda (IBRASA)**, see IBRASA (Instituicao Brasileira de Difusao Cultural Ltda)

**Editora Interciencia Ltda**
Rua Verna Magalhaes, 66, Engenho Novo, 20710-290 Rio de Janeiro-RJ
*Tel:* (021) 25819378 *Fax:* (021) 25014760
*Key Personnel*
Man Dir & Rights & Permissions: Edson G S Nascimento
Publicity: Nize Nascimento
Founded: 1969 (1975 as publisher)
Subjects: Science (General)
ISBN Prefix(es): 85-7193

**Interlivros Edicoes Ltda**
Rua Comandante Coelho 1085, 21250-510 Rio de Janeiro-RJ
*Tel:* (021) 3913134 *Fax:* (021) 3521005
*E-mail:* interlivros@ibm.net
*Key Personnel*
Executive: Abel Simoes de Morais
Subjects: Biological Sciences, Health, Nutrition, Medicine, Nursing, Dentistry, Psychology, Psychiatry
ISBN Prefix(es): 85-7236; 85-85891

**Irmaos Vitale S/A Industria e Comercio**
Rua Franca Pinto, 42, vila Mariana, 04704-000 Sao Paulo-SP
*Tel:* (011) 5574-7001 *Fax:* (011) 5574-7388
*E-mail:* irmaos@vitale.com.br
*Web Site:* www.vitale.com.br
ISBN Prefix(es): 85-7407; 85-85188
*Parent Company:* Irmaos Vitale S/A Ind E Comercio
Subsidiaries: Casa Vitale
Divisions: Edicoes musicais e Instrumentos musicais (Nacionais e importados)

**ISAEC**, see Editora Sinodal

**JUERP**, see Junta de Educacao Religiosa e Publicacoes da Convencao Batista Brasileira (JUERP)

**Junta de Educacao Religiosa e Publicacoes da Convencao Batista Brasileira (JUERP)+**
Rua Silva Vale, 781, 21370-360 Rio de Janeiro-RJ
*Tel:* (021) 2690772 *Fax:* (021) 2690296
*E-mail:* juerp@openlink.com.br
*Web Site:* www.juerp.org.br *Cable:* BATISTAS
*Key Personnel*
General Superintendent: Dr Claudio Mazzoni
Editorial & Rights & Permissions: Prof Joelcio Barreto
Marketing: Dr Oswaldo Paiao, Jr
Production: Dr Samuel Justino
Founded: 1907
Membership(s): Association of Brazilian Christian Publishers & Association of Brazilian Baptist Publishers.
Subjects: Religion - Other
ISBN Prefix(es): 85-350
*Branch Office(s)*
Filial Juerp, Ave Sao Joao 816/820, 01036-100 Sao Paulo-SP
Trav Padre Prudencio 61, 66000 Belem-PA
Rua Bahia 360 - Sobre loja, 30000 Belo Horizonte-MG
SDS B1 G - loja 17 - Conj Baracat, 70302 Brasilia-DF
Rua Treze de Maio 2659, 79100 Camop Grande-MS
Rua Rui Barbosa 139, 69007 Manaus-AM
Rua do Hospicio 187, 50000 Reclife-PE
Juerp Suese, Rua Silva Vale, 781 - Cavalcante, 21370-360 Rio de Janeiro-RJ

Av Sao Pantaleao 195, LJS A E B, Centro, 65015 Sao Kyis-MA
Abba Press Editora, Rua do Mar, 20 Interlagos, 04654-060 Sao Paulo-SP
Rua Barao de Itapemirim 208, 29000 Vitoria-ES
*Bookshop(s):* Ave Nil Pecanha 411, 25000 Caxais-RJ; Rua XV de Novembro 49, 24000 Niteroi-RJ; Rua Otavio Tarquinio 178, 26000 Nova Iguacu-RJ; Rua Cel Vicente 614, 90000 Porto Alegre-RS; Rua fo Rosario 141/216, Centro, 20041 Rio de Janeiro-RJ; Rua Mariz e Barris 39, Praca da Bandeira, 20270 Rio de Janeiro-RJ; Ave Viscondede Sao Lourenco 6, 40000 Salvador-BA

**Koinonia Comunidade Edicoes Ltda**
SCLN 203 - Bl A, 1 Andar, 70833-510 Brasilia-DF
*Tel:* (061) 3479431 *Fax:* (061) 3470972
*Key Personnel*
Contact: Divino Soares da Silva
Founded: 1992
Subjects: Biblical Studies, Religion - Protestant
ISBN Prefix(es): 85-85810
Divisions: Gravadora Koinonia Music
*Bookshop(s):* Praca Carlos Gomes, 01501-040 Sao Paulo-SP *Tel:* (011) 606-2644; Rua 4 N 906-Sector Central CEP, 74025-020 Gioania-GO

**Editora Koinonia Ltda**, see Koinonia Comunidade Edicoes Ltda

**Livraria Kosmos Editora Ltda**
Rua do Rosario 155, 20041-005 Rio de Janeiro-RJ
*Tel:* (021) 2224-8616 *Fax:* (021) 2221-4582
*E-mail:* livro-rio@kosmos.com.br
*Web Site:* www.kosmos.com.br *Cable:* EIKOS
*Key Personnel*
Man Dir: Stefan Geyerhahn; Luiz C Poppi
Founded: 1935
Subjects: Engineering (General), History, Language Arts, Linguistics, Music, Dance, Travel
ISBN Prefix(es): 85-7096

**Editora Kuarup Ltda+**
rua Diamantina, 381, 91040-460 Porto Alegre-RS
*Tel:* (051) 361-5522 *Fax:* (051) 361-3550
*E-mail:* kuarup@conex.com.br
*Key Personnel*
Director: Adalberto Felix Souto
Editor: Vera Miranda Ritter-Souto
Founded: 1983
Subjects: Astrology, Occult, Education, Religion - Other
ISBN Prefix(es): 85-269

**Francisco J Laissue Livros**
Prace Olavo Bilac 28, 201, 20041 Rio de Janeiro
*Tel:* (021) 509-7298
Founded: 1947
Bookshop specializing in Portuguese, Spanish, French & English.
Subjects: African American Studies, Anthropology, Archaeology, Asian Studies, Astrology, Occult, Religion - Buddhist, Religion - Hindu, Religion - Islamic, Religion - Jewish
Foreign Rep(s): Editorial Kier (Argentina)

**Lake-Livraria Editora Allan Kardec+**
Rua Assuncao, 45, Bras, 03005-020 Sao Paulo-SP
*Tel:* (011) 229-0526; (011) 229-1227; (011) 227-1396; (011) 229-0937; (011) 229-4592; (011) 229-0514 *Fax:* (011) 229-0935; (011) 227-5714
*E-mail:* lake@lake.com.br
*Web Site:* www.lake.com.br
*Key Personnel*
Contact: Roberto Francisco-Ferrero
Founded: 1937
ISBN Prefix(es): 85-7360

**LDA Editores Ltda+**
Rua Dias da Rocha Filho 1253, Unidade 03, 80410-510 Curitiba-PR
*Tel:* (041) 362-9173 *Fax:* (041) 262-3439
*E-mail:* lda.editores@uol.com.br
*Key Personnel*
Executive: Lionel de Almeida
Founded: 1991
Subjects: Architecture & Interior Design, Biography, Cookery, History, Journalism, Literature, Literary Criticism, Essays, Philosophy, Travel
Imprints: Peninsula

**Editora Leitura Ltda**
Rua Pedra Bonita, 870, Belo Horizonte-MG 30430-390
*Tel:* (031) 3371-4902 *Fax:* (031) 3714902
*E-mail:* leitura@editoraleitura.com.br
*Web Site:* www.editoraleitura.com.br
Subjects: Education
ISBN Prefix(es): 85-7358

**Libreria Editora Ltda+**
Rua Taquaritinga, 137/139, Mooca, 03170-010 Sao Paulo-SP
*Tel:* (011) 608-5411 *Fax:* (011) 948-1615
*E-mail:* portal@libreria.com.br; libreria@libreria.com.br
*Web Site:* www.libreria.com.br
*Key Personnel*
Dir Coml: Fiorentino S Mario
Founded: 1974
Membership(s): the Association of Brazilian Publishers; Association of Brazilian Distributors.
Subjects: Cookery, English as a Second Language, Geography, Geology, Language Arts, Linguistics, Natural History, Globes
ISBN Prefix(es): 85-85900

**Editora Lidador Ltda+**
Rua Hilario Ribeiro 154, Pca da Bandeira, 20270-180 Rio de Janeiro-RJ
*Tel:* (021) 2569-0594 *Fax:* (021) 2204-0684
*E-mail:* lidador@infolink.com.br
*Key Personnel*
Publicity Manager: Ruy Carvalho
Founded: 1960
Subjects: Communications, Economics, Education, Erotica, Fiction, Human Relations, Music, Dance, Parapsychology, Social Sciences, Sociology
ISBN Prefix(es): 85-7003
Number of titles published annually: 9 Print
Distributed by Topbook

**Waldir Lima Editora**
Rua 24 de Maio, 347, 20950-090 Rio de Janeiro-RJ
*Tel:* (05521) 581-5000 *Fax:* (05521) 581-3586
*E-mail:* geapo@ccaa.com.br
*Web Site:* www.ccaa.com.br
*Key Personnel*
Dir-General, Rights & Permissions: Waldyr Lima
Editorial, Research & Planning Dir: Rosane Roale
Sales, Production & Publicity Dir: Rogerio Gama
Founded: 1967
Specialize in English, Portuguese & Spanish language instruction.
Subjects: Education, English as a Second Language, Language Arts, Linguistics
ISBN Prefix(es): 85-341
Total Titles: 2,000,000 Print
*U.S. Office(s):* CCLS Publishing House, 3181 Coral Way, Miami, FL 33145, United States
*Showroom(s):* Publishing House, 3181 Coral Way, Miami, FL 33145, United States
*Orders to:* Publishing House, 3181 Coral Way, Miami, FL 33145, United States

**LISA (Livros Irradiantes SA)**
Rua Major Sertorio, 772, 01222-000 Sao Paulo-SP

*Tel:* (011) 2563755 *Fax:* (011) 2575776
*E-mail:* lerlisalivros@ig.com.br
*Key Personnel*
Man Dir: Leonidio Balbino da Silva
Sales Dir: Francisco de Paula Oliveira Filho
Founded: 1965
Subjects: Education
ISBN Prefix(es): 85-257

**Livraria Dos Advogados Editora Ltda**
Rua Riachuelo, 201, 3° andar, Sao Paulo-SP
*Tel:* (011) 3107-3979 *Fax:* (011) 3107-6878
*E-mail:* lael@lael.com.br
*Web Site:* www.lael.com.br
Subjects: Law

**Livraria e Editora Infobook SA+**
Rua do Mercado 34 Sala 1501, 20010-120 Rio de
    Janeiro-RJ
*Tel:* (021) 263-3807 *Fax:* (021) 263-3807
*E-mail:* infobook@ibpinet.com.br
*Key Personnel*
Contact: Virginia Maria Reeve Andrea
Founded: 1993
Subjects: Computer Science, Management
ISBN Prefix(es): 85-85588; 85-7331

**Livros Irradiantes SA**, see LISA (Livros
    Irradiantes SA)

**Oficina de Livros Ltda+**
Rua Tupinanbas, 360, 30120-070 Belo Horizonte
*Tel:* (061) 386-2355 *Toll Free Tel:* 800-644-3002
    *Fax:* (061) 386-9248
*E-mail:* nicanorsena2001@aol.com.br
*Key Personnel*
President: Bernardino Jose Monteiro Moniz
Commercial Dir: Geraldo Alberto Alvares
Editor: Antonio Roberto Bertelli
Founded: 1987
Subjects: Literature, Literary Criticism, Essays,
    Social Sciences, Sociology
ISBN Prefix(es): 85-85170
*Branch Office(s)*
Rua Genebra, 135-9 andar, 01316 Sao Paulo-SP
    *Tel:* (011) 379872

**Editora Logosofica**
Rua Coronel Oscar Porto, 818, Paraiso, 04003-
    004 Sao Paulo-SP
*Tel:* (011) 8851476; (011) 8856574 *Fax:* (011)
    8879480
*Key Personnel*
Man Dir, Editorial: Jose Antonio Antonini
Author: Carlos Bernardo Gonzalez Pecotche
Sales: Alayde Thereza Melloni
Production: Darcio Giavoni
Founded: 1964
Membership(s): Brazilian Book Association.
Subjects: Behavioral Sciences, Education, Philos-
    ophy
ISBN Prefix(es): 85-7097
*Branch Office(s)*
Argentina
Mexico
Uruguay
*U.S. Office(s):* Centro de Estudos Logosoficos,
    50 Woodfall Rd, Belmont, MA 02178, United
    States
*Bookshop(s):* SHCG - Norte, Area de Escolas
    Q704, 70000 Brasilia-DF; Rua Piaui 74 2,
    30000 Belo Horizonte-MG; Rua General Poli-
    doro 36, 22280 Rio de Janeiro-RJ

**Longman**, *imprint of* Pearson Education Do
    Brasil

**Edicoes Loyola SA+**
Rua 1822 No 347, 04216-000 Sao Paulo-SP
*Tel:* (011) 69141922 *Fax:* (011) 61634275
*E-mail:* editorial@loyola.com.br

*Web Site:* www.loyola.com.br
*Key Personnel*
Dir: Fidel Garcia Rodriguez *E-mail:* fidel@loyola.
    com.br
Editorial & Rights & Permissions: Marcos Mar-
    cionilo
Founded: 1965
Also acts as book packager.
Subjects: Anthropology, Art, Biblical Studies,
    Communications, Computer Science, Drama,
    Theater, Economics, Education, History, Law,
    Literature, Literary Criticism, Essays, Man-
    agement, Philosophy, Psychology, Psychiatry,
    Religion - Other, Self-Help, Social Sciences,
    Sociology
ISBN Prefix(es): 85-15
*Parent Company:* Seas Edicoes Loyola
Divisions: Loyola Multimidia

**LTC-Livros Tecnicos e Cientificos Editora
    S/A+**
Travessa do Ouvidor, 11, 6° Andar-Parte, 20040-
    040 Rio de Janeiro-RJ
*Tel:* (021) 2221-7106; (021) 224-5877 *Fax:* (021)
    252-2732; (021) 2221-5744
*Key Personnel*
Dir: Joao Pedro Lorch; Mauro Koogan Lorch
Rights & Permissions: Christina Noren
    *E-mail:* norenltc@unisys.com.br
Founded: 1968
Subjects: Chemistry, Chemical Engineering, Com-
    puter Science, Economics, Engineering (Gen-
    eral), Management, Mathematics, Physics,
    Technology
ISBN Prefix(es): 85-216

**LTR Editora Ltda**
Rua Jaguaribe, 585, 01224-001 Sao Paulo-SP
Mailing Address: CP 2112, 01224-001 Sao Paulo-
    SP
*Tel:* (011) 3667-1101 *Fax:* (011) 3825-6695
*E-mail:* ltr@ltr.com.br
*Web Site:* www.ltr.com.br/web/home.asp
*Key Personnel*
Man Dir: Vbiratan de Freitas Mesquita
Sales: Vbiratan de Freitas Mesquita
Founded: 1937
Subjects: Law
ISBN Prefix(es): 85-7322
*Branch Office(s)*
Guanabara Palace Hotel, Av Pres Vargas, 392,
    Rio de Janeiro-RJ *Tel:* (021) 2220-4744
    *Fax:* (021) 2533-1393

**Editora Lucre Comercio e Representacoes+**
Av. Paulista, 1159-Cj 507, 01311-200 Sao Paulo-
    SP
*Tel:* (019) 287-8593 *Fax:* (019) 287 8593
*E-mail:* lucre@mute.net.br
*Key Personnel*
Contact: Eduardo Montalban
Founded: 1996
Subjects: Career Development, Economics, Fi-
    nance, Management

**Madras Editora+**
Rua Paulo Goncalves, 88, 02403-020 Sao Paulo-
    SP
*Tel:* (011) 6959-1127 *Fax:* (011) 6959-3090
*E-mail:* editor@madras.com.br
*Web Site:* www.madras.com.br
*Key Personnel*
President: Wagner Veneziani Costa
Founded: 1991
Books for University students, professional people
    esoteric ones, self-help, mysticism, freema-
    sonry. Distribute for self & 30 publishing
    houses throughout Brazil.
Subjects: Astrology, Occult, Self-Help
ISBN Prefix(es): 85-7374
Total Titles: 300 Print

Imprints: WVC
Foreign Rights: H Katia Schumer (Brazil)

**Makron Books do Brasil Editora Ltda+**
Rua Tabapua 1348, 04533-044 Sao Paulo-SP
    20689
*Tel:* (011) 829-6879 *Fax:* (011) 829-8947
*E-mail:* makron@books.com.br
*Web Site:* www.makron.com.br
*Key Personnel*
President: Milton Assumplao *Fax:* (011) 8294970
    *E-mail:* milton@makron.com.be
Founded: 1985
Subjects: Business, Computer Science
ISBN Prefix(es): 85-346

**Editora Manole Ltda+**
Avenida Ceci, 672, 06460-120 Barueri-SP
*Tel:* (011) 4196-6000 *Fax:* (011) 4196 6007
*E-mail:* manole@virtual-net.com.br
*Web Site:* www.manole.com.br
*Key Personnel*
Editorial, Production, Rights & Permissions: Dinu
    Manole
Sales: Carlos Telles
Publicity: Ilma Manole
Production: Amarylis Manle
Founded: 1969
Subjects: Cookery, Crafts, Games, Hobbies,
    Health, Nutrition, Medicine, Nursing, Dentistry,
    Sports, Athletics, Veterinary Science
ISBN Prefix(es): 85-204
Total Titles: 120 Print
Distributed by Dina Livros

**Editora Mantiqueira de Ciencia e Arte+**
Av Eduardo Moreira da Cruz 295, 12460-000
    Campos do Jordao-SP
*Tel:* (0122) 621832 *Fax:* (0122) 622126
*Key Personnel*
Executive: Antonio Fernando Costella
Subjects: Animals, Pets, Art, Communications,
    Fiction, History, Journalism, Poetry, Travel
ISBN Prefix(es): 85-85681

**Editora Manuais Tecnicos de Seguros Ltda**
Rua Brigadeiro Galvao 288, 01151-00 Sao Paulo-
    SP
*Tel:* (011) 50835587 *Fax:* (011) 50835468
*E-mail:* editora@emts.com.br
*Web Site:* www.emts.com.br
*Key Personnel*
Contact: Christina Roncarati
Founded: 1970
Subjects: Securities
ISBN Prefix(es): 85-85549

**Marco Zero**, *imprint of* Livraria Nobel S/A

**Editora Marco Zero Ltda+**
Rua da Balsa, 559, 02910-000 Sao Paulo-SP
*Tel:* (011) 876-2822 *Fax:* (011) 257-2744
*E-mail:* marcozero@mutecnet.com.br
*Key Personnel*
International Rights: Maria Jose Silveria
Founded: 1980
Subjects: Biography, Child Care & Development,
    Cookery, How-to, Literature, Literary Criticism,
    Essays, Mysteries, Nonfiction (General), Travel
ISBN Prefix(es): 85-279
*Parent Company:* Nobel
*Associate Companies:* Studio Nobel

**McKids**, *imprint of* Editora Mundo Cristao

**Editora Meca Ltda**
Rua Araujo 81, 01220-020 Sao Paulo-SP
*Tel:* (011) 2599049; (011) 2599034; (011)
    2575346 *Fax:* (011) 2570312
*E-mail:* editora_meca@uol.com.br
*Web Site:* www.editorameca.com.br *Cable:*
    CABOGRAMA

*Key Personnel*
Man Dir & Editor: Cosmo Juvela
Sales: Anna Maria Santos Brasil
Publicity: Marcos Juvela
Rights & Permissions: Guarany Gallo
Founded: 1970
Subjects: English as a Second Language, Parapsychology
Imprints: Jogos Pedagogicos
*Warehouse:* Rio de Janeiro, 51 Campos Eliseos, Sao Paulo-SP

**Medicina Panamericana Editora Do Brasil Ltda+**
Rua Santa Isabel 265, 012221-010 Sao Paulo-SP
*Tel:* (011) 222-0366 *Fax:* (011) 222-0542
*Key Personnel*
Executive: Nivacir Carlos Emmerick
Founded: 1950
Subjects: Medicine, Nursing, Dentistry
ISBN Prefix(es): 85-303
*Parent Company:* Editorial Medica Panamericana SA, Buenos Aires, Argentina
Subsidiaries: RJ/MG/RS

**Medsi - Editora Medica e Cientifica Ltda**
Rua Visconde de Cairu, 165, 20270-050 Rio de Janeiro-RJ
*Tel:* (021) 5694342 *Fax:* (021) 2646392
*E-mail:* medsi@ism.com.br
*Key Personnel*
Dir: Jackson Alves de Oliveira
Founded: 1981
Subjects: Medicine, Nursing, Dentistry
ISBN Prefix(es): 85-7199; 85-85019
*Branch Office(s)*
Rua Dr Cesario Motta Jr, 179, 01221-020 Sao Paulo-SP

**Editora Melhoramentos Ltda+**
Subsidiary of Companhia Melhoramentos de Sao Paulo
Rua Tito, 479, 05051-000 Sao Paulo-SP
*Tel:* (011) 3874 0854 *Fax:* (011) 3874 0855
*E-mail:* blerner@melhoramentos.com.br
*Web Site:* melhoramentos.com.br
*Key Personnel*
Publishing Dir: Breno Lerner *E-mail:* blerner@melhoramentos.com.br
Contact: Alfredo Weiszflog *E-mail:* aweiszfl@melhoramentos.com.br
Founded: 1915
Specialize in reference books.
Subjects: Archaeology, Art, Cookery, English as a Second Language, History, Literature, Literary Criticism, Essays
ISBN Prefix(es): 85-06
Total Titles: 1,200 Print; 20 CD-ROM; 8 Audio
Distributed by ACME; Atlantida; Capeletti; Emece; L Rodrigues; SEP; Sigmar; Volcano Press
Distributor for Disney

**Memorias Futuras Edicoes Ltda+**
Rua Pereira da Silva 322, 22221-140 Rio de Janeiro-RJ
*Tel:* (021) 2053549 *Fax:* (021) 2252518
*E-mail:* memorias@br.homeshopping.com.br
*Key Personnel*
Contact: Hedy Costa de Oliveira
Founded: 1982
Subjects: Fiction
ISBN Prefix(es): 85-287

**Editora Mercado Aberto Ltda+**
Rua Dona Margarida, 894, Bairro Navegantes, 90240-610 Porto Alegre RS
*Tel:* (051) 3337-4833 *Fax:* (051) 3337-4905
*E-mail:* mercado@mercadoaberto.com.br
*Web Site:* www.mercadoaberto.com.br

*Key Personnel*
Executive: Roque Jacoby
Founded: 1977
Subjects: Anthropology, Education, Fiction, Health, Nutrition, History, Literature, Literary Criticism, Essays, Romance
ISBN Prefix(es): 85-280

**Mercuryo Jovem**, *imprint of* Editora Mercuryo Ltda

**Editora Mercuryo Ltda+**
Alameda dos Guaramomis, 1267, 04076-012 Sao Paulo-SP
*Tel:* (011) 5531-8222 *Fax:* (011) 5093-3265
*E-mail:* diretoraeditorial@mercuryo.com.br
*Web Site:* www.mercuryo.com.br
*Key Personnel*
Editor: Julia Barany
Founded: 1987
Subjects: Art, Biblical Studies, Biography, Fiction, History, Human Relations, Literature, Literary Criticism, Essays, Mysteries, Nonfiction (General), Parapsychology, Psychology, Psychiatry, Religion - Other, Science Fiction, Fantasy, Self-Help
ISBN Prefix(es): 85-7272
Number of titles published annually: 10 Print
Total Titles: 190 Print
Imprints: Unicornio Azul; Mercuryo Jovem

**MG Editores Associados Ltda**
Rua Itapicuru, 613-7° andar, Perdizes, 05006-000 Sao Paulo-SP
*Tel:* (011) 3872-3322 *Fax:* (011) 3872-7476
*E-mail:* mg@mgeditores.com.br; editor@mgeditores.com.br
*Web Site:* www.gruposummus.com.br/mgeditores/mg_fale.php
*Key Personnel*
Executive: Flavio Gikovate
Subjects: Behavioral Sciences, Education
ISBN Prefix(es): 85-7255

**Ministerio da Marinha Diretoria de Hidrografia Navegacao**
Rua Barao de Jaceguai, s/n Ponta da Areia, 24048-900 Niteroi-RJ
*Tel:* (021) 719-2626 (ext 147) *Fax:* (021) 719-4989
*E-mail:* 01@dhm.mar.mil.sr
*Telex:* 2133858/213220
*Key Personnel*
Bilingual Assistant: Jose Mauro F Lopes
  *E-mail:* 122@bhm.mar.mil.sr
ISBN Prefix(es): 85-7293

**Editora Moderna Ltda+**
Rua Padre Adelino, 758, 03303-904 Sao Paulo-SP
*Tel:* (011) 609-0130 *Fax:* (011) 608-3055
*E-mail:* moderna@moderna.com.br
*Web Site:* www.moderna.com.br
*Key Personnel*
President & Man Dir: Ricardo Arissa Feltre
  *Tel:* (011) 60901369 *E-mail:* ricardo@moderna.com.br
Man Editor: Geraldo Fernandes
Founded: 1968
Subjects: Education, Fiction, Health, Nutrition, History, Literature, Literary Criticism, Essays, Mathematics, Social Sciences, Sociology, Women's Studies
ISBN Prefix(es): 85-16
Total Titles: 1,515 Print; 12 CD-ROM
Subsidiaries: Rio Grande Do Sul
*Branch Office(s)*
Rua Sen Furtado 31, 20270 Rio de Janeiro-RJ

**Modulo Editora e Desenvolvimento Educacional Ltda**
Rua Albano Reis, 1093, Born Retiro, 80520-530 Curitiba-PR
*Tel:* (041) 2530077 *Fax:* (041) 2530103
*E-mail:* moduloed@moduloeditora.com.br
*Web Site:* www.moduloeditora.com.br
*Key Personnel*
Contact: Fausto Luiz Charneski
Founded: 1991
Subjects: Education, Geography, Geology, History, Mathematics, Science (General), Sports, Athletics
ISBN Prefix(es): 85-7397; 85-85764

**Editora Mundo Cristao+**
Rua Antonio Carlos Tacconi 79, 04810-020 Sao Paulo-SP
*Tel:* (011) 5668-1700 *Fax:* (011) 5666-4829
*E-mail:* editora@mundocristao.com.br
*Web Site:* www.mundocristao.com.br
*Key Personnel*
President: Mark L Carpenter
Founded: 1965
Subjects: Biblical Studies, Biography, Child Care & Development, Fiction, Religion - Protestant, Theology
ISBN Prefix(es): 85-7325
Imprints: Nexo; McKids

**Musa Editora Ltda**
Rua Monte Alegre, 1276, 05014-001 Perdizes-SP
*Tel:* (011) 62-2586 *Fax:* (011) 62-2586
*E-mail:* musaeditora@vol.com.br
*Key Personnel*
Executive: Ana Candida Costa
ISBN Prefix(es): 85-85653

**Musimed Edicoes Musicais Importacao E Exportacao Ltda+**
SCRS 505, Bloco A, Loja 65, 70350-510 Brasilia-DF
Mailing Address: CP 09693, Ag Central, 70001-970 Brasilia-DF
*Tel:* (061) 244-9799 *Fax:* (061) 226-0478
*E-mail:* cartas@musimed.com.br
*Web Site:* www.musimed.com.br
*Key Personnel*
Dir: Bohumil Med *E-mail:* bohumil@brnet.com.br
Purchasing Manager: Joselita Soares
Founded: 1984
Specialize in sheet music & music books.
Subjects: Music, Dance
ISBN Prefix(es): 85-7092; 85-85886
Total Titles: 23 Print
*Showroom(s):* SDS Ed Venaneio IV, Sobreloja, loja-14 Brasilia
*Orders to:* MusiMed Edicioes Musicias, SDS Edicioes Vanancio IV, Sobreloja, loja 14 Brasilia, Purchasing Managaer: Joselita Soares

**Companhia Editora Nacional**
Rua Joli, 294, 03016-020 Sao Paulo-SP
*Tel:* (011) 6099-7799 (ext 246) *Fax:* (011) 6694-5338
*Web Site:* www.ibep-nacional.com.br
*Key Personnel*
Editor: Mr Mauro Aristides *E-mail:* mauro@ibep-nacional.com.br
Founded: 1925
ISBN Prefix(es): 85-342
Number of titles published annually: 50 Print
Total Titles: 500 Print
*Parent Company:* Instituto Brasileiro de Edicoes Pedagogicas (IBEP)

**Nexo**, *imprint of* Editora Mundo Cristao

**Livraria Nobel S/A+**
Rua Pedroso Alvarenga, 1046 9 andar, Sao Paulo
  CEP 04531-004
*Tel:* (011) 3933-2822; (011) 3933-2811
  *Fax:* (011) 3218-2833; (011) 3931-3988
*E-mail:* ary@editoranobel.com.br
*Web Site:* www.livnobel.com.br
Founded: 1943
Subjects: Advertising, Agriculture, Animals, Pets,
  Architecture & Interior Design, Biography,
  Business, Cookery, Economics, Gardening,
  Plants, Health, Nutrition, House & Home, Ro-
  mance, Self-Help, Sports, Athletics, Technol-
  ogy, Travel
ISBN Prefix(es): 85-279; 85-213; 85-7553
Number of titles published annually: 80 Print
Total Titles: 230 Print
Imprints: Marco Zero; Studio Nobel
Subsidiaries: Editora Marco Zero; Editora Studio
  Nobel
Distributor for Harper Collins; Heinemann

**Editora Nova Aguilar SA+**
Rua Dona Mariana, 205-Casa 01, Botafogo,
  22280-020 Rio de Janeiro-RJ
*Tel:* (021) 537-7189; (021) 538-1406 *Fax:* (021)
  537-8275
*Telex:* 34695 Enfs *Cable:* AGUILAR
*Key Personnel*
President: Sebastiao Lacerda
Man Dir: Carlos Augusto Lacerda
Founded: 1958
ISBN Prefix(es): 85-210
*Parent Company:* Editora Nova Fronteira SA
*Branch Office(s)*
Ave Pedro Bueno 1509-1511, Jabaquara, 04342
  Sao Paulo-SP

**Editora Nova Alexandria Ltda+**
Rua Dionisio da Costa, 141, 04117-110 Sao
  Paulo-SP
*Tel:* (011) 5571-5637 *Fax:* (011) 5571-5637
*E-mail:* novaalexandria@novaalexandria.com.br
*Web Site:* www.novaalexandria.com.br
*Key Personnel*
Associate: Luiz Baggio-Neto *E-mail:* lbaggio@
  novaalexandria.com.br
Founded: 1992
Subjects: Biography, Cookery, Education, Fiction,
  History, Literature, Literary Criticism, Essays,
  Philosophy, Poetry, Romance, Sports, Athletics
ISBN Prefix(es): 85-7492
Number of titles published annually: 18 Print
Total Titles: 136 Print

**Editora Nova Era,** *imprint of* Distribuidora
  Record de Servicos de Imprensa SA

**Editora Nova Fronteira SA+**
Rua Bambina, 25, 22251-050 Rio de Janeiro-RJ
*Tel:* (021) 25 37 87 70; (021) 22 66 51 84
  *Fax:* (021) 22 86 67 55
*Web Site:* www.novafronteira.com.br
*Key Personnel*
General Dir & International Rights: Carlos Au-
  gusto Lacerda *E-mail:* caml@novafronteira.
  com.br
Foreign Rights Dir: Carlos Barbosa
Sales: Elson M da Rocha
Founded: 1965
Subjects: Art, Astrology, Occult, Astronomy, Bi-
  ography, Biological Sciences, Business, Ed-
  ucation, Fiction, Health, Nutrition, History,
  Language Arts, Linguistics, Literature, Liter-
  ary Criticism, Essays, Mysteries, Natural His-
  tory, Nonfiction (General), Philosophy, Poetry,
  Psychology, Psychiatry, Publishing & Book
  Trade Reference, Regional Interests, Romance,
  Science (General), Self-Help, Social Sciences,
  Sociology, Theology
ISBN Prefix(es): 85-209
Number of titles published annually: 90 Print

Total Titles: 1,200 Print
*Associate Companies:* Lexikon Informatica Ltd

**Editora Objetiva Ltda+**
Rua Cosme Velho, 103, 22241-090 Rio de
  Janeiro-RJ
*Tel:* (021) 2556-7824 *Fax:* (021) 2556-3322
*Web Site:* www.objetiva.com.br
*Key Personnel*
Publisher: Roberto Feith
Foreign Rights Acquisitions Manager: Alessandra
  Blocker *E-mail:* aless.blocker@ibm.net
Subjects: Behavioral Sciences, Biography, Fiction,
  Human Relations, Humor, Nonfiction (Gen-
  eral), Science (General), Self-Help
Number of titles published annually: 60 Print

**Off Set,** *imprint of* Centro de Estudos Juridicosdo
  Para (CEJUP)

**Olho D'Agua Comercio e Servicos Editoriais
Ltda+**
Rua Dr Homem de Melo, 1036, 05007-002 Sao
  Paulo-SP
*Tel:* (011) 2631287 *Fax:* (011) 2631287
*E-mail:* editora@olhodaguo.com.br
*Key Personnel*
Executive: Jorge Claudio Noel Ribeiro, Jr
Founded: 1991
Subjects: Behavioral Sciences, Education, Jour-
  nalism, Literature, Literary Criticism, Essays,
  Psychology, Psychiatry, Social Sciences, Soci-
  ology, Theology
ISBN Prefix(es): 85-85428
Distributed by Distribuidora Loyola

**Oliveira Rocha-Comercio e Servics Ltda
Dialetica+**
Av Bernardino de Campos, 327, cj 24, 04004-050
  Sao Paulo-SP
*Tel:* (011) 2845527; (011) 2886440 *Fax:* (011)
  2845362; (011) 2842096
*E-mail:* dialetic@virtual.net.com.br
*Key Personnel*
Contact: Valdir Oliveira Rocha
Founded: 1995
Subjects: Law
ISBN Prefix(es): 85-86208

**Organizacao Andrei Editora Ltda+**
Rua Conselheiro Nebias, 1071, 01203-002 Sao
  Paulo-SP
*Tel:* (011) 223-5111 *Fax:* (011) 221-0246
*E-mail:* diretoria@editora-andrei.com.br
*Web Site:* www.editora-andrei.com.br
*Key Personnel*
Executive: Edmundo Andrei
Founded: 1955
Subjects: Medicine, Nursing, Dentistry, Veterinary
  Science, Acupuncture, Homeopathy
Number of titles published annually: 30 Print
Total Titles: 650 Print; 3 CD-ROM

**Editora Ortiz SA**
Av Julio de Castilhos, 159 - SI 801, 90030-131
  Porto Alegre-RS
*Tel:* (051) 225-3026 *Fax:* (051) 225-3026
*Key Personnel*
President: Airton Ortiz
Founded: 1982
Subjects: Accounting, Agriculture, Business, Eco-
  nomics, Finance, Management, Marketing, Pub-
  lic Administration
ISBN Prefix(es): 85-85279

**Edit Palavra Magica+**
Rua Americo Brasiliense, 1205/1, Centro, 14015-
  050 Ribeirao Preto-SP
*Tel:* (016) 610-0204 *Fax:* (016) 625-4583
*E-mail:* editora@palavramagica.com.br
*Web Site:* www.palavramagica.com.br

*Key Personnel*
Dir: Galeno Amorim *E-mail:* galeno@
  palavramagica.com.br
Assistant Dir: Mariana Carla Magri
  *E-mail:* mariana@palavramagica.com.br
Man Dir, Financial: Luiz Antonio Ferraro
  *E-mail:* ferraro@palavramagica.com.br
Secretary: Maria Ivone Rodrigues dos Santos
  *E-mail:* ivone@palavramagica.com.br
Founded: 1995
Subjects: Behavioral Sciences, Earth Sciences,
  Human Relations, Regional Interests, Religion
  - Catholic, Religion - Other, Romance, Social
  Sciences, Sociology
ISBN Prefix(es): 85-85997

**Pallas Editora e Distribuidora Ltda+**
Rua Frederico de Albuquerque, 56, 44 Higienopo-
  lis, 21050-840 Rio de Janeiro-RJ
*Tel:* (021) 270-0186 *Fax:* (021) 590-6996; (21)
  5618007
*E-mail:* pallas@alternex.com.br
*Web Site:* www.pallaseditora.com.br
*Key Personnel*
Man Dir: Antonio Carlos Fernandes
Editorial, Rights & Permissions: Cristina Fernan-
  des Warth
Sales: Antonio Carlos Fernandes
Founded: 1975
SNEL - Sindicets Notional des Editores de
  Livros.
Subjects: African American Studies, Anthropol-
  ogy, Art, Biography, Ethnicity, Human Rela-
  tions, Music, Dance, Philosophy, Religion -
  Catholic, Religion - Other, Self-Help, Social
  Sciences, Sociology, Theology, Afro-Brasilian
  religions, culture, history, social sciences
ISBN Prefix(es): 85-347
Number of titles published annually: 30 Print
Total Titles: 200 Print

**Parma,** *imprint of* Global Editora e Distribuidora
  Ltda

**Paulinas Editorial+**
Rua Pedro de Toledo, 164, 04039-000 Sao Paulo-
  SP
*Tel:* (011) 50855199 *Fax:* (011) 50855198
*E-mail:* editora@paulinas.org.br
Subjects: Biblical Studies, Biography, Child Care
  & Development, Communications, Education,
  Human Relations, Psychology, Psychiatry, Re-
  ligion - Catholic, Self-Help, Social Sciences,
  Sociology, Theology
ISBN Prefix(es): 85-356; 85-7311

**Paulus Editora+**
Rua Francisco Cruz, 229, 04117-091 Sao Paulo-
  SP
*Tel:* (011) 50843066; (011) 5757362 *Fax:* (011)
  5703627
*E-mail:* dir.editorial@paulus.org.br
*Web Site:* www.paulus.com.br
*Telex:* 1139464 Pssp *Cable:* PAULINOS
*Key Personnel*
Man Dir, Publicity & Production: Arno Brustolin
Editorial & Rights & Permissions: Zolferino
  Tonon
Sales: A C D'Elboux
Founded: 1931
Bookshops throughout Brazil.
Subjects: Biblical Studies, Education, How-to,
  Music, Dance, Philosophy, Psychology, Psy-
  chiatry, Religion - Catholic, Religion - Other,
  Self-Help, Social Sciences, Sociology, Theol-
  ogy
ISBN Prefix(es): 85-05; 85-349
*Bookshop(s):* Praca da Se 180, Sao Paulo; Rua
  Mexico 111-B, Rio de Janeiro

**Editora Paz e Terra+**
Rua do Triunfo, 177, Sta Ifigenia, 01212-010 Sao
    Paulo-SP
*Tel:* (011) 3337-8399 *Fax:* (011) 223-6290
*E-mail:* vendas@pazeterra.com.br
*Web Site:* www.pazeterra.com.br
*Key Personnel*
General Manager, Sales & Editorial: Fernando
    Gasparian
Production, Publicity & Rights & Permissions:
    Marcus F Gasparian
Founded: 1966
Subjects: Drama, Theater, Government, Political
    Science, Literature, Literary Criticism, Essays,
    Philosophy, Regional Interests, Social Sciences,
    Sociology
ISBN Prefix(es): 85-219
Subsidiaries:
*Bookshop(s):* Livraria Argumento, Rua Oscar
    Freire 608, San Paulo-SP; Rua Dias Ferreira
    199, Rio de Janeiro-RJ; Livraria e Editora
    Livre, Rua Armando Penteado 44, Sao Paulo-
    SP

**Pearson Education Do Brasil**
Rua Emilio Goeldi, 747 Lapa, 05065-110 Sao
    Paulo-SP
*Tel:* (011) 3611 0740 *Fax:* (011) 3611 0444
*E-mail:* firstname.lastname@pearsoned.com.br
*Telex:* 2121799
*Key Personnel*
Interim General Manager/Commercial Dir: Jaime
    Carneiro
Finance Dir: Solange Beletatti
Promotion Manager ELT: Marco Malossi
Marketing Manager ELT: Helena Nagano
Administrative Assistant: Claudia Fisher
Representative, Higher Education: Luiz Henrique
Founded: 1996
Subjects: Accounting, Behavioral Sciences, Bio-
    logical Sciences, Business, Economics, Engi-
    neering (General), Marketing, Technology
ISBN Prefix(es): 85-7054; 85-87675
Number of titles published annually: 20 Print
*Parent Company:* Pearson Plc
Imprints: Addison Wesley; Longman; Prentice
    Hall; Scott Foresman
*Branch Office(s)*
Belo Horizonte, Rua Silva Jardim 235, Sao Paulo
    30150-010
Foreign Rights: Roger Trimer

**Jogos Pedagogicos**, *imprint of* Editora Meca Ltda

**Peninsula**, *imprint of* LDA Editores Ltda

**Editora Perspectiva**
Ave Brigadeiro Luis Antonio, 3025/3035, 01401-
    000 Sao Paulo-SP
*Tel:* (011) 8858388 *Fax:* (011) 3885-8388
*E-mail:* editora@editoraperspectiva.com.br
*Web Site:* www.editoraperspectiva.com.br
*Key Personnel*
Man Dir: Jaco Guinsburg
Founded: 1965
Subjects: Drama, Theater, Economics, Educa-
    tion, History, Human Relations, Music, Dance,
    Philosophy, Psychology, Psychiatry, Religion -
    Other, Social Sciences, Sociology
ISBN Prefix(es): 85-273

**Petit Editora e Distribuidora Ltda+**
Rua Atuai, 383 5 V Esperanca, 03646-000 Sao
    Paulo-SP
*Tel:* (011) 698 4162; (011) 691 7165 *Fax:* (011)
    292 4616
*E-mail:* petit@dialdata.com.br
*Web Site:* www.petit.com.br
*Key Personnel*
Contact: Flavio Machado
Founded: 1982

Subjects: Religion - Other
ISBN Prefix(es): 85-7253

**Pia Sociedade Filhas De Sao Paulo**, see
    Paulinas Editorial

**Editora Pini Ltda**
Rua Anhaia, 964, 01130-900 Sao Paulo-SP
*Tel:* (011) 224-8811 *Fax:* (011) 224-0314; (011)
    224-8541
*E-mail:* construcao@pini.com.br
*Web Site:* www.piniweb.com
*Telex:* 11-37803
*Key Personnel*
Contact: Ricardo Bertagnon
Founded: 1948
ISBN Prefix(es): 85-7266
*Bookshop(s):* R Vitoria, 486/496, 01210 Sao
    Paulo-SP; Rua Gentil de Moura, 128, 04278
    Sao Paulo-SP

**Livraria Pioneira Editora/Enio Matheus
    Guazzelli e Cia Ltd+**
Praca Dirceu de Lima 313, 02515-050 Sao Paulo-
    SP
*Tel:* (011) 858-3199 *Fax:* (011) 858-0443
*E-mail:* pioneira@virtual-net.com.br
*Key Personnel*
Editor & Rights & Permissions: Liliana Guazzelli
Dir, Finance: Roberto Guazzelli
Founded: 1960
Subjects: Accounting, Advertising, Agriculture,
    Architecture & Interior Design, Astrology, Oc-
    cult, Behavioral Sciences, Business, Computer
    Science, Economics, Education, History, Lan-
    guage Arts, Linguistics, Management, Mys-
    teries, Photography, Psychology, Psychiatry,
    Social Sciences, Sociology
ISBN Prefix(es): 85-221
*Associate Companies:* Disal, Distribuidores Asso-
    ciados de Livros Ltda

**Prentice Hall**, *imprint of* Pearson Education Do
    Brasil

**Casa Editora Presbiteriana SC+**
Rua Miguel Telles Junior, 382/394, Cambuci,
    01540-040 Sao Paulo-SP
*Tel:* (011) 270-7099 *Fax:* (011) 279-1255
*E-mail:* cep@cep.org.br
*Web Site:* www.cep.org.br
*Key Personnel*
Editor: Claudio A B Marra
Founded: 1948
Subjects: History, Religion - Other
ISBN Prefix(es): 85-86886

**Primor Editora Ltda**, see Grafica Editora Primor
    Ltda

**Editora Primor Ltda+**
Rodovia Presidente Dutra 2611, 21535-500 Rio
    de Janeiro-RJ
*Tel:* (021) 4744966
*Telex:* 22150 *Cable:* Primor
Subjects: Fiction, Humor, Nonfiction (General)
ISBN Prefix(es): 85-7024
Subsidiaries: Grafica Editora Primor SA

**Prol**, *imprint of* Global Editora e Distribuidora
    Ltda

**Proton Editora Ltda**
Ave Reboucas 3819, 05401-450 Sao Paulo-SP
*Tel:* (011) 2103616; (011) 8147922; (011)
    8159708 *Fax:* (011) 8159920
*E-mail:* sitaenk@uol.com.br
*Key Personnel*
President: Norberto R Keppe
Man Dir: Claudia S Pacheco

Founded: 1976
Subjects: Medicine, Nursing, Dentistry, Psychol-
    ogy, Psychiatry, Science (General)
ISBN Prefix(es): 85-7072; 85-85001

**Ediouro Publicacoes, SA+**
Rua Nova Jerusalem, 345, 21042-230 Rio de
    Janeiro-RJ
*Tel:* (021) 5606122 *Fax:* (011) 55893300
*E-mail:* ediourolivrosp@openlink.com.br; livros@
    ediouro.com.br
*Web Site:* www.ediouro.com.br
*Key Personnel*
President: Jorge Carneiro
Editor: Paul Christoph, Jr
Subjects: Animals, Pets, Biography, How-to, Jour-
    nalism, Literature, Literary Criticism, Essays,
    Mysteries, Science Fiction, Fantasy
ISBN Prefix(es): 85-00

**Editora de Publicacoes Medicas Ltda**
Rua do Russel, 404-grs 901/2-parte, 22210 Rio de
    Janeiro-RJ
*Tel:* (021) 2654047; (021) 2253516 *Fax:* (021)
    2613749
*Key Personnel*
Man Dir: Jose Maria de Sousa e Melo
Editorial: Dr Almir Lourenco da Fonseca
Sales & Publicity: Jose Ayrton de Souza Avila
Production: Edson de Oliveira Vilar
Founded: 1959
Subjects: Medicine, Nursing, Dentistry
*Branch Office(s)*
Rua Borges Lagoa 426, Sao Paulo
*Book Club(s):* Club do Livro Cientifico

**Qualitymark Editora Ltda+**
R Teixeira Junior, 441, Sao Cristovao, 20921-400
    Rio de Janeiro-RJ
*Tel:* (021) 3860-8422 *Fax:* (021) 3860-8424
*E-mail:* quality@qualitymark.com.br
*Web Site:* www.qualitymark.com.br
*Key Personnel*
Contact: Saidual Rahman Mahomed
Founded: 1991
Promote events dealing with seminars & lectures.
Subjects: Career Development, Economics, Edu-
    cation, Environmental Studies, Finance, Labor,
    Industrial Relations, Management, Medicine,
    Nursing, Dentistry, Nonfiction (General), Public
    Administration, Self-Help
ISBN Prefix(es): 85-7303; 85-85360

**Raboni Editora Ltda+**
Rua Sampaio Vidal, 629, Jardim Chapadao,
    13090-070 Campinas-SP
Mailing Address: CP 140, 13001-970 Campinas-
    SP
*Tel:* (019) 32428433 *Fax:* (019) 32428505
*E-mail:* raboni@raboni.com.br
*Web Site:* www.raboni.com.br
*Key Personnel*
Dir: Stella Castro *E-mail:* stella@raboni.com.br
Contact: Regis Castro
Founded: 1991
Publish & distribute Catholic books worldwide.
Subjects: Religion - Catholic
ISBN Prefix(es): 85-7345

**Editora Record**, *imprint of* Distribuidora Record
    de Servicos de Imprensa SA

**Distribuidora Record de Servicos de Imprensa
    SA+**
Rua Argentina 171, Sao Cristovao, 20921-380
    Rio de Janeiro-RJ
*Tel:* (021) 2585-2000 *Fax:* (021) 2580-4911
*E-mail:* record@record.com.br
*Web Site:* www.record.com.br
*Key Personnel*
Chairman, President & General Manager: Sergio
    C Machado

Vice President, Operations: Sonia M Sardim, Jr
Editorial Dir: Luciana Villas Boas
Founded: 1942
Subjects: Biography, Business, Fiction, History,
Nonfiction (General), Philosophy
ISBN Prefix(es): 85-01; 85-20
Number of titles published annually: 300 Print
Total Titles: 2,004 Print
Imprints: Editora Civilizacao Brasileira; Editora
Nova Era; Editora Record; Editora Rosa dos
Tempos
Subsidiaries: Editora Bertrand Brazil Ltd; Editora
BestSeller Ltda; Editora Jose Olympio Ltd
*Branch Office(s)*
Paraiso 139, 10 andar, 04103-000 Sao Paulo-SP,
Contact: Ms Francinete Zerbetto *Tel:* (011)
3286-0802 *Toll Free Tel:* (011) 0800-212380

**Rede Das Artes Industria, Comercio,
Importacaoe Exportacao Ltda+**
Rua Graham Bell 355, 04737-030 Sao Paulo-SP
*Tel:* (011) 246-5565 *Fax:* (011) 246-5565
*Key Personnel*
Executive: Andre Boccato *E-mail:* boccato@uol.
com.br
Founded: 1993
Subjects: Art, Cookery, Gardening, Plants, Health,
Nutrition, Photography, Sports, Athletics,
Travel, Wine & Spirits
ISBN Prefix(es): 85-85657

**Editora Resenha Tributaria Ltda**
Rua Quatinga, 12, 04140-020 Sao Paulo-SP
*Tel:* (011) 5772822 *Fax:* (011) 5772526
*Key Personnel*
Man Dir: Vaner Bicego
Editorial Dir: Valdyr Rezende Xavier
Commercial Dir: Jose Figueira da Cruz
Subjects: Education, Law
ISBN Prefix(es): 85-236

**Editora Revan Ltda+**
Av Paulo de Frontin, 163, Rio Comprido, 20260-
010 Rio de Janeiro-RJ
*Tel:* (021) 25027495 *Fax:* (021) 22736873
*E-mail:* editor@revan.com.br
*Web Site:* www.revan.com.br
*Key Personnel*
Contact: Dr Ing Renato Guimaraes-Cupertino
Founded: 1983
Subjects: Anthropology, Art, Behavioral Sciences,
Biography, Computer Science, Criminology,
Fiction, Military Science, Science (General),
Self-Help, Social Sciences, Sociology
ISBN Prefix(es): 85-7106
Number of titles published annually: 40 Print
Total Titles: 300 Print

**Livraria Editora Revinter Ltda+**
Rua do Matoso 170, Tijuca, 20270-131 Rio de
Janeiro-RJ
*Tel:* (021) 2563-9700 *Fax:* (021) 2563-9701
*E-mail:* livraria@revinter.com.br
*Web Site:* www.revinter.com.br
*Key Personnel*
Contact: Sergio Duarte Dortas
Subjects: Medicine, Nursing, Dentistry
ISBN Prefix(es): 85-7309
Distributor for Churchill Livingstone; Lippincott;
Mosby; W B Saunders; Georg Thieme

**RHJ Livros Ltda+**
Rua Cuiaba, 415, Prado, 30410-140 Belo
Horizonte-MG
*Tel:* (031) 3334-1566 *Fax:* (031) 3332-5823
*Web Site:* www.editorarhj.com.br
*Key Personnel*
Dir: Rafael Borges de Andrade
Founded: 1974
Membership(s): SNEL-457.

Subjects: Literature, Literary Criticism, Essays
ISBN Prefix(es): 85-7153

**Editora Rideel Ltda+**
Alameda Afonso Schmidt No 879, Santa Terez-
inha, 02450-001 Sao Paulo-SP
*Tel:* (011) 6977-8344 *Fax:* (011) 6976-7415
*E-mail:* rideel@virtual-net.com.br
*Web Site:* www.rideel.com.br
*Key Personnel*
Man Dir, Editorial: Italo Amadio
Production: Roberto Amadio
Founded: 1970
Subjects: Cookery, History, Language Arts, Lin-
guistics, Medicine, Nursing, Dentistry, Religion
- Other
ISBN Prefix(es): 85-339
*Bookshop(s):* Al Afonso Schmidt, No 877, Sta
Terezinha, 02450-001 Sao Paulo-SP

**Livraria Roca Ltda+**
Rua Dr Cesario Mota Jr 73, 01221-020 Sao
Paulo-SP
*Tel:* (011) 221-8609; (011) 221-6814 *Fax:* (011)
3331-8653
*E-mail:* edroca@uol.com.br
*Web Site:* www.editoraroca.com.br
*Key Personnel*
Contact: Casimiro Paya Piqueres
Founded: 1973
Subjects: Medicine, Nursing, Dentistry, Veterinary
Science
ISBN Prefix(es): 85-7241
*Associate Companies:* Livraria Paya Ltda

**Editora Rocco Ltda+**
Rua Rodrigo Silva 26-4 andar, 20011-040 Rio de
Janeiro-RJ
*Tel:* (021) 2507-2000 *Fax:* (021) 2507-2244
*E-mail:* rocco@rocco.com.br
*Web Site:* www.rocco.com.br
*Key Personnel*
Contact: Paulo Roberto Rocco
Founded: 1975
Subjects: Anthropology, Biography, Communi-
cations, Management, Science (General), Self-
Help, Social Sciences, Sociology, Women's
Studies
ISBN Prefix(es): 85-325
*Warehouse:* Av Brasil, 10-600, 21012-351 Rio de
Janeiro-RJ

**Editora Rosa dos Tempos**, *imprint of*
Distribuidora Record de Servicos de Imprensa
SA

**Salamandra Consultoria Editorial SA+**
Av Nilo Pecanha 155, Grupo 301, 20027-900 Rio
de Janeiro-RJ
*Tel:* (021) 2406306 *Fax:* (021) 2404775; (021)
5331622
*E-mail:* salprod@openlink.com.br
*Key Personnel*
Contact: Sir Geraldo Jordao Pereira
Founded: 1982
Subjects: Art
ISBN Prefix(es): 85-281

**Livraria Santos Editora Comercio e
Importacao Ltda+**
Rua Dona Brigida, 691/701, 04111-081 Sao
Paulo-SP
*Tel:* (011) 574-1200 *Fax:* (011) 573-8774
*E-mail:* editorasantos@terra.com.br
*Key Personnel*
Contact: Rui Santos
Founded: 1974
Subjects: Medicine, Nursing, Dentistry, Veterinary
Science
ISBN Prefix(es): 85-7288

Number of titles published annually: 60 Print
Total Titles: 510 Print

**Editora Santuario+**
Rua Padre Claro Monteiro 342, 12570-000 Sao
Paulo-SP
*Tel:* (012) 3104-2000 *Fax:* (012) 565 2141
*E-mail:* vendas@redemptor.com.br
*Web Site:* www.redemptor.com.br
*Key Personnel*
Administrative Manager: Padre Luis Rodrigues
Batista
Founded: 1900
Specialize in graphics.
Subjects: Literature, Literary Criticism, Essays,
Religion - Catholic
ISBN Prefix(es): 85-7200; 85-7265
*Parent Company:* Congregacao do Santissimo Re-
dentor
*Bookshop(s):* Praca Nossa Senhora Aparecida
292, Aparecida-SP

**Sao Paulo Editora**, *imprint of* Global Editora e
Distribuidora Ltda

**Saraiva SA, Livreiros Editores+**
Ave Marques de Sao Vicente 1697, 01139-904
Sao Paulo-SP
*Tel:* (011) 861-3344 *Fax:* (011) 861-3308
*E-mail:* diretoria.editora@editorasaraiva.com.br
*Web Site:* www.editorasaraiva.com.br
*Telex:* 1126789 *Cable:* ACADEMICA
*Key Personnel*
President: Jorge Eduardo Saraiva
Man Dir: Ruy Mendes Gono1alves; Jose Luiz M
A Prosper; Wander Soares
Editorial Dir, Education: Antonio Alexandre Fac-
cioli
Editorial Dir, Law: Juarez de Oliveira
Sales Dir: Nilson Lepera
Founded: 1914
17 Branches in Sao Paulo.
Subjects: Accounting, Business, Economics, Edu-
cation, Finance, Law, Management, Marketing,
Mathematics, Philosophy, Psychology, Psychia-
try, Securities
ISBN Prefix(es): 85-02
Subsidiaries: Saraiva Data-Informatica
*Branch Office(s)*
Ave Marechal Rondon 2231, Rio de Janeiro-RJ
Rua Celia de Souza 571, Belo Horizonte
Ave Princesa Isabel 1555, Curitiba
Ave Chicago 307, Porto Alegre

**Sarvier - Editora de Livros Medicos Ltda**
Rua Dr Amancio de Carvalho 459, 04012-090
Sao Paulo-SP
*Tel:* (011) 571-4570 *Fax:* (011) 571-3439
*Key Personnel*
Man Dir: Fernando Silva Xavier
Founded: 1965
Subjects: Medicine, Nursing, Dentistry
ISBN Prefix(es): 85-7378

**Karin Schindler Representante de Direitos
Autorais**
CP 19051, 04505-970 Sao Paulo-SP
*Tel:* (011) 241-9177 *Fax:* (011) 241-9077
*Key Personnel*
Executive: Karin Schindler *E-mail:* kschind@
terra.com.br

**Editora Scipione Ltda+**
Praca Carlos Gomes, 46, 01501-040 Sao Paulo-
SP
*Tel:* (011) 2392255 *Fax:* (011) 31053526
*E-mail:* info@scipione.com.br
*Web Site:* www.scipione.com.br
*Key Personnel*
General Dir: Luis Esteves Sallum
General Marketing: Maria Jose Rosolino

General Editorial: Aurelio Goncalves Filho
Founded: 1983
Specialize in books pre-school to second grade &
  also in technical & professional books.
Membership(s): Brazilian Book Association; Na-
  tional Book Foundation for Children & Juve-
  niles.
Subjects: Astronomy, Biological Sciences, Chem-
  istry, Chemical Engineering, Education, En-
  vironmental Studies, Fiction, Geography, Ge-
  ology, History, Literature, Literary Criticism,
  Essays, Mathematics, Mysteries, Nonfiction
  (General), Physics, Religion - Other, Romance,
  Science (General)
ISBN Prefix(es): 85-262
*Branch Office(s)*
S P R Teodoro da Silva, 1004 Rio de Janeiro-RJ
Av Visconde de Suassuna, 634 Recife-PE
Rua da Independecia, 21/13, Salvador-BA
Rua Gago Coutinho, 238, Lapa, Sao Paulo-SP
Distributor for Allca XX/Scipione Culture - Col-
  lection Archivos (South America)
*Showroom(s):* Rua Fagundes, 01508-030 Sao
  Paulo-SP
*Warehouse:* Via BR 116, 84 - km 291, 6 -
  Itapecerica da Serra, Sao Paulo-SP

**Scott Foresman**, *imprint of* Pearson Education
  Do Brasil

**Seculo XXI Editora e Comercio de Livros**
Rua Marcos Moreira, 119, Sala 201, 91350-040
  Porto Alegre-RS
*Tel:* (051) 3614459 *Fax:* (051) 3614459
*E-mail:* sewloxxi@poa-online.com.br
*Key Personnel*
Contact: Carlos Mauricio Igreja do Prado
Founded: 1993
ISBN Prefix(es): 85-86371

**Selecoes Eletronicas Editora Ltda+**
Ladeira Do Faria 23, 20221-380 Rio de Janeiro-
  RJ
*Tel:* (021) 2232442 *Fax:* (021) 2638840
*E-mail:* an-ep@pobox.com
*Key Personnel*
Man Dir: Maria B A Penna
Editorial: Gilberto A Penna, Jr
Publicity: Helio N Santos
Founded: 1960
Subjects: Computer Science, Electronics, Electri-
  cal Engineering, Microcomputers, Technology
ISBN Prefix(es): 85-7037
*Associate Companies:* Antenna Edicoes Tecnicas
  Ltda

**Selinunte Editora Ltda+**
Ave Miguel Stefano 183 Cj 01, 04301-010 Sao
  Paulo-SP
*Tel:* (011) 2760318
*Key Personnel*
Editorial Dir: Roberto Wilson
Administrative Dir, Financial: Arnaldo Majer
Founded: 1987
Membership(s): The Brazilian House of Books.
Subjects: Literature, Literary Criticism, Essays
ISBN Prefix(es): 85-85538

**SELTRON**, see Selecoes Eletronicas Editora Ltda

**Siciliano SA+**
Ave Raimundo Pereira de Magalhaes 3305,
  05145-200 Sao Paulo-SP
*Tel:* (011) 36494634; (011) 8319911 *Fax:* (011)
  8328616
*Telex:* 1180677
*Key Personnel*
Contact: Oswaldo Siciliano
Founded: 1952
Subjects: Literature, Literary Criticism, Essays

ISBN Prefix(es): 85-267
Divisions: Editorial, Livraria, Distribuidora de
  revistas

**Editora Sinodal+**
Rua Amadeo Rossi 467, 93001-970 Sao
  Leopoldo-RS
Mailing Address: CP 11, 93001-970 Sao
  Leopoldo-RS
*Tel:* (051) 590-2366 *Fax:* (051) 590-2664
*E-mail:* editora@editorasinodal.com.br
*Web Site:* www.editorasinodal.com.br
*Telex:* 511219 Xpsl *Cable:* SINODAL
*Key Personnel*
General Dir: Eloy Teckemeier *E-mail:* diretor@
  editorasinodal.com.br
Publishing Manager: Joao Artur M da Silva
  *E-mail:* editor@editorasinodal.com.br
Manager, Production: Silvio J dos Santos
  *E-mail:* grafica@editorasinodal.com.br
Manager, Vendas: Asciepiades Pomme
  *E-mail:* gerentedevendas@editorasinodal.com.br
Founded: 1949
Subjects: Education, Music, Dance, Religion -
  Other, Social Sciences, Sociology, Theology
ISBN Prefix(es): 85-233
*Parent Company:* Instituicao Sinodal de Assisten-
  cia, Educacao e Cultura (ISAEC)
*Associate Companies:* Colegio Sinodal
Subsidiaries: Escola Superior de Teologia
*Showroom(s):* Rua Buenos Aires, 123 Sao Paulo-
  SP
*Bookshop(s):* Editora Sinodal-Livraria; Livraria
  Volante

**Sobrindes Linha Grafica E Editora Ltda+**
Sig Sul Quadra 2 Lote 460, 70610-400 Brasilia-
  DF
*Tel:* (061) 2247778; (061) 2247706; (061)
  2247756 *Fax:* (061) 2241895
*E-mail:* linhagrafica@conectanet.com.br
Subjects: Fiction, History, Journalism, Religion -
  Other
ISBN Prefix(es): 85-7238

**Sociedade Distribuidora de Livros Ltda
(Sodilivro)+**
Rua Sa Freire 36/40, Parte, Sao Cristovao, 20930-
  430 Rio de Janeiro-RJ
*Tel:* (021) 580-1168; (021) 580-6230 *Fax:* (021)
  580-9955
*Key Personnel*
Executive: Reynaldo Max Paul Bluhm
ISBN Prefix(es): 85-215
*Parent Company:* Ao Livro Tecnico Ind e Com
  Ltda

**Spala Editora Ltda**
Rua Lauro Muller, 116-31 Andar S1 3101,
  22290-160 Rio de Janeiro-RJ
*Tel:* (021) 542-9995 *Fax:* (021) 542-4738
*Telex:* (021) 2664093
*Key Personnel*
Contact: Luis Fernando Freire
Founded: 1974
Subjects: Architecture & Interior Design, Art, Bi-
  ography
ISBN Prefix(es): 85-7048
Subsidiaries: Spala Publicidade; Spala Comunica-
  coes

**Studio Nobel**, *imprint of* Livraria Nobel S/A

**Livraria Sulina Editora+**
Av Borges de Medeiros 1030-1036, 90000 Porto
  Alegre-RS
Mailing Address: CP 357, 90000 Porto Alegre
*Tel:* (051) 254765; (051) 250287
*E-mail:* sulina@sulina.com.br *Cable:* ZIPASUL
*Key Personnel*
President: Vilson Nailon Noen

Editor: Luis Gomes
Founded: 1946
Subjects: Law, Psychology, Psychiatry, Science
  (General)
ISBN Prefix(es): 85-205
*Parent Company:* Organizacao Sulina de Repre-
  sentacoes SA, Rua Cel Gennino 290, 90010-
  350 Porto Alegre, RS
Subsidiaries: Editora Sulina
*Showroom(s):* Rua Deuetrio Ribeiro, 990 202
  Porta Alegre
*Bookshop(s):* Livraria Sulina, Rua Riachuelo,
  1218 Porta Alegre

**Summus Editorial Ltda+**
Rua Itapicuru 613 7° andar, 05006-000 Perdizes-
  SP
*Tel:* (011) 38723322 *Fax:* (011) 38727476
*E-mail:* summus@summus.com.br
*Web Site:* www.summus.com.br
*Key Personnel*
Dir: Raul Wassermann
Founded: 1974
Subjects: Advertising, Behavioral Sciences, Busi-
  ness, Communications, Education, Film, Video,
  Human Relations, Journalism, Marketing, Mu-
  sic, Dance, Psychology, Psychiatry, Radio, TV,
  Self-Help, Sports, Athletics, Women's Studies
ISBN Prefix(es): 85-323

**Edicoes Tabajara**
Rua dos Andradas 1774, 90000 Porto Alegre-RS
Mailing Address: CP 1918, 90000 Porto Alegre-
  RS
*Tel:* (0512) 241073; (0512) 247724
*Key Personnel*
Assistant Manager: Maria Azambuja
Subjects: Drama, Theater, Education, Language
  Arts, Linguistics, Mathematics, Science (Gen-
  eral), Social Sciences, Sociology
*Branch Office(s)*
Rua Santa Ifigenia 72, Sao Paulo

**Talento Publicacoes Editora e Grafica Ltda**
Rua Desembargador Joaquim Celidonio 33,
  01413-060 Sao Paulo-SP
*Tel:* (011) 3816-1718 *Fax:* (011) 2823752
*E-mail:* talento@talento.com.br
*Web Site:* www.talento.com.br
*Key Personnel*
Contact: Robert Henry Lennard Seadon
Subjects: Advertising, Communications
ISBN Prefix(es): 85-85062

**Livros Tecnicos e Cientificos Editora Ltda**, see
  LTC-Livros Tecnicos e Cientificos Editora S/A

**Temos Grafica Propria**, *imprint of* Editora
  Betania S/C

**Thex Editora e Distribuidora Ltda+**
Rua da Lapa 180, Conj 804/806, 20021-180 Rio
  de Janeiro-RJ
*Tel:* (021) 2221-4458 *Fax:* (021) 2252-9338
  *Fax on Demand:* (021) 252-9338
*E-mail:* atendimento@thexeditora.com.br
*Web Site:* www.thexeditora.com.br
*Key Personnel*
International Rights: Thex Correa da Silva
  *E-mail:* thex@domain.com.br
Founded: 1992
Subjects: Earth Sciences, Economics, Education,
  Fiction, Human Relations, Literature, Literary
  Criticism, Essays, Marketing, Mysteries, Po-
  etry, Self-Help, Social Sciences, Sociology
ISBN Prefix(es): 85-85575
Number of titles published annually: 10 Print
Total Titles: 50 Print

**34 Literatura S/C Ltda+**
Rua Hungria, 592, 01455-000 Sao Paulo-SP

*Tel:* (011) 3816-6777 *Fax:* (011) 3816-0078
*E-mail:* editora34@uol.com.br
*Key Personnel*
Contact: Beatriz Bracher
Founded: 1992
Subjects: Anthropology, Drama, Theater, Fiction, Literature, Literary Criticism, Essays, Music, Dance, Philosophy, Poetry, Romance, Science Fiction, Fantasy, Technology
ISBN Prefix(es): 85-85490; 85-7326
*Branch Office(s)*
Rua Massaca, 276 Alto de Pinheiros, 05465-050 Sao Paulo-SP *Tel:* (011) 2609738 *Fax:* (011) 8321041

**Totalidade Editora Ltda+**
Rua Eng Alcides Barbosa 29, Jardim America, 01430-010 Sao Paulo-SP
*Tel:* (011) 3064 3688 *Fax:* (011) 3081 9503
*E-mail:* totail@terra.com.br
*Web Site:* www.totalidade.com.br
*Key Personnel*
Contact: Elisa Guerra Malta Campos
Founded: 1989
Membership(s): Brazilian House of Books, National Syndication of Book Publishers, Astrological-Psychological Institute, English Huber School of Astrology, Seven Ray Institute & University of the Seven Rays & Meditation Mount.
Subjects: Art, Astrology, Occult, Psychology, Psychiatry, Self-Help
ISBN Prefix(es): 85-85293

**Triom Centro de Estudos Marina e Martin Hawey Editorial e Comercial Ltda+**
Rua Aracari, 218, 01453-020 Sao Paulo-SP
*Tel:* (011) 3168-8380 *Fax:* (011) 3845-0966
*E-mail:* info@triom.com.br
*Web Site:* www.triom.com.br
*Key Personnel*
Contact: Ruth Cunha-Cintra
Founded: 1991
Bookstore, publishing house.
Subjects: Alternative, Astrology, Occult, Music, Dance, Women's Studies
ISBN Prefix(es): 85-85464
Number of titles published annually: 5 Print
Total Titles: 40 Print; 2 Audio

**Editora UNESP+**
Praca Da Se, 108, 01001-900 Sao Paulo-SP
*Tel:* (011) 3242-7171 *Fax:* (011) 3242-7172
*E-mail:* feu@editora.unesp.br
*Web Site:* www.editora.unesp.br
*Key Personnel*
Dir: Jose Castilho Marques *E-mail:* castilho@editora.unesp.br
Executive Editor: Jezio H B Gutierre *E-mail:* jezio@editora.unesp.br
Founded: 1987
Membership(s): Camara Brasileira do Livro; Associacao Brasileira das Editoras Universitarias; Associacao Brasileira de Direitos Reprograficos; Asociacion de Editoriales de America Latina y el Caribe.
Subjects: Anthropology, Education, Government, Political Science, History, Philosophy, Psychology, Psychiatry, Social Sciences, Sociology
ISBN Prefix(es): 85-7139
Number of titles published annually: 100 Print
*Parent Company:* State University of Sao Paulo
*Bookshop(s):* Alameda Santos, 647, 01419-901 Sao Paulo-SP, Contact: Sandra Pedro
*Tel:* (011) 252 0630 *Fax:* (011) 252 0631
*E-mail:* livraria@editora.unesp.br

**Unicornio Azul**, *imprint of* Editora Mercuryo Ltda

**Editora Universidade de Brasilia**
SCS Quadra 2, Bloco C, No 78, 2° andar, Ed OK, 70300-500 Brasilia-DF
*Tel:* (061) 226-6874 *Fax:* (061) 323-1017
*E-mail:* editora@unb.br
*Web Site:* www.editora.unb.br
*Telex:* 611083 Unbs *Cable:* UNIVERBRASILIA EDITORA
*Key Personnel*
Chairman: Antonio A Briquet de Lemos
President: Alexandre Lima
Editorial Dir & Rights & Permissions: Airton Lugarinho
Production: Elmano Rodrigues Pinheiro
Founded: 1962
Subjects: Government, Political Science, Human Relations, Physical Sciences, Social Sciences, Sociology
ISBN Prefix(es): 85-230
*Branch Office(s)*
Escritorio de Representacao da Universidade de Brasilia, Ave Presidente Vargas 542 - 1309, 20210 Rio de Janeiro-RJ *Tel:* (021) 2636959
Rua Joao Adolfo 118 - 6° andar - sala 608, 01050 Sao Paulo-SP *Tel:* (011) 321413
*Bookshop(s):* SCS, Ed Anapolis, 70300 Brasilia-DF
*Book Club(s):* Clube do Livro da Universidade de Brasilia
*Warehouse:* Subsolo ICC-SUL, CP 04551, 70919 Brasilia-DF

**Editora da Universidade de Sao Paulo+**
Ave Prof Luciano Gualberto Travessau 374, 6 andar, 05508-900 Sao Paulo-SP
*Tel:* (011) 8184160; (011) 8138837 *Fax:* (011) 221-6988
*E-mail:* edusp@edu.usp.br
*Telex:* 36950 *Cable:* RUSPAULO
*Key Personnel*
President: Sergio Miceli Pessoa De Barros
Chairman: Heitor Ferraz
Publishing Dir: Plinio Martins Filho
Founded: 1962
Specialize in academic text.
Subjects: Anthropology, Art, Literature, Literary Criticism, Essays, Medicine, Nursing, Dentistry, Philosophy, Science (General), Social Sciences, Sociology
ISBN Prefix(es): 85-314
*Bookshop(s):* Antigo Predio da Reitoria, Avenida Prof Luciano Gualberto, Travessa J, n 374, Cidade Universitaria, 05508 Sao Paulo-SP; Centro de Convivencia da Reitoria, Rua da Reitoria, 74, Cidade Universitaria, 05508 Sao Paulo-SP; Escola Politecnica Avenida Prof Almeida Prado, Travessa 2, n 128, 05508 Sao Paulo; Escola Superior de Agricultura "Luis de Queiroz", Avenida Padua Dias, n 11, 13400 Piracicaba-SP; Faculdade de Educacao, Avenida da Universidade, Travessa 11, n 251, Cidade Universitaria, 05508 Sao Paulo; Faculdade de Medicina de Ribeirao Preto Predio da Biblioteca, Avenida Bandeirantes, n 3900, 14049 Ribeirao Preto-SP; FFLCH, Departamento de Historia e Geografia, Avenida Prof Lineu Prestes, n 338, Cidade Universitaria, 05508 Sao Paulo-SP; Instituto de Biociencias, Rua do Matao, 277; Instituto de Ciencias Biomedicas, Avenida Prof Lineu Prestes, 1524, Cidade Universitaria, 05508 Sao Paulo-SP

**Editora Universidade Federal do Rio de Janeiro+**
Forum de Ciencia e Cultura Avenida Pasteur, 250-Urca, Praia Vermelha, 22290-902 Rio de Janeiro-RJ
*Tel:* (021) 2542-7646 *Fax:* (021) 2295-0346
*E-mail:* livraria@editora.ufrj.br
*Web Site:* www.editora.ufrj.br; www.ufrj.br *Cable:* 22924
*Key Personnel*
Contact: Heloisa Buarque de Hollanda

Founded: 1986
Subjects: Anthropology, Architecture & Interior Design, Art, Economics, Education, History, Language Arts, Linguistics, Library & Information Sciences, Management, Physical Sciences, Social Sciences, Sociology
ISBN Prefix(es): 85-7108

**Livraria e Editora Universitaria de Direito Ltda**
Rua Benjamin Constant, 171, 1, andar, 01005-000 Sao Paulo-SP
*Tel:* (011) 3105-6374 *Fax:* (011) 3104-0317
*Key Personnel*
Man Dir, Production: Armando Luiz Almeida Martins
Editorial Dir: Pedro Gellindo Sommavilla
Sales Dir: Armando des Santos Mesquita Martins
Founded: 1968
Subjects: Law
ISBN Prefix(es): 85-7456

**Fundacao Getulio Vargas+**
Praia de Botafogo, 190-14° andar-Botafog, 22250-900 Rio de Janeiro-RJ
*Tel:* (021) 2559-5542; (021) 2559-5543; (021) 2559-5544 *Toll Free Tel:* 800-217777 *Fax:* (021) 2559-5532
*E-mail:* editora@fgv.br
*Web Site:* www.fgv.br
*Telex:* 36811 *Cable:* FUGEVAR
*Key Personnel*
Man Dir: Francisco de Castro Azevedo
Sales Dir: Juarez Nery de Souza
Subjects: Accounting, Business, Economics, Education, Marketing, Psychology, Psychiatry, Public Administration, Social Sciences, Sociology
ISBN Prefix(es): 85-225

**Editora Vecchi SA**
Rua do Resende 144, Esplanda do Senado, 20234 Rio de Janeiro-RJ
*Tel:* (021) 2444522
*Telex:* 32756 *Cable:* Vekieditora
*Key Personnel*
Dir-Superintendent: Delman Bonatto
Founded: 1913
Subjects: Astrology, Occult, Biography, Cookery, Philosophy, Religion - Other

**Editora Verbo Ltda**
Av Antonio Augusto Aguiar 148-6°, 1069 019 Lisbon
*Tel:* (021) 380 1100 *Fax:* (021) 386-5397
*E-mail:* verbo@virtual-net.com.br
*Web Site:* www.editorialverbo.pt *Cable:* Verbo
Founded: 1966
Subjects: Art, Education, Geography, Geology, History, Psychology, Psychiatry, Religion - Other, Social Sciences, Sociology
ISBN Prefix(es): 85-7230

**Editora Vida Crista Ltda+**
R Carlos Meira, 396 - Penha, 03605-010 Sao Paulo-SP
*Tel:* (011) 6647-7788 *Toll Free Tel:* 800-11-5074 *Fax:* (011) 6647-7125
*E-mail:* editora@vidacrista.com.br
*Web Site:* www.vidacrista.com.br
*Key Personnel*
Executive: Alan Leite
Founded: 1977
Subjects: Religion - Protestant
ISBN Prefix(es): 85-7163

**Editora Vigilia Ltda**
Rua Felipe dos Santos 508, Lourdes, 30180-160 Belo Horizonte-MG
*Tel:* (031) 3372744; (031) 3372363 *Fax:* (031) 3372834
Founded: 1960

Subjects: Education, Philosophy
ISBN Prefix(es): 85-259

**Vozes Editora Ltda**
Rua Frei Luis, 100, 25689-900 Petropolis-RJ
*Tel:* (024) 237 5112 *Fax:* (024) 231 4676
*E-mail:* editorial@vozes.com.br
*Web Site:* www.vozes.com.br *Cable:* VOZES
*Key Personnel*
Man Dir: Stephan Ottenbreit
Founded: 1901
Subjects: Communications, Language Arts, Linguistics, Philosophy, Psychology, Psychiatry, Public Administration, Religion - Other, Social Sciences, Sociology
ISBN Prefix(es): 85-326
*Branch Office(s)*
Rua Sergope, 120 Bairro Funcionarios, Belo Horizonte
Rua Tupis, 114, Belo Horizonte
SCLR/Norte, Q-704, bl A, N 16, Brasilia
Rua Barao de Jaguara, 1164, Campinas
Rua Dr Faivre, 1271, Curitiba
Rua Voluntarios da Patria, 41, Curitiba
Av Osmar Cunha, 183 Loja 15, Florianopolis
Rua Major Facundo, 730, Fortaleza
Rua 3, n 291, Goiania
Rua Espirito Santo, 963, Juiz de Fora
Rua Piaui, 72 Loja 1, Londrina
Rua Ramiro Barcelos, 386, Porto Alegre
Rua Riachuelo, 1280, Porto Alegre
Rua do Principe, 482, Recife
Rua Benedito Hipolito 1, Rio de Janeiro
Rua Senador Dantos, 118-I, Rio de Janeiro
Rua Carlos Gomes, 698-A, Salvador
Rua Luis Coelho, 295, Sao Paulo
Rua Senador Feijo, 168, Sao Paulo
Haddock Lobo, 360, Sao Paulo

**WVC**, *imprint of* Madras Editora

**Jorge Zahar Editor+**
Rua Mexico 31, Sobreloja Centro, 20031-144 Rio de Janeiro-RJ
*Tel:* (021) 2240-0226 *Fax:* (021) 2262-5123
*E-mail:* jze@zahar.com.br
*Web Site:* www.zahar.com.br
*Key Personnel*
General Manager: Jorge Zahar, Jr; Ana Cristina Zahar
Editorial: Mariana Zahar Ribeiro
  *E-mail:* mzahar@zahar.com.br
Founded: 1957
Subjects: Anthropology, Art, Behavioral Sciences, Biography, Economics, Education, Finance, History, Human Relations, Literature, Literary Criticism, Essays, Management, Marketing, Music, Dance, Philosophy, Psychology, Psychiatry, Science (General), Social Sciences, Sociology
ISBN Prefix(es): 85-7110; 85-85061
Number of titles published annually: 40 Print
Total Titles: 600 Print
*Warehouse:* Rua Cotia 35 (Rocha), 20960 Rio de Janeiro-RJ *Tel:* (021) 2218-3700 *Fax:* (021) 2581-2205 *E-mail:* comercial@zahar.com.br
*Distribution Center:* Companhia das Letias

**Zip Editora Ltda**
Rua Filomena Nunes 162, Olaria, 21021 Rio de Janeiro-RJ
Mailing Address: CP 20095, 21021 Rio de Janeiro-RJ
*Tel:* (021) 2807272
*Key Personnel*
Man Dir: Jan Rais
Marketing: Paul Margittai
Founded: 1978

# Brunei Darussalam

## General Information

*Capital:* Bandar Seri Begawan
*Language:* Malay, English & Chinese
*Religion:* Predominantly Sunni Muslim
*Population:* 369,000
*Bank Hours:* 0900-1200, 1400-1500 Monday-Friday; 0900-1100 Saturday
*Shop Hours:* 0730-1930 or 2000 Monday-Saturday in Bandar Seri Begawan, Tuesday-Sunday in Seria, Wednesday-Monday in Kuala Belait
*Currency:* 100 sen = 1 Brunei dollar
*Export/Import Information:* No tariff on books. No obscene literature allowed. Import licenses not required. No exchange controls.

**Leong Brothers**
52 Jl Bunga Kuning, Seria
Mailing Address: PO Box 164, Seria 7001
*Tel:* (03) 22381 *Fax:* (03) 222223
*Telex:* BU 3338 *Cable:* Leong

# Bulgaria

## General Information

*Capital:* Sofia
*Language:* Bulgarian
*Religion:* Bulgarian Orthodox & Islamic
*Population:* 8.9 million
*Bank Hours:* 0800-1200 Monday-Friday
*Shop Hours:* 0900-1230, 1300-1800 Monday-Saturday
*Currency:* 100 stotinki = 1 lev
*Export/Import Information:* Books imported by the foreign trade organization 'Hemus', pl Slavejkov 11, Sofia. Exchange controls. 18% VAT on books.
*Copyright:* UCC, Berne (see Copyright Conventions, pg xi)

**Abagar Pablioing+**
ul Golas 18, 1111 Sofia
*Tel:* (02) 702826 *Fax:* (02) 702926
*E-mail:* abagar@gti.bg
*Key Personnel*
Contact: Maria Arabadjieva
Founded: 1990
Subjects: Art, Fiction, History, Mathematics, Mysteries, Physical Sciences, Publishing & Book Trade Reference, Science (General), Science Fiction, Fantasy
ISBN Prefix(es): 954-584; 954-8004
Divisions: Abanas Ltd; Abhadon Ltd
*Showroom(s):* 55 Neofit Rilsui Str, Sofia 1000
*Bookshop(s):* Rousse Str, Rostislav Bluskov 1; Kjustendil Str, Tzar Osvoboditel 1; 55 Neofit Rilsui Str

**Abagar, Veliko Tarnovo+**
98 Nikola Gabrovski St, 5000 Veliko Tarnovo
*Tel:* (062) 43936; (062) 47814 *Fax:* (062) 46993
*E-mail:* abagar@dir.bg
*Key Personnel*
General Manager: Marian Kenarov
Founded: 1991
Membership(s): Bulgarian Book Publishers Association.
Subjects: Art, Education, Fiction, Health, Nutrition, History, Science (General)
ISBN Prefix(es): 954-427

Distributed by Damian Jacob (Sofia); Hermes (Plovdiv)
*Showroom(s):* 47N Tzarigradsko shose Str, Sofia

**AECD**, *imprint of* Agencija Za Ikonomicesko Programirane i Razvitie

**Agencija Za Ikonomicesko Programirane i Razvitie+**
ul Aksakov 31, 1000 Sofia
*Tel:* (02) 9816597 *Fax:* (02) 466110
*E-mail:* aecd@sf.cit.bg
*Key Personnel*
Vice President: Ms Mariel Nenova
International Rights: Ana-Maria Yankova
Head of Publications: Mr Ventsislav Voikov
Founded: 1991
Subjects: Economics
ISBN Prefix(es): 954-567
Imprints: AECD

**Agency for Economic Coordination & Development**, see Agencija Za Ikonomicesko Programirane i Razvitie

**Aleks Print Publishing House+**
ul Kavala 22, et 1, ap 1, 9000 Varna
*Tel:* (052) 823147 *Fax:* (052) 823147
*E-mail:* dstankov@ultranet.bg
*Key Personnel*
Contact: Anelia Stankova
Founded: 1992
Subjects: Romance, Science (General), Science Fiction, Fantasy, Travel
ISBN Prefix(es): 954-8261
*Parent Company:* Aleks Print & Tourism, Krali Marko 3, Varna
*Bookshop(s):* Alex Print & Tourism, Krali Marko 3, Varna 9000

**Aleks Soft+**
kv Banisora, ul ohrid, bl 32-36, vh A, et 5, 1000 Sofia
*Tel:* (02) 328855 *Fax:* (02) 328855
*E-mail:* info@alexsoft.net
*Key Personnel*
General Manager: Alexander Alexandrov
Founded: 1994
Subjects: Computer Science, Microcomputers
ISBN Prefix(es): 954-656
*Parent Company:* Aleks Soft Ltd

**Andina Publishing House**
ul Car Simeon I 10, 9000 Varna
*Tel:* (052) 630902
*Key Personnel*
Contact: Panko Anchev
ISBN Prefix(es): 954-432
Distributor for Longman (UK); Pengiun (UK)

**Antroposofsko Izdatelstvo Dimo R Daskalov OOD**
ul M Stanev 61-A, 6000 Stara Zagora
*Tel:* (042) 54481
*Key Personnel*
Contact: Dr Dimitar Dimchev
Founded: 1991
Subjects: Astrology, Occult, Biblical Studies, Education, Philosophy, Science (General), Social Sciences, Sociology
ISBN Prefix(es): 954-495

**Aratron, IK+**
pl Slavejkov 11, et 6, 1000 Sofia
Mailing Address: PO Box 1587, 1000 Sofia
*Tel:* (02) 9807455 *Fax:* (02) 958-19-31
*E-mail:* aratron@techno-link.com
*Key Personnel*
President: Dobrin Vassilev
Founded: 1993
Specialize in New Age books.

Subjects: Astrology, Occult, Business, Health, Nutrition, How-to, Nonfiction (General), Parapsychology, Psychology, Psychiatry, Self-Help
ISBN Prefix(es): 954-626

**Izdatelstvo na Balgarskata Akademija na Naukite**, see Marin Drinov Publishing House

**Bilblioteka Nov den - Sajuz na Svobodnite Demokrati (Union of Free Democrats)+**
Zk Mladost 4, bl 468, vh B, et 3, ap 41, 1715 Sofia
*Tel:* (02) 773982; (02) 9814280 *Fax:* (02) 327972
*Key Personnel*
President & Editor: Prof Ivan Kaltchev
   *E-mail:* ivan_kaltchev@yahoo.com
Founded: 1991
Specialize in theoretical books only.
Membership(s): Union of Bulgarian Foundations.
Subjects: Ethnicity, History, Philosophy, Religion - Other
ISBN Prefix(es): 954-8575
Number of titles published annually: 4 Print
Total Titles: 24 Print
*Parent Company:* Research Center for Direct Democracy
Imprints: Dimiter Blagoev; LIK
Subsidiaries: Bulgarian Philosophical Association
Distributed by Filvest; Dimiter Blagoev
Distributor for LIK
*Bookshop(s):* 15, Tzar Osvoboditel Blvd, 1000 Sofia, Contact: Sacho Savov *Tel:* (02) 85-81, code 003592
*Book Club(s):* Abagar, 47, Tzar Osvoboditel Blvd, 1000 Sofia, Contact: Stefan Vlakhov *Tel:* (02) 46-31, code 003592

**Bulgarski Houdozhnik Publishers+**
6 Shipka Str, et 1, 1504 Sofia
*Tel:* (02) 467285; (02) 43351; (02) 43278
   *Fax:* (02) 467285
*Key Personnel*
Dir: Bouyan Filchev *E-mail:* filchev@bulnet.bg
Founded: 1952 (reformation 1991)
ISBN Prefix(es): 954-406
Subsidiaries: Union of Bulgarian Artists

**Bulgarski Pissatel+**
6 Septemvri 35, 1000 Sofia
*Tel:* (02) 8708407; (02) 873454; (02) 874527
   *Fax:* (02) 872495
*Key Personnel*
Dir: Gertcho Atanasov
Publishing House of the Union of Bulgarian Writers.
Subjects: Fiction
ISBN Prefix(es): 954-443

**Bulvest 2000 Ltd+**
ul Serdika 13, vh A, et 3, 1000 Sofia
*Tel:* (02) 9833286; (02) 9833169 *Fax:* (02) 9815464
*E-mail:* bulvest@internet-bg.net
*Key Personnel*
President: Vladimir Topencharov
Founded: 1990
Subjects: Education, Fiction, Science (General)
ISBN Prefix(es): 954-18; 954-8112

**Ciela Publishing House+**
Member of Wolters Kluwer Group
80-A Patriarh Evtimii Blvd, 1463 Sofia
*Tel:* (02) 951 63 76; (02) 954 93 97; (02) 951 66 97 *Fax:* (02) 954 93 97
*E-mail:* ciela@bulnet.bg
*Web Site:* www.ciela.net
*Telex:* 24 611
*Key Personnel*
President: Vesselin Todorov *Tel:* (02) 954 93 98
   *E-mail:* vtodorov@ciela.net

Editor-in-Chief, Head of Law Editorial Dept: Yavor Mihaylov *Tel:* (02) 986 33 11; (02) 980 18 68
Publicity Manager: Violeta Igova *Tel:* (02) 986 33 11; (02) 980 18 68
Founded: 1990
Membership(s): Bulgarian Book Publishers Association.
Subjects: Accounting, Business, Economics, Education, Fiction, Finance, Law, Medicine, Nursing, Dentistry, Nonfiction (General), Psychology, Psychiatry, Publishing & Book Trade Reference, Technology
ISBN Prefix(es): 954-649
Number of titles published annually: 39 Print
Total Titles: 487 Print
*Associate Companies:* Ciela Consultancy, Ciela Printing House
Distributed by New Star; Sofi-R

**DA-Izdatelstvo Publishers+**
ul Patriarh Evtimij 26, 1000 Sofia
*Tel:* (02) 988 1208 *Fax:* (02) 986 6290
*Key Personnel*
Dir: Aleko Djankov *E-mail:* alekoda@aster.net
Founded: 1996
Subjects: Fiction, History, Medicine, Nursing, Dentistry, Psychology, Psychiatry, Transportation

**Hristo G Danov State Publishing House+**
ul Stojan Calakov 1, 4025 Plovdiv
*Tel:* (032) 632552; (032) 265421 *Fax:* (032) 260560
*Key Personnel*
Dir: Nacho Hristoskov
Editorial: Dimitur Stoilov
Founded: 1855
Subjects: Fiction, Poetry
ISBN Prefix(es): 954-442

**Darzhavno Izdatelstvo Zemizdat**
ul Georgi Benkovski 14, 1000 Sofia
*Tel:* (02) 9867895 *Fax:* (02) 9875454
*Key Personnel*
Dir: Petar Angelov
Chief Editor: Emil Krustev
Founded: 1949
State Agricultural Publishing House.
Subjects: Agriculture, Cookery, Crafts, Games, Hobbies, Environmental Studies, Nonfiction (General), Science (General)
ISBN Prefix(es): 954-05

**DATAMAP - Europe+**
22 Shandor Petiofi St, 1606 Sofia
*Tel:* (02) 510090 *Fax:* (02) 510090
*E-mail:* datamap@mail.techno-linek.com
*Key Personnel*
President: Chaudor Dinev
Founded: 1991
Specialize in digital & printed maps, atlases & catalogues.
ISBN Prefix(es): 87-17
Total Titles: 25 Print; 2 CD-ROM
*Associate Companies:* Datamap Review Ltd, Sofia, Contact: Christo Assenor *Tel:* (02) 510090 *Fax:* (02) 510090

**Dimiter Blagoev**, *imprint of* Bilblioteka Nov den - Sajuz na Svobodnite Demokrati (Union of Free Democrats)

**Dolphin Press Group Ltd+**
19 Botev St, 8000 Burgas
Mailing Address: POB 296, 8000 Burgas
*Tel:* (056) 844 044 *Fax:* (056) 844 077
*E-mail:* postmaster@dolphin-press.com
*Web Site:* www.dolphin-press.com
*Key Personnel*
Chairman: Valentin Fortunov, MA *Tel:* 888 206

530 *E-mail:* valentin.fortunov@dolphin-press.com
Founded: 1990
Subjects: Business, Career Development, Economics, Finance, Law, Management, Marketing, Public Administration
ISBN Prefix(es): 954-721
Subsidiaries: AB-Direct, Ltd; Eurobook Ltd
*Bookshop(s):* 17 Botev St, 8000 Bourgas
*Book Club(s):* The Golden Dolphin

**EA AD+**
ul San Stefano 43, 5800 Pleven
Mailing Address: PO Box 151, 5800 Pleven
*Tel:* (064) 822827 *Fax:* (064) 822528
*E-mail:* ea@famahold.com
*Key Personnel*
President: V Velikova
Editor-in-Chief: M Phillipova
Sales Manager: Y Raikova
Founded: 1991
Membership(s): the Bulgarian Publishers Association.
Subjects: Behavioral Sciences, Biography, Economics, Fiction, Literature, Literary Criticism, Essays, Philosophy, Poetry, Psychology, Psychiatry, Psychoanalysis
ISBN Prefix(es): 954-450
*Bookshop(s):* Ekvus Art, 2 Nikolai Rakitin Str, 1504 Sofia

**EnEffect, Center for Energy Efficiency**
One, Christo Smirnensky Blvd, 3rd floor, 1164 Sofia
Mailing Address: PO Box 43, 1606 Sofia
*Tel:* (02) 963 17 14; (02) 963 07 23; (02) 963 21 69 *Fax:* (02) 963 25 74
*E-mail:* eneffect@mail.orbitel.bg
*Web Site:* www.eneffect.bg
*Key Personnel*
Executive Dir: Dr Zdravko Genchev
Founded: 1992
Subjects: Energy, Environmental Studies

**Eurasia Academic Publishers+**
Lyulin bl 332, vh-b, ap 40, 1336 Sofia
Mailing Address: Lyulin 332 B-25, 1336 Sofia
*Tel:* (02) 241523
*E-mail:* eurasia@realsci.com
*Web Site:* www.biblio.hit.bg
*Key Personnel*
President: Plamen Gradinarov
Founded: 1990
Subjects: Asian Studies, Education, History, Natural History, Philosophy, Psychology, Psychiatry, Religion - Buddhist, Religion - Hindu
ISBN Prefix(es): 954-628

**Evrazija**, see Eurasia Academic Publishers

**Fama+**
ul Aksakov 10, ul Canko Cerkovski 23, 1000 Sofia
*Tel:* (02) 881175; (02) 657006 *Fax:* (02) 657006
*Key Personnel*
Editor: Maria Koeva; Igor Shemtov
Founded: 1992
Subjects: Literature, Literary Criticism, Essays
ISBN Prefix(es): 954-597

**Foi-Commerce+**
PO Box 775, 1000 Sofia
*Tel:* (02) 227116 *Fax:* (02) 227116
*E-mail:* foi@nlcv.net
*Key Personnel*
President: Markov Krassimir
Founded: 1990
Subjects: Accounting, Business, Computer Science, Library & Information Sciences, Mathematics, Science (General)
ISBN Prefix(es): 954-16

**Fondacija Zlatno Kljuce+**
Zk Mladost 1A, bl 523, vh 5, ap 115, Sofia 1729
*Tel:* (02) 760-671; (02) 623517 *Fax:* (02) 623517
*E-mail:* ynfirst@mat.bg
*Key Personnel*
President & International Rights: Mr M Tsvetanov
Founded: 1991
Promotion & subsidizing of miscellaneous pieces
of art-created by & addressed to children; puppet theatre.
Membership(s): ASIFA.
Subjects: Art, Child Care & Development,
Drama, Theater, Education
ISBN Prefix(es): 954-90237

**Galaktika Publishing House+**
ul Aleksandar Djakovic 25V, 9000 Varna
*Tel:* (052) 225077; (052) 241132; (052) 241156;
(052) 604716; (052) 604715 *Fax:* (052) 234750
*Key Personnel*
General Dir: Assya Kadreva
Publicity Manager: Dimitrichka Telezarova
Founded: 1960
Subjects: Economics, Literature, Literary Criticism, Essays, Science Fiction, Fantasy
ISBN Prefix(es): 954-418

**Gea-Libris Publishing House+**
Al Batenberg 16b, 1000 Sofia
Mailing Address: PO Box 365, 1000 Sofia
*Tel:* (02) 986678 *Fax:* (02) 9866900
*E-mail:* emilgea@techno-link.com; info@
gealibris.com
*Web Site:* www.gealibris.com
*Key Personnel*
Editor-in-Chief: Svetla Evstatieva
Dir: Emil Krastev *E-mail:* emio@gealibris.com
Computer & Design: Galina Krasteva
International Rights Contact: Milena Kardeleva
Founded: 1990
Publish in Bulgarian, English, German & Russian.
Subjects: Animals, Pets, Biological Sciences,
Chemistry, Chemical Engineering, Economics,
Environmental Studies, Fiction, Gardening,
Plants, Geography, Geology, Health, Nutrition,
Mathematics, Physical Sciences, Science (General), Zoology, Botany
Total Titles: 2,000 Print
*Branch Office(s)*
Boucher Str No 5, Varna, Contact: Anton Apostolov *Tel:* (052) 250452; (052) 824369

**Global Kontakts Balgarija**
34 Vladajska St, 1606 Sofia
*Tel:* (02) 540636 *Fax:* (02) 528790
*Key Personnel*
Man Dir: Maxim Behar *E-mail:* max@mbox.cit.
bg
Founded: 1997
Subjects: Advertising
ISBN Prefix(es): 954-90246

**Heliopol**
zk Mladost 1, bl 29, vh7, 1750 Sofia
*Tel:* (02) 746850; (02) 718513
*E-mail:* heliopol@heliopol.bg
ISBN Prefix(es): 954-578

**Hermes Publishing House+**
16 Dobry Voynikov St, 4000 Plovdiv
*Tel:* (032) 630630 *Fax:* (032) 634095
*E-mail:* hermes@plovdiv.techno-link.com
*Web Site:* www.hermesbooks.com
*Key Personnel*
President: Stoyo Vartolomeev
International Rights: Victoria Petrova
Founded: 1991
Membership(s): Bulgarian Bookpublishers Association.

Subjects: Education, Fiction, Health, Nutrition,
Nonfiction (General), Romance
ISBN Prefix(es): 954-459; 954-26
Subsidiaries: Hermes Publishers
*Book Club(s):* Friends of Hermes; Connoisseurs
of the Book

**Heron Press Publishing House+**
18 Oborishte St, 1504 Sofia
*Tel:* (02) 443368 *Fax:* (02) 443368
*E-mail:* heron_press@attglobal.net
*Key Personnel*
Contact: Ilia Petrov
Founded: 1993
Subjects: Fiction, Geography, Geology, History,
Mathematics, Medicine, Nursing, Dentistry,
Natural History, Nonfiction (General), Physical
Sciences, Physics, Science (General)
ISBN Prefix(es): 954-580
*Book Club(s):* Association of Bulgarian Publishers

**Hriker+**
Banichora, 17-A, vh b, et 5 ap 65, 1233 Sofia
*Tel:* (02) 319-217
*Key Personnel*
Contact: Ms Nevena Konstantinova Keremedchieva
Founded: 1994
Subjects: Art, Ethnicity, Literature, Literary Criticism, Essays, Philosophy, Poetry
ISBN Prefix(es): 954-8498
Number of titles published annually: 12 Print
Total Titles: 61 Print
*Book Club(s):* Club of Modern Bulgarian Poetry

**Publishing House Hristo Botev+**
ul Slavjanska 38 vh A et 1, 1000 Sofija
*Tel:* (02) 9817017 *Fax:* (02) 9817017
*Key Personnel*
Dir: Ivan Dinkov
Founded: 1944
Subjects: Biography, Fiction, Government, Political Science, History, Literature, Literary
Criticism, Essays, Philosophy, Social Sciences,
Sociology
ISBN Prefix(es): 954-445

**Interpres+**
1343, Ljulin-2 bl 214-d-102, 1343 Sofia
Mailing Address: PO Box 18, 1582 Sofia
*Tel:* (02) 517915 *Fax:* (02) 517915
*E-mail:* interpres@bis.bg; intrpres@usa.net
*Key Personnel*
President: Mariana Evlogieva
Founded: 1992
Subjects: Advertising, Business, Crafts, Games,
Hobbies, Education, Human Relations, Humor,
Language Arts, Linguistics, Literature, Literary
Criticism, Essays
ISBN Prefix(es): 954-664

**Izdatelstvo Ja**
ul Preslav 19, 8600 Jambol
*Tel:* (046) 26166; (046) 20077
ISBN Prefix(es): 954-615

**Izdatelstvo Lettera** (Lettera Publishers)+
ul Rhodope No 62, 4000 Plovdiv
Mailing Address: PO Box 802, 4000 Plovdiv
*Tel:* (032) 600 930 *Fax:* (032) 600 940
*E-mail:* lettera@plovdiv.techno-link.com; office@
lettera.bg
*Web Site:* www.lettera.bg
*Key Personnel*
President: Nadya Furnadzhieva
Founded: 1991
Membership(s): EEPG (European Educational
Publishers Group); ICC (International Certificate Conference); ABK (Association of Bulgarian Publishers).

Subjects: Education, English as a Second Language, Fiction, Humor, Language Arts, Linguistics, Mathematics
ISBN Prefix(es): 954-516
Distributed by Damian Yakov
*Showroom(s):* 10 Svetoslav Terter Str, 1124 Sofia
*Tel:* (02) 944 14 52
*Bookshop(s):* 10 Svetoslav Terter Str, 1124 Sofia

**Pejo K Javorov Publishing House+**
52 Dondukov Blvd, 1000 Sofia
*Tel:* (02) 875201; (02) 880137; (02) 876765
*Fax:* (02) 875592
*Key Personnel*
Man Dir: Julia Bouchkova
Founded: 1945
State owned publisher.
Subjects: Cookery, Fiction, History, Humor, Nonfiction (General), Poetry
ISBN Prefix(es): 954-525

**Kibea Publishing Co+**
Mailing Address: PO Box 70, 1336 Sofia
*Tel:* (02) 24 10 20; (02) 925 01 52 *Fax:* (02) 925
07 48
*E-mail:* kibea@internet-bg.net; office@kibea.net
*Web Site:* www.kibea.net
*Key Personnel*
Publisher: Dimitar Zlatarev
Founded: 1991
Subjects: Alternative, Anthropology, Art, Astrology, Occult, Biography, Cookery, Fiction,
Foreign Countries, Health, Nutrition, History,
How-to, Human Relations, Nonfiction (General), Parapsychology, Philosophy, Poetry, Psychology, Psychiatry, Religion - Buddhist, Religion - Other, Self-Help
ISBN Prefix(es): 954-474
Total Titles: 300 Print
*Bookshop(s):* Kibea Books & Health Centre
*Book Club(s):* Friends of Kibea Club

**Kolibri Publishing Group**
U1 Ivan Vazov 36, 1000 Sofia
*Tel:* (02) 988-87-81; (02) 955-84-81; (02) 955-91-
990 *Fax:* (02) 813625
*E-mail:* colibri@inet.bg; colibry@bgnet.bg
*Key Personnel*
President: Raymond Wagenstein
Editor: Zhechka Georgieva
Founded: 1990
Subjects: Fiction, Literature, Literary Criticism,
Essays, Nonfiction (General)
ISBN Prefix(es): 954-529
Distributor for Abrams, Thames & Hudson;
Larousse; Robert; Taschen; etc; Random House
Group
*Bookshop(s):* 2 Levski St, 1000 Sofia

**Kralica MAB** (Queen Mab)+
Mladost 1, bl 29A, vh 2 ap 21, 1750 Sofia
*Tel:* (02) 767357 *Fax:* (02) 767357
*E-mail:* mab@slovar.org
*Web Site:* www.slovar.org/mab
*Key Personnel*
President: Mariana Aretova
Senior Editor: Nikolay Aretov *E-mail:* naretov@
yahoo.com
Founded: 1992
Subjects: Astrology, Occult, Cookery, Literature,
Literary Criticism, Essays, Mysteries, Parapsychology, Philosophy, Psychology, Psychiatry,
Theology
ISBN Prefix(es): 954-533
Number of titles published annually: 20 Print
Total Titles: 110 Print

**LIK**, *imprint of* Bilblioteka Nov den - Sajuz na
Svobodnite Demokrati (Union of Free
Democrats)

**LIK Izdanija+**
ul Nikolaj Gogol 16, 1504 Sofia
*Tel:* (02) 9443181; (02) 943400; (02) 9434748
  *Fax:* (02) 9434400; (02) 9434748; (02)
  9443181
*E-mail:* lik@tea.bg
*Key Personnel*
President: Liuben Kosarev
Founded: 1993
Subjects: Anthropology, Education, Health, Nu-
  trition, History, Literature, Literary Criticism,
  Essays, Mathematics, Philosophy, Psychology,
  Psychiatry, Social Sciences, Sociology
ISBN Prefix(es): 954-607

**Litera Prima+**
Drouzhba-2, Bl 418, Entr 2, App 46, 1528 Sofia
Mailing Address: PO Box 38, 1528 Sofia
*Tel:* (02) 9731698; (02) 9745575
*E-mail:* mmihales@vmei.acad.bg
*Key Personnel*
Contact: Marin Naydenov *Fax:* (02) 9731698
  *E-mail:* mmihalev@vmei.acad.bg
Founded: 1993
Subjects: Anthropology, Archaeology, Astronomy,
  Mysteries, Natural History, Parapsychology,
  Physical Sciences, Science (General)
ISBN Prefix(es): 954-8163; 954-738

**Makros 2000 - Plovdiv+**
ul Zefir 6, 4019 Plovdiv
*Tel:* (032) 642900
*E-mail:* makros@makros.net
*Web Site:* www.makros.net
*Key Personnel*
President & Owner: Georgi Stanchev Nikolov
Founded: 1991
Subjects: Art, Astronomy, Biography, Biological
  Sciences, Business, Chemistry, Chemical Engi-
  neering, Computer Science, Economics, Edu-
  cation, Electronics, Electrical Engineering, Ge-
  ography, Geology, History, Literature, Literary
  Criticism, Essays, Management, Mathematics,
  Medicine, Nursing, Dentistry, Microcomputers,
  Music, Dance, Philosophy, Physical Sciences,
  Physics, Psychology, Psychiatry, Science (Gen-
  eral), Social Sciences, Sociology
ISBN Prefix(es): 954-561
*Bookshop(s):* Makros 2000, Tsar Assen 16, 4000
  Plovdiv

**Marin Drinov Publishing House**
Formerly Izdatelstvo na Balgarskata Akademija
  na Naukite
ul Akad Georgi Boncev 6, POB 113, 1113 Sofia
*Tel:* (02) 720-922; (02) 979-34-49; (02) 979-34-
  41 *Fax:* (02) 704-054
*Telex:* 32123 Izdban
*Key Personnel*
Editor-in-Chief: Todor Rangelov
Sales & Publicity Manager: Maria Arabadjieva
Production Manager: Peter Tsanev
Founded: 1869
Drinov Publishing House of the Bulgarian
  Academy of Sciences.
Subjects: Science (General)
ISBN Prefix(es): 954-430; 954-322
*Bookshop(s):* ul Rakovski 135, 1000 Sofia; ul V
  Kolarov 19, 4000 Plovdiv

**Mateks**, see MATEX

**MATEX+**
ul Han Omurtag 10, 1000 Sofia
*Tel:* (02) 430177
*E-mail:* mmk_fte@uacg.acad.bg
*Key Personnel*
President: Mihail Konstantinov
Manager: Emil Enchev
Founded: 1991

Subjects: Cookery, Education, Electronics, Elec-
  trical Engineering, Fiction, Health, Nutrition,
  Mathematics, Nonfiction (General), Science
  Fiction, Fantasy
ISBN Prefix(es): 954-508
*Associate Companies:* ELMA Publishing House
Subsidiaries: BIAR

**Medicina i Fizkultura EOOD**
pl Slavejkov 11, 1000 Sofia
*Tel:* (02) 884068 *Fax:* (02) 871308
Subjects: Biological Sciences, Geography, Ge-
  ology, Health, Nutrition, Medicine, Nursing,
  Dentistry, Sports, Athletics
ISBN Prefix(es): 954-420

**Mladezh IK+**
ul Car Kalojan 10, 1000 Sofia
*Tel:* (02) 882137 *Fax:* (02) 876135
*Key Personnel*
Dir: Stanimir Ilchev
Founded: 1945
Youth Publishing House.
Subjects: Fiction, Government, Political Science,
  Philosophy, Social Sciences, Sociology
ISBN Prefix(es): 954-413

**Musica EOOD**, see Musica Publishing House
Ltd

**Musica Publishing House Ltd+**
11 Slaveikov Sq, 1000 Sofia
*Tel:* (02) 877 963; (02) 892 642 *Fax:* (02) 877
  963
*E-mail:* musicaph@abv.bg
*Web Site:* www.geocities.com/
  musicapublishinghouse
*Key Personnel*
President: Neli Koulaksazova
Founded: 1975
Membership(s): Bulgarian Book Publishing Asso-
  ciation.
Subjects: Art, Biography, Child Care & Develop-
  ment, Education, Music, Dance, Poetry, Pub-
  lishing & Book Trade Reference
ISBN Prefix(es): 954-405

**Naouka i Izkoustvo, Ltd+**
11 Slaveikov, et 5, 1080 Sofia
*Tel:* (02) 9874790; (02) 9872496 *Fax:* (02)
  9872496
*E-mail:* nauk_izk@sigma–bg.com
*Key Personnel*
Dir: Loreta Poushkarova
Founded: 1948
Bulgarian & foreign scientific literature in the
  fields of philosophy, psychology, linguisitics,
  history, dictionaries & language learning mate-
  rials.
Subjects: Art, Business, Economics, History, Lan-
  guage Arts, Linguistics, Law, Mathematics,
  Philosophy, Physics, Psychology, Psychiatry,
  Science (General), Social Sciences, Sociology
ISBN Prefix(es): 954-02

**Narodna Kultura+**
One Angel Kunchev, 1000 Sofia
*Tel:* (02) 9878063; (02) 9872722; (02) 9871684
*E-mail:* peepcult@intemet-bg.bg
*Web Site:* web.narodnakultura.hit.bg
*Key Personnel*
Dir: Petar Manolov
Founded: 1944
Subjects: Literature, Literary Criticism, Essays,
  Poetry
ISBN Prefix(es): 954-04

**Narodna Kultura**
ul Angel Kanchev 1, 1000 Sofia
Mailing Address: PO Box 421, 1000 Sofia
*Tel:* (02) 981 4739 *Fax:* (02) 981 4739

*E-mail:* peepcult@internet-bg.net
*Web Site:* www.geocities.com/narodna_kultura
*Key Personnel*
Dir: Alexander Donev
Founded: 1944
Subjects: Social Sciences, Sociology
ISBN Prefix(es): 954-04

**Narodno delo OOD+**
Bul Hristo Botev 3, 9000 Varna
Mailing Address: PO Box 59, 9000 Varna
*Tel:* (052) 230241; (052) 288516
*Key Personnel*
Contact: Mr Konstantin Paskalev
Founded: 1990
Subjects: Advertising, Maritime, Regional Inter-
  ests, Travel
ISBN Prefix(es): 954-627
*Branch Office(s)*
Bourgas
Dobritch
Rouse
Shoumen
Sofia
*Orders to:* Festival & Congress Centre, Varna

**Nauka i Izkustovo EOOD**, see Naouka i
Izkoustvo, Ltd

**New Man Publishers**, *imprint of* Nov Covek
Publishing House

**Nov Covek Publishing House+**
28 Antim I St, 1303 Sofia
*Tel:* (02) 9863766 *Fax:* (02) 9863772
*E-mail:* newman@mbox.cit.bg; vogda@stratec.net
*Key Personnel*
President: Rumen Papratilov
Founded: 1990
Produces & distributes theological, reference &
  sociological literature.
Membership(s): International Literature Asso-
  ciates, Bulgarian Book Publishers Association.
Subjects: Biblical Studies, Child Care & Devel-
  opment, History, Human Relations, Philosophy,
  Psychology, Psychiatry, Social Sciences, Soci-
  ology, Theology
ISBN Prefix(es): 954-407
Imprints: New Man Publishers

**Universitetsko Izdatelstvo 'Kliment Ochridski'**
Blvd Carigradsko Sose 125, bl 4, 1113 Sofia
*Tel:* (02) 71288; (02) 71265; (02) 704271; (02)
  71151 *Fax:* (02) 704271
*E-mail:* gzisha@ns.sclg.uni-sofia.bg
*Key Personnel*
Dir: Dimitaz Tomov
Subjects: Science (General)
ISBN Prefix(es): 954-07

**Pensoft Publishers+**
Akad G Bonchevstr, Bldg 6, 1113 Sofia
*Tel:* (02) 716451 *Fax:* (02) 704508
*E-mail:* pensoft@mbox.infotel.bg; orders@
  pensoft.net; info@pensoft.net
*Web Site:* www.pensoft.net
*Key Personnel*
Man Dir: Dr Lyubomir D Penev, PhD
Publisher-in-Chief: Sergei I Golovatch
Founded: 1993
Also acts as book supplier for East European
  books.
Subjects: Agriculture, Archaeology, Biological
  Sciences, Business, Earth Sciences, Environ-
  mental Studies, Finance, History, Language
  Arts, Linguistics, Mathematics, Natural History,
  Physics, Religion - Other, Science (General),
  Botany, Zoology
ISBN Prefix(es): 954-642
Number of titles published annually: 60 Print
Total Titles: 160 Print
Divisions: Pensoft-Moscow

*Branch Office(s)*
Institute for Problems of Ecology & Education, Leninsky pr 33, V-71 Moscow, Russian Federation, Dr Sergei Golovatch *E-mail:* spol@orc.ru *Web Site:* www.pensoft.net
Distributed by Coronet Books Inc (USA); DA Information Services; Goecke & Evers Antiquariat (Germany); Kabourek; NHBS-Natural History Book Service
Distributor for Academic Publishing House-Sofia; Heron Press
*Orders to:* Coronet Books Inc, 311 Bainbridge St, Philadelphia, PA 19147, United States *Tel:* 215-925-2762 *Fax:* 215-925-1912 *E-mail:* jeffgolds@aol.com *Web Site:* www.coronetbooks.com

**Pet Plus+**
142 Rakovski St, 1000 Sofia
*Tel:* (02) 9874188
*E-mail:* editor@545plus.com; petplus@bnc.bg
*Web Site:* www.545plus.com
*Key Personnel*
President: Petyo Hristov
Founded: 1990
Specialize in books with cassette.
Membership(s): Association of the Bulgarian Editors.
Subjects: Biography, Literature, Literary Criticism, Essays, Poetry, Religion - Other
ISBN Prefix(es): 954-462
Total Titles: 2 Print
*Book Club(s):* Association of Book Publications

**Prohazka I Kacarmazov+**
ul Vasil Levski 50, 1000 Sofia
*Tel:* (02) 654969 *Fax:* (02) 654969
*E-mail:* eto@einet.bg
Subjects: Education, Language Arts, Linguistics, Literature, Literary Criticism, Essays, Poetry, Social Sciences, Sociology
ISBN Prefix(es): 954-603

**Prosveta Publishers AS+**
117, Bul Carigradsko Sose, 1184 Sofia
*Tel:* (02) 760651; (02) 9743696; (02) 761182 *Fax:* (02) 764451
*E-mail:* prosveta@intech.bg
*Key Personnel*
President: Joana Tomova
Founded: 1945
Specialize in school textbooks.
Subjects: Education
ISBN Prefix(es): 954-01
*Bookshop(s):* 39 Ivan Assen II Str, Sofia

**Prozoretz**, see Prozoretz Ltd Publishing House

**Prozoretz Ltd Publishing House** (Izdatelsica Kushta Prozoretz)+
117, Tzarigradsko Shousse Blvd, 1784 Sofia
*Tel:* (02) 765171; (02) 746053 *Fax:* (02) 746053
*E-mail:* prozor@tea.bg
*Key Personnel*
Man Dir: Joana Tomova
Subjects: English as a Second Language, Fiction, Health, Nutrition, Philosophy, Poetry, Religion - Other, Self-Help
ISBN Prefix(es): 954-733
*Bookshop(s):* 39 Ivan Assen II Str, Sofia

**Rakla+**
Zk Borovo, bl 222 A, vh D, et 6, ap 112, 1680 Sofia
*Tel:* (02) 580-569
*E-mail:* grigorit@yahoo.com
*Key Personnel*
Senior Manager: Velichka Bojinova *E-mail:* rakla.net@usa.net
Founded: 1993
Membership(s): Union of Bulgarian Journalists.

Subjects: Cookery, Gardening, Plants, History
ISBN Prefix(es): 954-90251

**Regalia 6 Publishing House+**
PO Box 172, 1700 Sofia
*Tel:* (02) 754111 *Fax:* (02) 566573
*E-mail:* vpruu@dir.bg
*Key Personnel*
Contact: Raicho Ushatov
Founded: 1991
Publication of school aids & supplementary materials for all levels of education, compiled by the specialists in the corresponding areas.
Subjects: Career Development, Computer Science, Crafts, Games, Hobbies, Education, English as a Second Language, Mathematics, Science (General)
ISBN Prefix(es): 954-8147

**Reporter+**
113 Tzarigradsko chausse, 1184 Sofia
*Tel:* (02) 760834; (02) 761084; (02) 769028 *Fax:* (02) 745114
*E-mail:* reporter@techno-link.com
*Key Personnel*
Manager: Krum Blagov *E-mail:* reporter@mail.techno-link.com
Founded: 1990
Nonfiction & fiction Bulgarian & foreign literature, planners & calendars.
Subjects: Advertising, Biography, Child Care & Development, Fiction, Health, Nutrition, Nonfiction (General)
ISBN Prefix(es): 954-8102
Number of titles published annually: 12 Print
Total Titles: 30 Print

**Sanra Book Trust**
ul Vezen 14, 1421 Sofia
Mailing Address: PO Box 47, 1408 Sofia
*Tel:* (02) 659594; (02) 9549481 *Fax:* (02) 657252
*Key Personnel*
Contact: Sasho Ranguelov
Founded: 1993
Subjects: English as a Second Language
ISBN Prefix(es): 954-662

**Seven Hills Publishers+**
ul Veliko Tarnovo 13, 4000 Plovdiv
*Tel:* (032) 262235 *Fax:* (032) 262235
*Key Personnel*
President: Valeri Nichevski
Vice President: Evelina Proeva
Founded: 1993
Subjects: Art, Business, English as a Second Language, Language Arts, Linguistics, Law, Medicine, Nursing, Dentistry, Psychology, Psychiatry
ISBN Prefix(es): 954-669

**Sibi+**
4 Slaveikov Sq, 1000 Sofia
*Tel:* (02) 9870141 *Fax:* (02) 9875709
*E-mail:* sibi@ind.interner-bg.bg
*Key Personnel*
President: Mr Vassil Tashev
Vice President & International Rights: Mrs Natalia Goudjeva
Founded: 1990
Sibi has own bookshops in major Bugarian cities.
Subjects: Labor, Industrial Relations, Law
ISBN Prefix(es): 954-8150; 954-730
*Bookshop(s):* City Court of Plovdiv, 6 Septemvri St 168, 4000 Plovdiv; Sibi Specialize Bookshop, Supreme Administrative Court Building, Stambolijski Blvd 18, 1000 Sofia
*Shipping Address:* 1799 Sofia, Mladost-2, bl 227, vh 5, et 2, ap 96
*Warehouse:* Mladost-2, bl 227, vh 5, et 2, ap 96, 1799 Sofia
*Orders to:* Mladost-2, bl 227, vh 5, et 2, ap 96, 1799 Sofia

**Sila & Zivot**
ul Dimitar Blagoev St, vh. 3, 8001 Burgas
Mailing Address: PO Box 609, 8001 Burgas
*Tel:* (056) 20965
*E-mail:* silajivot@bse.bg
*Key Personnel*
Publisher: Milka Kraleva
Founded: 1992
Specialize in books & music of Peter Deunov (1864-1944).
Subjects: Astrology, Occult, Biblical Studies, Child Care & Development, Education, Music, Dance, Parapsychology, Philosophy, Self-Help, Theology
ISBN Prefix(es): 954-8146

**Sinodalno Izdatelstvo na Balgarskata pravoslavna carkva**
ul Oboriste 4, 1000 Sofia
*Tel:* (02) 875611; (02) 875245
Synodal Publishing House.
Subjects: Religion - Other
ISBN Prefix(es): 954-8398

**Sita-MB+**
ul Vasil Drumev 47, vhA ap21, Varna 9002
*Tel:* (092) 872285
Founded: 1992
Subjects: Communications, Human Relations, Labor, Industrial Relations, Management
ISBN Prefix(es): 954-518

**Slance**, see Sluntse Publishing House

**Slavena+**
Radko Dimitriev St No 59A, 9000 Varna
*Tel:* (052) 602465; (052) 225935 *Fax:* (052) 225935
*E-mail:* slavena@triada.bg
*Web Site:* www.slavena.net
*Key Personnel*
Contact: Nasko Yakimov
Founded: 1990
Subjects: Art, Crafts, Games, Hobbies, Economics, Education, History, Law, Literature, Literary Criticism, Essays, Science (General)
ISBN Prefix(es): 954-579

**Sluntse Publishing House+**
11 Slaveykov Sq, 1000 Sofia
Mailing Address: PO Box 694, 1000 Sofia
*Tel:* (02) 988 37 97 *Fax:* (02) 987 14 05
*E-mail:* info@sluntse.com
*Web Site:* www.sluntse.com
*Key Personnel*
President: Nadia Kabakchieva
Founded: 1937
Subjects: Astrology, Occult, Biography, Child Care & Development, Education, Fiction, Foreign Countries, Gardening, Plants, Health, Nutrition, House & Home, Human Relations, Marketing, Native American Studies, Nonfiction (General), Publishing & Book Trade Reference, Romance, Autobiography, Memoirs, Letter & Beauty
ISBN Prefix(es): 954-8023; 954-742

**Srebaren lav+**
ul Plovdivsko pole, bl2 vhA ap3, 1756 Sofia
*Tel:* (02) 752298
Founded: 1991
Subjects: Literature, Literary Criticism, Essays
ISBN Prefix(es): 954-571

**Svetra Publishing House+**
Major Thompson St, Bl 12, entr 2, 1407 Sofia
*Tel:* (02) 62 27 39; (02) 983 45 42 *Fax:* (02) 23 49 66
*E-mail:* svetlev@cybernet.bg

*Key Personnel*
President: Nickolay Svetlev
Founded: 1993
Subjects: Advertising, Art, Biblical Studies, Fiction, Literature, Literary Criticism, Essays, Poetry, Science Fiction, Fantasy
ISBN Prefix(es): 954-8430
*Warehouse:* 83A Simeon St, 1000 Sofia *Tel:* (02) 834541

**Technica Publishing House+**
Slaveikov One Sq, 1000 Sofia
*Tel:* (02) 987 1283 *Fax:* (02) 987 4906
*E-mail:* technica@netel.bg; sales@technica-bg.com
*Web Site:* www.technica-bg.com
*Key Personnel*
Manager: Asen Milchev *E-mail:* upravitel@technica-bg.com
Marketing: Juliana Kovacheva
Founded: 1958
Subjects: Science (General)
ISBN Prefix(es): 954-03

**Tehnika EOOD**, see Technica Publishing House

**TEMTO**
Bul Gen Skobelev 35, Sofia 1463
*Tel:* (02) 524-924
*E-mail:* temto@sf.icn.bg
*Key Personnel*
President: Temenouga Todorova
Programmer: Kiril Voykov
Artist: Monika Voykova
Founded: 1991
Subjects: Advertising, Agriculture, Architecture & Interior Design, Computer Science, Health, Nutrition, Mathematics, Microcomputers, Poetry, Psychology, Psychiatry, Advertising, Programming
ISBN Prefix(es): 954-9566

**Todor Kableshkov University of Transport+**
158 Geo Milev St, 1574 Sofia
*Tel:* (02) 9709335; (02) 9709384; (02) 9709478 *Fax:* (02) 9709407
*E-mail:* office@vtu.bg
*Web Site:* www.vtu.bg
*Key Personnel*
Rector: Nencho Nenov, PhD *Tel:* (02) 97 09 406 *Fax:* (02) 97 09 242 *E-mail:* rector@vtu.bg
Vice Rector, Educational Activities: Detelin Vasilev, PhD *Tel:* (02) 97 09 406 *Fax:* (02) 97 09 407 *E-mail:* dvasilev@vtu.bg
Vice Rector, Research & International Relations: Rusko Valkov, PhD *Tel:* (02) 97 09 335 *Fax:* (02) 97 09 325 *E-mail:* rvalkov@vtu.bg
Founded: 1922
Subjects: Advertising, Behavioral Sciences, Business, Civil Engineering, Communications, Economics, Electronics, Electrical Engineering, Engineering (General), Mechanical Engineering, Transportation
ISBN Prefix(es): 954-12
Number of titles published annually: 45 Print
*Parent Company:* Ministry of Education & Science

**Trud - Izd kasta+**
15 Dunav Str, 1000 Sofia
*Tel:* (02) 9814110; (02) 9878261; (02) 9872924 *Fax:* (02) 467565
*E-mail:* book@cybernet.bg
*Web Site:* www.trud.bg
*Key Personnel*
President: Nikola Kitsevski *Tel:* (02) 9214157
Founded: 1994
Subjects: Biography, Fiction, History, Humor, Mysteries, Western Fiction
ISBN Prefix(es): 954-528
Number of titles published annually: 40 Print

Total Titles: 500 Print
*Parent Company:* Media Holding, 119 Ekzarh Joseph, 1000 Sofia
*Ultimate Parent Company:* WAZ- Germany
*Branch Office(s)*
Trud Publishing House, Contact: Krasimir Mirchev *Tel:* (02) 987-29-24

**Ivan Vazov Publishing House**
ul Georgi Benkovski 14, 1000 Sofia
*Tel:* (02) 878481; (02) 871572 *Fax:* (02) 878416
Founded: 1948
Subjects: Biography, Fiction, Government, Political Science, History, Humor, Literature, Literary Criticism, Essays, Nonfiction (General), Poetry, Science (General)
ISBN Prefix(es): 954-604

**Voenno Izdatelstvo**
ul Ivan Vazov 12, 1000 Sofia
*Tel:* (02) 9802766; (02) 9804186; (02) 9873934 *Fax:* (02) 9802779
*Web Site:* www.vi-books.com
Subjects: History, Military Science, Social Sciences, Sociology
ISBN Prefix(es): 954-509

**Zunica+**
Zk Bakston, bl 10, et 11, ap 48, 1618 Sofia
*Tel:* (02) 551-977
Subjects: Art, Drama, Theater, Fiction, Humor, Mysteries, Poetry, Romance, Science Fiction, Fantasy
ISBN Prefix(es): 954-9604

# Burundi

## General Information

*Capital:* Bujumbura
*Language:* French & Kirundi (Swahili & French commercially)
*Religion:* About half Roman Catholic; others follow traditional animist beliefs
*Population:* 6.0 million
*Bank Hours:* Normally closed for cash transactions in afternoon but open for all other business morning & afteroon
*Shop Hours:* 0800-1200, 1400-1630 Monday-Friday; 0800-1200 Saturday
*Currency:* 100 centimes = 1 Burundi franc
*Export/Import Information:* Import license required over value of 20,000 Burundi francs.

**Government Printer (INABU)**, see Imprimerie Nationale du Burundi

**Imprimerie Nationale du Burundi**
Formerly Government Printer (INABU)
BP 991, Bujumbura
*Tel:* (02) 22214; (02) 24046

**INABU**, see Imprimerie Nationale du Burundi

**Editions Intore+**
19 Matana Ave, Bujumbura
Mailing Address: BP 2524, Bujumbura
*Key Personnel*
Dir: Dr Andre Birabuza *E-mail:* anbirabuza@yahoo.fr
Founded: 1992
Subjects: Developing Countries, Ethnicity, History, Journalism, Literature, Literary Criticism, Essays, Philosophy, Social Sciences, Sociology
ISBN Prefix(es): 2-9506222
Divisions: Binensuel Intore; Librairie Papeterie Intore

**Les Presses Lavigerie**
5 Av de I'Uprona, BP 1640 Bujumbura
*Tel:* (02) 22368 *Fax:* (02) 220318
*E-mail:* lpl~bujumbura@cbinf.com
*Key Personnel*
Contact: Geiss Anton *Tel:* (02) 228508

# Cameroon

## General Information

*Capital:* Yaounde
*Language:* French & English (officially bilingual)
*Religion:* Christian, Islamic, traditional
*Population:* 12.7 million
*Bank Hours:* East: 0800-1130, 1430-1630 Monday-Friday; West: 0800-1330 Monday-Friday
*Shop Hours:* 0800-1200, 1430-1730 (earlier closing in West) Monday-Friday; 0800-1200 Saturday
*Currency:* 100 centimes = 1 CFA franc
*Export/Import Information:* Member of Customs & Economic Union of Central Africa. Import license, entitling holder to provision for necessary foreign exchange, required if value of import is over 500,000 CFA francs.
*Copyright:* UCC, Berne, Florence (see Copyright Conventions, pg xi)

**CAW Series**, *imprint of* Editions Buma Kor & Co Ltd

**Centre d'Edition et de Production pour l'Enseignement et la Recherche (CEPER)+**
BP 808, Yaounde
*Tel:* (023) 221323
*Telex:* 838 KN *Cable:* Cepmae Yaounde
*Key Personnel*
Dir General: Jean Claude Fouth
Sales Manager: Thomas Victor Mang Ngouni
Production Manager: Sonny Ekono
Contact: Theophile Maurice
Founded: 1967
Subjects: History, Nonfiction (General), Science (General), Social Sciences, Sociology, Technology
ISBN Prefix(es): 2-7405

**CEPER**, see Centre d'Edition et de Production pour l'Enseignement et la Recherche (CEPER)

**Editions CLE+**
BP 1501, Ave Marechal Foch, Yaounde
*Tel:* (0237) 22-35-54 *Fax:* (0237) 23-27-09
*E-mail:* edition@iccnet.cm *Cable:* CLE YAOUNDE
*Key Personnel*
Dir: Mr Comlan Prosper
Founded: 1963
Subjects: Drama, Theater, Fiction, How-to, Literature, Literary Criticism, Essays, Poetry, Religion - Protestant, Social Sciences, Sociology
ISBN Prefix(es): 2-7235
Distributed by CEC (Brussels); Editions ZOE (Geneva); L'Harmattan (Paris); Presence Africaine (Paris)
Distributor for CEDA (Ivory Coast); Editions Reynald Goulet (Quebec, Canada); Modulo Editeur (Quebec, Canada)
*Bookshop(s):* Librairie CLE, BP 1501, Yaounde

**Editions Buma Kor & Co Ltd+**
Box 727, Yaounde
*Tel:* (023) 22 48 99 *Fax:* (023) 23 29 03
*Telex:* 8438 KN

*Key Personnel*
Man Dir, Rights & Permissions: B D Buma Kor
Founded: 1977
Also act as representatives for Oxford University
    Press, Oxford, England.
Subjects: Drama, Theater, Economics, Fiction,
    Mathematics, Nonfiction (General), Poetry, Re-
    ligion - Protestant, Self-Help
*Parent Company:* Buma Kor & Co (Sarl)
*Associate Companies:* Speedymint Centres
Imprints: CAW Series
*Bookshop(s):* Librairie Bilingue/The Bilingual
    Bookshop

**Presses Universitaires d'Afrique+**
BP 71636, Yaounde
*Tel:* (023) 22 00 30 *Fax:* (023) 22 23 25
Founded: 1986
Membership(s): Cameroon Publisher Association.
Subjects: Economics, Education, Finance, Law,
    Literature, Literary Criticism, Essays, Public
    Administration, Social Sciences, Sociology,
    Theology
ISBN Prefix(es): 2-912086
*Parent Company:* L'Africaine D'Edition et de
    Services (AES)
Distributed by Editions CLE (West Africa); Li-
    brarie de France

**Semences Africaines+**
BP 5329, Yaounde Nlongkak
*Tel:* (023) 224058
*Key Personnel*
Man Dir, Production: Philippe-Louis Ombede
Editorial, Rights & Permissions: Martin King
    Mbida
Sales: Lea Ombede
Founded: 1974
Subjects: Drama, Theater, Fiction, History, Poetry,
    Regional Interests, Religion - Other
ISBN Prefix(es): 2-907553

# Cape Verde

## General Information

*Capital:* Praia
*Language:* Portuguese (official), French & En-
    glish are also widely spoken
*Religion:* Predominantly Roman Catholic
*Population:* 398,000
*Currency:* 100 centavos = 1 Cape Verde escudo =
    $0.82 US
*Export/Import Information:* Member of the Eco-
    nomic Community of the West African States
    (ECWAS) & the ACP.

**Centro de Documentacao e Informao para o
    Desenvolvimento**
CP 120, Praia
*Tel:* 613969 *Fax:* 1527
*Telex:* 6037 CV

# Chad

## General Information

*Capital:* N'Djamena
*Language:* French & Arabic
*Religion:* Islamic in north, traditional and some
    Christian in south
*Population:* 5.2 million
*Bank Hours:* 0700-1200 Monday-Saturday

*Shop Hours:* 0700 or 0800-1200 or 1230. 1600-
    1900 Monday-Saturday; some close Monday
*Currency:* 100 centimes = 1 CFA franc
*Export/Import Information:* No tariff on books.
    Consumption tax on children's picture-books &
    advertising. Import licenses required except for
    imports from the European Econimic Commu-
    nity & the Franc Zone.
*Copyright:* Berne (see Copyright Conventions, pg
    xi)

**Government Printer (Imprimerie National Du
    Tchad)**
BP 453, N'Djamena

# Chile

## General Information

*Capital:* Santiago
*Language:* Spanish
*Religion:* Roman Catholic
*Population:* 14 million
*Bank Hours:* 0900-1400 Monday-Friday
*Shop Hours:* 1000-1900 Monday-Friday; 1000-
    1800 Saturday-Sunday
*Currency:* 100 centavos = 1 Chilean peso
*Export/Import Information:* Member of Latin
    American Integration Association (ALADI).
    19% VAT on books, 11% tariff.
*Copyright:* UCC, Berne, Buenos Aires (see Copy-
    right Conventions, pg xi)

**Alfabeta Impresores Ltda**
Lira 140, Santiago
*Tel:* (02) 6397765 *Fax:* (02) 6391752
*Key Personnel*
Contact: Jaime Vicente Martinez

**Arrayan Editores**
Bernarda Morin 435, Providencia, Santiago
*Tel:* (02) 4314200 *Fax:* (02) 2741041
*E-mail:* web@arrayan.cl
*Web Site:* www.arrayan.cl
*Key Personnel*
President: Ramon Luis Undurraga Laso
Manager: Pablo Marinkovic
Editor: Juan Andres Pina Riquelme
Founded: 1982
Subjects: Accounting, Anthropology, Archaeol-
    ogy, Art, Astronomy, Biography, Biological
    Sciences, Chemistry, Chemical Engineering,
    Communications, Computer Science, Drama,
    Theater, Economics, Education, Engineering
    (General), Environmental Studies, Ethnicity,
    Geography, Geology, History, Journalism, Lan-
    guage Arts, Linguistics, Literature, Literary
    Criticism, Essays, Marketing, Mathematics,
    Medicine, Nursing, Dentistry, Music, Dance,
    Philosophy, Physical Sciences, Psychology,
    Psychiatry, Radio, TV, Regional Interests, Self-
    Help, Social Sciences, Sociology, Sports, Ath-
    letics, Technology, Travel, Veterinary Science,
    Customs, Design, Folklore, Mythology, Reli-
    gion, Zoology
ISBN Prefix(es): 956-240

**Ediciones Bat+**
Silvina Hurtado 1841-C, Providencia, Santiago
*Tel:* (02) 2743171 *Fax:* (02) 2250261
*Key Personnel*
Manager: Jose Cayuela Arzac
Founded: 1988
Subjects: Biography, History, Literature, Literary
    Criticism, Essays
ISBN Prefix(es): 956-7022

**Editorial Andres Bello/Editorial Juridica de
    Chile+**
Avda Ricardo Lyon 946, Providencia, Santiago
*Tel:* (02) 2049900; (02) 4619500 *Fax:* (02)
    2253600
*Web Site:* www.editorialjuridica.cl
*Telex:* 240901 Edjur *Cable:* EDIBEL
*Key Personnel*
General Manager: Julio Serrano Lamas
    *E-mail:* julio_serrano@entelchile.net
Dir: Ana Maria Garcia B
Publisher: Pilar de Iruarrizaga B; Karem Duffoo
    C
Founded: 1947
Subjects: Art, Education, History, Law, Literature,
    Literary Criticism, Essays, Medicine, Nursing,
    Dentistry
ISBN Prefix(es): 85-613
*Bookshop(s):* Libreria Andres Bello (under Major
    Booksellers)
*Book Club(s):* Clubs de Lectores 'Andres Bello'

**Bibliografica Internacional SA**
Monjitas 308, Santiago
*Tel:* (02) 6394057 *Fax:* (02) 6397693
*E-mail:* bibliograf@entelchile.net
*Key Personnel*
Manager: Ramon Trepat-Pinilla
ISBN Prefix(es): 956-7240; 956-8090

**Cesoc Ltda+**
Esmeralda 636, Santiago
*Tel:* (02) 6391081; (02) 6336992 *Fax:* (02)
    6325382
*E-mail:* cesoc@bellsouth.cl
*Key Personnel*
Manager: Julio Silva Solar
Founded: 1984
ISBN Prefix(es): 956-211
*U.S. Office(s):* Para Textor, 6 Avery St, Saratoga
    Springs, NY 12866, United States *Tel:* (518)
    587-3774 *Fax:* (518) 581-1859

**Cetal Ediciones**
Abtao 576, Cerro Concepcion, Valparaiso
*Tel:* (032) 213360 *Fax:* (032) 214851
*Key Personnel*
Manager: Pedro Berho Arteagotia
Founded: 1984
Services in technology.
Subjects: Environmental Studies
ISBN Prefix(es): 956-209

**Ediciones Cieplan**
Francisco Noguera 217, piso 4, depto 40, Provi-
    dencia, Santiago
*Tel:* (02) 2323212; (02) 2324558; (02) 6333836
    *Fax:* (02) 3340312
*E-mail:* cieplan@ctcreuna.cl
*Key Personnel*
President: Pablo Pinera
Subjects: Developing Countries, Economics, Pub-
    lic Administration, Technology
ISBN Prefix(es): 956-204

**Congregacion Paulinas - Hijas de San Pablo**
Vicuna Mackenna 6299, La Florida, Santiago
*Tel:* (02) 221 2832 *Fax:* (02) 221 2832
*E-mail:* paulinasedit@entelchile.net
*Key Personnel*
Sister Superior: Hortensia Lizama
Dir: Veronica Pinto Pasten
Subjects: Religion - Catholic, Theology
ISBN Prefix(es): 956-7433
*Bookshop(s):* Libreria San Pablo (under Major
    Booksellers); Centro Catequistico, Cienfuegos
    60, Casilla, 3429 Santiago
*Orders to:* Centro Catequistico Cienfuegos 60,
    Casilla, 3429 Santiago *Tel:* (02) 6964650
    *Fax:* (02) 6990327

**Corporacion de Promocion Universitaria**
Av Miguel Claro No 1460, Providencia, CP 664
    1209 Casilla 11 Correo 28, Santiago
*Tel:* (02) 2749022 *Fax:* (02) 2741828
ISBN Prefix(es): 956-229

**Editorial Cuarto Propio**
Keller 1175, Providencia, Santiago
*Tel:* (02) 204 7645 *Fax:* (02) 204 7622
*E-mail:* cuartopropio@cuartopropio.cl
*Web Site:* www.cuartopropio.cl
*Key Personnel*
General Manager: Marisol Vera
Founded: 1987
Membership(s): Chilean Chamber of the Book.
Subjects: Fiction, Nonfiction (General), Poetry,
    Women's Studies
Distributed by Paratextos (USA)
Distributor for Editorial Biblos (Argentina); Edi-
    torial La Marca (Argentina)
*Bookshop(s):* Libros sin Frontera, PO Box 2085,
    Olympia, WA 98507-2085, United States
*Orders to:* Paratextos, 6 Avery St, Saratoga
    Springs, NY 12866, United States

**Editorial Cuatro Vientos** (Cuatro Vientos
    Publishing House)+
Av Jaime Guzman Errazuriz 3293, Santiago
Mailing Address: Casilla 131 Correo 29, Santiago
*Tel:* (02) 2258381; (02) 269 5343 *Fax:* (02)
    3413107
*E-mail:* 4vientos@netline.cl
*Web Site:* www.cuatrovientos.net
*Key Personnel*
Manager: Dr Francisco Huneeus
Commercial Manager: Renato Valenzuela
Founded: 1980
Membership(s): The Chilean Association of Pub-
    lishers.
Subjects: Nonfiction (General), Psychology, Psy-
    chiatry
ISBN Prefix(es): 956-242
Number of titles published annually: 12 Print
Total Titles: 120 Print
Distributed by Edin (Argentina); Editorial Andres
    Bello (Chile); Editorial Universitaria (Chile)
Distributor for Be-Uve-Drais (Chile); Editorial
    Nuevo Extremo (Argentina); Editorial Troquel
    (Argentina); Luz De Luna (Argentina)

**Edeval (Universidad de Valparaiso)**
Errazuriz 2190, mesa central: 56-32-507000, Val-
    paraiso
*Tel:* (02) 250792 *Fax:* (02) 252125
*E-mail:* rrpp@uv.cl
*Web Site:* www.uv.cl
*Key Personnel*
International Rights: Arturo Salas Caceres
Founded: 1961
Subjects: Criminology, Economics, Government,
    Political Science, History, Human Relations,
    Labor, Industrial Relations, Law, Maritime,
    Philosophy, Publishing & Book Trade Refer-
    ence, Social Sciences, Sociology
ISBN Prefix(es): 956-200
*Bookshop(s):* Libreria Andres Bello, Huerfanos,
    1158 Santiago

**Instituto Geografico Militar**
Dieciocho N° 369, Santiago
*Tel:* (02) 4606863 *Fax:* (02) 4608294
*E-mail:* clientes@igm.cl
*Web Site:* www.igm.cl
*Telex:* 441677 16M C2
*Key Personnel*
Brig General: Enrique Gillmore Callejas
Contact: Mercedes Lucar
Founded: 1992
Specialized in cartography & topography of na-
    tional territory.
Subjects: Earth Sciences, Geography, Geology

ISBN Prefix(es): 956-202
Total Titles: 30 Print; 2 CD-ROM

**Grijalbo Mondadori SA**
Monjitas 392, Piso 11, Oficinas 1101-1102, Santi-
    ago
*Tel:* (02) 782-8200 *Fax:* (02) 782-8210
*E-mail:* editorial@randomhouse-mondadori.cl
*Web Site:* www.grijalbo.com
*Key Personnel*
Contact: Gian Carlo Corte Truffello
ISBN Prefix(es): 956-258
*Parent Company:* Ediciones Grijalbo SA
*Ultimate Parent Company:* Random House Mon-
    dadori

**Ediciones Mil Hojas Ltda**
Av Antonio Varas 1480, Providencia, Santiago
*Tel:* (02) 2743172 *Fax:* (02) 2250261
*Key Personnel*
Dir: David R Turkieltaub
Founded: 1991
Subjects: Anthropology, Art, Astrology, Occult,
    Education, Self-Help, Sports, Athletics, Travel
ISBN Prefix(es): 956-7741
Subsidiaries: Abanico Libros Ltda

**Editorial Juridica de Chile**, see Editorial Andres
    Bello/Editorial Juridica de Chile

**Libreria Libertad SA**
Rosas No 1281, Santiago
*Tel:* (02) 698 8773 *Fax:* (02) 672 6314
*Key Personnel*
Manager: Alejandro Melo
Founded: 1967
ISBN Prefix(es): 956-7348

**Ediciones Melquiades**
Bandera 341 of 352, Casilla 144/12, Santiago
*Tel:* (02) 2731545 *Fax:* (02) 2266602 *Cable:*
    240984
*Key Personnel*
Editor: Arturo Navarro
Founded: 1987
Subjects: Government, Political Science, Liter-
    ature, Literary Criticism, Essays, Social Sci-
    ences, Sociology
ISBN Prefix(es): 956-231

**Museo Chileno de Arte Precolombino**
Bandera 361, Casilla 3687, Santiago
*Tel:* (02) 6887078; (02) 6972779 *Fax:* (02)
    6972779
*E-mail:* bibmchap@ctcreuna.cl
*Web Site:* www.precolombino.cl
Specialize in Pre-Colombian Art.
Subjects: Archaeology, Art
ISBN Prefix(es): 84-89332; 956-243

**Norma de Chile**
Providencia 1760 Oficina 502, Santiago
*Tel:* (02) 236 3355 *Fax:* (02) 236 3362
*Web Site:* www.norma.com
*Key Personnel*
Manager: Elsy Salzar *E-mail:* esalazar@carvajal.
    cl
Contact: Octavio Alvarez Piedrahita
Subjects: Art, Literature, Literary Criticism, Es-
    says, Management, Marketing, Science Fiction,
    Fantasy, Self-Help
ISBN Prefix(es): 956-7250

**Editora Nueva Generacion**+
Casilla 22, Covero 30 Santiago
*Tel:* (02) 2183974 *Fax:* (02) 2182281
*Key Personnel*
Manager: Pablo Huneeus
Founded: 1982

Subjects: Cookery, Human Relations, Humor, So-
    cial Sciences, Sociology
ISBN Prefix(es): 956-226

**Editorial Patris SA**+
Jose Miguel Infante 132, Providencia, Santiago
*Tel:* (02) 2351343 *Fax:* (02) 2351343
*E-mail:* edit.patris@entelchile.net
*Web Site:* www.patris.cl
*Key Personnel*
Contact: German B Pumpin
Founded: 1974
Subjects: Religion - Other
ISBN Prefix(es): 956-246
Distributor for Edit Patris (Argentina)
*Bookshop(s):* Libreria Patris (Nazareth), Providen-
    cia, 1001 Santiago

**Pehuen Editores Ltda**+
Maria Luisa Santander 537, Providencia, Santiago
*Tel:* (02) 2049399 *Fax:* (02) 2049399
*E-mail:* pehuen@cmet.net
*Key Personnel*
Dir: Jorge T Barros
General Manager: Alicia Z Cerda
Sales Manager: J Sebastian Barros
Founded: 1983
Subjects: Biography, Literature, Literary Criti-
    cism, Essays, Philosophy, Poetry, Social Sci-
    ences, Sociology
ISBN Prefix(es): 956-16
Subsidiaries: Temuco

**Planeta SA**+
Member of Grupo Planeta
Santa Lucia 360, Piso 7, Santiago
*Tel:* (02) 6962374 *Fax:* (02) 6957260
*Telex:* 242514 EPCMI
*Key Personnel*
General Manager: Bartolo Ortiz Henriquez
ISBN Prefix(es): 956-247
Subsidiaries: Inversiones Planeta SA

**Editorial Planeta Chilena**, see Planeta SA

**Pontificia Universidad Catolica de Chile**+
Av Libertador Bernardo O'Higgins 340 of 311,
    Santiago
Mailing Address: Casilla 114-D, Santiago
*Tel:* (02) 2224516 (ext 2417) *Fax:* (02) 2225515
*Web Site:* www.puc.cl
*Telex:* 240395
*Key Personnel*
Dir & Editor: Gabriela Echeverria-Duco *Tel:* (02)
    6862424 *E-mail:* gechever@vra.puc.cl
Founded: 1981
50% University textbooks & 50% all reader.
Subjects: Art, Biological Sciences, Economics,
    Education, Engineering (General), History, Lit-
    erature, Literary Criticism, Essays, Philoso-
    phy, Psychology, Psychiatry, Religion - Other,
    Agronomy
ISBN Prefix(es): 956-14
Total Titles: 15 Print
Foreign Rep(s): Alfaomega Grupo Editor SA de
    CV (Argentina, Colombia, Mexico); Alfaomega
    Grupo Editor, S A de C V (Argentina, Colom-
    bia, Mexico)

**Proa SA**+
Mac Iver 140, Casilla 9935 Dir Postal, Santiago
*Tel:* (02) 633 65 34; (02) 633 98 54 *Fax:* (02)
    633 98 54
*E-mail:* proa@eutelchile.net
*Key Personnel*
Manager: Jose Luis Benavente; Guillermo Varas
    Valdes
Founded: 1954
Specialize in importing Reproductive Art.
Subsidiaries: Libreria Noray

**Publicaciones Lo Castillo SA**
Perez Valenzuela No 1620, Providencia, Santiago
*Tel:* (02) 235 2606 *Fax:* (02) 235 2007
*Key Personnel*
General Manager: Alvaro Perez
Editor: Bartolome Yankovic
Founded: 1982
Subjects: Education, House & Home, Journalism, Travel
ISBN Prefix(es): 956-237
Imprints: Revista DATO

**Publicaciones Nuevo Extremo**
Bombero Adolfo Ossa 1067, Santiago
*Tel:* (02) 698 1523; (02) 697 2337 *Fax:* (02) 697 2545
*E-mail:* nexxtremo@entelchile.net
*Key Personnel*
Managing Dir: Eduardo G Castillo
ISBN Prefix(es): 956-7063

**Red Internacional Del Libro+**
El Vergel 2882, of 11, Providencia, Santiago
*Tel:* (02) 2238100 *Fax:* (02) 2254269
*E-mail:* ril@rileditores.com
*Web Site:* www.rileditores.com
*Key Personnel*
Legal Representative: Ricardo Diaz Ramirez
Publisher: Daniel Calabrese; Eleonora Finkelstein
Sales: Emilio Campos
Founded: 1991
Subjects: Education, Literature, Literary Criticism, Essays, Poetry
ISBN Prefix(es): 956-284; 956-7159

**Ediciones Rehue Ltda**
Argomedo 40, Santiago
*Tel:* (02) 6344653; (02) 6341804 *Fax:* (02) 6351096
*Key Personnel*
Dir: Anibal Pastor Ninez
ISBN Prefix(es): 956-228

**Revista DATO**, *imprint of* Publicaciones Lo Castillo SA

**J.C. Saez Editor+**
Elretiro 4853, Santiago Vitacura
*Tel:* (02) 3260104
*E-mail:* jcsaezc@jcsaezeditor.cl
*Web Site:* www.jcsaezeditor.cl
*Key Personnel*
General Manager: Juan Carlos Saez Contreras
    *E-mail:* jcsaezc@vtr.net
Founded: 2002
Subjects: Education, Literature, Literary Criticism, Essays
ISBN Prefix(es): 956-7802

**Publicaciones Tecnicas Mediterraneo+**
Elidoro Yanez 2541, Providencia, Santiago
*Tel:* (02) 251 62 57; (02) 233 82 72 *Fax:* (02) 231 06 94
*E-mail:* msalinero@entelchile.net
*Key Personnel*
Manager: Ramon Alvarez Minder
Founded: 1981
Membership(s): Chilean Book Association.
Subjects: Medicine, Nursing, Dentistry
ISBN Prefix(es): 956-220

**Texido Ltda**, see Editorial Texido Ltda

**Editorial Texido Ltda+**
Av Einstein 921, Recoleta, Santiago
*Tel:* (02) 6224652 *Fax:* (02) 6224660
Founded: 1969
Subjects: Gardening, Plants, Human Relations, Nonfiction (General)

ISBN Prefix(es): 956-273
*Associate Companies:* Comercial Distribuidora Librimundi Ltda; Altima Ltda

**Ediciones de la Universidad de la Frontera**
Av Francisco Salazar, 01145 Temuco
Mailing Address: Casilla 54-D, Temuco
*Tel:* (045) 325000 *Fax:* (045) 325116
ISBN Prefix(es): 956-236

**Universidad de Valparaiso**, see Edeval (Universidad de Valparaiso)

**Editorial Universitaria SA+**
Maria Luisa Santander, 0447 Providencia, Santiago
*Tel:* (02) 487 0700 *Fax:* (02) 487 0702
*E-mail:* comunicaciones@universitaria.cl
*Web Site:* www.universitaria.cl/index.pl *Cable:* EDUNSA
*Key Personnel*
Man Dir: Rodrigo Castro
Editor: Braulio Fernandez
Founded: 1947
Subjects: Literature, Literary Criticism, Essays, Science (General), Social Sciences, Sociology
ISBN Prefix(es): 84-8340; 956-11
Subsidiaries: Talleres Graficos; Texto Libro
Distributed by Axius (Argentina); Contemporanea de Ediciones (Venezuela); Ediciones Coliguee (Argentina); Ericiencia (Ecuador); Maria Ester Garcia (Paraguay); Librerias Faustos (Argentina); Zulema Medina (Uruguay)
*Showroom(s):* Sala Matte, Av Libertador B O'Higgins, 1050 Santiago *Fax:* (02) 6956387
*Bookshop(s):* Latorre 2500, Local 4, Antofagasta *Fax:* (055) 494 864; El Roble 510, Chillan *Fax:* (042) 216 443; Bernardo O'Higgins 770, Local 33, Concepcion *Fax:* (041) 250 867; Cordovez 470, La Serena *Fax:* (051) 224 685; Cochrane 545, Osorno *Fax:* (064) 232 613; Av Dag Hammarskjold S/N, Santiago *Tel:* (02) 210 2477; Av Libertador B O'Higgins 1040, Santiago *Tel:* (02) 487 0991; (02) 487 0990; Av Libertador Bernardo O'Higgins 1050, Santiago *Tel:* (02) 487 0983 *Fax:* (02) 487 0972; Avda Providencia 2110, Santiago; Uno Sur 1111, Talca *Tel:* (071) 213 803; Diego Portales 861, Temuco *Fax:* (045) 215 330; Picarte 461, Local 1, Valdivia *Fax:* (063) 212 645; Esmeralda 1132, Valparaiso *Fax:* (032) 257 573
*Shipping Address:* Ricardo Matte Perez 04310, Casilla 10220, Providencia, Santiago *Tel:* (02) 2233765 *Fax:* (02) 2099455 (02) 2049058
*Orders to:* Ricardo Matte Perez 04310, Casilla, 10220 Providencia, Santiago *Tel:* (02) 2233765 *Fax:* (02) 2049058

**Ediciones Universitarias de Valparaiso+**
12 De Febrero 187, Valparaiso
*Tel:* (032) 273087; (02) 6332230 *Fax:* (032) 273429
*E-mail:* euvsa@aixl.uvc.cl
*Telex:* 230389 Ucval Cl
*Key Personnel*
Manager: Karlheinz H Laage
Founded: 1970
Subjects: Art, Education, Engineering (General), History, Law, Literature, Literary Criticism, Essays, Music, Dance, Philosophy, Science (General), Social Sciences, Sociology, Technology
ISBN Prefix(es): 956-17
*Parent Company:* Universidad Catolica de Valparaiso, 12 De Febrero 187, Valparaiso
*Branch Office(s)*
Moneda 673 - 8 piso, Santiago *Tel:* (02) 633233

**Zig-Zag SA+**
Los Conquistadores 1700, piso 17 of 17B, Providencia, Santiago
*Tel:* (02) 335 7477 *Fax:* (02) 335 7545

*E-mail:* zigzag@rdc.cl
*Web Site:* www.zigzag.cl
*Key Personnel*
General Manager: Francisco Perez Frugone
Publishing Manager: Jose Manuel Zanartu
Founded: 1934
Distribuidor en Chile de otros sellos editoriales.
Subjects: Literature, Literary Criticism, Essays
ISBN Prefix(es): 956-12
Distributor for Editorial Atlantida (Argentina); Editorial Voluntad (Colombia)
*Showroom(s):* Compania 2752, Santiago
*Orders to:* Compania 2752, Santiago

# China

## General Information

*Capital:* Beijing
*Language:* Principally Northern Chinese (Mandarin). Local dialects spoken in the south & southeast
*Religion:* Confucianism, Buddhism & Daoism with small Muslim & Christian minorities
*Population:* 1.2 billion
*Shop Hours:* Generally 0900-1900 every day
*Currency:* 100 fen = 10 jiao = 1 yuan
*Export/Import Information:* Foreign trade is a state monopoly. The foreign distributor for Chinese publications is Guoji Shudian, PO Box 399, Beijing. The importing organization is Waiwen Shudian, PO Box 88, Beijing.
*Copyright:* UCC, Berne (see Copyright Conventions, pg xi)

**Agricultural Publishing House**, see China Agriculture Press

**Anhui Children's Publishing House+**
One Yuejin Rd, Hefei, Anhui 230063
*Tel:* (0551) 2849306 *Fax:* (0551) 2849306
*E-mail:* ahsebwsh@mail.hf.ah.cn
*Web Site:* www.ahse.cn
*Key Personnel*
President: Jianwei Liu
Chief Editor: Zhirun Zhu
Rights: Li Wang
Founded: 1984
Subjects: Child Care & Development
ISBN Prefix(es): 7-5397
Number of titles published annually: 300 Print
Total Titles: 2,509 Print

**Anhui People's Publishing House+**
381 Jinzhailu, Hefei, Anhui Providence 230063
*Tel:* (0551) 257134; (0551) 2653673 *Cable:* 1344
*Key Personnel*
Dir: Mr Guo Minggang
Founded: 1952
Subjects: Accounting, Advertising, Behavioral Sciences, Economics, Government, Political Science, History, Law, Philosophy, Social Sciences, Sociology
ISBN Prefix(es): 7-212

**Aviation Industry Press+**
14 Xiaoguan Dongli, Anwai, Beijing 100029
Mailing Address: PO Box 9817, Beijing 100029
*Tel:* (010) 64918417 *Fax:* (010) 64922217
*Key Personnel*
Dir General, Editorial Dept: Tiejun Zhang
Founded: 1985
Subjects: Aeronautics, Aviation, Computer Science, Economics, English as a Second Language, Mechanical Engineering
ISBN Prefix(es): 7-80046

**Beijing Ancient Books Publishing House+**
6 Beisanhuan Zhonglu, Beijing 100011

*Tel:* (010) 2016699 313; (010) 2013122
  *Fax:* (010) 2012339
*E-mail:* geo@bph.com.cn *Cable:* 8909
*Key Personnel*
Rights Dir: Ms Jackie Huang
Founded: 1979
ISBN Prefix(es): 7-5300
*Parent Company:* Beijing Publishing House

**Beijing Arts & Crafts Publishing House**
30 Shatan Houjie, Beijing 100006
*Tel:* (010) 65230677; (010) 4031811
*Key Personnel*
President: Wang Zhen
Vice President: Wu Peng
Subjects: Art
ISBN Prefix(es): 7-80526
Subsidiaries: Beijing Stars Advertisement Co

**Beijing Education Publishing House+**
6 Beisanhuan Zhonglu, Beijing 100011
*Tel:* (010) 2016699-268; (010) 62013122
  *Fax:* (010) 2012339
*E-mail:* geo@bph.com.cn *Cable:* 8909
*Key Personnel*
Rights Dir: Ms Jackie Huang
Founded: 1983
Subjects: Education
ISBN Prefix(es): 7-5303
*Parent Company:* Beijing Publishing House

**Beijing Fine Arts & Photography Publishing House+**
6 Beisanhuan Zhonglu, Beijing 100011
*Tel:* (010) 2016699; (010) 62016699-315
  *Fax:* (010) 2012339
*E-mail:* geo@bph.com.cn *Cable:* 8909
*Key Personnel*
Rights Dir: Ms Jackie Huang
Founded: 1983
ISBN Prefix(es): 7-80501
*Parent Company:* Beijing Publishing House

**Beijing Juvenile & Children's Books Publishing House+**
6 Beisanhuan Zhonglu, Beijing 100011
*Tel:* (010) 2016699-350; (010) 62013122
  *Fax:* (010) 2012339
*E-mail:* geo@bph.com.cn *Cable:* 8909
*Key Personnel*
Rights Dir: Ms Jackie Huang
Founded: 1983
Subjects: Child Care & Development, Education, Self-Help
ISBN Prefix(es): 7-5301
*Parent Company:* Beijing Publishing House

**Beijing Medical University Press+**
Beijing Medical University, 38 Xue Yuan Rd, Beijing 100083
*Tel:* (010) 62092249 *Fax:* (010) 62029848
*E-mail:* bmupress@public.fhnet.cn.net
*Web Site:* www.bjmu.edu.cn
*Key Personnel*
Dir: Dr Lin An *E-mail:* cbi@mail.bjmu.edu.cn
Contacts: Yin-dao Lu; Dipl Ing Zheng-bao Lu
  *Tel:* (010) 62092405
Founded: 1989
Subjects: Biological Sciences, Environmental Studies, Health, Nutrition, Medicine, Nursing, Dentistry, Psychology, Psychiatry
ISBN Prefix(es): 7-81034
Number of titles published annually: 180 Print; 4 CD-ROM
Total Titles: 950 Print; 2 CD-ROM

**Beijing Publishing House+**
6 Beisanhuan Zhonglu, Beijing 100011
*Tel:* (010) 62003964 *Fax:* (010) 62012339; (010) 62016699
*E-mail:* geo@bph.com.cn; public@bphg.com.cn

*Web Site:* www.bph.com.cn *Cable:* 8909
Founded: 1956
Subjects: Agriculture, Antiques, Architecture & Interior Design, Art, Behavioral Sciences, Biography, Business, Child Care & Development, Computer Science, Cookery, Drama, Theater, Economics, Education, Engineering (General), English as a Second Language, Fiction, Finance, History, How-to, Human Relations, Language Arts, Linguistics, Law, Literature, Literary Criticism, Essays, Management, Marketing, Medicine, Nursing, Dentistry, Nonfiction (General), Philosophy, Physics, Poetry, Science (General), Self-Help, Social Sciences, Sociology, Western Fiction, Women's Studies
ISBN Prefix(es): 7-200

**Beijing University Press+**
Haidianqu, Beijing 100871
*Tel:* (010) 62752033 *Fax:* (010) 2564095
*E-mail:* psj@pup.pku.edu.cn
*Key Personnel*
President: Peng Songjian
Founded: 1979
Subjects: Biological Sciences, Chemistry, Chemical Engineering, Computer Science, Economics, Education, English as a Second Language, Finance
ISBN Prefix(es): 7-301

**CFERT,** see China Foreign Economic Relations & Trade Publishing House

**Chemical Industry Press+**
Huixinli No 3, Chaoyang District, Beijing 100029
*Tel:* (010) 64918054; (010) 4213641; (010) 4234411 *Fax:* (010) 64918054
*Web Site:* www.cip.com.cn
*Key Personnel*
President: Feng Peizong
Rights Manager: Liang Hong *E-mail:* liangh@cip.com.cn
Founded: 1953
Subjects: Agriculture, Biological Sciences, Chemistry, Chemical Engineering, Civil Engineering, Communications, Education, Electronics, Electrical Engineering, Energy, Engineering (General), Environmental Studies, Health, Nutrition, Mechanical Engineering, Medicine, Nursing, Dentistry, Technology, Transportation
ISBN Prefix(es): 7-5025
Number of titles published annually: 1,000 Print
Total Titles: 10,000 Print
Divisions: The Applied Chemistry & Agricultural Reader Publishing Center; Beijing Progress Periodical; The Environmental Science & Engineering Publishing Center; The Fine Chemical Publishing Center; The Industrial Equipment & Information Engineering Publishing Center; The Material Science & Engineering Publishing Center; The Modern Biotech & Medical Sci-Tech Publishing Center; The Multi-Media Publishing Center; The Textbook Publishing Center
*Bookshop(s):* Chemical Bookstore

**Chengdu Maps Publishing House+**
Longquanyi, Chengdu, Sichuan 610100
*Tel:* (028) 485 2177; (028) 445 3030
*E-mail:* ccph@public.cd.sc.cn *Cable:* 9570
*Key Personnel*
President: Yao Rusong
Founded: 1985
Membership(s): Sichuan Surveying & Mapping Bureau & Sichuan News Publishing Bureau.
Subjects: Advertising, Communications, Computer Science, Earth Sciences, Education, Foreign Countries, Geography, Geology, Travel
ISBN Prefix(es): 7-80544
Divisions: Mapping Dept, Printing Factory

Distributor for China Cartography Publishing House
*Shipping Address:* Chengdu Cartography Publishing House, 29 Yikuan N Rd, 3rd Section, Wholesale Dept., Chengdu, Sichuan, PR China

**China Agriculture Press+**
2 Nongzhanguan North Rd, Chaoyang Dist, Beijing 100026
*Tel:* (010) 5005665 *Fax:* (010) 5005894
*E-mail:* fcap@bj.col.com.cn
*Key Personnel*
President: Cai Shenglin
International Rights: Hui Xu
Founded: 1958
Specialize in agricultural, scientific & technological books.
Subjects: Agriculture, Animals, Pets, Biological Sciences, Gardening, Plants, Technology, Veterinary Science
ISBN Prefix(es): 7-109
Subsidiaries: Rural Readings Press

**China Braille Publishing House**
39 Chengnei St, Lu Gou Qiao, Beijing 100072
*Tel:* (010) 6382 5214; (010) 6381 7417
  *Fax:* (010) 6383 3585
*Key Personnel*
President: Song Jianmin
Founded: 1953
Production of books & magazines in braille & tapes for the blind.
Membership(s): Press & Publication Administration; specialize in braille books; also acts as China Library for the Blind.
Subjects: Animals, Pets, Art, Child Care & Development, Crafts, Games, Hobbies, Disability, Special Needs, Economics, Education, English as a Second Language
ISBN Prefix(es): 7-5002
Subsidiaries: Beijing Hengji Co
*Book Club(s):* China Library for the Blind; Reading Club

**China Cartographic Publishing House+**
3 Baizhifang Xijie, Xuanwu Dist, Beijing 100054
*Tel:* (010) 6356 4947 *Fax:* (010) 6352 9403
*E-mail:* fanyi@chinamap.com *Cable:* 1955
*Key Personnel*
President: Wang Jixian
International Rights: Fan Yi
Founded: 1954
Subjects: Earth Sciences, Geography, Geology, Transportation, Travel
ISBN Prefix(es): 7-5031; 7-900048

**China Film Press+**
22 Beisanhuan Donglu, Beijing 100013
*Tel:* (010) 4217845; (010) 4219917 *Fax:* (010) 4216415
*Telex:* 222669 CFP CN *Cable:* 8468 BEIJING
*Key Personnel*
Editor-in-Chief: Cui Junyan
Founded: 1956
Specialize in film.
Membership(s): International Film Exchange.
Subjects: Advertising, Art, Biography, Career Development, Crafts, Games, Hobbies, Drama, Theater, Fashion, Fiction, Film, Video, History, Law, Literature, Literary Criticism, Essays, Marketing, Outdoor Recreation, Photography
ISBN Prefix(es): 7-106
Subsidiaries: Beijing Film Book; Shanghai Film Services Co
*Bookshop(s):* China Film Bookshop

**China Foreign Economic Relations & Trade Publishing House+**
28 Donghouxiang, Andingmenwai Dajie, Main Bldg, Room 309, Beijing 100710

*Tel:* (010) 64248236; (010) 64219742; (010) 64245686 *Fax:* (010) 64219392
*E-mail:* cfertph@263.net
*Web Site:* www.caitec.org.cn/cfertph/indexv3.htm
*Key Personnel*
President: Yan Weijing *E-mail:* yanweijing@263.net
Vice President: Song Dongjin
Founded: 1980
Business Books & Magazines.
Subjects: Accounting, Business, Economics, English as a Second Language, Finance, Government, Political Science, Management, Marketing
ISBN Prefix(es): 7-80004

**China Forestry Publishing House+**
7 Liuhai Hutong, Xichengqu District, Beijing 100009
*Tel:* (010) 6013117; (010) 661884477 *Fax:* (010) 66180373
*E-mail:* cfph@public3.bta.net.cn *Cable:* 1010
*Key Personnel*
Vice Editor-in-Chief: Chen Li
Subjects: Agriculture, Animals, Pets, Biological Sciences, Chemistry, Chemical Engineering, Economics, Gardening, Plants
ISBN Prefix(es): 7-5038
Distributed by University of British Columbia Press (UBC Press) (North America)

**China Labour Publishing House+**
One Huixin Dongjie Chaoyangqu, Beijing 100029
*Tel:* (010) 64911180; (010) 4910488
*Key Personnel*
President: Yunqi Tang
Editor-in-Chief: Wang Jianxin
Deputy Editor-in-Chief: Mengxin Zhang
Sales Dir: Hongrui Li
Production Dir: Yongguang Xie
Publicity Dir: Zhang Jiasheng
Rights & Permissions: Chao Zhou
Founded: 1980
Subjects: Business, Labor, Industrial Relations
ISBN Prefix(es): 7-5045

**China Light Industry Press+**
6 Dongchanganjie St, Beijing 100740
*Tel:* (010) 65271562 *Fax:* (010) 65121371 *Cable:* 1508
*Key Personnel*
President: Zhao Ti-Qing
Founded: 1954
Subjects: Art, Cookery, Fashion, Film, Video, House & Home, Language Arts, Linguistics, Wine & Spirits
ISBN Prefix(es): 7-5019

**China Machine Press (CMP)+**
22 Baiwanzhuang Rd, Beijing 100037
*Tel:* (010) 88379973 *Fax:* (010) 68320405 (orders)
*E-mail:* cjhui@mail.machineinfo.gov.cn
*Web Site:* www.cmpbook.com; www.machineinfo.gov.cn
*Telex:* 222557 STIP CN
*Key Personnel*
President: Wang Wenbin
Vice President: Li Qi
Sales: Tang Xiaoming
Production: Cheng Jingning
Publicity: Xu Tong
Rights & Permissions, I D D Dir: Chen Jianhui
Founded: 1952
Subjects: Architecture & Interior Design, Automotive, Business, Computer Science, Electronics, Electrical Engineering, Management, Mechanical Engineering, Microcomputers, Technology, Foreign Languages, Telecommunications
ISBN Prefix(es): 7-111

Number of titles published annually: 3,000 Print; 130 CD-ROM
*Associate Companies:* Jingfeng Printing Company of China Machine Press, 88 Liuzhuangzi, Fengtai District, Beijing 100071 *Tel:* (010) 63793671; The Printing Company of China Machine Press, 4 Ganjiakou, Haidian District, Beijing 100037 *Tel:* (010) 68353476
*Subsidiaries:* Huazhang Graphics & Information Co
*Bookshop(s):* Jigong Bookstore *Tel:* (010) 88379641
*Warehouse:* Huaxiang, Beijing 100071

**China Materials Management Publishing House+**
25 Yuetan Beijie, Xichengqu District, Beijing 100834
*Tel:* (010) 68392913; (010) 68392825 *Fax:* (010) 8392911 *Cable:* 1444
*Key Personnel*
President: Fan Xiyi
General Editor: Zhang Lizhong
Founded: 1981
Subjects: Automotive, Behavioral Sciences, Business, Economics, Human Relations, Management, Marketing
ISBN Prefix(es): 7-5047
*Book Club(s):* China Copyright Association

**China Ocean Press+**
Subsidiary of State Oceanic Administration
8 Da Hui Si Rd, Haidian District, Beijing 100081
*Tel:* (010) 62112880-888 *Fax:* (010) 62112880-617
*E-mail:* zbs@oceanpress.com.cn
*Web Site:* www.oceanpress.com.cn
*Key Personnel*
President: Gai Guangsheng
Editor-in-Chief: Miss Yang Suihua
Dir, International Dept: Miss Yang Qing
*Tel:* (010) 62173322, ext 212
Founded: 1978
Publish mainly in English, other languages available; specialize in marine science & technology.
Subjects: Biography, Biological Sciences, Chemistry, Chemical Engineering, Civil Engineering, Computer Science, Earth Sciences, Environmental Studies, Geography, Geology, Management, Maritime, Mechanical Engineering, Physical Sciences, Physics, Real Estate, Religion - Buddhist, Religion - Islamic, Religion - Jewish, Science (General), Social Sciences, Sociology, Technology
ISBN Prefix(es): 7-5027
Number of titles published annually: 10 Print
Total Titles: 300 Print

**China Oil & Gas Periodical Office+**
One Lou, 2 Qu Anhuali, Andingmenwai, Beijing 100011
*Tel:* (010) 64219111
*Key Personnel*
Editor-in-Chief: Zhaoren Li
Distribution Manager: Baoguo Wu
Founded: 1994
Subjects: Energy
ISBN Prefix(es): 7-5021

**China Pictorial Publishing House**
33 Chegongzhuang Xilu, Haidian District, Beijing 100044
*Tel:* (010) 68412392; (010) 68414896; (010) 68412665 *Fax:* (010) 68413023
*E-mail:* wangjingtang@hotmail.com
*Web Site:* www.china-pictorial.com *Cable:* CHINAPIC 3973
*Key Personnel*
Contact: Li Lian
Founded: 1985
ISBN Prefix(es): 7-80024

**China Social Sciences Publishing House+**
A158 Gulou Xidajie, Beijing 100720
*Tel:* (010) 64031534 *Fax:* (010) 64074509
*Key Personnel*
Dir, Social Sciences: Wang Baochun
Dir, Reader Services: Wana Shan
Dir: Cui Yaqin
Founded: 1978
Specialize in the task of editing & publishing monographs, reference books, teaching materials & basic reading materials in the fields of philosophy & social sciences as well as Chinese translations of major foreign works, publisher for Social Sciences in China (Journal of Cass) & periodicals for several research institutes.
Subjects: Philosophy, Social Sciences, Sociology
ISBN Prefix(es): 7-5004
*Bookshop(s):* A62 Jianguomennei Dajie, Beijing 100005; 31 Book-Town Haidian Dajie, Beijing 10080

**China Textile Press+**
Subsidiary of China National Textile Industry Council (CNTIC)
No 6, Dongzhimen Nandajie, Beijing 100027
*Tel:* (010) 64168240 *Fax:* (010) 64168225
*Web Site:* www.c-textilep.com
*Key Personnel*
President: Chen Zhishan
Administrative Vice President: Li Lingshen
Editor-in-Chief: Zheng Qun
Copyright Manager: Li Jing *E-mail:* jing_lg@163.com
Textile & clothing technology, arts & crafts, business & management, culture & life style.
Membership(s): The Publishers Association of China.
Subjects: Business, Crafts, Games, Hobbies, Management
ISBN Prefix(es): 7-5064

**China Theatre Publishing House+**
A81 Dazhongsi Nancun, Haidianqu, Beijing 100086
*Tel:* (010) 62244207; (010) 62244208
*Key Personnel*
President: Li Haichuan
Founded: 1957
Subjects: Crafts, Games, Hobbies, Drama, Theater, Education, Fiction, History, Literature, Literary Criticism, Essays, Nonfiction (General)
ISBN Prefix(es): 7-104

**China Tibetology Publishing House+**
131 Beisihuandonglu, Beijing 100101
*Tel:* (010) 64917618; (010) 64932942 *Fax:* (010) 4917619
*Key Personnel*
Dir: Tendzin Sr
Editor-in-Chief: Liao Zugui
Specialize in Tibetan studies.
Subjects: Anthropology, Archaeology, Asian Studies, Economics, Education, Religion - Buddhist, Social Sciences, Sociology
ISBN Prefix(es): 7-80057
*Orders to:* China International Book Trading Corporation, PO Box 399, Beijing 100080

**China Translation & Publishing Corp+**
4 Taipingqiao Dajie, Xichengqu District, Beijing 100810
*Tel:* (010) 66168196; (010) 66168647 *Fax:* (010) 6022734
*E-mail:* ctpc@public.bta.net.cn
*Key Personnel*
Contact: Xu Jihong
International Rights & Deputy General Manager: Hsuan-chin Chou
Subjects: Economics, Education, Management
ISBN Prefix(es): 7-5001

**China Youth Publishing House+**
21 Dongsi Shiertiao, Beijing 100708
*Tel:* (010) 64033812; (010) 64032266 *Fax:* (010)
   4031803 *Cable:* 4357
*Key Personnel*
President: Cai Yun
Editor: Kan Daolong
Contact: Mr Bingbin Bi
Founded: 1950
Subjects: Education, Language Arts, Linguistics,
   Literature, Literary Criticism, Essays, Science
   (General), Social Sciences, Sociology
ISBN Prefix(es): 7-5006

**Chinese Literature Press+**
24 Baiwanzhuang Rd, Beijing 100037
*Tel:* (010) 68326678 *Fax:* (010) 68326678
*E-mail:* chinalit@public.east.cn.net
*Key Personnel*
Commissioning Editor: Zhang Shaoning
Contact: Shen Jieying
Founded: 1951 (English; 1964 French)
Subjects: Art, Fiction, Poetry
ISBN Prefix(es): 7-5071
*Parent Company:* China International Publishing
   Group
*Orders to:* China International Book Trading
   Corp (CIBTC), PO Box 399, Beijing 100044

**Chinese Pedagogics Publishing House+**
24 Baiwanzhuanglu Rd, Beijing 100037
Mailing Address: PO Box 399, Beijing 10004
*Tel:* (010) 68326333 *Fax:* (010) 8317390
*Telex:* 222475 FLP CN *Cable:* FOLAPRESS
   BEIJING
*Key Personnel*
President & Chief Executive: Shan Ying
   *Tel:* (010) 68994599
Editor-in-Chief: Jia Yinhuai
Sales (Overseas Dept Sinolingua) & Publicity:
   Hui Han
Rights & Permissions: Ling Yu
Founded: 1985
Specialize in teaching Chinese as a foreign lan-
   guage.
Membership(s): China International Publishing
   Group.
Subjects: Education, Language Arts, Linguistics
ISBN Prefix(es): 7-80052
Total Titles: 300 Print; 30 Audio
*Parent Company:* Foreign Languages Press
*Associate Companies:* China International Book
   Trading Corporation, 35 Chegong-zhuang
   Xilu, Beijing 100044 *Fax:* (010) 68412023
   *E-mail:* om@mail.cibtc.com.cn
*Branch Office(s)*
CBT China Book Trading GmbH, Max-Planck Str
   6-A, 63322 Rodermark, Germany *Fax:* (0674)
   95271 *E-mail:* chinabook@aol.com
Cypress Book Co Ltd, 10 Swinton St, London
   WC1X 9NX, United Kingdom *Fax:* (020) 7833
   0220
*U.S. Office(s):* Cypress Books (US) Co Inc, 450
   Third St, Unit 4B, San Francisco, CA 94124,
   United States
Distributed by China Books & Periodicals
*Shipping Address:* China International Book
   Trading Corporation, 35 Chegong-zhuang
   Xilu, Beijing 100044 *Fax:* (010) 68412023
   *E-mail:* om@mail.cibtc.com.cn; CBT China
   Book Trading GmbH, Max-Planck Str 6-A,
   63322 Rodermark, Germany *Fax:* (0674) 95271
   *E-mail:* chinabook@aol.com
*Warehouse:* China International Book Trading
   Corporation, 35 Chegong-zhuang Xilu, Beijing
   100044 *Fax:* (010) 68412023 *E-mail:* om@
   mail.cibtc.com.cn
CBT China Book Trading GmbH, Max-Planck Str
   6-A, 63322 Rodermark, Germany *Fax:* (0674)
   95271 *E-mail:* chinabook@aol.com
*Orders to:* Cypress Book Co (UK) Ltd, 10 Swin-
   ton St, London WC1X 9NX, United Kingdom
   *Fax:* (020) 7837 7768

CBT China Book Trading GmbH, Max-Planck Str
   6-A, 63322 Rodermark, Germany *Tel:* (0674)
   95271 *E-mail:* chinabook@aol.com
Cypress Books (US) Co Inc, 450 Third St, Unit
   4B, San Francisco, CA 94124, United States

**Chongqing University Press+**
No 174 Shapingba Zhengjie, Chongqing 400030
*Tel:* (023) 65111125 *Fax:* (023) 65106879
*E-mail:* chenxy@cqup.com.cn
*Web Site:* www.cqup.com.cn
*Key Personnel*
Dir: Zhang Gesheng
Founded: 1985
Subjects: Language Arts, Linguistics, Manage-
   ment, Science (General), Social Sciences, Soci-
   ology, Technology
ISBN Prefix(es): 7-5624
Number of titles published annually: 500 Print
Total Titles: 4,000 Print

**CITIC Publishing House+**
Ta Yuan Diplomatic Office Bldg, No 14,
   Liangmahe St, Chaoyang District, Beijing
   100600
*Tel:* (010) 85323366 *Fax:* (010) 85322508
*E-mail:* g-office@citic.com.cn; mail@citicpub.
   com
*Web Site:* www.citic.com.cn; www.publish.citic.
   com
*Telex:* 210026 CITIC CN
*Key Personnel*
Chairman: Wang Jun
Vice Chairman & President: Kong Dan
Chief Editor: Li Debao
Senior Revisor: Gong Yuang
Senior Editor: He Peihui
Founded: 1988
Specialize in both copyright transactions & co-
   publication of books with foreign publishers,
   bookdealers or any other relevant groups or
   individuals, & launching joint ventures on busi-
   ness in publication & distribution.
Subjects: Accounting, Business, Economics, Fi-
   nance, How-to, Law, Management, Marketing,
   Nonfiction (General)
ISBN Prefix(es): 7-80073
*Parent Company:* China International Trust & In-
   vestment Corporation (Holdings)
*Associate Companies:* CITIC Representative Office in Japan, 3/F, The Landic Third Akasaka
   Bldg, 2-3-2, Akasaka, Minato-Ku, Tokyo 107-
   0052, Japan *Tel:* (03) 35842636 *Fax:* (03)
   35056235 *E-mail:* citic.tyo@nifty.com; CITIC
   Representative Office in New York, 350
   Albany St, New York, NY 10280, United
   States *Tel:* 212-945-4068 *Fax:* 212-945-0273
   *E-mail:* citicny@msn.com; CITIC Representa-
   tive Office in Europe, HongKongstr 5, 3047
   BR Rotterdam, Netherlands *Tel:* (010) 4626
   588 *Fax:* (010) 2624 768

CMP, see China Machine Press (CMP)

**Cultural Relics Publishing House+**
Affiliate of Chinese Administration For Cultural
   Heritage
29 Wusi Dajie, Beijing 100009
*Tel:* (010) 64048057 *Fax:* (010) 64010698
*E-mail:* web@wenwu.com
*Web Site:* www.wenwu.com
*Key Personnel*
International Division: Mr Zhao Lihua *Tel:* (010)
   64048057
Founded: 1957
Subjects: Anthropology, Antiques, Archaeology,
   Art, Asian Studies, History
ISBN Prefix(es): 7-5010
Divisions: International Division
*Orders to:* International Division, 29 Wusi Dajie,
   Beijing 100009

CWPP, see Water Resources & Electric Power
   Press (CWPP)

**Dalian Maritime University Press+**
One Linghai Rd, Dalian 116026
*Tel:* (0411) 84729480; (0411) 84728394
   *Fax:* (0411) 84727996
*E-mail:* dmup@dmupress.com; cbs@dmupress.
   com
*Web Site:* www.dmupress.com
*Key Personnel*
Dir: Yuan Linxin
Founded: 1987
Subjects: Communications, Computer Science,
   Economics, Electronics, Electrical Engineering,
   English as a Second Language, Management,
   Maritime, Science (General)
ISBN Prefix(es): 7-5632

**Dolphin Books+**
24 Baiwanzhuanglu, Beijing 100037
*Tel:* (010) 68326332 *Fax:* (010) 8317390
*Telex:* 222475 Flp *Cable:* FOLAPRESS BEIJING
*Key Personnel*
Dir: Jiang Cheng'an
Publicity & Production: Zhangyun He
Founded: 1986
Specialize in illustrated children's books.
ISBN Prefix(es): 7-80051; 7-80138
*Parent Company:* Foreign Languages Press
*U.S. Office(s):* Cypress Book (US) Co Inc, 3450
   Third St, Unit 4B, San Francisco, CA 94124,
   United States *Tel:* 415-821-3582
*Shipping Address:* China International Book Trad-
   ing Corporation, 35 Chegong-zhuang Zilu, Bei-
   jing 100044
*Warehouse:* China International Book Trading
   Corporation, 35 Chegong-zhuang Zilu, Beijing
   100044
*Orders to:* Cypress Book Co (UK) Ltd, 10 Swin-
   ton St, London WC1X 9NX, United Kingdom
Cypress Book (US) Co Inc, 3450 Third St, Unit
   4B, San Francisco, CA 94124, United States
   *Tel:* 415-821-3582

**East China Normal University Press+**
N Zhongshan Rd 3663, Shanghai 200062
*Tel:* (021) 62232613 *Fax:* (021) 62864922
*E-mail:* lxb@ecnu.edu.cn
*Web Site:* www.ecnu.edu.cn
*Key Personnel*
President: Wang Jianpan
Editor: Jin Qin Xiang
Author: Kuan Guang Ye
Founded: 1957
ISBN Prefix(es): 7-5617
Subsidiaries: Da Hua Industry & Trade Co

**East China University of Science & Technology
Press**
130 Meilong Rd, Shanghai 200237
*Tel:* (021) 64132885 *Fax:* (021) 64250735
*E-mail:* ies@ecust.edu.cn
*Web Site:* www.ecust.edu.cn *Cable:* 9006
*Key Personnel*
President: Wang Xingyu
Founded: 1986
Subjects: Agriculture, Computer Science, Educa-
   tion, Engineering (General), English as a Sec-
   ond Language, Environmental Studies, Finance,
   Technology
ISBN Prefix(es): 7-5628

**Education Science Publishing House**
46 Beisanhuan Zhonglu, Beijing 100088
*Tel:* (010) 62102454; (010) 62013803 *Fax:* (010)
   62012454
*E-mail:* esph@public.net.china.com.cn
*Key Personnel*
International Rights: Ms Li Bin *Tel:* (010)
   62003353
Founded: 1980

Subjects: Education, English as a Second Language, Human Relations, Military Science, Natural History, Science Fiction, Fantasy
ISBN Prefix(es): 7-5041
Total Titles: 1,866 Print; 12 Audio
*Parent Company:* Yan-Li Gin
*Ultimate Parent Company:* Xu-Chang Fa

**Electronics Industry Publishing House**
PO Box 173, Wanshoulu, Beijing 100036
*Tel:* (010) 68159318; (010) 68159020 *Fax:* (010) 68159032
*Web Site:* www.phei.com.cn
*Key Personnel*
President: Mr Liang Xiang Feng
International Rights: Mr Huang Zhi Yu
Subjects: Communications, Computer Science, Electronics, Electrical Engineering, Microcomputers, Radio, TV
ISBN Prefix(es): 7-5053

**Encyclopedia of China Publishing House+**
17 Fuchengmen Bei Dajie, Beijing 100037
*Tel:* (010) 68315610 *Fax:* (010) 68316510
*E-mail:* ygh@bj.col.com.cn *Cable:* ECPH
*Key Personnel*
President. Shan Jifu
Founded: 1978
Subjects: Art, Education, Fiction, Technology
ISBN Prefix(es): 7-5000
Subsidiaries: Knowledge Publishing House

**First Edition,** *imprint of* Jinan Publishing House

**Foreign Language Teaching & Research Press+**
No 19, Xisanhuan Beilu, Beijing 100089
*Tel:* (010) 8881-7788 ext 3507 *Fax:* (010) 8881-7889
*E-mail:* international@fltrp.com
*Web Site:* www.fltrp.com
*Key Personnel*
President: Li Pengyi
Vice President, Sales & Publishing Manager: Zhao Wenyan
Assistant President & Head of the Inter-area & International Cooperation Dept: Yu Chunchi
Chief, General Editorial Office: Lei Hang
Chief, First Editorial Section: Wang Weiguo
Chief, Second Editorial Section: Cai Jianfeng
Chief, Third Editorial Section: Xu Jianzhong
Chief, Fourth Editorial Section: Xu Chunjian
Editorial Manager, Publicity & Rights & Permissions: Zheng Jiande
Head, Inter-Area & International Cooperation Dept: Yu Chanchi
Chief, Finance Section: Ge Jusheng
Founded: 1979
Subjects: English as a Second Language, Foreign Countries, History, Language Arts, Linguistics, Literature, Literary Criticism, Essays, Social Sciences, Sociology, Western Fiction
ISBN Prefix(es): 7-5600; 7-900626

**Foreign Languages Press+**
24 Baiwanzhuang Rd, Xicheng District, Beijing 100037
*Tel:* (010) 68995852; (010) 68996188
*E-mail:* flpcn@public3.bta.net.cn
*Web Site:* www.flp.com.cn
*Telex:* 222475 FLP CN *Cable:* FOLAPRESS BEIJING
*Key Personnel*
President: Xu Mingqiang
Vice President: Li Zhengno
Overseas Dept Dir & Rights & Permissions: Sun Haiyu
Founded: 1952
Published Languages (in addition to Chinese): Arabic, Bengali, English, French, German, Hindi, Indonesian, Italian, Japanese, Korean,

Myanmar, Portuguese, Russian, Spanish, Swahili, Urdu, & Vietnamese.
Subjects: Anthropology, Archaeology, Art, Biography, Cookery, Drama, Theater, Economics, Geography, Geology, Government, Political Science, History, Law, Literature, Literary Criticism, Essays, Medicine, Nursing, Dentistry, Philosophy, Science (General), Sports, Athletics, Travel
ISBN Prefix(es): 7-119
Total Titles: 1,500 Print; 40 Audio
*Parent Company:* China International Publishing Group
Imprints: Phoenix
Subsidiaries: Dolphin Books; Sinolingua
*U.S. Office(s):* Cypress Book Co Inc, 3450 Third St, Suite 4B, San Francisco, CA, United States
*Tel:* 415-821-3582
*Orders to:* Cypress Book (US) Co Inc, 3450 Third St, Suite 4B, San Francisco, CA 94124, United States
Cypress Book Co (UK) Ltd, 10 Swinton St, London WC1X 9NX, United Kingdom

**Fudan University Press+**
579 Guoquanlu, Shanghai 200433
*Tel:* (021) 5484906-2842 *Fax:* (021) 65104812; (021) 65642840
*E-mail:* fupirc@fudan.edu.cn
*Key Personnel*
President: Zhiwei Xu
Dir: Xianghua Lin
Founded: 1981
Subjects: Accounting, Advertising, Art, Asian Studies, Behavioral Sciences, Biography, Biological Sciences, Business, Chemistry, Chemical Engineering, Communications, Computer Science, Economics, Education, Electronics, Electrical Engineering, English as a Second Language, Finance, Genealogy, Geography, Geology, Government, Political Science, Health, Nutrition, History, How-to, Human Relations, Language Arts, Linguistics, Law, Library & Information Sciences, Literature, Literary Criticism, Essays, Management, Marketing, Mathematics, Microcomputers, Natural History, Philosophy, Photography, Physical Sciences, Physics, Poetry, Psychology, Psychiatry, Public Administration, Regional Interests, Religion - Buddhist, Science (General), Securities, Social Sciences, Sociology, Technology, Women's Studies, Comprehensive
ISBN Prefix(es): 7-309; 7-900606

**Fujian Children's Publishing House+**
59 Deguixiang, Fuzhou, Fujian Province 350001
*Fax:* (0591) 7539070
*E-mail:* fcph@163.net
Subjects: Art, Education, Humor, Literature, Literary Criticism, Essays
ISBN Prefix(es): 7-5395
Total Titles: 320 Print

**Fujian Science & Technology Publishing House+**
15F, Fujian Publishing Center Bldg, 76 Dongshui Rd, Fuzhou, Fujian 350001
*Tel:* (0591) 87538472 *Fax:* (0591) 87538472
*E-mail:* copyright@fjstp.com
*Web Site:* www.fjstp.com
Founded: 1979
Scientific & technological books & magazines provider.
Subjects: Agriculture, Architecture & Interior Design, Communications, Computer Science, Electronics, Electrical Engineering, Health, Nutrition, Medicine, Nursing, Dentistry, Science (General), Technology, Transportation
ISBN Prefix(es): 7-5335
Number of titles published annually: 400 Print; 100 CD-ROM

Total Titles: 4,000 Print; 300 CD-ROM
*Parent Company:* Fujian General Publishing House

**Geological Publishing House+**
Bldg 10, Section 7, Hepingli, Beijing 100083
*Tel:* (010) 62351944 *Fax:* (010) 6024523
*Telex:* 22531 MGMRC
*Key Personnel*
Man Dir & Rights & Permissions: Ma Qingyang
Editor-in-Chief: Shen Shurong
Sales Manager: Xu Yixiao
Production Manager: Wei Hongzhen
Founded: 1954
Subjects: Geography, Geology
ISBN Prefix(es): 7-116
*Bookshop(s):* Geological Bookshop, Xisi, Beijing

**Guangdong Science & Technology Press+**
13-14F/11 Shuiyin Rd, Guangzhou, Guangdong 510075
*Tel:* (020) 87768688; (020) 87618770 (Directorial Office); (020) 87769412 (Foreign Cooperation Editorial Office) *Fax:* (020) 87764169
*E-mail:* gdkjwb@ns.guangzhou.gb.com.cn
*Web Site:* www.xwcbj.gd.gov.cn *Cable:* 3934
*Key Personnel*
President: Ouyang Lian
International Rights: Yuntei (Violet) Ding
Founded: 1979
Subjects: Agriculture, Architecture & Interior Design, Computer Science, Cookery, English as a Second Language, Plants, Mathematics, Medicine, Nursing, Dentistry
ISBN Prefix(es): 7-5359; 7-900341

**Guizhou Education Publishing House**
289 Zhonghua Beilu, Guiyang, Guizhou Province 550001
*Tel:* (0851) 627904; (0851) 524211
*Key Personnel*
President: Jize Zhang
Founded: 1990
Subjects: Art, Chemistry, Chemical Engineering, Child Care & Development, Economics, Education, Gardening, Plants, History, Human Relations
ISBN Prefix(es): 7-80583

**Heilongjiang Science & Technology Press+**
41 Jianshejie Nangangqu, Harbin, Heilongjiang Province 150001
*Tel:* (0451) 3635613 *Fax:* (0451) 3642127
*Key Personnel*
President: Xiao Erbin
International Rights: Liu Zhong
Founded: 1979
Subjects: Advertising, Agriculture, Architecture & Interior Design, Business, Communications, Economics, Electronics, Electrical Engineering, Health, Nutrition, How-to, Management, Marketing, Medicine, Nursing, Dentistry, Photography, Physical Sciences, Science (General), Technology, Transportation, Veterinary Science
ISBN Prefix(es): 7-5388

**Henan Science & Technology Publishing House+**
66 Jingwu Rd, Zhengzhou, Henan Province 450002
*Tel:* (0371) 5727616; (0371) 5721756-643 *Fax:* (0371) 5727616
*E-mail:* hnkj565@public2.zz.ha.cn *Cable:* 5171
*Key Personnel*
President & Rights Contact: Li Jing-lin
Editor-in-Chief: Yuan Yuan *Tel:* (0371) 5727616
Rights Contact: Ms Liu Xin
Founded: 1980
Specialize in scientific & technological subjects.
Subjects: Architecture & Interior Design, Biological Sciences, Chemistry, Chemical Engineering,

Gardening, Plants, Mechanical Engineering, Medicine, Nursing, Dentistry, Physical Sciences, Living
ISBN Prefix(es): 7-5349
Total Titles: 300 Print
*Parent Company:* News & Publishing Bureau of Henan Province, Hong Kong
*Ultimate Parent Company:* News & Publicity Bureau of China

**HEP,** *imprint of* Higher Education Press

**Higher Education Press+**
4 Dewai Dajie, Xicheng District, Beijing 100011
*Tel:* (010) 58581862 *Fax:* (010) 82085552
*Web Site:* www.hep.edu.cn; www.hep.com.cn
*Cable:* 7559
*Key Personnel*
President: Liu Zhipeng
Vice President & Editor-in-Chief: Zhang Zeng-shun
Dir, International Cooperation Division: Li Min
*E-mail:* limin@hep.com.cn
Founded: 1954
Publications for textbooks & references in higher education, vocational & adult educational.
Subjects: Agriculture, Architecture & Interior Design, Biological Sciences, Civil Engineering, Computer Science, Cookery, Education, Engineering (General), English as a Second Language, Finance, Gardening, Plants, Geography, Geology, History, Language Arts, Linguistics, Management, Psychology, Psychiatry, Science (General), Social Sciences, Sociology, Technology, Travel, Women's Studies
ISBN Prefix(es): 7-04; 7-900076
Number of titles published annually: 4,000 Print
Total Titles: 12,000 Print
*Parent Company:* Ministry of Education
Imprints: HEP
Subsidiaries: Beijing Kewen Higher Education Co Ltd
Divisions: Shanghai Office

**Inner Mongolia Science & Technology Publishing House+**
4 Nanyiduan, Hadajie, Chifengshi, Inner Mongolia 024000
*Tel:* (0476) 82222 942 *Cable:* 5536
Founded: 1982
Subjects: Agriculture, Astronomy, Electronics, Electrical Engineering, Mathematics, Microcomputers, Physics, Publishing & Book Trade Reference, Science (General), Veterinary Science
ISBN Prefix(es): 7-5380

**International Culture Publishing Corp+**
40 Andingmennei Dajie, Beijing 100009
*Tel:* (010) 64013415 *Fax:* (010) 64013437
Founded: 1984
ISBN Prefix(es): 7-80049

**Jiangsu Juveniles & Children's Publishing House+**
14F Phoenix Palace Hotel, 47 Hunan Rd, Nanjing, Jiangsu 210009
*Tel:* (025) 83242938 *Fax:* (025) 83242350
*E-mail:* susao@public1.ptt.js.cn
*Key Personnel*
Copyright Dir: Xiao Hong Wu
Founded: 1984
Publish books for children under 15 years old including picture books, literature & parenting books.
ISBN Prefix(es): 7-5346
*Parent Company:* JiangSu Publishing Group

**Jiangsu People's Publishing House+**
165 Zhongyanglu, Jiangsu, Nanjing 210009
*Tel:* (025) 639780 *Fax:* (025) 83379766

*Web Site:* www.book-wind.com
*Telex:* 0512
ISBN Prefix(es): 7-214

**Jiangsu Science & Technology Publishing House+**
47 Hunan Road, Nanjing, Jiangsu 210009
*Tel:* (025) 83273033 *Fax:* (025) 83273111
*E-mail:* cnjsstph@publicl.ptt.js.cn
*Web Site:* www.jskjpub.com
*Key Personnel*
President: Ming Xiu Hu
International Dept: Helen Deng; LianMin Sun
Founded: 1978
Subjects: Chemistry, Chemical Engineering, Computer Science, Earth Sciences, Engineering (General), Environmental Studies, Geography, Geology, Health, Nutrition, Physical Sciences, Science (General), Technology
ISBN Prefix(es): 7-5345

**Jilin Science & Technology Publishing House+**
A22 Tongzhijie, Changchun, Jilin 130021
*Tel:* (0431) 5635185 *Fax:* (0431) 5635185
*E-mail:* jlkjcbs@public.ec.jl.cn
*Key Personnel*
Rights Director: Frank Young
*E-mail:* frankyoung@sina.com
Founded: 1984
Publishing house.
Subjects: Accounting, Advertising, Agriculture, Animals, Pets, Anthropology, Architecture & Interior Design, Astronomy, Automotive, Biography, Biological Sciences, Business, Career Development, Chemistry, Chemical Engineering, Child Care & Development, Civil Engineering, Computer Science, Cookery, Electronics, Electrical Engineering, Engineering (General), English as a Second Language, Environmental Studies, Health, Nutrition, House & Home, How-to, Management, Marketing, Mathematics, Mechanical Engineering, Medicine, Nursing, Dentistry, Microcomputers, Outdoor Recreation, Photography, Physical Sciences, Physics, Science (General), Science Fiction, Fantasy, Sports, Athletics, Technology, Travel, Veterinary Science
ISBN Prefix(es): 7-5384
Number of titles published annually: 200 Print
Total Titles: 500 Print

**Jinan Publishing House+**
251 Jingqilu, Jinan, Shandong 250001
*Tel:* (0531) 6913006
*Key Personnel*
President: Weng Cheng
Founded: 1988
Subjects: Agriculture, Cookery, Economics, Education, Medicine, Nursing, Dentistry, Nonfiction (General), Social Sciences, Sociology
ISBN Prefix(es): 7-80572; 7-80629
Imprints: First Edition

**Juvenile & Children's Publishing House**
1538 Yan'an Road W, Shanghai 200052
*Tel:* (021) 62823025 *Fax:* (021) 62526963
*Web Site:* www.jcph.com
ISBN Prefix(es): 7-5324

**Knowledge Press+**
17 Fuchengmen Beidajie, Beijing 100037
*Tel:* (010) 68315610 *Fax:* (010) 68316510
*E-mail:* ecphtdb@public3.bta.net.cn *Cable:* ECPH
*Key Personnel*
President: Zhai Defang
Subjects: Civil Engineering, Health, Nutrition, Human Relations, Science (General), Social Sciences, Sociology
ISBN Prefix(es): 7-5015

**Kunlun Publishing House+**
3A Maowu Hutong, Xishiku, Beijing 100034
*Tel:* (010) 6732721 *Fax:* (010) 62183683; (010) 66847703
*Key Personnel*
President: Cheng Bu-tao
Vice President: Fan Chuan-xin; Zhu Ya-nan
Founded: 1951
Subjects: Biography, Literature, Literary Criticism, Essays, Military Science, Nonfiction (General), Social Sciences, Sociology
ISBN Prefix(es): 7-80040
*Parent Company:* The Cultural Dept of the General Political Dep
*Bookshop(s):* 36 Middle North Sanhuan Rd, Beijing 100084

**Language Publishing House+**
51 Nanxiaojie Chaonei, Beijing 100010
*Tel:* (010) 65130349; (010) 65241766
*Key Personnel*
President: Li Xingjian
Founded: 1980
Subjects: Communications
ISBN Prefix(es): 7-80126

**Lanzhou University Press+**
216 Tianshuilu, Lanzhou, Gansu 730000
Mailing Address: General Edition Office, 308 Tianshui Rd, Lanzhou, Gansu 730000
*Tel:* (0931) 8843000-3514 *Fax:* (0931) 8615095
*E-mail:* press@lzu.edu.cn
*Key Personnel*
Chairman: Prof Li Ji-Jun *Tel:* (0931) 891-1282 *Fax:* (0931) 891-1282 *E-mail:* lijj@lzu.edu.cn
President: Mr Yu Zejun
Vice President: Mr Lei Hongchang; Mrs Rao Hui
General Editor: Mr Zhang Kefei
Founded: 1985
Subjects: Behavioral Sciences, Economics, Education, Government, Political Science, History, Law, Philosophy, Physics, Psychology, Psychiatry, Social Sciences, Sociology
ISBN Prefix(es): 7-311
*Bookshop(s):* 268 Tianshui Rd, Lanzhou University, Lanzhou, Gansu 730000

**The Law Publishing House**
17 Denglai Hutong, Guangneidajie, Xuanwuqu, Beijing 100073
*Tel:* (010) 63266796; (010) 63266790
*Key Personnel*
Executive Dir, Editorial: Lan Ming-Liang
Sales: Wang Jia-jing
Production, Publicity: Ling Yu-jie
Rights & Permissions: Jiang Xou Yuan
Founded: 1980
Also acts as book packager.
Subjects: Law
ISBN Prefix(es): 7-5036

**Liaoning People's Publishing House+**
108 Beiyi Malu, Hepingqu, Shenyang, Liaoning 110001
*Tel:* (024) 3861304 *Fax:* (024) 371472 *Cable:* 3652
*Key Personnel*
Chief Executive: Ren Huiying
Editorial Dir: Li Fan
Sales: Li Wenshan
Founded: 1951
Subjects: Economics, History
ISBN Prefix(es): 7-205
Subsidiaries: Liao-Shen Publishing House

**Metallurgical Industry Press (MIP)+**
2 Xinjiekouwai Dajie, Beijing 100008
*Tel:* (010) 62014832; (010) 64015599 *Fax:* (010) 62015019
*E-mail:* jrechina@public.fhnet.cn.net
*Telex:* 222753 CMMI CN *Cable:* 3658
*Key Personnel*
President: Qing Qiyun

Sales: Yang Jin
Editor-in-Chief: Yang Chuanfu; Liu Shan
Founded: 1953
Subjects: Chemistry, Chemical Engineering, Computer Science, Earth Sciences, Electronics, Electrical Engineering, Engineering (General), Environmental Studies, Geography, Geology, Management, Mathematics, Mechanical Engineering, Technology
ISBN Prefix(es): 7-5024

**MIP,** see Metallurgical Industry Press (MIP)

**Modern Press**
504 Anhuali, Andingmenwai, Beijing 100011
*Tel:* (010) 4215031-383 *Fax:* (010) 4214540
   *Cable:* 1200
*Key Personnel*
President: Lou Ming
ISBN Prefix(es): 7-80028

**Morning Glory Press+**
35 Chegongzhuang Xilu, Beijing 100044
*Tel:* (010) 68411973; (010) 68433187 *Fax:* (010) 68412023; (010) 68485739
*E-mail:* zh@mail.cibtc.com.cn; zh1@mail.cibtc.com.cn *Cable:* CIBTC BEIJING
*Key Personnel*
Contact: Ms Zheng Wenlei
Founded: 1982
Copyright transfer; purchase of entire editions.
Subjects: Art, Cookery, History, Photography
ISBN Prefix(es): 7-5054
*Parent Company:* China International Book Trading Corporation

**Nanjing University Press+**
Nanjing University, 22 Hankoulu Rd, Nanjing, Jiangsu 210093
*Tel:* (025) 83593450; (025) 83303347
*Web Site:* press.nju.edu.cn
*Key Personnel*
President: Shi Huirong
Founded: 1984
Subjects: Biography, Biological Sciences, Chemistry, Chemical Engineering, Computer Science, Earth Sciences, Economics, English as a Second Language, Environmental Studies
ISBN Prefix(es): 7-305

**National Defence Industry Press+**
23 Zizhuyuan Nanlu, Beijing 100044
*Tel:* (010) 68412244; (010) 6842577 *Fax:* (010) 68413125; (010) 68427707
*E-mail:* ndip@public3.bta.net.cn
*Key Personnel*
President: You Dong Zhang
Foreign Rights: Chen Bin *E-mail:* chenbin@public3.bta.net.cn
Founded: 1954
Subjects: Aeronautics, Aviation, Automotive, Computer Science, Electronics, Electrical Engineering, Microcomputers, Military Science, Science (General), Technology
ISBN Prefix(es): 7-118; 7-88704

**The Nationalities Publishing House+**
14 Hepingli Beijie, Beijing 100013
*Tel:* (010) 64212794; (010) 64212031
Founded: 1953
ISBN Prefix(es): 7-105
*Bookshop(s):* The Nationalities Culture Bookshop, 5 Hepingli Beijie, Beijing 100013

**New Times Press+**
23 Zizhuyuan Nanlu, Beijing 100044
*Tel:* (010) 68412244 *Fax:* (010) 68413125
*Key Personnel*
Foreign Rights: Chen Bin *E-mail:* chenbin@public3.bta.net.ca
Founded: 1980

Subjects: Education, Electronics, Electrical Engineering, English as a Second Language, Science (General), Technology
ISBN Prefix(es): 7-5042

**Patent Documentation Publishing House**
6 Xituchenglu, Jimenquiao Haidianqu, Beijing 100088
*Tel:* (010) 62362813; (010) 2026893 *Fax:* (010) 2019307
Subjects: Law, Science (General), Technology
ISBN Prefix(es): 7-80011

**Peking Union Medical College & Beijing Medical University Press,** see Beijing Medical University Press

**The People's Communications Publishing House+**
10 Hepingli St (E), Beijing 100013
*Tel:* (010) 64214479 *Fax:* (010) 64213713 *Cable:* 3652
*Key Personnel*
Contact: Gao Zhendu
Founded: 1952
Subjects: Automotive, Civil Engineering, Communications, Film, Video, Transportation, Shipbuilding & Repair
ISBN Prefix(es): 7-114

**People's Education Press+**
55 Sha Tan Hou St, Beijing 100009
*Tel:* (010) 6402 4555 *Fax:* (010) 6401 0370
*E-mail:* yaod@pep.com.cn (English); dongyj@pep.com.cn (Japanese)
*Web Site:* www.pep.com.cn/yingwenban; www.pep.com.cn/index.htm
*Key Personnel*
Editor-in-Chief: Wei Guodong
Dir: Han Shaoxiang
Founded: 1950
Subjects: Disability, Special Needs
ISBN Prefix(es): 7-900055
Number of titles published annually: 300 Print
Total Titles: 1,400 Print

**People's Fine Arts Publishing House+**
32 Beizongbu Hutong, Beijing 100735
*Tel:* (010) 65122375 *Fax:* (010) 65122370
*Key Personnel*
President: Yunhe Chen
Vice President: Youyuan Zhang
Founded: 1951
Membership(s): China Publishing Association.
Subjects: Art, Biography, History, Photography
ISBN Prefix(es): 7-102
*Book Club(s):* Art Books Research Association

**People's Health Publishing House,** see People's Medical Publishing House (PMPH)

**People's Literature Publishing House**
166 Chaonei Dajie, Beijing 100705
*Tel:* (010) 65138394 *Fax:* (010) 65138394
Founded: 1951
Subjects: Literature, Literary Criticism, Essays, Nonfiction (General), Poetry, Cultural history & studies; current events
ISBN Prefix(es): 7-02
*Branch Office(s)*
Shanghai

**People's Medical Publishing House (PMPH)+**
10 Tian Tanxili, Beijing 100050
*Tel:* (010) 67015812; (010) 67028822 *Fax:* (010) 67025429 *Cable:* 0427
*Key Personnel*
President: Dong Mianguo
Deputy Editor-in-Chief: Zhang Yuankang
Sales Dir: Yao Lingi

Production: Wang Duzhong
Head, Centre: Mr Liu Yiqing
Founded: 1953
Division of Ministry of Public Health.
Subjects: Health, Nutrition, Medicine, Nursing, Dentistry
ISBN Prefix(es): 7-117
*Bookshop(s):* 92 Dongdan Beidajie, Beijing

**The People's Posts & Telecommunication Publishing House**
4 Xizhaosi St Chongwenqu, Beijing 100016
*Tel:* (010) 65139968; (010) 65138129 *Fax:* (010) 65138139
*Key Personnel*
President: Niu Tianjia
Founded: 1953
Subjects: Communications, Computer Science, Crafts, Games, Hobbies, Electronics, Electrical Engineering
ISBN Prefix(es): 7-115

**People's Sports Publishing House+**
8 Tiyuguanlu Rd, Beijing 100061
*Tel:* (010) 67117673 *Fax:* (010) 67116129
*E-mail:* cbszbs@sohu.com
*Key Personnel*
Chief Executive: Liu Meng
Rights & Permissions: He Yang
Founded: 1954
Subjects: Crafts, Games, Hobbies, Sports, Athletics
ISBN Prefix(es): 7-5009
Number of titles published annually: 440 Print; 70 Audio
Total Titles: 3,800,000 Print; 70,000 Audio
*Bookshop(s):* Wu Huan Bookshops

**Petroleum Industry Publishing House,** see China Oil & Gas Periodical Office

**Phoenix,** *imprint of* Foreign Languages Press

**PMPH,** see People's Medical Publishing House (PMPH)

**Popular Science Press**
32 Baishiqiao Lu, Haidianqu, Beijing 100081
*Tel:* (010) 62178877
*Telex:* 5198
*Key Personnel*
President: Wen Zuning
Vice President: Gu Lizhi; Wu Zhijing
Editor-in-Chief: Jin Tao
ISBN Prefix(es): 7-110

**Printing Industry Publishing House+**
2 Cuiweilu Fuxingmenwai Wai, Beijing 100036
*Tel:* (010) 68218367 *Fax:* (010) 8214683
*E-mail:* capt@public3.bta.net.cn
*Key Personnel*
President: Shen Haixiang
Founded: 1981
Subjects: Chemistry, Chemical Engineering, Electronics, Electrical Engineering, Engineering (General), Management, Mechanical Engineering, Photography, Technology
ISBN Prefix(es): 7-80000

**Qi Lu Press**
39 Shengli Dajie, Jingjiulu, Jinan, Shandong 250001
*Tel:* (0531) 6910055-4920 *Fax:* (0531) 2906811
   *Cable:* 0427
*Key Personnel*
Dir: Meng Fan-Hai; Li Xin
Editorial: Zhao Bing-Nan; Sun Yan-Cheng
Founded: 1979
ISBN Prefix(es): 7-5333
*Branch Office(s)*
76 Jing-Shi Rd, Jinan

**Qingdao Publishing House+**
77 Xuzhoulu Qingdao, Shandong 266071
*Tel:* (0532) 5814611; (0532) 362524 *Fax:* (0532)
 515240
*Key Personnel*
President: Xu Cheng
Subjects: Accounting, Advertising, Aeronautics,
 Aviation, Agriculture, Alternative, Animals,
 Pets, Anthropology, Antiques, Archaeology, Ar-
 chitecture & Interior Design, Art, Asian Stud-
 ies, Astrology, Occult, Astronomy, Automotive,
 Behavioral Sciences, Biblical Studies, Biogra-
 phy, Biological Sciences, Business
ISBN Prefix(es): 7-5436
*Showroom(s):* Cui Zifan Art Gallery

**Science Press+**
16 Donghuangchenggen N St, Beijie, Beijing
 100717
*Tel:* (010) 64000246; (010) 64034558 *Fax:* (010)
 64030255
*E-mail:* mailorder@cspg.net
*Web Site:* www.sciencep.com
*Key Personnel*
President: Mr Wang Jixiang
Dir, International Sales & Marketing: Shi Xiong
 Zhao
Founded: 1954
Subjects: Animals, Pets, Archaeology, Biologi-
 cal Sciences, Chemistry, Chemical Engineer-
 ing, Computer Science, Earth Sciences, Elec-
 tronics, Electrical Engineering, Environmental
 Studies, Gardening, Plants, Law, Mathematics,
 Medicine, Nursing, Dentistry, Natural History,
 Physics, Science (General), Technology
ISBN Prefix(es): 7-03
Number of titles published annually: 500 Print;
 20 Audio
Total Titles: 5,000 Print
Subsidiaries: Science Press New York Ltd
*U.S. Office(s):* 84-04 58 Ave, Elmhurst, NY
 11373, United States, Contact: Mr Zhang Ju
 *Tel:* 718-476-0238 *Fax:* 718-476-0273

**SDX (Shenghuo-Dushu-Xinzhi) Joint
 Publishing Co**
166 Chaoyangmennei Dajie, Beijing 100010
*Tel:* (010) 64002730 *Fax:* (010) 64001122 *Cable:*
 1003
*Key Personnel*
President: Shen Changwen
Vice President: Dong Xiuyu
Rights & Permissions: Yang Jin; Ze Wei
Founded: 1932
Subjects: Biography, Economics, Government,
 Political Science, History, Literature, Literary
 Criticism, Essays, Management, Philosophy,
 Psychology, Psychiatry, Social Sciences, Soci-
 ology
ISBN Prefix(es): 7-108

**Shandong Education Publishing House+**
321 Jing Ba Weigi Rd, Jinan, Shandong Province
 250001
*Tel:* (0531) 2092661; (0531) 2092663 *Fax:* (0531)
 2092661
*E-mail:* sdjys@sjs.com.cn
*Web Site:* www.sjs.com.cn *Cable:* 0427
*Key Personnel*
Vice President: Yang Wen Hui *Tel:* (0531)
 2016904
Dir: Wang Hongxin
Chief Editor: Xie Rongdai
Editor-in-Chief: Sun Yong Da *Tel:* (0531)
 2907274
Founded: 1982
Subjects: Child Care & Development, Education,
 Fiction
ISBN Prefix(es): 7-5328
*Parent Company:* Shandong General Publication
 Bureau, 39 Shengli Dajie, Jingjiulu Shandong,
 Jinan 250001
*Orders to:* 39 Shengli St, Jinan, Shandong

**Shandong Fine Arts Publishing House+**
39 Shengli St, Jinan, Shandong 250001
*Tel:* (0531) 6910055 *Fax:* (021) 6911563 *Cable:*
 0427
*Key Personnel*
Dir & Editor-in-Chief: Liu Zhenqing
Deputy Dir: Jingchun Wang
Deputy General Editorial: Yarbo Jiang; Ying
 Wang
Founded: 1984
Books, commercial printing, engineering & archi-
 tectural services, newspapers.
ISBN Prefix(es): 7-5330
*Parent Company:* Shandong General Publication
 Bureau
*Bookshop(s):* Fine Arts Bookshop, Bldg No 1,
 Shunhe Commercial St, Jinan

**Shandong Friendship Publishing House+**
39 Shengli Dajie, Jinan, Shandong 250001
*Tel:* (0531) 2060055-7302 *Fax:* (0531) 2909354
*E-mail:* friendpub@sina.com
*Web Site:* www.sdpress.com.cn
*Key Personnel*
President: Yaping Li
Dir: Lui Tongshun
Deputy Dir: Chun Han
Deputy Editor-in-Chief: Yang Qizhang; Zhao
 Zhiping
Founded: 1986
ELT materials, travel, biography, fiction, lifestyle,
 Chinese culture.
Subjects: Fashion, Fiction, Travel, Comics/Car-
 toons, Lifestyle
ISBN Prefix(es): 7-80551; 7-80642
*Parent Company:* Shandong General Publica-
 tion House, 39 Shengli Dajie, Jinan, Shandong
 250001

**Shandong Literature & Art Publishing House+**
39 Shengli Dajie, Jinan, Shandong 250001
*Tel:* (0531) 6910052-7300 *Fax:* (0531) 613584
 *Cable:* 0427
*Key Personnel*
Dir: Guo Zhenming
Editor-in-Chief: Wang Shuguo
Founded: 1984
Subjects: Drama, Theater, Literature, Literary
 Criticism, Essays, Music, Dance
ISBN Prefix(es): 7-80551; 7-80642
*Parent Company:* Shandong General Publications
 Bureau
*Showroom(s):* 85 Culture Market, 46 Maarshan
 Rd, Jinan, Shandong PC 25001 *Tel:* (0531)
 6915710
*Warehouse:* 85 Culture Market, 46 Maarshan
 Rd, Jinan, Shandong PC 25001 *Tel:* (0531)
 6915710
*Orders to:* 85 Culture Market, 46 Maarshan
 Rd, Jinan, Shandong PC 25001 *Tel:* (0531)
 6915710

**Shandong People's Publishing House+**
39 Shengli Dajie, Jinan, Shandong 250001
*Tel:* (0531) 6910055 *Fax:* (0531) 613584
*Web Site:* www.sd-book.com.cn *Cable:* 0427
*Key Personnel*
Dir: Lui Tongshun
Deputy Dir: Tin Mingshan
Editor-in-Chief: Liu Dejiu
Deputy Editor-in-Chief: Yin Ming
Dir, General Editorial Affairs: Wang Xiaolin
Founded: 1951
Subjects: Economics, Government, Political Sci-
 ence, History, Law, Philosophy, Social Sci-
 ences, Sociology
ISBN Prefix(es): 7-209
*Associate Companies:* Shandong East Book Co

**Shandong Science & Technology Press+**
16 Yuhan Rd, Jinan, Shandong Province 250002
*Tel:* (0531) 6915110 *Fax:* (0531) 2023898

*E-mail:* li_yujn@sina.com *Cable:* 0067
*Key Personnel*
President: Xie Rongdai
Dir of International Cooperation: Li Yu
Founded: 1978
Subjects: Agriculture, Architecture & Interior De-
 sign, Business, Earth Sciences, Economics,
 Education, Electronics, Electrical Engineer-
 ing, Energy, Engineering (General), English
 as a Second Language, Environmental Stud-
 ies, Mechanical Engineering, Medicine, Nurs-
 ing, Dentistry, Technology, Computers, Foreign
 Language Study
ISBN Prefix(es): 7-5331
*Parent Company:* Shandong General Publishing
 House, 39 Shengli Dajie St, Jinan, Shandong
 250001

**Shandong University Press+**
Shanda Nanlu, 27, Jinan, Shandong 250100
*Tel:* (0531) 8902601
*E-mail:* hustpub@blue.hust.edu.cn
*Key Personnel*
Vice President: Li Qiuping
Founded: 1980
Subjects: Accounting, Architecture & Interior De-
 sign, Behavioral Sciences, Business, Chemistry,
 Chemical Engineering, Communications, Com-
 puter Science, Economics, Electronics, Electri-
 cal Engineering, Energy, Engineering (General),
 English as a Second Language, Environmental
 Studies, Finance, Geography, Geology, His-
 tory, Human Relations, Library & Information
 Sciences, Management, Mathematics, Mechan-
 ical Engineering, Microcomputers, Philosophy,
 Physical Sciences, Physics, Public Administration, Science (General), Technology
ISBN Prefix(es): 7-5607

**Shanghai Calligraphy & Painting Publishing
 House+**
237 Hengshan Lu, Shanghai 200031
*Tel:* (021) 64311905 *Fax:* (021) 3207505
*E-mail:* shcpph@online.sh.cn *Cable:* 5600
*Key Personnel*
President: Zhu Junbo
Founded: 1960
Subjects: Antiques, Art, Biography, Fashion, Pho-
 tography, Culural Studies, Lifestyles
ISBN Prefix(es): 7-80635; 7-80512
*Bookshop(s):* Shanghai

**Shanghai College of Traditional Chinese
 Medicine Press+**
530 Linglinglu, Shanghai 200032
*Tel:* (021) 64175039 *Fax:* (021) 64175039
*Key Personnel*
President: Hong Jiahe
Founded: 1985
Subjects: Asian Studies, Behavioral Sciences,
 Health, Nutrition, Science (General)
ISBN Prefix(es): 7-81010

**Shanghai Educational Publishing House+**
123 Yong Fu Rd, Shanghai 200031
*Tel:* (021) 64 37 71 65 *Fax:* (021) 64 33 99 95
*E-mail:* wuyiyang@public2.sta.net.cn *Cable:*
 3413
*Key Personnel*
Chief Executive, Production & International
 Rights: Chen He
Editorial: Bao Nan Ling
Adjoint Dir Editorial: M Zhang Wen-Jie
Founded: 1958
Subjects: Child Care & Development, Education,
 English as a Second Language, History, Micro-
 computers, Physics, Science (General), Social
 Sciences, Sociology
ISBN Prefix(es): 7-5320
Distributor for Xin Hua Book Store (Peoples Re-
 public of China)

**Shanghai Far East Publishers**
357 Xianxia Rd, Shanghai 200336
*Tel:* (021) 62247733-661 *Fax:* (021) 62414469
*E-mail:* ydbook@ydbook.com
*Web Site:* www.ydbook.com
*Key Personnel*
Vice Chief Editor: Zhang Anping
   *E-mail:* anping@ydbook.com
Editor: Zhao Jin
Subjects: Accounting, Animals, Pets, Art, Biography, Business, Career Development, Child Care
& Development, Communications, Economics,
English as a Second Language, Film, Video,
Health, Nutrition, Humor, Literature, Literary
Criticism, Essays, Management, Nonfiction
(General), Psychology, Psychiatry, Social Sciences, Sociology, Travel, Women's Studies
*Parent Company:* Shanghai Century Publishing
Group

**Shanghai Foreign Language Education Press+**
295 Zhongshan Bei Yi Lu, Shanghai 200083
*Tel:* (021) 65425300; (021) 65422896 *Fax:* (021)
35051287
*E-mail:* shudfk@online.sh.ca
*Web Site:* www.sflep.com
*Key Personnel*
President: Zhuang Zhixiang
International Rights: Zhang (John) Hong
   *E-mail:* johnhzhang@sflep.com
Founded: 1979
Subjects: Business, Education, English as a Second Language, Language Arts, Linguistics, Literature, Literary Criticism, Essays
ISBN Prefix(es): 7-81009
*Bookshop(s):* 564 Dalian Xi Rd, Shanghai 200083

**Shanghai People's Fine Arts Publishing House**
D Bldg, No 33, Lane 672, Changle Road, Shanghai 200040
*Tel:* (021) 54044520 *Fax:* (021) 54032331
*E-mail:* finearts@shi63.net
*Key Personnel*
Rights Manager: Summer Shao; Qian Simon
Established publisher with 50 years publishing
history on fine arts, visual arts (architecture,
design, photography) & children's books.
Subjects: Architecture & Interior Design, Art,
Photography
ISBN Prefix(es): 7-5322

**Shanghai Scientific & Technical Publishers+**
450 Ruijin Er Rd, Shanghai 200020
*Tel:* (021) 64736055; (021) 64184881; (021)
64174349 *Fax:* (021) 64730679
*E-mail:* gjb@sstp.cn
*Web Site:* www.sstp.com.cn; www.sstp.cn
*Telex:* 33384 Cpts
*Key Personnel*
President: Wu Zhiren
Editor-in-Chief: Hu Dawei
Sales: Wang Feng-ying
Founded: 1956
Subjects: Agriculture, Engineering (General),
Medicine, Nursing, Dentistry, Science (General), Technology
ISBN Prefix(es): 7-5323
*Bookshop(s):* SSTP Bookshop, 50 Ruijin Rd,
Shanghai 200020

**Shanghai Scientific & Technological Literature
Press**
2 Wukanglu, Shanghai 200031
*Tel:* (021) 64370782 *Cable:* 2115
*Key Personnel*
Chief Executive: Shu Feng Xiang
Editorial: Wen Jun Chi
Sales: Yi Liang Zhao
Production & Publicity: Cheng Qing Qu
Rights & Permissions: Jian Yue Sun
Founded: 1978

Subjects: Agriculture, Engineering (General),
Medicine, Nursing, Dentistry, Science (General)
ISBN Prefix(es): 7-5439
*Parent Company:* Science & Technology Commission of Shanghai Municipality, 30 Fu Zhou
Rd, Shanghai

**Sichuan Science & Technology Publishing
House+**
3 Yandaojie, Chengdu, Sichuan 610012
*Tel:* (028) 664982; (028) 662 5025 *Fax:* (028)
6654063 *Cable:* CHENGDU 1555
*Key Personnel*
President: Li Guangwei
International Rights: Luo Xiaoyan
Subjects: Agriculture, Crafts, Games, Hobbies,
Fashion, Health, Nutrition, Medicine, Nursing,
Dentistry, Science (General), Technology
ISBN Prefix(es): 7-5364

**Sichuan University Press+**
29 Wangjianglu, Chengdu, Sichuan 610064
*Tel:* (028) 583875-62529
*Key Personnel*
President: Wang Jintrou
Founded: 1985
Subjects: Accounting, Antiques, Computer Science, Economics, History, Marketing, Mathematics
ISBN Prefix(es): 7-5614

**South China University of Science &
Technology Press+**
Wushan Guangzhou, Guangdong 510640
*Tel:* (020) 87113489; (020) 87113484 *Cable:*
7003
*Key Personnel*
President: Zhou Shaohua
Founded: 1985
Subjects: Agriculture, Biological Sciences, Chemistry, Chemical Engineering, Civil Engineering, Computer Science, Economics, Education,
Electronics, Electrical Engineering
ISBN Prefix(es): 7-5623

**Southwest China Jiaotong University Press+**
Jiulidi, Chengdu, Sichuan 610031
*Tel:* (028) 784160-763 *Fax:* (028) 24377
*E-mail:* swju@swjtu.edu.cn
*Telex:* 600072 SWJUCN *Cable:* 6445
*Key Personnel*
President: Fan Ziliang
Vice President: Zhang Xue
Editor-in-Chief: Zhu Yonglin
Founded: 1985
Membership(s): Sichuan Publishers Association.
Subjects: Civil Engineering, Computer Science,
Electronics, Electrical Engineering, Engineering
(General), Management, Mathematics, Mechanical Engineering, Publishing & Book Trade
Reference, Science (General), Transportation
ISBN Prefix(es): 7-81022
Divisions: Division of Audiovisual Publication,
SWJU Press
*Bookshop(s):* SWJUP Readers Service, Chengdu,
Sichuan

**Tianjin Science & Technology Publishing
House+**
Unit of Bureau of Publications
189 Zhangzizhonglu Lu Hepingqu, Hepinggu,
Tianjin 300020
*Tel:* (022) 7312749 *Fax:* (022) 27312755
*E-mail:* tjstp@public.tpt.tj.on
*Key Personnel*
Dir: Wang Shu-Ze *Tel:* (022) 27301162
Editor-in-Chief: Kou Xiu-Rong *Tel:* (022)
27306821
Editor: Wu Chun-Li
Founded: 1979

Subjects: Agriculture, Architecture & Interior Design, Biological Sciences, Chemistry, Chemical
Engineering, Child Care & Development, Computer Science, Cookery, Electronics, Electrical
Engineering, Engineering (General), English as
a Second Language, Gardening, Plants, Health,
Nutrition, Mathematics, Medicine, Nursing,
Dentistry, Microcomputers, Physical Sciences,
Science (General), Technology
ISBN Prefix(es): 7-5308
Number of titles published annually: 300 Print
Total Titles: 1,000,000 Print

**Tomorrow Publishing House+**
39 Shengli Dajie, Jinan, Shandong 250001
*Tel:* (0531) 206 0055 *Fax:* (0531) 290 2094
*E-mail:* tomorrow@sdpress.com
*Web Site:* www.tomorrowpub.com *Cable:* 0427
*Key Personnel*
President & Editor-in-Chief: Liu Haiqi
Dir, Rights Section: David Fu
Founded: 1984
ISBN Prefix(es): 7-5332
*Parent Company:* Shandong General Press
*Associate Companies:* Shandong Xinhua Book
Store

**Tsinghua University Press+**
Tsinghua University, Haidiangu District, Beijing
100084
*Tel:* (010) 62783933; (010) 62594726 *Fax:* (010)
62770278
*E-mail:* right-tup@mail.tsinghua.edu.cn
*Telex:* 22617 QHTSC CN *Cable:* 1331 BEIJING
*Key Personnel*
President: Wang Minfu
Editor-in-Chief: Zhang Zhaoqi
Founded: 1980
Subjects: Architecture & Interior Design, Chemistry, Chemical Engineering, Civil Engineering, Computer Science, Education, Electronics,
Electrical Engineering, Engineering (General),
English as a Second Language, Mathematics,
Technology, Computers: Educational Software,
Operating Systems, Programming Languages &
Software
ISBN Prefix(es): 7-302
Number of titles published annually: 250 Print
Total Titles: 700 Print

**Universidade de Macau, Centro de Publicacoes**
(University of Macau, Publications Centre)
Av Padre Tomas Pereira, S J, Taipa, Macau
*Tel:* 397 4504 *Fax:* 397 4506
*E-mail:* pub_grp@umac.mo
*Web Site:* www.umac.mo
*Key Personnel*
Head: Dr Raymond Wong
Founded: 1993
Subjects: Art, Economics, Education, Government, Political Science, History, Literature, Literary Criticism, Essays, Management, Public
Administration, Social Sciences, Sociology
ISBN Prefix(es): 972-97631; 972-96791; 972-
97050; 972-97834
Number of titles published annually: 10 Print
Total Titles: 71 Print

**Water Resources & Electric Power Press
(CWPP)+**
6 Sanlihelu, Fuxingmenwai, Beijing 100044
*Tel:* (010) 898031 *Fax:* (010) 68353010
*Cable:* BEIJING 81605
*Key Personnel*
President: Mr Tang Xinhua
Vice President: Mr Liu Fengtong
Editor-in-Chief: Mr Jin Yan
International Cooperation Office & Project Manager: Ms Fang Ping
Founded: 1956
Subjects: Civil Engineering, Electronics, Electrical Engineering, Energy, Engineering (General),
Environmental Studies

ISBN Prefix(es): 7-120
*Orders to:* International Cooperation Div, 6 Sanlihe Rd, Beijing 100044

**World Affairs Press+**
A31 Waijiaobujie, Beijing 100005
*Tel:* (010) 65232695 *Fax:* (010) 5133181
*E-mail:* wap@bj.col.com.cn
*Key Personnel*
President: Mr An Guozheng
Founded: 1934
Subjects: Biography, Developing Countries, Fiction, Foreign Countries, Government, Political Science, History, Journalism, Social Sciences, Sociology
ISBN Prefix(es): 7-5012
Imprints: World Affairs Printing House

**World Affairs Printing House**, *imprint of* World Affairs Press

**World Books Publishing Corporation+**
137 Chaonei Dajie, Beijing 100010
*Tel:* (010) 64016320 *Fax:* (010) 4016320
*E-mail:* wpc@china.kw.co.cn
ISBN Prefix(es): 7-5062
*Branch Office(s)*
Beijing World Publishing Corp

**Writers' Publishing House+**
10 Nongzhanguan Nanli, Wenliandalou, Beijing 100026
*Tel:* (010) 65004079; (010) 65389244 *Fax:* (010) 65930761
*E-mail:* wrtspub@public.bta.net.cn
*Web Site:* www.zuojiachubanshe.com
Founded: 1953
A state enterprise publishing reprints of Chinese literature.
Subjects: Fiction, Poetry, Romance, Essay
ISBN Prefix(es): 7-5063
Number of titles published annually: 200 Print

**Wuhan University Press+**
Luojiashan, Wuhan, Hubei 430072
*Tel:* (027) 7870651; (010) 82001239 *Fax:* (027) 712661; (010) 82001248
*Telex:* 5678
*Key Personnel*
President: Xiong Yulian
Vice President: Li Haojie; Wang Wen-Hao
Founded: 1981
Subjects: Biological Sciences, Chemistry, Chemical Engineering, Computer Science, Economics, English as a Second Language, Government, Political Science, History, Law, Library & Information Sciences, Mathematics, Social Sciences, Sociology
ISBN Prefix(es): 7-307; 7-900634
Subsidiaries: Edit Computer Company; Wuhan University

**Xiamen University Press**
Xiamen University, Xiamen, 422 Siming Nanlu, Fujian 361005
*Tel:* (0592) 2186128
*E-mail:* chbanshe@jingxian.xmu.edu.cn; xmdx@fjbook.com
*Key Personnel*
Dir: Jiang Dongming
Chief Editor: Chen Fulang
Founded: 1985
ISBN Prefix(es): 7-5615

**Xi'an Cartography Publishing House+**
124 Youyi Donglu, Xi'an, Shaanxi 710054
*Tel:* (029) 7898962
*Key Personnel*
President: Xu Guohua
International Rights: Huang Meihua
Founded: 1985

Subjects: Earth Sciences, Environmental Studies, Geography, Geology, Nonfiction (General)
ISBN Prefix(es): 7-80545
Distributor for China Cartography Publishing House

**Xi'an Maps Publishing House**, see Xi'an Cartography Publishing House

**Xinhua Publishing House+**
Division of Xinhua News Agency
57 Xuanwumen Xidajie, Beijing 100803
*Tel:* (010) 3073880 *Fax:* (010) 3073880
*E-mail:* nianzh@xinhuanet.com
*Telex:* 22316 Xnabj *Cable:* 1631
*Key Personnel*
Dir: Qiu Yongsheng
Editor-in-Chief & Deputy Dir: Zhang Shoudi
Deputy Dir: Juo Bomin
Founded: 1979
Subjects: Biography, Economics, Ethnicity, Government, Political Science, Journalism, Social Sciences, Sociology, People's Republic of China Year Book
ISBN Prefix(es): 7-5011
*Bookshop(s):* China Journalism Bookstore

**Yunnan University Press+**
Yinghua Campus of Yunnan University, No 2 Cuihu Rd N, Kunming 650091
*Tel:* (0871) 5032001; (0871) 5031057 *Fax:* (0871) 5162823
*Web Site:* www.ynup.com
*Key Personnel*
President: Shi Weida *Tel:* (0871) 5033890
  *E-mail:* wds@ynup.com
Vice President: Zhang Yonghong *Tel:* (0871) 5032152 *E-mail:* zyh@ynup.com
Copyright Dir: Xiong Xiaoxia *E-mail:* helenx@ynup.com
Founded: 1988
Publishing house of Yunnan University. Over 1,700 titles published covering a wide variety of academic fields.
Subjects: Anthropology, Art, Business, Career Development, English as a Second Language, Ethnicity, Management, Marketing, Outdoor Recreation, Photography, Public Administration, Self-Help, Social Sciences, Sociology, Travel
ISBN Prefix(es): 7-81068
Number of titles published annually: 125 Print; 10 CD-ROM
Total Titles: 150 Print; 10 CD-ROM
*Parent Company:* Yunnan University

**Zhejiang Education Publishing House+**
347 Tiyuchanglu, Hangzhou, Zhejiang 310006
*Tel:* (0571) 5170300; (0571) 85103298
  *Fax:* (0571) 5176944
*E-mail:* zjjy@zjcb.com *Cable:* 2403
*Key Personnel*
Vice President: Shao Rouyu *E-mail:* shaory@zjcb.com
Founded: 1983
Subjects: Education, English as a Second Language
ISBN Prefix(es): 7-5338
*Parent Company:* Zhejiang General Publishing House

**Zhejiang University Press+**
20 Yugu Rd, Hangzhou, Zhejiang 310027
*Tel:* (0571) 88273066 *Fax:* (0571) 88273066
*E-mail:* zupress@zju.edu.cn
*Web Site:* www.zjupress.com
*Key Personnel*
President: Han Zhaoxiong
International Rights: You Jianzhong
Founded: 1984

Subjects: Accounting, Agriculture, Art, Biological Sciences, Business, Chemistry, Chemical Engineering, Civil Engineering, Computer Science, Education, History, How-to, Science (General), Technology, Computers, Electronic Media, Natural Sciences, Teaching Methods & Materials
ISBN Prefix(es): 7-308

**Zhong Hua Book Co**
36 Wangfujing Dajie, Beijing 100073
*Tel:* (010) 65134904 *Fax:* (010) 63458226
Founded: 1912
Also distribution.
Subjects: Anthropology, Fiction, History, Language Arts, Linguistics, Literature, Literary Criticism, Essays, Poetry, Travel
ISBN Prefix(es): 7-101
Number of titles published annually: 800 Print
Total Titles: 20,000 Print

# Colombia

## General Information

*Capital:* Bogota
*Language:* Spanish (English widely used in business)
*Religion:* Roman Catholic
*Population:* 34.3 million
*Bank Hours:* 0900-1500 Monday-Friday
*Shop Hours:* 0900-1230, 1430-1830 Monday-Saturday
*Currency:* 100 centavos = 1 Colombian peso
*Export/Import Information:* Member of Latin American Free Trade Association. Value added taxes on all imports; no sales tax on books. Ad valorem: none generally on books except on books bound in leather or similar materials, on photonovels of thrillers, detective stories, etc, on horoscopes, children's picture books, atlases & advertising catalogues. No import license for books. Exchange license from Banco de la Republica required.
*Copyright:* UCC, Berne, Buenos Aires (see Copyright Conventions, pg xi)

**ACPO**, see Dosmil Editora

**Amazonas Editores Ltda**
Carrera 11 No 94-02 Ofc 121, 47009 Bogota, DC
*Tel:* (091) 6180256; (091) 2182760 *Fax:* (091) 6180326
*Key Personnel*
Legal Representative: Ferrer Lucia Montano
Founded: 1991
Also acts as distributor.
Subjects: Archaeology, Architecture & Interior Design, Art, Environmental Studies, Government, Political Science, History, Poetry
ISBN Prefix(es): 958-95493
Distributor for Cridtina Uribe Editores; El Sello Editorial; Fondo FEN Colombia
*Book Club(s):* Camara Colombiana del Libro

**Asociacion Instituto Linguistico de Verano**
Calle 13 No 8-38, of 409, Apdo Aereo 27744, Bogota DC
*Tel:* (01) 2821047; (01) 3416185
*E-mail:* sil_colombia@sil.org
*Web Site:* www.sil.org/americas/colombia
Founded: 1962
All queries regarding activities in Colombia should be directed to the following: SIL International, Americas Area Office, 7500 W Camp Wisdom Rd, Dallas, TX 75236, USA. Tel: 972-708-7333, Fax: 972-708-7324.
Subjects: Language Arts, Linguistics
ISBN Prefix(es): 958-21

**Bedout Editores SA+**
Calle 61 No 51-04, Apdo Aereo 760, Medellin, Antioquia
*Tel:* (04) 5112900 *Fax:* (04) 2517946 *Cable:* BEDOUT
*Key Personnel*
President: Campuzano R Ilbgnacio
Manager: Mario Gutierrez
Founded: 1889
Subjects: Education, Literature, Literary Criticism, Essays, Social Sciences, Sociology
ISBN Prefix(es): 84-8274; 958-03
Divisions: Editora Beta SA
*Branch Office(s)*
Calle 13 No 21-51, Local 5, Bucaramanga
*Tel:* (076) 352171
Calle 25N No 3 bis-35, 200 piso, Cali *Tel:* (02) 672367
Calle 39 No 233-25, Santa Fe de Bogota DC
*Tel:* (01) 2445232

**Cekit SA+**
Calle 22, No 8-22, Piso 2, Pereira, Risaralda
*Tel:* (06) 3253033; (06) 3348179; (06) 3348189 *Fax:* (06) 3348020
*E-mail:* comercial@cekit.com.co
*Web Site:* www.cekit.com.co
*Key Personnel*
Contact: William Rojas
Founded: 1985
Specialize in learning material for the study of electronics.
Subjects: Electronics, Electrical Engineering
ISBN Prefix(es): 958-657
*Branch Office(s)*
Cekits Carrera 17 No 53-48, Piso 2, Bogota

**CELAM**, see Consejo Episcopal Latinoamericano (CELAM)

**Centro Regional para el Fomento del Libro en America Latina y el Caribe** (Regional Center for the Promotion of Books in Latin America & the Caribbean)
Calle 70 No 9-52, Bogota DC
*Tel:* (01) 212 6056; (01) 249 5141; (01) 321 7501; (01) 540 2071; (01) 312 5690 *Fax:* (01) 255 4614
*E-mail:* cerlalc@impsat.net.co; info@cerlalc.org; libro@cerlalc.org
*Web Site:* www.cerlalc.org
*Key Personnel*
Dir: Carmen Bravo
Founded: 1971
Subjects: Law, Literature, Literary Criticism, Essays, Editing, lecture promotion, production & circulation
ISBN Prefix(es): 92-9057; 958-671

**CERLALC**, see Centro Regional para el Fomento del Libro en America Latina y el Caribe

**CIAT - Centro Internacional de Agricultura Tropical**
Recta Cali-Palmira, km 17, Apdo Aereo 6713, Cali
*Tel:* (02) 445-0000 *Fax:* (02) 445-0073
*E-mail:* ciat@cgiar.org
*Web Site:* www.ciat.cgiar.org
*Telex:* 05769CIAT CO
*Key Personnel*
Contact: Luis Alberto Garcia *E-mail:* l.garcia-ciat@cgiar.org
Specialize in Investigation of Tropical Agriculture.
ISBN Prefix(es): 958-9183; 9972-856

**Editorial Cincel Kapelusz Ltda+**
Calle 37 N° 25-10, Bogota DC

*Tel:* (01) 2442035; (01) 3350031 *Fax:* (01) 3350042
*Telex:* 3350042 *Cable:* Kapelusz
*Key Personnel*
Man Dir, Sales & Rights & Permissions: Diego Tenorio
Founded: 1964
Subjects: Education, Physics, Psychology, Psychiatry
ISBN Prefix(es): 958-9010

**CINEP**, see Fundacion Centro de Investigacion y Educacion Popular (CINEP)

**Consejo Episcopal Latinoamericano (CELAM)+**
Transversal 67, Ave Boyaca No 173-71, Bogota
*Tel:* (01) 6670050; (01) 6706416
*E-mail:* editora@celam.org; celam@celam.org; itepal@celam.org
*Web Site:* www.celam.org
*Key Personnel*
Dir: Eduardo Pena Vanegas
Founded: 1970
Subjects: Biblical Studies, Child Care & Development, Education, Nonfiction (General), Philosophy, Regional Interests, Religion - Catholic, Theology
ISBN Prefix(es): 958-625

**Ediciones Cultural Colombiana Ltda**
Calle 72, No 16-15/21, Apdo Aereo 6307, Bogota
SAN: 001-6462
*Tel:* (01) 2116090 *Fax:* (01) 2176570 *Cable:* CULBIANA
*Key Personnel*
Man Dir: Jose Porto
Editorial: Jose Porto Vazquez
Sales Dir: Hernando Salazar
Production: Maximilian Nicolas
Founded: 1951
ISBN Prefix(es): 84-8273; 958-9013

**Ediciones Culturales Ver Ltda+**
Calle 37 No 16-64, Apdo Aereo 51095, Bogota
*Tel:* (01) 2859362; (01) 2859204 *Fax:* (01) 2859362
*Telex:* 45805
*Key Personnel*
Manager: Gaspar Alfonso Bacca
Founded: 1989
Membership(s): The House of Books.
Subjects: Education
ISBN Prefix(es): 958-9204

**Derecho Penal y Criminologia**, *imprint of* Universidad Externado de Colombia

**Dosmil Editora**
Carrera 39A, No 15-11, Bogota DC
*Tel:* (01) 2694800
*Telex:* 45623 Accpo *Cable:* Radiofonicas Bogota
*Key Personnel*
Man Dir: Hernando Bernal A
Editorial: Javier Martinez Naranjo
Sales & Rights & Permissions: Luis Felipe Delgado; Manuel Hoyos
Founded: 1947 (ACPO - Editora Dosmil 1964)
Formerly Accion Cultural Popular ACPO - Editora Dosmil.
Subjects: Art, Literature, Literary Criticism, Essays, Regional Interests, Social Sciences, Sociology
ISBN Prefix(es): 84-8275

**Ecoe Ediciones Ltda**
Calle 32 bis No 17-22, Bogota
*Tel:* (01) 2889821; (01) 2889871 *Fax:* (01) 3201377
*E-mail:* correo@ecoeediciones.com

*Web Site:* www.ecoeediciones.com
ISBN Prefix(es): 958-648

**Editorial Educativo Ltda**, see Fondo Educativo Interamericano SA

**El Ancora Editores+**
Ave 25c, No 3-99, Bosque Izquierdo, Bogota
*Tel:* (01) 283 9040; (01) 342 6224; (01) 283 9235 *Fax:* (01) 283 9235
*E-mail:* ancoraed@elancoraeditores.com
*Web Site:* www.elancoraeditores.com
*Key Personnel*
Man Dir: Patricia Hoher
Editorial, Rights & Permissions: Felipe Escobar Uribe
Founded: 1980
Subjects: Art, Economics, History, Humor, Journalism, Literature, Literary Criticism, Essays, Poetry, Social Sciences, Sociology
ISBN Prefix(es): 958-9044; 84-8277; 958-36; 958-96577; 958-8048

**Escala Ltda**
Calle 30 No 17-70, Bogota
*Tel:* (01) 2878200 *Fax:* (01) 2325148
*Key Personnel*
Contact: Ana Medina De Serna
Founded: 1962
Subjects: Architecture & Interior Design, Art, Engineering (General)
ISBN Prefix(es): 958-9082
*Branch Office(s)*
Ave San Antonio No 79 Of 101 Napoles, Mexico, DF, Mexico *Tel:* 5633672
Edif Tacagua piso 19 Apdo 19Q, Parque Central Ave Lecuna, Caracas, Venezuela
Apoquinto 4900 of 147-148 las Condes, Santiago de Chile *Tel:* 2466111

**Eurolibros Ltda+**
Affiliate of Camara de Comercio de Bogota
Calle 40 No 20-27, Bogota
*Tel:* (01) 2886400; (01) 3401837 *Fax:* (01) 2886400
*Telex:* 3 40 18 11; 3 40 18 37
*Key Personnel*
Legal Representative: Carlos Roberto Jimenez
*E-mail:* carlosji@latino.net.co
Founded: 1983
Membership(s): Camara Colombiana de la Industria Editorial.
Subjects: Education, Outdoor Recreation, Religion - Catholic
ISBN Prefix(es): 958-9417
Number of titles published annually: 2 Print
Total Titles: 12 Print
*Associate Companies:* Libros Leo Ltda
Distributed by Oriente (Argentina)

**Universidad Externado de Colombia+**
Calle 12 0-46 Este, Bogota
*Tel:* (01) 3428984; (01) 3420288 (ext 3151) *Fax:* (01) 3424948
*E-mail:* publicaciones@uexternado.edu.co
*Web Site:* www.uexternado.edu.co
*Key Personnel*
Dir: Conrado Zuluago
Founded: 1886
Subjects: Criminology, Education, Finance, Government, Political Science, Law, Management, Mathematics, Social Sciences, Sociology
ISBN Prefix(es): 958-616
Imprints: Derecho Penal y Criminologia; Informativo; Juridica
*Bookshop(s):* Calle 12 N° 1-17 Este, Bloque A Primer Piso, Bogota *Tel:* (01) 342 0288 (ext 3152)

**Fondo Educativo Interamericano SA+**
Calle 36 No 22-33, Apdo Aereo 29696, Bogota

*Tel:* (01) 3382577; (01) 3382877 *Fax:* (01)
2852891; (01) 2320191
*E-mail:* eeducativa@epm.net.co; educapyv@multi.
net.co
*Telex:* 45581 *Cable:* ADIWES BOGOTA
*Key Personnel*
Man Dir: Alvaro Toledo
Founded: 1970
ISBN Prefix(es): 958-610; 84-89220

**Fundacion Centro de Investigacion y**
**Educacion Popular (CINEP)+**
Carrera 5a No 33A-08, Apdo Aereo 25916, Bo-
gota
*Tel:* (01) 2456181 *Fax:* (01) 2879089
*E-mail:* info@cinep.org.co
*Web Site:* www.cinep.org.co
*Key Personnel*
Man Dir & Rights & Permissions: Francisco de
Roux
Production, Publicity & Publications Manager:
Helena Gardeazabal
Founded: 1959
Specialize in social science.
Subjects: Economics, Regional Interests, Social
Sciences, Sociology
ISBN Prefix(es): 958-644; 958-9027

**Fundacion Universidad de la Sabana Ediciones**
**INSE+**
Calle 70 No 12-08, Apdo Aereo 53753, Bogota
*Tel:* (01) 6760867
*E-mail:* susabana@col1.telcom.com.co
Founded: 1987
Subjects: Biological Sciences, Economics, Man-
agement, Philosophy, Religion - Catholic
ISBN Prefix(es): 958-12
*Bookshop(s):* Sede del Puente del Comon-Chia-
cundina-marca

**Ediciones Gamma+**
Calle 85, No 18-32, Piso 5, Bogota
*Tel:* (01) 6227054; (01) 6227076 *Fax:* (01)
6227129
*E-mail:* diners@cable.net.co
*Key Personnel*
Contact: Gustavo Casadiego
Founded: 1978
Subjects: Travel
ISBN Prefix(es): 958-95108; 958-95237; 958-
8177; 958-9308
*Parent Company:* Diners Club of Colombia

**Editora Guadalupe Ltda**
Carrera 42 No 10-57, Apdo Aereo 29765, Bogota
*Tel:* (01) 2690788; (01) 2690211 *Fax:* (01)
2685308
*Key Personnel*
Man Dir & Editorial: Marco A Moreno H
Sales: Mario E Joya Hernandez
Production: Jose Adel Lopez Q
Founded: 1969
Membership(s): The Colombian Booksellers As-
sociation.
Subjects: Literature, Literary Criticism, Essays,
Science (General), Technology
ISBN Prefix(es): 958-608

**Editorial Hispanoamerica+**
Carrera 56 B, No 45-27, Bogota DC
*Tel:* (01) 2216694 *Fax:* (01) 2213020
*Key Personnel*
Contact: Alvaro Pinzon
ISBN Prefix(es): 958-9104; 958-658

**Imprenta de la Universidad Nacional**
Ciudad Universitaria Edif 561, Apdo Aereo
37855, Bogota
*Tel:* (01) 2686965; (01) 2699111 *Fax:* (01)
2441035
ISBN Prefix(es): 958-628

**Informativo**, *imprint of* Universidad Externado de
Colombia

**Instituto Caro y Cuervo+**
Carrera 11 No 64-37, Apdo Aereo 51502, Bogota
DC
*Tel:* (01) 3456004 *Fax:* (01) 2170243; (01)
3422121
*E-mail:* direcciongeneral@caroycuervo.gov.co
*Web Site:* www.caroycuervo.gov.co
*Key Personnel*
Dir: Ignacio Chaves
Founded: 1942
Subjects: Education, Language Arts, Linguistics
ISBN Prefix(es): 958-611
*Bookshop(s):* Libreria Yerbabuena; Libreria
Cuervo

**Juridica**, *imprint of* Universidad Externado de
Colombia

**Editorial Juventud Colombiana Ltda**
Calle 58 Nº 19-41, Apdo Aereo 53694, Bogota
*Tel:* (01) 2557485; (01) 2490543 *Fax:* (01)
2557416
*Key Personnel*
Man Dir: Cecilia De Huidobro
ISBN Prefix(es): 958-23
*Parent Company:* Editorial Juventud SA, Spain

**LEGIS - Editores SA+**
Av El Dorado 81-10, Apdo Aereo 8646-9888,
Bogota
*Tel:* (01) 4255255 *Fax:* (01) 4255317
*E-mail:* scliente@legis.com.co
*Telex:* 43300 Legis *Cable:* LEGISLACION
*Key Personnel*
Man Dir: Mauricio Serna Melendez
Founded: 1952
Subjects: Economics, Law, Management, Market-
ing
ISBN Prefix(es): 958-653
Subsidiaries: Legislacion Economica Srl; URB
Industrial la Urbina
*Orders to:* CRA 16, No 98-62, Bogota

**Lerner Ediciones**
Calle 8A, No 68A-41, Apdo Aereo 8304, Bogota
Mailing Address: PO Box 8304, Bogota
*Tel:* (01) 4200650; (01) 2624224 *Fax:* (01)
2624459
*Telex:* 43195 *Cable:* Edilerner
*Key Personnel*
Man Dir: Jack A Grimberg Possin
Editorial: Juan Francisco di Domenico
Sales: Diego Jaramillo
Founded: 1959
Subjects: History, Literature, Literary Criticism,
Essays, Medicine, Nursing, Dentistry
ISBN Prefix(es): 958-95013; 958-9135
*Bookshop(s):* Libreria y Distribuidora Lerner Ltda

**Libros**, *imprint of* RAM Editores

**Editorial Libros y Libres SA+**
Ave Americus No 64A-39, Apdo Aero 006642,
Bogota DC, Cundinamarca
*Tel:* (01) 2907145; (01) 2907862; (01) 2886188
*Fax:* (01) 2696830
*E-mail:* edilibro@colomsat.net.co
*Key Personnel*
General: Rivero Samuel Diaz
Founded: 1985
Subjects: Behavioral Sciences, Biological Sci-
ences, Earth Sciences, Education, Science
(General), Social Sciences, Sociology
ISBN Prefix(es): 958-9253; 958-9008

**Libros y Libros Editorial SA+**
Calle 15 No 68D-52, Bogota

*Tel:* (01) 4117527; (01) 4117659; (01) 2886188
*Fax:* (01) 3124291
*E-mail:* edilibro@colomsat.net.co
*Key Personnel*
Man Dir, Sales, Publicity: Alberto Umana Carri-
zosa
Editorial: M C Jimero
Production: Jose B Restreps
ISBN Prefix(es): 958-9253; 958-9008

**Lito Technion Ltda**
Calle 21 No 43A-23, Apdo Aereo 80085, Bogota
*Tel:* (01) 2443502; (01) 2443177; (01) 2441538
*Telex:* 41456
*Key Personnel*
Man Dir: Benjamin Bursztyn V
Editorial: Samuel Bursztyn V
Sales: Ricardo Herrera G
Production: German Arias G
Publicity: Yonatan Bursztyn V
Founded: 1980
ISBN Prefix(es): 958-9007

**McGraw-Hill Colombia+**
Carrerall 11, No 93-46, Bogota D.C.
Mailing Address: Apdo 81078, Bogota DC
*Tel:* (01) 6003800; (01) 6003854 *Fax:* (01)
6003811
*E-mail:* servicioalcliente.co@mcgraw-hill.com
*Web Site:* www.mcgraw-hill.com.co
*Telex:* 43306 MNLACO
*Key Personnel*
Dir General: Carlos G Marquez H
*E-mail:* cmarquez@attmail.com
Professional Division Manager: Martha Edna
Suarez
College Division Manager: Luis Fernando Pinzon
Education Division Manager: Hector Zulauga
Controller: Luis Fernando Garavito
Production Manager: Consuelo Ruiz
Founded: 1974
Colombia, Venezuela, Ecuador, Peru & Bolivia.
Subjects: Accounting, Biological Sciences, Busi-
ness, Chemistry, Chemical Engineering, Eco-
nomics, Engineering (General), Physics, Psy-
chology, Psychiatry, Social Sciences, Sociology,
Technology
ISBN Prefix(es): 958-600; 84-8278; 958-41
*Parent Company:* The McGraw-Hill Companies,
1221 Avenue of the Americas, New York, NY
10020, United States
Subsidiaries: McGraw-Hill Interamericana de
Venezuela
Distributor for Harvard Business; Houghton Mif-
flin; Microsoft Press
*Warehouse:* Calle 22 No 90-27

**Migema Ediciones Ltda**
Calle 32 No 19-22, Bogota
*Tel:* (01) 2873158; (01) 2858538 *Fax:* (01)
2858538; (01) 2858224
*E-mail:* emigema@cc-net.net
*Key Personnel*
Legal Representative: Miguel Angel Torres Cam-
pos
ISBN Prefix(es): 958-681
*Orders to:* Calle 33A N 18-2D, Bogota

**Instituto Misionero Hijas De San Pablo+**
Carrera No 32A Nº 161A-04, Las Orquideas, Bo-
gota
*Tel:* (01) 6710992 *Fax:* (01) 6706378
*Key Personnel*
Editorial Dir: Lucero Patino
Superior Provincial: Yermy Castano
Founded: 1948
Subjects: Communications, Education, Philoso-
phy, Women's Studies
ISBN Prefix(es): 958-9335
*Branch Office(s)*
Barranquilla (two)
Bogota

Cali
Cucuta
Manizales
Medellin
*Bookshop(s):* Carrera No 32A N° 161A-04, Apdo
Aereo 6291, Santafe de Bogota Cundinamarca;
Carrera 13 No 72-41, Bogota

**Ediciones Monserrate+**
Calle 122 No 53A-29, Bogota
*Tel:* (01) 253 1347; (01) 253 3033 *Fax:* (01) 253
9517
*E-mail:* comercial@edimonserrate.com
*Web Site:* www.edimonserrate.com
*Key Personnel*
Man Dir & Editorial: P Enrique Fajardo
Sales: Maria Consuelo de Fajardo
Founded: 1977
Subjects: Law
ISBN Prefix(es): 958-95014

**Editorial Norma SA**
Calle 29N No 6A-40, Cali
*Tel:* (02) 660 1901 *Fax:* (02) 661 5278
*Web Site:* www.norma.com
*Telex:* 45584 NORMA *Cable:* Edinorma
*Key Personnel*
President: Fernando Gomez Campo *Tel:* (02) 660
1901 (ext 2740) *E-mail:* fernando.gomez@
norma.com
Editorial Dir, Trade Division: Maria del Mar
Ravassa
Editorial Dir, Textbook Division: Bernardo Pena
Editorial Dir, Periodicals Division: Maria C
Posada
Editorial Dir, International Division: Gustavo
Adolfo Carvajal
ISBN Prefix(es): 958-04
*Parent Company:* Carvajal SA
*Branch Office(s)*
Barranquilla
Bogota
Bucaramanga
Cartagena
Cucuta
Ibaque
Manizales
Medellin
Neiva

**Editorial Oveja Negra Ltda+**
Carrera 14 N° 79-17, Apdo Aereo 23940, Bogota
*Tel:* (01) 5309678 *Fax:* (01) 2577900
*Key Personnel*
Editor: Jose Vicente Katarain
Commercial Manager: Leyla Bibiana Cangrejo;
Victor Hugo Cangrejo
Founded: 1977
Subjects: Biography, Business, Humor, Litera-
ture, Literary Criticism, Essays, Poetry, Social
Sciences, Sociology
ISBN Prefix(es): 958-06

**Editorial Panamericana** (Panamericana
Publishing)+
Calle 12 No 34-20, Apdo Aereo No 6210, Bogota
*Tel:* (01) 360 30 77; (01) 277 01 00; (01)
3649000 (ext 213); (03) 5603831; (03)
5603832; (03) 5603833 *Fax:* (01) 2373805
*E-mail:* panaedit@panamericanaeditorial.com
*Web Site:* www.panamericanaeditorial.com
*Key Personnel*
Marketing Manager: Fernando Rojas
*E-mail:* frojas@panamericanaeditorial.com
Editor: Mireya Fonseca *E-mail:* mfonseca@
panamericanaeditorial.com; Gabriel Silva
*E-mail:* gsilva@panamericanaeditorial.com
Founded: 1993
Publish books of science & culture.
Subjects: Biography, Business, Communications,
Drama, Theater, English as a Second Lan-
guage, Fashion, History, Literature, Literary

Criticism, Essays, Poetry, Religion - Other,
Self-Help, Sports, Athletics
ISBN Prefix(es): 958-30
Number of titles published annually: 180 Print
Total Titles: 2,100 Print
*Parent Company:* Panamericana Editorial Ltda

**Pearson Educacion de Colombia Ltda+**
Carrera 68A No 22-55, Bogota DC
*Tel:* (01) 4059300 *Fax:* (01) 4059300
*Key Personnel*
President: Mauricio Mikan *E-mail:* mauricio.
mikan@pearsoned.com
Man Dir, Colombia: Antonio Ballesteros
*E-mail:* antonio-ballesteros@penhall.com
Manager, Operations: Hector Franco
Publisher & Manager, Escolar Division: Oscar E
Rodriguez
Publisher & Manager, College Division: Carlos E
Bermudez
Publisher & Manager, Professional/Trade: Liliana
Gonzalez
Founded: 1999
Educational texts in Spanish language.
Subjects: Computer Science, Education
ISBN Prefix(es): 958-9498
Number of titles published annually: 40 Print
*Parent Company:* Pearson Plc

**Procultura SA**
Ave 25C No 3-97, Apdo Aereo 044700, Bogota
*Tel:* (01) 2818254
*Key Personnel*
Manager: Ana Cristina Mejia
General Secretary: Lelia Arango
Founded: 1980
Nueva Biblioteca Colombiana de Cultura.
Subjects: Economics, History, Literature, Literary
Criticism, Essays, Poetry
ISBN Prefix(es): 958-9043

**RAM Editores+**
Calle 20 Sur No 60-24, Bogota DC, Cundina-
marca
*Tel:* (01) 2623067
*Key Personnel*
Man Dir: Jaime Ramirez Palmar
Sales: Luz Helena S de Ramirez
Production: Bernarda Sabogal Rodriguez
Founded: 1983
Also acts as book packager.
Subjects: Astrology, Occult, Crafts, Games, Hob-
bies, Fashion, Health, Nutrition, Regional Inter-
ests, Self-Help
ISBN Prefix(es): 958-9063
Imprints: Libros

**Editorial Santillana SA+**
Calle 80, No 10-23, Bogota
*Tel:* (01) 635 12 00 *Fax:* (01) 236 93 82
*E-mail:* alfaquar@latino.net.co
*Web Site:* www.santillana.com.co
*Key Personnel*
President: Gonzalo Arboleda
General Manager: Francisco Abbad
Founded: 1988
Membership(s): Colombia Book Association
Also acts as distributor.
Subjects: Animals, Pets, Antiques, Art, Cookery,
Management, Science Fiction, Fantasy, Self-
Help
ISBN Prefix(es): 958-24

**Siglo XXI Editores de Colombia Ltda**
Carrera 14 No 80-44, Bogota DC
*Tel:* (01) 6110787 *Fax:* (01) 6110757
*Key Personnel*
Man Dir: Santiago Pombo Vejarano
Contact: Lina Maria Perez Gaviria
Founded: 1976

Subjects: Anthropology, Architecture & Interior
Design, Art, Fiction, Government, Political
Science, History, Language Arts, Linguistics,
Philosophy, Psychology, Psychiatry, Social Sci-
ences, Sociology
ISBN Prefix(es): 958-606
*Parent Company:* Siglo XXI de Espana Editores
SA, Spain
*Associate Companies:* Siglo XXI Editores SA de
CV, Mexico

**Susaeta Ediciones**
Carrera 43A No 49B Sur-45, Apdo Aereo 1742-
596, Envigado
*Tel:* (01) 2884422; (01) 2885500 *Fax:* (01)
881472
*E-mail:* mdsusaet@medellin.impsat.net.co
*Key Personnel*
Contact: William Armando Rodriguez
ISBN Prefix(es): 958-07

**Tercer Mundo Editores S A**, *imprint of* Tercer
Mundo Editores SA

**Tercer Mundo Editores SA+**
Transversal 2A No 67-27, Bogota, Cundinamarca
*Tel:* (01) 2551539; (01) 2550737; (01) 2551695
*Fax:* (01) 2125976
*E-mail:* tmundo@polcola.com.co
*Telex:* 42192 *Cable:* TERCER MUNDO
*Key Personnel*
President: Santiago V Pombo
Editorial Dir: Maria Teresa Barajas
Founded: 1961
Editing, printing & distribution of book, mainly
in Colombia & Latino America, with or with-
out the company's name. Administration, man-
agement & city's studies.
Membership(s): Tercer Mundo Distribuidores S
A.
Subjects: Anthropology, Astrology, Occult, Eco-
nomics, Education, Environmental Studies,
Government, Political Science, History, Lit-
erature, Literary Criticism, Essays, Psychol-
ogy, Psychiatry, Science Fiction, Fantasy, Self-
Help, Social Sciences, Sociology, Technology,
Women's Studies
ISBN Prefix(es): 958-601
Number of titles published annually: 60 Print
Total Titles: 500 Print
Imprints: Tercer Mundo Editores S A
Divisions: Tercer Mundo Editores, Grafica
Distributed by Alfaomega Grupo Editor SA de
CV (Mexico & Central America); Centro de
Investigacion Para el Desarrollo Cid; Dolmen
Ediciones SA (Chile); Edisa, Ediciones Y Dis-
ribuciones Del Istmo SA (Costa Rica); La Fa-
milia (Peru); Latin American Book Source Inc
(United States); Libri Mundi (Equador); Presa
Peyran Editores CA (Venezuela)
Distributor for Tercer Mundo Distribuidores SA
*Bookshop(s):* Libreria Tercer Mundo, Car-
rera 7 No 16-91, Bogota, Clara Cortes
*Tel:* (01) 3340504 *Fax:* (01) 2125976
*E-mail:* tmundolib@polcola.com.co (Bolivia)
*Book Club(s):* Libreria Tercer Mundo,
CRA 13 No 44-70, Sandra Guerrero
*E-mail:* tmundolib@polcola.com.co
*Shipping Address:* Calle 69 No 6-46, Bogota

**UNISUR**, see Universidad Nacional Abierta y a
Distancia

**Universidad de Antioquia, Division
Publicaciones+**
Calle 67 No 53-108, Ciudad Universitaria, Bloque
28, oficina 233, Medellin
Mailing Address: Apdo Aereo 1226, Medellin
*Tel:* (04) 210 50 10 *Fax:* (04) 210 50 12
*E-mail:* direccion@editorialudea.com;
comunicaciones@editorialudea.com
*Web Site:* www.editorialudea.com

*Key Personnel*
Dir & Professor: Jorge Juan Franco
  *E-mail:* j_franco64@hotmail.com
Founded: 1984
Specialize in scientific & cultural texts, not only
  from the institution, but also from other intel-
  lectual & academic environments.
Membership(s): The University Editorial Associ-
  ation of Colombia - ASEUC; The Asociacion
  of Editorials.
Subjects: Art, Drama, Theater, Education, His-
  tory, Journalism, Literature, Literary Criticism,
  Essays, Medicine, Nursing, Dentistry, Music,
  Dance, Philosophy, Poetry, Social Sciences,
  Sociology
ISBN Prefix(es): 958-9021; 958-655
Number of titles published annually: 80 Print; 1
  CD-ROM
Total Titles: 79 Print

**Universidad de los Andes Editorial**
Carrera 1 No 19-27, Edificio Au 106, Bogota
SAN: 005-2027
*Tel:* (01) 3394949; (01) 3394999 *Fax:* (01)
  3394949 (ext 2158)
*E-mail:* infeduni@uniandes.edu.co
*Web Site:* ediciones.uniandes.edu.co
*Telex:* 42343 *Cable:* UNAND
*Key Personnel*
Dir: Martha Helena Esguerra Perez
  *E-mail:* maesguer@uniandes.edu.co
Founded: 1958
Subjects: Economics
ISBN Prefix(es): 958-695
Distributed by Libreria Uniandes (Colombia)

**Universidad Nacional Abierta y a Distancia**
Calle 53 No 14-39, Apdo Aereo 42891, Bogota
*Tel:* (01) 212 0159; (01) 346 0088 *Fax:* (01) 522
  3497
*E-mail:* unisur12@gaitana.interred.net.co
*Key Personnel*
Contact: Jesus Emilio Martinez Henao
Founded: 1981
Subjects: Accounting, Agriculture, Biological
  Sciences, Business, Chemistry, Chemical En-
  gineering, Communications, Computer Sci-
  ence, Economics, Environmental Studies, Film,
  Video, Finance, Management, Mathematics,
  Philosophy, Physics, Science (General), Social
  Sciences, Sociology
ISBN Prefix(es): 958-651
*Bookshop(s):* Cread Jose Acevedo y Gomex, Au-
  topista Sur No 16-38, Bogota

**Universidad Nacional Editorial**
Ciudad Universitaria, Torre Activa 602, Apdo
  Aereo 14490, Bogota
*Tel:* (01) 2448640
*Key Personnel*
Editor: Santiago Mutis Duran
ISBN Prefix(es): 958-17

**Editorial Universitaria de America Ltda**
Calle 41 No 20-39, Apdo Aereo 51820, Bogota
*Tel:* (01) 2566948; (01) 3201097 *Fax:* (01)
  3201097
ISBN Prefix(es): 958-613

**Carlos Valencia Editores+**
Ave 25C No 3-99, Apdo Aereo 5832, 56882, Bo-
  gota
*Tel:* (01) 2839040; (01) 3426224 *Fax:* (01)
  2839235
*E-mail:* ancoraed@elancoraeditores.com
*Key Personnel*
Man Dir: Patricia Hoher
Editorial, Rights & Permissions: Felipe Escobar
  Uribe
Founded: 1976
Specialize in literature for children & juveniles.

Subjects: Art, Economics, Government, Political
  Science, Regional Interests, Social Sciences,
  Sociology
ISBN Prefix(es): 958-9044; 84-8277; 958-36;
  958-96577; 958-8048

**Vertice Ltda**
Apdo Aereo 71137, Bogota
*Tel:* (01) 2437113
*Key Personnel*
General Manager: Jesus Antonio Villa Posse
Founded: 1980
ISBN Prefix(es): 84-8281

**Villegas Editores Ltda**
Ave 82 No 11-50, Bogota
*Tel:* (01) 6161788 *Fax:* (01) 6160020
*E-mail:* villedi@cable.net
*Web Site:* www.villegaseditores.com
*Key Personnel*
President & Editor: Benjamin Villegas
Subjects: Art, Cookery, Photography
ISBN Prefix(es): 958-8160; 958-9393

**Editorial Voluntad SA+**
Carrera 7 No 24-89 Pisos 21 & 24, Bogota
*Tel:* (01) 241 04 44 *Fax:* (01) 241 04 39
*E-mail:* voluntad@voluntad.com.co
*Web Site:* www.voluntad.com.co
*Key Personnel*
Man Dir: Gaston de Bedout-Arbelaez
Editorial Dir: William Gomez
Administration Dir: Hector Hurtado
Sales & Publicity Dir: Jairo Roldan
Founded: 1930
Subjects: Art, Communications, Cookery, Crafts,
  Games, Hobbies, Journalism, Language Arts,
  Linguistics, Music, Dance, Sports, Athletics
ISBN Prefix(es): 958-02
*Branch Office(s)*
Carrera 43B No 80-60, Barranquilla
  *Tel:* (095) 378 0955 *Fax:* (095) 373 5117
  *E-mail:* volbar01@voluntad.com.co
Zona Norte, Carrera 43B No 22A Bis 12, Bogota
  *Tel:* 368 3168; 368 3169; 268 3371 *Fax:* 368
  3168; 368 3169; 268 3371 *E-mail:* volbog03@
  andinet.com
Zona Sur, Calle 1 No 29-15, Bogota *Tel:* 247
  1617; 562 3390 *E-mail:* volbog01@andinet.
  com
Carrera 34 No 51-79, Bucaramanga
  *Tel:* (0976) 577 232 *Fax:* (0976) 573 502
  *E-mail:* volbuc01@andinet.com
Avenida 5a B Norte N, 21-69, Cali *Tel:* (092) 660
  1069; (092) 660 1070; (092) 660 1071; (092)
  667 3207; (092) 660-0653; (092) 661 5929
  *E-mail:* volcali@voluntad.com.co
Carrera 60 A No 30-47, Cartagena *Tel:* (0956)
  534 387; (0956) 531 254; (0956) 531 230;
  (0956) 531 296 *Fax:* (0956) 534 387; (0956)
  531 254; (0956) 531 230; (0956) 531 296
  *E-mail:* volcar01@voluntad.com.co
Avenida 2 E No 17 A 35, Cucuta *Tel:* (097) 571
  9984 *Fax:* (097) 583 3132 *E-mail:* volcuc01@
  telecom.com.co
Carrera 8 No 17 B 44, Duitama *Tel:* (098) 760
  3273 *Fax:* (098) 763 0999 *E-mail:* voldui01@
  telecom.com.co
Calle 18 No 7-21 Piso 1, Ibague *Tel:* (098)
  262 3895; (098) 263 5548; (098) 263 0899
  *Fax:* (098) 262 3895; (098) 263 5548; (098)
  263 0899 *E-mail:* vollba01@telecom.com.co
Calle 36 No 77-36, Medellin *Tel:* (094) 411 5916;
  (094) 411 5897; (094) 413 1665 *Fax:* (094)
  411 5767 *E-mail:* volmed01@voluntad.com.co
Carrera 6a No 27-36, Monteria *Tel:* (0947) 82
  1266 *Fax:* (0947) 82 1266 *E-mail:* volmon01@
  telecom.com.co
Calle 8a No 12-25, Neiva *Tel:* (0988) 715 276
  *Fax:* (0988) 715 276 *E-mail:* edivolnei@
  multiphone.net.co

Carrera 21 A No 17-10, Pasto *Tel:* (0927) 214
  128 *E-mail:* volpas01@etb.net.co
Calle 32 Bis No 13-09 piso 2, Pereira
  *Tel:* (096) 336 0095 *Fax:* (096) 266156
  *E-mail:* volper01@epm.net.co
Carrera 21B No 21-65, Santa Marta
  *Tel:* (095) 420 1601 *Fax:* (095) 420 1661
  *E-mail:* volsma01@celcaribe.net.co
Carrera 26 No 19-50, Sincelejo *Tel:* (095) 281
  8916; (095) 281 7050 *E-mail:* volunsjo@
  telecom.com.co
Carrera 5a No 14-69 Piso 1, Valledupar
  *Tel:* (0955) 742 153 *Fax:* (0955) 708 717
  *E-mail:* volva101@teleupar.net.co
Calle 39 B No 27-86 piso 2, Villavicencio
  *Tel:* (098) 670 4921 *Fax:* (098) 664 17 42
  *E-mail:* volvil01@andinet.com

**Ediciones Alfred y Cia Wild Ltda**
Calle 82 No 12A-35 Piso 2, Bogota
*Tel:* (01) 6218000 *Fax:* (01) 6114338
*E-mail:* info@galeriaalfredwild.com
*Web Site:* www.galeriaalfredwild.com
*Key Personnel*
Legal Representative: Alfred Wild Toro
ISBN Prefix(es): 958-95327; 958-96323
Subsidiaries: Casa Poblana (3 almacenes)

# The Democratic Republic of the Congo

## General Information

*Capital:* Kinshasa
*Language:* Officially French
*Religion:* Most follow traditional African beliefs;
  some Catholic and Protestant
*Population:* 39 million
*Shop Hours:* 0800-1200, 1500-1800 Monday-
  Friday; 0800-1200 Saturday
*Currency:* 100 makutu = 1 zaire
*Export/Import Information:* No tariff, but for
  books not of educational, scientific or cultural
  use there is a revenue tax; children's picture
  books and atlases are also taxed. Small quantities of advertising matter free. Statistical Tax
  on all imports. Goods subject to duty also
  subject to Turnover Tax of percentage of CIF
  value and customs and statistical tax. No import licences for books. Exchange controls.
*Copyright:* Berne, Florence (see Copyright Conventions, pg xi)

**CDPZ**, see Connaissance et Pratique du Droit
Zairos (CDPZ)

**Centre de Recherche, et Pedagogie Appliquee**
BP 8815, Kinshasa 1
*Key Personnel*
Dir: P Detienne *Tel:* (012) 22248
Adminstration: J Vannuffelen
Founded: 1959
Subjects: Accounting, Education, Geography,
  Geology, Language Arts, Linguistics, Mathe-
  matics, Medicine, Nursing, Dentistry, Physical
  Sciences
Distributor for L'Epiphamie
*Shipping Address:* 1142 11e Rue, Limete, Kin-
  shasa
*Warehouse:* 1142 11e Rue, Limete, Kinshasa
*Orders to:* 1142 11e Rue, Limete, Kinshasa

**Centre de Vulgarisation Agricole**
BP 4008, Kinshasa 2
*Tel:* (012) 71165 *Fax:* (012) 21351
*Key Personnel*
Dir General: Kimpianga Mahaniah
Publications: Ntanama Kamba
Subjects: Agriculture, Environmental Studies,
Gardening, Plants, Health, Nutrition
*Branch Office(s)*
1920 Roosevelt Dr, Apt 52, Northfield, MN,
United States
Distributed by Inades Formation (Zaire)

**Centre Protestant d'Editions et de Diffusion
(CEDI)+**
BP 11398, Kinshasa 1
*Key Personnel*
Man Dir: Henry Dirks
Founded: 1935
Subjects: Biography, Fiction, Poetry, Religion -
Other
*Bookshop(s):* CEDI Bookshop

**Connaissance et Pratique du Droit Zairos
(CDPZ)+**
BP 5502, Kinshasa, Gombe
*Key Personnel*
Editor: Dibunda Kabuinji
Founded: 1987
Subjects: Law
Total Titles: 6 Print; 6 Online
*Associate Companies:* Societe d'Etudes Juridiques
du Congo (SEJC)
Imprints: Reper Toire General be Jurisprudence
be la Cour Supreme be Justice; Revue Analy-
tiqu ebe Jurisprubencebu Congo; Revue Juri-
tique bu Congo
*Bookshop(s):* One rue Limete, Kinshasa/Masina-
Petro Congo, Republique Democratique du
Congo
*Warehouse:* One, rue Limete, Kinshasa-Masina/
Petro Congo

**Facultes Catholiques de Kinshasa**
2, Ave de l'Universite, 1534 Kinshasa
*Tel:* (088) 46 965 *Fax:* (088) 46 965
*E-mail:* facakin@ic.cd
*Web Site:* www.cenco.cd/facultescath/
*Key Personnel*
Dir: Prof Abbe Waswandi Kakule
Editorial: Prof Abbe Mukuna Wa Mutanda; Prof
Abbe Atal; Prof Pere Leon de Saint Moulin;
Prof Mweze
Founded: 1957
Subjects: Anthropology, Art, Biblical Studies,
Communications, Computer Science, Eco-
nomics, Government, Political Science, History
*Bookshop(s):* Librarie Saint Paul, Kinshasa-
Limete
*Orders to:* SEDIP (Service de Diffusion des Pub-
lications), Kinshasa-Limete

**Mediaspaul Afrique+**
10, rue Limete, Industriel No 18, Kinshasa
*E-mail:* diffusion@mediaspaul.org
*Web Site:* www.mediaspaul.org
*Key Personnel*
President: Charles Djunju-Simba
International Rights: M Claude Lechat
Founded: 1989
Subjects: Communications, Drama, Theater, Fic-
tion, Literature, Literary Criticism, Essays
ISBN Prefix(es): 2-7414
Distributed by Mediaspaul
*Bookshop(s):* Librairie Mediaspaul, Blvd National
nº83 Ville Basse, Kikwit; Librairie Mediaspaul,
c/o Ordre des Freres Mineurs, Kolwezi; Li-
brairie Mediaspaul, Blvd de l'independance
nº19, Likasi; Librairie Mediaspaul, Route
Kasapa-Carrefour, Lubumbashi; Route de Kin-
shasa nº5 (Rond point 2415), Matadi; Librairie
Mediaspaul, Av Odia David, Commune de

Muya Simis, Mbuji Mayi; Librairie Mediaspaul Kintambo, Av Kasa-Vubu nº 2, Commune
de Ngaliema, Kinshasa; Librairie Mediaspaul
Masina, Av Force Nationale nº 10, Commune
de Masina, Kinshasa; Librairie Mediaspaul Victoire, Av Bonga nº6172, Quartier Matonge,
Commune de Matonge, Kinshasa

**Presses Universitaires du Zaiire (PUZ)**
Blvd du 30 Juin 4113, Kinshasa 1
Mailing Address: BP 1682, Kinshasa 1
*Tel:* 30652
*Telex:* 21394 Bce Es *Cable:* PUZ Enseignement
*Key Personnel*
Man Dir, Rights & Permissions: Mumbanza mwa
Bawele
Editorial: Kabongo Kabongo
Sales: Nsolo Abeyingi
Production: Kawumbu Kabemba
Publicity: Bisimwa Nabintu
Founded: 1972
Subjects: Biography, Economics, Education, Eth-
nicity, Foreign Countries, History, Law, Lit-
erature, Literary Criticism, Essays, Medicine,
Nursing, Dentistry, Philosophy, Poetry, Psy-
chology, Psychiatry, Religion - Other, Science
(General), Social Sciences, Sociology, Technol-
ogy
*Parent Company:* Enseignement Superieu, Uni-
versitaire et Recherche Scientifique, BP 1682,
Kinshasa-Gombe
Imprints: PUZ
*Branch Office(s)*
Lubumbashi
*Bookshop(s):* Librairie des Presses Universitaires;
Librairie Universitaire de l'ISP/Kawanga; Li-
brairie du 'Groupe du Mukuba', Lubumbashi

**PUZ**, *imprint of* Presses Universitaires du Zaiire
(PUZ)

**Reper Toire General be Jurisprubence be la
Cour Supreme be Justice**, *imprint of*
Connaissance et Pratique du Droit Zairos
(CDPZ)

**Revue Analytiqu ebe Jurisprubencebu Congo**,
*imprint of* Connaissance et Pratique du Droit
Zairos (CDPZ)

**Revue Juritique bu Congo**, *imprint of*
Connaissance et Pratique du Droit Zairos
(CDPZ)

# Costa Rica

## General Information

*Capital:* San Jose
*Language:* Spanish
*Religion:* Roman Catholic
*Population:* 3.2 million
*Bank Hours:* 0900-1500 Monday-Friday
*Shop Hours:* 0800-1200, 1400-1800 Monday-
Saturday (some close Saturday afternoon)
*Currency:* 100 centimos = 1 Costa Rican colon
*Export/Import Information:* No import licenses,
but statistical recording prior to importation
necessary. Imports of a certain value must be
registered with Banco Central to be eligible for
foreign exchange allocation.
*Copyright:* Berne, UCC, Buenos Aires (see Copy-
right Conventions, pg xi)

**Academia de Centro America+**
Apdo 6347, 1000 San Jose
*Tel:* 283-1847 *Fax:* 283-1848

*E-mail:* info@academiaca.or.cr; rherrera@
acedmiaca.or.cr
*Key Personnel*
President: Eduardo Lizano
Subjects: Agriculture, Business, Economics, Envi-
ronmental Studies, Finance, Health, Nutrition,
Labor, Industrial Relations
ISBN Prefix(es): 9977-21

**Artex+**
Formerly Litografia Artex, SA
Apdo 7111, 1000 Heredia
*Tel:* 2373144 *Fax:* 2379568
*Key Personnel*
Contact: Gilbert Campos Gamboa
Founded: 1971
Subjects: Advertising, Medicine, Nursing, Den-
tistry, Poetry, Religion - Catholic
ISBN Prefix(es): 9977-86

**Asamblea Legislativa, Biblioteca Monsenor
Sanabria**
Apdo 1013, 1000 San Jose
*Tel:* 223-2396 *Fax:* 243-2400
*E-mail:* jvolio@congreso.aleg.go.cr; vvargas@
congreso.aleg.go.cr; epaniagu@congreso.aleg.
go.cr
Subjects: Economics, Education, Social Sciences,
Sociology
ISBN Prefix(es): 9977-916

**CATIE**, see Centro Agronomico Tropical de
Investigacion y Ensenanza (CATIE)

**CCCCA**, see Confederacion de Cooperativas del
Caribe y Centro America (CCCCA)

**Centro Agronomico Tropical de Investigacion y
Ensenanza (CATIE)**
Apdo 7170, 150 Turrialba
*Tel:* 556-6431 *Fax:* 556-1533
*E-mail:* comunicacion@catie.ac.cr
*Web Site:* www.catie.ac.cr
*Telex:* 8005 CATIE CR *Cable:* CATIE
TURRIALBA
*Key Personnel*
Editor: Eli Rodriguez *E-mail:* erodrigu@catie.ac.
cr
Founded: 1942
Research & Higher Educational Center
Specialize in scientific investigation & techniques
of Tropical America, Research & Training of
Tropical Agriculture & Natural Resouces.
Subjects: Agriculture, Biological Sciences, De-
veloping Countries, Economics, Education,
Engineering (General), Environmental Stud-
ies, Gardening, Plants, How-to, Natural History,
Social Sciences, Sociology, Technology
ISBN Prefix(es): 9977-57; 9977-951

**Confederacion de Cooperativas del Caribe y
Centro America (CCCCA)+**
400 mts este contiguo a Kilates, del Edificio el
ICE en Tibas, Apdo 3658, San Jose
*Tel:* 2404592 *Fax:* 2333122
*E-mail:* ccocca@sol.racsa.co.cr
*Key Personnel*
Executive Director: Felix J Cristia
Subjects: Finance, Public Administration
ISBN Prefix(es): 9977-82
Subsidiaries: Sistema de Informacion Cooperativa
(REDI-COOP)
*Branch Office(s)*
CCC-CA/Oficina Subrregional, PO Box 360707,
San Juan 00936-0707, Puerto Rico

**Editorial Costa Rica**
Apdo 10010, 1000 San Jose
*Tel:* 253-5354 *Fax:* 253-5091
*E-mail:* ventas@editorialcostarica.com; difusion@
editorialcostarica.com
*Web Site:* www.editorialcostarica.com

*Key Personnel*
Management: Habib Succar *E-mail:* editocr@
racsa.co.cr
Sales: Enilda Campos Barrantes
Production: Dennis Mesen Segura
Publicity Manager: Gustavo Adolfo Gonazalez
Mederas
Founded: 1959
Subjects: Regional Interests
ISBN Prefix(es): 84-8361; 9977-23

**Editorial DEI (Departamento Ecumenico de Investigaciones)+**
Apdo 390-2070, Sabanilla, Montes de Oca, San
Jose
*Tel:* 253-0229; 253-9124 *Fax:* 2531541
*E-mail:* publicaciones@dei-cr.org
*Web Site:* www.dei-cr.org
*Telex:* 3472 ADEI
*Key Personnel*
General Manager: Jose Duque
Founded: 1977
Subjects: Economics, Government, Political Sci-
ence, History, Theology, Women's Studies
ISBN Prefix(es): 9977-904; 9977-83
Imprints: Revista Pasos
*Bookshop(s):* Libreria Horizonte, Apdo 447-2070,
San Jose

**Fundacion Omar Dengo**
Apdo 1032-2050, San Jose
*Tel:* 257 6263 *Fax:* 2221654
*E-mail:* info@fod.ac.cr
*Web Site:* www.fod.ac.cr
*Key Personnel*
President: Alfonso Gutierrez Cerdas
Founded: 1987
ISBN Prefix(es): 9977-11

**Departamento Ecumenico de Investigaciones**,
see Editorial DEI (Departamento Ecumenico de
Investigaciones)

**EDUCA**, see Editorial Universitaria
Centroamericana (EDUCA)

**Fundacion Escuela Para Todos+**
Apdo 4757, 1000 San Jose
*Tel:* 2255438; 2255338; 2340530; 2341339
*Fax:* 2243014
*Key Personnel*
President: Manuela Tattenbach
Founded: 1963
ISBN Prefix(es): 9977-51

**EUNA**, see Editorial Universidad Nacional
(EUNA)

**Ediciones FLACSO Costa Rica**
675 este de la Iglesia, Santa Teresita No 3571,
1000 San Jose
Mailing Address: Apdo 11747, 1000 San Jose
*Tel:* 2248059; 2346890 *Fax:* 2256779
*E-mail:* libros@flacso.or.cr
*Web Site:* www.flacso.or.cr
*Key Personnel*
Contact: Olga Alvarado
ISBN Prefix(es): 9977-68; 84-89401

**Garcia Hermanos Imprenta y Litografia**
Apdo 10015, 1000 Santa Ana, San Jose
*Tel:* 2202003; 2212223 *Fax:* 2310675
*E-mail:* info@novanet.co.cr
*Web Site:* www.novanet.co.cr
*Key Personnel*
Contact: Juan Carlos Caamano Umana
*E-mail:* jcc@novanet.co.cr
ISBN Prefix(es): 9977-38

**IICA**, see Instituto Interamericano de
Cooperacion para la Agricultura (IICA)

**Imprenta y Litografia Trejos SA**
Apdo 10-096, 1000 San Jose
*Tel:* 2242411 *Fax:* 2241528
*Key Personnel*
President: Alvaro Trejos
ISBN Prefix(es): 9977-54

**INCAE**, see Insituto Centroamericano de
Administracion de Empresas (INCAE)

**Insituto Centroamericano de Administracion de Empresas (INCAE)**
Del Vivero Procesa No 1, 2 Km al Oeste, La
Garita, Alajuela
*Tel:* 433-9908; 433-9961; 437-2305 *Fax:* 433-
9989; 433-9983
*E-mail:* incaecr@mail.incae.ac.cr
*Web Site:* www.incae.ac.cr
*Key Personnel*
Chief Marketing: Sonia Jimenez
*E-mail:* jimenezs@mail.incae.ac.cr
ISBN Prefix(es): 9977-71

**Instituto Interamericano de Cooperacion para la Agricultura (IICA)**
PO Box 55-2200, San Isidro de Coronado, San
Jose
*Tel:* (0506) 216-0222 *Fax:* (0506) 216-0233
*E-mail:* iicahq@iica.ac.cr
*Web Site:* www.iica.int
*Key Personnel*
Dir, Information & Communication: Jorge
Sariego *E-mail:* jsariego@iica.ac.cr
Subjects: Agriculture, Computer Science, Devel-
oping Countries, Earth Sciences, Environmental
Studies, Marketing, Technology, Veterinary Sci-
ence, Women's Studies
ISBN Prefix(es): 956-212

**Jose Alfonso Sandoval Nunez+**
100 mts este de la Municipalidad, Residencia El
Carmen San Pedro de Montes de Oca, San Jose
*Tel:* 2252331; 8-326-426
*E-mail:* asandova@alpha.emate.ucr.ac.cr;
k_sanny@hotmail.com
Subjects: Education, Mathematics
ISBN Prefix(es): 9968-9882
Total Titles: 5 Print

**Juricom+**
De la Pops Curridabat, 100 mts sur, Apdo 4387,
1000 San Jose
*Tel:* 2836942 *Fax:* 2253800
*E-mail:* juricom@sol.racsa.co.cr
*Key Personnel*
Contact: Alejandra Linner de Silva
Founded: 1996
Subjects: Law
ISBN Prefix(es): 9968-769

**Libreria Imprenta y Litografia Lehmann SA**
Apdo 10011, San Jose
*Tel:* 2231212
*Telex:* 2540 Lill Eh
*Key Personnel*
Man Dir: Antonio Lehmann Struve
Publicity: Orlando Mora
Founded: 1894
Subjects: Fiction, Nonfiction (General)
ISBN Prefix(es): 9977-949

**Litografia Artex, SA**, see Artex

**Litografia e Imprenta LIL SA**
Apdo 75, 1100 Tibas
*Tel:* 2350011; 2213622 *Fax:* 2407814

*Key Personnel*
Contact: Mario Salazar Fonseca
Founded: 1974
ISBN Prefix(es): 9977-47

**Museo Historico Cultural Juan Santamaria**
Apdo 785, 4050 Alajuela
*Tel:* 441-4775; 442-1838 *Fax:* 441-6926
*E-mail:* mhcjscr@racsa.co.cr
*Web Site:* www.museojuansantamaria.go.cr
*Key Personnel*
Dir: Raul Aguilar
Founded: 1980
Subjects: Genealogy, History
ISBN Prefix(es): 9977-953

**Editorial Nacional de Salud y Seguridad Social Ednass**
Caja Costarricense de Seguridad Social, Apdo
10105, 1000 San Jose
*Tel:* 231-2214 *Fax:* 232-7451
*E-mail:* cendeiss@info.ccss.sa.cr
*Key Personnel*
Contact: Gerardo Campos Gamboa
Founded: 1988
Subjects: Behavioral Sciences, Biological Sci-
ences, Health, Nutrition, Medicine, Nursing,
Dentistry, Public Administration, Social Sci-
ences, Sociology
ISBN Prefix(es): 9977-984
Number of titles published annually: 10 Print
Total Titles: 2 Print

**Revista Pasos**, *imprint of* Editorial DEI
(Departamento Ecumenico de Investigaciones)

**Editorial Porvenir**
300 este de la escuela Franklin D Roosevelt, Bar-
rio La Granja, San Pedro
Mailing Address: Apdo 447-2050, Montes de Oca
*Tel:* 224-8119; 224-1052; 225-3115 *Fax:* 283-
8893; 224-8119
*E-mail:* porvenir@racsa.co.cr
*Telex:* 3220 CECADE CR
*Key Personnel*
President: William Reuben
Dir: Victoria Paris
Founded: 1979
Subjects: Economics, History, Law, Psychology,
Psychiatry, Social Sciences, Sociology
ISBN Prefix(es): 9977-944; 9968-764

**Ediciones Promesa+**
Contiguo a Taco Bell, Barrio Dent, Apdo 4300,
San Jose
*Tel:* 253-3759; 225-1511; 283-3033 *Fax:* 225-
1286
*E-mail:* edicionespromesa@hotmail.com
*Key Personnel*
President: Helena Ospina *E-mail:* helenaospina@
hotmail.com
Manager: Erika Chinchilla
Founded: 1982
Publishing, video, CD & documentation cultural
center
Cultural project interrelating the arts.
Membership(s): Camara Costarricense del Libro.
Subjects: Anthropology, Art, Behavioral Sciences,
Biography, Child Care & Development, Drama,
Theater, Education, Fashion, Film, Video, His-
tory, Human Relations, Language Arts, Lin-
guistics, Literature, Literary Criticism, Essays,
Music, Dance, Philosophy, Poetry, Psychology,
Psychiatry, Religion - Catholic, Self-Help, So-
cial Sciences, Sociology, Theology, Women's
Studies
ISBN Prefix(es): 9977-947; 9968-41
Number of titles published annually: 24 Print; 6
Audio
Total Titles: 85 Print; 2 E-Book; 20 Audio
*Parent Company:* Promotora de Medios de Comu-
nicacion SA

*Associate Companies:* Electronic Engineering, PO Box 4300, 1000 San Jose, Contact: Helena Maria Fonseca
*U.S. Office(s):* Ma Rosa Noda, 9022 SW 123 Court 0-109, Miami, FL 33186, United States, Contact: Maria Rosa Noda *Tel:* 305-279-9997 *E-mail:* mrnoda@un.int
*Showroom(s):* Edificio Electronic Engineering, Frente a Rectoria, Universidad de Costa Rica, Carretera a Sabanilla, 1000 San Jose, Contact: Helena Maria Fonseca *Tel:* (305) 283-3033 *Fax:* (305) 225-1286 *E-mail:* hf@eecrica.com *Web Site:* www.eecrica.com
*Bookshop(s):* Libreria Universal, Libreria Lehmann, San Jose

**Editorial Tecnologica de Costa Rica+**
Apdo 159, 7050 Cartago
*Tel:* 552-5333 ext 2297 *Fax:* 552-5354; 551-5348
*E-mail:* editec@itcr.ac.cr
*Web Site:* www.itcr.ac.cr
*Key Personnel*
Dir: Mario Castillo-Mendez
Founded: 1978
Membership(s): EULAC (Association of University Publishers of Latin American & the Caribbean).
Subjects: Science (General), Technology
ISBN Prefix(es): 9977-66; 84-89400

**Editorial Texto Ltda+**
Apdo 2988, 1000 San Jose
*Tel:* 2316643 *Fax:* 2962429
*Key Personnel*
President: Frank Thomas Gallardo
  *E-mail:* gallardo@sol.racsa.co.cr
Vice President: Renee Echeverria Rodriguez de Luz
Founded: 1963
Private Company
Online translating from Spanish to English & vice versa.
Subjects: Animals, Pets, Real Estate, Regional Interests
ISBN Prefix(es): 9977-29
Total Titles: 8 Print

**UICN,** see Union Mundial para la Naturaleza (UICN), Oficina Regional para Mesoamerica

**Union Mundial para la Naturaleza (UICN), Oficina Regional para Mesoamerica**
Apdo 146-2150, San Jose
*Tel:* 241-0101 *Fax:* 240-9934
*E-mail:* correo@iucn.org
*Web Site:* www.iucn.org/places/orma
*Key Personnel*
Contact: Dr Enrique J Lahmann
Founded: 1988
Subjects: Biological Sciences, Developing Countries, Environmental Studies, Coastal Zone Management, Wetlands, Gender & Development, Nature Conservation, Sustainable Development, Wildlife Management, Forest Management
ISBN Prefix(es): 9968-743
*Branch Office(s)*
IUCN Canada, 555 Rene Levesque Blvd W, Suite 500, Montreal, QC H2Z 1B1, Canada *Tel:* 514-287-9704 *Fax:* 514-287-6987 *E-mail:* canada@iucn.org *Web Site:* www.iucn.org/places/canada
IUCN Laguna Lachua National Park Project Office, 7a, av 6-80, Zona 13, Guatemala, Guatemala *Tel:* (0247) 35214 *Fax:* (0247) 35214 *E-mail:* proy.lachua@starnet.net.gt
IUCN Manglares del Pacifico de Guatemala Project Office, 7a, av 6-80, Zona 13, Guatemala, Guatemala *Tel:* (0247) 35213 *Fax:* (0247) 35213 *E-mail:* proy.manglares@starnet.net.gt
UICN Oficina Regional para America del Sur, Av De Los Shyris 2680 y Gaspar de Villar-

roel, Edificio Mita-Cobadelsa, Penthouse, PH, Casilla 17-17-626, Quito, Ecuador *Tel:* (02) 2261-075 *Fax:* (02) 2261-075 (ext 230) *E-mail:* samerica@sur.iucn.org *Web Site:* www.sur.iucn.org (South America)
*U.S. Office(s):* IUCN US Multilateral Office, 1630 Connecticut Ave NW, 3rd floor, Washington, DC 20009-1053, United States *Tel:* 202-387-4826 *Fax:* 202-387-4823 *E-mail:* postmaster@iucnus.org *Web Site:* www.iucn.org/places/usa

**Editorial de la Universidad de Costa Rica+**
Imprint of University of Costa Rica
Ciudad Universitaria Rodrigo Facio, 2060 Montes de Oca
*Tel:* 207-5006; 207-5837 *Fax:* 224-9367
*E-mail:* direccion@editorial.ucr.ac.cr
*Web Site:* www.editorial.ucr.ac.cr
*Telex:* 2544 Unicori
*Key Personnel*
Dir: Fernando Duran
Administrative Coordinator: Ruben Chacon
  *Tel:* 207-5624 *E-mail:* administracion@editorial.ucr.ac.cr
Founded: 1975
Subjects: Agriculture, Anthropology, Archaeology, Architecture & Interior Design, Art, Behavioral Sciences, Biological Sciences, Career Development, Civil Engineering, Computer Science, Cookery, Earth Sciences, Economics, Education, Energy, Engineering (General), English as a Second Language, Environmental Studies, Government, Political Science, Health, Nutrition, History, Language Arts, Linguistics, Law, Management, Natural History, Physical Sciences, Poetry, Public Administration, Science (General), Social Sciences, Sociology, Sports, Athletics
ISBN Prefix(es): 9977-67
Total Titles: 40 Print; 1 CD-ROM

**Editorial Universidad Estatal a Distancia (EUNED)**
Apdo 474-2050, San Pedro de Montes De Oca, San Jose
*Tel:* 234-7954; 253-2121 (ext 2440) *Fax:* 257-5042; 234-9138
*E-mail:* editoria@uned.ac.cr
*Web Site:* www.uned.ac.cr/ejecutiva/editorial/
*Telex:* 3003 *Cable:* UNED
*Key Personnel*
President, Rights & Permissions: Dr Alberto Canas Escalante
Editorial Dir: Rene Muinos Gual
Sales Dir: Hernan Mora Gonzalez
Production: Carlos Zamora-Murillo
Publicity: Annie Umana Campos
Founded: 1977
Subjects: Agriculture, Economics, Education, Government, Political Science, History, Medicine, Nursing, Dentistry, Philosophy
ISBN Prefix(es): 9977-64; 84-8362; 9968-31
*Showroom(s):* Calle 11, Ave 12-14, San Jose *Fax:* 331601
*Bookshop(s):* Libreria UNED; Calle 11, Ave 12-14, San Jose

**Editorial Universidad Nacional (EUNA)**
Apdo 86, 3000 Heredia
*Tel:* 277-3204; 277-3825 *Fax:* 277-3204
*E-mail:* editoria@una.ac.cr
*Web Site:* www.una.ac.cr/euna
*Key Personnel*
Contact: Sr Francisco Carballo
Founded: 1978
Membership(s): EULAC-CERLAC.
Subjects: Education, History, Literature, Literary Criticism, Essays, Poetry
ISBN Prefix(es): 9977-65
Number of titles published annually: 45 Print
Total Titles: 250 Print
Distributed by ACAL

**Universidad para la Paz** (University for Peace)
Apdo 138, 6100 Ciudad Colon, San Jose
*Tel:* 205-9000; 249-1511 (ext 20) *Fax:* 249-1929
*E-mail:* info@upeace.org
*Web Site:* www.upeace.org
ISBN Prefix(es): 9977-925

**Editorial Universitaria Centroamericana (EDUCA)+**
Ciudad Universitaria Rodrigo Facio, Apdo 64, 2060 San Jose
*Tel:* 2258740 *Fax:* 2340071
*E-mail:* educacr@sol.racsa.co.cr
*Telex:* 3011 COSUCA
*Key Personnel*
Dir: Sebastian Vaquerano
Sales: Anita de Formoso
Founded: 1969
Subjects: History, Poetry, Regional Interests, Romance, Social Sciences, Sociology
ISBN Prefix(es): 9977-30; 84-8360

# Cote d'Ivoire

## General Information

*Capital:* Yamoussoukro
*Language:* French (officially) and several African languages
*Religion:* Traditional, 20% Islamic, 20% Christian (mostly Roman Catholic)
*Population:* 13.5 million
*Bank Hours:* 0800-1200, 1500-1900 Monday-Friday
*Shop Hours:* 0800-1200, 1530-1830 or 1900 Monday-Friday; 0800-1200, 1430-1730 Saturday
*Currency:* 100 centimes = 1 CFA franc
*Export/Import Information:* Member of West African Economic Community. No tariff on books; single copies free but most advertising subject to customs duty, fiscal duty and VAT. No import licenses required for imports from EEC or Franc Zone.
*Copyright:* Berne, Florence (see Copyright Conventions, pg xi)

**Universite d'Abidjan+**
BP V 34, Abidjan 01
*Tel:* 441285 *Fax:* 434254
*E-mail:* puci@africaonline.co.ci
*Telex:* 3469
*Key Personnel*
Publications Dir: Alain Poiri
Founded: 1964
Subjects: Biography, Communications, Developing Countries, Economics, Environmental Studies, Law, Microcomputers, Public Administration, Social Sciences, Sociology
ISBN Prefix(es): 2-7166
Number of titles published annually: 50 Print

**Akohi Editions**
13 BP 585, Abidjan 13
*Tel:* 24 39 54 79 *Fax:* 24 39 75 58
*Key Personnel*
President: Bosson Brou Evariste *Tel:* 24 39 58 01; 05 99 25 52
Founded: 1995
Subjects: Drama, Theater, Human Relations, Literature, Literary Criticism, Essays, Music, Dance, Poetry
ISBN Prefix(es): 2-9507542; 2-910569
Total Titles: 10 Print
*Associate Companies:* Biennale Internationale des Arts Lettres et du Tourisme, 13 BP, 585 Abidjan, Contact: Bosson Brou Evariste *Tel:* 24 39 58 01; 24 99 25 52; 24 39 40 37

Subsidiaries: Imprimerie Akohi
Divisions: Akohi Diffusion
Distributed by Ed Passerelle Abidjan
Distributor for Ed Baudhouat Abidjan; Ed
 Passerelle Abidjan
Book Club(s): Association des Ecrivains, Contact:
 Josetti Abondio Tel: 24 39 10 37; Association
 des Editeurs-Ivoiriens, Contact: Mariam Sy Di-
 awara Tel: 35 35 35 Fax: 39 75 58
Shipping Address: Abobo, 2e Arret Sotra, 500M
 apres Brigade Gendarmerie Route, Anyama,
 Contact: Bosson Brou Evariste Kowouka


**CEDA**, see Centre d'Edition et de Diffusion
 Africaines

### Centre de Publications Evangeliques
BP 900, Abidjan 08
Tel: 444805 Fax: 445817
Key Personnel
Dir: Jules Ouoba
Founded: 1970
Subjects: Biblical Studies, Nonfiction (General),
 Religion - Protestant, Religion - Other
ISBN Prefix(es): 2-910307

### Centre d'Edition et de Diffusion Africaines
17 rue des Carrossiers, Abidjan 04
Mailing Address: 04 BP 541, Abidjan 04
Tel: 21 24 65 10; 21 24 65 11 Fax: 21 25 05 67
E-mail: infos@ceda-ci.com
Web Site: www.ceda-ci.com
Key Personnel
Editorial Dir: Marie Agathe Amoikon
Dir: Mr Venance Kacou
Founded: 1961
Distributors on behalf of INADES, the National
 University of the Ivory Coast & the Biblio-
 theque nationale.
Subjects: Biography, History, Law, Nonfiction
 (General), Philosophy, Regional Interests, Sci-
 ence (General), Social Sciences, Sociology
ISBN Prefix(es): 2-86394

### Heritage Publishing Co+
BP 54, Cidex 3 Abidjan-Riviera
Tel: 433056 Fax: 433056
Key Personnel
Contact: Tah Asongwed
Founded: 1993
Subjects: Biography, Developing Countries, Fic-
 tion, Government, Political Science, Language
 Arts, Linguistics, Nonfiction (General)
ISBN Prefix(es): 2-910021
Imprints: HP
U.S. Office(s): Heritage Publshing Company, 1015
 Stirling Rd, Silver Spring, MD 20901, United
 States Tel: 301-593-6450
Distributed by Waterville Publishing House
 (Ghana)
Distributor for Three Dimensional Publishing
 (USA)


**HP**, imprint of Heritage Publishing Co


**NEI**, see Les Nouvelles Editions Ivoiriennes
 (NEI)

### Les Nouvelles Editions Ivoiriennes+
One blvd de Marseille, Abidjan 01
Mailing Address: BP 1818, Abidjan 01
Tel: 21 24 07 66; 21 24 08 25 Fax: 21 24 24 56
E-mail: edition@nei-ci.com
Web Site: www.nei-ci.com
Telex: 22564 Nea CI
Key Personnel
Commercial Dir: M Oze G Roger
Founded: 1972
Subjects: Art, Drama, Theater, History, Literature,
 Literary Criticism, Essays, Religion - Other
ISBN Prefix(es): 2-7236

Parent Company: Les Nouvelles Editions
 Africaines du Senegal, 10, rue Amadou
 Assane-Ndoye, BP 260, Dakar, Senegal
Associate Companies: Togo

### Les Nouvelles Editions Ivoiriennes (NEI)+
Subsidiary of Hachette Livre International
One blvd de Marseille, 01 Abidjan
Mailing Address: 01 BP 1818, Abidjan 01
Tel: 21 24 92 12; 21 24 07 66; 21 24 08 25
 Fax: 21 24 24 56
Key Personnel
Dir General: Guy Lambin
Founded: 1992
Subjects: Art, Literature, Literary Criticism, Es-
 says, Poetry
ISBN Prefix(es): 2-910190; 2-911725; 2-84487
Distributed by EDICEF (France)
Distributor for Classiques Hachette sur Cote
 d'Ivoire; Hachette Livres


**PUCI**, see Universite d'Abidjan


# Croatia

## General Information

Capital: Zagreb
Language: Croatian
Religion: Predominantly Roman Catholic & East-
 ern Orthodox
Population: 4.8 million
Bank Hours: 0700-1900 Monday-Friday; 0700-
 1200 Saturday; 0800-1600 in the small towns
Shop Hours: 0800-1900 Monday-Friday & 0800-
 1300 Saturday
Currency: kuna, divisible into 100 lipa
Export/Import Information: Firms trade freely
 with foreign partners in accordance with international agreements & treaties, and with mea-
 sures which are in line with the principles &
 demands of the World Trade Organization.
Copyright: UCC, Berne (see Copyright Conventions, page xi)

### AGM doo+
Mihanoviceva 28, 10000 Zagreb
Tel: (01) 4856309; (01) 4856307 Fax: (01)
 4856316
E-mail: agm@agm.hr
Web Site: www.agm.hr
Key Personnel
Dir: Janislav Saban E-mail: janislav.saban@agm.
 hr
Subjects: Art, Drama, Theater, History, Literature,
 Literary Criticism, Essays, Nonfiction (Gen-
 eral), Philosophy, Social Sciences, Sociology
ISBN Prefix(es): 953-174

### ALFA dd za izdavacke, graficke i trgovacke
 poslove+
Nova Ves 23/a, 10000 Zagreb
Tel: (01) 4666 066; (01) 4666 077 Fax: (01) 4666
 258
E-mail: alfa-zg@zg.tel.hr
Key Personnel
Manager: Miro Petric
Editor: Bozidar Petrac
Public Relations & Marketing: Ana Maria Bogisic
Founded: 1971
Subjects: Cookery, Education, Fiction, Gardening,
 Plants, Government, Political Science, Litera-
 ture, Literary Criticism, Essays, Poetry, Reli-
 gion - Catholic
Bookshop(s): Krjizara (bookshop), ALFA, Impor-
 tanne Centar, 1000 Zagreb
Shipping Address: Platana bb, 10000 Zagreb
Warehouse: Platana bb, 10000 Zagreb

### ArTresor naklada+
Amruseva, 9, 10000 Zagreb
Tel: (01) 487 2917 Fax: (01) 487 2916
E-mail: artresor@zg.tel.hr
Key Personnel
Manager: Silva Tomanic Kis
Founded: 1996
Subjects: History, Language Arts, Linguistics, Lit-
 erature, Literary Criticism, Essays, Philosophy,
 Poetry
ISBN Prefix(es): 953-6522

### Drzavna Uprava za Zastitu Prirode i Okolisa
 (State Directorate for the Protection of
 Nature & Environment)
Ulica Grada Vukovara 78/111, 10000 Zagreb
Tel: (01) 613 3444 Fax: (01) 611 2073
E-mail: duzo@ring.net
Web Site: www.mzopu.hr
Key Personnel
Dir: Ante Kutle, MD
Founded: 1991
Subjects: Environmental Studies
ISBN Prefix(es): 953-97087; 953-6793

### Durieux d o o+
Sulekova 23, 10000 Zagreb
Tel: (01) 23 00 337; (01) 23 21 178 Fax: (01) 23
 00 337
E-mail: durieux@durieux.hr
Web Site: www.durieux.hr
Key Personnel
President: Drazen Toncic
Editor: Nenad Popovic
Founded: 1990
Subjects: Drama, Theater, Fiction, History, Liter-
 ature, Literary Criticism, Essays, Philosophy,
 Poetry
ISBN Prefix(es): 953-188

### Edit (Edizioni Italiane)
Ulica kralja Zvonimira 20a, 51 000 Rijeka
Tel: (051) 672 119; (051) 672 153 Fax: (051) 672
 151
E-mail: edit@edit.hr
Web Site: www.edit.hr
Key Personnel
Dir: Ennio Machin
ISBN Prefix(es): 86-7127; 953-6150; 953-230
Bookshop(s): Korzo Narodne Revolucije 37,
 51000 Rijeka

### Faust Vrancic+
Preradoviceva ul 25, 10000 Zagreb
Tel: (01) 4817-123; (01) 4558-469 Fax: (01)
 4817-123
E-mail: fv@faust-vrancic.com
Web Site: 90-stupnjeva.com; www.faust-vrancic.
 com
Key Personnel
Dir: Valerij Juresic
Editor: Katarina Mazuran E-mail: katarina.
 mazuran@pontes.com
Founded: 1995
Specialize in new literature, promotion of Croat-
 ian literature & new authors from abroad.
Membership(s): Croatian Independent Publishers.
Subjects: Fiction, Journalism, Literature, Literary
 Criticism, Essays, Music, Dance, Philosophy,
 Poetry, Science Fiction, Fantasy
ISBN Prefix(es): 953-6804
Number of titles published annually: 8 Print
Total Titles: 5 Print

### Filozofski Fakultet Sveucilista u Zagrebu
Ivana Lucica 3, 10000 Zagreb
Tel: (01) 6120111 Fax: (01) 6156879
E-mail: tajnik_fakultet@ffzg.hr
Web Site: www.ffzg.hr

*Key Personnel*
Editor & Author: Ms Jadranka Brncic
 *E-mail:* jbrncic@mudrac.ftzg.hr
Subjects: History, Language Arts, Linguistics,
 Literature, Literary Criticism, Essays, Social
 Sciences, Sociology
ISBN Prefix(es): 86-80279; 953-175

**Globus-Nakladni zavod DOO**
Vlaska 109, 10000 Zagreb
*Tel:* (01) 462 8400 *Fax:* (01) 462 8400 *Cable:*
 GLOBUS ZAGREB
*Key Personnel*
President & Editor: Tomislav Pusek
Founded: 1969
Subjects: Art, Fiction, Government, Political Sci-
 ence, History, Philosophy, Social Sciences, So-
 ciology
ISBN Prefix(es): 86-343; 953-167

**Graficki zavod Hrvatske**
Preobrazenska 4, 10000 Zagreb
*Tel:* (01) 430 300; (01) 240 7166 *Fax:* (01) 430
 331
*Telex:* 21606 Yu Gzh *Cable:* GZH ZAGREB
*Key Personnel*
Man Dir: Zdravko Zidovec
Editor: Branko Matan
Sales: Vilma Lopuh
Rights & Permissions: Maja Kotur
Production: Boro Brekalo
Founded: 1874
Subjects: Art, Biography, Fiction
ISBN Prefix(es): 86-399; 953-6009

**Hercegtisak doo**
Put Znjana 3, 21000 Split
*Tel:* (021) 320 663 *Fax:* (021) 320 663
*E-mail:* nakladnistvo@hercegtisak.ba
*Web Site:* www.hercegtisak.ba
*Key Personnel*
Contact: Dragan Simovic *E-mail:* d.simovic@
 hercegtisak.ba

**Izdavacka Delatnost Hrvatske Akademije
 Znanosti I Umjetnosti**
Zrinski trg 11, 10000 Zagreb
*Tel:* (01) 49 22 373; (01) 48 72 902 *Fax:* (01) 48
 19 979
*E-mail:* stross@mahazu.hazu.hr
*Key Personnel*
Man Dir: Gordana Poletto Ruzic
Founded: 1861
Subjects: Education, Government, Political Sci-
 ence, History, Medicine, Nursing, Dentistry,
 Philosophy, Science (General)
ISBN Prefix(es): 86-407; 953-154

**Hrvatsko filozofsko drustvo** (Croatian
 Philosophy Society)+
Ivana Lucica 3, 10000 Zagreb
*Tel:* (01) 612 0156 *Fax:* (01) 617 0682
*E-mail:* filozofska-istrazivanja@zg.tel.hr
*Key Personnel*
President: Milan Polio
Vice President: Dubravka Kuzina
Founded: 1957
Subjects: Ethnicity, Philosophy, Psychology, Psy-
 chiatry, Social Sciences, Sociology
ISBN Prefix(es): 86-81173; 953-164
Divisions: Journal Filozofska Istrazivanja/Synthe-
 sis Philosophica
*Warehouse:* Krcka 1, 10000 Zagreb

**Informator dd+**
Gunduliceva 19, 10000 Zagreb
*Tel:* (01) 4852 665; (01) 4852 668 *Fax:* (01) 4852
 673
*E-mail:* informator@informator.hr
*Web Site:* www.informator.hr
*Telex:* 21264 *Cable:* YU INF

*Key Personnel*
Manager: Dr Ivo Buric
Editor-in-Chief: Jasna Vukoja
Sales Manager: Milan Jerbic
Subjects: Economics, Finance, Government, Polit-
 ical Science, Law, Marketing, Social Sciences,
 Sociology
ISBN Prefix(es): 86-301; 953-170
*Bookshop(s):* M Visnsic, 7800 Banja Luka,
 Bosnia and Herzegovina; Vojv, Putnika 16B,
 71000 Sarajevo, Bosnia and Herzegovina;
 Kej M Pijade 8, 21000 Novi Sad; Trg Lava
 Mirskog 3, 54000 Osijek; Dj Djakovica 30,
 51000 Rijeka; Ilica 24, 41000 Zagreb
*Warehouse:* Janka Gredelja 3, 41000 Zagreb
*Orders to:* Odjel Prodaje Knjiga, Ilica 24, 41000
 Zagreb *Tel:* (041) 433666

**Knjizevni Krug Split**
Ispod Ure 3/11, 21000 Split
*Tel:* (021) 342 226; (021) 361 081 *Fax:* (021) 342
 226
*E-mail:* bratislav.lucin@public.srce.hr
*Key Personnel*
President: Prof Nenad Cambi, PhD
Vice President: Prof Ivo Petrinovic, PhD
Editor: Prof Bratislav Lucin
Founded: 1979
Subjects: Archaeology, Drama, Theater, History,
 Language Arts, Linguistics, Law, Literature,
 Literary Criticism, Essays, Maritime, Poetry
ISBN Prefix(es): 86-7397; 953-163

**Krscanska sadasnjost**
Marulicev trg 14, 10000 Zagreb
*Tel:* (01) 48 28 219; (01) 48 28 222 *Fax:* (01) 48
 28 227
*E-mail:* ks@zg.tel.hr
*Web Site:* www.ks.hr
Also acts as a press agency.
Subjects: Art, Biblical Studies, Religion - Other,
 Theology
ISBN Prefix(es): 86-397; 953-151

**Leksikografski Zavod Miroslav Krleza** (The
 Miroslav Krleza Lexicographic Institute)
Frankopanska 26, 10000 Zagreb
*Tel:* (01) 4800 492; (01) 4800 494 *Fax:* (01) 4800
 399
*E-mail:* lzmk@lzmk.hr
*Web Site:* www.lzmk.hr
*Key Personnel*
Dir: Vlaho Bogisic *Tel:* (01) 4800 398
 *E-mail:* vlaho.bogisic@lzmk.hr; Tomislav
 Ladan *Tel:* (01) 4800 398 *E-mail:* tomislav.
 ladan@lzmk.hr
Assistant Dir: Damir Boras *Tel:* (01) 4800 424
 *E-mail:* damir.boras@lzmk.hr; Ankica Karacic
 *Tel:* (01) 4800 319 *E-mail:* ankica.karacic@
 lzmk.hr; Zdenka Ozic *Tel:* (01) 4800 392
 *E-mail:* zdenka.ozic@lzmk.hr; Tomislav Vi-
 rovic *Tel:* (01) 4800 353 *E-mail:* tomislav.
 virovic@lzmk.hr
Contact: Vedrana Martinovic *Tel:* (01) 4800 331
 *E-mail:* vedrana.martinovic@lzmk.hr
Founded: 1950
ISBN Prefix(es): 953-6036

**Masmedia+**
Baruna Trenka 13, 10000 Zagreb
*Tel:* (01) 457-7400 *Fax:* (01) 457 7769
*E-mail:* masmedia@zg.tel.hr; mm@masmedia.hr
*Web Site:* www.masmedia.hr
*Key Personnel*
President: Stjepan Andrasic *E-mail:* stjepan.
 andrasic@zg.tel.hr
Contact: Romina Belak
Founded: 1990
Subjects: Business, Economics, Finance, Manage-
 ment, Marketing
ISBN Prefix(es): 953-157

*Associate Companies:* Andratom; Creditreform;
 GBMA; Rimedia
Subsidiaries: Masmedia-Split
*U.S. Office(s):* Associated Book Publishers Inc,
 PO Box 5657, Scottsdale, AZ 85261-5657,
 United States
Distributed by Associated Book Publishers
Distributor for Braun Verlag; Euredit (Europages)
 BDI; Gentner Verlag; Herold
*Bookshop(s):* Masmedia Rijeka, Dolac 9A, 51000
 Rijeka
*Book Club(s):* Croatian Book Clubs

**Matica hrvatska+**
Matice hrvatska 2, Strossmayerov trg 4, 10000
 Zagreb
*Tel:* (01) 4878-360; (01) 4878-354; (01) 4878-362
 *Fax:* (01) 4819-319
*E-mail:* matica@matica.hr
*Web Site:* www.matica.hr
*Key Personnel*
President: Igor Zidic
International Rights: Vera Cicin-Sain
Founded: 1842
Publisher of Biweekly Newspaper *Vijenac*.
Subjects: Agriculture, Archaeology, Art, Drama,
 Theater, History, Language Arts, Linguis-
 tics, Literature, Literary Criticism, Essays,
 Medicine, Nursing, Dentistry, Natural History,
 Nonfiction (General), Philosophy, Poetry, Re-
 gional Interests, Science (General), Social Sci-
 ences, Sociology
ISBN Prefix(es): 86-401; 86-7807
*Bookshop(s):* Maticina 2, 10000 Zagreb

**Mladost d d Izdavacku graficku i informaticku
 djelatnost**
Borongajska 69, 10000 Zagreb
*Tel:* (01) 215-853; (01) 229-811 *Fax:* (01) 239-
 5336
*Telex:* 21263 yu mladzg *Cable:* IRO ZAGREB
*Key Personnel*
Man Dir: Branko Juricevic
Import-Export Dir: Branko Vukovic
Publisher: Josip Fruk
Production Manager: Stipan Medak
Marketing Manager: Eduard Osredecki
Founded: 1948
Subjects: Art, Crafts, Games, Hobbies, Fiction,
 History, How-to, Music, Dance, Philosophy,
 Poetry, Science (General), Social Sciences, So-
 ciology, Sports, Athletics
ISBN Prefix(es): 86-05; 953-152
*Book Club(s):* Mladost's Book Fans Club

**Muzicka Naklada**
Nikole Tesle 10/I, 41000 Zagreb
*Tel:* (01) 424 099; (01) 424 019
*Telex:* 22430
*Key Personnel*
Dir: Rajko Latinovic
Founded: 1952
Publish music editions & scores.
Subjects: Music, Dance
ISBN Prefix(es): 86-80637

**Naklada Ljevak doo**
Palmoticeva 30/1, 10000 Zagreb
*Tel:* (01) 4804-000 *Fax:* (01) 4804-001
*E-mail:* naklada-ljevak@zg.hinet.hr
*Web Site:* www.naklada-ljevak.hr
*Telex:* 21449 Yu Ikpnzg *Cable:* Izdavacko
 Naprijed
*Key Personnel*
Dir: Nives Tomasevic
Subjects: Art, Economics, Fiction, Government,
 Political Science, History, Philosophy, Psy-
 chology, Psychiatry, Science (General), Social
 Sciences, Sociology
ISBN Prefix(es): 86-349; 953-178
*Bookshop(s):* Cetinska bb, 21, 21 310 Omis
 *Tel:* (021) 757-344 *Fax:* (021) 757-345
 *E-mail:* knjizara-ljevak-omis@zg.htnet.hr;

Trg bana Jelacica 17, 10 000 Zagreb *Tel:* (01) 4812-992; (01) 4812-963 *Fax:* (01) 4812-970
*E-mail:* knjizara-ljevak@zg.htnet.hr

**Narodne Novine**
Odjel oglasa i pretplate, Ulica Kralja Drzislava 14, 10000 Zagreb
*Tel:* (01) 4501-310 *Fax:* (01) 4501-348; (01) 4501-349
*E-mail:* e-pretplata@nn.hr
*Web Site:* www.nn.hr
*Key Personnel*
Dir: Ilija Dautovic
Subjects: Career Development, Law, Science (General)
ISBN Prefix(es): 86-337; 953-6053

**Nasa Djeca Publishing+**
Gunduliseva 40, 10000 Zagreb
*Tel:* (01) 485 6056; (01) 485 6046 *Fax:* (01) 485 6613
*E-mail:* nasa-djeca@zg.tel.hr
*Key Personnel*
Dir: Prof Drago Kozina
Secretary, Editorial Office: Verica Ozimec
Founded: 1951
Also publish children's periodical *Radost.*
Subjects: Literature, Literary Criticism, Essays, Poetry
ISBN Prefix(es): 86-7037; 953-171
Number of titles published annually: 30 Print

**Otokar Kersovani**
Janeza Trdine 2/11, 51000 Rijeka
*Tel:* (051) 338 558; (051) 338 016 *Fax:* (051) 331 690
*E-mail:* otokar-kersovani@ri.tel.hr
*Web Site:* www.o-k.hr *Cable:* Otokar Kersovani
*Key Personnel*
Man Dir & Editor-in-Chief: Tomislav Pilepic
Founded: 1954
Subjects: Biography, Fiction
ISBN Prefix(es): 86-385; 953-153
*Branch Office(s)*
Mehmed-pase Soholovica 24, Sarajevo, Bosnia and Herzegovina
Slavise Vajiera-Cice 3, Rijeka
Biankinijeva, 11 Zagreb
Zrmanjska 2/a, Belgrade, Serbia and Montenegro
Nade Tomic 15, Nis, Serbia and Montenegro

**Prosvjeta d d Bjelovar**
Nazorova 25, 43000 Bjelovar
*Tel:* (043) 245-222; (043) 245-223 *Fax:* (043) 245-220 *Cable:* Nisp Prosvjeta Bjelovar
*Key Personnel*
Dir: Branimir Premuzic *Tel:* (043) 245 224
Production: Ivan Ninic
ISBN Prefix(es): 86-80823; 953-6340
*Branch Office(s)*
Mose Pijade 31, Zagreb

**Prosvjeta doo**
Berislaviceva 10, 10000 Zagreb
*Tel:* (01) 4872-477 *Fax:* (01) 4872-481
*E-mail:* redakcija@prosvjeta-zg.hr *Cable:* Prosvjeta Zagreb
*Key Personnel*
Dir: Mile Radovic *Tel:* (01) 4872-475
Subjects: Business, Journalism
ISBN Prefix(es): 86-353; 953-6279
*Bookshop(s):* trg Bratstva i Jedinstva 5, Zagreb

**Skolska Knjiga**
Masarykova 28, 10000 Zagreb
*Tel:* (01) 48 30 491; (01) 48 30 511 *Fax:* (01) 48 30 506
*E-mail:* skolska@skolskaknjiga.hr
*Web Site:* www.skolskaknjiga.hr
*Telex:* 21894 *Cable:* SKOLSKA KNJIGA ZAGREB

*Key Personnel*
President: Ante Zuzul
Founded: 1950
Subjects: Art, Biography, Education, Engineering (General), History, How-to, Medicine, Nursing, Dentistry, Music, Dance, Philosophy, Poetry, Psychology, Psychiatry, Science (General), Social Sciences, Sociology
ISBN Prefix(es): 86-03; 953-0
*Bookshop(s):* Knjizara Skolska knjiga *Tel:* (01) 48 30 488; Knjizara Skolske knjige, Bogoviceva 1/a, 41000 Zagreb *Tel:* (01) 48 10 989

**Privlacica Slavonska Naklada+**
Ruzina 5 a, 32100 Vinkovci
*Tel:* (032) 306 068; (032) 306 069; (032) 306 070 *Fax:* (032) 331735
*E-mail:* privlacica@vk.tel.hr
*Key Personnel*
Contact: Martin Grgurovac
ISBN Prefix(es): 953-156

**Sveucilisna naklada Liber**
Trg marsala Tita 14, 10000 Zagreb
*Tel:* (01) 4564430; (01) 4564428 *Fax:* (01) 4564427
*Key Personnel*
Editor: Vera C Sain; Nikola Petrak
Publishing service of Zagreb University.
Subjects: Ethnicity, Language Arts, Linguistics, Literature, Literary Criticism, Essays, Science (General)
ISBN Prefix(es): 86-7819; 86-329; 953-6231

**Tehnicka Knjiga**
Jurisiceva 10, 10000 Zagreb
*Tel:* (01) 481 0819 *Fax:* (01) 481 0821 *Cable:* Tehnoknjiga
*Key Personnel*
Man Dir, Chief Editor: Zvonimir Vistricka
Founded: 1947
Subjects: Engineering (General), Literature, Literary Criticism, Essays, Science (General)
ISBN Prefix(es): 86-7059; 953-172
*Bookshop(s):* Antikvarijat, Zagreb; Gunduliceva 19, Zagreb; Knjizara Tehnicka Knjiga, Masarykova 17

**Vitagraf+**
Dubrovacka 4, 51000 Rijeka
*Tel:* (051) 322880 *Fax:* (051) 212622
*E-mail:* kontakt@novo.hr
*Web Site:* www.novo.hr
*Key Personnel*
President: Prof Boze Mimica
Author: Ivan Sokolic; Jeurem Brkovic; Lujo Margetic; Zjonimie Dusper
Founded: 1990
Specialize in Numismatic, History, Vine Books, Gastronomy Guide.
Subjects: Cookery, Crafts, Games, Hobbies, History, Radio, TV, Wine & Spirits
ISBN Prefix(es): 953-6059; 953-7030

**Znaci Vremena, Institut Za Istrazivanje Biblije**
Marulevec 82 E, 42243 Marulevec
*Tel:* (042) 729 977 *Fax:* (042) 729 977
*Key Personnel*
Dir: Karlo Lenart
Subjects: Archaeology, Biblical Studies, Health, Nutrition, Human Relations, Religion - Protestant, Theology
ISBN Prefix(es): 86-425; 953-183

**Znanje d d+**
Zvonimira 17, Ulica Kralja 10000 Zagreb 1000
*Tel:* (01) 4551500 *Fax:* (01) 4553-652
*E-mail:* znanje@zg.tel.hr *Cable:* ZNANJE ZAGREB
*Key Personnel*
President: Zarko Sepetavc

Vice President: Branko Jazbec
Founded: 1946
Subjects: Textbooks
ISBN Prefix(es): 86-313; 953-195; 953-6124; 953-6473
Divisions: Printing House
*Branch Office(s)*
Riva 8, Rijeka
Znanje d o o Mostar, Stjepana Radica 76E, 88000 Mostar, Bosnia and Herzegovina
Osijek, Vukovarska 71, 31000 Osijeck
*Showroom(s):* Vojnoviceva, 42 Zagreb
*Bookshop(s):* AG Matos stationary & bookstore, Frankopanska 5; I G Kovacic stationary & bookstore, Marticeva 12; Miroslav Krleza bookstore, Trg bana J Jelacica 17; Tin Ujevic second-hand bookstore, Zrinjevac 16; Znanje stationary & book store, Llica 17; Znanje stationary & bookstore, Ozaljska 102; Znanje stationary/paper shop, Gajeva 2

# Cuba

## General Information

*Capital:* Havana
*Language:* Spanish
*Religion:* Predominantly Roman Catholic
*Population:* 10.8 million
*Bank Hours:* 0800-1200, 1415-1615 Monday-Friday; 0800-1200 Saturday
*Currency:* 100 centavos = 1 Cuban peso
*Export/Import Information:* Control of all import & export by Ministry of Foreign Trade; books imported & exported by Ediciones Cubanas, Apdo 605, Havana. No commercial advertising permitted in Cuba; brochures etc must be sent to the appropriate foreign trade organization. Exchange controlled by National Bank of Cuba.
*Copyright:* UCC, Florence (see Copyright Conventions, pg xi)

**Apocalipis Digital+**
Calle 47 No 869, 3er Piso, Apto 6 entre 26 y Sta Ana, Plaza de la Revolucion, Havana
*Tel:* (07) 816625
*E-mail:* adigital@tinored.cu; adigital@colombus.cu
*Key Personnel*
President: Pedro E Garcia
Founded: 1987
Membership(s): Comicion Nacional de Proteccion de Datos.
Subjects: Computer Science, Microcomputers
ISBN Prefix(es): 959-231

**Editorial Capitan San Luis+**
Av 25 No 3406 entre 34 y 36, La Habana, Playa
*Tel:* (07) 2034475 *Fax:* (07) 332070
*Key Personnel*
Dir: Juan Carlos Rodriguez
Founded: 1989
Subjects: Government, Political Science, Literature, Literary Criticism, Essays
ISBN Prefix(es): 959-211
*Warehouse:* Ave 41 No 1410 entre 14 y 18, Playa, La Havana

**Casa de las Americas**
3ra y G, El Vedado, CP 10400 Havana
*Tel:* (07) 55 2706; (07) 55 2709 *Fax:* (07) 33 4554; (07) 32 7272
*E-mail:* revista@casa.cult.cu
*Web Site:* www.casadelasamericas.com
*Telex:* 511019
*Key Personnel*
Founder: Haydee Santamaria

Dir: Roberto Fernandez Retamar
Assistant Dir: Luis Toledo Sande
Founded: 1959
Subjects: Art, Ethnicity, Social Sciences, Sociology
ISBN Prefix(es): 959-04

**Casa Editora Abril+**
Prado 553 esq a Tte Rey, CP 10200 Habana Vieja, Havana
*Tel:* (07) 8627871; (07) 8624359 *Fax:* (07) 335282
*E-mail:* eabril@jcc.org.cu
*Web Site:* www.almamater.cu
*Key Personnel*
Dir: Mario Vizcaino Serrat
Sub-Dir: Silvio Gutierrez Perez
Publisher: Eduardo Jimenez Garcia
Founded: 1980
Subjects: Advertising, Film, Video, History, Humor, Journalism, Literature, Literary Criticism, Essays, Microcomputers, Philosophy, Poetry, Science Fiction, Fantasy
ISBN Prefix(es): 959-210

**Editorial de Ciencias Sociales**
Calle 14, No 4104, entre 41 y 43, Playa, Ciudad de la Havana
*Tel:* (07) 2036090; (07) 333441 *Fax:* (07) 2304801
*E-mail:* nuevomil@icl.cult.cu
*Key Personnel*
Dir: Ricardo Garcia Pampin
Founded: 1967
Subjects: Social Sciences, Sociology
ISBN Prefix(es): 959-06
*Orders to:* Ediciones Cubanas, Obispo y Bernaza, La Habana Vieja

**Editorial Cientifico Tecnica+**
Calle 14, No 4104 entre 41 y 43, Playa, Havana 10400
*Tel:* (07) 2036090 *Fax:* (07) 333441
*E-mail:* nuevomil@icl.cult.cu
*Key Personnel*
Dir: Isidro Fernandez Rodriguez
Founded: 1965
Subjects: Engineering (General), Science (General)
ISBN Prefix(es): 959-05

**Editora Cultura Popular**, *imprint of* Editora Politica

**Editorial Gente Nueva+**
O'Reilly No 4 esq a Tacon, Habana Vieja, CP 10100 Havana
*Tel:* (07) 833-7676 *Fax:* (07) 33-8187
*E-mail:* gentenueva@icl.cult
*Key Personnel*
Dir: Elenia Rodriguez Oliva
Founded: 1967
ISBN Prefix(es): 959-08

**Holguin, Ediciones**
Arias No 144, esq a Fomento, CP 80100, Holguin
*Tel:* (024) 424974
*E-mail:* promotoraliteraria@baibrama.cult.cu
Founded: 1986
Subjects: Art, Biography, Drama, Theater, History, Literature, Literary Criticism, Essays, Poetry
ISBN Prefix(es): 959-221
*Book Club(s):* SCAL (Sociedad Cabana de Amigos del Libro)

**IDICT**, see Instituto de Informacion Cientifica y Tecnologica (IDICT)

**Instituto de Informacion Cientifica y Tecnologica (IDICT)+**
Prado entre Dragones y San Jose, CP 10200 La Habana, Habana Vieja
*Tel:* (07) 862-6531; (07) 860-3411 *Fax:* (07) 862-6531
*E-mail:* andresdt@idict.cu; comercial@idict.cu
*Web Site:* www.idict.cu
Subjects: Career Development, Library & Information Sciences, Technology
ISBN Prefix(es): 959-234

**ISCAH Fructuoso Rodriguez**
Carretera de Tapaste y Autopista Nacional, San Jose de las Lajas, Havana 32700
*Tel:* (07) 62936 *Fax:* (07) 330942
*Key Personnel*
Contact: Julian Garcia Gomex *E-mail:* julian@reduniv.edu.cu
Subjects: Agriculture, Alternative, Economics, Education, Environmental Studies, Management, Sports, Athletics, Veterinary Science
ISBN Prefix(es): 959-232

**Editorial Letras Cubanas+**
O'Reilly No 4 esq Tacon, Habana Vieja, La Habana, Havana 10100
*Tel:* (07) 862-6864 *Fax:* (07) 33-8187
*E-mail:* elc@icl.cult.cu
*Telex:* 511881
*Key Personnel*
Dir: Juan Nicolas Padron Barquin; Daniel Garcia Santos
Sub-Dir: Basilia Papastamatiu; Esther Acosta Testa
Founded: 1977
Membership(s): Instituto Cubano del Libro.
Subjects: Art, Drama, Theater, Fiction, Literature, Literary Criticism, Essays, Poetry, Romance, Science Fiction, Fantasy
ISBN Prefix(es): 959-10
Number of titles published annually: 70 Print
Total Titles: 70 Print
*Distribution Center:* Ediciones Cubanas Empresa de Comercio Exterior de Publicaciones, Obispo 527 esq, a Bernaza, La Habana 10100, Dir: Jorge Paz *Tel:* (07) 631989; (07) 338942 *Fax:* (07) 338943 *E-mail:* edicuba@artsoft.cult.cu

**Editorial Oriente+**
Santa Lucia No 356, CP 90100 Santiago de Cuba
*Tel:* (0226) 22496; (0226) 28096 *Fax:* (0226) 86111
*E-mail:* edoriente@cultstgo.cult.cu
*Telex:* 061170
*Key Personnel*
President: Aida Bahr
Editorial: Consuel Muniz
Production: Sergio Daquin
Publicity: Ana Maria Rodriguez
Rights & Permissions: Omar Betancourt
Founded: 1971
Subjects: African American Studies, Cookery, Crafts, Games, Hobbies, Fiction, Health, Nutrition, History, House & Home, Literature, Literary Criticism, Essays, Poetry, Self-Help, Sports, Athletics
ISBN Prefix(es): 959-11
Total Titles: 821 Print
*Parent Company:* Vicepresidencia Editorial
*Ultimate Parent Company:* Instituto Cubano del Libro

**Editora Politica+**
Calle Belascoain No 864, esq a Desague, Municipio Centro Habana, CP 10300 Havana
*Tel:* (07) 79 8553-59 *Fax:* (07) 811024
*E-mail:* editora@ns.cc.cu; edit63@enet.cu
*Web Site:* www.pcc.cu/pccweb/publicaciones/editorapolitica.php
*Telex:* 1380

*Key Personnel*
Dir: Santiago Dorquez Perez
Chief Editor: Anolan Aguila
Founded: 1963
Subjects: Biography, Economics, Education, Government, Political Science, Health, Nutrition, History, Human Relations, Law, Philosophy, Poetry, Psychology, Psychiatry, Religion - Catholic, Religion - Other, Science (General), Social Sciences, Sociology
ISBN Prefix(es): 959-01
*Associate Companies:* Editora Cultura Popular
Imprints: Editora Cultura Popular
*Showroom(s):* Pabelloo Medios de Difusion EX-POCUBA, Tienda 11 y Paseo
*Bookshop(s):* Centro Internacional de Prensa, Calle 23 esq O Vedado

**Pueblo y Educacion Editorial (PE)+**
Ave 3A No 4605 entre 46 y 60, Playa, Havana 11300
*Tel:* (07) 20021490 *Fax:* (07) 2040844
*E-mail:* epe@ceniai.inf.cu
*Key Personnel*
Dir: Catalina Lajud
Sub-Dir: Juan Alberto Andino
Founded: 1971
Subjects: Computer Science, Education, Literature, Literary Criticism, Essays, Psychology, Psychiatry, Science (General), Social Sciences, Sociology, Sports, Athletics, Technology
ISBN Prefix(es): 959-13
Number of titles published annually: 476 Print
Total Titles: 8 Print
Distributed by Ediciones Cubanas Empresa de Comercio Exterior de Publicaciones

**Union de Escritores y Artistas de Cuba** (Union of Writers & Artists of Cuba)+
Calle 17 No 354,e/ G y H, Vedado, Plaza de la Revolucion, Havana CP 10400
*Tel:* (07) 8324551; (07) 8324571; (07) 553111; (07) 553113 *Fax:* (07) 333158
*E-mail:* uneac@cubarte.cult.cu
*Web Site:* www.uneac.com
*Telex:* 051156364
*Key Personnel*
Dir: Daniel Garcia Santos
Production: Jose Raul Garrido
Publicity: Emilio Comas Paret
Founded: 1961
Rights & Permissions, National Center of Author Rights, Linea y G, Vedado.
Subjects: Art, Literature, Literary Criticism, Essays, Regional Interests

# Cyprus

## General Information

*Capital:* Nicosia
*Language:* Greek & Turkish (English widely spoken)
*Religion:* Greek Orthodox & Islamic (among Turks)
*Population:* 716,000
*Bank Hours:* 0830-1200 Monday-Saturday
*Shop Hours:* Winter: 0800-1300, 1430-1700 Monday-Friday; 0730-1300 Saturday. Summer: 0730-1300, 1600-1830 Monday-Friday. Closed Wednesday afternoon (both winter & summer)
*Currency:* 100 cents = 1 Cyprus pound
*Export/Import Information:* No tariffs on books or advertising matter. No import license specially required. Exchange control administered by Central Bank of Cyprus.
*Copyright:* UCC, Berne, Florence (see Copyright Conventions, pg xi)

**Action Publications**
PO Box 24676, Lefkosia
*Tel:* (022) 818884 *Fax:* (022) 873634
*Key Personnel*
President: Tony Christodoulou
Vice President: Mickey Christodoulou
Production Dir: Dina Wilde
Founded: 1971
Subjects: Travel, Airline
ISBN Prefix(es): 9963-7587
*Parent Company:* Action Public Relations & Publishing Ltd
Subsidiaries: Action Media
*Orders to:* 6 Kondilakis St, 1090 Lefkosia

**Air Larko Panorama ALP**
11 Nicos Antonlades, 8046 Paphos
*Tel:* (06) 236181 *Fax:* (06) 245046
ISBN Prefix(es): 9963-574

**ALITHIA Publishing Co**
Pindarou & Androkleous, Nicosia 1060
*Tel:* (022) 463040 *Fax:* (022) 463945 *Cable:* ALITHIA
ISBN Prefix(es): 9963-586

**Andreou Chr Publishers**
64A Regenas, Nicosia
*Tel:* (022) 666877 *Fax:* (022) 666878
*E-mail:* andzeou2@cytanet.com.cy
Founded: 1979
Specialize in Cypress History, Literature, Biography & Bibliographies.
Subjects: Biography, History, Literature, Literary Criticism, Essays, Regional Interests
ISBN Prefix(es): 9963-563
*Associate Companies:* Practorion Vivliou; Chr Andreou Co Ltd
*Bookshop(s):* Rigenis 64a, Nicosia; Rigenis 67A, Nicosia *Fax:* (02) 666563

**James Bendon Ltd**
PO Box 56484, 3307 Limassol
*Fax:* (025) 632352
*E-mail:* books@jamesbendon.com
*Web Site:* www.jamesbendon.com
*Key Personnel*
President: James Bendon
Vice President: Rida Bendon
Founded: 1988
Subjects: Crafts, Games, Hobbies, History
ISBN Prefix(es): 9963-579; 9963-7624
Distributor for Christie's Robson Lowe

**Chrysopolitissa Publishers**
27 Al Papadiamanti, 2400 Nicosia
*Tel:* (022) 353929 *Fax:* (022) 353929
*Key Personnel*
Dir: Rina Catselli *E-mail:* rina@spidernet.com.cy
Founded: 1973
Subjects: Drama, Theater, Literature, Literary Criticism, Essays
ISBN Prefix(es): 9963-559
Number of titles published annually: 4 Print
*Showroom(s):* 9 Othello's St, 2018 Nicosia; MAM, C Paleologos St, No 10, Nicosia
*Bookshop(s):* Kypriaka Themata, PO Box 3835, Nicosia; MAM, PO Box 21722, Nicosia

**Cyprus Telecommunications Authority (CYTA)**
Telecommunications Str, Strovolos, TK 24929, 1396 Nicosia
*Tel:* (022) 701000 *Fax:* (022) 497155
*E-mail:* enquiries@cyta.com.cy
*Web Site:* www.cyta.com.cy
*Telex:* 2288 CYTA ENAC CY
*Key Personnel*
Chairman: Mr Stathis Papadakis
Vice Chairman: Markos Drakos
General Manager: Nicos M Timotheou
Deputy General Manager: Mr Photios Savvides

Assistant General Manager, Operations: Christos C Chappas
Assistant General Manager, Administration: Michael I Economides
ISBN Prefix(es): 9963-43

**CYTA**, see Cyprus Telecommunications Authority (CYTA)

**Kenek Ltd**
21 E Papaloannou, 1075 Nicosia
*Tel:* (022) 365842 *Fax:* (022) 475150
ISBN Prefix(es): 9963-596

**KY KE M+**
PO Box 4108, Nicosia
*Tel:* (022) 450302 *Fax:* (022) 463624
*Telex:* 4022
*Key Personnel*
President: Nicos Koutsou
Vice President: Soula Zavou
Founded: 1983
ISBN Prefix(es): 9963-562

**Kyrenia Municipality+**
Division of Chrysopolitissa Publishers
M Drakou, Nicosia
*Tel:* (022) 818040 *Fax:* (022) 818228
*Key Personnel*
Editor: Rina Catselli
ISBN Prefix(es): 9963-559
*Showroom(s):* 9 Othello's St, Nicosia
*Bookshop(s):* Kypriaka Themata, PO Box 3835, Nicosia

**MAM (The House of Cyprus & Cyprological Publications)+**
Leoforos Konstantinou Palaiologou 19, 1015 Nicosia
*Tel:* (022) 753536 *Fax:* (022) 375802
*E-mail:* mam@mam.com.cy
*Web Site:* www.mam.com.cy
*Key Personnel*
Secretary: Mr Mikis A Michaelides
Founded: 1965
Specialize in all kinds of publications on Cyprus & in all publications by Cypriots. Supplying all over the world to bookstores, libraries & anyone interested in these types of publications.
Subjects: Ethnicity, Cyprus
ISBN Prefix(es): 9963-625
*Bookshop(s):* MAM Kypriakes Ekdoseis, Stoa tou Vivliou ap 16, Odos Pesmazoglon 5, 105 64 Athens, Greece
*Book Club(s):* Cyprus Bibliophiles Association

**The Moufflon Book & Art Centre**, see Romantic Cyprus Publications

**Nikoklis Publishers+**
PO Box 23697, 1905 Nicosia
*Tel:* (022) 452079 *Fax:* (022) 360668
*Key Personnel*
Editor: Ellada Sophocleous
Founded: 1978
Subjects: Ethnicity, Travel
ISBN Prefix(es): 9963-566

**Omilos Pnevmatikis Ananeoseos**
One Omirou Engomi, Nicosia 2407
*Tel:* (022) 772898 *Fax:* (022) 311931
Subjects: Literature, Literary Criticism, Essays
ISBN Prefix(es): 9963-552

**Pierides Foundation**
4, Zennonos Kitieos, 6300 Larnaka
Mailing Address: PO Box 25, 6300 Larnaka
*Tel:* (02) 651345 *Fax:* (02) 657227
*Telex:* 4498

*Key Personnel*
Contact: Peter H Ashdjian
Founded: 1974
ISBN Prefix(es): 9963-560

**POLTE (Pancyprian Organization of Tertiary Education)**
c/o Higher Technical Institute, Nicosia
*Tel:* (022) 305030 *Fax:* (022) 494953
*Key Personnel*
President: Costas Neocleous
ISBN Prefix(es): 9963-564

**Romantic Cyprus Publications**
One Sofouli, 1096 Lefkosia
*Tel:* 22665155
ISBN Prefix(es): 9963-571
*Bookshop(s):* One Bophoulis St, PO Box 2375, Nicosia

# Czech Republic

## General Information

*Capital:* Prague
*Language:* Czech (official)
*Religion:* Predominantly Christian (mostly Roman Catholic)
*Population:* 10.4 million
*Currency:* 100 halerue = 1 koruna
*Export/Import Information:* 5% VAT on books.
*Copyright:* UCC, Berne (see Copyright Conventions, pg xi)

**Academia**
Legerova 61, 120 00 Prague 2
*Tel:* (02) 24 941 976 *Fax:* (02) 24 212 582
*E-mail:* academia@academia.cz
*Web Site:* www.academia.cz *Cable:* ACADEMY BOOKS PRAGUE
*Key Personnel*
Dir: Alexander Tomsky *Tel:* (02) 24 942 584 *Fax:* (02) 24 941 982 *E-mail:* director@academia.cz
Founded: 1953
Subjects: Archaeology, Chemistry, Chemical Engineering, Economics, Engineering (General), Geography, Geology, History, Language Arts, Linguistics, Mathematics, Philosophy, Physics
ISBN Prefix(es): 80-200
*Bookshop(s):* nam Svobody 13, Brno *Tel:* (05) 42 217 954 *E-mail:* knihy.brno@academia.cz; Zamecka 2, Ostrava *Tel:* (069) 596 114 578; (069) 596 114 580; (069) 596 116 692 *Fax:* (069) 596 123 097; Vaclavske nam 34, Prague *Tel:* (02) 24 223 511 *E-mail:* knihy.vaclavskenam@academia.cz; Narodni trida 7, Prague *Tel:* (02) 24 240 547 *E-mail:* knihy.narodni@academia.cz; Na Florenci 3, Prague *Tel:* (02) 24 814 621 *E-mail:* knihy.naflorenci@academia.cz

**Albatros AS+**
Member of Bonton Group
Pankraci 30, 140 00 Prague 4
*Tel:* (02) 34633261 *Fax:* (02) 34633262
*E-mail:* albatros@bonton.cz
*Web Site:* www.albatros.cz *Cable:* ALBATROS PRAHA
*Key Personnel*
Man Dir: Martin Slavik *E-mail:* martin.slavik@bonton.cz
Editorial Dir: Ondrej Muller *Tel:* (02) 24810850
Foreign Rights: Katerina Nicajasova *Tel:* (02) 34633271 *E-mail:* katerina.nicajasova@bonton.cz

Founded: 1949
ISBN Prefix(es): 80-00
Total Titles: 8,700 Print; 2 CD-ROM
*Bookshop(s):* Krizikova, Thamova 22, Prama 8
  *Tel:* (02) 24814725
*Book Club(s):* KMC (Young Readers' Club),
  Contact: Ludmila Hobova *Tel:* (02) 2319739
  *Fax:* (02) 2311178
*Warehouse:* 252 16 Nucice *Tel:* (0311) 678754
  *Fax:* (0311) 670525

**AMA nakladatelstvi+**
Gen Svobody 636, Trebic
*Tel:* (0618) 265 84 *Fax:* (0618) 228 31
*E-mail:* rstudio@login.cz
*Key Personnel*
Contact: Karel Karmasin
Founded: 1990
Specialize in desktop publishing & prepress tech-
  nology.
Subjects: Radio, TV
ISBN Prefix(es): 80-900232
*Associate Companies:* Ar Nakladatelstvi
*Orders to:* Eliscina 24, 67401 Trebic

**Amosium Servis**
Hladnovska 119 b, 712 00 Ostrava
*Tel:* (069) 624 55 01
*Key Personnel*
Dir: Karel Janak
Founded: 1990
ISBN Prefix(es): 80-85498

**Atlantis sro+**
PS 374, Ceska 15, 602 00 Brno
*Tel:* (05) 422 132 21 *Fax:* (05) 422 132 21
*E-mail:* atlantis-brno@volny.cz
*Web Site:* www.volny.cz/atlantis/
*Key Personnel*
Publisher & International Rights: Jana Uhdeova
Founded: 1989
Subjects: Biography, History, Literature, Literary
  Criticism, Essays
ISBN Prefix(es): 80-7108

**AULOS sro**
Kosarkovo nab. 1, 118 00 Prague 1
*Tel:* (02) 536863 *Fax:* (02) 90004536
*E-mail:* aulos@volny.cz
*Key Personnel*
Editor: Zdenek Krenek
Founded: 1992
Subjects: Fiction, Literature, Literary Criticism,
  Essays, Philosophy, Poetry
ISBN Prefix(es): 80-901261; 80-901895; 80-
  86184
*Showroom(s):* Michalska 21, 110 00 Prague 1
*Bookshop(s):* Michalska 21, 110 00 Prague 1
*Shipping Address:* Michalska 21, 110 00 Prague
  1, Czech Republic
*Warehouse:* Michalska 21, Prague 1, 110 00
  Czech Republic

**Aurora**
Opletalova 8, 110 00 Prague 1
*Tel:* (02) 24 21 43 26; (02) 24 21 46 24 *Fax:* (02)
  24 21 43 26
*E-mail:* eaurora@eaurora.cz
*Web Site:* www.eaurora.cz
*Key Personnel*
Owner: Eva Michalkova
Editor: Katerina Zavadova *E-mail:* zavadova@
  eaurora.cz
Founded: 1993
Subjects: Art, Fiction, Humor, Military Science,
  Nonfiction (General), Outdoor Recreation, Phi-
  losophy, Poetry
ISBN Prefix(es): 80-85974; 80-901603; 80-7299
Number of titles published annually: 50 Print
Total Titles: 75 Print

**AVCR Historicky ustav**
Prosecka 76, 190 00 Prague 9
*Tel:* (02) 868 821 21; (02) 838 813 73 *Fax:* (02)
  887 513
*E-mail:* panek@hiu.cas.cz
*Key Personnel*
Dir, Productions: Dr Pavla Vosahlikova
Founded: 1921
Subjects: History
ISBN Prefix(es): 80-85268; 80-7286

**Aventinum Nakladatelstvi spol sro+**
Nikoly Vapcarova 3274, 14300 Prague 4
*Tel:* (02) 41770660; (02) 441770616; (02)
  41767949 *Fax:* (02) 44402405
*Key Personnel*
Man Dir: Zdenek Pavlik
Founded: 1990
Specialize in illustrated books.
Subjects: Animals, Pets, Art, Astrology, Occult,
  Biological Sciences, Gardening, Plants, Natural
  History
ISBN Prefix(es): 80-7151; 80-85277

**Babtext Nakladatelska Spolecnost+**
Zirovnicka 2, 106 00 Prague 10
*Tel:* (02) 435 992 *Fax:* (02) 768992; (02)
  61221868
*Key Personnel*
Contact: Hilar Baburek
Founded: 1990
Subjects: Economics, Law
ISBN Prefix(es): 80-900178; 80-901444; 80-
  85816

**Barollet Publishers Inc**, see Baronet

**Baronet+**
Krizikova 16, 186 00 Prague 8
*Tel:* (02) 22310115 *Fax:* (02) 22310118
*E-mail:* baronet.odbyt@volny.cz
*Web Site:* www.baronet-knihy.cz; www.baronet.cz
*Key Personnel*
Publishing Dir: Mr Milan Soska, PhD
Founded: 1993
Specialize in historical romances, horoscopes &
  English/American fiction.
Subjects: Fiction, Military Science, Nonfiction
  (General), Romance, Science Fiction, Fantasy
ISBN Prefix(es): 80-7214; 80-85621; 80-85890;
  80-900765; 80-901068

**Barrister & Principal+**
Rybkova 23 Budova C 16, 602 00 Brno
*Tel:* (05) 45211015 *Fax:* (05) 45210607
*E-mail:* barrister@barrister.cz
*Web Site:* www.barrister.cz
*Key Personnel*
Manager: Ivo Lukas *E-mail:* lukas@barrister.cz
Founded: 1994
Subjects: Archaeology, Economics, Education,
  Government, Political Science, History, Jour-
  nalism, Language Arts, Linguistics, Philoso-
  phy, Poetry, Psychology, Psychiatry, Religion -
  Catholic, Social Sciences, Sociology, Theology
ISBN Prefix(es): 80-85947; 80-86598
Number of titles published annually: 20 Print
Total Titles: 5 Print

**Brody+**
Nakladatelství krásných knih, Spanelska 6/742,
  121 11 Prague 2
*Tel:* (02) 22252077 *Fax:* (02) 22252077
*E-mail:* brody@draha.czcom.cz
*Key Personnel*
Contact: Dita Horakova
Founded: 1995
Specialize in publishing books on the Far East &
  Russian Avant-Garde for reference markets in
  all areas of humanities.

Subjects: Art, Fiction, Literature, Literary Criticism, Essays, Nonfiction (General), Philosophy
ISBN Prefix(es): 80-86112; 80-902113

**Canis Vydavatelstvi a Nakladatelstvi+**
Korunni 9, 120 00 Prague 2
*Tel:* (02) 251096
*Key Personnel*
Editor & Publisher: Dr M Cisarovsky
Founded: 1990
ISBN Prefix(es): 80-900820
*Associate Companies:* Canis centrum, Vrsovicka
  7/27, Prague 10
Divisions: Manesova 48

**Ceska Biblicka Spolecnost** (Czech Bible
  Society)
Nahorni 12, 182 00 Prague 8
*Tel:* 284 693 925 *Fax:* 284 693 933
*E-mail:* cbs@dumbible.cz
*Web Site:* www.dumbible.cz
*Key Personnel*
General Secretary: Pavel Kral
Founded: 1990
Membership(s): United Bible Societies.
Subjects: Biblical Studies, Theology
ISBN Prefix(es): 80-85810; 80-900881

**Ceska Expedice+**
Jihozapadni III, 14, 141 00 Prague 4
*Tel:* (02) 727 612 04
*Key Personnel*
Contact: Jaromir Horec
Founded: 1989
Subjects: History, Literature, Literary Criticism,
  Essays, Poetry, Russie Subcarpatig
ISBN Prefix(es): 80-85281

**Chvojkova nakladatelstvi**
Halkova 11, 120 00 Prague 2
Mailing Address: Machova 22, 120 00 Prague 2
*Tel:* (02) 96202095; (02) 71743023 *Fax:* (02)
  96202095
*Key Personnel*
Contact: Jiri Chvojka
Subjects: Alternative, Astrology, Occult, History,
  Parapsychology, Psychology, Psychiatry
ISBN Prefix(es): 80-900239; 80-901270; 80-
  901622; 80-86183

**Cinema+**
Seifertova 47, 130 00 Prague 3
*Tel:* (02) 627 83 95-6 *Fax:* (02) 627 72 39
*E-mail:* schur@comp.cz
*Key Personnel*
International Rights: Roland Schuer
Founded: 1991
Subjects: Film, Video
ISBN Prefix(es): 80-85933; 80-901675

**Columbus+**
Nad Kolcavkov 8, 190 00 Prague 9
*Tel:* (02) 683 10 17; (02) 683 47 65; (02)
  74771407 *Fax:* (02) 683 10 17; (02) 683 08
  28
*E-mail:* columbus@alpha-net.cz
*Key Personnel*
Contact: Ivo Smoldas
Founded: 1991
Subjects: Biography, Geography, Geology, His-
  tory, Parapsychology
ISBN Prefix(es): 80-85928; 80-901578; 80-
  901696; 80-901727; 80-7249

**Concordia+**
Belohorska 99, 169 00 Prague 6
*Tel:* (02) 33357280; (02) 7929747 *Fax:* (02)
  7929747
*E-mail:* magdalenapechova@ahas.cz
*Key Personnel*
Executive: Ales Pech
Founded: 1990

Subjects: Literature, Literary Criticism, Essays
ISBN Prefix(es): 80-900124; 80-901389; 80-85997

**Diderot sro**
Jecna 12, 12000 Prague 2
*Tel:* (02) 55707711; (02) 55707703 *Fax:* (02) 55707700
*E-mail:* redakce@diderot.cz; obchod@bp.diderot.cz
*Web Site:* www.diderot.cz
*Key Personnel*
Contact: Martina Fialkova
Founded: 1988
Private publishing organization.
ISBN Prefix(es): 80-86613; 80-902555; 80-902723
Total Titles: 2 Print; 1 CD-ROM
*Branch Office(s)*
Moravian Branch, Sevcovska 1156, Ziln 76001
*Tel:* (067) 34156 *Fax:* (067) 779493

**Dimenze 2 Plus 2 Praha+**
Soukenicka 21, 110 00 Prague 1
*Tel:* (02) 231 11 41 *Fax:* (02) 231 11 41
*Web Site:* www.dub.cz/dimenze.html
*Key Personnel*
President: Tomas Pfeiffer
Founded: 1990
Subjects: Health, Nutrition, Philosophy
ISBN Prefix(es): 80-85238

**Divadelni Ustav** (Theatre Institute Prague)+
Subsidiary of Ministry of Culture, Czech Republic
Celetna 17, 110 00 Prague 1
*Tel:* (02) 24809111 *Fax:* (02) 24811452
*E-mail:* divadelni.ustav@czech-theatre.cz
*Web Site:* www.divadelni-ustav.cz
*Key Personnel*
Dir: Ondrej Cerny *Tel:* (02) 22315966
Founded: 1960
Subjects: Drama, Theater, Theatre Plays
ISBN Prefix(es): 80-7008
Number of titles published annually: 10 Print
*Bookshop(s):* Prospero Bookshop
*Tel:* (02) 24809156 *Fax:* (02) 24809156
*E-mail:* prospero@divadlo.cz *Web Site:* www.divadlo.cz/prospero

**Doplnek+**
Bratislavska 48/50, 602 00 Brno
*Tel:* (05) 452-424-55 *Fax:* (05) 452-424-55
*E-mail:* doplnek@doplnek.cz
*Web Site:* www.doplnek.cz
*Key Personnel*
Contact: Jan Sabata *E-mail:* sabata@sky.cz
Founded: 1991 (Founded in Bruo, Czech Republic)
Specialize in publishing of books with subject specialties.
Membership(s): The Association of Czech Booksellers & Publishers.
Subjects: Biography, Economics, Education, Environmental Studies, History, Humor, Journalism, Law, Literature, Literary Criticism, Essays, Psychology, Psychiatry, Science Fiction, Fantasy, Social Sciences, Sociology
ISBN Prefix(es): 80-7239; 80-85765; 80-901102
Number of titles published annually: 35 Print
Total Titles: 200 Print
Subsidiaries: Jan Sabata
Distributor for Jan Sabata
Foreign Rep(s): Andrew Nurberg Associate (Czech Republic); Thomas Perry (US)
*Bookshop(s):* Zerotinovo nam 9, 60200 Brno
*Tel:* (05) 42128382

**Erika spol sro+**
Jarnikova 1894, 148 00 Prague 4
Mailing Address: PO Box 27, 148 00 Prague 4

*Tel:* (02) 71913890 *Fax:* (02) 71913890
*Key Personnel*
Contact: Jan Suchl
Founded: 1990
Subjects: Health, Nutrition, Nonfiction (General)
ISBN Prefix(es): 80-900091; 80-85612; 80-7190
*Orders to:* Spira, Horska 10, 46014 Liberec

**Euromedia Group-Odeon+**
V Jamw 1, 111 21 Prague 1
*Fax:* (02) 241 623 28
*E-mail:* odeon@euromedia.cz *Cable:* ODEON PRAHA
*Key Personnel*
Man Dir: Ing Jiri Havlik
Editorial Rights & Permissions (Fiction): Dr Jiri Nasinec
Editorial Rights & Permissions (Art): Dr Milada Motlova
Publicity: Eva Svobodova
Production: Zdenek Suska
Founded: 1953
Publishing House of Literature & Art.
Subjects: Art, Biography, Fiction, Poetry
ISBN Prefix(es): 80-207
*Bookshop(s):* Na Florenci 3, 11586 Prague 1
*Book Club(s):* Odeon Book Club (Klub Ctenaru)

**Exemplare**, *imprint of* Granit sro

**Galaxie, vydavatelelstvi a nakladatelstvi+**
Petrska 29, 110 00 Prague 1
*Tel:* (02) 2317801; (02) 2317875 *Fax:* (02) 2311351
*Key Personnel*
Man Partner & Editor-in-Chief: Milan Pavek
Subjects: Education, Ethnicity, Fiction, Literature, Literary Criticism, Essays
ISBN Prefix(es): 80-85204

**Grada Publishing+**
U Pruhonu 22, 170 00 Prague 7
*Tel:* (02) 20386401; (02) 20386402 *Fax:* (02) 20386400
*E-mail:* info@gradapublishing.cz; obchod@gradapublishing.cz
*Web Site:* www.gradapublishing.cz; www.grada.cz
*Key Personnel*
Marketing: Zdenek Jaros *E-mail:* jaros@gradapublishing.cz
Foreign Rights: Magdalena Brenkova
*E-mail:* brenkova@gradapublishing.cz
Founded: 1993
Subjects: Computer Science, Economics, Law, Technology, Medicine
ISBN Prefix(es): 80-7169; 80-85424; 80-85623; 80-900250; 80-247
Total Titles: 850 Print

**Granit sro+**
Stefanikova 43, 150 00 Prague 5
*Tel:* (02) 27 018 361 *Fax:* (02) 27 018 361
*E-mail:* info@granit-publishing.cz
*Web Site:* www.granit-publishing.cz
*Key Personnel*
Dir: Lubomir Mlcoch *Tel:* (02) 57018361
Founded: 1992
Subjects: Animals, Pets, Biological Sciences, Crafts, Games, Hobbies, Education, Gardening, Plants, Geography, Geology, Health, Nutrition, Natural History, Science (General)
ISBN Prefix(es): 80-85805; 80-7296; 80-901195; 80-901443
Number of titles published annually: 12 Print
Total Titles: 80 Print
Imprints: Exemplare

**Galerie Hlavniho Mesta Prahy**
Mickiewiczova 3, 160 00 Prague 6
*Tel:* (02) 3332 1200 *Fax:* (02) 3332 3664
*E-mail:* ghmp@volny.cz

*Web Site:* www.citygalleryprague.cz
*Key Personnel*
Dir: Jaroslav Fatka
Founded: 1963
ISBN Prefix(es): 80-7010

**Horacek Ladislav-Paseka**
Chopinova 4, 120 00 Prague 2
*Tel:* (02) 222 710 751-3; (02) 222 718 886
*Fax:* (02) 22718886
*E-mail:* paseka@paseka.cz
*Web Site:* www.paseka.cz
*Key Personnel*
Publisher: Ladislav Horacek
Dir: Vladimir Pistorius
Founded: 1989
Subjects: Art, Biography, Fiction, History, Literature, Literary Criticism, Essays, Poetry
ISBN Prefix(es): 80-85192; 80-7185

**Josef Hribal+**
Na Vaclavce 10/1202, 150 21 Prague 5
Mailing Address: PO Box 210, 150 21 Prague 5
*Tel:* (02) 542731
*Key Personnel*
Contact: Zdenek Hribal
Founded: 1893
Subjects: Economics, Law, Nonfiction (General)
ISBN Prefix(es): 80-900132; 80-900892; 80-901381

**Infoa+**
Nova 141, 789 72 Dubicko
*Tel:* (0583) 449 091 *Fax:* (0583) 456 810
*E-mail:* infoa@infoa.cz
*Web Site:* www.infoa.cz
*Key Personnel*
Dir: Stanislav Sojak *Tel:* (0583) 456 811
Founded: 1992
Private company with its own distribution network in the Czech Republic, Slovakia & Poland.
Specialize in foreign languages.
ISBN Prefix(es): 80-7240; 86-85836; 80-86323; 88-901005; 1-900702
Total Titles: 250 Print
*Branch Office(s)*
Komenskeho 59, 90901 Skalica, Slovakia, Dir: Pavol Rehus *Tel:* (0801) 646172 *Fax:* (0801) 646172
Distributor for Express Publishing (Distribution rights for the Czech Republic & Slovakia)

**Inspirace+**
Volsinach 11, 100 00 Prague 10
*Tel:* (02) 7356615
*Key Personnel*
Contact: Alois Myslik
Founded: 1990
Subjects: Philosophy, Religion - Other
ISBN Prefix(es): 80-900119

**ISE**, see Institut Pro Stredoevropskou Kulturu A Politiku (ISE)

**Iuventus+**
Nedvezska 6, 100 00 Prague 10
*Tel:* (02) 7817314
*Key Personnel*
President: Dr Josef Smolka, CSC
Founded: 1990
Subjects: Government, Political Science
ISBN Prefix(es): 80-7123

**Nakladatelstvi Jan Vasut+**
Vitkova 10, 18621 Prague 8
*Tel:* (02) 22319 319 *Fax:* (02) 2481 1059
*E-mail:* vasut@mbox.vol.cz
*Web Site:* www.vasut.cz
*Key Personnel*
Publisher: Jan Vasut *Tel:* (02) 22 318 707
*E-mail:* jan.vasut@vasut.cz

Foreign Rights: Milena Taralezkovova
Founded: 1990
Subjects: Cookery, Crafts, Games, Hobbies, Humor, Sports, Athletics
ISBN Prefix(es): 80-7236
*Warehouse:* Grada Bohemia sro, Luzna 591, Prague 6 *Tel:* (02) 20121360

**Jednota Ceskych Matematiku A Fysiku**
Zitna 25, 117 10 Prague 1
*Tel:* (02) 222 111 54; (02) 220 907 08; (02) 220 907 09
*E-mail:* jcmf@math.cas.cz; predseda@jcmf.cz
*Web Site:* www.jcmf.cz
ISBN Prefix(es): 80-246; 80-7184; 80-7015
*Bookshop(s):* Celetna 18, 116 36 Prague 1
*Tel:* (02) 24491448 *Fax:* (02) 24491671

**Nakladatelstvi Jota spol sro+**
Krenova 19, Budova 1A, 602 00 Brno
*Tel:* (05) 37 014 203 *Fax:* (05) 37 014 213
*E-mail:* jota@jota.cz; books@bm.cesnet.cz
*Web Site:* www.jota.cz
*Key Personnel*
Contact: Marcel Nekvinda
Founded: 1990
Subjects: Alternative, Biography, Crafts, Games, Hobbies, Health, Nutrition, History, Military Science, Outdoor Recreation, Science Fiction, Fantasy
ISBN Prefix(es): 80-85617; 80-900281; 80-7217

**Kalich SRO**
Jungmannova 9, 111 21 Prague 1
Mailing Address: PO Box 220
*Tel:* (02) 24947505; (02) 24220296 *Fax:* (02) 24947504; (02) 24220296
*E-mail:* kalichpub@volny.cz
*Key Personnel*
Dir: Ema Snelia
Manager: Juan Vasin
Founded: 1922
Subjects: History, Philosophy, Religion - Catholic, Religion - Jewish, Religion - Protestant, Religion - Other, Social Sciences, Sociology, Theology
ISBN Prefix(es): 80-7017; 80-7072

**Jan Kanzelsberger Praha**
Jana Masaryka 56, 120 00 Prague 2
*Tel:* (02) 22 51 42 40; (02) 22 52 02 64 *Fax:* (02) 22 51 15 73
*E-mail:* masarykova@volny.cz
Founded: 1990
Subjects: Biography, Language Arts, Linguistics
ISBN Prefix(es): 80-900095; 80-85387; 80-900184
*Branch Office(s)*
Vaclavske nam 42, 110 00 Prague *Tel:* (02) 24217335 *Fax:* (02) 24221243
*Bookshop(s):* Knihkupectvi Orbis, Scobarova 5, 130 00 Prague

**Karmelitanske Nakladatelstvi+**
Kostelni Vydoi 58, Daeice 38001
*Tel:* 384 420 295 *Fax:* 384 420 295
*E-mail:* vydri@karmelitanske-nakladatelstvi.cz; zasilky@kna.cz
*Web Site:* www.karmelitanske-nakladatelstvi.cz; www.kna.cz
*Key Personnel*
Dir: Jan Fatka *Tel:* 220 181 350 *Fax:* 220 181 390 *E-mail:* fatka@kna.cz
Founded: 1991
Subjects: Biblical Studies, Biography, History, Poetry, Religion - Catholic, Theology
ISBN Prefix(es): 80-7192; 80-7195; 80-85527
Total Titles: 530 Print; 150 Audio
*Branch Office(s)*
Thakurova 3, 160 00 Prague 6 *Tel:* 220 181 350 *Fax:* 220 181 390

*Bookshop(s):* Mirove nam 15, Litomioice *Tel:* 416 732 458 *E-mail:* jonas@kna.cz; F Prochazky 101, Nova Paka *Tel:* 493 721 967 *E-mail:* nova.paka@kna.cz; Wurmova 6, Olomouc *Tel:* 587 405 336 *E-mail:* velehrad@kna.cz; Puchmajerova 10, Ostrava *Tel:* 596 121 463 *Fax:* 596 121 463 *E-mail:* caritas@kna.cz; Prokopova 19, Plzeo *Tel:* 377 237 253 *E-mail:* usvit@kna.cz; Jindoisska 23, Prague 1 *Tel:* 224 212 376 *E-mail:* sv.jindrich@kna.cz; Kolejni 4, Prague 6 *Tel:* 220 181 714 *E-mail:* sv.vojtech@kna.cz; Hradeanske namisti 16, Prague 1 *Tel:* 220 392 185 *E-mail:* sv.vit@kna.cz; Marianske nam 200, Uherske Hradisti *Tel:* 572 557 842 *E-mail:* uh.hradiste@kna.cz

**Karolinum, nakladatelstvi** (The Karolinum Press)+
Ovocny trh 3/5, 116 36 Prague 1
*Tel:* (02) 24491276 *Fax:* (02) 24212041
*E-mail:* cupress@ruk.cuni.cz; cupress@cuni.cz
*Web Site:* www.cupress.cuni.cz
*Key Personnel*
Dir: Jaroslav Jirsa *E-mail:* jaroslav.jirsa@ruk.cuni.cz
Production: Nadezda Lemochova *Tel:* (02) 24 491 271 *E-mail:* nadezda.lemochova@ruk.cuni.cz; Kamila Schullerova *Tel:* (02) 24 491 272 *E-mail:* kamila.schullerova@ruk.cuni.cz
Distribution: Jaroslava Stribrska *Tel:* (02) 24491275 *E-mail:* jaroslava.stribrska@ruk.cuni.cz
Editor: Renata Camska *Tel:* (02) 24 491 266 *E-mail:* renata.camska@ruk.cuni.cz; Zdenka Lubenova *Tel:* (02) 24 491 273; Milada Motlova *Tel:* (02) 24 491 266 *E-mail:* milada.motlova@ruk.cuni.cz; Petr Valo *Tel:* (02) 24 491 268 *E-mail:* petr.valo@ruk.cuni.cz; Jana Velova *Tel:* (02) 24 491 274 *E-mail:* jana.velova@ruk.cuni.cz
Foreign Rights: Martin Janecek *Tel:* (02) 24 491 269 *E-mail:* martin.janecek@ruk.cuni.cz
Promotion: Milan Susta *Tel:* (02) 24 491 265 *E-mail:* milan.susta@ruk.cuni.cz
Founded: 1990
Publishing House of Charles University, Prague.
Subjects: Architecture & Interior Design, Art, Business, Economics, Education, Fiction, Foreign Countries, History, Language Arts, Linguistics, Law, Mathematics, Medicine, Nursing, Dentistry, Philosophy, Physical Sciences, Religion - Other, Science (General), Social Sciences, Sociology, Political science
ISBN Prefix(es): 80-7066; 80-7184; 80-246
*Bookshop(s):* Celetna 18, 11636 Prague 1

**Kartografie Praha**
Ostrovni 30, 11000 Prague 1
*Tel:* (02) 21969411 *Fax:* (02) 21969428
*E-mail:* info@kartografie.cz
*Web Site:* www.kartografie.cz
*Telex:* 121471 guvs c *Cable:* GEOKART
*Key Personnel*
Man Dir: Miroslav Miksovsky
Editor-in-Chief: Ales Hasek
Founded: 1954
Geodetic & Cartographic Enterprise in Prague.
ISBN Prefix(es): 80-7011
*Orders to:* Artia, Foreign Trade Corporation, Ve Smeckach 30, 11127 Prague 1

**Knihovna A Tiskarna Pro Nevidome**
Ve Smeckach 15, 115 17 Prague 1
*Tel:* (02) 22 21 04 92; (02) 22 21 15 23 *Fax:* (02) 22 21 04 94
*E-mail:* ktn@ktn.cz
*Web Site:* www.ktn.cz
*Key Personnel*
Dir: Dr Josef Doksansky
Subjects: Biography, Fiction, Humor, Mysteries, Poetry, Psychology, Psychiatry, Religion - Other, Science Fiction, Fantasy
ISBN Prefix(es): 80-7061

**Konias+**
Waltrova 26, 318 14 Plzen
*Tel:* (019) 28 06 90 *Fax:* (019) 28 06 90
*E-mail:* konias@literaplzen.cz
*Key Personnel*
Contact: Miroslav Moravek
Founded: 1990
Subjects: Travel
ISBN Prefix(es): 80-900167; 80-901379

**Konsultace spol sro+**
Bilkova 8, 110 00 Prague 1
*Tel:* (02) 2310363 *Fax:* (02) 2310363
*Key Personnel*
Publisher (Oberengstringen): Antonin Pasek
Publisher (Zurich): Sarka Pasek
Dir: Antonin Seda
Founded: 1990
Subjects: Government, Political Science, History, Humor, Philosophy, Poetry
ISBN Prefix(es): 80-7124
*Associate Companies:* Consultation Verlag, Oberengstringen, Switzerland
*Orders to:* S Pasek, Consultation, Regensdorfestr 175, 8049 Zurich, Switzerland

**Kosik**
Hajecka 184, Chyne, 253 01 Hostivice
*Tel:* (311) 670929 *Fax:* (02) 2359403
*Key Personnel*
Contact: Jiri Kosik
ISBN Prefix(es): 80-900248; 80-902007

**Labyrint+**
Dittrichova 5, 120 00 Prague 2
Mailing Address: PO Box 52, Jablonecka 715, 190 00 Prague 9
*Tel:* (02) 24 922 422 *Fax:* (02) 24 922 422
*E-mail:* labyrint@wo.cz
*Web Site:* www.labyrint.net
*Key Personnel*
Contact: Joachim Dvorak
Founded: 1992
Subjects: Art, Fiction, Library & Information Sciences, Poetry
ISBN Prefix(es): 80-85935
Number of titles published annually: 10 Print; 1 E-Book
Total Titles: 100 Print; 2 E-Book
Subsidiaries: RAKETA (Children's books)

**Libri spol sro** (Libri Ltd)+
Na Hutmance 7, 158 00 Prague 5
*Tel:* (02) 5161 3113; (02) 5161 2302 *Fax:* (02) 5161 1013
*E-mail:* libri@libri.cz
*Web Site:* www.libri.cz
*Key Personnel*
Manager: Marie Honzakova
Founded: 1993
Original Czech encyclopedia, popularization.
Membership(s): Federation of Czech Publishers & Booksellers.
Subjects: Archaeology, Architecture & Interior Design, Economics, Foreign Countries, Geography, Geology, History, Literature, Literary Criticism, Essays, Social Sciences, Sociology
ISBN Prefix(es): 80-901579; 80-85983; 80-7277
Number of titles published annually: 50 Print
Total Titles: 300 Print; 3 CD-ROM; 25 E-Book

**Lidove Noviny Publishing House+**
Jana Masaryka 56, 120 00 Prague 2
*Tel:* (02) 225 223 50; (02) 222 510 845 *Fax:* (02) 225 240 12; (02) 222 514 012
*E-mail:* nln@nln.cz; nln@iol.cz
*Web Site:* www.nln.cz
*Key Personnel*
Editor-in-Chief: Eva Pleskova *Tel:* 603 810 506 *E-mail:* pleskova@nln.cz
Founded: 1993

Subjects: Archaeology, Art, Biography, Fiction, History, Language Arts, Linguistics, Nonfiction (General), Poetry, Science (General), Social Sciences, Sociology, Travel
ISBN Prefix(es): 80-7106
Number of titles published annually: 100 Print; 2 CD-ROM
Total Titles: 10 CD-ROM

**Josef Lukasik A Spol sro+**
Snopkova 481/3, 142 00 Prague 4
*Tel:* (02) 471 22 19; (02) 83 22 84; (0603) 95 52 55
*Key Personnel*
Contact: Marie Lukasikova
Founded: 1939
Subjects: Humor, Mysteries, Nonfiction (General), Romance
ISBN Prefix(es): 80-900303; 80-901763; 80-902508

**Luxpress VOS+**
Maliiska 6, 170 00 Prague 7
*Tel:* (02) 203 972 60 *Fax:* (02) 203 972 60
*E-mail:* ibs.czech@iol.cz
Founded: 1990
Subjects: Health, Nutrition, Human Relations, Religion - Other
ISBN Prefix(es): 80-7130

**Lyra Pragensis Obecne Prospelna Spolecnost**
Adamovska 1/803, 140 00 Prague 4
*Tel:* 224 910 787; 261 220 516; 602 683 500
*Fax:* 261 218 570
*E-mail:* info@lyrapragensis.cz
*Web Site:* www.lyrapragensis.cz
*Key Personnel*
Manager: Ivana Tetourova *E-mail:* tetourova@lyrapragensis.cz
Production: Ruzena Cizkova *E-mail:* cizkova@lyrapragensis.cz
Founded: 1967
Subjects: Drama, Theater, Fiction, Music, Dance, Philosophy, Poetry, Religion - Buddhist
ISBN Prefix(es): 80-7059
Subsidiaries: Spolecnost pratel kultury slova

**Mariadan+**
Klobroucnicka 7, 140 00 Prague 4
*Tel:* (02) 41 40 83 91
*Key Personnel*
Contact: Marie Jehlickova-Gucklerova
Founded: 1990
Subjects: Archaeology, Art, Astronomy, Earth Sciences, Fiction, Foreign Countries, History, Medicine, Nursing, Dentistry, Science Fiction, Fantasy
ISBN Prefix(es): 80-900304
Imprints: Tesinska
*Distribution Center:* Bookshop Kanzelberger, Vaclavske namesti, Prague 1

**Maxdorf Ltd+**
Na Sejdru 247, 142 00 Prague 4
*Tel:* (02) 444 710 37; (02) 41 011 680; (02) 41 011 681 *Fax:* (02) 41 710 245
*E-mail:* info@maxdorf.cz
*Web Site:* www.maxdorf.cz
*Key Personnel*
Editor-in-Chief: Jan Hugo *E-mail:* hugo@maxdorf.cz
Founded: 1993
Publishing house of scientific & professional literature.
Subjects: Art, Health, Nutrition, History, Medicine, Nursing, Dentistry, Science (General), Specialize in medicine, monograhies & handbooks
ISBN Prefix(es): 80-85800; 80-85912
Number of titles published annually: 40 Print
Total Titles: 105 Print; 1 E-Book

**Medica Publishing-Pavla Momcilova+**
V Zahradach 146, Cestlice, 251 01 Ricany
*Tel:* 272680919; 602271393 *Fax:* 272680919
*E-mail:* momcilova@volny.cz
*Key Personnel*
Publisher: Mrs Pavla Momcilova
Founded: 1990
Subjects: Child Care & Development, Cookery, Education, Health, Nutrition, Medicine, Nursing, Dentistry, Self-Help
ISBN Prefix(es): 80-900140; 80-901137; 80-85936
Number of titles published annually: 5 Print
Total Titles: 60 Print

**Melantrich, akc spol**
Vaclavske nam 36, 112 12 Prague 1
*Tel:* (02) 24227258 *Fax:* (02) 24213176
*Telex:* 121422 *Cable:* Melantrich
*Key Personnel*
Man Dir: Petr Zantovsky
Sales Dir: K Volesky
Editorial: Dr K Houba
Production: M Nevole
Founded: 1898
Subjects: Biography, Philosophy, Poetry
ISBN Prefix(es): 80-7023
*Bookshop(s):* Na prikope 3, Prague 1; Jilska 9, Prague 1

**Mendelova zemedelska a lesnicka univerzita v Brne** (Mendel University of Agriculture & Forestry Brno)
Zemedelska 1, 613 00 Brno
*Tel:* (05) 4513 1111; (05) 4513 2678 *Fax:* (05) 4513 5008
*Web Site:* www.mendelu.cz
*Key Personnel*
Contact: Dr Jiri Potacek *E-mail:* potacek@mendelu.cz
Founded: 1992
Subjects: Agriculture, Animals, Pets, Biological Sciences, Earth Sciences, Economics, Physical Sciences
ISBN Prefix(es): 80-7157
Number of titles published annually: 70 Print; 30 Audio
Total Titles: 400 Print; 2,000 Audio

**Mlada fronta+**
Division of Mlada fronta a s
Mezi Vodami 1952/9, 143 00 Prague 4
*Tel:* (02) 49 240 315 *Fax:* (02) 25 276 278
*Web Site:* www.mf.cz
*Key Personnel*
Dir: Dr Jiri Kolecko *E-mail:* kolecko@mf.cz
Editor-in-Chief: Vlastimil Fiala *Tel:* (02) 25 276 282 *E-mail:* fiala@mf.cz
Sec: Marcela Biersakova *E-mail:* biersakova@mf.cz
Founded: 1945
Subjects: Art, Astronomy, Biography, Fiction, History, Nonfiction (General), Philosophy, Poetry, Science (General), Science Fiction, Fantasy, Travel
ISBN Prefix(es): 80-204
Number of titles published annually: 100 Print
Total Titles: 6,500 Print

**Editio Moravia-Moravske hudebni vydavatelstvi+**
Sosnova 18, 637 00 Brno
*Tel:* (05) 41220025
*E-mail:* emdl@vtx.cz *Cable:* CS-61300 BRNO 13
*Key Personnel*
Publishing Dir: Dr Jaromir Dlouhy
Marketing Manager: Mag Martin Dlouhy
Founded: 1990
Specialize in music literature for schools.
Subjects: Education, Music, Dance
ISBN Prefix(es): 80-85322

**Moravska Galerie v Brne** (Moravian Gallery in Brno)
Husova 18, 66226 Brno
*Tel:* 532 169 131 *Fax:* 532 169 180
*E-mail:* m-gal@moravska-galerie.cz
*Web Site:* www.moravska-galerie.cz
*Key Personnel*
Dir: Marek Pokorny
Administration: Katerina Tlachova
Founded: 1873
Subjects: Architecture & Interior Design, Art, Photography, Applied Art, Design, Fine Art
ISBN Prefix(es): 80-7027
Number of titles published annually: 6 Print
Total Titles: 30 Print

**Narodni filmovy archiv** (National Film Archive)+
Malesicka 12, 130 00 Prague 3
Mailing Address: Bartolomejska 11, 110 00 Prague 1
*Tel:* 271 770 500; 271 770 502-9 *Fax:* 271 770 501
*E-mail:* nfa@nfa.cz
*Web Site:* www.nfa.cz
*Key Personnel*
President: Vladimir Opela
Founded: 1970
Subjects: Film, Video
ISBN Prefix(es): 80-7004

**Narodni Knihovna CR** (The National Library of the Czech Republic)+
c/o The National Library of the Czech Republic, Klementinum 190, 110 01 Prague 1
*Tel:* (02) 2810 13 316; (02) 2810 13 317
*Fax:* (02) 216 632 61; (02) 2810 13 333
*E-mail:* sekret.ur@nkp.cz; mirosovsky.ivo@cdh.nkp.cz
*Web Site:* www.nkp.cz
*Key Personnel*
Head, Publishing Division: Milena Redinova, PhD *E-mail:* redinova.milena@cdh.nkp.cz
The publishing division manages & coordinates publishing activities of the National Library in the areas of librarianship, bibliography & scientific information. The division is responsible for editorial planning, production, sales & shipping.
Membership(s): Conference of European National Librarians (CENL); Czech Association of Booksellers & Publishers; Czech Association of Librarian & Information Professionals; International Federation of Library Associations & Institutions (IFLA); Lique des Bibliotheques Europeennes de Recherche (LIBER).
Subjects: Library & Information Sciences
ISBN Prefix(es): 80-7050
Number of titles published annually: 32 Print; 2 CD-ROM; 1 Online
Total Titles: 94 Print; 2 CD-ROM; 1 Online
Imprints: National Library of the Czech Republic
Distributed by National Library of the Czech Republic
*Shipping Address:* National Library of the Czech Republic, Publishing Division, Central Depository Hostivar, Sodomkova 2, 102 00 Prague 10
*Tel:* (02) 2810 13 230
*Orders to:* National Library of the Czech Republic, Publishing Division, Central Depository Hostivar, Sodomkova 2, 102 00 Prague 10
*Returns:* National Library of the Czech Republic, Publishing Division, Central Depository Hostivar, Sodomkova 2, 102 00 Prague 10

**Narodni Muzeum**
Vaclavske namisti 68, 115 79 Prague 1
*Tel:* (02) 24497111; (02) 24226488 *Fax:* (02) 22246047
*E-mail:* ais@nm.anet.cz
*Web Site:* www.nm.cz

*Key Personnel*
Dir: Dipl Ing Milan Placek *Tel:* (02) 24497235 *Fax:* (02) 24224940 *E-mail:* milan.placek@nm.cz; Dr Milan Stloukal; Lukas Viktora *E-mail:* lukas.viktora@nm.cz
Founded: 1818
Subjects: Animals, Pets, Anthropology, Archaeology, Art, Asian Studies, Biological Sciences, Drama, Theater, Earth Sciences, History, Music, Dance, Natural History, Science (General), Sports, Athletics
ISBN Prefix(es): 80-7036

**Nase vojsko, nakladatelstvi a knizni obchod+**
Vitezne nam 4, 16000 Prague 6
*Tel:* (02) 243 130 71; (02) 243 112 04; (02) 249 171 47 *Fax:* (02) 243 112 04
*E-mail:* info@nasevojsko.com; info@nasevojsko.cz
*Web Site:* www.nasevojsko.com
*Key Personnel*
Dir: Jakub Cisar
Editorial: Dr Zdenka Alanova
Sales: Miroslav Ambros
Rights & Permissions: Marie Kutilkkova
Founded: 1945
Subjects: History, Humor, Maritime, Military Science, Mysteries, Nonfiction (General), Philosophy
ISBN Prefix(es): 80-206
*Warehouse:* Ostrovni 32, Prague 1

**National Library of the Czech Republic**, *imprint of* Narodni Knihovna CR

**Nava+**
Hankova 6, nam Republiky 17, 301 00 Plzen
*Tel:* (0377) 235721; (0377) 324189 *Fax:* (0377) 324189
*E-mail:* nakladatelstvi@nava.cz
*Web Site:* www.nava.cz
*Key Personnel*
Contact: Ota Rubner
Founded: 1990
Specializes in children's books.
Subjects: Fiction, History, Humor
ISBN Prefix(es): 80-85254; 80-7211

**NLN Ltd**, see Lidove Noviny Publishing House

**Cesky normalizacni institut** (Czech Standards Institute)
Biskupsky dvur 5, 110 02 Prague 1
*Tel:* (02) 21 80 21 11 *Fax:* (02) 21 80 23 10
*E-mail:* info@csni.cz
*Web Site:* www.csni.cz *Cable:* NORMALIZACE PRAHA
*Key Personnel*
Contact: Jan Jelinek; Otakar Kunc; Ms Bures ova Zdenka
Founded: 1922
Membership(s): CEN; CENELEC; ETSi; IEC; ISO.
Subjects: Automotive, Chemistry, Chemical Engineering, Electronics, Electrical Engineering, Engineering (General), Environmental Studies, Mechanical Engineering, Medicine, Nursing, Dentistry
ISBN Prefix(es): 80-85111; 80-7283
*Bookshop(s):* Prodejna norem, Hornomecholupska 40, 102 04 Prague 10 *Tel:* (02) 71 96 17 70 *Fax:* (02) 74 86 69 51; (02) 71 96 20 43 *E-mail:* odbyt@csni.cz; Prodejna norem, Biskupsky dvur c 5, 110 02 Prague 1 *Fax:* (02) 74 86 69 51; (02) 71 96 20 43 *E-mail:* odbyt@csni.cz

**Nakladatelstvi Olympia AS+**
Klimentska 1246/1, 110 15 Prague 1
*Tel:* (02) 224 810 146 *Fax:* (02) 222 312 137
*E-mail:* olympia@mbox.vol.cz

*Telex:* 121717 *Cable:* OLYMPIA PRAGUE
*Key Personnel*
Man Dir: Karel Zelnicek
Dir: Alexander Zurman
Sales Dir: Zdenek Pobuda
Publicity & Advertising: Monika Charvatova
Editor: Josef Smatlak
Founded: 1954
Publishing house of sports & tourism.
Subjects: Sports, Athletics, Travel
ISBN Prefix(es): 80-7033
*Bookshop(s):* Opletalova 59, Prague 1

**Omnipress Praha+**
Na Sypcine 9, 147 00 Prague 4
*Tel:* (02) 61211406 *Fax:* (02) 61211856
*E-mail:* dcf.clock@omnipress.cz
*Web Site:* www.omnipress.cz
*Key Personnel*
Contact: Dr Metodej K Chytil *E-mail:* m.chytil@omnipress.cz
Founded: 1990
Subjects: Communications, Medicine, Nursing, Dentistry, Philosophy, Science (General)
ISBN Prefix(es): 80-900153
*Associate Companies:* Omikron Desk-Top Publishing
*Orders to:* PO Box 106, 140 00 Prague

**P & R Centrum Vydavateistvi a Nakladateistvi**
Pod Barvirkou 14, 150 00 Prague 5
*Tel:* (02) 542901 *Fax:* (02) 51554485
*E-mail:* olda@katapult.cz
*Key Personnel*
Publisher: Milan Nestaval
Founded: 1990
Also a music agency.
Subjects: Language Arts, Linguistics, Literature, Literary Criticism, Essays, Music, Dance
ISBN Prefix(es): 80-85333
Imprints: P R Centrum
Divisions: Zborovska 60
*Bookshop(s):* Belgicka 36, 120 00 Prague 2

**P R Centrum**, *imprint of* P & R Centrum Vydavateistvi a Nakladateistvi

**Portal**, *imprint of* Portal spol sro

**Portal spol sro+**
Klapkova 2, 182 00 Prague 8
*Tel:* (02) 83028111 *Fax:* (02) 83028112
*E-mail:* naklad@portal.cz
*Web Site:* www.portal.cz
*Key Personnel*
Dir: Jaroslav Kuchar
Rights: Dominik Dvorak *Tel:* (02) 83028111 (ext 602) *E-mail:* dvorak@portal.cz
Founded: 1990
Membership(s): Association of Catholic Publishers & Booksellers.
Subjects: Child Care & Development, Communications, Disability, Special Needs, Education, Human Relations, Psychology, Psychiatry, Religion - Catholic
ISBN Prefix(es): 80-7178; 80-85282
Number of titles published annually: 90 Print
Total Titles: 450 Print
Imprints: Portal
Foreign Rep(s): Artforum sro (Slovak Republic)
*Bookshop(s):* Dominikanske nam 8, 602 00 Brno *Tel:* (05) 42213140 *E-mail:* brno@studovna.cz; Jindrisska 30, 11000 Prague 1 *Tel:* (02) 24213415 *E-mail:* praha@studovna.cz; Klapkova 2, 182 00 Prague 8 *Tel:* (02) 83028203 *E-mail:* obchod@portal.cz; Kostelni nam 2, Ostrava *Tel:* (05) 95136508 *Fax:* (05) 95136508

**Pragma 4+**
V Hodkoviekach 2/20, 147 00 Prague 4

*Tel:* 241 768 565; 241 768 566; 603 205 099 *Fax:* 241 768 561
*E-mail:* pragma@pragma.cz
*Web Site:* www.pragma.cz
*Key Personnel*
Business Manager: Ivan Marinec
Contact: Robert Nemec
Founded: 1989
Specialize in US publishers.
Subjects: Business, Health, Nutrition, Philosophy, Self-Help
ISBN Prefix(es): 80-7205; 80-85213
Total Titles: 480 Print; 20 Audio
*Parent Company:* Pragma
Distributed by Kanzelsberger

**Prazske nakladatelstvi Pluto**
Kremencova 1, 110 00 Prague 1
*Tel:* (02) 249 301 89; (02) 43 25 05 *Fax:* (02) 249 301 89
*Key Personnel*
Owner: Jiri Polacek; Leontina Polackova
Founded: 1990
Subjects: Art, History, Travel
ISBN Prefix(es): 80-900192; 80-901224; 80-901544; 80-86435; 80-902183

**PressArt Nakladatelstvi+**
Aloisina vyhlidka 628/100, 460 05 Liberec
*Tel:* (048) 29377 *Fax:* (048) 27958
*Key Personnel*
President: Jiri Oplt
Vice President: Petr Bartos
Founded: 1990
Subjects: Advertising, Business, Drama, Theater
ISBN Prefix(es): 80-900367
*Parent Company:* PressART
*Associate Companies:* Bohemia Union
Subsidiaries: M-Print; Eurotip
Divisions: Exportabt, Innlandabt

**Pressfoto Vydavatelstvi Ceske Tiskove Kancelare**
Zirovnicka 2389, 106 00 Prague 10
*Tel:* (02) 727 700 10 *Fax:* (02) 727 700 10
*Telex:* 122908 ctKC
Founded: 1963
Subjects: History, Regional Interests
ISBN Prefix(es): 80-7046

**Prostor, nakladatelstvi sro+**
Tynska 21, 110 00 Prague 1
*Tel:* (02) 224 826 688 *Fax:* (02) 242 441 694
*E-mail:* prostor@ini.cz
*Web Site:* www.prostor-nakladatelstvi.cz
*Key Personnel*
International Rights: Sylva Kurdiovska
Foreign Rights Agent: Kristin Olson *Tel:* (02) 222 580 048 *Fax:* 222 582 042 *E-mail:* kolson@vol.cz
Founded: 1990
Specialize in Czech & German history.
Membership(s): Svaz ceskych knihkupcu a nakladatelu
Subjects: Biography, Fiction, Government, Political Science, History, Nonfiction (General), Philosophy, Photography
ISBN Prefix(es): 80-7260
Number of titles published annually: 25 Print
Total Titles: 210 Print

**Psychoanalyticke Nakladatelstvi+**
Vinohradska 71, 120 00 Prague 2
*Tel:* (02) 33340305; (02) 545 97 12; (02) 627 1855 *Fax:* (02) 312 03 05
*Key Personnel*
Assistant Professor: Jiri Kocourek, PhD *E-mail:* kocourek@serverpha.czcom.cz
Founded: 1992
Subjects: Education, Medicine, Nursing, Dentistry, Psychology, Psychiatry, Psychoanalysis, Psychotherapy, Scientific & Popular
ISBN Prefix(es): 80-901601; 80-86123

Number of titles published annually: 10 Print
Total Titles: 40 Print
*Branch Office(s)*
Vitezne nam 10, 16000 Prague 6
Distributed by Grada, Mata, Kolporter

**Verlag Harry Putz+**
Oldichova 89/28, 460 03 Liberec
Mailing Address: PO Box 89, 460 31 Liberec
*Tel:* (048) 515 21 20; (048) 510 32 75 *Fax:* (048)
    510 32 75
*E-mail:* harrputz@mbox.vol.cz
Subjects: Language Arts, Linguistics
ISBN Prefix(es): 80-901119; 80-902165

**Simon Rysavy**
Ceska 31, 602 00 Brno
*Tel:* (05) 42 212 052; (05) 42 213 849 *Fax:* (05)
    42 216 633
*E-mail:* info@rysavy.cz
*Web Site:* www.itn.cz/rysavy-books; www.rysavy.
    cz
ISBN Prefix(es): 80-86137; 80-902143

**SEVT**, see Statisticke a evidencni vydavatelstvi
    tiskopisu (SEVT)

**Slon Sociologicke Nakladatelstvi+**
Jilska 1, 110 00 Prague 1
*Tel:* (02) 222 220 025 *Fax:* (02) 222 220 025
*E-mail:* redakce@slon-knihy.cz
*Web Site:* www.slon-knihy.cz
*Key Personnel*
Contact: Alena Miltova
Founded: 1991
Subjects: Anthropology, Government, Political
    Science, History, Philosophy, Psychology, Psy-
    chiatry, Social Sciences, Sociology
ISBN Prefix(es): 80-85850; 80-901059; 80-
    901424; 80-86429
Number of titles published annually: 17 Print
Total Titles: 146 Print

**Sofiprin+**
PO Box 1006, 111 21 Prague 1
*Tel:* (0602) 30 87 21 *Fax:* (02) 758280
*Key Personnel*
Dir: Jiri Horak
Foreign Relations Officer: Jan Spousta
Founded: 1991
ISBN Prefix(es): 80-85391

**Statisticke a evidencni vydavatelstvi tiskopisu
    (SEVT)**
Pekarova 4, 181 06 Prague 8
*Tel:* 233 551 711; 283 090 352 *Fax:* 233 543 918
*E-mail:* sevt@sevt.cz
*Web Site:* www.sevt.cz
*Key Personnel*
Head of Production: Jarmila Frysova *Tel:* 283 090
    339 *E-mail:* frysova@sevt.cz
General Manager: Jaroslav Cizek
Publishing House of Statistics & Data.
ISBN Prefix(es): 80-7049

**Statni Vedecka Knihovna Usti Nad Labem**
W Churchilla 3, 401 34 Usti Nad Labem
*Tel:* (047) 5200045; (047) 5209126 *Fax:* (047)
    5200045
*E-mail:* library@svkul.cz
*Web Site:* www.svkul.cz
*Key Personnel*
Library Dir: Mr Brozek Ales *E-mail:* brozeka@
    svkul.cz
Founded: 1945
Subjects: Library & Information Sciences
ISBN Prefix(es): 80-7055

**Institut Pro Stredoevropskou Kulturu A
    Politiku (ISE)**
Vysehradska 2, 128 00 Prague 2
*Tel:* (02) 249 168 60 *Fax:* (02) 249 168 60
*E-mail:* panevropa@iol.cz
ISBN Prefix(es): 80-85241; 80-86130

**NS Svoboda spol sro+**
Jungmannova 12, 113 03 Prague 1
Mailing Address: K Safine 145, 149 00 Prague 4
    *Tel:* (02) 24 22 98
*Tel:* (02) 449 132 58; (02) 23 06 14 *Fax:* (02)
    449 132 58
*E-mail:* nssvobod@centrum.cz
*Key Personnel*
Dir: Stefan Szerynski
Rights & Permissions: Michal Bencok
Founded: 1970
Publishing house in state ownership.
Subjects: Finance, History, Management, Market-
    ing, Mysteries, Nonfiction (General)
ISBN Prefix(es): 80-205
*Book Club(s):* Friends of Antiquity; Readers Club
    of Svoboda

**Svoboda Servis sro+**
Politickych vizou 9, 111 21 Prague 1
*Tel:* 222897347 *Fax:* 222897346
*E-mail:* svobserv@volny.cz
*Key Personnel*
Dir: Stefan Szerynski
Foreign Rights Representative: Michal Beneok
    *Tel:* 224009277 *Fax:* 222247383 *E-mail:* ak.
    bencok@cmail.cz
Founded: 1994
Subjects: Business, Management, Mysteries, Phi-
    losophy, Science Fiction, Fantasy
ISBN Prefix(es): 80-205
Number of titles published annually: 4 Print
Total Titles: 30 Print

**SystemConsult+**
Bartolomejska 89, CZ 530 02 Pardubice
*Tel:* (040) 466 501 585 *Fax:* (040) 466 501 585
*E-mail:* system.consult@tiscali.cz
*Web Site:* www.systemconsult.cz
*Key Personnel*
Contact: Ivo Machacka
Founded: 1990
Specialize in Computer Dictionaries (German-
    Czech, English-Czech), Road-Transport Tech-
    niques & Automotive Industry Dictionaries
    (German-English-Czech), Travel Dictionaries
    (English & German) & Road Transport, Traffic
    Signs in Europe.
Subjects: Business, Computer Science, History,
    Transportation, Travel
ISBN Prefix(es): 80-900344; 80-85629
Number of titles published annually: 5 Print; 1
    CD-ROM
Total Titles: 50 Print; 2 CD-ROM

**Tesinska**, *imprint of* Mariadan

**Touzimsky & Moravec**
Pod Lazni 12, 140 00 Prague 4
*Tel:* (02) 612 13 631; (02) 612 12 458 *Fax:* (02)
    612 12 458
*Key Personnel*
Contact: Michal Moravec
Subjects: Science Fiction, Fantasy, Western Fic-
    tion
ISBN Prefix(es): 80-900955; 80-900137; 80-
    85773; 80-7264

**Trizonia**
U Sipku 15, 15400 Prague 5
*Tel:* (02) 5816502
*Telex:* Trizonia Prag 2
*Key Personnel*
President: Dr Jindrich Jirka

Founded: 1990
Subjects: Economics, Law
ISBN Prefix(es): 80-900953; 80-900117; 80-
    85573

**Evzen Uher, Musikverlag UHER+**
Kollarova 404, 686 01 Uherske Hradiste
*Tel:* 572540376
*Key Personnel*
Contact: Evzen Uher
Founded: 1990
Subjects: Music, Dance
ISBN Prefix(es): 80-900136; 80-901386

**Univerzity Karlovy**, see Karolinum,
    nakladatelstvi

**Ladislav Vasicek+**
Pellicova 17, 602 00 Brno
*Tel:* 518611422
*Key Personnel*
Contact: Ladislav Vasicek
Founded: 1990
Subjects: Poetry
ISBN Prefix(es): 80-900164
*Bookshop(s):* Ing Vasicek, Kr Pole Berkova 46,
    61200 Brno
*Orders to:* Kvetinarska 1, 600 00 Brno

**Vitalis sro+**
U Zelezne lavky 568/10, 118 00 Prague 1
*Tel:* (02) 57530732 *Fax:* (02) 57531974
*E-mail:* info@vitalis-verlag.com
*Web Site:* www.vitalis-verlag.com
*Key Personnel*
Publisher: Dr Harald Salfellner
Sales Manager: Dr Gabriela Salfellner
Founded: 1992
Specialize in Bohemica.
Subjects: Biography, Cookery, Fiction, Foreign
    Countries, Poetry
ISBN Prefix(es): 80-85938; 80-901621; 80-
    901370; 80-7253
Number of titles published annually: 40 Print
Total Titles: 300 Print
*Warehouse:* LKG, Potzschauer Weg, 04579 Es-
    penhain, Germany
*Orders to:* LKG, Potzschauer Weg, 04579 Espen-
    hain, Germany

**Vodnar**
Kosicka 34, 101 00 Prague
*E-mail:* naklvodnar@volny.cz
*Web Site:* www.volny.cz/naklvodnar
*Key Personnel*
Contact: Vladimir Kvasnicka
Founded: 1990
Subjects: Astrology, Occult, Philosophy
ISBN Prefix(es): 80-85255; 80-86226
Number of titles published annually: 15 Print

**Volvox Globator Nakladatelstvi &
    vydavatelstvi**
One Pluku 7, 186 00 Prague 8
*Tel:* 224 236 268 *Fax:* 224 217 721
*E-mail:* volvox@volvox.cz
*Web Site:* www.volvox.cz
*Key Personnel*
Contact: Vit Houska
Founded: 1990
ISBN Prefix(es): 80-7207; 80-85769; 80-900906;
    80-901226
*Bookshop(s):* Knihkupectvi VOLVOX GLOBA-
    TOR s literarni kavarnou, Stitneho 16, 130 00
    Praque 3

**Votobia sro+**
Lazecka 70a, 771 00 Olomouc
Mailing Address: PO Box 214, 771 00 Olomouc
*Tel:* (068) 522 46 21 *Fax:* (068) 523 18 90
*E-mail:* votobia@mbox.vol.cz

*Key Personnel*
Contact: Tomas Koudela
Founded: 1991
Subjects: Alternative, Art, Astrology, Occult, Bi-
ography, Computer Science, Cookery, History,
Literature, Literary Criticism, Essays, Music,
Dance, Philosophy, Poetry, Religion - Buddhist
ISBN Prefix(es): 80-7198; 80-85619; 80-85885;
80-900614
*Bookshop(s):* Riegrova 33, 77100 Olomouc

**Vydavatelstvi Cesky Geologicky Ustav**
Klarov 3, 118 21 Prague 1
*Tel:* 257 089 411 *Fax:* 257 531 376
*E-mail:* sekret@cgu.cz
*Web Site:* www.cgu.cz
Founded: 1919
Subjects: Chemistry, Chemical Engineering, Earth
Sciences, Geography, Geology, Physical Sci-
ences
ISBN Prefix(es): 80-7075
*Branch Office(s)*
Leitnerova 22, 658 69 Brno *Tel:* 543 429 200
*Fax:* 543 212 370

**Vysehrad spol sro+**
Vita Nejedleho 15, 130 00 Prague 3
*Tel:* 224 221 703 *Fax:* 224 221 703
*E-mail:* info@ivysehrad.cz
*Web Site:* www.ivysehrad.cz
*Key Personnel*
Dir: Pravomil Novak *E-mail:* novak@ivysehrad.cz
Founded: 1934
Specialize in Christian-oriented books.
Subjects: Ethnicity, Philosophy, Poetry, Pub-
lic Administration, Religion - Other, Science
(General)
ISBN Prefix(es): 80-7021

# Denmark

## General Information

*Capital:* Copenhagen
*Language:* Danish (English and German widely
spoken). Faeroese in the Faroes. Greenlandic in
Greenland
*Religion:* Evangelical Lutheran
*Population:* 5.2 million
*Bank Hours:* 0930-1600 Monday-Friday; open
until 1800 Thursday
*Shop Hours:* 0800 or 0900-1700 or 1730
Monday-Thursday; open until 1900 Friday;
open until 1300 or 1700 Saturday
*Currency:* 100 ore = 1 krone
*Export/Import Information:* Denmark is a member
of the European Union, Faroes and Greenland
are not. No tariff on books except children's
picture-books from non-EU. No import licenses
required. Importers must use longest of alter-
native credit terms in contract, otherwise no
exchange controls. 25% VAT on books.
*Copyright:* UCC, Berne, Florence (see Copyright
Conventions, pg xi)

**Aarhus Universitetsforlag** (Aarhus University
Press)+
Langelandsgade 177, 8200 Aarhus N
*Tel:* 89425370 *Fax:* 89425380
*E-mail:* unipress@au.dk
*Web Site:* www.unipress.dk
*Key Personnel*
Man Dir: Claes Hvidbak *Tel:* 89425377
*E-mail:* ch@unipress.au.dk
Marketing Coordinator & Editor: Sanne Lind
Hansen *Tel:* 89425376 *E-mail:* slh@unipress.
au.dk
Editor: Carsten Fenger-Gren *Tel:* 89425379
*E-mail:* cfg@unipress.au.dk; Anette Juul

Hansen *Tel:* 89425374 *E-mail:* ajh@unipress.
au.dk; Pernille Pennington *Tel:* 89425373
*E-mail:* pp@unipress.au.dk
English Editor: Mary Waters Lund *Tel:* 89425375
*E-mail:* mwl@unipress.au.dk
Founded: 1985
Membership(s): International Association of
Scholarly Publishers.
Subjects: Anthropology, Archaeology, Asian Stud-
ies, Biblical Studies, Drama, Theater, Language
Arts, Linguistics, Literature, Literary Criticism,
Essays, Philosophy, Psychology, Psychiatry,
Religion - Other, Social Sciences, Sociology,
Theology
ISBN Prefix(es): 87-7288; 87-7934
Number of titles published annually: 40 Print
Total Titles: 650 Print
Distributed by David Brown Book Co (USA &
Canada); Lavis Marketing (UK & Ireland)
Distributor for Aalborg University Press; Jutland
Archaeological Society
*Warehouse:* Katrinebjergvej 89B, 8200 Aarhus N

**Academic Press**, see Akademisk Forlag A/S

**Agertofts Forlag A/S+**
Hinbjerg 9, 2690 Karlsunde
*Tel:* 4615 1248 *Fax:* 4615 2404
*Key Personnel*
Man Dir: Ejnar Agertoft
Founded: 1986
ISBN Prefix(es): 87-88014; 87-89970; 87-7878
*Bookshop(s):* The Children's Bookshop, Kob-
magergade 50, 1150 Copenhagen K

**Akademisk Forlag A/S+**
PO Box 54, 1002 Copenhagen K
*Tel:* 33 43 40 80 *Fax:* 33 43 40 99
*E-mail:* akademisk@akademisk.dk
*Web Site:* www.akademisk.dk
*Key Personnel*
Man Dir: Helle Lehrmann Madsen
Marketing: Gitte Kolbaek Jensen
Founded: 1962
Subjects: Economics, Education, Engineering
(General), History, Language Arts, Linguistics,
Law, Medicine, Nursing, Dentistry, Philoso-
phy, Psychology, Psychiatry, Science (General),
Social Sciences, Sociology
ISBN Prefix(es): 87-500
Subsidiaries: Akademisk Forlag

**Alinea A/S+**
Ewaldsgade 9, 2200 Copenhagen N
Mailing Address: Postboks 599, 2200 Copen-
hagen N
*Tel:* 33 69 46 66 *Fax:* 33 69 46 60
*E-mail:* alinea@alinea.dk; skoleservice@alinea.dk
*Web Site:* www.alinea.dk
*Key Personnel*
Administrative Dir: Ebbe Dam Nielsen
*E-mail:* edn@alinea.dk
Founded: 1996
ISBN Prefix(es): 87-23
*Parent Company:* Egmont Aschehoug

**Alma+**
Kaalundsvej 13, 3400 Hillerod
*Tel:* 48 25 54 41 *Fax:* 48 25 20 41
*Key Personnel*
Chief Executive: Susanne Vebel
Founded: 1984
Specialize in picture books.
Subjects: Fiction
ISBN Prefix(es): 87-7243; 87-985145
*Shipping Address:* Stabrand Spedition, Billedvej
8, Frihavnen, 2100 Copenhagen O
*Warehouse:* Jernholmen 29, 2650 Hvidovre
*Orders to:* DBK, Siljangade 2-8, Box 1731, 2300
Copenhagen S

**Forlaget alokke AS+**
Porskaervej 15, Nim, 8700 Horsens
*Tel:* 75671119 *Fax:* 75671074
*E-mail:* alokke@get2net.dk
*Key Personnel*
President: Bertil Toft Hansen
Founded: 1977
Membership(s): Danish Publishers Association.
Subjects: Advertising, English as a Second Lan-
guage
ISBN Prefix(es): 87-592; 87-87777

**Amanda**
Rathsacksvej 7, 1862 Frederiksberg C
*Tel:* 3379-0110 *Fax:* 33790011
*E-mail:* forlag@dansklf.dk
*Key Personnel*
Editorial Dir: Emborg Uhd Gert
ISBN Prefix(es): 87-89537

**Forlaget Apostrof ApS+**
Berggreensgade 24, 2100 Copenhagen O
Mailing Address: Postboks 2580, 2100 Copen-
hagen O
*Tel:* 3920 8420 *Fax:* 3920 8453
*E-mail:* info1@apostrof.dk
*Web Site:* www.apostrof.dk
*Key Personnel*
Publisher: Mia Thestrup *E-mail:* mt@apostrof.dk;
Ole Thestrup *E-mail:* ot@apostrof.dk
Founded: 1980
Specialize in psychology books, children's books
& quality children's books.
Subjects: Psychology, Psychiatry
ISBN Prefix(es): 87-591; 87-88002
Number of titles published annually: 30 Print
Total Titles: 400 Print
*Warehouse:* Dbks Forlagsekspedition, Mimersuej
4, 4600 Koge

**Arkitektens Forlag**
Overgaden oven Vandet 10, 1, 1415 Copenhagen
K
*Tel:* 32836970 *Fax:* 32836940
*E-mail:* eksp@arkfo.dk; red@arkfo.dk
*Web Site:* www.arkfo.dk
*Key Personnel*
Dir: Kim Dirckinck-Holmfeld
Founded: 1949
Subjects: Architecture & Interior Design
ISBN Prefix(es): 87-7407

**Arnkrone Forlaget A/S**
Fuglebakvej 4, 2770 Kastrup K
*Tel:* 31507000 *Fax:* 32522652
*Key Personnel*
Man Dir: J Juul Rasmussen
Founded: 1941
Subjects: Art, Ethnicity, Medicine, Nursing, Den-
tistry
ISBN Prefix(es): 87-87007

**Aschehoug Dansk Forlag A/S+**
Division of Egmont
8, Landemaerket, 1119 Copenhagen K
Mailing Address: PO Box 2179, 1017 Copen-
hagen K
*Tel:* 33305522; 33305822 *Fax:* 33305823
*E-mail:* info@ash.egmont.com
*Web Site:* www.aschehoug.dk
*Key Personnel*
Man Dir: Henrik Kristensen
Publishing Dir: Anette Wad
Founded: 1977
Subjects: Biography, Cookery, Fiction, Health,
Nutrition, How-to, Maritime
ISBN Prefix(es): 87-11; 87-429; 87-7512
Total Titles: 900 Print
Imprints: Sesam

**Atuakkiorfik A/S Det Greenland Publishers+**
Hans Egedesvej 3, 3900 Nuuk (Greenland)

Mailing Address: Postboks 840, 3900 Nuuk
(Greenland)
*Tel:* 32 21 22 *Fax:* 32 25 00
*E-mail:* henri@atuakkiorfik.gl
*Web Site:* www.atuakkiorfik.gl
*Key Personnel*
Man Dir: Nukaaraq Eugenius
Manager: Ove-Karl Berthelsen
Editor: Pauline Abelsen *E-mail:* pa@atuakkiorfik.
gl
Founded: 1956
Also acts as educational book publisher, public
relations.
Subjects: Art, Education, Fiction, Nonfiction
(General)
ISBN Prefix(es): 87-558
Number of titles published annually: 35 Print

**Bibelselskabets Forlag og Det Kgl Vajsenhus'**
**Forlag,** see Det Danske Bibelselskab

**Bierman og Bierman I/S**
Vestergade 126, 7200 Grindsted
*Tel:* 75 32 02 88 *Fax:* 75 32 15 48
*E-mail:* mail@bierman.dk
*Web Site:* www.bierman.dk
*Key Personnel*
Man Dir: Bo Lorentzen; Tom Selmer-Petersen
Founded: 1968
Subjects: Management

**Bogan's Forlag+**
8, Kastaniebakken, 3540 Lynge
*Tel:* 42 18 80 55 *Fax:* 42 18 87 69
*E-mail:* bogan@tele.dk
*Key Personnel*
Owner & Publisher: Evan Bogan
Founded: 1974
Subjects: Astrology, Occult, Health, Nutrition,
Humor, Nonfiction (General), Religion - Other,
Science (General)
ISBN Prefix(es): 87-87533; 87-7466; 87-7525
Number of titles published annually: 30 Print
Total Titles: 250 Print
Imprints: My Best Book
*Warehouse:* DBK, Siljangade 6, 2300 Copen-
hagen S *Tel:* 32697788 *Fax:* 32697789

**Bogfabrikken Fakta ApS**
Jacob Dannefaerdsvej 6 B/1, 1973 Frederiksberg
C
*Tel:* 3537 3533 *Fax:* 3537 3299
*E-mail:* bm@kd-consult.dk
Subjects: Crafts, Games, Hobbies, Environmental
Studies, Fashion, Nonfiction (General), Science
(General), Transportation
ISBN Prefix(es): 87-7771
*Parent Company:* K D - Consult A/S

**Bogklubben for Laeger,** *imprint of* Gyldendalske
Boghandel - Nordisk Forlag A/S

**Bogklubben for Sygeplejersker,** *imprint of*
Gyldendalske Boghandel - Nordisk Forlag A/S

**Bonnier Publications A/S+**
130 Strandboulevarden, 2100 Copenhagen OE
*Tel:* 3917 2000 *Fax:* 3929 0199
*Web Site:* www.bonnierpublications.com; www.
bonnier.dk
*Key Personnel*
President & Chief Executive Officer: Michael
Cordsen
Executive Vice President: Jens Henneberg
Vice President Marketing: Jesper Buchvald
Vice President Finance: Morten Kaiser
Sales Manager: Lars Guldager
Founded: 1959
Subjects: Criminology, Fiction, Military Science,
Western Fiction
ISBN Prefix(es): 82-535

*Parent Company:* Bonnier AB
*Branch Office(s)*
Bonnier Julkaisut Oy, 71 Valitalontie, 00660
Helsinki, Finland *Tel:* (09) 756 770 *Fax:* (09)
756 774 00
Bonnier Publications International AS, PB 433
Sentrum, 0107 Oslo, Norway *Tel:* 2240 1200
Bonnier Responsmedier AB, 2 A Bodalsvagen,
181 04 Lidingo, Sweden *Tel:* (08) 731 2940
*Fax:* (08) 731 0022 *Web Site:* www.brm.se

**Bonniers Specialmagasiner A/S Bogdivisionen+**
Strandboulevarden 130, 2100 Copenhagen 0
*Tel:* 39295500 *Fax:* 39172300
*Telex:* 15712 bonmag dk
*Key Personnel*
Publisher: Jette Juliusson
Founded: 1989
Subjects: Fiction, Nonfiction (General)
ISBN Prefix(es): 87-7741
*Parent Company:* Bonnier Publication A/S
Subsidiaries: Autour Du Fil, Editions Bonnier;
Bonniers Blade OG Boker
*Book Club(s):* Bogklubben 12 Boger A/S (jointly
owned with Lindhardt Ringhof) & Munksgaard
*Warehouse:* Bonniers Boger, Islevdalvej 148,
2610 Rodovre

**Borgens Forlag A/S+**
Valbygardsvej 33, 2500 Valby
*Tel:* 36 15 36 15 *Fax:* 36 15 36 16
*E-mail:* post@borgen.dk
*Web Site:* www.borgen.dk
*Key Personnel*
Man Dir: Niels Borgen *E-mail:* nborgen@borgen.
dk
Editorial Dir: Helle Borgen *E-mail:* hborgen@
borgen.dk
Production: Dennis Stovring *E-mail:* dstovring@
borgen.dk
Rights & Permissions Manager: Mette Nymark
*E-mail:* mnymark@borgen.dk
Founded: 1948
Subjects: Alternative, Animals, Pets, Art, Astrol-
ogy, Occult, Behavioral Sciences, Child Care
& Development, Crafts, Games, Hobbies, Edu-
cation, Environmental Studies, Fiction, Health,
Nutrition, How-to, Human Relations, Humor,
Literature, Literary Criticism, Essays, Music,
Dance, Nonfiction (General), Philosophy, Po-
etry, Psychology, Psychiatry, Regional Interests,
Religion - Other, Self-Help
ISBN Prefix(es): 87-418; 87-21; 87-7895; 87-
982973
Number of titles published annually: 250 Print; 5
Audio
Total Titles: 2,000 Print; 10 Audio
Subsidiaries: Hekla; Maaholms Forlag; Sommer
& Sorensen; Forlaget Vindrose A/S
*Book Club(s):* Borgens Bogklub
*Orders to:* DBK-Logistik Service, Mimersvej 4,
4600 Koge

**Bornegudstjeneste-Forlaget+**
25 Korskaervej, 7000 Fredericia
*Tel:* 75934455 *Fax:* 75924275
*E-mail:* lohse@imh.dk
*Key Personnel*
Dir: Finn Andersen
Founded: 1868
ISBN Prefix(es): 87-87828; 87-89682

**Borsen Forlag**
Montergade 19, 1140 Copenhagen K
*Tel:* 33 32 01 02 *Fax:* 33 12 24 45
*E-mail:* redaktionen@borsen.dk
*Web Site:* www.borsen.dk
*Key Personnel*
Editor-in-Chief & Chief Executive Officer: Leif
Beck Fallesen
Chief Sub-Editor: Bent Sorenson

Subjects: Management
ISBN Prefix(es): 87-7553; 87-7664; 87-7901; 87-
88184; 87-90790; 87-91157

**Ca Luna Forlaget+**
Frischsvej 40a, 1 sal, 8600 Silkeborg
*Tel:* 86 82 86 88; 26 20 24 68 *Fax:* 86 82 86 64
*E-mail:* caluna@caluna.dk
*Web Site:* www.caluna.dk
Founded: 1995
Specialize in New Age books.
Subjects: New Age
ISBN Prefix(es): 87-90312
Total Titles: 10 Print

**Carit Andersens Forlag A/S**
Subsidiary of Mercantila Publishers A/S
18 Upsalagade, 2100 Copenhagen
*Tel:* 35436222 *Fax:* 35435151
*E-mail:* info@caritandersen.dk
*Web Site:* www.caritandersen.dk
*Key Personnel*
Publisher: Erik Albrechtsen
Founded: 1982
ISBN Prefix(es): 87-424

**Forlaget Carlsen A/S+**
Krogshojvej 32, 2880 Bagsvaerd
*Tel:* 4444 3233 *Fax:* 4444 3633
*E-mail:* carlsen@carlsen.dk
*Web Site:* www.carlsen.dk
*Key Personnel*
Man Dir: Jesper Holm
Founded: 1942
Subjects: Humor
ISBN Prefix(es): 87-562; 87-456; 87-7529
Number of titles published annually: 300 Print; 3
CD-ROM; 75 Audio
Total Titles: 2,000 Print; 8 CD-ROM; 120 Audio
*Parent Company:* Bonniers Forlagene A/S
*Ultimate Parent Company:* Bonnier Media ATS
Imprints: Carlsen Comics
Subsidiaries: Carlsen Book Production
*Book Club(s):* Bogklubben Rasmus & Den Fak-
tyrlige Boklub
*Warehouse:* Holme Forlags Service, Lise Lundvej
4, 4791 Borre *Tel:* 55812252 *Fax:* 55 812078
Holme Forlag Service APS
Semil Forlag NE A/S

**Carlsen Comics,** *imprint of* Forlaget Carlsen A/S

**Forlaget Centrum** (Central Publishers)+
Imprint of Bonnier
St Kongensgade 92, 3, 1264 Copenhagen K
*Tel:* 33 32 12 06 *Fax:* 33 32 12 07
*E-mail:* info@forlaget-centrum.dk
*Web Site:* www.forlaget-centrum.dk
*Key Personnel*
Publisher: Lisbeth Moller-Madsen
Founded: 1979
Subjects: Fiction, Nonfiction (General)
ISBN Prefix(es): 87-583; 87-87123; 87-87810

**Cicero-Chr Erichsens**
Vester Voldgade 83, 2, 1552 Copenhagen V
*Tel:* 3316-0308 *Fax:* 33160307
*E-mail:* info@cicero.dk
*Web Site:* www.cicero.dk *Cable:* BOGERICH
*Key Personnel*
Dir: Alis Caspersen; Niels Gudbergsen
Editor: Marie Louise Valeur Jaques; Anders Mejl-
bjerg
Founded: 1902
Subjects: Fiction, Mysteries
ISBN Prefix(es): 87-7714; 87-555

**Copenhagen,** *imprint of* Spektrum
Forlagsaktieselskab

**Copenhagen Business School Press**
Virginiavej 11, 2000 Copenhagen F

*Tel:* 38153960 *Fax:* 38153962
*E-mail:* cbspress@cbs.dk
*Web Site:* www.cbspress.dk
*Key Personnel*
Man Dir & Marketing Manager: Axel Schultz-
Nielsen *E-mail:* asn.press@cbs.dk
Marketing Coordinator: Hanne Thorninger Ipsen
*E-mail:* hti.press@cbs.dk

**Dafolo Forlag+**
Division of Dafolo A/S
Dafolo A/S, Suderbovej 22-24, 9900 Frederik-
shavn
*Tel:* 9620 6666 *Fax:* 9842 9711
*E-mail:* dafolo@dafolo.dk
*Web Site:* www.dafolo.dk; www.dafaloforlag.dk
*Key Personnel*
Man Dir: Michael Schelde *E-mail:* ms@dafolo.dk
Administrative Dir: Jorgen Ulrik Jensen
Founded: 1960
Specialize in elementary textbooks.
Subjects: Education, Foreign Countries, History
ISBN Prefix(es): 87-7794; 87-7281; 87-7320; 87-
7846; 87-89460; 87-982569; 87-984669

**Dahlgaard Media BV**
c/o KD - Consults A/S, Jakob Dannefaerds Vej
6B, 1973 Frederiksberg C
*Tel:* 3537 3533 *Fax:* 3537 3299
Subsidiaries: Bogfabrikken Fakta ApS

**The Danish Literature Centre**
Kongens Nytorv 3, 1022 Copenhagen
Mailing Address: Postboks 9012, 1022 Copen-
hagen
*Tel:* 33744500 *Fax:* 33744565
*E-mail:* danlit@danlit.dk
*Web Site:* www.literaturenet.dk
*Key Personnel*
Chief Sub-Editor: Annette Bach
Founded: 1990
Promotion of Danish literature abroad & founda-
tion for translation grants.
Subjects: Drama, Theater, Fiction, Literature, Lit-
erary Criticism, Essays, Poetry

**Danmarks Forvaltningshojskole Forlaget**
Lindevangs Alle 6-12, 2000 Frederiksberg
*Tel:* 38 14 52 00 *Fax:* 38 14 53 45
*E-mail:* dhf@dhfnet.dk; dspa@dspa.dk
*Web Site:* www.dkdfh.dk
*Key Personnel*
Dir: Inge Maerkdahl
ISBN Prefix(es): 87-7392

**Dansk Biblioteks Center** (Danish Bibliographic
Centre)+
Tempovej 7-11, 2750 Ballerup
*Tel:* 44 86 77 77 *Fax:* 44 86 78 91
*E-mail:* dbc@dbc.dk
*Web Site:* www.dbc.dk
*Key Personnel*
Man Dir: Mogens Brabrand Jensen *Tel:* 44 86 77
00 *E-mail:* mbj@dbc.dk
Editor: Kirsten Waneck *E-mail:* kwh@dbc.dk
Secretary: Ann Sogaard Jensen *E-mail:* aj@dbc.
dk
Founded: 1991
Subjects: Library & Information Sciences
ISBN Prefix(es): 87-552

**Dansk Historisk Handbogsforlag ApS**
Buddingevej 87 A, 2800 Lyngby
*Tel:* 45 93 48 00 *Fax:* 45 93 47 47
*E-mail:* genos@worldonline.dk
*Key Personnel*
Owner, Man Dir: Henning Jensen
Founded: 1976
Subjects: Biography, Ethnicity, Genealogy, His-
tory, Law, Regional Interests
ISBN Prefix(es): 87-85207; 87-88742; 87-90222

*Parent Company:* Tordenskjold Forlag ApS
Subsidiaries: Juridisk Forlag

**Dansk Psykologisk Forlag**
Kongevejen 155, 2830 Virum
*Tel:* 3538 1665 *Fax:* 3538 1655
*E-mail:* salg@dpf.dk; dk-psych@dpf.dk
*Web Site:* www.dpf.dk
*Key Personnel*
Man Dir: Hans Gerhardt *E-mail:* hg@dpf.dk
Chief Editor: Lone Berg Jensen *E-mail:* lbj@dpf.
dk
Membership(s): European Test Publishers Group.
Subjects: Psychology, Psychiatry
ISBN Prefix(es): 87-7706; 87-87580

**Dansk Teknologisk Institut, Forlaget**
Gregersensvej, 2630 Taastrup
*Tel:* 42 99 66 11 *Fax:* 42 99 54 36
*E-mail:* info@teknologisk.dk
*Telex:* 33416 ti dk *Cable:* TEKNOLOGISK
*Key Personnel*
Contact: Ulrik Spanager *Tel:* 72 20 20 07
*E-mail:* ulrik.spanager@teknologisk.dk
Subjects: Crafts, Games, Hobbies, Labor, Indus-
trial Relations
ISBN Prefix(es): 87-7511; 87-7756

**Det Danske Bibelselskab+**
50 Frederiksborggade, 1360 Copenhagen K
*Tel:* 33 12 78 35 *Fax:* 33 93 21 50
*E-mail:* bibelselskabet@bibelselskabet.dk
*Web Site:* www.bibelselskabet.dk
*Key Personnel*
General Secretary: Rev Tine Lindhardt
Publishing Secretary International Rights: Lene
Trap-Lind *E-mail:* lene@bibelselskab.dk
Founded: 1814
ISBN Prefix(es): 87-7523; 87-7524

**Djof Publishing Jurist-og Okonomforbundets
Forlag**
17, Lyngbyvej, 2100 Copenhagen O
Mailing Address: Postboks 2702, 2100 Copen-
hagen O
*Tel:* 39 13 55 00 *Fax:* 39 13 55 55
*E-mail:* fl@djoef.dk
*Web Site:* www.djoef-forlag.dk
*Key Personnel*
President: Rolf Tvedt
Founded: 1959
Membership(s): IUS-Nordica, Nordic Legal Pub-
lishers Group.
Subjects: Economics, Finance, Law, Social Sci-
ences, Sociology
ISBN Prefix(es): 87-574; 87-629
Subsidiaries: Handelshojskolens Forlag; Nyt Ju-
ridisk Forlag
Distributed by Enfield Publishing (US)
*Orders to:* Enfield Publishing (US)

**Egmont International Holding A/S**
Vognmagergade 11, 1148 Copenhagen K
*Tel:* 33 30 55 50 *Fax:* 33 32 19 02
*E-mail:* egmont@egmont.com
*Web Site:* www.egmont.com
*Key Personnel*
Vice President, Corporate Communications:
Sascha Amarasinha *Tel:* 33 30 51 40
*E-mail:* sas@egmont.com
ISBN Prefix(es): 87-982380

**Egmont Lademann A/S**, see Aschehoug Dansk
Forlag A/S

**Egmont Serieforlaget A/S**
Vognmagergade 11, 1148 Copenhagen K
*Tel:* 70 20 50 35 *Fax:* 33 30 57 60; 36 18 58 90
*E-mail:* abonnement@tsf.egmont.com
*Web Site:* www.serieforlaget.dk

*Key Personnel*
Marketing Dir: Jesper Christiansen
ISBN Prefix(es): 87-89601

**Christian Ejlers' Forlag aps+**
Solvgade 38/3, 1307 Copenhagen K
Mailing Address: Postboks 2228, 1307 Copen-
hagen K
*Tel:* 3312 2114 *Fax:* 3312 2884
*E-mail:* liber@ce-publishers.dk
*Web Site:* www.ejlers.dk
*Key Personnel*
Publisher: Christian Ejlers
Founded: 1967
Subjects: Architecture & Interior Design, Art,
Biography, Cookery, Education, History, Law,
Nonfiction (General)
ISBN Prefix(es): 87-7241
Number of titles published annually: 20 Print; 1
CD-ROM; 1 Audio
Total Titles: 100 Print; 3 CD-ROM; 3 Audio

**FADL's Forlag A/S+**
Blegdamsvej 30, 2200 Copenhagen N
*Tel:* 35 35 62 87 *Fax:* 35 36 62 29
*E-mail:* forlag@fadl.dk
*Web Site:* forlag.fadl.dk
*Key Personnel*
Man Dir: Jan Frejlev *E-mail:* jan@fadl.dk
Founded: 1962
Membership(s): STM.
Subjects: Biological Sciences, Medicine, Nursing,
Dentistry
ISBN Prefix(es): 87-7437; 87-7749

**Forlaget for Faglitteratur A/S**
Vandkunsten 6, 1467 Copenhagen K
*Tel:* 33137900 *Fax:* 33145156
Subjects: Medicine, Nursing, Dentistry, Technol-
ogy
ISBN Prefix(es): 87-573

**Faktor Funf**, *imprint of* Kaleidoscope Publishers
Ltd

**Ficcion Espanola**, *imprint of* Kaleidoscope
Publishers Ltd

**Fiction Factory**, *imprint of* Kaleidoscope
Publishers Ltd

**Fiction Francaise**, *imprint of* Kaleidoscope
Publishers Ltd

**Foreningen af danske Laegestuderendes
Forlag**, see FADL's Forlag A/S

**Forlaget Forum** (Forum Publishers)
Imprint of Gyldendalske Boghandel - Nordisk
Forlag A/S
Kobmagergade 62 4 sal, 1019 Copenhagen K
Mailing Address: PO Box 2252, 1019 Copen-
hagen K
*Tel:* 33411830 *Fax:* 33411831
*E-mail:* kontakt@forlagetforum.dk
*Web Site:* www.forlagetforum.dk *Cable:*
FORUMBOOKS COPENHAGEN
*Key Personnel*
Man Dir: Werner Svendsen
Editor, Juvenile & Children: Lotte Nyholm
Founded: 1940
Subjects: Fiction, History, Humor, Mysteries
ISBN Prefix(es): 87-553
Divisions: Spektrum Publishers

**Forum Publishers**, *imprint of* Gyldendalske
Boghandel - Nordisk Forlag A/S

**Fremad A/S**, *imprint of* Gyldendalske Boghandel
- Nordisk Forlag A/S

**Fremad A/S**
Imprint of Gyldendalske Boghandel - Nordisk
  Forlage A/S
Kobmagergade 62, 1150 Copenhagen K
*Tel:* 33 41 18 10 *Fax:* 33 41 18 11
*Web Site:* www.fremad.dk *Cable:* Bogfremad
*Key Personnel*
Man Dir: Niels Kolle E-mail: niels_koelle@
  gyldendal.dk
Founded: 1912
Subjects: Astronomy, Business, Child Care &
  Development, Economics, Fiction, Health, Nu-
  trition, History, Language Arts, Linguistics,
  Mathematics, Science (General), Social Sci-
  ences, Sociology, Political science
ISBN Prefix(es): 87-557
*Bookshop(s):* Boghandelen Fremad, Fred-
  erikssundsvej 168, Bronshoj, 2700 Copenhagen

**J Frimodt Forlag+**
Korskaervej 25, 7000 Fredericia
*Tel:* 75934455 *Fax:* 75924275
*E-mail:* lohse@imh.dk
*Key Personnel*
Man Dir: Finn Andersen
Subjects: Fiction, Religion - Protestant
ISBN Prefix(es): 87-7446
*Associate Companies:* Lohses Forlag

**Gads Forlag**
Klosterstraede 9, 1157 Copenhagen K
*Tel:* 7766 6000 *Fax:* 7766 6001
*E-mail:* kuneservice@gads-forlag.dk
*Web Site:* www.gads-forlag.dk *Cable:* BOGGAD
*Key Personnel*
Man Dir: Peter Hartman
International Rights: Lars Boesgaard
Founded: 1855
Subjects: Biological Sciences, Cookery, Crafts,
  Games, Hobbies, Economics, Education, En-
  glish as a Second Language, Environmental
  Studies, Gardening, Plants, History, Mathe-
  matics, Natural History, Nonfiction (General),
  Physics, Travel
ISBN Prefix(es): 87-12; 87-13; 87-557
*Associate Companies:* Alinea A/S; Systime A/S
*Bookshop(s):* G E C Gads Boglader A/S GADs,
  Antikuariat Fiolstr 31-33, Copenhagen

**Forlaget GMT+**
Havet 66 A, 8585 Glaesborg
*Tel:* 86386095
*Key Personnel*
Publishers: Hans Jorn Christensen; Erik Bjorn
  Olsen
Founded: 1971
Subjects: Education, Fiction, Government, Polit-
  ical Science, History, Philosophy, Psychology,
  Psychiatry, Social Sciences, Sociology
ISBN Prefix(es): 87-7330

**Greenland Publishers**, see Atuakkiorfik A/S Det
  Greenland Publishers

**Grevas Forlag**
Auningvej 33, Sdr Kastrup, 8544 Morke
*Tel:* 86997065 *Fax:* 86997265
*E-mail:* info@grevas.dk; skrodhoj@worldonline.
  dk
*Web Site:* www.grevas.dk
*Key Personnel*
Sales & Man Dir: Luise Hemmer Pihl
Founded: 1966
Subjects: Art, Biography, Fiction, Poetry
ISBN Prefix(es): 87-7235

**Gyldendalske Boghandel - Nordisk Forlag A/S**
Klareboderne 3, 1001 Copenhagen K
Mailing Address: PO Box 11, 1001 Copenhagen
  K
*Tel:* 33755555 *Fax:* 33755556

*E-mail:* gyldendal@gyldendal.dk
*Web Site:* www.gyldendal.dk
*Telex:* 15887 Gyldaldk *Cable:*
  GYLDENDALSKE
*Key Personnel*
Dir: Per Hedeman
Man Dir: Stig Andersen
Literary Dir: Johannes Riis
Marketing Manager: Tine Smedegaard Andersen
Sales Dir: Jan H Schmith
Rights & Permissions, Juveniles: Louise Langhoff
  Koch
Rights & Permissions, Adult Fiction & Nonfic-
  tion: Esthi Kunz; Ingelise Korsholm
Founded: 1770
Subjects: Art, Biography, Education, Fiction, His-
  tory, How-to, Medicine, Nursing, Dentistry,
  Music, Dance, Philosophy, Poetry, Psychology,
  Psychiatry, Science (General), Social Sciences,
  Sociology
ISBN Prefix(es): 87-01; 87-00; 87-02
Imprints: Bogklubben for Laeger; Bogklubben
  for Sygeplejersker; Forum Publishers; Fremad
  A/S; Host & Son Publishers Ltd; Munksgaard
  Danmark; Paedagogisk Bogklub; Hans Re-
  itzels Forlag; Rosinante; Samlerens Forlag A/S;
  Spektrum Forlagsaktieselskab
Subsidiaries: G-B-Forlagene A/S; Gyldendal
  Akademisk A/S; Gyldendals Akademiske
  Bogklubber
*Book Club(s):* Gyldendals Baby Bogklub;
  Gyldendals Bogklub; Gyldendals Bornebog-
  lub; Gyldendals Junior Bogklub; Klassikere
  (Gyldendals Bogklubber); Laerer Bogklubben;
  Samlerens Bogklub

**P Haase & Sons Forlag A/S+**
Loevstraede 8, 2 tv, 1152 Copenhagen K
*Tel:* 33 18 10 80 *Fax:* 33 11 59 59
*E-mail:* haase@haase.dk
*Web Site:* www.haase.dk
*Key Personnel*
Man Dir: Michael Haase E-mail: mh@haase.dk
Foreign Rights: Nina Jensen E-mail: nj@haase.dk
Founded: 1877
Subjects: Education, Fiction, Health, Nutrition,
  Humor, Maritime, Nonfiction (General)
ISBN Prefix(es): 87-559
Imprints: Rasmus Naver

**Edition Wilhelm Hansen AS**
Bornholmsgade 1, 1266 Copenhagen K
*Tel:* 33 11 78 88 *Fax:* 33 14 81 78
*E-mail:* ewh@ewh.dk
*Web Site:* www.ewh.dk; www.wilhelm-hansen.dk
  *Cable:* MUSIKHANSEN
*Key Personnel*
Man Dir: Tine Birger Christensen E-mail: tbc@
  ewh.dk
Sales: Tina Andersen *Tel:* 33 70 15 05
  *E-mail:* ta@ewh.dk
Promotion: Marlene S Ottosen *Tel:* 33 70 15 11
  *E-mail:* mo@ewh.dk; Eline W Sigfusson
  *Tel:* 33 70 15 09 *E-mail:* ews@ewh.dk
Production (education): Rene Jensen *Tel:* 33 70
  15 06 *E-mail:* rj@ewh.dk
Founded: 1857
Subjects: Art, Education, Music, Dance
ISBN Prefix(es): 87-7455; 87-598
*Parent Company:* Music Sales Ltd, 8/9 Frith St,
  London W1V 5TZ, United Kingdom

**Hekla Forlag+**
Valbygaardsvej 33, 2500 Valby
*Tel:* 36 15 36 15 *Fax:* 36 15 36 16
*E-mail:* post@borgen.dk
*Web Site:* www.borgen.dk
*Key Personnel*
Publisher: Helle Borgen
Founded: 1979
Subjects: Fiction, Nonfiction (General)
ISBN Prefix(es): 87-7474

Number of titles published annually: 5 Print
Total Titles: 20 Print
*Parent Company:* Borgens Forlag A/S
*Orders to:* DBK-Logistik Service, Mimersvej 4,
  4600 Koge

**Hernovs Forlag+**
Norrebakken 25, 2820 Gentofte
*Tel:* 32963314 *Fax:* 32960446
*E-mail:* admin@hernov.dk
*Web Site:* www.hernov.dk
*Key Personnel*
Managing Editor: Else Hernov
Founded: 1941
Membership(s): Independent Danish Publishers.
Subjects: Fiction, Nonfiction (General)
ISBN Prefix(es): 87-7215; 87-590
Subsidiaries: Vinimport ApS
*Warehouse:* DBK-Dansk Boghandleres Kommis-
  sionsanstalt, Siljangade 6, 2300 Copenhagen
  S

**Forlaget Hjulet**
Bakkegardsalle 9 kld, 1804 Frederiksberg C
*Tel:* 31310900 *Fax:* 31310900
*E-mail:* aloa@gte2net.dk
*Key Personnel*
Contact: Vagn Plenge
Founded: 1976
Subjects: Cookery, Developing Countries, Fiction,
  Literature, Literary Criticism, Essays, Travel
ISBN Prefix(es): 87-87403; 87-89213
Subsidiaries: Foerlaget Hjule

**Holkenfeldt 3**
Fuglevadsvej 71, 2800 Lyngby
*Tel:* 931221 *Fax:* 938241
*E-mail:* holkenfeldt@mail.dk
*Key Personnel*
Man Dir: Kay Holkenfeldt
Subjects: Nonfiction (General)
ISBN Prefix(es): 87-90368; 87-7720; 87-89906;
  87-91014

**Host & Son Publishers Ltd**, *imprint of*
  Gyldendalske Boghandel - Nordisk Forlag A/S

**Host & Son Publishers Ltd+**
Imprint of Gyldendalske Boghandel - Nordisk
  Forlag A/S
Kobmagergade 62, 1018 Copenhagen
Mailing Address: PO Box 2212, 1018 Copen-
  hagen K
*Tel:* 33382888 *Fax:* 33382898
*E-mail:* host@euroconnect.dk *Cable:*
  BOOKHOST
*Key Personnel*
Man Dir: Erik C Lindgren
Editorial, Reference Books: Kirsten Fasmer; Hans
  Kristian Harbo
Editorial, Juvenile Books: Christel Amundsen
Editorial, Young Adults: Anne Morch-Hansen;
  Nanna Gyldenkaerne
Founded: 1836
Subjects: Crafts, Games, Hobbies, Environmental
  Studies, Fiction, History, Regional Interests
ISBN Prefix(es): 87-14
*Warehouse:* NBC, Bokvej 10-12, 4690 Haslev

**Forlaget Hovedland+**
Elsdyrvej 4, 8270 Hojbjerg
*Tel:* 86276500 *Fax:* 86276537
*E-mail:* mail@hovedland.dk
*Web Site:* www.hovedland.dk
*Key Personnel*
Publisher: Steen Piper
Founded: 1984
Subjects: Biography, Crafts, Games, Hobbies,
  Economics, Environmental Studies, Fiction,
  History, Humor, Literature, Literary Criticism,
  Essays, Mysteries, Nonfiction (General), Phi-

losophy, Self-Help, Social Sciences, Sociology, Sports, Athletics, Theology
ISBN Prefix(es): 87-7739; 87-88589

**IBIS**
Norrebrogade 68B, 2200 Copenhagen N
*Tel:* 35358788 *Fax:* 35350696
*E-mail:* ibis@ibis.dk
*Web Site:* www.ibis.dk
*Telex:* 1585 0 wus dk
*Key Personnel*
Editorial Dir, Rights & Permissions: Virginia Allen Jensen
Founded: 1972
ISBN Prefix(es): 87-87804
*Parent Company:* International Children's Book Service (ICBS)
*Branch Office(s)*
Odensegade 4B, 8000, Aarhus C *Tel:* 86181412
*E-mail:* aarhus@ibis.dk

**Ingenioeren/Boger** (Engineering Books Danish Technical Press)+
Ingerslevsgade 44, 1705 Copenhagen V
*Tel:* 63 15 17 00 *Fax:* 63 15 17 33
*E-mail:* info@nyttf.dk
*Web Site:* www.nyttf.dk
*Key Personnel*
Manager, Book Dept: Henrik Larsen *E-mail:* hl@nyttf.dk
Founded: 1948
Subjects: Business, Computer Science, Engineering (General)
ISBN Prefix(es): 87-571; 87-88939; 87-987965
Number of titles published annually: 80 Print; 4 CD-ROM; 3 E-Book
*Parent Company:* Erhvervsskolernes Forlag A/S
*Book Club(s):* Ingenioeren/Bogklubben

**Interpresse A/S+**
Ronnegade 1/5, 2100 Copenhagen
*Tel:* 39160200 *Fax:* 39272402
*Web Site:* www.interpresse.dk
*Key Personnel*
Man Dir: Haahon W Isachsen
Founded: 1954
Subjects: Fiction, Film, Video, Humor, Comic books
ISBN Prefix(es): 87-456; 87-7529; 87-90008
*Parent Company:* Semic International AB, Sweden
*Shipping Address:* Bent Bagger Spedition, Peder Skrams Gade 11, 1054 Copenhagen K

**IT-og Telestyrelsen**
Holsteinsgade 63, 2100 Copenhagen 0
*Tel:* 35 45 00 00 *Fax:* 35 45 00 10; 33 37 92 99
*E-mail:* itst@itst.dk
*Web Site:* www.denmark.dk; www.si.dk
*Key Personnel*
Head, Media Center: Hugo Prestegaard
Also acts as agent for official government publications.
Subjects: Environmental Studies, Government, Political Science, Library & Information Sciences, Public Administration
ISBN Prefix(es): 87-503; 87-601

**Jespersen og Pio**, see Lindhardt og Ringhof Forlag A/S

**Kaleidoscope Publishers Ltd+**
3 Klareboderne, 1001 Copenhagen K
*Tel:* 33755555 *Fax:* 33755544
*E-mail:* gujbt@gyldendal.dk
*Web Site:* www.kaleidoscope.publishers.dk; www.gyldendal.dk *Cable:* GYLDENDALSKE
*Key Personnel*
Publisher: Jens Bendtsen *Tel:* 33755509
*E-mail:* jens_bendtsen@gyldendal.dk
Founded: 1983

Subjects: Education, English as a Second Language, Film, Video, Language Arts, Linguistics, Literature, Literary Criticism, Essays
ISBN Prefix(es): 87-7565; 87-431
*Parent Company:* Gyldendal
Imprints: Faktor Funf; Ficcion Espanola; Fiction Factory; Fiction Francaise
Subsidiaries: Fiction Factory International Ltd/APS
*Warehouse:* Baekvej
Gyldendal
Haslev

**Forlaget Klematis A/S+**
Ostre Skovvej 1, 8240 Risskov
*Tel:* 86175455 *Fax:* 86175959
*E-mail:* klematis@klematis.dk; production@klematis.dk
*Web Site:* www.klematis.dk
*Key Personnel*
President: Claus Dalby
Editor: Mette Jorgensen
Founded: 1987
Specialize in children's books, craft, fiction & nonfiction.
Subjects: Crafts, Games, Hobbies, Fiction, Nonfiction (General)
ISBN Prefix(es): 87-7721; 87-7905
*Shipping Address:* JEURO Danmark, Baggeskaervej 6, 7400 Herning, Contact: M Stausholm
*Warehouse:* D B K, Siljangade 6-8, 2300 Copenhagen S

**Kraks Forlag AS**
Virumgardsvej 21, 2830 Virum
*Tel:* 95 65 00 *Fax:* 95 65 55
*E-mail:* krak@krak.dk
*Web Site:* www.krak.dk
*Key Personnel*
Administration Dir: Ove Leth-Sorensen
Founded: 1770
Subjects: Regional Interests
ISBN Prefix(es): 87-7225

**Lindhardt og Ringhof Forlag A/S+**
Frederiksborggade 1, 1360 Copenhagen K
*Tel:* 33 69 50 00 *Fax:* 33695001
*E-mail:* lr@lrforlag.dk
*Web Site:* www.lrforlag.dk *Cable:* ELETEREDIT
*Key Personnel*
Dir: Morten Hesseldahl
Dir, Sales & Marketing: Michael Bach-Marklund
Founded: 1971
Subjects: Fiction, Nonfiction (General)
ISBN Prefix(es): 87-595; 87-7560
*Parent Company:* Bonniers & Stockholm
Divisions: Jespersen og Pio
*U.S. Office(s):* Maria B Campbell Associates, United States
*Book Club(s):* Bogklubben 12 Boger (part owner)

**Lohse Forlag+**
Korskaervej 25, 7000 Fredericia
*Tel:* 7593 4455 *Fax:* 7592 4275
*E-mail:* lohse@imh.dk
*Web Site:* www.lohse.dk
*Key Personnel*
Dir: Finn Andersen
Founded: 1868
Subjects: Biblical Studies, Fiction, Religion - Other
ISBN Prefix(es): 87-564
*Associate Companies:* J Frimodts Forlag

**Mallings ApS**
Forlaget Carlsen, Krogshujvej 32, 2880 Bagsvaerd
*Tel:* 4444 3233 *Fax:* 4444 3633
*E-mail:* carlsen@carlsen.dk
*Telex:* 15817 Jmco *Cable:* Mallingbook

*Key Personnel*
Man Dir, Editorial, Rights & Permissions: Joachim Malling
Owner: Hannah Malling
Production: Michael Malling
Publicity: Dorthe Malling
Founded: 1975
Subjects: Education
ISBN Prefix(es): 87-7333

**Mellemfolkeligt Samvirke+**
Borgergade 14, 1300 Copenhagen K
*Tel:* 7731 0000 *Fax:* 7731 0101
*E-mail:* ms@ms.dk
*Web Site:* www.ms.dk
Subjects: Developing Countries, Education, Ethnicity, Foreign Countries, Publishing & Book Trade Reference, Travel
ISBN Prefix(es): 87-7028; 87-7907
*Bookshop(s):* Verdensbutikken *E-mail:* butik@ms.dk *Web Site:* www.verdensbutikken.dk

**Mercantila Publishers A/S**
18 Upsalagade, 2100 Copenhagen
*Tel:* 35436222 *Fax:* 35435151
*E-mail:* info@mercantila.dk
*Web Site:* www.gtft.dk
*Key Personnel*
Man Dir: Erik Albrechtsen
Founded: 1986
The guides to food transport are reference books with basic information about transporting perishables.
Subjects: Transportation, Food & Perishable Transport
ISBN Prefix(es): 87-89010
*Associate Companies:* Carit Andersens Forlag A/S

**MIKRO**, *imprint of* Wisby & Wilkens

**Forlaget Modtryk AMBA+**
Anholtsgade 4-6, 8000 Aarhus C
*Tel:* 8731 7600 *Fax:* 8731 7601
*E-mail:* forlaget@modtryk.dk
*Web Site:* www.modtryk.dk
*Telex:* Mod
*Key Personnel*
Man Dir, Rights & Permissions (Textbooks): Ilse Norr *E-mail:* in@modtryk.dk
Sales: Niels Jorn Jensen *E-mail:* njj@modtryk.dk
Production: Henning Morck Jensen *E-mail:* hmj@modtryk.dk
Founded: 1972
Subjects: Fiction, Mysteries, Nonfiction (General)
ISBN Prefix(es): 87-87458; 87-7394; 87-87620; 87-87817; 87-88135

**Munksgaard Danmark**, *imprint of* Gyldendalske Boghandel - Nordisk Forlag A/S

**Museum Tusculanum Press+**
University of Copenhagen, Njalsgade 92, 2300 Copenhagen S
*Tel:* 35 32 91 09 *Fax:* 35 32 91 13
*E-mail:* mtp@mtp.dk
*Web Site:* www.mtp.dk
*Key Personnel*
Dir & Man Dir: Marianne Alenius *Tel:* 35 32 91 10 *E-mail:* alenius@mtp.dk
Marketing & Promotion Manager: Nana Klitgaard *Tel:* 35 32 91 10 *E-mail:* nana@mtp.dk
Founded: 1975
Subjects: Anthropology, Antiques, Archaeology, Art, Asian Studies, Foreign Countries, History, Language Arts, Linguistics, Literature, Literary Criticism, Essays, Philosophy, Religion - Other, Social Sciences, Sociology, Women's Studies
ISBN Prefix(es): 87-980131; 87-88073; 87-7289
Number of titles published annually: 50 Print
Total Titles: 600 Print

Distributed by Gazelle Book Service Ltd (Europe, excluding Scandinavia & Germany); ISBS International Specialized Bookservices (USA & Canada)

**My Best Book**, *imprint of* Bogan's Forlag

**Rasmus Naver**, *imprint of* P Haase & Sons Forlag A/S

**New Era Publications International ApS+**
Subsidiary of New Era Publications Private Ltd
Store Kongensgade 55, 1264 Copenhagen K
*Tel:* 33736666 *Fax:* 33736633
*E-mail:* books@newerapublications.com
*Web Site:* www.newerapublications.com
*Key Personnel*
Man Dir: Ruth Lanciai
Senior Vice President: Thomas Bucher; Christiane Dumas
Publicity Dir & Foreign Rights Dir: Stephen Shinn
Founded: 1969
Subjects: Art, Education, Management, Philosophy, Science Fiction, Fantasy, Self-Help
ISBN Prefix(es): 87-7336; 87-87347; 87-7816; 87-7968
Subsidiaries: New Era Publications Australia Pty Ltd; New Era Publications Deutschland GmbH; New Era Publications Italia Srl; New Era Publications Japan Inc; New Era Publications Group; Continental Publications Pty Ltd; New Era Publications UK Ltd

**Nyt Nordisk Forlag Arnold Busck A/S+**
Kobmagergade 49, 1150 Copenhagen K
*Tel:* 33733575 *Fax:* 33733576
*E-mail:* nnf@nytnordiskforlag.dk
*Web Site:* www.nytnordiskforlag.dk
*Key Personnel*
Man Dir: Ole Arnold Busck
Dir: Jesper Toft Fensrig
Founded: 1896
Subjects: Art, Biography, Fiction, History, How-to, Medicine, Nursing, Dentistry, Music, Dance, Philosophy, Psychology, Psychiatry, Religion - Other, Science (General), Social Sciences, Sociology
ISBN Prefix(es): 87-17
Subsidiaries: Det Schonbergske Forlag A/S; Haandbog for Bygningsindustrien, HFB
*Bookshop(s):* Arnold Busck International Boghandel A/S *Tel:* 33733500 *Fax:* 33733535; Birkerod Boghandel & Kontorforsyning Arnold Busck A/S, Hovedgaden 37, 3460 Birkerod; Arnold Busck Antiquarian A/S, Fiolstraede 24, 1171 Copenhagen K *Tel:* 33733545 *Fax:* 33733587; Arnold Busck Boghandel A/S, Ballerup Centret, PO Box 604, 2750 Ballerup *Tel:* 44979009 *Fax:* 44682327; Arnold Busck Boghandel A/S, Stengade 51, PO Box 167, 3000 Helsingor *Tel:* 49210128 *Fax:* 49210111; Arnold Busck Boghandel A/S, Bredgade 18, 7400 Herning *Tel:* 97120299 *Fax:* 97120521; Arnold Busck Boghandel A/S, Norregade 13, 7500 Holstebro *Tel:* 97423433 *Fax:* 97427722; Arnold Busck Boghandel A/S, Norregade 5, 4600 Koge *Tel:* 56650254 *Fax:* 56636005; Arnold Busck Boghandel A/S, Vestergade 54, 5000 Odense C *Tel:* 66126803 *Fax:* 66114670; Arnold Busck Boghandel A/S, Perlegade 8, 6400 Sonderborg *Tel:* 74423800 *Fax:* 74432240; Arnold Busck Boghandel A/S, Haderslev, Apotekergade 4, 6100 Haderslev *Tel:* 74522703 *Fax:* 74530582; Arnold Busck Boghandel, Nakskov, Sondergade 24, 4900 Nakskov *Tel:* 54923246; Arnold Busck Boghandel, Nykobing F, Lilletorv, 4800 Nykobing F *Tel:* 54850255; Arnold Busck Boghandel, Randers, Radhusstraede 2, 8900 Randers *Tel:* 86420113 *Fax:* 86409113; Bornenes Boghandel ApS,

Kobmagergade 50, 1150 Copenhagen K
*Tel:* 33154466 *Fax:* 33931460; Arnold Busck Boghandel, Maribo, Ostergade 5, 4930 Maribo
*Tel:* 53881244 *Fax:* 53881525
*Orders to:* Nordisk Bog Center, Baekvej 2, 4690 Haslev *Tel:* 56364010 *Fax:* 56364038

**Nyt Teknisk Forlag,** see Ingenioeren/Boger

**Olivia**, *imprint of* Politikens Forlag A/S

**Paedagogisk Bogklub**, *imprint of* Gyldendalske Boghandel - Nordisk Forlag A/S

**Palle Fogtdal A/S**
Ostergade 22, 1100 Copenhagen K
*Tel:* 3315 3915 *Fax:* 3393 3505
*E-mail:* pallefogtdal@pallefogtdal.dk
*Key Personnel*
Man Dir: Palle Fogtdal
ISBN Prefix(es): 87-7248

**Joergen Paludan Forlag ApS**
Straedet 4, Borsholm, 3100 Hornbaek
*Tel:* 4975-1536 *Fax:* 4975-1537
*E-mail:* paludans.forlag@mobilixnet.dk
*Key Personnel*
Man Dir: Joergen Paludan
Subjects: Economics, Education, Government, Political Science, History, Nonfiction (General), Psychology, Psychiatry, Self-Help
ISBN Prefix(es): 87-7230

**Politiken**, *imprint of* Politikens Forlag A/S

**Politikens Forlag A/S+**
Vestergade 26, 1456 Copenhagen K
*Tel:* 33 47 07 07 *Fax:* 33 47 07 08
*E-mail:* politikensforlag@pol.dk
*Web Site:* www.politikensforlag.dk
*Key Personnel*
Publisher-Olivia: Kirsten Skaarup *E-mail:* kirsten.skaarup@pol.dk
Administrative Dir: Karsten Blauert
Founded: 1986
Subjects: Alternative, Cookery, Crafts, Games, Hobbies, Health, Nutrition, Psychology, Psychiatry, Self-Help
ISBN Prefix(es): 87-89019; 87-90181; 87-7963
Imprints: Olivia; Politiken
*Warehouse:* D B K Bogdistribution, Siljangade 2-8, 2300 Copenhagen S

**Politisk Revy+**
Nansensgade 70/st, 1366 Copenhagen K
*Tel:* 33 91 41 41 *Fax:* 33 91 51 15
*E-mail:* politiskrevy@forlagene.dk
*Web Site:* www.forlagene.dk/politiskrevy
*Key Personnel*
Publisher: Johannes Sohlman *E-mail:* sohlman@danbbs.dk
Founded: 1963
Small press, Independent publisher.
Subjects: Fiction, Government, Political Science, Literature, Literary Criticism, Essays, Nonfiction (General), Philosophy, Photography, Poetry, Psychology, Psychiatry, Social Sciences, Sociology
ISBN Prefix(es): 87-7378; 87-85186
Number of titles published annually: 12 Print
Total Titles: 250 Print
*Warehouse:* Nordisk Bogcenter A/S, Baekvej 2, Haslev 4690

**Polyteknisk Boghandel & Forlag+**
Anker Engelunds Vej 1, Bygn 101 A, 2800 Lyngby
*Tel:* 77 42 43 44 *Fax:* 77 42 43 54
*E-mail:* forlag@poly.dtu.dk
*Web Site:* www.polyteknisk.dk

*Key Personnel*
Dir: Lotte Lonver *E-mail:* lotte@poly.dtu.dk
Founded: 1962
Subjects: Engineering (General), Science (General)
ISBN Prefix(es): 87-502

**C A Reitzel Boghandel & Forlag A/S+**
Norregade 20, 1165 Copenhagen K
*Tel:* 33 12 24 00 *Fax:* 33 14 02 70
*E-mail:* info@careitzel.dk
*Web Site:* www.careitzel.dk
*Key Personnel*
Man Dir: Svend Olufsen
Founded: 1819
Subjects: Human Relations, Literature, Literary Criticism, Essays, Nonfiction (General), Philosophy, Science (General)
ISBN Prefix(es): 87-421; 87-7421; 87-7876; 87-87504

**Hans Reitzel Publishers Ltd+**
Ostergade 13, 1008 Copenhagen K
Mailing Address: PO Box 1073, 1008 Copenhagen K
*Tel:* 33382800 *Fax:* 33382808
*E-mail:* hrf@hansreitzel.dk
*Web Site:* www.hansreitzel.dk *Cable:* REITZELBOOKS
*Key Personnel*
Publishing Dir: Hanne Salomonsen *Tel:* 3338 2813 *E-mail:* hs@hansreitzel.dk
Founded: 1949
Subjects: Education, Philosophy, Psychology, Psychiatry, Social Sciences, Sociology
ISBN Prefix(es): 87-412
Total Titles: 350 Print
*Parent Company:* Gyldendalske Boghandel
*Ultimate Parent Company:* Nordisk Forlag Ltd, United Kingdom
*Warehouse:* Nordisk Bog Center, Bcekvej 10-12, 4690 Haslev

**Hans Reitzels Forlag**, *imprint of* Gyldendalske Boghandel - Nordisk Forlag A/S

**Rhodos, International Science & Art Publishers**
Holtegaard Horsholmvej 17, 3050 Humlebaek K
*Tel:* 32543020 *Fax:* 32543022
*E-mail:* rhodos@rhodos.com
*Web Site:* www.rhodos.dk *Cable:* SCIENCEBOOKS
*Key Personnel*
Man Dir: Ruben Blaedel
ISBN Prefix(es): 87-7245; 87-7496

**Rosenkilde & Bagger**
Kronprinsensgade 3, 1114 Copenhagen K
Mailing Address: PO Box 111, 2920 Charlottenlund
*Tel:* 33157044 *Fax:* 33937007
*E-mail:* r-b@rosenkilde-bagger.dk
*Web Site:* www.rosenkilde-bagger.dk
*Key Personnel*
Proprietor: Hans Bagger; Soren Bagger
Founded: 1941
Also has a rare book department.
Subjects: Science (General)
ISBN Prefix(es): 87-423

**Rosinante**, *imprint of* Gyldendalske Boghandel - Nordisk Forlag A/S

**Samfundslitteratur+**
Rosenorns Alle 9-11, 1970 Frederiksberg C
*Tel:* 38153880 *Fax:* 35357822
*E-mail:* samfundslitteratur@sl.cbs.dk; slforlag@sl.cbs.dk
*Web Site:* www.samfundslitteratur.dk

*Key Personnel*
Man Dir: Mogens Eliasson *Tel:* 35356399
    *E-mail:* me@sl.cbs.dk
Editorial Dir, Rights & Permissions: Birgit Vra
    *Tel:* 35356399 *E-mail:* bv@sl.cbs.dk
Founded: 1967
Publishers at Copenhagen Business School.
Subjects: Accounting, Advertising, Business,
    Communications, Developing Countries, Eco-
    nomics, Education, English as a Second Lan-
    guage, Environmental Studies, Finance, His-
    tory, Journalism, Language Arts, Linguistics,
    Management, Marketing, Public Administra-
    tion, Religion - Protestant, Social Sciences,
    Sociology
ISBN Prefix(es): 87-593; 87-7313; 87-87322
Total Titles: 600 Print; 3 CD-ROM
*Parent Company:* Samfundslitterator
Distributor for The World Bank (Denmark)
*Bookshop(s):* Dalgas Have 15, 2000 Frederiksberg
    C; Rosenorns Alle 11, 1970 Frederiksberg C;
    RUC, Bygn 01, Marbjergvej 35, 4000 Roskilde
*Book Club(s):* Erhverislitteratur

**Samlerens Forlag A/S**, *imprint of* Gyldendalske
    Boghandel - Nordisk Forlag A/S

**Samlerens Forlag A/S+**
Imprint of Gyldendalske Boghandel - Nordisk
    Forlag A/S
Kobmagergade 62, 4, 1019 Copenhagen K
Mailing Address: Postboks 2252, 1019 Copen-
    hagen K
*Tel:* 3341 1800 *Fax:* 3341 1801
*E-mail:* samleren@samleren.dk
*Web Site:* www.samleren.dk
*Key Personnel*
Dir: Torben Madsen *E-mail:* torben_madsen@
    samleren.dk
Foreign Rights: Ingelise Korsholm
Founded: 1943
Subjects: Fiction, Government, Political Science,
    History, Literature, Literary Criticism, Essays
ISBN Prefix(es): 87-568
Total Titles: 150 Print

**Scan-Globe A/S**
25 Ulvevej, 4622 Havdrup
*Tel:* 46 18 54 00 *Fax:* 46 18 52 70
*E-mail:* info@scanglobe.dk
*Telex:* 40275
*Key Personnel*
Man Dir: Mr Per Lund-Hansen
Founded: 1963
Subjects: Geography, Geology
ISBN Prefix(es): 87-87343; 87-90468; 87-91154

**Scandinavia Publishing House+**
Drejervej 15-3, 2400 Copenhagen NV
*Tel:* 35 31 03 30 *Fax:* 35 31 03 34
*E-mail:* info@scanpublishing.dk
*Web Site:* www.scanpublishing.dk
*Key Personnel*
President & Publisher: Jorgen Vium Olesen
    *E-mail:* jvo@scanpublishing.dk
Editor & Secretary: Jytte Larsen *Tel:* 35 31 03 31
    *E-mail:* jytte@scanpublishing.dk
Sales & Marketing: Anthony Hoglind
Founded: 1979
Specialize in education & religion.
Subjects: Biblical Studies, Biography, Education,
    Theology
ISBN Prefix(es): 87-7247; 87-87732
Total Titles: 323 Print
*Book Club(s):* Den Kristne Bogklub, Contact: Bo
    Nielsen *Tel:* 35 31 03 36

**Det Schonbergske Forlag A/S+**
Subsidiary of Nyt Nordisk Forlag Arnold Busck
    A/S
Landemaerket 5, 1119 Copenhagen K

*Tel:* 33 73 35 85 *Fax:* 33 73 35 76
*E-mail:* Schoenberg@nytnordiskforlag.dk
*Web Site:* www.nytnordiskforlag.dk *Cable:*
    SCHOENBOOK
*Key Personnel*
Dir: Joakim Werner
Production Manager: Arvid Honore
Sales Manager: Max-Erik Reinhold
Founded: 1857
Subjects: Art, Biography, Career Development,
    Fiction, History, Humor, Philosophy, Poetry,
    Psychology, Psychiatry, Travel
ISBN Prefix(es): 87-570
Divisions: Woeldike

**Schultz Information+**
Herstedvang 12, 2620 Albertslund
*Tel:* 43632300 *Fax:* 43631969
*E-mail:* schultz@schultz.dk
*Web Site:* www.schultz.dk
*Key Personnel*
Man Dir: Henrik Christiansen
Division Manager: Gert Eriksen *E-mail:* ge@
    schultz.dk
Contact: Anette Klubien
Founded: 1661
Specialize in law information.
Subjects: Business, Environmental Studies, Law,
    Nonfiction (General)
ISBN Prefix(es): 87-569; 87-609
*Parent Company:* J H Schultz Holding A/S
*Ultimate Parent Company:* J H Schultz-Fondeu
*Associate Companies:* Schultz Interactive In-
    formation A/S; J H Schultz Grafisk A/S
    *Fax:* 4635329; Synergi Data A/S
*Bookshop(s):* Schultz Boghandel, Hersted-
    vang 4, 2620 Albertslund *Tel:* 33734747
    *Fax:* 43155772 *E-mail:* boghandel@schultz.dk

**Sesam**, *imprint of* Aschehoug Dansk Forlag A/S

**Forlaget Sesam**
Aschehoug Dansk Forlag A/S, Vognmagergade 7,
    1120 Copenhagen K
*Tel:* 3330-5044; 3330-5522 *Fax:* 3391-3878
*E-mail:* aschehoug@ash.egmont.com
*Key Personnel*
Publishing Dir: Per Kolle *Fax:* 3330-5824
ISBN Prefix(es): 87-7258; 87-7324; 87-7801
Divisions: Aschehoug, Egmont

**A/S Skattekartoteket**
Palaegade 4, 1022 Copenhagen K
Mailing Address: Postboks 9026, 1022 Copen-
    hagen K
*Tel:* 33117874 *Fax:* 33938025
*E-mail:* magnus@cddk.dk
*Key Personnel*
Man Dir: Peter Taarnhoj
Subjects: Public Administration
ISBN Prefix(es): 87-87451; 87-7762
*Parent Company:* CD-Danmark A/S

**Sommer & Sorensen**
Valbygaardsvej 33, 2500 Valby
*Tel:* 36153615 *Fax:* 36153616
*E-mail:* post@borgen.dk
*Key Personnel*
Dir: Niels Borgen
Editorial Dir: Jens Christiansen
Contact: Mette Nymark
Subjects: Fiction
ISBN Prefix(es): 87-7499; 87-90189
Number of titles published annually: 5 Print
Total Titles: 10 Print
*Parent Company:* Borgens Forlag A/S

**Spektrum Forlagsaktieselskab**, *imprint of*
    Gyldendalske Boghandel - Nordisk Forlag A/S

**Spektrum Forlagsaktieselskab+**
Imprint of Gyldendalske Boghandel - Nordisk
    Forlage A/S
Skindergade 14, 1159 Copenhagen K
*Tel:* 33 32 63 22 *Fax:* 33 32 64 54
*Key Personnel*
Man Dir: Werner Svendsen
Founded: 1990
Subjects: Nonfiction (General)
ISBN Prefix(es): 87-7763
Imprints: Copenhagen

**Square Dance Partners Forlag+**
Hasselvej 18, 2830 Virum
*Tel:* 45 83 99 83
*Key Personnel*
President & International Rights Contact: Margot
    Gunzenhauser *E-mail:* mgunz@worldonline.dk
Founded: 1987
Specialize in the publishing of books, tapes &
    CD's dealing with traditional style American
    square & contra dancing, related dance forms
    & their music.
Subjects: Crafts, Games, Hobbies, How-to, Mu-
    sic, Dance
ISBN Prefix(es): 87-982674
Total Titles: 4 Print
*U.S. Office(s):* K-113 Pennswood Village, 1382
    Newtown-Langhorne Rd, Newtown, PA 18940,
    United States, Contact: Dorothy Gunzenhauser
    *Tel:* 215-579-2298 *E-mail:* deg@tradenet.net
Distributed by Barn Dance Publications Ltd (UK)

**Strandbergs Forlag+**
Vedbaek Strandvej 475, 2950 Vedbaek
*Tel:* 4589 4760 *Fax:* 4589 4701
*E-mail:* strandberg.publishing@get2net.dk
*Key Personnel*
Publisher: Hans Joergen Strandberg
Founded: 1861
Also book packager.
Subjects: Ethnicity, Humor
ISBN Prefix(es): 87-7717; 87-87200
*Parent Company:* Strandberg

**Strubes Forlag og Boghandel ApS**
Dag Hammarskjolds Alle 36, 2100 Copenhagen
*Tel:* 3142 5300 *Fax:* 3142 2398 *Cable:*
    STRABEBOOKS
*Key Personnel*
Man Dir: Jonna Strube
Subjects: Social Sciences, Sociology, Human Sci-
    ences, Religion

**Syddansk Universitetsforlag** (University Press of
    Southern Denmark)+
Campusvej 55, 5230 Odense M
*Tel:* 66 15 79 99 *Fax:* 66 15 81 26
*E-mail:* press@forlag.sdu.dk
*Web Site:* www.universitypress.dk
*Key Personnel*
Man Dir: Thomas Kaarsted *E-mail:* thk@forlag.
    sdu.dk
Founded: 1966
Subjects: Archaeology, Fiction, History, Liter-
    ature, Literary Criticism, Essays, Medicine,
    Nursing, Dentistry, Philosophy, Technology
ISBN Prefix(es): 87-7492; 87-7838

**Systime+**
Skt Pauls Gade 25, 8000 Aarhus C
*Tel:* 70 12 11 00 *Fax:* 70 12 11 05
*E-mail:* systime@systime.dk
*Web Site:* www.systime.dk
*Key Personnel*
Man Dir: P H Mikkelsen
Editor: Stefan Emkjaer; Birte Annette Noerre-
    gaard; Christine Ohlenschlaeger; Claes Soen-
    derriis
Rights & Permissions: Inga-Lill Amini
Founded: 1980
Specialize in educational materials.

Subjects: Accounting, Chemistry, Chemical Engineering, Computer Science, Economics, English as a Second Language, Film, Video, Geography, Geology, History, Mathematics, Philosophy, Physics, Religion - Other, Technology
ISBN Prefix(es): 87-616; 87-7351; 87-7783; 87-87454
Total Titles: 100 Print
*Parent Company:* GEC Gad

**Teaterforlaget Drama**
Nygade 15, 6300 Grasten
*Tel:* 70 25 11 41 *Fax:* 74 65 20 93
*E-mail:* drama@drama.dk
*Web Site:* www.drama.dk
*Key Personnel*
Dir: Liselotte Lunding *E-mail:* ll@drama.dk
Founded: 1977
Specialize in drama & theatre, books & manuscripts.
Subjects: Drama, Theater
*Associate Companies:* Teater Hjornet; International Teater Boghandel, Vesterbrogade 175, 1800 Frederisberg *Tel:* 33222247 *Fax:* 33225847 *E-mail:* drama@dats.dk

**Forlaget Thomson A/S+**
Nytorv 5, 1450 Copenhagen K
*Tel:* 33 74 07 00 *Fax:* 33 12 16 36
*E-mail:* thomson@thomson.dk
*Web Site:* www.thomson.dk
*Key Personnel*
Administrative Dir: Thomas Hegelund
Chief Sales & Marketing: Per Holst-Hansen
Subjects: Accounting, Business, Education, Law
ISBN Prefix(es): 87-619; 87-7747; 87-88109; 87-980953
*Parent Company:* The Thomson Corporation

**Tiderne Skifter Forlag A/S+**
Laederstraede 5, 1, 1201 Copenhagen K
*Tel:* 33 18 63 90 *Fax:* 33 18 63 91
*E-mail:* tiderneskifter@tiderneskifter.dk
*Web Site:* www.tiderneskifter.dk
*Key Personnel*
Man Dir: Claus Clausen
Founded: 1973
Subjects: Ethnicity, Fiction, Literature, Literary Criticism, Essays, Photography
ISBN Prefix(es): 87-7445; 87-7973
Number of titles published annually: 40 Print
Total Titles: 1,000 Print
*Orders to:* Nordisk Bog Center, Baekvej 10-12, 4690 Haslev *Tel:* 56364000 *Fax:* 56384038

**Unitas Forlag+**
Peter Bangs Vej 1D, 2000 Frederiksberg
*Tel:* 36166481 *Fax:* 38116481
*E-mail:* forlag@unitas.dk
*Web Site:* forlag.unitas.dk
*Key Personnel*
Publisher: Peder Gundersen *E-mail:* pg@forlag.unitas.dk
Founded: 1914
Subjects: Biblical Studies, Biography, Fiction, Religion - Protestant, Theology
ISBN Prefix(es): 87-7517
*Parent Company:* YMCA/YWCA

**Vandrer mod Lysets Forlag Aps**
Solvgade 10. 6 sal, 1307 Copenhagen K
*Tel:* 3315 7815 *Fax:* 3311 8030
*E-mail:* vml@vandrer-mod-lyset.dk
*Web Site:* www.vandrer-mod-lyset.dk
*Key Personnel*
Dir: Boerge Broennum
Publisher: Mrs Konny Falck
ISBN Prefix(es): 87-87871; 87-980350

**Forlaget Vindrose A/S+**
Valbygardsvej 33, 2500 Valby

*Tel:* 36153615 *Fax:* 36153616
*E-mail:* post@borgen.dk
*Web Site:* www.borgen.dk
*Key Personnel*
Publisher: Jens Christiansen
Man Dir: Niels Borgen
Rights & Permissions Manager: Mette Nymark *E-mail:* mnymark@borgen.dk
Production: Dennis Stovring
Founded: 1980
Subjects: Fiction, Poetry, Science (General), Social Sciences, Sociology
ISBN Prefix(es): 87-7456
Number of titles published annually: 20 Print
Total Titles: 200 Print
*Parent Company:* Borgens Forlag A/S
*Warehouse:* DBK-Logistik Service, Mimersvej 4, 4600 Koge
*Orders to:* D B K-bogdistribution, Siljangade 2-8, 2300 Copenhagen S

**Wisby & Wilkens+**
Vesterled 45, 8300 Odder
Mailing Address: PO Box 98, 8464 Galten
*Tel:* 7023 4622 *Fax:* 7043 4722
*E-mail:* mail@bogshop.dk
*Web Site:* www.wisby-wilkens.com; www.bogshop.dk
*Key Personnel*
Dir: Jacob Wisby
Founded: 1986
Membership(s): Danish Publishers Association.
Subjects: Crafts, Games, Hobbies, Fiction, Humor, Literature, Literary Criticism, Essays, Nonfiction (General), Outdoor Recreation, Science Fiction, Fantasy
ISBN Prefix(es): 87-89190; 87-89191; 87-7046
Number of titles published annually: 24 Print
Total Titles: 200 Print
Imprints: MIKRO
Distributor for Grandview USA (Scandinavia)
*Warehouse:* DBK, Siljangade 2, 2300 Copenhagen S

**Forlaget Woldike K/S**
c/o Det Schonbergske Forlag, 13 Stagers Alle, 2000 Frederiksberg C
*Tel:* 31 86 39 54 *Fax:* 38 33 70 80
Founded: 1969
Subjects: Art, Economics, Fiction, Government, Political Science, History, Law, Management, Medicine, Nursing, Dentistry, Nonfiction (General), Religion - Other, Social Sciences, Sociology, Technology, Children's & Comic Books, Leisure, Reference, Teaching
ISBN Prefix(es): 87-7233

# Dominican Republic

## General Information

*Capital:* Santo Domingo
*Language:* Spanish
*Religion:* Predominantly Roman Catholic
*Population:* 7.5 million
*Bank Hours:* 0830-1230 Monday-Friday; some open 0830-1130 Saturday
*Shop Hours:* 0800-1200, 1400 or 1500-1800 Monday-Friday; some open Saturday
*Currency:* 100 centavos = 1 Dominican Republic peso. US currency is widely used
*Export/Import Information:* No import licenses required for books. Exchange license and approval from Central Bank required.
*Copyright:* UCC, Berne, Buenos Aires (see Copyright Conventions, pg xi)

**Editorama SA**
Calle Eugenio Contreras No 54, Los Trinitarios, Santo Domingo
Mailing Address: Apartado Postal 2074, Santo Domingo
*Tel:* 596-6669; 596-4274 *Fax:* 594-1421
*E-mail:* editorama@codetel.net.do
*Web Site:* www.editorama.com
*Key Personnel*
Dir: Juan R Quinones
Founded: 1970
ISBN Prefix(es): 9977-88

**Editora Listin Diario**
Calle Paseo de los Periodistas, No 52, Ensanche Miraflores, Santo Domingo 1455
*Tel:* (0809) 686-6688 *Fax:* (0809) 686-6595
*E-mail:* webmaster.listin@listindiario.com.do
*Web Site:* www.listindiario.com.do
*Telex:* (809) 346-0206 *Cable:* LISTIN
*Key Personnel*
President: Eduardo Pellerano
Executive Dir: Osvaldo Santana
Dir: Miguel Franjul
Editor-in-Chief: Fabio Cabra

**Pontificia Universidad Catolica Madre y Maestra+**
Departamento de Puplicaciones, Autopista Duparte, km 1 1/2, Santiago de los Caballeros
SAN: 004-5527
*Tel:* (809) 5801962; (809) 5350111 *Fax:* (809) 5824549; (809) 5350053
*Web Site:* www.pucmmsti.edu.do
*Telex:* 3461032 PUCMM
*Key Personnel*
Editorial: Carmen Perez de Cabral
Founded: 1962
Membership(s): University Editorial Association of Latin America & the Caribbean.
Subjects: Accounting, Agriculture, Archaeology, Architecture & Interior Design, Biblical Studies, Biography, Biological Sciences, Business, Career Development, Chemistry, Chemical Engineering, Civil Engineering, Communications, Developing Countries, Drama, Theater, Economics, Education, Electronics, Electrical Engineering, Energy, Engineering (General), English as a Second Language, Environmental Studies, Geography, Geology, Government, Political Science, Health, Nutrition, History, Language Arts, Linguistics, Law, Library & Information Sciences, Literature, Literary Criticism, Essays, Management, Marketing, Mathematics, Mechanical Engineering, Medicine, Nursing, Dentistry, Philosophy, Physical Sciences, Physics, Poetry, Regional Interests, Religion - Catholic, Social Sciences, Sociology, Technology, Theology
ISBN Prefix(es): 84-89548; 99934-832; 99934-870
*Warehouse:* Economato Universitario, PUCMM

**Sociedad Editorial Americana+**
Ramon Santana No 2-B, esquina Benito Moncion Gazcue, Santo Domingo DN
*Tel:* 689 7813 *Fax:* 688 9378
*E-mail:* fco.franco@codetel.net.do *Cable:* FRANKLIN FRANCO
*Key Personnel*
President: Franklin Franco
Founded: 1975
Subjects: Economics, History, Law, Literature, Literary Criticism, Essays, Philosophy, Social Sciences, Sociology
ISBN Prefix(es): 99934-0
Total Titles: 2 CD-ROM
*Parent Company:* Credilibros, Apdo 559, Calle Ramon Santana 2B, Santo Domingo

**Editora Taller+**
Calle Juan vallenilla esq Jauncio Dolores, Zona
Industrial de Herrera, Apdo 1, 190 Santo
Domingo
SAN: 002-2136
*Tel:* 531-7975 *Fax:* 531-7979
*E-mail:* editora.taller@codetel.net.do
*Key Personnel*
Contact: Lourdes Cuello
Founded: 1971
Subjects: Economics, History, Literature, Literary
Criticism, Essays
ISBN Prefix(es): 84-8400; 99934-846
Distributor for Editora Vicens Vives
*Orders to:* Vicente Celestino Duarte, No 2

# Ecuador

## General Information

*Capital:* Quito
*Language:* Spanish
*Religion:* Predominantly Roman Catholic
*Population:* 10.9 million
*Bank Hours:* 0900-1330 Monday-Friday
*Shop Hours:* 0930-1300, 1500-1900 Monday-
Friday; 0930-1300 Saturday
*Currency:* 100 centavos = 1 sucre
*Export/Import Information:* Member of the Latin
American Free Trade Association. Books and
most advertising catalogues not dutiable. No
import licenses or exchange controls for books.
*Copyright:* UCC, Buenos Aires (see Copyright
Conventions, pg xi)

**Ediciones Abya-Yala+**
Ave 12 de Octubre 1430 y Wilson, Casilla 17-12-
719 Quito
*Tel:* (02) 2506251; (02) 2506247 *Fax:* (02)
2506255
*E-mail:* editorial@abyayala.org
*Web Site:* www.abyayala.org
*Key Personnel*
Dir: Padre Juan Bottasso *E-mail:* jbottasso@
abyayala.org
Dir General: P Xavier Herran
Founded: 1975
Membership(s): Quito Book Association.
Subjects: Anthropology, Environmental Studies,
Language Arts, Linguistics, Theology
ISBN Prefix(es): 9978-04; 9978-22
Total Titles: 1,060 Print; 2 CD-ROM; 900 E-
Book

**Centro De Educacion Popular**
Av America 3584, Quito
Mailing Address: Casilla Postal 17-08-8604,
Quito
*Tel:* (02) 525 521 *Fax:* (02) 542 818
*E-mail:* cedep@fmlaluna.com
*Web Site:* www.jacomenet.com/laluna/cedep.html
*Key Personnel*
Dir: Diego Landazuri
Founded: 1978
Subjects: Communications, Economics
ISBN Prefix(es): 9978-00

**Centro de Planificacion y Estudios Sociales
(CEPLAES)**
Av 6 de Diciembre y Alpallana, Quito
*Tel:* (02) 548-547 *Fax:* (02) 566-207
*E-mail:* ceplaes@ceplaes.ec
*Key Personnel*
Executive Dir: Alexandra Ayala Marin
Founded: 1978
Subjects: Agriculture, Anthropology, Child Care
& Development, Education, Health, Nutrition,
Social Sciences, Sociology, Women's Studies
ISBN Prefix(es): 9978-93

**Centro Internacional de Estudios Superiores
de Comunicacion para America Latina**, see
CIESPAL (Centro Internacional de Estudios
Superiores de Comunicacion para America
Latina)

**CEPLAES**, see Centro de Planificacion y
Estudios Sociales (CEPLAES)

**CIDAP**
Calle Hermano Miguel 3-23, La Escalinata,
Cuenca
*Tel:* (07) 829-451; (07) 828-878 *Fax:* (07) 831-
450
*E-mail:* ciesa@pi.pro.ec
*Key Personnel*
Dir: Claudio Malo Gonzalez
Subjects: Art, Crafts, Games, Hobbies
ISBN Prefix(es): 84-89420; 9978-85

**CIESPAL (Centro Internacional de Estudios
Superiores de Comunicacion para America
Latina)**
Av Diego de Almagro N32-133 y Andrade Marin,
Quito
Mailing Address: Apdo 17-01-584, Quito
*Tel:* (02) 2524177 *Fax:* (02) 2502487
*E-mail:* publicaciones@ciespal.net
*Web Site:* www.ciespal.net
*Telex:* 2474 Ciespl *Cable:* Ciespal
*Key Personnel*
Dir: Dr Edgar Jaramillo
Dir, Orders: Jorge Jarrin
Founded: 1959
Subjects: Biography, Communications, Journal-
ism, Publishing & Book Trade Reference, Ra-
dio, TV, Technology
ISBN Prefix(es): 9978-55

**Corporacion de Estudios y Publicaciones**
Acuna 168 y Agama, 17-21-00186 Quito, Casilla
*Tel:* (02) 221-711 *Fax:* (02) 226-256
*E-mail:* cep@accessinter.net
Founded: 1963
Subjects: Law, Public Administration
ISBN Prefix(es): 9978-86

**Biblioteca Ecuatoriana Aurelio Espinosa Polit'**
Jose Nogales 220 y Francisco Arcos, Cotocollao,
Quito
Mailing Address: Apdo 17-01-160, Quito
*Tel:* (02) 2491 157; (02) 2491 156 *Fax:* (02)
493928
*E-mail:* beaep@uio.satnet.net
*Web Site:* www.beaep.org.ec
*Key Personnel*
Dir: Rev Julian G Bravo *E-mail:* director@beaep.
org.ec
Founded: 1929
Specialize in all publications by Ecuadorians &/or
about Ecuador.
Subjects: Ecuador
ISBN Prefix(es): 9978-971

**Corporacion Editora Nacional**
Roca 230 y Tamayo, Casilla 17-12-88, Quito
*Tel:* (02) 554358; (02) 554558; (02) 554658
*Fax:* (02) 566340
*E-mail:* cen@accessinter.net
*Key Personnel*
President: Ernesto Alban Gomez
Founded: 1978
Editorial corporation with non-profits.
Subjects: Archaeology, Biography, Economics,
Education, Geography, Geology, Government,
Political Science, History, Law, Literature, Lit-
erary Criticism, Essays, Philosophy, Social Sci-
ences, Sociology
ISBN Prefix(es): 9978-84; 9978-958
Total Titles: 332 Print

**Ediciones Legales SA**
Unit of Corporacion Myl
Polonia N31-134 y Vancouver, Quito
Mailing Address: Apdo 1703-186, Quito
*Tel:* (02) 250-7729 *Fax:* (02) 250-8490
*E-mail:* edicioneslegales@corpmyl.com
*Web Site:* www.edicioneslegales.com
*Key Personnel*
President: Manuel Mejia Dalmau
General Manager: Ernesto Alban Gomez
Founded: 1989
Subjects: Law
ISBN Prefix(es): 9978-81
Total Titles: 28 Print; 2 CD-ROM

**Libresa S A+**
Murgeon 346 y Uloa, Quito
*Tel:* (02) 230925; (02) 525581 *Fax:* (02) 502992
*E-mail:* libresa@interactive.net.ec
*Key Personnel*
President: Fausto Coba Estrella
General: Jaime Pena Novoa
Founded: 1979
Subjects: Education, Literature, Literary Criti-
cism, Essays, Philosophy
ISBN Prefix(es): 9978-80; 9978-952
*Associate Companies:* Delibresa, Librerias Es-
panolas

**Pontificia Universidad Catolica del Ecuador,
Centro de Publicaciones**
Ave 12 de Octubre y Carrion, Quito
*Tel:* (02) 2991700; (02) 2565627
*E-mail:* wjimenez@puceuio.puce.edu.ec
*Web Site:* www.puce.edu.ec
*Key Personnel*
Dir: Dr Marco Vinicio Rueda
Founded: 1946
Subjects: Anthropology, Archaeology, Art, Eco-
nomics, Government, Political Science, History,
Law, Literature, Literary Criticism, Essays, Phi-
losophy, Science (General), Social Sciences,
Sociology, Theology
ISBN Prefix(es): 9978-77

**Pudeleco/Publicaciones de Legislacion**
Reina Victoria 447 y Roca, Primer Piso Office 1-
C, Quito
*Tel:* (02) 543273 *Fax:* (02) 2543607
*E-mail:* pudeleco@uio.satnet.net
*Key Personnel*
Manager: Ramiro Arias Gerente
ISBN Prefix(es): 9978-966

**SECAP**
Gral Francisco Oleary No 264 y Macuma, Quito
*Fax:* (02) 2 283-851
*E-mail:* secap@plus.net.ec
*Web Site:* www.secap.gov.ec
Founded: 1966
Subjects: Agriculture, Automotive, Education,
Library & Information Sciences, Public Admin-
istration
ISBN Prefix(es): 9978-64

**Servicio Ecuatoriano de Capacitacion
Profesional**, see SECAP

**Universidad Central del Ecuador,
Departamento de Publicaciones**
Avda America y A Perez, Quito
Mailing Address: Apdo 3291, Quito
*Tel:* (02) 2234 722 *Fax:* (02) 2236 367; (02) 2521
925
*Web Site:* www.ucentral.edu.ec
*Key Personnel*
Academic Dir: Tiberio Juado Cevallos

# Egypt (Arab Republic of Egypt)

## General Information

*Capital:* Cairo
*Language:* Arabic (English and French widely used)
*Religion:* Predominantly Muslim (of the Sunni sect)
*Population:* 56.4 million
*Bank Hours:* Generally 0830-1230 Monday-Thursday; 1000-1200 Saturday
*Shop Hours:* 0830-1330, 1630-1900 Monday-Saturday
*Currency:* 1,000 milliemes = 100 piastres = 5 tallaris = 1 Egyptian pound
*Export/Import Information:* Exchange rate set by individual banks. No longer government monopoly but some book importing done by Foreign Trade Company, Misr Import & Export Co, 6 Adly St, Cairo.
*Copyright:* Berne, Florence (see Copyright Conventions, pg xi)

### Al Ahram Establishment
6 Al-Galaa' St, Cairo
*Tel:* (02) 748248 *Fax:* (02) 745888
*E-mail:* ahram@ahram.org.eg
*Telex:* 20185-92544
*Key Personnel*
Editor-in-Chief: Ibrahim Nafei
General Manager: Hany Tolba
Production: Fathi Al Charkawi
Rights & Permissions: Mrs Nawal El Mahallawi
Founded: 1875
Also translation agency, printer, distributor, importer, exporter.
Membership(s) Distripreso STM.
Subjects: Human Relations, Science (General)
ISBN Prefix(es): 977-13
*Associate Companies:* Al Ahram Commercial Press; Al Ahram Agency for Distribution
Subsidiaries: Al Ahram Center for Strategic & Political Studies; Al Ahram Center for Scientific Translation & Publishing; Al Ahram Center for Microfilm & Organization; Al Ahram Center for Computer & Management; Al Ahram Advertising Agency; Al Ahram Org 8 Information Technology Center; Al Ahram Commercial Press; Al Ahram Press Agency
*Bookshop(s):* Al Ahram Bookshop, 165 Mohamed Faird St, Cairo
*Book Club(s):* Al Ahram Book Club; ARL (Al-Ahram Research Library)

### American University in Cairo Press+
113 Sharia Kasr el Aini, Cairo 11511
*Tel:* (02) 797 6926; (02) 797 6895 (orders) *Fax:* (02) 794 1440
*E-mail:* aucpress@aucegypt.edu
*Web Site:* aucpress.com
*Telex:* 92224 Aucai un *Cable:* VICTORIOUS
*Key Personnel*
Dir: Mark Linz *Tel:* (02) 797-6888 *E-mail:* linz@aucegypt.edu
Associate Dir, Finance & Administration: Laila Ghali *Tel:* (02) 797-6890 *E-mail:* lailag@aucegypt.edu
Man Editor: Neil Hewison *Tel:* (02) 797-6892 *E-mail:* rnh@aucegypt.edu
Marketing Manager: Atef el-Hoteiby *Tel:* (02) 797-6981 *E-mail:* ahoteiby@aucegypt.edu
Sales & Distribution Manager: Tahany el-Shammaa *Tel:* (02) 797-6895 *E-mail:* tahanys@aucegypt.edu
Promotion Manager: Nabila Akl *Tel:* (02) 797-6896 *E-mail:* akl@aucegypt.edu
Managing Publications Services: Miriam Naim Atef Fahmi *Tel:* (02) 797-6937 *E-mail:* miriam@aucegypt.edu
Rights & Permissions Coordinator: Hala Ganayni *Tel:* (02) 797-6889 *E-mail:* halag@aucegypt.edu
Founded: 1960
Membership(s): AAUP.
Subjects: Anthropology, Architecture & Interior Design, Art, Earth Sciences, History, Language Arts, Linguistics, Literature, Literary Criticism, Essays, Social Sciences, Sociology
ISBN Prefix(es): 977-424
*U.S. Office(s):* 420 Fifth Ave, New York, NY 10018-2729, United States *Tel:* 212-730-8800 *Fax:* 212-730-1600 *E-mail:* ct_aucpress@aucnyo.edu
Distributed by Columbia University Press
*Orders to:* Books International, PO Box 605, Hendon, VA 20172, United States *Tel:* 703-661-1570 *Fax:* 703-661-1501 *E-mail:* bimail@presswarehouse.com (North America)
Eurospan (EDS), 3 Henrietta St, London WC2E 8LU, United Kingdom *Tel:* (020) 7240 0856 *Fax:* (020) 7379 0609 *E-mail:* orders@edspubs.co.uk *Web Site:* www.eurospan.co.uk (UK & Europe)
Rassan Trading Co Pty Ltd, PO Box 44, Kingsway West, NSW 2208, Australia *Tel:* (02) 9159 4411 *Fax:* (02) 9502 2711 (Australasia & Far East)

### Al Arab Publishing House+
23 Faggalah St, Cairo
*Tel:* (02) 908027
*Key Personnel*
Man Dir: Prof Saladin Boustany, PhD
Sales Manager: George G Edde
Founded: 1900
Specialize in modern, contemporary & out-of-print Arabic monographs & periodicals.
Subjects: Developing Countries, Economics, Fiction, Government, Political Science, History, Journalism, Language Arts, Linguistics, Law, Literature, Literary Criticism, Essays, Philosophy, Poetry, Psychology, Psychiatry, Religion - Islamic, Religion - Other, Social Sciences, Sociology

### Cairo University Press
Al-Giza, Cairo
*Tel:* (02) 846144
ISBN Prefix(es): 977-223

**CEDEJ**, see Centre d'Etudes et Documentation Economique Juridique et Sociale (CEDEJ)

### Centre d'Etudes et Documentation Economique Juridique et Sociale (CEDEJ)
2, Sikkat al-Fadl, Qasr al-Nil, Cairo
Mailing Address: PO Box 392, Muhhamad Farid, Cairo
*Tel:* (02) 392 87 11; (02) 392 87 16; (02) 392 87 39; (02) 704641 *Fax:* (02) 392 87 91
*E-mail:* cedej@idsc.net.eg
*Web Site:* www.cedej.org.eg
*Key Personnel*
Dir: Philippe Fargues
Founded: 1970
ISBN Prefix(es): 2-905838

### Dar Al-Kitab Al-Masri+
33 Kasr El Nile St, 11511 Cairo
Mailing Address: PO Box 156 Atabah, 11511 Cairo
*Tel:* (02) 742168; (02) 754301; (02) 744657 *Fax:* (02) 3924657
*E-mail:* info@daralkitab-online.com *Cable:* KITAMISR

*Key Personnel*
President & Man Dir: El-Zein Hassan *E-mail:* hlelzein@datum.com.eg
Founded: 1929
Also distributor & printer.
Membership(s): Time Life Time Warner.
Subjects: Education, Regional Interests
ISBN Prefix(es): 977-238
*Parent Company:* Dar Al-Kitab Al-Lubnani
*Associate Companies:* Dar Al-Kitab Al-Lubnani, Madame Kuri St in front of Hotel Bristol, PO Box 11, 8330 Beirut, Lebanon *Tel:* (01) 735731, (01) 735732 *Fax:* (01) 351433
*Branch Office(s)*
Cairo
Paris, France
Beirut, Lebanon
Casablanca, Morocco
Madrid, Spain
Geneva, Switzerland

### Dar Al-Matbo at Al-Gadidah
5 Saint Mark St, Alexandria
*Tel:* (03) 4825508 *Fax:* (03) 4833819
Subjects: Agriculture, Animals, Pets, Library & Information Sciences, Social Sciences, Sociology
ISBN Prefix(es): 977-207

### Dar al-Nahda al Arabia
32 Abdel Khalek Sarwat St, Cairo
Founded: 1960
Also distributor.
Subjects: Law, Literature, Literary Criticism, Essays
ISBN Prefix(es): 977-04

### Dar Al-Thakafia Publishing+
32 Sabry Abou-Alam St, Cairo
*Tel:* (02) 42718 *Fax:* (02) 4034694
*E-mail:* nassar@hotmail.com
*Key Personnel*
President: Mohamed Youssef Elguindi
Founded: 1968
Publishes Arabic books in a variety of disciplines including comparative literature & regional political issues.
Subjects: Child Care & Development, Computer Science, History, Theology, Religion
ISBN Prefix(es): 977-221

### Dar El Shorouk+
8 Sebaweh El Masry St, Rabaa El Adawia, Nasr City, Cairo
*Tel:* (02) 4023399; (02) 4037567 *Fax:* (02) 3934814
*E-mail:* dar@shorouk.com
*Web Site:* www.shorouk.com
*Telex:* 93091 Shrok *Cable:* SHOROUK
*Key Personnel*
Chief Executive, Editorial, Rights & Permissions: Ibrahim El Moallim
Sales: Ahmad El Sawy
Production: Ahmed El Zayadi
Children's Books: Amira Aboulmadg
Founded: 1976
Subjects: Behavioral Sciences, Biography, Business, Computer Science, Education, English as a Second Language, Fiction, History, Law, Literature, Literary Criticism, Essays, Management, Mysteries, Nonfiction (General), Poetry, Psychology, Psychiatry, Religion - Islamic
ISBN Prefix(es): 977-09
*Associate Companies:* Shorouk Press
Subsidiaries: Shorouk Bookshop
*Bookshop(s):* The First Mall, 25 Giza St, Giza; One Soliman Pasha Sq, Cairo

### The Egyptian Society for the Dissemination of Universal Culture & Knowledge (ESDUCK)
1081 Corniche El Nil, Garden City, Cairo
Mailing Address: PO Box 21, Cairo

*Tel:* (02) 35425079; (02) 3542 0295 *Fax:* (02) 3540295 *Cable:* ESDUCK
*Key Personnel*
Executive Manager: Dr Amin El-Gamal
Production: Amal Kilany
Rights & Permissions: Inas Effat
Founded: 1953
Co-publisher with local & American firms. Also translation agency.

**Elias Modern Publishing House+**
One Kenisset El-Rum el Kathulik St, Cairo 11271
*Tel:* (02) 5903756; (02) 5939544 *Fax:* (02) 5880091
*E-mail:* eliasmph@gega.net
*Web Site:* www.eliaspublishing.com
*Key Personnel*
Man Dir: Laura Kfoury
Founded: 1913
Subjects: Language Arts, Linguistics, Literature, Literary Criticism, Essays, Poetry
ISBN Prefix(es): 977-5028
Subsidiaries: Elias Modern Press

**ESDUCK**, see The Egyptian Society for the Dissemination of Universal Culture & Knowledge (ESDUCK)

**General Egyptian Book Organization+**
Corniche el-Nil - Ramlet Boulac, Cairo 11221
*Tel:* (02) 5765436; (02) 5775228; (02) 5775109; (02) 5775367; (02) 5775436; (02) 5775545; (02) 5775000 *Fax:* (02) 5765058
*E-mail:* info@egyptianbook.org
*Web Site:* www.egyptianbook.org
*Key Personnel*
Chmn: Dr Nasser El Ansary
VChmn: Dr Waheed Abdel Majeed
General Manager, Marketing: Mr Samir Saad
Founded: 1961
26 Branches throughout Egypt.
ISBN Prefix(es): 977-01
*Bookshop(s):* International Book Centre, 3, 26 July St, Cairo *Tel:* (02) 5788431

**Dar Al Hilal Publishing Institution**
16 Mohamed Ezz Al-Arab St, Cairo 11511
*Tel:* (02) 362 5450 *Fax:* (02) 362 5469
*Telex:* 92703 Hilal *Cable:* Al Mussawar Cairo
*Key Personnel*
Chairman of the Board & Editor-in-Chief: Makram Muhammad Ahmed
Founded: 1892
Subjects: Fiction, Nonfiction (General)
ISBN Prefix(es): 977-07

**Lehnert & Landrock Bookshop**
44 Sherif St, Cairo 11511
*Tel:* (02) 3927606 *Fax:* (02) 3934421
*Key Personnel*
Manager: Dr E Lambelet
Founded: 1924
Subjects: Archaeology, History, Travel
ISBN Prefix(es): 977-243
Number of titles published annually: 2 Print

**Dar Al Maaref+**
1119 Courniche EL Nil, Cairo
*Tel:* (02) 759411; (02) 759552 *Fax:* (02) 5744999
*E-mail:* maaref@idsc.gov.eg
*Telex:* 92199 Marefun *Cable:* Damaref
*Key Personnel*
Chairman & Man Dir: Ragab Al-Banna
Founded: 1890
Also co-publishers, importers & exporters.
Subjects: Education, Regional Interests, Science (General)
ISBN Prefix(es): 977-02

Subsidiaries: Dar Al-Maaref Liban Sarl
*Bookshop(s):* Alexandria; El Arish; Assiut; Asswan; Cairo; Ismailia; Mansoura; Qena; Shebin El kom; Sohage; Suez; Tanta; Zagazig

**Middle East Book Centre**
45 Kasr Al-Nil St, Cairo
*Tel:* (02) 910980
*Key Personnel*
Man Dir: Dr A M Mosharrafa
Sales Manager: A Ismail
Founded: 1954
Subjects: Biography, Fiction, History, Language Arts, Linguistics, Literature, Literary Criticism, Essays, Philosophy, Poetry, Regional Interests, Religion - Other, Science (General), Social Sciences, Sociology

**Senouhy Publishers**
54 Sharia Abdel-Khalek, Tharwat, Cairo
*Key Personnel*
Man Dir: Leila A Fadel
Founded: 1956
Subjects: History, Nonfiction (General), Poetry, Regional Interests, Religion - Other

**Sphinx Publishing Co**
3 Shawarby St, 3rd Floor, Cairo
*Tel:* (02) 392 4616 *Fax:* (02) 391 8802
*E-mail:* sphinx@intouch.com
*Telex:* 93927
*Key Personnel*
Man Dir: Habib Sayegh
Founded: 1958
Part of Librairie du Liban Group, Lebanon.
Subjects: Education
*Parent Company:* Pearson Plc

**Ummah Press+**
24 Degla St-Flat 9, Off Shehab St, Mohandiseen, Cairo
*Tel:* (02) 337-8556
*E-mail:* ghurabh@internetegypt.com
*Key Personnel*
President: Ahmad El Shazly
Publishing & translation service.
Subjects: Business, Economics, Government, Political Science, Journalism, Regional Interests, Religion - Islamic

# El Salvador

## General Information

*Capital:* San Salvador
*Language:* Spanish
*Religion:* Predominantly Roman Catholic
*Population:* 5.6 million
*Bank Hours:* 0900-1200, 1345-1530 Monday-Friday
*Shop Hours:* 0800-1200, 1400-1800 Monday-Friday; 0800-1200 Saturday
*Currency:* 100 centavos = 1 Salvadorean colon
*Export/Import Information:* Member of the Central American Common Market. No import licenses but exchange license from Exchange Control Department of Central Reserve Bank required, if goods coming from outside Central America. Commercial banks authorize certain import payments.
*Copyright:* UCC, Berne, Buenos Aires, Florence (see Copyright Conventions, pg xi)

**Clasicos Roxsil Editorial SA de CV+**
4A Ave Sur Nº 2-3, Santa Tecla
*Tel:* 2228-1832; 2288-2646; 2229-6742 *Fax:* 2228-1212

*Key Personnel*
Manager: Rosa Serrano de Lopez
Chief Editorial Dept: Roxana Beatriz Lopez
　*E-mail:* roxanabe@navegante.com.sv
Founded: 1976
Subjects: Biography, Literature, Literary Criticism, Essays, Poetry
ISBN Prefix(es): 84-89541; 84-89899; 99923-24
Number of titles published annually: 10 Print
Total Titles: 173 Print
Distributor for Fondo Editorial UNESCO (El Salvador)
*Book Club(s):* Club de Lectores de Clasicos Roxsil, Contact: Marco Antonio Barraza

**UCA Editores+**
Blvd Los Proceres, San Salvador
*Tel:* 210-6600 *Fax:* 210-6655
*E-mail:* info@uca.edu.sv
*Web Site:* www.uca.edu.sv
*Key Personnel*
Dir: Rodolfo Cardenal SJ
Sub Dir: Carolina Cordova
Founded: 1975
Subjects: Philosophy, Religion - Other, Social Sciences, Sociology, Theology
ISBN Prefix(es): 99923-34
Number of titles published annually: 10 Print
*Bookshop(s):* Libreria UCA (under Major Booksellers)
*Orders to:* Distribuidora de Publicaciones de la Universidad Centroamericana, Universidad Centroamericana Jose Simeon Canas, Apdo 01-575, Autopista Sur, Jardinesde Guadalupe, San Salvador

**Editorial Universitaria de la Universidad de El Salvador**
Ciudad Universitaria, Apdo de Correos 3110, San Salvador
*Tel:* 2558826 *Fax:* 254208
*Key Personnel*
Dir: Armando Herrara
Contact: Francisco Guzman Argueta
Founded: 1923
Subjects: Gardening, Plants, Government, Political Science, Literature, Literary Criticism, Essays, Philosophy, Poetry, Regional Interests, Social Sciences, Sociology
ISBN Prefix(es): 84-89540

# Estonia

## General Information

*Capital:* Tallinn
*Language:* Estonian, Russian, Finnish & English
*Religion:* Evangelical Lutheran
*Population:* 1.5 million
*Currency:* 100 cents = 1 kroon (eek); 8 eek = 1 dem
*Export/Import Information:* No export/import duties. 18% VAT on books (except educational & medical).
*Copyright:* Berne (see Copyright Conventions, pg xi)

**Academic Library of Tallinn Pedagogical University** (Tallinna Pedagoogikaulikooli Akadeemiline Raamatukogu)
10 Raevala Ave, 15042 Tallinn
*Tel:* (02) 6659 401 *Fax:* (02) 6659 400
*E-mail:* ear@ear.ee
*Web Site:* www.ear.ee
*Key Personnel*
Head Librarian: Andres Kollist *E-mail:* andres.kollist@ear.ee
Learned Secretary: Aita Kraut *Tel:* (02) 6659 404
　*E-mail:* aita.kraut@ear.ee

Founded: 1946
Subjects: Biological Sciences, Ethnicity, Geography, Geology, History, Library & Information Sciences, Exhibition Catalogues, Yearbooks
Number of titles published annually: 6 Print; 1 CD-ROM
*Parent Company:* Tallinn Pedagogical University, Narva St 25, 10120 Tallinn

**Eesti Entsuklopeediakirjastus** (Estonian Encyclopaedia Publishers)+
Narva mnt 4, 10117 Tallinn
*Tel:* 6999 620 *Fax:* 6999 621
*E-mail:* ene@ene.ee
*Web Site:* www.ene.ee
*Key Personnel*
Chairman of the Board: Hardo Aasmae
International Rights: Aili Saks
Founded: 1991 (as the successor of former Encyclopedia Editorial Board, founded 1963)
Specialize in reference books for all age groups.
Membership(s): Estonian Publishers Association.
Subjects: Agriculture, Art, Astronomy, Biography, Biological Sciences, Earth Sciences, Economics, Geography, Geology, History, Military Science, Music, Dance, Natural History, Nonfiction (General), Philosophy, Physical Sciences, Science (General), Social Sciences, Sociology, Sports, Athletics, Technology
ISBN Prefix(es): 5-89900; 9985-70
Number of titles published annually: 40 Print
Total Titles: 240 Print
*Bookshop(s):* A&O Reference Book Shop

**Eesti Piibliselts+**
Kaarli pst 9, 10119 Tallinn
*Tel:* 631 1671 *Fax:* 631 1438
*E-mail:* eps@eps.ee
*Web Site:* www.eps.ee
*Key Personnel*
Head of Publications: Sra Tarmo Lilleoja
  *E-mail:* tarmo@eps.ee
Founded: 1813
Specialize in Estonian bibles, new testaments & portions, bible related literature.
Membership(s): United Bible Societies.
Subjects: Biblical Studies, History
ISBN Prefix(es): 9985-889; 9985-9027
Number of titles published annually: 4 Print; 1 CD-ROM
Total Titles: 2 Print

**Eesti Rahvusraamatukogu** (National Library of Estonia)
Tonismagi 2, 15189 Tallinn
*Tel:* 630 7611 *Fax:* 631 1410
*E-mail:* nlib@nlib.ee
*Web Site:* www.nlib.ee
*Key Personnel*
Dir General: Tiiu Valm *Tel:* 630 7600
  *E-mail:* tiiu.valm@nlib.ee
Marketing Manager: Triin Soone *Tel:* 630 7271
  *E-mail:* triin@nlib.ee
Founded: 1918
Information services on humanities & social sciences; exhibition & conference service; book binding & conservation; photocopying; publishing.
Membership(s): CDNL, CENL, EIA, IALL, IAML, IFLA, International Council of Archives, International Paper Conservation Institute & LIBER.
Subjects: Art, History, Law, Library & Information Sciences, Music, Dance, Specialize in information services, exhibition & conference services, preservation, publishing for Parliament & other libraries. Specialize in dictionaries & reference books
ISBN Prefix(es): 9985-803; 9985-9217; 9985-9265; 9985-9334

Number of titles published annually: 50 Print; 13 CD-ROM; 2 E-Book
Total Titles: 13 CD-ROM; 8 E-Book

**Estonian Academy Publishers** (Eesti Teaduste Akadeemia Kirjastus)
Unit of Estonian Academy of Sciences
Kohtu Stz 6, 10130 Tallinn
*Tel:* 645 4504 *Fax:* 646 6026
*E-mail:* niine@kirj.ee
*Web Site:* www.kirj.ee
*Key Personnel*
Dir: Ulo Niine
Executive Editor: Virve Kurnitski *Tel:* 645 4156
  *E-mail:* virve@kirj.ee
Marketing Manager: Asta Tikerpae *E-mail:* asta@kirj.ee
Founded: 1994
Subjects: Science (General)
ISBN Prefix(es): 9985-50
Number of titles published annually: 30 Print
Total Titles: 360 Print; 8 Online

**Estonian ISBN Agency**
Tonismaegi 2, 15189 Tallinn
*Tel:* 630 7372 *Fax:* 631 1200
*E-mail:* eraamat@nlib.ee
*Web Site:* www.nlib.ee
*Key Personnel*
Contact: Mai Valtna
*Parent Company:* National Library of Estonia

**Ilmamaa+**
Vanemuise 19, 51014 Tartu
*Tel:* (07) 427 290 *Fax:* (07) 427 320
*E-mail:* ilmamaa@ilmamaa.ee
*Web Site:* www.ilmamaa.ee
*Key Personnel*
Chairman: Hando Runnel
Dir: Mart Jagomagi *E-mail:* mj@ilmamaa.ee
Founded: 1993
Subjects: Fiction, History, Literature, Literary Criticism, Essays, Nonfiction (General), Philosophy, Poetry
ISBN Prefix(es): 9985-821; 9985-878; 9985-77
Number of titles published annually: 30 Print; 6 Online
Total Titles: 105 Print; 23 Online

**Kirjastus Kunst** (Kunst Publishers)+
Lai t 34, 10133 Tallinn
*Tel:* 6411764; 6411766 *Fax:* 6411762
*E-mail:* kunst.myyk@mail.ee
*Web Site:* www.kirjastused.com/kunst
*Key Personnel*
Editorial Dir: Katre Oim
Marketing: Asta Pajumaee
Design: Tiiu Allikvee
Finance: Marika Kirbits
Foreign Rights Manager: Eve Kork *Tel:* (02) 6411363
Founded: 1957
Specialize in Art.
Subjects: Architecture & Interior Design, Art, Biography, Fiction, History
ISBN Prefix(es): 5-89920; 9949-407
Number of titles published annually: 40 Print
Total Titles: 8 Print

**Koolibri+**
Lehola 8 / Hiiu 38, 11620 Tallinn
*Tel:* 651 5300 *Fax:* 651 5301
*E-mail:* koolibri@koolibri.ee
*Web Site:* www.koolibri.ee
*Key Personnel*
Dir: Kalle Kaljurand *Tel:* 651 5325
  *E-mail:* kalle@koolibri.ee; Ants Lang *Tel:* 651 5302 *E-mail:* ants@koolibri.ee
Assistant Dir: Valve Kruusma *Tel:* 651 5303
  *E-mail:* valve@koolibri.ee

Publicity Manager: Maire Tanna *Tel:* 651 5318
  *E-mail:* maire@koolibri.ee
ISBN Prefix(es): 9985-0
Total Titles: 300 Print

**Kupar Publishers+**
Pamu mnt 67a, 10134 Tallinn
*Tel:* (02) 628 6173; (02) 628 6175 *Fax:* (02) 646 2076
*E-mail:* kupar@netexpress.ee
*Key Personnel*
Chairman: Mihkel Mutt
Man Dir: Ivo Sandre
Editor-in-Chief: Marilin Lips
Founded: 1987
Subjects: Fiction, Human Relations, Parapsychology, Social Sciences, Sociology, Western Fiction
ISBN Prefix(es): 9985-61
*Bookshop(s):* Kupar, Lossi 9, Poltsamaa; Kupar, Harju 1, EE0001 Tallinn

**Mats Publishers Ltd+**
Laki 15, EE 12915 Tallinn
*Tel:* (O2) 6563589
*Key Personnel*
President & Man Dir: Heido Ots
Founded: 1991
Subjects: Automotive, History, House & Home, Transportation
ISBN Prefix(es): 9985-51
Number of titles published annually: 10 Print
Total Titles: 30 Print
Imprints: Mats Tallinn

**Mats Tallinn,** *imprint of* Mats Publishers Ltd

**AS Medicina+**
Laki 26, 12915 Tallinn
*Tel:* (06) 567660 *Fax:* (06) 567620
*E-mail:* medicina@hot.ee
*Web Site:* medicina.co.ee
*Key Personnel*
Man Dir: Kaja Uska
Founded: 1993
Membership(s): the Estonian Book Publishers Association.
Subjects: Medicine, Nursing, Dentistry
ISBN Prefix(es): 9985-829
*Parent Company:* Kustannus Oy Duodecim, Helsinki, Finland

**Olion Publishers+**
Laki 26, 12915 Tallinn
*Tel:* 655 0175 *Fax:* 655 0173
*E-mail:* olion@not.ee
*Key Personnel*
Dir: Hulle Unt
Editor-in-Chief: Veiko Talts *Tel:* 644 4347
Founded: 1989
Subjects: Biography, Business, Economics, Education, Fiction, History, Law, Nonfiction (General), Philosophy, Social Sciences, Sociology, Western Fiction
ISBN Prefix(es): 5-460; 9985-66
Number of titles published annually: 40 Print

**Oue Eesti Raamat**
Laki tn 26, Tallinn 12915
*Tel:* 658 7885; 658 7886; 658 7887; 658 7889
  *Fax:* 658 7889
*E-mail:* helgi.gailit@mail.ee
*Web Site:* www.eestiraamat.ee
*Key Personnel*
Dir: Anne Kask *E-mail:* anne.kask.003@mail.ee
Rights & Contract Manager: Georg Grunberg
  *E-mail:* georg.grynberg@mail.ee
Founded: 1964
Subjects: Biography, Fiction, Poetry
ISBN Prefix(es): 9985-65
Number of titles published annually: 50 Print

## Perioodika+
Voorimehe 9, PO Box 3648, Tallinn 10507
*Tel:* 644 1262 *Fax:* 644 2484
*E-mail:* perioodika@hot.ee
*Key Personnel*
Manager, Editorial Board: Ivar Sinimets
Dir: Uuno Sillajoe
Founded: 1973
Subjects: Astrology, Occult, Cookery, Romance,
  Women's Studies
ISBN Prefix(es): 5-7979
Number of titles published annually: 30 Print
Total Titles: 90 Print

## Sinisukk+
Tueri 9, Tallinn 11314
*Tel:* 656 1872 *Fax:* 656 1872
*E-mail:* sinisukk@vorguvara.ee
*Key Personnel*
President & International Rights: Marie Edala
  *E-mail:* marie@sinisukk.ee
Founded: 1992
Subjects: Animals, Pets, Astrology, Occult, Bi-
  ography, Child Care & Development, Cookery,
  Crafts, Games, Hobbies, Fiction, Film, Video,
  Gardening, Plants, House & Home, How-to,
  Nonfiction (General), Psychology, Psychiatry,
  Self-Help
ISBN Prefix(es): 9985-73; 9985-812
Number of titles published annually: 180 Print
Total Titles: 212 Print

## Tael Ltd
Ruutli 6, Tallinn EE0001
*Tel:* (02) 6314162 *Fax:* (02) 6314162
*E-mail:* tael@teleport.ee
*Key Personnel*
Publisher: Vladimir Sokolovski
Founded: 1991
Subjects: Archaeology
Total Titles: 1 Print

## TEA Kirjastus (Tea Publishers)+
Liivalaia 28, 10118 Tallinn
*Tel:* 644 9253; 645 9206 *Fax:* 645 9208
*E-mail:* info@tea.ee
*Web Site:* www.tea.ee
*Key Personnel*
President: Mrs Silva Tomingas *E-mail:* silva.
  tomingas@tea.ee
General Manager: Mr Olavi Valner
International Rights Manager: Kersti Neiman
  *E-mail:* kersti.neiman@tea.ee
Founded: 1992
Publishing & design of books & dictionaries on
  diskettes. Subject specialties include textbooks,
  practice books & grammar books.
ISBN Prefix(es): 9985-71; 9985-843; 9985-9003;
  9985-9029
Number of titles published annually: 50 Print; 1
  CD-ROM
Total Titles: 130 Print; 1 CD-ROM; 10 Audio
*Branch Office(s)*
Parnu, Sirje Manna *Tel:* (02) 4476303
TARTU, Botooni 9 *Tel:* (02) 7307959 *Fax:* (02)
  7307970
*Bookshop(s):* 27 Narva Mnt, Tallinn, Contact:
  Mrs Ene Tiidelepp *Tel:* (02) 6426019

## Tuum+
Harju 1, 10146 Tallinn
*Tel:* 627 6427; (051) 41 290 *Fax:* 641 8054
*E-mail:* enelier@yahoo.com
*Key Personnel*
Contact: Piret Viires
Founded: 1992
Subjects: Human Relations, Literature, Literary
  Criticism, Essays, Natural History, Philosophy,
  Poetry, Psychology, Psychiatry, Science Fiction,
  Fantasy
ISBN Prefix(es): 9985-802

## Valgus Publishers+
Tulika 19, Tallinn 10613
*Tel:* 650 5025; (050) 59 958 *Fax:* 650 5104
*E-mail:* info@kirjastusvalgus.ee
*Key Personnel*
Dir: Ants Sild
Founded: 1965
Subjects: Agriculture, Animals, Pets, Archaeol-
  ogy, Architecture & Interior Design, Biological
  Sciences, Child Care & Development, Cookery,
  Crafts, Games, Hobbies, Electronics, Electrical
  Engineering, Engineering (General), English as
  a Second Language, Gardening, Plants, Geog-
  raphy, Geology, Health, Nutrition, Medicine,
  Nursing, Dentistry, Science (General), Hand-
  books, Healthcare, Popular-science
ISBN Prefix(es): 5-440; 9985-68

# Ethiopia

## General Information

*Capital:* Addis Ababa
*Language:* Amharic (official), English also widely
  used
*Religion:* Ethiopian Orthodox
*Population:* 51.1 million
*Bank Hours:* 0830-1230, 1430-1730 Monday-
  Friday; 0830-1230 Saturday
*Shop Hours:* Addis Ababa: 0900-1300, 1500-
  2000 Monday-Saturday. Asmara: 0800-1300,
  1600-2000 Monday-Friday
*Currency:* 100 cents = 1 birr
*Export/Import Information:* No tarriff on books,
  but additional taxes. Advertising subject to cus-
  toms and same taxes. No import license re-
  quired but Exchange Payment License neces-
  sary.
*Copyright:* No copyright conventions signed

## Addis Ababa University Press
PO Box 1176, Addis Ababa
*Tel:* (01) 239746; (01) 239800 (ext 227) *Fax:* (01)
  239729
*E-mail:* aau.pres@telecom.net.et *Cable:* AA
  UNIV
*Key Personnel*
General Editor & Dir: Prof Darge Wole
Assistant General Dir: Messelech Habte
Founded: 1968
Publishing House of the Addis Ababa University.
Membership(s): Ethiopian Publishers Associa-
  tion; African Association of Science Editors;
  APNET; ABC.
Subjects: Biography, Chemistry, Chemical En-
  gineering, Geography, Geology, Health, Nu-
  trition, History, Language Arts, Linguistics,
  Literature, Literary Criticism, Essays, Science
  (General), Technology, Botany, Climatology,
  Diary, Hydrology, Public Health
Total Titles: 15 Print
*Associate Companies:* James Currey Publishers,
  United Kingdom; Illinois University Press, IL,
  United States; Lund University Press, Sweden;
  Norwegian University of Science & Technol-
  ogy, Norway

**ENI**, see Ethiopian Nutrition Institute (ENI)

## Ethiopian Nutrition Institute (ENI)
PO Box 5654, Addis Ababa
*Tel:* (01) 151600 *Fax:* (01) 754744 *Cable:*
  NUTRITION
*Key Personnel*
Dir: Dr Zewdie Wolde-Gebriel
*Parent Company:* Ministry of Health
Divisions: Medical, Laboratory, Training, Food
  Science & Technology

## Government Printer
Government Printing Press, Addis Ababa
Mailing Address: PO Box 1241, Addis Ababa

# Fiji

## General Information

*Capital:* Suva
*Language:* Fijian & Hindi. English widely spoken
*Religion:* Christian (mainly Methodist) with large
  minority of Hindus
*Population:* 800,000
*Bank Hours:* 1000-1500 Monday-Thursday; 1000-
  1600 Friday
*Shop Hours:* 0800-1630 or later Monday-Friday;
  early closing Wednesday or Saturday
*Currency:* 100 cents = 1 Fiji dollar
*Export/Import Information:* No tariffs on books
  and advertising. No import licenses. Exchange
  control by Reserve Bank of Fiji; no specific
  Exchange license required and authorized
  banks perform transaction upon application.
*Copyright:* Berne, UCC (see Copyright Conven-
  tions, pg xi)

## Islands Business International Ltd
46 Gordon St, Suva
Mailing Address: PO Box 12718, Suva
*Tel:* 312 040 *Fax:* 301 423
*E-mail:* 75070.2637@compuserve.com
*Telex:* 2350
*Key Personnel*
Man Dir: Godfrey Scoullar
Publisher: Robert Keith-Reid
Editor: Peter Lomas
Senior Writer: Vasiti Waqa
Advertising Manager: Ganga Gounder
Circulation Manager: Davina Hughes
ISBN Prefix(es): 982-206
Publication(s): *Fiji Islands Business*

## Library Service of Fiji
Government Bldgs, Suva
Mailing Address: PO Box 2526, Suva
*Tel:* 315 344 *Fax:* 314 994
*Key Personnel*
Chief Librarian: Humesh Prasad
Founded: 1981
Oversees the management of public, government
  department & school libraries in Fiji. Operates
  37 government department libraries, 28 school
  media centers & 5 mobile libraries.
Listing & information service.
*Branch Office(s)*
Nausori Library, Nausori *Tel:* 476387
  *Fax:* 400048
Northern Regional Library, Ministry of Education,
  Labasa *Tel:* 812894 *Fax:* 814770
Raki Raki Branch Library, PO Box 1, Raki Raki
  *Tel:* 694153 *Fax:* 694855
Savu Savu Branch Library, Savu Savu
  *Tel:* 850154 *Fax:* 850154
Tavua Branch Library, Tauna *Tel:* 694153
  *Fax:* 681390
Western Regional Library, PO Box 150, Lautokia
  *Tel:* 660091 *Fax:* 668195

## Lotu Pacifika Productions
Government Bldgs, Suva
Mailing Address: PO Box 2401, Suva
*Tel:* 301314 *Fax:* 301183 *Cable:* LOTUPAK
*Key Personnel*
Manager: Seru L Verebalavu
Founded: 1973
Subjects: Cookery, Education, Ethnicity, Poetry,
  Religion - Other

**University of the South Pacific+**
PO Box 1168, Laucala Campus, Suva
*Tel:* (033) 3232077 *Fax:* (033) 3232038
*Web Site:* www.usp.ac.fj
*Telex:* 2276 usp fj *Cable:* UNIVERSITY SUVA
Founded: 1968
Subjects: Education, Environmental Studies, Natural History, Regional Interests
ISBN Prefix(es): 982-302; 982-03; 982-01

# Finland

## General Information

*Capital:* Helsinki
*Language:* Finnish and Swedish (officially bilingual); English and German spoken widely
*Religion:* Predominantly Evangelical Lutheran
*Population:* 5.2 million
*Bank Hours:* 0915-1615 Monday-Friday
*Shop Hours:* 0900-1700 or later Monday-Friday; 0900-1600 (1400 in summer) Saturday
*Currency:* 100 Eurocents = 1 Euro; 5.94573 markkas = 1 Euro
*Export/Import Information:* Member of the European Union. 12% VAT on books. No import licenses required on books. No exchange controls.
*Copyright:* UCC, Berne, Florence (see Copyright Conventions, pg xi)

**AB Svenska Laromedel-Editum+**
Rusthaellargatan 1, 02270 Esbo
*Tel:* (09) 88704017 *Fax:* (09) 8043257
*E-mail:* jjohnson@schildts.fi
*Key Personnel*
Chief Executive: Jan-Peter Kullberg
Founded: 1971
Subjects: Education, Fiction, Nonfiction (General)
ISBN Prefix(es): 951-553
*Showroom(s):* Kyruoesplanaden 9, 65100 Vasa

**Abo Akademis forlag - Abo Akademi University Press**
Tavastgatan 30 C, 20700 Abo
*Tel:* (02) 215 3292 *Fax:* (02) 215 4490
*E-mail:* forlaget@abo.fi
*Web Site:* www.abo.fi/stiftelsen/forlag
*Key Personnel*
Secretary: Inger Hassel
Founded: 1987
Subjects: Science (General), Doctoral Dissertations
ISBN Prefix(es): 951-9498; 952-9616; 951-765
Number of titles published annually: 20 Print
*Orders to:* Oy Tibo-Trading Ab, PO Box 33, 21601 Pargas *Tel:* (02) 454 9200 *Fax:* (02) 454 9220 *E-mail:* tibo@tibo.net *Web Site:* www.tibo.net

**Akateeminen Kustannusliike Oy+**
Arkadiankatu 12 A 5, 00100 Helsinki
*Tel:* (09) 434 2320 *Fax:* (09) 43423234
*Web Site:* www.spes.fi
*Key Personnel*
Manager: Tapani Mattila
Sales: Ulla-Riitta Tuulenmaki
Founded: 1927
Subjects: History, Language Arts, Linguistics, Religion - Protestant
ISBN Prefix(es): 951-9023

**Art House Group**
Bulevardi 19 C, 00120 Helsinki
*Tel:* (09) 9800 2500 *Fax:* (09) 693 3762
*Web Site:* www.arthouse.fi
Founded: 1975

Publish Finnish & translated literature, science books, health books, cookbooks & Roald Dahl's children's books. Specialize in historical books.
Subjects: Biological Sciences, Chemistry, Chemical Engineering, Cookery, Film, Video, Health, Nutrition, History, Mathematics, Music, Dance, Physics, Science (General)
ISBN Prefix(es): 951-884; 951-96086; 951-96135

**Atena Kustannus Oy+**
PL 436, 40101 Jyvaskyla
*Tel:* (014) 620192 *Fax:* (014) 620190
*E-mail:* atena@atenakustannus.fi
*Web Site:* www.atenakustannus.fi
*Key Personnel*
Contact: Pekka Maekelae
Founded: 1986
Subjects: History, Nonfiction (General)
ISBN Prefix(es): 951-9362; 951-796

**Basam Books Oy+**
Hameentie 155 A 7, 00561 Helsinki
Mailing Address: PL 42, 00561 Helsinki
*Tel:* (09) 7579 3839 *Fax:* (09) 7579 3838
*E-mail:* bs@basambooks.com
*Web Site:* www.basambooks.com
*Key Personnel*
Man Dir & International Rights: Batu Samaletdin
Founded: 1993
Subjects: Fiction, Literature, Literary Criticism, Essays, Philosophy, Poetry, Psychology, Psychiatry
ISBN Prefix(es): 952-9842; 952-5534

**Building Information Ltd**
Runeberginkatu 5, 00101 Helsinki
Mailing Address: PO Box 1004, 00101 Helsinki
*Tel:* (09) 549 5570 *Fax:* (09) 5495 5320
*E-mail:* rakennustieto@rakennustieto.fi
*Web Site:* www.rakennustieto.fi
*Key Personnel*
Man Dir: Markku Salmi *Tel:* (09) 5495 5333 *E-mail:* markku.salmi@rakennustieto.fi
Assistant Man Dir: Heimo Salo *Tel:* (09) 5495 5395 *E-mail:* heimo.salo@rakennustieto.fi
Subjects: Architecture & Interior Design, Building & Construction
Total Titles: 8 CD-ROM; 2 Online; 1 E-Book
*Parent Company:* The Building Information Foundation RTS, Helsinki
*Associate Companies:* Helsinki Building Centre *Tel:* (09) 5495 5426 *Fax:* (09) 5495 5420; Lappeenranta Building Centre, Raatimiehenkatu 20, 53100 Lappeenranta *Tel:* (05) 415 0990 *Fax:* (05) 415 2600; Kuopio Building Centre, Kauppakatu 40-42, 70110 Kuopio *Tel:* (017) 261 6109 *Fax:* (017) 261 8666; Oulu Building Centre, Uusikatu 32, 90100 Oulu *Tel:* (08) 311 6122 *Fax:* (08) 377 334; Tampere Building Centre, Satakunnankatu 18, 33210 Tampere *Tel:* (03) 212 6961 *Fax:* (03) 212 6989
Foreign Rep(s): Latvian Building Centre Ltd (LBC) (Latvia); Estonian Building Centre (Estonia); Moscow Construction Centre ZAO (Russia); St Petersburg Construction Centre Ltd (Russia)
*Bookshop(s):* The Building Bookshop, Helsinki *Tel:* (09) 5495 5400 *Fax:* (09) 5495 5340

**Docendo Finland Oy+**
Vapaaherrantie 2, 40100 Jyvaskyla
*Tel:* (014) 339 7700 *Fax:* (014) 339 7755
*E-mail:* info@docendo.fi
*Web Site:* www.docendo.fi
*Key Personnel*
Man Dir: Sahlman Mika
Founded: 1990
Subjects: Civil Engineering, Computer Science, Engineering (General), Microcomputers

ISBN Prefix(es): 952-9823; 952-5159; 951-96321; 951-846
*Parent Company:* Werner Soderstrom Oy

**Kustannus Oy Duodecim** (Duodecim Medical Publications Ltd)+
Kalevankatu 11 A, 00100 Helsinki
Mailing Address: PO Box 713, 00101 Helsinki
*Tel:* (09) 618851 *Fax:* (09) 61885400
*E-mail:* etunimi.sukunimi@duodecim.fi
*Web Site:* www.duodecim.fi
*Key Personnel*
Secretary: Raija Orndahl *E-mail:* raija.orndahl@duodecim.ti
Man Dir: Pekka Mustongn *E-mail:* pekka.mustongn@duodecim.ti
Information Officer: Annakaisa Tavast *E-mail:* annakaisa.tavast@duodecim.fi
Founded: 1984
Membership(s): Finnish Book Publishers Association.
Subjects: Medicine, Nursing, Dentistry, Psychology, Psychiatry
ISBN Prefix(es): 951-656; 951-8917; 951-9347
Number of titles published annually: 15 Print
*Associate Companies:* AS Medicina, Gonsiori 29, Tallinn, Estonia *Tel:* (06) 484 679

**Edita Publishing Oy+**
Siltasaarenkatu 14, 00043 Helsinki
Mailing Address: PL 700, 00043 Edita
*Tel:* (020) 450 00 *Fax:* (020) 450 2396
*E-mail:* etunimi.sukunimi@edita.fi
*Web Site:* www1.edita.fi
*Telex:* 123458 Vapk
*Key Personnel*
Dir-General: Mikko Suotsalo *E-mail:* mikko.suotsalo@edita.fi
Dir, Publication: Leo Eskola *E-mail:* leo.eskola@edita.fi
Editorial Dir: Lauri Veijola *E-mail:* lauri.veijola@edita.fi; Timo Lepisto *Tel:* (020) 450 2355 *E-mail:* timo.lepisto@edita.fi
Marketing Dir & Rights & Permissions: Pauli Niemi-Jaskari *E-mail:* pauli.niemi-jaskari@edita.fi
Founded: 1859
ISBN Prefix(es): 951-37; 951-859; 951-860; 951-861
*Bookshop(s):* Annankatu 44, 00100 Helsinki; Etelaeesplanadi 4

**Ekenas Tryckeri AB**
PB 26, 10601 Ekenaes
*Tel:* (019) 222 800 *Fax:* (019) 222 815
*E-mail:* leif.rex@eta.fi
*Key Personnel*
Man Dir: Sven Sundstroem
Founded: 1881
Subjects: Government, Political Science, History
ISBN Prefix(es): 951-9000; 951-9001

**Fenix-Kustannus Oy+**
PL 11, 02211 Espoo
*Tel:* (09) 420 8190 *Fax:* (09) 420 8045
*Key Personnel*
Chief Executive, Rights & Permissions: Reima T A Luoto *E-mail:* reima.luoto@matkailutoimittajat.fi
Editorial: Kalevi Viljanen
Sales: Tapio Vaekevaeinen
Production: Matti Saarinen
Founded: 1993
Subjects: Nonfiction (General)
ISBN Prefix(es): 951-862

**Finnish Lawyers' Publishing Co**, see Kauppakaari Oyj

**Forsamlingsforbundets Forlags AB+**
Bangatan 29 A, 00120 Helsingfors

Mailing Address: PO Box 285, 00121 Helsingfors
*Tel:* (09) 61261546 *Fax:* (09) 603963
*E-mail:* bokhandel@ff-forlag.fi
*Key Personnel*
Man Dir: Leif Westerling *E-mail:* leif.
westerling@ff-forlag.fi
Sales: Asa Nordstrom
Founded: 1920
Subjects: Biblical Studies, Psychology, Psychiatry,
Religion - Protestant
ISBN Prefix(es): 951-550
Distributor for Verbum-Sweden

**Frenckellin Kirjapaino Oy** (Frenckell Printing
Works)
Niittyrinne 4, 02270 Espoo
*Tel:* (09) 887 3611 *Fax:* (09) 887 3670
*E-mail:* etunimi.sukunimi@frenckell.fi
*Web Site:* www.frenckell.fi
*Key Personnel*
Chief Executive Officer: Berndt von Frenckell
*Tel:* (09) 887 3622
Marketing Manager: Jari Mikola *Tel:* (09) 887
3627 *E-mail:* jari.mikola@frenckell.fi
Sales Manager: Harri Nikulainen *Tel:* (09) 887
3625 *E-mail:* harri.nikulainen@frenckell.
fi; Lauri Silvennoinen *Tel:* (09) 887 3631
*E-mail:* lauri.silvennoinen@frenckell.fi
Founded: 1642
ISBN Prefix(es): 951-9417; 951-95311

**Gummerus Publishers+**
Arkadiankatu 23 B, 00100 Helsinki
Mailing Address: PO Box 749, 00101 Helsinki
*Tel:* (09) 584 301 *Fax:* (09) 5843 0200
*Web Site:* www.gummerus.fi
*Key Personnel*
Man Dir: Ilkka Kylmala *E-mail:* ilkka.kylmala@
gummerus.fi
Publishing Dir, Nonfiction: Risto Vaisanen
*E-mail:* risto.vaisanen@gummerus.fi
Publishing Manager, Ajatus Kirjat (Nonfiction):
Jan Erola *E-mail:* jan.erola@gummerus.fi
Publishing Dir, Fiction: Anna Baijars
*E-mail:* anna.baijars@gummerus.fi
Publishing Manager, Dictionaries: Virpi Kallioku-
usi *E-mail:* virpi.kalliokuusi@gummerus.fi
Rights & Permissions: Paula Peltola
*E-mail:* paula.peltola@gummerus.fi
Founded: 1872
Subjects: Fiction, Nonfiction (General)
ISBN Prefix(es): 951-20
*Parent Company:* Gummerus Oy

**Herattaja-yhdistys Ry**
PL 21, 62101 Lapuan
*Tel:* (06) 438 8911 *Fax:* (06) 438 7430
*E-mail:* jormakka@nic.fi
*Key Personnel*
Executive Dir: Jouko Kuusinen
Founded: 1892
Subjects: Biblical Studies, History, Literature,
Literary Criticism, Essays, Poetry, Religion -
Protestant, Theology
ISBN Prefix(es): 951-878; 951-9012; 951-9013;
951-9014

**Kaantopiiri Oy+**
Meritullinkatu 21, 00170 Helsinki
*Tel:* (09) 622 9970 *Fax:* (09) 135 1372
*E-mail:* like@likekustannus.fi
*Web Site:* www.likekustannus.fi
*Key Personnel*
Editor & Foreign Rights: Saara Karvinen
*Tel:* (09) 68746077
Founded: 1987
Specialize in literature by women in Third World
countries.
Subjects: Fiction, Foreign Countries, Literature,
Literary Criticism, Essays, Nonfiction (Gen-
eral), Women's Studies

ISBN Prefix(es): 951-8989
*Parent Company:* Like Kustannus Oy

**Karas-Sana Oy+**
Kaisaniemenkatu 8, 4 krs, 00100 Helsinki
*Tel:* (09) 6815 5600 *Fax:* (09) 6815 5611
*E-mail:* toimitus@sana.fi
*Web Site:* www.karas-sana.fi/sana
*Key Personnel*
Man Dir: Hans Krause *E-mail:* hans.krause@
karas-sana.fi
Publishing Manager: Paivi Karri *E-mail:* paivi.
karri@karas-sana.fi
Founded: 1974
Subjects: Human Relations, Religion - Protestant,
Self-Help
ISBN Prefix(es): 951-655; 951-851
Number of titles published annually: 15 Print
Total Titles: 172 Print; 1 Audio
*Parent Company:* Kansan Raamattuseuran Saeae-
tioe, PO Box 48, Vivamo SF-08101 Lohja

**Karisto Oy+**
Paroistentie 2, 13600 Hameenlinna
*Tel:* (03) 63 151 *Fax:* (03) 616 1565
*E-mail:* kustannusliike@karisto.fi
*Web Site:* www.karisto.fi
*Key Personnel*
Man Dir: Simo Moisio
Publishing Dir, Editorial & Foreign Rights:
Pirkko Mikkola *Tel:* (03) 631 5210
Founded: 1900
Subjects: Fiction, Nonfiction (General)
ISBN Prefix(es): 951-23
*Warehouse:* Kirjavalitys Oy, Hakakalliontie 10,
05800 Hyvinkaeae

**Kauppakaari Oyj**
Uudenmaankatu 4-6A, 00120 Helsinki
*Tel:* (020) 442 4730 *Fax:* (020) 442 4723
*E-mail:* etunimi.sukunimi@talentum.fi
*Web Site:* www.talentum.fi/kirjat
*Key Personnel*
Publishing Dir: Mr Tuomo Rasanen
Sales Secretary: Ms Taija Haapaniemi
Founded: 1958
Subjects: Business, Law
ISBN Prefix(es): 951-640; 952-14; 951-8986;
951-762
*Bookshop(s):* Lakipiste, Uudenmaankatu 4-6A,
00120 Helsinki *Tel:* (09) 54212230 *Fax:* (09)
54212223

**Kirja-Leitzinger+**
Kytoesuontie 8 D 47, 00300 Helsinki
*Tel:* (09) 588 3377 *Fax:* (09) 588 3373
*E-mail:* leitzinger@luukku.com
*Key Personnel*
Man Dir: Antero Leitzinger
Founded: 1993
Subjects: Asian Studies, Ethnicity, Foreign Coun-
tries, Genealogy, Government, Political Sci-
ence, History, Music, Dance, Travel
ISBN Prefix(es): 952-9752
Total Titles: 15 Print

**Kirjatoimi+**
Ketarantie 4, 33680 Tampere
Mailing Address: PL 94, 33101 Tampere
*Tel:* (03) 360 0000 *Fax:* (03) 360 0454
*E-mail:* kirjatoimi@sdafin.org *Cable:*
KIRJATOIMI
*Key Personnel*
Man Dir & Chief Editor: Kalliokoski Klaus
Office Manager: Kallman Maarit
*E-mail:* wellwoma@sdafin.org
Founded: 1897
Subjects: Health, Nutrition, Religion - Protestant
ISBN Prefix(es): 951-629
*Parent Company:* Seventh-Day Adventist Church
in Finland

**Kirjayhtyma Oy**
Urho Kekkosen Katu 4-6E, 00100 Helsinki
*Tel:* (09) 6937641 *Fax:* (09) 69376366
*E-mail:* oppimateriaauit@tammi.net *Cable:*
KIRJAYHTYMAe
*Key Personnel*
Man Dir: Olli Arrakoski
Publishing Dir, Textbooks: Tuija Nurmiranta
Publishing Dir, Fiction & Nonfiction: Jaakko
Tapaninen
Contact: Haarala Paeivi
Founded: 1958
Subjects: Fiction, Nonfiction (General)
ISBN Prefix(es): 951-26
*Parent Company:* Tammi Publishers
*Bookshop(s):* Kirjava Satama, Urho Kekkosen
Katu 4-6E, 00100 Helsinki
*Warehouse:* Libri-Logistiikka Oy, Hakakalliontie
10, 05800 Hyvinkaa
*Orders to:* Libri-Logistiikka Oy, Hakakalliontie
10, 05800 Hyvinkaa

**Koala-Kustannus Oy** (Greenbay House
Publishing Ltd)+
Kulosaarentie 8 C 20, 00570 Helsinki
*Tel:* (050) 408 1590 *Fax:* (09) 6845034
*E-mail:* info@koalakustannus.fi
*Web Site:* www.koalakustannus.fi
*Key Personnel*
Man Dir & International Rights: Lassi Eskola
*E-mail:* lassi.eskola@koalakustannus.fi
Founded: 1997
Membership(s): Finnish Book Publishers Associa-
tion.
Subjects: Aeronautics, Aviation, Film, Video, His-
tory, Maritime, Military Science, Music, Dance,
Nonfiction (General), Sports, Athletics
ISBN Prefix(es): 952-5186
Number of titles published annually: 20 Print; 1
CD-ROM
Total Titles: 40 Print

**Kustannus Oy Kolibri+**
Office Center, Lautatarhankatu 6A, 00581
Helsinki
Mailing Address: PL 399, 00101 Helsinki
*Tel:* (09) 774 5310 *Fax:* (09) 701 9351
*E-mail:* susanna.frankenhaeuser@
kolibrikustannus.fi
*Key Personnel*
Man Dir: Rauno Malmstrom
Founded: 1989
Subjects: Nonfiction (General), Wine & Spirits
ISBN Prefix(es): 951-576; 952-16

**Rakentajain Kustannus Oy (Building
Publications Ltd)+**
Rahakamarinportti 3A, 00240 Helsinki
*Tel:* (09) 142855 *Fax:* (09) 5032542
*Key Personnel*
Chief Executive Officer: Pertti Sarmala
Publishing Dir: Eeva Kalin
Founded: 1916
Specialize in books on all fields & levels of con-
struction.
Subjects: Architecture & Interior Design, How-to
ISBN Prefix(es): 951-676
*Bookshop(s):* Fredrikinkatu 53, 00100 Helsinki

**Kustannus Oy Semic**
PL 317, 33101 Tampere
*Tel:* (03) 273 8111 *Fax:* (031) 243 8287
*E-mail:* minna.alanko@egmont-kustannus.fi
*Telex:* Semic
*Key Personnel*
Chief Executive & Publicity: Pentti Molander
Editorial, Production: Marjaana Tulosmaa
Founded: 1971
ISBN Prefix(es): 951-9112; 951-876; 951-95793;
951-95794; 951-95231; 951-95232
*Parent Company:* Semic International AB, Swe-
den

**Kustannus Oy Uusi Tie+**
Opistotie 1, 12310 Ryttylae
*Tel:* (019) 77 920 *Fax:* (019) 779 2300
*E-mail:* uusitie@uusitie.com
*Web Site:* www.uusitie.com
*Key Personnel*
Editor-at-Large: Vuokko Vanska
Sales: Raimo Raukko
Founded: 1965
Subjects: Fiction, Religion - Other, Theology
ISBN Prefix(es): 951-619

**Kustannuskiila Oy**
Vuorikatu 21-23, 70100 Kuopio
Mailing Address: PL 68, 70101 Kuopio
*Tel:* (017) 303 111 *Fax:* (017) 303 242
*E-mail:* anneli-siimes@savonsanomat.fi
*Telex:* 42111 Sasan
*Key Personnel*
President, Editorial, Production, Publicity &
    Sales: Juhani Pitkaenen *E-mail:* juhani.
    pitkaenen@savonsanomat.fi
Founded: 1964
Subjects: History
ISBN Prefix(es): 951-657
*Parent Company:* Savon Sanomat

**Kustannusosakeyhtio Tammi** (Tammi
    Publishers)
Urho Kekkosen katu 4-6 E, 00100 Helsinki
Mailing Address: PL 410, 00101 Helsinki
*Tel:* (09) 6937 621 *Fax:* (09) 6937 6266
*E-mail:* tammi@tammi.net
*Web Site:* www.tammi.net *Cable:* TAMMI
*Key Personnel*
Man Dir: Pentti Molander
Manager, Children's & Juvenile: Terttu Toiviainen
Literary Dir: Jaakko Tapaninen *E-mail:* jaakko.
    tapaninen@tammi.net
Founded: 1943
Subjects: Fiction, Nonfiction (General)
ISBN Prefix(es): 951-30; 951-31
Number of titles published annually: 400 Print
*Parent Company:* Bonnier Media AB, Sweden
*Associate Companies:* Libri-Logistiikka Oy
*Subsidiaries:* Kirjayhtymae Oy; Kirjasuomi Oy;
    Kustannus Oy Kolibri; Oy Opifer Ltd; Oy
    Satusiivet-Sagovingar AB
*Bookshop(s):* Kirjava Satama, Urho Kekkosen
    katu 4-6 E, 00100 Helsinki
*Book Club(s):* ExLibris; Lasten Parhaat Kirjat
*Warehouse:* Libri-Logistiikka Oy, Hakakalliontie
    10, 05800 Hvyinkaa
*Orders to:* Libri-Logistiikka Oy, Hakakalliontie
    10, 05800 Hvyinkaa

**Kuva ja Sana+**
PL 86, 00381 Helsinki
*Tel:* (09) 477 4920 *Fax:* (09) 4774 9250
*E-mail:* kuva.sana@patmos.fi
*Key Personnel*
Chief Executive Officer, President, Editor-in-
    Chief, Rights & Permissions: Leo Meller
Production & Publicity: Olli Palen
Founded: 1942
Subjects: Government, Political Science, Religion
    - Other, Social Sciences, Sociology
ISBN Prefix(es): 951-9024; 951-9072; 951-9073;
    951-9203; 951-585
*Associate Companies:* Patmos International
*Subsidiaries:* Ideakustannus
*Bookshop(s):* Christian Center, Harjukatu 2,
    00500 Helsinki

**Lasten Keskus Oy**
Saerkiniementie 7 A, 00210 Helsinki
*Tel:* (09) 6877 450 *Fax:* (09) 6877 4545
*E-mail:* tilaukset@lastenkeskus.fi
*Web Site:* www.lastenkeskus.fi *Cable:* LASTEN
    KESKUS
*Key Personnel*
Man Dir: Pertti Rosenholm *Tel:* (09) 6877 4540

Manager: Maisa Tonteri *Tel:* (09) 6877 4542
Manager Children's Books & Juveniles: Arja
    Kanerva *Tel:* (09) 6877 4535
Founded: 1974
Subjects: Biblical Studies, Child Care & Devel-
    opment, Crafts, Games, Hobbies, Education,
    Human Relations, Religion - Protestant
ISBN Prefix(es): 951-627; 951-626
*Associate Companies:* Suomen Kirkko-Mediat Oy
*Subsidiaries:* Pentella Oy
*Bookshop(s):* Lasten Kirjakauppa, Fredrikinkatu
    61, 00100 Helsinki (Children's Bookstore)

**Oy LIKE Kustannus** (Like Publishing Ltd)+
Meritullinkatu 21, 00170 Helsinki
*Tel:* (09) 622 9970 *Fax:* (09) 135 1372
*E-mail:* like@like.fi
*Web Site:* www.likekustannus.fi
*Key Personnel*
Man Dir: Hannu Paloviita *E-mail:* hannu.
    paloviita@likekustannus.fi
Founded: 1987
The leading independent publishing house in Fin-
    land. Publishes a cultural magazine, circulation
    700,000 copies.
Subjects: Fiction, Nonfiction (General), Science
    Fiction, Fantasy
ISBN Prefix(es): 951-578; 951-8929; 951-96078;
    952-471
Number of titles published annually: 100 Print
Total Titles: 600 Print
*Bookshop(s):* Like Kirjakauppe, Vuorikatu
    5, 00100 Helsinki, Contact: Otto Sallinen
    *Tel:* (09) 2600288

**Otava Publishing Co Ltd+**
Affiliate of Otava Books & Magazines Group Ltd
Uudenmaankatu 10, 00120 Helsinki
Mailing Address: PO Box 134, 00121 Helsinki
*Tel:* (09) 19961 *Fax:* (09) 643 136
*Web Site:* www.otava.fi *Cable:* OTAVA
    HELSINKI
*Key Personnel*
Chairman: Olli Reenpaa *E-mail:* olli.reenpaa@
    otava.fi
Man Dir: Antti Reenpaa *E-mail:* antti.reenpaa@
    otava.fi
Publishing Dir, General Books: Leena Majander
    *E-mail:* leena.majander@otava.fi
Publishing Dir, Educational Books: Jukka Vahtola
    *E-mail:* jukka.vahtola@otava.fi
Publishing Manager, Children's Books: Katriina
    Kauppila *E-mail:* katriina.kauppila@otava.fi
Publishing Manager, General Nonfiction: Tero
    Norkola *E-mail:* tero.norkola@otava.fi
Publishing Manager, Handbooks: Heli Hottinen
    *E-mail:* heli.hottinen@otava.fi
Publishing Manager, Reference Books: Irja
    Hamalainen *E-mail:* irja.hamalainen@otava.fi
Publishing Manager, Special Books: Eva Reenpaa
    *E-mail:* eva.reenpaa@otava.fi
Publishing Manager, Translated Fiction: Minna
    Castren *E-mail:* minna.castren@otava.fi
Publishing Manager, Otava Education/Adult
    Education: Heikki Hiltunen *E-mail:* heikki.
    hiltunen@otava.fi
Publishing Manager, Otava Education/Basic Edu-
    cation: Maarit Pyotsia *E-mail:* maarit.pyotsia@
    otava.fi
Publishing Manager, Otava Education/Humanities
    & Arts Dept: Helena Ruuska *E-mail:* helena.
    ruuska@otava.fi
Publishing Manager, Otava Education/Modern
    Languages Dept: Selja Saarialho *E-mail:* selja.
    saarialho@otava.fi
Publishing Manager, Otava Education/Science
    Dept: Teuvo Sankila *E-mail:* teuvo.sankila@
    otava.fi
Foreign Rights Manager, Selling: Eila Mellin
    *Tel:* (09) 1996 445 *Fax:* (09) 1996 440
    *E-mail:* eila.mellin@otava.fi
Founded: 1890

Subjects: Architecture & Interior Design, Art,
    Fiction, History, How-to, Nonfiction (General)
ISBN Prefix(es): 951-1
*Subsidiaries:* Otavan Kirjapaino Oy (Otava Book
    Printing Ltd); Suuri Suomalainen Kirjak-
    erho Oy (The Great Finnish Book Club Ltd);
    Yhtyneet Kuvalehdet Oy (United Magazines
    Ltd)

**Paiva Osakeyhtio+**
Lukiokatu 15, 13101 Hameenlinna
Mailing Address: PL 10, 13101 Hameenlinna
*Tel:* (03) 644 6110 *Fax:* (03) 612 2109
*E-mail:* paiva@paiva.fi
*Web Site:* www.paiva.fi
*Key Personnel*
Man Dir: Merja Pitkanen *Tel:* (03) 644 6111
    *E-mail:* merja.pitkanen@paiva.fr
Founded: 1962
Subjects: Religion - Protestant, Religion - Other
ISBN Prefix(es): 951-622

**Pohjoinen**
Lekatie 1, 90150 Oulu
Mailing Address: PL 170, 90401 Oulu
*Tel:* (08) 5377 111 *Fax:* (08) 5377 572
*E-mail:* pohjoinen@kaleva.fi
*Web Site:* www.kaleva.fi
*Key Personnel*
Publishing Manager: Peerit Tahtinen *Tel:* (08)
    5377 570 *E-mail:* peerit.tahtinen@kaleva.fi
Founded: 1964
ISBN Prefix(es): 951-749; 951-9099; 951-9152
*Parent Company:* Kirjapaino Osakeyhito Kaleva

**Rakennusalan Kustantajat RAK+**
Kaupintie 13, 00440 Helsinki
*Tel:* (09) 503 2540 *Fax:* (09) 503 2542
*E-mail:* info@sarmala.com
*Web Site:* www.sarmala.com
*Key Personnel*
Publisher: Pertti Sarmala
Founded: 1991
ISBN Prefix(es): 952-9687; 951-664

**Rakennustieto Oy** (Building Information Ltd)+
Runeberginkatu 5, 00100 Helsinki
Mailing Address: PL 1004, 00101 Helsinki
*Tel:* (09) 549 5570 *Fax:* (09) 5495 5320
*E-mail:* rakennustieto@rakennustieto.fi
*Web Site:* www.rakennustieto.fi
*Key Personnel*
Man Dir: Markku Salmi
Assistant Man Dir: Heimo Salo
Founded: 1974
Subjects: Architecture & Interior Design
ISBN Prefix(es): 951-682
*Parent Company:* Rakennustietosaeaetio - Build-
    ing Information Foundation RTS

**Recallmed Oy+**
Valkjarventie 45, 01800 Klaukkala
*Tel:* (09) 8797177 *Fax:* (09) 8797088
*E-mail:* recallmed@recallmed.fi
*Key Personnel*
Publishing Dir: Timo Saarinen
Chairman of the Board: Dr Bruno Taajamaa
Founded: 1981
Subjects: Biography, Medicine, Nursing, Den-
    tistry, Music, Dance, Sports, Athletics
ISBN Prefix(es): 951-9221; 951-847

**Sairaanhoitajien Koulutussaatio+**
Sitratori 5, 00420 Helsinki
*Tel:* (09) 5666788 *Fax:* (09) 531504
*Key Personnel*
Executive Dir: Paivi Huopalahti
Financial Manager: Raija Jarvio
Chief Editor: Maija Tupala
Founded: 1944
Subjects: Medicine, Nursing, Dentistry
ISBN Prefix(es): 951-8963; 951-9105

**Schildts Forlags AB+**
Rusthallargatan 1, 02270 Esbo
Mailing Address: PO Box 86, 02271 Esbo
*Tel:* (09) 88 70 400 *Fax:* (09) 804 32 57
*E-mail:* schildts@schildts.fi
*Web Site:* www.schildts.fi *Cable:* BOKSCHILDT
*Key Personnel*
Man Dir: Mr Johan Johnson *Tel:* (09) 88 70 40
 17 *E-mail:* jjohnson@schildts.fi
Rights & Permissions: Helen Svensson *Tel:* (09)
 88 70 40 33 *E-mail:* helens@schildts.fi
Marketing Dir: Elisabeth Jansson *Tel:* (09) 88 70
 40 20 *E-mail:* bettan@schildts.fi
Founded: 1913
Subjects: Art, Biography, Fiction, History, Music,
 Dance, Philosophy, Poetry
ISBN Prefix(es): 951-50
*Associate Companies:* Pagina
*Orders to:* Foerlagssystem Finland Ab *Tel:* (09)
 88 70 40 52 *Fax:* (09) 88 70 40 55

**Scriptum Forlags AB**
Handelsesplanaden 23 A, 65100 Vasa
*Fax:* (06) 3242 210
*E-mail:* scriptum@svof.fi
*Web Site:* www.svof.fi/scriptum
*Key Personnel*
Chairman: Vivan Lygdback *Tel:* (06) 3242 226
 *E-mail:* vivan.lygdback@svof.fi
Founded: 1987
Subjects: Archaeology, Fiction, Poetry, Essays
ISBN Prefix(es): 951-8902; 952-5496
Number of titles published annually: 9 Print
Total Titles: 100 Print

**Soderstroms Forlag**
Georgsgatan 29 A, 2 van, 00101 Helsingfors
Mailing Address: PB 870, 00101 Helsingfors
*Tel:* (09) 6841 8620 *Fax:* (09) 6841 8621
*E-mail:* soderstrom@soderstrom.fi
*Web Site:* www.soderstrom.fi *Cable:*
 SOeDERSTROeMS
*Key Personnel*
Man Dir: Marianne Bargum *Tel:* (09) 6841 8644
 *E-mail:* marianne.bargum@soderstrom.fi
Editorial Dir: Tapani Ritamaki *Tel:* (09) 6841
 8616 *E-mail:* ritamaki@soderstrom.fi
Editorial Dir, School Books: Kenneth Nykvist
 *Tel:* (09) 6841 8633 *E-mail:* nykvist@
 soderstrom.fi
Information & Marketing: Susanna Sucksdorff
 *Tel:* (09) 6841 8622 *E-mail:* sucksdorff@
 soderstrom.fi
Founded: 1891
Subjects: Art, Biography, Fiction, History, How-
 to, Philosophy, Poetry, Psychology, Psychiatry,
 Religion - Other, Science (General)
ISBN Prefix(es): 951-52
Total Titles: 30 Print
*Orders to:* Foerlagssystem Finland Ab *Tel:* (09)
 8870 4052 *Fax:* (09) 8870 4055

**Suomalaisen Kirjallisuuden Seura** (Finnish
 Literature Society)
Hallituskatu 1, 00170 Helsinki
Mailing Address: PL 259, 00171 Helsinki
*Tel:* (0201) 131 231 *Fax:* (09) 1312 3219
*Key Personnel*
Secretary-General-Dir: Tuomas M S Lehtonen
Publisher: Paivi Vallisaari *Tel:* (09) 131 23 210
 *E-mail:* paivi.vallisaari@finlit.fi
Founded: 1831
Subjects: Anthropology, History, Language Arts,
 Linguistics, Literature, Literary Criticism, Es-
 says
ISBN Prefix(es): 951-717; 951-746
Number of titles published annually: 100 Print
Total Titles: 1,500 Print

**Suomen Matkailuliitto ry** (The Finish Travel
 Association)
Atomitie 5 C, 00370 Helsinki

*Tel:* (09) 622 6280 *Fax:* (09) 654 358
*E-mail:* matkailuliitto@matkailuliitto.org
*Web Site:* www.matkailuliitto.org
Founded: 1887
Subjects: Travel
ISBN Prefix(es): 951-838

**Suomen Pipliaseura RY+**
Kauppiaankatu 7, 00161 Helsinki
Mailing Address: PL 173, 00161 Helsinki
*Tel:* (09) 612 9350 *Fax:* (09) 612 935 11
*E-mail:* info@bible.fi; etunimi.sukunimi@bible.fi
*Web Site:* www.bible.fi
Founded: 1812
Specialize in Bibles, fund raising for Bible Soci-
 ety & development of teaching methods of the
 Bible.
Subjects: Biblical Studies
ISBN Prefix(es): 951-9010; 951-577

**SV-Kauppiaskanava Oy+**
Kruunuvuorenkatu 5A, 00160 Helsinki
*Tel:* (09) 10 53010 *Fax:* (09) 10 5336238
*E-mail:* kaija.tynkkynen@k-kauppasuitto.fi
*Web Site:* www.k-kauppasliitto.fi
*Key Personnel*
Man Dir: Rinta Perttu
Publishing Manager: Tommi Tanhuanpaa
 *Tel:* (09) 105336218 *Fax:* (09) 105336206
 *E-mail:* tommi.tanhuanpaa@k-kauppasliitto.fi
Founded: 1912
Publishing House of the Finnish Retailers Associ-
 ation
Groceries, food, shoes, clothes, sports equipment,
 builders' & agricultural supplies.
Subjects: Cookery, Crafts, Games, Hobbies,
 House & Home
ISBN Prefix(es): 951-635

**Svenska Oesterbottens Litteraturfoerening**
Stagnas Vagen 85, 66640 Maxmo
*Tel:* (06) 3450286
*Key Personnel*
Contact: Gun Anderssen
Subjects: Poetry
ISBN Prefix(es): 951-95007

**Tietoteos Publishing Co**
PL 22, 02881 Veikkola
*Tel:* (09) 2564475 *Fax:* (09) 8136361
*E-mail:* tt@jkttietoteos.fi
*Web Site:* www.jkttietoteos.fi
*Key Personnel*
Man Dir: Jyrki K Talvitie *E-mail:* jyrki.talvitie@
 tt.inet.fi
Founded: 1948
Subjects: Economics, Travel
ISBN Prefix(es): 951-9035; 951-8919

**Ursa ry+**
Raatimiehenkatu 3A2, 00140 Helsinki
*Tel:* (09) 684 0400 *Fax:* (09) 6840 4040
*E-mail:* ursa@ursa.fi
*Web Site:* www.ursa.fi
*Key Personnel*
Publications Dir: Markku Sarimaa *Tel:* (09) 6840
 4060 *E-mail:* markku.sarimaa@ursa.fi
Founded: 1921
Subjects: Earth Sciences, Physical Sciences, Sci-
 ence (General)
ISBN Prefix(es): 951-9269; 952-5329

**Osuuskunta Vastapaino+**
Yliopistonkatu 60 A, 33100 Tampere
*Tel:* (03) 214 6246 *Fax:* (03) 214 6646
*E-mail:* vastapaino@vastapaino.fi
*Web Site:* www.vastapaino.fi
*Key Personnel*
Man Dir: Teijo Makkonen *E-mail:* teijo.
 makkonen@vastapaino.fi
Founded: 1981

Subjects: Behavioral Sciences, Education, History,
 Journalism, Literature, Literary Criticism, Es-
 says, Philosophy, Social Sciences, Sociology,
 Women's Studies
ISBN Prefix(es): 951-9066; 951-768
Number of titles published annually: 25 Print
Total Titles: 180 Print

**Watti-Kustannus Oy**
Meritullinkatu 11 C, 00170 Helsinki
*Tel:* (09) 1356878 *Fax:* (09) 1356437
ISBN Prefix(es): 951-95945

**Weilin & Goos Oy+**
Subsidiary of Werner Soederstrom Osakeyhtio
 (WSOY )
Kappelitie 8, 02200 Espoo
Mailing Address: PL 123, 02201 Espoo
*Tel:* (09) 4377 603 *Fax:* (00) 4377 334
*E-mail:* asiakaspalvelu@wg.fi
*Web Site:* www.wg.fi
*Key Personnel*
President: Koskinen Olle
Publishing Dir: Juhani Mikola
Editorial Manager, Nonfiction: Kuosmanen Riitta-
 Liisa
Information Officer: Irmeli Kotkavuori
Founded: 1872
Subjects: Animals, Pets, Art, Health, Nutrition,
 History, Nonfiction (General)
ISBN Prefix(es): 951-35
Subsidiaries: Bertmark Media AB

**Werner Soederstrom Osakeyhtio (WSOY)+**
Division of SanomaWSOY Corporation
Bulevardi 12, 00120 Helsinki
Mailing Address: PO Box 222, 00121 Helsinki
*Tel:* (09) 61 681 *Fax:* (09) 6168 3566
*Key Personnel*
Man Dir: Jorma Kaimio *E-mail:* jorma.kaimio@
 wsoy.fi
Foreign Rights Manager: Sirkku Klemola
 *E-mail:* sirkku.klemola@wsoy.fi
Literary Dir: Touko Siltala *E-mail:* touko.siltala@
 wsoy.fi
Educational Division: Hannu Laukkanen
 *E-mail:* hannu.laukkanen@wsoy.fi
Founded: 1878
Subjects: Education, Fiction, Nonfiction (General)
ISBN Prefix(es): 951-0
*Associate Companies:* Rautakirja Oy, Koivu-
 vaarankuja 2, 01640 Vantaa *Tel:* (09) 85281
 *Fax:* (09) 8533281; WS Bookwell, Teollisuustie
 4, 06100 Porvoo *Tel:* (019) 21941 *Fax:* (019)
 219 4802
Subsidiaries: Ajasto Osakeyhtio; Bertmark A/S;
 Bertmark Media AB; Bertmark Norge AS;
 Bertmarks Forlag AB; Weilin & Goos Oy
*Book Club(s):* Uudet Kirjat

**WSOY**, see Werner Soederstrom Osakeyhtio
 (WSOY)

**Yliopistopaino/Helsinki University Press+**
Teollisuuskatu 23B, 00014 University of Helsinki
Mailing Address: PO Box 26, 00014 University
 of Helsinki
*Tel:* (09) 7010 230; (09) 7010 2360 *Fax:* (09)
 7010 2370
*E-mail:* sst@yopaino.yliopistopaino.helsinki.fi
*Web Site:* www.yliopistopaino.helsinki.fi
*Key Personnel*
Chief Executive: Reino Lantto
Dir of Publishing: Minna Laukkanen
Founded: 1987
Subjects: Behavioral Sciences, Biological Sci-
 ences, Communications, Drama, Theater, Ed-
 ucation, Environmental Studies, Gay & Les-
 bian, Health, Nutrition, History, Journalism,
 Language Arts, Linguistics, Literature, Liter-
 ary Criticism, Essays, Mathematics, Medicine,
 Nursing, Dentistry, Music, Dance, Psychology,

Psychiatry, Social Sciences, Sociology, Theology, Travel, Women's Studies
ISBN Prefix(es): 951-570; 951-95164; 952-442
*Parent Company:* Helsinki University

**Yritystieto Oy - Foretagsdata AB**
PO Box 148, 00181 Helsinki
*Tel:* (09) 648292 *Fax:* (09) 648250
*Key Personnel*
Publisher: Boerje Thilman
Founded: 1972
Subjects: Business
ISBN Prefix(es): 951-9102

# France

## General Information

*Capital:* Paris
*Language:* French (regional dialects), Basque in the Basque country of the southwest, Breton in Brittany, Catalan in Roussillon, Corsican in Corsica, Dutch along parts of border with Belgium, German in Alsace, Occitan in south; most people in these minority linguistic groups also speak French
*Religion:* Predominantly Roman Catholic
*Population:* 59.3 million
*Bank Hours:* 0900-1200, 1400-1600 Monday-Friday. Some closed Monday.
*Shop Hours:* 0900-1930 Monday-Saturday. Many closed Monday
*Currency:* 100 Eurocents = 1 Euro; 6.55957 French francs = 1 Euro
*Export/Import Information:* Member of the European Economic Community. 5.5% VAT on books. Import licenses not required. There is a control of the book trade based on a number of legal and regulating provisions applying to the import of pirated publications, articles and writings that offend against morality and public order, publications harmful to youth, writings forbidden by the Minister for the Interior; the customs official must submit articles subject to control for examination by the General Information Service of the Ministry of the Interior.
*Copyright:* UCC, Berne, Buenos Aires, Florence (see Copyright Conventions, pg xi)

**ABES,** see Agence Bibliographique de l'Enseignement Superieur

**Academie Nationale de Reims**
17 rue du Jard, 51100 Reims
*Tel:* (0326) 910449 *Fax:* (0326) 910449
*E-mail:* academie.nationale.reims@wanadoo.fr
*Key Personnel*
Secretary General: Patrick Demouy *Tel:* (0326) 479819 *E-mail:* patrick.demouy@laposte.net
Administrative Secretary: Philippe Petit-Stervinou
Founded: 1841
Founded by Cardinal Gousset, archeveque de Reims.
Subjects: Biography, Communications, History
Total Titles: 500 Print
Foreign Rep(s): Champagne

**Editions Accarias L'Originel+**
cite Industrielle, 75011 Paris
*Tel:* (01) 43 48 73 07 *Fax:* (01) 43 48 73 07
*E-mail:* originel-accarias@club-internet.fr
*Key Personnel*
Dir: Jean-Louis Accarias
Founded: 1980
Subjects: Philosophy, Religion - Buddhist, Religion - Hindu, Religion - Other, Social Sciences, Sociology
ISBN Prefix(es): 2-86316

*Shipping Address:* Dilisco, 128 bis avenue Jean Jaures, 94200 Ivry-sur-Seine
*Orders to:* Dilisco, 128 bis avenue Jean Jaures, 94200 Ivry-sur-Seine

**Editions ACLA+**
5 bis, blvd Saint Paul, 75004 Paris
*Tel:* (01) 48 04 00 75 *Fax:* (01) 42 77 72 98
*Telex:* 613814
*Key Personnel*
Man Dir: Thierry Schimpff
Founded: 1980
Subjects: Sports, Athletics
ISBN Prefix(es): 2-86519

**ACR Edition+**
20 ter, rue de Bezons, 92400 Courbevoie, Paris
*Tel:* (01) 47 88 14 92 *Fax:* (01) 43 33 38 81
*E-mail:* acredition@acr-edition.com
*Web Site:* www.acr-edition.com
*Key Personnel*
Man Dir, Rights & Permissions: A Rafif
Editorial: Mrs M P Kerbrat
Founded: 1983
Membership(s): Syndicat de L'Edition Groupe Art.
Subjects: Art
ISBN Prefix(es): 2-86770
Foreign Rep(s): Artbook International (London)

**Actes-Graphiques+**
67 ter Cours Fauriel, 42010 Saint-Etienne Cedex 2
Mailing Address: BP 81, 42010 Saint-Etienne Cedex 2
*Tel:* (04) 77 21 23 80; (06) 09 42 21 13 *Fax:* (04) 77 25 39 28
*Web Site:* www.actes-graphiques.com
*Key Personnel*
Dir: Georges Callet *E-mail:* georges.callet@free.fr
Founded: 1994
Subjects: Geography, Geology, Government, Political Science, Humor, Literature, Literary Criticism, Essays, Mysteries, Photography, Regional Interests, Religion - Catholic, Religion - Other
ISBN Prefix(es): 2-910868
Subsidiaries: Le Henaff-Action Graphique
Distributor for Action Graphique; Le Henaff

**Editions Actes Sud+**
BP 38, 13633 Arles Cedex
*Tel:* (04) 90 49 86 91 *Fax:* (04) 90 96 95 25
*E-mail:* contact@actes-sud.fr
*Web Site:* www.actes-sud.fr
*Key Personnel*
President: Hubert Nyssen
Man Dir: Francoise Nyssen
Editorial: Bertrand Py
Rights: Franck Benalloul
Foreign Rights: Elisabeth Beyer *Tel:* (04) 90 49 56 66 *E-mail:* e.beyer@actes-sud.fr
Financial Dir: Jean Paul Capitani
Founded: 1978
Subjects: Biography, Drama, Theater, Literature, Literary Criticism, Essays, Poetry
ISBN Prefix(es): 2-7427; 2-86869; 2-86943; 2-7274; 2-85376; 2-901567
Number of titles published annually: 300 Print
Imprints: Babel (paperback); Solin (nonfiction: essays, biographies & foreign literature); Travel Aventure; Cactus
Subsidiaries: Actes Sud Junior (Children books & literature); Babel (paperback); Sinbad (Arabv literatures & Islam); Solin (nonfiction: essays, biographies & foreign literature)
*Branch Office(s)*
18 rue Seguier, 75006 Paris *Tel:* (01) 55 42 63 00 *Fax:* (01) 55 42 63 01 *E-mail:* accueil.paris@actes-sud.fr
Distributor for Andre Dimanche; Lemeac; Paris-Musees

*Bookshop(s):* 47, rue du Docteur Fanton, 13200 Arles *Tel:* (04) 90495677 *E-mail:* librairie@actes-sud.fr; Le Mejan, Pl Nina Berberova, 13200 Arles *E-mail:* mejan@actes-sud.fr
*Orders to:* U D Union Distributors Flammarion, 2A Delta, 29-31 ave Guynemer, BP 403, Chevilly Lorue, 94152 Rungis Cedex

**Action Artistique de la Ville de Paris**
25 rue Saint-Louis-en-l'Ile, 75004 Paris
*Tel:* (01) 43 25 30 30 *Fax:* (01) 43 25 17 69
*E-mail:* aavp@club-internet.fr; edition@aavp.com
*Web Site:* www.aavp.com
Founded: 1977
Also specializes in Urbanism.
Subjects: Architecture & Interior Design, Art, History
ISBN Prefix(es): 2-905118; 2-913246
Total Titles: 70 Print
Distributor for CiD

**ADPF Publications** (Association pour la Diffusion de la Pensee Francaise)
6, rue Ferrus, 75683 Paris Cedex 14
*Tel:* (01) 43 13 11 00 *Fax:* (01) 43 13 11 25
*E-mail:* adpfpublications@adpf.asso.fr
*Web Site:* www.france.diplomatie.fr; www.adpf.asso.fr
*Key Personnel*
President: Pierrette Bonnaud
Dir: Francois Neuville
Editorial Dir: Anne Parian
Service Communication: Anne du Parquet
Founded: 1996
Subjects: Art, Biography, Literature, Literary Criticism, Essays, Philosophy, Photography, Poetry
ISBN Prefix(es): 2-911127

**Adrian+**
12 rue Bachaumont, 75002 Paris
*Tel:* (01) 42 36 44 29 *Fax:* (01) 42 36 44 29
*Key Personnel*
Publisher: Paul Adrian
Specialize in spectacles of circus, cinema or variety.
ISBN Prefix(es): 2-900107
Total Titles: 9 Print

**Adverbum SARL+**
La Fresquiere, 04340 Meolans-Revel
*Tel:* (04) 92 81 28 81 *Fax:* (04) 92 81 37 11
*E-mail:* info@adverbum.fr
*Web Site:* www.adverbum.fr
*Key Personnel*
Manager: Michel Mirale
Founded: 1989
Subjects: Anthropology, Behavioral Sciences, Biblical Studies, Health, Nutrition, How-to, Language Arts, Linguistics, Medicine, Nursing, Dentistry, Religion - Catholic
ISBN Prefix(es): 2-907653; 2-911328; 2-914338; 2-911220
Number of titles published annually: 18 Print
Total Titles: 120 Print
Imprints: Editions Desiris; Editions Gregoriennes; Atelier Perrousseaux Editeur; Editions le Sureau

**Agence Bibliographique de l'Enseignement Superieur**
Unit of French Ministry for Higher Education
25, rue Guillaume Dupuytren, BP 4367, 34196 Montpellier Cedex 5
*Tel:* (04) 67 54 84 10 *Fax:* (04) 67 54 84 14
*E-mail:* nom@abes.fr
*Web Site:* www.abes.fr
*Key Personnel*
Dir: Sabine Barral *E-mail:* barral@abes.fr
Librarian: Anne Brigant *E-mail:* brigant@abes.fr
Founded: 1994
Membership(s): GFII, ADBS, IFLA, EUSIDIC & AFUGI.

Subjects: Library & Information Sciences
ISBN Prefix(es): 2-912292
Total Titles: 2 CD-ROM
Imprints: CCNPS
*Branch Office(s)*
Repertoire des bibliotheque
Distributed by Bibliopolis

**Editions Al Liamm**
venelle Poulbriken, 29200 Brest
*Tel:* (0298) 02 10 84
*Key Personnel*
Man Dir: Ronan Huon
Founded: 1949
This is a non-commercial organization specializing in the Breton Language.
Subjects: Drama, Theater, Education, Fiction, Literature, Literary Criticism, Essays, Poetry
ISBN Prefix(es): 2-7368; 2-902427
*Parent Company:* Association Al Liamm, 2 Venelle Poulbriquen, 29200 Brest
*U.S. Office(s):* Schoenhof's Foreign Books, Catalogue Dept, 76A Mount Auburn St, Cambridge, MA 02138, United States *Tel:* 617-547-8855 *Fax:* 617-547-8551
Stephen Griffin, 9 Irvington Rd, Medford, MA, United States
*Orders to:* R Huon L Vennelle Poulbriquen, 29200 Brest

**Editions Albatros**, see Editions Copernic

**Alliance Biblique Universelle**, *imprint of* Societe Biblique Francaise

**Alsatia SA**
4, rue de Fesches, 25490 Dampierre les Bois
Mailing Address: BP 1066, 68051 Mulhouse Cedex
*Tel:* (03) 89 45 21 53; (03) 89 56 97 60 *Fax:* (03) 89 45 18 98; (03) 89 56 97 63
*Web Site:* www.forum-alsatia.com
*Key Personnel*
President: Eric de Valence
Sales, Publicity, Advertising, Rights & Permissions: Virginie Poussier
Founded: 1896
Subjects: Biography, Education, History, How-to, Medicine, Nursing, Dentistry, Poetry, Religion - Other
ISBN Prefix(es): 2-7032
*Bookshop(s):* Librairie Alsatia, 31 pl de la Cathedrale, 67000 Strasbourg *Tel:* (03) 88 32 13 93; Librairie Union, 28 rue des Tetes, 68000 Colmar; 26 rue Charles de Gaulle, 68130 Altkirch; 108 ruede la Republique, 68500 Guebwiller; 4 place de la Reunion, Mulhouse Cedex

**Editions Alternatives+**
5 rue de Pontoise, 75005 Paris
*Tel:* (01) 43 29 88 64 *Fax:* (01) 43 29 02 70
*E-mail:* info@editionsalternatives.com
*Web Site:* www.editionsalternatives.com
*Key Personnel*
President: Gerard Aime *Tel:* (01) 46 33 49 22
Founded: 1975
Subjects: Alternative, Architecture & Interior Design, Art, House & Home, How-to, Music, Dance, Photography
ISBN Prefix(es): 2-86227
*Orders to:* CDE, 17 rue de Tournon, 75006 Paris

**Editions ALTESS+**
4 rue des Petits Hotels, espace Harmonie, 75010 Paris
*Tel:* (01) 47 70 78 79 *Fax:* (01) 47 70 78 77
*E-mail:* eliaur@club-internet.fr
*Web Site:* www.ifrance.com/3eMillenaire/altess/index.htm
*Key Personnel*
Contact: Alain-Rene Gelineau

Founded: 1990
Subjects: Biography, Health, Nutrition, Poetry, Psychology, Psychiatry, Religion - Other, Spirituality; personal development
ISBN Prefix(es): 2-84243; 2-905219
Number of titles published annually: 15 Print
Total Titles: 160 Print
Distributed by LAVAL Distribution (Quebec Canada)
Distributor for Editions Voici la Clef (Here's the Key) (France)
*Showroom(s):* Espace Harmonie, 4 rue des Petits Hotels, 75010 Paris *Tel:* (01) 47 70 78 79 *Fax:* (01) 47 70 78 77
*Warehouse:* ALTESS-AR Gelineau, 95 Residence Vincennes, 77330 Ozoir-la-Ferriere *Tel:* (01) 64 40 35 89 *Fax:* (01) 64 40 27 57
*Orders to:* ALTESS-AR Gelineau, 95 Residence Vincennes, 77330 Ozoir-la-Ferriere *Tel:* (01) 64 40 35 89 *Fax:* (01) 64 40 27 57

**Editions Alzieu+**
BP 3045, 38816 Grenoble Cedex 1
*Tel:* (04) 76 51 09 51 *Fax:* (04) 76 51 09 51
*E-mail:* admin@editions-alzieu.com
*Web Site:* www.editions-alzieu.com
*Key Personnel*
Dir: Claude Alzieu
Founded: 1991
ISBN Prefix(es): 2-910717; 2-914093
Distributed by Brepols

**Editions de l'Amateur+**
43 bis, rue des Entrepreneurs, 75015 Paris
*Tel:* (01) 56 77 06 20
*Key Personnel*
President-Dir General: Nuria Boussac
Subjects: Art
ISBN Prefix(es): 2-85917; 2-84647

**Editions d'Amerique et d'Orient, Adrien Maisonneuve+**
11 rue St-Sulpice, 75006 Paris
*Tel:* (01) 43 26 86 35 *Fax:* (01) 43 54 59 54
*E-mail:* maisonneuve@maisonneuve-adrien.com
*Web Site:* www.maisonneuve-adrien.com
*Key Personnel*
Man Dir: Jean Maisonneuve
Founded: 1926
Subjects: Art, Ethnicity, History, Philosophy, Religion - Other, Social Sciences, Sociology
ISBN Prefix(es): 2-7200
Imprints: Librairie D'Amerique Et D'Orient
*Bookshop(s):* 3 bis, place de la Sorbonne, 75005 Paris *Tel:* (01) 43 26 19 50 *Fax:* (01) 43 54 59 54

**Editions Amez+**
One Sq de l'Aiguillage, 67100 Strasbourg
*Tel:* (03) 88 84 56 56 *Fax:* (03) 88 84 56 84
*Key Personnel*
Associate Editor: Christine Vanet
Founded: 1991
Subjects: Art
ISBN Prefix(es): 2-909242

**L'Amitie par le Livre+**
13 ave du 60 Ri, 25001 Cedex, Besancon
Mailing Address: BP 1031, 25001 Cedex, Besancon
*Tel:* (03) 81820894 *Fax:* (03) 81820894
*Key Personnel*
Dir General: Gerard Varin
Founded: 1930
Subjects: Biography, Education, Humor, Literature, Literary Criticism, Essays, Natural History, Photography, Poetry
ISBN Prefix(es): 2-7121

**Editions Amphora SA+**
14 rue de l'Odeon, 75006 Paris

Mailing Address: 27 rue Saint Andre des Arts, 75006 Paris
*Tel:* (01) 43 26 10 87 *Fax:* (01) 40 46 85 76
*E-mail:* sports@ed-amphora.fr
*Web Site:* www.ed-amphora.fr
*Key Personnel*
Man Dir & Publicity: Bernard Dubois
Founded: 1954
Subjects: Crafts, Games, Hobbies, Sports, Athletics
ISBN Prefix(es): 2-85180
*Branch Office(s)*
27, rue Saint Andre des Arts, 75006 Paris *Tel:* (01) 43 29 03 04 *Fax:* (01) 43 29 49 49
Distributed by Dimedia (Canada); Interforum Benelux (Belgium); OLF Diffusion (Switzerland)
Distributor for Editions Actio; Editions du Puits Fleuri

**Editions Amrita SA+**
Les Cheyroux, 24580 Plazac-Rouffignac
*Tel:* (05) 53 50 79 54 *Fax:* (05) 53 50 80 20
*E-mail:* amrita.editions@perigord.com
*Key Personnel*
PDG: Anne Meurois-Givaudan
Founded: 1984
Subjects: Art, Astrology, Occult, Health, Nutrition, How-to, Parapsychology, Philosophy, Religion - Other
ISBN Prefix(es): 2-904616; 2-911022

**L'Anabase+**
284 rue de Croisades, Les Jardins du Ponant, 11 bat H, 34280 La Grande-Motte
*Tel:* (04) 67 56 13 38; (01) 30 41 07 47 *Fax:* (01) 34 85 80 73
*Key Personnel*
Contact: Christian Molinier
Founded: 1991
Subjects: Literature, Literary Criticism, Essays, Philosophy, Psychology, Psychiatry, Social Sciences, Sociology
ISBN Prefix(es): 2-909535
*Bookshop(s):* Librairie Roudil, 53, rue Saint Jacques, 75005 Paris
*Distribution Center:* 8 rue des ecoles, 75005 Paris

**Anako Editions+**
236 Ave Victor Hugo, 94120 Fontenay-Sous-Bois
*Tel:* (01) 43 94 92 88 *Fax:* (01) 43 94 02 45
*E-mail:* anako.editions@anako.com
*Web Site:* www.anako.com
*Key Personnel*
Dir: Patrick Bernard
Sales & Administration: Jean-Marie Gehin
Founded: 1988
Subjects: Anthropology, Photography, Travel
ISBN Prefix(es): 2-907754

**Editions l'Ancre de Marine+**
11 rue au Coq, 27400 Louviers
*Tel:* (02) 32 25 45 97
*E-mail:* service-clients@ancre-de-marine.com
*Web Site:* www.ancre-de-marine.com
*Key Personnel*
Dir: Bertrand de Queretain
Founded: 1985
Subjects: History, Maritime, Regional Interests
ISBN Prefix(es): 2-905970; 2-84141
Number of titles published annually: 20 Print
Total Titles: 200 Print
*Parent Company:* Syndicat National de l'edition
Imprints: Cifonit Figle
Distributed by Edilarge Ouest France

**Editions d'Annabelle+**
8 rue d'Anjou, 75008 Paris
Mailing Address: 11, rue Tronchet, 75008 Paris
*Tel:* (01) 47 42 01 61 *Fax:* (01) 47 42 42 14
*Key Personnel*
Manager: Lydia Rolland

Founded: 1991
Subjects: Animals, Pets
ISBN Prefix(es): 2-909660
*Bookshop(s):* Sofedis, 29 rue St, Sulpice 6e, Paris
*Warehouse:* Sodis

**Annales de l'Est**, *imprint of* Presses
Universitaires de Nancy

**Annales du Bac**, *imprint of* Librairie Vuibert

**l'ANRT**, see Atelier National de Reproduction
des Theses

**Edition Anthese+**
30 ave Jean-Jaures, 94117 Arcueil Cedex
*Tel:* (01) 46 56 06 67 *Fax:* (01) 49 85 09 92
*Telex:* 202382 F
*Key Personnel*
Man Dir: Claude Draeger
Sales: Fransoise Benoit-Latour
Press: Cristina Campodonico
Founded: 1983
Subjects: Architecture & Interior Design, Art, Bi-
ography
ISBN Prefix(es): 2-904420; 2-912257
*Orders to:* Generale du Livre, 13 rue Ernest Cres-
sou, 75014 Paris

**APRD**, see Association pour la Recherche et
l'Information demographiques (APRD)

**L'Arbalete**
8 rue Paul-Bert, 69150 Decines
*Tel:* (04) 72933434 *Fax:* (04) 72933400
Subjects: Art, Literature, Literary Criticism, Es-
says
ISBN Prefix(es): 2-902375

**Editions Arcam**
40 rue de Bretagne, 75003 Paris
*Tel:* (01) 42729312
*E-mail:* phreatiq@multimania.com
*Key Personnel*
Man Dir: Lorris Murail
Editorial, Sales, Production & Publicity: Gerard
Murail
Founded: 1971
Subjects: Art, Poetry
ISBN Prefix(es): 2-86476

**L'Arche Editeur**
86, rue Bonaparte, 75006 Paris
*Tel:* (01) 46 33 46 45 *Fax:* (01) 46 33 56 40
*E-mail:* contact@arche-editeur.com
*Web Site:* www.arche-editeur.com
*Key Personnel*
Dir: Rachel Rudolf
Stage Rights: Katharina Bismarck *Tel:* (01) 46 33
63 26
Bookstore Dept: Laurence Dorveaux *Tel:* (01) 46
33 57 47 *E-mail:* commande@arche-editeur.
com
Founded: 1947
Publishes some of the most famous dramatic au-
thors of the 19th & 20th centuries, also con-
temporary texts. Essays on art, music, cinema
& philosophy.
Membership(s): SNE (Syndicate National de
L'Edition).
Subjects: Art, Biography, Drama, Theater, Litera-
ture, Literary Criticism, Essays, Music, Dance,
Philosophy, Psychology, Psychiatry, Social Sci-
ences, Sociology
ISBN Prefix(es): 2-85181
Number of titles published annually: 15 Print
Total Titles: 436 Print
Foreign Rep(s): Claude M Diffusion (Canada)

**Editions de l'Archipel+**
34 rue des Bourdonnais, 75001 Paris
*Tel:* (01) 55 80 77 40 *Fax:* (01) 55 80 77 41
*E-mail:* ecricom@wanadoo.fr
*Key Personnel*
Dir: Jean-Daniel Belfond
Founded: 1991
Subjects: Biography, Fiction, Literature, Literary
Criticism, Essays
ISBN Prefix(es): 2-84187; 2-909241
Number of titles published annually: 80 Print
Total Titles: 300 Print
Divisions: Editions Ecriture; Presses du Chatelet
Foreign Rep(s): Chloe Ataroff (US); Arabella
Cruse (Netherlands, Scandinavia); Anna
Droumeva (Bulgaria, Romania, Serbia and
Montenegro); Catherine Fragou-Rassinier
(Greece); Laura Grandi (Italy); Judit Hermann
(Croatia, Hungary); Jackie Huang (China);
Asli Karasuil (Turkey); Pauline Kim (Ko-
rea); Eva Koralnik (Germany); Efrat Lev (Is-
rael); Corinne Quentin (Japan); Ingrida Sniedze
(Baltic States); Maria Strarz-Kanska (Poland);
Ludmilla Sushkova (Russia); Petra Tobiskova
(Czech Republic, Slovenia); Anne-Marie Vallat
(Spain)

**Architecture-Modelisme**, *imprint of* Editions
l'Instant Durable

**Publications Aredit+**
357 blvd Gambetta, 59200 Tourcoing
*Tel:* (03) 20 26 79 81
*Telex:* 130372 F
*Key Personnel*
Editor: Emile Keirsbilk
Editorial, Publicity: Yves Cattelain
Subjects: Fiction, Military Science, Romance,
Science Fiction, Fantasy, Western Fiction
ISBN Prefix(es): 2-7346; 2-7311

**Editions de l'Armancon+**
24, rue de l'Hotel-de-Ville, 21390 Precy-sous-Thil
Mailing Address: BP 14, 21390 Precy-sous-Thil
*Tel:* (03) 80 64 41 87 *Fax:* (03) 80 64 46 96
*E-mail:* info@editions-armancon.fr
*Web Site:* www.editions-armancon.fr
*Key Personnel*
Dir: Gerard Gautier
Founded: 1987
Subjects: Art, Biography, Cookery, History, Liter-
ature, Literary Criticism, Essays, Photography,
Regional Interests, Wine & Spirits
ISBN Prefix(es): 2-906594; 2-84479
Number of titles published annually: 10 Print
Total Titles: 110 Print

**Armand Colin Drott**, *imprint of* Editions Dalloz
Sirey

**Arnette Blackwell SA+**
224, blvd Saint-Germain, 75007 Paris
*Tel:* (01) 45 49 65 00 *Fax:* (01) 45 49 12 88
*Telex:* 270150F TXFRA 690
*Key Personnel*
General Dir: Gil Raveux
Founded: 1915
Subjects: Medicine, Nursing, Dentistry
ISBN Prefix(es): 2-7184
*Parent Company:* Blackwell Scientific Publica-
tions, United Kingdom
*U.S. Office(s):* Blackwell Scientific Publication,
Boston, MA, United States
*Orders to:* One rue d Lille, 75007 Paris *Tel:* (01)
44 86 07 70 *Fax:* (01) 44 86 07 66

**Art Creation Realisation**, see ACR Edition

**Arthaud**, *imprint of* Flammarion Groupe

**Artprice+**
BP 69, 69270 Saint-Romain-au-Mont-d'Or
*Tel:* (04) 72 421 706 *Fax:* (04) 78 220 606
*Web Site:* www.artprice.com
*Key Personnel*
Dir General: Jacques Madina
ISBN Prefix(es): 2-909711
*Parent Company:* Groupe Serveur

**ASA Editions**
18, rue Laffitte, 75009 Paris
*Tel:* (01) 47 70 42 90 *Fax:* (01) 47 70 42 98
*E-mail:* info@asaeditions.fr
*Web Site:* www.asaeditions.fr
*Key Personnel*
Administrative & Sales Manager: Marc Wiltz
Dir Commercial/Export: Catherine Sas
ISBN Prefix(es): 2-911589

**L'Asiatheque**, see Langues &
Mondes-L'Asiatheque

**Editions Assimil SA**
13 rue Gay-Lussac, 94431 Chennevieres-sur-
Marne Cedex
Mailing Address: BP 25, 94331 Chennevieres-sur-
Marne Cedex
*Tel:* (01) 45 76 87 37 *Fax:* (01) 45 94 06 55
*E-mail:* contact@assimil.com
*Web Site:* www.assimil.com
*Key Personnel*
Dir & Editorial: J L Cherel
Sales, Advertising: J P Vandenhende
Production: A Blanquet
Founded: 1929
Subjects: Language Arts, Linguistics
ISBN Prefix(es): 90-74996; 2-7005; 88-86968
*Bookshop(s):* Boutique Assimil, 11, rue des Pyra-
mides, 75001 Paris *Tel:* (01) 42 60 40 66
*Fax:* (01) 40 20 02 17

**L'Association**
16 rue de la Pierre-Levee, 75011 Paris
*Tel:* (01) 43558587 *Fax:* (01) 43558621
*E-mail:* lassocia@club-internet.fr
*Key Personnel*
President: Jean-Christophe Menu
Founded: 1990
ISBN Prefix(es): 2-909020; 2-84414

**Association pour la Recherche et l'Information
demographiques (APRD)**
Universite de Paris-Sorbonne, 191 rue Saint-
Jacques, 75005 Paris
*Tel:* (01) 44321400 *Fax:* (01) 40462588
*Key Personnel*
Chairman & President: Gerard-Francois Dumont
*E-mail:* Gerard-Francois.Dumont@paris4.
sorbonne.fr
Founded: 1976
Subjects: Social Sciences, Sociology
ISBN Prefix(es): 2-86419
Total Titles: 27 Print

**Editions de l'Atelier+**
12 ave Soeur Rosalie, 75013 Paris
*Tel:* (01) 44 08 95 15 *Fax:* (01) 44 08 95 00
*Key Personnel*
President: Daniel Prin
Editor: Bernard Stephan
Foreign Rights: Valerie Francois
Sales Manager: Patrick Merrant
Founded: 1939
Subjects: Biblical Studies, Biography, Economics,
Government, Political Science, History, Reli-
gion - Catholic, Social Sciences, Sociology
ISBN Prefix(es): 2-7082

**Atelier National de Reproduction des Theses**
9 rue Auguste Angellier, 59046 Lille Cedex
*Tel:* (03) 20 30 86 73 *Fax:* (03) 20 54 21 95
*E-mail:* anrt@univ-lille3.fr

*Web Site:* www.anrtheses.com.fr
*Key Personnel*
Dir: Elisabeth Fichez
Founded: 1971
Reproduction sur micro-fiches et numerisation de theses universitaires soutenues en France.
Subjects: Art, Geography, Geology, History, Language Arts, Linguistics, Law, Literature, Literary Criticism, Essays, Philosophy, Psychology, Psychiatry, Social Sciences, Sociology
ISBN Prefix(es): 2-284; 2-7295
Distributed by Presses du Septentrion (Universite Lille III at Villeneuve d'Ascq)

**Ateliers et Presses de Taize+**
71250 Taize-Communaute
*Tel:* (03) 85 50 30 50 *Fax:* (03) 85 50 30 55
*E-mail:* editions@taize.fr
*Web Site:* www.taize.fr
*Key Personnel*
Contact: Reynold Gallusser
Founded: 1959
Subjects: Religion - Catholic, Religion - Protestant
ISBN Prefix(es): 2-85040
Number of titles published annually: 2 Print
Imprints: Les Presses de Taize

**Editions Atlantica Seguier+**
Rue du Loustalot, Blvd du BAB, 64600 Anglet
*Tel:* (05) 59 52 84 00 *Fax:* (05) 59 52 84 01
*E-mail:* atlantica@atlantica.fr
*Web Site:* www.atlantica.fr
*Key Personnel*
Literary Dir: Marie-Helene Saphore *Tel:* (05) 59 52 84 07 *E-mail:* mhs@atlantica.fr
Founded: 1992
Subjects: Art, Biography, Drama, Theater, Fiction, Literature, Literary Criticism, Essays
ISBN Prefix(es): 2-84049

**Editions Atlas**
89 rue de la Boetie, 75008 Paris
*Tel:* (01) 40 74 38 38 *Fax:* (01) 45 61 19 85
*E-mail:* contact@editionsatlas.fr
*Web Site:* www.editionsatlas.fr
*Telex:* 642481F
*Key Personnel*
Contact: Patrick Lemarchand
ISBN Prefix(es): 2-7234; 2-7312
*Branch Office(s)*
1186, rue de Cocherel, Evreux *Tel:* (02) 32 29 29 29 *E-mail:* serviceclients@editionsatlas.fr

**ATP - Packager+**
ZA les Vignettes, 63405 Chamalieres Cedex
Mailing Address: BP 75, 63405 Chamalieres Cedex
*Tel:* (0473) 19 58 80 *Fax:* (0473) 195899
*E-mail:* atp.chamalieres@wanadoo.fr
*Key Personnel*
Dir: Herve Chaumeton
International Rights: Isabelle Leyris-Chambon *Tel:* 473195896
Founded: 1984
Subjects: Aeronautics, Aviation, Animals, Pets, Archaeology, Automotive, Cookery, Earth Sciences, Gardening, Plants, Health, Nutrition, History, House & Home, Natural History, Outdoor Recreation, Wine & Spirits
Number of titles published annually: 100 Print

**Aubanel Editions+**
7, rue d'Assas, 75014 Paris
*Tel:* (01) 53 03 31 00 *Fax:* (01) 45 49 17 00
*Web Site:* www.lamartiniere.fr/groupe/aubanel.htm
*Key Personnel*
Man Dir: Laurent Theodore-Aubanel
Founded: 1744
Subjects: Fiction, Psychology, Psychiatry, Regional Interests, Travel

ISBN Prefix(es): 2-7006
*Parent Company:* La Martiniere Groupe
*Branch Office(s)*
4, rue Pedro Meylan, 1208 Geneva, Switzerland
*Tel:* (022) 7365110 *Fax:* (022) 7352402

**Editions de l'Aube+**
BP 32, Le Moulin de Chateau, 84240 La-Tour-d'Aigues
*Tel:* (04) 90 07 46 60 *Fax:* (04) 90 07 53 02
*Web Site:* www.aube-editions.com/
*Key Personnel*
Man Dir: Jean Viard
Literary Dir: Marion Hennebert
Founded: 1987
Subjects: Cookery, Economics, Environmental Studies, Foreign Countries, Literature, Literary Criticism, Essays, Mysteries, Philosophy, Social Sciences, Sociology
ISBN Prefix(es): 2-87678; 2-7526
Distributed by Editions Zoe (Switzerland)

**Aubie,** *imprint of* Flammarion Groupe

**Editions Aubier-Montaigne SA**
26, rue Racine, 75278 Paris Cedex 06
*Tel:* (01) 40 51 31 00 *Fax:* (01) 43 29 21 48
*Key Personnel*
Man Dir: Mrs M Aubier-Gabail
Sales Manager, Rights & Permissions: Patrice Mentha
Founded: 1924
Subjects: Education, History, Language Arts, Linguistics, Philosophy, Poetry, Psychology, Psychiatry, Religion - Other, Social Sciences, Sociology
ISBN Prefix(es): 2-7007
*Parent Company:* Flammarion et Cie

**Etudes Augustiniennes,** see Institut d'Etudes Augustiniennes

**Editions d'Aujourd'hui (Les Introuvables)**
c/o L'Harmattan, 7 rue de l'Ecole-Polytechnique, 75005 Paris
*Tel:* (01) 43 54 79 10 *Fax:* (01) 43 29 86 20
*Key Personnel*
Man Dir: Odette Charriere
Founded: 1974
Subjects: Drama, Theater, Ethnicity, Fiction, Film, Video, Human Relations, Literature, Literary Criticism, Essays, Music, Dance, Poetry
ISBN Prefix(es): 2-7307; 2-85775
Distributed by UNIVERS (Canada)
*Bookshop(s):* 16 rue des ecoles, 75005 Paris
*Tel:* (01) 40 46 79 11; (01) 40 46 79 20

**Aurore Editions D'Art,** *imprint of* Editions Cercle d'Art SA

**Autrement Editions**
77 rue du Faubourg Saint-Antoine, 75011 Paris
*Tel:* (01) 44 73 80 00 *Fax:* (01) 44 73 00 12
*E-mail:* contact@autrement.com
*Web Site:* www.autrement.com
*Key Personnel*
President, Chief Executive Officer & Dir, Publication: Henry Dougier *E-mail:* henry.dougier@autrement.com
Sales & Transfer of Rights: Anne-Marie Bellard *E-mail:* commercial@autrement.com
Founded: 1975
Subjects: Anthropology, Behavioral Sciences, Fiction, Foreign Countries, History, Literature, Literary Criticism, Essays, Natural History, Nonfiction (General), Philosophy, Psychology, Psychiatry, Regional Interests, Social Sciences, Sociology, Travel
ISBN Prefix(es): 2-86260; 2-7467
Total Titles: 700 Print
Distributed by Editions du le Seuil

**Autres Temps+**
97, ave de la Gouffonne, 13009 Marseille
*Tel:* (0491) 26 80 33 *Fax:* (0491) 41 11 01
*E-mail:* editions.autrestemps@free.fr
Founded: 1990
Subjects: Literature, Literary Criticism, Essays
ISBN Prefix(es): 2-908805; 2-911873; 2-84521
Total Titles: 200 Print
Imprints: Litterature Generale

**Editions Philippe Auzou+**
24-32 rue des Amandiers, 75020 Paris
*Tel:* (01) 40 33 84 00 *Fax:* (01) 47 97 20 08
*E-mail:* editions@auzou.fr
*Web Site:* www.auzoueditions.com
*Telex:* Auzou Sofradif 220686 F
*Key Personnel*
President: M Philippe Auzou
Administrative Dir: Michele Halimi
Marketing Manager: Louise Darme
Founded: 1978
Subjects: Art
ISBN Prefix(es): 2-7338
Subsidiaries: Editions & Diffusions Internationales

**Editions l'Avant-Scene Theatre+**
6 rue Git-le-Coeur, 75006 Paris
*Tel:* (01) 46 34 28 20 *Fax:* (01) 43 54 50 14
*Web Site:* www.avant-scene-theatre.com
*Key Personnel*
Man Dir: Jacques Leclere
Founded: 1949
Subjects: Drama, Theater, Film, Video, Music, Dance
ISBN Prefix(es): 2-907468; 2-7498; 2-900130
Imprints: Editions des Quatre-Vents
*Warehouse:* 6 Mail Nord, 5350 Boynes

**Babel,** *imprint of* Editions Actes Sud

**Bac en Poche,** *imprint of* Librairie Vuibert

**Editions J B Bailliere**
2, cite Paradis, 75010 Paris
*Tel:* (01) 55 33 69 00 *Fax:* (01) 55 33 68 07
*Telex:* Livrcom 201326 F
*Key Personnel*
Dir General: Dr Philippe Le Due
Rights & Permissions: Arlette Hertig
Advertising: Marika Papageoriou
Founded: 1802
Subjects: Agriculture, Labor, Industrial Relations, Medicine, Nursing, Dentistry, Technology
ISBN Prefix(es): 2-7008

**La Baleine,** *imprint of* Editions du Seuil

**Editions Balland+**
33 rue Saint-Andre des Arts, 75006 Paris
*Tel:* (01) 43 25 74 40 *Fax:* (01) 46 33 56 21
*E-mail:* info@balland.fr
*Web Site:* www.balland.fr
*Key Personnel*
Publisher: Jean-Jacque Auj-ier
Sales: Jean-Paul Hirsch
Founded: 1966
Subjects: Biography, Fiction, Film, Video, Humor
ISBN Prefix(es): 2-7158

**La Bartavelle**
8, rue des Tanneries, 42190 Charlieu
*Tel:* (04) 77 69 01 50 *Fax:* (04) 77 60 11 94
*Key Personnel*
Publications Dir: Eric Ballandras
Subjects: Literature, Literary Criticism, Essays, Photography
ISBN Prefix(es): 2-87744; 2-84414; 2-70094

**Editions A Barthelemy+**
Domaine de Fontvert, 84132 Le Pontet Cedex
Mailing Address: BP 50, 84132 Le Pontet Cedex
*Tel:* (04) 90 03 60 00 *Fax:* (04) 90036009
*E-mail:* infos@editions-barthelemy.com
*Web Site:* www.editions-barthelemy.com
*Key Personnel*
Editor: Alain Barthelemy; Odile Barthelemy
Founded: 1978
Subjects: Cookery, Health, Nutrition, Regional
  Interests, Travel
ISBN Prefix(es): 2-87923

**Societe Nouvelle Rene Baudouin+**
10, rue de Nesle, 75006 Paris
*Tel:* (01) 43290050 *Fax:* (01) 43257241
*Key Personnel*
President: Alain Levy *E-mail:* al.levy@wanadoo.
  fr
Founded: 1974
Remainder dealer.
Subjects: Antiques, Art, Cookery
ISBN Prefix(es): 2-86396
Total Titles: 4 Print
Divisions: Le Dernier Terrain Vague; Levy; Edi-
  tions Charles Moreau

**Bayard Editions**, *imprint of* Bayard Presse

**Bayard Presse+**
3, rue Bayard, 75008 Paris
*Tel:* (01) 44 35 60 60; (01) 44 35 64 20 *Fax:* (01)
  44 35 61 61; (01) 44 35 60 73
*E-mail:* communication@bayard-presse.com
*Web Site:* www.bayardpresse.com
*Key Personnel*
President: Alain Cordier
Dir: Patrick Zago
Marketing Dir: H Sauzay
Dir, Communication: Emmanuelle Duthu
Founded: 1873
Specialize in essays & adult Books.
Subjects: Art, Education, History, Religion -
  Other, Social Sciences, Sociology, Humanities
ISBN Prefix(es): 2-227; 2-7009; 2-915480; 2-
  9518356
Number of titles published annually: 60 Print
Imprints: Bayard Editions; Centurion
*Orders to:* Sofedis, The Soufflot, 75005 Paris

**Editions des Beatitudes, Pneumatheque+**
Burtin, 41600 Nouan le Fuzelier
*Tel:* (02) 54 88 21 18 *Fax:* (02) 54 88 97 73
*E-mail:* infos2@editions-beatitudes.fr
*Web Site:* www.editions-beatitudes.fr
*Key Personnel*
Foreign Rights Manager: Laurence de Feydean
Founded: 1984
Subjects: Religion - Catholic
ISBN Prefix(es): 2-905480; 2-84024; 2-85847
Distributed by Alliance Service (Belgium); Albert
  Legrand SA (Switzerland); Editions Mediaspaul
  (Canada)
*Bookshop(s):* Logos-Beatitudes Diffusion,
  Monastere Notre-Dame des Sept Douleurs
  Preville, 21600 Ouges *Tel:* (03) 80 36 91 15
  *Fax:* (03) 80 36 91 15 *Web Site:* www.logos-
  beatitudes.com

**Beauchesne Editeur+**
7 cite du Cardinal Lemoine, 75005 Paris
*Tel:* (01) 53 10 08 18 *Fax:* (01) 53 10 85 19
*E-mail:* beauchesne2@wanadoo.fr
*Web Site:* www.editions-beauchesne.com
*Key Personnel*
President: Mr Jean Pierre Druaud
Dir General: Jean-Etienne Mittlelmann
Founded: 1851
Subjects: Biography, Government, Political Sci-
  ence, History, Human Relations, Journalism,

Literature, Literary Criticism, Essays, Religion
  - Other, Social Sciences, Sociology, Theology
ISBN Prefix(es): 2-7010
Total Titles: 800 Print; 1 CD-ROM; 1 Audio
Distributed by O L F S A (Suisse)
Distributor for Anne Sigier France (Belgique &
  Luxembourg); Anne Sigier (Canada)

**Editions Belin+**
8, rue Ferou, 75278 Paris Cedex 06
*Tel:* (01) 55 42 84 00 *Fax:* (01) 43 25 18 29
*E-mail:* contact@edition-belin.fr
*Web Site:* www.editions-belin.com
*Key Personnel*
President: Marie Claude Brossollet
Documentation: Soraya Eghbal-Dupouey
Marketing: Emmanuel Fouquet
Rights & Permissions: Anne Vignau
  *E-mail:* anne.vignau@editions-belin.fr
Founded: 1777
Subjects: Art, Education, Gardening, Plants, Lit-
  erature, Literary Criticism, Essays, Poetry, Sci-
  ence (General)
ISBN Prefix(es): 2-7011
Number of titles published annually: 150 Print; 5
  CD-ROM; 10 Audio
Total Titles: 2,000 Print; 40 Audio
Subsidiaries: Editions Herscher; Pour la Science
  SARL
*Shipping Address:* Editions Belin, 4 rue Ferdinand
  de Lesseps, 91420 Morangis
*Warehouse:* Editions Belin, 4 rue Ferdinand de
  Lesseps, 91420 Morangis *Tel:* (01) 69090097
  *Fax:* (01) 69348198

**Societe d'Edition Les Belles Lettres+**
95 Blvd Raspail, 75006 Paris
*Tel:* (01) 44398420 *Fax:* (01) 45449288
*E-mail:* courrier@lesbelleslettres.com
*Web Site:* www.lesbelleslettres.com
*Key Personnel*
President & Man Dir: Michel Desgranges
International Rights: Marie Jose D'Hoop
Founded: 1919
Subjects: Education, Fiction, History, Language
  Arts, Linguistics, Literature, Literary Criticism,
  Essays, Philosophy, Religion - Other, Classical
  studies
ISBN Prefix(es): 2-251
Imprints: Manitoba; Sortileges
*Bookshop(s):* Librairie Guillaume Bude, Paris

**Berg International Editeur+**
129 blvd Saint-Michel, 75005 Paris
*Tel:* (01) 43267273 *Fax:* (01) 46339499
*Cable:* BERGEDIT PARIS
*Key Personnel*
Man Dir: Georges Nataf
Contact: Marie Gougaud
Founded: 1969
Subjects: Anthropology, History, Literature, Lit-
  erary Criticism, Essays, Philosophy, Religion -
  Islamic, Religion - Jewish, Religion - Other
ISBN Prefix(es): 2-900269; 2-911289
*Orders to:* Press Universitairs de France, 14 Ave
  du Boisdel' Epi, 91003 Evry

**Berger-Levrault Editions SAS**
5, rue Andre Ampere, 54250 Champigneulles
Mailing Address: BP 79, 54250 Champigneulles
*Tel:* (03) 83 38 83 83 *Fax:* (03) 83 38 86 10; (03)
  83 38 37 12
*E-mail:* ble@berger-levrault.fr
*Web Site:* www.berger-levrault.fr
*Telex:* 270797 F
*Key Personnel*
President Dir General: Alain Sourisseau
Dir General: Gilles Brochen
Founded: 1676
Subjects: Architecture & Interior Design, Art,
  Ethnicity, History, Social Sciences, Sociology
ISBN Prefix(es): 2-7013

*Parent Company:* Berger-Levrault Imprimerie,
  Nancy
*Branch Office(s)*
3, rue Ferrus, 75014 Paris *Tel:* (01) 40644232
  *Fax:* (01) 40644230 *E-mail:* ble@berger-
  levrault.fr
*Bookshop(s):* Librairie Berger-Levrault, 23 pl
  Broglie, F-67000 Strasbourg

**Editions Bertout**
6 rue Gutenberg, 76810 Luneray
Mailing Address: BP 7, 76810 Luneray
*Tel:* (02) 35 04 69 68 *Fax:* (02) 35 04 69 65
*Web Site:* www.editionsbertout.com
*Key Personnel*
President: Josette Bertout
Dir: Florence Bertout
Founded: 1934
Subjects: Cookery, Genealogy, History, Regional
  Interests
ISBN Prefix(es): 2-86743
Imprints: La Memoire Normande

**Editions Bertrand-Lacoste+**
36 rue Saint-Germain-l'Auxerrois, 75041 Paris
  Cedex 01
*Tel:* (01) 53 40 53 53 *Fax:* (01) 42 33 82 47
*E-mail:* contact@bertrand-lacoste.fr
*Web Site:* www.bertrand-lacoste.fr
Founded: 1980
Subjects: Accounting, Computer Science, Eco-
  nomics, Law
ISBN Prefix(es): 2-7399; 2-7352

**La Bibliotheque des Arts+**
3, Place de l'Odeon, 75006 Paris
*Tel:* (01) 46331818 *Fax:* (01) 40469596
*Key Personnel*
Chairman: Francois Daulte
Founded: 1954
Subjects: Architecture & Interior Design, Art,
  Literature, Literary Criticism, Essays, Poetry,
  Travel
ISBN Prefix(es): 2-85047; 2-88453
Distributor for Ides & Calendes

**Bibliotheque Nationale de France** (National
  Library of France)+
58, rue de Richelieu, 75084 Paris Cedex 02
*Tel:* (01) 53 79 59 59; (01) 53 79 81 75; (01) 53
  79 87 94 *Fax:* (01) 53 79 81 72
*E-mail:* commercial@bnf.fr
*Web Site:* www.bnf.fr
*Key Personnel*
President: Jean-Noel Jeanneney
Head, Publications & Sales: Christopher Beslon
  *Tel:* (01) 53 79 88 01 *E-mail:* christopher.
  beslon@bnf.fr
Publishing department of the French National Li-
  brary.
Subjects: History, Library & Information Sci-
  ences, Literature, Literary Criticism, Essays
ISBN Prefix(es): 2-7177
Number of titles published annually: 30 Print
Total Titles: 500 Print
Foreign Rep(s): Sevil (Worldwide)

**Societe Biblique Francaise+**
5 Ave des Erables, 95400 Villiers-le-Bel
Mailing Address: BP 47, 95400 Villiers-le-Bel
*Tel:* (01) 39945051 *Fax:* (01) 39905351
*E-mail:* contacts@alliance-biblique-fr.org
*Web Site:* www.la-bible.net
*Key Personnel*
Editorial: Elsbeth Scherrer
  *E-mail:* elsbethscherrer@wanadoo.fr
Sales & Production: Pascal Dubs
Founded: 1818
Membership(s): United Bible Societies/Alliance
  Biblique Universelle.

Subjects: Religion - Catholic, Religion - Protestant
ISBN Prefix(es): 2-85300
Total Titles: 140 Print
Imprints: Alliance Biblique Universelle
*U.S. Office(s):* American Bible Society, 1865 Broadway, New York, NY 10023-9980, United States
Distributed by CERF; Excelsis; Oberlin
Distributor for Brepols; CERF; CLC; Desclee de Brower; Farel; Vie et Sante

**Adam Biro Editions+**
Division of Le Baron Perche
28, rue de Sevigne, 75004 Paris
*Tel:* (01) 44 59 84 59 *Fax:* (01) 44 59 87 17
*E-mail:* edibiro@freesurf.fr
*Key Personnel*
Editor: Adam Biro
Editor & Publicity: Laurence Golstennel
Author: Daniel Arasse; Bernard Comment; Georges Didi-Huberman; Ernst Gombrich; Tzvetan Todorov
Founded: 1987
Subjects: Antiques, Architecture & Interior Design, Art, Fashion, Photography
ISBN Prefix(es): 2-87660
Number of titles published annually: 20 Print
Total Titles: 285 Print
Distributor for Office du Livre (Switzerland); Presse de Belgique (Beligum)
*Warehouse:* Vilo, 21 Leval 11 ave Arago, Morangis
*Orders to:* Vilo, 25 rue Ginoux, 75015 Paris

**William Blake & Co+**
15, rue Maubec, 33037 Bordeaux Cedex
Mailing Address: BP 4, 33037 Bordeaux Cedex
*Tel:* (05) 56 31 42 20 *Fax:* (05) 56 31 45 47
*E-mail:* editions.william.blake@wanadoo.fr
*Web Site:* www.editions-william-blake-and-co.com
*Key Personnel*
Publications Dir: Jean-Paul Michel
Founded: 1976
Subjects: Architecture & Interior Design, Art, Literature, Literary Criticism, Essays, Philosophy, Photography, Poetry
ISBN Prefix(es): 2-84103; 2-905810
Imprints: L'Invention du Lecteur; La Pharmacie de Platon
Distributor for Arts & Arts

**Librairie Scientifique et Technique Albert Blanchard**, see Librairie Scientifique et Technique Albert Blanchard

**Blay Foldex**
40-48 rue des Meuniers, 93108 Montreuil Cedex
*Tel:* (01) 49 88 92 10 *Fax:* (01) 49 88 92 09
*Key Personnel*
Contact: Martin Kryn *E-mail:* martin.krynitz@jrc.lt
Founded: 1934
Private mapping company.
Subjects: How-to
*Parent Company:* Langenscheidt Publishing Group, Munich, Germany

**Blondel La Rougery SARL**
268, rue de Brement, 93561 Rosny-Sous-Bois Cedex
*Tel:* (01) 48 94 94 52 *Fax:* (01) 48 94 94 38
*Key Personnel*
Chairman: J Barbotte
Founded: 1902
Subjects: Advertising, Foreign Countries, Geography, Geology, How-to, Public Administration, Transportation
ISBN Prefix(es): 2-903862

**De Boccard Edition-Diffusion**
11, rue de Medicis, 75006 Paris
*Tel:* (01) 43 26 00 37 *Fax:* (01) 43 54 85 83
*Key Personnel*
Man Dir: Dominique Chaulet
Manager: Jean-Bernard Chaulet
Founded: 1866
Subjects: Archaeology, Art, Asian Studies, History, Religion - Other
ISBN Prefix(es): 2-7018

**Editions Andre Bonne+**
29 rue Marceau, 94200 Ivry-sur-Seine
*Tel:* (01) 45150061 *Fax:* (01) 45218175
*Key Personnel*
Dir General: Annet-Georges Aupois
Dir, Literature: Alain Armand-Villoy
Subjects: Art, Biography, Crafts, Games, Hobbies, History, Literature, Literary Criticism, Essays, Poetry, Travel
ISBN Prefix(es): 2-7019

**Bookmaker+**
12, rue Servandoni, 75006 Paris
*Tel:* (01) 43 54 84 34 *Fax:* (01) 43 54 71 02
*E-mail:* bookmake@club-internet.fr
*Key Personnel*
Editor: Jean-Loup Chiflet
Founded: 1985
Specialize in packaging.
Subjects: Art, Astronomy, Gardening, Plants, Bookart & Artist's Books, Edutainment, Picture Books
ISBN Prefix(es): 2-906986

**Bordas**, *imprint of* Editions Bordas

**Editions Bordas+**
89 blvd Blanqui, 75013 Paris
*Tel:* (01) 72 36 40 00 *Fax:* (01) 72 36 40 10
*Web Site:* www.editions-bordas.fr
*Key Personnel*
General Manager: Jean Lissarrague
Man Dir: Dominique Desmottes; Didier Tetaud
Editorial, Trade: Philippe Fournier-Bourdier
Editorial, School: Alain Cardona
Sales, France: Jean-Michel Angenault
Sales, Export: Alain Guilermin
Production: Francoise Barbera
Publicity, Trade: Dominique de Romanet
Publicity, School: Isabelle Brunelin
Rights & Permissions: Mireille Debenne
Founded: 1945
Subjects: Education, Nonfiction (General)
ISBN Prefix(es): 2-04; 2-7294; 2-7109
*Parent Company:* Groupe de la Cite, 20 ave Hoche, 75008 Paris
Imprints: Bordas; Pedagogie Modern; Technique et Vulgarisation
Subsidiaries: Societe Gauthier-Villars; Privat SA; Dunod Editeur SA (all France); Bordas-Dunod Bruxelles
*Bookshop(s):* Librairie Beranger, Liege, Belgium; Librairie Dunod, 30 rue St-Sulpice, 75006 Paris
*Warehouse:* Route d'Etampes, 45330 Malesherbes *Tel:* (01) 38349249 *Fax:* (01) 38347385
*Orders to:* 11 rue Gossin, 92543 Montrouge Cedex *Tel:* (01) 46 56 52 66 *Fax:* (01) 46 56 04 76

**Pierre Bordas & Fils, Editions**
25 rue Saint Sulpice, 75006 Paris
*Tel:* (01) 43 25 04 51 *Fax:* (01) 43 25 47 84
*E-mail:* pierre.bordas.filsd@wanadoo.fr
*Key Personnel*
Man Dir: Nicole Bordas
Editorial, Rights & Permissions: Pierre Bordas
Founded: 1978
Subjects: Art, Cookery, Crafts, Games, Hobbies, Education, Environmental Studies, Literature, Literary Criticism, Essays, Poetry, Travel

ISBN Prefix(es): 2-86311
*Distribution Center:* NQL, 78 Bd Saint Michel, 75280 Paris Cedex 06

**Presses Universitaires de Bordeaux (PUB)+**
Universite Michel de Montaigne Bordeaux 3, Domaine Universitaire, 33607 Pessac Cedex
*Tel:* (05) 57 12 44 22 *Fax:* (05) 57 12 45 34
*E-mail:* pub@u-bordeaux3.fr
*Web Site:* www.pub.montaigne.u-bordeaux.fr
*Key Personnel*
Dir General: Bernard Gilbert *Tel:* (05) 5712 4421
Dir Commercial: Antoine Poli *Tel:* (05) 5712 4634
Founded: 1983
Subjects: Anthropology, Education, Environmental Studies, Geography, Geology, History, Law, Literature, Literary Criticism, Essays, Philosophy, Wine & Spirits
ISBN Prefix(es): 2-86781
*Orders to:* CID, 131 blvd Saint-Michel, 75005 Paris *Tel:* (01) 43 54 47 15 *Fax:* (01) 43 54 80 73 *E-mail:* cid@msh-paris.fr
Nord-Sud, 150, rue Berthelot, 1190 Brussels, Belgium *Tel:* (02) 343 10 13 *Fax:* (02) 343 42 91
University of Exeter Press, Reed Hall, Streatham Drive, Exeter EX4 4QR, United Kingdom *Tel:* (01392) 263066 *Fax:* (01392) 263064 *E-mail:* uep@exeter.ac.uk *Web Site:* www.ex.ac.uk/uep/

**Bornemann**, *imprint of* Editions Sang de la Terre

**Editions Bornemann**
Imprint of Editions Sang de la Terre
62, rue Blanche, 75009 Paris
*Tel:* (01) 42 82 08 16 *Fax:* (01) 48 74 14 88
*Web Site:* www.sangdelaterre.com
*Key Personnel*
Dir: Dominique Bigourdan
Founded: 1829
Subjects: Animals, Pets, Art, Environmental Studies, How-to, Sports, Athletics
ISBN Prefix(es): 2-85182

**Bottin SA**
31, rue Anatole France, 92300 Levallois-Perret
*Tel:* (01) 47 48 75 75 *Fax:* (01) 47 48 75 50
*Telex:* 262401
*Key Personnel*
President: Jean Paul Devai
Founded: 1796
Subjects: Agriculture, Business, Finance, Human Relations, Medicine, Nursing, Dentistry, Sports, Athletics
ISBN Prefix(es): 2-7039
*Parent Company:* Editions du Juris-Classeur
*Ultimate Parent Company:* Reed Elsevier plc

**Christian Bourgois**, see Presses de la Cite

**Christian Bourgois Editeur**
116 rue du bac, Paris 75007
*Tel:* (01) 45 44 09 13 *Fax:* (01) 45 44 87 86
*E-mail:* bourgois-editeur@wanadoo.fr
*Web Site:* www.christianbourgois-editeur.fr
*Key Personnel*
Contact: Dominique Bourgois *E-mail:* dominique.bourgois2@wanadoo.fr
Subjects: Fiction, Essays, Music
ISBN Prefix(es): 2-267

**Editions Colin Bourrelier**, see Armand Colin, Editeur

**Bragelonne+**
15 rue Girard, 93100 Montreuil
*Tel:* (01) 48 18 19 70; (01) 48 18 19 71 *Fax:* (01) 48 18 02 47
*E-mail:* info@bragelonne.fr

*Web Site:* www.bragelonne.fr
*Key Personnel*
Senior Editor: Stephane Marsan *E-mail:* s.
  marsan@bragelonne.fr; Alain Nevant *Tel:* (01)
  4818 1971 *E-mail:* a.nevant@bragelonne.fr
Founded: 2000
Subjects: Crafts, Games, Hobbies, Fiction, Film,
  Video, History, Humor, Literature, Literary
  Criticism, Essays, Mysteries, Radio, TV, Sci-
  ence Fiction, Fantasy
ISBN Prefix(es): 2-914370
Number of titles published annually: 16 Print
Total Titles: 8 Print
Foreign Rights: L'Agebce de l'Est (Bulgaria,
  Croatia, Czech Republic, Estonia, Germany,
  Latvia, Lithuania, Poland, Slovak Republic,
  Slovenia)
*Distribution Center:* Harmonia Mundi, Mas de
  Vert, BP 150, 13631 Arles Cedex, Frederic Sal-
  bans *Tel:* (04) 9049 9049 *Fax:* (04) 9049 9614
  *E-mail:* fsalbans@harmoniamundi.com

**Editions Breal**
One rue de Rome, 93561 Rosny-sous-Bois Cedex
*Tel:* (01) 48 12 22 22 *Fax:* (01) 48 12 22 39
*E-mail:* infos@editions-breal.fr
*Web Site:* www.editions-breal.fr
*Key Personnel*
Man Dir: Jean-Michel Zunquin
Founded: 1969
Subjects: Accounting, Advertising, Biological Sci-
  ences, Communications, Computer Science,
  Economics, Electronics, Electrical Engineering,
  History, Language Arts, Linguistics, Law, Man-
  agement, Marketing, Mathematics, Philosophy,
  Physical Sciences, Physics
ISBN Prefix(es): 2-85394; 2-84291; 2-7495
*Associate Companies:* ABC Editions
*Bookshop(s):* Librairie Des Prepas, 34 rue Ser-
  pente, 75006 Paris *Tel:* (01) 43 26 85 04
  *Fax:* (01) 46 33 98 15
*Orders to:* Breal Diffusion, Bat No 9, 20 rue Es-
  coffier, 94671 Charenton Cedex *Tel:* (01) 49 77
  88 55 *Fax:* (01) 49 77 88 51

**Emgleo Breiz+**
10 rue de Quimper, 29200 Brest
*Tel:* (02) 98 44 89 42 *Fax:* (02) 98 02 68 17
*E-mail:* andrelemercier@hotmail.com; brud.
  nevez@wanadoo.fr
*Web Site:* emgleo.breiz.online.fr
*Key Personnel*
Man Dir, Rights & Permissions: M le Mercier
Sales: Miss Allain
Production: M le Gall
Publicity: M Keravel
Founded: 1954
ISBN Prefix(es): 2-900828; 2-911210

**Editions Jacques Bremond+**
Le Clos de la Cournilhe, 30210 Remoulins-sur-
  Gardon
*Tel:* (04) 66 57 45 61; (06) 78 51 48 15 *Fax:* (04)
  66 37 27 40
*E-mail:* editions-jacques-bremond@wanadoo.fr
*Key Personnel*
Chairman: Jacques Bremond
Founded: 1975
Subjects: Drama, Theater, Literature, Literary
  Criticism, Essays, Poetry
ISBN Prefix(es): 2-910063; 2-903108; 2-915519
Number of titles published annually: 10 Print
Total Titles: 300 Print

**Alain Brethes Editions+**
7, rue du Port, 44470 Thouare-sur-Loire
Mailing Address: 3, rue de la Liberte Le Parc,
  78280 Guyancourt
*Tel:* (02) 40 77 35 11; (02) 51 13 04 55
*Key Personnel*
Editor: Alain Brethes

Subjects: Astrology, Occult, Health, Nutrition,
  Human Relations, Philosophy, Psychology, Psy-
  chiatry
ISBN Prefix(es): 2-906803

**Editions BRGM+**
3 Ave Claude-Guillemin, 45060 Orleans Cedex
  02
Mailing Address: PO Box 6009, 45060 Orleans
  Cedex 02
*Tel:* (02) 38 64 30 28 *Fax:* (02) 38 64 36 82
*E-mail:* editions@brgm.fr
*Web Site:* editions.brgm.fr
*Key Personnel*
Dir: Florence Jaudin *Tel:* (02) 38 64 31 61
  *E-mail:* f.jaudin@brgm.fr
Founded: 1962
BRGM is the Office of Geological & Mineral Re-
  search in France & French Geological Survey.
Subjects: Earth Sciences, Environmental Studies,
  Geography, Geology
ISBN Prefix(es): 2-7159; 2-901709
Number of titles published annually: 20 Print
Total Titles: 800 Print; 80 E-Book; 3 Audio
*Parent Company:* BRGM, 39-43 quai Andre Cit-
  roen, 75739 Paris Cedex 15

**Brud Nevez**
10 rue de Quimper, 29200 Brest
*Tel:* (02) 98 02 68 17 *Fax:* (02) 98 02 68 17
*E-mail:* brud.nevez@wandoo.fr
*Web Site:* www.emgleobreiz.com
*Key Personnel*
Man Dir: M Le Mercier
Subjects: Education, Fiction, Geography, Geology,
  Language Arts, Linguistics, Literature, Literary
  Criticism, Essays, Maritime, Poetry, Travel
ISBN Prefix(es): 2-90637; 2-86775
Total Titles: 250 Print
Divisions: Ar Skol Vrezoneg, Engelo Breiz, Li-
  ogam

**Editions Buchet-Chastel Pierre Zech Editeur+**
18 rue de Conde, 75006 Paris
*Tel:* (01) 44 32 05 60 *Fax:* (01) 44 32 05 61
*E-mail:* buchet.chastel@wanadoo.fr
*Web Site:* www.theatre-contemporain.net/editions/
  buchet/buchet.htm
*Key Personnel*
Dir: Pierre Zech
Founded: 1986
Subjects: Art, Biblical Studies, Crafts, Games,
  Hobbies, Education, Photography, Religion -
  Catholic, Theology
ISBN Prefix(es): 2-7020; 2-283
Imprints: Le Seneve; Le Temps apprivoise;
  Lethielleux
Subsidiaries: Marque le Temps Apprivoise

**Editions du Buot**
chez Acte 3 212, rue Saint-Maur, 75010 Paris
*Tel:* (01) 53388110 *Fax:* (01) 53388119
Founded: 1975
Subjects: Art, Travel
ISBN Prefix(es): 2-908480

**Bureau des Longitudes**
3, rue Mazarine, 75006 Paris
*Tel:* (01) 43 26 59 02 *Fax:* (01) 43 26 80 90
*E-mail:* contact@bureau-des-longitudes.fr
*Web Site:* www.bureau-des-longitudes.fr
*Key Personnel*
President: Suzanne Debarbat
Vice President: Francois Barlier
Founded: 1795
Subjects: Earth Sciences, Science (General),
  Space Science

**Cactus**, *imprint of* Editions Actes Sud

**Editions du Cadratin+**
Division of MCP Sarl
Quai de l'Ource, 10360 Essoyes
*Tel:* (03) 25 38 60 24 *Fax:* (03) 25 38 60 24
*Key Personnel*
Editor: Marie-Claude Dufourneaud
Founded: 1979
Subjects: Art, History, Literature, Literary Criti-
  cism, Essays
ISBN Prefix(es): 2-86549

**Editions des Cahiers Bourbonnais+**
rue de l'Horloge, 03140 Charroux
*Tel:* (0470) 568 061 *Fax:* (0470) 568 080
*Web Site:* www.cahiers-bourbonnais.com
*Key Personnel*
Dir: Jean-Pierre Petit *E-mail:* j-p.petit@cahiers-
  bourbonnais.com
Founded: 1957
Subjects: Agriculture, Archaeology, Art, Business,
  History, Literature, Literary Criticism, Essays,
  Poetry, Publishing & Book Trade Reference
ISBN Prefix(es): 2-85370

**Editions Cahiers d'Art**
14 rue du Dragon, 75006 Paris
*Tel:* (01) 45487673 *Fax:* (01) 45449850
*E-mail:* cahiersart@aol.com
*Key Personnel*
Man Dir: Yves de Fontbrune
Founded: 1926
Subjects: Art
ISBN Prefix(es): 2-85117

**Cahiers du Cinema+**
9, passage de la Boule-Blanche, 75012 Paris
*Tel:* (01) 53 44 75 77 *Fax:* (01) 43 43 95 04
*E-mail:* cducinema@lemonde.fr
*Web Site:* www.cahiersducinema.com
*Key Personnel*
Dir General: Claudine Paquot; Serge Toubiana
Contact: Pierre Zins
Founded: 1951
Subjects: Art, Drama, Theater, Religion - Other,
  Social Sciences, Sociology, Human Sciences
ISBN Prefix(es): 2-86642

**Les Cahiers Fiscaux Europeens+**
51 Ave Reine Victoria, 06000 Nice
*Tel:* (04) 93 53 89 39 *Fax:* (04) 93 53 66 28
*E-mail:* auteurs@fontaneau.com
*Web Site:* www.cahiers-fiscoux.com
*Key Personnel*
Dir, Publication: Pierre Marie Fontaneau
Founded: 1968
Subjects: Economics
ISBN Prefix(es): 2-85444
*Parent Company:* Societe d'Etudes Juridiques In-
  ternationales et Fiscales, Nice
Subsidiaries: CFE Belgique

**Cahiers Rouges**, *imprint of* Societe des Editions
  Grasset et Fasquelle

**Editions Calmann-Levy SA+**
31, rue de Fleurus, 75006 Paris
*Tel:* (01) 49 54 36 00 *Fax:* (01) 45 44 86 32
*E-mail:* editions@calmann-levy.com
*Web Site:* www.editions-calmann-levy.com
*Key Personnel*
President & Man Dir: Denis Bourgeois
  *E-mail:* dbourgeois@calmann_levy.fr
Sales Dir: Marc Grinsztajn
Rights & Permissions: Heidi Warneke
  *E-mail:* hwarneke@calmann_levy.fr
Founded: 1836
Subjects: Biography, Economics, Fiction, History,
  Humor, Philosophy, Psychology, Psychiatry,
  Science Fiction, Fantasy, Social Sciences, Soci-
  ology, Sports, Athletics

ISBN Prefix(es): 2-7021
*Orders to:* Hachette Distribution, ZA de Coignieres, One Avenue Gutenberg, 78316 Maurepas Cedex

**Editions Canal+**
8 av du Maine, 75015 Paris
*Tel:* (01) 42222730 *Fax:* (01) 42223025
*Key Personnel*
Man Dir: Richard Ducousset
Editorial Dir: Herve Desinge
Public Relations: Soraya Devisscher
Rights & Permissions: Joschi Guitton
Founded: 1991
Subjects: Humor, Nonfiction (General), Sports, Athletics
ISBN Prefix(es): 2-911493

**Canal+ Editions**, see Editions Canal

**Editions Canope+**
20 Bd Gambetta, 63400 Chamalieres
*Tel:* (04) 73 93 82 90 *Fax:* (04) 73 39 33 00
*Key Personnel*
Dir: Marcel Antonio
Founded: 1984
Subjects: Art, Biography, History, Regional Interests
ISBN Prefix(es): 2-906320
Number of titles published annually: 2 CD-ROM
Total Titles: 30 Print

**La Capitelle**, *imprint of* Editions Casteilla

**Editions Caracteres+**
7, rue de l'Arbalete, 75005 Paris
*Tel:* (01) 43 37 96 98 *Fax:* (01) 43 37 26 10
*E-mail:* contact@editions-caracteres.fr
*Web Site:* www.editions-caracteres.fr
*Key Personnel*
Contact: Bruno Durocher
Founded: 1950
Subjects: Philosophy, Poetry
ISBN Prefix(es): 2-85446
Distributed by Alterdis

**Editions Didier Carpentier**
7 rue Saint-Lazare, 75009 Paris
*Tel:* (01) 48 78 85 81 *Fax:* (01) 42 82 91 99
*Key Personnel*
Manager: Didier Carpentier
Founded: 1982
Subjects: Crafts, Games, Hobbies, House & Home
ISBN Prefix(es): 2-84167; 2-906962
Total Titles: 250 Print

**Editions Casteilla+**
10, rue Leon Foucault, 78184 Saint-Quentin en Yvelines Cedex
*Tel:* (01) 30 14 19 30 *Fax:* (01) 34 60 31 32
*E-mail:* info@casteilla.fr
*Web Site:* www.casteilla.fr
*Key Personnel*
Manager: Marinus Visser *Tel:* (01) 30 14 19 45
    *E-mail:* visser@chiron.as
Founded: 1950
Specialize in textbooks, vocational training.
Subjects: Art, Economics, Law, Vocational Training
ISBN Prefix(es): 2-7135
Number of titles published annually: 100 Print
Total Titles: 800 Print
*Parent Company:* VisLand SA
Imprints: La Capitelle; Desforges; Educalivre; Techniplus
*Bookshop(s):* Librairie Casteilla, 25 rue Monge, 75005, Paris

**Le Castor Astral+**
53, rue Carnot, 33130 Begles
Mailing Address: BP 11, 33038 Bordeaux Cedex
*Tel:* (01) 48 40 14 95 *Fax:* (01) 48 45 97 52
*E-mail:* swproduction@magic.fr
*Key Personnel*
Man Editor: Marc Torralba
Founded: 1975
Subjects: Literature, Literary Criticism, Essays
ISBN Prefix(es): 2-85920

**CCNPS**, *imprint of* Agence Bibliographique de l'Enseignement Superieur

**CELSE**, see Compagnie d'Editions Libres, Sociales et Economiques (CELSE)

**Cemagref Editions+**
Parc de Tourvoie, 92163 Antony Cedex
Mailing Address: BP 44, 92163 Antony Cedex
*Tel:* (01) 4096 61 21 *Fax:* (01) 4096 60 36
*E-mail:* info@cemagref.fr
*Web Site:* www.cemagref.fr
*Key Personnel*
Regional Dir: Gerard Sachon
Dir General: Patrick Ravarde
Dir: M Nicolas de Menthiere *Tel:* (01) 40 96 61 87 *Fax:* (01) 40 96 61 39 *E-mail:* nicolas.de-menthiere@cemagref.fr
Chief of Service: Mdme Odile Hologne *Tel:* (01) 40 96 60 96 *E-mail:* odile.hologne@cemagref.fr
Subjects: Agriculture, Earth Sciences, Engineering (General), Environmental Studies, Mechanical Engineering
ISBN Prefix(es): 2-85362

**Editions Cenomane+**
33-39 rue des Ponts Neufs, 72000 Le Mans
*Tel:* (02) 43242157 *Fax:* (02) 43771916
*Key Personnel*
Dir General: Alain Mala
Founded: 1986
Subjects: Art, History, Literature, Literary Criticism, Essays, Military Science, Regional Interests, Transportation
ISBN Prefix(es): 2-905596
Number of titles published annually: 5 Print
Total Titles: 100 Print

**Cent Pages**
27, rue Nicolas-Chorier, 38009 Grenoble Cedex
Mailing Address: BP 291, 38009 Grenoble Cedex
*Tel:* (04) 38 12 16 20 *Fax:* (04) 38 12 16 29
*E-mail:* editions@editions-centpages.fr
*Web Site:* www.editions-centpages.fr
*Key Personnel*
Literary Dir: Gadet Olivier
    *E-mail:* aministrateur@editions-centpages.fr
ISBN Prefix(es): 2-906724
Distributed by Les Belles Lettres

**Center Technique Industriel de la Fonderie**, see CTIF (Center Technique Industriel de la Fonderie)

**Centre de Formation et de Perfectionnement des Journalistes**, see Les Editions du CFPJ (Centre de Formation et de Perfectionnement des Journalistes) - Sarl Presse et Formation

**Centre de Librairie et d'Editions Techniques (CLET)**
c/o Dunod, 15 rue Gossin, 92543 Montrouge Cedex
*Tel:* (01) 40926500 *Fax:* (01) 40926550
*Telex:* 634916
*Key Personnel*
Man Dir: Binnen Dyke
Editorial & Sales: Philippe Gualino

Founded: 1975
Subjects: Accounting, Economics, Finance, Law, Management
ISBN Prefix(es): 2-85354
*Bookshop(s):* Librairie CLET, 15 rue Gossin, 92543 Montrouge

**Centre National de Documentation Pedagogique (CNDP)+**
29, rue d'Ulm, 75230 Paris Cedex 05
*Tel:* (01) 55 43 60 00 *Fax:* (01) 55 43 60 01
*Web Site:* www.cndp.fr/cndp_reseau
*Key Personnel*
Dir: Alain Coulon
Publisher of multimedia works under direction of the Minister of Education.
Subjects: Education
ISBN Prefix(es): 2-240
*Bookshop(s):* 13, rue du Four, 75006 Paris
    *Tel:* (01) 46 34 54 80 *Fax:* (01) 46 34 82 01
*Distribution Center:* 4, ave du Futuroscope Teleport 1, BP 80158, 86961 Futuroscope Cedex
    *Tel:* (05) 49 49 78 09

**Centre national de la recherche scientifique editions**, see CNRS Editions

**Centre pour l'Innovation et la Recherche en Communication de l'Entreprise (CIRCE)+**
Polytems Conseil, 20 rue de l'Arcade, 75008 Paris
*Tel:* (01) 49 24 96 76
*Key Personnel*
Dir: Claude Lutz
Founded: 1988
Subjects: Drama, Theater, Fiction, Literature, Literary Criticism, Essays, Nonfiction (General), Philosophy, Poetry
ISBN Prefix(es): 2-9505426
*Orders to:* Harmonia Mundi, Le Mas de Vert, 13200 Arles

**Centre Technique National d'Etudes et de Recherches sur les Handicaps et les Inadaptations**, see CTNERHI - Centre Technique National d'Etudes et de Recherches sur les Handicaps et les Inadaptations

**Centurion**, *imprint of* Bayard Presse

**CEP Editions**
17 rue d'Uzes, 75108 Paris Cedex 02
*Tel:* (01) 40 13 30 05 *Fax:* (01) 48 24 34 89
*Telex:* 680 876 f
*Key Personnel*
President: Christian Bregou
Subjects: Architecture & Interior Design, Technology
ISBN Prefix(es): 2-281; 2-7327; 2-902302
*Parent Company:* Editions du Moniteur
Subsidiaries: Librairie Larousse

**Cepadues Editions SA+**
111, rue Nicolas Vauquelin, 31100 Toulouse
*Tel:* (05) 61 40 57 36 *Fax:* (05) 61 41 79 89
*E-mail:* cepadues@cepadues.com
*Web Site:* www.cepadues.com
*Key Personnel*
President: Jean-Claude Joly
Dir: Annie Joly
Sales Manager & International Rights: Jean-Pierre Marson
Founded: 1969
Specialize in scientific & technical books.
Subjects: Aeronautics, Aviation, Computer Science, Education, Mathematics, Mechanical Engineering, Science (General), Technology, Transportation
ISBN Prefix(es): 2-85428
Total Titles: 200 Print

**Editions Cercle d'Art SA+**
10, rue Sainte-Anastase, 75003 Paris
*Tel:* (01) 48 87 92 12 *Fax:* (01) 48 87 47 79
*E-mail:* info@officieldesarts.com
*Web Site:* www.officieldesarts.com/cercledart/
*Telex:* 206685 Cerdart
*Key Personnel*
Man Dir: Philippe Monsel
Founded: 1950
Subjects: Art
ISBN Prefix(es): 2-7022
Imprints: Diagonales; Aurore Editions D'Art

**CERDIC-Publications+**
11 Rue Jean Sturm, 67520 Nordheim
*Tel:* (0388) 877107 *Fax:* (0388) 877125
*E-mail:* cerdic@wanadoo.fr
*Key Personnel*
Man Dir: Marie Zimmerman
Founded: 1968
Subjects: History, Law, Religion - Catholic, Religion - Islamic, Religion - Jewish, Religion - Protestant, Religion - Other, Social Sciences, Sociology, Women's Studies
ISBN Prefix(es): 2-85097
Total Titles: 1 Print

**Editions du Cerf**
29 bd La Tour-Maubourg, 75340 Paris Cedex 07
*Tel:* (01) 44 18 12 12 *Fax:* (01) 45 56 04 27
*Web Site:* www.editionsducerf.fr
*Key Personnel*
General Dir: P Moity
Editorial Dir: D Barrios-Delgado; F D Boespflug; B Lauret; N J Sed
Sales Dir, Publicity & Advertising: P Marion
Rights & Permissions: Mrs F de Chassey
Founded: 1929
Subjects: Biblical Studies, History, Philosophy, Religion - Other, Social Sciences, Sociology
ISBN Prefix(es): 2-204
Distributed by Fides; Labor & Fides Medialogue; Novalis; Saint Paul
*Warehouse:* 3 Chemin de Prunais, 94350 Villiers sp Marne

**CF**, *imprint of* References cf

**CF**, *see* References cf

**CFAG**, *imprint of* Compagnie Francaise des Arts Graphiques SA

**CGT Total Exploration-Production+**
Ave Larribau, 64018 Pau Cedex
*Tel:* (05) 59 83 65 80 *Fax:* (05) 59 83 57 88
*E-mail:* contact.ep@cgt-total.org
*Web Site:* www.cgt-total.org/ncgt-ep/
*Key Personnel*
Editor: Jean-Francois Raynaud
Founded: 1967
Subjects: Earth Sciences, Geography, Geology
ISBN Prefix(es): 2-901026; 2-85843
*Book Club(s):* France Edition; Syndicate National de L'Edition; Unipresse

**Chadwyck-Healey France (CHF)+**
50 rue de Paradis, 75010 Paris
*Tel:* (01) 44 83 81 81 *Fax:* (01) 44 83 81 83
*Key Personnel*
Man Dir: Jean-Pierre Sakoun
Sales: Charles Myara
Founded: 1985
Publisher of CD-ROMs.
ISBN Prefix(es): 2-86976
*Parent Company:* Chadwyck-Healey Ltd, United Kingdom
*Associate Companies:* Chadwyck-Healey, Spain
*U.S. Office(s):* Chadwyck-Healey Inc, 1101 King St, Alexandria, VA 22314, United States

**Editions du Chalet+**
15-27, rue de Moussorgski, 75018 Paris
*Tel:* (01) 53 26 33 35 *Fax:* (01) 53 26 33 36
*Telex:* 202036 F (Begedis SA)
*Key Personnel*
Publishing Manager: Bernard Le Bras
Founded: 1946
Subjects: Biblical Studies, Religion - Catholic, Religion - Other, Theology
ISBN Prefix(es): 2-7023
*Associate Companies:* Editions Desclee et Cie; Editions Gamma; Nouvelles Editions Mame; Editions Universitaires
*Orders to:* Begedis, 11 rue Duguay-Trouin, 75006 Paris
Arc-en-Ciel International, ZI Tournai Ouest, 7713 Marquain, Belgium (Foreign)

**Editions Jacqueline Chambon+**
18 rue Seguier, 75006 Paris
*Tel:* (01) 44 27 01 16 *Fax:* (01) 43 54 30 05
Founded: 1988
Subjects: Art, Literature, Literary Criticism, Essays, Philosophy, Photography
ISBN Prefix(es): 2-87711
Total Titles: 150 Print
*Shipping Address:* Harmonia Mundi, BP 150, 13631 Arles Cedex *E-mail:* webmaster@ harmoniamundi.com
*Orders to:* Harmonia Mundi, BP 150, 13631 Arles Cedex

**Champ Libre**, *imprint of* Ivrea

**Editions Champ Vallon+**
01420 Seyssel
*Tel:* (04) 50 56 15 51 *Fax:* (04) 50 56 15 64
*E-mail:* info@champ-vallon.com
*Web Site:* www.champ-vallon.com
*Key Personnel*
Editor: Patrick Beaune
International Rights: Myriam Monteiro-Braz *E-mail:* myriam.monteiro@champ-vallon.com
Founded: 1980
Subjects: Biography, Fiction, History, Literature, Literary Criticism, Essays, Philosophy, Poetry, Psychology, Psychiatry, Social Sciences, Sociology
ISBN Prefix(es): 2-87673; 2-903528
Total Titles: 440 Print
Distributed by Presses Universitaires de France; Union Diffusion
Foreign Rights: Marion Colas

**Champs Dominos**, *imprint of* Flammarion Groupe

**Librairie des Champs-Elysees/Le Masque+**
17, rue Jacob, 75006 Paris
*Tel:* (01) 44 41 74 50; (01) 44 41 74 00 *Fax:* (01) 43 26 91 04
*Web Site:* www.lemasque.com
*Key Personnel*
Dir General: Isabelle Laffont
Editorial Dir: Helene Bihery
Collection Dir: Marie-Caroline Aubert
Founded: 1927
Subjects: Criminology, Mysteries
ISBN Prefix(es): 2-7024
*Parent Company:* Hachette Livre
Imprints: Editions du Masque; Club des Masques

**Philippe Chancerel Editeur**
17, route de Meulan, 78480 Verneuil-sur-Seine
*Tel:* (01) 39 65 69 18
*Telex:* 314235 F
*Key Personnel*
Chairman: Philippe Chancerel
Founded: 1960
Subjects: Crafts, Games, Hobbies, Humor, Sports, Athletics

ISBN Prefix(es): 2-907390
*Associate Companies:* Chancerel Publishers Ltd, United Kingdom

**Editions Chardon Bleu+**
29 rue Charton, 69600 Oullins
*Mailing Address:* BP 3050, 14018 Caen Cedex 02
*Tel:* (02) 31 94 49 59 *Fax:* (02) 31 93 23 92
*E-mail:* chardonbleued@aol.com
*Web Site:* www.chardonbleu.com
*Key Personnel*
Responsible: Claude Four; Dominique Isnard
Founded: 1983
ISBN Prefix(es): 2-86833
*Orders to:* BP 3050, 14018 Caen Cedex *Tel:* (02) 31 94 49 59

**Editions du Chariot+**
BP 14, 28190 Saint Georges S/Eure
*Tel:* (02) 37258989 *Fax:* (02) 37258900
*E-mail:* edchariot@aol.com
*Web Site:* members.aol.com/edchariot/
*Key Personnel*
Publisher & Editor: Liliane Genin-Muchery *Tel:* (02) 37258662
Founded: 1927
Subjects: Astrology, Occult, Parapsychology
ISBN Prefix(es): 2-85371

**Editions Charles-Lavauzelle SA+**
Le Prouet, BP 8, 87350 Panazol
*Tel:* (05) 55 58 45 45 *Fax:* (05) 55 58 45 25
*Web Site:* lavauzelle.com
*Key Personnel*
Man Dir: Jean Claude Mazaud
Publicity & Production: Henri Chabrier
Founded: 1830
Subjects: Law, Military Science, Sports, Athletics
ISBN Prefix(es): 2-7025
*Branch Office(s)*
20 rue de Saint Petersbourg, 75008 Paris Cedex *Tel:* (01) 43 87 42 30

**Chasse Maree**
Abri du Marin, rue Henri Barbusse, 29177 Douarnenez Cedex
*Tel:* (02) 98 92 66 33 *Fax:* (02) 98 92 04 34
*E-mail:* chasse-maree@glenat.com
*Web Site:* www.chasse-maree.com
*Key Personnel*
Dir: Jacques Glenat
Dir General: Olivier Blanche
Founded: 1981
Subjects: Art, Crafts, Games, Hobbies, History, How-to, Maritime, Music, Dance
ISBN Prefix(es): 2-903708; 2-914208

**Editions du Chene+**
43 Quai de Grenelle, 75905 Paris Cedex 15
*Tel:* (01) 43 92 30 00 *Fax:* (01) 43 92 33 81
*Web Site:* www.editionsduchene.fr
*Key Personnel*
Man Dir: Isabelle Jendron
Rights & Co-Editions Manager: Sherri Aldis
Editorial Dir: Philippe Pierrelee
Marketing: Clara Engel
Press: Helene Maurice
Founded: 1941
Specializes in illustrated books.
Subjects: Architecture & Interior Design, Art, Cookery, History, Travel
ISBN Prefix(es): 2-85108; 2-84277
Number of titles published annually: 65 Print
*Parent Company:* Hachette Livre SA
Imprints: Editions du Chene EPA
*Orders to:* Hachette Livre SA

**Editions du Chene EPA**, *imprint of* Editions du Chene

**Le Cherche Midi Editeur+**
23 rue du Cherche-Midi, 75006 Paris
*Tel:* (01) 42 22 71 20 *Fax:* (01) 45 44 08 38
*E-mail:* infos@cherche-midi.com
*Web Site:* www.cherche-midi.com
*Key Personnel*
President, General Binding: Philippe Heracles
General Dir: Jean Orizet
Founded: 1978
Subjects: Aeronautics, Aviation, Animals, Pets, Astrology, Occult, Biography, Cookery, Fiction, History, Humor, Journalism, Literature, Literary Criticism, Essays, Nonfiction (General), Poetry, Romance, Science (General), Social Sciences, Sociology, Sports, Athletics, Transportation
ISBN Prefix(es): 2-86274; 2-7491
Distributed by Servidis for Switzerland; ADP for Canada; Dilibel for Belgium
Foreign Rights: Chantal Galtier Roussel (Brazil, China, Eastern Europe, Greece, Japan); Patricia Berg (Australia, Africa, UK, Netherlands, Germany, Israel, Italy, Portugal, South Africa, South America, Scandinavia, Spain, Turkey, US)

**CHF**, see Chadwyck-Healey France (CHF)

**Editions Chiron+**
10, rue Leon-Foucault, 78180 Montigny-le-Bretonneux
*Tel:* (01) 30141930 *Fax:* (01) 34603132
*E-mail:* info@editionschiron.com
*Web Site:* www.editionschiron.com/fr/
*Key Personnel*
Chairman: Denys Ferrando-Durfort
Promotion & Foreign Rights: Chantal Ferrando-Durfort
Founded: 1906
Subjects: Aeronautics, Aviation, Automotive, Health, Nutrition, How-to, Music, Dance, Outdoor Recreation, Psychology, Psychiatry, Sports, Athletics
ISBN Prefix(es): 2-7027

**Chotard et Associes Editeurs**
One av Edouard-Belin, 92856 Rueil-Malmaison
*Tel:* (01) 41 29 96 05 *Fax:* (01) 41 29 98 15
*Key Personnel*
Man Dir: Nicole Boinet
Founded: 1969
Subjects: Economics, Engineering (General), Management, Marketing, Psychology, Psychiatry, Social Sciences, Sociology
ISBN Prefix(es): 2-7127
*Orders to:* Sofedis, 29 rue St Sulpice, 75006 Paris

**Chronique Sociale+**
7, rue du Plat, 69288 Lyon Cedex 02
*Tel:* (04) 78372212 *Fax:* (04) 78420318
*E-mail:* chroniquesociale@wanadoo.fr
*Web Site:* www.chroniquesociale.com
*Key Personnel*
Commercial Dir: Andre Soutrenon
Founded: 1920
Subjects: Human Relations, Philosophy, Psychology, Psychiatry, Religion - Other, Self-Help, Social Sciences, Sociology
ISBN Prefix(es): 2-85008
Number of titles published annually: 25 Print
Total Titles: 550 Print
Distributor for Couleurs Savoirs (Brussels); Beauchemin (Canada); Presses Universite Laval (PUL) (Canada)

**Cicero Editeurs+**
6, rue de la Sorbonne, 75005 Paris
*Tel:* (01) 43544757 *Fax:* (01) 40517385
Founded: 1989
Subjects: Art, Drama, Theater, Literature, Literary Criticism, Essays, Music, Dance

ISBN Prefix(es): 2-908369
*Orders to:* Klincksicck, 18 rue de Lille, 75007 Paris

**Cifonit Figle**, *imprint of* Editions l'Ancre de Marine

**CILF**, see Conseil International de la Langue Francaise

**Cimaise sarl**
95 rue Vieille du Temple, 75003 Paris
*Tel:* (01) 45437045 *Fax:* (01) 45437045
*Key Personnel*
Publication Dir: Nartine Arnault-tran
Founded: 1953
Art magazine (contemporary art).

**Cirad+**
Avenue Agropolis, 34398 Montpellier Cedex 5
*Tel:* (04) 67 61 58 00 *Fax:* (04) 67 61 55 47
*Web Site:* www.cirad.fr
*Key Personnel*
Head, Publication Unit: Martine Seguier-Guis
   *Tel:* (0467) 61 44 86 *E-mail:* seguier@cirad.fr
Promotion & Export: Christiane Jacquet
   *E-mail:* christiane.jacquet@cirad.fr
Founded: 1985
Subjects: Agriculture, Veterinary Science, Tropical Agronomy, Scientific & Technical Books
ISBN Prefix(es): 2-87614
Total Titles: 250 Print; 50 CD-ROM

**CIRCE**, see Centre pour l'Innovation et la Recherche en Communication de l'Entreprise (CIRCE)

**Editions Circonflexe+**
12 rue de la Montagne Sainte Genevieve, 75005 Paris
*Tel:* (01) 46 34 77 77 *Fax:* (01) 43 25 34 67
*E-mail:* info@circonflexe.fr
*Web Site:* www.circonflexe.fr
*Telex:* 200128
*Key Personnel*
Dir: Paul Fustier
Commercial Dir: Benoit Rouillard
Founded: 1989
Subjects: Art, Education, Fiction, History, Humor, Language Arts, Linguistics
ISBN Prefix(es): 2-87833
*Parent Company:* Info Media Communication
*Orders to:* Disilsco, 122 rue Marcel Hartmann, 92400 Ivry sur Seine

**Editions Citadelles & Mazenod+**
33 rue de Naples, 75008 Paris
*Tel:* (01) 53043060 *Fax:* (01) 45220427
*E-mail:* info@citadelles-mazenod.com
*Web Site:* www.citadelles-mazenod.com
*Key Personnel*
President & Dir General: Francois de Waresquiel
Editorial Manager: Agnes de Gorter *Tel:* (01) 53043064 *E-mail:* a.degorter@citadelles-mazenod.com
Commercial Manager: Ludovic du Ranquet
   *Tel:* (01) 53043066 *E-mail:* l.duranquet@citadelles-mazenod.com
Foreign Rights: Clair Morizet *Tel:* (01) 53043070
   *E-mail:* c.morizet@citadelles-mazenod.com
Founded: 1936
Specialize in architecture & art.
Subjects: Architecture & Interior Design, Art
ISBN Prefix(es): 2-85088
Number of titles published annually: 12 Print
Total Titles: 80 Print
Distributed by Hachette Diffusion International; Dilibel (Belgium); Diffulivre (Switzerland); Hachette Canada Inc (Canada); CELF

**Editions de la Cite**, *imprint of* Editions Ouest-France

**CLD+**
42 avenue des Platanes, 37172 Chambray-les-Tours cedex
Mailing Address: BP 203, 37172 Chambray-les-Tours cedex
*Tel:* (02) 47282068 *Fax:* (02) 47288548
*Key Personnel*
Man Dir, Editorial: Michel Magat
Deputy Manager: Michel Jacquet
Production: Emmanuel Magat
Founded: 1961
Subjects: Architecture & Interior Design, Ethnicity, History, Regional Interests, Religion - Other, Travel
ISBN Prefix(es): 2-85443
Total Titles: 300 Print

**Cle International+**
27 rue de la Glaciere, 75013 Paris
*Tel:* (01) 45 87 44 00 *Fax:* (01) 45 87 44 10
*E-mail:* cle@cle-inter.com
*Web Site:* www.cle-inter.com
*Key Personnel*
Dir: Jean-Luc Wollensack
Sales Dir: Dominique Richard
Editorial Dir: Michele Grandmangin
Founded: 1973
Subjects: Education, Language Arts, Linguistics
ISBN Prefix(es): 2-19; 2-09
*Showroom(s):* Espace Luxembourg, 103 Boulevard Saint-Michel, 75005 Paris *Tel:* (01) 53104120 *Fax:* (01) 45874425

**CLET**, see Centre de Librairie et d'Editions Techniques (CLET)

**CLET**, *imprint of* Dunod Editeur

**Climapoche**, *imprint of* SEDIT (Societe d'Etudes et de Diffusion des Industries Thermiques et Aerauliques)

**Editions Climats+**
470 chemin des Pins, 34170 Castelnau-le-Lez
*Tel:* (04) 99 58 30 91; (04) 67 45 37 90 *Fax:* (04) 99 58 30 92
*E-mail:* contact@editions-climats.com
*Web Site:* www.editions-climats.com
*Key Personnel*
Man Editor: Alain Martin
Founded: 1988
Subjects: Film, Video, Literature, Literary Criticism, Essays, Music, Dance, Mysteries
ISBN Prefix(es): 2-84158; 2-907563
*Shipping Address:* Harmonia Mundi, BP 150, 13631 Arles Cedex *Tel:* (04) 90499049 *Fax:* (04) 90499614
*Warehouse:* Harmonia Mundi, BP 150, 13631 Arles Cedex
*Orders to:* Harmonia Mundi, BP 150, 13631 Arles Cedex *Tel:* (04) 90499049 *Fax:* (04) 90499614

**Club J G**, *imprint of* Sarl Editions Jean Grassin

**CNDP**, see Centre National de Documentation Pedagogique (CNDP)

**CNE**, see Comite National d'Evaluation (CNE)

**CNRS Editions+**
15 rue Malebranche, 75005 Paris
*Tel:* (01) 53 10 27 00 *Fax:* (01) 53 10 27 27
*E-mail:* cnrseditions@cnrseditions.fr
*Web Site:* www.cnrseditions.fr
*Key Personnel*
Man Dir: Danielle Saffar *Tel:* (01) 53 10 27 15
   *E-mail:* danielle.saffar@cnrseditions.fr

Publicity & Advertising Manager: Liliane Bruneau *Tel:* (01) 53 10 27 11 *E-mail:* liliane.bruneau@cnrseditions.fr
Editorial: Pascal Rouleau *E-mail:* pascal.rouleau@cnrseditions.fr
Founded: 1986
Specializes in scientific books.
Subjects: Archaeology, Art, Astrology, Occult, Biological Sciences, Chemistry, Chemical Engineering, Communications, Economics, Education, Environmental Studies, Ethnicity, Geography, Geology, History, Language Arts, Linguistics, Law, Literature, Literary Criticism, Essays, Mathematics, Music, Dance, Philosophy, Physics, Psychology, Psychiatry, Religion - Other, Science (General), Social Sciences, Sociology
ISBN Prefix(es): 2-222; 2-271
Number of titles published annually: 100 Print
Total Titles: 2 CD-ROM
*Parent Company:* Centre National de la Recherche Scientifique
*Bookshop(s):* 151 bis, rue Saint-Jacques, 75005 Paris *Tel:* (01) 53 10 05 05 *Fax:* (01) 53 10 05 07 *E-mail:* lib.cnrseditions@wanadoo.fr

**Codes Rousseau**
BP 80093, 85109 Les Sables d'Olonne Cedex
*Tel:* (02) 51 23 11 00 *Fax:* (02) 51 21 31 02
*E-mail:* info@codes-rousseau.fr
*Web Site:* www.codesrousseau.fr
*Key Personnel*
President: Mr C Czajka
Dir General: M Goepp
Subjects: Education, Electronics, Electrical Engineering, Law, Transportation
ISBN Prefix(es): 2-7095
*Parent Company:* Bertelsmann A G
Subsidiaries: La Baule; Les Editions du Bateau, Les Editions; Rousseau Diffusion, Sables d' Olonne

**Armand Colin, Editeur**
21, rue Montparnasse, 75283 Paris cedex 6
*Tel:* (01) 44395447 *Fax:* (01) 44394343
*E-mail:* infos@armand-colin.com
*Web Site:* www.armand-colin.com
*Telex:* Acolin 201269 F
*Key Personnel*
Man Dir: Guillaume Dervieux *E-mail:* gdervieux@sejer.fr
Sales Dir: Remy Bourrelier
Publicity & Advertising: Yvette Dardenne
Rights & Permissions: Antoine Bonfait *E-mail:* abonfait@sejer.fr
Editor: Armand Colin
General Manager: Alain Cardona *E-mail:* acardona@vuef.fr
Founded: 1870
Incorporates publications of former separate company, Editions Armand Colin Bourrelier.
Subjects: Education, Geography, Geology, History, Literature, Literary Criticism, Essays, Philosophy, Psychology, Psychiatry, Social Sciences, Sociology
ISBN Prefix(es): 2-200
*Orders to:* BP 107, 75663 Paris Cedex 14

**College de Philosophie**, *imprint of* Societe des Editions Grasset et Fasquelle

**Editions du Comite des Travaux Historiques et Scientifiques (CTHS)+**
One rue Descartes, 75005 Paris Cedex
*Tel:* (01) 55 55 97 64 *Fax:* (01) 55 55 97 60
*E-mail:* cths.ventes@recherche.gouv.fr
*Web Site:* www.cths.fr
*Key Personnel*
President: Leon Pressouyre
Vice President: Bruno Delmas
Secretary: Olivier Guyotjeannin; Pierre Pinon
Founded: 1834

Subjects: Archaeology, Art, Ethnicity, Geography, Geology, History
ISBN Prefix(es): 2-7355
*Shipping Address:* Distique, 5 rue du Marechal Leclerc, 28600 Luisant

**Comite National d'Evaluation (CNE)**
43, rue de la Procession, 75015 Paris
*Tel:* (01) 55 55 60 97 *Fax:* (01) 55 55 63 94
*Web Site:* www.cne-evaluation.fr
*Key Personnel*
Publisher: Francine Sarrazin *Tel:* (01) 55 55 63 63 *E-mail:* francine.sarrazin@cne-evaluation.fr
President: Gilles Bertrand *Tel:* (01) 55 55 69 80 *E-mail:* pdtcne@cne-evaluation.fr
Deputy General: Jolivet Jean-Wolf *E-mail:* sgcne@cne-evaluation.fr
Founded: 1986
Subjects: Education
Number of titles published annually: 15 Print; 15 E-Book
Total Titles: 230 Print; 165 E-Book
Divisions: Service Publications

**Communication Par Livre (CPL)**
3, square du Croisic, 75015 Paris
Mailing Address: 28 rue Vaneau, 75007 Paris
*Tel:* (01) 42733047 *Fax:* (01) 42733047
*Key Personnel*
General Dir: Philippe Leclerc
Founded: 1989
Subjects: Advertising, Architecture & Interior Design, Art, History, Real Estate
ISBN Prefix(es): 2-908867

**Editions Comp'Act+**
157, Carre Curial, 73000 Chambery
*Tel:* (04) 79 85 27 85 *Fax:* (04) 79 85 29 34
*E-mail:* editionscomp.act@wanadoo.fr
*Web Site:* www.editionscompact.com
*Key Personnel*
Literary Dir: Henri Poncet
Founded: 1986
Subjects: Literature, Literary Criticism, Essays, Photography, Poetry
ISBN Prefix(es): 2-87661
Number of titles published annually: 30 Print
Total Titles: 30 Print
*Distribution Center:* Union Distribution (Flammarion), Paris

**Compagnie d'Editions Libres, Sociales et Economiques (CELSE)**
10 rue Leon Coqniet, 75821 Paris Cedex 17
Mailing Address: BP 106, 75821 Paris Cedex 17
*Tel:* (01) 42674123 *Fax:* (01) 42274020
*E-mail:* celse@celsedit.com
*Web Site:* www.celsedit.com
*Key Personnel*
Dir General: Marc Lamoussiere
Founded: 1957
Subjects: Transportation
ISBN Prefix(es): 2-85009
Total Titles: 72 Print

**Compagnie Europeenne de Publication**, see CEP Editions

**Compagnie Francaise des Arts Graphiques SA+**
47 rue des Murs, 45300 Ecrennes
*Tel:* (05) 46243925
*Key Personnel*
President: V P Victor-Michel
Founded: 1939
Subjects: Art, Drama, Theater, Music, Dance
ISBN Prefix(es): 2-85001
Imprints: CFAG
*Orders to:* 129 Ave Achille Peretti, 92200 Neuilly sur Seine

**Compagnie 12+**
33, av du Maine, 75015 Paris
Mailing Address: BP 34, 75755 Paris Cedex 15
*Tel:* (01) 56 54 27 37 *Fax:* (01) 56 54 27 38
Founded: 1981
ISBN Prefix(es): 2-903866
*U.S. Office(s):* Company 12 Inc, 190 E 56 St, New York, NY 10017, United States
*Orders to:* 22, rue des Canettes, 75006 Paris

**Editions de Compostelle+**
BP 7, 77890 Beaumont-du-Gatinais
*Tel:* (01) 64299404
*Key Personnel*
Contact: Francois-Xavier Chaboche
Founded: 1988
Subjects: Human Relations, Parapsychology, Philosophy, Religion - Other, Theology
ISBN Prefix(es): 2-907449
Total Titles: 10 Print

**Conseil International de la Langue Francaise**
11 rue de Navarin, 75009 Paris
*Tel:* (01) 48787395 *Fax:* (01) 48784928
*E-mail:* cilf@cilf.org
*Web Site:* www.cilf.org
*Key Personnel*
Secretary-General: Hubert Joly
Founded: 1968
Specialize in multilingual scientific dictionaries.
Subjects: Agriculture, Architecture & Interior Design, Language Arts, Linguistics, Medicine, Nursing, Dentistry, Public Administration
ISBN Prefix(es): 2-85319

**Le Conseiller Juridique Pour Tous**, *imprint of* Editions du Puits Fleuri

**Continent Europe**, *imprint of* Editions Hermes Science Publications

**Cooperative Regionale de l'Enseignement Religieux (CRER)**
22 blvd Jacques-Millot, 49008 Angers Cedex 01
Mailing Address: BP 848, 49008 Angers Cedex 01
*Tel:* (02) 41689140 *Fax:* (02) 41689141
*E-mail:* crer49@wanadoo.fr
*Key Personnel*
Man Dir: Michel Pourrias
Founded: 1968
Subjects: Religion - Other
ISBN Prefix(es): 2-85733

**Editions Copernic**
25 rue Barque, 75015 Paris
*Tel:* (01) 40 61 97 67 *Fax:* (01) 40 61 96 33
*Key Personnel*
Man Dir: Bertrand Sorlot
Sales, Production, Rights & Permissions, Publicity: Jeanne Bordeau
Founded: 1976
Subjects: Film, Video, History, Philosophy, Religion - Other, Science Fiction, Fantasy
ISBN Prefix(es): 2-85984
*Associate Companies:* Editions Albatross, Publeditec

**Editions Coprur+**
34 rue du Wacken, 67000 Strasbourg
*Tel:* (03) 88 14 72 41 *Fax:* (03) 88 14 72 39
*E-mail:* coprur@editions-coprur.fr
*Key Personnel*
Dir: Bernard Sadoun
Founded: 1871
Subjects: History, Natural History, Regional Interests
ISBN Prefix(es): 2-84208; 2-903297
Number of titles published annually: 25 Print
Total Titles: 300 Print

**Corsaire Editions+**
One rue Royale, 45000 Orleans
*Tel:* (02) 38 53 15 00 *Fax:* (02) 38 54 08 92
*E-mail:* corsaire.editions@wanadoo.fr
*Web Site:* www.corsaire-editions.com
*Key Personnel*
President: Gilbert Trompas
Founded: 1994
Subjects: Biography, Biological Sciences, Earth
Sciences, History, Humor, Literature, Literary
Criticism, Essays, Poetry, Social Sciences, So-
ciology
ISBN Prefix(es): 2-910475
Distributed by Diffusion Transat (Switzerland)

**Editions Jose Corti+**
11 rue de Medicis, 75006 Paris
*Tel:* (01) 43 26 63 00; (01) 43 26 80 48 *Fax:* (01)
40 46 89 24
*E-mail:* corti@noos.fr
*Web Site:* www.jose-corti.fr
*Key Personnel*
Man Dir: Bertrand Fillaudeau
Editorial: Fabienne Raphoz-Fillaudeau
Publicity, Rights & Permissions: Isabelle Dibie
Founded: 1938
Subjects: Fiction, Literature, Literary Criticism,
Essays, Poetry
ISBN Prefix(es): 2-7143
Total Titles: 799 Print
*Orders to:* Edition du Seuil, 27 rue Jacob, 75006
Paris

**Council of Europe Publishing+**
Division of Council of Europe
Palais de l'Europe, 67075 Strasbourg Cedex
*Tel:* (0388) 41 25 81 *Fax:* (0388) 41 39 10
*E-mail:* publishing@coe.int
*Web Site:* book.coe.int
*Telex:* 870943F
*Key Personnel*
Commercial Manager: Sophie Lobey *Tel:* (0388)
412263 *E-mail:* sophie.lobey@coe.int
Rights & Permissions Manager: Charalam-
bos Papadopoulos *Tel:* (03) 88 412952
*E-mail:* charalambos.papadopoulos@coe.int
Editorial Manager: Annick Pachod *Tel:* (0388)
412249 *E-mail:* annick.pachod@coe.int;
Francine Raveney *Tel:* (0388) 415114
*E-mail:* francine.raveney@coe.int
Founded: 1949
Official publisher of the Council of Europe & re-
flects many different aspects of the Council's
work, addressing the main challenges facing
European society & the world today. Our cata-
logue of over 1500 titles in French & English
includes topics ranging from international law,
human rights, ethical & moral issues, society,
environment, health, education & culture.
Subjects: Law, Medicine, Nursing, Dentistry, Social Sciences, Sociology, Human Rights, Criminology, Sociology, Nature, Consumer Protection, Education, Sports, Culture, Social Security, Youth, Local Authorities
ISBN Prefix(es): 92-871
Number of titles published annually: 120 Print
Total Titles: 1,500 Print
Distributed by Manhattan Publishing Co
Foreign Rep(s): Akademika A/S Universitets-
bokhandel; Akateeminen Asta Liimen (Fin-
land); Bersy (Switzerland); Bookshop Jean de
Lannoy (Belgium); De Lindeboom Int Pub-
likaties/Inor (Netherlands); Euro Information
Service (Hungary); European Bookshop SA
(Belgium); Glowna Ksiegarnia Naukowa im
B Prusa (Poland); Hunter Publications (Aus-
tralia); Kauffmann Bookshop (Greece); Libreria
Commissionaria Sansoni (Italy); Livraria Portu-
gal (Portugal); Manhattan Publishing Co (US);
Mundi-Prensa Libros SA (Spain); Munksgaard
Book & Subscription Service (Denmark); Re-
nouf Publishing Co Ltd (Canada); TSO (UK);
UNO Verlag (Austria, Germany)

*Shipping Address:* T S O, 51 Nine Elms Lane,
London SW8 5DR, United Kingdom *Tel:* (020)
7873 8200
*Returns:* Mundi-Prensa Libros SA, Castell6
37, E-28001 Madrid, Spain *Fax:* (01) 575
3998 *E-mail:* libreria@mundiprensa.es *Web
Site:* www.mundiprensa.es

**CPL,** see Communication Par Livre (CPL)

**Editeurs Crepin-Leblond**
14, rue du Patronage Laique, 52000 Chaumont
*Tel:* (03) 25 03 87 48 *Fax:* (03) 25 03 87 40
*E-mail:* crepin-leblond@graphycom.com
*Web Site:* www.graphycom.com
*Key Personnel*
Man Dir: Jean Bletner
Publicity: Laurent Picart *Tel:* (032) 5038749;
Francoise Pelletier *Tel:* (032) 5038749;
Christophe Inoux *Tel:* (032) 5038645
*Fax:* (032) 5038652
Founded: 1952
Subjects: Animals, Pets, Environmental Studies,
Sports, Athletics
ISBN Prefix(es): 2-7030

**CRER,** see Cooperative Regionale de
l'Enseignement Religieux (CRER)

**Editions Criterion+**
15-27 rue Moussorgski, 75895 Paris Cedex 18
*Tel:* (01) 53 26 33 35 *Fax:* (01)53 26 33 39
*Key Personnel*
Dir General: Pierre-Marie Dumont
Founded: 1990
Subjects: Biography, History, Literature, Literary
Criticism, Essays, Social Sciences, Sociology
ISBN Prefix(es): 2-903702; 2-7413; 2-903701; 2-
902105

**CTHS,** see Editions du Comite des Travaux
Historiques et Scientifiques (CTHS)

**CTIF (Center Technique Industriel de la
Fonderie)**
44 ave de la Division Leclerc, 92318 Sevres
Cedex
*Tel:* (01) 41 14 63 00 *Fax:* (01) 45 34 14 34
*E-mail:* contact@ctif.com
*Web Site:* www.ctif.com
*Key Personnel*
Contact: Michel Guiny *E-mail:* guiny_mi@ctif.
com
Subjects: Technology
ISBN Prefix(es): 2-7119

**CTNERHI - Centre Technique National
d'Etudes et de Recherches sur les Handicaps
et les Inadaptations**
236 Bis rue de Tolbiac, 75013 Paris
*Tel:* (01) 45 65 59 00 *Fax:* (01) 45 65 44 94
*E-mail:* ctnerhi@club-internet.fr
*Web Site:* perso.club-internet.fr/ctnerhi
*Key Personnel*
President: Marc Dupont
Dir: Marc Maudinet
Subjects: Disability, Special Needs, Psychology,
Psychiatry, Social Sciences, Sociology
ISBN Prefix(es): 2-87710
Distributed by Presses Universitaires de France

**Editions Cujas+**
4/8, rue de la Maison Blanche, 75013 Paris
Mailing Address: BP 417, 75626 Paris Cedex 13
*Tel:* (01) 44 24 24 36; (01) 44 24 24 37 *Fax:* (01)
44 24 24 38
*E-mail:* cujas@cujas.fr
*Web Site:* www.cujas.com
*Telex:* 200513

*Key Personnel*
Man Dir: Pierre Joly
Founded: 1946
Subjects: Economics, Education, Government, Po-
litical Science, History, Law, Social Sciences,
Sociology
ISBN Prefix(es): 2-254
*Bookshop(s):* Cujjas Librairie, 2 rue de Rouen,
92000 Nanterre

**Culture et Bibliotheque pour Tous**
212, rue Lecourbe, 75015 Paris
*Tel:* (01) 45 33 07 07 *Fax:* (01) 45 33 45 76
*E-mail:* uncbpt.services@wanadoo.fr
*Key Personnel*
Publication Dir: Marie-Francoise Cathala
Founded: 1943
Monthly periodicals.
Subjects: Biography, Fiction, History, Human Re-
lations, Literature, Literary Criticism, Essays,
Mysteries, Publishing & Book Trade Refer-
ence, Romance

**Les Editions Roger Dacosta+**
19 blvd Raspail, 75006 Paris
*Tel:* (01) 45 44 14 91
*Key Personnel*
Man Dir: Marie-Madeleine Dacosta
Sales Dir: Isabelle Dacosta
Founded: 1912
Subjects: Medicine, Nursing, Dentistry
ISBN Prefix(es): 2-85128

**DAFSA**
117 quai de Valmy, 75010 Paris
*Tel:* (01) 55 45 26 00 *Fax:* (01) 55 45 26 35
*E-mail:* dorra.medjani@dri-wefa.com
*Web Site:* www.dafsa.fr
*Telex:* 640472 Daf Doc
*Key Personnel*
Chairman: Pierre Cabon
Man Dir: Yves Wilmors
Subjects: Economics, Finance
ISBN Prefix(es): 2-270

**Dalloz,** *imprint of* Editions Dalloz Sirey

**Editions Dalloz Sirey+**
31-35, rue Froidevaux, 75685 Paris Cedex 14
*Tel:* (01) 40 64 54 54 *Fax:* (01) 40 64 54 60
*E-mail:* ventes@dalloz.fr
*Web Site:* www.dalloz.fr
*Telex:* 206446 F
*Key Personnel*
President: Charles Vallee *Tel:* (01) 40655436
Chief Executive Officer: Philippe Chagnon
*Tel:* (01) 40645434
Dir General: Nathalie De Baudry D'Asson
Marketing: Nathalie Thouny *Tel:* (01) 40645438
Foreign Rights: Muriel Funel *Tel:* (01) 40645420
Founded: 1845 (Sirey, 1845 Dalloz)
Administration Office: 35 rue Tournefort, 75240
Paris, Cedex 05. Tel: (01) 40515454
Online publishing.
Subjects: Advertising, Economics, Finance, Law,
Marketing
ISBN Prefix(es): 2-247
Total Titles: 2,000 Print; 50 CD-ROM; 10 E-
Book
*Parent Company:* Havas Vivendi
Imprints: Armand Colin Drott; Dalloz; Delmas;
Sirey
Distributor for Groupe Revue Fiduciaire
*Bookshop(s):* 14 rue Soufflot, 75005 Paris; 22 rue
Soufflot, 75005 Paris
*Distribution Center:* Livredis, 11-15 Rue Pierre
Rig-Aud, 94854 Ivry S/Jeine

**Librairie D'Amerique Et D'Orient,** *imprint of*
Editions d'Amerique et d'Orient, Adrien
Maisonneuve

**Editions Dangles SA-Edilarge SA+**
18, rue Lavoisier, 45801 Saint Jean-de-Braye
Mailing Address: BP 30 039, 45801 Saint Jean-de-Braye
*Tel:* (02) 38864180 *Fax:* (02) 38837234
*E-mail:* info@editions-dangles.com
*Web Site:* www.editions-dangles.com
*Key Personnel*
Man Dir, Rights & Permissions: J Y Anstet Dangles
Sales: Alain Queant
Contact: Berangere Lemaiitre
Founded: 1926
Subjects: Medicine, Nursing, Dentistry, Parapsychology, Psychology, Psychiatry
ISBN Prefix(es): 2-7033
*Branch Office(s)*
30 rue des Freres Lumiere, 94260 Fresnes

**Dargaud+**
15/27 rue Moussorgski, 75018 Paris
*Tel:* (01) 53 26 32 32 *Fax:* (01) 53 26 32 00
*E-mail:* contact@dargaud.fr
*Web Site:* www.dargaud.fr
*Key Personnel*
President & Publisher: Claude de Saint Vincent
Editorial: Guy Vidal
Rights & Permissions: Sophie Castille
   *E-mail:* castille@dargaud.fr
Dir, Commercial & International: Eric de Moutlivault
Founded: 1943
Subjects: Fiction, Humor, Mysteries, Science Fiction, Fantasy, Western Fiction, Comics
ISBN Prefix(es): 2-205
*Parent Company:* Sofidar
Subsidiaries: Citel Video; Dargaud Benelux; Dargaud Publishing International; Dargard Suisse; Delta Verlag; Editions Blake et mortimer; Editions du Lombard; Grijalbo-Dargaud; Hodder-Dargaud; Marina Productions; Millesime Productions
Distributor for Blake et Mortimer; Lombard
*Orders to:* MDS, ZI de la Gaudree, 91417 Dourdan Cedex *Tel:* (01) 60818700 *Fax:* (01) 64593063

**Editions du Dauphin+**
43-45, rue Tombe-Issoire, 75014 Paris
*Tel:* (01) 43 27 79 00 *Fax:* (01) 43 27 76 31
*Key Personnel*
Publishing Manager: Anne Tromelin
Founded: 1935
Subjects: Fiction, How-to, Psychology, Psychiatry
ISBN Prefix(es): 2-7163
Subsidiaries: Editions Jacqueline Renard
*Distribution Center:* Diffedit, 96 bd du Montparnasse, 75014 Paris, Contact: Francois Bera *Tel:* (0144) 107575 *Fax:* (0144) 107580

**Michel De Maule Editions+**
41, rue de Richelieu, 75001 Paris
*Tel:* (01) 42 97 93 56; (01) 42 97 93 48 *Fax:* (01) 42 97 94 90
*Key Personnel*
President: Hubert de Bouville
Founded: 1997
Specialize in Latin & Greek publications.
ISBN Prefix(es): 2-87623
*Parent Company:* Editions Tum

**De Vecchi Editions SA**
52, rue Montmartre, 75002 Paris
Mailing Address: 29 rue Gustave-Eiffel, Zlle Val, 91420 Morangis
*Tel:* (01) 69 34 12 01; (01) 44 76 88 88 *Fax:* (01) 64 48 24 97; (01) 44 76 88 89
*Key Personnel*
Dir: J M Gosselin
Founded: 1971

Subjects: Animals, Pets, Astrology, Occult, Business, Health, Nutrition, How-to, Outdoor Recreation, Parapsychology, Sports, Athletics
ISBN Prefix(es): 2-7328; 2-85177

**Nouvelles Editions Debresse**
17 rue Duguay-Trouin, 75006 Paris
*Tel:* (01) 45481047
*Key Personnel*
Man Dir: Pierre Moulin
Editorial, Sales & Publicity: Vincent Moulin
Founded: 1933
Subjects: Astrology, Occult, Fiction, History, Poetry, Religion - Other, Social Sciences, Sociology
ISBN Prefix(es): 2-7164

**Decanord**
30 rue de Verlinghem, 59130 Lambersart Cedex
Mailing Address: BP 139, 59832 Lambersart Cedex
*Tel:* (03) 20 09 90 60 *Fax:* (03) 20 09 92 75
*E-mail:* decanord@wanadoo.fr
*Web Site:* www.decanord.fr
*Key Personnel*
General Dir: Luc Jonghmans
Founded: 1948
Subjects: Religion - Catholic
ISBN Prefix(es): 2-903898

**Editions La Decouverte+**
9 bis, rue Abel-Hovelacque, 75013 Paris
*Tel:* (01) 44 08 84 01 *Fax:* (01) 44 08 84 17
*E-mail:* ladecouverte@editionsladecouverte.com
*Web Site:* www.editionsladecouverte.fr
*Key Personnel*
Man Dir: Francois Geze
Foreign Rights Manager: Delphine Ribouchon
Founded: 1959
Membership(s): SNE.
Subjects: Communications, Developing Countries, Economics, Fiction, Foreign Countries, History, Philosophy, Social Sciences, Sociology
ISBN Prefix(es): 2-7071
*Parent Company:* Vivendi Universal Publishing
Subsidiaries: Le Monde-Editions

**Editions Delcourt+**
54, rue d'Hauteville, 75010 Paris
*Tel:* (01) 56 03 92 20 *Fax:* (01) 56 03 92 30
*Web Site:* www.editions-delcourt.fr
*Key Personnel*
Dir: Guy Delcourt
Dir Marketing & Communication: Francois Capuron
Foreign Rights: Claire Wilson
Founded: 1986
Children's & comic books.
ISBN Prefix(es): 2-906187; 2-84055; 2-84789
Distributed by Diffulivre (Switzerland); Evadix Logistics (Benelux); Flammarion; Flammarion-Casterman (Benelux); Flammarion Export (Switzerland); OLF (Switzerland); Union-Distribution; Vertige Graphic

**La Delirante**
8, rue des Ecoles Rondil SA, 75005 Paris
*Tel:* (01) 43 54 47 97 *Fax:* (01) 43 54 06 97
*Key Personnel*
President: Patrick Genevaz
Founded: 1967
Subjects: Drama, Theater, Literature, Literary Criticism, Essays, Poetry
ISBN Prefix(es): 2-85745
*Orders to:* 112, rue Rambuteau, 75001 Paris *Tel:* (01) 45 08 86 65

**Delmas**, *imprint of* Editions Dalloz Sirey

**Editions Delmas**
31-35 rue Froidevaux, 75685 Paris Cedex 14

*Tel:* (08) 20 80 00 17 *Fax:* (01) 40 64 89 90
*E-mail:* delmas@dalloz.fr
*Web Site:* www.editions-delmas.com
*Key Personnel*
Man Dir: Charles Vallee
Dir Sales: Philippe Nani
Publicity: Monique Remillieux
International Rights: Christian Roblin
Founded: 1947
Subjects: Accounting, Economics, Law, Public Administration, Real Estate, Securities
ISBN Prefix(es): 2-247; 2-7034
*Parent Company:* Editions Dalloz Sirey

**Jean-P Delville Editions+**
40 rue du Four, 75006 Paris
*Tel:* (01) 42 22 72 90 *Fax:* (01) 42 22 65 62
*E-mail:* editions.delville@wanadoo.fr
*Key Personnel*
Man Dir: Jean-Pierre Delville
Founded: 1976
Subjects: Aeronautics, Aviation, Automotive, Cookery, History, How-to
ISBN Prefix(es): 2-85922

**Editions du Demi-Cercle+**
29 rue Jean-Jacques-Rousseau, 75001 Paris
*Tel:* (01) 42330685 *Fax:* (01) 42330862
*Key Personnel*
Manager: Veronique Hartmann
Founded: 1987
Subjects: Archaeology, Architecture & Interior Design, Environmental Studies
ISBN Prefix(es): 2-907757

**Editions Denoel+**
9, rue du Cherche-Midi, 75006 Paris
*Tel:* (01) 44 39 73 73 *Fax:* (01) 44 39 73 90
*E-mail:* denoel@denoel.fr *Cable:* Edepege
*Key Personnel*
Man Dir: Olivier Rubinstein
Rights & Permissions: Marie-Fransoise Bothorel; Juliette Moreau
Foreign Rights: Marie Ledereg
Founded: 1932
Subjects: Art, Economics, Fiction, Government, Political Science, History, Philosophy, Psychology, Psychiatry, Science Fiction, Fantasy
ISBN Prefix(es): 2-207
*Parent Company:* Editions Gallimard, 5, rue Sebastien-Bottin, 75328 Paris Cedex 07
*Associate Companies:* Mercure de France

**Dervy**, *imprint of* Dervy Editions

**Dervy Editions+**
204, blvd Raspail, 75014 Paris
*Tel:* (01) 42 79 25 21 *Fax:* (01) 42 78 25 39
*E-mail:* contact@dervy.fr
*Key Personnel*
Manager: Bernard Renaud de la Faverie
Founded: 1946
Subjects: History, Human Relations, Psychology, Psychiatry, Religion - Other, Social Sciences, Sociology, Free Masonry, Personnel Development, Spiritualities
ISBN Prefix(es): 2-85076; 2-84454
Number of titles published annually: 40 Print
Total Titles: 600 Print
*Parent Company:* SFPI
Imprints: Dervy
Subsidiaries: CQFDL
*Warehouse:* Dilisco, Parc Mure 2, Batiment 4.4, 128 Ave Jean Jaures, BP 102, 94208 Ivry Sur Seine

**Desclee de Brouwer SA+**
76 bis, rue des Saint-Peres, 75007 Paris
*Tel:* (01) 45 49 61 92 *Fax:* (01) 42 22 61 41
*E-mail:* direction@descleedebrouwer.com
*Web Site:* www.descleedebrouwer.com

*Key Personnel*
President: Marc Leboucher
General Manager: Etienne Leroy
Founded: 1877
Subjects: History, Literature, Literary Criticism,
    Essays, Religion - Other, Social Sciences, Soci-
    ology, Theology
ISBN Prefix(es): 2-220; 2-7045
Divisions: (Social Sciences) Epi

**Desclee Editions**
15-27 rue Moussorgski, 75018 Paris
*Tel:* (01) 53 26 33 35 *Fax:* (01) 53 26 33 36
    *Cable:* Desclee Marquain
*Key Personnel*
Literary Dir: A Paul
Founded: 1872
Subjects: Literature, Literary Criticism, Essays,
    Philosophy, Religion - Other
ISBN Prefix(es): 2-7189
*Associate Companies:* Editions Desclee; Droquet
    & Ardant; Editions Gamma, Belgium; Mame
Divisions: Groupe Mame

**Desforges,** *imprint of* Editions Casteilla

**Editions Desiris,** *imprint of* Adverbum SARL

**Dessain et Tolra SA+**
21, rue du Montparnasse, 75283 Paris Cedex 06
*Tel:* (01) 44 39 44 00 *Fax:* (01) 44 39 43 43
*Telex:* 260776F
*Key Personnel*
Dir: Marie-Pierre Levallois
General Manager: Philippe Fournier-Bourdier
Editorial Manager: Jean Gueret
Founded: 1964
Subjects: Architecture & Interior Design, Art,
    Crafts, Games, Hobbies, How-to
ISBN Prefix(es): 2-249; 2-04
*Bookshop(s):* Diff-edi, 96 BD DU Montparnasse,
    75680 Paris Cedex 14

**Editions Desvigne**
10, rue Leon Foucault, 78184 Saint-Quentin Yve-
    lines Cedex
*Tel:* (01) 30 14 19 30 *Fax:* (01) 34 60 31 32
*E-mail:* info@casteilla.fr
*Web Site:* www.casteilla.fr
*Key Personnel*
President: Visser Marinus *Tel:* (01) 30141945
    *Fax:* (01) 30141946
Subjects: Education
ISBN Prefix(es): 2-7037
Total Titles: 800 Print
*Ultimate Parent Company:* Editions Casteilla

**Les Editions des Deux Coqs d'Or+**
43 Quai de Grenelle, 75905 Paris Cedex 15
*Tel:* (01) 43 92 34 55 *Fax:* (01) 43 92 33 38
*Telex:* 650780 Deucodo *Cable:* Deucodo Paris
*Key Personnel*
Man Dir: Frederique de Buron
Editor: Christine Foulquies
Art Manager: Maryvonne Denizet
Rights & Permissions: Monique Lantelme
Founded: 1949
Membership(s): The Syndicat National de
    l'Edition Francaise.
Subjects: Animals, Pets, Fiction, History, Religion
    - Catholic, Religion - Other
ISBN Prefix(es): 2-01; 2-7192; 2-906017
*Parent Company:* Hachette Livre SA
*Warehouse:* Centre de Distribution du Livre, Z A
    de Coignieres-Maurepas, 1 avenue Gutenberg,
    78316 Maurepas Cedex
*Orders to:* Hachette Livre, 43 Quai de Grenelle,
    75905 Paris Cedex 15

**Deux Coqs d'Or,** *imprint of* Hachette Jeunesse

**Institut pour le Developpement Forestier**
    (Institute for Forestry Development)
23 ave Bosquet, 75007 Paris
*Tel:* (01) 40622280 *Fax:* (01) 45559854
*E-mail:* paris@association-idf.com
*Key Personnel*
President: Roland Martin
Founded: 1960
Subjects: Agriculture, Environmental Studies
ISBN Prefix(es): 2-904740

**Les Devenirs Visuels+**
56 rue du Faubourg Poissonniere, 75010 Paris
*Tel:* (01) 47 70 60 02 *Fax:* (01) 47 70 60 03
*Key Personnel*
Contact: Claive Rius
Founded: 1987
Specialize in packaging.
Subjects: Economics, Geography, Geology, Physi-
    cal Sciences
ISBN Prefix(es): 2-910745

**Diagonales,** *imprint of* Editions Cercle d'Art SA

**Editions de la Difference+**
47 rue de la Villette, 75019 Paris
*Tel:* (01) 53 38 85 38 *Fax:* (01) 42 45 34 94
*E-mail:* editions-de-la-difference@wanadoo.fr
*Web Site:* www.ladifference.fr
*Key Personnel*
Dir: Colette Lambrichs; Joaquim Vital
Press: Frederique Martinie
Administration: Parcidio Gonclaves
Founded: 1976
Subjects: Art, Literature, Literary Criticism, Es-
    says, Poetry
ISBN Prefix(es): 2-7291

**Le Dilettante+**
9-11 rue du Champ-de-l'Alouette, 75013 Paris
    13e
*Tel:* (01) 43 37 98 98 *Fax:* (01) 43 37 06 10
*E-mail:* info@ledilettante.com
*Web Site:* www.ledilettante.com
*Key Personnel*
President: Dominique Gaultier *E-mail:* gaultier@
    ledilettante.com
Foreign Rights: Claude Tarrene *E-mail:* claude.
    tarrene@ledilettante.com
Founded: 1985
Subjects: Literature, Literary Criticism, Essays,
    Science (General)
ISBN Prefix(es): 2-84263; 2-905344
*Branch Office(s)*
Impasse du Ferradou, 11170 Montolieu

**Dilicom**
20, rue des Grands-Augustins, 75006 Paris
*Tel:* (01) 43254335 *Fax:* (01) 43297688
*E-mail:* contact@dilicom.net
*Web Site:* www.dilicom.net
*Key Personnel*
President: Eric Hardin
Dir General: Bernard de Freminville

**Editions Dis Voir+**
One Cite Riverain, 75010 Paris
*Tel:* (01) 48 87 07 09 *Fax:* (01) 48 87 07 14
*E-mail:* disvoir@aol.com
*Web Site:* www.disvoir.com
*Key Personnel*
Dir General & Editor: Daniele Riviere
    *E-mail:* daniele.riviere@free.fr
Founded: 1986
Subjects: Architecture & Interior Design, Art,
    Fiction, Film, Video, Literature, Literary Criti-
    cism, Essays, Music, Dance, Philosophy
ISBN Prefix(es): 2-906571; 2-914563
Total Titles: 100 Print; 55 Online
*U.S. Office(s):* DAP, 155 Avenue of the Amer-
    icas, 2nd floor, New York, NY, United

States *Tel:* 212-627-1999 *Fax:* 212-627-9484
    *E-mail:* dap@dapinc.com *Web Site:* www.
    artbook.com
Distributed by CELF (South America, Italy,
    Spain, Japan, Germany, Greece, Portugal);
    Central Books (UK); DAP (USA); Exhibi-
    tions International (Netherlands); Manic Ex-
    Poseur/BAM (Australia); NORD-SUD (Bel-
    gium)

**Disney Hachette Edition+**
Quai de Grenelle, 75015 Paris
*Tel:* (01) 43 92 38 50 *Fax:* (01) 43 92 38 61
*Key Personnel*
President: Pierre Sissmann
Dir: Catherine Teissandier
Founded: 1992
Subjects: Child Care & Development
ISBN Prefix(es): 2-230
*Parent Company:* The Walt Disney Company
    France/Hachette Groupe Livre
*Shipping Address:* Centre de distribution du Livre,
    One ave Gutenberg, 78316 Maurepas
*Warehouse:* Centre de distribution du Livre, One
    ave Gutenberg, 78316 Maurepas
*Orders to:* Hachette - Service Commercial, 79
    blvd St Germain, 75006 Paris

**Documentation en Economie de la Sante,** see
    IRDES - Institut de Recherche et

**Societe de Documentation et d'Analyses
    Financieres,** see DAFSA

**La Documentation Francaise+**
29 Quai Voltaire, 75007 Paris Cedex 07
*Tel:* (01) 40 15 70 00 *Fax:* (01) 40 15 67 83
*E-mail:* contact@ladocumentationfrancaise.fr
*Web Site:* www.ladocfrancaise.gouv.fr
*Telex:* 204826 Docfran Paris
*Key Personnel*
Man Dir: Sophie Moati *E-mail:* s-moati@
    ladocfrancaise.gouv.fr
Sales, Promotion: Alain-Marie Bassy *Tel:* (01) 40
    15 70 80 *E-mail:* am-bassy@ladocfrancaise.
    gouv.fr; Sophie Seyer *E-mail:* s-seyer@
    ladocfrancaise.gouv.fr
Publicity: Laura Esterhazy
Foreign Rights: Francoise Bacnus *E-mail:* f-
    bacnus@ladocfrancaise.gouv.fr; Bernard Meu-
    nier *E-mail:* b-meunier@ladocfrancaise.gouv.fr
Founded: 1945
Publications of the General Secretary's Office of
    the French Government.
Membership(s): Syndicat National de l'Edition.
Subjects: Art, Economics, Environmental Studies,
    Government, Political Science, Law, Manage-
    ment, Technology
ISBN Prefix(es): 2-11
Number of titles published annually: 500 Print; 3
    CD-ROM; 200 E-Book
Total Titles: 6,000 Print; 5 CD-ROM; 500 E-
    Book
Foreign Rep(s): Distribudora Bertrand (Portugal);
    DPLU Inc (Canada); Jean de Lannoy (Bel-
    gium, Luxembourg); Librairie Kauffmann SA
    (Greece); Licosa (Italy); Maruzen Co (Japan);
    Mundi Prensa Libros SA (Spain); Servidis SA
    (Switzerland)
*Bookshop(s):* 165 rue Garibaldi, 69401 Lyon
    Cedex 03 *Tel:* (01) 78 63 23 02 *Fax:* (01) 78
    63 32 24 *E-mail:* docfr2@easynet.fr
*Orders to:* 124 rue Henri Barbusse, 93308
    Aubervilliers Cedex, Contact: Charles Mbanda
    *Tel:* (01) 40 15 68 74 *Fax:* (01) 40 15 68 01
    *E-mail:* libauber@ladocumentationfrancaise.fr

**Doin Editeurs+**
1, av Edouard-Belin, 92856 Ruel Malmaison
    Cedex
*Tel:* (01) 41 29 99 99 *Fax:* (01) 41 29 77 05

*Key Personnel*
President: M Jean-Francois Roure; M Thierry Verret
Founded: 1874
Subjects: Biological Sciences, Chemistry, Chemical Engineering, Earth Sciences, Education, Health, Nutrition, How-to, Medicine, Nursing, Dentistry, Psychology, Psychiatry, Science (General), Social Sciences, Sociology
ISBN Prefix(es): 2-7040
*Parent Company:* Groupe Lamarre
*Warehouse:* Editions Maisonneuve, 386 route de Paris, Sainte-Ruffine, 57162 Moulins-les-Metz
*Orders to:* Tothemes, 47 rue Saint-Andre-des-Arts, 75006 Paris

**Les Dossiers d'Aquitaine**
5, impasse Bardos, 33800 Bordeaux
*Tel:* (05) 56 91 84 98 *Fax:* (05) 56 91 64 92
*E-mail:* ddabx@wanadoo.fr
*Web Site:* www.ddabordeaux.com
*Key Personnel*
President: Andre Desforges
Founded: 1978
Publisher.
Subjects: Biography, History, How-to, Literature, Literary Criticism, Essays, Poetry, Publishing & Book Trade Reference
ISBN Prefix(es): 2-905212; 2-84622
Number of titles published annually: 50 Print
Total Titles: 200 Print

**Draeger Editeur**, see Edition Anthese

**Dreamland Editeur+**
60, rue Blanche, 75009 Paris
*Tel:* (01) 53 20 46 66 *Fax:* (01) 53 20 46 67
*E-mail:* dreamland@nous.fr
Subjects: Art, Film, Video, Radio, TV
ISBN Prefix(es): 2-910027; 2-84808
Total Titles: 70 Print; 33 E-Book
*Distribution Center:* Vilo

**Editions Droguet et Ardant**
15-27 rue Moussorgski, 75018 Paris
*Tel:* (01)53 26 33 35 *Fax:* (01) 53 26 33 36
*Telex:* 580934
*Key Personnel*
Man Dir: Robert Ardant
Publicity Dir: Suzanne Ardant
Subjects: Religion - Catholic
ISBN Prefix(es): 2-7041

**B Drouaud Editions**, see Editions J H Paillet et B Drouaud

**Du May+**
20, rue de la Saussiere, 92100 Boulogne-Billancourt
*Tel:* (01) 41 31 80 50 *Fax:* (01) 41 31 80 51
*Key Personnel*
Dir General: Jacques Peron
Founded: 1986
ISBN Prefix(es): 2-84102
*Returns:* 65, rue Etienne-Bezout Zl du chateau d'eau, 77550 Moissy-Cramayel *Tel:* (01) 64887510 *Fax:* (01) 64887618

**Dunod Editeur+**
5 rue Laromiguiere, 75005 Paris
*Tel:* (01) 40 46 35 00 *Fax:* (01) 40 46 49 95
*E-mail:* infos@dunod.com
*Web Site:* www.dunod.com
*Key Personnel*
President: Charles Vallee
General Manager: Nathalie de Baudry d'Asson
Assistant General Manager: Pierre-Andre Michel
Editorial, Information & Electronics: Jean-Luc Sensi
Editorial, Reference: Eileen Lignot
Marketing: Marc Laforge

Rights & Permissions: Maryvonne Vitry
Technical Education: Francoise Menasce
Founded: 1800
Subjects: Computer Science, Economics, Education, Electronics, Electrical Engineering, Film, Video, Language Arts, Linguistics, Literature, Literary Criticism, Essays, Management, Microcomputers, Photography, Psychology, Psychiatry, Science (General)
ISBN Prefix(es): 2-10
*Parent Company:* Editions Bordas, 17 rue Remy Dumoncel, BP 50, 75661 Paris Cedex 14
Imprints: CLET; Gauthier-Villars; Privat-Garnier; PSI; Radio; Editions Techniques et Scientifiques Francaises (ETSF)
Subsidiaries: Classiques Garnier
*U.S. Office(s):* Gauthier-Villars North America Inc, 875-81 Massachusetts Ave, Cambridge, MA 02139, United States
*Showroom(s):* 5 rue Mabillon, 75006 Paris
*Bookshop(s):* Librairie des Arts et Metiers, 33 rue Reaumur, 75003 Paris; Librairie Dauphine, Place du Marechal de Lattre de Tasigny, 75016 Paris; Librairie Saint-Sulpice, 30 rue St Sulpice, 75006 Paris
*Warehouse:* Route d'Etampes, 45330 Malesherbes
*Orders to:* 11 rue Gossin, 92543 Montrouge Cedex

**Duo, Harlequin**, *imprint of* Harlequin SA

**Editions J Dupuis+**
57, blvd de la Villette, 75010 Paris
*Tel:* (01) 44 84 40 80 *Fax:* (01) 44 84 40 99
*E-mail:* info@dupuis.com
*Web Site:* www.dupuis.com
*Key Personnel*
President & General Manager: Jean-Manuel Bourgois
Founded: 1898
Subjects: Humor
ISBN Prefix(es): 2-8001; 90-314; 90-6574
*Parent Company:* Editions Dupuis SA, Rue Destree, 52, B-6001 Marcinelle, Belgium

**Editions de l'Eclat+**
25, rue Ginoux, 75015 Paris
*Tel:* (01) 45 77 04 04 *Fax:* (01) 45 75 92 51
*E-mail:* eclat@lyber-eclat.net
*Web Site:* www.lyber-eclat.net
*Key Personnel*
General Dir: Michel Valensi
Contact: Elodie Dathis *Tel:* (01) 45 77 85 92 *E-mail:* elodie@lyber-eclat.net
Founded: 1985
Subjects: Philosophy, Religion - Islamic, Religion - Jewish
ISBN Prefix(es): 2-84162; 2-905372
Total Titles: 160 Print
Distributed by Caravelle (Belgium); Dimedia (Canada); Harmonia Mundi (France); Zoe (Switzerland)

**Editions de l'Ecole**
11 rue de Sevres, 75278 Paris Cedex 06
*Tel:* (01) 42 22 94 10 *Fax:* (01) 45 48 04 99
*E-mail:* edl@ecoledesloisirs.com
*Web Site:* www.ecoledesloisirs.fr
*Telex:* Ecolois 205735 F *Cable:* LIBRECOLE
*Key Personnel*
Man Dir: Jean Fabre
Export Sales Manager, Rights & Permissions: S Sevray
Publicity & Advertising: Jean Delas
Subjects: Education
ISBN Prefix(es): 2-211
Divisions: Pastel A

**Editions de l'Ecole des Hautes Etudes en Sciences Sociales (EHESS)+**
Unit of E HESS

54 blvd Raspail, 75006 Paris
*Tel:* (01) 49 54 25 25 *Fax:* (01) 45 44 93 11
*E-mail:* editions@ehess.fr
*Web Site:* www.ehess.fr
*Key Personnel*
President: M Jacques Revel *Tel:* (01) 49 54 25 01 *Fax:* (01) 49 54 24 96 *E-mail:* preside@ehess.fr
Founded: 1959
Subjects: Anthropology, Asian Studies, Economics, History, Social Sciences, Sociology
ISBN Prefix(es): 2-7132
Number of titles published annually: 15 Print
Total Titles: 650 Print
Distributed by CID; Seuil; Vrin
*Bookshop(s):* 131 blvd Saint-Michel, 75005 Paris *Tel:* (01) 40 46 70 80 *Fax:* (01) 44 07 08 89
*Orders to:* 5-7 rue Marcelin-Berthelot, 92762 Antony Cedex *Tel:* (01) 55 59 52 53 *Fax:* (01) 55 59 52 50 *E-mail:* info@aboservices.com

**Editions et Publications de l'Ecole Lacanienne (EPEL)+**
29, rue Madame, 75006 Paris
*Tel:* (01) 45 44 24 00 *Fax:* (01) 45 44 22 85
*E-mail:* contact@epel-edition.com
*Web Site:* 60gp.ovh.net/~sartorio/epel/site/
*Key Personnel*
Dir: Jean Allouch *E-mail:* jean.allouch@epel-edition.com
Founded: 1990
Subjects: Philosophy, Psychology, Psychiatry
ISBN Prefix(es): 2-908855

**Ecole Nationale Superieure des Beaux-Arts+**
14, rue Bonaparte, 75006 Paris
*Tel:* (01) 47035000 *Fax:* (01) 47035080
*E-mail:* info@ensba.fr
*Web Site:* www.ensba.fr
*Key Personnel*
Dir: Henry-Claude Cousseau
Dean: Alfred Pacquement
Editor: Pascale Le Thorel-Daviot *E-mail:* pascale.lethoreldaviot@ensba.fr
Subjects: Art
ISBN Prefix(es): 2-84056; 2-903639
Number of titles published annually: 15 Print; 1 CD-ROM
Total Titles: 100 Print
*Parent Company:* Ministery of Culture
*Bookshop(s):* 13, quai Malaquais, 75506 Paris

**EDHIS**, see Editions d'Histoire Sociale (EDHIS)

**Editions Edisud+**
La Calade, 3120 Route d'Avignon, 13090 Aix-en-Provence
*Tel:* (04) 42 21 61 44 *Fax:* (04) 42 21 56 20
*E-mail:* info@edisud.com
*Web Site:* www.edisud.com
*Key Personnel*
Man Dir, Sales, Production: Charly-Yves Chaudoreille
Editorial: Anne-Marie Lapillonne
Rights & Permissions: Marie-Noelle Boudon
Founded: 1971
Subjects: Agriculture, Anthropology, Archaeology, Architecture & Interior Design, Art, Cookery, Energy, Environmental Studies, Ethnicity, Gardening, Plants, Geography, Geology, History, How-to, Music, Dance, Outdoor Recreation, Regional Interests, Sports, Athletics, Wine & Spirits
ISBN Prefix(es): 2-85744; 2-7449

**Institute Editeur**
63, rue Edouard-Vaillant, 92300 Levallois-Perret
*Tel:* (01) 40 87 17 17 *Fax:* (01) 40 87 17 18
*Key Personnel*
Dir: Claudine Muller
Founded: 1989

Subjects: Advertising, Architecture & Interior Design, Electronics, Electrical Engineering, History, Management
ISBN Prefix(es): 2-907904
Imprints: Histoire D'Entreprises

**Les Editeurs Reunis+**
Division of YMCA-Press
11, rue de la Montagne-Sainte-Genevieve, 75005 Paris
*Tel:* (01) 43 54 74 46; (01) 43 54 43 81 *Fax:* (01) 43 25 34 79
Founded: 1932
The company acts as sole agent for YMCA Press in publishing a comprehensive list of Russian books in the original Russian.
Subjects: Literature, Literary Criticism, Essays, Religion - Other
ISBN Prefix(es): 2-85065

**Edition1+**
31, rue de Fleurus, 75006 Paris
*Tel:* (01) 49 54 36 00 *Fax:* (01) 45 44 86 32
*Key Personnel*
Publisher, Editor, Man Dir & Right & Permissions: Rene Guitton
Editor: Isabelle Brossard
Founded: 1979
Subjects: Biography, Literature, Literary Criticism, Essays, Nonfiction (General), Self-Help, Sports, Athletics
ISBN Prefix(es): 2-86391; 2-84612
*Parent Company:* Hachette Group

**Les Editions de Minuit SA+**
7, rue Bernard-Palissy, 75006 Paris
*Tel:* (01) 44 39 39 20 *Fax:* (01) 45 44 82 36
*E-mail:* contact@leseditionsdeminuit.fr
*Web Site:* www.leseditionsdeminuit.fr
*Key Personnel*
President & Dir General: Irene Lindon *Tel:* (01) 44 39 39 22
Founded: 1942
Subjects: Fiction, Literature, Literary Criticism, Essays, Philosophy, Social Sciences, Sociology
ISBN Prefix(es): 2-7073
Number of titles published annually: 20 Print
Total Titles: 600 Print
Distributed by La Cite - L'Age d'Homme (Switzerland); Dimedia Inc (Canada)
*Bookshop(s):* Compagnie, 58 rue des Ecoles, 75005 Paris
*Orders to:* Le Seuil, 27 rue Jacob, 75006 Paris *Tel:* (01) 43547486

**Editions d'Organisation+**
61 bd Saint-Germain, 75240 Paris Cedex 05
*Tel:* (01) 44 41 11 11 *Fax:* (01) 44 41 11 85
*E-mail:* service-lecteurs@editions-organisation.com
*Web Site:* www.editions-organisation.com
*Key Personnel*
President: Serge Eyrolles
General Manager: Jean Pierre Tissier
Founded: 1952
Subjects: Business, Computer Science, Electronics, Electrical Engineering, Engineering (General), House & Home, How-to, Law, Management, Social Sciences, Sociology
ISBN Prefix(es): 2-7081
Number of titles published annually: 550 Print
*Parent Company:* Groupe Eyrolles SA, 57 bd Saint Germain, 75240 Paris Cedex 05
*Bookshop(s):* Librairie De Provence, 31 Cours Mirabeau, 13100 Aix-en-Provence *Tel:* (042) 42 26 07 23; Librarie Des Entreprises, Av Bernard Hirsch, BP 105, 95021 Cergy Pontoise Cedex *Tel:* (01) 30 38 14 52; Librairie Des Entreprises, One rue de la Liberation, Centre HEC-ISA, Jouy-en-Josas *Tel:* (01) 39 67 94 59; Librairie Des Entreprises, 79 ave de la

Republique, ESCP Hall Blondeau, 75543 Paris Cedex 11 *Tel:* (01) 43 38 26 71; Librairie Eyrolles, Paris *Tel:* (01) 44 41 11 74

**Les Editions du CFPJ (Centre de Formation et de Perfectionnement des Journalistes) - Sarl Presse et Formation+**
Affiliate of CFPJ
35 rue du Louvre, 75002 Paris
*Tel:* (01) 44 82 20 00 *Fax:* (01) 44 82 20 01
*E-mail:* cfpj@cfpj.com
*Web Site:* www.cfpj.com
*Key Personnel*
General Dir: Marie Ducastel
Contact: Carole Boyer *Tel:* (01) 44 82 20 55
 *E-mail:* cboyer@cfpj.com
Founded: 1988
Subjects: Communications, Journalism
ISBN Prefix(es): 2-85900; 2-902734
Imprints: Presse et Formation

**Editions du Conseil de l'Europe**, see Council of Europe Publishing

**Editions ELOR**
10 rue du Chandelier, 56350 Saint-Vincent-sur-Oust
*Tel:* (02) 99 91 22 80 *Fax:* (02) 99 91 34 45
*E-mail:* edit.elor@wanadoo.fr
*Web Site:* www.elor.com
*Key Personnel*
Dir: Jacqueline Frain
Founded: 1976
Subjects: Crafts, Games, Hobbies, Religion - Catholic
ISBN Prefix(es): 2-907524; 2-912214
Imprints: Editions de Iorme Rond
Distributed by Duquesne Diffusion

**Les Editions ESF+**
2 rue Maurice Hartmann, 92133 Issy-les-Moulineaux Cedex
Mailing Address: BP 62, 92133 Issy-les-Moulineaux Cedex
*Tel:* (02) 37 29 69 20 *Fax:* (02) 37 29 69 35
*E-mail:* info@esf-editeur.fr
*Web Site:* www.esf-editeur.fr
*Key Personnel*
President: Dominique Prat
Man Dir: Vincent Wackenheim
Founded: 1947
Subjects: Business, Communications, Economics, Education, Finance, Law, Management, Marketing, Microcomputers, Psychology, Psychiatry, Technology
ISBN Prefix(es): 2-7101
*Parent Company:* Reed Business Information
Warehouse: PRAT, Zi de Comhre, 28481 Thiron
*Orders to:* CDE, 17 rue de Tournon, 75006 Paris
Dimedia, Canada
Presses de Belgique, Belgium
Servidis, Switzerland

**Editions Grund+**
60 rue Mazarine, 75006 Paris
*Tel:* (01) 53103600 *Fax:* (01) 43294986
*E-mail:* grund@grund.fr
*Web Site:* www.grund.fr *Cable:* GRUND PARIS
*Key Personnel*
President: Alain Grund
Sales: Yannick Lemonnier
Chief Editor: Monique Souchon
Public Relations: Chantal Janisson *Tel:* (01) 53103612 *E-mail:* chantal.janisson@grund.fr
Founded: 1880
Subjects: Animals, Pets, Art, Environmental Studies, How-to, Travel
ISBN Prefix(es): 2-7000; 2-85205
Number of titles published annually: 180 Print
*Associate Companies:* Editions Alpina; Editions Guy Le Prat

**Editions Litteraires et Linguistiques de l'Universite de Grenoble III**, see ELLUG (Editions Litteraires et Linguistiques de l'Universite de Grenoble III)

**Editions Recherche sur les Civilisations (ERC)**
Unit of ADPF
6, rue Ferrus, 75683 Paris Cedex 14
*Tel:* (01) 43 13 11 00 *Fax:* (01) 43 13 11 25
*E-mail:* erc.edit@adpf.asso.fr
*Web Site:* www.france.diplomatie.fr; www.adpf.asso.fr/edition/
*Key Personnel*
Editorial Dir: Hina Descat
Contact: Guillaume Desanges
Founded: 1980
Subjects: Anthropology, Archaeology, Ethnicity, History, Social Sciences, Sociology
ISBN Prefix(es): 2-86538
Total Titles: 268 Print

**Editions rue d'Ulm**
45 rue d'Ulm, 75005 Paris
*Tel:* (01) 44 32 30 29 *Fax:* (01) 44 32 36 86
*E-mail:* ulm-editions@ens.fr
*Web Site:* www.presses.ens.fr
*Key Personnel*
Man Dir: Laure Leveille
Editorial: Frederique Matonti
Sales: Angustinee Belsoeur
Production: Pascale Lehec
Founded: 1975
Subjects: Archaeology, Economics, History, Literature, Literary Criticism, Essays, Philosophy, Science (General), Social Sciences, Sociology
ISBN Prefix(es): 2-7288
*Bookshop(s):* 29, rue d'Ulm, 75005 Paris *Tel:* (01) 44 32 29 70 *Fax:* (01) 44 32 29 72

**Editions Techniques et Scientifiques Francaises (ETSF)**, *imprint of* Dunod Editeur

**Editions Terrail/Finest SA**
43 bis, rue des Entrepreneurs, 75015 Paris
*Tel:* (01) 56 77 06 20 *Fax:* (01) 56 77 06 26
 *Fax on Demand:* (01) 45 75 08 98
*Key Personnel*
Dir, Editorial: Jean-Francois Gonthier
Dir, Ventes & Marketing: Erik Boursier
Specialize in art books.
Subjects: Archaeology, Architecture & Interior Design, Art
ISBN Prefix(es): 2-87939
*Parent Company:* Groupe Bayard Presse

**Editions Unes+**
BP 205, 83006 Draguignan cedex
*Tel:* (04) 94673158 *Fax:* (04) 94673175
*Key Personnel*
Contact: Jean-Pierre Sintive
Founded: 1981
Subjects: Library & Information Sciences, Literature, Literary Criticism, Essays, Poetry
ISBN Prefix(es): 2-87704
*Branch Office(s)*
Raphaille Dedourge, 15 rue ar Maire, 75003 Cedex Paris *Tel:* (01) 42 77 25 82
 *E-mail:* raphaellededourge2@compuses.com

**Editions Verticales**, *imprint of* Editions du Seuil

**EDJA**, *imprint of* Editions Juridiques Africaines

**EDP Sciences+**
Subsidiary of Societe Francaise de Physique
17, ave du Hoggar, Parc d'Activities de Courtaboeuf, 91944 Les Ulis Cedex A
Mailing Address: BP 112, 91944 Les Ulis Cedex A
*Tel:* (01) 69 18 75 75 *Fax:* (01) 69 28 84 91
*E-mail:* edps@edpsciences.org

*Web Site:* www.edpsciences.org
*Key Personnel*
Man Dir & Publications Manager: Jean-Marc
   Quilbe *E-mail:* quilbe@edpsciences.org
Founded: 1920
Services for electronic publications, web site de-
   velopment & printing.
Subjects: Astronomy, Engineering (General),
   Mathematics, Mechanical Engineering, Physics,
   Science (General), Technology, Life Sciences
ISBN Prefix(es): 2-86883; 2-902731
Number of titles published annually: 45 Print
Total Titles: 20 E-Book
*U.S. Office(s):* 875-81 Massachusetts Ave, Cam-
   bridge, MA 02139, United States, Contact:
   Doug Wright *Tel:* 617-395-4070 *Fax:* 617-354-
   6875 *E-mail:* dwright@pcgplus.com


**Educalivre,** *imprint of* Editions Casteilla


**EHESS,** see Editions de l'Ecole des Hautes
   Etudes en Sciences Sociales (EHESS)


**Electre**
35 rue Gregoire-de-Tours, 75279 Paris
*Tel:* (01) 44 41 28 00 *Fax:* (01) 44 41 28 65
*E-mail:* biblio@electre.com
*Web Site:* www.electre.com
*Key Personnel*
Man Dir: Jean-Marie Doublet
Dir Development: Pascal Fouche
Founded: 1983
Subjects: Library & Information Sciences
ISBN Prefix(es): 2-7654


**Ellebore Editions**
18, Impasse Mousset, 75560 Paris Cedex 12
Mailing Address: PO Box 01, 75560 Paris Cedex
   12
*Tel:* (01) 40 01 09 49 *Fax:* (01) 40 01 09 94
*E-mail:* ellebore@wfi.fr; info@ellebore.fr
*Web Site:* www.wfi.fr/ellebore
*Telex:* 213907 Parac
*Key Personnel*
Manager: Jean-Paul Barriolade
Founded: 1980
Subjects: Health, Nutrition, Psychology, Psychia-
   try
ISBN Prefix(es): 2-86898


**Ellipses - Edition Marketing SA**
32, rue Bargue, 75740 Paris Cedex 15
*Tel:* (01) 45 67 74 19 *Fax:* (01) 47 34 67 94
*E-mail:* infos@editions-ellipses.com
*Web Site:* www.editions-ellipses.fr
*Key Personnel*
Man Dir: Jean-Pierre Benezet
Founded: 1973
Subjects: Medicine, Nursing, Dentistry, Science
   (General)
ISBN Prefix(es): 2-7298


**ELLUG (Editions Litteraires et Linguistiques
   de l'Universite de Grenoble III)** (University
   Stendhal-Grenoble III Press)+
Universite Stendhal, 1180 ave Centrale-Domaine
   Universitaire, 38400 Saint Martin d'Heres
Mailing Address: BP 25, 38040 Grenoble Cedex
   9
*Tel:* (04) 76 82 43 72; (04) 76 82 77 74 *Fax:* (04)
   76 82 41 85
*E-mail:* ellug@u-grenoble3.fr
*Web Site:* www.ellug.u-grenoble3.fr/ellug
*Key Personnel*
Man Dir: Pierre Morere
Editor: Elisabeth Greslou *E-mail:* elisabeth.
   greslou@u-grenoble3.fr
Founded: 1978
Membership(s): International Association of
   Scholarly Publishers.

Subjects: Antiques, Communications, Language
   Arts, Linguistics, Literature, Literary Criticism,
   Essays
ISBN Prefix(es): 2-902709; 2-84310
Number of titles published annually: 10 Print
Total Titles: 120 Print
*Distribution Center:* CID, 131 bd Saint Michel,
   Paris 75005 *Tel:* (01) 43 54 47 15 *Fax:* (01)
   43 54 80 73 *E-mail:* cid@msh_paris.fr *Web
   Site:* www.u-grenoble3.fr


**Elsevier SAS (Editions Scientifiques et
   Medicales Elsevier)**
23, rue Linois, 75724 Paris Cedex 15
*Tel:* (01) 71 72 46 50 *Fax:* (01) 71 72 46 50
*Web Site:* www.elsevier.fr
*Key Personnel*
President & Dir-General: Catherine Lucet
Finance Dir: Patrick Regnier
Founded: 1984
Subjects: Mathematics, Medicine, Nursing, Den-
   tistry, Physics
ISBN Prefix(es): 2-84299; 2-906077


**EM Inter,** *imprint of* Editions Lavoisier


**Encres Vives**
2, allee des Allobroges, 31770 Colomiers
*Tel:* (05) 62740787
*E-mail:* encres@mygale.org
*Key Personnel*
Dir: Michel Cosem
Founded: 1960
Subjects: Poetry
ISBN Prefix(es): 2-85550


**Encyclopedia Universalis France SA+**
18 rue de Tilsitt, 75809 Paris Cedex 17
*Tel:* (01) 45 72 72 72 *Fax:* (01) 45 72 03 43
*E-mail:* contact@universalis.fr
*Web Site:* www.universalis.fr
*Key Personnel*
President: Giuseppe Annoscia
Editorial: Bernard Couvelaire
Financial Manager: Herve Rouanet
Export Manager: Speranta Gallage *Tel:* (01) 45
   72 72 52 *E-mail:* sgallage@universalis.fr
Production Manager: Dominique Reyren
Founded: 1968
ISBN Prefix(es): 2-85229


**L'encyclopedie Poetique,** *imprint of* Sarl Editions
   Jean Grassin


**Les Encyclopedies du Patrimoine**
2 rue de Valois, 75001 Paris
*Tel:* (01) 42 60 66 63 *Fax:* (01) 42 60 66 73
*Key Personnel*
Dir: Wanda Diebolt
ISBN Prefix(es): 2-911200


**Editions Entente+**
12, rue Honore-Chevalier, 75006 Paris
*Tel:* (01) 55 42 84 00 *Fax:* (01) 40 49 01 02
*Key Personnel*
Man Dir: Edouard Esmerian
Founded: 1975
Publish *La Gazette du Livre* (La Tribune des Pe-
   tits Editeurs).
Membership(s): Association des Petits Editeurs
   Francophones.
Subjects: Cookery, Developing Countries, Eco-
   nomics, Education, Energy, Environmental
   Studies, Human Relations, Literature, Literary
   Criticism, Essays, Poetry, Science (General),
   Technology
ISBN Prefix(es): 2-7266
Total Titles: 102 Print; 1 Audio
Distributor for l'Athanor; Editions d'En-Bas;
   Robert Jauze; Jacques Laget; Lierre &

Coudrier; Mamamelis; Le Nid; La Pleine Lune;
   Le Signet
*Bookshop(s):* Librairie Entente12 rue Honore-
   Chevalier, 75006 Paris


**Histoire D'Entreprises,** *imprint of* Institute
   Editeur


**EPA (Editions Pratiques Automobiles)+**
Imprint of Editions du Chene
43 Quai de Grenelle, 75905 Paris Cedex 15
*Tel:* (01) 43 92 30 00 *Fax:* (01) 43 92 33 81
*Web Site:* www.editionsduchene.fr
*Key Personnel*
President: Fatine Layt
Man Dir: Isabelle Jendron
Editorial Dir: Philippe Pierrelee
Rights Manager: Sherri Aldis
Founded: 1972
Subjects: Aeronautics, Aviation, Architecture &
   Interior Design, Automotive, Cookery, History,
   Maritime, Military Science, Sports, Athletics,
   Transportation, Wine & Spirits
ISBN Prefix(es): 2-85120
*Parent Company:* Hachette Livre


**Epanouissement,** *imprint of* Jouvence Editions


**Editions de l'Epargne+**
18-24 rue Cabanis, 12 villa Lourcine, 75014 Paris
*Tel:* (01) 44 16 95 80 *Fax:* (01) 44 16 95 99
*Key Personnel*
Man Dir: Dominique Therond
Founded: 1957
Subjects: Architecture & Interior Design, Art,
   Economics, Finance, History, How-to, Law
ISBN Prefix(es): 2-85015


**EPEL,** see Editions et Publications de l'Ecole
   Lacanienne (EPEL)


**ERC,** see Editions Recherche sur les Civilisations
   (ERC)


**L'Ere Nouvelle+**
BP 171, 06407 Cannes Cedex
*Tel:* (04) 93 99 30 13
*E-mail:* lerenouvelle@wanadoo.fr
*Web Site:* assoc.wanadoo.fr/lerenouvelle/pub
*Key Personnel*
Dir: Pierre Lance *E-mail:* pierre.lance@wanadoo.
   fr
Founded: 1980
Subjects: Energy, Health, Nutrition, Philosophy,
   Psychology, Psychiatry, Social Sciences, Soci-
   ology
ISBN Prefix(es): 2-905825


**Editions Eres+**
11 rue des Alouettes, 31520 Ramonville
*Tel:* (05) 61 75 15 76 *Fax:* (05) 61 73 52 89
*E-mail:* eres@edition-eres.com
*Web Site:* www.edition-eres.com
*Key Personnel*
Manager: Jean Sacrispeyre *E-mail:* jean.
   sacrispeyre@editions-eres.com
Editorial Dir: Marie-Francoise Dubois-Sacrispeyre
   *E-mail:* mf.dubois-sacrispeyre@editions-eres.
   com
Marketing Dir: Liliane Gestermann *E-mail:* l.
   gestermann@editions-eres.com
Founded: 1980
Subjects: Criminology, Law, Philosophy, Psychol-
   ogy, Psychiatry, Social Sciences, Sociology
ISBN Prefix(es): 2-86586; 2-7492
Number of titles published annually: 60 Print


**Editions Errance**
7 rue Jean du Bellay, 75004 Paris
*Tel:* (01) 43 26 85 82 *Fax:* (01) 43 29 34 88
*Key Personnel*
Editor: Frederic Lontcho

Founded: 1982
Subjects: Archaeology, History
ISBN Prefix(es): 2-87772; 2-903442

**Editions Eska**
12, rue du Quatre Septembre, 75002 Paris
*Tel:* (01) 42 86 55 93 *Fax:* (01) 42 60 45 35
*E-mail:* eska@eska.fr
*Web Site:* www.eska.fr
*Key Personnel*
Sales Dir: Patricia Fousweray
Subjects: Aeronautics, Aviation, Economics, Engineering (General), Labor, Industrial Relations, Law, Management, Medicine, Nursing, Dentistry
ISBN Prefix(es): 2-86911; 2-7472
Distributor for Presses Universitaires du Quebec (Canada)

**Eska Interactive-Sybex France+**
12 rue du Quatre-Septembre, 75002 Paris
*Tel:* (01) 42 86 55 73 *Fax:* (01) 42 60 45 35
*E-mail:* eska@eska.fr
*Web Site:* www.sybex.fr
*Key Personnel*
President: Francois-Xavier Chaussonniere
Founded: 1976
Subjects: Microcomputers
ISBN Prefix(es): 2-7361; 2-902414
*Parent Company:* Sybex Inc, 1151 Marina Village Parkway, Alameda, CA 94501, United States
Foreign Rep(s): Acorn Publishing Co (Korea); BPB Publications (Bangladesh, India, Pakistan); Express Trains Distributors Computer (Caribbean, Latin America); Firefly Books Ltd (Canada); International Sybex (UK, Europe, Middle East, North Africa); Intersoft (South Africa); Lidel Edicoes Tecnicas Lda (Portugal); Livraria Cultura (Brazil); Sulcor Investindo (Indonesia); TransQuest Publishers Pte Ltd (Hong Kong, Malaysia, Singapore, Thailand); Woodslane Pty Limited (Australia, New Zealand)

**ESME,** see Elsevier SAS (Editions Scientifiques et Medicales Elsevier)

**Editions Espaces 34+**
BP 2080, 34025 Montpellier Cedex
*Tel:* (04) 67 84 11 23 *Fax:* (04) 67 84 00 74
*E-mail:* chesp34@club-internet.fr
*Web Site:* www.editions-espaces34.fr
*Key Personnel*
President: Laurent Chevallier
Subjects: Biological Sciences, Drama, Theater, Literature, Literary Criticism, Essays, Mathematics, Medicine, Nursing, Dentistry, Social Sciences, Sociology
ISBN Prefix(es): 2-907293; 2-84705
Total Titles: 110 Print

**L'Esprit Du Temps+**
115 ave Anatole France, 33491 Le Bouscat Cedex
Mailing Address: BP 107, 33491 Le Bouscat Cedex
*Tel:* (0556) 02 84 19 *Fax:* (0556) 02 91 31
*E-mail:* espritemp@aol.com
*Web Site:* www.psy-book.net
*Key Personnel*
Manager: Eleonore Brenot
Literary Dir: Philippe Brenot
Founded: 1989
Subjects: Literature, Literary Criticism, Essays, Medicine, Nursing, Dentistry, Psychology, Psychiatry, Psychoanalysis, Reviews
ISBN Prefix(es): 2-908206; 2-913062; 2-84795
Number of titles published annually: 30 Print
Total Titles: 250 Print
*Orders to:* PUF, 14 ave du Bois de l'Epiue, BP 90, 91003 Evry Cedex

**Editions de L'Est+**
Rue Theophraste-Renaudot, 54185 Heillecourt Cedex
*Tel:* (03) 88 15 77 27 *Fax:* (03) 88 75 16 21
*E-mail:* nueebleue@dna.fr
*Telex:* 961749F
*Key Personnel*
President: Pascal Chipot
Dir General: Gerard Gabriel
Contact: Pascal More Schweitzer
ISBN Prefix(es): 2-86955; 2-7165

**Institut d'Ethnologie du Museum National d'Histoire Naturelle**
Service des Publications Scientifiques, 57, rue Cuvier, 75231 Paris Cedex 05
*Tel:* (01) 40 79 48 38 *Fax:* (01) 40 79 38 58
*E-mail:* diff.pub@mnhn.fr
*Web Site:* www.mnhn.fr/publication
*Key Personnel*
Head: Philippe Bouchet
Founded: 1925
Subjects: Archaeology, Ethnicity, Language Arts, Linguistics
ISBN Prefix(es): 2-85653; 2-85265
Number of titles published annually: 1 Print
Total Titles: 125 Print

**ETSF,** see Editions Techniques et Scientifiques Francaises

**Institut d'Etudes Augustiniennes**
3 rue de l'Abbaye, 75006 Paris
*Tel:* (01) 43 54 80 25 *Fax:* (01) 43 54 39 55
*E-mail:* iea@wanadoo.fr
*Key Personnel*
Man Dir: Jean-Claude Fredouille
Contact: Claudine Croyere
Founded: 1954
Subjects: Antiques, Archaeology, History, Philosophy, Religion - Catholic, Theology
ISBN Prefix(es): 2-85121
*Shipping Address:* Brepols Steen Weg op Tielen 68, 2300 Turnhout, Belgium *Tel:* (014) 40 27 00 *Fax:* (014) 42 89 19 *E-mail:* publishers@brepols.com
*Warehouse:* Brepols Steen Weg op Tielen 68, 2300 Turnhout, Belgium *Tel:* (014) 40 27 00 *Fax:* (014) 42 89 19 *E-mail:* publishers@brepols.com
*Orders to:* Brepols Steen Weg op Tielen 68, 2300 Turnhout, Belgium *Tel:* (014) 40 27 00 *Fax:* (014) 42 89 19 *E-mail:* publishers@brepols.com

**Institut d'Etudes Slaves IES+**
9, rue Michelet, 75006 Paris
*Tel:* (01) 43 26 50 89; (01) 43 26 79 18 *Fax:* (01) 43 26 16 23; (01) 55 42 14 66
*E-mail:* etudes.slaves@paris4.sorbonne.fr
*Web Site:* www.etudes-slaves.paris4.sorbonne.fr
*Key Personnel*
Dir: Pierre Gonneau
Founded: 1920
Subjects: History, Language Arts, Linguistics, Literature, Literary Criticism, Essays, Slavic Studies
ISBN Prefix(es): 2-7204

**l'Europeenne,** *imprint of* Editions de Septembre

**L'Expansion Scientifique Francaise**
15, rue Saint-Benoit, 75278 Paris Cedex 06
*Tel:* (01) 45 48 42 60 *Fax:* (01) 45 44 81 55
*E-mail:* expansionscientifiquefrancaise@wanadoo.fr
*Web Site:* www.expansionscientifique.com
*Key Personnel*
Man Dir: Pierre Bergeaud
Founded: 1925

Subjects: Biological Sciences, Medicine, Nursing, Dentistry
ISBN Prefix(es): 2-7046
*Bookshop(s):* Librairie des Facultes de Medecine et de Pharmacie, 174 blvd St-Germain, 75297 Paris Cedex 06 *Tel:* (01) 45 48 54 48 *Fax:* (01) 45 48 84 10

**Groupe Express-Expansion**
17, rue de l'Arrivee, 75733 Paris Cedex 15
*Tel:* (01) 53 91 11 11 *Fax:* (01) 53 91 10 06
*Web Site:* www.groupe-expansion.com
*Telex:* 205581 f
*Key Personnel*
President & Man Dir: Jean-Louis Servan-Schreiber
General Manager: Damien Dufour *Tel:* (01) 40 60 44 12 *Fax:* (01) 40 60 41 29
Publicity, International Advertising Dir: Vincent Perrote
Subjects: Architecture & Interior Design, Economics, Education, Government, Political Science, Law, Literature, Literary Criticism, Essays, Science (General), Social Sciences, Sociology, Technology
ISBN Prefix(es): 2-904833
*Parent Company:* Socpresse, 12, rue de Presbourg, 75016 Paris

**Editions Eyrolles+**
61 blvd Saint-Germain, 75240 Paris Cedex 05
*Tel:* (01) 44 41 11 11 *Fax:* (01) 44 41 11 85
*E-mail:* service-lecteurs@editions-eyrolles.com
*Web Site:* www.editions-eyrolles.com
*Telex:* Eyrotp 203385 F
*Key Personnel*
Man Dir: Jean-Pierre Tissier
Editorials: Eric Sulpice; Jean-Jacques Brisebarre
Foreign Rights: Marlyne Tolentino *Tel:* (01) 44 41 11 16 *Fax:* (01) 44 41 46 00 *E-mail:* foreignrights@eyrolles.com
Contact: Miguel Tejedor
Founded: 1918
Subjects: Architecture & Interior Design, Computer Science, Crafts, Games, Hobbies, Earth Sciences, Electronics, Electrical Engineering, Management, Mechanical Engineering, Physical Sciences
ISBN Prefix(es): 2-212
*Parent Company:* Ecole Speciale des Travaux Publics
*Associate Companies:* Editions d'Organisation
Distributor for Microsoft Press France

**FAC Editions,** see Federation d'Activities Culturelles, Fac Editions

**Falguiere 36,** see Galerie Esther Woerdehoff

**Editions Fallois**
22 rue La Boetie, 75008 Paris
*Tel:* (01) 42669195 *Fax:* (01) 49240637
Founded: 1987
Subjects: Literature, Literary Criticism, Essays
ISBN Prefix(es): 2-87706
*Orders to:* Hachette Export, 58 rue Jean Bleuzen, 92178 Vanves Cedex

**Editions Pierre Fanlac+**
12 Rue du Professeur-Peyrot, 24002 Perigueux Cedex
Mailing Address: BP 2043, 24002 Perigueux Cedex
*Tel:* (05) 53-53-41-90 *Fax:* (05) 53-08-05-85
*E-mail:* info@fanlac.com
*Web Site:* www.fanlac.com
*Key Personnel*
Dir General: Bernard Tardien
Founded: 1943

Subjects: Art, Cookery, Literature, Literary Criticism, Essays, Photography, Poetry, Regional Interests, Travel
ISBN Prefix(es): 2-86577; 2-85122
Number of titles published annually: 10 Print
*Branch Office(s)*
31 rue Faidherbe, 75011 Paris *Tel:* (01) 43-67-51-32 *Fax:* (01) 40-09-94-00
*Distribution Center:* Fanlac Editions

**Editions Farel+**
BP 20, 77421 Marne-la-Vallee Cedex 2
*Tel:* (01) 64 68 46 44 *Fax:* (01) 64 68 39 90
*E-mail:* lire@editionsfarel.com
*Web Site:* www.editionsfarel.com
*Key Personnel*
Dir: D Steven Dixon
Founded: 1978
Subjects: Religion - Protestant
ISBN Prefix(es): 2-86314
Number of titles published annually: 20 Print
Total Titles: 220 Print
Distributed by Le Bon Livre (Belgium); Diffusion Emmaues (Switzerland); Inter-livres LLB (Canada)
Distributor for G-Lu Publishing House; Janz Team/Peniel

**Editions Fata Morgana+**
Fontfroide le Haut, 34980 Saint-Clement
*Tel:* (04) 67 54 40 40 *Fax:* (04) 67 04 14 91
*E-mail:* davidini@wanadoo.fr
*Web Site:* perso.wanadoo.fr/fatamorgana
*Key Personnel*
President: Roy Bruno
International Rights: David Massabuau
Founded: 1966
Subjects: Art, Asian Studies, Literature, Literary Criticism, Essays, Philosophy, Religion - Catholic, Religion - Hindu, Religion - Islamic, Religion - Jewish, Religion - Other
ISBN Prefix(es): 2-85194
Subsidiaries: Fakir Press; Bibliotheque Artistique & Litteraire
Distributed by DPLU (Canada); L'Age-D'Homme (Switzerland); Nouvelle Diffusion (Belgium)
*Bookshop(s):* Librairie Freecyb, 41 rue Basfroi, Paris, Jean-Francois Poupelin *E-mail:* yanndortin@freecyb.com *Web Site:* freecyb.com
*Orders to:* Les Belles Lettres, 95 Bd Raspail, 75006 Paris *Tel:* (01) 44-39-84-20 *Fax:* (01) 45-44-92-88

**Editions Faton+**
25 rue Berbisey, BP 669, 21017 Dijon Cedex
*Tel:* (03) 80 40 41 00 *Fax:* (03) 80 30 15 37
*E-mail:* infos@faton.fr
*Web Site:* www.art-metiers-du-livre.com
*Key Personnel*
Dir: Louis Faton
Secretary: Marguerite Dugat *E-mail:* dugat@faton.fr
Sales Manager: Olivier Fabre *E-mail:* olivier-fabre@faton.fr
Founded: 1994
Subjects: Art, Presse-edition
ISBN Prefix(es): 2-911071
Total Titles: 3 Print
*Orders to:* One, rue des Artisans, BP 190, 21803 Quetigny Cedex *Tel:* (03) 80 48 98 48 *Fax:* (03) 80 48 98 46

**Librairie Artheme Fayard+**
75, rue des Saints-Peres, 75279 Paris Cedex 6
*Tel:* (01) 45498200 *Fax:* (01) 42224017
*Web Site:* www.editions-fayard.fr
*Telex:* 264918 trace
*Key Personnel*
President & Man Dir: Claude Durand
Publicity: Caroline Gutmann
Advertising Dir: Frederique Larvor

Rights & Permissions: Martine Bertea
*E-mail:* rights@editions-fayard.fr
Founded: 1854
Subjects: Biography, Fiction, History, Music, Dance, Philosophy, Religion - Other, Science (General), Social Sciences, Sociology, Technology
ISBN Prefix(es): 2-213
*Parent Company:* Hachette

**FBT de R Editions**
49, av de la Reistance, 92370 Chaville
*Tel:* (01) 41 15 19 69; (06) 07 68 33 71 *Fax:* (01) 41 15 19 69
*Key Personnel*
President: Francoise Thiam
Founded: 1995
Subjects: Art, Criminology, Economics, Fiction, Foreign Countries, Government, Political Science, Human Relations, Literature, Literary Criticism, Essays, Travel
ISBN Prefix(es): 2-911064

**Federation d'Activities Culturelles, Fac Editions**
Formerly FAC Editions
30, rue Madame, 75006 Paris
*Tel:* (01) 45 48 76 51 *Fax:* (01) 42 22 22 31
*Key Personnel*
General Dir: Max Huot De Longchamp
Subjects: Philosophy, Religion - Catholic, Theology
ISBN Prefix(es): 2-903422
Imprints: Paroisse & Famille
Distributor for CLD

**Federation Francaise de la Randonnee Pedestre+**
14, rue Riquet, 75019 Paris
*Tel:* (01) 44 89 93 90 *Fax:* (01) 40 35 85 48
*E-mail:* info@ffrp.asso.fr
*Web Site:* www.ffrp.asso.fr
*Key Personnel*
President: Maurice Bruzek
Founded: 1947
Subjects: Outdoor Recreation, Sports, Athletics
ISBN Prefix(es): 2-85699
*Shipping Address:* IGN, lamp des Landes, 41200 Villefranche s/cher
*Warehouse:* IGN, lamp des Landes, 41200 Villefranche s/cher
*Orders to:* IGN, lamp des Landes, 41200 Villefranche s/cher

**Editions Des Femmes+**
6, rue de Mezieres, 75006 Paris Cedex 6
*Tel:* (01) 42 22 60 74 *Fax:* (01) 42 22 62 73
*E-mail:* info@desfemmes.fr
*Web Site:* www.desfemmes.fr
*Key Personnel*
Proprietor & Man Dir: Antoinette Fouque
General Manager: Marie-Claude Grumbach
Founded: 1974
Subjects: Art, Biography, Drama, Theater, Fiction, History, Literature, Literary Criticism, Essays, Photography, Poetry
ISBN Prefix(es): 2-7210
Number of titles published annually: 5 Print; 2 Audio
Total Titles: 450 Print; 100 Audio
Distributor for Sonjis

**Editions du Feu Nouveau+**
3, rue du Chateau, 60390 Troussures
*Tel:* (01) 44844797
*Key Personnel*
Man Dir: Henri Caffarel
Founded: 1946
Subjects: Literature, Literary Criticism, Essays, Religion - Catholic, Religion - Other

ISBN Prefix(es): 2-85017
*Shipping Address:* SOFEDIS (Diffuseur), 29 rue Saint-Sulpice, 75006 Paris

**Figures**, *imprint of* Societe des Editions Grasset et Fasquelle

**Editions Filipacchi-Sonodip+**
10, rue Thierry LeLuron, 92592 Levallois-Perret
*Tel:* (01) 41 34 90 69; (01) 41 34 90 55 *Fax:* (01) 41 34 90 70
*E-mail:* sonodip@hfp.fr
*Key Personnel*
Manager, Editorial: Marie-Francoise Acdouard
Founded: 1970
Subjects: Art, Cookery, House & Home, Photography, Travel, Leisure
ISBN Prefix(es): 2-85018

**Editions First+**
27, rue Cassette, 75006 Paris
*Tel:* (01) 45 49 60 00 *Fax:* (01) 45 49 60 01
*E-mail:* firstinfo@efirst.com
*Web Site:* www.efirst.com
*Key Personnel*
Editorial Dir: Henri Bovet
Production & Administration: Jean Fontanieu
Rights: Stephanie Koch
Founded: 1985
Subjects: Computer Science, Health, Nutrition, Humor, Marketing
ISBN Prefix(es): 2-87691

**Librairie Fischbacher**
33, rue de Seine, 75006 Paris
*Tel:* (01) 43 26 84 87 *Fax:* (01) 43 26 48 87
*E-mail:* info@librairiefischbacher.fr
*Web Site:* www.librairiefischbacher.fr
*Key Personnel*
Dir, Production, Publicity, Rights & Permissions: Marie-Colette Galand
Sales: P Diani-Garel
Founded: 1850
Specialize in original art.
Membership(s): Library of Fine Arts.
Subjects: Art, History, Music, Dance, Philosophy, Religion - Protestant, Social Sciences, Sociology, Theology
ISBN Prefix(es): 2-7179

**Editions Fivedit**
96 rue du Faubourg-Poissonniere, 75010 Paris
Mailing Address: BP 146, 74941 Annecy Le Vieux Cedex
*Tel:* (04) 50 66 33 78 *Fax:* (04) 50 23 33 08
*E-mail:* fivedit.sa@wanadoo.fr
*Key Personnel*
Man Dir: Rene Fivel-Demoret
Founded: 1976
Subjects: How-to, Travel
ISBN Prefix(es): 2-904394
Total Titles: 30 Print
*Branch Office(s)*
Distribution Ulysse, 4176 Saint Denis, Montreal, QC, Canada
Distributed by Vivendi Universal Publishing Services
Distributor for APCA Bienvenue a la Ferme; Gites de France; Logis de Belgique; Logis de France; Logis D' Italia; Tables et Auberges de France

**Flammarion Groupe+**
87, quai Panhard et Levassor, 75647 Paris Cedex 13
*Tel:* (01) 40 51 31 00 *Fax:* (01) 43 29 43 43
*Web Site:* www.flammarion.com
*Telex:* flamedit 205641 *Cable:* 205146
*Key Personnel*
Chairman: Charles-Henri Flammarion
Man Dir: Danielle Nees

Sales Manager: Alain Flammarion
Publicity, Advertising: Catherine Bachelez
Rights & Permissions: Renata Morteo
Press: Francine Brobeil *Fax:* (01) 40 51 31 29
   *E-mail:* fbr@flammarion.fr
Founded: 1875
Subjects: Architecture & Interior Design,
   Art, Fiction, Gardening, Plants, House &
   Home, Literature, Literary Criticism, Essays,
   Medicine, Nursing, Dentistry, Nonfiction (General), Wine & Spirits
ISBN Prefix(es): 2-257
*Associate Companies:* Pygnalion
Imprints: Arthaud; Aubie; Champs Dominos; GF;
   Glacial; Fluide; Librio; Medecine-Sciences;
   Pere Castor
Subsidiaries: Aubie; Editions Aubier, Flammarion
   Canada; Beau Arts SA; Delagrave; Flammarion
   4; Flammarion Presse; Flammarion 2; Flammarion Switzerland; Flammarion USA Inc; J'ai
   Lu
*U.S. Office(s):* Flammarion USA Inc, 200 Park
   Ave S, Suite 1406, New York, NY 10003,
   United States *Tel:* 212-777-6888 *Fax:* 212-777-3438
Distributed by Abbeville (USA); Thames & Hudson (UK)
Distributor for Abbeville; Actes Sud; Assouline;
   CNAC; Delcourt; Flohic; Hoebeke; Horay; Bibliotheque de l'Image; Le Petit Fute; Pygnalion;
   Revue du Vin de France; Zulma
*Bookshop(s):* Flammarion 4, 19 Rue Visconti,
   75006 Paris
*Warehouse:* UD-Union Distribution, 06 rue Petit
   le roy, Chevilly-Larue, 94152 Rungis Cedex
   *Tel:* (01) 41 80 20 20 *Fax:* (01) 46 87 51 04
*Orders to:* UD-Union Distribution, 106 rue Petit
   le roy, Chevilly-Larue, 94152 Rungis Cedex
   *Tel:* (01) 41 80 20 20 *Fax:* (01) 46 87 51 80

**FLE**, see Hachette francais langue etrangere -
   FLE

**Editions Fleurus+**
15-27 rue Moussorgski, 75895 Paris Cedex 18
*Tel:* (01) 53 26 33 35 *Fax:* (01) 53 26 33 36
*Telex:* 201650 F
*Key Personnel*
Man Dir: Pierre-Marie Dumont
Eitorial Dir: Christophe Savoure
Editorial: Janine Boudineau
Sales Dir: Dominique Delage
Foreign Rights: Euriel Donval; Chantal Hourcade
Founded: 1944
Subjects: Architecture & Interior Design, Art,
   Crafts, Games, Hobbies, Fiction, Psychology,
   Psychiatry, Religion - Other, Social Sciences,
   Sociology
ISBN Prefix(es): 2-215

**Fleuve No ite Editions**, see Presses de la Cite

**Fluide**, *imprint of* Flammarion Groupe

**Folklore Comtois**
Musee des Maisons Comtoises, 25360 Nancray
*Tel:* (03) 81 55 29 77 *Fax:* (03) 81 55 23 97
*E-mail:* musee@maisons-comtoises.org
*Web Site:* www.maisons-comtoises.org
*Key Personnel*
President: Jean Louis Clade
Vice President: Pierre Bourgin
Subjects: Agriculture, Architecture & Interior Design, History, House & Home

**Editions Foucher**
Subsidiary of Hachette
58 rue Jean Bleuzen, 92178 Vanves Cedex
*Tel:* (01) 41 23 65 60 *Fax:* (01) 41 23 65 03
*E-mail:* contact@editions-foucher.fr
*Web Site:* www.editions-foucher.fr

*Key Personnel*
President: Christine Breiteinstein
General Manager: Daniel Segala
Founded: 1936
Subjects: Accounting, Economics, Education,
   Medicine, Nursing, Dentistry, Public Administration
ISBN Prefix(es): 2-216
Total Titles: 1,000 Print

**Editions Fragments**
5, rue de Charonne, 75011 Paris
*Tel:* (01) 47 00 76 48 *Fax:* (01) 47 00 22 04
*E-mail:* art@fragmentseditions.com
*Web Site:* www.fragmentseditions.com
*Key Personnel*
Dir: Francois de Villandry
Publishing Coordinator: Julie Alinquant
Press & Public Relations: Sophie Godard
Founded: 1989
Specialize in contemporary art.
Subjects: Art, Photography
ISBN Prefix(es): 2-908066; 2-912964
Number of titles published annually: 7 Print
Total Titles: 80 Print
Distributed by Goutal-Darly (Europe); Vilo
   (China, Europe, Japan, Korea, North America,
   South America)
*Warehouse:* Zone Industrielle Leval, 11 ave
   Arago, 91420 Morangis
*Orders to:* Vilo Diffusion, 25 rue Ginoux, 75015
   Paris

**Institut Francais de Recherche pour
   l'Exploitation de la Mer (IFREMER)** (French
   Research Institute for Exploitation of the Sea)
155, rue Jean-Jacques Rousseau, 92138 Issy-les-
   Moulineaux Cedex
Mailing Address: BP 70, 29280 Plouzane Cedex
*Tel:* (02) 98 22 40 13 *Fax:* (02) 98 22 45 86
*E-mail:* editions@ifremer.fr
*Web Site:* www.ifremer.fr
*Key Personnel*
Chief Executive Officer: Jean-Francois Minster
Editorial & Promotion: Courtay Nelly
   *E-mail:* nelly.courtay@ifremer.fr
Founded: 1984
Specialize in scientific & technical publications.
Subjects: Environmental Studies, Maritime, Outdoor Recreation, Technology, Transportation
ISBN Prefix(es): 2-905434; 2-84433
Total Titles: 4 CD-ROM; 40 Audio
*Orders to:* ALT Brest Service Logistique, 3, rue
   Edouard Belin BP 23, 29801 Brest Cedex 9
   *Tel:* (02) 98 02 42 34 *Fax:* (02) 98 41 49 43
   *E-mail:* logistique.brest@alt.sa.com (for booksellers)
INRA Editions, RD 10, 78026 Versailles Cedex
   *Tel:* (01) 30 83 34 06 *Fax:* (01) 30 83 34 49
   *E-mail:* intra.editions@versailles.inra.fr (mail
   order)

**Association Francaise de Normalisation+**
11, ave Francis de Pressense, 93571 Saint-Denis
   La Plaine Cedex
*Tel:* (01) 41 62 80 00 *Fax:* (01) 49 17 90 00
*E-mail:* info.formation@afnor.fr
*Web Site:* www.afnor.fr
*Key Personnel*
Dir, Publication & General Manager: Olivier
   Peyrat
Administrator & International Rights: Gildas
   Bourdais
Subjects: Management
ISBN Prefix(es): 2-12

**France Edition Office de Promotion
   Internationale**
Association d'editeurs, 115, Blvd Saint-Germain,
   75006 Paris
*Tel:* (01) 44 41 13 13 *Fax:* (01) 46 34 63 83
*E-mail:* info@franceedition.com

*Web Site:* bief.org
*Key Personnel*
President: Alain Grund
Managing Dir: Jean-Guy Boin *E-mail:* jgboin@
   bief.org
Specialize in all subjects.
*Branch Office(s)*
France Edition Vietnam, Mlle Ho Thi Ngoc
   Lan, 30 rue Dinh Ngaug, Hanoi, Viet Nam
   *Tel:* (04) 826 48 62 *Fax:* (04) 825 34 11
   *E-mail:* lanfevn@hn.vnn.vn
*U.S. Office(s):* France Edition Inc, 853 Broadway,
   Suite 1509, New York, NY 10003-4703, United
   States, Contact: Lucinda Karter *Tel:* 212-254-
   4540 *Fax:* 212-254-4540 *Web Site:* www.
   frenchpubagency.com
Foreign Rights: France Edition Inc

**Editions France-Empire+**
13, rue Le Sueur, 75116 Paris
*Tel:* (01) 45 00 33 00 *Fax:* (01) 45 00 20 77
*E-mail:* france-empire@france-empire.fr
*Web Site:* www.france-empire.fr
*Key Personnel*
Contact: Jean-Louis Giral
Founded: 1945
ISBN Prefix(es): 2-7048
*Parent Company:* Desquenne et Giral
*Bookshop(s):* Librairie France-Empire, 30 rue
   Washington, 75008 Paris

**France-Loisirs**
123 blvd de Grenelle, 75725 Paris Cedex 15
*Tel:* (01) 45 68 60 00 *Fax:* (01) 42 73 14 38
*E-mail:* serviceclub@france-loisirs.com
*Web Site:* www.franceloisirs.com
*Telex:* 202 459 f
*Key Personnel*
Publicity: A Cinar
Subjects: Art, Literature, Literary Criticism, Essays
ISBN Prefix(es): 2-7242; 2-7441

**Les Editions Franciscaines SA**
9, rue Marie-Rose, 75014 Paris
*Tel:* (01) 45407351 *Fax:* (01) 40447504
*E-mail:* editions-franciscaines@wanadoo.fr
*Key Personnel*
President: Michel Deleu
Founded: 1932
Specialize in books.
Subjects: Religion - Catholic, Theology, Franciscan Spirituality
ISBN Prefix(es): 2-85020
Number of titles published annually: 5 Print
Total Titles: 105 Print
Distributed by Alliances Service (Belgium);
   Univers (Canada)
Distributor for Franciscan Printing Press

**Association Frank+**
c/o Frank Books, BP 29, 94301 Vincennes Cedex
*Tel:* (01) 43656405 *Fax:* (01) 48596668
*Key Personnel*
President: David Applefield *E-mail:* david@paris-
   anglo.com
Founded: 1990
A special group called Lawyers for Literature
   functions as honorary publishers for Frank, The
   Literary Journal.
Subjects: Drama, Theater, Fashion, Fiction, Howto, Labor, Industrial Relations, Literature, Literary Criticism, Essays, Poetry
ISBN Prefix(es): 2-908171
*Associate Companies:* Anglophone SA
*U.S. Office(s):* Mosaic Press, 85 River Rock
   Drive, No 202, Buffalo, NY 14207-2170,
   United States
Distributed by Houghton-Mifflin (UK)

**Futuribles SARL+**
55, rue de Varenne, 75007 Paris

*Tel:* (01) 53 63 37 70 *Fax:* (01) 42 22 65 54
*E-mail:* revue@futuribles.com
*Web Site:* www.futuribles.com
*Key Personnel*
General Dir: Hugues de Jouvenel *Tel:* (01) 53 63
37 73 *E-mail:* hjouvenel@futuribles.com
International Rights & General Secretary: Corinne
Roels *Tel:* (01) 53 63 37 71
Founded: 1975
Publish a monthly independent transdisciplinary
policy oriented journal.
Subjects: Developing Countries, Economics, En-
vironmental Studies, Government, Political Sci-
ence, Labor, Industrial Relations, Management,
Social Sciences, Sociology, Technology
ISBN Prefix(es): 2-84387
Number of titles published annually: 11 Print
Total Titles: 300 Print
*Associate Companies:* Association Futuribles In-
ternational

**Les Editions Gabalda et Cie**
18, rue Pierre et Marie Curie, 75005 Paris
*Tel:* (01) 43 26 53 55 *Fax:* (01) 43 25 04 71
*E-mail:* editions@gabalda.com
*Web Site:* www.gabalda.com
*Key Personnel*
Proprietor: J Gabalda
Founded: 1845
Subjects: Religion - Other, Theology
ISBN Prefix(es): 2-85021
*Parent Company:* Librarie Lecoffre

**Editions Jacques Gabay+**
151 bis, rue Saint-Jacques, 75005 Paris
*Tel:* (01) 43 54 64 64 *Fax:* (01) 43 54 87 00
*E-mail:* infos@gabay.com
*Web Site:* www.gabay.com
*Key Personnel*
Man Dir: Jacques Gabay
Founded: 1987
Subjects: Astronomy, Chemistry, Chemical Engi-
neering, Economics, Mathematics, Philosophy,
Physical Sciences, Physics, Science (General)
ISBN Prefix(es): 2-87647
Total Titles: 230 Print
Imprints: Oblong

**Editions Galilee+**
9, rue de Linne, 75005 Paris
*Tel:* (01) 43 31 23 84 *Fax:* (01) 45 35 53 68
*E-mail:* editions.galilee@free.fr
*Key Personnel*
Man Dir: Michel Delorme
Founded: 1971
Subjects: Art, History, Literature, Literary Criti-
cism, Essays, Philosophy, Poetry, Psychology,
Psychiatry, Social Sciences, Sociology
ISBN Prefix(es): 2-7186
*Shipping Address:* 128 ave du Marechalde Laltre-
de-Tattiguy, 77400 Lagny
*Warehouse:* 128 ave du Marechalde Laltre-de-
Tattiguy, 77400 Lagny
*Orders to:* Sodis, BP 142, 77403 Lagny sur
Marne *Tel:* (01) 45 31 16 06

**Editions Gallimard**
5, rue Sebastien-Bottin, 75328 Paris Cedex 07
*Tel:* (01) 49 54 42 00 *Fax:* (01) 45 44 94 03
*Web Site:* www.gallimard.fr
*Telex:* GALLIM 204121F *Cable:* Enerefene Paris
044
*Key Personnel*
President: Antoine Gallimard
Editorial Dir: Teresa Cremisi
Sales Dir: Bruno Caillet
Rights & Permissions: Prune Berge; Anne
Solange Noble
Editor: Jean-Loup Champion; Francoise Cibiel;
Colline Faure-Poiree; Yvon Girard; Gustavo
Guerrero; Veronique Jacob; Christine Jordis;

Bernard Lortholary; Jean Mattern; Patrick Ray-
nal; Eric Vigne
Art Dir: Jacques Maillot
Export: Jean-Charles Grunstein
Founded: 1911
Subjects: Art, Biography, Fiction, History, Music,
Dance, Philosophy, Poetry
ISBN Prefix(es): 2-07
Subsidiaries: Editions Denoel; Editions Gallimard
Images (Canada); Editions Gallimard Jeunesse;
Editions Mercure de France; Schoenhof's For-
eign Books (USA); Les Editions de la Table
Ronde
Distributed by Centre de Diffusion de l'Edition;
France Export Diffusion; La SODIS
*Bookshop(s):* Le Divan, 203, rue la convention,
75015 Paris *Tel:* (01) 53 68 90 68 *Fax:* (01)
42 50 84 68; Librairie Delamain, 155, rue
Saint Honore, 75001 Paris *Tel:* (01) 42 61 48
78 *Fax:* (01) 40 15 91 69; Librairie des Fac-
ultes, Strasbourg; Librairie Gallimard, 15 blvd
Raspail, 75007 Paris *Tel:* (01) 45 48 24 84
*Fax:* (01) 42 84 16 97; Librairie Kleber, 1,
rue des Francs Bourgeois, 67000 Strasbourg
*Tel:* (03) 88 15 78 88 *Fax:* (03) 88 15 78 80;
Librairie de Paris, 7, 9, 11 Place de Clichy,
75017 Paris *Tel:* (01) 45 22 47 81 *Fax:* (01) 40
08 08 50

**Editions Gamma**
BP 10, Bonneuil-les-Eaux, 60121 Breteuil Cedex
*Tel:* (03) 44 80 68 63 *Fax:* (03) 44 80 68 60
*E-mail:* contact@editions-gamma.com
*Web Site:* www.editions-gamma.com
*Telex:* 202036 (Begedis SA)
*Key Personnel*
President: Bernard Ramspaxher
Editor: Jean Nicolas Moreau
Founded: 1963
Subjects: Social Sciences, Sociology
ISBN Prefix(es): 2-7130
*Parent Company:* Gedit SA Tournai
*Associate Companies:* Editions du Chalet, Paris;
Desclee Editeurs, Belgium; Editions Desclee
et Cie, Paris; Editions Gamma, Belgium; Nou-
velles Editions Mame, Paris; Editions Universi-
taires, Paris
*Orders to:* Begedis, 11 rue Duquay-Trouin, 75006
Paris
Arc-en-Ciel International, 2 I Tournai Ouest, B-
7713 Marquain, Belgium (Foreign)

**Gammaprim+**
78, rue de Dunkerque, 75009 Paris
*Tel:* (01) 49959492 *Fax:* (01) 40230134
*E-mail:* fgosselin@gammaprim.fr
*Key Personnel*
Editor: Franck Gosselin
Founded: 1982
Subjects: Biological Sciences, Chemistry, Chem-
ical Engineering, Economics, Geography, Ge-
ology, History, Literature, Literary Criticism,
Essays, Mathematics, Philosophy, Physics
ISBN Prefix(es): 2-903908; 2-84391
Distributed by Sodis; Sofedis
*Warehouse:* Sodis, 128 ave du Mal de lattre de
Tassigny, 77400 Lagny Sur Marne
*Orders to:* Sodis, 128 ave du Mal de Lattre de
Tassigny, 77400 Lagny sur Marne

**Editions Ganymede+**
PO Box 12, 77220 Presles-en-Brie
*Tel:* (01) 64 25 83 01 *Fax:* (01) 64 42 86 68
*E-mail:* rozeille.hatem@wanadoo.fr
*Web Site:* www.hatem.com/librairie.htm
*Key Personnel*
Dir & International Rights: Frank Hatem
Founded: 1973
Subjects: Philosophy, Physics, Psychology, Psy-
chiatry, Science (General)
ISBN Prefix(es): 2-9500999; 2-85824

**Editions du Garde-Temps+**
106, rue Vieille-du-Temple, 75003 Paris
*Tel:* (01) 44788477 *Fax:* (01) 44788479
*E-mail:* studio-magnet@calva.net
*Key Personnel*
Contact: Michel Le Louarn
Founded: 1995
Subjects: Travel
ISBN Prefix(es): 2-9509273; 2-913545
*Warehouse:* Vilo, 25 rue Gihoux, 75737 Paris
Cedex 15, Contact: Sophie Praquin *Tel:* (01)
45770805 *Fax:* (01) 45799715

**Imprimerie Librairie Gardet**
Unit of Edimontagne
La Mollard, 74400 Chamonix
*Tel:* (04) 50 53 67 47 *Fax:* (04) 50 53 67 47
*E-mail:* edimontagne@wanadoo.fr
*Key Personnel*
Editor: Jacques Gendrault
Founded: 1836
Subjects: Art, Crafts, Games, Hobbies, Education,
History, Regional Interests
ISBN Prefix(es): 2-7049
Total Titles: 70 Print

**Gauthier-Villars**, *imprint of* Dunod Editeur

**Gautier Languereau**, *imprint of* Hachette
Jeunesse

**Librairie Generale Francaise SA**
43, Quai de Grenelle, 75905 Paris Cedex 15
*Tel:* (01) 43 92 30 00 *Fax:* (01) 43 92 35 90
The above is the Head Office. Editorial & pro-
duction are run from Le Livre de Poche.
ISBN Prefix(es): 2-253

**Editions Gerard de Villiers**
43 Quai de Grenelle, 75905 Paris Cedex 15
*Tel:* (01) 43 92 30 00 *Fax:* (01) 43 92 35 80
*Web Site:* www.editionsgerarddevilliers.com
*Telex:* 204434
*Key Personnel*
President & Dir General: M Gerard de Villiers
Editorial Dir: Christine de Grandmaison
Founded: 1988
Subjects: Fiction, Mysteries
ISBN Prefix(es): 2-7386

**Paul Geuthner Librairie Orientaliste+**
12, rue Vavin, 75006 Paris
*Tel:* (01) 46 34 71 30 *Fax:* (01) 43 29 75 64
*E-mail:* geuthner@geuthner.com
*Web Site:* www.geuthner.com *Cable:* LIBORIENT
PARIS
*Key Personnel*
Man Dir: Marc F Seidl-Geuthner
Founded: 1901
Subjects: Anthropology, Antiques, Art, Biblical
Studies, Biography, Foreign Countries, Geog-
raphy, Geology, History, Law, Music, Dance,
Philosophy, Religion - Buddhist, Religion -
Catholic, Religion - Hindu, Religion - Islamic,
Religion - Jewish, Religion - Protestant, Social
Sciences, Sociology
ISBN Prefix(es): 2-7053

**GF**, *imprint of* Flammarion Groupe

**GIPPE**, see Groupement d'Information
Promotion Presse Edition (GIPPE)

**Gippe-Les Amoureux des Livres**, *imprint of*
Groupement d'Information Promotion Presse
Edition (GIPPE)

**Editions Jean Paul Gisserot+**
10, rue Gracieuse, 75005 Paris
*Tel:* (01) 43 31 80 04 *Fax:* (01) 43 31 88 15
*E-mail:* editions@editions-gisserot.com

*Web Site:* www.editions-gisserot.com
*Key Personnel*
Dir: Thibault Chattard *E-mail:* thibault.chattard@
editions-gisserot.com
Founded: 1988
Subjects: Aeronautics, Aviation, Animals, Pets,
Anthropology, Archaeology, Architecture &
Interior Design, Art, Astronomy, Biography,
Cookery, Education, English as a Second Lan-
guage, Foreign Countries, Gardening, Plants,
Genealogy, History, How-to, Humor, Maritime,
Music, Dance, Natural History, Regional Inter-
ests, Religion - Catholic, Religion - Protestant,
Travel, Wine & Spirits
ISBN Prefix(es): 2-87747
Number of titles published annually: 50 Print
Total Titles: 560 Print
Subsidiaries: Telegiss Distribution (France)
*Shipping Address:* TeleGiss Distribution, Z I de
Saint Eloi, 29800 Plouedern *Tel:* (02) 9821
3663 *Fax:* (02) 9821 5631
*Orders to:* TeleGiss Distribution, Z I de Saint
Eloi, 29800 Plouedern *Tel:* (02) 9821 3663
*Fax:* (02) 9821 5631
*Returns:* TeleGiss Distribution, Z I de Saint Eloi,
29800 Plouedern *Tel:* (02) 9821 3663 *Fax:* (02)
9821 5631

**Glacial**, *imprint of* Flammarion Groupe

**Editions Glenat+**
6, rue Lieutenant-Chanaron, 38000 Grenoble
Mailing Address: BP 177, 38008 Grenoble Cedex
*Tel:* (04) 76 88 75 75 *Fax:* (04) 76 88 75 70
*Web Site:* www.glenat.com
*Telex:* 320030 glenat
*Key Personnel*
President & Joint Man Dir: Jacques Glenat
Editorial: Dominique Burdot; Jean-Claude Ca-
mano
Sales (Export): Christine Glenat
Production: Francis Bernard
Rights & Permissions: Jean-Brice Roux
Founded: 1969
Subjects: Cookery, Fiction, Humor, Science Fic-
tion, Fantasy, Sports, Athletics, Travel, Comics,
Leisure
ISBN Prefix(es): 2-7234
Subsidiaries: Glenat-Benelux; Glenat Espagne;
Glenat-Images
*Bookshop(s):* Glenat-Librairie, 16 Lafayette,
75009 Paris *Tel:* (01) 42 46 98 81

**Editions Jacques Grancher+**
98, rue de Vaugirard, 75006 Paris
*Tel:* (01) 42 22 64 80 *Fax:* (01) 45 48 25 03
*E-mail:* info@grancher.com
*Web Site:* www.grancher.com *Cable:* SCE DE
VENTE/LIBRAIRIES 5480317
*Key Personnel*
Man Dir: Jacques Grancher
Editor: Michel Grancher *E-mail:* m.grancher@
worldonline.fr; Philippe Grancher
*E-mail:* grancher@worldonline.fr
Founded: 1952
Subjects: Astrology, Occult, Cookery, Health, Nu-
trition, How-to, Humor, Military Science, Non-
fiction (General), Parapsychology, Psychology,
Psychiatry, Religion - Catholic, Religion - Is-
lamic, Religion - Jewish, Religion - Protestant,
Religion - Other, Travel
ISBN Prefix(es): 2-7339
Number of titles published annually: 40 Print
Total Titles: 400 Print
Distributed by Hachette
*Distribution Center:* Hachette

**Grand Angle**, *imprint of* Editions l'Instant
Durable

**Les Grandes Anthologies**, *imprint of* Sarl
Editions Jean Grassin

**Editions Grandir** (To Grow)+
Impasse des soucis, 30000 Nimes
*Tel:* (04) 66 84 01 19 *Fax:* (04) 66 26 14 50
*Key Personnel*
Manager: Rene Turc
Founded: 1978
Subjects: Art, Fiction, Physical Sciences
ISBN Prefix(es): 2-84166; 2-904292
Total Titles: 350 Print

**Granit Editions**
2, rue Frederic-Schneider Hall 8/143, 75018 Paris
*Tel:* (01) 42 54 08 00 *Fax:* (01) 42 54 73 04
*Key Personnel*
Dir: Francois Xavier Jaujard
ISBN Prefix(es): 2-86281
*Orders to:* Distique, 5 rue du Marechal Leclerc,
28600 Luisant

**Sarl Editions Jean Grassin**
Place de Port-en-Dro, 56342 Carnac-Plage
Mailing Address: BP 75, 56342 Carnac Cedex
*Tel:* (02) 97 52 93 63 *Fax:* (02) 97 52 83 90
*E-mail:* j.grassin@wanadoo.fr
*Web Site:* www.editions-grassin.com
*Key Personnel*
Man Dir: Jean Grassin
Founded: 1957
Subjects: History, Literature, Literary Criticism,
Essays, Poetry
ISBN Prefix(es): 2-7055
Imprints: Club J G; L'encyclopedie Poetique; Les
Grandes Anthologies; Sequences
*Book Club(s):* Poetes Presents

**Editions Gregoriennes**, *imprint of* Adverbum
SARL

**GRET**, see Groupe de Recherche et d'Echanges
Technologiques (GRET)

**Groupe de Recherche et d'Echanges
Technologiques (GRET)**
211-213 rue La Fayette, 75010 Paris
*Tel:* (01) 40 05 61 61 *Fax:* (01) 40 05 61 10
*E-mail:* gret@gret.org; librairie@gret.org
*Web Site:* www.gret.org
*Key Personnel*
President: Herve Bichat
Dir: Serge Allou
Founded: 1976
Subjects: Agriculture, Anthropology, Developing
Countries, Finance, Journalism, Technology
ISBN Prefix(es): 2-86844
Total Titles: 110 Print
*Distribution Center:* CELF

**Groupe Hatier International+**
Subsidiary of Groupe Alexandre Hatier
31 rue de Fleurus, 75006 Paris
*Tel:* (01) 44 39 28 00 *Fax:* (01) 45 44 84 54
*E-mail:* hatier@intl.com
*Key Personnel*
Man Dir: Patrick C Dubs *Fax:* (01) 44 39 28 16
*E-mail:* pdubs@hatier.intl.com
Promotion: Nathalie Hernandez *Tel:* (01)
44 39 28 14 *Fax:* (01) 42 84 03 19
*E-mail:* nhernandez@hatier-intl.com
Specialize in export & textbook publishing for
French & Arabic speaking countries. Educa-
tional materials, maps.
ISBN Prefix(es): 2-7473
Number of titles published annually: 60 Print
Total Titles: 300 Print
*Ultimate Parent Company:* Hachette SA
Distributor for Editions Didier

**Groupe Revue Fiduciaire+**
100 rue La Fayette, 75010 Paris Cedex 10
*Tel:* (01) 47 70 42 42 *Fax:* (01) 48 24 12 93
*E-mail:* courrier@grouperf.com

*Web Site:* www.grouperf.com
*Key Personnel*
Dir General: Yves-Robert De la Villeguerin
ISBN Prefix(es): 2-86521
*Associate Companies:* Societe Europeenne de
Presse Fiscale, Juridique
*Orders to:* 45 rue Victor Hugo, 93507 Pantin
*Tel:* (01) 48 40 01 11

**Groupement d'Information Promotion Presse
Edition (GIPPE)**
60, rue Dombasle, 75015 Paris
*Tel:* (01) 45 32 12 75
*E-mail:* gippe@free.fr
*Web Site:* gippe.free.fr
*Key Personnel*
General Secretary: Rene Froment
Founded: 1987
Subjects: Literature, Literary Criticism, Essays
ISBN Prefix(es): 2-9508635
*Parent Company:* Les Amoureux des Livres-
Gippe (Publisher)
Imprints: Gippe-Les Amoureux des Livres

**Librairie Guenegaud**
Subsidiary of P M C
10, rue de l'Odeon, 75006 Paris
*Tel:* (01) 43260791 *Fax:* (01) 40468872
*E-mail:* librairie.guenegaud@wanadoo.fr
*Key Personnel*
Man Dir: Philippe Barrault
Founded: 1910
Subjects: Biography, Genealogy, History, Outdoor
Recreation, Regional Interests, Romance
ISBN Prefix(es): 2-85023
Number of titles published annually: 10 Print
Total Titles: 95 Print
*Associate Companies:* La Societe et le High Life

**Guide Franck**, *imprint of* Editions Franck
Mercier

**Guide Pratique**, *imprint of* Les Presses du
Management

**Guides Gallimard**, *imprint of* Les Nouveaux
Loisirs

**Editions d'Art Albert Guillot**
4 rue de Seze, 69006 Lyon
*Tel:* (04) 78521026
Subjects: Art
ISBN Prefix(es): 2-85096

**Hachette Education+**
43 Quai de Grenelle, 75905 Paris Cedex 15
*Tel:* (01) 43 92 30 00; (01) 43 92 31 12 *Fax:* (01)
43 92 30 30
*Web Site:* www.hachette-education.com
*Key Personnel*
Dir: Isabelle Jeuge-Maynart
Press: Martine Monchanin *Tel:* (01) 43 92 31 91
*Fax:* (01) 43 92 16 38 *E-mail:* mmonchanin@
hachette-livre.fr
Founded: 1826
Specialize in CD-ROMs & reference books.
Subjects: Education, French as a Second Lan-
guage
ISBN Prefix(es): 2-01
Total Titles: 4,000 Print
*Parent Company:* Hachette Livre
*Ultimate Parent Company:* Lagardere Groupe
Subsidiaries: Edicef; Sylemma-Andrieu; Hachette
Diffusion Internationale
*Showroom(s):* Espace Enseignant, 8 rue Haute
Jenille, 75006 Paris

**Hachette francais langue etrangere - FLE+**
58, rue Jean-Bleuzen, 92178 Vanves Cedex

*Tel:* (01) 43 92 30 00 *Fax:* (01) 43 92 39 20
*E-mail:* fle@hachette-livre.fr
*Web Site:* www.fle.hachette-livre.fr
*Key Personnel*
Publishing Dir: Anne Reberioux *Tel:* (01) 46 62
   10 58 *E-mail:* anneberioux@hachette.lane.fr
ISBN Prefix(es): 2-01
Number of titles published annually: 50 Print; 4
   Audio
Total Titles: 50 Print
*Parent Company:* Hachette Livre SA, Paris

**Hachette Jeunesse+**
43 quai de Grenelle, 75905 Paris Cedex 15
*Tel:* (01) 43923000 *Fax:* (01) 43923338
*Web Site:* www.hachettejeunesse.com
*Key Personnel*
Dir: Frederique de Buron
Editorial Dir: Emmanuelle Massonaud
International Rights Manager: Evelyne Dil
Founded: 1885
Subjects: Nonfiction (General), Picture & Charac-
   ter Books
ISBN Prefix(es): 2-01; 2-217
*Parent Company:* Hachette Livre SA
Imprints: Gautier Languereau; Deux Coqs d'Or
*Warehouse:* Centre de Distribution du Livre, Z
   A Coignieres-Maurepas, One ave Gutenberg,
   78316 Maurepas Cedex

**Hachette Jeunesse Roman+**
43, quai de Grenelle, 75905 Paris Cedex 15
*Tel:* (01) 43 92 30 00 *Fax:* (01) 443 92 33 38
   *Cable:* HACHECI-PARIS 25
*Key Personnel*
Dir: Catherine Tessandier
International Rights Manager: Monique Lantelme
Founded: 1856
ISBN Prefix(es): 2-01
*Parent Company:* Hachette

**Hachette Livre+**
43, quai de Grenelle, 75905 Paris Cedex 15
*Tel:* (01) 43 92 30 00 *Fax:* (01) 43 92 30 30
*Web Site:* www.hatchette-livre.fr
*Key Personnel*
Chief Executive Officer: Arnaud Nourry
Founded: 1826
Subjects: Architecture & Interior Design, Art,
   Economics, Education, Engineering (General),
   Fiction, Government, Political Science, History,
   Language Arts, Linguistics, Nonfiction (Gen-
   eral), Philosophy, Science (General), Self-Help,
   Social Sciences, Sociology, Sports, Athletics,
   Travel
ISBN Prefix(es): 2-01
Number of titles published annually: 5,000 Print
*Ultimate Parent Company:* Lagardere Groupe
Subsidiaries: Editions du Chene; Hachette Littera-
   tures; Hachette Pratique

**Hachette Livre International+**
58 rue Jean Bleuzen, 92178 Vanves Cedex
*Tel:* (01) 55 00 11 00 *Fax:* (01) 55 00 11 60
*Key Personnel*
Dir General, Africa & Indian Ocean: Laurent
   Loric
Subjects: Economics, Education, English as a
   Second Language, Environmental Studies, Law,
   Literature, Literary Criticism, Essays, Mathe-
   matics, Physics
ISBN Prefix(es): 2-84129; 2-85069
*Parent Company:* Hachette Livre SA
*Associate Companies:* EDICEF; Hatier Interna-
   tional
Subsidiaries: NEI (Nouvelles Editions Ivoiri-
   ennes)
Distributor for EDICEF; Hatier International

**Hachette Pratiques+**
43, quai de Grenelle, 75905 Paris Cedex 15

*Tel:* (01) 43 92 30 00 *Fax:* (01) 43 92 30 39
*Key Personnel*
Dir: Jean Arcache *E-mail:* jarcache@hachette-
   livre.fr
Editorial: Pierre Baron
Publicity: Cecile Boyer
Foreign Rights: Monique Lanthelme
Coeditions & Foreign Rights: David Inman
Founded: 1826
Subjects: Animals, Pets, Astrology, Occult, Bi-
   ography, Cookery, Crafts, Games, Hobbies,
   Fashion, Gardening, Plants, Health, Nutrition,
   Management, Sports, Athletics, Wine & Spirits
ISBN Prefix(es): 2-01
*Warehouse:* Hachette Distribution, ZA Coigni-
   etires, One avenue Gutenberg, 78316 Maurepas
   Cedex

**Editions Viviane Hamy+**
89 rue du Faubourg Saint Antoine, 75011 Paris
*Tel:* (01) 53171600 *Fax:* (01) 53171609
*E-mail:* information@viviane-hamy.fr
*Web Site:* www.viviane-hamy.fr/0000.html
*Key Personnel*
Contact: Viviane Hamy; Frederic Martin
   *E-mail:* frederic.martin@viviane-hamy.fr
Founded: 1990
Subjects: Literature, Literary Criticism, Essays
ISBN Prefix(es): 2-87858
Number of titles published annually: 12 Print
Total Titles: 120 Print
Distributed by Flammarion

**Harlequin SA**
83-85 blvd Vincent-Auriol, 75013 Paris
*Tel:* (01) 42166363 *Fax:* (01) 45828694
*Key Personnel*
Man Dir: Frederique Sarfati
Editorial Manager: Anne Coquet
Founded: 1978
Subjects: Astrology, Occult, Romance
ISBN Prefix(es): 2-280; 2-86259
*Parent Company:* Hachette SA
Imprints: Duo, Harlequin

**L'Harmattan+**
5-7 rue de l'Ecole-Polytechnique, 75005 Paris
*Tel:* (01) 40 46 79 11; (01) 40 46 79 20 *Fax:* (01)
   43 25 82 03
*E-mail:* harmat@worldnet.fr
*Web Site:* www.editions-harmattan.fr
*Key Personnel*
Man Editor: Denis Pryen
Foreign Relations: Armelle Riche
Founded: 1975
Subjects: African American Studies, Asian Stud-
   ies, Developing Countries, Foreign Countries,
   History, Human Relations, Language Arts, Lin-
   guistics, Literature, Literary Criticism, Essays,
   Science (General), Social Sciences, Sociology
ISBN Prefix(es): 2-7384; 2-85802; 2-7475
Total Titles: 1,400 Print
Subsidiaries: Diffusion Nord-Sud (Belgium);
   L'Harmattan Hongrie; L'Harmattan Inc
   (Canada); L'Harmattan Italia SRL; L'Age
   d'Homme
Distributed by Distribution de Livres Univers
   (Canada)
*Bookshop(s):* 16 rue des Ecoles, 75005 Paris
   *Tel:* (01) 40467911 *Fax:* (01) 43298620 *Web
   Site:* www.librairieharmattan.com

**Harmonia Mundi**, *imprint of* Lettres Vives
Editions

**Editions Hatier SA+**
8, rue d'Assas, 75278 Paris Cedex 06
*Tel:* (01) 49 54 49 54 *Fax:* (01) 40 49 00 45
*E-mail:* enseignants@editions-hatier.fr
*Web Site:* www.editions-hatier.fr
*Telex:* 202732 F

*Key Personnel*
Man Dir: Bernard Foulon
Sales & Distribution: Fabienne Fera *Tel:* (01) 49
   54 48 04 *Fax:* (01) 49 54 49 71 *E-mail:* ffera@
   editions-hatier.fr
Foreign Rights: Anne Risaliti *Tel:* (01) 49 54 48
   99 *Fax:* (01) 49 54 47 30 *E-mail:* arisaliti@
   editions-hatier.fr
Human Resources Dir: Alain Bergdoll *Fax:* (01)
   49 54 49 51 *E-mail:* drh@editions-hatier.fr
Founded: 1880
Subjects: Architecture & Interior Design, Biolog-
   ical Sciences, Economics, Education, English
   as a Second Language, Environmental Studies,
   Self-Help
ISBN Prefix(es): 2-11
*Parent Company:* Groupe Hachette Livre
Imprints: Rageot Editeur
*Bookshop(s):* 59 blvd Raspail, 75006 Paris, Con-
   tact: Christian Reynaud *Tel:* (05) 49 91 80 50
   *E-mail:* creynaud@editions-hatier.fr

**Pierre Hautot Editions**
36, rue du Bac, 75007 Paris
*Tel:* (01) 42 61 10 15 *Fax:* (01) 49 27 00 06
*Telex:* 214293
Founded: 1952
Subjects: Art

**Editions Hazan+**
Imprint of Hachette Illustrated
64 Quai Marcel Cachin, 94290 Villeneuve-le-Roi
Mailing Address: BP 26, 94290 Villeneuve-le-Roi
*Tel:* (01) 49 61 92 08; (01) 49 61 90 90 *Fax:* (01)
   45 97 83 47; (01) 45 97 83 45
*Telex:* 250769
*Key Personnel*
Dir: Jean-Francois Barrielle
Rights Manager: Sherri Aldis
Founded: 1945
Subjects: Architecture & Interior Design, Art
ISBN Prefix(es): 2-85025; 2-7198
*Bookshop(s):* Editions Fernand Hazan, 35-37 rue
   de Seine, 75006 Paris
*Distribution Center:* Diffulivre Suisse
Dilibel Belgique
Hachette Canada
Hachette Diffusion Internationale
Hachette-Livre

**Editions Herault**
BP 14, 49360 Maulevrier
*Tel:* (02) 41554590 *Fax:* (02) 41554590
*Key Personnel*
General Manager: Andre Hubert Herault
Founded: 1971
Subjects: Biography, Genealogy, History, Re-
   gional Interests
ISBN Prefix(es): 2-7407; 2-903851

**Hermann editeurs des Sciences et des Arts
SA+**
293 rue Lecourbe, 75015 Paris
*Tel:* (01) 45 57 45 40 *Fax:* (01) 40 60 12 93
*E-mail:* hermann.sa@wanadoo.fr
*Key Personnel*
Man Dir: Pierre Beres
Foreign Rights: Nissa Bernard
Founded: 1870
Subjects: Art, Chemistry, Chemical Engineering,
   Mathematics, Medicine, Nursing, Dentistry,
   Physics, Science (General), Technology
ISBN Prefix(es): 2-7056
Number of titles published annually: 50 Print
Total Titles: 1,000 Print
Subsidiaries: Pierre Beres; Richard Masse (mu-
   sic); La Palme
*Showroom(s):* 6 rue de la Sorbonne, 75005 Paris
*Bookshop(s):* 6 rue de la Sorbonne, 75005 Paris

**Hermes Science**, *imprint of* Editions Lavoisier

**Editions Hermes Science Publications+**
14 rue de Provigny, 94236 Cachan Cedex
*Tel:* (01) 47 40 67 00 *Fax:* (01) 47 40 67 02
*E-mail:* livres@lavoisier.fr
*Web Site:* www.hermes-science.com; www.
editions-hermes.fr
*Key Personnel*
Man Dir: Sami Menasce
Marketing Dir: Jean Philippe
Founded: 1981
Membership(s): French Publishers Association.
Subjects: Chemistry, Chemical Engineering, Civil
Engineering, Electronics, Electrical Engineer-
ing, Engineering (General), Geography, Geol-
ogy, Health, Nutrition, Language Arts, Linguis-
tics, Law
ISBN Prefix(es): 2-86601; 2-7462
Number of titles published annually: 300 Print;
150 Online; 150 E-Book
Total Titles: 1,200 Print; 1 CD-ROM; 15 Online;
15 E-Book
*Parent Company:* Lavoisier
*Associate Companies:* Hermes Science Publishing
Ltd, 6 Fitzroy Public Garden, W1T 5DX Lon-
don, United Kingdom, Contact: Sami Menasce
*Tel:* (020) 73 801051 *Fax:* (020) 78 376348
*E-mail:* menasce@hermes-science.com
Imprints: Continent Europe
Distributed by Editions Continent Europe
*Bookshop(s):* 11 St Lavoisier, 75008 Paris
*Tel:* (01) 42 65 39 95 *Fax:* (01) 42 65 02 46

**Editions de l'Herne**
41, rue de Verneuil, 75007 Paris
*Tel:* (01) 42 61 25 06 *Fax:* (01) 42 60 10 00
*E-mail:* lherne@freesurf.fr
*Key Personnel*
Chairman, Rights & Permissions: Constantin
Tacou
Dir: Laurence Tacou
Editorial, Press Agent: Alexandre Tacou
Founded: 1964
Subjects: Art, Fiction, Government, Political Sci-
ence, Philosophy, Poetry, Social Sciences, Soci-
ology
ISBN Prefix(es): 2-85197

**Herscher+**
8 rue Ferou, 75278 Paris Cedex 6
*Tel:* (08) 25 82 01 11 *Fax:* (01) 43 25 18 29
*E-mail:* contact@editions-belin.fr
*Web Site:* www.editions-belin.fr
*Key Personnel*
President: Marie-Claude Brossollet
Subjects: Art
ISBN Prefix(es): 2-7335
Total Titles: 1,200 Print; 50 Audio
*Parent Company:* Editions Belin
*Bookshop(s):* 8, rue Ferou, 75278 Paris Cedex 6
*Tel:* (01) 55 42 84 55 *Fax:* (01) 55 42 84 58
*Shipping Address:* 4 rue Ferdinand de Lesseps,
91420 Morangis
*Warehouse:* 4 rue Ferdinand de Lesseps, 91420
Morangis

**Editions Hervas**
Division of Industries Graphiques de Paris
123, ave Philippe-Auguste, 75011 Paris
*Tel:* (01) 43 79 10 95 *Fax:* (01) 43 79 77 10
ISBN Prefix(es): 2-903118; 2-84334

**Editions d'Histoire Sociale (EDHIS)**
23 rue de Valois, 75001 Paris
*Tel:* (01) 42614778
*Key Personnel*
Man Dir: Anne Centner
Founded: 1967
Subjects: Economics, Foreign Countries, History,
Social Sciences, Sociology
ISBN Prefix(es): 2-7156
*Bookshop(s):* 144 Galerie de Valois, Paris

**Editions Hoebeke+**
12 rue du Dragon, 75006 Paris
*Tel:* (01) 42 22 83 81 *Fax:* (01) 45 44 04 96
*E-mail:* contact@hoebeke.fr
*Web Site:* www.hoebeke.fr
*Key Personnel*
Dir: Lionel Hoebeke
Dir, Commercial/Export: Mdme Aline Goujon
Subjects: Art, Fiction, Humor, Photography
ISBN Prefix(es): 2-905292; 2-84230

**Editions Honore Champion**
7, quai Malaquais, 75006 Paris
*Tel:* (01) 46340729 *Fax:* (01) 46346406
*E-mail:* champion@honorechampion.com
*Web Site:* www.honorechampion.com
*Key Personnel*
Man Dir: Michel Slatkine
Founded: 1874
Subjects: History, Comparative Literature,
Freemasonry, French Literature, Grammar, Jew-
ish Studies, Lexicography, Linguistics, Music
ISBN Prefix(es): 2-85203; 2-7453

**Pierre Horay Editeur**
22 bis, passage Dauphine, 75006 Paris
*Tel:* (01) 43 54 53 90 *Fax:* (01) 43 54 63 50
*E-mail:* editions@horay-editeur.fr
*Web Site:* www.horay-editeur.fr
*Key Personnel*
Man Dir & Rights & Permissions: Sophie Horay
Founded: 1946
Subjects: Art, Biography, Fiction, History, How-
to, Music, Dance
ISBN Prefix(es): 2-7058
*Orders to:* Flammarion, 26 rue Racine, 75006
Paris

**Editions Humblot**, *imprint of* Presses
Universitaires de Nancy

**IBE**, *imprint of* UNESCO Publishing

**Ici et Ailleurs-Vents d'Ailleurs**
4, allee des Argelas-la-Gavotte, 13790
Chateauneuf-le-Rouge
*Tel:* (04) 42533087 *Fax:* (04) 42533097
*E-mail:* info@kaona.com
*Web Site:* www.kaona.com
*Key Personnel*
General Dir: Gilles Colleu *E-mail:* gcolleu@
kaona.com
International Rights: Jutta Hepka
*E-mail:* jhepka@kaona.com
Assistant: David Barrel *E-mail:* dbarrel@kaona.
com; Sebastian Mengin *E-mail:* smengin@
kaona.com
Founded: 1995
Publisher of multimedia & Caribbean literature.
Subjects: Literature, Literary Criticism, Essays
ISBN Prefix(es): 2-911412

**Editions Ifremer,** see Institut Francais de
Recherche pour l'Exploitation de la Mer
(IFREMER)

**IGN,** see Institut Geographique National IGN

**IIEP,** *imprint of* UNESCO Publishing

**Image/Magie+**
4, rue Diderot, 92150 Suresnes
*Tel:* (01) 66 80 34 02 *Fax:* (01) 66 80 34 56
*Key Personnel*
Editor: Jean-Paul Menges
Subjects: Art, Photography, Travel
ISBN Prefix(es): 2-907059

**Editions Imago+**
7, rue Suger, 75006 Paris
*Tel:* (01) 46 33 15 33 *Fax:* (01) 60 23 87 51
*E-mail:* info@editions-imago.fr
*Web Site:* www.editions-imago.fr
*Key Personnel*
Dir General: Thierry Auzas
Subjects: Anthropology, History, Literature, Liter-
ary Criticism, Essays, Philosophy, Psychology,
Psychiatry, Social Sciences, Sociology, Ethnol-
ogy, Fine Arts, Religions, Romance
ISBN Prefix(es): 2-902702; 2-911416
Number of titles published annually: 20 Print
Total Titles: 200 Print
Distributed by Diffusion Dimedia Inc (Canada);
Nouvelle Diffusion (Belgium); Office du Livre
(Switzerland); Presses Universitaires de France
*Distribution Center:* Union-Distribution, 6 avenue
de l'Europe, 45300 Sermaises *Tel:* (02) 38 39
00 43 *Fax:* (02) 38 39 03 08

**IMEC+**
9 rue Bleue, 75009 Paris
*Tel:* (01) 53 34 23 23 *Fax:* (01) 53 34 23 00
*E-mail:* paris@imec-archives.com
*Web Site:* www.imec-archives.com
*Key Personnel*
General Manager: Olivier Corpet *E-mail:* olivier.
corpet@imec-archives.com
Founded: 1989
Preserves & manages archives & studies linked to
the writing & book world of the 20th century
allowing academic researches in intellectual,
artistic & literary domains.
Subjects: History of literature & publications
ISBN Prefix(es): 2-908295
Number of titles published annually: 4 Print
Total Titles: 30 Print
*Branch Office(s)*
l'abbaye d'Ardenne, St Germain-La-Blanche-
Herbe, F-14280 Caen, Contact: Catherine Gir-
erd *Tel:* (02) 31 29 37 37 *Fax:* (02) 31 29 37
36 *E-mail:* ardenne@imec-archives.com

**Indigo & Cote-Femmes Editions+**
4 rue de la Petite Pierre, 75011 Paris
*Tel:* (01) 43 79 74 79 *Fax:* (01) 43 79 46 87
*E-mail:* indigo.cote-femmes.edition@wanadoo.fr
*Web Site:* www.indigo-cf.com
*Key Personnel*
Dir: Milagros Palma
Founded: 1989
Subjects: Anthropology, Art, Biography, Litera-
ture, Literary Criticism, Essays, Women's Stud-
ies
ISBN Prefix(es): 2-907883; 2-911571; 2-914378
Number of titles published annually: 20 Print

**Editions Infrarouge+**
79 rue Vitruve, 75020 Paris
*Tel:* (01) 44 93 45 64 *Fax:* (01) 49 95 08 74
*E-mail:* editionsinfrarouge@libertysurf.fr;
editions.infrarouge@caramail.com
*Web Site:* www.chez.com/editinfrarouge
*Key Personnel*
President: Yves Soubrillard *E-mail:* yves.
soubrillard@libertysurf.fr
Literature Dir: Isabelle Soubrillard
Founded: 1996
Subjects: Drama, Theater, Fiction, Humor, Lit-
erature, Literary Criticism, Essays, Religion
- Other, Science Fiction, Fantasy, Social Sci-
ences, Sociology, Novels
ISBN Prefix(es): 2-908614
Number of titles published annually: 6 Print
Total Titles: 50 Print

**INRA Editions (Institut National de la
Recherche Agronomique)+**
Route de Saint-Cyr, 78026 Versailles Cedex
*Tel:* (01) 30 83 34 06 *Fax:* (01) 30 83 34 49
*E-mail:* inra-editions@versailles.inra.fr
*Web Site:* www.inra.fr/editions

*Key Personnel*
Service Dir: Claudine Geynet
International Rights: Christiane Colon
Founded: 1946
Subjects: Agriculture, Biological Sciences, Earth Sciences, Economics, Environmental Studies, Geography, Geology, Health, Nutrition, Social Sciences, Sociology, Veterinary Science
ISBN Prefix(es): 2-7380; 2-85340
Number of titles published annually: 25 Print
Distributed by Backhuys Publishers (Germany, Netherlands, Scandinavia); De Lannoy (Benelux); Dokumente Verlag (Germany); DPLU (Canada); Interscientia (Italy); Librairie Albert le Grand (Switzerland); Librairie Antoine (Lebanon); Librairie Internationale (Morocco); Librairie le Point (Lebanon); Mundi-Prensa Libros (Spain); Patrimoine (Benelux); Le Triangle Universitaire (Morocco)

**Editions INSERM+**
Member of STM Group
101 rue de Tolbiac, 75654 Paris Cedex 13
*Tel:* (01) 44 23 60 82 *Fax:* (01) 44 23 60 69
*Web Site:* www.inserm.fr
*Key Personnel*
Man Dir, Editorial, Rights & Permissions: Stephanie Lux *E-mail:* lux@tolbiac.inserm.fr
Contact: Brigitte Durrande *E-mail:* durrande@tolbiac.inserm.fr
Founded: 1970
Subjects: Biological Sciences, Health, Nutrition, Medicine, Nursing, Dentistry, Social Sciences, Sociology, Biomedical Research, Public Health
ISBN Prefix(es): 2-85598
Total Titles: 2 Print
*Parent Company:* Institut National de la Sante et de la Recherche Medicale
Distributed by Lavoisier (France)

**Editions l'Instant Durable+**
PO Box 234, 63007 Clermont-Ferrand Cedex 1
*Tel:* (04) 73 91 13 87 *Fax:* (04) 73 91 13 87
*E-mail:* art@instantdurable.com
*Web Site:* www.instantdurable.com
*Key Personnel*
Publisher: Alain de Bussac
Founded: 1983
Membership(s): SNE (Syndicat National de L'Edition - Paris).
Subjects: Architecture & Interior Design, Art
ISBN Prefix(es): 2-86404
Imprints: Architecture-Modelisme; Grand Angle

**Institut de Recherche Scientifique pour le Developpement**, see IRD Editions

**Institut Geographique National IGN**
136 bis, rue de Grenelle, 75700 Paris O7 SP
*Tel:* (01) 43988000 *Fax:* (01) 43988400
*Web Site:* www.ign.fr
*Key Personnel*
Man Dir: J F Carrez
Sales: J P Grelot
Production: J Moschetti
Publicity: A C Ferrari
Rights & Permissions: C Dupre
Founded: 1940
ISBN Prefix(es): 2-85595

**InterEditions+**
Division of Dunod Editor
5, rue Laromiguiere, 75005 Paris
*Tel:* (01) 40 46 35 00 *Fax:* (01) 40 46 49 95
*Web Site:* www.intereditions.com
*Key Personnel*
Man Dir: Lidy Arslan
Rights & Permissions: Valere Talamon
Publicity: Veronique Bernier
Founded: 1976

Subjects: Biological Sciences, Business, Chemistry, Chemical Engineering, Computer Science, Management, Mathematics, Medicine, Nursing, Dentistry, Physics, Psychology, Psychiatry
ISBN Prefix(es): 2-10; 2-7296; 2-225

**Les Editions Interferences**
4 rue Cesar Franck, 75015 Paris
*Tel:* (01) 45 67 33 56
*E-mail:* interferences@editions-interferences.com
*Web Site:* www.editions-interferences.com
*Key Personnel*
Translator: Sophie Benech
Publisher-Bookseller: Alain Benech
Founded: 1992
Subjects: Literature, Literary Criticism, Essays
ISBN Prefix(es): 2-909589
*Distribution Center:* maison Belin, 8 rue Ferou, 75006 Paris *Tel:* (01) 55 42 84 00 *Fax:* (01) 55 42 84 30 *Web Site:* www.editions-belin.com

**Institut International de la Marionnette**
7 pl Winston Churchill, 08000 Charleville-Mezieres
*Tel:* (03) 24 33 72 50 *Fax:* (03) 24 33 72 69
*E-mail:* institut@marionnette.com
*Web Site:* www.marionnette.com
*Key Personnel*
President: Jacques Felix
Dir: Lucile Bodson
Founded: 1981
Subjects: Art, Drama, Theater
ISBN Prefix(es): 2-9505282

**L'Invention du Lecteur**, *imprint of* William Blake & Co

**Editions de Iorme Rond**, *imprint of* Editions ELOR

**IRD Editions**
213 rue La Fayette, 75480 Paris Cedex 10
*Tel:* (01) 48 03 76 06 *Fax:* (01) 48 02 79 09
*E-mail:* editions@paris.ird.fr
*Web Site:* www.editions.ird.fr *Cable:* ORSTOM PARIS
*Key Personnel*
Dir: Thomas Mourier *E-mail:* mourier@paris.ird.fr
Editorial: Elisabeth Lorne
Founded: 1962
Subjects: Archaeology, Biological Sciences, Developing Countries, Earth Sciences, Environmental Studies, Geography, Geology, Health, Nutrition, History, Science (General), Social Sciences, Sociology, Technology, Ecology
ISBN Prefix(es): 2-7099
Number of titles published annually: 35 Print; 2 CD-ROM
Total Titles: 830 Print; 5 CD-ROM
*Shipping Address:* IRD Editions-Diffusion, 32 ave Henri-Varagnat, 93143 Bondy Cedex, Contact: Alain Morliere *Tel:* (01) 48 02 56 49 *Fax:* (01) 48 02 79 09 *E-mail:* diffusion@bondy.ird.fr *Web Site:* www.bondy.ird.fr

**IRDES - Institut de Recherche et**
10 rue Vauvenargues, 75018 Paris
*Tel:* (01) 53 93 43 00 *Fax:* (01) 53 93 43 50
*E-mail:* contact@irdes.fr
*Web Site:* www.credes.fr; www.irdes.fr
*Key Personnel*
Chair: Francois Joliclerc
Dir: Dominique Polton
Founded: 1985
ISBN Prefix(es): 2-87812

**Editions Isoete**
13 Av Amiral Lemonnier, 50100 Cherbourg-Octeville
*Tel:* (02) 33 43 36 64 *Fax:* (02) 33 43 37 13

*Key Personnel*
Dir: Alain Fleury
Founded: 1984
Subjects: History, Literature, Literary Criticism, Essays, Photography, Regional Interests
ISBN Prefix(es): 2-905385; 2-913920
Distributor for Distique

**Ivrea+**
27, rue de Sommerard, 75005 Paris
*Tel:* (01) 43 26 06 21 *Fax:* (01) 43 26 11 68
*Key Personnel*
Contact: Valentin Lorenzo
International Rights: Dodart Jacques
*E-mail:* jacques.dodart@liane.net
Founded: 1970
Subjects: History, Literature, Literary Criticism, Essays, Military Science, Poetry, Social Sciences, Sociology
ISBN Prefix(es): 2-85184
Imprints: Champ Libre
*Warehouse:* SODIS, 128 ave du Marechal de Lattre de Tassigny, BP 142, 77400 Lagny
*Orders to:* CDE, 17 rue de Tounon, 75006 Paris

**Editions du Jaguar**
57 bis rue d'Auteuil, 75016 Paris
*Tel:* (01) 44301970 *Fax:* (01) 44301979
*E-mail:* Jaguar@jeuneafrique.com
*Web Site:* www.useditionsdujaguar.com
*Telex:* 651 105F
*Key Personnel*
Deputy Manager: Nicole Houstin *E-mail:* n.houstin@jeuneafrique.com
Founded: 1985
Subjects: Art, Cookery, Geography, Geology, Government, Political Science, Health, Nutrition, History, How-to, Human Relations, Regional Interests, Religion - Islamic, Social Sciences, Sociology, Travel
ISBN Prefix(es): 2-86950; 2-85258

**Editions J'ai Lu**
Subsidiary of Flammarion Groupe
84 rue de Grenelle, 75007 Paris
*Tel:* (01) 44 39 34 70 *Fax:* (01) 44 39 65 52
*E-mail:* ajasmin@jailu.com
*Web Site:* www.jailu.com
*Telex:* Jailu 202765
Founded: 1958
Subjects: Fiction, Science Fiction, Fantasy
ISBN Prefix(es): 2-277; 2-290; 2-292

**Editions Jannink, SARL**
127 rue de la Galciere, 75013 Paris
*Tel:* (01) 45 89 14 02 *Fax:* (01) 45 89 14 02
*E-mail:* jannink@noos.fr
*Web Site:* www.editionsjannink.com
*Key Personnel*
Dir: Baudouin Jannink
Literary Dir: Marie Caroline Aubert
Commercial Dir: Antoine Soriano
Production: Claire Bonnevie
Founded: 1977
Subjects: Art, History, Adult books; contemporary art
ISBN Prefix(es): 2-902462
Number of titles published annually: 6 Print
Total Titles: 70 Print
*Associate Companies:* SIPEL

**Editions Jean-Claude Lattes+**
17 rue Jacob, F-75006 Paris
*Tel:* (01) 44417400 *Fax:* (01) 43253047
*E-mail:* jpeguillam@editions-jclattes.fr
*Key Personnel*
Man Dir: Isabelle Laffont *Fax:* (01) 43 26 91 04
Editorial: Laurent Laffont *Fax:* (01) 43 26 91 04
Foreign Rights: Eva Bredin *Tel:* (01) 44 41 74 34 *Fax:* (01) 43 26 91 04 *E-mail:* ebredin@editions-jclattes.fr
Founded: 1968
General trade publisher.

Subjects: Fiction, Nonfiction (General)
ISBN Prefix(es): 2-7096
Number of titles published annually: 100 Print
Total Titles: 1,250 Print
*Parent Company:* Hachette Livre
*Ultimate Parent Company:* Hachette/Lagardere

**Editions du Jeu de Paume**
One Place de la Concorde, Jardin des Tuileries,
 75001 Paris
*Tel:* (01) 47 03 13 25 *Fax:* (01) 42 61 26 10
*Key Personnel*
Dir General: Regis Durand
Editor & International Rights: Francoise Bon-
 nefoy *E-mail:* francoisebonnefoy@jeudepaume.
 org
Founded: 1991
Specialize in exhibitions catalogues.
Subjects: Art, Film, Video, Photography
ISBN Prefix(es): 2-915704
Number of titles published annually: 5 Print
Total Titles: 80 Print

**Joly Editions+**
31 rue Falguiere, 75741 Paris Cedex 15
*Tel:* (01) 56 54 16 00 *Fax:* (01) 56 54 16 46
*E-mail:* loic.even@eja.fr
*Web Site:* www.editions-joly.com
*Key Personnel*
Manager: Nathalic Jouven
Subjects: Law, Securities
ISBN Prefix(es): 2-907512
*Parent Company:* EJA
Distributed by EJA

**Le Jour, Editeur+**
Division of Sogides
Immeuble Paryseine, 3, Alle de la Seine, 94854
 Ivry Cedex
*Tel:* (01) 49 59 11 89; (01) 49 59 11 91 *Fax:* (01)
 49 59 11 96
*Web Site:* www.edjour.com
*Key Personnel*
Contact: H Laurent *E-mail:* hlaurent@sogides.
 com
Subjects: Animals, Pets, Astrology, Occult, Ca-
 reer Development, Health, Nutrition, How-to,
 Medicine, Nursing, Dentistry, Psychology, Psy-
 chiatry, Women's Studies
ISBN Prefix(es): 0-7760; 2-89044
*Branch Office(s)*
955 rue Amherst, Montreal, QC H2L 3K4,
 Canada, Contact: Pierre Lesperance
 *Tel:* 514-523-1182 *Fax:* 514-597-0370
 *E-mail:* edhomme@sogides.com
Foreign Rights: Chantal Galtier-Roussel

**Jouvence Editions+**
BP 7, 74161 St Julien-en-Genevois
*Tel:* (04) 50 43 28 60 *Fax:* (04) 50 43 29 24
*E-mail:* info@editions-jouvence.com
*Web Site:* www.editions-jouvence.com
*Key Personnel*
Manager & International Rights: Nelly Irniger
Founded: 1991
Subjects: Cookery, Earth Sciences, Education,
 Health, Nutrition, How-to, Human Relations,
 Medicine, Nursing, Dentistry, Philosophy, Psy-
 chology, Psychiatry, Self-Help, Social Sciences,
 Sociology, Sports, Athletics
ISBN Prefix(es): 2-88353; 2-909206
Imprints: Epanouissement; Pratique Sante; Sante
 Spiritualite
Distributor for Carthame editions

**Jupiter**, *imprint of* Les Editions
 LGDJ-Montchrestien

**Editions Juridiques Associees**, see Les Editions
 LGDJ-Montchrestien

**Editions Juridiques Africaines**
44 rue Poliveau, 75005 Paris
*Tel:* (01) 43370401 *Fax:* (01) 43370401
Founded: 1987
Subjects: Foreign Countries, Law
ISBN Prefix(es): 2-87838
Imprints: EDJA
Divisions:

**Editions Juridiques et Techniques Lamy SA**
21-23 rue des Ardennes, 75935 Paris Cedex 19
*Tel:* (01) 44 72 12 00 *Fax:* (01) 44 72 18 26
*Telex:* 214398
*Key Personnel*
President: Jean-Marc Detailleur
Sales: Jean-Luc Cretal; Eric Forein
Publicity: Jean-Pierre Benedi
Founded: 1949
Subjects: Law, Social Sciences, Sociology
ISBN Prefix(es): 2-7212
*Parent Company:* Wolters Kluwer NV

**Jurif (Societe d' Etudes Juridiques
 Internationales et Fiscales)**, see Les Cahiers
 Fiscaux Europeens

**Editions du Juris-Classeur**
141 rue de Javel, 75747 Paris Cedex 15
*Tel:* (01) 45 58 92 00 *Fax:* (01) 45 58 94 00
*E-mail:* editorial@juris-classeur.com; relations-
 clients@juris-classeur.com
*Web Site:* www.juris-classeur.fr
*Key Personnel*
President: Martin Desprez
Editorial Dir: Bernard Bonjean; Christophe Veyrin
 Forrer
Marketing: Bruno DecLementi
Subjects: Law
ISBN Prefix(es): 2-7110
*Parent Company:* LexisNexis Group
*Ultimate Parent Company:* Reed Elsevier plc
*Warehouse:* 14 rue de la Passerelle, 31200
 Toulouse Cedex

**Editions Juris Service**
12 Quai Andre Lassagne, 69001 Lyon
*Tel:* (04) 72 98 18 40 *Fax:* (04) 78 28 93 83
*E-mail:* info@editionsjuris.com
*Web Site:* www.editionsjuris.com
*Key Personnel*
President: Philippe Chagnon
Founded: 1983
Specialize in tourism & law, non-profit sector,
 real estate joint ownership, liberal professions.
Subjects: Communications, Law, Management,
 Real Estate
ISBN Prefix(es): 2-907648; 2-910992
Number of titles published annually: 5 Print
Total Titles: 70 Print; 2 CD-ROM

**Kailash Editions+**
69 rue Saint-Jacques, 75005 Paris
*Tel:* (01) 43.29.52.52 *Fax:* (01) 46.34.03.29
*E-mail:* kailash@imaginet.fr
*Key Personnel*
Dir: Raj de Condappa
Founded: 1991
Subjects: Anthropology, Archaeology, Art, Asian
 Studies, Biography, History, Literature, Literary
 Criticism, Essays, Travel, Specialize in Asia &
 Indian continent
ISBN Prefix(es): 2-909052; 2-84268
Distributor for Kwokon
*Bookshop(s):* Librairie Kailash, 69 rue Saint-
 Jacques, 75005 Paris

**Editions Kaleidoscope+**
11 Rue de Sevres, 75006 Paris
*Tel:* (01) 45 44 07 08 *Fax:* (01) 45 44 53 71
*E-mail:* infos@editions-kaleidoscope.com
*Web Site:* www.editions-kaleidoscope.com

*Key Personnel*
President: Isabel Finkenstaedt
 *Fax:* isabel@editions-kaleidoscope.com
Founded: 1988
ISBN Prefix(es): 2-87767
*Warehouse:* Ecole des loisirs, Lotissment de la
 Butte, 11 rue Gutenberg, 91620 Nozay
*Orders to:* L'Ecole des Loisirs, 11 rue de Sevres,
 75278 Paris cedex 06 *Tel:* (01) 42 22 94 10

**Karger**, *imprint of* Librairie Luginbuhl

**Karthala Editions-Diffusion+**
22-24 Blvd Arago, 75013 Paris
*Tel:* (01) 43 31 15 59 *Fax:* (01) 45 35 27 05
*E-mail:* karthala@wanadoo.fr
*Telex:* 250303 Public Paris
*Key Personnel*
Man Dir, Editorial, Rights & Permissions, & Pro-
 duction: Robert Ageneau
Publicity: Farida Benbelaid
Founded: 1980
Subjects: Anthropology, Asian Studies, Develop-
 ing Countries, Economics, Education, Geog-
 raphy, Geology, Literature, Literary Criticism,
 Essays, Religion - Catholic, Religion - Islamic,
 Religion - Protestant, Social Sciences, Sociol-
 ogy, Travel
ISBN Prefix(es): 2-86537; 2-84586
*Branch Office(s)*
Editions Hurthbise, 7360 Blvd Newtian, La Salle,
 QC H8N 1X2, Canada
Distributor for Codesria; CRA; Haho; Hurthbise;
 Inades; Institut Royal des Tropiques; Jasor

**Editions Klincksieck**
6 rue de la Sorbonne, 75005 Paris
*Tel:* (01) 43 54 47 57 *Fax:* (01) 40 51 73 85
*E-mail:* courrier@klincksieck.com
*Web Site:* www.klincksieck.com
*Key Personnel*
Joint Man Dir: Alain Baudry
Founded: 1842
Subjects: Archaeology, Art, History, Language
 Arts, Linguistics, Literature, Literary Criticism,
 Essays, Music, Dance, Science (General), So-
 cial Sciences, Sociology
ISBN Prefix(es): 2-252
*Associate Companies:* Aux Amateurs De Livres

**Eric Koehler+**
16 rue Arthur-Groussier, 75010 Paris
*Tel:* (01) 49 27 06 37; (01) 44 55 37 50 *Fax:* (01)
 47 03 39 86; (01) 40 20 99 74
Founded: 1987
Subjects: Photography
ISBN Prefix(es): 2-7107; 2-907220

**Editions Lacour-Olle+**
25 blvd Amiral Courbet, 30000 Nimes
*Tel:* (04) 66 67 30 30 *Fax:* (04) 66 21 11 23
*E-mail:* c.lacour@editions-lacour.com
*Web Site:* www.editions-lacour.com
*Key Personnel*
Contact: Christian Lacour
Founded: 1791
Subjects: Astrology, Occult, Cookery, Para-
 psychology, Regional Interests, Religion -
 Catholic, Religion - Protestant, Religion -
 Other
ISBN Prefix(es): 2-86971; 2-84149; 2-84406; 2-
 84692; 2-84691; 2-7504

**L'Adret editions+**
Route de Soueiche, Encausse-les-Thermes, 31160
 Aspet
*Key Personnel*
Man Dir: Jean Mandion
Founded: 1983
Subjects: History, Regional Interests
ISBN Prefix(es): 2-904458

**Les Editions Jeanne Laffitte**
25, cours d'Estienne d'Orves, 13001 Marseille
Mailing Address: BP 1903, Marseille Cedex 02
*Tel:* (04) 91 59 80 43 *Fax:* (04) 91 54 25 64
*E-mail:* editions@jeanne-laffitte.com
*Web Site:* www.jeanne-laffitte.com/editions/
*Key Personnel*
President: Jeanne Laffitte
Founded: 1980
Subjects: Ethnicity, History, Regional Interests
ISBN Prefix(es): 2-86276; 2-7348; 2-86604
Distributed by CELF

**Editions Robert Laffont+**
24 ave Marceau, 75381 Paris Cedex 08
*Tel:* (01) 53 67 14 00 *Fax:* (01) 53 67 14 14
*Web Site:* www.laffont.fr
*Telex:* 260 808
*Key Personnel*
Pres & Dir General: Leonello Brandolini
Founded: 1987
Subjects: Fiction
ISBN Prefix(es): 2-221; 2-87645
*Associate Companies:* Bellitz Fixot

**Editions Jacques Lafitte - Who's Who in France**
16, rue Camille Pelletan, 92300 Levallois-Perret
*Tel:* (0141) 272 830 *Fax:* (0141) 272 840
*E-mail:* whoswho@whoswho.fr
*Web Site:* www.whoswho.fr
*Key Personnel*
President: Antoine Hebrard *E-mail:* antoine.
  hebrard@whoswho.fr
Dir General: Eleonore de Dampierre
  *E-mail:* eleonore.de.dampierre@whoswho.fr
Publicity: Marion Poussielgue
  *E-mail:* mpoussielgue@whoswho.fr
Founded: 1951
Subjects: Biographical Dictionary
ISBN Prefix(es): 2-85784
Number of titles published annually: 1 Print; 1
  Online

**Michel Lafon Publishing+**
7-13 blvd Paul-Emile Victor, 92521 Neuilly
  Cedex
*Tel:* (01) 41 43 85 85 *Fax:* (01) 46 24 00 95
*Key Personnel*
Publisher: Pierre Fery-Zendel; Michel Lafon
Publicity: Nathalie Ladurantie
Rights & Permissions: Patricia Nadal
Founded: 1983
Subjects: Biography, Cookery, Drama, Theater,
  Fiction, Film, Video, History, Sports, Athletics,
  Autobiography, Testimony, Thriller
ISBN Prefix(es): 2-84098; 2-908652; 2-7499

**Librairie Leonce Laget**
88, rue Bonaparte, 75006 Paris
*Tel:* (01) 43 29 90 04 *Fax:* (01) 43 26 89 68
*E-mail:* contact@librairieleoncelaget.fr
*Web Site:* www.librairieleoncelaget.fr *Cable:*
  LIBLAGET PARIS 110
*Key Personnel*
President: Veronique Delvaux
Founded: 1955
Subjects: Architecture & Interior Design, Art,
  Career Development, Crafts, Games, Hobbies,
  History
ISBN Prefix(es): 2-85204

**Editions Lamarre SA**
One, av Edouard Belin, 92856 Rueil-Malmaison
  Cedex
Mailing Address: BP 60, 78141 Velizy Cedex
*Tel:* (01) 41 29 99 99 *Fax:* (01) 41 29 77 05
*Key Personnel*
Dir: Marie Laure Dechatre *Tel:* (01) 41 29 76 76
  *E-mail:* mldechatre@groupeliaisons.fr
Sales Manager: Thierry de Puniet de Parry

Marketing: Nelly Couret *Tel:* (01) 41 29 77 03
  *E-mail:* ncouret@groupeliaisons.fr
Commercial: Philippe Hamel *Tel:* (01) 41 29 96
  89 *E-mail:* phamel@groupeliaisons.fr
Founded: 1957
Subjects: Medicine, Nursing, Dentistry
ISBN Prefix(es): 2-85030

**Langues & Mondes-L'Asiatheque+**
Cite Veron 11, 75018 Paris
*Tel:* (01) 42 62 04 00 *Fax:* (01) 42 62 12 34
*E-mail:* info@asiatheque.com
*Web Site:* www.asiatheque.com
*Key Personnel*
General & Editorial Dir: Mdme Christiane Thiol-
  lier
Editorial Dir: Alain Thiollier
Editorial Assistant: Elizabeth Eldin
Founded: 1973
Specialize in material for learning of foreign lan-
  guages & books about cultures & civilizations
  of the whole world.
Subjects: Asian Studies, Cookery, Education, For-
  eign Countries, Language Arts, Linguistics,
  Literature, Literary Criticism, Essays, Religion
  - Buddhist, Religion - Hindu, Self-Help
ISBN Prefix(es): 2-911053; 2-901795; 2-915255
Total Titles: 130 Print; 23 Audio
Distributor for Presses Universitaires de France
  (PUF); Union Distribution Flammarion (UD)

**Editions Fernand Lanore Sarl+**
One rue Palatine, 75006 Paris
*Tel:* (01) 43 25 66 61; (01) 46 33 97 65 *Fax:* (01)
  43 29 69 81
*Key Personnel*
Dir: Francois Sorlot
Founded: 1920
Subjects: Education, History, Language Arts, Lin-
  guistics, Outdoor Recreation, Philosophy, Reli-
  gion - Other, Travel
ISBN Prefix(es): 2-85157

**Editions du Laquet+**
Le Bourg, 46600 Floirac
*Tel:* (05) 65 37 43 54 *Fax:* (05) 65 37 43 55
*E-mail:* contact@editions-dulaquet.fr
*Web Site:* www.editions-dulaquet.fr
*Key Personnel*
Sales Manager: Dominique Barbier
Founded: 1990
Subjects: Art, Cookery, Drama, Theater, Fiction,
  Literature, Literary Criticism, Essays, Travel
ISBN Prefix(es): 2-910333; 2-84523
Number of titles published annually: 25 Print
Total Titles: 170 Print

**Editions Larousse+**
21 rue du Montparnasse, 75283 Paris Cedex 06
*Tel:* (01) 44 39 44 00 *Fax:* (01) 44 39 43 43
*Web Site:* www.larousse.fr
*Telex:* 250828 LAROUS PARIS *Cable:* Liblarous
  43 Paris
*Key Personnel*
Chairman & Man Dir: Christian Bregou
Foreign Rights Dir: Evelyne Le Bourse
Founded: 1852
Subjects: Animals, Pets, Art, Child Care & De-
  velopment, Cookery, Gardening, Plants, His-
  tory, Language Arts, Linguistics, Medicine,
  Nursing, Dentistry, Music, Dance, Psychology,
  Psychiatry, Regional Interests, Science (Gen-
  eral), Self-Help, Social Sciences, Sociology,
  Sports, Athletics, Technology
ISBN Prefix(es): 2-03
*Parent Company:* Vivendi Universal Publishing
Subsidiaries: Ediciones Larousse Argentina SA;
  Ediciones Larousse Colombiana Ltda; Edi-
  ciones Larousse SA; Editions Francaises Inc;
  Editora Larousse do Brazil; Larousse-Belgique;
  Larousse (Suisse) SA

**Editions Le Laurier**
19, Passage Jean Nicot, 75007 Paris
*Tel:* (01) 45 51 55 08 *Fax:* (01) 45 51 81 83
*E-mail:* editions@lelaurier.fr
*Web Site:* www.lelaurier.fr
*Key Personnel*
Manager: Nicolas Macarez
Founded: 1981
Subjects: Religion - Catholic
ISBN Prefix(es): 2-86495; 2-910095

**Editions Lavoisier+**
11 rue Lavoisier, 75008 Paris 08
*Tel:* (01) 47 40 67 00 *Fax:* (01) 47 40 67 88
*E-mail:* edition@tec-et-doc.com
*Web Site:* www.tec-et-doc.com
*Key Personnel*
Man Dir: Patrick Fenouil
Import Manager: Romuald Verrier
Editorial: Jean-Marc Bocabeille; Philippe Zawieja
Marketing & Publicity: Christine Cardinal
  *E-mail:* cardinal@lavoisier.fr
Founded: 1947
Subjects: Agriculture, Biological Sciences, Chem-
  istry, Chemical Engineering, Cookery, Elec-
  tronics, Electrical Engineering, Engineering
  (General), Environmental Studies, Geography,
  Geology, Labor, Industrial Relations, Maritime,
  Medicine, Nursing, Dentistry, Technology, New
  Communication & Information Technologies
ISBN Prefix(es): 2-85206; 2-7430
Number of titles published annually: 100 Print
Imprints: EM Inter; Hermes Science; Tec & Doc
*Branch Office(s)*
Intercept Ltd, PO Box 716, Andover, Hants SP10
  1YG, United Kingdom *Tel:* (01264) 334748
  *Fax:* (01264) 334058 *E-mail:* intercept@
  andover.co.uk
*U.S. Office(s):* Lavoisier Publishing Inc, Springer
  Verlag Customer Services, PO Box 2485,
  Secaucus, NJ 07096-2485, United States
  *Fax:* 201-348-4505 *E-mail:* orders@springer-
  ny.com
*Shipping Address:* 14 rue de Provigny, 94236
  Cachan Cedex *Tel:* (01) 47406700 *Fax:* (01)
  47406702

**Editions Universitaires LCF**
Passage des Graves, 33000 Bordeaux Cedex
*Tel:* (05) 56 51 51 37 *Fax:* (05) 56 51 51 37
*Key Personnel*
Dir: Alain Yagues
Founded: 1989
Subjects: Health, Nutrition, History, Law, Wine &
  Spirits
ISBN Prefix(es): 2-908193

**Editions Francis Lefebvre**
42 rue de Villiers, 92532 Levallois, Cedex
*Tel:* (01) 41 05 22 00; (01) 41 05 22 06 *Fax:* (01)
  41 05 36 80
*Web Site:* www.efl.fr/
*Telex:* 649470
*Key Personnel*
Dir: J Icart
Contact: Y Chareton
Founded: 1930
Subjects: Law
ISBN Prefix(es): 2-85115; 2-85786
Foreign Rep(s): Nathalie Le Garff

**Editions Legislatives+**
80, ave de la Marne, 92546 Montrouge Cedex
*Tel:* (01) 40 92 36 36 *Fax:* (01) 40 92 36 63
*E-mail:* infocom@editions-legislatives.fr
*Web Site:* www.editions-legislatives.fr
*Telex:* 632855F
*Key Personnel*
General Dir: Oliver Gaultier
Dir, Foreign Relations: Michel Blanc
Founded: 1947
Subjects: Agriculture, Business, Career Devel-
  opment, Economics, Environmental Studies,

Labor, Industrial Relations, Law, Library &
Information Sciences, Medicine, Nursing, Den-
tistry, Real Estate
ISBN Prefix(es): 2-85086

**Editions Dominique Leroy+**
3, rue Docteur Andre Ragot, BP 313, 89103 Sens
Cedex
*Tel:* (03) 86 64 15 24 *Fax:* (03) 86 64 15 24
*Web Site:* www.enfer.com
*Key Personnel*
Man Dir: Dominique Leroy *E-mail:* domleroy@
enfer.com
Founded: 1970
Subjects: Art, Erotica, Fiction, Humor, Literature,
Literary Criticism, Essays
ISBN Prefix(es): 2-86688
Number of titles published annually: 4 CD-ROM;
12 E-Book
Total Titles: 110 Print; 10 CD-ROM; 42 E-Book
Imprints: Vertiges Bulles
*Bookshop(s):* Librairie Curiosa - MBD, Contact:
Daniele Masson *E-mail:* curiosa@enfer.com

**Lethielleux,** *imprint of* Editions Buchet-Chastel
Pierre Zech Editeur

**P Lethielleux Editions+**
54, rue Michel-Ange, 75016 Paris
*Tel:* (01) 44 32 05 60 *Fax:* (01) 44 32 05 61
*Telex:* ELITA 283155 F
*Key Personnel*
Dir: M Pierre Zech
International Rights: Sophie Zech
Subjects: Biblical Studies, Religion - Catholic,
Theology
ISBN Prefix(es): 2-249; 2-283
*Parent Company:* Pierre Zech Editeur

**Letouzey et Ane Editeurs**
87, blvd Raspail, 75006 Paris
*Tel:* (01) 45 48 80 14 *Fax:* (01) 45 49 03 43
*E-mail:* letouzey@tree.tr
*Key Personnel*
General Dir: Florence Letouzey-Dumont
Founded: 1885
Subjects: Biblical Studies, Biography, History,
Religion - Catholic, Religion - Islamic, Reli-
gion - Other
ISBN Prefix(es): 2-7063
Number of titles published annually: 10 Print
Distributor for L'Annee Canonique

**Lettres Modernes Minard**
10 rue de Valence, 75005 Paris
*Tel:* (01) 43 36 25 83 *Fax:* (02) 31 84 48 09
*E-mail:* editorat.lettresmodernes@wanadoo.fr
*Key Personnel*
Contact: Dominique Alice Minard
Founded: 1954
Subjects: Film, Video, Literature, Literary Criti-
cism, Essays
ISBN Prefix(es): 2-256
Number of titles published annually: 20 Print
*Shipping Address:* Minard Distribution, 45
rue de Saint Andre, 14123 Fleury Sur Orne
*Tel:* (02) 31 84 47 06 *Fax:* (02) 31 84 48 09
*E-mail:* minarddistribution@wanadoo.fr
*Warehouse:* Minard Distribution, 45 rue
de Saint Andre, 14123 Fleury Sur Orne
*Tel:* (02) 31 84 47 06 *Fax:* (02) 31 84 48 09
*E-mail:* minarddistribution@wanadoo.fr
*Orders to:* Minard Distribution, 45 rue de
Saint Andre, 14123 Fleury Sur Orne
*Tel:* (02) 31 84 47 06 *Fax:* (02) 31 84 48 09
*E-mail:* minarddistribution@wanadoo.fr

**Lettres Vives Editions+**
Campu Magnu, 20213 Castellare-di-Casinca
Mailing Address: PO Box 7, 20213 Folelli
*Tel:* (04) 95 36 40 93 *Fax:* (04) 95 36 59 92

*E-mail:* lettresvives@mic.fr
*Key Personnel*
Editor: Claire Tievant
Founded: 1981
Subjects: Literature, Literary Criticism, Essays,
Poetry
ISBN Prefix(es): 2-903721; 2-914577
Number of titles published annually: 5 Print
Total Titles: 120 Print
Imprints: Harmonia Mundi

**Liana Levi Editions+**
One Paul Painleve Pl, 75005 Paris
*Tel:* (01) 44 32 19 30 *Fax:* (01) 46 33 69 56
*E-mail:* liana.levi@wanadoo.fr
*Web Site:* www.lianalevi.fr
*Key Personnel*
Man Dir: Liana Levi *E-mail:* llevi@club-internet.
fr
Rights & Permissions: Colette Fradin
Foreign Rights: Sylvie Mouches
Founded: 1983
Subjects: Art, Fiction, History, Nonfiction (Gen-
eral)
ISBN Prefix(es): 2-86746

**Les Editions LGDJ-Montchrestien+**
31 rue Falguiere, 75741 Paris Cedex 15
*Tel:* (01) 56 54 16 00 *Fax:* (01) 56 54 16 49
*Web Site:* www.lgdj.fr/lgdj/accueil.php
*Key Personnel*
Man Dir: Vincent Marty
Man Dir & Sales Manager, Rights & Permissions:
Nathalie Jouven
Sales Manager: Piene Coustols
Founded: 1836
Subjects: Economics, Government, Political Sci-
ence, History, Law, Public Administration, So-
cial Sciences, Sociology
ISBN Prefix(es): 2-275
*Parent Company:* Petites Affiches
Imprints: Jupiter; Navarre
Distributed by Bruylant; Patrimoine
Distributor for L'Abecedaire parlementaire;
Academia; AENGDE; ATOL; Bruylant; City
& York; Comite pour l'histoire economique et
financiere de la France; Delta; Edition For-
mation Entreprise; Georg; Imprimerie Na-
tionale; MB Edition; Pantheon-Assas Paris II;
Presses Universitaires de la Faculte de droit
de Clermont; Presses Universitaires de Laval;
SCHULTHESS; Staempfli
*Bookshop(s):* 20 rue Soufflot, 75005 Paris
*Tel:* (01) 46 33 89 85 *Fax:* (01) 40 51 81 85
*E-mail:* librairie-lgdj@eja.fr
*Orders to:* 160 rue Saint-Jacques, 75005 Paris

**Editions John Libbey Eurotext+**
Subsidiary of John Libbey Co Ltd
127, ave de la Republique, 92120 Montrouge
*Tel:* (01) 46 73 06 60 *Fax:* (01) 40 84 09 99
*E-mail:* contact@john-libbey-eurotext.fr
*Web Site:* www.john-libbey-eurotext.fr
*Key Personnel*
Dir, Publications: Gilles Cahn *Tel:* (01) 46 73 06
79 *E-mail:* gilles.cahn@jle.com
Dir, Marketing: Perrine Sentilhes *Tel:* (01) 46 73
01 35 *E-mail:* perrine.sentilhes@jle.com
Advertising Dir: Anne Coche *Tel:* (01) 46 73 06
77 *E-mail:* anne.coche@jle.com
Editorial & Development Manager: Marie-Anne
Lambert *Tel:* (01) 46 73 06 70 *E-mail:* marie-
anne.lambert@jle.com
Founded: 1986
Subjects: Agriculture, Economics, Environmen-
tal Studies, Medicine, Nursing, Dentistry, Life
Sciences
ISBN Prefix(es): 2-7420

**Editions Librairie-Galerie Racine+**
23 rue Racine, 75006 Paris
*Tel:* (01) 43269724 *Fax:* (01) 43269724

*E-mail:* lgr@librairie-galerie-racine.com
*Key Personnel*
Editorial: Jean Breton
Publicity: Philippe Heracles
Founded: 1969
Subjects: Poetry
ISBN Prefix(es): 2-243; 2-84328

**Librairie Luginbuhl**
36 blvd de Latour-Maubourg, 75007 Paris
*Tel:* (01) 45 51 42 58 *Fax:* (01) 45 56 07 80
*E-mail:* liblug@club-internet.fr
*Key Personnel*
Contact: Jean Luginbuhl
Subjects: Medicine, Nursing, Dentistry
Imprints: Karger

**Librairie Scientifique et Technique Albert
Blanchard**
9, Rue de Medicis, 75006 Paris
*Tel:* (01) 43 26 90 34 *Fax:* (01) 43 29 97 31
*E-mail:* librairie.blanchard@wanadoo.fr
*Web Site:* www.blanchard75.fr
*Key Personnel*
Contact: Laurent Debruyne
Subjects: Astronomy, Chemistry, Chemical Engi-
neering, Earth Sciences, Mathematics, Natural
History, Philosophy, Physics, Science (General)
ISBN Prefix(es): 2-85367
Number of titles published annually: 3 Print
Total Titles: 1,721 Print

**Librarie Maritime Outremer**
17 rue Jacob, 75006 Paris
*Tel:* (04) 91 54 79 40 *Fax:* (04) 91 54 79 49
*E-mail:* webmaster@librairie-outremer.com
*Web Site:* www.librairie-outremer.com
*Telex:* 205652 JCLates
*Key Personnel*
Man Editor: Pierre Gutelle
Rights & Permissions: Emilie Levi
Founded: 1839
Subjects: Maritime, Sports, Athletics
ISBN Prefix(es): 2-7070
*Parent Company:* Editions Jean-Claude Lattes

**Libraries Techniques SA,** see LiTec (Librairies
Techniques SA)

**Librio,** *imprint of* Flammarion Groupe

**Le Lierre et Le Coudrier+**
83, rue Lamarck, 75018 Paris
Mailing Address: PO Box 54, 75861 Paris Cedex
18
*Tel:* (01) 42 55 00 27 *Fax:* (01) 42 57 04 97
ISBN Prefix(es): 2-907975; 2-9502146
*Associate Companies:* La Lonave-vue, 363 b,
Chaunic de Waterloo, 1060 Bruyelle, Belgium

**Lignes De Vie,** *imprint of* Editions de Septembre

**Ligue pour la Lecture de la Bible,** see LLB
France (Ligue pour la Lecture de la Bible)

**Editions des Limbes d'Or FBT de R Editions**
49, av de la Reistance, 92370 Chaville
*Tel:* (01) 41151969 *Fax:* (01) 41151969
*Key Personnel*
President: Francoise Thiam
Founded: 1995
Subjects: Art, Criminology, Economics, Fiction,
Foreign Countries, Government, Political Sci-
ence, Human Relations, Literature, Literary
Criticism, Essays, Travel
ISBN Prefix(es): 2-911064

**LiTec (Librairies Techniques SA)+**
141, rue de Javel, 75747 Paris
*Tel:* (01) 45 58 92 70 *Fax:* (01) 45 58 94 00

E-mail: libraries@juris-classeur.com
Web Site: www.lexisnexis.fr
Key Personnel
Dir: Alexandre Guegan
Sales Manager: Marie Oneissi
Founded: 1927
Subjects: Accounting, Government, Political Science, Labor, Industrial Relations, Law
ISBN Prefix(es): 2-7111
Parent Company: Editions du Juris-Classeur
Ultimate Parent Company: Reed Elsevier plc/LexisNexis
Branch Office(s)
26 rue Soufflot, 75005 Paris Tel: (01) 43 29 07 71 Fax: (01) 40 51 83 72 E-mail: librairie@soufflot@juris-classeur.com
27 Place Dauphine, 75001 Paris Tel: (01) 43 26 60 90 Fax: (01) 46 34 22 98 E-mail: librairie.dauphine@juris-classeur.com
Warehouse: Zone Artisanale-Route de Niort, 85205 Fontenay le Comte Cedex

**Editions Lito**
41, rue de Verdun, 94503 Champigny-sur-Marne Cedex
Mailing Address: BP 363, 94503 Champigny-sur-Marne, Cedex
Tel: (01) 45161700 Fax: (01) 48820085
E-mail: annick.cabrelli@editionslito.com
Key Personnel
Man Dir, Editorial, Rights & Permissions: Pierre Rosdahl
Founded: 1958
Subjects: Crafts, Games, Hobbies, Nonfiction (General)
ISBN Prefix(es): 2-244
Subsidiaries: Lito Editrice

**Litterature Generale**, imprint of Autres Temps

**Le Livre de Paris+**
58, rue Jean Bleuzen, 92178 Vanves Cedex
Tel: (01) 41 23 65 00 Fax: (01) 41 45 34 42
E-mail: ldpsiege@hachette-livre.fr
Web Site: www.livre-de-paris.com
Key Personnel
General Dir: Patrice Burckel de Tell
International Rights Contact: Monica Mondardini
Founded: 1935
Membership(s): the Syndicat National de L'Edition.
Subjects: Art, How-to
ISBN Prefix(es): 2-245
Parent Company: Hachette Livre
Imprints: Livres de Paris; Quillet; Tout L'Univers

**Le Livre de Poche-L G F (Librairie Generale Francaise)+**
43, Quai de Grenelle, 75905 Paris Cedex 15
Tel: (01) 43923000 Fax: (01) 43923590
Web Site: www.livredepoche.com; www.hachette.com
Key Personnel
Man Dir & Dir, Foreign Rights & International Development: Dominique Goust
Founded: 1953
Subjects: Biography, Drama, Theater, Environmental Studies, Fiction, Government, Political Science, History, Language Arts, Linguistics, Literature, Literary Criticism, Essays, Philosophy, Poetry, Science (General), Science Fiction, Fantasy, Social Sciences, Sociology
ISBN Prefix(es): 2-253
Parent Company: Hachette

**Livre des Vacances**, imprint of Librairie Vuibert

**Livres de Paris**, imprint of Le Livre de Paris

**Les Livres du Dragon d'Or+**
60, rue Mazarine, 75006 Paris

Tel: (01) 53 10 36 37 Fax: (01) 53 10 36 39
E-mail: dragondor@gruend.fr
Key Personnel
Man Dir: Nathalie Perrin
Founded: 1989
Specialize in license publishing & book packaging for the international market.
ISBN Prefix(es): 2-87881
Number of titles published annually: 10 Print
Total Titles: 100 Print
Parent Company: Editions Gruend
Orders to: Editions Gruend, 60, rue Mazarine, 75006 Paris Tel: (01) 53 10 36 00 Fax: (01) 43 29 49 86 Web Site: www.grund.fr

**LLB France (Ligue pour la Lecture de la Bible)+**
51 Blvd Gustave-Andre, 26007 Valence, Cedex
Mailing Address: BP 728, 26007 Valence, Cedex
Tel: (04) 75 56 02 68 Fax: (04) 75 56 02 97
E-mail: contact@llbfrance.com
Web Site: www.llbfrance.com
Key Personnel
President: Pierre Berthoud
General Dir: Marc Deroeux
Editor: Eric Denimal E-mail: eric.denimal@llbfrance.com
Founded: 1946
Subjects: Archaeology, How-to, Religion - Protestant, Theology
ISBN Prefix(es): 2-85031
U.S. Office(s): Scripture Union, Suite 115, 150 Shafford Ave, Wayne, PA 19087, United States
Distributed by Cedis; CLC; Vida (France)

**Lonely Planet**
1 rue du Dahomey, 75011 Paris
Tel: (01) 55 25 33 00 Fax: (01) 55 25 33 01
E-mail: bip@lonelyplanet.fr
Web Site: www.lonelyplanet.fr
Key Personnel
General Dir: Benoit Del planque E-mail: benoit.delplanque@lonelyplanet.fr
Founded: 1992
Subjects: Travel
ISBN Prefix(es): 2-84070
Parent Company: Lonely Planet Publications, Australia
U.S. Office(s): Autre Filiale de Lonely Planet-Aux E-U Cette Fois, 150 Linden St, Oakland, CA 94607-2538, United States Tel: 510-893-8555 Fax: 510-893-8563 E-mail: info@lonelyplanet.com Web Site: www.lonelyplanet.com
Orders to: Vilo Diffusion, 25 rue Ginoux, 75015 Paris

**Editions Loubatieres+**
10 bis rue de l'Europe, 31190 Portet-sur Garonne Cedex
Mailing Address: BP 27, 31122 Portet-sur Garonne Cedex
Tel: (05) 61 72 83 53 Fax: (05) 61 72 83 50
E-mail: loubatieres@club-internet.fr
Key Personnel
Dir: Francis Loubatieres
Founded: 1970
Subjects: Art, Geography, Geology, History, Regional Interests, Travel
ISBN Prefix(es): 2-86266
Divisions: Librairie Loubatieres

**LPM**, see Les Presses du Management

**LT Editions-Jacques Lanore+**
15, rue Soufflot, 75254 Paris Cedex 05
Tel: (01) 44 41 89 30 Fax: (01) 44 41 89 39
E-mail: lanore@lanore.com
Web Site: www.lanore.com
Key Personnel
Contact: A M Tabaste

Subjects: Architecture & Interior Design, Career Development, Child Care & Development, Cookery, Health, Nutrition, House & Home, Law, Technology, Travel
ISBN Prefix(es): 2-86268
Parent Company: Groupe Flammarion
Bookshop(s): Librairie-Editions J Lanore, 4 rue de Tournon, 75006 Paris Tel: (01) 43 29 43 50

**LT Editors**, see LT Editions-Jacques Lanore

**Lumiere Biblique series**, imprint of Les Editions de la Source Sarl

**Editions Josette Lyon+**
Division of Editions La Maisnie
19, rue Saint-Severin, 75005 Paris
Tel: (01) 44 41 81 60 Fax: (01) 45 42 30 99
E-mail: editions.josette.lyon@wanadoo.fr
Web Site: www.editions-josette-lyon.com
Key Personnel
Man Dir: Sophie Gillot
Founded: 1986
Subjects: Health, Nutrition
ISBN Prefix(es): 2-906757; 2-84319

**Editions Lyonnaises d'Art et d'Histoire**
2, Quai Claude Bernard, 69007 Lyon 07
Tel: (04) 78 72 49 00 Fax: (04) 78 69 00 48
Web Site: www.achatlyon.com/editionslyonnaises
Key Personnel
General Dir: Corinne Poirieux
Founded: 1995
Subjects: Archaeology, Biography, Genealogy, History, How-to, Literature, Literary Criticism, Essays
ISBN Prefix(es): 2-84147
Distributor for Ed Nichel Chomarer; Ed Nichel Repnier

**Macula+**
6, rue Coetlogon, 75006 Paris
Tel: (01) 45 48 58 70 Fax: (01) 45 44 45 89
Key Personnel
Dir: Jean Clay
Founded: 1980
Subjects: Antiques, Art, Film, Video, History, Literature, Literary Criticism, Essays, Photography, Psychology, Psychiatry
ISBN Prefix(es): 2-86589
Total Titles: 58 Print

**Magnard**
20 rue Berbier-du-Mets, 75647 Paris Cedex 13
Tel: (01) 44 08 85 85 Fax: (01) 44 08 49 79
Web Site: www.magnard.fr
Telex: 202294 F
Key Personnel
Contact: Jean-Manuel Bourgois
Founded: 1933
Subjects: Education
ISBN Prefix(es): 2-210
Subsidiaries: Dilisco (Diffusion du Livre Scolaire)

**Maison de la Revelation+**
46 av de la Liberation, 33740 Ares
Mailing Address: BP 16, 33740 Ares
Tel: (05) 56249381 Fax: (05) 56931631
Key Personnel
President: Dominique Mottas
Author: Michel Potay
Founded: 1974
Subjects: Philosophy, Religion - Other
ISBN Prefix(es): 2-901821

**La Maison des Instituteurs**, see Editions MDI (La Maison des Instituteurs)

**Editions de la Maison des Sciences de l'Homme, Paris**
54, blvd Raspail, 75270 Paris Cedex 06

*Tel:* (01) 49 54 20 30; (01) 49 54 20 31 *Fax:* (01) 49 54 21 33
*E-mail:* public@msh-paris.fr
*Web Site:* www.editions.msh-paris.fr
*Telex:* 203104 F
*Key Personnel*
Dir: Maurice Aymard
Head of Services: F Kahn *E-mail:* kahn@msh-paris.fr
Production: R Arcier; S Farraut; Jacky Thowmine
Founded: 1975
Specializes in French-German Programs.
Subjects: Anthropology, Archaeology, Economics, History, Music, Dance, Psychology, Psychiatry, Social Sciences, Sociology
ISBN Prefix(es): 2-7351; 2-901725
*Orders to:* CID, 131 blvd St-Michel, 75005 Paris

**La Maison du Dictionnaire+**
98 Bd du Montparnasse, 75014 Paris
*Tel:* (01) 43 22 12 93 *Fax:* (01) 43 22 01 77
*E-mail:* service-client@dicoland.com
*Web Site:* www.dicoland.com
*Key Personnel*
Man Dir: Michel Feutry
Founded: 1976
Specialize in software aides, electronic dictionaries & CD-ROMs.
ISBN Prefix(es): 2-85608
*Branch Office(s)*
DPLU, 5165 Ouest Rue Sherbrooke, Montreal, QC H4A 1T6, Canada
*U.S. Office(s):* International Book Distributor Ltd, 24 Hudson St, Kinderhook, NY 12106, United States

**Adrien Maisonneuve**, see Editions d'Amerique et d'Orient, Adrien Maisonneuve

**Editions Adrien Maisonneuve**
Librairie d'Amerique et d'Orient, 11 rue Saint Sulpice, 75006 Paris
*Tel:* (01) 43 26 19 50 *Fax:* (01) 43 54 59 54
*E-mail:* maisonneuve@maisonneuve-adrien.com
*Web Site:* www.maisonneuve-adrien.com
*Key Personnel*
Dir General: Jean Maisonneuve
ISBN Prefix(es): 2-7200

**Maisonneuve Editeur**
26, Av de l'Europe, 78141 Velizy Cedex
Mailing Address: BP 60, 78141 Velizy Cedex
*Tel:* (01) 34 63 33 33 *Fax:* (01) 34 65 39 70
*Key Personnel*
Man Dir: Andre G Maisonneuve
Founded: 1959
Subjects: Health, Nutrition, Medicine, Nursing, Dentistry
ISBN Prefix(es): 2-7160

**Maisonneuve et Larose+**
15 rue Victor-Cousin, 75005 Paris
*Tel:* (01) 44414930 *Fax:* (01) 43257741
*E-mail:* servedit1@wanadoo.fr
*Key Personnel*
President: Ms France Roque
Man Dir: Alain Jauson
Founded: 1835 (& 1860 respectively, merged 1961)
Subjects: Agriculture, Animals, Pets, Astrology, Occult, Language Arts, Linguistics, Regional Interests, Religion - Jewish
ISBN Prefix(es): 2-7068
Distributed by Belles Lettres; Servedit
Distributor for Ecole Francais d'Extreme Orient

**Editions Maloine+**
23, rue de l'Ecole de Medecine, 75006 Paris
*Tel:* (01) 43 25 60 45; (01) 43 29 54 50 *Fax:* (03) 44 23 02 27
*E-mail:* vpc@vigot.fr

*Web Site:* www.vigotmaloine.fr
*Telex:* 203215 F
*Key Personnel*
President, Man Dir, Rights & Permissions: Daniel Vigot
Dir: Christian Vigot
Sales, Publicity & Advertising: Thierry de Puniet
Production, Publicity & Advertising: Jean Phillipart
Founded: 1881
Subjects: Medicine, Nursing, Dentistry, Veterinary Science
ISBN Prefix(es): 2-224

**Editions Mango+**
4, rue Caroline, 75017 Paris
*Tel:* (01) 55 30 40 50 *Fax:* (01) 55 30 40 50
*E-mail:* mango@editions-mango.fr
*Web Site:* www.editions-mango.fr
*Key Personnel*
Dir General: Hugues de Saint Vincent
International Rights: Sophie Thunierelle
Founded: 1990
Subjects: Art, Child Care & Development, Crafts, Games, Hobbies, Gardening, Plants, Health, Nutrition, House & Home, How-to, Microcomputers, Outdoor Recreation, Sports, Athletics, Wine & Spirits
ISBN Prefix(es): 2-7404; 2-84270
*Parent Company:* Editions Fleurus
Distributed by SODIS

**Manitoba**, *imprint of* Societe d'Edition Les Belles Lettres

**Editions Marcus**
25, rue Ginoux, 75015 Paris
*Tel:* (01) 45770404 *Fax:* (01) 45759251
*Telex:* 643841
*Key Personnel*
Man Dir: Patrick Arfi
Sales: Mrs Gaubert
Founded: 1963
Subjects: Travel
ISBN Prefix(es): 2-7131

**La Marge+**
4 rue Emmanuel Arene, 20000 Ajaccio, Corsica
*Tel:* (04) 95512367 *Fax:* (04) 95500900
*Key Personnel*
Dir: Jean Jacques Colonna d'Istria
Founded: 1986
ISBN Prefix(es): 2-86523

**Editions Marie-Noelle+**
7, rue de la Liberte, 39700 Orchamps
*Tel:* (03) 81877500; (03) 84812891 *Fax:* (03) 81875669
*Key Personnel*
General Dir: Michel Siegwart
Founded: 1993
Subjects: Fiction, Literature, Literary Criticism, Essays, Science Fiction, Fantasy
ISBN Prefix(es): 2-910186

**Editions Maritimes et D'Outremer**, *imprint of* Editions Ouest-France

**Martelle**
3, rue des Vergeaux, 80005 Amiens Cedex 1
Mailing Address: BP 0540, 80005 Amiens Cedex 1
*Tel:* (03) 22 71 54 55 *Fax:* (03) 22 92 89 33
*Telex:* 145306
*Key Personnel*
Contact: M Cochard
Founded: 1990
Subjects: Regional Interests
ISBN Prefix(es): 2-87890
*Bookshop(s):* Centre Amiens, 2 le Fleure, 94 rue St Lazare, Paris

**Editions de la Martiniere**
2, rue Christine, 75006 Paris
*Tel:* (01) 40 51 52 00 *Fax:* (01) 40 51 52 05
*E-mail:* coedition@lamartiniere.fr
*Web Site:* www.lamartiniere.fr
*Key Personnel*
President: Herve De La Martiniere
General Dir: Olivier d' Arrouzat
Editorial: Philippe Gadesaude
Foreign Rights: Marianne Lassandro
ISBN Prefix(es): 2-7324; 2-84675
*Showroom(s):* 6, rue Christine, 75006 Paris
*Tel:* (01) 43 25 55 26

**Editions Marval+**
30 rue de Charonne, 75011 Paris
*Tel:* (01) 48 07 50 40 *Fax:* (01) 48 07 01 08
*E-mail:* info@marval.com
*Web Site:* www.marval.com
*Key Personnel*
Manager: Yves-Marie Marchand
*E-mail:* ymarval@noos.fr
Founded: 1942 (New company 1999)
Subjects: Art, Photography
ISBN Prefix(es): 2-86234
Total Titles: 180 Print
*Ultimate Parent Company:* Vilo, 25, rue Ginoux, 75015 Paris
*Distribution Center:* CELF *Tel:* (01) 43 47 30 03 *Fax:* (01) 43 47 59 43
Edipress, 945, ave Beaumont, Montreal, QC H3N 1W3, Canada (Canada)
Nouvelle Diffusion, 24, rue de Bosnie, 1060 Brussels, Belgium *Tel:* (02) 538 88 46 *Fax:* (02) 538 88 42 (Belgium)
OLF, ZI 3 Corminboeuf, 1701 Fribourg, Switzerland *Tel:* (026) 46 75 111 *Fax:* (026) 46 75 444 (Switzerland)
Vilo, 25, rue Ginoux, 75015 Paris *Tel:* (01) 45 77 08 05 *Fax:* (01) 45 79 97 15

**Le Masque**, see Librairie des Champs-Elysees/Le Masque

**Editions du Masque**, *imprint of* Librairie des Champs-Elysees/Le Masque

**Club des Masques**, *imprint of* Librairie des Champs-Elysees/Le Masque

**Editions Charles Massin et Cie**
16-18 rue de l'Amiral Mouchez, 75686 Paris Cedex 14
*Tel:* (01) 45 65 48 55 *Fax:* (01) 45 65 47 00
*E-mail:* info@massin.fr
*Web Site:* www.massin.fr
*Telex:* 4264918 Trace
Founded: 1910
Subjects: Architecture & Interior Design, Art, House & Home
ISBN Prefix(es): 2-7072

**Masson Editeur+**
21, rue Camille Desmoulins, Issy Les Moulineaux, 92789 Paris Cedex 9
*Tel:* (01) 73 28 16 34 *Fax:* (01) 73 28 16 49
*E-mail:* infos@masson.fr
*Web Site:* www.masson.fr; www.e2med.com
*Telex:* Massoned 260946 *Cable:* GEMAS PARIS 025
*Key Personnel*
Chairman & Dir, Publication: Daniel Rodriguez
Foreign Rights Manager: Gail Markham
*Tel:* (01) 40 13 40 04 *Fax:* (01) 40 13 40 16
*E-mail:* gmarkham.icon@medimedia.com
Founded: 1804
Publish medicine & health care-related subjects & 50 journals in paper & on-line versions; dictionaries.

Subjects: Medicine, Nursing, Dentistry, Psychology, Psychiatry, Veterinary Science
ISBN Prefix(es): 2-225; 2-294
Number of titles published annually: 200 Print
Total Titles: 3,000 Print
*Ultimate Parent Company:* Groupe MediMedia
Subsidiaries: Masson SA; Masson SpA
Distributed by Havas Diffusion International; Havas Services Suisse; Livredis; O L F; Presses de Belgique; Somabec

**Masson-Williams et Wilkins+**
3-5, rue Laromiguiere, 75005 Paris
*Tel:* (01) 40466000 *Fax:* (01) 40466126
*E-mail:* pradel@lsicom.fr
*Key Personnel*
Contact: Mariette Guena; Ray Pitt
Founded: 1988
Subjects: Biological Sciences, Medicine, Nursing, Dentistry
ISBN Prefix(es): 2-907516; 2-84360
*Parent Company:* Wolters Kluwer NV

**Matrice**
71, rue des Camelias, 91270 Vigneux
*Tel:* (01) 69 42 13 02 *Fax:* (01) 69 40 21 57
*Key Personnel*
President: Jacques Pain
Founded: 1984
Subjects: Human Relations
ISBN Prefix(es): 2-905642
*Showroom(s):* Casteilla, 10, rue Leon-Foucault, 78180 Montigny le Bretonneux *Tel:* (01) 30 14 19 30

**Maxima Laurent du Mesnil Editeur+**
192, bd Saint-Germain, 75007 Paris
*Tel:* (01) 44 39 74 00 *Fax:* (01) 45 48 46 88
*E-mail:* edition@maxima.fr
*Web Site:* www.maxima.fr
*Key Personnel*
President & General Dir: Laurent du Mesnil du Buisson
Dir: Stephane Derville *Tel:* (01) 44 39 74 04
  *E-mail:* sderville@maxima.fr
Founded: 1990
Subjects: Business, Career Development, Economics, Finance, Human Relations, Law, Management, Marketing
ISBN Prefix(es): 2-84001
Number of titles published annually: 20 Print; 5 E-Book
Total Titles: 250 Print; 20 E-Book
*Associate Companies:* Editions Francis Lefebvre
Distributed by Interforum-Editis

**Editions MDI (La Maison des Instituteurs)**
56-60 rue de la Glaciere, 75640 Paris 13
*Tel:* (01) 45 87 52 11 *Fax:* (01) 45 87 51 97
*E-mail:* serviceclient@mdi-editions.com; mpetit@vuef.fr
*Web Site:* www.mdi-editions.com
*Telex:* MDI Edit 698094 F
*Key Personnel*
Man Dir: Marc Baudry
Export Dir: Daniel Beaudat
Founded: 1954
Subjects: Education, Geography, Geology, History, Science (General)
ISBN Prefix(es): 2-223
*Parent Company:* Editions Bordas

**Medecine-Sciences,** *imprint of* Flammarion Groupe

**Editions Medianes+**
72 rue d'Amiens, 76000 Rouen
*Tel:* (02) 35 88 85 71 *Fax:* (02) 35 15 28 44
*E-mail:* medianesconseil@wanadoo.fr
*Key Personnel*
Dir General: Jean-Marie Tiercelin

Contact: Christian de Chanteloup
Founded: 1989
Membership(s): SNE.
Subjects: Art, Biography, Drama, Theater, History, Literature, Literary Criticism, Essays, Photography, Regional Interests
ISBN Prefix(es): 2-908345

**Editions Mediaspaul+**
48, rue du Four, 75006 Paris
*Tel:* (01) 45 48 71 93 *Fax:* (01) 42 22 47 46
*E-mail:* mediaspaul.com@wanadoo.fr
Founded: 1981
Subjects: Biblical Studies, Religion - Catholic, Theology
ISBN Prefix(es): 2-7122
*Bookshop(s):* 16 rue de la Visitation, 71600 Paray Le Monial *Tel:* (03) 85 81 08 93 *Fax:* (03) 85 81 08 93
*Warehouse:* BP 26, 62 rue de Chanteloup, 91291 Arpajon Cedex *Tel:* (01) 64 90 87 40 *Fax:* (01) 64 90 96 09 *E-mail:* media.arp@wanadoo.fr

**Medius Editions**
204, blvd Raspail, 75014 Paris
*Tel:* (01) 42 79 25 21 *Fax:* (01) 42 78 25 39
*E-mail:* contact@dervy.fr
*Key Personnel*
Manager: Bernard Renaud de la Faverie
Subjects: Astrology, Occult, Psychology, Psychiatry, Bach Flowers, Feng Shui, Reiki, Self Medicine, Yi King Chakras
ISBN Prefix(es): 2-85327
Number of titles published annually: 12 Print
Total Titles: 120 Print
*Warehouse:* Dilisco, Parc Mure 2, Batiment 4.4, 128 Ave Jean Jaures, BP 102, 94208 Ivry Sur Seine

**Editions MeMo+**
4, rue des Olivettes Passage Douard, 44000 Nantes
*Tel:* (02) 40 47 98 19 *Fax:* (02) 40 47 98 21
*E-mail:* contactweb@editionsmemo.fr
*Web Site:* www.editionsmemo.fr
*Key Personnel*
General Dir: Mdme Christine Morault
Founded: 1993
Subjects: Art
ISBN Prefix(es): 2-910391

**Editions Memoire des Arts+**
BP 4553, 69244 Lyon Cedex 04
*Tel:* (04) 78 83 22 62 *Fax:* (04) 72 19 48 74
*Key Personnel*
General Dir: Alain Vollerin *E-mail:* alain.vollerin@wanadoo.fr
Founded: 1991
Subjects: Art
ISBN Prefix(es): 2-912544

**La Memoire Normande,** *imprint of* Editions Bertout

**Editions Menges**
6, rue du Mail, 75002 Paris
*Tel:* (01) 44 55 37 50 *Fax:* (01) 40 20 99 74
*E-mail:* info@editions-menges.com
*Web Site:* www.editions-menges.com
*Telex:* Cflglm 630385
*Key Personnel*
Manager, Admin & Finance: Carl Van Eiszner
Editorial Dir & Foreign Rights: Isabelle de Tinguy
Sales Manager: Guillaume Dopffer
Public Relations: Carole Brianchon
Founded: 1975
Subjects: Cookery, Gardening, Plants, Health, Nutrition, Sports, Athletics
ISBN Prefix(es): 2-85620

*Parent Company:* Editions Sand
Distributed by Vivendi Universal Publishing Services

**Editions Franck Mercier+**
One bis rue du Forum, 74013 Annecy, cedex
Mailing Address: BP 404, 74013 Annecy cedex
*Tel:* (04) 50 57 16 50 *Fax:* (01) 450579301
*E-mail:* franck@mercier.com.ch
*Key Personnel*
Contact: Franck Mercier
Founded: 1985
Subjects: Geography, Geology, How-to, Outdoor Recreation, Sports, Athletics, Travel
ISBN Prefix(es): 2-86868
Total Titles: 120 Print
Imprints: Guide Franck

**Mercure de France SA**
26, rue de Conde, 75006 Paris
*Tel:* (01) 55 42 61 90 *Fax:* (01) 43 54 49 91
*E-mail:* mercure@mercure.fr
*Web Site:* www.mercuredefrance.fr
*Key Personnel*
Production Dir: Brigitte Duverger
Foreign Rights & Permissions: Nicole Boyer
Editor: Nicolas Brehal; Jean-Marc Roberts
Founded: 1891
Subjects: Astrology, Occult, Biography, Fiction, History, Literature, Literary Criticism, Essays, Philosophy, Poetry
ISBN Prefix(es): 2-7152
*Parent Company:* Editions Gallimard, 5, rue Sebastien-Bottin, 75328 Paris Cedex 07
*Associate Companies:* Editions Denoel Sarl

**Editions A M Metailie+**
5 rue de Savoie, 75006 Paris
*Tel:* (01) 55 42 83 00 *Fax:* (01) 55 42 83 04
*E-mail:* presse@metailie.info
*Web Site:* www.metailie.info
*Key Personnel*
Man Dir & Editor: Anne Marie Metailie
  *E-mail:* presse@metailie.info
Manager: Jocelyne Valle
Literary Dir: P Dibie; P Leglise-Costa
Communication & Foreign Rights: Marie Descourtieux
Founded: 1979
Subjects: Anthropology, Fiction, Literature, Literary Criticism, Essays, Mysteries, Social Sciences, Sociology
ISBN Prefix(es): 2-86424
Total Titles: 550 Print
*Warehouse:* Seuil, 13 ave du General Leclere, 91120 L Ballainvilliers, Longjumeau
*Orders to:* Seuil, 27 rue Jacob, 75261 Paris Cedex 06

**Editions Albin Michel+**
22, rue Huyghens, 75014 Paris Cedex 14
*Tel:* (01) 42 79 10 00 *Fax:* (01) 43 27 21 58
*Web Site:* www.albin-michel.fr
*Key Personnel*
President: Francis Esmenard
Vice President: Richard Ducousset
General Secretary: Agnes Fruman
  *E-mail:* afrumen@aldin-michel.fr; Thierry Pfister
Man Dir: Alexis Esmenard; Henri Esmenard; Patrice Gueriy
Sales Dir: Jean-Yves Bry
Dir, Advertising & Promotion: Sylvie Hoare
Foreign Rights: Jacqueline Favero
Subsidiary Rights: Marie Dormann
Dir, Foreign Dept: Tony Cartano
Public Relations: Regine Billot; Florence Godfernaux
Children's Books: Marion Jablonski
Foreign Rights (Children's books): Aurelie Lapautre
Founded: 1902

Subjects: Art, Biography, Child Care & Development, Cookery, Fiction, History, How-to, Humor, Literature, Literary Criticism, Essays, Music, Dance, Nonfiction (General), Philosophy, Religion - Other, Social Sciences, Sociology
ISBN Prefix(es): 2-226

**Michelin Editions des Voyages**
46, ave de Breteuil, 75324 Paris Cedex 07
*Tel:* (01) 45 66 22 22 *Fax:* (01) 45 66 15 53
*Telex:* 270 789 F
*Key Personnel*
Contact: M Alain Arnaud
Founded: 1900
Subjects: Travel
ISBN Prefix(es): 2-06
*Associate Companies:* Elastika Michelin, Greece; Michelin Asia Co PTE Ltd, Singapore; Michelin Asia Ltd, Hong Kong; Michelin Companhia Luso Pneu LDA Portugal; Michelin Reifenwerke, Austria; Michelin Reifenwerke, Germany; Michelin Travel Publications; Michelin Tyre PLC, United Kingdom; Nihon Michelin Tire KK, Japan; S A Belge du Pneumatique Michelin, Belgium; SA des Pneumatiques Michelin, Switzerland; SAFE de Neumaticos Michelin, Spain; S P A Michelin Italiana, Italy; Ste Canadienne des Pneus Michelin

**Microsoft Press France**
18, ave du Quebec, 91957 Courtaboeuf Cedex
*Tel:* (0825) 827 829 *Fax:* (01) 64 46 06 60
*E-mail:* msfrance@microsoft.com
*Web Site:* www.microsoft.com/france
Founded: 1992
Subjects: Computer Science
ISBN Prefix(es): 2-84082

**Mille et Une Nuits+**
37, rue du Four, 75006 Paris
*Tel:* (01) 45 49 82 00 *Fax:* (01) 45 49 79 96
*E-mail:* info1001nuits@editions-fayard.fr
*Web Site:* www.1001nuits.com
*Key Personnel*
President: Monsieur Maurizio Medico
International Rights: Monsieur Olivier Rubinstein
Founded: 1993
Subjects: Literature, Literary Criticism, Essays
ISBN Prefix(es): 2-84205; 2-910233

**Librairie Minard**
45 rue de St-Andre, 14 123 Fleury/Orne
*Tel:* (02) 31844706 *Fax:* (02) 31844809
*Key Personnel*
Man Dir: Michel J Minard
Contact: Daniele Minard
Founded: 1978
Subjects: Film, Video, Literature, Literary Criticism, Essays
ISBN Prefix(es): 2-85210
Distributor for Lettres Modernes

**Editions Minerva**
Subsidiary of La Martiniere Groupe
96 bd du Montparnasse, 75014 Paris
*Tel:* (01) 44 10 75 75 *Fax:* (01) 44 10 75 80
*Web Site:* www.lamartiniere.fr
*Key Personnel*
President: Herve De La Martiniere
ISBN Prefix(es): 2-7324

**Presses Universitaires du Mirail+**
Universite Toulouse-Le Mirail, 5 allees Antonio Machado, 31058 Toulouse Cedex 9
*Tel:* (05) 61 50 38 10 *Fax:* (05) 61 50 38 00
*E-mail:* pum@univ-tlse2.fr
*Web Site:* www.univ-tlse2.fr/pum
*Key Personnel*
Administration & Sales: Marie-Pierre Sales
    *E-mail:* sales@univ-tlse2.fr
Founded: 1987

University press that publishes books written mainly by academics.
Subjects: Geography, Geology, History, Language Arts, Linguistics, Literature, Literary Criticism, Essays, Philosophy, Psychology, Psychiatry, Social Sciences, Sociology, Women's Studies
ISBN Prefix(es): 2-85816
Number of titles published annually: 30 Print
Total Titles: 600 Print; 1 CD-ROM; 1 E-Book
Imprints: PUM Toulouse

**Miroir Sprint Publications**, see Les Editions Vaillant-Miroir-Sprint Publications

**Editions Modernes Media+**
12, rue Haudriettes, 75003 Paris
*Tel:* (01) 44 54 90 42 *Fax:* (01) 44 54 90 47
*E-mail:* ed.mod.media@wanadoo.fr
*Key Personnel*
Literary Dir: A M Marina Mediavilla
Founded: 1972
Subjects: Education, Language Arts, Linguistics, Literature, Literary Criticism, Essays, Philosophy
ISBN Prefix(es): 2-85398

**Gerard Monfort Editeur Sarl+**
BP 20, 27800 Brionne
*Tel:* (01) 40 27 95 54 *Fax:* (01) 40 27 95 60
*E-mail:* contact@gerard-monfort.com
*Web Site:* www.gerard-monfort.com
Founded: 1960
Subjects: Art, History, Literature, Literary Criticism, Essays, Specialize in Art History
ISBN Prefix(es): 2-85226

**Editions du Moniteur+**
17, rue d'Uzes, 75108 Paris Cedex 02
*Tel:* (01) 40 13 33 72 *Fax:* (01) 40 41 08 87
*E-mail:* clients@editionsdumoniteur.com
*Web Site:* www.editionsdumoniteur.com
*Telex:* 680876 F
*Key Personnel*
President: Jacques Guy *Tel:* (01) 40 13 32 31
Man Dir: Frederic Lenne *Tel:* (01) 40 13 34 34
Commercial Manager: Florence Delouche
    *Tel:* (01) 40 13 37 34
Editor: Jean-Marc Joannes *Tel:* (01) 40 13 32 62
Founded: 1981
Subjects: Architecture & Interior Design, Law, Technology, Construction/Building
ISBN Prefix(es): 2-281; 2-7327; 2-902302
Number of titles published annually: 30 Print; 1 CD-ROM
Total Titles: 160 Print; 4 CD-ROM
*Bookshop(s):* Librairies du Moniteur, 15 rue d'Uzes, 75002 Paris; 7 pl de l'Odeon, 75006 Paris
*Distribution Center:* Interforum

**Editions Paul Montel**
11, rue Gossin, 92543 Montrouge Cedex
*Tel:* (01) 46565266
*Key Personnel*
Man Dir: Marc Vigier
Dir: Guy de Dampierre
Sales: Yves-Louis Walle
Subjects: Film, Video, Photography
ISBN Prefix(es): 2-7075

**Muller Edition+**
BP 122, 92134 Issy-les-Moulineaux Cedex
*Tel:* (01) 40 90 09 65 *Fax:* (01) 47 76 33 97
*E-mail:* courrier@muller-edition.com
*Web Site:* www.muller-edition.com
*Key Personnel*
President: Joseph Muller
Founded: 1990
Subjects: Archaeology, History, How-to, Military Science
ISBN Prefix(es): 2-904255

Total Titles: 500 Print; 300 E-Book
Distributed by Editions Picard; Goutiere diffusioer; Histoire et documents
Distributor for Editions Bertout; Editions Jean Curutchet; Editions des Ecrivains Associes; Editions Domens; Editions Etoile De La Pensee; Editions L' Harmattan; Editions Charles Lavauzelle; Martelle; Ouest-France
*Distribution Center:* Muller, 123 av Publo Picasso, Nanterre, 2 etage, Porte 3024

**Editions de la Reunion des Musees Nationaux+**
49, rue Etienne Marcel, 75039 Paris Cedex 01
*Tel:* (01) 40 13 49 66 *Fax:* (01) 40 13 49 73
*E-mail:* editions@rmn.fr
*Web Site:* www.rmn.fr
*Key Personnel*
Dir: J J Lugbull
Founded: 1931
Subjects: Antiques, Archaeology, Architecture & Interior Design, Art, Ethnicity, History
ISBN Prefix(es): 2-7118
*Branch Office(s)*
Reumusnat Paris *Fax:* (01) 42225073 (Telex: Rm 200115 F)
Distributed by Editions du Seuie
*Bookshop(s):* Grand Louvre, 75001 Paris; Librairie du Musee d'Orsay, 60ter rue de Lille, 75001 Paris
*Warehouse:* Centre de Distribution de la R M N, 1-31, allee du 12 fevrier 1934, 77186 Noisiel

**Editions Maurice Nadeau, Les Lettres Nouvelles+**
135, rue Saint-Martin, 75194 Paris Cedex 04
*Tel:* (01) 48 87 75 87 *Fax:* (01) 48 87 13 01
*Key Personnel*
President: Bernard Coutaz
Manager: Maurice Nadeau
Subjects: Literature, Literary Criticism, Essays
ISBN Prefix(es): 2-86231
*Parent Company:* Societe D'Editions Litteraires et Scientifiques (SELIS)
*Orders to:* Harmonia Mundi, 13200 Arles

**Nanga**
BP 62, 22430 Erquy
*Tel:* (02) 96 72 32 16 *Fax:* (02) 96 72 08 48
*E-mail:* nanga@nanga.fr; nangaw@wanadoo.fr
*Web Site:* www.nanga.info
*Key Personnel*
Publisher: Jerome Feugereux *E-mail:* jerome@feugereux.com
Founded: 1991
Subjects: Art, Earth Sciences, Literature, Literary Criticism, Essays, Poetry
ISBN Prefix(es): 2-909152
Number of titles published annually: 4 Print; 2 E-Book
Total Titles: 20 Print; 3 E-Book

**Editions Fernand Nathan**
Subsidiary of Vivendi Universal Publishing
9, rue Mechain, 75104 Paris Cedex 13
*Tel:* (01) 45 87 50 00; (0825) 00 11 67 *Fax:* (01) 45 87 53 43
*Web Site:* www.nathan.fr; www.nathan.fr/contacts
*Telex:* Nataned 204525 F *Cable:* NATHANED PARIS
*Key Personnel*
Dir General: Catherine Lucet
Executive Vice President: Jean-Paul Baudouin
Elementary Dir: Arnaud Langlois-Meurinne
Educational Dir: Michel Legrain
Educational Aids & University Dir: Philippe Merlet
Dir, Children's Books: Marc Baudry
Languages Dir: Marc Gudimard
Sales Dir: Alain Carita; Patrick de Porcaro
Marketing Dir: Emilie Carelli
Finance Dir: Serge Grand

Rights & Permissions: Evelyne Mathiaud
  *Tel:* (01) 45 87 51 54 *Fax:* (01) 45 87 57 80
  *E-mail:* emathiaud@nathan.fr
Founded: 1881
Specialize in Children & Pedagogy.
Subjects: Education, History, Philosophy, Psychology, Psychiatry, Science (General), Social Sciences, Sociology
ISBN Prefix(es): 2-09
Subsidiaries: CLE; Retz; Le Robert

**Nathan International**
9, rue Mechain, 75014 Paris
*Tel:* (01) 45 87 50 00 *Fax:* (01) 45 87 57 57
*Web Site:* www.nathan.fr
*Telex:* 201426
ISBN Prefix(es): 2-288
*Parent Company:* Vivendi Universal Publishing

**Centre National de la Photographie+**
11, rue Berryer, Hoetel Salomon de Rothschild, 75008 Paris
*Tel:* (01) 53 76 12 31 *Fax:* (01) 53 76 12 33
*E-mail:* centre.national.de.la.photographie@wanadoo.fr
*Web Site:* www.cnp-photographie.com
*Key Personnel*
Dir: Regis Durand *Tel:* (01) 53 76 86 66
Commercial Dir: Benoit Rivero
Publishing Manager: Maurice Lecomte *Tel:* (01) 53 76 86 76
Production Manager: Annie Girard *Tel:* (01) 53 76 86 77 *E-mail:* a.girard@cnp-photo.com
Founded: 1982
Subjects: Photography
ISBN Prefix(es): 2-86754

**Institut National de Recherche Pedagogique INRP**
Place du Pentacle, BP 17, 69195 Saint-Fons Cedex Cedex 05
*Tel:* (04) 72 89 83 00 *Fax:* (04) 72 89 83 29
*E-mail:* publica@inrp.fr
*Web Site:* www.inrp.fr *Cable:* INATREP
*Key Personnel*
Dir: Marie-Claude Lartigot *Tel:* (04) 72 89 83 40
Secretary General: Martine Muller *E-mail:* sg@inrp.fr
Founded: 1879
Subjects: Education
ISBN Prefix(es): 2-7342
*Parent Company:* Ministere de l'Education Nationale, 110 rue de Grenelle, 75357 Paris
*Branch Office(s)*
29, rue d'Ulm, 75230 Paris Cedex 05 *Tel:* (01) 46 34 90 00 *Fax:* (01) 43 54 32 01
*Bookshop(s):* Librairie du CRDP, 37 rue Jacob, 75006 Paris *Tel:* (01) 44 56 62 34

**Navarre,** *imprint of* Les Editions LGDJ-Montchrestien

**NEF,** see Nouvelles Editions Francaises

**NEL,** *imprint of* Nouvelles Editions Latines

**Nil Editions+**
24, Ave Marceau, 75381 Paris Cedex 08
*Tel:* (01) 53 67 14 00 *Fax:* (01) 53 67 14 90
*Web Site:* www.laffont.fr; www.nil-editions.fr
*Key Personnel*
President: Nicole Lattes
International Rights: Celine Chiflet
Foreign Rights: Olga Begin *E-mail:* obegin@robert-laffont.fr; Renata de La Chapelle *E-mail:* rdelachapelle@robert-laffont.fr; Benita Edzard *E-mail:* bedzard@robert-laffont.fr; Gwenael Gouiffes *E-mail:* ggouiffes@robert-laffont.fr; Camille Schyrr *E-mail:* cschyrr@robert-laffont.fr
Founded: 1993

Subjects: Biography, Fiction, Literature, Literary Criticism, Essays, Philosophy, French literature, Spirituality
ISBN Prefix(es): 2-84111
*Orders to:* Edition du Sevil, BP 281, 911621 Longjumeau Cedex *Tel:* (01) 64 48 49 63

**Librairie A-G Nizet Sarl+**
41, rue de l'Auberdiere, 37510 Saint Genouph
*Tel:* (02) 47 45 50 41 *Fax:* (02) 47 45 50 15
*E-mail:* librairie-a.g-nizet@wanadoo.fr
*Key Personnel*
Man Dir & General Manager: Daniel Nizet
Founded: 1945
Also acts as Bookseller.
Membership(s): Edition Syndication, Group "Scholarship".
Subjects: Drama, Theater, Literature, Literary Criticism, Essays
ISBN Prefix(es): 2-7078
Number of titles published annually: 6 Print
Total Titles: 762 Print
Distributed by D P L U (North America); L'Age d'homme (Switzerland); Nord-Sud (Benelux)
Distributor for France Tosho

**Librairie F de Nobele**
35 rue Bonaparte, 75006 Paris
*Tel:* (01) 43 26 08 62 *Fax:* (01) 40 46 85 96
*E-mail:* librairie.f.de.nobele@wanadoo.fr *Cable:* Denobelef Paris 110
*Key Personnel*
Man Dir: F de Nobele
Founded: 1885
Subjects: Art
ISBN Prefix(es): 2-85189

**Noir Sur Blanc+**
One rue Garnier, 92200 Neuilly sur Seine
*Tel:* (01) 41 43 72 70 *Fax:* (01) 41 43 72 71
*E-mail:* noirsurblanc@noirsurblanc.com
*Web Site:* www.noirsurblanc.com
*Key Personnel*
Literary Dir: Jan Michalski
Dir: Vera Michalski
Founded: 1990
Subjects: Biography, Cookery, Drama, Theater, Fiction, Literature, Literary Criticism, Essays
ISBN Prefix(es): 2-88250
*Parent Company:* Editions Noir sur Blanc

**Editions Nord-Sud** (North-South Editions)
Imprint of Nord-Sud Verlag
2, rue Racine, 78100 Saint-Germain-en-Laye
*Tel:* (01) 39 21 90 40 *Fax:* (01) 39 21 90 42
*E-mail:* nord-sud@editions-nord-sud.com
*Key Personnel*
President: Davy Sidjanski
Dir: Didier Teyras
Founded: 1981
ISBN Prefix(es): 3-85825; 3-314; 2-8311; 3-03733; 3-03703

**Editions Norma+**
149, rue de Rennes, 75006 Paris
*Tel:* (01) 45 48 70 96 *Fax:* (01) 45 48 05 84
*E-mail:* norma@freesurf.fr
*Key Personnel*
Manager: Maiite Hudry
Founded: 1991
Subjects: Architecture & Interior Design, Art, Drama, Theater, Foreign Countries, History, House & Home, Regional Interests, 20th Century Decorative Arts
ISBN Prefix(es): 2-909283
*Warehouse:* ETAI, 20 rue de la Saussiere, 92100 Boulogne *Tel:* (01) 46992424

**Editions Mare Nostrum**
12 bis, rue Jeanne d'Arc, 66000 Perpignan
*Tel:* (04) 68 51 17 50 *Fax:* (05) 61 41 15 43

*E-mail:* mare.nost@wanadoo.fr
*Telex:* 34421415
*Key Personnel*
President: Philippe Salus
Treasurer: Henri Taverner
Founded: 1990
Subjects: Literature, Literary Criticism, Essays, Philosophy, Poetry, Religion - Jewish
ISBN Prefix(es): 2-908476
*Warehouse:* Taye, 28110 Luce
*Orders to:* Taye, 28110 Luce

**Les Nouveaux Loisirs+**
5, rue Sebastien-Bottin, 75328 Paris Cedex 07
*Tel:* (01) 49 54 42 00 *Fax:* (01) 45 44 94 03
*Web Site:* www.gallimard.fr
*Key Personnel*
Dir of Development: Ghislain de Compreignac
International Rights: Hedwige Pasquet
Founded: 1992
Subjects: Architecture & Interior Design, Art, Environmental Studies, Geography, Geology, History, How-to, Regional Interests
ISBN Prefix(es): 2-7424
*Parent Company:* Editions Gallimard
*Associate Companies:* Gallimard Jeunesse
*Imprints:* Guides Gallimard
Distributed by Dohosna (Japan); Dumont (Germany); Everytian (UK); Knopf (USA); Owl Publishing (China, Taiwan); SM-Acento (Spain); Standard (Netherlands); TCI (Italy)

**Nouvelle Cite+**
37, Ave de la Marne, 92120 Montrouge
*Tel:* (01) 40927085 *Fax:* (01) 40921168
*Key Personnel*
Man Dir, Rights & Permissions: Henri-Louis Roche
Sales: Christian Charnay
Founded: 1963
Subjects: Education, Literature, Literary Criticism, Essays, Religion - Other
ISBN Prefix(es): 2-85313

**Nouvelles Editions Fiduciaires**
2 bis, rue de Villiers, 92 300 Levallois Perret
*Tel:* (01) 46 39 47 13; (01) 46 39 47 00 *Fax:* (01) 47 58 00 63
*Key Personnel*
Dir: Sophie Robert
Founded: 1980
Subjects: Economics, Law, Management
ISBN Prefix(es): 2-86544

**Nouvelles Editions Francaises+**
152, rue de Picpus, 75583 Paris Cedex 12
*Tel:* (01) 44 74 16 00 *Fax:* (01) 44 04 98 03
*Key Personnel*
Man Dir: Eliane Allegret
Founded: 1843
Subjects: Art, History, House & Home
ISBN Prefix(es): 2-7079

**Nouvelles Editions Latines+**
One, rue Palatine, 75006 Paris
*Tel:* (01) 43 54 77 42 *Fax:* (01) 43 29 69 81
*E-mail:* info@editions-nel.com
*Web Site:* www.editions-nel.com
*Key Personnel*
Man Dir: Jean Sorlot
Founded: 1928
Subjects: Fiction, History, Poetry, Religion - Other, Travel
ISBN Prefix(es): 2-7233; 2-85147
*Imprints:* NEL

**La Nuee Bleue - Dernieres Nouvelles d'Alsace**
3 rue saint Pierre-le-Jeune, 67000 Strasbourg
*Tel:* (03) 88 15 77 27 *Fax:* (03) 88 75 16 21
*E-mail:* nuee-bleue@sdv.fr
*Web Site:* www.sdv.fr/nuee-bleue/
ISBN Prefix(es): 2-7165

**Oblong**, *imprint of* Editions Jacques Gabay

**Editions Obsidiane+**
11, rue Andre Gateau, 89100 Sens
*Tel:* (03) 86965218 *Fax:* (03) 86870112
*E-mail:* genevieve.bigant@wanadoo.fr
*Key Personnel*
Manager: Francois Boddaert
Founded: 1985
Subjects: Literature, Literary Criticism, Essays, Poetry
ISBN Prefix(es): 2-904469; 2-911914
Number of titles published annually: 10 Print
Total Titles: 200 Print
Distributed by Les Belles-Lettres
*Distribution Center:* Farandole Diffusion (Belgium)
Librairie Gallimard a Montreal (Canada)

**Editions Odile Jacob+**
15, rue Soufflot, 75005 Paris
*Tel:* (01) 44 41 64 93 *Fax:* (01) 44 41 46 90; (01) 43 29 88 77
*Web Site:* www.odilejacob.fr
*Key Personnel*
President: Odile Jacob
Rights & Permissions: Claire Teeuwissen
*Tel:* (01) 44 41 64 80
Founded: 1985
Subjects: Biography, Economics, Fiction, Government, Political Science, History, How-to, Law, Philosophy, Psychology, Psychiatry, Science (General), Social Sciences, Sociology
ISBN Prefix(es): 2-7381
Number of titles published annually: 120 Print
Imprints: Poches Odile Jacob

**OGC Michele Broutta Editeur**
31 rue des Bergers, 75015 Paris
*Tel:* (01) 45779371 *Fax:* (01) 40590432
*Key Personnel*
Man Dir: Michele Broutta *E-mail:* m.broutta@wanadoo.fr
Founded: 1970
Subjects: Art, Library & Information Sciences
ISBN Prefix(es): 2-900332; 2-902886

**L' Olivier**, *imprint of* Editions du Seuil

**Editions Omnibus+**
12 ave d'Italie, 75013 Paris
*Tel:* (01) 44 16 05 00 *Fax:* (01) 44 16 05 18
*E-mail:* omnibus@psb-editions.com
*Web Site:* www.omnibus.tm.fr
*Telex:* preci 204 807 f
*Key Personnel*
Man Dir: Georges Leser
Dir, Literature: Jean-Louis Festjens
International Rights: Florence De Bourgues
Founded: 1993
Subjects: Humor
ISBN Prefix(es): 2-258; 2-84119
Number of titles published annually: 250 Print
*Parent Company:* Presses/Solar

**Editions Ophrys+**
5 allee du Torrent, 05000 Gap
*Tel:* (04) 92 53 85 72 *Fax:* (04) 92 51 78 65
*E-mail:* edition.ophrys@ophrys.fr; infos@ophrys.fr
*Web Site:* www.ophrys-editions.com
*Key Personnel*
Man Dir, Publicity & Advertising: Mrs B Monnier
Founded: 1934
Subjects: Earth Sciences, Education, English as a Second Language, Genealogy, Geography, Geology, History, Language Arts, Linguistics, Regional Interests, Self-Help, Social Sciences, Sociology, Travel
ISBN Prefix(es): 2-7080

*Bookshop(s):* Succursale de Paris, 10 rue de Nesle, 75006 Paris *Tel:* (01) 44 41 63 75 *Fax:* (01) 46 33 15 97
*Orders to:* 10 rue de Nesle, 75006 Paris
*Tel:* (01) 44 41 63 75 *Fax:* (01) 46 33 15 97
*E-mail:* ophrys4@wanadoo.fr

**Opsys Operating System**
3 rue Paul-Valerien-Perrin, 38172 Seyssinet-Pariset
*Tel:* (04) 76 84 34 20; (04) 76 84 34 34 *Fax:* (04) 76 84 34 21
*E-mail:* opsys@opsys.fr
*Web Site:* www.opsys.fr
*Key Personnel*
President & Dir General: Alain Gagne
*E-mail:* agagne@opsys.fr
Commercial Dir: Thierry Ponset
*E-mail:* tponset@opsys.fr
Operations Dir: Jean-Pierre Schmitt
*E-mail:* jpschmit@opsys.fr
Development Dir: Joseph Ramblas
*E-mail:* jramblas@opsys.fr
Research Dir: Jacques Kergomard
*E-mail:* jkergomard@opsys.fr
Subjects: Library & Information Sciences

**Editions de l'Orante+**
6 rue du General-Bertrand, 75007 Paris
*Tel:* (01) 47 83 55 02 *Fax:* (01) 45 66 00 16
*Key Personnel*
Man Dir: Jacques Lafarge
Founded: 1940
Membership(s): Syndicat National de l'Edition.
Subjects: History, Philosophy, Poetry, Religion - Other
ISBN Prefix(es): 2-7031
Total Titles: 80 Print

**Organisation for Economic Co-operation & Development OECD+**
2, rue Andre Pascal, 75775 Paris Cedex 16
*Tel:* (01) 45 24 82 00 *Fax:* (01) 45 24 85 00
*E-mail:* sales@oecd.org
*Web Site:* www.oecd.org/bookshop; www.sourceoecd.org
*Key Personnel*
Head of Dissemination & Marketing: Toby Green
*Tel:* (01) 45 24 94 15 *Fax:* (01) 45 24 19 50
*E-mail:* toby.green@oecd.org
International Rights: Laurence Gerrer *Tel:* (01) 45 24 13 90 *Fax:* (01) 45 24 13 91
*E-mail:* laurence.gerrer@oecd.org
Founded: 1960 (Successor organization to the Organization for European Economic Co-operation)
OECD is the forum where the governments of 30 democracies work together to address the economic, social & environmental challenges of our times. OECD Publishing disseminates the results of the Organization's statistics gathering & research on economic, social & environmental issues, as well as the conventions, guidelines & standards agreed by its members.
Subjects: Agriculture, Business, Child Care & Development, Communications, Developing Countries, Economics, Education, Energy, Environmental Studies, Government, Political Science, Labor, Industrial Relations, Management, Public Administration, Science (General), Social Sciences, Sociology, Technology, Transportation
ISBN Prefix(es): 92-64; 92-821
Number of titles published annually: 250 Print; 12 CD-ROM; 250 Online; 250 E-Book
Total Titles: 12 CD-ROM; 250 Online; 250 E-Book
*Branch Office(s)*
OECD Berlin Centre, Albrechtstr 9, 3 OG, 10117 Berlin-Mitte, Germany, Marketing Manager: Damon Allen *Tel:* (030) 2888 353 *Fax:* (030) 2888 35 45 *E-mail:* berlin.contact@oecd.org

*Web Site:* www.oecd.org/deutschland (Austria, Germany & Switzerland)
OECD Mexico Centre, av Presidente Mazaryk 526, Colonia, Polanco, 11560 Mexico, DF, Mexico, Marketing Manager: Alejandro Camacho *Tel:* (0525) 138 6233 *Fax:* (0525) 280 0480 *E-mail:* mexico.contact@oecd.org *Web Site:* www.oecdmexico.org.mx (Mexico & Latin America)
OECD Tokyo Centre, Nippon Press Center Bldg, 2-2-1, 3rd floor, Uchisaiwaicho, Chiyoda-ku, Tokyo 100-0011, Japan, Marketing Manager: Shunji Onada *Tel:* (03) 5532 0021 *Fax:* (03) 5532 0035; (03) 5532 6298 (direct) *E-mail:* centre@oecdtokyo.org *Web Site:* www.oecdtokyo.org (Asia)
*U.S. Office(s):* OECD Washington Center, 2001 "L" St NW, Suite 650, Washington, DC 20036-4922, United States, Marketing Officer: Suzanne Edam *Tel:* 202-785-0350 *Fax:* 202-785-6323 *E-mail:* washington.contact@oecd.org *Web Site:* www.oecdwash.org
Distributor for European Conference of Ministers of Transport; International Energy Agency; Nuclear Energy Agency
Foreign Rep(s): ADECO - Van Diermen Editions Techniques (Switzerland); Akademibokhandeln (Sweden); Akademika AS (Norway); Anvil Publishing Inc (Philippines); Ars Polona (Poland); Bernan Associates (US); Bookwell (India); Charlesworth China (China); Co-operative Bookshop Ltd (Malaysia); DA Information Services (Australia); Dandy Booksellers (UK); Data Beuro (UK); La Documentation Francaise (France); Dynapresse Marketing SA (Switzerland); Euro Info Service (Hungary); Federal Publications Inc (Canada); GAD Direct (Denmark); GV Zalozba doo (Slovenia); Infoenlace Ltda (Colombia); International Tax Institute (Canada, US); Librairie Internationale (Morocco); Izdatelstvo VES MIR (Russia); JSC MK-Periodica (Russia); Librairie Kauffmann (Greece); KINS Inc (Korea); Jean De Lannoy (Belgium); Legislation Direct (New Zealand); Liberalia (Chile); Les Editions La Liberte Inc (Canada); Librotrade Kft (Hungary); De Lindeboom Internationale Publikaties bv (Netherlands); MERIC-The Middle East Readers' Information Center (Egypt); Miller Distributors Ltd (Malta); Mundi-Prensa Barcelona (Spain); Mundi-Prensa Libros SA (Spain); Overseas Press (India); Librairie Payot SA (Switzerland); PDII-LIPI (Indonesia); Livraria Portugal (Portugal); PrioInfo AB (Sweden); Les Publications Gouvernementales (Canada); Renouf Publishing Co Ltd (Canada, US); Libreria Commissionaria Sansoni (Italy); J H Schultz Information (Denmark); SDU Uitgevers Externe Fondsen (Netherlands); SLOVART GTG sro (Slovak Republic); The Stationery Office (UK); Suksit Siam Co Ltd (Thailand); Suomalainen Kirjakauppa Oy (Finland); Swindon Book Co Ltd (Hong Kong); Systematics Studies Ltd (Caribbean, Trinidad & Tobago); Tycoon Information Inc (China); UNO Verlag GmbH (Germany); World Publications SA (Argentina); Xunhasaba (Vietnam)
*Distribution Center:* Turpin Distribution Services, 143 West St, New Milford, CT 06776, United States *Tel:* 860-350-0041 *Fax:* 781-829-9052; 860-350-0039 (orders) *E-mail:* oecdna@turpin-distribution.com
OECD Turpin Distribution Services Ltd, Stratton Business Park, Pegasus Drive, Biggleswade, Beds SG18 8QB, United Kingdom *Fax:* (01767) 60140 *E-mail:* oecdrow@extenza-turpin.com *Web Site:* www.extenza-turpin.com

**Librairie Orientaliste**, see Paul Geuthner Librairie Orientaliste

**Ouest Editions**
3 rue des Freres Coustou, 78000 Versailles
*Tel:* (01) 39 02 11 82 *Fax:* (01) 39 50 19 44
*E-mail:* contact@ouest-editions.com
*Web Site:* www.ouest-editions.com
*Key Personnel*
Dir General: Yves Suaudeau
Founded: 1989
Subjects: Accounting, Biological Sciences, Chemistry, Chemical Engineering, Civil Engineering, Earth Sciences, Economics, Geography, Geology, History, Regional Interests
ISBN Prefix(es): 2-908261
Distributed by Alena Libert Inc (Canada); Boinemouth (UK); Chinon Diffusion (Europe); Continental Books

**Editions Ouest-France+**
Subsidiary of Sofiouest
13 rue du Breil, 35063 Rennes Cedex
*Tel:* (02) 99 32 58 23 *Fax:* (02) 99 32 58 30
*Web Site:* www.edilarge.com
*Key Personnel*
Dir General: Servane Biguais
Founded: 1975
Subjects: Cookery, History, Science (General), Travel, Creative Leisures
ISBN Prefix(es): 2-7373; 2-85882
Number of titles published annually: 150 Print
Total Titles: 1,800 Print
*Parent Company:* Ouest France
Imprints: Editions de la Cite; Editions Maritimes et D'Outremer

**Editions J H Paillet et B Drouaud+**
73 rue de La Varenne, 41120 Cellettes
*Tel:* 54704303
*Key Personnel*
Editor: Jean-Hubert Paillet; Brigitte Drouaud
Founded: 1989
Subjects: Literature, Literary Criticism, Essays
ISBN Prefix(es): 2-9504241; 2-909565

**Editions du Papyrus**
17, bd Rouget de Lisle, 93189 Montreuil
*Tel:* (01) 48 57 27 05 *Fax:* (01) 48 57 26 79
*E-mail:* papyrus@netfly.fr
*Web Site:* www.editions-papyrus.com
Founded: 1986
Subjects: Law
ISBN Prefix(es): 2-86541

**Editions Paradigme**
14 Quai Saint Laurent, 45000 Orleans
*Tel:* (02) 38 70 84 44 *Fax:* (02) 38 70 56 76
*Web Site:* paradigme.com; cpuniv.com
*Key Personnel*
President & Editor: Bernard Legrand
    *E-mail:* blegrand@wanadoo.fr
Founded: 1983
Specialize in erudition & law.
Subjects: Energy, Geography, Geology, History, Law, Literature, Literary Criticism, Essays, Philosophy, Erudition
ISBN Prefix(es): 2-86878; 2-911377
Total Titles: 170 Print
*Parent Company:* FAB

**Editions Pardes+**
9 rue Jules Dumesnil, 45390 Puisseaux
*Tel:* (02) 38 33 53 28 *Fax:* (02) 38 33 58 99
*Key Personnel*
Managing Editor: Georges Gondinet
Founded: 1982
Subjects: Archaeology, Astrology, Occult, Health, Nutrition, History, Religion - Buddhist, Religion - Hindu, Social Sciences, Sociology
ISBN Prefix(es): 2-86714

**Editions Parentheses**
72, cours Julien, 13006 Marseille

*Tel:* (0495) 08 18 20 *Fax:* (0495) 08 18 24
*E-mail:* ed.parentheses@wanadoo.fr
*Key Personnel*
General Dir: Varoujan Arzoumanian
Dir: Patrick Bardou
Founded: 1978
Subjects: Anthropology, Architecture & Interior Design, Art, Ethnicity, Music, Dance
ISBN Prefix(es): 2-86364
Total Titles: 150 Print
*Distribution Center:* Diffusion Dimedia, 539 blvd Lebeau, Ville Saint-Laurent, ON N4N 1S2, Canada
Harmonia Mundi, Mas de Vert, BP 150, 13631 Arles Cedex *Tel:* (0490) 49 90 49 *Fax:* (0490) 49 96 14
Nouvelle Diffusion, 24, rue de Bosnie, 1060 Brussels, Belgium
Office du Livre, Route de Villars 101, 1701 Fribourg, Switzerland

**Association Paris-Musees+**
28, rue Notre Dame des Victoires, 75002 Paris
*Tel:* (01) 44 58 99 19 *Fax:* (01) 47 03 36 44
*Key Personnel*
Publisher: Arnauld Pontier
Distribution: Emmanuelle Sarrazin
Founded: 1985
Specialize in art-exhibition's catalogues & children's books.
Subjects: Architecture & Interior Design, Art, Fashion, History, Photography
ISBN Prefix(es): 2-87900
Foreign Rights: Cecile Capelle (Worldwide)

**Paroisse & Famille**, *imprint of* Federation d'Activities Culturelles, Fac Editions

**Le Parvis des Arts**, *imprint of* Presses Universitaires de Nancy

**Payot & Rivages+**
106, Blvd Saint-Germain, 75006 Paris
*Tel:* (01) 44413990 *Fax:* (01) 44413969
*E-mail:* editions@payotrivages.com
*Key Personnel*
Man Dir: Jean-Francois Lamuniere
Foreign Rights: Marie-Martine Serrano-Lavau
Founded: 1984
Subjects: Anthropology, Biography, Cookery, Fiction, History, Humor, Language Arts, Linguistics, Literature, Literary Criticism, Essays, Mysteries, Nonfiction (General), Philosophy, Religion - Other, Science Fiction, Fantasy, Social Sciences, Sociology, Technology, Transportation, Travel, Contemporary History, Cultural Studies, Ethnology, Fantasy, Modern History, Political Science, Sexuality Short Stories, Thriller
ISBN Prefix(es): 2-7436; 2-903059; 2-86930
*Parent Company:* Eol Rivagei
*Orders to:* Le Seuil, 27 rue Jacod, 75006 Paris

**Pearson Education/CampusPress**, *imprint of* Pearson Education France

**Pearson Education France+**
47 bis, rue des Vinargriers, 75010 Paris
*Tel:* (01) 7274 9000 *Fax:* (01) 4804 5361 (sales); (01) 4887 7130 (finance); (01) 4205 2217
*E-mail:* infos@pearsoned.fr
*Web Site:* www.pearsoneducation.fr
*Key Personnel*
President: Helene Dennery
Vice President, Finance & Operations: Patricia Gasquet
Editor, CampusPress Man Dir: Patrick Ussunet
Editor, Village Mondail Man Dir: Geoff Staines
Founded: 1995
Publisher of computer books.

Subjects: Business, Computer Science, Education, Finance, Microcomputers
ISBN Prefix(es): 2-7440
Total Titles: 300 Print
*Parent Company:* Pearson Education
*Ultimate Parent Company:* Pearson Plc
Imprints: Pearson Education/CampusPress; Pearson Education/Les Echos; Pearson Education/Les Echos.fr Press

**Pearson Education/Les Echos**, *imprint of* Pearson Education France

**Pearson Education/Les Echos.fr Press**, *imprint of* Pearson Education France

**Pedagogie Modern**, *imprint of* Editions Bordas

**Editions A Pedone+**
13 rue Soufflot, 75005 Paris
*Tel:* (01) 43 54 05 97 *Fax:* (01) 46 34 07 60
*E-mail:* editions-pedone@wanadoo.fr
*Key Personnel*
Man Dir: Denis Pedone
Founded: 1837
Subjects: Agriculture, Earth Sciences, Economics, Engineering (General), Law, Management, Maritime, Air Law, Criminal Philosophy, Diplomatic History, International Law, International Relations, Penal Sciences, Philosophy of the Right, Right European, Right of the Sea
ISBN Prefix(es): 2-233

**Peeters-France**
52 Blvd Saint-Michel, 75006 Paris
*Tel:* (01) 6 23 51 70 *Fax:* (01) 6 22 85 00
*E-mail:* peeters@peeters-leuven.be
*Web Site:* www.peeters-leuven.be
*Key Personnel*
Editor: Vladimir Randa
Specialize in Classical Studies, Eastern Studies, Egyptology, History of Art, Medicine, Oriental Studies & Ethics, Patristics.
Subjects: Anthropology, Archaeology, Biblical Studies, History, Language Arts, Linguistics, Literature, Literary Criticism, Essays, Philosophy, Theology
ISBN Prefix(es): 2-87723; 90-6831; 90-429
Number of titles published annually: 120 Print; 2 CD-ROM
*Parent Company:* Peeters, Bondgenoten Laan 153, 3000 Leuven, Belgium
*U.S. Office(s):* Peeters Academic Publishers Inc, 6 Ash Lane, Dudley, MA 07517, United States, Contact: Catherine Cornille *Fax:* 508-949-0557
    *E-mail:* peeters@charter.net
Distributed by BR&D
*Bookshop(s):* Bondgenotenlaan 153, 3000 Leuven, Belgium, I Huenaerts *Tel:* (016) 23 51 70 *Fax:* (016) 22 85 00 *E-mail:* peeters-leuven.be; Grand rue 56, 1348 Louvain-la-Neuve, Belgium
*Shipping Address:* Kolonel Begaultlaan 61, 3000 Leuven, Belgium *Tel:* (016) 24 40 00 *Fax:* (016) 22 85 00 *E-mail:* peeters@peeters-leuven.be
*Warehouse:* Kolonel Begaultlaan 61, 3000 Leuven, Belgium
*Orders to:* Bondgenotenlaan 153, 3000 Leuven, Belgium, I Huenaerts *Tel:* (016) 23 51 70 *Fax:* (016) 22 85 00 *E-mail:* peeters@peeters-leuven.be

**PEMF**, see Editions Publications de l'Ecole Moderne Francaise sa (PEMF)

**Pere Castor**, *imprint of* Flammarion Groupe

**Atelier Perrousseaux Editeur**, *imprint of* Adverbum SARL

**La Pharmacie de Platon**, *imprint of* William Blake & Co

**Editions Phebus**
12 rue Gregoire de Tours, 75006 Paris
*Tel:* (01) 46 33 36 36 *Fax:* (01) 43 25 67 69
*E-mail:* phebedit@wanadoo.fr
*Web Site:* www.phebus-editions.com
*Key Personnel*
Man Dir: Jean-Pierre Sicre
Founded: 1976
Subjects: Art, Literature, Literary Criticism, Essays
ISBN Prefix(es): 2-85940
*Orders to:* SEUIL Diffusion, 27 rue Jacob, 75006 Paris

**Editions A et J Picard SA**
82, rue Bonaparte, 75006 Paris
*Tel:* (01) 43 26 97 78 *Fax:* (01) 43 26 42 64
*E-mail:* livres@librairie-picard.com
*Web Site:* www.abebooks.com/home/libpicard/
*Telex:* Bsc Picaredit 305551 F
*Key Personnel*
Man Dir: Chantal Pasini-Picard
Founded: 1869
Subjects: Antiques, Archaeology, Architecture & Interior Design, Art, Education, Ethnicity, History, Language Arts, Linguistics, Literature, Literary Criticism, Essays, Music, Dance, Religion - Other
ISBN Prefix(es): 2-7084

**Editions Jean Picollec+**
47, rue Auguste Lancon, 75013 Paris
*Tel:* (01) 45 89 73 04 *Fax:* (01) 45 89 40 72
*E-mail:* jean.picollec@noos.fr
*Key Personnel*
Publisher & Man Dir: Jean Picollec
Publishing Consultant: Helene Simon
Public Relations & Sales: Corinne Saulneron
Founded: 1979
Specialize in reference books & documents - Celtic World.
Subjects: Biography, Ethnicity, Fiction, Government, Political Science, History, Literature, Literary Criticism, Essays, Nonfiction (General), Regional Interests, Travel
ISBN Prefix(es): 2-86477
Number of titles published annually: 12 Print
Total Titles: 25 Print
Distributed by Age d'Homme (Switzerland); Nouvelle Diffusion (Belgium)
Foreign Rep(s): L'age d'Homme (Switzerland); Nouvelle Diffusion (Belgium)
Foreign Rights: Arabella Cruse (Scandinavia); Laura Dail (North America); Catherine Fragou (Greece); Patricia Pasqualini (Eastern Europe, Central Europe)
*Distribution Center:* Alterdis, 5, Rue du Marechal-Leclerc, 28600 Luisant *Tel:* (02) 37 30 57 00 *Fax:* (02) 37 30 57 12
*Orders to:* CED, 73 quai Auguste Deshaies, 94200 Ivry-Sur-Seine *Tel:* (01) 46 58 38 40 *Fax:* (01) 46 71 25 59

**Editions Philippe Picquier+**
Le Mas De Vert, 13200 Arles
*Tel:* (04) 90496156 *Fax:* (04) 90499615
*E-mail:* editions-philippepicquier@harmoniamundi.com
*Key Personnel*
Dir: Philippe Picquier
Founded: 1986
Subjects: Erotica, Literature, Literary Criticism, Essays
ISBN Prefix(es): 2-87730
Total Titles: 400 Print
*Orders to:* Harmonia Mundi Diffusion Livres

**Editions Pierron+**
2, rue Gutenberg, 57206 Sarreguemines

Mailing Address: BP 80609, 57206 Sarreguemines
*Tel:* (03) 87 95 10 89 *Fax:* (03) 87 95 60 95
*E-mail:* editions@pierron.fr
*Web Site:* www.editions-pierron.com
*Telex:* 860495 F
*Key Personnel*
Dir: Jeannie Jung-Pierron
Subjects: Education, History
ISBN Prefix(es): 2-7085
*Parent Company:* Pierron Entreprise SA

**Editions Christian Pirot+**
13 rue Maurice-Adrien, 37540 Saint-Cyr-Sur-Loire
*Tel:* (02) 47 54 54 20 *Fax:* (02) 47 51 57 96
*E-mail:* editionspirot@friendship-first.com
*Web Site:* www.friendship-first.com
*Key Personnel*
Dir: Christian Pirot *E-mail:* christianpirot@friendship-first.com
Founded: 1979
Subjects: Biography, Cookery, Fiction, Literature, Literary Criticism, Essays, Music, Dance, Poetry, Travel
ISBN Prefix(es): 2-86808
Number of titles published annually: 12 Print
Total Titles: 160 Print
*Branch Office(s)*
Diffusion Canada, Diffusion DIMEDIA, 539 Blvd Libeau, Ville Saint Laurent, Quebec, ON H4N 1S2, Canada *Tel:* 514-336-3941 *Fax:* 514-331-3916 *E-mail:* dimedia@infopuq.uquebec.ca
*U.S. Office(s):* Diffusion USA, University Press of the South, 5500 Prytania St, Suite 421, New Orleans, LA 70115, United States *Tel:* 504-866-2791 *Fax:* 504-866-2750 *E-mail:* unprsouth@aol.com
Distributed by Harmonia Mundi Diffusion; University Press of the South (USA)
*Orders to:* Harmonia Mundi Diffusion, BP 150, 13631 Arles Cedex *Tel:* (04) 90499049 *Fax:* (04) 90499614

**Jean-Michel Place+**
3, rue Lhomond, 75005 Paris
*Tel:* (01) 44 32 05 90 *Fax:* (01) 44 32 05 91
*E-mail:* place@jmplace.com
*Web Site:* www.jmplace.com
*Key Personnel*
Dir: Jean-Michel Place
Founded: 1973
Subjects: Anthropology, Art, Literature, Literary Criticism, Essays, Philosophy, Photography, Publishing & Book Trade Reference
ISBN Prefix(es): 2-85893

**Plon-Perrin**
76, rue Bonaparte, 75006 Paris
*Tel:* (01) 44 41 35 00 *Fax:* (01) 44 41 35 02
*Web Site:* www.editions-perrin.fr
*Key Personnel*
Man Dir: Xavier de Bartillat
Foreign Rights: Sylvie Breguet
ISBN Prefix(es): 2-259

**Editions Plume+**
26, rue Racine, 75278 Paris Cedex 06
*Tel:* (01) 40 51 31 00 *Fax:* (01) 43 14 02 01
*Key Personnel*
Director: Nathalie Peillard
Editor & Publicity: Catherine Laulhere-Vigneau
Chief of Manufacturing: Julie Rouart
Author: Michel Boujut; Frederic Mitterand; Isabel Munoz
Founded: 1989
Subjects: Drama, Theater, Fashion, Film, Video, Music, Dance, Photography
ISBN Prefix(es): 2-84110; 2-908034
*Orders to:* Harmonia Mundi, Petite Route de Saint Gilles, Mas de Vert, 13200 Arles

**Poches Odile Jacob**, *imprint of* Editions Odile Jacob

**POF**, see Publications Orientalistes de France (POF)

**Point Hors Ligne Editions**
28, rue Barbet de Jouy, 75007 Paris
*Tel:* (01) 43544964 *Fax:* (01) 43253032
Subjects: Psychology, Psychiatry
ISBN Prefix(es): 2-904821

**Les Editions du Point Veterinaire+**
9, rue Alexandre, BP 233, 94702 Maisons-Alfort Cedex
*Tel:* (01) 45 17 02 61 *Fax:* (01) 45 17 02 60
*E-mail:* serviceclients@pointveterinaire.com
*Web Site:* www.pointveterinaire.com
*Key Personnel*
President: Patrick Join-Lambert
International Rights: Christine Graffard-Lenormand
Subjects: Animals, Pets, Veterinary Science
ISBN Prefix(es): 2-86326

**Editions POL+**
33, rue Saint-Andre-des-Arts, 75006 Paris
*Tel:* (01) 43 54 21 20 *Fax:* (01) 43 54 11 31
*E-mail:* pol@pol-editeur.fr
*Web Site:* www.pol-editeur.fr
*Key Personnel*
President: Paul Otchakovsky-Laurens
Founded: 1983
Subjects: Drama, Theater, Fiction, Literature, Literary Criticism, Essays, Poetry
ISBN Prefix(es): 2-86744; 2-84682
Foreign Rep(s): Gallimard/La Caravelle (Belgium); Gallimard Limitee (Canada); Gallimard/Office du Livre (Switzerland); SODIS (France)
*Orders to:* Sodis, BP 142, 77403 Lagny sur Maine Cedex

**Pole de Recherche pour l'Organisation et la Diffusion de l'Information Geographique**, see PRODIG

**Polytechnica SA+**
49, rue Hericart, 75015 Paris
*Tel:* (01) 45 78 12 92 *Fax:* (01) 45 75 05 67
*Key Personnel*
President: Daniel Loizeau
Promotion & International Rights: Isabelle Doal
Founded: 1992
Subjects: Agriculture, Biological Sciences, Chemistry, Chemical Engineering, Electronics, Electrical Engineering, Energy, Engineering (General), Health, Nutrition, Mechanical Engineering, Physical Sciences, Physics, Science (General), Technology
ISBN Prefix(es): 2-7178; 2-84054
Distributor for AIA; CIIA; INA

**Editions du Centre Pompidou+**
Centre Pompidou, 75191 Paris Cedex 04
*Tel:* (01) 44 78 12 33 *Fax:* (01) 44 78 12 05
*Web Site:* www.centrepompidou.fr
*Key Personnel*
President: Jean-Jacques Aillagon
Head of Publications & Sales: Martin Bethenod
Deputy Manager: Philippe Bidaine
Sales Manager & Foreign Rights: Benoit Collier
Founded: 1977
Subjects: Architecture & Interior Design, Art, Film, Video, Gay & Lesbian
ISBN Prefix(es): 2-85850; 2-84426
Distributed by Art Data (Great Britain); Flammarion (Canada); Flammarion Export (Greece, Turkey, Syria); Idea Books (Holland); Union

Distribution (France, Belgium & Switzerland); Yohan (Japan)
Distributor for BPI
*Foreign Rep(s):* Richard Bowen (Denmark, Finland, Norway, Sweden); Phillip Galgiani (US)
*Orders to:* Service Commercial, 75191 Paris Cedex 04

**Pratique Sante**, *imprint of* Jouvence Editions

**Editions Pratiques Automobiles**, see EPA (Editions Pratiques Automobiles)

**Le Pre-aux-clercs+**
12, ave D'ltalie, 75013 Paris
*Tel:* (01) 44 16 05 00; (01) 44 16 05 80 *Fax:* (01) 44 16 05 01
*Web Site:* www.horscollection.com
*Key Personnel*
Chairman: Jerome Talamon
Vice President: Jean Manuel Bourgois
Dir General Adjoint: Fabienne Delmote
Rights & Permissions: Frederique Polet
Founded: 1963
Subjects: Art, Biography, Fiction, Health, Nutrition, History, How-to, Human Relations, Literature, Literary Criticism, Essays, Music, Dance, Mysteries, Nonfiction (General), Poetry, Romance
ISBN Prefix(es): 2-7144; 2-84228
*Parent Company:* Masson

**Presence Africaine Editions+**
25bis, rue des Ecoles, 75005 Paris
*Tel:* (01) 43 54 13 74; (01) 43 54 15 88 *Fax:* (01) 43 25 96 67
*E-mail:* presaf@club-internet.fr
*Web Site:* www.letissu.com *Cable:* PRESAFRIC PARIS
*Key Personnel*
Dir, Publicity, Rights & Permissions: Mrs Yande Christiane Diop
Press Relations: R J Agonse
Manufacturing: D Alliot
Founded: 1947
Subjects: Fiction, History, Philosophy, Poetry, Religion - Other
ISBN Prefix(es): 2-7087
Distributed by Nord-Sud (Benelux); Zoe (Switzerland)

**Presse et Formation**, *imprint of* Les Editions du CFPJ (Centre de Formation et de Perfectionnement des Journalistes) - Sarl Presse et Formation

**Presses**, *imprint of* Presses de la Cite

**Presses de la Cite+**
Imprint of Belfond
12 Ave d'Italie, 75627 Paris Cedex 13
*Tel:* (01) 44160500 *Fax:* (01) 44160505
*Web Site:* www.pressesdelacite.com
*Telex:* preci 204 807 f *Cable:* SVENNIL PARIS
*Key Personnel*
Man Dir: Georges Leser
General Dir: Pierre Dutilleul
Founded: 1947
Subjects: Biography, Fiction, History, Mysteries, Nonfiction (General), Romance, Science Fiction, Fantasy, Family Saga, Horror, Humor, Mystery & Detective, Thriller, Science Fiction
ISBN Prefix(es): 2-258
Total Titles: 300 Print
*Parent Company:* Havas
*Ultimate Parent Company:* Vivendi
Imprints: Presses; Solar

**Presses de la Renaissance+**
Subsidiary of Havas

12, Ave d'Italie, 75627 Paris Cedex 13
*Tel:* (01) 44 16 05 00 *Fax:* (01) 44 16 05 64
*Web Site:* www.presses-renaissance.fr
*Key Personnel*
Man Dir: Pierre Dutilleul
Publication Dir: Alain Noel *Tel:* (01) 44 16 05 96
    *E-mail:* alainoel@aol.com
Rights Manager: Delphina Ribouchon *Tel:* (01) 44 08 84 35 *Fax:* (01) 44 08 84 05
Founded: 1997
Subjects: Biography, Philosophy, Spirituality, Novels, Documents & Testimonials
ISBN Prefix(es): 2-85616; 2-7509
Total Titles: 40 Print
*Ultimate Parent Company:* Vivendi

**Presses de la Sorbonne Nouvelle/PSN**
Universite Paris III, 8 rue de la Sorbonne, 75005 Paris
*Tel:* (01) 40 46 48 02 *Fax:* (01) 40 46 48 04
*E-mail:* psn@univ-paris3.fr
*Web Site:* www.univ-paris3.fr/recherche/psn/
*Key Personnel*
General Dir: Pierre Vilar
Founded: 1982
Subjects: Drama, Theater, History, Language Arts, Linguistics, Literature, Literary Criticism, Essays
ISBN Prefix(es): 2-87854; 2-903019
Number of titles published annually: 20 Print
Total Titles: 20 Print
Distributor for Cid (France)
*Bookshop(s):* CID, 131 Blvd St Michel, 75005 Paris, Contact: Michel Zumkir *Tel:* (01) 43544745 *Fax:* (01) 43548073 *E-mail:* cid@msh-paris.fr

**Presses de l'Ecole Nationale des Ponts et Chaussees+**
Unit of Ponts Formation Edition SA
28, rue des Saints-Peres, 75343 Paris Cedex 07
*Tel:* (01) 44 58 27 40 *Fax:* (01) 44 58 27 44
*Web Site:* www.enpc.fr
*Key Personnel*
Dir: Guy Coronio *Tel:* (01) 44 58 24 60
    *E-mail:* coronio@enpc.fr
Marketing: Laurent Deschryver *Tel:* (01) 44 58 28 32 *E-mail:* laurent.deschryver@mail.enpc.fr
Founded: 1977
Specialize in scientific, technical & professional subjects.
Membership(s): Syndicat National de l'Edition.
Subjects: Civil Engineering, Computer Science, Earth Sciences, Real Estate, Transportation
ISBN Prefix(es): 2-85978
Total Titles: 200 Print; 2 CD-ROM
Distributed by Geodif

**Presses de Sciences Politiques+**
44 rue du Four, 75006 Paris
*Tel:* (01) 44 39 39 60 *Fax:* (01) 45 48 04 41
*E-mail:* info.presses@sciences-po.fr
*Web Site:* www.sciences.po.fr/edition/
*Telex:* Scipol 201002 F
*Key Personnel*
Executive Dir: Marie-Genevieve Vandesande
    *E-mail:* mariegenevieve.vandesande@sciences-po.fr
Secretary: Fabien Crespin *Tel:* (01) 44 39 39 72
    *E-mail:* fabien.crespin@sciences-po.fr
Founded: 1975
Subjects: Economics, Government, Political Science, History, Social Sciences, Sociology
ISBN Prefix(es): 2-7246

**Les Presses de Taize**, *imprint of* Ateliers et Presses de Taize

**Les Presses d'Ile-de-France Sarl+**
54 Ave Jean-Jaures, 75940 Paris Cedex 19
*Tel:* (01) 44 52 37 24 *Fax:* (01) 42 38 09 87

*E-mail:* contact@presses-idf.fr
*Web Site:* www.scouts-france.fr
*Key Personnel*
Man Dir: Pierre Tremeau
Manager: Bernard Le Roux
Founded: 1929
Subjects: Crafts, Games, Hobbies, Music, Dance, Outdoor Recreation, Religion - Catholic
ISBN Prefix(es): 2-7088

**Les Presses du Management+**
41, rue Greneta, 75002 Paris
*Tel:* (01) 53 00 11 71 *Fax:* (01) 53 00 10 08
*Key Personnel*
Contact: Jacques Descubes Marie
Founded: 1989
Subjects: Business, Career Development, Economics, How-to, Management, Marketing, Psychology, Psychiatry, Self-Help
ISBN Prefix(es): 2-87845
*Parent Company:* Editions Michel Lafon
Imprints: Guide Pratique; Turbo
*Orders to:* 7, rue de Malte, 75011 Paris

**Presses-Pocket**, see Presses de la Cite

**Presses Universitaires de Caen**
14032 Caen Cedex
*Tel:* (02) 31 56 62 20 *Fax:* (02) 31 56 62 25
*E-mail:* puc@mrsh.unicaen.fr
*Web Site:* www.unicaen.fr/mrsh/puc
*Key Personnel*
Dir, University Press: Michel Zuinghedau
Founded: 1984
Subjects: Accounting, Antiques, Biological Sciences, Geography, Geology, History, Language Arts, Linguistics, Literature, Literary Criticism, Essays, Philosophy, Social Sciences, Sociology
ISBN Prefix(es): 2-84133; 2-905461

**Presses Universitaires de France (PUF)+**
6, Ave Reille, 75685 Paris Cedex 14
*Tel:* (01) 58 10 31 00 *Fax:* (01) 58 10 31 82
*E-mail:* puf.com@puf.com
*Web Site:* www.puf.com
*Key Personnel*
President & Dir General: Michel Prigent *Tel:* (01) 53 10 00 07 *Fax:* (01) 53 10 41 79
Dir: Eric Amaudry *Tel:* (01) 43 26 7741
    *Fax:* (01) 46 33 21 94; Bruno Clerc *Tel:* (01) 44 41 17 20 *Fax:* (01) 44 33 61 21
Sales Dir: Jean-Pierre Giband *Tel:* (01) 60 87 30 00 *Fax:* (01) 60 79 20 45
Technical Dir: Bruno Clerc
Dir, Development: Dominique Morel *Tel:* (01) 55 02 20 61
Publicity, Advertising: Alain Papillaud *Tel:* (01) 44 41 39 39 *Fax:* (01) 43 54 78 87
Foreign Rights: Marion Colas *E-mail:* colas@puf.com
Press: Dominique Reymond *Tel:* (01) 58 10 31 80
Editorial: Corinne Decalonne; Catherine DeLage
Founded: 1921
Administration & Editorial offices are located at the above main address; Public Relations & Publicity departments are at 90 Blvd St-Germain, 75005 Paris.
Subjects: Art, Biography, Engineering (General), Geography, Geology, Government, Political Science, History, Human Relations, Law, Medicine, Nursing, Dentistry, Music, Dance, Philosophy, Psychology, Psychiatry, Religion - Other, Social Sciences, Sociology
ISBN Prefix(es): 2-13
*Bookshop(s):* Librairie generale des PUF, 49, Bd Saint Michel, 75005 Paris, Contact: Dominique Morel *Tel:* (01) 44 41 81 20 *Fax:* (01) 43 54 64 81 (Under Major Booksellers); La Pochotheque, 17 rue Soufflot, 75005 Paris *Tel:* (01) 43267741 *Fax:* (01) 46332196

*Orders to:* 14 Ave du Bois de l'Epine, BP 90, 91003 Evry Cedex, Contact: Jean-Pierre Giband *Tel:* (01) 60 87 30 00 *Fax:* (01) 60 79 20 45

**Presses Universitaires de Grenoble+**
1041, rue de Residences, 38400 Saint-Martin-d'Heres 9
Mailing Address: BP 47, 38040 Grenoble Cedex 9
*Tel:* (04) 76 82 56 51; (04) 76 82 56 52 *Fax:* (04) 76 82 78 35
*E-mail:* pug@pug.fr
*Web Site:* www.pug.fr
*Telex:* Unisog 980910
*Key Personnel*
General Manager: Bernard Wirbel
    *E-mail:* bernard.wirbel@pug.fr
Editorial Manager: Rene Bourgeois
    *Fax:* rene.bourgeois@pug.fr
Finance Manager: Corine Desbenoit
    *E-mail:* corine.desbenoit@pug.fr
Sales Manager: Barbara Muller *E-mail:* barbara.muller@pug.fr
Manufacturing: Muriel Girard *E-mail:* muriel.girard@pug.fr
Founded: 1972
Subjects: Accounting, Chemistry, Chemical Engineering, Communications, Economics, History, Language Arts, Linguistics, Law, Literature, Literary Criticism, Essays, Management, Marketing, Mathematics, Psychology, Psychiatry, Social Sciences, Sociology, Sports, Athletics, Economics, Europe, French Language, Political Science
ISBN Prefix(es): 2-7061
Number of titles published annually: 45 Print
Total Titles: 1,000 Print
Imprints: PUG
*Orders to:* Sofedis, 11 rue Soufflot, 75005 Paris
    *Tel:* (01) 53 10 25 26

**Presses Universitaires de Lyon+**
80, Blvd de la Croix-Rousse, BP 4371, 69242 Lyon Cedex 04
*Tel:* (04) 78 29 39 39 *Fax:* (04) 78 29 39 41
*Web Site:* sites.univ-lyon2.fr/pul
*Key Personnel*
Man Dir: Andre Pelletier *E-mail:* andre.pelletier@univ-lyon2.fr
Sales & Marketing: Norbert Fauvet
    *E-mail:* norbert.fauvet@univ-lyon2.fr
Founded: 1976
Membership(s): Syndicat National de l'Edition
Subjects: Economics, Government, Political Science, History, Human Relations, Language Arts, Linguistics, Law, Literature, Literary Criticism, Essays, Management
ISBN Prefix(es): 2-7297
Distributor for Editions W a Macon; Editions Lyonnaises d'Art et d'Histoire a'Lyon

**Presses Universitaires de Nancy+**
42-44 ave de la Liberation, 54014 Nancy Cedex
Mailing Address: BP 3347, 54014 Nancy Cedex
*Tel:* (03) 83 96 84 30 *Fax:* (03) 83 96 84 39
*E-mail:* pun@univ-nancy2.fr
*Web Site:* www.univ-nancy2.fr
*Key Personnel*
Chairman: Jean-Marie Bonnet
Man Dir: Alain Trognon
General Manager: Jeanne Weill
Editorial Manager: Daniele Silvy-Leligois
Sales: Sophie Izorche
Publicity, Rights & Permissions: Daniele Silvy-Leligois
Founded: 1976
Subjects: Communications, Drama, Theater, Economics, Education, Geography, Geology, Government, Political Science, History, Language Arts, Linguistics, Law, Literature, Literary Criticism, Essays, Philosophy, Psychology, Psychi-

atry, Religion - Other, Social Sciences, Sociology
ISBN Prefix(es): 2-86480
*Associate Companies:* Editions Serpenoise, BP 89, 57140 Metz-Woippy
Imprints: Annales de l'Est; Editions Humblot; Le Parvis des Arts
Warehouse: Sodis-128, ave de Lattre de Tassigny, 77400 Lagny-Sur-Marne
*Orders to:* Sofedis, 29 rue Saint-Sulpice, 75006 Paris

**Presses Universitaires de Strasbourg**
Palais Universitaire, 9, place de l'Universite, 67084 Strasbourg Cedex
*Tel:* (03) 88 25 97 21 *Fax:* (03) 88 35 65 23
*E-mail:* info@pu-strasourg.com
*Web Site:* www.pu-strasbourg.com
*Key Personnel*
President: Lucien Braun
Founded: 1920
Subjects: Art, History, Literature, Literary Criticism, Essays, Philosophy, Social Sciences, Sociology
ISBN Prefix(es): 2-86820

**Presses Universitaires du Septentrion+**
Rue du Barreau, 59654 Villeneuve d'Ascq, Cedex
Mailing Address: BP 199, 59654 Villeneuve d'Ascq, Cedex
*Tel:* (03) 20 41 66 80 *Fax:* (03) 20 41 66 90
*E-mail:* septentrion@septentrion.com
*Web Site:* www.septentrion.com
*Key Personnel*
Editorial & Production: Jerome Vaillant
Sales, Publicity, Rights & Permissions: Jean-Gabriel Caby
Founded: 1971
Subjects: History, Language Arts, Linguistics, Law, Literature, Literary Criticism, Essays, Philosophy, Psychology, Psychiatry, Social Sciences, Sociology
ISBN Prefix(es): 2-284; 2-85939; 2-86531; 2-907170

**Privat-Garnier**, *imprint of* Dunod Editeur

**PRODIG+**
191, rue Saint-Jacques, 75005 Paris
*Tel:* (01) 44 32 14 81; (01) 42 34 56 21 *Fax:* (01) 43 29 63 83
*E-mail:* prodig@univ-paris1.fr
*Web Site:* prodig.univ-paris1.fr/umr
*Key Personnel*
Dir: Jean Louis Chaleard *E-mail:* jl.chaleard@wanadoo.fr
Contact: Beatrice Velard *E-mail:* bvelard@univ-paris1.fr
Founded: 1947
Subjects: Geography, Geology, Library & Information Sciences
ISBN Prefix(es): 2-901560
*Parent Company:* Centre national de la recherche scientifique (CNRS)
*Associate Companies:* Universite de Paris One; Universite de Paris Four; Universite de Paris Seven

**Propos 2 Editions+**
MJC, Allee de Provence, 04100 Manosque
*Tel:* (04) 92 73 08 94 *Fax:* (04) 92 73 08 94
*E-mail:* ProposdeC@aol.com
*Web Site:* www.propos2editions.net
*Key Personnel*
Publications Dir: Samuel Autexier
Founded: 1993
Revue d art et de Poesie.
Subjects: Art, Poetry
ISBN Prefix(es): 2-912144

**Editions Prosveta**
BP 12, 83601 Frejus Cedex
*Tel:* (04) 94 19 33 33 *Fax:* (04) 94 19 33 34
*E-mail:* international@prosvesta.com
*Web Site:* www.prosveta.com
*Telex:* 970809F
*Key Personnel*
President: Marcel Cieutat
Author: Mikhael Aivanhov
Founded: 1976
Subjects: Education, Philosophy, Religion - Other
ISBN Prefix(es): 2-85566
*U.S. Office(s):* Prosveta USA, PO Box 49614, Los Angeles, CA 90049, United States

**PSI**, *imprint of* Dunod Editeur

**PUB**, see Presses Universitaires de Bordeaux (PUB)

**Publi-Fusion+**
Village Artisanal de Regourd, 46000 Cahors
*Tel:* (05) 65220303 *Fax:* (05) 65220322
*E-mail:* publi-fusion@wanadoo.fr
*Key Personnel*
Contact: Jean-Claude Delmas
Founded: 1987
Subjects: Automotive, Literature, Literary Criticism, Essays
ISBN Prefix(es): 2-907265
Total Titles: 43 Print

**Publi Union**, *imprint of* Editions Village Mondial

**Editions Publications de l'Ecole Moderne Francaise sa (PEMF)+**
Parc d'activites de l'Argile, 06376 Mouans Sartoux Cedex
*Tel:* (04) 92 28 42 84 *Fax:* (04) 92 28 42 99
*Key Personnel*
Man Dir & Editorial: Robert Poitrenaud
Man Dir: Norbert Jouve
Founded: 1986
ISBN Prefix(es): 2-87785; 2-84526

**Publications de l'Universite de Rouen**
One, rue Lavoisier, 76821 Mont-Saint-Aignan Cedex
*Tel:* (02) 35 14 63 43; (02) 35 14 65 31 *Fax:* (02) 35 14 63 47
*Web Site:* www.univ-rouen.fr
*Key Personnel*
Communications: Patricia Lanoe *E-mail:* patricia.lanoe@univ-rouen.fr
Founded: 1968
Subjects: Geography, Geology, History, Law, Literature, Literary Criticism, Essays, Psychology, Psychiatry
ISBN Prefix(es): 2-87775
*Orders to:* CID, 131 Blvd St-Michel, 75005 Paris

**Publications Orientalistes de France (POF)+**
14, Ave du Garric, 15000 Aurillac
*Tel:* (04) 71 43 23 78 *Fax:* (04) 71 43 23 78
*E-mail:* sieffert@pofjapon.com
*Web Site:* www.pofjapon.com
*Key Personnel*
Dir: Simone Sieffert
Founded: 1973
Subjects: Drama, Theater, History, Language Arts, Linguistics, Literature, Literary Criticism, Essays, Music, Dance, Poetry, Social Sciences, Sociology
ISBN Prefix(es): 2-7169
*Orders to:* Distique, 5, rue du Mal Leclerc, 28600 Luisant

**Publisud Editions+**
15 rue des Cinq-diamants, 75013 Paris
*Tel:* (01) 45 80 78 50 *Fax:* (01) 45 89 94 15
*E-mail:* publisud@compuserve.com; edipublisud@wanadoo.fr

*Key Personnel*
Man Editor: Marybel Boix
Founded: 1980
ISBN Prefix(es): 2-86600

**PUF**, see Presses Universitaires de France (PUF)

**PUG**, *imprint of* Presses Universitaires de Grenoble

**Editions du Puits Fleuri+**
22 Ave Fontainebleau, 77850 Hericy
*Tel:* (01) 64 23 61 46 *Fax:* (01) 64 23 69 42
*E-mail:* puitsfleuri@wanadoo.fr
*Web Site:* www.puitsfleuri.com
*Key Personnel*
Literary Dir: Emile Guchet
Founded: 1981
Subjects: How-to, Law
ISBN Prefix(es): 2-86739
Imprints: Le Conseiller Juridique Pour Tous
*Showroom(s):* Amphora, 14 rue de l'Odeon, 75006 Paris

**PUM Toulouse**, *imprint of* Presses Universitaires du Mirail

**PUS**, see Presses Universitaires du Septentrion

**PYC Edition+**
16-18 Pl de La Chapelle, 75018 Paris
*Tel:* (01) 53 26 48 00 *Fax:* (01) 53 26 48 01
*E-mail:* info@pyc.fr
*Web Site:* www.pyc.fr
*Key Personnel*
Man Dir: Pierre Benichou
Founded: 1934
Subjects: Energy, Mechanical Engineering
ISBN Prefix(es): 2-85330; 2-911008; 2-84651

**Editions Pygmalion+**
70 Ave de Breteuil, 75007 Paris
*Tel:* (01) 45 67 40 77 *Fax:* (01) 47 34 51 52
*E-mail:* pygmalion@pygmalion.fr
*Key Personnel*
General Manager: Gilles Haeri
Sales & Foreign Rights: Sylvie Goguel
Founded: 1974
Subjects: Archaeology, Art, Biography, Fiction, History, Literature, Literary Criticism, Essays, Parapsychology
ISBN Prefix(es): 2-85704
Total Titles: 500 Print
*Warehouse:* Union Distribution, 106 rue Petit Leroy, Cherilly-La rue, 94152 Rungis Cedex
*Distribution Center:* Flammarion, 26 rue Racine, 75278 Paris Cedex 06, Marketing Dir: Patrick Du Fant *Tel:* (01) 40513100

**Editions des Quatre-Vents**, *imprint of* Editions l'Avant-Scene Theatre

**Quillet**, *imprint of* Le Livre de Paris

**Radio**, *imprint of* Dunod Editeur

**Rageot Editeur**, *imprint of* Editions Hatier SA

**Rageot Editeur+**
6, rue d'Assas, 75006 Paris
*Tel:* (01) 45 48 07 31 *Fax:* (01) 42 22 68 01
*E-mail:* rageotediteur@editions-hatier.fr
*Web Site:* www.rageotediteur.fr
*Key Personnel*
Dir: Caroline Westberg
Manager: Arnaud Nourry
Founded: 1941

ISBN Prefix(es): 2-7002
*Orders to:* Librairie Hatier SA, 8 rue d'Assas, 75006 Paris *Tel:* (01) 30 66 20 66 *Fax:* (01) 49 54 49 71 *Web Site:* www.editions-hatier.com

**Editions Ramsay**
60, rue Saint Andres des Arts, 75006 Paris
*Tel:* (01) 53 10 02 80 *Fax:* (01) 53 10 02 88
*Key Personnel*
Man Dir: Jean-Claude Gawsewitch
Rights & Permissions: Zeline Guena
Founded: 1976
Subjects: Drama, Theater, Fiction, History, Literature, Literary Criticism, Essays, Nonfiction (General)
ISBN Prefix(es): 2-84114

**Realisations pour l'Enseignement Multilingue International (REMI)**
70, rue du Theatre, 75015 Paris
*Tel:* (01) 45 75 78 49 *Fax:* (01) 45 79 06 66
*Key Personnel*
Man Dir: Mrs D Holtzer
Founded: 1966
ISBN Prefix(es): 2-85134

**Refclim**, *imprint of* SEDIT (Societe d'Etudes et de Diffusion des Industries Thermiques et Aerauliques)

**References cf**
26340 Saint Nazaire le Desert
*Tel:* (04) 75 27 52 59 *Fax:* (04) 75 27 52 59
*Key Personnel*
Publisher: Bernard Dermineur
Founded: 1984
Subjects: Art, Genealogy, History, Library & Information Sciences
ISBN Prefix(es): 2-908302
Total Titles: 20 Print; 3 CD-ROM
Imprints: CF
*Bookshop(s):* Librairie la Stravaganza, 32 rue Traversiere, 75012 Paris *Tel:* (01) 43 45 80 83 *Fax:* (01) 43 45 50 96

**REMI**, see Realisations pour l'Enseignement Multilingue International (REMI)

**Les Editions Albert Rene+**
26, Ave Victor Hugo, 75116 Paris
*Tel:* (01) 45 00 41 41 *Fax:* (01) 40 67 95 12
*E-mail:* rene.cominfo@editions-albert-rene.com
*Web Site:* www.editions-albert-rene.com
*Telex:* 613160 F
*Key Personnel*
Dir: Sylvie Uderz
Founded: 1979
Subjects: Humor
ISBN Prefix(es): 2-86497
Distributed by Hachette
*Orders to:* Les Presses de la Cite, 8 rue Garanciere, 75006 Paris

**Editions Revue EPS+**
11, Ave of Tremblay, 75571 Paris Cedex 12
*Tel:* (01) 41 74 82 82 *Fax:* (01) 43 98 37 38
*E-mail:* revue@revue-eps.com
*Web Site:* www.revue-eps.com
*Key Personnel*
President: Jean Eisenbeis
Subjects: Education, Sports, Athletics
ISBN Prefix(es): 2-86713

**Revue Espaces et Societes+**
Universite de Toulouse-Le-Mirail, 5, allee Antonio-Machado, 31058 Toulouse Cedex 9
*Tel:* (05) 61 50 35 65 *Fax:* (05) 61 50 49 61
*E-mail:* espacesetsocietes@msh-paris.fr
*Web Site:* www.espacesetsocietes.msh-paris.fr

*Key Personnel*
Editor-in-Chief: Maurice Blanc *E-mail:* blanc@umb.u-strasbg.fr
Editorial: Joelle Jacquin *E-mail:* jjacquin@espacesetsocietes.com
Founded: 1968
2 or 3 installments/year in 16 x 24 cm format (about 600 pages/year).
Subjects: Anthropology, Environmental Studies, Social Sciences, Sociology
Distributed by L' Harmattan

**Revue Noire**
8 rue Cels, 75014 Paris
*Tel:* (01) 43 20 92 00 *Fax:* (01) 43 22 92 60
*E-mail:* redaction@revuenoire.com
*Web Site:* www.revuenoire.com
*Key Personnel*
President: Michelle Rakotoson
Dir, Publications & Editor: Jeau Loup Pivin *Tel:* (01) 43 20 78 38
Editor: Simon Njami *Tel:* (01) 43 20 79 56
Distribution & Web Dir: N'Gone Fall *Tel:* (01) 43 20 82 34
Art Dir: Pascal Martin St Leon *Tel:* (01) 43 20 83 02
Editor Member: Bruno Tilliette
Administration Dir: Gwendal Vaillant *Tel:* (01) 43 20 80 07 *E-mail:* order@revuenoire.com
Founded: 1991
Subjects: African American Studies, Architecture & Interior Design, Art, Fashion, Literature, Literary Criticism, Essays, Music, Dance, Photography, Poetry
ISBN Prefix(es): 2-909571
*Parent Company:* Revue Noire Sarl
Distributed by Editions Hazan Distribution (France, Belgium, Switzerland, Canada)
Distributor for DAP

**Yves Riviere Editeur+**
117 rue Vieille-du-Temple, 75003 Paris
*Tel:* (01) 42 74 77 84 *Fax:* (01) 42 78 12 65
*E-mail:* yvestri@mail.club.internet.fr
Founded: 1971
Specialize in catalogues & reference books, art posters & prints signed & numbered.
Subjects: Art
ISBN Prefix(es): 2-85666
Total Titles: 75 Print

**Le Robert**
27, rue de la Glaciere, 75640 Paris Cedex 13
*Tel:* (01) 45 87 43 00 *Fax:* (01) 45 35 76 06
*Web Site:* www.lerobert.com
*Telex:* Dicorob 240763 F
*Key Personnel*
President, Man Dir: Bertrand Eveno
Publicity: Denis A Fasse
Technical Manager: Jacques Pierre
Export Manager: Michel Terrier
Founded: 1951
ISBN Prefix(es): 2-85036; 2-84902

**Editions du Rocher**
6 pl St-Sulpice, 75006 Paris
*Tel:* (01) 40 46 54 00 *Fax:* (01) 46 34 64 26
*E-mail:* info@editionsdurocher.net
*Key Personnel*
President: Jean-Paul Bertrand *E-mail:* jpb@post.club-internet.fr
Subjects: History, Literature, Literary Criticism, Essays, Religion - Other, Social Sciences, Sociology, Humanities, Human Sciences, Leisure
ISBN Prefix(es): 2-268

**Editions Rombaldi SA**
58 rue Jean Bleuzen, 92178 Vanves Cedex
*Tel:* (01) 41 23 65 00 *Fax:* (01) 46 45 34 42
*Telex:* 631 253

*Key Personnel*
President: Etienne Vendroux
Commercial Dir & Production Manager: Henri Kaufman
Commercial Dir: Francis Petit
Founded: 1920
Subjects: Cookery, Crafts, Games, Hobbies, Humor
ISBN Prefix(es): 2-231

**Guide Rosenwald**
10 rue Vineuse, 75784 Paris Cedex 16
*Tel:* (01) 44 30 81 00 *Fax:* (01) 44 30 81 11
*E-mail:* info@rosenwald.com
*Web Site:* www.rosenwald.com
*Key Personnel*
Editor: Afif Ben Yedder *E-mail:* benyedder@icpublications.com
Founded: 1887
Subjects: Health, Nutrition, Medicine, Nursing, Dentistry
ISBN Prefix(es): 2-907749
Number of titles published annually: 5 Print; 5 CD-ROM; 5 Online
Total Titles: 20 Print; 20 CD-ROM; 20 Online
*Parent Company:* I C Publications

**Editions Roudil SA**
8, rue des Ecoles, 75005 Paris
*Tel:* (01) 43 54 47 97 *Fax:* (01) 43 54 06 97
*Key Personnel*
Man Dir: Henry Roudil
Founded: 1954
Subjects: Fiction, History, Philosophy
ISBN Prefix(es): 2-85044

**Editions du Rouergue+**
Parc Saint-Joseph, BP 3522, 12035 Rodez Cedex 9
*Tel:* (05) 65.77.73.70 *Fax:* (05) 65.77.73.71
*E-mail:* info@lerouergue.com
*Web Site:* www.lerouergue.com
*Key Personnel*
Contact: Danielle Dastugue; Anne Marcy
Founded: 1986
Subjects: Cookery, Fiction, Gardening, Plants, Health, Nutrition, How-to, Romance, Wine & Spirits
ISBN Prefix(es): 2-84156; 2-905209

**Editions Saint-Michel SA+**
Fougerolles, La Reserve de Gamillon Saint-Michel-de-Boulogne, 07200 Saint-Michel-de-Boulogne
*Tel:* (04) 75 87 10 50 *Fax:* (04) 75 87 10 61
*Key Personnel*
Contact: Guy Dupuis
Subjects: Astrology, Occult, Behavioral Sciences, Medicine, Nursing, Dentistry, Parapsychology
ISBN Prefix(es): 2-902450

**Editions Saint-Paul SA+**
3, rue de la Porte de Buc, 78000 Versailles
Mailing Address: BP 652, 78006 Versailles
*Tel:* (01) 39 67 16 00 *Fax:* (01) 30 21 41 95
*Key Personnel*
Man Dir: M Lerozier
Dir, Religous Edition: M Larive
Founded: 1879
Subjects: Philosophy, Religion - Other, Theology
ISBN Prefix(es): 2-85049
Total Titles: 150 Print
Subsidiaries: Editions Saint-Paul SA
Distributed by CERF

**Editions Salvator Sarl+**
103, rue Notre-Dame-des-Champs, 75006 Paris
*Tel:* (01) 53 10 38 38 *Fax:* (01) 53 10 38 39
*E-mail:* salvator.editions@wanadoo.fr
Founded: 1924

Subjects: Human Relations, Religion - Other
ISBN Prefix(es): 2-7067

**Salvy Editeur+**
33 rue Saint Andre des Arts, 75006 Paris
*Tel:* (01) 43 25 74 40 *Fax:* (01) 46 33 56 21
*Key Personnel*
President: Gerard-Julien Salvy
Founded: 1989
Subjects: Literature, Literary Criticism, Essays
ISBN Prefix(es): 2-905899

**Editions Sand et Tchou SA**
6 rue du Mail, 75002 Paris
*Tel:* (01) 44 55 37 50 *Fax:* (01) 40 20 99 74
*E-mail:* info@editions-menges.com
*Key Personnel*
Man Dir: Carl van Eiszner
Rights & Permissions: Isabelle de Tinguy
Founded: 1979
Subjects: Astrology, Occult, Biography, Fiction, Health, Nutrition, How-to, Music, Dance, Psychology, Psychiatry, Social Sciences, Sociology
ISBN Prefix(es): 2-7107
Subsidiaries: Editions Menges

**Editions Sang de la Terre+**
62, rue Blanche, 75009 Paris
*Tel:* (01) 42 82 08 16 *Fax:* (01) 48 74 14 88
*E-mail:* editeur@sangdelaterre.com
*Web Site:* www.sangdelaterre.com
*Key Personnel*
Publications Dir: Dominique Bigourdan
Editor: Karine Reysset
Founded: 1986
Subjects: Agriculture, Animals, Pets, Cookery, Crafts, Games, Hobbies, Environmental Studies, Gardening, Plants, Health, Nutrition, How-to
ISBN Prefix(es): 2-86985
Imprints: Bornemann
Subsidiaries: 670 Bornemann

**Sante Spiritualite**, *imprint of* Jouvence Editions

**Sarment/Editions du Jubile+**
8 Villa Poirier, 75015 Paris
*Tel:* (01) 53 58 06 07 *Fax:* (01) 53 58 06 08
*E-mail:* contact@editionsdujubile.com
*Web Site:* www.editionsdujubile.com
*Key Personnel*
Dir: Jean-Claude Didelot
Foreign Rights: Marc Moingeon
Founded: 1980
Subjects: Religion - Catholic
ISBN Prefix(es): 2-86679
Number of titles published annually: 30 Print

**Sauramps Medical+**
11 blvd Henri IV, 34000 Montpellier
*Tel:* (04) 67 63 68 80 *Fax:* (04) 67 52 59 05
*E-mail:* sauramps.medical@livres-medicaux.com
*Web Site:* www.livres-medicaux.com
*Key Personnel*
Man Dir: Dominique Torreilles
Founded: 1985
Subjects: Medicine, Nursing, Dentistry, Gynecology-Obstetrics, Orthopaedic Surgery, Radiology
ISBN Prefix(es): 2-905030; 2-84023
Number of titles published annually: 35 Print
Total Titles: 500 Print
Distributed by Lidel (Portugal); SODIS (France); Somabec (Canada); Vivendi (Belgium)
*Bookshop(s):* Librairie Sauramps Medical (under Major Booksellers); 30, rue Godefroy Cavaignac, 75011 Paris, Contact: George Lauret *Tel:* (01) 40092771 *Fax:* (01) 40038071

**Editions Scala+**
Passage Lhomme, 26 rue de Charonne, 75011 Paris
*Tel:* (01) 49 29 42 25 *Fax:* (01) 49 29 99 33
*E-mail:* editions.scala@wanadoo.fr
*Key Personnel*
Contact: Chantal Desmazieres
Founded: 1980
Subjects: Antiques, Art
ISBN Prefix(es): 2-86656
Total Titles: 110 Print

**SEDIT (Societe d'Etudes et de Diffusion des Industries Thermiques et Aerauliques)**
Domaine de St-Paul, 102 Route de Limours - Bat 16_, 78471 St-Remy-les-Chevreuse Cedex
*Tel:* (01) 30 85 20 10 *Fax:* (01) 30 85 20 38
*E-mail:* sedit@costic.com
*Web Site:* www.costic.com
*Key Personnel*
Contact: Armel Jegou; Odette Guibert
ISBN Prefix(es): 2-236
Imprints: Refclim; Climapoche

**Editions Seghers**
Imprint of Editions Robert Laffont
24 Ave Marceau, 75008 Paris
*Tel:* (01) 53 67 14 00 *Fax:* (01) 53 67 14 14
*Web Site:* www.laffont.fr/seghers
*Key Personnel*
President & Man Dir: Leonello Brandolini
Literary Manager: Alain Beiastein
Rights & Permissions: Beatrix Vernet *Tel:* (01) 53 67 14 89 *E-mail:* bvernet@robert.laffont.fr
Founded: 1944
Subjects: Poetry
ISBN Prefix(es): 2-232
*Orders to:* Inter Forum, 46 route de Sermaires, BP 11, 45337 Nalesherbes Cedex *Tel:* (02) 38 32 71 00

**Selection du Reader's Digest SA**
5/7 Ave Louis Pasteur, 92220 Bagneux
Mailing Address: BP 101, 92225 Bagneux Cedex
*Tel:* (01) 46748484 *Fax:* (01) 46748580
*E-mail:* serviceclients@readersdigest.tm.fr
*Web Site:* www.selectionclic.com/srd/; www.rd.com/international/shared/?countryid=fr
*Cable:* Readigest Paris
*Key Personnel*
President & Dir General: Patricia Killen
Founded: 1947
Subjects: Architecture & Interior Design, Art, Economics, Environmental Studies, Fiction, History, How-to, Medicine, Nursing, Dentistry, Science (General), Social Sciences, Sociology, Technology, Travel
ISBN Prefix(es): 2-7098

**Editions Selection J Jacobs SA+**
66 rue Falguiere, 75015 Paris
Subjects: Art, How-to, Technology
ISBN Prefix(es): 2-7174

**Le Seneve**, *imprint of* Editions Buchet-Chastel Pierre Zech Editeur

**Sepia Editions**
6 Ave du Gouverneur General Binger, 94100 St-Maur
*Tel:* (01) 43 97 22 14 *Fax:* (01) 43 97 32 62
*E-mail:* sepia@editions-sepia.com
*Web Site:* www.editions-sepia.com
*Key Personnel*
Dir: Patrick Merand
Founded: 1987
Specialize in Africa.
Subjects: Archaeology, Art, Ethnicity, Fiction, Foreign Countries, Social Sciences, Sociology
ISBN Prefix(es): 2-84280; 2-907888

**Editions de Septembre+**
34 rue de l'Abbe-Groult, 75015 Paris
*Tel:* (01) 53 68 96 20 *Fax:* (01) 53 68 96 21
*Key Personnel*
Dir: Christophe Roux; Jean-Luc Simonin
Editor: Rodolphe Fouano; Alain Vuyet
Founded: 1990
Membership(s): SNE.
Subjects: Biography, Fiction, Humor, Journalism,
   Literature, Literary Criticism, Essays, Science
   (General), Social Sciences, Sociology
ISBN Prefix(es): 2-87914
Imprints: l'Europeenne; Lignes De Vie
Divisions: Atelier Graphique des Editions de
   Septembre; Septembre Communication

**Sequences,** *imprint of* Sarl Editions Jean Grassin

**Editions Le Serpent a Plumes**
20 rue des Petits Champs, 75002 Paris
*Tel:* (01) 55 35 95 85 *Fax:* (01) 42 61 17 46
*E-mail:* contact@serpentaplumes.com
*Key Personnel*
Dir, Editorial: Pierre Astier
Sales: Xavier Belrose
Production: Sylvia Lohr
Rights: Laure Pecher
Founded: 1988
Subjects: Fiction, Foreign Countries, Literature,
   Literary Criticism, Essays
ISBN Prefix(es): 2-908957; 2-84261
Distributed by CDE; Foliade-La Caravelle; Galli-
   mard Export; Gallimard Ltee; Office du Livre;
   SODIS

**Servedit+**
15, rue Victor-Cousin, 75005 Paris
*Tel:* (01) 44 41 49 30 *Fax:* (01) 43 25 77 41
*E-mail:* servedit@wanadoo.fr
*Key Personnel*
President: Alain Jauson
ISBN Prefix(es): 2-86877

**Service des Publications Scientifiques du
   Museum National d 'Histoire Naturelle**
57 rue Cuvier, 75231 Paris Cedex 05
*Tel:* (01) 40 79 48 38 *Fax:* (01) 40 79 38 40
*E-mail:* diff.pub@mnhn.fr
*Web Site:* www.mnhn.fr/publication
*Key Personnel*
Dir: Philippe Bouchet
Founded: 1802
Subjects: Earth Sciences, Environmental Studies,
   Natural History, Also bilingual
ISBN Prefix(es): 2-85653; 2-86515
Number of titles published annually: 314 Print
*Warehouse:* Bibliotheque Centrale du Museum
   National d, 38 rue Geoffroy, Saint Hilaire,
   75005 Paris
*Orders to:* Universal Book Services, Dr Back-
   huys, PO Box 321, 2300 AH Leiden, Nether-
   lands (Only for the memoires collection/series,
   except geology)

**Service Hydrographique et Oceanographique
   de la Marine (SHOM)**
3 avenue Octave Greard, Paris 7eme
Mailing Address: BP 5, 00307 Armees
*Tel:* (01) 44 38 41 16
*E-mail:* cartespa@shom.fr
*Web Site:* www.shom.fr
*Key Personnel*
Contact: Gilles Bessero *E-mail:* gilles.bessero@
   shom.fr
ISBN Prefix(es): 2-11
*Distribution Center:* 13, rue du Chatellier,
   29603 Brest Cedex *Tel:* (02) 98 03 09 17
*E-mail:* distribution@shom.fr

**Service Technique pour l'Education**
19 blvd Poissonniere, 75002 Paris

*Tel:* (01) 45084756
*Key Personnel*
Man Dir: Mrs Gradvohl
Founded: 1962
Subjects: Art, Biography, Education, Fiction, His-
   tory, Music, Dance, Philosophy, Poetry, Reli-
   gion - Jewish, Religion - Other
ISBN Prefix(es): 2-901041

**Editions du Seuil+**
27 rue Jacob, 75006 Paris
*Tel:* (01) 40 46 50 50 *Fax:* (01) 40 46 43 00
*E-mail:* contact@seuil.com
*Web Site:* www.seuil.com *Cable:* EDISEUIL
*Key Personnel*
Chairman: Claude Cherki
General Manager: Pascal Flamand
Chairman & Editorial Advisor: Olivier Cohen
Chairman & Advisor: Francoise Peyrot
Marketing Manager: Ludovic Girod
   *E-mail:* lgirod@seuil.com
Executive Dir: Marie-France Fontaine
Publicity: Nathalie Cordier
Production: Daniel Glorel
Rights & Permissions Manager: Mireille Reis-
   soulet *Tel:* (01) 40465103 *E-mail:* mreissou@
   sevil.com
Editorial: Vincent Bardet; Jacques Binsztok; Eve-
   lyne Cazade; Rene de Ceccatty; Richard Figu-
   ier; Anne Freyer; Louis Gardel; Martine van
   Geertruyden; Jean-Luc Giribone; Jean-Claude
   Guillebaud; Claude Henard; Jean-Marc Levy-
   Leblond; Thierry Marchaisse; Annie Morvan;
   Maurice Olender; Christelle Paris; Robert
   Pepin; Denis Roche; Jean-Louis Schlegel;
   Michel Winock
Founded: 1935
Subjects: Art, Biography, Fiction, Government,
   Political Science, History, How-to, Literature,
   Literary Criticism, Essays, Music, Dance, Phi-
   losophy, Photography, Poetry, Psychology, Psy-
   chiatry, Religion - Other, Science (General),
   Social Sciences, Sociology
ISBN Prefix(es): 2-02
*Parent Company:* Editions de l'Olivier
Imprints: La Baleine; L' Olivier; Editions Verti-
   cales
Subsidiaries: Societe d'Editions Scientifiques; Bo-
   real (Montreal, Canada); College de France
Distributor for Alliage; L'Ane; Arlea; Autrement;
   Baleine; Belin; Bibliotheque Nationale de
   France; Boreal; Bourgois; Cahiers Cinema
   du; Calliecphale; Cause Freudienne; Corti; Es-
   prit; Les 400 coups; Genre Humain; Hoebeke;
   L'Homme; O Jacob; Liana Levi; Maison des
   Roches; A M Metailie; Milan; Minuit; Mol-
   lat; Montparnasse Editions Video; Navarin;
   Noir sur Blanc; Olivier; Panoramiques; Payot-
   Rivages; Phebus; Raisons d'Agir; Regard;
   RMN; Sept Video Arte; Taize; Textuel; Thames
   & Hudson; Verticales
*Orders to:* 13 rue du General Leclerc, Ballainvil-
   liers, 91160 Longjumeau

**SHOM,** see Service Hydrographique et
   Oceanographique de la Marine (SHOM)

**Editions Siloe+**
18 rue des Carmelites, 44000 Nantes
*Tel:* (02) 43 53 26 01 *Fax:* (02) 43 53 56 01
*E-mail:* contact@siloe.fr
*Web Site:* www.siloe.fr
*Key Personnel*
Man Dir: Michel Thierry *Tel:* (02) 43 53 89 30
   *E-mail:* michel.thierry@siloe.fr
Founded: 1982
Subjects: Geography, Geology, History, How-to,
   Literature, Literary Criticism, Essays, Photog-
   raphy, Regional Interests, Religion - Catholic,
   Travel, Wine & Spirits
ISBN Prefix(es): 2-905259; 2-84231
Total Titles: 250 Print

*Branch Office(s)*
4 rue Souchu-Serviniere, BP 939, 53009 Laval
   Cedex *Tel:* (02) 40 98 61 10
La Rinjardiene, 44370 Varades, Contact: Yves
   Brien *Tel:* (0240) 98 61 10 *Fax:* (0240) 98 61
   10
*Distribution Center:* Litteral Diffusion, ZI
   du Bois Imbert, BP 12, 85280 La Ferriere
   *Tel:* (02) 51 98 33 34 *Fax:* (02) 51 98 42 11
   *E-mail:* contact@litteral-diffusion.com *Web
   Site:* www.litteral-diffusion.com

**Editions Andre Silvaire Sarl+**
20 rue Domat, 75005 Paris
*Tel:* (01) 43 26 72 34 *Fax:* (01) 55 42 16 69
Founded: 1944
Subjects: Drama, Theater, Fiction, Literature, Lit-
   erary Criticism, Essays, Philosophy, Poetry,
   Social Sciences, Sociology
ISBN Prefix(es): 2-85055

**Sirey,** *imprint of* Editions Dalloz Sirey

**Slavonic,** see Institut d'Etudes Slaves IES

**Societe des Editions Grasset et Fasquelle+**
61 rue des Sts-Peres, 75006 Paris
*Tel:* (01) 44392200 *Fax:* (01) 42226418
*E-mail:* editorial@grasset.fr
*Web Site:* www.grasset.fr
*Telex:* 615887
*Key Personnel*
Chairman: Jean-Claude Fasquelle
Man Dir: Yves Berger; Manuel Carcassonne;
   Jean-Paul Enthoven
Sales: Jean-Pierre Pigeard
General Manager, Publicity & Advertising: Denis
   Bourgeois
Production: Jean-Pierre Decaens
Administrative Dir: Denis Lepeu
Rights & Permissions: Marie-Helene d'Ovidio
Public Relations: Claude Dalla-Torre; Joelle
   Faure; Martine Savary
Founded: 1907
Subjects: Fiction, Literature, Literary Criticism,
   Essays, Nonfiction (General), Philosophy
ISBN Prefix(es): 2-246
Imprints: Figures; College de Philosophie;
   Cahiers Rouges
*U.S. Office(s):* c/o Sanford & Greenburger Asso-
   ciates, 55 Fifth Ave, 15th floor, New York, NY
   10003, United States

**Societe des Editions Privat SA+**
10, rue des Arts, 31000 Toulouse
Mailing Address: BP 828, 31080 Toulouse Cedex
*Tel:* (05) 34 31 81 81; (05) 34 31 81 88 *Fax:* (05)
   34 31 64 44
*E-mail:* editionsprivat@wanadoo.fr
*Key Personnel*
Dir: Dominique Porte
Publicity & Press Relations: Anne-Marie Bagieu
Editor: Veronique Sucere
Foreign Rights: Chantal Galtier Roussel
Founded: 1839
Subjects: Regional Interests, Patrimony, Health,
   National & International, Southern History
ISBN Prefix(es): 2-7089
Number of titles published annually: 70 Print
*Parent Company:* Laboratoires Pierre Fabre, Le
   Carla-Burlats, 81106 Castres Cedex

**Societe d'Etudes et de Diffusion des Industries
   Thermiques et Aerauliques,** see SEDIT
   (Societe d'Etudes et de Diffusion des Industries
   Thermiques et Aerauliques)

**Societe d'Etudes Juridiques Internationales et
   Fiscales,** see Les Cahiers Fiscaux Europeens

**Societe Francaise des Imprimeries Administratives Centrales**, see Sofiac (Societe Francaise des Imprimeries Administratives Centrales)

**Societe Mathematique de France - Institut Henri Poincare**
11 rue Pierre-et-Marie-Curie, 75231 Paris Cedex 05
*Tel:* (01) 44 27 67 96 *Fax:* (01) 40 46 90 96
*E-mail:* smf@dma.ens.fr
*Web Site:* smf.emath.fr
*Key Personnel*
President: M Waldschmidt
Secretary General: Claire Ropartz
Founded: 1872
Subjects: Mathematics
Number of titles published annually: 20 Print
*Bookshop(s):* Maison de la SMF, BP 67, 13276 Marseille Cedex 9, Contact: C Munusami *Tel:* (0491) 833025 *Fax:* (0491) 411751 *E-mail:* smf@smf.univ-mrs.fr

**Sofiac (Societe Francaise des Imprimeries Administratives Centrales)+**
3, rue Ferrus, 75014 Paris Cedex
*Tel:* (01) 40 64 42 42 *Fax:* (01) 40 64 42 40
*E-mail:* ble@berger-levrault.fr
*Web Site:* www.editions.berger-levrault.fr
*Key Personnel*
President: Bruno Declementi
Publisher: Veronique Fastrez
Subjects: Accounting, Business, Law, Public Administration
ISBN Prefix(es): 2-85130
*Parent Company:* Groupe Berger-Levrault
*Orders to:* 5, rue Andre Ampere, BP 79, 54250 Champigneulles *Tel:* (03) 83 38 83 83 *Fax:* (03) 83 38 37 12

**Solar**, *imprint of* Presses de la Cite

**Solin**, *imprint of* Editions Actes Sud

**Editions Soline+**
10, blvd de la paix, 92400 Courbevoie
*Tel:* (01) 43 33 74 24 *Fax:* (01) 43 33 67 37
*E-mail:* contact@soline.fr
*Web Site:* perso.wanadoo.fr/soline
*Key Personnel*
Manager: Nicole Pialet
Founded: 1988
Subjects: Automotive, Fashion, Gardening, Plants, House & Home, Wine & Spirits
ISBN Prefix(es): 2-87677
Total Titles: 90 Print
Distributed by VILO
*Warehouse:* 19-23 rue Pierre Curie, 92400 Courbevoie

**Somogy editions d'art+**
57, rue de la Roquette, 75011 Paris
*Tel:* (01) 48 05 70 10 *Fax:* (01) 48 05 71 70
*E-mail:* somogy@magic.fr
*Key Personnel*
Man Dir: Nicolas Neumann
Editorial: Veronique le Dosseur
International Rights: Jana Navratil-Nanent
Founded: 1937
Subjects: Antiques, Archaeology, Architecture & Interior Design, Art, Biography, Photography
ISBN Prefix(es): 2-84598; 2-85056

**Publications de la Sorbonne**
212, rue Saint-Jacques, 75005 Paris
*Tel:* (01) 43 25 80 15 *Fax:* (01) 43 54 03 24
*E-mail:* publisor@univ-paris1.fr
*Web Site:* www.univ-paris1.fr/recherche/rubrique46.html
*Key Personnel*
Dir: Elisabeth Mornet

Founded: 1971
Subjects: Archaeology, Art, Economics, Geography, Geology, Government, Political Science, History, Law, Literature, Literary Criticism, Essays, Philosophy, Social Sciences, Sociology
ISBN Prefix(es): 2-85944
Number of titles published annually: 25 Print
Total Titles: 25 Print
*Orders to:* Diffusion CID, 131 blvd Saint Michel, 75005 Paris *Tel:* (01) 43 54 47 15 *Fax:* (01) 40 51 02 80 *E-mail:* cid@msh-paris.fr

**Association d'Editions Sorg**
54 rue de l'Est, 92100 Boulogne
*Tel:* (01) 48252524 *Fax:* (01) 46052563
*Key Personnel*
Chairman & International Rights: Jacques Sorg
Founded: 1986
Subjects: Aeronautics, Aviation, Fiction, History, Humor, Philosophy
ISBN Prefix(es): 2-906794

**Sortileges**, *imprint of* Societe d'Edition Les Belles Lettres

**Editions SOS (Editions du Secours Catholique)**
11, rue de Cambrai Batiment 28, 2E Etage, 75019 Paris
*Tel:* (01) 40 35 44 65 *Fax:* (01) 40 35 42 73
*Key Personnel*
Man Dir: Maurice Herr
Publicity & Advertising: Georges Fanucchi
Founded: 1949
Subjects: History, Philosophy, Religion - Other, Social Sciences, Sociology
ISBN Prefix(es): 2-7185

**Souffles+**
157 rue des Blains, 92220 Bagneux
*Tel:* (01) 45 36 44 30 *Fax:* (01) 45 36 44 39
*Key Personnel*
President: Thomas Jallaud
Founded: 1987
Subjects: Literature, Literary Criticism, Essays
ISBN Prefix(es): 2-87658

**Les Editions de la Source Sarl**
5 rue de la Source, 75016 Paris
*Tel:* (01) 45 25 30 07
*Key Personnel*
Man Dir: Rev Father Dom Gozier
All Other Offices: Rev Father Dom Balladur
Founded: 1927
Subjects: Biblical Studies, Religion - Other, Theology
ISBN Prefix(es): 2-900005
Imprints: Lumiere Biblique series
*Bookshop(s):* Librairie Sainte Marie, 5 rue de la Source, 75016 Paris
*Orders to:* Office General du Livre, 14 bis rue Jean-Ferrandi, 75006 Paris *Tel:* (01) 45 48 38 28

**Spectres Familiers**
29, rue Barthelemy, 13001 Marseille
*Tel:* (0491) 912645 *Fax:* (0491) 909951
*Key Personnel*
Literature Dir: Emmanuel Ponsart
Subjects: Literature, Literary Criticism, Essays, Poetry
ISBN Prefix(es): 2-909097; 2-909857
*Distribution Center:* 2, rue de la Charite, 13002 Marseille

**Spengler Editeur+**
130 blvd Saint Germain, 75006 Paris
*Tel:* (01) 49 70 15 55 *Fax:* (01) 49 70 15 50
Founded: 1992
Subjects: Fiction, Literature, Literary Criticism, Essays

ISBN Prefix(es): 2-909997
Distributed by Prologue (Canada)

**Editions Spratbrow+**
10 rue Leon Foucault, 78180 Montigny-le-Bretonneux Cedex
*Tel:* (01) 30 14 19 30 *Fax:* (01) 34 60 31 32
*Key Personnel*
President: Francoise Begrand
Founded: 1990
Subjects: Education, English as a Second Language, Language Arts, Linguistics, Self-Help
ISBN Prefix(es): 2-903891
*Parent Company:* Editions Casteilla
Distributed by Groupe Deboeck a Louvin (Belgium)
Distributor for Santillana (France)
*Bookshop(s):* Librairie Casteilla, 25, rue Monge, 75005 Paris

**Editions Springer France+**
One, rue Paul Cezanne, 75008 Paris
*Tel:* (01) 5393 3647 *Fax:* (01) 53933729
*Web Site:* www.springer-paris.fr
Founded: 1986
Subjects: Astronomy, Chemistry, Chemical Engineering, Civil Engineering, Computer Science, Earth Sciences, Economics, Electronics, Electrical Engineering, Engineering (General), Mathematics, Mechanical Engineering, Medicine, Nursing, Dentistry, Physics, Psychology, Psychiatry
ISBN Prefix(es): 2-287; 3-540
*Parent Company:* Springer-Verlag GmbH & Co KG, Heidelberger Platz 3, 14197 Berlin, Germany

**Editions Stil**
22, blvd Saint-Denis, 75010 Paris
*Tel:* (01) 48009224; (06) 85024238 *Fax:* (01) 48009336
*Key Personnel*
Editor: Alain Villain
Founded: 1971
Subjects: Art, Literature, Literary Criticism, Essays, Music, Dance
ISBN Prefix(es): 2-85254

**Editions Stock+**
31 rue de Fleurus, 75006 Paris
*Tel:* (01) 49543655 *Fax:* (01) 49543662
*Web Site:* www.editions-stock.fr/
*Key Personnel*
President: Claude Durand
Rights & Permissions: Fabienne Roussel
Founded: 1708
Subjects: Biography, Child Care & Development, Fiction, Film, Video, Literature, Literary Criticism, Essays, Nonfiction (General), Poetry, Social Sciences, Sociology
ISBN Prefix(es): 2-234
*Parent Company:* Librairie Hachette
*U.S. Office(s):* Bureau du Livre Francais, 583 Broadway, New York, New York, NY 10003, United States

**Editions Subervie**
Parc des Moutiers, 12032 Rodez Cedex 09
*Tel:* (05) 65 67 20 17 *Fax:* (05) 65 67 36 38
*E-mail:* contact@subervie.com
*Web Site:* www.subervie.com
*Key Personnel*
Contact: Jo Subevio
ISBN Prefix(es): 2-85644; 2-911381

**SUD+**
62 rue Sainte, BP 38, 13484 Marseille Cedex 20
*Tel:* (0491) 336068 *Fax:* (0491) 336068
*Key Personnel*
Man Dir: Yves Broussard
Founded: 1970

Subjects: Literature, Literary Criticism, Essays, Poetry
ISBN Prefix(es): 2-86446

**Editions Sud Ouest**
6, rue de la Merci, 33000 Bordeaux
Mailing Address: BP 130, 33036 Bordeaux Cedex
*Tel:* (0556) 44 68 21 *Fax:* (0556) 44 40 83
*E-mail:* contact@editions-sudouest.com
*Web Site:* www.editions-sudouest.com
*Key Personnel*
Contact: Catherine Dubourg *Tel:* (0556) 003508
   *E-mail:* c.dubourg@sudouest.com
Founded: 1988
Subjects: Cookery, History, How-to, Outdoor Recreation, Regional Interests
ISBN Prefix(es): 2-87901
Number of titles published annually: 60 Print
Total Titles: 500 Print
*Parent Company:* Groupe Sud-Ouest, 8 rue de Cheverus, 33000 Bordeaux
Distributor for Editions Jean Paul Gisserot
*Warehouse:* Rando SA, Queeynes, 33000 Bordeaux

**Editions le Sureau,** *imprint of* Adverbum SARL

**Les Editions de la Table Ronde**
7 rue Corneille, 75006 Paris
*Tel:* (01) 40 46 70 70 *Fax:* (01) 40 46 71 01
*E-mail:* editionslatableronde@wanadoo.fr
*Key Personnel*
President & Dir General: Denis Tillinac
Publisher: Olivier Frebourg
Rights & Permissions: Marie-Therese Caloni
Founded: 1944
Subjects: Biography, Fiction, History, Nonfiction (General), Psychology, Psychiatry, Religion - Other
ISBN Prefix(es): 2-7103
*Associate Companies:* Editione la Palatine

**Editeurs Tacor International**
13 rue Saint-Honore, 78000 Versailles
Mailing Address: BP 1, 78170 La Celle-Saint Cloud
*Tel:* (01) 39 18 29 39 *Fax:* (01) 30 82 43 90
*Key Personnel*
Man Dir: Annette Riis-Zahrai
Founded: 1988
Subjects: Human Relations, Religion - Other, Social Sciences, Sociology
ISBN Prefix(es): 2-907308

**Editions Tallandier+**
18, rue Dauphine, 75006 Paris
*Tel:* (01) 40 46 43 88 *Fax:* (01) 40 46 43 98
*Web Site:* www.tallandier.com
Founded: 1865
Subjects: Art, Fiction, Geography, Geology, History
ISBN Prefix(es): 2-235
*Warehouse:* BP 65, 45390 Puiseaux
*Orders to:* BP 65, 45390 Puiseaux

**Editions Tardy SA+**
15-27, rue Moussorgski, 75018 Paris
*Tel:* (01) 53 26 33 35 *Fax:* (01) 53 26 33 36
*Telex:* 205781
*Key Personnel*
Man Dir, Rights & Permissions: Pierre Penet
Dir: Pierre-Marie Dumont
Founded: 1938
Subjects: Religion - Catholic, Religion - Other
ISBN Prefix(es): 2-7105
*Warehouse:* 48 rue Galande, 75005 Paris

**Taride Editions+**
Division of ULISSE Edition
15 rue Mansart, 75009 Paris
*Tel:* (01) 48 78 40 74 *Fax:* (01) 48 78 40 77

*Web Site:* www.taride.com
*Key Personnel*
Man Dir: Pierre-Alain Imhof
General Manager: Frederique Imhof
Founded: 1852
Subjects: Cookery, Geography, Geology, Travel
ISBN Prefix(es): 2-7106

**Editions Tarmeye+**
Roudon, 43520 Mazet Saint Voy
*Tel:* (0471) 650153 *Fax:* (0471) 650154
*Key Personnel*
Publisher: Jacqueline Tartar; Jean-Marc Tartar
Founded: 1986
Subjects: Humor
ISBN Prefix(es): 2-906029

**Tec & Doc,** *imprint of* Editions Lavoisier

**Editions Technip SA+**
27 rue Ginoux, 75737 Paris Cedex 15
*Tel:* (01) 45 78 33 80 *Fax:* (01) 45 75 37 11
*E-mail:* info@editionstechnip.com
*Web Site:* www.editionstechnip.com
*Key Personnel*
President & Dir General: Jean-Pierre Sabbagh
Sales Manager: Corinne Herran
Founded: 1956
Specialize in the publishing of scientific & technical books on the oil & gas industry.
Subjects: Automotive, Chemistry, Chemical Engineering, Computer Science, Earth Sciences, Electronics, Electrical Engineering, Energy, Engineering (General), Mathematics, Technology
ISBN Prefix(es): 2-7108
Number of titles published annually: 20 Print
Total Titles: 1,000 Print; 3 CD-ROM
*Parent Company:* Institut Francais du Petrole, 1-4, ave de Bois Preau, 92852 Rueil-Malmaison Cedex
*Bookshop(s):* Brown Book Shop, 1517 San Jacinto, Houston, TX 77002, United States *Tel:* 713-652-3937 *Fax:* 713-652-1914 *E-mail:* info@brownbookshop.com; J A Majors Co, 8961 Interchange Dr, Houston, TX 77054, United States *Tel:* 713-662-3984 *Fax:* 713-662-9627 *E-mail:* houston@majors.com; DeMille Technical Books, 120 Eighth Ave SW, Calgary, AB T2P 1B3, Canada *Tel:* 403-264-7411 *Fax:* 403-262-1445 *E-mail:* sales@calgary. mcnallyrobison.ca
*Distribution Center:* DA Information Services, 648 Whitehorse Rd, Mitcham, Victoria 3132, Australia *Tel:* (03) 9210 7777 *Fax:* (03) 9210 7788 *E-mail:* service@dadirect.com.au
Enfield Publishing & Distribution Co, PO Box 699, May St, Enfield, NH 03748, United States *Tel:* 603-632-7377 *Fax:* 603-632-5611 *E-mail:* info@enfieldbooks.com *Web Site:* www.enfieldbooks.com
Hikari Book Trading Co Ltd, Nagatani Bldg, Room 201, 26 Sakamachi, Shinjuku-ku, Tokyo 160 *Tel:* (03) 3353 5201 *Fax:* (03) 3353 5203 *E-mail:* yoshikal@sepia.ocn.ne.jp
PF Book, jl Dr Setia Budhi 274, Bandung 40143, Indonesia *Tel:* (022) 2011149 *Fax:* (022) 2012840 *E-mail:* pfbook@bandung.wasantara. net.id
Presses Internationales Polytechnique, 1170 Beaumont, Mont-Royal, QC H3P 3E5, Canada *Tel:* 514-340-3286 *Fax:* 514-340-5882 *E-mail:* pip@polymlt.ca *Web Site:* www. polymlt.ca/pub/
Progressive International Agencies (Pvt) Limited, 174-X, Block 2, PECH Society, Off Tarig Rd, PO Box N°=8069, Karachi 75400, Pakistan *Tel:* (021) 452 5544-6 *Fax:* (021) 2454 6687 *E-mail:* gaziani@super.net.pk
Shankar's Book Agency Private Ltd, 133, Lenin Sarani, Kolkata 700 013, India *Tel:* (033) 246 8993 *Fax:* (033) 246 3257 *E-mail:* davinder@ vsnl.com

Shankar's Book Agency Private Ltd, 103, Munish Plaza, 20, Ansari Rd, Darya Ganj, New Delhi 110 002, India *Tel:* (011) 3279 967 *Fax:* (012) 6322 806 *E-mail:* sbapld@de12.vsnl.net.in

**Techniplus,** *imprint of* Editions Casteilla

**Technique et Vulgarisation,** *imprint of* Editions Bordas

**Editions Techniques et Scientifiques Francaises**
Imprint of Dunod Editeur
5 rue Laromiguiere, 75005 Paris
*Tel:* (01) 40 46 35 00 *Fax:* (01) 40 46 49 95
*E-mail:* infos@dunod.com
*Web Site:* www.dunod.com
*Telex:* pgv230472f
*Key Personnel*
President: Charles Vallee
ISBN Prefix(es): 2-85535

**Le Temps apprivoise,** *imprint of* Editions Buchet-Chastel Pierre Zech Editeur

**10/18+**
Imprint of Havas Poche
12 avenue d'Italie, 75013 Paris
*Tel:* (01) 44 16 05 00 *Fax:* (01) 44 16 05 03
*E-mail:* editeur@10-18.fr; commercial@10-18.fr
*Web Site:* www.10-18.fr
*Telex:* 204807F
*Key Personnel*
Publisher: Jean-Claude Dubost
Editor: Pauline de Margerie
Founded: 1961
Quality paperbacks.
Subjects: Fiction, Government, Political Science, Literature, Literary Criticism, Essays, Mysteries, International fiction & mysteries (mostly historical crime)
ISBN Prefix(es): 2-264
*Parent Company:* Vivendi Universal Publishing Group

**Librairie Pierre Tequi et Editions Tequi**
82 rue Bonaparte, 75006 Paris
*Tel:* (01) 40 46 72 90 *Fax:* (01) 40 46 72 93
*E-mail:* pierre.tequi@wanadoo.fr
*Web Site:* www.editionstequi.com
*Key Personnel*
Dir: Pierre Lemaire
Literary Manager: G Cerbelaud Salagnac
Founded: 1845
Subjects: Education, Philosophy, Religion - Catholic, Social Sciences, Sociology, Theology
ISBN Prefix(es): 2-7403; 2-85244
*Bookshop(s):* S A Vander (Belgium); Iris Diffusion (Canada); Editions Saint-Augustin (Switzerland)

**Terre Vivante+**
Domaine de Raud, 38710 Mens
*Tel:* (04) 76 34 80 80 *Fax:* (04) 76 34 84 02
*E-mail:* infos@terrevivante.org
*Web Site:* www.terrevivante.org
*Key Personnel*
Man Dir: Claude Aubert
Founded: 1980
Subjects: Agriculture, Cookery, Energy, Gardening, Plants, Health, Nutrition, House & Home, Technology
ISBN Prefix(es): 2-904082; 2-914717
Total Titles: 2 Print; 60 Audio

**Editions Thames & Hudson+**
12, rue de Seine, 75006 Paris
*Tel:* (01) 56240450 *Fax:* (01) 56240458
*E-mail:* thameshudson@wanadoo.fr
*Web Site:* www.thameshudson.fr
*Key Personnel*
Dir: Thomas Neurath

Editor: Helene Borraz *E-mail:* h.borraz.
thameshudson@wanadoo.fr; Frederique Popet
*E-mail:* f.popet.thameshudson@wanadoo.fr;
Anne Levine *E-mail:* a.levine.thameshudson@
wanadoo.fr
Publicity: Perrine Auclair *E-mail:* p.auclair.
thameshudson@wanadoo.fr
Founded: 1989
Subjects: Archaeology, Architecture & Interior
Design, Art, Fashion, Photography, Religion -
Jewish
ISBN Prefix(es): 2-87811
*Parent Company:* Thames & Hudson Londres
*Orders to:* Hazan *Tel:* (01) 49619207 *Fax:* (01)
45978347

**Editions Theatrales+**
38, rue du Faubourg Saint-Jacques, 75014 Paris
*Tel:* (01) 53 10 23 00 *Fax:* (01) 53 10 23 01
*E-mail:* info@editionstheatrales.fr
*Web Site:* www.editionstheatrales.fr
*Key Personnel*
Dir: J P Engelbach
Founded: 1990
Subjects: Drama, Theater
ISBN Prefix(es): 2-907810; 2-84260
Distributed by Distique
Distributor for CNDP collection Theatre Aujourd-
hui; Theatre du Soleil

**Alain Thomas Editeur+**
18 passage Foubert, 75013 Paris
*Tel:* (01) 45 88 28 03 *Fax:* (01) 45 88 49 24
*Web Site:* alainthomasimages.com
*Key Personnel*
Editor: Alain Thomas *E-mail:* alain-thomas@
wanadoo.fr
Founded: 1991
Subjects: Photography, Travel, Western Fiction
ISBN Prefix(es): 2-9503864
Total Titles: 3 Print
*Parent Company:* Alain Thomas Images
Distributed by Centre Cartographique (in Belgium
only)

**Editions Tiresias Michel Reynaud+**
21, rue Letort, 75018 Paris
Mailing Address: BP 249, 75866 Paris Cedex 18
*Tel:* (01) 42 23 47 27 *Fax:* (01) 42 23 73 27
*E-mail:* editions.tiresias@club-internet.fr
*Web Site:* www.editions-tiresias.fr.tc
*Key Personnel*
Contact: Michel Reynaud
Founded: 1990
Subjects: Biography, History, Literature, Literary
Criticism, Essays
ISBN Prefix(es): 2-908527
*Branch Office(s)*
12 rue de Nombonnet, 28160 Unverre

**TOP Editions+**
Member of Casteilla
10, rue Leon-Foucault, 78184 Montigny-le-
Bretonneux
*Tel:* (01) 30 14 19 30 *Fax:* (01) 34 60 31 32
*E-mail:* info@editionschiron.com
*Web Site:* www.editionschiron.com
*Key Personnel*
Dir General: Marinus Visser
Founded: 1982
Subjects: Accounting, Career Development, Com-
munications, Finance, How-to, Management,
Marketing, Securities
ISBN Prefix(es): 2-87731
Number of titles published annually: 25 Print
Total Titles: 75 Print

**Tout L'Univers,** *imprint of* Le Livre de Paris

**Transedition ASBL**
11 rue d'Odessa, 75014 Paris

*Tel:* (01) 43211080 *Fax:* (01) 43211079
*Key Personnel*
Man Dir, Editorial: Marc Dachy
Sales: Anne Barres
Production: Paule Pousseele
Publicity: Stephanie Gregoire
Rights & Permissions: Jacques Bekaert
Founded: 1972
Subjects: Art, Literature, Literary Criticism, Es-
says
ISBN Prefix(es): 2-8025
*Associate Companies:* Montfaucon Research Cen-
ter, 8 rue d'Anjou, 75008 Paris
*Subsidiaries:* Editions Luna-Park

**Transeuropeennes/RCE+**
c/o Maison de l'Europe, Hotel de Coulanges, 35,
rue des Francs Bourgeois, 75004 Paris
*Tel:* (01) 55 07 88 90 *Fax:* (01) 55 07 97 38
*E-mail:* te.revue@transeuropeennes.org; contact@
transeuropeennes.org
*Web Site:* www.transeuropeennes.org
*Key Personnel*
Editor-in-Chief: Ghislaine Glasson Deschaumes
Man Dir: Gaele de la Brosse
Distribution Manager: Yacine Saadi
Founded: 1993
Comprehensive & interdisciplinary review.
Subjects: Art, Drama, Theater, Foreign Countries,
History, Literature, Literary Criticism, Essays,
Philosophy, Photography, Social Sciences, Soci-
ology
ISBN Prefix(es): 2-912002
Number of titles published annually: 3 Print
Total Titles: 14 Print

**Travel Aventure,** *imprint of* Editions Actes Sud

**Guy Tredaniel Editeur-Editions Courrier du
Livre**
65 rue Claude Bernard, 75005 Paris
*Tel:* (01) 43 36 41 05 *Fax:* (01) 43 31 07 45
*E-mail:* tredaniel-courrier@wanadoo.fr
*Web Site:* www.livre-edition-tredaniel.com
Subjects: Environmental Studies, Gardening,
Plants, Health, Nutrition, Philosophy, Religion -
Other, Sports, Athletics
ISBN Prefix(es): 2-7029; 2-84445; 2-85707

**Turbo,** *imprint of* Les Presses du Management

**Ulisse Editions+**
15 rue Mansart, 75009 Paris
*Tel:* (01) 48 78 40 74 *Fax:* (01) 48 78 40 77
*Web Site:* www.ulisseditions.com
*Key Personnel*
Managing Editor: Gerard Boulanger
Founded: 1990
Subjects: Architecture & Interior Design, Art,
Crafts, Games, Hobbies, House & Home,
Sports, Athletics
ISBN Prefix(es): 2-907601; 2-84415; 2-921403

**UNESCO Publishing+**
Imprint of UNESCO Publishing
7 place de Fontenoy, 75352 Paris 07-SP
*Tel:* (01) 45 68 10 00 *Fax:* (01) 45 67 16 90
*E-mail:* publishing.promotion@unesco.org
*Web Site:* www.upo.unesco.org
*Telex:* 204461; 270602
*Key Personnel*
Dir General: Koichiro Matsuura
Chief, Promotion & Sales: Chandran Nair
Chief Publisher: Michiko Tanaka
Promotion: Cristina Laje
Founded: 1946
Subjects: Art, Communications, Education, Hu-
man Relations, Science (General), Social Sci-
ences, Sociology
ISBN Prefix(es): 92-3

Imprints: IBE; IIEP
Distributed by Bernan Associate (USA); Stationery Office Books (UK)

**Universitas**
Subsidiary of Buchverlage Langen-Mueller/Her-
big
62 ave de Suffren, 75015 Paris
*Tel:* (01) 45 67 18 38 *Fax:* (01) 45 66 50 70
*E-mail:* info@universitas.fr
*Key Personnel*
Dir: Andrew Brown
Founded: 1989
Subjects: History, Language Arts, Linguistics, Lit-
erature, Literary Criticism, Essays, Philosophy
ISBN Prefix(es): 2-7400

**Publications de l'Universite de Pau**
Av de l'Universite, 64000 Pau
Mailing Address: BP 576, 64012 Pau Cedex
*Tel:* (05) 59 40 70 00 *Fax:* (05) 59 80 83 29
*Web Site:* www.univ-pau.fr
*Key Personnel*
Dir: Bertrand Rouge
Man Dir: Alain Andreucci
Founded: 1992
Subjects: Art, Geography, Geology, Language
Arts, Linguistics, Law, Literature, Literary Crit-
icism, Essays, Photography, Poetry, Social Sci-
ences, Sociology
ISBN Prefix(es): 2-908930

**La Vague a l'ame+**
BP 22, 38701 La Tronche Cedex
*Tel:* (04) 76470784
*Key Personnel*
President: Georges Elisee
Founded: 1980
Subjects: Cookery, Drama, Theater, Humor, Pho-
tography, Poetry, Religion - Catholic, Travel
ISBN Prefix(es): 2-84063

**Editions Vague Verte+**
271 rue du Haut, 80460 Woignarue
*Tel:* (03) 22 30 72 50 *Fax:* (03) 22 26 58 73
*E-mail:* edlavagueverte@wanadoo.fr
*Web Site:* perso.wanadoo.fr/editionslavagueverte
*Key Personnel*
Dir: Jimmy Grandsire
Founded: 1989
Subjects: Art, Biography, Earth Sciences, Envi-
ronmental Studies, History, Literature, Literary
Criticism, Essays, Mysteries, Natural History,
Poetry, Regional Interests, Travel
ISBN Prefix(es): 2-908227
Number of titles published annually: 25 Print

**Les Editions Vaillant-Miroir-Sprint
Publications**
146 rue du Faubourg-Poissoniere, 75010 Paris
*Tel:* (01) 42819103
*Telex:* f 281353f
*Key Personnel*
International Sales Manager: Alain Lesaint
Subjects: Humor, Sports, Athletics
ISBN Prefix(es): 2-7325

**Editions Van de Velde+**
26 rue George-Sand, 75016 Paris
*Tel:* (01) 56 68 86 64 *Fax:* (01) 56 68 90 66
*E-mail:* vandevelde.editions@wanadoo.fr
*Web Site:* www.musicollege.com
*Key Personnel*
Dir: Francis Van de Velde
Copyrights: Ursula Van de Velde
Founded: 1898
Subjects: Music, Dance
ISBN Prefix(es): 2-85868; 2-86299
Number of titles published annually: 20 Print
Total Titles: 197 Print
Distributor for Konemann Music Budapest

**Gerard Varin**, see L'Amitie par le Livre

**Vents d'Ouest+**
31-33 rue Ernest Renan, 92130 Issy-les-
   Moulineaux
*Tel:* (01) 41 46 11 46 *Fax:* (01) 40 93 05 58
*Web Site:* www.ventsdouest.com
*Key Personnel*
Contact: Estelle Revelant *E-mail:* estelle.
   revelant@glenat.com
International Rights: Annick Briard
Subjects: Humor, Science Fiction, Fantasy
ISBN Prefix(es): 2-86967; 2-7493

**Editions Verdier**
234, rue du Faubourg-Saint-Antoine, 75012 Paris
*Tel:* (04) 68 24 05 75; (01) 43 79 20 45 *Fax:* (04)
   68 24 00 89; (01) 43 79 84 20
*E-mail:* contact@editions-verdier.fr
*Web Site:* www.editions-verdier.fr
*Key Personnel*
Dir, Literature: Gerard Bobillier
Founded: 1979
Subjects: Literature, Literary Criticism, Essays,
   Philosophy, Religion - Islamic, Religion - Jew-
   ish
ISBN Prefix(es): 2-86432
Number of titles published annually: 25 Print
Total Titles: 400 Print
Distributed by SODIS

**Editions de Vergeures+**
23 ave Villemain, 75014 Paris
*Tel:* (01) 45 43 82 60 *Fax:* (01) 45 43 81 40
*Key Personnel*
Manager: Robert Cauchuix
Founded: 1979
Subjects: Art, How-to
ISBN Prefix(es): 2-7309; 2-909175

**Vertiges Bulles**, *imprint of* Editions Dominique
   Leroy

**Editions Vigot Universitaire**
23 rue de l'Ecole de Medecine, 75006 Paris
*Tel:* (01) 43 29 54 50 *Fax:* (01) 46 34 05 89
*E-mail:* vpc@vigot.fr
*Web Site:* www.vigotmaloine.fr
*Telex:* 201708 F
*Key Personnel*
Man Dir: Daniel Vigot
Founded: 1890
Subjects: Medicine, Nursing, Dentistry, Sports,
   Athletics, Veterinary Science
ISBN Prefix(es): 2-7114
*Bookshop(s):* Librairie Vigot Maloine *Tel:* (01) 43
   25 60 45

**Editions Village Mondial+**
47 bis, rue des Vinaigriers, 75010 Paris
*Tel:* (01) 72 74 90 00 *Fax:* (01) 42 05 22 17
*E-mail:* infos@pearsoned.fr
*Web Site:* www.pearsoneducation.fr
*Key Personnel*
President: Geoffrey Staines
Founded: 1995
Specialize in higher education textbooks.
Subjects: Economics, Finance, Human Relations,
   Management, Marketing
ISBN Prefix(es): 2-84211; 2-7440
Total Titles: 100 Print
*Parent Company:* Pearson Education France
Imprints: Publi Union

**Editions Vilo SA**
25 rue Ginoux, 75015 Paris
*Tel:* (01) 45 77 08 05 *Fax:* (01) 45 79 97 15
*Telex:* 200305 F *Cable:* Edivilo Paris
*Key Personnel*
Man Dir: Mme Larfillon

Subjects: Architecture & Interior Design, Art, Automotive, History, Language Arts, Linguistics,
   Literature, Literary Criticism, Essays, Nonfiction (General), Religion - Other, Sports, Athletics, Travel
ISBN Prefix(es): 2-7191

**Editions VM+**
61 bd Saint-Germain, 75240 Paris Cedex 05
*Tel:* (01) 44 41 11 11 *Fax:* (01) 44 41 11 85
*Web Site:* www.editions-vm.com
Founded: 1965
Subjects: Photography
ISBN Prefix(es): 2-86258
*Parent Company:* Groupe Eyrolles
*Bookshop(s):* La Photo Librairie, 49 Ave de Vil-
   liers, 75017 Paris

**La Voix du Regard**
11 rue Henri Martin, 94200 Ivry-sur-Seine, Paris
*Tel:* (01) 46 70 88 69 *Fax:* (01) 46 70 88 69
*E-mail:* voixduregard@9online.fr
*Key Personnel*
President: Jocelyn Maixent *E-mail:* jocelyn.
   maixent@wanadoo.fr
International Rights: Pauline Jacquey
Founded: 1991
Subjects: Art, Drama, Theater, Fiction, Film,
   Video, Literature, Literary Criticism, Essays,
   Photography, Poetry, Radio, TV
ISBN Prefix(es): 2-9517982

**Librairie Philosophique J Vrin+**
6 place de la Sorbonne, 75005 Paris
*Tel:* (01) 43 54 03 47 *Fax:* (01) 43 54 48 18
*E-mail:* contact@vrin.fr
*Web Site:* www.vrin.fr
*Key Personnel*
Man Dir: Anne-Marie Arnaud
Founded: 1920
Publisher & Bookseller of New Books, Book-
   seller of Secondhand Books.
Subjects: History, Philosophy, Psychology, Psy-
   chiatry, Religion - Other, *Specializes in philos-
   ophy*
ISBN Prefix(es): 2-7116
Number of titles published annually: 50 Print; 1
   CD-ROM
Total Titles: 1,500 Print
*Bookshop(s):* Philosophy, Law, Religion, Litera-
   ture, Art & History, 75005 Paris

**Librairie Vuibert+**
20 rue Berbier-du-Mets, 75647 Paris Cedex 13
*Tel:* (01) 44 08 49 00 *Fax:* (01) 44 08 49 39
*Web Site:* www.vuibert.com
*Telex:* 201005 F Vuibpar *Cable:* VUIBERT
   PARIS
*Key Personnel*
President: Philippe Sylvestre
Founded: 1877
Subjects: Biological Sciences, Chemistry, Chem-
   ical Engineering, Earth Sciences, Economics,
   Law, Mathematics, Physics
ISBN Prefix(es): 2-7117
Imprints: Annales du Bac; Bac en Poche; Livre
   des Vacances

**Galerie Lucie Weill-Seligmann**
6 rue Bonaparte, 75006 Paris
*Tel:* (01) 43 54 71 95 *Fax:* (01) 40 51 82 88
*Key Personnel*
President: France Faure-Seligmann
Founded: 1930
*Book Club(s):* Nouveau Cercle Parisien du Livre

**Editions Weka**
249, rue de Crimee, 75935 Paris Cedex 19
*Tel:* (01) 53 35 16 16; (01) 53 35 17 17 *Fax:* (01)
   53 35 17 01
*E-mail:* infos@weka.fr

*Web Site:* www.weka.fr
*Telex:* 210 504 f
*Key Personnel*
Dir: Andre Blanc
General Man: Robert Christian
Editorial: Philippe Dorenlot
Commercial (Sales Direct Marketing): Jean-Pierre
   Chauvet
Founded: 1979
Subjects: Computer Science, Electronics, Elec-
   trical Engineering, Labor, Industrial Relations,
   Law, Management, Social Sciences, Sociology
ISBN Prefix(es): 2-7337
*Parent Company:* Weka-Verlag, Postfach 1180,
   8901 Kissing, Germany
*Associate Companies:* Weka Presse, 82 rue Cu-
   rial, 75935 Paris
*U.S. Office(s):* Weka Publishing Inc, 97 Indian
   Field Rd, Greenwich, CT 06830, United States
50 Main St, Suite 1000, White Plains, NY 10606,
   United States

**Galerie Esther Woerdehoff**
36 rue Falguiere, 75015 Paris
*Tel:* (01) 43 21 44 83 *Fax:* (01) 43 21 45 03
*E-mail:* galerie@ewgalerie.com
*Web Site:* www.ewgalerie.com

**YMCA-Press**
11 rue de la Montagne Ste-Genevieve, 75005
   Paris
*Tel:* (01) 43 54 74 46 *Fax:* (01) 43 25 34 79
See also Les Editeurs Reunis.
Subjects: Literature, Literary Criticism, Essays,
   Religion - Other
ISBN Prefix(es): 2-85065

**Editions Philateliques Yvert et Tellier**
37 rue des Jacobins, 80036 Amiens Cedex 1
*Tel:* (03) 22717171 *Fax:* (03) 22717189
*Telex:* 145010f
Subjects: Sports, Athletics
ISBN Prefix(es): 2-86814

# French Guiana

## General Information

*Capital:* Cayenne
*Language:* French and Creole
*Religion:* Roman Catholic
*Population:* 133,000
*Bank Hours:* 0700-1130, 1400-1600 Monday-
   Friday
*Shop Hours:* 0800-1300, 1500-1800 Monday-
   Friday
*Currency:* 100 centimes = 1 French franc
*Export/Import Information:* Overseas department
   of France, which is a member of the European
   Economic Community. Tariff as for France.
   See France for domiciliation of documents. No
   import licenses required. Same exchange re-
   strictions as France.
*Copyright:* Berne, UCC (see Copyright Conven-
   tions, pg xi)

**Guy Delabergerie Editions Sarl**
BP 682, 97303 Cayenne
*Tel:* 311162 *Fax:* 311759
ISBN Prefix(es): 2-906262
*Warehouse:* ZI du Larivot Lot, Dalmuzin Haugar
   Briot, 97351 Matoury

# French Polynesia

## General Information

*Capital:* Papeete
*Language:* French (official) & Polynesian languages
*Religion:* Mainly Protestant & Roman Catholic
*Population:* 199,031
*Bank Hours:* 0730-1530 Monday-Friday; some 0730-1130 Saturday
*Shop Hours:* 0730-1100, 1400-1700 Monday-Friday; 0730-1130 Saturday
*Currency:* 100 centimes = 1 CFA franc
*Export/Import Information:* No tariff on books other than children's picture books; advertising matter subject to customs duty, import duty, although catalogues generally considered printed books. Advertising subject to Statistical Tax. Miscellaneous tax of 2% of customs value on books and advertising. No import license required. Exchange controls.

**Ancre de Polynesie,** *imprint of* Simone Sanchez

**Scoop/Au Vent des Iles+**
BP 5670, 98716 Pirae, Tahiti
*Tel:* 50 95 95 *Fax:* 50 95 97
*E-mail:* mail@auventdesiles.pf
*Web Site:* www.auventdesiles.pf
*Key Personnel*
Manager: Christian Robert *E-mail:* christian@auventdesiles.pf
Founded: 1992
Membership(s): Ligne Editoriale Rattachee au Pacifique Sud, Pacific Islands Book Council.
Subjects: Biography, Cookery, Fiction, Geography, Geology, History, How-to, Literature, Literary Criticism, Essays, Mysteries, South Pacific
ISBN Prefix(es): 2-909790
Imprints: Nouvelles du Pacifique

**Collection Moemoea,** *imprint of* Simone Sanchez

**Haere Po Editions+**
BP 1958, 8713 Papeete Tahiti
*Tel:* 582636 *Fax:* 582333
*E-mail:* haerepotahiti@mail.pf
*Key Personnel*
Man Dir: L Shan
Founded: 1981
Subjects: Anthropology, Earth Sciences, Ethnicity, History, Language Arts, Linguistics, Natural History, Travel
ISBN Prefix(es): 2-904171

**Nouvelles du Pacifique,** *imprint of* Scoop/Au Vent des Iles

**Simone Sanchez**
BP 13973, Punaauia, Tahiti
*Tel:* (0689) 533260
*Key Personnel*
Contact: Simone Sanchez
Founded: 1993
Subjects: Fiction, History, Regional Interests
ISBN Prefix(es): 2-910256
Imprints: Ancre de Polynesie; Collection Moemoea

**Scoop,** see Scoop/Au Vent des Iles

# Gambia

## General Information

*Capital:* Banjul
*Language:* English
*Religion:* Predominantly Islamic
*Population:* 1,026,000
*Bank Hours:* 0800-1300 Monday-Thursday; 0800-1000 Friday-Saturday
*Shop Hours:* 0800 or 0900-1200, 1400-1700 Monday-Thursday; 0800 or 0900-1200, 1500-1700 Friday; 0800 or 0900-1200 Saturday
*Currency:* 100 butut = 1 dalasi
*Export/Import Information:* No tariff on books. Import tax on all. No import license required. National Trading Corporation has no monopoly. Exchange controls.
*Copyright:* Berne (see Copyright Conventions, pg xi)

**Government Printer**
PO Box 898, Printing Dept, Banjul
*Tel:* 227399
*Telex:* 2204
ISBN Prefix(es): 9983-86

# Georgia

## General Information

*Capital:* Tbilisi
*Language:* Georgian
*Religion:* Predominantly Georgian Orthodox
*Population:* 5.6 million
*Currency:* 100 tetri = 1 lari; 1 dollar = 2.23 lari
*Export/Import Information:* Customs duty for import, 12% to 20% of VAT.

**Merani Publishing House**
42, Shota Rustaveli Ave, 380008 Tbilisi
*Tel:* (032) 996492; (032) 935396; (032) 935554; (032) 935514 *Fax:* (032) 932996
*Key Personnel*
President & Dir: G E Gvertfsiteli
Editor-in-Chief: G I Alhazishvili
Commercial Manager: E G Gamezardashvili
Founded: 1925
Subjects: Regional Interests
ISBN Prefix(es): 5-515; 99928-947; 99928-946; 99928-16; 99928-948; 99928-949; 99928-950

**Sakartvelo Publishing House**
5 Marjanishvili St, Tbilisi
*Tel:* 954201; 952927
*Key Personnel*
Dir: D A Tcharkviani
Chief Editor: V R Djavakhadze
Founded: 1921
Subjects: Agriculture, Government, Political Science, Science (General), Social Sciences, Sociology
ISBN Prefix(es): 5-529; 99928-29

# Germany

## General Information

*Capital:* Berlin
*Language:* German. Sorbian speaking minority. Danish spoken by a Danish minority in South Schleswig, North Frisian in North Frisian Islands
*Religion:* Predominately Protestant and Roman Catholic
*Population:* 82.7 million
*Bank Hours:* 0900-1300, 1430-1600 Monday-Friday
*Shop Hours:* 0900-1830 Monday-Friday; 0900-1400 Saturday
*Currency:* 100 Eurocents = 1 Euro; 1.95583 Deutsche marks = 1 Euro
*Export/Import Information:* Member of the European Economic Community. No tariff on books except children's picture books from non-EEC. None on advertising to be distributed free, if exporter's country grants reciprocal treatment, otherwise charged. Import turnover tax on books and advertising. Also, 7% VAT on books. No import license required. No exchange controls.
*Copyright:* UCC, Berne, Florence (see Copyright Conventions, pg ix)

**A Francke Verlag (Tubingen und Basel)+**
Hans-Graessel-weg 13, 81375 Munich
Mailing Address: Postfach 701067, 81310 Munich
*Tel:* (089) 718 747 *Fax:* (089) 7142039
*E-mail:* info@iudicium.de
*Web Site:* www.geist.de
*Key Personnel*
Publisher: Gunter Narr
Manufacturing: Horst Schmid
Founded: 1831
Subjects: Drama, Theater, Economics, Government, Political Science, Literature, Literary Criticism, Essays, Philosophy, Psychology, Psychiatry, Social Sciences, Sociology, Theology
ISBN Prefix(es): 3-7720
*Associate Companies:* Gunter Narr Verlag
*Branch Office(s)*
Gerbergasse 48, 4001 Basel, Switzerland

**Abakus Musik Barbara Fietz**
Haversbach 1, 35753 Greifenstein
*Tel:* (06478) 2250 *Fax:* (06478) 1355
*E-mail:* hotline@abakus-musik.de
*Web Site:* www.abakus-musik.de
*Key Personnel*
Man Dir: Barbara Fietz *Tel:* (06478) 911060
Man Dir, Production: Siegfried Fietz
Founded: 1974
Specialize in musical & notebook publications.
Membership(s): JFPI; Borsenverein; DMV.
Subjects: Music, Dance, Religion - Other
ISBN Prefix(es): 3-88124
Total Titles: 100 E-Book; 250 Audio
Distributed by BMK Wartburg Vertriebsges mbH (Austria); Herder AG Basel (Switzerland)

**ABC der Deutschen Wirtschaft, Verlagsgesellschaft mbH**
Berliner Allee 8, 64295 Darmstadt
Mailing Address: Postfach 100264, 64202 Darmstadt
*Tel:* (06151) 38920 *Fax:* (06151) 33164; (06151) 389280
*E-mail:* info@abconline.de
*Web Site:* www.abconline.de
*Key Personnel*
Man Dir: Margit Selka
Publisher of industrial reference directories.
ISBN Prefix(es): 3-87000
Number of titles published annually: 3 Print
Total Titles: 5 Print
*Associate Companies:* ABC Europe Production; Industrischow Verlags GmbH

**Accedo Verlagsgesellschaft mbH+**
Gnesenerstr 1, 81929 Munich
*Tel:* (089) 935714 *Fax:* (089) 9294109
*E-mail:* accedoverlag@web.de
*Web Site:* www.accedoverlag.de
*Key Personnel*
Manager: Dr Manfred Holler *E-mail:* holler@
econ.uni-hamburg.de
Marketing: Dr Barbara Klose-Ullmann
Founded: 1988
Subjects: Art, Economics, Geography, Geology,
Government, Political Science, History, Man-
agement, Medicine, Nursing, Dentistry, Phi-
losophy, Science (General), Social Sciences,
Sociology, Art history, Medicine
ISBN Prefix(es): 3-89265
Total Titles: 50 Print
*Associate Companies:* Verlag Holler
Imprints: Homo Oeconomicus
Distributor for Verlag Holler

**Achterbahn AG Buch+**
Werftbahnstr 8, 24143 Kiel
*Tel:* (0431) 7028-209 *Fax:* (0431) 7028-228
*E-mail:* info@achterbahn.de
*Web Site:* www.achterbahn.de
*Key Personnel*
Publisher: Christian Dreller *Tel:* (0431) 7028 201
*E-mail:* christiandreller@achterbahn.de
Manager: Jens Nieswand
Rights: Hans Kettwig
Founded: 1991
Subjects: Humor
ISBN Prefix(es): 3-928950; 3-89719; 3-89982
*Warehouse:* KVA Verlagsauslieferung, Specken-
beker Weg 116, 24113 Kiel

**Joh van Acken GmbH & Co KG**
Magdeburgerstr 5, 47800 Krefeld
Mailing Address: Postfach 105, 47701 Krefeld
*Tel:* (02151) 44 00-0 *Fax:* (02151) 44 00-11
*E-mail:* verlag@van-acken.de
*Web Site:* www.www.van-acken.de
*Key Personnel*
Publisher & International Rights: Ulrich Kalten-
meier
Founded: 1890
Subjects: Regional Interests
ISBN Prefix(es): 3-923140

**F A Ackermanns Kunstverlag GmbH**
Meglinger Str 60, 81477 Munich
Mailing Address: Postfach 71 01 08, 81451 Mu-
nich
*Tel:* (089) 78580826 *Fax:* (089) 78580828
*E-mail:* info@ackermann-kalender.de
*Web Site:* www.ackermann-kalender.de *Cable:*
KUNSTACKERMANN MUNICH
*Key Personnel*
Man Dir: Michael G Kathan
Founded: 1806
Specialize in calendars.
Subjects: Art, Photography
ISBN Prefix(es): 3-8173; 3-87002
Number of titles published annually: 100 Print

**Addison Wesley Verlag**, see Pearson Education
Deutschland GmbH

**Adyar Edition**, *imprint of* Aquamarin Verlag

**Adyar Verlag**, *imprint of* Aquamarin Verlag

**Aerogie-Verlag+**
Fliessstr 20/21, 12526 Berlin
*Tel:* (030) 6 76 32 00 *Fax:* (030) 6 76 32 00
*Key Personnel*
Man Dir: Gerd Otto
Founded: 1990
Specialize in Environmental Energy.

Subjects: Energy, Engineering (General), Environ-
mental Studies, Science (General), Transporta-
tion
ISBN Prefix(es): 3-910142
*Associate Companies:* Ingenieurbuero fuer
Windenergie und Schadstofffreie Energetik

**Aethera**, *imprint of* Verlag Freies Geistesleben

**The African Literature Club**, see Books on
African Studies

**Agentur des Rauhen Hauses Hamburg GmbH**
Beim Bruederhof 8, 22844 Norderstedt
*Tel:* (040) 53 53 88-0 *Fax:* (040) 53 53 88-43
*E-mail:* kundenservice@agentur-rauhes-haus.de
*Web Site:* www.agentur-rauhes-haus.de
*Key Personnel*
Man Dir: Willi Kohlmann
Rights & Permissions: Hans-Heinrich Holm
Cataloging: Ms Schrom
Founded: 1842
Subjects: Religion - Protestant, Religion - Other,
Theology
ISBN Prefix(es): 3-7600
Divisions: Reise-und Versandbuchhandlung des
Rauhen Hauses

**AGIS Verlag GmbH**
Ooser Luisenstr 23, 76532 Baden-Baden
Mailing Address: Postfach 22 20, 76492 Baden-
Baden
*Tel:* (07221) 95 75-0 *Fax:* (07221) 6 68 10
*E-mail:* info@agis-verlag.de
*Web Site:* www.agis-verlag.de *Cable:* AGIS
BADEN BADEN
*Key Personnel*
Man Dir: Karl G Fischer; Karin Grochowiak
Media consulting.
Subjects: Art, Philosophy, Science (General)
ISBN Prefix(es): 3-87007

**Ahriman-Verlag GmbH+**
Stuebeweg 60, 79108 Freiburg
Mailing Address: Postfach 6569, 79041 Freiburg
*Tel:* (0761) 502303 *Fax:* (0761) 502247
*E-mail:* ahriman@t-online.de
*Web Site:* www.ahriman.com
*Key Personnel*
Man Dir: Edeltraud Rudow *E-mail:* thanilo@t-
online.de
Founded: 1983
Subjects: Government, Political Science, History,
Psychology, Psychiatry, Religion - Other, Sci-
ence (General)
ISBN Prefix(es): 3-922774; 3-89484
Total Titles: 1 Print; 1 CD-ROM; 20 Audio

**aid infodienst - Verbraucherdienst,
Ernaehrung, Landwirtschaft eV**
Friedrich-Ebert-Str 3, 53177 Bonn - Bad Godes-
berg
*Tel:* (0228) 8499-0 *Fax:* (0228) 8499-177
*E-mail:* aid@aid.de
*Web Site:* www.aid.de
*Key Personnel*
Man Dir: Dr Margret Buening-Fesel

**Air Gallery Edition, Helmut Kreuzer**
Goethestr 8, 85435 Erding
Mailing Address: Postfach 1526, 85425 Erding
*Tel:* (08122) 84487 *Fax:* (08122) 84487
*Key Personnel*
President: Helmut Kreuzer
Founded: 1988
Subjects: Aeronautics, Aviation
ISBN Prefix(es): 3-9802101; 3-9805934

**Aisthesis Verlag+**
Oberntorwall 21 (Eingang Mauerstr), 33602
Bielefeld
*Tel:* (0521) 172604 *Fax:* (0521) 172812
*E-mail:* aisthesis@bitel.net
*Web Site:* www.aisthesis.de
*Key Personnel*
Man Dir, Rights & Permissions: Dr Detlev Kopp;
Dr Michael Vogt
Founded: 1985
Subjects: Art, History, Literature, Literary Criti-
cism, Essays, Philosophy, Science (General)
ISBN Prefix(es): 3-925670; 3-89528

**Akademie Schloss Solitude**, see Merz &
Solitude - Akademie Schloss Solitude

**Akademie Verlag GmbH+**
Palisadenstr 40, 10243 Berlin
*Tel:* (030) 4 22 00 60 *Fax:* (030) 422 00 657
*E-mail:* info@akademie-verlag.de
*Web Site:* www.akademie-verlag.de
*Key Personnel*
Man Dir: Dr Gerd Giesler *E-mail:* giesler@
akademie-verlag.de
Founded: 1946
Membership(s): the Association of German Book-
sellers.
Subjects: History, Language Arts, Linguistics, Lit-
erature, Literary Criticism, Essays, Philosophy,
Social Sciences, Sociology
ISBN Prefix(es): 3-05; 3-922251
*Parent Company:* R Oldenbourg Verlag
Muenchen, Rosenheimerstr 145, 81671 Munich
*Distribution Center:* Publisher Service Munich,
PO Box 1280, 82197 Munich *Fax:* (08105) 388
100
*Orders to:* Verlegerdienst Muenchen, Gutenbergstr
1, 82205 Gilching

**akg-images gmbh+**
Teutonenstr 22, 14129 Berlin
*Tel:* (030) 80485200 *Fax:* (030) 80485500
*E-mail:* info@akg.de; info@akg-images.com
*Web Site:* www.akg-images.com
*Key Personnel*
Contact: Kathrin Goepel
Founded: 1945
Picture library, collection, documentation.
Subjects: Art, History, Photojournalism
ISBN Prefix(es): 3-88912
*Associate Companies:* akg-images Ltd, London,
United Kingdom; akg-images SAR, Paris,
France

**M Akselrad+**
Hauptstr 190, 69117 Heidelberg
*Tel:* (06221) 183030 *Fax:* (06221) 181223
*E-mail:* makselrad@gmx.net
*Key Personnel*
Dir: Michael Akselrad
Founded: 1972
Subjects: Literature, Literary Criticism, Essays,
Nonfiction (General)
ISBN Prefix(es): 3-921265

**Alba Fachverlag GmbH & Co KG+**
Willstaetterstr 9, 40549 Duesseldorf
Mailing Address: Postfach 11 01 50, 40501 Dues-
seldorf
*Tel:* (0211) 5 20 13-0 *Fax:* (0211) 5 20 13-28
*E-mail:* oepnv@alba.verlag.de
*Web Site:* www.alba-verlag.de
*Telex:* 8585536
*Key Personnel*
Publishing Dir: Robert Braun
Man Dir, Rights & Permissions: Alf Teloeken
*Tel:* (0211) 5 20 13-10 *E-mail:* at@alba-verlag.
de
Manager: Tim Teloeken *Tel:* (0211) 5 20 13-12
*E-mail:* teloeken@alba-verlag.de

Sales, Publicity: Willi Lennartz; Cornelia Honekamp
Production: P Gerens
Founded: 1951
Subjects: Crafts, Games, Hobbies, Film, Video, Outdoor Recreation
ISBN Prefix(es): 3-87094
*Associate Companies:* Alba Publikation Alf Teloeken GmbH und Co KG; Schwesternge-sellschaft: Alba Fachverlag GmbH & Co KG

**Albarello Verlag GmbH+**
Dornaper Str 23, 42327 Wuppertal
*Tel:* (02058) 8279 *Fax:* (02058) 80534
*E-mail:* email@albarello.de
*Web Site:* www.albarello.de
*Key Personnel*
Man Dir: Frank Zimmermann
Founded: 2001
ISBN Prefix(es): 3-930299; 3-9801855; 3-86559

**Verlag Karl Alber GmbH+**
Hermann-Herder-Str 4, 79104 Freiburg im Breis-gau
*Tel:* (0761) 27 17-436 *Fax:* (0761) 27 17-212
*E-mail:* info@verlag-alber.de
*Web Site:* www.verlag-alber.de
*Key Personnel*
Man Dir: Lukas Trabert
Founded: 1939
Subjects: History, Philosophy
ISBN Prefix(es): 3-495
Number of titles published annually: 30 Print
Total Titles: 400 Print
*Parent Company:* Verlag Herder
*Orders to:* Verlagsauslieferung Koch, Neff & Oetinger, Schockenriedstr 39, Postfach 800620, 70565 Stuttgart

**Albert Nauck & Co**
Gutenbergstr 6, 10587 Berlin
*Tel:* (030) 3980640
*Key Personnel*
Contact: A Gallus; J Kuth
ISBN Prefix(es): 3-87574

**Albino Verlag,** *imprint of* Bruno Gmuender Verlag GmbH

**E Albrecht Verlags-KG+**
Freihamer Str 2, 82166 Graefelfing
Mailing Address: Postfach 11 40, 82153 Graefelf-ing
*Tel:* (089) 85853-0 *Fax:* (089) 85853199
*E-mail:* av@albrecht.de
*Key Personnel*
Man Dir & Publisher: Hansgeorg Albrecht
Publisher: Oliver Albrecht
Founded: 1927
Subjects: Career Development, Sports, Athletics
ISBN Prefix(es): 3-87014

**Verlag und Antiquariat Frank Albrecht**
Panoramastr 4, 69198 Schriesheim
*Tel:* (06203) 65713 *Fax:* (06203) 65311
*E-mail:* albrecht@antiquariat.com
*Web Site:* www.antiquariat.com
*Key Personnel*
Publisher: Frank Albrecht
Founded: 1985
Membership(s): PEN International & German An-tiques.
Subjects: Government, Political Science, History, Literature, Literary Criticism, Essays
ISBN Prefix(es): 3-926360
Total Titles: 1 Print

**Alexander Verlag Berlin+**
Postfach 191824, 14008 Berlin
*Tel:* (030) 3021826 *Fax:* (030) 3029408
*E-mail:* info@alexander-verlag.com

*Web Site:* www.alexander-verlag.com
*Key Personnel*
Owner: Alexander Wewerka *E-mail:* wewerka@ alexander-verlag.com
Founded: 1983
Subjects: Drama, Theater, Film, Video, Literature, Literary Criticism, Essays, Music, Dance
ISBN Prefix(es): 3-923854; 3-89581
Total Titles: 85 Print; 8 CD-ROM; 3 Audio
Distributed by AVA-Buch 2000 (Switzerland); AS Verlagsservice Holler (Austria)
*Orders to:* Sova, Friesstr 20-24, 60388 Frankfurt am Main, Contact: Brigitte Platteel *Tel:* (069) 410211 *Fax:* (069) 410280 *E-mail:* sovaffm@t-online.de

**Alkor-Edition Kassel GmbH+**
Heinrich-Schuetz-Allee 35, 34131 Kassel
*Tel:* (0561) 3105-282 *Fax:* (0561) 37755
*E-mail:* alkor-edition@baerenreiter.com
*Web Site:* www.alkor-edition.com
*Key Personnel*
Man Dir: Barbara Scheuch-Voetterle
Founded: 1934
Subjects: Music, Dance
ISBN Prefix(es): 3-920018
Distributed by Baerenreiter Ltd (Great Britain, Ireland, New Zealand & Australia); Baerenre-iter Music Corporation (Canada & US); Edi-tio Baerenreiter Praha (Slovakian & Czech Republic); Casa Musicale Sonzogno (Italy); Faber Music Distribution (Great Britain, Ire-land, New Zealand & Australia); Hartai Music Agency (Hungary); Muziekhandel Albersen & Co (Netherlands); Polskie Wydawnictwo Muzy-czne (PWM) (Germany & Austria); SEEMSA (Spain & Portugal); Zamp (Croatia & Slovenia)
Distributor for Editio Baerenreiter Praha (Ger-many, Austria & Switzerland); Baerenreiter Verlag Kassel (Basel, London, New York, Prag) (Worldwide); Gustav Bosse Verlag Kas-sel (Worldwide); Dilia Prag (Germany, Aus-tria, Switerland, Benelux countries, Scandi-navia); Faber Music London (Germany, Aus-tria & Switzerland); Henle Verlag Muenchen (Worldwide); Henschel Verlag fuer Musik Berlin (Worldwide); Editions Henry Lemoine Paris (Germany, Austria & Switzerland); Musikwissenschaftlicher Verlag Wien (World-wide with the exception of Austria); Polskie Wydawnictwo Muzyczne (PWM) (Germany & Austria); Slowakischer Musikfonds Bratislava (Germany, Austria, Switerland, Benelux coun-tries); Strauss Edition Wien (Worldwide); Sued-deutscher Musikverlag Heidelberg (Worldwide); Tschechischer Musikfonds Praha (Germany, Austria, Switzerland, Benelux countries, Scan-dinavia, Spain & Portugal)

**Alouette Verlag+**
Uferstr 41, 22113 Oststeinbek
*Tel:* (040) 712 23 53 *Fax:* (040) 713 41 88
*E-mail:* webmaster@alouette-verlag.de
*Web Site:* www.alouette-verlag.de
*Key Personnel*
President & Publisher: Juergen F Boden
  *E-mail:* juergen.boden@alouette-verlag.de
Editor: Elke Emshoff
Art Dir: Petra Horn
Founded: 1983
Book & film publishers
Specialize in nature-oriented picture & text books (pictorials with profound text matter) mainly about North America, the Arctic & Siberia, TV documentaries & cultural books.
Subjects: Natural History, Travel, Foreign Cul-tures
ISBN Prefix(es): 3-924324
Number of titles published annually: 2 Print; 2 Audio
Total Titles: 20 Print; 4 Audio

**Alpha Literatur Verlag/Alpha Presse**
August-Siebertstr 9, 60323 Frankfurt
*Tel:* (069) 555325 *Fax:* (069) 955130-99
*Key Personnel*
Man Dir: Dr Gisela Philipps
Founded: 1969
Subjects: Drama, Theater, Poetry
ISBN Prefix(es): 3-924510

**ALS-Verlag GmbH+**
Voltastr 3, 63128 Dietzenbach
Mailing Address: Postfach 1440, 63114 Dietzen-bach
*Tel:* (06074) 82 16-0; (06074) 82 16-50 (orders) *Fax:* (06074) 2 73 22
*E-mail:* info@als-verlag.de
*Web Site:* www.als-verlag.de
*Key Personnel*
Man Dir: Juergen Hils
Founded: 1967
Subjects: Art, Crafts, Games, Hobbies, Educa-tion, Environmental Studies, How-to, Outdoor Recreation
ISBN Prefix(es): 3-89135; 3-921366
Imprints: Dietzenbach

**Altberliner Verlag GmbH+**
Akademiestrabe 19, 80799 Munich
*Tel:* (089) 2101 1913 *Fax:* (089) 2101 1923
*E-mail:* info@altberliner.de
*Web Site:* www.altberliner.de
*Key Personnel*
Owner: Dr Stephan Schmidt
Owner & Dir: Renate Nickl
Founded: 1945
Subjects: Developing Countries, Fiction, Litera-ture, Literary Criticism, Essays, Mysteries
ISBN Prefix(es): 3-357
*Branch Office(s)*
Zentuerstr 19, 80798 Munich *Tel:* (089) 1 23 62-59 *Fax:* (089) 12 779 954 *E-mail:* vertrieb@ altberliner.de

**Anneliese Althoff,** see Asso Verlag

**Aluminium-Verlag Marketing & Kommunikation GmbH**
Aachener Str 172, 40223 Duesseldorf
*Fax:* (0211) 15 91-379
*E-mail:* info@alu-verlag.de
*Web Site:* www.alu-verlag.de
*Key Personnel*
Man Dir: Werner Lenzen *Tel:* (0211) 15 91-370
  *E-mail:* w.lenzen@alu-verlag.de
Sales Manager: Anne Tappen *Tel:* (0211) 15 91-371 *E-mail:* a.tappen@alu-verlag.de
Seminar & Advertising Manager: Christiane Czech *Tel:* (0211) 15 91-372 *E-mail:* c.czech@ alu-verlag.de
Founded: 1953
Subjects: Earth Sciences
ISBN Prefix(es): 3-87017
Number of titles published annually: 3 CD-ROM
Total Titles: 17 Print; 3 CD-ROM

**Anabas-Verlag Guenter Kaempf GmbH & Co KG+**
Friesstr 20-24, 60388 Frankfurt
*Tel:* (069) 94 21 98 71 *Fax:* (069) 94 21 98 72
*E-mail:* info@anabas-verlag.com
*Key Personnel*
Man Dir: Guenter Kaempf
Founded: 1966
Membership(s): Borsenverein des Deutschen Buchandles, Hessischer Buchhandler- und Ver-legerverband.
Subjects: Art, History, Poetry, Travel
ISBN Prefix(es): 3-87038
Number of titles published annually: 10 Print
Total Titles: 315 Print
Foreign Rep(s): Pierre Bachofner (Switzerland); Seth Meyer-Bruhns (Austria)

*Orders to:* Sozialistische Verlagsauslieferung GmbH, Friesstr 20-22, 60388 Frankfurt am Main *Tel:* (069) 410211 *Fax:* (069) 410280 *E-mail:* sovaffm@t-online.de

**Angelika und Lothar Binding**
Gaisbergstr 68, 69115 Heidelberg
*Tel:* (06221) 20955 *Fax:* (06221) 181846
*E-mail:* Angelika.Binding@gmx.net
*Web Site:* www.binding-singles.de
*Key Personnel*
Owner: Angelika Binding *E-mail:* angelika. binding@gmx.net; Lothar Binding
Founded: 1984
Subjects: Music, Dance
ISBN Prefix(es): 3-9804710
Total Titles: 2 Print

**Anrich Verlag GmbH+**
Werderstr 10, 69469 Weinheim
Mailing Address: Postfach 100154, 69441 Weinheim
*Tel:* (06201) 6007-0 *Fax:* (06201) 17464
*Key Personnel*
Man Dir: Gerold Anrich *E-mail:* g.anrich@beltz.de
Founded: 1970
Membership(s): Arbeitsgemeinschaft von Jugend Buchverlegern in Der Brd eV.
ISBN Prefix(es): 3-920110; 3-89106

**Antex Verlag-Hans Joachin Schuhmacher+**
Am Gabelsee, 15306 Falkenhagen
*Tel:* (033603) 40410 *Fax:* (033603) 40400
*Key Personnel*
Publisher: Hajo Schuhmacher
Sales: Heidi Schuhmacher
Author: Tina Rau
Founded: 1988
ISBN Prefix(es): 3-9801871; 3-9809302

**Antiqua-Verlag GmbH**
Dorneckstr 3a, 79793 Wutoeschingen-Horheim
*Tel:* (07746) 2273 *Fax:* (07746) 2260
*Key Personnel*
Manager: Ottfried Ludwig
Founded: 1977
Subjects: Geography, Geology, Medicine, Nursing, Dentistry
ISBN Prefix(es): 3-88210

**Antiquariats-Union Vertriebs GmbH & Co KG**
Luener Rennbahn 14, 21339 Lueneburg
*Tel:* (04131) 983504 *Fax:* (04131) 9835595
*Web Site:* www.restauflagen.de
*Key Personnel*
Contact: Jens Harelberg *E-mail:* harelberg@antiquariats-union.de
Number of titles published annually: 15 Print
Total Titles: 70 Print

**Anzeigenverwaltung & Herstellung**, *imprint of* Johann Wolfgang Goethe Universitat

**AOL-Verlag Frohmut Menze**
Waldstr 18, 77839 Lichtenau-Scherzheim
*Tel:* (07227) 95 88-0 *Fax:* (07227) 95 88-95
*E-mail:* info@aol-verlag.de; bestellung@aol-verlag.de
*Web Site:* www.aol-verlag.de
*Key Personnel*
Man Dir: Frohmut Menze *Fax:* (07227) 95 88-22 *E-mail:* frohmut.menze@aol-verlag.de
Advertising: Ute Hettel *Fax:* (07227) 95 88-21 *E-mail:* ute.hettel@aol-verlag.de
Sales: Thomas Hofmann *Tel:* (07227) 95 88-94 *E-mail:* thomas.hofmann@aol-verlag.de; Gisela Korn *Tel:* (07227) 95 88-31 *E-mail:* gisela.korn@aol-verlag.de
Subjects: Advertising, Art, Biological Sciences, Career Development, Chemistry, Chemical En-

gineering, Child Care & Development, Computer Science, Drama, Theater, Education, Energy, English as a Second Language, Environmental Studies, Fiction, Film, Video, Foreign Countries, Government, Political Science, Health, Nutrition, History, Literature, Literary Criticism, Essays, Management, Mathematics, Natural History, Nonfiction (General), Outdoor Recreation, Physical Sciences, Physics, Science (General), Sports, Athletics, Transportation
ISBN Prefix(es): 3-89111

**Verlag APHAIA Svea Haske, Sonja Schumann GbR**
Radickestr 44, 12489 Berlin-Treptow
*Tel:* (030) 813 39 98 *Fax:* (030) 813 39 98
*E-mail:* info@aphaia-verlag.de
*Web Site:* www.aphaia-verlag.de
*Key Personnel*
Contact: Svea Haske; Sonja Schumann
Founded: 1986
Subjects: Art, Literature, Literary Criticism, Essays, Music, Dance, Poetry, Bookart, Literature, Lyrics, Music
ISBN Prefix(es): 3-926677
Number of titles published annually: 5 Print
Total Titles: 125 Print
Distributor for Friedrich Nolte Verlag; Paian Verlag
*Orders to:* Aphaia Verlag, Berlin-Treptow

**Apollo-Verlag Paul Lincke GmbH**
Weihergarten 5, 55116 Mainz
Mailing Address: Postfach 3640, 55026 Mainz
*Tel:* (06131) 246300 *Fax:* (06131) 246861
*E-mail:* apollo@schott-musik.de
*Key Personnel*
Contact: Dr Christian Sprang
Subjects: Music, Dance
ISBN Prefix(es): 3-920030
*Sales Office(s):* SMD Schott Music Distribution GmbH, Carl Zeissstr 1, 55129 Mainz

**Aquamarin Verlag+**
Muehlenstr 43, 85567 Grafing
*Tel:* (08092) 9444 *Fax:* (08092) 1614
*E-mail:* aquamarin_verlag@t-online.de
*Key Personnel*
Man Dir: Dr Peter Michel
Founded: 1980
Subjects: Art, Astrology, Occult, Parapsychology, Philosophy, Religion - Buddhist, Religion - Hindu, Science (General)
ISBN Prefix(es): 3-922936; 3-89427
Imprints: Adyar Edition; Adyar Verlag; Sulamith Wulfing Edition; Sulamith Wulfing Verlag
*U.S. Office(s):* Bluestar, 160 Camino Don Miguel, Orinda, CA 94563, United States, Contact: Petra Michel *Tel:* 925-386-0440 *Fax:* 925-386-0386 *Web Site:* www.bluestar.com
Foreign Rep(s): Dr Fiuliana Bernardi (Italy)
Foreign Rights: Katia Schume (Portugal, South America, Spain)

**Aragon GmbH+**
Formerly Edition Aragon-Verlagsgesellschaft mbH
Amselstr 8, 47445 Moers
*Tel:* (02841) 16561 *Fax:* (02841) 24336
*Key Personnel*
President & Publisher: Willi Klauke
Founded: 1984
Subjects: Art, Drama, Theater, Travel
ISBN Prefix(es): 3-89535
Distributed by AVA b+i (Switzerland)
*Orders to:* Prolit, Siemensstr 18a, 35463 Fernwald/Annerod

**arani-Verlag GmbH+**
Gneisenaustr 23, 10961 Berlin
*Tel:* (030) 691-7073 *Fax:* (030) 691-4067

*Key Personnel*
Man Dir: Volker Spiess
Founded: 1947
Subjects: History, Regional Interests, Religion - Jewish, Judaica
ISBN Prefix(es): 3-7605
*Associate Companies:* Haude und Spenersche Verlagsbuchhandlung; Wissenschaftsverlag Volker Spiess GmbH
*Orders to:* VAH-Jager Verlagsauslieferungen, Miraustr 54, 13509 Berlin

**Arbeiterpresse Verlags- und Vertriebsgesellschaft mbH+**
Postfach 500105, 45055 Essen
Mailing Address: Dickmannstr 2-4, Essenruhr 45143
*Tel:* (0201) 6462106 *Fax:* (0201) 6462108
*E-mail:* info@arbeiterpresse.de
*Web Site:* www.arbeiterpresse.de
*Key Personnel*
Contact: Wolfgang Zimmermann *E-mail:* wz@arbeiterpresse.de
Founded: 1979
Subjects: Government, Political Science, History, Labor, Industrial Relations, Social Sciences, Sociology
ISBN Prefix(es): 3-88634
Number of titles published annually: 4 Print
Total Titles: 32 Print
*U.S. Office(s):* Mehring Books, PO Box 48377, Oak Park, MI 48237, United States *Tel:* 967-2924 *Fax:* 967-3023 *E-mail:* inquiries@mehring.com

**Arbeitsgruppe LOK Report eV**
Sigmaringerstr 26, 10713 Berlin
*Tel:* (030) 86 40 92 63 *Fax:* (030) 86 40 92 64
*E-mail:* redaktion@lok-report.de
*Web Site:* www.lok-report.de
*Key Personnel*
Chief Editor: Martin Stertz
Founded: 1972
Specialize in transport, railways, locomotive, German & Eastern European railways
Publish monthly railway magazine *Lok Report*.
Subjects: Transportation, Locomotives, Railways
ISBN Prefix(es): 3-921980
Number of titles published annually: 2 Print
Total Titles: 6 Print

**Arcadia Verlag GmbH+**
Johnsallee 23, 20148 Hamburg
*Tel:* (040) 4141000 *Fax:* (040) 41410041
*E-mail:* contact@sikorski.de
*Web Site:* www.sikorski.de
*Key Personnel*
Man Dir: Dagmar Sikorski; Prof Hans-Wilfred Sikorski
Rights & Permissions: Karl-Hermann Adrio
Founded: 1935
Subjects: Drama, Theater, Music, Dance
ISBN Prefix(es): 3-920033
*Parent Company:* Buehnen-und Musikverlage Dr Sikorski KG

**ARCult Media+**
Affiliate of ERICarts - European Institute for Comparative Cultural Research
Dahlmannstr 26, 53113 Bonn
*Tel:* (0228) 211059 *Fax:* (0228) 217493
*E-mail:* info@arcultmedia.de
*Web Site:* www.arcultmedia.de; www.kulturforschung.de; www.ericarts.org
*Key Personnel*
Dir: Dr Andreas Joh Wiesand
Contact: Ingo Bruenglinghaus
Founded: 1969
Publications & research documents in all fields of the arts & culture industries.
Subjects: Art, Developing Countries, Drama, Theater, Journalism, Management, Music, Dance, Outdoor Recreation, Publishing & Book Trade

Reference, Radio, TV, Social Sciences, Sociology, Women's Studies
ISBN Prefix(es): 3-930395
Total Titles: 60 Print; 2 CD-ROM; 5 Online
*Branch Office(s)*
Vienna, Austria
Berlin
Distributed by C H Beck (Munich); Leske & Budrich (Opladen); Sam's Books (Services for Arts Management)

**Ardey-Verlag GmbH**
An den Speichern 6, 48157 Muenster
*Tel:* (0251) 4132-0 *Fax:* (0251) 4132-20
*E-mail:* ardey@muenster.de
*Web Site:* www.ardey-verlag.de
*Key Personnel*
Man Dir: Bodo Strototte
Publisher: Ulrich Grabowsky
Founded: 1951
Subjects: Architecture & Interior Design, Art, Geography, Geology, History, Literature, Literary Criticism, Essays, Nonfiction (General), Regional Interests, Religion - Other
ISBN Prefix(es): 3-87023
*Orders to:* CVK, Kammeratsheide 66, 33609 Bielefeld

**Arena Verlag GmbH+**
Rottendorferstr 16, 97074 Wuerzburg
Mailing Address: Postfach 5169, 97001 Wuerzburg
*Tel:* (0931) 79 644-0 *Fax:* (0931) 79 644-13
*Key Personnel*
Man Dir: Juergen Weidenbach
Publicity: Dirk Meyer
Sales Dir: Albrecht Oldenbourg
Production: Winfried Popp
Foreign Rights: Monika Obrist *Tel:* (0931) 73644-62 *E-mail:* monika.obrist@arena-verlag.de
Founded: 1949
Subjects: Fiction, Nonfiction (General)
ISBN Prefix(es): 3-401; 3-88155
Number of titles published annually: 500 Print
Total Titles: 2,000 Print
*Parent Company:* Georg Westermann GmbH & Co, Georg-Westermann-Allee 66, 38104 Braunschweig
Imprints: Edition Buecherbar im Arena Verlag; Ensslin Verlag im Arena Verlag
*Warehouse:* VSB Verlagsservice Braunschweig GmbH, Georg-Westermann-Allee 66, 38104 Braunschweig

**Argon Verlag GmbH+**
Unit of S Fischer Verlag
Neuenburgerstr 17, 10969 Berlin
*Tel:* (030) 25 37 38-0 *Fax:* (030) 25 37 38-99
*E-mail:* info.argon@fischerverlage.de
*Web Site:* www.fischerverlage.de
*Key Personnel*
Editor-in-Chief: Hans Christian Rohr *Tel:* (030) 25 37 38-24 *E-mail:* christian.rohr@fischerverlage.de
Founded: 1952
Subjects: Fiction, Nonfiction (General)
ISBN Prefix(es): 3-87024; 3-930088
*Orders to:* S Fischer Verlag, 60591 Frankfurt/Main *Tel:* (069) 60620 *Fax:* (069) 6062214 *E-mail:* verkauf@fischerverlage.de

**Argument-Verlag+**
Eppendorfer Weg 95a, 20259 Hamburg
*Tel:* (040) 401800-0 *Fax:* (040) 401800-20
*E-mail:* verlag@argument.de
*Web Site:* www.argument.de
*Key Personnel*
Contact: Bettina Fischer; Wolfgang Fritz Haug; Frigga Haug
Founded: 1959
Subjects: Fiction, Gay & Lesbian, Government, Political Science, Philosophy, Science Fiction,

Fantasy, Social Sciences, Sociology, Women's Studies
ISBN Prefix(es): 3-88619; 3-920037
Divisions: Redaktion

**Aries-Verlag Paul Johannes Muller+**
Ringstr 32a, 83355 Grabenstaett
Mailing Address: Postfach 166, 83355 Grabenstaett
*Tel:* (08661) 8209 *Fax:* (08661) 985980
*Key Personnel*
Owner: Paul J Mueller *E-mail:* pjm@aires-verlag.de
Founded: 1965
Subjects: Architecture & Interior Design, Art
ISBN Prefix(es): 3-920041

**Ariston,** *imprint of* Heinrich Hugendubel Verlag GmbH

**Arkana Verlag Tete Boettger Rainer Wunderlich GmbH+**
Hainbundstr 17, 37085 Goettingen
Mailing Address: Postfach 1140, 37001 Goettingen
*Tel:* (0551) 41709 *Fax:* (0551) 43868
*Key Personnel*
Owner: Mr T Boettger *E-mail:* teteboettger@t-online.de
Founded: 1981
Subjects: Art, History, Science (General), History of Science
ISBN Prefix(es): 3-923257

**Arnoldsche Verlagsanstalt GmbH** (Arnoldsche Art Publishers)+
Liststr 9, 70180 Stuttgart
*Tel:* (0711) 645618-0 *Fax:* (0711) 645618-79
*E-mail:* art@arnoldsche.com
*Web Site:* www.arnoldsche.com
*Key Personnel*
International Rights: Dieter Zuehlsdorff
Marketing, Distribution & Public Relations: Dirk Allgaier *Tel:* (0711) 645618-20 *E-mail:* allgaier@arnoldsche.com
Founded: 1988
Subjects: Antiques, Architecture & Interior Design, Art, Fashion, Photography, Specialize in jewelry, glass, porcelain, Asian art & Non-European Art
ISBN Prefix(es): 3-925369; 3-89790
Number of titles published annually: 15 Print
Total Titles: 80 Print
*Associate Companies:* Forum fuer Europaeische Kunst und Kultur, Stuttgart
*U.S. Office(s):* Antique Collectors' Club Ltd, 51 Market St, Industrial Park, Wappings Falls, NY 12590, United States *Tel:* 845-297-0003 *Fax:* 845-297-0068

**Ars Edition GmbH+**
Friedrichstr 9, 80801 Munich
Mailing Address: Postfach 430151, 80731 Munich
*Tel:* (089) 3810060 *Fax:* (089) 381006-58
*Key Personnel*
Man Dir: Marcel Nauer
Man Dir, Rights & Permissions: Sabine Lippert
Production: Gregor Schulze
Public Relations: Birgit Welzel
Founded: 1896
Subjects: Art, Child Care & Development, Cookery, Crafts, Games, Hobbies, Fiction, House & Home, Nonfiction (General), Romance
ISBN Prefix(es): 3-7607
Subsidiaries: Ars Edition

**Ars Vivendi Verlag+**
Bauhof 1, 90556 Cadolzburg
Mailing Address: Postfach 9, 90553 Cadolzburg
*Tel:* (09103) 719 29 0 *Fax:* (09103) 719 59 19

*E-mail:* ars@arsvivendi.com
*Web Site:* www.arsvivendi.com
*Key Personnel*
Owner: Norbert Treuheit
Founded: 1988
Subjects: Cookery, Nonfiction (General), Travel
ISBN Prefix(es): 3-927482; 3-931043; 3-89716

**Art Directors Club Verlag GmbH**
Leibnizstr 65, 10629 Berlin-Charlottenburg
*Tel:* (030) 59 00 31 0 *Fax:* (030) 59 00 31 0
*E-mail:* adc@adc.de
*Web Site:* www.adc.de
*Key Personnel*
Manager: Elly Koszytorz; Susann Schronen *Tel:* (030) 59 22 31 0-21 *Fax:* (030) 59 22 31 0-21 *E-mail:* susann.schronen@adc.de
Project Manager: Astrid Hegenauer *Tel:* (030) 59 00 31 0-21 *Fax:* (030) 59 00 31 0-21 *E-mail:* astrid.hegenauer@adc.de
Project Management Events/Seminars: Katrin Puelacher *Tel:* (030) 59 00 31 0-21 *Fax:* (030) 59 00 31 0-21 *E-mail:* katrin.puelacher@adc.de
Founded: 1964
Art Directors Club is only licenser.
Subjects: Advertising, Communications
*Orders to:* Universitaetsdruckerei und Verlag Hermann Schmidt Mainz, Robert-Kochstr 8, 55214 Mainz *Tel:* (06131) 506030 *Fax:* (06131) 506080

**Arun-Verlag+**
Engerda 28, 07407 Engerda
*Tel:* (036743) 233-0 *Fax:* (036743) 233-17
*E-mail:* info@arun-verlag.de
*Web Site:* www.arun-verlag.de
*Key Personnel*
Publisher: Stefan Ulbrich
Founded: 1989
Subjects: Astrology, Occult, Native American Studies, Philosophy, Religion - Other
ISBN Prefix(es): 3-927940; 3-935581
Total Titles: 50 Print

**Roland Asanger Verlag GmbH**
Boedldorf 3, 84178 Kroening
*Tel:* (08744) 7262 *Fax:* (08744) 967755
*E-mail:* verlag@asanger.de
*Web Site:* www.asanger.de
*Key Personnel*
Publisher: Dr Gerd Wenninger
Founded: 1987
Subjects: Environmental Studies, Health, Nutrition, Psychology, Psychiatry, Social Sciences, Sociology
ISBN Prefix(es): 3-89334
Distributed by Herder AG Basel
*Distribution Center:* Publishing House Service Southwest *Tel:* (07254) 507-0 *Fax:* (07254) 507-24 *E-mail:* verlagsservicesw@tonline.de
*Orders to:* Verlagsservice Suedwest, Boschstr 2, 68753 Waghaeusel *Tel:* (07254) 507 13 *Fax:* (07254) 507 24 *E-mail:* verlagsservice-sw@t-online.de

**Aschendorffsche Verlagsbuchhandlung GmbH & Co KG+**
Soester Str 13, 48135 Muenster
*Tel:* (0251) 690136 *Fax:* (0251) 690143
*E-mail:* buchverlag@aschendorff.de
*Web Site:* www.aschendorff.de/buch
*Telex:* 892555
*Key Personnel*
Contact: Dr Eduard Huffer; Dr Jurgeu Beuedikt Huffer
Founded: 1720
Membership(s): VGS - Verlagsgesellschaft mbH & Co KG.
Subjects: History, Language Arts, Linguistics, Philosophy, Psychology, Psychiatry, Regional Interests, Religion - Other, Theology

ISBN Prefix(es): 3-402
Number of titles published annually: 80 Print; 2
  CD-ROM


**Asclepios Edition Lothar Baus+**
Zum Lappentascher Hof 65, 66424 Homburg/Saar
*Tel:* (06841) 71863
*Web Site:* www.asclepiosedition.de
*Key Personnel*
Contact: Lothar Baus *E-mail:* lotharbaus@web.de
Founded: 1985
Specialize in Goethe-Studies, Friedrich Nietzsche
  & Stoic Philosophie.
Subjects: Biography, Literature, Literary Criti-
  cism, Essays, Philosophy
ISBN Prefix(es): 3-925101; 3-935288


**Asgard-Verlag Dr Werner Hippe GmbH**
Einsteinstr 10, 53757 Sankt Augustin
Mailing Address: Postfach 1465, 53732 Sankt
  Augustin
*Tel:* (02241) 3164-0 *Fax:* (02241) 316436
*E-mail:* service@asgard.de
*Key Personnel*
Man Dir: Stefan Maus; Uwe Schliebusch
Founded: 1947
Subjects: Government, Political Science, Health,
  Nutrition, Medicine, Nursing, Dentistry, Public
  Administration, Social Sciences, Sociology
ISBN Prefix(es): 3-537
Subsidiaries: Siegler & Co Verlag fur Zeitarchive
  GmbH


**Assimil GmbH**
Hinter den Hagen 1, 52388 Noervenich
Mailing Address: Postfach 47, 52386 Noervenich
*Tel:* (02426) 94000 *Fax:* (02426) 4862
*E-mail:* kontakt@assimil.com
*Web Site:* www.assimil.com
Founded: 1988
Specialize in textbooks-foreign languages.
Subjects: Language Arts, Linguistics
ISBN Prefix(es): 3-89625


**Asso Verlag+**
Martin-Heix-Platz 3, 46045 Oberhausen
*Tel:* (0208) 802356 *Fax:* (0208) 809882
*E-mail:* info@asso-verlag-oberhausen.de
*Key Personnel*
Contact: Anneliese Althoff
Founded: 1970
Subjects: Labor, Industrial Relations, Poetry, Re-
  gional Interests, Social Sciences, Sociology
ISBN Prefix(es): 3-921541
*Warehouse:* Lothringerstr 64, 46045 Oberhausen


**Verlag Atelier im Bauernhaus Fischerhude
  Wolf-Dietmar Stock+**
In der Bredenau 6, 28870 Ottersberg-Fischerhude
*Tel:* (04293) 491; (04293) 493 *Fax:* (04293) 1238
*Key Personnel*
Publisher: Wolf-Dietmar Stock
Rights & Permissions: Hans-Guenther Pawelzik
Founded: 1976
Subjects: Art, Fiction, Regional Interests
ISBN Prefix(es): 3-88132
*Orders to:* VVA, An der Autobahn, 33310
  Guetersloh


**Atelier Verlag Andernach (AVA)+**
Antel 74, 56626 Andernach
*Tel:* (02632) 44432 *Fax:* (02632) 31383
*E-mail:* info@atelierverlag-andernach.de
*Web Site:* www.atelierverlag-andernach.de
*Key Personnel*
Man Dir, Rights & Permissions: Fritz Werf
Founded: 1966
Subjects: Art, Poetry
ISBN Prefix(es): 3-921042

**AUE-Verlag GmbH+**
Korgerstr 20, 74219 Moeckmuehl
Mailing Address: Postfach 1108, 74215 Moeck-
  muehl
*Tel:* (06298) 1328 *Fax:* (06298) 4298
*E-mail:* info@aue-verlag.com
*Web Site:* www.aue-verlag.com
*Key Personnel*
Manager: Thomas Gauger
Founded: 1919
Subjects: Crafts, Games, Hobbies, Education, Re-
  ligion - Protestant, Religion - Other
ISBN Prefix(es): 3-87029
Divisions: Redaktion


**Auer Verlag GmbH+**
Heilig-Kreuzstr 16, 86609 Donauwoerth
Mailing Address: Postfach 1152, 86601 Donau-
  woerth
*Tel:* (0906) 73-240 *Fax:* (0906) 73177; (0906)
  73178
*E-mail:* info@auer-verlag.de
*Web Site:* www.auer-verlag.de *Cable:* AUER
  DONAUWORTH
*Key Personnel*
Man Dir: Herr Buechler *Tel:* (0906) 73242
Contact: Tanja Auernhamer *Tel:* (0906) 73152
  *E-mail:* auernhamer@auer-verlag.de
Founded: 1875
Membership(s): TR-Verlagsunion GmbH.
Subjects: Education, History, Mathematics, Mu-
  sic, Dance, Psychology, Psychiatry, Religion -
  Catholic, Science (General), Sports, Athletics,
  Theology
ISBN Prefix(es): 3-403; 3-87904
Number of titles published annually: 100 Print;
  20 CD-ROM; 5 Audio
Total Titles: 1,800 Print; 60 CD-ROM; 20 Audio
*Branch Office(s)*
Westenhellweg 126, 44137 Dortmund *Tel:* (0231)
  5844830 *Fax:* (0231) 58448320
August-Bebelstr 43, 04275 Leipzig *Tel:* (0341)
  3026270 *Fax:* (0341) 3026271


**Aufbau Taschenbuch Verlag GmbH**
Neue Promenade 6, 10178 Berlin
Mailing Address: Postfach 193, 10105 Berlin
*Tel:* (030) 283 94-0 *Fax:* (030) 283 94 100
*E-mail:* info@aufbau-verlag.de
*Web Site:* www.aufbau-verlag.de
*Key Personnel*
Program Manager: Rene Strien
Manager: Peter Dempewolf
International Rights: Astrid Poppenhusen
  *Tel:* (030) 283 94 212 *E-mail:* poppenhusen@
  aufbau-verlag.de
Contact: Barbara Stang
Rights & Permissions: Kathrin Schulz
Founded: 1994
Subjects: Fiction, Film, Video, Government, Po-
  litical Science, Literature, Literary Criticism,
  Essays, Poetry, Romance
ISBN Prefix(es): 3-7466
Number of titles published annually: 150 Print
Total Titles: 500 Print
*Shipping Address:* Mohr Morawa, Buchvertrieb
  Gesellschaft mbH, Postfach 260, 1101 Vienna,
  Austria; Buecher Balmer Verlagsausliefrung,
  Neugasse 12, 6301 Zurich, Switzerland
*Warehouse:* Libri-Distributions GmbH, August-
  Schanzstr 33, 60433 Frankfurt
*Orders to:* Libri-Distributions GmbH, August-
  Schanzstr 33, 60433 Frankfurt


**Aufbau-Verlag GmbH+**
Neue Promenade 6, 10178 Berlin
Mailing Address: Postfach 193, 10105 Berlin
*Tel:* (030) 28 394-0 *Fax:* (030) 28 394-100
*E-mail:* info@aufbau-verlag.de
*Web Site:* www2.aufbauverlag.de
*Key Personnel*
Program Manager: Rene Strien

Manager: Peter Dempewolf
International Rights: Astrid Poppenhusen
  *Tel:* (030) 28394212 *E-mail:* poppenhussen@
  aufbau-verlag.de
Contact: Barbara Stang
Rights & Permissions: Kathrin Schulz
Founded: 1945
Subjects: Fiction, Film, Video, Government, Po-
  litical Science, Literature, Literary Criticism,
  Essays, Mysteries, Poetry, Romance
ISBN Prefix(es): 3-351
Number of titles published annually: 80 Print; 20
  Audio
Total Titles: 400 Print
*Shipping Address:* Mohr Morawa, Buchvertrieb
  Gesellschaft mbH, Postfach 260, 1101 Vienna,
  Austria; Buecher Balmer Verlagsausliefrung,
  Neugasse 12, 6301 Zurich, Switzerland
*Warehouse:* Libri-Distributions-GmbH, August-
  Schanz-Str 33, 60433 Frankfurt
*Orders to:* Libri-Distributions-GmbH, August-
  Schanz-Str 33, 60433 Frankfurt


**Aufstieg-Verlag GmbH**
Isarweg 37, 84028 Landshut
*Tel:* (0871) 54112 *Fax:* (0871) 54112
*Web Site:* www.aufstieg-verlag.de
*Key Personnel*
Man Dir & International Rights: Gisela Werner
Founded: 1947
Subjects: Cookery, Fiction, Foreign Countries,
  History, Humor
ISBN Prefix(es): 3-7612; 3-920235


**August Guese Verlag GmbH**
Am Spitzacker 10, 61184 Karben
*Tel:* (06039) 48 01 10 *Fax:* (06039) 48 01 48
*E-mail:* info@guese.de
*Web Site:* www.guese.de
*Key Personnel*
Man Dir: Johannes Guese
Founded: 1954
Subjects: Gardening, Plants
ISBN Prefix(es): 3-87278


**J J Augustin Verlag GmbH**
Am Fleth 36-37, 25348 Glueckstadt
Mailing Address: Postfach 1106, 25342 Glueck-
  stadt
*Tel:* (04124) 20 44-46 *Fax:* (04124) 47 09
*Key Personnel*
President & International Rights: Walter Pruess
Founded: 1920
Subjects: Asian Studies, Literature, Literary Criti-
  cism, Essays, Religion - Islamic, Science (Gen-
  eral)
ISBN Prefix(es): 3-87030


**Augustinus-Verlag Wurzburg Inh
  Augustinerprovinz**
Grabenberg 2, 97070 Wuerzburg
*Tel:* (0931) 3097-400 *Fax:* (0931) 3097-401
*E-mail:* verlag@augustiner.de
*Web Site:* www.augustiner.de
*Key Personnel*
Publishing Dir: Eric Englert
Contact: Jrina Nebel
Founded: 1922
Subjects: Religion - Other
ISBN Prefix(es): 3-7613
*Bookshop(s):* Buch und Kumst, Dominikanerplarz
  4, 97070 Wuerzburg


**Augustus Verlag+**
Hilblestr 54, 80636 Munich
*Tel:* (089) 9271-0 *Fax:* (089) 9271-168
*Web Site:* www.droemer-weltbild.de
*Key Personnel*
Publisher: Dr Hans-Peter Uebleis
Man Dir: Ralf Mueller
Marketing: Christian Tesch
Founded: 1989

Subjects: Animals, Pets, Architecture & Interior Design, Crafts, Games, Hobbies, Gardening, Plants, Photography
ISBN Prefix(es): 3-8043
*Parent Company:* Verlagsgruppe Droemer Weltbild
*Orders to:* VVA-Bertelsmann Distribution GmbH, Postfach 7600, 33310 Guetersloh

**Aulis Verlag Deubner & Co KG+**
Antwerpener Str 6-12, 50672 Cologne
*Tel:* (0221) 9514540 *Fax:* (0221) 518443
*E-mail:* info@aulis.de
*Web Site:* www.aulis.de
*Key Personnel*
Publisher: Wolfgang Deubner
Founded: 1950
Subjects: Biological Sciences, Chemistry, Chemical Engineering, Geography, Geology, History, Mathematics, Nonfiction (General), Physics, Science (General)
ISBN Prefix(es): 3-7614

**Aussaat Verlag+**
Andreas-Braem-Str 18/20, 47506 Neukirchen-Vluyn
Mailing Address: Postfach 101265, 47497 Neukirchen-Vluyn
*Tel:* (02845) 392222 *Fax:* (02845) 33689
*E-mail:* info@neukirchener-verlag.de
*Web Site:* www.aussaat-verlag.de
*Key Personnel*
Man Dir: Klaus Guenther
Sales Manager: Christoph Siepermann
   *E-mail:* vertrieb@neukirchener-verlagshaus.de
Founded: 1978
Subjects: Biblical Studies, Education, Fiction, Religion - Protestant, Religion - Other, Theology
ISBN Prefix(es): 3-7615
Number of titles published annually: 50 Print
Total Titles: 400 Print
*Parent Company:* Verlagsgesellschaft des Erziehungsvereins mbH
Divisions: Edition Sonnenweg, Friedrich Bahn Verlag

**Verlag der Autoren GmbH & Co KG+**
Schleusenstr 15, 60327 Frankfurt am Main
Mailing Address: Postfach 111 963, 60054 Frankfurt am Main
*Tel:* (069) 23 85 74-0 *Fax:* (069) 24 27 76 44
*E-mail:* buch@verlag-der-autoren.de
*Web Site:* www.verlag-der-autoren.de *Cable:* AUTORENVERLAG FRANKFURT
*Key Personnel*
Contact: Brigitte Pfannmoeller *Tel:* (069) 23857441; Annette Reschke *Tel:* (069) 23857423
Founded: 1969
One of Germany's theatre & film agencies, publishing a line of titles on theatre & film.
Subjects: Drama, Theater, Film, Video
ISBN Prefix(es): 3-920983; 3-88661
Number of titles published annually: 8 Print
Total Titles: 190 Print
Foreign Rep(s): International Editors (Argentina, South America, Spain); Marton Agency of New York (US); Orion Library Agency of Tokyo (Japan); Rosica Colin Ltd (Canada, London)
*Orders to:* Edition Text und Kritik, Levelingstr 6a, 81673 Munich, Contact: Mrs Ingmann *Tel:* (089) 432929 *Fax:* (089) 433997
   *E-mail:* etk.muenchen@t-online.de

**Autovision Verlag Guenther & Co+**
Kronprinzenstr 54, 22587 Hamburg
*Tel:* (040) 810327 *Fax:* (040) 87932995
*E-mail:* mail@autovision.de
*Web Site:* www.autovision-verlag.de
*Key Personnel*
Publisher: Dieter Guenther
Founded: 1992

Subjects: Automotive, Technology
ISBN Prefix(es): 3-9802766; 3-9805832
*Orders to:* VAL, Luener Dennbahn 16, 21339 Luneburg

**AVA,** see Atelier Verlag Andernach (AVA)

**Aviatic Verlag GmbH+**
Kolpingring 16, 82041 Oberhaching
*Tel:* (089) 613890-0 *Fax:* (089) 613890-10
*E-mail:* aviatic@aviatic.de
*Web Site:* www.aviatic.de
*Key Personnel*
Manager: Peter Pletschacher
Founded: 1985
Specialize in aeronautics.
Subjects: Aeronautics, Aviation
ISBN Prefix(es): 3-925505
Total Titles: 35 Print
Distributed by Schiffer Publishing (USA)

**AvivA Britta Jurgs GmbH**
Emdener Str 33, 10551 Berlin
*Tel:* (030) 39 73 13 72 *Fax:* (030) 39 73 13 71
*E-mail:* aviva@txt.de
*Web Site:* www2.txt.de
*Key Personnel*
Publisher: Jurgs Britta
Founded: 1997
Subjects: Art, Literature, Literary Criticism, Essays, Women's Studies
ISBN Prefix(es): 3-932338

**Axel Juncker Verlag Jacobi KG**
Member of The Langenscheidt Group
Mies-van-der-Rohestr 1, 80807 Munich
Mailing Address: Postfach 401120, 80711 Munich
*Tel:* (089) 360960 *Fax:* (089) 36096432; (089) 36096258
*Telex:* 5215379 lkgmd
*Key Personnel*
Man Dir: Karl Ernst Tielebier-Langenscheidt; Andreas Langenscheidt
Founded: 1902
Sales & promotion through Langenscheidt KG.
ISBN Prefix(es): 3-558
*Orders to:* Langenscheidt KG, Neusserstr 3, 80807 Munich

**AZ Bertelsmann Direct GmbH**
Division of Bertelsmann Services Group
Unit of Avarto AG
Carl-Bertelsmann-Str 161S, 33311 Guetersloh
*Tel:* (05241) 805438 *Fax:* (05241) 8066962
*E-mail:* az@bertelsmann.de
*Web Site:* www.az.bertelsmann.de
Founded: 1966
International full-service direct marketing.
Subjects: Business, Marketing
ISBN Prefix(es): 3-573

**Babel Verlag Kevin Perryman**
Lorenz Paulstr 4, 86920 Denklingen
Mailing Address: PO Box 1, 86920 Denklingen
*Tel:* (08243) 961691 *Fax:* (08243) 961614
*E-mail:* info@babel-verlag.de
*Web Site:* www.babel-verlag.de
*Key Personnel*
Publisher: Kevin Perryman
Founded: 1983
Specializes in poetry, bilingual poetry & translations.
Subjects: Poetry
ISBN Prefix(es): 3-931798
Number of titles published annually: 2 Print
Total Titles: 39 Print
*Distribution Center:* GVA, Goettingen

**J P Bachem Verlag GmbH+**
Ursulaplatz 1, 50668 Cologne

*Tel:* (0221) 1619-0 *Fax:* (0221) 1619-159
*E-mail:* info@bachem-verlag.de
*Web Site:* www.bachem-verlag.de
*Telex:* 8881128 *Cable:* BACHEMHAUS COLOGNE
*Key Personnel*
Dir: Dipl Kfm Lambert Bachem
Publisher: Reinhard Metz
Founded: 1818
Subjects: Regional Interests
ISBN Prefix(es): 3-7616
*Parent Company:* Bachem Publishing Group

**Dr Bachmaier Verlag GmbH+**
Kagerstr 8B, 81669 Munich
*Tel:* (089) 685120 *Fax:* (089) 685120
*E-mail:* contact@verlag-drbachmaier.de
*Web Site:* www.verlag-drbachmaier.de
*Key Personnel*
Man Dir: Dr Peter Bachmaier
Contact: Barbara Bachmaier
Also acts as Bookseller.
Subjects: History, Literature, Literary Criticism, Essays, Poetry, Science (General), Science Fiction, Fantasy
ISBN Prefix(es): 3-931680; 3-88605
Number of titles published annually: 7 Print
Total Titles: 34 Print
Foreign Rights: Dr Doglioli (Italy)

**Badenia Verlag und Druckerei GmbH+**
Rudolf-Freytag-Str 6, 76189 Karlsruhe
*Tel:* (0721) 95 45-0 *Fax:* (0721) 95 45-125
*E-mail:* verlag@badeniaverlag.de
*Web Site:* www.badeniaverlag.badeniaonline.de
*Key Personnel*
Publisher: Angelika Schmidt *E-mail:* schmidt@ badeniaverlag.de
Founded: 1874
Subjects: Regional Interests, Travel
ISBN Prefix(es): 3-7617

**Badischer Landwirtschafts-Verlag GmbH**
Friedrichstr 43, 79098 Freiburg
Mailing Address: Postfach 209, 79002 Freiburg
*Tel:* (0761) 271330 *Fax:* (0761) 2713372
*E-mail:* redaktion@blv-freiburg.de *Cable:* BBZ FRBG
*Key Personnel*
Assistant Editor-in-Chief: Richard Briskowski
Rights: Manfred Zimper
Founded: 1947
Subjects: Agriculture
ISBN Prefix(es): 3-9801818

**Baedeker,** *imprint of* Mairs Geographischer Verlag

**Hans A Baensch,** see Mergus Verlag GmbH Hans A Baensch

**Baerenreiter-Spieltexte,** *imprint of* Otto Teich

**Baha'i Verlag GmbH+**
Eppsteiner Str 89, 65719 Hofheim
*Tel:* (06192) 22921 *Fax:* (06192) 22936
*E-mail:* info@bahai-verlag.de
*Web Site:* www.bahaipublishers.org
*Key Personnel*
Man Dir, Rights & Permissions: F Ardalan
Founded: 1925
Subjects: Religion - Other
ISBN Prefix(es): 3-87037

**Bahnsport Aktuell Verlag GmbH**
Birkenweiherstr 14, 63505 Langenselbold
*Tel:* (06184) 9233-30 *Fax:* (06184) 9233-50
*E-mail:* mce-aktuell@mce-online.de
Founded: 1971
ISBN Prefix(es): 3-9800965

**Baken-Verlag Walter Schnoor+**
Kastanienallee 16, 25548 Rosdorf Holstein
*Tel:* (04822) 1671; (04192) 1784 *Cable:* BAKEN
*Key Personnel*
Owner: Uwe Jens Schnoor
Founded: 1951
Subjects: Environmental Studies, History, Regional Interests
ISBN Prefix(es): 3-7622
*Bookshop(s):* Buecherstube, Maienbeeck 4, 24576 Bad Bramstedt

**C Bange GmbH & Co KG+**
Marienplatz 12, 96142 Hollfeld
Mailing Address: Postfach 1160, 96139 Hollfeld
*Tel:* (09274) 94130 *Fax:* (09274) 94132
*E-mail:* service@bange-verlag.de
*Web Site:* www.bange-verlag.de
*Key Personnel*
Manager: Thomas Appel
Assistant Manager: Kerstin Lange
Founded: 1871
Subjects: Education, Fiction
ISBN Prefix(es): 3-8044
Number of titles published annually: 20 Print
Total Titles: 850 Print
Imprints: Bange Lernhilfen; Koenigs Erlaeuterungen; Koenigs Lektueren; Kon & Bundig

**Bange Lernhilfen**, *imprint of* C Bange GmbH & Co KG

**Bank-Verlag GmbH+**
Wendelinstr 1, 50933 Cologne
Mailing Address: Postfach 450209, 50877 Cologne
*Tel:* (0221) 54 90-0 *Fax:* (0221) 54 90-120
*E-mail:* bank-verlag@bank-verlag.de
*Web Site:* www.bank-verlag.de
*Key Personnel*
Manager: Helmut Gsanger
Founded: 1961
Subjects: Business, Economics, Finance, Law, Management, Securities
ISBN Prefix(es): 3-00

**Dr Richard Bar di animali**
Kopernikusplatz 36, 90459 Nurnberg
*Tel:* (0911) 951 9490 *Fax:* (0911) 951 9489
*E-mail:* di.animali@web.de
*Web Site:* www.zivilist.it
ISBN Prefix(es): 3-00

**Barenreiter-Verlag Karl-Votterle GmbH & Co KG+**
Heinrich-Schuetz-Allee 35, 34131 Kassel
*Tel:* (0561) 3105-0 *Fax:* (0561) 3105-176
*E-mail:* info@baerenreiter.com
*Web Site:* www.baerenreiter.com
*Key Personnel*
Man Dir: Leonhard Scheuch *E-mail:* lscheuch@baerenreiter.com; Barbara Scheuch-Voetterle *E-mail:* bscheuch@baerenreiter.com
Dir, Finances: Anne Schaefer *E-mail:* schaefer@baerenreiter.com
Publishing Dir: Dr Wendelin Goebel *E-mail:* goebel@baerenreiter.com
Dir, Sales & Marketing: Christine Husemann *E-mail:* husemann@baerenreiter.com
Sales Manager: Uta Dangelmaier *E-mail:* dangelmaier@baerenreiter.com; Dr Christiane Loskant *E-mail:* loskant@baerenreiter.com; Corinne Votteler *E-mail:* votteler@baerenreiter.com; Petra Woodfull-Harris *E-mail:* pwoodfull-harris@baerenreiter.com
Product Information: Ilse-Lore Krummel-Laartz *E-mail:* krummel-laartz@baerenreiter.com
International Rights: Thomas Tietze
Founded: 1923
Subjects: Music, Dance

ISBN Prefix(es): 3-7618
*Associate Companies:* Baerenreiter Verlag Basel
Subsidiaries: Gustav Bosse Verlag; KGA, Verlags-Service GmbH; Sueddeutscher Musikverlag, Alkor-Edition, Henschel Verlag Fuer Musik
*Branch Office(s)*
Basel, Switzerland
Prague, Czech Republic
London, United Kingdom
*U.S. Office(s):* Music Associates of America, 224 King St, Englewood, NJ 07631, United States, Contact: George Strum *Tel:* 201-569-2898 *Fax:* 201-569-7023
Distributed by Barenreiter Ltd (UK); Baerenreiter Verlag Basel AG (Switzerland)
*Bookshop(s):* Neuwerk-Buch-und Musikalien-handlung
*Shipping Address:* KGA-technischer Betrieb, Brandaustr 10, 34127 Kassel
*Warehouse:* KGA-technischer Betrieb, Brandaustr 10, 34127 Kassel
*Orders to:* KGA, Postfach 102180, 34021 Kassel

**Verlag Dr Albert Bartens KG**
Lueckhoffstr 16, 14129 Berlin
Mailing Address: Postfach 380250, 14112 Berlin
*Tel:* (030) 803 56 78 *Fax:* (030) 803 20 49
*E-mail:* info@bartens.com
*Web Site:* www.bartens.com
*Key Personnel*
Editor: Dr Juergen Bruhns
Founded: 1951
Subjects: Agriculture, Economics, Energy, Technology
ISBN Prefix(es): 3-87040

**Otto Wilhelm Barth-Verlag KG**
Hilblestr 54, 80636 Munich
*Tel:* (089) 9271-0 *Fax:* (089) 9271-168
*Key Personnel*
Man Dir: Peter Lohmann; Andreas Wiedmann
Sales: Wolfgang Radaj
Editor: Graf Eckhard
Rights & Permissions: Barbara Fankhauser
Founded: 1924
Subjects: Astrology, Occult, Philosophy, Religion - Other
ISBN Prefix(es): 3-502; 3-89304
*Parent Company:* Scherz Verlag AG, Marktgasse 25 Postf 66, 3000 Bern, Switzerland
*Associate Companies:* Scherz Verlag GmbH, Munich

**Bartkowiaks Forum Book Art**
Koernerstr 24, 22301 Hamburg
*Tel:* (040) 2793674 *Fax:* (040) 2704397
*E-mail:* info@forumbookart.de
*Web Site:* www.forumbookart.com
*Key Personnel*
Man Dir: Heinz Stefan Bartkowiak
Founded: 1988
Subjects: Art
ISBN Prefix(es): 3-9802035; 3-935462; 3-9803534

**Basilisken-Presse Marburg+**
Hirschberg 5, 35037 Marburg
Mailing Address: Postfach 561, 35017 Marburg
*Tel:* 06421 15188
*Key Personnel*
Owner, Rights & Permissions: Armin Geus
Founded: 1976
Specialize in medicine, nursing & history of science.
Subjects: Art, History, Medicine, Nursing, Dentistry
ISBN Prefix(es): 3-925347; 3-9800020

**BasisDruck Verlag GmbH**
Schliemannstr 23, 10437 Berlin

*Tel:* (030) 445 76 80 *Fax:* (030) 445 95 99
*E-mail:* basisdruck@onlinehome.de
*Web Site:* www.basisdruck.de
*Key Personnel*
Man Dir: Michael Kukutz
Founded: 1990
Subjects: Government, Political Science, History
ISBN Prefix(es): 3-86163

**Bassermann Verlag+**
Neumarkterstr 28, 81673 Munich
*Tel:* (089) 41 360
*E-mail:* vertrieb.verlagsgruppe@randomhouse.de
*Web Site:* www.randomhouse.de/bassermann
*Key Personnel*
Publisher: Stefan Ewald *E-mail:* stefan.ewald@bertelsmann.de
Foreign Rights: Silke Bruenink *Tel:* (089) 43 72-26 48 *Fax:* (089) 43 72-27 47 *E-mail:* silke.bruenink@bertelsmann.de
Founded: 1843
Subjects: Cookery, Crafts, Games, Hobbies, Gardening, Plants, Nonfiction (General), Outdoor Recreation
ISBN Prefix(es): 3-8094

**Bastei Luebbe Taschenbuecher**, *imprint of* Verlagsgruppe Luebbe GmbH & Co KG

**Bastei Luebbe Taschenbuecher+**
Imprint of Verlagsgruppe Luebbe GmbH & Co KG
Scheidtbachstr 23-31, 51469 Bergisch Gladbach
Mailing Address: Postfach 200180, 51431 Bergisch Gladbach
*Tel:* (02202) 121-293; (02202) 121-544 *Fax:* (02202) 121-927
*E-mail:* bastei.luebbe@luebbe.de
*Web Site:* www.luebbe.de
*Key Personnel*
Man Dir: Karlheinz Jungbeck
Founded: 1963
Subjects: Fiction, Nonfiction (General)
ISBN Prefix(es): 3-404
Total Titles: 500 Print

**Bastei Verlag**, *imprint of* Verlagsgruppe Luebbe GmbH & Co KG

**Bastei Verlag+**
Imprint of Verlagsgruppe Luebbe GmbH & Co KG
Scheidtbachstr 23-31, 51431 Bergisch Gladbach
Mailing Address: Postfach 200180, 51431 Bergisch Gladbach
*Tel:* (02202) 121-0 *Fax:* (02202) 121-936
*E-mail:* info@bastei.de
*Web Site:* www.bastei.de *Cable:* SCHEIDTBACHSTR 23-31
*Key Personnel*
Man Dir: Karlheinz Jungbeck
Founded: 1949
Subjects: Fiction, Science Fiction, Fantasy, Western Fiction
ISBN Prefix(es): 3-404
Number of titles published annually: 80 Print
*Associate Companies:* Gustav Luebbe Verlag

**Baumann GmbH & Co KG+**
E-C-Baumann-Str 5, 95326 Kulmbach
*Tel:* (09221) 949-0 *Fax:* (09221) 949-378
*E-mail:* info@bayerische_rundschau.de
*Key Personnel*
Publisher: Helmuth Jungbauer
Man Dir: Bernd Mueller *Tel:* (09921) 949 208 *E-mail:* b.mueller@bayerische_rundschau.de
Editor: Thomas Lange
Founded: 1902
ISBN Prefix(es): 3-922091
Subsidiaries: Coburger Tageblatt; Filialbetrieb Naila

**Dr Wolfgang Baur Verlag Kunst & Alltag+**
Poignring 24c, 82515 Wolfratshausen
*Tel:* (08171) 217514 *Fax:* (08171) 217515
*E-mail:* verlag@kunstalltag.de
*Web Site:* www.kunstalltag.de
*Key Personnel*
Owner: Dr Wolfgang Baur
Founded: 1977
Subjects: Art, Environmental Studies, Ethnicity,
    Humor, Philosophy, Poetry, Science (General)
ISBN Prefix(es): 3-88410
Imprints: Edition Jonas; Edition U

**Bautz Traugott**
Eisenacher Str 15, 37412 Herzberg
*Tel:* (05521) 57 00; (05521) 55 88 *Fax:* (05521)
    16 73; (05521) 57 80
*E-mail:* bautz@bautz.de
*Web Site:* www.bautz.de
*Key Personnel*
Contact: Traugott Bautz
Founded: 1971
Subjects: Regional Interests, Theology
ISBN Prefix(es): 3-88309

**Bauverlag GmbH+**
Avenwedderstr 55, 33311 Guetersloh
*Tel:* (05241) 802119 *Fax:* (05241) 809582
*E-mail:* info@bauverlag.de
*Web Site:* www.bauverlag.de *Cable:*
    BAUVERLAG WALL&U14FF
*Key Personnel*
Dir: Stefan Ruehling; Ulrike Mattern
Founded: 1929
Subjects: Architecture & Interior Design, Civil
    Engineering, Energy, Environmental Studies
ISBN Prefix(es): 3-7625
*Parent Company:* Emap
Imprints: LBO-Dienst
*Branch Office(s)*
Nikolsburger Str 11, 10717 Berlin

**Bayerische Akademie der Wissenschaften**
    (Bavarian Academy of Sciences & Humanities)
Marstallplatz 8, 80539 Munich
*Tel:* (089) 23031-0 *Fax:* (089) 23031-100
*E-mail:* info@badw.de
*Web Site:* www.badw.de
*Key Personnel*
President: Noeth Heinrich
Secretary General: Monika Stoermer
Librarian: Heldegard Glaser *Tel:* (089) 23037746
    *E-mail:* glaser@bsb.badw-muencher.de
Founded: 1759
Subjects: Science (General)
ISBN Prefix(es): 3-7696
Number of titles published annually: 130 Print
*Orders to:* CH Beck'sche Verlags Buchhand-
    lung, Postfach 400340, 80703 Munich, Con-
    tact: Oscar Beck *Tel:* (089) 381890 *Fax:* (089)
    38189/381398

**Bayerischer Schulbuch-Verlag GmbH**
Rosenheimer Str 145, 81671 Munich
Mailing Address: Postfach 801360, 81613 Mu-
    nich
*Tel:* (089) 450510 *Fax:* (089) 45051-200
*E-mail:* info@oldenbourg-bsv.de
*Web Site:* www.oldenbourg-bsv.de
*Key Personnel*
Dir: Hartmut Koeppelmann; Roland Mayr
Subjects: Biological Sciences, Business, Chem-
    istry, Chemical Engineering, English as a Sec-
    ond Language, Environmental Studies, Geog-
    raphy, Geology, History, Literature, Literary
    Criticism, Essays, Mathematics, Music, Dance,
    Philosophy, Physics
ISBN Prefix(es): 3-7627
*Warehouse:* Bayerischer Schulbuch-Verlag, Ohm-
    str 10, 85757 Karlsfeld

**BDS**, see Bund Deutscher Schriftsteller (BDS)

**BdWi**, see Bund demokratischer
    Wissenschaftlerinnen und Wissenschafler eV
    (BdWi)

**be.bra verlag GmbH+**
KulturBrauerei Haus S, Schoenhauser Allee 37,
    10435 Berlin
*Tel:* (030) 440 23-810 *Fax:* (030) 440 23-819
*E-mail:* post@bebraverlag.de
*Web Site:* www.bebraverlag.de
*Key Personnel*
Publisher: Ulrich Hopp
Press Manager: Regine Buczek *Tel:* (030) 440 23-
    812
Sales Managers: Antje Steinriede *Tel:* (030) 440
    23-813
Founded: 1994
Membership(s): Borsenverein des Deutschen
    Buchhandels.
Subjects: Architecture & Interior Design, Govern-
    ment, Political Science, Regional Interests
ISBN Prefix(es): 3-930863; 3-89809
Number of titles published annually: 20 Print
Total Titles: 46 Print

**Ludwig Bechauf Verlag**
Hermelinstr 16, 33803 Steinhagen Westf
*Tel:* (05204) 888776 *Fax:* (05204) 888775
*Key Personnel*
Owner: Wilfried Carlmeyer
Founded: 1893
Subjects: Theology
ISBN Prefix(es): 3-8076

**Bechtermuenz Verlag**
Hilblestr 54, 80636 Munich
*Tel:* (089) 9271 312 *Fax:* (0821) 70 04-179
ISBN Prefix(es): 3-86047; 3-8289; 3-89350; 3-
    927117
*Parent Company:* Weltbild Verlag GmbH

**Bechtle Graphische Betriebe und
    Verlagsgesellschaft GmbH und Co KG**
Zeppelinstr 116, 73730 Esslingen
Mailing Address: Postfach 100209, 73702 Esslin-
    gen
*Tel:* (0711) 9310-0
*Key Personnel*
Manager, International Rights: Otto W Bechtle;
    Dr Christine Bechtle-Koberg
Manager: Ulrich Gottlieb
Founded: 1868
Subjects: Biography
ISBN Prefix(es): 3-7628
Subsidiaries: Rotenberg Verlag GmbH

**Verlag C H Beck oHG+**
Wilhelmstr 9, 80801 Munich
Mailing Address: Postfach 400340, 80703 Mu-
    nich
*Tel:* (089) 38189-0 *Fax:* (089) 38189-402
*E-mail:* kundenservice@beck-shop.de
*Web Site:* www.beck.de
*Telex:* 5215085 beck d
*Key Personnel*
Dir: Dr Hans D Beck; Wolfgang Beck
Editorial, Fiction, Humanities: Dr Detlef Felueu
Rights & Permissions: Susanne Simor
    *Tel:* (089) 38189-228 *Fax:* (089) 38189-699
    *E-mail:* susanne.simor@beck.de
Editorial Law & Taxation Economy: Burkail
    Schulz
Founded: 1763
Subjects: Anthropology, Archaeology, Art, Eco-
    nomics, History, Language Arts, Linguistics,
    Law, Literature, Literary Criticism, Essays,
    Management, Music, Dance, Nonfiction (Gen-
    eral), Philosophy, Social Sciences, Sociology,
    Theology
ISBN Prefix(es): 3-406

*Associate Companies:* Verlag Franz Vahlen
    GmbH
*Branch Office(s)*
Palmengartenstr 14, 60325 Frankfurt am Main

**Edition Monika Beck**
Schwedenhof/Am Roemermuseum, 66424 Hom-
    burg/Saar
*Tel:* (06848) 72152 *Fax:* (06848) 72159
*E-mail:* info@mathbeck.de
*Web Site:* www.mathbeck.de/edmb
*Key Personnel*
Man Dir & Proprietor: Mathias Beck
    *E-mail:* mathiasbeck@mathbeck.de
Editorial & Publicity Dir: Susanna Eckenfels
Founded: 1967
Edition for Contemporary Art.
Subjects: Art
ISBN Prefix(es): 3-924360
Number of titles published annually: 8 Print
Total Titles: 248 Print
*Parent Company:* Mathias Beck Kulturmanage-
    ment Ltd

**Beerenverlag**
Morfelder Landstr 109, 60598 Frankfurt
*Tel:* (069) 61009551 *Fax:* (069) 61009560
*Key Personnel*
Manager: Bernard Rensinghoff
Art Dir: Thomas Majevszky
Editorial: Andreas Golm
Founded: 1992
Subjects: Fiction, Humor, Poetry, Travel
ISBN Prefix(es): 3-929198
Imprints: Kleine Reike; Rudi der Bar ist las
Distributed by Harrassourk Verlag

**M P Belaieff**, *imprint of* C F Peters Musikverlag
    GmbH & Co KG

**Verlag Beleke KG+**
Kronprinzenstr 13, 45128 Essen
*Tel:* (0201) 8130-0 *Fax:* (0201) 8130-108
*E-mail:* info@beleke.de
*Web Site:* www.beleke.de
*Key Personnel*
Owner & Man Dir: Norbert Beleke
Man Dir: Heike Bogott
International Rights: Dr Michael Platzkoester
    *Tel:* (0201) 8130-118 *Fax:* (0201) 8130-130
    *E-mail:* mplatzkoester@beleke.de
Founded: 1964
Membership(s): Verband Deutscher Auskunfts
    und Verzeichnismedien eV; European Asso-
    ciation of Directory & Database Publishers;
    Boersenverein des Deutschen Buchhandels eV.
Subjects: Biography, Business, Criminology,
    Medicine, Nursing, Dentistry, Nonfiction (Gen-
    eral), Regional Interests
ISBN Prefix(es): 3-8215
*Associate Companies:* ELVIKOM Film-Verlag
    GmbH, Essen; Hansisches Verlagskontor, Post-
    fach 2051, 23508 Luebeck *Tel:* (0451) 703101
    *Fax:* (0451) 7031281; NOBEL-Verlag GmbH,
    Postfach 103952, 45039 Essen; ntv neue televi-
    sion FILM-TV-PRODUKTION GmbH, Essen;
    Das Rathaus Verlagsgesellschaft mbH & Co
    KG; Verlag Schmidt-Roemhild, Luebeck
*Showroom(s):* Hohe Str 56, 44139 Dortmund 1;
    Redaktionsbuero Duesseldorf, Berliner Allee
    30, 40212 Duesseldorf; Drei-Lilien-Platz 1,
    65183 Wiesbaden; Verlag Schmidt-Roemhild,
    Prinzregentenstr 42, 10715 Berlin; Verlag
    Schmidt-Roemhild, Mengstr 16, 23552 Lue-
    beck

**Edition Belletriste**, *imprint of* Weidler
    Buchverlag Berlin

**Belser GmbH & Co KG - Wissenschaftlicher Dienst**
Affiliate of Belser Wissenschaftlicher Dienst Ltd, Ireland
Postfach 126, 72218 Wildberg
*Tel:* (07054) 2475
*E-mail:* belser@compuserve.com
*Key Personnel*
Executive Dir: Dr Rolf D Schmid, PhD
*E-mail:* bwd@belser.com
Founded: 1989
Specialize in conversion medieval manuscripts, rare books, pamphlets, paintings & drawings of the 16th - early 20th centuries into microfiche, ebooks or CD-ROMs with various electronic access options.
Subjects: Art, Behavioral Sciences, Biblical Studies, Drama, Theater, Fiction, History, Labor, Industrial Relations, Library & Information Sciences, Literature, Literary Criticism, Essays, Philosophy, Poetry, Psychology, Psychiatry, Religion - Catholic, Social Sciences, Sociology, Theology, Women's Studies, English, French & German Literature, Fine Art, Mysticism, Politics, Psychoanalysis
ISBN Prefix(es): 3-628
Total Titles: 24,500 CD-ROM; 35,000 E-Book
*Associate Companies:* Belser Wissenschaftlicher Dienst Ltd


**Chr Belser GmbH & Co KG**, see Belser GmbH & Co KG - Wissenschaftlicher Dienst


**Julius Beltz GmbH & Co KG+**
Werderstr 10, 69469 Weinheim
*Tel:* (06201) 60070
*E-mail:* info@beltz.de
*Web Site:* www.beltz.de
*Key Personnel*
Man Dir: Joachim Radmer; Dr Manfred Beltz Ruebelmann
Marketing: Eckhard Mueller
Rights: Charlotte Larat
Marketing: Rosemarie Bornholt *Tel:* (06201) 6007-433 *Fax:* (06201) 6007-493 *E-mail:* r.bornholt@beltz.de
Founded: 1841
Membership(s): VGS - Verlagsgessellschaft mbH & Co KG.
Subjects: Science (General)
ISBN Prefix(es): 3-407; 3-621
Subsidiaries: Beltz Athenaeum Verlag, Anrich Verlag; Deutscher Studien Verlag; PsychologieVerlagsUnion
*Warehouse:* Koch, Neff & Oetinger Verlagsauslieferung, 70551 Stuttgart *Tel:* (0711) 7899 20 30 *Fax:* (0711) 7899 10 10 *E-mail:* order@kno-va.de


**Petra Bornhauber Benleo Verlag+**
Bahnstr 16, 50126 Bergheim
*Tel:* (02271) 4782-0 *Fax:* (02271) 4782-20
*Web Site:* www.benleo.de
*Key Personnel*
International Rights: Petra Bornhauber
Founded: 1996
ISBN Prefix(es): 3-9805061


**Bergmoser & Holler Verlag AG**
Karl-Friedrich-Str 76, 52072 Aachen
Mailing Address: Postfach 50 04 04, 52088 Aachen
*Tel:* (0241) 93888-10 *Fax:* (0241) 93888-134
*E-mail:* kontakt@buhv.de
*Web Site:* www.buhv.de
*Key Personnel*
Man Dir: Josef Bergmoser
Founded: 1971
ISBN Prefix(es): 3-88997
*U.S. Office(s):* ci Publishing Inc, 230 Fifth Ave NE, Hickory, NC 28601, United States


**Bergverlag Rother GmbH+**
Haidgraben 3, 85521 Ottobrunn
*Tel:* (089) 608669-0 *Fax:* (089) 608669-69
*E-mail:* bergverlag@rother.de
*Web Site:* www.rother.de
*Key Personnel*
Manager: Dr Christian Halbwachs
*E-mail:* halbwachs@freytagberndt.at
Founded: 1920
Specialize in Alpine literature, documents & guidebooks.
Subjects: Nonfiction (General), Outdoor Recreation, Sports, Athletics, Travel
ISBN Prefix(es): 3-7633
Number of titles published annually: 50 Print; 1 CD-ROM
Total Titles: 300 Print; 13 CD-ROM
*Parent Company:* Freytag-Berndt u Artaria KG, Brunner Str 63, 1231 Vienna, Austria
Distributed by Cordee (UK)


**Berliner Debatte Wissenschafts Verlag, GSFP-Gesellschaft fur Sozialwissen-schaftliche Forschung und Publizistik mbH & Co KG**
Erich-Weinert-Str 19, 10439 Berlin
*Tel:* (030) 44651355 *Fax:* (030) 44651358
*E-mail:* web@berlinerdebatte.de
*Web Site:* www.berlinerdebatte.de
*Key Personnel*
Manager: Dr Rainer Land; Dr Erhard Crome
Founded: 1992
Subjects: Government, Political Science, History, Philosophy, Social Sciences, Sociology
ISBN Prefix(es): 3-929666; 3-931703; 3-936382
*Orders to:* Bugrim, Saalburgstr 3, 12099 Berlin


**Berliner Handpresse Wolfgang Joerg und Erich Schonig**
Prinzessinenstr 20, 10969 Berlin
*Tel:* (030) 6148728; (030) 6142605
*Key Personnel*
Publisher: Wolfgang Joerg
Founded: 1961
Subjects: Art, Fiction


**Berliner Wissenschafts-Verlag GmbH (BWV)+**
Axel-Springer-Str 54b, 10117 Berlin
*Tel:* (030) 84 17 70-0 *Fax:* (030) 84 17 70-21
*E-mail:* bwv@bwv-verlag.de
*Web Site:* www.bwv-verlag.de
*Key Personnel*
Man Dir: Dr Volker Schwarz
Manager: Dr Brigitta Weiss
Founded: 1962
Subjects: Business, Economics, Environmental Studies, Government, Political Science, History, Law, Library & Information Sciences, Management, Marketing, Mathematics, Medicine, Nursing, Dentistry, Music, Dance, Philosophy, Public Administration, Publishing & Book Trade Reference, Real Estate, Theology
ISBN Prefix(es): 3-87061; 3-8305
*Parent Company:* Nomos Verlagsgesellschaft GmbH, Waidseestr 3-5, 76530 Baden-Baden
Imprints: Ostrecht
*Warehouse:* Nomos Verlagsgesellschaft GmbH, Waidseestr 3-5, 76530 Baden-Baden
*Orders to:* Nomos Verlagsgesellschaft GmbH, Waidseestr 3-5, 76530 Baden-Baden


**Bernard und Graefe Verlag+**
Heilsbachstr 26, 53123 Bonn
*Tel:* (0228) 64830 *Fax:* (0228) 6483109
*E-mail:* 101336.245@compuserve.com
*Key Personnel*
Man Dir: Manfred Sadlowski
Rights & Permissions (Sales): Jung Horst
Founded: 1918
Subjects: Military Science
ISBN Prefix(es): 3-7637


**Bernecker Mediagruppe**
Unter dem Schoeneberg 1, 34212 Melsungen
*Tel:* (05661) 731-0 *Fax:* (05661) 731-111
*Web Site:* www.bernecker.de
*Key Personnel*
Manager: Conrad Fischer *E-mail:* fischer@bernecker.de
Assistant Editor-in-Chief: Mr Roennfranz
Founded: 1869
ISBN Prefix(es): 3-87064
Subsidiaries: A Bernecker GmbH & Co Druckerei KG; Agentur Bernecker Media Ware GmbH


**C Bertelsmann Verlag GmbH**
Neumarkterstr 28, 81673 Munich 80
Mailing Address: Postfach 800360, 81603 Munich
*Tel:* (089) 41360; (1805) 990505 (hotline for literature & nonfiction) *Fax:* (089) 4372-2812
*E-mail:* vertrieb.verlagsgruppe@randomhouse.de
*Web Site:* www.randomhouse.de
*Telex:* 523259 vbm ve d
*Key Personnel*
Press Dir: Margrit Schoenberger
Founded: 1835
Membership(s): TR- Verlagsunion GmbH.
Subjects: Art, Biography, Fiction, Government, Political Science, Nonfiction (General)
ISBN Prefix(es): 3-570
*Parent Company:* Verlagsgruppe Bertelsmann GmbH
*Associate Companies:* Verlagsgruppe Bertelsmann GmbH
*U.S. Office(s):* Bettina Schrewe Literary Scouting, 101 Fifth Ave, Suite 11B, New York, NY 10003, United States (US Scout)


**Bertelsmann Lexikon Verlag GmbH**
Avenwedderstr 55, 33311 Gutersloh
Mailing Address: Postfach 800360, 81603 Munich
*Tel:* (05241) 802286 *Fax:* (05241) 73075
*E-mail:* info@wissenmediaverlag.de
*Web Site:* www.lexiconverlag.de/lexiconverlag.html
*Telex:* 933646 *Cable:* BERTELSMANN GUTERSLOH
*Key Personnel*
President & Chief Executive Officer: Dr Mark Woessner
Division President, Bertelsmann Publishing Group International: Bernhard von Minckwitz
Division President: Frank Woessner
Division President, Electronic Media: Manfred Lahnstein
Division President, Printing & Manufacturing: Dr Gunter Thielen
Vice Chairman & Chief Executive Officer, Gruner & Jahr AG: Gerd Schulte-Hillen
Chairman & Chief Executive Officer, Bertelsmann Music Group (BMG), New York: Dr Michael Dornemann
Subjects: Anthropology, Art, Biography, Business, Career Development, Communications, Economics, Fiction, Film, Video, Foreign Countries, History, How-to, Law, Management, Marketing, Medicine, Nursing, Dentistry, Radio, TV, Technology, Travel
ISBN Prefix(es): 3-570; 3-576
*Parent Company:* Bertelsmann HG
*Associate Companies:* Bertelsmann Inc, 1540 Broadway, New York, NY 10036, United States
Divisions: International Book & Record Clubs; Book Germany; Bertelsmann Publishing Group International Printing & Manufacturing; Bertelsmann Music Group, Electronic Media; Gruner + Jahr; Book Germany
*U.S. Office(s):* Bettina Schrewe Literary Scouting, 101 Fifth Ave, Suite 11B, NY 10003, United States (US Scout)
*Book Club(s):* Bertelsmann Club; Bertelsmann Club Vertrieb; Buchgemeinschaft Donauland, Kremayr & Scheriau; Buch-und Schallplat-

tenfreunde; Deutsche Buch-Gemeinschaft; Deutscher Buecherbund; EBG Buch & Musik; Hallo RTL; Ring der Musikfreunde; Club Top 13; Doubleday Australia, Australia; ECI voor Boeken en Platen, Belgium; France Loisirs Belgique, Belgium; Doubleday Book & Music Clubs; Quebec Loisirs; France Loisirs, France; Librarie Papeterie Marigny et Joly, France; Setradis, France; SGED, France; Bookclub of Ireland; Euroclub Italia, Italy; Librum, Italy; ECI voor Boeken en Platen, Netherlands; Eurobook, Netherlands; Grambo BV, Netherlands; Nederlandse Lezerskring Boek en Plaat, Netherlands; Doubleday New Zealand, New Zealand; Circulo de Leitores, Portugal; Circulo de Lectores, Spain; France Loisirs Suisse, Switzerland; Book Club Associates, United Kingdom; Doubleday Book & Music Club, New York, NY, United States; Magyar Konyvklub, Budapest, Hungary; Magyar Konyvklub, Budapest, Hungary

**Verlag Bertelsmann Stiftung** (Bertelsmann Foundation Publishers)+
Carl-Bertelsmannstr 256, 33311 Gutersloh
Mailing Address: Postfach 103, 33311 Gutersloh
*Tel:* (05241) 81-81175 *Fax:* (05241) 81-81931
*Web Site:* www.bertelsmann-stiftung.de/verlag
*Key Personnel*
Publisher: Sabine Reimann *E-mail:* sabine. reimann@bertelsmann.de
Subjects: Education, Government, Political Science
ISBN Prefix(es): 3-89204
Number of titles published annually: 50 Print
Total Titles: 308 Print
*Orders to:* Brookings Institution Press, 1775 Massachusetts Ave NW, Washington, DC 20036, United States, Contact: Jessica Howard *Tel:* 202-797-6468 *Fax:* 202-797-6195 *E-mail:* jhoward@brookings.edu

**W Bertelsmann Verlag GmbH & Co KG**
Auf dem Esch 4, 33619 Bielefeld
Mailing Address: Postfach 100633, 33506 Bielefeld
*Tel:* (0521) 911-01-0 *Fax:* (0521) 911 01-79
*E-mail:* service@wbv.de
*Web Site:* www.wbv.de; www.berufsbildung.de; www.berufe.net
*Key Personnel*
Dir: Thomas Kellersohn *Tel:* (0521) 91101-38 *E-mail:* thomas.kellersohn@wbv.de
Founded: 1864
Subjects: Career Development, Education, Foreign Countries, Labor, Industrial Relations, Law, Management, Public Administration, Science (General), Social Sciences, Sociology, Vocational Training
ISBN Prefix(es): 3-7639
Distributor for Bundesanstalt fuer Arbeit; Bundesinstitut fuer Berufsbildung; Deutsches Institute fuer Erwachsenenbildung

**Verlag Beruf und Schule Belz KG+**
Albert-Schweitzer-Ring 45, 25524 Itzehoe
Mailing Address: Postfach 2008, 25510 Itzehoe
*Tel:* (04821) 40140 *Fax:* (04821) 4941
*E-mail:* info@vbus.de
*Web Site:* www.verlag-beruf-schule.de
*Key Personnel*
Contact: Renate Golpon
Founded: 1970
Subjects: Career Development, Chemistry, Chemical Engineering, Computer Science, Humor, Mathematics, Poetry, Publishing & Book Trade Reference
ISBN Prefix(es): 3-88013
Imprints: Edition Heitere Poetik
Divisions: Edition Heitere Poetik; Buchdienst B & S
*Orders to:* VVA Bertelsmann Distribution GmbH, Postfach 7777, 33310 Guetersloh

**Betzel Verlag GmbH+**
Schumannstr 16, 31582 Nienburg
*Tel:* (05021) 91 48 69 *Fax:* (05021) 914868
*E-mail:* betzelverlag@proximedia.de
*Key Personnel*
Man Dir, Rights & Permissions: Anita Kubicek
Formerly Gruppe Hinterhaus.
Subjects: Art, Drama, Theater, Fiction, Philosophy, Poetry
ISBN Prefix(es): 3-929017; 3-932069

**Beust Verlag GmbH+**
Fraunhoferstr 13, 80469 Munich
*Tel:* (089) 230895-0 *Fax:* (089) 230895-131
*E-mail:* mail@beustverlag.de
*Web Site:* www.beustverlag.de
Founded: 1994
Subjects: Child Care & Development, Psychology, Psychiatry
ISBN Prefix(es): 3-89530
Subsidiaries: Gaia Text Publishing

**Beuth Verlag GmbH**
Burggrafenstr 6, 10787 Berlin
*Tel:* (030) 26010 *Fax:* (030) 26011260
*E-mail:* info@beuth.de
*Web Site:* www.beuth.de; www.mybeuth.de
*Telex:* 183622 bvb d; 185730 bvb d *Cable:* DEUTSCHNORMEN BERLIN
*Key Personnel*
Man Dir: Georg Gruetzner; Claudia Michalski
Publicity Dir: Peter Anthony
Founded: 1924
Specialize in technical & scientific literature.
Subjects: Architecture & Interior Design, Chemistry, Chemical Engineering, Communications, Electronics, Electrical Engineering, Energy, Engineering (General), Environmental Studies, Health, Nutrition, Management, Mathematics, Mechanical Engineering, Physics, Securities, Technology, Theology, Transportation
ISBN Prefix(es): 3-410
*Parent Company:* DIN Deutsches Institut fuer Normung eV
*Orders to:* Osterreichisches Normungsinstitut, Heinestr 38, 1021 Vienna 2, Austria (Austrian orders)
Schweizerische Normenvereinigung, Muehlebachstr 54, 8008 Zurich, Switzerland (Swiss orders)

**Bewusster Leben**, *imprint of* Koenigsfurt Verlag, Evelin Buerger et Johannes Fiebig

**Joachim Beyer Verlag+**
Langgasse 25, 96142 Hollfeld
*Tel:* (09274) 95051 *Fax:* (09274) 95053
*E-mail:* info@beyerverlag.de
*Web Site:* www.derschachladen.de
*Key Personnel*
Owner: Joachim Beyer
Founded: 1972
Subjects: Crafts, Games, Hobbies
ISBN Prefix(es): 3-88805; 3-921202

**Bezugsbedingungen**, *imprint of* Johann Wolfgang Goethe Universitat

**Biblio Verlag**
Subsidiary of Zeller Verlag GmbH & Co
Auf dem Busch 2, 49143 Bissendorf
*Tel:* (05402) 641720 *Fax:* (05402) 641722
*E-mail:* info@militaria-biblio.de
*Web Site:* www.militaria-biblio.de
*Key Personnel*
Man Dir: Wolfram Zeller
Subjects: Archaeology, Art, History, Language Arts, Linguistics, Law, Military Science, Philosophy, Religion - Other
ISBN Prefix(es): 3-7648

**Bibliographisches Institut & F A Brockhaus AG+**
Duden Route 6, 68167 Mannheim
Mailing Address: Postfach 10 03 11, 68003 Mannheim
*Tel:* (0621) 3901-01 *Fax:* (0621) 3901-3 91
*Web Site:* www.brockhaus.de *Cable:* BIFAB
*Key Personnel*
Man Dir: Albrecht Kiel; Andreas Langenscheidt; Dr Florian Langenscheidt; Dr Karl-Josef Schmidt; Dr Michael Wegner
Sales: Rosita Throm
Publicity Manager: Hans Gareis
Sales Dir, Rights & Permissions: Claus Greuner
Public Relations: Anja zum Hingst
Product Informations: Michaela Thuerling *Tel:* (0621) 3901-650 *Fax:* (0621) 3901-633
Pressing & Public Work: Klaus Holoch *Tel:* (0621) 3901-385 *Fax:* (0621) 3901-395
Personnel: Wolf of Zobeltitz *Tel:* (0621) 3901-267
Founded: 1805
Publishers of the Duden Series of Dictionaries, Brockhaus und Meyer Series of Encyclopedias.
Subjects: Engineering (General), Geography, Geology, Language Arts, Linguistics, Medicine, Nursing, Dentistry, Science (General)
ISBN Prefix(es): 3-411
*Associate Companies:* Thueringer Verlagsauslieferung Langenscheidt KG, Langenscheidtstr 10, 99867 Gotha; Mohr MORAWA, Sulzengasse 2, 1232 Vienna, Austria; Schweizer Buchzentrum, Postfach 522, 4600 Olten, Switzerland
Subsidiaries: Bibliographisches Institut GmbH (Mannheim); Dr Helmuth Buecking GmbH (Mannheim); Brockhaus Direkt Gmbh (Mannheim); Suedbuch-Vertriebsgesellschaft mbH (Mannheim); Thueringer Verlagsauslieferung Langenscheidt SK (Mannheim); Bibliographisches Institut & F A Brockhaus (Salzburg, Austria); VBH-Verlagsbuchhandelsgesellschaft mbH (Salzburg, Austria); Bibliographisches Institut & F A Brockhaus AG (Zug, Switzerland); Suedbuch Vertrieb AG (Zurich, Switzerland)

**Bibliographisches Institut GmbH+**
Subsidiary of Bibliographisches Institut und F A Brockhaus AG
Querstr 18, 04103 Leipzig
Mailing Address: Postfach 100130, 04001 Leipzig
*Tel:* (0341) 97 86-30 *Fax:* (0341) 97 86-5 60
*Web Site:* www.bifab.de
*Key Personnel*
Man Dir: Dieter Baer
Dir, Rights & Permissions: Dr Karl-Josef Schmidt; Dr Michael Wegner
Founded: 1826
ISBN Prefix(es): 3-323

**Bibliomed - Medizinische Verlagsgesellschaft mbH**
Stadtwaldpark 10, 34212 Melsungen
Mailing Address: Postfach 1150, 34202 Melsungen
*Tel:* (05661) 73440 *Fax:* (05661) 8360
*E-mail:* info@bibliomed.de
*Web Site:* www.bibliomed.de
*Key Personnel*
Man Dir: Uta Meurer
Dir: Dr Annette Beller
Editorial: Markus Boucsein
Sales, Rights & Permissions: Harald Horchler
Founded: 1977
Subjects: Medicine, Nursing, Dentistry
ISBN Prefix(es): 3-89556; 3-921958
Total Titles: 8 CD-ROM
Imprints: Krankenpflegeforschung; Melsunger Medizinische Mitteilungen

**Bibliothek Klassischer Texte**, *imprint of* Wissenschaftliche Buchgesellschaft

**Bibliothek Natur & Wissenschaft**, *imprint of*
Verlag Natur & Wissenschaft Harro
Hieronimus & Dr Jurgen Schmidt

**Edition Bielefelden Kunstverein**, *imprint of*
Pendragon Verlag

**Bielefelder Verlagsanstalt GmbH & Co KG
Richard Kaselowsky+**
Ravensbergerstr 10 F, 33602 Bielefeld
Mailing Address: Postfach 100653, 33506 Biele-
feld
*Tel:* (0521) 595 514 *Fax:* (0521) 595 518
*E-mail:* kontakt@bva-bielefeld.de
*Web Site:* www.bva-bielefeld.de
*Key Personnel*
Publishing Dir: Hans-Joerg Kaiser *Tel:* (0521)
510-514
Books & Maps: Ralph Plum *Tel:* (0521) 521-510
Public Services: Miriam Flacke *Tel:* (0521) 595
542
Founded: 1946
Publish books & maps for cyclists (travel guides)
& in Germany bicycle report books.
Membership(s): Borsenverein.
Subjects: How-to, Outdoor Recreation, Travel
ISBN Prefix(es): 3-87073
Total Titles: 170 Print
*Parent Company:* E Gundlach GmbH & Co KG
Distributed by Mairs Geographischer Verlag

**Biermann Verlag GmbH**
Otto-Hahn-Str 7, 50997 Cologne
*Tel:* (02236) 376-0 *Fax:* (02236) 376-999
*E-mail:* info@biermann.net
*Web Site:* www.biermann-online.de
*Key Personnel*
Contact: Dr Hans Biermann
Man Dir: Ernst-Uwe Kopperf
Leader: Christoph Dusse *Tel:* (02236) 376-202
*Fax:* (02236) 376-203 *E-mail:* du@biermann-
verlag.de
Editor: Bernd Schunk *Tel:* (02236) 376-400
*Fax:* (02236) 376-401 *E-mail:* sk@biermann-
verlag.de
CVD Print: Axel Viola *Tel:* (02236) 376-402
*Fax:* (02236) 376-403 *E-mail:* av@biermann-
verlag.de
Graphics: Heike Dargel *Tel:* (02236) 376-151
*E-mail:* hd@biermann-verlag.de
Marketing: Jan-Hendrik Wiedemann *Tel:* (02236)
376-300 *Fax:* (02236) 376-301 *E-mail:* wi@
biermann-verlag.de
EDP: Thomas Narres *Tel:* (02236) 376-260
*Fax:* (02236) 376-261 *E-mail:* it@biermann-
verlag.de
Founded: 1989
Subjects: Medicine, Nursing, Dentistry
ISBN Prefix(es): 3-924469; 3-930505

**Bild und Heimat Verlagsgesellschaft GmbH**
Zwickauerstr 68, 08468 Reichenbach
Mailing Address: Postfach 1143, 08461 Reichen-
bach
*Tel:* (03765) 78 15-0 *Fax:* (03765) 1 22 45
*Key Personnel*
Man Dir & Owner: Harald Guenther; Stephan
Treuleben
Man Dir: Sven Hoefgen
Founded: 1964
ISBN Prefix(es): 3-7310
*Parent Company:* Treuleben & Bischof Beteili-
gungsgesellschaft, Planegg

**Bild und Text**, *imprint of* Wilhelm Fink GmbH
& Co Verlags-KG

**Bildarchiv Preussischer Kulturbesitz bpk+**
Maerkisches Ufer 16-18, 10179 Berlin (Mitte)
*Tel:* (030) 278 792 0 *Fax:* (030) 278 792 39
*E-mail:* bildarchiv@bpk.spk-berlin.de

*Web Site:* www.bildarchiv-bpk.de
*Key Personnel*
Man Dir, Rights & Permissions: Dr Karl H Puetz
Founded: 1965
Subjects: Photography, Prussian picture archives
*Parent Company:* Stiftung Preussischer Kulturbe-
sitz

**BW Bildung und Wissen Verlag und Software
GmbH+**
Suedwestpark 82, 90449 Nuremberg
Mailing Address: Postfach 820150, 90252
Nuremberg
*Tel:* (0911) 96 76-175 *Fax:* (0911) 96 76-189
*E-mail:* info@bwverlag.de
*Web Site:* www.bwverlag.de
*Key Personnel*
Man Dir & International Rights Contact: L
Lodter; U Sippel
Contact for Orders: Thomas Preuss
*E-mail:* thomas.preuss@bwverlag.de
Contact: Silke Radzuweit *Tel:* (0911) 9676158
*E-mail:* silke.radzuweit@bwverlag.de
Founded: 1975
Specialist publishers for initial & further training,
occupation & employment.
Membership(s): Stock Exchange of German
Booksellers, Bavarian Booksellers & Publishers
Association.
Subjects: Career Development, Education
ISBN Prefix(es): 3-8214

**Bindernagelsche Buchhandlung**
Kaiserstr 72, 61169 Friedberg
Mailing Address: Postfach 100153, 61141 Fried-
berg
*Tel:* (06031) 7323-0 *Fax:* (06031) 734949
*Key Personnel*
Owner: Karl C Herrmann
Founded: 1834
Subjects: Regional Interests
ISBN Prefix(es): 3-87076

**Birkner & Co Zweigniederlassung
Mecklenburg-Vorpommern**
Winsbergring 38, 22525 Hamburg
Mailing Address: Postfach 540750, 22507 Ham-
burg
*Tel:* (040) 85308502 *Fax:* (040) 85308381
*Key Personnel*
Man Dir: Dr Christoph Dunnrath
Contact: Stefan Otto
Founded: 1904
Also acts as Internationale Zellstoff- und Pa-
pierindustrie.
ISBN Prefix(es): 3-923543; 3-929467
*Parent Company:* Dumrath & Fassnacht Komm
Gesellschaft

**BKV-Brasilienkunde Verlag GmbH**
Sunderstr 15, 49497 Mettingen
Mailing Address: Postfach 1220, 49494 Mettin-
gen
*Tel:* (05452) 4598 *Fax:* (05452) 4357
*E-mail:* brasilien@T-Online.de
*Web Site:* www.brasilienkunde.de
*Key Personnel*
Man Dir, Rights & Permissions: P O Gogolok
Founded: 1979
Subjects: Ethnicity, Foreign Countries, Regional
Interests, Religion - Other, Social Sciences, So-
ciology
ISBN Prefix(es): 3-88559
Imprints: Aspekter der Brasilienkunde; BTB

**Blackwell Wissenschafts-Verlag GmbH+**
Kurfuerstendamm 58, 10707 Berlin
*Tel:* (030) 32 79 06-0 *Fax:* (030) 32 79 06-10
*E-mail:* verlag@blackwell.de
*Web Site:* www.blackwis.de

*Key Personnel*
Man Dir: Elisabeth Kukla *Tel:* (030) 32 79 06-16
Marketing Manager: Tobias Przybilla *Tel:* (030)
32 79 06-11
Founded: 1989
Integration in 1994 of the Scientific Program of
Paul Parey Publishers (Berlin/Hamburg) &
1996 Integration of the Professional List of
Paul Parey Publishers (Berlin/Hamburg).
Subjects: Agriculture, Animals, Pets, Biological
Sciences, Environmental Studies, Gardening,
Plants, Medicine, Nursing, Dentistry, Natural
History, Nonfiction (General), Physical Sci-
ences, Veterinary Science
ISBN Prefix(es): 3-89412; 3-8263
*Parent Company:* Blackwell Science, Ltd, Osney
Mead, Oxford OX2 OEL
Imprints: Parey Buchverlag
Subsidiaries: Blackwell Wissenschafts-Verlag
*U.S. Office(s):* Blackwell Science Inc, Com-
merce Place, 350 Main St, Malden, MA 02148,
United States
*Orders to:* Koch, Neff & Oetinger, Schockenried-
str 39, 70565 Stuttgart

**Blanvalet Verlag GmbH+**
Neumarkter Str 28, 81673 Munich
*Tel:* (089) 41360; (089) 990505 (literature hot-
line) *Fax:* (089) 4372-2812
*E-mail:* vertrieb.verlagsgruppe@randomhouse.de
*Web Site:* www.blanvalet-verlag.de
*Telex:* 529965 wg vmn d *Cable:* Bertelsmann
Muenchen
Founded: 1935
Subjects: Biography
ISBN Prefix(es): 3-7645
*Parent Company:* Verlagsgruppe Bertelsmann
GmbH
*U.S. Office(s):* Bettina Schrewe Literary Scout-
ing, 101 Fifth Ave, Suite 11B, New York, NY
10003, United States (US Scout)

**Verlag Die Blaue Eule**
Annastr 74, 45130 Essen
*Tel:* (0201) 8 77 69 63 *Fax:* (0201) 8 77 69 64
*E-mail:* info@die-blaue-eule.de
*Web Site:* www.die-blaue-eule.de
*Key Personnel*
Publisher: Dr W L Hohmann
Contact: Eva Wunsch
Founded: 1983
Galeria.
Subjects: Art, Education, History, Language Arts,
Linguistics, Music, Dance, Philosophy, Psy-
chology, Psychiatry, Science (General), Social
Sciences, Sociology, Theology, Mythology
ISBN Prefix(es): 3-924368; 3-89206; 3-89924
Total Titles: 1,000 Print
Distributed by Engros Buchhandlung Dessauer;
Freihofer AG Verlagsauslieferung Wissenschaft

**Die Blauen Buecher (The Blue Book)**, *imprint
of* Karl Robert Langewiesche Nachfolger Hans
Koester KG

**Blaukreuz-Verlag Wuppertal+**
Freiligrathstr 27, 42289 Wuppertal
Mailing Address: Postfach 200252, 42202 Wup-
pertal
*Tel:* (0202) 6200370 *Fax:* (0202) 6200381
*E-mail:* bkv@blaukreuz.de
*Web Site:* www.blaukreuz.de
*Key Personnel*
Publisher: Horst Westmeier *E-mail:* westmeier@
blaukreuz.de
Founded: 1892
Subjects: Health, Nutrition, Human Relations, Lit-
erature, Literary Criticism, Essays, Self-Help,
Addiction & Assistance
ISBN Prefix(es): 3-920106; 3-89175
Number of titles published annually: 7 Print
Total Titles: 70 Audio

*Parent Company:* Blaues Kreuz in Deutschland eV, Wuppertal
Distributed by Blaukreuz-Verlag Bern (Switzerland); BMK Wartburg Vertriebsges.mbH (Austria)
Distributor for Nicol-Verlag Kassel
*Distribution Center:* Chris Media GmbH, Staufenberg


**Bleicher Verlag GmbH+**
Weilimdorfstr 76, 70839 Gerlingen
Mailing Address: Postfach 10 01 23, 70826 Gerlingen
*Tel:* (07156) 43 08-0 *Fax:* (07156) 43 08-27
*E-mail:* info@bleicher-verlag.de
*Web Site:* www.bleicher-verlag.de
*Key Personnel*
Dir: Rainer Abel
Publisher, Editorial: Ev Marie Bartolitius
Publisher, Editorial, Rights & Permissions: Thomas Bleicher
Sales: Klaus Vahlbruch
Press Relations: Edda Bournot
Founded: 1968
Subjects: Fiction, Government, Political Science, History, Social Sciences, Sociology
ISBN Prefix(es): 3-88350; 3-7953; 3-7988; 3-921097
Number of titles published annually: 20 Print
Subsidiaries: Hoffmann Verlag GmbH


**BLISTA,** see Deutsche Blinden-Bibliothek


**Eberhard Blottner Verlag GmbH+**
Silberbachstr 9, 65232 Taunusstein
Mailing Address: Postfach 1104, 65219 Taunusstein
*Tel:* (06128) 2 36 00 *Fax:* (06128) 21180
*E-mail:* blottner@blottner.de
*Web Site:* www.blottner.de *Cable:* BLOTTNERTAUNUSSTEIN
*Key Personnel*
Publisher, Rights & Permissions: Eberhard Blottner
Marketing: Britta Blottner
Founded: 1988
Subjects: Architecture & Interior Design, Crafts, Games, Hobbies, Earth Sciences, Environmental Studies, House & Home
ISBN Prefix(es): 3-89367
Total Titles: 28 Print
*Associate Companies:* Blottner Fachverlag GmbH & Co KG


**BLT,** *imprint of* Verlagsgruppe Luebbe GmbH & Co KG


**BLV Verlagsgesellschaft mbH+**
Lothstr 29, 80797 Munich
Mailing Address: PO Box 400220, 80702 Munich
*Tel:* (089) 127050 *Fax:* (089) 12705354
*E-mail:* blv.verlag@blv.de
*Web Site:* www.blv.de *Cable:* BLV VERLAG
*Key Personnel*
Man Dir, Book Division: Hartwig Schneider
Marketing & Distribution Manager: Michael Wellbrock
Editorial, Nature: Wilhelm Eisenreich
Editorial, Sports: Juergen Kemmler
Foreign Rights: Undine Hoegl *Tel:* (089) 12705-417 *Fax:* (089) 12705-415 *E-mail:* undine.hoegl@blv.de; Hannelore Koenig *Tel:* (089) 12705-416 *Fax:* (089) 12705-415 *E-mail:* hannelore.koenig@blv.de
Book Trade: Karin Herbschleb *E-mail:* karin.herbschleb@blv.de
Warehouse & Specialty Shop: Helga Weingartner *E-mail:* helga.weingartner@blv.de
Delivery Trade: Eva Bednarek *E-mail:* eva.bednarek@blv.de
Founded: 1946

Membership(s): TR-Verlagsunion GmbH.
Subjects: Agriculture, Animals, Pets, Astronomy, Gardening, Plants, Natural History, Outdoor Recreation, Sports, Athletics, Travel
ISBN Prefix(es): 3-405; 3-331
Number of titles published annually: 80 Print
Total Titles: 600 Print
Imprints: VUA (agricultural titles)
Subsidiaries: DLV Deutscher Landwirtschaftsverlag GmbH
*Branch Office(s)*
BLV Verlagsgesellschaft mbH, Verlagsbuero Berlin, Gurtelstr 29a-30, 10247 Berlin
Distributed by Athesia Buch GmbH (Italy)
Distributor for Ceres Verlag
*Warehouse:* BLV Auslieferung, Rotwandweg 2, 82024 Taufkirchen


**Verlag Erwin Bochinsky GmbH & Co KG+**
Muenchener Str 45, 60329 Frankfurt am Main
*Tel:* (069) 27 13 78 90 *Fax:* (069) 27 13 789 94
*Web Site:* www.bochinsky.de
*Key Personnel*
Man Dir: Helmut Amberg; Thilo M Kramny
Founded: 1952
Specialize in musical instruments (acoustic & electronic).
Membership(s): Europiano.
Subjects: Electronics, Electrical Engineering, Music, Dance, Nonfiction (General)
ISBN Prefix(es): 3-920112; 3-923639
*Parent Company:* PPVMEDIEN GmbH, Dachauer Str 376, 85232 Feldgeding


**Bock und Herchen Verlag**
Reichenbergerstr 11e, 53604 Bad Honnef
Mailing Address: Postfach 11 45, 53581 Bad Honnef
*Tel:* (02224) 57 75 *Fax:* (02224) 7 83 10
*E-mail:* buh@bock-net.de
*Web Site:* www.b-u-b.de
*Key Personnel*
Man Dir, Rights & Permissions: Prof Karl Heinrich Bock
Founded: 1977
Subjects: Library & Information Sciences, Science (General)
ISBN Prefix(es): 3-88347


**Boehlau-Verlag GmbH & Cie+**
Ursulaplatz 1, 50668 Cologne
*Tel:* (0221) 91 39 0-0 *Fax:* (0221) 91 39 0-32
*E-mail:* vertrieb@boehlau.de
*Web Site:* www.boehlau.de *Cable:* BOHLAU, COLOGNE
*Key Personnel*
Man Dir: Dr Peter Rauch *E-mail:* peter.rauch@boehlau.at
Sales & Distribution: Joachim Bischofs *Tel:* (0221) 91390-16
Founded: 1951
Subjects: Anthropology, Archaeology, Art, Education, History, Journalism, Language Arts, Linguistics, Social Sciences, Sociology, Women's Studies
ISBN Prefix(es): 3-412
Number of titles published annually: 180 Print
Total Titles: 1,800 Print
*Associate Companies:* Boehlau Verlag GmbH, Sachsenplatz 4-6, 1201 Vienna, Austria *Tel:* (01) 33024270 *Fax:* (01) 3302432 *E-mail:* boehlau@boehlau.at *Web Site:* www.boehlau.at
*Branch Office(s)*
Boehlau Verlag GmbH & Cie, Eisfeld 5, 99423 Weimar
*Orders to:* Koch, Neff und Oetinger & Co, Postfach 800620, 70506 Stuttgart


**Verlag Hermann Boehlaus Nachfolger Weimar GmbH & Co+**
Prellerstr 2a, 99423 Weimar

Mailing Address: Postfach 2260, 99403 Weimar
*Tel:* (03643) 8508-90; (03643) 8508-91 *Fax:* (03643) 8508-92
*Key Personnel*
Editor & International Rights: Gunter Lauterbach
Founded: 1624
Subjects: Architecture & Interior Design, Art, Foreign Countries, History, Law, Literature, Literary Criticism, Essays, Poetry, Science (General), Theology
ISBN Prefix(es): 3-7400
*Orders to:* Verlagsaurlieferung Karlstr 10, Postfach 546, 72488 Sigmaringen


**Klaus Boer Verlag+**
Vokartstr 30, 80634 Munich
*Tel:* (089) 13938099 *Fax:* (089) 13938098
*E-mail:* boerv@onlinehome.de
*Web Site:* www.boerverlag.de
*Key Personnel*
Owner: Klaus Boer
Founded: 1984
Subjects: Art, History, Literature, Literary Criticism, Essays, Philosophy
ISBN Prefix(es): 3-924963
*Orders to:* Buchvertrieb Grimmstr, Saalburgstr 3, 12099 Berlin


**Edition Boiselle+**
Wormsestr 30, 67346 Speyer
*Tel:* (06232) 629662 *Fax:* (06232) 629664
*E-mail:* info@edition-boiselle.de
*Web Site:* www.edition-boiselle.de
*Key Personnel*
Man Dir: Gabriele Boiselle
Founded: 1990
Subjects: Calendars, Equestrian
ISBN Prefix(es): 3-927589
*Sales Office(s):* Kraemer Pferdesportversandhaus, 68764 Hockenheim *Tel:* (0180) 5949400 *Fax:* (06205) 949488 *E-mail:* info@kraemer-pferdesport.de *Web Site:* www.kraemer-pferdesport.de
Distributed by Buecher Zentrum (Austria); Edition Boiselle (UK, US, France & Spain); Islandpferdehof Plarenga (Switzerland); Mias Ridsport (Sweden)


**Bolanz Verlag fur Alle**
Friedrichstr, Moltkestr 11/1, 88046 Friedrichshafen
Mailing Address: Postfach 2580, 88045 Friedrichshafen
*Tel:* (07541) 33 6 99 *Fax:* (07541) 32467
Specialize in calendars.
ISBN Prefix(es): 3-927744; 3-932640; 3-936673
*Bookshop(s):* Christliche Buchhandlung Buecherecke, Ailingerstr 11, 88046 Friedrichshafen; Christliche Buchhandlung Buecherecke, Zeppelinstr 2, 88212 Ravensburg; Christliche Buchhandlung Buecherecke, Ambrosius-Blaresstr 3, 78532 Tuttlingen


**CB-Verlag Carl Boldt**
Baseler Str 80, 12205 Berlin
Mailing Address: Postfach 45 02 07, 12172 Berlin
*Tel:* (030) 833 70 87 *Fax:* (030) 833 91 25
*E-mail:* cb-verlag@t-online.de
*Key Personnel*
Contact: Wolf P Gesellius
Founded: 1904
Subjects: Law, Medicine, Nursing, Dentistry
ISBN Prefix(es): 3-920731


**Bollmann-Bildkarten-Verlag GmbH & Co KG**
Lilienthalplatz 1, 38108 Braunschweig
*Tel:* (0531) 332069 *Fax:* (0531) 353064
*E-mail:* info@bollmann-bildkarten.de
*Web Site:* www.bollmann-bildkarten.de

*Key Personnel*
Man Dir, Rights & Permissions: Friedrich Boll-
mann
Founded: 1948


**Dr Bolte KG**, see Polyglott-Verlag


**Bonifatius GmbH Druck-Buch-Verlag+**
Karl-Schurzstr 26, 33100 Paderborn
Mailing Address: Postfach 1280, 33042 Pader-
born
*Tel:* (05251) 153 0 *Fax:* (05251) 153 104
*E-mail:* mail@bonifatius.de
*Web Site:* www.bonifatius.de
*Key Personnel*
Manager: Rainer Beseler; Gerd Geliner
Founded: 1869
Subjects: Art, Literature, Literary Criticism, Es-
says, Music, Dance, Theology
ISBN Prefix(es): 3-87088; 3-00; 3-89710
Imprints: Kontur; Creator


**Bonsai-Centrum**
Mannheimerstr 401, 69123 Heidelberg-
Weiblingen
*Tel:* (06221) 8491-0 *Fax:* (06221) 849130
*E-mail:* info@bonsai-centrum.de
*Web Site:* www.bonsai-centrum.de
*Key Personnel*
President, Publisher & Author: Paul Lesniewicz
Subjects: Gardening, Plants
ISBN Prefix(es): 3-924982; 3-9800345


**Books on African Studies+**
Formerly The African Literature Club
Ladenburgerstr 50, 69120 Heidelberg
Mailing Address: Postfach 1320, 69193
Schriesheim
*Tel:* (06221) 411861 *Fax:* (06221) 411861
*Key Personnel*
Man Dir: Jerry Bedu-Addo *E-mail:* jbeduaddo@
aol.com
Founded: 1982
Book publication & distribution.
Subjects: Africa
ISBN Prefix(es): 3-927198
*Associate Companies:* Timbuktu, Ladenburgerstr
50, 69120 Heidelberg
*Branch Office(s)*
Books on African Studies, PO Box BT, 328,
Tema, Ghana *Tel:* (022) 206135 *Fax:* (022)
206134 *E-mail:* beaddo@ghana.com
*Book Club(s):* African Literature Club, Laden-
burgerstr 50, Heidelberg 69120, Contact:
Eva Groppenbaecher *Tel:* (06221) 411861
*Fax:* (06221) 473946 *E-mail:* evagroppe@aol.
com


**Richard Boorberg Verlag GmbH & Co**
Scharrstr 2, 70563 Stuttgart
*Tel:* (0711) 73 85-0 *Fax:* (0711) 73 85-100
*Web Site:* www.boorberg.de
*Key Personnel*
Manager: Dr Berndt Oesterhelt
Administration: Markus Ott
Production: Werner Frasch
Sales: Hermann Ruckdeschel
International Rights: Roderich Dohse
Founded: 1927
Subjects: Law
ISBN Prefix(es): 3-415
Subsidiaries: Josef Moll Verlag GmbH & Co
*Branch Office(s)*
Berlin
Hanover
Levelingstr 6a, 81673 Munich *Tel:* (089) 43 60
00-0 *Fax:* (089) 4 36 15 64
Weimar


**Boosey & Hawkes Music Publishers LTD,
London+**
Luetzowufer 26, 10787 Berlin
*Tel:* (030) 25001300 *Fax:* (030) 25001399
*E-mail:* musikverlag@boosey.com
*Web Site:* www.boosey.com/publishing
*Key Personnel*
Man Dir: Winfried Jacobs
Founded: 1838
Subjects: Music, Dance
ISBN Prefix(es): 3-7931
*Parent Company:* Boosey & Hawkes Music Pub-
lishers Ltd, London
*Branch Office(s)*
Boosey & Hawkes Pty Ltd, Unit 12/6 Campbell
St, Artarmon, NSW 2076, Australia *Tel:* (02)
9439 4144 *Fax:* (02) 9439 2912 *E-mail:* info@
boosey.au.com
Buffet Crampon Limited, 8-17, Toyo-4, Koto-
ku, Tokyo 135-0016, Japan *Tel:* (05632) 5511
*Fax:* (05632) 5527 *E-mail:* tokyo@boosey.com
Boosey & Hawkes Music Publishers LTD, 295
Regent St, London W1B 2JH, United Kingdom
*Tel:* (020) 7580 2060 *Fax:* (020) 7637 7109
*E-mail:* composers@boosey.com
*U.S. Office(s):* Boosey & Hawkes New York Inc,
35 East 21 St, New York, NY 10010-6216,
United States *Tel:* 212-358-5300 *Fax:* 212-358-
5301 *E-mail:* info.ny@boosey.com
*Bookshop(s):* 10623 Berlin *Tel:* (030) 31100310


**Born-Verlag+**
Leuschnerstr 72-74, 34134 Kassel
Mailing Address: Postfach 420220, 34071 Kassel
*Tel:* (0561) 4095107 *Fax:* (0561) 4095112
*E-mail:* info.born@ec-jugend.de
*Web Site:* www.born-buch.de
*Key Personnel*
Publishing Manager: Claudia Siebert
*E-mail:* siebert.born@ec-jugend.de
Founded: 1898
Subjects: Religion - Catholic, Religion - Protes-
tant
ISBN Prefix(es): 3-87092


**Borntraeger Verlagsbuchhandlung**, *imprint of*
Gebrueder Borntraeger Science Publishers


**Gustav Bosse GmbH & Co KG+**
Heinrich-Schutz-Allee 35, 34131 Kassel
Mailing Address: Postfach 101420, 34014 Kassel
*Tel:* (0561) 31 05-0 *Fax:* (0561) 31 05-2 40
*E-mail:* info@bosse-verlag.de
*Web Site:* www.bosse-verlag.de
*Key Personnel*
Man Dir: Barbara Scheuch-Voetterle; Leonhard
Scheuch
Rights & Permissions: Thomas Tietze
Editor: Berthold Kloss
Founded: 1912
Subjects: Education, Music, Dance
ISBN Prefix(es): 3-7649
*Parent Company:* Verlag Baerenreiter, Kassel
*Distributed by* Barenreiter Ltd (UK); Barenreiter
Verlag Basel AG (Switzerland)
*Warehouse:* KGA-Technischer Betrieb, Brandaustr
10, 34127 Kassel
*Orders to:* KGA, Postfach 102180, 34021 Kassel


**Bote & Bock Musikalienhandelsgesellschaft
mbH+**
Lutzowufer 26, 10787 Berlin
*Tel:* (030) 2500-1300 *Fax:* (030) 2500-1399
*E-mail:* musikverlag@boosey.com
*Web Site:* www.boosey.com
*Key Personnel*
Dir: Winfried Jacobs
Founded: 1838
Primarily a music store.
Subjects: Music, Dance
ISBN Prefix(es): 3-7931


**Bouvier Verlag+**
Am Hof 28, 53113 Bonn
Mailing Address: Postfach 1268, 53002 Bonn
*Tel:* (0228) 72901124 *Fax:* (0228) 637909
*E-mail:* verlag@books.de
*Web Site:* www.bouvier-online.de
*Key Personnel*
Publishing Dir & International Rights: Peter
Parusel
Sales, Press: Elisabeth Keuthen-Nuechel
Sales, President: Sabine Taeffner
Manager & Publishing Dir: Thomas Grundmonn
Founded: 1828
Subjects: Government, Political Science, Regional
Interests, Science (General)
ISBN Prefix(es): 3-416
*Orders to:* Koch, Neff, Oetinger & Co, Schock-
enriedstr 39, 70565 Stuttgart *Tel:* (0711)
78991120 *Fax:* (0711) 78991155


**Verlag Brandenburger Tor GmbH**
Wittestr 30 K, 13509 Berlin
*Tel:* (030) 8557511 *Fax:* (030) 85605332
*E-mail:* info@verlag-brandenburger-tor.de
*Key Personnel*
Publisher: Klaus-Juergen Holzapfel; Andreas
Holzapfel
Founded: 1973
Subjects: Government, Political Science
Subsidiaries: Verlag Brandenburger Tor
*Orders to:* NDV Neue Darmstaedter Ver-
lagsanstalt, Postfach 1560, 53585 Bad Hon-
nef *Tel:* (022241) 3232 *Fax:* (022241) 78639
*E-mail:* ndv@ndvverlag.de


**Brandenburgisches Verlagshaus**, *imprint of*
Verlagsgruppe Dornier GmbH


**Brandenburgisches Verlagshaus in der Dornier
Medienholding GmbH+**
Liebknechtstr 33, 70565 Stuttgart
*Tel:* (0711) 78803-0 *Fax:* (0711) 78803-0
*E-mail:* info@dornier-verlage.de
*Web Site:* www.dornier-verlage.de
*Key Personnel*
Man Dir: Olaf Carstons; Roland Grimmelsmann
Founded: 1956
Subjects: Biography, Engineering (General), For-
eign Countries, History, Management, Mar-
itime, Military Science, Nonfiction (General),
Regional Interests, Travel
ISBN Prefix(es): 3-89488
*Parent Company:* Dormier Medienholding GmbH


**Brandes & Apsel Verlag GmbH+**
Scheidswaldstr 33, 60385 Frankfurt am Main
*Tel:* (069) 957 301 86 *Fax:* (069) 957 301 87
*E-mail:* brandes-apsel@doodees.de
*Web Site:* www.brandes-apsel-verlag.de
Founded: 1986
Subjects: Anthropology, Developing Countries,
Education, Ethnicity, Fiction, Government, Po-
litical Science, Human Relations, Literature,
Literary Criticism, Essays, Poetry, Psychology,
Psychiatry, Social Sciences, Sociology, Dance,
Psychoanalysis, Theater, Self Psychology
ISBN Prefix(es): 3-925798; 3-86099
Number of titles published annually: 40 Print
Total Titles: 300 Print
*Orders to:* Prolit Verlagsauslieferung, Siemensstr
16, 35463 Fernwald-Annerod *Tel:* (0641)
94393-22, (0641) 94393-23 *Fax:* (0641) 94393-
29


**Oscar Brandstetter Verlag GmbH & Co KG+**
Wilhelminenstr 1a, 65193 Wiesbaden
Mailing Address: Postfach 1708, 65007 Wies-
baden
*Tel:* (0611) 9 91 20-0 *Fax:* (0611) 3 08 37 85
*E-mail:* brandstetter-verlag@t-online.de
*Web Site:* www.brandstetter-verlag.de

*Key Personnel*
Man Dir: Guenther H Froehlen
Founded: 1862
Subjects: Chemistry, Chemical Engineering, Communications, Computer Science, Economics, Electronics, Electrical Engineering, Engineering (General), Language Arts, Linguistics, Law, Medicine, Nursing, Dentistry, Physical Sciences, Technology
ISBN Prefix(es): 3-87097
*Shipping Address:* Koch, Neff & Oetinger & Co, Verlagsauslieferung Smlt, 70551 Stuttgart, Contact: Erika Vogelmann *Tel:* (0711) 78992123 *Fax:* (0711) 78991010
*Warehouse:* Koch, Neff & Oetinger & Co, Verlagsauslieferung Smlt, 70551 Stuttgart, Contact: Erika Vogelmann *Tel:* (0711) 78992123 *Fax:* (0711) 78991010
*Orders to:* Koch, Neff & Oetinger & Co, Verlagsauslieferung Smlt, 70551 Stuttgart, Contact: Erika Vogelmann *Tel:* (0711) 78992123 *Fax:* (0711) 78991010

**Aspekter der Brasilienkunde**, *imprint of*
BKV-Brasilienkunde Verlag GmbH

**Brasilienkunde Verlag GmbH**, see
BKV-Brasilienkunde Verlag GmbH

**G Braun GmbH & Co KG+**
Karl-Friedrich-Str 14-18, 76133 Karlsruhe
*Tel:* (0721) 1607320 *Fax:* (0721) 1607321
*E-mail:* info@gbraun-immo.de
*Web Site:* www.gbraun.de
*Telex:* 7826904
*Key Personnel*
Publisher: Klaus Kapp
Dir: Georg van Griesheim; Peter Scheuble
Founded: 1813
Subjects: Art, History, Regional Interests, Travel
ISBN Prefix(es): 3-7650

**Breitkopf & Hartel+**
Walkmuehlstr 52, 65195 Wiesbaden
Mailing Address: Postfach 1707, 65007 Wiesbaden
*Tel:* (0611) 450080 *Fax:* (0611) 4500859; (0611) 4500860; (0611) 4500861
*E-mail:* info@brcitkopf.com
*Web Site:* www.breitkopf.com; www.breitkopf.de
*Cable:* BREITKOPFS WIESBADEN
*Key Personnel*
Man Dir: Gottfried Moeckel; Lieselotte Sievers
International Rights: Vivian Rehman
  *Tel:* (0611) 45008 36 *Fax:* (0611) 45008 60
  *E-mail:* rehman@breitkopf.de
UK Sales Representative: Robin Winter
  *Tel:* (01263) 768732 *Fax:* (01263) 768733
  *E-mail:* sales@breitkopf.com
Founded: 1719
Music publisher.
Subjects: Music, Dance
ISBN Prefix(es): 3-7651
*Branch Office(s)*
22 rue Chauchat, 75009 Paris, France, Contact: Mr Farid Aich *Tel:* (01) 48 01 01 33 *Fax:* (01) 48 01 01 66 *E-mail:* breitkopf.aich@wanadoo.fr
Deutscher Verlag fuer Musik, Bauhofstr 3-5, 04103 Leipzig *Tel:* (0341) 997190 *Fax:* (0341) 9971930 *E-mail:* leipzig@breitkopf.com
Obere Waldstr 30, 65232 Taunusstein
  *Tel:* (06128) 9663 0 *Fax:* (06128) 9663 50; (06128) 966360 *E-mail:* sales@breitkopf.com
Broome Cottage, The Street, Suffield Norwich NR 11 7EQ, United Kingdom, Contact: Robin Winter *Tel:* (01263) 768732 *Fax:* (01263) 768733 *E-mail:* sales@breitkopf.com

**Breklumer Buchhandlung und Verlag**
Kirchenstr 1, 25821 Breklum

*Tel:* (04671) 910020 *Fax:* (04671) 910030
*E-mail:* verlag@breklumer.de
*Web Site:* www.breklumer.de *Cable:*
  BREKLUMER VERLAG BREKLUM
*Key Personnel*
Publisher: Manfred Siegel
Founded: 1875
Subjects: Religion - Other
ISBN Prefix(es): 3-7793

**Joh & Sohn Brendow Verlag GmbH+**
Gutenbergstr 1, 47443 Moers
*Tel:* (02841) 809-0 *Fax:* (02841) 809-291
*E-mail:* info@brendow-verlag.de
*Web Site:* www.brendow.de
*Key Personnel*
Man Dir: Friedr-Wilh Seinsche
Founded: 1849
Subjects: Religion - Other
ISBN Prefix(es): 3-87067

**Verlag Das Brennglas+**
Roettbacherstr 61, 97892 Kreuzwertheim
*Tel:* (09342) 915843 *Fax:* (09342) 915843
*E-mail:* info@brennglas.com
*Web Site:* www.brennglas.com
Founded: 1981
Subjects: Art, Literature, Literary Criticism, Essays
ISBN Prefix(es): 3-924243

**Brigg Verlag Franz-Joset Buchler KG**
Zusamstr 9, 86165 Augsburg
*Tel:* (0821) 78094660 *Fax:* (0821) 78094661
*Key Personnel*
Man Dir: Franz-Josef Buechler
Founded: 1950
Subjects: Poetry, Regional Interests
ISBN Prefix(es): 3-87101

**Brockhaus Commission GmbH**
Kreidlerstr 9, 70803 Kornwestheim
*Tel:* (07154) 1327-33 *Fax:* (07154) 1327-13
*E-mail:* bro@brockhaus-commission.de
*Key Personnel*
Man Dir: Dr Wolfgang Berg; Steffen Goehler
Founded: 1805
Subjects: Geography, Geology
ISBN Prefix(es): 3-87103

**Verlag Ekkehard & Ulrich Brockhaus GmbH & Co KG**
Am Wolfshahn 31, 42117 Wuppertal
*Tel:* (0202) 44 74 74; (0172) 2 55 59 61
  *Fax:* (0202) 42 82 82
*E-mail:* mail@verlag-brockhaus.de
*Web Site:* www.verlag-brockhaus.de
Subjects: Genealogy, Cultural History
ISBN Prefix(es): 3-930132

**F A Brockhaus GmbH**
Dudenstr 6, 68167 Mannheim
*Tel:* (0621) 3901-01 *Fax:* (0621) 3901-391
*Web Site:* www.brockhaus.de
*Key Personnel*
Contact: Dieter Baer; Dr Karl-Josef Schmidt; Dr Michael Wegner
Founded: 1805
ISBN Prefix(es): 3-411
*Parent Company:* Bibliographisches Institut & F A Brockhaus AG, Mannheim

**R Brockhaus Verlag+**
Bodenborn 43, 58452 Witten
*Tel:* (02302) 930 93 800 *Fax:* (02302) 930 93 801
*E-mail:* info@brockhaus-verlag.de
*Web Site:* www.brockhaus-verlag.de
*Key Personnel*
Chief Executive Officer & Publisher: Erhard Diehl
Editorial: Hans-Werner Durau

International Rights: Christina Schneider
Founded: 1853
Membership(s): Stiftung Christliche Medien.
Subjects: Biography, Fiction, Music, Dance, Psychology, Psychiatry, Religion - Other, Theology
ISBN Prefix(es): 3-417
*Associate Companies:* Oncken Verlag KG
*Subsidiaries:* R Brockhaus Verlag AG

**F Bruckmann Munchen Verlag & Druck GmbH & Co Produkt KG+**
Innsbrucker Ring 15, 81673 Munich
Mailing Address: Postfach 80 02 40, 81602 Munich
*Tel:* (089) 13 06 99 11 *Fax:* (089) 13 06 99 10
*E-mail:* info@bruckmann.de
*Web Site:* www.bruckmann-verlag.de *Cable:*
  BRUCKMANNKOGE MUNICH
*Key Personnel*
Editor & Publishing Manager: Dr Joerg D Stiebner
Editor: Michael Wellbrock
Sales Manager: Dr Klaus Beckschulte *Tel:* (089) 13 06 99 48 *E-mail:* klaus.beckschulte@bruckmann.de; Andreas von Bleichert *Tel:* (089) 13 06 99 49 *E-mail:* andreas.vonbleichert@bruckmann.de
Marketing Manager: Thilo Heller *Tel:* (089) 89 13 06 99 45 *E-mail:* thilo.heller@bruckmann.de
Manager, Magazines & Periodicals: Dr Regine Hahn *Tel:* (089) 13 06 99 17 *E-mail:* regine.hahn@bruckmann.de
Sales: Maria Elisabeth Jantzer
Publicity: Barbara Aschenberner
Production: Helmut Huber
Sales & Trade Service: Nina Baier *Tel:* (089) 13 06 99 14 *E-mail:* nina.baier@bruckmann.de; Angelika Maerz *Tel:* (089) 13 06 99 15 *E-mail:* angelika.maerz@bruckmann.de
Customer Service: Sabine Korb *Tel:* (089) 13 06 99 15 *E-mail:* sabine.korb@bruckmann.de
Press: Carola Schindler *Tel:* (089) 13 06 99 27 *E-mail:* carola.schindler@bruckmann.de
Product Management: Martina Appich *E-mail:* martina.appich@geranova.de; Sabine Klingan *E-mail:* sabine.klingan@bruckmann.de; Sonya Mayer *E-mail:* sonya.mayer@geranova.de
Founded: 1858
Membership(s): TR - Verlagsunion GmbH.
Subjects: Art, Film, Video, Gardening, Plants, History, Humor, Outdoor Recreation, Regional Interests, Science (General), Travel
ISBN Prefix(es): 3-7654; 3-932785

**Bruecke-Verlag Kurt Schmersow**
Arnekenstr 22-25, 31134 Hildesheim
*Tel:* (05121) 91 92 0 *Fax:* (05121) 91 92 20
*E-mail:* buchhaltung@bruecke-verlag.de
*Web Site:* www.bruecke-verlag.de
*Key Personnel*
Owner: Gerda Niemz
Founded: 1920
ISBN Prefix(es): 3-87105

**Bruehlsche Uni-Druckerei Verlag, der Giessener Anzeiger GmbH & Co KG**
Am Urnenfeld 12, 35396 Giessen
Mailing Address: Postfach 100451, 35334 Giessen
*Tel:* (0641) 95040 *Fax:* (0641) 9504100
*Telex:* 482859 bruel
*Key Personnel*
Manager & International Rights: Dr Wolfgang Maass
ISBN Prefix(es): 3-922300

**BRUEN-Verlag, Gorenflo**
Weserstr 22, 65428 Ruesselsheim
Mailing Address: Postfach 1356, 65403 Ruesselsheim
*Tel:* (06142) 61434 *Fax:* (06142) 61259

*E-mail:* 0614261434-1@t-online.de
*Key Personnel*
Man Dir: R Gorenflo
Founded: 1987
Subjects: Art, Fiction, History, Nonfiction (General), Poetry, Regional Interests
ISBN Prefix(es): 3-926759

**Brunnen-Verlag GmbH+**
Gottlieb-Daimler Str 22, 35398 Giessen
*Tel:* (0641) 6059-0 *Fax:* (0641) 6059-100
*E-mail:* info@brunnen-verlag.de
*Web Site:* www.brunnen-verlag.de
*Key Personnel*
Man Dir: Detlef Holtgrefe
Editorial: Eva-Maria Busch; Irmgard Froese-Schreer; Renate Huebsch; Helmut Jablonski; Petra Luetjen
International Rights & Editorial: Ralf Tibusek
    *E-mail:* ralf.tibusek@brunnen-verlag.de
Sales Manager: Reinhard Engeln
    *E-mail:* reinhard.engeln@brunnen-verlag.de
Founded: 1919
Subjects: Religion - Other, Theology
ISBN Prefix(es): 3-7655
Number of titles published annually: 120 Print
Total Titles: 800 Print
*Associate Companies:* Brunnen Verlag, Basel, Switzerland
*Distribution Center:* ChrisMedia *Tel:* (06406) 8346-100 *E-mail:* bestellung@chrismedia24.de

**BTB**, *imprint of* BKV-Brasilienkunde Verlag GmbH

**Buch- und Kunstverlag Kleinheinrich+**
Koenigsstr 42, 48143 Muenster
*Tel:* (0251) 4840193 *Fax:* (0251) 4840194
*Key Personnel*
International Rights: Dr Josef Kleinheinrich
Founded: 1986
Subjects: Art, Literature, Literary Criticism, Essays
ISBN Prefix(es): 3-926608; 3-930754

**Bucharchiv**, see Deutsches Bucharchiv Muenchen, Institut fur Buchwissenschaften

**Verlag C J Bucher GmbH+**
Innsbrucker ring 15, 81673 Munich
Mailing Address: PO Box 80 02 40, 81602 Munich
*Tel:* (089) 51480 *Fax:* (089) 5148-2229
*E-mail:* info@bucher-verlag.de
*Key Personnel*
Man Dir: Axel Schenck
Sales & Publicity: Alexander Herrmann
Production: Angelika Kerscher
Publisher: Christian Strasser
Rights & Permissions: Bettina Breitling
Publicity: Michael Then
Founded: 1956
Subjects: Art, Nonfiction (General), Photography, Travel
ISBN Prefix(es): 3-7658
*Associate Companies:* Paul List Verlag; Suedwest Verlag; W Ludwig Verlag
*Orders to:* Koch, Neff, Oetinger & Co Verlagsauslieferung GmbH, Schockenriedstr 39, 70506 Stuttgart

**Buchheim-Verlag**
Biersackstr 23, 82340 Feldafing
*Tel:* (08157) 1221 *Fax:* (08157) 3143
*Key Personnel*
Owner & International Rights: Lothar-Guenther Buchheim
Founded: 1951
Subjects: Art
ISBN Prefix(es): 3-7659

**BuchMarkt Verlag K Werner GmbH**
    (Bookmarket)
Sperberweg 4a, 40668 Meerbusch
*Tel:* (02150) 9191-0 *Fax:* (02150) 919191
*E-mail:* redaktion@buchmarkt.de
*Web Site:* www.buchmarkt.de
*Key Personnel*
Dir, International Rights: Christian Von Zittwitz
Founded: 1966
Publishers of the trade magazine Buchmart for the booktrade.
Subjects: Publishing & Book Trade Reference
ISBN Prefix(es): 3-920518

**C C Buchners Verlag GmbH & Co KG**
Laubanger 8, 96052 Bamberg
Mailing Address: Postfach 1269, 96003 Bamberg
*Tel:* (0951) 96 501-0 *Fax:* (0951) 61-774
*E-mail:* service@ccbuchner.de
*Web Site:* www.ccbuchner.de
*Key Personnel*
Dir, Rights & Permissions: Gunnar Gruenke
Founded: 1832
Subjects: Earth Sciences, Government, Political Science, History, Regional Interests
ISBN Prefix(es): 3-7661

**Buchverlag Junge Welt GmbH**
Oranienburgerstr 65, 10117 Berlin
*Tel:* (030) 231079 0 *Fax:* (030) 2826989
*E-mail:* info@bvjw.de
*Web Site:* www.bvjw.de
*Key Personnel*
Manager: Dr Thomas Seng; Eberhard Tackenberg
Founded: 1991
Subjects: Education, Science (General), Technology
ISBN Prefix(es): 3-7302

**Buchverlage Langen-Mueller/Herbig+**
Thomas-Wimmer-Ring 11, 80539 Munich
*Tel:* (089) 2 90 88-0 *Fax:* (089) 29088-144
*E-mail:* info@herbig.net
*Web Site:* www.herbig.net
*Key Personnel*
Man Dir: Dr Herbert Fleissner
International Rights: Frauke Hoppen *E-mail:* f.hoppenaherbig@net
Subjects: Cookery, Economics, Fiction, Health, Nutrition, Parapsychology, Self-Help
ISBN Prefix(es): 3-7766; 3-7844
Subsidiaries: Amalthea; Bechtle; F A Herbig Verlagsbuchhandlung GmbH; Langen Mueller; Mary Hahn; Nymphenburger; Signum; Terra Magica; Universitas; Wirtschaftsverlag
*Warehouse:* Vereinigte Verlagsauslieferung, Guetersloh

**Edition Buecherbaer im Arena Verlag**, see Arena Verlag GmbH

**Edition Buecherbar im Arena Verlag**, *imprint of* Arena Verlag GmbH

**Buchergilde Gutenberg Verlagsgesellschaft mbH**
Untermainkai 66, 60329 Frankfurt am Main
Mailing Address: Postfach 160165, 60064 Frankfurt am Main
*Tel:* (069) 27 39 08-0 *Fax:* (069) 27 39 08-26; (069) 27 39 08-25
*E-mail:* service@buechergilde.de
*Web Site:* www.buechergilde.de
*Key Personnel*
Man Dir, Editorial, Rights & Permsissions: Mario Frueh
Sales & Publicity: Carol Mueller
Production: Grit Fischer
Founded: 1924
Primarily a Book Club, but also a publisher.

Subjects: Art, Government, Political Science, History, Literature, Literary Criticism, Essays
ISBN Prefix(es): 3-7632
*Book Club(s):* Buechergilde Gutenberg

**Buechse der Pandora Verlags-GmbH+**
Schulstr 20, 35579 Wetzlar, OT Steindorf
Mailing Address: Postfach 2820, 35538 Wetzlar OT Steindorf
*Tel:* (06441) 911312 *Fax:* (06441) 911314 *Cable:* 35579 WETZLAR-STEINDORF
*Key Personnel*
Man Dir: Peter Grosshaus
Founded: 1977
Subjects: Art, Education, Literature, Literary Criticism, Essays, Philosophy
ISBN Prefix(es): 3-88178
*Orders to:* Rotation Verlagsauslieferung, Mehringdamm 51, 10961 Berlin

**Bund demokratischer Wissenschaftlerinnen und Wissenschafler eV (BdWi)+**
Gisselbergstr 7, 35037 Marburg
*Tel:* (06421) 2 13 95 *Fax:* (06421) 2 46 54
*E-mail:* verlag@bdwi.de
*Web Site:* www.bdwi.de
*Key Personnel*
Manager: Dr Rainer Rilling
Founded: 1993
Subjects: Government, Political Science, Psychology, Psychiatry, Social Sciences, Sociology, Women's Studies
ISBN Prefix(es): 3-924684
*Associate Companies:* Informationsstelle Wissenschaft und Frieden (IWIF), 53113 Bonn *Tel:* (0228) 210744 *Fax:* (0228) 214924; Informationsdienst Wissenschaft und Frieden ev, Reuterstr 44, 5300 Bonn 1 *Tel:* (0228) 213334 *Fax:* (0228) 214924
*Imprints:* Forum Wissenschaft Studien; Internationale Studien zen Fatigkeititleone; Sammlung; Schriftenfeibe Wissenschaft und Frieden
*Branch Office(s)*
BdWi Bonn ev, Reuterstr 44, 53115 Bonn 1 *Tel:* (0228) 219946 *Fax:* (0228) 214924
*Orders to:* Bugtiur-Verlagsanslieferung, Sodelburgstr 3, 12099 Berlin

**Bund Deutscher Schriftsteller (BDS)** (German Writers Association)
Romerstr 2, 63128 Dietzenbach
*Tel:* (06074) 47566 *Fax:* (06074) 47540
Founded: 1997
Also acts as Literary Agent.
Membership(s): World Writers Association, London.
ISBN Prefix(es): 3-00
Total Titles: 2 Print
Publication(s): *Authors Yearbook*; *Register of German Authors*

**Bund fuer deutsche Schrift und Sprache**
Postfach 1145, 38711 Seesen
*Tel:* (05381) 46355 *Fax:* (05381) 46355
*E-mail:* verwaltung@bfds.de
*Web Site:* www.bfds.de
*Key Personnel*
Man Dir: Helmut Delbanco
Founded: 1918
ISBN Prefix(es): 3-930540

**Bund-Verlag GmbH+**
Heddernheimer Landstr 144, 60439 Frankfurt am Main
*Tel:* (069) 79 50 10 20 *Fax:* (069) 79 50 10 10
*E-mail:* kontakt@bund-verlag.de
*Web Site:* www.bund-verlag.de
*Key Personnel*
Man Dir: Christian Paulsen
Sales: Tamara Kellberg
Production: Birgit Gast; Inga Tomalla
Rights & Permissions: Dr Angermund Schroeder
Founded: 1947

Subjects: Economics, Fiction, Finance, Government, Political Science, Law, Poetry
ISBN Prefix(es): 3-7663; 3-930453

**Bundes-Verlag GmbH**
Bodenborn 43, 58452 Witten
*Tel:* (02302) 930 93-0
*E-mail:* info@bundesverlag.de
*Web Site:* www.bundes-verlag.de
*Key Personnel*
Man Dir: Erhard Diehl
Founded: 1887
Subjects: Religion - Catholic
ISBN Prefix(es): 3-926417; 3-933660

**Bundesanzeiger Verlagsgesellschaft**
Amsterdamerstr 192, 50735 Cologne
Mailing Address: Postfach 10 05 34, 50445
    Cologne
*Tel:* (0221) 9 76 68-0 *Fax:* (0221) 9 76 68-278
*E-mail:* vcotiicb@bundesanzeiger.de
*Web Site:* www.bundesanzeiger.de
*Key Personnel*
Man Dir: Rainier Diesem
Contact: Birgit Drehsen
Founded: 1948
Subjects: Government, Political Science, History,
    Law, Regional Interests
ISBN Prefix(es): 3-88784; 3-89817
Subsidiaries: Deutscher Bundesverlag

**Burckhardthaus-Laetare Verlag GmbH+**
Schumannstr 161, 63069 Offenbach
*Tel:* (069) 8400030 *Fax:* (069) 84000333
*Key Personnel*
Publisher & Manager: Andre Juenger
Rights & Permissions: Alexandra Cordes
Founded: 1918
Subjects: Education, Psychology, Psychiatry, Religion - Other
ISBN Prefix(es): 3-7664

**Aenne Burda Verlag**
Am Kestendamm 2, 77652 Offenburg
Mailing Address: Postfach 1160, 77601 Offenburg
*Tel:* (0781) 843322 *Fax:* (0781) 843386
*Telex:* 752804 *Cable:* BURDAMODEN
    OFFENBURG
Founded: 1949
Subjects: Cookery, Crafts, Games, Hobbies
ISBN Prefix(es): 3-920158; 3-88978
Subsidiaries: Burda Patterns Inc; Dipa SA; ZVB
    Zeitschriften Vertriebs AB

**Ulrich Burgdorf/Homeopathic Publishing House+**
Tegeler Weg 8, 37085 Goettingen
*Tel:* (0551) 796050 *Fax:* (0551) 796955
*E-mail:* Burgdorf-Verlag@t-online.de
*Web Site:* www.burgdorf-verlag.de
*Key Personnel*
Contact: Dons Scheleper
Founded: 1979
Subjects: Philosophy, Photography, Psychology,
    Psychiatry
ISBN Prefix(es): 3-922345; 3-89762

**Kartographischer Verlag Busche GmbH**
Schleefstr 1, 44287 Dortmund
*Tel:* (0231) 4 44 77-0 *Fax:* (0231) 4 44 77-77
*E-mail:* info@busche.de
*Web Site:* www.kvbusche.de
*Key Personnel*
Man Dir, Publicity: Juergen Ruediger Klaffka
Editorial: Barbara Roemer
Marketing Management: Ulrike Rudolph
    *Tel:* (05221) 775-275
Founded: 1972
Subjects: Travel

ISBN Prefix(es): 3-88584; 3-921143; 3-89764; 3-925086
*Parent Company:* Busche KG

**Anita und Klaus Buscher B & B Verlag+**
Erika-Koth-Str 56, 67435 Neustadt-Konigsbach
*Tel:* (06321) 968485 *Fax:* (06321) 968486
*Key Personnel*
Man Dir: Anita Buscher
Founded: 1988
ISBN Prefix(es): 3-927419

**Helmut Buske Verlag GmbH+**
Richardstr 47, 22081 Hamburg
Mailing Address: Postfach 760244, 22052 Hamburg
*Tel:* (040) 2999580 *Fax:* (040) 29995820
*E-mail:* info@buske.de
*Web Site:* www.buske.de
*Key Personnel*
Man Dir: Manfred Meiner
Publishing Dir: Michael Hechinger
Rights, Marketing: Johannes Kambylis *Tel:* (040)
    299958-23 *E-mail:* kambylis@buske.de
Founded: 1959
Subjects: Language Arts, Linguistics
ISBN Prefix(es): 3-87118; 3-87548
*Ultimate Parent Company:* Felix Meiner Verlag
    GmbH

**Verlag Busse und Seewald GmbH+**
Ahmserstr 190, 32052 Herford
Mailing Address: Postfach 1344, 32003 Herford
*Tel:* (05221) 775266; (05221) 775276
    *Fax:* (05221) 775204
*E-mail:* info@busse-seewald.de
*Web Site:* www.busse-seewald.de
*Key Personnel*
Manager: Michael Best; Harald Busse
Sales & Advertising: Regina Benecke
Rights & Permissions: Ulrike Rudolph
    *Tel:* (05221) 775-275
Founded: 1947
Subjects: Architecture & Interior Design, Maritime, Nonfiction (General), Outdoor Recreation, Regional Interests, Travel, Wine & Spirits
ISBN Prefix(es): 3-512; 3-87120
*Associate Companies:* Buchdruckerei und Verlag
    Busse; Westdeutsche Verlagsanstalt GmbH
Distributor for DSV-Verlag (Germany, Austria,
    Switzerland)

**Butzon & Bercker GmbH+**
Hoogeweg 71, 47623 Kevelaer
Mailing Address: Postfach 1355, 47623 Kevelaer
*Tel:* (02832) 929-0 *Fax:* (02832) 929-112
*E-mail:* service@butzonbercker.de
*Web Site:* www.butzonbercker.de *Cable:*
    BUTZONBERCKER
*Key Personnel*
Dir: Dr Edmund J Bercker *E-mail:* edmund.
    bercker@bube.de; Klaus Bercker
Editorial: Pit Stenmans
Sales: Helga Behr
Publicity: Helmut Kaiser
Rights & Permissions: Anne Moore
Founded: 1870
Subjects: Religion - Catholic, Theology
ISBN Prefix(es): 3-7666
Distributor for Lahn (Limburg); Styria (Graz/
    Cologne)

**BWV**, see Berliner Wissenschafts-Verlag GmbH
    (BWV)

**Caann Verlag, Klaus Wagner**
Am Anger 11, 85570 Ottenhofen
*Tel:* (08121) 9 32 71 *Fax:* (08121) 9 32 78
*E-mail:* info@caann-verlag.de
*Web Site:* www.caann-verlag.de

*Key Personnel*
Man Dir: Klaus Wagner
Founded: 1969
Subjects: Nonfiction (General), Philosophy, Social
    Sciences, Sociology
ISBN Prefix(es): 3-87121

**Cadmos Verlag GmbH+**
Imdorfe 11, 22946 Brunsbek
*Tel:* (04107) 8517-0 *Fax:* (041307 8517-0
*E-mail:* info@cadmos.de
*Web Site:* www.cadmos.de
*Key Personnel*
Publisher: Hans J Schmidtke
Founded: 1986
Subjects: Dogs, Equestrian, Horses
ISBN Prefix(es): 3-925760; 3-86127
Number of titles published annually: 50 Print; 2
    Audio
Total Titles: 150 Print; 8 Audio
Foreign Rep(s): Hans Schmidtke

**Verlag Georg D W Callwey GmbH & Co+**
Streitfeldstr 35, 81673 Munich
*Tel:* (089) 436005-0 *Fax:* (089) 436005-117
*E-mail:* info@callwey.de
*Web Site:* www.callwey.de *Cable:*
    CALLWEYVERLAG
*Key Personnel*
Man Dir: Amos Kotte *E-mail:* a.kotte@callwey.de
Editorial: Dr Stefan Granzow *E-mail:* s.
    granzow@callwey.de
Rights & Permissions, Publicity & Sales: Jens-
    Peter Arndt *E-mail:* jp.arndt@callwey.de
Publicity: Andreas Hagenkord
Founded: 1884
Subjects: Architecture & Interior Design, Crafts,
    Games, Hobbies, Gardening, Plants, House &
    Home, How-to
ISBN Prefix(es): 3-7667

**Calwer Verlag GmbH+**
Balingerstr 31, 70567 Stuttgart
Mailing Address: Postfach 810293, 70519
    Stuttgart
*Tel:* (0711) 167 22-0 *Fax:* (0711) 167 22 77
*E-mail:* info@calwer.com
*Web Site:* www.calwer.com
*Key Personnel*
Dir: Dr Berthold Brohm *E-mail:* brohm@calwer.
    com; Joachim Hinderer *E-mail:* hinderer@
    calwer.com
Marketing: Beatrice Basgier *E-mail:* basgier@
    calwer.com
Production: Karin Klopfer *E-mail:* klopfer@
    calwer.com
Rights: Susanne Hien *E-mail:* hien@calwer.com
Founded: 1836
Subjects: Education, Religion - Other, Theology
ISBN Prefix(es): 3-7668
*Orders to:* Brockhans Kommission, Kreidlestr 9,
    70806 Kornwestheim *Fax:* (07154) 13 27 13

**Campus Verlag GmbH+**
49 Kurfuerstenstr, 60486 Frankfurt am Main
*Tel:* (069) 976 516-0 *Fax:* (069) 976 516-78
*E-mail:* info@campus.de
*Web Site:* www.campus.de
*Key Personnel*
Executive Dir, Publisher & Rights & Permissions:
    Thomas Carl Schwoerer *Tel:* (069) 976 516-43
    *E-mail:* schwoerer@campus.de
Foreign Rights: Franziska Stadler *Tel:* (069) 976
    516-15 *E-mail:* stadler@campus.de
Editor-in-Chief: Britta Kroker *Tel:* (069) 976 516-
    56 *E-mail:* kroker@campus.de
Editor-in-Chief, Science: Adalbert Hepp
    *Tel:* (069) 976 516-52 *E-mail:* hepp@campus.
    de
Sales Dir: Andreas Horn *Tel:* (069) 976 516-14
    *E-mail:* horn@campus.de
Production: Klaus Schoeffner *Tel:* (069) 976 516-
    64; Ulrich Begemeier *Tel:* (069) 976 516-66

Advertising: Markus J Karsten *Tel:* (069) 976
516-32
Publicity: Margit Knauer *Tel:* (069) 976 516-21
Founded: 1975
Specialize also in cultural studies.
Subjects: Business, Career Development, Eco-
nomics, Government, Political Science, History,
Management, Philosophy, Social Sciences, So-
ciology, Women's Studies
ISBN Prefix(es): 3-593
Number of titles published annually: 240 Print;
10 Audio
*Orders to:* Brockhaus Commission, Kreidlerstr
9, 70806 Kornwestheim *Tel:* (07154) 1327-76
*Fax:* (07154) 1327-13 *E-mail:* bestell@brocom.
de *Web Site:* www.brocom.de

**Campusbooks Medien AG+**
Bonner Platz 4, 80803 Munich
*Tel:* (089) 18921730 *Fax:* (089) 18921731
*E-mail:* info@campusbooks.de
*Web Site:* www.campusbooks.de/partner_main.
html
*Key Personnel*
Dir Business Development: Juergen Reuter
Founded: 2000
Bookseller for corporate customers & publishing
house for theses & magazines.
Number of titles published annually: 10 Print

**Dr Cantz'sche Druckerei GmbH & Co+**
Senefelderstr 12, 73760 Ostfildern
*Tel:* (0711) 4405-0; (0711) 4405-121 (Marketing
& Sales) *Fax:* (0711) 4405-111
*E-mail:* bklein@jfink.de
*Web Site:* www.jfink.de
*Key Personnel*
Publisher & International Rights: Annette Ku-
lenkanpff
Publisher: Bernd Barde
Man Dir & Sales Dir: Markus Hartmann
Founded: 1980
Distributor of Art Books.
Subjects: Architecture & Interior Design, Art,
Photography
ISBN Prefix(es): 3-89322; 3-922608
*U.S. Office(s):* DAP (Distributed Art Publish-
ers), 636 Broadway, Rm 1200, New York,
NY 10012, United States *Tel:* 212-627-1999
*Fax:* 212-627-9484
Distributed by Thames & Hudson Ltd (London)
Distributor for Guggenheim Museum; Skira Edi-
tore (Milano)
*Orders to:* Cantz Verlag, Senefelderstr 12, 73760
Ostfildern-Ruit
Koch, Neff, Oetinger & Co, Postfach 800620,
70565 Stuttgart

**Carl-Auer-Systeme Verlag+**
Weberstr 2, 69120 Heidelberg
*Tel:* (06221) 64380 *Fax:* (06221) 643822
*E-mail:* info@carl-auer.de
*Web Site:* www.carl-auer.de
*Key Personnel*
Man Dir: Dr Fritz B Simon
Program & Production: Beate Ch Ulrich
*Tel:* (06221) 6438-15 *E-mail:* ulrich@carl-
auer.de
Publishing: Klaus W Muller *Tel:* (06221) 6438-16
*E-mail:* mueller@carl-auer.de
Sales: Johannes Altrock *Tel:* (06221) 6438-20
*E-mail:* altrock@carl-auer.de
Publicity: Francoise Jaouiche *Tel:* (06221) 6438-
17 *E-mail:* jaouiche@carl-auer.de
Founded: 1989
Subjects: Child Care & Development, Human Re-
lations, Management, Philosophy, Psychology,
Psychiatry
ISBN Prefix(es): 3-927809; 3-931574; 3-89670
Total Titles: 110 Print; 90 Audio

**Fachverlag Hans Carl GmbH+**
Andernacher Str 33a, 90411 Nuremberg
Mailing Address: Postfach 990153, 90268
Nuremberg
*Tel:* (0911) 95285-0 *Fax:* (0911) 95285-48;
(0911) 95285-71; (0911) 95285-61
*E-mail:* info@hanscarl.com
*Web Site:* www.hanscarl.com
*Key Personnel*
Man Dir, Editorial: Dr Karl-Ullrich Heyse
*Tel:* (0911) 95285-22 *Fax:* (0911) 95285-60
*E-mail:* heyse@hanscarl.com
Man Dir: Wolfgang Illguth *Tel:* (0911) 95285-20
*E-mail:* illguth@hanscarl.com
Board: Michael Schmitt *E-mail:* m.schmitt@
hanscarl.com
Founded: 1861
Subjects: Art, Chemistry, Chemical Engineering,
Fiction, History, Outdoor Recreation, Philoso-
phy, Poetry, Regional Interests, Science (Gen-
eral), Wine & Spirits
ISBN Prefix(es): 3-418
*Bookshop(s):* Fachbuchhandlung Hans Carl,
Wolf-Dieter Schoyerer *Tel:* (0911) 9528531
*E-mail:* fachbuchhandlung@hanscarl.com

**Carl Link Verlag-Gesellschaft mbH Fachverlag
fur Verwaltungsrecht**
Adolf - Kolping Str 10, 96317 Kronach
*Tel:* (09261) 969 4000 *Fax:* (09261) 969 4111
*E-mail:* info@carllink.de
*Web Site:* www.carllink.de
*Key Personnel*
Man Dir & International Rights: Dr Wilhelm
Warth
Founded: 1884
Subjects: Law
ISBN Prefix(es): 3-556
*Parent Company:* Carl Link
*Associate Companies:* Bueromarkt, Kronach; Carl
Link Druck GmbH, Kronach
*Bookshop(s):* Buchdienst, Gueterstr 7, 96317 Kro-
nach
*Warehouse:* Carl Link Bueromarkt, Gueterstr 7,
96317 Kronach

**Carlsen Verlag GmbH+**
Voelckersstr 14-20, 22765 Hamburg
Mailing Address: Postfach 500380, 22703 Ham-
burg
*Tel:* (040) 39 804 0 *Fax:* (040) 39 804 390
*Key Personnel*
Dir: Klaus Humann; Klaus Kaempfe-Burghardt
Editorial: Anne Bender; Barbara Koenig; Frank
Kuehne; Ulrike Schuldes; Katja Schultze
Sales: Ann Oelkers
Production: Wiebke Duesedau
Advertising: Marianne Ohmann
Public Relations: Cornelia Berger
Press Manager: Katrin Hogrebe *E-mail:* katrin.
hogrebe@carlsen.de
Foreign Rights: Erdmut Gross
Founded: 1953
Specialize in children's books & comics.
Subjects: Fiction, Humor
ISBN Prefix(es): 3-551
*Parent Company:* Bonnier Media Holding GmbH,
Hamburg
*Associate Companies:* ARS Edition; Piper Verlag;
Thienemann Verlag

**CartoTravel Verlag GmbH & Co KG+**
Auf der Krautweide 24, 65812 Bad Soden/Taunus
*Tel:* (06196) 6096-0 *Fax:* (06196) 27450
*E-mail:* info@cartotravel.de
*Web Site:* www.cartotravel.de *Cable:*
ADACVERLAG
*Key Personnel*
Man Dir: Thomas Haupka; Thomas Mueller
Founded: 1958
Also carry magazines & travel guides.

Subjects: Automotive, Travel
ISBN Prefix(es): 3-87003; 3-8264

**Catia Monser Eggcup-Verlag**
Werstener Feld 235, 40591 Duesseldorf
*Tel:* (0211) 215122 *Fax:* (0211) 215122
*E-mail:* cmonserev@aol.com
*Web Site:* members.aol.com/CMonserEV
*Key Personnel*
Contact: Catia Monser
Founded: 1992
Subjects: Disability, Special Needs, Health, Nu-
trition, Human Relations, Medicine, Nursing,
Dentistry, Mysteries
ISBN Prefix(es): 3-930004

**Centaurus-Verlagsgesellschaft GmbH**
Bugstr 7-9, 79336 Herbolzheim
*Tel:* (07643) 93 39-0 *Fax:* (07643) 93 39-11
*E-mail:* info@centaurus-verlag.de
*Web Site:* www.centaurus-verlag.de
*Key Personnel*
Manager: Petra Sanft; Britta Schulz
Founded: 1983
Membership(s): The Stock Exchange of German
Booksellers.
Subjects: Criminology, Education, History, Law,
Psychology, Psychiatry, Religion - Other, So-
cial Sciences, Sociology, Women's Studies
ISBN Prefix(es): 3-89085; 3-8255

**Chancerel International Publishers Ltd+**
Rotebuhstr 77, Stuttgart 70178
*Tel:* (049711) 6672 5728 *Fax:* (049711) 6672
2004
*E-mail:* tvandree@klett-mail.de
*Web Site:* www.chancerel.com
*Key Personnel*
Man Dir: W D B Prowse
Founded: 1976
Specialize in language teaching materials: English
(British & American), German, French, Span-
ish, Italian & Japanese.
Subjects: Education, Language Arts, Linguistics
ISBN Prefix(es): 0-905703; 1-899888; 1-903749
*Parent Company:* Klett Languages London Ltd
*Ultimate Parent Company:* Ernst Klett Sprachen
GmbH
Distributed by BEBC (UK)

**Verlag fur chemische Industrie H Ziolkowsky
GmbH**
Beethovenstr 16, 86150 Augsburg
Mailing Address: Postfach 10 25 65, 86015
Augsburg
*Tel:* (0821) 325-830 *Fax:* (0821) 325-8323
*E-mail:* info@kosmet.com
*Key Personnel*
Contact: Bernd Ziolkowsky
ISBN Prefix(es): 3-87846

**Chiron-Verlag Reinhardt Stiehle+**
Staeudach 6/1, 72074 Tuebingen
*Tel:* (07071) 8884150 *Fax:* (07071) 8884151
*E-mail:* info@chironverlag.de
*Web Site:* www.chironverlag.de
*Key Personnel*
President & Publisher: Reinhardt Stiehle
Founded: 1985
Membership(s): The Stock Exchange of German
Booksellers.
Subjects: Astrology, Occult
ISBN Prefix(es): 3-925100; 3-89997
*Orders to:* Brockhaus Commission, Kreidler-
strasse 9, 70806 Kornwestheim

**Chmielorz GmbH Verlag+**
Marktplatz 13, 65183 Wiesbaden
Mailing Address: Postfach 22 29, 65183 Wies-
baden
*Tel:* (0611) 360980 *Fax:* (0611) 36098-17

*E-mail:* tme@chmielorz.de
*Web Site:* www.chmielorz.de
*Key Personnel*
Man Dir: Thomas Mueller-Eggersgluess
Founded: 1949
Publish professional magazines (trade press), handbooks, loose-leaf books (law commentaries), CD-ROMs, databases.
Subjects: Business, Civil Engineering, Cookery, Earth Sciences, Economics, Fiction, Geography, Geology, Health, Nutrition, Law, Medicine, Nursing, Dentistry, Public Administration, Publishing & Book Trade Reference, Social Sciences, Sociology, Sports, Athletics, Cinema, Film Industry, Food, International Law, Movies, Sport (Trade, Industry)
ISBN Prefix(es): 3-87124
*Branch Office(s)*
Druckhaus Chmielorz, Ostring 13, 65205 Wiesbaden-Nordenstadt, Contact: Carsten Augsburger *Tel:* (06122) 7709-01 *Fax:* (06122) 7709-181 *E-mail:* dc@chmielorz.de
Distributor for EuBuCo-Verlag; mhp-Verlag

### Chorus-Verlag
Wichernweg 22 A, 81737 Munich
*Tel:* (089) 634 999 60 *Fax:* (089) 634 999 61
*Web Site:* www.chorus-verlag.de
*Key Personnel*
Dir: Martin van der Koelen *E-mail:* mvdk@ chorus-verlag.de
Founded: 1995
Subjects: Art, Specialize in museum catalogues & catalog raisonnes
ISBN Prefix(es): 3-931876
Total Titles: 60 Print
Distributed by Arteko Galeria de Arte (Spain); AVA-Buch 2000 Verlagsauslieferung (Switzerland); Bugrim Verlagsauslieferung (Germany & Austria); Continent Books (Benelux); Joker Art Diffusion (France); Hurtado de Ediciones (Spain)

### Chr Belser AG fur Verlagsgeschaefte und Co KG+
Pfizerstr 5-7, 70184 Stuttgart
Mailing Address: Postfach 100561, 70004 Stuttgart
*Tel:* (0711) 2191-0 *Fax:* (0711) 2191-330 *Cable:* BELSERVERLAG
*Key Personnel*
Publisher: Dr Herbert Fleissner
Manager: Axel Meffert
Rights & Permissions: Andrea Ahlers
Publicity: Renate Palmer
Production: Ulrich Dotzauer
Founded: 1835
Subjects: Art, History, Music, Dance, Nonfiction (General), Religion - Other, Theology, Travel
ISBN Prefix(es): 3-7630
*Parent Company:* Chr Belser AG Zuerich
Subsidiaries: Amalthea; Bechtle; Kronos; Langen Mueller; Lentz; Mahnert-Lueg; Mary Hahn; Meyster; Nymphenburger; Reich; Universitas; USM Soft Media; Wirtschaftsverlag
*Warehouse:* VVA, An der Autobahn, 33310 Gutersloh

### Christian Verlag GmbH+
Amalienstr 62, 80799 Munich
*Tel:* (089) 381803-17; (089) 381803-31 *Fax:* (089) 38180381
*E-mail:* info@christian-verlag.de
*Web Site:* www.christian-verlag.de
*Key Personnel*
Manager: Martin Dort; Johannes Heyne
Chief Editor: Florentine Schwabbauer
Sales & Advertising: Barbara Thieme *Tel:* (089) 38 18 03-30 *Fax:* (089) 38 18 03-81; Dr Ingeborg Kluge *Tel:* (089) 38 18 03-17; Susanne Pietsch *Tel:* (089) 38 18 03-31
Editorial Rights: Claudia Bitz; Tanja Germann

Public Relations: Gudrun Schroeder *Tel:* (089) 2 01 40 10 *Fax:* (089) 2 01 40 11 *E-mail:* g. schroeder.muc@t-online.de
Founded: 1979
Subjects: Architecture & Interior Design, Cookery, Gardening, Plants, Nonfiction (General), Photography, Wine & Spirits
ISBN Prefix(es): 3-88472

### Hans Christians Druckerei und Verlag GmbH & Co KG+
Behringstr 28 a, 22765 Hamburg
*Tel:* (040) 35 60 06-0 *Fax:* (040) 35 60 06-26
*E-mail:* verlag@christians.de
*Web Site:* www.christians.de *Cable:* CHRISTIANS DRUCK
*Key Personnel*
Man Dir: Susanne Liebelt *Tel:* (040) 35 60 06-11 *E-mail:* susanne.liebelt@christians.de
Manager: Martin Lind *Tel:* (040) 35 60 06-27 *E-mail:* martin.lind@christians.de
Public Relations, Rights & Permissions: Sabine Bayer *Tel:* (040) 35 60 06-15 *E-mail:* sabine. bayer@christians.de
Sales: Petra Jehnichen *Tel:* (040) 35 60 06-35 *E-mail:* petra.jehnichen@christians.de
Founded: 1740
Subjects: Architecture & Interior Design, Art, Biography, Communications, Cookery, Education, Ethnicity, Gardening, Plants, Geography, Geology, History, Music, Dance, Natural History, Nonfiction (General), Outdoor Recreation, Photography, Regional Interests, Religion - Jewish, Social Sciences, Sociology, Travel
ISBN Prefix(es): 3-7672
Distributor for CCV; Eylers; Verlag Gronenberg; Land & Meer Verlag; Verlag fuer Medienliteratur; Verlag Robert Wenzel
*Warehouse:* Vull-Service GmbH, Werftbahnstr 8, 24143 Kiel *Tel:* (0431) 702 82 70 *Fax:* (0431) 702 82 99

### Christliche Verlagsgesellschaft mbH+
Molkestr 1, 35683 Dillenburg
*Tel:* (02771) 8302-0 *Fax:* (02771) 8302-30
*E-mail:* info@cv-dillenburg.de
*Web Site:* www.cb-buchshop.de
*Key Personnel*
Editorial, Publicity, Production: Hartmut Jaeger
Sales: Bernd-Udo Flick
Rights & Permissions: Mirko Merten
Founded: 1957
Subjects: Religion - Other
ISBN Prefix(es): 3-89436
Subsidiaries: Christliche Buecherstuben GmbH
Distributed by CB Medienvertrieb (Germany); Schwengeler Verlag (Switzerland)
Distributor for CLV; Daniel Verlag; KEB; Leuchtturm Verlag; Media C; Schwengeler; 3L Verlag
*Bookshop(s):* Lennestr 25, 58762 Altena; Molkestr 1, 35683 Dillenburg; Friedrichsstr 10, Duesseldorf; Rosenallee, 52249 Eschweiler; Dreikoenigenstr 21, 47799 Krefeld 1; Poststr 24, 4780 Lippstadt; Muensterstr 27, 46316 Luenen; Lindauerstr 8, 87700 Memmingen; Am Koenigshof 43, 40822 Mettman; Hofgarten 4, 52249 Neunkirchen; Im Kobbenrod 3, 58840 Plettenberg; Harschbacherstr 12, 56316 Raubach; Koenigstr 20, Rendsburg; Alte Poststr 7, 57072 Siegen 1; Zwingergasse 1, 74889 Sinsheim; Kirchstr 19, 52531 Uebach-Palenberg; Neustadtstr 12, 58791 Werdohl; Schwelmerstr 48, 42389 Wuppertal 22

### Christliches Verlagshaus GmbH+
Motorstr 36, 70499 Stuttgart
Mailing Address: Postfach 311141, 70471 Stuttgart
*Tel:* (0711) 830000 *Fax:* (0711) 830010
*Key Personnel*
Man Dir: Armin Jetter
Founded: 1872

Subjects: Literature, Literary Criticism, Essays, Religion - Other
ISBN Prefix(es): 3-7675
Subsidiaries: Anker Buch und Medien GmbH; Druckhaus West GmbH

### Christophorus-Verlag GmbH+
Subsidiary of Verlag Herder GmbH & Co KG
Hermann-Herderstr 4, 79104 Freiburg im Breisgau
*Tel:* (0761) 27170 *Fax:* (0761) 2717352
*Key Personnel*
Man Dir: Dr Klaus-Christoph Scheffels
International Rights: Norbert Landa
Founded: 1935
Subjects: Crafts, Games, Hobbies, How-to, Outdoor Recreation
ISBN Prefix(es): 3-419
*Book Club(s):* Bertelsmann; Weltbild
*Shipping Address:* Koch, Neff & Oetinger, Schockenriedstr 39, 70565 Stuttgart
*Warehouse:* Koch, Neff & Oetinger, Schockenriedstr 39, 70565 Stuttgart
*Orders to:* Koch, Neff & Oetinger, Schockenriedstr 39, 70565 Stuttgart

### Christusbruderschaft Selbitz ev, Abt Verlag
Wildenberg 23, 95152 Selbitz
Mailing Address: Postfach 1260, 95147 Selbitz
*Tel:* (09280) 68-34 *Fax:* (09280) 68-68
*E-mail:* info@verlag-christusbruderschaft.de
*Web Site:* www.verlag-christusbruderschaft.de
*Key Personnel*
International Rights: Sr Baerbel Quarg
Founded: 1953
Subjects: Art, Poetry, Religion - Protestant, Theology
ISBN Prefix(es): 3-928745

### Cicero Presse Verlag & Antiquariat
25980 Morsum/Sylt
*Tel:* (04651) 890305 *Fax:* (04651) 890885
*E-mail:* ciceropresse@t-online.de
*Web Site:* www.zvab.com
Founded: 1965
Membership(s): International League of Antiquarian Booksellers (ILAB) & Verband Deutscher Antiquarc (VDA).
ISBN Prefix(es): 8-9120
Total Titles: 20 Print

### Verlag Marianne Cieslik+
Stresemannstr 20-22, 47051 Duisburg
*Tel:* (0203) 30527-0 *Fax:* (0203) 30527-820
*Web Site:* www.verlag-cieslik.de
*Key Personnel*
Owner: Marianne Cieslik *E-mail:* verlagmariannecieslik@t-online.de
Manager: Jurgen Cieslik
Founded: 1975
Publishers for collector books & magazines (dolls, toys, teddy bears).
Subjects: Crafts, Games, Hobbies, Price guides
ISBN Prefix(es): 3-921844

### Claassen Verlag GmbH+
Friedrichstr 126, 10117 Berlin
*Tel:* (030) 23456-300 *Fax:* (030) 23456-303
*Web Site:* www.claassen-verlag.de
*Telex:* 927108
*Key Personnel*
Man Dir: Hubertus Meyer-Burckhardt; Christian Strasser
Founded: 1934
Subjects: Biography, Fiction, Literature, Literary Criticism, Essays, Nonfiction (General)
ISBN Prefix(es): 3-546
*Parent Company:* Gebrueder Gerstenberg GmbH & Co

**Claudius Verlag+**
Birkerstr 22, 80636 Munich
*Tel:* (089) 12172-123 *Fax:* (089) 12172-138
*E-mail:* info@claudius.de
*Web Site:* www.claudius.de
*Key Personnel*
Dir: Hartmut Joisten *Tel:* (089) 12172112
Publisher: Dr Manuel Zelger *Tel:* (089) 12172136
 *E-mail:* mzelger@epv.de
International Rights: Antje Fritsch-Brown
 *Tel:* (089) 12172132 *E-mail:* afritsch@epv.de
Founded: 1954
Subjects: Developing Countries, Humor, Religion
 - Protestant, Religion - Other, Self-Help, Theol-
 ogy
ISBN Prefix(es): 3-532
Number of titles published annually: 30 Print
Total Titles: 300 Print
*Parent Company:* Evangelischer Presseverband
 fuer Bayern eV
*Bookshop(s):* Claudius Versandbuchhandlung,
 Contact: Regine Zendrek *Tel:* (089) 12172119
 *Fax:* (089) 12172138 *E-mail:* vsb@epv.de

**CMA Edition+**
Roter Brach Weg 54b, 93049 Regensburg
*Tel:* (0941) 23939; (0941) 34003; (08458) 8960
 *Fax:* (08458) 8960; (0941) 34003
*Key Personnel*
Contact: Christine Adlhoch; Dietrich Leisching
Founded: 1984
Subjects: Biography, Poetry
ISBN Prefix(es): 3-9801025

**Charles Coleman Verlag GmbH & Co KG**
Stolberger Str 84, 50933 Cologne
Mailing Address: Postfach 41 09 49, 50869
 Cologne
*Tel:* (0221) 5497-0 *Fax:* (0221) 5497-326
*E-mail:* coleman@rudolf.mueller.de
*Web Site:* www.coleman-verlag.de; www.rudolf-
 mueller.de
*Key Personnel*
Man Dir: Rudolf M Bleser; Dr Christoph Mueller
Founded: 1894
Subjects: Career Development, Engineering (Gen-
 eral), Mechanical Engineering
ISBN Prefix(es): 3-87128
*Parent Company:* Verlagsgesellschaft Rudolf
 Mueller GmbH, Stolbergerstr 84, 50933
 Cologne

**Collection b,** *imprint of* Deutsche
 Bibelgesellschaft

**Columbus Verlag Paul Oestergaard GmbH+**
Am Bahnhof 2, 72505 Krauchenwies
*Tel:* (07576) 96 03-0 *Fax:* (07576) 96 03-29
*E-mail:* info@columbus-verlag.de
*Web Site:* www.columbus-verlag.de *Cable:*
 COLUMBUS-VERLAG
*Key Personnel*
Publisher: Torsten Oestergaard
Founded: 1909
Subjects: Astronomy, Geography, Geology, House
 & Home, Globes
ISBN Prefix(es): 3-87129
Subsidiaries: Leipziger Globusmanufaktur
*Orders to:* Columbus Haus, an der Station 2,
 72505 Krauchenwies

**ComMedia & Arte Verlag Bernd Mayer+**
Am Hang 27, 74626 Bretzfeld
Mailing Address: Postfach 1117, 74622 Bretzfeld
*Tel:* (07945) 950719 *Fax:* (07945) 950718
*Key Personnel*
Owner: Bernd Mayer
Founded: 1982
Subjects: Fiction, Gay & Lesbian
ISBN Prefix(es): 3-924244
*Orders to:* Rotation, Mehringdamm 51, 10000
 Berlin *Tel:* (030) 6927934 *Fax:* (030) 6942006

**Compact Verlag GmbH+**
Zuericherstr 29, 81476 Munich
*Tel:* (089) 7451610 *Fax:* (089) 756095
*E-mail:* info@compactverlag.de
*Web Site:* www.compactverlag.de
*Key Personnel*
Publisher, Manager & International Rights:
 Friedrich Niendieck
Man Dir: Bernd Steier
Foreign Rights: Sandra Brack *Tel:* (089)
 74516183 *E-mail:* sandra.brack@
 compactverlag.de
Founded: 1976
Specialize in nonfiction books.
Subjects: Business, Cookery, Crafts, Games, Hob-
 bies, Education, English as a Second Language,
 Gardening, Plants, Health, Nutrition, History,
 House & Home, How-to, Law, Nonfiction
 (General), Real Estate, Travel
ISBN Prefix(es): 3-8174
Number of titles published annually: 180 Print
Total Titles: 1,000 Print
*Warehouse:* CDC GmbH, Rotwandweg 1, 82024
 Taufkirchen-Potzham

**Concordia-Buchhandlung & Verlag+**
Bahnhofstr 8, 08056 Zwickau
Mailing Address: Postfach 200226, 08002
 Zwickau
*Tel:* (0375) 21 28 50 *Fax:* (0375) 29 80 80;
 (0375) 21 28 50
*E-mail:* concordia@t-online.de
*Web Site:* www.concordiabuch.de
*Key Personnel*
Business Associate: Dr Gottfried Herrmann
Founded: 1990
Subjects: Religion - Other, Theology
ISBN Prefix(es): 3-910153

**Connection Medien GmbH+**
Hauptstr 5, 84494 Niedertaufkirchen
*Tel:* (08639) 98 34-0 *Fax:* (08639) 1219
*E-mail:* seminare@connection.de
*Web Site:* www.connection.de; www.seminar-
 connection.de
*Key Personnel*
Contact: Wolf Schneider *E-mail:* schneider@
 connection.de
Founded: 1985
Subjects: Human Relations, Parapsychology, Reli-
 gion - Buddhist, Religion - Other, Self-Help
ISBN Prefix(es): 3-928248
Number of titles published annually: 5 Print
*Parent Company:* Connection Medien GmbH
Divisions: Satzstudio, Seminar-und organisation,
 Vertrieb

**Copernicus,** *imprint of* Springer
 Science+Business Media GmbH & Co KG

**Coppenrath Verlag+**
Subsidiary of Verlag Wolfgang Hoelker
Hafenweg 30, 48155 Muenster
*Tel:* (0251) 41411-0 *Fax:* (0251) 4141120
*E-mail:* info@coppenrath.de
*Web Site:* www.coppenrath.de
*Key Personnel*
Man Dir: Wolfgang Hoelker
Production: Wolfgang Foerster
Publicity: Tomas Rensing
Sales: Hubert Bergmoser
Rights & Permissions: Anette Riedel
Founded: 1768
Subjects: Architecture & Interior Design, Art,
 Nonfiction (General)
ISBN Prefix(es): 3-88547; 3-8157
Divisions: Edition Spiegelburg
*Warehouse:* Coppenrath-Hoelker Distribu-
 tion, 48612 Horstmar *Tel:* (02558) 98818
 *Fax:* (02558) 98819

**Copress Verlag+**
Imprint of Stiebner Verlag GmbH
Nymphenburgerstr 86, 80636 Munich
*Tel:* (089) 1257414 *Fax:* (089) 12162282
*E-mail:* verlag@stiebner.com
*Web Site:* www.stiebner.com *Cable:* COPRESS
 MUNCHEN
Subjects: Health, Nutrition, History, Outdoor
 Recreation, Sports, Athletics
ISBN Prefix(es): 3-7679; 3-8307

**Corian-Verlag Heinrich Wimmer**
Bernhard-Monath-Str 28, 86405 Meitingen
Mailing Address: Postfach 1169, 86400 Meitin-
 gen
*Tel:* (08271) 5951 *Fax:* (08271) 6931
*E-mail:* 082716941-0001@t-online.de; 101374.
 1022@compuserve.com
*Key Personnel*
Man Dir: Heinrich Wimmer
Founded: 1983
Subjects: Film, Video, Science Fiction, Fantasy
ISBN Prefix(es): 3-89048

**Cornelsen und Oxford University Press GmbH
 & Co**
Mecklenburgische Str 53, 14197 Berlin
Mailing Address: Postfach 330109, Berlin 14197
*Tel:* (030) 897 850 *Fax:* (030) 897 85 499
*E-mail:* c-mail@cornelsen.de
*Web Site:* www.cornelsen.de
*Telex:* 184968 cvk b
*Key Personnel*
Dir: Jesus Lezcano; Alfred Predhumean
Founded: 1971
Subjects: Education
ISBN Prefix(es): 3-8109
Subsidiaries: Cornelsen Verlag GmbH & Co

**Cornelsen Verlag GmbH & Co OHG+**
Mecklenburgischestr 53, 14197 Berlin
*Tel:* (030) 897 85-0 *Fax:* (030) 897 85-299
*E-mail:* c-mail@cornelsen.de
*Web Site:* www.cornelsen.com
*Key Personnel*
Man Dir: Hans-Joerg Duellmann; Wolf-Rudiger
 Feldmann; Walter Funken; Alfred Gruener;
 Martin Hueppe
International Relations & Foreign Rights: Holger
 Behm *Tel:* (030) 897 85-341 *E-mail:* holger.
 behm@cornelsen.de
Founded: 1946
Textbook publisher in all areas of learning.
Membership(s): European Educational Publishers
 Group (EEPG); Association of German Book-
 sellers.
Subjects: Accounting, Advertising, Biological Sci-
 ences, Career Development, Chemistry, Chemi-
 cal Engineering, Communications, Economics,
 Education, English as a Second Language,
 Geography, Geology, History, Management,
 Marketing, Mathematics, Physical Sciences,
 Physics, Technology
ISBN Prefix(es): 3-464
Total Titles: 8,000 Print; 100 CD-ROM; 150 Au-
 dio
*Parent Company:* Cornelsen Verlagsholding
 GmbH & Co
*Associate Companies:* ALL-Group, Bucharest,
 Romania; Cornelsen Experimenta, Berlin; Cor-
 nelsen Verlagskontor GmbH Co KG; CS Druck
 Cornelsen Stuertz, Berlin; Nakladatelstri Fraus,
 Plzen, Czech Republic; Kamp Schulbuchver-
 lag Due sseldorf; PZV Berlin; VERITAS, Linz,
 Austria
Subsidiaries: Cornelsen Verlag Scriptor; Sauer-
 laender Verlage AG
*Orders to:* CVK Cornelsen Verlagskontor, Kam-
 merratsheide 66, 33609 Bielefeld

**Cornelsen Verlag Scriptor GmbH & Co KG+**
Subsidiary of Cornelsen Verlag
Mecklenburgische Str 53, 14197 Berlin
*Tel:* (030) 89 7858700 *Fax:* (030) 89 7858799
*E-mail:* c-mail@cornelsen.de
*Web Site:* www.cornelsen.de
*Key Personnel*
General Manager: Alfred Gruener; Horst Linder
Founded: 1973
Subjects: Education
ISBN Prefix(es): 3-589
*Orders to:* CVK Cornelsen Verlagskontor, Kammerratsheide 66, 33598 Bielefeld

**Corona Verlag+**
Saselbekstr 35, 22393 Hamburg
*Tel:* (040) 6424144 *Fax:* (040) 64221023
*Key Personnel*
Publisher: Halina Kamm
Editor: Joachim Stiller
Founded: 1990
Subjects: Music, Dance, Psychology, Psychiatry, Esoteric, Meditation, Natural Science
ISBN Prefix(es): 3-928084; 3-934438
Total Titles: 100 Print; 100 CD-ROM; 100 Audio

**J G Cotta'sche Buchhandlung Nachfolger GmbH+**
Rotebuehlstr 77, 70178 Stuttgart
Mailing Address: Postfach 106016, 70049 Stuttgart
*Tel:* (0711) 6672-1256 *Fax:* (0711) 6672-2031
*E-mail:* info@klett-cotta.de
*Web Site:* www.klett-cotta.de
*Telex:* 7222232 klet d
*Key Personnel*
Publisher: Michael Klett
Man Dir: Rainer Just *E-mail:* r.just@klett-cotta.de
Foreign Relations: Derrik Jenkins
Foreign Rights: Roland Knappe *E-mail:* r.knappe@klett-cotta.de
Founded: 1659
Subjects: Child Care & Development, Education, Fiction, History, Human Relations, Literature, Literary Criticism, Essays, Management, Nonfiction (General), Philosophy, Poetry, Psychology, Psychiatry, Science (General)
ISBN Prefix(es): 3-12; 3-7681; 3-608; 3-7885; 3-7835
Total Titles: 3,000 Print
*Parent Company:* Ernst Klett AG
Imprints: Pfeiffer bei Klett-Cotta
*Warehouse:* BDK Bucherdienst GmbH, Kolnerstr 248, Cologne

**Creator**, *imprint of* Bonifatius GmbH Druck-Buch-Verlag

**CTL-Presse Clemens-Tobias Lange**
Borselstr 9-11, 22765 Hamburg
*Tel:* (040) 39902223 *Fax:* (040) 39902224
*E-mail:* ctl@europe.com
*Web Site:* www.ctl-presse.de
Founded: 1989
Subjects: Art, Photography, Poetry, Artist's Books, Literature
Number of titles published annually: 2 Print
Total Titles: 79 Print

**Daco Verlag Guenter Blase oHG+**
Christophstr 40-42, 70180 Stuttgart
*Tel:* (0711) 96421-0 *Fax:* (0711) 96421-10
*E-mail:* info@daco-verlag.de
*Web Site:* www.daco-verlag.de
*Key Personnel*
Publishing Dir, Rights & Permissions: Stephan Goetz
Founded: 1943
Subjects: Art
ISBN Prefix(es): 3-87135
Imprints: Hanfstaengl-Verlag; Nadif

**Daedalus Verlag+**
Oderstr 25, 48145 Muenster
*Tel:* (0251) 231355 *Fax:* (0251) 232631
*E-mail:* info@daedalus-verlag.de
*Web Site:* www.daedalus-verlag.com
*Key Personnel*
Publisher, Rights & Permissions: Joachim Herbst
Founded: 1984
Subjects: Communications, Government, Political Science, Nonfiction (General), Psychology, Psychiatry, Social Sciences, Sociology
ISBN Prefix(es): 3-89126

**Dagmar Dreves Verlag+**
Spangenbergstr 29, 21337 Lueneburg
*Tel:* (04131) 248100 *Fax:* (04131) 248102
*Key Personnel*
Manager: Horst Ernst
Founded: 1989
Subjects: Mysteries, Nonfiction (General), Parapsychology
ISBN Prefix(es): 3-924532; 3-936269
*Bookshop(s):* Dagmar Dreves Verlag, Knoopstr 8, Hamburg 21073
*Warehouse:* Dagmar Dreves Verlag, Knoopstr 8, 21073 Hamburg
*Orders to:* Dagmar Dreves Verlag, Knoopstr 8, 21073 Hamburg

**Dana Verlag**
Campemoorweg 8, 49565 Bram
*Tel:* (05468) 1813 *Fax:* (05468) 239
*Key Personnel*
Contact: Gonda Sewald; Wolfgang Sewald
Founded: 1988
Subjects: Science Fiction, Fantasy
ISBN Prefix(es): 3-9801976; 3-931335

**Dareschta Consulting und Handels GmbH+**
Bahnhofstr 41, 65185 Wiesbaden
*Tel:* (0611) 9310992 *Fax:* (0611) 3082096
*Key Personnel*
International Rights: Beatrix Siebel
Founded: 1988
Subjects: Anthropology, Biological Sciences, Medicine, Nursing, Dentistry, Psychology, Psychiatry, Religion - Catholic, Religion - Protestant, Social Sciences, Sociology, Women's Studies
ISBN Prefix(es): 3-89379; 3-9801744

**Verlag Darmstaedter Blaetter Schwarz und Co**
Haubachweg 5, 64285 Darmstadt
*Tel:* (06151) 48196
*Key Personnel*
Man Dir: Dr Guenther Schwarz
Founded: 1967
Subjects: Language Arts, Linguistics, Philosophy, Psychology, Psychiatry, Religion - Jewish, Social Sciences, Sociology
ISBN Prefix(es): 3-87139

**Das Arsenal, Verlag fuer Kultur und Politik GmbH+**
Tegeler Weg 97, 10589 Berlin
*Tel:* (030) 3441827; (030) 34651360 *Fax:* (030) 34651362
*Key Personnel*
Man Dir: Dr Peter Moses-Krause
Publisher: Jutta Siegert
Founded: 1977
Membership(s): Stock Exchange of German Booksellers.
Subjects: Art, Drama, Theater, Fiction, History, Philosophy
ISBN Prefix(es): 3-921810; 3-931109
*Orders to:* Bugrim, Saalburgstr 3, 12099 Berlin

**Data Becker GmbH & Co KG+**
Merowingerstr 30, 40223 Duesseldorf

Mailing Address: Postfach 102044, 40011 Duesseldorf
*Tel:* (0211) 9331 800; (0211) 9334 900 (orders) *Fax:* (0211) 9331 444; (0211) 9334 999 (orders)
*E-mail:* info@databecker.de
*Web Site:* www.databecker.de
*Key Personnel*
President: Harald Becker
President & Marketing: Dr Achim Becker
Founded: 1981
Subjects: Computer Science, Microcomputers
ISBN Prefix(es): 3-8158; 3-89011

**DBV**, *imprint of* Don Bosco Verlag

**R v Decker's Verlag, G Schenck GmbH**, see Huthig GmbH & Co KG

**Degener & Co, Manfred Dreiss Verlag+**
Nuernbergerstr 27, 91413 Neustadt an der Aisch
*Tel:* (09161) 886039 *Fax:* (09161) 886057
*E-mail:* degener@degener-verlag.com
*Web Site:* www.degener-verlag.com
*Key Personnel*
Contact: Manfred Dreiss
Founded: 1910
Subjects: Genealogy, History, Military Science, Regional Interests
ISBN Prefix(es): 3-7686
*Associate Companies:* Verlag Bauer & Raspe; Heinz Reise-Verlag
Distributor for Bauer & Raspe; Heinz-Reise-Verlag
*Distribution Center:* Stuttgarter Verlagskoutor, SVK-VA, PO Box 106016, 70049 Stuttgart
*Orders to:* Verlag Degener & Co, Nurnbergerstr 27, 91413 Neustadt

**Verlag Horst Deike KG+**
Gottlieb-Daimlerstr 5, 78467 Konstanz
Mailing Address: Postfach 100452, 78404 Konstanz
*Tel:* (07531) 81550 *Fax:* (07531) 815581
*E-mail:* info@deike-verlag.de
*Web Site:* www.deike-verlag.de
*Key Personnel*
President: Wolfgang Deike
Founded: 1923
Subjects: Art, Literature, Literary Criticism, Essays, Music, Dance
ISBN Prefix(es): 3-87142
Subsidiaries: Deike AG
*U.S. Office(s):* Horst Deike KG Verlag, 463 State St, Santa Barbara, CA 93101-2304, United States

**Delius, Klasing und Co+**
Siekerwall 21, 33602 Bielefeld
*Tel:* (0521) 55 90 *Fax:* (0521) 55 91 13
*E-mail:* info@delius-klasing.de
*Web Site:* www.delius-klasing.de
*Telex:* 0932934 Dekla *Cable:* BUCHKLASING BIELEFELD
*Key Personnel*
Dir: Konrad-Wilhelm Delius; Kurt Delius
Production: Hermann Ludewig
Publicity: Susanne Lange
Rights & Permissions: Petra Trueltzsch
Founded: 1911
Subjects: Automotive, Maritime, Outdoor Recreation
ISBN Prefix(es): 3-7688; 3-87412
*Associate Companies:* Edition Maritim Hamburg; Moby Dick Kiel
Distributed by Ermatingen; Lechner & Sohn (Austria); Neptun Verlag; Schweiz
*Orders to:* Delius Klasing Verlag GmbH, Siekerwall 21, 33602 Bielefeld

**Delius Klasing Verlag GmbH+**
Siekerwall 21, 33602 Bielefeld

*Tel:* (0521) 55 90 *Fax:* (0521) 55 91 13
*E-mail:* info@delius-klasing.de
*Web Site:* www.delius-klasing.de *Cable:*
  BUCHKLASING BIELEFELD
*Key Personnel*
Librarian: Baerbel Schubel
Publisher: Kurt Delius
Sales & Publicity Manager: Susanne Lange
Rights & Permissions: Petra Trueltzsch
Producer: Hermann Ludewig
Founded: 1911
Subjects: Maritime
ISBN Prefix(es): 3-7688; 3-87412
*Parent Company:* Delius, Klasing und Co
*Associate Companies:* Edition Maritim Hamburg;
  Moby Dick Verlag Uiel
Distributed by Ermatingeni; Lechner & Sohn
  (Austria); Neptun Verlag; Schweiz

**Delphin Verlag GmbH+**
Postfach 501863, 50978 Cologne
*Tel:* (02236) 39990 *Fax:* (02236) 399997
*Telex:* 8886642/2236364kvg
*Key Personnel*
Man Dir: Guenter Goebel; Juergen Naumann
Founded: 1962
ISBN Prefix(es): 3-7735; 3-8184; 3-88971
*Parent Company:* Naumann & Goebel Verlagsge-
  sellschaft mbH
*Associate Companies:* Daumueller Werbeges
  mbH; Delphin AG; Naturalis Verlags und Ver-
  triebsgesellschaft mbH; Neuer Pawlak Verlag
  GmbH; Tigris Verlag GmbH; V & M Verlags
  & Medienges Koeln mbH; VEMAG Verlags-
  und Medien AG; Verlag 'Das persoenliche
  Geburtstagsbuch' GmbH

**Delp'sche Verlagsbuchhandlung**
Kegetstr 11, 91438 Bad Windsheim
Mailing Address: Postfach 140, 91424 Bad Wind-
  sheim
*Tel:* (09841) 9030 *Fax:* (09841) 90315
*Telex:* 61524
*Key Personnel*
Man Dir: Heinrich Delp
Founded: 1961
Subjects: Art, Regional Interests
ISBN Prefix(es): 3-7689

**Delta**, *imprint of* Egmont EHAPA Verlag GmbH

**Engelbert Dessart Verlag KG**, see Siebert
  Verlag GmbH

**Verlag Harri Deutsch+**
Graefstr 47, 60486 Frankfurt am Main
*Tel:* (069) 77015860 *Fax:* (069) 77015869
*E-mail:* verlag@harri-deutsch.de
*Web Site:* www.harri-deutsch.de/verlag
*Key Personnel*
Man Dir: Martin Kegel
Dir, Rights & Permissions: Harri Deutsch
Editor: Bernd Mueller
Production: Torsten Hellbusch
Founded: 1960
Subjects: Biological Sciences, Chemistry, Chem-
  ical Engineering, Earth Sciences, Economics,
  Electronics, Electrical Engineering, Engineer-
  ing (General), Mathematics, Natural History,
  Physical Sciences, Physics, Sports, Athletics
ISBN Prefix(es): 3-87144; 3-8171
Subsidiaries: Verlag Harri Deutsch AG
*Bookshop(s):* Naturwissenschaftliche Fachbuch-
  handlung Harri Deutsch, Graefstr 47/51, 60486
  Frankfurt am Main

**Deutsche Bibelgesellschaft+**
Balingerstr 31, 70567 Stuttgart
*Tel:* (0711) 7181-0 *Fax:* (0711) 7181-250
*E-mail:* infoabt@dbg.de
*Web Site:* www.dbg.de

*Telex:* 7255299 Bibl d *Cable:* BIBELHAUS
  STUTTGART
*Key Personnel*
Dir & International Rights: Dr Volkmar J Loebel
Dir: Rev Jan A Buehner, PhD
Founded: 1812 (1981)
German Bible Society.
Subjects: Biblical Studies
ISBN Prefix(es): 3-438
Imprints: Collection b
*U.S. Office(s):* American Bible Society, 1865
  Broadway, New York, NY 10023-7505, United
  States *Fax:* 212-408-1456 *Web Site:* www.
  americanbible.org

**Die Deutsche Bibliothek**
Adickesallee 1, 60322 Frankfurt am Main
*Tel:* (069) 1525-0 *Fax:* (069) 1525-1010
*E-mail:* postfach@dbf.ddb.de
*Web Site:* www.ddb.de
*Key Personnel*
Dir: Dr Elisabeth Niggemann
Contact: Kathrin Ansorge *Tel:* (069) 15251004
  *E-mail:* ansorge@dbf.ddb.de
Founded: 1912
ISBN Prefix(es): 3-922051; 3-933641

**Deutsche Bibliothek der
  Wissenschaften/German Library of Sciences**,
  *imprint of* Frankfurter Literaturverlag GmbH

**Deutsche Blinden-Bibliothek+**
Am Schlag 8, 35037 Marburg
Mailing Address: Postfach 1160, 35001 Marburg
*Tel:* (06421) 6060 *Fax:* (06421) 606259
*E-mail:* info@blista.de
*Web Site:* www.blista.de
*Key Personnel*
Man Dir: Juergen Hertlein *Tel:* (06421) 606101
  *E-mail:* hertlein@blista.de
Library Dir, Publishing Manager & International
  Rights: Rainer F V Witte *Tel:* (06421) 606103
  *Fax:* (06421) 606269 *E-mail:* witte@blista.de
Founded: 1916
German Library for the Blind.
ISBN Prefix(es): 3-89642
*Parent Company:* Deutsche Blindenstudienanstalt
  eV (DBSTA)
Divisions: Archiv und Internat Dokumentation
  zzuum Blinden-und Sehbehindertenwesen;
  Bibliographic Centre; Deutsche Blindenhoer-
  buecherei (aufgesprochene Literatur/talking
  books); Emil-Krueckmann-Bibliothek (Blinden-
  schift/Braille)

**Deutsche Gesellschaft fuer
  Eisenbahngeschichte eV**
Kleinsorgenring 14, 59457 Werl
*Tel:* (02922) 84970 *Fax:* (02922) 84927
*E-mail:* info@dgeg.de
*Web Site:* www.dgeg.de
*Key Personnel*
Contact: Guenter Krause
Founded: 1967
Subjects: Transportation
ISBN Prefix(es): 3-921700; 3-936619

**Deutsche Gesellschaft fuer Luft-und
  Raumfahrt Lilienthal Oberth eV**
Godesberger Allee 70, 53175 Bonn
*Tel:* (0228) 30 80 5-0 *Fax:* (0228) 30 80 5-24
*E-mail:* geschaeftsstelle@dglr.de
*Web Site:* www.dglr.de
*Key Personnel*
Secretary General: Hans Luttgen
ISBN Prefix(es): 3-922010; 3-932182

**Deutsche Hochschulschriften/German
  University Studies**, *imprint of* Frankfurter
  Literaturverlag GmbH

**Deutsche Landwirtschafts-Gesellschaft
  VerlagsgesGmbH+**
Eschborner Landstr 122, 60489 Frankfurt
*Tel:* (069) 24 788-451 *Fax:* (069) 24 788-484
*E-mail:* dlg-verlag@dlg-frankfurt.de
*Web Site:* www.dlg-verlag.de
*Telex:* veber 413185 dig.ffm
*Key Personnel*
President & International Rights: Karin Scheller
Marketing Manager: Stefan Pierre-Louis
  *Tel:* (069) 24 788-466 *E-mail:* s.pierrelouis@
  dlg-frankfurt.de
Founded: 1952
Subjects: Agriculture, Health, Nutrition, Travel
ISBN Prefix(es): 3-7690
Number of titles published annually: 15 Print
Total Titles: 350 Print
*Parent Company:* DLG eV
Distributed by Verlagsunion Agrar
*Distribution Center:* SuedOst Verlags Service,
  Am Steinfeld 4, 94065 Waldkirchen
*Returns:* SuedOst Verlags Service, Am Steinfeld
  4, 94065 Waldkirchen

**Verlag Deutsche Unitarier+**
Birkenstr 4, 88214 Ravensburg
*Tel:* (0751) 625 96 *Fax:* (0751) 672 01
*E-mail:* verlag@unitarier.de
*Web Site:* www.unitarier.de
*Key Personnel*
Publisher: Micha Ramm
Founded: 1950
Membership(s): International Association for Re-
  ligious Freedom (IARF); International Council
  of Unitarians & Universalists (ICUU).
Subjects: Philosophy, Religion - Other
ISBN Prefix(es): 3-922483
Total Titles: 15 Print
*Parent Company:* Deutsche Unitarier Religionsge-
  meinschaft eV, Hamburg

**Deutsche Verlags-Anstalt GmbH (DVA)+**
Koeniginstr 9, 80539 Munich
*Tel:* (089) 45554-0 *Fax:* (089) 45554-100; (089)
  45554-111
*E-mail:* info@dva.de; buch@dva.de
*Web Site:* www.dva.de
*Telex:* 7111193DVA d *Cable:* DEVA
  STUTTGART
*Key Personnel*
Man Dir: Juergen Horbach *E-mail:* juergen.
  horbach@dva.de; Dr Ulrich Quiel
Marketing: Susanne Lange *E-mail:* susanne.
  lange@dva.de
Publisher: Michael Neher
Rights & Licenses: Susanne Seggewiss
  *E-mail:* susanne.seggewiss@dva.de
Advertising: Ulrike Bachmann *E-mail:* ulrike.
  bachmann@dva.de
Public Relations: Markus Desaga *E-mail:* markus.
  desaga@dva.de; Christine Liebl
  *E-mail:* christine.liebl@dva.de
Founded: 1831
Subjects: Architecture & Interior Design, Astron-
  omy, Biography, Earth Sciences, Fiction, Gov-
  ernment, Political Science, History, Literature,
  Literary Criticism, Essays, Music, Dance, Phi-
  losophy, Poetry, Psychology, Psychiatry, Sci-
  ence (General)
ISBN Prefix(es): 3-421
*Parent Company:* Verlagsgruppe, Frankfurter All-
  gemeine Zeitung GmbH, Frankfurt am Main
Subsidiaries: Engelhorn Verlag GmbH; Julius
  Hoffmann Verlag GmbH; Manesse Verlag
  GmbH
*U.S. Office(s):* Del Commune Enterprises, Inc,
  285 W Broadway, Suite 310, New York,
  NY 10013, United States *Tel:* 212-226-6664
  *Fax:* 212-965-9294
*Warehouse:* Verlegerdienst Muenchen, Guten-
  bergstr 1, 82205 Gilching

**Deutscher Aerzte-Verlag GmbH+**
Dieselstr 2, 50859 Cologne
*Tel:* (02234) 7011-0 *Fax:* (02234) 7011-398;
 (02234) 7011-475
*E-mail:* zielinka@aerzteverlag.de
*Web Site:* www.aerzteverlag.de
*Key Personnel*
Man Dir: Jurgen Fuhrer
Man Dir & International Rights: Dieter Weber
Founded: 1949
Subjects: Medicine, Nursing, Dentistry
ISBN Prefix(es): 3-7961
Subsidiaries: CEDIP Verlags GmbH; J F
 Lehmanns Med Buchhandlung GmbH; Otto
 Spatz GmbH & Co KG; Schwarzeck-Verlag
 GmbH

**Deutscher Apotheker Verlag Dr Roland
 Schmiedel GmbH & Co** (German Pharmacists
 Publishers)+
Birkenwaldstr 44, 70191 Stuttgart
Mailing Address: Postfach 101061, 70009
 Stuttgart
*Tel:* (0711) 2582-0 *Fax:* (0711) 2582-290
*E-mail:* service@deutscher-apotheker-verlag.de
*Web Site:* www.deutscher-apotheker-verlag.de
*Key Personnel*
Man Dir: Dr Klaus G Brauer; Andre Caro; Dr
 Christian Rotta
International Rights: Sabine Koerner
Marketing Manager: Siegmar Bauer
 *E-mail:* sbauer@deutscher-apotheker-verlag.de
Founded: 1861
Subjects: Medicine, Nursing, Dentistry, Pharmacy
ISBN Prefix(es): 3-7692
Subsidiaries: S Hirzel Verlag GmbH & Co; Med-
 pharm Scientific Publishers; Franz Steiner Ver-
 lag Wiesbaden GmbH; Wissenschaftliche Ver-
 lagsgesellschaft mbH
Distributor for American Society of Hospital
 Pharmacists; Drug Intelligence Publications
 (Europe); Pharmaceutical Press (London, UK);
 United States Pharmacopeial Convention Inc
 (USA)
Foreign Rights: Sabine Koerner

**Deutscher Betriebswirte-Verlag GmbH+**
Bleichstr 20-22, 76593 Gernsbach
Mailing Address: Postfach 1332, 76586 Gerns-
 bach
*Tel:* (07224) 9397-151 *Fax:* (07224) 9397-905
*E-mail:* info@betriebswirte-verlag.de
*Web Site:* www.betriebswirte-verlag.de
*Telex:* 78915 dbv d *Cable:* DBV GERNSBACH
*Key Personnel*
Man Dir: Dr Casimir Katz; Christel Katz
Editor, Rights & Permissions, Publicity: Regina
 Meier
Founded: 1926
Subjects: Business, Economics, Public Adminis-
 tration
ISBN Prefix(es): 3-921099; 3-88640

**Deutscher Drucker Verlagsgesellschaft mbH &
 Co KG** (German Printer Publishing House)
Riedstr 25, 73760 Ostfildern
Mailing Address: Postfach 4125, 73744 Ostfildern
*Tel:* (0711) 448170 *Fax:* (0711) 442099
*E-mail:* info@publish.de
*Web Site:* www.publish.de
*Key Personnel*
Man Dir: Martin Metzger *E-mail:* m.metzger@
 publish.de
Information for professionals, dealing with all as-
 pects of digital workflow. Print communication,
 colour publishing & packaging.
ISBN Prefix(es): 3-920226
*Parent Company:* Ebner Verlag
Foreign Rep(s): Babel Marketing (UK); Ebner
 Publishing (US); Andrew Karning (Scotland)

**Deutscher EC-Verband**
Leuschnerstr 74, 34134 Kassel
Mailing Address: PO Box 42020, 34071 Kassel
*Tel:* (0561) 40950 *Fax:* (0561) 4095112
*E-mail:* info.dv@ec-jugend.de
*Web Site:* www.ec-jugend.de
*Key Personnel*
President: Gerald Pauly
Man Dir: Rolf Trauernicht
Subjects: Religion - Catholic, Religion - Protes-
 tant

**Deutscher Fachverlag GmbH**
Mainzer Landstr 251, 60326 Frankfurt am Main
*Tel:* (069) 7595-01 *Fax:* (069) 75952999
*E-mail:* info@dfv.de
*Web Site:* www.dfv.de
*Key Personnel*
Man Dir: Klaus Kottmeier; Peter Russ; Michael
 Schellenberger
Manager: Joerg Hintz
Founded: 1946
Sportswear International New York.
Subjects: Advertising, Agriculture, Business,
 Communications, Engineering (General), Fash-
 ion, Marketing, Nonfiction (General)
ISBN Prefix(es): 3-87150
*Associate Companies:* Manstein Zeitschnfton Ver-
 lag, Perchtoldsdorf B Wein, Austria; Edizioni
 Ecomarket SpA, 1-20121 Milan
Subsidiaries: Verlag Alfred Strothe GmbH & Co

**Deutscher Gemeindeverlag GmbH**
Hebruhlstr 69, 70549 Stuttgart
*Tel:* (0711) 78630 *Fax:* (0711) 7863400
Founded: 1925
Subjects: Government, Political Science
ISBN Prefix(es): 3-555
*Parent Company:* Verlag W Kohlhammer GmbH
*Branch Office(s)*
Rudolf-Leonhardstr 28, 01097 Dresden
 *Tel:* (0351) 5022685 *Fax:* (0351) 5670664
Gustav-Freytag Str 59, 99096 Erfurt *Tel:* (0361)
 3735379 *Fax:* (0361) 3460537
Postfach 1465, 30014 Hannover *Tel:* (0511)
 327029 *Fax:* (0511) 320143
Postfach 1865, 24017 Kiel *Tel:* (0431) 554857
 *Fax:* (0431) 554944
Schleinufes 14, 39104 Magdeburg *Tel:* (0391)
 597080 *Fax:* (0391) 5970813
Postfach 261134/55057, Mainz *Tel:* (06131)
 891540 *Fax:* (06131) 891624
Sellostr 19, 14471 Potsdam *Tel:* (0331) 964670
 *Fax:* (0331) 964672 (German Municipality
 Publishing Company)
Postfach 040204, 19026 Schwerin *Tel:* (0385)
 616105 *Fax:* (0385) 616146
*Warehouse:* Verlagsvertrieb Stuttgart GmbH, Hep-
 bruehlstr 69, 76565 Stuttgart

**Deutscher Instituts-Verlag GmbH+**
Subsidiary of Koelner Universitaetsverlag GmbH
Gustav-Heinemann Ufer 84-88, 50968 Cologne
Mailing Address: Postfach 510670, 50942
 Cologne
*Tel:* (0221) 49 81-0 *Fax:* (0221) 49 81
*E-mail:* div@iwkoeln.de
*Web Site:* www.divkoeln.de
*Key Personnel*
Man Dir, Rights & Permissions: Dr Franz Josef
 Link *Tel:* (0221) 49 81-410 *Fax:* (0221) 49 81-
 501; Ulrich Brodersen *Tel:* (0221) 49 81-420
 *Fax:* (0221) 49 81-501
Marketing: Michael Opferkuch *Tel:* (0221) 49 81-
 285 *Fax:* (0221) 49 81-286
Man Dir, Rights & Permissions: Axel Rhein
 *Tel:* (0221) 49 81-510 *Fax:* (0221) 49 81-533
 *E-mail:* geisler@iwkoeln.de
Founded: 1951
Subjects: Developing Countries, Economics, La-
 bor, Industrial Relations
ISBN Prefix(es): 3-602; 3-931206; 3-88054

Number of titles published annually: 100 Print
Total Titles: 148 Print
*Parent Company:* Institut der Deutschen
 Wirtschaft, Cologne (German Economics In-
 stitute)
Subsidiaries: Alpha Omega GmbH; Berolino.pr
 GmbH; Edition Agrippa GmbH; Rheinsiteme-
 dia GmbH

**Deutscher Klassiker Verlag**
Lindenstr 29-35, 60325 Frankfurt am Main
Mailing Address: Postfach 101945, 60019 Frank-
 furt am Main
*Tel:* (069) 75601-0 *Fax:* (069) 75601-522
*Web Site:* www.suhrkamp.de
*Key Personnel*
Publisher: Ulla Unseld-Berkewicz
Man Dir: Philip Roeder *Tel:* (069) 75601-500
 *E-mail:* roeder@suhrkamp.de
Rights & Permissions: Dr Petra Hardt
Founded: 1981
ISBN Prefix(es): 3-618
*Parent Company:* Insel Verlag
*Associate Companies:* Suhrkamp Verlag;
 Suhrkamp Verlag AG, Switzerland

**Deutscher Kunstverlag GmbH**
Nymphenburger Str 84, 80636 Munich
Mailing Address: Postfach 190354, 80603 Mu-
 nich
*Tel:* (089) 121516-0 *Fax:* (089) 121516-10; (089)
 121516-16
*E-mail:* vertrieb@deutscher-kunstverlag.ccn.de
*Key Personnel*
Man Dir: Albert Hirmer; Juergen Kleidt
Rights & Permissions: Rudolf Winterstein
Founded: 1921
Subjects: Art
ISBN Prefix(es): 3-422
*Orders to:* Koch, Neff, Oetinger & Co, Schocken-
 riedstr 39, Postfach 800620, 70565 Stuttgart
Buch 2000, Affolten 8910, Switzerland

**Deutscher Psychologen Verlag GmbH (DPV)**
Oberer Lindweg 2, 53129 Bonn
*Tel:* (0228) 987310 *Fax:* (0228) 641023
*E-mail:* service@bdp-verband.org
*Web Site:* www.bdp-verband.org
*Key Personnel*
Man Dir: Jan Frederichs *Tel:* (0228) 19873118
 *E-mail:* dpv@bdp-verband.org
Founded: 1984
Subjects: Psychology, Psychiatry
ISBN Prefix(es): 3-925559; 3-931589
Number of titles published annually: 5 Print
Total Titles: 65 Print
*Parent Company:* Berufsverband Deutscher Psy-
 chologinnen und Psychologen eV
*Warehouse:* Deutscher Psychologen Verlag, Ver-
 lagsauslieferung, Holzwiesenstr 2, 72127 Kus-
 terdingen, Jan Frederichs

**Deutscher Sparkassenverlag GmbH**
Am Wallgraben 115, 70565 Stuttgart
Mailing Address: Postfach 70547, 70565 Stuttgart
*Tel:* (0711) 782-0 *Fax:* (0711) 782-16 35
*E-mail:* webredaktion@dsv-gruppe.de
*Web Site:* www.dsv-gruppe.de
*Key Personnel*
Man Dir: Bernd Kobarg
Founded: 1947
Membership(s): Boersenverein des Deutschen
 Buchhandels; Suedwestdeutsches
 Zeitschriftenverleger-Verband; Verband der
 Verlage und Buchhandlungen; Specialize in
 Literature on Banking Business Management.
ISBN Prefix(es): 3-09
*Associate Companies:* Deutsche Sparkassen-
 Datendienste GmbH; AM-Werbegesellschaft
 mbH

**Deutscher Studien Verlag+**
Werderstr 10, 69469 Weinheim
*Tel:* (06201) 60070
*E-mail:* info@beltz.de
*Web Site:* www.beltz.de
*Key Personnel*
Man Dir: Dr Manfred Beltz Ruebelmann;
   Joachim Radmer
Contact: Rosemarie Bornholt *Tel:* (06201) 6007
   433 *E-mail:* r.bornholt@beltz.de
Rights: Charlotte Larat
Subjects: Psychology, Psychiatry, Social Sciences,
   Sociology
ISBN Prefix(es): 3-89271
*Parent Company:* Julius Beltz GmbH
*Warehouse:* Koch, Neff & Detringer, Verlagsaus-
   lieferung, 70551 Stuttgart *Tel:* (0711) 7899 20
   30 *Fax:* (0711) 7899 10 10


**Deutscher Taschenbuch Verlag GmbH & Co
   KG (dtv)+**
Friedrichstr 1a, 80801 Munich
Mailing Address: Postfach 400422, 80704 Mu-
   nich
*Tel:* (089) 38167-0 *Fax:* (089) 346428
*E-mail:* verlag@dtv.de
*Web Site:* www.dtv.de
*Key Personnel*
Man Dir: Wolfgang Balk
Finance Dir: Markus Angst
Rights & Permissions: Constance Chory; Elke
   Feistauer
Founded: 1961
Subjects: Art, Astronomy, Behavioral Sciences,
   Biography, Child Care & Development, Edu-
   cation, Fiction, Government, Political Science,
   Health, Nutrition, History, Humor, Law, Litera-
   ture, Literary Criticism, Essays, Music, Dance,
   Nonfiction (General), Philosophy, Poetry, Psy-
   chology, Psychiatry, Religion - Other, Science
   (General), Science Fiction, Fantasy, Self-Help,
   Social Sciences, Sociology
ISBN Prefix(es): 3-423
*Orders to:* Koch, Neff, Oetinger & Co, Schock-
   enriedstr 39, 70506 Stuttgart *Tel:* (0711)
   78603322


**Deutscher Universitats-Verlag**
Unit of GWV Fachverlage GmbH
Abraham-Lincoln-Str 46, 65189 Wiesbaden
*Tel:* (0611) 7878-0 *Fax:* (0611) 7878-400
*Web Site:* www.duv.de; www.gwv-fachverlage.de
*Key Personnel*
General Manager: Dr Hans-Dieter Haenel
Man Dir: Dr Heinz Weinheimer
Editorial: Ute Wrasmann *E-mail:* ute.wrasmann@
   gwv-fachverlage.de
Founded: 1968
Subjects: Economics, Science (General), Social
   Sciences, Sociology
ISBN Prefix(es): 3-8244
*Parent Company:* Springer Science & Business
   Media
*Distribution Center:* VVA Bertelsmann Distribu-
   tion, Postfach 7777, 33310 Guetersloh


**Deutscher Verlag fur Grundstoffindustrie
   GmbH+**
Ruedigerstr 14, 70469 Stuttgart
Mailing Address: Postfach 301120, 70451
   Stuttgart
*Tel:* (0711) 8931-0 *Fax:* (0711) 8931-298
*E-mail:* kunden.service@thieme.de
*Web Site:* www.thieme.de
*Key Personnel*
Editor: Christoph Iven *E-mail:* christoph.iven@
   thieme.de
Foreign Rights: Barbara Pfeifer *Tel:* (0711)
   8931184 *E-mail:* barbara.pfeifer@thieme.de
Contact: Martin Spencker
Founded: 1960

Subjects: Chemistry, Chemical Engineering, Earth
   Sciences, Energy, Engineering (General), En-
   vironmental Studies, Geography, Geology, Me-
   chanical Engineering, Nonfiction (General),
   Technology
ISBN Prefix(es): 3-342
Number of titles published annually: 3 Print
Total Titles: 90 Print
*Parent Company:* Georg Thieme Verlag KG


**Deutscher Verlag fur Kunstwissenschaft
   GmbH+**
Zimmerstr 26-27, 10969 Berlin
*Tel:* (030) 259173589 *Fax:* (030) 25913537
*Key Personnel*
Man Dir: Holger Beer
Publishing Dir: Andreas A Catsch
Founded: 1964
Subjects: Art
ISBN Prefix(es): 3-87157
*Parent Company:* Springer-Verlag
*Associate Companies:* Gebr Mann Verlag, Char-
   lottenstr 13, 10969 Berlin
*Orders to:* Koch, Neff, Oetinger & Co Ver-
   lagsauslieferung GmbH, Schockenriedstr 39,
   Postfach 800620, 70565 Stuttgart


**Deutscher Wanderverlag Dr Mair & Schnabel
   & Co+**
Gutenbergstr 13, 73760 Ostfildern
*Tel:* (0711) 455005 *Fax:* (0711) 4569952
*Key Personnel*
Publisher: Rudolf K Fr Schnabel
Founded: 1978
Subjects: Outdoor Recreation, Travel
ISBN Prefix(es): 3-8134


**Deutscher Wirtschaftsdienst John von Freyend
   GmbH+**
Imprint of Wolters Kluwer Deutschland GmbH
Marienburger Str 22, 50968 Cologne
*Tel:* (0221) 93763-0 *Fax:* (0221) 93763-99
*E-mail:* box@dwd-verlag.de
*Web Site:* www.dwd-verlag.de
*Key Personnel*
Sales, Rights & Permissions Dir: Peter John von
   Freyend
Editorial & Publicity: Michael Rieck
Editorial: Dr Reinhardt Spindler
Founded: 1949
Membership(s): The Stock Exchange of German
   Publishers.
Subjects: Business, Career Development, Com-
   munications, Energy, Environmental Studies,
   Finance, Management, Technology
ISBN Prefix(es): 3-87156
Subsidiaries: VWV Verlag fuer Wirtschaft und
   Verwaltung GmbH; Weltforum Verlag fuer
   Politik und Auslandskunde GmbH; Kontaplan
   Werbegesellschaft mbH


**Deutsches Bucharchiv Muenchen, Institut fur
   Buchwissenschaften**
Salvatorplatz 1, 80333 Munich
*Tel:* (089) 291951-90; (089) 291951-91
   *Fax:* (089) 291951-95
*E-mail:* kontakt@bucharchiv.de
*Web Site:* www.bucharchiv.de
*Key Personnel*
Dir: Prof Ludwig Delp *Tel:* (089) 790 11 90
Founded: 1948
Membership(s): Boersenverein des Deutschen
   Buchhandels eV.
Subjects: Communications, Journalism, Library
   & Information Sciences, Publishing & Book
   Trade Reference
ISBN Prefix(es): 3-447
Total Titles: 72 Print
Distributed by Otto Harrassowitz Verlag

**Deutsches Jugendinstitut (DJI)** (German Youth
   Institute)
Nockherstr 2, 81541 Munich
*Tel:* (089) 62306-0 *Fax:* (089) 62306-265
*E-mail:* dji@dji.de
*Web Site:* www.dji.de
*Key Personnel*
Man Dir: Dr Thomas Rauschenbach
Editorial, Publicity & Rights: Hans-Hermann
   Schwarzer
Sales & Production: Maria-Anne Weber
Sales: Natascha Wolf *E-mail:* nwolf@dji.de
Founded: 1963
Subjects: Education, Social Sciences, Sociology
ISBN Prefix(es): 3-87966; 3-935701


**Dharma Edition, Tibetisches Zentrum+**
Hermann Balkstr 106, 22147 Hamburg
*Tel:* (040) 6443585 *Fax:* (040) 6443515
*E-mail:* tz@tibet.de
*Web Site:* www.tibet.de
*Key Personnel*
President: Axel Prosch
Publisher: Rolf Kraemer
Founded: 1979
Subjects: Religion - Buddhist
ISBN Prefix(es): 3-927862
*Bookshop(s):* Tsongkang Buddhistische Buecher
   *Tel:* (040) 6449828 *E-mail:* tk@tibet.de


**Edition Dia+**
Fidicinstr 9, 10965 Berlin
*Tel:* (030) 6235021; (030) 6235022 *Fax:* (030)
   6235023
*E-mail:* info@editiondia.de
*Web Site:* www.editiondia.de
*Key Personnel*
Man Dir: Helmut Lotz *E-mail:* lotz@editiondia.de
Man Dir, International Rights: Kai Precht
Founded: 1984
Subjects: Biography, Cookery, Gay & Lesbian,
   Nonfiction (General)
ISBN Prefix(es): 3-86034


**Diagonal-Verlag GbR Rink-Schweer+**
Alte Kasselerstr 43, 35039 Marburg
Mailing Address: Postfach 1248, 35002 Marburg
*Tel:* (06421) 681936 *Fax:* (06421) 681944
*E-mail:* info@diagonal-verlag.de
*Web Site:* www.diagonal-verlag.de
*Key Personnel*
Publisher: Steffen Rink *E-mail:* rink@diagonal-
   verlag.de; Thomas Schweer *E-mail:* schweer@
   diagonal-verlag.de
Founded: 1988
Specialize in science of religion.
Subjects: Literature, Literary Criticism, Essays,
   Poetry, Religion - Other, Science (General)
ISBN Prefix(es): 3-927165
Total Titles: 35 Print


**Dialog-Verlag GmbH**
Haidkoppelweg 24a, 21465 Reinbek
*Tel:* (040) 7111424 *Fax:* (040) 7101267
Founded: 1982
Subjects: Regional Interests, Travel
ISBN Prefix(es): 3-923707


**Die Andere Bibliothek,** *imprint of* Eichborn AG


**Die Verlag H Schafer GmbH+**
Industriestr 16, 61381 Friedrichsdorf, Taunus
*Tel:* (06172) 95830 *Fax:* (06172) 71288
*E-mail:* dieverlag@t-online.de
*Key Personnel*
Man Dir: Peter Vollrath-Kuhne
Founded: 1923
Subjects: Economics, Government, Political Sci-
   ence, Law, Management, Radio, TV

ISBN Prefix(es): 3-920826
*Associate Companies:* Menschund Leben Verlagsgesellschaft, Postfach 2243, 61292 Bad Homburg

**Diederichs**, *imprint of* Heinrich Hugendubel Verlag GmbH

**Diesterweg, Moritz Verlag+**
Heddrichstr 108-110, 60596 Frankfurt am Main
Mailing Address: Postfach 701161, 60561 Frankfurt am Main
*Tel:* (069) 42081-0 *Fax:* (069) 42081-200
*Web Site:* www.diesterweg.de
*Key Personnel*
Man Dir: Ralf Meier; Karl Slipek
Founded: 1860
Subjects: Education, Language Arts, Linguistics, Social Sciences, Sociology
ISBN Prefix(es): 3-425
Distributed by European Book Co (USA); IBIS (USA)
*Warehouse:* Sigloch GmbH, Zeppelinstr 35, 74653 Kuenzelsau
*Orders to:* Schroedel Verlag, Hildesheimerstr 202-206, 30517 Hannover

**Sammlung Dieterich Verlagsgesellschaft mbH**
Gerichtsweg 28, 04103 Leipzig
Mailing Address: Postfach 101563, 04015 Leipzig
*Tel:* (0341) 9954600 *Fax:* (0341) 9954620
*E-mail:* info@aufbau-verlag.de
*Web Site:* www.aufbau-verlag.de
*Key Personnel*
Man Dir: Peter Birgit; Peter Dempewolf
Founded: 1991
Subjects: Literature, Literary Criticism, Essays, Philosophy
ISBN Prefix(es): 3-7350
*Parent Company:* Leipziger Verlags- und Vertriebsgesellschaft mbH
*Associate Companies:* Gustav Kiepenheuer Verlag Leipzig und Weimar GmbH
*Shipping Address:* Mohr-Morava Buchrertrieb Gesellschatt mbH, Sulzengasse 2, 1101 Vienna, Austria; Pegasus-Stichting, Uitgeverijen-Boekhandel, Rhijuvis Feithstr 28, PO Box 59687, 1054 PZ Amsterdam, Netherlands; Verlaapauslieferung Balmer, Bosch 41, Huenenberg, 6331 Olten, Switzerland

**Dieterichsche Verlagsbuchhandlung Mainz+**
Beuthenerstr 17, 55131 Mainz
*Tel:* (06131) 573276 *Fax:* (06131) 571061
*E-mail:* DVB-mainz@t-online.de
*Web Site:* www.dvb-mainz.de
*Key Personnel*
Publisher: Prof Alfred Klemm, PhD
Founded: 1766
Subjects: Art, Asian Studies, History, Literature, Literary Criticism, Essays, Philosophy, Poetry, Religion - Other
ISBN Prefix(es): 3-87162
Number of titles published annually: 3 Print
*Orders to:* A Eipper, Kirchensteig 12, 71126 Gaeufelden
GVA Postfach 2021, 37010 Gottingen *Tel:* (0551) 487177 *Fax:* (0551) 41392

**Maximilian Dietrich Verlag+**
Weberstr 36, 87700 Memmingen
Mailing Address: Postfach 1636, 87686 Memmingen
*Tel:* (08331) 2853 *Fax:* (08331) 490364
*E-mail:* dietrich-verlag@freenet.de
*Web Site:* www.maximilian-dietrich-verlag.de/index.htm
*Telex:* ueber 54524 mzdruk d
*Key Personnel*
Man Dir: Curt Visel
Sales: Jurgen Schweitzer

Founded: 1946
Subjects: Biography, Human Relations, Regional Interests
ISBN Prefix(es): 3-87164
Subsidiaries: Edition Curt Visel

**Dietrich zu Klampen Verlag+**
Hermannshof Voelksen Roese 21, 31832 Springe
*Tel:* (5041) 801133 *Fax:* (5041) 801336
*E-mail:* info@zuklampen.de
*Web Site:* www.dan4u.de/zuklampen
*Key Personnel*
Owner: Dietrich zu Klampen
Publisher: Dr Rolf Johannes
Founded: 1983
Subjects: Government, Political Science, Philosophy, Poetry, Psychology, Psychiatry, Science (General), Social Sciences, Sociology
ISBN Prefix(es): 3-924245; 3-933156

**Verlag J H W Dietz Nachf GmbH+**
Dreitehnmorgenweg 24, 53129 Bonn
*Tel:* (0228) 23 80 83 *Fax:* (0228) 23 41 04
*E-mail:* info@dietz-verlag.de
*Web Site:* www.dietz-verlag.de
*Key Personnel*
Manager: Dr Gerhard Fischer
Dir, Sales: Hilde Holthamp *E-mail:* hilde.holtkamp@dietz-verlag.de
Editorial, Rights & Permissions: Daniela Mueller *E-mail:* daniela.mueller@dietz-verlag.de
Founded: 1881
Subjects: Developing Countries, Environmental Studies, Government, Political Science, History, Nonfiction (General), Social Sciences, Sociology
ISBN Prefix(es): 3-8012; 3-87831
Foreign Rep(s): Elisabeth Anintah-Hirt (Austria)
*Distribution Center:* Beat Eberle buch 2000 Verlagsauslieferung AVA, Centralweg 16, Postfach 27, 8910 Affoltern am Albis, Switzerland *Tel:* (04117) 62 42 60 *Fax:* (04117) 62 42 10 (Switzerland)
Far Eastern Book Sellers, PO Box 72, Kanda, Tokyo, Japan (Japan)
LIBRI Distributions GmbH, Postfach 10 14 34, 60014 Frankfurt *Tel:* (069) 95 42 22 24 *Fax:* (069) 54 20 13 (Germany & Austria)

**Dietz Verlag Berlin GmbH+**
Weydingerstr 14-16, 10178 Berlin
Mailing Address: Postfach 273, 10124 Berlin
*Tel:* (030) 24 00 92 90 *Fax:* (030) 24 00 95 90
*E-mail:* info@dietzverlag.de
*Web Site:* www.dietzverlag.de
*Key Personnel*
Man Dir: Dr Reinhard Semmelmann
Sales Dir: Hartmut Goetze
Editorial, Rights & Permissions: Christine Krauss
Founded: 1945
Subjects: Biography, Government, Political Science, History, Social Sciences, Sociology
ISBN Prefix(es): 3-320
*Shipping Address:* Bugrim Verlagsauslieferung, Saalburgstr 3, 12099 Berlin
*Warehouse:* Bugrim Verlagsauslieferung, Saalburgstr 3, 12099 Berlin
*Orders to:* Bugrim Verlagsauslieferung, Saalburgstr 3, 12099 Berlin

**Dietzenbach**, *imprint of* ALS-Verlag GmbH

**Digital Publishing+**
Tumblingerstr 32, 80337 Munich
*Tel:* (089) 747482-0 *Fax:* (089) 74792308
*E-mail:* info@digitalpublishing.de
*Web Site:* www.digitalpublishing.de
*Key Personnel*
International Market: Elsa Blume
Public Relations Manager: Sina Wolf
Founded: 1994

Independent publisher.
ISBN Prefix(es): 3-89477; 3-930947
Total Titles: 65 CD-ROM
Distributor for M8 das medieu team (Bookstores/Germany)

**Discordia Verlagsgesellschaft mbH**
Wiehlerstr 5, 51545 Waldbroel
*Tel:* (02291) 911024 *Fax:* (02291) 911925
Founded: 1978
ISBN Prefix(es): 3-922733

**Edition Diskord**
Schwaerzlocherstr 104/b, 72070 Tuebingen
*Tel:* (07071) 40102 *Fax:* (07071) 44710
*E-mail:* ed.diskord@t-online.de
*Web Site:* www.edition-diskord.de
*Key Personnel*
Man Dir: Gerd Kimmerle
Founded: 1985
Subjects: Biography, History, Philosophy, Psychology, Psychiatry, Social Sciences, Sociology, Women's Studies
ISBN Prefix(es): 3-89295

**Divyanand Verlags GmbH+**
Saegestr 37, 79737 Herrischried
*Tel:* (07764) 93 97-0 *Fax:* (07764) 93 97-39
*E-mail:* info@sandila.de
*Web Site:* www.sandila.de
*Key Personnel*
Man Dir: Gerlinde Gloeckner
Founded: 1987
Specialize in spirituality.
Subjects: Parapsychology, Philosophy, Religion - Other, Self-Help
ISBN Prefix(es): 3-926696
Number of titles published annually: 2 Print
Total Titles: 23 Print
*U.S. Office(s):* 129 Juneberry Court, San Jose, CA 95136, United States

**DJI**, see Deutsches Jugendinstitut (DJI)

**DLV Deutscher Landwirtschaftsverlag GmbH**
(German Agriculture Publishing House)
Subsidiary of BLV Verlagsgesellschaft mbH
Kabelkamp 6, 30179 Hannover
Mailing Address: Postfach 14 40, 30014 Hannover
*Tel:* (0511) 678 06-0 *Fax:* (0511) 678 06-110
*E-mail:* dlv.hannover@dlv.de
*Web Site:* www.dlv.de
*Key Personnel*
Man Dir: Hans-Peter Kliemann; Bernd Kuhrmeier; Hans Mueller
Founded: 2001
Subjects: Agriculture, Animals, Pets, Environmental Studies, Gardening, Plants, Country Life with Garden, Nature, Environment, Beekeeping/Apiculture & Folk Music, Farming, Forestry, Hunting
ISBN Prefix(es): 3-331
*Ultimate Parent Company:* Landbuch-Verlagsgesellschaft mbH, Hannover
*Branch Office(s)*
Berliner Str 112A, 13189 Berlin *Tel:* (030) 29 39 74-50 *Fax:* (030) 29 39 74-59 *E-mail:* dlv.berlin@dlv.de
Lothstr 29, 80797 Munich *Tel:* (089) 12 70 5-1 *Fax:* (089) 1 27 05-355 *E-mail:* dlv.muenchen@dlv.de

**Christoph Dohr**
Kasselberger Weg 120, 50769 Cologne
*Tel:* (0221) 70 70 02 *Fax:* (0221) 70 43 95
*E-mail:* info@dohr.de
*Web Site:* www.dohr.de
*Key Personnel*
Contact: Christoph Dohr
Founded: 1990

Music publisher.
Subjects: Music, Dance
ISBN Prefix(es): 3-925366
Number of titles published annually: 80 Print
Total Titles: 1,100 Print

**Dolling und Galitz Verlag GmbH+**
Grosse Bergstr 253, 22767 Hamburg
*Tel:* (040) 3893515 *Fax:* (040) 38904945
*E-mail:* doellingundgalitzverlag@compuserve.com
*Web Site:* www.doellingundgalitz.de
*Key Personnel*
Editor: Dr Peter Dolling; Dr Robert Galitz
Press: Brita Reimers
Manager: Sabine Niemann
Founded: 1986
Subjects: Architecture & Interior Design, Art,
  History, Literature, Literary Criticism, Essays,
  Music, Dance, Photography, Religion - Jewish,
  Religion - Other
ISBN Prefix(es): 3-926174; 3-930802; 3-933374;
  3-935549
*Warehouse:* Siemensstra 16, 35463 Fernwald (An-
  nerod) *Fax:* 06419439329
*Orders to:* PROLIT Verlagsauslieferung

**agenda Verlag Thomas Dominikowski+**
Drubbel 4, 48153 Muenster
*Tel:* (0251) 79 96 10 *Fax:* (0251) 79 95 19
*E-mail:* info@agenda.de
*Web Site:* www.agenda.de
*Key Personnel*
Publisher: Thomas Dominikowski
International Rights: Michael Alfs
Founded: 1992
Subjects: Developing Countries, Environmental
  Studies, Government, Political Science, History,
  Journalism, Regional Interests, Social Sciences,
  Sociology, Women's Studies
ISBN Prefix(es): 3-929440; 3-89688

**Domino Verlag, Guenther Brinek GmbH**
Menzinger Str 13, 80638 Munich
*Tel:* (089) 179130
*E-mail:* info@domino-verlag.de
*Web Site:* www.domino-verlag.de
*Key Personnel*
Manager: Guenther Brinek
Founded: 1964
Subjects: Drama, Theater
ISBN Prefix(es): 3-926123

**Domowina Verlag GmbH**
Tuchmacherstr 27, 02625 Bautzen
*Tel:* (03591) 5770 *Fax:* (03591) 577243
*E-mail:* domowinaverlag@t-online.de
*Web Site:* www.buchhandel.de/domowinaverlag
*Key Personnel*
Man Dir: Ludmila Budar *Tel:* (03591) 577 241
Marketing & Management: Manja Bujnowska
  *Tel:* (03591) 577 262
Press: Mirana Mieth *Tel:* (03591) 577 256
  *E-mail:* Werbung.LND@t-online.de
Publications & Bookshop: Dr Ruth Thiemann
  *Tel:* (03591) 422 32
Founded: 1958
Subjects: Ethnicity, Scientific, Technical Litera-
  ture
ISBN Prefix(es): 3-7420

**Don Bosco Verlag+**
Sieboldstr 11, 81669 Munich
*Tel:* (089) 48008300 *Fax:* (089) 48008309
*Web Site:* www.donbosco.de
*Key Personnel*
Dir: Alfons Friedrich
Editorial: Reinhold Storkenmaier
Sales: Gerhard Sacher
Founded: 1948
Subjects: Education, Religion - Other
ISBN Prefix(es): 3-7698

Imprints: DBV
*Branch Office(s)*
Rixdorferstr 15, 51063 Cologne
Kaulbachstr 63a, 805369 Munich

**Donat Verlag+**
Borgfelder Heerstr 29, 28357 Bremen
*Tel:* (0421) 274886 *Fax:* (0421) 275106
*E-mail:* donatverlag@excite.de
*Key Personnel*
Publisher: Helmut Donat
Founded: 1988
Membership(s): Bvrsenverein des Deutschen
  Buchhandels.
Subjects: Art, Government, Political Science, His-
  tory, Regional Interests, Religion - Jewish
ISBN Prefix(es): 3-924444; 3-931737; 3-934836
Number of titles published annually: 35 Print
Total Titles: 220 Print

**Verlagsgruppe Dornier GmbH** (Publishing
  Group Dornier)+
Liebknechtstr 33, 70565 Stuttgart
*Tel:* (0711) 78803-0 *Fax:* (0711) 78803-10
*E-mail:* info@verlagsgruppe-dornier.de
*Web Site:* www.verlagsgruppe-dornier.de
  *Cable:* EDILEIP
*Key Personnel*
Man Dir: Olaf Carstens; Roland Grimmelsmann
*Parent Company:* Verlagsgruppe Dornier, Dirck-
  senstr 48, 10178 Berlin
*Associate Companies:* Cross Publishing House,
  Postfach 80 06 69, 70506 Stuttgart *Tel:* (0711)
  788 03-0; Kreuz Verlag, Breitwiesenstr
  30, 70565 Stuttgart *Tel:* (0711) 78803-
  91 *Fax:* (0711) 78803-10 *E-mail:* info@
  kreuzverlag.de *Web Site:* www.kreuzverlag.de
  (religion, self-help, spiritual giftbooks); Theseus Verlag, Dircksenstr 48, 10178 Berlin,
  Contact: Ursula Richard *Tel:* (030) 28447-
  100 *Fax:* (030) 28447-103 *E-mail:* theseus@
  dornier-verlage.de *Web Site:* www.theseus-
  verlage.de (Buddhist publisher); Urania Verlag,
  Berlin (parenting, home improvement, arts &
  crafts)
Imprints: Brandenburgisches Verlagshaus (military
  history); EA Seemann Verlag (art, photography); Edition Leipzig (regional art, architecture
  & history books (Saxonia), official publisher of
  books on Meissen porcelaine); Henschel Verlag (performing arts: theater, cinema, music,
  ballet); Alf Luechow Verlag (advaita, spiritual
  health, self-help)
*Orders to:* Leipziger Kommissions und Grossbuchhandelsgesellschaft mbH, Poetzschauer
  Weg, 04579 Espenhain

**DPV,** see Deutscher Psychologen Verlag GmbH
  (DPV)

**Drei Brunnen Verlag GmbH & Co**
Heusee 19, 73655 Pluederhausen
*Tel:* (0711) 86020 *Fax:* (0711) 860229
*E-mail:* mail@drei-brunnen-verlag.de
*Web Site:* www.drei-brunnen-verlag.de
*Key Personnel*
Man Publisher: Emmerich Mueller
Publisher: Dieter Rath
Contact: Thomas Mueller
Founded: 1950
Subjects: Outdoor Recreation, Travel
ISBN Prefix(es): 3-7956
Number of titles published annually: 10 Print
Total Titles: 60 Print
*Shipping Address:* Geo Center, Schockenriedstr
  44, 70565 Stuttgart
*Orders to:* Geo Center, Schockenriedstr 44, 70565
  Stuttgart

**Drei Eichen Verlag Manuel Kissener+**
Bahnhofstr 36, 97762 Hammelburg

Mailing Address: Postfach 1147, 97754 Hammel-
  burg
*Tel:* (09732) 9142-0 *Fax:* (09732) 9142-20
*E-mail:* info@drei-eichen.de
*Web Site:* www.drei-eichen.de
*Key Personnel*
Owner: Manuel Kissener
Founded: 1931
Subjects: Philosophy, Science Fiction, Fantasy,
  Self-Help
ISBN Prefix(es): 3-7699
Number of titles published annually: 10 Print
Total Titles: 200 Print
Imprints: Edition Kima; Politik und Spiritualitaet

**Drei Ulmen Verlag GmbH+**
Schleissheimer Str 274, 80809 Munich
*Tel:* (089) 3087911; (089) 3088343
*Key Personnel*
Publisher: Dr Hermann Schreiber
Founded: 1985
Membership(s): Small Publishers Study Group.
Subjects: Biography, Literature, Literary Criti-
  cism, Essays, Travel
ISBN Prefix(es): 3-926087
*Associate Companies:* AVA-GmbH, Seeblickstr
  46, 82211 Herrsching

**Dreisam Ratgeber in der Rutsker Verlag
  GmbH+**
Schreberstr 2, 51105 Cologne
*Tel:* (0221) 921635-0 *Fax:* (0221) 921635-24
*E-mail:* kontakt@hayit.com
*Web Site:* www.hayit.com
*Key Personnel*
International Rights: Ertay Hayit *E-mail:* hayit@
  hayit.com
Editorial: Cornelia Auschra *Tel:* (0221) 921635-
  13 *E-mail:* cornelia.auschra@hayit.com; Mike
  Gahn *E-mail:* mike@hayit.com; Ute Hayit
  *Tel:* (0221) 921635-11 *E-mail:* ute.hayit@
  hayit.com; Simone Kruger-Naujoks *Tel:* (0221)
  921635-22 *E-mail:* simone-naujoks@hayit.com
Founded: 1988
Subjects: Biological Sciences, Career Develop-
  ment, Cookery, Economics, Education, Envi-
  ronmental Studies, Health, Nutrition, Human
  Relations, Law, Medicine, Nursing, Dentistry,
  Psychology, Psychiatry, Religion - Islamic
ISBN Prefix(es): 3-89607

**Cecilie Dressler Verlag GmbH & Co KG+**
Poppenbuetteler Chaussee 53, 22397 Hamburg
Mailing Address: Postfach 658230, 22374 Ham-
  burg
*Tel:* (040) 607909-03 *Fax:* (040) 6072326
*E-mail:* dressler@vsg-hamburg.de
*Web Site:* www.cecilie-dressler.de
*Key Personnel*
Man Dir & Sales: Thomas Huggle
Man Dir, Rights & Permissions: Silke Weitendorf
Editorial: Ursula Heckel
Publicity: Katja Muissus
International Rights: Renate Reichstein
  *Tel:* (040) 607909-13 *Fax:* (040) 607909-51
  *E-mail:* lizenzen@vsg.hamburg.de
Press: Judith Richter *Tel:* (040) 607909-65
  *Fax:* (040) 607909-40 *E-mail:* presse@vsg-
  hamburg.de; Frauke Wedler *Tel:* (040) 607909-
  23 *Fax:* (040) 607909-40 *E-mail:* presse@vsg-
  hamburg.de
Internet Editor: Svenja David *Tel:* (040)
  607909-48 *Fax:* (040) 607909-51
  *E-mail:* internetredaktion@vsg-hamburg.de
Marketing: Dr Juergen Huebner *Tel:* (040)
  607909-55 *Fax:* (040) 607909-50
  *E-mail:* werbung@vsg-hamburg.de
Founded: 1928
Subjects: Fiction
ISBN Prefix(es): 3-7915
*Associate Companies:* Atrium Verlag
*Warehouse:* Runge Verlagsauslieferung, Bergstr 2,
  33803 Steinhagen

## Verlagsgruppe Droemer Knaur GmbH & Co KG+

Hilblestr 54, 80636 Munich
*Tel:* (089) 9271-0 *Fax:* (089) 9271-168
*E-mail:* info@droemer-knaur.de
*Web Site:* www.droemer-knaur.de *Cable:*
DROEMERVERLAG
*Key Personnel*
Publisher & Man Dir: Dr Hans Peter Uebleis
Commercial Man Dir: Ralf Mueller
Man Dir Sales & Marketing: Christian Tesch
Public Relations: Susanne Klein
Rights: Renate Abrasch
Sales: Iris Haas
Founded: 1901
Also known as Droemer Knaur Verlag.
Subjects: Biography, Business, Cookery, Erotica,
Fiction, How-to, Humor, Mysteries, Nonfiction
(General), Science (General), Self-Help, Wine
& Spirits, Anthology, Fairy Tales, Family Saga,
Fantasy, Food/Drink, Horror, Movie or Televi-
sion, Thriller
ISBN Prefix(es): 3-426
*Parent Company:* Verlagsgruppe Droemer Welt-
bild GmbH & Co KG
*Associate Companies:* Augustus Verlag; Knaur
Taschenbuecher; Midena Verlag; Pattloch Ver-
lag; Schneekluth Verlag GmbH
Imprints: MenSana
*Shipping Address:* VVA Bertelsmann Distribution

## Droste Verlag GmbH

Martin-Luther-Platz 26, 40212 Duesseldorf
Mailing Address: Postfach 104251, 40033 Dues-
seldorf
*Tel:* (0211) 8605220 *Fax:* (0211) 3230098
*Telex:* 8582495 dv d *Cable:* DROSTEVERLAG
DUSSELDORF
*Key Personnel*
Chairman & Man Dir: Clemens Bauer
Man Dir: Dieter Reichel
Publishing Dir: Dr Manfred Lotsch
Editorial: Heidemarie Alertz
Production, Publicity: Helmut Schwanen
Founded: 1711
Subjects: Art, Economics, Government, Politi-
cal Science, History, Humor, Social Sciences,
Sociology
ISBN Prefix(es): 3-7700
Subsidiaries: Wilhelm Knapp Verlag
*Warehouse:* Xantheuerstr 3a, 41460 Neuss

## Karl Elser Druck GmbH

Kisslingweg 35, 75417 Muehlacker
*Tel:* (07041) 805-41 *Fax:* (07041) 805-50
*E-mail:* info@elserdruck.de
*Web Site:* www.elserdruck.de
*Key Personnel*
Man Dir & International Rights: Brigitte Wetzel-
Haendle
Man Dir: Else Haendle
Founded: 1890
Also acts as newspaper & printing office.
Subjects: Biography, Fiction, Regional Interests
ISBN Prefix(es): 3-7987
*Associate Companies:* Karl Elser Druck GmbH
*Bookshop(s):* Buch-Elser, Bahnhofstr 62, 75417
Muehlacker

## Druckerei u Verlagsanstalt Bayerland GmbH

Konrad-Adenauerstr 19, 85221 Dachau
Mailing Address: Postfach 1868, 85208 Dachau
*Tel:* (08131) 7 20 66 *Fax:* (08131) 73 53 99
*E-mail:* zentrale@bayerland-amperbote.de
*Web Site:* www.bayerland.de
*Key Personnel*
Contact: Klaus Kiermeier
ISBN Prefix(es): 3-89251; 3-922394; 3-9800040
Number of titles published annually: 20 Print
Total Titles: 250 Print

## Druffel-Verlag+

Landsbergerstr 57, 82266 Inning
*Tel:* (08143) 992160 *Fax:* (08143) 992241;
(08143) 992161
*Key Personnel*
Publisher: Dr Gert Suedholt
Founded: 1952
Subjects: Government, Political Science, History
ISBN Prefix(es): 3-8061

## DRW-Verlag Weinbrenner-GmbH & Co+

Fasanenweg 18, 70771 Leinfelden-Echterdingen
Mailing Address: PO Box 100354, 70747
Leinfelden-Echterdingen
*Tel:* (0711) 75 91-0 *Fax:* (0711) 75 91-333
*E-mail:* info@weinbrenner.de
*Web Site:* www.drw-verlag.de; www.weinbrenner.
de
*Key Personnel*
Dir: Karl-Heinz Weinbrenner
Business Manager: Bernhard Driehaus
Founded: 1874
Subjects: Nonfiction (General), Physical Sciences,
Regional Interests
ISBN Prefix(es): 3-87181
Subsidiaries: BIT-Verlag Weinbrenner; Ver-
lagsanstalt Alexander Koch GmbH
Divisions: Fachbuch Service
*Orders to:* Koch, Neff & Oetinger Verlagsaus-
lieferung, Schockenriedstr 39, 70565 Stuttgart

## DSI Data Service & Information

Xantener Str 51a, 47495 Rheinberg
*Tel:* (049) 2843 3220 *Fax:* (049) 2843 3230
*E-mail:* dsi@dsidata.com
*Web Site:* www.dsidata.com
*Key Personnel*
Manager: Dr Wilhelm Hennerkes
Contact: Konrad Wilms *E-mail:* konrad.wilms@
dsidata.com
Founded: 1985
Electronic preparation & publishing of national &
international statistical information (numerical
databases) on CD-ROM & on the internet.
Subjects: Economics, Social Sciences, Sociology
Distributor for Bernan; Enerdata SA; European
Union; International Bank for Reconstruction &
Development; Organization for Economic Co-
Operation & Development; Smartal Solutions
Ltd
Foreign Rep(s): ABE Marketing (Poland); Al-
bertina Data SRO (Czech Republic, Slovak
Republic); Albertina Incone Praha (Czech
Republic); BH Sistemas de Informacao (Por-
tugal); Diaz de Santos SA (Spain); Edutech
(United Arab Emirates); Far Eastern Book-
sellers (Kyokuto Shoten) (Japan); Greendata
(Spain); IBS Buke SDN BHD (Malaysia); Info
Access & Distribution Pte Ltd (Singapore);
Info Technology Supply Ltd (UK); Kaiga
Kyozai Center (Japan); Kinokuniya Co Ltd
(Japan); Kyobo Book Centre (Korea); Leader
Books SA (Greece); Licosa SpA (Italy); Lo-
giser SA (Portugal); LUSODOC (Portugal);
Maruzen Co, IRN Import (Books) (Japan);
Mundi-Prensa Libros SA (Spain); Paradox Li-
bros (Spain); RoweCom Espana (Spain); Sis-
temas Documentales SL (Spain)

**dtv**, see Deutscher Taschenbuch Verlag GmbH &
Co KG (dtv)

## Verlag Duerr & Kessler GmbH+

Sieglarer Str 2, 53842 Troisdorf
*Tel:* (0180) 304 14 20 *Fax:* (02241) 39 76 190
*E-mail:* info@wolfverlag.de
*Web Site:* www.wolfverlag.de
*Key Personnel*
Publisher: Siegfried Brunner
Marketing: Alexandra Ried *Tel:* (02241) 39 76-
806 *E-mail:* aried@by-1.de
Founded: 1953

Subjects: Education, Language Arts, Linguistics
ISBN Prefix(es): 3-8181
*Parent Company:* WoltersKluwer Co

## Dumjahn Verlag

Immenhof 12, 55128 Mainz
*Tel:* (06131) 330810 *Fax:* (06131) 330811
*E-mail:* railway@dumjahn.de
*Web Site:* www.dumjahn.de
Founded: 1974
Specialize in railway.
Membership(s): Borsenverein des Deutschen
Buchhandels.
Subjects: Publishing & Book Trade Reference,
Transportation, Travel
ISBN Prefix(es): 3-921426; 3-88992
Number of titles published annually: 2 Print; 2 E-
Book
Total Titles: 18 Print
*Bookshop(s):* Versandbuchhandlung und Anti-
quariat Horst-Werner Dumjahn, Immenhof 12,
55128 Mainz

## DuMont monte Verlag GmbH & Co KG+

Neven DuMont Haus, Amsterdamer Str 192,
50735 Cologne
*Tel:* (0221) 224-1823 *Fax:* (0221) 224-1812
*E-mail:* info@dumontmonte.de
*Web Site:* www.dumontmonte.de
*Telex:* 8882975 dbeb d
*Key Personnel*
Manager: Dieter Eickel *Tel:* (0221) 224-2931
*E-mail:* eickel@dumontmonte.de
Sales Manager: Anke Hardt *Tel:* (0221) 224-
1964 *E-mail:* hardt@dumontmonte.de;
Jan Scherberich *Tel:* (0221) 224-1821
*E-mail:* scherberich@dumontmonte.de
Founded: 1998
Subjects: Architecture & Interior Design, Art,
Cookery, Crafts, Games, Hobbies, Gardening,
Plants, House & Home, How-to
ISBN Prefix(es): 3-8320
Total Titles: 75 Print
*Parent Company:* Dumont

## DuMont Reiseverlag GmbH & Co KG+

Amsterdamer Str 192, 50735 Cologne
Mailing Address: Postfach 101045, 50450
Cologne
*Tel:* (0221) 224-1839 *Fax:* (0221) 224-1855
*E-mail:* info@dumontreise.de
*Web Site:* www.dumontreise.de
*Telex:* 8882 975 dbeb d
*Key Personnel*
Man Dir: Uwe Distelrath; Andreas von Stedman
Marketing Manager: Udo Zimmermann
*Tel:* (0221) 224-1894 *E-mail:* zimmermann@
dumontreise.de
Sales Manager: Katharina Hokema *Tel:* (0221)
224-1833 *E-mail:* hokema@dumontreise.de
Public Relations: Angelika Trippe *Tel:* (0221)
224-1835 *E-mail:* trippe@dumontreise.de
Rights: Yvonne Paris
Founded: 1956
Subjects: Archaeology, Art, Cookery, Gardening,
Plants, Travel
ISBN Prefix(es): 3-8320
*Orders to:* BDK Buecherdienst, Koelner 87 248,
50859 Cologne

## Duncker und Humblot GmbH+

Carl-Heinrich-Becker-Weg 9, 12165 Berlin
Mailing Address: Postfach 410329, 12113 Berlin
*Tel:* (030) 79 00 06-0 *Fax:* (030) 79 00 06-31
*E-mail:* info@duncker-humblot.de
*Web Site:* www.duncker-humblot.de
*Key Personnel*
Publisher & International Rights: Prof H C
Norbert Simon, PhD *Tel:* (030) 790006-19
*Fax:* (030) 790006-43 *E-mail:* verlag@duncker-
humblot.de

Marketing: Ingrid Buehrig *Tel:* (030) 790006-30 *Fax:* (030) 790006-53 *E-mail:* werbung@ duncker-humblot.de
Founded: 1798
Subjects: Asian Studies, Biography, Criminology, Developing Countries, Economics, Environmental Studies, Finance, Government, Political Science, History, Law, Literature, Literary Criticism, Essays, Marketing, Military Science, Philosophy, Science (General), Social Sciences, Sociology, Theology
ISBN Prefix(es): 3-428
Number of titles published annually: 350 Print
Total Titles: 9,300 Print
Subsidiaries: Speyer & Peters GmbH; Berliner Buchdruckerei Union Gmb

**Dustri-Verlag Dr Karl Feistle+**
Bajuwarenring 4, 82041 Oberhaching-Munich
Mailing Address: Postfach 1351, 82032 Deisenhofen-Munich
*Tel:* (089) 61 38 61-0 *Fax:* (089) 613 54 12
*E-mail:* info@dustri.de
*Web Site:* www.dustri.de
*Key Personnel*
Dir: Frank Feistle; Joerg Feistle *Tel:* (089) 61 38 61-30 *E-mail:* joerg.feistle@dustri.de
Founded: 1965
Subjects: Medicine, Nursing, Dentistry
ISBN Prefix(es): 3-87185

**Klaus D Dutz+**
Lingener Str 7, 48155 Muenster
Mailing Address: Postfach 5725, 48031 Muenster
*Tel:* (0251) 65514; (0251) 661692 *Fax:* (0251) 661692
*E-mail:* dutz.nodus@t-online.de
*Key Personnel*
Contact: Klaus D Dutz
Founded: 1987
Subjects: Film, Video, Language Arts, Linguistics, Philosophy, Science (General)
ISBN Prefix(es): 3-89323
Subsidiaries: Stichting Neerlandistiek VU; Stichting Uitgeverij De Keltische Draak

**DVA**, see Deutsche Verlags-Anstalt GmbH (DVA)

**DVG-Deutsche Verlagsgesellschaft mbH+**
Postfach 1180, 32352 Preubisch Oldendorf
*Tel:* (08031) 15643 *Fax:* (08031) 380662
*Key Personnel*
Contact: Waldemar Schuetz
Founded: 1969
Subjects: Government, Political Science, History, Military Science
ISBN Prefix(es): 3-920722
*Associate Companies:* Verlag fuer Aussergewoehnlichen Perspektiven
*Orders to:* VAP Verlagsauslieferung, Mindenerstr 34, 32361 Preussisch Oldendorf

**DVS-Verlag GmbH**, see Verlag fur Schweissen und Verwandte Verfahren

**Ebenhausen bei Muenchen**, *imprint of* Verlag Langewiesche-Brandt KG

**Ebersberg**, *imprint of* Eironeia-Verlag

**Echo Verlag+**
Lotzestr 24a, 37083 Gottingen
Mailing Address: Postfach 1704, 37007 Goettingen
*Tel:* (0551) 796824 *Fax:* (0551) 74035
*E-mail:* clages.echoverlag@t-online.de
*Web Site:* www.echoverlag.de
*Key Personnel*
Man Dir, Rights & Permissions: Andrea Clages
Founded: 1985

Membership(s): The Stock Exchange of German Booksellers; Land Association Lower Saxony.
Subjects: Animals, Pets, Environmental Studies
ISBN Prefix(es): 3-9801216; 3-926914

**Echter Wurzburg Frankische Gesellschaftsdruckerei und Verlag GmbH+**
Dominikanerplatz 8, 97070 Wuerzburg
*Tel:* (0931) 66068-0 *Fax:* (0931) 66068-23
*E-mail:* info@echterverlag.de
*Web Site:* www.echter-verlag.de *Cable:* ECHTERVERLAG
*Key Personnel*
Dir: Gerhard Schaefer *Tel:* (0931) 6671-220 *Fax:* (0931) 6671-295 *E-mail:* g.schaefer@ echter.de; Albrecht Siedler *Tel:* (0931) 6671-216 *Fax:* (0931) 6671-295 *E-mail:* a.siedler@ echter.de
Publisher: Thomas Haeussner *Tel:* (0931) 6671-158 *Fax:* (0931) 6671-151 *E-mail:* th. haeussner@echter.de
Founded: 1900
Subjects: Art, Biblical Studies, Fiction, History, Regional Interests, Religion - Catholic, Religion - Other, Theology, Wine & Spirits
ISBN Prefix(es): 3-429
Total Titles: 600 Print

**Ecomed Verlagsgesellschaft AG & Co KG+**
Justus-Von-Liebig Str 1, 86899 Landsberg
*Tel:* (08191) 1250 *Fax:* (08191) 125492
*E-mail:* info@ecomed.de
*Web Site:* www.ecomed.de
*Key Personnel*
Publishing Manager: Udo Graf *Tel:* (08191) 125208
Foreign Rights Manager: Gerlinde Stanglmeier *Tel:* (08191) 125571 *E-mail:* g.stanglmeier@ ecomed.de
Marketing: Gerhard Heinzmann *Tel:* (08191) 125399
Product Management: Manuela Czech *Tel:* (08191) 125420; Bernhard Gall *Tel:* (08191) 125564; Dr Iris Korn *Tel:* (08191) 125191; Susanne Kuehbandner *Tel:* (08191) 125500; Dr Norbert Schueller *Tel:* (08191) 125804
Sales: Nina Karlsdorfer *Tel:* (08191) 125800
Customer Service: Gabriele Honzu *Tel:* (08191) 125152
Founded: 1979
Subjects: Biological Sciences, Chemistry, Chemical Engineering, Engineering (General), Environmental Studies, Gardening, Plants, Labor, Industrial Relations, Medicine, Nursing, Dentistry, Technology, Transportation
ISBN Prefix(es): 3-609
Total Titles: 700 Print
*Parent Company:* verlag moderne industrie AG

**Econ Taschenbuchverlag+**
Subsidiary of Econ Verlag GmbH
Bayerstr 71-73, 80335 Munich
Mailing Address: Postfach 151329, 80048 Munich
*Tel:* (0211) 43596
*Key Personnel*
Chief Executive Officer & Publisher: Dr Dietrich Oppenberg
Marketing & Sales: Felicitas Wendt
Rights & Permissions: Herbert Borgartz
Founded: 1951
Publishing group comprised of: Econ-Verlag GmbH; Econ Taschenbuch Verlag GmbH. The group forms part of the newspaper publishing concern Rheinisch-Westfaelische Verlagsgesellschaft mbH, Pressehaus NRZ, Sachsenstr 30, 45128 Essen
Representative: Christina McInerney International Ltd, 730 Fifth Ave, Suite 402, New York, NY 10019, USA.

Subjects: Career Development, Computer Science, Economics, Health, Nutrition, Mysteries, Nonfiction (General), Self-Help
ISBN Prefix(es): 3-430; 3-612; 3-547
*Associate Companies:* Groethe str 43, 80336 Munich
*Warehouse:* VVA, Guetersloh

**Econ Verlag GmbH+**
Friedrichstr 126, 10117 Berlin
*Tel:* (030) 23456-300 *Fax:* (030) 23456-303
*Web Site:* www.econ-verlag.de *Cable:* ECONVERLAG
*Key Personnel*
Chief Executive Officers & Publishers: Heinrich Meyer; Christian Strasser
Marketing: Herbert Borgartz
Rights & Permissions: Felicitas Wendt
Founded: 1950
Subjects: Economics, Fiction, Nonfiction (General), Science (General)
ISBN Prefix(es): 3-430; 3-612; 3-547
Subsidiaries: Econ Taschenbuch Verlag GmbH; Marion von Schroeder Verlag GmbH
*U.S. Office(s):* Jane Starr, Planetarium Station, PO Box 907, New York, NY 10024, United States
Distributor for Stiftung Warentest GmbH (Berlin/ Germany)
*Warehouse:* VVA, An der Autobahn, 33310 Guetersloh

**Ede Vau Verlag GmbH**
Halskestr 3-5, 47877 Willich
*Tel:* (02154) 490080 *Fax:* (02154) 490081
*E-mail:* evvgmbh@t-online.de
*Key Personnel*
Manager: Horst Stuhlweissenburg
Founded: 1989
ISBN Prefix(es): 3-89428

**Edition Aragon-Verlagsgesellschaft mbH**, see Aragon GmbH

**Edition Tranvia**, see Verlag Walter Frey

**editionLuebbe**, *imprint of* Verlagsgruppe Luebbe GmbH & Co KG

**Egmont EHAPA Verlag GmbH+**
Wallstr 59, 10179 Berlin
Mailing Address: Postfach 040740, 10064 Berlin
*Tel:* (030) 24008-0 *Fax:* (030) 24008-599
*Web Site:* www.ehapa.de
*Key Personnel*
Man Dir: Frank Knau
International Rights: Peter M Schmitz
Public Relations Manager: Marion Egenberger *E-mail:* kontakt@ehapa.de
Founded: 1951
Children's magazines.
Subjects: Humor, Comics
ISBN Prefix(es): 3-7704; 3-89343; 3-928108
Number of titles published annually: 200 Print
Total Titles: 1,000 Print
*Parent Company:* Egmont Holding GmbH
Imprints: Delta
Subsidiaries: Cultfish Entertainment (Teen Label)
Divisions: OU Character Kids (Comic Magazine & Juvenile Journals); OU Disney Kids (Disney Publication); Egmont Manga & Anime Europe (Manga)

**Egmont Franz Schneider Verlag GmbH+**
Schleissheimer Str 267, 80809 Munich
*Tel:* (089) 3 58 11-6 *Fax:* (089) 3 58 11-7 55
*E-mail:* postmaster@schneiderbuch.de
*Web Site:* www.schneiderbuch.de
*Telex:* 05215804
*Key Personnel*
Man Dir: Rehne Herzig
Marketing: Hans-Juergen Schneider

Account: Matthias Allendorff
Production: Karl-Heinz Bezold
Publicity: Dr Andrea Hilbk
Founded: 1913
Specialize in Disney books, Television/Film re-
lated books.
Subjects: Fiction, Film, Video, History, Nonfiction
(General), Science Fiction, Fantasy
ISBN Prefix(es): 3-505
Number of titles published annually: 150 Print
Total Titles: 700 Print
*Parent Company:* Egmont

**Egmont Pestalozzi-Verlag+**
Schleissheimer Str 267, 80809 Munich
Mailing Address: Postfach 460725, 80915 Mu-
nich
*Tel:* (089) 35811 *Fax:* (089) 5811-869
*Telex:* 629766 Pevau *Cable:* PESTALOZZI
ERLANGEN
*Key Personnel*
Man Dir: Rehne Herzig
Editorial, Rights & Permissions: Sibylle Lehmann
Founded: 1844
Subjects: Crafts, Games, Hobbies
ISBN Prefix(es): 3-614; 3-87624
Subsidiaries: Boje-Verlag
Distributed by Groupe de la Cite (France); Guten-
berghus (Scandinavia); Arnoldo Mondadori
(Italy); Simon & Schuster (USA)

**Egmont vgs verlagsgesellschaft mbH+**
Gertrudenstr 30-36, 50667 Cologne
Mailing Address: Postfach 101251, 50452
Cologne
*Tel:* (0221) 20811-0 *Fax:* (0221) 20811-66
*E-mail:* info@vgs.de
*Web Site:* www.vgs.de
*Key Personnel*
Man Dir: Dr Bernward Malaka *E-mail:* b.
malaka@vgs.de
Man Dir & Publisher: Michael Schweins
Communications: Dr Juergen Puetz *E-mail:* j.
puetz@vgs.de
Sales: Andrea Rueller
Advertising: Ingrid Reisner
Editorial Dir: Kurt-Juergen Heering; Stefanie
Koch
Press Manager: Simone Altheim
Founded: 1970
Market-leading TV tie-in publisher in the
German-speaking territory; popular nonfiction
on health subjects, illustrated books.
Subjects: Animals, Pets, Art, Asian Studies, Biog-
raphy, Crafts, Games, Hobbies, Fiction, Film,
Video, Foreign Countries, Gardening, Plants,
Health, Nutrition, History, House & Home,
Music, Dance, Mysteries, Natural History, Non-
fiction (General), Outdoor Recreation, Radio,
TV, Science Fiction, Fantasy, Travel
ISBN Prefix(es): 3-8025
Number of titles published annually: 120 Print
Total Titles: 500 Print
*Parent Company:* Egmont Holding GmbH
(Berlin)
*Warehouse:* Cornelsen Verlagskontor, Kammerrat-
sheide 66, 33609 Bielefeld
*Orders to:* Cornelsen Verlagskontor, Kammerrat-
sheide 66, 33609 Bielefeld

**Ehrenwirth Verlag**, *imprint of* Verlagsgruppe
Luebbe GmbH & Co KG

**Ehrenwirth Verlag+**
Imprint of Verlagsgruppe Luebbe GmbH & Co
KG
Scheidtbachstr 23-31, 51469 Bergisch Gladbach
Mailing Address: Postfach 200180, 51431 Ber-
gisch Gladbach
*Tel:* (02202) 121-330 *Fax:* (02202) 121-920
*E-mail:* ehrenwirth@luebbe.de
*Web Site:* www.luebbe.de

*Key Personnel*
Man Dir: Karlheinz Jungbeck
Founded: 1945
Subjects: Fiction, How-to, Nonfiction (General)
ISBN Prefix(es): 3-431
Number of titles published annually: 25 Print

**Ehrenwirth Verlag GmbH+**
Scheidtbachstr 23-31, 51469 Bergisch Gladbach
*Tel:* (02202) 121-0 *Fax:* (02202) 121 928
*Web Site:* www.ehrenwirth.de
*Key Personnel*
Man Dir: Karlheinz Jungbeck
Founded: 1945
Membership(s): TR-Verlagsunion GmbH.
Subjects: Biography, Crafts, Games, Hobbies,
Fiction, History, How-to, Poetry, Psychology,
Psychiatry, Social Sciences, Sociology
ISBN Prefix(es): 3-431
*Parent Company:* Veritas-Verlag und Handelsge-
sellschaft mbH, Linz, Austria
*Orders to:* Verlegerdienst Muenchen, Postfach
1280, 82205 Gilching

**Eichborn AG+**
Kaiserstr 66, 60329 Frankfurt
*Tel:* (069) 256003-0 *Fax:* (069) 256003-30
*E-mail:* rights@eichborn.de; vertrieb@eichborn.de
*Web Site:* www.eichborn.de
*Key Personnel*
Chief Executive: Matthias Kierzek
Publishing Dir: Dr Wolfgang Hoeruer; Matthias
Bischoff
Production: Ulrike Bettermann
Sales & Publicity: Ute Hollmann
Founded: 1980
Subjects: Fiction, History, Humor, Literature, Lit-
erary Criticism, Essays, Mysteries, Nonfiction
(General)
ISBN Prefix(es): 3-8218
Number of titles published annually: 200 Print;
30 Audio
Imprints: Die Andere Bibliothek
Foreign Rights: ACER (Latin America, Portugal,
Spain); Agence Hoffman (Belgium, France);
Hercules Business & Culture Development
GmbH (China, Taiwan); Imrie & Dervis Lit-
erary Agency (UK, Greece); International Lit-
eratuur Bureau BV (Belgium, Netherlands);
Leonhardt & Hoier (Denmark, Finland, Iceland,
Norway, Sweden); Onk Agency Ltd (Turkey);
Orion Literary Agency (Japan); Pikarski Ltd
Literary Agency (Israel); Studio Nabu (Italy);
Writers House LLC (US)

**Eiland-Verlag Sylt Frank Roseman**
Friesische Str 53, 25980 Westerland
*Tel:* (04651) 936212 *Fax:* (04651) 936214
*E-mail:* info@eiland-verlag.de
*Web Site:* www.eiland-verlag.de
Founded: 1975
ISBN Prefix(es): 3-922753

**EinfallsReich Verlagsgesellschaft MbH+**
Breitenkamp 43, 37619 Kirchbrak
*Tel:* (05533) 2017
Founded: 1987
Subjects: Art, Environmental Studies, Fiction,
Humor, Literature, Literary Criticism, Essays,
Music, Dance, Nonfiction (General), Travel
ISBN Prefix(es): 3-926207

**Einfuehrungen**, *imprint of* Wissenschaftliche
Buchgesellschaft

**Eironeia-Verlag**
Sonnhalde 37, 79194 Gundelfingen
*Tel:* (0761) 581617 *Fax:* (0761) 3603474529
*Key Personnel*
Man Dir: Thomas Ebersberg
Founded: 1987

Subjects: History, Human Relations, Literature,
Literary Criticism, Essays, Philosophy
ISBN Prefix(es): 3-926607
Imprints: Ebersberg; Th Kirchbaum, K

**Eisenbahn-Kurier Verlag**, see EK-Verlag GmbH

**EK-Verlag GmbH+**
H-V Stephanstr 15, 79100 Freiburg
Mailing Address: Postfach 500111, 79027
Freiburg
*Tel:* (0761) 70310-31 *Fax:* (0761) 70310-50
*Key Personnel*
Man Dir: Rudolf Wesemann
Man Dir & Production: Wolfgang Schumacher
Editorial & Publicity: Klaus Eckert
Editorial: Ingo Seifert
Sales: Karin Klemm
Rights & Permissions: Hansjuergen Wenzel
Founded: 1966
Subjects: Film, Video, Transportation
ISBN Prefix(es): 3-88255

**Elektor-Verlag**, *imprint of* Elektor-Verlag GmbH

**Elektor-Verlag GmbH+**
Susterfeldstr 25, 52072 Aachen
*Tel:* (0241) 889090 *Fax:* (0241) 8890988
*E-mail:* redaktion@elektor.de
*Web Site:* www.elektor.de
*Key Personnel*
Man Dir: M M F Landman
Publications Man: A Schommers
Marketing Man: G Klein
Founded: 1972
Membership(s): German Association of Book
Distributors.
Subjects: Electronics, Electrical Engineering, En-
gineering (General), Environmental Studies,
Microcomputers, Nonfiction (General), Physical
Sciences, Technology, Travel
ISBN Prefix(es): 3-921608; 3-928051
*Parent Company:* Elektuur BV
Imprints: Elektor-Verlag

**Verlag Heinrich Ellermann GmbH & Co KG+**
Poppenbuetteler Chaussee 53, 22397 Hamburg
Mailing Address: Postfach 658220, 22374 Ham-
burg
*Tel:* (040) 607909-08 *Fax:* (040) 607909-59
*E-mail:* ellermann@vsg-hamburg.de
*Web Site:* www.ellermann.de
*Key Personnel*
Press: Frauke Wedler *Tel:* (040) 607909-23
*Fax:* (040) 607909-40 *E-mail:* wedler@vsg-
hamburg.de
Marketing: Dr Juergen Huebner *Tel:* (040)
607909-55 *Fax:* (040) 607909-50
*E-mail:* marketing@vsg-hamburg.de; Su-
sanne Weiss *Tel:* (040) 607909-777 *Fax:* (040)
607909-50 *E-mail:* vertrieb@vsg-hamburg.de
Advertising: Katja Muissus *Tel:* (040) 607909-30
*Fax:* (040) 607909-40 *E-mail:* werbung@vsg-
hamburg.de
Rights & Licensing: Renate Reichstein
*Tel:* (040) 607909-13 *Fax:* (040) 607909-51
*E-mail:* lizenzen@vsg-hamburg.de
Founded: 1934
ISBN Prefix(es): 3-7707
*Parent Company:* Koesel-Verlag GmbH & Co
*Orders to:* Moderne Industrie Verlagsservice,
Landsberg

**Ellert & Richter Verlag GmbH+**
Grosse Brunnenstr 116-120, 22763 Hamburg
*Tel:* (040) 39 84 77-0 *Fax:* (040) 39 84 77-23
*E-mail:* info@ellert-richter.de
*Web Site:* www.ellert-richter.de
*Key Personnel*
International Rights: Marita Ellert-Richter
Founded: 1979

Subjects: Architecture & Interior Design, Art, Foreign Countries, Gardening, Plants, History, Nonfiction (General), Travel
ISBN Prefix(es): 3-89234
*Warehouse:* Runge GmbH, Bergstr 2, 4803 Steinhagen *Web Site:* www.rungeva.de

**Elpis Verlag GmbH+**
Rohrbacherstr 20, 69115 Heidelberg
*Tel:* (06221) 165789
*Key Personnel*
Dir: Lothar Faas; Dr Manfred Thiel
Founded: 1977
Subjects: Philosophy, Poetry, Religion - Islamic, Theology
ISBN Prefix(es): 3-921806
Number of titles published annually: 2 Print

**Elsevier GmbH/Urban & Fischer Verlag+**
Karlstr 45, 80333 Munich
Mailing Address: Postfach 201930, 80019 Munich
*Tel:* (089) 5383-0 *Fax:* (089) 5383-939
*E-mail:* info@elsevier-deutschland.de
*Web Site:* www.elsevier.de
*Key Personnel*
Man Dir: Angelika Lex
Rights & Permissions: Cathrin Korz *E-mail:* c.korz@elsevier.com
Founded: 1866
Subjects: Health, Nutrition, Medicine, Nursing, Dentistry, Science (General)
ISBN Prefix(es): 3-437
Number of titles published annually: 220 Print
*Parent Company:* Reed Elsevier GmbH, Munich
*Branch Office(s)*
Urban & Partner Wydawnictno Medyene nl, Curie-Skldowskiei 55/61, Instytut Elektrotechniki 50, 950 Wroclaw, Poland
Urban & Schwarzenberg GesmbH, Frankgasse 4, 1096 Vienna, Austria
*Bookshop(s):* Oscar Rothacker Versandbuchhandlung GmbH, Fraunhoferstr 10, 82152 Martinsried
*Shipping Address:* Servicecenter Fachverlage, Holzwiesenstr 2, 72127 Kusterdingen

**N G Elwert Verlag+**
Reitgasse 7-9, Pilgrimstein 30, 35037 Marburg
*Tel:* (06421) 17090 *Fax:* (06421) 15487
*E-mail:* elwertmail@elwert.de
*Web Site:* www.elwert.de *Cable:* ELWERT MARBURG
*Key Personnel*
Man Dir: Rudolph Braun-Elwert
Founded: 1726
Subjects: History, Law, Literature, Literary Criticism, Essays, Religion - Other, Social Sciences, Sociology
ISBN Prefix(es): 3-7708
*Bookshop(s):* N G Elwert Universitaetsbuchhandlung GmbH & Co KG, Reitgasse 7-9, Pilgrimstein 30, 35037 Marburg/Lahn

**Gholam Emami**
Fritz-von-Rothstr 25, 90249 Nurnberg
Mailing Address: Postfach 810451, 90249 Nurnberg
*Tel:* (0911) 288356 *Fax:* (0911) 288356
ISBN Prefix(es): 3-9801145

**Emons Verlag+**
Luetticher Str 38, 50674 Cologne
*Tel:* (0221) 56977-0 *Fax:* (0221) 524937
*E-mail:* info@emons-verlag.de
*Web Site:* www.emons-verlag.de
*Key Personnel*
Publisher: Hejo Emons *E-mail:* emons@emons-verlag.de
Press: Dr Britta Schmitz *E-mail:* schmitz@emons-verlag.de

Sales: Dorothee Junck *E-mail:* junck@emons-verlag.de
Founded: 1984
Subjects: Film, Video, Mysteries
ISBN Prefix(es): 3-924491; 3-89705
Total Titles: 120 Print

**Encyclopedia Britannica**
Rosenstr 12/13, 48143 Munster
*Tel:* (0251) 48 227-0 *Fax:* (0251) 48 227-27
*E-mail:* lexikadienst@aol.com
*Web Site:* www.britannica.de
*Key Personnel*
Contact: Hans-Dieter Blatter

**Engel & Bengel Verlag+**
Haardtweg 3, 67273 Bobenheim
*Tel:* (06353) 8107 *Fax:* (06353) 507057
*E-mail:* verlag@engelundbengel.de
*Web Site:* www.engelundbengel.de
Founded: 1990
Subjects: Animals, Pets, Disability, Special Needs, Fiction, How-to, Human Relations
ISBN Prefix(es): 3-928129
*Orders to:* Verlag Koch, Neff & Oetinger, Stuttgart
Koehler & Volckmar, Cologne

**Engelhorn Verlag GmbH+**
Koniginstr 9, 80539 Munich
*Tel:* (089) 45554-0 *Fax:* (089) 45554-111
*Telex:* uber 71 11193-DVA
*Key Personnel*
Publisher: Jurgen Horbach
Founded: 1860
Subjects: Biography
ISBN Prefix(es): 3-87203
*Parent Company:* Deutsche Verlags-Anstalt GmbH

**Englisch Verlag GmbH+**
Toepferstr 14, 65191 Wiesbaden
*Tel:* (0611) 9 427 2-0 *Fax:* (0611) 9 42 72 30
*E-mail:* info@englisch-verlag.de
*Web Site:* www.englisch-verlag.de
*Key Personnel*
Publisher: Iring F Englisch *E-mail:* iring.englisch@englischverlag.de
Program Management: Britta Sopp *Tel:* (0611) 9 42 72-15 *E-mail:* programm@englischverlag.de
Sales: Alexander Leidl *Tel:* (0611) 9 42 72-11 *E-mail:* alexander.leidl@englischverlag.de
Press: Sandra Will *Tel:* (0611) 9 42 72-17 *E-mail:* presse@englischverlag.de
Founded: 1973
Membership(s): Boersenverein des Deutschen Buchhandels.
Subjects: Art, Crafts, Games, Hobbies, How-to
ISBN Prefix(es): 3-8241
Number of titles published annually: 80 Print
Total Titles: 300 Print
Foreign Rep(s): Schweizer Buchzentrum (Switzerland); Dr Franz Hain (Austria)
*Warehouse:* VVA Vereinigte Verlagsauslieferung, 33310 Guetersloh, Contact: Ms Riediger *Tel:* (05241) 803893 *Fax:* (05241) 46750
*Orders to:* VVA Bertelsmann Distribution, Postfach 7777, 33310 Guetersloh

**Verlag Peter Engstler**
Oberwaldbehrungen 10, 97645 Ostheim/Rhoen
*Tel:* (09774) 858490 *Fax:* (09774) 858491
*E-mail:* engstler-verlag@t-online.de
*Web Site:* www.engstler-verlag.de
*Key Personnel*
Contact: Peter Engstler
Founded: 1988
Subjects: Art, Fiction, Government, Political Science, Literature, Literary Criticism, Essays, Poetry
ISBN Prefix(es): 3-929375; 3-9801770; 3-9802826

**Enke**, *imprint of* Georg Thieme Verlag KG

**Ensslin Jugendbuchverlag**, see Ensslin und Laiblin Verlag GmbH & Co KG

**Ensslin und Laiblin Verlag GmbH & Co KG+**
Harretstr 6, 72800 Eningen
*Tel:* (07121) 98 98 0 *Fax:* (07121) 98 98 44
*E-mail:* ensslin-verlag@t-online.de
*Web Site:* www.ensslin-verlag.de *Cable:* BUCHHAUS REUTLINGEN
*Key Personnel*
Man Dir, Rights & Permissions: Ariane Hanfstein *Tel:* (07121) 989822
Sales Dir: Joachim Hanfstein *Tel:* (01721) 989825
Production: Birgit Weber *Tel:* (07121) 989831
Public Relations, Advertising: Friederike Tiemann *Tel:* (07121) 989829
Founded: 1818
Specialize in children's & juvenile literature & in highly qualified teaching materials for preschool & elementary school children. A special focus of the program is on "playing & learning" educational aids like the "Ensslin-Lernpuck®" or the "New learning games" (NELS) which enable children to exercise topics of various subjects at their very own pace. A new kind of educational aid are the "Duesenberg-Kids" - funny comics combined with detailed information & activity-tips which encourage children to have self-confidence & sense of responsibility.
Membership(s): Association of Children's Books.
Subjects: Education, Fiction, Literature, Literary Criticism, Essays, Nonfiction (General), Science Fiction, Fantasy
ISBN Prefix(es): 3-7709
Total Titles: 180 Print
*Warehouse:* Libri Distributions GmbH, August-Schanz-Str 33, 60433 Frankfurt *Tel:* (069) 95422219 *Fax:* (069) 542013

**Ensslin Verlag im Arena Verlag**, *imprint of* Arena Verlag GmbH

**EOS Verlag der Benefiktiner der Erzabtei St. Ottilien+**
86941 St Ottilien
*Tel:* (08193) 71261 *Fax:* (08193) 6844
*E-mail:* mail@eos-verlag.de
*Web Site:* www.eos-verlag.de
*Key Personnel*
Man Dir: P Walter Sedlmeier
Founded: 1885
Subjects: Art, Fiction, History, Religion - Other, Theology
ISBN Prefix(es): 3-88096; 3-920289
Subsidiaries: Druckerei
Divisions: Satz, Repro, Druckerei, Buchbiudeve
*Bookshop(s):* Klosterladen, Erzabtei St Ottilien, 86941 Sankt Ottilien

**Eppinger-Verlag OHG**
Stauffenbergstr 18, 74523 Schwaebisch Hall
*Tel:* (0791) 95061-0 *Fax:* (0791) 95061-41
*E-mail:* info@eppinger-verlag.de *Cable:* EPPINGER-VERLAG SCHWAEBISCH HALL
*Key Personnel*
Man Dir: Hans Paul Eppinger
Founded: 1970
Subjects: Business, Career Development, Developing Countries, Economics, Foreign Countries, Management, Regional Interests, Technology
ISBN Prefix(es): 3-87176

**Erasmus Grasser-Verlag GmbH**
Bachtal 6, 86978 Hohenfurch
*Tel:* (08861) 241900 *Fax:* (08861) 241901
*Web Site:* www.eg-v.de

*Key Personnel*
Manager: Wolfgang Vogelsgesang
Founded: 1974
ISBN Prefix(es): 3-925967

## Eremiten-Presse und Verlag GmbH

Fortunastr 11, 40235 Duesseldorf
Mailing Address: Postfach 170143, 40082 Duesseldorf
*Tel:* (0211) 66 05 90 *Fax:* (0211) 698 94 70
*Key Personnel*
Man Dir: Friedolin Reske; Jens D Olsson
Founded: 1949
Subjects: Art, Fiction, Poetry
ISBN Prefix(es): 3-87365

## Eres Editions-Horst Schubert Musikverlag

Haupstr 35, 28865 Lilienthal
Mailing Address: Postfach 1220, 28859 Lilienthal
*Tel:* (04298) 1676 *Fax:* (04298) 5312
*E-mail:* info@eres-musik.de
*Web Site:* www.eres-musik.de
*Key Personnel*
Man Dir: Horst Schubert
Founded: 1946
Subjects: Music, Dance
ISBN Prefix(es): 3-87204

## ERF-Verlag GmbH+

Berliner Ring 62, 35576 Wetzlar
*Tel:* (06441) 9570 *Fax:* (06441) 957120
*E-mail:* info@erf.de
*Web Site:* www.erf.de
*Key Personnel*
Chairman: Ulrich Ruesch
Chairman & Dir: Juergen Werth
Founded: 1978
Specialize in audio & video.
Subjects: Music, Dance, Religion - Other
ISBN Prefix(es): 3-89562
*Parent Company:* Evangeliums-Rundfunk eV
*Branch Office(s)*
Vienna, Austria
Zurich, Switzerland
*U.S. Office(s):* Trans World Radio, Cary, NC, United States

## Ergebnisse Verlag GmbH+

Abendrothsweg 58, 20251 Hamburg
*Tel:* (040) 4801027 *Fax:* (040) 4801592
*Key Personnel*
Editor: Dietrich Lueders; Wolfgang Schwibbe; Michael Wildt
Sales, Rights & Permissions: Dr Thomas Neumann
Sales, Advertising & Publicity: Ingc Busch
Founded: 1978
Subjects: Health, Nutrition, History, Medicine, Nursing, Dentistry, Psychology, Psychiatry, Regional Interests
ISBN Prefix(es): 3-87916
*Orders to:* PNV Petersen und Nieswand Vertriebsservice GmbH, Werftbahnstr 8, 24143 Kiel

## Ergon Verlag Dr H J Dietrich+

Grombuehlstr 7, 97080 Wurzburg
*Tel:* (0931) 280084 *Fax:* (0931) 282872
*E-mail:* service@ergon-verlag.de
*Web Site:* www.ergon-verlag.de
*Key Personnel*
Press: Brigitte Miebach-Schrader
  *E-mail:* miebach-schrader@ergon-verlag.de
Contact: Dr Hans-Juergen Dietrich *E-mail:* dr. dietrich@ergon-verlag.de
ISBN Prefix(es): 3-928034; 3-932004; 3-933563; 3-89913; 3-935556
*Distribution Center:* Hora-Verlags-Gesselschaft m.b.H., Hackhofergasse 8-10, Postfach 24,

1195 Vienna-Nussdorf, Austria *Tel:* (0222) 67 15 80 *Fax:* (0222) 37 63 93
Schweizer Buchzentrum, 4601 Olten 1, Switzerland *Tel:* (062) 209 25 25 *Fax:* (062) 209 26 27

## Erlanger Verlag Fuer Mission und Okumene

(Erlanger Publishing House for Missions & Ecumerics)+
Hauptstr 2, 91564 Neuendettelsau
Mailing Address: Postfach 68, 91561 Neuendettelsau
*Tel:* (09874) 9 17 00 *Fax:* (09874) 9 33 70
*E-mail:* verlagsleitung@erlanger-verlag.de
*Web Site:* www.erlanger-verlag.de
*Key Personnel*
Director: Dr Johannes Triebel
Founded: 1897
Subjects: Asian Studies, Developing Countries, Religion - Islamic, Religion - Other, Theology, Specialize in African studies
ISBN Prefix(es): 3-87214
Total Titles: 106 Print
*Parent Company:* Evang Luth Church in Bavaria, Germany

## Ernst Kabel Verlag GmbH+

Imprint of Piper Verlag Gmbh
Georgeustr 4, 80799 Munich
Mailing Address: Postfach 430861, 80731 Munich
*Tel:* (089) 381801-0 *Fax:* (089) 338704
*E-mail:* info@piper.de
*Web Site:* www.piper.de
*Key Personnel*
Publisher: Victor Niemann
Man Dir: Hartmyt Jedicke
Editorial: Bettiva Feldweg
Founded: 1977
Specialize in gift books.
Subjects: Biography, Fiction, Nonfiction (General), Psychology, Psychiatry, Self-Help
ISBN Prefix(es): 3-8225
Number of titles published annually: 25 Print
*Ultimate Parent Company:* Bounier Media Holding GmbH
*Orders to:* Koch Neff Ogtinger & Co, Schockenriedstr 39, 7055A Stuttgart

## Ernst Klett Verlag Gmbh+

Formerly Manz G J Verlag und Druckerei
Rotebuehlstr 77, 70178 Stuttgart
*Tel:* (0711) 6151790 *Fax:* (0711) 6151791
*Web Site:* www.klett-verlag.de
*Key Personnel*
Dir, Publisher & Editorial: Lydia Franzelius
Foundcd: 1830
Subjects: Education
ISBN Prefix(es): 3-12; 3-7863; 3-8213; 3-88447
Subsidiaries: Verlag J Pfeiffer; Erich Wewel Verlag
*Orders to:* Verlagsgruppe MANZ, AG, Anzingerstr 15, 81671 Munich

## Ernst, Wilhelm & Sohn, Verlag Architektur und technische Wissenschaft GmbH & Co+

Buhringstr 10, 13086 Berlin
*Tel:* (030) 47031-200 *Fax:* (030) 47031-270
*E-mail:* info@ernst-und-sohn.de
*Web Site:* www.wiley.vch.de/ernstsohn
*Key Personnel*
Dir: Dagmar Stehle
Editorial, Rights & Permissions: Monika Herr
Founded: 1851
Subjects: Architecture & Interior Design, Civil Engineering, Technology
ISBN Prefix(es): 3-433
*Parent Company:* Wiley-VCH Verlag GmbH, Boschstr 12, 69469 Weinheim

*Shipping Address:* VSW GmbH, Postfach 1355, 68745 Waghaeusel
*Warehouse:* Wiley-VCH Verlag GmbH, Boschstr 12, 69469 Weinheim

## Ertraege der Forschung zur Forschung-,

*imprint of* Wissenschaftliche Buchgesellschaft

## Verlagsgesellschaft des Erziehungsvereins GmbH+

Andreas-Braem-Str 18-20, 47506 Neukirchen-Vluyn
*Tel:* (02845) 392-0 *Fax:* (02845) 392392
*E-mail:* info@neukirchener-verlag.de
*Web Site:* www.neukirchener-verlag.de *Cable:* VERLAGSHAUS NEUKIRCHEN VLUYN
*Key Personnel*
Man Dir: Jochen Boeckler; Dr Rudolf Weth
Publishing Manager: Dr Volker Hampel
  *E-mail:* verlagsleitung@neukirchener-verlag.de
Sales Representative: Stefan Schubert
  *E-mail:* schubert@neukirchener-verlag.de
Lecturer: Ekkehard Starke *E-mail:* letkorat@ neukirchener-verlag.de
Production: Hans Hegner *E-mail:* herstellung@ neukirchener-verlag.de; Karin Jacobs *E-mail:* herstellung@neukirchener-verlag. de; Volker Kuschnik *E-mail:* herstellung@ neukirchener-verlag.de
Advertising: Christoph Siepermann
  *E-mail:* vertrieb@neukirchener-verlag.de
Dispatch Bookshop: Angelika Boos *Tel:* (02845) 392-218 *E-mail:* vsb@neukirchener-verlag.de
Subjects: Religion - Protestant, Theology
ISBN Prefix(es): 3-7615; 3-7887; 3-7621; 3-7673; 3-7958
*Associate Companies:* Aussaat Verlag; Kalenderverlag des Erziehungsvereins; Neukirchener Verlag

## Verlag am Eschbach GmbH+

Im Alten Rathaus, Haupstr 37, 79427 Eschbach/ Markgraeflerland
*Tel:* (07634) 1088 *Fax:* (07634) 3796
*E-mail:* vertrieb@verlag-am-eschbach.de
*Web Site:* www.verlag-am-eschbach.de
*Key Personnel*
Gesellschafter-Geschaeftsfuehrers: Heribert Mohr; Martin Schmeisser; Juergen Schwarz
Founded: 1979
Subjects: Art, Religion - Catholic, Religion - Protestant
ISBN Prefix(es): 3-88671

## Esogetics GmbH+

Hildastr 8, 76646 Bruchsal
*Tel:* (07251) 8001-40 *Fax:* (07251) 8001-55
*E-mail:* info-de@esogetics.com
*Web Site:* www.esogetics.com
*Key Personnel*
Man Dir: Sophocles Amanatidis *E-mail:* sa@ esogetics.com; Markus Wunderlich
Founded: 1988
Subjects: Health, Nutrition, Medicine, Nursing, Dentistry, Science (General)
ISBN Prefix(es): 3-925806
Total Titles: 2 Print
Foreign Rep(s): Techiche Nuove, Hay
Foreign Rights: Techiche Nuove, Hay (Spain)

## Verlag Esoterische Philosophie GmbH

Goedekeweg 8, 30419 Hannover
*Tel:* (0511) 755331 *Fax:* (0511) 755334
*E-mail:* info@esoterische-philosophie.de
*Web Site:* www.esoterische-philosophie.de
*Key Personnel*
Man Dir: Baerbel Ackermann
Art Dir: Matthias Winter
Founded: 1984
Specialize in translations of English literature.

Subjects: Anthropology, Astrology, Occult, Parapsychology, Philosophy, Religion - Buddhist, Religion - Other, Science (General), Cosmology, Science of Religions
ISBN Prefix(es): 3-924849

**Espresso Verlag GmbH+**
Am Treptower Park 28-30, 12435 Berlin
*Tel:* (030) 5333 4444 *Fax:* (030) 5333 4159
*E-mail:* info@espresso-verlag.de
*Web Site:* www.espresso-verlag.de
*Key Personnel*
Manager: Maruta Schmidt
Sales Manager: Martina Hayo
Public Relations & Rights: Claudia Schulz
Founded: 1977
Subjects: Art, Developing Countries, Government, Political Science, History, Humor, Literature, Literary Criticism, Essays, Mysteries, Photography, Social Sciences, Sociology, Women's Studies
ISBN Prefix(es): 3-88520
Total Titles: 200 Print

**Esslinger Verlag J F Schreiber GmbH+**
Marktplatz 19, 73728 Esslingen
Mailing Address: Postfach 10 03 25, 73703 Esslingen
*Tel:* (0711) 310594-6 *Fax:* (0711) 310594-77; (0711) 310594-65
*E-mail:* esslinger@klett-mail.de
*Key Personnel*
Man Dir: Franz Scharetzer
Man Dir & Publishing Dir: Mathias Berg
Editor, Publicity: Sabine Frankholz
Editor: Urte Fiutak
Founded: 1831
Children's book publisher.
Specialize in nostalgic children's books, reprints & fairy tales.
ISBN Prefix(es): 3-480; 3-87286
*Parent Company:* Ernst Klett Information

**Eulen Verlag+**
Einsteinstr 167, 81675 Munich
*Tel:* (089) 47 07 77 44 *Fax:* (089) 47 07 77 42
*E-mail:* info@eulenverlag.de
*Web Site:* www.eulen-verlag.de
*Key Personnel*
Owner & Publisher: Harald Glaeser
Founded: 1983
Subjects: Art, Crafts, Games, Hobbies, Outdoor Recreation, Photography, Regional Interests, Travel
ISBN Prefix(es): 3-89102
Total Titles: 125 Print
*Warehouse:* Libri Distributions Gmbh, August-Schanzstr 33, 60433 Frankfurt am Main

**Eulenhof-Verlag Wolfgang Ehrhardt Heinold+**
Appener Weg 3b, 20251 Hamburg
*Tel:* (040) 490005-14 *Fax:* (040) 490005-15
*E-mail:* w.e.heinold@eulenhof.de
*Web Site:* www.eulenhof.de
*Key Personnel*
Man Dir: Iris Wolf *Tel:* (0171) 4181248
Founded: 1981
Specialize in information on children's media.
Membership(s): Borsenverein des Deutschen Buchhandels & Arbetskreis Fur Jugendliteratur EV.
Subjects: Library & Information Sciences
ISBN Prefix(es): 3-88710
Number of titles published annually: 1 Print
Total Titles: 3 Print
*Associate Companies:* Eulenhof Institut, WE Heinold Beratungs Gesellschaft mbH, Contact: Wolfgang Ehrhardt Heinold *Tel:* (040) 4900050 *Fax:* (040) 49000515 *E-mail:* eulenwolf@compuserve.com

*Branch Office(s)*
Nuernbergerstr 25, 86609 Donauwoerth
*Tel:* (0906) 2461-17 *Fax:* (0906) 2461-16
*E-mail:* m.j.bock@eulenhof.de

**Europ Export Edition GmbH**
Berliner Allee 8, 64295 Darmstadt
Mailing Address: Postfach 100264, 64202 Darmstadt
*Tel:* (06151) 38920 *Fax:* (06151) 38 92 80
*E-mail:* info@abconline.de
*Web Site:* www.abconline.de
*Key Personnel*
Publisher: Margit Selka
Founded: 1958
ISBN Prefix(es): 3-87208
Foreign Rep(s): Export Edition SA (France, Italy, Switzerland)

**Verlag Europa-Lehrmittel GmbH & Co KG+**
Nourney, Vollmer GmbH & Co KG, Duesselberger Str 23, 42781 Haan-Gruiten
Mailing Address: Postfach 420464, 42404 Haan-Gruiten
*Tel:* (02104) 6916-0 *Fax:* (02104) 6916-27
*E-mail:* info@europa-lehrmittle.de
*Web Site:* www.europa-lehrmittel.de
*Key Personnel*
General Manager, Rights & Permissions: Joachim Nourney
Editor: Armin Steinmueller
Sales: Wolfgang Baldauf
Founded: 1948
Subjects: Automotive, Computer Science, Economics, Electronics, Electrical Engineering, Geography, Geology, Physics
ISBN Prefix(es): 3-8085

**Europa Union Verlag GmbH+**
Holtorfer Str 35, 53229 Bonn
Mailing Address: Postfach 33 01 49, 53203 Bonn
*Tel:* (0228) 7 29 00 0
*E-mail:* Service@euverlag.de
*Web Site:* www.europa-union-verlag.de
*Key Personnel*
Man Dir, Rights & Permissions: Gisbert Karsten
Sales: Rainer Mertens; Wolfgang Schuefer
Founded: 1959
Subjects: Government, Political Science
ISBN Prefix(es): 3-7713
Subsidiaries: Verlag fur Internationale Politik GmbH
*Warehouse:* VVA, Postfach 7777, 33310 Guetersloh

**Europa Verlag GmbH+**
Neuer Wall 10, 20354 Hamburg
*Tel:* (040) 355434-0 *Fax:* (040) 355434-66
*E-mail:* info@europaverlag.de
*Web Site:* www.europaverlag.de *Cable:* EUROPAVERLAG
*Key Personnel*
Manager: Vito von Eichborn
Marketing: Dirk Kaufmann
International Rights: Peter Hahn
  *E-mail:* lizenzen@europaverlag.de
Publisher Reader: Dr Edgar Bracht; Afra Margaretha
Press: Leslie Middelmann *E-mail:* presse@europaverlag.de
Programmer: Aenne Glienke
Production: Frank Wagner *E-mail:* herstellung@europaverlag.de
Founded: 1933
Subjects: Biography, Fiction, Government, Political Science, Literature, Literary Criticism, Essays, Mysteries, Nonfiction (General), Philosophy
ISBN Prefix(es): 3-203
*Parent Company:* Europaverlag GmbH Muenich
Subsidiaries: Europaverlag GmbH

Foreign Rep(s): Tom Franke (Germany); Gabriele Funcke (Germany); Barbara Haab (Switzerland); Mareile Handrich (Germany); Peter Handrich (Germany); Juergen Niemeier (Germany); Guenther Poelking-Henkel (Germany); Achim Reigel (Germany); Raimund Thomas (Germany); Guenter Weber (Germany); Okkar Wuthe (Austria)
*Distribution Center:* Dr Franz Hain GmbH Verlagsauslieferungen, Dr Otto Neurathstr 3-5, 1220 Vienna, Austria *Tel:* (0282) 65 65-24 *Fax:* (0282) 65 65-75
Koch, Neff & Oetinger Co GmbH, Schockenriedstr 39, 70565 Stuggart *Tel:* (0711) 7899-20 36 *Fax:* (0711) 7899-10 10
Schweizer Buchzentrum, 4601 Olten, Switzerland *Tel:* (062) 209 23-44 *Fax:* (062) 209 27 60

**Europaeische Verlagsanstalt GmbH & Rotbuch Verlag GmbH & Co KG+**
Bei den Muehren 70, 20457 Hamburg
*Tel:* (040) 450194-0 *Fax:* (040) 450194-50
*E-mail:* info@rotbuch.de
*Web Site:* www.rotbuch.de; www.europaeische-verlagsanstalt.de
*Key Personnel*
Publisher: Dr Sabine Groenewold *E-mail:* info@sabine-groenewold-verlage.de
Editor: Irlen Kauser
Lektorat - Literature: Olaf Irlenkaeuser
  *E-mail:* irlenkaeuser@rotbuch.de
Foreign Rights: Andrea Schlotfeldt *Tel:* (040) 450194-13 *E-mail:* rechte@sabine-groenewold-verlage.de
Founded: 1946
Subjects: Anthropology, Architecture & Interior Design, Biography, Criminology, Government, Political Science, History, Literature, Literary Criticism, Essays, Philosophy
ISBN Prefix(es): 3-434; 3-88022
Total Titles: 600 Print; 2 CD-ROM
Subsidiaries: Rotbuch Verlag; Syndikat Autoren und Verlagsgesellschaft
Foreign Rep(s): Rolf-Peter Baacke (Germany); Richard Bhend (Switzerland); Fina Bothur (Germany); Fritz Denke (Germany); Karlheinz Flessenkemper (Germany); Edwin Gantert (Germany); Stefan Moedritscher (Austria); Guenther Raunjak (Austria); Juergen Stelling (Germany); Verena Suery (Switzerland)

**Verlag Europaeische Wehrkunde+**
Steintorwall 17, 32052 Herford
*Tel:* (0228) 340884 *Fax:* (040) 79713304
*Key Personnel*
Publisher: Peter Tamm
Manager: Lothar Lichtenheldt
*Associate Companies:* Verlagsgruppe Koehler/Mittler, Steintorwall 17, 32052 Herford
*Branch Office(s)*
Austr 19, 53179 Bonn *Tel:* (0228) 530962-64 *Fax:* (0228) 230102

**Evangelische Haupt-Bibelgesellschaft und von Cansteinsche Bibelanstalt+**
Ziegelstr 30, 10117 Berlin
*Tel:* (030) 28878850-0 *Fax:* (030) 28878850-8
*E-mail:* kontakt@ehbg.de
*Web Site:* www.ehbg.de
*Key Personnel*
Church President: Helge Klasson
Man Dir & Pastor: Friedrich Delius
  *E-mail:* delius@ehbg.de
Founded: 1814
Subjects: Literature, Literary Criticism, Essays
ISBN Prefix(es): 3-7461

**Evangelische Verlagsanstalt GmbH+**
Blumenstr 76, 04155 Leipzig
*Tel:* (0341) 71141-0 *Fax:* (0341) 7114150
*E-mail:* info@eva-leipzig.de

*Web Site:* www.eva-leipzig.de *Cable:*
EVAVERLAG LEIPZIG
*Key Personnel*
Dir: Ulrich Roebbelen
Founded: 1946
Subjects: Biblical Studies, Biography, Fiction, Religion - Protestant, Religion - Other, Theology
ISBN Prefix(es): 3-374
Total Titles: 270 Print
*Bookshop(s):* Buchhandlung an der
Thomaskirche, Burgstr 1, 04109 Leipzig; C L
Ungelenk Nachfolger, Kreuzstr 7, 01067 Dresden *Tel:* (0351) 4969804
*Warehouse:* Leipziger Kommissions- und Grossbuchhandelsgesellschaft, Potzschauer Weg, 04579 Espenhain
*Orders to:* Leipziger Kommissions- und Grossbuchhandelsgesellschaft, Potzschauer Weg, 04579 Espenhain

**Evangelischer Presseverband fuer Baden eV**
Vorholzstr 7, 76137 Karlsruhe
Mailing Address: Postfach 2280, 76010 Karlsruhe
*Tel:* (0721) 93 27 50 *Fax:* (0721) 9 32 75 20
*Key Personnel*
Manager: Herwig Schelling
Subjects: Religion - Protestant
ISBN Prefix(es): 3-87210
Subsidiaries: Hans Thoma Verlag

**Evangelischer Presseverband fuer Bayern eV+**
Birkerstr 22, 80636 Munich
*Tel:* (089) 121 72-0 *Fax:* (089) 121 72-138
*E-mail:* info@epv.de
*Web Site:* www.epv.de
*Telex:* 523718
*Key Personnel*
Dir: Hartmut Joisten
Publisher: Dr Manuel Zelger
International Rights: Antje Fritsch-Brown
*Tel:* (089) 121 72-132 *E-mail:* afritsch@epv.de
Founded: 1932
Bavarian Evangelical Press Union.
Subjects: Philosophy, Theology
ISBN Prefix(es): 3-583
Total Titles: 60 Print

**EVT Energy Video Training & Verlag GmbH**
Borsigallee 37, 60388 Frankfurt
*Tel:* (069) 431575 *Fax:* (069) 4950974
*Key Personnel*
Author: Marianne Uhl
International Rights: Karsten Schloberg
*E-mail:* kschloberg@aol.com
Founded: 1991
Subjects: Alternative, Astrology, Occult,
Medicine, Nursing, Dentistry, Music, Dance,
Parapsychology, Psychology, Psychiatry, Self-Help, Esoteric, Healing, Meditation
ISBN Prefix(es): 3-930255

**Exil Verlag+**
Rheinstr 20, 60325 Frankfurt
*Tel:* (069) 751102 *Fax:* (069) 751547
*E-mail:* fs7a020@uni-hamburg.de
*Key Personnel*
Publisher: Edita Koch *Tel:* (069) 751102
Founded: 1981
Publisher of books about German theater in exile
1933-1945 & a journal about literature, arts,
theater, film & science of Germans in exile
1933-1945.
Total Titles: 36 Print
Distributed by Otto Harrassowitz

**expert verlag GmbH, Fachverlag fuer
Wirtschaft & Technik+**
Wankelstr 13, 71272 Renningen
*Tel:* (07159) 92 65-0 *Fax:* (07159) 92 65-20
*E-mail:* expert@expertverlag.de
*Web Site:* www.expertverlag.de

*Key Personnel*
Publisher: Elmar Wippler
Editor: Dr Arnulf Krais *Tel:* (07159) 92 65-12
*E-mail:* krais@expertverlag.de
Advertising: Rainer Paulsen *Tel:* (07159) 92 65-16 *E-mail:* paulsen@expertverlag.de
Press: Christa Beran *Tel:* (07159) 92 65-16
*E-mail:* presse@expertverlag.de
Founded: 1979
Subjects: Electronics, Electrical Engineering, Energy, Environmental Studies, Management, Mechanical Engineering
ISBN Prefix(es): 3-8169
Number of titles published annually: 100 Print
Total Titles: 800 Print
Distributed by Baufachverlag (Switzerland); Lindeverlag (Austria); Schweizer Baudokumentation (Switzerland)
*Distribution Center:* Dessauer Engros Buchhandlung, 8046 Zurich, Switzerland *Tel:* (01) 466 96 66 *Fax:* (01) 466 96 69 *E-mail:* dessauer@dessauer.ch
Dr Franz Hain Verlagsauslieferungen, Dr Otto Neurath Gasse 5, 1220 Vienna, Austria
*Tel:* (01) 2 82 65 65 *Fax:* (01) 2 82 52 82
*E-mail:* office@hain.at

**Expolibri GmbH**
Buchwebung & Austellungen/Gerichtsweg 26, 04103 Leipzig
*Tel:* (0341) 2113 231 *Fax:* (0341) 2115 996
*Key Personnel*
Man Dir: Marion Renker
Founded: 1991

**Extent Verlag und Service Wolfgang M
Flamm+**
Pestalozzistr 64, 10627 Berlin-Charlottenburg
Mailing Address: Postfach 120429, 10594 Berlin
*Tel:* (030) 3279805-0; (030) 3279805-11
*Fax:* (030) 3279805-35
*E-mail:* extent@t-online.de
*Key Personnel*
International Rights: Flamm Wolfgang-Martin
Founded: 1987
Subjects: Art, Astrology, Occult, Communications, Fashion, Human Relations, Literature, Literary Criticism, Essays, Music, Dance
ISBN Prefix(es): 3-926671
Imprints: Pixel Transfer Design Studio

**Fabel-Verlag Gudrun Liebchen+**
Kirchenstr 6, 97657 Sandberg
*Tel:* (09701) 1463 *Fax:* (09701) 1463
*Key Personnel*
Dir: Gudrun Liebchen
Founded: 1989
Subjects: Drama, Theater, Environmental Studies, Literature, Literary Criticism, Essays, Nonfiction (General), Poetry
ISBN Prefix(es): 3-9802142

**Fabylon-Verlag+**
Forststr 10-12, 80997 Munich
*Tel:* (0172) 8211847 *Fax:* (089) 8110882
*E-mail:* fabylon@t-online.de
*Web Site:* www.fabylonzeitspur.de
*Key Personnel*
Publisher, Editor, Rights & Permissions: Gerald Jambor
Publisher & Authoress: Uschi Zietsch-Jambor
Founded: 1987
Membership(s): Stock Exchange of German Booksellers.
Subjects: Mysteries, Science Fiction, Fantasy
ISBN Prefix(es): 3-927071

**Fachbuchverlag Leipzig GmbH**
Naumburger Str 26, 04229 Leipzig
*Tel:* (0341) 4 90 34-0 *Fax:* (0341) 4 80 62 20
*E-mail:* voigt@hanser.de

*Web Site:* www.hanser.de
*Key Personnel*
Editorial: Christine Fritzsch *E-mail:* fritzsch@hanser.de; Yochen Horn; Erika Hotho
*E-mail:* hotho@hanser.de
Founded: 1949
*Parent Company:* Carl Hanser Verlag

**Fachbuchverlag Pfanneberg & Co**
Duesselbergerstr 23, 42781 Haan-Gruiten
Mailing Address: Postfach 4204 64, 42404 Haan-Gruiten
*Tel:* (02104) 6916-0 *Fax:* (02104) 6916-27
*E-mail:* info@pfanneberg.de
*Web Site:* www.pfanneberg.de
*Key Personnel*
Man Dir, Rights & Permissions: Dr Guenther Pfanneberg
Production: Gerhard Duske
Founded: 1949
Subjects: Business, Career Development, Cookery, Health, Nutrition
ISBN Prefix(es): 3-8057

**Fachmedien Verlag Winfried Ruf (FMV)+**
Parsevalstr 20, 86415 Mering
Mailing Address: Postfach 1248, 86407 Mering
*Tel:* (08233) 4924 *Fax:* (08233) 4789
*Key Personnel*
Contact: Winfried Ruf
Founded: 1990
ISBN Prefix(es): 3-928752

**Fachverlag fur das graphische Gewerbe GmbH**
Friedrichstr 22, 80801 Munich
Mailing Address: Postfach 401929, 80719 Munich
*Tel:* (089) 33036131 *Fax:* (089) 33036100
*Key Personnel*
Man Dir & International Rights: Dr Klaus Beichel
Founded: 1955
Subjects: Business
ISBN Prefix(es): 3-87218
Imprints: Mitteilungsblatt der Verbandes deds bayerischen Druckincleestrie eV

**Fachverlag Schiele & Schoen GmbH+**
Markgrafenstr 11, 10969 Berlin
Mailing Address: Postfach 610280, Berlin 10924
*Tel:* (030) 253 75 20 *Fax:* (030) 251 72 48
*E-mail:* service@schiele-schoen.de
*Web Site:* www.schiele-schoen.de
*Key Personnel*
Man Dir, Rights & Permissions: Karl-Michael Mehnert *E-mail:* peter.schoen@schiele-schoen.de
Sales: Ingrid Bade
Production: Lutz Stehr
Founded: 1946
Publishers of technical & scientifical publications.
Subjects: Biological Sciences, Communications, Crafts, Games, Hobbies, Engineering (General), Medicine, Nursing, Dentistry, Technology
ISBN Prefix(es): 3-7949
Foreign Rep(s): Norwin A Merens Ltd (North America)

**Fackeltrager-Verlag GmbH+**
Wurzburgerstr 14, 26121 Oldenburg
Mailing Address: Postfach 3407, 26024 Oldenburg
*Tel:* (0441) 980 66-0 *Fax:* (0441) 980 66-34
*E-mail:* info@lappan.de
*Web Site:* www.lappan.de
*Key Personnel*
Editorial Dir: Peter Baumann; Dieter Schwalm
Marketing: Michael Bohme *E-mail:* vertrieb@lappan.de; Heike Kroner
International Rights: Heidtun Viampl
Publicity: Elke Horstmann
Rights: Nicola Heinrichs

Advertising: Andrea Groteluschen
  *E-mail:* presse@lappan.de
Founded: 1949
Subjects: Art, History, Humor
ISBN Prefix(es): 3-89082; 3-8303
*Parent Company:* Lappan Verlag GmbH

**Christa Falk-Verlag+**
Ischl 11, 83370 Seeon
*Tel:* (08667) 14 13 *Fax:* (08667) 14 17
*E-mail:* email@chfalk-verlag.de
*Web Site:* www.chfalk-verlag.de
*Key Personnel*
Publisher: Christa Falk
Founded: 1982
Specialize in esoteric books.
ISBN Prefix(es): 3-924161; 3-89568
Number of titles published annually: 10 Print; 2
  CD-ROM; 1 Audio
Total Titles: 240 Print; 196 Online; 16 Audio
Foreign Rep(s): AS Hoeller (Austria)

**Falken-Verlag GmbH+**
Neumarkterstr 28, 81673 Munich
Mailing Address: Postfach 1120, 65521 Niedern-
  hausen
*Tel:* (01805) 990505 *Fax:* (04136) 3333
*E-mail:* vertrieb.verlagsgruppe@bertelsmann.de
*Web Site:* www.randomhouse.de/falken
*Key Personnel*
Man Dir: Frank Sicker
Publishing Manager: Manfred Abrahamsberg
Production: Josef Jung
Publicity: Stefan Becht *Tel:* (06127) 702-190
  *Fax:* (06127) 702-248 *E-mail:* presse@falken.
  de
Foreign Rights: Silke Bruenink *Tel:* (06127) 702-
  178 *Fax:* (06127) 702-277
Founded: 1923
Subjects: Cookery, Crafts, Games, Hobbies, Ed-
  ucation, Gardening, Plants, Health, Nutrition,
  History, How-to, Humor, Photography, Sports,
  Athletics
ISBN Prefix(es): 3-8068
*Associate Companies:* Moeller Verlag
Subsidiaries: Falken Taschenbuch Verlag;
  Friedrich Bassermann'sche Verlagsbuchhand-
  lung
*Orders to:* KNO, Schockenriedstr 39, 70565
  Stuttgart 80

**Ekkehard Faude Verlag**
Postfach 100524, 78405 Konstanz
*Tel:* (041 71) 6883555 *Fax:* (041 71) 6883565
ISBN Prefix(es): 3-922305

**Favorit-Verlag Huntemann und Markus & Co
  GmbH+**
Stettinerstr 16, 76437 Rastatt
*Tel:* (07222) 2 22 54 *Fax:* (07222) 2 98 38
*E-mail:* info@favorit-verlag.de
*Web Site:* www.favorit-verlag.de
*Telex:* 786630 *Cable:* FAVORITVERLAG
*Key Personnel*
Man Dir: Trudel Huntemann; Ilse Markus;
  Michael Markus
Founded: 1965
ISBN Prefix(es): 3-921102; 3-8227

**Feinschmecker**, *imprint of* Graefe und Unzer
  Verlag GmbH

**Dr Karl Feistle**, see Dustri-Verlag Dr Karl
  Feistle

**Feltron-Elektronik Zeissler & Co GmbH**
Auf dem Schellerod 22, 53842 Troisdorf
Mailing Address: Postfach 1263, 53822 Troisdorf
*Tel:* (02241) 48670 *Fax:* (02241) 404241
*Key Personnel*
Owner: M Zeissler

Founded: 1947
Subjects: Communications, Computer Science,
  Electronics, Electrical Engineering, Microcom-
  puters
ISBN Prefix(es): 3-88050

**Ferd Dummler's Verlag+**
Fuggerstr 7, 51149 Cologne
*Tel:* (02203) 3029-0 *Fax:* (02203) 3029-40
*Key Personnel*
Man Dir: Helmut Lehmann
Founded: 1808
Membership(s): VGS - Verlagsgesellschaft mbH
  & Co KG
Subjects: Chemistry, Chemical Engineering, Civil
  Engineering, Computer Science, Crafts, Games,
  Hobbies, Earth Sciences, Government, Political
  Science, History, Language Arts, Linguistics,
  Mathematics, Mechanical Engineering, Physical
  Sciences, Physics, Sports, Athletics
ISBN Prefix(es): 3-427

**Franz Ferzak World & Space Publications+**
Am Bachl 1, 93336 Altmannstein
*Tel:* (09446) 1403
*Key Personnel*
Owner: Franz Ferzak *Tel:* (089) 82089393
Founded: 1987
Subjects: Astronomy, Electronics, Electrical Engi-
  neering, Energy, Engineering (General), Physi-
  cal Sciences, Physics, Science (General), Tech-
  nology
ISBN Prefix(es): 3-9801465; 3-9805835
Number of titles published annually: 2 Print
Total Titles: 11 Print
*Orders to:* Michaels Verlag, 86971 Peiting
  *Tel:* (08861) 59018 *Fax:* (08861) 67091
  *E-mail:* mvv@michaelsverlag.de

**Festland Verlag GmbH**
Basteistr 88, 53173 Bonn
Mailing Address: Postfach 200561, 53135 Bonn
*Tel:* (0228) 36 20 21-23 *Fax:* (0228) 35 17 71
*E-mail:* verlag@festland-verlag.de
*Web Site:* www.oeckl-online.de
*Key Personnel*
International Rights: Heinz H Hey
Founded: 1950
Subjects: Communications, Economics, Educa-
  tion, Government, Political Science, Social Sci-
  ences, Sociology
ISBN Prefix(es): 3-87224
Number of titles published annually: 2 Print; 2
  CD-ROM; 1 Online
*Parent Company:* C W Niemeyer GmbH & Co
  KG, 31784 Hameln

**Festo Didactic GmbH & Co KG**
Rechbergstr 3, 73770 Denkendorf
*Tel:* (0711) 3467-1253 *Toll Free Tel:* 800 560-
  0967 (orders) *Fax:* (0711) 34754-1253
  *Toll Free Fax:* 800 560-0843 (orders)
*E-mail:* did@festo.com
*Web Site:* www.festo.com/didactic
*Key Personnel*
Man Dir: Dr Theodor Niehaus; Dr Wilfried Stoll
Founded: 1980
Membership(s): Association of German Publish-
  ing Companies.
Subjects: Career Development, Education, Elec-
  tronics, Electrical Engineering, Engineering
  (General)
ISBN Prefix(es): 3-8127
*U.S. Office(s):* Festo Corporation, 395 More-
  land Rd, Hauppauge, NY 11788, United States
  *Tel:* 516-435-0800 *Fax:* 516-435-8026

**Fibre Verlag**
Martinistr 37, 49080 Osnabrueck
*Tel:* (0541) 431838 *Fax:* (0541) 432786
*E-mail:* info@fibre-verlag.de

*Web Site:* www.fibre-verlag.de
ISBN Prefix(es): 3-929759

**Wolfgang Fietkau Verlag+**
Ernst-Thaelmannstr 152, 14532 Kleinmachnow
*Tel:* (033203) 71 105 *Fax:* (033203) 71 109
*E-mail:* post@fietkau.de
*Web Site:* www.fietkau.de
*Key Personnel*
Publisher, Rights & Permissions: Wolfgang Fi-
  etkau
Founded: 1959
Acts as booktrader on German Stockmarket.
Subjects: Poetry
ISBN Prefix(es): 3-87352

**Barbara Fietz**, see Abakus Musik Barbara Fietz

**Emil Fink Verlag**
Siemensstr 52, 70469 Stuttgart
*Tel:* (0711) 814646 *Fax:* (0711) 8106070
*E-mail:* info@fink-verlag.de
*Web Site:* www.fink-verlag.de
*Key Personnel*
Publisher, Rights & Permissions: Stefan Scheibel
Founded: 1919
Specialize in calendars, greeting cards & post-
  cards.
Subjects: Art
ISBN Prefix(es): 3-7717
Foreign Rep(s): Arcaldion (Austria, Netherlands,
  France, Switzerland); Art Bula; Calandars-
  Cards; Edition Classic Art; Verlagsauslieferung
  R & B

**Verlagsgruppe J Fink GmbH & Co KG+**
Siemensstr 52, 70469 Stuttgart
*Tel:* (0711) 81 4646 *Fax:* (0711) 81 06070
*E-mail:* info@fink-verlag.de
*Web Site:* www.fink-verlag.de
*Telex:* 723737 fkf d *Cable:* Buch-Fink
*Key Personnel*
Man Dir: Bodo Neiss; Wolfgang Titze
Man Dir, Rights & Permissions: Sigmund Zip-
  perle
Rights & Permissions: Beatrice Weber
Public Relations: Helmut Braun
Founded: 1935
Firm has developed from an association between
  the German company J Fink (founded 1894)
  & the Swiss cartographic company Kuem-
  merly und Frey (founded 1852). The latter firm
  also continues as an independent company in
  Switzerland.
Subjects: Health, Nutrition, Nonfiction (General),
  Outdoor Recreation, Sports, Athletics
ISBN Prefix(es): 3-7718; 3-350; 3-89142; 3-
  9801113
*Parent Company:* Kummerly und Frey Verlag,
  Bern, Switzerland

**Wilhelm Fink GmbH & Co Verlags-KG+**
Juehenplatz 1-3, 33098 Paderborn
*Tel:* (05251) 127-5; (05251) 127-842
  *Fax:* (05251) 127-860
*E-mail:* kontakt@fink.de
*Web Site:* www.fink.de *Cable:* FINK MUNCHEN
*Key Personnel*
Publisher: Ferdinand Schoeningh *Tel:* (05251)
  127-777 *Fax:* (05252) 127-670 *E-mail:* info@
  schoeningh.de
Editor & Man Dir: Dr Raimar Zons
Founded: 1962
Subjects: Archaeology, Art, History, Language
  Arts, Linguistics, Literature, Literary Criticism,
  Essays, Music, Dance, Philosophy, Psychology,
  Psychiatry, Social Sciences, Sociology
ISBN Prefix(es): 3-7705
Imprints: Poetik und Hermeneutik; Bild und Text

*Orders to:* Ferdinand Schoeningh Verlag, Jue-henplatz 1-3, 33098 Paderborn *Tel:* (05251) 1 27-777 *Fax:* (05251) 1 27-670 *E-mail:* info@ schoeningh.de

**Finken Junior**, *imprint of* Finken Verlag GmbH

**Finken-Verlag**, see Finken Verlag GmbH

**Finken Verlag GmbH+**
Zimmersmuhlenweg 40, 61440 Oberursel
Mailing Address: Postfach 1546, 61405 Oberursel
*Tel:* (06171) 6388-0 *Fax:* (06171) 6388-44
*E-mail:* info@finken.de
*Web Site:* www.finken.de *Cable:* NEUER
FINKENVERLAG OBERURSEL
*Key Personnel*
Dir: Manfred Krick
Foreign Rights: Karoline Jockel *E-mail:* karoline.
jockel@finken.de
Founded: 1985
Specialize in learning & teaching material for children from 3 to 12 years-old at school & at home, LOGICO™-the new learning system with selfchecking; also reading skills & early learning.
Membership(s): Deutscher Didacta Verband-Germany, Worlddidac Association, Boersen-verein des deutschen Buchhandels Germany.
Subjects: Education, English as a Second Language, Mathematics, Natural History
ISBN Prefix(es): 3-8084
Imprints: Finken Junior

**Harald Fischer Verlag GmbH+**
Theaterplatz 31, 91054 Erlangen
Mailing Address: Postfach 1565, 91005 Erlangen
*Tel:* (09131) 205620 *Fax:* (09131) 206028
*E-mail:* info@haraldfischerverlag.de
*Web Site:* www.haraldfischerverlag.de
*Key Personnel*
Contact: Dr Claudia Schorcht
Founded: 1984
Microfiche Editions.
Membership(s): Boersenverein des dt Buchhandels.
Subjects: Disability, Special Needs, Engineering (General), History, Language Arts, Linguistics, Library & Information Sciences, Medicine, Nursing, Dentistry, Philosophy, Publishing & Book Trade Reference, Religion - Jewish, Science (General), Women's Studies
ISBN Prefix(es): 3-89131
Total Titles: 350 Print; 2 CD-ROM

**Verkehrs-Verlag J Fischer GmbH & Co KG**
Paulusstr 1, 40237 Duesseldorf
Mailing Address: Postfach 140265, 40072 Duesseldorf
*Tel:* (0211) 99193-0 *Fax:* (0211) 6801544; (0211) 9919327
*E-mail:* vvf@verkehrsverlag-fischer.de
*Web Site:* www.verkehrsverlag-fischer.de
*Key Personnel*
Publisher: Paul Urban *Tel:* (0211) 9919311
*E-mail:* paul.urban@verkehrsverlag-fischer.de
Founded: 1904
Subjects: Transportation
ISBN Prefix(es): 3-87841

**Karin Fischer Verlag GmbH+**
Wallstr 50, 52064 Aachen
Mailing Address: Postfach 10 21 32, 52021 Aachen
*Tel:* (0241) 960 90 90 *Fax:* (0241) 960 90 99
*E-mail:* info@karin-fischer-verlag.de
*Web Site:* www.karin-fischer-verlag.de
*Key Personnel*
President & Editor: Karin Fischer
Reader: Dr Manfred S Fischer
Founded: 1989

Subjects: Fiction, Literature, Literary Criticism, Essays, Nonfiction (General), Philosophy, Poetry, Social Sciences, Sociology
ISBN Prefix(es): 3-927854; 3-89514

**Verlag Reinhard Fischer**
Weltistr 34, 81477 Munich
*Tel:* (089) 791 88 92 *Fax:* (089) 791 83 10
*E-mail:* verlagfischer@compuserve.de
*Web Site:* www.verlag-reinhard-fischer.de
*Key Personnel*
Owner: Reinhard Fischer
Founded: 1982
Subjects: Communications, Journalism, Marketing, Radio, TV
ISBN Prefix(es): 3-88927

**Rita G Fischer Verlag+**
Orberstr 30, 60386 Frankfurt
*Tel:* (069) 941942-0 *Fax:* (069) 941942-99; (069) 941942-98
*E-mail:* r.g.fischer.verlag@t-online.de
*Web Site:* www.buchhandel.de/r.g.fischer/
*Key Personnel*
Man Dir: Rita G Fischer *E-mail:* r.g.fisher. verlag@t-online.de
Founded: 1977
Subjects: Engineering (General), Fiction, Government, Political Science, How-to, Medicine, Nursing, Dentistry, Poetry, Psychology, Psychiatry, Social Sciences, Sociology
ISBN Prefix(es): 3-88323; 3-89406; 3-89501; 3-8301

**S Fischer Verlag GmbH+**
Formerly Fischer Taschenbuch Verlag GmbH
Subsidiary of S Fischer Verlag GmbH
Hedderichstr 114, 60596 Frankfurt am Main
*Tel:* (069) 6062-0 *Fax:* (069) 6062-319
*Web Site:* www.s-fischer.de
*Key Personnel*
Man Dir: Monika Schoeller; Dr Hubertus Schenkel
Man Dir, Rights & Permissions: Wolfgang Mertz
Sales: Ralf Alkenbrecher
Publicity: Margarete Schwind
Production: Wilfried Meiner
Editorial: Martin Bauer; Dr Ursula Koehler
Founded: 1952
Subjects: Biography, History, Literature, Literary Criticism, Essays, Nonfiction (General), Psychology, Psychiatry, Women's Studies
ISBN Prefix(es): 3-596

**S Fischer Verlag GmbH+**
Hedderichstr 114, 60596 Frankfurt am Main
Mailing Address: Postfach 700355, 60553 Frankfurt am Main
*Tel:* (069) 6062-0 *Fax:* (069) 6062-214
*Web Site:* www.fischerverlage.de *Cable:* BUCHFISCHER
*Key Personnel*
Man Dir: Dr Joerg Bong; Lothar Kleiner; Peter Lohmann; Monika Schoeller
Founded: 1886
Subjects: Fiction, Literature, Literary Criticism, Essays, Nonfiction (General)
ISBN Prefix(es): 3-10
Subsidiaries: Wolfgang Krueger Verlag; Fischer Taschenbuch Verlag

**Fischer Taschenbuch Verlag GmbH**, see S Fischer Verlag GmbH

**Fit fuers Leben Verlag**, *imprint of* NaturaViva Verlags GmbH

**Flaschenpost**, *imprint of* Keysersche Verlagsbuchhandlung GmbH

**Flechsig Buchvertrieb**
Imprint of Verlagshaus Wurzburg
Beethovenstr 5, 97070 Wurzburg
*Tel:* (0931) 385235 *Fax:* (0931) 385305
*E-mail:* info@verlagshaus.com
*Web Site:* www.verlagshaus.com
*Key Personnel*
Publishing Dir: Dieter Krause
Dir, Production: Juergen Roth
Sales Dir: Johannes Glesius
Subjects: Travel

**Erich Fleischer Verlag**
Postfach 1264, 28818 Achim
*Tel:* (04202) 517-0 *Fax:* (04202) 517-41
*E-mail:* info@efv-online.de
*Web Site:* www.efv-online.de
*Key Personnel*
Contact: Gerhard Schroeter *Tel:* (04202) 51729
*E-mail:* schroeter@efv-online.de
Founded: 1954
Subjects: Law
ISBN Prefix(es): 3-8168
Number of titles published annually: 10 Print; 2 CD-ROM
Total Titles: 50 Print; 9 CD-ROM

**Fleischhauer & Spohn GmbH & Co**
Mundelsheimerstr 3, 74321 Bietigsheim-Bissingen
Mailing Address: Postfach 1764, 74307 Bietigsheim-Bissingen
*Tel:* (07142) 596161 *Fax:* (07142) 596280
*E-mail:* info@verlag-fleischhauer.de
*Web Site:* www.verlag-fleischhauer.de
*Telex:* 724237 umco d
*Key Personnel*
Marketing: Dieter Keilbach
Man Dir: Dr Max Bez; Thomas Bez; Martin Roth; Simone Roth
Founded: 1830
Subjects: History, Regional Interests, Travel
ISBN Prefix(es): 3-87230
*Associate Companies:* Barsortiment G Umbreit GmbH & Co (book wholesaler)

**Flensburger Hefte Verlag GmbH+**
Holm 64, 24937 Flensburg
*Tel:* (0461) 2 63 63; (0461) 2 14 72 *Fax:* (0461) 2 69 12
*E-mail:* flensburgerhefte@t-online.de
*Web Site:* www.flensburgerhefte.de
*Key Personnel*
Man Dir: Wolfgang Weirauch
Founded: 1987
Subjects: Education, Health, Nutrition, History, Human Relations, Philosophy, Religion - Other, Social Sciences, Sociology
ISBN Prefix(es): 3-926841; 3-935679
*Warehouse:* Helemenallee 4, 24937 Flensburg

**Flugzeug Publikations GmbH+**
Thomas Mannstr 3, 89257 Illertissen
Mailing Address: Postfach 3055, 89253 Illertissen
*Tel:* (07303) 964220 *Fax:* (07303) 964141
*Key Personnel*
Sales: Manfred Franzke; Werner Richter
Founded: 1985
Subjects: Aeronautics, Aviation, History
ISBN Prefix(es): 3-927132
Total Titles: 4 Print

**FN-Verlag der Deutschen Reiterlichen Vereinigung GmbH+**
Freiherr-von-Langenstr 8a, 48231 Warendorf
*Tel:* (02581) 63 62-115 *Fax:* (02581) 63 31 46
*Web Site:* www.fnverlag.de
*Telex:* 258113 FENGER
*Key Personnel*
Manager: Siegmund Friedrich; Rainer Reisloh
*Tel:* (02581) 63 62-205
Marketing: Heike Ourajini *Tel:* (02581) 63 62-221
*E-mail:* hourajini@fn-dokr.de

Sales: Tamara Erkelenz *Tel:* (02581) 63 62-154
  *E-mail:* terkelenz@fn-dokr.de; Tanja Kneupper
  *Tel:* (02851) 63 62-254 *E-mail:* tkneupper@fn-
  dokr.de
Founded: 1977
Subjects: Film, Video
ISBN Prefix(es): 3-88542

**Focus-Verlag Gesellschaft mbH+**
Unterer Hardthof 29, 35398 Giessen
*Tel:* (0641) 76031; (0641) 68225 (orders)
  *Fax:* (0641) 76031; (0641) 68331 (orders)
*E-mail:* info@focus-verlag.de
*Web Site:* www.focus-verlag.de
*Key Personnel*
Man Dir, Sales, Rights & Permissions: Mr
  Schmid
Publicity, Advertising Dir: Mr Neuhofer
Founded: 1970
Subjects: Environmental Studies, History, Psy-
  chology, Psychiatry, Social Sciences, Sociology
ISBN Prefix(es): 3-920352; 3-88349

**Forum**, *imprint of* Wissenschaftliche
  Buchgesellschaft

**Forum Verlag GmbH & Co**
Schrempfstr 8, 70597 Stuttgart
*Tel:* (0711) 76727-0 *Fax:* (0711) 76727-28
*E-mail:* info@forumverlag.de
*Web Site:* www.forumverlag.de
*Key Personnel*
Man Dir: Dr Werner Schumacher
Founded: 1964
Our journal *Deutsches Architektenblatt* is sent
  to every architect who is a member of the
  German Architektenkammer, approximately
  110,000 monthly.
Subjects: Architecture & Interior Design
ISBN Prefix(es): 3-8091

**Forum Verlag Leipzig Buch-Gesellschaft mbH+**
Gottschedstr 30, 04109 Leipzig
*Tel:* (0341) 9 80 50 08 *Fax:* (0341) 9 80 50 07
*E-mail:* info@forumverlagleipzig.de
*Web Site:* www.forumverlagleipzig.de
*Key Personnel*
Publisher: Helen Jannsen
Founded: 1995
Membership(s): Boersenverein des Deutschen
  Buchhandels eV.
Subjects: Biography, History, Humor, Nonfiction
  (General), Regional Interests
ISBN Prefix(es): 3-931801
Number of titles published annually: 7 Print
Total Titles: 50 Print; 1 Audio
*Orders to:* LKG Verlagsauslieferung mbH, Po-
  etzschauer Weg, 04579 Espenhain, Con-
  tact: Frank Waldhelm *Tel:* (034206) 65132
  *Fax:* (034206) 65130 *E-mail:* fwaldhelm@lkg-
  service.de *Web Site:* www.lkg-va.de

**Forum Wissenschaft Studien**, *imprint of* Bund
  demokratischer Wissenschaftlerinnen und
  Wissenschafler eV (BdWi)

**Fouque-Literaturverlag**, *imprint of* Frankfurter
  Literaturverlag GmbH

**Fouque-Publishers Inc**, *imprint of* Frankfurter
  Literaturverlag GmbH

**Verlag der Francke Buchhandlung GmbH+**
Am Schwanhof 19, 35037 Marburg
Mailing Address: Postfach 200640, 35018 Mar-
  burg
*Tel:* (06421) 17 25-0 *Fax:* (06421) 17 25-30
*E-mail:* info@francke-buch.de
*Web Site:* www.francke-buch.de

*Key Personnel*
Man Dir, Editorial & Publicity: Uwe Schmidt
Sales: Margot Agel
Founded: 1934
Firm is contributor to the Telos series of evangeli-
  cal paperbacks.
Subjects: Theology
ISBN Prefix(es): 3-88224; 3-86122; 3-920345
*Bookshop(s):* Gunzenhausen; Velbert; Lemfoerde;
  Oberursel; Elbingerode; Neustadt

**Franckh-Kosmos Verlags-GmbH & Co+**
Pfizerstr 5-7, 70184 Stuttgart
Mailing Address: Postfach 10 60 11, 70049
  Stuttgart
*Tel:* (0711) 2191-0 *Fax:* (0711) 2191-422
*E-mail:* info@kosmos.de
*Web Site:* www.kosmos.de
*Telex:* 721669 Kosm d *Cable:* KOSMOS
  VERLAG STUTTGART
*Key Personnel*
President: Axel Meffert *Tel:* (0711) 2191341
Publicity Dir: Bettina Schaub *Tel:* (0711)
  2191341 *Fax:* (0711) 2191141 *E-mail:* b.
  schaub@kosmos.de
Production Dir: Juergen Bischoff *Tel:* (0711)
  2191221 *Fax:* (0711) 2191121 *E-mail:* j.
  bischoff@kosmos.de
Foreign Rights Dir: Andrea D Ahlers *Tel:* (0711)
  2191254 *Fax:* (0711) 2191154 *E-mail:* a.
  ahlers@kosmos.de
Marketing Dir: Manfred Haarer *Tel:* (0711)
  2191401 *Fax:* (0711) 2191101 *E-mail:* m.
  haarer@kosmos.de; Heiko Windfelder
  *Tel:* (0711) 2191322 *Fax:* (0711) 2191122; Birgit Carlsen *Tel:* (0711) 21911205 *Fax:* (0711)
  21911205 *E-mail:* b.carlsen@kosmos.de
Founded: 1822
Specialize in fishing & hunting.
Subjects: Animals, Pets, Astronomy, Biological
  Sciences, Chemistry, Chemical Engineering,
  Crafts, Games, Hobbies, Electronics, Electri-
  cal Engineering, Engineering (General), Envi-
  ronmental Studies, Fiction, Gardening, Plants,
  Geography, Geology, House & Home, Natural
  History, Nonfiction (General), Outdoor Recre-
  ation, Physics, Science (General), Technology
ISBN Prefix(es): 3-440
Number of titles published annually: 120 Print
Total Titles: 600 Print
*Parent Company:* Buchverlage Langen Mueller
  Herbig
*Associate Companies:* F A Herbig (Munich);
  Klee-Spiele GmbH (Fuerth)
*Warehouse:* VVA, An der Autobahn, 33310
  Guetersloh

**Verlag Frankfurter Buecher**, *imprint of*
  Societaets-Verlag

**Frankfurter Literaturverlag GmbH** (Frankfurt
  Publishing Group)+
Hanauer Landstr 338, 60314 Frankfurt am Main
*Tel:* (069) 40894-0 *Fax:* (069) 40894-194
*E-mail:* info@haensel-hohenhausen.de
*Web Site:* www.cgl-verlag.de
Founded: 1987
Membership(s): AAP; ABA; World Union of
  Publishers.
ISBN Prefix(es): 3-8267; 3-89349
Number of titles published annually: 250 Print
Total Titles: 2,000 Print
Imprints: Deutsche Bibliothek der Wis-
  senschaften/German Library of Sciences;
  Deutsche Hochschulschriften/German Univer-
  sity Studies; Fouque-Literaturverlag; Fouque-
  Publishers Inc; Cornelia Goethe Literaturverlag
Foreign Rep(s): Fouque London Publishers

**Frankfurter Societaets-Druckerei GmbH**, see
  Societaets-Verlag

**FVA-Frankfurter Verlagsanstalt GmbH+**
Wildungerstr 6A, 60487 Frankfurt am Main
*Tel:* (069) 96220610 *Fax:* (069) 96220630
*E-mail:* info@frankfurter-verlagsanstalt.de
*Web Site:* www.frankfurter-verlagsanstalt.de
*Key Personnel*
Publisher: Dr Joachim Unseld
Manager: Dagmar Fretter *E-mail:* fretter@
  frankfurter-verlagsanstalt.de
Foreign Rights: Ricarda von Bergen *Tel:* (069)
  962206 15
Founded: 1986
Subjects: Biography
ISBN Prefix(es): 3-627
*Parent Company:* Unseld
*Associate Companies:* Sophienbuchhandlung
*Orders to:* Libri Distribution, August-Schanz-Str
  33, 60433 Frankfurt am Main

**Franz-Sales-Verlag+**
Rosental 1, 85072 Eichstaett
*Tel:* (08421) 9 34 89-31 *Fax:* (08421) 9 34 89-35
*E-mail:* info@franz-sales-verlag.de
*Web Site:* www.franz-sales-verlag.de
*Key Personnel*
President & Editor: P Herbert Winklehner
  *E-mail:* herbert.winklehner@franz-sales-verlag.
  de
Founded: 1931
Disseminate the work of St Francis de Soles
  (1567-1622) into the modern world.
Membership(s): VKB, AKB, Borsenverein Des
  Deutschen Buchhandels & Verband Bayrischer
  Verleger Und Buchhandler
Subjects: Art, Biography, Religion - Catholic,
  Theology
ISBN Prefix(es): 3-7721
Total Titles: 100 Print

**Verlag Franz Vahlen GmbH+**
Wilhelmstr 9, 80801 Munich
*Tel:* (089) 38189-381 *Fax:* (089) 38189-402
*E-mail:* info@vahlen.de
*Web Site:* www.vahlen.de
*Key Personnel*
Manager: Dr Hans D Beck
Founded: 1870
Subjects: Economics, Finance, Law, Management,
  Marketing
ISBN Prefix(es): 3-8006
*Associate Companies:* Verlag C H Beck (OHG)

**Franzis-Verlag GmbH+**
Gruberstr 46a, 85586 Poing
*Tel:* (08121) 95 0 *Fax:* (08121) 95 16 96
*E-mail:* info@franzis.de
*Web Site:* www.franzis.de
*Key Personnel*
Man Dir: Dr Ruediger Hennings; Werner Muetzel
Founded: 1924
Subjects: Communications, Computer Science,
  Electronics, Electrical Engineering
ISBN Prefix(es): 3-7723
*Parent Company:* WEKA Firmengruppe GmbH &
  Co KG

**Frauenoffensive Verlagsgesellschaft MbH+**
Metzstr 14C, 81667 Munich
*Tel:* (089) 489500-48 *Fax:* (089) 489500-49
*E-mail:* info@verlag-frauenoffensive.de
*Web Site:* www.verlag-frauenoffensive.de
*Key Personnel*
Dir, Rights & Permissions: Gerlinde Kowitzke
Editorial: H Schlaeger
Sales: S Kohlstadt
Founded: 1974
Subjects: Women's Studies
ISBN Prefix(es): 3-88104

**Fraunhofer IRB Verlag Fraunhofer
  Informationszentrum Raum und Bau+**
Division of Fraunhofer-Gesellschaft
Nobelstr 12, 70569 Stuttgart

Mailing Address: Postfach 800469, 70504 Stuttgart
*Tel:* (0711) 9 70-25 00 *Fax:* (0711) 9 70-25 07
*E-mail:* irb@irb.fhg.de
*Web Site:* www.irbdirekt.de
*Key Personnel*
Man Dir: Dr Wilhelm Wissmann
Sales Manager: Barbara Scherer
Founded: 1947
Specialize in literature on building construction, building damages & regional planning.
Subjects: Architecture & Interior Design, Civil Engineering, Earth Sciences, Environmental Studies, House & Home, Outdoor Recreation, Regional Interests
ISBN Prefix(es): 3-8167; 3-924068; 3-9800658
Number of titles published annually: 100 Print; 6 CD-ROM
Total Titles: 20 Print; 6 CD-ROM

**frechverlag GmbH+**
Turbinenstr 7, 70499 Stuttgart
*Tel:* (0711) 83086-11 *Fax:* (0711) 83086-86
*E-mail:* kundenservice@frechverlag.de
*Web Site:* www.frech.de
*Key Personnel*
Man Dir: Marion Milkau; Werner Muetzel
Business Manager & Sales: Berud Leuz
Founded: 1955
Specialize in hobby & leisure activities.
Subjects: Crafts, Games, Hobbies, Electronics, Electrical Engineering
ISBN Prefix(es): 3-7724

**Frederking & Thaler Verlag GmbH+**
Infanteriestr 19, Haus 2, 80797 Munich
*Tel:* (089) 4372-0 *Fax:* (089) 4372-2854
*Key Personnel*
Owner, Publisher & International Rights: Monika Thaler *Tel:* (089) 12113 11
    *E-mail:* monikathaler@frederking-thaler.de
Founded: 1988 (as independent publisher, 1998-2001 Bertelsmann/Random House Publishing Group, in 2002 independent publisher)
Specialize in high quality illustrated books in the realm of wonders of nature, foreign cultures & their spiritual worlds. Also nonfiction narrative reports (culture, nature & travel).
Subjects: Archaeology, Art, Foreign Countries, Photography, Travel, World Religions
ISBN Prefix(es): 3-89405
Number of titles published annually: 30 Print
Total Titles: 120 Print; 120 E-Book
Imprints: Villa Arceno; Sierra
*Warehouse:* VVA Bertelsmann Distribution, 33310 Gutersloh

**Erika G Freese Verlag+**
Potsdamerstr 16, 12205 Berlin
*Tel:* (030) 8333077 *Fax:* (030) 8333077
*E-mail:* eg.freese@t-online.de
*Key Personnel*
Man Dir, Rights & Permissions: Erika Freese
Founded: 1982
Membership(s): the Stock Market of German Booksellers.
ISBN Prefix(es): 3-88942
*Orders to:* Buchvertrieb Grimmstrasse, Grimmstrasse 27, 12305 Berlin 16

**Verlag Freies Geistesleben+**
Division of Verlag Freies Geistesleben & Urachhaus GmbH
Postfach 131122, 70069 Stuttgart
*Tel:* (0711) 28532 00 *Fax:* (0711) 28532 10
*E-mail:* info@geistesleben.com
*Web Site:* www.geistesleben.com
*Key Personnel*
Publishing Dir: Jean-Claude Lin *Tel:* (0711) 2853221 *E-mail:* lin@geistesleben.com; Andreas Neider *E-mail:* a.neider@geistesleben.com

Sales: Reinhardt Stiehle *Tel:* (0711) 2853232
    *E-mail:* r.steihle@geistesleben.com
Founded: 1947
Membership(s): Community of Youth Book Publishers.
Subjects: Art, Biography, Education, History, How-to, Medicine, Nursing, Dentistry, Music, Dance, Philosophy, Psychology, Psychiatry, Religion - Other, Science (General), Social Sciences, Sociology, Picture books
ISBN Prefix(es): 3-7725; 3-87838; 3-8251
Number of titles published annually: 60 Print
Total Titles: 800 Print
Imprints: Aethera
*Orders to:* Koch, Neff & Oetinger, Schockenriedstr 39, Postfach 800620, Stuttgart *Tel:* (0711) 78992140 *Fax:* (0711) 78991010

**Freiherr von Stein Gedaechtnisausgabe**, *imprint of* Wissenschaftliche Buchgesellschaft

**Freimund-Verlag der Gesellschaft fur Innere und Aeussere Mission im Sinne der Lutherischen Kirche eV**
Ringstr 15, 91564 Neuendettelsau
Mailing Address: Postfach 48, 91561 Neuendettelsau
*Tel:* (09874) 6 89 39 80 *Fax:* (09874) 6 89 39 99
*E-mail:* info@freimund-verlag.de
*Web Site:* www.freimund-buchhandlung.de/verlag
*Key Personnel*
Man Dir: Dr Martin Kobler; Hildegard Wickert
Founded: 1933
Subjects: Religion - Other
ISBN Prefix(es): 3-7726
*Bookshop(s):* Freimund-Buchhandlung, Hauptstr 2, 91564 Neuendettelsau

**Margarethe Freudenberger - selbstverlag fur jedermann+**
Gartenstr 22, 97906 Faulbach
*Tel:* (09392) 8449
Founded: 1979
Subjects: Art, Fiction, How-to, Human Relations, Humor, Poetry
ISBN Prefix(es): 3-924711

**Verlag Walter Frey+**
Dusseldorfer Str 49, 10666 Berlin
Mailing Address: Postfach 150455, 10666 Berlin
*Tel:* (030) 883 25 61 *Fax:* (030) 883 25 61
*E-mail:* tranvia@aol.com
*Key Personnel*
Man Dir: Walter Frey
Founded: 1985
Publish literature of & about Spain, Portugal & Latin America.
Subjects: Regional Interests, Spain, Portugal, Latin America
ISBN Prefix(es): 3-925867
Number of titles published annually: 10 Print

**Frick Verlag GmbH+**
Postfach 447, 75104, Pforzheim
*Tel:* (07231) 102842 *Fax:* (07231) 357744
*E-mail:* info@frickverlag.de
*Web Site:* www.frickverlag.de
*Key Personnel*
Man Dir: Beate D Frick
Founded: 1970
Specialize in religion, metaphysics, esoteric.
Membership(s): Deutschief Bosenverlise.
Subjects: Religion - Other, Metaphysics, Esoteric
ISBN Prefix(es): 3-920780
Number of titles published annually: 3 Print
Total Titles: 3 Print
*Branch Office(s)*
Haupt, Str 279, Rosrath, Contact: Thele Jung *Tel:* (02205) 3308 *Fax:* (02205) 53308
Witere Weinberg, Str 11-1, Eisengen, Contact: Peter D'Orazio *Tel:* (07232) 383083 *Fax:* (07232) 383084

**Erhard Friedrich Verlag**
Im Brande 17, 30926 Seelze
Mailing Address: Postfach 10 01 50, 30917 Seelze
*Tel:* (0511) 400040 *Fax:* (0511) 40004-119
*E-mail:* info@friedrich-verlag.de
*Web Site:* www.friedrich-verlagsgruppe.de
*Telex:* 0922923 *Cable:* FRIEDRICH
*Key Personnel*
International Rights: Uwe Brinkmann
Publisher: Erhard Friedrich
Founded: 1960
Subjects: Art, Drama, Theater, Education
ISBN Prefix(es): 3-617

**Friedrich Kiehl Verlag+**
Postfach 140108, 67021 Ludwigshafen
*Tel:* (0621) 6 35 02-0 *Fax:* (0621) 6 35 02-22
*E-mail:* hotline@kiehl.de
*Web Site:* www.kiehl.de
*Telex:* 464810 Kiehl d
*Key Personnel*
Dir: Ernst-Otto Kleyboldt; Dr Karl-Friedrich Peter
Sales Manager: Klaus Bissinger
Rights & Permissions, International Rights: Adolf Schmidt
Founded: 1932
Subjects: Advertising, Business, Career Development, Computer Science, Economics, Education, Finance, Law, Marketing, Medicine, Nursing, Dentistry
ISBN Prefix(es): 3-470
*Parent Company:* Verlag Neue Wirtschafts-Briefe GmbH
Distributed by Linde-Verlag
Distributor for Linde-Verlag Ostereicl
*Warehouse:* Schuechtermannstr 180, 44628 Herne

**Frieling & Partner GmbH**
Huenefeldzeile 18, 12247 Berlin-Steglitz
*Tel:* (030) 7 66 99 90 *Fax:* (030) 7 74 41 03
*Web Site:* www.frieling.de *Cable:* FRIELING BERLIN
*Key Personnel*
Publisher: Wilhelm Ruprecht Frieling
Man Dir: Dr Johann-Friedrich Huffmann
    *E-mail:* gf@frieling.de
Editor: Peter Hehr *E-mail:* redaktion@frieling.de
Founded: 1871
ISBN Prefix(es): 3-89009; 3-8280

**Verlag A Fromm im Druck- u Verlagshaus Fromm GmbH & Co KG+**
Breiter Gang 10-16, 49074 Osnabrueck
Mailing Address: Postfach 1948, 49009 Osnabrueck
*Tel:* (0541) 3100 *Fax:* (0541) 310315; (0541) 310440
*Telex:* 94916 fromm d
*Key Personnel*
Publisher: Leo V Fromm
Chief Executive Officer & International Rights: Annette Harms-Hunold
Sales Manager: Annegret Busch
Public Relations: Ursula Malzahn
Founded: 1868 (Parent Company)
Subjects: Economics, Education, Environmental Studies, Ethnicity, Government, Political Science, History, Science (General), Social Sciences, Sociology
ISBN Prefix(es): 3-7729
*Parent Company:* Druck- und Verlagshaus Fromm GmbH & Co KG
*Associate Companies:* Fromm International Publishing Corp, 560 Lexington Ave, New York, NY 10022, United States
Imprints: Osnabrueck
*Branch Office(s)*
Edition Interfrom AG, Postfach 5005, Zurich, Switzerland *Tel:* (0041) 1 202 0900

**Friedrich Frommann Verlag+**
Koenig-Karlstr 27, 70372 Stuttgart
*Tel:* (0711) 955969-0 *Fax:* (0711) 955969-1
*E-mail:* info@frommann-holzboog.de
*Web Site:* www.frommann-holzboog.de
*Key Personnel*
Man Dir: Eckhart Holzboog *E-mail:* eckhart.
holzboog@frommann-holzboog.de
Editor: Tina Koch *E-mail:* lekorat@frommann-
holzboog.de
Press & Promotion Manager: Sybille Wittmann
*E-mail:* werbung-presse@frommann-holzboog.
de
Production Manager: Karl-Heinz Paczkowski
*E-mail:* herstellung@frommann-holzboog.de
Rights & Permissions: Kerstin Hamm
Marketing Assistant: Ulrike Doerr
Founded: 1727
Specialize in fine editions & textbooks. Indepen-
dent publisher of arts & humanities. Titles with
a focus in philosophy, psychoanalysis & theol-
ogy.
Subjects: History, Language Arts, Linguistics,
Law, Literature, Literary Criticism, Essays,
Mathematics, Philosophy, Psychology, Psy-
chiatry, Religion - Protestant, Social Sciences,
Sociology, Theology
ISBN Prefix(es): 3-7728
Number of titles published annually: 40 Print
Total Titles: 1,300 Print

**Fuldaer Verlagsanstalt GmbH & Co KG**
Rangstr 3-7, 36037 Fulda
*Tel:* (0661) 295-0 *Fax:* (0661) 295-70
*E-mail:* info@fva.de
*Web Site:* www.fva.de
*Telex:* 49739-FVAD
*Key Personnel*
Contact: Reinhold Hartwich
Subsidiaries: Vito von Eichborn GmbH & Co,
Verlag KG

**FVA,** see FVA-Frankfurter Verlagsanstalt GmbH

**Gabal-Verlag GmbH+**
Schumannstr 163, 63069 Offenbach
Mailing Address: Postfach 200252, 63077 Offen-
bach
*Tel:* (069) 84 000 66-0 *Fax:* (069) 84 000 66-66
*E-mail:* support@gabal-verlag.de
*Web Site:* www.gabal-verlag.de
*Key Personnel*
Man Editor: Helmut Juergen
Founded: 1979 (Vorlaufer)
Subjects: How-to, Literature, Literary Criticism,
Essays, Management
ISBN Prefix(es): 3-923984; 3-89749; 3-930799
*Parent Company:* Juergen Verlag GmbH
*Associate Companies:* PLS Sprachen, 176
Solothurn, Switzerland
Subsidiaries: Rot Gelb Grain Verlag
Divisions: Verlag

**Betriebswirtschaftlicher Verlag Dr Th Gabler+**
Unit of GWV Fachverlage GMBH
Abraham-Lincoln-Str 46, 65189 Wiesbaden
Mailing Address: Postfach 1546, 65173 Wies-
baden
*Tel:* (0611) 7878470 *Fax:* (0611) 787878400
*Web Site:* www.gwv-fachverlage.de
*Key Personnel*
General Manager: Dr Hans-Dieter Haenel
*E-mail:* hans-dieter.haenel@gwv-fachverlage.de
Man Dir: Dr Heinz Weinheimer
Editorial: Claudia Splittgerber; Ulrike Vetter
Sales & Marketing Manager: Rolf-Guenther
Hobbeling
Rights & Permissions: Angelika Bolisega
*Tel:* (0611) 7878361 *Fax:* 0611 7878470
*E-mail:* angelike.bolisega@gwv-fachverlage.de
Editorial: Maria Akhavan
Founded: 1929

Professional information for managers, personal
assistants; textbooks for students, encyclope-
dias.
Subjects: Accounting, Business, Economics, Fi-
nance, Management, Marketing
ISBN Prefix(es): 3-409
Total Titles: 1,500 Print
*Parent Company:* Springer Science & Business
Media
*Distribution Center:* VVA Bertelsmann Distribu-
tion, Postfach 7777, D-33310 Guetersloh

**Gabriel Verlag,** *imprint of* Thienemann Verlag
GmbH

**Galerie Der Spiegel-Dr E Stunke Nachfolge
GmbH**
Richartzstr 10, 50667 Cologne
*Tel:* (0221) 25 55 52 *Fax:* (0221) 25 55 53
*E-mail:* der-spiegel@galerie.de
*Web Site:* www.galerie.de/der-spiegel
Founded: 1945
Specialize in international art editions & book
catalogue portfolios.
Membership(s): Bundesverband Deutscher Galerie
& Boisenverein Des Deutschen Buchhandels.
Subjects: Art
ISBN Prefix(es): 3-87285

**Galrev Druck-und Verlagsgesellschaft Hesse &
Partner OHG+**
Lychenerstr 73, 10437 Berlin
*Tel:* (030) 44 65 01 83 *Fax:* (030) 44 65 01 84
*E-mail:* galrev@galrev.com
*Web Site:* www.galrev.com
*Key Personnel*
Manager: Egmont Hesse; Rainer Schedlinski
Founded: 1989
Subjects: Poetry
ISBN Prefix(es): 3-910161; 3-933149

**Gatzanis Verlags GmbH**
Alte Weinsteige 28, 70180 Stuttgart
*Tel:* (0711) 9640570 *Fax:* (0711) 9640572
*E-mail:* info@gatzanis.de
*Web Site:* www.gatzanis.de
*Key Personnel*
Owner: Jolanta Gatzanis
Founded: 1995
Subjects: Art, Biography, Child Care & Devel-
opment, Gay & Lesbian, Human Relations,
Humor, Self-Help
ISBN Prefix(es): 3-932855; 3-9803897
Number of titles published annually: 2 Print
Total Titles: 13 Print

**Gebrueder Borntraeger Science Publishers+**
Affiliate of E Schweizerbart'sche Verlagsbuch-
handlung
Johannesstr 3 A, 70176 Stuttgart
*Tel:* (0711) 3514560 *Fax:* (0711) 35145699
*E-mail:* mail@schweizerbart.de
*Web Site:* www.schweizerbart.de
*Key Personnel*
Man Dir, Sales: Dr Walter Obermiller
Man Dir, Production: Dr Erhard Naegele
Exhibition Manager: Martina Ihringer
Founded: 1790
Subjects: Biological Sciences, Earth Sciences,
Geography, Geology, Maritime
ISBN Prefix(es): 3-443
Imprints: Borntraeger Verlagsbuchhandlung

**Konkursbuch Verlag Claudia Gehrke+**
Hechingerstr 203, im Sudhaus, 72072 Tuebingen
*Tel:* (07071) 78779 *Fax:* (07071) 763780
*E-mail:* office@konkursbuch.com
*Web Site:* www.konkursbuch.com
*Key Personnel*
International Rights: Claudia Gehrke
Founded: 1978

Subjects: Literature, Literary Criticism, Essays,
Travel, Women's Studies
ISBN Prefix(es): 3-88769

**Verlag Junge Gemeinde E Schwinghammer
GmbH & Co KG+**
Max-Eyth-Str 13, 70771 Leinfelden-Echterdingen
Mailing Address: Postfach 100355, 70747
Leinfelden-Echterdingen
*Tel:* (0711) 99078-0 *Fax:* (0711) 99078-25 *Cable:*
JUNGEGEMEINDEVERLAG
*Key Personnel*
Manager: Siegfried Krumrey
Founded: 1928
Specialize in books for Sunday school.
Subjects: Education, Religion - Protestant
ISBN Prefix(es): 3-7797

**Genius Verlag** (Genius Publishing House)+
Aach 34, 87534 Oberstaufen
*Tel:* (08386) 960401 *Fax:* (08386) 960402
*E-mail:* contact@genius-verlag.de
*Web Site:* www.genius-verlag.de
*Key Personnel*
Contact: Dagmar Neubronner
Founded: 1997
Publish spiritual books.
Subjects: Biblical Studies, Biography, Career De-
velopment, Human Relations, Music, Dance,
Philosophy, Science (General), Self-Help, The-
ology
ISBN Prefix(es): 3-9806106; 3-934719
Number of titles published annually: 3 Print
Total Titles: 12 Print

**Alfons W Gentner Verlag GmbH & Co KG+**
Forststr 131, 70193 Stuttgart
*Tel:* (0711) 63672-0 *Fax:* (0711) 63672747
*E-mail:* gentner@gentnerverlag.de
*Web Site:* www.gentnerverlag.de
*Key Personnel*
Publisher: E F Reisch
Founded: 1927
Subjects: Automotive, Business, Career Devel-
opment, Engineering (General), Environmental
Studies, Medicine, Nursing, Dentistry
ISBN Prefix(es): 3-87247
Subsidiaries: B & V Kiado Kft; CNTL spool sra;
EUROMEDIA; GEMA Strucna Naklada; Insta-
lator Polski zoo; Magyar Mediprint Szakkiado
Kft; Technischer Fachverlag GmbH; Verbatim
Publishers (Pvt) Ltd

**Georgi GmbH+**
Theaterstr 77, 52062 Aachen
*Key Personnel*
Man Dir: Manfred Georgi; Werner Georgi
Rights & Permissions: Adriane Georgi
Sales: Josef Brauers
Founded: 1928
Subjects: History, How-to, Music, Dance, Science
(General)
ISBN Prefix(es): 3-87248; 3-8292
Subsidiaries: Georgi Publishers

**Carl Gerber Verlag,** see Schwaneberger Verlag
GmbH

**Gerhard Wolf Janus-Press GmbH+**
Amalienpark 7, 13187 Berlin
*Tel:* (030) 47535220 *Fax:* (030) 47533790
Founded: 1990
ISBN Prefix(es): 3-928942; 3-00

**Germanisches Nationalmuseum**
Kartausergasse 1, 90402 Nuernberg
*Tel:* (0911) 13310 *Fax:* (0911) 1331 200
*E-mail:* info@gnm.de
*Web Site:* www.gnm.de
*Key Personnel*
Chief, Publishing Dept: Dr Hermann Maue

Founded: 1853
Books & catalogues about artistic & cultural history from German speaking regions from prehistoric times to present, related to the museum's collections.
Subjects: Archaeology, Art, History, Science (General), Musical Instruments
ISBN Prefix(es): 3-926982; 3-936688
Number of titles published annually: 10 Print
Total Titles: 180 Print; 2 CD-ROM

**Gerstenberg Verlag+**
Rathausstr 18-20, 31134 Hildesheim
Mailing Address: Postfach 100555, 31105 Hildesheim
*Tel:* (05121) 1060 *Fax:* (05121) 106498
*E-mail:* verlag@gerstenberg-verlag.de
*Web Site:* www.gerstenberg-verlag.de
*Telex:* 927108 gberg d
*Key Personnel*
Man Dir: Dr Edmund Jacoby *Tel:* (05121) 106451 *E-mail:* dr.edmund.jacoby@gerstenberg-verlag.de
Editorial: Petra Albers *Tel:* (05121) 106460 *E-mail:* petra.albers@gerstenberg-verlag.de
Manager, Sales & Advertising: Wolfgang J Dietrich *Tel:* (05121) 106470 *E-mail:* wolfgang.dietrich@gerstenberg-verlag.de
Production: Friedrich Weskott *Tel:* (05121) 106465 *E-mail:* friedrich.weskott@gerstenberg-verlag.de
Rights & Permissions: Ina Feist *Tel:* (05121) 106454 *E-mail:* ina.feist@gerstenberg-verlag.de
Publicity: Andrea Deyerling-Baier *Tel:* (05121) 106456 *E-mail:* andrea.deyerlingbaier@gerstenberg-verlag.de
Founded: 1792
Subjects: Architecture & Interior Design, Gardening, Plants, Nonfiction (General)
ISBN Prefix(es): 3-8067

**Klaus Gerth Musikverlag+**
Dillerberg 2, 35614 Asslar
Mailing Address: Postfach 1148, 35607 Asslar
*Tel:* (06443) 68-0 *Fax:* (06443) 68-34
*E-mail:* info@gerth.de
*Web Site:* www.gerth.de
*Key Personnel*
Man Dir & International Rights: Klaus Gerth *Tel:* (06443) 6811 *Fax:* (06443) 6813 *E-mail:* gerth@gerth.de
Man Dir: Dieter Spahn
Founded: 1949
Subjects: Music, Dance, Religion - Other, Theology
ISBN Prefix(es): 3-89615; 3-922283
Distributor for Ganzteam Music

**Gerth Medien GmbH+**
Dillerberg 2, 35614 Asslar
Mailing Address: Postfach 1148, 35607 Asslar-Berghausen
*Tel:* (06443) 68-0 *Fax:* (06443) 68-34
*E-mail:* info@gerth.de
*Web Site:* www.gerth.de
*Key Personnel*
Man Dir: Klaus Gerth *E-mail:* gerth@gerth.de
Sales Dir: Rolf Fischer *E-mail:* fischer@gerth.de
Marketing Dir: Stefanie Goemmer *E-mail:* goemmer@gerth.de; Hannes Boehm *E-mail:* boehm@gerth.de
Founded: 1949
Subjects: Biography, Fiction, Nonfiction (General), Religion - Other, Self-Help
ISBN Prefix(es): 3-89437
Number of titles published annually: 90 Print; 5 Audio
Total Titles: 500 Print; 25 Audio

**Verlag fuer Geschichte der Naturwissenschaften und der Technik+**
Schlossstr 1, 49356 Diepholz

*Tel:* (05441) 92 71 29 *Fax:* (05441) 92 71 27
*E-mail:* info@gnt-verlag.de
*Web Site:* www.gnt-verlag.de
*Key Personnel*
Publisher: Reinald Schroeder
Founded: 1990
Specialize in scientific publications.
Subjects: History, History of Science & Technology
ISBN Prefix(es): 3-928186
*Shipping Address:* LKG, Bestellannahme, Potzschauer Weg, 04579 Espenhain
*Warehouse:* LKG, Bestellannahme, Potzschauer Weg, 04579 Espenhain
*Orders to:* LKG Bestellannahme, Poetzschauer Weg, 04579 Espenhain

**Gesellschaft fuer Organisationswissenschaft e V+**
Haus No 18 A, 95490 Mistelgau-Truppach
*Tel:* (09206) 480 *Fax:* (09206) 628
*Key Personnel*
Chairman: Ruediger W Monz
Vice Chairman: Theodor Koenig
Founded: 1956
Spreading of Organization Science according to (& authorized by) the late Dr.techn. Kurt von Wieser, Vienna, by instruction & books. Sell rights of non-English translations.
Subjects: Social Sciences, Sociology
ISBN Prefix(es): 3-926980
Total Titles: 24 Print

**Gesundheits-Dialog Verlag GmbH+**
Gaenslerweg 1, 82041 Oberhaching
Mailing Address: Postfach 1453, 82033 Oberhaching
*Tel:* (089) 6 13 40 24 *Fax:* (089) 6 13 37 87
*E-mail:* dialog.top@t-online.de
*Web Site:* www.gesundheits-dialog.de
*Key Personnel*
Publisher: Franz Woellzenmueller
Subjects: Child Care & Development, Health, Nutrition, Medicine, Nursing, Dentistry, Sports, Athletics
ISBN Prefix(es): 3-929732

**Gieck-Verlag GmbH+**
Nimrodstr 26, 82110 Germering
*Tel:* (089) 8415906 *Fax:* (089) 8403310
*Key Personnel*
Contact: R Gieck
Founded: 1931
Subjects: Engineering (General), Mechanical Engineering
ISBN Prefix(es): 3-920379
*Orders to:* Alfaomega Grupo Editor SA, Pitagoras 1139, Col Del Valle 03100, Mexico
Brockhaus Commission, Postfach 1220, 70806 Kornwestheim
Delta Press, Endseweg 3 NL, 3959 AT Amerongen, Overberg, Netherlands
Dunod, 5, rue Laromiguiere, 75241 Paris Cedex 05, France
McGraw Hill Inc, 1221 Avenue of the Americas, New York, NY 10020, United States

**Verlag Ernst und Werner Gieseking GmbH**
Deckertstr 30, 33617 Bielefeld
Mailing Address: Postfach 13 01 20, 33617 Bielefeld
*Tel:* (0521) 1 46 74 *Fax:* (0521) 14 37 15
*E-mail:* gieseking-verlag@t-online.de
*Web Site:* www.gieseking-verlag.de
*Key Personnel*
Man Dir & Publisher: Dr Klaus Schleicher
Founded: 1937
Subjects: Law, Music, Dance
ISBN Prefix(es): 3-7694
*Orders to:* VVA

**H Gietl Verlag & Publikationsservice GmbH+**
Pfaelzerstr 11, 93128 Regenstauf
Mailing Address: Postfach 166, 93122 Regenstauf
*Tel:* (09402) 93 37-0 *Fax:* (09402) 93 37-24
*Web Site:* www.gietl-verlag.de
*Key Personnel*
Man Dir: Heinrich Gietl *Tel:* (09402) 93 37-15 *E-mail:* heinrich.gietl@gietl-verlag.de; Josef Roidl *Tel:* (09402) 93 37-13 *E-mail:* josef.roidl@gietl-verlag.de
Advertising Manager: Kurt Fischer *Tel:* (09402) 93 37-14 *E-mail:* kurt.fischer@gietl-verlag.de
Special publishing house for numismatic literature.
Subjects: Crafts, Games, Hobbies, History

**Gildefachverlag GmbH & Co KG+**
Foehrster Str 8, 31061 Alfeld
Mailing Address: Postfach 1351, 31043 Alfeld
*Tel:* (05181) 8004-0 *Fax:* (05181) 8004-90
*Key Personnel*
Man Dir: Wilhelm Schlame
Founded: 1949
Specialize in gastronomy & crafts.
Subjects: Cookery, Crafts, Games, Hobbies, Health, Nutrition
ISBN Prefix(es): 3-7734
Imprints: IWT Magazine Publishing House GmbH
Subsidiaries: Gildebuchverlag

**Gilles und Francke Verlag+**
Blumenstr 67-69, 47057 Duisburg
*Tel:* (0203) 362787 *Fax:* (0203) 355520
*E-mail:* verlag@gilles-francke.de
*Web Site:* www.gilles-francke.de
*Key Personnel*
Publisher & Proprietor: Werner Francke
Sales: Barbara Francke
Founded: 1900
Subjects: Fiction, Literature, Literary Criticism, Essays, Poetry
ISBN Prefix(es): 3-921104; 3-925348
Number of titles published annually: 4 Print
Total Titles: 3 Print
*Bookshop(s):* G & F Buch und Zeitschriftenhandlung *E-mail:* buchversand@gilles-francke.de *Web Site:* www.gilles-francke.de

**GLB Parkland Verlags-und Vertriebs GmbH+**
Schanzenstr 33, 51063 Cologne
*Tel:* (0221) 96493-0 *Fax:* (0221) 964933
*Telex:* 721907
*Key Personnel*
Man Dir: Gerd Fiegweil; Heiner Taubert
Founded: 1974
Subjects: Antiques, Architecture & Interior Design, Art, Gardening, Plants, Poetry, Travel
ISBN Prefix(es): 3-88059; 3-89340
*Warehouse:* VSB Verlagsservice Braunschweig GmbH, Georg-Westermann-Allee 66, 38104 Braunschweig, Postfach 4738, 38037 Braunschweig
*Orders to:* VSB Verlagsservice Braunschweig GmbH, Georg-Westermann-Allee 66, 38104 Braunschweig

**Gloatz, Hille GmbH & Co KG fur Mehrfarben und Zellglasdruck**
Ebereschenallee 18, 14050 Berlin
Mailing Address: Postfach 191362, 14003 Berlin
*Tel:* (030) 721 99 12; (030) 723 254 93 *Fax:* (030) 721 95 65
*E-mail:* gloatz.hille.gmbh@gmx.de; info@gloatz-hille.de
*Web Site:* www.gloatz-hille.de *Cable:* GEHACO D
*Key Personnel*
Manager: Hans-Peter Gloatz
Founded: 1936
Subjects: Engineering (General), Geography, Geology, Medicine, Nursing, Dentistry
ISBN Prefix(es): 3-920956

**Verlag Glueckauf GmbH+**
Montebruchstr 2, 45219 Essen
Mailing Address: Postfach 185620, 45206 Essen
*Tel:* (02054) 924120 *Fax:* (02054) 924129
*E-mail:* info@vge.de; vertrieb@vge.de
*Web Site:* www.vge.de
*Key Personnel*
Man Dir, Editorial, Rights & Permissions: Bernd Litke
Founded: 1918
Membership(s): German Society for Geotechnical Engineering (DGGT) & Austrian Society for Geomechanics (OEGG).
Subjects: Earth Sciences, Energy, Environmental Studies
ISBN Prefix(es): 3-7739

**Gmelin Verlag GmbH+**
Erlinger Hohe 9, 82346 Andechs
*Tel:* (08152) 6671 *Fax:* (08152) 5120
*E-mail:* gerd.gmelin@gmelin-verlag.de
*Web Site:* www.gmelin-verlag.de
*Key Personnel*
Owner, Rights & Permissions: Gerd E Gmelin
Founded: 1949
Subjects: Fiction, Health, Nutrition, Literature, Literary Criticism, Essays, Medicine, Nursing, Dentistry, Nonfiction (General), Philosophy, Physical Sciences, Science (General)
ISBN Prefix(es): 3-926253

**Bruno Gmuender Verlag GmbH+**
Kleiststr 23-26, 10787 Berlin
*Tel:* (030) 615003-0 *Fax:* (030) 615003-20
*E-mail:* info@brunogmuender.com
*Web Site:* www.brunogmuender.com
*Key Personnel*
Man Dir: B Gmuender
Founded: 1981
Subjects: Gay & Lesbian
ISBN Prefix(es): 3-86187; 3-924163; 3-9800578
Imprints: Albino Verlag
*Bookshop(s):* Bruno's in Berlin, Nuernbergerstr 53, 10789 Berlin; Bruno's in Cologne, Friesenwall 24, 50672 Cologne
*Distribution Center:* Abt Vertrieb, Wrangelstr 100, 10997 Berlin *Tel:* (030) 61001-100 *Fax:* (030) 6159008 *E-mail:* vertrieb@brunogmuender.com

**GNT-Verlag,** see Verlag fuer Geschichte der Naturwissenschaften und der Technik

**Cornelia Goethe Literaturverlag,** *imprint of* Frankfurter Literaturverlag GmbH

**Cornelia Goethe Literaturverlag** (Cornelia Goethe Publishers)+
Hanauer Landstr 338, 60314 Frankfurt am Main
*Tel:* (069) 40894-0 *Fax:* (069) 40894-169
*E-mail:* literatur@fouque-verlag.de
*Web Site:* www.cornelia-goethe.de; www.fouque-verlag.de
Founded: 1987
Publisher for new authors.
ISBN Prefix(es): 3-8267
Number of titles published annually: 200 Print
Total Titles: 1,000 Print
*Branch Office(s)*
70 Fortune Green Rd, London NW6 1DS, United Kingdom

**Wilhelm Goldmann Verlag GmbH**
Neumarkterstr 28, 81673 Munich
Mailing Address: Postfach 800709, 81607 Munich
*Tel:* (089) 4136-0; (01805) 990505 (hot line)
*Fax:* (089) 43722812
*E-mail:* vertrieb.verlagsgruppe@bertelsmann.de
*Telex:* 529965 wgvmn d

*Key Personnel*
Man Dir: Klaus Eck
Editorial: Dr Georg Reuchlein-Diehl
Publicity: Brigitte Nunner
Founded: 1922
Subjects: Art, Astrology, Occult, Biography, Criminology, Education, Fiction, Film, Video, History, How-to, Law, Medicine, Nursing, Dentistry, Psychology, Psychiatry, Science (General), Science Fiction, Fantasy, Social Sciences, Sociology
ISBN Prefix(es): 3-442
*Parent Company:* Verlagsgruppe Bertelsmann GmbH
*U.S. Office(s):* Bettina Schrewe Literary Scouting, 101 Fifth Ave, Suite 11B, NY 10003, United States (US Scout)
Foreign Rep(s): Angelika Straus-Fischer

**Goldschneck Verlag+**
Industriepark 3, 56291 Wiebelsheim
*Tel:* (06766) 903140 *Fax:* (06766) 903320
*Web Site:* www.goldschneck.de
*Key Personnel*
Owner: Werner Weidert
Founded: 1983
Specialize in paleontology.
Subjects: Geography, Geology, Paleontology
ISBN Prefix(es): 3-926129
Number of titles published annually: 2 Print
Total Titles: 1 Print

**Goll Bruno Verlag fur Aussergewoehnliche Perspektiven (VAP)+**
Postfach 1180, 32352 Preussisch Oldendorf
*Tel:* (05742) 93 04 44 *Fax:* (05742) 93 04 55
*Web Site:* www.vap-buch.de
Founded: 1972
Subjects: Government, Political Science
ISBN Prefix(es): 3-922367
Divisions: Edition ScienTerra; Edition Freie Energie; Edition Life Energie
*Shipping Address:* VAP-Verlagsauslieferung, Postfach 1180, 32352 PreuBisch Oldendorf & Mindenerstr 34, PreuBisch Oldendorf

**Gondrom Verlag GmbH & Co KG+**
Buehlstr 4, 95463 Bindlach
Mailing Address: Postfach 1, 95463 Bindlach
*Tel:* (09208) 51-0 *Fax:* (09208) 51-21
*E-mail:* service@gondrom.de
*Web Site:* www.gondrom.de
*Telex:* 920882
*Key Personnel*
President: Volker Gondrom
Man Dir: Jens Brase
Editorial, Rights & Permissions: Reinhard Fabian
Founded: 1974
Subjects: Art, History, Literature, Literary Criticism, Essays, Nonfiction (General)
ISBN Prefix(es): 3-8112
*Associate Companies:* Loewe Verlag, Buehlstr 4, 95461 Bindlach

**Govi-Verlag Pharmazeutischer Verlag GmbH+**
Carl-Mannich-Str 26, 65760 Eschborn
Mailing Address: Postfach 5360, 65728 Eschborn
*Tel:* (06196) 9 28-2 50 *Fax:* (06196) 9 28-2 59
*E-mail:* service@govi.de
*Web Site:* www.govi.de
*Key Personnel*
Man Dir: Peter J Egenolf *Tel:* (06196) 928 201 *Fax:* (06196) 928 203
Founded: 1949
Subjects: Specialized in Pharmaceuticals & Medicine
ISBN Prefix(es): 3-7741
Total Titles: 140 Print; 20 CD-ROM
*Parent Company:* Bundesvereinigung Deutscher Apothekerverbaende, Ginnheimer Str 26, 65760 Echborn Tannus

*Associate Companies:* Werbe-und Vertriebsgesellschaft Deutscher Apotheker mbH; Zentrallaboratorium Deutscher Apotheker; Marketing-Gesellschaft Deutscher Apotheker mbH
Distributor for WHO World-Health-Organization
*Bookshop(s):* Versandbuchhandlung, 65760 Eschborn Taunus *E-mail:* service@govi.de
*Warehouse:* Industriestr 1, Eschborn
*Returns:* Industriestr 1, 65760 Eschborn

**Grabert-Verlag+**
Am Apfelberg 18, 72076 Tuebingen
Mailing Address: Postfach 1629, 72006 Tuebingen
*Tel:* (07071) 40700 *Fax:* (07071) 407026 *Cable:* GRABERT-TUBINGEN
*Key Personnel*
Man Dir & Owner: Wigbert Grabert
Founded: 1953
Subjects: Art, Biography, History
ISBN Prefix(es): 3-87847
Number of titles published annually: 10 Print
Total Titles: 200 Print
*Book Club(s):* Deutscher Buchkreis

**Graefe und Unzer Verlag GmbH+**
Grillparzerstr 12, 81675 Munich
*Tel:* (089) 4 19 81-0 *Fax:* (089) 4 19 81-113
*E-mail:* leserservice@graefe-und-unzer.de
*Web Site:* www.graefe-und-unzer.de
*Key Personnel*
Publisher & Man Dir: Georg Kessler *Tel:* (089) 41981404 *E-mail:* kessler@graefe-und-unzer.de
Man Dir, Distribution & Sales: Guenter Kopietz *Tel:* (089) 41981307 *E-mail:* kopietz@graefe-und-unzer.de
Man Dir, Finances: Urban Meister *Tel:* (089) 41981300 *E-mail:* meister@graefe-und-unzer.de
Rights Dir: Annette Beetz *Tel:* (089) 41981150 *E-mail:* beetz@graefe-und-unzer.de
Foreign Rights Manager (US, UK, Latin America, Spain & Portugal): Manuela Kerkhoff *Tel:* (089) 41981153 *E-mail:* kerkhoff@graefe-und-unzer.de
Foreign Rights Manager (France, Italy, Eastern EU, Asia): Gabriella Hoffman *Tel:* (089) 41981419 *E-mail:* hoffmann@graefe-und-unzer.de
Foreign Rights Manager (Germany & Northern Europe): Ingrid Puchner *Tel:* (089) 41981412 *E-mail:* puchner@graefe-und-unzer.de
Man Editor GU: Doris Birk *Tel:* (089) 41981409 *E-mail:* birk@graefe-und-unzer.de
Editorial Dir, Cookery: Birgit Rademacker *Tel:* (089) 41981401 *E-mail:* rademacker@graefe-und-unzer.de
Editorial Dir, Gardening: Anne Hahnstein *Tel:* (089) 41981319 *E-mail:* hahnstein@graefe-und-unzer.de
Editorial Dir, Pets: Anita Zellner *Tel:* (089) 41981215 *E-mail:* zellner@graefe-und-unzer.de
Editorial Dir, Health: Ulrich Ehrlenspiel *Tel:* (089) 41981118 *E-mail:* ehrlenspiel@graefe-und-unzer.de
Editorial Dir, Travel: Veronica Reisenegger *Tel:* (089) 41981426 *E-mail:* reisenegger@graefe-und-unzer.de
Editorial Dir, Business: Steffen Haselbach *Tel:* (089) 41981486 *E-mail:* haselbach@graefe-und-unzer.de
Distribution & Sales, Trade: Jan Wiesemann *Tel:* (089) 41981305 *E-mail:* wiesemann@graefe-und-unzer.de
Distribution & Sales, Non-Trade: Erik Vogel *Tel:* (089) 41981302 *E-mail:* vogel@graefe-und-unzer.de
Marketing Dir: Kerstin Moskon *Tel:* (089) 41981205 *E-mail:* moskon@graefe-und-unzer.de
Production Manager: Thomas Narr *Tel:* (089) 41981402 *E-mail:* narr@graefe-und-unzer.de
Founded: 1722

Subjects: Animals, Pets, Business, Cookery, Gardening, Plants, Health, Nutrition, Natural History, Self-Help, Travel
ISBN Prefix(es): 3-7742
Number of titles published annually: 120 Print
Total Titles: 1,050 Print
Imprints: Feinschmecker (Gourmet Cookery); Hallwag (Wine); Merian (Travel Guide Series); Teubner Edition (Cookery)
*Warehouse:* Verlegerdienst Munchen, Gutenbergstr 1, 82205 Gilching

**Graf Editions**
Elisabethstr 29, 80796 Munich
*Tel:* (089) 27 159 57 *Fax:* (089) 27 159 97
*E-mail:* info@graf-editions.de
*Web Site:* www.graf-editions.de
*Key Personnel*
Contact: Dieter Graf
Founded: 1993
Subjects: Language Arts, Linguistics, Travel, Hiking
ISBN Prefix(es): 3-9803130
Total Titles: 4 Print
Distributed by Baseline Book Co (UK); Ennsthaler Verlagsauslieferung (Austria); Fotofolio (USA); Geo Center (Germany); Map Link (USA); Museum of Contemporary Art (Australia); Schweizer Buchzentrum (Switzerland); Willems Adventure (Netherlands)
Foreign Rep(s): Baseline Book Company (UK); Cordee Distributors (UK); Fotofolio (US); Hellenic Distribution Agency (Greece); MapLink (US); Willems Adventure (Netherlands)
*Bookshop(s):* Museum of Contemporary Art Bookstore, 250 S Grand Ave, Los Angeles, CA 90012, United States

**Grafit Verlag GmbH+**
Chemnitzer Str 31, 44139 Dortmund
*Tel:* (0231) 7214650 *Fax:* (0231) 7214677
*E-mail:* info@grafit.de
*Web Site:* www.grafit.de
*Key Personnel*
Man Dir: Dr Rutger Booss
Founded: 1989
Membership(s): Boersenverein des deutschen Buchhandels.
Subjects: Fiction, Mysteries, Modern detective stories, crime fiction
ISBN Prefix(es): 3-89425
Number of titles published annually: 20 Print
Total Titles: 150 Print
*Orders to:* CVK Cornelsen, Postfach 100271, 33502 Bielefeld

**Verlag der Stiftung Gralsbotschaft GmbH+**
Lenzhalde 15, 70192 Stuttgart
*Tel:* (0711) 294355 *Fax:* (07156) 18663
*E-mail:* info@gral.de
*Web Site:* www.gral.de
*Key Personnel*
Man Dir & Editor: Juergen Sprick
Founded: 1928
Subjects: Health, Nutrition, Human Relations, Nonfiction (General), Parapsychology, Philosophy, Religion - Other, Self-Help
ISBN Prefix(es): 3-87860
*U.S. Office(s):* Grail Foundation Press, PO Box 45, Gambier, OH 43022, United States

**Grass-Verlag**
Bleerstr 107, 40789 Monheim
Mailing Address: Postfach 100219, 40766 Monheim
*Tel:* (02173) 51305 *Fax:* (02224) 770515
*Key Personnel*
Publisher: Aloys Grass
Founded: 1984
Subjects: Religion - Protestant
ISBN Prefix(es): 3-924974

**Greuthof Verlag und Vertrieb GmbH+**
Herrenweg 2, 79261 Gutach im Breisgau
*Tel:* (07681) 6025 *Fax:* (07681) 6027
ISBN Prefix(es): 3-923662

**Greven Verlag Koeln GmbH+**
Neue Weyerstr 1-3, 50676 Cologne
Mailing Address: Postfach 101644, 50478 Cologne
*Tel:* (0221) 20 33-161 *Fax:* (0221) 20 33-162
*E-mail:* greven.verlag@greven.de
*Web Site:* www.greven-verlag.de
*Telex:* 8882249 grev d *Cable:* GREVENVERLAG KOLN
*Key Personnel*
Man Dir, Rights & Permissions: Irene Greven
Publishing Managers: Dr Diethelm Schmidt; Manfred vom Stein
Founded: 1827
Subjects: Art, Regional Interests
ISBN Prefix(es): 3-7743

**Grote'sche Verlagsbuchhandlung GmbH & Co KG**
Max-Planckstr 12, 50858 Cologne
Mailing Address: Postfach 400263, 50832 Cologne
*Tel:* (02234) 1060 *Fax:* (02234) 106284
*Cable:* GROTEVERLAG
*Key Personnel*
Publisher: Dr Juergen Gutbrod
Founded: 1661
Subjects: History
ISBN Prefix(es): 3-7745
*Parent Company:* W Kohlhammer GmbH, Hessbruehlstr 69, 70565 Stuttgart
*Warehouse:* Verlagsvertrieb Stuttgart GmbH, 70549 Stuttgart
*Orders to:* W Kohlhammer GmbH, 70549 Stuttgart

**Verlag Grundlagen und Praxis GmbH & Co+**
Bergmannstr 20, 26789 Leer
*Tel:* (0491) 6 18 86 *Fax:* (0491) 36 34
*E-mail:* info@grundlagen-praxis.de
*Web Site:* www.grundlagen-praxis.de
*Key Personnel*
Man Dir, Rights & Permissions: Axel Camici
Founded: 1972
Subjects: Language Arts, Linguistics, Medicine, Nursing, Dentistry
ISBN Prefix(es): 3-921229

**Gruner + Jahr AG & Co**
Am Baumwall 11, 20459 Hamburg
*Tel:* (040) 37030 *Fax:* (040) 37036000
*E-mail:* oeffentlichkeiharbeit@guj.de
*Web Site:* www.guj.de
*Key Personnel*
President & Chief Executive Officer: J Russell Denson
Subjects: Human Relations, Photography
ISBN Prefix(es): 3-570; 3-00

**Gruppe 21 GmbH+**
Landsberger Str 101, 45219 Essen
*Tel:* (02054) 10489-0 *Fax:* (02054) 10489-29
*E-mail:* redaktion@info21.de
*Web Site:* www.gruppe21.de
*Key Personnel*
Manager: Gerhard Klaes
Founded: 1986
Specialize in Database & Electronic Publishing Services.
ISBN Prefix(es): 3-928930
*Parent Company:* Advanstar Communications GmbH & Co KG
*Orders to:* Siehe Zeile 010

**Verlag Gruppenpaedagogischer Literatur+**
Rudolf-Diesel-Str 8, 61273 Wehrheim

Mailing Address: Postfach 1252, 61269 Wehrheim
*Tel:* (06081) 5 67 40 *Fax:* (06081) 5 74 38
*E-mail:* info@vglw.de
*Web Site:* www.vglw.de
Founded: 1976
Membership(s): Boersenverein des deutschen Buchhandels.
Subjects: Career Development, Child Care & Development, Crafts, Games, Hobbies, Education, Music, Dance, Outdoor Recreation, Sports, Athletics
ISBN Prefix(es): 3-921496; 3-89544

**Walter de Gruyter GmbH & Co KG+**
Genthinerstr 13, 10785 Berlin
*Tel:* (030) 260 05-0 *Fax:* (030) 260 05-251
*E-mail:* wdg-info@degruyter.de
*Web Site:* www.degruyter.de *Cable:* WISSENSCHAFT BERLIN 0184027
*Key Personnel*
Man Dir: Reinhold Tokar
Marketing Dir: Dorothea Kern *E-mail:* kern@degruyter.de
Marketing: Paul Osborn
Advertising: Dietlind Makswitat *E-mail:* ad@degruyter.de
Public Relations: Ulrike Lippe *E-mail:* ulrike.lippe@degruyter.com
Sales: Harald Hoffmann
Founded: 1919
Subjects: Archaeology, Biological Sciences, History, Language Arts, Linguistics, Law, Literature, Literary Criticism, Essays, Management, Marketing, Mathematics, Medicine, Nursing, Dentistry, Philosophy, Physical Sciences, Physics, Science (General), Social Sciences, Sociology, Theology
ISBN Prefix(es): 0-202; 3-11
Total Titles: 8,500 Print
Subsidiaries: Aldine de Gruyter; Mouton de Gruyter
*U.S. Office(s):* Walter de Gruyter, Inc, 200 Saw Mill River Rd, Hawthorne, NY 10532, United States *Tel:* 914-747-0110 *Fax:* 914-747-1326

**Arthur L Sellier & Co KG-Walter de Gruyter GmbH & Co KG**, see Dr Arthur L Sellier & Co KG-Walter de Gruyter GmbH & Co KG OHG

**Gunter Olzog Verlag GmbH+**
Fuerstenriederstr 250, 81377 Munich
*Tel:* (089) 71 04 66 60 *Fax:* (089) 71 04 66 61
*E-mail:* olzog.verlag@t-online.de
*Web Site:* www.olzog.de
*Key Personnel*
Publisher: Dr Reinhard Moestl *Tel:* (089) 71 04 66 64 *E-mail:* moestl@olzog.de
Man Dir, Rights & Permissions: Dr Dirk F Passmann
Sales: Stefan Keim *Tel:* (089) 71 04 66 65 *E-mail:* keim@olzog.de
Rights & Permissions: Gerlinde Stanglmeier
Advertising: Martina Gesierich
Publicity: Claudia Franz *E-mail:* franz@olzog.de
Founded: 1949
Membership(s): TR- Verlagsunion GmbH.
Subjects: Economics, Film, Video, Foreign Countries, Government, Political Science, History, Journalism, Management, Marketing, Publishing & Book Trade Reference, Social Sciences, Sociology
ISBN Prefix(es): 3-7892
*Parent Company:* Verlag Moderne Industrie AG

**Guenther Butkus+**
Stapenhorststr 15, 33615 Bielefeld
*Tel:* (0521) 69689 *Fax:* (0521) 174470
*E-mail:* pendragon.verlag@t-online.de
*Web Site:* www.pendragon.de

*Key Personnel*
Publisher: Gunther Butkus
Founded: 1981
Subjects: Art, Fiction, Poetry, Novels, poems & music
ISBN Prefix(es): 3-929096; 3-934872
Total Titles: 250 Print; 20 Audio
Distributed by Prolit

**Verlag Klaus Guhl**
Akazienallee 27A, 14050 Berlin
Mailing Address: Postfach 191532, 14005 Berlin
*Tel:* (030) 3213062 *Fax:* (030) 30823868
*Key Personnel*
Man Dir: Dr Klaus-Dieter Guhl
Editorial: Fabian Carlos Guhl
Sales: Florian Robert Guhl
Production: Hans Paul Guhl
Publicity: Dr Kurt Kreiler
Rights & Permissions: Dr Thomas Bark
Founded: 1974
Subjects: Art, Government, Political Science, Literature, Literary Criticism, Essays
ISBN Prefix(es): 3-88220
Subsidiaries: Buchladen Bunter Baer GmbH; Fanel GmbH
*Bookshop(s):* Bunter Baer-Guhl, Knobelsdorffstr 8, 14059 Berlin

**Verlag des Gustav-Adolf-Werks**
Pistorisstr 6, 04229 Leipzig
Mailing Address: Postfach 310763, 04211 Leipzig
*Tel:* (0341) 490 62 0 *Fax:* (0341) 4770505
*E-mail:* info@gustav-adolf-werk.de
*Web Site:* www.gustav-adolf-werk.de
*Key Personnel*
Publishing Manager: Evelin Hoehne
Founded: 1968
Subjects: Developing Countries, Religion - Protestant, Theology
ISBN Prefix(es): 3-87593

**Gutenberg-Gesellschaft eV** (Gutenberg Society)
Liebfrauenplatz 5, 55116 Mainz
*Tel:* (06131) 22 64 20 *Fax:* (06131) 23 35 30
*E-mail:* gutenberg-gesellschaft@freenet.de
*Web Site:* www.gutenberg-gesellschaft.uni-mainz. de
*Key Personnel*
President: Jens Beutel
Vice President: Hannetraud Schultheiss
Editor-in-Chief: Dr Stephan Fuessel
Secretary General: Dr Cornelia Fischer
Founded: 1900
International association for past & present history of the art of printing & of the book.
Subjects: Publishing & Book Trade Reference
ISBN Prefix(es): 3-7755
Number of titles published annually: 1 Print
Distributed by Otto Harrassowitz (Yearbook only)

**Gutersloher Verlaghaus GmbH /Chr Kaiser/Kiefel/Quell+**
Carl-Miele-Str 214, 33311 Guetersloh
*Tel:* (05241) 74050 *Fax:* (05241) 740548
*E-mail:* info@gtvh.de
*Web Site:* www.gtvh.de
*Telex:* 933868 bert d
*Key Personnel*
Man Dir, Rights & Permissions: Hans Juergen Meurer
International Rights Contact: Heike Daut-Ruenger
Founded: 1845
Subjects: Religion - Other, Theology
ISBN Prefix(es): 3-579; 3-7811

**H B Verlags und Vertriebs-Gesellschaft mbH**
Marco-Polo-Str 1, 73760 Ostfildern
*Tel:* (040) 4151-04 *Fax:* (040) 41513231
*Key Personnel*
Dir: Kurt Bortz; Dr Joachim Dreyer; Eike Schmidt

Founded: 1979
ISBN Prefix(es): 3-616; 3-922822

**H L Schlapp Buch- und Antiquariatshandlung GmbH und Co KG Abt Verlag**
Ludwigsplatz 3, 64283 Darmstadt
*Tel:* (06151) 17 90-0 *Fax:* (06151) 17 90 40
*E-mail:* darmstadt@schlapp.de
*Web Site:* www.schlapp.de
*Key Personnel*
Owner: Karl-Eugen Schlapp; Eckart Schlapp
Founded: 1836
Subjects: Regional Interests
ISBN Prefix(es): 3-87704

**Verlag H M Hauschild GmbH**
Hans-Bredow-Str 7, 28307 Bremen
Mailing Address: Postfach 45 02 35, 28296 Bremen
*Tel:* (0421) 1785-0 *Fax:* (0421) 1785-285
*E-mail:* info@hauschild-werbedruck.de
*Web Site:* www.hauschild.werbedruck.de
*Key Personnel*
Man Dir: Hartmut Schneider; Ingo Steinmeyer
Rights & Permissions: Ernst-August Echtermann
Founded: 1854
Subjects: Art, Regional Interests
ISBN Prefix(es): 3-920699; 3-926598; 3-929902; 3-89757; 3-931785
*Parent Company:* Werbedruck Bremen Grafischer Betrieb GmbH

**Haack,** *imprint of* Justus Perthes Verlag Gotha GmbH

**Haag und Herchen Verlag GmbH+**
Fichardstr 30, 60322 Frankfurt am Main
*Tel:* (069) 550911-13 *Fax:* (069) 552601; (069) 554922
*E-mail:* verlag@haagundherchen.de
*Web Site:* www.haagundherchen.de
*Key Personnel*
Man Dir, Rights & Permissions: Hans-Alfred Herchen
Founded: 1975
Subjects: Engineering (General), Government, Political Science, How-to, Medicine, Nursing, Dentistry, Psychology, Psychiatry, Science (General), Social Sciences, Sociology
ISBN Prefix(es): 3-88129; 3-86137; 3-89228; 3-89846

**C W Haarfeld GmbH & Co**
Annastr 32-36, 45130 Essen
Mailing Address: Postfach 101562, 45015 Essen
*Tel:* (0201) 720950 *Fax:* (0201) 7209533
*Key Personnel*
Man Dir: Wolfgang Otto
Founded: 1867
ISBN Prefix(es): 3-7747
*Parent Company:* Wolters Kluwer NV, Netherlands

**Wolfgang G Haas - Musikverlag Koeln ek+**
Rheinbergstr 92, 51143 Cologne
*Tel:* (02203) 98 88 3-0 *Fax:* (02203) 98 88 3-50
*E-mail:* info@haas-koeln.de
*Web Site:* www.haas-koeln.de
*Key Personnel*
Contact: Wolfgang G Haas
Founded: 1985
Membership(s): International Trumpet Guild & German Society of Music Publishers.
Subjects: Music, Dance
ISBN Prefix(es): 3-928453

**Dr Rudolf Habelt GmbH**
Am Buchenhang 1, 53115 Bonn
Mailing Address: Postfach 150104, 53040 Bonn
*Tel:* (0228) 9 23 83-22 *Fax:* (0228) 9 23 83-23

*E-mail:* info@habelt.de *Web Site:* www.habelt. de
*Tel:* (0228) 9 23 83-0 *Fax:* (0228) 9 23 83-6
*E-mail:* info@habelt.de
*Web Site:* www.habelt.de
*Key Personnel*
Man Dir: Wolfgang Habelt
Editorial, Production: Dr Susanne Biegert
Founded: 1954
Subjects: Archaeology, History, Regional Interests
ISBN Prefix(es): 3-7749
Number of titles published annually: 30 Print
*Bookshop(s):* Antiquarian Bookshop, Am Buchenhang 1, 53115 Bonn, Contact: Wolfgang Habelt
*Tel:* (0228) 9 23 83-33 *Fax:* (0228) 9 23 83-6

**Hachmeister Verlag+**
Klosterstr 12, 48143 Munster
*Tel:* (0251) 51210 *Fax:* (0251) 57217
*E-mail:* hachmeister.galerie@t-online.de
*Web Site:* www.hachmeister-galerie.de
*Key Personnel*
Dir: Dr Heiner Hachmeister
Founded: 1979
Catalogues & books.
Subjects: Art
ISBN Prefix(es): 3-88829
Number of titles published annually: 2 Print
Total Titles: 35 Print
*Parent Company:* Hachmeister Galerie

**Walter Haedecke Verlag+**
Lukas-Moser-Weg 2, 71263 Weil der Stadt
Mailing Address: Postfach 1203, 71256 Weil der Stadt
*Tel:* (07033) 138080 *Fax:* (07033) 1380813
*E-mail:* haedecke_vlg@t-online.de
*Key Personnel*
Owner & Publisher: Joachim Graff
Founded: 1919
Subjects: Cookery, Health, Nutrition, Self-Help, Wine & Spirits
ISBN Prefix(es): 3-7750
Number of titles published annually: 16 Print
Total Titles: 112 Print
Distributor for NaturaViva Verlags GmbH

**Dr Curt Haefner-Verlag GmbH+**
Bachstr 14-16, 69121 Heidelberg
Mailing Address: Postfach 106060, 69050 Heidelberg
*Tel:* (06221) 6446-0 *Fax:* (06221) 6446-40
*E-mail:* info@haefner-verlag.de
*Web Site:* www.haefner-verlag.de
*Key Personnel*
President: Dieter Neumann *E-mail:* d.eumann@ haefner-verlag.de
Founded: 1956
Medicine, Nursing & Social Sciences.
Subjects: Business, Child Care & Development, Education, Health, Nutrition, Human Relations, Medicine, Nursing, Dentistry, Public Administration, Science (General), Social Sciences, Sociology, Safety on Work & Occupational Health
ISBN Prefix(es): 3-87284
Total Titles: 22 Print
Subsidiaries: Werkschriften Verlag GmbH

**Haenssler Verlag GmbH+**
Max-Eyth-Str 41, 71088 Holzgerlingen
*Tel:* (07031) 7414-177 *Fax:* (07031) 7414-119
*E-mail:* info@haenssler.de
*Web Site:* www.haenssler.de
*Key Personnel*
Publisher: Joachim Beyer
Founded: 1919
Membership(s): the Telos Group.
Publishes all publications of the American Institute of Musicology.
Subjects: Art, Film, Video, Literature, Literary Criticism, Essays, Music, Dance, Religion - Other

ISBN Prefix(es): 3-7751
Bookshop(s): Hanssler Verlag-Buchhandlung

**Heinz-Jurgen Hausser+**
Frankfurterstr 64, 64293 Darmstadt
Tel: (06151) 22824 Fax: (06151) 26854
Founded: 1989
Subjects: Architecture & Interior Design, Art, Literature, Literary Criticism, Essays
ISBN Prefix(es): 3-927902; 3-89552
Orders to: Lamuv, Nikolaikirchhof 7, 37073
Goettingen

**Lehrmittelverlag Wilhelm Hagemann GmbH+**
Karlstr 20, 40210 Duesseldorf
Mailing Address: Postfach 103545, 40026 Duesseldorf
Tel: (0211) 17 92 70-0 Fax: (0211) 17 92 70-70
E-mail: aktuell@hagemann.de
Web Site: www.hagemann.de Cable:
HAGEMANNVERLAG DUSSELDORF
Key Personnel
General Manager: Maria Schuette-Hagemann
Sales: Walter Kils-Huetten
Founded: 1929
Membership(s): VGS (Verlagsgesellschaft mbH & Co KG); Association of School Book Publishers; German Didactic Associations; Worlddidac.
Subjects: Biological Sciences, Environmental Studies, Health, Nutrition, Physical Sciences
ISBN Prefix(es): 3-544
Subsidiaries: Hagemann & Partner; Bildungsmedien Verlagsges mbH
Warehouse: Karlstr 16, 40210 Duesseldorf

**Hahner Verlagsgesellschaft mbH+**
Heidchenberg 11, 52076 Aachen-Hahn
Tel: (02408) 55 05 Fax: (02408) 58081
E-mail: office@hvg.de
Key Personnel
Manager: Peter Brand
Founded: 1986
Subjects: Science (General)
ISBN Prefix(es): 3-89294
Parent Company: IZOP-Institut zur Objektivierung von Lern-und Pruefungsverfahren GmbH

**Mary Hahn's Kochbuchverlag+**
Subsidiary of Buchverlage Langen-Mueller/Herbig
Thomas-Wimmer-Ring 11, 80539 Munich
Tel: (089) 2 90 88-0
E-mail: l.eggs@herbig.net
Web Site: www.herbig.net
Key Personnel
Sales, Publicity Manager: Eva Ohser E-mail: e.ohser@herbig.net
Subjects: Cookery, House & Home
ISBN Prefix(es): 3-87287
Orders to: VVA, An der Autobahn, 33310
Guetersloh

**Hahnsche Buchhandlung+**
Leinstr 32, 30159 Hannover
Mailing Address: Postfach 2460, 30024 Hannover
Tel: (0511) 80 71 80 40 Fax: (0511) 36 36 98
E-mail: verlag@hahnsche-buchhandlung.de
Web Site: www.hahnsche-buchhandlung.de
Key Personnel
Manager, Rights & Permissions: Dr Horst Zimmerhackl
Founded: 1792
Specialize in German history.
Membership(s): Stock Exchange of German Booksellers; Association of German Magazine Publishers.
Subjects: Education, History, Regional Interests
ISBN Prefix(es): 3-7752
Bookshop(s): Abt Verlag

**Herbert von Halem Verlag**
Lindenstr 19, 50674 Cologne
Tel: (0221) 92 58 29 0 Fax: (0221) 92 58 29 29
E-mail: info@halem-verlag.de
Web Site: www.halem-verlag.de; www.inpunkto.de
Key Personnel
Contact: Herbert von Halem
Subjects: Communications, Journalism, Library & Information Sciences, Philosophy, Radio, TV, Social Sciences, Sociology, Cultural Studies, Political Science
ISBN Prefix(es): 3-931606
Number of titles published annually: 25 Print
Total Titles: 54 Print

**Hallwag**, imprint of Graefe und Unzer Verlag GmbH

**Hamburger Lesehefte Verlag Iselt & Co Nfl mbH+**
Subsidiary of Husum Druck- und Verlagsgesellschaft mbH & Co KG
Nordbahnhofstr 2, 25813 Husum
Mailing Address: Postfach 1480, 25804 Husum
Tel: (04841) 8352-0 Fax: (04841) 8352-10
E-mail: verlagsgruppe.husum@t-online.de
Web Site: www.verlagsgruppe.de
Key Personnel
Man Dir, Editorial, Rights & Permissions: Ingwert Paulsen
Founded: 1953
ISBN Prefix(es): 3-87291
Associate Companies: Hansa Verlag Ingwert Paulsen Jr; Matthiesen Verlag Ingwert Paulsen Jr; Verlag der Nation

**Liselotte Hamecher**
Goethestr 18, 34119 Kassel
Tel: (0561) 16611 Fax: (0561) 775262
Key Personnel
Owner: Liselotte Hamecher
Founded: 1947
Subjects: History, Maritime, Military Science
ISBN Prefix(es): 3-920307
Shipping Address: Goethestr 74, 34119 Kassel
Warehouse: Goethestr 74, 34119 Kassel

**Alfred Hammer+**
EJARM Publishing House, Curtigasse 4, 64823
Gross-Umstadt
Tel: (06078) 71622 Fax: (06078) 71655
Key Personnel
Man Dir: Freddy Hammer
Founded: 1996
Subjects: Aeronautics, Aviation, Law, Management, European Joint Aviation Requirements
ISBN Prefix(es): 3-9805586

**Peter Hammer Verlag GmbH+**
Foehrenstr 33-35, 42283 Wuppertal
Mailing Address: Postfach 200963, 42209 Wuppertal
Tel: (0202) 505066; (0202) 505067 Fax: (0202) 509252
E-mail: info@peter-hammer-verlag.de
Web Site: www.peter-hammer-verlag.de
Key Personnel
Dir: Hermann Schulz
International Rights: Monika Bilstein
Advertising, Press: Dr Claudia Putz
Founded: 1966
Subjects: Developing Countries, Foreign Countries, Literature, Literary Criticism, Essays
ISBN Prefix(es): 3-87294; 3-7795
Associate Companies: Jugenddienst Verlag, Foehrenstr 33-35, 42283 Wuppertal
Distributed by Prolit Verlagsauslieferung GmbH

**Hammonia-Verlag GmbH Fachverlag der Wohnungswirtschaft+**
Tangstedter Landstr 83, 22415 Hamburg
Mailing Address: Postfach 620228, 22402 Hamburg
Tel: (040) 520103-0 Fax: (040) 520103-30
E-mail: info@hammonia.de
Web Site: www.hvh.de
Key Personnel
Man Dir, Publisher & International Rights: Guenther Hegemann
Sales Manager: Rolf Roemer Tel: (040) 520103-35 E-mail: rolf.roemer@hammonia.de
Founded: 1946
Subjects: House & Home
ISBN Prefix(es): 3-87292

**Verlag Handwerk und Technik GmbH+**
Lademannbogen 135, 22339 Hamburg
Mailing Address: Postfach 630500, 22331 Hamburg
Tel: (040) 5 38 08-0 Fax: (040) 5 38 08-101
E-mail: info@handwerk-technik.de
Web Site: www.handwerk-technik-shop.de
Key Personnel
Dir, Rights & Permissions: Johann Carl Buechner
Dir: Oskar Kummer
Founded: 1949
Subjects: Career Development, Education, Labor, Industrial Relations
ISBN Prefix(es): 3-582
Subsidiaries: Holland & Josenhans Gmbh & Co
Showroom(s): Informationsbuero Leipzig mit Verlagsausstellung, August- Bebel-Str 65, 04275 Leipzig; Informationsbuero Stuttgart mit Verlagsausstellung, Feuerseeplatz 2, 70176 Stuttgart
Orders to: Techn Fachbuch - Vertrieb AG M Studer, Spitalstr 12, Postfach 119, 2501 Biel, Switzerland Tel: (032) 322 61 41 Fax: (032) 322 61 30 E-mail: info@tfv.ch (Switzerland)
Veritas - Verlags und Handelsgessellschaft mbH & Co OHG, Hafenstra 1-3, 4010 Linz, Austria Tel: (0732) 776451-280 Fax: (0732) 776451-239 E-mail: veritas@veritas.at Web Site: www.veritas.at (Austria)

**Hanfstaengl-Verlag**, imprint of Daco Verlag Guenter Blase oHG

**Edition Hannemann**, imprint of Verlag Stephanie Naglschmid

**Hannibal-Verlag+**
Lochhamerstr 9, 82152 Planegg
Tel: (089) 24 245 415 Fax: (089) 24 245 294
E-mail: info@hannibal-verlag.de
Web Site: www.hannibal-verlag.de
Key Personnel
Man Dir & Publisher: Francoise Degrave E-mail: francoise.degrave@kochbooks.com
Founded: 1986
Subjects: Literature, Literary Criticism, Essays, Musical Biographies
ISBN Prefix(es): 3-85445
Number of titles published annually: 12 Print
Total Titles: 240 Print
Parent Company: Verlagsgruppe Koch, Gewerbegebiet, 6600 Hoefen/Tirol, Austria
Warehouse: b & i buch und information ag, Centralweg 16, 8910 Affoltern, Switzerland
Prolit Verlagsauslieferung, Siemensstr 16, 35463 Fernwald-Annerod

**Hansa Verlag Ingwert Paulsen Jr**
Nordbahnhofstr 2, 25813 Husum
Mailing Address: Postfach 1480, 25804 Husum
Tel: (04841) 8352-0 Fax: (04841) 8352-10
E-mail: verlagsgruppe.husum@t-online.de
Web Site: www.verlagsgruppe.de

*Key Personnel*
International Rights: J Paulsen
Founded: 1954
Subjects: Literature, Literary Criticism, Essays
ISBN Prefix(es): 3-920421
*Parent Company:* Husum Druck-und Verlagsgesellschaft
*Associate Companies:* Hamburger Lesehefte Verlag Nachf Iselt & Co Nfl mbH; Husum Druck- und Verlagsgesellschaft mbH & Co KG; Matthiesen Verlag Ingwert Paulsen Jr; Verlag der Nation

**Carl Hanser Verlag+**
Kolbergerstr 22, 81679 Munich
*Tel:* (089) 9 98 30 0 *Fax:* (089) 98 48 09
*E-mail:* info@hanser.de
*Web Site:* www.hanser.de/verlag
*Key Personnel*
Man Dir & Publisher, Fiction & Non-Fiction: Michael Krueger *E-mail:* krueger@hanser.de
Man Dir & Publisher, Technical & Science: Wolfgang Beisler *E-mail:* beisler@hanser.de
Publishing Dir, Professional Books: Dr Hermann Riedel *E-mail:* riedel@hanser.de
Publishing Dir, Professional Magazines: Michael Himmelstoss *E-mail:* himmelstoss@hanser.de
Man Dir, Financial: Stephan D Joss *E-mail:* joss@hanser.de
Sales Dir, Fiction & Nonfiction: Felicitas Feilhauer *E-mail:* feilhauer@hanser.de
Sales Dir, Technical & Science: Barbara Kothe *E-mail:* kothe@hanser.de
Advertising Dir, Technical & Science: Guenter Scheffel *E-mail:* scheffel@hanser.de
Publicity, Fiction & Nonfiction: Christina Knecht *E-mail:* knecht@hanser.de
Foreign Rights, Fiction & Nonfiction: Susanne Bauknecht *E-mail:* bauknecht@hanser.de
Foreign Rights, Technical & Science: Evelyn Waizenegger
Founded: 1928
Subjects: Computer Science, Economics, Electronics, Electrical Engineering, Engineering (General), Environmental Studies, Fiction, Management, Mathematics, Mechanical Engineering, Microcomputers, Nonfiction (General), Philosophy, Physics, Poetry, Plastics
ISBN Prefix(es): 3-446
Imprints: Zsolnay
*U.S. Office(s):* Hanser Publishers, 6915 Valley Ave, Cincinnati, OH 45244, United States
Hanser/Gardner Publishers Inc, 6915 Valley Ave, Cincinnati, OH 45244, United States

**Happy Mental Buch- und Musik Verlag**
Am Hoehenberg 21, 82327 Tutzing
*Tel:* (08158) 993303 *Fax:* (08158) 993305
Subjects: Health, Nutrition, Music, Dance, Religion - Buddhist, Religion - Hindu
ISBN Prefix(es): 3-9805692
*Book Club(s):* Bertelsmann; Weltbild

**Hardt und Worner Marketing fur das Buch+**
Saalburgstr 20, 61381 Friedrichsdorf
*Tel:* (06172) 7005 *Fax:* (01672) 71547
*E-mail:* hardt.woerner@t-online.de
Founded: 1993
Subjects: Publishing & Book Trade Reference
ISBN Prefix(es): 3-930120
Total Titles: 12 Print
Distributor for Blueprint (Germany)
*Distribution Center:* LKG, Potsahower Weg, 04579 Espenhain *Tel:* (0206) 165-121 *Fax:* (0206) 65-110
*Orders to:* LKG, Potsahower Weg, 04579 Espenhain

**Harenberg Kommunikation Verlags- und Medien-GmbH & Co KG+**
Koenigswall 21, 44137 Dortmund
*Tel:* (0231) 9056-0 *Fax:* (0231) 9056-110
*E-mail:* post@harenberg.de

*Web Site:* www.harenberg.de
*Key Personnel*
Man Dir: Bodo Harenberg; Sven Merten
Founded: 1973
Subjects: Architecture & Interior Design, Art, History, Music, Dance, Travel
ISBN Prefix(es): 3-88379; 3-611; 3-921846

**Siegfried Haring Literatten-Verlag Ulm+**
Weichselstr 21, 89231 Neu-Ulm
*Tel:* (0731) 9806040 *Fax:* (0731) 9806042
*E-mail:* ratart.edition@t-online.de
*Key Personnel*
Man Dir: Siegfried Haering
Founded: 1986
Subjects: Drama, Theater
ISBN Prefix(es): 3-926217

**Harmonie Verlag** (Harmony Publications)
Gunterstalstr 12, 79100 Freiburg
*Tel:* (0761) 709667 *Fax:* (0761) 709662
*E-mail:* harmonieverlag@aol.com
*Key Personnel*
Dir: Regina Gaus
Subjects: Religion - Other
ISBN Prefix(es): 3-929474

**Harrassowitz Verlag+**
Taunusstr 14, 65183 Wiesbaden
*Tel:* (0611) 530-0 *Fax:* (0611) 530-560 (orders)
*E-mail:* service@harrassowitz.de
*Web Site:* www.harrassowitz.de *Cable:* HARRASSOWITZ VERLAG WIESBADEN
*Key Personnel*
Man Dir & International Rights: Dr Knut Dorn
Man Dir: Ruth Becker-Scheicher; Friedmann Weigel
Founded: 1872
Specialize in Slavic studies & Eastern European research.
Subjects: Asian Studies, Language Arts, Linguistics, Library & Information Sciences, Linguistics, Eastern European Research, Civic Studies
ISBN Prefix(es): 3-447; 3-8086
Total Titles: 2,600 Print

**Harth Musik Verlag-Pro musica Verlag GmbH**
Frankenforsterstr 40, 51427 Bergisch Gladbach
*Tel:* (02204) 2003-0 *Fax:* (02204) 2003-33 *Cable:* Musica Leipzig
*Key Personnel*
Manager: Rita Preiss
Founded: 1946
Subjects: Music, Dance
ISBN Prefix(es): 3-7334

**Litteraturverlag Karlheinz Hartmann**
Schneckenhofstr 17-19, 60596 Frankfurt am Main
*Tel:* (069) 60 32 52 02 *Fax:* (069) 60 32 52 01
*E-mail:* litteraturverlag@web.de
*Key Personnel*
Man Dir: M A Karlheinz Hartmann
Founded: 1976
Subjects: Film, Video, Literature, Literary Criticism, Essays, Poetry
ISBN Prefix(es): 3-87293

**Haschemi Edition Cologne Kunstverlag fuer Fotografie+**
Mechternstr 44, 50823 Cologne
*Tel:* (0221) 561007; (0221) 561008 *Fax:* (0221) 529282
*E-mail:* info@haschemi.de
*Web Site:* www.haschemi.de
*Key Personnel*
International Rights: Baback Haschemi
Founded: 1983
Subjects: Photography, Travel
ISBN Prefix(es): 3-924169; 3-931282; 3-936222
Subsidiaries: Haschemi Edition Virginia

**von Hase & Koehler Verlag KG+**
Bahnhofstr 4-6, 55116 Mainz
Mailing Address: Postfach 2269, 55012 Mainz
*Tel:* (06131) 232334 *Fax:* (06131) 227952
*Key Personnel*
Publisher, Rights & Permissions: Volker Hansen
Founded: 1964
Subjects: Biography, Communications, Education, Finance, Literature, Literary Criticism, Essays, Poetry, Radio, TV
ISBN Prefix(es): 3-7758; 3-920324
Subsidiaries: Niederlassung Munchen

**Hatje Cantz Verlag** (Hatje Cantz Publishers)+
Senefelderstr 12, 73760 Ostfildern
Mailing Address: PO Box 4259, 73745 Ostfildern
*Tel:* (0711) 44 05-0 *Fax:* (0711) 44 05-220
*E-mail:* contact@hatjecantz.de
*Web Site:* www.hatjecantz.de
*Key Personnel*
Senior Publisher: Gerd Hatje *Tel:* (0711) 44 05-200
Man Dir & Publisher: Annette Kulenkampff *Tel:* (0711) 44 05-200
International Sales Dir & Foreign Rights: Markus Hartmann *Tel:* (0711) 44 05-203 *E-mail:* m.hartmann@hatjecantz.de
International Sales Manager & Foreign Rights: Evelin Georgi *Tel:* (0711) 44 05-218 *E-mail:* e.georgi@hatjecantz.de
Promotion: Stefanie Gommel *Tel:* (0711) 44 05-208 *E-mail:* s.gommel@hatjecantz.de; Martina Reitz *Tel:* (0711) 44 05-213 *E-mail:* m.reitz@hatjecantz.de
Press: Meike Gatermann *Tel:* (0711) 6 57 32 95 *Fax:* (0711) 65 02 12 *E-mail:* presse@hatjecantz.de
Founded: 1945
Publisher of art books, books on architecture, design & photography, exhibition catalogues.
Subjects: Architecture & Interior Design, Art, Photography
ISBN Prefix(es): 3-7757
Number of titles published annually: 150 Print
Total Titles: 1,000 Print
*Parent Company:* Dr Cantz'sche Druckerei
*Associate Companies:* belser kunst quartal *Tel:* (0711) 4405226; (0711) 4405227 *Fax:* (0711) 4405228 *E-mail:* belser@hatjecantz.de
*Warehouse:* Koch, Neff & Oetinger
*Orders to:* Koch, Neff & Oetinger, Schockenriedstr 39, 70565 Stuttgart *Tel:* (0711) 78992031 *Fax:* (0711) 78991010
*Returns:* Koch, Neff & Oetinger

**Haude und Spenersche Verlagsbuchhandlung+**
Gneisenaustr 33, 10961 Berlin
Mailing Address: Postfach 610494, 10928 Berlin
*Tel:* (030) 6917073 *Fax:* (030) 6914067
*Cable:* HAUDE
*Key Personnel*
Owner, Manager, Rights & Permissions: Volker Spiess
Founded: 1614
Subjects: History, Nonfiction (General), Regional Interests, Religion - Jewish, Travel
ISBN Prefix(es): 3-7759
*Associate Companies:* Arani-Verlag GmbH; Wissenschaftsverlag Volker Spiess
*Orders to:* VAH-Jager Verlagsauslieferungen, Miraustr 54, 13509 Berlin

**Haufe Mediengruppe,** see Rudolf Haufe Verlag GmbH & Co KG

**Rudolf Haufe Verlag GmbH & Co KG+**
Hindenburgstr 64, 79102 Freiburg
Mailing Address: Postfach 740, 79007 Freiburg
*Tel:* (0761) 3683-0 *Fax:* (0761) 3683-195
*E-mail:* online@haufe.de
*Web Site:* www.haufe.de *Cable:* HAUFEVERLAG

*Key Personnel*
Man Dir: Helmuth Hopfner; Martin Laqua; Uwe
  Renald Mueller
Founded: 1934
Subjects: Accounting, Business, Computer Sci-
  ence, Economics, Finance, Law, Management,
  Marketing, Real Estate
ISBN Prefix(es): 3-448
Subsidiaries: Lexware Gesellschaft fur Softwa-
  reentwicklung der rechts- und steuerberatenden
  Berufe mbH; WRS Verlag Wirtschaft, Recht
  und Steuern GmbH & Co
*Branch Office(s)*
Haufe Berlin, Albrechtstr 146, 10117 Berlin


**Haug**, *imprint of* Georg Thieme Verlag KG


**Dr Ernst Hauswedell & Co+**
Haldenstr 30, 70376 Stuttgart
Mailing Address: Postfach 140155, 70071
  Stuttgart
*Tel:* (0711) 54 99 71-0; (0711) 54 99 71-11
  *Fax:* (0711) 54 99 71-21
*E-mail:* verlag@hiersemann.de
*Web Site:* www.hauswedell.de
*Key Personnel*
President: Charles Gerd Hiersemann
Founded: 1927
Subjects: Antiques, Art, Library & Information
  Sciences, Publishing & Book Trade Reference,
  Science (General), Literature, Typography
ISBN Prefix(es): 3-7762
Number of titles published annually: 10 Print
Total Titles: 200 Print; 8 CD-ROM
*Associate Companies:* Anton Hiersemann KG
  - Verlag, Haldenstr 30, D - 70376 Stuttgart
  *E-mail:* verlag@hiersemann.de *Web Site:* www.
  hiersenmann.de
Distributor for Staats-und Universitaets-Bibliothek
  Hamburg
*Book Club(s):* Maximilian Gesellschaft Hamburg


**Hayit Reisefuhrer in der Rutsker Verlag
  GmbH+**
c/o Mundo Media GmbH, Schreberstr 2, 51105
  Cologne
*Tel:* (0221) 921635-0 *Fax:* (0221) 921635-24
*E-mail:* kontakt@hayit.com
*Web Site:* www.hayit.com
*Key Personnel*
Man Dir, Publicity, Rights & Permissions &
  Sales: Ertay Hayit *E-mail:* ertay.hayit@hayit.
  com
Editorial: Cornelia Auschra *Tel:* (0221) 921635-
  13 *E-mail:* cornelia.auschra@hayit.com; Mike
  Gahn *E-mail:* mike@hayit.com, Ute Hayit
  *Tel:* (0221) 921635-11 *E-mail:* ute.hayit@hayit.
  com
Founded: 1988
Subjects: Travel
ISBN Prefix(es): 3-89607; 3-88676; 3-89210; 3-
  922145; 3-925727
*Associate Companies:* Adl Hayit, Amsterdam,
  Netherlands
*U.S. Office(s):* County Route 9, PO Box 357,
  Chatham, NY 12037, United States *Tel:* 518-
  392-4526 *Fax:* 518-392-4557
Hayit Publishing USA Inc, c/o Pratley Interna-
  tional, 30 East 81 St, New York, NY 10028,
  United States *Tel:* 212-772-2267 *Fax:* 212-772-
  3692 (Telex: 277258)


**Heckners Verlag**
Harzstr 22/23, 38300 Wolfenbuettel
Mailing Address: Postfach 1559, 38285 Wolfen-
  buettel
*Tel:* (05331) 8008-0 *Fax:* (05331) 8008-58
*Key Personnel*
Dir, Rights & Permissions: Siegfried Mathea
Founded: 1895
Subjects: Career Development, Economics
ISBN Prefix(es): 3-449

*Parent Company:* Kieser Verlag GmbH, Neusaess
Distributed by Orell Fuessli (Switzerland)


**Heel Verlag GmbH+**
Gut Pottscheidt, 53639 Koenigswinter
*Tel:* (02223) 9230-0 *Fax:* (02223) 9230-13;
  (02223) 9230-26
*Web Site:* www.heel-verlag.de
*Key Personnel*
President: Franz-Christoph Heel
Foreign Rights Dir: Karin Michelberger
  *Tel:* (02223) 9230-46 *E-mail:* k.michelberger@
  heel-verlag.de
Founded: 1980
Subjects: Aeronautics, Aviation, Automotive,
  Cookery, Crafts, Games, Hobbies, Film, Video,
  Gardening, Plants, Humor, Maritime, Music,
  Dance, Nonfiction (General), Outdoor Recre-
  ation, Photography, Science Fiction, Fantasy,
  Sports, Athletics, Transportation, Travel
ISBN Prefix(es): 3-922858; 3-89365; 3-89880
Number of titles published annually: 120 Print
Total Titles: 600 Print
Distributor for Edition Anderweit; Bear Family
  Records; Highlights Verlag
*Shipping Address:* VSB Lager/Wareneingang,
  Helmstedter Str 99, 38126 Braunschweig
*Warehouse:* VSB Verlagsservice, Georg-
  Westermann-Allee 66, 38104 Braunschweig,
  Contact: Herr Wandert *Tel:* (0531) 708650
  *Fax:* (0531) 708608


**Joh Heider Verlag GmbH**
Paffratherstr 102-116, 51465 Bergisch Gladbach
*Tel:* (02202) 95 40-35 *Fax:* (02202) 2 15 31
*E-mail:* anzeigen@marburger-bund.de
*Web Site:* www.heider-verlag.de/mb/mediadaten/
*Key Personnel*
Man Dir: Hans Heider
Publisher: Dr Dieter Boeck; Dr Dieter Mitrenga
Editorial: Anna von Borstell; Barbara Huen-
  nighausen; Dr Lutz Retzlaff; Angelika Steimer-
  Schmid
Founded: 1889
Subjects: Economics, Law, Social Sciences, Soci-
  ology
ISBN Prefix(es): 3-87314
*Sales Office(s):* Burgstr 122, 51427 Ber-
  gisch Gladbach, Contact: Christine Kaffka
  *Tel:* (02204) 96 18 18 *Fax:* (02204) 96 29 50


**Heigl Verlag, Horst Edition+**
Oberhaslach 6, 88633 Heiligenberg
*Tel:* (07554) 283 *Fax:* (07552) 938756
*E-mail:* info@heigl-verlag.de
*Web Site:* www.heigl-verlag.de
*Key Personnel*
Manager: Horst Heigl
Author: Horst Lozynski
Founded: 1987
Subjects: Art, Astrology, Occult, Physical Sci-
  ences, Religion - Other
ISBN Prefix(es): 3-89316


**Verlag Otto Heinevetter Lehrmittel GmbH**
Papenstr 41, 22089 Hamburg
*Tel:* (040) 25 90 19 *Fax:* (040) 251 2128
*E-mail:* info@heinevetter-verlag.de
*Web Site:* www.heinevetter-verlag.de
*Key Personnel*
Manager: Werner Klopfer
Founded: 1947
ISBN Prefix(es): 3-87474


**Wolfgang Heinold**, see Eulenhof-Verlag
  Wolfgang Ehrhardt Heinold


**Heinrichshofen-Books**, see Florian Noetzel
  Verlag

**Heinrichshofen's Verlag GmbH & Co KG+**
Liebigstr 16, 26389 Wilhelmshaven
*Tel:* (04421) 9267-0 *Fax:* (04421) 9267-99
*E-mail:* info@heinrichshofen.de
*Web Site:* www.heinrichshofen.de
*Key Personnel*
President: Juergen Etzoldt
Production, Printing: Peter Hensel *Tel:* (04421)
  9267-11
Marketing: Michael Etzoldt
Founded: 1797
Also publish music, printing shop & bindery.
Subjects: Music
Number of titles published annually: 25 Print; 15
  CD-ROM
Total Titles: 3,500 Print; 40 CD-ROM
*Associate Companies:* Otto Heinrich Noetzel Ver-
  lag; C F Peters Corporation, 70-30 80 St, Glen-
  dale, NY 11385, United States
Distributed by CPEA; C F Peters Corporation
  (New York); Peters Edition (London)


**Heinz-Theo Gremme Verlag+**
Tobiaspark 2, 44534 Lunen
*Tel:* (02592) 984200
*E-mail:* theo@gremme-verlag.de
*Web Site:* www.gremme-verlag.de
Founded: 1991
Subjects: Fiction, Human Relations, Poetry, Sci-
  ence Fiction, Fantasy, Self-Help
ISBN Prefix(es): 3-9802679


**Heinze GmbH**
Bremer Weg 184, 29223 Celle
*Tel:* (01805) 339833 *Fax:* (01805) 119877
*E-mail:* info@heinze.de; kundenservice@heinze.
  de
*Web Site:* www.heinze.de/; www.heinzebauoffice.
  de
*Telex:* 925202
*Key Personnel*
President: Michael Hoelker
Founded: 1964
Subjects: Advertising
ISBN Prefix(es): 3-921724
*Parent Company:* Bertelsmann Fachinformationen
  Munich


**Edition Heitere Poetik**, *imprint of* Verlag Beruf
  und Schule Belz KG


**Heitz Librarie**, *imprint of* Verlag Valentin
  Koerner GmbH


**HelfRecht Verlag und Druck**
Markgrafenstr 32, 95680 Bad Alexandersbad
*Tel:* (09232) 6010 *Fax:* (09232) 601280
*E-mail:* info@helfrecht.de
*Web Site:* www.helfrecht.de
*Key Personnel*
Man Dir: Manfred Helfrecht; Gottfried
  Haberkorn; Werner Bayer
Public Relations & International Rights:
  Christoph Beck
Public Relations Assistant: Theresa Kraupner
Founded: 1975
Subjects: Career Development, Economics
ISBN Prefix(es): 3-920400
*Parent Company:* Firmengruppe HelfRecht GmbH
  & Co-Holding KG
*Branch Office(s)*
Rittet-von-Eitzeuberger-Str 25, 95448 Bayreuth
  *Tel:* (0921) 9088 *Fax:* (0921) 9088


**Heliopolis-Verlag+**
Schellingstr 41, 72072 Tuebingen
Mailing Address: PO Box 1827, 72008 Tuebingen
*Tel:* (07473) 5427 *Fax:* (07473) 5427
*Key Personnel*
Manager: Dr Volker Katzmann
Founded: 1949

ISBN Prefix(es): 3-87324
*Associate Companies:* Katzmann-Verlag KG,
Schellingstr 41, 72072 Tuebingen

**Hellerau-Verlag Dresden GmbH**
Koenigstr 12, 01097 Dresden
*Tel:* (0351) 803 5293 *Fax:* (0351) 826 0130
*E-mail:* info@hellerau-verlag.de
*Web Site:* www.hellerau-verlag.de/
*Key Personnel*
Publisher: Lothar Dunsch
Founded: 1990
Subjects: Fiction, History, Regional Interests
ISBN Prefix(es): 3-910184

**G Henle Verlag**
Forstenrieder Allee 122, 81476 Munich
*Tel:* (089) 759820 *Fax:* (089) 7598240
*E-mail:* info@henle.de
*Web Site:* www.henle.de
*Key Personnel*
Chief Executive Officer & President: Dr
Wolf-Dieter Seiffert *Tel:* (089) 75982-21
*E-mail:* seiffert@henle.de
Editor-in-Chief: Dr Norbert Gertsch
*E-mail:* gertsch@henle.de
Head of Manufacturing: Gerhard Fischl
*E-mail:* fischl@henle.de
Head of Sales & Marketing: Ulrike Lucht-Lorenz
*E-mail:* lucht-lorenz@henle.de
Founded: 1948
Subjects: Music, Dance, Complete Editions
(Brahms, Haydn & Beethoven), Music Books
& Catalogs, Urtext Editions of Classical Music
ISBN Prefix(es): 3-87328
Total Titles: 50 Print
Subsidiaries: G Henle USA Inc

**Henschel Verlag**, *imprint of* Verlagsgruppe
Dornier GmbH

**Edition Hentrich Druck & Verlag Gebr
Hentrich und Tank GmbH & Co KG+**
Hindenburgdamm 78, 12203 Berlin
*Tel:* (030) 84410001 *Fax:* (030) 84410002
*Key Personnel*
Publisher & Manager: Werner Buchwald
Founded: 1982
Subjects: Art, Biography, Drama, Theater, Gov-
ernment, Political Science, History, Nonfiction
(General), Religion - Jewish, Social Sciences,
Sociology
ISBN Prefix(es): 3-89468; 3-926175

**Herausgeber**, *imprint of* Johann Wolfgang
Goethe Universitat

**F A Herbig Verlagsbuchhandlung GmbH+**
Subsidiary of Buchverlage Langen-Mueller/Her-
big
Thomas-Wimmer-Ring 11, 80539 Munich
*Tel:* (089) 2 90 88-0
*E-mail:* l.eggs@herbig.net
*Web Site:* www.herbig.net *Cable:*
LANGENMULLER
*Key Personnel*
Man Dir & Publisher: Dr Herbert Fleissner
Man Dir: Dr Brigitte Sinhuber
Sales: Eva Ohser *E-mail:* e.ohser@herbig.net
Rights & Permissions: Dorothea Estermann;
Frauke Hoppen *Tel:* (089) 2 90 88-156
*Fax:* (089) 2 90 88-178 *E-mail:* f.hoppen@
herbig.net
Editorial: Dr Bernhard Struckmeyer
Founded: 1821
Subjects: Art, Astronomy, Biography, Cookery,
Health, Nutrition, History, Nonfiction (Gen-
eral), Physical Sciences, Travel
ISBN Prefix(es): 3-7766
*Orders to:* VVA, An der Autobahn, 33310
Guetersloh

**Hans-Alfred Herchen & Co Verlag KG**
Fichardstr 30, 60322 Frankfurt am Main
*Tel:* (069) 550911-13 *Fax:* (069) 552601; (069)
554922
*Key Personnel*
Contact: Hans-Alfred Herchen
Founded: 1984
Subjects: Government, Political Science, Social
Sciences, Sociology
ISBN Prefix(es): 3-89184

**Verlag Herder GmbH & Co KG+**
Hermann-Herder-Str 4, 79104 Freiburg
*Tel:* (0761) 2717440 *Fax:* (0761) 2717360
*E-mail:* kundenservice@herder.de
*Web Site:* www.herder.de/ *Cable:* HERDER
FREIBURGBREISGAU
*Key Personnel*
Man Dir: Dr Hermann Herder; Manuel-Gregor
Herder; Ulrich Peters; Dr Klaus-Christoph
Scheffels
Rights & Permissions: Franziska Komm
Sales Dir: Rainer Lege
Export: Peter Pagendarm
Founded: 1801
Subjects: Biblical Studies, Education, Govern-
ment, Political Science, History, Nonfiction
(General), Religion - Buddhist, Religion -
Catholic, Religion - Islamic, Religion - Other,
Self-Help, Theology
ISBN Prefix(es): 3-451
*Associate Companies:* Herder Editrice e Libreria,
Italy; Editorial Herder SA, Spain; Herder Ag,
Switzerland
*Imprints:* Herderbuecherei; Herder/Spektrum;
Uerle Verlag; Verlag Ploetz
*Subsidiaries:* Verlag Karl Alber GmbH;
Christophorus-Verlag GmbH
*Divisions:* Kerle-Verlag; Ploetz
*Bookshop(s):* Carolus Buchrandlung Herder,
Frankfurt am Main
*Book Club(s):* Herder Buchgemeinde
*Shipping Address:* Koch, Neff & Oetinger,
Schockenriedstr 39, 70565 Stuttgart
*Warehouse:* Koch, Neff & Oetinger, Schocken-
riedstr 39, 70565 Stuttgart

**Herder/Spektrum**, *imprint of* Verlag Herder
GmbH & Co KG

**Herderbuecherei**, *imprint of* Verlag Herder
GmbH & Co KG

**Hermetische Truhe Buchhandlung fuer
Esoterische Literatur Barbara Dethlefsen**
Gaertnerplatz 1, 80469 Munich
*Tel:* (089) 2710650 *Fax:* (089) 2724627
*Key Personnel*
Owner: Barbara Dethlefsen
Founded: 1983
ISBN Prefix(es): 3-927183

**Herold Verlag Dr Wetzel+**
Kirchbachweg 16, 81479 Munich
*Tel:* (089) 7915774
*E-mail:* wetzel@herold-verlag.de
*Web Site:* www.herold-verlag.de
*Key Personnel*
Man Dir & Publisher: Hans Meisinger
Rights & Publicity: Christiane Schneider
Founded: 1871
ISBN Prefix(es): 3-7767
*Orders to:* MVS Meisinger Verlagsservice
GmbH, Am Steinfeld 4, 94065 Waldkirchen
*Tel:* (08581) 9605-0 *Fax:* (08581) 754

**Axel Hertenstein, Hertenstein-Presse**
Mathystr 36, 75173 Pforzheim
*Tel:* (07231) 2 70 84 *Fax:* (07231) 2 70 84
*Key Personnel*
Publicity Manager: Ulrike Hertenstein

Founded: 1967
Specialize in library books & maps.
Subjects: Poetry

**Hertenstein-Presse**, see Axel Hertenstein,
Hertenstein-Presse

**Hessisches Ministerium fuer Umwelt,
Landwirtschaft und Forsten**
Mainzerstr 80, 65189 Wiesbaden
*Tel:* (0611) 8150 *Fax:* (0611) 8151941
*Web Site:* www.mulf.hessen.de
*Telex:* 4182011 HMUE D
*Key Personnel*
Contact: Manuela Scharfenberg
Specialize in ecology.
Subjects: Agriculture, Energy, Environmental
Studies, Ecology
ISBN Prefix(es): 3-89274; 3-89277
Total Titles: 120 Print; 3 CD-ROM

**Hestra-Verlag Hernichel & Dr Strauss GmbH
& Co KG+**
Holzhofallee 33, 64295 Darmstadt
Mailing Address: Postfach 100751, 64207 Darm-
stadt
*Tel:* (06151) 39070 *Fax:* (06151) 390777
*Key Personnel*
Man Dir & International Rights: Holger Musset
*Tel:* (06151) 390731 *E-mail:* musset@hestra.de
Founded: 1948
Subjects: Civil Engineering, Engineering (Gen-
eral), Law, Transportation
ISBN Prefix(es): 3-7771

**Hexaglot Holding GmbH+**
Sportallee 41, 22335 Hamburg
*Tel:* (040) 514560 *Fax:* (040) 51456991
*E-mail:* info@hexaglot.de
*Web Site:* www.hexaglot.de/ *Cable:* HEXAGER
*Key Personnel*
Manager: Dr Hans-Werner Scholz
Founded: 1989
ISBN Prefix(es): 3-928824; 3-931535; 3-935996;
3-9802552
*Parent Company:* Langenscheidt KG
*Subsidiaries:* Sita Daten-und Kommunikations
GmbH

**Friedrich W Heye Verlag GmbH+**
Oberweg 8, 82008 Unterhaching
*Tel:* (089) 6653201 *Fax:* (089) 66532210
*E-mail:* verlag@heye.de
*Web Site:* www.heye-verlag.de
*Key Personnel*
Man Dir: Peter Keil; Claudia Knauss; Juergen
Knauss
Founded: 1962
ISBN Prefix(es): 3-88141; 3-89400; 3-8318; 3-
89529; 3-89768
*Associate Companies:* Heye Top Present GmbH
*Warehouse:* Kapellenstr 13, 85622 Feldkirchen

**Carl Heymanns Verlag KG+**
Luxemburgerstr 449, 50939 Cologne
*Tel:* (0221) 94373-0 *Fax:* (0221) 94373-901
*E-mail:* marketing@heymanns.com
*Web Site:* www.heymanns.com
*Key Personnel*
Man Dir, Rights & Permissions: Andreas Gallus
*Tel:* (0221) 94373-101 *Fax:* (0221) 94373-105
*E-mail:* a.gallus@heymanns.com
Editorial: K Endlich *Tel:* (089) 224811
*E-mail:* endlich@heymanns.com; P Halter
*Tel:* (0221) 94373-160 *E-mail:* halter@
heymanns.com; H Kruppa *Tel:* (0221) 94373-
134 *E-mail:* kruppa@heymanns.com; K Pompe
*Tel:* (0221) 94373-600 *E-mail:* pompe@
heymanns.com; M Sauerwald *Tel:* (0221)
94373-138 *E-mail:* sauerwald@heymanns.com

Production: M Voges *Tel:* (0221) 94373-200
*E-mail:* voges@heymanns.com
Editorial: K-L Steinhaeuser *Tel:* (0221) 94373-
132 *E-mail:* steinhaeuser@heymanns.com
Marketing Manager: Gerd Welb *Tel:* (0221)
94373-300 *Fax:* (0221) 94373-310
*E-mail:* welb@heymanns.com
Founded: 1815
Subjects: Economics, Engineering (General),
Government, Political Science, Law, Manage-
ment, Public Administration
ISBN Prefix(es): 3-452
Total Titles: 2,000 Print; 70 CD-ROM
Subsidiaries: Euroliber Verlags- und Vertriebs-
GmbH; Gallus Druckerei KG; Albert Nauck &
Co
*Branch Office(s)*
Gutenbergstr 3-4, Berlin *Tel:* (030) 3914081
*Fax:* (030) 3912861
Steinsdorfstr 10, Postfach 26, 80538 Munich
*Tel:* (089) 224811

**Wilhelm Heyne Verlag+**
Neumarkterstr 28, 81673 Munich
Mailing Address: Postfach 200143, 80001 Mu-
nich
*Tel:* (089) 41 36 0 *Fax:* (089) 51 48 2229
*E-mail:* heyne-suedwest@randomhouse.de
*Web Site:* www.heyne.de *Cable:*
HEYNEVERLAG MUNCHEN
*Key Personnel*
Publisher: Rolf Heyne
Editorial Dir: Lothar Menne
Editorial: Ulrich Genzler; Wolfgang Jeschke; Dr
Theda Krohm-Linke; Ria Lottermoser; Bern-
hard Matt; Ingeborg Meier
Sales Dir: Christian Tesch
Advertising Manager: David Hauptmann
Rights & Permissions: Traudel Eckardt
Founded: 1934
Subjects: Astrology, Occult, Biography, Cookery,
Fiction, Film, Video, History, How-to, Humor,
Mysteries, Psychology, Psychiatry, Romance,
Science Fiction, Fantasy
ISBN Prefix(es): 3-453
Subsidiaries: Collection Rolf Heyne, Diana Ver-
lag; Zabert Sandmann
*U.S. Office(s):* Franklin & Siegal Associates Inc,
1350 Broadway, Suite 2015, New York, NY
10018, United States
*Orders to:* Schleissheimerstr 106, 85748
Garching-Hochbrueck

**Max Hieber KG+**
Liebfrauenstr 1, 80331 Munich
Mailing Address: Postfach 330429, 80064 Mu-
nich
*Tel:* (089) 29008023 *Fax:* (089) 229782
*E-mail:* info@eminent-orgeln.de
*Web Site:* www.eminent-orgeln.de/kontakte.htm
*Key Personnel*
Contact: Daniel Stieb
Founded: 1884
Subjects: Music, Dance
ISBN Prefix(es): 3-920456
*Branch Office(s)*
Max Hieber Musikverlag, Verlagsauslieferung
Einkauf, Musikalien-Versand Loewengrube 10,
80331 Munich
Distributed by Musikverlag Preissler

**Anton Hiersemann, Verlag+**
Haldenstr 30, 70376 Stuttgart
Mailing Address: Postfach 14 01 55, 70071
Stuttgart
*Tel:* (0711) 54 99 71-0; (0711) 54 99 71-11
*Fax:* (0711) 54 99 71-21
*E-mail:* verlag@hiersemann.de
*Web Site:* www.hiersemann.de *Cable:* (0711) 54
99 71-21

*Key Personnel*
President & Dir, Rights & Permissions: Gerd Hi-
ersemann
Founded: 1884
Also specialize in monographs, publishing &
book trade reference.
Subjects: Art, Astronomy, Biography, Drama,
Theater, Genealogy, History, Library & In-
formation Sciences, Literature, Literary Criti-
cism, Essays, Religion - Buddhist, Religion -
Catholic, Religion - Hindu, Religion - Islamic,
Religion - Jewish, Religion - Protestant, Re-
ligion - Other, Science (General), Theology,
Bookmaking
ISBN Prefix(es): 3-7772
Number of titles published annually: 45 Print
Total Titles: 1,200 Print; 7 CD-ROM
*Associate Companies:* Dr Ernst Hauswedell & Co
Imprints: Maximilian Gesellschaft eV
Subsidiaries: Karl W Hiersemann
*Book Club(s):* Geschaeftsstelle von: Literarischer
Verein in Stuttgart eV

**AIG I Hilbinger Verlag GmbH+**
Frauensteiner Str 70, 65199 Wiesbaden
*Tel:* (0611) 4190088; (0611) 7239233 *Fax:* (0611)
7239209
*Key Personnel*
Man Dir, Rights & Permissions: Immo A
Hilbinger
Founded: 1989
Subjects: Astrology, Occult, Parapsychology, Self-
Help
ISBN Prefix(es): 3-927110
*Associate Companies:* Agentur fuer Informations-
gestaltung, Zum Dornhachtal, 65321 Heidenrod

**Himmelsturmer Verlag+**
Kirchenweg 12, 20099 Hamburg
*Tel:* (040) 48061717 *Fax:* (040) 48061799
*E-mail:* himmelstuermer@gmx.de
Founded: 1998
Specialize in gay novels & documentaries.
Subjects: Gay & Lesbian
ISBN Prefix(es): 3-934825; 3-9806249
Number of titles published annually: 6 Print
Total Titles: 25 Print

**Verlag Hinder und Deelmann+**
Postfach 1206, 35068 Gladenbach
*Tel:* (06462) 1301 *Fax:* (06462) 3307
*Web Site:* www.hinderunddeelmann.de/
*Key Personnel*
Publisher: Johannes Deelmann; Dr Rolf Hinder
Founded: 1953
Subjects: History, Philosophy, Religion - Other,
Social Sciences, Sociology
ISBN Prefix(es): 3-87348
Distributor for Pondicherry (India); Sabda (India)

**Hinstorff Verlag GmbH+**
Lagerstr 7, 18055 Rostock
*Tel:* (0381) 49 69-0 *Fax:* (0381) 49 69-103
*E-mail:* sekretariat@hinstorff.de
*Web Site:* www.hinstorff.de
*Key Personnel*
Manager: Birgit Heinze
Contact: Birgit Kruggel
Founded: 1831
Subjects: Literature, Literary Criticism, Essays
ISBN Prefix(es): 3-356
*Parent Company:* Heinz Heise Verlag GmbH &
Co KG, Hannover
*Warehouse:* VSB Verlagsservice Braunschweig
GmbH, Helmstedterstr 99, 38126 Braunschweig
*Orders to:* VSB Verlagsservice Braunschweig
GmbH, Postfach 4738, 38037 Braunschweig
Georg Westermann Allee 66, 38104 Braun-
schweig

**Hippokrates,** *imprint of* Georg Thieme Verlag
KG

**Hippokrates-Verlag GmbH,** see MVS
Medizinverlage Stuttgart GmbH & Co KG

**Hirmer Verlag GmbH+**
Member of Weltkunst Verlagsgruppe
Nymphenburgerstr 84, 80636 Munich
Mailing Address: Postfach 190454, 80604 Mu-
nich
*Tel:* (089) 1215160 *Fax:* (089) 12151610; (089)
12151616 (distribution)
*E-mail:* vertrieb@hirmerverlag.de
*Web Site:* www.hirmerverlag.de; www.
weltkunstverlag.de
*Key Personnel*
Man Dir & Editorial: Albert Hirmer
Man Dir: Juergen Kleidt
Editorial: Dr Veronika Birbaumer; Margret Haase
Founded: 1948
Subjects: Archaeology, Art
ISBN Prefix(es): 3-7774

**Harro V Hirschheydt**
Neue Wiesen 6, 30900 Wedemark-Elze
*Tel:* (05130) 36758 *Fax:* (05130) 36799
*E-mail:* kontakt@hirschheydt-online.de
*Key Personnel*
Owner, Rights & Permissions: Harro V
Hirschheydt
Founded: 1950
Subjects: Regional Interests
ISBN Prefix(es): 3-7777

**F Hirthammer Verlag GmbH+**
Raiffeisenallee 10, 82041 Oberhaching
*Tel:* (089) 3233360 *Fax:* (089) 3241728
*E-mail:* info@hirthammerverlag.de
*Web Site:* www.hirthammerverlag.de
*Key Personnel*
Manager: Franz Hirthammer
Founded: 1965
Subjects: Animals, Pets, Astrology, Occult, Envi-
ronmental Studies, Health, Nutrition, Medicine,
Nursing, Dentistry, Parapsychology, Philosophy,
Religion - Buddhist, Religion - Hindu, Religion
- Other, Theosophy
ISBN Prefix(es): 3-88721; 3-921288
Number of titles published annually: 15 Print
Total Titles: 200 Print

**S Hirzel Verlag GmbH und Co+**
Birkenwaldstr 44, 70191 Stuttgart
Mailing Address: Postfach 101061, 70009
Stuttgart
*Tel:* (0711) 25820 *Fax:* (0711) 2582290
*E-mail:* service@hirzel.de
*Web Site:* www.hirzel.de *Cable:*
HIRZELVERLAG, STUTTGART
*Key Personnel*
Man Dir: Dr Klaus Brauer; Andre Caro; Dr
Christian Rotta; Dr Thomas Schaber
Rights: Sabine Koerner
Sales: Siegmar Bauer *E-mail:* sbauer@hirzel.de
Founded: 1853
Subjects: Chemistry, Chemical Engineering, Engi-
neering (General), Language Arts, Linguistics,
Natural History, Philosophy, Psychology, Psy-
chiatry, Regional Interests, Science (General)
ISBN Prefix(es): 3-7776
*Parent Company:* Deutscher Apotheker Verlag,
Postfach 101061, 70009 Stuttgart
*Associate Companies:* Medpharm Scientific
Publishers; Franz Steiner Verlag Wiesbaden
GmbH; Wissenschaftliche Verlagagsellschaft
mbH

**Verlag Wolfgang Hoelker+**
Hafenweg 30, 48155 Muenster
Mailing Address: Postfach 3820, 48021 Muenster
*Tel:* (0251) 414110 *Fax:* (0251) 4141140
*E-mail:* info@coppenrath.de
*Web Site:* www.coppenrath.de
*Key Personnel*
Man Dir: Wolfgang Hoelker

Sales: Hubert Bergmoser
Production: Wolfgang Foerster
Publicity: Tomas Rensiny
International Rights: Christiane Leesker
Founded: 1973
Subjects: Cookery
ISBN Prefix(es): 3-88117; 3-9800058
Subsidiaries: Coppenrath Verlag
*Warehouse:* Coppenrath-Hoelker Distribution, Textilstrasse, 48612 Horstmar *Tel:* (02558) 98818 *Fax:* (02558) 98819

**Verlag Peter Hoell+**
Darmstaedterstr 14 b, 64397 Modautal
*Tel:* (06167) 912220 *Fax:* (06167) 912221
*E-mail:* hoell.verlag@t-online.de
*Web Site:* www.hoell.de.vu
Founded: 1987
Subjects: Anthropology, Astrology, Occult, Human Relations, Literature, Literary Criticism, Essays
ISBN Prefix(es): 3-9801439; 3-928564
Total Titles: 5 Print

**Hofbauer, Christoph und Trojanow Ilia, Akademischer Verlag Muenchen+**
Paul-Heysestr 3la, 80336 Munich
*Tel:* (089) 51616151 *Fax:* (089) 51616199
*E-mail:* avm@druckmedien.de
*Key Personnel*
Contact: Christoph Hofbauer; Ilija Trojanow
Founded: 1991
Subjects: Anthropology, Business, Economics, Literature, Literary Criticism, Essays, Physical Sciences
ISBN Prefix(es): 3-929115; 3-932965
*Associate Companies:* Marino Verlag, c/o Frederking & Thaler, Neumarkter Str 18, Munich
Distributor for GBI-Verlag; Faktum

**Edgar Hoff Verlag**, see Reise Know-How

**Edition Hoffmann & Co**
Goerbelheimer Muehle, 61169 Friedberg
*Tel:* (06031) 2443 *Fax:* (06031) 62965
Founded: 1967
Subjects: Architecture & Interior Design, Art
ISBN Prefix(es): 3-926026

**Dieter Hoffmann Verlag**
Senefelderstr 75, 55129 Mainz
*Tel:* (06136) 95100 *Fax:* (06136) 951037
*Key Personnel*
Man Dir, Rights & Permissions: Dieter Hoffman
Founded: 1960
Subjects: History, Outdoor Recreation
ISBN Prefix(es): 3-87341

**H Hoffmann GmbH**
An der Stammbahn 53, 14532 Kleinmachnow
*Tel:* (033203) 305810 *Fax:* (033203) 305820
*E-mail:* hhvberlin@t-online.de
ISBN Prefix(es): 3-87344

**Hoffmann und Campe Verlag GmbH+**
Harvestehuder Weg 42, 20149 Hamburg
*Tel:* (040) 441880 *Fax:* (040) 44188290
*E-mail:* email@hoca.de
*Web Site:* www.hoca.de
*Telex:* 0214259 HoCa
*Key Personnel*
Man Dir: Thomas Hackenberg; Uwe Marsen; Dr Rainer Moritz; Manfred Bissinger; Thomas Ganske; Dr Kai Laakmann
Editorial: Hubertus Rabe; Tania Schlie
Marketing Dir: Margrit Osterwold
Production: Roland Kraft
Publicity Dir: Dr Joachim Koehler
Rights & Permissions: Sibylle Chory; Ingeborg Rose
Rights: Nadja Kossack

Founded: 1781
Subjects: Art, Biography, Fiction, History, Music, Dance, Nonfiction (General), Philosophy, Poetry, Psychology, Psychiatry, Science (General), Social Sciences, Sociology
ISBN Prefix(es): 3-455
Foreign Rep(s): Dagmar Bhend (Switzerland); Herbert Pamminger (Austria); Helga Riegler (Austria)

**Verlag Karl Hofmann GmbH & Co+**
Steinwasenstr 6-8, 73614 Schorndorf
Mailing Address: Postfach 1360, 73603 Schorndorf
*Tel:* (07181) 4020 *Fax:* (07181) 402111
*E-mail:* info@hofmann-verlag.de
*Web Site:* www.hofmann-verlag.de
*Key Personnel*
Man Dir, Rights & Permissions: Ottmar Hecht
Man Dir, Sales: Thomas Hecht
Founded: 1904
Subjects: Sports, Athletics
ISBN Prefix(es): 3-7780

**Friedrich Hofmeister Musikverlag+**
Buettnerstr 10, 04103 Leipzig
*Tel:* (0341) 960 07 50 *Fax:* (0341) 960 30 55
*E-mail:* info@hofmeister-musikverlag.de
*Web Site:* www.friedrich-hofmeister.de; www.hofmeister-musikverlag.com
*Key Personnel*
Manager: Karl Heinz Schwarze
Founded: 1807
Subjects: Music, Dance
ISBN Prefix(es): 3-7331; 3-87350

**Hogrefe Verlag GmbH & Co Kg+**
Rohnsweg 25, 37085 Goettingen
*Tel:* (0551) 496090 *Fax:* (0551) 4960988
*E-mail:* verlag@hogrefe.de
*Web Site:* www.hogrefe.de/
*Key Personnel*
Proprietor: Dr Dr G-Juergen Hogrefe
    *E-mail:* hogrefe@hogrefe.de
Man Dir: Dr Michael Vogtmeier *Tel:* (0551) 4960921 *E-mail:* vogtmeier@hogrefe.de
Sales Dir: Reinhard Dornieden
Production: B Otto
Promotion: S Otto
Founded: 1949
Subjects: Medicine, Nursing, Dentistry, Psychology, Psychiatry
ISBN Prefix(es): 3-8017; 3-87844
Subsidiaries: Verlag fur Angewandte Psychologie
*U.S. Office(s):* Hogrefe & Huber Publishing, Seattle Regional Headquarters, PO Box 2487, Kirkland, WA 98083-2487, United States
*Bookshop(s):* Oettinger & Hogrefe GmbH, Buchhandlung fuer Medizin und Psychologie, Robert-Bosch-Breite 25, 37079 Goettingen
*Warehouse:* Robert-Bosch-Breite 25, 37079 Goettingen
*Orders to:* Brockhaus Commission, Kreidlerstr 9, 70806 Kornwestheim

**Hohenrain-Verlag GmbH+**
Am Apfelberg 18, 72076 Tuebingen
Mailing Address: Postfach 1611, 72006 Tuebingen
*Tel:* (07071) 40700 *Fax:* (07071) 407026
*Key Personnel*
Man Dir: Wigbert Grabert
Founded: 1985
Subjects: Art, Biography, Fiction, Government, Political Science, History
ISBN Prefix(es): 3-89180
Number of titles published annually: 3 Print
Total Titles: 70 Print

**Matth Hohner AG Verlag**
Andreas-Kochstr 9, 78647 Trossingen

*Tel:* (07425) 200 *Fax:* (07425) 249
*E-mail:* info@hohner.de
*Web Site:* www.hohner.de
*Telex:* 760727 hohnd
*Key Personnel*
Manager: Dr Ing Horst Braeuning
Founded: 1857
ISBN Prefix(es): 3-920468
*Warehouse:* Hohnerstr 8, 78647 Trossingen

**Buchhandlung Holl & Knoll KG, Verlag Alte Uni**
Brettenerstr 30, 75031 Eppingen
*Tel:* (07262) 4417 *Fax:* (07262) 7942
*E-mail:* alteuni@aol.com
*Key Personnel*
Contact: Karl Knoll
Founded: 1986
Subjects: Art, Cookery, Medicine, Nursing, Dentistry, Music, Dance, Regional Interests
ISBN Prefix(es): 3-926315

**Holland & Josenhans GmbH & Co+**
Subsidiary of Verlag Handwerk und Technik GmbH
Feuerseeplatz 2, 70176 Stuttgart
Mailing Address: Postfach 1023 52, 70019 Stuttgart
*Tel:* (0711) 6143920 *Fax:* (0711) 6143922
*E-mail:* verlag@huj.03.net
*Web Site:* www.holland-josenhans.de/
*Key Personnel*
Marketing: Heidi Scheurle *Tel:* (0711) 6143925 *Fax:* (0711) 6143955 *E-mail:* marketing@huj.03.net
Founded: 1861
Subjects: Education
ISBN Prefix(es): 3-7782
Foreign Rep(s): Technischer Fachbuchvertrieb AG (Switzerland)

**Holos Verlag+**
Ermekeilstr 15, 53113 Bonn
*Tel:* (0228) 263020; (0228) 262332 *Fax:* (0228) 212435
Founded: 1987
Specialize in humanities.
Subjects: Anthropology, Archaeology, Fiction, Gay & Lesbian, Geography, Geology, History, Language Arts, Linguistics, Philosophy, Psychology, Psychiatry, Social Sciences, Sociology
ISBN Prefix(es): 3-926216; 3-86097

**Verlagsgruppe Georg von Holtzbrinck GmbH**
Gaensheidestr 26, 70184 Stuttgart
Mailing Address: Postfach 105039, 70044 Stuttgart
*Tel:* (0711) 2150-0 *Fax:* (0711) 2150-269
*E-mail:* info@holtzbrinck.com
*Web Site:* www.holtzbrinck.com
Founded: 1971
Subjects: Education, Fiction, Nonfiction (General), Science (General), Newspapers

**Guenther Holzboog**, see Friedrich Frommann Verlag

**Hans Holzmann Verlag GmbH und Co KG**
Gewerbestr 2, 86825 Bad Woerishofen
Mailing Address: Postfach 1342, 86816 Bad Woerishofen
*Tel:* (08247) 35401 *Fax:* (08247) 354170
*E-mail:* info@holzmannverlag.de
*Web Site:* www.holzmannverlag.de/
*Telex:* 539331 *Cable:* HOLZMANN VERLAG
*Key Personnel*
Man Dir: Alexander Holzmann *E-mail:* alexander.holzmann@holzmannverlag.de
Production Dir: Helmut Mauritz
Publishing Dir: Harald Bos *E-mail:* harald.bos@holzmannverlag.de
Finances: Arthur Fostmaier

Founded: 1936
Subjects: Business, Education, Law, Marketing
ISBN Prefix(es): 3-7783; 3-920416
Subsidiaries: Druck und Werbung Holzmann GmbH
Divisions: Abt Buchverlag; Abt Fach-Zeitschriften; Abt Anzeigen

**Homo Oeconomicus**, *imprint of* Accedo Verlagsgesellschaft mbH

**Hoppenstedt GmbH & Co KG**
Havelstr 9, 64295 Darmstadt
Mailing Address: Postfach 100139, 64201 Darmstadt
*Tel:* (06151) 380-0 *Fax:* (06151) 380-360
*E-mail:* info@hoppenstedt.de
*Web Site:* www.hoppenstedt.de
*Key Personnel*
Man Dir: Werner Reiber; Roland Repp
Contact: Silke Braun *Tel:* (06151) 380-261
Founded: 1926
Subjects: Finance, Marketing, Securities
ISBN Prefix(es): 3-8203
*Associate Companies:* Druckhaus Darmstadt GmbH, Darmstadt *Tel:* (06151) 80550 *Fax:* (06151) 8055200; Hoppenstedt Bonnier Information GmbH, Darmstadt *Tel:* (06151) 380367 *Fax:* (06151) 380488 *E-mail:* info@catalogic.de; ComHouse AG, Wuerzburg *Tel:* (0931) 3561-0 *Fax:* (0931) 3561-140 *E-mail:* mail@comhouse.com; Belgisch ABC voor Handel en Industrie Bv, Asse, Belgium *Tel:* (021) 4630213 *Fax:* (021) 4630885 *E-mail:* info@abc-de.be; HBI sro, Prague, Czech Republic *Tel:* (02) 6316624 *Fax:* (02) 6516616 *E-mail:* hoppenstedt@televom.cz; Hoppenstedt Bonnier & Tarsa Informacios Kft, Budapest, Hungary *Tel:* (01) 2761333 *Fax:* (01) 2760933 *E-mail:* mail@hoppbonn.hu; HBI SpA Bassano del Grappa, Bassano del Grappa, Italy *Tel:* (0424) 529088 *Fax:* (0424) 529191 *E-mail:* info@hbiitaly.it; ABC voor Handel en Industrie CV, Haarlem, Netherlands *Tel:* (023) 5533533 *Fax:* (023) 5327033 *E-mail:* info@abc-de.nl; Hoppenstedt Bonnier Information Polska Sp zoo, ul Kwiatka 12, 09-400 Plock, Poland *Tel:* (024) 366 33 10 *Fax:* (024) 366 33 33 *E-mail:* hbi@hbi.pl *Web Site:* www.hbi.pl
Subsidiaries: Seibt Verlag GmbH; Verlag Hoppenstedt & Co Wirtschajtsverlag Ges mbH; Hoppenstedt France SNC Compiegne; Hoppenstedt Nederland BV; Hoppenstedt AG Kilchberg

**Horlemann Verlag+**
Postfach 1307, 53583 Bad Honnef
*Tel:* (02224) 5589 *Fax:* (02224) 5429
*E-mail:* horlemann@aol.com
*Web Site:* www.horlemann-verlag.de/
*Key Personnel*
Owner & International Rights: Beate Horlemann
Founded: 1990
Membership(s): The Stock Exchange of German Booksellers.
Subjects: Asian Studies, Developing Countries, Education, Environmental Studies, Fiction, Foreign Countries, Government, Political Science, Literature, Literary Criticism, Essays, Nonfiction (General), Philosophy, Poetry, Religion - Islamic, Social Sciences, Sociology
ISBN Prefix(es): 3-927905; 3-89502

**Hans Huber+**
Laenggass-Str 76, 3000 Bern 9
*Tel:* (031) 3004500 *Fax:* (031) 3004590
*E-mail:* verlag@hanshuber.com
*Web Site:* www.hanshuber.com *Cable:* HUBERVERLAG BERN
*Key Personnel*
Man Dir: Dr G-Juergen Hogrefe
Editorial Dir: Juerg Flury
Marketing: Christian Liengme

Advertising: Anina Burkhalter
Founded: 1927
Subjects: Education, Medicine, Nursing, Dentistry, Psychology, Psychiatry
ISBN Prefix(es): 3-456
Subsidiaries: Hogrefe & Huber Publishers Inc, Seattle/Toronto; Psychodiagnostika, Brno/Czechia & Bratislava/Slovakia; Testzentrale der Schweizer Psychologen AG
*U.S. Office(s):* Hogrefe & Huber Publishers Inc, PO Box 2487, Kirkland, WA 98083-2487, United States *Tel:* 425-820-1500 *Fax:* 425-823-8324
*Bookshop(s):* Schanzenstr 1, 3000 Bern 9, Switzerland *Tel:* (031) 3004646 *Fax:* (031) 3004656 *E-mail:* contactbern@huberlang.com; Zeltweg 6, 8032 Zurich, Switzerland *Tel:* (01) 2683939 *Fax:* (01) 2683920 *E-mail:* contactzurich@huberlang.com

**Volker Huber Edition & Galerie+**
Berlinerstr 218, 63067 Offenbach
Mailing Address: Postfach 101153, 63011 Offenbach
*Tel:* (069) 814523 *Fax:* (069) 880155
*E-mail:* edition-huber@t-online.de
*Web Site:* www.volkerhuber.de
*Key Personnel*
Owner: Volker Huber
Founded: 1965
Subjects: Art
ISBN Prefix(es): 3-921785

**Max Hueber Verlag GmbH & Co KG+**
Max-Hueber Str 4, 85737 Ismaning
Mailing Address: Postfach 1142, 85729 Ismaning
*Tel:* (089) 9602-0 *Fax:* (089) 9602-358
*E-mail:* kundenservice@hueber.de
*Web Site:* www.hueber.de
*Telex:* 523613 hueb d
*Key Personnel*
Dir: Wolf Dieter Eggert; Michaela Hueber
Rights: Claudia Harbauer
Founded: 1921
Subjects: Education, Language Arts, Linguistics, Adult Education in Foreign Languages, German as a Foreign Language
ISBN Prefix(es): 3-19
*U.S. Office(s):* Alder's Foreign Books Inc, 915 Foster St, Evanston, IL, United States
Continental Book Company Inc, 625E 70 Ave, Suite 5, Denver, CO 80229, United States
German Book Center, NA Inc, PO Box 99, Mountaindale, NY 12763-0099, United States
International Book Import Service Inc, 161 Main St, Lynchburg, TN 37352-8188, United States
Schoenhof's Foreign Books, Inc, 76A Mount Auburn St, Cambridge, MA 02138-5051, United States
Distributed by Editorial Idiomas (Spain); Hueber-Hellas (Greece)

**Felicitas Huebner Verlag+**
Warolderstr 1, 34513 Waldeck
*Tel:* (05695) 1028 *Fax:* (05695) 1027
*Key Personnel*
Publisher: Felicitas Huebner
Founded: 1981
Subjects: Film, Video, Health, Nutrition, Sports, Athletics
ISBN Prefix(es): 3-927359
*Orders to:* Bugrim Verlagsauslieferung Dr Laube & Partner, Saalburgstr 3, 12099 Berlin

**Verlag Uta Huelsey**
Hansaring 52, 46483 Wesel
Mailing Address: Postfach 101034, 46470 Wesel
*Tel:* (0281) 27227 *Fax:* (0281) 24682
*E-mail:* uta.hulsey@t-online.de
ISBN Prefix(es): 3-923185

**Heinrich Hugendubel Verlag GmbH+**
Holzstr 28, 80469 Munich
*Tel:* (089) 235586-0 *Fax:* (089) 235586-111
*Web Site:* www.hugendubel.de
*Key Personnel*
Managing Partner: Heinrich Hugendubel; Dr Monika Roell
Publishing Dir: Stephanie Ehrenschwendner
Rights & Permissions: Susanna Schoeni
Subjects: Astrology, Occult, Government, Political Science, Health, Nutrition, Human Relations, Management, Nonfiction (General), Psychology, Psychiatry, Religion - Other, Self-Help
ISBN Prefix(es): 3-7205; 3-7162; 3-8267; 3-88034; 3-424
Total Titles: 100 Print
Imprints: Ariston; Diederichs; Irisiana; Kailash
*Orders to:* VVA-Vereinigte Verlagsanslieferung, An der Antobahn, Postfach 1111, 33310 Guetersloh *Fax:* (05241) 460367

**Edition Humanistische Psychologie (EHP)+**
Johannesstr 22, 51465 Bergisch Gladbach
Mailing Address: PO Box 200 222, 51432 Bergisch Gladbach
*Tel:* (02202) 981236 *Fax:* (02202) 981237
*E-mail:* info@ehp-koeln.de
*Web Site:* www.ehp-koeln.com; www.ehp.biz
*Key Personnel*
Vice President & Manager: Michels Kohlhage *Tel:* (0221) 5303817 *E-mail:* mmk@ehp-koeln.com
Editor: Andreas Kohlhage *E-mail:* andrea.kohlhage@ehp-koeln.com
Founded: 1986
Subjects: Human Relations, Literature, Literary Criticism, Essays, Management, Nonfiction (General), Psychology, Psychiatry, Science (General), Social Sciences, Sociology
ISBN Prefix(es): 3-926176; 3-9804784; 3-89797
Number of titles published annually: 5 Print
Total Titles: 60 Print
*Orders to:* Brockhaus Commission, Kreidlerstr 9, 70806 Kornwestheim, Contract: Mrs Schlayh *Tel:* (07154) 13270 *Fax:* (07154) 132713 *E-mail:* bestell@brocom.de
Hans Huber AG, Langgass-str 76, 3012 Bern, Switzerland, Contract: Mrs Keller *Tel:* (031) 3004-500 *Fax:* (031) 3004-590 *E-mail:* verlag@huberag.com

**Humanistischer Verband Deutschlands, Landesverband Berlin eV**
Wallstr 61-65, 10179 Berlin
*Tel:* (030) 6139040 *Fax:* (030) 61390450
*E-mail:* lvd@humanismus.de
*Web Site:* www.humanismus.de
*Key Personnel*
Manager: Wolfgang Hecht
ISBN Prefix(es): 3-924041
Number of titles published annually: 4 Print
Total Titles: 55 Print

**Humboldt-Taschenbuch Verlag Jacobi KG+**
Member of The Langenscheidt Group
Neusserstr 3, 80807 Munich
Mailing Address: Postfach 401120, 80711 Munich
*Tel:* (089) 360960 *Fax:* (089) 36096-222 (general); (089) 36096-258 (orders)
*E-mail:* redaktion@humboldt.de
*Key Personnel*
Man Dir: Karl Ernst Tielebier-Langenscheidt *E-mail:* redaktion@humboldt.de; Andreas Langenscheidt
Publishing Dir: Rolf Muller
Chief Editor: Claus-Ulrich Schmidt
Sales Dir: Dr Matti Schusseler
Advertising: Brigitte Pasch
Founded: 1953
Sales & promotion through Langenscheidt KG.
Subjects: Nonfiction (General), Travel

ISBN Prefix(es): 3-581
*Orders to:* Langenscheidt KG, Neusser Str 3,
80807 Munich

**Edition Hundertmark**
Bruesselerstr 29, 50674 Cologne
*Tel:* (0221) 237944 *Fax:* (0221) 249146
*E-mail:* info@hundertmark-gallery.com
*Web Site:* www.hundertmark-gallery.com
*Key Personnel*
Man Dir: Armin Hundertmark
Founded: 1970
Subjects: Art, Literature, Literary Criticism, Essays
*Showroom(s):* Galerie und Edition Hundermark,
Brusseler Str 29, 50674 Cologne

**Huss-Medien GmbH**
Am Friedrichshain 22, 10407 Berlin
*Tel:* (030) 421510 *Fax:* (030) 42151332
*E-mail:* huss.medien@hussberlin.de
*Web Site:* huss-medien.de *Cable:*
TECHNIKVERLAG BERLIN
*Key Personnel*
Dir: Guenther Schwarz *Tel:* (030) 42151203
*E-mail:* guenther.schwarz@hussberlin.de
Secretary: Monika Ebert *Tel:* (030) 42151302
*E-mail:* monika.ebert@hussberlin.de
Founded: 1946
Subjects: Career Development, Electronics, Electrical Engineering, Mechanical Engineering,
Radio, TV, Technology
ISBN Prefix(es): 3-341
*Parent Company:* Huss-Verlag GmbH, Munich
*Orders to:* LKG-Leipziger Kommissions-und
Grossbuchhandel mbH, Poetzschauer Weg,
04579 Espenhain
Zeitschriftenvertrieb, Am Friedrichshain 22,
10400 Berlin

**Huss-Verlag GmbH+**
Joseph-Dollinger-Bogen 5, 80807 Munich
Mailing Address: Postfach 460480, 80192 Munich
*Tel:* (089) 323910 *Fax:* (089) 32391416
*E-mail:* management@huss-verlag.de
*Web Site:* www.huss-verlag.de/
*Key Personnel*
President: Wolfgang Huss
Public Relations: Monica-Ines Oppel
Founded: 1975
Subjects: Automotive, Business, Electronics,
Electrical Engineering, Engineering (General),
Transportation
ISBN Prefix(es): 3-921455
*Associate Companies:* Huss GmbH,
Friedrichshain 22, 10407 Berlin
Subsidiaries: Verlag Technik GmbH; Verlag
Die Wirtschaft GmbH; Verlag fuer Bauwesen
GmbH
*Orders to:* Huss-GmbH, Am Friedrichshain 22,
10407 Berlin

**Husum Druck- und Verlagsgesellschaft mbH Co KG+**
Nordbahnhofstr 2, 25813 Husum
Mailing Address: Postfach 1480, 25804 Husum
*Tel:* (04841) 83520 *Fax:* (04841) 835210
*E-mail:* verlagsgruppe.husum@t-online.de
*Web Site:* www.verlagsgruppe.de/
*Key Personnel*
Man Dir, Editorial, Production, Rights & Permissions: Ingwert Paulsen
Founded: 1973
Subjects: Regional Interests
ISBN Prefix(es): 3-88042; 3-89876
*Associate Companies:* Hansa Verlag Ingwert
Paulsen Jr; Matthiesen Verlag Ingwert Paulsen
Jr; Verlag der Nation
Subsidiaries: Hamburger Lesehefte Verlag Iselt &
Co Nfl mbH

**Huthig GmbH & Co KG+**
Im Weiher 10, 69121 Heidelberg
Mailing Address: Postfach 102869, 69018 Heidelberg
*Tel:* (06221) 4890 *Fax:* (06221) 489279
*E-mail:* info@huethig.de
*Web Site:* www.huethig.de
*Key Personnel*
Man Dir: Hans-Joern Hoffmann; Huethig Holger;
Bernhard Kessler; Clemens Koehler
Marketing: Joseph Weisbrod
Founded: 1925
Subjects: Architecture & Interior Design, Business, Chemistry, Chemical Engineering, Civil
Engineering, Communications, Computer Science, Criminology, Earth Sciences, Electronics,
Electrical Engineering, Energy, Film, Video,
Health, Nutrition, Law, Medicine, Nursing,
Dentistry, Science (General), Technology
ISBN Prefix(es): 3-929471; 3-7785; 3-7832; 3-8226; 3-87541
Subsidiaries: Barth Verlag; C F Mue Verlag; Rv
Decker's Verlag; G Schenck; dpunkt Verlag;
Economica Verlag; Forkel Verlag; Haug Verlagstuppe; Heidelberg, Wichmann Verlag; tuer
digitale Technologie
*U.S. Office(s):* Hennig Wriedt, 29 MacIntosh Dr,
Oxford, CT 06478, United States *Tel:* 203-881-2467 *Fax:* 203-881-2795
*Warehouse:* Verlagsservice Suedwest, Boschstr 2,
68753 Waghaeusel, Kirrlach
*Orders to:* Heidelberger Verlagsservice GmbH,
Im Weiher 10, 69121 Heidelberg

**Edition ID-Archiv/ID-Verlag+**
Gneisenaustr 2a, 10961 Berlin
*Tel:* (030) 6947703 *Fax:* (030) 6947808
*E-mail:* id-verlag@mail.nadir.org
*Web Site:* www.txt.de/id-verlag/
*Key Personnel*
Contact: Andreas Fanizadeh; Wolfgang Tawereit
Founded: 1988
Subjects: Communications, Developing Countries,
Government, Political Science, History, Literature, Literary Criticism, Essays, Publishing &
Book Trade Reference
ISBN Prefix(es): 3-89408
Foreign Rep(s): Sebastian Count (Switzerland);
Seth Meyer Bruhns (Austria)
*Orders to:* Sova, Friesstr 20-24, 60388 Frankfurt
am Main

**Idea Verlag GmbH+**
Ringstr 40, 82223 Eichenau
Mailing Address: Postfach 1361, 82169 Puchheim
*Tel:* (08141) 80939 *Fax:* (08141) 80939
*E-mail:* info@idea-verlag.de
*Web Site:* www.idea-verlag.de
*Key Personnel*
Man Dir & Rights: Hariet Paschke
Founded: 1980
Subjects: Crafts, Games, Hobbies, Literature,
Literary Criticism, Essays, Science (General),
Sports, Athletics, Technology
ISBN Prefix(es): 3-88793; 3-9800371

**IDW-Verlag GmbH+**
Tersteegenstr 14, 40474 Duesseldorf
Mailing Address: Postfach 320580, 40420 Duesseldorf
*Tel:* (0211) 45610 *Fax:* (0211) 4561206
*E-mail:* post@idw-verlag.de
*Web Site:* www.idw-verlag.de *Cable:*
IDEWEVERLAG
*Key Personnel*
Man Dir: Rainer von Buechau
Founded: 1950
Subjects: Accounting, Business, Finance
ISBN Prefix(es): 3-8021
Subsidiaries: WPA- Wirtschaftsakademie

**Igel Verlag Literatur Michael Matthias Schardt**
Uhlhornsweg 99A, 26129 Oldenburg
*Tel:* (0441) 6640262 *Fax:* (0441) 6640263
*E-mail:* igelverlag@t-online.de
*Key Personnel*
Contact: Michael Schardt
ISBN Prefix(es): 3-89621; 3-927104

**Ikarus - Buchverlag+**
Schuhgasse 6, 36142 Tann Rhoen
*Tel:* (06682) 919383 *Fax:* (06682) 919385
*E-mail:* ikarus-verlag@t-online.de
*Web Site:* www.ikarus-verlag.de
*Key Personnel*
Man Dir: Dr Wolfgang Hautumm
Founded: 1982
Subjects: Archaeology, History, Literature, Literary Criticism, Essays, Travel
ISBN Prefix(es): 3-9802064; 3-9800471
Number of titles published annually: 2 Print
Total Titles: 25 Print

**IKO Verlag fur Interkulturelle Kommunikation+**
Assencheimerstr 17, 60489 Frankfurt am Main
Mailing Address: Postfach 900421, 60444 Frankfurt/Main
*Tel:* (069) 784808 *Fax:* (069) 7896575
*E-mail:* info@iko-verlag.de
*Web Site:* www.iko-verlag.de
*Key Personnel*
Man Dir: Walter Suelberg
Founded: 1982
Subjects: Alternative, Anthropology, Asian Studies, Business, Developing Countries, Education,
Environmental Studies, Ethnicity, Labor, Industrial Relations, Science (General), Women's
Studies
ISBN Prefix(es): 3-88939
*Associate Companies:* Holger Ehluig Publishers
at Tho-Verlag fur Tutor-Kultaelle Kouieriko-hou, 4T Leroy House, 436 Essex Rd, London
N1 3QP, United Kingdom *Tel:* (020) 7688 1688
*Fax:* (020) 7688 1699

**ILS**, see Institut fuer Landes- und
Stadtentwicklungsforschung des Landes
Nordrhein-Westfalen

**Impuls-Theater-Verlag+**
Postfach 1147, 82141 Planegg
*Tel:* (089) 8597577 *Fax:* (089) 8593044
*E-mail:* info@buschfunk.de
*Web Site:* www.buschfunk.de
*Key Personnel*
Contact: Florian Laber
Founded: 1932
Specialize in theatre: plays & books.
Subjects: Drama, Theater, Film, Video, Music,
Dance
ISBN Prefix(es): 3-7660
Distributed by Teaterverlag elgg (Switzerland)
Distributor for Stutz-Velag (Germany & Austria)

**IMSF**, see Institut fuer Marxistische Studien und
Forschungen eV (IMSF)

**Industria-Verlagsbuchhandlung GmbH**
Eschstr 22, 44629 Herne
Mailing Address: Postfach 101849, 44621 Herne
*Tel:* (02323) 1410 *Fax:* (02323) 141123
*Telex:* 8229870
*Key Personnel*
Manager: Ernst-Otto Kleyboldt
Subjects: Accounting, Law
ISBN Prefix(es): 3-87373

**Industrieschau Verlagsgesellschaft mbH**
Berliner Allee 8, 64295 Darmstadt
Mailing Address: Postfach 100264, 64202 Darmstadt

*Tel:* (06151) 38920 *Fax:* (06151) 389280
*E-mail:* info@abconline.de
*Web Site:* www.abconline.de
*Key Personnel*
Man Dir: Margit Selka
Reference & product directories about German
   industrial groups.
ISBN Prefix(es): 3-7790
*Parent Company:* ABC der Deutschen Wirtschaft
   Verlagsgesellschaft mbH
*Branch Office(s)*
PO Box 75, 1095 Vienna, Austria *Tel:* (0222)
   4053327
*U.S. Office(s):* Western Hemisphere Publishing
   Corp, PO Box 847, Hillsboro, OR 97123-0847,
   United States *Tel:* 503-640-3736 *Fax:* 503-640-
   2748

**Mediteg-Gesellschaft fuer Informatik Technik
   und Systeme Verlag+**
Limesstr 5, 61273 Wehrheim
*Tel:* (06081) 5171 *Fax:* (06081) 56017
*Key Personnel*
Manager: Rudolf Putz
Founded: 1984
Subjects: Medicine, Nursing, Dentistry
ISBN Prefix(es): 3-924373

**Informationsstelle Suedliches Afrika eV (ISSA)**
   (Information Centre on Southern Africa)
Koenigswinterer Str 116, 53227 Bonn
*Tel:* (0228) 464369 *Fax:* (0228) 468177
*E-mail:* issa@comlink.org
*Web Site:* www.issa-bonn.org
*Key Personnel*
Man Dir: Hein Moellers
Founded: 1971
Subjects: Developing Countries, Literature, Liter-
   ary Criticism, Essays
ISBN Prefix(es): 3-921614

**Infostelle Industrieverband Deutscher
   Schmieden e V**, see Infostelle Industrieverband
   Massivumformung e V

**Infostelle Industrieverband Massivumformung
   e V**
Formerly Infostelle Industrieverband Deutscher
   Schmieden e V
Goldene Pforte 1, 58093 Hagen
*Tel:* (02331) 958828 *Fax:* (02331) 958728
*E-mail:* cpair@imu.wsm-net.de
*Web Site:* www.metalform.de
*Key Personnel*
Management: Dr Theodore L Tutmann
   *Tel:* (02331) 958812 *E-mail:* ltutmann@imu.
   wsm-net.de
Marketing: Heinrich Benneker *Tel:* (02331)
   958821 *E-mail:* benneker@iht.wsm-net.de
ISBN Prefix(es): 3-928726; 3-9800981

**Inno Vatio Verlags AG**
Kurt Schumacherstr 2, 53113 Bonn
*Tel:* (0228) 93-444-33 *Fax:* (0228) 93-444-93
*E-mail:* medien-tenor@innovatio.de
*Web Site:* www.innovatio.de; www.medien-tenor.
   de
Founded: 1985
Subjects: Business, History, Specialize in monthly
   & quarterly newsletters on media content anal-
   ysis
Total Titles: 25 Print

**Insel Verlag+**
Lindenstr 29-35, 60325 Frankfurt am Main
Mailing Address: Postfach 101945, 60019 Frank-
   furt am Main
*Tel:* (069) 75601-0 *Fax:* (069) 75601-522
*Web Site:* www.suhrkamp.de *Cable:*
   INSELVERLAG

*Key Personnel*
Publisher: Ulla Unseld-Berkewicz
Man Dir: Philip Roeder *Tel:* (069) 75601-500
   *E-mail:* roeder@suhrkamp.de
Editorial Director: Dr Rainer Weiss
Sales & Marketing Dir: Dr Georg Rieppel
Rights & Permissions: Dr Petra Hardt
Founded: 1899
Subjects: Art, Ethnicity, Literature, Literary Criti-
   cism, Essays
ISBN Prefix(es): 3-458
*Associate Companies:* Deutscher Klassiker Ver-
   lag; Suhrkamp Verlag; Suhrkamp Verlag AG,
   Switzerland
*Branch Office(s)*
Liviastr 2, 04105 Leipzig *Tel:* (0341) 988980
   *Fax:* (0341) 9889820
Foreign Rep(s): Claudia Brandes (Netherlands,
   Europe, Scandinavia); Ulrich Breth (Asia,
   Greece, Turkey); Michael Griesinger (Latin
   America, Portugal, Spain); Petra Hardt (Aus-
   tralia, China, France, Israel, Italy, Middle East,
   Taiwan, US)
Foreign Rights: Agenzia (Italy); Balla & Co
   Literary Agents (Hungary); Bardon Chinese
   Media Agency (Taiwan); Hercules Business
   (China); Internationaal Literatuur Bureau
   (Netherlands); International Editors (Brazil,
   Latin America, Spain); Leonhardt & Hoier Lit-
   erary (Scandinavia); Sakai Agency (Japan)

**Institut fuer Baustoffe, Massivbau und
   Brandschutz/Bibliothek** (Institute for Building
   Materials, Reinforced Concrete Construction &
   Fire Protection Library)
Beethovenstr 52, 38106 Braunschweig
*Tel:* (0531) 391 5400 *Fax:* (0531) 391 5900
*E-mail:* ibmb@tu-bs.de
*Web Site:* www.ibmb.tu-bs.de
*Key Personnel*
Librarian: Oliver Dienelt *E-mail:* o.dienelt@tu-bs.
   de
Founded: 1963
Subjects: Civil Engineering, Proceedings, Reports,
   Theses
ISBN Prefix(es): 3-89288
Number of titles published annually: 8 Print
Total Titles: 180 Print

**Interconnections Reisen und Arbeiten Georg
   Beckmann+**
Schilerstr 44, 79102 Freiburg
*Tel:* (0761) 700650 *Fax:* (0761) 700688
*Key Personnel*
Owner: Georg Beckmann
Founded: 1985
Subjects: Travel
ISBN Prefix(es): 3-924586; 3-86040
*Orders to:* Internationaler Land Kartenhaus,
   Schockenreidstr 44a, 705655 Stuttgart

**International Thomson Publishing (ITP)+**
Koenigswintererstr 418, 53227 Bonn
*Tel:* (0228) 970240 *Fax:* (0228) 441342
*E-mail:* info@vmi-buch.de
*Web Site:* www.mitp.de
*Key Personnel*
President: Hartmut Gante
International Rights: H J Beese
Sales Dir: Markus Kanderer
Founded: 1992
Subjects: Computer Science
ISBN Prefix(es): 3-8266
Subsidiaries: Datacom; ITP - IWT; Wolframs
*Warehouse:* VVA Bertelsmann, Postfach 7777,
   33310 Guetersloh

**Verlag fuer Internationale Politik GmbH+**
Rauchstr 17-8, 10787 Berlin
*Tel:* (030) 254 231 46 *Fax:* (030) 254 231 16
*E-mail:* ip@dgap.org
*Web Site:* www.internationalepolitik.de

*Key Personnel*
Partner: Otto Wolff von Amerongen; Alfred Frhr
   von Oppenheim
Man Dir: Gerhard Eickhorn
Man Dir Assistant: Ulrike Rothe
Sales: Rainer Mertens
Founded: 1971
Subjects: Government, Political Science
ISBN Prefix(es): 3-921011
*Parent Company:* Europa Union Verlag GmbH

**Internationale Studien zen Fatigkeititleone**,
   *imprint of* Bund demokratischer
   Wissenschaftlerinnen und Wissenschafler eV
   (BdWi)

**Internationale Vereinigung fuer Geschichte
   und Gegenwart der Druckkunst eV**, see
   Gutenberg-Gesellschaft eV

**Intertrans-Verlag GmbH+**
Neckarstr 37, 63071 Offenbach
*Tel:* (069) 871500 *Fax:* (069) 852894
*Key Personnel*
Manager & International Rights: Bernhard
   Mueller
Founded: 1982
Subjects: Language Arts, Linguistics
ISBN Prefix(es): 3-8223; 3-922718
Distributor for Edition-Disque Omnivox
*Orders to:* Kurfuenstenstr 7, 67061 Ludwigshafen

**Irisiana**, *imprint of* Heinrich Hugendubel Verlag
   GmbH

**Klaus Isele+**
Heidelstr 9, 79805 Eggingen
*Tel:* (07746) 91116 *Fax:* (07746) 91117
*E-mail:* klaus.isele@t-online.de
*Key Personnel*
Owner: Klaus Isele
Editorial Dir: Eva Taubert
Founded: 1984
Subjects: Art, Fiction, Literature, Literary Crit-
   icism, Essays, Poetry, Religion - Buddhist,
   Travel
ISBN Prefix(es): 3-925016; 3-86142
Number of titles published annually: 18 Print; 6
   Audio
Total Titles: 200 Print; 20 Audio
*Orders to:* Kock, Neff & Oetinger & Co Ver-
   lagsauslieferung GmbH, Schockenriedstr 59,
   70565 Stuttgart *Tel:* (0711) 78990

**Iselt und Co Nfl mbH**, see Hamburger Lesehefte
   Verlag Iselt & Co Nfl mbH

**Verlag der Islam+**
Genfer Str 11, 60437 Frankfurt
*Tel:* (069) 50688-651 *Fax:* (069) 50688-655
*Telex:* 416187 Islam d *Cable:* ISLAM
   FRANKFURT MAIN
*Key Personnel*
Editor: Hadayatullah Huebsch *Tel:* (069) 314596
Founded: 1949
Subjects: Nonfiction (General), Religion - Islamic
ISBN Prefix(es): 3-921458; 3-932244
Total Titles: 110 Print
*U.S. Office(s):* The Ahmadiyya Movement in Is-
   lam Inc, Masjid Bait-ur-Rehman, 15000 Good
   Hope Rd, Silver Spring, MD, United States
   *Tel:* (301) 879-0110 *Fax:* (301) 879-0115
*Warehouse:* Hanauer Landstr 50, 60314 Frankfurt,
   Contact: Mr Munir *Tel:* (069) 43059519

**ISSA**, see Informationsstelle Suedliches Afrika
   eV (ISSA)

**ITP**, see International Thomson Publishing (ITP)

**ITpress Verlag+**
Mozartweg 24, 76646 Bruchsal
Mailing Address: Postfach 1744, 76607 Bruchsal
*Tel:* (07251) 300575 *Fax:* (07251) 14823
*E-mail:* itpress@acm.org
*Web Site:* www.itpress.com
*Key Personnel*
Prof: Dr Reiner Hartenstein *Tel:* (0631) 2052606
Founded: 1994
Subjects: Computer Science, Electronics, Electrical Engineering, Microcomputers, Nonfiction (General), Public Administration
ISBN Prefix(es): 3-929814
Number of titles published annually: 10 Print
Total Titles: 10 Print
Subsidiaries: ITpressHartenstein

**Iudicium Verlag GmbH+**
Hans-Graessel-Weg 13, 81375 Munich
Mailing Address: Postfach 701067, 81310 Munich
*Tel:* (089) 718747 *Fax:* (089) 7142039
*E-mail:* info@iudicium.de
*Web Site:* www.iudicium.de
*Key Personnel*
Man Dir: Dr Phil Habil
Manager: Dr Peter Kapitza
Contact: Dominique Colmont-Freisinger; Kiyoko Kapitza; Elisabeth Schaidhammer; Dr Lucia Schwellinger
Founded: 1983
Subjects: Anthropology, Art, Asian Studies, Biography, Communications, Drama, Theater, Education, Fiction, Foreign Countries, History, Language Arts, Linguistics, Library & Information Sciences, Literature, Literary Criticism, Essays, Music, Dance, Mysteries, Philosophy, Poetry, Psychology, Psychiatry, Religion - Catholic, Social Sciences, Sociology, Theology, Women's Studies
ISBN Prefix(es): 3-89129

**Reisebuchverlag Iwanowski GmbH**
Salm-Reifferscheidt-Allee 37, 41540 Dormagen
*Tel:* (02133) 26030 *Fax:* (02133) 260333
*E-mail:* info@iwanowski.de
*Web Site:* www.iwanowski.de
Founded: 1984
Subjects: Travel
ISBN Prefix(es): 3-933041; 3-923975
Number of titles published annually: 5 Print
Total Titles: 70 Print

**IWT Magazine Publishing House GmbH,**
*imprint of* Gildefachverlag GmbH & Co KG

**J Ch Mellinger Verlag GmbH+**
Burgholzstr 25, 70376 Stuttgart
*Tel:* (0711) 543787 *Fax:* (0711) 556889
*E-mail:* mellinger@sambo.de
*Key Personnel*
Manager: Wolfgang Militz; Tobias Sambo; Gudrun Emmert
Founded: 1926
Subjects: Biography, Education, Fiction
ISBN Prefix(es): 3-88069

**Verlag J P Peter, Gebr Holstein GmbH & Co KG**
Erlbacher Str 104, 91541 Rothenburg
*Tel:* (09861) 4 00-3 81 *Fax:* (09861) 4 00-70
*E-mail:* peter-verlag@rotabene.de
*Web Site:* www.peter-verlag.de
*Key Personnel*
Man Dir: Dr Gerhard Prinz; Wolfgang Schneider
Publisher: Dekan Christoph Schmerl
Founded: 1884
Subjects: Poetry, Religion - Other
ISBN Prefix(es): 3-87625; 3-87311
*Bookshop(s):* Evangel Bucherdrenst Rothenburg

**Jahreszeiten-Verlag GmbH+**
Possmoorweg 5, 22301 Hamburg
*Tel:* (040) 2717-0 *Fax:* (040) 2717-2056
*E-mail:* jahreszeitenverlag@jalag.de
*Web Site:* www.jalag.de *Cable:* JALAG
*Key Personnel*
Publisher: Thomas Ganske
Man Dir: Dr Vlla Kopp; Jorg Hausendorf; Peter Rensmann
International Advertising Dir: Oliver Schnoor
    *Tel:* (040) 2712-2296 *E-mail:* oliver.schnoor@jalag.de
Founded: 1948
Subjects: Architecture & Interior Design, Automotive, Cookery, Crafts, Games, Hobbies, Fashion, Foreign Countries, Gardening, Plants, Health, Nutrition, House & Home, How-to, Journalism, Travel, Wine & Spirits, Women's Studies
ISBN Prefix(es): 3-87383
*Parent Company:* Verlagsgruppe Ganske
*Associate Companies:* Hoffmann & Campe; Prinz Kommunikations GmbH; DLS GmbH; Graefe & Onzer; Die Woche
*U.S. Office(s):* Publicitas Globe Media, 261 Madison Ave, 19th floor, New York, NY 10016, United States, Contact: John Moncure *Tel:* 212-599-5057 *Fax:* 212-599-8298
*Bookshop(s):* Buchhaus Campe, Karolinenstr 13, 90402 Nuremberg; Medienhaus Prinz, T11-3, 68161 Mannheim; Schrobsdorff sche Buchhandlung, Koenigsallee 22, 40212 Dusseldorf

**Janus Verlagsgesellschaft, Dr Norbert Meder & Co+**
Am Rottmannshof 6, 33619 Bielefeld
*Tel:* (0521) 1369236 *Fax:* (0521) 1369237
Founded: 1980
Subjects: History, Language Arts, Linguistics, Science (General), Social Sciences, Sociology
ISBN Prefix(es): 3-922607; 3-922977
*Orders to:* Prolit Buchvertrieb GmbH, Siemensstr 16, 35463 Fernwald

**Verlag Winfried Jenior**
Lassallestr 15, 34119 Kassel
*Tel:* (0561) 7391621 *Fax:* (0561) 774148
*E-mail:* jenior@aol.com
*Web Site:* www.jenior.de
Publish book series of Kassel University, travel books on Spain, Spanish cookery books, yearbook & books on Kassel & region.
Subjects: Cookery, Regional Interests, Travel
ISBN Prefix(es): 3-9801438; 3-928172; 3-934377
Distributor for Moll Verlag

**JKL Publikationen GmbH+**
Klausenpas 14, 12107 Berlin
*Tel:* (030) 74104624 *Fax:* (030) 74104626
*E-mail:* info@zeitgut.com
*Web Site:* www.zeitgut.com
*Key Personnel*
Contact: Juergen Kleindienst *E-mail:* j.kleindienst@zeitgut.com
Membership(s): Boersenverlin des Deutschen Buchhandels.
Subjects: Biography, History
ISBN Prefix(es): 3-933336

**Wolfgang Joerg und Ingrid Joerg,** see Berliner Handpresse Wolfgang Joerg und Erich Schonig

**Johann Wolfgang Goethe Universitat**
Senckenberganlage 31-33, 60325 Frankfurt am Main
*Tel:* (069) 798-0 *Fax:* (069) 798-28383
*E-mail:* praesident@uni-frankfurt.de
*Web Site:* www.rz.uni-frankfurt.de
*Key Personnel*
President: Dr Rudolf Steinberg
    *E-mail:* praesident@uni-frankfurt.de

Founded: 1983
Subjects: Science (General)
Imprints: Anzeigenverwaltung & Herstellung; Bezugsbedingungen; Herausgeber; Redaktion & Gestaltung

**Johannes Berchmans Verlagsbuchhandlung GmbH**
Kaulbachstr 33, 80539 Munich
*Tel:* (089) 38185-244
*Key Personnel*
Manager: Manfred Hanke
ISBN Prefix(es): 3-87056

**Johannes Verlag Einsiedeln, Freiburg+**
Lindenmattenstr 29, 79117 Freiburg
*Tel:* (0761) 640168 *Fax:* (0761) 640169
*E-mail:* johverlag@aol.com
*Key Personnel*
Contact: Susanne Greiner; Cornelia Capol
Founded: 1947
Subjects: Philosophy, Religion - Catholic, Theology
ISBN Prefix(es): 3-89411
Number of titles published annually: 10 Print
Total Titles: 340 Print

**Johannis+**
Heiligenstr 24, 77933 Lahr
*Tel:* (07821) 5810 *Fax:* (07821) 581-26
*E-mail:* johannis-druck@t-online.de
*Web Site:* www.johannis-verlag.de
*Key Personnel*
Owner: Reinhold Fels
Publisher: Karlheinz Kern
Founded: 1896
Also publish gift books, booklets, stationery & greeting cards.
Subjects: Biblical Studies, Photography, Religion - Protestant, Theology
ISBN Prefix(es): 3-501
Total Titles: 1,100 Print

**Edition Jonas,** *imprint of* Dr Wolfgang Baur Verlag Kunst & Alltag

**Jonas Verlag fuer Kunst und Literatur GmbH**
Weidenhaeuser Str 88, 35037 Marburg
*Tel:* (06421) 25132 *Fax:* (06421) 210572
*E-mail:* jonas@jonas-verlag.de
*Web Site:* www.jonas-verlag.de
*Key Personnel*
Manager: Dieter Mayer-Guerr
Founded: 1978
Subjects: Art, History
ISBN Prefix(es): 3-89445
*Orders to:* Prolit *Fax:* (0641) 9439389

**Dr Werner Jopp Verlag+**
Leibnizstr 26, 65191 Wiesbaden
*Tel:* (0611) 547116 *Fax:* (0611) 542762
*Key Personnel*
Publisher: Dr Werner Jopp
Founded: 1987
Specialize in health advice.
Subjects: Health, Nutrition
ISBN Prefix(es): 3-926955; 3-89698

**Jovis Verlag GmbH+**
Kurfuerstenstr 15/16, 10785 Berlin
*Tel:* (030) 2636720 *Fax:* (030) 26367272
*E-mail:* jovis@jovis.de
*Web Site:* www.jovis.de
*Key Personnel*
Publisher: Jochen Visscher *E-mail:* visscher@jovis.de
Sales & Marketing Manager: Jutta Bornholdt-Cassetti *E-mail:* bornholdt@jovis.de
Founded: 1994
Subjects: Art, Film, Video, History, Nonfiction (General), Photography, Architecture, History of Art

ISBN Prefix(es): 3-931321; 9-936314
Number of titles published annually: 18 Print
Total Titles: 91 Print
*Distribution Center:* LKG, Poetzschauer Weg, 04579 Espenhain *Tel:* (034206) 65106 *Fax:* (034206) 65130 *E-mail:* kobarski@lkg-service.de
*Orders to:* Distributed Art Publishers (DAP), 155 Sixth Ave, New York, NY 10013-1507, United States *Tel:* 212-627-1999 *Fax:* 212-627-9484 *E-mail:* dwingate@dapinc.com

**Jowi-Verlag+**
Muehlbacher Str 5, 97753 Karlstadt-Laudenbach
*Tel:* (09353) 2921
Founded: 1991
ISBN Prefix(es): 3-9802897

**Joy Verlag GmbH+**
Am Fichtelholz 5, 87477 Sulzberg
*Tel:* (08376) 97383 *Fax:* (08376) 8845
*E-mail:* joy_verlag@compuserve.com
*Key Personnel*
Manager: Thomas Kettenring
Founded: 1989
Subjects: Health, Nutrition, Religion - Buddhist, Self-Help
ISBN Prefix(es): 3-928554; 3-9801624

**Juedischer Verlag GmbH+**
Lindenstr 29-35, 60325 Frankfurt am Main
Mailing Address: Postfach 101945, 60019 Frankfurt am Main
*Tel:* (069) 75601-0 *Fax:* (069) 75601-522
*Web Site:* www.suhrkamp.de
*Key Personnel*
Publisher: Ulla Unseld-Berkewicz
Man Dir: Philip Roeder *Tel:* (069) 75601-500 *E-mail:* roeder@suhrkamp.de
Rights & Permissions: Dr Petra Hardt
Founded: 1902
Subjects: Religion - Jewish
ISBN Prefix(es): 3-633
*Parent Company:* Suhrkamp Verlag

**Jugenddienst-Verlag**, see Peter Hammer Verlag GmbH

**Julius Klinkhardt Verlagsbuchhandlung+**
Ramsauer Weg 5, 83670 Bad Heilbrunn
*Tel:* (08046) 9304 *Fax:* (08046) 9306
*E-mail:* info@klinkhardt.de
*Web Site:* www.klinkhardt.de
*Key Personnel*
Contact: Andreas Klinkhardt; Rudiger Hartmann
Founded: 1834
Membership(s): The Stock Exchange of German Booksellers & Association of School Book Publishers.
Subjects: Education, Psychology, Psychiatry
ISBN Prefix(es): 3-7815

**Junfermann-Verlag+**
Imadstr 40, 33102 Paderborn
Mailing Address: Postfach 1840, 33048 Paderborn
*Tel:* (05251) 1 34 40 *Fax:* (05251) 13 44 44
*E-mail:* infoteam@junfermann.de
*Web Site:* www.junfermann.de
*Key Personnel*
Contact: Heike Carstensen *Tel:* (05251) 13 44 18 *E-mail:* carstensen@junfermann.de
Founded: 1659
Specialize in psychology & psychotherapy.
Subjects: Management, Psychology, Psychiatry, Self-Help
ISBN Prefix(es): 3-87387
Number of titles published annually: 30 Print
Total Titles: 250 Print

**Junius Verlag GmbH+**
Stresemannstr 375, 22761 Hamburg
Mailing Address: Postfach 500727, 22707 Hamburg
*Tel:* (040) 892599 *Fax:* (040) 891224
*E-mail:* info@junius-verlag.de
*Web Site:* www.junius-verlag.de
*Key Personnel*
Man Dir: Karl Olaf Petters *E-mail:* petters@junius-verlag.de
Founded: 1979
Subjects: Architecture & Interior Design, Government, Political Science, Philosophy, Social Sciences, Sociology
ISBN Prefix(es): 3-88506
Number of titles published annually: 30 Print
Total Titles: 200 Print
Distributed by AVA Book 2000 (Switzerland)
Foreign Rep(s): Idea Books, Amsterdam (Worldwide)
*Orders to:* LKG, Poetzschauer Weg, 04529 Esperhain *Tel:* (034206) 65720 *Fax:* (034206) 65770

**Justus-Liebig-Universitat Giessen**
Ludwigstr 23, 35390 Giessen
*Tel:* (0641) 99-0 *Fax:* (0641) 99-12259
*E-mail:* michael.kost@admin.uni-giessen.de
*Web Site:* www.uni-giessen.de
*Key Personnel*
President: Dr Stefan Hormuth *Tel:* (0641) 99-12000 *Fax:* (0641) 99-12009
Research institution (international economic & social development & environment).
Subjects: Agriculture, Environmental Studies
ISBN Prefix(es): 3-924840

**Jutta Pohl Verlag+**
Konigsbacherstr 51, 75196 Remchingen
*Tel:* (07232) 2239 *Fax:* (07202) 3879
*E-mail:* jutta@pohlverlag.de
*Web Site:* www.pohl-verlag.de *Cable:* POHL, CELLE
*Key Personnel*
Dir: Udo Meyer *Tel:* (05141) 9889-15
Subjects: Health, Nutrition, Music, Dance, Outdoor Recreation, Sports, Athletics
ISBN Prefix(es): 3-7911
Total Titles: 60 Print; 2 Audio
*Parent Company:* Cellesche Zeitung Schweiger & Pick Verlag, Pfingsten GmbH & Co KG
Foreign Rep(s): As Bartsch-Holler Gmbh (Austria); Schweizer Buchzentruun (Switzerland); Uitgeverij de Vraseborch (Netherlands)

**Juventa Verlag GmbH+**
Ehretstr 3, 69469 Weinheim
*Tel:* (06201) 9020-0 *Fax:* (06201) 9020-13
*E-mail:* juventa@juventa.de
*Web Site:* www.juventa.de
*Key Personnel*
Man Dir: Lothar Schweim *Tel:* (06201) 9020-10 *E-mail:* schweim@juventa.de
Advertising: Andrea Biernatzki *Tel:* (06201) 9020-15 *E-mail:* biernatzki@juventa.de
Founded: 1953
Subjects: Criminology, Education, Health, Nutrition, History, Psychology, Psychiatry, Social Sciences, Sociology
ISBN Prefix(es): 3-7799
Number of titles published annually: 70 Print
Total Titles: 800 Print
*Warehouse:* Justus-von-Liebigstr 1, 86899 Landsberg/Lech *Tel:* (08191) 125 243 *Fax:* (08191) 125 198
*Orders to:* WMi Verlags Service *Tel:* (08191) 125 243 *Fax:* (08191) 125 198

**K + G Verlagsgesellschaft**, see Karto + Grafik Verlagsgesellschaft (K & G Verlagsgesellschaft)

**Kabel Verlag**, *imprint of* Piper Verlag GmbH

**Kailash**, *imprint of* Heinrich Hugendubel Verlag GmbH

**KaJo Verlag+**
Imprint of Verlagshaus Wurzburg
Beethovenstr 5, 97070 Wurzburg
*Tel:* (0931) 385235 *Fax:* (0931) 385305
*E-mail:* info@verlagshaus.com
*Web Site:* www.verlagshaus.com
*Key Personnel*
Publishing Dir: Dieter Krause
Dir, Production: Juergen Roth
Sales Dir: Johannes Glesius
Founded: 1985
Subjects: Travel
ISBN Prefix(es): 3-925544

**Kallmeyer'sche Verlagsbuchhandlung GmbH+**
Im Brande 19, 30926 Seelze
*Tel:* (0511) 4 00 04-1 75 *Fax:* (0511) 4 00 04-1 76
*E-mail:* leserservice@kallmeyer.de
*Web Site:* www.kallmeyer.de
*Key Personnel*
Man Dir: Uwe Brinkman
Founded: 1986
Specialize in elementary drawings, rhythm & teaching goods.
Subjects: Career Development, Crafts, Games, Hobbies, Education, Engineering (General), Environmental Studies, Music, Dance, Nonfiction (General), Sports, Athletics
ISBN Prefix(es): 3-7800

**J Kamphausen Verlag & Distribution GmbH+**
Buddestr 15, 33602 Bielefeld
Mailing Address: Postfach 101849, 33518 Bielefeld
*Tel:* (0521) 56052-0 *Fax:* (0521) 56052-29
*Key Personnel*
Contact: Joachim Kamphausen
Founded: 1989
Subjects: Health, Nutrition, Medicine, Nursing, Dentistry
ISBN Prefix(es): 3-928430; 3-89901; 3-933496
*Orders to:* Jollenbeckerstr 29, 33613 Bielefeld

**S Karger GmbH Verlag fuer Medizin und Naturwissenschaften+**
Loerracher Str 16A, 79115 Freiburg
*Tel:* (0761) 45 20 70 *Fax:* (0761) 45 20 714
*E-mail:* information@karger.de
*Web Site:* www.karger.com; www.karger.de
*Cable:* KARGERMEDBOOKS
*Key Personnel*
Man Dir, International Rights: S Karger
Founded: 1890
Subjects: Medicine, Nursing, Dentistry, Psychology, Psychiatry, Science (General)
ISBN Prefix(es): 3-8055
*Parent Company:* S Karger AG, Allschwilerstr 10, 4009 Basel, Switzerland
*U.S. Office(s):* S Karger Publishers Inc, 26 W Avon Rd, PO Box 529, Farmington, CT 06085, United States
*Bookshop(s):* Karger-Buchhandlung Ausstellung und Vertrieb internationaler medizinischer Fachliteratur, Loerracher Str 16a, 79115 Freiburg

**Verlag Karl Baedeker GmbH**
Member of Mair Dumont
Marco-Polo-Zentrum 1, 73760 Ostfildern
Mailing Address: Postfach 3162, 73751 Ostfildern
*Tel:* (0711) 4502262 *Fax:* (0711) 4502343
*E-mail:* baedeker@mairdumont.com
*Web Site:* www.baedeker.de
*Key Personnel*
Man Dir: Dr Volkmar Mair
Chief Editor: Ranier Eisenschmid
Founded: 1827

Publshes travel guides worldwide & in many languages.
Subjects: Travel
ISBN Prefix(es): 3-87504; 3-89525; 3-8297
*Parent Company:* Mair Dumont

**Karl-May-Verlag Lothar Schmid GmbH+**
Schuetzenstr 30, 96047 Bamberg
*Tel:* (0951) 98 20 60 *Fax:* (0951) 2 43 67
*E-mail:* info@karl-may.de
*Web Site:* www.karl-may.de
*Key Personnel*
Man Dir, Publicity, Rights & Permissions: Lothar
    Schmid
Man Dir & Publicity: Bernhard Schmid
Founded: 1913
Subjects: Fiction, Western Fiction
ISBN Prefix(es): 3-7802
Number of titles published annually: 7 Print
Total Titles: 200 Print
Imprints: Edition Ustad
Subsidiaries: Karl May Verwaltungs-und
    Vertriebs-GmbH

**Karto + Grafik Verlagsgesellschaft (K & G
    Verlagsgesellschaft)+**
Schoenberger Weg 15, 60488 Frankfurt
*Tel:* (069) 76 20 31 *Fax:* (069) 76 91 06
*E-mail:* info@hildebrunds.de
*Web Site:* www.hildebrands.de
*Key Personnel*
Publisher: Volker Hildebrand
Man Dir: Hr Stefan Beyer
Founded: 1980
Subjects: Travel
ISBN Prefix(es): 3-88989
Total Titles: 100 Print
Distributed by Map Link; Librairie Ulysse Inc;
    ITMB Publishing Ltd; World Leisure Marketing

**Kartographischer Verlag Reinhard Ryborsch+**
Laubenstr 3, 63179 Obertshausen
Mailing Address: Postfach 2105, 63170
    Oberthausen
*Tel:* (06104) 79039 *Fax:* (06104) 75356
*Key Personnel*
Dir: Reinhard Ryborsch
Founded: 1987
Membership(s): Boersenverein des Deutschen
    Buchhandels; Deutsche Gesellschaft fuer Kartographie.
Subjects: Aeronautics, Aviation, Geography, Geology, Travel
ISBN Prefix(es): 3-920339; 3-927549

**Kastell Verlag GmbH+**
Giselastr 15, 80802 Munich
Mailing Address: Postfach 440312, 80752 Munich
*Tel:* (089) 33 21 75; (089) 399742 *Fax:* (089) 340
    11 78
*E-mail:* kastell-verlag@t-online.de
*Key Personnel*
Man Dir, Rights & Permissions: Christoph Burgauner
Founded: 1984
Subjects: History, Music, Dance
ISBN Prefix(es): 3-924592

**Verlag Katholisches Bibelwerk GmbH+**
Silberburgstr 121, 70176 Stuttgart
*Tel:* (0711) 619200 *Fax:* (0711) 6192044
*E-mail:* verlag@bibelwerk.de
*Web Site:* www.bibelwerk.de
*Key Personnel*
Editor, Rights & Permissions: Herbert Wilfart *Tel:* (0711) 6192027 *E-mail:* wilfart@
    bibelwerk.de
Man Dir: Juergen M Schymura MA *Tel:* (0711)
    6192020-21 *E-mail:* schymura@bibelwerk.de

Editor: Dr Winfried Bader *Tel:* (0711) 6192036
    *E-mail:* bader@bibelwerk.de
Founded: 1937
Membership(s): KMV.
Subjects: Biblical Studies, Religion - Catholic
ISBN Prefix(es): 3-460

**Katzmann Verlag KG+**
Schellingstr 41, 72072 Tuebingen
Mailing Address: Postfach 1827, 72008 Tuebingen
*Tel:* (07473) 5427 *Fax:* (07473) 5427 *Cable:*
    KATZMANN VERLAG
*Key Personnel*
Man Dir, Production, Publicity, Rights & Permissions: Dr Volker Katzmann
Sales Dir: Sibylle Katzmann
Founded: 1945
Specialize in scientific literature.
Subjects: Art, Education, Religion - Other, Social
    Sciences, Sociology, Theology
ISBN Prefix(es): 3-7805
*Associate Companies:* Heliopolis-Verlag Ewald
    Katzmann

**Verlag Ernst Kaufmann GmbH+**
Alleestr 2, 77933 Lahr
*Tel:* (07821) 93 90-0 *Fax:* (07821) 9390-11
*E-mail:* info@kaufmann-verlag.de
*Web Site:* www.kaufmann-verlag.de
*Key Personnel*
Man Dir: Michael Jacob
Chief Editor: Renate Schupp
Founded: 1816
Membership(s): Verlagsring Religionsunterricht
    (VRU), ATV & AVJ.
Subjects: Religion - Protestant, Religion - Other
ISBN Prefix(es): 3-7806

**KBV Verlags-und Medien - GmbH+**
Augustinerstr 1, 54576 Hillesheim
*Tel:* (06593) 998668 *Fax:* (06593) 998701
*E-mail:* info@kbv-verlag.de
*Web Site:* www.kbv-verlag.de
*Key Personnel*
Man Dir: Herbert Klein
Founded: 1989
Subjects: Fiction, Gay & Lesbian, Government,
    Political Science, Mysteries, Nonfiction (General), Adventure, Anthologies, Historical, Short
    Stories, Thriller
ISBN Prefix(es): 3-927658
*Warehouse:* LKG Leipziges Komissions-
    und Grosbuchhandels Gesellschaft mbH,
    Plotzschauer Wey, 04579 Espenhain
*Orders to:* LKG Leipziges Kommissions-
    und Grossbuchhandels Gesellchaft mbH,
    Plotzschauer Wey, 04579 Espenhain

**Keip GmbH+**
Bayernstr 9, 63773 Goldbach
*Tel:* (06021) 59 05 0 *Fax:* (06021) 59 05 42
*E-mail:* info@keip.net
*Web Site:* www.keip.net
*Key Personnel*
Manager: Ulrich Keip *Fax:* (06021) 59 05 32
    *E-mail:* ulrich@keip.net
Manager & Publisher: Dr Michael Simon
    *Fax:* (06021) 59 05 24 *E-mail:* simon@keip.net
Founded: 1967
Also antiquarian bookseller.
Membership(s): ILAB.
Subjects: Economics, History, Law, Social Sciences, Sociology
ISBN Prefix(es): 3-8051

**SachBuchVerlag Kellner** (Kellner Publishing
    House)+
St-Pauli-Deich 3, 28199 Bremen
*Tel:* (0421) 77866 *Fax:* (0421) 704058
*E-mail:* kellner-verlag@t-online.de

*Web Site:* kellner-verlag.de
*Key Personnel*
Editor: Klaus Kellner
Founded: 1988
Also acts as shipping house.
Subjects: Government, Political Science, Labor,
    Industrial Relations, Law, Nonfiction (General),
    Outdoor Recreation, Public Administration,
    Travel
ISBN Prefix(es): 3-927155
Number of titles published annually: 6 Print

**Martin Kelter Verlag GmbH u Co**
Postfach 70 10 09, 22010 Hamburg
*Tel:* (040) 68 28 95-0 *Fax:* (040) 68 28 95 50
*E-mail:* info@kelter.de
*Web Site:* www.kelter.de
*Telex:* 213126
*Key Personnel*
Man Dir: Gerhard Melchert
Founded: 1938
ISBN Prefix(es): 3-88832
*Associate Companies:* Mero-Druck Otto Melchert
    GmbH & Co KG

**P Keppler Verlag GmbH & Co KG**
Industriestr 2, 63150 Heusenstamm
Mailing Address: Postfach 1353, 63151 Heusenstamm
*Tel:* (06104) 606 0 *Fax:* (06104) 606 121
*E-mail:* info@kepplermediengruppe.de
*Web Site:* www.kepplermediengruppe.de
*Key Personnel*
Man Dir: Heinz Egon Schmitt
ISBN Prefix(es): 3-87398

**Kerber Verlag**
Windelsbleicherstr 166-170, 33659 Bielefeld
*Tel:* (0521) 95008-10 *Fax:* (0521) 95008-88
*E-mail:* info@kerber-verlag.de
*Web Site:* www.kerber-verlag.de
*Key Personnel*
Publisher: Christof Kerber *Tel:* (0521) 95008-11
    *Fax:* (0521) 95008-18
Editor: Tanja Kemmer *Tel:* (0521) 96768-30
    *Fax:* (0521) 96768-32
Production: Wolfgang Gros *Tel:* (0521) 95008-20
Marketing: Grit Schewe
Specialize in paintings & art.
Subjects: Architecture & Interior Design, Art,
    History
ISBN Prefix(es): 3-924639; 3-933040; 3-936646
Foreign Rep(s): DAP

**Verlag Kerle im Verlag Herder+**
Hermann Herder Str 4, 79104 Freiburg
*Tel:* (0761) 2717-0 *Fax:* (0761) 2717-520
*E-mail:* info@kerle.de
*Web Site:* www.kerle.de
*Key Personnel*
Man Dir: Dr Klaus-Christoph Scheffel
Editorial: C Soltau; B Wurster
Sales: W Reisterer
Press, Rights: Helga Theile
Founded: 1886
ISBN Prefix(es): 3-210; 3-85303
*Associate Companies:* Verlag Herder GmbH
    & Co KG; Verlag A G Ploetz GmbH & Co
    KG; Herder Editrice e Libreria, Italy; Editorial Herder SA, Spain; Libraria Herder, Spain;
    Herder AG
*Bookshop(s):* Herder Verlag

**Keysersche Verlagsbuchhandlung GmbH+**
Geibelstr 6, 81679 Munich
*Tel:* (089) 455540 *Fax:* (089) 45554111
*Key Personnel*
Publisher, Rights & Permissions: Hermann Farnung
Publisher: Klaus Rudloff
Advertising: Michaela Beck
Sales: Gudrun Shutzenberger
Founded: 1777

Subjects: Science (General)
ISBN Prefix(es): 3-87405
*Parent Company:* Frankfurter Allgemeine Zeitung GmbH
*Associate Companies:* BVU Buchverlage Union GmbH; Koehler & Amelang Verlagsgesellschaft mbH
Imprints: Flaschenpost

**Kidemus Verlag GmbH+**
Ruenderotherstr 15, 51109 Cologne
Mailing Address: Postfach 940225, 51090 Cologne
*Tel:* (0221) 84 20 97 *Fax:* (0221) 84 20 98
*E-mail:* info@kidemus.de
*Web Site:* www.kidemus.de
*Key Personnel*
Man Dir: Reinhold Schulze
Founded: 1995
ISBN Prefix(es): 3-9804821; 3-9806910
Number of titles published annually: 3 Print
Total Titles: 17 Print

**Verlag Kiepenheuer & Witsch+**
Rondorfer Str 5, 50968 Cologne
*Tel:* (0221) 376 85-0 *Fax:* (0221) 38 85 95
*E-mail:* verlag@kiwi-koeln.de
*Web Site:* www.kiwi-koeln.de *Cable:* KIEPENBUCHER COLOGNE
*Key Personnel*
Man Dir: Gaby Callenberg *E-mail:* gcallenberg@kiwi-koeln.de
Foreign Rights & Permissions: Gudrun Fahndrich *E-mail:* gfaehndrich@kiwi-koeln.de
Advertising: Susanne Beck *E-mail:* sbeck@kiwi-koeln.de
Founded: 1949
Subjects: Biography, Fiction, History, Nonfiction (General), Social Sciences, Sociology
ISBN Prefix(es): 3-462
Imprints: Kiwi-Reihe
*U.S. Office(s):* 171 W 79 St, New York, NY 10024, United States, Scout: Alison M Bond
Joan Daves Agency, 21 W 26th St, New York, NY 10010, United States, Agent: Jennifer Lyons

**Gustav Kiepenheuer Verlag GmbH+**
Gerichtsweg 28, 04103 Leipzig
Mailing Address: Postfach 101563, 04015 Leipzig
*Tel:* (0341) 9954600 *Fax:* (0341) 9954620
*E-mail:* info@aufbau-verlag.de
*Web Site:* www.aufbau-verlag.de
*Key Personnel*
Program Manager: Peter Birgit
Foreign Rights & Permissions: Astrid Poppenhusen *E-mail:* poppenhusen@aufbau-verlag.de
German Rights & Permissions: Martin Lorento *Tel:* (030) 28394-118 *E-mail:* lorentz@aufbau-verlag.de
Founded: 1909
Subjects: Biography, Nonfiction (General), Regional Interests
ISBN Prefix(es): 3-378
*Parent Company:* Leipziger Verlags- und Vertriebsgesellschaft mbH
*Associate Companies:* Sammlung Dieterich Verlagsgesellschaft mbH, Leipzig
*Shipping Address:* Mohr-Morava Buchvertrieb Gesellschaft mbH, Postfach 260, 1101 Vienna, Austria; Pegasus-Stichting, Uitgeverijen-Boekhandel, Rhijuvis Feithstr 28, PO Box 59687, 1054 PZ Amsterdam, Netherlands; Verlagsauslieferung Balmer, Boesch 41, Huenenberg
*Orders to:* Hans Heinrich Petersen GmbH, Bredowstr 20, 22113 Hamburg

**Kierdorf Ute Verlag+**
Gut Dohrgaul, 51688 Wipperfuerth
*Tel:* (02267) 2888 *Fax:* (02267) 4458
*E-mail:* Kierdorfverlag@t-online.de

*Web Site:* www.kierdorfverlag.de
*Key Personnel*
Owner: Ute Kierdorf
International Rights: Wolfgang Kierdorf
Founded: 1978
Subjects: Equestrian & Fung Shui
ISBN Prefix(es): 3-89118
*Orders to:* Grossohaus Wehling, Friedr Hajewann-Str 5560, 33719 Bielefeld

**Kilda Verlag+**
Muensterstr 71, 48268 Greven
*Tel:* (02571) 52115 *Fax:* (02571) 953269
*E-mail:* info@kildaverlag.de
*Web Site:* www.kildaverlag.com
*Key Personnel*
Man Dir: Fritz Poelking
Founded: 1969
Subjects: Photography, Nature
ISBN Prefix(es): 3-921427; 3-88949
Total Titles: 41 Print
*Orders to:* KSS, Zur Landwehr 2, 33824 Werther *Tel:* (05203) 9189-0 *Fax:* (05203) 9189-25 *E-mail:* info@ks-fotoliteratur.de *Web Site:* www.ks-fotoliteratur.de

**Verlag im Kilian GmbH+**
Nikolaistr 3, 35037 Marburg
*Tel:* (06421) 2 93 30 *Fax:* (06421) 16 38 94
*E-mail:* verlag@kilian.de
*Web Site:* www.kilian-verlag.de
*Telex:* 482381
*Key Personnel*
Man Dir: Barbara von Stackelberg *E-mail:* barbara.vonstackelberg@kilian.de
Founded: 1994
Specialize in health information & advice to professionals & the general public.
Subjects: Child Care & Development, Health, Nutrition, Medicine, Nursing, Dentistry
ISBN Prefix(es): 3-932091; 3-9803688; 3-9804445
*Parent Company:* Deutsches Gruenes Kreuz

**Edition Kima**, *imprint of* Drei Eichen Verlag Manuel Kissener

**Kinderbuchverlag**
Werderstr 10, 69469 Weinheim
*Tel:* (06201) 6007-0 *Fax:* (06201) 6007-310
*Key Personnel*
Man Dir: Joachim Radmer
Publicity: Ulrich Stoeriko-Blume
Rights: Charlotte Larat; Kerstin Michaelis
Founded: 1880
Subjects: Nonfiction (General)
ISBN Prefix(es): 3-358
*Parent Company:* Verlagsgruppe Beltz

**Kindler Verlag**, *imprint of* Rowohlt Verlag GmbH

**Th Kirchbaum, K**, *imprint of* Eironeia-Verlag

**P Kirchheim Verlag+**
Postfach 14 04 32, 80454 Munich
*Tel:* (089) 267474 *Fax:* (089) 2605528
*E-mail:* info@kirchheimverlag.de
*Web Site:* www.kirchheimverlag.de
*Key Personnel*
Owner: Peter Kirchheim
Founded: 1977
Publish books & CDs.
Subjects: Literature, Literary Criticism, Essays, Poetry, Regional Interests, Self-Help
ISBN Prefix(es): 3-87410
Number of titles published annually: 5 Print; 1 CD-ROM

Total Titles: 100 Print; 2 CD-ROM
*Warehouse:* LKG Leipziger Kommissions - und Grossbuchhandels GmbH, Poetzschauer Weg, 04579 Espenhain (Leipzig)

**Kirschbaum Verlag GmbH+**
Siegfriedstr 28, 53179 Bonn
Mailing Address: Postfach 210209, 53157 Bonn
*Tel:* (0228) 9 54 53-0 *Fax:* (0228) 9 54 53-27
*E-mail:* info@kirschbaum.de
*Web Site:* www.kirschbaum.de
*Key Personnel*
Man Dir: Bernhard Kirschbaum *E-mail:* b.kirschbaum@kirschbaum.de
Founded: 1949
Subjects: Automotive, Civil Engineering, Geography, Geology, Law, Transportation
ISBN Prefix(es): 3-7812
Total Titles: 195 Print

**Kiwi-Reihe**, *imprint of* Verlag Kiepenheuer & Witsch

**Klages-Verlag**
Eckermannstr 8, 30625 Hannover
*Tel:* (0511) 5358936 *Fax:* (0511) 5358928
*E-mail:* kv@lsz.de
*Key Personnel*
Contact: August-Wilhelm Klages
Founded: 1917
Membership(s): German Electronic Book Committee.
Subjects: Economics, Law, Public Administration
ISBN Prefix(es): 3-7813

**Klartext Verlagsgesellschaft mbH+**
Heblerstr 37, 45329 Essen
*Tel:* (0201) 86 206-0 *Fax:* (0201) 86 206-22
*E-mail:* info@klartext-verlag.de
*Web Site:* www.klartext-verlag.de
*Key Personnel*
Man Dir, Rights & Permissions & Editorial: Dr Ludger Classen *Tel:* (0201) 86206-59 *E-mail:* classen@klartext-verlag.de
Sales: Ariane Rump *Tel:* (0201) 86206-33 *E-mail:* rump@klartext-verlag.de
Advertising: Melanie Brockes *Tel:* (0201) 86206-29 *E-mail:* brockes@klartext-verlag.de
Production: Frank Muenschke *Tel:* (0201) 96206-60 *E-mail:* muenschke@klartext-verlag.de
Founded: 1982
Subjects: Government, Political Science, History, Nonfiction (General), Regional Interests, Self-Help, Social Sciences, Sociology, Sports, Athletics
ISBN Prefix(es): 3-88474; 3-89861
Distributed by Prolit Verlagsauslieferung GmbH (Germany & Austria); Schweizer Buchzentrum (Switzerland)
Foreign Rep(s): Jutta Leitner (Austria)
*Warehouse:* Postfach 9, 6301 Fernwald (Annerod) *Tel:* (0641) 43071 *Fax:* (0641) 42773
*Orders to:* Prolit Buchvertrieb, Siemensstr 16

**Ingrid Klein Verlag GmbH+**
Georgenstr 4, 80799 Munich
*Tel:* (089) 3818010 *Fax:* (089) 338704
*E-mail:* info@piper.de
*Web Site:* www.piper.de
*Key Personnel*
Man Dirs, Editorial: Joachim Jessen; Ingrid Klein
Man Dir: Detlef Lerch
Sales: Heike Latendorf-Janzen
Founded: 1993
Subjects: How-to, Psychology, Psychiatry, Self-Help, Body, Mind & Spirit, Esoterics, New Age
ISBN Prefix(es): 3-89521
*Orders to:* VVA Bertelsmann Distribution A: Klein Verlag, Postfach 7777, 33310 Guetersloh

**Kleine Reike**, *imprint of* Beerenverlag

**Verlag Kleine Schritte Ursula Dahm & Co**
(Little Steps Publisher)+
Medardstr 105, 54294 Trier
*Tel:* (0651) 309 010 *Fax:* (0651) 300 699
*E-mail:* mail@kleine-schritte.de
*Web Site:* www.kleine-schritte.de
*Key Personnel*
Man Dir: Ursula Dahm
Founded: 1980
Subjects: Astrology, Occult, Biography, Fiction, Gay & Lesbian, Human Relations, Nonfiction (General), Poetry, Psychology, Psychiatry, Self-Help, Women's Studies
ISBN Prefix(es): 3-923261; 3-89968

**Kleiner Bachmann Verlag fur Kinder und Umwelt+**
Hauptstr 279, 51503 Rosrath
*Tel:* (02205) 904-79 51 *Fax:* (02205) 910 855
*E-mail:* buch@kleinerbachmann.de
*Web Site:* www.kleinerbachmann.de
*Key Personnel*
Editor: Helmut Bachmann
Publishing Editor: Felicitas Jung
Founded: 1997
Specialize in picture books, Scandinavian authors, travel books for children, young authors under 18 years of age. The picture books try to awake sensitivity for environmental issues in a playful & uncomplicated manner.
Membership(s): AVJ (Arbeitsgemeinschaft von Jugendbuchverlagen).
Subjects: Environmental Studies, Fiction, Human Relations, Travel
ISBN Prefix(es): 3-933160
Number of titles published annually: 6 Print
Total Titles: 10 Print; 2 Audio
*Distribution Center:* Umbreit GmbH & Co KG Verlagsauslieferung, Mundelsheimer Str 3, 74321 Bietigheim-Bissingen, Contact: Ms Haberlandt *Tel:* (07142) 596-385 *Fax:* (07142) 596-387 *E-mail:* umbreit-verlagsauslieferung@t-online.de

**Unterwegs Verlag, Manfred Klemann+**
Dr Andlerstr 28, 78224 Singen
*Tel:* (07731) 63544 *Fax:* (07731) 62401
*E-mail:* uv@reisefuehrer.com
*Web Site:* www.reisefuehrer.com
*Key Personnel*
President & Rights: Manfred Klemann
Founded: 1983
ISBN Prefix(es): 3-924334; 3-86112
Subsidiaries: Hohentwiel-Verlag GmbH
*Warehouse:* VVA-Bertelsmann Distribution GmbH, An der Autonbahn, 33310 Guetersloh

**Klens Verlag GmbH+**
Carl-Mosterts-Platz 1, 40477 Duesseldorf
Mailing Address: Postfach 320620, 40421 Duesseldorf
*Tel:* (0211) 944794-0 *Fax:* (0211) 944794-30
*E-mail:* info@klensverlag.de
*Key Personnel*
Publisher: Doris Henseler
Founded: 1916
Subjects: Education, Religion - Other
ISBN Prefix(es): 3-87309
*Bookshop(s):* Buecher & Kunst KlensVerlag

**Verlag Klett-Cotta+**
Rotebuehlstr 77, 70178 Stuttgart
*Tel:* (0711) 6672-1256 *Fax:* (0711) 6672-2031
*E-mail:* info@klett-cotta.de
*Web Site:* www.klett-cotta.de
*Telex:* 722225 klet d
*Key Personnel*
Publisher: Michael Klett
Man Dir: Rainer Just *E-mail:* r.just@klett-cotta.de
Sales & Advertising: Hans-Werner Serwe
*E-mail:* h.serwe@klett-cotta.de

Sales Promotion: Horst Flinspach *Tel:* (0711) 6672-1533 *E-mail:* h.flinspach@klett-cotta.de
Advertising: Kirsten Brueckmann *Tel:* (0711) 6672-1429 *E-mail:* k.brueckmann@klett-cotta.de; Axel Loesdau *Tel:* (0711) 6672-1905 *E-mail:* a.loesdau@klett-cotta.de
Sales: Gaby Schuska *Tel:* (0711) 6672-1519 *E-mail:* g.schuska@klett-cotta.de
Public Relations: Ilona Jakobs *Tel:* (0711) 6672-1716 *Fax:* (0711) 6672-2032 *E-mail:* i.jakobs@klett-cotta.de; Katharina Wilts *Tel:* (0711) 6672-1258 *Fax:* (0711) 6672-2032 *E-mail:* k.wilts@klett-cotta.de
Rights & Permissions: Jasmin Fallahi *Tel:* (0711) 6672-1938 *E-mail:* j.fallahi@klett-cotta.de; Susanne Habermann *Tel:* (9711) 6672-1344 *E-mail:* s.habermann@klett-cotta.de; Roland Knappe *Tel:* (0711) 6672-1257 *Fax:* (0711) 6672-2033 *E-mail:* r.knappe@klett-cotta.de
Founded: 1659
Foreign Rep(s): Heinz-Andrea Spychiger & Heinz Marti (Switzerland); Eleonore Littasy (Austria); OBV - Klett-Cotta Verlagsgesellschaft mbH (Austria)
*Distribution Center:* BDK Buecherdienst Koeln, Koelner Str 248, 51149 Cologne *Tel:* (02203) 1002-0 *Fax:* (02203) 1002-146
Buchauslieferungsgesellschaft mbH & Co KG, Postfach 133, 2355 Wiener Neudorf, Austria *Tel:* (02236) 63535-244 *Fax:* (02236) 63535-243
Buecher Balmer, Boesch 41, 6331 Huenenberg, Switzerland *Tel:* (041) 7807100 *Fax:* (041) 7811520

**Ernst Klett Verlag GmbH+**
Rotebuehlstr 77, 70178 Stuttgart
Mailing Address: Postfach 106016, 70049 Stuttgart
*Tel:* (0711) 66 720 *Fax:* (0711) 66 72-20 00
*E-mail:* klett-kundenservice@klett-mail.de
*Web Site:* www.klett-verlag.de
*Telex:* 722232 kletd
*Key Personnel*
Publisher: Michael Klett
Rights & Export Sales, Klett International: Derrick Jenkins
Founded: 1897
Subjects: Education, Geography, Geology, Educational software
ISBN Prefix(es): 3-12; 3-7863; 3-8213; 3-88447; 3-88448
*Associate Companies:* Klett International GmbH

**Kley, Werner, Beteilgungs GmbH+**
Werlerstr 304, 59069 Hamm
*Tel:* (02381) 9504030 *Fax:* (02381) 9504019
*Key Personnel*
Publisher, Rights & Permissions: Kley Werner
Author: Wilhelm Sohlote
ISBN Prefix(es): 3-924607

**Erika Klopp Verlag GmbH+**
Member of Oetinger Group
Poppenbuetteler Chaussee 53, 22397 Hamburg
*Tel:* (040) 60790907 *Fax:* (040) 60790959
*E-mail:* klopp@vsg-hamburg.de
*Web Site:* www.erika-klopp.de; www.klopp.biz
*Key Personnel*
Publisher, Rights & Permissions: Jan Weitendorf
Founded: 1925
ISBN Prefix(es): 3-7817
Total Titles: 150 Print
*Parent Company:* VSG Verlags-Service Gesselschaft mbH
*Warehouse:* Runge Verlagsauslieferung/Steinhagen *Tel:* (05204) 9181-0 *Fax:* (05204) 9181-93

**Klosterhaus-Verlagsbuchhandlung Dr Grimm KG**
Klosterhaus, 37194 Wahlsburg
*Tel:* (05572) 7310 *Fax:* (05572) 999823

*Key Personnel*
President: Dr Holle Grimm
Founded: 1951
Subjects: History
ISBN Prefix(es): 3-87418

**Vittorio Klostermann GmbH+**
Frauenlobstr 22, 60487 Frankfurt am Main
Mailing Address: Postfach 90 06 01, 60446 Frankfurt am Main
*Tel:* (069) 97 08 16-0 *Fax:* (069) 70 80 38
*E-mail:* verlag@klostermann.de
*Web Site:* www.klostermann.de
*Key Personnel*
Man Dir & Publisher: Vittorio E Klostermann
International Rights: Anastasia Urban *Tel:* (069) 97 08 16-17
Marketing: Martin Warny *Tel:* (069) 97 08 16-12 *E-mail:* m.warny@klostermann.de
Publicity: Ms Friedrike Haertling *Tel:* (069) 97 08 16-11 *E-mail:* f.haertling@klostermann.de
Founded: 1930
Subjects: Genealogy, History, Law, Library & Information Sciences, Literature, Literary Criticism, Essays, Philosophy, Publishing & Book Trade Reference, Science (General)
ISBN Prefix(es): 3-465

**Verlag Fritz Knapp GmbH+**
Aschaffenburger Str 19, 60599 Frankfurt am Main
Mailing Address: Postfach 11 11 51, 60046 Frankfurt
*Tel:* (069) 97 08 33-0 *Fax:* (069) 7 07 84 00
*E-mail:* info@kreditwesen.de
*Web Site:* www.kreditwesen.de
*Telex:* 411397 Knapp d *Cable:* SCHAUINSLAND
*Key Personnel*
Man Dir: Klaus-Friedrich Otto
Marketing, Sales & Publicity: Werner Scholz
Production, Rights & Permissions: Claus Wonneberger
Founded: 1949
Subjects: Economics, Finance
ISBN Prefix(es): 3-7819; 3-8314
*Associate Companies:* Verlag Helmut Richardi GmbH, Theodor-Heuss-Allee 106, 60486 Frankfurt am Main
Subsidiaries: Kreditwesen Service GmbH
*Orders to:* Koch, Neff & Oetinger, Schockenriedstr 37, 70565 Stuttgart

**Albrecht Knaus Verlag GmbH+**
Neumarkterstr 28, 81673 Munich
*Tel:* (01805) 990505 *Fax:* (089) 4136-3333
*Telex:* 529965
*Key Personnel*
Publisher: Klaus Eck
Production: Peter Sturm
Publicity: Margit Schoenberger
Founded: 1978
Subjects: Art, Biography, Fiction, History, Nonfiction (General)
ISBN Prefix(es): 3-8135
*Parent Company:* Verlagsgruppe Bertelsmann GmbH
*Orders to:* VVA Bertelsmann Distribution, Postfach 7777, 33310 Guetersloh

**Verlag Josef Knecht+**
Liebfrauenberg 37, 60313 Frankfurt
*Tel:* (069) 281767; (069) 281768 *Fax:* (069) 296653
*Key Personnel*
Man Dir: Dr Hermann Herder; Dr Marianne Regnier
Rights & Permissions: Dieter Naveau
Founded: 1946
Specialize in religion, philosphy, social problems, human sciences. Special interest: the situation of mankind in post modern times.

Subjects: Philosophy, Regional Interests, Religion
- Other, Social Sciences, Sociology, Theology,
Travel, Cultural History
ISBN Prefix(es): 3-7820

**Knesebeck Verlag+**
Holzstr 26, 80469 Munich
Mailing Address: Postfach 140560, 80455 Munich
*Tel:* (089) 264059 *Fax:* (089) 269258
*E-mail:* sekretariat@knesebeck-verlag.de
*Web Site:* www.knesebeck-verlag.de
*Key Personnel*
Publisher & International Rights: Dr Rosemarie
von dem Knesebeck *E-mail:* rknesebeck@
knesebeck-verlag.de
Publisher: Herneid von dem Knesebeck
Founded: 1987
Subjects: Architecture & Interior Design, Biography, Photography
ISBN Prefix(es): 3-926901; 3-89660
Number of titles published annually: 20 Print
Total Titles: 70 Print

**Knowledge Media International+**
Division of Bertelsmann Arvato AG
Weihenstephaner Str 7, 81673 Munich
*Tel:* (089) 4136-8433 *Fax:* (089) 4136-8411
*Web Site:* www.k-m-i.com
*Key Personnel*
International Rights Dir: Vanessa Nowak
*E-mail:* vanessa.nowak@bertelsmann.de
International Rights Manager: Ines Killat
*E-mail:* ines.killat@bertelsmann.de
Licensing of books & multimedia products to international publishers; IT services & solutions.
Subjects: Animals, Pets, Architecture & Interior
Design, Child Care & Development, English
as a Second Language, Foreign Countries, Gardening, Plants, Geography, Geology, Health,
Nutrition, History, Mysteries, Natural History,
Nonfiction (General), Sports, Athletics, Travel

**Verlag Knut Reim, Jugendpresseverlag**
Steenwisch 24, 22527 Hamburg
Mailing Address: Postfach 302824, 20310 Hamburg
*Tel:* (040) 34 26 41 *Fax:* (040) 34 46 87
*Key Personnel*
General Manager: Jens Christians; Knut Reim
Founded: 1958
Subjects: Economics, Fiction, Law
ISBN Prefix(es): 3-87950
*Parent Company:* Jugend-Presse-Verlag, Dammtorstr 30, 20354 Hamburg

**Verlagsanstalt Alexander Koch GmbH+**
Fasanenweg 18, 70771 Leinfelden-Echterdingen
Mailing Address: Postfach 100256, 70746
Leinfelden-Echterdingen
*Tel:* (0711) 7591-0 *Fax:* (0711) 7591-380
*Web Site:* www.koch-verlag.de
*Key Personnel*
Man Dir: Karl-Heinz Weinbrenner; Liselotte
Drabarczyk
Founded: 1890
Subjects: Architecture & Interior Design
ISBN Prefix(es): 3-87422
*Associate Companies:* DRW-Verlag Weinbrenner
GmbH & Co; Bit-Verlag Weinbrenner GmbH
& Co KG

**Kochbuch Verlag Olga Leeb+**
Landsbergerstr 238, 80687 Munich
Mailing Address: Postfach 210628, Munich
80676
*Tel:* (089) 58998303; (089) 583094 *Fax:* (089)
560208; (089) 58995303
*Telex:* 5212486
*Key Personnel*
Man Dir: Olli Leeb

Founded: 1976
Subjects: Cookery
ISBN Prefix(es): 3-921799

**Koehler & Amelang Verlagsgesellschaft+**
c/o Deutsche Verlags-Anstalt GmbH, Koeniginstr
9, 80539 Munich
*Tel:* (089) 455 54-0 *Fax:* (089) 455 54-100
*E-mail:* buch@dva.de
*Web Site:* www.dva.de
*Key Personnel*
Publisher: Juergen Horbach *Tel:* (089) 455 54-
200 *Fax:* (089) 455 54-106 *E-mail:* juergen.
horbach@dva.de
Marketing Manager: Susanne Lange *Tel:* (089)
455 54-400 *E-mail:* susanne.lange@dva.de
Sales: Bernhard Fetsch *Tel:* (089) 455 54-406
*E-mail:* bernhard.fetsch@dva.de
Advertising: Ulrike Bachmann *Tel:* (089) 455 54-
405 *E-mail:* ulrike.bachmann@dva.de
Public Relations: Markus Desaga *Tel:* (089) 455
54-300 *Fax:* (089) 455 54-115 *E-mail:* markus.
desaga@dva.de
Rights: Susanne Seggewiss *Tel:* (089) 455 54-
310 *Fax:* (089) 455 54-113 *E-mail:* susanne.
seggewiss@dva.de
Founded: 1925
Subjects: Architecture & Interior Design, Art, Biography, History, Regional Interests
ISBN Prefix(es): 3-7338

**K F Koehler Verlag GmbH**
Am Wallgraben 110, 70565 Stuttgart
Mailing Address: Postfach 800569, 70553
Stuttgart
*Tel:* (0711) 7892 130 *Fax:* (0711) 7892 132
*E-mail:* info@kfk.de; sabine.haegele@kfk.de
*Telex:* ueber 7255344 kno d
*Key Personnel*
Man Dir: Joachim Herkert
Founded: 1789
Subjects: Biography, Geography, Geology, Government, Political Science, History, Law, Publishing & Book Trade Reference, Social Sciences, Sociology
ISBN Prefix(es): 3-87425

**Verlagsgruppe Koehler/Mittler+**
Striepenweg 31, 21147 Hamburg
*Tel:* (040) 7971303 *Fax:* (040) 79713324
*E-mail:* vertrieb@koehler-mittler.de
*Web Site:* www.koehler-mittler.de
*Key Personnel*
Publisher: Peter Tamm; Wolf O Storck
Production: Hans-Peter Herfs-George
Manager: Thomas Bantle
Sales & Publicity: Hans-Focko Koehler
Founded: 1789
Group Members: Verlag E S Mittler und Sohn
GmbH, Koehlers Verlagsgesellschaft mbH,
Verlag Offene Worte, Verlag Europaeische
Wehrkunde.
Subjects: Aeronautics, Aviation, Film, Video, History, Law, Maritime, Military Science, Philosophy, Public Administration, Social Sciences,
Sociology
ISBN Prefix(es): 3-8132; 3-7822
*Branch Office(s)*
Godesberger Allee 91, 53175 Bonn *Tel:* (0228)
30789-0 *Fax:* (0228) 30789-15 (for all members of group)

**Koehlers Verlagsgesellschaft mbH+**
Member of Verlagsgruppe Koehler/Mittler
Striepenweg 31, 21147 Hamburg
*Tel:* (040) 79713-03 *Fax:* (040) 79713324
*E-mail:* vertrieb@koehler-mittler.de
*Web Site:* www.koehler-mittler.de *Cable:*
KOEHLERS VLG D-21447 HAMBURG
*Key Personnel*
Publisher: Wolf O Storck; Peter Tamm
Manager: Thomas Bantle

Sales: Hans-Focko Koehler
Subjects: Fiction, Maritime, Nonfiction (General)
ISBN Prefix(es): 3-7822
*Associate Companies:* Maximilian-Verlag; E S
Mittler und Sohn GmbH; Verlag Offene Worte
Verlag Europaeische Wehrkunde
*Branch Office(s)*
Godesberger Allee 91, 53175 Bonn *Tel:* (0228)
307890 *Fax:* (0228) 3078915

**Koelner Universitaets-Verlag GmbH+**
Subsidiary of Deutscher Instituts-Verlag
Gustav-Heinemann-Ufer 84-88, 50968 Cologne
*Tel:* (0221) 48 81-1 *Fax:* (0221) 49 81-533
*E-mail:* welcome@iwkoeln.de
*Web Site:* www.iwkoeln.de
*Telex:* 8882071
*Key Personnel*
Man Dir & International Rights: Dr Michael
Huther
Founded: 1953
Subjects: Business, Economics, Education, Government, Political Science, Social Sciences,
Sociology
ISBN Prefix(es): 3-87427
*Parent Company:* Aktiv-informedia verlag GmbH

**Koenigs Erlaeuterungen**, *imprint of* C Bange
GmbH & Co KG

**Koenigs Lektueren**, *imprint of* C Bange GmbH
& Co KG

**Koenigsfurt Verlag, Evelin Buerger et
Johannes Fiebig+**
Koenigsfurt 6, Klein Koenigsfoerde am Nord-
Ostsee-Kanal, 24796 Krummwisch
*Tel:* (04334) 18 99 02; (04334) 18 22 010
*Fax:* (04334) 18 22 011
*E-mail:* info@koenigsfurt.com
*Web Site:* www.koenigsfurt.com
*Key Personnel*
Contact: Evelin Buerger
Founded: 1989
Also German market leader for Tarot & Co nonbooks.
Subjects: Astrology, Occult, Nonfiction (General),
Psychology, Psychiatry, Self-Help
ISBN Prefix(es): 3-927808; 3-933939; 3-89875
Number of titles published annually: 100 Print
Total Titles: 500 Print
Imprints: Bewusster Leben

**Verlag Koenigshausen und Neumann GmbH+**
Theodor Koernerstr 3a, 97072 Wuerzburg
*Tel:* (0931) 78 40-7 00
*E-mail:* info@koenigshausen-neumann.de
*Web Site:* www.koenigshausen-neumann.de/
*Key Personnel*
Man Dir: Dr Johannes Koenigshausen; Dr
Thomas Neumann
Founded: 1979
Subjects: Archaeology, Economics, Education,
Ethnicity, Law, Literature, Literary Criticism,
Essays, Philosophy, Psychology, Psychiatry,
Social Sciences, Sociology
ISBN Prefix(es): 3-88479; 3-8260

**Lucy Koerner Verlag+**
Bahnhofstr 49, 70734 Fellbach
Mailing Address: Postfach 1106, 70701 Fellbach
*Tel:* (0711) 588472 *Fax:* (0711) 5789634
*Key Personnel*
Man Dir: Lucy Koerner
Subjects: Fiction
ISBN Prefix(es): 3-922028

**Verlag Valentin Koerner GmbH**
Postfach 100164, 76482 Baden-Baden
*Tel:* (07221) 22423 *Fax:* (07221) 38697
*E-mail:* info@koernerverlag.de

*Web Site:* www.koernerverlag.de/ *Cable:*
KOERNERVERLAG
*Key Personnel*
Publisher: Tobias Koerner
Founded: 1954
Subjects: Art, History, Music, Dance, Theology
ISBN Prefix(es): 3-87320
Number of titles published annually: 20 Print
Total Titles: 500 Print
Imprints: Heitz Librarie

**Koesel-Verlag GmbH & Co+**
Flueggenstr 2, 80639 Munich
*Tel:* (089) 17801-0 *Fax:* (089) 17801-111
*E-mail:* leserservice@koesel.de
*Web Site:* www.koesel.de/ *Cable:*
KOESELVERLAG MUNICH
*Key Personnel*
Man Dir: Juergen Horbach; Winfried Nonhoff
Production: Armin Koehler
Sales: Kathrin Doering
Rights & Permissions: Ingrid Fink
Advertising: Marion Riedl
Founded: 1593
Membership(s): TR-Verlagsunion GmbH;
Gesellschafter of Deutscher Taschenbuch Ver-
lag (dtv).
Subjects: Education, Philosophy, Psychology, Psy-
chiatry, Religion - Other
ISBN Prefix(es): 3-466
Distributed by Verlagsauslieferung Balmer
(Switzerland); WMI Verlagsservice GmbH &
Co KG (Germany)
*Bookshop(s):* Koeselsche Buchhandlung, Roncalli-
platz 2, 50667 Cologne
*Orders to:* Moderne Industrie Verlagsservice,
Landsberg

**W Kohlhammer GmbH+**
Hessbruehlstr 69, 70565 Stuttgart
*Tel:* (0711) 7863-0 *Fax:* (0711) 7863-8204
*E-mail:* redaktion@kohlhammer.de
*Web Site:* www.kohlhammer.de *Cable:*
KOHLHAMMER STUTTGART
*Key Personnel*
Man Dir: Dr Juergen Gutbrod; Hans-Joachim
Nagel
Sales Dir: Joerg Neumann
Editorial Dir, Rights & Permissions: Dr Alexan-
der Schweickert
Contact: Gerda Schmid
Founded: 1866
Subjects: Architecture & Interior Design, Busi-
ness, Economics, Education, Engineering (Gen-
eral), Government, Political Science, History,
Language Arts, Linguistics, Law, Management,
Marketing, Medicine, Nursing, Dentistry, Phi-
losophy, Psychology, Psychiatry, Public Ad-
ministration, Religion - Catholic, Religion -
Islamic, Religion - Jewish, Religion - Protestant,
Religion - Other, Social Sciences, Sociology,
Theology
ISBN Prefix(es): 3-17
Total Titles: 3,400 Print
Subsidiaries: Deutscher Gemeindeverlag GmbH;
Grote'sche Verlagsbuchhandlung GmbH & Co
KG; Kohlhammer und Wallishauser GmbH;
W Kohlhammer Druckerei GmbH & Co; W
Kohlhammer Communication GmbH; Bruell-
mann GmbH & Co Repro-und Systemtechnik;
Data Images Audiovisuelle Kommunikation;
Verlagsvertrieb Stuttgart GmbH; Dienst am
Buch GmbH
Divisions: W Kohlhammer Intermedia GmbH
*Branch Office(s)*
Ernst-Reuter-Haus, Strasse des 17, Juni 110-114,
10623 Berlin
Cologne
Rudolf-Leonhard-Str 28, 01097 Dresden
*Tel:* (0351) 8022685 *Fax:* (0351) 8020664
Gustav-Freytag-Str 59, 99096 Erfurt *Tel:* (0361)
3735379 *Fax:* (0361) 3460537

Alexanderstr 3, 30159 Hannover *Tel:* (0511)
327029 *Fax:* (0511) 320143
Jagersberg 17, 24103 Kiel *Tel:* (0431) 554857
*Fax:* (0431) 554944
Schleinufer 14, 39104 Magdeburg *Tel:* (0391)
597080 *Fax:* (0391) 5970813
Alexander-Diehl-Str 10, 55130 Mainz
*Tel:* (06131) 891540 *Fax:* (06131) 891624
Werkstr 209, 19061 Schwerin *Tel:* (0385) 616105
*Fax:* (0385) 616146
*Warehouse:* Verlagsvertrieb Stuttgart GmbH,
Hessbruhlstr 69, 70565 Stuttgart

**Kolibri-Verlag GmbH+**
Wielandstr 37, 22089 Hamburg
*Tel:* (040) 2202243 *Fax:* (040) 2276368
*E-mail:* infos@kolibriverlag.de
*Key Personnel*
International Rights: Mr Foen Tjoeng Lie
Founded: 1990
Subjects: Asian Studies, Health, Nutrition, Non-
fiction (General), Philosophy, Religion - Bud-
dhist, Sports, Athletics
ISBN Prefix(es): 3-928288
Number of titles published annually: 5 Print
Total Titles: 50 Print
Subsidiaries: Kolibri Seminare

**Kommentator,** *imprint of* Wolters Kluwer
Deutschland GmbH

**Kon & Bundig,** *imprint of* C Bange GmbH & Co
KG

**Konkordia Verlag GmbH**
Eisenbahnstr 31, 77815 Buehl
*Tel:* (07223) 98 89-0 *Fax:* (07223) 98 89-45
*E-mail:* verlag@konkordia.de
*Web Site:* www.konkordia.de
Founded: 1881
Subjects: Education, Mathematics, Regional Inter-
ests
ISBN Prefix(es): 3-934873

**Konkret Literatur Verlag+**
Hoheluftchaussee 74, 20253 Hamburg
*Tel:* (040) 47 52 34 *Fax:* (040) 47 84 15
*E-mail:* info@konkret-literatur-verlag.de
*Web Site:* www.konkret-verlage.de
*Key Personnel*
Man Dir, Rights & Permissions: Dr Dorothee
Gremliza
Founded: 1978
Subjects: Developing Countries, Government,
Political Science, Health, Nutrition, History,
Medicine, Nursing, Dentistry, Nonfiction
(General), Poetry, Social Sciences, Sociology,
Women's Studies
ISBN Prefix(es): 3-922144; 3-89458
Distributed by B&I (Switzerland); Herder & Co
(Austria)
*Shipping Address:* Bertelsmann Distribution/VVA,
Postfach 7777, 33310 Guetersloh *Tel:* (05241)
801499 *Fax:* (05241) 809352
*Warehouse:* Bertelsmann Distribution/VVA, Post-
fach 7777, 33310 Guetersloh *Tel:* (05241)
801499 *Fax:* (05241) 809352
*Orders to:* Bertelsmann Distribution/VVA, Post-
fach 7777, 33310 Guetersloh *Tel:* (05241)
801499 *Fax:* (05241) 809352

**Anton H Konrad Verlag**
Schulstr 5, 89264 Weissenhorn
Mailing Address: Postfach 1206, 89259 Weis-
senhorn
*Tel:* (07309) 26 57 *Fax:* (07309) 60 69
*E-mail:* info@konrad-verlag.de
*Web Site:* www.konrad-verlag.de/
*Key Personnel*
Man Dir, Rights & Permissions: Anton H Konrad
Founded: 1961

Subjects: Art, Biography, Geography, Geology,
History, Philosophy, Regional Interests
ISBN Prefix(es): 3-87437

**Konradin-Verlagsgruppe+**
Ernst-Mey-Str 8, 70771 Leinfelden-Echterdingen
*Tel:* (0711) 7594-0 *Fax:* (0711) 7594-390
*E-mail:* info@konradin.de
*Web Site:* www.konradin.de
*Key Personnel*
Manager: Katja Kohlhammer
Founded: 1929
Subjects: Architecture & Interior Design, Chem-
istry, Chemical Engineering, Computer Science,
Electronics, Electrical Engineering, Engineering
(General), Technology
ISBN Prefix(es): 3-920560
*U.S. Office(s):* Trade Media International Corp,
421 Seventh Ave, Suite 607, New York, NY
10001-2002, United States *Tel:* 212-564-3380
*E-mail:* cdgtmicor@cs.com
*Shipping Address:* PVS, Sonnengasse 2, 74172
Neckarsulm

**KONTEXTverlag+**
Lindenhoekweg 2, 10409 Berlin
*Tel:* (030) 94415444 *Fax:* (030) 94415445
*E-mail:* service@kontextverlag.de
*Web Site:* www.kontextverlag.de
*Key Personnel*
Owner: Torsten Metelka *E-mail:* metelka@
kontextverlag.de
Founded: 1990
Subjects: Art, Government, Political Science, Lit-
erature, Literary Criticism, Essays, Philosophy
ISBN Prefix(es): 3-86161; 3-931337

**Kontur,** *imprint of* Bonifatius GmbH
Druck-Buch-Verlag

**kopaed verlagsgmbh**
Pfaelzer-Wald-Str 64, 81539 Munich
*Tel:* (089) 68890098 *Fax:* (089) 6891912
*E-mail:* info@kopaed.de
*Web Site:* www.kopaed.de
*Key Personnel*
Contact: Dr Ludwig Schlump
Subjects: Communications, Education, Film,
Video, Nonfiction (General), Radio, TV
ISBN Prefix(es): 3-935686; 3-929061; 3-934079
Number of titles published annually: 25 Print
Total Titles: 180 Print

**Koptisch-Orthodoxes Zentrum**
St Antonius-Kloster, Pater Michael Hauptstr 10,
35647 Waldsolms-Kroeffelbach
*Tel:* (06085) 23 17 *Fax:* (06085) 26 66
*E-mail:* jugend@kopten.de
*Web Site:* www.kopten.de
*Key Personnel*
Contact: St Antonius Kloster
Subjects: Nonfiction (General), Religion - Other
ISBN Prefix(es): 3-927464

**Bergstadtverlag Wilhelm Gottlieb Korn GmbH
Wuerzburg+**
Hermann-Herder-Str 4, 79104 Freiburg im Breis-
gau
*Tel:* (0711) 4406-193 *Fax:* (0711) 4406-199
*Key Personnel*
Dir: Dr Joachim Bensch
Founded: 1732
Subjects: Art, Biography, History, Literature, Lit-
erary Criticism, Essays, Poetry, Regional Inter-
ests, Travel
ISBN Prefix(es): 3-87057

**Kosmos-Verlag,** see Franckh-Kosmos
Verlags-GmbH & Co

**Dr Anton Kovac Slavica Verlag+**
Elizabethstr 22, 80796 Munich

*Tel:* (089) 2725612 *Fax:* (089) 2716594
*E-mail:* 101566.2450@compuserve.com
*Key Personnel*
Owner: Anton Kovac
Founded: 1987
Subjects: Anthropology, Ethnicity, Fiction, Foreign Countries, Government, Political Science, History, Language Arts, Linguistics, Literature, Literary Criticism, Essays, Philosophy, Poetry, Religion - Other
ISBN Prefix(es): 3-927077

**Roman Kovar Verlag+**
Hauptstr 13, 86492 Egling an der Paar
*Tel:* (08206) 961977 *Fax:* (08206) 961978
*E-mail:* romankovar@gmx.net
*Web Site:* www.kovar-verlag.com
*Key Personnel*
Publisher: Roman Kovar
Founded: 1986
Subjects: Art, Library & Information Sciences, Literature, Literary Criticism, Essays, Religion - Jewish
ISBN Prefix(es): 3-925845

**Karl Kraemer Verlag GmbH und Co+**
Schulze-Delitzsch-Str 15, 70565 Stuttgart
Mailing Address: Postfach 80 06 50, 70506 Stuttgart
*Tel:* (0711) 7 84 96-0 *Fax:* (0711) 7 84 96-20
*E-mail:* info@kraemerverlag.com
*Web Site:* www.kraemerverlag.com
*Key Personnel*
President: Karl H Kraemer *E-mail:* karl.kraemer@kraemerverlag.com
Dir: Gudrun Kraemer *E-mail:* gudrun.kraemer@kraemerverlag.com; Lutz Kraemer *E-mail:* lutz.kraemer@kraemerverlag.com
Founded: 1930
Subjects: Architecture & Interior Design
ISBN Prefix(es): 3-7828
Total Titles: 118 Print
*Associate Companies:* Verlag Karl Kraemer & Co, Postfach 1209, 8034, Switzerland
*Bookshop(s):* Fachbuchhandlung Karl Kraemer, Rotebuehlstr 40, Postfach 102842, 701784 Stuttgart *Tel:* (0711) 669930 *Fax:* (0711) 628955 *Web Site:* www.karl.kraemer.de
*Orders to:* Koch, Neff, Oetinger & Co, Postfach 800620, 70506 Stuttgart

**Reinhold Kraemer Verlag+**
Rothenbaumchaussee 103F, 20148 Hamburg
*Tel:* (040) 4101429 *Fax:* (040) 455770
*E-mail:* info@kraemer-verlag.de
*Web Site:* www.kraemer-verlag.de
*Key Personnel*
Man Dir: Dr Reinhold Kraemer
Founded: 1987
Subjects: Science (General)
ISBN Prefix(es): 3-926952; 3-89622

**Adam Kraft Verlag+**
Imprint of Verlagshaus Wurzburg
Beethovenstr 5, 97070 Wurzburg
*Tel:* (0931) 385235 *Fax:* (0931) 385305
*E-mail:* info@verlagshaus.com
*Web Site:* www.verlagshaus.com
*Key Personnel*
Publishing Dir: Dieter Krause
Dir of Production: Juergen Roth
Sales Dir: Johannes Glesius
Founded: 1927
Subjects: Foreign Countries, Regional Interests, Travel
ISBN Prefix(es): 3-8083

**Krafthand Verlag Walter Schultz GmbH**
Walter-Schulz Str 1, 86825 Bad Woerishofen
Mailing Address: Postfach 1462, 86817 Bad Worishofen

*Tel:* (08247) 30070 *Fax:* (08247) 300770
*E-mail:* info@krafthand.de
*Web Site:* www.krafthand.de
*Key Personnel*
President, Man Dir & Public Relations: Gottfried Karpstein
Man Dir & Editorial Chief: Walter G Schweizer
Founded: 1927
Subjects: Civil Engineering
ISBN Prefix(es): 3-87441

**Verlag Edition Kraftpunkt Anton Fedrigotti+**
Steinerne Furt 78, 86167 Augsburg
*Tel:* (0821) 705011 *Fax:* (0821) 705008
*Key Personnel*
Owner: Toni Fedrigotti
Founded: 1982
ISBN Prefix(es): 3-925557; 3-928086; 3-89647
*U.S. Office(s):* Dr Eldon Taylor, 816 W Big Bear Blvd, Big Bear City, CA 92314, United States
*Tel:* (909) 585-6065 *Fax:* (909) 585-6365

**Karin Kramer Verlag+**
Postfach 440417, 12004 Berlin
*Tel:* (030) 6845055; (030) 6842598 *Fax:* (030) 6858577
*E-mail:* kramer@virtualitas.com
*Web Site:* www.anares.org/kramer/
*Key Personnel*
Editorial & Publicity: Bernd Kramer
Founded: 1970
Subjects: Alternative, Art, Biography, Government, Political Science, History, Literature, Literary Criticism, Essays, Nonfiction (General), Philosophy, Poetry, Science Fiction, Fantasy, Social Sciences, Sociology
ISBN Prefix(es): 3-87956

**Verlag Waldemar Kramer+**
Orberstr 38, 60386 Frankfurt am Main
Mailing Address: Berlinerstr 8a, 61440 Oberursel
*Tel:* (069) 449045 *Fax:* (069) 449064
*E-mail:* info@frankfurtbuecher.de
*Web Site:* www.frankfurtbuecher.de
*Key Personnel*
Publisher: Dr Henriette Kramer
Founded: 1939
Subjects: Art, Biological Sciences, Education, Environmental Studies, Geography, Geology, History, Natural History, Science (General)
ISBN Prefix(es): 3-7829
Total Titles: 200 Print

**Krankenpflegeforschung,** *imprint of* Bibliomed - Medizinische Verlagsgesellschaft mbH

**Nara Verlag Josef Krauthaeuser+**
Akazienring 6a, 85391 Allershausen
Mailing Address: Postfach 1241, 85388 Allershausen
*Tel:* (08166) 8530; (08166) 8531 *Fax:* (08166) 8530
*E-mail:* info@nara-verlag.de
*Web Site:* www.nara-international.de; www.nara-verlag.de
*Key Personnel*
Manager, Rights & Permissions: Josef Krauthaeuser
Founded: 1982
Subjects: Aeronautics, Aviation
ISBN Prefix(es): 3-925671

**Hubert Kretschmar Leipziger Verlagsgesellschaft+**
Gerichtsweg 28, 04103 Leipzig
*Tel:* (0341) 2210229 *Fax:* (0341) 2210226
*Key Personnel*
Proprietor, Rights & Permissions: Hubert Kretschmar
Founded: 1990
Specialize in high quality catalogs & art books.

Subjects: Art, History, Literature, Literary Criticism, Essays, Regional Interests
ISBN Prefix(es): 3-910143

**Verlag Hubert Kretschmer+**
Nymphenburgerstr 34, 80336 Munich
Mailing Address: Postfach 260117, 80058 Munich
*Tel:* (089) 1234530 *Fax:* (089) 1238638
*E-mail:* hubert.kretschmer@t-online.de
*Web Site:* www.verlag-hubert-kretschmer.de
Founded: 1980
Specialize in artist's books, catalogs, new & abstract photography.
Subjects: Art, Photography
ISBN Prefix(es): 3-923205
Total Titles: 40 Print
Distributor for ICON

**Kriebel Verlag GmbH**
Auf der Hoehe 14, 86923 Finning
*Tel:* (08806) 93 60 *Fax:* (08806) 93 61
*E-mail:* info@kriebelverlag.de
*Web Site:* www.kriebel-sat.de; www.kriebelverlag.de
*Key Personnel*
Manager: Henning Kriebel
Founded: 1986
Subjects: Communications
ISBN Prefix(es): 3-927617
Divisions: Media Service

**Alfred Kroner Verlag+**
Reinsburgstr 56, 70178 Stuttgart
*Tel:* (0711) 6155363 *Fax:* (0711) 61553646
*E-mail:* kontakt@kroener-verlag.de
*Web Site:* www.kroener-verlag.de
*Key Personnel*
Man Dir: Arno Klemm; Dr Imma Klemm; Walter Kohrs
Founded: 1904
Subjects: Art, Drama, Theater, History, Language Arts, Linguistics, Literature, Literary Criticism, Essays, Music, Dance, Philosophy, Religion - Other
ISBN Prefix(es): 3-520
Total Titles: 180 Print
*Orders to:* VA/KNO Stuttgart

**Krueger Verlag GmbH+**
Hedderichstr 114, 60596 Frankfurt am Main
*Tel:* (069) 6062-0 *Fax:* (069) 6062-214
*Web Site:* www.fischerverlage.de
*Key Personnel*
Man Dir: Monika Schoeller; Dr Hubertus Schenkel
Man Dir, Rights & Permissions: Wolfgang Mertz
Sales: Joerg Alkenbrecher
Publicity: Margarete Schwind
Production: Wilfried Meiner
Editorial: Peter Wilfert
Subjects: Fiction, Humor, Nonfiction (General)
ISBN Prefix(es): 3-8105
*Parent Company:* S Fischer Verlag GmbH

**Krug & Schadenberg+**
Arndtstr 34, 10965 Berlin
*Tel:* (030) 61625752 *Fax:* (030) 61625751
*E-mail:* info@krugschadenberg.de
*Web Site:* www.krugschadenberg.de
*Key Personnel*
International Rights: Andrea Krug
Founded: 1993
Membership(s): Women in Publishing.
Subjects: Fiction, Gay & Lesbian, Human Relations, Literature, Literary Criticism, Essays, Self-Help, Women's Studies
ISBN Prefix(es): 3-930041
Number of titles published annually: 6 Print
Total Titles: 30 Print

**Verlag Ernst Kuhn+**
Mendelssohnstr 7, 10405 Berlin
Mailing Address: PO Box 080147, 10001 Berlin
*Tel:* (030) 44342230 *Fax:* (030) 4424732
*E-mail:* ernst-kuhn-verlag@t-online.de
*Web Site:* www.vek.de
*Key Personnel*
Publisher: Ernst Kuhn *E-mail:* kuhn@vek.de
Man Dir: Baerbel Bruder *E-mail:* bruder@vek.de
Founded: 1991
Specialize in books on Russian music; also
   online-bookshop (books on music, sheet mu-
   sic, scores).
Subjects: Biography, History, Music, Dance
ISBN Prefix(es): 3-928864; 3-936637
*Orders to:* LKG mbH, Potzschauer Weg, 04579
   Espenhain bei Leipzig

**Kulturbuch-Verlag GmbH**
Sprosserweg 3, 12351 Berlin
Mailing Address: Postfach 470449, 12313 Berlin
*Tel:* (030) 6618484 *Fax:* (030) 6617828
*E-mail:* kbvinfo@kulturbuch-verlag.de
*Web Site:* www.kulturbuch-verlag.de
*Key Personnel*
Manager: Lothar Seikrit
Founded: 1949
Subjects: Environmental Studies, Law, Regional
   Interests
ISBN Prefix(es): 3-88961

**Kulturstiftung der deutschen Vertriebenen**
Kaiserstr 113, 53113 Bonn
*Tel:* (0228) 915120 *Fax:* (0228) 218397
*E-mail:* kulturstiftung@t-online.de
*Web Site:* www.kulturstiftung-der-deutschen-
   vertriebenen.de
*Key Personnel*
Chairperson: Dr Reinold Schleifenbaum
Man Dir: Dr Hans-Jakob Tebarth
Founded: 1974
Subjects: Art, Government, Political Science, His-
   tory, Law, Literature, Literary Criticism, Essays
ISBN Prefix(es): 3-88557
Number of titles published annually: 12 Print
Total Titles: 200 Print

**Verlag der Kunst/G+B Fine Arts Verlag
   GmbH+**
Rosa-Menzerstr 12, 01309 Dresden
Mailing Address: Postfach 190154, 01281 Dres-
   den
*Tel:* (0351) 3360742; (0351) 3100052 *Fax:* (0351)
   3105245
*E-mail:* verlag-der-kunst@t-online.de
*Web Site:* www.verlag-der-kunst.de
*Key Personnel*
Editor: Martina Buder
Marketing Manager: Dr Barbara Schmidt
Founded: 1952
Specialize in architecture.
Subjects: Architecture & Interior Design, Art,
   Photography, Regional Interests
ISBN Prefix(es): 3-364; 90-5705
Total Titles: 120 Print
*Associate Companies:* G+B Arts International
Distributed by IPD
*Warehouse:* SOVA, Friesstr 20-24, 60388 Frank-
   furt
*Distribution Center:* SOVA, Friesstr 20-24, 60388
   Frankfurt

**Kunst und Wohnen Verlag GmbH**, see Dr
   Wolfgang Schwarze Verlag

**Verlag Antje Kunstmann GmbH+**
Georgenstr 123, 80743 Munich
Mailing Address: Postfach 431351, Munich
   80743
*Tel:* (089) 1211930 *Fax:* (089) 12119320
*E-mail:* info@kunstmann.de

*Web Site:* www.kunstmann.de
*Key Personnel*
Man Dir, Editorial: Antje Kunstmann
Sales: Ulrich Deurer
Founded: 1970
Subjects: Drama, Theater, Education, Fiction,
   Government, Political Science, Humor, Liter-
   ature, Literary Criticism, Essays, Nonfiction
   (General)
ISBN Prefix(es): 3-921040; 3-88897
*Orders to:* LKG, Potzschaues Weg, 04579 Espen-
   hain
B & I, Obfelderstr 35, 8910 Affoltern a A,
   Switzerland
Mohr-Morawa, Sulzengasse 2, 1230 Vienna, Aus-
   tria

**Kunstverlag Maria Laach**
56653 Maria Laach
*Tel:* (02652) 59360 *Fax:* (02652) 59383
*E-mail:* verlag@maria_laach.de; versand@
   maria_laach.de
*Web Site:* www.ars-liturgica.de/verlag
*Key Personnel*
Dir: P Cremer

**Kunstverlag Weingarten GmbH+**
Laegelerstr 31, 88250 Weingarten
*Tel:* (0751) 561290 *Fax:* (0751) 5612920
*E-mail:* kunstverlag@weingarten-verlag.de
*Web Site:* www.kv-weingarten.de
*Key Personnel*
President: Rainer Berger
Publisher & International Rights: Hero Schiefer
   *Tel:* (0751) 5612940 *E-mail:* hschiefer@
   weingarten-verlag.de
Founded: 1976
Publishers of art & photo calendars.
Subjects: Animals, Pets, Antiques, Architecture
   & Interior Design, Art, Cookery, Health, Nu-
   trition, Literature, Literary Criticism, Essays,
   Music, Dance, Photography
ISBN Prefix(es): 3-8170; 3-921617
Total Titles: 180 Print

**Kupfergraben Verlagsgesellschaft mbH+**
Luetzowstr 105, 10785 Berlin
*Tel:* (030) 2622097 *Fax:* (030) 2621990
*Key Personnel*
Man Dir: Wolfgang Stapp
Founded: 1984
Subjects: Art, Literature, Literary Criticism, Es-
   says
ISBN Prefix(es): 3-89181

**Kynos Verlag Dr Dieter Fleig GmbH+**
Am Remelsbach 30, 54570 Muerlenbach/Eifel
*Tel:* (06594) 653 *Fax:* (06594) 452
*E-mail:* info@kynos-verlag.de
*Web Site:* www.kynos-verlag.de
*Key Personnel*
Dir: Herbert Wolter
Foreign Rights: Gisela Rau
Founded: 1980
Subjects: Animals, Pets
ISBN Prefix(es): 3-929545; 3-924008; 3-933228
Total Titles: 210 Print

**Laaber-Verlag GmbH+**
Regensburgerstr 19, 93164 Laaber
*Tel:* (09498) 2307 *Fax:* (09498) 2543
*E-mail:* info@laaber-verlag.de
*Web Site:* www.laaber-verlag.de
*Key Personnel*
Man Dir: Dr Henning Mueller-Buscher
Editor: Susanne Boehm
Founded: 1977
Subjects: Music, Dance
ISBN Prefix(es): 3-89007; 3-921518
Total Titles: 1,000 Print

**Labyrinth Verlag Gisela Ottmer**
Yorckstr 3, 38102 Braunschweig
*Tel:* (0531) 64259 *Fax:* (0531) 681358
*E-mail:* labyrinthbraunschweig@t-online.de
*Web Site:* www.frauenart.
   de/labyrinthbraunschweig
ISBN Prefix(es): 3-9801010; 3-9806542; 3-
   9807707

**Ambro Lacus, Buch- und Bildverlag Walter A
   Kremnitz**
Frieding-Hurtenstr 25, 82346 Andechs
*Tel:* (08152) 1332 *Fax:* (08152) 40186 *Cable:*
   KREMNITZ-FRIEDING
*Key Personnel*
Man Dir, Rights & Permissions: Walter Kremnitz
Bookkeeping: P Kremnitz
Founded: 1974
Subjects: Earth Sciences, Gardening, Plants, Law,
   Nonfiction (General), Science (General), Travel
ISBN Prefix(es): 3-921445
Number of titles published annually: 2 Print

**Lahn-Verlag GmbH+**
Hoogeweg 71, 47623 Kevelaer
*Tel:* (02832) 929-0 *Fax:* (02832) 929-211
*E-mail:* service@lahn-verlag.de
*Web Site:* www.lahn-verlag.de *Cable:* LAHN-
   VERLAG
*Key Personnel*
Publisher: Dr Gerhard Hartmann *E-mail:* gerhard.
   hartmann@lahn-verlag.de; Engelbert Tauscher
Editorial: Dr Stefan Ohnesorge; Anne Voorhoeve
Sales: Helmut Kaiser *E-mail:* helmut.kaiser@
   lahn-verlag.de
Founded: 1900
Subjects: Poetry, Religion - Catholic, Theology
ISBN Prefix(es): 3-7840
Total Titles: 200 Print; 50 Audio
*Orders to:* Butzon & Bercker GmbH, Hoogeweg
   71, 47623 Kevelaer *Tel:* (02832) 9290
   *Fax:* (02832) 929 211 *E-mail:* service@
   butzonbercker.de

**Johannis Lahr**, see Verlag der
   Sankt-Johannis-Druckerei C Schweickhardt

**Lambda Edition GmbH+**
Clemens-Schultzstr 77, 20359 Hamburg
Mailing Address: Postfach 304171, 20324 Ham-
   burg
*Tel:* (040) 312836 *Fax:* (040) 3192096
*Key Personnel*
Publisher: Michael P Hartleben
Founded: 1980
Membership(s): the Stock Exchange of German
   Booksellers.
Subjects: Fiction
ISBN Prefix(es): 3-925495

**Lambertus Verlag GmbH+**
Mitscherlichstr 8, 79108 Freiburg
Mailing Address: Postfach 1026, 79010 Freiburg
*Tel:* (0761) 368250 *Fax:* (0761) 3682533
*E-mail:* info@lambertus.de
*Web Site:* www.lambertus.de
*Key Personnel*
Man Dir: Fritz Boll; Gerhild Neugart
Founded: 1898
ISBN Prefix(es): 3-7841
Subsidiaries: Freiburge Buchedienst (verlagsbuch-
   handlung)
*Bookshop(s):* Freiburger Buecherdienst, Wolfinstr
   4, 79104 Freiburg

**Lamuv Verlag GmbH+**
Gromerstr 20, 37073 Goettingen
Mailing Address: Postfach 2605, 37016 Goettin-
   gen
*Tel:* (0551) 44024 *Fax:* (0551) 41392
*E-mail:* info@lamuv.de
*Web Site:* www.lamuv.de

*Key Personnel*
Man Dir, Editorial: Karl-Klaus Rabe
Sales: Leonore Frester
Founded: 1976
Subjects: Developing Countries, Government, Political Science, Literature, Literary Criticism, Essays, Regional Interests
ISBN Prefix(es): 3-921521; 3-88977

**Landbuch-Verlagsgesellschaft mbH**
(Countrybook-Publishing House)+
Kabelkamp 6, 30179 Hannover
Mailing Address: Postfach 160, 30001 Hannover
*Tel:* (0511) 27046-153 *Fax:* (0511) 27046-150
*E-mail:* info@landbuch.de
*Web Site:* www.landbuch.de *Cable:* LANDBUCH HANOVER
*Key Personnel*
Man Dir: Bernd Kuhrmeier
Sales: Elvira Frede
Sales & Marketing: Rene Busse
Production, Rights & Permissions: Dieter Brodbeck
Public Relations: Ulrike Clever
Founded: 1945
Subjects: Agriculture, Animals, Pets, Cookery, Crafts, Games, Hobbies, House & Home, Humor, Nonfiction (General), Outdoor Recreation, Regional Interests, Travel, Country Cooking, Country Life, Guides for Northern Germany
ISBN Prefix(es): 3-7842

**Institut fuer Landes- und Stadtentwicklungsforschung des Landes Nordrhein-Westfalen** (Research Institute for Regional & Urban Development of the Federal State of North Rhine-Westphalia)+
Deutsche Str 5, 44339 Dortmund
*Tel:* (0231) 90 51-0 *Fax:* (0231) 90 51-1 55
*E-mail:* postelle@ils.nrw.de
*Web Site:* www.ils.nrw.de
*Key Personnel*
Dir: Sierau Ullrich
Founded: 1971
Subjects: Architecture & Interior Design, Energy, Environmental Studies, Law, Outdoor Recreation, Physical Sciences, Public Administration, Regional Interests, Social Sciences, Sociology, Technology, Transportation, Women's Studies
ISBN Prefix(es): 3-8176
Distributed by WAZ-Vertrieb Bitte streichen

**Peter Lang GmbH Europaeischer Verlag der Wissenschaften+**
Eschborner Landstr 42-50, 60489 Frankfurt am Main
Mailing Address: Postfach 940225, 60460 Frankfurt am Main
*Tel:* (069) 7807050 *Fax:* (069) 780705-50
*E-mail:* zentrale.frankfurt@peterlang.com
*Web Site:* www.peterlang.de
*Key Personnel*
Man Dir: Ruprecht Sickel; Juergen-Matthias Springer
Licenses: Ruediger Brunsch *Tel:* (069) 78070520
*E-mail:* r.brunsch@peterlang.com
Founded: 1971
Subjects: Education, Government, Political Science, History, Language Arts, Linguistics, Law, Literature, Literary Criticism, Essays, Philosophy, Science (General), Theology
ISBN Prefix(es): 3-631; 3-8204
*Parent Company:* Verlag Peter Lang AG, Switzerland
*Associate Companies:* Peter Lang Publishing Inc, 275 Seventh Ave, 28th floor, New York, NY 10001-6708, United States *Tel:* 212-647-7706 *Fax:* 212-647-7707 *E-mail:* customerservice@plang.com *Web Site:* www.peterlang.com
*Orders to:* Peter Lang AG, Moosstr 1, 2542 Pieterlen, Switzerland *Tel:* (032)

376 17 17 *Fax:* (032) 376 17 27
*E-mail:* customerservice@peterlang.com *Web Site:* www.peterlang.ch

**Langenscheidt Fachverlag GmbH+**
Mies-van-der-Rohestr 1, 80807 Munich
*Tel:* (089) 36096-0 *Fax:* (089) 36096-222
*E-mail:* kundenservice@langenscheidt.de
*Web Site:* www.langenscheidt.de
*Key Personnel*
Manager: Marie-Jeanne Derouin *Tel:* (089) 36096 475 *E-mail:* marie-jeanne.derouin@langenscheidt.de
Founded: 1991
Subjects: Specialized bilingual & multilingual print & electronic versions
ISBN Prefix(es): 3-86117
*Parent Company:* Langenscheidt KG
*Warehouse:* TVA Gotha, Langenscheidtstr 70, 99867 Gotha
*Orders to:* Langenscheidt Fachverlag, Postfach 401120, 80711 Munich

**The Langenscheidt Group+**
Mies-van-der-Rohestr 1, 80807 Munich
Mailing Address: Postfach 401120, 80711 Munich
*Tel:* (089) 36096-0; (089) 36096-258 (orders) *Fax:* (089) 36096-222; (089) 36096-258
*E-mail:* kundenservice@langenscheidt.de
*Web Site:* www.langenscheidt.de
*Key Personnel*
General Partner: Andreas Langenscheidt; Nare Ernst Tidebier-Langenscheidt
Publishing Dir: Rolf Mueller
Sales Dir & Marketing: Dr Matt Schuesseler
Financial Dir: Dr Eugene Saller
Founded: 1856
The Group consists of: Bibliographisches Institut und F A Brockhaus AG; Axel Juncker Verlag; Langenscheidt KG; Langenscheidt-Hachette GmbH; Langenscheidt-Longman GmbH; Mentor-Verlag; Polyglott Verlag GmbH; Langenscheidt Fachverlag GmbH (all in Germany); Langenscheidt-Verlag GmbH, Austria; Apa Publications; GmbH & Co Verlag KG; Langenscheidt AG, Switzerland; Langenscheidt Publishers, Inc; Creative Sales Corp; American Map Corp; ADC; Trakker Maps Inc Nationwide; Arrow Map Inc; Hagstrom Map Co Inc; The Map Store Inc; Ha ADC Map & Travel Center; Berlitz Publishing; Hammond: Blay Folder SAS France; Langenscheidt Polska; Geo Center International UK.
ISBN Prefix(es): 3-468; 3-86117; 3-595; 3-526; 3-493

**Langenscheidt-Hachette+**
Mies-van-der-Rohestr 1, 80807 Munich
Mailing Address: Postfach 401120, 80711 Munich
*Tel:* (089) 360960 *Fax:* (089) 36096-222; (089) 36096-472 (general); (089) 36096-258 (orders)
*E-mail:* kundenservice@langenscheidt.de
*Web Site:* www.langenscheidt.de
*Key Personnel*
Man Dir: Karl Ernst Tielebier-Langenscheidt; Marc Moingeon
Editorial: Dr Herbert Bornebusch
Founded: 1977
Sales & Promotion through Langenscheidt KG.
Membership(s): the Langenscheidt Group.
Subjects: Education, Language Arts, Linguistics
ISBN Prefix(es): 3-595

**Langenscheidt KG+**
Member of The Langenscheidt Group
Mies-van-der-Roehstr 1, 80807 Munich
Mailing Address: Postfach 401120, 80711 Munich
*Tel:* (089) 36096-0; (089) 36096-258 (orders) *Fax:* (089) 36096-222

*E-mail:* kundenservice@langenscheidt.de
*Web Site:* www.langenscheidt.de
*Telex:* Munich 5215379 lkgmd *Cable:* LANGENSCHEIDT MUNICH
*Key Personnel*
Man Dir: Karl Ernst Tielebier-Langenscheidt; Andreas Langenscheidt
Program Manager: Dr Wolfgang Wieter
Chief Editor, English language: Wolfgang Kaul
Chief Editor, Slavonic languages: Dr Paul Ruehl
Chief Editor, German as a Foreign language: Dr Herbert Bornebusch
Chief Editor, Roman languages: Dieter Meier
Production: Helmut Wahl
Sales Dir: Michael Staehler
Advertising: Brigitte Pasch
Publicity: Margrit Philipp
Export: Alan Francis Roberts
Electronic Publishing: Dr Hans Werner Scholz
Rights & Permissions: Walburga Hallet-Wolters
Legal Dept: Dr Martin Wagner
Founded: 1856
Membership(s): TR- Verlagsunion GmbH.
ISBN Prefix(es): 3-526
Subsidiaries: Langenscheidt-Longman GmbH; Langenscheidt-Hachette GmbH; Polyglott-Verlag Dr Bolte KG; Humboldt-Taschenbuchverlag Jacobi KG; Mentor Verlag Dr Ramdohu KG; Karl Baedeker GmbH; Bibliographisches Institut und F L Brockhaus AG; Verlag Enzyklopaedie; Langenscheidt-Verlag GmbH; Langenscheidt AG; Trakker Maps Inc; Arrow Map Inc; Creative Sales Corp; Langenscheidt Publishers Inc; American Map Corp; Hagstrom Map Co; ADC; Apa Publications (HK) Ltd

**Verlag Langewiesche-Brandt KG+**
Lechnerstr 27, 82067 Ebenhausen (Schaeftlarn)
*Tel:* (08178) 4857 *Fax:* (08178) 7388
*E-mail:* textura@langewiesche-brandt.de
*Web Site:* www.langewiesche-brandt.de
*Key Personnel*
Man Dir: Kristof Wachinger *E-mail:* wachinger@langewiesche-brandt.de
Founded: 1906
Subjects: Poetry
ISBN Prefix(es): 3-7846
Number of titles published annually: 4 Print
Total Titles: 60 Print
Imprints: Ebenhausen bei Muenchen

**Karl Robert Langewiesche Nachfolger Hans Koester KG+**
Gruener Weg 6, 61462 Koenigstein
*Tel:* (06174) 7333 *Fax:* (06174) 933 039
*E-mail:* info@langewiesche-verlag.de
*Web Site:* www.langewiesche-verlag.de *Cable:* LANGEWIESCHE KOENIGSTEINTAUNUS
*Key Personnel*
Publisher & Man Dir, Production: Hans-Curt Koester *E-mail:* koester@langewiesche-verlag.de
Editorial: Gabriele Klempert
Founded: 1902
Specialize in books, journals & calendars.
Membership(s): Motovun Group Association, Lucerne.
Subjects: Antiques, Archaeology, Architecture & Interior Design, Art, History, How-to, Photography
ISBN Prefix(es): 3-7845
Number of titles published annually: 5 Print
Total Titles: 120 Print
Imprints: Die Blauen Buecher (The Blue Book)
Distributed by Abaris Books (USA); Penfield Books (USA)

**Ingrid Langner**
Buchentwiete 24 A, 25355 Barmstedt
Mailing Address: Postfach 1125, 25349 Barmstedt

*Tel:* (04123) 7780 *Fax:* (04123) 7885
*Key Personnel*
Owner: Manfred Langner
Founded: 1985
Subjects: Fiction, Language Arts, Linguistics, Literature, Literary Criticism, Essays
ISBN Prefix(es): 3-9801131

**Lappan Verlag GmbH+**
Wuerzburger Str 14, 26121 Oldenburg
Mailing Address: Postfach 3407, 26024 Oldenburg
*Tel:* (0441) 980660 *Fax:* (0441) 9806622; (0441) 9806624; (0441) 9806634
*E-mail:* info@lappan.de
*Web Site:* www.lappan.de
*Key Personnel*
Man Dir: Dieter Schwalm
Editorial Dir: Peter Baumann
Sales: Michael Boehme
International Rights: Heidrun Kaempf
Founded: 1983
Publisher of books for children & humor gift books for adults.
Subjects: Cartoon Books of Uli Stein, Humor
ISBN Prefix(es): 3-89082; 3-8303
Number of titles published annually: 80 Print
Total Titles: 470 Print
*Associate Companies:* Achterbahn Verlag GmbH
Distributor for Edition C (Switzerland)
*Distribution Center:* LKG, Poetzschauer Weg, 04579 Espenhain

**Michael Lassleben Verlag und Druckerei**
(Michael Lassleben Publishing House & Printing Office)
Lange Gasse 19, 93183 Kallmuenz
Mailing Address: Postfach 20, 93183 Kallmunz
*Tel:* (09473) 205 *Fax:* (09473) 8357
*E-mail:* druckerei@oberpfalzverlag-lassleben.de
*Web Site:* www.oberpfalzverlag-lassleben.de
*Key Personnel*
Owner: Erich Lassleben, Sr
Founded: 1907
Subjects: Archaeology, Geography, Geology, History, Literature, Literary Criticism, Essays
ISBN Prefix(es): 3-7847
Number of titles published annually: 20 Print

**J Latka Verlag GmbH+**
Heilsbachstr 32, 53123 Bonn
*Tel:* (0228) 919320 *Fax:* (0228) 9193217
*E-mail:* info@latka.de
*Web Site:* www.latka.de
*Key Personnel*
President, Rights & Permissions: Joachim Latka
*E-mail:* jlatka@latka.de
Founded: 1984
Subjects: History, Travel
ISBN Prefix(es): 3-925068
Total Titles: 30 Print
*U.S. Office(s):* Cosmedia Inc, 560 Sutter St, Suite 300, San Francisco, CA 94102, United States, Contact: Ms E A Olesen *Tel:* 415-677-9700 *Fax:* 415-677-9300 *E-mail:* cosmedia@sirius.com
Foreign Rep(s): Elizabeth A Olesen (North America)
*Orders to:* Herold, Kolpingring 4, 82041 Oberhaching, Contact: Ms Stanglmeier *Tel:* (089) 6138710 *Fax:* (089) 61387120

**H Lauppsche Buchhandlung**, *imprint of* Mohr Siebeck

**LBO-Dienst**, *imprint of* Bauverlag GmbH

**Lebenshilfe-Verlag Marburg, Verlag der Bundesvereinigung Lebenshilfe fuer Menschen mit geistiger Behinderung eV+**
Raiffeisenstr 18, 35043 Marburg

*Tel:* (06421) 4 91-0 *Fax:* (06421) 4 91-1 67
*E-mail:* bundesvereinigung@lebenshilfe.de
*Web Site:* www.lebenshilfe.de
*Key Personnel*
Publishing Dir: Dr Bernhard Conrads
Founded: 1958
Subjects: Disability, Special Needs, Health, Nutrition, Law, Medicine, Nursing, Dentistry, Nonfiction (General), Self-Help, Social Sciences, Sociology
ISBN Prefix(es): 3-88617

**Lebensstrom eV**
Graefestr 71, 10967 Berlin
Mailing Address: Postfach 12 03 07, 10593 Berlin
*Tel:* (030) 3131247 *Fax:* (030) 3121098
*E-mail:* info@lebensstrom.com
*Web Site:* www.lebensstrom.com
*Parent Company:* Living Stream Ministry

**Verlag fuer Lehrmittel Poessneck GmbH+**
Neustaedterstr 63, 07381 Poessneck
*Tel:* (03647) 425018 *Fax:* (03647) 425020
*Key Personnel*
Manager: Lothar Stein
Founded: 1947
ISBN Prefix(es): 3-7493

**Leibniz Verlag+**
Auf dem Haehnchen 34, 56329 St Goar
*Tel:* (06741) 1720 *Fax:* (06741) 1749
*E-mail:* reichl-verlag@telda.net
*Key Personnel*
Man Dir: Matthias Draeger
Founded: 1994
Subjects: Human Relations, Language Arts, Linguistics, Philosophy, Science (General)
ISBN Prefix(es): 3-931155

**Leibniz-Buecherwarte+**
Robert-Koch-Str 12, 31848 Bad Muender
Mailing Address: Postfach 1214, 31842 Bad Muender
*Tel:* (05042) 15 28 *Fax:* (05042) 15 28
*E-mail:* leibniz-buecherwarte@t-online.de
*Web Site:* www.leibniz-buecherwarte.com
*Key Personnel*
Contact: Gabrielle Spaeth
Founded: 1985
Specialize in philosophy with children.
Subjects: Literature, Literary Criticism, Essays, Philosophy, Religion - Other
ISBN Prefix(es): 3-925237

**Edition Leipzig**, *imprint of* Verlagsgruppe Dornier GmbH

**Leipziger Universitaetsverlag GmbH+**
Oststr 41, 04317 Leipzig
*Tel:* (0341) 9900440 *Fax:* (0341) 9900440
*E-mail:* info@univerlag-leipzig.de
*Web Site:* www.univerlag-leipzig.de
*Key Personnel*
International Rights: Dr Gerald Diesener
Founded: 1992
Subjects: Communications, History, Law, Medicine, Nursing, Dentistry, Philosophy, Science (General), Women's Studies
ISBN Prefix(es): 3-929031; 3-931922; 3-933240; 3-934565; 3-935693; 3-936522; 3-937209

**Leitfadenverlag Verlag Dieter Sudholt+**
Oberlandstr 26a, 82335 Berg
*Tel:* (08151) 51045 *Fax:* (08151) 50357
*Key Personnel*
Publisher: Dipl Kfm Volker Sudholt
Founded: 1957
Subjects: Business, Economics, Law

ISBN Prefix(es): 3-543
*Associate Companies:* Leitfadenverlag Gesellschaft mbH, Innsbruck, Austria

**Anton G Leitner Verlag (AGLV)+**
Buchenweg 3 b, 82234 Wessling
*Tel:* (08153) 9525-22 *Fax:* (08153) 9525-24
*E-mail:* info@aglv.com
*Web Site:* www.dasgedicht.de
*Key Personnel*
Author: Anton G Leitner
Founded: 1992
Subjects: Education, Literature, Literary Criticism, Essays, Mathematics, Poetry
ISBN Prefix(es): 3-929433
Distributor for Initiative Junger Autoren eV
Foreign Rep(s): Manford Chobot (Austria); Dr Margit Ohuhumma; Markus Hedigo; Jean Portank

**Verlag Otto Lembeck+**
Gaertnerweg 16, 60322 Frankfurt am Main
*Tel:* (069) 5970988 *Fax:* (069) 5975742
*E-mail:* verlag@lembeck.de
*Web Site:* www.lembeck.de *Cable:* LEMBECKDRUCK FRANKFURTMAIN
*Key Personnel*
Contact: Dr Wolfgang Neumann
Founded: 1945
Subjects: Religion - Protestant, Religion - Other
ISBN Prefix(es): 3-87476
*Warehouse:* Stuttgarter Verlagskontor, Expedition Westrampe, Fritz-Klett-Str 61-65, 71404 Korb
*Orders to:* Stuttgarter Verlagskontor, Rotebuehlstr 77, 70178 Stuttgart, Contact: Ingelborg Hoepner *Tel:* (0711) 66721604 *Fax:* (0711) 66724974 *E-mail:* Ihoepner@svk.de

**Lentz Verlag+**
Subsidiary of Buchverlage Langen-Mueller/Herbig
Thomas-Wimmer-Ring 11, 80539 Munich
*Tel:* (089) 290880 *Fax:* (089) 29088-144
*E-mail:* l.eggs@herbig.net
*Web Site:* www.herbig.net
*Key Personnel*
Man Dir & Publisher: Brigitte Fleissner-Mikorey
Rights & Permissions: Frauke Hoppen *Fax:* (089) 29088178
Founded: 1953
Subjects: Fiction, Nonfiction (General)
ISBN Prefix(es): 3-88010
Total Titles: 10 Print
Distributed by Mohr Morawa Buchvertrieb; Schweizer Buchzentrum
*Warehouse:* VVA-Bertelsmann Distribution GmbH, Warenannahme 100, An der Autobahn, 33310 Guetersloh
*Orders to:* VVA-Vereinigte, Postfach 7600, 33310 Guetersloh, Contact: Mr Borgartz *Tel:* (05241) 805403 *Fax:* (05241) 806643

**Dr Gisela Lermann+**
Am Heiligenhaus 18, 55122 Mainz
*Tel:* (06131) 31149 *Fax:* (06131) 387945
*Web Site:* www.lermann-verlag.de
*Key Personnel*
Owner & Dir: Dr Gisela Lermann *E-mail:* dr-gisela-lermann@lermann-verlag.de
Founded: 1988
Subjects: Biography, Fiction, Government, Political Science, Human Relations, Literature, Literary Criticism, Essays, Mysteries, Nonfiction (General), Philosophy, Poetry, Psychology, Psychiatry, Romance, Women's Studies
ISBN Prefix(es): 3-927223
*Shipping Address:* Herold Verlagsauslieferung, Kolpingring 4, 82041 Oberhaching *Tel:* (089) 6138710 *Fax:* (089) 61387120 *E-mail:* herold-oberhaching@t-online.de
*Warehouse:* Herold Verlagsauslieferung, Kolpringring 4, 82041 Oberhaching *Tel:* (089)

6138710 *Fax:* (089) 61387120 *E-mail:* herold-
oberhaching@t-online.de
*Orders to:* Herold Verlagsauslieferung, Kolpringring 4, 82041 Oberhaching *Tel:* (089)
6138710 *Fax:* (089) 61387120 *E-mail:* herold-
oberhaching@t-online.de

**Lettre International Kulturzeitung+**
Elisabethhof, Portal 3B, Erkelenzdamm 59/61,
10999 Berlin
*Tel:* (030) 30870441 *Fax:* (030) 2833128
*E-mail:* lettre@lettre.de
*Web Site:* www.lettre.de
*Key Personnel*
Editor-in-Chief: Frank Berberich
Founded: 1988
Subjects: Ethnicity, Government, Political Sci-
ence, Literature, Literary Criticism, Essays
*Branch Office(s)*
c/o Kalina Garelova, Metropolis, blvd V Levski
87, 1000 Sofia, Bulgaria *Tel:* (02) 988 86 32
*Fax:* (02) 988 86 62 *E-mail:* letera@hotmail.
com
Kozarska ulica 16, 10 000 Zagreb, Croatia
*Tel:* (01) 42 43 41 *Fax:* (01) 42 04 12
La Nouvelle Lettre Internationale, 41, rue
Bobillot, 75013 Paris, France *Tel:* (01)
45 65 29 29 *Fax:* (01) 45 65 90 01
*E-mail:* lettre_internationale@hotmail.com
Magyar Lettre Internationale, Karolyl Mihaly u
16, Budapest 1053, Hungary *Tel:* (01) 30 30
384 *Fax:* (01) 30 30 384 *E-mail:* letter@c3.hu
c/o Lelio Basso Foundation, Via della Do-
gana Vecchia 5, 00186 Rome, Italy
*Tel:* (06) 68 30 06 44 *Fax:* (06) 687 61 63
*E-mail:* lettera.int@tiscalinet.it *Web Site:* www.
letterainternazionale.it
ul 11 Oktomvri 2/6-2, 91000 Skopje, The
Former Yugoslav Republic of Macedonia
*E-mail:* jvladova@soros.org.mk
Fundatia Culturala Romana, Aleea Alexandru
38, sector 1, Bucharest, Romania *Tel:* (01)
230 13 73 *Fax:* (01) 230 75 59 *E-mail:* lettre-
internationale@yahoo.com *Web Site:* www.fcr.
ro
Lettre Internationale - Wsemirnoe Slowo, ulica
Spalernaja 18, St Petersburg 191187, Russian
Federation *Tel:* (0812) 274 54 62 *Fax:* (0812)
274 54 62 *E-mail:* vsslovo@8m.com
Claka Liubina1/V, 11000 Belgrade, Serbia and
Montenegro
Letra Internacional, Editorial Pablo Iglesias,
Monte Esquinza 30, 2º dcha, 28010 Madrid,
Spain *Tel:* (01) 310 46 96 *Fax:* (01) 319 45 85
*E-mail:* fpl@infornet.es *Web Site:* www.arce.
es/indicesarce.htm#5

**LEU-VERLAG Wolfgang Leupelt+**
Herweg 34, 51429 Bergisch Gladbach
*Tel:* (02204) 981141 *Fax:* (02204) 981143
*E-mail:* info@leu-verlag.net
*Web Site:* www.leu-verlag.net
*Key Personnel*
Publisher: Wolfgang Leupelt
Founded: 1990
Specialize in music play along books with CD.
Subjects: Education, Music, Dance, Sheet Music,
Music Education Books with CD
ISBN Prefix(es): 3-928825; 3-89775
Number of titles published annually: 10 Print; 5
Audio
Total Titles: 100 Print; 20 Audio

**Leuchter-Verlag EG+**
Industriestr 6-8, 64390 Erzhausen
Mailing Address: Postfach 1161, 64386
Erzhausen
*Tel:* (06150) 97360 *Fax:* (06150) 9736-36
*Key Personnel*
Man Dir, Sales, Rights & Permissions: Karl-
Heinz Neumann
Founded: 1946

Subjects: Religion - Other
ISBN Prefix(es): 3-87482

**Verlag Gerald Leue+**
Kanzlerweg 24, 12101 Berlin
*Tel:* (030) 7865020 *Fax:* (030) 78913876
*E-mail:* vertrieb@leue-verlag.de
*Web Site:* www.leue-verlag.de
*Key Personnel*
Publisher: Gerald Leue
Founded: 1982
Subjects: How-to, Humor
ISBN Prefix(es): 3-923421

**Libertas- Europaeisches Institut GmbH+**
Vaihinger Str 24, 71063 Sindelfingen
Mailing Address: Postfach 5 67, 71047 Sindelfin-
gen
*Tel:* (07031) 6186-80 *Fax:* (07031) 6186-86
*E-mail:* info@libertas-institut.com
*Web Site:* www.libertas-institut.com
*Key Personnel*
President: Hans-Juergen Zahorka *E-mail:* hj.
zahorka@libertas-institut.com
Man Dir: Ute Hirschburger *E-mail:* ute.
hirschburger@libertas-institut.com
Founded: 1976
Think-tank on European & international economy
& politics with publication division.
Subjects: Business, Developing Countries, Eco-
nomics, Environmental Studies, Fiction, Fi-
nance, Government, Political Science, History,
Law, Management, Nonfiction (General), Phi-
losophy, Regional Interests, Social Sciences,
Sociology, Transportation
ISBN Prefix(es): 3-921929
Number of titles published annually: 20 Print; 5
CD-ROM; 5 Audio
Total Titles: 50 Print; 2 CD-ROM

**Edition Libri Illustri GmbH**
Neissestr 31, 71638 Ludwigsburg
*Tel:* (07141) 84720 *Fax:* (07141) 875117
*E-mail:* info@libri-illustri.de
*Web Site:* www.edition-libri-illustri.de
*Key Personnel*
Publisher: Peter Teicher
Founded: 1987
Subjects: History, Religion - Other, Nuremberg
Chronicle, Aesopus, Apocalypsis
ISBN Prefix(es): 3-927506; 3-9806441
Number of titles published annually: 1 Print
Total Titles: 8 Print; 1 Audio
*U.S. Office(s):* Peter KeLehnert, 510 W Forest Dr,
Houston, TX 77079-6914, United States

**Edition Lidiarte**
Knesebeckstr 13/14, 10623 Berlin
*Tel:* (030) 3137420 *Fax:* (030) 3127117
*E-mail:* edition@lidiarte.de
*Web Site:* www.lidiarte.de
*Key Personnel*
President: Dieter Marx
Founded: 1980
Specialize in architectural posters & postcards.
Subjects: Architecture & Interior Design
ISBN Prefix(es): 3-9801862
Number of titles published annually: 10 Print
Total Titles: 220 Print

**Hildegard Liebaug-Dartmann+**
J Sebastian Bach Weg 15, 53340 Meckenheim
*Tel:* (02225) 909343 *Fax:* (02225) 909345
*E-mail:* liebaug-dartmann@t-online.de
*Web Site:* www.liebaug-dartmann.de
*Key Personnel*
Owner: Hildegard Liebaug-Dartmann
Founded: 1982
Membership(s): Boersenveriene des Deutschen
Buchhandels.
Subjects: Physics, German as a Foreign Language

ISBN Prefix(es): 3-922989
Distributed by KNO; KV

**Liebenzeller Mission, GmbH, Abt. Verlag+**
Liobastr 8, 75378 Bad Liebenzell
*Tel:* (07052) 17-163 *Fax:* (07052) 17-170
*E-mail:* buch@liebenzell.org
*Web Site:* www.liebenzell.org/blm/index.htm
*Key Personnel*
Publishing Dir: Arthur Klenk
Man Dir: Martin Auch
Founded: 1906
Also produce games & radio games for children.
Subjects: Biography, Fiction, Theology
ISBN Prefix(es): 3-88002; 3-921113
*Orders to:* Ausl Edition VLM, Postfach 5, 7630
Lahr, Contact: Johannis Lahr *Tel:* (07821) 581-
32 *Fax:* (07821) 581-26

**Robert Lienau GmbH & Co KG**
Strubbergstr 80, 60489 Frankfurt am Main
*Tel:* (069) 9782866 *Fax:* (069) 97828689
*E-mail:* info@lienau-frankfurt.de
*Web Site:* www.lienau-frankfurt.de
*Key Personnel*
Manager: Cornelia Grossmann; Michael Voily
Founded: 1810
Music publisher.
Subjects: Drama, Theater, Music, Dance
ISBN Prefix(es): 3-87484

**Lienhard Pallast Verlag**
Stoeckerfeld 7, 53773 Hennef
*Tel:* (02244) 5863 *Fax:* (02244) 5863
*E-mail:* lienhard@pallast-publisher.com
*Web Site:* www.pallast-publisher.com
Subjects: Literature, Literary Criticism, Essays,
Poetry

**Limpert Verlag+**
Industriepark 3, 56291 Wiebelsheim
Mailing Address: Postfach 1004, 56291
Wiebelsheim
*Tel:* (06766) 903160 *Fax:* (06766) 903320
*E-mail:* vertrieb@limpert.de
*Telex:* 0418135 limp
*Key Personnel*
Man Dir, Rights & Permissions: Dr Irmgard
Meissl *Tel:* (06766) 903242 *Fax:* (06766)
903360 *E-mail:* meissl@aula-verlag.de
Founded: 1921
Subjects: Sports, Athletics
ISBN Prefix(es): 3-7853
*Bookshop(s):* Humanitas Buchversand

**J Lindauer Verlag+**
Kaufingerstr 16, 80331 Munich
Mailing Address: Postfach 330 626, 80066 Mu-
nich
*Tel:* (089) 223041 *Fax:* (089) 224315
*E-mail:* info@lindauer-gmbh.de
*Web Site:* www.lindauer-verlag.de
*Key Personnel*
Owner, Rights & Permissions: Renate Schaefer
ISBN Prefix(es): 3-87488

**H Lindemanns Buchhandlung**
Nadlerstr 4, 70173 Stuttgart
*Tel:* (0711) 248999-0 *Fax:* (0711) 233320
*E-mail:* lindemannsbuch@t-online.de
*Web Site:* www.lindemanns-buchhandlung.de
*Key Personnel*
Contact: Werner Goetze
ISBN Prefix(es): 3-89506; 3-928126

**Linden-Verlag+**
Kasseler Str 25, 04155 Leipzig
*Tel:* (0341) 5902024 *Fax:* (0341) 5904436
*E-mail:* verlag@linden-buch.de
*Web Site:* www.linden-buch.de
*Key Personnel*
International Rights: Thomas Loest

Founded: 1989
Specialize in books by Buecher von Erich Loest.
ISBN Prefix(es): 3-9802139; 3-86152

**Martha Lindner Verlags-GmbH+**
Jahnstr 22, 76133 Karlsruhe
*Tel:* (0721) 843965 *Fax:* (0721) 8303716
*Key Personnel*
Manager: Martha Lindner
Founded: 1975
Subjects: Music, Dance, Science (General), Theology
ISBN Prefix(es): 3-921653

**Christoph Links Verlag - LinksDruck GmbH+**
Schoenhauser Allee 36 - Haus S, 10435 Berlin
*Tel:* (030) 440232-0 *Fax:* (030) 44023229
*E-mail:* mail@linksverlag.de
*Web Site:* www.linksverlag.de
*Key Personnel*
Publisher: Christoph Links *E-mail:* links@
  linksverlag.de
Founded: 1990
Subjects: Biography, Government, Political Science, History, Nonfiction (General), Self-Help
ISBN Prefix(es): 3-86153
Number of titles published annually: 30 Print
Total Titles: 330 Print
*Orders to:* Prolit Verlagsauslieferung, Siemensstr
  16, 35463 Fernwald, Contact: Gaby Kraft
  *Tel:* (0641) 94393-21 *Fax:* (0641) 94393-29
  *E-mail:* g.kraft@prolit.de

**Siegbert Linnemann Verlag+**
Ohlbrocksweg 61, 33330 Guetersloh
*Tel:* (05241) 14061 *Fax:* (05241) 26439
*E-mail:* info@linnemann-verlag.com
*Web Site:* www.linnemann-verlag.com
*Key Personnel*
Man Dir: Siegbert Linnemann
Founded: 1986
Specialize in travel picture wall calendars.
Subjects: Geography, Geology, Travel
ISBN Prefix(es): 3-926466; 3-89523
Number of titles published annually: 90 Print
*U.S. Office(s):* Sormani Calendars, Box
  6059, Chelsea, MA 02150, United States
  *Tel:* 617-889-9300 *Fax:* 617-889-9306
  *E-mail:* sormani@mindspring.com *Web
  Site:* www.sormanicalendars.com

**LIT Verlag+**
Grevenerstr/Fresnostr 2, 48159 Muenster
*Tel:* (0251) 235091 *Fax:* (0251) 231972
*E-mail:* lit@lit-verlag.de
*Web Site:* www.lit-verlag.de
*Key Personnel*
Man Dir & International Rights: Dr Wilhelm
  Hopf
Founded: 1981
Subjects: Art, Asian Studies, Economics, Ethnicity, Fashion, Public Administration, Science
  (General), Social Sciences, Sociology
ISBN Prefix(es): 3-88660; 3-89473; 3-8258
Subsidiaries: LII Verlag Muenster-Hamburg
*U.S. Office(s):* c/o J Bach, 610 W 115 St, No
  53B, New York, NY 10025, United States
  *Tel:* 212-666-7674 *Fax:* 212-666-7674

**Henry Litolff's Verlag,** *imprint of* C F Peters
  Musikverlag GmbH & Co KG

**Rainer Loessl Verlag**
Johann-Fichtestr 11, 80805 Munich
*Tel:* (089) 362646
ISBN Prefix(es): 3-9800376

**Antiquariat Oskar Loewe**
Subsidiary of Latvijas Nacionala Biblioteka, LV-
  Riga
Sauerbruchstr 8d, 45661 Recklinghausen-Sued

*Tel:* (02361) 960813 *Fax:* (02361) 960815
*E-mail:* loewe.bochum@t-online.de
*Web Site:* www.antiquariat.net/loewe
*Key Personnel*
Owner: Oskar Loewe
Founded: 1876
Subjects: Antiquarian (News, Old Books)
Distributed by Zentralverzeichnis Antiquarischer
  Buecher (ZVAB)

**Loewe Verlag GmbH+**
Buehlstr 4, 95463 Bindlach
Mailing Address: Postfach 1, 95461 Bindlach
*Tel:* (09208) 51-0 *Fax:* (09208) 51-309
*E-mail:* presse@loewe-verlag.de
*Web Site:* www.loewe-verlag.de
*Telex:* 920882
*Key Personnel*
Publisher & Man Dir: Volker Gondrom
Editorial: Alexandra Borisch; Christiane Duering
Publicity, Sales Dir: Hajo Schwabe
Foreign Rights Manager: Jeannette Hammer-
  schmidt *Tel:* (09208) 51202 *E-mail:* lizenzen@
  loewe-verlag.de
Founded: 1863
ISBN Prefix(es): 3-7855

**Logophon Verlag und Bildungsreisen GmbH+**
Affiliate of Euro-Schulen-Organisation
Alte Gaertnerei 2, 55128 Mainz
*Tel:* (06131) 71645 *Fax:* (06131) 72596
*E-mail:* verlag@logophon.de
*Web Site:* www.logophon.de
*Key Personnel*
Man Dir: Jean-Pierre Jouteux; Pierre Semidei
Founded: 1979
Subjects: Business, English as a Second Language, Human Relations, Language Arts, Linguistics
ISBN Prefix(es): 3-922514
Number of titles published annually: 8 Print
Total Titles: 80 Print; 2 CD-ROM

**Logos Verlag GmbH+**
Ehlenbrucherstr 96, 32791 Lage
*Tel:* (05232) 960120; (05232) 960124
  *Fax:* (05232) 960121
*E-mail:* info@logos-verlag.de
*Web Site:* www.logos-verlag.de
*Key Personnel*
Manager: Johannes Reimer
Purchasing, Sales Manager: Andreas Bergen
Founded: 1989
Christian books in German & Russian.
Subjects: History, Religion - Protestant, Theology,
  Autobiography, Memoirs, Letters, Bibliography
ISBN Prefix(es): 3-927767; 3-933828; 3-936850

**Logos-Verlag Literatur & Layout GmbH+**
Auf der Adt 14 Villa Fledermaus, 66130 Saar-
  bruecken
*Tel:* (06893) 986096 *Fax:* (06893) 986095
*Key Personnel*
Publisher: Friedhelm Schneidecrond
Founded: 1983
Subjects: Biological Sciences, Fiction, Geography, Geology, Literature, Literary Criticism,
  Essays, Mysteries, Nonfiction (General), Poetry,
  Regional Interests, Science Fiction, Fantasy,
  Social Sciences, Sociology
ISBN Prefix(es): 3-928598; 3-9801790

**Lokrundschau Verlag GmbH**
Ellernreihe 80, 22179 Hamburg
*Fax:* (40) 69692321
*E-mail:* verlag@lokrundschau.de
*Web Site:* www.lokrundschau.de
*Key Personnel*
Man Dir: Jan Borchers *E-mail:* jan.borchers@
  lokrundschau.de
Founded: 1995

Specialize in books about German railway &
  journals.
ISBN Prefix(es): 3-931647

**Stefan Loose Verlag+**
Zossenerstr 55/2, 10961 Berlin
*Tel:* (030) 6 91 37 89 *Fax:* (030) 6 93 01 71
*E-mail:* info@loose-verlag.de
*Web Site:* www.loose-verlag.de
*Key Personnel*
President: Renate Ramb
Publisher: Stefan Loose
Founded: 1978
Subjects: Travel
ISBN Prefix(es): 3-922025; 3-935021

**Lorber-Verlag & Turm-Verlag Otto Zluhan**
Hindenburgstr 5, 74321 Bietigheim Bissingen
*Tel:* (07142) 940843 *Fax:* (07142) 940844
*E-mail:* info@lorber-verlag.de; bestellen@lorber-
  verlag.de
*Web Site:* www.lorber-verlag.de *Cable:* LORBER,
  BIETIGHEIM
*Key Personnel*
Man Dir, Publisher, Rights & Permissions:
  Friedrich Zluhan
Founded: 1854
Subjects: Parapsychology, Religion - Other
ISBN Prefix(es): 3-87495

**Johannes Loriz Verlag der Kooperative
  Duernau**
Im Winkel 11, 88422 Duernau
*Tel:* (07582) 93000 *Fax:* (07582) 930020
*Web Site:* www.kooperative.de
*Key Personnel*
Owner: Johannes Loriz
Subjects: Natural History
ISBN Prefix(es): 3-88861

**Verlag an der Lottbek+**
Susterfedlstr 83, 52072 Aachen
*Tel:* (0241) 873434 *Fax:* (0241) 875577
*Key Personnel*
Editor: Peter Jensen
Founded: 1988
Membership(s): the Stock Exchange of German
  Booksellers.
Subjects: Science (General)
ISBN Prefix(es): 3-926987; 3-86130
Subsidiaries: Edition Hathor
Divisions: Belletriotik
*Showroom(s):* Bundes Str 74, 2000 Hamburg 13
*Warehouse:* Bundes Str 74, 2000 Hamburg 13

**Hermann Luchterhand Verlag GmbH,** see
  Wolters Kluwer Deutschland GmbH

**Luchterhand Literaturverlag GmbH/Verlag
  Volk & Welt GmbH+**
Neumarkterstr 28, 81673 Munich
*Tel:* (089) 4136-0; (01805) 990505 *Fax:* (089)
  21215250
*E-mail:* vertrieb.verlagsgruppe@randomhouse.de
*Web Site:* www.randomhouse.de/luchterhand
*Key Personnel*
Owner: Dietrich von Boetticher
Publisher: Gerald J Trageiser
Founded: 1924
Subjects: Fiction, Literature, Literary Criticism,
  Essays, Nonfiction (General)
ISBN Prefix(es): 3-630
Number of titles published annually: 50 Print
Total Titles: 500 Print
*Parent Company:* Verlagsgruppe Random House
  GmbH
*Ultimate Parent Company:* Bertelsmann AG
Distributor for Gerhard Wolf Janus Press
*Orders to:* Vereinigte Verlagsauslieferung, An der
  Autobahn, 33310 Guetersloh

**Lucius & Lucius Verlagsgesellschaft mbH+**
Gerokstr 51, 70184 Stuttgart
*Tel:* (0711) 242060 *Fax:* (0711) 242088
*E-mail:* lucius@luciusverlag.com
*Web Site:* www.luciusverlag.com
*Key Personnel*
Publisher: Dr Wulf D von Lucius
Founded: 1996
Specialize in academic books & journals in eco-
nomics, social sciences & sociology; research
monographs & proceedings
Privately owned.
Membership(s): Borsenverein & STM.
Subjects: Economics, Social Sciences, Sociology
ISBN Prefix(es): 3-8282
Number of titles published annually: 35 Print
Total Titles: 420 Print
*Warehouse:* Brockhaus/Commission, Kreidlerstr
9, 70803 Kornwestheim, Contact: Mrs Rother
*Tel:* (07154) 132737 *Fax:* (07154) 132713
*E-mail:* bro@brockhaus-commission.de (Or-
ders)

**Luebbe Audio,** *imprint of* Verlagsgruppe Luebbe
GmbH & Co KG

**Gustav Luebbe Verlag,** *imprint of* Verlagsgruppe
Luebbe GmbH & Co KG

**Gustav Luebbe Verlag+**
Imprint of Verlagsgruppe Luebbe GmbH & Co
KG
Scheidtbachstr 23-31, 51469 Bergisch Gladbach
Mailing Address: Postfach 200180, 51431 Ber-
gisch Gladbach
*Tel:* (02202) 121-330 *Fax:* (02202) 121-920
*E-mail:* glv@luebbe.de
*Web Site:* www.luebbe.de
*Key Personnel*
Man Dir: Peter Molden; Karlheinz Jungbeck
Founded: 1963
Subjects: Archaeology, Biography, Fiction, His-
tory, How-to, Nonfiction (General)
ISBN Prefix(es): 3-404; 3-7857; 3-89185
*Associate Companies:* Bastei Verlag

**Verlagsgruppe Luebbe GmbH & Co KG+**
Scheidtbachstr 23-31, 51469 Bergisch Gladbach
Mailing Address: Postfach 200180, 51431 Ber-
gisch Gladbach
*Tel:* (02202) 121-0 *Fax:* (02202) 121-920
*E-mail:* info@luebbe.de
*Web Site:* www.luebbe.de
*Key Personnel*
Man Dir: Karlheinz Jungbeck; Peter Molden
Founded: 1953
Subjects: Biography, Fiction, Nonfiction (Gen-
eral), Romance
ISBN Prefix(es): 3-404; 3-431; 3-7857; 3-89185
Imprints: Bastei Luebbe Taschenbuecher; Bastei
Verlag; BLT; editionLuebbe; Ehrenwirth Ver-
lag; Luebbe Audio; Gustav Luebbe Verlag

**Alf Luechow Verlag,** *imprint of* Verlagsgruppe
Dornier GmbH

**Lukas Verlag fur Kunst- und Geistesgeschichte**
Kollwitzstr 57, 10405 Berlin
*Tel:* (030) 44049220 *Fax:* (030) 4428177
*E-mail:* lukas.verlag@t-online.de
*Web Site:* www.lukasverlag.com
*Key Personnel*
Contact: Dr Frank Bottcher
Founded: 1995
Specialize in art history, cistercians, medieval art
& GDR.
Subjects: Archaeology, History, Philosophy, So-
cial Sciences, Sociology
ISBN Prefix(es): 3-931836; 3-936872
Total Titles: 30 Print

**Lusatia Verlag-Dr Stuebner & Co KG+**
Toepferstr 35, 02625 Bautzen
*Tel:* (03591) 532400; (03591) 532401
*Fax:* (03591) 532400
*E-mail:* lusatiaverlag@t-online.de
Founded: 1992
Membership(s): Association of German Book-
sellers.
Subjects: Art, Fiction, Regional Interests, Travel
ISBN Prefix(es): 3-929091; 3-936758
Number of titles published annually: 10 Print
Total Titles: 115 Print
Distributed by Domowina-Verlag
Distributor for Domowina-Verlag

**Luther-Verlag GmbH+**
Cansteinstr 1, 33647 Bielefeld
*Tel:* (0521) 94 40-137 *Fax:* (0521) 94 40-136
*E-mail:* vertrieb@luther-verlag.de
*Web Site:* www.ekvw.de/pressehaus/lv/
*Telex:* 937325 epdgi
*Key Personnel*
Man Dir, Rights & Permissions: Wolfgang Riewe
Founded: 1911
Subjects: Religion - Protestant
ISBN Prefix(es): 3-7858

**Lutherische Verlagsgesellschaft mbH**
Gartenstr 20, 24103 Kiel
Mailing Address: Postfach 3169, 24030 Kiel
*Tel:* (0431) 55779-285 *Fax:* (0431) 55779-292
*Key Personnel*
Manager: Rainer Thun
Founded: 1956
Subjects: Regional Interests, Theology
ISBN Prefix(es): 3-87503
*Parent Company:* Evangelischer Presseverband
Nord ev, Postfach 3466, 24033 Kiel

**Lutherisches Verlagshaus GmbH+**
Knochenhauerstr 38-40, 30159 Hannover
Mailing Address: Postfach 3849, 30038 Hannover
*Tel:* (0511) 1241-716 *Fax:* (0511) 1241-948
*E-mail:* lvh@lvh.de
*Web Site:* www.lvh.de
*Telex:* 922686
*Key Personnel*
Man Dir, Rights & Permissions: Klaus Woehleke
General Manager: Werner Sass
Management: Dr Hasko von Bassi *Tel:* (0511)
1241720 *Fax:* (0511) 3681098
Marketing: Ralf Mueller *Tel:* (0511) 1241-726
*Fax:* (0511) 3681098; (0511) 3 68 10 98
Sales: Andrea Roecher *Fax:* (0511) 3681098
Advertising: Hannelore Splitt *Tel:* (0511) 1241
710 *Fax:* (0511) 3681098
Founded: 1948
Subjects: Religion - Other, Theology
ISBN Prefix(es): 3-7859
Distributed by CVK Cornelsen Verlagskontor
Gmbh & Co KG (Germany); Felix A Gaugler
(Switzerland)
*Orders to:* Cornelsen Verlagskontor, Kammerat-
sheide 66, 4800 Bielefeld 1

**Verlag Waldemar Lutz**
Baslerstr 130, 79540 Loerrach
*Tel:* (07621) 88812 *Fax:* (07621) 12599
*E-mail:* wlutz@verlag-lutz.de
*Web Site:* www.verlag-lutz.de
*Key Personnel*
Man Dir, Rights & Permissions: Waldemar Lutz
Founded: 1978
Subjects: Literature, Literary Criticism, Essays,
Regional Interests
ISBN Prefix(es): 3-922107
*Bookshop(s):* Lutz-Die Buchhandlung, Tumringer-
str 179, D-79540 Loerrach

**Karin Mader**
Mittelsmoorerstr 80, 28879 Grasberg

*Tel:* (04208) 556 *Fax:* (04208) 3429
*E-mail:* info@mader-verlag.de
*Web Site:* www.mader-verlag.de
Founded: 1978
Subjects: Travel
ISBN Prefix(es): 3-921957
Distributed by VAH Jager Verlagsauslieferung
*Orders to:* VAH Jager Verlagsauslieferung, Post-
fach 3248, 10729 Berlin

**Maeander Verlag GmbH+**
Diepoltsberg 2, 84326 Falkenberg
*Tel:* (08727) 1657 *Fax:* (08727) 1569
*Key Personnel*
Man Dir, Rights & Permissions: Dr Renate Piel
Founded: 1977
Specialize in monographs & art history in gen-
eral.
Subjects: Archaeology, Art, Philosophy
ISBN Prefix(es): 3-88219
Total Titles: 78 Print
*Orders to:* Koch, Neff und Oetinger & Co
GmbH, Schockenriedstr 39, 80807 Stuttgart

**Annemarie Maeger+**
Ebertallee 6, 22607 Hamburg
*Tel:* (040) 8992480 *Fax:* (040) 8994475
*E-mail:* re@a-maeger-verlag.de
*Web Site:* www.a-maeger-verlag.de
*Key Personnel*
Contact: A Maeger
Founded: 1993
Subjects: Drama, Theater, History, Mathemat-
ics, Philosophy, Science (General), Theology,
Women's Studies
ISBN Prefix(es): 3-929805

**Magdalenen-Verlag GmbH**
Gewerbering 14a, 83607 Holzkirchen
*Tel:* (08024) 5051 *Fax:* (08024) 7064
*E-mail:* info@magdalenen-verlag.de
*Web Site:* www.magdalenen-verlag.de
*Key Personnel*
Manager: Clemens Kopp
ISBN Prefix(es): 3-930350; 3-9800186; 3-936317

**Magnus Verlag+**
Im Teelbruch 60-62, 45219 Essen
Mailing Address: Postfach 185528, 45205 Essen
*Tel:* (02054) 5080; (02054) 5094; (02327) 292 0
*Fax:* (02054) 83762
*Key Personnel*
Man Dir: Walter Stender
Rights & Permissions: Michael Salzwedel
ISBN Prefix(es): 3-88400; 3-920617

**Karl Mahnke, Dierk Mahnke+**
Grossestr 108, 27283 Verden-Aller
*Tel:* (04231) 3011-0 *Fax:* (04231) 3011-11
*E-mail:* info@mahnke-verlag.de
*Web Site:* www.mahnke-verlag.de
*Key Personnel*
Owner: Dierk Mahnke
Editor: Dieter Jorschik
Founded: 1841
Specialize in Amateur Theater Publishing.
ISBN Prefix(es): 3-920613

**Otto Maier Verlag,** see Ravensburger Buchverlag
Otto Maier GmbH

**Mairs Geographischer Verlag+**
Marco-Polo-Zentrum, 73760 Ostfildern
*Tel:* (0711) 45020 *Fax:* (0711) 4502340
*E-mail:* info@mairs.de
*Web Site:* www.mairs.de
*Telex:* 721796 *Cable:* MAIRVERLAG
*Key Personnel*
Man Dir: Dr Volkmar Mair
Sales Dir: Claus Benath
Founded: 1948
Subjects: Regional Interests, Travel

ISBN Prefix(es): 3-87504
Imprints: Baedeker; Marco Polo
Distributed by Fleischmann (Austria); Hallwag
    AG (Switzerland)
Distributor for ADAC Verlag

**Mairs Geographischer Verlag, Kurt Mair
    GmbH & Co+**
Formerly RV Reise- und Verkehrsverlag
Marco-Polo-Zentrum, 73760 Ostfildern
Mailing Address: Postfach 800360, 81603 Mu-
    nich
*Tel:* (0711) 4502-0 *Fax:* (0711) 4502-340
*Telex:* 523259
*Key Personnel*
Dir: Wolfgang Kunth; Klaus Juergens
Editorial Dir: Dieter Meinhardt
Sales Manager: Michael Maap
Foreign Rights: Konrad Weinstock-Adorno
ISBN Prefix(es): 3-88445; 3-8279; 3-575; 3-
    920317; 3-87504; 3-89525; 3-8297; 3-87505
*Parent Company:* Verlagsgruppe Bertelsmann
    GmbH, 81664 Munich
Subsidiaries: Guetersloh; Potsdam/Werder
*Orders to:* Geo Center Verlagsvertrieb GmbH,
    Neumarkterstr 18, 81603 Munich

**Mairs Geographischer Verlag Kurt Mair
    GmbH & Co**
Marco Polo Zentrum, 73760 Ostfildern
*Tel:* (0711) 4502-0 *Fax:* (0711) 4502-340
*Key Personnel*
Chief Executive Officer: Hans J Moock
Editorial: Dr Helge Lintzhoeft
Technical: Christoph Riess
Sales & Marketing: Michael Staehler
Founded: 1945
Specialize in, cartography (city maps & atlases,
    road maps & road atlases).
ISBN Prefix(es): 3-88445; 3-8279; 3-920317
Subsidiaries: GeoData, GmbH & Co KG
*Branch Office(s)*
Berlin
Hamburg
Lepzig
Stuttgart
Distributor for Berlitz; DCC; Gruner & Jahr;
    Iwanowski; Ravenstein

**Malik Verlag,** *imprint of* Piper Verlag GmbH

**Manholt Verlag+**
Fedelhoeren 88, 28203 Bremen
*Tel:* (0421) 32 35 94 *Fax:* (0421) 3 36 54 63
*E-mail:* manholtverlag@t-online.de
*Web Site:* www.manholt.de
*Key Personnel*
Editor, Rights & Permissions: Dr Dirk Hemjeolt-
    manns
Founded: 1985
Publishes French Literature in German.
ISBN Prefix(es): 3-924903

**Gebr Mann Verlag GmbH & Co+**
Zimmerstr 26-27, 10969 Berlin
*Tel:* (030) 259171570 *Fax:* (030) 259171577;
    (030) 259173537
*E-mail:* vertrieb-kunstverlage@reimer-verlag.de
*Key Personnel*
Man Dir, Rights & Permissions: Holger Beer
Publishing Dir: Andreas A Catsch
Founded: 1917
Subjects: Archaeology, Architecture & Interior
    Design, Art, Crafts, Games, Hobbies, History
ISBN Prefix(es): 3-496; 3-7861
*Associate Companies:* Deutscher Verlag fuer
    Kunstwissenschaft
*Orders to:* Koch, Neff & Oetinger & Co Ver-
    lagsauslieferung GmbH, Schockenriedstr 39,
    Postfach 800620, 70565 Stuttgart

**Mannerschwarm Skript Verlag GmbH+**
Lange Reihe 102, 20099 Hamburg
*Tel:* (040) 4302650 *Fax:* (040) 4302932
*E-mail:* verlag@maennerschwarm.de
*Web Site:* www.maennerschwarm.de
*Key Personnel*
Publisher: Joachim Bartholomae; Detlef Grum-
    bach
Founded: 1992
Subjects: Gay & Lesbian
ISBN Prefix(es): 3-928983; 3-935596
Number of titles published annually: 15 Print
Total Titles: 150 Print
Imprints: Schwul Lesbische Studien Universitat
    Bremen; Edition Waldschloesschen; Bibliothek
    rosa Winkel
*Shipping Address:* So Va, Friesstr 20-24, 60388
    Frankfurt *Tel:* (069) 410 211 *Fax:* (069) 410
    280
*Warehouse:* So Va, Friesstr 20-24, 60388 Frank-
    furt
*Orders to:* So Va, Friesstr 20-24, 60388 Frankfurt

**Manutius Verlag+**
Eselspfad 2, 69117 Heidelberg
*Tel:* (06221) 163290 *Fax:* (06221) 167143
*E-mail:* kontakt@manutius-verlag.de
*Web Site:* www.manutius-verlag.de
*Key Personnel*
Publisher: Frank Wuerker
Founded: 1985
Subjects: Art, History, Literature, Literary Criti-
    cism, Essays, Music, Dance, Philosophy, Hu-
    manist, Jurisprudence, Political Science
ISBN Prefix(es): 3-925678; 3-934877
Total Titles: 80 Print

**Manz G J Verlag und Druckerei,** see Ernst
    Klett Verlag Gmbh

**Marco Polo,** *imprint of* Mairs Geographischer
    Verlag

**Margraf Verlag**
Kanalstr 21, 97990 Weikersheim
*Tel:* (07934) 3071 *Fax:* (07934) 8156
*E-mail:* info@margraf-verlag.de
*Web Site:* www.margraf-verlag.de
*Key Personnel*
Contact: Dirk Hangstein *E-mail:* hangstein@
    margraf-verlag.de
Founded: 1985
Subjects: Agriculture, Biological Sciences, De-
    veloping Countries, Environmental Studies,
    Geography, Geology
ISBN Prefix(es): 3-8236; 3-924333
*Associate Companies:* Backhuys Publishers,
    PO Box 321, 2300 AH Leiden, Holland,
    Netherlands, Contact: Mike Ruijsenaars *Web
    Site:* www.backhuys.com
Distributed by DA Books & Journals

**Edition Maritim GmbH+**
Raboisen 8, 20095 Hamburg
*Tel:* (040) 3396670 *Fax:* (040) 33966777
*E-mail:* mail@edition-maritim.de
*Key Personnel*
Dir: Konrad Delius *Tel:* (0521) 559-210
    *Fax:* (0521) 559-116 *E-mail:* info@delius-
    klasing.de
Dir, Rights & Permissions: Frank Grube
Founded: 1978
Subjects: Crafts, Games, Hobbies, Fiction, Mar-
    itime, Sports, Athletics, Transportation, Travel
ISBN Prefix(es): 3-922117; 3-89225
*Parent Company:* Delius Klasing Verlag, Sieker-
    wall 21, 33602 Bielefeld

**Marketing & Wirtschaft Verlagsges, Flade &
    Partner mbH+**
Elisabethstr 34, 80796 Munich

*Tel:* (089) 27813417 *Fax:* (089) 2710156
*Key Personnel*
Publisher: Frido Flade
Chief Editor: Fabian Flade
Founded: 1979
Subjects: Economics, Energy
ISBN Prefix(es): 3-922804
Subsidiaries: Edition Wissen & Literatur
*Warehouse:* Revilak Verlags-Service, Gutenbergstr
    5, 822056 Gilching

**Markt & Technik,** see Pearson Education
    Deutschland GmbH

**Maro Verlag und Druck, Benno Kaesmayr**
Zirbelstr 57a, 86154 Augsburg
*Tel:* (0821) 416034 *Fax:* (0821) 416036
*E-mail:* info@maroverlag.de
*Web Site:* www.maroverlag.de
*Key Personnel*
Proprietor: Benno Kaesmayr
Founded: 1969
Subjects: Fiction, Poetry
ISBN Prefix(es): 3-87512
Number of titles published annually: 5 Print
Total Titles: 120 Print

**Institut fuer Marxistische Studien und
    Forschungen eV (IMSF)**
Postfach 500936, 60397 Frankfurt
*Tel:* (069) 7392934
*Key Personnel*
Honorary President: Juergen Reusch
Founded: 1968
ISBN Prefix(es): 3-88807

**Mattes Verlag GmbH**
Steigerweg 69, 69115 Heidelberg
Mailing Address: Postfach 103866, 69028 Heidel-
    berg
*Tel:* (06221) 459321; (06221) 437853
    *Fax:* (06221) 459322
*E-mail:* verlag@mattes.de
*Web Site:* www.mattes.de
*Key Personnel*
Publisher: Kurt Mattes *E-mail:* info@ameria.de
Founded: 1990
Subjects: Literature, Literary Criticism, Essays,
    Medicine, Nursing, Dentistry, Psychology, Psy-
    chiatry
ISBN Prefix(es): 3-9802440; 3-930978

**Matthaes Verlag GmbH**
Olgastr 87, 70180 Stuttgart
Mailing Address: Postfach 103144, 70027
    Stuttgart
*Tel:* (0711) 21 33-0 *Fax:* (0711) 21 33-320
*E-mail:* info@matthaes.de
*Web Site:* www.matthaes.de *Cable:*
    MATTHAESVERLAG
*Key Personnel*
Man Dir: Hugo Matthaes; Dr Clemens Knoll
Founded: 1905
Subjects: Cookery
*Branch Office(s)*
Frankfurt
Hamburg
Munich

**Matthes und Seitz Verlag GmbH+**
Huebnerstr 11, 80637 Munich
Mailing Address: Postfach 190624, 80606 Mu-
    nich
*Tel:* (089) 1232510 *Fax:* (089) 187534
*Key Personnel*
Man Dir, Rights & Permissions: Axel Matthes
Founded: 1977
Subjects: Art, Fiction, History, Literature, Literary
    Criticism, Essays, Music, Dance, Philosophy,
    Poetry, Theology, autobiography, memoirs, let-
    ters

ISBN Prefix(es): 3-88221
*Orders to:* Koch, Neff & Oetinger, Postfach 800620, 70506 Stuttgart

**Matthias-Gruenewald-Verlag GmbH**
Member of Verlagsgruppe Engagement
Max Hufschmidtstr 4a, 55130 Mainz
Mailing Address: Postfach 3080, 55020 Mainz
*Tel:* (06131) 92860 *Fax:* (06131) 928626
*E-mail:* mail@gruenewaldverlag.de
*Web Site:* members.aol.com/matthgruen
*Key Personnel*
Publisher: Josef Wagner
Publisher Editorial: Hiltraud Laubach
Man Dir: Josef Wagner
Sales Dir: Jeanine Glaesser
Production: Ellen Schneider
Publicity: Silvia Schumacher
Founded: 1918
Subjects: Biography, Psychology, Psychiatry, Religion - Other, Theology
ISBN Prefix(es): 3-7867
Number of titles published annually: 60 Print; 3 Audio
Total Titles: 840 Print; 40 Audio

**Matthiesen Verlag Ingwert Paulsen Jr+**
Nordbahnhofstr 2, 25813 Husum
Mailing Address: Postfach 1480, 25804 Husum
*Tel:* (04841) 83520 *Fax:* (04841) 835210
*E-mail:* info@verlagsgruppe.de
*Web Site:* www.verlagsgruppe.de
*Key Personnel*
Man Dir, Editorial, Rights & Permissions: Ingwert Paulsen
Founded: 1892
Subjects: Science (General)
ISBN Prefix(es): 3-7868
*Associate Companies:* Hamburger Lesehefte Verlag Iselt & Co Nfl mbH; Hansa Verlag Ingwert Paulsen Jr; Husum Druck- und Verlagsgesellschaft mbH & Co KG; Verlag der Nation

**Hans K Matussek Buchhandlung & Antiquariat+**
Marktstr 13, 41334 Nettetal
*Tel:* (02153) 91 64 30 *Fax:* (02153) 1 33 63
*Web Site:* www.buchkatalog.de/matussek
*Key Personnel*
Contact: Hans K Matussek; Fabian Matussek *E-mail:* fabian.matussek@t-online.de
Founded: 1961
ISBN Prefix(es): 3-920743

**Matzker Verlag DiA**
Osternburger Str 30, 28237 Bremen
Mailing Address: Postfach 130193, 13601 Berlin
*Tel:* (0421) 6207934
*Key Personnel*
Contact: Dr Reiner Matzker
Founded: 1985
Subjects: Art, Education, Fiction, Poetry
ISBN Prefix(es): 3-925789

**Max Schimmel Verlag**
Im Kreuz 9, 97076 Wuerzburg
Mailing Address: Postfach 94 44, 97094 Wuerzburg
*Tel:* (0931) 27 91 400 *Fax:* (0931) 27 91 444
*E-mail:* info@schimmelverlag.de
*Web Site:* www.schimmelverlag.de
*Key Personnel*
Man Dir: Helmuth Hopfner; Ingo Schloo
Subjects: Marketing
ISBN Prefix(es): 3-920834

**Maximilian Gesellschaft eV**, *imprint of* Anton Hiersemann, Verlag

**J A Mayersche Buchhandlung GmbH & Co KG Abt Verlag**
Matthiashofstr 28-30, 52064 Aachen
*Tel:* (0241) 4777 499 *Fax:* (0241) 4777 467
*E-mail:* vertrieb@mayersche.de
*Web Site:* www.mayersche.de *Cable:* MAYER AACHEN
*Key Personnel*
Man Dir, Publicity: Helmut Falter
Membership(s): AWS-JASV.
Subjects: Regional Interests
ISBN Prefix(es): 3-87519
*Branch Office(s)*
Anlage, 5100 Aachen
*Bookshop(s):* Ursulinerstr 17-19, 52062 Aachen
*Tel:* (0241) 4777 0 *Fax:* (0241) 4777 167
*E-mail:* aachenurs@mayersche.de; Neumarkt 1B, 50667 Cologne; Hohe Str 68-82, 50667 Cologne; Kuhstr 33, 47051 Duisburg; Hindenburgstr 75, 41061 Moenchengladbach 1; Stresemannstr 43, 41236 Moenchengladbach 2; Bahnhofstr 55-65, 45879 Gelsenkirchen; Pontstr 131, 52062 Aachen *Tel:* (0241) 47494 0 *Fax:* (0241) 47494 1 *E-mail:* aachenth@mayersche.de

**Mayr Miesbach Druckerei und Verlag GmbH**
Am Windfeld 15, 83714 Miesbach
*Tel:* (08025) 294-0 *Fax:* (08025) 294-235
*E-mail:* info@mayrmiesbach.de
*Web Site:* www.mayrmiesbach.de
*Key Personnel*
Man Dir: Wilhelm Friedrich Mayr
Man Dir, Sales & International Rights: Dieter Bergemann
Sales & International Rights: Ulrich Herzog *Tel:* (08025) 294-232
*Parent Company:* Schattauer GmbH - Verlag fuer Medizin und Naturwissenschaften, Hoelderlinstr 3, 70174 Stuttgart
Subsidiaries: Verlag Freizeit & Wassersport GmbH

**Dr Norbert Meder & Co**, see Janus Verlagsgesellschaft, Dr Norbert Meder & Co

**Mediapress GmbH+**
Gewerbepark 10/1, 83052 Bruckmuehl
*Tel:* (08062) 78770 *Fax:* (08062) 6122
*Telex:* 781217
*Key Personnel*
Man Dir, Rights & Permissions: Dieter Brinzer
Founded: 1982

**Medico International eV**
Obermainanlage 7, 60314 Frankfurt/Main
*Tel:* (069) 94438-0 *Fax:* (069) 436002
*E-mail:* info@medico.de
*Web Site:* www.medico.de
*Telex:* 416153 merco d
*Key Personnel*
Publishing: Gudrun Kortas
Founded: 1968
Subjects: Developing Countries, Health, Nutrition
ISBN Prefix(es): 3-923363

**Medien-Verlag Bernhard Gregor GmbH**
Rosengasse 7, 36272 Niederaula
*Tel:* (06625) 5011; (0171) 7723972 *Fax:* (06625) 919743
*E-mail:* gregor-medien@t-online.de; mail@gregor-medien.de
*Web Site:* www.gregor-medien.de
*Key Personnel*
Man Dir: Bernhard Gregor
Founded: 1982
Subjects: Biography, Religion - Catholic, Theology
ISBN Prefix(es): 3-89150; 3-87391; 3-922770
Number of titles published annually: 3 Print

Total Titles: 60 Print
Distributed by Christiana (Switzerland)

**Medium-Buchmarkt+**
Rosenstr 5-6, D-48143 Munster
*Tel:* (0251) 46 000 *Fax:* (0251) 46 745
*E-mail:* info@mediumbooks.com
*Web Site:* www.mediumbooks.com
*Key Personnel*
International Rights: Friedrich W Bitzhenner
Editorial: Carsten Schulte
Specialize in books on pop music.
Subjects: Music, Dance
ISBN Prefix(es): 3-933642

**Medizinisch-Literarische Verlagsgesellschaft mbH+**
Postfach 1151/1152, 29501 Uelzen
*Tel:* (0581) 808-151 *Fax:* (0581) 808-158
*E-mail:* mlverlag@mlverlag.de
*Web Site:* www.mlverlag.de *Cable:* ML-VERLAG 29525 UELZEN
*Key Personnel*
Chief: Dr D Ippen
Publisher: Helmut Block
Founded: 1957
Subjects: Alternative, Cookery, Health, Nutrition, Medicine, Nursing, Dentistry, Sports, Athletics
ISBN Prefix(es): 3-88136; 3-87522
*Parent Company:* C Beckers Buchdruckerei, 29525 Uelzen

**Medpharm Scientific Publishers+**
Birkenwaldstr 44, 70191 Stuttgart
Mailing Address: Postfach 101061, 70009 Stuttgart
*Tel:* (0711) 2582-0 *Fax:* (0711) 2582-290
*E-mail:* service@medpharm.de
*Web Site:* www.medpharm.de
*Key Personnel*
Man Dir: Dr Klaus Brauer; Andre Caro; Dr Christian Rotta
Contact: Siegmar Bauer
Founded: 1981
Subjects: Medicine, Nursing, Dentistry, Pharmacy
ISBN Prefix(es): 3-88763
*Parent Company:* Deutscher Apotheker Verlag
Subsidiaries: S Hirzel Verlag GmbH & Co; Franz Steiner Verlag Wiesbaden GmbH; Wissenschaftliche Verlagsgesellschaft mbH
Foreign Rights: Sabine Koerner

**Felix Meiner Verlag GmbH+**
Richardstr 47, 22081 Hamburg
Mailing Address: Postfach 760742, 22057 Hamburg
*Tel:* (040) 298756-0 *Fax:* (040) 298756-20
*E-mail:* info@meiner.de
*Web Site:* www.meiner.de
*Key Personnel*
Man Dir: Manfred Meiner *E-mail:* meiner@meiner.de
Rights, Marketing: Johannes Kambylis *Tel:* (040) 298756-23 *E-mail:* kambylis@meiner.de
Founded: 1911
Membership(s): the German Book Trade Association.
Subjects: Philosophy
ISBN Prefix(es): 3-7873
Subsidiaries: Helmut Buske Verlag GmbH

**Meisenbach Verlag GmbH**
Franz-Ludwigstr 7a, 96047 Bamberg
*Tel:* (0951) 861-0 *Fax:* (0951) 861-158
*E-mail:* geschltg@meisenbach.de
*Web Site:* www.meisenbach.de
*Key Personnel*
Man Dir: Hans Limmer *E-mail:* h.limmer@meisenbach.de
Founded: 1922

Subjects: Technology
ISBN Prefix(es): 3-87525

**Otto Meissner Verlag+**
Bingerstr 29, 14197 Berlin
*Tel:* (030) 8249558 *Fax:* (030) 8233338
*Key Personnel*
Dir, Rights & Permissions: Dieter Beuermann
Founded: 1848
Subjects: Crafts, Games, Hobbies, Human Relations, Nonfiction (General)
ISBN Prefix(es): 3-87527

**Melsunger Medizinische Mitteilungen**, *imprint of* Bibliomed - Medizinische Verlagsgesellschaft mbH

**Idime Verlag Inge Melzer**
Kienestr 37/1, 88045 Friedrichshafen
*Tel:* (07541) 55220 *Fax:* (07541) 55201
*E-mail:* idime@t-online.de
*Web Site:* www.idime.de
*Key Personnel*
Man Dir: Inge Melzer
Founded: 1983
Subjects: Anthropology, Foreign Countries
ISBN Prefix(es): 3-924026; 3-933937

**Edition Axel Menges GmbH**
Esslingerstr 24, 70736 Fellbach
*Tel:* (0711) 574759 *Fax:* (0711) 574784
*Key Personnel*
International Rights: Axel Menges *Tel:* (0711) 574753 *E-mail:* axelmenges@aol.com; Dorothea Dune *Tel:* (0711) 514753 *E-mail:* ddune@aol.com
Founded: 1994
Subjects: Architecture & Interior Design, Art, Film, Video, Photography, Travel
ISBN Prefix(es): 3-930698; 3-932565
Number of titles published annually: 20 Print
Total Titles: 10 Print
*Associate Companies:* Michal Robinson, 125 Stamford Court, Goldhawk Rd, London W6 OXE, United Kingdom *Tel:* (020) 8995 8340 *Fax:* (020) 8995 0113 *E-mail:* mrrobinson@compuserve.com
*Distribution Center:* National Book Network, 4720 Boston Way, Lanham, MD, United States, Contact: Marianne Bohr *Tel:* 301-459-3366 *Fax:* 301-459-2118 *E-mail:* mbohr@nbnbooks.com (also US representative)

**MenSana**, *imprint of* Verlagsgruppe Droemer Knaur GmbH & Co KG

**Menschenkinder Verlag und Vertrieb GmbH+**
An der Kleimannbruecke 97, 48157 Muenster
*Tel:* (0251) 932520 *Fax:* (0251) 9325290
*E-mail:* info@menschenkinder.de
*Web Site:* www.menschenkinder.de
*Key Personnel*
Man Dir: Detlev Joecker
Subjects: Music, Dance
ISBN Prefix(es): 3-927497; 3-89516; 3-9801811

**mentis Verlag GmbH+**
Schulze-Delitzschstr 19, 33100 Paderborn
*Tel:* (05251) 687902; (05251) 687904 *Fax:* (05251) 687905
*E-mail:* info@mentis.de
*Web Site:* www.mentis.de
Founded: 1998
Subjects: Language Arts, Linguistics, Literature, Literary Criticism, Essays, Philosophy
ISBN Prefix(es): 3-89785
Number of titles published annually: 35 Print
Total Titles: 260 Print; 2 CD-ROM
*Distribution Center:* VSB Verlagsservice Braunschweig

*Orders to:* VSB Verlagsservice Braunschweig
*Returns:* VSB Verlagsservice Braunschweig

**Mentor-Verlag Dr Ramdohr KG+**
Member of The Langenscheidt Group
Mies-van-der-Rohe-Str 1, 80807 Munich
Mailing Address: Postfach 401120, 80711 Munich
*Tel:* (089) 360960 *Fax:* (089) 36096-222 (general); (089) 36096-258 (orders)
*E-mail:* mentor@langenscheidt.de
*Key Personnel*
Man Dirs: Karl Ernst Tielebier-Langenscheidt; Andreas Langenscheidt
Chief Editor: Dr Brigitte Abel
Sales Dir: Dr Matti Schusseler
Advertising: Brigitte Pasch
Founded: 1904
Sales & Promotion through Langenscheidt KG.
ISBN Prefix(es): 3-580

**Mercator-Verlag**, *imprint of* Verlagshaus Wohlfarth

**Mergus Verlag GmbH Hans A Baensch+**
Im Wiele 27, 49328 Melle
*Tel:* (05422) 3636 *Fax:* (05422) 1404
*E-mail:* info@mergus.de
*Web Site:* www.mergus.com *Cable:* MERGUS MELLE
*Key Personnel*
Man Dir, Rights & Permissions: Hans A Baensch
Founded: 1977
Subjects: Animals, Pets, Natural History
ISBN Prefix(es): 3-88244
Distributed by Rolf C Hagen Inc (Canada); Rolf C Hagen (UK) Ltd; ICA SA (Canary Islands, Spain); IMAZO OFF (Sweden); Microcosm Ltd (USA); Tetra Sales (Warner Lamber Co) (USA); Pet Pacific Pty Ltd (Australia); Primaris, Edizioni d'Accuariofilia (Italy); SAVAC Sa; Taikong Trading Corp (Taiwan)

**Merian**, *imprint of* Graefe und Unzer Verlag GmbH

**Merit**, *imprint of* Xenos Verlagsgesellschaft mbH

**Merlin Verlag Andreas Meyer Verlags GmbH und Co KG+**
Gifkendorf Nr 38, 21397 Gifkendorf
*Tel:* (04137) 7207 *Fax:* (04137) 7948
*E-mail:* info@merlin-verlag.de
*Web Site:* www.merlin-verlag.de
*Key Personnel*
Publisher: Andreas J Meyer
Sales Manager: Ilse K Meyer
Manager, Theater Dept: Lilli Nitsche
Junior Publisher, License & Press: Dr Katharina E Meyer
Founded: 1957
Subjects: Anthropology, Art, Biography, Drama, Theater, Fiction, Gay & Lesbian, Government, Political Science, Literature, Literary Criticism, Essays, Parapsychology, Philosophy, Poetry
ISBN Prefix(es): 3-87536; 3-926112
Number of titles published annually: 12 Print
Total Titles: 200 Print; 3 Audio
*Associate Companies:* Little Tiger Verlag GmbH, Poppenbuetteler Chausee 53, 22397 Hamburg

**Verlag Merseburger Berlin GmbH+**
Motzstr 9, 34117 Kassel
Mailing Address: Postfach 103880, 34038 Kassel
*Tel:* (0561) 789809-0 *Fax:* (0561) 789809-16
*E-mail:* info@merseburger.de; order@merseburger.de
*Web Site:* www.merseburger.de
*Key Personnel*
Contact: Corinne Votteler *Tel:* (0561) 78980311 *E-mail:* corinne.votteler@merseburger.de

Founded: 1849
Specialize in sheet music & books.
Subjects: Music
ISBN Prefix(es): 3-87537

**Merve Verlag**
Crellestr 22, 10827 Berlin
*Tel:* (030) 784 8433 *Fax:* (030) 788 1074
*E-mail:* merve@merve.de
*Web Site:* www.merve.de
*Key Personnel*
Man Dir, Rights & Permissions: Hans-Peter Gente; Heidi Paris
Founded: 1970
ISBN Prefix(es): 3-88396; 3-920986

**Merz & Solitude - Akademie Schloss Solitude**
Solitude 3, 70197 Stuttgart
*Tel:* (0711) 99 619-471 *Fax:* (0711) 99 619-50
*E-mail:* mr@akademie-solitude.de
*Web Site:* www.akademie-solitude.de
*Key Personnel*
Academy Dir: Jean-Baptiste Joly
Founded: 1989
Publish literary books, artists' books & catalogs by the Akademie Schloss Solitude fellows only.
Subjects: Architecture & Interior Design, Art, Drama, Theater, Fiction, Music, Dance, Photography
ISBN Prefix(es): 3-929085
Number of titles published annually: 12 Print
Total Titles: 110 Print
*Distribution Center:* GVA, Goettingen

**Gustav Mesmer Stiftung**, *imprint of* Silberburg-Verlag Titus Haeussermann GmbH

**Verlag fuer Messepublikationen**, see Verlag fuer Messepublikationen Thomas Neureuter KG

**Metropolis- Verlag fur Okonomie, Gesellschaft und Politik GmbH**
Bahnhofstr 16a, 35037 Marburg
*Tel:* (06421) 67377 *Fax:* (06421) 681918
*E-mail:* info@metropolis-verlag.de
*Web Site:* www.metropolis-verlag.de
*Key Personnel*
Man Dir: Hubert Hoffmann *E-mail:* hoffman@metropolis-verlag.de
Founded: 1987
Subjects: Business, Economics, Environmental Studies, Government, Political Science, Philosophy, Social Sciences, Sociology
ISBN Prefix(es): 3-89518; 3-926570

**Metropolitan Verlag+**
Haus an der Eisemen Bruecke, 93042 Regensburg
*Tel:* (0941) 56840 *Fax:* (0941) 5684111
*E-mail:* walhalla@walhalla.de
*Web Site:* www.metropolitan.de
*Key Personnel*
Publisher: Eva-Maria Steckenleiter *E-mail:* walhalla@walhalla.de
Founded: 1995
Also specializing in rights.
Subjects: Economics
ISBN Prefix(es): 3-8029; 3-89623
Total Titles: 180 Print; 1 CD-ROM; 1 Online; 1 E-Book; 1 Audio

**Karl-Heinz Metz**
Josef-Hollerbachstr 14, 76571 Gaggenau
*Tel:* (07225) 74098 *Fax:* (07225) 74098
*E-mail:* info@metz-verlag.de
*Web Site:* www.metz-verlag.de
*Key Personnel*
Owner: Karl-Heinz Metz
Subjects: Animals, Pets, History, Mysteries, Social Sciences, Sociology, Adventure, Social Situations, Horror & Ghost, Love & Sexuality
ISBN Prefix(es): 3-927655

**J B Metzlersche Verlagsbuchhandlung+**
Werastr 21-23, 70182 Stuttgart
Mailing Address: Postfach 103241, 70028
Stuttgart
*Tel:* (0711) 2194-0 *Fax:* (0711) 2194-249
*E-mail:* info@metzlerverlag.de
*Web Site:* www.metzlerverlag.de *Cable:*
METZLERVERLAG STUTTGART
*Key Personnel*
Man Dir: Michael Justus *E-mail:* justus@
metzlerverlag.de; Dr Bernd Lutz *Tel:* (0711)
2194-220 *E-mail:* lutz@metzlerverlag.de
Marketing & Sales Dir: Michael Schmid
*E-mail:* schmid@metzlerverlag.de
Advertising: Sabine Zobeley *E-mail:* zobeley@
metzlerverlag.de
Licensing & Rights: Andrea Rupp *Tel:* (0711)
2194 225 *E-mail:* rupp@metzlerverlag.de
Press: Joachim Bader *E-mail:* bader@
metzlerverlag.de
Founded: 1682
Membership(s): T R- Verlagsunion GmbH.
Subjects: Antiques, Art, Film, Video, History,
Language Arts, Linguistics, Literature, Literary
Criticism, Essays, Music, Dance, Philosophy
ISBN Prefix(es): 3-476
Number of titles published annually: 80 Print; 2
CD-ROM
*Parent Company:* Georg von Holtzbrinck GmbH
& Co
Distributor for SFG - Servicecenter Fachverlage
GmbH

**Alfred Metzner**, *imprint of* Wolters Kluwer
Deutschland GmbH

**Verlag Gisela Meussling+**
Dixstr 29, 53225 Bonn
*Tel:* (0228) 466347 *Fax:* (0228) 466347
*Web Site:* www.meussling-verlag.de
*Key Personnel*
Man Dir, Rights & Permissions: Gisela Meussling
Founded: 1978
Subjects: Anthropology, History, Philosophy,
Physical Sciences, Women's Studies, Esoter-
ics/New Age, Ethnology
ISBN Prefix(es): 3-922129
*Warehouse:* Stiftsstr 39, 53225 Bonn

**Meyer & Meyer Verlag+**
Von-Coels Str 390, 52080 Aachen
*Tel:* (0241) 95810-0 *Fax:* (0241) 95810-10
*E-mail:* verlag@m-m-sports.com
*Web Site:* www.m-m-sports.com
*Key Personnel*
Man Dir: Hans Juergen Meyer *E-mail:* hjm@m-
m-sports.com; Irmgard Meyer-Purpar *E-mail:* i.
meyer-purpar@m-m-sports.com
Founded: 1984
Also acts as President of WSA (World Sportpub-
lisher Association).
Subjects: Disability, Special Needs, Drama, The-
ater, Health, Nutrition, Music, Dance, Nonfic-
tion (General), Sports, Athletics, Travel
ISBN Prefix(es): 3-89124; 3-89899
Number of titles published annually: 120 Print
Total Titles: 960 Print
Divisions: Aachener Buch Service
*U.S. Office(s):* Lewis International, 2201 NW 102
Pl, No 1, PO Box 5076, Miami, FL 33172,
United States
Foreign Rep(s): Continental Sales (US)
*Warehouse:* Aachener Buch Service, Tempelhofer-
str 21, 52068 Aachen
*Distribution Center:* Bookwide Asia Pte Ltd, 29
Tampines St, 92, Singapore 528779, Singapore
(Southeast Asia)
Bookwise International, PO Box 8892, Symonds
Post Office, Auckland, New Zealand *Tel:* (09)
6 23 23 48 *Fax:* (09) 6 23 21 40 (New
Zealand)

Bookwise International (Pty) Ltd, 174 Cormack
Rd, Winfield, SA 5013, Australia *Tel:* (08268)
82 22 *Fax:* (08268) 87 04 *E-mail:* orders@
bookwise.com.au (Australia)
Buchzentrum AG, Postfach, 4601 Olten, Switzer-
land *Tel:* (062) 2 09 27 05 *Fax:* (062) 2 09 27
88 *Web Site:* www.buchzentrum.de
Commerce Logistic Center, Am Steinfeld 4,
94065 Waldkirchen *Tel:* (085) 81-96 05-0
*Fax:* (085) 81-7 54
Fair Play Sport Bt, Hungary, Contact: Nora
Bendiner *Tel:* (01) 4 71 4 325 *E-mail:* nora.
bendiner@helka.iif.hu (Hungary)
AS Hoeller GmbH, Schaldorferstr 16, 8641 Saint
Marein im Muerztal, Austria *Tel:* (038) 64-67
77 *Fax:* (038) 64-38 88 (Austria/South Tyrol)
Megaform-Sport- & Freetime Equipment, Rue
Haute, 177, 4700 Eupen, Belgium *Tel:* (087)
32 17 17 *Fax:* (087) 31 29 99 *E-mail:* info@
megaform.be *Web Site:* www.megaform.be
(Beglium)
Windsor Books International, 11 The Boundary, Wheatley Rd, Garsington, Oxford OX44
9EJ, United Kingdom *Tel:* (01865) 36 11
22 *Fax:* (01865) 36 11 33 *E-mail:* sales@
windsorbooks.co.uk (Great Britain, France,
Greece, Ireland, Italy, The Netherlands, Portugal, Scandinavia, Spain, South Africa)

**Peter Meyer Verlag (pmv)+**
Schopenhauerstr 11, 60316 Frankfurt am Main
*Tel:* (069) 49 44 49 *Fax:* (069) 44 51 35
*E-mail:* info@PeterMeyerVerlag.de
*Web Site:* www.petermeyerverlag.de
*Key Personnel*
International Rights & Man Dir: Peter Meyer
Man Dir: Annette Sievers
Founded: 1976
Subjects: Language Arts, Linguistics, Regional
Interests, Travel
ISBN Prefix(es): 3-922057; 3-89859
Number of titles published annually: 16 Print
Total Titles: 50 Print
*Orders to:* Prolit Verlagsauslieferung GmbH,
Postfach 9, 35461 Fernwald *Tel:* (0641) 943
93-0 *Fax:* (0641) 943 93-93 *E-mail:* service@
prolit.de *Web Site:* www.prolit.de

**Ursala Meyer und Dr Manfred Duker
Ein-Fach-Verlag+**
Monheimsallee 21, 52062 Aachen
*Tel:* (0241) 405501 *Fax:* (0241) 400 96 67
*E-mail:* einfachverlag@gmx.de
Founded: 1989
Membership(s): Boersenverein.
Subjects: Language Arts, Linguistics, Philosophy,
Religion - Hindu, Science (General), Women's
Studies, Feminist Philosophy
ISBN Prefix(es): 3-928089
Total Titles: 26 Print
*Orders to:* GVA - Gemeinsame Verlagsaus-
lieferung, Postfach 20 21, 37010 Gottin-
gen *Tel:* (0551) 487177 *Fax:* (0551) 41392
*E-mail:* rabe@gva-verlage.de

**Edition Meyster**, *imprint of* nymphenburger

**MICHEL/Schwaneberger Verlag**, see
Schwaneberger Verlag GmbH

**Gertraud Middelhauve Verlag GmbH & Co
KG+**
Lucile-Grahn Str 39, 81675 Munich
*Tel:* (089) 41 94 02-0 *Fax:* (089) 47 01 08-1
*Key Personnel*
Man Dir: Hans Meisinger
Founded: 1947
ISBN Prefix(es): 3-7876
*Parent Company:* Meisinger Verlagsgruppe
*Orders to:* MVS Meisinger Verlagsservice
GmbH, Am Steinfeld 4, 94065 Waldkirchen
*Tel:* (08581) 9605-0 *Fax:* (08581) 754

**Midena Verlag+**
Hilbestr 54, 80636 Munich
*Tel:* (089) 9271-0 *Fax:* (089) 9271-168
*Web Site:* www.droemer-knaur.de
*Key Personnel*
Editorial Dir: Erhard Held
Rights & Permissions: Silke Breitlaender
Founded: 1981
Subjects: Child Care & Development, Cookery,
Education, Health, Nutrition, Human Relations,
Medicine, Nursing, Dentistry, Psychology, Psy-
chiatry, Self-Help
*Parent Company:* Verlagsgruppe Droemer Weltbild
GmbH & Co KG

**Militzke Verlag+**
Huttenstr 5, 04249 Leipzig
*Tel:* (0341) 42643-0 *Fax:* (0341) 42643-99
*E-mail:* info@militzke.de
*Web Site:* www.militzke.de
*Key Personnel*
Editorial: Dr Siegfried Kaetzel *E-mail:* lektorat@
militzke.de
Public Relations, Press & Licensing: Christiane
Voelkel *Tel:* (0341) 42643-20 *Fax:* (0341)
42643-26 *E-mail:* presse@militzke.de
Contact for Orders: Melitta Siebert *Tel:* (0341)
42643-12
Founded: 1990 (First privately founded publisher
on former GDR territory since 1989)
National & international rights bought & sold,
publication of textbooks & special interest
hardcovers.
Membership(s): German Publishers & Booksellers
Association & Association of Publishers &
Bookshops.
Subjects: Biography, Government, Political Sci-
ence, Special Interest Hardcover, Authentic
Criminal Cases, Historical & Political Popular
Science & Detective Novels
ISBN Prefix(es): 3-86189
Number of titles published annually: 50 Print
Total Titles: 637 Print; 1 Audio

**Minerva Edition Wissen Medizinischer und
Naturwissenschaftlicher Verlag und Vertieb+**
Kirchheimer Str 60, 67269 Gruenstadt-Pfalz
*Tel:* (0700) 96 389 352 *Fax:* (0700) 96 389 353
*E-mail:* info@woetzel.de
*Web Site:* www.woetzel.de
*Key Personnel*
President: Martin M Preuss *Tel:* (06351) 41000
Founded: 1987
STM - Books, health, psychology.
ISBN Prefix(es): 3-936611
Total Titles: 32 Print; 1 CD-ROM; 3 Audio
*Bookshop(s):* Akademische Buchhandlung Woet-
zel *Tel:* (06359) 924726 *Fax:* (06359) 924723

**Miranda-Verlag Stefan Ehlert+**
Humboldtstr 145, 28203 Bremen
Mailing Address: PO Box 101021, 28010 Bremen
*Tel:* (0421) 7943226 *Fax:* (0421) 7943226
*E-mail:* miranda-verlag@t-online.de
*Web Site:* www.miranda-verlag.de
Founded: 1997
Subjects: Biography, Literature, Literary Criti-
cism, Essays
ISBN Prefix(es): 3-934790
Number of titles published annually: 2 Print
Total Titles: 6 Print

**Missio eV+**
Goethestr 43, 52064 Aachen
Mailing Address: Postfach 101253, Aachen 52012
*Tel:* (0241) 75 07-00 *Fax:* (0241) 75 07-336
*E-mail:* info@missio-aachen.de
*Web Site:* www.missio-aachen.de
*Telex:* 832719 mira d
Subjects: Developing Countries, Religion -
Catholic, Religion - Other
ISBN Prefix(es): 3-930556

*Bookshop(s):* Missio am Dom, Muensterplatz, 52064 Aachen
*Warehouse:* missio eV, Industriestr 12, 52146 Wuerselen

**Missionshandlung**
Georg-Haccius-Str 9, 29320 Hermannsburg
Mailing Address: Postfach 1109, 29314 Hermannsburg
*Tel:* (05052) 69-0 *Fax:* (05052) 69-222
*E-mail:* central_de@elm.mission.net
*Web Site:* www.missionshandlung.de
*Key Personnel*
Contact: Hans Peter Schiebe; Wilfried Schulte
Founded: 1856
Subjects: Regional Interests
ISBN Prefix(es): 3-87546
*Parent Company:* Ev luth Missionswerk in Niedersachsen (ELM)

**Mitteilungsblatt der Verbandes deds bayerischen Druckincleestrie eV,** *imprint of* Fachverlag fur das graphische Gewerbe GmbH

**Mitteldeutscher Verlag GmbH+**
Am Steintor 23, 06112 Halle
*Tel:* (0345) 23322-0 *Fax:* (0345) 23322-66
*E-mail:* mitteldeutscher.verlag@t-online.de
*Web Site:* www.buecherkisten.de
*Key Personnel*
Man Dir: Veronika Schneides
Founded: 1946
Subjects: Art, Fiction, History, Literature, Literary Criticism, Essays, Nonfiction (General), Photography, Poetry, Regional Interests, Travel
ISBN Prefix(es): 3-932776

**E S Mittler und Sohn GmbH+**
Member of Verlagsgruppe Koehler/Mittler
Striepenweg 31, 21147 Hamburg
Mailing Address: Postfach 920463, 21134 Hamburg
*Tel:* (040) 7 97 13-03 *Fax:* (040) 79713324
*Cable:* MITTLER & SOHN, HERFORD/WESTF
*Key Personnel*
Publisher: Wolf O Storck; Peter Tamm
Sales: Hans-Focko Koehler
Manager: Thomas Bantle
Founded: 1789
Subjects: Aeronautics, Aviation, Government, Political Science, Maritime, Military Science
ISBN Prefix(es): 3-87547; 3-8132
*Associate Companies:* Verlag Europaeische Wehrkunde; Koehlers Verlagsgesellschaft; Maximilian-Verlag; Verlag Offene Worte
*Branch Office(s)*
Godesberger Allee 91, 53175 Bonn *Tel:* (0228) 307890 *Fax:* (0228) 3078915

**MMV Medizin Verlag GmbH Munich,** see Urban & Vogel Medien und Medizin Verlagsgesellschaft mbH & Co KG

**Moby Dick Verlag+**
Kaistr 33, Eckmann-Speicher, 24103 Kiel
Mailing Address: Postfach 3369, 24032 Kiel
*Tel:* (0431) 640110 *Fax:* (0431) 6401112
*E-mail:* mobybook@aol.com
*Key Personnel*
Publisher: Konrad Delius
Editor: Klaus Bartelt
Subjects: Automotive, Crafts, Games, Hobbies, Mysteries, Outdoor Recreation, Sports, Athletics, Technology, Transportation, Travel
ISBN Prefix(es): 3-922843; 3-930392; 3-89595
Total Titles: 20 Print
*Parent Company:* Delius Klasing Verlag

**mode information Heinz Kramer GmbH**
Pilgerstr 20, 51491 Overath

*Tel:* (02206) 60070 *Fax:* (02206) 600717
*E-mail:* info@modeinfo.com
*Web Site:* www.modeinfo.com
Subjects: Architecture & Interior Design, Fashion, Management, Marketing
ISBN Prefix(es): 3-00
Foreign Rights: Eastgate House (UK); Inter Fashion Express (Greece); H Kramer GmbH (Germany); Masolo Representacoes SA (Portugal); Mode Gallery BAJ Oy (Finland); Pej Gruppen Aps (Denmark)

**Modellsport Verlag GmbH+**
Schulstr 12, 76532 Baden-Baden
*Tel:* (07221) 95 21-0 *Fax:* (07221) 95 21-45
*E-mail:* modellsport@modellsport.de
*Web Site:* www.modellsport.de
*Key Personnel*
Manager: Heinz Ongsieck
Founded: 1977
ISBN Prefix(es): 3-923142

**Moderne Buchkunst und Graphie Wolfgang Tiessen**
Meisenstr 9, 63263 Neu-Isenburg
Mailing Address: Postfach 2179, 63243 Neu-Isenburg
*Tel:* (06102) 53335 *Fax:* (06102) 53335
Founded: 1977
Specialize in limited editions finely printed with illustrations in original graphic.
ISBN Prefix(es): 3-920947; 3-928395

**modo verlag GmbH**
Runzstr 62, 79102 Freiburg
*Tel:* (0761) 2022875 *Fax:* (0761) 2022876
*E-mail:* info@modoverlag.de
*Web Site:* www.modoverlag.de
Subjects: Architecture & Interior Design, Art, Contemporary Art, Late 20th Century Art
ISBN Prefix(es): 3-922675; 3-937014
Number of titles published annually: 8 Print
Total Titles: 45 Print

**Moeck Verlag und Musikinstrumentenwerk, Inhaber Dr Hermann Moeck**
Lueckenweg 4, 29227 Celle
Mailing Address: Postfach 3131, 29231 Celle
*Tel:* (05141) 88 53-0 *Fax:* (05141) 88 53-42
*E-mail:* info@moeck-music.de
*Web Site:* www.moeck-music.de
*Key Personnel*
Owner: Dr Hermann Moeck
ISBN Prefix(es): 3-87549

**Karl Heinrich Moeseler Verlag+**
Hoffmann-von-Fallerslebenstr 8, 38304 Wolfenbuettel
*Tel:* (05331) 95970 *Fax:* (05331) 9597-20
*Key Personnel*
President & International Rights: Dietrich Moeseler
Founded: 1949
Subjects: Music, Dance
ISBN Prefix(es): 3-7877

**Moewig,** *imprint of* Pabel-Moewig Verlag KG

**Mohr Siebeck+**
Wilhelmstr 18, 72074 Tuebingen
Mailing Address: Postfach 2040, 72010 Tuebingen
*Tel:* (07071) 923-0 *Fax:* (07071) 5 11 04
*E-mail:* info@mohr.de
*Web Site:* www.mohr.de *Cable:* SIEBECK TUBINGEN
*Key Personnel*
Owner & Publisher: Georg Siebeck *Tel:* (07071) 923 32 *Fax:* (07071) 923 67 *E-mail:* siebeck@mohr.de

Sales & Marketing Dir: Sabine Stehle *Tel:* (07071) 923 56 *E-mail:* sabine.stehle@mohr.de
Production: Matthias Spitzner *Tel:* (07071) 923 43 *E-mail:* matthias.spitzner@mohr.de
Rights & Permissions: Jill Sopper *Tel:* (07071) 923 61 *E-mail:* jill.sopper@mohr.de
Editorial Dir Law: Dr Franz-Peter Gillig *Tel:* (07071) 923 50 *Fax:* (07071) 923 67 *E-mail:* franz-peter.gillig@mohr.de
Editorial Dir Theology: Dr Henning Ziebritzki *Tel:* (07071) 923 59 *Fax:* (07071) 511 04 *E-mail:* henning.ziebritzki@mohr.de
Founded: 1801
Academic Books & Journals. Encyclopedias, Historical-critical Editions & Monographs.
Subjects: Economics, History, Law, Philosophy, Religion - Protestant, Religion - Other, Social Sciences, Sociology, Theology, Judaism
ISBN Prefix(es): 3-16
Number of titles published annually: 180 Print
Total Titles: 3,210 Print
Imprints: H Lauppsche Buchhandlung
*Warehouse:* Christophstr 32, 72072 Tuebingen

**Monastica,** *imprint of* Verein der Benediktiner zu Beuron- Beuroner Kunstverlag

**Monia Verlag+**
Strobelallee 62, 66953 Pirmasens
Mailing Address: Postfach 2120, 66929 Pirmasens
*Tel:* (06331) 41425 *Fax:* (06331) 41425
*Key Personnel*
Contact: Elisabeth Dillenburger
Founded: 1971
Novels & bilingual poetry for adults.
Subjects: Biography, Fiction, Literature, Literary Criticism, Essays, Poetry
ISBN Prefix(es): 3-926753; 3-9800383

**Moritz Verlag+**
Kantstr 12, 60316 Frankfurt am Main
*Tel:* (069) 4305084 *Fax:* (069) 4305083
*E-mail:* MoritzVerlag@t-online.de
*Key Personnel*
Contact: Markus Weber
Founded: 1994
ISBN Prefix(es): 3-89565
*Parent Company:* l'ecole des loisirs, Paris, France
*Warehouse:* Koch, Neff & Oetinger, 70551 Stuttgart
*Orders to:* Koch, Neff & Oetinger, 70551 Stuttgart *Tel:* (0711) 78 99 10 10 *E-mail:* order@kno-va.de

**Morsak Verlag+**
Wittelsbacherstr 2-8, 94481 Grafenau
Mailing Address: Postfach 1262, 94476 Grafenau
*Tel:* (08552) 4200 *Fax:* (08552) 42050
*E-mail:* morsak@morsak.de
*Web Site:* www.morsak.de
*Key Personnel*
Man Dir, Production: Erich Stecher
Sales: Rosa Zarham
Founded: 1884
Subjects: Regional Interests
ISBN Prefix(es): 3-87553

**Morus-Verlag GmbH**
Gotzstr 65, 12099 Berlin
*Tel:* (030) 89 79 37-0 *Fax:* (030) 75 70 81 12
*E-mail:* mail@morusverlag.de
*Web Site:* www.morusverlag.de
*Key Personnel*
Dir: Olaf Lezinsky
Founded: 1945
Subjects: Religion - Other
ISBN Prefix(es): 3-87554

**Mosaik Verlag GmbH**
Neumarkterstr 28, 81673 Munich

Mailing Address: Postfach 800360, 81673 Munich

*Tel:* (089) 4372-0; (089) 4136-0; (01805) 990505 (hot line) *Fax:* (089) 4372-2812

*E-mail:* vertrieb.verlagsgruppe@randomhouse.de

*Web Site:* www.randomhouse.de/mosaik

*Telex:* 523259 vbmue d

*Key Personnel*

Man Dir: Georg Kessler; Lothar Beyer

Publicity: Helga Mahmoud-Treimer

Rights & Permissions: Angelika Straus-Fischer

Subjects: Animals, Pets, Antiques, Architecture & Interior Design, Career Development, Child Care & Development, Cookery, Crafts, Games, Hobbies, Economics, Film, Video, Finance, Gardening, Plants, Health, Nutrition, House & Home, Human Relations, Self-Help, Sports, Athletics, Wine & Spirits, Women's Studies

ISBN Prefix(es): 3-576

*Parent Company:* Verlagsgruppe Bertelsmann GmbH

*U.S. Office(s):* Bettina Schrewe Literary Scouting, 101 Fifth Ave, Suite 11B, New York, NY 10003, United States (US Scout)

**Motorbuch-Verlag+**

Division of Paul Pietsch Verlage GmbH & Co

Olgastr 86, 70180 Stuttgart

*Tel:* (0711) 210 80 65 *Fax:* (0711) 210 80 70

*E-mail:* versand@motorbuch.de

*Web Site:* www.motorbuch-versand.de *Cable:* PICO D

*Key Personnel*

Man Dir: Paul Pietsch; Dr Patricia Scholten

Sales, Publicity: Thomas Guenther

Rights & Permissions: Patricia Hofmann

Editorial: Martin Benz; Claus-Guergen Jacobson; Joachim Kuch; Oliver Schwarz

Marketing: Jarg Ebert

Founded: 1962

Subjects: Aeronautics, Aviation, Automotive, History, Military Science, Nonfiction (General)

ISBN Prefix(es): 3-87943

*Orders to:* Koch, Neff, Oetinger & Co Verlagsauslieferung GmbH, Postfach 800620, 70506 Stuttgart

**Mueller & Schindler Verlag ek**

Rotwiesenstr 22, 70599 Stuttgart

*Tel:* (0711) 233204 *Fax:* (0711) 2369977

*Key Personnel*

Owner: Rolf Mueller

Founded: 1965

Subjects: Art, History, Religion - Other

ISBN Prefix(es): 3-87560

**C F Mueller Verlag, Huethig Gmb H & Co+**

Im Weiher 10, 69121 Heidelberg

Mailing Address: Postfach 10 28 69, 69121 Heidelberg

*Tel:* (06221) 489 395 *Fax:* (06221) 489623

*E-mail:* cfmueller@huethig.de

*Web Site:* www.huethig.de

Founded: 1797

Subjects: Architecture & Interior Design, Energy, Engineering (General), Technology, Technical books

ISBN Prefix(es): 3-7880

Number of titles published annually: 16 Print

*Parent Company:* Huethig GmbH & Co KG

**Verlag Karl Mueller GmbH+**

Nattermann Allee 1, 50829 Cologne

*Tel:* (0221) 130 65-0 *Fax:* (0221) 130 65-299

*E-mail:* info@karl-mueller-verlag.de

*Web Site:* www.karl-mueller-verlag.de

*Key Personnel*

Man Dir: Guido Zanolli

Founded: 1980

ISBN Prefix(es): 3-86070

**Verlag Norbert Mueller AG & Co KG+**

Emmy-Noetherstr 2, 80992 Munich

*Tel:* (089) 5485201 *Fax:* (089) 54852192

*E-mail:* info@vnm.de

*Web Site:* www.vnm.de

*Key Personnel*

Publications Manager: Traude Wuest *Tel:* (089) 35093213 *E-mail:* t.west@vnm.de

Advertising Manager: Gabriele David *Tel:* (089) 35093204 *E-mail:* g.david@vnm.de

Rights Director, Foreign Affairs: Maria Pinto-Peuckmann *Tel:* (089) 548 52-84 26 *Fax:* (089) 548 52-84 21

Contact: Christian Luetgenau

Founded: 1968

Publisher of newsletters.

Subjects: Finance, Management, Marketing, Real Estate

ISBN Prefix(es): 3-920663; 3-89486

*Parent Company:* Verlag Moderne Industrie, Justus-Von-Liebig Str 1, 86899 Landsberg am Lech

*U.S. Office(s):* Verlag Norbert Mueller, 15775 Hillcrest, Suite 508, Dallas, TX 75248-4106, United States

*Shipping Address:* Verlag Moderne Industrie, Justus-Von-Liebig Str 1, 86899 Landsberg am Lech

*Warehouse:* Verlag Moderne Industrie, Justus-Von-Liebig Str 1, 86899 Landsberg am Lech

**Mueller und Steinicke Verlag**

Aidenbachstr 78, 81379 Munich

*Tel:* (089) 74 99 156 *Fax:* (089) 74 99 157

*E-mail:* info@mueller-und-steinicke.de

*Web Site:* www.mueller-und-steinicke.de

*Key Personnel*

Manager: Werner Gissler

Founded: 1903

Subjects: Medicine, Nursing, Dentistry

ISBN Prefix(es): 3-87569

**Muensterschwarzacher Kleinschriften,** *imprint* *of* Vier Tuerme GmbH Verlag Klosterbetriebe

**Muensterschwarzacher Studien,** *imprint of* Vier Tuerme GmbH Verlag Klosterbetriebe

**Multi Media Kunst Verlag Dresden+**

Sarrasanistr 13, 01097 Dresden

*Tel:* (0351) 8041291 *Fax:* (0351) 8041291

*Key Personnel*

Author, Publisher: Hans Kromer

Founded: 1990

Subjects: Art, Literature, Literary Criticism, Essays

ISBN Prefix(es): 3-9700002

**Mundo Verlag GmbH**

Schreberstr 2, 51105 Cologne

*Tel:* (0180) 9216350 *Fax:* (0180) 921635-24

*E-mail:* info@mundo-media.de

*Web Site:* www.mundo-text.de

*Key Personnel*

Man Dir: Ertay Hayit *E-mail:* ertay.hayit@mundo-media.de

Editorial: Cornelia Auschra *Tel:* (0221) 921635-13 *E-mail:* auschra@mundo-media.de; Ute Hayit *Tel:* (0221) 921635-11 *E-mail:* ute.hayit@mundo-media.de

Founded: 1982

Subjects: Travel

ISBN Prefix(es): 3-87322

**Munich, Edition, Verlag, Handels-und Dienstleistungskontar GmbH**

Angererstr 12, 80796 Munich

Mailing Address: Postfach 400128, 80701 Munich

*Tel:* (089) 349830 *Fax:* (089) 349834

*E-mail:* bzit99e@benezit.de

*Key Personnel*

Manager: Harry Blattel

Founded: 1990

Subjects: Art, Wine & Spirits

ISBN Prefix(es): 3-928263

**Munzinger-Archiv GmbH Archiv fuer publizistische Arbeit+**

Albersfelderstr 34, 88213 Ravensburg

*Tel:* (0751) 76931-0 *Fax:* (0751) 65 24 24

*E-mail:* box@munzinger.de

*Web Site:* www.munzinger.de

*Key Personnel*

Manager: Ernst Munzinger

Founded: 1913

Subjects: Biography, Economics, Foreign Countries, Government, Political Science, History, Music, Dance, Sports, Athletics

**Musikantiquariat und Dr Hans Schneider Verlag GmbH+**

Mozartstr 6, 82323 Tutzing

*Tel:* (08158) 3050; (08158) 6967 *Fax:* (08158) 7636

*E-mail:* musikbuch@aol.com; musikantiquar@aol.com *Cable:* MUSIKANTIQUAR

*Key Personnel*

Manager: Dr Hans Schneider

Founded: 1949

Subjects: Antiques, Biography, History, Music, Dance, Science (General)

ISBN Prefix(es): 3-7952

**Musikverlag Zimmermann+**

Strubbergstr 80, 60489 Frankfurt am Main

*Tel:* (069) 978286-6 *Fax:* (069) 978286-89

*E-mail:* info@zimmermann-frankfurt.de; lektorat@zimmermann-frankfurt.de

*Web Site:* www.zimmermann-frankfurt.de

*Key Personnel*

Man Dir: Cornelia Grossmann *Tel:* (069) 978 286-79 *E-mail:* grossmann@zimmermann-frankfurt.de; Michael Kary *Fax:* (069) 978 286-79 *E-mail:* kary@zimmermann-frankfurt.de

International Rights: Saskia Herchenroeder

Sales & Distribution: Aynalem Gebremedhim *Tel:* (069) 978 286-86 *E-mail:* info@zimmermann-frankfurt.de; Michael Henne *Tel:* (069) 978 826-86 *E-mail:* henne@zimmermann-frankfurt.de

Rights & Licensing: Saskia Bieber *Tel:* (069) 978 286-72 *Fax:* (069) 978 286-79 *E-mail:* bieber@zimmermann-frankfurt.de

Advertising, Public Relations: Ulrike Osterhage *Tel:* (069) 978 286-75 *Fax:* (069) 978 286-79 *E-mail:* osterhage@zimmermann-frankfurt.de

Editorial & Production: Friedhelm Neubert *Tel:* (069) 978 286-79 *E-mail:* neubert@zimmermann-frankfurt.de; Judith Picard *Tel:* (069) 978 286-76 *Fax:* (069) 978 286-79 *E-mail:* picard@lienau-frankfurt.de; Peter Ruecker *Tel:* (069) 978 286-73 *Fax:* (069) 978 286-79 *E-mail:* ruecker@zimmermann-frankfurt.de

Subjects: Music, Dance

ISBN Prefix(es): 3-921729

*Associate Companies:* Robert Lienau Musikverlag, Frankfurt

**Muster-Schmidt Verlag+**

Schuhstr, 37154 Sudheim

*Tel:* (05551) 908420 *Fax:* (05551) 9084229

*E-mail:* info@muster-schmidt.de

*Web Site:* www.muster-schmidt.de *Cable:* MUSTERSCHMIDT

*Key Personnel*

Dir: Eva Maria Gerhardy-Loecken *E-mail:* muster-schmidt@t-online.de

Founded: 1905

Subjects: Biography, History, Color

ISBN Prefix(es): 3-7881

*Branch Office(s)*
Nansenstr 1, 8050 Zurich, Switzerland *Tel:* (01) 251 75 71 *Fax:* (01) 252 44 68 *E-mail:* info@ muster-schmidt.de

**MUT Verlag+**
Bahnhofstr 1, 27330 Asendorf
Mailing Address: Postfach 1, 27328 Asendorf
*Tel:* (04253) 566; (04253) 672 *Fax:* (04253) 16 03
*Key Personnel*
Man Dir, Rights & Permissions: Bernhard C Wintzek
Founded: 1972
Subjects: Government, Political Science, History, Culture
ISBN Prefix(es): 3-89182

**MVB Marketing- und Verlagsservice des Buchhandels GmbH**
Grosser Hirschgraben 17/21, 60311 Frankfurt
Mailing Address: Postfach 10 04 42, 60004 Frankfurt
*Tel:* (069) 1306-0; (069) 1306-339 (Boersenblatt); (069) 1306-340 (Boersenblatt) *Fax:* (069) 1306-201
*E-mail:* info@mvb-online.de
*Web Site:* www.mvb-online.de
*Key Personnel*
Management: Dr Michael Schoen *Tel:* (069) 1306-225 *Fax:* (069) 1306-545
Advertising Manager: Lilli Fleck *Tel:* (069) 1306-217 *E-mail:* l.fleck@mvb-online.de
Founded: 1947
Subjects: Publishing & Book Trade Reference
ISBN Prefix(es): 3-7657
Total Titles: 200 Print; 15 CD-ROM
*Parent Company:* Boersenverein des Deutschen Buchhandels ev

**MVS Medizinverlage Stuttgart GmbH & Co KG+**
Formerly Hippokrates-Verlag GmbH
Oswalt-Hessestr 50, 70469 Stuttgart
*Tel:* (0711) 8931-0 *Fax:* (0711) 8931-706
*Web Site:* www.medizinverlage.de
*Telex:* 7252275 gtvd
*Key Personnel*
Man Dir: Dr Thomas Scherb
Marketing: Sigrid Lesch *E-mail:* sigrid.lesch@ thieme.de
Founded: 1925
Subjects: Medicine, Nursing, Dentistry
ISBN Prefix(es): 3-7773; 3-87758; 3-8304
*Parent Company:* Georg Thieme Verlag KG
*Subsidiaries:* Sonntag Verlag
*Shipping Address:* c/o Koch, Neff, Oetinger & Co, Postfach 210, 7000 Stuttgart
*Warehouse:* c/o Koch, Neff, Oetinger & Co, Postfach 210, 7000 Stuttgart
*Orders to:* c/o Koch, Neff, Oetinger & Co, Postfach 210, 7000 Stuttgart

**Nadif,** *imprint of* Daco Verlag Guenter Blase oHG

**Verlag Stephanie Naglschmid+**
Senefelderstr 10, 70178 Stuttgart
*Tel:* (0711) 62 68 78 *Fax:* (0711) 61 23 23
*E-mail:* naglschmid.vsn@t-online.de
*Web Site:* www.naglschmid.de
*Key Personnel*
Contact: Dr Friedrich Naglschmid; Stephanie Naglschmid
Founded: 1984
Also acts as book dealer for Diving Literature.
Subjects: Biological Sciences, Environmental Studies, Film, Video, Natural History, Outdoor Recreation, Photography, Physical Sciences, Sports, Athletics, Travel
ISBN Prefix(es): 3-927913; 3-89594; 3-925342

*Associate Companies:* JLVA Internationale Lizenzvewertungs-Agentur; MTI (Medien - und Touristik Informations Services); Divemaster (Touchmagatin)
Imprints: Edition Hannemann; Edition Schwab

**Verlag Natur & Wissenschaft Harro Hieronimus & Dr Jurgen Schmidt** (Nature & Science Publishing)+
Dompfaffweg 53, 42659 Solingen
Mailing Address: Postfach 170209, 42624 Solingen
*Tel:* (0212) 819878 *Fax:* (0212) 816216
*E-mail:* info@verlagnw.de
*Key Personnel*
Contact: Harro Hieronimus
Founded: 1989
Membership(s): the Stock Exchange of German Booksellers.
Subjects: Animals, Pets, Biological Sciences, Earth Sciences, Environmental Studies, Gardening, Plants, Geography, Geology, Natural History
ISBN Prefix(es): 3-927889; 3-936616
Imprints: Bibliothek Natur & Wissenschaft
Distributor for ACS-Verlag

**NaturaViva Verlags GmbH+**
Lukas-Moser-Weg 4, 71263 Weil der Stadt
Mailing Address: Postfach 1203, 71256 Weil der Stadt
*Tel:* (07033) 1380816 *Fax:* (07033) 1380817
*E-mail:* naturaviva@t-online.de
*Key Personnel*
Man Dir: Simone Graff
Founded: 1999
Membership(s): Borsenverein des Deutschen Buchhandels eV.
Subjects: Health, Nutrition
ISBN Prefix(es): 3-89881; 3-935407
Number of titles published annually: 6 Print
Total Titles: 80 Print
Imprints: Fit fuers Leben Verlag; Waldthausen Verlag
Distributed by Walter Haedecke Verlag

**Naumann & Goebel Verlagsgesellschaft mbH**
Emil-Hoffmann Str 1, 50996 Cologne
Mailing Address: Postfach 501863, 50978 Cologne
*Tel:* (02236) 39990 *Fax:* (02236) 399997
*E-mail:* einstieg@aol.com; fdvemag@netcologne. de
*Telex:* 8886642
*Key Personnel*
Manager: Guenter Goebel; Juergen Naumann; Juergen Krause
Subjects: Animals, Pets, Art, Biblical Studies, Computer Science, Cookery, Crafts, Games, Hobbies, Education, Fashion, Fiction, Gardening, Plants, Health, Nutrition, History, House & Home, How-to, Mathematics, Medicine, Nursing, Dentistry, Science (General), Travel, Family & Relationships, Foreign Language Study, Nature
ISBN Prefix(es): 3-625; 3-632; 3-8247; 3-88703; 3-923723
*Associate Companies:* Delphin AG; Delphin Verlag GmbH; Tigris Verlag GmbH; Naturalis Verlags- u Vertriebsges mbH; Daumueller Werbeges mbH; Reichenbach Verlag GmbH; Verlag Das persoenliche Geburtstagsbuch GmbH; V & M Verlags & Mediengesellschaft Koeln mbH; Neuer Pawlak Verlag GmbH; MZ Medien Zentrum GmbH

**Edition Nautilus Verlag+**
Alte Hostenstr 22, 21031 Hamburg
*Tel:* (040) 7213536 *Fax:* (040) 7218399
*E-mail:* edition-nautilus@t-online.de
*Web Site:* www.edition-nautilus.de

*Key Personnel*
Owner: Lutz Schulenburg
Rights & Permissions: Hanna Mittelstaedt
Editiorial & Press: Katharina Leunig
Production: Klaus Voss
Founded: 1974
Subjects: Art, Biography, Government, Political Science, Literature, Literary Criticism, Essays
ISBN Prefix(es): 3-89401; 3-921523
Distributed by Mohr/Morawa (Austria); Scheidegger & Co AG (Switzerland); SoVa Gmbh

**NDV Neue Darmstadter Verlagsanstalt**
Hauptstr 74, 53619 Rheinbreitbach
Mailing Address: Postfach 1560, 53585 Bad Honnef
*Tel:* (02224) 3232 *Fax:* (02224) 78639
*E-mail:* ndv@ndv.info
*Web Site:* www.ndv-verlag.de
*Key Personnel*
Publisher, Rights & Permissions: Klaus J Holzapfel; Andreas Holzapfel
Editor: Susanne Dirkwinkel
Sales: Sylke Beyer
Marketing, Sales: Markus Fleischer
Founded: 1949
Subjects: Government, Political Science
ISBN Prefix(es): 3-87576
*Branch Office(s)*
Wittestr 30 K, 13509 Berlin *Tel:* (030) 8557511 *Fax:* (030) 85605332

**Nebel Verlag GmbH**
Bahnhofsplatz 4, 86919 Utting
Mailing Address: Postfach 1153, 86917 Utting
*Tel:* (08806) 9215-0 *Fax:* (08806) 9215-22
*Key Personnel*
Contact: Pirmin Nebel
Founded: 1989
Subjects: Cookery, Gardening, Plants, History, Literature, Literary Criticism, Essays, Romance, Travel
ISBN Prefix(es): 3-89555

**Neckar Verlag GmbH+**
Klosterring 1, 78008 Villingen-Schwenningen
Mailing Address: Postfach 1820, 78008 Villingen-Schwenningen
*Tel:* (07721) 89 87-0 *Fax:* (07721) 89 87-50
*E-mail:* service@neckar-verlag.de
*Web Site:* www.neckar-verlag.de
*Key Personnel*
Man Dir: Inge Holtzhauer; Dr Heinz Loercher
Marketing: Peter Walter *Tel:* (07721) 87 87-45 *E-mail:* walter@neckar-verlag.de
Founded: 1945
Subjects: Aeronautics, Aviation, Literature, Literary Criticism, Essays, Literature & Plans for RC-Model Aircraft & RC-Model Ship
ISBN Prefix(es): 3-7883

**Neff,** *imprint of* Pabel-Moewig Verlag KG

**Nelles Verlag GmbH+**
Schleissheimerstr 371b, 80935 Munich
*Tel:* (089) 357 19 40 *Fax:* (089) 357 19 430
*E-mail:* info@nelles-verlag.de
*Web Site:* www.nelles-verlag.de
*Key Personnel*
Man Dir, Rights & Permissions: Guenter Nelles
Man Dir: Martin Nelles
Founded: 1975
Subjects: Travel
ISBN Prefix(es): 3-88618; 3-920397; 3-922539
*Orders to:* Geocenter/ILH, Postfach 800830, 70508 Stuttgart

**Neue Darmstadter Verlagsanstalt,** see NDV Neue Darmstadter Verlagsanstalt

**Neue Erde Verlags GmbH+**
Cecilienstr 29, 66111 Saarbruecken
*Tel:* (0681) 372313 *Fax:* (0681) 3904102
*E-mail:* info@neueerde.de
*Key Personnel*
Publisher: Andreas Lentz
Founded: 1984
Subjects: Environmental Studies, Parapsychology,
   Self-Help
ISBN Prefix(es): 3-89060
Imprints: Ryvellus

**Verlag Neue Kritik KG+**
Kettenhofweg 53, 60325 Frankfurt
*Tel:* (069) 727576 *Fax:* (069) 726585
*E-mail:* neuekritik@compuserve.com
*Key Personnel*
Man Dir: Dorothea Rein
Founded: 1965
Subjects: Art, Fiction, Philosophy, Poetry,
   Women's Studies, Judaica
ISBN Prefix(es): 3-8015
*Orders to:* Sozialistische Verlagsauslieferung
   GmbH, Franziusstr 44, 60314 Frankfurt am
   Main

**Verlag Neue Musik GmbH**
Grabbeallee 15, 13156 Berlin
*Tel:* (030) 616981-0 *Fax:* (030) 616981-21
*E-mail:* vnm@verlag-neue-musik.de
*Web Site:* www.verlag-neue-musik.de
*Key Personnel*
Dir: Detlef Kessler
Manager: Axel Muetze-Kern
Founded: 1957
Subjects: Music, Dance
ISBN Prefix(es): 3-7333
Subsidiaries: Edition Margaux

**Verlag Neue Musikzeitung GmbH**
Brunnstr 23, 93053 Regensburg
*Tel:* (0941) 94 59 30 *Fax:* (0941) 94 59 350
*E-mail:* nmz@nmz.de
*Web Site:* www.nmz.de
*Key Personnel*
Publisher & Chief Editor: Theo Geissler
Editor-in-Chief: Gerhard Rohde
Editorial Manager: Andreas Kolb
Founded: 1993
Subjects: Art, Ethnicity, Music, Dance
*Parent Company:* Con Brio Verlagsgesellschaft
   mbH, Postfach 100245, Brunnstr 23, 93053
   Regensburg

**Verlag Neue Stadt GmbH+**
Mangfallstr 29, 81547 Munich
*Tel:* (08093) 2091 *Fax:* (08093) 2096 *Cable:*
   NEUE STADT
*Key Personnel*
Man Dir: Wolfgang Bader
Sales, Publicity & Advertising: Gabriele Hartl
Rights: Stefan Liesenfeld
Founded: 1961
Subjects: Biblical Studies, Biography, Fiction,
   How-to, Music, Dance, Religion - Other, The-
   ology, Autobiography, Family & Relationships
ISBN Prefix(es): 3-87996
*Parent Company:* Citta Nuova Editrice, Italy
*Branch Office(s)*
Trostr 116, 1100 Vienna, Austria
Seestr 426, Postfach 435, 8038 Zurich, Switzer-
   land

**Verlag Neue Wirtschafts-Briefe GmbH & Co+**
Eschstr 22, 44629 Herne
*Tel:* (02323) 141-900 *Fax:* (02323) 141-123
*E-mail:* info@nwb.de
*Web Site:* www.nwb.de *Cable:* STEUERBRIEFE
   HERNE
*Key Personnel*
Publisher: Dr Karl-Friedrich Peter

Man Dir: E O Kleyboldt
Sales & Advertising Dir: J Mueller-Grote
Founded: 1947
Subjects: Accounting, Business, Career Develop-
   ment, Law
ISBN Prefix(es): 3-482
*Associate Companies:* Verlag fuer die Rechts- und
   Anwaltspraxis GmbH & Co KG
Subsidiaries: Friedrich Kiehl Verlag GmbH
*Shipping Address:* Schuechtermannstr 180, 44628
   Herne
*Warehouse:* Schuechtermannstr 180, 44628 Herne
*Orders to:* Postfach 101849, 44621 Herne

**Neuer Honos Verlag GmbH+**
Emil-Hoffmann- Str 1, 50996 Cologne
*Tel:* (0221) 3 36 20-0 *Fax:* (0221) 3 36 20-99
*E-mail:* nhonos@netcologne.de
*Key Personnel*
Chief Executive Officer: Stefan Sommer
   *Tel:* (0221) 336200
Founded: 1998
Subjects: Animals, Pets, Biblical Studies, Com-
   puter Science, Cookery, Health, Nutrition, Nu-
   trition, How-to, Language Arts, Linguistics,
   Nonfiction (General), Travel, Health & Fitness,
   Foreign Language Study, Nature
ISBN Prefix(es): 3-8299
*Warehouse:* GVA, Gesellschaft fur Verlagsaus-
   lieferung & Logistik mbH, Heideweg 8a,
   36160 Bad-Bwischenahn *Tel:* (0441) 969412
   *Fax:* (0441) 969415

**Neuer ISP Verlag GmbH**
Marienstr 15, 76137 Karlsruhe
*Tel:* (0721) 31 183 *Fax:* (0721) 31 250
*E-mail:* contact@sterneck.net
*Web Site:* www.sterneck.net/alive/isp
*Key Personnel*
Manager, Rights & Permissions: Wolfgang Feik-
   ert
Subjects: Economics, Government, Political Sci-
   ence, History, Philosophy, Social Sciences, So-
   ciology
ISBN Prefix(es): 3-929008; 3-89900
*Orders to:* Buro Frankfurt Im, Kassler Str 1 a,
   60486 Frankfurt

**Verlag Neuer Weg GmbH+**
Alte Bottroper Str 42, 45356 Essen
*Tel:* (0201) 2 59 15 *Fax:* (0201) 61 444 62
*E-mail:* verlag@neuerweg.de
*Web Site:* www.neuerweg.de
*Key Personnel*
Rights & Permissions: Gert Bierikoven
Dir: Christoph Klug
Founded: 1971
Subjects: Developing Countries, Education, En-
   vironmental Studies, Government, Political
   Science, Health, Nutrition, History, Physical
   Sciences, Women's Studies
ISBN Prefix(es): 3-88021
*Bookshop(s):* Buchladen NeuerWeg, Reuterstr 15,
   12053 Berlin; Ernst-Thaelmann-Buchhandlung,
   Hauptstaetter Str 39, 70173 Stuttgart

**Verlag Neues Leben GmbH+**
Max-Beerstr 13, 10119 Berlin
Mailing Address: Postfach 35, 10121 Berlin
*Tel:* (030) 2827148; (020) 2827020 *Fax:* (030)
   28388075 *Cable:* NEUESLEBEN BERLIN
*Key Personnel*
Man Dir, Rights & Permissions: Rudolf
   Chowanetz
Production: Hannelore Lange
Sales: Walter Toelg
Founded: 1946
Subjects: Biography, Cookery, Fiction, Gay &
   Lesbian, History, Human Relations, Nonfiction
   (General), Religion - Jewish
ISBN Prefix(es): 3-355

*Warehouse:* Moor Morawa Buchvertriebsges
   mbH, Sulzengasse 2, 1232 Vienna, Austria
Schweizer Bucherzentrum, Postfach, 4601 Olten,
   Switzerland
*Orders to:* LKG-Verlagsauslieferung, Poet-
   zschauer Weg, 04579 Espenhain

**Neues Literaturkontor+**
Goldstr 15, 48147 Muenster
*Tel:* (0251) 45343 *Fax:* (0251) 40565
*E-mail:* neues-literaturkontor@t-online.de
*Web Site:* www.neues-literaturkontor.de
*Key Personnel*
Contact: Dr Hans D Mummendey
International Rights: Dorothea Potthoff
Founded: 1990
Specialize in novels & short stories.
Subjects: Poetry
ISBN Prefix(es): 3-920591
Number of titles published annually: 5 Print
Total Titles: 60 Print

**Neuland-Verlagsgesellschaft mbH+**
Markt 24-26, 21502 Geesthacht
Mailing Address: Postfach 1422, 21496
   Geesthacht
*Tel:* (04152) 8 13 42 *Fax:* (04152) 8 13 43
*E-mail:* vertrieb@neuland.com
*Web Site:* www.neuland.com
*Key Personnel*
Manager: Jens Burmester *E-mail:* gf@neuland.
   com
Founded: 1889
Specialize in the area of addictions.
Subjects: Health, Nutrition, Medicine, Nursing,
   Dentistry, Psychology, Psychiatry, Self-Help,
   Social Sciences, Sociology
ISBN Prefix(es): 3-87581

**Verlag J Neumann-Neudamm GmbH & Co
KG+**
Schwalbenweg 1, 34212 Melsungen
*Tel:* (05661) 52222 *Fax:* (05661) 6008
*E-mail:* info@neumann-neudamm.de
*Web Site:* www.neumann-neudamm.cfmx.de
*Key Personnel*
Dir: Walter Schwartz
Foreign Rights: Rolf Roosen
Founded: 1872
Subjects: Outdoor Recreation, Science (General),
   Sports, Athletics
ISBN Prefix(es): 3-7888
Subsidiaries: JANA (Gesellschaft fur Jagd und
   Natur GmbH)

**Verlag fuer Messepublikationen Thomas
Neureuter KG**
Sueskindstr 4, 81929 Munich
*Tel:* (089) 99 30 91-0 *Fax:* (089) 93 78 96
*E-mail:* info@neureuter.de
*Web Site:* www.neureuter.de
*Telex:* 522918 mesu d
*Key Personnel*
Publisher: Thomas Neureuter
Founded: 1948
ISBN Prefix(es): 3-921362
*Branch Office(s)*
Leipziger Messe Verlag und Vertriebsge-
   sellschaft mbH, Messe-Allee 1, 04358 Leipzig
   *Tel:* (0341) 67 877-0 *Fax:* (0341) 67 877-12
   *E-mail:* info@leipziger-messeverlag.de *Web
   Site:* www.leipziger-messeverlag.de
Chuang's Enterprises Bldg, Room 1003, 10/F,
   382 Lockhart Rd, Wanchai, Hong Kong
   *Tel:* 2519 3581 *Fax:* 2519 6941 *E-mail:* info@
   neureuter.com.hk *Web Site:* www.neureuter.
   com.hk
Binterimstr 13, Duesseldorf *Tel:* (0211) 34 20 26
   *Fax:* (0211) 33 34 85

**Neuthor - Verlag+**
Obere Pfarrgasse 31, 64720 Michelstadt

*Tel:* (06061) 40 79 *Fax:* (06061) 26 46
*Web Site:* www.neuthor-verlag.de
*Key Personnel*
Publisher: Peter-Jochen Bosse *E-mail:* bosse@
neuthor-verlag.de
Founded: 1980
Subjects: Architecture & Interior Design, Biography, Fiction, Foreign Countries, History, Mysteries, Travel
ISBN Prefix(es): 3-88758

**New Era Publications Deutschland GmbH**
Hittfelder Kirchweg 5a, 21220 Seevetal-Maschen
*Tel:* (04105) 68330 *Fax:* (04150) 683322
*E-mail:* buch@newerapublications.de
*Web Site:* www.newerapublications.com
*Key Personnel*
Manager: Thomas Goeldenitz
Founded: 1985
Subjects: Religion - Other, Science Fiction, Fantasy, Self-Help
ISBN Prefix(es): 3-929284
*Parent Company:* New Era Publications Int Aps, Stove Kangensgade 55, 1264 Copenhagen, Denmark

**Nicolaische Verlagsbuchhandlung Beuermann GmbH+**
Neuenburger Str 17, 10969 Berlin
*Tel:* (030) 253738-0 *Fax:* (030) 253738-39
*E-mail:* info@nicolai-verlag.de
*Web Site:* www.nicolai-verlag.de
*Key Personnel*
Publisher: Dr Hans von Trotha
Marketing: Susanne Boger *Tel:* (030) 253738-12
*Fax:* (030) 253738-40 *E-mail:* susanne.boger@
nicolai-verlag.de
Rights & Licenses: Irene von Trotha *Tel:* (030)
253738-33 *Fax:* (030) 253738-39 *E-mail:* irene.
trotha@nicolai-verlag.de
Subjects: Architecture & Interior Design, Art, Biography, Photography, Regional Interests
ISBN Prefix(es): 3-87584; 3-89479; 3-9803217
*Orders to:* S Fischer Velope, 60591 Frankfurt/Main *Tel:* (069) 6062-0 *Fax:* (069) 6062-21X

**Nie/Nie/Sagen-Verlag+**
Silvanerweg 17, 78464 Konstanz
*Tel:* (07531) 53570 *Fax:* (07531) 64496
*E-mail:* haberkern-imz@t-online.de
*Web Site:* www.nie-nie-sagen-verlag.de
*Key Personnel*
Publisher: Atina Haberkern
Founded: 1977
Subjects: Literature, Literary Criticism, Essays, Poetry, Religion - Buddhist, Religion - Other, Self-Help
ISBN Prefix(es): 3-921778

**Niederland-Verlag Helmut Michel**
Winnendestr 20, 71522 Backnang
Mailing Address: Postfach 1480, 71504 Backnang
*Tel:* (07191) 3277-200 *Fax:* (07191) 3277-15
*E-mail:* micheldruck@t-online.de
*Key Personnel*
Owner: Helmut Michel
Subjects: History, Regional Interests
ISBN Prefix(es): 3-923947

**Nielsen Frederic W**, see Toleranz Verlag, Nielsen Frederic W

**C W Niemeyer Buchverlage GmbH+**
Osterstr 19, 31785 Hameln
*Tel:* (05151) 200-312 *Fax:* (05151) 200-319
*E-mail:* info@niemeyer-buch.de
*Web Site:* www.niemeyer-buch.de
*Key Personnel*
Publisher: Hans Freiwald
Founded: 1797

Membership(s): Borsenverein des Deutschen Buchhandels.
Subjects: Architecture & Interior Design, Art, Fiction, History, Humor, Library & Information Sciences, Literature, Literary Criticism, Essays, Mysteries
ISBN Prefix(es): 3-8271; 3-87585
Subsidiaries: Adolf Sponholtz Verlag
*Orders to:* VSB - Verlagsservice Braunschweig GmbH, Postfach 4738, 38037 Braunschweig
*Tel:* (0531) 708650 *Fax:* (0531) 708608

**Max Niemeyer Verlag GmbH+**
Pfrondorferstr 6, 72074 Tuebingen
Mailing Address: Postfach 2140, 72011 Tuebingen
*Tel:* (07071) 98 94 0 *Fax:* (07071) 98 94 50
*E-mail:* max@niemeyer.de; info@niemeyer.de
*Web Site:* www.niemeyer.de *Cable:* NIEMEYER TUBINGEN
*Key Personnel*
Man Dir: Robert Harsch-Niemeyer; Nikolaus Steinberg
Publicity & Marketing: Karin Wenzel
*Tel:* (07071) 989413 *E-mail:* wenzel@
niemeyer.de
Editorial Dir: Birgitta Zeller *E-mail:* zeller@
niemeyer.de
International Rights: Marlene Kirton *Tel:* (07071)
989427 *E-mail:* kirton@niemeyer.de
Marketing: Barbara Opel *E-mail:* opel@niemeyer.
de
Sales: Nikolaus Steinberg
Founded: 1870
Subjects: History, Language Arts, Linguistics, Literature, Literary Criticism, Essays, Philosophy
ISBN Prefix(es): 3-484
Number of titles published annually: 160 Print

**Nieswand-Verlag GmbH+**
Werftbahnstr 8, 24143 Kiel
*Tel:* (0431) 7028 200 *Fax:* (0431) 7028 228
*E-mail:* vertrieb@nieswandverlag.de
*Web Site:* www.nieswandverlag.de
*Key Personnel*
Manager: Jens Nieswand
Co-Editor: Ingo Wulff
Marketing: Ines Heinrich
Rights & Permissions: Melanie Voss
Sales: Carola Dreller *Tel:* (0431) 7028 218
*E-mail:* caroladreller@nieswandverlag.de
Founded: 1986
Membership(s): the Stock Exchange of German Booksellers.
Subjects: Art, Music, Dance, Photography
ISBN Prefix(es): 3-926048; 3-89567
*Orders to:* Coen Sligting Bookimport, Paulus Potterstraat 20, 1071 DA Amsterdam, Netherlands (International Distributor)
PNV Vertriebsservice GmbH, Werftbahnstr 8, 24143 Kiel
DAP Distributed Art Publishers, 155 Avenue of the Americas, 2nd floor, New York, NY 10013-1507, United States *Tel:* 212-627-1999

**Hans-Nietsch-Verlag+**
Poststr 3, 79098 Freiburg
Mailing Address: PO Box 228, 79002 Freiburg
*Tel:* (0761) 2966930 *Fax:* (0761) 2966960
*E-mail:* mail@nietsch.de
*Web Site:* www.nietsch.de
*Key Personnel*
Contact: Hans Nietsch
Subjects: Religion - Other, Health, Occult
ISBN Prefix(es): 3-934647; 3-929475
Number of titles published annually: 10 Print
Total Titles: 100 Print
Imprints: Edition Sternenprinz
Distributor for Verlag Hans-Juergen Maurer; Edition Synthese
*Distribution Center:* Val Silberschnur, Steinstr 1, 56593 Guellesheim

**Rainar Nitzsche Verlag+**
Gasstr 34, 67655 Kaiserslautern
*Tel:* (0631) 61305 *Fax:* (0631) 61305
*E-mail:* rainar.nitzscheverlag@t-online.de
*Web Site:* nitzscheverlag.de.vu; www.
nitzscheverlag.homepage.t-online.de
*Key Personnel*
Contact: Dr Rainar Nitzsche
*E-mail:* drrainarnitzsche@web.de
Founded: 1989
Subjects: Behavioral Sciences, Biological Sciences, Science Fiction, Fantasy
ISBN Prefix(es): 3-9802102; 3-930304

**Nobel-Verlag GmbH Vertrieb Neue Medien+**
Kronprinzenstr 13, 45128 Essen
*Tel:* (0201) 81300 *Fax:* (0201) 8130108
*E-mail:* mplatzkoester@beleke.de
*Web Site:* www.gewusst-wo.de; www.nobel.de
*Key Personnel*
Contact: Dr Michael Platzkoester
ISBN Prefix(es): 3-922785

**Florian Noetzel Verlag+**
Holtermannstr 32, 26384 Wilhelmshaven
Mailing Address: Postfach 1443, 26353 Wilhelmshaven
*Tel:* (04421) 4 30 03 *Fax:* (04421) 4 29 85
*E-mail:* florian.noetzel@t-online.de
*Key Personnel*
Contact: Florian Noetzel
Founded: 1986
Subjects: Music, Dance, Theatre
ISBN Prefix(es): 3-7959
Number of titles published annually: 30 Print
Total Titles: 650 Print

**Nomos Verlagsgesellschaft mbH und Co KG**
Waldseestr 3-5, 76530 Baden-Baden
*Tel:* (07221) 2104-0 *Fax:* (07221) 210427
*E mail:* nomos@nomos.de
*Web Site:* www.nomos.de
*Key Personnel*
Man Dir: Dr Alfred Hoffmann
Publicity: Christian Kamradt
Founded: 1936
Subjects: Business, Economics, Government, Political Science, Law, Social Sciences, Sociology
ISBN Prefix(es): 3-7890; 3-8329

**nymphenburger+**
Subsidiary of Buchverlage Langen-Mueller/Herbig
Thomas-Wimmer-Ring 11, 80539 Munich
*Tel:* (089) 2 90 88-0 *Fax:* (089) 2 90 88-1 44
*E-mail:* nymphenburger@herbig.net
*Web Site:* www.herbig.net
*Key Personnel*
Man Dir & Publisher: Brigitte Fleissner-Mikorey
Rights & Permissions: Frauke Hoppen *Fax:* (089)
2 90 88-1 78 *E-mail:* fhoppen@herbig.net
Founded: 1946
Subjects: Art, Biography, Child Care & Development, Crafts, Games, Hobbies, Fiction, Health, Nutrition, Nonfiction (General), Outdoor Recreation, Philosophy, Photography, Religion - Buddhist, Self-Help, Sports, Athletics, True life stories
ISBN Prefix(es): 3-485
Total Titles: 25 Print
*Parent Company:* F A Herbig Verlagsbuchhandlung GmbH (Germany)
*Associate Companies:* Langen Mueller Herbig, Thomas-Wimmer-Ring 11, 80539 Munich, Contact: Lydia Eggs *Tel:* (089) 290880
*Fax:* (089) 29088155
Imprints: Edition Meyster
Distributed by Mohr Morawa Buchvertrieb; Schweizer Buchzentrum
*Warehouse:* VVA-Bertelsmann Distribution GmbH, Warenannahme 100, An der Autobahn, 33310 Gutersloh

*Orders to:* VVA-Vereinigte Verlagsauslieferung, Postfach 7600, 33310 Gutersloh, Contact: Renate Fechtelhoff *Tel:* (05209) 805403 *Fax:* (05209) 806643

**Oberbaum Verlag GmbH+**
Friedelstr 6, 12047 Berlin
*Tel:* (030) 624 69 21 *Fax:* (030) 624 69 21
*Key Personnel*
Man Dir: Siegfried Heinrichs
Founded: 1966
Subjects: Government, Political Science, History, Literature, Literary Criticism, Essays, Regional Interests
ISBN Prefix(es): 3-926409; 3-928254; 3-933314

**Oeko-Test Verlag GmbH & Co KG Betriebsgesellschaft**
Kasslerstr 1A, 60486 Frankfurt am Main
Mailing Address: Postfach 90 07 66, 60447 Frankfurt am Main
*Tel:* (069) 9 77 77-0 *Fax:* (069) 9 77 77-139
*E-mail:* oet.verlag@oekotest.de
*Web Site:* www.oekotest.de
*Key Personnel*
Man Dir: Bernd Waeltz; Albrecht Martin
Editor: Juergen Stellpflug
Publicity & Marketing: Anette Elnain *Tel:* (069) 9 77 77-133 *E-mail:* anette.elnain@oekotest.de; Friederike Elnain *Tel:* (069) 9 77 77-138 *E-mail:* friederike.elnain@oekotest.de
Founded: 1985
Subjects: Environmental Studies, Health, Nutrition
ISBN Prefix(es): 3-929530

**Oekobuch Verlag & Versand GmbH+**
Gewerbestr 15a, 79219 Staufen
Mailing Address: Postfach 1126, 79216 Staufen
*Tel:* (07633) 50613 *Fax:* (07633) 50870
*E-mail:* oekobuch@t-online.de
*Web Site:* www.oekobuch.de
*Key Personnel*
Man Dir: Claudia Ladener
Contact: Heinz Ladener
Founded: 1979
Subjects: Architecture & Interior Design, Civil Engineering, Crafts, Games, Hobbies, Energy, Environmental Studies, House & Home
ISBN Prefix(es): 3-922964
Total Titles: 42 Print

**Oekotopia Verlag, Wolfgang Hoffman GmbH & Co KG+**
Hafenweg 26a, 48155 Muenster
*Tel:* (0251) 48198-0 *Fax:* (0251) 48198-29
*E-mail:* info@oekotopia-verlag.de
*Web Site:* www.oekotopia-verlag.de
*Key Personnel*
Man Dir: Wolfgang Hoffmann; Stefan Scholz *E-mail:* scholz@oekotopia-verlag.de
Founded: 1983
Specialize in Environmental/Education.
Subjects: Drama, Theater, Education, Environmental Studies, Fiction, History, Human Relations, Humor, Music, Dance, Nonfiction (General), Outdoor Recreation, Psychology, Psychiatry
ISBN Prefix(es): 3-925169; 3-931902; 3-936286
Foreign Rights: Hercules Business & Culture Development GmbH (People's Republic of China, Taiwan); Living (Italy); Ute Korner Literary Agent, SL (Brazil, Latin America, Portugal, Spain)

**Oekumenischer Verlag Dr R-F Edel**
Rathmecker Weg 13, 58513 Luedenscheid
*Tel:* (02351) 51547 *Fax:* (02351) 568908
*Key Personnel*
Manager: Klaus Busenius
Founded: 1976

Subjects: Art, Biblical Studies, Ethnicity, History, Language Arts, Linguistics, Philosophy, Religion - Other, Theology
ISBN Prefix(es): 3-87598
*Orders to:* Verlagsauslieferung Klaus Busenius, Rathmecker Weg 13, 58513 Lundenscheid

**Oertel & Sporer GmbH & Co+**
Burgstr 1-7, 72764 Reutlingen
Mailing Address: PO Box 1642, D-72706 Reutlingen
*Tel:* (07121) 302 555; (07121) 302 552 *Fax:* (07121) 302 558
*Telex:* 729634
*Key Personnel*
Member of General Management: Mr Ermo Lehari *Tel:* (07121) 302 122 *Fax:* (07121) 302 123 *E-mail:* lehari@compuserve.com
Founded: 1888
Publishing & printing company
Books & Periodicals.
Subjects: Animals, Pets, Cookery, Crafts, Games, Hobbies, Nonfiction (General)
ISBN Prefix(es): 3-921017; 3-88627
Total Titles: 140 Print

**Paul Oestergaard GmbH**, see Columbus Verlag Paul Oestergaard GmbH

**Verlag Friedrich Oetinger GmbH+**
Poppenbuetteler Chaussee 53, 22397 Hamburg
Mailing Address: Postfach 658220, 22374 Hamburg
*Tel:* (040) 607909-02 *Fax:* (040) 6072326
*E-mail:* oetinger@vsg-hamburg.de
*Web Site:* www.oetinger.de
*Key Personnel*
Man Dir & Editorial: Silke Weitendorf
Man Dir & Sales: Thomas Huggle
Editorial: Marleus Niesen
Publicity: Judith Richter *Tel:* (040) 607909-65 *E-mail:* richter@vsg-hamburg.de; Frauke Wedler *Tel:* (040) 607909-23 *E-mail:* wedler@vsg-hamburg.de
Rights & Licensing: Renate Reichstein *Tel:* (040) 607909-13 *Fax:* (040) 607909-51 *E-mail:* lizenzen@vsg-hamburg.de
Sales & Marketing: Dr Juergen Huebner *Tel:* (040) 607909-55 *Fax:* (040) 607909-50 *E-mail:* marketing@vsg-hamburg.de
Marketing: Susanne Weiss *Tel:* (040) 607909-777 *Fax:* (040) 607909-50 *E-mail:* vertrieb@vsg-hamburg.de
Founded: 1946
Subjects: Fiction
ISBN Prefix(es): 3-7891
Subsidiaries: Cecilie Dressler Verlag GmbH

**Dr Oetker Verlag KG+**
Lutterstr 14, 33617 Bielefeld
*Tel:* (0521) 521 155-0 *Fax:* (0521) 521 155-2995
*E-mail:* presse@oetker.de
*Web Site:* www.oetker-gruppe.de
*Key Personnel*
Man Dir: Annelore Strullkoetter *Tel:* (0521) 520643 *E-mail:* strullkoetter@oetker-verlag.de
Founded: 1951
Subjects: Cookery
ISBN Prefix(es): 3-7670
*Parent Company:* August Oetker, Bielefeld

**Verlag Offene Worte+**
Striepenweg 31, 21147 Hamburg
*Tel:* (040) 79713-03 *Fax:* (040) 79713-324
*E-mail:* vertrieb@koehler-mittler.de
*Web Site:* www.koehler-mittler.de *Cable:* VLG OFFENE WORTE, HAMBURG/W
*Key Personnel*
Publisher: Wolf O Storck; Peter Tamm
Manager: Thomas Bantle
Sales: Hans-Focko Koehler

Subjects: Government, Political Science, Military Science
ISBN Prefix(es): 3-87599
*Associate Companies:* Koehlers Verlagsgesellschaft
*Branch Office(s)*
Godesberger Allee 91, 53175 Bonn *Tel:* (0228) 307890 *Fax:* (0228) 3078915

**Oktagon Verlagsgesellschaft mbH+**
Albertusstr 1, 50667 Cologne
*Tel:* (0221) 2059653-54 *Fax:* (0221) 2059660
*E-mail:* oktagon@buchhandlung-walterkoenig.de
*Key Personnel*
Manager: Paul Johannes Mueller
Founded: 1989
Subjects: Architecture & Interior Design, Art
ISBN Prefix(es): 3-927789; 3-89611
*Bookshop(s):* Ehrenstr 4, 50672 Cologne *Tel:* (0221) 20 59 6-0 *Fax:* (0221) 20 59 6-40 *E-mail:* order@buchhandlung-walther-koenig.de

**R Oldenbourg Verlag GmbH+**
Rosenheimerstr 145, 81671 Munich
Mailing Address: Postfach 801360, 81613 Munich
*Tel:* (089) 45 05 10; (089) 45 05 12 04 *Fax:* (089) 45051333 (Zeitschriften); (089) 4505200 (Schulbuch); (089) 4505333 (Fachbuch)
*Key Personnel*
Dir: Dr Thomas von Cornides; Wolfgang Dick; Dr Dieter Hohm; Johannes Oldenbourg
Founded: 1858
Membership(s): TR-Verlagsunion GmbH.
Subjects: Education, Electronics, Electrical Engineering, Engineering (General), History, Psychology, Psychiatry, Science (General), Social Sciences, Sociology, Technology
ISBN Prefix(es): 3-486
Subsidiaries: Verlag Oldenbourg; Michael Proegel Verlag; Vulkan Verlag Essen
*Showroom(s):* Oldenbourg Verlag Informationszentrum, Kaufingerstr 29, 80331 Munich
*Orders to:* Verlegerdienst Muenchen, Auslieferung R Oldenbourg Verlag, Gutenbergstr 1, Postfach 1280, 82205 Gilching *Tel:* (08105) 3880 *Fax:* (08105) 388100

**Georg Olms Verlag AG+**
Hagentorwall 7, 31134 Hildesheim
*Tel:* (05121) 15010 *Fax:* (05121) 150150; (05121) 32007
*E-mail:* info@olms.de
*Web Site:* www.olms.de *Cable:* HILDESHEIM
*Key Personnel*
Publisher: Dietrich Olms *E-mail:* dietrich.olms@olms.de
Editorial: Dr Peter Guyot *E-mail:* guyot@olms.de; Doris Wendt *E-mail:* wendt@olms.de
Production: Andreas Maybaum
Rights & Permissions: Christiane Busch
Marketing, Editorial (Equestrian Titles): Danielle Schons *E-mail:* marketing@olms.de
Founded: 1945
Subjects: Antiques, Biography, Drama, Theater, Economics, Education, Gardening, Plants, Geography, Geology, Government, Political Science, History, Language Arts, Linguistics, Law, Library & Information Sciences, Literature, Literary Criticism, Essays, Music, Dance, Philosophy, Religion - Islamic, Religion - Jewish, Religion - Protestant, Romance, Science (General), Social Sciences, Sociology, Theology, Travel, Classical Studies, History of Art
ISBN Prefix(es): 3-487
Number of titles published annually: 250 Print; 3 CD-ROM
Total Titles: 5,000 Print
*Parent Company:* Georg Olms AG, Zurich, Switzerland

*Associate Companies:* Weidmannsche Verlags-
buchhandlung
Imprints: Olms New Media; Olms Presse
Subsidiaries: Edition Olms AG
*U.S. Office(s):* Georg Olms Verlag, Empire State
Bldg, 350 Fifth Ave, Suite 3304, New York,
NY 10118-0069, United States
*Warehouse:* VVA, Bertelsmann Distribution,
33399 Verl, Contact: Monika Hermesmeier
*Tel:* (05241) 803844 *Fax:* (05241) 8060220

**Olms New Media**, *imprint of* Georg Olms Verlag
AG

**Olms Presse**, *imprint of* Georg Olms Verlag AG

**Oncken Verlag KG+**
Bodenborn 43, 58452 Witten
*Tel:* (02302) 930 93 800 *Fax:* (02302) 930 93 801
*E-mail:* info@brockhaus-verlag.de
*Web Site:* www.brockhaus-verlag.de
*Key Personnel*
Chief Executive Officer & Publisher: Erhard
Diehl
Editor & Publicity Manager: Hans-Werner Durau
International Rights: Christina Schneider
Founded: 1828
Membership(s): Stiftung Christliche Medien.
Subjects: Fiction, Religion - Other
ISBN Prefix(es): 3-7893
*Associate Companies:* R Brockhaus Verlag
Distributed by BMU (Austria); Brunnen (Switzer-
land)

**Orbis Verlag fur Publizistik GmbH+**
Neumarkter Str 28, 81673 Munich
Mailing Address: Postfach 800360, 81603 Mu-
nich
*Tel:* (01805) 990 505 *Fax:* (089) 4136-3333
*Key Personnel*
Man Dir: Wolfgang Kunth; Ortner Werner
Founded: 1987
Subjects: Animals, Pets, Archaeology, Cookery,
English as a Second Language, Gardening,
Plants, Health, Nutrition, History, Language
Arts, Linguistics
ISBN Prefix(es): 3-572
*Parent Company:* Verlagsgruppe Bertelsmann
GmbH

**Oreos Verlag GmbH+**
Krottenthal 9, 83666 Waakirchen
*Tel:* (08021) 86 68 *Fax:* (08021) 17 50
*E-mail:* lachenmann@oreos.de
*Web Site:* www.oreos.de
*Key Personnel*
Publisher: Walter Lachenmann
*E-mail:* lachenmann@oreos.de
Founded: 1982
Subjects: Biography, Music, Dance, Regional In-
terests
ISBN Prefix(es): 3-923657

**Orlanda Frauenverlag+**
Zossenerstr 55-58, 10961 Berlin
*Tel:* (030) 216-3566; (030) 216-2960 *Fax:* (030)
2153958
*E-mail:* post@orlanda.de
*Web Site:* www.orlanda.de
*Key Personnel*
Manager, Rights & Permissions: Prof Dagmar
Schultz, PhD
Contact: Ekpenyong Aui
Founded: 1974
Subjects: Developing Countries, Ethnicity, Gay &
Lesbian, Health, Nutrition, Literature, Literary
Criticism, Essays, Psychology, Psychiatry, Self-
Help, Social Sciences, Sociology
ISBN Prefix(es): 3-922166; 3-929823; 3-936937

**Oros Verlag+**
Borghorster Str 6, 48341 Altenberge
Mailing Address: Postfach 11 45, 48337 Al-
tenberge
*Tel:* (02505) 947191 *Fax:* (02505) 3534
*Key Personnel*
Manager: Prof Adel Th Khoury, PhD
Founded: 1988
Subjects: Literature, Literary Criticism, Essays,
Philosophy, Theology
ISBN Prefix(es): 3-89375

**Osho Verlag GmbH**
Gilbachstr 29A, 50672 Cologne
*Tel:* (0221) 278 04-0 *Fax:* (0221) 278 04-66
*E-mail:* info@oshoverlag.de
*Web Site:* www.oshoverlag.de
*Key Personnel*
Manager: Dr Hansjoerg Sieberer; Joachim Spoh
Founded: 1988
Subjects: Behavioral Sciences, Human Relations,
Philosophy, Psychology, Psychiatry, Religion
- Buddhist, Religion - Catholic, Religion -
Hindu, Religion - Islamic, Religion - Jewish,
Religion - Protestant, Religion - Other, Self-
Help
ISBN Prefix(es): 3-925205; 3-933556; 3-9800883
Divisions: Osho Times International, Deutsche
Ausgabe

**Osnabrueck**, *imprint of* Verlag A Fromm im
Druck- u Verlagshaus Fromm GmbH & Co KG

**Ostfalia-Verlag Jurgen Schierer+**
Kornbergweg 13, 31224 Peine
*Tel:* (05171) 41763 *Fax:* (05171) 41769
*E-mail:* juergen.schierer@t-online.de
*Web Site:* www.ostfalia-verlag.de
*Key Personnel*
Manager: Juergen Schierer
Founded: 1980
Subjects: Fiction, Poetry, Regional Interests
ISBN Prefix(es): 3-926560
Number of titles published annually: 2 Print
Total Titles: 32 Print

**Ostrecht**, *imprint of* Berliner
Wissenschafts-Verlag GmbH (BWV)

**Erzabtei Sankt Ottilien**, see EOS Verlag der
Benefiktiner der Erzabtei St. Ottilien

**Otto-Friedrich Universitat Bamberg**
Kapuzinerstr 20, Room 221-223, 96045 Bamberg
*Tel:* (0951) 863-1021 *Fax:* (0951) 863-4021
*E-mail:* presse@uni-bamberg.de
*Web Site:* www.uni-bamberg.de/zuv/presse/
mitarbeiter

**Pabel-Moewig Verlag KG+**
Postfach 2352, 76413 Rastatt
*Tel:* (07222) 13 0 *Fax:* (07222) 13 218
*E-mail:* kontakt@moewig.de
*Web Site:* www.vpm-online.de
*Key Personnel*
Book Manager: Eckhard Schwettmann
*E-mail:* esch@pobox.com
ISBN Prefix(es): 3-8118
Number of titles published annually: 120 Print
Total Titles: 350 Print
*Parent Company:* Heinrich Bauer Verlag
Imprints: Moewig; Neff
Subsidiaries: Hestia Verlag; Paul Neff Verlag

**Pahl-Rugenstein Verlag Nachfolger-GmbH+**
Breitestr 47, 53111 Bonn
*Tel:* (0228) 632306 *Fax:* (0228) 634968
*E-mail:* prv@che-chandler.com
*Key Personnel*
Manager & International Rights: Arnold Bruns

Founded: 1990
Subjects: Biography, Developing Countries, Government, Political Science, History, Philosophy,
Religion - Protestant, Social Sciences, Sociology, Theology
ISBN Prefix(es): 3-89144; 3-88142; 3-87682; 3-
7609

**Pal Verlagsgesellschaft mbH+**
Am Oberen Luisenpark 33, 68165 Mannheim
*Tel:* (0621) 415741 *Fax:* (0621) 415101
*E-mail:* info@palverlag.de
*Web Site:* www.pal-verlag.de
*Key Personnel*
Manager: Dr Rolf Merkle
Founded: 1986
Subjects: Biography, Psychology, Psychiatry
ISBN Prefix(es): 3-923614

**Pala-Verlag GmbH+**
Rheinstr 37, 64283 Darmstadt
*Tel:* (06151) 23028 *Fax:* (06151) 292713
*E-mail:* info@pala-verlag.de
*Web Site:* www.pala-verlag.de
*Key Personnel*
Man Dir: Wolfgang Hertling *E-mail:* w.hertling@
pala-verlag.de
Editorial: Barbara Reis *E-mail:* b.reis@pala-
verlag.de
Sales: Katrin Kolb *E-mail:* k.kolb@pala-verlag.de
Founded: 1980
Subjects: Cookery, Environmental Studies, Gar-
dening, Plants, Health, Nutrition, Medicine,
Nursing, Dentistry, Sports, Athletics
ISBN Prefix(es): 3-923176; 3-89566

**Palazzi Verlag GmbH+**
Ostertorsteinweg 36, 28195 Bremen
*Tel:* (0421) 32 11 00 *Fax:* (0421) 32 13 00
*Web Site:* www.palazzi-kalerder.de
*Key Personnel*
Manager: Volker Hedwig
Founded: 1989
Subjects: Aeronautics, Aviation, Earth Sciences,
Environmental Studies, Foreign Countries, Ge-
ography, Geology, Natural History, Physical
Sciences, Travel
ISBN Prefix(es): 3-927956; 3-936421

**Palmyra Verlag+**
Haupstr 64, 69117 Heidelberg
*Tel:* (06221) 165409 *Fax:* (06221) 167310
*E-mail:* palmyra-verlag@t-online.de
*Web Site:* www.palmyra-verlag.de
*Key Personnel*
President: Georg Stein
Founded: 1989
Subjects: Anthropology, Foreign Countries, Gov-
ernment, Political Science, Music, Dance, Non-
fiction (General)
ISBN Prefix(es): 3-9802298; 3-930378

**Pandion-Verlag, Ulrike Schmoll+**
Gartenstr 10, 55469 Simmern
*Tel:* (06761) 7142 *Fax:* (06761) 77172
*E-mail:* pandion@t-online.de; info@pandion-
verlag.de
*Web Site:* www.pandion-verlag.de
Founded: 1954
Subjects: Art, Fiction, Poetry, Regional Interests,
Religion - Other
ISBN Prefix(es): 3-922929

**PapyRossa Verlags GmbH & Co
Kommanditgesellschaft KG+**
Luxemburger Str 202, 50937 Cologne
*Tel:* (0221) 44 85 45 *Fax:* (0221) 44 43 05
*E-mail:* mail@papyrossa.de
*Web Site:* www.papyrossa.de
*Key Personnel*
Manager: Dr Jurgen Harrer
Founded: 1990

Subjects: Developing Countries, Government, Political Science, History, Human Relations, Social Sciences, Sociology, Women's Studies
ISBN Prefix(es): 3-89438
*Orders to:* SOVA, Friesstr 20-24, 60388 Frankfurt

**Edition Parabolis**
Schliemannstr 23, 10437 Berlin
*Tel:* (030) 44 65 10 65 *Fax:* (030) 444 10 85
*E-mail:* info@emz-berlin.de
*Web Site:* www.emz-berlin.de
Publishing section of the Berlin Institute for Comparative Social Research (BIVS).
Membership(s): European Migration Centre.
Subjects: Anthropology, Ethnicity, Nonfiction (General), Social Sciences, Sociology, Migration
ISBN Prefix(es): 3-88402
Number of titles published annually: 20 Print

**Paranus Verlag - Bruecke Neumuenster GmbH**
Ehndorfer Str 13-17, 24537 Neumuenster
Mailing Address: Postfach 1264, 24502 Neumuenster
*Tel:* (04321) 2004-500 *Fax:* (04321) 2004-411
*E-mail:* verlag@paranus.de
*Web Site:* www.paranus.de
*Key Personnel*
International Rights: Fritz Bremer
Founded: 1989
Publishing project which involves mentally ill persons in the editing, producing, printing & distribution of books & periodicals.
Subjects: Art, Literature, Literary Criticism, Essays, Psychology, Psychiatry
ISBN Prefix(es): 3-926200

**Parey**, *imprint of* Georg Thieme Verlag KG

**Parey Buchverlag**, *imprint of* Blackwell Wissenschafts-Verlag GmbH

**Verlag Parzeller GmbH & Co KG+**
Frankfurterstr 8, 36043 Fulda
*Tel:* (0661) 280-663 *Fax:* (0661) 280-285
*E-mail:* verlag@parzeller.de
*Web Site:* www.buchkatalog.de/parzeller
*Telex:* 49838
*Key Personnel*
Contact: Rainer Klitsch *Tel:* (0661) 280361 *E-mail:* rainer.klitsch@parzeller.de
Founded: 1874
Subjects: Regional Interests, Religion - Catholic, Religion - Protestant, Religion - Other
ISBN Prefix(es): 3-7900
Subsidiaries: Druckerei Parzeller GmbH & Co KG

**Passavia Druckerei GmbH, Verlag**
Medienstr 5b, 94036 Passau
*Tel:* (0851) 802670 *Fax:* (0851) 802680
*E-mail:* contact@just-print-it.com
*Web Site:* www.passavia.de; www.just-print-it.com
*Key Personnel*
Man Dir: Erwin Neudecker
Publishing Dir, Rights & Permissions: Peter Oeller
Founded: 1888
Subjects: Fiction, House & Home, Humor, Travel
ISBN Prefix(es): 3-87616
Subsidiaries: Passavia Universitaetsverlag und-Druck GmbH

**Passavia Universitaetsverlag und -Druck GmbH**
St Englmarstr 11, 94034 Passau
*Tel:* (0851) 700226 *Fax:* (0851) 700277
*Key Personnel*
Publishing Dir, Rights & Permissions: Bernd Kammerer
Subjects: Science (General)

ISBN Prefix(es): 3-922016; 3-86036
*Parent Company:* Passavia Druckerei GmbH

**Patio, Galerie und Druckwerkstatt+**
Laubestr 24H, 60594 Frankfurt
*Tel:* (06150) 84566
*Key Personnel*
Man Dir: Klaus Muenchschwander
Editorial: David Ward
Sales: Regine Behrends; Franz Gaber
Production: Volker Mueller; Walter Zimbrich
Publicity: Yves Daniel Zimbrich
Rights & Permissions: Manfred Linke; Renate Kafitz-Pfeuffer
Founded: 1963

**Patmos Verlag GmbH & Co KG+**
Am Wehrhahn 100, 40211 Duesseldorf
*Tel:* (0211) 16795-0 *Fax:* (0211) 16795-75
*E-mail:* info@patmos.de
*Web Site:* www.patmos.de *Cable:* PATMOS VERLAG
*Key Personnel*
Dir: Dr Tullio Aurelio *Tel:* (0211) 1679569 *E-mail:* fauth@patmos.de
Publicity: Ralf Pollmann
Founded: 1910
Subjects: Antiques, Art, History, Literature, Literary Criticism, Essays, Religion - Other, Theology
ISBN Prefix(es): 3-491
Subsidiaries: Walter Verlag AG; Artemis & Winkler Verlag AG; Benziger Verlag AG

**Pattloch Verlag GmbH & Co KG+**
Hilblestr 54, 80636 Munich
*Tel:* (089) 9271-0 *Fax:* (089) 9271-168
*E-mail:* vertrieb@droemer-knaur.de
*Web Site:* www.droemer-weltbild.de
Founded: 1965
Subjects: Nonfiction (General)
ISBN Prefix(es): 3-629
*Parent Company:* Verlagsgruppe Droemer Weltbild GmbH & Co KG
*Orders to:* VVA Bertelsmann Distribution, Postfach 7600, 33310 Guetersloh, Contact: Jennifer Strebinger *Tel:* (05241) 801754 *Fax:* (05241) 8060260 *E-mail:* jennifer.strebinger@bertelsmann.de

**Paulinus Verlag GmbH+**
Maximineracht 11c, 54295 Trier
*Tel:* (0651) 4608-0 *Fax:* (0651) 4608-221
*E-mail:* service@paulinus.de
*Web Site:* www.paulinus.de
*Key Personnel*
Publisher: Siegfried Faeth
Man Dir: Thomas Juncker
Rights & Permissions: Dr Harald Baulig
Founded: 1875
Subjects: Religion - Other, Theology
ISBN Prefix(es): 3-7902; 3-87760
*Parent Company:* Paulinus Druckerei GmbH, Fleischstr 62-65, 54290 Trier
*Associate Companies:* Spee Buchverlag GmbH

**Paulinus Verlag GmbH+**
Formerly Spee Buchverlag GmbH
Maximineracht 11C, 54295 Trier
Mailing Address: Postfach 3040, 54220 Trier
*Tel:* (0651) 4608-0; (0651) 4608-121; (0651) 4608-120 *Fax:* (0651) 4608220
*Key Personnel*
Publisher: Dr Harold Boulig; Siegfried Faeth
Founded: 1967
Subjects: Art, History
ISBN Prefix(es): 3-7902; 3-87760
*Parent Company:* Paulinus GmbH Verlag
*Associate Companies:* Paulinus Verlag

**Ingwert Paulsen Jr**, see Hansa Verlag Ingwert Paulsen Jr

**Pawel Panpresse+**
Zum Seemenbach Nr 1, 63654 Budingen
*Tel:* (06041) 5822
*Key Personnel*
Man Dir, Production, Rights: Sascha Juritz
Founded: 1972
Subjects: Art, Literature, Literary Criticism, Essays, Poetry
ISBN Prefix(es): 3-921454
*Associate Companies:* Edition Druckhuette No 2
*Orders to:* Siehe Pawel Panpresse

**Pearson Education Deutschland GmbH+**
Martin-Kollar-Str 10-12, 81829 Munich
Mailing Address: Postfach 820461, 81804 Munich
*Tel:* (089) 46003-0 *Fax:* (089) 46003-120
*E-mail:* firstinitiallastname@pearson.de; info@pearson.de
*Web Site:* www.pearsoned.de
*Key Personnel*
President: Axel Nehen *Tel:* (089) 46003 401 *Fax:* (089) 46003 410
Vice President, Finance & Operations: Rudolf Nertinger *Tel:* (089) 46003 123
Foreign Rights: Ines Killat *Tel:* (089) 46003 124
Assistant to the President: Britta Tiedtke-Heimers *Tel:* (089) 46003 405
Editorial Dir, M & T: Catherine Magdolen *Tel:* (089) 46003 336 *Fax:* (089) 46003 330
Editorial Dir, Addison Wesley: Christian Rauscher *Tel:* (089) 46003 331 *Fax:* (089) 46003 330
Human Resources Manager: Uschi Jacob *Tel:* (089) 46003 122
Founded: 1993
Subjects: Computer Science
ISBN Prefix(es): 3-89090; 3-87791; 3-922120; 3-8273; 3-8272; 3-89319; 3-925118
Imprints: Que; SAMS; Prentice Hall; X-Games
Distributor for Macmillan Computer Publishing USA; Prentice Hall
*Warehouse:* Adelmannstr 5, 81827 Munich

**Pelikan Vertriebsgesellschaft mbH & Co KG+**
Werftstr 9, 30163 Hannover
*Tel:* (0511) 6969-0 *Fax:* (0511) 6969-212
*E-mail:* info@pelikan.de
*Web Site:* www.pelikan.de
*Telex:* 175118481 Pelikan
*Key Personnel*
Man Dir & Marketing Manager: Terry Edwards
Marketing: Michael Fey *E-mail:* m.fey@pelikan.de
Founded: 1978
Subjects: Fiction
ISBN Prefix(es): 3-8144
*Parent Company:* Pelikan Holding, Switzerland
*Associate Companies:* Franz-Buttner, AG/Pelikan-Vertrieb, Wollerau, Switzerland
Distributor for Diverse

**Pendragon Verlag+**
Stapenhorststr 15, 33615 Bielefeld
*Tel:* (0521) 69689 *Fax:* (0521) 174470
*E-mail:* pendragon.verlag@t-online.de
*Web Site:* www.pendragon.de
*Key Personnel*
Man Dir, Sales, Rights & Permissions: Guenther Butkus
Production & Publicity: Michael Baltus
Founded: 1981
Subjects: Art, Criminology, Fiction, History, Literature, Literary Criticism, Essays, Poetry
ISBN Prefix(es): 3-923306; 3-929096; 3-934872
Imprints: Edition Bielefelden Kunstverein

**Perryman**, see Babel Verlag Kevin Perryman

**Verlag Sigrid Persen**
Dorfstr 14, 21640 Horneburg, Niederelbe
Mailing Address: Postfach 260, 21637 Horneburg,
   Niederelbe
*Tel:* (04163) 81400 *Fax:* (04163) 814050
*E-mail:* info@persen.de
*Web Site:* www.persen.de
*Key Personnel*
Man Dir: Franz-Josef Buechler
Founded: 1976
Subjects: English as a Second Language, Lan-
   guage Arts, Linguistics, Mathematics, Music,
   Dance
ISBN Prefix(es): 3-921809; 2-89358

**Justus Perthes Verlag Gotha GmbH+**
Justus-Perthes-Str 1-5, 99867 Gotha
Mailing Address: Postfach 100452, 99854 Gotha
*Tel:* (03621) 385-0 *Fax:* (03621) 385-102;
   (03621) 385-103
*E-mail:* perthes@klett-mail.de
*Web Site:* www.klett-verlag.de/klett-perthes *Cable:*
   PERTHES GOTHA
*Key Personnel*
Dir: Volker Streibel
Founded: 1785
Subjects: Geography, Geology, History, Cartogra-
   phy
ISBN Prefix(es): 3-7301; 3-623
*Parent Company:* Ernst Klett Verlag GmbH,
   Stuttgart
Imprints: Haack; Schreiber-Naturtafeln

**Klett Perthes**, see Justus Perthes Verlag Gotha
   GmbH

**C F Peters Musikverlag GmbH & Co KG**
Kennedyallee 101, 60596 Frankfurt am Main
Mailing Address: Postfach 700851, 60558 Frank-
   furt am Main
*Tel:* (069) 6300990 *Fax:* (069) 635401
*E-mail:* vertrieb@musia.de; info@musia.de
*Web Site:* www.musia.de *Cable:* PETERSEDIT
*Key Personnel*
Partner: Dr Johannes Petschull; Roland Schied
Founded: 1800
Subjects: Music, Dance
ISBN Prefix(es): 3-87626; 3-920735
*Associate Companies:* C F Peters Corp, NY,
   United States; Hinrichsen Edition Ltd, London,
   United Kingdom
Imprints: M P Belaieff; Henry Litolff's Verlag;
   Edition Peters; Edition Schwann

**Edition Peters**, *imprint of* C F Peters
   Musikverlag GmbH & Co KG

**Jens Peters Publikationen+**
Gotenstr 65, 10829 Berlin
*Tel:* (030) 7847265 *Fax:* (030) 7883127
*E-mail:* jens.peters@usa.net
*Web Site:* www.jenspeters.de
*Key Personnel*
President, Rights & Permissions: Jens Peters
Founded: 1977
Subjects: Travel
ISBN Prefix(es): 3-923821; 3-9800154
*Orders to:* Osterholzer Dorfstr 45, 28307 Bremen
   *Tel:* (0421) 451743 *Fax:* (0421) 455406

**Pfaffenweiler Presse+**
MittlereStr 23, 79292 Pfaffenweiler
*Tel:* (07664) 8999 *Fax:* (07664) 8999
*E-mail:* info@pfaffenweiler-presse.de
*Web Site:* www.pfaffenweiler-presse.de
*Key Personnel*
Owner: Herta Flicker
Founded: 1974
ISBN Prefix(es): 3-921365; 3-927702

**Pfalzische Verlagsanstalt GmbH**
Industriestr 15, 76829 Landau
Mailing Address: Postfach 1950, 76809 Landau
*Tel:* (06341) 142-0 *Fax:* (06341) 142-265
*Key Personnel*
Publisher: Herr Karl-Friedrich Geissler
Manager: Rolf Schaefer; Horst K Neubauer
Founded: 1892
Subjects: Art, Biography, Fiction, Foreign Coun-
   tries, Wine & Spirits
ISBN Prefix(es): 3-87629
*Orders to:* VSB-Braunschweig, Postfach 4738,
   3300 Braunschweig

**Pfeiffer bei Klett-Cotta**, *imprint of* J G
   Cotta'sche Buchhandlung Nachfolger GmbH

**J Pfeiffer Verlag+**
Anzingerstr 15, 81671 Munich
*Tel:* (089) 4130010
*Key Personnel*
Publisher & Editorial: Lydia Franzelius
Editor: Dr Christine Treml
Production: Siegbert Seitz
Founded: 1882
Subjects: Psychology, Psychiatry, Religion - Other
ISBN Prefix(es): 3-7904
*Parent Company:* Manz Verlag
*Shipping Address:* mi-Verlags Service GmbH,
   Justus-von-Liebig-Str 1, 8689 Landsberg-Lech
*Warehouse:* mi-Verlags Service GmbH, Justus-
   von-Liebig-Str 1, 86898 Landsberg-Lech
*Orders to:* Verlagsgruppe Manz

**Verlag Dr Friedrich Pfeil**
Wolfratshauser Str 27, 81379 Munich
*Tel:* (089) 7428270 *Fax:* (089) 7242772
*E-mail:* info@pfeil-verlag.de
*Web Site:* www.pfeil-verlag.de
*Key Personnel*
Editor: Dr Friedrich Pfeil
Founded: 1981
Subjects: Biological Sciences, Philosophy
ISBN Prefix(es): 3-923871; 3-931516; 3-89937
*Branch Office(s)*
Falkweg 37, 81243 Munich

**Richard Pflaum Verlag GmbH & Co KG+**
Lazarettstr 4, 80636 Munich
Mailing Address: Postfach 190737, 80607 Mu-
   nich
*Tel:* (089) 12607-0 *Fax:* (089) 12607-333
*E-mail:* info@pflaum.de
*Web Site:* www.pflaum.de
*Key Personnel*
Manager: Beda Bohinger
Head Book Dept: Helmut Brackebusch
Founded: 1919
Subjects: Communications, Electronics, Electrical
   Engineering, Medicine, Nursing, Dentistry
ISBN Prefix(es): 3-7905
Subsidiaries: Gastgewerbe Verlag GmbH & Co
   KG; Huethig und Pflaum Verlag GmbH & Co
   KG Laenderdienst Verlag GmbH
*Branch Office(s)*
Bad Kissingen
Berlin
Dusseldorf
Heidelberg

**Helker Pflug**, see Verlag Wissenschaft und
   Politik

**Philipp Reclam Jun Verlag GmbH+**
Siemensstr 32, 71254 Ditzingen
Mailing Address: Postfach 1349, 71252 Ditzingen
*Tel:* (07156) 163 0 *Fax:* (07156) 163 197
*E-mail:* info@reclam.de
*Web Site:* www.reclam.de *Cable:* RECLAM
   DITZINGEN

*Key Personnel*
Publisher: Dr Frank R Max
Publicity Dir: Dr Karl-Heinz Fallbacher
Sales Manager: Juergen Bernardi; Anja Krauss
Rights & Permissions: Dr Stephan Koranyi
Founded: 1828
Subjects: Art, Fiction, Film, Video, History, Mu-
   sic, Dance, Philosophy, Poetry, Religion -
   Other, Jazz
ISBN Prefix(es): 3-15
*Parent Company:* Philipp Reclam jun GmbH &
   Co, Stuttgart
Distributor for Reclam Verlag Leipzig

**Philippka-Sportverlag+**
Rektoratsweg 36, 48159 Muenster
Mailing Address: Postfach 150105, 48061 Muen-
   ster
*Tel:* (0251) 23005-0 *Fax:* (0251) 23005-79
*E-mail:* info@philippka.de
*Web Site:* www.philippka.de
*Key Personnel*
Publisher: Konrad Honig *Tel:* (0251) 23005-25
Publicity: Peter Moellers *Tel:* (0251) 23005-28
   *E-mail:* moellers@philippka.de
Founded: 1978
Subjects: Sports, Athletics
ISBN Prefix(es): 3-922067
Number of titles published annually: 3 Print; 1
   CD-ROM
Total Titles: 50 Print; 2 CD-ROM
*Associate Companies:* Success in Soccer, Albu-
   querque, NM, United States
Foreign Rep(s): Manni Klar (US)
*Warehouse:* Albuquerque, NM, United States

**Philipps-Universitaet Marburg**
Biegenstr 10, 35032 Marburg
*Tel:* (06421) 28-20 *Fax:* (06421) 28-22500
*E-mail:* pressestell@verwaltung.uni.marburg.de
*Web Site:* www.uni-marburg.de
*Telex:* 482-372
*Key Personnel*
President: Prof Dr Kern
Public Relations: Klaus Walter
Librarian: Heino Krueger
Subjects: Anthropology, Archaeology, History,
   Library & Information Sciences, Psychology,
   Psychiatry, Science (General)
ISBN Prefix(es): 3-8185

**Philosophia Verlag GmbH+**
Gundelindenstr 4, 80805 Munich
Mailing Address: Postfach 221362, 80503 Mu-
   nich
*Tel:* (089) 299975 *Fax:* (089) 299975
*E-mail:* info@philosophiaverlag.com
*Web Site:* www.philosophiaverlag.com
*Key Personnel*
Man Dir & Publisher: Ulrich Staudinger
Editorial Board: Hans Burkhardt; Barry Smith;
   Ignacio Angelelli; Christian Thiel
Sales & Marketing: Frank Kiesebrink
Founded: 1966
Publishers for philosophy & economics.
Membership(s): Stock Exchange of German
   Booksellers; Association of Bavarian Publishers
   & Booksellers.
Subjects: Economics, Philosophy
ISBN Prefix(es): 3-88405
Number of titles published annually: 3 Print
Total Titles: 70 Print
Divisions: Medienbuero Muenchen
Distributed by Vrin (France)
*Orders to:* Herold Verlagsauslieferung, Kolping-
   gring 4, 82041 Oberhaching/Munich, Contact:
   A Stanglmeier *Tel:* (089) 613871-0 *Fax:* (089)
   61387120 *E-mail:* herold-oberhaching@t-
   online.de *Web Site:* www.herold-va.de

**Physica**, *imprint of* Springer Science+Business
   Media GmbH & Co KG

**Physica-Verlag+**
Imprint of Springer-Verlag
Tiergartenstr 17, 69121 Heidelberg
Mailing Address: PO Box 105280, 69042 Heidelberg
*Tel:* (06221) 4878-0; (06221) 4878-345 (customer service)
*E-mail:* physica@springer.de
*Web Site:* www.springer.de
*Key Personnel*
Man Dir: Dr Dietrich Goetze *Tel:* (06221) 4878-345
Dir, Division Sales/Marketing & Corporate Development: Arnoud de Kemp *Tel:* (06221) 487-397 *Fax:* (06221) 487-288 *E-mail:* dekemp@springer.de
Journals/LINK Dir: Gertraud Griepke *Tel:* (06221) 487-457 *Fax:* (06221) 487-288 *E-mail:* griepke@springer.de
Territory Manager (Middle East, Africa, Greece, Turkey): Franziska Sachsse *Tel:* (06221) 487-628 *Fax:* (06221) 487-620 *E-mail:* sachsse@springer.de
Marketing Communications Dir: Michael Lechler *Tel:* (06221) 487-515 *Fax:* (06221) 487-156 *E-mail:* lechler@springer.de
Sales & Marketing Manager, Client Presses: Sandra Cortes-Hemmerich *Tel:* (06221) 487-289 *Fax:* (06221) 487-620 *E-mail:* cortes@springer.de
Territory Manager (Scandinavia): Bettina Schies *Tel:* (06221) 487-309 *Fax:* (06221) 487-620 *E-mail:* schies@springer.de
Territory Manager (Belgium, The Netherlands): Marc Puma *Tel:* (01) 53 93 37 79 *Fax:* (01) 53 93 36 83 *E-mail:* puma@springer-paris.fr
Specialize in Statistics & Information Systems.
Subjects: Business, Economics, Finance, Regional Interests, Science (General), Econometrics, Information Systems
ISBN Prefix(es): 3-7908
Number of titles published annually: 100 Print
Total Titles: 500 Print
*Branch Office(s)*
Springer-Verlag Wien New York, Sachsenplatz 4-6, 1201 Vienna, Austria *Tel:* (01) 330 24 15 *Fax:* (01) 330 24 26
Foreign Rep(s): Academic Marketing Services (Pty) Ltd (South Africa); Eastern Book Service Inc (Japan); Michael Lechler (Austria, Germany, Luxembourg, Switzerland); Behruz Neirami (Iran); Springer-Verlag (Australia, Africa, Baltic States, Bangladesh, CIS, Eastern Europe, Egypt, India, Israel, Middle East, New Zealand, Nepal, Pakistan, Russia, Sri Lanka, Turkey); Springer-Verlag France (France, Morocco, Tunisia, Algeria); Springer-Verlag Hong Kong Ltd (China, Hong Kong, Indonesia, Malaysia, Myanmar, Philippines, South Korea, Singapore, Thailand, Vietnam, Macao); Springer-Verlag Iberica SAI (Portugal, Spain); Springer-Verlag Italia Srl (Greece, Italy); Springer-Verlag Liaison Office (Bangladesh, India, Nepal, Pakistan, Sri Lanka); Springer-Verlag London Ltd (Belgium, UK, Netherlands, Ireland, Scandinavia); Springer-Verlag New York Inc (North America, South America); Springer-Verlag Singapore Pte Ltd (Malaysia, Singapore, Thailand, Southeast Asia); Springer-Verlag Taipei (Taiwan)
*Shipping Address:* Springer Shipping Centre, Hatschekstr 8, 69126 Heidelberg
*Orders to:* Customer Service, Haberstr 7, 69126 Heidelberg *Tel:* (06221) 345221 *Fax:* (06221) 345229

**PIAG**, see PIAG Presse Informations AG

**Heinz Pier+**
Carl-Schurz-Str 98, 50374 Erftstadt
Mailing Address: Postfach 2462, Erftstadt 50358
*Tel:* (02235) 3998 *Fax:* (02235) 41654

*Key Personnel*
Owner: Heinz Pier *Tel:* (02235) 44808
Founded: 1922
ISBN Prefix(es): 3-924576
*Branch Office(s)*
Bonnerstr 26, Lechenich, 50374 Erftstadt, Contact: Hedwig Pier *Tel:* (02235) 71959 *Fax:* (02235) 953753

**Paul Pietsch Verlage GmbH & Co+**
Olgastr 86, 70180 Stuttgart
Mailing Address: Postfach 103743, 70032 Stuttgart
*Tel:* (0711) 2 10 80-0 *Fax:* (0711) 2 10 80-82; (0711) 2 36 04-15
*E-mail:* ppv@motorbuch.de
*Web Site:* www.motorbuch.de
*Key Personnel*
Man Dir: Paul Pietsch
Man Dir & Editorial: Dr Patricia Scholten
Rights & Permissions: Patricia Hofmann *E-mail:* p.hoffmann@motorbuch.de
Founded: 1962
Subjects: Aeronautics, Aviation, Automotive, How-to, Maritime, Military Science, Travel
ISBN Prefix(es): 3-87943; 3-613; 3-344
*Associate Companies:* Verlag Mueller-Rueschlikon
Divisions: Motorbuch-Verlag; Pietsch-Verlag; Schrader-Verlag; Transpress
Distributed by Bucheli-Verlag (Switzerland); Mueller-Rueschlikon (Switzerland)
*Warehouse:* Koch, Neff & Oetinger & Co, Schockenriedstr 39, 70565 Stuttgart

**Piper Verlag GmbH+**
Georgenstr 4, 80799 Munich
*Tel:* (089) 381801-0 *Fax:* (089) 338704
*E-mail:* info@piper.de
*Web Site:* www.piper.de
*Key Personnel*
Publisher: Viktor Niemann
Man Dir: Hartmut Jedicke
Editorial: Ulrike Buergel-Goodwin; Bettina Feldweg; Tanja Graf; Thomas Tebbe; Dr Klaus Stadler; Ulrich Wank
Foreign Rights: Ingrid Fuehrer
Contracts & Rights: Annette Sabelus
Sales Manager: Christa Beiling
Press Manager: Eva Brenndorfer
Advertising Manager: Ingrid Ullrich
Founded: 1904
Specialize in music.
Subjects: Biography, Fiction, History, Music, Dance, Philosophy, Psychology, Psychiatry, Science (General), Theology
ISBN Prefix(es): 3-8225; 3-89521; 3-89029; 3-492; 3-921909
Number of titles published annually: 300 Print
*Parent Company:* Bonnier Media Holding GmbH
Imprints: Kabel Verlag; Malik Verlag
*Orders to:* Koch, Neff, Oetinger & Co, Schockenriedstr 39, 70551 Stuttgart

**Pixel Transfer Design Studio**, *imprint of* Extent Verlag und Service Wolfgang M Flamm

**Verlag Ploetz**, *imprint of* Verlag Herder GmbH & Co KG

**pmv**, see Peter Meyer Verlag (pmv)

**Verlag Walter Podszun Burobedarf-Bucher Abt+**
Bahnhofstr 9, 59929 Brilon
*Tel:* (02961) 2507 *Fax:* (02961) 2508
*E-mail:* verlag.podszun@t-online.de
*Key Personnel*
Editor: Walter Podszun
International Rights: Brigitte Podszun
Founded: 1969

Subjects: Automotive, Engineering (General), Humor, Transportation
ISBN Prefix(es): 3-86133; 3-923448
*Bookshop(s):* Buchhandlung Podszun

**Podzun-Pallas Verlag GmbH+**
Kohlhaeuserstr 8, 61200 Woelfersheim
*Tel:* (06036) 9436 *Fax:* (06036) 6270
*Web Site:* www.podzun-pallas.de
*Key Personnel*
Man Dir, Rights & Permissions: Beate Danker
Editorial & Sales: Mrs Karin Kuenzel
Founded: 1979
Subjects: Military Science
ISBN Prefix(es): 3-7909

**Poetik und Hermeneutik**, *imprint of* Wilhelm Fink GmbH & Co Verlags-KG

**Politik und Spiritualitaet**, *imprint of* Drei Eichen Verlag Manuel Kissener

**Galerie Eva Poll**
Luetzowplatz 7, 10785 Berlin
*Tel:* (030) 261 70 91 *Fax:* (030) 261 70 92
*E-mail:* galerie@poll-berlin.de
*Web Site:* www.germangalleries.com/poll
*Key Personnel*
International Rights: Lothar C Poll
Founded: 1968
Subjects: Art

**POLLeditionen Verlag**, see Galerie Eva Poll

**Pollner Verlag+**
Rotdornstr 7, 85764 Oberschleissheim
*Tel:* (089) 3151890 *Fax:* (089) 3151890
*E-mail:* info@pollner-verlag.de
*Web Site:* www.pollner-verlag.de
*Key Personnel*
Contact: Max Pollner
Schwerpunkt Kanuliteratur Outdoor Sports.
Subjects: Environmental Studies, Humor, Outdoor Recreation, Travel, Sport, Kanu, Kajak
ISBN Prefix(es): 3-925660

**Polyband Gesellschaft fur Bild Tontraeger mbH & Co Betriebs KG**
Am Moosfeld 37, 81829 Munich
*Tel:* (089) 420 03-0 *Fax:* (089) 420 03-42
*E-mail:* contact@polyband.de
*Web Site:* www.polyband.de
*Telex:* 522636 pdy d
*Key Personnel*
Man Dir: Swetlana Winkel
Marketing: Marco Koesling *E-mail:* marco.koesling@polyband.de
Publicity: Elza Kronthaler *E-mail:* elza.kronthaler@polyband.de
Founded: 1963
Subjects: Film, Video
ISBN Prefix(es): 3-89276

**Polyglott-Verlag+**
Member of The Langenscheidt Group
Mies-van-der-Rohe-Str 1, 80807 Munich
Mailing Address: Postfach 401120, 80711 Munich
*Tel:* (089) 360960 *Fax:* (089) 36096-222 (general); (089) 36096-258 (orders)
*E-mail:* kundenservice@langenscheidt.de; redaktion@polyglott.de
*Web Site:* www.polyglott.de
*Key Personnel*
Man Dir: Karl Ernst Tielebier-Langenscheidt *E-mail:* redaktion@polyglott.de; Andreas Langenscheidt
Publishing Dir: Rolf Muller
Advertising: Brigitte Pasch
Editorial: Barbara Lennartz
Founded: 1902
Sales & promotion through Langenscheidt KG.

Subjects: Travel
ISBN Prefix(es): 3-493
*Orders to:* Langenscheidt KG, Neusserstr 3, 80807 Munich

**Portikus**
Weckmarkt 17, 60311 Frankfurt am Main
*Tel:* (069) 219 987-60; (069) 219 987-59
    *Fax:* (069) 219 987-61
*E-mail:* portikus@pop.stadt-frankfurt.de
*Web Site:* www.portikus.de
*Key Personnel*
Dir: Dr Daniel Birnbaum
Curator: Jochen Volz
Founded: 1987
Specialize in exhibition catalogues.
Subjects: Art
ISBN Prefix(es): 3-928071
Number of titles published annually: 8 Print
Total Titles: 90 Print
*Parent Company:* Staedelschule

**Possev-Verlag GmbH+**
Flurscheideweg 15, 65936 Frankfurt
*Tel:* (069) 34-12-65 *Fax:* (069) 34-38-41
*E-mail:* possev-ffm@t-online.de
*Key Personnel*
Manager: Leonid Mueller
Founded: 1945
Also runs a translation agency.
ISBN Prefix(es): 3-7912
*Branch Office(s)*
Redaktion Possev, Postfach 325, 117602 Moscow, Russian Federation *Tel:* (095) 2831090

**Prasenz Verlag der Jesus Bruderschaft eV+**
Gnadenthal, 65597 Huenfelden
*Tel:* (06438) 81281 *Fax:* (06438) 81282
*Web Site:* www.uni-giessen.de
*Key Personnel*
Dir: Jens Oertel
Founded: 1962
Subjects: Art, Poetry, Religion - Jewish
ISBN Prefix(es): 3-87630

**Premop Verlag GmbH+**
Kuechelstr 5, 81375 Munich
*Tel:* (089) 562257 *Fax:* (089) 5803214
*E-mail:* premop@mnet-online.de
*Key Personnel*
Manager: Bernard Schenkel
Founded: 1988
Subjects: Music, Dance
ISBN Prefix(es): 3-927724
Subsidiaries: Edition Premop

**Prentice Hall**, *imprint of* Pearson Education Deutschland GmbH

**PIAG Presse Informations AG+**
Landstr 67a, 76547 Sinzheim Baden
*Tel:* (07221) 301 7560 *Fax:* (07221) 301 7570
*E-mail:* office@piag.de
*Web Site:* www.piag.de
*Key Personnel*
Publisher & Man Dir: Dieter Brinzer
Marketing: Jens Hoeppner *Tel:* (0721) 301 7568
    *E-mail:* jhoeppner@piag.de
Sales & Advertising Dir: Sven Kadow
    *Tel:* (07721) 301 7563 *E-mail:* s.kadow@piag. de
Editor: Dr Stefan Hartmann *Tel:* (07221) 301 7564 *E-mail:* s.hartmann@piag.de
Administration: Christiane Kist *Tel:* (07221) 301 7562 *E-mail:* office@piag.de
Founded: 1963
Publisher of specialized books & magazines for the trade of published photography.
Subjects: Law, Photo law & photo prices in Europe
ISBN Prefix(es): 3-921864; 3-922725

**Presse Verlagsgesellschaft mbH+**
Ludwigstr 33-37, 60327 Frankfurt am Main
*Tel:* (069) 97460-0 *Fax:* (069) 97460-400
*E-mail:* journal@mmg.de
*Web Site:* www.journal-frankfurt.de
*Key Personnel*
Man Dir, International Rights: Dr Carsten Brandt
    *Tel:* (01) 61886 *E-mail:* grundlagen-praxis@t-online.de; Carsten Lienemann
Founded: 1980
Subjects: Regional Interests, Homeopathy
ISBN Prefix(es): 3-928789
Number of titles published annually: 2 Print
Total Titles: 7 Print
*Parent Company:* MMG - Medieu Marketing Gruppe
Subsidiaries: K/C/E Marketing GmbH

**Guido Pressler Verlag+**
Auf dem Strifft 19, 52393 Huertgenwald
*Tel:* (02429) 1385; (02408) 929692 *Fax:* (02408) 955931
*E-mail:* info@pressler-verlag.com
*Web Site:* www.pressler-verlag.com
Founded: 1957
Subjects: Art, History, Literature, Literary Criticism, Essays, Philosophy, Psychology, Psychiatry
ISBN Prefix(es): 3-87646

**Prestel Verlag+**
Koeniginstr 9, 80539 Munich
*Tel:* (089) 38 17 09 0 *Fax:* (089) 33 51 75
*E-mail:* info@prestel.de
*Web Site:* www.prestel.de *Cable:* PRESTELVERLAG
*Key Personnel*
Publisher: Juergen Tesch
Sales Dir: Juergen Krieger *Tel:* (089) 38 17 09 48
Publicity Dir: Pia Werner *Tel:* (089) 38 17 09 55
    *E-mail:* werner@prestel.de
Financial Dir: Rolf Alkenbredner
Founded: 1924
Subjects: Architecture & Interior Design, Art, Photography
ISBN Prefix(es): 3-7913
*Branch Office(s)*
Prestel Publishing Ltd, 4 Bloomsbury Place, London WC1A 2QA, United Kingdom, Contact: Andrew Hansen *Tel:* (020) 7323 5004 *Fax:* (020) 7636 8004 *E-mail:* sales@prestel-uk.co.uk
*U.S. Office(s):* Prestel Publishing, 175 Fifth Ave, Suite 402, New York, NY 10010, United States, Contact: Stephen Hulburt *Tel:* 212-995-2720 *Fax:* 212-995-2733 *E-mail:* sales@prestel-usa.com

**Preussische Koepfe**, *imprint of* Stapp Verlag GmbH

**Helmut Preussler Verlag+**
Dagmarstr 8, 90482 Nuernberg
*Tel:* (0911) 95478 0 *Fax:* (0911) 542486
*E-mail:* preussler_verlag@t_online.de *Cable:* PREUSSLER-VERLAG
*Key Personnel*
Man Dir, Editorial, Production & Rights & Permissions: Achin Raak
Sales, Publicity: Annemarie Seeberger
Founded: 1973
ISBN Prefix(es): 3-921332; 3-925362; 3-934679
*Associate Companies:* Preussler Druck & Versand GmbH
Subsidiaries: Versandbuchhandlung Gebhart; Polizei Verlag Heinz Krause
*Bookshop(s):* Ernst Gebhard, Dagmarstr 8, 90482 Nuremberg

**Pro Natur Verlag GmbH+**
Ziegelhuettenweg 43A, 60598 Frankfurt am Main

*Tel:* (069) 9688610 *Fax:* (069) 96886124
*Key Personnel*
Manager: Rudolf L Schreiber
Founded: 1979
Subjects: Environmental Studies
ISBN Prefix(es): 3-88582
*Parent Company:* Pro Natur Gesellschaft zur Foerderung des Umweltschutzes mbH

**Projektion J Buch- und Musikverlag GmbH+**
Dillerberg 2, 35614 Asslar
*Tel:* (06443) 68-0 *Fax:* (06443) 68-34
*E-mail:* info@gerth.de
*Web Site:* www.gerth.de
*Key Personnel*
International Rights: Christian Goelker
Founded: 1989
Subjects: Fiction, How-to, Human Relations, Management, Music, Dance, Nonfiction (General), Religion - Other, Self-Help, Theology, Western Fiction, study aids
ISBN Prefix(es): 3-89490; 3-925352; 3-9800258
*Showroom(s):* Rheingaustr 85A, 65203 Wiesbaden
*Bookshop(s):* Rheingaustr 85A, 65203 Wiesbaden
*Shipping Address:* Rheingaustr 85A, 65203 Wiesbaden
*Warehouse:* Rheingaustr 85A, 65203 Wiesbaden
*Orders to:* Rheingaustr 85A, 65203 Wiesbaden

**Propylaeen Verlag, Zweigniederlassung Berlin der Ullstein Buchverlage GmbH+**
Charlottenstr 13, 10969 Berlin
*Tel:* (030) 2591-3570 *Fax:* (030) 2591-3533
    *Cable:* ULLSTEINBUCH BERLIN
*Key Personnel*
Man Dir: Dr Wolfram Goebel
Sales Dir: Karl-Heinz Reimann
Chief Editor (Hardcover): Dr Uwe Heldt
Chief Editor (Paperbacks): Dr Juergen Mueller
Rights: Heidi Walitza
Founded: 1903
Subjects: Architecture & Interior Design, Art, Biography, Education, Ethnicity, Fiction, Film, Video, Geography, Geology, Government, Political Science, Health, Nutrition, History, How-to, Humor, Literature, Literary Criticism, Essays, Maritime, Military Science, Music, Dance, Mysteries, Nonfiction (General), Poetry, Romance, Science (General), Social Sciences, Sociology, Travel
ISBN Prefix(es): 3-549
*Parent Company:* Ullstein Buchverlage GmbH & Co KG
*Associate Companies:* SVB Sportverlag Berlin
Subsidiaries: Propylaeen Verlag; Ullstein Taschenbuchverlag; Verlag Gesundheit
*U.S. Office(s):* 439 Ninth St, No 2, New York, NY 10009, United States, Contact: Liz Fried *Tel:* 212-533-2296
*Warehouse:* VVA Bertelsmann Distribution GmbH, An der Autobahn, 33310 Gutersloh

**Psychiatrie-Verlag GmbH+**
Thomas-Mannstr 49a, 53111 Bonn
*Tel:* (0228) 725340 *Fax:* (0228) 7253420
*E-mail:* verlag@psychiatrie.de
*Web Site:* www.psychiatrie.de/verlag
*Key Personnel*
Publishing Manager: York Bieger
    *E-mail:* bieger@psychiatrie.de; Ute Hueper
Founded: 1978
Subjects: Health, Nutrition, Psychology, Psychiatry
ISBN Prefix(es): 3-88414
*Orders to:* VVA, Fr Bienne, Postfach 7777, 33310 Gutersloh

**Psychologie Verlags Union GmbH+**
Werderstr 10, 69469 Weinheim
*Tel:* (06201) 60070
*E-mail:* info@beltz.de
*Web Site:* www.beltz.de

*Key Personnel*
Man Dir: Dr Manfred Beltz Ruebelmann
Publishing Manager: Dr Heike Berger
  *Tel:* (06201) 6007370 *Fax:* (06201) 6007395
  *E-mail:* h.berger@beltz.de
Contact: Michaela Frommherz *E-mail:* m.
  frommherz@beltz.de
Founded: 1986
Subjects: Behavioral Sciences, Biological Sciences, Business, Child Care & Development, Communications, Education, Environmental Studies, Psychology, Psychiatry, Social Sciences, Sociology
ISBN Prefix(es): 3-621
*Parent Company:* Beltz Verlag, Werderstr 10, 69469 Weinheim

**Psychosozial-Verlag+**
Goethestr 29, 35390 Giessen
*Tel:* (0641) 77819 *Fax:* (0641) 77742
*E-mail:* info@psychosozial-verlag.de;
  bestellung@psychosozial-verlag.de
*Web Site:* www.psychosozial-verlag.de
*Key Personnel*
Publisher: Dr Hans-Jurgen Wirth
Founded: 1991
Specialize in psychoanalysis.
Subjects: History, Psychology, Psychiatry, Social Sciences, Sociology
ISBN Prefix(es): 3-932133; 3-930096; 3-89806
Total Titles: 210 Print

**Publik-Forum-Verlagsgesellschaft mbH**
Krebsmuehle, 61440 Oberursel
Mailing Address: Postfach 2010, 61410 Oberursel
*Tel:* (06171) 70030 *Fax:* (06171) 700340
*Key Personnel*
Manager: Dieter Grohmann
ISBN Prefix(es): 3-88095; 3-921807

**Pulp Master Frank Nowatzki Verlag+**
Imprint of Maas Verlag
Samariterstr 6, 10247 Berlin
*Tel:* (030) 6868292 *Fax:* (030) 6868292
*E-mail:* master@txt.de
*Web Site:* www.maasmedia.de
*Key Personnel*
Man Dir, Rights & Permissions: Frank Nowatzki
Founded: 1989
Subjects: Fiction, Mysteries
ISBN Prefix(es): 3-927734
*Orders to:* Bugrim, Saalburgstr 3, 12099 Berlin

**Verlag Friedrich Pustet GmbH & Co Kg**
Gutenbergstr 8, 93051 Regensburg
Mailing Address: Postfach 100862, 93008 Regensburg
*Tel:* (0941) 94 24 105 *Fax:* (0941) 94 24 100
*E-mail:* buecher@pustet.de
*Web Site:* www.pustet.de *Cable:* PUSTET
*Key Personnel*
Man Dir: Elisabeth Pustet
Editorial: Fritz Pustet
Founded: 1826
Subjects: Archaeology, Art, Biography, History, Religion - Catholic, Theology
ISBN Prefix(es): 3-7917
*Bookshop(s):* Buchhandlung Friedrich Pustet, Gesandtenstr 6, Regensburg; Kleiner Exerzierplatz 4, Passau; Karolinenstr 12, Augsburg, Theresieuplatz 41, Straubing; Altstadt 28, Landshut, Residentstr 2-6, 91522 Ausbach

**edition q Berlin Edition in der Quintessenz Verlags-GmbH+**
Division of Quintessenz Verlags GmbH
Ifenpfad 2-4, 12107 Berlin
Mailing Address: Postfach 42 04 52, 12064 Berlin
*Tel:* (030) 761 80-5 *Fax:* (030) 761 80-680

*E-mail:* editionq@quintessenz.de; info@
  quintessenz.de
*Web Site:* www.quintessenz.de
*Telex:* 500/183815
*Key Personnel*
Publisher: Horst-Wolfgang Haase *Tel:* (030) 761
  80-622 *Fax:* (030) 761 80-691
Publishing Dir: Johannes W Wolters *Tel:* (030)
  761 80-670 *Fax:* (030) 761 80-692
Editor, Berlin Edition: Bernhard Thieme
  *Tel:* (030) 761 80-640
Online Editor: Joachim Liebers *Tel:* (030) 761
  80-604 *Fax:* (030) 761 80-693
International Rights: Bernd Burkart *Tel:* (030)
  761 80-608 *Fax:* (030) 761 80-693
Sales Manager: Cornelia Gross *Tel:* (030) 761 80-
  635 *Fax:* (030) 761 80-692
Marketing: Uwe Janssen *Tel:* (030) 761 80-614
Commercial Manager: Thomas Fritz *Tel:* (030)
  761 80-658 *Fax:* (030) 761 80-692
Manager Electronic Publishing: Andreas Mueller
  *E-mail:* mueller@quintessenz.de
Advertising: Gudrun Matthes *Tel:* (030) 761 80-
  629 *Fax:* (030) 761 80-691 *E-mail:* anzeigen@
  quintessenz.de
Product Manager Offline-Media: Martin Hecklinger *Tel:* (030) 761 80-677
  *E-mail:* hecklinger@quintessenz.de
Assistant Manager: Christian Haase *Tel:* (030)
  761 80-605
Subscriptions: Angela Koethe *E-mail:* abo@
  quintessenz.de
Book Orders: Leo Korff *E-mail:* buch@
  quintessenz.de
Graphics: Ines Bluemel *Tel:* (030) 761 80-608
Founded: 1990
Membership(s): Boersenverein des Deutschen Buchhandels eV.
Subjects: Art, History, Literature, Literary Criticism, Essays, Arts & Culture, Contemporary History, Japanese Literature
ISBN Prefix(es): 3-86124; 3-928024; 3-8148
Total Titles: 200 Print
*U.S. Office(s):* Quintessence Publishing Co Inc/Edition q Inc, 551 N Kimberly Dr, Carol Stream, IL 60188-1881, United States *Tel:* 630-682-3223 *Fax:* 630-682-3288 *E-mail:* quintpub@aol.com *Web Site:* www. quintpub.com
Foreign Rep(s): Edition q Inc (US); Quintessence Publishing Co Inc (US)
Foreign Rights: Quintessence Publishing Co Ltd (UK)
*Shipping Address:* Prolit Verlagsaulieferin GmbH, Siemensstr 16, 35463 Fernwald-Annerod, Contact: Gabriele Boehnen *Tel:* (0641) 94393 21 *Fax:* (0641) 94393 29
*Warehouse:* Prolit Verlagsaulieferin GmbH, Siemensstr 16, 35463 Fernwald-Annerod, Contact: Gabriele Boehnen *Tel:* (0641) 94393 21 *Fax:* (0641) 94393 29
*Orders to:* Edition Guides, Quintessenz Verlags GmbH, Berlin, Contact: Helga Schebera *Tel:* (030) 761 80-635 *Fax:* (030) 761 80-692

**Que,** *imprint of* Pearson Education Deutschland GmbH

**Quell Verlag+**
Augustenstr 124, 70197 Stuttgart
*Tel:* (0711) 601000 *Fax:* (0711) 6010076
*Key Personnel*
Dir, Editorial, Publicity, Rights & Permissions: Walter Waldbauer
Founded: 1830
Subjects: Biography, Fiction, History, Philosophy, Religion - Other
ISBN Prefix(es): 3-7918
*Parent Company:* Evangelische Gesellschaft, Postfach 103852, 70033 Stuttgart

Subsidiaries: Evangelische Gemeindepresse GmbH; Wartburg Verlag GmbH iG
*Bookshop(s):* Buchhandlung der Evangelischen Gesellschaft in Heidenheim, Heilbronn Ludwigsburg, Schaebisch Hall, Stuttgart

**Quelle und Meyer Verlag GmbH & Co+**
Industriepark 3, 56291 Wiebelsheim
*Tel:* (06766) 903200 *Fax:* (06766) 903320
*E-mail:* service@humanitas-book.de
*Web Site:* www.quelle-meyer.de
*Key Personnel*
Man Dir: Gerhard Stahl
Sales: Ralf Simolka
Rights & Permissions: Dr Jrmgard Meissl
Founded: 1906
Subjects: Biological Sciences, Education, History, Language Arts, Linguistics, Literature, Literary Criticism, Essays, Philosophy, Psychology, Psychiatry, Religion - Other, Social Sciences, Sociology
ISBN Prefix(es): 3-494; 3-88988
*Associate Companies:* AULA-Verlag GmbH, Industrie Park 3, Wiebelsheim 56291 *Tel:* (06766) 903141 *Fax:* (06766) 903320 *E-mail:* vertrieb@aula-verlag.de; Limpert Verlag GmbH, Industrie Park 3, 56291 Wiebelsheim *Tel:* (06766) 903160 *Fax:* (06766) 903360 *E-mail:* vertrieb@limpert.de

**Querverlag GmbH**
Akazienstr 25, 10823 Berlin
*Tel:* (030) 78 70 23 39; (030) 78702340
  *Fax:* (030) 788 49 50
*E-mail:* mail@querverlag.de
*Web Site:* www.querverlag.de
*Key Personnel*
Publisher: Jim Baker *E-mail:* jim@querverlag.de
Founded: 1995
Germany's first & only gay & lesbian book publisher.
Membership(s): Borsenverein des Deutschen Buchhandels.
Subjects: Fiction, Gay & Lesbian, Nonfiction (General), Gay & Lesbian Fiction & Nonfiction, Homosexuality, Queer Studies
ISBN Prefix(es): 3-89656
*Shipping Address:* Prolit Verlagsauslieferung, Siemensstr 16, 35463 Fernwald, Contact: Andrea Willenberg *Tel:* (0641) 9439-335 *Fax:* (0641) 9439-339 *E-mail:* a.willenberg@ prolit.de *Web Site:* www.prolit.de

**Quintessenz Verlags-GmbH+**
Ifenpfad 2-4, 12107 Berlin
Mailing Address: Postfach 420452, 12064 Berlin
*Tel:* (030) 761805 *Fax:* (030) 76180680
*E-mail:* info@quintessenz.de
*Web Site:* www.quintessenz.de
*Telex:* 183815 quint d
*Key Personnel*
Publisher: H W Haase
International Rights: Gerda Steinmeyer
  *E-mail:* steinmeyer@quintessenz.de
Founded: 1949
Subjects: Biography, Career Development, Communications, Fiction, Film, Video, Health, Nutrition, Literature, Literary Criticism, Essays, Management, Medicine, Nursing, Dentistry, Mysteries
ISBN Prefix(es): 3-86124; 3-928024; 3-8148; 3-87652; 3-9801163
Subsidiaries: Edition Q
*U.S. Office(s):* Quintessence Publishing Co Inc, 551 N Kimberly Dr, Carol Stream, IL 60188, United States

**Dr Josef Raabe-Verlags GmbH**
Postfach 103922, 70034 Stuttgart
*Tel:* (0711) 62900-0 *Fax:* (0711) 6290010
*Web Site:* www.raabe.de

*Key Personnel*
Man Dir: Dr Reinhard Sander; Wolfgang Schulz
Founded: 1985
Specialize in loose leaf editions, universities, school management.
Subjects: Education, Environmental Studies, Management, Public Administration, Science (General)
ISBN Prefix(es): 3-88649; 3-8183
*Parent Company:* Ernst Klett Information GmbH, Rotebuehlstr 77, 70178 Stuttgart
*Ultimate Parent Company:* Ernst Klett AG
Subsidiaries: RAABE Bulgarien; Dr Josef Raabe Spolka Wydawnicza; Nakladatelstvi RAABE; RAABE Fachverlag fur Bildungsmanagement; RAABE Fachverlag fur Oeffentliche Verwaltung Duesseldorf; RAABE Fachverlag fur Wissenschaftsinformation; RAABE Fachverlag fur die Schule; RAABE Koenyvkiado
*Warehouse:* BDK Buecherdienst Koeln, Koelner Str 248, 51149 Koeln
*Orders to:* Dr Josef Raabe Verlags-GmbH, Kundenservice, Postfach 103922, 70034 Stuttgart
*Tel:* (0711) 62900-0 *Fax:* (0711) 62900-10
*E-mail:* info@raabe.de

**Raben Verlag von Wittern KG+**
Frohschammerstr 14, 80807 Munich
*Tel:* (089) 3594879 *Fax:* (089) 3596622
*Key Personnel*
Contact: York von Wittern
Founded: 1980
ISBN Prefix(es): 3-922696

**Radius-Verlag GmbH+**
Olgastr 114, 70180 Stuttgart
*Tel:* (0711) 6076666; (0172) 7126573 *Fax:* (0711) 6075555
*E-mail:* radiusverlag@freenet.de
*Key Personnel*
Man Dir: Wolfgang Erk
Founded: 1962
Subjects: Fiction, Philosophy, Psychology, Psychiatry, Religion - Other
ISBN Prefix(es): 3-87173

**Rake Verlag GmbH+**
Koenigsweg 20, 24103 Kiel
*Tel:* (0431) 6611515 *Fax:* (0431) 6611517
*E-mail:* info@rake.de
*Web Site:* www.rake.de
*Key Personnel*
Publisher: Micha Rau *E-mail:* rau@rake.de
Sales: Peter Keune *E-mail:* keune@rake.de
Public Relations: Annette Borchers *E-mail:* borchers@rake.de
Founded: 1994
Subjects: Fiction, Humor, Self-Help, Specialize in contemporary German authors
ISBN Prefix(es): 3-931476
Number of titles published annually: 20 Print
Total Titles: 35 Print; 1 Audio
*Branch Office(s)*
MediaPartner, Hofackerstr 13, 8032 Zurich, Switzerland *Tel:* (01) 385 55 10 *Fax:* (01) 385 55 19 *E-mail:* mediapartner@access.ch
Distributed by PNV Vertriebs Service

**Dr Mohan Krischke Ramaswamy Edition RE+**
RE Wolfgang-Doringstr 4, 37077 Goettingen
*Tel:* (0171) 8026882 *Fax:* (0171) 5311065
*E-mail:* edition.re@epost.de
*Key Personnel*
Owner: Dr Mohan Krischke Ramaswamy *E-mail:* ramaswamy@epost.de
Founded: 1979
Subjects: Ethnicity, Music, Dance, Social Sciences, Sociology
ISBN Prefix(es): 3-927636; 3-937031

**Dr Ramdohr KG**, see Mentor-Verlag Dr Ramdohr KG

**Rationalisierungs-Kuratorium der Deutschen Wirtschaft eV (RKW)**
Sohnstr 70, 40237 Duesseldorf
*Tel:* (0211) 680010 *Fax:* (0211) 68001 68; (0211) 68001 69
*E-mail:* info@rkw-nrw.de
*Web Site:* www.rkwnrw.de
*Telex:* 4072755 rkw d *Cable:* ERKAWE
*Key Personnel*
Manager: Dr Gerhard Schrick; Dr H Mueller
Publicity Manager: H Degenhard
Publications, Rights: Dr Natascha Breme
Founded: 1921
Registered Society of the German Industrial Rationalization Board.
Subjects: Business, Economics, Engineering (General), Labor, Industrial Relations, Management, Technology
ISBN Prefix(es): 3-926984; 3-921451; 3-929796; 3-89644

**Werner Rau Verlag+**
Feldbergstr 54 D, 70569 Stuttgart
*Tel:* (0711) 7819 4610 *Fax:* (0711) 7819 4654
*E-mail:* info@rau-verlag.de
*Web Site:* www.rau-verlag.de
Founded: 1986
Subjects: Travel
ISBN Prefix(es): 3-926145
*Orders to:* Bertelsmann Distribution GmbH, Postfach 7777, 33310 Gutersloh 100

**Gerhard Rautenberg Druckerei und Verlag GmbH & Co KG**
Imprint of Verlagshaus Wurzburg
Beethovenstr 5, 97070 Wurzburg
*Tel:* (0931) 385235 *Fax:* (0931) 385305
*E-mail:* info@verlagshaus.com
*Web Site:* www.verlagshaus.com
*Key Personnel*
Publishing Dir: Dieter Krause
Dir of Production: Juergen Roth
Sales Dir: Johannes Glesius
Founded: 1825
Subjects: Drama, Theater, Fiction, Humor, Regional Interests
ISBN Prefix(es): 3-7921
*Bookshop(s):* Rautenbergsche Buchhandlung, Blinke 8, 26767 Leer

**Ravensburger Buchverlag Otto Maier GmbH+**
Postfach 1860, 88188 Ravensburg
*Tel:* (0751) 86 1717 *Fax:* (0751) 861818
*E-mail:* info@ravensburger.de
*Web Site:* www.ravensburger.de *Cable:* MAIERVERLAG
*Key Personnel*
President: Otto Julius Maier; Dorothee Hess-Maier
Man Dir: Claus Runge
Editorial: Michael Kohlhammer; Cornelius Retting; Valeska Schneider-Finke
Production: Max Weishaupt
International Sales: Michael Bartl
Marketing: Michael Pfleiderer
Publicity: Anja Fahs
Rights & Permissions: Michael Ramm; Florence Roux
Founded: 1883
Subjects: Art, Crafts, Games, Hobbies, Education, Fiction, Nonfiction (General)
ISBN Prefix(es): 3-473
*Parent Company:* Ravensburger AG
*Associate Companies:* Ravensburger Verlag GmbH; Ravensburger GmbH, Vienna, Austria; Editions Ravensburger SA, Attenschwiller, France; Ravensburger SpA, Milan, Italy; Ravensburger BV, Amersfoort, Netherlands; Carlit und Ravensburger AG, Wueenlos, Switzerland; Ravensburger Ltd, Bicester, United Kingdom

Divisions: Ravensburger SpieleVerlag GmbH; Ravensburger Interactive Media GmbH; Ravensburger Freizeit & Promotion Service GmbH; Ravensburger Film & TV GmbH

**Ravenstein Verlag GmbH+**
Auf der Krautweide 24, 65812 Bad Soden
*Tel:* (06196) 609630 *Fax:* (06196) 63619
*E-mail:* g.koenig@ravenstein-verlag.de
*Telex:* 4072538 haco d *Cable:* RAVENSTEINVERLAG
*Key Personnel*
Man Dir: Ruediger Bosse
Founded: 1830
ISBN Prefix(es): 3-87660
*U.S. Office(s):* Seven Hills Book Div, 49 Central Ave, Cincinnati, OH 45202, United States

**Reader's Digest Deutschland Verlag Das Beste GmbH**
Augustenstr 1, 70178 Stuttgart
Mailing Address: Postfach 106020, 70049 Stuttgart
*Tel:* (0711) 66020 *Fax:* (0711) 6602547
*E-mail:* verlag@readersdigest.de
*Web Site:* www.readersdigest.de *Cable:* READIGEST STUTTGART
*Key Personnel*
Man Dir: Werner Neunzig
Founded: 1948
Also publish music & video editions.
ISBN Prefix(es): 3-87070
*Parent Company:* The Reader's Digest Association Inc, Reader's Digest Rd, Pleasantville, NY 10570-7000, United States
Subsidiaries: Optimail Direktwerbeservice GmbH; Pegasus Buch- und Zeischriften-Vertriebs-GmbH

**Verlag Recht und Wirtschaft GmbH+**
Haeusserstr 14, 69115 Heidelberg
Mailing Address: Postfach 105960, 69049 Heidelberg
*Tel:* (06221) 9060 *Fax:* (06221) 906259
*E-mail:* verlag@ruw.de; info@ruw.de
*Web Site:* www.ruw-ruw.de *Cable:* RECHTWIRTSCHAFT HEIDELBERG
*Key Personnel*
Man Dir: Michael Giesecke
Publisher: Angelika Sauer
Contact: Norbert Konda
Founded: 1946
Subjects: Economics, Law, Social Sciences, Sociology
ISBN Prefix(es): 3-8005
Subsidiaries: I H Sauer Verlag GmbH

**Reclam Verlag Leipzig+**
Inselstr 26, 04103 Leipzig
*Tel:* (0341) 997170 *Fax:* (0341) 9971730
*E-mail:* info@reclam-leipzig.de
*Web Site:* www.reclam.de *Cable:* RECLAM LEIPZIG
*Key Personnel*
Man Dir: Dr Frank Rainer Max; Franz Schaefer
International Rights: Dr Stephan Koranyi
Founded: 1828
Subjects: Biography, History, Literature, Literary Criticism, Essays, Philosophy
ISBN Prefix(es): 3-379
*Parent Company:* Philipp Reclam jun GmbH & Co, Stuttgart
*Orders to:* Philipp Reclam Jun, 71252 Ditzingen

**Redaktion & Gestaltung**, *imprint of* Johann Wolfgang Goethe Universitat

**Reed Elsevier Deutschland GmbH+**
Gabrielenstr 9, 80636 Grafelfing, Munich
Mailing Address: Postfach 201663, 80016 Munich

Tel: (089) 898170 Fax: (089) 89817-300
Web Site: www.reedbusiness.de
Key Personnel
Man Dir: Burkhard Bierschenck
Editor: Wolfram Haase
Founded: 1938
Subjects: Environmental Studies, Medicine, Nursing, Dentistry
ISBN Prefix(es): 3-8040
Parent Company: Reed Elsevier, Netherlands
Subsidiaries: ipc magazin verlag GmbH

**REGENSBERG Druck & Verlag GmbH & Co**
Daimlerweg 58, 48163 Muenster
Mailing Address: Postfach 6667, 48035 Muenster
Tel: (0251) 749800 Fax: (0251) 7498040
Key Personnel
Manager: Bernhard Lucas
Founded: 1591
Subjects: Regional Interests
ISBN Prefix(es): 3-7923

**Verlag fuer Regionalgeschichte+**
Windelsbleicher Str 13, 33335 Gutersloh
Mailing Address: Postfach 120423, 33653 Bielefeld
Tel: (05209) 6714; (05209) 980266 Fax: (05209) 6519; (05209) 980277
E-mail: regionalgeschichte@t-online.de
Web Site: www.regionalgeschichte.de
Key Personnel
Publisher: Olaf Eimer
Founded: 1987
Subjects: Art, History, Regional Interests, Social Sciences, Sociology
ISBN Prefix(es): 3-927085; 3-89534
Number of titles published annually: 40 Print
Total Titles: 350 Print

**Regura Verlag**
Karim Zia, Reza Haidari Kahkesh, Kirchgarten Str, 4A, 60439 Frankfurt
Tel: (0711) 2269835 Fax: (0711) 2238829
Web Site: www.regura.de
Founded: 1997
Digital publications, internet solutions & services for publishers
International cultural exchange, priority: Orient, Persia & Germany.
Subjects: Art, Cookery, Fiction
ISBN Prefix(es): 3-932814

**Konrad Reich Verlag GmbH+**
Kaeppen-Pott-Weg 6, 18055 Rostock Brinckmansdorf
Tel: (0381) 693020 Fax: (0381) 693021
Key Personnel
Man Dir, Rights & Permissions: Konrad Reich
Founded: 1990
Subjects: Art, Ethnicity, Fiction, Geography, Geology, Travel
ISBN Prefix(es): 3-86167

**Dr Ludwig Reichert Verlag+**
Tauernstr 11, 65199 Wiesbaden
Tel: (0611) 461851 Fax: (0611) 468613
E-mail: info@reichert-verlag.de
Web Site: www.reichert-verlag.de
Key Personnel
Publisher: Ursula Reichert
Founded: 1970
Worldwide distribution.
Subjects: Archaeology, Art, Asian Studies, Geography, Geology, History, Language Arts, Linguistics, Library & Information Sciences, Music, Dance, Religion - Jewish, Science (General)
ISBN Prefix(es): 3-920153; 3-88226; 3-89500
Warehouse: Brockhaus Commission, Kreidlerstr 9, 70806 Kornwestheim, Contact: Mrs Wunder-

lich Tel: (07154) 132726 Fax: (07154) 132713
E-mail: reichert@brocom.de
Orders to: Brockhaus Commission, Kreidlerstr 9, 70806 Kornwestheim, Contact: Mrs Wunderlich Tel: (07154) 132726 Fax: (07154) 132713
E-mail: reichert@brocom.de

**Reichl Verlag Der Leuchter+**
Auf dem Haehnchen 34, 56329 St Goar
Tel: (06741) 1720 Fax: (06741) 1749
E-mail: reichl-verlag@telda.net
Web Site: www.reichl-verlag.de
Key Personnel
Man Dir: Matthias Draeger
Founded: 1909
Subjects: Astrology, Occult, Medicine, Nursing, Dentistry, Parapsychology, Religion - Other, Self-Help
ISBN Prefix(es): 3-87667
Subsidiaries: Leibniz Verlag
Divisions: Edition Asklepios

**Dietrich Reimer Verlag GmbH+**
Zimmerstr 26-27, 10969 Berlin
Tel: (030) 25 91 15 70 Fax: (030) 25 91 15 77
E-mail: vertrieb-kunstverlage@reimer-verlag.de
Web Site: www.reimer-verlag.de
Key Personnel
Publisher, Rights & Permissions: Dr Friedrich Kaufmann
Editorial & International Rights: Beate Behrens
Sales & Publicity: Gabriele Dornemann
Production: Dieter Eckert; Nicola Willam
Secretary: Brigitte Struck
Founded: 1845
Subjects: Anthropology, Art, Ethnicity, Cartography, Customs & Traditions, Dance, Television, Theatre
ISBN Prefix(es): 3-496; 3-7861
Bookshop(s): Nautische Buchhandlung Dietrich Reimer, Unter den Eichen 57, 12203 Berlin, Contact: Fr Haberey Tel: (030) 8312341 Fax: (030) 8313873; Dietrich Reimer Wissenschaftliche Fachbuchhandlung, 12203 Berlin, Contact: Mrs Carina Ebert Tel: (030) 8314082 Fax: (030) 8313873
Orders to: Koch, Neff, Oetinger & Co Verlagsauslieferung GmbH, Schockenriedstr 39, 70506 Stuttgart

**Ernst Reinhardt Verlag GmbH & Co KG+**
Kemnatenstr 46, 80639 Munich
Mailing Address: Postfach 380280, 80615 Munich
Tel: (089) 17 80 16 0 Fax: (089) 17 80 16 30
E-mail: webmaster@reinhardt-verlag.de
Web Site: www.reinhardt-verlag.de
Key Personnel
Man Dir: Hildegard Wehler E-mail: wehler@reinhardt-verlag.de
Production: Dorothea Roll Tel: (089) 17 80 16 20 E-mail: roll@reinhardt-verlag.de
Finance: Peter Dietz Tel: (089) 17 80 16 17 E-mail: dietz@reinhardt-verlag.de
Sales: Daniela Postleb Tel: (089) 17 80 16 22 E-mail: postleb@reinhardt-verlag.de
Founded: 1899
Subjects: Child Care & Development, Education, Management, Medicine, Nursing, Dentistry, Music, Dance, Philosophy, Psychology, Psychiatry, Religion - Other, Science (General), Social Sciences, Sociology, Medicine, Nursing
ISBN Prefix(es): 3-497
Distributed by Buch und Medienvertriebs AG (Switzerland); Koch, Neff & Oetinger & Co (Germany); Mohr Morawa Wien (Australia)
Orders to: Koch, Neff, Oetinger & Co Verlagsauslieferung GmbH, Schockenriedstr 39, 70565 Stuttgart

**E Reinhold Verlag** (E Reinhold Publishing)
Hillgasse 15, 04600 Altenburg

Tel: (03447) 311889 Fax: (03447) 375611
E-mail: erv@querstand.de
Web Site: www.querstand.de
Key Personnel
Publisher: Klaus-Juergen Kamprad
Founded: 1990
Subjects: Biography, History, Photography, Regional Interests, Travel, Regional Interests of East Germany
ISBN Prefix(es): 3-910166; 3-937940
Number of titles published annually: 10 Print
Total Titles: 100 Print

**Reise Know-How**, imprint of Reise Know-How Verlag Peter Rump GmbH

**Reise Know-How+**
Zwalbacherstr 3, 66709 Rappweiler
Tel: (06872) 91737 Fax: (06872) 91738
E-mail: hoff-verlag@reise-know-how.com
Web Site: www.reise-know-how.com
Key Personnel
Man Dir: Edgar P Hoff E-mail: edgarhoff@aol.com
Founded: 1981
Publisher of travel guides.
Subjects: Travel, Travel Guides
ISBN Prefix(es): 3-923716
Total Titles: 13 Print
Subsidiaries: Backpacker Information Service

**Reise Know-How Verlag-Daerr GmbH+**
Osnabruecker Str 79, 33649 Bielefeld
Tel: (0521) 946490 Fax: (0521) 441047
E-mail: info@reise-know-how.de
Web Site: www.reise-know-how.de
Key Personnel
Man Dir: Peter Rump
Founded: 1987
Subjects: Travel
ISBN Prefix(es): 3-921497; 3-89662
Associate Companies: Reise-Know-How, Rump-Verlag, Haupt Str 198, 33647 Bielefeld Tel: (0521) 440835; Reise-Know-How Verlag Tondok, Nadistr 18, 808009 Munich; Reise-Know-Verlag, Dr HR Grundmann, Heinrich-Schwarz-Weg 36, 27777 Ganderkesee Tel: (04222) 8799; Reise-Know-How-Verlag Hermann, Untere Muehle, 71706 Markgroeningen Tel: (07145) 8278
Shipping Address: Prolit, Postfach 9, 35461 Fernwald Tel: (0641) 43071 Fax: (0641) 42773
Warehouse: Prolit, Postfach 9, 35461 Fernwald Tel: (0641) 43071 Fax: (0641) 42773
Orders to: Prolit, Postfach 9, 35461 Fernwald Tel: (0641) 43071 Fax: (0641) 42773

**Reise Know-How Verlag Dr Hans-R Grundmann GmbH**
Member of Verlagsgruppe Reise Know-How
Am Hamjebusch 29, 26655 Westerstede
Tel: (04488) 761994 Fax: (04488) 761030
E-mail: reisebuch@aol.com
Founded: 1988
Specialize in North America travel publications.
ISBN Prefix(es): 3-927554; 3-9800151

**Reise Know-How Verlag Helmut Hermann**
Member of Verlagsgruppe Reise Know-How
Untere Muhle, 71706 Markgroningen
Tel: (07145) 8278 Fax: (07145) 26736
Key Personnel
Contact: H Hermann E-mail: rkhhermann@aol.com
Founded: 1986
Subjects: Photography, Travel
ISBN Prefix(es): 3-929920; 3-9800975; 3-9803296
Orders to: Prolit, Postfach 9, 35463 Fernwald

**Reise Know-How Verlag Peter Rump GmbH+**
Member of Verlagsgruppe Reise Know-How
Osnabrucker Str 79, 33649 Bielefeld
*Tel:* (0521) 94649-0 *Fax:* (0521) 441047
*E-mail:* info@reise-know-how.de
*Web Site:* www.reise-know-how.de
*Key Personnel*
Man Dir: Peter Rump
Founded: 1981
Subjects: Foreign Countries, Geography, Geology,
   Language Arts, Linguistics, Travel
ISBN Prefix(es): 3-922376; 3-89416; 3-8317
Imprints: Reise Know-How
*U.S. Office(s):* SCB Distributors, PO Box 5446,
   Carson, CA 90749-5446, United States
*Orders to:* Prolit GmbH, Siemensstr 16, Postfach
   9, 35463 Fernwald (Annerod)

**Reise Know-How Verlag Tondok**
Member of Verlagsgruppe Reise Know-How
Nadistr 18, 80809 Munich
*Tel:* (089) 3514857 *Fax:* (089) 3518485
*E-mail:* rhk@tondok-verlag.de
*Web Site:* www.tondok-verlag.de
*Key Personnel*
Contact: Wil Tondok
Subjects: Travel
ISBN Prefix(es): 3-921838

**Verlagsgruppe Reise Know-How+**
Osnabruecker str 79, 33649 Bielefeld
*Tel:* (0521) 946490 *Fax:* (0521) 441047
*E-mail:* info@reise-know-how.de
*Web Site:* www.reise-know-how.de
*Key Personnel*
Rights & Permissions: Peter Rump
Founded: 1981
Subjects: Language Arts, Linguistics, Travel
ISBN Prefix(es): 3-922376; 3-89416; 3-8317
*Associate Companies:* Reise Know-How Ver-
   lag Peter Rump Gmbh, Osnabrucker Str
   79, 33649 Bielefeld *Tel:* (0521) 94649-0
   *Fax:* (0521) 44104-7 *E-mail:* info@reise-
   know-how.dc; Reise Know-How Verlag Hel-
   mut Hermann, Untere Muhle, 71706 Mark-
   groningen *Tel:* (07145) 8278 *Fax:* (07145)
   26736 *E-mail:* rkhhermann@aol.com; Reise
   Know-How Verlag Tondok, Nadistr 18,
   80809 Munich *Tel:* (089) 3514857 *Fax:* (089)
   3518485 *E-mail:* rkh@tondok-verlag.de;
   Reise Know-How Verlag/Hans Grundmann
   GmbH, Am Hamjebusch 29, 26655 Westerstede *Tel:* (04488) 761994 *Fax:* (04488) 761030
   *E-mail:* reisebuch@aol.com
*Orders to:* Prolit Verlagsauslieferung, Siemensstr
   16, 35463 Fernwald (Annerod)

**Verlag Norman Rentrop+**
Ruengsdorferstr 2e, 53173 Bonn
*Tel:* (0228) 36 88 40 *Fax:* (0228) 36 58 75
*E-mail:* jra@rentrop.com
*Web Site:* www.normanrentrop.de
*Key Personnel*
Man Dir: Norman Rentrop
Publisher: Janine Rasche
Founded: 1975
Specialize in looseleaf services.
Subjects: Business, Finance, Public Administra-
   tion, Real Estate
*Branch Office(s)*
Arenbergstr 33, 5020 Salzburg, Austria
Sagestr 14, 5600 Lenzburg/Zurich, Switzerland
One Place du Lycee, 68005 Colmar, France
27A Old Gloucester St, London WC1N 3XX,
   United Kingdom
*U.S. Office(s):* Georgetown Publishing House,
   1101 30 St NW, Washington, DC 20007,
   United States *Tel:* 202-337-5960 *Fax:* 202-337-
   1512
117 W Harrison, Suite R-246, Chicago, IL 60605,
   United States
*Orders to:* Buchhandel Deutschland an Buecher-
   dienst Cologne, 51169 Cologne

**Respublica Verlag**
Kaiserstr 99-101, 53721 Siegburg
Mailing Address: Postfach 1831, 53708 Siegburg
*Tel:* (02241) 62925; (02241) 64039 *Fax:* (02241)
   53891
*Key Personnel*
President, International Rights: Franz Schmitt
Founded: 1932
Subjects: Music, Dance, Regional Interests
ISBN Prefix(es): 3-87710

**Verlagsgruppe Rhein Main GmbH & Co KG**
Erich Dombrowskistr 2, 55127 Mainz-Marienborn
*Tel:* (06131) 48-46-94
*E-mail:* info@main-rheiner.de
*Web Site:* www.main-rheiner.de
*Key Personnel*
Manager: Holger Albaum *Tel:* (06131) 48 41 80
   *Fax:* (06131) 48 41 73 *E-mail:* halbaum@vrm.
   de
ISBN Prefix(es): 3-920615

**Verlag Rheinischer Merkur GmbH**
Godesberger Allee 91, 53175 Bonn
Mailing Address: Postfach 201164, 53141 Bonn
*Tel:* (0228) 884-0 *Fax:* (0228) 88 41 70 (sales);
   (0228) 88 41 99 (editorial); (0228) 88 42 99
   (advertising)
*E-mail:* abo@merkur.de
*Web Site:* www.merkur.de
*Key Personnel*
Man Dir: Bert G Wegener
ISBN Prefix(es): 3-9801913

**RVBG Rheinland-Verlag-und
   Betriebsgesellschaft des
   Landschaftsverbandes Rheinland mbH+**
Abtei Brauweiler, 50259 Pulheim
Mailing Address: Postfach 2140, 50250 Pulheim
*Tel:* (02234) 9854265 *Fax:* (02234) 82503
*Telex:* uber 8873335 Lvrkd
*Key Personnel*
Man Dir: Christian Buepel
Founded: 1958
Subjects: Archaeology, History, Regional Interests
ISBN Prefix(es): 3-7927
Subsidiaries: Rhein Eifel Mosel Verlag
*Bookshop(s):* Versandbuchhandlung, Abtei
   Brauweiler, 50259 Pulheim
*Shipping Address:* Dr Rudolf Habelt Verlag, Am
   Buchenhang 2, 53315 Bonn

**Richardi Helmut Verlag GmbH+**
Aschaffenburger Str 19, 60599 Frankfurt am
   Main
Mailing Address: Postfach 111151, 60046 Frank-
   furt am Main
*Tel:* (069) 9708330 *Fax:* (069) 7078400
*E-mail:* kreditwesen@t-online.de
*Key Personnel*
Owner: Klaus-Friedrich Otto
Publisher: Claus Wonneberger; Werner Scholz
Founded: 1955
Subjects: Finance, Real Estate
ISBN Prefix(es): 3-921722
*Associate Companies:* Friz Knapp Verlag

**Edition Riesenrad,** *imprint of* Xenos
   Verlagsgesellschaft mbH

**Rigodon-Verlag Norbert Wehr+**
Nieberdingstr 18, 45147 Essen
*Tel:* (0201) 77 81 11; (0221) 360 21 92
   *Fax:* (0201) 77 51 74; (0221) 360 21 92
*E-mail:* Schreibheft@NetCologne.de
*Web Site:* www.schreibheft.de
*Key Personnel*
Manager: Norbert Wehr
Founded: 1977
Subjects: Literature, Literary Criticism, Essays
ISBN Prefix(es): 3-924071

**Rimbaud Verlagsgesellschaft mbH+**
Oppenhoffalle 20, 52066 Aachen
Mailing Address: Postfach 10 01 44, 52001
   Aachen
*Tel:* (0241) 54 25 32; (0241) 9019583
   *Fax:* (0241) 514117
*E-mail:* info@rimbaud.de
*Web Site:* www.rimbaud.de
*Key Personnel*
Man Dir, Sales, Publicity: Walter Hoerner
Editorial: Dr Reinhard Kiefer
International Rights: Dr Bernard Albers
Founded: 1983
Subjects: Literature, Literary Criticism, Essays,
   Music, Dance, Photography, Poetry
ISBN Prefix(es): 3-89086
Distributed by Pegasus Verlagsauslieferung
   (Switzerland); Hora-Verlag (Austria)

**Ritterbach Verlag GmbH**
Rudolf-Dieselstr 5-7, 50226 Frechen
Mailing Address: Postfach 1820, 50208 Frechen
*Tel:* (02234) 18 66 0 *Fax:* (02234) 18 66 90
*E-mail:* service@ritterbach.de; coeln.ml@
   ritterbach.de
*Web Site:* www.ritterbach.de
Founded: 1987
Subjects: Architecture & Interior Design, Art,
   Career Development, Crafts, Games, Hobbies,
   Education
ISBN Prefix(es): 3-89314

**Ritzau KG Verlag Zeit und Eisenbahn+**
Landsbergerstr 24, 86932 Puergen
*Tel:* (08196) 252 *Fax:* (08196) 1240
*E-mail:* mail@ritzau.kg.de
*Web Site:* www.ritzau-kg.de
Founded: 1968
Subjects: History, Transportation
ISBN Prefix(es): 3-921304; 3-935101

**RKW,** see Rationalisierungs-Kuratorium der
   Deutschen Wirtschaft eV (RKW)

**Roehrig Universitaets Verlag Gmbh**
Eichendorffstr 37, 66386 Sankt Ingbert
*Tel:* (06894) 8 79 57 *Fax:* (06894) 87 03 30
*E-mail:* info@roehrig-verlag.de
*Web Site:* www.roehrig-verlag.de
*Key Personnel*
Publisher: Werner J Roehrig
Founded: 1984
Membership(s): Provincial Federation of Book-
   sellers & Publishers; National Federation of
   Booksellers & Publishers; Boersenverein des
   Deutschen Buchhandels.
Subjects: Government, Political Science, History,
   Language Arts, Linguistics, Literature, Literary
   Criticism, Essays, Science (General)
ISBN Prefix(es): 3-924555; 3-86110
Number of titles published annually: 40 Print
Total Titles: 400 Print

**Erich Roeth-Verlag+**
Kastanienweg 4, 39343 Rottmersleben
*Tel:* (039206) 90103 *Fax:* (039206) 90103 *Cable:*
   ROTHVERLAG
*Key Personnel*
Man Dir, Rights & Permissions: Manfred Kaiser
Founded: 1921
Specialize in fairytales.
Subjects: Art, Music, Dance
ISBN Prefix(es): 3-87680
Number of titles published annually: 3 Print; 1
   CD-ROM; 1 Audio

**Rogner und Bernhard GmbH & Co Verlags KG+**
Ferdinand-Porsche-Str 37-39, 60386 Frankfurt
*Tel:* (069) 420 8000 *Fax:* (069) 420 800 198
*E-mail:* service@zweitausendeins.de
*Web Site:* www.zweitausendeins.de
*Key Personnel*
Manager: Jarchow Klaas *E-mail:* jarchow@
rogner-bernhard.de; Antje Landshoff
*E-mail:* jarchow@rogner-bernhard.de
Assistant to the Editor: Marlies Hebler
Founded: 1968
Specialize in popular culture.
Subjects: Art, Fiction, Photography
ISBN Prefix(es): 3-8077; 3-920802
Total Titles: 100 Print
*Orders to:* Zweitausendeins Versand
*Tel:* (069) 4208000 *Fax:* (069) 420800198
*E-mail:* service@zweitausendeins.de

**Verlag und Buchversand Wolfgang Roller**
Goethestr 15, 63225 Langen
*Tel:* (06103) 71886 *Fax:* (06103) 929501
*E-mail:* verlag-roller@t-online.de
*Web Site:* www.verlag-roller.de
ISBN Prefix(es): 3-923620

**Rombach GmbH Druck und Verlagshaus & Co+**
Unterwerkstr 5, 79115 Freiburg
*Tel:* (0761) 4500 0 *Fax:* (0761) 4500 2125
*E-mail:* info@buchverlag.rombach.de
*Web Site:* www.rombach.de
*Key Personnel*
Man Dirs: Dr Christian H Hodeige
Management: Andreas Hodeige
Dir: Willi Mandery
International Rights: Dr Edelgard Spaude
*E-mail:* spaude@buchverlag.rombach.de
Sales: Melanie Panzer *Tel:* (0761) 4500-2135
*E-mail:* panzer@buchverlag.rombach.de
Founded: 1936
Subjects: Art, Government, Political Science, History, Literature, Literary Criticism, Essays, Regional Interests, Social Sciences, Sociology
ISBN Prefix(es): 3-7930
*Associate Companies:* Rombach Druckhaus KG, Bertoldstr 10, 79098 Freiburg; Rombach Handelshaus KG, Bertoldstr 10, 79098 Freiburg; Rombach Medienhaus KG, Bertoldstr 10, 79098 Freiburg
*Bookshop(s):* Rombach Buchhandlung, Bertoldstr 10, 79098 Freiburg
*Orders to:* Waltesverlagsauslieferung, Blochmattstr 11, 7843 Herkesheim

**Romiosini Verlag+**
Nordstrabe 11, 38106 Braunschweig
*Tel:* (0531) 336050 *Fax:* (0531) 336049
*E-mail:* romiosini@unisolo.de
*Web Site:* www.unisolo.de/pls/romiosini/griechische_literatur
*Key Personnel*
Publisher: Niki Eideneier
Founded: 1982
Specialize in Greek literature in German translation.
Subjects: Cookery, Fiction, History, Literature, Literary Criticism, Essays, Music, Dance, Poetry, Travel
ISBN Prefix(es): 3-923728; 3-929889
Distributed by PHOIBOS Verlag (Austria); MAM (Cypress); Athener Bookshop AG (Greece); Greek Books Elyki (Switzerland)
*Orders to:* Unisolo/Despina Kazantzidou, Nordohr 11, 38106 Braunschweig *Tel:* (0531) 336050 *Fax:* (0531) 336049 *E-mail:* despina.kazantzidou@unisolo.de *Web Site:* www.unisolo.de/romiosini.htm

**Rosenheimer Verlagshaus GmbH & Co KG+**
Am Stocket 12, 83022 Rosenheim
*Tel:* (08031) 2838 0 *Fax:* (08031) 2838 44
*E-mail:* info@rosenheimer.com
*Web Site:* www.rosenheimer.com *Cable:* ROSENHEIMER VERLAGSHAUS ROSENHEIM
*Key Personnel*
Man Dir: Klaus G Foerg
Chief Editor: Dagmar Becker-Goethel
Sales, Rights, Permissions & Publicity: Bernhard Edlmann
Marketing Manager: Uta Lamp *Tel:* (08031) 2838 60
Sales: Angelika Krichbaumer *Tel:* (08031) 2838 61; Regina Rogger *Tel:* (08031) 2838 61
Founded: 1949
Subjects: Crafts, Games, Hobbies, Fiction, History, Regional Interests
ISBN Prefix(es): 3-475
Total Titles: 200 Print; 30 Audio

**Rossipaul Kommunikation GmbH+**
Menzingerstr 37, 80638 Munich
Mailing Address: Postfach 38 0164, 80614 Munich
*Tel:* (089) 17 91 06 0 *Fax:* (089) 17 91 06 22
*E-mail:* info@rossipaul.de
*Web Site:* www.rossipaul.de
*Key Personnel*
Man Dir, Rights & Permissions: Rainer Rossipaul
Publicity: Ingo Neubert
Founded: 1952
Subjects: Advertising, Career Development, Computer Science, Finance, Health, Nutrition, Language Arts, Linguistics, Law, Management, Nonfiction (General), Outdoor Recreation
ISBN Prefix(es): 3-87686

**Rowohlt Berlin Verlag GmbH**, *imprint of* Rowohlt Verlag GmbH

**Rowohlt Berlin Verlag GmbH+**
Imprint of Rowohlt Verlag GmbH
Kreuzberger Str 30, 10965 Berlin
*Tel:* (030) 2853840 *Fax:* (040) 28538422
*E-mail:* info@rowohlt.de
*Web Site:* www.rowohlt.de
*Key Personnel*
Man Dir: Dr Helmut Daehne; Alexander Fest; Lutz Kettmann
Editorial Dir: Gunnar Schmidt *E-mail:* gunnar.schmidt@rowohlt.de
Rights & Permissions: Kristina Krombholz
Founded: 1990
Specialize in fiction from East & Central Europe; political nonfiction.
Subjects: Fiction, Nonfiction (General)
ISBN Prefix(es): 3-87134
Number of titles published annually: 30 Print
Total Titles: 160 Print

**Rowohlt Taschenbuch Verlag**, *imprint of* Rowohlt Verlag GmbH

**Rowohlt Verlag GmbH+**
Hamburgerstr 17, 21465 Reinbek
*Tel:* (040) 72720 *Fax:* (040) 7272319
*E-mail:* info@rowohlt.de
*Web Site:* www.rowohlt.de
*Key Personnel*
Man Dir: Dr Helmut Daehne; Alexander Fest; Lutz Kettmann
Rights & Permissions: Kristina Krombholz
Contact: Eckhard Kloos *Tel:* (040) 7272214 *E-mail:* eckhard.kloos@rowohlt.de
Founded: 1908
Subjects: Fiction, Nonfiction (General)
ISBN Prefix(es): 3-498; 3-499; 3-8052
Imprints: Kindler Verlag; Rowohlt Berlin Verlag GmbH; Rowohlt Taschenbuch Verlag; Wunderlich Verlag
*U.S. Office(s):* Greenburger New York, 55 Fifth Ave, New York, NY 10003, United States

**Rudi der Bar ist las**, *imprint of* Beerenverlag

**Rudolf Haufe Verlag GmbH & Co KG**
Formerly Haufe Mediengruppe
Hindenburgstr 64, 79102 Freiburg
*Tel:* (0761) 3683-0 *Fax:* (0761) 3683-195
*E-mail:* online@haufe.de
*Web Site:* www.haufe.de
*Key Personnel*
Executive Board: Helmuth Hopfner; Martin Laqua
Chairman: Uwe Renald Mueller
Founded: 1934 (by Rudolf Haufe in Berlin)
Subjects: Business, Education, Law, Information Management, Taxation
Number of titles published annually: 150 Print
*Associate Companies:* Haufe Akademie, Freiburg; Haufe + Kisling Verlag AG, Zurich, Switzerland; Haufe Publishing, Planegg; Haufe Service Center, Freiburg; Intuit Inc (US); LEGIOS, Frankfurt; Lexware, Freiburg; Memento Verlag AG, Freiburg; Mobilecom AG; Openshop AG, Munich; Max Schimmel Verlag, Wuerzburg; Soft-Use, Freiburg; WRS Verlag, Planegg

**Ruetten & Loening Berlin GmbH+**
Neue Promenade 6, 10178 Berlin
Mailing Address: Postfach 193, 10105 Berlin
*Tel:* (030) 283 94 0 *Fax:* (030) 283 94 100
*E-mail:* info@aufbau-verlag.de
*Web Site:* www.aufbau-verlag.de
*Key Personnel*
Program Manager: Rene Strien
Manager: Peter Dempewolf
International Rights: Astrid Poppenhusen *Tel:* (030) 283 94 212 *E-mail:* poppenhusen@aufbau-verlag.de
Contact: Barbara Stang
Rights & Permissions: Kathrin Schulz
Founded: 1844
Subjects: Fiction, Government, Political Science, History, Literature, Literary Criticism, Essays, Mysteries, Poetry, Romance
ISBN Prefix(es): 3-352
Number of titles published annually: 30 Print
Total Titles: 100 Print
*Shipping Address:* Mohr Morawa, Buchvertrieb Gesellschaft mbH, Postfach 260, A-1101 Vienna, Austria; Buecher Balmer, Verlagsauslieferung, Neugasse 12, 6301 Zurich, Switzerland
*Warehouse:* Libri-Distributions GmbH, August-Schanzstr 33, 60433 Frankfurt
*Orders to:* Libri-Distributions GmbH, August-Schanzstr 33, 60433 Frankfurt

**Winfried Ruf**, see Fachmedien Verlag Winfried Ruf (FMV)

**Dieter Ruggeberg Verlagsbuchhandlung+**
Wuppermannstr 28, 42275 Wuppertal
Mailing Address: Postfach 13 08 44, 42035 Wuppertal
*Tel:* (0202) 592811 *Fax:* (0202) 592811
*E-mail:* vrggeberg@aol.com
*Web Site:* www.vbdr.de
*Key Personnel*
Man Dir, Rights & Permissions: Dieter Rueggeberg *E-mail:* vrggeberg@aol.com
Founded: 1968
Subjects: Astrology, Occult, Government, Political Science, Religion - Other
ISBN Prefix(es): 3-921338

**Ruhland Verlag Gimblt**
Berliner Str 2, 63065 Offenbach Am Main
*Tel:* (069) 811768 *Fax:* (069) 811769
*Key Personnel*
Man Dir, Publicity, Rights & Permissions: Margitta Kieltsch-weidl
Founded: 1968

Subjects: Business, Management
ISBN Prefix(es): 3-88509; 3-920793

**Verlag an der Ruhr GmbH+**
Alexanderstr 54, 45472 Muelheim an der Ruhr
Mailing Address: Postfach 102251, 45422 Muel-
heim
*Tel:* (0208) 4395454 *Fax:* (0208) 4395439
*E-mail:* info@verlagruhr.de
*Web Site:* www.verlagruhr.de
*Key Personnel*
Man Dir & Publisher: Wilfried Stascheit
Man Dir: Annelie Loeber-Stascheit
Founded: 1981
Books & worksheets for pedagogical & educa-
tional work in school & extracurricular work.
Unconventional methods, innovative contents &
topical themes.
Membership(s): German Booksellers Association.
Subjects: Art, Communications, Developing
Countries, Education, English as a Second Lan-
guage, Environmental Studies, Geography, Ge-
ology, History, Human Relations, Literature,
Literary Criticism, Essays, Mathematics, Phi-
losophy, Physical Sciences, Religion - Other
ISBN Prefix(es): 3-86072; 3-927279; 3-924884
Total Titles: 500 Print
Distributed by Schulverlag blmv AG; Veritas
*Orders to:* Paedexpress GmbH & Co KG
*Tel:* (0208) 495040 *Fax:* (0208) 4950495
*E-mail:* info@paedexpress.de

**RV**, see Mairs Geographischer Verlag, Kurt Mair
GmbH & Co

**RV Reise- und Verkehrsverlag**, see Mairs
Geographischer Verlag, Kurt Mair GmbH & Co

**RVBG**, see RVBG Rheinland-Verlag-und
Betriebsgesellschaft des Landschaftsverbandes
Rheinland mbH

**Reinhard Ryborsch**, see Kartographischer Verlag
Reinhard Ryborsch

**Ryvellus**, *imprint of* Neue Erde Verlags GmbH

**Ryvellus Medienagentur Dopfer+**
Cecilienstr 29, 66111 Saarbrueken
*Tel:* (0681) 372313 *Fax:* (0681) 3904102
*Key Personnel*
Manager: Manfred Dopfer
Founded: 1989
Subjects: Environmental Studies, Health, Nutri-
tion, Nonfiction (General), Psychology, Psychi-
atry, Body, Mind & Spirit, Esoterics/New Age,
Popular, Non-Fiction
ISBN Prefix(es): 3-89453

**Saarbrucker Druckerei und Verlag GmbH
(SDV)**
Halbergstr 3, 66121 Saarbruecken
Mailing Address: Postfach 102745, 66027 Saar-
bruecken
*Tel:* (0681) 66501-0 *Fax:* (0681) 66501-10
*Web Site:* www.sdv-saar.de
*Key Personnel*
Man Dir & Editorial: Olanfred Wagner
Sales Manager: Corinne Wuest *E-mail:* cwuest@
sdv-saar.de
Founded: 1922
Subjects: Antiques, Archaeology, Art, History,
Language Arts, Linguistics, Literature
ISBN Prefix(es): 3-921646; 3-925036; 3-930843

**Saatkorn-Verlag GmbH**
Luener Rennbahn 14, 21339 Lueneburg
*Tel:* (04131) 98 35-02 *Fax:* (04131) 98 35 505
*E-mail:* info@saatkornverlag.de
*Web Site:* wwww.saatkorn-verlag.de

*Key Personnel*
Man Dir: Eckhard Boettge *E-mail:* boettge@
saatkorn-verlag.de
Editorial, Rights & Permissions Secretary: Eli
Diez
Sales: Erhard Knirr
Printing Works: Peter Streit
Founded: 1895
Subjects: Health, Nutrition, Theology
ISBN Prefix(es): 3-8150; 3-87689
Subsidiaries: Grindeldruck GmbH
*Warehouse:* Auf dem Salzstock 11, 21217
Seevetal-Meckelfeld

**Verlag Werner Sachon GmbH & Co**
Schloss Mindelburg, 87714 Mindelheim
*Tel:* (08261) 999-0 *Fax:* (08261) 999 391
*E-mail:* info@sachon.de
*Web Site:* www.sachon.de
*Telex:* 539624
*Key Personnel*
Contact: Wolfgang Burkart; Werner Sachon
Subjects: Engineering (General), Health, Nutri-
tion, Management, Marketing, Mechanical En-
gineering, Wine & Spirits
ISBN Prefix(es): 3-920819; 3-929032

**Sachsenbuch Verlagsgesellschaft Mbh**
Bruehl 76, 04109 Leipzig
*Tel:* (0341) 9784259; (0341) 9784261 *Fax:* (0341)
9784259
*Key Personnel*
Manager: Wolf-Diethelm Zastrutzki
Editor: Klaus Hoerhold
Public Relations: W U Schuette
Founded: 1990
Membership(s): Stock Exchange of German
Booksellers.
Subjects: Art, Regional Interests
ISBN Prefix(es): 3-910148; 3-89664
*Branch Office(s)*
Neuer Sachsenverlag Leipzig, Coppistr 36, 04157
Leipzig
*Bookshop(s):* Neue Leipzigerstr 16, 04205
Leipzig; Schwarzackerstr, 04229 Leipzig
*Shipping Address:* Buchhandlung Sachsenbuch,
Bruhl 76, Postfach 461, 04109 Leipzig

**Verlag Otto Sagner**
Subsidiary of Kubon & Sagner Buchexport-
Import GmbH
Hessstr 39/41, 80798 Munich
*Tel:* (089) 54 218-0 *Fax:* (089) 54 218-218
*E-mail:* postmaster@kubon-sagner.de
*Web Site:* www.kubon-sagner.de
*Key Personnel*
Man Dir: Petrols Sagner; Sabine Sagner-Weigl
*E-mail:* sabine.sagnerweigl@kubon-sagner.de
Publisher: Otto Sagner
Editorial: Prof Peter Rehder, PhD
Founded: 1947
Book export import publishing company.
Subjects: Language Arts, Linguistics, Literature,
Literary Criticism, Essays
ISBN Prefix(es): 3-87690

**Sammlung**, *imprint of* Bund demokratischer
Wissenschaftlerinnen und Wissenschafler eV
(BdWi)

**SAMS**, *imprint of* Pearson Education Deutschland
GmbH

**Verlag der Sankt-Johannis-Druckerei C
Schweickhardt+**
Heiligenstr 24, 77933 Lahr
*Tel:* (07821) 5810 *Fax:* (07821) 58126
*E-mail:* johannis-druck@t-online.de
*Web Site:* www.johannis-verlag.de *Cable:*
VERITAS LAHR SCHWARZWALD

*Key Personnel*
Man Dir: Walter Guthmann
Editorial, Publicity, Rights & Permissions: Dr
Thomas Baumann
Sales: Karl Heinz Kern
Production: Helmut Schlegel
Founded: 1896
Membership(s): the Telos Group Publishing Evan-
gelical Paperbacks.
Subjects: Art, Biography, Fiction, Religion -
Protestant
ISBN Prefix(es): 3-501
*Associate Companies:* Edition VLM; SKV-Edition
Distributed by BMK Verlagsauslieferung (Aus-
tria); Brunnen Verlag (Switzerland)

**Sassafras Verlag**
Dreikoenigenstr 146, 47798 Krefeld
*Tel:* (02151) 787770 *Fax:* (02151) 771302
*Key Personnel*
Man Dir, International Rights: Klaus Ulrich Dues-
selberg
Founded: 1975
Subjects: Literature, Literary Criticism, Essays,
Poetry
ISBN Prefix(es): 3-922690

**I H Sauer Verlag GmbH+**
Hausserstr 14, 69115 Heidelberg
Mailing Address: Postfach 105960, 69049 Heidel-
berg
*Tel:* (06221) 9060 *Fax:* (06221) 906259
*E-mail:* sauer-verlag@ruw.de
*Web Site:* www.ruw-ruw.de
*Telex:* 461665rewhihd
*Key Personnel*
Man Dir: Michael Giesecke
Publisher: Angelika Sauer
Contact: Norbert Konda
Founded: 1964
Subjects: Career Development, Communications,
Economics, Labor, Industrial Relations, Man-
agement, Marketing, Psychology, Psychiatry
ISBN Prefix(es): 3-7938
*Associate Companies:* Verlag Recht und
Wirtschaft GmbH

**Verlag Sauerlaender GmbH+**
Am Wehrhahn 100, 40211 Duesseldorf
Mailing Address: Postfach 630247, 60352 Frank-
furt
*Tel:* (0211) 16795-0 *Fax:* (0211) 16795-75
*Key Personnel*
Publisher: Hans C Sauerlaender
Founded: 1807
Subjects: Fiction, Science (General)
ISBN Prefix(es): 3-7941
*Parent Company:* Sauerlaender AG, 5001 Aarau,
Switzerland
*Associate Companies:* Verlag Sauerlaender,
Muenzgasse 1, A-5020 Salzburg, Austria
*Showroom(s):* Infortiationsstelle Schlilbuch, Lau-
rentenvorstadt 85, 5001 Arau
*Orders to:* Sauerlander AG, Laurentenvorstadt 89,
5001 Karan, Switzerland *Tel:* (062) 836 8686
*Fax:* (062) 836 8620

**J D Sauerlaender's Verlag+**
Finkenhofstr 21, 60322 Frankfurt
*Tel:* (069) 555217 *Fax:* (069) 5964344
*E-mail:* j.d.sauerlaenders.verlag@t-online.de
*Web Site:* www.sauerlaender-verlag.com
*Key Personnel*
Publisher: Stephanie Aulbach
Founded: 1816
Specialize in forest genetics.
Subjects: Agriculture, Language Arts, Linguistics
ISBN Prefix(es): 3-7939
Number of titles published annually: 6 Print

**K G Saur Verlag GmbH, A Gale/Thomson
Learning Company+**
Unit of Thomson Learning

Ortlerstr 8, 81373 Munich
Mailing Address: Postfach 70 16 20, 81316 Munich
*Tel:* (089) 76902-0 *Fax:* (089) 76902-150
*E-mail:* saur.info@thomson.com
*Web Site:* www.saur.de
*Key Personnel*
Man Dir: Prof Dr h c mult Klaus G Saur
   *E-mail:* K.Saur@saur.de
Sales Dir: Paul Fertl *E-mail:* P.Fertl@saur.de
Promotion & Press Service: Petra Huetter
   *E-mail:* P.Huetter@saur.de
Production Dir: Manfred Link *E-mail:* M.Link@
   saur.de
Publishing Dir: Clara Waldrich *E-mail:* C.
   Waldrich@saur.de
Commercial Dir: Christoph Hahne *E-mail:* C.
   Hahne@saur.de
Rights & Permissions: Christina Hofmann
   *E-mail:* C.Hofmann@saur.de
Editorial Dir: Barbara Fischer *E-mail:* b.fischer@
   saur.de
Founded: 1949
Subjects: Art, Biography, Communications, History, Library & Information Sciences, Literature, Literary Criticism, Essays, Music, Dance, Philosophy, Publishing & Book Trade Reference, Social Sciences, Sociology
ISBN Prefix(es): 3-598; 3-7940; 3-907820; 3-908255; 2-86294
Total Titles: 2,500 Print; 100 CD-ROM; 6 E-Book
*Parent Company:* Gale
*Ultimate Parent Company:* The Thomson Corporation

**Sax-Verlag Beucha**
An der Halde 12, 04824 Beucha
*Tel:* (034292) 75210 *Fax:* (034292) 75220
*E-mail:* info@sax-verlag.de
*Web Site:* www.sax-verlag.de
*Key Personnel*
Contact: Erika Heydick
Founded: 1992
Subjects: Biography, Education, History, Nonfiction (General), Regional Interests, Science (General), Social Sciences, Sociology
ISBN Prefix(es): 3-930076; 3-934544; 3-9802997
Number of titles published annually: 15 Print
Total Titles: 100 Print

**scaneg Verlag**
Heiglhofstr 24, 81377 Munich
Mailing Address: Postfach 701606, 81316 Munich
*Tel:* (089) 759 33 36 *Fax:* (089) 759 39 14
*E-mail:* verlag@scaneg.de
*Web Site:* www.scaneg.de
Founded: 1983
Subjects: Art, History, Literature, Literary Criticism, Essays, Poetry, Art History
ISBN Prefix(es): 3-89235; 3-9800671

**Verlag Th Schaefer im Vicentz Verlag KG**
Stockholmer Allee 5, 30539 Hannover
Mailing Address: Postfach 721306, 30533 Hannover
*Tel:* (0511) 87575-075 *Fax:* (0511) 87575-079
*Key Personnel*
Publisher: Werner Geisselbrecht
Founded: 1980
Specialize in reprints of professional books.
Subjects: Architecture & Interior Design, Art, Crafts, Games, Hobbies, House & Home
ISBN Prefix(es): 3-88746
*Parent Company:* Th Schaefer Verlag im Vincentz Verlag KG
*Orders to:* Vincentz Verlag KG, Postfach 6247, 30062 Hannover *Tel:* (0511) 9910-012 *Fax:* (0511) 9910-013 *Web Site:* www.libri_rari. de

**Verlag Anke Schaefer**
Ortsstr 43, 56379 Charlottenberg bei Holzappel, Rhein-Lahn-K
*Tel:* (06439) 7870
*Key Personnel*
Owner: Anke Schaefer
Founded: 1978
Subjects: Gay & Lesbian, Women's Studies
ISBN Prefix(es): 3-922229
Divisions: Feministischer Buchverlag
*Bookshop(s):* Frauenbuchversand, Luxemburgstr 2, 65185 Wiesbaden

**Schaeffer-Poeschel Verlag fuer Wirtschaft Steuern Recht+**
Werastr 21-23, 70182 Stuttgart
Mailing Address: Postfach 10 32 41, 70028 Stuttgart
*Tel:* (0711) 2194-0 *Fax:* (0711) 2194-119
*E-mail:* info@schaeffer-poeschel.de
*Web Site:* www.schaeffer-poeschel.de
*Key Personnel*
Man Dir: Michael Justus *E-mail:* justus@ schaeffer-poeschel.de
General Manager: Volker Dabelstein; Marita Rollnik Mollenhauer
Sales Dir: Michael Schmid
Marketing Manager: Michael Schmid
Rights Manager: Andrea Rupp
Advertising: Sabine Zobeley
Press: Joachim Bader
Electronic Publishing: Ursula Chwalisz
Founded: 1902
Subjects: Accounting, Business, Economics, Finance, Management, Marketing
ISBN Prefix(es): 3-7910; 3-8202; 3-7992
Number of titles published annually: 200 Print
Total Titles: 800 Print
*Parent Company:* Verlagsgruppe Handelsblatt
*Ultimate Parent Company:* Verlagsgruppe Georg Von Holtzbrinck

**Schangrila Verlags und Vertriebs GmbH+**
Lindenstr 45, 87648 Aitrang
*Tel:* (08343) 581 *Fax:* (08343) 657
*E-mail:* info@schangrila.com
*Web Site:* www.schangrila.com
Founded: 1984
Subjects: Cookery, Medicine, Nursing, Dentistry, Philosophy
ISBN Prefix(es): 3-924624

**Schapen Edition, H W Louis+**
Gartenweg 6b, 38104 Braunschweig
*Tel:* (0531) 360921 *Fax:* (0531) 363190
*E-mail:* schapen.edition@t-online.de
*Key Personnel*
International Rights: Dr Hans Walter Louis
Founded: 1990
Subjects: Environmental Studies, Law
ISBN Prefix(es): 3-927942

**M & H Schaper GmbH & Co KG+**
Borsigstr 5, 31061 Alfeld-Leine
Mailing Address: Postfach 1642, 31046 Alfeld-Leine
*Tel:* (05181) 8009-0 *Fax:* (05181) 8009-33
*E-mail:* info@schaper-verlag.de
*Web Site:* www.schaper-verlag.de
*Key Personnel*
International Rights: Wolfgang Habeck
Marketing Manager: Dieter Meyer *Tel:* (05181) 8009-40 *E-mail:* d.meyer@schaper-verlag. de; Rainer Paland *Tel:* (05181) 8009-14 *E-mail:* info@schaper-verlag.de
Sales Manager: Carsten Sadlau *Tel:* (05181) 8009-16 *E-mail:* c.sadlau@schaper-verlag.de
Founded: 1897
Subjects: Animals, Pets, Crafts, Games, Hobbies, Veterinary Science
ISBN Prefix(es): 3-7944

**Schattauer GmbH Verlag fuer Medizin und Naturwissenschaften+**
Hoelderlinstr 3, 70174 Stuttgart
*Tel:* (0711) 2 29 87-0 *Fax:* (0711) 2 29 87-50
*E-mail:* info@schattauer.de
*Web Site:* www.schattauer.de
*Key Personnel*
Man Dir: Dieter Bergemann
Founded: 1949
Publishing house for medicine & natural sciences.
Subjects: Medicine, Nursing, Dentistry, Science (General)
ISBN Prefix(es): 3-7945
*Shipping Address:* Koch, Neff & Oetinger & Co Verlagsauslieferungen, Schockenriedstr 39, 70565 Stuttgart *Tel:* (0711) 78603365
*Warehouse:* Koch, Neff & Oetinger & Co Verlagsauslieferungen, Schockenriedstr 39, 70565 Stuttgart *Tel:* (0711) 78603365
*Orders to:* D A Book Depot Pty Ltd, 648 Whitehorse Rd, Mitcham, Victoria 3132, Australia *Tel:* (03) 873 4411 *Fax:* (03) 873 5679
Mohr-Morawa Gesellschaft mbH, Sulzengasse 2, 1232 Vienna, Austria *Tel:* (0222) 684614 *Fax:* (0222) 687130
Allied Publishers Pvt Ltd, 13/14 Asaf Ali Rd, PO Box 155, New Delhi 110002, India *Tel:* 2750001
Verlag Hans Huber AG, Langgassstr 76, 3000 Bern 9, Switzerland *Tel:* (031) 262533 *Fax:* (031) 43380
John Wiley & Sons Inc, Wiley-Liss Division, 111 River St, Hoboken, NJ 07030, United States *Tel:* 201-748-6000 *Fax:* 201-748-6088

**Verlag Heinrich Scheffler**, *imprint of* Societaets-Verlag

**Scheffler-Verlag+**
Goethestr 26, 58313 Herdecke
Mailing Address: Postfach 1449, 58304 Herdecke
*Tel:* (02330) 1743 *Fax:* (02330) 2281
*Key Personnel*
President: Lothor Scheffler
Vice President: Barbel Scheffler
Founded: 1989
ISBN Prefix(es): 3-89704; 3-9802922; 3-9803249; 3-929885
Total Titles: 15 Print

**Schelzky & Jeep, Verlag fuer Reisen und Wissen+**
Fidicinstr 29, 10965 Berlin
*Tel:* (030) 6939495 *Fax:* (030) 6914697
*E-mail:* schelzky.jeep@t-online.de
Founded: 1981
Subjects: Architecture & Interior Design, Regional Interests, Social Sciences, Sociology, Travel
ISBN Prefix(es): 3-89541; 3-923024

**Renate Schenk Verlag+**
Heinkstr 10, 04347 Leipzig
*Tel:* (0341) 2300825 *Fax:* (0341) 2300826
*E-mail:* schenk-verlag@t-online.de
*Web Site:* www.schenk-verlag.de
Founded: 1984
Membership(s): Australian Book Publishers Association (ABPA). Specialize in books about Australia, Australian Books, Antiquariat Aboroginal Art.
Subjects: Anthropology, Earth Sciences, Natural History, Travel
ISBN Prefix(es): 3-924759
Divisions: Winjeel Shop Alice Springs Australia
Distributor for Magabala (Lansdown); Reader's Digest (Australia); Reed Books (Australia)
*Bookshop(s):* Koala Trade
*Orders to:* Geo Center Touristik Medien Service GmbH, Schockenriedstr 44, 70565 Stuttgart, Contact: Cornelia Braun *Tel:* (0711) 781946-41143 *Fax:* (0711) 781946-56

**Richard Scherpe Verlag GmbH**
Glockenspitz 140, 47800 Krefeld
Mailing Address: Postfach 2630, 47726 Krefeld
*Tel:* (02151) 539-0 *Fax:* (02151) 505390
*E-mail:* info@scherpe.de
*Web Site:* www.scherpe.de
*Key Personnel*
Owner: Richard Scherpe
International Rights: Mrs Wendt
Subjects: Education, Fiction, Government, Political Science
ISBN Prefix(es): 3-7948

**Ulrich Schiefer bahn Verlag+**
Fuerstenriederstr 44, 80686 Munich
Mailing Address: Postfach 210620, 80676 Munich
*Tel:* (089) 89020999 *Fax:* (089) 89020087
*Key Personnel*
Owner: Ulrich Schiefer
Founded: 1985
Subjects: Crafts, Games, Hobbies, Film, Video, Transportation
ISBN Prefix(es): 3-924969

**Schiffahrts-Verlag**
Striepenweg 31, 21147 Hamburg
Mailing Address: PO Box 920655, 21147 Hamburg
*Tel:* (040) 79713-02 *Fax:* (040) 79713-324; (040) 79713-208; (040) 79713-214
*Web Site:* www.hansa-online.de
*Key Personnel*
Senior Editor: Claus Wilde *E-mail:* c_wilde@hansa-online.de
Specialize in shipbuilding & ship technology, shipping.
ISBN Prefix(es): 3-87700
Number of titles published annually: 2 Print
Total Titles: 20 Print

**Schild-Verlag GmbH+**
Henschelstr 7, 81249 Munich
*Tel:* (089) 8 64 1189 *Fax:* (089) 8 63 2310
*Key Personnel*
Man Dir: Gunther Damerau
Founded: 1951
Subjects: Antiques, History, Literature, Literary Criticism, Essays, Military Science
ISBN Prefix(es): 3-88014
Total Titles: 35 Print

**Verlag der Schillerbuchhandlung Hans Banger OHG**
Guldenbachstr 1, 50935 Cologne
*Tel:* (0221) 46014-0 *Fax:* (0221) 46014-25; (0221) 46014-26
*E-mail:* banger@banger.de
*Web Site:* www.banger.de
*Key Personnel*
Man Dir: Ruth Jepsen; Elisabeth Mueller
Founded: 1950
ISBN Prefix(es): 3-87856

**Schillinger Verlag GmbH+**
Wallstr 14, 79098 Freiburg
Mailing Address: Postfach 1502, 79015 Freiburg
*Tel:* (0761) 33233 *Fax:* (0762) 39055
*E-mail:* schillingerverlag@t-online.de
*Web Site:* schillingerverlag.de
*Key Personnel*
Man Dir: Helga Schillinger; Wolfgang Schillinger
Founded: 1984
Membership(s): the Stock Exchange of German Booksellers.
Subjects: Art, Asian Studies, Environmental Studies, Fiction, Foreign Countries, History, Regional Interests, Travel
ISBN Prefix(es): 3-89155
Number of titles published annually: 15 Print
Total Titles: 214 Print

**Schirmer/Mosel Verlag GmbH+**
Widenmayerstr 16, 80538 Munich
Mailing Address: Postfach 221641, 80506 Munich
*Tel:* (089) 2126700 *Fax:* (089) 338695
*E-mail:* mail@schirmer-mosel.com
*Web Site:* www.schirmer-mosel.com
*Key Personnel*
Executive Dir: Lothar Schirmer
Production: Roland Hepp
International Rights: Dr Franz Ringel
Founded: 1975
Specialize in Collector's Editions.
Subjects: Art, Photography
ISBN Prefix(es): 3-88814; 3-8296; 3-921375
*U.S. Office(s):* PO Box 457, New York, NY 10012, United States, US Representative: Phillip Galgiani

**Schirner Verlag+**
Zerninstr 7, 64297 Darmstadt
*Tel:* (06151) 29 39 59 *Fax:* (06151) 29 39 87
*E-mail:* verlag@schirner.com
*Web Site:* www.schirner.com
*Key Personnel*
Man Dir: Kirsten Glueck *Tel:* (06151) 29 39 52; Markus Schirner
Bookkeeper: Erika Furbush *Tel:* (06151) 29 33 69
Contact: Gabriele Olschok; Uta Wagner
Founded: 1994
Subjects: Buddhist , Ethno-dictionaries, Mandala Painting Books, Practical Workbooks & Spiritual Self-Help
ISBN Prefix(es): 3-930944; 3-89767
Total Titles: 300 Print; 35 Audio
Foreign Rep(s): Dessauer (Switzerland); Hartmut Gindler Verlagsvertretur (Germany); Verlagsvertretung Klaus-Dieter Guhl (Germany); Verlagsvertretur Mareile & Peter Handrich (Germany); AS Hoeller Gmbh (Austria); Verlagsvertretung Martina & Detief Jessen (Germany); Verlagsagentur Reinhard Lieber (Germany); Handelsvertretung Hannelore Lindemann (Germany); Verlagsvertretung Herbert Pamminger (Austria); Walter Stolte Verlagsvertretung mH Herz (Germany)
Foreign Rights: Daniel Doglioli (Italy); Peter Schmidt Media Service International (France, Spain)

**Agora Verlag Manfred Schlosser+**
Grunewaldstr 53, 10825 Berlin
*Tel:* (030) 8545372; (030) 8545915 *Fax:* (030) 8545372
*E-mail:* agora2@gmx.net *Cable:* AGORA BERLIN
*Key Personnel*
Man Dir, Production: Manfred Schloesser
Sales & Publicity: Monika Schloesser-Fischer
Founded: 1960
Subjects: Fiction, Literature, Literary Criticism, Essays, Music, Dance, Poetry, Religion - Jewish
ISBN Prefix(es): 3-87008
Total Titles: 140 Print
Subsidiaries: Erato-Presse
*Orders to:* Bugrim Saalburgstr 3, 712099 Berlin

**Schmetterling Verlag Jorg Hunger und Paul Sander+**
Lindenspuerstr 38B, 70176 Stuttgart
*Tel:* (0711) 62 67 79 *Fax:* (0711) 62 69 92
*E-mail:* info@schmetterling-verlag.de
*Web Site:* www.schmetterling-verlag.de
*Key Personnel*
Production: Paul Sander
Public Speaker: Joerg Hunger
Contact: Joerg Exner
Subjects: Culture, Politics
ISBN Prefix(es): 3-926369; 3-89657

**Schmid Verlag GmbH**
Hedwigstr 13b, 93049 Regensburg
*Tel:* (0941) 21519 *Fax:* (0941) 28766
*E-mail:* info@schmid-verlag.de
*Web Site:* www.schmid-verlag.de
*Key Personnel*
Owner: Irmigard Schmid
Founded: 1947
Subjects: Travel
ISBN Prefix(es): 3-930572; 3-921657
*Branch Office(s)*
Karl-Wurmbstr 3, 5020 Salzburg, Austria

**Schmidmusic**, *imprint of* Silberburg-Verlag Titus Haeussermann GmbH

**Verlag Dr Otto Schmidt KG+**
Unter den Ulmen 96-98, 50968 Cologne (Marienburg)
*Tel:* (0221) 9 37 38-01 *Fax:* (0221) 9 37 38 00
*E-mail:* info@otto-schmidt.de
*Web Site:* www.otto-schmidt.de
*Telex:* 8883381 osvd *Cable:* SCHMIDTVERLAG
*Key Personnel*
Man Dir: K P Winters
Editorial: Dr Katherine Knauth
Sales, Publicity & Advertising: Michael Rieck
Organization, Financial: Arno Harms
Founded: 1905
Subjects: Business, Finance, Law
ISBN Prefix(es): 3-504
*Associate Companies:* Centrale fur GmbH Dr Otto Schmidt
Subsidiaries: Anwalt-Suchservice GmbH; Centrale fur Verbaende und Vereine Verlag Dr Otto Schmidt GmbH
*Branch Office(s)*
Haus Bayenthalguertel, Bayenthalguertel 13, 50968 Cologne (Marienburg)
Buerocenter Bonnerstr 484-486, 50968 Cologne (Marienburg)
*Bookshop(s):* Friedrich-Verlegerstr 7, 33602 Bielefeld; Am Yustizzentrum 3, 50939 Cologne 47; Buchhandlung Hermann Sack, Klosterstr 22, 40211 Duesseldorf; Buchhandlung Hermann Sack, Guenthersburgallee 1, 60316 Frankfurt am Main; Harkortstr 7, 04107 Leipzig; Struppe u Winckler, Postfach 10 24 91, 33527 Bielefeld
*Distribution Center:* Kirschbaumweg 18a, 50966 Cologne (Rodenkirchen)

**Erich Schmidt Verlag GmbH & Co**
Genthiner Str 30 G, 10785 Berlin
Mailing Address: Postfach 304240, 10724 Berlin
*Tel:* (030) 25 00 85-0 *Fax:* (030) 25 00 85-305
*E-mail:* esv@esvmedien.de
*Web Site:* www.erich-schmidt-verlag.de
*Key Personnel*
Man Dir: Claus-Michael Rast *E-mail:* c.rast@esvmedien.de; Dr Joachim Schmidt *E-mail:* j.schmidt@esvmedien.de
Sales Manager: Sibylle Boehler *E-mail:* s.boehler@esvmedian.de
Founded: 1924
Subjects: Accounting, Business, Finance, Law, Philological Topics
ISBN Prefix(es): 3-503; 3-89161
Number of titles published annually: 220 Print

**Verlag Hermann Schmidt Universitatsdruckerei GmbH & Co+**
Robert Kochstr 8, 55129 Mainz-Hechtsheim (Gewerbegebiet)
Mailing Address: Postfach 105020, 55136 Mainz
*Tel:* (06131) 506030 *Fax:* (06131) 506080
*E-mail:* info@typografie.de
*Web Site:* www.typografie.de
*Key Personnel*
Contact: Karin Schmidt-Friderichs *Tel:* (06131) 506029 *E-mail:* ksf@typografie.de
Founded: 1950
Specialize in typography & design.

Subjects: Art
ISBN Prefix(es): 3-87439
*Orders to:* Verlag Hermann Schmidt Mainz,
Luisenstr 6, 55124 Mainz

**Schmidt Periodicals GmbH**
Dettendorf Romerring 12, 83075 Bad Feilnbach
*Tel:* (08064) 221 *Fax:* (08064) 557
*E-mail:* schmidt@periodicals.com
*Web Site:* www.periodicals.com
*Key Personnel*
Dir: Gerhard Schmidt
Sales & Marketing: Victoria Smith *Tel:* (0034)
921 412194 *Fax:* (0034) 921 412625
*E-mail:* vsmith@periodicals.com
Founded: 1962
Specialize in back sets, volumes & issues of pe-
riodicals, serials & reference works in all sub-
jects & languages.
Subjects: Science (General), Medical, Technical
Total Titles: 9,999 Print
*U.S. Office(s):* Periodicals Service Company, 11
Main St, Germantown, NY 12526, United
States, Contact: James Curran *Tel:* 518-
537-4700 *Fax:* 518-537-5899 *E-mail:* psc@
periodicals.com

**Max Schmidt-Roemhild Verlag+**
Mengstr 16, 23552 Luebeck
*Tel:* (0451) 70 31-01 *Fax:* (0451) 70 31-253
*E-mail:* msr-luebeck@t-online.de
*Web Site:* www.schmidt-roemhild.de
*Key Personnel*
Publisher: Norbert Beleke
Man Dir, Rights & Permissions: Hans-Juergen
Sperling
Editorship: Dr Edwin Kube *Tel:* (0228) 28044-40
*Fax:* (0228) 28044-41 *E-mail:* kube@forum-
kriminalpraevention.de
Layout: Peter Koesling *Tel:* (0201) 8130-200
*Fax:* (0201) 8130-196
Contact: Dr M Platzkoester
Founded: 1579
Subjects: Criminology, History, Law, Medicine,
Nursing, Dentistry, Regional Interests, Social
Sciences, Sociology, Sports, Athletics
ISBN Prefix(es): 3-7950; 3-8016
*Associate Companies:* Schmidt-Roemhild
Verlagsgesellschaft mbH Brandenburg,
August-Bebelstr 23-27, 14470 Brandenburg
*Tel:* (03381) 3693-0
Subsidiaries: Hansisches Verlags Kontor
*Branch Office(s)*
Schmidt-Roemhild Verlagsgesellschaft mbH
Leipzig, Coppistr 2, 04129 Leipzig *Tel:* (0341)
90 48 50
Schmidt-Roemhild Verlagsgesellschaft mbH Ros-
tock, Platz der Freundschaft 1, 18059 Rostock
*Tel:* (0381) 44 84 55
Schmidt-Roemhild Verlagsgesellschaft mbH
Schwerin, Graf-Schack-Allee 6, 19053 Schw-
erin *Tel:* (0385) 5 91 88-0
Verlag fur Polizeiliches Fachschrifttum Georg
Schmidt- Roemhild, Mengstr 16, 23552 Lue-
beck

**Wilhelm Schmitz Verlag+**
Am Weidacker 12, 35435 Wettenberg-Launsbach
*Tel:* (0641) 877 3939
*E-mail:* kontakt@wilhelm-schmitz-verlag.de
*Web Site:* www.wilhelm-schmitz-verlag.de
*Key Personnel*
Man Dir, Rights & Permissions: Siegfried
Schmitz
Founded: 1847
Subjects: Art, Ethnicity, Foreign Countries, Lan-
guage Arts, Linguistics, Literature, Literary
Criticism, Essays, Medicine, Nursing, Dentistry
ISBN Prefix(es): 3-87711

**Schneekluth Verlag+**
Hilblestr 54, 80636 Munich

*Tel:* (089) 9271-0 *Fax:* (089) 9271-168
*Web Site:* www.schneekluth.de
*Key Personnel*
Man Dir: Ralf Mueller; Christian Tesch; Dr Hans-
Peter Uebleis
Founded: 1949
ISBN Prefix(es): 3-7951
Number of titles published annually: 30 Print
*Parent Company:* Verlagsgruppe Droemer Knaur

**Rudolf Schneider Verlag**, see Wolf Schneider

**Wolf Schneider+**
Formerly Rudolf Schneider Verlag
Luitpoldstr 16, 91781 Weissenburg
*Tel:* (089) 8113466 *Fax:* (089) 8110619
*Key Personnel*
Publisher & Man Dir: Karl-Heinz Biebl
Founded: 1926
Divisions: Edition Hohenstaufen

**Verlag Schnell und Steiner GmbH+**
Leibnizstr 13, 93055 Regensburg
Mailing Address: Postfach 200429, 93063 Re-
gensburg
*Tel:* (0941) 787850 *Fax:* (0941) 7878516
*E-mail:* susvertrieb@t-online.de *Cable:*
SCHNELLSTEINER REGENSBURG
*Key Personnel*
Publisher: Conrad Lienhardt
Sales & Marketing: Rainer Boos; Christian Pflug
Founded: 1934
Subjects: Archaeology, Art, Biblical Studies,
Biography, History, Music, Dance, Religion
- Catholic, Religion - Protestant, Theology,
Travel
ISBN Prefix(es): 3-7954
Number of titles published annually: 45 Print
Total Titles: 3,500 Print
Imprints: Zodiaque
Distributed by Rex Verlag (Switzerland)

**Schnitzer GmbH & Co KG+**
Feldbergstr 11, 78112 St Georgen
*Tel:* (07724) 9432-0 *Fax:* (07724) 9432-20
Founded: 1966
Subjects: Health, Nutrition
ISBN Prefix(es): 3-922894; 3-921123

**Schoeffling & Co+**
Kaiserstr 79, 60329 Frankfurt am Main
*Tel:* (069) 92 07 87-0 *Fax:* (069) 92 07 87-20
*E-mail:* info@schoeffling.de
*Web Site:* www.schoeffling.de
*Key Personnel*
Publisher: Klaus Schoeffling
Publicity, Editorial: Ida Schoeffling
Rights & Permissions, International Rights:
Kathrin Scheel
Founded: 1993
Subjects: Biography, Fiction, Literature, Literary
Criticism, Essays, Travel
ISBN Prefix(es): 3-89561
Number of titles published annually: 30 Print

**Verlag Hans Schoener GmbH+**
Walther-Rathenaustr 13, 75203 Koenigsbach-Stein
Mailing Address: Postfach 69, 75197
Koenigsbach-Stein
*Tel:* (07232) 4007-0 *Fax:* (07232) 4007-99
*E-mail:* info@verlag-schoener.de
*Web Site:* www.verlag-schoener.de
*Key Personnel*
Man Dir: Elke Schoener *Tel:* (07232) 40 07-20
*E-mail:* es@verlag-schoener.de; Jourg Schoener
*Tel:* (07232) 40 07-11 *E-mail:* js@verlag-
schoener.de
Founded: 1971
Subjects: Fashion, Music, Dance, Photography
ISBN Prefix(es): 3-923765

**Ferdinand Schoeningh Verlag GmbH+**
Am Juhenplatz 1-3, 33098 Paderborn
Mailing Address: Postfach 2540, 33055 Pader-
born
*Tel:* (05251) 1275 *Fax:* (05251) 127860; (05251)
127670
*E-mail:* info@schoeningh.de
*Web Site:* www.schoeningh.de
*Key Personnel*
Man Dir: Ferdinand Schoeningh
Press: Hansgeorg Enzian
Production: Friedhelm Meyer
Editor, Scholarly Books: Dr Hans Jacobs; Dr Di-
atlund Sawicki; Michael Werner
Founded: 1847
Specialize in scholarly books.
Subjects: Biography, Government, Political Sci-
ence, History, Language Arts, Linguistics, Lit-
erature, Literary Criticism, Essays, Philosophy,
Religion - Catholic, Theology
ISBN Prefix(es): 3-506
Number of titles published annually: 100 Print
Total Titles: 1,500 Print
*Warehouse:* F Schoeningh GmbH, Otto-Stadler-
Str 6, 33100 Paderborn

**Schott Musik International GmbH & Co KG+**
Weihergarten 5, 55116 Mainz
*Tel:* (06131) 246-0 *Fax:* (06131) 246-211
*E-mail:* info@schott-musik.de
*Web Site:* www.schott-online.com *Cable:*
SCOTSON
*Key Personnel*
President: Dr Peter Hanser-Strecker
Man Dir: Michael Petry
Press Relations Manager: Dr Christiane
Krautscheid
Financial: Wolfgang Emmerich
Legal: Volker Landtag
Marketing: Susanne Hain
Founded: 1770
Subjects: Biography, Education, Music, Dance
ISBN Prefix(es): 3-7957
*Associate Companies:* Wiener Urtext Edition-
Musikverlag GmbH & Co KG, Australia
(jointly owned with Universal Edition AG,
Austria)
Subsidiaries: Ars-Viva-Verlag GmbH; Atlantis
Musikbuch-Verlag GmbH; Cranz GmbH; Ernst
Eulenburg & Co GmbH; Eulenburg AG; Fuer-
stner Musikverlag GmbH; Arnold Schoenberg
Gesamtausgabe GmbH; Music Factory GmbH;
Musikverlag Kompositor International GmbH;
Panton International GmbH; Schotta Wergo
Music Media GmbH; SMD Schott Music Dis-
tribution GmbH; Wega Verlag GmbH
*Branch Office(s)*
Espanola de Ediciones Musicales Schott SL, Al-
cala 70, 28009 Madrid, Spain
Schott & Co Ltd, 48 Great Marlborough St, Lon-
don W1V 2BN, United Kingdom
Schott Japan Co Ltd, Toyko, Japan
Schott Paris SARL, 40 rue Blomet, 75015 Paris,
France
*U.S. Office(s):* European American Music Distrib-
utors Corp, Valley Forge, PA, United States
*Bookshop(s):* Mainzer Musikalienzentrum, Wei-
hergarten 9, Mainz
*Orders to:* SMD Schott Music Distribu-
tion GmbH, Postfach 3640, 55026 Mainz
*Tel:* (06131) 5050 *Fax:* (06131) 505115

**Schrader Verlag**
Olgastr 86, 70180 Stuttgart
*Tel:* (0711) 210 80 0 *Fax:* (0711) 236 04 15
*E-mail:* verlag@motorbuch.de
*Web Site:* www.motorbuch.de
*Key Personnel*
Man Dir: Paul Pietsch
ISBN Prefix(es): 3-344
*Parent Company:* Paul Pietsch Verlage GmbH &
Co KG

**Schreiber-Naturtafeln**, *imprint of* Justus Perthes Verlag Gotha GmbH

**Verlag Silke Schreiber+**
Agnesstr 12, 80798 Munich
Mailing Address: Postfach 431161, 80741 Munich
*Tel:* (089) 2710180 *Fax:* (089) 2716957
*E-mail:* metzel@verlag-Silke-schreiber.de
*Web Site:* www.verlag-silke-schreiber.de
*Key Personnel*
Manager, Rights & Permissions: Dr Luise Metzel
    *E-mail:* metzel@t.online.de
Founded: 1982
Subjects: Art, Modern Art
ISBN Prefix(es): 3-88960
*U.S. Office(s):* Chris Pichler, Fulfillment Services, 1355 West Grand Rd, Suite 230, Tucson, AZ 85745, United States
*Orders to:* Vice Versa, Waldemarstr 81, 10997 Berlin, Contact: Gabriela Wachter *Tel:* (030) 61609237 *Fax:* (030) 61609238

**Schriften zur Kontemplation**, *imprint of* Vier Tuerme GmbH Verlag Klosterbetriebe

**Schriftenfeibe Wissenschaft und Frieden**, *imprint of* Bund demokratischer Wissenschaftlerinnen und Wissenschafler eV (BdWi)

**Verlag und Schriftenmission der Evangelischen Gesellschaft Wuppertal+**
Kaiserstr 78, 42329 Wuppertal
Mailing Address: Postfach 110533, 42305 Wuppertal
*Tel:* (0202) 278500 *Fax:* (0202) 2785040
*Key Personnel*
Man Dir: Hans Mohr
Sales, Production: Herbert Becker
Founded: 1954
Membership(s): the Telos group publishing evangelical paperbacks. Publishing House & Scriptural Mission of the German Evangelical Society.
Subjects: Literature, Literary Criticism, Essays, Religion - Other
ISBN Prefix(es): 3-87857

**Schroedel Schulbuchverlag GmbH**
Georg-Westermann-Allee 66, 38104 Braunschweig
*Tel:* (531) 708-0 *Fax:* (0531) 708-209
*E-mail:* sco@schroedel.de
*Web Site:* www.schroedel.de
*Key Personnel*
Man Dir: Ilrike Juergens; Thomas Michael; Dr Peter Schell; Michael Wolf
ISBN Prefix(es): 3-285

**Ferdinand Schroll**, see Titania-Verlag Ferdinand Schroll

**Carl Ed Schuenemann KG**
Zweite Schlachtpforte 7, 28195 Bremen
Mailing Address: Postfach 10 60 67, 28060 Bremen
*Tel:* (0421) 369030 *Fax:* (0421) 3690339
*Web Site:* www2.schuenemann-verlag.de
*Key Personnel*
Man Dir, Sales & Publicity: Klaus Kirchner
Founded: 1810
Subjects: Art, Regional Interests
ISBN Prefix(es): 3-7961

**Schueren Verlag GmbH+**
Universitaetsstr 55, 35037 Marburg
*Tel:* (06421) 6 30 84; (06421) 6 30 85
    *Fax:* (06421) 68 11 90
*E-mail:* info@schueren-verlag.de

*Web Site:* www.schueren-verlag.de
*Key Personnel*
Manager: Dr Annette Schueren
Founded: 1985
Subjects: Biography, Communications, Economics, Film, Video, Government, Political Science, Labor, Industrial Relations, Nonfiction (General), Radio, TV, Regional Interests, Science (General), Self-Help, Social Sciences, Sociology
ISBN Prefix(es): 3-89472
Number of titles published annually: 20 Print
Total Titles: 150 Print

**Verlag Karl Waldemar Schuetz+**
Postfach 1433, 96404 Coburg
*Tel:* (09561) 80780 *Fax:* (09561) 807820
*Key Personnel*
Man Dir, Rights & Permissions: Peter Dehoust
Editorial: Karl Richter
Founded: 1948
Subjects: History, Military Science
ISBN Prefix(es): 3-87725
*Parent Company:* Nation Europa Verlags GmbH, Bahnhofstr 25, 96450 Coburg

**Schulz-Kirchner Verlag GmbH+**
Mollweg 2, 65510 Idstein
Mailing Address: Postfach 1275, 65502 Idstein
*Tel:* (06126) 93200 *Fax:* (06126) 9320-50
*E-mail:* info@schulz-kirchner.de
*Web Site:* www.schulz-kirchner.de
*Key Personnel*
Manager: Berit Felgentreff
Founded: 1984
Subjects: Business, Economics, Energy, Finance, Health, Nutrition, History, Labor, Industrial Relations, Language Arts, Linguistics, Marketing, Medicine, Nursing, Dentistry, Philosophy, Science (General), Social Sciences, Sociology
ISBN Prefix(es): 3-8248; 3-925196

**Verlag R S Schulz GmbH+**
Enzianstr 4a, 82319 Starnberg
Mailing Address: Postfach 1780, 82317 Starnberg
*Tel:* (089) 36007-0 *Fax:* (089) 36007-3310
*E-mail:* rss@rss.de
*Web Site:* www.rss.de
*Key Personnel*
Man Dir: Dr Wilhelm Warth
Subjects: Architecture & Interior Design, Fiction, Health, Nutrition, Law, Social Sciences, Sociology, Veterinary Science
ISBN Prefix(es): 3-7962

**H O Schulze KG**
Laurenzistr 2, 96215 Lichtenfels
*Tel:* (09571) 7800 *Fax:* (09571) 78055
*E-mail:* verkauf@schulze-kg.de
*Web Site:* www.schulze-kg.de
*Key Personnel*
Publisher: Heinrich Schulze
Founded: 1865
Subjects: Art, Fiction, Geography, Geology, History, Nonfiction (General), Travel
ISBN Prefix(es): 3-87735
Distributed by Colloquium Historicum Wirsbergense; Verlag des Historischen Vereins Bamberg

**Theodor Schuster**
Muehlenstr 15/17, 26789 Leer
Mailing Address: Postfach 1944, 26769 Leer
*Tel:* (0491) 925900 *Fax:* (0491) 9259059
*E-mail:* buchhandlung-Schuster@t-online.de
*Key Personnel*
Contact: Theo Schuster
Subjects: Fiction, Humor, Nonfiction (General), Poetry
ISBN Prefix(es): 3-7963
Number of titles published annually: 5 Print; 1 CD-ROM; 2 Audio

**Edition Schwab**, *imprint of* Verlag Stephanie Naglschmid

**Heinrich Schwab Verlag KG+**
Eglofstal 42, 88260 Argenbuehl
Mailing Address: Gschwend 77, 6932 Langen bei Bregenz, Austria
*Tel:* (05575) 20101 *Fax:* (05575) 4745
*E-mail:* heinrichschwabverlag@aon.at
*Web Site:* www.heinrichschwabverlag.de
*Key Personnel*
Manager: Verena Brocksieper
Founded: 1926
Subjects: Parapsychology, Philosophy, Psychology, Psychiatry, Religion - Other, Alternative Medicine, Biological Horticulture, Breathe Therapies, Border Sciences, Esoteric Works & Meditation, Life Assistance, Life-Wise, Medicine, Mental Healing, Naturopathy, Positive Thinking, Religion Science, Spirituality, Yoga
ISBN Prefix(es): 3-7964
Total Titles: 130 Print; 5 CD-ROM; 10 Audio

**Schwabenverlag Aktiengesellschaft+**
Senefelderstr 12, 73760 Ostfildern
*Tel:* (0711) 4406-0 *Fax:* (0711) 4406-177
*E-mail:* info@schwabenverlag.de
*Web Site:* www.schwabenverlag.de
*Key Personnel*
President: Ulrich Peters
International Rights: Gertrud Widmann
Founded: 1848
Subjects: Art, Regional Interests, Religion - Catholic, Religion - Other, Theology
ISBN Prefix(es): 3-7966
Subsidiaries: Rottenburger Druckerei; Sueddeutsche Verlagsgesellschaft mbH Ulm
Distributed by Auslieferung (Austria & Germany); Auslieferung Schweiz Herder; Brockhaus/Commission; Österreichisches Katholisches Bibelwerk
*Bookshop(s):* Schwabenverlag Buchhandlung, Bahnhofstr 20, 89073 Ulm; Schwabenverlag Buchhandlung, Spitalstr 19, 73479 Ellwangen; TheoBuch Rottenburg, Karmeliterstr 2, 72108 Rottenburg

**Schwaneberger Verlag GmbH**
Muthmannstr 4, 80939 Munich
*Tel:* (089) 3239302 *Fax:* (089) 3232402
*E-mail:* webmaster@michel.de
*Web Site:* www.michel.de
*Key Personnel*
Man Dir, Rights & Permissions: Hans Hohenester
Editorial: Jochen Stenzke
Sales: Joachim Stolz
Publicity: Werner Maier
Founded: 1910
Subjects: Crafts, Games, Hobbies
ISBN Prefix(es): 3-87858
*Associate Companies:* Carl Gerber Verlag GmbH

**Edition Schwann**, *imprint of* C F Peters Musikverlag GmbH & Co KG

**Otto Schwartz Fachbochhandlung GmbH+**
Annastr 7, 37075 Goettingen
*Tel:* (0551) 31051 *Fax:* (0551) 372812
*E-mail:* schwartz.stadt@t-online.de
*Key Personnel*
Man Dir: Dr Herbert Weisser
Man Dir, Rights & Permissions: Konrad Weisser
Rights & Permissions: Ernst Leopold
Branch Manager: Marlis Potthast *Tel:* (0551) 5085978
Sales: Mrs Barke *Tel:* (0551) 5085978; Mrs Beuermann *Tel:* (0551) 5085978; Ms Willgerodt *Tel:* (0551) 5085978
Founded: 1871

Subjects: Ethnicity, Law, Public Administration, Social Sciences, Sociology
ISBN Prefix(es): 3-509
*Bookshop(s):* Fachbuchhandlung Otto Schwartz & Co

**Dr Wolfgang Schwarze Verlag+**
Richard Strauss Allee 35, 42289 Wuppertal
Mailing Address: Postfach 201744, 42217 Wuppertal
*Tel:* (0202) 622005; (0202) 622006 *Fax:* (0202) 63631
*Key Personnel*
Man Dir, Rights & Permissions: Dr Wolfgang Schwarze
Sales, Office Chief: Ursula Schwarze
Founded: 1968
Subjects: Antiques, Architecture & Interior Design, Art, House & Home
ISBN Prefix(es): 3-87741

**Verlag Schweers + Wall GmbH+**
Rudolfstr 65-67, 52070 Aachen
Mailing Address: Postfach 1586, 52016 Aachen
*Tel:* (0241) 87 22 51 *Fax:* (0241) 8 52 06
*E-mail:* schweers.wall@t-online.de
Founded: 1986
Subjects: Transportation, Travel
ISBN Prefix(es): 3-921679; 3-89494

**E Schweizerbart'sche Verlagsbuchhandlung (Naegele und Obermiller)+**
Affiliate of Gebrueder Borntraeger Verlagsbuchhandlung
Johannesstr 3A, 70176 Stuttgart
*Tel:* (0711) 3514560 *Fax:* (0711) 351456-99
*E-mail:* mail@schweizerbart.de
*Web Site:* www.schweizerbart.de
*Key Personnel*
Man Dir, Production: Dr Erhard Naegele
Man Dir, Sales: Dr Walter Obermiller
Exhibition Manager: Martina Ihringer
Founded: 1826
Subjects: Anthropology, Archaeology, Biological Sciences, Earth Sciences, Environmental Studies, Geography, Geology, Maritime, Science (General)
ISBN Prefix(es): 3-510 (Schweizerbart); 3-443 (Borntraeger)
*U.S. Office(s):* Balogh International Inc, 1911 N Duncan Rd, Champaign, IL 61822, United States, Contact: Pamela Burns-Balogh *Tel:* 217-355-9331 *Fax:* 217-355-9413 *E-mail:* balogh@balogh.com *Web Site:* www.balogh.com
Distributor for Bundesanstalt fuer Geowissenschaften und Rohstoffe; Senckenbergische Naturforschende Gesellschaft

**Schwul Lesbische Studien Universitat Bremen,** *imprint of* Mannerschwarm Skript Verlag GmbH

**Scientia Verlag und Antiquariat Schilling OHG**
Adlerstr 65, 73434 Wurtt
Mailing Address: Postfach 1660, 73406 Wurtt
*Tel:* (07361) 41700 *Fax:* (07361) 45620
*Cable:* SCIENTIA AALENWUERTT
*Key Personnel*
Man Dir: Guenter Schilling
Founded: 1953
Subjects: Archaeology, Economics, Education, History, Law, Philosophy, Religion - Other, Social Sciences, Sociology, Theology
ISBN Prefix(es): 3-511

**SDV,** see Saarbrucker Druckerei und Verlag GmbH (SDV)

**EA Seemann Verlag,** *imprint of* Verlagsgruppe Dornier GmbH

**Seibt Verlag GmbH**
Havelstr 9, 64295 Darmstadt
*Tel:* (06151) 380-140 *Fax:* (06151) 380-141
*E-mail:* info@seibt.com
*Web Site:* www.seibt.de
*Key Personnel*
Man Dir: Alfred Augustine; Werner Reiber; Roland Repp
Advertising Dir: Brita Graef
Founded: 1921
Membership(s): VDAV (Verband Deutscher Adressbuchveleger) & EADP (European Association of Directory Publishers).
Subjects: Environmental Studies, Mechanical Engineering, Medicine, Nursing, Dentistry
ISBN Prefix(es): 3-922948; 3-931336; 3-936865
*Parent Company:* Hoppenstedt GmbH & Co

**Dr Arthur L Sellier & Co KG-Walter de Gruyter GmbH & Co KG OHG+**
Genthinerstr 13, 10785 Berlin
Mailing Address: PO Box 303421, 10728 Berlin
*Tel:* (030) 26005-0 *Fax:* (030) 260 05-251
*E-mail:* wdq-info@degruyter.de
*Web Site:* www.degruyter.de
*Telex:* 184027 *Cable:* WISSENSCHAFT BERLIN
*Key Personnel*
Contact: Georg Broeckelmann
Founded: 1990
Subjects: Law, Commentary to the German Civil Code
ISBN Prefix(es): 3-8059
*U.S. Office(s):* 200 Saw Mill River Rd, Hawthorne, NY 10532, United States *Tel:* 914-747-0110 *Fax:* 914-747-1326

**Siebeck,** see Mohr Siebeck

**Siebenberg-Verlag+**
Warolder Str 1, 34513 Waldeck-Dehringhausen
*Tel:* (05695) 1028 *Fax:* (05695) 1027
*E-mail:* fh@huebner-books.de
*Web Site:* www.huebner-books.de
*Key Personnel*
Publisher: Felicitas Huebner
Founded: 1936
Subjects: Art, Asian Studies, Poetry
ISBN Prefix(es): 3-87747
*Orders to:* Bugrim Verlagsauslieferung Dr Laube & Partner, Saalburgstr 3, 12099 Berlin

**Siebert Verlag GmbH+**
Werderstr 10, 69469 Weinheim
*Tel:* (06201) 6007-0
*E-mail:* info@beltz.de
*Web Site:* www.beltz.de
*Key Personnel*
Man Dir & Publisher: Hans Meisinger
Rights & Publicity: Christiane Schneider
Founded: 1967
Subjects: Crafts, Games, Hobbies
ISBN Prefix(es): 3-8089; 3-920215; 3-89050
*Parent Company:* Verlagsgruppe Beltz
*Orders to:* MVS Meisinger Verlagsservice GmbH, Am Steinfeld 4, 94065 Waldkirchen *Tel:* (08581) 9605-0 *Fax:* (08581) 754

**Siedler Verlag+**
Neumarkter Str 28, 81673 Munich
*Tel:* (089) 41 36-0
*E-mail:* vertrieb.verlagsgruppe@randomhouse.de
*Web Site:* www.randomhouse.de/siedler
*Key Personnel*
Press: Isabel Thielen
Founded: 1982
Subjects: Biography, Government, Political Science, History, Journalism, Nonfiction (General)
ISBN Prefix(es): 3-88680; 3-8275
*Parent Company:* Bertelsmann Verlagsgruppe GmbH, Postfach 800360, 81603 Munich
*Orders to:* Siedler Verlag Vertiel, Neumarkterstr 18, 81673 Munich

**Siegler & Co Verlag fuer Zeitarchive GmbH+**
Einsteinstr 10, 53757 St Augustin
Mailing Address: Postfach 1455, 53732 St Augustin
*Tel:* (02241) 3164-0
*Key Personnel*
Manager & International Rights: Dr Werner Hippe
Publishing Dir: Gerd Meiser
Founded: 1931
Subjects: Government, Political Science, History
ISBN Prefix(es): 3-87748
*Parent Company:* Asgard Verlag Dr Werner Hippe KG

**Georg Siemens Verlagsbuchhandlung**
Boothstr 11, 12207 Berlin
Mailing Address: Postfach 450169, 12171 Berlin
*Tel:* (030) 769904-0 *Fax:* (030) 769904-18
*E-mail:* gsiemensv@t-online.de
*Key Personnel*
Contact: Hans Klessinger *Tel:* (030) 76990412
Founded: 1891
Subjects: Specializes in Railway transportation & Craft Sanitary facilities & heating
ISBN Prefix(es): 3-87749

**Sierra,** *imprint of* Frederking & Thaler Verlag GmbH

**Sigloch Edition Helmut Sigloch GmbH & Co KG+**
Am Buchberg 8, 74572 Blaufelden
Mailing Address: Postfach 1201, Blaufelden 74568
*Tel:* (07953) 883-0 *Fax:* (07953) 883-320
*E-mail:* info@sigloch.de
*Web Site:* www.sigloch.de
*Telex:* 74 161
*Key Personnel*
President: Helmut Sigloch
Production Manager: Michael Sanny
Founded: 1972
Subjects: Cookery, Technology
ISBN Prefix(es): 3-89393
*Warehouse:* Sigloch Distribution GmbH

**Edition Sigma e.Kfm+**
Karl-Marxstr 17, 12043 Berlin
*Tel:* (030) 623 23 63 *Fax:* (030) 623 93 93
*E mail:* verlag@edition-sigma.de
*Web Site:* www.edition-sigma.de
*Key Personnel*
Contact: Mr R Bohn
Founded: 1984
Subjects: Social Sciences, Sociology
ISBN Prefix(es): 3-924859; 3-89404

**Silberburg-Verlag Titus Haeussermann GmbH+**
Schoenbuchstr 48, 72074 Tuebingen-Bebenhausen
*Tel:* (07071) 6885-0 *Fax:* (07071) 6885-20
*E-mail:* info@silberburg.de
*Web Site:* www.silberburg.com
*Key Personnel*
Editor-in-Chief: Titus Haeussermann
Sales & Advertising: Christel Werner
Founded: 1985
Membership(s): Stock Exchange of German Booksellers & Association of Publishers & Booksellers in Baden-Wuerttemberg.
Subjects: Regional Interests
ISBN Prefix(es): 3-925344; 3-87407
Number of titles published annually: 50 Print; 20 Audio
Total Titles: 300 Print; 50 Audio
Imprints: Gustav Mesmer Stiftung; Schmidmusic
Distributed by Maule & Gosch Tontragervertrieb

Distributor for JS Film-Produktion GmbH;
Maeule & Gosch Tontragervertrieb; Musekater
Musikverlag; Schwoissfuass GmbH
*Warehouse:* Silberburg-Verlag, c/o Koch, Neff &
Oetinger & Co, Verlagsauslieferung GmbH,
Schockenriedstr 39, 70565 Stuttgart-Vaihingen
*Tel:* (0711) 78600

**Die Silberschnur Verlag GmbH+**
Steinstr 1, 56593 Guellesheim
*Tel:* (02687) 929068 *Fax:* (02687) 929524
*E-mail:* info@silberschnur.de
*Web Site:* www.silberschnur.de
*Key Personnel*
Man Dir: Tom Hockemeyer; Manfred Huber
Publisher's Reader: N Kugberg *Tel:* (02687)
929089
Founded: 1982
Subjects: Alternative, Astrology, Occult, Parapsy-
chology, Alternative healing, Esoteric Teach-
ings & Life After Death
ISBN Prefix(es): 3-923781; 3-931652; 3-89845
Number of titles published annually: 20 Print
Total Titles: 300 Print
Distributor for Adwaita; Arun; Corona; Coudris;
Devas Edition; Dude; EVT; Genius; Grasmuck;
Heindel; Hubner; ICH; Kopp; 1 zu l; Larimar;
Lichtring; Medicum Keg; Naam; Nietsch; NLS;
Omega; Ostergaard; PAN; Quadropol; Riechel;
Rocke; Sequoyah; Silberschnur; Simeunovic;
Sternentor; Subtilis; Weltenhuter

**Buchkonzept Simon KG+**
Kaiserstr 33, 80801 Munich
Mailing Address: Postfach 431062, 80740 Mu-
nich
*Tel:* (089) 21939012 *Fax:* (089) 21939014
*Key Personnel*
Man Dir: Claudia Magiera; Gerd Simon
Founded: 1979
Subjects: Asian Studies, Fiction, Foreign Coun-
tries, Travel
ISBN Prefix(cs): 3-88676
Subsidiaries: Tutto Mondo

**Rudolf G Smend+**
Mainzerstr 31, 50678 Cologne
*Tel:* (0221) 312047 *Fax:* (0221) 9 32 07 18
*E-mail:* smend@smend.de
*Key Personnel*
Contact: Rudolf G Smend
Founded: 1973
Art gallery & publisher of catalogues.
Subjects: Art, Asian Studies, Indonesian art, tex-
tile art
ISBN Prefix(es): 3-926779
Number of titles published annually: 1 Print
Total Titles: 10 Print
*Orders to:* Mainzerstr 33, Cologne *Fax:* (0221)
325134

**Societaets-Verlag+**
Frankenallee 71-81, 60327 Frankfurt am Main
*Tel:* (069) 75 01-0 *Fax:* (069) 75 01-48 77
*Web Site:* www.societaets-verlag.de
*Telex:* 0411655 *Cable:* Zeitung Frankfurtmain
*Key Personnel*
Publisher: Dr Juergen Kron *Tel:* (069) 75 01-45
11 *E-mail:* juergen.kron@fsd.de
Sales: Henrike Brueck *Tel:* (069) 75 01-42 97
*Fax:* (069) 75 01-45 11 *E-mail:* henrike.
brueck@fsd.de
Production: Cordula Tippkoetter *Tel:* (069) 75 01-
42 98 *Fax:* (069) 75 01-45 11 *E-mail:* cordula.
tippkoetter@fsd.de
Publicity: Silvie Horch *Tel:* (069) 75 01-45 71
*Fax:* (069) 75 01-45 11 *E-mail:* silvie.horch@
fsd.de
Founded: 1921
Subjects: Art, Business, Economics, History, Lit-
erature, Literary Criticism, Essays

ISBN Prefix(es): 3-7973; 3-87235
Imprints: Verlag Frankfurter Buecher; Verlag
Heinrich Scheffler

**Soldi-Verlag im Drockzentrum Harburg**
Steinbeckerstr 97, 21244 Buchholz id Nordheide
*Tel:* (04181) 29 16 22 *Fax:* (04181) 29 16 23
*E-mail:* kontakt@karismaverlag.de
*Web Site:* www.karismaverlag.de
*Key Personnel*
Man Dir: Horst Ernst
Founded: 1977
ISBN Prefix(es): 3-928028; 3-923744; 3-931877

**Sonnentanz-Verlag Roland Kron+**
Waterloostr 25, 86165 Augsburg
*Tel:* (0821) 311070 *Fax:* (0821) 158979
*E-mail:* sonnentanz@t-online.de
*Key Personnel*
Contact: Roland Kron
Founded: 1988
Specialize in rock literature & rock biographies.
Subjects: Biography, Music, Dance
ISBN Prefix(es): 3-926794

**Sonntag,** *imprint of* Georg Thieme Verlag KG

**Johannes Sonntag Verlagsbuchhandlung
GmbH+**
Oswalt-Hesse-Str 50, 70469 Stuttgart
*Tel:* (0711) 8931-0 *Fax:* (0711) 8931-706
*Web Site:* www.sonntag-verlag.com
*Key Personnel*
Man Dir: Dr Thomas Scherb
Marketing: Sigrid Lesch *E-mail:* sigrid.lesch@
thieme.de
Founded: 1927
Specialize in books, magazines, medicine, com-
plementary medicine.
ISBN Prefix(es): 3-87758
Number of titles published annually: 25 Print
Total Titles: 150 Print
*Parent Company:* Hippokrates Verlag

**Spee Buchverlag GmbH,** see Paulinus Verlag
GmbH

**Spektrum der Wissenschaft Verlagsgesellschaft
mbH**
Slevogtstr 3-5, 69126 Heidelberg
Mailing Address: PO Box 10 48 40, 69038 Hei-
delberg
*Tel:* (06221) 9126600 *Fax:* (06221) 9126751
*E-mail:* marketing@spektrum.com
*Web Site:* www.spektrum.de
*Key Personnel*
Man Dir: Markus Bossle
Publicity: Barbara Kuhn
Founded: 1978
Subjects: Science (General), Technology
*Parent Company:* Scientific American Inc, 415
Madison Ave, New York, NY 10017, United
States

**Spiegel-Verlag Rudolf Augstein GmbH & Co
KG+**
Brandstwiete 19, 20457 Hamburg
Mailing Address: Postfach 110413, 20404 Ham-
burg
*Tel:* (040) 3007-0 *Fax:* (040) 3007-2247
*E-mail:* spiegel@spiegel.de
*Telex:* 2161221
*Key Personnel*
Man Dir: Karl-Dietrich Seikel
International Rights: Dietrich Krause
Founded: 1946
ISBN Prefix(es): 3-87763
Subsidiaries: a+i art and information GmbH &
Co KG; manager magazine Verlagsgesellschaft
mbH; manager magazin ONLINE GmbH;

Quality Channel GmbH; SPIEGELnet GmbH;
SPIEGEL ONLINE GmbH; Spiegel TV GmbH
*Orders to:* Postfach 105840, 20039 Hamburg

**Spiess Volker Wissenschaftsverlag GmbH+**
Gneisenaustr 33, 10961 Berlin
Mailing Address: Postfach 610494, 10928 Berlin
*Tel:* (030) 6917073-74 *Fax:* (030) 6914067
*Cable:* SPIESSVERLAG
*Key Personnel*
Publisher: Volker Spiess
Founded: 1967
Subjects: Communications, Film, Video, History,
Journalism, Language Arts, Linguistics, Social
Sciences, Sociology
ISBN Prefix(es): 3-89166; 3-89776
*Associate Companies:* Haude und Spenersche
VerlagsBuchhandlung, Postfach 303046, 10928
Berlin *Tel:* (030) 2165061 *Fax:* (030) 2165064
Subsidiaries: Edition Marhold; Edition collo-
quium

**Wissenschaftsverlag Volker Spiess Gmbh**
Gneisenaustr 33, 10961 Berlin
Mailing Address: Postfach 610494, 10928 Berlin
*Tel:* (030) 6917073 *Fax:* (030) 6914067
*E-mail:* info@spiess-verlage.de
*Web Site:* www.spiess-verlage.de
*Key Personnel*
Contact: Volker Spiess
Subjects: Disability, Special Needs
ISBN Prefix(es): 3-89166; 3-89776
*Associate Companies:* arani-verlag GmbH; Haude
und Spenersche Verlagsbuchhandlung

**Spieth-Verlag Verlag fuer Symbolforschung+**
Postfach 31 13 08, 10643 Berlin
*Tel:* (0331) 2705199 *Fax:* (0331) 2010849
*Key Personnel*
Owner: Rudolf Arnold Spieth
Founded: 1969
Subjects: Anthropology, Astrology, Occult, Para-
psychology, Philosophy, Psychology, Psychia-
try, Religion - Other, Self-Help
ISBN Prefix(es): 3-88093
Subsidiaries: Bund der Runenforscher Deutsch-
lands (BRD)/Internationaler Zentralverband
Germanischer Runenforscher (IZGR)

**Spiridon-Verlags GmbH+**
Dorfstr 18A, 40699 Erkrath
*Tel:* (02104) 47260 *Fax:* (0211) 786823
*Key Personnel*
Publisher: Manfred Steffny
Founded: 1974
Subjects: Health, Nutrition, Sports, Athletics
ISBN Prefix(es): 3-922011
*Bookshop(s):* Steffnys Laufladen, Linienstr 12,
40227 Dusseldorf

**Adolf Sponholtz Verlag+**
Subsidiary of C W Niemeyer Buchverlage GmbH
c/o C W Niemeyer Buchverlage GmbH, Osterstr
19, 31785 Hameln
Mailing Address: Postfach 100752, 31763
Hameln
*Tel:* (05151) 200312 *Fax:* (05151) 200319
*Web Site:* www.niemeyer-buch.de
*Key Personnel*
Dir: Hans Freiwald
Founded: 1894
Subjects: Animals, Pets, Energy, Environmental
Studies, Fiction, History, Literature, Literary
Criticism, Essays, Nonfiction (General), Out-
door Recreation
ISBN Prefix(es): 3-87766
*Orders to:* VSB Verlagsservice Braunschweig
GmbH, Westerman- Allee 66, 38104 Braun-
schweig *Tel:* (0531) 708650 *Fax:* (0531)
708608

## Sportverlag Berlin GmbH SVB+
Hohenzollerndamm 56, 14199 Berlin
*Tel:* (030) 8973666 *Fax:* (030) 2591-3516
*E-mail:* marketing@sportverlag-berlin.de *Cable:*
UND SPORTVERLAG BERLIN
*Key Personnel*
Man Dir: Dr Wolfram Goeibel
Sales, Rights & Permissions: Brigitte Kummer
Marketing Manager: Helmut Krueger
Editor-in-Chief: Raymund Stolze
Founded: 1947
Subjects: How-to, Sports, Athletics
ISBN Prefix(es): 3-328; 3-333
*Warehouse:* VVA, A64 DFB/F An der Autobahn,
33370 Gutersloh

## Axel Springer Verlag AG
Axel-Springer-Platz 1, 20350 Hamburg
*Tel:* (040) 347-00 *Fax:* (040) 345811
*E-mail:* information@axelspringer.de
*Web Site:* www.asv.de
*Telex:* 2170010; 402255
*Key Personnel*
Contact: Edda Fels
Founded: 1946
ISBN Prefix(es): 3-921305

## Springer Science+Business Media GmbH & Co KG+
Tiergartenstr 17, 69121 Heidelberg
Mailing Address: Postfach 105280, 69042 Heidelberg
*Tel:* (06221) 487-0 *Fax:* (06221) 487-8366
*E-mail:* orders@springer.de
*Web Site:* www.springer.de
*Key Personnel*
Chairman, Supervisory Board of the Springer Group: Derk Haank
Man Dir: Rudiger Gebauer; Peter Hendriks; Martin Mos; Dr Ulrich Vest
Founded: 1991
Membership(s): TR- Verlagsunion GmbH.
Subjects: Agriculture, Architecture & Interior Design, Art, Astronomy, Behavioral Sciences, Biography, Biological Sciences, Business, Chemistry, Chemical Engineering, Child Care & Development, Civil Engineering, Computer Science, Cookery, Criminology, Earth Sciences, Economics, Electronics, Electrical Engineering, Energy, Engineering (General), Environmental Studies, Finance, Geography, Geology, Government, Political Science, Health, Nutrition, History, Law, Management, Marketing, Mathematics, Mechanical Engineering, Medicine, Nursing, Dentistry, Nonfiction (General), Philosophy, Physical Sciences, Physics, Psychology, Psychiatry, Science (General), Social Sciences, Sociology, Technology
ISBN Prefix(es): 0-8194; 0-387; 3-7643; 3-7985; 2-287; 3-540; 3-211; 4-431; 3-7908; 84-07; 1-85233; 3-18; 88-470; 3-88537; 0-8716; 0-907259; 981-3083
*Parent Company:* Springer Science+Business Media GmbH & Co KG, Berlin
*Associate Companies:* Springer-Verlag New York LLC, 175 Fifth Ave, New York, NY 10010, United States *Tel:* 212-460-1500 *Fax:* 212-473-6272; Springer-Verlag London Ltd, Sweetapple House, Cateshall Rd, Surrey, Godalming GU7 3DJ, United Kingdom *Tel:* (01483) 418822 *Fax:* (01483) 415151; Springer-Verlag France, One rue Paul Cezanne, 75375 Paris, France *Tel:* (01) 5393-3644 *Fax:* (01) 5393-3683; Springer-Verlag Tokyo Inc, 3-13, Hougo 3-chome, Bunkyo-ku, Tokyo, Japan *Tel:* (03) 38120337 *Fax:* (03) 38187454; Eastern Book Service Inc, 3-13, Hongo 3-chome, Bunkyo-ku, Tokyo 113, Japan *Tel:* (03) 38180861 *Fax:* (03) 38180864; Springer-Verlag Hong Kong Ltd, Unit 1702 Tower I, Enterprise Square, 9 Sheung Yuet Rd, Kowloon Bay, Hong Kong *Tel:* 27239698 *Fax:* 27242366; Springer-Verlag Iberica SA, Corcega 505, entlo 3, 08025

Barcelona, Spain; Springer-VDI-Verlag GmbH & Co KG, Heinrichstr, 40239 Duesseldorf *Tel:* (0211) 6103-222 *Fax:* (0211) 6103-113; Springer-Verlag Wien, Sachsenpl 4-6, 1201 Vienna, Austria *Tel:* (01) 3302415 *Fax:* (01) 3302426; Springer Italia, Via Podgora 14, 20122 Mailand, Italy *Tel:* (02) 54259721 *Fax:* (02) 55193360; Springer-Verlag GmbH & Co KG, Indian Liaison Office, 906-907, Akash Deep Bldg, Barakhamba Rd, 110001 New Delhi, India *Tel:* (011) 3358590 *Fax:* (011) 3358716; Urban and Vogel Medien und Medizin Verlagsgesellschaft GmbH, Neumarkter Str 43, 81673 Munich; Springer PWN Ltd, Warsaw, Poland
Imprints: Copernicus; Physica; TELOS
Distributor for AIP Press (American Institute of Physics)
*Bookshop(s):* Minerva Wissenschaftliche Buchhandlung GmbH, Sachsenplatz 4-6, 7207 Vienna, Austria *Tel:* (01) 330 2433 *Fax:* (01) 330 2439
*Warehouse:* Springer GmbH & Co Auslieferungs-Gesellschaft, Haberstr 7, 69126 Heidelberg *Tel:* (06221) 345-112 *Fax:* (06221) 345-182 *E-mail:* orders@springer.de

## Springer Science+Business Media GmbH & Co KG, Berlin+
Heidelberger Platz 3, 14197 Berlin
Mailing Address: Postfach 140201, 14302 Berlin
*Tel:* (030) 82787-0; (030) 82787 5282 (press & public relations) *Fax:* (030) 8214091; (030) 82787 5707 (press & public relations)
*E-mail:* press@springer-sbm.com
*Web Site:* www.springer-sbm.de
*Key Personnel*
Chief Executive Officer: Derk Haank
Chief Operating Officer: Martin Mos
Chief Financial Officer: Dr Ulrich Vest
Founded: 1842
Publisher of scientific & specialist literature. In addition to scientific literature provides competent information service for the B-to-B (business to business) market.
Subjects: Architecture & Interior Design, Economics, Engineering (General), Medicine, Nursing, Dentistry, Science (General), Transportation, Construction
ISBN Prefix(es): 0-306 (Kluwer Academic Publishers); 1-56898 (Princeton Architectural Press); 0-387 (Springer-Verlag New York); 3-519 (Teubner); 3-409 (Gabler); 3-7643 (Birkhaeuser); 3-528 (Vieweg); 3-540 (Springer-Verlag Berlin/Heidelberg); 3-7908 (Physica); 1-4020 (Kluwer Academic Publishers)
Number of titles published annually: 5,000 Print
Total Titles: 40,000 Print
*Branch Office(s)*
ArchiPoint, Draaiboomstr 6, 2160 Wommelgem, Belgium *Tel:* (03) 3555010 *Fax:* (03) 3555020
Artze Woche Zeitungsverlagsgesellschaft mbH, Wiesingerstr 1, 1010 Vienna, Austria, Contact: Rodolf Siegle *Tel:* (01) 3302415 *Fax:* (01) 3302426 *E-mail:* siegle@springer.at
Artze Zeitung Verlagsgesellschaft mbH, Am Forsthaus Gravenbruch 5, 63263 Neu-Isenburg, Contact: Gerald Kosaris *Tel:* (06102) 506-150 *Fax:* (06102) 506-100 *E-mail:* gerald.kosaris@aerztezeitung.de
Auto Business Verlag GmbH & Co KG, Robert-Bosch-Str 7, 85521 Ottobrunn, Contact: Dr Carsten Thies *Tel:* (089) 4372 1130 *Fax:* (089) 4372 1275 *E-mail:* carsten.thies@springer-sbm.de
Bau-Data Osterreich GmbH, Langgasse 182, 5400 Hallein-Vigaun, Austria, Contact: Bernhard Bogensperger *Tel:* (062) 45 797 18 *Fax:* (062) 45 797 90 *E-mail:* bernhard.bogensperger@bau-data.co.at
BauDatenbank GmbH, Bremer Weg 184, 29219 Celle, Contact: Michael Hoelker *Tel:* (05141)

50 370; (05141) 50 233 *Fax:* (05141) 50 374 *E-mail:* michael.hoelker@heinze.de
BauNetz Online-Dienst GmbH & Co KG, Schluterstr 42, 10707 Berlin, Contact: Jurgen Paul *Tel:* (030) 887 26 301 *Fax:* (030) 887 26 303 *E-mail:* paul@baunetz.de
Bauverlag GmbH, Avenwedder Str 55, 33311 Gutersloh, Contact: Stefan Ruehling *Tel:* (05241) 80 24 76 *Fax:* (05241) 80 95 82 *E-mail:* stefan.ruehling@bauverlag.der
Business Solutions Medicine (BSMO), Johannisberger Str 74, 14197 Berlin, France, Contact: Dr Joerg Zorn *Tel:* (030) 884 293 18 *Fax:* (030) 884 293 41 *E-mail:* joerg.zorn@bsmo.de
Birkhauser Verlag AG, Viadukstr 42, 4051 Basel, Switzerland, Contact: Sven Fund *Tel:* (061) 20 50 710 *Fax:* (061) 20 50 790 *E-mail:* fund@birkhauser.ch
Birkhauser Verlag GmbH, Am Forsthaus Gravenbrunch 5, 63263 Neu-Isenburg, Contact: Anja Beyersdorff *Tel:* (06102) 59980 10 *Fax:* (06102) 59980 99 *E-mail:* anja.beyersdorff@form.de
CoboSystems NV, Draaiboomstr 6, 2160 Wommelgem, Belgium *Tel:* (03) 3555010 *Fax:* (03) 3555020
Codes Rosseau SAS, 135 rue de Plesses, BP93, 85510 Les Sables d'Olonne Cedex, France, Contact: Michel Goepp *Tel:* (0251) 231 117 *Fax:* (0251) 220 525 *E-mail:* michel.goepp@code-rousseau.fr
Deutscher Universitats-Verlag GmbH, Abraham-Lincoln Str 46, 65189 Wiesbaden, Contact: Dr Hans-Dieter Haenel *Tel:* (0611) 78 78 102 *Fax:* (0611) 78 78 104 *E-mail:* hans-dieter.haenel@gwv-fachverlage.de
ETRASA - Editorial Trafico Vial SA, C/Puerto de Navacerrada 128, Pol Ind Las Nieves, 28935 Mostoles, Madrid, Spain, Contact: Efa Rimoldi *Tel:* (091) 665 80 01 *Fax:* (091) 665 80 03 *E-mail:* efa@estrasa.com
Eurosoft, C/Puerto de Navacerrada 128, Pol Ind Las Nieves, 28935 Mostoles, Madrid, Spain, Contact: Efa Rimoldi *Tel:* (091) 665 80 01 *Fax:* (091) 665 80 03 *E-mail:* efa@etrasa.com
FachMediaCom AG, Rutistra 2, 8952 Schlieren, Switzerland, Contact: Heike Findeis *Tel:* (01) 7385 252 *Fax:* (01) 7385 128 *E-mail:* heike.findeis@fachmediacom.ch
Fachmedien Verlag GmbH, Inkustra 16, 3403 Klosterneuburg, Austria, Contact: Ferenc Papp *Tel:* (02243) 30111 235 *Fax:* (02243) 30111 222 *E-mail:* papp@technopress.at
Dr Hans Fuchs GmbH Verlag Fuchsbriefe, Albrechtstr 22, 10117 Berlin, Contact: Ralf Vielhaber *Tel:* (030) 28 88 17 0 *Fax:* (030) 28 04 55 76 *E-mail:* ralf.vielhaber@fuchsbriefe.de
Betriebswirtschaftlicher Verlag Dr Th Gabler, Abraham-Lincoln Str 46, 65189 Wiesbaden, Contact: Hans-Dieter Haenel *Tel:* (0611) 78 78 102 *Fax:* (0611) 78 78 104 *E-mail:* hans-dieter.haenel@gwv-fachverlage.de
GOF Verlag, Inkustra 16, 3403 Klosterneuburg, Austria, Contact: Ferenc Papp *Tel:* (02243) 30111 235 *Fax:* (02243) 30111 222 *E-mail:* papp@technopress.at
Grupa Image Sp zoo, ul Witkiewicza 14, 03-305 Warsaw, Poland, Contact: Witold Wisniewski *Tel:* (022) 811 01 99 *Fax:* (022) 811 19 93 *E-mail:* witold@grupaimage.com.pl
GWV Fachverlage GmbH, Abraham-Lincoln Str 46, 65189 Wiesbaden, Contact: Dr Hans-Dieter Haenel *Tel:* (0611) 78 78 102 *Fax:* (0611) 78 78 104 *E-mail:* hans-dieter.haenel@gwv-fachverlage.de
Heinrich Vogel Verlag Schweiz, Rutistra 22, 8952 Schlieren, Switzerland, Contact: Heike Findeis *Tel:* (01) 73 85 252 *Fax:* (01) 73 85 128 *E-mail:* heike.findeis@fachmediacom.ch
Heinze GmbH, Bremer Weg 184, 29219 Celle, Contact: Michael Hoelker *Tel:* (05141) 50 370 *Fax:* (05141) 50 374 *E-mail:* michael.hoelker@heinze.de

ibau Informationsdienst fur den Baumarkt GmbH, Anton-Bruchausen Str, Munster 48147, Contact: Dr Roland Ehrenfels *Tel:* (0251) 78 05 116 *Fax:* (0251) 78 05 244 *E-mail:* r. ehrenfels@ibau.de

ICW Publications Ltd, The Chapter House, Hinderton Hall Estate, Neston, South Wirral CH64 7UX, United Kingdom, Contact: Simon Mahoney *Tel:* (0151) 353 35 11 *Fax:* (0151) 353 35 02 *E-mail:* simon.mahoney@ abibuildingdata.com

IMS Investitions Media Service Werbe- & Public Relations GmbH, Inkustra 16, 3403 Klosterneuburg, Austria, Contact: Ferenc Papp *Tel:* (022) 43 301 11 235 *Fax:* (022) 43 301 11 222 *E-mail:* papp@technopress.at

Infobuild nv, Groeningestr 39 boite 21, 8500 Kortrijk, Belgium *Tel:* (056) 24 37 30 *Fax:* (056) 24 37 31 *E-mail:* info@infobuild.be *Web Site:* www.infobuild.be

InfoChem Gesellschaft fur chemische Information mbH, Landsberger Str 408, 81241 Munich, Contact: Dr Peter Low *Tel:* (089) 58 93 91 14 *Fax:* (089) 58 93 91 30 *E-mail:* infochem@t-online.de

Kluwer Academic Publishers (KAP), Van Godewijckstr 30, 3311 Dordrecht, Netherlands, Contact: Peter Hendriks *Tel:* (078) 6576283 *Fax:* (078) 6576322 *E-mail:* peter.hendriks@ wkap.nl

Kompetenz Interkon doo, MB 3876608, Bosutska 9, 10000 Zagreb, Croatia, Contact: Nenad Zunec *Tel:* (01) 6311 800 *Fax:* (01) 6311 810 *E-mail:* direktor@kompetenz-interkon.hr

Kompetenz-Verlag, Prenterweg 9, 8045 Weinitzen, Austria, Contact: Wolfgang Hasenhuetl *Tel:* (03132) 4660 33 *Fax:* (03132) 4660 32 *E-mail:* hasenhuetl@kompetenz.at

Media-Daten Ag, Kanzleistr 80, 8026 Zurich, Switzerland, Contact: Heike Findeis *Tel:* (01) 29 69 798 *Fax:* (01) 29 69 702 *E-mail:* heike. findeis@fachmediacom.ch

Media-Daten Verlag, Abraham-Lincoln Str 46, 65189 Wiesbaden, Contact: Jan Peter Kruse *Tel:* (0611) 78 78 *Fax:* (0611) 78 78 *E-mail:* jan-peter.kruse@gwv-fachverlage.de

Mediacom Springer-Verlag Italia, Via Decembrio 28, 20137 Milan, Italy, Contact: Dr Madeleine Hofmann *Tel:* (02) 54209741 *Fax:* (02) 55193360 *E-mail:* m.hofmann@springer.it

MED.Komm Gesellschaft fur medizinische Kommunikation mbH, Neumarkter Str 43, 81673 Munich, Contact: Dr Georg Ralle *Tel:* (089) 43 72 13 72 *Fax:* (089) 43 72 13 70 *E-mail:* ralle@urban-vogel.de

MMV Medien & Medizin Verlag AG, Viadukstr 42, 4051 Basel, Switzerland, Contact: Eleonore E Droux *Tel:* (061) 205 01 73 *Fax:* (061) 205 01 75 *E-mail:* droux@medien-medizin.ch

Physica-Verlag, Tiergartenstr 17, 69121 Heidelberg, Contact: Dr Werner A Mueller *Tel:* (06221) 487 83 45 *Fax:* (06221) 487 81 77 *E-mail:* w.a.mueller@springer.de

Scientific Publishing Services (SPS), 195 Double Rd, Indira nagar, Bangalore 560038, India, Contact: Sharad Wasani *Tel:* (080) 25259595 *Fax:* (080) 25259961 *E-mail:* sharad.wasani@ sps.sify.net

Springer Science+Business Media Benelux NV, Draaiboomstr 6, 2160 Wommelgen, Belgium *Tel:* (03) 3555010 *Fax:* (03) 3555020

Springer Science+Business Media Czech Republic sro, Nadrazni 32, 15000 Prague, Czech Republic, Contact: Tomas Tkacik *Tel:* (02) 25351 111 *Fax:* (02) 25351 151 *E-mail:* tkacik@ springermedia.cz

Springer Science+Business Magyarorszag Kft, Neumann Janos u 1, 2040 Budaors, Hungary, Contact: Janos Adam *Tel:* (023) 422 455 *Fax:* (023) 422 383 *E-mail:* janos.adam@ springermedia.hu

Springer Science+Business Media Schweiz AG, Rutistra 22, 8952 Schkieren, Switzerland, Contact: Heike Findeis *Tel:* (01) 73 85 252

*Fax:* (01) 73 85 128 *E-mail:* heike.findeis@ fachmediacom.ch

Springer-Verlag Berlin/Heidelberg, Heidelberger Platz 3, 14197 Berlin, Contact: Derk Haank *Tel:* (030) 827 87 0 *Fax:* (030) 8214091 *E-mail:* derk.haank@springer-sbm.com

Springer-Verlag France SARL, One rue Paul Cezanne, 75375 Paris Cedex 08, France, Contact: Dr Rolf Lange *Tel:* (06221) 487 8145 *Fax:* (06221) 487 8572 *E-mail:* lange@ springer.de

Springer-Verlag Hong Kong Ltd, Unit 1702 Tower l, Enterprise Square, 9 Sheung Yuet Rd, Kowloon Bay, Kowloon, Hong Kong, Contact: Maurice Kwong *Tel:* 2723 9698 *Fax:* 2724 2366 *E-mail:* mauricek@springer.com.hk

Springer-Verlag GmbH & Co KG Indian Liaison Office, 906-907 Akash Deep Bldg, Barakhamba Rd, New Delhi 110 001, India, Contact: Sanjiv Goswami *Tel:* (011) 335 85 90 *Fax:* (011) 335 87 16 *E-mail:* sanjiv.goswami@springer.firm.in

Springer-Verlag Italia Srl, Via Decembrio 28, 20137 Milan, Italy, Contact: Dr Madeleine Hofmann *Tel:* (02) 54 25 97 21 *Fax:* (02) 55 19 33 60 *E-mail:* m.hofmann@springer.it

Springer-Verlag London Ltd, Sweetapple House, Catteshall Rd, Godalming GU7 3DJ, United Kingdom, Contact: John Watson *Tel:* (014) 83 52 70 51 *Fax:* (014) 83 41 51 44 *E-mail:* john@svl.co.uk

Springer-Verlag KG Wein New York, Sachsenplatz 4-6, 1201 Vienna, Austria, Contact: Rudolf Siegle *Tel:* (01) 330 24 15 *Fax:* (01) 330 24 26 *E-mail:* siegle@springer.at

Springer-Verlag Tokyo Inc, 3-13 Hongo 3-chome, Bunkyo-ku, Toyko 113-0033, Japan, Contact: Terumasa Hirano *Tel:* (03) 38 12 03 31 *Fax:* (03) 38 18 74 54 *E-mail:* t-hirano@svt-ebs.co.jp

Springer-VDI-Verlag GmbH & Co KG, Heinrich-str 24, 40239 Dusseldorf, Contact: Christian W Scheyko *Tel:* (0211) 61 03 222 *Fax:* (0211) 61 03 113 *E-mail:* scheyko@technikwissen.de

Steinkopff-Verlag, Poststr 9, 64293 Darmstadt, Contact: Dr Thomas Thiekoetter *Tel:* (06151) 828 99 0 *Fax:* (06151) 828 99 30 *E-mail:* thiekoetter.steinkopff@springer.de

technopress Fachzeitschriftenverlags-Ges m b H, Inkustra 16, 3403 Klosterneuburg, Austria, Contact: Ferenc Papp *Tel:* (02243) 30111 235 *Fax:* (02243) 30111 222 *E-mail:* papp@ technopress.at

B G Teubner GmbH, Abraham-Lincoln Str 46, 65189 Wiesbaden, Contact: Dr Hans-Dieter Haenel *Tel:* (0611) 78 78 102 *Fax:* (0611) 78 78 104 *E-mail:* hans-dieter.haenel@gwv-fachverlage.de

Universitatsdruckerei H Sturz AG, Beethovenstr 5, 97080 Wurzburg, Contact: Dr Konrad Hartmann *Tel:* (0931) 385 255 359 *Fax:* (0931) 385 359 *E-mail:* drkhartmann@stuertz.de

Urban & Vogel Medien und Medizin Verlagsgesellschaft mbH, Neumarkter Str 43, 81673 Munich, Contact: Dr Georg Ralle *Tel:* (089) 43 72 13 72 *Fax:* (089) 43 72 13 70 *E-mail:* ralle@ urban-vogel.de

Verlag Aktuelle Information GmbH der Platow Brief, Stuttgarter Str 25-29, 60329 Frankfurt am Main, Contact: Albrecht Schirmacher *Tel:* (069) 24 26 39 15 *Fax:* (069) 23 69 09 *E-mail:* albrecht.schirmacher@platow.de

Verlag Dieter Zimpel, Lucile-Grahn Str 37, 81675 Munich, Contact: Dr Hans-Dieter Haenel *Tel:* (089) 306385 21 *Fax:* (089) 306385 77 *E-mail:* hans-dieter.haenel@gwv-fachverlage.de

Verlag Heinrich Vogel GmbH Fachverlag, Neumarkter Str 18, 81664 Munich, Contact: Andreas Koesters *Tel:* (089) 43 72 28 77 *Fax:* (089) 43 72 28 79 *E-mail:* andreas. koesters@bertelsmann.de

Friedr Vieweg & Sohn Verlagsgesellschaft, Abraham-Lincoln Str 46, 65189 Wiesbaden, Contact: Hans-Dieter Haenel *Tel:* (0611) 78

78 102 *Fax:* (0611) 78 78 104 *E-mail:* hans-dieter.haenel@gwv-fachverlage.de

VS Verlag fur Sozialwissenschaften, Abraham-Lincoln Str 46, 65189 Wiesbaden, Contact: Hans-Dieter Haenel *Tel:* (0611) 78 78 102 *Fax:* (0611) 78 78 104 *E-mail:* hans-dieter. haenel@gwv-fachverlage.de

Wendel-Verlag GmbH, Giebergstr 41-45, 34117 Kassel, Contact: Gaby Kraus-Nitsch *Tel:* (0561) 860 02 *Fax:* (0561) 860 03 *E-mail:* gaby.kraus-nitsch@bertelsmann.de

*U.S. Office(s):* Key Curriculum Press, 1150 65 St, Emeryville, CA 94608, United States *Tel:* 510-595-7000 *Fax:* 510-595-7040 *E-mail:* srasmussen@keypress.com

Birkhauser Verlag Boston, 675 Massachusetts Ave, Cambridge, MA 02139-3309, United States, Contact: Rudiger *Tel:* 617-876-2333 *Fax:* 617-876-1272 *E-mail:* rgebauer@springer-ny.com

Princeton Architectural Press, 37 E Seventh St, New York, NY 10011, United States, Contact: Kevin Lippert *Tel:* 212-995-9620 *Fax:* 212-995-9454 *E-mail:* lippert@papress.com

Springer-Verlag New York Inc, 175 Fifth Ave, New York, NY 10010, United States, Contact: Rudiger Gebauer *Tel:* 212-460-1501 *Fax:* 212-505-6528 *E-mail:* rgebauer@springer-ny.com

## L Staackmann Verlag KG+

Lochenerstr 6, 83623 Dietramszell-Linden
*Tel:* (08027) 337; (089) 342248 *Fax:* (08027) 816
*Key Personnel*
Man Dir: Dr Friedrich Vogel
Founded: 1869
Second Address: Verlagsbuero Dr Vogel, Lochener Str 6, 83623 Linden/Obb.
Subjects: Fiction
ISBN Prefix(es): 3-920897; 3-88675

## Staatliche Museen Kassel

Schloss Wilhelmshoehe, 34131 Kassel
Mailing Address: Postfach 410420, 34066 Kassel
*Tel:* (0561) 316-800 *Fax:* (0561) 31680-111
*E-mail:* info@museum-kassel.de
*Web Site:* www.museum-kassel.de
*Key Personnel*
Contact: S Naumer *E-mail:* bibliothek@museum-kussel.de
Subjects: Antiques, Architecture & Interior Design, Art, History
ISBN Prefix(es): 3-931787
Divisions: Museums Bibliothek

## Staatsbibliothek zu Berlin - Preussischer Kulturbesitz (Berlin State Library - Prussian Cultural Foundation)

Unter den Linden 8, 10117 Berlin
Mailing Address: Potsdamer Str 33, 10785 Berlin
*Tel:* (030) 266-0
*E-mail:* webserveradmin@sbb.spk-berlin.de
*Web Site:* www.sbb.spk-berlin.de; www.staatsbibliothek-berlin.de
*Telex:* 183160 staab d
*Key Personnel*
General Dir: Dipl Ing Barbara Schneider-Kempf *E-mail:* barbara.schneider-kempf@sbb.spk-berlin.de
Founded: 1661
Subjects: Library & Information Sciences
ISBN Prefix(es): 3-88053; 3-7361

## Stadler Verlagsgesellschaft mbH+

Max-Stromeyerstr 172, 78467 Konstanz
*Tel:* (07531) 898-0 *Fax:* (07531) 898-103
*E-mail:* info@verlag-stadler.de
*Web Site:* www.verlag-stadler.de
Founded: 1815
Membership(s): Berscuvevcin des Deutschen Buchhandels ev.

Subjects: Art, Geography, Geology, History, Maritime, Music, Dance, Nonfiction (General), Outdoor Recreation, Regional Interests
ISBN Prefix(es): 3-7977

**Stadt Duisburg - Amt Fuer Statistik, Stadtforschung und Europaangelegenheiten**
Bismarckstr 150-158, 47049 Duisburg
*Tel:* (0203) 283 4502 *Fax:* (0203) 288 4404
*E-mail:* amt12@stadt-duisburg.de
*Key Personnel*
Dir: German Bensch
Administrator: Anita Rauser *E-mail:* a.rauser@stadt-duisburg.de
Specialize in public administration-abstracting, statistics & bibliographies.
Periodicals & irregulars.
Subjects: Public Administration
ISBN Prefix(es): 3-89279
Total Titles: 15 Print

**Staedte-Verlag, E v Wagner und J Mitterhuber GmbH+**
Steinbeisstr 9, 70736 Fellbach b Stuttgart
Mailing Address: Postfach 2080, 70710 Fellbach b Stuttgart
*Tel:* (0711) 576201 *Fax:* (0711) 5762199
*E-mail:* info@staedte-verlag.de
*Web Site:* www.staedte-verlag.de *Cable:* STAEDTEVERLAG
*Key Personnel*
Man Dir: Meinhard Mitterhuber; Michael Mitterhuber; Manfred von Wagner
Publicity Dir: Rolf Mueller
Rights Dir: Ulrich Groh
Founded: 1951
Subjects: Geography, Geology, Outdoor Recreation
ISBN Prefix(es): 3-8164; 3-920900
Number of titles published annually: 500 Print
Subsidiaries: NovoPrint Verlags GmbH

**Verlag Stahleisen GmbH+**
Sohnstr 65, 40237 Duesseldorf
Mailing Address: Postfach 105164, 40042 Duesseldorf
*Tel:* (0211) 6707-0 *Fax:* (0211) 6707-117
*E-mail:* stahleisen@stahleisen.de
*Web Site:* www.stahleisen.de *Cable:* STAHLEISEN DUSSELDORF
*Key Personnel*
Man Dir, Rights Permissions: Dipl Ing Adrian Schommers *E-mail:* adrian.schommers@stahleisen.de
Founded: 1908
Specialize in Steel, Casting-Practice.
Subjects: Chemistry, Chemical Engineering, Civil Engineering, Engineering (General), Mechanical Engineering, Technology
ISBN Prefix(es): 3-514
*Associate Companies:* Giesserei-Verlag GmbH, Postfach 102532, 40016 Duesseldorf *E-mail:* giesserei@stahleisen.de
Subsidiaries: Montan- und Wirtschaftsverlag GmbH

**Verlag fuer Standesamtswesen GmbH**
Hanauer Landstr 197, 60314 Frankfurt am Main
*Tel:* (069) 40 58 94 0 *Fax:* (069) 40 58 94 900
*E-mail:* info@vfst.de
*Web Site:* www.vfst.de
*Key Personnel*
Manager: Klaudia Metzner
Founded: 1929
Subjects: Law
ISBN Prefix(es): 3-8019

**Stapp Verlag GmbH+**
Neue Promenade 6, 10178 Berlin
*Tel:* (030) 28304350 *Fax:* (030) 28304353

*Key Personnel*
Owner, Rights & Permissions: Wolfgang Stapp
Founded: 1953
Subjects: Biography, Geography, Geology, History, Literature, Literary Criticism, Essays, Music, Dance, Natural History, Nonfiction (General), Outdoor Recreation, Regional Interests, Travel
ISBN Prefix(es): 3-87776
*Associate Companies:* Kupfergraben Verlags Gesellschaft mbH, Lutzowstr 105, 10785 Berlin *Tel:* (030) 2622097 *Fax:* (030) 2621990
Imprints: Preussische Koepfe
Distributed by Neue Buecher (Switzerland)
Distributor for Kupfergraben Verlag

**C A Starke Verlag+**
Zeppelinstr 2, 65549 Limburg
*Tel:* (06431) 96 15-0 *Fax:* (06431) 96 15 15
*E-mail:* starkeverlag@t-online.de
*Web Site:* www.starkeverlag.de
*Key Personnel*
Manager Dipl Kfm: Rasched Salem
Founded: 1847
Subjects: Biography, Genealogy, History, Nonfiction (General), Heraldry, Family
ISBN Prefix(es): 3-7980

**Stattbuch Verlag GmbH+**
Gneisenaustr 2a, 10961 Berlin
*Tel:* (030) 6913094; (030) 6913095 *Fax:* (030) 6943354
Founded: 1978
Subjects: Literature, Literary Criticism, Essays, Travel
ISBN Prefix(es): 3-922778
*Orders to:* Rotation, Mehringdamm 51, 10961 Berlin

**Stauffenburg Verlag Brigitte Narr GmbH+**
Stauffenbergstr 42, 72074 Tuebingen
Mailing Address: Julius Groos Verlag, Postfach 2525, 72015 Tuebingen
*Tel:* (07071) 9730-0 *Fax:* (07071) 973030
*E-mail:* info@stauffenburg.de
*Web Site:* www.stauffenburg.de
*Key Personnel*
Man Dir & Publisher: Brigitte Narr *Tel:* (07071) 973097 *E-mail:* narr@stauffenburg.de
Founded: 1982
Subjects: Communications, English as a Second Language, Language Arts, Linguistics, Literature, Literary Criticism, Essays, Women's Studies
ISBN Prefix(es): 3-923721; 3-86057
Number of titles published annually: 70 Print
Total Titles: 800 Print
*Associate Companies:* Julius Groos Verlag, Postfach 2525, 72015 Tuebingen

**Steidl Verlag+**
Duestere Str 4, 37073 Goettingen
*Tel:* (0551) 49 60 60 *Fax:* (0551) 49 60 649
*E-mail:* mail@steidl.de
*Web Site:* www.steidl.de
*Key Personnel*
Marketing & International Rights: Jan Menkens *Tel:* (0551) 49 60 618 *Fax:* (0551) 49 60 617 *E-mail:* jmenkens@steidl.de
Public Relations: Claudia Glenewinkel *Tel:* (0551) 49 60 650 *Fax:* (0551) 49 60 644 *E-mail:* cglenewinkel@steidl.de
Sales: Friederike Sprenger *Tel:* (0551) 49 60 616 *E-mail:* fsprenger@steidl.de
Founded: 1968
Hauseigene Druckerei
Specializes in marketing.
Subjects: Art, Biography, Fiction, History, Literature, Literary Criticism, Essays, Marketing, Nonfiction (General), Philosophy, Photography, Poetry, Psychology, Psychiatry
ISBN Prefix(es): 3-88243; 3-86521

Distributed by DAP Book Distribution Center (USA); Gemeinsame Verlagsauslieferung Goettingen (GVA) (Germany, Switzerland & Austria); Thames & Hudson Ltd; VILO DIFFUSION (France)

**Steiger Verlag+**
Hilblestr 54, 80636 Munich
Mailing Address: Postfach 80632, Munich
*Tel:* (089) 9271-0 *Fax:* (089) 9271-68
*Key Personnel*
Man Dir: Dr Petra Altmann
Editor: Frank Heins
Rights & Permissions: Silke Breitlaender
Founded: 1979
Subjects: Astronomy, Earth Sciences, Foreign Countries, Geography, Geology, Outdoor Recreation, Regional Interests, Sports, Athletics, Travel
ISBN Prefix(es): 3-8043; 3-89441; 3-89440; 3-89652
*Parent Company:* Weltbild Verlag GmbH
*Book Club(s):* Weltbild-Versandhandel

**Conrad Stein Verlag GmbH+**
Dorfstr 3a, 59514 Welver
Mailing Address: Postfach 1233, 59512 Welver
*Tel:* (02384) 963912 *Fax:* (02384) 963913
*E-mail:* outdoor@tng.de
*Web Site:* outdoor.tng.de
*Key Personnel*
Rights & Permissions: Conrad Stein
Founded: 1980
Subjects: Outdoor Recreation, Travel
ISBN Prefix(es): 3-922965; 3-89392
Total Titles: 150 Print

**Franz Steiner Verlag Wiesbaden GmbH+**
Birkenwaldstr 44, 70191 Stuttgart
Mailing Address: Postfach 101061, 70009 Stuttgart
*Tel:* (0711) 2582 0 *Fax:* (0711) 2582 290
*E-mail:* service@steiner-verlag.de
*Web Site:* www.steiner-verlag.de
*Key Personnel*
Publishing Dir: Dr Thomas Schaber
Man Dir: Dr Klaus Brauer *Tel:* (0711) 2582 226 *Fax:* (0711) 2582 296 *E-mail:* Service@Deutscher-Apotheker-Verlag.de; Andre Caro *Tel:* (0711) 2582 364 *Fax:* (0711) 2582 296 *E-mail:* Service@Deutscher-Apotheker-Verlag.de; Dr Christian Rotta *Tel:* (0711) 2582 225 *E-mail:* Service@Wissenschaftliche-Verlagsgesellschaft.de
Publicity: Susanne Szoradi *Tel:* (0711) 2582 321 *E-mail:* sszoradi@steiner-verlag.de
Distribution: Siegmar Bauer *Tel:* (0711) 2582 219 *E-mail:* Service@Deutscher-Apotheker-Verlag.de
Production: Gregor Hoppen *Tel:* (0711) 2582 305 *E-mail:* ghoppen@steiner-verlag.de
Founded: 1949
Membership(s): Borsenverein des Deutschen Buchhandels.
Subjects: African American Studies, Archaeology, Art, Asian Studies, Developing Countries, Earth Sciences, Education, Foreign Countries, Geography, Geology, History, Language Arts, Linguistics, Law, Music, Dance, Philosophy, Religion - Buddhist, Religion - Hindu, Religion - Islamic, Classical Studies, History of Science
ISBN Prefix(es): 3-515
Number of titles published annually: 180 Print
Total Titles: 4,800 Print
*Parent Company:* Deutscher Apotheker Verlag
*Associate Companies:* S Hirzel Verlag GmbH & Co *E-mail:* service@hirzel.de; Wissenschaftliche Verlagsgesellschaft mbH *E-mail:* service@wissenschaftliche-Verlagegesellschaft.de

Subsidiaries: Medpharm Scientific Publishers
*Warehouse:* Brockhaus/Commission, Kornwest-
heim *Tel:* (07154) 1327-0 *Fax:* (07154) 132713
*E-mail:* bestell@brocom.de

**J F Steinkopf Verlag GmbH+**
Gartenstr 20, 24103 Kiel
Mailing Address: Postfach 3169, 24030 Kiel
*Key Personnel*
Man Dir: Rainer Thun
International Rights: Johannes Keussen
Founded: 1792
Subjects: Art, Biblical Studies, History, How-to,
Literature, Literary Criticism, Essays, Religion
- Other, Social Sciences, Sociology
ISBN Prefix(es): 3-7984

**Dr Dietrich Steinkopff Verlag GmbH & Co+**
Poststr 9, 64293 Darmstadt
Mailing Address: Postfach 100462, 64204 Darm-
stadt
*Tel:* (06151) 82899-0 (bestellungen) *Fax:* (06151)
82899-40
*E-mail:* info.steinkopff@springer.de
*Web Site:* www.steinkopff.springer.de *Cable:*
STEINKOPFF
*Key Personnel*
Chief Executive Officer: Dr Thomas Thiekoetter
*E-mail:* thiekoetter.steinkopff@springer.de
Marketing & Product Manager: Sabine Scheffler
*E-mail:* scheffler.steinkopff@springer.de
Founded: 1908
Advertising through Springer-Verlag.
Subjects: Health, Nutrition, Medicine, Nursing,
Dentistry, Psychology, Psychiatry
ISBN Prefix(es): 3-7985
Total Titles: 850 Print; 2 CD-ROM
*Parent Company:* Springer-Verlag GmbH & Co
KG, Tiesgastenstr 17, Heidelberg 69121
*U.S. Office(s):* Springer Verlag New York Inc,
175 Fifth Avenue, New York, NY 10010,
United States *Tel:* 212-493-6272
Distributed by Springer-Verlag
*Warehouse:* Springer GmbH & Co,
Auslieferungs-Gesellschaft, Haberstr 7, 69126
Heidelberg *Tel:* (06221) 345-0 *E-mail:* orders@
springer.de

**Steintor Verlag GmbH**
Grapengiesserstr 30, 23556 Luebeck
*Tel:* (0451) 8798849 *Fax:* (0451) 8798837
*E-mail:* info@steintor-verlag.de
*Web Site:* www.steintor-verlag.de
*Key Personnel*
Owner: Rudolf Juedes
Founded: 1969
Subjects: Art
ISBN Prefix(es): 3-9801506
*Bookshop(s):* Gallerie Meiborssen, 37647 Mei-
borssen *Tel:* (05535) 8851

**Steinweg-Verlag, Jurgen vomHoff+**
Fasanenstr 6, 38102 Braunschweig
*Tel:* (0531) 2339197 *Fax:* (0531) 2336649
*Key Personnel*
Contact: Juergen Vom Hoff
Founded: 1986
Subjects: Art, History, Photography, Regional In-
terests, Social Sciences, Sociology
ISBN Prefix(es): 3-925151

**Verlag Stendel+**
Untere Sackgasse 9, 71332 Waiblingen
Mailing Address: Postfach 1713, 71307 Waiblin-
gen
*Tel:* (07151) 956603 *Fax:* (07151) 956605
*E-mail:* info@stendel-verlag.de; verlag.stendel@t-
online.de
*Web Site:* www.verlag-stendel.de
*Key Personnel*
Manager: Dagmar Kuebler

Editor: Roland Kuebler
Founded: 1987
Subjects: Fiction, Literature, Literary Criticism,
Essays, Psychology, Psychiatry, Science Fic-
tion, Fantasy
ISBN Prefix(es): 3-926789

**Stephanus Edition Verlags GmbH+**
Gebhardsweiler 10, 88690 Uhldingen-Muehlofen
Mailing Address: Postfach 1280, 88683
Uhldingen-Muehlofen
*Tel:* (07556) 8331 *Fax:* (07556) 8373
*E-mail:* 0755692110@tonline.de
*Key Personnel*
Man Dir: Sabastian Braun
Editorial: Hans Braun
Founded: 1978
Subjects: Religion - Other
ISBN Prefix(es): 3-921213; 3-922816; 3-932880

**Annemarie Stern,** see Asso Verlag

**Stern-Verlag Janssen & Co+**
Friedrichstr 24-26, 40001 Duesseldorf
Mailing Address: Postfach 101053, 40217 Dues-
seldorf
*Tel:* (0211) 3881-0 *Fax:* (0211) 3881-280
*E-mail:* webmaster@buchhaus-sternverlag.de
*Web Site:* www.buchsv.de
*Key Personnel*
Man Partner: Horst Janssen; Klaus Janssen
Founded: 1900
Subjects: Biography, History, Language Arts, Lin-
guistics, Nonfiction (General), Philosophy
ISBN Prefix(es): 3-87784
*Associate Companies:* Artibus et Literis
*Bookshop(s):* Universitaetsbuchhandlung, Univer-
sitaetstr 1, 40225 Duesseldorf

**Sternberg-Verlag bei Ernst Franz+**
Industriestr 8, 72585 Riederich
*Tel:* (07123) 938922 *Fax:* (07123) 938920
*Key Personnel*
Manager: Gerhard Heinzelmann
Founded: 1950
Subjects: Biblical Studies, Biography, History,
Religion - Protestant, Theology
ISBN Prefix(es): 3-87785
*Parent Company:* Ernst Franz Verlag
Distributed by Haenssler; KNO; K&V; Libri;
Umbreit (D)

**Edition Sternenprinz,** *imprint of*
Hans-Nietsch-Verlag

**Steyler Verlag+**
Postfach 2460, 41311 Nettetal
*Tel:* (02157) 120220 *Fax:* (02157) 120260
*E-mail:* verlag@steyler.de
*Web Site:* www.steyler.de
*Key Personnel*
Man Dir: Andreas Heider; Paul Langer
Founded: 1927
Subjects: Anthropology, Biography, Developing
Countries, Language Arts, Linguistics, Religion
- Catholic, Science (General)
ISBN Prefix(es): 3-87787; 3-8050
*Parent Company:* Steyler Verlagsbuchhandlung
GmbH, Bahnofstr 9, 41334 Nettetal

**Stiebner Verlag GmbH+**
Nymphenburger Str 86, 80636 Munich
*Tel:* (089) 1257414 *Fax:* (089) 12162282
*E-mail:* verlag@stiebner.com
*Web Site:* www.stiebner.com
Founded: 1998
Specialize in reproductions.
Subjects: Art, Sports, Athletics
ISBN Prefix(es): 3-7679; 3-8307

**Stiefel Eurocart GmbH+**
Felix-Wankel-Ring 13a, 85101 Lenting
*Tel:* (08456) 924100 *Fax:* (08456) 924134
*E-mail:* stiefel.gmbH@stiefel-online.de
*Web Site:* www.stiefel-online.com
*Key Personnel*
Manager: Heinrich Stiefel
International Rights: Franz Hofherr
Founded: 1982
Membership(s): World Didac Borsezvenez.
Subjects: Biological Sciences, English as a Sec-
ond Language, Environmental Studies, Geogra-
phy, Geology, History, Language Arts, Linguis-
tics, Mathematics, Religion - Other, French
ISBN Prefix(es): 3-929627
Subsidiaries: Stiefel Digitalprint GmbH (Austria);
Stiefel Digitalprint GmbH (Germany); Stiefel
Eurocart Kft; Stiefel Eurocart KG/SAS; Stiefel
Eurocart Spzoo; Stiefel Eurocart srl; Stiefel Eu-
rocart sro (Czech Republic); Stiefel Eurocart
sro (Slovakia); Stiefel Verlag; Steinberger Verlag GmbH

**Stiftung Buchkunst** (Book Art Foundation)
Adickesallee 1, 60322 Frankfurt am Main
*Tel:* (069) 1525-1800 *Fax:* (069) 1525-1805
*E-mail:* buchkunst@dbf.ddb.de
*Web Site:* www.stiftung-buchkunst.de
*Key Personnel*
Man Dir: Uta Schneider
Founded: 1966
*Branch Office(s)*
Buero Leipzig, Gerichtsweg 26, Leipzig
*Tel:* (0341) 9954-210 *Fax:* (0341) 9954-211

**Edition Gunter Stoberlein**
Niethammerstr 15, 80997 Munich
*Tel:* (089) 8115289
*Key Personnel*
Owner: Gunter Stoberlein
Founded: 1972
Membership(s): Boirsenverein Des Deutschen
Buchhandels.
Subjects: Art, Literature, Literary Criticism, Es-
says, Poetry
ISBN Prefix(es): 3-88045; 3-921430

**Stollfuss Verlag Bonn GmbH & Co KG+**
Dechenstr 7, 53115 Bonn
Mailing Address: Postfach 2428, 53014 Bonn
*Tel:* (0228) 7 24-0 *Fax:* (0228) 7 24-9 11 81
*E-mail:* info@stollfuss.de
*Web Site:* www.stollfuss.de *Cable:*
STOLLFUSSVERLAG
*Key Personnel*
Man Dir: Michael Stollfuss; Wolfgang Stollfuss
Editorial: Hans-Josef Metz
Rights & Permissions, Production: Reinhard Just
Founded: 1913
Specialize in Tax & Fiscal Law.
Subjects: Accounting, Economics, Finance, Law,
Public Administration
ISBN Prefix(es): 3-08
Distributor for Schriften des BMF und BMA
*Warehouse:* Justus-von Liebig Str 6, 53121 Bonn

**Straelener Manuskripte Verlag GmbH+**
Venloerstr 45, 47638 Straelen
Mailing Address: Postfach 1324, 47630 Straelen
*Tel:* (02834) 6588 *Fax:* (02834) 6588
*Web Site:* www.straelener-manuskripte.de
*Key Personnel*
Manager: Renate Birkenhauer, PhD *E-mail:* r.
birkenhauer@straelener-manuskripte.de
Founded: 1983
Subjects: Literature, Literary Criticism, Essays,
Poetry
ISBN Prefix(es): 3-89107
Number of titles published annually: 2 Print
Total Titles: 33 Print

**Stroemfeld/Nexus,** *imprint of* Stroemfeld Verlag

**Stroemfeld/Roter Stern**, *imprint of* Stroemfeld Verlag

**Stroemfeld Verlag+**
Holzhausenstr 4, 60322 Frankfurt
*Tel:* (069) 955 226-0 *Fax:* (069) 955 226-22
*E-mail:* info@stroemfeld.de
*Web Site:* www.stroemfeld.de
*Key Personnel*
Publisher: Karl D Wolff
International Rights: Doris Kern
Founded: 1981 (Nexus)
Subjects: Literature, Literary Criticism, Essays, Psychology, Psychiatry
ISBN Prefix(es): 3-87877; 3-86109
*Parent Company:* Stroemfeld Verlag AG, Basel, Switzerland
*Imprints:* Stroemfeld/Roter Stern; Stroemfeld/Nexus
*Branch Office(s)*
Basel, Switzerland
*Orders to:* SOVA, Friesstr 20-24, 60388 Frankfurt

**STS Standard Tabellen und Software Verlag GmbH**
Subsidiary of Rudolf Haufe Verlag GmbH & Co KG
Fraunhoferstr 5, 82152 Planegg
Mailing Address: Postfach 1363, 82142 Planegg
*Tel:* (089) 89517-0 *Fax:* (089) 89517290
*Key Personnel*
Dir: Helmuth Hopfner; Martin Lagua; Uwe Renald Muller
Founded: 1939
ISBN Prefix(es): 3-86027

**Sturtz Verlag GmbH**
Imprint of Verlagshaus Wurzburg
Beethovenstr 5, 97070 Wurzburg
*Tel:* (0931) 385235 *Fax:* (0931) 385305
*E-mail:* info@verlagshaus.de
*Web Site:* www.verlagshaus.com
*Key Personnel*
Publishing Dir: Dieter Krause
Dir, Production: Juergen Roth
Sales Dir: Johannes Glesius
Founded: 1830
Subjects: Travel
ISBN Prefix(es): 3-8003

**Sueddeutsche Verlagsgesellschaft mbH+**
Sendlingerstr 8, 80331 Munich
*Tel:* (089) 2183-0 *Fax:* (089) 2183-787
*E-mail:* verlag@sueddeutsche.de; redaktion@sueddeutsche.de
*Web Site:* www.sueddeutsche.de
*Key Personnel*
Man Dir, Rights & Permissions: Udo Vogt
Contact: Reinhard Keller
Founded: 1898
Subjects: Art, History, Nonfiction (General), Regional Interests, Religion - Catholic
ISBN Prefix(es): 3-88294; 3-920921
*Parent Company:* Schwabenverlag AG, Senefelderstr 12, Ostfildern
*Branch Office(s)*
Schwabenverlag AG, Abt Buchhandlung, Bahnhofstr 21, Aalen
*Bookshop(s):* Sueddeutsche Verlagsges mbH, Sedelhofgasse, 89073 Ulm/Donau; Schwabenverlag AG, Abt Buchhandlung, Spital Str 19, 73479 Ellwangen

**Suedverlag GmbH+**
Schuetzenstr 24, 78462 Konstanz
Mailing Address: Postfach 10 20 51, 78420 Konstanz
*Tel:* (07531) 9053-0 *Fax:* (07531) 9053-98
*E-mail:* willkommen@uvk.de
*Web Site:* www.suedverlag.de

*Key Personnel*
Publishing Manager: Walter Engstle *Tel:* (07531) 905312 *E-mail:* walter.engstle@uvk.de
Founded: 1945
Subjects: Biography, Humor, Regional Interests
ISBN Prefix(es): 3-87800
*Associate Companies:* UVK Verlagsgesellschaft mbH
*Orders to:* Brockhaus Commission Verlagsauslieferung, Kreidlerstr 9, 70806 Kornwestheim

**Suedwest Verlag GmbH & Co KG+**
Bayerstr 71-73, 80335 Munich
*Tel:* (089) 4136-0; (01805) 990505 (hotline) *Fax:* (089) 5148-2229
*E-mail:* heyne-suedwest@randomhouse.de
*Web Site:* www.suedwest-verlag.de
*Key Personnel*
Man Partner: Christian Strasser
Publicity & Co-production: Bettina Breitling
Founded: 1945
Subjects: Cookery, Health, Nutrition, Nonfiction (General), Travel
*Associate Companies:* Paul List Verlag GmbH; W Ludwig Verlag GmbH; C J Bucher Verlag GmbH

**Suhrkamp Verlag+**
Lindenstr 29-35, 60325 Frankfurt am Main
Mailing Address: Postfach 101945, 60019 Frankfurt am Main
*Tel:* (069) 75601-0 *Fax:* (069) 75601-522; (069) 75601-314
*Web Site:* www.suhrkamp.de *Cable:* SUHRKAMPVERLAG
*Key Personnel*
Publisher: Ulla Unseld-Berkewicz
Man Dir: Philip Roeder *Tel:* (069) 75601-500 *E-mail:* roeder@suhrkamp.de
Editorial Dir: Dr Raines Weiss
Sales & Marketing Dir: Georg Rieppel
Rights & Permissions: Dr Petra Hardt
Founded: 1950
Subjects: Biography, Fiction, Philosophy, Poetry, Psychology, Psychiatry, Science (General)
ISBN Prefix(es): 3-518
*Associate Companies:* Deutscher Klassiker Verlag; Insel Verlag; Juedischer Verlag; Suhrkamp Verlag AG, Switzerland
Foreign Rep(s): Agenzia Letteraria Internazionale (Italy); Balla & Co Literary Agents (Hungary); Bardon Chinese Media Agency (Taiwan); Claudia Brandes (Netherlands, Eastern Europe, Scandinavia); Ulrich Breth (Asia, Greece, Turkey); Michael Griesinger (Africa, Latin America, Portugal, South America, Spain); Petra Christina Hardt (Australia, UK, British Commonwealth, China, France, Israel, Italy, Middle East, US); Hercules Business (China); International Editors (Latin America, Portugal, Spain); International Literature Bureau (Netherlands); Leohardt & Hoier Literary Agency (Scandinavia); Sakai Agency (Japan)

**Suin Buch-Verlag**
Kappstr 29, 64678 Lindenfels
*Tel:* (06255) 2657 *Fax:* (06255) 9596875
*Key Personnel*
Owner: Dr Bernhard Suin de Boutemard
Founded: 1975
Subjects: Alternative, Anthropology, Civil Engineering, Education, History, Human Relations, Philosophy, Religion - Catholic, Religion - Protestant, Religion - Other, Self-Help, Social Sciences, Sociology, Theology
ISBN Prefix(es): 3-921559

**Sulamith Wulfing Edition**, *imprint of* Aquamarin Verlag

**Sulamith Wulfing Verlag**, *imprint of* Aquamarin Verlag

**Svato Zapletal+**
Missundestr 18, 22769 Hamburg
*Tel:* (040) 4390004 *Fax:* (040) 4390004
*Key Personnel*
Contact: Svato Zapletal
Founded: 1976
Subjects: Art, Fiction, Poetry
ISBN Prefix(es): 3-924283

**Sybex Verlag GmbH+**
Postfach 501253, 50972 Cologne
*Tel:* (02236) 399920-0 *Fax:* (02236) 399922-9
*E-mail:* sybex@sybex.de
*Web Site:* www.sybex.de
*Key Personnel*
Manager: Gerhard Prollius
Founded: 1981
Subjects: Computer Science
ISBN Prefix(es): 3-88745; 3-8155
*Associate Companies:* Sybex Uitgeverij BV, Birkstr 95, 3768 HD Soest, Netherlands *Tel:* (031) 3560 27625 *Fax:* (031) 3560 26556 *E-mail:* sybex@sybex.nl; Sybex SARL, 76 Ave Pierre Brossolette, 92247 Malakoff Paris Cedex 14, France *Tel:* (01) 55 58 4000 *Fax:* (01) 49 65 0410 *Web Site:* www.sybex.fr
*U.S. Office(s):* Sybex Inc, 1151 Marine Village Parkway, Alameda, CA 94501, United States *Tel:* 510-523-8233 *Fax:* 510-523-2373 *E-mail:* info@sybex.com
*Orders to:* VVA, Postfach 7777, 33310 Gutersloh *Tel:* (05) 2410805906 *Fax:* (05) 2410460130

**Synthesis Verlag+**
Postfach 14 32 06, 45262 Essen
*Tel:* (0201) 51 01 88 *Fax:* (0201) 51 10 49
*E-mail:* synthesis@synthesis-verlag.com
*Web Site:* www.synthesis-verlag.com
Founded: 1979
Subjects: Health, Nutrition, Science (General)
ISBN Prefix(es): 3-922026; 3-936503
*Orders to:* VSB-Verlagsservice Braunschweig GmbH, Georg-Westermann-Allee 66, 38104 Braunschweig *Tel:* (0531) 7080708277 *Fax:* (0531) 708 619

**Taoasis Verlag, Birgit Meyer+**
Bismarckstr 23, 32657 Lemgo
Mailing Address: PO Box 824, 32638 Lemgo
*Tel:* (05261) 9383-0 *Fax:* (05261) 9383-21
*E-mail:* info@taoasis.de
*Web Site:* www.taoasis.de
*Key Personnel*
Man Dir: Axel Meyer
ISBN Prefix(es): 3-926014

**TASCHEN GmbH**
Hohenzollernring 53, 50672 Cologne
*Tel:* (0221) 201 80 0 *Fax:* (0221) 25 49 19
*E-mail:* contact@taschen.com
*Web Site:* www.taschen.com
*Key Personnel*
Dir: Benedikt Taschen
Chief Editor: Dr Angelika Taschen
Founded: 1980
Subjects: Architecture & Interior Design, Art, Erotica, Photography
ISBN Prefix(es): 3-8228
*Subsidiaries:* TASCHEN America; TASCHEN Deutschland; TASCHEN Espana; TASCHEN France; TASCHEN Japan; TASCHEN UK
*Bookshop(s):* 2 rue de Buci, 75006 Paris, France *Tel:* (01) 40 51 79 22 *E-mail:* store@taschen-france.com; Hohenzollernring 28, 50672 Cologne *Tel:* (0221) 2573304 *Fax:* (0221) 254968 *E-mail:* store@taschen.com; 354 N Beverly Hills Dr, Beverly Hills, CA 90210, United States *Tel:* 310-274-4300 *Fax:* 310-274-4040 *E-mail:* store-la@taschen.com

**Verlag fuer Technik und Wirtschaft GmbH & Co KG**, see Vereinigte Fachverlage GmbH

**Hochschule fur Technik Wirtschaft und Kultur Leipzig (FH)**
Karl Liebknechtstr 132, 04277 Leipzig
Mailing Address: Postfach 30 11 66, 04251 Leipzig
*Tel:* (0341) 3076-0 *Fax:* (0341) 3076-6456
*E-mail:* dekan@htwk.leipzig.de
*Web Site:* www.htwk-leipzig.de
*Key Personnel*
Contact: Prof Torsten Seela
Founded: 1992

**Otto Teich+**
Hilpertstr 9, 64295 Darmstadt
Mailing Address: Postfach 200144, 64300 Darmstadt
*Tel:* (06151) 824120 *Fax:* (06151) 895656
*Key Personnel*
Man Dir & International Rights: Christine Otto
Founded: 1889
Specialize in humorous performances.
Subjects: Drama, Theater, Humor
ISBN Prefix(es): 3-8069
*Associate Companies:* Eduard Bloch Verlag, Hilpertstr 9, 64295 Darmstadt; Bergwald Verlag, Hilpertstr 9, 64295 Darmstadt
Imprints: Baerenreiter-Spieltexte

**Alf Teloeken Verlag KG**, see Alba Fachverlag GmbH & Co KG

**TELOS**, *imprint of* Springer Science+Business Media GmbH & Co KG

**Edition Temmen+**
Hohenlohestr 21, 28209 Bremen
*Tel:* (0421) 34843-0 *Fax:* (0421) 348094
*E-mail:* info@edition-temmen.de
*Web Site:* www.edition-temmen.de
*Key Personnel*
Owner: Horst Temmen
Founded: 1983
Subjects: Government, Political Science, History, Literature, Literary Criticism, Essays, Maritime, Military Science, Nonfiction (General), Social Sciences, Sociology, Travel
ISBN Prefix(es): 3-926958; 3-86108

**teNeues Verlag GmbH & Co KG+**
Am Selder 37, 47906 Kempen
*Tel:* (02152) 916-0 *Fax:* (02152) 916-111
*E-mail:* verlag@teneues.com
*Web Site:* www.teneues.com
*Key Personnel*
Publisher & Man Dir: Hendrik te Neues
   *Tel:* (02152) 916210 *E-mail:* hteneues@aol.com
Man Dir, Marketing: Hartmut Rau *Tel:* (02152) 916126 *E-mail:* hrau@teneues.de
Man Dir, International Division: Marcus Herfort *Tel:* (02152) 916117 *E-mail:* mherfort@teneues.de
Dir, Sales & Marketing Book Trade: Ralf Daab *Tel:* (02152) 916120
Man Dir, Product Development: Sebastian te Neues
Dir, Editorial Dept: Kristina Kruger; Sabine Wurfel *Tel:* (02152) 916245
Man Dir, Chief Financial Officer/Administration: Dieter Schepers
Founded: 1950
International publishing group with offices in Kempen, New York & London, world wide distribution in over 60 countries
Calendars, art merchandise & internet reference guides.
Subjects: Architecture & Interior Design, Art, Fashion, Photography, Travel
ISBN Prefix(es): 3-8238; 3-87580; 3-8377; 3-89865
Total Titles: 20 E-Book

*Parent Company:* teNeues Publishing Co, c/o Macmillan Canada, 29 Birch Ave, Toronto, ON M4V 1E2, Canada
*Associate Companies:* teNeues Publishing UK, Aldwych House, 71-91 Aldwych, London WC2B 4HN, United Kingdom *Tel:* (020) 8283 6426 *Fax:* (020) 8283 6426; teNeues France, 140 rue de la Croix Nivert, 75015 Paris, France *Tel:* (01) 55-766205 *Fax:* (01) 55-766419 *E-mail:* teneuesfrance@wanadoo.fr
Divisions: teNeues Publishing Canada
*U.S. Office(s):* teNeues Publishing Company, 16 W 22 St, New York, NY 10010, United States, Dir, Sales & Marketing: Stephen Hulburt *Tel:* 212-627-9090 *Fax:* 212-627-9534
*Orders to:* teNeues Publishing Co New York, 16 W 22 St, New York, NY 10010, United States *Tel:* 212-627-9090 *Fax:* 212-627-9511 *E-mail:* tnp@teneues-usa.com (USA orders)

**Terra-Verlag GmbH**
Neuhauserstr 21, 78464 Konstanz
Mailing Address: Postfach 102144, 78421 Konstanz
*Tel:* (07531) 81220 *Fax:* (07531) 812299
*E-mail:* info@terra-verlag.de
*Web Site:* www.terra-verlag.de
*Key Personnel*
Publisher: Eberhard Heizmann
Founded: 1946
ISBN Prefix(es): 3-920942
Total Titles: 10 Print
Subsidiaries: Terra Media Kft

**Tessloff Verlag Ragnar Tessloff GmbH & Co KG**
Burgschmietstr 2-4, 90419 Nuernberg
*Tel:* (0911) 39906-0 *Fax:* (0911) 39906-39
*E-mail:* tessloff@osn.de
*Web Site:* www.tessloff.com
*Key Personnel*
General Manager: Dr Thomas Seng
ISBN Prefix(es): 3-7886

**Tetra Verlag Gmbh+**
Berliner Str 8, 16727 Berlin-Velten
*Tel:* (03304) 20 22-0 *Fax:* (03304) 20 22-20
*E-mail:* info@tetra-verlag.de
*Web Site:* www.tetra-verlag.de
*Key Personnel*
Publisher: Dr Hans-Joachim Herrmann
   *E-mail:* hermann@tetra-verlag.de
Founded: 1972
Publish calendars.
Membership(s): Boersenverein des Deutsche Buchhandels.
Subjects: Animals, Pets, Maritime, Popular Scientific & Lobbyist Literature
ISBN Prefix(es): 3-89745
Number of titles published annually: 8 Print
Total Titles: 93 Print

**Tetzlaff Verlag**
Nordkanalstr 36, 20097 Hamburg
Mailing Address: Postfach 101609, 20010 Hamburg
*Tel:* (040) 237 14-03 *Fax:* (040) 237 14-233
*Web Site:* www.eurailpress.com
*Key Personnel*
Man Dir: Detlev K Suchanek *Tel:* (040) 237 14-228 *Fax:* (040) 237 14-236 *E-mail:* suchanek@eurailpress.com
Editor: Christoph Mueller *Tel:* (040) 237 14-152 *Fax:* (040) 237 14-205 *E-mail:* mueller@eurailpress.com
Sales: Riccardo di Stefano *Tel:* (040) 237 14-101 *Fax:* (040) 237 14-233 *E-mail:* distefano@eurailpress.com; Sophie Elfendahl *Tel:* (040) 237 14-220 *Fax:* (040) 237 14-236 *E-mail:* elfendahl@eurailpress.com
Founded: 1906

Subjects: Transportation
ISBN Prefix(es): 3-87814

**B G Teubner Verlag+**
Unit of GWV Fachverlage Gmbh
Abraham-Lincoln-Str 46, 65189 Wiesbaden
*Tel:* (0611) 78780 *Fax:* (0611) 7878470
*Web Site:* www.teubner.de; www.gwv-fachverlage.de
*Key Personnel*
Man Dir: Dr Heinz Weinheimer
Rights & Permissions Manager: Mrs Angelika Bolisega *E-mail:* angelika.bolisega@gwv-fachverlage.de
General Manager: Hans-Dieter Haenel
Editorial: Ulrike Schmickler-Hirzebruch; Ewald Schmitt
Founded: 1811
Subjects: Chemistry, Chemical Engineering, Civil Engineering, Computer Science, Electronics, Electrical Engineering, Mathematics, Mechanical Engineering, Physics, Technology
ISBN Prefix(es): 3-519; 3-8154
Total Titles: 1,500 Print; 14 Online
*Parent Company:* Springer Science & Business Media
*Orders to:* VVA Bertelsmann Distribution, Postfach 7777, 33310 Guetersloh

**Teubner Edition**, *imprint of* Graefe und Unzer Verlag GmbH

**edition Text & Kritik im Richard Boorberg Verlag GmbH & Co+**
Levelingstr 6a, 81673 Munich
Mailing Address: Postfach 800529, 81605 Munich
*Tel:* (089) 43600012 *Fax:* (089) 43600019
*E-mail:* info@etk-muenchen.de
*Web Site:* www.etk-muenchen.de
*Key Personnel*
Man Dir: Dr Berndt Oesterhelt
International Rights: Dr Monika Bopp *E-mail:* m.bopp-edition-text+kritik@boorberg.de
Founded: 1975
Subjects: Film, Video, Literature, Literary Criticism, Essays, Music, Dance
ISBN Prefix(es): 3-921402; 3-88377
Divisions: Auslieferung von Verlag der Autoren

**Thalacker Medien GmbH Co KG+**
Member of Horti Media Europe (HME)
Postfach 83 64, 38133 Braunschweig
*Tel:* (0531) 38004 0 *Fax:* (0531) 38004 25
*E-mail:* info@thalackermedien.de
*Web Site:* www.thalackermedien.de
*Key Personnel*
Contact: Brigitte Mayr *Tel:* (0531) 3800447 *Fax:* (0531) 38004830 *E-mail:* b.mayr@thalackermedien.de
Founded: 1867
Specialize in technical literature of gardening & floral design, newspapers, magazines, technical books & reference books.
Membership(s): Boersenverein des Deutschen Buchhandels & Verband Deutscher Zeitschriften Verleger.
Subjects: Agriculture, Gardening, Plants
ISBN Prefix(es): 3-87815
Number of titles published annually: 10 Print
Total Titles: 80 Print

**Thauros Verlag GmbH**
Jakob-Huberstr 9, 88171 Weiler-Simmerberg
Mailing Address: Postfach 1141, 88168 Weiler im Allgaeu
*Tel:* (08387) 2510 *Fax:* (08387) 3731
*E-mail:* thaurosverlag@t-online.de
*Key Personnel*
Editor: Christian Schneider
Founded: 1978

Subjects: Astrology, Occult, Biblical Studies, Biography, Religion - Jewish, Religion - Other
ISBN Prefix(es): 3-88411

**Konrad Theiss Verlag GmbH+**
Moenchhaldenstr 28, 70191 Stuttgart
*Tel:* (0711) 255 27-0 *Fax:* (0711) 255 27-17
*E-mail:* service@theiss.de
*Web Site:* www.theiss.de *Cable:*
THEISSVERLAG STUTTGART
*Key Personnel*
Man Dir: Christian Rieker *Tel:* (0711) 255 27-12
Sales: Ruth Kessler *E-mail:* kessler@theiss.de
Production: Karin Dechow *Tel:* (0711) 255 27-18
 *E-mail:* dechow@theiss.de
Program Manager: Jurgen Beckedorf *Tel:* (0711)
 255 27-16 *E-mail:* beckedorf@theiss.de
Founded: 1997
Subjects: Archaeology, Art, History, Nonfiction
 (General)
ISBN Prefix(es): 3-8062
Total Titles: 2 CD-ROM
Distributed by Wissenschiftliche Buchgesellschaft

**Druck-und Verlagshaus Thiele & Schwarz GmbH+**
Werner-Heisenbergstr 7, 34123 Kassel
*Tel:* (0561) 9 59 25-0 *Fax:* (0561) 9 59 25-68
*E-mail:* info@thiele-schwarz.de
*Web Site:* www.thiele-schwarz.de *Cable:* THIELE
 & SCHWARZ KASSEL-WALDAU
*Key Personnel*
Proprietor: Rolf Schwarz
Founded: 1879
ISBN Prefix(es): 3-87816
*Associate Companies:* Verlag Schule und Elternhaus
*Bookshop(s):* Buch und Musik Center Wilhelmshoehe, Wilhelmshoeheer Allee 256, 34119 Kassel; Buchhandlung Am Markt, Marktstr 10, 99310 Armkstadt

**Georg Thieme Verlag KG+**
Ruedigerstr 14, 70469 Stuttgart
Mailing Address: Postfach 301120, 70451
 Stuttgart
*Tel:* (0711) 8931-0 *Fax:* (0711) 8931-298
*E-mail:* kunden.service@thieme.de
*Web Site:* www.thieme.de; www.thieme.com
 *Cable:* THIEMEBUCH
*Key Personnel*
Publisher: Albrecht Hauff
Man Dir: Dr Wolfgang Knueppe
Press: Anne-Katrin Doebler
Division Head, Marketing & Sales: Dr Harald
 Steiner
Dir, International Marketing & Sales: Malik
 Lechelt *E-mail:* malik.lechelt@thieme.de
International Rights Manager: Barbara Pfeifer
 *Tel:* (0711) 8931-184 *Fax:* (0711) 8931-143
 *E-mail:* barbara.pfeifer@thieme.de
Founded: 1886
Subjects: Biological Sciences, Chemistry, Chemical Engineering, Health, Nutrition, Medicine, Nursing, Dentistry, Psychology, Psychiatry, Physiotherapy
ISBN Prefix(es): 3-13; 3-8304; 1-58890
Number of titles published annually: 600 Print;
 20 CD-ROM; 10 Audio
Total Titles: 5,100 Print; 100 CD-ROM; 50 Audio
*Associate Companies:* MVS Medizinverlage
 Stuttgart GmbH & Co KG, Oswald-Hesse-Str
 50, 70469 Stuttgart, Foreign Rights: Susanne
 Seeger *Tel:* (0711) 8931-147 *Fax:* (0711) 8931-143
Imprints: Enke; Haug; Hippokrates; Parey; Sonntag; TRIAS
*U.S. Office(s):* Thieme Medical Publishers, 333
 Seventh Ave, 5th Floor, New York, NY 10001,
 United States
Distributed by Baker & Taylor (US); Miguel Concha SA (Chile); Elsevier Australia (Australia &

New Zealand); Hwa Eng Trading Co (Taiwan - books only); Jaypee Brothers Medical Publishers (P) Ltd (India - medicine & dentistry only); Lidel Edicoes Tecnicas LDA (Portugal, Angola, Mozambique, Guinea-Bissau, Cape Verde Islands, Sao Tome - books & journals); Login Brothers Canada (Canada); J A Majors Co (US); Matthews Medical Books (US); Nobel Tip Kitabevleri (Turkey); PF Book Importer (Indonesia - books only); Ernesto Reichmann Distribuidora de Livros Ltda (Brazil); Rittenhouse Book Distributors (US); Seoul Medical Scientific Books Co (South Korea - books only)
Distributor for AANS; Martin Dunitz
Foreign Rep(s): Academic Marketing Services (Pty) Ltd (Botswana, Namibia, South Africa); Amin Al-Abini (North Africa, Middle East exc Iran); Jamshid Fattahi (Iran); Michael Goh (Brunei, Burma, Cambodia, China, Indonesia, Korea, Laos, Malaysia, Philippines, Singapore, Taiwan, Thailand, Vietnam); Laszlo Horvath (Eastern Europe, Russia); Aiko Hosoya (Japan); Anwer Iqbal (Pakistan); Momenta Publishing Ltd (Belgium, UK, Netherlands, Ireland); David Towle International (Baltic States, Scandinavia); Trinidad Lopez Gonzalez (Spain); Katia Zevelekakis (Cyprus, Greece)
*Bookshop(s):* Frohberg Buchhandlung fuer Medizin, Tempelhofer Weg 11-12, 10829 Berlin
 *Tel:* (030) 8390030
*Warehouse:* Koch, Neff & Oetinger & Co, Verlagsauslieferung, Schockenriedstr 39, Postfach 800620, 70506 Stuttgart

**Thien, Hans-Gunter, u Hanns Wienold**
Verlag Westfalisches Dampfboot, Hafenweg 26a,
 48145 Muenster
*Tel:* (0251) 3900480 *Fax:* (0251) 39004850
*E-mail:* info@dampfboot-verlag.de
*Web Site:* www.dampfboot-verlag.de
*Key Personnel*
Man Dir: Dr Hans-Guenther Thien; Dr Hanns
 Wienold
Founded: 1984
ISBN Prefix(es): 3-89691
Number of titles published annually: 40 Print
Distributor for Prolit Verlagaushieferung

**Thienemann Verlag GmbH+**
Blumenstr 36, 70182 Stuttgart
*Tel:* (0711) 210 55-0 *Fax:* (0711) 210 55 39
*E-mail:* info@thienemann.de
*Web Site:* www.thienemann.de
*Key Personnel*
Man Dir: Klaus Willberg
Editor-in-Chief: Stefan Wendel
Foreign & Domestic Rights: Doris Keller-Riehm
Founded: 1849
Subjects: Fiction
ISBN Prefix(es): 3-522
Number of titles published annually: 100 Print
Total Titles: 800 Print
Imprints: Gabriel Verlag (religious children's
 books)
*Distribution Center:* Koch, Neff & Oetinger &
 Co GmbH, Stuttgart

**Verlag Theodor Thoben**
Langestr 77-79, 49610 Quakenbrueck
*Tel:* (05431) 3486 *Fax:* (05431) 3584
*E-mail:* info@buecher-thoben.de
*Web Site:* www.buecher-thoben.de
*Key Personnel*
Publisher: Theodor Thoben
Founded: 1903
Subjects: Regional Interests
ISBN Prefix(es): 3-921176
*Bookshop(s):* Buecher-Thoben, Lange Str 77-79,
 49610 Quakenbrueck

**Hans Thoma Verlag GmbH Kunst und Buchverlag**
Vorholzstr 7, 76137 Karlsruhe
Mailing Address: Postfach 6345, 76043 Karlsruhe
*Tel:* (0721) 932750 *Fax:* (0721) 9327520
*E-mail:* htv@pv_medien.de
*Web Site:* www.pv_medien.de/htv/ueberuns.htm
*Key Personnel*
Manager: Herwig Schelling
Subjects: Art
ISBN Prefix(es): 3-87297
*Parent Company:* Evangelischer Presseverband

**Jan Thorbecke Verlag GmbH & Co+**
Senefelderstr 12, 73760 Ostfildern
Mailing Address: Postfach 4201, 73745 Ostfildern
*Tel:* (0711) 44 06-0 *Fax:* (0711) 44 06-199
*E-mail:* info@thorbecke.de
*Web Site:* www.thorbecke.de *Cable:*
THORBECKE
*Key Personnel*
Manager: Bardo Jensch; Ulrich Peters
Publisher: Dr Joern Laakman *Tel:* (0711) 44 06-
 191 *E-mail:* joern.laakmann@thorbecke.de
Marketing: Matthias Reimann *Tel:* (0711) 44 06-
 195 *E-mail:* matthias.reimann@thorbecke.de
Founded: 1946
Subjects: Archaeology, Art, Foreign Countries,
 History, Literature, Literary Criticism, Essays,
 Regional Interests, Theology, Travel
ISBN Prefix(es): 3-7995
*Associate Companies:* Bergstadtverlag Wilhelm Gottlieb Korn GmbH, Wuerzburg;
 Bergstadtverlag Wilhelm Gottlieb Korn GmbH,
 Karlstr 10, Postfach 546, 75488 Sigmaringen
 (correspondence & distribution)
*Distribution Center:* Brockhaus / Commission, Kreidlerstr 9, 70806 Kornwestheim
 *Tel:* (07154) 13 27-54 *Fax:* (07154) 13 27-
 13 *E-mail:* info@brocom.de *Web Site:* www.
 brocom.de
Buch- und Medienvertriebs AG, Hochstr 357,
 8200 Schaffhausen, Switzerland *Tel:* (052) 6 43
 54 30 *Fax:* (052) 6 43 54 35 *E-mail:* order@
 buch-medien.ch (Switzerland)

**Tipp Creative**, *imprint of* Xenos
Verlagsgesellschaft mbH

**Tipress Deutschland**, *imprint of* Tipress
Dienstleistungen fuer das Verlagswesen GmbH

**Tipress Dienstleistungen fuer das Verlagswesen GmbH+**
Johannes-Fecht Str 2, Hauptstr 66, 79295
 Sulzburg
*Tel:* (07634) 591193 *Fax:* (07634) 591192
*E-mail:* tipress@tipress.com
*Web Site:* www.tipress.com
*Key Personnel*
President: Roberto Toso
Literary agency & services for publishers in four
 languages; projects of series of books, realization of books & consultants.
Subjects: Business, Crafts, Games, Hobbies, Fiction, Nonfiction (General)
Imprints: Tipress Deutschland
*Branch Office(s)*
Via Cernaia 34, 10122 Turin, Italy *Tel:* (011)
 533487 *Fax:* (011) 535283

**Titania-Verlag Ferdinand Schroll+**
Forststr 104B, 70193 Stuttgart
Mailing Address: Postfach 104832, 70042
 Stuttgart
*Tel:* (0711) 63 81 25 *Fax:* (0711) 63 69 872
 *Cable:* TITANIAVERLAG STUTTGART
*Key Personnel*
Publisher, International Rights: Wolfgang Schroll
Publisher: Gerdi Schroll
Founded: 1949
Subjects: Fiction
ISBN Prefix(es): 3-7996

**S Toeche-Mittler Verlag GmbH**
Hindenburgstr 33, 64295 Darmstadt
*Tel:* (06151) 33665 *Fax:* (06151) 314048
*E-mail:* info@net-library.de
*Web Site:* www.net-library.de
*Key Personnel*
Sales Manager: Albrecht Lueft
Founded: 1789
Subjects: Economics, Law, Nonfiction (General),
    Sports, Athletics
ISBN Prefix(es): 3-87820
Divisions: TRIOPS, Tropical Scientific Books

**Toleranz Verlag, Nielsen Frederic W**
Sundgauallee 19, 79114 Freiburg im Breisgau
Mailing Address: Postfach 6009, 79114 Freiburg
    im Breisgau
*Tel:* (0761) 81415
*E-mail:* irenenielsen@web.de
Founded: 1971
Subjects: Biography, Government, Political Sci-
    ence, History, Poetry
ISBN Prefix(es): 3-925745; 3-9800069

**Tomus Verlag GmbH+**
Am Steinfeld 4, 94065 Waldkirchen Niederbay
*Tel:* (08581) 910666 *Fax:* (08581) 910668
*E-mail:* info@tomus.de
*Web Site:* www.tomus.de
*Key Personnel*
Publisher: Dr Gerhard Braunsperger
Dir: Oliver A Frank
Founded: 1962
Membership(s): Stockmarket Association.
Subjects: Animals, Pets, Cookery, Crafts, Games,
    Hobbies, Humor, Science (General), Travel
ISBN Prefix(es): 3-8231
*Associate Companies:* Telelit Verlag AG/Fakt Ver-
    lag AG
*Branch Office(s)*
Dr Wernerstr 5, 82194 Groebenzell
*Warehouse:* VVΛ, An der Autobahn, 33310
    Gutersloh

**P J Tonger Musikverlag GmbH & Co**
Auf dem Brand 10, 50996 Cologne
*Tel:* (0221) 935564-0 *Fax:* (0221) 935564-11
*E-mail:* musikverlag@tonger.de
*Web Site:* www.tonger.de
*Key Personnel*
Man Dir & Publicity: Peter Tonger
Founded: 1822
Subjects: Sheet Music books
ISBN Prefix(es): 3-920950
Subsidiaries: Carl Engels Musikverlag; Musikver-
    lage Gerhard Rabe; Fritz Spies GmbH

**TR - Verlagsunion GmbH+**
Thierschstr 11/III Stock, 80538 Munich
Mailing Address: Postfach 260202, 80059 Mu-
    nich
*Tel:* (089) 2121 390 *Fax:* (089) 296129; (089)
    296357
*E-mail:* vertrieb@tr-verlag.de
*Web Site:* www.tr-verlag.de
*Key Personnel*
Man Dir, Rights & Permissions: Andreas Keiser
    *E-mail:* andreaskeiser@tr-verlag.de
Editorial: Gabriele Rieth-Winterherbst
    *Tel:* (089) 212139-13 *E-mail:* rieth@tr-verlag.
    de; Inga Dopatka *Tel:* (089) 212139-29
    *E-mail:* dopatka@tr-verlag.de
Publicity: Cornelia Wiedemann *Tel:* (089)
    212139-18 *E-mail:* wiedemann@tr-verlag.de;
    Elke Funke *Tel:* (089) 212139-25
Sales: Imogen Fries *Tel:* (089) 212139-17
    *E-mail:* fries@tr-verlag.de; Elisabeth Kroier
    *Tel:* (089) 212139-20 *E-mail:* kroier@tr.verlag.
    de
Founded: 1968

The Union publishes & distributes books, audio
    & videocassette, software, sets of lessons etc to
    link up with TV & radio programs.
The TR (Television & Radio) Publishing Union
    comprises two broadcasting companies (Bay-
    erischer Rundfunk & Suedwest und Funk)
    & the following publishing companies: Lud-
    wig Auer GmbH; BLV Verlagsgesellschaft
    mbH; Verlag C H Beck; C Bertelsmann Ver-
    lag GmbH; Verlag Bruckmann Muenchen;
    Ernst Klett Verlag; Koesel-Verlag GmbH &
    Co; Langenscheidt KG; Suddeutscher Verlag,
    Buchverlag GmbH; JB Metzler Poeschel; R
    Oldenbourg Verlag GmbH; Guenter Olzog Ver-
    lag; K G Saur Verlag; Springer Verlag.
Subjects: Architecture & Interior Design, Edu-
    cation, English as a Second Language, Film,
    Video, Health, Nutrition, Radio, TV, Religion -
    Other, Travel
ISBN Prefix(es): 3-8058
Total Titles: 150 Print; 5 CD-ROM; 50 Audio
*Branch Office(s)*
TR-Verlagsunion Buero Potsdam, August-Bebel-
    Str 16, Potsdam, Contact: Harald Smeja
    *Tel:* (0331) 7312815 *Fax:* (0331) 7312815
*Orders to:* Moderne Industrie Verlagsservice,
    Justus-von-Liebig-Str 1, 86899 Landsberg

**Traditionell Bogenschiessen Verlag Angelika
    Hornig**
Siebenpfeifferstr 16, 67071 Ludwigshafen
*Tel:* (0621) 68 94 41 *Fax:* (0621) 68 94 42
*E-mail:* info@bogenschiessen.de
*Web Site:* www.bogenschiessen.de
*Key Personnel*
Editor: Angelika Hoernig *E-mail:* ah@
    bogenschiessen.de
Subjects: Archaeology, History, How-to, Outdoor
    Recreation, Sports, Athletics

**Trans Tech Publications+**
Freibergerstr 1, 38678 Clausthal-Zellerfeld
*Tel:* (05323) 96970 *Fax:* (05323) 969796
*E-mail:* ttp@transtech-online.com
*Web Site:* www.transtech-online.com
*Key Personnel*
Publisher: Reiner Grochowski
Founded: 1972
International journals for the powder & bulk in-
    dustry.
Subjects: Chemistry, Chemical Engineering, Civil
    Engineering, Earth Sciences, Mechanical Engi-
    neering
ISBN Prefix(es): 0-87849

**Transpress+**
Olgastr 86, 70180 Stuttgart
*Tel:* (0711) 210 80 65 *Fax:* (0711) 210 80 70
*E-mail:* versand@motorbuch.de
*Web Site:* www.motorbuch-versand.de *Cable:*
    TRANSPRESS STUTTGART
*Key Personnel*
Man Dir: Paul Pietsch; Dr Patricia Schotten
Founded: 1990
Subjects: Automotive, Transportation
ISBN Prefix(es): 3-344
*Parent Company:* Paul Pietsch Verlage GmbH &
    Co
*Bookshop(s):* Transpress Buchhandlung, Haupt-
    bahnhof, Mittelbau-Ladenstr, 04103 Leipzig
*Shipping Address:* Koch, Neff & Oetinger & Co,
    Postfach 800620, 70506 Stuttgart
*Warehouse:* Koch, Neff & Oetinger & Co, Post-
    fach 800620, 70506 Stuttgart

**Trautvetter & Fischer Nachf**
Gladenbacher Way 57, 35037 Marburg
*Tel:* (06421) 33309 *Fax:* (06421) 34959
*E-mail:* bestell@trautvetterfischerverlag.de
*Web Site:* www.trautvetterfischerverlag.de

*Key Personnel*
Publisher: Dr Wilhelm A Eckhardt
    *E-mail:* eckhardt@trautvetterfischerverlag.de
Founded: 1941
Specialize in history of Hessen.
Membership(s): Borsenverein Des Deutschen
    Buchhandels.
Subjects: History, Regional Interests
ISBN Prefix(es): 3-87822
Number of titles published annually: 2 Print
Total Titles: 50 Print

**Trees Wolfgang Triangel Verlag+**
Fuchserde 44, 52066 Aachen, Permony
*Tel:* (0241) 6 99 00 *Fax:* (0241) 6 99 15
*E-mail:* info@triangelverlag.de
*Web Site:* www.triangel-verlag.de
*Key Personnel*
Owner: Wolfgang Trees
Founded: 1981
Membership(s): Borsenverein de deutschen Buch-
    handels.
Subjects: History, Military Science, Regional
    Interests, Travel, Books about the history &
    tourism in Euregio Meuse-Rhine, ie Aachen
    (D), Maastricht (NL) & Liege (B). Especially:
    WWII 1933-1945, Rhineland, Huertpen Forest
    & smugglings 1545-1953
ISBN Prefix(es): 3-922974
Number of titles published annually: 2 Print
Total Titles: 12 Print

**Trescher Verlag GmbH**
Reinhardtstr 9, 10117 Berlin
*Tel:* (030) 2 83 24 96 *Fax:* (030) 2 81 59 94
*E-mail:* post@trescherverlag.de
*Web Site:* www.trescherverlag.de
*Key Personnel*
Sales: Bernd Schwenkros
Production: Tom Schuelke
Dir: Detlev Von Oppeln
Founded: 1993
Subjects: Film, Video, Nonfiction (General), Out-
    door Recreation, Travel
ISBN Prefix(es): 3-928409; 3-89794

**Treves Editions Verein Zur Foerderung der
    Kuenstlerischen Taetigkeiten** (Club for the
    Promotion of Artistic Work)+
Medardstr 105, 54294 Trier
Mailing Address: Postfach 1550, 54205 Trier
*Tel:* (0651) 309 010 *Fax:* (0651) 300 699
*E-mail:* mail@treves.de
*Web Site:* www.treves.de
*Key Personnel*
Man Dir: Rainer Breuer
Man Dir, Rights & Permissions: Ursula Dahm
Founded: 1974
Subjects: Art, Erotica, Fiction, Health, Nutrition,
    History, Literature, Literary Criticism, Essays,
    Music, Dance, Mysteries, Nonfiction (General),
    Poetry, Travel
ISBN Prefix(es): 3-88081

**TRIAS,** *imprint of* Georg Thieme Verlag KG

**Trias Verlag in MVS Medizinverlage Stuttgart
    GmbH & Co KG+**
Subsidiary of Georg Thieme Verlag KG
Oswald-Hesse-Str 50, 70469 Stuttgart
*Tel:* (0711) 8931-0 *Fax:* (0711) 8931-298
*E-mail:* kunden.service@thieme.de
*Web Site:* www.thieme.de; www.medizinverlage.
    de
*Key Personnel*
Man Dir: Dr Thomas Scherb
Foreign Rights: Susanne Seeger *Tel:* (0711) 8931-
    147 *Fax:* (0711) 8931-143 *E-mail:* susanne.
    seeger@thieme.de
Founded: 1989

Subjects: Health, Nutrition, Nonfiction (General), Psychology, Psychiatry
ISBN Prefix(es): 3-8304
*Associate Companies:* Enke Verlag; Karl F Haug Verlag; Hippokrates Verlag; Parey Verlag; Sonntag Verlag

**Trotzdem-Verlags Genossenschaft eG+**
Postfach 1159, 71117 Grafenau
*Tel:* (07033) 44273 *Fax:* (07033) 45264
*E-mail:* trotzdemusf@t-online.e
*Web Site:* www.trotzdem-verlag.de; www.txt.de/trotzdem
*Key Personnel*
Contact: Wolfgang Haug *E-mail:* wolfganghaug@aol.com
Founded: 1978
Publishing of books & magazines from a libertarian viewpoint.
Subjects: Alternative, Biography, Drama, Theater, Education, Government, Political Science, History, Photography, Social Sciences, Sociology
ISBN Prefix(es): 3-922209; 3-931786
Divisions: Redaktion Schwarzer Faden
Distributor for Anares; Anarchijtische Buchhandlung

**Mario Truant Verlag+**
Frauenlobstr 95, 55118 Mainz/Rhein
*Tel:* (06131) 961660 *Fax:* (0721) 151222306
*E-mail:* viva@truant.de
*Web Site:* www.truant.de
*Key Personnel*
Publisher: Mario Truant
Founded: 1990
Subjects: Crafts, Games, Hobbies, Fiction, Parapsychology, Science Fiction, Fantasy
ISBN Prefix(es): 3-926801; 3-934282

**Tuduv Verlagsgesellschaft mbH+**
Zieblandstr 7, 80799 Munich
Mailing Address: Postfach 340163, 80098 Munich
*Tel:* (089) 280 90 95 *Fax:* (089) 280 95 28
*E-mail:* info@tuduv.de
*Web Site:* www.tuduv.de
*Key Personnel*
Manager: Sonya Rosnovsky
Founded: 1974
Subjects: Art, Biography, Communications, Ethnicity, Government, Political Science, History, Language Arts, Linguistics, Literature, Literary Criticism, Essays, Medicine, Nursing, Dentistry, Social Sciences, Sociology, Technology
ISBN Prefix(es): 3-88073
*Associate Companies:* Verlag V Florentz GmbH (WF)

**Tuebinger Vereinigung fur Volkskunde eV (TVV)**
Ludwig-Uhland-Institut, Schloss Hohentuebingen, 72070 Tuebingen
*Tel:* (07071) 295449; (07071) 2972374 (orders) *Fax:* (07071) 295330
*E-mail:* info@tvv-verlag.de
*Web Site:* www.tvv-verlag.de
*Key Personnel*
Man Dir, Editorial, Production & Sales: Bernd Juergen Warneken
Editorial, Production & Sales: Utz Jeggle; Hermann Bausinger; Ute Bechdolf; Gottfried Korff
Founded: 1963
Subjects: Ethnicity, Film, Video, History, Language Arts, Linguistics, Regional Interests, Social Sciences, Sociology, Women's Studies
ISBN Prefix(es): 3-925340; 3-932512

**TUeV-Verlag GmbH**
Am Grauen Stein, 51105 Cologne
*Tel:* (0221) 806-3535 *Fax:* (0221) 806-3510
*E-mail:* tuev-verlag@de.tuv.com

*Web Site:* www.tuev-verlag.de; www.qm-aktuell.de; www.mt-medizintechnik.de
*Key Personnel*
Manager: Dr Anton Reiter
Founded: 1971
Subjects: Energy, Environmental Studies, Regional Interests, Technology, Transportation
ISBN Prefix(es): 3-8249; 3-88585; 3-921059
*Parent Company:* TUeV Rheinland Holding AG

**Turkischer Schulbuchverlag Onel Cengiz+**
Silchesto 13, 50827 Cologne
*Tel:* (0221) 5879084; (0221) 5879085 *Fax:* (0221) 488093; (0221) 5879004
*Key Personnel*
Vice President: Ibrahim Ilbasi
Publisher: C Hayati Oenel
Founded: 1981
Subjects: Travel
ISBN Prefix(es): 3-924542; 3-929490; 3-933348

**Edition U**, *imprint of* Dr Wolfgang Baur Verlag Kunst & Alltag

**Wirtschaftsverlag Carl Ueberreuter+**
Lurgialle 6-8, 60439 Frankfurt am Main
*Tel:* (069) 580905-80 *Fax:* (069) 580905-10
*E-mail:* info@redline-wirtschaft.de
*Web Site:* www.redline-wirtschaft.de
*Key Personnel*
Manager: Hans-Joachim Hartmann
Publisher: Juergen Diessl
Rights Director, Foreign Affairs: Maria Pinto-Peuckmann *Tel:* (089) 548 52-84 26 *Fax:* (089) 548 52-84 21
Founded: 1988
Subjects: Accounting, Business, Law, Management
ISBN Prefix(es): 3-220

**Uerle Verlag**, *imprint of* Verlag Herder GmbH & Co KG

**Verlag Dr Alfons Uhl+**
Mittlere Gerbergasse 1, 86720 Noerdlingen
*Tel:* (09081) 87248 *Fax:* (09081) 23710
*E-mail:* dr.uhl@uhl-verlag.de
*Web Site:* www.uhl-verlag.com
*Key Personnel*
Dir, Rights & Permissions: Dr Alfons Uhl
Subjects: Architecture & Interior Design, Art, Geography, Geology
ISBN Prefix(es): 3 921503

**Ullstein Heyne List GmbH & Co KG+**
Bayerstr 71-73, 80335 Munich
*Tel:* (089) 51 48 0 *Fax:* (089) 51 48 2229
*Web Site:* www.ullstein.de
*Key Personnel*
Managing Partner: Hubertus Meyer-Burckhardt; Christian Strasser
Publicity: Claus Martin Carlsberg
Founded: 1894
Membership(s): TR-Verlagsunion GmbH.
Subjects: Art, Biography, Fiction, History, Literature, Literary Criticism, Essays, Philosophy, Psychology, Psychiatry, Religion - Other, Science (General), Social Sciences, Sociology
ISBN Prefix(es): 3-89834
*Associate Companies:* Bucher Verlag GmbH; W Ludwig Verlag GmbH; Suedwest Verlag

**Guenter Albert Ulmer Verlag**
Hauptstr 16, 78609 Tuningen
*Tel:* (07464) 98740 *Fax:* (07464) 3054
*E-mail:* info@ulmertuningen.de
*Web Site:* www.ulmertuningen.de
*Key Personnel*
Man Dir: Guenter Albert Ulmer
Founded: 1983

Subjects: Earth Sciences, Environmental Studies, Gardening, Plants, Health, Nutrition, Human Relations, Natural History, Nonfiction (General), Poetry, Regional Interests, Religion - Protestant, Theology, Meditation
ISBN Prefix(es): 3-924191; 3-932346

**Verlag Eugen Ulmer GmbH & Co** (Eugen Ulmer Publishers)+
Wollgrasweg 41, 70599 Stuttgart, BRD
Mailing Address: Potfach 700561, 70574 Stuttgart
*Tel:* (0711) 4507-0 *Fax:* (0711) 4507-120
*E-mail:* info@ulmer.de
*Web Site:* www.ulmer.de
*Telex:* 723634
*Key Personnel*
Man Dir: Roland Ulmer
Deputy Dir: Matthias Ulmer *E-mail:* mulmer@ulmer.de
Production: Dieter Kleinschrot
Reader: Dr Nadja Kneissler *E-mail:* lektorat@ulmer.de
Sales Dir: Michael Kurzer
Rights & Permissions Man: Sigrun Wagner *E-mail:* wagner@ulmer.de
Founded: 1868
Membership(s): VGS - Verlagsgesellschaft mbH & Co KG.
Subjects: Agriculture, Animals, Pets, Environmental Studies, Gardening, Plants, How-to, Science (General), Veterinary Science
ISBN Prefix(es): 3-8001
Total Titles: 900 Print
Subsidiaries: Editions Eugen Ulmer; Neumann Verlag, Radebeul

**Ulrike Helmer Verlag+**
Altkoenigstr 6a, 61462 Koenigstein
*Tel:* (06174) 936060 *Fax:* (06174) 936065
*E-mail:* info@ulrike-helmer-verlag.de
*Web Site:* www.ulrike-helmer-verlag.de
*Key Personnel*
Man Dir: Ulrike Helmer
Founded: 1988
Subjects: Fiction, Gay & Lesbian, History, Literature, Literary Criticism, Essays, Philosophy, Social Sciences, Sociology, Women's Studies
ISBN Prefix(es): 3-927164; 3-89741
*Warehouse:* SOVA, Friesstr 20-24, 60388 Frankfurt/M

**Neuer Umschau Buchverlag+**
Maximilianstr 35, 67433 Neustadt/Weinstr
Mailing Address: Postfach 110262, 60037 Frankfurt am Main
*Tel:* (06321) 877850 *Fax:* (06321) 877859
*E-mail:* info@umschau-buchverlag.de
*Web Site:* www.umschau-buchverlag.de
*Key Personnel*
Man Dir, Publisher: Katharina Toebben
Sales: Cornelia Pendt
Founded: 1850
Also acts as distributor.
Membership(s): Boersenverein.
Subjects: Cookery, Health, Nutrition, Nonfiction (General), Science (General)
ISBN Prefix(es): 3-524
*Parent Company:* Unternehmensgruppe Niederberger

**Uni-Taschenbuecher UTB Fuer Wissenchaft CmbH,** see UTB fuer Wissenschaft Uni Taschenbuecher GmbH

**Universitaetsverlag Winter GmbH Heidelberg GmbH+**
Dassenheimer Landstra 13, 69121 Heidelberg
Mailing Address: Postfach 10 61 40, 69051 Heidelberg
*Tel:* (06221) 7702-60 *Fax:* (06221) 7702-69
*E-mail:* info@winter-verlag-hd.de
*Web Site:* www.winter-verlag-hd.de

*Key Personnel*
President & Editor: Dr Andreas Barth
 *Tel:* (06221) 7702-63 *E-mail:* a.barth@winter-verlag-hd.de
Production: Ralf Stemper *Tel:* (06221) 7702-67 *E-mail:* r.stemper@winter-verlag-hd.de
Sales Manager: Klaus Philipp Mertens
 *Tel:* (06221) 7702-65 *E-mail:* kp.mertens@winter-verlag-hd.de
Customer Service: Rotraud Hohlbein *E-mail:* r.hohlbein@winter-verlag-hd.de
Founded: 1993
Subjects: Language Arts, Linguistics, Literature, Literary Criticism, Essays
ISBN Prefix(es): 3-8253
Total Titles: 2,600 Print
*Associate Companies:* Heidelberger Verlagsanstalt (HVA) & Edition S
*Distribution Center:* Engros-Buchhandlung Dessauer, Raffelstr 32, 8036 Zurich, Switzerland *Tel:* (01) 4 66 96 66 *Fax:* (01) 4 66 96 69 (Switzerland)

**Universitatsverlag Ulm GmbH**
Bahnhofstr 20, 89073 Ulm
*Tel:* (0731) 15 28 60 *Fax:* (0731) 15 28 62
*E-mail:* info@uni-verlag-ulm.de
*Web Site:* www.uni-verlag-ulm.de
*Key Personnel*
Manager: Alexander Schraut
Founded: 1988
Specialize in neurology, psychiatry & brain research.
Subjects: Medicine, Nursing, Dentistry, Physical Sciences
ISBN Prefix(es): 3-927402; 3-89559
*Parent Company:* Schwaebischer Verlag KG, 7970 Leutkirch
*Shipping Address:* Dalnheph 20, 89073 Ulm

**UNO-Verlag GmbH**
Am Hofgarten 10, 53113 Bonn
*Tel:* (0228) 94 90 2-0 *Fax:* (0228) 94 90 2-22
*E-mail:* info@uno-verlag.de
*Web Site:* www.uno-verlag.de
*Key Personnel*
Man Dir: Wolfgang Fischer
Founded: 1982
Subjects: Aeronautics, Aviation, Agriculture, Developing Countries, Economics, Education, Energy, Environmental Studies, Finance, Government, Political Science, Health, Nutrition, Labor, Industrial Relations, Social Sciences, Sociology
ISBN Prefix(es): 3-923904
Distributor for Asian Development Bank; Council of Europe; FAO; Inter-American Development Bank; International Atomic Energy Agency; International Civil Aviation Organization; International Monetary Fund (IMF); Nordic Council of Ministers Publications; OECD; UNDP; UNESCO; UNIDO; United Nations Publications; WHO; Worldbank; World Intellectual Property Organization; World Tourism Organization; World Trade Organization

**Unrast Verlag e V+**
Postfach 8020, 48043 Munster
*Tel:* (0251) 666293 *Fax:* (0251) 666120
*E-mail:* kontakt@unrast-verlag.de
*Web Site:* www.unrast-verlag.de
*Key Personnel*
International Rights: Martin Schuering
Founded: 1989
Subjects: Developing Countries, Fiction, Government, Political Science, Women's Studies
ISBN Prefix(es): 3-89771; 3-928300

**Urania Verlag mit Ravensburger Ratgebern+**
Liebknechtstr 33, 70565 Stuttgart
*Tel:* (0) 711-78803-0 *Fax:* (0) 711-78803-10
*E-mail:* urania@verlagsgruppe-dornier.de

*Web Site:* www.urania-ravensburger.de *Cable:* URANIA LEIPZIG
*Key Personnel*
Dir: Olaf Carstens; Roland Grimmelsmann
Founded: 1924
Subjects: Biological Sciences, Nonfiction (General)
ISBN Prefix(es): 3-332
*Parent Company:* Dornier Medienholding
*Shipping Address:* Leipziger Kommissions- und Grosbuchhandelsgesellschaft mbH, Polzschauer Weg, 04579 Espenhain
*Orders to:* Leipziger Kommissions- und Grosbuchhandelsgesellschaft mbH, Polzchauer Weg, 04579 Espenhain

**Urban & Vogel Medien und Medizin Verlagsgesellschaft mbH & Co KG**
Neumarkterstr 43, 81673 Munich
*Tel:* (089) 4372-0 *Fax:* (089) 4372-2633
*E-mail:* verlag@urban-vogel.de
*Web Site:* www.urban-vogel.de
*Telex:* 524631 vervo d
*Key Personnel*
Manager: Dr George Ralle
Sales & Marketing: Frank Niemann
Founded: 1972
Subjects: Medicine, Nursing, Dentistry
ISBN Prefix(es): 3-8208
*Parent Company:* Verlagsgruppe Bertelsmann International GmbH
Distributed by Vleweg Verlag (Germany)

**Edition Ustad**, *imprint of* Karl-May-Verlag Lothar Schmid GmbH

**UTAS-Verlag fur Moderne Lernmethoden Uta Stechl+**
Kellerstr 15, 84577 Tussling
Mailing Address: Postfach 62, 84577 Tussling
*Tel:* (08633) 1450 *Fax:* (08633) 7805
*Key Personnel*
Owner: Uta Stechl
Founded: 1981
ISBN Prefix(es): 3-925220

**UTB fuer Wissenschaft Uni Taschenbuecher GmbH**
Breitwiesenstr 9, 70565 Stuttgart
*Tel:* (0711) 7 82 95 55-0 *Fax:* (0711) 7 80 13 76
*E-mail:* utb@utb-stuttgart.de
*Web Site:* www.utb.de
*Key Personnel*
Man Dir: Volker Huehn
Manager: Ferdinand Schoeningh; Dr Michael Schoeningh
Founded: 1970
The company represents a group of 13 publishers (shareholders) producing paperbacks of a general academic/technical/scientific nature.
Subjects: Agriculture, Biological Sciences, Business, Chemistry, Chemical Engineering, Computer Science, Economics, Electronics, Electrical Engineering, Engineering (General), Government, Political Science, Health, Nutrition, History, Language Arts, Linguistics, Library & Information Sciences, Literature, Literary Criticism, Essays, Medicine, Nursing, Dentistry, Philosophy, Physics, Psychology, Psychiatry, Religion - Other, Social Sciences, Sociology, Veterinary Science
ISBN Prefix(es): 3-8252; 3-920971
Distributed by Mohr Morawa (Austria); Reinhardt Media-Service (Switzerland)
*Warehouse:* Brockhaus Commission, Kreidlerstr 9, Postfach 1220, 708016 Kornwestheim

**UVK Universitatsverlag Konstanz GmbH+**
Schuetzenstr 24, 78462 Konstanz
Mailing Address: PO Box 10 20 51, 78420 Konstanz

*Tel:* (07531) 90530 *Fax:* (07531) 905398
*E-mail:* willkommen@uvk.de
*Web Site:* www.uvk.de
*Key Personnel*
Publishing Manager & International Rights Contact: Walter Engstle *Tel:* (07531) 905312 *E-mail:* walter.engstle@uvk.de
Founded: 1963
Subjects: Archaeology, History, Literature, Literary Criticism, Essays, Philosophy, Science (General)
ISBN Prefix(es): 3-89669; 3-87940
Number of titles published annually: 10 Print
Total Titles: 700 Print
*Associate Companies:* Suedverlag GmbH/uvk Verlagsgesellschaft mbH
*Orders to:* Brockhaus Commission Verlagsauslieferung, Kreidlerstr 9, 70806 Kornwestheim

**UVK Verlagsgesellschaft mbH+**
Schutzenstr 24, 78462 Konstanz
Mailing Address: PO Box 10 20 51, 78420 Konstanz
*Tel:* (07531) 90530 *Fax:* (07531) 905398
*E-mail:* willkommen@uvk.de
*Web Site:* www.uvk.de
*Key Personnel*
Publishing Manager & International Rights: Walter Engstle *Tel:* (07531) 905312 *E-mail:* walter.engstle@uvk.de
Founded: 1995
Subjects: Communications, Film, Video, History, Journalism, Radio, TV, Social Sciences, Sociology
ISBN Prefix(es): 3-89669
Number of titles published annually: 80 Print
Total Titles: 650 Print
*Associate Companies:* UVK Universitaetsverlag Konstanz GmbH (University Press)
*Orders to:* Brockhaus Commission Verlagsauslieferung, Kreidlerstr 9, 70806 Kornwestheim bei Stuttgart

**Dorothea van der Koelen**
Hinter der Kapelle 54, 55128 Mainz
*Tel:* (06131) 346 64 *Fax:* (06131) 36 90 76
*E-mail:* dvanderkoelen@xterna-net.de
*Key Personnel*
Contact: Dorothea van der Koelen
Founded: 1986
Art publisher & art gallery.
Subjects: Art, Science (General), Art History
ISBN Prefix(es): 3-926663
*Parent Company:* Vander Koelen Verlag
*Distribution Center:* Austria
France
Switzerland

**Vandenhoeck & Ruprecht+**
Robert Bosch-Breite 6, 37070 Gottingen
*Tel:* (0551) 5084-40 *Fax:* (0551) 5084-422
*E-mail:* info@v-r.de
*Web Site:* www.v-r.de
*Key Personnel*
Man Dir: Dr Dietrich Ruprecht
Man Dir, Editorial Theology & Religion: Jorg Persch
Man Dir, International Rights & Permissions: Reinhilde Ruprecht
Man Dir, Rights & Permissions: Dr Arndt Ruprecht
Marketing Dir: Carola Mueller *Tel:* (0551) 5084-470 *E-mail:* c.mueller@v-r.de
Sales: Ingo Halscheidt
Publicity: Regina Lange
Editorial German Literature, Classics/Antiquity, Philosophy: Dr Ulrike Giessmann
Editorial History & Economics: Martin Rethmeier
Editorial Psychology: Dr Bernd Rachel
Founded: 1735

Subjects: Education, History, Language Arts, Linguistics, Philosophy, Psychology, Psychiatry, Religion - Other, Theology
ISBN Prefix(es): 3-525
*Associate Companies:* Buchhandlung Deuerlich
Subsidiaries: Druckerei Hubert & Company; V&R Unipress GmbH
Distributor for V&R Unipress GmbH; Wallstein Verlag; Weidle Verlag

**VAP-Verlag**, see Goll Bruno Verlag fur Aussergewoehnliche Perspektiven (VAP)

**VAS-Verlag fuer Akademische Schriften+**
Wielandstr 10, 60318 Frankfurt am Main
*Tel:* (069) 77 93 66 *Fax:* (069) 7073967
*E-mail:* info@vas-verlag.de
*Web Site:* www.vas-verlag.de
*Key Personnel*
International Rights: Karl-Heinz Balon
Founded: 1982
Subjects: Education, Environmental Studies, Government, Political Science, History, Human Relations, Language Arts, Linguistics, Psychology, Psychiatry, Social Sciences, Sociology, Women's Studies
ISBN Prefix(es): 3-88864

**VDE-Verlag GmbH+**
Bismarckstr 33, 10625 Berlin
Mailing Address: PO Box 120143, 10591 Berlin
*Tel:* (030) 34 80 01 0 *Fax:* (030) 341 70 93
*E-mail:* voss@vde-verlag.de
*Web Site:* www.vde-verlag.de
*Telex:* 181683 vde d
*Key Personnel*
Manager: Dr Ing A Gruetz
Founded: 1929
Subjects: Communications, Electronics, Electrical Engineering
ISBN Prefix(es): 3-8007
*U.S. Office(s):* Hallenbook, County Route 9, PO Box 357, Chatham, NY 12037, United States

**VDI Verlag GmbH+**
Heinrichstr 24, 40239 Duesseldorf
*Tel:* (0211) 61 88-0 *Fax:* (0211) 61 88-306
*E-mail:* info@vdi-nachrichten.com
*Web Site:* www.vdi-nachrichten.com *Cable:* INGENIEURVERLAG DUSSELDORF
*Key Personnel*
Man Dir: Raymond Johnson-Ohla
    *E-mail:* geschaeftsfuehrung@vdi-nachrichten.com
Founded: 1923
Subjects: Engineering (General), Science (General), Technology
ISBN Prefix(es): 3-18

**Verein der Benediktiner zu Beuron- Beuroner Kunstverlag+**
Abteistr 2, 88631 Beuron
*Tel:* (07466) 17-0 *Fax:* (07466) 17-107
*E-mail:* bibliothek@erzabtei-beuron.de
*Web Site:* www.erzabtei-beuron.de *Cable:* BEURONER KUNSTVERLAG
*Key Personnel*
Dir: Gabriel Gawletta
Publicity Manager: Siegfried Studer
Founded: 1898
Subjects: Art, Biblical Studies, Humor, Religion - Catholic, Religion - Protestant, Religion - Other
ISBN Prefix(es): 3-87071
Imprints: Monastica

**Vereinigte Fachverlage GmbH**
Lise-Meitner-Str 2, 55129 Mainz
Mailing Address: Postfach 100465, 55135 Mainz
*Tel:* (06131) 992-0 *Fax:* (06131) 992-100

*Key Personnel*
Manager: Manfred Grunenberg
Founded: 1937
ISBN Prefix(es): 3-7830
Subsidiaries: VF Verlagsgesellschaft GmbH

**Vereinte Evangelische Mission, Abt Verlag**
    (United Evangelical Mission)
Rudolfstr 137, 42285 Wuppertal
Mailing Address: Postfach 20 19 63, 42219 Wuppertal
*Tel:* (0202) 89004 0 *Fax:* (0202) 89004 79
*E-mail:* info@vemission.org
*Web Site:* www.vemission.org
*Key Personnel*
Editor-in-chief: Thomas Sandner
Founded: 1828
Communion of churches in 3 continents.
Subjects: Theology
ISBN Prefix(es): 3-87855; 3-921900
Total Titles: 2 Print

**Verkehrs-Verlag J Fischer**, see Verkehrs-Verlag J Fischer GmbH & Co KG

**Verlag Beltz & Gelberg+**
Werderstr 10, 69469 Weinheim
*Tel:* (06201) 60070
*E-mail:* info@beltz.de
*Web Site:* www.beltz.de
*Key Personnel*
Man Dir: Joachim Radmer
Publishing Dir: Ulrich Stoeriko-Blume
Rights: Charlotte Larat; Kerstin Michaelis
ISBN Prefix(es): 3-407
*Parent Company:* Beltz Publishing Group

**Verlag fur die Rechts- und Anwaltspraxis GmbH & Co+**
Beisingerweg 1a, 45657 Recklinghausen
Mailing Address: Postfach 101953, 45619 Recklinghausen
*Tel:* (02361) 9142-0 *Fax:* (02361) 9142-35
*E-mail:* hotline@zap-verlag.de
*Web Site:* www.zap-verlag.de
*Key Personnel*
Publisher: Dr Karl-Friedrich Peter
Man Dir: Hermann Boger
Founded: 1989
Subjects: Law
ISBN Prefix(es): 3-927935; 3-89655
*Shipping Address:* Schuechtermannstr 180, 44628 Herne
*Warehouse:* Schuechtermannstr 180, 44628 Herne
*Orders to:* Postfach 101849, 44621 Herne

**Verlag fur Schweissen und Verwandte Verfahren** (Publishing House for Welding)+
Subsidiary of Deutscher Verband fur Schweissen und verwandte Verfahren eV
Aachenerstr 172, 40223 Duesseldorf
Mailing Address: Postfach 101965, 40010 Duesseldorf
*Tel:* (0211) 15910 *Fax:* (0211) 1591150
*E-mail:* verlag@dvs-hg.de
*Web Site:* www.dvs-verlag.de
*Key Personnel*
Manager: M Stumpf; Dr Ing D von Hofe
Founded: 1955
Subjects: Engineering (General), Mechanical Engineering, Technology, Welding & Allied Processes
ISBN Prefix(es): 3-87155
Number of titles published annually: 15 Print; 3 CD-ROM
Total Titles: 419 Print; 10 CD-ROM
*Parent Company:* German Welding Society

**Verlag Moderne Industrie AG & Co KG+**
Emmy-Noetherstr 2, 80992 Munich
*Tel:* (089) 5484202 *Fax:* (089) 548428428

*E-mail:* info@mi-verlag.de
*Web Site:* www.mi-verlag.de
*Telex:* 527114 moin d
*Key Personnel*
President: Klaus Hengster *Fax:* (08191) 125-542
Publisher: Evelyn Boos *E-mail:* e.boos@mvg-verlag.de
Rights Dir, Foreign Affairs: Maria Pinto-Peuckmann *Tel:* (089) 548 52-84 26 *Fax:* (089) 548 52-84 21 *E-mail:* m.pinto-p@redline-wirtschaft.de
Marketing & Sales: Martin Brueninghaus *E-mail:* m.brueninghaus@mvg-verlag.de
Founded: 1952
Also publishes loose-leaf editions.
Membership(s): EBP-Network.
Subjects: Advertising, Business, Career Development, Communications, Computer Science, Economics, Management, Marketing, Technology, Investment, Money, Success Stories
ISBN Prefix(es): 3-478; 3-87957; 3-920716; 3-87959
*Associate Companies:* mvg Verlag *Fax:* (089) 548 52-84 21 *E-mail:* info@mvg-verlag.de (career development, communications, motivation & self-help; ISBN 3-478); Verlag Moderne Industrie Buch AG & Co KG, Koenigswintererstr 418, 53227 Bonn *Tel:* (0228) 97024 41 *Fax:* (0228) 97024 21 *E-mail:* info@vmi-buch.de

**Verlag Puppen & Spielzeug**, *imprint of* Verlagshaus Wohlfarth

**Verlag und Druckkontor Kamp GmbH**
Kurfuerstenstr 4a, 44791 Bochum
*Tel:* (0234) 51617-0 *Fax:* (0234) 51617-18
*E-mail:* mail@kamp-verlag.de
*Web Site:* www.kamp-verlag.de
*Key Personnel*
Owner: Dr Ferdinand Kamp
Founded: 1996
Subjects: Education
ISBN Prefix(es): 3-89709

**Verlag und Studio fuer Hoerbuchproduktionen+**
Bahnhofstr 24, 35037 Marburg/Lahn
*Tel:* (06421) 889-110 *Fax:* (06421) 889-1111
*E-mail:* verlag@hoerbuch.de; info@hoerbuch.de
*Web Site:* www.hoerbuch.de; www.hoerbuch.com
*Key Personnel*
Publisher: Hans Eckardt; Heidemarie Eckardt
Founded: 1987
Subjects: Biblical Studies, Career Development, Management, Marketing, Mysteries, Poetry
ISBN Prefix(es): 3-89614
Total Titles: 200 Audio
*Distribution Center:* Koch, Neff & Oettinger

**Verlag Volk & Welt GmbH**, see Luchterhand Literaturverlag GmbH/Verlag Volk & Welt GmbH

**Verlagsbereich Bau**, *imprint of* Verlagshaus Wohlfarth

**Verlagsgruppe Jehle-Rehm GmbH**
Emmy-Noetherstr 2, 80992 Munich
Mailing Address: Postfach 500699, 80976 Munich
*Tel:* (089) 54 8 52-06 *Fax:* (089) 54 8 52-82 30
*E-mail:* info@HJR-verlag.de
*Web Site:* www.jehle-rehm.de
*Key Personnel*
Manager: Wolfgang Quadflieg
Publisher: Peter Habit
Founded: 1988
Subjects: Business, Economics, Law
ISBN Prefix(es): 3-8073; 3-7825; 3-87253
*Parent Company:* Sueddeutscher Verlag, Munich
Divisions: Fachbuchhandlung Kova

*Branch Office(s)*
Friedrichstr 130a, 10117 Berlin *Tel:* (030)
    283098-0 *Fax:* (030) 283098-10
*E-mail:* verlagsgruppe@jehle-rehm.de
*Bookshop(s):* Kova & Rau, Einsteinstr 172, 81675
    Munich

**Vervuert Verlagsgesellschaft**
Wielandstr 40, 60318 Frankfurt
*Tel:* (069) 597 4617 *Fax:* (069) 5978743
*E-mail:* info@iberoamericanalibros.com
*Web Site:* www.ibero-americana.net
*Key Personnel*
Manager: Klaus Dieter Vervuert
Founded: 1988
Also bookshop & library supplier.
Subjects: Developing Countries, Drama, Theater,
    Ethnicity, Foreign Countries, Language Arts,
    Linguistics, Literature, Literary Criticism, Es-
    says, Social Sciences, Sociology
ISBN Prefix(es): 3-89354; 3-921600; 3-86527;
    84-8489; 84-95107
Distributor for Iberoamericana (Madrid, Spain);
    Latin American Bookstore (USA)

**Vice Versa Verlag+**
Leuschnerdamm 5, 10999 Berlin
*Tel:* (030) 61609237 *Fax:* (030) 61609238
*E-mail:* viceversa@comp.de
*Key Personnel*
Publisher: Gabriela Wachter
Founded: 1992
Subjects: Architecture & Interior Design, Art
ISBN Prefix(es): 3-9803212; 3-932809
*Associate Companies:* Vice Versa Vertrieb; Vice
    Versa Vertretung

**Vier Tuerme GmbH Verlag Klosterbetriebe+**
Schweinfurterstr 40, 97359 Muensterschwarzach
    Abtei
*Tel:* (09324) 20292 *Fax:* (09324) 20495
*E-mail:* info@vier-tuerme.de
*Web Site:* www.vier-tuerme.de
*Key Personnel*
Publisher: Dr Mauritius Wilde
Man Dir: Christoph Gerhard
Founded: 1955
Subjects: How-to, Religion - Catholic, Theology
ISBN Prefix(es): 3-87868
Number of titles published annually: 15 Print; 10
    Audio
Total Titles: 35 Audio
Imprints: Muensterschwarzacher Kleinschriften;
    Muensterschwarzacher Studien; Schriften zur
    Kontemplation

**Friedr Vieweg & Sohn Verlag+**
Unit of GWV Fachverlage GMBH
Abraham-Lincolnstr 46, 65189 Wiesbaden
Mailing Address: Postfach 1546, 65173 Wies-
    baden
*Tel:* (0611) 7878-0 *Fax:* (0611) 7878-470
*E-mail:* vieweg.service@bertelsmann.de
*Web Site:* www.vieweg.de; www.gwv-fachverlage.
    de
*Key Personnel*
General Manager: Dr Hans-Dieter Haenel
    *E-mail:* hans-dieter.haenel@gwv-fachverlage.de
Man Dir: Dr Heinz Weinheimer
Editorial: Dr Reinald Klockenbusch; Ulrike
    Schmickler-Hirzebruch; Ewald Schmitt
Sales Marketing Manager: Rolf-Guenther Hobbel-
    ing
Rights & Permissions: Angelika Bolisega
    *Fax:* (0611) 7878361 *E-mail:* angelika.
    bolisega@gwv-fachverlage.de
Founded: 1786
Professional information for engineers & techni-
    cians; textbooks for students in technology &
    mathematics.

Subjects: Civil Engineering, Computer Science,
    Electronics, Electrical Engineering, Mathemat-
    ics, Mechanical Engineering, Technology
ISBN Prefix(es): 3-528
Number of titles published annually: 5 CD-ROM
Total Titles: 1,500 Print; 25 CD-ROM
*Parent Company:* Springer Science+Business Me-
    dia
*Orders to:* VVA Bertelsmann Distribution, Post-
    fach 7777, D-33310 Guetersloh

**Villa Arceno**, *imprint of* Frederking & Thaler
    Verlag GmbH

**Edition Vincent Klink**
Alte Weinsteige 71, 70597 Stuttgart
*Tel:* (0711) 62007211 *Fax:* (0711) 6409408
*E-mail:* edition@vincent-klink.de
Founded: 1988
Subjects: Fiction, Music, Dance, Poetry, Religion
    - Buddhist
ISBN Prefix(es): 3-927350; 3-00

**Curt R Vincentz Verlag+**
Schiffgraben 43, 30175 Hannover
Mailing Address: Postfach 6247, 30062 Hannover
*Tel:* (0511) 9910000 *Fax:* (0511) 9910099
*E-mail:* info@vincentz.de
*Web Site:* www.vincentz.de *Cable:* VINHA
*Key Personnel*
Man Dir, Rights & Permissions: Dr Lothar Vin-
    centz
Commercial Dir: Helmut Fitting
Sales: Ina Baatz
Founded: 1893
Subjects: Chemistry, Chemical Engineering,
    Medicine, Nursing, Dentistry
ISBN Prefix(es): 3-87870
*Warehouse:* Emil-Meyer-Str 22, 30165 Hannover

**Edition Curt Visel+**
Weberstr 36, 87700 Memmingen
*Tel:* (08331) 2853 *Fax:* (08331) 490364
*E-mail:* info@edition-curt-visel.de
*Web Site:* www.edition-curt-visel.de
*Key Personnel*
Owner: Juergen Schweitzer
Founded: 1963
Subjects: Art, Biography
ISBN Prefix(es): 3-922406
*Parent Company:* Maximilian Dietrich Verlag

**Vista Point Verlag GmbH+**
Haendelstr 25-29, 50674 Cologne
Mailing Address: Postfach 270572, 50511
    Cologne
*Tel:* (0221) 921613-0 *Fax:* (0221) 921613-14
*E-mail:* info@vistapoint.de
*Web Site:* www.vistapoint.de
*Key Personnel*
Manager: Dr Horst Schmidt-Bruemmer *E-mail:* h.
    schmidt-bruemmer@vistapoint.de; Andreas
    Schulz
Founded: 1977
Subjects: Travel
ISBN Prefix(es): 3-88973

**VJK**, see Verlag Josef Knecht

**VNW**, see Verlag Neuer Weg GmbH

**Vogel Medien GmbH & Co KG+**
Max-Planckstr 7/9, 97082 Wuerzburg
*Tel:* (0931) 418-2590 *Fax:* (0931) 418-2860
*E-mail:* info@vogel-medien.de
*Web Site:* www.vogel.de *Cable:* VOGELVERLAG
    WURZBURG
*Key Personnel*
Man Dir: Dietmar Salein; Claus Wuestenhagen
Founded: 1891

Subjects: Automotive, Chemistry, Chemical En-
    gineering, Civil Engineering, Communications,
    Computer Science, Electronics, Electrical Engi-
    neering, Environmental Studies, Management,
    Mechanical Engineering
ISBN Prefix(es): 3-8023
*U.S. Office(s):* Vogel Europublishing, 632 Sun-
    flower Court, San Ramon, CA 94583, United
    States, Contact: Mark Hauser *Tel:* 510-648-
    1170 *Fax:* 510-648-1171

**Voggenreiter-Verlag+**
Viktoriastr 25, 53173 Bonn-Bad Godesberg
*Tel:* (0228) 93 575-0 *Fax:* (0228) 35 50 53
*E-mail:* info@voggenreiter.de
*Web Site:* www.voggenreiter.de
*Key Personnel*
Proprietor: Charles Voggenreiter; Ralph Voggen-
    reiter
Founded: 1919
Music publisher of Rock & Pop
Also specialize in full tutorials, reference books,
    sheet music & videos.
Membership(s): NAMM, RPMDA, DMV.
Subjects: Music, Dance
ISBN Prefix(es): 3-8024
Total Titles: 200 Print; 5 CD-ROM; 15 Audio
*U.S. Office(s):* MTC, 495 Lorimer St, Brooklyn,
    NY 11211, United States, Contact: Marcus De-
    muth *Tel:* 718-963-2777 *Fax:* 718-302-4890
    *E-mail:* mtc@inditec.com
*Distribution Center:* Voggenreiter Logistikeen-
    tuim, Wittfelder Stich 1, 53343 Wachtberg-
    Villip *Tel:* (0228) 34 10 43 *Fax:* (0228) 95 16
    334

**Ellen Vogt Garbe Verlag+**
Kinkelstr 15, 90482 Nuernberg
*Tel:* (0911) 5430983 *Fax:* (0911) 5430983
*Key Personnel*
Contact: Ellen Vogt
Founded: 1994
Subjects: Environmental Studies, Humor, Philoso-
    phy, Poetry
ISBN Prefix(es): 3-930143

**Verlag Volk & Welt GmbH+**
Neumarkterstr 18, 81673 Munich
*Tel:* (089) 4372 2769 *Fax:* (089) 4372 2743
    *Cable:* VOLKWELT BERLIN
*Key Personnel*
Dir: Dierich von Boetticher; Dietrich Simon
Sales Dir: Monika Mueller
Founded: 1947
Membership(s): Stock Exchange of German
    Booksellers.
Subjects: Fiction, History, Nonfiction (General)
ISBN Prefix(es): 3-353
Distributor for Janus Press
*Shipping Address:* VSB Verlagsservice Braun-
    schweig, Georg-Westermann-Allee 66, 38104
    Braunschweig
*Warehouse:* VSB Verlagsservice Braunschweig,
    Georg-Westermann-Allee 66, 38104 Braun-
    schweig
*Orders to:* VSB Verlagsservice Braunschweig,
    Georg-Westermann-Allee 66, 38104 Braun-
    schweig

**Volk und Wissen Verlag GmbH & Co+**
Mecklenburgische Strabe 53, 14197 Berlin
*Tel:* (030) 89785-0
*E-mail:* email@cornelsen.de
*Web Site:* www.vwv.de
*Telex:* 112181 vowiv dd *Cable:* VOLKWISSEN
    BERLIN
*Key Personnel*
Man Dir: Hans-Jorg Dullmann
Founded: 1945
Subjects: Biological Sciences, Chemistry, Chem-
    ical Engineering, Education, Geography, Geol-
    ogy, Mathematics, Physical Sciences, Physics
ISBN Prefix(es): 3-06

*Parent Company:* Franz-Cornelsen-Stiftung, Berlin
Subsidiaries: Paedagogischer Zeitschriftenverlag GmbH & Co

**Verlag Deutsches Volksheimstaettenwerk GmbH+**
Neefestr 2a, 53115 Bonn
*Tel:* (0228) 7259930; (0228) 7259931 *Fax:* (0228) 7259919
*E-mail:* ibn@bonn.ihk.de
*Web Site:* www.ibn.ihk-bonn.de
*Key Personnel*
Contact: I Hilderbrand
Founded: 1982
Subjects: House & Home, Law
ISBN Prefix(es): 3-87941

**Dokument und Analyse Verlag Bogislaw von Randow**
Barer Str 43, 80799 Munich
*Tel:* (089) 2720100 *Fax:* (089) 2720311
*Key Personnel*
Publisher: Bogislaw von Randow
Founded: 1972
Subjects: Economics, Government, Political Science, Law, Science (General), Social Sciences, Sociology

**Votum Verlag GmbH+**
Grevenerstr 89-91, 48159 Muenster
*Tel:* (0251) 26514-0 *Fax:* (0251) 26514-20
*E-mail:* info@votum-verlag.de
*Web Site:* www.votum-verlag.de
*Key Personnel*
Man Dir: Dr Klaus Muenstermann
Founded: 1986
Subjects: Law, Psychology, Psychiatry, Social Sciences, Sociology, Women's Studies
ISBN Prefix(es): 3-926549; 3-930405; 3-933158; 3-935984

**VS Verlag fur Sozialwissenschaften+**
Unit of GWV Fachverlage GMBH
Abraham-Lincoln-Str 46, 65189 Wiesbaden
*Tel:* (0611) 78780 *Fax:* (0611) 7878-470
*Web Site:* www.vs-verlag.de; www.gwv-fachverlage.de
*Key Personnel*
General Manager: Dr Hans-Dieter Haenel *E-mail:* hans-dieter.haenel@gwv-fachverlage.de
Editorial: Annette Kirsch *Tel:* (0611) 7878-368 *Fax:* (0611) 7878-368 *E-mail:* annette.kirsch@gwv-fachverlage.de
Rights & Permissions: Angelika Bolisega *Fax:* (0611) 7878-470 *E-mail:* angelika.bolisega@gwv-fachverlage.de
Founded: 1947
Books & periodicals which cover all important topics in the social sciences.
Subjects: Communications, Social Sciences, Sociology
ISBN Prefix(es): 3-8100; 3-531
Total Titles: 2,000 Print
*Parent Company:* Springer Science+Business Media
*Orders to:* VVA Bertelsmann Distribution, Postfach 7777, D-33311 Guetersloh

**VUA (agricultural titles),** *imprint of* BLV Verlagsgesellschaft mbH

**Vulkan-Verlag GmbH+**
Huyssenalle 52-54, 45128 Essen
Mailing Address: Postfach 10 39 62, 45039 Essen
*Tel:* (0201) 82002-0 *Fax:* (0201) 82002-34
*Web Site:* www.oldenbourg.de/vulkan-verlag
*Key Personnel*
Man Dir: Dr Dieter Hohm *E-mail:* d.hohm@vulkan-verlag.de

Marketing Manager: Thomas Steinbach *E-mail:* t.steinbach@vulkan-verlag.de
Sales: Silvia Spies *E-mail:* s.spies@vulkan-verlag.de
Founded: 1928
Subjects: Chemistry, Chemical Engineering, Energy, Engineering (General), Environmental Studies, Mechanical Engineering
ISBN Prefix(es): 3-8027
*Parent Company:* R Oldenbourg Verlag, Rosenheimerstr 145, 81671 Munich

**VVF Verlag V Florentz GmbH+**
Furstenstr 15, 80333 Munich
Mailing Address: Postfach 34 01 63, 80098 Munich
*Tel:* (089) 2809095 *Fax:* (089) 2809528
*Key Personnel*
Manager: Franz Frank
Rights & Permissions: Hans Frank
Founded: 1975
Subjects: Government, Political Science, Labor, Industrial Relations, Law, Regional Interests
ISBN Prefix(es): 3-88259; 3-89481; 3-921491
*Associate Companies:* Tuduv Verlagsgesellschaft mbH

**VWB-Verlag fur Wissenschaft & Bildung, Amand Aglaster**
Zossenerstr 55, 10833 Berlin
Mailing Address: PO Box 11 03 68, 10833 Berlin
*Tel:* (030) 251 04 15 *Fax:* (030) 251 11 36
*E-mail:* 100615.1565@compuserve.com
*Web Site:* www.vwb-verlag.com
*Key Personnel*
Owner: Amand Aglaster
Founded: 1988
Subjects: Anthropology, Art, Biological Sciences, Education, Ethnicity, Geography, Geology, Medicine, Nursing, Dentistry, Music, Dance, Psychology, Psychiatry, Science (General), Social Sciences, Sociology, Women's Studies
ISBN Prefix(es): 3-927408; 3-86135

**W Ludwig Verlag GmbH+**
Bayerstr 71-73, 80335 Munich
*Tel:* (089) 41360; (01805) 990505 (hotline)
*E-mail:* heyne-suedwest@randomhouse.de
*Web Site:* www.ludwig-verlag.de
*Telex:* 151329
*Key Personnel*
Managing Partner: Bettina Breitling; Christian Strasser
Founded: 1945
Subjects: Art, Fiction, History, Nonfiction (General), Travel
ISBN Prefix(es): 3-7787
*Associate Companies:* C J Bucher Verlag GmbH; Paul List Verlag GmbH; Suedwest Verlag GmbH & Co KG

**Wachholtz Verlag GmbH**
Rungestr 4, 24537 Neumuenster
*Tel:* (04321) 250-930 *Fax:* (04321) 906-275
*E-mail:* info@wachholtz.de
*Web Site:* www.wachholtz.de
*Key Personnel*
Man Dir & Permissions: Gabriele Wachholtz; Dr Gisela Wachholtz
Production: Renate Braus; Henner Wachholtz
Founded: 1871
Subjects: Archaeology, Art, History, Language Arts, Linguistics, Social Sciences, Sociology
ISBN Prefix(es): 3-529

**Friedenauer Presse Katharina Wagenbach-Wolff+**
Carmerstr 10, 10623 Berlin
*Tel:* (030) 312 99 23 *Fax:* (030) 312 99 02
*Web Site:* www.friedenauer-press.de

*Key Personnel*
Man Dir & International Rights: Katharina Wagenbach-Wolff
Founded: 1963
Subjects: Literature, Literary Criticism, Essays
ISBN Prefix(es): 3-921592; 3-932109

**Edition Waldschloesschen,** *imprint of* Mannerschwarm Skript Verlag GmbH

**Waldthausen Verlag,** *imprint of* NaturaViva Verlags GmbH

**Walhalla Fachverlag GmbH & Co KG Praetoria+**
Haus an der Eisernen Bruecke, 93042 Regensburg
Mailing Address: Postfach 10 10 53, 93010 Regensburg
*Tel:* (0941) 5684-0 *Fax:* (0941) 5684-111
*E-mail:* walhalla@walhalla.de
*Web Site:* www.walhalla.de
*Key Personnel*
Manager: Bernhard Roloff
Founded: 1949
Subjects: Business, Career Development, Law, Public Administration
ISBN Prefix(es): 3-8029

**Uwe Warnke Verlag+**
Sonntagstr 22, 10245 Berlin
*Tel:* (030) 29049903
*E-mail:* warnke@snafu.de
*Key Personnel*
Publisher/Author: Uwe Warnke *E-mail:* warnke@snafu.de
Founded: 1982
Subjects: Art, Literature, Literary Criticism, Essays, Photography, Poetry
ISBN Prefix(es): 3-910165
Total Titles: 100 Print; 1 CD-ROM

**Wartburg Verlag GmbH+**
Lisztstr 2 A, 99423 Weimar
*Tel:* (03643) 24 61-44 *Fax:* (03643) 24 61-18
*E-mail:* buch@wartburgverlag.de
*Web Site:* www.wartburgverlag.de
*Key Personnel*
Man Dir: Torsten Bolduan; Barbara Harnisch
Founded: 1990
Subjects: Art, Literature, Literary Criticism, Essays, Regional Interests, Religion - Protestant
ISBN Prefix(es): 3-86160
Number of titles published annually: 12 Print
Total Titles: 90 Print

**Ernst Wasmuth Verlag GmbH & Co+**
Fuerststr 133, 72072 Tuebingen
Mailing Address: Postfach 27 28, 72017 Tuebingen
*Tel:* (07071) 97 55 00 *Fax:* (07071) 97 55 013
*E-mail:* info@wasmuth-verlag.de
*Web Site:* www.wasmuth-verlag.de
*Key Personnel*
Man Dir: Ernst-Juergen Wasmuth
Sales: Annerose Fischer
Rights & Permissions: Dorah Schneider
Editorial Dir: Dr Sigrid Hauser
Production: Rosa Wagner
Founded: 1872
Subjects: Archaeology, Architecture & Interior Design, Art
ISBN Prefix(es): 3-8030
Number of titles published annually: 20 Print
Total Titles: 250 Print
Distributor for L'Arcaedizioni
*Bookshop(s):* Wasmuth Buchhandlung & Antiquariat GmbH & Co, Pfalzburgerstr 43-44, 10717 Berlin *Tel:* (030) 8 63 09 90 *Fax:* (030) 86 30 99 99 *E-mail:* info@wasmuth.de *Web Site:* www.wasmuth.de

**Waxmann Verlag GmbH+**
Steinfurterstr 555, 48046 Muenster
Mailing Address: Postfach 8603, 48046 Muenster
*Tel:* (0251) 265040 *Fax:* (0251) 2650426
*E-mail:* info@waxmann.com
*Web Site:* www.waxmann.com
*Key Personnel*
Man Dir: Dr Ursula Heckel *E-mail:* heckel@
waxmann.com
Contact: Beate Plugge *E-mail:* plugge@waxmann.
com
Founded: 1987
Subjects: Education, Ethnicity, History, Literature, Literary Criticism, Essays, Psychology, Psychiatry, Science (General), Social Sciences, Sociology, Theology, Women's Studies
ISBN Prefix(es): 3-89325; 3-8309
Number of titles published annually: 120 Print
Total Titles: 1,200 Print
*Branch Office(s)*
Torstr 195, 10115 Berlin *Tel:* (030) 283900-
49 *Fax:* (030) 283900-59 *E-mail:* berlin@
waxmann.com
*U.S. Office(s):* Waxmann Publishing Co, PO Box 1318, New York, NY 10028, United States

**WDV Wirtschaftsdienst Gesellschaft fur Medien & Kommunikation mbH & Co OHG+**
Siemensstr 6, 61352 Bad Homburg
Mailing Address: Postfach 2551, 61295 Bad Homburg
*Tel:* (06172) 670-0 *Fax:* (01672) 670144
*E-mail:* info@wdv.de
*Web Site:* www.wdv.de
*Telex:* 414452 widi d
*Key Personnel*
Managers: Adolf Hilger; Thomas Kuhn; Rolf M Laufer
Marketing: Klaus Tonello
Founded: 1948
Subjects: Health, Nutrition, Travel
ISBN Prefix(es): 3-926181
*Parent Company:* Zeitschriften VVG Verlags- und Verwaltungsgesellschaft mbH & Co KG
Subsidiaries: Analyse & Concept Kommunikationsberatung GmbH; Montan-Wirtschaftsverlag GmbH
*U.S. Office(s):* Conover Brown, International Media, 21 E 40 St, Suite 901, New York, NY 10016, United States
*Warehouse:* Hertzweg 4, 63071 Offenbach am Main

**Weber Zucht & Co+**
Steinbruchweg 14a, 34123 Kassel
*Tel:* (0561) 519194; (0561) 515953 *Fax:* (0561) 5102514
*E-mail:* wezuco@t-online.de
*Key Personnel*
International Rights: Helga Weber
Contact: Wolfgang Zucht
Founded: 1980
Subjects: Alternative, Biography, Education, Environmental Studies, Government, Political Science, History, Military Science, Nonfiction (General), Philosophy, Science (General), Self-Help, Social Sciences, Sociology
ISBN Prefix(es): 3-88713

**Wege der Forschung**, *imprint of*
Wissenschaftliche Buchgesellschaft

**Weidler Buchverlag Berlin+**
Luebecker Str 8, 10559 Berlin
Mailing Address: Postfach 21 03 15, 10503 Berlin
*Tel:* (030) 394 86 68 *Fax:* (030) 394 86 98
*E-mail:* weidler_verlag@yahoo.de
*Web Site:* www.weidler-verlag.de
*Key Personnel*
Man Dir: Joachim Weidler

Founded: 1985
Membership(s): Boersenverein des Deutschen Buchhandels.
Subjects: Drama, Theater, Earth Sciences, Education, Fiction, Geography, Geology, Language Arts, Linguistics, Literature, Literary Criticism, Essays, Management, Marketing, Nonfiction (General), Philosophy, Poetry, Psychology, Psychiatry, Regional Interests, Science (General), Social Sciences, Sociology
ISBN Prefix(es): 3-925191; 3-89693
Number of titles published annually: 30 Print
Total Titles: 215 Print
Imprints: Edition Belletriste

**Weidlich Verlag+**
Imprint of Verlagshaus Wurzburg
Beethovenstr 5, 97070 Wurzburg
*Tel:* (0931) 385235 *Fax:* (0931) 385305
*E-mail:* info@verlagshaus.com
*Web Site:* www.verlagshaus.com
*Key Personnel*
Publishing Dir: Dieter Krause
Dir, Production: Juergen Roth
Sales Dir: Johannes Glesius
Subjects: Foreign Countries, Travel
ISBN Prefix(es): 3-8035

**Weidmannsche Verlagsbuchhandlung GmbH+**
Hagentorwall 7, 31134 Hildesheim
*Tel:* (05121) 15010 *Fax:* (05121) 150150
*E-mail:* info@olms.de
*Web Site:* www.olms.de
*Key Personnel*
Publisher: Dr W Georg Olms
Publishing Dir: Dietrich Olms
Founded: 1680
Subjects: Antiques, History, Language Arts, Linguistics, Philosophy, Romance, Classical Studies, Medieval Studies
ISBN Prefix(es): 3-615; 3-296
Number of titles published annually: 20 Print
Total Titles: 450 Print
*U.S. Office(s):* Empire State Bldg, 350 Fifth Ave, Suite 3304, New York, NY 10118-0069, United States
*Warehouse:* VVA, PO Box 1254, 33399 Verl, Contact: Herr Stronz *Tel:* (05241) 803844 *Fax:* (05241) 8060220

**Verlag W Weinmann+**
Beckerstr 7, 12157 Berlin
*Tel:* (030) 855 48 95 *Fax:* (030) 8 55 94 64
*E-mail:* info@weinmann-verlag.de
*Web Site:* www.weinmann-verlag.de
*Key Personnel*
Man Dir: Dr Weinmann
Founded: 1961
Membership(s): Boersenverein.
Subjects: Humor, Sports, Athletics, Martial Arts
ISBN Prefix(es): 3-87892
Total Titles: 70 Print
Foreign Rep(s): Dessauer CH; Ennsthaler A

**Weisser Ring, Gemeinnutzige Verlagsgesellschaft mbH**
Bundesgeschaeftsstelle, Weberstr 16, 55130 Mainz
*Tel:* (06131) 83 03 01 *Fax:* (06131) 83 03 45
*E-mail:* info@weisser ring.de
*Web Site:* www.weisser-ring.de
*Key Personnel*
Editor: Dieter Eppenstein
Founded: 1989
Specializing in the production of books (Mainzer Schriften) relating to issues concerning victims of crime.
ISBN Prefix(es): 3-9802412; 3-9803526; 3-9806463; 3-9807624
Total Titles: 20 Print
*Parent Company:* Weisser Ring eV

**WEKA Firmengruppe GmbH & Co KG+**
Roemerstr 4, 86438 Kissing
*Tel:* (08233) 23-0 *Fax:* (08233) 23-7500
*E-mail:* service@weka.de
*Web Site:* www.weka.de; www.weka-group.de; www.weka-group.com
*Telex:* 533287
*Key Personnel*
Chairman: Werner Muetzel; Rainer B Wozny
Man Dir: Robert Boss; Wolfgang Materna; Taap Mulder; Gerhard Schierbling
Founded: 1973
Subjects: Architecture & Interior Design, Behavioral Sciences, Business, Career Development, Civil Engineering, Communications, Electronics, Electrical Engineering, Energy, Engineering (General), Environmental Studies, How-to, Law, Management, Mechanical Engineering, Medicine, Nursing, Dentistry, Outdoor Recreation, Real Estate, Technology
ISBN Prefix(es): 3-8111; 3-825; 3-8276; 3-8277
Subsidiaries: Demeter Verlag GmbH & Co KG, Batinger; DMV Daten-und Medien-Verlag GmbH & Co KG; ECPA; Editions WEKA SA; Editions WEKA SARL; Edizioni WEKA SpA; Franzis-Verlag GmbH & Co KG; Interest-Verlag GmbH; Nidderau und Busborn; Spitta Verlag GmbH; Turnus GmbH; Uitgeverij BV; Verlag Recht & Praxis GmbH; Verwaltungs-Verlag GmbH; WAGO-Curadata Steuerberatungs-Systeme GmbH; WEKA Baufach-Software GmbH; WEKA Baufachverlage GmbH; WEKA Fachverlag fuer Behoerden und Institutionen; WEKA Fachverlag fur technische Fuhrungskrafte GmbH; WEKA Handels-GmbH; WEKA Informationsschriften- und Werbefachverlag GmbH; WEKA Management Fachverlag GmbH; WEKA Publishing Inc; WEKA-Verlag AG; WEKA Verlag Ges mbH; WEKA Verlagsgesellschaft fuer aktuelle Publikationen mbH; WEKA Verlagsservice GmbH
*U.S. Office(s):* WEKA Publishing Inc, Huntington Point, 1077 Bridgeport Ave, Sheldon, CT 06484, United States *Tel:* 203-925-1711

**Verlagsgruppe Weltbild GmbH** (Publishing Group Weltbild GmbH)+
Steinerne Furt, 86167 Augsburg
*Tel:* (0821) 70 04-70 00 *Fax:* (0821) 70 04-17 90
*E-mail:* info@weltbild.com
*Web Site:* www.weltbild.com
*Key Personnel*
President: Carel Halff
Man Dir: Dr Klaus Driever; Werner Ortner; Herbert Zoch
Founded: 1949
Subjects: Animals, Pets, Art, Cookery, Crafts, Games, Hobbies, Environmental Studies, Ethnicity, Fashion, Fiction, Gardening, Plants, Health, Nutrition, History, Nonfiction (General), Philosophy
ISBN Prefix(es): 3-86047; 3-8289; 3-89350; 3-89604; 3-927117
*Associate Companies:* Verlagsgruppe Droemer Weltbild GmbH & Co KG, Hilblestr 54, 80636 Munich *Tel:* (0821) 92 71-0 *Fax:* (0821) 92 71-168 *E-mail:* info@droemer-weltbild.org *Web Site:* www.droemer-weltbild.de; Bechtermuenz Verlag; Weltbild Verlag
Subsidiaries: Andreas & Dr Mueller Verlagsbuchhandel GmbH; Bauer-Weltbild Media Spzoo, SpK; Booxtra GmbH & Co Kg; DMC Direkt Marketing Consulting GmbH; Olzog Verlag GmbH; Publica-Data-Service GmbH; Sailer Verlag GmbH & Co KG; Weltbildplus Medienvertriebs GmbH & Co KG; Weltbild Verlag Schweiz GmbH
*Shipping Address:* VVA-Bertelsmann Distribution GmbH, Postfach 7600, 33310 Gutersloh
*Warehouse:* VVA-Bertelsmann Distribution GmbH, Postfach 7600, 33310 Gutersloh

**Weltforum Verlag GmbH+**
Subsidiary of Deutscher Wirtschaftsdienst John von Freyend GmbH
Hohenzollernplatz 3, 53173 Bonn
*Tel:* (0228) 3682436 *Fax:* (0228) 3682436
*E-mail:* wfv@internationsafrikaforum.de
*Key Personnel*
Dir, Sales, Rights & Permissions: Peter John von Freyend
Publicity: Deonika Langer
Founded: 1963
Subjects: Developing Countries
ISBN Prefix(es): 3-8039

**Weltkunst Verlag GmbH+**
Nymphenburgerstr 84, 80636 Munich
*Tel:* (089) 1269900 *Fax:* (089) 12699011
*E-mail:* info@weltkunstverlag.de
*Web Site:* www.weltkunstverlag.de
*Key Personnel*
Contact: Felix Frohn-Bernau
Founded: 1930
Subjects: Art
ISBN Prefix(es): 3-921669
*Parent Company:* Time Beteiligungs AG, Starnberg
Subsidiaries: Antiquitaeten-Zeitung Verlag; Hirmer Verlag GmbH; W B Verlag
*U.S. Office(s):* Axel Springer Group Inc, 500 Fifth Ave, Suite 2800, New York, NY 10110, United States *Tel:* 212-972-1720 *Fax:* 212-972-1724 *E-mail:* asg-usa@msn.com

**Wer liefert was? GmbH** (Who Supplies What?)
Normannenweg, 16-20, 20537 Hamburg
Mailing Address: Postfach 100549, 20004 Hamburg
*Tel:* (040) 25440-0 *Fax:* (040) 25440-100
*E-mail:* info@wlw.de
*Web Site:* www.wlw.de
*Key Personnel*
Man Dir: Andrew Pylyp; Peter Schulze
Founded: 1948
Membership(s): Informationsgemeinschaft zur Feststellung der Verbreitung von Wer bertraegern eV; Verband Deutscher Andressbuchverleger eV; Europaeischen Andressbuchverleger-Verband; Verband Deutscher Wirtschaftsnachschlagewerke eV.
Subjects: Business, Marketing
ISBN Prefix(es): 3-923878
Total Titles: 1 Print; 5 CD-ROM; 1 Online; 1 E-Book
*Parent Company:* Eniro AB, Stockholm, Sweden
*Branch Office(s)*
Wer liefert was? Ges mbH, Inkustr 1-7/6/1 OG, 3400 Klosterneuburg, Austria *Tel:* (02243) 33765 *Fax:* (02243) 33765-88 *E-mail:* info@wlw.at *Web Site:* www.wlw.at
Wer liefert was? GmbH, succ belge, Louiza-laan 65/11, 1050 Brussels, Belgium *Tel:* (02) 2452228 *Fax:* (02) 2456213 *E-mail:* info@wlw.be *Web Site:* www.wlw.be
Wer liefert was? spol s r o, Sokolska 52, 120 00 Prague-2, Czech Republic *Tel:* (02) 96330-200 *Fax:* (02) 96330-201 *E-mail:* info@wlw.cz *Web Site:* www.wlw.cz
Wer liefert was? doo, Fallerovo setaliste 22, 10000 Zagreb, Croatia *Tel:* (01) 3030500 *Fax:* (01) 3030501 *E-mail:* info@wlw.hr *Web Site:* www.wlw.hr
Wer liefert was? Nederlandse Vestiging, Hoogoorddreef 9, 1101 BA Amsterdam, Netherlands *Tel:* (020) 6960706 *Fax:* (020) 6968866 *E-mail:* info@wlw.nl *Web Site:* www.wlw.nl
Wer liefert was? Doo, Gregorciceva ulica 7, 3000 Celje, Slovenia *Tel:* (03) 42508 00 *Fax:* (03) 42508 01 *E-mail:* info@wlw.si *Web Site:* www.wlw.si
Wer liefert was AG, Blegistr 15, 6340 Baar-Walterswil, Switzerland *Tel:* (041) 7603438 *Fax:* (041) 7603430 *E-mail:* info@wlw.ch *Web Site:* www.wlw.ch

**Werner Verlag GmbH & Co KG+**
Karl-Rudolf-Str 172, 40215 Duesseldorf
Mailing Address: Postfach 10 53 54, 40044 Duesseldorf
*Tel:* (0211) 3 87 98-0 *Fax:* (0211) 3 87 98-11
*E-mail:* info@werner-verlag.de
*Key Personnel*
Publishing Dir: Klaus-Juergen Schneider
Founded: 1945
Subjects: Economics, Engineering (General), Law
ISBN Prefix(es): 3-8041
*Parent Company:* Wolters Kluwer

**Georg Westermann Verlag GmbH+**
Georg-Westermann-Allee 66, 38104 Braunschweig
*Tel:* (0531) 708-0 *Fax:* (0531) 708-209
*E-mail:* schulservice@westermann.de
*Web Site:* www.westermann.de *Cable:* GEWEBUCH
*Key Personnel*
Man Dir: Ulrike Jurgens; Thomas Michael; Dr Peter Schell; Michael Wolf
Founded: 1838
Subjects: Nonfiction (General)
ISBN Prefix(es): 3-07
*Parent Company:* Georg Westermann Verlag, Druckerei und Kartographische Anstalt GmbH & Co, Brunswick (printing & publishing management company)
*Orders to:* VSB Verlagsservice Braunschweig GmbH, Postfach 4925, 38039 Braunschweig *Tel:* (0531) 708-0

**Westermann Schulbuchverlag GmbH**
Georg-Westermann-Allee 66, 38104 Braunschweig
*Tel:* (0531) 7 08-0 *Fax:* (0531) 70 82 09
*E-mail:* schulservice@westermann.de
*Web Site:* www.westermann.de
*Telex:* 0952841 wbuch d *Cable:* GEWEBUCH
*Key Personnel*
Editorial, Production: Juergen Grimm
Sales, Publicity: Hartmut Becker
Subjects: Education, History
ISBN Prefix(es): 3-14; 3-8045
*Parent Company:* Georg Westermann Verlag, Druckerei und Kartographische Anstalt GmbH & Co, (Printing & Publishing Management Co), Brunswick

**Verlag Westfaelisches Dampfboot+**
Hafenweg 26a, 48155 Muenster
*Tel:* (0251) 3900480 *Fax:* (0251) 39004850
*E-mail:* info@dampfboot-verlag.de
*Web Site:* www.dampfboot-verlag.de
*Key Personnel*
Editor: Prof H G Thien, PhD; Prof H Wienold, PhD
Founded: 1984
Subjects: Labor, Industrial Relations, Law, Social Sciences, Sociology, Women's Studies
ISBN Prefix(es): 3-924550; 3-929586; 3-89691
*Orders to:* Prolit Verlagsauslieferung, Siemensstr 13, 35463 Fernwald *Tel:* (0641) 9439333 *Fax:* (0641) 9439339 *Web Site:* www.prolit.de

**Westholsteinische Verlagsanstalt und Verlagsdruckerei Boyens & Co+**
Wulf-Isebrand-Platz, 25746 Heide
*Tel:* (0481) 6886-0 *Fax:* (0481) 6886-467
*E-mail:* buchhandlung@sh-nordsee.de
*Web Site:* www.sh-nordsee.de/buchverlag.html
*Telex:* 28833 boyens d
*Key Personnel*
Dir: Dipl Kfm Boyens Uwe
Man Dir: Bernd Rachuth
Sales Dir: Reinhard Lipinski
Technical Dir: Heinz Fuhrberg
Founded: 1869
Subjects: Cookery, Literature, Literary Criticism, Essays, Regional Interests

ISBN Prefix(es): 3-8042
Subsidiaries: Brunsbuetteler Zeitung GmbH
*Branch Office(s)*
Albersdorf
Busum
Marne
Meldorf Wesselburen
St Michaelisdorn
*Orders to:* PO Box 1880, 25738 Heath

**Erich Wewel Verlag GmbH+**
Heilig-Kreuz-Str 16, 86609 Donauwoerth
Mailing Address: Postfach 1152, 86601 Donauwoerth
*Tel:* (0906) 73-1240 *Fax:* (0906) 73-1 77
*Web Site:* www.klett.de/geschaeftsbereiche/grundschule.html
*Key Personnel*
Dir & Editorial: Lydia Franzelius
Founded: 1936
Subjects: Philosophy, Religion - Other, Theology
ISBN Prefix(es): 3-403; 3-87904
*Parent Company:* Klett Gruppe

**Wichern Verlag GmbH+**
Georgenkirchstr 69-70, 10249 Berlin
*Tel:* (030) 28 87 48 10 *Fax:* (030) 28 87 48 12
*E-mail:* info@wichern.de
*Web Site:* www.wichern.de
*Key Personnel*
Contact: Dr Elke Rutzenhofer
Founded: 1880
Specialize in Christian Literature.
Membership(s): the Stock Exchange of German Booksellers & the Association of Publishers & Bookstores in Berlin-Brandenburg.
Subjects: Biography, History, Religion - Other, Theology
ISBN Prefix(es): 3-88981; 3-7674
Distributed by BMK Buchauslieferung (Austria); Evangelische Verlagsauslieferung

**Wichern-Verlag GmbH+**
Georgenkirchstr 69-70, 10249 Berlin
Mailing Address: Postfach 350954, 10218 Berlin
*Tel:* (030) 288748-0 *Fax:* (030) 28874812
*E-mail:* 101711.1207@compuserve.com
*Key Personnel*
Publisher: Wolfgang Fietkau
Founded: 1982
Membership(s): the Stock Exchange of German Booksellers & the Association of Publishers & Bookstores in Berlin-Brandenburg.
Subjects: History, Religion - Other
ISBN Prefix(es): 3-88981; 3-7674
Divisions: CZV-Verlag
Distributed by BMK Buchauslieferung (Austria); Evangelische Verlagsauslieferung (Switzerland)
*Warehouse:* Mehringdamm 32-34, 10961 Berlin

**Herbert Wichmann Verlag+**
Im Weiher 10, 69121 Heidelberg
Mailing Address: Postfach 102869, 69018 Heidelberg
*Tel:* (06221) 4890 *Fax:* (06221) 489279
*E-mail:* wichmann@huethig.de
*Web Site:* www.huethig.de
Founded: 1889
Subjects: Aeronautics, Aviation, Communications, Earth Sciences, Geography, Geology
ISBN Prefix(es): 3-87907
Number of titles published annually: 11 Print
*Parent Company:* Huethig GmbH & Co KG

**Wiechmann-Verlag Betriebs GmbH**
Deggenhauser Str 8, 88693 Deggenhausertal
*Tel:* (0700) 08000035 *Fax:* (0700) 08000036
*Key Personnel*
Manager: Carsta Korhammer; Heidi Wiechmann
Founded: 1893
ISBN Prefix(es): 3-87908

**Wiley-VCH Verlag GmbH+**
Boschstr 12, 69469 Weinheim
Mailing Address: Postfach 101161, 69451 Weinheim
*Tel:* (06201) 606 0 *Fax:* (06201) 606 328
*E-mail:* info@wiley-vch.de
*Web Site:* www.wiley-vch.de
*Telex:* 467-155-vchwh d
*Key Personnel*
Publishing Dir: Dr Eva E Wille *Tel:* (030) 6201-606272 *Fax:* (030) 6201-606205 *E-mail:* ewille@wiley-vch.de
Human Resources Dir: Sven Kroeger *Tel:* (030) 6201-606159 *Fax:* (030) 6201-606192 *E-mail:* skroeger@wiley-vch.de
Marketing & Sales Dir: Juergen Boos *E-mail:* j-boos@wiley-vch.de
Finance & Administration Dir: Bijan Ghawami
Information Technology: Petra Wyrwa
Editorial Dir, Business: Bettina Querfurth
Founded: 1921
Subjects: Biological Sciences, Chemistry, Chemical Engineering, Law, Physical Sciences, Physics, Science (General)
ISBN Prefix(es): 3-527
Total Titles: 1,580 Print
*Parent Company:* John Wiley & Sons Inc, 111 River St, Hoboken, NJ 07030, United States
Subsidiaries: Wilhelm Ernst & Sohn Verlag fuer Architektur und technische Wissenschaft; Chemical Concepts; Verlagsservice Suedwest; Verlag Helvetica Chimica Actc AG

**Windmuehle GmbH Verlag und Vertrieb von Medien+**
Gosslerstr 22/24, 22587 Hamburg
Mailing Address: Postfach 551080, 22570 Hamburg
*Tel:* (040) 86 83 07 *Fax:* (040) 866 31 23
*E-mail:* info@windmuehle-verlag.de
*Web Site:* www.windmuehle-verlag.de
*Key Personnel*
Manager: Rita Bolte
Founded: 1981
Specialize in furthering education in organization & management.
Subjects: Education, Management
ISBN Prefix(es): 3-922789
*Warehouse:* Metzler-Poeschel, Hermann Leins Auslieferungsdienst, Postfach 7, 7408 Kusterdingen *Tel:* (07071) 93530 *Fax:* (07071) 93530

**Windpferd Verlagsgesellschaft mbH+**
Friesenriederstr 45, 87648 Aitrang
Mailing Address: Postfach 87648, Aitrang
*Tel:* (08343) 1404 *Fax:* (08343) 1403
*E-mail:* info@windpferd.de
*Web Site:* www.windpferd.de
*Key Personnel*
Manager: Monika Junemann
Founded: 1987
Subjects: Psychology, Psychiatry
ISBN Prefix(es): 3-89385

**Bibliothek rosa Winkel**, *imprint of* Mannerschwarm Skript Verlag GmbH

**Rosa Winkel Verlag GmbH+**
Kufsteinerstr 12, 10825 Berlin
Mailing Address: Postfach 302949, 10777 Berlin
*Tel:* (030) 85729295 *Fax:* (030) 85729296
*E-mail:* rosawinkel@t-online.de
*Key Personnel*
Publisher: Egmont Fassbinder
Subjects: Gay & Lesbian, Nonfiction (General)
ISBN Prefix(es): 3-921495; 3-86149

**Dr Dieter Winkler+**
Katharinastr 37, 44793 Bochum
Mailing Address: Postfach 102665, 44726 Bochum

*Tel:* (0234) 9650200 *Fax:* (0234) 9650201
*E-mail:* winkler-verlag.bochum@tonline.de
*Web Site:* www.winklerverlag.de
*Key Personnel*
Owner: Dr Dieter Winkler
Founded: 1984
Membership(s): Boersenverein des Dt Buchhandels.
Subjects: Education, History, Nonfiction (General), Regional Interests, Science (General), Social Sciences, Sociology
ISBN Prefix(es): 3-924517; 3-930083; 3-89911
Number of titles published annually: 10 Print
Total Titles: 115 Print

**Winklers Verlag Gebrueder Grimm**
Alsfelderstr 7, 64289 Darmstadt
Mailing Address: Postfach 111552, 64230 Darmstadt
*Tel:* (06151) 87 68-0 *Fax:* (06151) 87 68-61
*E-mail:* service@winklers.de
*Web Site:* www.winklers.de
*Key Personnel*
Manager: Ulrike Jurgens; Thomas Michael
Manager, Rights & Permissions: Michael Wolf
Founded: 1902
Subjects: Career Development
ISBN Prefix(es): 3-8045
*Shipping Address:* Elisabethenstr 34, 64283 Darmstadt

**Verlag fuer Wirtschaft & Verwaltung Hubert Wingen GmbH & Co KG+**
Alfredistr 32, 45127 Essen
Mailing Address: Postfach 103824, 45038 Essen
*Tel:* (0201) 22 25 41; (0201) 22 25 42; (0201) 221451-52 *Fax:* (0201) 229660
*Key Personnel*
Manager: Martha Wingen; Rainer Wingen
Founded: 1958
Subjects: Architecture & Interior Design, Civil Engineering, Law, Public Administration, Real Estate, Religion - Catholic
ISBN Prefix(es): 3-8028
Subsidiaries: Lugerus Verlag GmbH & Co KG

**Wirtschaft, Recht & Steuern**, see WRS Verlag Wirtschaft, Recht und Steuern GmbH & Co KG

**Verlag fuer Wissenschaft & Bildung**, see VWB-Verlag fur Wissenschaft & Bildung, Amand Aglaster

**Verlag Wissenschaft und Politik**
Markt 13, 06785 Oranienbaum
Mailing Address: PO Box 1107, 06782 Oranienbaum
*Tel:* (034904) 32946 *Fax:* (034904) 32946
*E-mail:* helker.pflug@t-online.de
*Key Personnel*
Owner & Man Dir: Helker Pflug
Founded: 1961
Specialize in books on Central & Eastern Europe.
Subjects: Ethnicity, Genealogy, Government, Political Science, History, Language Arts, Linguistics, Law, Religion - Jewish, Science (General), Social Sciences, Sociology
ISBN Prefix(es): 3-8046
Number of titles published annually: 8 Print
Total Titles: 120 Print

**Wissenschaftliche Buchgesellschaft** (Scientific Book Society)+
Hindenburgstr 40, 64295 Darmstadt
*Tel:* (06151) 33 08-127 *Fax:* (06151) 33 08 208
*E-mail:* service@wbg-darmstadt.de
*Web Site:* www.wbg-darmstadt.de
*Key Personnel*
Acting Dir: Andreas Auth
Chief Reader: Martin Bredol

Rights & Permissions: Friedericke Ludolph
Press: Barbara Gese *Tel:* (06151) 3308-161 *E-mail:* gese@wbg-darmstadt.de
Founded: 1949
Subjects: Archaeology, Art, Economics, Education, History, Language Arts, Linguistics, Law, Literature, Literary Criticism, Essays, Mathematics, Medicine, Nursing, Dentistry, Music, Dance, Philosophy, Psychology, Psychiatry, Religion - Other, Science (General), Social Sciences, Sociology
ISBN Prefix(es): 3-534
Imprints: Bibliothek Klassischer Texte; Einfuehrungen; Ertraege der Forschung zur Forschung-; Forum; Freiherr von Stein Gedaechtnisausgabe; Wege der Forschung
Distributor for AVA B&I (Switzerland); Dr Franz Hain Verlagsauslieferung (Austria)
*Book Club(s):* Wissenschaftliche Buchgesellschaft

**Wissenschaftliche Verlagsgesellschaft mbH+**
Birkenwaldstr 44, 70191 Stuttgart
Mailing Address: Postfach 101061, 70009 Stuttgart
*Tel:* (0711) 2582-325 *Fax:* (0711) 2582-290
*E-mail:* service@dav-buchhandlung.de
*Web Site:* www.dav-buchhandlung.de
*Key Personnel*
Man Dir: Dr Klaus Brauer; R Hack; Dr Christian Rotta
Contact: Siegmar Bauer
Founded: 1921
Subjects: Biological Sciences, Medicine, Nursing, Dentistry, Science (General), Pharmacy
ISBN Prefix(es): 3-8047
*Parent Company:* Deutscher Apotheker Verlag
Subsidiaries: S Hirzel Verlag GmbH & Co; Medpharm Scientific Publishers; Franz Steiner Verlag Wiesbaden GmbH

**Wissenschaftlicher Autoren Verlag KG**, see Verlag Grundlagen und Praxis GmbH & Co

**Wissenschaftsrat**
Brohlerstr 11, 50968 Cologne
*Tel:* (0221) 3776-0 *Fax:* (0221) 38 84 40
*E-mail:* post@wissenschaftsrat.de
*Web Site:* www.wissenschaftsrat.de
Founded: 1957
ISBN Prefix(es): 3-923203; 3-935353

**Verlag Claus Wittal**
Fliednerstr 27, 65195 Wiesbaden-Bierstadt
*Tel:* (0611) 502907 *Fax:* (0611) 503021
*E-mail:* cw@exlibrisart.com
*Web Site:* www.exlibrisart.com
Founded: 1979
Subjects: Art, Exlibris/bookplates
ISBN Prefix(es): 3-922835

**Friedrich Wittig Verlag GmbH+**
Gartenstr 20, 24103 Kiel
Mailing Address: Postfach 3169, 24030 Kiel
*Tel:* (0431) 55779 206 *Fax:* (0431) 55779 292
*E-mail:* vertrieb@wittig-verlag.de
*Web Site:* www.wittig-verlag.de *Cable:* WITTIGVERLAG
*Key Personnel*
Man Dir: Rainer Thun
Sales: Wolfgang Steinmeier
International Rights: Johannes Keussen
Founded: 1946
Subjects: Art, Biblical Studies, History, Religion - Other
ISBN Prefix(es): 3-8048
*Associate Companies:* J F Steinkopf Verlag GmbH

**Verlag Konrad Wittwer GmbH+**
Postfach 105343, 70046 Stuttgart
*Tel:* (0711) 25 07 0 *Fax:* (0711) 25 07 145
*E-mail:* info@wittwer.de

*Web Site:* www.wittwer.de
*Key Personnel*
Man Dir: Christian Wittwer; Dr Konrad M Wittwer; Konrad P Wittwer; Michael Wittwer
Founded: 1867
Subjects: Earth Sciences, Mathematics, Nonfiction (General), Science (General)
ISBN Prefix(es): 3-87919
*Bookshop(s):* Koenigstr 30, 70173 Stuttgart

**WLW,** see Wer liefert was? GmbH

**Wochenschau,** *imprint of* Wochenschau Verlag, Dr Kurt Debus GmbH

**Wochenschau Verlag, Dr Kurt Debus GmbH+**
Adolf-Damaschkestr 10, 65824 Schwalbach-Taunus
*Tel:* (06196) 8 60 65 *Fax:* (06196) 8 60 60
*E-mail:* info@wochenschau-verlag.de
*Web Site:* www.wochenschau-verlag.de
*Key Personnel*
Publishing Dir: Bernward Debus
Manager & Editor-in-Chief: Ursula Buch
Founded: 1949
Subjects: Education, Geography, Geology, Government, Political Science, History
ISBN Prefix(es): 3-87920
Imprints: Wochenschau

**Verlagshaus Wohlfarth+**
Stresemannstr 20-22, 47051 Duisburg
*Tel:* (0203) 3 05 27-0 *Fax:* (0203) 3 05 27-820
*E-mail:* info@wohlfarth.de
*Web Site:* www.wohlfarth.de
*Key Personnel*
Man Dir, Publishing: Frank Wohlfarth
Man Dir, Editorial: Uwe Hennig
Book Sales Manager: Lothar Koopmann
*E-mail:* l.koopmann@wohlfarth.de
Contact: Stephen Hasselbach *E-mail:* s.hasselbach@wohlfarth.de
Founded: 1953
Membership(s): Borsenverein des Deutschen Buchhandels.
Subjects: Architecture & Interior Design, Crafts, Games, Hobbies, House & Home, Regional Interests
ISBN Prefix(es): 3-87463
Total Titles: 5 Print
Imprints: Mercator-Verlag; Verlag Puppen & Spielzeug; Verlagsbereich Bau

**Wolf's-Verlag Berlin+**
Bergedorferstr 180, 12623 Berlin
*Tel:* (030) 5675190
*Key Personnel*
Publishing Manager: Evelyn Wolf
Founded: 1990
Subjects: Fiction, Literature, Literary Criticism, Essays, Travel
ISBN Prefix(es): 3-86164

**Wolke Verlags GmbH+**
Niederhofheimerstr 45 a-c, 65719 Hofheim
*Tel:* (06192) 7243 *Fax:* (06192) 952939
*E-mail:* wolke-verlag@t-online.de
*Web Site:* www.wolke-verlag.de
*Key Personnel*
Man Dir: Peter Mischung
Subjects: Music, Dance
ISBN Prefix(es): 3-923997; 3-936000

**Wolters Kluwer Deutschland GmbH**
Formerly Hermann Luchterhand Verlag GmbH
Heddesdorfer Str 31, 56564 Neuwied
Mailing Address: Postfach 2352, 56513 Neuwied
*Tel:* (02631) 8010 *Fax:* (02631) 801210
*E-mail:* info@luchterhand.de
*Web Site:* www.luchterhand.de

*Key Personnel*
Man Dir: Juergen M Luczak *Tel:* (02631) 801-330 *Fax:* (02631) 801-225 *E-mail:* juergen.luczak@luchterhand.de
Publication Manager: Elke Richter-Weiland *Tel:* (02631) 801-264 *Fax:* (02631) 801-353 *E-mail:* elke.richter-weiland@luchterhand.de; Stefan Wiemuth *Tel:* (06192) 408-229 *Fax:* (06192) 408-248 *E-mail:* 100537.357@compuserve.com; Rainer Joede *Tel:* (06192) 408-200 *Fax:* (06192) 408-248 *E-mail:* rainer.joede@dwd-verlag.de; Rainer Winkler *Tel:* (02631) 801-232 *Fax:* (02631) 801-204; Walter Kastor *Tel:* (02631) 801-239 *Fax:* (02631) 801-415 *E-mail:* walter.kastor@luchterhand.de
Sales Manager: Erminold Malzbender *Tel:* (02631) 801-318 *Fax:* (02631) 801-381
Contact: Evelin Gerlach *Tel:* (02631) 801 275 *Fax:* (02631) 801 225 *E-mail:* evelin.gerlach@luchterhand.de
Founded: 1924
Subjects: Business, Education, Law, Management
ISBN Prefix(es): 3-472
*Parent Company:* Wolters Kluwer Deutschland GmbH
*Ultimate Parent Company:* Wolters Kluwer NV, Netherlands
Imprints: Kommentator; Alfred Metzner
Subsidiaries: Werner Verlag GmbH & Co KG
Divisions: Fachverlag Deutscher Wirtschaftsdienst GmbH, Koeln
*Branch Office(s)*
Pestalozzistr 5-8 13187, Berlin *Tel:* (030) 48839011 *Fax:* (030) 48839020
Gutenbergstr 8, Kriftel *Tel:* (06192) 4080 *Fax:* (06192) 408248

**The World of Books Literaturverlag+**
Friedrich-Ebert-Str 80, 67549 Worms
*Tel:* (0174) 8382269 *Fax:* (06241) 954926
*Web Site:* www.twobl-online.de
*Key Personnel*
Contact: Reinhard Becker *E-mail:* reinhard.becker@twobl-online.de
Founded: 1981
ISBN Prefix(es): 3-88325

**The World Society of Victimology eV+**
Richard-Wagner Str 101, 41065 Moenchengladbach
*Tel:* (02161) 186 609 *Fax:* (02161) 186 633
*Web Site.* www.world-society-victimology.de/
*Key Personnel*
Director: Dr Gerd Ferdinand Kirchhoff *E-mail:* kirchhoff@bigfoot.de
Founded: 1979
ISBN Prefix(es): 3-929441
Number of titles published annually: 1 Print; 4 Audio

**Verlag DAS WORT GmbH** (The Word Publishing House)
Max-Braunstr 2, 97828 Martheidenfeld-Altfeld
*Tel:* (09391) 504135 *Fax:* (09391) 504133
*E-mail:* info@das-wort.com
*Web Site:* www.das-wort.com; www.universal-spirit.cc
*Key Personnel*
General Manager: Christine Schulte *Tel:* (09391) 504132
Membership(s): Borsenverein.
Subjects: Health, Nutrition, Human Relations, Philosophy, Religion - Other, Self-Help
ISBN Prefix(es): 3-89201
Total Titles: 68 Print
*U.S. Office(s):* Universal Life, The Inner Religion, PO Box 651, Gilford, CT 06437, United States *Fax:* 203-457-9693 *Web Site:* www.universal-life.com

**WRS Verlag Wirtschaft, Recht und Steuern GmbH & Co KG**
Subsidiary of Rudolf Haufe Verlag GmbH & Co KG
Fraunhoferstr 5, 82152 Planegg
Mailing Address: Postfach 1363, 82142 Planegg
*Tel:* (089) 89 517-0 *Fax:* (089) 89 517-250
*E-mail:* info@wrs.de
*Web Site:* www.wrs.de *Cable:* WRS VERLAG
*Key Personnel*
Dir: Martin Laqua; Helmuth Hopfner; Mueller Uwe Renald
Founded: 1973
Subjects: Accounting, Advertising, Business, Computer Science, Economics, House & Home, Law, Management, Marketing, Nonfiction (General)
ISBN Prefix(es): 3-8092
Subsidiaries: STS Standard Tabellen-und Software Verlag

**Das Wunderhorn Verlag GmbH**
Bergstr 21, 69120 Heidelberg
*Tel:* (06221) 402428 *Fax:* (06221) 402483
*E-mail:* info@wunderhorn.de
*Web Site:* www.wunderhorn.de
*Key Personnel*
Publisher: Manfred Metzner *E-mail:* metzner@wunderhorn.de
Founded: 1978
Subjects: Art, Biography, Fiction, Film, Video, History, Literature, Literary Criticism, Essays, Poetry, Science (General), Women's Studies
ISBN Prefix(es): 3-88423
Number of titles published annually: 16 Print
Total Titles: 230 Print
Distributed by Rudi Deuble; Leitner Verlagsvertretungen (Austria); Prolit Buchvertrieb GmbH (Austria & Germany); Scheidegger & Co AG

**Wunderlich Verlag,** *imprint of* Rowohlt Verlag GmbH

**Wunderlich Verlag+**
Hamburgerstr 17, 21453 Reinbek
*Tel:* (040) 72 72 0 *Fax:* (040) 72 72 319
*E-mail:* info@rowohlt.de
*Web Site:* www.rowohlt.de
*Key Personnel*
Man Dir: Helmut Daehne; Alexander Fest; Lutz Kettmann
Contact: Eckhard Kloos
Rights & Permissions: Kristina Krombholz
Subjects: Biography, Fiction, History, Nonfiction (General)
*Parent Company:* Rowohlt Verlag GmbH

**Fachbuchverlag Armin W Wuth,** see Wuth-Gruppe

**Wuth-Gruppe+**
Formerly Fachbuchverlag Armin W Wuth
Im Blenze 31, 31515 Wunstorf
Mailing Address: Postfach 6110, 31509 Wunstorf
*Tel:* (05031) 91 69 81 *Fax:* (05031) 91 69 82
*E-mail:* zentrale@wuth-gruppe.de
*Web Site:* www.wuth-gruppe.de
*Key Personnel*
Man Dir: Dr Armin W Wuth *E-mail:* a.wuth@wuth-grupper.de
Founded: 1982
Specializes in Stock Exchange.
Subjects: Business, Computer Science, Economics, Medicine, Nursing, Dentistry
ISBN Prefix(es): 3-924018; 3-87082
*Branch Office(s)*
c/o GBB eV, Karl Liebknecht-Str 32, 10178 Berlin *E-mail:* berlin@wuth-gruppe.de
WUTH India, c/o ADI Infotech Pvt Ltd, No 567, Huda Sector 23, Gurgaon, Haryana 122001, India *E-mail:* india@wuth-gruppe.de

WUTH Singapore, Servcorb S V Office TM, 16 Raffles Quay, Singapore 048581, Singapore *Tel:* (0322) 85 88 *Fax:* (0322) 85 58
*E-mail:* singapore@wuth-gruppe.de
WUTH Thailand, c/o MBE Pattaya, MBE Suite 125, 269/2 Soi Potisarn M00 6, Naklua Banglamung, Chonburi 20150, Thailand
*E-mail:* thailand@wuth-gruppe.de
*U.S. Office(s):* WUTH USA I, 28 Vesey St, PO Box 2133, New York, NY 10007, United States
*E-mail:* usa@wuth-gruppe.de

**X-Games**, *imprint of* Pearson Education Deutschland GmbH

**Xenos Verlagsgesellschaft mbH** (Xenos Publishing)+
Affiliate of Lies & Spiel Publishing Co
Am Hehsel 40, 22339 Hamburg
*Tel:* (040) 538093-0 *Fax:* (040) 5386000
*E-mail:* xenos.verlag@t-online.de
*Web Site:* www.xenosverlag.de
*Key Personnel*
Man Dir: Bjoern Heimberger *Tel:* (040) 53809329; Erwin Heimberger *Tel:* (040) 53809320
Sales, Germany: Wolfgang Steigner
Sales Manager, Germany: Oliver Draeger *Tel:* (040) 53809344
Production: Meino Dorbandt *Tel:* (040) 53809340 *Fax:* (040) 5387863
Founded: 1975
Children's book publishers specializing in wall charts, colony & activity books, atlases.
Also acts as book packager.
Membership(s): Borsenverein Chamber of Commerce.
Subjects: Nonfiction (General)
ISBN Prefix(es): 3-8212; 3-933697; 3-935746
Number of titles published annually: 180 Print
*Parent Company:* Frankfurter Allgemeine Zeitung, Hellerhofstr 2-4, Frankfurt am Main
Imprints: Edition Riesenrad; Merit; Tipp Creative
Subsidiaries: Lies & Spiel Hausparty GmbH
*Shipping Address:* Spedition Rapid, Wilhelm-Iwan-Ring 5, 21035 Hamburg *Tel:* (040) 734130
*Warehouse:* PVS Fulfillment Service, Werner-Hassstr 5, 74172 Neckarsulm, Contact: Mr Jurgens *Tel:* (07132) 9690 *Fax:* (07132) 969170
*Distribution Center:* PVS Fulfillment, Werner-Haas-Str 5, 74172 Neckarsulm *Tel:* (07132) 969166 *Fax:* (07132) 969170

**Verlag Philipp von Zabern**
Philipp-von-Zabern Platz 1-3, 55116 Mainz
*Tel:* (06131) 28747-0 *Fax:* (06131) 28747-44
*E-mail:* zabern@zabern.de
*Web Site:* www.zabern.de
*Key Personnel*
Man Dir: Dr Annette Nuennerich Asmus
Management: Felix Frohn-Bernau
Sales: Christine Vorhoelzer *Tel:* (089) 121516-61; (089) 121516-26 *Fax:* (089) 121516116
*E-mail:* vertrieb@verlagvonzabern.de
Advertising: Ms Manuela Dressen *Tel:* (06131) 28747 11 *E-mail:* m.dressen@zabern.de
Founded: 1802
Subjects: Archaeology, Art, History, Regional Interests
ISBN Prefix(es): 3-8053
Number of titles published annually: 100 Print
*Orders to:* PO Box 190930, 80689 Munich, Sales: Christine Vorhoelzer *Tel:* (089) 121516-61; (089) 121516-26 *Fax:* (089) 121516-16
*E-mail:* vertrieb@verlagvonzabern.de

**Zambon Verlag+**
Leipziger Str 24, 60487 Frankfurt am Main
*Tel:* (069) 773054 *Fax:* (069) 773054
*E-mail:* zambon@online.de
*Web Site:* www.zambonverlag.de

*Key Personnel*
Publisher: Dr Giuseppe Zambon
Founded: 1974
Subjects: Cookery, Developing Countries, Government, Political Science, History, Poetry, Regional Interests, Travel
ISBN Prefix(es): 3-88975
*Bookshop(s):* Internationale Buchhandlung, Kaiserstr 55, 60329 Frankfurt *Fax:* (069) 23 02 77

**Zebulon Verlag GmbH & Co KG+**
Wormserstr 37, 50677 Cologne
Mailing Address: Postfach 250 369, 50519 Cologne
*Tel:* (0221) 3405620 *Fax:* (0221) 3405622
*E-mail:* zebulon-koeln@t-online.de
*Key Personnel*
Man Dir & Publishing Dir: Hajo Leib
Founded: 1992
Subjects: Criminology, Environmental Studies, Government, Political Science, Health, Nutrition, Nonfiction (General), Women's Studies
ISBN Prefix(es): 3-928679
*Warehouse:* Prolit Verlagsausliefrung GmbH, Siemensstr 16, 35463 Fernwald (Annerod)

**Zeitgeist Media GmbH+**
Duesseldorfer Str 60, 40545 Duesseldorf
*Tel:* (0211) 55 62 55 *Fax:* (0211) 57 51 67
*E-mail:* info@zeitgeistmedia.de
*Web Site:* www.zeitgeistverlag.de
*Key Personnel*
Man Dir, Rights & Permissions: Hubert Buecken *E-mail:* hb@zeitgeistmedia.de
Founded: 1989
Subjects: Human Relations, Humor, Outdoor Recreation, Travel
ISBN Prefix(es): 3-926224; 3-934046

**Verlag Zeitschrift fur Naturforschung**
Uhlandstr 11, 72072 Tuebingen
Mailing Address: Postfach 2645, 72016 Tuebingen
*Tel:* (07071) 31555 *Fax:* (07071) 360571
*E-mail:* mail@znaturforsch.com
*Web Site:* www.znaturforsch.com
*Key Personnel*
Man Dir: Tamina Greifeld *Tel:* (089) 3541485 *E-mail:* greifeld@znaturforsch.com
Founded: 1946
Publish scientific periodicals.
Subjects: Biological Sciences, Chemistry, Chemical Engineering, Physical Sciences
Total Titles: 3 Print; 3 Online
*Branch Office(s)*
Beuthenerstr 17, 55131 Mainz *Tel:* (06131) 573276 *Fax:* (06131) 571061

**Verlag Clemens Zerling+**
Goethestr 9, 83435 Bad Reichenhall
*Tel:* (08651) 602295 *Fax:* (08651) 602295
*Key Personnel*
Man Dir, Editorial: Clemens Zerling
Sales: Daniela Moeser
Founded: 1979
Subjects: Anthropology, Astrology, Occult, Biography, History, Religion - Other
ISBN Prefix(es): 3-88468
*Associate Companies:* Edition Weber, Berlin

**Zettner Verlag GmbH & Co KG+**
Hofweg 12, 97209 Veitshoechheim
*Tel:* (0931) 91970 *Fax:* (0931) 960 097
*E-mail:* info@zettnerverlag.com
*Web Site:* www.zettnerverlag.com
Founded: 1955
Subjects: Art, Erotica, Fiction, Science (General)
ISBN Prefix(es): 3-87931
Number of titles published annually: 30 Print
Total Titles: 500 Print

**ZfKf-Zentrum fur Kulturforschung**, see ARCult Media

**Verlag im Ziegelhaus Ulrich Gohl+**
Pflasteraeckerstr 20, 70186 Stuttgart
*Tel:* (0711) 46 63 63 *Fax:* (0711) 46 13 41
*E-mail:* gohl@n.zgs.de
*Key Personnel*
Owner: Ulrich Gohl
Founded: 1984
Subjects: History
ISBN Prefix(es): 3-925440
Number of titles published annually: 3 Print

**Ziethen-Panorama Verlag GmbH+**
Flurweg 15, 53902 Bad Muenstereifel
*Tel:* (02253) 6047 *Fax:* (02253) 6756
*E-mail:* mail@ziethen-panoramaverlag.de
*Web Site:* www.ziethen-panoramaverlag.de
*Key Personnel*
Owner: Horst Ziethen
Bookkeeping: Karin Gallmann *Tel:* (02236) 3989-15 *Fax:* (02236)3989-39
Founded: 1992
Publisher for picture landscape books.
Subjects: Foreign Countries, Photography, Regional Interests, Travel
ISBN Prefix(es): 3-921268; 3-929932; 3-934328
*Parent Company:* Ziethen-Medien GmbH & Co KG
*Warehouse:* Unter Buschweg 17, 50999 Cologne

**Zodiaque**, *imprint of* Verlag Schnell und Steiner GmbH

**ZS Verlag Zabert Sandmann GmbH+**
Barerstr 9, 80333 Munich
*Tel:* (089) 548 25 15-0 *Fax:* (089) 550 18 19
*E-mail:* contact@zsverlag.de
*Web Site:* www.zsverlag.de
*Telex:* 114 Jekret
*Key Personnel*
Man Dir: Friedrich-Karl Sandmann
Licensing Manager: Dr Katrin Bernhard
Editorial Manager: Kathrin Ullerich
Press: Claudia Limmer
Production: Karin Mayer
Founded: 1983
Subjects: Cookery, Health, Nutrition, Wine & Spirits
ISBN Prefix(es): 3-924678; 3-932023; 3-89883
*Associate Companies:* Verlag Elisabeth Sandmann
*Warehouse:* Schleissheimerstr 106, 85748 Garching-Hochbrueck
*Orders to:* Schleissheimerstr 106, 85748 Garching-Hochbrueck

**Zsolnay**, *imprint of* Carl Hanser Verlag

**Zweipunkt Verlag K Kaiser KG+**
Gestuet Rossbacher Hof, 64711 Erbach
*Tel:* (06062) 61108 *Fax:* (06062) 63422
*Key Personnel*
Partner, Rights & Permissions: Kurt Kaiser
Subjects: Crafts, Games, Hobbies
ISBN Prefix(es): 3-88168

# Ghana

## General Information

*Capital:* Accra
*Language:* English
*Religion:* About 42% Christian, remainder follow traditional beliefs
*Population:* 16.2 million

*Bank Hours:* 0830-1400 Monday-Thursday; 0830-1500 Friday
*Shop Hours:* 0830-1230, 1330-1730 Monday, Tuesday, Thursday, Friday; 0830-1330 Wednesday & Saturday
*Currency:* 100 pesawas = 1 new cedi
*Export/Import Information:* No tariffs on books; advertising matter over 1 kg gross weight 50%. Import license required, but single copies of books under Open General License. Levy charged on import licenses required. Credit terms not permitted.
*Copyright:* UCC, Berne, Florence (see Copyright Conventions, pg xi)

**Adaex Educational Publications Ltd+**
Gicel Block No 18, Rooms 162/163, Accra
*Tel:* (024) 367145; (021) 854188; (021) 854189
  *Fax on Demand:* 001-661-761-9001
*E-mail:* epublication@yahoo.com
*Key Personnel*
Publisher: Asare Konadu Yamoah
  *E-mail:* "asareyamoah"epublication@yahoo.com
Founded: 1995
Also acts as printer, book & literary agent.
Membership(s): Ghana Book Publishers Association.
Subjects: Cookery, Fiction, Health, Nutrition, History, How-to
ISBN Prefix(es): 9988-573
Number of titles published annually: 5 Print
Total Titles: 37 Print
*Orders to:* PO Box AO252, Accra

**The Advent Press+**
PO Box 0102, Osu PO, Osu, Accra
*Tel:* (021) 777861 *Fax:* (021) 2119
*Telex:* 2119 *Cable:* ADVENT GH
*Key Personnel*
General Manager: E C Tetteh
Founded: 1937
Subjects: Religion - Other
ISBN Prefix(es): 9964-962

**Adwinsa Publications (Ghana) Ltd+**
PO Box M 18, Accra
*Tel:* (021) 221654; (021) 21577
*Key Personnel*
Man Dir, Rights & Permissions: Kwabena Amponsah
General Manager & Production: Kofi Kyere-Amponsah
Accountant & Sales: Kwadwo Oppong-Kyeremeh
Editorial & Personnel: Grace Amponsah
Founded: 1977
Membership(s): Ghana Book Publishers Association.
ISBN Prefix(es): 9964-955; 9964-975
*Branch Office(s)*
Adwinsa Bookstand (Eredec Hotel), PO Box 845, Koforidua
*Bookshop(s):* Adwinsa Distribution Agency Ltd, Adwinsa House (North Legon), PO Box 92, Legon
*Orders to:* Adwinsa Distribution Agency Ltd, PO Box M18, Accra

**Afram Publications**, *imprint of* Afram Publications (Ghana) Ltd

**Afram Publications (Ghana) Ltd+**
C 184/22 Midway Lane, Abofu, Achimota, Accra
Mailing Address: PO Box M18, Accra
*Tel:* (021) 412561; (021) 406060
*E-mail:* aframpub@punchgh.com *Cable:* AFRAMBOOKS
*Key Personnel*
Man Dir, Rights & Permissions: Eric Ofei
  *E-mail:* ericofei@yahoo.co.uk
Editorial Manager: Mr E C Tetteh
Founded: 1974

Membership(s): Ghana Book Publishers Association; Afro-Asian Book Council.
Subjects: Fiction, Nonfiction (General)
ISBN Prefix(es): 9964-70
Imprints: Afram Publications
Distributed by African Books Collective

**Africa Christian Press+**
PO Box 30, Achimota
*Tel:* (021) 220271 *Fax:* (021) 220271; (021) 6681155
*E-mail:* acpbooks@ghana.com
*Key Personnel*
General Manager: Richard Crabbe
Deputy General Manager: Mork Eiwuley
Founded: 1964
Specialize in Christian literature & children's books.
Membership(s): Ghana Publishers Association.
Subjects: Biography, Fiction, Nonfiction (General), Religion - Other
ISBN Prefix(es): 9964-87
Number of titles published annually: 12 Print
Total Titles: 110 Print
Imprints: Children's Activity Series; Student's Series
*Branch Office(s)*
50 Loxwood Ave, Worthing, Sussex BN14 7RA, United Kingdom
*U.S. Office(s):* 130 N Bloomingdale Rd, Suite 101, Bloomingdale, IL 60108, United States

**Anowuo Educational Publications+**
PO Box 3918, Accra
*Tel:* (021) 669961 *Cable:* ANOWUO PUBS, ACCRA
*Key Personnel*
Publisher: S A Konadu
Sales Manager: Yamoah Konadu
Founded: 1966
Also acts as copyright broker.
Membership(s): Ghana Publishers Association.
Subjects: Fiction, History, How-to, Poetry, Regional Interests, Science (General)
ISBN Prefix(es): 9964-79
*Branch Office(s)*
PO Box 1, Asamang Ashanti Region
*Showroom(s):* 2R McCarthy Hill, PO Box 3918, Accra

**Asempa Publishers+**
PO Box 919, Accra
*Tel:* (021) 221706
*E-mail:* asempa@ghana.com
*Key Personnel*
General Manager: Rev Emmanuel Borlabi Bortey
Production: Sarah Apronti
Finance: Stephen K Darku
International Rights: E B Bortey; S Apronti
Founded: 1970
Membership(s): Ghana Book Publishers Association.
Subjects: Biblical Studies, Biography, Fiction, Music, Dance, Nonfiction (General), Poetry, Religion - Protestant, Religion - Other, Social Sciences, Sociology, Theology
ISBN Prefix(es): 9964-78; 9964-91
Number of titles published annually: 20 Print
Total Titles: 112 Print
*Parent Company:* Christian Council of Ghana
Imprints: IBRA (Ghana)

**Beginners Publishers+**
Box CT 785, Cantonments, Accra
*Tel:* (021) 503040 *Fax:* (051) 772642 *Attn:* Beginners Publishers
*Telex:* 3047 *Attn:* Beginners Publishers
*Key Personnel*
President & Editor: Nana Opoku Ankama-Fofie
Publisher & Author: Akosua Gyamfuaa-Fofie
Vice President: Kwabena Owusu-Peprah
Founded: 1988

Subjects: English as a Second Language, Fiction, Language Arts, Linguistics, Mathematics, Romance
ISBN Prefix(es): 9964-995
*Associate Companies:* Hope & Faith Agencies, Box C 1096, Cantonments, Accra
*Branch Office(s)*
Cape Coast
Sunyani
Tamale
Tema
Distributed by Makna Publications
Distributor for Makna Publications; Speedy Variety Publications
*Showroom(s):* House No 020, North Suntresu, Kumasi; House No Wab-34 TI; New Ashaley Botwe, Madina, Accra
*Bookshop(s):* Adwen Pa, Madina, Winners & Nsempii-Kumasi; Afram, Box N18, Accra; Catholic Bookshop, Kumasi; Dorilad Bookshop, Abeka, Accra; Gyawu Bookshop, Tamale; Legon Bookshop, Box 1, Legon, Accra; Makna, Box 9820 Airport, Accra; Methodist Bookshops, Accra, Kumasi, Cape-Coast; Obrapa Bookshop, Tema; Omari Bookshop, Labone, Accra; Presbyterian Bookshops, Accra, Kumasi, Cape-Coast, Swedru; Speedy Variety Agencies Ltd, Box 5337, Accra; Topman Book Center, Accra
*Warehouse:* Box BP 313, Bohyen-Kumasi

**Black Mask Ltd+**
PO Box 252, Fante New Town, Kumasi
*Tel:* (021) 500178 *Fax:* (021) 667701
*E-mail:* balme@ug.gn.apc.org *Cable:* BML
*Key Personnel*
Man Dir: Yaw Owusu Asante
Publicity: Kwasi Asante
Rights & Permissions: Opia-Mensah Kumah
Founded: 1979
Subjects: Cookery, Drama, Theater, Economics, Education, Social Sciences, Sociology
ISBN Prefix(es): 9964-960

**BP**, see Beginners Publishers

**BRRI**, see Building & Road Research Institute (BRRI)

**Building & Road Research Institute (BRRI)**
University of Science & Technology, PO Box 40, Kumasi
*Tel:* (051) 60064; (051) 60065 *Fax:* (051) 60080
*E-mail:* brri@ghana.com
*Web Site:* www.csir.org.gh/brri.html
*Key Personnel*
Dir: Dr K Amoah-Mensah
Founded: 1952
Subjects: Architecture & Interior Design, Civil Engineering, Computer Science, Earth Sciences, Real Estate, Technology, Transportation
ISBN Prefix(es): 9964-86; 9964-977
*Parent Company:* Council for Scientific & Industrial Research (CSIR)

**Bureau of Ghana Languages**
PO Box 1851, Accra
*Tel:* (021) 665461; (021) 65194
*Key Personnel*
Dir, Rights & Permissions: J N Nanor
Sales Manager: J C Abbey
Founded: 1951
Also acts as a translation agency/association.
Subjects: Biography, Drama, Theater, Fiction, Poetry, Science (General)
ISBN Prefix(es): 9964-2
*Branch Office(s)*
PO Box 177, Tamale, Northern Region

**Children's Activity Series**, *imprint of* Africa Christian Press

**Educational Press & Manufacturers Ltd+**
PO Box 4434, Kumasi
*Tel:* (051) 5003; (051) 5845 *Fax:* (051) 227572
*Telex:* 2236 gh
*Key Personnel*
International Rights: George Koduah
Founded: 1979
Subjects: Fiction
ISBN Prefix(es): 9964-89
Subsidiaries: Knowledge Publishing & Trading
  Ltd
*Branch Office(s)*
PO Box 5381, Accra-North

**Educational Publishers Ltd**
PO Box 9184, Accra-Airport
*Tel:* (021) 220395 *Fax:* (021) 227572
*Telex:* 2236GH *Cable:* EDU PRESS
ISBN Prefix(es): 9964-953
*Parent Company:* Halko Book & Educational As-
  sories Ltd

**Ekab Business Ltd+**
PO Box 6262, Accra-North
*Tel:* (021) 225318 *Cable:* Emmapus Accra
*Key Personnel*
Dir: Emmanuel K Nsiah
Founded: 1978
Company has reprint arrangements in Ghana for
  Oxford University Press publications.
Subjects: Education
ISBN Prefix(es): 9964-91; 9964-73
*Bookshop(s):* Mayan Book Centre, PO Box 6173,
  Accra

**EPP Books Services+**
PMB TUC Post Office, La Education Centre
  Bldg, Behind Ghana Trade Fair Centre, La,
  Accra
Mailing Address: PO Box TF 490, Accra
*Tel:* (021) 778853; (021) 778347 *Fax:* (021)
  779099
*E-mail:* info@eppbooks.com
*Web Site:* www.eppbooks.com
*Key Personnel*
Executive Dir: Gibrine Adam
Founded: 1991
Also acts as bookseller & stationery distributor.
Subjects: Accounting, Mathematics, Social Sci-
  ences, Sociology
ISBN Prefix(es): 9964-997
*Associate Companies:* Excellent Publishing &
  Printing; Staples Systems Ghana Ltd
Foreign Rep(s): Epp Books Services (Nigeria)
Foreign Rights: Sterling Publishers Pvt (India)
*Bookshop(s):* EPP Bookshop, Accra-Nsawam Rd,
  Achimota-Accra, Mutawakilu Adam *Tel:* (021)
  408885 *Fax:* (021) 779099 *E-mail:* epp@
  africaonline.com.gh *Web Site:* www.eppbooks.
  com; EPP Bookshop, PO Box TF 490, La, Accra, Koforidua *Tel:* (021) 779099 *E-mail:* epp@
  africaonline.com.gh *Web Site:* www.eppbooks.
  com; EPP Bookshop, Behind Kumasi Polytechnic, Amakom-Kumasi, Kumasi, Constance Nuamah *Tel:* (051) 23367 *Fax:* (021)
  779099 *E-mail:* epp@africaonline.com.gh *Web
  Site:* www.eppbooks.com

**Frank Publishing Ltd+**
PO Box M414, Ministry Branch Post Office, Ac-
  cra
*Tel:* (021) 240711 *Cable:* KNOWLEDGE
*Key Personnel*
Man Dir, Editorial, Production: Francis K
  Dzokoto
Sales, Public Relations: Moses K Dzokoto
Founded: 1976
Specialize in school textbooks & typesetting for
  other publishing houses.
Membership(s): Ghana Publishers Association;
  Ghana Association of Book Editors.

Subjects: Economics, English as a Second Lan-
  guage, Government, Political Science, Religion
  - Catholic, Religion - Protestant, Religion -
  Other
ISBN Prefix(es): 9964-959

**Ghana Academy of Arts & Sciences+**
PO Box M32, Accra
*Tel:* (021) 777651
*E-mail:* gaas@ghastinet.gn.apc.org
*Key Personnel*
President: D A Bekoe
Founded: 1959
Subjects: Art, Literature, Literary Criticism, Es-
  says, Music, Dance, Science (General)
ISBN Prefix(es): 9964-90; 9964-969; 9964-950

**Ghana Institute of Linguistics Literacy &
  Bible Translation (GILLBT)**
PO Box 7271, Accra North
*Tel:* (021) 777525
Founded: 1962
Subjects: Anthropology, Biblical Studies, English
  as a Second Language, Environmental Studies,
  Health, Nutrition, Language Arts, Linguistics,
  Religion - Protestant, Women's Studies
ISBN Prefix(es): 9964-92; 9988-7525

**Ghana Publishing Corporation**
Private Post Bag, Tema
*Tel:* (021) 812921 *Fax:* (021) 664330
*E-mail:* asspcom@africaonline.com.gh
*Telex:* Publishing Tema
*Key Personnel*
Man Dir: F K Nyarko
General Manager (Publishing Division): K B
  Arkorful
Editor-in-Chief: J K Fuachie-Sobreh
Rights & Permissions: Miss O Agbenyega
Sales Manager: W D Opare
Production: Fred Odametey
Publicity: Fidelis D Adzakey
Founded: 1965
Subjects: Biography, Ethnicity, Fiction, History,
  Language Arts, Linguistics, Nonfiction (Gen-
  eral), Poetry, Science (General), Social Sci-
  ences, Sociology, Technology
ISBN Prefix(es): 9964-1
*Parent Company:* Ghana Publishing Corporation,
  Head Office, PO Box 4348, Accra
*Branch Office(s)*
Accra
Bolgatanga
Cape Coast
Ho
Hohoe
Koforidua
Sunyani
Swedru
Tamale
Wa
*Sales Office(s):* PO Box 3632, Accra
*Distribution Center:* PO Box 3632, Accura

**Ghana Standards Board**, see GSB (Ghana
  Standards Board)

**Ghana Universities Press (GUP)+**
PO Box GP 2419, Accra
*Tel:* (021) 22532
*Telex:* Univpress Accra
*Key Personnel*
Dir: K M Ganu *Tel:* (020) 8178075
  *E-mail:* balme@libr.ug.edu.gh
Senior Business Manger: J K Bosomtwe
Founded: 1962
Membership(s): Ghana Book Publishers Associ-
  ation, International Association of Scholarly
  Publishers, African Books Collective.
Subjects: Agriculture, Biological Sciences, Com-
  munications, Government, Political Science,

History, Language Arts, Linguistics, Medicine,
  Nursing, Dentistry, Social Sciences, Sociology
ISBN Prefix(es): 9964-3
*Associate Companies:* African Books Collective
  Ltd, Oxford

**GILLBT**, see Ghana Institute of Linguistics
  Literacy & Bible Translation (GILLBT)

**Goodbooks Publishing Co+**
PO Box 10416, Accra North
*Tel:* (021) 665629 *Fax:* (021) 302993
*E-mail:* allgoodbooks@hotmail.com
*Key Personnel*
Contact: Alberta Asirifi; Mary Asirifi
Founded: 1992
ISBN Prefix(es): 9964-88
*Bookshop(s):* D803/4 Granville Ave, Okaishie,
  Accra

**GSB (Ghana Standards Board)**
PO Box MB 245, Accra
*Tel:* (021) 662942; (021) 665461
*Telex:* 2545 MINCOM Attn GSB
ISBN Prefix(es): 9964-990

**IBRA (Ghana)**, *imprint of* Asempa Publishers

**Kwamfori Publishing Enterprise+**
Dansoman-Estates, Accra
Mailing Address: PO Box 1325, Accra
*Key Personnel*
Proprietor: Ofori Akuamoah
Founded: 1991
Subjects: Economics, English as a Second Lan-
  guage, Humor
ISBN Prefix(es): 9964-987

**Manhill Publication+**
PO Box 548, Madina, Accra
*Tel:* (021) 508251 *Fax:* (021) 669078
*Key Personnel*
President & Author: Paul N Maanoh
Vice President: Hilda Maanoh
Editor & Author: Asuma Karikari
Author: Ferkah Ahenkorah; George Amable;
  Chris Darkwaa
Founded: 1986
Also distributes wares for Ghana Bible Society.
  Dealers in printing materials.
Membership(s): Ghana Bible Society.
Subjects: English as a Second Language, Fiction,
  Literature, Literary Criticism, Essays
ISBN Prefix(es): 9964-999
*Associate Companies:* Manhill Enterprise
*Branch Office(s)*
Kumasi
Sunyani
Distributed by Gospel Tracts Information (USA)
*Orders to:* Manhill Publications, PO Box 1075,
  Madina-Accra

**Moxon Paperbacks**
PO Box M 160, Osu, Accra
*Tel:* (021) 665397
*Key Personnel*
Man Dir: James Moxon
Founded: 1967
Subjects: Ethnicity, Fiction, History, Nonfiction
  (General), Poetry, Travel
ISBN Prefix(es): 9964-954
*Branch Office(s)*
28 Corve St, Dudlow, Shropshire SY8 IDA,
  United Kingdom
*Bookshop(s):* The Atlas Bookshop

**Osimpam Educational Books**
PO Box 1851, Accra
*Key Personnel*
Man Editor: Armah Asiedu
Founded: 1991
ISBN Prefix(es): 9964-994

**Quick Service Books Ltd+**
PO Box 15403, Accra North
*Tel:* (021) 224236
*Key Personnel*
Man Dir: Isaac Mensah Dankyi
Editor: D A Addo
Marketing Manager: Kwasi Saka-Dankyi
Founded: 1986
Subjects: Education
ISBN Prefix(es): 9964-90; 9964-985

**Sam Woode Ltd+**
House No 1, Adole Abla Link, Sahara-Dansoman
Mailing Address: PO Box 12719, Accra North
*Tel:* (021) 229487 *Fax:* (021) 310482
*E-mail:* samwoode@ghana.com *Cable:* SAM
WOODE ACCRA
*Key Personnel*
Executive Chairman: Kwesi Sam-Woode
Publishing Manager: Pamela Woode
Marketing Manager: Luke Dery
Founded: 1986
Membership(s): Ghana Book Publishers Association.
Subjects: Agriculture, Career Development, English as a Second Language, Mathematics, Physical Sciences, Science (General)
ISBN Prefix(es): 9964-979; 9988-609
Imprints: SWL Books
Distributed by West African Book Publishers Ltd (Nigeria)

**Sedco**, *imprint of* Sedco Publishing Ltd

**Sedco Publishing Ltd+**
Sedco House, Labon St, Off Ring Rd Central North Ridge, Accra
Mailing Address: PO Box 2051, Accra
*Tel:* (021) 221332 *Fax:* (021) 220107
*E-mail:* sedco@africaonline.com.gh
*Telex:* 2456
*Key Personnel*
Man Dir: Courage Kwami Segbawu
Marketing Dir: Frank Segbawu
Founded: 1975
Educational materials for all levels.
Subjects: Agriculture, Biological Sciences, Chemistry, Chemical Engineering, Education, English as a Second Language, Fiction, History, Law, Mathematics, Physics, Science (General)
ISBN Prefix(es): 9964-72
Number of titles published annually: 5 Print
Total Titles: 145 Print
*Parent Company:* Pearson Plc
Imprints: Sedco

**Student's Series**, *imprint of* Africa Christian Press

**Sub-Saharan Publishers+**
PO Box 358, Legon-Accra
*Tel:* (021) 228398
*E-mail:* sub-saharan@ighmail.com
*Key Personnel*
Man Dir: Akoss Ofori-Mensah
Founded: 1992
Membership(s): Ghana Publishers Association.
Subjects: Education, Environmental Studies, African Literature
ISBN Prefix(es): 9988-550
Total Titles: 30 Print
Distributed by African Books Collective
*Orders to:* Sub-Saharan Publishers, PO Box 1176, Cantonments, Accra

**SWL Books**, *imprint of* Sam Woode Ltd

**Unimax Macmillan Ltd**
42 Ring Rd South, Industrial Area, Accra North
Mailing Address: PO Box 10722, Accra North

*Tel:* (021) 227 443; (021) 223 709 *Fax:* (021) 225 215
*E-mail:* info@unimacmillan.com
*Web Site:* www.macmillan-africa.com; www. unimacmillan.com
*Key Personnel*
Man Dir: Edward Addo
Marketing Manager: Abubakari Wumbei
Founded: 1985
International education division of Macmillan Publishers Ltd.
Subjects: Agriculture, Environmental Studies, Mathematics, Science (General)
ISBN Prefix(es): 9988-553; 9988-0; 9988-601
*Parent Company:* Macmillan Publishers Ltd
*Branch Office(s)*
Unicorn House, Prempah 11 St, PO Box KS, 1169 Kumasi, Manager: Edward Udzu
*Tel:* (051) 39284; (051) 39286 *Fax:* (051) 39285
*Showroom(s):* Unicorn House, Prempah 11 St, PO Box KS, 1169 Kumasi, Manager: Edward Udzu *Tel:* (051) 39284; (051) 39286 *Fax:* (051) 39285
*Warehouse:* Unicorn House, Prempah 11 St, PO Box KS, 1169 Kumasi, Manager: Edward Udzu *Tel:* (051) 39284; (051) 39286 *Fax:* (051) 39285

**Waterville Publishing House+**
Thorpe Rd, Accra
Mailing Address: PO Box 195, Accra
*Tel:* (01) 663124; (01) 662415 *Cable:* BOOKS ACCRA
*Key Personnel*
Man Dir: H W O Okai
Founded: 1963
Subjects: Biography, Ethnicity, Fiction, History, Nonfiction (General), Poetry, Religion - Other, Science (General), Social Sciences, Sociology
ISBN Prefix(es): 9964-5
*Parent Company:* Presbyterian Book Depot Ltd
Divisions: Presbyterian Press

**Woeli Publishing Services**
PO Box K601, Accra-New Town
*Tel:* (021) 227182; (021) 229294 *Fax:* (021) 777098; (021) 229294
*E-mail:* woeli@libr.ug.edu.gh; asempa@ghana. com
*Key Personnel*
Publisher: Mr Woeli Dekutsey
Founded: 1984
Membership(s): Ghana Book Publishers Association.
Subjects: Drama, Theater, Fiction, Poetry, Women's Studies
ISBN Prefix(es): 9964-90; 9964-970; 9964-978
Total Titles: 6 Print
*Orders to:* African Books Collective, 27 Park End St, Oxford 0X1 1HU, United Kingdom

**World Literature Project**
PO Box 290, Legon, Accra
*Tel:* (022) 2119 *Fax:* (022) 2119
*Key Personnel*
Publisher: Friedolin Ankrama-Afarie
Founded: 1991
Specialize in dissemination of vital information on better health, welfare, new books, literature, etc.
Subjects: Advertising, Biblical Studies, Child Care & Development, Cookery, Developing Countries, Film, Video, Health, Nutrition, How-to, Human Relations, Humor, Marketing, Medicine, Nursing, Dentistry, Mysteries, Outdoor Recreation, Psychology, Psychiatry, Publishing & Book Trade Reference, Religion - Other, Securities, Self-Help, Women's Studies
ISBN Prefix(es): 9964-986

# Greece

## General Information

*Capital:* Athens
*Language:* Greek (official), English, French
*Religion:* Predominately Greek Orthodox
*Population:* 10.6 million
*Bank Hours:* 0800-1400 Monday-Friday
*Shop Hours:* Vary. Generally 0800-1500 Monday, Wednesday, Saturday; 0800-1400, 1730-2030 Tuesday, Thursday, Friday
*Currency:* 100 Eurocents = 1 Euro; 340.750 Greek drachmas = 1 Euro
*Export/Import Information:* Member of the European Economic Community. No tariff on non-Greek books except children's picture books (free from EEC). Foreign-language advertising catalogues & other advertising matter free from EEC. Children's picture books & advertising matter subject to stamp duty, and books & advertising subject to small additional taxes, University Tax & Bank Fee, Contribution for Farmer's Social Assistance. Only books printed in Greek need import license; all advertising matter other than price lists require license. No special exchange controls. 4% VAT on books.
*Copyright:* UCC, Berne, Florence (see Copyright Conventions, pg xi)

**AE Expaideftikon Vivlion Kai Diskon**
19 Antinoros, 116 34 Athens
*Tel:* 2107239474 *Fax:* 2107239483
*Key Personnel*
President & Man Dir: John Drossos
Founded: 1963
ISBN Prefix(es): 960-7351; 960-7972
*Parent Company:* Educational Books & Records SA

**Akritas+**
24 Efesou, 171 21 N Smyrni, Athens
*Tel:* 2109314968; 2109334554 *Fax:* 210 9311436
*Key Personnel*
Contact: Maria Kokkinou
Founded: 1979
Subjects: Art, Child Care & Development, Cookery, History, Human Relations, Psychology, Psychiatry, Religion - Other, Theology
ISBN Prefix(es): 960-7006; 960-328

**Alamo Ellas+**
6, Sarantaporou St, 111 44 Athens
*Tel:* 2102280027 *Fax:* 2102280027
*Key Personnel*
President: Dr Ath I Delikastopoulos
Subjects: Biblical Studies, Cookery, English as a Second Language, Gardening, Plants, Law, Philosophy, Religion - Catholic, Religion - Islamic, Religion - Jewish, Religion - Protestant, Theology, Travel
ISBN Prefix(es): 960-7639
*Associate Companies:* Alpha Delta

**Vefa Alexiadou Editions+**
4 Leonidou Str, 144 52 Metmorphos, Athens
*Tel:* 2102840086 *Fax:* 2102849689
*E-mail:* vefaeditions@ath.forthnet.gr
*Web Site:* www.addgr.com/comp/vefa/index.htm
*Key Personnel*
Marketing & Sales Dir: Alexia Alexiadou
Founded: 1979
Membership(s): IACP.
Subjects: Cookery
ISBN Prefix(es): 960-85018; 960-8125; 960-90137; 960-91230
*Associate Companies:* Vefa's House, Alba Editions
*Branch Office(s)*
16, Nevrokopiou Str, 552 26 Thessaloniui

Distributed by Howell Press (USA & Canada);
Tower Books (Australia)
Distributor for Sterling Editions (USA)
*Bookshop(s):* One Kresnas St, 141 23 Ly Kovrisi,
Athens

**Anemonylos**, *imprint of* Ilias Kambanas
Publishing Organization, SA

**Anixis Publications+**
23 Viltanioti Str, Kifisia, 145 64 Athens
*Tel:* 2106205436 *Fax:* 2108079357
*Key Personnel*
International Rights: Mr Aristotelis Papadimitriou
　*E-mail:* apapa@hol.gr
Founded: 1993
Subjects: Child Care & Development, Geography,
Geology, History
Total Titles: 105 Print

**Apostoliki Diakonia tis Ekklisias tis Hellados**
One Iassiou St, 115 21 Athens
*Tel:* 2107239417; 2107248681-9
　*Fax:* 2107238149
*E-mail:* editions@apostoliki-diakoria.gr
*Web Site:* www.apostoliki-diakonia.gr
*Key Personnel*
Chief Executive: Archim Agathaggelos Chara-
mantidis
Editorial Manager, Rights & Permissions: Evan-
gelos Lekkos
Production: Socrates Mavrogonatos
Founded: 1936
Subjects: Biblical Studies, Film, Video, History,
Music, Dance, Religion - Other, Social Sci-
ences, Sociology, Theology
ISBN Prefix(es): 960-315
*Bookshop(s):* 2 Dragatsaniou St, 105 59 Athens
*Tel:* 2103228637; 2103310977 *Fax:* 210
3228637; 9-A Ethnikis Aminis & Tsimiski
Str, 546 21 Thessaloniki *Tel:* 2310275126
*Fax:* 2310278559; 143 Riga Ferreou Str,
Filopimenos, Patra *Tel:* 2610223110
*Fax:* 2610223110

**Aquarius Ekdotiki Etaireia**
39 Valtetsiou, 106 81 Athens
*Tel:* 2103842354 *Fax:* 2108826060
ISBN Prefix(es): 960-7002; 960-7628

**D I Arsenidis Publications**
57, Akademias Str, 106 79 Athens
*Tel:* 2103629538; 2103633923
　*Fax:* 2103618707
*Web Site:* www.arsenidis.gr
*Key Personnel*
Man Dir: John Arsenides
Subjects: Biography, History, Philosophy, Social
Sciences, Sociology
ISBN Prefix(es): 960-253

**Ekdoseis Athina-Mavrogianni+**
37 Arachovis, 106 81 Athens
*Tel:* 2103821308; 2103304628 *Fax:* 210
3838228
*Key Personnel*
Contact: G Mavrogiannis
Subjects: Education, Language Arts, Linguistics,
Mathematics, Physics
ISBN Prefix(es): 960-7319; 960-514; 960-7819
Total Titles: 150 Print

**Atlantis M Pechlivanides & Co SA+**
23 Leontiou Str & 37 Fr Smit, Neos Kosmos, 117
45 Athens
*Tel:* 2109220071; 2109220073 *Fax:* 210
9025773
Founded: 1927
Subjects: Art, Education, Fiction, Nonfiction
(General)

ISBN Prefix(es): 960-07
*Bookshop(s):* Korai 8, 105 64 Athens *Tel:* 210
3231624

**Atlas**
Tzavella 96, Nafpactos, TK 3300
*Tel:* 2103627342 *Fax:* 2103300257
*E-mail:* c_poulos@hotmail.com

**Axiotelis G+**
18 Char Trikaupi, Akadimias, 106 79 Athens
*Tel:* 2103610091; 2103636264; 210
3634264
*Key Personnel*
Contact: George Axiotelis
Founded: 1974
Membership(s): European Educational Publishers
Group.
Subjects: Education, Government, Political Sci-
ence
ISBN Prefix(es): 960-7053; 960-7807

**Bell Best-Seller**, *imprint of* Harlenic Hellas
Publishing SA

**Bell Literature**, *imprint of* Harlenic Hellas
Publishing SA

**Bergadis**
Mavromichali 4, 106 79 Athens
*Tel:* 2103614263
Subjects: History, Social Sciences, Sociology
*Branch Office(s)*
Doryleou 22, Athens *Tel:* 2103614263

**Beta Medical Publishers+**
3 Adrianiou St, 115 25 Athens
*Tel:* 2106714340; 2106714371 *Fax:* 210
6715015
*E-mail:* betamedarts@hol.gr
*Web Site:* www.betamedarts.gr
*Key Personnel*
General Manager: Anastasia Vassilakou
Founded: 1976
Subjects: Medicine, Nursing, Dentistry, Veterinary
Science
ISBN Prefix(es): 960-7308; 960-8071
Total Titles: 106 Print

**Blaze**, *imprint of* Harlenic Hellas Publishing SA

**Boukoumanis' Editions+**
One Mavromichalistr, 106 79 Athens
*Tel:* 2103618502; 2103637436 *Fax:* 210
3630669
*E-mail:* info@boukoumanis.gr
*Web Site:* www.boukoumanis.gr *Cable:* 214422
RC GR
*Key Personnel*
Man Dir: Elias Boukoumanis
Rights & Permissions: Mrs Trisevgeni Vour-
garides
Founded: 1968
Subjects: Education, Environmental Studies, Gov-
ernment, Political Science, History, Philosophy,
Psychology, Psychiatry, Social Sciences, Soci-
ology
ISBN Prefix(es): 960-7458

**Chrysi Penna - Golden Pen Books+**
16, Zoodohou Pigis Str, 106 81 Athens
*Tel:* 2103805672 *Fax:* 2103825205
*E-mail:* info@chrissipenna.com
*Web Site:* www.chrissipenna.com
*Key Personnel*
Man Dir: Anne Hood; K Papachrysanthou
Founded: 1964
Specializes in cookbooks & paperback books.
Subjects: Animals, Pets, Astrology, Occult, Child
Care & Development, Cookery, Education, Fic-

tion, Health, Nutrition, Nonfiction (General),
Technology
ISBN Prefix(es): 960-245
Number of titles published annually: 18 Print
Total Titles: 120 Print
*Warehouse:* H Trikoupi Str 157, 114 72 Athens

**Chryssos Typos AE Ekodeis**
7 Z Pigis St, 106 78 Athens
*Tel:* 2103637945 *Fax:* 2103824417
Subjects: Art, History, Medicine, Nursing, Dentistry, Photography, Science (General)

**Diachronikes Ekdoseis+**
77 Vas Sofias, 115 21 Athens
*Tel:* 2107213225; 2107213387 *Fax:* 210
7246180
*Key Personnel*
President: Costas Sioras
ISBN Prefix(es): 960-85630
*Parent Company:* ASCENT Ltd - Public
Relations-Publications, Athens

**Diavlos+**
10 Valtetsiou St, 106 80 Athens
*Tel:* 2103631169 *Fax:* 2103617473
*E-mail:* info@diavlos-books.gr
*Web Site:* www.diavlos-books.gr
*Key Personnel*
Man Dir: Emmanuel Deligiannakis
Founded: 1988
Subjects: Astronomy, Computer Science, How-
to, Humor, Mathematics, Nonfiction (General),
Physical Sciences, Physics, Science (General),
Science Fiction, Fantasy
ISBN Prefix(es): 960-7140; 960-531
*Bookshop(s):* 5 Pezmazoglou St, Athens 105 64,
Contact: Mr D Gongos *Tel:* 2103312413

**Difros Publications**
57 Akadimias St, 106 79 Athens
*Tel:* 2103610811
Subjects: Literature, Literary Criticism, Essays
ISBN Prefix(es): 960-314

**Dioptra Publishing**
9 Zalongou str, 106 78 Athens
*Tel:* 2103302828 *Fax:* 2103302882
*E-mail:* info@dioptra.gov
*Web Site:* www.dioptra.gr
*Key Personnel*
Manager: George Papadopoulos *E-mail:* george@
dioptra.gr
Rights Manager: Costas Papadopoulos
　*E-mail:* costas@dioptra.gr
Sales Manager: Helen Papadopoulos
　*E-mail:* helen@dioptra.gr
Founded: 1985
Specialize in alternative therapies, metaphysics &
esotericism.
Subjects: Literature, Literary Criticism, Essays,
Psychology, Psychiatry
ISBN Prefix(es): 960-364
Total Titles: 100 Print
*Distribution Center:* 27 Zoodochou Str, 106 81
Athens *Tel:* 2103805228 *Fax:* 2103300439
　*E-mail:* sales@dioptra.gr

**Dodoni Publications**
Asklipiou 3, 106 79 Athens
*Tel:* 2103636312; 2103637973 *Fax:* 210
3637067
*E-mail:* dodoni@elea.gr
Subjects: Fiction, History, Nonfiction (General)
ISBN Prefix(es): 960-248; 960-385

**Ekdoseis Domi AE+**
Ippokratous 67, Arachovis, 106 80 Athens
*Tel:* 2103637389; 2103672056 *Fax:* 210
3601782
*Key Personnel*
President: Elias Maniateas

Marketing Manager: George Dimitropoulos
International Rights: Aris Petropoulos
Subjects: Cookery, Geography, Geology
ISBN Prefix(es): 960-8177

**Dorikos Publishing House+**
9-11 Charalampi Sotiriou, 114 72 Athens
*Tel:* 2106454726 *Fax:* 2103301866
*Key Personnel*
Man Dir, Rights & Permissions: Aristides Klados
Editor: Roussos Vranas
Founded: 1958
Subjects: Biography, Crafts, Games, Hobbies, Drama, Theater, Fiction, Government, Political Science, History, Literature, Literary Criticism, Essays, Philosophy, Poetry, Psychology, Psychiatry
ISBN Prefix(es): 960-279
*Associate Companies:* Aposperitis Editions, Eressou 9, 106 80 Athens *Tel:* 2103604161

**E Mokas - Morfotiki+**
Formerly Morfotiki Estia AE
50 Veranzerou, 104 38 Athens
*Tel:* 2105227830 *Fax:* 2105200534
*Key Personnel*
Contact: Makas
Founded: 1975
ISBN Prefix(es): 960-215
*Bookshop(s):* 49 Har Tricoupi St, Athens 10681
*Warehouse:* 13 Haralambous St, Athens

**Ecole francaise d'Athenes+**
Didotou 6, 106 80 Athens
*Tel:* 2103679900 *Fax:* 2103632101
*E-mail:* efa@efa.gr
*Web Site:* www.efa.gr *Cable:* ECOFRANCE
*Key Personnel*
Man Dir, Editorial: Dominique Mulliez
Publications: Gilles Touchais *Tel:* 2103679921
  *E-mail:* gilles.touchais@efa.gr
Founded: 1846
Subjects: Archaeology, Architecture & Interior Design, Art, History, Social Sciences, Sociology, Ancient History, Ancient Religions, Greek Archaeology & History, Mythology, Sculpture, Town Planning
ISBN Prefix(es): 2-86958
Number of titles published annually: 6 Print
Total Titles: 200 Print; 2 CD-ROM
Distributed by De Boccard Edition-Diffusion
*Orders to:* Diffusion de Boccard, 11 rue de Medicis, 75006 Paris, France, Contact: Mr J B Chaulet *Tel:* (01) 43260037 *Fax:* (01) 43548583 *E-mail:* deboccard@deboccard.com
  *Web Site:* www.deboccard.com

**Ekdoseis Kazantzaki (Kazantzakis Publications)+**
116 Charilaou Trikoupi, 114 72 Athens
*Tel:* 2103642829 *Fax:* 2103642830
*Key Personnel*
Owner & Editor: Mr Patroklos Stavrou
Publish only works by Nickos Kazantzakis & his wife Helen.
Subjects: Drama, Theater, Fiction, Literature, Literary Criticism, Essays, Philosophy, Poetry, Travel
ISBN Prefix(es): 960-7948

**Ekdoseis Thetili**
16 Emm Benaki, 106 78 Athens
*Tel:* 2103302229; 2107511300
Founded: 1983
Subjects: History, Psychology, Psychiatry, Women's Studies, Drugs
ISBN Prefix(es): 960-85198

**Ekdotike Athenon SA+**
34 Akadimias, 106 72 Athens
*Tel:* 2103608911 *Fax:* 2103606157

*Key Personnel*
President: George A Christopoulos
Man Dir: John C Bastias
Founded: 1961
Specialize in books on Greek history & culture.
Subjects: Archaeology, Art, History, Travel
ISBN Prefix(es): 960-213
*Associate Companies:* Ekdotike Hellados SA, Philadelphias 8, Athens (printer)

**Ekdotikos Oikos Adelfon Kyriakidi A E+**
5K Melenikou, 546 35 Thessaloniki
*Tel:* 2310208540 *Fax:* 2310245541
*E-mail:* johnkyr@the.forthnet.gr
*Key Personnel*
President: Dimitrios Kyriakidis
Vice President: Anastasios Kyriakidis
Founded: 1970
Subjects: Accounting, Chemistry, Chemical Engineering, Economics, History, Mathematics, Theology
ISBN Prefix(es): 960-343

**Eleftheroudakis, GCSA International Bookstore**
37 Panepistimiou, 105 63 Athens
*Tel:* 2103229388
*E-mail:* elebooks@netor.gr
*Key Personnel*
Man Dir: Virginia Eleftheroudakis-Gregos
Founded: 1915
Subjects: Fiction
ISBN Prefix(es): 960-200

**Elliniki Leschi Tou Vivliou**
3, A Tsocha St, 115 21 Athens
*Tel:* 2106463888 *Fax:* 2106463263
*E-mail:* elli@gezmanosnet.gr
Subjects: Fiction, History, Human Relations, Nonfiction (General), Philosophy, Poetry, Romance, Science Fiction, Fantasy
ISBN Prefix(es): 960-85570

**Epikerotita+**
42 Mavromihali Str, 106 80 Athens
*Tel:* 2103636083; 2103607382 *Fax:* 210 3636083
*Key Personnel*
Contact: Michalis Mpakirtzis
Founded: 1980
Subjects: Computer Science
ISBN Prefix(es): 960-205

**Etaireia Spoudon Neoellinikou Politismou Kai Genikis Paideias** (The Moraitis Foundation for Literary & Cultural Studies)+
A Papanastasiou & A Dimitriou St, 154 52 Athens
*Tel:* 2106795000 *Fax:* 21006795090
*E-mail:* admin@moraitis.edu.gr
*Web Site:* www.moraitis.edu.gr
*Key Personnel*
President: Prof N Hourmouziadis
Founded: 1972
Subjects: Drama, Theater, Education, History, Literature, Literary Criticism, Essays, Poetry, Social Sciences, Sociology
ISBN Prefix(es): 960-259

**Eurotyp,** *imprint of* Stochastis

**Evrodiastasi**
49 Kallifrona St, 113 64 Athens
*Tel:* 2108611303 *Fax:* 2108611303
Founded: 1992
Folios with collection of engravings & texts. Ideal for libraries, museums, universities, schools & collections.
Subjects: Archaeology, Art, History, Travel
ISBN Prefix(es): 960-85724; 960-86262; 960-8212

**Exandas Publishers**
Didotou, 57, 106 81 Athens
*Tel:* 2103822064; 2103084885 *Fax:* 210 3813065
*Web Site:* www.exandasbooks.gr
*Key Personnel*
President: Magda N Kotzia
Vice President: Lena Philippou
Editor: Manuela Berki; Alexander Panoussis
Founded: 1975
Subjects: Art, Cookery, Economics, Environmental Studies, Erotica, Fiction, Government, Political Science, History, Literature, Literary Criticism, Essays, Mysteries, Psychology, Psychiatry, Public Administration, Romance, Science Fiction, Fantasy, Social Sciences, Sociology, Fairy Tales, Horror
ISBN Prefix(es): 960-256

**F & D Stephanides OE,** see Sigma

**Ekdoseis Filon** (Friends' Publications)
10 Panepistimiou St, 106 71 Athens
*Tel:* 2103618705 *Fax:* 2103618705
*Key Personnel*
Publisher: Antonios Tsakiris; Kostas Tsiropoulos
Founded: 1961
Subjects: Literature, Literary Criticism, Essays, Philosophy, Poetry
ISBN Prefix(es): 960-289 (Filon); 960-8150 (Eythini Publications)
Number of titles published annually: 20 Print
Total Titles: 915 Print
*Parent Company:* Eythini

**Forma Edkotiki E P E+**
One Klimenis, L Ionias, 104 45 Athens
*Tel:* 2108327008
*Key Personnel*
President: Peter Cottis
Vice President: Themis Sfaellos
Editor: Aristidis Liakouras; Zaphiria Cotti MSc
Founded: 1980
Membership(s): Cooperative of Greek Publishers.
Subjects: Architecture & Interior Design, Economics, History, Literature, Literary Criticism, Essays, Poetry
ISBN Prefix(es): 960-271

**Gartaganis D**
3 Kon Melenikou, 540 06 Thessaloniki
*Tel:* 2310209680
Founded: 1934
Subjects: Agriculture, Veterinary Science, Food Technology
ISBN Prefix(es): 960-7013

**Giourdas Moschos+**
4 Sergiou Patriarchou St, 114 72 Athens
*Tel:* 2103624947; 2103630219 *Fax:* 210 3624947
*E-mail:* mgiurdas@acci.gr
*Web Site:* www.mgiurdas.gr
*Key Personnel*
Foreign Rights & Sales Manager: Panagiotis Assonitis *E-mail:* notisass@hotmail.com
Founded: 1967
Translations from USA & German titles
Self ruling publishing company.
Subjects: Architecture & Interior Design, Computer Science, Engineering (General)
ISBN Prefix(es): 960-512
Total Titles: 500 Print; 18 Online; 25 E-Book

**Giovanis Publications, Pangosmios Ekdotikos Organismos**
Zoodohou Pigis 7, 106 78 Athens
*Tel:* 2103825798; 2103301511 *Fax:* 210 3824417
*E-mail:* giovani1@otenet.gr

*Web Site:* www.geocities.com/giovanis_pub/
en_main1.htm
Subjects: Geography, Geology, History, Medicine,
Nursing, Dentistry, Photography, Religion -
Other, Science (General)

**Govostis Publishing SA+**
21 Zoodohou Pigis, 106 81 Athens
*Tel:* 2103815433; 2103822251
*Web Site:* www.govostis.gr
*Key Personnel*
President: Costas Govostis *E-mail:* cotsos@
gorostis.gr
Founded: 1926
Subjects: Art, Astrology, Occult, Biography,
Child Care & Development, Computer Science,
Drama, Theater, Fiction, Government, Political
Science, History, Nonfiction (General), Physics,
Poetry
ISBN Prefix(es): 960-270
*Warehouse:* 58-60 Laskareos, 114 72 Athens

**Gutenberg Dardanos,** see Gutenberg
Publications

**Gutenberg Publications+**
37 Didotou, 106 81 Athens
*Tel:* 2103642003; 2103800798; 2103843511
*Fax:* 2103642030; 2103800127; 21038
29402
*E-mail:* gutenberg@internet.gr
*Key Personnel*
Man Dir, Editorial & Sales in Bookshops: George
Dardanos
Production: Christos Stavropoulos
Retail Sales: Karakatsanis Haralambos
Founded: 1963
Specialize in books for education at all degrees.
Membership(s): POEV, SEVA, PFPB.
Subjects: Art, Economics, Education, Govern-
ment, Political Science, History, Literature,
Literary Criticism, Essays, Philosophy, Psy-
chology, Psychiatry, Social Sciences, Sociology
ISBN Prefix(es): 960-01
*Associate Companies:* Spoudi; Typothito
Distributor for Litera
*Bookshop(s):* Solonos 103, 106 79 Athens

**Harlenic Hellas Publishing SA+**
57 Ippokratous St, 106 80 Athens
*Tel:* 2103610218 *Fax:* 2103614846
*E-mail:* info@harlenic.gr
*Web Site:* www.harlenic.gr
*Key Personnel*
Man Dir: Constantine N Ordolis *Tel:* 2103610
218 *E-mail:* c.n.ordolis@harlenic.gr
Financial Manager: Eleftheria Chrissicopoulou
Marketing Manager: Evily Sakkalis
Sales Manager: Costas Apostolakis
Editorial Manager: Marina Kouloumoundra
Production Manager: Charalambos Rigas
Founded: 1979
Subjects: Fiction, Literature, Literary Criticism,
Essays, Romance
ISBN Prefix(es): 960-450; 960-620
Number of titles published annually: 450 Print
*Parent Company:* Harlequin Enterprises Ltd, 225
Duncan Mill Rd, Don Mills, ON M3B 3K9,
Canada
*Associate Companies:* Cora Verlag, Germany;
Forlaget Harlequin AB, Sweden; Harlequin SA,
France; Harlequin Iberica SA, Spain; Harlequin
Holland, Netherlands; Harlequin Japan, Japan;
Harlequin Mills & Boon (London); Harlequin
Mondadori
Imprints: Bell Best-Seller; Bell Literature; Mira;
Harlequin; Red Dress Ink; Blaze

**Harlequin,** *imprint of* Harlenic Hellas Publishing
SA

**Denise Harvey**
Katounia, 340 05 Limni, Evia
*Tel:* 2227031154 *Fax:* 2227031154
*Key Personnel*
Man Dir: Denise Harvey *E-mail:* denise@
teledomenet.gr
Founded: 1972
Subjects: Biography, Ethnicity, Literature, Lit-
erary Criticism, Essays, Nonfiction (General),
Philosophy, Poetry, Theology
ISBN Prefix(es): 960-7120
Number of titles published annually: 3 Print
Total Titles: 50 Print
Imprints: Romiosyni (series)
Distributed by Cosmos Publishing Co Inc (United
States); Orthodox Christian Books Ltd (UK &
Europe)

**Hestia-I D Hestia-Kollaros & Co Corporation+**
Odos Solonos 60, 106 72 Athens
*Tel:* 2103635970; 2103615077; 210360574
*Fax:* 2103606758; 2103606759
*Web Site:* www.ianos.gr
*Key Personnel*
Publicity Manager: Eva Karaitidi
President: Marina Karaitidi
Founded: 1885
Subjects: Animals, Pets, Anthropology, Archae-
ology, Architecture & Interior Design, Art, As-
trology, Occult, Behavioral Sciences, Biblical
Studies, Biography, Business, Career Devel-
opment, Child Care & Development, Com-
munications, Drama, Theater, Education, En-
ergy, Fiction, Geography, Geology, History,
Human Relations, Journalism, Language Arts,
Linguistics, Law, Library & Information Sci-
ences, Literature, Literary Criticism, Essays,
Management, Music, Dance, Mysteries, Natu-
ral History, Philosophy, Photography, Poetry,
Psychology, Psychiatry, Public Administration,
Romance, Science Fiction, Fantasy, Social Sci-
ences, Sociology, Travel, Veterinary Science,
Women's Studies
ISBN Prefix(es): 960-05
Divisions: Hestia
*Bookshop(s):* Hestia Bookstore, 60 Solonas St,
106 72 Athens
*Warehouse:* 85, Evripidou Str, Athens

**I Prooptiki, Ekdoseis+**
152 G Septemvriou, 112 51 Athens
*Tel:* 2108226254 *Fax:* 2108226254
*E-mail:* info@prooptikibooks.gr
*Web Site:* wwws.prooptikibooks.gr
*Key Personnel*
Contact: Polychronis Papacristou
Founded: 1991
Specialize in educational books & editions.
Subjects: Education
ISBN Prefix(es): 960-7331
Total Titles: 8 Print

**Ianos+**
Aristotelous 7, 546 24 Thessaloniki
*Tel:* 2310284833 *Fax:* 2310284832
*E-mail:* internet@ianos.gr
*Web Site:* www.ianos.gr
*Key Personnel*
Contact: N Karatzas
Founded: 1984
Membership(s): Thessaloniki's Booksellers Asso-
ciation.
Subjects: Biography, Ethnicity, History, Literature,
Literary Criticism, Essays, Philosophy
ISBN Prefix(es): 960-7771; 960-7827
*Parent Company:* Bookstore Ianos AE
Subsidiaries: Gallery Ianos
*Branch Office(s)*
Metamorphoseos 24 Kalamaria, 551 31 Thessa-
loniki *Tel:* 2310426780 *Fax:* 2310426780
Filippoupoleos 57 Ambelokipi, 561 23 Thessa-
loniki *Tel:* 2310727075 *Fax:* 2310727075

**Idmon Publications+**
106 Ag Glykerias, 132 31 Athens
Mailing Address: PO Box 48030, 132 31
Petroupoli, Athens
*Tel:* 2105015550 *Fax:* 2105015550
*E-mail:* idmon@in.gr
*Key Personnel*
Editor: Nikos Deligiannis
Subjects: History, Literature, Literary Criticism,
Essays, Poetry
ISBN Prefix(es): 960-85270; 960-7547

**Idryma Meleton Chersonisou tou Aimou**
(Institute for Balkan Studies)
Meg Alexandrou 31A, 546 41 Thessaloniki
Mailing Address: PO Box 50932, 540 14 Thessa-
loniki
*Tel:* 2310832143 *Fax:* 2310831429
*E-mail:* imxa@imxa.gr
Founded: 1953
Subjects: Art, Economics, Education, Ethnicity,
History, Social Sciences, Sociology, Balkan
Area from Ancient Times to Present Day
ISBN Prefix(es): 960-7387
Number of titles published annually: 6 Print
Total Titles: 276 Print
*Distribution Center:* Pournaras Panagiotis, Kas-
tritsiou 12, 546 23 Thessaloniki *Fax:* 2310
270941 *E-mail:* pournarasbooks@theforthnet.gr

**Ikaros Ekdotiki**
4 Voulis St, 105 62 Athens
*Tel:* 2103225152 *Fax:* 2103235262
Founded: 1943
Subjects: Literature, Literary Criticism, Essays
ISBN Prefix(es): 960-7233; 960-7721

**Institute of Neohellenic Studies, Manolis
Triantaphyllidis Foundation+**
Aristotelcio Parepistimio Thessalonikis, 540 06
Thessaloniki
*Tel:* 2310997128 *Fax:* 2310997122
*E-mail:* ins@phil.auth.gr
*Telex:* 418562
*Key Personnel*
Contact: K Prokovas
Founded: 1959
Subjects: Education, Language Arts, Linguistics
ISBN Prefix(es): 960-231
*Orders to:* S Patakis, Valtetsiou 14, 10680 Athens
*Fax:* 2103628950

**Irini Publishing House - Vassilis G Katsikeas
SA+**
130 Solonos str, 106 81 Athens
*Tel:* 2103839259; 2103810465 *Fax:* 2103800
651; 2103805113
*E-mail:* katsikgr@hol.gr
*Web Site:* www.infomedacoop.gr
*Telex:* 223639 Kats gr *Cable:* CATGROUP
ATHENS
*Key Personnel*
President, Rights & Permissions: Vassilis G Kat-
sikeas
Editorial, Production, Publicity: Vicky Pantazopou-
lou
Sales: Georges V Katsikeas; Konstantin V Kat-
sikeas
Subjects: Biography, Economics, Fiction, Govern-
ment, Political Science, History, Poetry, Social
Sciences, Sociology
*Associate Companies:* K and K Ltd *Tel:* 210
3609489 *Fax:* 2103606669
Subsidiaries: Ekdotiki Irini Ltd; Irini Foundation
*Branch Office(s)*
Aristotelous 7, 546 24 Salonika *Tel:* 2310261069

**Kalentis & Sia+**
Mavromichali 11, 106 79 Athens
*Tel:* 2103601551 *Fax:* 2103623553
*E-mail:* kalendis@ath.forthnet.gr

*Key Personnel*
Contact: Alexandros Kalentis; Marianna Kalentis;
Nikos Kalentis; Emily Stamou
Founded: 1983
Subjects: Biological Sciences, Child Care & Development, Cookery, Erotica, Fiction, Health, Nutrition, History, Medicine, Nursing, Dentistry, Philosophy, Poetry
ISBN Prefix(es): 960-219
Number of titles published annually: 40 Print; 10 CD-ROM; 10 Online
Total Titles: 822 Print; 32 CD-ROM; 32 Online
Distributor for Delithanasis Publications;
Ereynites Publications; Kirki Publicatitons;
Malliaris Publications
*Showroom(s):* CR Smirnis A Korai, 162 32 Biron
*Bookshop(s):* Parametros No I, 62 Metonos
Str, 155 61 Holargos *Tel:* 2106523145; Parametros No II, 56 Perikleous Str, 155 61 Holargos
*Tel:* 2106528176
*Warehouse:* A Kalendis-A Stamou, 62 Metonos
Str, 155 61 Holargos
*Orders to:* A Kalendis-A Stamou, 62 Metonos
Str, 155 61 Holargos

**Ilias Kambanas Publishing Organization, SA+**
66 Paparrigopoulou St, 121 33 Peristeri-Athens
*Tel:* 2105762791 *Fax:* 2105743988
*E-mail:* kambanas@internet.gr
*Key Personnel*
President: Thalia Kambana
Vice President & Man Dir: Sophia Charokopou
Marketing Manager: Kirsten Janz
Founded: 1969
Specialize in textbooks for elementary schools, atlases, dictionaries, educational materials, novelty books, picture books, cut-out models.
Membership(s): Panhellenic Federation of Publishers & Booksellers.
Subjects: Crafts, Games, Hobbies
ISBN Prefix(es): 960-257
Imprints: Anemonylos; Superkids
*Bookshop(s):* 49 Char Trikoupi St, 106 81 Athens
*Tel:* 2103647600 *Fax:* 2105743988
*Warehouse:* 65 Paparrigopoulou St, 121 33
Peristeri-Athens

**Dionysuis P Karavias Ekdoseis**
35 Asklipiou, 106 80 Athens
*Tel:* 2103620465 *Fax:* 2103620465
Subjects: History
ISBN Prefix(es): 960-258

**Kardamitsa A+**
Ippokratous 8, 106 79 Athens
*Tel:* 2103615156 *Fax:* 2103631100
*E-mail:* info@kardamitsa.gr
*Web Site:* kardamitsa.gr
*Key Personnel*
Contact: Mina Kardamitsa-Psychoyos; Basil Psychoyos
Founded: 1970
Subjects: Archaeology, History, Literature, Literary Criticism, Essays, Philosophy
ISBN Prefix(es): 960-7262; 960-354
Number of titles published annually: 10 Print
Total Titles: 270 Print
*Parent Company:* Institut du Livre, A Kardamitsa, 10679 Athens

**Kastaniotis Editions SA+**
11 Zalogou St, 106 78 Athens
*Tel:* 2103301208; 2103301327 *Fax:* 2103822
530
*E-mail:* info@kastaniotis.com
*Web Site:* www.kastaniotis.com
*Key Personnel*
Man Dir, Editorial: Athanasios Kastaniotis
Editorial: Anna Stamatopoulou
Sales: Stelios Kanakis
Production: Voula Vrachati
Publicity, Rights & Permissions: Sophie Catris

Founded: 1968
Membership(s): Association of Publishers & Booksellers of Athens.
Subjects: Anthropology, Architecture & Interior Design, Art, Astrology, Occult, Biography, Business, Child Care & Development, Computer Science, Cookery, Crafts, Games, Hobbies, Drama, Theater, Economics, Education, Fiction, Film, Video, Government, Political Science, Health, Nutrition, History, Humor, Literature, Literary Criticism, Essays, Philosophy, Poetry, Psychology, Psychiatry, Astrology, Beauty, Cartoons & Comics, Esoterics & New Age
ISBN Prefix(es): 960-03
*Associate Companies:* Ath Kastaniotis & Co General Partnership
*Subsidiaries:* Ath A Kastaniotis & Co Ltd Partnership

**Katoptro Publications+**
8, Korizi Str, 117 43 Athens
*Tel:* 2109244827; 2109244852 *Fax:* 2109244
756
*E-mail:* info@katoptro.gr
*Web Site:* www.katoptro.gr
Founded: 1987
Specialize in sciences.
Subjects: Mathematics, Nonfiction (General), Philosophy, Science (General)
ISBN Prefix(es): 960-7023; 960-7778
*Bookshop(s):* 5, Pesmazogloustr, 105 64 Athens
*Tel:* 2103247785

**Kedros Publishers+**
3, G Gennadiou Str, 106 78 Athens
*Tel:* 2103809712 *Fax:* 2103302655
*E-mail:* books@kedros.gr
*Web Site:* www.kedros.gr
*Key Personnel*
Man Dir: Evangelos Papathanassopoulos
Foreign Rights: Laura McDowell
Founded: 1954
Subjects: Biography, Child Care & Development, Drama, Theater, Fiction, History, Humor, Literature, Literary Criticism, Essays, Philosophy, Poetry, Psychology, Psychiatry, Romance, Science (General), Self-Help, Social Sciences, Sociology, Travel
ISBN Prefix(es): 960-04
Distributed by Cosmos Publishing Co (USA)

**Kentro Byzantinon Erevnon**
12 Kastritsiou Str, 546 23 Thessaloniki
*Tel:* 2310270941 *Fax:* 2310228922

**Kleidarithmos, Ekdoseis+**
27V Stournari, 106 82 Athens
*Tel:* 2103832044
*Key Personnel*
Man Dir: Giannis Faldamis
Founded: 1985
Subjects: Architecture & Interior Design, Automotive, Civil Engineering, Computer Science, Electronics, Electrical Engineering, Management, Marketing, Mechanical Engineering, Microcomputers
ISBN Prefix(es): 960-209
*Bookshop(s):* Stournari 37, 106 82 Athens
*Tel:* 2103829629

**Knossos Publications**
8 Soultani, 106 83 Athens
*Tel:* 2103810108
Founded: 1972
Subjects: Biography, History, Literature, Literary Criticism, Essays, Poetry, Travel
ISBN Prefix(es): 960-207
*Parent Company:* Stelios Chalkiadakis
*Bookshop(s):* 29, Evans Str, 712 10 Iraklion Kreta

**Kritiki Publishing+**
1-3 Tsamadou Str, 106 83 Athens
*Tel:* 2103803730 *Fax:* 2103803740
*E-mail:* biblia@kritiki.gr
*Web Site:* www.kritiki.gr
*Key Personnel*
Directing Manager: Yannis Zirinis
Founded: 1987
Specialize in social sciences.
Subjects: Anthropology, Business, Economics, Fiction, Finance, Government, Political Science, History, Literature, Literary Criticism, Essays, Management, Marketing, Nonfiction (General), Philosophy, Self-Help, Social Sciences, Sociology
ISBN Prefix(es): 960-218
Number of titles published annually: 60 Print
Total Titles: 300 Print

**Leon,** *imprint of* Vivliofilia K Ch Spanos

**A G Leventis Foundation**
9 Fragoklissias St, 15 125 Maroussi
*Tel:* 2106165232 *Fax:* 2106165235
*E-mail:* leventcy@zenon.logos.cy.net; eleni.
mariolea@leventis.net
*Web Site:* www.leventisfoundation.org
Founded: 1979
Subjects: Archaeology, Art, History
ISBN Prefix(es): 9963-560
*Branch Office(s)*
40 Gladstonos St, PO Box 2543, 1095 Nicosia, Cyprus *Tel:* (022) 667706; (022) 674018 *Fax:* (022) 675002

**Libro Ltd**
10-12 Glykonos, 106 75 Athens
*Tel:* 2107247116; 2107228647 *Fax:* 210
7226648
*E-mail:* libro@hol.gr
ISBN Prefix(es): 960-7009; 960-490

**Livani Publishing Organization SA,** see Nea Synora Publications

**Longman,** *imprint of* Longman-Pearson Education Hellas SA

**Longman-Pearson Education Hellas SA**
Formerly Pearson Education Hellas SA
229 Syngrou Ave, Nea Smyrni, 171 21 Athens
*Fax:* 2109373206
*E-mail:* publ.pass@longman.gr
*Key Personnel*
Man Dir: Themis Zoulias
Sales Manager: Liz Hammon
Publisher: Loukas Ioannou
Founded: 1985
ELT supplementary titles.
Number of titles published annually: 10 Print
Total Titles: 20 Print
*Parent Company:* Pearson Plc
Imprints: Longman
*Branch Office(s)*
12 Mackenzie King St, 546 22 Thessaloniki
*Tel:* 2310271163 *Fax:* 2310241056
Foreign Rights: Loukas Ioannou

**Lycabettus Press**
Afaias 54, P Psychiko, 154 52 Athens
*Tel:* 2106741788 *Fax:* 2106710666
*E-mail:* services@lycabettus.com
*Web Site:* lycabettus.com
*Key Personnel*
Editor: John Chapple *E-mail:* j.chapple@
lycabettus.com
Founded: 1968
ISBN Prefix(es): 960-7269

**Mamuth Comix EPE+**
130 Solonos, 106 81 Athens

Tel: 2103625054 Fax: 2103625055
E-mail: themask@athena.gr
Key Personnel
International Rights: Irene Tzourou
Founded: 1982
Subjects: Humor
ISBN Prefix(es): 960-321
Distributed by Ehapa Verlag Germany

**Medusa/Selas Publishers+**
Didotou 26, 106 80 Athens
Tel: 21036483234 Fax: 2103648321
Key Personnel
Contact: Yannis Perdikogiannis
Founded: 1994
Subjects: Art, Fiction, Film, Video, Health, Nu-
trition, Music, Dance, Nonfiction (General),
Science Fiction, Fantasy, Comics & Cartoons,
Humor
ISBN Prefix(es): 960-7246; 960-85004
Associate Companies: Topos, Lithi
Imprints: Topos, Lithi
Bookshop(s): Synergasia Andrea Metaxa 4,
Athens
Warehouse: 63 Eressou Str, 10683 Athens

**Melissa Publishing House+**
58 Skoufa St, 106 80 Athens
Tel: 2103611692 Fax: 2103600865
E-mail: sales@melissabooks.com
Web Site: www.melissabooks.com
Key Personnel
Man Dir: George Ragias
Sales Dir: Chrys Ragias
Contact: Annie Ragia E-mail: annieragia@
melissabooks.com
Founded: 1954
Book publishers.
Subjects: Architecture & Interior Design, Art,
History, Maritime, Greek Civilization
ISBN Prefix(es): 960-204
Subsidiaries:
Divisions: Dictionary of Greek Artists
Distributed by Harry N Abrams Inc

**Minoas SA+**
One Poseidonos St, 141 21 Athens-Iraklei
Tel: (2210) 2711222 Fax: (2210) 2711056
E-mail: info@minoas.gr
Web Site: www.minoas.gr
Key Personnel
Man Dir: Yannis Konstantaropoulos
Executive Manager: Andreas Konstantaropoulos
Sales Manager: Christos Hatzipantelides
Founded: 1958
Publications.
Subjects: Art, Biography, Fiction, History, Music,
Dance, Nonfiction (General)
ISBN Prefix(es): 960-240; 960-542; 960-699
Number of titles published annually: 80 Print
Total Titles: 800 Print
Bookshop(s): Patission 126, 112 57 Athens
Tel: 2108215664 Fax: 2108215664

**Mira**, imprint of Harlenic Hellas Publishing SA

**Editions Moressopoulos+**
2 Chairefonts, 103 10 Athens
Tel: 2103234217
E-mail: hcp@photography.gr
Telex: 216465 masgr
Key Personnel
Man Dir: Stavros Moressopoulos
Rights & Permissions: Voula Moressopoulos
Founded: 1977
Membership(s): Union of Book Publishers
(Athens), Association of Photo Biennials (Paris,
France), Union of Journalists, Owners of Peri-
odical Press (Athens).
Subjects: Animals, Pets, Crafts, Games, Hobbies,
How-to, Music, Dance, Photography, Sports,
Athletics, Travel, Wine & Spirits

ISBN Prefix(es): 960-366
Parent Company: Moressopoulos SA
Associate Companies: Hellenic Centre of Photog-
raphy (nonprofit making) European School of
Photography, Iperidou 19, 105 58 Athens
Subsidiaries: Photografia Magazine

**Morfotiki Estia AE**, see E Mokas - Morfotiki

**Morfotiko Idryma Ethnikis Trapezas** (National
Bank Cultural Foundation)+
13 Thoukydidou, 105 58 Athens
Tel: 2103230841; 2103221335 Fax: 210324
5089
Founded: 1966
Subjects: Archaeology, History, Language Arts,
Linguistics, Literature, Literary Criticism, Es-
says, Nonfiction (General), Philosophy, Science
(General)
ISBN Prefix(es): 960-250

**Mouseio Benaki**
One Koumpari, 106 74 Athens
Tel: 2103626215; 2103612694 Fax: 210
3622547
E-mail: belesioti@benaki.gr
ISBN Prefix(es): 960-7671; 960-85160; 960-8347;
960-8452

**Nakas Music House+**
147 Skiathou Skokou, 112 55 Athens
Tel: 2103647111; 2102282160
Fax: (2210) 2112302
E-mail: bookw@nakas.gr
Web Site: www.nakas.gr
Telex: 8018NAKAGR
Key Personnel
Contact: George Nakas
Founded: 1937
Subjects: Music, Dance
ISBN Prefix(es): 960-290
Distributor for Boosey & Hawkes; Henley Verlag;
Ricordi

**Ed Nea Acropolis+**
29 Ag Meletiou, 113 61 Athens
Tel: 2108231301; 2108817900 Fax: 210
8810830
Key Personnel
President: Panagiotis Goumas
Vice President: Peter Kostinis
Editor: Costula Giannopulu
Founded: 1981
Subjects: Anthropology, Archaeology, Drama,
Theater, History, Music, Dance, Mysteries,
Parapsychology, Philosophy
ISBN Prefix(es): 960-8407
Branch Office(s)
Hania
Heraklion
Ioannina
Kallithea
Kavala
Patras
Rethymno
Salonica
Volos

**Nea Synora Publications+**
98 Solonos St, 106 80 Athens
Tel: 2106435709 Fax: 2108815275
E-mail: neasynora@otenet.gr
Web Site: www.nea-synora.gr
Telex: 21812269spa
Key Personnel
President: Giota Livani; Ilias Livani
Editor: Tonia Chourchouli
Founded: 1972
ISBN Prefix(es): 960-236; 960-237; 960-238;
960-14

Parent Company: Livani Publishing Organization
SA
Associate Companies: Mythos, Klydi
Subsidiaries: Multimedia Electronic Publishing
SA
Warehouse: 135 Platonos St, 176 73 Athens

**Nea Thesis - Evrotas+**
Ippokratoys St 65, 106 80 Athens
Tel: 2103643932 Fax: 2103617592
Key Personnel
Contact: John Schinas
Subjects: Archaeology, Ethnicity, Government,
Political Science, History, Philosophy
ISBN Prefix(es): 960-7076

**Nikas**
Solonos 102, 106 80 Athens
Tel: 2103634686; 2103633754
ISBN Prefix(es): 960-297

**Nikolopoulos**
96 Solonos, 106 80 Athens
Tel: 2103607725
E-mail: bkyriakid@otenet.gr
Key Personnel
Publisher: Sotiris Nikolopoulos
Founded: 1994
Publish books for Greek language as a foreign
language.
Membership(s): Book Publishers Association.
Subjects: History, Literature, Literary Criticism,
Essays, Psychology, Psychiatry, Social Sci-
ences, Sociology, Grammar, Vocabulary, Or-
thography, Ancient Greek History, Byzantine,
European, Global, Ancient Greek Literature
ISBN Prefix(es): 960-7634
Total Titles: 100 Print

**Nomiki Vivliothiki+**
51 Mavromichali St, 106 80 Athens
Tel: 2103600968 Fax: 2103636422
E-mail: legalinn@otenet.gr
Key Personnel
Man Dir & International Rights Contract: Adonis
Karatzas Tel: (01) 3678856 E-mail: adonik@
nb.org
Founded: 1977
Internet & legal services, professional training
courses & seminars.
Subjects: Economics, Labor, Industrial Relations,
Law, Publishing & Book Trade Reference
ISBN Prefix(es): 960-272

**Notos**
Omirou 15, 106 72 Athens
Tel: 2103636577; 2103629746 Fax: 210
3636737
Telex: 515418
ISBN Prefix(es): 960-8491

**Oceanida+**
38 Dervenion St, 106 81 Athens
Tel: 2103806137 Fax: 2103805531
E-mail: oceanida@internet.gr
Key Personnel
Publisher: Louisa Zaoussi
Founded: 1986
Subjects: Art, History, Literature, Literary Criti-
cism, Essays
ISBN Prefix(es): 960-7213; 960-410
Number of titles published annually: 30 Print
Total Titles: 250 Print
Distributor for Erevnites
Distribution Center: 25 Solomon St, 106 82
Athens Tel: 2103827341

**Odysseas Publications Ltd+**
3 Moraitou, 114 71 Athens
Tel: 2103624326; 2103625575 Fax: 210
3648030

*Key Personnel*
Contact: Titos Mylonopoulos
Founded: 1973
Subjects: Biography, Child Care & Development, History, Human Relations, Philosophy, Psychology, Psychiatry, Romance, Women's Studies
ISBN Prefix(es): 960-210

**Opera**
23 Koletti, 106 77 Athens
*Tel:* 2103304546 *Fax:* 2103303634
*E-mail:* opera@acci.gr
*Key Personnel*
Contact & Opera Editions: George Miressiotis
Founded: 1989 (Private book publishing house)
Literary Books & Translations
Specialize in European & Latin American authors.
ISBN Prefix(es): 960-7073
Total Titles: 90 Print

**Orfanidis Publications+**
8 Lontou St, 106 81 Athens
*Tel:* 2103836925 *Fax:* 2103845623
Founded: 1940
Subjects: Astrology, Occult, Automotive, Cookery, Gardening, Plants, Geography, Geology, Mysteries, Philosophy

**Pagoulatos Bros+**
56 Panepistimiou St, 106 78 Athens
*Tel:* 2103818780; 2103801485 *Fax:* 21 03838028
*E-mail:* pagoulatos_publ@ath.forthnet.gr
Founded: 1965
Subjects: Biography, English as a Second Language, Mathematics
ISBN Prefix(es): 960-7208

**Pagoulatos G-G P Publications**
50 Sina, 106 72 Athens
*Tel:* 2103604895; 2103600720 *Fax:* 210 3604897
*Key Personnel*
Editor: Gerasimos Pagoulatos
Subjects: English as a Second Language
ISBN Prefix(es): 960-294

**Panepistimio Ioanninon**
PO Box 1186, 451 10 Ioannina
*Tel:* 2651097122 *Fax:* 2651097015
*E-mail:* intlrel@uoi.gr
*Web Site:* www.uoi.gr
*Key Personnel*
Publications Office: Mrs E Gouma
Subjects: Anthropology, Archaeology, Chemistry, Chemical Engineering, Education, History, Physics, Psychology, Psychiatry, Social Sciences, Sociology
ISBN Prefix(es): 960-233

**D Papadimas+**
8 Ippokratous, 106 79 Athens
*Tel:* 2103627318 *Fax:* 2103610271
Subjects: Antiques, Archaeology, Geography, Geology, History, Regional Interests, Theology
ISBN Prefix(es): 960-206

**Kyr I Papadopoulos E E+**
9, Kapodistriou St, 14452 Athens
*Tel:* 2102816134; 2102846074; 2102846075 *Fax:* 2102817127
*E-mail:* info@picturebooks.gr
*Web Site:* www.picturebooks.gr
*Telex:* 225176 Book Gr
*Key Personnel*
Man Dir: Kyr Papadopoulos
Sales: P Hatjibodojis
Production: George Papadopoulos
Rights & Permissions: Yiannis Papadopoulos

Founded: 1953
Subjects: Animals, Pets, Fiction, History, Literature, Literary Criticism, Essays, Nonfiction (General), Adventure, Classics, Social Situations
ISBN Prefix(es): 960-261; 960-412
Number of titles published annually: 100 Print
Total Titles: 600 Print

**Papazissis Publishers SA**
2 Nikitara, 106 78 Athens
*Tel:* 2103838020; 2103822496 *Fax:* 210 3809150
*Telex:* 219807 Itec
*Key Personnel*
Man Dir: Victor Papazissis
Sales, Advertising: Thalia Papazissis
Rights & Permissions: Stefanos Vlachos
Founded: 1929
Subjects: Economics, Education, Environmental Studies, Government, Political Science, History, Law, Regional Interests, Social Sciences, Sociology
ISBN Prefix(es): 960-02
*Parent Company:* Corais Ltd

**Patakis Publishers+**
16 Emm Benaki, 106 78 Athens
*Tel:* 2103831078; 2103811850; 210 3650000 *Fax:* 2103628950
*E-mail:* info@patakis.gr
*Web Site:* www.patakis.gr
*Key Personnel*
President: Stefanos Patakis
Production: Alexander Patakis
Sales: Peter Lazaridis
Publicity: Hara Mavrogonatou
Rights & Permissions: Yiannis Ntzoufras
Editorial: Nikitas Stellas
Foreign Rights Assistant: Vicky Stamatopoulou
   *Tel:* 2103615356 *E-mail:* vstamat@patakis.gr
Founded: 1974
Subjects: Anthropology, Art, Biography, Business, Child Care & Development, Cookery, Drama, Theater, Education, Fiction, Health, Nutrition, History, Language Arts, Linguistics, Literature, Literary Criticism, Essays, Management, Nonfiction (General), Philosophy, Poetry, Psychology, Psychiatry, Social Sciences, Sociology, Travel
ISBN Prefix(es): 960-293; 960-360; 960-600; 960-378; 960-16
Number of titles published annually: 500 Print
Total Titles: 3,000 Print
*Branch Office(s)*
N Monastiriou 122, Thessaloniki *Tel:* 2310 706354 *Fax:* 2310706355
Distributor for Conceptum (CD-ROM); Goulandri-Horn Institute; Iolkos Publications; Triantafyllidis Institute
*Bookshop(s):* Akadimias 65, 106 78 Athens *Tel:* 2103811740 *Fax:* 2103811850
*Warehouse:* These Tzaverdela, Aspropyrgos 19300
*Distribution Center:* Em Benaki 16, Athens *Tel:* 2103831078 (also showroom)

**Pearson Education Hellas SA**, see Longman-Pearson Education Hellas SA

**Pergamini**, *imprint of* Vivliofilia K Ch Spanos

**Galousis P Petros**
48 Solomou, 106 82 Athens
*Tel:* 2103605004

**Pontiki Publications SA+**
10 Massalias, 106 80 Athens
*Tel:* 2103609531; 2103609533 *Fax:* 210 3645406

*Key Personnel*
Publisher: Kostas Papayoannou
Man Dir: Kostas Yabanis
Editorial Dir: Roussos Vranas
Founded: 1979
Subjects: Government, Political Science, History
ISBN Prefix(es): 960-8402

**Proskinio Spyros Ch Marinis**
76 Solonos, 106 81 Athens
*Tel:* 2103648170 *Fax:* 2103648033
*Key Personnel*
President: A Sideratos
Founded: 1990
Subjects: Government, Political Science, History
ISBN Prefix(es): 960-7107; 960-8342

**M Psaropoulos & Co EE+**
3 Kriezotou, 106 71 Athens
*Tel:* 2103606808 *Fax:* 2103609645
*Key Personnel*
Man Dir: Tassos Psaropoulos
Editorial: Thalia Iacovidis
Sales: John Psaropoulos
Production: D Mavromatis
Publicity: P Pissanos
Rights & Permissions: M Psaropoulos
Founded: 1962
Subjects: Fiction, Medicine, Nursing, Dentistry
ISBN Prefix(es): 960-7147
*Parent Company:* Althayia SA
Subsidiaries: Finedawn Publishers

**Psichogios Publications SA+**
Mavromichali 1, 106 79 Athens
Mailing Address: Zaimi 8, 106 83 Athens
*Tel:* 2103302535; 2103302234 *Fax:* 210 3640683; 2103302098
*E-mail:* psicho@otenet.gr
*Telex:* 225874 Mps Gr
*Key Personnel*
Man Dir: Athanassios Psichogios
   *E-mail:* thanospsicho@otenet.gr
Editorial, Rights & Permission: Elly Solomon
Founded: 1978
Subjects: Fiction, Philosophy, Human Science
ISBN Prefix(es): 960-7020; 960-274; 960-7021
Number of titles published annually: 100 Print
Total Titles: 800 Print
*Branch Office(s)*
Vassileos Irakliou 32, 546 24 Thessaloniki
*Bookshop(s):* Pesmazoglou 5, 105 64 Athens
*Warehouse:* Edessis 29, 118 55 Votanikos

**Red Dress Ink**, *imprint of* Harlenic Hellas Publishing SA

**Romiosyni (series)**, *imprint of* Denise Harvey

**Rossi, E Kdoseis Eleni Rossi-Petsiou+**
5 Kiafas, 106 76 Athens
*Tel:* 2103304440; 2103301854 *Fax:* 210 3304410
Founded: 1895
Subjects: Education, Student's Aid
ISBN Prefix(es): 960-225

**Sakkoulas Publications SA+**
23, Ippokratous Str, 106 79 Athens
*Tel:* 2103387500 *Fax:* 2103390075
*E-mail:* info@sakkoulas.gr
*Web Site:* www.sakkoulas.gr
*Key Personnel*
Man Dir: Panagiotis I Sakkoulas
Founded: 1958
Subjects: Business, Economics, Labor, Industrial Relations, Law, Management, Maritime, Public Administration, Social Sciences, Sociology
ISBN Prefix(es): 960-301
*Branch Office(s)*
42, Ethnikis Amyis Str, 546 21 Thessaloniki

*Tel:* 2310244228; 2310244229
*Fax:* 2310244230
Distributor for Nomos Verlagsgesellschaft; Verlag
  Recht und Wirtschaft mbH
*Bookshop(s):* 42, Ethnikis Amyis Str, 546 21
  Thessaloniki *Tel:* 2310244228; 2310244
  229 *Fax:* (22310) 244 230; One Fragon Str,
  546 26 Thessaloniki *Tel:* 2310535381
  *Fax:* 2310546812

**Scripta Theofilus Palevratzis-Ashover+**
25 3is Septemvriou, 104 32 Athens
*Tel:* 2105230382 *Fax:* 2105233574
*Key Personnel*
Contact: Theophilos Palevratzis-Ashover
Founded: 1980
Subjects: English as a Second Language
ISBN Prefix(es): 960-7166; 960-8341

**Siamantas VA A Ouvas**
60 Lpeirou & 1-3 Akakiou, 104 39 Athens
*Tel:* 2108824960 *Fax:* 2108824960
Subjects: Fiction, History, Nonfiction (General)
ISBN Prefix(es): 960-87184

**J Sideris OE Ekdoseis**
115 Alexandreias, 104 41 Athens, Akadimia
  Platonos
*Tel:* 2103833434; 2105140627 *Fax:* 210
  3832294
*Key Personnel*
Contact: Andreas Sideris
Subjects: Language Arts, Linguistics, Literature,
  Literary Criticism, Essays, Science (General)
ISBN Prefix(es): 960-08

**Michalis Sideris**
Andr Metaxa 28 & Themistokleous, 106 81
  Athens
*Tel:* 2103301165; 21003301161 (bookstore)
  *Fax:* 2103301164
Founded: 1978
Subjects: Earth Sciences, Education, Energy,
  English as a Second Language, Mathematics,
  Physics
ISBN Prefix(es): 960-7012

**Sigma+**
20, Mavromihali St, 106 80 Athens
*Tel:* 2103638941; 2103607667 *Fax:* 210
  3638941
*E-mail:* sigma@sigmabooks.gr
*Web Site:* www.sigmabooks.gr
*Key Personnel*
Contact: Dimitris Stephanides
Founded: 1973
Subjects: Art, Fiction, Folk Tales, Mythology
ISBN Prefix(es): 960-425
Total Titles: 95 Print
Distributed by Cosmos Publishing Co Inc (US);
  Hellidon Press (UK)
Foreign Rep(s): Cosmos Publishing Co Inc
  (Canada, US)
Foreign Rights: Shin Won Agency Co (China,
  Japan, Korea)

**Alex Siokis & Co+**
54 Alex Svolou, 500 41 Thessaloniki
*Tel:* 2310230257; 2310287016
  *Fax:* 2310281014
*E-mail:* siokis@spark.net.gr
*Key Personnel*
Medical Publisher: Niki Sioki
Founded: 1960
Subjects: Medicine, Nursing, Dentistry
ISBN Prefix(es): 960-7461

**Society for Macedonian Studies**
4 Ethnikis Amynis Ave, 546 21 Thessaloniki
*Tel:* 2310268710 *Fax:* 2310971501
*E-mail:* ems@hyper.gr

Founded: 1939
Promotes the research in the topics of history, ar-
  chaeology, linguistics & folklore concerning
  the region of Macedonia.
Subjects: Anthropology, Archaeology, History,
  Philosophy, Humanities
Total Titles: 4 Print
Foreign Rights: Ebsco; Faxon; Wasmuth; Daw-
  son; Raabe; Readmore; Dokomente-Verlag;
  Sweis

**Vivliofilia K Ch Spanos**
7 Mavromichali, 106 79 Athens
*Tel:* 2103623917; 2103614332 *Fax:* 210
  8953076
*E-mail:* biblioph@otenet.gr *Cable:* Bibliospan
*Key Personnel*
Man Dir, Editorial: C Spanos
Sales: John Papadakis
Publicity: Sophia Tjimoianni
Subjects: Regional Interests
ISBN Prefix(es): 960-262
Imprints: Leon; Pergamini

**Spyropoulos A+**
74, Ag Georgiou, 154 51 Neo Psychico
*Tel:* 2106712991 *Fax:* 2106719622
Founded: 1972
Specialize in ELT material.
ISBN Prefix(es): 960-7302

**Stochastis+**
39 Mavromichali, 106 80 Athens
*Tel:* 2103601956; 2103610445 *Fax:* 210
  3610445
*Key Personnel*
President: Loukas Axelos
Founded: 1969
Subjects: Ethnicity, History, Literature, Literary
  Criticism, Essays, Philosophy, Social Sciences,
  Sociology, Travel
ISBN Prefix(es): 960-303
*Associate Companies:* Koinopraktiki (Union of
  Greek Publishers)
Imprints: Eurotyp
*Book Club(s):* Cosmos Book Club; Mos Book
  Club; The Friends of Book Book Club

**Superkids**, *imprint of* Ilias Kambanas Publishing
  Organization, SA

**Technical Chamber of Greece**
4 Karageorgi Servias Str, 102 48 Athens
*Tel:* 2103254591; 2103314403 *Fax:* 210
  3314403
*E-mail:* registry@central.tee.gr
*Telex:* 218374 Teegr
*Key Personnel*
General Dir: V Torolopoulos
Founded: 1923
The Technical Chamber of Greece (TEE) is a cor-
  porate body, under public law, supervised by
  the Ministry of Public Works.
Subjects: Science (General), Technology
ISBN Prefix(es): 960-7018

**Tekmirio**
17 Z Pigis, 106 81 Athens
*Tel:* 2103637912; 2102287548

**Thymari Publications+**
24 Har Trikoupi Str, 106 79 Athens
*Tel:* 2103634901; 2103643015 *Fax:* 210
  3636591
*E-mail:* thymari@thymari.gr
*Web Site:* thymari.gr
*Key Personnel*
Dir & Editor-in-Chief: T H Grammenou
Psychologist, Marketing: I Grammenou
Key Author: G Pinteris PhD
Editorial Advisor: A Grammenou

Psychologist, Translator: M Koulentianou
Founded: 1978
Subjects: Human Relations, Psychology, Psychia-
  try, Social Sciences, Sociology
ISBN Prefix(es): 960-7161; 960-349
*Warehouse:* Sarantaporou 98, 155 61 Holargos
  *Tel:* 2106512216; 2106540811 *Fax:* 210
  6549207

**To Rodakio+**
Apollonos 35, 105 56 Athens
*Tel:* 2103221700; 2103221742 *Fax:* 210
  3221700
*E-mail:* rodakio@otenet.gz
*Key Personnel*
International Rights: Julia Tsiakiris
Founded: 1992
Subjects: Art, Drama, Theater, Fiction, Literature,
  Literary Criticism, Essays, Poetry
ISBN Prefix(es): 960-7360; 960-8372
Number of titles published annually: 10 Print
Total Titles: 110 Print
Foreign Rights: Kleoniki Douqe (France)

**Topos, Lithi**, *imprint of* Medusa/Selas Publishers

**Toubis M**
519 Vouliagmenis Ave, 163 41 Athens
*Tel:* 2109923876; 2109923806 *Fax:* 2109923
  867
*E-mail:* toubis@otenet.gr
*Key Personnel*
Secretary: Katerina Koumarianou
Founded: 1965
Development, production & distribution of high
  quality tourist publication.

**Tropos Zois+**
One Solomou St, 152 32 Athens, Chalandri
*Tel:* 2106840156; 2106858852 *Fax:* 210
  6858851
Subjects: Alternative medicine, natural eating &
  living, nutrition, yoga, reflexology
ISBN Prefix(es): 960-7118
Number of titles published annually: 6 Print; 1
  CD-ROM
Total Titles: 10 Print; 2 CD-ROM; 50 Audio

**Typos**
3-5 Gravias, 106 78 Athens
*Tel:* 2103819083; 2103819085; 2103619083
  *Fax:* (21) 3825012
ISBN Prefix(es): 960-246

**D & J Vardikos Vivliotechnica Hellas**
2 A Metaxa, 106 81 Athens
*Tel:* 2103631148 *Fax:* 2109564354
*Key Personnel*
Man Dir: Dimitrios Vardikos
Founded: 1978
Subjects: Aeronautics, Aviation
ISBN Prefix(es): 960-7810
*Branch Office(s)*
Davaki 34, Kallithea, Athens
*Bookshop(s):* Inter-Attica, Davaki 34, Kallithea,
  Athens

**J Vassiliou Bibliopolein+**
15e Ippokratous St, 106 79 Athens
*Tel:* 2103623382; 2103623480 *Fax:* 210
  3623598
*Key Personnel*
President: J Vassiliou
Founded: 1913
Membership(s): Association of Publishers &
  Booksellers of Athens.
Subjects: Fiction, History, Philosophy

**Vivliothiki Eftychia Galeou+**
39 Chalandriou, 151 25 Maroussi, Athens

*Tel:* 2106841191 *Fax:* 2106825862
*Key Personnel*
Contact: N S Galeos
Subjects: Advertising, Business, Finance, Management, Marketing
ISBN Prefix(es): 960-7126
*Bookshop(s):* 19 Kolokotroni St, Athens *Tel:* 210 3227840

**Vlassis+**
2-4 Lontou, 106 81 Athens
*Tel:* 2103812900; 2103827557 *Fax:* 210 3827557
*E-mail:* amvlassi@otenet.gr
*Key Personnel*
General Manager: Nickos Vlassis
Publisher, Marketing Manager & International Rights Contact: Anna-Maria Vlassis *Tel:* 210 3833013 *E-mail:* amvlassi@otenet.gr
Founded: 1964
Hard cover & paper back.
Subjects: Biography, Fiction, Literature, Literary Criticism, Essays
ISBN Prefix(es): 960-302
Total Titles: 600 Print

**S J Zacharopoulos SA Publishing Co+**
Parodos Leof Kryoneriou, Agio Stefanos, 145 65 Athens
*Tel:* 2103231525; 2103225011; 2108142611
   *Fax:* 2103243814
*Key Personnel*
President, Publicity, Rights & Permissions: Stavros Zacharopoulos
Production: Loucas Zacharopoulos
Editorial: Stefanos Zacharopoulos
Sales: George Zacharopoulos
Founded: 1959
Subjects: Drama, Theater, History, Poetry, Science (General)
ISBN Prefix(es): 960-208
*Bookshop(s):* Praxitelous 141, 185 35 Piraeus

**Zacharopoulos Z & G**
22-24 Atlantos k patisia, 112 54 Athens
*Tel:* 2102111895-7 *Fax:* 2102111897
*E-mail:* zachapub@otenet.gr
ISBN Prefix(es): 960-281

**ZOI**
Subsidiary of "Zoe", Brotherhood of Theologians
14 Karytsi, 105 61 Athens
*Tel:* 2103223560 *Fax:* 2103221283
*Key Personnel*
Man Dir: P Anastopoulos
Founded: 1907
Subjects: Religion - Other
*Bookshop(s):* St Sophia 41, Salonika *Tel:* 2310 54623 (also in three other Greek cities)

**Har Zolindakis**
65 Panepistimiou, 105 64 Athens
*Tel:* 2103216504
Subjects: History

**Zyrichidi Bros**
30 Aristotelous, 546 23 Thessaloniki
*Tel:* 2310227915; 2310266036 *Fax:* 2310 266036
*Key Personnel*
Contact: Zyrichidi Bros *Tel:* 2310285856
Founded: 1959
Publisher of books, selling all other book publishing companies
General Partnership.
Subjects: Literature, Literary Criticism, Essays
Total Titles: 15 Print

*Branch Office(s)*
Zsimiski 115 *Tel:* 2310285856 *Fax:* 2310 266036
*Bookshop(s):* Zsimiski 115 *Tel:* 2310266036
   *Fax:* 2310266036

# Guadeloupe

## General Information

*Capital:* Basse-Terre
*Language:* French, Creole patois
*Religion:* Roman Catholic
*Population:* 400,000
*Bank Hours:* 0800-1200, 1400-1600 Monday-Friday
*Shop Hours:* 0900-1300, 1500-1800 Monday-Friday
*Currency:* 100 centimes = 1 French franc

**JASOR**
46 rue Schoelcher, 97110 Pointe-a-Pitre
*Tel:* 911848 *Fax:* 210701
*Telex:* 919-2333
Subjects: Language Arts, Linguistics, Literature, Literary Criticism, Essays
ISBN Prefix(es): 2-912594

# Guatemala

## General Information

*Capital:* Guatemala City
*Language:* Spanish
*Religion:* Roman Catholic
*Population:* 10 million
*Bank Hours:* 0900-1500 Monday-Friday
*Shop Hours:* 0900-1300, 1500-1900 Monday-Friday; 0900-1300 Saturday
*Currency:* 100 centavos = 1 quetzal
*Export/Import Information:* Member of the Central American Common Market. Duty on catalogues is Q 0.03 per gross kilo. No import licenses, no exchange control.
*Copyright:* UCC, Buenos Aires, Florence (see Copyright Conventions, pg xi)

**Cultura de La Universidad,** *imprint of* Grupo Editorial RIN-78

**Editorial Cultura**
O Calle 16-40, Zona 15, Guatemala
*Tel:* (02) 692080 *Fax:* (02) 346135
*Telex:* 5805 *Cable:* CAN EXO

**Fundacion para la Cultura y el Desarrollo**
9 calle 2-75, zona 1, 01001 Guatemala
SAN: 003-1429
*Tel:* (02) 500216 *Fax:* (02) 325508
*Key Personnel*
General Manager: Carlos I Castaneda Acuna
   *E-mail:* ccast@intelnet.net.gt
Founded: 1986
Subjects: History
ISBN Prefix(es): 84-88622
*Parent Company:* Asociacion de Amigos del Pais

**Grupo Editorial RIN-78+**
O Calle 16-40, Zona 15, Guatemala 692080
*Tel:* (02) 692080 *Fax:* (02) 601834
*Key Personnel*
Contact: Juan F Cifuentes
Founded: 1984

Subjects: Archaeology, Fiction, History, Literature, Literary Criticism, Essays, Military Science, Philosophy, Poetry, Science Fiction, Fantasy, Social Sciences, Sociology
*Associate Companies:* Servicios Editoriales "Palabra Tras Palabra"
Imprints: Cultura de La Universidad; Pedernal; Ymoescuento
Subsidiaries: Editorial "Palo de Hormigo"
Divisions: Centro de Documentacion de Estudios Literarios
*U.S. Office(s):* Roberto Quezada, 3442 N Delta Ave, Rosemead, CA 91770, United States
   *Fax:* 818-572-0964
Distributed by Oscar de Leon Castillo
Distributor for Artemis y Edimter

**Editorial del Ministerio de Educacion**
15 Ave 3-22, Zona 1, Guatemala

**Pedernal,** *imprint of* Grupo Editorial RIN-78

**Editorial Piedra Santa**
5 Calle, Zona 1, 7-55 Guatemala
SAN: 002-6204
*Tel:* (02) 29053
*E-mail:* piedrasanta.sal@salnet.net
*Key Personnel*
President: Irene Piedra Santa
   *E-mail:* irene_piedra_santa@hotmail.com
Founded: 1947
ISBN Prefix(es): 84-8377; 99922-1; 99922-58
Subsidiaries: Editorial y Libreria Piedra Santa SA de CV
*Bookshop(s):* 11 Calle 6-50, Zona 1

**Ymoescuento,** *imprint of* Grupo Editorial RIN-78

# Guinea-Bissau

## General Information

*Capital:* Bissau
*Language:* Portuguese (official), Criolo, Tribal Languages
*Religion:* Indigenous Beliefs (65%), Muslim (30%), Christian (5%)
*Population:* 1 million
*Currency:* Peso (12,068 = $1 US)
*Copyright:* Berne (see Copyright Conventions, pg xi)

**Instituto Nacional de Estudos e Pesquisa (INEP)**
PO Box 112, Bairro Cobornel, Bissau
*Tel:* 21 17 15; 21 44 97; 21 13 01 *Fax:* 25 11 25
*Web Site:* www.inep.gov.br
*Key Personnel*
Dir: Mamadu Jao *E-mail:* mama_jao@hotmail.com
Founded: 1984
Subjects: Agriculture, Anthropology, Developing Countries, Environmental Studies, Health, Nutrition, History, Social Sciences, Sociology, Technology

# Guyana

## General Information

*Capital:* Georgetown
*Language:* English & Amerindian dialects
*Religion:* Christian, Hindu, Islamic

*Population:* 739,000
*Shop Hours:* 0800-1130, 1300-1600 Monday-Friday; 0800-1130 Saturday
*Currency:* 100 cents = 1 Guyana dollar
*Export/Import Information:* No tariff on books. Only advertising of commercial value, subject to duty. There are numerous businesses that import books. Import license required. Nominal exchange controls.
*Copyright:* Berne (see Copyright Conventions, pg xi)

**Amerindian Research Unit**
University of Guyana, PO Box 101110, Georgetown
*Tel:* (02) 4930 *Fax:* (02) 54885
*Web Site:* www.wisard.org

**Caribbean Community Secretariat**
Bank of Guyana Bldg, Ave of the Republic, PO Box 10827, Georgetown
*Tel:* (02) 26-9280; (02) 26-9281; (02) 26-9282; (02) 26-9283; (02) 26-9284; (02) 26-9285; (02) 26-9286; (02) 26-9287; (02) 26-9288; (02) 26-9289 *Fax:* (02) 26-7816; (02) 25-7341; (02) 25-8031
*E-mail:* carisec1@caricom.org; carisec2@caricom.org; carisec3@caricom.org
*Web Site:* www.caricom.org *Cable:* CARIBSEC GUYANA
*Key Personnel*
Senior Project Officer (Documentation Center): Maureen Newton
Founded: 1973
Regional integration movement whose ultimate goal is the improvement of the standard of living of all peoples in the Community. At present the Community has 14 member states. The Secretariat is the administrative arm of the Community.
ISBN Prefix(es): 976-600
Total Titles: 24 Print; 1 CD-ROM

**Guyana Community Based Rehabilitation Progeamme**
c/o European Union, 72 High St, Georgetown
*Tel:* (022) 64004 *Fax:* (022) 62615
Founded: 1986
Subjects: Child Care & Development, Developing Countries, Disability, Special Needs, Education
ISBN Prefix(es): 976-8107

**The Hamburgh Register+**
c/o Walter Roth Museum of Anthropology, 61 Main St, Georgetown
Mailing Address: PO Box 10187, Georgetown
*Tel:* (02) 258486 *Fax:* (02) 258511
*E-mail:* wrma@sdup.org.gy
*Key Personnel*
Contact: Jennifer Wishart
Founded: 1996
Subjects: Anthropology, Archaeology
ISBN Prefix(es): 976-8152

**New Guyana Co Ltd**
Lot 8, Industrial Site, Ruimveldt, Georgetown
Mailing Address: PO Box 101088
*Tel:* (02) 262471 *Cable:* NEWCO GEORGETOWN GUYANA
Printers of Mirror Newspaper.
ISBN Prefix(es): 976-8000

**Roraima Publishers Ltd**
76 Robb St, Lacytown, Georgetown
Mailing Address: PO Box 10322, Georgetown
*Tel:* (02) 2-73551; (02) 2-2363; (02) 2-5057 *Fax:* (02) 62319; (02) 58844
*E-mail:* roraima-distributors@solutions2000.net
*Key Personnel*
Man Dir: David Yhann
Founded: 1994

Subjects: Fiction, Nonfiction (General), Guyanese Works
ISBN Prefix(es): 976-8147
*Associate Companies:* Roraima Distributors

# Haiti

## General Information

*Capital:* Port-au-Prince
*Language:* French and Creole
*Religion:* Predominantly Roman Catholic (about 75%)
*Population:* 6.4 million
*Bank Hours:* 0900-1300 Monday-Friday
*Currency:* 100 centimes = 1 gourde. US currency is widely used
*Export/Import Information:* Books charged ad valorem, children's picture books per kilo net. Advertising matter under 1 kilo gross weight duty-free. No import licenses or exchange controls, other than occasional exchange rationing, leading to delays.
*Copyright:* UCC (see Copyright Conventions, pg xi)

**Editions Caraibes SA**
Lalue, Port-au-Prince
Mailing Address: PO Box 2013, Port-au-Prince
*Tel:* 23179
*Telex:* ITT 2030198
*Key Personnel*
Contact: Pierre J Elie
Founded: 1973
Subjects: Agriculture, Business, English as a Second Language, History, Marketing, Physics
Distributor for L'Ecole SA; Hatier International; LeRobert; LaRousse

**Deschamps Imprimerie**
Rue Jean Gilles Varneux, Port-au-Prince
Mailing Address: PO Box 164, Port-au-Prince
*Tel:* 2461 905; 2501 474; 56-3853; 56-2253 *Fax:* 2491 225
*E-mail:* henrid@acn2.net
*Key Personnel*
Man Dir: Jacques Deschamps
Editorial Dir: Henri R Deschamps; Mael Fouchard
Production Dir: Claude Deschamps; Wilhelm Frisch, Jr
Financial Dir: Jacques Deschamps, Jr
Sales Dir: Peter J Frisch
Read extensively in English & French.
Subjects: Education, Fiction, Literature, Literary Criticism, Essays, Religion - Other
ISBN Prefix(es): 99935-0
Divisions: Imprimerie Henri Deschamps

**Editions du Soleil**
Rue du Centre, Port-au-Prince
Mailing Address: PO Box 2471, Port-au-Prince
*Tel:* (01) 23147
*Telex:* Ppbooth 2030001 attn Lisocial *Cable:* LISOCIAL
*Key Personnel*
Contact: Edouard A Tardieu
Founded: 1952
Subjects: Education

**Theodor (Imprimerie)**
rue Dantes Destouches, Port-au-Prince
Subjects: Fiction, History, Literature, Literary Criticism, Essays

# Holy See (Vatican City State)

## General Information

*Language:* Italian and Latin
*Religion:* Roman Catholic
*Population:* 802
*Currency:* Vatican lira = Italian lira. Italian currency is used
*Copyright:* UCC, Berne (see Copyright Conventions, pg xi)

**Biblioteca Apostolica Vaticana** (Vatican Apostolic Library)
Cortile del Belvedere, 00120 Citta del Vaticano
*Tel:* (06) 6987 9402 *Fax:* (06) 6988 4795
*E-mail:* bav@vatlib.it
*Telex:* 2024 Dirgental VA
*Key Personnel*
Dir & Chief Executive: Don Raffaele Farina
Subjects: Art, History, Language Arts, Linguistics, Law, Philosophy, Theology
ISBN Prefix(es): 88-210

**Archivio Segreto Vaticano**
Cortile del Belvedre, 00120 Citta del Vaticano
*Tel:* (06) 69883314 *Fax:* (06) 69885574
ISBN Prefix(es): 88-85042

**LEV**, *imprint of* Libreria Editrice Vaticana

**Pontificia Academia Scientiarum** (The Pontifical Academy of Sciences)
Casina Pio IV, V-00120 Vatican City S
*Tel:* 0669883195 *Fax:* 0669885218
*E-mail:* academy.sciences@acdscience.va
*Web Site:* www.vatican.va/roman_curia/pontifical_academies/index_it.htm
*Telex:* 2024
*Key Personnel*
President: Prof Nicola Cabibbo
Founded: 1936
"To promote the progress of the mathematical, physical & natural sciences & the study of epistemological problems relating thereto".
Subjects: Biological Sciences, Chemistry, Chemical Engineering, Earth Sciences, Environmental Studies, Mathematics, Medicine, Nursing, Dentistry, Physics, Science (General)
ISBN Prefix(es): 88-7761
Number of titles published annually: 3 Print
Total Titles: 100 Print

**Scuola Vaticana Paleografia - Scuola Vaticana di Paleografia Diplomatica e Archivistica**
Cortile del Belvedere, 00120 Citt a del Vaticano
*Tel:* (06) 69883595 *Fax:* (06) 69881377
*E-mail:* pagano@librs6k.vatlib.it
*Key Personnel*
Dir: Rev Sergio B Pagano *E-mail:* pagano@librs6k.vatlib.it
Founded: 1884
Subjects: Human Relations, Language Arts, Linguistics, Library & Information Sciences
ISBN Prefix(es): 88-85054

**Libreria Editrice Vaticana+**
Via Della Tipografia, 00120 Vatican City
*Tel:* (06) 698-85003 *Fax:* (06) 698-84716
*Telex:* 5042024 Dirgentel Va
*Key Personnel*
Dir: Don Nicolo Suffi
Founded: 1926

Subjects: Art, History, Literature, Literary Criticism, Essays, Philosophy, Religion - Other, Theology
ISBN Prefix(es): 88-209
Imprints: LEV

# Honduras

## General Information

*Capital:* Tegucigalpa
*Language:* Spanish (English on northern coast)
*Religion:* Predominantly Roman Catholic
*Population:* 5.0 million
*Bank Hours:* 0900-1200, 1400-1630 Monday-Friday
*Shop Hours:* Tegucigalpa: 0800-1800, 1330-1800 Monday-Friday; 0800-1200 Saturday; San Pedro Sula: 0700-1200, 1400-1900 Monday-Friday; 0800-1200 Saturday
*Currency:* 100 centavos = 1 lempira
*Export/Import Information:* Member of the Central American Common Market but has applied tariffs to imports from other CACM countries since December 1970. No tariff on books. Duty on catalogues is per kilo. No import licenses. No exchange controls.
*Copyright:* Berne, Buenos Aires (see Copyright Conventions, pg xi)

### Editorial Guaymuras+
Calle Adolfo Zuniga, Bo La Ronda, PO Box 1843, Tegucigalpa
Mailing Address: Apdo Postal 1843, Tegucigalpa
*Tel:* 237 54 33 *Fax:* 238 45 78
*E-mail:* editorial@sigmanet.hn
*Key Personnel*
Dir: Isolda Arita Melzer
Manager: Rosendo Antunez *Tel:* 2375433
Founded: 1980
Also acts as printer, bookseller & distributor.
Membership(s): Library Group of America.
Subjects: Anthropology, Education, Environmental Studies, Ethnicity, Government, Political Science, History, Language Arts, Linguistics, Social Sciences, Sociology
ISBN Prefix(es): 99926-15
Number of titles published annually: 54 Print
Total Titles: 320 Print
Distributed by Abya-Yala de Ecuador; Arco Iris de El Salvador; Libros sin Fronteras (USA); Piedra Santa de Guatemala
Distributor for Centro Editorial; ENLACE y Nuevos Libros de Nicaragua; Libreria de la UNAH; Roxsil; UCA de El Salvador
*Bookshop(s):* Libreria Guaymuras, Ave Cervantes No 1055, Tegucigalpa *Tel:* 2224140

### Editorial Nuevo Continente
Ave Cervantes, Tegucigalpa
*Tel:* 22-5073
*Key Personnel*
Dir: Leticia Oyuela

### Editorial Universitaria
c/o Universidad de Honduras, Tegucigalpa
Mailing Address: PO Box 3560, Tegucigalpa
*Tel:* 312110
*Telex:* 1289

# Hong Kong

## General Information

*Language:* English and Chinese (Cantonese Chinese community)
*Religion:* Predominately Buddhist, also some Confucianism, Islamic, Hinduism & Daoism
*Population:* 5.8 million
*Bank Hours:* 0900-1640 Monday-Friday; 0900-1200 Saturday
*Shop Hours:* 1000-2000 Monday-Saturday
*Currency:* 100 cents = 1 Hong Kong dollar
*Export/Import Information:* No tariffs on books and advertising. No import licenses required. No exchange controls.
*Copyright:* Berne, UCC (see Copyright Conventions, pg xi)

### Adsale Publishing Co Ltd
Units 1101-1106, 11/F, Island Place Tower, 510 King's Rd, North Point, Hong Kong
*Tel:* 2811 8897 *Fax:* 2516 5024
*E-mail:* publicity@adsale.com.hk
*Web Site:* www.adsale.com.hk
*Key Personnel*
Contact: Annie Chu; Ms P Y Ho
Publish Chinese & English industrial trade magazines to foster trade links between foreign companies & China.
Subjects: Automotive, Technology (packaging, plastics, rubber, textile)
ISBN Prefix(es): 962-7036
Number of titles published annually: 26 Print; 4 Online
Total Titles: 624 Print; 8 Online
*U.S. Office(s):* 21070 Homestead Rd, Suite 100, Cupertino, CA 95014, United States, Contact: Monica Kan *Tel:* 408-737-2820 *Fax:* 408-737-2369 *E-mail:* info@us.adsale.com.hk

### Asia Pacific Communications Ltd
Fook Lee Community Centre, Suite 2803, 33 Lockhart Rd, Wanchai
*Tel:* 2861 0102 *Fax:* 2529 6816
*E-mail:* asiapac@attglobal.net
*Key Personnel*
Editor & Publisher: Kathleen Ng
Founded: 1991
Subjects: Finance, Asian Private Equity, Venture Capital
ISBN Prefix(es): 962-85096
Subsidiaries: Institute of Asian Private Equity Investment

### Asia 2000 Ltd+
Tung Yiu Commercial Bldg, 5th floor, 31A Wyndham St Central, Hong Kong
*Tel:* 2530 1409 *Fax:* 2526 1107
*E-mail:* info@asia2000.com.hk; editor@asia2000.com.hk
*Web Site:* www.asia2000.com.hk
*Key Personnel*
Publisher: Michael Morrow *E-mail:* mmorrow@asia2000.com.hk
Marketing, Distribution Manager: Edowan Bersma
Founded: 1980
Independent publisher of English language books
Distributor for overseas publishers.
Subjects: Art, Asian Studies, Fiction, Government, Political Science, Photography, Regional Interests
ISBN Prefix(es): 962-7160; 962-8783
*Parent Company:* Asia 2000 Group
*Associate Companies:* Manager Media, China
Subsidiaries: Asia Inc
Distributor for St Martens Press; World Bank; World Trade Press

**B & I Publication Co Ltd**, see Business & Industrial Publication Co Ltd

### Benefit Publishing Co+
PO Box 92310, Tsim Sha Tsui Post Office, Kowloon
Founded: 1994
Subjects: Art, Film, Video, Music, Dance, Publishing & Book Trade Reference
ISBN Prefix(es): 962-598
*Book Club(s):* Hong Kong Book & Magazine Trade Association Ltd

### Book Marketing Ltd+
North Point Industrial Bldg, Flat A, 17F, 499 King's Rd, North Point, Hong Kong
*Tel:* (02) 5620121 *Fax:* (02) 5650187
*Key Personnel*
Man Dir: Bernard King Sum Chiu
Founded: 1973
Wholesaler.
Subjects: English as a Second Language, Self-Help
ISBN Prefix(es): 962-211
*Associate Companies:* Leo Publications Ltd, 499 King's Rd, 17F, Flat A, Hong Kong

### Breakthrough Ltd - Breakthrough Publishers+
Breakthrough Village, 11th floor, 33A Kung Kok Shan Rd, New Territories
*Tel:* 2632 0257 *Fax:* 2632 0288
*Web Site:* www.teachlikethis.com
*Key Personnel*
Contact: Karen Chan
Founded: 1973
Membership(s): Hong Kong Book & Magazine Trade Association Ltd, Hong Kong Article Numbering Association.
Subjects: Fiction, How-to, Human Relations, Humor, Literature, Literary Criticism, Essays, Poetry
ISBN Prefix(es): 962-264; 962-8791
*Warehouse:* Flats A, S-V, 14/F, Haribest Industrial Bldg, Shatin Town Lot 173, Fo Tan, Shatin

### Business & Industrial Publication Co Ltd+
China Overseas Bldg, Rm B-C 5/F, 139 Hennessy Rd, Wan Chai, Hong Kong
*Tel:* 25273377 *Fax:* 28667732
*Key Personnel*
Dir: Alan Kwok
Founded: 1974
Subjects: Mechanical Engineering, Technology
ISBN Prefix(es): 962-7701
*Associate Companies:* Business & Industrial Trade Fairs Ltd

### Butterworths Hong Kong
12/F, Hennessey Centre, 500 Hennessey Rd, Causeway Bay
*Tel:* 2965-1400 *Fax:* 2976-0840
*E-mail:* customer.care@butterworths-hk.com
*Web Site:* www.butterworths-hk.com
*Key Personnel*
Commissioning Editor: Anisha Sakhrani
Senior Editor (Hong Kong Cases): Victoria Lai
Advertising Sales Manager: Simon King
General Manager, Customer Service: Wong Wai Cheng
Subjects: Law
*Parent Company:* Reed Elsevier
*Associate Companies:* Butterworths India, 14th floor, Vijaya Bldg, 17, Barakhamba Rd, New Delhi 110001, India, Publishing Manager: Ambika Nair *Tel:* (011) 373 9614 *Fax:* (011) 332 6456 *Web Site:* www.butterworths-india.com; Malayan Law Journal Sdn Bhd, Unit A-5-1, 5th floor, Wisman HB, Megan Phileo Ave, 12 Jalan Yap Kwan Seng, 50450 Kuala Lumpur, Malaysia, Managing Editor, New Product Development: Julie Anne Thomas *Tel:* (03) 2162-

2882 *Fax:* (03) 2162-3811 *Web Site:* www. mlj.com.my; Butterworths Singapore, No 1 Temasek Ave, 17-01 Millenia Tower, Singapore 039192, Singapore, Regional Publishing Dir: Conita Leung *Tel:* 336 9661 *Fax:* 336 9662 *Web Site:* www.butterworths.com.sg

**Celeluck Co Ltd+**
Rm 603, Opulent Bldg, 402 Hennessy Rd, Wan Chai
*Tel:* 2893 9197; 2893 9147 *Fax:* 2891 5591
*E-mail:* open@open.com.hk
*Web Site:* www.open.com.hk
*Key Personnel*
Chief Editor: Jin Zhong
Subjects: Asian Studies, Government, Political Science, History, Journalism, Specializes in China affairs
ISBN Prefix(es): 962-7934

**CFW Publications Ltd+**
130 Connaught Rd Central, Hong Kong
*Tel:* 2554 3004 *Fax:* 2543 8007
Founded: 1979
Subjects: Cookery, Travel
ISBN Prefix(es): 962-7031

**China Express Media Ltd**
Flat/Room 07-10, 26F, North Point MLC Millennia Plaza, 663 King's Rd, Hong Kong
*Tel:* 2575 7288 *Fax:* 2575 7088
*E-mail:* kcchan@ossima.com
ISBN Prefix(es): 962-86560

**Chinese Christian Literature Council Ltd+**
Flat A, 4/F, 138 Nathan Rd, Kowloon
*Tel:* 2367 8031
*Key Personnel*
Contact: Mr Sau-Chung Fung
Administration Secretary: Ms Yvonne Mak
*E-mail:* yvonne@cclc.biz.com.hk
An interdenominational publishing house-mainly in the Chinese Language & also a nonprofit making organization.
Membership(s): WACC; UK.
Subjects: Literature, Literary Criticism, Essays, Music, Dance, Religion - Protestant, Theology
ISBN Prefix(es): 962-294
*Bookshop(s):* 10 Tung Fong St G/F, Kowloon
*Warehouse:* 77 Wong Chuk Yeung St, Room 702, Yan Hing Centre, Fo Tan, Shatin

**The Chinese University Press+**
The Chinese University of Hong Kong, Sha Tin, New Territories
*Tel:* 2609 6508 *Fax:* 2603 6692; 2603 7355
*E-mail:* cup@cuhk.edu.hk
*Web Site:* www.cuhk.edu.hk/cupress.w1.htm; www.chineseupress.com
*Telex:* 50301 cuhk hx *Cable:* SINOVERSITY
*Key Personnel*
Dir: Steven K Luk *Tel:* 2609 6460
*E-mail:* stevenkluk@cuhk.edu.hk
Sales, Rights & Permissions & Business Manager: Angelina Wong *Tel:* 2609 6500
*E-mail:* laifunwong@cuhk.edu.hk
Production Manager: Kingsley Ma *Tel:* 2609 6467 *E-mail:* kwaihungma@cuhk.edu.hk
Editorial: Esther Tsang *Tel:* 2609 6499
*E-mail:* esthertsang@cuhk.edu.hk
Founded: 1977
Membership(s): Association of American University Press; Association for Asian Studies; International Association of Scholarly Publishers; Society of Scholarly Publishing.
Subjects: Art, Asian Studies, Business, Child Care & Development, Education, Geography, Geology, Government, Political Science, History, Journalism, Language Arts, Linguistics, Law, Literature, Literary Criticism, Essays,

Philosophy, Psychology, Psychiatry, Science (General), Social Sciences, Sociology
ISBN Prefix(es): 962-201; 962-996
Number of titles published annually: 60 Print
Total Titles: 900 Print; 4 CD-ROM; 2 Audio
Distributed by Columbia University Press (North America); The Eurospan Group (UK, Europe, Middle East, Africa & Central Asia)
Distributor for The Chinese University of Hong Kong
Foreign Rep(s): Columbia University Press (North America); The Eurospan Group (Africa, Europe, Middle East, Central Asia)

**Chopsticks Publications Ltd+**
8A Soares Ave, Ground floor, Kowloon
*Tel:* 2336-8433 *Fax:* 2338-1462
*E-mail:* chopsticks1971@netvigator.com
*Key Personnel*
Manager: Caroline Au-Yeung
Founder & Dir, Rights & Permissions: Cecilia Jennie Au-Yang *E-mail:* cauyeung@netvigator.com
Sales, Production & Publicity: Chiu Mei Au-Yeung
Founded: 1971
Train caterers in the art of Chinese cooking. Offers classes that last one, four, eight & 13 weeks as well as a 17-week teacher training course.
Membership(s): International Association of Culinary Professionals, USA; Specialize in Oriental cuisine.
Subjects: Cookery, Oriental Cuisine, Dim Sum, Health Cookery
ISBN Prefix(es): 962-7018
*Associate Companies:* Cherrytree Press Ltd
Distributed by Gazelle Book Services Ltd (UK)

**Christian Communications Ltd**
3/F, 128 Castle Peak Rd, Kowloon
*Tel:* 2725-8558 *Fax:* 2386-1804
*Web Site:* www.ccfellow.org
*Key Personnel*
General Secretary: Thomas Tang
Founded: 1971
Also acts as bookseller & printing service.
Subjects: Biblical Studies, Religion - Protestant
ISBN Prefix(es): 962-202; 962-8740; 962-8810
*U.S. Office(s):* 1711 Branham Lane, Suite A-4A, San Jose, CA 95118, United States
*Bookshop(s):* 1/F 46 Morrison Hill Rd, Wan Chai; 2/F Hing Pong Commercial Bldg, 749A Nathan Rd, Kowloon; 1/F Kolok Bldg, 722 Nathan Rd, Kowloon; 1/F Hong Lok House, 475 Nathan Rd, Kowloon
*Shipping Address:* Block D, 18/F, Tsuen Tung Factory Bldg, 38-40 Chai Wai Kok St, Tsuen Wan, New Territories
*Warehouse:* Block D, 18/F, Tsuen Tung Factory Bldg, 38-40 Chai Wai Kok St, Tsuen Wan, New Territories
*Orders to:* Block D, 18/F, Tsuen Tung Factory Bldg, 38-40 Chai Wai Kok St, Tsuen Wan, New Territories

**Chung Hwa Book Co (HK) Ltd+**
Unit 1, 2F Fu Hang Bldg, One Hok Yuen St E, Hung Hom, Kowloon
*Tel:* 2715 0176 *Fax:* 2713 8202; 2713 4675
*E-mail:* info@chunghwabook.com.hk; pub-dept@chunghwabook.com.hk
*Web Site:* www.chunghwabook.com.hk *Cable:* 5494
*Key Personnel*
Man Dir & Editor-in-Chief: Kwok-fai Chan
Publishing Manager: Shirley Cheung
Sales Manager: Belgrid Wong
Founded: 1927
Membership(s): Hong Kong Publishing Professionals Society Ltd; Hong Kong Publishing Federation Ltd (permanent member).

Subjects: Antiques, Art, Asian Studies, Business, Career Development, Computer Science, English as a Second Language, History, Language Arts, Linguistics, Literature, Literary Criticism, Essays, Management, Marketing, Philosophy, Religion - Buddhist, Self-Help, Social Sciences, Sociology
ISBN Prefix(es): 962-231; 962-8820
*Parent Company:* Sino United Publishing (Holdings) Ltd
Divisions: Publishing, Marketing & Sales, Retail
Distributor for Longman Asia Ltd; Open Learning Univeristy of Hong Kong (Macau & Hong Kong); Oxford University Press (Hong Kong); Publications (Holding) Ltd; University of H K Press
*Bookshop(s):* 5B Ma Hang Chung Rd, 2nd floor, Tokwawan, Kowloon; Reader's Service Centre, 450-452 Nathan Rd, Kowloon; Mongkok Branch, 740A Nathan Rd, Kowloon; 88 Fu Yan St, Kwun Tong, Kowloon; Tsuen Wan Branch, 245 Sha Tsui Rd, Tsuen Wan, NT

**Commercial Press (Hong Kong) Ltd+**
8/F, Eastern Central Plaza, 3 Yiu Hing Rd, Shau Kei Wan
*Tel:* 25651371 *Fax:* 25651113; 25654277
*E-mail:* info@commercialpress.com.hk
*Web Site:* www.commercialpress.com.hk
*Telex:* 86564 Cmprs HX *Cable:* COMPRESS
*Key Personnel*
Man Dir & Chief Editor: Chan Man Hung
Deputy General Manager: Chan Kwok Fai
Assistant General Manager: Leung Chung Ho; Tseng Kwok Tai
Marketing Manager & Copyright Controller: Charlemagne Choi
Production Manager: Yam Kin Wah
Founded: 1897
Subjects: Art, Education, Ethnicity, How-to, Language Arts, Linguistics, Medicine, Nursing, Dentistry
ISBN Prefix(es): 962-07
Subsidiaries: Hong Kong Educational Publishing Co
*Branch Office(s)*
KL Commercial Book Malaysia Sdn. Bhd Co, Malaysia
Commercial Press Ltd, Republic of Singapore, Singapore
*Bookshop(s):* Book Centre, 9-15 Yee Wo St, Causeway Bay, China *Tel:* (05) 8908028 *Fax:* (05) 8951027; Central Branch & Stamp Centre, 28 Wellington St, Central, China *Tel:* (05) 5250315 *Fax:* (05) 8450035; Shatin Book Plaza, 165 Level 1 & 266-270 Level 2, Phase 1, Shatin, China; North Point Branch, 395 King's Rd, North Point *Tel:* (05) 5620266 *Fax:* (05) 5656763; Mongkok Branch, 608 Nathan Rd, Kowloon, China *Tel:* (05) 3848228 *Fax:* (05) 7703861; Tuen Mun Branch, G/F, Yaohan Stores, Tuen Mun Town Plaza, NT, Tuen Mun, NT, China *Tel:* (05) 4589332 *Fax:* (05) 4591925; Kornhill Branch, 3/F, Jusco Stores, Quarry Bay, China *Tel:* (05) 5600238 *Fax:* (05) 5679801; Tai Po Branch, 212-215, 1/F Tai Wo Shopping Mall, Tai Po, NT, China *Tel:* (05) 6502628; New Town Plaza, Shatin, China *Tel:* (05) 6931933 *Fax:* (05) 6912064
*Orders to:* 2/F, Heng Ngai Jewelry Centre, 4 Hok Yuen St E, Hunghom, Kowloon

**Courseguides International Ltd**
1505, Seaview Centre, 139-141 Hoi Bun Rd, Kwun Tong, Kowloon
*Tel:* 2737 3322 *Fax:* 2793 1188
*Key Personnel*
Publisher: T P C Street
Founded: 1982
Subjects: Sports, Athletics
Subsidiaries: Courseguides International (UK) Ltd

**Design Human Resources Training & Development+**
10C, Mountain View Ct, Discovery Bay, Lantau Island, Hong Kong
*Tel:* 29877018 *Fax:* 29877018
*Key Personnel*
Author & International Rights: Robert Wright
  *E-mail:* wright@hkusua.hku.hk
Subjects: Management, Self-Help
ISBN Prefix(es): 962-85036
Distributor for Asia 2000
*Orders to:* Robert Wright School of Business, University of Hong Kong, 7/F Men Wah Complex, Pokfulam Rd, Hong Kong

**The Dharmasthiti Buddist Institute Ltd+**
Block A, 2nd floor, Cambridge Court, 84 Waterloo Rd, Kowloon
*Tel:* 2760 8878 *Fax:* 2760 1223
*Key Personnel*
Contact: Ms Lai Jill; Cho Karen
Founded: 1982
A registered nonprofit, religious & cultural organization; also participates in cultural education.
Subjects: Education, Ethnicity, Philosophy, Regional Interests, Religion - Buddhist, Academic, Chinese Culture, Life Growth
ISBN Prefix(es): 962-7541

**Easy Finder Ltd**
10 Tseung Kwan O Industrial Estate W, 8 Chun Ying St, Tseung Kwan O
*Tel:* 2990 7100 *Fax:* 2623 9315
*E-mail:* easybook@nextmedia.com.hk
*Web Site:* www.nextmedia.com.hk
ISBN Prefix(es): 962-85324; 962-85533; 962-8751

**Economy and Press**
A1, 5/F, Lo Yong Court Commercial Bldg, 220 Lockhart Road, Room 210, Wanchai
*Tel:* 28917556
ISBN Prefix(es): 962-7277

**The Educational Publishing House Ltd**
16/F Tsuen Wan Industrial Centre, 220-248 Texaco Rd, Tsuen Wan, New Territories
*Tel:* 24088801 *Fax:* 2810 4201
*Telex:* 35330 eph hx
ISBN Prefix(es): 962-12
*Associate Companies:* Fook Hing Offset Printing Co Ltd; The World Publishing Co; Kam Pui Enterprises Ltd; The Seashore Publishing Co; Harris Book Co Ltd; Hong Kong Housing Projects Corp Ltd; Pan-Lloyds (HK) Ltd

**Electronic Technology Publishing Co Ltd+**
9/F, Room 1, 15 Shing Yip St, Kwun Tong, Kowloon
*Tel:* 2342 8298; 2342 8299; 2342 9845 *Fax:* 2341 4247
*E-mail:* info@electronictechnology.com
*Web Site:* www.electronictechnology.com
*Key Personnel*
General Manager: Peter Luk
Founded: 1969
Branch offices located in China & Taiwan, Province of China.
Subjects: Communications, Computer Science, Electronics, Electrical Engineering, How-to, Marketing, Radio, TV, Technology
ISBN Prefix(es): 962-7007
Subsidiaries: Modern Electronic & Computing Publishing Co Ltd

**FormAsia Books Ltd+**
706 Yu Yuet Lai Bldg, 45 Wyndham St, Central Hong Kong
*Tel:* (02) 2525 8572 *Fax:* (02) 2522 4234
*E-mail:* formasia@hkstar.com
*Web Site:* www.formasiabooks.com

*Key Personnel*
Dir: Frank Fischbeck
Founded: 1985
Essentially Hong Kong.
Subjects: Art, History, Specialize in Chinese colonial arts, culture & history
ISBN Prefix(es): 962-7283
Distributed by Weatherhill

**Friends of the Earth (Charity) Ltd**
53-55 Lockhart Road, 2/F, Wan Chai
*Tel:* 2528 5588 *Fax:* 2529 2777
*E-mail:* foehk@hk.super.net
Subjects: Agriculture, Energy, Environmental Studies, Government, Political Science, Health, Nutrition
ISBN Prefix(es): 962-8119

**Geocarto International Centre**
Wah Ming Centre, 2nd floor, Rooms 16 & 17, 421 Queen's Rd W, Hong Kong
*Tel:* 2546-4262 *Fax:* 2559-3419
*E-mail:* geocarto@geocarto.com
*Web Site:* www.geocarto.com
*Key Personnel*
Contact: K N Au
Subjects: Earth Sciences, Geography, Geology
ISBN Prefix(es): 962-8226

**Good Earth Publishing Co Ltd**
Flat A 10/F Chiap King Industrial Bldg, 714 Prince Edward Rd, San Po Kong, Kowloon
*Tel:* 2338 6103 *Fax:* 2338 3610
*Key Personnel*
General Manager: Yu Chen Fan
ISBN Prefix(es): 962-7878

**Hong Kong China Tourism Press**
24/F Westlands Centre, 20 Westlands Rd, Quarry Bay
*Tel:* 2561 8001 *Fax:* 2561 8196
*E-mail:* edit-e@hkctp.com.hk
*Web Site:* www.hkctp.com.hk
*Key Personnel*
Editor-in-Chief: Wang Miao
Vice General Manager & International Rights: Catherine Lee
Founded: 1980
Subjects: Travel
ISBN Prefix(es): 962-7799; 962-7166; 962-8746
Subsidiaries: HK China Tourism Company Ltd

**Hong Kong Publishing Co Ltd**
307 Yue Yuet Lai Bldg, 43-45 Wyndham St, Central Hong Kong
*Tel:* 25259053
*Telex:* 78018 stkhx hx *Cable:* Hkpublish
*Key Personnel*
Man Dir: Dean Barrett
Editor: Julia Birch
Founded: 1975
Subjects: Asian Studies, Fiction, Travel
ISBN Prefix(es): 962-7035

**Hong Kong University Press+**
14/F Hing Wai Centre, 7 Tin Wan Praya Rd, Aberdeen
*Tel:* 2550 2703 *Fax:* 2875 0734
*E-mail:* upweb@hkucc.hku.hk
*Web Site:* www.hkupress.org *Cable:* University, Hong Kong
*Key Personnel*
Publisher, Rights & Permissions: Colin Day
Editor: Dennis Cheung
Marketing: Winnie Chau *E-mail:* hkupress@hkucc.hku.hk
Founded: 1956
Specialize in academic Publishing in Chinese & English.
Subjects: Anthropology, Art, Asian Studies, Behavioral Sciences, Biography, Biological Sci-

ences, Child Care & Development, Communications, Criminology, Disability, Special Needs, Education, English as a Second Language, Environmental Studies, Film, Video, Geography, Geology, Government, Political Science, History, Labor, Industrial Relations, Language Arts, Linguistics, Law, Library & Information Sciences, Medicine, Nursing, Dentistry, Natural History, Philosophy, Public Administration, Real Estate, Religion - Buddhist, Social Sciences, Sociology, Women's Studies
ISBN Prefix(es): 962-209
Total Titles: 250 Print
Distributed by Apac Publishers Services Pte Ltd (Singapore); Eleanor Brasch Enterprises (Australia & New Zealand); The Eurospan Group (Europe); University of Washington Press (USA)
Distributor for Centre of Asian Studies at the University of Hong Kong (Hong Kong, Macau, UK); Comparative Education Research Centre (at the University of Hong Kong); Department of Comparative Literature at the University of Hong Kong (at the University of Hong Kong); Department of Social Work & Social Administration at the University of Hong Kong (at the University of Hong Kong); INSTEP Faculty of Education (at the University of Hong Kong); Oriental Ceramic Society of Hong Kong (Worldwide); University Museum & Art Gallery at the University of Hong Kong (Worldwide); Zed Books Ltd (UK, Hong Kong & Macau)

**Island Press+**
3/F, Flat A, 33 Hill Rd, Hong Kong
*Tel:* 28588176 *Fax:* 2482 9889
*Key Personnel*
Man Dir: Ho Leung-mau
Founded: 1983 (originally founded under the names Li Weijia, Lee Chik-Yuet, Ho Leung-mau)
Subjects: Education, Environmental Studies, Journalism, Literature, Literary Criticism, Essays, Publishing & Book Trade Reference, Travel
ISBN Prefix(es): 962-431

**Joint Publishing (HK) Co Ltd**
10/F, 9 Queen Victoria St, Central Hong Kong
Mailing Address: 10/F, Tsuen Wan Industrial, Bldg, 220-248 Texaco Rd, Tsuen Wan, New Territories
*Tel:* 2523 0105 *Fax:* 2525 8355
*E-mail:* jpchk@hk.super.net
*Web Site:* www.jointpublishing.com *Cable:* JOINT PCO
*Key Personnel*
Man Dir: Mr Zhao Bin
Deputy General Manager: Mr Au Kang Lam
Assistant General Manager: Mr Li Chi Kin; Mr Ho Pui Tong
Dir & Deputy Chief Editor: Mr Li Xin
Rights & Permissions: Judith Luk
Bookshop Manager: Mr Wong Ming Pang
Founded: 1948
Overseas Office: Guangzhou, China.
Subjects: Architecture & Interior Design, Art, Asian Studies, Business, Environmental Studies, Film, Video, Finance, Health, Nutrition, History, Language Arts, Linguistics, Law, Literature, Literary Criticism, Essays, Management, Marketing, Medicine, Nursing, Dentistry
ISBN Prefix(es): 962-04
*Parent Company:* Sino United Publishing (Holdings) Ltd
Subsidiaries: JPC Collection Ltd (Flags & Gifts); JPC Data Chu Ltd
*Bookshop(s):* BC & Sino United Publishing (Toronto) Ltd; Eastwind Books & Arts Inc, San Francisco, CA, United States; Foshan H, China; Foshan United Book Co Ltd, China; Guangzhou, China; Joint Publishing Co, Bejing; JPC Bookstore & SUP Bookstore, China;

Kwai Chung; Kwai-Fong Branch; Lam Tin
Branch, Kowloon; Oriental Culture Enterprise,
New York, NY, United States; Readers Ser-
vice Centre, 9/F Chung Sheung Bldg, 9 Queen
Victoria St, Central Hong Kong; Sino United
(Canada) Ltd; Sino United Publishing (LA)
Ltd, Monterey Park, CA, United States; Wham-
poa Branch; Tsuen Wan Cultural Plaza, Tsuen
Wan, New Territories

**Lands Department, Survey & Mapping Office**
Murray Bldg, 14/F, Garden Rd, Central Hong
Kong
*Tel:* 2848 2182 *Fax:* 2521 8726
Subjects: Air photo
ISBN Prefix(es): 962-567

**Lea Publications Ltd+**
499 King's Rd, 17/F, Flat A, North Point, Hong
Kong
*Tel:* 25-620121 *Fax:* 2565 0187
*Key Personnel*
Chairman: Bernard K S Chiu
Founded: 1976
Subjects: English as a Second Language, Fiction
ISBN Prefix(es): 962-213
*Associate Companies:* Book Marketing Ltd
Distributed by Book Marketing Ltd (Hong Kong)

**Ling Kee Publishing Group+**
Top floor, Zung Fu Industrial Bldg, 1067 King's
Rd, Quarry Bay, Hong Kong
*Tel:* 25616151 *Fax:* 2811 1980
*Web Site:* www.lingkee.com *Cable:* BOOKLAND
*Key Personnel*
Founder-owner, Chairman & Chief Executive:
Bak Ling Au
Man Dir: Albert Au
Founded: 1945
Membership(s): Hong Kong Educational Publish-
ers Association.
Subjects: Antiques, Education, English as a Sec-
ond Language, History, How-to, Nonfiction
(General)
ISBN Prefix(es): 962-605; 962-608; 962-609;
962-610
*Parent Company:* Ling Kee Group Ltd
Subsidiaries: Ling Kee Publishing Co Ltd; Ling
Kee Book Store Ltd; Unicorn Books Ltd; Uni-
corn Book (S) Ltd; Ling Lee Publishing Co (S)
Ltd; Ling Kee (UK) Ltd; Ward Lock Educa-
tional Co Ltd; BLA Publishing Ltd; Thames
Head Publishers; Unicorn Publications Inc;
Ling Kee Publishing Co Inc
Distributor for Encyclopedia of China Publishing
House (Beijing, China)
*Showroom(s):* 755 Nathan Rd, Kowloon
*Bookshop(s):* Ling Kee Bookstore Ltd, 127-131
Des Voeux Rd, Central Hong Kong *Tel:* 2545
1540 *Fax:* 2541 1383; Ling Kee Bookstore
Ltd, 755 Nathan Rd, Mongkok *Tel:* 2394 1800
*Fax:* 2393 3288

**Steve Lu Publishing Ltd**
Rm 1203, Man Yee Bldg, 60-68 Des Voeux Rd
Central, Hong Kong
*Tel:* 25210681 *Fax:* 28450492
*E-mail:* ltlahk@netvigator.com
*Key Personnel*
Dir: Steve Lu
Subjects: Art, Natural History, Photography,
Travel
ISBN Prefix(es): 962-85043

**Macmillan Publishers (China) Ltd**
Unit 1812, 18/F Paul Y Centre, 51 Hung To Rd,
Kwun Tong, Kowloon
*Tel:* 2811 8781 *Fax:* 2811 0743
*Web Site:* www.macmillan.com.hk
*Key Personnel*
Man Dir: Yiu Hei Kan *E-mail:* yhk@macmillan.
com.hk

Founded: 1969
Subjects: Foreign Countries
ISBN Prefix(es): 962-03
*Parent Company:* Macmillan Publishers Ltd,
United Kingdom

**Med Info Publishing Co**
401 Man Yee Bldg, 60 Des Voeux Rd, C, Hong
Kong
*Tel:* 2522 2713
*Key Personnel*
Sales Manager: Stella Ng
ISBN Prefix(es): 962-363

**Ming Pao Publications Ltd+**
Subsidiary of Ming Pao Enterprise Corp Ltd
Ming Pao Industrial Centre, 15/F, Block A, 18 Ka
Yip St, Hong Kong
*Tel:* 2595 3084 *Fax:* 2898 2646
*E-mail:* geocomm@mingpao.com
*Web Site:* security.mingpao.com/books
*Key Personnel*
General Man & Chief Editor: Mr Poon Yiu Ming
*Tel:* 2595 3318
Dir: Tiong Kiew Chiong
Founded: 1986
Subjects: Biography, Business, Child Care &
Development, Cookery, Economics, Fiction,
Health, Nutrition, Management, Nonfiction
(General), Philosophy, Psychology, Psychiatry,
Regional Interests, Comics, Investment
ISBN Prefix(es): 962-357; 962-973
*Associate Companies:* Ming Pao Magazines
Ltd, Mr Lung King Cheong *Tel:* 2515 5111
*Fax:* 2505 7841 *Web Site:* www.mpweekly.
com; Ming Pao Newspapers Ltd, Mr Che-
ung Kin Bor *Fax:* 2898 3282 *Web Site:* www.
mingpao.com; Yazhou Zhoukan Ltd, Mr Yau
Lop Poon *Fax:* 2505 9662 *Web Site:* www.
yzzk.com
*Book Club(s):* Ming Pao Book Club, Mr Poon
Yiu Ming

**Modern Electronic & Computing Publishing
Co Ltd+**
Blk 1, 9/F, 15 Shing Yip St, Kwun Tong,
Kowloon
*Tel:* 2342 8299 *Fax:* 2341 4247
*E-mail:* info@computertoday.com.hk
*Web Site:* www.computertoday.com.hk
*Key Personnel*
General Manager: Peter Luk *Tel:* 2342 9844
Founded: 1989
Subjects: Communications, Computer Science,
Education, How-to, Microcomputers, Technol-
ogy
ISBN Prefix(es): 962-7007
*Parent Company:* Electronic Technology Publica-
tion Co
*Branch Office(s)*
China
Taiwan, Province of China

**Next Magazine Advertising Ltd**
8 Chun Ying St, TKO Industial Estate West, Tse-
ung Kwan O
*Tel:* 2990-8588 *Fax:* 2623-9278
*E-mail:* subdesk@appledaily.com
*Web Site:* www.nextmedia.com.hk
ISBN Prefix(es): 962-86411

**Peace Book Co Ltd+**
Rm 1502 Wing On House, 71 Des Voeuk Rd C,
Central Hong Kong
*Tel:* 2804-6687 *Fax:* 2804-6409 *Cable:*
PEACEBOOK
*Key Personnel*
Dir: Qian Wangsi
Founded: 1979
Subjects: Asian Studies, Health, Nutrition
ISBN Prefix(es): 962-7176

**Pearson Education China Ltd**
18/F Cornwall House, Taikoo Place, 979 King's
Rd, Quarry Bay
*Tel:* 3181 0000 *Fax:* 2565 7440
*E-mail:* info@ilongman.com
*Web Site:* www.pearsoned.com.hk
*Key Personnel*
President, North Asia: T C Goh
Finance Dir, North Asia: Marion Cameron
Marketing & Sales Dir: KP Tse
Publishing Dir: Cynthia Lam; Kenneth Ma
Dir, Bilingual Dictionaries & Home Edudation: T
C Wong
Dir, Asia ELT: Farrah Ching

**Philopsychy Press+**
PO Box 1224, Shatin, NT
*Tel:* 2604 4403
*E-mail:* ppp@net1.hkbu.edu.hk
*Web Site:* www.hkbu.edu.hk
*Key Personnel*
International Rights: Dr Stephen R Palmquist
*E-mail:* stevepq@hkbu.edu.hk
Founded: 1993
Philopsychy means soul-loving. The society is
a global, internet-based community of writers
& those interested in supporting the society's
principles.
Subjects: Biblical Studies, Philosophy, Psychol-
ogy, Psychiatry, Religion - Protestant, Self-
Help, Theology
ISBN Prefix(es): 962-7770

**Photoart Ltd+**
Flat D, 8/F, 51 Paterson St, Causeway Bay, Hong
Kong
*Tel:* 2117 1198 *Fax:* 2507 2878
*E-mail:* info@photoart.com.hk
*Web Site:* www.photoart.com.hk
*Key Personnel*
Man Dir: Mr Lee Georming
Founded: 1960
Subjects: Photography, Publishing & Book Trade
Reference
ISBN Prefix(es): 962-8165

**Press Mark Media Ltd+**
Flat D, 1/F, Prospect Mansion, 66-72 Paterson St,
Causeway Bay
*Tel:* 28822230 *Fax:* 2882 3949; 2882 2471
*E-mail:* magazine@todayliving.com
Founded: 1987
Publishing & advertising.
Subjects: Architecture & Interior Design, Art,
House & Home, Publishing & Book Trade Ref-
erence, Regional Interests, Sports, Athletics,
Travel, Wine & Spirits
ISBN Prefix(es): 962-7608

**Research Centre for Translation+**
Institute of Chinese Studies, Chinese University
of Hong Kong, Shatin, New Territories
*Tel:* 2609 7399; 2609 7407 *Fax:* 2603 5110; 2603
5195
*E-mail:* rct@cuhk.edu.hk
*Web Site:* www.cuhk.edu.hk/rct/home.html
*Telex:* 50301 CUHK HX *Cable:* SINOVERSITY
*Key Personnel*
Dir & Editor: Eva Hung *Tel:* 2609 7385
*E-mail:* evahung@cuhk.edu.hk
Man Editor: David E Pollard *E-mail:* pollard-
david@cuhk.edu.hk
Production Assistant: Cecilia Ip *E-mail:* ceci@
cuhk.edu.hk
Founded: 1971
Specialize in English translations of Chinese liter-
ature.
Subjects: Asian Studies, Fiction, Literature, Liter-
ary Criticism, Essays, Poetry

ISBN Prefix(es): 962-7255
Distributed by China Books (Australia); Chinese University Press (Worldwide)

**Ringier Pacific**
6F, Right Emperor Commercial Bldg, 122-124 Wellington St, Central SAR
*Tel:* 2369-8788 *Fax:* 2869-5919
*E-mail:* thaihoa@ringierasia.com
*Web Site:* www.ringierpacific.com
*Key Personnel*
Manager: Peter Siau
Founded: 1998
Publishes trade journals which help to satisfy the need for specialized business information in China.
*Parent Company:* TPL & Ringier AG

**SCMP Book Publishing Ltd+**
No 1 Leighton Rd, Causeway Bay, Hong Kong
*Tel:* 2836 6088 *Fax:* 2838 4061
*Key Personnel*
Publishing Manager: Leung Ka Kei
Editor: Ms Tse Yin Fong
Marketing Manager: Mr Fung Ka Wai
Founded: 1980
Subjects: Accounting, Advertising, Animals, Pets, Antiques, Astrology, Occult, Business, Career Development, Child Care & Development, Cookery, Crafts, Games, Hobbies, Fiction, Finance, Gardening, Plants, Health, Nutrition, How-to, Management, Marketing, Mysteries, Nonfiction (General), Psychology, Psychiatry, Travel
ISBN Prefix(es): 962-17
*Parent Company:* TVE International Ltd
*Associate Companies:* CV Idayus; TV Week Ltd; Retail Corp Ltd; Audio-Visual Travel Ltd; Highlight Tours Ltd

**Sesame Publication Co+**
Room 505, 4/F, Winner House, 310 King's Rd, North Point, Hong Kong
*Tel:* 2508 9920; 2508 9311 *Fax:* 2508 9603
*E-mail:* sesame01@hkstar.hk
*Key Personnel*
Man Dir: Dick Paul Wong
Founded: 1987
Specialize in children's books & printing services.
Subjects: Animals, Pets, Child Care & Development, English as a Second Language, Fiction
ISBN Prefix(es): 962-347; 962-8795; 962-983; 962-8811; 962-8818
*Warehouse:* Blk B, 23/F, Jing Ho Ind Bldg, 78-84 Wang Lung St, Tsuen Wan, New Territories
*Tel:* 2408 7685 *Fax:* 2407 2565

**Shanghai Book Co Ltd**
5th floor, Block A, 345 Des Voeux Rd, West, Hong Kong
*Tel:* 2548 6160
*Key Personnel*
Man Dir: Lap Shan Wong
Founded: 1946
Subjects: Music, Dance
ISBN Prefix(es): 962-239
*Associate Companies:* Shanghai Book Co (Pte) Ltd, Singapore; Shanghai Book Co, (KL) Sdn Bhd, Malaysia; China Cultural Corporation
Imprints: The Won Yit Book Co
Distributor for People's Music Publishing House

**Sin Min Chu Publishing Co**
Hunghom Commercial Centre, Room 1015, Hunghom, 39 Ma Tau Wai Rd, Tower A, Kowloon
*Tel:* (02) 2334 9327 *Fax:* (02) 76 58 471
ISBN Prefix(es): 962-336

**South China Morning Post Ltd+**
22 Dai Fat St, Tai Po

*Tel:* 2680 8888
*Web Site:* www.scmp.com
*Telex:* hx 86008 *Cable:* Postscript Hong Kong
*Key Personnel*
Editor: Adrian Oosthuizen
Publisher: Christopher Axberg
Marketing Manager: Sharon Galistan
Founded: 1976
Subjects: Asian Studies, Radio, TV
ISBN Prefix(es): 962-10
*Bookshop(s):* SCM Post Family Bookshops in Star Ferry, Furama Hotel, Ocean Centre

**Springer-Verlag Hong Kong Ltd**
Room 701, Mirror Tower, 61 Mody Rd, Tsim Sha Tsui, Kowloon Bay, Kowloon
*Tel:* 27 23 96 98 *Fax:* 27 24 23 66
Founded: 1986
ISBN Prefix(es): 962-430
*Parent Company:* Springer-Verlag GmbH & Co KG, Heidelberger Platz 3, 14197 Berlin, Germany

**Summerson Eastern Publishers Ltd+**
4/F, Block B, 434 Queen's Rd W, Hong Kong
*Tel:* 25408123 *Fax:* 2559 7869
*Key Personnel*
Man Dir: Mr M K Woo
Executive Dir: Ms M M Chong
Senior Manager: Bill M P Lo
Founded: 1976
Membership(s): Hong Kong Educational Publishers Association Ltd.
ISBN Prefix(es): 962-221

**Sun Mui Press**
PO Box 366, Shatin, NT
*Tel:* 2694 8525 *Fax:* 2610 1202
*E-mail:* auly@chevalier.net
*Key Personnel*
Contact: Au Loong-Yu
Subjects: Economics, Government, Political Science, History
ISBN Prefix(es): 962-7529

**Sun Ya Publications (HK) Ltd+**
Rm 1306, Eastern Centre, 1065 King's Rd, Hong Kong
*Tel:* 2562 0161 *Fax:* 2565 9951
*E-mail:* info@sunya.com.hk
*Web Site:* www.sunya.com.hk
*Telex:* 85849 Clwso Hx *Cable:* 6386
*Key Personnel*
Man Dir, Editorial, Rights & Permissions: Irene Yim
Man Dir: Yim Ng Seen Ha
Sales: Chan Chung-Chiu
Production: Miss Tsang Suet-Ying
Publicity: Wai Kim-Hung
Founded: 1961
Subjects: Fiction, Nonfiction (General)
ISBN Prefix(es): 962-08
*Parent Company:* Sino United Publishing (Holdings) Ltd
Subsidiaries: Sunbeam Publications (HK) Ltd
*Bookshop(s):* 111 N Atlantic Blvd, Suite 228, Monterey Park, CA 91754, United States

**Ta Kung Pao (HK) Ltd**
6/F 342 Hennessy Rd, Hong Kong
*Tel:* 25737213; 25757181 *Fax:* 257463316
*Key Personnel*
Marketing Manager, Circulation & Marketing Executive: Summy Ho
Subjects: China
ISBN Prefix(es): 962-582

**Tai Yip Co+**
1/F Capitol Plaza, 2-10 Lyndhurst Terrace, Central Hong Kong
*Tel:* 2524-5963 *Fax:* 2845-3296

*E-mail:* tybook@taiyipart.com.hk
*Web Site:* www.taiyipart.com.hk
*Key Personnel*
Dir: Ying-Lau Cheung
Subjects: Art
ISBN Prefix(es): 962-7239
*Bookshop(s):* Tai Yip Art Book Centre, 1/F, Hong Kong Museum of Art, 10 Salisbury Rd, Tsim Sha Tsui, Kowloon *Tel:* 2732-2088 *Fax:* 2312-1208

**Technology Exchange Ltd+**
Fo Tan Industrial Centre, 26-28 Au Pui Wan St, Suite 1102, Fotan Sha Tin, New Territories, Hong Kong
*Tel:* 2602 6300 *Fax:* 2609 1687
*Key Personnel*
General Manager: Francis K F Ng
*E-mail:* publication@tech-ex.com
Founded: 1987
Specialize also in medical devices, instrumentation of automation & cable tv.
Subjects: Communications, Electronics, Electrical Engineering, Radio, TV
ISBN Prefix(es): 962-452
Total Titles: 6 Print

**Thomson Corporation**
17/F Lyndhurst Tower, One Lyndhurst Terrace, Central Hong Kong
*Tel:* 2533 5416 *Fax:* 2530 3588
*Web Site:* www.tfibcm.com
*Key Personnel*
Editor-in-Chief: Tony Shale
General Manager & International Rights: Geoff Defreitas
Subjects: Finance

**Times Publishing (Hong Kong) Ltd+**
9-10/F, Block C, Seaview Est, 2-8 Watson Rd, North Point, Hong Kong
*Tel:* 23342421 *Fax:* 27645095; 23657834
*E-mail:* admin@federalbooks.com
*Key Personnel*
Man Dir: Tom Y L Ng
Founded: 1959
Membership(s): Hong Kong Educational P A, Educational Booksellers Association.
Subjects: Biblical Studies, Biological Sciences, Computer Science, Geography, Geology, Health, Nutrition, Mathematics, Religion - Protestant, Science (General)
ISBN Prefix(es): 962-302; 962-8781
*Parent Company:* Times Publishing Ltd, Singapore
*Associate Companies:* Federal Publications Sdn Bhd, Malaysia; Federal Publications (S) Pte Ltd; Times Books International
*Bookshop(s):* The Times Book Centre, Centre, Shops C & E, Mitlon Mansion, 96 Nathan Rd, Kowloon; The Times Book Centre, Shop G31, Hutchison House, Central District; Howard Book Store, G/F 74 Argyle St, Kowloon
*Warehouse:* Federal Publications Ltd, 2D Freder Centre, 68 Sung Wong Toi Rd, Kowloon

**Unicorn Books Ltd+**
14/F Zung Fu Industrial Bldg, 1067 King's Rd, Hong Kong
*Tel:* 2561 6151 *Fax:* 2811 1980
*Key Personnel*
Chief Operating Officer: Albert K W Au
Membership(s): The Ling Kee Group, Hong Kong.
Subjects: Antiques, Child Care & Development, Crafts, Games, Hobbies, Gardening, Plants, How-to, Self-Help, Chinese Language, Encyclopedia, Hong Kong History
ISBN Prefix(es): 962-232
*Parent Company:* Ling Kee Publishing Group
Distributed by Encyclopeida Publishing House of China (Beijing, China)

**Union Press Ltd**
3/F, Hong Lok Mansion, 74 Argyle St, Kowloon
*Tel:* 2567 3762 *Fax:* 2394 5084
ISBN Prefix(es): 962-207

**The University of Hong Kong, Department of Philosophy**
Pokfulam Rd, Hong Kong
*Tel:* 28592797 *Fax:* 2559 8452
*E-mail:* fctmoore@hkuxa.hku.hk
*Key Personnel*
Contact: Prof Laurence Goldstein
Subjects: Computer Science, Philosophy
ISBN Prefix(es): 962-375

**Vision Pub Co Ltd+**
Flat 33, 5/F, Tower B, Cambridge Plaza, 510 King's Rd, North Point, New Territories
*Tel:* 23147627; 92676502 *Fax:* 29078838
*E-mail:* pcgameos@pcgame.com.hk
*Web Site:* www.pcgame.com.hk
*Key Personnel*
Manager: Kai-man Pang
Founded: 1987
Membership(s): HK Educational Publishers Association Ltd.
Subjects: Mathematics, Technology
ISBN Prefix(es): 962-407

**Vista Productions Ltd**
Room A 7/F, Melbourne Industrial Bldg, 16 Westlands Rd, Hong Kong
*Tel:* 25632492 *Fax:* 25655803
*Telex:* 63321 Timbk Hx
Subjects: Education
ISBN Prefix(es): 962-05
*Associate Companies:* Times Educational Co Sdn Bhd, Malaysia

**Wellday Ltd**
Rm 1901, Kai Tak Commercial Bldg, 317-321 Des Voeux Rd Central, Hong Kong
*Tel:* 23628489 *Fax:* 23628564
*Key Personnel*
General Manager: Ms Shen Miao
Subjects: Advertising, Business
ISBN Prefix(es): 962-85051
Distributor for Miller Freeman Publishers Ltd

**Witman Publishing Co (HK) Ltd+**
9-11 Tsat Tse Mui Rd, North Point, Hong Kong
*Tel:* 2562 6279 *Fax:* 2565 5482
*E-mail:* witmanp@hk.star.com
*Key Personnel*
Dir: Yau Suk Ching
Founded: 1978
Specialize in English language books, cassettes, videos & diskettes.
Membership(s): ACTPO.
Subjects: Fiction, History, Language Arts, Linguistics, Mathematics
ISBN Prefix(es): 962-7044; 962-304

**The Won Yit Book Co,** *imprint of* Shanghai Book Co Ltd

**Yazhou Zhoukan Ltd**
15/F, Blk A, Ming Pao Industrial Centre, 18 Ka Yip St, Chai Wan
*Tel:* 2515 5483 *Fax:* 2595 0497
*E-mail:* yzad@mingpao.com
*Web Site:* www.yzzk.com
*Key Personnel*
Contact: Tracy Cheung; Patrick Lo; Ruby Lo; Ivy Sze
Founded: 1987
Subjects: Asian Studies, Business, Economics, Finance, Regional Interests
ISBN Prefix(es): 962-85434
*Parent Company:* Ming Pao Grou

**Zie Yongder Co Ltd**
14/F, Aik San Bldg, 14 Westlands Road, Quarry Bay, Hong Kong
*Tel:* 29630111
ISBN Prefix(es): 962-7359

**ZYC Holding Ltd**
Aik San Factory Bldg 14 Westlands Rd, Quarry Bay, Hong Kong
*Tel:* 2963 0111

# Hungary

## General Information

*Capital:* Budapest
*Language:* Hungarian (German widely known)
*Religion:* Predominantly Roman Catholic, also Hungarian Reformed, Lutheran & Hungarian Orthodox
*Population:* 10.3 million
*Bank Hours:* 0800-1630 Monday-Friday
*Shop Hours:* 1000-1800 Monday-Friday; 1000-1500 Saturday
*Currency:* 100 filler = 1 forint
*Export/Import Information:* Any companies should be registered at the Registry Court. 12% VAT on books. Book importing & exporting is through Kultura - Hungarian Foreign Trading Co, H-1389 Budapest 62, Postfi0k 149; atlases through Cartographica, H-1443 Budapest, Postafiok 132. Magyar Hirdeto, Budapest, is a full service advertising agency.
*Copyright:* UCC, Berne (see Copyright Conventions, pg xi)

**Advent Kiado+**
Borsfa u 55, 1171 Budapest
*Tel:* (01) 256-5205 *Fax:* (01) 2565205
*E-mail:* advent12@matavnet.hu
*Key Personnel*
Publishing Dir: Laszlo Erdelyi
Founded: 1988
Subjects: Astrology, Occult, Biblical Studies, Cookery, Education, Health, Nutrition, Medicine, Nursing, Dentistry, Poetry, Religion - Protestant
ISBN Prefix(es): 963-7817; 963-9122

**Agape Ferences Nyomda es Konyvkiado Kft**
Matyas ter 26, 6725 Szeged
*Tel:* (062) 444-002; (062) 323-002 *Fax:* (062) 442-592
*E-mail:* agape@tiszanet.hu
*Key Personnel*
Dir: Karoly Harmath
Founded: 1991
Subjects: Religion - Catholic
ISBN Prefix(es): 963-458; 963-8112
*Parent Company:* Agape, Cara Dusana 4, Novi Sad, Serbia and Montenegro

**Agrargazdsagi Kutato es Informatikai Intezet**
Zsil u 3/5, 1093 Budapest
Mailing Address: Postfach 5, 1355 Budapest
*Tel:* (01) 2171011 *Fax:* (01) 1177037
*Telex:* 22-6923
ISBN Prefix(es): 963-491

**Akademiai Kiado+**
Prielle Korneila u 19, 1117 Budapest
Mailing Address: PO Box 245, 1519 Budapest
*Tel:* (01) 4648220; (01) 4648282; (01) 4648221; (01) 4648231
*Key Personnel*
President & Man Dir: Zsolt Bucsi Szabo

Sales, Promotion, Home & International: Rita Nemeth
Editorial Dir: Peter Bajor; Gyongyi Pomazi
Founded: 1828
Publishing House of the Hungarian Academy of Sciences.
Subjects: Archaeology, Art, Biological Sciences, Earth Sciences, Economics, Engineering (General), History, Language Arts, Linguistics, Law, Literature, Literary Criticism, Essays, Medicine, Nursing, Dentistry, Music, Dance, Philosophy, Science (General), Social Sciences, Sociology, Veterinary Science
ISBN Prefix(es): 963-05
*U.S. Office(s):* ISBS (International Specialized Book Service Inc), 5804 NE Hassolo St, Portland, OR 97213-3644, United States

**Aranyhal Konyvkiado Goldfish Publishing+**
Dolmany u 5-7, 1131 Budapest
*Tel:* (01) 239-6721 *Fax:* (01) 239-6730
*E-mail:* sprinter@com.kibernet.hu
*Key Personnel*
Owner & Manager: Gandor Radvan
Marketing Manager: Zulton Takacs
Artistic & Design Manager: Xenia Radvan
International Rights Contact: S Emege David
Founded: 1993
Specialize in children's books, mainly board books & activity books.
Membership(s): MKKE (Association of Hungarian Book Publishers & Distributors).
Subjects: Animals, Pets, Child Care & Development, Cookery, Crafts, Games, Hobbies, Education, Humor, Language Arts, Linguistics, Literature, Literary Criticism, Essays, Nonfiction (General), Outdoor Recreation, Physics
ISBN Prefix(es): 963-348; 963-8366; 963-9196; 963-9268; 963-9394
Number of titles published annually: 70 Print; 2 CD-ROM
Total Titles: 35 Print
*Ultimate Parent Company:* MKKE (Association of Hungarian Book Publishers & Distributors)
Subsidiaries: Sprinter Prest Romania SRL
Distributed by Sprinter Rft
Foreign Rep(s): Sprinter Prest Romania SRL (Romania)
*Distribution Center:* SICC Nagykereskede's

**Atlantisz Kiado+**
Gerloczy u 4, 1052 Budapest
*Tel:* (01) 4065645 *Fax:* (01) 4065645
*E-mail:* atlantis@budapest.hu
*Key Personnel*
Publisher: Dr Tamas Miklos
Founded: 1990
Also International Bookshop.
Subjects: History, Philosophy, Religion - Other, Social Sciences, Sociology, Theology
ISBN Prefix(es): 963-7978; 963-9165

**Balassi Kiado Kft+**
Muranyi u 61, 1078 Budapest
*Tel:* (01) 3518075; (01) 3518343
*E-mail:* balassi@mail.datanet.hu
*Key Personnel*
Dir: Peter Koeszeghy
International Rights: Judit Borus
Founded: 1990
Membership(s): Hungarian Publishers & Booksellers Association.
Subjects: Art, History, Language Arts, Linguistics, Literature, Literary Criticism, Essays, Nonfiction (General), Philosophy, Social Sciences, Sociology
ISBN Prefix(es): 963-506; 963-7873
Total Titles: 533 Print; 1 CD-ROM
Distributed by Harrassowitz; Polis (Romania)
Distributor for Cambridge UP; Kaligram (Romania, Slovakia); Polis (Romania)

*Bookshop(s):* Margit u 1, Budapest 1023, Contact: Hannus Zsuzaa *Tel:* (01) 212-0214 *Fax:* (01) 212-0214
*Book Club(s):* Balassi-Klub, Margit u 1, Budapest 1023 *Tel:* (01) 335-2885 *Fax:* (01) 335-2885

**Budapesti Muszaki es Gazdasagtudomanyi Egyetem**
Muegyetem rkp 3, 1111 Budapest
Mailing Address: Postfach 91, 1521 Budapest
*Tel:* (01) 4632441; (01) 4632440
*Telex:* 224944 omikk h
*Key Personnel*
Dir General: Dr Peter Horvath
Dir: Lajos Janszky
ISBN Prefix(es): 963-420; 963-421

**Cartographia Ltd+**
Bosnyak Ter 5, 1149 Budapest
Mailing Address: PO Box 80, 1590 Budapest
*Tel:* (01) 222-6727 *Fax:* (01) 222-6728
*E-mail:* mail@cartographia.hu
*Web Site:* www.cartographia.hu *Cable:* CARTOGRAPHIA
*Key Personnel*
Man Dir: Dr Arpad Papp-Vary *Tel:* (01) 252-8507 *Fax:* (01) 363-3649 *E-mail:* apappvary@cartographia.hu
Sales, Publicity, Rights & Permissions: Ms Zsuzsa Nemenyi
Founded: 1954
ISBN Prefix(es): 963-350; 963-350; 963-351; 963-353
*Bookshop(s):* Bajcsy-Zsilinszky u 37, Budapest 1067

**Central European University Press+**
Szent Istvan ter 11b, 2nd floor, 1051 Budapest
Mailing Address: Postfach 519/2, 1397 Budapest
*Tel:* (01) 327 3000 *Fax:* (01) 327 3183
*E-mail:* ceupress@ceupress.com
*Web Site:* www.ceupress.com
*Key Personnel*
Dir: Istvan Bart *Tel:* (01) 327 3270 *E-mail:* barti@ceu.hu
Executive Manager: Peter Inkei *Tel:* (01) 327 3181 *E-mail:* inkeip@ceu.hu
Founded: 1994
Dedicated to broadening the range of literature available in English or topics concerning the past & present history & culture of people living in the countries of central & eastern Europe.
Subjects: Economics, Government, Political Science, History, Literature, Literary Criticism, Essays, Social Sciences, Sociology, Cultural studies & medieval history
ISBN Prefix(es): 1-85866; 963-9116; 963-9241
Total Titles: 98 Print; 1 Online
*U.S. Office(s):* 400 W 59 St, New York, NY 10019, United States, Contact: Martin Greenwald *Tel:* 212-547-6932 *Fax:* 646-557-2416 *E-mail:* mgreenwald@sorosny.org (USA & Canada)
*Orders to:* Books International, PO Box 605, Herndon, VA 20172, United States *Tel:* 703-661-1500 *Fax:* 703-661-1501 (Orders for USA & Canada)
Plymbridge Distributors Ltd, Estover Rd, Plymbridge, United Kingdom *Tel:* (01752) 202301 *Fax:* (01752) 202333 (Orders for UK & Western Europe)

**Corvina Books Ltd+**
Rakoczi ut 16, 1072 Budapest
Mailing Address: PO Box 108, 1364 Budapest 4
*Tel:* (01) 1184347 *Fax:* (01) 1184410
*E-mail:* corvina@axelero.hu *Cable:* CORVINA BUDAPEST
*Key Personnel*
General Manager: Laszlo Kunos
Founded: 1955

Subjects: Art, Cookery, History, Language Arts, Linguistics, Social Sciences, Sociology
ISBN Prefix(es): 963-13

**Edito Musica Budapest**, see Zenemukiado

**Europa Konyvkiado+**
Kossuth Lajos ter 13-15, 1055 Budapest
Mailing Address: Postfach 65, 1363 Budapest
*Tel:* (01) 331-2700 *Fax:* (01) 331-4162
*E-mail:* info@europakiado.hu
*Web Site:* www.europakiado.hu
*Telex:* 225645 *Cable:* EUROLIBER
*Key Personnel*
Publisher: Levente Osztovits
Executive Dir: Dr P Roman
Production: T Nevery
Sales: M Kertesz
Publicity: G Joo
Founded: 1945
Subjects: Biography, Fiction, Philosophy, Poetry
ISBN Prefix(es): 963-07

**Foldmuvelesugyi Miniszterium Muszaki Intezet**
Tessedik S u 4, 2101 Godollo
Mailing Address: Postfach 103, 2101 Godollo
*Tel:* (028) 320-644 *Fax:* (028) 320-960
*E-mail:* dekani@eng.gau.hu
*Telex:* 022-5816 *Cable:* FMMI GODOLLO
*Key Personnel*
Dir: Dr Fozsef Hajdu
Founded: 1954
Subjects: Agriculture, Electronics, Electrical Engineering, Energy, Engineering (General), Environmental Studies, Mechanical Engineering, Science (General), Technology
ISBN Prefix(es): 963-611
Imprints: Mezogazdasagi; Technika
*Orders to:* FMMI, Postfach 103, 2101 Godollo

**Gondolat Kiado**
Brody S u16, 1088 Budapest
Mailing Address: Postfach 225, 1368 Budapest
*Tel:* (01) 38-3358 *Fax:* (01) 138-4540
*Key Personnel*
Editor-in-Chief: Miklos Hernadi, PhD
Dir: Gyorgy Feher
Subjects: Nonfiction (General)
ISBN Prefix(es): 963-280; 963-281; 963-282

**Greger-Delacroix**
Amfiteatrum u3, Budapest 1031
*Tel:* (01) 608936
*E-mail:* gregerdelacroix@compuserve.com; greger@elender.hu
*Key Personnel*
President & Dir: Andras J Kereszty *E-mail:* biograph@greger.hu
Bureau Chief: Erika Kormendy *Tel:* (01) 302-5149 *E-mail:* delacroix@greger.hu
Founded: 1990
Reliable books.
ISBN Prefix(es): 963-85811; 963-86144

**Hatagu Sip Alapitvany**
Vaci ut 100, Budapest 1133
*Tel:* (01) 1403728
ISBN Prefix(es): 963-7615

**Hatter Lap- es Konyvkiado Kft+**
Vaci ut 19, 1134 Budapest
Mailing Address: Postfach 97, 1525 Budapest
*Tel:* (01) 3208230; (01) 3297293 *Fax:* (01) 3208230; (01) 3297293
*E-mail:* hatterkiado@matavnet.hu
*Telex:* 1311343
*Key Personnel*
Dir: Kalman Lantos
Founded: 1985

Subjects: Science (General), Transportation
ISBN Prefix(es): 963-7403; 963-7455; 963-8128; 963-9365

**Helikon Kiado+**
Bajcsy-Zsilinsky ut 37, 1065 Budapest
*Tel:* (01) 428-9450; (01) 428-9429 *Fax:* (01) 428-9481
*E-mail:* helikon@helikon.hu
*Web Site:* www.helikon.hu
*Key Personnel*
Man Dir: Janos Szilagyi
Founded: 1982
Subjects: Art, History
ISBN Prefix(es): 963-207; 963-208
*Bookshop(s):* Helikon Bookshop, Suetoe u 2, 1052 Budapest; Litea Bookshop & Teagarden, Hess A ter 4, 1014 Budapest

**Holnap Kiado Vallalat**
Zenta u 5, 1111 Budapest
*Tel:* (01) 666928 *Fax:* (01) 656624
*Key Personnel*
Dir: Dr Eszter Milkovich
ISBN Prefix(es): 963-345; 963-346

**Idegenforgalmi Propaganda es Kiado Vallalat+**
Angol u 22, 1149 Budapest
Mailing Address: Postfach 164, 1440 Budapest
*Tel:* (01) 633652; (01) 633653 *Fax:* (01) 1837320
*Telex:* 225309 *Cable:* 1PV-BUDAPEST
*Key Personnel*
General Dir: Istvan Fazekas
Assistant Dir: Tamas Moldovan; Andras Vaczi
Founded: 1971
32 different services in sport & Congressional events.
Membership(s): WTO.
Subjects: Science (General), Travel
ISBN Prefix(es): 963-316
Imprints: IPV Herausgeben
*Branch Office(s)*
Brussels, Belgium
Milan, Italy
*Warehouse:* IPV Buecherlager, 1135 Budapest

**Ifjusagi Lap-es Konyvkiado Vallalat** (Youth Publishing House)+
Revay utca 16, 1374 Budapest
*Tel:* (01) 1116660 *Fax:* (01) 1530959
*Telex:* 226183
*Key Personnel*
Dir: Bela Koncz
Assistant Dir: Jozsef Gebler
Founded: 1957
Subjects: Crafts, Games, Hobbies, Fiction, House & Home, Mysteries, Romance, Science Fiction, Fantasy
ISBN Prefix(es): 963-422; 963-423

**Ikon Publishing Ltd**
Toeroekvesz ut 46/d, 1025 Budapest
*Tel:* (01) 1764401; (01) 1758183 *Fax:* (01) 1158089
*Key Personnel*
Man Dir: Dr Andras Renyi
ISBN Prefix(es): 963-7948

**IPV Herausgeben**, *imprint of* Idegenforgalmi Propaganda es Kiado Vallalat

**Janus Pannonius Tudomanyegyetem**
Postfach 9, 7601 Pecs
*Tel:* (072) 411 433 *Fax:* (072) 15738
*Key Personnel*
President of Publishing Committee: Lovasz Gyoergy
Founded: 1991
Subjects: Earth Sciences, History, Law, Management, Marketing, Philosophy, Physical Sciences, Social Sciences, Sociology
ISBN Prefix(es): 963-641

**Jelenkor Verlag+**
Munkacsy Mihaly u 30/A, 7621 Pecs
*Tel:* (072) 314-782; (072) 335-767 *Fax:* (072)
    532-047
*E-mail:* jelenkor@mail.datanet.hu
*Web Site:* www.jelenkor.com
*Key Personnel*
Dir: Dr Gabor Csordas *E-mail:* jk.csg@freemail.
    hu
Founded: 1993
Promote contemporary Hungarian poetry, fiction
    & philosophy.
Subjects: Art, Drama, Theater, Fiction, Film,
    Video, History, Literature, Literary Criticism,
    Essays, Philosophy, Poetry
ISBN Prefix(es): 963-676; 963-7770
*Branch Office(s)*
Rakoczi ut 59 II/9, 1081 Budapest *Tel:* (01)
    3133804 *Fax:* (01) 3230376

**Joszoveg Muhely Kiado+**
Ibrik u 3a, 1222 Budapest
*Tel:* (01) 226-5935 *Fax:* (01) 226-5935
*E-mail:* info@joszoveg.hu
*Web Site:* www.joszoveg.hu
*Key Personnel*
Publications Manager: Dr Peter Foti
Distribution Manager: Eva Fay
Founded: 1997
Specialize in bilingual books & ethnography.
Subjects: Government, Political Science, Philos-
    ophy, Psychology, Psychiatry, Social Sciences,
    Sociology, Ethnography
ISBN Prefix(es): 963-9134
Total Titles: 5 Print

**Kepzoemueveszeti Kiado+**
Kelemen L u 9 11/1, 1026 Budapest
*Tel:* (01) 3980036; (01) 3980037 *Fax:* (01)
    3980036; (01) 3980037
*Telex:* 22405
*Key Personnel*
Manager: Kemenczey Zolt an
Founded: 1954
Fine arts publishing house.
ISBN Prefix(es): 963-336
*Bookshop(s):* Poszterhaz, V, Bajcsy-Zsilinszky ut
    62; Kepesbolt, Budapest V; 1, Deak Ferenc ter
    6
*Orders to:* Kerepesi ut 62, 1148 Budapest

**Vince Kiado Kft+**
Margit korut 64/B, 1027 Budapest
*Tel:* (01) 375-7288 *Fax:* (01) 202-7145
*E-mail:* hl2618vin@ella.hu
*Key Personnel*
Publisher & General Manager: Gabor Vince
Publishing Dir: Magda Molnar
Founded: 1991
Membership(s): Museum Store Association.
Subjects: Art, Health, Nutrition, How-to, Physical
    Sciences
ISBN Prefix(es): 963-7826; 963-9069; 963-9192;
    963-9323
Distributor for Bonechi; Konemann; Taschen In-
    ternational
*Showroom(s):* Muecsarnox, Konyvesbolt, Dozsa
    Cyoergy ut37, 1146 Budapest; Budacyongye
    Bevagarouozpont, 1026 Budapest
*Bookshop(s):* Kulturtrade Konyvesbolt, Krisztina
    Urt 34, 1013 Budapest
*Warehouse:* Bakfark Balint u 1-3, 1027 Budapest

**Kiiarat Konyvdiado**
Verder u 20, 1035 Budapest
*Tel:* (01) 388-6312 *Fax:* (01) 388-6312
*Key Personnel*
Manager: Gyorgy Palinkas
Founded: 1995
Three book series: Hungarian architecture, philo-
    sophical essays & youngest generation of Hun-
    garian literature.

Limited Partnership.
Membership(s): MKKE-Budapest.
Subjects: Architecture & Interior Design, Litera-
    ture, Literary Criticism, Essays, Philosophy
ISBN Prefix(es): 963-85415; 963-85696; 963-
    9136
Total Titles: 69 Print
Foreign Rights: Agency Balla & Co (Hungary)
*Showroom(s):* Mucsarnok Kunsthalle, Dozsa gy-
    u-37, 1146 Budapest, Contact: Gabriella Nagy
    *Tel:* (01) 3437401 *Fax:* (01) 3435205
*Bookshop(s):* Irok Boltja, Andrassy ut 45, 1061
    Budapest, Contact: Bernadette Nagy *Tel:* (01)
    3221645
*Warehouse:* Helikon Bookhouse, Bajosy-zs. u 37,
    1065 Budapest, Contact: Ipdiko Hortobagyi
    *Tel:* (01) 3312329

**Kijarat**, see Kiiarat Konyvdiado

**KJK-Kerszov+**
Prielle Kornelia u 21-35, 1117 Budapest
Mailing Address: Postfach 101, 1518 Budapest
*Tel:* (01) 464-5656 *Fax:* (01) 464-5657
*E-mail:* complex@kjk-kerszov.hu
*Web Site:* www.kerszov.hu
*Key Personnel*
Man Dir: David G Young
Editorial: Judit Fogarasi
Contact: Bucsi Szabo Zsolt
Founded: 1955
*Rights & Permissions/Distribution:* Artisjus, Bu-
    dapest Bookstore for Specialists.
Subjects: Business, Economics, Education, Gov-
    ernment, Political Science, Journalism, Law,
    Marketing, Psychology, Psychiatry, Social Sci-
    ences, Sociology
ISBN Prefix(es): 963-222; 963-220; 963-221;
    963-224
Total Titles: 500 Print; 10 CD-ROM; 5 Online; 5
    E-Book
*Bookshop(s):* Economy & Law, Nador utca 8,
    1051 Budapest; Szechenyi Istvan Bookstore,
    Szent Istvan ter 4, 1064 Budapest V
*Warehouse:* 1106 Jaszberenyi ut 29, Budapest

**Koenyveshaz Kft+**
Vaci ut 19, 1134 Budapest
*Tel:* (01) 1311566 *Fax:* (01) 1311566
*Key Personnel*
President: Mr Jozsef Ronga
Also a distribution house.

**Magyar Tudomanyos Akademia Koezponti
    Fizikai Kutato Intezet Koenyvtara**
Konkoly Thege M ut 29-33, 1121 Budapest
Mailing Address: Postfach 49, 1525 Budapest
*Tel:* (01) 1382344 (ext 44) *Fax:* (01) 1316954
*E-mail:* kolcs@sunserv.kfki.hu *Cable:* MTA
    KFKI KOENYVTAR
*Key Personnel*
Head of Library: Erika Eory
Systems Librarian: Zsolt Banhegyi
    *E-mail:* zsolt@vax.mtak.hu
Founded: 1950
Subjects: Chemistry, Chemical Engineering, Com-
    puter Science, Electronics, Electrical Engineer-
    ing, Mathematics, Microcomputers, Physical
    Sciences, Physics
ISBN Prefix(es): 84-7248; 84-9768
*Orders to:* KFKI Konyvtara, Spain

**Kossuth Kiado RT** (Kossuth Publishing)+
Csanyi Laszlo utca 34, 1043 Budapest
Mailing Address: PO Box 55, 1327 Budapest
*Tel:* (01) 3700607 *Fax:* (01) 3700602
*E-mail:* rt@kossuted.hu
*Web Site:* www.kossuth.hu
*Key Personnel*
Man Dir: Mr Andras Sandor Kocsis *Tel:* (01)
    3700600 *E-mail:* andrass@kossuted.hu

Book Publishing Dir: Mrs Jolanta Szabone Szuba
    *Tel:* (01) 3700603 *E-mail:* jolanta@kossuted.hu
Multimedia Manager: Mr Laszlo Foldes *Tel:* (01)
    3700608 *E-mail:* hobo@kossuted.hu
International Relations Manager: Mr Balint Or-
    dogh *E-mail:* balinto@kossuted.hu
Rights Manager: Eszter Gyorfi
    *E-mail:* rightskossuth@axelero.hu
Subjects: Business, Child Care & Development,
    Communications, Education, Finance, Geogra-
    phy, Geology, Health, Nutrition, Management,
    Natural History, Philosophy, Psychology, Psy-
    chiatry, Religion - Catholic, Travel, Wine &
    Spirits
Number of titles published annually: 80 Print; 12
    CD-ROM
Total Titles: 80 Print; 45 CD-ROM
*Showroom(s):* Andrassy Ut 13, 1061 Budapest
    *Tel:* (01) 266-3514 *Fax:* (01) 266-3515

**Lang Kiado+**
Balassi Balint u 7, 1055 Budapest
*Tel:* (01) 301-3888 *Fax:* (01) 301-3833
*E-mail:* holding@lang.hu
*Web Site:* www.lang.hu *Cable:* 1055 BUDAPEST,
    BALASSI BALINT U 7
*Key Personnel*
President: Dr Erdoes Akos
Vice President: Zsuzsanna Vadas
Founded: 1988
Subjects: Business, Literature, Literary Criticism,
    Essays, Public Administration
ISBN Prefix(es): 963-8054; 963-7840
Subsidiaries: Kner Printing House; Victoria Kft;
    Sorger-Kolon Kft: B & W Kft; Wien- Bu-
    dapest Kft; Publicitas Kft; Cash Flow Kft;
    Europrospekt Kft; Indikator Kft; Magyar In-
    stallateur Kft; CompAlmanach CSFR; Televital
    Kft; Repro Express Kft
*Bookshop(s):* Pozsonyi ut 5 Ungarn, 1134 Bu-
    dapest

**Magveto Koenyvkiado+**
Szervita ter 5, 1052 Budapest
Mailing Address: Postfach 123, 1806 Budapest
*Tel:* (01) 302 2798; (01) 302 2799 *Fax:* (01) 302
    2800
*E-mail:* magveto@mail.datanet.hu
*Telex:* 22-3502-Magve H
*Key Personnel*
Man Dir: Geza Morcsanyi
Chief Dir: Zsuzsa Koermendy
Sales & Publicity: Rozalia Janos
Founded: 1955
Rights & Permissions: Artisjus (under Literary
    Agents).
Membership(s): MKKE.
Subjects: Art, Fiction, History, Music, Dance,
    Philosophy, Poetry
ISBN Prefix(es): 963-14; 963-270; 963-271
*Bookshop(s):* Magvetoe Koenyvesbolt, Szent Ist-
    van Koerut 26, 1137 Budapest
*Warehouse:* Vaci ut 19, 1134 Budapest

**Magyar Kemikusok Egyesulete** (Hungarian
    Chemical Society)
Fo utca 68, 1027 Budapest
Mailing Address: Postfach 451, 1372 Budapest
*Tel:* (01) 2016883 *Fax:* (01) 343 25 41
*E-mail:* webinfo@mtesz.hu
*Web Site:* www.mtesz.hu
*Telex:* 224343 MTESZ H
*Key Personnel*
President: Dr Alajos Kalman
Vice President: Dr Laszlo Pallos
Secretary General: Dr Gyula Koertvelyessy
Subjects: Travel
ISBN Prefix(es): 963-8191

**Magyar Koenyvkiadok es Koenyvterjesztoek
    Egyesuelese Vereinigung der Ungarischen
    Buchverlage & Vertriebsunternehmen**

(Association of Hungarian Publishers &
Booksellers)
Kertesz u 41 I/4, 1073 Budapest
Mailing Address: Postfach 130, 1367 Budapest
*Tel:* (01) 343-25-40 *Fax:* (01) 343 25 41
*E-mail:* mkke@mkke.hu
*Web Site:* www.mkke.hu
*Key Personnel*
President: Peter Laszlo *E-mail:* zpl@mkke.hu
ISBN Prefix(es): 963-7002; 963-7409

**Marton Aron Kiado Publishing House**
Division of The Hungarian Pastoral Institute
Korhaz u 37, 1035 Budapest
*Tel:* (01) 3689527; (01) 3678415 *Fax:* (01)
1689869
*E-mail:* oli@hcbc.hu
*Key Personnel*
Dir: Miklos Blanckenstein
Founded: 1992
Subjects: Education, Human Relations, Religion -
Catholic, Theology
ISBN Prefix(es): 963-7947; 963-9011; 963-9439

**Medicina Koenyvkiado+**
Zoltan utca 8, 1054 Budapest
Mailing Address: Postfach 1012, 1245 Budapest
*Tel:* (01) 312-2650 *Fax:* (01) 312-2450
*Cable:* MEDICINA H-1054 BUDAPEST,
BELOISNNISZ 8
*Key Personnel*
Man Dir: Prof Istvan Arky, PhD
Editor: Dr Bulcsu Buda; Bela Ortutay
Production: Marton Orlai
Founded: 1957
Publishing house of medical literature.
Membership(s): Hungarian Publishers & Book-
sellers Association (MKKE-HPBA).
Subjects: Medicine, Nursing, Dentistry, Sports,
Athletics, Travel
ISBN Prefix(es): 963-240; 963-242; 963-241

**Mezogazda Kiado** (Farmer Publishing House)
Koronafurt u 44, 1165 Budapest
*Tel:* (01) 4071018 *Fax:* (01) 4071787
*E-mail:* mezogazda@matavnet.hu
*Key Personnel*
Dir: Dr Lajos Lelkes
Founded: 1992
Subjects: Agriculture, Animals, Pets, Environmen-
tal Studies, Gardening, Plants, Science (Gen-
eral), Veterinary Science, Wine & Spirits
ISBN Prefix(es): 963-7362; 963-8160; 963-8439;
963-9121; 963-9239; 963-9358
Number of titles published annually: 50 Print
Total Titles: 150 Print

**Mezogazdasagi**, *imprint of* Foldmuvelesugyi
Miniszterium Muszaki Intezet

**Mora Ferenc Ifjusagi Koenyvkiado Rt+**
Vaci ut 19, 1134 Budapest
*Tel:* (01) 320 4740 *Fax:* (01) 320 5328
*E-mail:* mora.kiado@elender.hu
*Telex:* 227027
*Key Personnel*
Contact: Dr Janos Cs Toth
Founded: 1950
Intellectual workshop of the Hungarian literature
for children & the young by bringing out qual-
ity new books.
Subjects: Science Fiction, Fantasy
ISBN Prefix(es): 963-11
*Bookshop(s):* Bobita Koenyvesbolt, Bajcsy-
Zsilinszky ut 27, 1065 Budapest; Mora Fer-
enc Koenyvesbolt, Szabadsag ter 3/A, 6000
Kecskemet
*Book Club(s):* Mora Koenyvklub (Mora
Bucklub)-Kinderbuecher

**Mueszaki Koenyvkiado Ltd+**
Szentendrei u 89-93, 1033 Budapest
Mailing Address: Postfach 385, 1536 Budapest
*Tel:* (01) 1557122
*E-mail:* berczis@muzakikiado.hu
*Telex:* 226490
*Key Personnel*
Man Dir: Sandor Berczi *E-mail:* berczis@
muszakikiado.hu
BCI, Textbooks: Maria Kekes
BC2, Vocational Textbooks: Norbert Baranyi
Rights & BC3, Professional: Zoltan Lakatos
Founded: 1955
Subjects: Architecture & Interior Design, Career
Development, Chemistry, Chemical Engineer-
ing, Computer Science, Electronics, Electri-
cal Engineering, Management, Mathematics,
Physics, Science (General), Technology
ISBN Prefix(es): 963-10; 963-16

**Mult es Jovo Kiado+**
Keleti Karoly u 27, 1024 Budapest
*Tel:* (01) 316-70-19; (01) 438-38-06; (01) 438-38-
07 *Fax:* (01) 316-70-19
*E-mail:* mandj@multesjovo.hu
*Web Site:* www.multesjovo.hu
*Key Personnel*
Dir & Chief Editor: Janos Kobanyai
Founded: 1989
Subjects: History, Literature, Literary Criticism,
Essays, Social Sciences, Sociology, Jewish Lit-
erature, History & Culture
ISBN Prefix(es): 963-85295; 963-85697; 963-
85817; 963-9171
Foreign Rep(s): Liepman AG Literary Agency

**Nemzeti Tankoenyvkiado+**
Szobranc u 6-8, 1143 Budapest
Mailing Address: Postfach 620, 1439 Budapest
*Tel:* (01) 460-1800 *Fax:* (01) 460-1862
*E-mail:* public@ntk.hu
*Web Site:* www.ntk.hu
*Key Personnel*
Man Dir: Dr Abraham Istvan
Editorial: Mr Rethy Endre
Sales: Dr Danka Attila
Production: Mrs Etclka Babies Vasvan
International Rights Contact: Mrs Fudit Farago
*Tel:* (01) 460-1868
Founded: 1949
Textbook Publishing House.
Subjects: Biological Sciences, Education, Geogra-
phy, Geology, History, Language Arts, Linguis-
tics, Law, Literature, Literary Criticism, Essays,
Marketing, Mathematics, Mechanical Engi-
neering, Music, Dance, Philosophy, Physics,
Psychology, Psychiatry
ISBN Prefix(es): 963-17; 963-18; 963-19
*Shipping Address:* Pontus Book Shop & Delivery
Service, Gat u 25, 1095 Budapest

**Nemzetkozi Szinhazi Intezet Magyar
Kozpontja**
Krisztina krt 57, 1013 Budapest
*Tel:* (01) 1752372 *Fax:* (01) 1751184
*Key Personnel*
President: Gyoergy Lengyel
Dir: Erzsebet Bereczky
Subjects: Drama, Theater, Literature, Literary
Criticism, Essays
ISBN Prefix(es): 963-691

**Novorg International Szervezo es Kiado kft+**
Csanadi u 7, 1132 Budapest
Mailing Address: Postfach 52, 1553 Budapest
*Tel:* (01) 603790; (01) 603596; (01) 602300
*Fax:* (01) 495581
*E-mail:* info@hu.inter.net
*Key Personnel*
Manager: P Boris
Founded: 1986

Subjects: Business, Cookery, Economics, Finance,
How-to, Law, Management, Marketing, Public
Administration, Real Estate
ISBN Prefix(es): 963-485
*Parent Company:* Wolters Kluwer
*Associate Companies:* Koezgazdasagi Es Jogi Koe
nyvkiado
*Showroom(s):* W K Koenyvkereskedelmi
Koezpont, Szentendrei ut 89-93, 1033 Budapest
*Warehouse:* W K Koenyvkereskedelmi Koezpont,
Szentendrei ut 89-93, 1033 Budapest

**Officina Nova Konyvek+**
Marvany u 17, 1012 Budapest
*Tel:* (01) 557282 *Fax:* (01) 1686674
*Key Personnel*
Dir: Katalin Balogh
Editor-in-Chief: Andras Szekely
Founded: 1987
Subjects: Antiques, Art, Cookery, Gardening,
Plants, Health, Nutrition, History, Humor,
Travel
ISBN Prefix(es): 963-7835; 963-7836; 963-8185;
963-477
*Parent Company:* Bertelsmann Verlagsgruppe
GmbH, Munich,, Germany
*Associate Companies:* Bertelsmann Professional
Information
Divisions: Media Nova

**OKKER Kiado**
Csengery u 68, 1067 Budapest
*Tel:* (01) 3324587
*Key Personnel*
Dir: Susanna Nouakne Gal
ISBN Prefix(es): 963-7315; 963-85136; 963-
85351; 963-85206; 963-9228

**Osiris Kiado** (Osiris Publishing)+
Egyeten Ter 5, 2/10a, 1053 Budapest
*Tel:* (01) 266-6560 *Fax:* (01) 267-0935
*E-mail:* kiado@osirismail.hu
*Web Site:* www.osiriskiado.hu
*Key Personnel*
Dir: Janos Gyurgyak *Tel:* (01) 266-6560, Ext 106
Founded: 1993
Subjects: Anthropology, Communications, Eco-
nomics, Film, Video, Government, Political
Science, History, Language Arts, Linguistics,
Law, Library & Information Sciences, Liter-
ature, Literary Criticism, Essays, Philosophy,
Psychology, Psychiatry, Religion - Catholic,
Religion - Protestant, Social Sciences, Sociol-
ogy, Theology
Number of titles published annually: 200 Print
*Distribution Center:* Vaci ut 100, 1133 Budapest

**Panem+**
Ov u 146, 1147 Budapest
Mailing Address: Postafiok 809, 1385 Budapest
*Tel:* (01) 460-0273 *Fax:* (01) 460-0274
*E-mail:* panem@mail.datanet.hu
*Web Site:* www.panem.hu
*Key Personnel*
Dir: Ms Zsuzsa Tarr
Founded: 1990
Subjects: Computer Science, Economics, Engi-
neering (General), Science (General)
ISBN Prefix(es): 963-545; 963-7628

**Park Konyvkiado Kft (Park Publisher)+**
Keleti K u 29, 1024 Budapest
*Tel:* (01) 2125534; (01) 2125535; (01) 2124363
*E-mail:* park@mail.matav.hu
*Key Personnel*
Manager: Andras Rochlitz
Marketing: Mr Aniko Zambo
Founded: 1989
Subjects: Art, Child Care & Development, Gar-
dening, Plants, History, House & Home, Man-
agement, Nonfiction (General), Self-Help
ISBN Prefix(es): 963-7737; 963-7970; 963-8227
Total Titles: 110 Print

**Planetas Kiadoi es Kereskedelmi Kft**
Koronafurt u 44, 1165 Budapest
*Tel:* (01) 4071018 *Fax:* (01) 4071787
*Key Personnel*
Dir: Dr Lajos Lelkes
Founded: 1990
Specialist art publications.
Subjects: Art, Music, Dance, Folk art
ISBN Prefix(es): 963-7931; 963-9014; 963-9414

**Polgart Kft+**
Baross u 11-15, 1047 Budapest
*Tel:* (01) 399 0859 *Fax:* (01) 399 0859
*E-mail:* polgart@elender.hu
*Key Personnel*
Editor-in-Chief: Tamas Bekes
Founded: 1994
Provides values & guidance for the slowly developing Hungarian middle classes.
Subjects: Literature, Literary Criticism, Essays, Science (General)
ISBN Prefix(es): 963-9002
Subsidiaries: Polgar Video Ltd

**Pro Natura+**
Bathori u 10, 1054 Budapest
*Tel:* (01) 1317330 *Fax:* (01) 1117270
*Telex:* 61 20 2536
*Key Personnel*
Manager: Dr Csaba Gallyas
Founded: 1950
Agricultural publishing house.
Subjects: Agriculture, Science (General)
ISBN Prefix(es): 963-7518
Subsidiaries: Natura
*Bookshop(s):* Agricultural Bookshop, Vecsei u 5, Budapest

**Saldo Penzugyi Tanacsado es Informatikai Rt+**
Mor u 2-4, 1135 Budapest
Mailing Address: Pf 397, 1394 Budapest
*Tel:* (01) 237-9800 *Fax:* (01) 237-9841
*E-mail:* kiado@saldo.hu
*Web Site:* www.saldo.hu
*Telex:* 226387
*Key Personnel*
General Dir: Dr Andras Mohos
Marketing Manager: Dr Jozsef Racz
Founded: 1959
Subjects: Accounting, Economics, Finance, Law, Public Administration
ISBN Prefix(es): 963-621; 963-638

**SH Kiado**, see Springer Tudomanyos Kiado Kft

**Springer Tudomanyos Kiado Kft**
Formerly SH Kiado
Muzeum u 9, 1088 Budapest
Mailing Address: Postfach 94, 1327 Budapest
*Tel:* (01) 2664776
*Telex:* 2515973
Founded: 1990
Subjects: Earth Sciences, Engineering (General), Medicine, Nursing, Dentistry
ISBN Prefix(es): 963-7775; 963-7922; 963-699; 963-8455

**Statiqum Kiado es Nyomda Kft+**
Kaszasdulo u 2, 1033 Budapest
Mailing Address: Postfach 99, 1300 Budapest
*Tel:* (01) 1803311 *Fax:* (01) 1688635
*Telex:* 226699 Skv h
*Key Personnel*
Man Dir: Benedek Belecz
Sales Dir: Gyoergy Szehr
Founded: 1991 (predecessor 1954)
Legal successor of Statistical Publishing House.
Subjects: Computer Science, Economics, Mathematics, Social Sciences, Sociology
ISBN Prefix(es): 963-340

*Parent Company:* State Property Agency, Vigado u 6, 1051 Budapest
*Bookshop(s):* Statistical & Computing Bookshop, Keleti Karoly u 10, Budapest *Tel:* (01) 1158018
*Orders to:* KULTURA Aussenhandelsunternehmen fur Bucher und Zeintschriften, PO Box 149, 1389 Budapest

**Szabad Ter Kiado+**
Postfach 95, 1525 Budapest
*Tel:* (01) 3561565; (01) 3755922 *Fax:* (01) 1560998
*Telex:* 223553
*Key Personnel*
Dir: Gabor Koltay
Deputy Dir, Productions Dir: Jozsef Lovasi
Founded: 1988
Cultural Service Guidance, Expense Sheet.
Subjects: Fashion, Government, Political Science, Literature, Literary Criticism, Essays, Mysteries
ISBN Prefix(es): 963-7810; 963-9201

**Szabvanykiado+**
Ulloi u 25, 1091 Budapest
Mailing Address: Postfach 24, 1450 Budapest
*Tel:* (01) 1183011; (01) 1183442 *Fax:* (01) 1185125
*Telex:* 225723 norm h
Founded: 1972
Subjects: Nonfiction (General)
ISBN Prefix(es): 963-402

**Szarvas Andras Cartographic Agency+**
Repassy jeno u, 2, 1149 Budapest
*Tel:* (01) 363 0672; (01) 221 68 30 *Fax:* (01) 363 0672; (01) 221 68 30
*E-mail:* szarvas.andras@mail.datanet.hu
*Key Personnel*
Owner: Szarvas Andras *E-mail:* szarvas.andras@mail.datanet.hu
Founded: 1991
Map publishing & distribution.
Subjects: Earth Sciences, Geography, Geology, Regional Interests, Transportation, Travel
ISBN Prefix(es): 963-9251
Number of titles published annually: 20 Print
Total Titles: 40 Print

**Szazadveg**
U Benczur u 33, 1068 Budapest
Mailing Address: Menesi ut 12, 1118 Budapest
*Tel:* (01) 4795280 *Fax:* (01) 479 5290
*E-mail:* szazadveg@szazadveg.hu
*Web Site:* www.szazadveg.hu
*Key Personnel*
Marketing Manager: Pesti Zsuzsa
Pres, Szazadveg Foundation: Dr Istvan Stumpf
Founded: 1990
Nonpartisan, nonprofit organization financed by the contributions of its supporters & the sale of its publications & services.
ISBN Prefix(es): 963-379; 963-7911; 963-8384

**Szepirodalmi Koenyvkiado Kiado**
Gyongyvirag u 41, 1038 Budapest
Mailing Address: Postfach 58, 1428 Budapest
*Tel:* (01) 3117293
*Key Personnel*
Man Dir: Marton Tarnoc
Founded: 1950
Subjects: Education, Fiction, Poetry
ISBN Prefix(es): 963-15; 963-86184

**Magyar Eszperanto Szoevetseg**
Kenyermezw u 6, 1081 Budapest
Mailing Address: Postfach 193, 1368 Budapest
*Tel:* (01) 1334343; (01) 1563659 *Cable:* ESPERANTOCENTRO, BUDAPEST

*Key Personnel*
Dir: Mr Oszkar Princz
ISBN Prefix(es): 963-571

**Tajak Korok Muzeumok Egyesuelet**
Konyves K krt 40, 1087 Budapest
Mailing Address: Postfach 54, 1476 Budapest
*Tel:* (01) 303 4069 *Fax:* (01) 303 4069
*E-mail:* tkmets@elender.hu
*Key Personnel*
Publisher: Istvan Eri
Founded: 1977
Organizes the movements which play a significant role in popularizing Hungary's natural resources, monuments & exhibitions.
Subjects: Archaeology, Architecture & Interior Design, Art, History, Natural History
ISBN Prefix(es): 963-554; 963-555

**Taltos Kiadasszervezesi Ltd**
Bajza u 1, 1071 Budapest
*Tel:* (01) 1213515; (01) 1420676
ISBN Prefix(es): 963-7825

**Technika**, *imprint of* Foldmuvelesugyi Miniszterium Muszaki Intezet

**Tevan Kiado Vallalat+**
Luther u 12, Bekescsaba 5600
*Tel:* 66441181
*Key Personnel*
Dir: Dr Janos Cs Toth
Deputy Dir: Kantor Zsolt
Founded: 1989
Subjects: Fiction, Poetry
ISBN Prefix(es): 963-7900; 963-7278

**Typotex Kft Elektronikus Kiado+**
Retek u 33-35, 1024 Budapest
*Tel:* (01) 316-2473; (01) 316-3759 *Fax:* (01) 316-3759
*E-mail:* info@typotex.hu
*Web Site:* www.typotex.hu
*Key Personnel*
Man Dir: Zsuzsa Votisky *E-mail:* votis@typotex.hu
Editor-in-Chief: Kinga Nemeth *E-mail:* kinga@typotex.hu
Sales Manager: Zsolt Nemeth *E-mail:* nezsolt@typotex.hu
Marketing: Borbala Pinter *E-mail:* bori@typotex.hu
Founded: 1989
Subjects: Mathematics, Philosophy, Physics
ISBN Prefix(es): 963-7546; 963-9132; 963-9326
Total Titles: 100 Print
Subsidiaries: Index Buchladen

**Magyar Tudomanyos Akademia VilagGazdasagi Kutato Intezet**
Kallo esp u 15, 1124 Budapest
Mailing Address: PO Box 936, 1535 Budapest
*Tel:* (01) 1668433 *Fax:* (01) 1620661
*Telex:* 227713 *Cable:* BUWORLDINST
*Key Personnel*
Dir: Prof Andras Inotai
ISBN Prefix(es): 963-301

**Zenemukiado+**
Hugo St 11-15, 1132 Budapest
*Tel:* (01) 2361 100 *Fax:* (01) 2361 101
*E-mail:* musicpubl@emb.hu
*Web Site:* www.emb.hu
*Telex:* 225500 *Cable:* EDITIOMUSICA
*Key Personnel*
Man Dir: Istvan Homolya
International Rights: Antal Boronkay
Founded: 1950
Subjects: Biography, Music, Dance
ISBN Prefix(es): 963-330
*Bookshop(s):* Andrassy ut h5, 1061 Budapest
*Tel:* (01) 322-4091 *Fax:* (01) 322-4091

**Zrinyi Kiado**
Kerepesi u 29/b, 1087 Budapest
*Tel:* (01) 4595371; (01) 3339113
*Key Personnel*
Manager: Mate Eszes
Publishing House of the Hungarian Army.
Subjects: Military Science, Science (General)
ISBN Prefix(es): 963-327; 963-326

# Iceland

## General Information

*Capital:* Reykjavik
*Language:* Icelandic (widespread knowledge of English
*Religion:* Lutheran
*Population:* 259,000
*Bank Hours:* 0915-1600 Monday-Friday (winter); 0800-1600 (summer); some open 1700-1800 Thursday
*Shop Hours:* 0900-1800 Monday-Thursday; 0900-1700/1900 Friday; most open 0900-1600 Saturday (winter)
*Currency:* 100 aurar = 1 krona
*Export/Import Information:* Member of the European Economic Area. 14% VAT on books. Sales Tax. No import licenses required. No exchange controls for books but they may not be imported on credit.
*Copyright:* UCC, Berne, Florence (see Copyright Conventions, pg xi)

**AEskan**
Stangarhyl 4, 110 Reykjavik
*Tel:* 530-5400 *Fax:* 530-5407
*E-mail:* aeskan@aeskan.is
*Web Site:* www.aeskan.is
*Key Personnel*
Editor: Karl Helgason
Founded: 1930
ISBN Prefix(es): 9979-808; 9979-9395; 9979-9411; 9979-9416; 9979-767; 9979-9443; 9979-9472

**Almenna Bokafelagid**
Suourlandsbraut 12, 108 Reykjavik
*Tel:* 522-2000 *Fax:* 522-2025
*Web Site:* www.edda.is
*Key Personnel*
Man Dir: Fridriksson Fridrik
Editor: Bjarni Thorsteinsson *E-mail:* bjarni.thorsteinsson@edda.is
Editorial: Eirikur Hreinn Finnbogason
Sales Dir: Andri Thor Gudmundsson
Rights & Permissions: Stefania Petursdottir
Founded: 1955
Subjects: Biography, Fiction, History, Nonfiction (General), Poetry
ISBN Prefix(es): 9979-4
*Parent Company:* EDDA
*Book Club(s):* The AB Book Club (BAB); The MAT Cookery Book Club; TAB (Music Club)

**Arnamagnaean Institute in Iceland**, see Stofnun Arna Magnussonar a Islandi

**Hjalmar R Bardarson**
Hrauntunga vio Alftanesveg, 210 Garoabaer
Mailing Address: Postholf 998, 121 Reykjavik
*Tel:* 555-0729
*Key Personnel*
Editor: Hjalmar R Bardarson
ISBN Prefix(es): 9979-818
*Warehouse:* Sidumuli 21, PO Box 8181, IS-128 Reykjavik
*Orders to:* Islensk Bokadrefin HF

**Bifrost hf Bokaforlag, Bokaklubbur Birtings+**
Formerly Bokaforlag Birtingur
Laugavegur 66, 101 Reykjavik
*Tel:* 562-7700 *Fax:* 562-7710
Founded: 1988
Subjects: Astrology, Occult, Health, Nutrition, Mysteries, Parapsychology, Philosophy, Psychology, Psychiatry, Religion - Other
ISBN Prefix(es): 9979-815; 9979-9002

**Bokaforlag Birtingur**, see Bifrost hf Bokaforlag, Bokaklubbur Birtings

**Bokaklubbur DV**
Formerly Frjals fjolmiolun hf-Urvalsbaekur
Skaftahlio 24, 105 Reykjavik
*Tel:* 550-5000; 550-5999 *Fax:* 550-5022
*Key Personnel*
Editor: Sig Hreidar Hreidarsson
Founded: 1981 (an amalgamation of firms from 1910)
Subjects: Fiction, Mysteries, Romance
ISBN Prefix(es): 9979-9006; 9979-9023; 9979-840; 9979-9493

**Bokautgafan Orn og Orlygur ehf+**
Dvergshoefoi 27, 112 Reykjavik
*Tel:* 568-4866 *Fax:* 5671240
*Telex:* 2197
*Key Personnel*
Man Dir: Pall Bragi Kristjonsson *E-mail:* pbk@centrum.is
Founded: 1966
Subjects: Biography, Cookery, Gardening, Plants, Health, Nutrition, How-to
ISBN Prefix(es): 9979-55

**Bokaverslun Sigfusar Eymundssonar**
Austurstr 18, 101 Reykjavik
*Tel:* 13135 *Fax:* 15078
Subjects: Education

**Draupnisutgafan, Loegberg**, *imprint of* Idunn

**Filadelfia forlag**
Hatuni 2, 105 Reykjavik
Mailing Address: Postholf 5135, 125 Reykjavik
*Tel:* 552-5155; 552-0735 *Fax:* 562-0735
*E-mail:* filadelfia-forlag@gospel.is
*Telex:* 3000 simtexisforlag
*Key Personnel*
Man Dir: Hronn Svansdottir
ISBN Prefix(es): 9979-803

**Fjolvi**
Njoervasundi 15 A, 104 Reykjavik
*Tel:* 5688433 *Fax:* 5588142
*E-mail:* fjolvi@fjolvi.is
*Web Site:* www.fjolvi.is
*Telex:* 2159 Rethor
*Key Personnel*
Man Dir: Sturla Eiriksson
Dir: Ingunn Thorarensen; Thorsteinn Thorarensen
Founded: 1966
Subjects: Fiction, Nonfiction (General)
ISBN Prefix(es): 9979-58
*Book Club(s):* Bokaklubbur Fjolva; Particip 'Verold'

**Forlagid+**
Sudurlandsbraut 12, 108 Reykjavik
*Tel:* 522-2000 *Fax:* 522-2022
*E-mail:* edda@edda.is
*Web Site:* www.edda.is
*Key Personnel*
Publishing Dir: Kristjan B Jonasson
Founded: 1984
Subjects: Photography, Travel
ISBN Prefix(es): 9979-53
*Parent Company:* EDDA

**Frjals fjolmiolun hf-Urvalsbaekur**, see Bokaklubbur DV

**Godord**
Hringbraut 81, 107 Reykjavik
*Tel:* 551-6998
*Key Personnel*
Editor: Brynjar Viborg
Founded: 1989
Subjects: Poetry
ISBN Prefix(es): 9979-9017

**Haskolautgafan - University of Iceland Press**
Haskoli Islands, Adalbygging v/Sudurgoetu, 107 Reykjavik
*Tel:* 5254003 *Fax:* 525-5255
*Web Site:* www.haskolautgafan.hi.is
*Key Personnel*
Dir: Joerundur Godmundsson *E-mail:* jorig@hi.is
Contact: Bryndis Erla Hjalmarsdottir *E-mail:* bryndihj@hi.is
Founded: 1988
Subjects: History, Philosophy, English & Icelandic titles on Norse studies
ISBN Prefix(es): 9979-54

**Hid Islenzka Bokmenntafelag** (Icelandic Literary Society)+
Skeifan 3B, 128 Reykjavik
*Tel:* 5889060 *Fax:* 5889095
*E-mail:* hib@islandia.is
*Web Site:* www.hib.is
*Key Personnel*
President: Sigurdur Lindal
Dir: Sverrir Kristinsson
Man Dir: Gunnar H Ingimundarson
Founded: 1816
Subjects: Art, Government, Political Science, History, Language Arts, Linguistics, Literature, Literary Criticism, Essays, Natural History, Psychology, Psychiatry, Social Sciences, Sociology, Icelandic Art, Literature, Philosophy & Saga
ISBN Prefix(es): 9979-804; 9979-66

**Iceland Review+**
Borgartuni 23, 105 Reykjavik
*Tel:* 512-7575 *Fax:* 561-8646
*E-mail:* icelandreview@icelandreview.com
*Web Site:* www.icelandreview.com
*Telex:* 2121
*Key Personnel*
Chairman of the Board: Haraldur J Hamar
Founded: 1963
Subjects: Art, Literature, Literary Criticism, Essays, Regional Interests
ISBN Prefix(es): 9979-51

**Idunn+**
Suourlandsbraut 12, 108 Reykjavik
*Tel:* 522-2000 *Fax:* 522-2022
*E-mail:* idunn@idunn.is
*Web Site:* www.idunn.is
*Telex:* 2308 *Cable:* REYKJAVIK PUBLISHERS
*Key Personnel*
Dir: Jon Karlsson *E-mail:* jk@idunn.is
Editor: Thorgunnur Skuladottir *E-mail:* thorgunnur@idunn.is
Founded: 1945
Subjects: Biography, Fiction, History, Nonfiction (General), Poetry
ISBN Prefix(es): 9979-1
*Parent Company:* EDDA
Imprints: Draupnisutgafan, Loegberg
*Book Club(s):* Draupnisutgafan

**Independent Media Inc**, see Bokaklubbur DV

**Isafoldarprentsmidja hf+**
Tverholti 9, 105 Reykjavik

*Tel:* 550-5990 *Fax:* 550-5994
*E-mail:* isafold@isafold.is
*Web Site:* www.isafold.is
*Key Personnel*
Contact: Ragnar Ragnarsson *E-mail:* ragnar@
  isafold.is
Founded: 1877
Subjects: Education, Fiction
ISBN Prefix(es): 9979-809

**Katholska kirkjan a Islandi - Landakot
  Publishers Thorlakssjodur**
Landakoti, 101 Reykjavik
*Tel:* 555-0188
*Key Personnel*
Contact: Torfi Olafsson
Founded: 1987
Subjects: Religion - Catholic
ISBN Prefix(es): 9979-9261

**Landakot Publishers Thorlakssjodur**, see
  Katholska kirkjan a Islandi - Landakot
  Publishers Thorlakssjodur

**Mal og menning+**
Imprint of Edda Publishing
Sudurlandsbraut 12, 108 Reykjavik
*Tel:* 522 2500 *Fax:* 522 2505
*E-mail:* edda@edda.is
*Web Site:* www.edda.is
*Key Personnel*
Man Dir: Pall Bragi Kristjonsson *E-mail:* pall.
  bragi@edda.is
Editorial Dir: Sigurdur Svavarsson
  *E-mail:* sigurdur.svavarsson@edda.is
Founded: 1937
Subjects: Education, Fiction, Literature, Literary
  Criticism, Essays, Nonfiction (General), Poetry,
  Travel
ISBN Prefix(es): 9979-3
*Associate Companies:* Vaka-Helgafell, Sudur-
  landsbraut 12, 108 Reykjavik *Tel:* 522 2000
  *Fax:* 522 2022
Imprints: Uglan Paperback Bookclub
Subsidiaries: Heimskringla
*Book Club(s):* Mal og menning; Uglan

**Namsgagnastofnun**
Laugavegi 166, 105 Reykjavik
*Tel:* 5528088 *Fax:* 5624137
*E-mail:* upplysingar@nams.is
*Web Site:* www.namsgagnastofnun.is
*Telex:* 3000 Simtext Is-Edice *Cable:* EDICE
*Key Personnel*
Dir: Ingibjoerg Asgeirsdottir *E-mail:* ingibjorg@
  nams.is; Asgeir Gudmundsson
Editor: Bogi Indridason *E-mail:* bogi@nams.is
Rights & Permissions: Eirikur Grimsson
Publicity, Sales: Hoerour Ragnarsson
Editor: Tryggvi Jakobsson *E-mail:* tryggvij@
  nams.is
Founded: 1937
National Centre for Educational Materials is a
  nonprofit publishing house run by the Icelandic
  government.
Membership(s): International Council for Educa-
  tional Media (ICEM).
Subjects: Disability, Special Needs, Education
ISBN Prefix(es): 9979-0

**Ormstunga+**
Ranargotu 20, 101 Reykjavik
*Tel:* 561 0055 *Fax:* 552 4650
*E-mail:* books@ormstunga.is
*Web Site:* www.ormstunga.is
*Key Personnel*
Man Dir: Gisli Mar Gislason
Founded: 1992
ISBN Prefix(es): 9979-63; 9979-9048

**Prentsmidjan Oddi**
Hofdabakka 3-7, 110 Reykjavik
*Tel:* 5155000 *Fax:* 5155001
*E-mail:* oddi@oddi.is
*Web Site:* www.oddi.is
*Key Personnel*
Dir: Thorgeir Baldursson *E-mail:* thorgeir@oddi.
  is
Vice President: Hilmar Baldursson
Founded: 1943
*U.S. Office(s):* PO Box 415, Lincroft, NJ 07738,
  United States

**Setberg**
Freyjugoetu 14, IS-101 Reykjavik
Mailing Address: Postholf 619, 121 Reykjavik
*Tel:* 5517667; 552-9150 *Fax:* 5526640
*Telex:* 3000 Simtex ls *Cable:* Setbergpublish
*Key Personnel*
Dir: Arnbjoern Kristinsson
Subjects: Cookery, Education, Fiction, Nonfiction
  (General)
ISBN Prefix(es): 9979-52

**Skjaldborg Ltd+**
Grensasvegur 14, 108 Reykjavik
*Tel:* 5882400 *Fax:* 5888994
*E-mail:* skjaldborg@skjaldborg.is
*Key Personnel*
Dir: Bjorn Eiriksson *E-mail:* bjorn@skjaldborg.is
Editorial Manager: Helgi Magnusson
Subjects: Animals, Pets, Astrology, Occult, Biog-
  raphy, Crafts, Games, Hobbies, Fiction, Gar-
  dening, Plants, How-to, Humor, Nonfiction
  (General)
ISBN Prefix(es): 9979-57
*Associate Companies:* Heima er bezt
Subsidiaries: Childrens Educational Bookclub
*Book Club(s):* Educational Book Club for Chil-
  dren

**Stofnun Arna Magnussonar a Islandi** (Arni
  Magnusson Manuscript Institute)
Unit of University of Iceland
Arnagaroi v/Suourgoetu, 101 Reykjavik
*Tel:* 525-4010 *Fax:* 525-4035
*E-mail:* rosat@hi.is
*Web Site:* www.am.hi.is
*Key Personnel*
Dir: Vesteinn Olason *E-mail:* vesteinn@hi.is
Founded: 1972
Specialize in research & publication of Icelandic
  manuscripts & folklore.
Membership(s): FIDEM.
Subjects: History, Language Arts, Linguistics,
  Literature, Literary Criticism, Essays, Music,
  Dance, Poetry, Regional Interests
ISBN Prefix(es): 9979-819
Number of titles published annually: 4 Print
Total Titles: 70 Print; 7 CD-ROM
Distributed by University of Iceland Press

**Thjodsagao ehf**
Dvergshofda 27, IS-112 Reykjavik
*Tel:* 567-1777 *Fax:* 567-1240
*E-mail:* pbk@centrum.is

**Uglan Paperback Bookclub**, *imprint of* Mal og
  menning

**Vaka-Helgafell**
Sueurlandsbraut 12, 108 Reykjavik
*Tel:* 522 2000 *Fax:* 522 2022
*E-mail:* edda@edda.is
*Web Site:* www.vaka.is
*Telex:* 3190 vakice
*Key Personnel*
International Rights: Petur Mar Olafsson
Marketing Dir: Edda Bjorgvinsdottir
Chairman of the Board: Olafur Ragnarsson
Founded: 1981

Preserves, promotes & enriches the Icelandic language & the cultural heritage of the Icelandic
  people.
ISBN Prefix(es): 9979-2

# India

## General Information

*Capital:* New Delhi
*Language:* Hindi & English are used for official
  purposes. Seventeen regional languages are
  accorded recognition by the constitution. Generally each administrative state includes speakers of a particular major language. In all, over
  1500 languages & dialects are spoken
*Religion:* Predominantly Hindu, some Muslims
  (about 11%)
*Population:* 886.4 million
*Bank Hours:* 1000-1400 (1100-1500 Mumbai)
  Monday-Friday; 1000-1200 (1100-1300 Mumbai) Saturday
*Shop Hours:* Delhi: 0930-1930; Kolkata & Mumbai: 1000-1830; Chennai: 0900-1930. All effective Monday-Saturday, some open Sunday.
  Many close 2 hours for lunch
*Currency:* 100 paise = 1 Indian rupee
*Export/Import Information:* No tariff on books
  but advertising matter is dutied. Import Licenses required. Educational books may be
  imported by booksellers under open general
  license. Exchange transactions restricted.
*Copyright:* UCC, Berne, Buenos Aires (see Copyright Conventions, pg xi)

**A L Publishers+**
44 Bhimangar, Opp Indira Park, Hyderabad
  500380
*Tel:* (040) 7611600
*Key Personnel*
President: Mrs K Rama Dev
Author: Prof K M Lakshmana Rao
Founded: 1987
Subjects: Medicine, Nursing, Dentistry
ISBN Prefix(es): 81-900416

**Aarti Books**, *imprint of* Spectrum Publications

**ABC**, see Allied Book Centre

**Abhinav Publications+**
E-37 Hauz Khas, New Delhi 110016
*Tel:* (011) 26566387; (011) 26524658 *Fax:* (011)
  26857009
*Web Site:* www.abhinavexports.com
*Key Personnel*
Dir: Shakti Malik *E-mail:* shakti@nde.vsnl.net.in
Founded: 1972
Subjects: Archaeology, Architecture & Interior
  Design, Art, Criminology, Drama, Theater, Eth-
  nicity, Government, Political Science, History,
  Human Relations, Literature, Literary Criti-
  cism, Essays, Music, Dance, Philosophy, Reli-
  gion - Other, Social Sciences, Sociology
ISBN Prefix(es): 81-7017
Number of titles published annually: 18 Print
Distributed by South Asia Books (USA)

**Abhishek Publications**
SCO 57-59 Sector 17-C, Chandigarh 160 017
Mailing Address: PO Box 34, Chandigarh 160017
*Tel:* (0172) 707562 *Fax:* (0172) 704668
*Key Personnel*
Chief Executive, Production, Publicity: SLM
  Prachand
Editorial: Mrs Geeta Mehndiratta
Sales, Rights & Permissions: Bharat Bhushan
Founded: 1977

Subjects: Government, Political Science, History, Philosophy
ISBN Prefix(es): 81-85733
*Associate Companies:* Nirjhar Prakashan, 3625 Sector 23-D, Chandigarh 160023

**Academic Book Corporation+**
C-1491, Rajaji Puram, Lucknow 226 017
*Tel:* (0522) 418421; (0522) 416584 *Fax:* (0522) 22061; (0522) 210376 *Cable:* ACADEMIC
Founded: 1982
Subjects: Law, Management
ISBN Prefix(es): 81-238

**The Academic Press+**
Old Subzi Mandi, Gurgaon, Haryana 122 001
*Tel:* (0124) 6322779; (0124) 6322005 *Fax:* (0124) 6324782
*E-mail:* indoc@indiatimes.com
*Key Personnel*
Dir: Pankaj Jain *E-mail:* pancoj@indiatimes.com
Editorial: Satya Prakash
Sales: Kapil Jain
Production, Rights & Permissions: Sanjeev Jain Satyaprakash
Founded: 1968
Subjects: History, Human Relations, Philosophy, Religion - Other, Social Sciences, Sociology
ISBN Prefix(es): 81-85260

**Academic Publishers**
12/1A Bankim Chatterjee St, Kolkata 700073
Mailing Address: PO Box 12341, Kolkata 700073
*Tel:* (033) 241-4857 *Fax:* (033) 241-3702
*E-mail:* acabooks@cal.vsnl.net.in *Cable:* ACABOOKS
*Key Personnel*
Man Dir: Bimal Kumar Dhur
Sales Dir: B L Dutta
Founded: 1958
Subjects: Accounting, Business, Management, Medicine, Nursing, Dentistry
ISBN Prefix(es): 81-86358; 81-85086; 81-87504
Distributed by UBS Publishers Distributors Ltd (outside Kolkata)

**Addison Wesley**, *imprint of* Addison-Wesley Pte Ltd

**Addison-Wesley Pte Ltd+**
India Branch, 482 FIE Patparganj, Delhi 110 092
*Tel:* (011) 214 6067 *Fax:* (011) 214 6071
*E-mail:* info@pearsoned.co.in
*Web Site:* www.pearsonedindia.com
*Key Personnel*
General Manager: Subroto Mozumdar
   *E-mail:* subroto.mozumdar@pearsonedindia.com
Finance: Dipankar Rose
Founded: 1997
One of the world's largest educational publishers. It has played a very important role in publishing both higher education/academic titles as well as school products. The India Office is a liaison office, headquartered in Singapore. Since its inception in 1997, Addison Wesley Longman India has reprinted classic higher academic & professional titles & recently dictionaries & ELT products to make them available to students in India at affordable prices.
Subjects: Biological Sciences, Business, Chemistry, Chemical Engineering, Civil Engineering, Computer Science, Economics, Electronics, Electrical Engineering, English as a Second Language, Management, Mathematics, Physics, Science (General), Social Sciences, Sociology
Number of titles published annually: 200 Print
Total Titles: 303 Print
*Parent Company:* Pearson Plc
Imprints: Addison Wesley; Scott Foresman; Peachpit Press; Benjamin Cummings; Pren-

tice Hall; Allyn & Bacon; Globe Fearon; Silver Burdett Ginn; Longman; Prentice Hall; Benjamin Cummings; SAMS; PTR; QUE; New Riders; Penguin Longman Publishing; Pitman; Financial Times PH; Merrill Education

**Advaita Ashrama+**
5 Dehi Entally Rd, Kolkata 700 014
*Tel:* (033) 22440898; (033) 22452383; (033) 22164000 *Fax:* (033) 22450050
*E-mail:* advaita@vsnl.com
*Web Site:* www.advaitaonline.com
*Key Personnel*
Manager: Swami Bodhasarananda
Founded: 1899
Publication department of Ramakrishina Mission.
Subjects: Art, Religion - Hindu
ISBN Prefix(es): 81-85301; 81-7505
Number of titles published annually: 150 Print
Total Titles: 400 Print; 2 CD-ROM; 2 Online
*Ultimate Parent Company:* Ramakrishna Math
Distributed by Ramakrishna Vedanta Centre (UK); Vedanta Society of Southern California (USA); Vivekananda Vedanta Society (USA)

**Affiliated East West Press Pvt Ltd+**
105 Nirmal Tower, 26 Barakhamba Rd, New Delhi 110001
*Tel:* (011) 23315398; (011) 23279113; (011) 23264180 *Fax:* (011) 23260538
*E-mail:* aewp.newdel@axcess.net.in; affiliat@vsnl.com
*Key Personnel*
Man Dir: Sunny Malik
Dir: Kamil Malik
Founded: 1962
Membership(s): Delhi State Booksellers' & Publishers Association; Federation of Publishers & Booksellers Associations of India; Federation of Indian Publishers.
Subjects: Aeronautics, Aviation, Agriculture, Anthropology, Biological Sciences, Chemistry, Chemical Engineering, Civil Engineering, Computer Science, Economics, Electronics, Electrical Engineering, Environmental Studies, Geography, Geology, Management, Mathematics, Mechanical Engineering, Microcomputers, Physical Sciences, Physics, Poetry, Psychology, Psychiatry, Science (General), Veterinary Science, Women's Studies
ISBN Prefix(es): 81-85095; 81-85336; 81-85938; 81-7671
Imprints: EWP
Distributor for Academic Press; American Association of Petroleum Geologists; American Ceramic Society; American Society for Quality; American Water Works Association; William Andrew; ASM International; Blackwell Science; Converor Equipment Manufacturers Association; CRC Press; Elsevier Science; FAO (Food & Agriculture Organization); Geological Society Publishing House; HarperCollins Publishers; Horwood Publishing; Humana Press; IEEE; Institute of Petroleum; Lippincott Williams Wolkins; MIT Press; Palgrave; Pira; Portland; Prentice-Hall; RAPRA Technology; Routledge; W B Saunders; Society for Mining, Metallurgy & Exploration; Society of Manufacturing Engineers; TAPPI Press; Thomson Learning; John Wiley
*Orders to:* G-1/16 Ansari Rd, Darya Ganj, New Delhi 110 002

**Agam Kala Prakashan**
34, Central Market, Ashok Vihar, New Delhi 110 005
*Tel:* (011) 713395 *Fax:* (011) 7401485
*Key Personnel*
Editorial, Sales, Publicity, Rights & Permissions: Agam Prasad
Founded: 1977
Membership(s): Capexal & Intach.

Subjects: Anthropology, Antiques, Archaeology, Art, Asian Studies, Earth Sciences, History, Language Arts, Linguistics
ISBN Prefix(es): 81-85415; 81-7186; 81-7320
*Associate Companies:* Agam Prakashan; Rahul Publishing House; Swati Publication
Distributed by M/S, Munshiram Manoharlal (P) Ltd; M/S, UBS Publishers & Distributors Ltd
Distributor for Rahul Publishing House; Swati Publications

**Agricole Publishing Academy+**
208, Shopping Complex, Defence Colony Flyover, New Delhi 110024
*Tel:* (011) 692703 *Cable:* AGRIPUBLIS
*Key Personnel*
Dir: Lalita Jain
Chief Executive: T C Jain
Founded: 1978
Subjects: Agriculture, Behavioral Sciences, Biological Sciences, Economics, Education, Energy, Engineering (General), Environmental Studies, Health, Nutrition, Labor, Industrial Relations, Real Estate, Social Sciences, Sociology, Technology
ISBN Prefix(es): 81-85005
*Associate Companies:* Yatan Publications; Agricole Reprints Corp

**Ajanta Publications (India)+**
One UB Jawahar Nagar, Bangalow Rd, New Delhi 110 007
Mailing Address: 1743 Outram Lane, SGTB Nagar, Delhi 110 009
*Tel:* (011) 2917375; (011) 2926182 *Fax:* (011) 741 5016; (011) 713 2908; (011) 7213076
*Key Personnel*
Chief Executive: Atwal Amit
Founded: 1975
Also acts as Academic/General/Literary Agent & Printer.
Membership(s): FIP.
Subjects: Anthropology, Archaeology, Art, Ethnicity, Government, Political Science, Language Arts, Linguistics, Literature, Literary Criticism, Essays, Management, Philosophy, Public Administration, Religion - Other, Social Sciences, Sociology
ISBN Prefix(es): 81-202
*Parent Company:* Ajanta Books International

**Akshat Publications+**
B-250, Ashok Vihar, Phase I, Delhi 110052
*Tel:* (011) 7247234; (011) 7114425; (011) 7240483 *Fax:* (011) 7254734; (011) 7218836 *Cable:* SAYONARA
*Key Personnel*
Contact: Dr Roopa Vohra; Mr K L Jain
Founded: 1985
ISBN Prefix(es): 81-85069
*Parent Company:* Sayonara Group

**Allied Book Centre+**
9/5 Rajpur Rd, 1st floor, Dehra Dun, Uttaranchal 248001
*Tel:* (0135) 656526; (0135) 650949; (0135) 9837066875 *Fax:* (0135) 656554
*E-mail:* abc_book@rediffmail.com
*Key Personnel*
Proprietor: Mohit Gahlot *E-mail:* gahlotmohit@rediffmail.com
Founded: 1995
Also acts as printer & distributor.
Membership(s): Association of Indian Publishers & Booksellers.
Subjects: Agriculture, Animals, Pets, Biological Sciences, Computer Science, Earth Sciences, Energy, Environmental Studies, Gardening, Plants, Geography, Geology, Natural History, Science (General), Technology, Veterinary Science, Botany, Forestry, Hydrology, Remote Sensing, Wildlife, Zoology
ISBN Prefix(es): 81-7089

Number of titles published annually: 10 Print
Total Titles: 20 Print

**Allied Publishers Pvt Ltd+**
1-13/14 Asaf Ali Rd, New Delhi 110 002
Mailing Address: PO Box 7203, New Delhi 110 002
*Tel:* (011) 3239001; (011) 3233002; (011) 5402792 *Fax:* (011) 3235967
*E-mail:* allied.delhi@vsnl.com; delhi.allied@excess.net.in
*Web Site:* www.alliedpublishers.com
*Telex:* 315153
*Key Personnel*
Man Dir: S M Sachdev
Editorial, Rights & Permissions: Sunil Sachdev
Manager: R N Purwar
Production: Ravi Sachdev
Publicity: S Banerjee
Founded: 1934
Subjects: Agriculture, Economics, Education, Energy, Government, Political Science, Management
ISBN Prefix(es): 81-7023; 81-7764
*Associate Companies:* Allied Publishers Subscription Agency
*Branch Office(s)*
15, J N Heredia Marg, Ballard Estate, Mumbai 400038 *Tel:* (022) 2617926; (022) 2617927 *Fax:* (022) 2617928 *E-mail:* allredpl@vsnl.com
17 Chittaranjan Ave, Kolkata 700072 *Tel:* (033) 2257023; (033) 2252514 *Fax:* (033) 261158 *E-mail:* alliedcal@vsnl.com
3-5-1129 Kachiguda Cross Rd, Hyderabad 500027 *Tel:* (040) 4619079; (040) 4619081 *Fax:* (040) 4619079; (040) 4619081
Patiala House, 16-A, Ashok Marg, Lucknow 226 001 (UP) *Tel:* (0522) 214253; (0522) 280358 *Fax:* (0522) 214253
Prarthana Flats, Opposite Thakor Baug, Navrangpura, Ahmedabad 380009 *Tel:* (079) 6465916; (079) 6630079 *Fax:* (079) 6465916 *E-mail:* alliedad@ad1.vsnl.net.in
81 Hill Rd, Ramnagar, Nagpur 440010 *Tel:* (0712) 52122; (0712) 542625 *Fax:* (0712) 542625

**Allyn & Bacon,** *imprint of* Addison-Wesley Pte Ltd

**Amar Prakashan+**
A-1/139-B Lawrence Rd, New Delhi 110035
*Tel:* (011) 713182 *Cable:* AMARPRA
*Key Personnel*
Chief Executive: M S Juneja
Editorial: Ganesh Rao
Sales: Maheep Singh
Publicity: Priya Chibbar
Production: Harbajan Singh
Founded: 1977
Membership(s): FPBAI.
Subjects: Economics, Ethnicity, Government, Political Science, History, Management, Social Sciences, Sociology
ISBN Prefix(es): 81-85061; 81-85420
Divisions: Ideal Publications, Eternal Books
*Branch Office(s)*
UBS Publishers Dist, 5 Ansari Rd, Darya Ganj, Delhi 110002

**Ambar Prakashan+**
88, East Park Rd, Karol Bagh, New Delhi 110 005
*Tel:* (011) 2362 5528 *Fax:* (011) 2574 3569
*E-mail:* pitambar@bol.net.in
*Key Personnel*
Partner: Ved Bhushan *Tel:* (011) 23535406 *Fax:* (011) 23676058
Founded: 1977
Subjects: Education, English as a Second Language, Mathematics, Science (General)
ISBN Prefix(es): 81-7289

Total Titles: 100 Print
*Parent Company:* Pitambar Publishing Co Pvt Ltd
Distributed by Pitambar Publishing Co Pvt Ltd

**Anand Paperbacks,** *imprint of* Orient Paperbacks

**Ananda Publishers Pvt Ltd+**
45 Beniatola Lane, Kolkata 700 009
*Tel:* (033) 2241 4352; (033) 2241 3417 *Fax:* (033) 2253240; (033) 2253241
*E-mail:* ananda@cal3.vsnl.net.in
*Web Site:* www.anandapub.com
*Key Personnel*
Manager: Dwijendranath Basu
Subjects: Anthropology, Art, Biography, Cookery, Drama, Theater, Economics, Fiction, Finance, Gardening, Plants, History, Music, Dance, Mysteries, Philosophy, Photography, Poetry, Psychology, Psychiatry, Science (General), Science Fiction, Fantasy, Social Sciences, Sociology, Sports, Athletics
ISBN Prefix(es): 81-7215; 81-7066; 81-7756

**Ankur Publishing Co**
C/1, Anandvan, Anandpark, Thane (West), Maharashtra, Mumbai 400 601
*Tel:* (022) 543 2817; (022) 536 9907 *Fax:* (022) 543 2817
*E-mail:* ankur@bom3.vsnl.net.in
*Web Site:* www.satyamplastics.com/ankurpublishing/
*Key Personnel*
Man Dir: Mrs Seema Mukherjee
Founded: 1976
Subjects: Government, Political Science, Literature, Literary Criticism, Essays, Science (General)
ISBN Prefix(es): 81-85043
*Associate Companies:* Sanjay Composers & Printers, Uphar Cinema Bldg, Green Park Extension, New Delhi 110016

**Anmol Publications Pvt Ltd+**
4374/4B, Ansari Rd, Daryaganj, New Dehli 110 002
*Tel:* (011) 3255577; (011) 3261597; (011) 3278000 *Fax:* (011) 3280289
*E-mail:* anmol@nde.vsnl.net.in
Founded: 1985
Subjects: Education, Environmental Studies, Geography, Geology, Library & Information Sciences, Management, Science (General), Social Sciences, Sociology, Women's Studies
ISBN Prefix(es): 81-7041; 81-7488; 81-261

**APH Publishing Corp+**
5 Ansari Rd, Darya Ganj, New Delhi 110026
*Tel:* (011) 5100581; (011) 5410924; (011) 3285807 *Fax:* (011) 3274050
*E-mail:* aph@mantrasonline.com
*Key Personnel*
Editorial & International Rights: S B Nangia
Sales: Gopal Sharma
Founded: 1974
Also acts as distributor.
Membership(s): Federation of Indian Publishers.
Subjects: Accounting, Agriculture, Archaeology, Architecture & Interior Design, Biography, Chemistry, Chemical Engineering, Criminology, Economics, Education, Energy, Environmental Studies, Ethnicity, Fiction, Geography, Geology, Government, Political Science, Health, Nutrition, History, Labor, Industrial Relations, Law, Library & Information Sciences, Management, Marketing, Natural History, Philosophy, Public Administration, Religion - Hindu, Religion - Islamic, Religion - Other, Science (General), Social Sciences, Sociology, Travel, Women's Studies
ISBN Prefix(es): 81-7024; 81-7648
Number of titles published annually: 100 Print

Total Titles: 1,200 Print
*Branch Office(s)*
8/81, Punjabi Bagh, New Delhi 110026
Distributed by UBS Publishers & Distributors Ltd

**Arihant Publishers+**
Opp Rajasthan University, Jawahar Lal Nehru Marg, Jaipur 302004
*Tel:* (0141) 515192
*Key Personnel*
Contact: Sumer Jain
Also acts as distributor.
Membership(s): The Federation of Publishers & Booksellers Associations in India.
Subjects: Biological Sciences, Human Relations, Social Sciences, Sociology
ISBN Prefix(es): 81-7230
*Parent Company:* Bookmen Associates, 9 Opp Rajasthab University, JLN Marg, Jaipur 302004

**Arya Medi Publishing House**
c/o Arya Book Depot, 4805/24 Bharat Ram Rd, Darya Ganj, New Delhi 110002
*Tel:* (011) 5717012 *Fax:* (011) 5715850
*Key Personnel*
Man Dir: Naveen Gupta
Founded: 1980
Subjects: Science (General), Social Sciences, Sociology
ISBN Prefix(es): 81-7063; 81-7064; 81-86809

**Asia Pacific Business Press Inc+**
c/o National Institute of Industrial Research, 106-E, Kamla Nagar, New Delhi 110 007
Mailing Address: PO Box No 2162, New Delhi 110 007
*Tel:* (011) 23845886; (011) 23845654; (011) 23843955; (011) 23844729 *Fax:* (011) 23841561
*E-mail:* niir@vsnl.com
*Web Site:* www.niir.org
*Key Personnel*
Chief Executive Officer & President: Mr Ajay Kr Gupta
Senior Vice President: Mr P K Tripathi
Senior Project Consultant: Mr P K Chattopadhyay
Founded: 2000
Subjects: Business, Chemistry, Chemical Engineering, Science (General), Technology
ISBN Prefix(es): 81-7833
Number of titles published annually: 50 Print
Distributed by National Institute of Industrial Research

**Asian Educational Services+**
C-2/15, SDA, New Delhi 110016
Mailing Address: PO Box 4534, New Delhi 110016
*Tel:* (011) 661493 *Fax:* (011) 6852805; (011) 6855499
*E-mail:* asianeds@nda.vsnl.net.in *Cable:* ASIABOOKS NEW DELHI
*Key Personnel*
Publisher: Jagdish Jetley
Chief Executive: Gaurav Jetley
Publicity, Rights & Permissions: Mrs Saroj Jetley; Gautam Jetley
Founded: 1972
Subjects: Anthropology, Archaeology, Asian Studies, Astrology, Occult, Biography, Ethnicity, History, Language Arts, Linguistics, Military Science, Music, Dance, Natural History, Philosophy, Religion - Buddhist, Religion - Hindu, Religion - Islamic, Religion - Other, Social Sciences, Sociology, Theology, Travel
ISBN Prefix(es): 81-206
Subsidiaries: Antiquarian Publication and Reprographic Services Pvt Ltd
*Branch Office(s)*
31 Hauzkhas Village, New Delhi 110016 *Tel:* (011) 668594
PO Box 4534, 5 Scripuram First St, Chennai *Tel:* (044) 8265040 *Fax:* (044) 8211291

Distributed by Alexandra & Leigh Copeland; Bay Foreign Language Books; Editions Kailash; French & European Publications; Hippocrene Books, Inc; Jeremy Tenniswood; Kalaimahal Book Depot; Lake House Bookshop; La Librairie Du Trefle; Laurier Books Ltd; Libri Dall'Asia; Messages of Gods Love Multi; Sarasavi Book Shop (Pvt) Ltd; Schoenhof's Foreign Books; Selous Books Ltd; South Asia Books; Vijitha Yapa Book Shop; West Port Books; Wuest GmbH & Co Kg
*Warehouse:* 17 Shahpur Jat, New Delhi 110 017

**Asian Trading Corporation+**
58, Second Cross, Da Costa Layout, St Mary's Town, Bangalore 560 084
Mailing Address: PO Box 8444, Bangalore 560 084
*Tel:* (080) 5487444; (080) 5490444 *Fax:* (080) 5479444
*E-mail:* mail@atcbooks.net; sales@atcbooks.net
*Web Site:* www.atcbooks.net *Cable:* PASPIN
*Key Personnel*
Partner: C C Pais *Tel:* (080) 216846 *Fax:* (080) 216944; Nigel Fernandes
Founded: 1946
Also exporters, importers & booksellers.
Subjects: Communications, Philosophy, Religion - Catholic, Religion - Other, Social Sciences, Sociology, Theology
ISBN Prefix(es): 81-7086
Total Titles: 125 Print
Imprints: Nil
*Branch Office(s)*
Mallikatte, Mangalore *Tel:* (0824) 216846 *Fax:* (0824) 216944

**Associated Publishing House+**
New Market, Karol Bagh, New Delhi 110005
*Tel:* (011) 2429392
*Key Personnel*
Man Dir, Sales: Ravinder K Paul
Editorial, Production Dir: Ashok K Paul
Publicity Dir, Rights & Permissions: Sharda Paul
Founded: 1966
Subjects: Art, Business, Economics, History, Philosophy, Poetry, Public Administration, Religion - Other, Social Sciences, Sociology, Travel
ISBN Prefix(es): 81-7045
Imprints: Associated Travel Series

**Associated Travel Series**, *imprint of* Associated Publishing House

**Atma Ram & Sons**
1376 Kashmere Gate, Delhi 110006
Mailing Address: PO Box 1429, Delhi 110006
*Tel:* (011) 223092
*E-mail:* yogesh2@ndf.vsnl.net.in *Cable:* BOOKS
*Key Personnel*
Man Dir, Publicity, Rights & Permissions: Sushil Kumar Puri
Sales: Ashutosh Pury
Founded: 1909
Subjects: Art, Education, Engineering (General), History, How-to, Medicine, Nursing, Dentistry, Philosophy, Science (General), Social Sciences, Sociology, Technology
ISBN Prefix(es): 81-7043
*Branch Office(s)*
17 Ashok Marg, Lucknow

**Authorspress**
C-102, Pandav Nagar Complex, Ganesh Nagar, Delhi 110092
*Tel:* (011) 22436299; (011) 22460145 *Fax:* (011) 22460145
*E-mail:* authorspress@yahoo.com
*Key Personnel*
Contact: Mr H S Negi
Publishers of Scholarly Books.

Subjects: Asian Studies, Computer Science, Economics, Education, Finance, History, Journalism, Library & Information Sciences, Philosophy, Religion - Islamic, Social Sciences, Sociology, Technology, Women's Studies
ISBN Prefix(es): 81-7273
Total Titles: 84 Print

**Avinash Reference Publications+**
W-70, MIDC, Shirali, Kolhapur 416122
*Tel:* (0231) 21024 *Fax:* (0231) 27262
*Telex:* 195272 IN
*Key Personnel*
Chief Editor: Dr J A Naik
Manager: Rajesh Naik
Founded: 1978
Subjects: Agriculture, Economics, Social Sciences, Sociology
ISBN Prefix(es): 81-85175
*Associate Companies:* Dr Naik & Co, W-70, MIDC, Shirali, Kolhapur 416122

**B I Churchill Livingstone**, *imprint of* B I Publications Pvt Ltd

**B I Publications Pvt Ltd+**
54 Janpath, New Delhi 110 001
*Tel:* (011) 3274443; (011) 3259352; (011) 3255118 *Fax:* (011) 3261290
*E-mail:* bigroup@del3.vsnl.net.in
*Telex:* 31-63352
*Key Personnel*
Chairman: R D Bhagat
Chief Executive: K S Mani
Publishing Dir: Y R Chadha *E-mail:* yrchadha@bipgroup.com
Founded: 1959
Subjects: Biological Sciences, Chemistry, Chemical Engineering, Electronics, Electrical Engineering, Engineering (General), Health, Nutrition, Mechanical Engineering, Medicine, Nursing, Dentistry, Physics
ISBN Prefix(es): 81-7225; 81-7042; 81-7431
*Associate Companies:* British Institute of Eng Technology (India) Pvt Ltd, 359, D N Rd, Mumbai 400 023
Imprints: B I Churchill Livingstone; B I Waverly
Subsidiaries: B I Churchill Livingstone Pvt Ltd (BICL); B I Waverly Pvt Ltd (BIW)
*Branch Office(s)*
One Aishwarya Apts 9/B, Kumkum Society Stadium Rd, Ahmedabad 380014 *Tel:* (079) 459847
147, Infantry Rd, Bangalore 560 001 *Tel:* (080) 2204652 *Fax:* (080) 2205696
35 Mount Rd, Chennai 600 002 *Tel:* (044) 8521851 *Fax:* (044) 8525361
13-1A, Govt Pl East, Kolkata 700001 *Tel:* (033) 2488742 *Fax:* (033) 2488743
18 Landsdowne Rd, Mumbai 400 039 *Tel:* (020) 2021766 *Fax:* (020) 2046778
13 Daryaganj, New Delhi 110 002 *Tel:* (011) 3274443 *Fax:* (011) 3261290
Dharhara House, Nayatola (Police Chowki), Patna 800 004 *Tel:* (0612) 657814 *Fax:* (0612) 663794
Distributor for Edward Arnold; ASM International; Elsevier Science; Lippincott-Williams & Wilkins; Macmillan Group; Routledge Chapman & Hall; Roskill

**B I Waverly**, *imprint of* B I Publications Pvt Ltd

**K P Bagchi & Co+**
286 BB, Ganguli St, Kolkata 700012
*Tel:* (033) 267474; (033) 269496 *Fax:* (033) 2482973 *Cable:* KHPIBEE
*Key Personnel*
Chief Executive, Publicity, Rights & Permissions: P K Bagchi
Editorial, Sales, Production: K K Bagchi

Founded: 1972
Subjects: Anthropology, Economics, Government, Political Science, History, Language Arts, Linguistics, Literature, Literary Criticism, Essays, Social Sciences, Sociology
ISBN Prefix(es): 81-7074
*Associate Companies:* Kusum Book Agency, Kalyan Nagar, PO Pansila 743180, Dist North 24, Parganas, Bengla

**Baha'i Publishing Trust of India+**
F-3/6 Okhla Industrial Area, Phase-I, New Delhi 110 020
*Tel:* (011) 26819391; (011) 26818990 *Fax:* (011) 26812703
*E-mail:* publisher@bahaindia.org; bptindia@del3.vsnl.net.in; nsaindia@bahaindia.org
*Web Site:* www.bahaindia.org
*Telex:* 0314881 Nsa In *Cable:* BAHAIFAITH
*Key Personnel*
General Manager: Mr Jiten Mishra
Founded: 1954
Subjects: Education, Religion - Other, Social Sciences, Sociology
ISBN Prefix(es): 81-85091; 81-7896; 81-86953
*Parent Company:* National Spiritual Assembly of the Baha'is of India, 6-Shrimant Madhavrao Scindia Marg, New Delhi 110 001
*U.S. Office(s):* Baha'i Publishing Trust, 415 Linden Ave, Wilmette, IL 60091, United States

**The Bangalore Printing & Publishing Co Ltd+**
88 Mysore Rd, Bangalore 560018
*Tel:* (080) 6709638; (080) 6709027 *Fax:* (080) 6704053
*E-mail:* marketing@bangalorepress.com
*Web Site:* www.bangalorepress.com *Cable:* MUDRASALA
*Key Personnel*
Man Dir: H R Ananth
General Marketing Manager: C A Krishnaswamy
Founded: 1916
Membership(s): Federation of Indian Publishers.
Subjects: Agriculture, Biography, Fiction, Health, Nutrition, Philosophy, Psychology, Psychiatry, Religion - Other, Social Sciences, Sociology
ISBN Prefix(es): 81-87145
*Branch Office(s)*
The Bangalore Press, Statue Sq, Mysore *Tel:* 570-001
Distributed by U B S Publishers' Distributors Ltd (India)

**Bani Mandir, Book-Sellers, Publishers & Educational Suppliers+**
Ranibari, Panbazar, Guwahati 781 001
*Tel:* (0361) 520241; (0361) 513886
*E-mail:* utpal@gwl.vsnl.net.in
*Web Site:* www.banimandir.cjb.net
*Telex:* 235-2455 NEWS IN *Cable:* LABANYA GUWAHATI
*Key Personnel*
Chief Executive: Chandra Kanta Hazarika
Editorial, Rights & Permissions: Surjya Kanta Hazarika
Sales: Ujjal Kumar Hazarika
Publicity: Utpal Kumar Hazarika
Founded: 1949
Membership(s): Federation of Indian Publishers; Federations of Indian Booksellers & Publishers Association.
Subjects: Anthropology, Biological Sciences, Chemistry, Chemical Engineering, Cookery, Economics, Education, Environmental Studies, Ethnicity
ISBN Prefix(es): 81-7206
Subsidiaries: Chandra Kanta Press Pvt Ltd

**Benjamin Cummings**, *imprint of* Addison-Wesley Pte Ltd

**Bharat Law House Pvt Ltd+**
T-1/95 Mangolpuri Industrial Area, New Delhi
110 083
*Tel:* (011) 791 0001; (011) 791 0002; (011) 791
0003 *Fax:* (011) 791 0004
*E-mail:* blh@nda.vsnl.net.in
*Key Personnel*
Chairman, Man Dir, Rights & Permissions: D C
Puliani
Sales: Ashok Puliani
Editorial: Ravi Puliani
Publicity, Production: Mahesh Puliani
Founded: 1957
Subjects: Law
ISBN Prefix(es): 81-85397; 81-7737
*Branch Office(s)*
Shop 6, 1st floor, Amar Towers 1, First Cross,
Gandhinagar, Bangalore 560009 *Tel:* (080)
2263434
*Showroom(s):* 4779/23 Ansari Rd, Daryaganj,
New Delhi 110002 *Tel:* (011) 3275884; (011)
3278282

**Bharat Publishing House+**
Flat No 123, Durga Chambers, Desh Bandhu
Gupta Rd, Karol Bagh, New Delhi 110005
*Tel:* (011) 25757081; (011) 23670067 *Fax:* (011)
23676058
*E-mail:* pitambar@bol.net.in
*Key Personnel*
Contact: Manish Aggarwal
Founded: 1990
Membership(s): Federation of Indian Publishers,
New Delhi (India).
Subjects: Geography, Geology, Language Arts,
Linguistics, Mathematics, Physics, Science
(General)
ISBN Prefix(es): 81-86378
*Parent Company:* Pitambar Publishing Co (P)
Ltd, 888 E Park Rd, Karol Bagh, New Delhi
11005
*Associate Companies:* Ambar Parkashan
Distributed by Pitambar Publishing Co (P) Ltd
Foreign Rep(s): S Rattan (Middle East)

**Bharatiya Vidya Bhavan**
Munshi Sadan Marg Kulapathikm, Mumbai 400
007
*Tel:* (022) 3631261; (022) 8118261; (022)
8118262 *Fax:* (022) 3630058 *Cable:*
BHAVIDYA BOMBAY GIRGAON
*Key Personnel*
Executive Secretary, Editorial, Rights & Permis-
sions: S Ramakrishnan
Founded: 1938
Subjects: Art, Biography, Ethnicity, Fiction, His-
tory, Literature, Literary Criticism, Essays, Phi-
losophy, Religion - Other, Social Sciences, So-
ciology
ISBN Prefix(es): 81-7276
*Branch Office(s)*
Ahmedabad
Bangalore
Baroda
Belgaum
Bharuch
Bharwari
Bhatpara
Bhimavaram
Bhopal
Bhubaneswar
Calicut
Cannanore
Chandigarh
Chennai
Coimbatore
Dakor
Delhi
Ernakulam
Guntur
Hyderabad
Jaipur
Jammu

Jamnagar
Jodhpur
Kakinada
Kannyakumari
Kanpur
Kodaikanal
Kolkata
Kurkunta
Lucknow
Mangalore
Mukundgarth
Nagpur
New Delhi
Palghat
Patna
Pune
Ramachandrapuram
Ratangarh
Renukoot
Rourkela
Serampore
Tadapalligudam
Trichur
Trivandrum
Varanasi
Visakhapatnam
4-A Castle Town Rd, London W14 9HQ, United
Kingdom *Tel:* (020) 8381 3086
*U.S. Office(s):* 79 Milk St, Boston, MA, United
States *Tel:* 617-426-4525
65-09 Queens Blvd, Woodside, NY 11377,
United States

**Bhawan Book Service, Publishers &
Distributors+**
13/2 Pant Nagar, New Delhi 110014
*Tel:* 2258836; 271559; 612-67-2506 *Fax:* 265315;
612-67-0010
*E-mail:* bbpdpat@glascl01.vsnl.net.in
*Key Personnel*
Contact: Sanjay Bose
Founded: 1942
Membership(s): Federation of Indian Publishers;
Federation of Educational Publishers.
Subjects: Agriculture, Chemistry, Chemical En-
gineering, Computer Science, Earth Sciences,
Economics, Education, English as a Second
Language, Geography, Geology
ISBN Prefix(es): 81-87090
*Branch Office(s)*
Darbhanga
Kolkata
Muzaffarpur
New Delhi
Ranchi

**Biblia Impex Pvt Ltd**
2/18 Ansari Rd, New Delhi 110002
*Tel:* (011) 23278034; (011) 23262515 *Fax:* (011)
2328-2047
*E-mail:* info@bibliaimpex.com
*Web Site:* www.bibliaimpex.com *Cable:* ELYSI
UM
*Key Personnel*
Man Dir: P K Goel
Founded: 1980
Also export Indian publications.
ISBN Prefix(es): 81-85012

**Big Database Publishing Pvt Ltd**
36-C Connaught Pl, New Delhi 110001
*Key Personnel*
Man Dir, Publicity: Sudhir Malhorta
Editorial: Arun Coyal
Sales: S Khanna
Production: K D Sharma
Founded: 1984
Subjects: Economics
ISBN Prefix(es): 81-85166
*Associate Companies:* Orient Paperbacks; Vision
Books Pvt Ltd

**Bihar Hindi Granth Akademi**
One Premchand Marg, Rajender Nagar, Patna
800016
*Tel:* (0612) 50390
*Key Personnel*
Chairman: Lokesh Nath Jha
Dir, Rights & Permissions: Dr B N Thakur
Editorial: Yoganand Jha
Sales, Production & Publicity: Ramchandra Singh
Founded: 1970
Subjects: Human Relations, Science (General)
ISBN Prefix(es): 81-7351

**Book Circle**
Subsidiary of Disha Prakashan
Prakash Mahal, 109, Daryaganj, New Delhi
110002
*Tel:* (011) 23266258; (011) 23288283; (011)
23257798 *Fax:* (011) 23263050
*E-mail:* info@meditechbooks.com
*Web Site:* www.meditechbooks.com
*Key Personnel*
Proprietor: Himanshu Chawla
Specialize in medical & technical books.
Subjects: Agriculture, Architecture & Interior De-
sign, Asian Studies, Criminology, Engineering
(General), Mathematics, Mechanical Engineer-
ing, Medicine, Nursing, Dentistry, Philosophy,
Religion - Buddhist, Social Sciences, Sociol-
ogy, Veterinary Science, Women's Studies
*Ultimate Parent Company:* Heritage Publishers

**Book Faith India+**
Flat No 416, Express Tower, Azadpur Commer-
cial Complex, Delhi 110033
*Tel:* (011) 713-2459 *Fax:* (011) 724-9674
*E-mail:* pilgrim@del2.vsml.net.in
*Key Personnel*
Publisher: Rawa Tiwari
Man Editor: Praveen Sareen *Tel:* (011) 7462427
Executive Editor: John Snyder Jr
Founded: 1990
Membership(s): New Delhi Association of Pub-
lishers.
Subjects: Asian Studies, Religion - Buddhist, Re-
ligion - Hindu
ISBN Prefix(es): 81-7303
*Associate Companies:* Pilgrim Book House, B-
27/98 A-8 Durgakund, Habasganj, Varanasi
*E-mail:* Pilgrim@RW1.vsnl.net.in
*U.S. Office(s):* Pilgrims Book Distributors, PO
Box 72, Lake City, MI 49651-0072, United
States
Distributed by Moving Books; Pilgrims Book
House (Nepal)
*Orders to:* PO Box 3872, Kathmandu, Nepal

**Book Field Centre**, *imprint of* Era Books

**Bookionics**
Member of The Book Syndicate
3-5 1114/7, Opp Hotel Traveller Kachiguda X
Rd, Hyderabad 500 027
*Tel:* (040) 593654 *Fax:* (040) 595678
*E-mail:* bookionics@yahoo.com
*Key Personnel*
Owner: Chandrakant P Shah
Founded: 1985
Subjects: Computer Science, Engineering (Gen-
eral), Management

**Booklinks Corporation**
3-4-423/5 & 6 Narayanguda, Hyderabad 500029
*Tel:* (0842) 65021; (0842) 62282; (0842) 65550
*Cable:* BOOKLINKS
*Key Personnel*
Chief Executive, Editorial: K B Satyanarayana
Sales, Production, Publicity: K Ramakrishna
Founded: 1965
Subjects: Social Sciences, Sociology, Humanities
ISBN Prefix(es): 81-85194

**Books & Books+**
C4A/20A, Janakpuri, New Delhi 110058
*Tel:* (011) 551252
*Key Personnel*
Contact: Indramohan Sharma; Aniruddha Bhaskar
Founded: 1980
Membership(s): Federation of Indian Publishers;
  Specializes in Archaeology & Art.
Subjects: Anthropology, Archaeology, Architec-
  ture & Interior Design, Art, History, Philos-
  ophy, Religion - Buddhist, Religion - Hindu,
  Religion - Islamic
ISBN Prefix(es): 81-85016

**BPB Publications+**
20 Munish Plaza, 20 Ansari Rd, Darya Ganj,
  New Delhi 110002
*Tel:* (011) 3281723; (011) 3254990; (011)
  3254991 *Fax:* (011) 3266427
*E-mail:* admin@bpbonline.com
*Web Site:* www.bpbonline.com
*Telex:* 31 66971qyanin *Cable:* Radiocraft
*Key Personnel*
President: Manish Jain
Founded: 1958
Subjects: Computer Science, Electronics, Electri-
  cal Engineering
ISBN Prefix(es): 81-7029; 81-7656
*Branch Office(s)*
8/1 Ritchie St, Mount Rd, Chennai 600002
4-3-269 Giriraj Lane, Bank St, Hyderabad 500001
*Bookshop(s):* Radio & Craft Publications, 4794
  Bharat Ram Rd, 23 Daryaganj, New Delhi
  110002

**BR Publishing Corporation+**
A-6, Nimri Commercial Centrem, Ashok Vihar
  Phase IV, Shastri Nagar, Delhi 110052
*Tel:* (011) 7430113; (011) 7143353
*Telex:* 31-66778 DK IN *Cable:* INDLIT
*Key Personnel*
Chief Executive, Editorial, Production & Public-
  ity: Praveen Mittal
Founded: 1974
Subjects: Agriculture, Anthropology, Archaeol-
  ogy, Art, Economics, Government, Political
  Science, Health, Nutrition, History, Literature,
  Literary Criticism, Essays, Social Sciences, So-
  ciology
ISBN Prefix(es): 81-7018; 81-7646
*Parent Company:* BRPC (India) Ltd
*Associate Companies:* Books for All; Low Price
  Publications
*U.S. Office(s):* South Asia Books, PO Box 502,
  Columbia, MO, United States
*Showroom(s):* One Ansari Rd, Daryaganj, New
  Delhi 110002
*Orders to:* D K Publisher's Distributors Pvt Ltd,
  One Ansari Rd, New Delhi 2

**Brijbasi Printers Pvt Ltd+**
E-46/11 Okhia Industrial Area, Phase II, New
  Delhi 110020
*Tel:* (011) 6914115; (011) 6841897 *Fax:* (011)
  6837835
*Key Personnel*
Dir: Saurabh Garg; M L Garg
Founded: 1980
Subjects: Art, Cookery, Natural History, Religion
  - Hindu, Travel
ISBN Prefix(es): 81-7107
*Associate Companies:* S S Brijbasl & Sons

**BS Publications+**
Member of The Book Syndicate
Sultan Bazaar, Girraj Lane, 4-4-309, 2nd floor,
  500 095 Hyderabad
*Tel:* (040) 23445600; (040) 23445601 *Fax:* (040)
  23445611
*E-mail:* contactus@bspublications.net
*Key Personnel*
Owner: Nikhil Nandan C Shah

Founded: 1999
Subjects: Biological Sciences, Chemistry, Chem-
  ical Engineering, Communications, Computer
  Science, Earth Sciences, Electronics, Electri-
  cal Engineering, Energy, Engineering (Gen-
  eral), Environmental Studies, Geography, Ge-
  ology, Management, Mechanical Engineering,
  Medicine, Nursing, Dentistry, Microcomputers,
  Physical Sciences, Physics, Transportation
ISBN Prefix(es): 81-7800
Total Titles: 25 Print

**BSMPS - M/s Bishen Singh Mahendra Pal
  Singh+**
23A Connaught Pl, Dehra Dun 248 001
Mailing Address: PO Box 137, Dehra Dun 248
  001
*Tel:* (0135) 24048 *Fax:* (0135) 650107
*Key Personnel*
Man Dir, Sales: Gajendra Singh Gahlot
Editorial, Publicity, Rights & Permissions: R G S
  Gahlot
Production: Srimati Jaswanti Devi
Founded: 1957
Subjects: Agriculture, Biological Sciences, Earth
  Sciences, Environmental Studies, Geography,
  Geology, Natural History
ISBN Prefix(es): 81-211
Distributed by Koeltz Scientific Books (Germany)

**Business Information Group,** see Big Database
Publishing Pvt Ltd

**Central Tibetan Secretariat**
c/o Library of Tibetan Works & Archives,
  Gangchen Kyishong, Dharamsala 176215
*Tel:* (01892) 22467 *Fax:* (01892) 23723
*E-mail:* ltwa@ndf.vsnl.net.in
*Key Personnel*
General Secretary: Sonam Topgyal
Sales Manager: Pasang Tsering
Production, Publicity, Rights & Permissions: Lodi
  G Gyari
Founded: 1961
Subjects: Ethnicity, Journalism, Religion - Other
Subsidiaries: Sheja Press, McLeod Ganj, Dharam-
  sala Cantt, Himachal Pradesh; Tibetan Bulletin,
  c/o Library of Tibetan Works & Archives; Ti-
  betan Freedom Press, Toon Soong, Tenzin Nor-
  gay Rd, Darjeeling, Bengla

**Chanakya Publications+**
F 10/14, Model Town, Delhi 110009
*Tel:* (011) 711976 *Cable:* CHANAKYA
*Key Personnel*
Proprieter: Akhileshwar Jha
Sales: R P Maurya
Production: Chakradhar
Editorial, Publicity, Rights & Permissions: S K
  Jha
Founded: 1980
Subjects: Ethnicity, Fiction, Human Relations,
  Poetry, Social Sciences, Sociology
ISBN Prefix(es): 81-7001
Subsidiaries: Prism India Paperbacks

**S Chand & Co Ltd+**
Ram Nagar, Hotel Tourist Complex, New Delhi
  110 055
Mailing Address: PO Box 5733, Ram Nagar, New
  Delhi 110 055
*Tel:* (011) 3672080; (011) 3672081; (011)
  3672082 *Fax:* (011) 3677446
*E-mail:* schand@vsnl.com
*Telex:* 31-61310 *Cable:* ESCHAND, NEW
  DELHI
*Key Personnel*
Man Dir, Editorial & Publishing Dir, Rights &
  Permissions: Rajendra Kumar Gupta
General Administration & Export: B N Chatterjee
Sales & Marketing: R K Sahni

Founded: 1917
Subjects: Art, Business, Economics, Government,
  Political Science, Medicine, Nursing, Dentistry,
  Philosophy, Science (General), Social Sciences,
  Sociology, Technology
ISBN Prefix(es): 81-219
*Associate Companies:* Rajendra Ravindra Printers
  Pvt Ltd, New Delhi; Shyamlal Charitable Trust,
  New Delhi (Publications)
Subsidiaries: Eurasia Publishing House Pvt Ltd
Divisions: S Chand Education Worldwide (direct
  sales for Encyclopeadia Britannica products)
*Branch Office(s)*
No 6, Ahuja Chambers, 1st Cross, Kumara
  Krupa Rd, Bangalore 560001, Contact:
  Mr P Rajalingam *Fax:* (080) 2268048
  *E-mail:* schandpublish@vsnl.net
SCO 6, 7 & 8, Sector 9D, Chandigarh 160016,
  Contact: B L Ghai *Tel:* (0712) 692680
152, Anna Salai, Chennai 600002, Contact:
  A M Arunachalam *Fax:* (044) 8460026
  *E-mail:* mdschand@del6.vsnl.net.in
613-7, M G Rd, Ernakulam, Kochi, Contact:
  Mr Mohan Das Menon *Tel:* (0484) 381740
  *E-mail:* schandco@md4.vsnl.net.in
Dilip Commercial, 1st floor, M N Rd, Pan
  Bazaar, Guwahati 780001, Contact: S K Ba-
  gal *Fax:* (0361) 522155 *E-mail:* guschand@
  gw1.vsnl.net.in
Sultan Bazaar, Hyderabad 500195, Contact: Mr
  I J Talwar *Tel:* (040) 4744815 *Fax:* (040)
  4651135 *E-mail:* schand@hd2.dot.net.in
Mai Hiran Gate, Jalandhar 144008, Contact: M P
  J Singh *Tel:* (0181) 401630 *E-mail:* jaschand@
  vsnl.com
285/j Bipin Bihari, Ganguly St, Kolkata 700012,
  Contact: Mrs R M Nath *Tel:* (033) 2367459
  *Fax:* (033) 2373914 *E-mail:* clschnd@del6.
  vsnl.net.in
Mahavir Market, 25-Gwynne Rd, Aminabad,
  Lucknow 226801, Contact: Mr Vipin Kr
  Gupta *Tel:* (0522) 284815 *Fax:* (0522) 226801
  *E-mail:* schand_luk@ayadh.net
Blackie House, 103/5 Walchand Hirachand Marg,
  Opp GPO, Mumbai 400001, Contact: Mr D R
  Parab *Tel:* (022) 2690881 *Fax:* (022) 2610885
  *E-mail:* schand@del6.vsnl.net.in
Gandhi Sagar E, Nagpur 440002, Con-
  tact: Mr B Kaushik *Tel:* (0712) 723901
  *E-mail:* naschand@nagpur.dot.net.in
104 CitiCentre Ashok, Govind Mitra Rd, Patna
  800004, Contact: Mr R C Bhatt *Tel:* (0612)
  671366 *E-mail:* paschand@dte.vsnl.net.in
Distributor for Britannica (India)
*Orders to:* Nirja Construction & Development
  Co (P) Ltd, Publishers, Ram Nagar, New Delhi
  110055

**Charotar Publishing House**
Opp Amul Dairy, Civil Court Rd, PO Box 65,
  Anand Gujarat 388001
*Tel:* (02692) 256237 *Fax:* (02692) 240089
*E-mail:* charotar@icenet.net; charotar@cphbooks.
  com
*Web Site:* www.cphbooks.com
*Key Personnel*
Chief Executive, Publicity, Right & Permissions:
  Ramanbhai C Patel
Sales: Bhavin R Patel; Pradeep R Patel
Founded: 1944
Subjects: Civil Engineering, Engineering (Gen-
  eral)
ISBN Prefix(es): 81-85594
Total Titles: 50 Print
*Parent Company:* Charotar Associate, Charotar
  Books Distributors
Subsidiaries: Charotar Book Distributors
*Bookshop(s):* Charotar Book Stall, nr Post Office,
  Vallabh Vidyanagar, Via Anand Gujarat 388120

**Chetana Private Ltd Publishers &
  International Booksellers**
K Dubash Marg, Kala Ghoda, Mumbai 400023

*Tel:* (022) 228 81159; (022) 282 4983 *Fax:* (022) 262 4316
*E-mail:* orders@chetana.com; chetana1946@ chetana.com
*Web Site:* www.chetana.com *Cable:* Indology
*Key Personnel*
Man Dir: Sudhakar S Dikshit
Publicity: K T Vaidya
Founded: 1946
Subjects: Philosophy, Religion - Other
ISBN Prefix(es): 81-85300

**Children's Book Trust+**
Nehru House, 4 Bahadur Shah Zafar Marg, New Delhi 110 002
*Tel:* (011) 23316974; (011) 23316970 *Fax:* (011) 23721090
*E-mail:* cbtnd@vsnl.com
*Web Site:* www.childrensbooktrust.com *Cable:* CHILDTRUST
*Key Personnel*
Chief Executive: Yamuna Shankar
General Manager, Rights & Permissions: Ravi Shankar
Sales Manager & Publicity: H R Khurana
Founded: 1957
ISBN Prefix(es): 81-7011
*Branch Office(s)*
18-C, Rayala Towers, Anna Salai, Chennai 600002, Contact: V Badrinarynan *Tel:* (044) 28521850
G-14, Kamalalaya Centre, 156-A, Lenin Sarani, Kolkata 700013, Contact: Bimal Datta *Tel:* (033) 22155094

**Chowkhamba Sanskrit Series Office**
K-37/99 Gopal Mandir Lane, Varanasi 221 001
Mailing Address: PO Box 1008, Varanasi 221 001
*Tel:* (0542) 2333458 *Fax:* (0542) 2333458
*E-mail:* cssoffice@satyam.net.in
*Web Site:* www.chowkhambaseries.com *Cable:* CHOWKHAMBA SERIES VARANASI
*Key Personnel*
Man Dir, Publicity: Brajmohan Das Gupta *Tel:* (0542) 2335020
Sales, Production: Kamalesh Kumar Gupta *Tel:* (0542) 2334032
Founded: 1892
Printing & selling Ayurvedic books & books on Indology.
Subjects: Anthropology, Archaeology, Architecture & Interior Design, Art, Asian Studies, Astrology, Occult, Astronomy, Biography, Economics, Geography, Geology, Health, Nutrition, History, Music, Dance, Philosophy, Physical Sciences, Poetry, Religion - Other
ISBN Prefix(es): 81-7080
Number of titles published annually: 20 Print
Total Titles: 450 Print
*Associate Companies:* Chowkhamba Krishnadas Academy, K-37/118 Gopal Mandir Lane, PO Box 1118, Varanasi 221001 *Tel:* (0542) 2335020 *E-mail:* cssoffice@satyam.net.in

**The Christian Literature Society+**
No 68, Evening Bazaar Rd, Park Town, Chennai 600 003
Mailing Address: PO Box No 501, Park Town, Tamil Nadu 600 003
*Tel:* (044) 25354296; (044) 25354297 *Fax:* (044) 25354297 *Cable:* Vedic
*Key Personnel*
Contact: Joshua J Singh
Founded: 1858
Subjects: Asian Studies, Biblical Studies, Biography, Philosophy, Religion - Protestant, Technology, Women's Studies
ISBN Prefix(es): 81-85884
Distributed by ISPCK
*Bookshop(s):* CLS Bookshop, The Estate, Ground floor, Rear Block, 121, Dickenson Rd, Banga-

lore 560 042 *Tel:* (080) 25582729; CLS Bookshop, PO Box 501, Park Town, Chennai 600 003; CLS Bookshop, M G Rd, Cochin 682 011 *Tel:* (0484) 2381677; CLS Bookshop, 775, Avanashi Rd, Coimbatore 641 018 *Tel:* (0422) 2301609; CLS Bookshop, Nampally Station Rd, Hyderabad 500 001 *Tel:* (040) 23202046; CLS Bookshop, 15-D, W Veli St, Madurai 625 001 *Tel:* (0452) 2342405; CLS Bookshop, M G Rd, Pulimood, Trivandrum 695 001 *Tel:* (0471) 478115

**Chugh Publications**
2, Strachey Rd, Civil Lines, Allahabad 211001
*Tel:* (0532) 623561
*Key Personnel*
Chief Executive, Production, Publicity, Rights & Permissions: Ramesh Chugh
Sales: Suman Chugh
Founded: 1973
Subjects: Human Relations, Social Sciences, Sociology
ISBN Prefix(es): 81-85076; 81-85613
*Associate Companies:* R S Publishing House, 20 Mahatma Gandhi Marg, Allahabad
*Bookshop(s):* Universal Book Shop

**CICC Book House, Leading Publishers & Booksellers**
Press Club Rd, Cochin, Kerala 682011
*Tel:* (0484) 353557; (0484) 355658
*Key Personnel*
Contact: T Jayachandran
Founded: 1962
Subjects: Drama, Theater, Fiction, Literature, Literary Criticism, Essays
ISBN Prefix(es): 81-7174
*Book Club(s):* Crime Book Club

**Clarion**, *imprint of* Hind Pocket Books Private Ltd

**Clarion Books**, *imprint of* Full Circle Publishing

**Classical Publishing Co**
c/o Indological Publishers & Booksellers, 28 Shopping Centre, Karampura, New Delhi 110015
*Tel:* (011) 563689
*Key Personnel*
Man Dir, Editorial: Bal Krishan Taneja
Marketing: Miss Suman Sharma
Production: Nirmal Rani
Publicity: R P Singh
Founded: 1976
Subjects: Social Sciences, Sociology
ISBN Prefix(es): 81-7054

**Comdex Computer Publishing**, *imprint of* Pustak Mahal

**Concept Publishing Co+**
A/15-16, Commercial Block, Mohan Garden, New Delhi 110059
Mailing Address: PO Box 6274, New Delhi 11015
*Tel:* (011) 5648039 *Fax:* (011) 5648053
*E-mail:* publishing@conceptpub.com
*Web Site:* www.conceptpub.com *Cable:* CONPUBCO, New Delhi-59
*Key Personnel*
Proprietor & Chief Executive: Ashok Kumar Mittal
Editorial, Sales, Publicity: Nitin Mittal
Founded: 1974
Subjects: Alternative, Anthropology, Asian Studies, Behavioral Sciences, Communications, Earth Sciences, Economics, Education, Energy, Environmental Studies, Ethnicity, Geography, Geology, History, Journalism, Library & Information Sciences, Management, Philoso-

phy, Psychology, Psychiatry, Public Administration, Self-Help, Social Sciences, Sociology, Women's Studies
ISBN Prefix(es): 81-7022; 81-8069
Number of titles published annually: 50 Print
Total Titles: 1,400 Print
*Parent Company:* D K Agencies (P) Ltd
Subsidiaries: Logos Press
*Showroom(s):* 23 Ansari Rd, New Delhi 110002 *Tel:* (011) 3272187
*Bookshop(s):* 23 Ansari Rd, New Delhi 110002 *Tel:* (011) 3272187

**Cosmo Publications+**
24-B Ansari Rd, Daryaganj, New Delhi 110002
Mailing Address: PO Box 7206, New Delhi 110002
*Tel:* (011) 3278779; (011) 3280455 *Fax:* (011) 3274597
*E-mail:* genesis.cosmo@axcess.net.in; genesis@ ndb.vsnl.net.in
*Key Personnel*
Chairman & Man Dir: Rani Kapoor
Chief Editor & Sales Dir: Subodh Kapoor
Dir Foreign Sales, Rights & Permissions: Sunil Kapoor
Founded: 1972
Membership(s): Federation of Indian Publishers; Federation of Publishers & Booksellers Association in India; Chemicals & Allied Export Promotions Council.
Subjects: Agriculture, Anthropology, Archaeology, Art, Asian Studies, Developing Countries, Drama, Theater, Economics, Education, Ethnicity, Government, Political Science, History, Language Arts, Linguistics, Library & Information Sciences, Literature, Literary Criticism, Essays, Music, Dance, Natural History, Nonfiction (General), Philosophy, Religion - Buddhist, Religion - Hindu, Religion - Islamic, Social Sciences, Sociology, Veterinary Science
ISBN Prefix(es): 81-7020; 81-7755
Total Titles: 1,225 Print
*Parent Company:* Genesis Publishing Pvt Ltd
Imprints: Siddhi Books
Subsidiaries: Cosmopolitan Book House
Divisions: Cosmo Dictionaries; Falcon Books
*Warehouse:* 4/16 West Patel Nagar, New Delhi 110 008

**Current Books**
D C Bookshop Poorna Complex, Thrissur 680001
*Tel:* (0487) 2444322
*E-mail:* info@dcbooks.com
*Web Site:* www.dcbooks.com/currentbooks.htm *Cable:* Current Books
*Key Personnel*
Chief Executive: D C Kizhakemuri
Editorial: M S Chandrasekhara Warrier
Sales: Kiliroor Radhakrishnan
Production, Publicity: Vadayar Vijayakumar
Rights & Permissions: Ponnamma Deecee
Founded: 1952
Subjects: Fiction, Nonfiction (General)
ISBN Prefix(es): 81-226
*Associate Companies:* D C Books; Kairali Children's Book Trust; Kairali Mudralayam
*Branch Office(s)*
Alappuzha *Tel:* (0477) 2261197
Aluva *Tel:* (0484) 2626006
Ernakulam *Tel:* (0484) 2351590
Irinjalakuda *Tel:* (0480) 2820667
Kalpetta *Tel:* (0493) 6203766
Kollam *Tel:* (0474) 2749055
Kottayam *Tel:* (0481) 2560342
Kozhikode *Tel:* (0495) 2727299
Palakkad *Tel:* (0491) 2535314
Pathanamthitta *Tel:* (0468) 2321268
Thalassery *Tel:* (0490) 2320668
Thiruvanathapuram *Tel:* (0471) 2477693
Thodupuzha *Tel:* (0486) 2223915
Vadakara *Tel:* (0496) 2523810
*Book Club(s):* VIP Book Club

**D C Press**, *imprint of* Kairali Children's Book Trust

**Dastane Ramchandra & Co+**
830, Sadashiv Peth, Chitrashala Chowk, Pune, Maharashtra 411 030
*Tel:* (020) 447 8193; (020) 448 5950; (020) 551 1964 *Fax:* (020) 4478193
*Key Personnel*
Man Dir, Editorial, Production: Vishwas Dastane
Sales, Publicity, Rights & Permissions: Mrs Bharati Dastane
Founded: 1960
Membership(s): Marathi Publishers' Association; Specialize in Social Sciences, Career Development & Help-books.
Subjects: Career Development, Economics, History, Library & Information Sciences, Literature, Literary Criticism, Essays, Science (General), Science Fiction, Fantasy, Self-Help, Social Sciences, Sociology, Sports, Athletics, Women's Studies
ISBN Prefix(es): 81-85080
*Associate Companies:* Abhang Stores, Printers & Stationers, 830 Sadashiv Peth, Chitrashala Chowk, Pune 411030; Sports Publications, 830 Sadashiv Peth, Chitrashala Chowk, Pune 411030; Anuja Prakashan Publishers, 13A, Abhang Poona-Bombay Rd, Pune
*Bookshop(s):* 456 Raviwar Peth, Pune 411002

**Daya Publishing House+**
4762-63/23, Ansari Rd, Darya Ganj, New Delhi 110 002
*Tel:* (011) 23245578; (011) 23244987 *Fax:* (011) 23244987
*E-mail:* dayabooks@vsnl.com
*Web Site:* www.dayabooks.com
*Key Personnel*
Contact: Anil Mittal
Founded: 1986
Subjects: Agriculture, Biological Sciences, Earth Sciences, Environmental Studies, Geography, Geology, Natural History, Veterinary Science
ISBN Prefix(es): 81-7035
Number of titles published annually: 25 Print

**DC Books+**
Good Shepherd St, Kottayam, Kerala 686001
Mailing Address: PO Box 214, Kottayam, Kerala 686001
*Tel:* (0481) 2563114; (0481) 2301614
*Web Site:* www.dcbooks.com *Cable:* Deecibooks
*Key Personnel*
Chief Executive, Rights & Permissions: D C Kizhakemuri
Editorial: M S Chandrasekhara Warrier
Sales: T K Murukesan
Production, Publicity: D Sreekumar
Founded: 1974
Subjects: Fiction, Literature, Literary Criticism, Essays, Poetry
ISBN Prefix(es): 81-7130; 81-264
*Associate Companies:* Current Books; Kairali Children's Book Trust; Kairali Mudralayam
*Book Club(s):* Classics Club; D C Book Club

**Diamond Comics (P) Ltd+**
A-22, Sector-63, Gobird Villa, Phase-3, Noida-201 301, Uttar Pradesh
*Tel:* 9810003062 (Mobile) *Fax:* (0120) 2401093; (0120) 2401094; (0120) 2401095; (0120) 2401073
*E-mail:* comicsdiamond@mantraonline.com
*Web Site:* www.comicsdiamond.com
*Key Personnel*
Man Dir: Narender Kumar
Editorial: Gulshan Rai
International Rights: Mr Marrish Verma
Founded: 1948

Subjects: Cookery, Crafts, Games, Hobbies, Criminology, Fiction, Health, Nutrition, How-to, Religion - Hindu
ISBN Prefix(es): 81-7184
*Associate Companies:* Diamond Books International, X-30, Okhala Industrial Estate Phase II, New Delhi 110020; Diamond Pocket (P) Ltd Books, X-30, Okhala Industrial Estate Phase II, New Delhi 110020; Punjabi Pustak Bhandar
Subsidiaries: Diamond Magazines
*Book Club(s):* Diamond Book Club

**Disha Prakashan**
138/16 Onkar Nagar-B, Tri Nagar, Delhi 110035
*Tel:* 7108832
*Key Personnel*
Man Dir, Publicity: B R Chawla
Founded: 1973
Subjects: Biography, Economics, History, Language Arts, Linguistics, Literature, Literary Criticism, Essays, Philosophy, Religion - Other, Social Sciences, Sociology
ISBN Prefix(es): 81-85045; 81-88081
*Parent Company:* Heritage Publishers
*Associate Companies:* Intellectuals' Rendezvous, Aggarwal Bhawa, 4C Ansari Rd, New Delhi 110002; Pankaj Publications International
Subsidiaries: Book Circle

**DK Printworld (P) Ltd+**
Srikunj, F-52 Bali Nagar, New Delhi 110015
*Tel:* (011) 25453975; (011) 25466019 *Fax:* (011) 25465926
*E-mail:* dkprintworld@vsnl.net
*Key Personnel*
Dir: Mr Susheel K Mittal
Founded: 1992
Specialize in books on Indology.
Subjects: Archaeology, Art, Asian Studies, Astrology, Occult, Drama, Theater, History, Music, Dance, Philosophy, Religion - Buddhist, Religion - Hindu, Religion - Islamic
ISBN Prefix(es): 81-246
Total Titles: 300 Print

**Doaba Publications**
4497/14 Guru Nanak Market, Nai Sarak, New Delhi 110 006
*Tel:* (011) 3274669; (011) 3259753
*Key Personnel*
Chief Executive, Editorial, Sales, Rights & Permissions: S N Malhotra
Production, Publicity: Rajiv Malhotra; A C Seth
Founded: 1924
Subjects: Education, English as a Second Language, Literature, Literary Criticism, Essays
ISBN Prefix(es): 81-85173; 81-87764

**Dolphin Publications+**
203-5 Shiv Darshan M G Rd, Opp Station Santacruz (West), Mumbai 400054
*Tel:* (022) 6490184 *Fax:* (022) 6233674
*Key Personnel*
Editor: Mrs Renu Nauriyal
Founded: 1986
Membership(s): Federation of Indian Publishers & Export Promotion Council; Specialize in children's books, general & nonfiction books.
Subjects: Animals, Pets, Biblical Studies, Crafts, Games, Hobbies, History, Mathematics, Natural History, Nonfiction (General)
ISBN Prefix(es): 81-85523
*Associate Companies:* India Book House, 203-5 Shiv Darshan M G Rd, Opp Station Santacruz (West), Mumbai 400054
Subsidiaries: J Moolur & Co

**Dreamland Publications+**
J-128, Kirti Nagar, New Delhi 110015
*Tel:* (011) 25106050; (011) 25435657 *Fax:* (011) 25428283

*E-mail:* dreamland@vsnl.com
*Web Site:* www.dreamlandpublications.com
*Key Personnel*
Contact: Ved Chawla
Founded: 1986
ISBN Prefix(es): 81-7301
*Parent Company:* Indian Book Depot

**Dutta Publishing Co Ltd+**
College Hostel Rd, Panbazar, Guwahati-1, Assam 781 001
*Tel:* (0361) 543995
*Key Personnel*
Man Dir: J N Dutta Baruah
Founded: 1938
Also act as distributors.
Membership(s): Federation of Indian Publishers.
Subjects: Art, Cookery, Language Arts, Linguistics, Literature, Literary Criticism, Essays, Poetry, Religion - Hindu, Religion - Other, Sports, Athletics
ISBN Prefix(es): 81-7373
Subsidiaries: M/S Parbati Prakashan

**Eastern Book Centre+**
Publishers Distributors & Library Suppliers, F-26, Shankar Market Connaught Circus, New Delhi 110001
*Tel:* (011) 3314191
*Key Personnel*
Contact: Subir Ghosh
Founded: 1989
Membership(s): Federation of Indian Publishers.
Subjects: Social Sciences, Sociology
ISBN Prefix(es): 81-85186

**Eastern Book Co+**
34 Lalbagh, Lucknow 226 001
*Tel:* (0522) 2223171; (0522) 2226517 *Fax:* (0522) 2224328
*E-mail:* sales@ebc-india.com
*Web Site:* www.ebc-india.com *Cable:* LAWBOOK; LUCKNOW
*Key Personnel*
Chief Executive: P L Malik
Editorial: Surendra Malik
Production, Publicity & Exports: Vijay Malik
Founded: 1947
Specialize in law books & law reports in print media & electronic media (CD-ROM).
Membership(s): Federation of Publishers & Booksellers Association of India, New Delhi; Avadh Chamber of Commerce & Industry; Lucknow Management Association; Indian Industries Association; Lalbagh Vyapar Mandal; Chemicals & Allied Products Export Promotion Council.
Subjects: Law
ISBN Prefix(es): 81-7012
Number of titles published annually: 100 Print; 2 CD-ROM
Total Titles: 1,200 Print; 8 CD-ROM
*Associate Companies:* Eastern Book Co, 5-B, Atma Ram House, 1, Tolstoy Marg, Connaught Pl, Delhi 110054, Contact: Vijay Malik *Tel:* (011) 23752321 *Fax:* (011) 23752320; Eastern Book Company Pvt Ltd, Contact: Sumain Malik *E-mail:* sales@scconline.com *Web Site:* www.scconline.com; EBC Publishing Pvt Ltd; Manav Law House, 8-10, MG Marg, Opp Bishop Johnson School, Allahabad 211001 *Tel:* (0532) 2623551; (0532) 2560710 *Fax:* (0532) 2623584
Distributed by Anupam Gyan Bhandar (Bangladesh); Blackwell's (Periodicals Division) (UK); Gurley & Associates (Trinidad & Tobago); Kokusai Shobo Ltd (Japan); Law Book Traders (Malaysia); Mabrochi International Co Ltd (Nigeria); Pakistan Law House (Pakistan); State Mutual Book & Periodical Services Ltd (US)

**Eastern Law House Pvt Ltd+**
54 Ganesh Chunder Ave, Kolkata 700 013
*Tel:* (033) 237 4989; (033) 237 2301 *Fax:* (033) 215 0491
*E-mail:* elh@cal.vsnl.net.in
*Web Site:* easternlawhouse.com
*Key Personnel*
Director: Asok De
Founded: 1918
Subjects: Accounting, Government, Political Science, Law, Social Sciences, Sociology
ISBN Prefix(es): 81-7177
Number of titles published annually: 20 Print
Total Titles: 1,000 Print
*Bookshop(s):* 36 Netaji Subhash Marg, Daryaganj, New Delhi 11002
*Orders to:* 36 Netaji Subhash Marg, Daryaganj, New Delhi 110002 *Tel:* (011) 327 9982 *Fax:* (011) 325 3844

**Enkay Publishers Pvt Ltd**
Enkay House, 3-4 Malcha Marg, Shopping Centre, Diplomatic Enclave, New Delhi 110021
*Tel:* (011) 301-6994; (011) 301-2314 *Fax:* (011) 301-2314
*Telex:* 031-6312nkayin *Cable:* ENTRAVEL
*Key Personnel*
Contact: S Narinder Singh Kohli
Membership(s): Federation of Indian Publishers.
Subjects: Biography, History, Religion - Other, Social Sciences, Sociology
ISBN Prefix(es): 81-85148
Subsidiaries: Enkay International Pvt Ltd

**Era Books**
52/47 Ramjas Rd, Karol Bagh, New Delhi 110005
*Tel:* (011) 473993; (022) 5741764 *Cable:* Goldenhill
*Key Personnel*
Chief Executive, Rights & Permissions: Eranna R Jinde
Editorial: C V Bhimasankaram
Sales: V R Jinde
Production: B Ramakumar
Publicity: J E Rao
Founded: 1979
Subjects: Education, Mathematics
ISBN Prefix(es): 81-900270
Imprints: Book Field Centre
Subsidiaries: Book Field Centre
*Branch Office(s)*
2-30 Khariboudi St, Adoni 518301

**Ess Ess Publications+**
CA 100929, Allahabad Bank, Darya Ganj Branch, Ansari Rd, New Delhi 110 002
*Tel:* (011) 3260807 *Fax:* (011) 3274173
*E-mail:* sumitsethi@vsnl.com
*Web Site:* www.essess.8m.com *Cable:* ESS ESS PUBLICATIONS
*Key Personnel*
Man Dir, Publicity, Rights & Permissions: Mrs Sheel Sethi
Editorial, Sales, Production: Sumit Sethi
 *E-mail:* sumitsethi@vsnl.com
Founded: 1974
Specialize in all Indian books on library & information science.
Subjects: Economics, History, Human Relations, Library & Information Sciences, Management, Philosophy, Religion - Hindu, Social Sciences, Sociology
ISBN Prefix(es): 81-7000
*Parent Company:* Ess Ess Publishers' Distributors, KD-6A Ashok Vihar, Delhi 110052
Subsidiaries: Sumit Publications
*Orders to:* Ess Ess Publishers' Distributors, KD-6A Ashok Vihar, Delhi 110052 *Tel:* (011) 7437308

**Eurasia Publishing House Private Ltd**
PO Box 5733, Ram Nagar, New Delhi 110 055
*Tel:* (011) 7779891 *Fax:* (011) 7777446
*E-mail:* schandco@giasdl.net.in
*Telex:* 3161310 Sccl In *Cable:* escahand
*Key Personnel*
Man Dir, Sales Dir, Rights & Permissions: Rajendra Kumar Gupta
Founded: 1960
Subjects: Education, Engineering (General), Psychology, Psychiatry, Science (General), Social Sciences, Sociology
ISBN Prefix(es): 81-219
*Parent Company:* S Chand & Co Ltd, Ram Nagar, New Delhi 110055
*Shipping Address:* S Chand & Co Ltd, Ram Nagar, New Delhi 110055
*Warehouse:* S Chand & Co Ltd, Ram Nagar, New Delhi 110055
*Orders to:* S Chand & Co Ltd, Ram Nagar, New Delhi 110055

**EWP**, *imprint of* Affiliated East West Press Pvt Ltd

**Financial Times PH**, *imprint of* Addison-Wesley Pte Ltd

**Firewall Media**, *imprint of* Laxmi Publications Pvt Ltd

**Firma KLM Privatee Ltd, Publishers & International Booksellers+**
257-B BB Ganguly St, Kolkata 700012
*Tel:* (033) 274391; (033) 4681209 *Fax:* (033) 276544
*Key Personnel*
Man Dir, Rights & Permissions: R N Mukherti
Editorial, Production: K Roy
Founded: 1950
Subjects: Alternative, Human Relations, Social Sciences, Sociology, Humanities, Indology
ISBN Prefix(es): 81-7102
*Associate Companies:* Firma Mukhopadhyay, 2/1 Dr Aksay Pal Rd, Kolkata 700034
Distributed by Blue Dove Press (USA); Malshow Co Ltd (Japan); South Asia Books (USA)
Distributor for Asiatic Society Calcutta Publications; Burdwan University; Sanskrit College (Kolkata)

**Focus**, *imprint of* Popular Prakashan Pvt Ltd

**Frank Brothers & Co Publishers Ltd+**
4675-A Ansari Rd, 21 Darya Ganj, New Delhi 110002
*Tel:* (011) 263393; (011) 279936; (011) 278150; (011) 260796 *Fax:* (011) 3269032
*E-mail:* fbros@ndb.vsnl.net.in
*Telex:* 0313265 Fran In
*Key Personnel*
Chairman: R C Govil
Dir: Neeraj Govil
Founded: 1930
Subjects: Accounting, Art, Biological Sciences, Business, Computer Science, Cookery, Economics, Education, English as a Second Language, Environmental Studies, Fiction, Geography, Geology, Government, Political Science, Health, Nutrition, History, Management, Mathematics, Nonfiction (General), Physics, Science (General)
ISBN Prefix(es): 81-7170
Number of titles published annually: 50 Print
Total Titles: 1,000 Print
*Bookshop(s):* IV/85 Chandni Chowk, Delhi 110006 *Tel:* (011) 3276791

**Full Circle Publishing+**
J-40 Jorbagh Lane, New Delhi 110003
*Tel:* (011) 55654197 *Fax:* (011) 24645795

*E-mail:* gbp@del2.vsnl.com; fullcircle@vsnl.com
*Web Site:* www.atfullcircle.com
*Key Personnel*
Chairman: D N Malhotra
Founded: 1970
Membership(s): Federation of Indian Publishers.
Subjects: Archaeology, Asian Studies, Astrology, Occult, Child Care & Development, Cookery, Economics, Gardening, Plants, Health, Nutrition, How-to, Humor, Language Arts, Linguistics, Law, Management, Marketing, Nonfiction (General), Poetry, Religion - Other, Self-Help, Arts of India, Indology, Mind/Body/Spirit
ISBN Prefix(es): 81-85120
*Parent Company:* Hind Pocket Books (P) Ltd
Imprints: Clarion Books; Mainstreet Books
Distributor for Embassy Books; Manjul Publications; Pentagon Press; Wilco

**Galgotia Publications Pvt Ltd+**
5 Ansari Rd, Daryaganj, New Delhi 110002
Mailing Address: PO Box 7221, New Delhi 110002
*Tel:* (011) 589334 *Fax:* (011) 3281909; (011) 321909
*E-mail:* gppl.galgtia@axcess.net.in
*Telex:* 03171161 Star In
*Key Personnel*
Chief Executive, Editorial: Suneel Galgotia
Sales: Vinod Behl
Founded: 1972
Subjects: Computer Science, Engineering (General), Management, Medicine, Nursing, Dentistry
ISBN Prefix(es): 81-7515; 81-85623; 81-86011; 81-86340
*Branch Office(s)*
Galgotia Towers, G-64, Manserovar Business Complex Sector 18, Noida
*Showroom(s):* 17B Conn Pl, New Delhi 110001
*Bookshop(s):* E D Galgotia & Sons

**Ganesh & Co+**
38 Thanikachalam Rd T Nagar, Chennai 600017
*Tel:* (044) 4344519 *Fax:* (044) 4342009
*E-mail:* ksm@md2.vsnl.net.in; service@kkbooks.com
*Key Personnel*
Dir: K Srinivasamurthy
Founded: 1910
Subjects: Philosophy, Religion - Other
ISBN Prefix(es): 81-85988
*Parent Company:* Productivity & Quality Publishing Pvt Ltd

**Geeta Prakashan**
Hindi Book Centre, 4-5-769, 1st floor, Badichowdi 500027
*Tel:* (0821) 33589
*Key Personnel*
General Manager: Gopala Krishna
Sales Manager: Gururaja Rao
Rights & Permissions: Sathyanarayana Rao
Founded: 1958
Subjects: Biography, History, Literature, Literary Criticism, Essays, Philosophy, Poetry, Religion - Other, Science (General), Social Sciences, Sociology
ISBN Prefix(es): 81-900754

**General Book Depot+**
1691, Nai Sarak, Delhi 110006
Mailing Address: PO Box 1220, Delhi 110006
*Tel:* (011) 2326 3695; (011) 2325 0635
 *Fax:* (011) 2394 0861
*E-mail:* contact@goyalbookshop.com
*Web Site:* www.goyalbookshop.com
*Key Personnel*
Contact: Kaushal Goyal
Founded: 1936
Specialize in English & German language reprints & French language books.

Subjects: Business, Career Development, English as a Second Language, How-to, Language Arts, Linguistics, Nonfiction (General), Self-Help, Travel
ISBN Prefix(es): 81-85288
Imprints: GOYL Saab Publishers & Distributors
Distributor for Oscar Brandstetter Verlag (Indian Sub-continent)

**General Printers & Publishers+**
263/F Raja Rammohan Roy Rd, Girgaon, Mumbai 400 004
*Tel:* (022) 2387 3113; (022) 2382 6854
*Fax:* (022) 2382 7197
*Key Personnel*
Executive Dir: Vijay P Thakker *E-mail:* thakker@bom3.vsnl.net.in
Founded: 1952
Membership(s): Federation of Indian Publishers, Federation of Educational Publishers in India.
Subjects: Education, Workbooks, Testpapers
ISBN Prefix(es): 81-85619
Number of titles published annually: 20 Print
Total Titles: 100 Print

**Gitanjali Publishing House**
2/12 Vikram Vihar, Lajpat Nagar-IV, New Delhi 110024
*Tel:* (011) 621991; (011) 6237555
Founded: 1962
Subjects: Economics, Government, Political Science, History, Human Relations, Social Sciences, Sociology
ISBN Prefix(es): 81-85060
*Bookshop(s):* Indian Book Service, 2/12 Vikram Vihar, Lajpat Nagar-IV, New Delhi 110024

**Globe Fearon**, *imprint of* Addison-Wesley Pte Ltd

**Goel Prakashen**
359, Alam Geri Ganj, Bareilly, UP 250 002
*Tel:* (0121) 642946; (0121) 644766 *Fax:* (0121) 645855
*Key Personnel*
Man Dir, Editorial: B D Rastogi
Sales: Atul Krishna
Production: K Krishna
Publicity & Advertising Dir: Kamalni Rastogi
Founded: 1948
Subjects: Art, Chemistry, Chemical Engineering, Economics, Government, Political Science, History, Mathematics
ISBN Prefix(es): 81-85932
Subsidiaries: Krishna Prakashan Mandir
*Bookshop(s):* Goel Publishing, Krishna Prakashan Mandir, Subhash Bazar, Meerut 250002 UP

**Golden Bells**, *imprint of* Laxmi Publications Pvt Ltd

**GOYL Saab Publishers & Distributors**, *imprint of* General Book Depot

**GOYL Saab, Publishers & Distributors**, see General Book Depot

**Gyan Bharati**, *imprint of* National Publishing House

**Gyan Books (P) Ltd**, see Gyan Publishing House

**Gyan Publishing House+**
5 Ansari Rd, Daryaganj, New Delhi 110002
*Tel:* (011) 23261060; (011) 23282060 *Fax:* (011) 23285914
*E-mail:* gyanbook@del2.vsnl.net.in
*Web Site:* www.gyanbooks.com

*Key Personnel*
Chief Executive: B P Garg
Dir, Publications & International Rights: Amit Garg
Founded: 1984
Specialize in humanities & social science books.
Membership(s): Federation of Indian Publishers, Federation of Indian Publishers & Booksellers Association, Delhi State Booksellers & Publishers Association.
Subjects: Agriculture, Anthropology, Archaeology, Art, Asian Studies, Astrology, Occult, Astronomy, Biography, Career Development, Child Care & Development, Communications, Cookery, Crafts, Games, Hobbies, Developing Countries, Drama, Theater, Earth Sciences, Economics, Education, Environmental Studies, Geography, Geology, Government, Political Science, History, Human Relations, Journalism, Language Arts, Linguistics, Law, Library & Information Sciences, Management, Music, Dance, Natural History, Philosophy, Psychology, Psychiatry, Public Administration, Religion - Buddhist, Religion - Hindu, Religion - Islamic, Self-Help, Social Sciences, Sociology, Sports, Athletics, Travel, Women's Studies
ISBN Prefix(es): 81-212
Number of titles published annually: 150 Print
Total Titles: 2,000 Print
*Associate Companies:* Gyan Books (P) Ltd; Gyan Exports
*Warehouse:* 30-C, Satyawati Colony, Ashok Vihar, Phase III, New Delhi 110052
*E-mail:* gyanbook@vsnl.com

**Hans Prakashan**
18 Nyaya Marg, Allahabad, Uttar Pradesh 211001
Mailing Address: PO Box 103, Allahabad 211001
*Tel:* (0532) 623077
*E-mail:* ar@nde.vsnl.net.in
*Key Personnel*
Chief Executive: Mahendra Pal Jha
Production: Amrit Rai
Founded: 1950
Subjects: Fiction
ISBN Prefix(es): 81-85954

**Health-Harmony**, *imprint of* B Jain Publishers Overseas

**Arnold Heinman Publishers (India) Pvt Ltd**
AB/9, 1st floor Safdaoung Enclave, New Delhi 110029
*Tel:* (011) 6383422; (011) 60780; (011) 664256 *Fax:* (011) 6877571
*Telex:* 31-72370ahpiin *Cable:* Heinemann
*Key Personnel*
Man Dir: G A Vazirani
Editorial, Rights & Permissions: Ms Rashmi Bhushan
Production: Mukesh Vazirani
Publicity: Ms Rani Roy
Sales: R K Rana
Founded: 1969
Subjects: Art, Engineering (General), Fiction, Government, Political Science, Literature, Literary Criticism, Essays, Medicine, Nursing, Dentistry, Philosophy, Poetry, Religion - Other, Social Sciences, Sociology
ISBN Prefix(es): 81-7031
*Associate Companies:* Edward Arnold (Publishers) Ltd, United Kingdom
Imprints: Mayfair Paperbacks; Sanskriti; Zebra Books for Children

**Heritage Publishers+**
32 Prakash Apt, 5, Ansari Rd, Darya Ganj, Delhi 110002
*Tel:* (011) 23266258 *Fax:* (011) 23263050
*E-mail:* heritage@nda.vsnl.net.in; info@meditechbooks.com *Cable:* HERIPUB

*Key Personnel*
Proprietor: B R Chawla
Founded: 1973
Subjects: Aeronautics, Aviation, Agriculture, Architecture & Interior Design, Art, Astronomy, Automotive, Biography, Chemistry, Chemical Engineering, Civil Engineering, Computer Science, Crafts, Games, Hobbies, Disability, Special Needs, Economics, Education, Electronics, Electrical Engineering, Engineering (General), Health, Nutrition, History, Language Arts, Linguistics, Literature, Literary Criticism, Essays, Medicine, Nursing, Dentistry, Military Science, Philosophy, Physics, Religion - Other, Social Sciences, Sociology, Medical & Technical Books
ISBN Prefix(es): 81-7026
*Associate Companies:* Heritage Impex Worldwide
Subsidiaries: Book Circle; Intellectuals' Rendezvous, K-3/5
Distributor for Blackwell; CRC Press; Routledge; Taylor & Francis; Thames & Hudson

**Himalaya Publishing House**
Pooja Apartment, 4B Murarilai S, Ansari Rd, Daryaganj, New Delhi 110002
*Tel:* (011) 3270392; (011) 652225 *Fax:* (022) 3956286
*Key Personnel*
Chief Executive, Editorial, Publicity: D P Pandey
Production: Anuj Pandey
Rights & Permissions: Mrs Meena Pandey
Sales: Sudhir Joshi; K N Pandey
Founded: 1976
Subjects: Art, Business, Law, Management, Psychology, Psychiatry, Science (General), Social Sciences, Sociology
ISBN Prefix(es): 81-7040
*Parent Company:* Randoot, Kelewadi, Girgaon, Mumbai 400004
*Associate Companies:* Geetanjali Press Pvt Ltd, Kundanlal Chandak Industrial Estate, Ghat Rd, Nagpur *Tel:* (0712) 24747
*Branch Office(s)*
Kudanlal Chandak Industrial Estate, Ghat Rd, Nagpur *Tel:* (0712) 24747
*Bookshop(s):* Randoot, Kelewadi, Girgaon, Mumbai 400004
*Shipping Address:* Randoot, Kelewadi, Girgaon, Mumbai 400004 *Tel:* (022) 360170 (022) 355798 (022) 363863
*Warehouse:* Randoot, Kelewadi, Girgaon, Mumbai 400004 *Tel:* (022) 360170 (022) 355798 (022) 363863
*Orders to:* Randoot, Kelewadi, Girgaon, Mumbai 400004

**Himalayan Books+**
17-L, Connaught Circus, New Delhi 110 001
*Tel:* (011) 352126; (011) 351731 *Fax:* (011) 332-1731
*E-mail:* ebs@vsnl.com *Cable:* HIMALAYAN BOOKS
*Key Personnel*
Chief Executive Officer, Man Dir, Editorial: Ms Pawan Chowdhri
Sales, Production, Publicity, Rights & Permissions: Ms P Chowdhri
Founded: 1986
Specializes in aviation, Indian art & culture, travel, religion & philosophy.
Subjects: Aeronautics, Aviation, Architecture & Interior Design, Military Science, Philosophy, Regional Interests, Religion - Other, Travel
ISBN Prefix(es): 81-7002
Number of titles published annually: 12 Print
Total Titles: 200 Print
*Associate Companies:* English Book Store

**Hind Pocket Books Private Ltd+**
18/19 Dilshad Garden, G T Rd, Shahdar, Delhi 110095

*Tel:* (011) 202046; (011) 202332; (011) 202467
  *Fax:* (011) 2282332 *Cable:* POCKETBOOK
  DELHI
*Key Personnel*
Man Dir: Dina N Malhotra
Marketing, Rights & Permissions: Shekhar Mal-
hotra
Founded: 1957
Membership(s): Federation of Indian Publishers.
Subjects: Biography, Fiction, How-to, Nonfiction
  (General), Self-Help
ISBN Prefix(es): 81-216
*Associate Companies:* Clarion Books; Global
  Business Press; Indian Book Company; Sar-
  swati
*Imprints:* Clarion
*Book Club(s):* Clarion Book Club; Gharelu Li-
  brary Yojna

**Hindi Pracharak Sansthan+**
C/21/30 Pisachmochan, Varanasi 220010
Mailing Address: PO Box 1106, Varanasi
*Tel:* (0542) 54470; (0542) 52425; (0542) 52670;
  (0542) 355168; (0542) 56850; (0542) 361452
*Key Personnel*
Editorial: K C Beri; V P Beri; R P Beri; A K
  Beri
Sales: Vivek Beri
Subjects: Fiction
ISBN Prefix(es): 81-7337
*Parent Company:* Hindi Pracharak Sansthan
*Associate Companies:* Sahitya Bharati Publica-
  tions Pvt Ltd; H P S Publications Pvt Ltd;
  Hindi Pracharak Publications Pvt Ltd
*Subsidiaries:* Kashi Offset Printers Pvt Ltd
*Branch Office(s)*
Pishach Mochan, Varanass (UP)
Cal Sahitya Bharati Publications Pvt Ltd, 211/1,
  Bidhan Sarin

**IBD**, see International Book Distributors

**IBD Publisher & Distributors+**
S-5, 3rd floor, Akarshan Bhawan, 23, Ansari Rd,
  Darya Ganj, New Delhi 110002
*Tel:* (011) 23251094 *Fax:* (011) 23259102
*E-mail:* piyush_gahlot@rediffmail.com
Founded: 2001
Also distributor.
Membership(s): Delhi State Booksellers & Pub-
  lisher Association (DSBPA).
Subjects: Agriculture, Biological Sciences, Envi-
  ronmental Studies, Science (General), Technol-
  ogy
ISBN Prefix(es): 81-7089
Number of titles published annually: 15 Print
*Associate Companies:* Allied Book Centre; Inter-
  national Book Distributors
*Distributed by* DAYA; DK Publishers; Koeltz Sci-
  entific; Kramer; UBS Publishers
*Distributor for* CAB International; Koeltz Scien-
  tific
*Showroom(s):* Dehra Dun, New Delhi
*Warehouse:* Dehra Dun, New Delhi

**IBH Publishing Services**
Unit of India Book House Pvt Ltd
Fleet Bldg, Marol Naka, M V Rd, Mumbai 400
  059
*Tel:* (022) 2852-7619 *Fax:* (022) 2852-9473
*Web Site:* www.ibhsolves.com
*Key Personnel*
Chief Executive: Dilip Mirchandani *Tel:* 917-
  779-8255 *Fax:* 973-783-7164 *E-mail:* dkm@
  ibhsolves.com
Production Manager: Nizam Ahmed *Tel:* (022)
  2850-7189 *E-mail:* nizam.a@ibhsolves.com
Sales Manager: Madhukar Gandhi *Tel:* (022)
  2852-1921 *E-mail:* madhukar.g@ibhsolves.com
Technology Manager: Samuel Vinodkumar
  *Tel:* (022) 2850-8644 *E-mail:* sam.v@
  ibhsolves.com

End-to-end publishing solutions—composition,
  editing, proofreading, typesetting, printing—for
  book & journal publishers. Primarily STM
  (Scientific, Technical, Medical) & digital services, such as e-book & xml conversions, electronic page/data input & management & repur-
  posing content for other media.

**ICSSR**, see Indian Council of Social Science
  Research (ICSSR)

**Idara Ishaat-E-Diniyat Ltd**
168/2 Jha House, Hazrat Nizamuddin, New Delhi
  110 013
*Tel:* (011) 26926832; (011) 26926833 (office);
  (011) 461676; (011) 4631786 (showroom)
  *Fax:* (011) 26932787; (011) 4632786
*E-mail:* sales@idara.com; idara@yahoo.com
*Web Site:* www.idara.com *Cable:* DINIYAT
*Key Personnel*
Man Dir: Mohammad Anas
Dir, Exports: Mohammad Yunus
Dir: Mohammad Yusuf
Founded: 1950
Specialize in Holy Qur'an & Islamic Religious
  Books. Cover Urdu, Arabic, English, French,
  Hindi & Gujrati Languages.
ISBN Prefix(es): 81-7101
*Warehouse:* D 80-81, Near Masjid Bilal, Abul
  Fazal Enclave Phase-I, Jamia Nagar, New Delhi
  110 025

**India Book House Pvt Ltd+**
Mahalaxmi Chambers, 5th floor, 22 Bhulabhai
  Desai Rd, Mumbai 400026
*Tel:* (022) 2840165 *Fax:* (022) 2835099
*Key Personnel*
Man Dir: Deepak Mirchandani
Editorial & Publishing Dir: Padmini Mirchandani
  *E-mail:* padmini@ibhindia.com
Founded: 1952
Distripress.
Subjects: Architecture & Interior Design, Art
ISBN Prefix(es): 81-7508; 81-85028
*Parent Company:* Mirchandani & Co Pvt Ltd
*Associate Companies:* IBH Magazine Services,
  Jesia House, 137 Modi St, Fort, Mumbai 400
  001, Contact: Lata Vasvani *Tel:* (022) 2840165
  *Fax:* (022) 2633067 *E-mail:* subscriptions@
  ibhworld.com; IBH Subscription Agency, Fleet
  Fasteners Bldg, MV Rd, Marol Naka, Andheri
  (East), Mumbai 400 059, Contact: Moti Wad-
  hwani *Tel:* (022) 8501999 *Fax:* (022) 8500645
  *E-mail:* journals@ibhworld.com; Rishi Exports,
  Arch 29, Below Mahalaxmi Bridge, Maha-
  laxmi, Mumbai 400 034, Contact: Mohan Sha-
  hani *Tel:* (022) 4927463 *Fax:* (022) 4950392
*Distributed by* Antique Collectors' Club (UK)
*Distributor for* HarperCollins (USA); Hodder &
  Stoughton Ltd (UK); Litle Hampton Publish-
  ers (UK); Random House Inc (USA); Simon &
  Schuster (USA & UK); Transworld Publishers
  Ltd (UK)

**The Indian Anthropological Society**, see Indian
  Museum

**Indian Book Depot+**
J-128, Kirti Nagar, New Delhi 110015
*Tel:* (011) 3673927; (011) 3523635 *Fax:* (011)
  3552096
*E-mail:* ibdmaps@ndb.vsnl.net.in; indiabo@
  indiabookfair.net
*Key Personnel*
Proprietor: Harish Chawla
Subjects: Mathematics, Travel
ISBN Prefix(es): 81-87172
Total Titles: 464 Print
*Warehouse:* 2937 Bahadur Garh Rd, New Delhi
  110006
*Orders to:* 2937 Bahadur Garth Rd, New Delhi
  110006

**Indian Council for Cultural Relations**
Azad Bhavan, Indraprastha Estate, New Delhi
  110002
*Tel:* (011) 3370732; (011) 3378647 *Fax:* (011)
  3712639
*E-mail:* iccr@vsnl.com
*Web Site:* education.vsnl.com/iccr
*Telex:* 3161860; 3166004 *Cable:* Culture
Founded: 1950
Subjects: Art, Drama, Theater, Ethnicity, Litera-
  ture, Literary Criticism, Essays
ISBN Prefix(es): 81-85434
*Branch Office(s)*
Bangalore
Chandigarth
Chennai
Kolkata
Mumbai
Varanasi

**Indian Council of Agricultural Research**
Krishi Anusandhan Bhavan Dr, New Delhi
  110001
*Tel:* (011) 388991 (ext 496); (011) 23382306
  *Fax:* (011) 387293
*E-mail:* jssamra@icar.delhi.nic.in
*Web Site:* www.icar.org.in
*Telex:* 03162249 Icar In *Cable:* Agrisec
*Key Personnel*
Dir: Sh A Chatravarty *Tel:* 257-16010
  *E-mail:* dirdipa@kab.delhi.nic.in
Business, Advertising: S K Joshi *Tel:* 257-13657
  *E-mail:* bmicar@kab.delhi.nic.in
Publicity & Public Relations: S K Sharma
  *Tel:* 258-54649 *E-mail:* kuldeep@kab.delhi.
  nic.in
Subjects: Agriculture, Animals, Pets
ISBN Prefix(es): 81-7164

**Indian Council of Social Science Research
  (ICSSR)**
35, Ferozeshah Rd, New Delhi 110 001
Mailing Address: PO Box 10528, Aruna Asfa Ali
  Marg, New Delhi 110 067
*Tel:* (011) 23385959; (011) 26717066 *Fax:* (011)
  26179836
*E-mail:* info@icssr.org
*Web Site:* www.icssr.org *Cable:* ICSORES
*Key Personnel*
Chief Executive, Editorial, Production, Rights
  & Permissions & Chairman: Prof V R Panch-
  mukhi
Director, NASSDOC: Dr P R Goswami
  *E-mail:* prgoswami@icssr.org
Founded: 1969
Promote, sponsor & support social science re-
  search & social science information activities
  in India by providing financial assistance in the
  form of fellowship, sponsorship, study grants
  & grants-in-aid to individuals as well as institu-
  tions.
Subjects: Anthropology, Business, Criminology,
  Economics, Education, Geography, Geology,
  History, Law, Management, Psychology, Psy-
  chiatry, Public Administration, Social Sciences,
  Sociology
ISBN Prefix(es): 81-85008
Total Titles: 500 Print
*Branch Office(s)*
Dr Baba Sahib Ambedkar National Institute of
  Social Sciences, Dongargaon AB Rd, Mhow
  Cantonment, Mhow 453441, Contact: Prof
  Nandu Ram *Tel:* (07324) 272830; (07324)
  274377; (07324) 272534 *Fax:* (07324) 273645
  *E-mail:* solanki_baniss@rediff.com
AN Sinha Institute of Social Studies, Patna 800
  001, Contact: Dr B B Srivastava *Tel:* (0612)
  221395; (0612) 223320; (0612) 227856
  *Fax:* (0612) 226226; (0612) 226227
Centre for Development Studies, Ulloor, Thiru-
  vananthapuram 695 011, Contact: Dr K P Kan-

nan *Tel:* (0471) 2448881 *Fax:* (0471) 2447137 *E-mail:* cdsedp@vsnl.com

Centre for Economic & Social Studies, Nizamia Observatory Campus, Begumpet, Hyderabad 500 016, Contact: Prof S Mahendra Dev *Tel:* (040) 23402789; (040) 23416780 *Fax:* (040) 23406808 *E-mail:* cesshyd@hd1.vsnl.net.in

Centre for Policy Research, Dharma Marg, Chanakyapuri, New Delhi 110 021, Contact: Dr Charan Wadhwa *Tel:* (011) 26114797; (011) 26115273 *Fax:* (011) 26872746; (011) 26886902 *E-mail:* president_cpr@vsnl.com

Centre for Research in Rural & Industrial Development, 21, Sector, 19-A, Madhya Marg, Chandigarh 160 019, Contact: Rashpal Malhotra *Tel:* (0172) 549450 *Fax:* (0172) 725215 *E-mail:* sscrrid@ren.nic.in

Centre for Social Studies, South Gujarat University Campus, Udhna-Magdalla Rd, Surat 395 007, Acting Dir: Prof Biswaroop Das *Tel:* (0261) 2227173; (0261) 2227174; (0261) 3210503 *Fax:* (0261) 2223851 *E-mail:* css_surat@satyam.net.in

Centre for Studies in Social Sciences, R1, Baishnabghata, Patuli Township, Kolkata 700 094, Contact: Prof Partha Chatterjee *Tel:* (033) 24627252; (033) 24625794 *Fax:* (033) 24626183 *E-mail:* cssscal@vsnl.net

Centre for the Study of Developing Societies, 29, Rajpur Rd, Delhi 110 054, Contact: Dr R K Shrivastava *Tel:* (011) 23951190; (011) 23942199 *Fax:* (011) 23943450 *E-mail:* csds@del2.vsnl.net.in

Council for Social Development-Southern Regional Office, Plot No 230, Shiva Nagar Colony, Hydderguda Village, Rajendranagar Rd, Bahadurpura Post Office, Hyderabad 500 064, Contact: Prof K S Bhat *Tel:* (040) 24016395 *Fax:* (040) 24001958 *E-mail:* csdhyd@hotmail.com

Giri Institute of Development Studies, Sector 'O', Aliganj Housing Scheme, Lucknow 226024, Contact: Dr G P Mishra *Tel:* (0522) 2373640; (0522) 2325021 *Fax:* (0522) 2373640 *E-mail:* gids@sancharnet.in

Gujarat Institute of Development Research, Sarkhej, Gandhinagar Highway, Gota Char Rasta, PO High Court, Gota, Ahmedabad 380 060, Contact: Prof Sudarshan Iyengar *Tel:* (079) 3742366 *Fax:* (079) 3742365 *E-mail:* gidrad1@sancharnet.in

ICSSR Eastern Regional Centre, R1, Baishnabghata, Patuli Township, Kolkata 700 094, Contact: Prof Partha Chatterjee *Tel:* (033) 24512482; (033) 24625795; (033) 24627252 *Fax:* (033) 24626183 *E-mail:* cssscal@vsnl.net

ICSSR North Eastern Regional Centre, Upper Nongthymmai, Shillong 793014, Contact: Prof David Reid Syiemlieh *Tel:* (0364) 2231173 *Fax:* (0364) 2231631 *E-mail:* icssrnerc@sancharnet.in

ICSSR Northern Regional Centre, JNU, Central Library Bldg, New Campus, NW Mehrauli Rd, New Delhi 110067, Contact: Prof M H Qureshi *Tel:* (011) 26167557; (011) 26107676 (ext 2536) *Fax:* (011) 26165886 *E-mail:* ssnrc@rec.nic.in

ICSSR North-Western Regional Centre, Punjab University Library Bldg, Chandigarh 160 014, Acting Dir: P K Saini *Tel:* (0172) 2541015; (0172) 2541491 *Fax:* (0172) 2541022 *E-mail:* icssr@pu.ac.in

ICSSR Southern Regional Centre, Osmania University Library, Hyderabad 500007, Acting Dir: Dr Masood Ali Khan *Tel:* (040) 27098756; (040) 27098951 (ext 306) *Fax:* (040) 27098754 *E-mail:* csr@icssr.cmc.net.in

ICSSR Western Regional Centre, J P Nayak Bhavan, Vidyanagari, Vidyanagari Marg, Mumbai 400098, Acting Dir: M R Prabhu *Tel:* (022) 26526050; (022) 26113091 (ext 375) *Fax:* (022) 26528712 *E-mail:* wrcicssr@vsnl.in

Indian Institute of Education, 128/2, J P Naik Rd, Kothrud, Pune 411 029, Contact: Dr S R Kakade *Tel:* (020) 5436980; (020) 5424580 *Fax:* (020) 5435239 *E-mail:* iiepune@giaspn01.vsnl.net.in

Institute of Development Studies, 8-B, Jhalana Institutional Area, Jaipur 302 004, Contact: Prof S S Acharya *Tel:* (0141) 2705726 *Fax:* (0141) 2705348 *E-mail:* ids@sancharnet.in

Institute of Economic Growth, University Enclave, Delhi 110 007, Contact: Prof B B Bhattacharya *Tel:* (011) 27667288 *Fax:* (011) 27667401 *E-mail:* bbb@ieg.ernet.in

Institute of Public Enterprise, Osmania University Campus, Hyderabad 500 007, Contact: Dr K Harigopal *Tel:* (040) 27097445 *Fax:* (040) 27095478 *E-mail:* ipeouc@vsnl.in

Institute of Social & Economic Change, Nagarbhabhavi, Bangalore 560072, Contact: Prof Gopal Kadekodi *Tel:* (080) 3215519; (080) 3215468 *Fax:* (080) 3217008; (080) 3211798 *E-mail:* registrar@isec.ac.in

Institute of Studies in Industrial Development, PO Box 7151, Narendra Niketan, Indraprastha Estate, New Delhi 110 002, Contact: Prof S K Goyal *Tel:* (011) 23702449 *Fax:* (011) 23702448 *E-mail:* info@vidur.delhi.nic.in

Madhya Pradesh Institute of Social Science Research, 19-20, Mahasweta Nagar, Ujjain 456010, Contact: Dr D C Sah *Tel:* (0734) 2510978 *Fax:* (0734) 2512450 *E-mail:* mpissr@epatra.com

Madras Institute of Development Studies, 79, Second Main Rd, PO Box 948, Gandhinagar, Adyar, Chennai 600 020, Contact: Prof V K Natraj *Tel:* (044) 24412589 *Fax:* (044) 24910872 *E-mail:* director@mids.tn.nic.in

NKC Centre for Development Studies, Plot No A, Chandrasekharpur, Bhubaneswar 751 013, Contact: Prof G C Kar *Tel:* (0674) 2300471; (0674) 2301094 *Fax:* (0674) 2300471 *E-mail:* ncdsvc@sancharnet.in

OKD Institute of Social Change & Development, K K Bhatta Rd, Chenikuthi, Guwahati 781 003, Contact: Dr Abu Nasar Saied Ahmed *Tel:* (0361) 2667493; (0361) 2665903; (0361) 2668321 *Fax:* (0361) 2663589 *E-mail:* dkdscd@hotmail.com

G B Pant Social Science Institute, 3 No Yamuna Enclave, Jhusi, Sangam Nagar, Allahabad 221 019, Contact: Prof R C Tripathi *Tel:* (0532) 2667206 *Fax:* (0532) 2667207 *E-mail:* rctripathi@rediffmail.com

Sardar Patel Institute of Economic & Social Research, Thaltej Rd, Ahmedabad 380 054, Acting Dir: R G Nambiar *Tel:* (079) 6850598 *Fax:* (079) 6851714; (079) 6850714 *E-mail:* arpu@x400nicgw.nic.in

*Bookshop(s):* Centre for Multi-Disciplinary Development Research, D B Rodda Rd, Jubilee Circle, Dharwad 580001, Contact: Prof P R Panchamukhi *Tel:* (0836) 2745273; (0836) 2447639 *Fax:* (0836) 2447627 *E-mail:* cmdr@sancharnet.in; Centre for Women's Development Studies, 25, Bhai Vir Singh Marg, New Delhi 110 001, Contact: N K Banerjee *Tel:* (011) 23345530; (011) 23365541; (011) 23366930 *Fax:* (011) 23346044 *E-mail:* cwds@ndb.vsnl.net.in

**Indian Defence Review**, *imprint of* Lancer Publisher's & Distributors

**Indian Documentation Service+**
2 Ansari Rd, Panna Bhawan Daryaganj, New Delhi 110 002
Mailing Address: PO Box 13, Nai Subzi Mandi, Gurgaon 122 001
*Tel:* (0124) 6322005; (0124) 6322779 *Fax:* (0124) 6324782
*E-mail:* indoc@indiatimes.com
*Key Personnel*
Dir: Pankaj Jain

Editorial, Production, Rights & Permissions: Mr Satyaprakash
Sales, Publicity: Pankaj Kumar
Founded: 1970
Membership(s): Federation of Indian Publishers & Booksellers.
ISBN Prefix(es): 81-85258

**Indian Institute of Advanced Study**
Rashtrapati Nivas, Shimla, Himachal Pradesh 171005
*Tel:* (0177) 72303; (0177) 75139 *Fax:* (0177) 75139
*E-mail:* info@iias.org
*Web Site:* www.iias.org *Cable:* INSTITUTE
*Key Personnel*
Dir: Prof V C Srivastava
Sales: A K Sharma
Founded: 1965
Subjects: Social Sciences, Sociology
ISBN Prefix(es): 81-85952; 81-7986

**Indian Institute of World Culture+**
6 B P Wadia Rd, Basavangudi, Bangalore 560 004
*Tel:* (080) 6678581
*Web Site:* www.ultindia.org/culture.htm
*Key Personnel*
Vice President: Prof V K Doraswamy
Honorary Secretary: Y M Balakrishna
Founded: 1945
Subjects: Ethnicity

**Indian Museum**
27 Jawaharlal Nehru Rd, Kolkata 700016
*Tel:* (033) 249 9902; (033) 249 9979; (033) 249 8948; (033) 249 8931 *Fax:* (033) 249 5699
*E-mail:* imbot@cal2.vsnl.net.in
*Web Site:* www.indianmuseum-calcutta.org
*Telex:* 0021-4472IMIN *Cable:* Imbot
*Key Personnel*
Dir: Dr Sakti Kali Basu
Founded: 1814
Subjects: Anthropology, Archaeology, Art, Geography, Geology, Science (General)
ISBN Prefix(es): 81-85525

**Indian Society for Promoting Christian Knowledge (ISPCK)+**
PO Box 1585, 1654, Madarsa Rd, Kashmere Gate, Delhi 110 006
*Tel:* (011) 23866323 *Fax:* (011) 23865490
*E-mail:* ispck@nde.vsnl.net.in
*Web Site:* ispck.org.in *Cable:* LITHOUSE DELHI
*Key Personnel*
Dir: Rev Ashish Amos
Financial & Administrative Secretary: Rev Dr J D M Stuart
Marketing & Distribution Manager: Mr Sundeep Chowdhry
Founded: 1957 (as autonomous body 1958)
Subjects: Biblical Studies, Biography, Government, Political Science, Religion - Other, Social Sciences, Sociology, Theology
ISBN Prefix(es): 81-7214
Subsidiaries: Navdin Prakashan Kendra
*Branch Office(s)*
Andrhra Christian Theological College, Lower Tank Bund Rd, Gandhi Nagar (PO), Hyderabad, Andhra Pradesh 500080 *Tel:* (033) 22421804 *E-mail:* sales@ispck.org.in
Christian Book Depot, Diocese of Eastern Himilaya CNI, Diocesan Centre, Gandhi Rd, Darjeeling, Bengla *Tel:* 0354256389 *Fax:* 91113865490 *E-mail:* ispck@nde.vsnl.net.in
The Church of South India, CSI Center, No 5, White Rd, Royapettah, Chennai, Tamilnadu 600014
Leonard Theological College, Post Box 36, Civil Lines, Jabalpur, Madhya Pradesh 482001

*Bookshop(s):* 51, Chowringhee Rd, Kolkata, Bengla 700071 *Tel:* (033) 22821804 *E-mail:* sales@ispck.org.in; Opp Liberty Cinema, Residency Rd, Sadar, Nagpur, Maharastra 440001 *Tel:* (0712) 2543425 *E-mail:* sales@ispck.org.in; Chotanagpur Diocesan Bookshop, PO Church Rd, Ranchi, Bihar 834001; Jabalpur Diocesan Bookshop, Mission Boys Hostel, Jarbhata, Bilashpur, Madhya Pradesh 495001

**Indus Publishing Co+**
FS-5 Tagore Garden, New Delhi 110027
*Tel:* (011) 25935289; (011) 25151333 *Fax:* (011) 25922102
*E-mail:* indus@indusbooks.com
*Web Site:* www.indusbooks.com
*Key Personnel*
Man Dir: M L Gidwani
Dir Sales & Product Development: Lokesh Gidwani *E-mail:* lgidwani@indusbooks.com
Founded: 1987
Publishers, booksellers & exporters. Specialize in Himalayan Studies, Forestry, Environment, Mountaineering & Trekking.
Membership(s): Delhi State Booksellers' & Publishers' Association.
Subjects: Agriculture, Archaeology, Environmental Studies, History, Natural History, Religion - Buddhist, Religion - Hindu, Social Sciences, Sociology, Travel, Botany, Himalayan Studies, Horticulture
ISBN Prefix(es): 81-85182; 81-7387
Number of titles published annually: 25 Print
Total Titles: 250 Print
*Associate Companies:* Indus International, 5-A (MIG), Rajouri Garden, New Delhi 110027, Contact: Lokesh Gidwani *Tel:* (011) 5151333 *Fax:* (011) 5449682 *E-mail:* mail@indus-intl.com *Web Site:* www.indus-intl.com (exporters of Indian books & journals; worldwide delivery)
*Book Club(s):* Indus Club (special discount for members)

**Institute of Book Publishing,** *imprint of* Sterling Publishers Pvt Ltd

**Intellectual Publishing House+**
23 Darya Ganj, Pratap Gali, New Delhi 110002
*Tel:* (011) 3275860
*Key Personnel*
International Rights: D R Chopra
Founded: 1974
Subjects: Archaeology, Art, Government, Political Science, History, Literature, Literary Criticism, Essays, Philosophy, Religion - Other, Social Sciences, Sociology
ISBN Prefix(es): 81-7076
*Parent Company:* Intellectual Book Corner Pvt Ltd

**Inter-India Publications+**
D-17 Raja Garden, New Delhi 110015
*Tel:* (011) 5441120; (011) 5467082
*Key Personnel*
Chief Executive, Editorial, Rights & Permissions: M C Mittal
Sales: Praveen Mittal
Founded: 1975
Membership(s): Federation of Indian Publishers, New Delhi; specialize in tribes, women & forests.
Subjects: Agriculture, Anthropology, Archaeology, Art, Asian Studies, Crafts, Games, Hobbies, Economics, Ethnicity, Geography, Geology, Government, Political Science, History, Philosophy, Religion - Other, Social Sciences, Sociology, Transportation, Women's Studies
ISBN Prefix(es): 81-210
*Parent Company:* DK Publishers' Distributors Pvt Ltd

**International Book Distributors+**
9/3 Rajpur Rd, 1st floor, Dehra Dun, Uttaranchal 248001
*Tel:* (0135) 2656526; (0135) 2657497; (0135) 2650949 *Fax:* (0135) 2656554
*E-mail:* ibdbooks@sancharnet.in
*Web Site:* ibdbooks.com
*Key Personnel*
Proprietor: R P Singh *E-mail:* rpsinghgahlot@yahoo.co.in
Founded: 1976
Specialize in printing, scanning & planning. Also distributor & publisher of scientific & technical books & journals.
Membership(s): All India Federation of Booksellers & Publishers, New Delhi.
Subjects: Agriculture, Animals, Pets, Biological Sciences, Crafts, Games, Hobbies, Environmental Studies, Gardening, Plants, Natural History, Science (General), Technology, Veterinary Science, Botany, Forestry, Wildlife
ISBN Prefix(es): 81-7089
Number of titles published annually: 50 Print
Total Titles: 500 Print
*Associate Companies:* IBD Publisher & Distributors, 23 Ansari Rd, Daryaganj, New Delhi 110002 *Tel:* (011) 23251094 *Fax:* (011) 23259102 *E-mail:* piyush_gahlot@rediffmail.com; Valley Offset Printers & Publishers, 15/2 B, Rajpur Rd, Dehra Dun, Uttranchal 248001, Contact: Mr Prashant Gahlot *Tel:* (0135) 2653998; (0135) 2656172 *Fax:* (0135) 2656554 *E-mail:* ibdbooks2003@yahoo.co.in
*Bookshop(s):* Allied Book Centre, 9/5 Rajpur Rd, Dehra Dun, Uttranchal 248001

**Interprint,** *imprint of* Mehta Publishing House

**Intertrade Publications Pvt Ltd+**
55 Gariahat Rd, Ballygunge, Kolkata 700019
Mailing Address: PO Box 10210, Kolkata 700 019
*Tel:* (033) 474872; (033) 475069 *Cable:* HELBELL
*Key Personnel*
Man Dir, Rights & Permissions: Dr K K Roy
Sales Dir: S Paul
Publicity Dir: Renu Kochhar
Advertising Dir: Pradip Raj
Founded: 1954
Subjects: Biography, History, Medicine, Nursing, Dentistry, Philosophy, Poetry, Religion - Other
Subsidiaries: Intertrade Publications (India) Pvt Ltd

**Islamic Publishing House+**
Islamic Service Trust Bldgs, 10-529 Maideen Pali Rd Calicut, Kerala 673 001
*Tel:* (0495) 720092; (0495) 724618 *Fax:* (0495) 724524
*E-mail:* iphcalicut@eth.net
*Key Personnel*
International Rights: Sheikh Mohamed
Manager: A P Moosa-Koya
Founded: 1945
Subjects: Biography, Government, Political Science, Health, Nutrition, History, Human Relations, Law, Philosophy, Religion - Islamic, Travel
ISBN Prefix(es): 81-7204
Number of titles published annually: 150 Print
*Parent Company:* Islamic Service Trust, Kerala
Distributed by Current Books Kottayam
Distributor for Markazi Maktaba Islami (India)

**ISPCK,** see Indian Society for Promoting Christian Knowledge (ISPCK)

**Jaico Publishing House**
127 Mahatma Gandhi Rd, Mumbai 400 023

*Tel:* (022) 2676702; (022) 2676802; (022) 2674501 *Fax:* (022) 2656412
*E-mail:* jaicowbd@vsnl.com
*Web Site:* www.jaicobooks.com
*Telex:* 113369 Jai In *Cable:* JAICOBOOKS
*Key Personnel*
Man Dir: Ashwin J Shah
Executive Dir: S C Sethi
Editor: R H Sharma
Founded: 1946
Subjects: Astrology, Occult, Behavioral Sciences, Biography, Cookery, Criminology, Economics, Engineering (General), Ethnicity, Government, Political Science, Health, Nutrition, History, Humor, Language Arts, Linguistics, Law, Management, Philosophy, Psychology, Psychiatry, Religion - Other, Self-Help
ISBN Prefix(es): 81-7224
Subsidiaries: Jaico Press Pvt Ltd
*Branch Office(s)*
Jaico Book Agency, No 57, Dr Giri Rd, T Nagr, Chennai 600 017 *Tel:* (044) 2826 2874 *E-mail:* jaicoche@md3.vsnl.net.in
Jaico Book Distributors, 194, Patpur Ganj Indl Area, Delhi *Tel:* (011) 2214 4204; (011) 2214 4205 *Fax:* (011) 224 4206 *E-mail:* jaicobook@vsnl.net
Jaico Book Distributors, G-2, 16 Ansari Rd, Daryaganj, New Delhi 110 002 *Tel:* (011) 2326 0651 *Fax:* (011) 2327 8469 *E-mail:* sethidel@del6.vsnl.net.in
Jaico Book Enterprises, 302 Acharya Prafulla Chandra Roy Rd, Park Circus, Kolkata 700 009 *Tel:* (033) 2360 0542; (033) 2360 0543 *E-mail:* jaicocal@cal2.vsnl.net.in
Jaico Book House, 14-1 1st Main Rd, 6th Cross, Gandhi Nagar, Bangalore 560 009 *Tel:* (080) 226 7016; (080) 225 7083 *Fax:* (080) 228 5492 *E-mail:* jaicobgr@blr.vsnl.net.in
Jaico Book House, 3-4-494/1/2, Barkatpura, Hyderabad 500 027 *Tel:* (040) 2755 1992 *E-mail:* hyd1_jaicohyd@sancharnet.in
Jaicos' Wholesale Book Distributors, ELGI House, 2 Mill Officers' Colony, Opp Times of India, Ashram Rd, Ahmedabad 380 009 *Tel:* (079) 657 9865; (079) 657 5262 *E-mail:* jaicoahm@vsnl.com
*Bookshop(s):* Jaicos

**B Jain Publishers Overseas+**
Subsidiary of B Jain Publishers (P) Ltd
1921 Street No 10, Chuna Mandi, Paharganj, New Delhi 110055
*Tel:* (011) 2358 0800; (011) 5169 8991; (011) 2358 3100 *Fax:* (011) 2358 0471; (011) 5169 8993
*E-mail:* bjain@vsnl.com
*Web Site:* www.bjainbooks.com *Cable:* BOOKCENTRE
*Key Personnel*
CEO: Kuldeep Jain
Dir & Editorial, Rights & Permissions: Ashok Jain
Dir Sales & Publicity: Nishant Jain *E-mail:* nishant@bjainbooks.com
Founded: 1972
Subjects: Alternative, Health, Nutrition, Medicine, Nursing, Dentistry, Self-Help
ISBN Prefix(es): 81-7021; 81-8056
Number of titles published annually: 80 Print
Total Titles: 1,250 Print
Imprints: Health-Harmony

**B Jain Publishers (P) Ltd+**
1921 Street No 10, Chuna Mandi Paharganj, New Delhi 110055
*Tel:* (011) 23580800; (011) 23581100; (011) 23583100 *Fax:* (011) 23580471
*E-mail:* bjain@vsnl.com
*Web Site:* www.bjainbooks.com *Cable:* Bookcentre
*Key Personnel*
Chief Executive Officer: Sh Kuldeep Jain

Man Dir: Dr Premnath Jain *Tel:* (011) 2169633
Dir & Editorial, Rights & Permissions: Ashok
Jain
Founded: 1967
Subjects: Health, Nutrition, Medicine, Nurs-
ing, Dentistry, Religion - Buddhist, Religion
- Hindu
ISBN Prefix(es): 81-7021
Number of titles published annually: 40 Print
Total Titles: 1,330 Print
*Associate Companies:* B Jain Exports India
Subsidiaries: B Jain Publishers Overseas
*Distribution Center:* New Leaf Distributors,
401 Thoronton Rd, Atlanta, GA 30122-1557,
United States (USA)

**Jaipur Publishing House**
5, Lalji Sand Ka Rasta, Chaura Rasta, Jaipur 302
004
*Tel:* (0141) 319198; (0141) 319094
*E-mail:* jph@indiaresult.com
*Key Personnel*
Manager: Rajesh Agarwal
Production: R C Agarwal
Sales: Dhoop Chand Jain
Founded: 1960
ISBN Prefix(es): 81-8047

**Jaypee Brothers Medical Publishers Pvt Ltd+**
B-3 EMCA House, 23/23B Ansari Rd, Daryaganj,
New Delhi 110002
Mailing Address: PO Box 7193, New Delhi 110
002
*Tel:* (011) 3272143; (011) 3282021; (011)
3272703 *Fax:* (011) 3276490
*E-mail:* jpmedpub@del2.vsnl.net.in
*Web Site:* www.jpbros.20m.com
*Key Personnel*
Editorial: Jitendar Vij
Sales: Pawaninder Vij
Subjects: Medicine, Nursing, Dentistry
ISBN Prefix(es): 81-7179; 81-8061
*Associate Companies:* BMJ; F A Davis Co;
Mosby Year Book
*Branch Office(s)*
202 Batavia Chambers, 8 Kumara Kruppa
Rd, Kumara Park East, Bangalore 560 001
*Tel:* (080) 2281761 *Fax:* (080) 2382956
*E-mail:* jaypeebc@bgl.vsnl.net.in
282, 3rd floor, Khaleel Shirazi Estate, Foun-
tain Plaza, Pantheon Rd, Chennai 600 008
*Tel:* (044) 8262665 *Fax:* (044) 8262331
*E-mail:* jpmedpub@md3.vsnl.net.in
One-A Indian Mirror St, Wellington Sq, PO Box
8880, Kolkata 700 013 *Tel:* (033) 2451926
*Fax:* (033) 2456075 *E-mail:* jpbcal@cal.vsnl.
net.in
106 Amit Industrial Estate, 61 Dr SS Rao Rd,
Near MGM Hospital, Parel, Mumbai 400 012
*Tel:* (022) 4124863 *Fax:* (022) 4160828; (022)
4104532 *E-mail:* jpmedpub@bom7.vsnl.net.in

**Kairali Children's Book Trust**
PO Box 624- Railway Station Rd, Current Books
Bldg, Kottayam, Kerala 686 001
*Tel:* (0481) 563226; (0481) 560918 *Fax:* (0481)
564758
*Web Site:* www.dcbooks.com/kcbt.htm
*Key Personnel*
Chief Executive, Rights & Permissions: D C
Kizhakemuri
Editorial: Dr K Velayudhan Nair
Production: V P Sreedharan Nayanar
Publicity: G Sreekumar
Founded: 1980
Subjects: Biography, Fiction, Foreign Countries
ISBN Prefix(es): 81-7152
*Associate Companies:* Current Books; DC Books;
Kairali Mudralayam
Imprints: D C Press

*Book Club(s):* Kairali Club
*Orders to:* Current Books, VIII/493 Railway Station Rd, Kottayam 686001

**Kairalee Mudralayam**
D C Books Complex, Good Shepherd St, Kot-
tayam 686001
*Tel:* (0481) 2563114; (0481) 2301614 *Fax:* (0481)
2564758
*E-mail:* info@dcbooks.com
*Web Site:* www.dcbooks.com/kairali.htm
*Key Personnel*
Manager: D C Kizhakemuri
Editorial: M S Chandrasekhara Warrier
Sales: D C Ponnamma
Production, Publicity, Rights & Permissions:
Mary John
Founded: 1978
Subjects: Biography, Fiction, Humor
ISBN Prefix(es): 81-85226
*Associate Companies:* Current Books; D C
Books; Kairali Children's Book Trust

**Kali For Women+**
K-92, Hauz Khas Enclave, 1st floor, New Delhi
10016
*Tel:* (011) 6864497; (011) 6852530 *Fax:* (011)
6864497
*E-mail:* kaliw@del2.vsnl.net.in
*Web Site:* www.kalibooks.com
*Key Personnel*
Contact: Ritu Menon; Urvashi Butalia
Editor: Preeti Gill
Founded: 1984
Subjects: Art, Biography, Drama, Theater, Envi-
ronmental Studies, Fiction, Health, Nutrition,
History, Law, Nonfiction (General), Social Sci-
ences, Sociology, Women's Studies
ISBN Prefix(es): 81-85107; 81-86706

**Kalyani Publishers+**
4863-2B Bharat Ram Rd, 24 Daryaganj, New
Delhi 110002
*Tel:* (011) 3274393; (011) 3271469
*Key Personnel*
Man Dir: Raj Kumar
Subjects: Science (General), Humanities
ISBN Prefix(es): 81-272; 81-7663
*Bookshop(s):* Lyall Book Depot, Chaura Bazar,
Ludhiana *Tel:* (0161) 2760031; (0161) 2745872

**Kerala University, Department of Publications**
Thiruvananthapuram, Kerala 695 034
*Tel:* (0471) 306422; (0471) 305931 *Fax:* (0471)
307158
*E-mail:* unikereg@md4.vsnl.net.in
*Web Site:* www.collegeskerala.com
*Key Personnel*
Chief Executive: Dr A Razaludeen
Production: Dr P Balachandran
Sales: Dr M A Karim
Founded: 1939
ISBN Prefix(es): 81-86397

**Khanna Publishers+**
2-B Nath Market, Nai Sarak, New Delhi 110 006
*Tel:* (011) 2912380; (011) 7224179
*Key Personnel*
Dir: R C Khanna; Vineet Khanna
Founded: 1959
Subjects: Civil Engineering, Communications,
Computer Science, Electronics, Electrical Engi-
neering, Energy, Engineering (General), Envi-
ronmental Studies, Management, Mathematics,
Mechanical Engineering, Technology
ISBN Prefix(es): 81-7409
*Branch Office(s)*
11 Community Centre, Ashok Vihar, Phase Il,
Delhi 110052 *Tel:* (011) 7224179

**Kitab Ghar**
24/4855 Ansari Rd, Darya Ganj, New Delhi 110
002
*Tel:* (011) 213206
*Key Personnel*
Chief Executive, Rights & Permissions: Satya
Brat Sharma
Editorial, Production: Jagat Ram Sharma
Sales, Publicity: Dev Datt
Founded: 1970
Subjects: Biography, Drama, Theater, Fiction,
Poetry, Science (General), Social Sciences, So-
ciology
ISBN Prefix(es): 81-7016; 81-7891

**Konark Publishers Pvt Ltd+**
A-149, Main Vikas Marg, Shakarpur, Delhi
110092
*Tel:* (011) 22504101; (011) 22455731; (011)
22507103 *Fax:* (011) 22507103
*E-mail:* kppl23@eth.net; konarkpublishers@
hotmail.com *Cable:* THE KONARK DELHI
*Key Personnel*
Man Dir: KPR Nair *E-mail:* kprn07@hotmail.
com
Founded: 1986
Membership(s): Federation of Publishers & Book-
sellers Association in India.
Subjects: Government, Political Science, Human
Relations, Labor, Industrial Relations, Social
Sciences, Sociology
ISBN Prefix(es): 81-220
Number of titles published annually: 40 Print
Total Titles: 750 Print

**Kosi Books**, *imprint of* Vidyarthi Mithram Press

**Krishna Prakashan Media (P) Ltd**, see Goel
Prakashen

**Lalit Kala Akademi**
Rabindar Bhavan, 35 Ferozshah Rd, New Delhi
110001
*Tel:* (011) 23387241; (011) 23387243; (011)
23387242 *Fax:* (011) 23782485
*E-mail:* lka@lalitkala.org.in
*Web Site:* www.lalitkala.org.in *Cable:* Artakademi
*Key Personnel*
Chairman: Prof Sankho Chaudhuri
Acting Secretary: M Rajaram
Sales: Kewal Krishan
Founded: 1954
Subjects: Art, Ethnicity
ISBN Prefix(es): 81-87507

**Lancer International**, *imprint of* Lancer
Publisher's & Distributors

**Lancer Paperbacks**, *imprint of* Lancer
Publisher's & Distributors

**Lancer Publishers**, *imprint of* Lancer Publisher's
& Distributors

**Lancer Publisher's & Distributors+**
56 Gautam Nagar, New Delhi 110049
*Tel:* (011) 6867339; (011) 6854691 *Fax:* (011)
6862077
*Web Site:* www.geocites.com/TheTropics/3328/
lancer.htm
*Key Personnel*
Man Dir & International Rights: Capt Bharat
Verma
Founded: 1983
Also acts as printer & manufacturer for foreign
publishers, importers, exporters & distributors.
Subjects: Asian Studies, Military Science, Self-
Help
ISBN Prefix(es): 81-7062; 81-85096

*Associate Companies:* Spantech & Lancer, Spantech House Lagham Rd, South Godstone, Surrey RH9 8HB, United Kingdom *Tel:* (01342) 893239 *Fax:* (01342) 892584; Spantech & Lancer, 3986 Ernst Rd, Hartford, WI 53027, United States *Tel:* 414-673-9064 *Fax:* 414-673-9064
*Imprints:* Lancer Paperbacks; Lancer International; Lancer Publishers; Indian Defence Review
Divisions: Indian Defence Review
*Distributor* for Raweltte Books (UK); Greenhill Books (UK)
*Orders to:* Spantech & Lancer, Spantech House, Lagham Rd, South Godstone, Surrey RH9 8H8, United Kingdom
Spantech & Lancer, 3986 Ernst Rd, Hartford, WI 53027, United States

**Law Publishers+**
Sardar Patel Marg, Civil Lines, Allahabad 211 001
Mailing Address: PO Box 1077, Allahabad 211 001
*Tel:* (0532) 2622758; (0532) 2420974 *Fax:* (0532) 2622781; (0532) 2609943
*E-mail:* lawpub@vsnl.com; lawpub@sancharnet.in
*Web Site:* www.law-publishers.com *Cable:* PUBLISHERS
*Key Personnel*
Chief Executive: Naresh Sagar
Manager: Shekhar Srivastava
Founded: 1961
Export of law & non-law journals & subscription service on back sets.
Subjects: Agriculture, Business, Criminology, Economics, Engineering (General), Environmental Studies, Government, Political Science, History, Law, Library & Information Sciences, Management, Mechanical Engineering, Physical Sciences, Psychology, Psychiatry, Religion - Buddhist, Religion - Hindu, Religion - Islamic, Science (General), Technology, Women's Studies
ISBN Prefix(es): 81-7111

**Laxmi Publications Pvt Ltd+**
22, Prakashdeep Bldg, Daryaganj, New Delhi 110 002
*Tel:* (011) 23262368; (011) 23262370 *Fax:* (011) 23262279
*E-mail:* colaxmi@hotmail.com
*Web Site:* www.laxmipublications.com
*Key Personnel*
Chairman: Mr R K Gupta
Man Dir: Mr Saurabh Gupta *E-mail:* guptas@global.t-bird.edu
Founded: 1974
Specialize in computer books, engineering, college & school textbooks.
Membership(s): Federation of Indian Publishers.
Subjects: Civil Engineering, Computer Science, Electronics, Electrical Engineering, Mathematics, Mechanical Engineering
ISBN Prefix(es): 81-7008
Number of titles published annually: 50 Print
Total Titles: 900 Print
Imprints: Firewall Media; Golden Bells; New Age International

**Learners Press Private Ltd+**
A-59, Okhla Industrial Area Phase II, New Delhi 110020
*Tel:* (011) 26387070; (011) 26386209 *Fax:* (011) 26383788
*E-mail:* info@sterlingpublishers.com
*Web Site:* www.sterlingpublishers.com *Cable:* PAPERBACKS
*Key Personnel*
Rights & Permissions: Vikas Ghai
Editorial: Marry Joseph
Production: Shammi Kapoor

Founded: 1990
Membership(s): Federation of Indian Publishers.
ISBN Prefix(es): 81-7181

**LexisNexis India**
14th floor, Vijaya Bldg, 17, Barakhamba Rd, New Delhi 110001
*Tel:* (011) 373 9614; (011) 373 9615; (011) 373 9616; (011) 332 6454 customer service; (011) 332 6455 customer service *Fax:* (011) 332 6456
*E-mail:* info@lexisnexis.co.in; customer.care@lexisnexis.co.in
*Web Site:* www.lexisnexis.co.in
*Key Personnel*
Publishing Manager: Ambika Nair
  *E-mail:* ambika.nair@lexisnexis.co.in
Editorial Manager: Sandeep Joshi
  *E-mail:* sandeep.joshi@lexisnexis.co.in
Commissioning Editor: Vidyaranya Chakravarthy
  *E-mail:* vidyaranya.chakravarthy@lexisnexis.co.in
General Manager: Sudarshan Sharma
  *E-mail:* sudarshan.sharma@lexisnexis.co.in
Assistant Manager, Customer Service: Ruchika Malik *E-mail:* ruchika.malik@lexisnexis.co.in
Assistant Manager, Sales: Vikas Saddar
  *E-mail:* vikas.saddar@lexisnexis.co.in
Publishers of law, taxation & business books.
Subjects: Business, Law, Taxation
*Parent Company:* Reed Elsevier
*Associate Companies:* LexisNexis Hong Kong, 12/F, Hennessey Centre, 500 Hennessey Rd, Causeway Bay, Hong Kong, Commissioning Editor: Anisha Sakhrani *Tel:* 2965 1400 *Fax:* 2976 0840 *Web Site:* www.lexisnexis.com.uk; Malayan Law Journal Sdn Bhd, Unit A-5-1, 5th floor, Wisma HB, Megan Phileo Ave, 12 Jalan Yap Kwan Seng, 50450 Kuala Lumpur, Malaysia, Managing Editor, New Product Development: Julie Ann Thomas *Tel:* (03) 2166-7558 *Fax:* (03) 2166-7550 *Web Site:* www.mlj.com.my; LexisNexis Singapore, 3 Killiney Rd, 08-08, Winsland House 1, Singapore 239519, Singapore, Regional Publishing Dir: Conita Leung *Tel:* 6733 1380 *Fax:* 6733 1175 *Web Site:* www.lexisnexis.com.sg; LexisNexis Butterworths Australia, Tower 2, 475-495 Victoria Ave, Chatswood, NSW 2067, Australia *Tel:* (02) 9422-2222 *Fax:* (02) 9422-2444; LexisNexis China, LexisNexis China Representative Office, Rm 1808, 18/F, Tower E3, Oriental Plaza No.1, East Chang An Ave, Dong Cheng District, Beijing, China *Tel:* (010) 8518 5801 *Fax:* (010) 8518 9287; LexisNexis Japan, Toranomon 19, Mori Bldg 9F 1-2-20, 105-0001 Minato-ku, Tokyo *Tel:* (03) 3509-1844 *Fax:* (03) 3509-1845; LexisNexis Korea, 1119 Punglim Bldg, Gongduck-Dong, Mapo Gu, Seoul 121-718, Republic of Korea *Tel:* (02) 713 8605 *Fax:* (02) 713 8602; LexisNexis Malaysia, Unit A-5-1, 5th fl, Wisma HB, Megan Phileo Ave, 12 Jalan Yap Kwan Seng, 50450 Kuala Lumpur, Malaysia *Tel:* (03) 2166 7558 *Fax:* (03) 2166 7550; LexisNexis Butterworths New Zealand, 205-207 Victoria St, PO Box 472, Wellington, New Zealand *Tel:* (04) 385 1479 *Fax:* (04) 385 1598 *E-mail:* customer.service@lexisnexis.co.nz *Web Site:* www.lexisnexis.com.au/nz; LexisNexis Taiwan, 17 F/B, No 167 Tun Hwa N Rd, Hung Kuo Bldg, 105, Taipei, Taiwan, Province of China *Tel:* (02) 2717 1999 ext 1111 *Fax:* (02) 2717 2886

**Lokvangmaya Griha Pvt Ltd**
Bhupesh Gupta Bhavan, 85, Sayan Rd, Prabha devi, Mumbai 400025
*Tel:* (022) 4362474 *Fax:* (022) 4313220
*E-mail:* lokvang@bol.net.in
*Key Personnel*
General Manager: Sukumar Damle
Founded: 1973

Subjects: Human Relations, Social Sciences, Sociology
ISBN Prefix(es): 81-86995; 81-88284
*Bookshop(s):* 5-22-32 Tilak Path, Aurangabad 431001; People's Book House, IS Cawasji Patel St, Fort Bombay 400001; Red Flag Bldg, Bindu Chowk, Kolhapur 416002; 562 Sadashiv Peth, Chirtashala Prakalp, Pune 411030

**Longman,** *imprint of* Addison-Wesley Pte Ltd

**Lotus,** *imprint of* Roli Books Pvt Ltd

**Lustre Press,** *imprint of* Roli Books Pvt Ltd

**Lustre Press Pvt Ltd,** see Roli Books Pvt Ltd

**M/S Family Books Pvt Ltd,** *imprint of* Pustak Mahal

**M/S Motilal Banarsidass Publishing (P) Ltd**
41-UA Bungalow Rd, Jawahar Nagar, New Delhi 110 007
*Tel:* (011) 23851985; (011) 23858335; (011) 23854826; (011) 23852747 *Fax:* (011) 23850689; (011) 25797221
*E-mail:* mail@mlbd.com
*Web Site:* www.mlbd.com
*Key Personnel*
Chairperson: Leela Jain
Founded: 1903
ISBN Prefix(es): 81-208

**Mahajan Publishers Pvt Ltd+**
Super Market Basement, Near Natraj Cinema, Ashram Rd, Ahmedabad 380009
*Tel:* 78547 *Fax:* (079) 6589101
*E-mail:* mahajan2000@hotmail.com *Cable:* PERIODICAL
*Key Personnel*
Man Dir: Mr Dinker Mahajan
  *E-mail:* mahajan2000@hotmail.com
Founded: 1953
Specializes in textiles.
ISBN Prefix(es): 81-85401
*Associate Companies:* Mahajan Book Distributors

**Mainstreet Books,** *imprint of* Full Circle Publishing

**Manohar Publishers & Distributors+**
4753/23 Ansari Rd, Daryaganj, New Delhi 110 002
*Tel:* (011) 23284848; (011) 23289100; (011) 23262796; (011) 23260774 *Fax:* (011) 23265162
*E-mail:* manbooks@vsnl.com; sales@manoharbooks.com
*Web Site:* www.manoharbooks.com
*Key Personnel*
Man Dir, Rights & Permissions, Publicity: Ajay Jain
Editorial: B N Varma
Publicity: Siddharth Chowdhury
Founded: 1969
Subjects: Anthropology, Architecture & Interior Design, Art, Economics, Education, Ethnicity, Government, Political Science, History, Literature, Literary Criticism, Essays, Philosophy, Religion - Other, Science (General), Social Sciences, Sociology, Politics
ISBN Prefix(es): 81-85054; 81-85425; 81-7304
Number of titles published annually: 50 Print
*Associate Companies:* Manohar Book Service, 2/6 Ansari Rd, Daryaganj, New Delhi 110 002
Distributed by South Asia Books

**Manosabdam Books,** *imprint of* Vidyarthi Mithram Press

**Mapin Publishing Pvt Ltd+**
31 Somnath Rd, Usmanpura, Ahmedabad, Gujarat 380013
*Tel:* (079) 2755-1793; (079) 2755-1833
*Fax:* (079) 2755-0955
*E-mail:* info@mapinpub.com
*Web Site:* www.mapinpub.com
*Key Personnel*
Man Dir: Mallika Sarabhai
International Rights: Bipin Shah
Founded: 1985
Specialize in books on art, crafts, architecture, culture of India, heritage & archaeology.
Membership(s): Federation of Indian Publishers.
Subjects: Archaeology, Architecture & Interior Design, Art, Asian Studies, Crafts, Games, Hobbies, Photography, Religion - Hindu, Religion - Islamic
ISBN Prefix(es): 81-85822; 81-7380; 81-88204
Number of titles published annually: 15 Print; 2 CD-ROM
Total Titles: 70 Print; 2 CD-ROM
*Associate Companies:* Grantha Corp, 77 Daniele Drive, Ocean, NJ 07712, United States *Tel:* 732-493-3466 *Fax:* 309-409-6399 *E-mail:* mapinpub@aol.com
*Orders to:* Antique Collector's Club Ltd, 91 Market St Industrial Park, Wappingers' Falls, NY 12590, United States *Tel:* 800-252-5231 *Fax:* 845-297-0068 *E-mail:* info@antiquecc.com *Web Site:* www.antiquecc.com (North America)
Art Books International, Unit 007, The Chandlery, 50 Westminster Bridge Rd, London SE1 7QY, United Kingdom *Tel:* (020) 7953 8290 *Fax:* (020) 7953 8290 *E-mail:* sales@art-bks.com *Web Site:* www.art-bks.com (UK & Europe)
MapinLit, 31 Somnath Rd, Usmanpura, Ahmedabad 380013 *Tel:* (079) 2755-1793 *Fax:* (079) 2755-0955 *E-mail:* mapin@icenet.net

**Marg Publications**
Army & Navy Bldg, 3rd floor, 148 Mahatma Gandhi Rd, Mumbai 400001
*Tel:* (022) 2821151; (022) 2045947-8; (022) 842520 *Fax:* (022) 047102
*E-mail:* margpub@tata.com
*Web Site:* www.tata.com/marg
*Telex:* 118-2618, 118-2731 TATA IN
*Key Personnel*
Publisher: J J Bhabha
Editorial: Ms Chandiramani Savita
Sales, Publicity: Baptist Sequeira
Design: Miss Naju Hirani
Contact: Radhika Sabavala
Business Development Manager: Baptist Sequeira
Founded: 1946
Marg meaning pathway leads the reader through the cultural heritage of India & its neighboring countries.
Publisher of books & magazines.
Subjects: Architecture & Interior Design, Art, Music, Dance, Indian Art, Paintings, Sculpture
ISBN Prefix(es): 81-85026
*Parent Company:* National Centre for the Performing Arts, Nariman Point, Mumbai 400021
*Branch Office(s)*
Tata Services Ltd, Jeevan Bharati Tower No 1, 10th floor, 124 Connaught Circus, New Delhi, Contact: Mr R K Gupta *Tel:* (011) 3327072-76 *Fax:* (011) 3226265
Distributed by Art Media Resources Ltd/Paragon Book Gallery

**Sri Ramakrishna Math**
31 Ramakrishna Math Rd, Mylapore, Chennai 600 004
*Tel:* (044) 24621110 *Fax:* (044) 24934589
*E-mail:* srkmath@vsnl.com
*Web Site:* www.sriramakrishnamath.org
*Key Personnel*
President: Sri Ramakrishna Math

Founded: 1897
Subjects: Biography, Philosophy, Religion - Hindu
ISBN Prefix(es): 81-7120; 81-7823
Distributor for Advaita Ashrama (Kolkata)
*Showroom(s):* 99, Pondy Baza, T Nagar, Chennai 600 017; Chennai Central Railway Station, Chennai 600 004
*Bookshop(s):* 16 Ramakrishna Math Rd, Mylapore, Chennai 600 004; No 26, S Mada St, Mylapore, Chennai 600 004

**Maya Publishers Pvt Ltd+**
303/4 Kawshalya Park, New Delhi 110 016
*Tel:* (011) 6494878; (011) 6494850; (011) 649 0451; (011) 649 0959 *Fax:* (011) 6491039; (011) 686 4614
*E-mail:* surit@del2.vsnl.net.in
*Key Personnel*
Contact: Surit Mitra
ISBN Prefix(es): 81-86268
*Associate Companies:* Gulmohur Press Pvt Ltd

**Mayfair Paperbacks**, *imprint of* Arnold Heinman Publishers (India) Pvt Ltd

**Mayoor Paperbacks**, *imprint of* National Publishing House

**Mehta Publishing House+**
1941 Sadashiv Peth, Madiwale Colony, Pune, Maharashtra 411030
*Tel:* (020) 24476924; (020) 24463048 *Fax:* (020) 24475462
*E-mail:* mehpubl@vsnl.com
*Web Site:* www.mehtapublishinghouse.com
*Key Personnel*
Proprietor: Sunil Mehta
Man Dir, Production, Rights & Permissions: Gautam Mehta
Publicity & Marketing Manager: G P S Bawa
Founded: 1971
Subjects: Agriculture, Asian Studies, Computer Science, Education, Medicine, Nursing, Dentistry, Orientalia
ISBN Prefix(es): 81-7161; 81-7766
Number of titles published annually: 200 Print
Total Titles: 2,000 Print
*Parent Company:* Mehta Offset Pvt Ltd
Imprints: Interprint
Subsidiaries: Mehta Book Sellers
*Book Club(s):* T Book Club

**Merrill Education**, *imprint of* Addison-Wesley Pte Ltd

**Minerva Associates (Publications) Pvt Ltd+**
7-B Lake Pl, Kolkata 700 029
*Tel:* (033) 2466 3783
*Key Personnel*
Chairman, Publicity, Rights & Permissions: Sushil Mukherjea
Editorial Dir: O K Ghosh
Sales: T K Mukherjee
Founded: 1973
Publication of serious studies.
Subjects: Agriculture, Anthropology, Asian Studies, Economics, Education, Ethnicity, Government, Political Science, History, Journalism, Labor, Industrial Relations, Literature, Literary Criticism, Essays, Natural History, Philosophy, Psychology, Psychiatry, Public Administration, Religion - Buddhist, Religion - Hindu, Social Sciences, Sociology
ISBN Prefix(es): 81-7715
Number of titles published annually: 7 Print
Total Titles: 175 Print

**Ministry of Information & Broadcasting**
Publications Division, Patiala House, Tilak Marg, New Delhi 110 001

*Tel:* (011) 3387983; (011) 3386879; (011) 3387069; (011) 3386452 *Fax:* (011) 3387341
*E-mail:* indiapub@nda.vsnl.net.in; dpd@sb.nic.in
*Web Site:* mib.nic.in *Cable:* EXINFOR
*Key Personnel*
Dir: Shri S Jaipal Reddy
Subjects: Art, Biography, Environmental Studies, Ethnicity, History, Science (General), Social Sciences, Sociology
ISBN Prefix(es): 81-230
*Branch Office(s)*
Government Press, Press Rd, Thiruvananthapuram
LL Auditorium, Anna Salai, Chennai
State Archaeological Museum Bldg, Public Garden, Hyderabad
8 Esplanade East, Kolkata
Commerce House, Currimbhoy Rd, Ballard Pier, Mumbai
Super Bazar, 2nd floor, Connaught Circus, New Delhi
Bihar State Co-operative Bank Bldg, Ashoka Rajpath, Patna

**Mittal Publications**
B-2/19-B Lawrence Rd, Delhi 110035
*Tel:* (011) 5163610; (011) 5648028; (011) 3250398 *Fax:* (011) 5648725
*E-mail:* mittalp@ndf.vsnl.net.in
*Key Personnel*
Contact: K M Mittal
Founded: 1979
Membership(s): India Federation of Publishers' & Booksellers' Association.
Subjects: Social Sciences, Sociology
ISBN Prefix(es): 81-7099
*Orders to:* A-110 Mohan Garden, New Delhi 110059

**Motilal Banarsidass Publishers Pvt Ltd+**
41 U A Bungalow Rd, Jawahar, Nagar, Delhi 110007
*Tel:* (011) 23911985; (011) 23918335; (011) 23974826 *Fax:* (011) 23930689; (011) 25797221
*E-mail:* mlbd@vsnl
*Web Site:* www.mlbd.com
*Telex:* 03166053 Enky In; 03165367 Kkrc In
*Cable:* GLORYINDIA
*Key Personnel*
Dir, Editorial, Rights & Permissions & Publishing: N P Jain
Home Sales: J P Jain
Finance: Ravi P Jain
Publishing: Anurag Jain
Founded: 1903
Subjects: History, Language Arts, Linguistics, Literature, Literary Criticism, Essays, Medicine, Nursing, Dentistry, Philosophy, Religion - Other
ISBN Prefix(es): 81-208
*Branch Office(s)*
16, St Mark's Rd, Bangalore, Karnataka 560001
PO Box 75, Chowk, Varanasi 221 001 *Tel:* (0542) 62898
Ashok Raipath, opposite Patna College, Patna, Bihar 800 004 *Tel:* (0612) 51442
120 Royapettah High Rd, Mylapore, Chennai 600004
*Warehouse:* 45 A, Naraina Industrial Area phase-I, New Delhi 28

**Mudgala Trust+**
Kaveri 12, Fourth Cross St, Ramakrishna Nagar, Chennai 600028
*Tel:* (044) 837257
*Key Personnel*
Founder: S R Balasubrahmanyam
President: Meenakshi Natarajan
Joint Secretary & Treasurer: B Natarajan; Dr B Venkataraman
Founded: 1965

Subjects: Architecture & Interior Design, Art, Drama, Theater, Ethnicity, Music, Dance, Philosophy, Religion - Other
ISBN Prefix(es): 81-86392
*U.S. Office(s):* Mohan Venkataraman, 361 Bancroft Court, No 2, Rockford, IL 61107, United States *Tel:* 815-227-4553

**Mudrak Publishers & Distributors+**
W-152 Greater Kailash-1, New Delhi 110 048
*Tel:* (011) 3730818; (011) 3738319; (011) 6416317
*Key Personnel*
Prop: S P Kumria
Books of academic interest on subjects of humanities.
ISBN Prefix(es): 81-87161
Total Titles: 5 Print

**A Mukherjee & Co Pvt Ltd**
2, Bankim Chatterjee St, Kolkata 700 073
*Tel:* (033) 2417406; (033) 2418199 *Fax:* (033) 440-8641
*Key Personnel*
Dir: Rajeev Neogi
Founded: 1940
Subjects: Education, Government, Political Science, Nonfiction (General), Religion - Other, Travel
ISBN Prefix(es): 81-86043

**Multitech Publishing Co+**
15 Yogesh Hingwala Lane, Ghatkopar East, Mumbai 400077
*Tel:* (022) 5118820; (022) 5154206 *Fax:* (022) 5115904
*Key Personnel*
Contact: Sevantilal Shah
Founded: 1978
Membership(s): Federation of India Publishers.
Subjects: Chemistry, Chemical Engineering, Engineering (General), Management, Mechanical Engineering, Technology
*Branch Office(s)*
Ahmedabad Book Centre, D/122, Mahavir Chamber, Near Relief Cinema, Salapose Rd, Ahmedabad 380 001

**Munshiram Manoharlal Publishers Pvt Ltd+**
54 Rani Jhansi Rd, New Delhi 110055
Mailing Address: PO Box 5715, New Delhi 110055
*Tel:* (011) 3671668; (011) 3673650 *Fax:* (011) 3612745
*E-mail:* mrml@mantraonline.com
*Web Site:* www.mrmlbooks.com
*Key Personnel*
Chief Executive, Man Dir: Devendra Jain
Production, Publicity: Pankaj D Jain
    *E-mail:* pankaj.mrml@mantraonline.com
Sales Dir: Ashok Jain
Founded: 1952
Also major book dealer.
Subjects: Anthropology, Archaeology, Architecture & Interior Design, Art, Asian Studies, Astrology, Occult, Drama, Theater, History, Language Arts, Linguistics, Music, Dance, Philosophy, Religion - Buddhist, Religion - Hindu, Religion - Islamic, Religion - Other
ISBN Prefix(es): 81-215
Number of titles published annually: 80 Print
Total Titles: 1,200 Print
*Bookshop(s):* 4416 Nai Sarak, Delhi 110006 (Amir Chand Marg)

**M/S Gulshan Nanda Publications+**
7 Sheesh Mahal, 5A Pali Hill, Bandra, Mumbai 50
*Tel:* (022) 6406994 *Fax:* (022) 4303696
*Key Personnel*
President: Himanshu Nanda

Vice President: Rahul Nanda
Founded: 1984
Membership(s): Federation of Indian Publishers' Association.
Subjects: Fiction
ISBN Prefix(es): 81-7241
*Associate Companies:* Sonex Marketing & Publishing, United Kingdom *Tel:* (081) 4225172

**Naresh Publishers+**
111 Shankar Rd Market, New Rajendra Nagar, New Delhi 110016
*Tel:* (011) 572-3235; (011) 575-4442 *Fax:* (011) 574-6485
*Key Personnel*
Contact: Mohinder Kumar Chowdhry
Founded: 1972
Membership(s): Federation of Educational Publishers in India, Federation of Indian Publishers, & Federation of Publishers & Booksellers in India.
ISBN Prefix(es): 81-7005
*Associate Companies:* Paramount Sales (India) Pvt Ltd, 484 Double Storey, PO Box 2860, New Rajinder Nagar, New Delhi 110060
*Tel:* (011) 5723235 *Fax:* (011) 5746485

**Narosa Publishing House+**
22, Daryaganj, Delhi Medical Association Rd, Delhi 110002
*Tel:* (011) 23243224; (011) 23243415; (011) 23243416 *Fax:* (011) 23243225; (011) 23258934
*E-mail:* narosa@ndc.vsnl.net.in; narosadl@nda.vsnl.net.in
*Web Site:* www.narosa.com *Cable:* Narosa New Delhi
*Key Personnel*
Man Dir: N K Mehra
Senior Executive: P K Chopra
Marketing Manager: S Mehra
Founded: 1977
Subjects: Biological Sciences, Chemistry, Chemical Engineering, Computer Science, Engineering (General), Environmental Studies, Mathematics, Medicine, Nursing, Dentistry, Physics
ISBN Prefix(es): 81-85015; 81-85198; 81-7319
*Associate Companies:* Narosa Book Distributors Pvt Ltd
*Branch Office(s)*
35-36 Greams Rd, Thousand Lights, Chennai 600006 *Tel:* (044) 28295362 *Fax:* (044) 28290377 *E-mail:* narosamds@vsnl.net
2F-2G Shivam Chambers, 53 Syed Amir Ali Ave, Kolkata 700019 *Tel:* (033) 22814809 *Fax:* (033) 22814778
306 Shiv Centre, D B C Sector 17 PO KU Bazar, New Bombay 400705 *Tel:* (022) 27890977 *Fax:* (022) 27891930

**National Academy of Art**, see Lalit Kala Akademi

**National Academy of Letters, India**, see Sahitya Akademi

**National Book Organization+**
A-5 Green Park, New Delhi 110016
*Tel:* (011) 6518378 *Fax:* (011) 6851795
*E-mail:* nbtindia@ndb.vsnl.net.in
*Web Site:* www.nbtindia.com
*Telex:* 031 73034nbt-in
Founded: 1984
Acts also as distributor.
Subjects: Agriculture, Anthropology, Archaeology, Architecture & Interior Design, Behavioral Sciences, Child Care & Development, Developing Countries, Economics, Education, Environmental Studies, Geography, Geology, Government, Political Science, History, Human Relations, Labor, Industrial Relations, Law, Man-

agement, Military Science, Religion - Other, Social Sciences, Sociology, Women's Studies
ISBN Prefix(es): 81-85135; 81-237; 81-87521
*Branch Office(s)*
Delhi
Distributed by UBS Publishers & Distributors Ltd
*Bookshop(s):* Municipal Flat No 18, Bungalos Rd, Delhi 110007

**National Book Trust**, see National Book Organization

**National Book Trust India**
A5 Green Park, New Delhi 110016
*Tel:* (011) 6518378; (011) 23379868 *Fax:* (011) 6851795
*E-mail:* nbtindia@ndb.vsnl.net.in
*Web Site:* www.nbtindia.com
*Telex:* 031-73034 *Cable:* Nabotrust
*Key Personnel*
Chairman: Anand Sarub
Dir: Arvind Kumar
Joint Dir, Administration & Finance: S N Madan
Deputy Dir, Arts: Jyotish Datta Gupta
Deputy Dir, Exhibitions: Talewar Giri
Deputy Dir, Subsidies: R Gupta
Deputy Dir, Information & Publicity: D Das Gupta
Deputy Dir, Production: Dhruv Bhargava
Founded: 1957
Subjects: Foreign Countries, Human Relations
ISBN Prefix(es): 81-85135; 81-237; 81-87521
*Bookshop(s):* Jayanagar Shopping Complex, Bangalore; S A Bhabari, Dutt Lane, Kolkata; A-4 Green Park, New Delhi; CIDCO Bldg, Sector 1, 2nd floor, Vashi, Mumbai

**National Council of Applied Economic Research, Publications Division**
Parisila Bhawan, 11, Indraprastha Estate, New Delhi 110 002
*Tel:* (011) 23379861; (011) 23379862; (011) 23379863; (011) 23379865; (011) 23379866; (011) 23379868 *Fax:* (011) 23370164
*E-mail:* infor@ncaer.org
*Web Site:* www.ncaer.org
*Key Personnel*
Dir-General: Mr Suman Bery
Founded: 1956
Subjects: Agriculture, Business, Economics
ISBN Prefix(es): 81-85877

**National Council of Educational Research & Training, Publication Department**
Sri Aurobindo Marg, New Delhi 110016
*Tel:* (011) 6851070; (011) 662708 *Fax:* (011) 6868419
*E-mail:* crc@giasdlo1.vsnl.net.in
*Web Site:* ncert.nic.in
*Telex:* 31-73024 NCRT-IN *Cable:* EDUPRINT, NEW DELHI
*Key Personnel*
Dir: Dr K Gopalan
Founded: 1962
Membership(s): Afro-Asian Book Council. Specializes in school textbooks, research monographs, supplementary readers.
Subjects: Education
ISBN Prefix(es): 81-7450

**National Institute of Industrial Research (NIIR)**
Affiliate of NIIR Project Exports India (P) Ltd
106-E Kamla Nagar, Delhi 110 007
Mailing Address: PB No 2162, Delhi 110 007
*Tel:* (011) 3923955; (011) 3935654; (011) 3945886 *Fax:* (011) 3941561
*E-mail:* niir@usnl.com
*Web Site:* www.niir.org
*Key Personnel*
President & Chief Executive Officer: Mr Ajay Kumar Gupta *E-mail:* akgupta@niir.org

Senior Vice President: Mr P K Tripathi
   *E-mail:* pktripathi@niir.org
Senior Project Consultant: Mr P K Chattopadhyay
   *E-mail:* chattopadhyay@niir.org
Founded: 1994
Publishers of process technology books, Business
   & Industrial Directory, Worldwide Importers
   Directory & Industrial Monthly Magazine.
Subjects: Business, Chemistry, Chemical Engi-
   neering, Science (General), Technology
ISBN Prefix(es): 81-86623
Number of titles published annually: 20 Print
Total Titles: 70 Print
Distributor for M/S Small Industry Research In-
   stitute

**National Museum**
Janpath, New Delhi 110 011
*Tel:* (011) 3018415; (011) 3019272; (011)
   3019237
*E-mail:* rdchoudh@ndf.vsnl.net.in
*Web Site:* www.nationalmuseumindia.org
*Key Personnel*
Public Relations: Mr U Das
Subjects: Art, Ethnicity
ISBN Prefix(es): 81-85832

**National Publishing House**
23, Daryaganj, New Delhi 110002
*Tel:* (011) 3274161; (011) 3275267
*Key Personnel*
Man Dir: K L Malik
Editorial, Production, Rights & Permissions: S K
   Malik
Sales: M K Malik
Founded: 1950
A-95 Sector 5, Noida 201301 (UP) Tel:
   3683/4507.
Subjects: Ethnicity, Human Relations, Social Sci-
   ences, Sociology
ISBN Prefix(es): 81-214
*Parent Company:* K L Malik & Sons Pvt Ltd, 23
   Daryaganj, New Delhi 110 002
Imprints: Mayoor Paperbacks; Gyan Bharati
*Branch Office(s)*
K L Malik & Sons Pvt Ltd, 34 Netaji Subhash
   Marg, Allahabad 3
Malik & Co, Chaura Rasta, Jaipur 302003
*Bookshop(s):* 23 Daryaganj, New Delhi 110002

**Natraj Prakashan, Publishers & Exporters+**
A-98, Ashok Vihar, Phase 1, Delhi 110052
*Telex:* 316 5503 FXRS IN
*Key Personnel*
Owner: Mrs Kusum Goyanka
Founded: 1987
Subjects: Biography, Fiction, Literature, Literary
   Criticism, Essays, Poetry, Religion - Hindu
ISBN Prefix(es): 81-85979

**Navajivan Trust+**
Post Navajivan, Ahmedabad, Gujarat 380 014
*Tel:* (079) 27541329; (079) 27542634; (079)
   27540635 *Fax:* (079) 27541329
*Web Site:* www.navajivantrust.org
*Key Personnel*
Chairman: Biharibhai P Shah
Managing Trustee: Jitendar T Desai
   *E-mail:* jdesai@navajivantrust.org
Manager, Sales & Permissions: Kapil Rawal
Founded: 1919
Printing, publishing & distribution of Gandhian
   literature.
Subjects: Biography, History, Philosophy, Reli-
   gion - Other
ISBN Prefix(es): 81-7229
*Branch Office(s)*
130 Princess St, Mumbai 400 002

**Navrang Booksellers & Publishers+**
RB-7 Inderpuri, New Delhi 110 012

*Tel:* (011) 5835914; (011) 5836197 *Fax:* (011)
   5836113; (011) 5836761
*E-mail:* navrang@del2.vsn.net.in
*Key Personnel*
Proprietor: Mrs Nirmal Singal
Founded: 1968
Subjects: Archaeology, Art, Developing Coun-
   tries, Education, Ethnicity, History, Philosophy,
   Religion - Buddhist, Religion - Hindu
ISBN Prefix(es): 81-7013

**Navyug Publishers**
K-24 Hauz Khas, New Delhi 110 016
*Tel:* (011) 278370
*Key Personnel*
Editorial: Pritam Singh
Sales: Gurbachan Singh
Founded: 1949
Subjects: Ethnicity
ISBN Prefix(es): 81-7599; 81-85267; 81-86216

**Naya Prokash+**
206 Bidhan Sarani, Kolkata 700 006
*Tel:* 349566 *Fax:* (033) 5523366; (033) 5524053
   *Cable:* Napkas
*Key Personnel*
Production, Rights & Permissions, Editorial:
   Barin Mitra
Partner, Sales, Publicity: D Roy
Founded: 1962
Subjects: Agriculture, Environmental Studies,
   Gardening, Plants, Government, Political Sci-
   ence, History, Language Arts, Linguistics,
   Management, Military Science, Science (Gen-
   eral), Social Sciences, Sociology
ISBN Prefix(es): 81-85109; 81-85421
*Parent Company:* Darbari Offset Pvt Ltd
*Associate Companies:* Mitrata Offset Print;
   Prokash Pvt Ltd
Subsidiaries: NP Sales Pvt Ltd

**Neeta Prakashan+**
A-4 Ring Rd, South Extension Part-1, New Delhi
   110 049
Mailing Address: PO Box 3853, New Delhi
   110049
*Tel:* (011) 692013 *Fax:* (011) 4636011
*E-mail:* neeta@giasdl01.vsnl.net.in *Cable:*
   Loveneeta
*Key Personnel*
Man Proprietor: Shanti Devi
Sales, Production, Publicity, Rights & Permis-
   sions Executive: Rakesh Gupta
Founded: 1960
Subjects: Education
ISBN Prefix(es): 81-7202

**Neha Mini Katha**, *imprint of* Spectrum
   Publications

**Nem Chand & Brothers+**
Civil Lines, Roorkee 247667 U P
*Tel:* (01332) 72258; (01332) 72752; (01332)
   74343 *Fax:* (01332) 73258 *Cable:*
   ENGINJOUR
*Key Personnel*
Man Dir, Rights & Permissions: N C Jain
Editorial Dir: Dr Ashok K Jain
Sales Dir: Anil Jain
Production Dir: Shanil Jain
Publicity, Advertising Dir: Mrs Shashi Jain
Founded: 1951
Membership(s): Chemical & Allied Products Ex-
   port Promotion Council (Books Division); Also
   book packager.
Subjects: Agriculture, Architecture & Interior
   Design, Career Development, Earth Sciences,
   Fashion, Gardening, Plants, House & Home,
   Women's Studies
ISBN Prefix(es): 81-85240

Subsidiaries: Roorkee Press
*Warehouse:* Opposite Old Dy S P Office, Roorkee
   247667

**New Age International**, *imprint of* Laxmi
   Publications Pvt Ltd

**New Light Publishers+**
B-8 Rattan Jyoti, 18 Rajendra Pl, New Delhi
   110008
*Tel:* (011) 5712137 *Fax:* (011) 5812385
*E-mail:* newlight@vsnl.net *Cable:* ENELPEE
*Key Personnel*
Man Partner: Vikas Chowdhary
Editorial: Prof R P Chopra
Publicity, Advertising: R K Chowdhry
Founded: 1963
Subjects: Language Arts, Linguistics, Self-Help
ISBN Prefix(es): 81-85018; 81-86332

**New Riders**, *imprint of* Addison-Wesley Pte Ltd

**Newspread International+**
E 2 Greater Kailish II, New Delhi 110048
*Tel:* (011) 2331402 *Fax:* (011) 2607252
*Telex:* 22143 Bureau *Cable:* NEWSPREAD
*Key Personnel*
Executive Editor: Kul Bhushan
Production Manager: Benedict Mutisya Nzomo
Founded: 1971
ISBN Prefix(es): 81-86858
*Showroom(s):* Leader House, Moi Ave, Kenya

**Nil**, *imprint of* Asian Trading Corporation

**Niyo Software**
Unit 1B, Devgiri Ind Estate, S No 17/1B Plot
   No14 Kothrud, Pune 411029
*Tel:* (020) 546 7296; (020) 400 1603 *Fax:* (020)
   400 1603
*E-mail:* info@niyoindia.com
*Web Site:* www.niyoindia.com
*Key Personnel*
President: Milind Chudgar
Founded: 1995
Document conversion & e-enabling services,
   animation & graphic generation. Various for-
   mats including LIT, Adobe PDF, Palm Devices
   (PDB), XML, OEB & all possible ebook for-
   mats.
ISBN Prefix(es): 81-88303

**Omsons Publications+**
Publishers & Distributors, T-7, Rajouri Garden,
   New Delhi 110027
*Tel:* (011) 5412452 *Fax:* (011) 3289353
*E-mail:* omsons@satyam.net.in
*Key Personnel*
Contact: Ramesh Kumar Virmani
Founded: 1983
Subjects: Agriculture, Anthropology, Behavioral
   Sciences, Biography, Business, Career Devel-
   opment, Drama, Theater, Economics, Educa-
   tion, Environmental Studies, Fiction, Foreign
   Countries, Geography, Geology, Government,
   Political Science, History, Humor, Library &
   Information Sciences, Literature, Literary Criti-
   cism, Essays, Management, Marketing, Philos-
   ophy, Psychology, Psychiatry, Social Sciences,
   Sociology, Travel, Veterinary Science, Women's
   Studies
ISBN Prefix(es): 81-7117
*Parent Company:* Western Book Depot, Panbazar,
   Guwahati 781001
*Branch Office(s)*
Jasomanta Rd, Panbazar, Guwahati 781001
*Bookshop(s):* Western Book Depot, Panbazar,
   Guwahati 781001
*Orders to:* Omsons, Prakash House, 4379/4B
   Ansari Rd, New Delhi 110002

**Orient Paperbacks+**
Imprint of Vision Books Pvt Ltd
1590 Madarsa Rd, Kashmere Gate, Delhi 110006
*Tel:* (011) 2386-2267; (011) 2386-2201
 *Fax:* (011) 2386-2935
*E-mail:* orientpbk@vsnl.com
*Web Site:* www.orientpaperbacks.com *Cable:*
 VISIONBOOK, DELHI 110006
*Key Personnel*
Man Dir: Vishwa Nath
Editorial, Production: Kapil Malhotra
Sales, Publicity, Rights & Permissions: Sudhir
 Malhotra *E-mail:* smalhotra@orientpaperbacks.
 com
Exports, Mideast & Asia: Sidharth Malhotra
Founded: 1977
Specialize in fitness.
Subjects: Astrology, Occult, Business, Career De-
 velopment, Cookery, Crafts, Games, Hobbies,
 Drama, Theater, Fiction, Health, Nutrition,
 How-to, Humor, Nonfiction (General), Poetry,
 Self-Help, Sports, Athletics, Fitness
ISBN Prefix(es): 81-222
Number of titles published annually: 50 Print
Total Titles: 650 Print
*Associate Companies:* Rajpal & Sons; Ravin-
 dra Printing Press; Shiksha Bharati; Shiksha
 Bharati Press, G T Rd, Shadara, Delhi 110 032
Imprints: Anand Paperbacks
*Branch Office(s)*
3-6-280/A/5 Himayatnagar, Hyderabad, K M
 Govindan *Tel:* (040) 2322-3252
Vasant, Ground floor, 3-B Pedder Rd, Mumbai
 400026 *Tel:* (022) 2351-0343 *Fax:* (022) 2351-
 0229
24 Feroze Gandhi Marg, Lajpat Nagar, New
 Delhi 110024 *Tel:* (011) 2983-6470; (011)
 2983-6480 *Fax:* (011) 2983-6490
*Book Club(s):* Orient Book Club

**Oxford & IBH Publishing Co Pvt Ltd+**
66 Janpath, 2nd floor, New Delhi 110001
*Tel:* (011) 2332 45 78; (011) 2332 05 18
 *Fax:* (011) 2371 0090
*E-mail:* oxford@vsnl.com
*Key Personnel*
Dir: Mohan Primlani; Raju Primlani; Vijay Prim-
 lani
Founded: 1962
Subjects: Agriculture, Asian Studies, Biological
 Sciences, Civil Engineering, Earth Sciences,
 Engineering (General), Mechanical Engineer-
 ing, Natural History, Psychology, Psychiatry,
 Science (General)
ISBN Prefix(es): 81-204; 81-205; 81-7087
Subsidiaries: Science Publishers Inc
*Branch Office(s)*
22 Park Mansion, Park St, Kolkata 700016

**Oxford University Press+**
YMCA Library Bldg, 1st floor, One Jai Singh Rd,
 New Delhi 110 001
*Tel:* (011) 2021029; (011) 2021198; (011)
 2021396 *Fax:* (011) 3732312; (011) 3360897
*E-mail:* admin.in@oup.com
*Telex:* OXORIENT
*Key Personnel*
Man Dir: Manzar Khan
Finance Dir: Vivek Dayal
Educational & Higher Educational Publishing Dir:
 Ranjan Kaul
Educational Marketing Dir: K.M. Thomas
Academic Publishing Dir: Nitasha Devasar
Dir HR & Administration: Sanjay Gaur
Academic Marketing Dir: Yogesh Saxena
Regional Sales Dir, North: Shammi Manik
Regional Sales Dir, West: Vimal Kohli
Regional Manager, East: Anindya Sengupta
Regional Manager, South: Venugopal Bhaskaran
Publicity Manager: Rowena Kapparath
Founded: 1912
Subjects: Biography, Business, Developing Coun-
 tries, Economics, History, Literature, Literary

Criticism, Essays, Natural History, Philoso-
 phy, Religion - Hindu, Politics, Sociology, Cul-
 ture Studies, Gender Studies. Ecology, Science,
 Medicine
ISBN Prefix(es): 81-7025; 0-19-56
*Parent Company:* Oxford University Press, United
 Kingdom
*Branch Office(s)*
Oxford House, 289 Anna Salai, Chennai 600006
 *Tel:* (044) 28110832; (044) 28111861; (044)
 28112107 *Fax:* (044) 28110962
2/11 Ansari Rd, Daryaganj, New Delhi 110002
 *Tel:* (011) 23273841; (011) 23273842; (011)
 23253647 *Fax:* (011) 23277812
Plot No A1-5, Block GP, Sector V, Salt Lake
 Electronics Complex, Kolkata 700091
 *Tel:* (033) 23573739; (033) 23573740; (033)
 23573741 *Fax:* (033) 23573738
167, Vidyanagari Marg, Kalina, Santacruz (East),
 Mumbai 400098 *Tel:* (022) 26521034; (022)
 26521035; (022) 56973891; (022) 56973892
 *Fax:* (022) 26521133
*U.S. Office(s):* US University Press, 198 Madison
 Ave, New York, NY 11016, United States
*Showroom(s):* 94 Industrial Area, 4th B Cross,
 Fifth Block, Koramangala, Bangalore 560095
 *Tel:* (080) 5534286 *Fax:* (080) 5538736; SCO
 45 & 46, First fl, Sector 8C, Madhya Marg,
 Chandigarh 160009 *Tel:* (0172) 2545794; Dan-
 ish Rd, Panbazar, Guwahati 781001 *Tel:* (0361)
 2524050 *Fax:* (0361) 2513310; 8-2-577, First
 fl, Rd No 7, Banjara Hills, Hyderabad 500029
 *Tel:* (040) 23356425 *Fax:* (040) 23356424;
 A-19, Main Sahakar Path, Jaipur 302001
 *Tel:* (0141) 5179892; (0141) 2743816; B-
 7/18, Sector K, Aliganj, Lucknow 226024
 *Tel:* (0522) 2364215; (0522) 762472; H/o Mr
 M.K. Sinha, 178/B, S.K. Puri, Patna 800001;
 Gayatri Sadan, 2060 Sadashiv Peth, V N
 Colony, Pune 411030 *Tel:* (020) 4334537
 *Fax:* (020) 4337262; Kesava Bldgs, First fl,
 TC No 25/1437 (2), Thampanoor, Thiruvanan-
 thapuram 695001 *Tel:* (0471) 2330995

**Oxonian Press (P) Ltd+**
N-66 Connaught Circus, New Delhi 110001
*Tel:* (011) 44957; (011) 3313584 *Fax:* (011)
 3322639
*E-mail:* oxford.publ@axcess.net.in *Cable:*
 INDAMER
*Key Personnel*
Dir, Rights & Permissions: Gulab Primlani
Sales Dir: Dr A M Primlani
Publicity Manager: Ms Chandra Naharwar
Subjects: Engineering (General), Music, Dance,
 Science (General)
ISBN Prefix(es): 81-7087
*Parent Company:* Oxford & IBH Publishing Co
 Pvt Ltd
*Associate Companies:* Amerind Publishing Co P
 Ltd
*Branch Office(s)*
17 Park St, Kolkata 700016
29 Wodehouse Rd, Mumbai
165 Golf Links, New Delhi 110003
*Showroom(s):* Oxford Book & Stationery Co,
 Scindia House, New Delhi 110 001
*Warehouse:* Plot No 6, Sector 27A, Industrial
 Area, Faridabad

**Paico Publishing House+**
M G Rd, Cochin, Kerala 682035
Mailing Address: PO Box 2560, Ernakulam,
 Cochin 682035
*Tel:* (0484) 355835
*Web Site:* www.paicoindia.com *Cable:* PAICO
*Key Personnel*
Man Dir: Kanchana V Pai
Founded: 1955
Subjects: Fiction, History, Science (General)
*Associate Companies:* Broadway; Ernakulam; Pai
 & Co

*Branch Office(s)*
New Rd, Mattancherry, Cochin 682002
Paico Buildings, Press Rd, Trivandrum 1
*Bookshop(s):* 181 Mount Rd, Chennai 600002;
 Paico Books & Arts, Cochin; Kallai Rd, Cali-
 cut 673002; K K Rd, Kottayam 686002

**Panchasheel Prakashan**
Film Colony, Chaura Rasta, Jaipur 302 003
*Tel:* (0141) 65072 *Fax:* (0141) 326554
*Key Personnel*
Editorial: M C Gupta
Sales: O P Agarwal
Founded: 1968
Subjects: Fiction
ISBN Prefix(es): 81-7056

**Pankaj Publications+**
3 Regal Bldg, Sansad Marg, New Delhi 110001
*Tel:* (011) 3363395; (011) 3348805 *Fax:* (011)
 5163525; (01) 5511684
*E-mail:* pankajbooks@hotmail.com
*Key Personnel*
Manager: Vikas Bajaj *E-mail:* bajajvikas@
 hotmail.com
Subjects: Crafts, Games, Hobbies, Ethnicity, Mu-
 sic, Dance
ISBN Prefix(es): 81-87155
Number of titles published annually: 20 Print
Total Titles: 150 Print
*Bookshop(s):* Cambridge Book Depot, 3 Regal
 Bldg, Connaught Circus, New Delhi 110001,
 Mr Ranjana Bajaj *E-mail:* cambridgebooks@
 hotmail.com

**Paramount Sales (India) Pvt Ltd+**
484, Double Storey, New Rajinder Nagar, New
 Delhi 110060
*Tel:* (011) 7776821; (011) 5746485 *Fax:* (011)
 5746485
*Key Personnel*
Dir: Naresh Kumar Chowdhry
Founded: 1986
Subjects: Art, Language Arts, Linguistics
ISBN Prefix(es): 81-7103
*Associate Companies:* Naresh Publishers, 111
 Shankar Rd Market, New Rajinder Nagar, New
 Delhi 110060 *Tel:* (011) 5723235 *Fax:* (011)
 5746485

**Parimal Prakashan+**
Parimal Bldg, Khadkeshwar, Maharashtra, Au-
 rangabad 431001
*Tel:* (0240) 4556
*Key Personnel*
Man Dir, Production: A B Dashrathe
Sales: S B Padalkar
Founded: 1974
Subjects: Archaeology, Astrology, Occult, Career
 Development, Education, Ethnicity, Human Re-
 lations, Literature, Literary Criticism, Essays,
 Medicine, Nursing, Dentistry, Social Sciences,
 Sociology
ISBN Prefix(es): 81-7088
*Branch Office(s)*
159/2 Shaniwar Peth Pune, Kennedy Bridge,
 Mumbai
*Bookshop(s):* Marathwada Book Distributors,
 Parimal Bldg, Khadkeshwar, Maharashtra, Au-
 rangabad 431001

**Peachpit Press**, *imprint of* Addison-Wesley Pte
Ltd

**Penguin Longman Publishing**, *imprint of*
Addison-Wesley Pte Ltd

**People's Publishing House (P) Ltd**
5-E Rani Jhansi Rd, New Delhi 110 055
*Tel:* (011) 529365 *Cable:* QUAMIKITAB
*Key Personnel*
Chairman: T Madhavan

General Manager: P P C Joshi
Founded: 1948
Subjects: Biography, Engineering (General), History, Philosophy, Poetry, Social Sciences, Sociology
ISBN Prefix(es): 81-7007
*Bookshop(s):* 2 Marina Arcade, Connaught Pl, New Delhi 110001 *Tel:* (011) 344064

**Pitambar Publishing Co (P) Ltd+**
888 E Park Rd, Karol Bagh, New Delhi 110 005
*Tel:* (011) 776058; (011) 776067 *Fax:* (011) 2367 6058
*E-mail:* pitambar@bol.net.in *Cable:* PITAMBAR NEW DELHI
*Key Personnel*
Man Dir, Production, Rights & Permissions: Ved Bhushan
Man Dir, Publicity: Anand Bhushan
Sales: Manish Aggarwal; V P Jugaan
Production: Jaideep Aggarwal
Founded: 1947
Membership(s): Federation of Indian Publishers, New Delhi, Akhil Bhartia Hindi Prakashak Sangh, New Delhi.
Subjects: Accounting, Chemistry, Chemical Engineering, Computer Science, Economics, Electronics, Electrical Engineering, Fiction, History, Mathematics, Microcomputers, Religion - Buddhist, Religion - Hindu
ISBN Prefix(es): 81-209
Total Titles: 800 Print
*Associate Companies:* Ambar Prakashan, 888 E Park Rd, New Delhi 110 005, Contact: Ved Bhushan; Bharat Publishing House, 123 Durga Chambers, Desh Bandhu Gupta Rd, New Delhi 110005, Contact: Karol Bagh; Computel Systems & Services, 10 Community Centre, Mayapuri, Phase I, New Delhi, Contact: Dr V B Aggarwal *Tel:* (011) 25136652 *Fax:* (011) 25133088; Piyush Printers Publishers Pvt Ltd, G-12 Udyog Nagar, Rohtak Road Industrial Area, New Delhi 110041, Contact: Jaideep Aggarwal; Reliant Microsystems Pvt Ltd, 10 Community Centre, Mayapuri, Phase-I, New Delhi 64, Contact: Prof V B Aggarwal
*Branch Office(s)*
H No 6/2, III Main Rd, SK Garden, Bensen Town Post, Bangalore 560046 *Tel:* (080) 3534673
1-1-230/6 (407) Vivek Nagar, Chikkadapally, Hyderabad 500020 *Tel:* (04) 7645614
*Warehouse:* 415-1-3, Mundika, New Delhi 110041

**Pitman**, *imprint of* Addison-Wesley Pte Ltd

**Pointer Publishers+**
807, Vyas Bldg, SMS Highway, Jaipur 302 003
*Tel:* (0141) 2568159 *Fax:* (0141) 2568159
*E-mail:* info@pointerpublishers.com; pointerpub@hotmail.com
*Web Site:* www.pointerpublishers.com
*Key Personnel*
Manager: Vipin Jain
Founded: 1986
Publish reference & general books in agriculture, humanities arts, science & commerce.
Subjects: Accounting, Agriculture, Biological Sciences, Child Care & Development, Economics, Education, Environmental Studies, Gardening, Plants, Geography, Geology, Government, Political Science, History, Journalism, Library & Information Sciences, Literature, Literary Criticism, Essays, Management, Military Science, Philosophy, Psychology, Psychiatry, Social Sciences, Sociology, Women's Studies
ISBN Prefix(es): 81-7132
Total Titles: 200 Print

**Popular Prakashan Pvt Ltd+**
35C Pandit Madan Mohan, Malviya Marg, Popular Press Bldg, Tardeo, Mumbai 400 034
*Tel:* (022) 494 1656 *Fax:* (022) 24945294
*E-mail:* info@popularprakashan.com
*Web Site:* www.popularprakashan.com *Cable:* NANDIBOOK
*Key Personnel*
Chairman: Sadanand Ganesh Bhatkal
Man Dir: Ramdas Ganesh Bhatkal
Dir: Harsha Ramdas Bhatkal
Founded: 1926
Subjects: Anthropology, Biography, Computer Science, Cookery, Economics, Government, Political Science, Health, Nutrition, History, Management, Medicine, Nursing, Dentistry, Music, Dance, Social Sciences, Sociology, Women's Studies
ISBN Prefix(es): 81-7154
*Parent Company:* Popular Book Depot
*Associate Companies:* Bhatkal & Sen; Indiancookery.com Pvt Ltd, 501, Damini, Plot No 889, Juhu Tara Rd, Juhu, Mumbai 400049 *Tel:* (022) 26171070 *Fax:* (022) 26132416
Imprints: Focus
*Branch Office(s)*
16 Southern Ave, Kolkata 700026 *Tel:* (033) 761413
4648-1 Ansari Rd, 21 Daryaganj, New Delhi 110002 *Tel:* (011) 3265245

**Prabhat Prakashan+**
4-19 Asaf Ali Rd, New Delhi 110002
*Tel:* (011) 3264676; (011) 3289555; (011) 3289666 *Fax:* (011) 3253233
*E-mail:* prabhat@indianabooks.com; prabhat1@vsnl.com
*Web Site:* www.indianabooks.com
*Key Personnel*
Chief Executive: Shyam Sunder
Executive: Pawan Agrawal
Editorial: Shyam Bahadur Verma
Sales: Raghuvir Verma
Production: Dharam Vir
Founded: 1958
Subjects: Art, Biography, Cookery, Fiction, Humor, Library & Information Sciences, Nonfiction (General), Poetry
ISBN Prefix(es): 81-7315
*Branch Office(s)*
Mathura
*Bookshop(s):* 4-19 Asaf Ali Rd, New Delhi 110002

**Pratibha Pratishthan+**
1685 Dakhnirai St, Netaji Subhash Marg, New Delhi 110 002
*Tel:* (011) 3289666 *Toll Free Tel:* (011) 3253233
*Key Personnel*
President: Prabhat Kumar
Vice President: Piyush Agrawal
Sales Executive: Ajay Kumar; D S Negi
Founded: 1981
Subjects: Art, Biography, Cookery, Fiction, Humor, Library & Information Sciences, Nonfiction (General), Poetry
ISBN Prefix(es): 81-85827; 81-88266

**Prentice Hall**, *imprint of* Addison-Wesley Pte Ltd

**Prima Communications Inc**, *imprint of* Rajendra Publishing House Pvt Ltd

**Promilla & Publishers**
Sonali, C-127 Sarvodaya Enclave, New Delhi 110017
*Tel:* (011) 668720 *Fax:* (011) 6448947
*Key Personnel*
President & Editor: Prof D H Butani
Production, Rights & Permissions Dir: Ashok Butani
General Manager: M M Khanna
Sales Manager: Sutikshan Naithani
Chief Executive: Nirmala Butani

Founded: 1970
Subjects: Art, Biography, Economics, Government, Political Science, History, Religion - Other, Social Sciences, Sociology, Women's Studies
ISBN Prefix(es): 81-85002

**PTR**, *imprint of* Addison-Wesley Pte Ltd

**Publication Bureau**
Punjabi University, Patiala Panjab, Chandigarh 160 014
*Tel:* (0172) 541782; (0172) 534373
*Key Personnel*
Manager: H R Grover
Founded: 1948
Membership(s): Federation of Indian Publishers.
Subjects: Biography, History, Philosophy, Poetry, Religion - Other, Social Sciences, Sociology
ISBN Prefix(es): 81-85822; 81-7380

**Publications & Information Directorate, CSIR+**
Hillside Rd, New Delhi 110012
*Tel:* (011) 5785359; (011) 5786301 (ext 288) *Fax:* (011) 5787062
*Telex:* 031-77271pidin *Cable:* PUBLIFORM
*Key Personnel*
Editorial: G P Phondka
Sales: A K Srivastava
Founded: 1942
Subjects: Biological Sciences, Chemistry, Chemical Engineering, Physics, Science (General), Technology
ISBN Prefix(es): 81-7236; 81-85038
*Parent Company:* Council of Scientific & Industrial Research, New Delhi

**Pustak Mahal+**
F2/16, Anasari Rd, Darya Ganj, New Delhi 110 002
*Tel:* (011) 23276539; (011) 23272783; (011) 23272784 *Fax:* (011) 3260518
*E-mail:* pustakmahal@vsnl.net.in
*Web Site:* www.pustakmahal.com
*Telex:* 031-78090 SBP IN
*Key Personnel*
Chairman: T R Gupta
Man Dir: Ram Avtar Gupta
Marketing & Publishing Dir: Vikas Gupta
Dir, Sales: Ramesh Kumar Gupta
Dir, Marketing: Dr Ashok Kumar Gupta
Production Dir: Venod Gupta
Founded: 1974
Specialize in supplementary educational literature for children & informative books of mass appeal. Publishes in twelve languages.
Membership(s): Delhi State Booksellers Association; Federation of Educational Publishers of India; Federation of Indian Publishers; Federation of Publishers; Publishers of South India.
Subjects: Architecture & Interior Design, Astrology, Occult, Biography, Computer Science, Cookery, Crafts, Games, Hobbies, Health, Nutrition, History, House & Home, Language Arts, Linguistics, Medicine, Nursing, Dentistry, Music, Dance, Parapsychology, Romance, Science (General)
ISBN Prefix(es): 81-223
Imprints: M/S Family Books Pvt Ltd; Comdex Computer Publishing
Subsidiaries: M/S Hind Pustak Bhandar
Divisions: Industrial Books Division
*Branch Office(s)*
22/2, Mission Rd, Bangalore *Tel:* (080) 2234025 *Fax:* (080) 2240209 (Shama Rao's Compound)
23-25 Zaoba Wadi, Thakurdwar, Mumbai 400 002 *Tel:* (022) 2010941 *Fax:* (022) 2053387 *E-mail:* rapidex@bom5.net.in
Khemka House, Ashok Rajpath, Patna 4 *Tel:* (0612) 653644 *Fax:* (0612) 653644
*Book Club(s):* Comdex Book Club

QUE, *imprint of* Addison-Wesley Pte Ltd

**Radiant Publishers+**
E-155, State Bank of India Bldg, Kalkaji, New Delhi 110019
*Tel:* (011) 6435477; (011) 6482861 *Fax:* (011) 6479870
*E-mail:* rpbooksind@yahoo.com
*Key Personnel*
Man Dir, Sales, Production, Publicity & Editorial, Rights & Permissions: Sunita Jain
Founded: 1973
Subjects: Economics, Education, Environmental Studies, Government, Political Science, Religion - Other, Social Sciences, Sociology, Women's Studies
ISBN Prefix(es): 81-7027
Number of titles published annually: 10 Print
Total Titles: 200 Print

**Rahul Publishing House**
3348, Naisadak, Shastri Nagar, Meerut 250005
*Tel:* (0121) 2774518
*Key Personnel*
Editorial & Production: Rahul Singhal
Founded: 1993
Subjects: Anthropology, Antiques, Archaeology, Art, Asian Studies, Earth Sciences, History, Language Arts, Linguistics, Regional Interests
ISBN Prefix(es): 81-7388
*Associate Companies:* Agam Kala Prakashan; Agam Prakashan; Swati Publication

**Rajasthan Hindi Granth Academy+**
A-26/2, Vidya laya Marg, Tilak Nagar, Jaipur 302 004
*Tel:* (0141) 61410; (0141) 511129
*Key Personnel*
Dir: Dr Ved Prakash *Tel:* (0141) 510341
Sales, Publicity: K N Agrawal
Production: Mahesh Jain
Founded: 1969
Subjects: Agriculture, Art, Chemistry, Chemical Engineering, Economics, Education, Human Relations, Language Arts, Linguistics, Law, Library & Information Sciences, Medicine, Nursing, Dentistry, Philosophy, Physics, Science (General), Social Sciences, Sociology
ISBN Prefix(es): 81-7137

**Rajendra Publishing House Pvt Ltd+**
202 Patel Estate, B-40, New Link Rd, Andheri (W), Mumbai Worii 400053
*Tel:* (022) 6300741; (022) 6300742; (022) 6301930 *Fax:* (022) 6301940; (022) 6322146
*E-mail:* books@rajendrabooks.com
*Web Site:* www.rajendrabooks.com
*Key Personnel*
Chairman: Mr R K Tandon
Man Dir: Ms Swarn Tandon
Executive Dir: Ms Bindu Swaminathan Tandon; Mr Vivek Tandon *Tel:* (022) 8755935 *Fax:* (022) 8738551
Founded: 1989
Specialize in direct mail sale of high quality books.
Subjects: Astronomy, Geography, Geology, Health, Nutrition, History, How-to, Management, Science (General), Self-Help, Social Sciences, Sociology
ISBN Prefix(es): 81-900085; 81-86406; 81-900279
Total Titles: 10 Print
Imprints: Prima Communications Inc
Distributed by Gazelle Book Services Ltd
Distributor for Conari Press; Dorling Kindersley; Elements Books Ltd; Rodale Press Inc

**Rajesh Publications+**
One Ansari Rd, Daryaganj, New Delhi 110002
*Tel:* (011) 274550

*Key Personnel*
Man Dir: Mohan Lal *Tel:* 981111605 (mobile)
Contact: Sanjay Gupta
Founded: 1970
Subjects: Economics, Education, Geography, Geology, History, Management, Philosophy, Religion - Other
ISBN Prefix(es): 81-85891
Distributed by Janki Prakashan
Distributor for Seema Publications

**Rajkamal Prakashan Pvt Ltd**
One-B, Netaji Subhash Marg, Darya Ganj, New Delhi 110002
*Tel:* (011) 3288769; (011) 3274463 *Fax:* (011) 3278144
Subjects: Education
ISBN Prefix(es): 81-7178
*Branch Office(s)*
M/D Ravkamal Prakashan Pvt Ltd

**Rajpal & Sons+**
1590 Madarasa Rd, Kashmere Gate, Delhi 110006
*Tel:* 223904; 229174 *Fax:* (0141) 2967791 *Cable:* RAJPALSONS DELHI
*Key Personnel*
Man Dir: Vishwa Nath
Sales: Satish Kumar
Editorial: Meera Johri
Publicity, Rights & Permissions: Kapil Malhotra
Founded: 1947
Specialize in dictionaries.
Subjects: Fiction, Human Relations, Literature, Literary Criticism, Essays, Science (General)
ISBN Prefix(es): 81-7028
*Associate Companies:* Orient Paperbacks; Shiksha Bharati; Vision Books Pvt Ltd
*Branch Office(s)*
3-6-280/A5, Himayat Nagar, Hyderabad 500 029
3B Peddar Rd, Mumbai 400026 *Tel:* (022) 4929343
*Bookshop(s):* Lothian Rd, Kashmere Gate, Delhi 110006 *Tel:* (011) 2516602

**Rastogi Publications+**
Gangotri Shivaji Rd, Meerut 250 002
*Tel:* 24142; 24688
*E-mail:* vrastogi@vsnl.com; info@ indianbookmart.com
*Telex:* 0549-209 *Cable:* RASTOGICO
*Key Personnel*
Editorial, Production, Rights & Permissions: R K Rastogi
Sales, Publicity: H K Rastogi
Sales, Publicitiy: Vivek Rastogi
Founded: 1966
Subjects: Agriculture, Animals, Pets, Biological Sciences, Earth Sciences, Education, Government, Political Science, Science (General)
ISBN Prefix(es): 81-7133; 81-85711
Subsidiaries: Pioneer Printers

**Rebel Publishing House Pvt Ltd**
50 Koregaon Park, Pune 411001
*Tel:* (0212) 628562 *Fax:* (0212) 624181
*Key Personnel*
Contact: Narain Das; Anando Ma Deva; Yoga Amit Swami
Founded: 1988
Subjects: Philosophy, Religion - Other, Theology
ISBN Prefix(es): 81-7261
*Orders to:* Sadhana Foundation, 17 Koreganon Park, Pune 411001

**Regency Publications+**
20/36-G Old Market, West Patel Nagar, New Delhi 110008
*Tel:* (011) 5712539; (011) 5740038 *Fax:* (011) 5783571
*E-mail:* regency@satyam.net.in

*Key Personnel*
Owner: Arun Verma
Founded: 1993
Membership(s): Delphi State Publishers & Booksellers Association.
Subjects: Agriculture, Anthropology, Archaeology, Art, Biological Sciences, Education, Environmental Studies, Ethnicity, Fiction, Geography, Geology, Government, Political Science, History, Language Arts, Linguistics, Law, Philosophy, Regional Interests, Religion - Other, Social Sciences, Sociology, Sports, Athletics, Women's Studies
ISBN Prefix(es): 81-86030; 81-87498
Number of titles published annually: 20 Print
Total Titles: 150 Print
Distributed by DK Agencies; D K Publishers/Distributors; UBS Publishers' Distributors

**Rekha Prakashan+**
16 Daryaganj, New Delhi 110 002
*Tel:* (011) 23279907; (011) 23279904 *Fax:* (011) 2321783
*E-mail:* rprakashan@satyam.net.in
*Web Site:* www.museumoffolkandtribalart.org
*Key Personnel*
Chief Executive, Rights & Permissions: K C Aryan
Editorial: S Aryan
Sales: B N Aryan
Publicity Dir: G D Aryan
Founded: 1973
Membership(s): Delhi State Booksellers' & Publishers' Association.
Subjects: Art, Regional Interests, History of Art (India); Indian Folk & Tribal Art
ISBN Prefix(es): 81-900002; 81-900003
Number of titles published annually: 3 Print
Total Titles: 27 Print

**Reliance Publishing House+**
3026/7-H, Ranjit Nagar, New Delhi 110008
*Tel:* (011) 5852605; (011) 5772768; (011) 5737377 *Fax:* (011) 5786769
*Fax on Demand:* (011) 5852605
*E-mail:* reliance@indiatimes.com
*Key Personnel*
Man Dir, Rights & Permissions: Dr S K Bhatia
Sales: M K Bhatia
Publicity: Geeta Saxena *Tel:* (011) 5786769
Editorial: Bhatia Durgesh *Tel:* (011) 5737377
Founded: 1985
Publishers of reference books on the Indian book industry, humanities & social sciences.
Subjects: Accounting, Advertising, Agriculture, Anthropology, Archaeology, Architecture & Interior Design, Art, Asian Studies, Astrology, Occult, Astronomy, Behavioral Sciences, Biography, Biological Sciences, Business, Career Development, Child Care & Development, Communications, Criminology, Developing Countries, Disability, Special Needs, Drama, Theater, Earth Sciences, Economics, Education, Energy, Environmental Studies, Ethnicity, Fiction, Finance, Geography, Geology, Government, Political Science, History, Human Relations, Humor, Journalism, Labor, Industrial Relations, Library & Information Sciences, Literature, Literary Criticism, Essays, Management, Marketing, Medicine, Nursing, Dentistry, Military Science, Music, Dance, Mysteries, Nonfiction (General), Philosophy, Poetry, Psychology, Psychiatry, Public Administration, Publishing & Book Trade Reference, Regional Interests, Religion - Buddhist, Religion - Hindu, Science Fiction, Fantasy, Social Sciences, Sociology, Sports, Athletics, Technology, Travel, Women's Studies, Mythology
ISBN Prefix(es): 81-85047; 81-85972; 81-7510
Total Titles: 525 Print; 4 Online; 4 E-Book
*Associate Companies:* Geeta Graphics, J436, Baljit Nagar, New Delhi 110008, Contact: Manish K Bhatia *Tel:* (011) 25845330

*Fax:* (011) 25842605; (011) 25846769; Geeta Enterprises, J436, Baljit Nagar, New Delhi 110008 *Tel:* (011) 5772748; (011) 5875330 *Fax:* (011) 5786769
Distributed by DK Publishers' Distributors; UBS Publishers Distributors Ltd
*Warehouse:* J-436, Baljit Nagar, New Delhi 110008 *Tel:* (011) 25845330 *Fax:* (011) 25846769; (011) 25842748 *E-mail:* reliance@indiatimes.com
*Distribution Center:* 3026/7H, Shiv Chowk, S Patel Nagar, New Delhi 110008 *Tel:* (011) 5852605 *Fax:* (011) 5786769

**Research Signpost**
37/661(2), Fort, PO, Thiruvananthapuram, Kerala 695023
*Tel:* (0471) 2460384 *Fax:* (0471) 2573051
*E-mail:* ggcom@vsnl.com
*Web Site:* www.researchsignpost.com
*Key Personnel*
Man Editor: Shankar Pandalai
Publications Manager: Anandavalli Gayathri
Publishers of scientific, technical, medical & agricultural books & journals. Also produces CD-ROMs.
Subjects: Agriculture, Medicine, Nursing, Dentistry, Science (General)
ISBN Prefix(es): 81-86481
Number of titles published annually: 150 Print

**Researchco Reprints+**
25-B/2, New Rohtak Rd, Near Liberty Cinema, New Dehli 110005
*Tel:* (011) 28712565; (011) 55150446; (011) 28714057 *Fax:* (011) 28716134
*Telex:* 31-79055 *Cable:* SEARCHBOOK
*Key Personnel*
Dir: Anil Jain *E-mail:* akjain@de12.vsnl.net.in; Arvind Jain
Founded: 1969
Specialize in stocking & supplying of books & back volume journals.
Subjects: Science (General), Technology
*Warehouse:* 1865 Trinagar, Delhi 110035

**Response**, *imprint of* SAGE Publications India Pvt Ltd

**Roli Books Pvt Ltd+**
M-75 Greater Kailash-II (Mkt), New Delhi 110 048
*Tel:* (011) 6462782; (011) 6442271; (011) 6460886 *Fax:* (011) 6467185
*E-mail:* roli@vsnl.com
*Web Site:* rolibooks.com
*Key Personnel*
Publishing Manager & Managing Editor: Renuka Chaudmury *Tel:* (011) 6420516
Contact: Kiran Kapoor *Tel:* (011) 29215924; Pramod Kapoor *Tel:* (011) 29212271
Founded: 1978
Publishing house & distributor for foreign publishers. Sells titles to other houses under their logo. Specializes in plain text & coffee table books, destinations & monuments & politics.
Subjects: Art, Business, Cookery, Erotica, Fiction, Government, Political Science, History, Management, Music, Dance, Religion - Buddhist, Religion - Hindu, Religion - Islamic, Religion - Jewish, Travel
ISBN Prefix(es): 81-7437
Total Titles: 122 Print; 122 Online; 4 Audio
*Parent Company:* Roli Books
Imprints: Lotus; Lustre Press

**Roorkee Press**, see Nem Chand & Brothers

**Rupa & Co+**
15 Bankim Chatterjee St, College Sq, Kolkata 700 073

Mailing Address: PO Box 7071, New Delhi 110002
*Tel:* (011) 344821; (011) 346305 *Fax:* (011) 327 7294
*E-mail:* rupa@ndb.vsnl.net.in; del.rupaco@axcess.net.in *Cable:* RUPANCO
*Key Personnel*
Man Dir: D Mehra
Sales: R N Barman
Productions & International Rights: R K Mehra
Accounts: S K Mehra
Publicity: C K Mehra
Founded: 1936
Subjects: Art, Crafts, Games, Hobbies, Education, Fiction, History, Literature, Literary Criticism, Essays, Philosophy, Religion - Other, Sports, Athletics
ISBN Prefix(es): 81-7167
*Associate Companies:* HarperCollins Publishers India
Imprints: Rupa Paperbacks
*Branch Office(s)*
94 South Malaka, Allahabad *Tel:* (0532) 53936
G1 & 2 Ghaswalla Tower, P G Solanki Path, Mumbai 400007
7/16 Makhanlal St, Ansari Rd, Daryaganj, New Delhi 2
Distributor for Affiliated East-West (India); Elbs titles (UK); Faber & Faber (UK); Hamlyn (UK); Ladybird (UK); Macmillan (UK); McGraw-Hill Kogakusha (Singapore); Penguin (UK); Prentice-Hall (India); Tata McGraw-Hill (India); Unwin Hyman (UK); Wiley Eastern (India)

**Rupa Paperbacks**, *imprint of* Rupa & Co

**SABDA+**
Unit of Sri Aurobindo Ashram Trust
No 123, S V Patel Salai, Pondicherry 605 002
*Tel:* (0413) 2334980; (0413) 2223328 *Fax:* (0413) 2223328
*E-mail:* sabda@sriaurobindoashram.org
*Web Site:* sabda.sriaurobindoashram.org
*Telex:* 0469221 Sas In *Cable:* SABDA
*Key Personnel*
Manager: Mira Gupta; Jay Raichura
International Rights & Permissions: Manoj Das Gupta
Founded: 1952
Specialize in works by or on the philosopher Sri Aurobindo & his spiritual collaborator known as "the Mother".
Membership(s): Federation of Indian Publishers; Akhil Bharatiya Hindi Prakashak Sangh; CAPEXIL (Export Promotion Council).
Subjects: Asian Studies, Education, Government, Political Science, Literature, Literary Criticism, Essays, Philosophy, Poetry, Psychology, Psychiatry, Religion - Hindu, Religion - Other, Social Sciences, Sociology, The spritual teachings & system of "Integral Yoga" of Sri Aurobindo
ISBN Prefix(es): 81-7058; 81-7060; 81-86413
Total Titles: 1,700 Print
*Branch Office(s)*
Sri Aurobindo Bhavan, 8 Shakespeare Sarani, Kolkata 700071 *Tel:* (033) 22829261
*E-mail:* sabdacalcutta@vsnl.net
Distributed by Auromere (USA only); East-West Cultural Center (USA only); Lotus Press (USA only); Matagiri (USA only)
Distributor for Sri Aurobindo Ashram; Sri Aurobindo Society; Sri Mira Trust
*Showroom(s):* 13 Marine St, Pondicherry *Tel:* (0413) 2334072 *Fax:* (0413) 2223328 *E-mail:* sabda@sriaurobindoashram.org
*Bookshop(s):* Sri Aurobindo Society, 11 Sahakar, B Rd, Churchgate, Mumbai 400 020 *Tel:* (022) 22043076; Sri Aurobindo Marg, New Delhi 110 016 *Tel:* (011) 26524810 *Fax:* (011) 26857449 *E-mail:* aurobindo@vsnl.com

**Ratna Sagar Pvt Ltd+**
A-8 Mukherjee Nagar, Commercial Complex, Delhi 110009
*Tel:* (011) 7654095; (011) 7654099 *Fax:* (011) 7250787
*E-mail:* rsagar@giasdlo1.vsnl.net.in; rsagar@nda.vsnl.net.in
*Telex:* 61604 AEROIN *Cable:* RATNABOOKS
*Key Personnel*
Contact: Dhanesh Jain
Founded: 1982
ISBN Prefix(es): 81-7070

**SAGE Publications India Pvt Ltd+**
B-42 Panchsheel Enclave, New Delhi 110 017
Mailing Address: PO Box 4109, New Delhi 110 017
*Tel:* (011) 2649 1290 *Fax:* (011) 2649 2117
*E-mail:* sage@vsnl.com; marketing@indiasage.com; editors@indiasage.com
*Web Site:* www.indiasage.com *Cable:* SAGEPUB NEW DELHI 110048
*Key Personnel*
Man Dir & Sales: Tejeshwar Singh
Editorial: Omita Goyal
Marketing: Sunanda Ghosh
Founded: 1981
Subjects: Anthropology, Asian Studies, Behavioral Sciences, Business, Communications, Developing Countries, Economics, Environmental Studies, Government, Political Science, Management, Psychology, Psychiatry, Public Administration, Social Sciences, Sociology, Women's Studies
ISBN Prefix(es): 81-7036; 81-7829
Total Titles: 900 Print
*Associate Companies:* Sage Publications Inc, 2455 Teller Rd, Thousand Oaks, CA 91320, United States *E-mail:* info@sagepub.com *Web Site:* www.sagepub.com; Sage Publications Ltd, One Oliver's Yard, 55 City Rd, London EC1Y 1SP, United Kingdom *Tel:* (020) 7324 8500 *Fax:* (020) 7324 8600 *E-mail:* info@sagepub.co.uk *Web Site:* www.sagepub.co.uk
Imprints: Response; Vistaar
*Branch Office(s)*
11 Sararana St, T Nagar, Chennai 600 017 *Tel:* (044) 2434 5822 *E-mail:* sage.chennai@vsnl.net *Web Site:* www.indiasage.net
31, LB Stadium, Post Box 131, Hyderabad 500 001 *Tel:* (040) 2323 1447 *E-mail:* sage.hyderabad@vsnl.net *Web Site:* www.indiasage.com
59-5 Prince Baktiar Shah Rd, Ground floor, Tollygunge, Kolkata 700 033 *Tel:* (033) 2417 2642 *E-mail:* sage.kolkata@vsnl.net *Web Site:* www.indiasage.com
1187/37 Ameya, Shivajinagar, Off Ghole Rd, Pune 411 005 *Tel:* (020) 2551 3407 *E-mail:* sagepune@vsnl.net

**Sahasrara Publications+**
1143, Sector 37, Arun Vihar, Noida 201303
*Tel:* (011) 2432617
*E-mail:* sahasrarapublications@yahoo.co.in
*Key Personnel*
Contact: Opender Nath Karir
Founded: 1996
Encyclopedia Bharatam Series: *The A's of India, The B's of India, The C's of India, The D's of India, The E's, F's, G's of India; Treasury of Indian Quotations & Extracts; Democracy is Demon-o-cracy, Selectocracy is Heaven.*
Membership(s): Federation of Publishers & Booksellers Association of India.
Subjects: Regional Interests
ISBN Prefix(es): 81-86568
Number of titles published annually: 2 Print
Total Titles: 7 Print; 2 E-Book
*Parent Company:* Sahasrara Publications
*Branch Office(s)*
1340, Sector 37, Arun Vihar, Noida 201303, Con-

tact: Daya Mukherjee *Tel:* (0981) 8326771
*E-mail:* daya_jsr@satyam.net.in
Distributed by DK Publishers Distributors;
Manohar Book Service (New Delhi); UBS Publishers' Distribution (New Delhi)

**Sahitya Akademi** (National Academy of Letters)
Rabindra Bhawan, 35, Ferozeshah Rd, New Delhi 110001
*Tel:* (011) 3386626; (011) 3735297; (011) 3364207 (sales); (011) 3386629 *Fax:* (011) 3382428; (011) 3364207
*E-mail:* sesy@ndl.vsnl.net.in *Cable:* SAHITYAKAR
Founded: 1955
Subjects: Literature, Literary Criticism, Essays
ISBN Prefix(es): 81-7201; 81-260

**Sahitya Pravarthaka Co-operative Society Ltd**
PO Box 94, Kottayam, Kerala 686001
*Tel:* (0481) 4111; (0481) 4112 *Cable:* Sahithyam
*Key Personnel*
Secretary: P Gopinadh
Sales: N C Rayi
Production: Yalath Mopasang
Founded: 1945
Subjects: Literature, Literary Criticism, Essays
ISBN Prefix(es): 81-213
*Bookshop(s):* National Book Stall, PO Box 40, Kottayam 686001 (with branches throughout Kerala)
*Orders to:* National Book Stall, c/o Sales Manager, Kottayam

**Sai Early Learners (P) Ltd**, *imprint of* Sterling Publishers Pvt Ltd

**Samkaleen Prakashan**
2762, Rajguru Marg, Paharganj, New Delhi 110055
*Tel:* (011) 3523520; (011) 3518197
*Key Personnel*
Editor: Krishan Khullar
Founded: 1976
Specialize in Indology.
Subjects: Art, Language Arts, Linguistics, Law, Poetry, Religion - Other, Technology, Indology
ISBN Prefix(es): 81-7083
Total Titles: 180 Print

**SAMS**, *imprint of* Addison-Wesley Pte Ltd

**Samya**, *imprint of* Stree

**Sanskriti**, *imprint of* Arnold Heinman Publishers (India) Pvt Ltd

**Saraswati Publishers & Distributors+**
434, Avadh Bihari Ki Gali, Govind Rao Ji Ka Rasta, Jaipur 302001
*Key Personnel*
Contact: Onkar Nath Tripathi
Founded: 1986
ISBN Prefix(es): 81-85808

**M C Sarkar & Sons (P) Ltd+**
14 Bankim Chatterjee St, Kolkata 700 012
*Tel:* (033) 2417490
Founded: 1910
Subjects: Fiction, Nonfiction (General)
ISBN Prefix(es): 81-7157

**Sasta Sahitya Mandal+**
N-77 Connaught Circus, New Delhi 110 001
*Tel:* (011) 3310505 *Cable:* SATSAHITYA
*Key Personnel*
President: Dharam Vira
Secretary: Yashpal Jain
Founded: 1925

Subjects: Agriculture, Animals, Pets, Biography, Economics, Education, Ethnicity, History, Literature, Literary Criticism, Essays, Philosophy, Religion - Hindu, Politics
ISBN Prefix(es): 81-7309
*Branch Office(s)*
Zero Rd, Allahabad *Tel:* (0532) 50034

**Sat Sahitya Prakashan+**
205-B, Chawri Bazar, Delhi 110006
*Tel:* (011) 3276316
*Key Personnel*
Chief Executive: S Sunder
Editorial: Nabab Singh Chauhan
Sales: P N Tiwari
Production: Rajan Chaudhary; P Kumar
Founded: 1970
Subjects: Art, Biography, Cookery, Fiction, Humor, Library & Information Sciences, Nonfiction (General), Poetry
ISBN Prefix(es): 81-7721; 81-85830

**Sri Satguru Publications+**
40/5 Shakti Nagar, 1st floor, Delhi 110007
*Tel:* (011) 716497; (011) 7434930 *Fax:* (011) 7227336
*E-mail:* ibcindia@vsnl.com
*Web Site:* www.indianbookscentre.com
*Key Personnel*
Man Dir, Rights & Permissions: Anil Gupta
Export, Sales: Naresh Gupta
Publicity: Virender Gupta
Founded: 1980
Subjects: Art, History, Language Arts, Linguistics, Literature, Literary Criticism, Essays, Medicine, Nursing, Dentistry, Music, Dance, Philosophy, Religion - Buddhist, Religion - Other, Indology, Ayurveda
ISBN Prefix(es): 81-7030
*Parent Company:* Indian Books Centre
*Associate Companies:* Bibliotheca Indo-Buddhica Series; Sri Garib Dass Oriental Series

**Satprakashan Sanchar Kendra+**
Division of Divine Word Society
Bhanwarkna Chowraha, Indore M P 452 001
Mailing Address: PO Box 507, Indore 452001
*Tel:* (0731) 475744; (0731) 475637 *Fax:* (0731) 47573
*E-mail:* sskin@sancharnet.in
*Key Personnel*
Dir: Sony Sebastian
Founded: 1980
Subjects: Biblical Studies, Communications, Religion - Catholic
ISBN Prefix(es): 81-85357; 81-85428
Number of titles published annually: 10 Print
Total Titles: 108 Print; 48 Audio

**Sawan Kirpal Publications**
H-11 Vi'jay Nagar, New Delhi 110009
*Tel:* (011) 7110722; (011) 7222244 *Fax:* (011) 7210720
*Key Personnel*
Man Dir: Sant Rajinder Singh
Editorial: Dr Vinod Sena
Sales Dir: Rajesh Seth
Production: Jay Linksman
Publicity: Gary Moed
Founded: 1977
Subjects: Religion - Other
ISBN Prefix(es): 81-85380
*Parent Company:* Sawan Kirpal Publications Spiritual Society
*U.S. Office(s):* SK Publications, 4S 175 Naperville Rd, Naperville, IL 60563, United States
PO Box 24, Bowling Green, VA 22427-0004, United States

**SBW Publishers+**
7/9A Makhab Lal St, Ansari Rd, Daryaganj, New Delhi 110002
*Tel:* (011) 3279603
*Key Personnel*
Contact: K L Sabharwal
Founded: 1980
Subjects: Philosophy, Regional Interests, Religion - Other, Social Sciences, Sociology
ISBN Prefix(es): 81-85708
*Parent Company:* Sabharwal Book Wholesalers

**Scientific Publishers India+**
Maan Bhawan, Ratanda Rd, Jodhpur 342001
Mailing Address: PO Box 91, Jodhpur 342001
*Tel:* (0291) 512712; (0291) 433323 *Fax:* (0291) 512580
*E-mail:* scienti@sancharnet.in *Cable:* SCIENTIFIC-JODHPUR 342001
*Key Personnel*
Man Dir, Editorial: Pawan Kumar
Sales: Dawal Gawr
Founded: 1978
Also acts as booksellers & subscription agents.
Subjects: Agriculture, Biological Sciences, Engineering (General), Natural History, Social Sciences, Sociology
ISBN Prefix(es): 81-85046; 81-7233; 81-85519
Total Titles: 350 Print
*Parent Company:* United Book Traders, 5A, New Pali Rd, Jodhpur 342001
Divisions: Publications & Export

**Scott Foresman**, *imprint of* Addison-Wesley Pte Ltd

**Selina Publishers**
4725/21A Dayanand Marg, Daryaganj, New Delhi 110002
*Tel:* (011) 3280711 *Fax:* (011) 3277230
*Key Personnel*
Man Dir, Publicity, Rights & Permissions: H L Gupta
Editorial: Preeti Mehra
Production: Subhash Arora
Sales: D M D'Bras
Founded: 1975
Subjects: Education
ISBN Prefix(es): 81-85612
*Associate Companies:* Granth Bharati (printing press)
Subsidiaries: Mudra Prakashan
*Branch Office(s)*
48 Daryaganj, New Delhi 110002
*Book Club(s):* Sanket Library Yojna

**Shaibya Prakashan Bibhag+**
86/1, Mahatma Gandhi Rd, Kolkata 700009
*Tel:* (033) 388268; (033) 2411748
Founded: 1984
Subjects: Biography, Computer Science, Electronics, Electrical Engineering, English as a Second Language, Publishing & Book Trade Reference, Religion - Hindu, Science (General), Science Fiction, Fantasy
ISBN Prefix(es): 81-87051

**Sharda Prakashan**
33/1, Bhul Bhullaian Rd, Mehrauli, New Delhi 110030
*Tel:* (011) 653982
*Key Personnel*
Chief Executive, Production, Rights & Permissions: Vijay Dev Jhari
Editorial, Publicity: Ravinder Jhari
Sales: R D Jhari
Founded: 1971
Subjects: Biography, Drama, Theater, Fiction, Literature, Literary Criticism, Essays
ISBN Prefix(es): 81-85023
*Associate Companies:* Itihas Shodh Sansthan, 33/1 Mehrauli, New Delhi 110030; Jharison, Bhullehullian Rd, Mehrauli, New Delhi 110030

Subsidiaries: Nalanda Prakashan
Bookshop(s): 16-F3 Ansari Rd, Daryaganj, New Delhi 110002 Tel: (011) 279853

**R R Sheth & Co+**
110-112 Princess St, Keshav Baug, Mumbai 400 002
Tel: (022) 2013441 Fax: (079) 5321732
E-mail: chintan@rrsheth.com
Web Site: www.rrsheth.com
Key Personnel
Proprietor: Bhagatbhai Bhuralal Sheth Tel: (022) 6183182
Founded: 1926
Publisher, bookseller & exporter. Specialize in Gujarati language.
Subjects: Fiction, Literature, Literary Criticism, Essays
Total Titles: 100 Print
Associate Companies: Lokpriya Prakashan, 110, Princess St, Mumbai 400 002 Tel: (022) 2058293
Branch Office(s)
Opp Phuvara, Gandhi Rd, Ahmedabad Tel: (079) 5356573 E-mail: rrsheth_co@hotmail.com

**Shiksha Bharati+**
Kashmere Gate, Delhi 110006
Tel: (011) 386-7791 Fax on Demand: (011) 386-7791
Key Personnel
Man Dir, Rights & Permissions: Sudhir Malhotra
Editorial: Meera Johri
Founded: 1959
Subjects: Education
ISBN Prefix(es): 81-7483
Associate Companies: Orient Paperbacks; Rajpal & Sons; Vision Books Pvt Ltd
Subsidiaries: Shiksha Bharati Press
Bookshop(s): Lothian Rd, Kashmere Gate, Delhi 110006 Tel: (011) 2516602

**Siddhi Books**, imprint of Cosmo Publications

**Silver Burdett Ginn**, imprint of Addison-Wesley Pte Ltd

**SIRI**, see Small Industry Research Institute (SIRI)

**Sita Books & Periodicals Pvt Ltd+**
308, Arjun Centre, Govandi Station Rd, Govandi (E), Govandi, Mumbai 400 088
Mailing Address: PO Box TF B-8, Govandi, Mumbai 400 088
Tel: (022) 5555589; (022) 5973281; (022) 5973282; (022) 5973283 Fax: (022) 5561622
E-mail: ssrao@bom5.vsnl.net.in; sitabook@bom7. vsnl.net.in
Web Site: www.sitabooks.com
Telex: SITAJAB
Key Personnel
Man Dir: Mrs Pushpa S Rao
Founded: 1987
Importers of international books & journals. Publishers of text books & general & technical books.
Subjects: Accounting, Advertising, Aeronautics, Aviation, Agriculture, Architecture & Interior Design, Automotive, Biological Sciences, Business, Chemistry, Chemical Engineering, Child Care & Development, Civil Engineering, Computer Science, Economics, Education, Electronics, Electrical Engineering, Energy, Engineering (General), Environmental Studies, Fashion, Finance, Labor, Industrial Relations, Library & Information Sciences, Literature, Literary Criticism, Essays, Management, Maritime, Marketing, Mathematics, Mechanical Engineering, Microcomputers, Physics, Psychology, Psy-

chiatry, Publishing & Book Trade Reference, Technology
ISBN Prefix(es): 81-86052
Parent Company: Sita Books
Associate Companies: Sita Books & Periodicals Pvt Ltd, 308, Arjun Centre, Govandi(E), Mumbai 400 088 Tel: (022) 5561622 Fax: (022) 5561622
Branch Office(s)
Sita Books & Periodicals, 'Sita Villa', Chakrapani Rd, Mangalore 575 001 Tel: (0824) 426968 (behind K M C Hospital)
Bookshop(s): Herikripa,, 3 Krishna, Govandi(E), Mumbai 400 088

**Small Industry Research Institute (SIRI)+**
Gali No 6, 4/43, Roop Nagar, New Delhi 110007
Tel: (011) 23841893; (011) 2916804 Fax: (011) 2910805
E-mail: siri@ndf.vsnl.net.in; siricon@vsnl.com
Key Personnel
Dir: D C Gupta
Founded: 1972
Industrial consultancy, publishing & exporting of industrial process technology books, directories, project reports, etc.
Membership(s): Capexil; FIP; DSBPA; JBC (FICCI); ITA (London) Niesbud; BIS (Lib); Indo German Chamber of Commerce & Industry; Indo Italian Chamber of Commerce.
Subjects: Technology
ISBN Prefix(es): 81-85480
Number of titles published annually: 15 Print
Total Titles: 120 Print
Subsidiaries: SIRI Consultants & Engineers
Showroom(s): Small Industry Research Institute, 4/43, Roop Nagar, Delhi 110007

**Somaiya Publications Pvt Ltd+**
Fazalbhoy Bldg, 45/47 M G Rd, Fort Mumbai 400 001
Tel: (022) 2048272 Fax: (022) 2047297
Web Site: www.somaiya.com
Telex: 0118-4588 SOC IN Cable: MANIKAKA
Key Personnel
Chairman: Dr S K Somaiya E-mail: mridughar@ bol.net.in
Mumbai Executive: K S Hattangadi
Delhi Executive: T V Kunni Krishnan
Ordering Contact: Mr N S Narayanan
Founded: 1967
Membership(s): Federation of Indian Publishers.
Subjects: Agriculture, Anthropology, Archaeology, Asian Studies, Astrology, Occult, Behavioral Sciences, Business, Communications, Disability, Special Needs, Economics, Education, Engineering (General), English as a Second Language, Fiction, Government, Political Science, History, Journalism, Labor, Industrial Relations, Language Arts, Linguistics, Management, Marketing, Mechanical Engineering, Music, Dance, Nonfiction (General), Parapsychology, Philosophy, Psychology, Psychiatry, Religion - Buddhist, Religion - Hindu, Social Sciences, Sociology, Technology, Women's Studies
ISBN Prefix(es): 81-7039
Total Titles: 300 Print
Parent Company: The Godavari Sugar Mills Ltd
Associate Companies: The Book Centre Ltd, Ranade Rd, Dadar, Mumbai 400028 (Book Sales Division); The Book Centre Ltd, Plot No 103, Sixth Rd, Sion, Mumbai, Contact: S S Sathe Tel: (022) 4076812; (022) 4077416 (Printing Press Division)
Branch Office(s)
Bank of Baroda Bldg, 6th floor, Parliament St, New Delhi 110 001 Tel: (011) 3324929; (011) 3324939; (011) 3325134 Fax: (011) 3723351

**South Asia Publications+**
29, Central Market, Ashok Vihar, Delhi 110052

Tel: (011) 7241869; (011) 7235539
Key Personnel
Contact: S P Garg
Founded: 1986
Subjects: Advertising, Agriculture, Anthropology, Art, Business, Economics, Finance, History, Management, Religion - Other
ISBN Prefix(es): 81-7433
Associate Companies: SanPark Press Pvt Ltd

**South Asian Publishers Pvt Ltd+**
36, Netaji Subhash Marg, Darya Ganj, New Delhi 110002
Tel: (011) 276292; (011) 276740
E-mail: vchigs@giasdla.vsnl.net.in
Key Personnel
Chief Executive, Editorial, Rights & Permissions: Vinod Kumar
Production, Publicity: K A Rastogi
Founded: 1980
Specialize in International Relations.
Subjects: Anthropology, Asian Studies, Biological Sciences, Chemistry, Chemical Engineering, Civil Engineering, Developing Countries, Electronics, Electrical Engineering, Engineering (General), Environmental Studies, Government, Political Science, Labor, Industrial Relations, Mathematics, Physics, Religion - Buddhist, Religion - Hindu, Science (General), Social Sciences, Sociology, Technology
ISBN Prefix(es): 81-7003
Warehouse: Sector IX, H 65, UP India

**Spectrum Publications+**
Hembarua Rd, Pan Bazar, Guwahati, Assam 781001
Mailing Address: PO Box 45, Guwahati, Assam 781001
Tel: (0361) 26381; (0361) 24791 Fax: (0361) 544791 Cable: UNIPUB GUWAHATI
Key Personnel
Publisher: Krishan Kumar
Editorial: Ms Aarti Kumar
Sales: Ms Anita Kumar
Publicity: Ms Neha Kumar
Founded: 1976
Membership(s): Federation of Indian Publishers.
Subjects: Anthropology, Asian Studies, Social Sciences, Sociology, Travel
ISBN Prefix(es): 81-85319; 81-87502; 81-900396; 81-900750
Imprints: Aarti Books; Neha Mini Katha; Sunny Classics
Branch Office(s)
298 Tagore Park, Model Town 1, Delhi 110009 Tel: (011) 7122641
GS Rd, Shilcong 793001 Tel: (0364) 223476
Distributor for Abilac; DIPR Arunachal Pradesh; Law Research Institute; Nehu Publications
Showroom(s): 4754-57 Daryaganj, 23 Ansari Rd, New Delhi 110002
Bookshop(s): The Modern Book Depot, Panbazar, Main Rd, Guwahati 781 001; United Publishers
Orders to: United Publishers, Panbazar, PO Box 82, Guwahati 781001

**Sree Rama Publishers**
15-1-513 Siddiamber Bazar, Hyderabad 50012
Tel: (040) 2522609
E-mail: thehindu@usnl.com
Web Site: www.hinduonnet.com Cable: BOOKS SECUNDERABAD
Key Personnel
Man Dir: Shiva Ramaiah Pabba
Editorial: Sreenivas Prabhu Pabba
Sales: Subash Chandra Sekhar Pabba
Production, Publicity, Rights & Permissions: Shivarajaiah Pabba
Contact: P Bhaskar Rao
Founded: 1916
Subjects: Theology
ISBN Prefix(es): 81-7275

*Parent Company:* Sree Rama Book Depot, Market St, Secunderabad
*Associate Companies:* Popular Book House; Secunderabad; Sree Sita Rama Book Depot
*Bookshop(s):* Sree Rama Book Depot, Gunfoundry, Hyderabad 500001; Sree Rama Book Depot, Siddiamber Bazar, Hyderabad
*Orders to:* 113 Sarojinin Devi Rd, Secunderabad 500003

**Sri Satguru Publications+**
40/5 Shakti Nagar, 1st floor, Delhi 110 007
*Tel:* (011) 27126497; (011) 27434930 *Fax:* (011) 27227336
*E-mail:* ibcindia@giasdlo1.vsnl.net.in or ibcindia@ibcindia.com
*Key Personnel*
Man Dir, Rights & Permissions: Naresh Gupta
Export Dir: Sunil Gupta
Sales: Anil Gupta
Publicity: Virender Gupta
Founded: 1976
Subjects: Asian Studies, Music, Dance, Regional Interests, Religion - Buddhist
ISBN Prefix(es): 81-7030
*Associate Companies:* Bibliotheca Indo-Buddhica Series, 40/5 Shakti Nagar, Delhi 110 007; Sri Garib Dass Oriental Series, 40/5 Shakti Nagar, Delhi 110 007

**Star Publications (P) Ltd+**
4/5 B Asaf Ali Rd, New Delhi 110002
*Tel:* (011) 23268651; (011) 23286757; (011) 23258993; (011) 23261696 *Fax:* (011) 23273335; (011) 26481565
*Web Site:* www.starpublic.com
*Key Personnel*
Chairman & Man Dir: Amar N Varma
Chief Executive: Anil K Varma *Tel:* (011) 3258993
Production, Publicity: Sanjay Varma *Tel:* (011) 3274874
Dir: Sunil Varma *Tel:* (011) 6468427
Founded: 1957
Publisher & distributor of English & Indian language books.
Subjects: English as a Second Language, History, Language Arts, Linguistics, Literature, Literary Criticism, Essays, Religion - Hindu, Politics, Religion-Islam, Religion-Jain, Religion-Sikh
ISBN Prefix(es): 81-85243
Total Titles: 600 Print; 50 Audio
*Associate Companies:* Star Book Centre, 4/5B Asaf Ali Rd, New Delhi 110002
*Subsidiaries:* Publications India; Hindi Book Centre; Star Publishers Distributors
*Showroom(s):* Hindi Book Centre, Star Publications (P) Ltd
*Bookshop(s):* Hindi Book Centre
*Shipping Address:* D-92/3 Okhla Industrial Area I, New Delhi 110020

**Sterling Information Technologies+**
L-11, Green Park Extension, New Delhi 110 016
*Tel:* (011) 669560 *Fax:* (011) 26383788
*Cable:* PAPERBACKS
*Key Personnel*
Rights & Permission: Vikas Ghai
Editorial: Malhotra Vandana
Founded: 1993
Subjects: Computer Science, Management, Marketing, Microcomputers, Technology
Distributed by Goodwill Book Store (Philippines); S S Mubaruks Bros Pte Ltd (Singapore); Vanguard Books Ltd (Pakistan)

**Sterling Press (P) Ltd**, *imprint of* Sterling Publishers Pvt Ltd

**Sterling Publishers Pvt Ltd+**
A-59 Okhla Industrial Area, Phase II, New Delhi 110020

*Tel:* (011) 26387070; (011) 26386209; (011) 26386165; (011) 26385677 *Fax:* (011) 26383788
*E-mail:* info@sterlingpublishers.com
*Web Site:* www.sterlingpublishers.com *Cable:* PAPERBACKS
*Key Personnel*
Chairman & Man Dir: S K Ghai *E-mail:* ghai@nde.vsnl.net.in
Rights & Permissions: Shuchita Ghai
Editorial: Marry Joseph
Sales: Vikas Ghai
Production: Shreeh Kumar
Publicity: Mr Mohammed Khan
Export: Kusum Malik
Founded: 1965
Specialize in humanities & social science.
Membership(s): Afro Asian Book Council; Asian Association of Scholarly Publishers; Federation of Indian Publishers.
Subjects: Agriculture, Art, Asian Studies, Astrology, Occult, Biography, Communications, Developing Countries, Economics, Education, English as a Second Language, Fiction, Gardening, Plants, Government, Political Science, History, Journalism, Library & Information Sciences, Literature, Literary Criticism, Essays, Management, Medicine, Nursing, Dentistry, Philosophy, Public Administration, Religion - Hindu, Religion - Islamic, Religion - Other, Science (General), Social Sciences, Sociology, Technology, Women's Studies, Humanities
*Associate Companies:* Learners Press (P) Ltd, Sterling House, New Delhi
*Imprints:* Institute of Book Publishing; Sai Early Learners (P) Ltd; Sterling Press (P) Ltd

**Stree+**
Imprint of Bhatkal & Sen
16 Southern Ave, Kolkata 700 026
*Tel:* (033) 2466 0812 *Fax:* (033) 2464 4614; (033) 2466 6677
*E-mail:* stree@vsnl.com
*Web Site:* www.streebooks.com
*Key Personnel*
Dir: Mandira Sen *E-mail:* stree@cal2.vsnl.net.it
Founded: 1990
Publish women's studies in English & Bengali, also culture & dissent (under Samya imprint).
Jointly founded by popular Prakashan, Mumbii & Mandira, Kolkata, who formed Bhatkal & Sen.
Subjects: Asian Studies, Women's Studies
ISBN Prefix(es): 81-85604
Total Titles: 30 Print
Imprints: Samya
*Branch Office(s)*
Popular Prakashan, 46481 Ansari Rd, 21 Daryaganj, Delhi 110002, Contact: C Kothari *Tel:* (011) 23265245 *E-mail:* populardel@mantraonline.com *Web Site:* www.samyabooks.com
Popular Prakashan, 35C Pandit MM Malariya Marq, Popular Press Bldg, Tardeo, Mumbai 400034, Contact: Harsha Bhatkal *Tel:* (022) 24941556 *E-mail:* harshab@hotmail.com
Distributed by Gazelle Book Services (UK, Europe & USA)

**Sultan Chand & Sons Pvt Ltd**
4859/24 Darya Ganj, New Delhi 110002
*Tel:* (011) 3266105; (011) 3277843; (011) 3281876 *Fax:* (011) 3266357
*E-mail:* nbcnd@ndb.vsnl.net.in
*Key Personnel*
Man Dir: Vivek Agarwal *Tel:* (011) 3278018
Founded: 1950
Membership(s): Federation of Publishers & Booksellers Associations of India.
Subjects: Accounting, Behavioral Sciences, Biological Sciences, Business, Career Development, Chemistry, Chemical Engineering, Computer Science, Economics, Education, Electronics, Electrical Engineering, Engineering (Gen-

eral), English as a Second Language, Finance, Geography, Geology, Government, Political Science, Health, Nutrition, History, How-to, Human Relations, Labor, Industrial Relations, Law, Management, Marketing, Mathematics, Physics, Public Administration, Self-Help, Social Sciences, Sociology, Technology
*Parent Company:* Northern Book Centre, 4221/1 Daryaganj, Ansari Road, New Delhi 110002 (Publishers of Scholarly Reference Books)
Distributed by Prakash Sons

**Suman Prakashan Pvt Ltd+**
24B/9, Desh Bandhu Gupta Rd, Dev Nagar, New Delhi 110 005
*Tel:* (011) 5842253; (011) 5721750 *Fax:* (011) 5754739
*E-mail:* info@sumanprakashan.com
*Web Site:* www.sumanprakashan.com
*Key Personnel*
Dir: R N Malhotra
Founded: 1970
Specialize in children's textbooks.
Membership(s): PHDCCI; FICCI.
Subjects: Art, History, Mathematics, Science (General)
ISBN Prefix(es): 81-85869; 81-7795
*Associate Companies:* Pearl (India) Publishing House (P) Ltd
*Branch Office(s)*
108, Lingapur Bldg, Amrutha Estate, Himayat Naggar, Hyderabad 500029 *Tel:* (040) 3224078
2, Bankim Chatterjee St, 2nd floor, Kolkata 700073 *Tel:* (033) 2190463
1st floor, Shiv Vindhaya Complex, Sector-22, mrapali Bazaar, Indira Nagar, Lucknow 226016
10 Kitab Bhavan Rd, North Shri Krishnapura, Patna 800013 *Tel:* (0612) 261093

**Sunny Classics**, *imprint of* Spectrum Publications

**Surjeet Publications+**
7-K Kolhapur Rd, Kamla Nagar, Delhi 110 007
Mailing Address: PO Box 2157, Kamla Nagar, Delhi 110 007
*Tel:* (011) 3914746; (011) 3914174 *Fax:* (011) 3918475
*E-mail:* surpub@del3.vsnl.net.in
*Telex:* 31-78101asiain
*Key Personnel*
Managing Partner: Harnam Singh
Founded: 1976
Also acts as bookseller, distributor & remainder dealer.
Subjects: Literature, Literary Criticism, Essays, Social Sciences, Sociology
ISBN Prefix(es): 81-229

**Tara Publishing+**
38/GA, Shoreham, Fifth Ave, Besant Nagar, Chennai 600090
*Tel:* (044) 24401696; (044) 24912846 *Fax:* (044) 24453658
*E-mail:* mail@tarabooks.com
*Web Site:* www.tarabooks.com
*Key Personnel*
Publisher: Gita Wolf *E-mail:* gita.wolf@tarabooks.com
Editorial Dir: V Geetha *E-mail:* v.geetha@tarabooks.com
Editorial Dir & Rights Manager: Sirish Rao *E-mail:* sirish.rao@tarabooks.com
Founded: 1994
Independent publishing house.
Subjects: Art, Asian Studies, Crafts, Games, Hobbies, Education, Fiction, History, How-to, Religion - Buddhist, Religion - Hindu
ISBN Prefix(es): 81-86211
Number of titles published annually: 15 Print
Total Titles: 50 Print
Foreign Rights: The English Agency (Japan); Alice Gruenfelder (Germany); Motovun (Japan);

Sea of Stories (France, Spain); Servizi Editoriali (Italy); Sigma (Korea)
*Shipping Address:* Consortium Book Sales & Distribution, 1045 Westgate Drive, Saint Paul, MN 55114, United States, Contact: John Baynes
*E-mail:* jbaynes@cbsd.com
*Warehouse:* Consortium Book Sales & Distribution, 1045 Westgate Drive, Saint Paul, MN 55114, United States, Contact: John Baynes
*E-mail:* jbaynes@cbsd.com
*Distribution Center:* Consortium Book Sales & Distribution, 1045 Westgate Drive, Saint Paul, MN 55114, United States
*Orders to:* Consortium Book Sales & Distribution, 1045 Westgate Drive, Saint Paul, MN 55114, United States *Fax:* 651-221-0124
*E-mail:* nliberty@cbsd.com
*Returns:* Consortium Book Sales & Distribution, 1045 Westgate Drive, Saint Paul, MN 55114, United States, Contact: John Baynes
*E-mail:* jbaynes@cbsd.com

**DB Taraporevala Sons & Co Pvt Ltd**
210 Dr D Naoroji Rd, Fort, Mumbai 400001
*Tel:* 2041433; 2041434 *Cable:* BOOKSHOP BOMBAY
*Key Personnel*
Chief Executive: Prof Russi J Taraporevala
Dir: Mrs Manekbai J Taraporevala; Miss Sooni J Taraporevala
Founded: 1864
Subjects: Art, Ethnicity, History, Social Sciences, Sociology

**Tata McGraw-Hill Publishing Co Ltd+**
Subsidiary of The McGraw-Hill Companies Inc
7, West Patel Nagar, New Delhi 110 008
*Tel:* (011) 2588 2743; (011) 2588 2746; (011) 2588 9304; (011) 2588 9307
*E-mail:* info_india@mcgraw-hill.com
*Web Site:* www.tatamcgrawhill.com
*Key Personnel*
Chairman: Dr F.A. Mehta
Founded: 1970
40% owned by McGraw-Hill Book Co, 1221 Ave of the Americas, New York, NY 10020, USA.
Subjects: Business, Engineering (General), Management, Science (General), Social Sciences, Sociology
ISBN Prefix(es): 0-07

**Theosophical Publishing House**
Division of Theosophical Society (Worldwide)
Adyar, Chennai 600020
*Tel:* (044) 412904 *Fax:* (044) 4901399; (044) 4902706
*E-mail:* intl-hq@ts-adyar.org
*Web Site:* ts-adyar.org *Cable:* THEOTHECA
*Key Personnel*
Manager: D K Govindaraj *E-mail:* theos.soc@gems.vsnl.net.in
Publications Officer: T Albert Echikwa
*E-mail:* theos.soc@gems.vsnl.net.in
Founded: 1913
Provide books on Theosophy & Allied subjects at easily affordable prices. Do not buy rights but permit the use of excerpts conditionally.
Subjects: Biography, History, Human Relations, Mysteries, Parapsychology, Philosophy, Religion - Other, Science (General), Theology
ISBN Prefix(es): 81-7059
Total Titles: 291 Print
*Associate Companies:* TPH Manila, Iba St, Quezon City, Metro, Manila, Philippines
*Tel:* (02) 741-5740 *Fax:* (02) 740-3751
*E-mail:* tspeace@mnl.sequel.net; Theosophical Publishing House, 306 W Geneva Rd, PO Box 270, Wheaton, IL 60189, United States *Tel:* 630-665-0130 *Fax:* 630-665-8791
*E-mail:* olcott@theosophia.org
*Bookshop(s):* Adelaide, Australia; Brisbane, Australia; Perth, Australia; Sydney, Australia; Vic-

toria, Australia; Accra, Ghana; Amsterdam, Netherlands; Manila, Philippines; Quezon City, Philippines; Stockholm, Sweden; London, United Kingdom; CA, United States

**Today & Tomorrow's Printers & Publishers+**
24-b/5 Desh Bandhu, Gupta Marg, Karol Bagh, New Delhi 110005
*Tel:* (011) 5721928; (011) 5727770
*Key Personnel*
Man Dir, Editorial, Rights & Permissions: R K Jain
Sales, Publicity, Production: S K Jain
Founded: 1960
Membership(s): Federation of Publishers & Booksellers Associations in India.
Subjects: Agriculture, Natural History, Science (General)
ISBN Prefix(es): 81-7019
*U.S. Office(s):* Scholarly Publications, 2825 Wilcrest, Suite 255, Houston, TX 77042, United States *Tel:* 713-781-0070 *Fax:* 713-781-2112
Distributed by Scholarly Pub (USA)

**Transworld Research Network**
37/661(2), Fort PO, Thiruvananthapuram, Kerala 695023
*Tel:* (0471) 2460384 *Fax:* (0491) 2573051
*E-mail:* ggcom@vsnl
*Web Site:* www.transworldresearch.com
*Key Personnel*
Man Editor: Shankar Pandalai
Publications Manager: Anandavalli Gayathri
Founded: 1996
Publishes review books in all areas of science, agriculture, medicine, pure science & technology. Also does CD-ROM production & software development.
Subjects: Agriculture, Medicine, Nursing, Dentistry, Science (General)
ISBN Prefix(es): 81-86846; 81-7895

**N M Tripathi Pvt Ltd Publishers & Booksellers**
164 Shamaldas Gandhi Marg, Mumbai 400002
*Tel:* (022) 22013651 *Fax:* (022) 22050048
*Key Personnel*
Man Dir & Executive Manager: K R Tripathi
Founded: 1888
Gujrati language & literature, poetry & novels.
Subjects: Business, Ethnicity, Religion - Hindu
ISBN Prefix(es): 81-7118
Total Titles: 50 Print
*Parent Company:* Bombay Booksellers & Publishers' Association, Mumbai
*Ultimate Parent Company:* Federation of Publishers' & Booksellers' Associations, Delhi

**UBS Publishers Distributors Ltd**
5 Ansari Rd, Darya Ganj, New Delhi 110 002
*Tel:* (011) 273601; (011) 3266646 *Fax:* (011) 3276593; (011) 3274261
*E-mail:* ubspd@ubspd.com
*Web Site:* www.ubspd.com *Cable:* ALLBOOKS
*Key Personnel*
Man Dir: C M Chawla
Exec Dir: Sukumar Das
Gen Mgr: Vivek Ahuja
Publish political, current affairs, cookery, religion, biography, fiction, self-improvement, management & general books. Distribute all types of books.
Subjects: Biography, Cookery, Fiction, Government, Political Science, Management, Religion - Other, Current Affairs, Self Improvement
ISBN Prefix(es): 81-7476; 81-85273; 81-85674; 81-85944; 81-86112
*Branch Office(s)*
80 Noronha Rd, Cantonment Kanpur 208 004
*Tel:* (0512) 369124; (0512) 362665; (0512) 352665, 357488 *Fax:* (0512) 315122

6 First Main Rd, PO Box 9713, Ghandi-Nagar Bangalore 560 009 *Tel:* (0172) 2263901; (0172) 2263902; (0172) 2253903 *Fax:* (0172) 2263904
6 Sivaganga Rd, Nugambakkam, Chennai 700 016 *Tel:* (044) 8276355; (044) 8270189 *Fax:* (044) 8278920
8/1-B Chowringhee Lane, Kolkata 700-016 *Tel:* (033) 2441821; (033) 2442910; (033) 244973 *Fax:* (033) 2450027
*E-mail:* ubspdcal@cal.vsnl.net.in
5 A Rajendra Nagar, Patna 800 016 *Tel:* (0612) 672856; (0612) 673973; (0612) 656170 *Fax:* (0612) 656169

**UBSPD,** see UBS Publishers Distributors Ltd

**Vakils Feffer & Simons Ltd+**
Hague Bldg, 9 Sprott Rd, Ballard Estate, Maharashtra, Mumbai 400001
*Tel:* (022) 2611221; (022) 2619121 *Fax:* (022) 2614924; (022) 2610432
*Telex:* oil83668vkilin *Cable:* FLEETBOOKS
*Key Personnel*
Dir: Mr Arun K Mehta
Founded: 1960
Subjects: Art, Cookery, Gardening, Plants, Management, Religion - Hindu, Religion - Islamic, Religion - Other, Travel
ISBN Prefix(es): 81-87111
*Showroom(s):* Vakil & Sons Ltd, Vakils House, 18 Ballard Estate, Mumbai 400001
*Bookshop(s):* Vakil & Sons Ltd, Vakils House, 18 Ballard Estate, Mumbia 400001

**Vani Prakashan+**
4697/5, 21-A Daryaganj, Ansari Rd, New Delhi 110002
*Tel:* (011) 23273167 *Fax:* (011) 23275710
*E-mail:* vani-prakashan@yahoo.com
*Key Personnel*
Chief Executive, Editorial, Production, Publicity & Sales: Arun Kumar Maheshwari
Founded: 1968
Subjects: Ethnicity, Fiction, History, Literature, Literary Criticism, Essays, Poetry, Hindi (with various subjects)
ISBN Prefix(es): 81-7055; 81-8143
*Associate Companies:* Navodaya Sales, 35, A, DDA Flat, Mansarovar Park, Shadhara, Delhi 32; Swarn Jyanti, 1/5971, Kabool Nagar, Shadhara, Delhi 32
*Branch Office(s)*
Book Corner, Sri Ram Center, Safdar Hashni Marg, New Delhi
*Book Club(s):* Jan Sulakh Pathak Manch

**Vastu Gyan Publication**
9/1, Institutional Area, Aruna Asat All Rd (opp Jnu East Gate), New Delhi 110067
*Tel:* (011) 3318730
*Key Personnel*
Author: Mr BB Puri
Subjects: Architecture & Interior Design
ISBN Prefix(es): 81-900614

**Vidhi**
Vibhagiya Prakashan Bikri Kendra, Vikas Bhawan, Secretariate, Patna 800015
*Tel:* (011) 389001 *Cable:* PATRIKA
*Key Personnel*
Sales Manager: C B Deogam
Assistant Manager: Ram Labhaya
Founded: 1975
Specialize in publications of the Acts in diglot form.
Subjects: Law
ISBN Prefix(es): 81-85956
Divisions: Vidhi Sahitya Prakashan

**Vidhi Sahitya Prakashan,** see Vidhi

**Vidya Puri+**
Balu Bazar, Cuttack 753002
*Tel:* (0671) 620637; (0671) 617260 *Cable:*
VIDYAPURI
*Key Personnel*
Man Partner, Edit: Pitamber Mishra
Partner: Ramananda Mishra; Rupananda Mishra;
Bhabananda Mishra; Jivananda Mishra
Sales: S K Sarangi
Founded: 1961
Subjects: Accounting, Animals, Pets, Biography, Biological Sciences, Business, Chemistry, Chemical Engineering, Computer Science, Literature, Literary Criticism, Essays
ISBN Prefix(es): 81-7411
*Associate Companies:* Goswami Press, Alamchand Bazar, Cuttack 753002; Graftek Pvt Ltd, Bhubaneswar 751002; Rainbow Offset (P) Ltd, Bhubaneswar 751002
Divisions: Vidyashre DTP Centre

**Vidyarthi Mithram Press+**
Vidyarthi Mathram Bldg, Bakar Rd, Kottayarn 686001
*Tel:* (0481) 563281; (0481) 563282; (0481) 561713; (0481) 562616 (after office hours) *Fax:* (0481) 562616 *Cable:* VIDYARTHI
*Key Personnel*
Man Dir: Koshy P John
Founded: 1928
Subjects: Biography, Biological Sciences, Chemistry, Chemical Engineering, Child Care & Development, Computer Science, Cookery, Drama, Theater, Economics
*Associate Companies:* Auroville Publishers, Kottayam
Imprints: Kosi Books; Manosabdam Books
*Branch Office(s)*
Ernakulam
Kollam
Kozhikode
Palakkad
Thiruvalla
Thiruvananthapuram
Thrissur
*Bookshop(s):* Vidyarthi Mithram Book Depot, Baker Rd, Kottayam
*Book Club(s):* Vidyarthi Mithram Novel Club

**Vikas Higher Education Books/Madhubun Educational Books**, *imprint of* Vikas Publishing House Pvt Ltd

**Vikas Publishing House Pvt Ltd+**
576, Masjid Rd, Jangpura, New Delhi 110 014
*Tel:* (011) 24315313; (011) 24315570; (011) 24317857 *Fax:* (011) 24310879
*E-mail:* helpline@vikaspublishing.com
*Key Personnel*
Dir: Piyush Chawla; Sajili Shirodkar
Founded: 1969
Vikas focuses on textbooks & professional books on management, computers, engineering & technology. Madhubun, the children's book imprint, offers a high quality range from preschool upwards.
Subjects: Chemistry, Chemical Engineering, Computer Science, Economics, Education, Engineering (General), Management, Mathematics, Physics, Science (General), Technology
ISBN Prefix(es): 81-259
Number of titles published annually: 100 Print
Total Titles: 1,200 Print
Imprints: Vikas Higher Education Books/Madhubun Educational Books
Distributor for Thomson Learning (Routledge)

**Vision Books Pvt Ltd+**
24 Feroze Gandhi Rd, Lajpat Nagar-III, New Delhi 110024
*Tel:* (011) 2386-2267; (011) 2386-2201
*Fax:* (011) 2386-2935

*E-mail:* mail@orientpaperbacks.com *Cable:*
VISIONBOOK DELHI
*Key Personnel*
Chairman: Vishwa Nath
Man Dir, Rights & Permissions, Sales: Sudhir Malhotra
Publishing Dir: Kapil Malhotra
Publicity, Exports: Sidharth Malhotra
Editor: Dr O P Jaggi
Founded: 1975
Membership(s): Federation of Indian Publishers, Delhi State Booksellers & Publishers Association.
Subjects: Anthropology, Cookery, Education, Fiction, Health, Nutrition, History, How-to, Humor, Management, Medicine, Nursing, Dentistry, Military Science, Nonfiction (General), Religion - Other, Science (General), Travel, Career Guides, Fitness, Puzzle Books
ISBN Prefix(es): 81-7094
Total Titles: 700 Print
*Associate Companies:* Rajpal & Sons; Ravindra Printing Press; Shiksha Bharati; Vision Enterprises
*Subsidiaries:* Anand Paperbacks; Orient Paperbacks
*Branch Office(s)*
3-6-280/A/5 Himayatnagar, Hyderabad *Tel:* (040) 2322-3252
24 Firoze Gandhi Rd, Lajpat, Nagar *Tel:* (011) 2983-6470-80 *Fax:* (011) 2983-6490
3-B Peddar Rd, Vasant Ground floor, Mumbai *Tel:* (022) 492 9343 *Fax:* (022) 496 0229
*Book Club(s):* Anand Book Club; Orient Book Club

**Vistaar**, *imprint of* SAGE Publications India Pvt Ltd

**S Viswanathan (Printers & Publishers) Pvt Ltd+**
38, McNichols Rd, Chetput, Chennai 600 031
*Tel:* (044) 826 5623; (044) 826 5633 *Fax:* (044) 825 6002
*E-mail:* svprint@md2.vsnl.net.in
*Key Personnel*
Contact: Mr V Subramanian
Founded: 1971
Subjects: Biological Sciences, Chemistry, Chemical Engineering, Computer Science, English as a Second Language, History, Mathematics, Medicine, Nursing, Dentistry, Physics, Religion - Hindu, Science (General)
ISBN Prefix(es): 81-87156
*Associate Companies:* Beta Photo-Comps Pvt Ltd
*Bookshop(s):* Ananda Book Depot, 38, McNichols Rd, Chetput, Chennai 600 031

**Viva Books Pvt Ltd+**
4262/3 Ansari Rd, Daryaganj, New Delhi 110 002
*Tel:* (011) 3258325; (011) 3283121 *Fax:* (011) 3267224
*E-mail:* viva@mantraonline.com
*Web Site:* www.vivagroupindia.com
*Key Personnel*
Man Dir: Vinod Vasishtha
Subjects: Business, Career Development, Chemistry, Chemical Engineering, Child Care & Development, Civil Engineering, Communications, Earth Sciences, Economics, Education, Electronics, Electrical Engineering, Energy, Engineering (General), English as a Second Language, Environmental Studies, Management, Marketing, Mechanical Engineering, Military Science, Psychology, Psychiatry, Public Administration, Science (General), Social Sciences, Sociology, Technology, Travel
ISBN Prefix(es): 81-7649; 81-85617
Number of titles published annually: 100 Print
Total Titles: 500 Print

**Vivek Prakashan**
7-UA Jawahar Nagar, Delhi 110007
*Tel:* (011) 2529649; (011) 2944014 *Fax:* (011) 6827347
*Key Personnel*
Contact: Asha Rani
Founded: 1980
Subjects: Economics, Fiction, Literature, Literary Criticism, Essays, Social Sciences, Sociology
ISBN Prefix(es): 81-7004

**A H Wheeler & Co Ltd+**
23 Lal Bahadur Shastri Marg, Allahabad 211 001
*Tel:* (011) 3312629; (011) 3318537 *Fax:* (011) 3357798
*E-mail:* wheelerpub@mantraonline.com
*Key Personnel*
Contact: Arunjeet Banerjee
Founded: 1879
Membership(s): Federation of Indian Publishers.
Subjects: Accounting, Advertising, Behavioral Sciences, Business, Career Development, Civil Engineering, Communications, Computer Science
ISBN Prefix(es): 81-7544; 81-85614; 81-85814
*Associate Companies:* Wheeler Leather Corporation Ltd
*Subsidiaries:* Symonds & Co
Divisions: Wheeler Exports; Wheeler Offset Press; Wheeler Publishing
*Branch Office(s)*
Bangalore
Chennai
Delhi
Kolkata
Mumbai

**Zebra Books for Children**, *imprint of* Arnold Heinman Publishers (India) Pvt Ltd

# Indonesia

## General Information

*Capital:* Jakarta
*Language:* Bahasa Indonesia (a form of Malay) is official language. English is common second language. About 25 local languages & over 250 dialects are spoken
*Religion:* About 87% Islamic, 10% Christian & some Hindu & Buddhist
*Population:* 195 million
*Bank Hours:* Generally 0800-1400 Monday-Thursday; 0800-1500 Friday; 0800-1300 Saturday
*Currency:* Rupiah
*Export/Import Information:* Books subject to import tax & VAT tax. No exchange control. Books & printed matter using Indonesian languages prohibited. Importers require no license but are categorized into four groups for credit arrangement controls.
*Copyright:* No copyright conventions signed but Indonesia has recently enacted tougher domestic copyright laws

**Mandira Jaya Abadi+**
Jl Letjen, Mt Haryono 501, Semarang, Jawa Tengah 50241
*Tel:* (024) 3519547; (024) 3519548 *Fax:* (024) 3542189
Founded: 1984
ISBN Prefix(es): 979-490

**Advent Indonesia Publishing**
Jalan Raya Cimindi No 72, Yogyakarta
*Tel:* (022) 630392; (022) 642006 *Fax:* (022) 630588 *Cable:* Indopub

*Key Personnel*
Manager: Djinan Sinaga
Chief Editor: Jahotner F Manullang
Treasurer: Agus Ricky
Founded: 1954
Subjects: Child Care & Development, Health, Nutrition, Human Relations, Religion - Protestant, Religion - Other
ISBN Prefix(es): 979-504

**Akadoma CV**
Jl Kalasan No 1, Jakarta Pusat
*Tel:* (021) 3904323
*Key Personnel*
Man Dir: Adam Saleh

**Al-Bayan**, *imprint of* Mizan

**Alma'Arif PT**
Jl Tamblong No 48-50, Bandung 40112
*Tel:* (022) 4207177; (022) 4203708 *Fax:* (022) 439194
*Key Personnel*
Man Dir: H M Baharthah
ISBN Prefix(es): 979-400

**Alumni PT**
Jl Dr Djundjunan, Bandung 40197
*Tel:* (022) 2501251; (022) 2503039; (022) 2503038 *Fax:* (022) 2503044
*Telex:* 28640
*Key Personnel*
Man Dir, Rights & Permissions: Eddy Damian
Editorial: Yayat Ruchiyat
Sales: Punomo
Production Manager: Philips
Founded: 1966
Subjects: Economics, Law, Medicine, Nursing, Dentistry, Psychology, Psychiatry, Social Sciences, Sociology
ISBN Prefix(es): 979-414
*Branch Office(s)*
Jl Jend A Yani 206E, Banjarmasin
Wisma Sawah Besar, 8th floor, Jl Sukarjo Wiryopranoto 30, Jakarta *Tel:* (021) 372730 (Telex: 46810 Alumni Ia)
Putri Hijaubaru 37, Medan *Tel:* (061) 510615
Jl Kartini 22B, Tanjungkarang *Tel:* (0721) 53135
*Bookshop(s):* H Juanda St 54, Bandung *Tel:* (022) 58290

**Andi Offset+**
Jln Beo No 38-40, Yogyakarta 55281
*Tel:* (0274) 561881 *Fax:* (0274) 588282
*E-mail:* andi_pub@indo.net.id
*Key Personnel*
Dir: J H Gondowijoyo
Founded: 1980
Membership(s): Indonesian Publishers Association.
Subjects: Accounting, Chemistry, Chemical Engineering, Computer Science, Electronics, Electrical Engineering, Management, Marketing, Science (General), Technology
ISBN Prefix(es): 979-533
Distributor for Prenhallindo

**Angkasa CV+**
Jl Merdeka, No 6, Bandung 40111
Mailing Address: PO Box 354/Ed, Bandung
*Tel:* (022) 4208955; (022) 4204795 *Fax:* (022) 439183
*Telex:* 28276 Panghegar Bandung
*Key Personnel*
Chief Executive: Dr Fachri Said
Editorial Manager, Rights & Permissions: R Djajoesman
Sales Manager: Kofindar
Production Manager: Tom Gunadi
Founded: 1966

Subjects: Fiction, Nonfiction (General), Religion - Other
ISBN Prefix(es): 979-404; 979-547; 979-665
*Associate Companies:* PT Mutiara Sumber Widya
*Bookshop(s):* Balai Buku Angkasa, Jl Merdeka, No 6, Jawa Barat, Bandung

**PT Pustaka Antara Publishing & Printing+**
Taman Kebon Sirih III/13, 10250 Jakarta Pusat
*Tel:* (021) 3156994; (021) 3156995 *Fax:* (021) 322745
*E-mail:* nacelod@indo.net.id
*Key Personnel*
Dir: Aida Joesoef Ahmad
Founded: 1952
Membership(s): Board of IKAPI (Indonesian Publishers Association)
Also acts as Director of Research, Training & International Relations.
Subjects: Religion - Islamic
ISBN Prefix(es): 979-8013
*Associate Companies:* CV Idayus *Tel:* (06221) 322745
*Warehouse:* P T Demina, Jl Rempoa Mulya, No 12, Bintaro, Jakarta Selatan *Tel:* (021) 7370966; (021) 7370967

**Aries Lima**, see New Aqua Press

**Aurora+**
Jln Bambu Betung VII No 8, Bojong Indah, Jakarta 11740
*Tel:* (021) 5810413
*Key Personnel*
International Rights: Ms Nanik Hardjono
Subjects: Asian Studies, Biblical Studies, Education, Religion - Catholic, Religion - Protestant
ISBN Prefix(es): 979-564

**Badan Penerbit Kristen Gunung Mulia**
(Gunung Mulia Christian Publishing House Ltd Co)+
Jalan Kwitang 22-23, Jakarta 10420
*Tel:* (021) 3901208 *Fax:* (021) 3901633
*E-mail:* corp.off@bpkgm.com
*Web Site:* www.bpkgm.com
*Key Personnel*
President: Ichsan Gunawan *E-mail:* ichsan@bpkgm.com
Dir: Viveka Nanda Leimena
Founded: 1951
Membership(s): CBA.
Subjects: Christian, Theological General Literature
ISBN Prefix(es): 979-415; 979-9290
Number of titles published annually: 100 Print
Total Titles: 900 Print

**Balai Pustaka+**
Jl Gunung Sahari Raya No 4, Jakarta Pusat 10710
*Tel:* (021) 3447003; (021) 3447006 *Fax:* (021) 3446555
*E-mail:* mail@balaiperaga.com
*Web Site:* www.balaiperaga.com
*Telex:* 45905 Pnbp Jkt *Cable:* PERUM BALAI PUSTAKA
*Key Personnel*
President, Dir: Dr Zakaria Idris
Editorial, Production Dir: Kuntjono Sastrodarmodjo
Sales, Publicity Dir: Dr Chasan Mintara
Rights & Permissions Dir: Ismu Amran
Founded: 1917
Subjects: Education, Ethnicity
ISBN Prefix(es): 979-651
*Branch Office(s)*
Jl Pulogadung Kav Jl5, Pulogadung, Jakarta Timur
Jl Rawagate 17, Pulogadung, Jakarta Timur
*Book Club(s):* KPI (Klub Perpustakaan Indonesia)

**Bhratara Karya Aksara+**
Jl Rawabal, Kawawan Industri Pulogadung, Jakarta, Timur 13340
*Tel:* 021 81858
*Telex:* 48292 Bhranmia
*Key Personnel*
President: Ahmad Jayusman
Dir: Adit Jayusman; Robinson Rusdi
Founded: 1958
Sales agent for UNU, UNESCO, ICPE, Journal IMMA, IDRC Pubs. Also printer & book importer/exporter.
Membership(s): Association of Indonesian Publishers (IKAPI).
Subjects: Agriculture, Economics, Education, Health, Nutrition, History, Language Arts, Linguistics, Science (General), Social Sciences, Sociology, Technology
ISBN Prefix(es): 979-410
Subsidiaries: P T Bhratara Tekno Komputer
Divisions: P T Karya Upaya Arta
*Branch Office(s)*
Jogja
Malang
Medan
Padang
Surabaya Ujung Pandang
Distributor for ICPE; IDRC; Journal Muslin Minority Affairs; UNESCO
*Showroom(s):* Bhratara Bookshop, Jl Otista III/29, Jakarta, Timur *Tel:* (021) 8191858
*Bookshop(s):* Bhratara Bookshop, Jl Otista III/29, Jakarta, Timur *Tel:* (021) 8191858
*Shipping Address:* Bhratara Bookshop, Jl Otista III/29, Jakarta, Timur *Tel:* (021) 8191858
*Warehouse:* Bhratara Bookshop, Jl Otista III/29, Jakarta, Timur *Tel:* (021) 8191858
*Orders to:* Bhratara Bookshop, Jl Otista III/29, Jakarta, Timur *Tel:* (021) 8191858

**Bina Aksara Parta+**
Jln Raya Ubud, 80571 Bali
*Tel:* (361) 95240
*Key Personnel*
Contact: Silvio Santosa
Founded: 1983
Subjects: Fiction, Music, Dance, Religion - Hindu, Travel
ISBN Prefix(es): 979-8042
*Associate Companies:* Orti Co, Jl Sandat 22, Ubud, Bali 80571
*Orders to:* Orti Co, PO Box 20, Ubud, Bali 80571

**Bina Cipta PT**
Jl Ganesha No 4, Bandung
*Tel:* (022) 2504319 *Fax:* (022) 2504319
*Key Personnel*
Dir: O Bardin
ISBN Prefix(es): 979-8928

**Bina Ilmu**
Jl Tunjungan No 53 E-F, Surabaya 60275
*Tel:* (031) 5323214; (031) 5340076 *Fax:* (031) 5315421
*Key Personnel*
Man Dir: H Mc Ariefin Noor
ISBN Prefix(es): 979-422

**Bina Rena Pariwara**
Jl Pejaten Raya No 5-E, Pasar Minggu, Jakarta Selatan 12510
*Tel:* (021) 7901938 *Fax:* (021) 7901939
*Key Personnel*
President & Dir: Yullia Himawati
Founded: 1988
Membership(s): Indonesian Publishers Association (IKAPI).
Subjects: Communications, Economics, Education, Finance, Government, Political Science, Nonfiction (General), Religion - Islamic, Travel
ISBN Prefix(es): 979-8175; 979-9056

*Parent Company:* Yayasan Bina Pembangunan
(Development Foundation)
*Associate Companies:* Center for Fiscal & Monetary Studies-CFMS
Divisions: BRP Consultant Division
Distributor for Pt Penakencana Nusadwipa
*Bookshop(s):* Most Big Book Stores in the Capital Cities of All Provinces in Indonesia
*Book Club(s):* Indonesian Publishers Association (IKAPI)
*Warehouse:* Depok Bogor

**Biro Pusat Statistik** (Bureau of Statistical
Information System)
Jl dr Sutomo No 8, Kotak Pos 1003, Jakarta
10010
*Tel:* (021) 3507057 *Fax:* (021) 3857046
*E-mail:* bpsha@bps.go.id
*Web Site:* www.bps.go.id
*Telex:* 45159 *Cable:* KBPS
*Key Personnel*
Chief of Bureau: Yuwono Hadipramono

**PT Bulan Bintang+**
Jl Kramat Kitang I/8, Jakarta Pusat 10420
*Tel:* (021) 3901651; (021) 3901652 *Fax:* (021)
3107027 *Cable:* BULANBINTANG
*Key Personnel*
President: Amran Zamzami
Vice President, Editor-in-Chief: Fauzi Amelz
Founded: 1954
Subjects: Art, Business, Economics, Education, Engineering (General), Fiction, Finance, Government, Political Science, History, Law, Literature, Literary Criticism, Essays, Nonfiction (General), Philosophy, Psychology, Psychiatry, Religion - Islamic, Science (General), Social Sciences, Sociology, Sports, Athletics, Technology
ISBN Prefix(es): 979-418

**Bumi Aksara PT+**
Jl Sawo Raya No 18, Rawamangun, Jakarta
Timur 13220
*Tel:* (021) 4717049; (021) 4700988 *Fax:* (021)
4700989
*Key Personnel*
Dir: H Amir Hamzah
Founded: 1990
Membership(s): Indonesian Book Association.
Subjects: Accounting, Agriculture, Business, Economics, Law, Management, Marketing, Religion - Islamic
ISBN Prefix(es): 979-526

**Institut Dagang Muchtar**
Jl Embong Wungu 8, Surabaya
*Tel:* (031) 42973
ISBN Prefix(es): 979-417

**PT Dian Rakyat+**
Kawasan Industri Pulogadung, Jl Rawa Gelam I
No 4, Jakarta Timur
*Tel:* (021) 460-4444
*Telex:* 62338 Fega Ia *Cable:* DIAN RAKYAT
*Key Personnel*
Dir: H Mohammad Ais
Publishing Division Man: Mlle Harmiel M
Soekardjo
Founded: 1963
Subjects: Cookery, Economics, Literature, Literary Criticism, Essays, Medicine, Nursing, Dentistry
ISBN Prefix(es): 979-523

**Dinastindo+**
Jl Senopati No 54, Kebayoran Baru, Jakarta
12110
*Tel:* (021) 7250002; (021) 72799307 *Fax:* (021)
7262145
*E-mail:* dinastindo@yahoo.com

*Key Personnel*
Contact: Rijanto Tosin
Founded: 1984
Membership(s): ASP: IKAPI; Apkomindo.
Subjects: Business, Career Development, Computer Science, Management, Self-Help
ISBN Prefix(es): 979-552
*Branch Office(s)*
Surabaya & Bandung
Distributor for Abdi Tandu Publisher; Der Die
Das; Pisi 2 Ribu Software; Solid Pro Publisher

**Dioma, Kanisius, Obor,** *imprint of* Nusa Indah

**Diponegoro CV+**
Jl Mohammad Toha 44-46, Bandung 40252
*Tel:* (022) 5201215 *Fax:* (022) 5201215 *Cable:* C
V DIPONEGORO BANDUNG
*Key Personnel*
Man Dir: H A Dahlan
Editorial, Sales, Production, Publicity: Dr Anwaruddin
Founded: 1963
Membership(s): Indonesian Publishers Association.
Subjects: Religion - Other
ISBN Prefix(es): 979-8155; 979-9405

**Djambatan PT**
Jl Kramat Raya, Jakarta 10430
*Tel:* (021) 7203199 *Fax:* (021) 7208562
*Key Personnel*
Manager: Roswitha Pamoentjak
Founded: 1958
Subjects: Art, Literature, Literary Criticism, Essays, Philosophy, Religion - Other, Social Sciences, Sociology
ISBN Prefix(es): 979-428

**Dunia Pustaka Jaya PT**
Jl Kramat Raya 5-K, Jakarta Pusat 10450
*Tel:* (021) 3909322; (021) 3909284 *Fax:* (021)
3909320 *Cable:* Depeje
*Key Personnel*
Dir: Ahad Rifai
Editor: S W Rukasah; Sugiarta Sriwibawa
Founded: 1971
Subjects: Art, Drama, Theater, Ethnicity, Fiction, Literature, Literary Criticism, Essays, Philosophy, Poetry
ISBN Prefix(es): 979-419

**Duta Wacana University Press+**
Jl Dr Wahidin 5-19, Yogyakarta 55224
*Tel:* (0274) 563929 *Fax:* (0274) 513235
*E-mail:* humas@ukdw.ac.id
*Web Site:* www.ukdw.ac.id
*Telex:* 25486 UKDW IA
*Key Personnel*
Dir: S H Hadi Purnomo
Founded: 1989
ISBN Prefix(es): 979-8139

**Eresco PT**
Jl Megger Girang No 98, Bandung 40254
*Tel:* (022) 5205985 *Fax:* (022) 5205984
*Cable:* Erescopete Bandung
*Key Personnel*
Man Dir: Dr Arfan Razali
Editorial: Dr H Rochmat Soemitro
Sales: Mr Amun; Mr Harsono
Founded: 1956
Subjects: Economics, Law, Philosophy, Psychology, Psychiatry
ISBN Prefix(es): 979-8020
*Bookshop(s):* Jl Perapatan 22 Pav, Jakarta
*Tel:* (021) 368000
*Book Club(s):* Himpunan Masyarakat Pencinta
Buku (HMPB)

**Fortunajaya+**
Jl Diponegoro 11, Klaten
*Tel:* (0272) 22030 *Fax:* (0272) 22543
Founded: 1985
ISBN Prefix(es): 979-557
*Showroom(s):* Jln Pemuda, Selatan 44 B, Klaten

**Gaya Favorit Press+**
Jl HR Rasuna Said, Kav B 32-33, Jakarta Selatan
12910
*Mailing Address:* Kuningan
*Tel:* (021) 513816 *Fax:* (021) 5209366; (021)
4609115
*E-mail:* ptgfp1@rad.net.id
*Telex:* 62338 Fega IA
*Key Personnel*
Man Dir: Mirta Kartohadiprodjo
Editorial: Wied Harry Apriadji
Sales: Irwan SLT
Editorial, Publicity, Rights & Permissions: R H
Yus Kayam
Founded: 1972
Subjects: Crafts, Games, Hobbies, Fiction, Nonfiction (General)
ISBN Prefix(es): 979-515
*Parent Company:* PT Gaya Favorit Press, Jln HR
Rasuna Said blok B, Kav 32-33, Jakarta 12910

**Gramedia+**
Jl Palmerah Selatan 22-28, Jakarta Pusat 10270
*Tel:* (021) 5483008; (021) 5490666 *Fax:* (021)
5300545
*Web Site:* www.gramedia.co.id
*Telex:* Kompas Jkt 46327 *Cable:* KOMPAS
JAKARTA
*Key Personnel*
President: Jakob Detama
Group Director: Teddy Surianto
Executive Manager: Al Adhi Mardhiyond
Production: Slamet M Jaeni
Rights & Permissions: Puspita Dewi
Publicity: Y Suliantoro
Founded: 1985
Publisher, software house, multimedia.
Specialize in educational software & comics.
Subjects: Accounting, Animals, Pets, Antiques, Child Care & Development, Computer Science, Cookery, Crafts, Games, Hobbies, Electronics, Electrical Engineering, Fiction, Gardening, Plants, How-to, Management, Microcomputers, Mysteries, Technology
ISBN Prefix(es): 979-511; 979-605; 979-655;
979-686
*Parent Company:* Kompas-Gramedia Group

**PT BPK Gunung Mulia** (Gunung Mulia
Christian Publishing House Limited
Company)+
Jl Kwitang 22-23, Jakarta Pusat 10420
*Tel:* (021) 3901208 *Fax:* (021) 3901633
*E-mail:* corp.off@bpkgm.com
*Web Site:* www.bpkgm.com
*Key Personnel*
Dir: Budi Arlianto
Founded: 1950
Subjects: Religion - Other
ISBN Prefix(es): 979-415; 979-9290
*Bookshop(s):* Toko Buku PT BPK Gunung Mulia

**Harris+**
Jln Veteran GOR 6, Medan
*Tel:* (061) 22272
*Key Personnel*
Man Dir: Ny Maswari
Founded: 1952
Membership(s): Indonesian Publishers Association.

**ILMU-ILMU Islam,** *imprint of* Mizan

**PT Indira+**
Jl Borobudur No 20, Jakarta, Pusat 10320

*Tel:* (021) 3904290; (021) 3148868 *Fax:* (021)
  3929373
*E-mail:* indirawb@mweb.co.id
*Key Personnel*
Man Dir: Dr Bambang P Wahyudi
Founded: 1950
Subjects: Automotive, Business, Career Develop-
  ment, Computer Science, Crafts, Games, Hob-
  bies, Energy, English as a Second Language,
  Film, Video
ISBN Prefix(es): 979-8063
*Parent Company:* Grolier Inc, United States
*Associate Companies:* PT Widyadara
Subsidiaries: PT Radio Prambors-Commercial
  Radio Broadcasting

**Indrajaya CV**
Jl Jatibaru No 20, Jakarta Pusat
*Tel:* (021) 3457039; (021) 3457041 *Fax:* (021)
  3457039

**Institut Teknologi Bandung+**
Jl Tamansari 64, Bandung 40116
*Tel:* (022) 2550935 *Fax:* (022) 2550935
*E-mail:* info-center@itb.ac.id
*Web Site:* www.itb.ac.id
*Key Personnel*
Editor-in-Chief: Sofia Niksolihin
Founded: 1959
Subjects: Chemistry, Chemical Engineering, Ed-
  ucation, Electronics, Electrical Engineering,
  Engineering (General), Health, Nutrition, Math-
  ematics, Science (General), Technology
ISBN Prefix(es): 979-8001; 979-8591; 979-9299

**Islamiyah**
Jln Sutomo 329, Kotakpos 11, Medan
*Tel:* (061) 25421

**Karunia CV**
Jln Peneleh 18, Surabaya
*Tel:* (031) 5344120 *Fax:* (031) 5343409
ISBN Prefix(es): 979-9039

**Karya Anda, CV+**
Jl Praban No 55, Surabaya 60001
*Tel:* (031) 5344215; (031) 522580; (031) 5315402
  *Fax:* (031) 5310594
*Key Personnel*
Man Dir: Moechlis
Subjects: Agriculture, Anthropology, Automotive,
  Behavioral Sciences, Education, Environmental
  Studies, Fiction, Humor
ISBN Prefix(es): 979-8002

**Katalis PT Bina Mitra Plaosan**
Jl Pratama 111/18 Pulo Mas, Jakarta, Timur
  13220
*Tel:* (021) 7510477
*Key Personnel*
Publisher, Rights & Permissions: Elisabeth
  Soeprapto-Hastrich
Senior Editor: Ms Rasfiati Iskarno
Marketing Supervisor: Gertrud Moeljono
Business Manager, Production: Kisbandi
  Soeprapto
Editorial Assistant, Publicity: Gabriella Martiyah
Founded: 1986
Subjects: Career Development, How-to, Liter-
  ature, Literary Criticism, Essays, Nonfiction
  (General), Science (General)
ISBN Prefix(es): 979-8060
Imprints: Siemens-Penuntun Berencana

**Kesaint Blanc+**
Jl Lentong No 9, Narogong Raya Km 17116
*Tel:* (021) 4204847; (021) 4204851 *Fax:* (021)
  4216792
*Web Site:* www.kesaintblanc.com
*Key Personnel*
Dir: Antonius Bangun

Founded: 1979
ISBN Prefix(es): 979-8295; 979-593
*Associate Companies:* Kesaint Krakatau; Kesaint
  Sibayak; Mitra Utama
Imprints: Megapoin; Oriental; Renaisans; Tamtan
  Gabara; Visipro
*Branch Office(s)*
Bandar Lampung
Bandung
Medan
Surabaya
Yogyakarta
*Warehouse:* Jl Mekar Sari, Cimanggis, Bogor

**Kinta CV**
Jl Tengku Cikditiro 54A, Jakarta 10310
*Tel:* (021) 5494751
*Key Personnel*
Man Dir: Dr Mohammad Saleh
ISBN Prefix(es): 979-8004

**Kurnia Esanata**
Jl Jenderal Sudirman Kav 36A, Jakarta Pusat
  10420
*Tel:* (021) 361974; (021) 3104948
*Telex:* 44328
*Key Personnel*
Man Dir: Taufik H Das
ISBN Prefix(es): 979-446

**Lembaga Demografi Fakultas Ekonomi
  Universitas Indonesia**
Jl Salemba Raya 4, Jakarta Pusat, 10430
*Tel:* (021) 3900703; (021) 336434; (021) 336539
  *Fax:* (021) 3102457
*E-mail:* demofeui@indo.net.id *Cable:* FEKODEM
*Key Personnel*
Dir: Dr Haidy A Pasay
Founded: 1964
Subjects: Child Care & Development, Developing
  Countries, Economics, Education, Environmen-
  tal Studies, Ethnicity, Health, Nutrition, Labor,
  Industrial Relations, Library & Information
  Sciences, Social Sciences, Sociology, Women's
  Studies
ISBN Prefix(es): 979-525
*Parent Company:* Faculty of Economics Univer-
  sity of Indonesia

**Madju FA**
Jl Sisingamangaraja 25, Medan 20215
*Tel:* (061) 711990; (061) 710430 *Fax:* (061)
  717753
ISBN Prefix(es): 979-8005

**Marfiah, CV**
Jln Kalibutuh No 131, Surabaya
*Tel:* (031) 46023
*Key Personnel*
Man Dir: Ellyati Wahyuni

**Megapoin**, *imprint of* Kesaint Blanc

**Mizan+**
Jl Yodkali 16, Bekamin Suci, Bandung 40124
*Tel:* (022) 7200931
*E-mail:* info@mizan.com
*Web Site:* www.mizan.com
*Key Personnel*
President & Dir: Haidar Bagir
Man Dir: Putut Widjanarko *E-mail:* pututw@
  mizan.com
Founded: 1983
Membership(s): Association of Indonesian Pub-
  lishers (IKAPI).
Subjects: Asian Studies, Religion - Islamic
ISBN Prefix(es): 979-433
Imprints: Al-Bayan; ILMU-ILMU Islam; Mizan:
  Khazanah; Mizan Pustaka: Kronik Indonesia
  Baru; Mizan Sobat Bocah Muslim; Mizan Sa-
  habat Remaja Muslim

*Branch Office(s)*
Jl Duren Tiga Selatan WII 8A, Jakarta
*Bookshop(s):* (Many throughout Indonesia, Singa-
  pore, Malaysia & Brunei)

**Mizan: Khazanah**, *imprint of* Mizan

**Mizan Pustaka: Kronik Indonesia Baru**,
  *imprint of* Mizan

**Mizan Sahabat Remaja Muslim**, *imprint of*
  Mizan

**Mizan Sobat Bocah Muslim**, *imprint of* Mizan

**Mutiara Sumber Widya PT+**
Gedurg Maya Indah, Jakarta Pusat 10440
*Tel:* (021) 3909864; (021) 3909261; (021)
  3909247 *Fax:* (021) 3160313
*Telex:* 46709 Mutiara Ia
*Key Personnel*
Chief Executive: H Firdaus Oemar
Dir: Fahmi Umar
Subjects: Economics, Education, Mathematics,
  Music, Dance, Physics, Religion - Other
ISBN Prefix(es): 979-8011; 979-9331
*Associate Companies:* CV Angkasa (Publishers)
Subsidiaries: CV Mutiara Bhakti; Mutiara Per-
  mata Widya

**New Aqua Press**
Kawasan Indrustri Pulo Gadung, Jl Rawagela II/4,
  Jakarta Timur 13012
*Tel:* (021) 4897566
ISBN Prefix(es): 979-441

**Nusa Indah+**
Jl El Tari, Ende Flores-NTT 86318
*Tel:* (0381) 21502 *Fax:* (0381) 21645; (0381)
  22373 *Cable:* NUSAINDAHENDE
*Key Personnel*
Dir: Henri Daros *Tel:* (0381) 21081
Vice Dir & Sales Manager: Frans Ndoi
Man Editor: Lucas Lege
Production, Design: Eman Diaz
Library & Documents: Rofinus Jamin
Founded: 1970
Membership(s): Association of Indonesian Pub-
  lishers (IKAPI); Indonesian Christian Publish-
  ers' Association (PLKI).
Subjects: Biblical Studies, Human Relations, Lan-
  guage Arts, Linguistics, Literature, Literary
  Criticism, Essays, Poetry, Religion - Catholic,
  Theology
ISBN Prefix(es): 979-429
Total Titles: 350 Print
*Parent Company:* PT ANI
Imprints: Dioma, Kanisius, Obor (East Indonesia)
*Branch Office(s)*
Perwakilan Nusa Indah, Jln Matraman Raya 125,
  Jakarta *Tel:* (021) 8582447 *Fax:* (021) 8502403
Gudang Buku Nusa Indah, Jln Polisi Istimewa 9,
  Surabaya 60265 *Tel:* (031) 5617746 *Fax:* (031)
  5684307
Distributed by Dioma (East Java); Gramedia (all
  Gramedia bookshops in Jakarta, Surabaya,
  Kalimantan, Timor Timur, etc.); Kanisius (Cen-
  tral Java); Obor (Jakarta)
*Showroom(s):* Jln Matraman Raya 125, Jakarta
  13012; Jln Polisi Istimewa 9, Surabaya 60265
*Book Club(s):* Kanisius Reading Community

**Oriental**, *imprint of* Kesaint Blanc

**PATCO**
Jln Sawahan Sarimulyo 14, Surabaya
*Tel:* (031) 310021
*Key Personnel*
Man Dir: Adolf Pattyranie
Founded: 1972

Subjects: Regional Interests
*Bookshop(s):* TB Puncak Agung, Pasar Tambahrejo Blok A 21A, Jl Kapas Krampung, Surabaya

**Pelita Masa PT**
Jl Lodaya No 25, Bandung 40262
*Tel:* (022) 50823
*Key Personnel*
Man Dir: Rochdi Partamatmadja

**Pembimbing Masa PT**
Pusat Perdagangan Senen, Blok 1, Lantai IV No 2, Jakarta, Pusat
Mailing Address: PO Box 3281, Jakarta Pusat
*Tel:* (021) 367645; (021) 366042
*Key Personnel*
Man Dir: Setia Dharma Majiid
ISBN Prefix(es): 979-8023
*Bookshop(s):* Pembimbing Masa PT

**Penerbit Erlangga**
Jl H Baping Raya No 100, Ciracas, Jakarta 13740
*Tel:* (021) 8717006 *Fax:* (021) 8717011
*E-mail:* erlprom@rad.net.id
*Web Site:* www.erlangga.com
*Key Personnel*
Dir: Gunawan Hutauruk
ISBN Prefix(es): 979-411

**PT Bhakti Baru**
Jln Jend Akhmad Yani 15, Ujung Pandang
*Tel:* (0411) 5192 *Fax:* (0411) 7156
*Telex:* 7156 Hakalla UP *Cable:* Bhakti Baru
*Key Personnel*
Man Dir: Dr H M Jusuf Kalla
Publicity Manager: Alwi Hamu
Founded: 1972
Subjects: Religion - Other
*Branch Office(s)*
Jl Lembang 9, Jakarta, India *Tel:* (021) 336364

**PT Pradnya Paramita**
Jl Bunga No 8-8A, Jakarta 13140
*Tel:* (021) 8583369 *Fax:* (021) 8504944
  *Cable:* PRADNYA JKT
*Key Personnel*
President & Dir: Soenarto Sindopranoto
Production Dir: Dr Mimien Saleh
Sales Executive: J Josojuwono
Editorial: A F Julianto
Founded: 1973
ISBN Prefix(es): 979-408
*Bookshop(s):* (See under Major Booksellers)

**PT Pustaka LP3ES Indonesia**
Jl Letjen S Parman 81, Slipi, Jakarta Barat 11420
*Tel:* (021) 5674211; (021) 5667139; (021) 56967920 *Fax:* (021) 5683785
*Web Site:* www.lp3es.or.id
*Key Personnel*
Dir: Imam Ahmad
Man Dir: Sudar Dwi Atmanto
Founded: 1971
Membership(s): The Institute for Economics & Social Research, Education & Information.
Subjects: Science (General)
ISBN Prefix(es): 979-8015
*Parent Company:* LP3ES

**Pusat Penelitian Perkebunan Sumbawa+**
Palembang, 30001 Sumsel
Mailing Address: PO Box 1127, Palembang 30001
*Tel:* (0711) 312182; (0711) 361793 *Fax:* (0711) 361793
*Key Personnel*
Contact: Mr Anwar Chairil
ISBN Prefix(es): 979-529

**Pustaka Utama Grafiti, PT+**
Utan Kayu Utara, Jl Utan Kayu No 68, E, F, G, Jakarta Timur 13120
*Tel:* (021) 8567502 *Fax:* (021) 8582430
*Telex:* 62797 TEMPO IA
*Key Personnel*
Man Dir: Zulkifly Lubis
Production Manager: A Rahman Tolleng
Commercial Manager: Yusril Djalinus
Founded: 1986
Membership(s): IKAPI.
Subjects: Anthropology, Art, Biography, Business, Economics, Government, Political Science, History, Humor, Literature, Literary Criticism, Essays, Philosophy, Religion - Other, Social Sciences, Sociology
ISBN Prefix(es): 979-444
*Parent Company:* Grafiti Pers
*Bookshop(s):* Ancol, Pasar Seni, Jakarta Utara; Slipi Jaya Plaza, Basement, Jl S Parman Kav 17-18, Jakarta 11410; Pertokoan Italiano, Jl Margonda Raya No 166, Depok; J1 Sumatera 31 Block G-H, Surabaya
*Warehouse:* Jl Cipinang Kebembem I No 3 A, Jakarta Timur

**Remaja Rosdakarya CV**
Jl Ciateul 34-36, Bandung
*Tel:* (022) 5200287
ISBN Prefix(es): 979-514; 979-425; 979-692

**Renaisans,** *imprint of* Kesaint Blanc

**Rosda Jaya Putra**
Jl Kramat Raya 5J, Jakarta Pusat 10450
*Tel:* (021) 3904984; (021) 3901692; (021) 3904985 *Fax:* (021) 3901703
*Key Personnel*
Man Dir: H Rozali Usman
ISBN Prefix(es): 979-426

**Sastra Hudaya PT**
Jl Proklamasi 61, Jakarta Pusat
*Tel:* (021) 3904223
*Key Personnel*
Man Dir: Doddy Yudhista
ISBN Prefix(es): 979-8016

**Universitas Sebelas Maret**
Jl Ir Sutami No 36A, Surakarta
*Tel:* (0271) 646994; (0271) 646761; (0271) 646624 *Fax:* (0271) 46655
*E-mail:* due-uns@slo.mega.net.id; pptk-uns@slo.mega.net.id
*Web Site:* www.uns.ac.id
ISBN Prefix(es): 979-498
*Bookshop(s):* Toko Buku, Jln Ir Sutami 36A, Solo 57126

**Siemens-Penuntun Berencana,** *imprint of* Katalis PT Bina Mitra Plaosan

**Sumatera Utara University Press**
Jl Universitas 21A, Medan, Sumatera Utera 20155
Mailing Address: Sumatera Utara
*Tel:* (061) 811045 *Fax:* (061) 816264
*Telex:* 51753
*Key Personnel*
Chairman: Mukmin Saraan
ISBN Prefix(es): 979-458

**Tamtan Gabara,** *imprint of* Kesaint Blanc

**Tintamas Indonesia PT+**
Jl Kramat Raya No 60, Jakarta Pusat 10420
*Tel:* (021) 3107148; (021) 7393701 *Fax:* (021) 3911459; (021) 3107148
*Key Personnel*
Dir: Marhamah Djambek

Founded: 1947
Membership(s): IKAPI (Indonesian Publishers Association).
Subjects: Biography, History, Law, Philosophy, Religion - Other
ISBN Prefix(es): 979-590

**Usaha Baru CV**
Jln Apel Kedjoran 11/5, Surabaya
*Tel:* (031) 22128
*Key Personnel*
Man Dir: Imron Siregar

**Visipro,** *imprint of* Kesaint Blanc

**Widjaya Penerbit**
Jl Pecenongan No 48-C, Jakarta Pusat
*Tel:* (021) 3813446
*Branch Office(s)*
Jl Dalem Kaum 86, Bandung

**CV Yasaguna**
Jl Minangkabau, 44, Jakarta Selatan
*Tel:* (021) 8290422
*Key Personnel*
Manager: Hilman Madewa
Subjects: Agriculture
ISBN Prefix(es): 979-443

**Yayasan Jaya Baya**
Jln Penghela 2, Surabaya
Mailing Address: Kotakpos 250, Surabaya
*Tel:* (031) 41169

**Yayasan Kawanku**
Jln Setiabudi Raya, Gg Sumbangsih 11/3A, Jakarta
*Tel:* (021) 583100

**Yayasan Lontar** (Lontar Foundation)+
Jl Danau Laut Tawar No 53, Pejombongan, Jakarta 10210
*Tel:* (021) 574-6880 *Fax:* (021) 572-0353
*E-mail:* lontar@attglobal.net
*Web Site:* www.lontar.org
*Key Personnel*
Chairperson: Adila Suwarmo
Vice Chairperson: Indra Harbani
Secretary: Miriam Widodo
Treasurer: Fikri Jufri
Editor-in-Chief: John H McGlynn
Founded: 1987
Subjects: Art, Ethnicity, Literature, Literary Criticism, Essays
ISBN Prefix(es): 979-8083

**Yayasan Obor Indonesia+**
Jl Plaju, No 10, Jakarta Pusat 10230
*Tel:* (021) 3920114; (021) 31926978 *Fax:* (021) 31924488
*E-mail:* obor@ub.net.id
*Web Site:* www.obor.or.id
*Key Personnel*
Chairman & International Rights: Mochtar Lubis
General Manager: Kartini Nurdin
Founded: 1978
Subjects: Advertising, Asian Studies, Business, Child Care & Development, Developing Countries, Earth Sciences, Economics, Education, Environmental Studies, Government, Political Science, History, Literature, Literary Criticism, Essays, Military Science, Natural History, Nonfiction (General), Philosophy, Publishing & Book Trade Reference, Science (General), Social Sciences, Sociology, Technology, Global Issues, Human Rights
ISBN Prefix(es): 979-461
*U.S. Office(s):* Obor Inc, 501 Cherry St, Philadelphia, PA 19102, United States

# Islamic Republic of Iran

## General Information

*Capital:* Tehran
*Language:* Persian (Farsi), Turkish and Armenian in Northwest, Arabic in Southwest, Kurdish in Kurdistan (English or French also)
*Religion:* Islamic (Shi'a sect and some Sunni sect)
*Population:* 61.2 million
*Bank Hours:* Generally Winter: 0800-1300 Saturday-Thursday; 1600-1800 Saturday-Wednesday; Summer: 0730-1300, 1700-1900 Saturday-Wednesday, 0730-1130 Thursday
*Shop Hours:* Generally Winter: 0800-2000 Saturday-Thursday; 0800-1200 Friday; Summer: 0800-1300, 1700-2100 Saturday-Thursday, 0800-1200 Friday
*Currency:* 100 dinars = 1 Iranian rial
*Export/Import Information:* No tariff on books and advertising but catalogs subject to VAT. Import licenses required. Publications offending public order, official religion or morality prohibited. Exchange controls, with new regulations issued each March.
*Copyright:* No copyright conventions signed

**Amir Kabir Book Publishing & Distribution Co**
PO Box 1136-54191, Tehran
*Tel:* (021) 3933996; (021) 3933997; (021) 3900751-2; (021) 3112118 *Fax:* (021) 3903747
*Telex:* 212421 NJR IR
*Key Personnel*
Dir: H Anwary
Production: Masdjed-Jamee
Publicity: A Poormomtaz
Sales: Emany
Founded: 1948
ISBN Prefix(es): 964-00
*Parent Company:* Sasman-e Tablighat-e Eslami
Subsidiaries: Shokufeh Books

**Scientific and Cultural Publications**
Ministry of Culture & Higher Education, 64 St, Sayyed Jamal-E-Din Asad Abadi Ave, Tehran
*Tel:* (021) 685475; (021) 686278
Founded: 1953
Subjects: History, Philosophy, Religion - Other, Science (General)
*Bookshop(s):* Enghelab St, Tehran

**University of Tehran Publications & Printing Organization**
Univ of Tehran, Control Administration, Enghelab Ave & 16 Azar St, Tehran
*Tel:* (021) 6462699; (021) 6419831; (021) 6405047 *Fax:* (021) 6409348
*Web Site:* www.ut.ac.ir
*Key Personnel*
Man Dir: Dr A Rastgou
Sales & Publicity: Mr R Farahani
Rights & Permissions: J Qajarieh
Founded: 1944
*Bookshop(s):* Enqelab Ave, Tehran

# Iraq

## General Information

*Capital:* Baghdad
*Language:* Arabic (official), and some Kurdish (English is the principal foreign language in Baghdad)
*Religion:* Islamic (predominantly the Shiite sect)
*Population:* 18.4 million
*Bank Hours:* Winter: 0900-1300 Saturday-Wednesday; 0900-1200 Thursday; Summer: 0800-1200 Saturday-Wednesday, 0800-1100 Thursday
*Shop Hours:* Winter: 0830-1430, 1700-1900 Saturday-Wednesday, 0830-1330 Thursday; Summer: 0800-1400, 1700-1900 Saturday-Wednesday, 0800-1300 Thursday
*Currency:* 1,000 fils = 20 dirhams = 1 Iraqi dinar
*Export/Import Information:* No tariffs on books & advertising. Import licenses required. Exchange control, influenced by annual foreign exchange budget. Importation by state trading company or established importer. The state trading company is the National House for Publishing, Distributing & Advertising, Aljamhuria St, 624, Baghdad.
*Copyright:* No copyright conventions signed

**National House for Publishing, Distributing & Advertising**
Al-Jumhuriyah St, Baghdad
Mailing Address: PO Box 624, Baghdad
*Tel:* (01) 4251846
*Telex:* 2392 *Cable:* Donta
Founded: 1972
Firm is attached to the Ministry of Information & is the sole importer & distributor of newspapers, magazines, periodicals & books.
Subjects: Agriculture, Business, Economics, Education, Government, Political Science, Science (General), Social Sciences, Sociology

# Ireland

## General Information

*Capital:* Dublin
*Language:* English & Irish (Gaelic)
*Religion:* Predominately Roman Catholic, some Church of Ireland
*Population:* 3.8 million
*Bank Hours:* 1000-1230, 1330-1500 Monday-Friday. Open until 1700 one night a week
*Shop Hours:* 0900 or 0930-1730 Monday-Saturday
*Currency:* 100 Eurocents = 1 Euro; 0.787564 Irish pounds = 1 Euro
*Export/Import Information:* Member of the European Community. BH & VMcK No tariff on books except on prayer & similar books from non-UK & children's picture books from non-EC. Pamphlets dutied from non-EEC. VAT is charged. No import licenses. Exchange controls.
*Copyright:* UCC, Berne (see Copyright Conventions, pg xi)

**A & A Farmar+**
Beech House, 78 Ranelagh Village, Dublin 6
*Tel:* (01) 4963625 *Fax:* (01) 4970107
*E-mail:* afarmar@iol.ie
*Web Site:* www.farmarbooks.com
*Key Personnel*
International Rights & Dir: Anna Farmar
Founded: 1992

Specializes in general literature, food & wine, business & social history.
Subjects: Business, Child Care & Development, Cookery, Literature, Literary Criticism, Essays, Wine & Spirits
ISBN Prefix(es): 1-899047
Number of titles published annually: 12 Print
Total Titles: 50 Print
*U.S. Office(s):* Irish Books & Media Inc, 1433 Franklin Ave East, Minneapolis, MN 55404-2135, United States
*Orders to:* Columba Mercier Distribution Ltd, 55A Spruce Ave, Stillorgan Industrial Park, Blackrock, Dublin

**AIS,** see Bord na Gaeilge

**An Gum+**
44 Sraid Ui Chonaill Uacht, Baile Atha Cliath, Dublin 1
*Tel:* (01) 8734700 *Fax:* (01) 8731104
*E-mail:* gum@educ.irlgov.ie
*Telex:* 31136
*Key Personnel*
Editorial: Maire Nic Mhaolain
Production: John Dixon
Publicity: Seosamh O'Murchu
Founded: 1926
Subjects: Art, Cookery, Education, Geography, Geology, Mathematics, Science (General)
ISBN Prefix(es): 1-85791
*Parent Company:* The Department of Education, Dublin 1
*Imprints:* Oifig an tSolathair
*Bookshop(s):* Oifig Dhiolta Foilseachain Rialtais, Sr Theach Laighean, Dublin 2
*Warehouse:* Bishop S, Dublin 8
*Orders to:* An Ais, 31 Sr na bhFinini, Dublin 2

**Atrium,** *imprint of* Cork University Press

**Attic Press,** *imprint of* Cork University Press

**Attic Press+**
Imprint of Cork University Press (CUP)
c/o Cork University Press, Youngline Industrial Estate, Pouladuff Rd, Cork
*Tel:* (021) 490 2980 *Fax:* (021) 431 5329
*E-mail:* corkuniversitypress@ucc.ie
*Web Site:* www.corkuniversitypress.com
*Key Personnel*
Editorial Manager: Tom Dunne *E-mail:* t.dunne@ucc.ie
Founded: 1984
Subjects: Biography, Cookery, Government, Political Science, Health, Nutrition, History, Humor, Literature, Literary Criticism, Essays, Social Sciences, Sociology, Women's Studies
ISBN Prefix(es): 0-946211; 1-85594
*Orders to:* Dufour Editions Inc, Buyers Rd, PO Box 7, Chester Springs, PA 19425-0007, United States *Tel:* 610-458-5005 *Fax:* 610-458-7103 *Web Site:* www.dufoureditions.com
Gill & Macmillan, Goldenbridge Hume Ave, Park West, Dublin 12
Marston Book Services Ltd, PO Box 269, Abingdon OX14 4YN, United Kingdom *Tel:* (01235) 465500 *Fax:* (01235) 465555 *E-mail:* trade.orders@marston.co.uk

**Avoca Publications+**
Lonsdale Avoca Ave, Blackrock, Dublin
*Tel:* (01) 889218
Founded: 1983
Subjects: Aeronautics, Aviation
ISBN Prefix(es): 0-9509206

**Ballinakella Paperbacks,** *imprint of* Ballinakella Press

**Ballinakella Press+**
Whitegate, Clare
*Tel:* (061) 927030 *Fax:* (061) 927418
*E-mail:* info@ballinakella.com
*Key Personnel*
President: Dr Hugh W L Weir
Vice President: Mrs Hugh W L Weir
Founded: 1984
Specialize in Irish historical, topographical, genealogical & biographical books.
Subjects: Architecture & Interior Design, Biography, Genealogy, Geography, Geology, History, Regional Interests, Travel
ISBN Prefix(es): 0-946538
Number of titles published annually: 2 Print
Total Titles: 32 Print
*Parent Company:* Weir Publishing
Imprints: Ballinakella Paperbacks; Bell'acards; Weir's Guides
Subsidiaries: Bell'acards


**Beehive Books**, *imprint of* Veritas Co Ltd


**Bell'acards**, *imprint of* Ballinakella Press


**Blackwater Press**, *imprint of* Folens Publishers


**Blue Flag**, *imprint of* The O'Brien Press Ltd


**Bord na Gaeilge**
Formerly AIS
J H Newman Bldg, Room D213, University College Dublin, Belfield
*Tel:* (01) 716 8208
*Web Site:* www.ucd.ie/bnag
*Key Personnel*
Chairman: Prof Enda Hession
Vice Chairman: Dr Micheal O Dochartaigh
Also acts as distributor for all Irish language publications.
ISBN Prefix(es): 0-946339
*Parent Company:* Bord Na Gaeilge


**Brandon**, *imprint of* Mount Eagle Publications Ltd


**Brandon Book Publishers Ltd+**
Cooleen, Dingle, Co Kerry
*Tel:* (066) 9151463 *Fax:* (066) 9151234
*Web Site:* www.brandonbooks.com
*Key Personnel*
Man Dir, Editorial: Steve MacDonogh
Founded: 1982
Subjects: Biography, Fiction, Literature, Literary Criticism, Essays, Nonfiction (General)
ISBN Prefix(es): 0-86322
*Parent Company:* Mount Eagle Publications Ltd
*Orders to:* Gill & Macmillan Distribution, Goldenbridge, Inchicore, Dublin 8


**Edmund Burke Publisher+**
Division of De Burca Rare Books
27 Priory Dr, Blackrock, County Dublin
Mailing Address: 51 A Dawson St, Dublin 2
*Tel:* (01) 2882159; (01) 6719777 *Fax:* (01) 2834080
*E-mail:* deburca@indigo.ie
*Web Site:* www.deburcararebooks.com
*Key Personnel*
Contact: Eamonn de Burca; Regina McAuley
Founded: 1980
Historical, topographical & genealogical works on Ireland.
Subjects: Biography, History, Academic, Bibliography
ISBN Prefix(es): 0-946130


**Campus**, *imprint of* Campus Publishing Ltd


**Campus Publishing Ltd+**
26 Tirellan Heights, Galway City
*Tel:* (091) 524662; (091) 767408 *Fax:* (091) 527505
*Key Personnel*
Publisher: Kevin T Brophy
Founded: 1990
Subjects: Drama, Theater, Education, Literature, Literary Criticism, Essays, Religion - Catholic, Religion - Protestant, Religion - Other, Self-Help, Social Sciences, Sociology, Playscripts
ISBN Prefix(es): 1-873223
Imprints: Campus; Playscripts


**Careers & Educational Publishers Ltd+**
Lower James St, Claremorris, County Mayo
*Tel:* (094) 71093
*Key Personnel*
Man Dir, Editorial, Publicity, Rights & Permissions: Eamonn Patrick O'Boyle
Sales: Christina O'Boyle
Production: William J O'Keeffe
Founded: 1976
Subjects: Career Development, Cookery, Crafts, Games, Hobbies, Education
ISBN Prefix(es): 0-906121
Imprints: Heritage Books
*Bookshop(s):* Eamonn P O'Boyle's Book Sales, Lower James St, Claremorris, County Mayo; Kilcolman Press Bookshop, Convent Rd, Claremorris, County Mayo


**Cathedral Books Ltd**
4 Sackville Pl, Dublin 1
*Tel:* (01) 8787372 *Fax:* (01) 8787704
*E-mail:* cathedra@indigo.ie
Subjects: Biblical Studies, Philosophy, Psychology, Psychiatry, Religion - Catholic, Self-Help, Theology, Women's Studies
ISBN Prefix(es): 0-9517132; 1-871337


**Children's Poolbeg**, *imprint of* Poolbeg Press Ltd


**The Children's Press+**
45 Palmerston Rd, Dublin 6
*Tel:* (01) 497-3628 *Fax:* (01) 496-8263
*E-mail:* cle@iol.ie
*Web Site:* www.irelandseye.com *Cable:* CHILDREN'S PRESS DUBLIN
*Key Personnel*
Publisher: John Murphy
Founded: 1981
Subjects: Biography, Fiction, History
ISBN Prefix(es): 0-900068; 0-947962; 1-901737
*Parent Company:* Anvil Books Lts


**Clo Iar-Chonnachta Teo+**
Indreabhan, Conamara, Galway, County Galway
*Tel:* (091) 593 307 *Fax:* (091) 593 362
*E-mail:* cic@iol.ie
*Web Site:* www.cic.ie
*Key Personnel*
Man Dir: Michael O'Conghaile
General Manager: Deirdre Thuathail
Marketing Executive: Caitriona Bhaoill
Founded: 1985
Most publications are in the Irish language.
Subjects: Drama, Theater, Fiction, History, Music, Dance, Poetry, Regional Interests
ISBN Prefix(es): 1-874700; 1-900693; 1-902420
Number of titles published annually: 15 Print; 2 Audio
Total Titles: 300 Print; 20 Audio
Distributed by Dufour Editions
Foreign Rep(s): Dufour Editions (Canada, US)
Foreign Rights: AIS (Iceland); Maggie Doyle (France); Harry Smith (US); Hansevik Tonnheiu (Sweden)


**Clodhanna Teoranta**
Chonradh na Gaeilge, 6 Sraid Fhearchair, Dublin 2
*Key Personnel*
Publicity Manager: Donnchadh O Laodha
ISBN Prefix(es): 0-905027; 0-9501264


**The Collins Press+**
West Link Park, Doughcloyne, Wilton, Cork
*Tel:* (021) 4347717 *Fax:* (021) 4347720
*E-mail:* enquiries@collinspress.le
*Web Site:* www.collinspress.com
*Key Personnel*
Contact: Con Collins
Founded: 1990
Independent Book Publisher.
Membership(s): Irish Publishers Association (CLE).
Subjects: Archaeology, Biography, History, Human Relations, Natural History, Photography, Drama, Mind, Body & Spirit
ISBN Prefix(es): 0-9516036; 1-895256; 1-903464
Number of titles published annually: 17 Print
Total Titles: 91 Print
Distributed by Columbia Mercier Distribution (Ireland & Northern Ireland); Drake International Services (Britain, Common Wealth & Europe); Dufour Editions (US); Irish Books & Media (US)
Foreign Rep(s): Brookside Publishing Services (Ireland, Northern Ireland)
Foreign Rights: AMV Agencia Literaria SL; Gundhild Lenz-Mulligan


**The Columba Press+**
Imprint of The Columba Bookservice Ltd
55A Spruce Ave, Stillorgan Industrial Park, Blackrock, Dublin
*Tel:* (01) 2942556 *Fax:* (01) 2942564
*E-mail:* info@columba.ie
*Web Site:* www.columba.ie
*Key Personnel*
Publisher: Sean O'Boyle *E-mail:* sean@columba.ie
Sales Dir: Cecilia West *E-mail:* west@columba.ie
Public Relations & Marketing Manager: Brian Lynch *E-mail:* brian@columba.ie
Founded: 1985
Membership(s): Cle-The Irish Book Publishers' Association.
Subjects: Art, History, Religion - Catholic, Religion - Protestant, Self-Help, Theology
ISBN Prefix(es): 0-948183; 1-85607
Total Titles: 250 Print
Imprints: Currach Press; Gartan, Preas Cholmcille


**Cork University Press+**
Youngline Industrial Estate, Pouladuff Rd, Cork
*Tel:* (021) 490 2980 *Fax:* (021) 431 5329
*E-mail:* corkuniversitypress@ucc.ie
*Web Site:* www.corkuniversitypress.com
*Key Personnel*
Publications Dir: Mike Collins *E-mail:* mike.collins@ucc.ie
Editorial Manager: Tom Dunne *E-mail:* t.dunne@ucc.ie
Founded: 1925
Specialize in Irish studies, history, literature, cultural studies & politics.
Membership(s): Cle-The Irish Publishers' Association.
Subjects: Archaeology, Geography, Geology, History, Social Sciences, Sociology, Women's Studies
ISBN Prefix(es): 0-902561; 1-85918; 0-9502440
Number of titles published annually: 10 Print
Total Titles: 150 Print
Imprints: Atrium; Attic Press
*U.S. Office(s):* Stylus Publishing LLC, 22883 Quicksilver Drive, Sterling, VA 20166-2012, United States, Contact: John von Knorring *Fax:* 703-661-1501 *E-mail:* stylusmail@

presswarehouse.com *Web Site:* www.styluspub.
com
Foreign Rep(s): Peter Prout (Portugal, Spain);
Stylus (US)

**Currach Press**, *imprint of* The Columba Press

**Dee-Jay Publications+**
3 Meadows Lane, Arklow, County Wicklow
*Tel:* (0402) 39125 *Fax:* (0402) 39064
*Key Personnel*
Contact: Jim Rees *E-mail:* jrees@eircom.net
Founded: 1992
Subjects: Biography, Genealogy, History, Mar-
itime, Nonfiction (General), Travel
ISBN Prefix(es): 0-9519239
*U.S. Office(s):* Irish Books & Media Inc, 1433-E
Franklin Ave, Minneapolis, MN 55404-2135,
United States
Distributor for Arklow Enterprise Centre

**Dominican Publications**
42 Parnell Sq, Dublin 1
*Tel:* (01) 872-1611; (01) 873-1355 *Fax:* (01) 873-
1760
*E-mail:* sales@dominicanpublications.com
*Web Site:* www.dominicanpublications.com
*Key Personnel*
Chief Executive, Editorial, Sales: Austin Flannery
Advertising, Production: Bernard Treacy
Founded: 1897
Subjects: Biography, History, Religion - Catholic,
Theology, Books & periodicals on theology
ISBN Prefix(es): 0-9504797; 0-907271; 1-871552
Total Titles: 20 Print; 2 CD-ROM
Distributed by Columba
*Book Club(s):* Doctrine & Life Book Club; Re-
ligious Life Review Book Club; Scripture in
Church Book Club

**Dublin Institute for Advanced Studies**
10 Burlington Rd, Dublin 4
*Tel:* (01) 6140100 *Fax:* (01) 6680561
*Web Site:* www.dias.ie
*Telex:* 31687 Dias Ei
*Key Personnel*
Registrar: John Duggan
Founded: 1940
Specialize in research & advanced study in Celtic
studies & physics.
Subjects: Ethnicity, Physics
ISBN Prefix(es): 0-901282; 1-85500

**Eason & Son Ltd**
66 Middle Abbey St, Dublin 1
*Tel:* (01) 873 3811 *Fax:* (01) 873 3545
*E-mail:* info@eason.ie
*Web Site:* www.eason.ie
*Telex:* 32566
*Key Personnel*
Man Dir: Gordon Bolton
Editorial, Sales, Production, Publicity, Rights &
Permissions: Tom Owens
Founded: 1886
Subjects: Regional Interests
ISBN Prefix(es): 0-900346; 1-873430
Imprints: Irish Heritage Series
Subsidiaries: Eason & Son (NI) Ltd; Eason Ad-
vertising
*Warehouse:* Brickfield Dr, Crumlin, Dublin 12

**The Economic & Social Research Institute**
4 Burlington Rd, Dublin 4
*Tel:* (01) 6671525 *Fax:* (01) 6686231
*E-mail:* admin@esri.ie
*Web Site:* www.esri.ie
*Key Personnel*
Dir: Prof Brendan J Whelan *E-mail:* brendan.
whelan@esri.ie
Assistant Dir, Secretary, Sales & Publicity:
Gillian Davidson *E-mail:* admin@esri.ie

Founded: 1960
Subjects: Economics, Education, Environmental
Studies, Finance, Health, Nutrition, Social Sci-
ences, Sociology
ISBN Prefix(es): 0-7070; 0-901809
Total Titles: 300 Print

**The Educational Company of Ireland**
Ballymount Rd, Walkinstown, Dublin 12
*Tel:* (01) 4500611 *Fax:* (01) 4500993
*E-mail:* info@edco.ie
*Web Site:* www.edco.ie
*Key Personnel*
Chief Executive: Frank Maguire
Executive Dir Sales & Marketing: Mr Oisin
Mulcahy
Executive Dir: R McLoughlin
Founded: 1910
Firm is a trading unit of Smurfit Ireland Ltd.
Subjects: Business, Career Development, Com-
puter Science, Ethnicity, Geography, Geology,
History, Mathematics, Religion - Other, Science
(General)
ISBN Prefix(es): 0-901802; 0-904916; 0-86167
*Branch Office(s)*
20-1 Talbot St, Dublin 1

**Emerald Publications+**
The Studio, 22 Summerstown Grove, Wilton Cork
*Tel:* (021) 962853 *Fax:* (021) 310983
*E-mail:* alongk@iol.ie
*Key Personnel*
Contact: Denis Linehan
Founded: 1980
Also acts as legal consultant.
Subjects: Criminology, Government, Political Sci-
ence, Health, Nutrition, Law, Theology
ISBN Prefix(es): 0-9525813

**Environmental Research Unit**
St Martin's House, Waterloo Rd, Dublin 4
*Tel:* (01) 660 25 11 *Fax:* (01) 668 00 09
*Telex:* 30846 *Cable:* Foras Dublin
*Key Personnel*
Chief Executive Officer: L M McCumiskey
Information & Training: S Smyth
Founded: 1964
National Institute for Physical Planning & Con-
struction Research.
Subjects: Environmental Studies
ISBN Prefix(es): 0-906120; 0-9500200; 0-
9501356; 1-85053; 0-900115

**Estragon Press Ltd+**
Durrus, County Cork 7
*Tel:* (027) 61186 *Fax:* (027) 61186
*E-mail:* estragon@iol.ie
*Key Personnel*
Dir, Publisher, Author: John McKenna; Sally
McKenna
Founded: 1991
Subjects: Cookery, Travel, Wine & Spirits
ISBN Prefix(es): 1-874076

**European Foundation for the Improvement of
Living & Working Conditions**
Wyattville Rd, Loughlinstown, Dublin
*Tel:* (01) 2043100 *Fax:* (01) 2826456
*E-mail:* postmaster@eurofound.eu.int
*Web Site:* www.eurofound.ie
*Key Personnel*
Press Officer: Mans Martensson
Founded: 1975
Subjects: EU Social Policy
ISBN Prefix(es): 92-897

**European Healthcare Management Association**
Vergemount Hall, Clonskeagh, Dublin 6
*Tel:* (01) 283 9299 *Fax:* (01) 283 8653
*E-mail:* office@ehma.org

*Web Site:* www.ehma.org
ISBN Prefix(es): 0-907727

**Fact Pack Ireland Guides**, *imprint of* Morrigan
Book Co

**C J Fallon**
Lucan Rd, Palmerston, Dublin 20
*E-mail:* sales@cjfallon.ie
*Web Site:* www.cjfallon.ie
*Key Personnel*
Man Dir: H McNicholas
Editorial: N White
Secretary: P Tolan
Founded: 1927
ISBN Prefix(es): 0-7144

**Fitzwilliam Publishing Co Ltd+**
1488 Assumpta Villas, Kildare
*Tel:* (01) 614575 *Fax:* (01) 614575
*Key Personnel*
Man Dir: Kevin McCaffrey
Marketing: Tom Madden
Subjects: Education, Ethnicity
ISBN Prefix(es): 1-871423

**Flyers**, *imprint of* The O'Brien Press Ltd

**Flyleaf Press+**
4 Spencer Villas, Glenageary, County Dublin
*Tel:* (01) 2845906 *Fax:* (01) 2831693
*E-mail:* flyleaf@indigo.ie
*Web Site:* www.flyleaf.ie
*Key Personnel*
Man Editor: James Ryan *E-mail:* jim.ryan@circa.
ie
Founded: 1982
Membership(s): Cle - Irish Book Publishers Asso-
ciation.
Subjects: Genealogy, Natural History, Family His-
tory
ISBN Prefix(es): 0-9508466; 0-9539974
Number of titles published annually: 2 Print
Total Titles: 16 Print
Distributed by Irish Books & Media (USA)

**Folens Publishers+**
Hibernian Industrial Estate, Greenhills Rd, Tal-
laght, Dublin 24
*Tel:* (01) 4137200 *Fax:* (01) 4137280
*E-mail:* info@folens.ie
*Web Site:* www.folens.ie
*Key Personnel*
Man Dir: John O'Connor *E-mail:* john.
o'connor@folens.ie
Financial Controller: Aoife Geraghty
Primary Publisher: Deirdre Whelan
Secondary Publisher: Anna O'Donovan
Founded: 1957
Subjects: Education
ISBN Prefix(es): 0-86121; 0-902592; 1-84131
*Associate Companies:* Folens Limited, United
Kingdom; JUKA-91 Spzoo, Poland
Imprints: Blackwater Press

**Four Courts Press Ltd+**
7 Malpas St, Dublin 8
*Tel:* (01) 453-4668 *Fax:* (01) 453-4672
*E-mail:* info@four-courts-press.ie
*Web Site:* www.four-courts-press.ie
*Key Personnel*
Man Dir: Michael Adams
Dir: Martin Healy *E-mail:* martin.healy@four-
courts-press.ie
Founded: 1970
Subjects: Art, History, Law, Literature, Liter-
ary Criticism, Essays, Philosophy, Religion -
Catholic, Theology, Celtic & Medieval Studies
ISBN Prefix(es): 0-906127; 1-85182
Number of titles published annually: 50 Print
Total Titles: 400 Print
Imprints: Open Air

*Warehouse:* Gill & Macmillan Book Distributors, Hume Ave, Park West, Dublin 12
*Distribution Center:* ISBS, 920 NE 58th Ave, Suite 300, Portland, OR 97213, United States (North America)
*Orders to:* Gill & Macmillan Book Distributors, Hume Ave, Park West, Dublin 12

**The Gallery Press**
Loughcrew, Oldcastle, Co Meath
*Tel:* (049) 8541779 *Fax:* (049) 8541779
*E-mail:* gallery@indigo.ie
*Web Site:* www.gallerypress.com
*Key Personnel*
Chief Executive, Editorial: Peter Fallon
Administration: Jean Barry
Administrator: Suella Wynne
Sales: Anne Duggan
Founded: 1970
Specialize in contemporary Irish literature by Irish authors only.
Subjects: Drama, Theater, Poetry
ISBN Prefix(es): 0-902996; 0-904011; 1-85235
Distributed by Dufour Editions Inc (USA)

**Gandon Editions+**
Oysterhaven, Kinsale, County Cork
*Tel:* (021) 770830 *Fax:* (021) 770755
*Key Personnel*
Editor & International Rights: John O'Regan
Founded: 1983
Specialize in art & architecture books.
Subjects: Archaeology, Architecture & Interior Design, Art, Environmental Studies, History, Nonfiction (General)
ISBN Prefix(es): 0-946641; 0-946846; 0-948037

**Gartan, Preas Cholmcille**, *imprint of* The Columba Press

**Gateway**, *imprint of* Gill & Macmillan Ltd

**Gill & Macmillan Ltd+**
10 Hume Ave, Park West, Dublin 12
*Tel:* (01) 500 9500 *Fax:* (01) 500 9599
*E-mail:* sales@gillmacmillan.ie
*Web Site:* www.gillmacmillan.ie
*Key Personnel*
Man Dir: Michael Gill *E-mail:* mhgill@gillmacmillan.ie
Publishing Dir, Educational Books: H J Mahony *E-mail:* hmahony@gillmacmillan.ie
Marketing & Sales Dir: P A Thew *E-mail:* pthew@gillmacmillan.ie
Finance Dir: M D O'Dwyer *E-mail:* dodwyer@gillmacmillan.ie
Production Dir: M O O'Keeffe *E-mail:* mokeefe@gillmacmillan.ie
Distribution Dir: J Manning *E-mail:* jmanning@gillmacmillan.ie
Publishing Dir, General Books: F M Tobin *E-mail:* ftobin@gillmacmillan.ie
Founded: 1968 (formerly Gill & Son)
*Representation Overseas*
Australia (Education titles): Macmillan Education Australia, Level 4 & 5, 627 Chapel St, Locked Bag 1400, South Yarra, Victoria 3141, Australia
Australia (General, Newleaf & Gateway titles): Banyan Tree Book Distributors, 13 College Rd, Kent Town, Adelaide, SA 5067, Australia
Canada (General, Newleaf & Gateway titles): Hushion House Publishing, 36 Northline Rd, Toronto, ON M4B 3E2, Canada
Europe (Switzerland, Germany, Austria, Belgium, Netherlands, France & Luxemburg): Michael Geoghegan, 14 Frognal Gardens, London NW3 6UX, UK
Scandinavia: Hanne Rotovnik, PO Box 5, Strandvejen 685B, 2930 Klampenbourg, Denmark

India, Pakistan, Sri Lanka (Newleaf & Gateway): Rajdeep Mukherjee, Pan Macmillan India, 5A/12 Ansari Rd, Daryaganj, New Delhi 110002, India
New Zealand: New Holland Publishers, Unit 1A, 218 Lake Rd, Northcote, Auckland, New Zealand
Singapore, Indonesia, Brunei & Malaysia: Pansing Distribution Sdn Bhd, 7 Tai Seng Dr, No 05-00, Nicosia Warehouse, Singapore 535217, Singapore
South Africa (Education Titles): Macmillan Boleswa, 2nd Floor, Old Trafford No 4, Isle of Houghton, Corner of Boundary & Carsed Gowrie Rds, Houghton, Johannesburg 2017, South Africa
South Africa (General, Newleaf & Gateway titles): Pan Macmillan South Africa, 2nd Floor, North Block, Hyde Park Corner, Corner Jan Smuts & First Rd, 2196 Hyde Park, Johannesburg, South Africa
UK (General, Newleaf & Gateway titles): Bounce Marketing, Islington Business Centre, 3-5 Islington High St, London N1 9LQ, UK
USA (General & Irish Interest titles): Irish Books & Media Inc, 1433 Franklin Ave East, Minneapolis, MN 55404-2102, USA
USA (Newleaf & Gateway titles): Hushion House Publishing, 36 Northline Rd, Toronto, ON M4B 3E2, Canada
West Indies: Macmillan Caribbean, Between Towns Rd, Oxford OX4 3PP, UK.
Subjects: Biography, Business, Child Care & Development, Cookery, Economics, Education, Fiction, Government, Political Science, Health, Nutrition, History, Law, Literature, Literary Criticism, Essays, Psychology, Psychiatry, Regional Interests, Self-Help, Travel
ISBN Prefix(es): 0-7171
Total Titles: 800 Print
*Associate Companies:* Macmillan Publishers Ltd, United Kingdom
Imprints: Gateway; Newleaf; Tivoli; Ri Ra
Foreign Rep(s): Hagenbach & Bender GmbH Literary and Media Agency

**The Goldsmith Press Ltd+**
Newbridge, Co Kildare
*Tel:* (045) 433613 *Fax:* (045) 434648
*E-mail:* de@iol.ie
*Key Personnel*
Publicity Manager: Peter Mulreid
Business Manager: V M Abbott
Company Secretary: Patricia McGuane
Founded: 1972
Publisher of Irish poetry & books of Irish interest.
Subjects: Art, Cookery, Fiction, History, Literature, Literary Criticism, Essays, Poetry, Regional Interests
ISBN Prefix(es): 0-904984; 1-870491
Number of titles published annually: 6 Print
Total Titles: 100 Print

**Government Publications Ireland**
Division of Government Supplies Agency
51 St Stephens Green, Dublin 2
*Tel:* (01) 6476000 *Fax:* (01) 6610747
*E-mail:* info@opw.ie
*Web Site:* www.opw.ie *Cable:* ENACTMENTS
*Key Personnel*
Contact: Fintan Butler *E-mail:* finton.butler@opw.ie
Founded: 1922
Heritage books, Irish language books, government reports, daily & senate debates.
Subjects: Government, Political Science
ISBN Prefix(es): 0-7076; 0-7557
*Ultimate Parent Company:* Office of Public Works

*Bookshop(s):* Government Publications Sale Office, Sun Alliance House, Molesworth St, Dublin 2
*Warehouse:* Mount Shannon Rd, Rialto Dublin 8

**The Hannon Press+**
5 Carriff Bridge, Ballivor, County Meath
*Tel:* (0405) 46089 *Fax:* (0405) 46089
*Key Personnel*
International Rights: Patricia Oliver *E-mail:* poliver@indigo.ie
Founded: 1995
Subjects: Biography, Business, How-to
ISBN Prefix(es): 0-9516472

**Harbinger House**, *imprint of* Roberts Rinehart Publishers

**Heritage Books**, *imprint of* Careers & Educational Publishers Ltd

**Heritage Maps & Guides**, *imprint of* Morrigan Book Co

**Herodotus Press+**
PO Box 4674, Dublin 8
*Tel:* (01) 4540120 *Fax:* (01) 4541134
Founded: 1995
Subjects: Archaeology, Genealogy, History, Maritime
ISBN Prefix(es): 0-9525414

**History House Publishing+**
5 Bindon St, Ennis, County Clare
Mailing Address: PO Box 50, Ennis, County Clare
*Tel:* (065) 24066 *Fax:* (065) 20388
*Key Personnel*
Man Dir: James Williams
Founded: 1983
Specialize in genealogy.
Subjects: Genealogy, History
ISBN Prefix(es): 0-86366

**IAP**, *imprint of* Irish Academic Press

**Institute of Public Administration**
Vergemount Hall, Clonskeagh, Dublin 6
*Tel:* (01) 240 3600 *Fax:* (01) 2698644
*E-mail:* information@ipa.ie
*Web Site:* www.ipa.ie
*Telex:* 90533 INPA EI *Cable:* ADMIN DUBLIN
*Key Personnel*
Publication Dir: Declan McDonagh
Production: Hannah Ryan
Sales: Eileen Kelly
Founded: 1957
Subjects: Economics, Education, Government, Political Science, Health, Nutrition, History, Law, Public Administration, Social Sciences, Sociology, International Affairs, Public Affairs
ISBN Prefix(es): 0-902173; 0-906980; 1-872002; 1-902448

**Irish Academic Press+**
44 Northumberland Rd, Ballsbridge, Dublin
*Tel:* (01) 668 8244 *Fax:* (01) 660 1610
*E-mail:* sales@iap.ie
*Web Site:* www.iap.ie
*Key Personnel*
Managing Editor: Linda Longmore
Founded: 1974
Subjects: Art, History, Literature, Literary Criticism, Essays, Military Science
ISBN Prefix(es): 0-7165
Imprints: IAP; Irish University Press

*U.S. Office(s):* ISBS, 5804 NE Hassalo St, Portland, OR 97213, United States *Tel:* 503-287-3093 *Fax:* 503-280-8832
*Orders to:* Gill & Macmillan Book Distributors, Goldenbridge, Inchicore, Dublin 8

**Irish Heritage Series,** *imprint of* Eason & Son Ltd

**Irish Management Institute+**
Sandyford Rd, Dublin 16
*Tel:* (01) 2078400 *Fax:* (01) 2955150
*E-mail:* 3025reception@imi.ie
*Web Site:* www.imi.ie
*Telex:* 30325
*Key Personnel*
Dir of Human Resources: Martin Farelly
Founded: 1952
The Institute is concerned with management, education, training & development. Publishing & bookselling are complementary activities.
Membership(s): Cle, The Irish Book Publishers' Association.
Subjects: Accounting, Business, Communications, Economics, Finance, Labor, Industrial Relations, Management
ISBN Prefix(es): 0-903352; 0-9500327; 1-902664

**Irish Texts Society (Cumann Na Scribeann nGaedhilge)**
31 Fenian St, Dublin 2
*Tel:* (01) 6616522 *Fax:* (01) 6612378
*E-mail:* shuttonseanfile@aol.com
*Key Personnel*
President: Prof Padraig ORiain
Honorary Treasurer: Michael J Burns
Founded: 1898
Specialize in educational charity publishing Irish language texts with translations, & a subsidiary series of supporting commentaries, studies, indexes, etc; organization of annual seminar in conjunction with the combined departments of Irish, University College, Cork, Ireland; publication of catalogue & newsletter.
Subjects: Anthropology, History, Poetry
ISBN Prefix(es): 1-870166
*Orders to:* Michael J Burns, Tibradden Rd, Rockbrook, Dublin 16 *E-mail:* burnsfam@iol.ie

**Irish Times Ltd+**
10-16 D'Olier St, Dublin 2
*Tel:* (01) 6758000 *Fax:* (01) 6773282
*E-mail:* lettersed@irish-times.ie
*Web Site:* www.ireland.com
*Telex:* 25167
*Key Personnel*
Prize Administrator: Gerard Cavanagh
Founded: 1859
Membership(s): Committee of Irish Book Publishers Association; Council Member Dublin City Center Business Association.
Subjects: Fiction, Genealogy, Literature, Literary Criticism, Essays
ISBN Prefix(es): 0-907011; 0-9503418
*Branch Office(s)*
Farum House, 10 Great Victoria St, Belfast BT27BE *Tel:* (01232) 04890-323324 *Fax:* (01232) 04890-231469
76 Shoe Lane, London EC4A 3JB, United Kingdom *Tel:* (020) 7353 8981 *Fax:* (020) 7353 8809
*U.S. Office(s):* Irish Trade Board, 880 Third Ave, 8th floor, New York, NY 10020, United States
*Showroom(s):* 16 D'Olier St, Dublin 2

**Irish University Press,** *imprint of* Irish Academic Press

**Irish YouthWork Press**
National Youth Federation, 20 Lower Dominick St, Dublin 1

*Tel:* (010) 8729933 *Fax:* (010) 8724183
*E-mail:* info@nyf.ie
*Web Site:* www.nyf.ie
*Key Personnel*
Services Executive: Mr Fran Bissett
Specialize in Youth Work Publications.
Subjects: Child Care & Development, Education, Social Sciences, Sociology
ISBN Prefix(es): 0-9522207; 1-900416
Total Titles: 17 Print

**Kells Publishing Company Ltd**
John St, Kells, Co Meath
*Tel:* (046) 40117; (046) 40255 *Fax:* (046) 41522
ISBN Prefix(es): 1-872490

**Albertine Kennedy Publishing**
5 Henrietta St, Dublin 1
*Tel:* (01) 6607090 *Fax:* (01) 6607090
*Key Personnel*
Man Dir: Tom Kennedy
ISBN Prefix(es): 0-906002

**Kerryman Ltd**
Clash, Tralee, Co Kerry
*Tel:* (066) 21666 *Fax:* (066) 21608
*E-mail:* info@kerryman.ie
*Web Site:* www.unison.ie/kerryman
*Telex:* 28100
*Key Personnel*
Man Dir: Bryan G Cunningham
Editorial: Gerard Colleran
Sales, Production: Brendan Doran
Founded: 1970
Subjects: History, Religion - Other
ISBN Prefix(es): 0-946277
*Parent Company:* Independent Newspapers Ltd, Middle Abbey St, Dublin 1

**Libra House Ltd**
PO Box 1127, Dublin 8
*Tel:* (01) 4542717
*Key Personnel*
Contact: Cathal Tyrrell
Founded: 1972
Subjects: Labor, Industrial Relations, Transportation, Travel
ISBN Prefix(es): 0-904169

**The Lilliput Press Ltd+**
62-63 Sitric Rd, Arbour Hill, Dublin 7
*Tel:* (01) 6711647 *Fax:* (01) 6711233
*E-mail:* info@lilliputpress.ie
*Web Site:* www.lilliputpress.ie
*Key Personnel*
Publisher: Antony Farrell
Founded: 1984
Membership(s): Cle-The Irish Book Publishers' Association.
Subjects: Architecture & Interior Design, Biography, Fiction, History, Literature, Literary Criticism, Essays, Natural History, Poetry, Regional Interests
ISBN Prefix(es): 0-946640; 1-874675; 1-901866; 1-84351

**Lindisfarne,** *imprint of* Veritas Co Ltd

**Little Rhino Books,** *imprint of* Roberts Rinehart Publishers

**Marino Books,** *imprint of* Mercier Press Ltd

**Mentor Publications+**
Sandyford Industrial Estate, 43 Furze Rd, Dublin 18
*Tel:* (01) 2952112 *Fax:* (01) 2952114
*E-mail:* admin@mentorbooks.ie
*Web Site:* www.mentorbooks.ie
Total Titles: 200 Print

**Mercier,** *imprint of* Mercier Press Ltd

**Mercier Press Ltd+**
Douglas Village, Cork
*Tel:* (021) 489 9858 *Fax:* (021) 489 9887
*E-mail:* books@mercierpress.ie
*Web Site:* www.mercierpress.ie
*Key Personnel*
Man Dir: John F Spillane
Founded: 1944
Subjects: Biography, Fiction, History, Humor, Nonfiction (General), Regional Interests, Religion - Catholic
ISBN Prefix(es): 0-85342; 1-85635; 1-86023
Number of titles published annually: 30 Print
Total Titles: 380 Print
Imprints: Marino Books; Mercier
*Branch Office(s)*
Mercier/Marino, Douglas Village, Cork
*Tel:* (021) 489 9858 *Fax:* (021) 489 9887
*E-mail:* books@mercierpress.ie
Distributed by Irish Books & Media (USA); Tower Books (Australia)
Foreign Rights: Amer-Asia (Asia); Lora Fountain (France); Natoli Stefan Oliva (Italy); Kristin Olson (Czech Republic); P&P Fritz (Germany); Rosenstone/Wender (US); Margit Schaleck (Denmark, Norway); Julio F Yanez (Latin America, Spain)
*Warehouse:* CMD (Columbia Mercier Distribution), 55a Spruce Ave, Stillorgan Industrial Park, Blackrock, Co Dublin *Tel:* (01) 2942560 *Fax:* (01) 2942564 *E-mail:* cmd@columbia.ie

**Messenger Publications**
37 Lower Leeson St, Dublin 2
*Tel:* (01) 6767 491; (01) 6767 492 *Fax:* (01) 661 16 06
*E-mail:* sales@messenger.ie
*Web Site:* www.messenger.ie
*Key Personnel*
Editor: Brendan Murray SJ
Assistant Editor: Anne Duff
Founded: 1888
ISBN Prefix(es): 0-901335; 1-872245

**Mizen Books,** *imprint of* Roberts Rinehart Publishers

**Morrigan Book Co+**
Gore St, Killala, Ballina, County Mayo
*Tel:* (096) 32555 *Fax:* (096) 32555
*E-mail:* admin@atlanticisland.ie
*Key Personnel*
Publisher: Gerald Conan Kennedy *E-mail:* gerry. kennedy@online.ie
Founded: 1982
Subjects: Archaeology, Folklore, Mythology & General Irish Interest
ISBN Prefix(es): 0-907677
*Parent Company:* Morigna Mediaco Teoranta
Imprints: Fact Pack Ireland Guides; Heritage Maps & Guides

**Mount Eagle Publications Ltd+**
Cooleen, Dingle, Co Kerry
Mailing Address: PO Box 32, Dingle, Co Kerry
*Tel:* (066) 9151463 *Fax:* (066) 9151234
*Web Site:* www.brandonbooks.com
*Key Personnel*
Publisher: Steve MacDonogh
Founded: 1997
Subjects: Biography, Fiction, History, Literature, Literary Criticism, Essays, Nonfiction (General)
ISBN Prefix(es): 0-86322; 1-902011
Imprints: Brandon
Subsidiaries: Brandon Book Publishers

**National Library of Ireland**
Kildare St, Dublin 2

*Tel:* (01) 603 02 00 *Fax:* (01) 6766690
*E-mail:* info@nli.ie
*Web Site:* www.nli.ie
*Key Personnel*
Dir: Aongus O hAonghusa
Founded: 1877
Subjects: Regional Interests
ISBN Prefix(es): 0-907328

**New Books/Connolly Books**
43 E Essex St, Temple Bar, Dublin 2
*Tel:* (01) 6711943 *Fax:* (01) 6711943
Subjects: Economics, Government, Political Science, History, Philosophy
ISBN Prefix(es): 0-902912

**New Writers' Press**
61 Clarence Mangan Rd, Dublin 8
*Key Personnel*
Man Dir: Michael Smith
Founded: 1967
Subjects: Literature, Literary Criticism, Essays, Poetry
ISBN Prefix(es): 0-905582

**Newleaf,** *imprint of* Gill & Macmillan Ltd

**Oak Tree Press+**
19 Rutland St, Cork
*Tel:* (021) 431 3855 *Fax:* (021) 431 3496
*E-mail:* info@oaktreepress.com
*Web Site:* www.oaktreepress.com
*Key Personnel*
Man Dir: Brian O'Kane *E-mail:* brian.okane@ oaktreepress.com
Founded: 1991
Business book publishers & developers of enterprise training & support materials.
Subjects: Accounting, Business, Career Development, Finance, Labor, Industrial Relations, Law, Management, Marketing
ISBN Prefix(es): 1-872853; 1-86076; 1-904887
Number of titles published annually: 15 Print
Total Titles: 170 Print
*Parent Company:* Cork Publishing

**O'Brien Educational**
20 Victoria Rd, Rathgar, Dublin 6
*Tel:* (01) 4923333 *Fax:* (01) 4922777
*E-mail:* books@obrien.ie
*Web Site:* www.obrien.ie
*Key Personnel*
Editorial, Rights & Permissions, Sales, Production: Michael O'Brien
Founded: 1974
Publishers to the Curriculum Development Unit, Trinity College, Dublin 2, & to other educational institutions in Ireland & the EEC.
Subjects: Art, Business, Career Development, Environmental Studies, History, Science (General)
ISBN Prefix(es): 0-905140; 0-86278; 0-9502046
*Associate Companies:* The O'Brien Press Ltd
*Orders to:* Gill & Macmillan Ltd, Goldenbridge Industrial Estate, Dublin 8 *Tel:* (01) 531005 *Fax:* (01) 541688
Keith Ainworth (Pty), 66A Abel St, Suite 4, Penrith, NSW 2750, Australia *Tel:* (047) 323411 *Fax:* (047) 218259
Riverwood Publishers Ltd, 6 Donlands Ave, PO Box 70, Sharon, ON L0G 1VO, Canada *Tel:* 416-478-8396 *Fax:* 416-478-8380
Central Books, 99 Wallis Rd, London E9 5LN, United Kingdom *Tel:* (020) 8986 4854 *Fax:* (020) 8533 5821
Michael Geoghegan, 15A Tower Terrace, Wood Green, London N22 6SX, United Kingdom *Tel:* (020) 8889 7094
Irish Books & Media, 1433 Franklin Ave E, Minneapolis, MN 55404-2135, United States *Tel:* 612-871-3505 *Fax:* 612-871-3358

**The O'Brien Press Ltd+**
20 Victoria Rd, Rathgar, Dublin 6
*Tel:* (01) 4923333 *Fax:* (01) 4922777
*E-mail:* books@obrien.ie
*Web Site:* www.obrien.ie
*Key Personnel*
Man Dir, Rights & Permissions: Michael O'Brien
Editorial: Ide ni Laoghaire
Sales Dir: Ivan O'Brien
Founded: 1974
Subjects: Architecture & Interior Design, Biography, Business, Cookery, Criminology, Fiction, History, Humor, Music, Dance, Nonfiction (General), Self-Help, Sports, Athletics, Travel, Wine & Spirits, Women's Studies
ISBN Prefix(es): 0-905140; 0-86278; 0-9502046
*Associate Companies:* O'Brien Educational
Imprints: Blue Flag; Flyers; Pandas; Red Flag; Solos
Foreign Rights: Agenzia Letteraria Internazionale SRL (Italy); Akcali Ltd (Turkey); Big Apple Tuttle-Mori (People's Republic of China); Valerie Hoskins & Associates (UK); Ilustrata SL (Portugal, Spain); Japan Foreign-Rights (Japan); Liepman AG (Germany); Lora Fountain (France, Russia); Kristin Olson Literary Agency (Czech Republic); Silkroad Agency (Thailand)
*Distribution Center:* Gill & MacMillan Distribution, Hume Ave, Park West, Dublin *Tel:* (01) 500 9500 *Fax:* (01) 500 9599 (Ireland & world excluding other territories listed)
Tower Books, Unit 9/19 Rodborough Rd, Frenchs Forest, NSW 2086, Australia *Tel:* (02) 99755566 *Fax:* (02) 9975599
David Forrester Books NZ, Private Bag 102907, MSMC, Auckland, New Zealand *Tel:* (09) 4152080 *Fax:* (09) 4152083 (New Zealand)
Compass Independent Book Sales, 6 Waldeck Rd, Strand on the Green, Chiswick, London W4 3NP, United Kingdom *Tel:* (020) 8995 6324 *Fax:* (020) 8558 1500 (Britain)
Independent Publishers Group (IPG), 814 N Franklin St, Chicago, IL 60610, United States *Tel:* 312-337-0747 *Fax:* 312-337-5985 *Web Site:* www.ipgbook.com (USA/Canada)
Irish Books & Media, 1433 Franklin Ave E, Minneapolis, MN 55404-2135, United States *Tel:* 612-871-3505 *Fax:* 612-871-3358 *E-mail:* irishbook@aol.com (Irish gift shops, North America)
*Orders to:* Gill & Macmillan Ltd, Hume Ave, Park West, Dublin 12 *Tel:* (01) 500 9500 *Fax:* (01) 500 9599
Irish Books & Media, 1433 Franklin Ave E, Minneapolis, MN 55404-2135, United States *Tel:* 612-871-3505 *Fax:* 612-871-3358

**Oifig an tSolathair,** *imprint of* An Gum

**The On Stream Local History Collection,** *imprint of* On Stream Publications Ltd

**On Stream Publications Ltd+**
Currabaha, Cloghroe, Blarney, County Cork
*Tel:* (021) 4385798 *Fax:* (021) 4385798
*E-mail:* info@onstream.ie
*Web Site:* www.onstream.ie
*Key Personnel*
Man Dir: Roz Crowley
Founded: 1992
Specialize in quality publications.
Subjects: Agriculture, Behavioral Sciences, Biography, Cookery, Developing Countries, Health, Nutrition, History, How-to, Medicine, Nursing, Dentistry, Nonfiction (General), Travel, Wine & Spirits
ISBN Prefix(es): 1-897685
Number of titles published annually: 3 Print
Total Titles: 13 Print
Imprints: The On Stream Local History Collection; Tackling Series of Practical Books

**Open Air,** *imprint of* Four Courts Press Ltd

**Ossian Publications+**
40 MacCurtain St, Cork, County Cork
Mailing Address: PO Box 84, Cork, County Cork
*Tel:* (021) 4502040 *Fax:* (021) 4502025
*E-mail:* ossian@iol.ie
*Web Site:* www.ossian.ie
*Key Personnel*
Dir: John Loesberg
Founded: 1989
Irish music publisher & distributor.
Subjects: Ethnicity, How-to, Music, Dance, Irish Music
ISBN Prefix(es): 0-946005; 1-900428
*Associate Companies:* Bookmark
*U.S. Office(s):* Ossian USA, 118 Beck Rd, Loudon, NH 03301, United States *E-mail:* ossianusa@attbi.com
Distributed by Dufour Editions; Music Exhange; Music Sales Corp; Soar Valley Music
Distributor for Halshaw; Dave Malinson Publications; Music Sales Corp; Waltons

**Pandas,** *imprint of* The O'Brien Press Ltd

**Playscripts,** *imprint of* Campus Publishing Ltd

**Poolbeg Press Ltd+**
Imprint of Auburn House
Poolbeg Group Services, 123 Baldoyle Industrial Estate, Baldoyle, Dublin 13
*Tel:* (01) 832 1477 *Fax:* (01) 832 1430
*E-mail:* info@poolbeg.com
*Web Site:* www.poolbeg.com
*Key Personnel*
Man Dir: Philip MacDermott
Finance Dir: Kieran Devlin
Editorial Dir: Kate Cruise O'Brien
Marketing Manager: Michael McLoughlin
Founded: 1976
Subjects: Fiction, History, Nonfiction (General)
ISBN Prefix(es): 1-85371; 0-905169; 1-84223
Imprints: Salmon; Torc; Children's Poolbeg
Subsidiaries: Torc Books Ltd; Salmon Publishing Ltd

**PSAI Press**
Political Studies Association of Ireland, c/o Dublin City University Business School, Glasnevin, Dublin 9
*Tel:* (01) 6081651
*E-mail:* nconnol4@tcd.ie
*Web Site:* www.politics.tcd.ie/psai
*Key Personnel*
Contact: Dr Gary Murphy *Tel:* (01) 7005664 *E-mail:* gary.murphy@dcu.ie
Founded: 1982
Specializes in: Political Science
Publications include: Journals & Irish Political Books.
ISBN Prefix(es): 0-9519748
*Ultimate Parent Company:* Political Studies Association of Ireland

**Publishers Group South West (Ireland)+**
Allihies, Bantry, Co Cork
*Tel:* (027) 73025 *Fax:* (027) 73131
*E-mail:* 73551.655@compuserve.com
*Key Personnel*
President: Tony Lowes
Vice President: Peter Haston
Secretary: Guy Cotten
Founded: 1984
Membership(s): An Taise, The National Trust; Specialize in promotional T-shirts, buttons & balloons.
Subjects: Fiction, Philosophy, Poetry
ISBN Prefix(es): 1-870618; 0-9511629

Imprints: Christa-Jo Utley
Divisions: Cod's Head Preservation Society; Friends of Allihies Artists

**Real Ireland Design**
27 Beechwood Close, Boghall Rd, Bray
*Tel:* (01) 2860799 *Fax:* (01) 2829962
*E-mail:* info@realireland.ie
*Web Site:* www.realireland.ie
*Key Personnel*
Man Dir: Leonard Desmond
Founded: 1981
Subjects: Photography, Travel
ISBN Prefix(es): 0-946887

**Red Flag**, *imprint of* The O'Brien Press Ltd

**Relay Books+**
Tyone, Nenagh Co Tipperary
*Tel:* (067) 31734 *Fax:* (067) 31734
*E-mail:* relaybooks@eiscom.net
*Key Personnel*
Dir & Editor: Donal A Murphy
Founded: 1982
Membership(s): Cle-The Irish Book Publishers' Association.
Subjects: History, Literature, Literary Criticism, Essays, Regional Interests
ISBN Prefix(es): 0-946327
Distributed by Irish Books & Media (USA)

**Rhino Books**, *imprint of* Roberts Rinehart Publishers

**Ri Ra**, *imprint of* Gill & Macmillan Ltd

**Roberts Rinehart Publishers+**
Trinity House, Charlestown Rd, Ranelagh, Dublin 6
*Tel:* (01) 497-6860 *Fax:* (01) 497-6861
*E-mail:* books@townhouse.ie
*Key Personnel*
President: Rick Rinehart
Vice President: Jack van Zandt
Rights Dir: Mary Hegarty
Founded: 1983
Subjects: Anthropology, Art, Biography, Environmental Studies, Ethnicity, Fiction, History, Natural History, Photography, Regional Interests, Travel
ISBN Prefix(es): 0-911797; 1-879373; 1-57098
*Parent Company:* 6309 Monarch Park Place, Nivot, CO 80503, United States
Imprints: Rhino Books; Little Rhino Books; Mizen Books; Harbinger House
*U.S. Office(s):* 5309 Monarch Park Pl, Niwot, CO 80503, United States *Tel:* 303-652 2685 *Fax:* 303-652 2689 *E-mail:* books@ robertrinehart.com

**Sean Ros Press**
Millquarter, Foulkesmill, Co Wexford
*Tel:* (051) 28666
*Key Personnel*
Contact: Bernard Browne
Founded: 1993
Subjects: Genealogy, History, Natural History
ISBN Prefix(es): 0-9525771; 1-903922
Total Titles: 9 Print

**Round Hall Sweet & Maxwell+**
43 Fitzwilliam Pl, Dublin 2
*Tel:* (01) 662 5301
*E-mail:* info@roundhall.ie
*Web Site:* www.roundhall.ie
*Key Personnel*
Dir: Catherine Dolan
Marketing Manager: Maura Smyth
Founded: 1982

Subjects: Criminology, Finance, Labor, Industrial Relations, Law
ISBN Prefix(es): 0-947686; 1-899738; 0-9508725; 0-85800
Total Titles: 200 Print
*Parent Company:* The Thomson Corporation
*Orders to:* Gill & Macmillan Distribution, Goldenbridge, Inchicore, Dublin 8, Contacts: Karen/ Karen Gallagher/ Donoghue *Tel:* (01) 4531005 *Fax:* (01) 4541688

**Royal Dublin Society**
Ballsbridge, Dublin 4
*Tel:* (01) 6680866 *Fax:* (01) 6604014
*E-mail:* info@rds.ie
*Web Site:* www.rds.ie *Cable:* SOCIETY DUBLIN
*Key Personnel*
Science Development Executive: Annette McDonnell *E-mail:* amcdonnell@rds.ie
Founded: 1731
Subjects: Biological Sciences, Science (General)
ISBN Prefix(es): 0-86027

**Royal Irish Academy+**
19 Dawson St, Dublin 2
*Tel:* (01) 6762570 *Fax:* (01) 6762346
*E-mail:* admin@ria.ie
*Web Site:* www.ria.ie
*Key Personnel*
Executive Secretary, Rights & Permissions: Patrick Buckley
Editor, Productions: Rachel McNicholl
Publications Officer: Hugh Shiels *Tel:* (01) 6380911 *E-mail:* h.shiels@ria.ie
Founded: 1785
Subjects: Archaeology, Biological Sciences, Earth Sciences, Environmental Studies, Ethnicity, Geography, Geology, Government, Political Science, History, Mathematics, Physical Sciences
ISBN Prefix(es): 0-901714; 1-874045; 0-9543855
Number of titles published annually: 6 Print
Distributor for Environmental Institute; University College Dublin

**Runa Press**
2 Belgrave Terrace, Monkstown, Co Dublin
*Tel:* (01) 2801869
Subjects: Philosophy, Poetry
ISBN Prefix(es): 0-903543

**Salmon**, *imprint of* Poolbeg Press Ltd

**Salmon Publishing+**
Cliffs of Moher, Co Clare
*Tel:* (065) 7081941 *Fax:* (065) 7081941
*E-mail:* info@salmonpoetry.com
*Web Site:* www.salmonpoetry.com
Founded: 1980
Subjects: Poetry
ISBN Prefix(es): 1-897648; 0-948339; 1-903392

**Solos**, *imprint of* The O'Brien Press Ltd

**Tackling Series of Practical Books**, *imprint of* On Stream Publications Ltd

**Tir Eolas** (Knowledge of the Land)
Newtownlynch, Doorus, Kinvara, Co Galway
*Tel:* (091) 637452 *Fax:* (091) 637452
*E-mail:* info@tireolas.com
*Web Site:* www.tireolas.com
*Key Personnel*
Dir: Anne Korff
Founded: 1987
Membership(s): Cle-The Irish Book Publishers' Association.
Subjects: Anthropology, Archaeology, Biography, Environmental Studies, History, Natural History, Outdoor Recreation
ISBN Prefix(es): 1-873821

Total Titles: 10 Print
Distributed by Eason & Son (Ireland); Irish Books & Media (USA); Colin Smythe Publisher (England)
*Orders to:* Colin Smythe Publishers, PO Box 6, Gerrards Cross, Bucks SL9 8XA, United Kingdom
Eason & Sons, Furry Park Industrial Esate, Santry, Dublin 9
Irish Books & Media, 1433 Franklin Ave E, Minneapolis, MN 55404-2123, United States

**Tivenan Publications+**
Dually, New Castle West, Co Limerick
*Tel:* (069) 62596 *Fax:* (069) 62933
*E-mail:* wellwoman@wellwoman.info
*Web Site:* www.wellwoman.info
*Key Personnel*
Publisher: Nancy Murphy
Founded: 1993
Specialize in health, pregnancy & women's health.
Subjects: Child Care & Development, Health, Nutrition, Self-Help, Childbirth & Pregnancy
ISBN Prefix(es): 0-9522578
Number of titles published annually: 1,000 Print
Total Titles: 1 E-Book
*Parent Company:* SIA
Distributed by Easons Dublin (Ireland)
*Bookshop(s):* Easons Wholesalers, Furry Park Industrial Estate, Santry, Dublin 9 (Books)

**Tivoli**, *imprint of* Gill & Macmillan Ltd

**Tomar Publishing Ltd+**
Bloom House, 78 Eccles St, Dublin 7
*Fax:* (01) 744697
*Key Personnel*
Publisher: Mr Tom Breen
Founded: 1982
Subjects: History
ISBN Prefix(es): 1-871793

**Topaz Publications+**
10 Haddington Lawn, Glenageary, Co Dublin
*Tel:* (01) 2800460 *Fax:* (01) 2800460
*Key Personnel*
Man Partner: Mrs Davida Murdoch
Founded: 1988
Subjects: Law
ISBN Prefix(es): 0-9514032
Distributed by LexisNexis Export Team

**Torc**, *imprint of* Poolbeg Press Ltd

**Town House & Country House**
Trinity House, Charleston Rd, Ranelagh, Dublin 6
*Tel:* (01) 4972399 *Fax:* (01) 4970927
*E-mail:* books@townhouse.ie
*Web Site:* www.irelandseye.com/cle/publish/ townhouse.html
*Key Personnel*
Man Dir, Rights & Permissions: Treasa Coady
Editorial: Siobhan Parkinson
Production: John McCurrie
Sales & Marketing: Brud Ni Chuilinn
Founded: 1984
Also acts as Publisher to Trinity College Dublin.
Subjects: Archaeology, Art, Biography, Fiction, Romance
*Associate Companies:* Town House Publications Ltd
Imprints: Trinity College Dublin Press
Distributed by Roberts Rinehart Publishers (Canada & USA)
Distributor for Roberts Rinehart Publishers (USA)
*Book Club(s):* BCA
*Warehouse:* Gill & Macmillan, Goldenbridge Industrial Estate, Ichicore, Dublin
*Orders to:* Gill & Macmillan, Goldenbridge Industrial Estate, Inchicore, Dublin 8

**Trinity College Dublin Press**, *imprint of* Town House & Country House

**Christa-Jo Utley**, *imprint of* Publishers Group South West (Ireland)

**Veritas Co Ltd+**
Veritas House, 7-8 Lower Abbey St, Dublin 1
*Tel:* (01) 878 8177 *Fax:* (01) 8786507
*E-mail:* publications@veritas.ie
*Web Site:* www.veritas.ie
*Key Personnel*
Dir: Maura Hyland
Editorial, Rights & Permissions: Helen Carr
Retail: Maureen Sanders
Marketing, Publicity: Amanda Conlon-McKenna
Founded: 1969
Veritas Publications is the publishing division of the Catholic Communications Institute of Ireland Inc.
Subjects: Biblical Studies, Biography, Child Care & Development, Developing Countries, Disability, Special Needs, Education, Environmental Studies, Nonfiction (General), Philosophy, Religion - Catholic, Religion - Protestant, Religion - Other, Theology, Catechetical
ISBN Prefix(es): 0-905092; 0-86217; 0-901810; 1-85390
Number of titles published annually: 40 Print; 1 CD-ROM
*Parent Company:* The Catholic Communications Institute of Ireland
Imprints: Beehive Books; Lindisfarne; Veritas Publications
*Branch Office(s)*
Cork
Dublin
Ennis
Letterkenny
Sligo
Leamington Spa, United Kingdom
*Warehouse:* 8 Hanover Quay, Dublin 2

**Veritas Publications**, *imprint of* Veritas Co Ltd

**Weir's Guides**, *imprint of* Ballinakella Press

**Wolfhound Press Ltd+**
Imprint of Merlin Publishing
16 Upper Pembroke St, Dublin 2
*Tel:* (01) 6764373 *Fax:* (01) 6764373
*E-mail:* websales@wolfhound.ie
*Key Personnel*
Publisher: Seamus Cashman
Sales, Marketing & Rights: Seamus O'Reilly
Founded: 1974
Subjects: Biography, Fiction, Photography
ISBN Prefix(es): 0-9503454; 0-905473; 0-86327
Total Titles: 300 Print
*Orders to:* Gill & Macmillan Ltd, Goldenbridge Industrial Estate, Inchicore, Dublin 8 *Tel:* (01) 4531005 *Fax:* (01) 4541688

# Israel

## General Information

*Capital:* Jerusalem
*Language:* Hebrew and Arabic (English and German widely known)
*Religion:* Predominantly Jewish (about 82%) and Muslim (about 14%)
*Population:* 4.7 million
*Bank Hours:* 0830-1230 Sunday-Thursday; also 1600-1700 Sunday-Tuesday & Thursday

*Shop Hours:* Usually Sunday 0900-1300, 1600-1800; weekdays 0900-1300, 1600-1900; many close Friday afternoon
*Currency:* 100 agorot = 1 new sheqel
*Export/Import Information:* Books (except for children's picture books) and advertising duty-free. 17% VAT on books. No import license required for books but must apply for importing number; exchange granted automatically. Import restrictions on Hebrew books.
*Copyright:* UCC, Berne, Florence (see Copyright Conventions, pg xi)

**Academon Publishing House**
Hebrew University, 91000 Jerusalem
Mailing Address: PO Box 24130, Jerusalem
*Tel:* (02) 5882163 *Fax:* (02) 5815558
Founded: 1952
ISBN Prefix(es): 965-350
*Bookshop(s):* Academon, at the four Hebrew University campuses, Jerusalem & Rehovot

**Academy of the Hebrew Language**
Givat Ram, 91034 Jerusalem
Mailing Address: PO Box 3449, 91034 Jerusalem
*Tel:* (02) 6493555 *Fax:* (02) 5617065
*E-mail:* acad2u@vms.huji.ac.il
*Web Site:* hebrew-academy.huji.ac.il
*Key Personnel*
President: Prof Moshe Bar-Asher
Man Dir: Dr Nathan Efrati
Founded: 1953
Specialize in research & development of the Hebrew language.
Subjects: Hebrew Language & Linguistics
ISBN Prefix(es): 965-481
Number of titles published annually: 12 Print

**Ach Publishing House+**
PO Box 170, Kiriat Bialik 27000
*Tel:* (04) 8727227 *Fax:* (04) 8417839
*Fax on Demand:* (03) 9342850
Founded: 1967
Subjects: Behavioral Sciences, Education
ISBN Prefix(es): 965-267

**Achiasaf Publishing House Ltd**
1A Zorn St, S Industrial Zone, Netanya
Mailing Address: PO Box 8414, 42504 Netanya
*Tel:* (09) 8851390 *Fax:* (09) 8851391
*E-mail:* info@achiasaf.co.il
*Web Site:* www.achiasaf.co.il
*Key Personnel*
Man Dir: Matan Achiasaf; Shachna Achiasaf
Founded: 1933
Subjects: Fiction, Nonfiction (General), Science (General)

**Achiever Ltd**
22 Hahistadrut St, Jerusalem 94230
*Tel:* (02) 6253627 *Fax:* (02) 6255740
*Key Personnel*
Manager: D Kessler
Man Dir: Ayala Atzmon; Sara Atzmon

**Agudat Sabah+**
PO Box 2415, Natanya 42123
*Tel:* (09) 8620544 *Fax:* (09) 8620546
*Key Personnel*
Author & Editor: Sidney Pimienta
Founded: 1978
Subjects: Anthropology, Genealogy, History, Language Arts, Linguistics, Management, Regional Interests, Religion - Jewish
ISBN Prefix(es): 965-453
Subsidiaries: SIIAC (Societe Internationale d'Intervention et d'Action Commerciale)
*Branch Office(s)*
SIIAC-Pimienta

**Am Oved Publishers Ltd**
22 Mazeh St, 65213 Tel Aviv
Mailing Address: PO Box 470, 61003 Tel Aviv
*Tel:* (03) 6291526 *Fax:* (03) 6298911
*E-mail:* info@am-oved.co.il
*Web Site:* www.am-oved.co.il
*Telex:* 1568 *Cable:* AMOVED TELAVIV
*Key Personnel*
Man Dir: Yaron Sadan
Founded: 1942
Subjects: Biography, Fiction, History, Philosophy, Poetry, Psychology, Psychiatry, Social Sciences, Sociology
ISBN Prefix(es): 965-13
*Orders to:* Distributor's Centre for Israeli Books Ltd, 22 Nachmani St, PO Box 2811, Tel Aviv

**Amichai Publishing House Ltd**
19 Yad Harotzim St, PO Box 8448, Netanyah 42505
*Tel:* (09) 8859099 *Fax:* (09) 8853464
*Key Personnel*
Man Dir: Dr Itzhak Oron *E-mail:* oron@idc.ac.ii
Founded: 1948
Subjects: Fiction, Language Arts, Linguistics, Science (General)

**Ariel Publishing House**
28 Nayqdot St, Pisgat Zeev, 91033 Jerusalem
*Tel:* (02) 6434540 *Fax:* (02) 6436164
*Key Personnel*
Chief Executive: Ely Schiller *E-mail:* elysch@netvision.net.il
Founded: 1976
Subjects: Geography, Geology, History, Regional Interests, Religion - Other
ISBN Prefix(es): 965-439

**Arsan Publishing House Ltd**, see Kivunim-Arsan Publishing House

**Astrolog Publishing House+**
PO Box 1123, 45111 Hod Hasharon
*Tel:* (09) 7412044 *Fax:* (09) 7442044
*Key Personnel*
Man Dir: Sara Ben-Mordechai *E-mail:* sarabm@netvision.net.il
Editor-In-Chief: Elisha Ben-Mordechai
Founded: 1994
A general publisher in the Hebrew language, New Age & alternative medicine in English & other languages. Also specializing in mysticism, prediction of the future, awareness & various religions.
Membership(s): Israel Publishers' Association.
Subjects: Astrology, Occult, Nonfiction (General), Religion - Other, Alternative Medicine, New Age
ISBN Prefix(es): 965-494
Total Titles: 600 Print
Distributed by Independent Publishers Group (IPG) (United States)

**Aurora Semanario Israeli de Actualidad+**
PO Box 18066, Tel Aviv 61180
*Tel:* (03) 5462785; (03) 5463297 *Fax:* (03) 5625082
*E-mail:* aurorail@netvision.net.il
Founded: 1963
ISBN Prefix(es): 965-333
*Parent Company:* Aurora
*Associate Companies:* Aurora Em Poreuquce
Subsidiaries: Isnet
Divisions: Internet
*Branch Office(s)*
Buenos-Aires

**Aviv Publishers Ltd**, *imprint of* Bitan Publishers Ltd

**Bar Ilan University Press**
Bar Ilan University, 52900 Ramat Gan
*Tel:* (03) 5318111 *Fax:* (03) 5353446
*E-mail:* press@mail.biu.ac.il
*Web Site:* www.biu.ac.il/Press
*Key Personnel*
General Manager: Margalit Avisar
Chairman, Book Committee: Prof Yehuda Fried-
lander
Founded: 1978
Membership(s): Israel Association of Publishers.
Subjects: Archaeology, Behavioral Sciences, Bib-
lical Studies, Economics, Education, Geogra-
phy, Geology, History, Language Arts, Linguis-
tics, Law, Literature, Literary Criticism, Essays,
Philosophy, Psychology, Psychiatry, Religion -
Jewish, Social Sciences, Sociology
ISBN Prefix(es): 965-226
Number of titles published annually: 25 Print

**Ben-Zvi Institute+**
12 Abarbanel St, 91076 Jerusalem
Mailing Address: PO Box 7660, 91076 Jerusalem
*Tel:* (02) 5398844; (02) 5398848 *Fax:* (02)
5612329
*E-mail:* mahonzvi@h2.hum.huji.ac.il
*Web Site:* www.ybz.org.il
*Key Personnel*
Dir: Menahem Ben-Sasson
Academic Secretary: Michael Glatzer
Founded: 1947
Specialize in Sephardi & Eastern Jewry.
Subjects: Ethnicity, Foreign Countries, History,
Language Arts, Linguistics, Literature, Literary
Criticism, Essays, Regional Interests, Religion -
Jewish
ISBN Prefix(es): 965-235
Total Titles: 100 Print
*Parent Company:* Yad Izhak Ben-Zvi & the He-
brew University of Jerusalem

**Bezalel Academy of Arts & Design**
Mt Scopus, PO Box 24046, 91240 Jerusalem
*Tel:* (02) 589 3333 *Fax:* (02) 582 3094
*E-mail:* mail@bezalel.ac.il
*Web Site:* www.bezalel.ac.il
Subjects: Architecture & Interior Design, Art,
Photography
ISBN Prefix(es): 965-324

**The Bialik Institute+**
PO Box 92, 91000 Jerusalem
*Tel:* (02) 6783554; (02) 6797942 *Fax:* (02)
6783706
*E-mail:* bialik@actcom.co.il
*Web Site:* www.bialik-publishing.com
*Key Personnel*
Man Dir: Yitzchak Taub
Founded: 1935
Subjects: Archaeology, Art, Biblical Studies, His-
tory, Literature, Literary Criticism, Essays, Phi-
losophy, Poetry, Religion - Jewish
ISBN Prefix(es): 965-342
Number of titles published annually: 46 Print
Distributor for Ben Gurion University of the
Neger Press; Moreshet (Holocaust publica-
tions); The Zionist Library

**Bitan Publishers Ltd+**
50 Yeshayahu St, 62494 Tel Aviv
Mailing Address: PO Box 3068, 47130 Ramat
Hasharon
*Tel:* (03) 6040089; (054) 664575 *Fax:* (03)
5404792
*Key Personnel*
Man Dir: Asher Bitan
Founded: 1965
Also acts as director of the Israeli Publisher As-
sociation & Optimum Educational Software
(1993) Ltd.
Subjects: Aeronautics, Aviation, Biography, Child
Care & Development, Fiction, How-to, Human

Relations, Literature, Literary Criticism, Es-
says, Mysteries, Nonfiction (General), Outdoor
Recreation, Poetry, Self-Help, Travel, Women's
Studies
*Parent Company:* ABM Publishers Ltd
Imprints: Orbach Editions Ltd; Aviv Publishers
Ltd
Subsidiaries: Bitan United Multimedia Ltd
Divisions: Multimedia
*Orders to:* 14 Valenberg St, 69719 Tel Aviv

**The Book Publishers Association of Israel**
29 Carlebach St, 67132 Tel Aviv
Mailing Address: PO Box 20123, 61201 Tel Aviv
*Tel:* (03) 5614121 *Fax:* (03) 5611996
*E-mail:* info@tbpai.co.il
*Web Site:* www.tbpai.co.il
*Key Personnel*
Man Dir: Amnon Ben-Shmuel
Founded: 1939

**Books in the Attic Publishers Ltd+**
PO Box 23146, Tel Aviv 61231
*Tel:* (03) 248324 *Fax:* (03) 623630
*Key Personnel*
President: Dr Yehuda Melzer
Founded: 1989
Subjects: Health, Nutrition, Medicine, Nursing,
Dentistry
ISBN Prefix(es): 965-419

**Boostan Publishing House**
36 Meskek, Ben-Shemen Moshav 73115
*Tel:* (03) 9221821 *Fax:* (03) 9221299 *Cable:*
Boostanmod Telaviv
*Key Personnel*
Man Dir: Mordechai Boostan
Sales Dir: Roni Birkenfield
Publicity Dir: Riva Almagor
Advertising Dir: Sara Wohlfeiler
Rights & Permissions: Dalia Sheingarten
Founded: 1969
Subjects: Biography, Education, Fiction, History,
How-to, Medicine, Nursing, Dentistry, Poetry,
Psychology, Psychiatry
ISBN Prefix(es): 965-275
Subsidiaries: Distributors' Centre for Israeli
Books Ltd

**Breslov Research Institute+**
PO Box 5370, Jerusalem 91053
*Tel:* (02) 5824641 *Fax:* (02) 5825542
*E-mail:* info@breslov.org
*Web Site:* www.breslov.org/catalog.html
*Key Personnel*
Executive Dir: Rabbi Chaim Kramer
Founded: 1979
Subjects: Biblical Studies, Biography, Education,
Health, Nutrition, History, Literature, Literary
Criticism, Essays, Nonfiction (General), Phi-
losophy, Psychology, Psychiatry, Religion -
Jewish, Self-Help, Theology, Specialize in writ-
ings in English, French, Spanish, Russian & in
Hebrew
ISBN Prefix(es): 965-290
Number of titles published annually: 5 Print
Total Titles: 70 Print; 70 Online; 70 E-Book
Imprints: Tsohar Publications
*U.S. Office(s):* PO Box 587, Monsey, NY 10952-
0587, United States *Tel:* 914-425-4258; 800-33-
BRESLOV *Fax:* 914-425-3018
Distributed by Jewish Lights

**Carta, The Israel Map & Publishing Co Ltd+**
18 Ha'uman St, Jerusalem 91024
Mailing Address: PO Box 2500, Jerusalem 91024
*Tel:* (02) 678 3355 *Fax:* (02) 678 2373
*E-mail:* carta@carta.co.il
*Web Site:* www.holyland-jerusalem.com
*Key Personnel*
Chairman: Emanuel Hausman

President, Chief Executive Officer: Shay Hausman
Editorial: Lorraine Kessel; Pirchia Cohen; Bar-
bara Ball
Art Dir: Eli Kellerman
Founded: 1958
Cartographic & foreign language publisher - En-
glish, German & Russian, Hebrew.
Subjects: Archaeology, Education, Health, Nutri-
tion, History
ISBN Prefix(es): 965-220
Number of titles published annually: 30 Print; 1
CD-ROM
Total Titles: 300 Print; 3 CD-ROM
Imprints: Nitzanim
Subsidiaries: Cana Publishing House; W Van Leer
Publishing Ltd
*Warehouse:* Lonnie Kahn Ltd, 20, Eliahu Eitan,
Rishon Le Zion 58851, Aaron Segal *Tel:* (03)
9520158/9518408 *Fax:* (03) 9520251/9518415/
9518416

**Center for Research & Study of Sephardi &
Oriental Jewish History**, see Misgav
Yerushalayim

**Centre for Educational Technology**
PO Box 39513, 61394 Tel Aviv
*Tel:* (03) 6460183 *Fax:* (03) 6460821
*Key Personnel*
Publishing Dir: Dani Dolev
ISBN Prefix(es): 965-354

**Classikaletet+**
22 Derekh Hashalom St, 67892 Tel Aviv
*Tel:* (03) 5616996 *Fax:* (03) 5615526
*E-mail:* kimbooks@netvision.net.it
*Key Personnel*
Man Dir: Yoram Ros
Founded: 1980
Subjects: Child Care & Development, Cook-
ery, House & Home, How-to, Humor, Music,
Dance, Nonfiction (General), Psychology, Psy-
chiatry, Travel
ISBN Prefix(es): 965-286; 965-509

**Cordinata Ltd (Holy Land 2000)**
27 Sutin St, 64684 Tel Aviv
*Tel:* (03) 5226885 *Fax:* (03) 5276661
*E-mail:* cordinata@isdn.net.il
*Key Personnel*
General Manager: Eliezer Sacks
Marketing Manager: Yaron Goldfisher
Founded: 1995
Specialize in books, mainly albums on the Holy
Land. Also produce old & new maps, CD-
ROM, videos & calendars - all about the Holy
Land.
ISBN Prefix(es): 965-7143
Number of titles published annually: 10 Print; 5
CD-ROM; 5 Online; 15 E-Book; 5 Audio
Total Titles: 10 Print; 5 CD-ROM; 5 Online; 15
E-Book; 5 Audio
*U.S. Office(s):* Argecy Co, 27280 Haggerty,
Farmington Hills, MI 48331, United States,
General Manager: Mr Coby Gutkovitch
*Tel:* 248-324-1800 (ext 124) *Fax:* 248-324-
1900 *E-mail:* argecy@msn.com
Distributed by Riverside Distributors

**Dalia Peled Publishers, Division of Modan+**
36 Moshav, Ben-Shemen 73115
*Tel:* (08) 4221821 *Fax:* (08) 4221299
*Key Personnel*
Man Dir, Publicity, Rights & Permissions: Dahlia
Peled
Editorial: Israel Peled
Sales: Raanan Rogel
Production: Ruti Bar-Lev
Founded: 1980
Subjects: Computer Science, Humor
ISBN Prefix(es): 965-269
Subsidiaries: People and Computers

**DAT Publications+**
PO Box 27019, Jaffa 61270
*Tel:* (03) 5071239 *Fax:* (03) 5070458
*E-mail:* dat@y-dat.co.il
*Web Site:* www.y-dat.co.il
*Key Personnel*
General Dir & Rights Contact: Yigal Miller
  *Tel:* (03) 5071239
Dir: Benci Sharon *Tel:* (03) 5072683
Public Relations: Gilah Bonen *Tel:* (03) 6095460
  *Fax:* (03) 6035460
Founded: 1969
Publishers of original fiction & nonfiction in
  Hebrew & English. Occasionally, we publish
  some gift & audio titles.
Publisher & international Agent of Shlomo Kalo's
  works (Sold in 15 countries). Privately owned.
Subjects: Biblical Studies, Fiction, History, Hu-
  mor, Literature, Literary Criticism, Essays,
  Nonfiction (General), Philosophy, Religion -
  Other, Self-Help, Theology
ISBN Prefix(es): 965-7028
Total Titles: 60 Print; 4 Audio
*U.S. Office(s):* Forevermore Bible Discov-
  ery Books, PO Box 92613, South Lake,
  TX 76092, United States, Contact: Moshe
  Haber *Tel:* 817-605-3688 *Fax:* 817-605-3684
  *E-mail:* ForEvrMor1@aol.com
*Foreign Rep(s):* Forevermore (US)
*Showroom(s):* 22 Dov Mimezeritz, Jaffa, Contact:
  Nizah Miller *Tel:* (03) 6580221
*Warehouse:* 22 Dov Mimezeritz, Jaffa, Contact:
  Nizah Miller *Tel:* (03) 5072149

**Dekel Academic Press**, *imprint of* Dekel
  Publishing House

**Dekel Publishing House+**
17 Motzkin St, 61450 Tel Aviv
Mailing Address: PO Box 45094, 61450 Tel Aviv
*Tel:* (03) 6045379 *Fax:* (03) 5440824
*E-mail:* dekelpbl@netvision.net.il
*Web Site:* www.dekelpublishing.com
*Key Personnel*
Man Dir: Zvi Morik
Founded: 1975
Membership(s): PMA.
Subjects: Cookery, Crafts, Games, Hobbies, Fic-
  tion, History, How-to, Mysteries, Securities,
  Self-Help, Sports, Athletics, Travel, Self-
  defense: Krav Maga
ISBN Prefix(es): 965-7178
Imprints: Dekel Academic Press; Duvdevan;
  Tamai Books
Distributed by Frog Co Ltd; North Atlantic Books

**Devora Publishing Co**, *imprint of* Pitspopany
  Press

**Doko Video Ltd**
33 Hayetzira St, 52521 Ramat Gan
*Tel:* (03) 5753555 *Fax:* (03) 5753189
*E-mail:* dokoa@ibm.net
*Key Personnel*
Sales & Marketing Manager: Sharon Moss
Founded: 1981
Subjects: Music, Dance, Religion - Other
ISBN Prefix(es): 965-478

**Domino**, *imprint of* Keter Publishing House Ltd

**Duvdevan**, *imprint of* Dekel Publishing House

**Dvir Publishing Ltd+**
11 Lev Pesach, 71293 N Industrial Area Lod
Mailing Address: PO Box 149, 61001 Tel Aviv
*Tel:* (08) 9246565 *Fax:* (08) 9251770
*E-mail:* info@zmora.co.il
*Key Personnel*
Man Dir & Editorial: Ohad Zmora
Sales: Eran Zmora

Founded: 1924
Subjects: Literature, Literary Criticism, Essays,
  Poetry, Religion - Jewish
ISBN Prefix(es): 965-01
Total Titles: 1,500 Print
*Parent Company:* Zmora-Bitan Publishers Ltd
*Subsidiaries:* Dvir Distribution; Karni Publishers
  Ltd; Megiddo Publishing Co Ltd

**Dyonon/Papyrus Publishing House of the
Tel-Aviv+**
Tel Aviv University, PO Box 39040, 69978 Tel
  Aviv
*Tel:* (03) 6408111 *Fax:* (03) 6423149
*Key Personnel*
General Manager: Eitan Zinger
Import Manager: Rachel Hamo
Editor-in-Chief: Raya Itzkovich
Founded: 1977
Membership(s): National Association of College
  Stores, USA.
Subjects: Behavioral Sciences, Business, Chem-
  istry, Chemical Engineering, Child Care &
  Development, Criminology, Economics, Edu-
  cation, Finance, Genealogy, History, Medicine,
  Nursing, Dentistry, Nonfiction (General), Phi-
  losophy, Social Sciences, Sociology
ISBN Prefix(es): 965-306
Imprints: Papyrus
*Branch Office(s)*
Ben Gurion (Beer Sheva) University Campus
*Bookshop(s):* Bar-Ilan University; Ben-Guryon
  University; Tel Aviv University

**Edanim Publishers Ltd+**
Division of Yedlot Aharonot Books
5 Mikunis St, 61376 Tel Aviv
Mailing Address: PO Box 37744, 61376 Tel Aviv
*Tel:* (03) 688-8466 *Fax:* (03) 537-7820
*Telex:* 33847
*Key Personnel*
Publisher: Asher Weill
Founded: 1975
Subjects: Biography, History, Regional Interests
ISBN Prefix(es): 965-248

**Encyclopedia Judaica**, *imprint of* Keter
  Publishing House Ltd

**Encyclopedia Judaica+**
Industrial Zone, Givat Shaul B, 91071 Jerusalem
Mailing Address: PO Box 7145, 91071 Jerusalem
*Tel:* (02) 6557822 *Fax:* (02) 6528962
*E-mail:* info@keter-books.co.il
*Web Site:* www.keter-books.co.il
*Key Personnel*
Man Dir: Yiftach Dekel
ISBN Prefix(es): 965-07
*Parent Company:* Keter Publishing House Ltd,
  Jerusalem

**Eretz Hemdah Institute for Advanced Jewish
Studies**
5 HaMem Gimmel St, 94428 Jerusalem
Mailing Address: PO Box 36236, 91360
  Jerusalem
*Tel:* (02) 537-1485 *Fax:* (02) 537-9626
*E-mail:* eretzhem@netvision.net.il
*Web Site:* www.eretzhemdah.org
*Key Personnel*
President: Harav Shaul Israeli
Founded: 1987
Subjects: Law, Religion - Jewish
ISBN Prefix(es): 965-436
Distributor for Rubin Mass Ltd (Israel)

**ESH (English for Speakers of Hebrew)**, *imprint
of* University Publishing Projects Ltd

**Eshkol Books Publishers & Printing Ltd**
24 Avodat Israel St, Jerusalem 95155

*Tel:* (02) 5370451; (02) 5370179 *Fax:* (02)
  5372732
*Key Personnel*
Manager: S Weinfeld
Subjects: Religion - Jewish

**Feldheim Publishers Ltd**
PO Box 35002, 91350 Jerusalem
*Tel:* (02) 6513947 *Fax:* (02) 6536061
*E-mail:* sales@feldheim.com
*Web Site:* www.feldheim.com
*Key Personnel*
Man Dir: Yaakov Feldheim
Sales Dir: Chaim Vomberg
Founded: 1939
Subjects: Biography, Cookery, Health, Nutrition,
  History, Philosophy, Religion - Jewish
ISBN Prefix(es): 0-87306; 1-58330
*U.S. Office(s):* 200 Airport Executive Park,
  Nanuet, NY 10954, United States *Tel:* 845-
  356-2282 *Fax:* 845-425-1908

**The Arnold & Leona Finkler Institute of
Holocaust Research**
Bar-Ilan University, 52900 Ramat-Gan
*Tel:* (03) 5340333 *Fax:* (03) 5351233
*E-mail:* michmad@mail.biu.ac.il
*Web Site:* www.biu.ac.il
*Key Personnel*
Prof & Chair: Dan Michman
Founded: 1979
Subjects: History, Religion - Jewish, Holocaust,
  20th Century Jewish History
Total Titles: 40 Print
*Parent Company:* Bar-Ilan University

**Rodney Franklin Agency**
53 Mazeh St, Tel Aviv 61376
Mailing Address: PO Box 37727, Tel Aviv 61376
*Tel:* (03) 5600724 *Fax:* (03) 5600479
*E-mail:* rodneyf@netvision.net.il
Founded: 1974
Publishers representatives, book & journal confer-
  ence exhibitions.

**Freund Publishing House Ltd+**
PO Box 35010, 61350 Tel Aviv
*Tel:* (03) 562-8540 *Fax:* (03) 562-8538
*Web Site:* www.freundpublishing.com
*Key Personnel*
Chief Executive Officer: Edmund Freund
Founded: 1970
Also translation agency.
Subjects: Aeronautics, Aviation, Behavioral Sci-
  ences, Biography, Chemistry, Chemical Engi-
  neering, Engineering (General), Environmental
  Studies, Mathematics, Mechanical Engineering,
  Medicine, Nursing, Dentistry, Science (Gen-
  eral), Social Sciences, Sociology
ISBN Prefix(es): 965-294
*Branch Office(s)*
Suite 500, Chesham House, 150 Regent St, Lon-
  don W1R 5FA, United Kingdom

**S Friedman Publishing House Ltd**
27 Gruzenberg St, Tel Aviv 61292
Mailing Address: PO Box 29350, 65152 Tel Aviv
*Tel:* (03) 5176091 *Fax:* (03) 5179756
*Key Personnel*
General Manager: Shmuel Friedman
Man Dir: Dov Friedman; Malka Friedman Shapir

**Gefen**, *imprint of* Gefen Publishing House Ltd

**Gefen Publishing House Ltd+**
7 Ariel St, 91060 Jerusalem
Mailing Address: PO Box 36004, 91060
  Jerusalem
*Tel:* (02) 5380247 *Fax:* (02) 5388423
*E-mail:* info@gefenpublishing.com
*Web Site:* www.israelbooks.com

## Key Personnel
Chief Executive, Publicity: Murray S Greenfield
Publisher: Dror Greenfield; Ilan Greenfield
Founded: 1981
Subjects: Archaeology, Art, Biblical Studies, Biography, Cookery, English as a Second Language, Fiction, Government, Political Science, Health, Nutrition, History, How-to, Language Arts, Linguistics, Law, Medicine, Nursing, Dentistry, Military Science, Nonfiction (General), Photography, Poetry, Psychology, Psychiatry, Religion - Jewish, Theology, Travel, Wine & Spirits
ISBN Prefix(es): 965-229
Imprints: Gefen
Subsidiaries: Israbook Purchasing Service
U.S. Office(s): Gefen Books, 12 New St, Hewlett, NY 11557, United States, Contact: Maury J Storch Tel: 516-295-2805 Fax: 516-295-2739 E-mail: gefenbooks@compuserve.com
Distributor for Magnes Press Ltd; MOD Publishing Ltd; Yad Uashem
Shipping Address: Gefen Books, 12 New St, Hewlett, NY 11557, United States, Contact: Maury J Storch Tel: 516-295-2805 Fax: 516-295-2739 E-mail: gefenbooks@compuserve.com
Warehouse: Gefen Books, 12 New St, Hewlett, NY 11557, United States, Contact: Maury J Storch Tel: 516-295-2805 Fax: 516-295-2739 E-mail: gefenbooks@compuserve.com
Orders to: Gefen Books, 12 New St, Hewlett, NY 11557, United States, Contact: Maury J Storch Tel: 516-295-2805 Fax: 516-295-2739 E-mail: gefenbooks@compuserve.com

## Gvanim Publishing House+
29 Bar Kochba St, Tel Aviv 61111
Mailing Address: PO Box 11138, 61111 Tel Aviv
Tel: (03) 5281044; (03) 5283648 Fax: (03) 5283648
E-mail: traklinm@zahav.net.il
Key Personnel
Man Dir: Maritza Rosman
Founded: 1959
Subjects: Fiction, Poetry
Number of titles published annually: 100 Print
Total Titles: 6,000 Print
Parent Company: Traklin Ltd, Halonot
Associate Companies: Traklin Ltd, Gvanim
Foreign Rights: Pikarsky

## Habermann Institute for Literary Research+
20 King David Blvd, 71103 Lod
Mailing Address: PO Box 383, 71103 Lod
Tel: (08) 9244569; (08) 9241160 Fax: (08) 9249466
E-mail: zmalachi@post.tau.ac.il
Key Personnel
Dir: Dr Michal Saraf
Founded: 1982
Subjects: Ethnicity, Literature, Literary Criticism, Essays, Poetry, Religion - Jewish
ISBN Prefix(es): 965-351
Number of titles published annually: 15 Print
Total Titles: 75 Print
Subsidiaries: MAHUT- Journal For Jewish Culture

## Hadar Publishing House Ltd
32 Schocken St, 66556 Tel Aviv
Tel: (03) 6812244 Fax: (03) 6826138
E-mail: info@zmora.co.il
Key Personnel
Manager: Uzi Shavit
Man Dir: Zvi Zmora
Founded: 1950
Subjects: History, Literature, Literary Criticism, Essays
ISBN Prefix(es): 965-211

## Haifa University Press
Mount Carmel, Haifa 31905
Tel: (04) 8240111 Fax: (04) 8342245
Web Site: www.haifa.ac.il
Key Personnel
Chairman: Prof Manfred Lahnstein
Subjects: Archaeology, Biblical Studies, Education, History, Language Arts, Linguistics, Literature, Literary Criticism, Essays, Philosophy, Public Administration
ISBN Prefix(es): 965-311
Distributed by University Press of New England (Outside of Israel)

## Hakibbutz Hameuchad Publishing House Ltd
Hayarkon 23, Bnei Brak 51114
Mailing Address: POB 1437, 51114 Bnei Brak
Tel: (03) 5785810 Fax: (03) 5785811
Key Personnel
Man Dir: Uzi Shavit
Sales Manager: Nahman Gil
Founded: 1940
Subjects: Agriculture, Archaeology, Art, Biblical Studies, Biography, Biological Sciences, Drama, Theater, Economics, Education, Fiction, Foreign Countries, Geography, Geology, Government, Political Science, Health, Nutrition, History, Human Relations, Literature, Literary Criticism, Essays, Music, Dance, Natural History, Nonfiction (General), Philosophy, Poetry, Psychology, Psychiatry, Regional Interests, Religion - Jewish, Social Sciences, Sociology, Theology, Travel, Women's Studies
ISBN Prefix(es): 965-02

## Otzar Hamore
c/o Israel Teachers' Union, 8 Ben Saruk St, Tel Aviv 62969
Tel: (03) 6922983 Fax: (03) 6922903
Key Personnel
Manager: Avigdor Biton
Man Dir: Joseph Salomon
Founded: 1951
Subjects: Education, Mathematics, Psychology, Psychiatry

## Hanitzotz A-Sharara Publishing House
PO Box 41199, 61411 Jaffa
Tel: (03) 6839145 Fax: (03) 6839148
E-mail: oda@netvision.net.il
Web Site: www.odaction.org; www.hanitzotz.com/challenge
Key Personnel
Publisher: Shimon Tzabar
Editor-in-Chief: Ms Roni Ben Efrat
Editor: Liz Leyh Levac
Language Editor: Stephen Langfur
Founded: 1985
Publishes a bimonthly magazine on the Israeli-Palestinian Conflict, Challenge.
Subjects: Developing Countries, Economics, Education, Film, Video, Foreign Countries, Labor, Industrial Relations, Social Sciences, Sociology, Politics; Israelai Palestinian Conflict

## Beth Hatefutsoth
Tel Aviv University Campus, Klausner St, 61392 Ramat Aviv
Mailing Address: PO Box 39359, 61392 Tel Aviv
Tel: (03) 640 8000 Fax: (03) 640 5727
E-mail: bhwebmas@post.tau.ac.il
Web Site: www.bh.org.il
Key Personnel
Contact: Yossi Avner E-mail: bhyavner@post.tau.ac.il
ISBN Prefix(es): 965-425

## Hod-Ami, Computer Books Ltd+
3 Bilu St, 46426 Herzliya
Mailing Address: PO Box 6108, 46160 Herzliya
Tel: (09) 9541207 Fax: (09) 9571582

E-mail: info@hod-ami.co.il
Web Site: www.hod-ami.co.il
Key Personnel
Chief Executive Officer: Itzhak Amihud
Founded: 1968
Subjects: Computer Science
ISBN Prefix(es): 965-361
Total Titles: 180 Print

**IMI**, see Israel Music Institute (IMI)

## Inbal Publishers+
24 Amal St, 48092 Park Afek-Rosh Haayin
Mailing Address: PO Box 11415, 48092 Park Afek-Rosh Haayin
Tel: (03) 9030111 Fax: (03) 9030888
E-mail: inbalpub@internet-zahav.net
Key Personnel
Man Dir: Shahrokh Sabzerov
Founded: 1980
Specialize in children's board books.
ISBN Prefix(es): 965-332
Distributor for Pestalozzi Verlan (Germany)

## Inbal Travel Information+
18 Hayet Zira St, 52521 Ramat Gan
Tel: (03) 5753032 Fax: (03) 5753130
Key Personnel
President: Michael Shichor
Founded: 1983
Subjects: Travel
ISBN Prefix(es): 965-288
Imprints: Michael's Guides

## The Institute for Israeli Arabs Studies
PO Box 810, Ra'anana 43107
Tel: (09) 7486738 Fax: (09) 7486341
Founded: 1995
Subjects: Anthropology, Economics, Ethnicity, Government, Political Science, Labor, Industrial Relations, Regional Interests, Religion - Islamic, Social Sciences, Sociology, Women's Studies
ISBN Prefix(es): 965-454

## The Institute for the Translation of Hebrew Literature+
23 Baruch Hirsch St, Bnei Brak
Mailing Address: PO Box 1005 1, 52001 Ramat Gan
Tel: (03) 5796830 Fax: (03) 5796832
E-mail: hamachon@inter.net.il; litscene@ithl.org.il
Web Site: www.ithl.org.il
Key Personnel
Man Dir: Mrs Nilli Cohen
Office Manager: Debbie Dagan
Founded: 1962
Subjects: Literature, Literary Criticism, Essays, Poetry
ISBN Prefix(es): 965-255

## Intermedia Audio, Video Book Publishing Ltd+
20 Ha-hashmal St, Tel Aviv 61367
Tel: (03) 5608501 Fax: (03) 5608513
E-mail: freed@inter.net.il
Key Personnel
Man Dir: Arie Fried
Founded: 1993
Subjects: Business, Education, English as a Second Language, Health, Nutrition, Journalism, Mathematics, Medicine, Nursing, Dentistry, Philosophy, Self-Help, Specialize in Alternative Medicine
ISBN Prefix(es): 965-7079
Total Titles: 25 Print; 6 Audio

## The Israel Academy of Sciences & Humanities+
43 Jabotinsky Rd, 91040 Jerusalem
Mailing Address: PO Box 4040, 91040 Jerusalem

*Tel:* (02) 5636211 *Fax:* (02) 5666059
*E-mail:* isracado@vms.huji.ac.il
*Key Personnel*
Man Dir: Dr Meir Zadok
Publications Dept: Tami Korman
Founded: 1959
Subjects: Biological Sciences, Environmental
  Studies, Geography, Geology, History, Philoso-
  phy, Religion - Jewish
ISBN Prefix(es): 965-208

**Israel Antiquities Authority**
Rockefeller Museum Bldg, PO Box 586,
  Jerusalem 91004
*Tel:* (02) 5638421 *Fax:* (02) 6289066
*Web Site:* www.israntique.org.il
*Key Personnel*
Editor-in-Chief: Tsvika Gal *Tel:* (02) 5638424
  *Fax:* (02) 5630526 *E-mail:* tsvika@israntique.
  org.il
Dir: Shuka Dorfman *Tel:* (02) 6204600/1/8
  *Fax:* (02) 6288391 *E-mail:* oshrat@israntique.
  org.il
Secretary: Harriet Menahem *Tel:* (02) 6204622
  *E-mail:* harriet@israntique.org.il
Founded: 1990 (Formerly a Department of the
  Israel Ministry of Education)
Designated by the government of Israel to ad-
  minister the Law of Antiquities, responsible
  for all archeological matters, custodianship of
  all archeological sites, conducts excavations
  & surveys, issues excavation permits, cura-
  torship, documentation & storage of all finds.
  Also, lends finds to museums, conservation &
  restoration of antiquities sites & antiquities,
  documentation, publication & education. Publications include excavation reports, surveys,
  bibliographies, monographs, guide books &
  video cassettes.
Subjects: Archaeology, Archaeology of Israel (the
  Holy Land)
ISBN Prefix(es): 965-406
Total Titles: 74 Print
*Orders to:* Eisenbrauns (USA)

**Israel Book & Printing Centre**
Industry House, 29 Hamered St, Tel Aviv 68125
*Tel:* (03) 5142916 *Fax:* (03) 5142881
*Web Site:* www.export.gov.il
*Key Personnel*
Executive: Ronit Adler *Tel:* (03) 5142916
  *Fax:* (03) 5142881 *E-mail:* adler@export.gov.il

**Israel Exploration Society+**
5 Avidah St, 91070 Jerusalem
Mailing Address: PO Box 7041, 91070 Jerusalem
*Tel:* (02) 6257991 *Fax:* (02) 6247772
*E-mail:* ies@vms.huji.ac.il
*Web Site:* www.hum.huji.ac.il/ies
*Key Personnel*
Man Dir: J Aviram
Founded: 1913
Subjects: Archaeology, Biblical Studies, Geogra-
  phy, Geology, History
ISBN Prefix(es): 965-221

**The Israel Institute for Occupational Safety &
  Hygiene**
22 Maze St, Tel Aviv
Mailing Address: PO Box 1122, 61010 Tel Aviv
*Tel:* (03) 6875037 *Fax:* (03) 6875038
*Web Site:* www.osh.org.il
*Key Personnel*
Dir: Menachem Schwartz *Tel:* (03) 5266444
  *E-mail:* menachem@osh.org.il
Deputy Dir: Chaim Eliyahu *Tel:* (03) 5266432
Head of Publishing: Andrei Matias *Tel:* (03)
  5266476 *Fax:* (03) 6208232
Distribution Manager: Hizkiya Israel *Tel:* (03)
  6575147 *Fax:* (03) 6575148

Subjects: Specialize in books about safety & hygiene in the work place
ISBN Prefix(es): 965-490

**Israel Museum Products Ltd**
PO Box 71117, Jerusalem 91710
*Tel:* (02) 6708811 *Fax:* (02) 6631833
*E-mail:* sb@imj.org.il
*Web Site:* www.imj.org.il
*Key Personnel*
Dir: Rita Gans
Founded: 1965
ISBN Prefix(es): 965-278

**Israel Music Institute (IMI)**
55 Menachem Begin Rd, 67138 Tel Aviv
Mailing Address: PO Box 51197, 67138 Tel Aviv
*Tel:* (03) 624 70 95 *Fax:* (03) 561 28 26
*E-mail:* musicinst@bezeqint.net
*Web Site:* www.imi.org.il
*Key Personnel*
Dir: Paul Landau
Founded: 1962
Membership(s): IAMIC; International Federation
  Serious Music Publishers.
Subjects: Music, Dance
Total Titles: 2,300 Print
Distributed by AB Nordiska Musikfoerlaget
  (Sweden); Albersen & Co BV (Holland);
  Cesky Hudebni Fond (Czech Republic, Hun-
  gary & Slovak Republik); Editions Musicales
  Europeennes (EME) (France, Belgium, Lux-
  embourg, Spain & Portugal); Engstrom & So-
  dring Musikforlag AS (Denmark); Harald &
  Lyche & Co AS (Norway); Peer Musikverlag
  GmbH (Germany, Austria & Switzerland); Ri-
  cordi Americana SAEC (Argentina); Theodore
  Presser Co (USA, Canada & Mexico)
Distributor for Th Presser & Co

**Israel Program for Scientific Translations,** see
  Keter Publishing House Ltd

**Israel Universities Press+**
Givat Shaul B, Jerusalem 91071
Mailing Address: PO Box 7145, Jerusalem 91071
*Tel:* (02) 6557822 *Fax:* (02) 6528962
*E-mail:* info@keter-books.co.il
*Web Site:* www.keter-books.co.il
*Key Personnel*
Man Dir: Yiftach Dekel
Founded: 1969
Subjects: Government, Political Science, Regional
  Interests, Social Sciences, Sociology
ISBN Prefix(es): 965-07
*Parent Company:* Keter Publishing House Ltd

**Israeli Music Publications Ltd**
25 Keren Hayesod St, 94188 Jerusalem
Mailing Address: PO Box 7681, 94188 Jerusalem
*Tel:* (02) 6241377; (02) 6241378 *Fax:* (02)
  62413708
*E-mail:* khanukaev@pop.isracom.net.il
*Key Personnel*
Dir: Sergei Khanukaev
Founded: 1949
Subjects: Music, Dance
ISBN Prefix(es): 965-259
Distributed by Theodore Presser Co (USA)

**Jabotinsky Institute in Israel**
38 King George St, Tel Aviv
Mailing Address: PO Box 23110, 61230 Tel Aviv
*Tel:* (03) 6210611; (03) 5287320 *Fax:* (03)
  5285587
*E-mail:* jabo@actcom.co.il
*Web Site:* www.jabotinsky.org
*Key Personnel*
Chairman: Peleg Tamir
Founded: 1937

Subjects: Government, Political Science, History
ISBN Prefix(es): 965-416

**(JDC) Brookdale Institute of Gerontology &
  Adult Human Development in Israel**
JDC Hill, Jerusalem 91130
Mailing Address: PO Box 13087, Jerusalem
  91130
*Tel:* (02) 6557445 *Fax:* (02) 5635851
*E-mail:* brook@jdc.org.il
*Web Site:* www.jdc.org.il/brookdale/
*Key Personnel*
Dir, Human Resources & Administration: Re-
  becca Caspi
Founded: 1974
Subjects: Health, Nutrition, Social Sciences, Soci-
  ology
ISBN Prefix(es): 965-353

**Jerusalem Center for Public Affairs**
c/o Beit Milken, 13 Tel Hai St, 92107 Jerusalem
*Tel:* (02) 5619281 *Fax:* (02) 5619112
*E-mail:* jcenter@jcpa.org
*Web Site:* www.jcpa.org
*Key Personnel*
President: Dr Dore Gold
Publications Coordinator: Mark Ami-El
Founded: 1976
Specialize in Israel, Jewish communities, Jewish
  political tradition & federalism.
ISBN Prefix(es): 965-218
Total Titles: 60 Print

**The Jerusalem Publishing House Ltd+**
39 Tchernichovsky St, Jerusalem 91071
Mailing Address: PO Box 7147, Jerusalem 91071
*Tel:* (02) 5617744 *Fax:* (02) 5634266
*E-mail:* jphgagi@netvision.net.il
*Key Personnel*
Man Dir: Shlomo S Gafni *Fax:* (02) 54346016
Man Editor: Rachel Gilon
Founded: 1966
Israel Export Institute.
Subjects: Archaeology, History, Religion - Jewish

**Biblioteca Judaica,** see L B Publishing Co

**K Dictionaries Ltd+**
10 Nahum St, Tel Aviv 63503
*Tel:* (03) 5468102 *Fax:* (03) 5468103
*E-mail:* kd@kdictionaries.com
*Web Site:* kdictionaries.com
*Key Personnel*
Chief Executive Officer: Ilan J Kernerman
  *E-mail:* contact@kdictionaries.com
Founded: 1993
Specialize in the development & global marketing
  of bilingual English learners dictionaries for
  different levels & all electronic applications,
  multilingual dictionaries & general bilingual
  (non-English) dictionaries. Local language ver-
  sions appear by local publishers worldwide.
Subjects: English as a Second Language, Lan-
  guage Arts, Linguistics
ISBN Prefix(es): 965-90207
*Associate Companies:* Kernerman Publishing Ltd
Imprints: Kernerman Semi-Bilingual Dictionaries
Distributed by Alma Littera (Lithuania); As-
  chehoug (Norway); Andrew Betsis, ELT
  (Greece); Bookman Books (Taiwan); Colibri
  (Bulgaria); DZS (Slovenia); EDDA (Iceland);
  ELI (Italy); Festart (Estonia); Fragment (Czech
  Republic); Inkilap (Turkey); Kernerman Pub-
  lishing (Israel); Kesaint Blanc (Indonesia);
  Kielikone (Finland); Martins Fontes Editora
  (Brazil); Mlada Fronta (Czech Republic); Mod-
  ulo Editeur (Canada); Nemzeti Tankonivki-
  ado (NTK) (Hungary); Niculescu (Romania);
  The Popular Group (USA); PWN (Poland);
  Rokus (Slovenia); Shanghai Lexicographical
  Publishing House (China); Skolska Knjiga

(Croatia); Ediciones SM (Spain); SPN - Mlada Leta (Slovak Republic); Studentlitteratur (Sweden); System Publishing House (Malaysia); TEA (Estonia); Thai Watana Panich (Thailand); Russky Yazyk (Russia); Sesame Publications (Hong Kong); Unistar Books (India); WSOY (Finland); YBM Si-sa-yong-o-sa (Korea); Zanichelli Editore (Italy); Zvaigzne ABC Publishers (Latvia)

**Karni Publishers Ltd**
32 Schocken St, 66556 Tel Aviv
*Tel:* (03) 812244 *Fax:* (03) 826138
*E-mail:* info@zmora.co.il
*Key Personnel*
Man Dir: Ohad Zmora
Founded: 1951
Subjects: Biography, Fiction, How-to, Poetry
ISBN Prefix(es): 965-254
*Parent Company:* Dvir Publishing House
Subsidiaries: Megiddo Publishing Co Ltd

**The Harry Karren Institute for the Analysis of Propaganda, Yad Labanim**
Yad Labanim, Wolfson Str, 46489 Herzliya
*Tel:* (09) 9573736 *Fax:* (09) 9546896
*Key Personnel*
Contact: Elisa Mermelstein
Subjects: Film, Video, Journalism
ISBN Prefix(es): 965-414

**Kernerman Semi-Bilingual Dictionaries,** *imprint of* Kernerman Publishing Ltd

**Kernerman/Password,** see K Dictionaries Ltd

**Kernerman Publishing Ltd+**
Affiliate of K Dictionaries Ltd
10 Nahum St, 63503 Tel Aviv
*Tel:* (03) 5468102 *Fax:* (03) 5468103
*E-mail:* kd@kdictionaries.com
*Web Site:* www.kdictionaries.com
*Key Personnel*
Chief Executive: Ari Kernerman
Production Manager: Nili Sadeh
Founded: 1969
Specialize in English learner's dictionaries for non-native speakers & general English-Hebrew dictionaries.
Subjects: Education, English as a Second Language
ISBN Prefix(es): 965-307
*Associate Companies:* Password Publishers Ltd
Imprints: Password; Kernerman Semi-Bilingual Dictionaries
Distributor for Chambers-Harrap; Oxford University Press (Israel); Simon & Schuster Education
*Orders to:* Lonnie Kahn Ltd, 20 Eliahu Eitan St, 75703 Rishon L'Tsion *Tel:* (03) 9518418 *Fax:* (03) 9518415 *E-mail:* kpu@internet-zahav.net

**Kernerman Semi-Bilingual Dictionaries,** *imprint of* K Dictionaries Ltd

**Keter,** *imprint of* Keter Publishing House Ltd

**Keter Publishing House Ltd+**
16th Beit Hadfus, Givat Sahul B, 91071 Jerusalem
Mailing Address: PO Box 7145, 91071 Jerusalem
*Tel:* (02) 6557822 *Fax:* (02) 6528962
*E-mail:* info@keter-books.co.il
*Web Site:* www.keter-books.co.il
*Key Personnel*
Man Dir: Yiftach Dekel
Publisher & Editor: Zvika Meir
Founded: 1959
Subjects: Art, Fiction, How-to, Philosophy, Psychology, Psychiatry, Social Sciences, Sociology

ISBN Prefix(es): 965-07
Imprints: Domino; Encyclopedia Judaica; Keter
Subsidiaries: Domino Press; Encyclopaedia Judaica; Israel Program for Scientific Translations

**Kiryat Sefer**
66 Allenby St, Tel Aviv 65812
*Tel:* (03) 5178922 *Fax:* (03) 5100227
*Key Personnel*
Man Dir: Avi Sivan
Founded: 1933
Subjects: Fiction, Poetry, Religion - Other
ISBN Prefix(es): 965-17

**Kivunim-Arsan Publishing House+**
21 Hgalgal St, Industrial Area, Rehovot 76488
*Tel:* (08) 9470791 *Fax:* (08) 9469740
*Key Personnel*
Man Dir: Arieh Sandler
Founded: 1980
Subjects: Humor, Management
ISBN Prefix(es): 965-276
*Showroom(s):* Elhad Haam 20, Rehovot 76260
*Bookshop(s):* Elhad Haam 20, Rehovot 76260

**Koren Publishers Jerusalem Ltd**
33 Herzog St, 42622 Jerusalem
Mailing Address: PO Box 4044, 91040 Jerusalem
*Tel:* (02) 5660188 *Fax:* (02) 5666658
*Web Site:* www.koren-publishers.co.il
*Key Personnel*
Dir: Eli Koren
Man Dir: Eli Kahn
Founded: 1962
Printing & publishing of the Korean Bible.
Subjects: Biblical Studies, Religion - Jewish
ISBN Prefix(es): 965-301
*Parent Company:* Maron Publishing Co Ltd
Distributed by Feldheim Publishers
Distributor for Maron Publishing Co Ltd

**L B Publishing,** *imprint of* L B Publishing Co

**L B Publishing Co+**
Imprint of Editorial D A Let C A
PO Box 32056, Jerusalem 91000
*Tel:* (02) 5664637 *Fax:* (02) 5290774
*E-mail:* editorial_lb@yahoo.com
*Key Personnel*
President: Lili Breziner
Editor-in-Chief: Salomon Lewinsky
Founded: 1993
Also acts as mediator & publisher for third parties; Specialize in Judaica.
Membership(s): Publishers Association (Israel).
Subjects: Regional Interests, Religion - Jewish, Israel Dispora, Jewish History
ISBN Prefix(es): 965-484
Number of titles published annually: 5 Print
Total Titles: 35 Print
*Parent Company:* Reencuentro L B Publishing Co
*Associate Companies:* Reencuentro L B Editorial C A, Calle Santa Clara, Edif Bertolini, Piso 3, Boleita Norte, Caracas, Venezuela *Tel:* 2345554 *Fax:* 2345555
Imprints: L B Publishing
Subsidiaries: Biblioteca Judaica
Distributed by Galerna (Buenos Aires); Nuevas Estructuras (Madrid)
Distributor for Anaya; Planeta; Universidad de Salamanca
Foreign Rep(s): Galerna (Argentina); Gandhi (Mexico); Nuevas Estructuras (Spain)

**Le'Dory Publishing House+**
6 Ginzburg St, 75150 Lezion
Mailing Address: PO Box 75092, 75150 Lezion
*Tel:* (03) 9612182
*Key Personnel*
Manager: Gil Gefner
ISBN Prefix(es): 965-402

**Maaliyot-Institute for Research Publications**
Mitzpeh Nevo, 90610 Maaleh Adumim
Mailing Address: PO Box 113, 90610 Maaleh Adumim
*Tel:* (02) 5353655 *Fax:* (02) 5353947
*E-mail:* ybm@virtual.co.il
Subjects: Religion - Jewish
ISBN Prefix(es): 965-417

**Ma'alot Publishing Company Ltd**
29 Carlebach St, 67132 Tel Aviv
Mailing Address: PO Box 20123, 61201 Tel Aviv
*Tel:* (03) 5614121 *Fax:* (03) 5611996
*E-mail:* maalot@tbpai.co.il
*Web Site:* www.tbpai.co.il
*Key Personnel*
Man Dir: Amnon Ben-Shmuel
Founded: 1969
Established by the Book Publishers' Association of Israel as a jointly-owned publishing house in which most of the members of the Association are shareholders.
*Parent Company:* Book Publishers Association of Israel

**Maarachot,** *imprint of* Ministry of Defence Publishing House

**Ma'ariv Book Guild (Sifriat Ma'ariv)**
3A Yoni Netanyahu St, 60376 Or Yehuda
*Tel:* (03) 5333333 *Fax:* (03) 5333619
*Telex:* 033735 *Cable:* Ma'ariv Telaviv
*Key Personnel*
Publisher & Editor-in-Chief: Aryeh Nir
Man Dir: Yitzhak Kfir
Founded: 1954
Subjects: Biography, Education, Fiction, Geography, Geology, Government, Political Science, History, Religion - Other, Science (General), Travel
ISBN Prefix(es): 965-239
*Book Club(s):* Ma'ariv Book Club

**Machbarot Lesifrut**
11 Lev Pesach St, North Industrial Area, Lod 71293
Mailing Address: PO Box 4020, Lod 71110
*Tel:* (08) 9246565 *Fax:* (08) 9251770
*E-mail:* info@zmora.co.il
*Key Personnel*
Man Dir: Zvi Zmora
Subjects: Fiction, Government, Political Science, History, Language Arts, Linguistics, Literature, Literary Criticism, Essays
Number of titles published annually: 20 Print
Total Titles: 250 Print
*Associate Companies:* Zmora Bitan-Publishing House

**The Magnes Press+**
The Hebrew University, PO Box 39099, 91390 Jerusalem
*Tel:* (02) 6586656 *Fax:* (02) 5633370
*E-mail:* magnes@vms.huji.ac.il
*Web Site:* www.huji.ac.il
*Key Personnel*
Man Dir: Dan Benovici
Founded: 1929
Subjects: Archaeology, Art, Biography, History, Law, Music, Dance, Philosophy, Psychology, Psychiatry, Science (General)
ISBN Prefix(es): 965-223; 965-493
*Parent Company:* The Hebrew University, Jerusalem
Imprints: Mount Scopus Press

**MAP-Mapping & Publishing Ltd+**
17 Tchernichovsky St, 61560 Tel Aviv
Mailing Address: PO Box 56024, 61560 Tel Aviv
*Tel:* (03) 6210500 *Fax:* (03) 5257725
*E-mail:* info@mapa.co.il

*Web Site:* www.mapa.co.il
*Key Personnel*
Man Dir: Dani Tracz
Editor-in-Chief: Mulli Meltzer
Founded: 1985
Subjects: History, Nonfiction (General), Travel
ISBN Prefix(es): 965-7009
Number of titles published annually: 35 Print
Total Titles: 200 Print
Imprints: Tel Aviv Books
*Book Club(s):* The Map Children Book Club

**Massada Press Ltd+**
PO Box 1232, 91000 Jerusalem
*Tel:* (02) 6719441 *Fax:* (02) 6719442 *Cable:*
ENCYCLOMAS
*Key Personnel*
Board Chairman, Chief Executive, Rights & Permissions: Alexander Peli
Man Dir: Nathan Regev
Founded: 1932
Subjects: Art, Biography, Cookery, Education, History, How-to, Music, Dance, Philosophy, Psychology, Psychiatry, Religion - Jewish, Religion - Other, Science (General), Social Sciences, Sociology
ISBN Prefix(es): 965-257
*Associate Companies:* Yeda Lakol Publishing Co Ltd

**Massada Publishers Ltd**
9 Bialik St, 53447 Givatayim
Mailing Address: PO Box 187, 53101 Givatayim
*Tel:* (03) 5716659; (03) 5712702 *Fax:* (03) 5716639
*Telex:* 361211 Mape Il *Cable:* PELIPRINT
*Key Personnel*
Man Dir: Yoav Barash
Founded: 1932
Subjects: Art, Cookery, Fiction, History, How-to
ISBN Prefix(es): 965-10
*Associate Companies:* Peli Printing Works Ltd; Reprocolor Ltd

**Matar Publishing House**
43 Brodetsky St, 69052 Tel Aviv
*Tel:* (03) 7441199 *Fax:* (03) 7441314
*E-mail:* mtriwaks@netvision.net.il
*Key Personnel*
Man Dir: Moshe Triwacks
Subsidiaries: Triwaks Books Ltd

**Medcom Ltd**
PO Box 751, 49107 Petach-Tikva
*Tel:* (03) 9343853 *Fax:* (03) 9343850
Founded: 1981
Subjects: Chemistry, Chemical Engineering, Medicine, Nursing, Dentistry
ISBN Prefix(es): 965-272

**Megiddo Publishing Co Ltd**, see Karni Publishers Ltd

**Michael's Guides**, *imprint of* Inbal Travel Information

**Midrashiat Naom, Pardess Hanna**
3 Achuzat Bayit St, Tel Aviv 65143
*Tel:* (09) 5172637 *Fax:* (09) 5100594
ISBN Prefix(es): 965-469

**Ministry of Defence Publishing House+**
27 David Elazar St, 67673 Hakiryah
Mailing Address: PO Box 7103, 67673 Tel Aviv
*Tel:* (03) 6917940 *Fax:* (03) 6375509
*Key Personnel*
Dir: Joseph Perlovitch
Deputy Dir & Chief Editor: Yishai Cordova
*Tel:* (03) 5655956
Founded: 1939

Subjects: Foreign Countries, History, Military Science, History of the Land of Israel & Geography; Holocaust; Albums, Picture Books
ISBN Prefix(es): 965-05
Total Titles: 1,500 Print
Imprints: MOD: Broadcast University; Maarachot; To Live (Holocaust)

**Mirkam Publishers+**
PO Box 10209, Nof-Kingreth, Post Office Rosh Pina 12000
*Tel:* (06) 6900967 *Fax:* (06) 6900967
*Key Personnel*
Owner, Chief Editor & General Manager: Yafa Shoham
Founded: 1993
Mostly translations of material to acquaint the Israeli reader with current metaphysical understanding & information
Privately owned enterprise.
Subjects: Spiritual Growth & Channeling
Total Titles: 15 Print
Distributed by Lior Sharf Marketing & Distribution

**Misgav Yerushalayim**
Unit of Faculty of Humanities
Faculty of Humanities, The Hebrew University of Jerusalem, Mount Scopus, 91905 Jerusalem
Mailing Address: PO Box 4035, 91040 Jerusalem
*Tel:* (02) 5883962 *Fax:* (02) 5815460
*E-mail:* misgav@h2.hum.huji.ac.il
*Web Site:* www.hum.huji.ac.il/misgav
*Key Personnel*
Dir: Prof Zeev W Harvey
Deputy Dir: Ms Nitza Genuth
Founded: 1972
University Research Center specializing in academic teaching & research on Shephardi & Oriental Jewry (multi-disciplinary).
Subjects: Art, Ethnicity, History, Language Arts, Linguistics, Literature, Literary Criticism, Essays, Philosophy, Religion - Jewish
ISBN Prefix(es): 965-296; 965-493
Total Titles: 1 Print
*Ultimate Parent Company:* The Hebrew University, Jerusalem

**Miskal Publishing Ltd+**
20 Magshimim St, Petah-Tikwa 49348
*Tel:* (03) 9246980 *Fax:* (03) 9246985
*Key Personnel*
President: Dov Eichenwald
Man Dir: Haim Eichenwald
Founded: 1984
*Parent Company:* Yedioth Ahronot
*Warehouse:* 19 Merkava St, Holon

**M Mizrahi Publishers**
67 Levinsky St, Tel Aviv 66855
*Tel:* (03) 6870936 *Fax:* (03) 5475399 *Cable:*
MIZEDITION TELAVIV
*Key Personnel*
Man Dir: Meir Mizrahi; Israel Mizrahi
Founded: 1960
Subjects: Fiction, History, Medicine, Nursing, Dentistry, Science (General)
*Branch Office(s)*
33 Hagivea St, Savyon *Tel:* 344661

**MOD: Broadcast University**, *imprint of* Ministry of Defence Publishing House

**Modan Publishers Ltd**
8 Meshek 33, 73115 Moshav Ben-Shemen
*Tel:* (08) 9221821 *Fax:* (08) 9221299
*E-mail:* modan@modan.co.il
*Web Site:* www.modan.co.il
*Key Personnel*
Man Dir: Oded Modan
Dir: A Friedman

Subjects: Cookery, Religion - Jewish, Classics
ISBN Prefix(es): 965-341; 965-7141

**Mosad Harav Kook**, see Rav Kook Institute

**The Moshe Dayan Center for Middle Eastern & African Studies**
Tel Aviv University, Ramat Aviv, Tel Aviv 69978
*Tel:* (03) 640-9646 *Fax:* (03) 641-5802
*E-mail:* dayancen@post.tau.ac.il
*Web Site:* www.dayan.org *Cable:* 342171 vesy il
*Key Personnel*
Head of Center: Dr Martin Kramer
Founded: 1959
Subjects: History, Modern Middle East
ISBN Prefix(es): 965-224
Distributed by Frank Cass; Oxford University Press; Syracuse University Press; Westview Press

**Mount Scopus Press**, *imprint of* The Magnes Press

**Nehora Press**
3 Kiryat Sara, Har Canaan, Safed 13410
Mailing Address: PO Box 2586, Safed 13410
*Tel:* (04) 6970255 *Fax:* (04) 6970255
*E-mail:* nehora@canaan.co.il
*Web Site:* www.nehorapress.com
*Key Personnel*
Publisher: Amanda Goodman-Cohen
Founded: 2002
Publish authentic translations of Kabbalah from Hebrew into English.
Membership(s): Publishers Marketing Association.
Subjects: Philosophy, Religion - Jewish
ISBN Prefix(es): 965-7222
Number of titles published annually: 3 Print
*Shipping Address:* 8153 Hansen Rd NE, Bainbridge Island, WA 98110, United States, Contact: D Steinecher *Tel:* 206-780-0124
*Returns:* 8153 Hansen Rd NE, Bainbridge Island, WA 98110, United States, Contact: D Steinecher

**Nitzanim**, *imprint of* Carta, The Israel Map & Publishing Co Ltd

**Open University of Israel+**
16 Klausner St, Ramat Aviv, Tel Aviv 61392
Mailing Address: PO Box 39328, Tel Aviv 61392
*Tel:* (03) 6460460 *Fax:* (03) 6419279
*E-mail:* englishsite@openu.ac.il
*Web Site:* www.openu.ac.il
*Key Personnel*
President: Prof Eliahu Nissim
Founded: 1974
Occasionally engages in joint publications with Yale University Press & Boston University
Specialize in Academic Publications & Textbooks in Hebrew.
Subjects: Accounting, Biblical Studies, Biological Sciences, Chemistry, Chemical Engineering, Computer Science, Economics, Education, Government, Political Science, History, Journalism, Literature, Literary Criticism, Essays, Management, Mathematics, Physics, Psychology, Psychiatry, Religion - Jewish, Social Sciences, Sociology
ISBN Prefix(es): 965-302; 965-06
*U.S. Office(s):* American Friends of the Open Univeristy of Israel, 180 W 80 St, New York, NY 10024, United States *Tel:* 212-712-1800 *Fax:* 212-496-3296

**Or-Teva**, *imprint of* Or'am Publishers

**Or'am Publishers+**
28 Itzhak Sade St, Tel Aviv 67212
*Tel:* (03) 5372277 *Fax:* (03) 5372281

*E-mail:* orampub@netvision.net.il
*Web Site:* www.oram.co.il
*Key Personnel*
Man Dir: Or'am Shatz; Shoshana Shatz
Founded: 1974
ISBN Prefix(es): 965-230
Total Titles: 1,700 Print; 10 Audio
Imprints: Or-Teva

**Orbach Editions Ltd**, *imprint of* Bitan
Publishers Ltd

**Papyrus**, *imprint of* Dyonon/Papyrus Publishing
House of the Tel-Aviv

**Password**, *imprint of* Kernerman Publishing Ltd

**Pitspopany Press+**
c/o Simcha Publishing Co, PO Box 4636,
Jerusalem 91044
*Tel:* (02) 6233507 *Fax:* (02) 6233510
*E-mail:* pitspop@netvision.net.il
*Web Site:* www.pitspopany.com
*Key Personnel*
President: Yaacov Peterseil
Administrator: Wendy Tohar
Founded: 1993
Subjects: Cookery, Fiction, Health, Nutrition, Hu-
mor, Mysteries, Religion - Jewish, Science Fic-
tion, Fantasy, Self-Help, Adult Fiction & Non-
Fiction
ISBN Prefix(es): 965-483; 1-930143; 0-943706
Number of titles published annually: 15 Print
Total Titles: 100 Print
Imprints: Devora Publishing Co; Simcha Pub
*U.S. Office(s):* 40 E 78 St, Suite 16D, New York,
NY 10021, United States *Tel:* 212-472-4959
*Fax:* 212-472-6253
*Shipping Address:* 7253 Grayson Rd, Harrisburg,
PA 17111, United States *Tel:* 712-564-2111
*Distribution Center:* Stackpole Distribution

**Prolog Publishing House**
PO Box 300, 48101 Rosh Ha'ayin
*Tel:* (03) 9022904 *Fax:* (03) 9022906
*E-mail:* info@prolog.co.il
*Web Site:* www.prolog.co.il
*Key Personnel*
Man Dir: Ben Naim Raanan
Founded: 1988
Specialize in language teaching audio-video cas-
sette courses, how-to books.
Subjects: How-to, Language Arts, Linguistics

**Rav Kook Institute+**
Shchunat Maimon St, Jerusalem 91006
Mailing Address: PO Box 642, Jerusalem 91006
*Tel:* (02) 6526231 *Fax:* (02) 6526968
*Key Personnel*
Dir General: Joseph Mowshovitz
Founded: 1937
Non-profit public corporation supported by the
Jewish Agency, Ministry of Education & Cul-
ture & Ministry of Religious Affairs. Also pro-
vides financial support for works in subjects
below.
Subjects: Biography, Philosophy, Religion - Jew-
ish, Religion - Other, Theology
ISBN Prefix(es): 965-7265
Number of titles published annually: 10 Print
Total Titles: 3,000 Print

**Rolnik Publishers+**
PO Box 17075, 61170 Tel Aviv
*Tel:* (03) 6496663 *Fax:* (03) 6478661
*E-mail:* rolknik@attglobal.net
*Web Site:* www.rolnik.com; www.bible2000.com
*Key Personnel*
Publisher: Amos Rolnik
Founded: 1970

Subjects: Art, Biblical Studies, Film, Video, Israel, Hebrew Studies
ISBN Prefix(es): 965-326

**Rubin Mass Ltd+**
PO Box 990, Jerusalem 91009
*Tel:* (02) 627-7863 *Fax:* (02) 627-7864
*E-mail:* rmass@barak.net.il
*Web Site:* www.rubin-mass.com
*Key Personnel*
Man Dir: Mr Oren Mass
Founded: 1927
Also acts as exporters of Israeli publications &
periodicals.
Subjects: Biblical Studies, Biography, Education,
Government, Political Science, Medicine, Nurs-
ing, Dentistry, Philosophy, Psychology, Psy-
chiatry, Publishing & Book Trade Reference,
Religion - Jewish, Religion - Other
ISBN Prefix(es): 965-09
Total Titles: 1,600 Print; 3 CD-ROM
Distributor for Carta; Yad Vashm

**Saar Publishing House**
39 Basel St, Tel Aviv 62744
Mailing Address: POB 26243, Tel Aviv 62744
*Tel:* (03) 5445292 *Fax:* (03) 5445293
*Key Personnel*
Man Dir: Saar Hanoch
Founded: 1979
Specialize in the publication of original & trans-
lated poetry.
Subjects: Fiction, Humor, Travel

**Sadan Publishing Ltd+**
One David Hamelech St, Tel Aviv 64953
Mailing Address: PO Box 16096, Tel Aviv 64953
*Tel:* (03) 6954402 *Fax:* (03) 6953122
*Key Personnel*
President: David Sadan
Founded: 1962
Firm is also an international co-publisher & pack-
ager.
Subjects: Archaeology, Biblical Studies, Law
ISBN Prefix(es): 965-234
Subsidiaries: Sadan Publication International Inc

**Schlesinger Institute**
Shaare Zedek Medical Center, PO Box 3235,
Jerusalem 91031
*Tel:* (02) 655-5266 *Fax:* (02) 655-5266
*E-mail:* medhal@szmc.org.il
*Web Site:* www.szmc.org.il
*Key Personnel*
Dir: Dr Mordechai Halperin
Subjects: Law, Medicine, Nursing, Dentistry, Re-
ligion - Jewish

**Schocken Publishing House for Children**,
*imprint of* Schocken Publishing House Ltd

**Schocken Publishing House Ltd+**
24 Nathan Yelin Mor St, Tel Aviv 67015
Mailing Address: POB 2316, Tel Aviv 61022
*Tel:* (03) 5610130 *Fax:* (03) 5622668
*E-mail:* find@schocken.co.il *Cable:*
SCHOCKENIS
*Key Personnel*
Man Dir: Racheli Edelman *E-mail:* racheli@
haaretz.co.il
Production: Dita Eliaz
Rights & Permissions: Ms Shira Asher
Founded: 1938
Membership(s): Israeli Book Publishers Associa-
tion.
Subjects: Anthropology, Behavioral Sciences,
Child Care & Development, Criminology,
Drama, Theater, Economics, Education, Fiction,
Health, Nutrition, History, Law, Literature, Lit-
erary Criticism, Essays, Nonfiction (General),

Philosophy, Poetry, Psychology, Psychiatry, Re-
ligion - Jewish, Travel, Women's Studies
ISBN Prefix(es): 965-19
Imprints: Schocken Publishing House for Chil-
dren; Shin, Shin, Shin
Divisions: Schocken Publishing House
*Warehouse:* Schocken Publishing House, 19
Lilienblum St, Tel Aviv

**Shalem Press**
22A Hatzfira St, 93102 Jerusalem
*Tel:* (02) 566-0601 *Fax:* (02) 566-0590
*E-mail:* shalem@shalem.org.il
*Web Site:* www.shalem.org.il
*Key Personnel*
Contact: Anat Altman *E-mail:* anata@shalem.org.
il; Shmnel Reisman *E-mail:* shmuelr@shalem.
org.il
Founded: 1994
Publish original books in Hebrew & English.
Translate books into Hebrew.
Subjects: Economics, Government, Political Sci-
ence, History, Philosophy, Cultural Issues
ISBN Prefix(es): 965-7052
Total Titles: 3 Print
*Parent Company:* The Shalem Center
*U.S. Office(s):* The Shalem Center, 1140 Con-
necticut Ave NW, Suite 801, Washington,
DC 20036, United States *Tel:* 202-887-1270
*Fax:* 202-887-1277
Distributed by Armony Ltd

**Shin, Shin, Shin**, *imprint of* Schocken Publishing
House Ltd

**Sifri**, *imprint of* Steimatzky Group Ltd

**Sifri Ltd**
PO Box 526, Tel Aviv 61004
*Tel:* (03) 5784679
*Key Personnel*
Dir: Yehoshua Matzliah; Eri M Steimatzky

**Sifriat Poalim Ltd**
24 Kibbutz Galuyot St, Merkazim Buil Gate 3,
Tel Aviv 68166
Mailing Address: PO Box 37068, Tel Aviv 61369
*Tel:* (03) 5183143 *Fax:* (03) 5183191
*E-mail:* akantor@inter.net.il
*Key Personnel*
Man Dir: Avram Kantor
Management: Shlomo Zur
Encyclopedias: Amram Gordon
Production: Yaakov Shaia
Rights & Permissions: Yona Herzberg
Founded: 1939
Subjects: Art, Fiction, History, Labor, Industrial
Relations, Philosophy, Social Sciences, Sociol-
ogy
ISBN Prefix(es): 965-04

**Simcha Pub**, *imprint of* Pitspopany Press

**Sinai Publishing Co**
72 Allenby St, 65812 Tel Aviv
*Tel:* (03) 5163672 *Fax:* (03) 5176783
*Key Personnel*
Man Dir: Moshe Schlesinger
Founded: 1853
Subjects: Religion - Jewish
ISBN Prefix(es): 965-7055
Subsidiaries: Sinai Export Co Ltd
*Bookshop(s):* Sinai Bookstore

**R Sirkis Publishers Ltd+**
13 Bialik St, 52523 Ramat-Gan
Mailing Address: POB 22027, 61220 Tel Aviv
*Tel:* (03) 7510792 *Fax:* (03) 7513750
*E-mail:* sirkispb@inter.net.il

*Key Personnel*
Man Dir: Rafael Sirkis
President & Chief Editor: Ruth Sirkis
Founded: 1983
Subjects: Archaeology, Art, Child Care & Development, Cookery, Crafts, Games, Hobbies, Fashion, Gardening, Plants, Health, Nutrition, How-to, Psychology, Psychiatry, Self-Help, Travel
ISBN Prefix(es): 965-387

**Y Sreberk+**
16 Balfour St, Tel Aviv 65211
*Tel:* (03) 6293343 *Fax:* (03) 6299297
*Key Personnel*
Man Dir: Zeev Namir
Production Manager: Y Namir
Founded: 1951
Subjects: Literature, Literary Criticism, Essays, Music, Dance, Classics

**Steimatzky,** *imprint of* Steimatzky Group Ltd

**Steimatzky Group Ltd+**
11 Hakishon St, Bnei-Brak 51114
Mailing Address: PO Box 1444, Bnei-Brak 51114
*Tel:* (03) 5775777 *Fax:* (03) 5794567
*E-mail:* info@steimatzky.co.il
*Web Site:* www.steimatzky.com
*Key Personnel*
Chief Executive Officer: Eri M Steimatzky
Man Dir: Yehoshua Matzliah
Founded: 1925
130 bookshops around the country. Also wholesaler, distributor, publisher, book club & mail order.
Subjects: Art, Biography, Cookery, Fiction, Religion - Jewish, Travel
ISBN Prefix(es): 965-236
*Associate Companies:* SIFRI Ltd
Imprints: Sifri; Steimatzky

**Steinhart-Katzir Publishers+**
PO Box 16540, 61164 Tel Aviv
*Tel:* (03) 6960995 *Toll Free Tel:* 800-22-5854
  *Fax:* (09) 8854771
*E-mail:* webmaster@haolam.co.il
*Web Site:* www.haolam.co.il
*Key Personnel*
Man Dir: Ohad Sharav
Founded: 1991
Subjects: Travel
ISBN Prefix(es): 965-420
Number of titles published annually: 20 Print
Total Titles: 100 Print
Distributor for Berndtson & Berndtson; Freytag & Berndt; ITM; Karto Alatier; National Geographic

**Talmudic Encyclopedia Publications**
One Hapisga St, 91160 Jerusalem
Mailing Address: PO Box 16066, 91160 Jerusalem
*Tel:* (02) 6423242 *Fax:* (02) 6423919
*Key Personnel*
Man Dir: Rabbi Yehoshua Hutner
Founded: 1949
Subjects: Religion - Jewish
ISBN Prefix(es): 965-445

**Tamai Books,** *imprint of* Dekel Publishing House

**Tcherikover Publishers Ltd**
12 Hasharon St, Tel Aviv 66185
*Tel:* (03) 6870621; (03) 6396099
  *Toll Free Tel:* 800-828-080 *Fax:* (03) 6874729
*E-mail:* barkay@inter.net.il
*Key Personnel*
Man Dir: Moshe Barkay *E-mail:* barkay@inter.net.il
Manager, Editorial: S Tcherikover

Subjects: Art, Criminology, Economics, Education, Geography, Geology, History, Language Arts, Linguistics, Literature, Literary Criticism, Essays, Management, Nonfiction (General), Psychology, Psychiatry
ISBN Prefix(es): 965-16

**Tel Aviv Books,** *imprint of* MAP-Mapping & Publishing Ltd

**Tel Aviv Books Ltd**
Imprint of MAP - Mapping & Publishing
17 Tchernikhovsky St, Tel Aviv 61560
*Tel:* (03) 6210500 *Fax:* (03) 5257725

**Tel Aviv University+**
The Jaffee Center for Strategic Studies, The Yariv Wing, Gilman Bldg, 69978 Tel Aviv
Mailing Address: PO Box 39040, 69978 Tel Aviv
*Tel:* (03) 6408111; (03) 6424571; (03) 6409200; (03) 6426682 *Fax:* (03) 6422404; (03) 6408355
*E-mail:* tauinfo@post.tau.ac.il
*Web Site:* www.tau.ac.il
*Key Personnel*
Prof: Zeev Maoz
Founded: 1977
Subjects: Foreign Countries, Government, Political Science, History, Military Science, Regional Interests, Social Sciences, Sociology
ISBN Prefix(es): 965-459
*U.S. Office(s):* Westview Press, Boulder, CO, United States
Distributed by Jerusalem Post (Israel); Westview Press

**Terra Sancta Arts+**
PO Box 10009, Tel Aviv 61100
*Tel:* (03) 6499520; (03) 6499525 *Fax:* (03) 6490532
*Key Personnel*
Man Dir: Gil Ran; Nachman Ran
Founded: 1972
Subjects: Biblical Studies, Religion - Other
ISBN Prefix(es): 965-260
*Shipping Address:* 31 Ehud Str, Tel Aviv 69936

**Tirosh Communication Ltd**
PO Box 6428, Tel Aviv 61063
*Tel:* (03) 6044959 *Fax:* (03) 6053840
*E-mail:* hgeffen@netvision.net.il
*Key Personnel*
International Rights: Amos Geffen
Founded: 1969
ISBN Prefix(es): 965-330

**To Live (Holocaust),** *imprint of* Ministry of Defence Publishing House

**Harry S Truman Research Institute for the Advancement for Peace+**
Hebrew University of Jerusalem, Mount Scopus, Jerusalem 91905
*Tel:* (02) 58823000; (02) 58823001; (02) 5882315 *Fax:* (02) 5828076
*E-mail:* mstruman@pluto.mscc.huji.ac.il
*Web Site:* truman.huji.ac.il
*Telex:* SCOPUS JERUSALEM
*Key Personnel*
Chairman: Ambassador William A Brown
Dir: Prof Eyal Ben-Ari
Administrative Dir: Dr Nauma Shpeter
Founded: 1966

**Tsohar Publications,** *imprint of* Breslov Research Institute

**University of Haifa Library**
Mount Carmel, 31905 Haifa
*Tel:* (04) 257753 *Fax:* (04) 342104
*E-mail:* webmaster@lib.haifa.ac.il

*Web Site:* lib.haifa.ac.il
*Key Personnel*
Dir: Baruch Kipnis *E-mail:* baruch@univ.haifa.ac.il
Head of Administration: Ms Humi Rekem
Subjects: Library & Information Sciences

**University Publishing Projects Ltd+**
10 Zarhin St, 43104 Raanana
Mailing Address: PO Box 393, 43104 Raanana
*Tel:* (09) 7459955 *Fax:* (09) 7459977
*E-mail:* upp@upp.co.il
*Web Site:* www.upp.co.il
*Key Personnel*
Dir: Nathan Eden
Founded: 1970
Subjects: English as a Second Language, Religion - Jewish, English as a Foreign Language (EFL)
ISBN Prefix(es): 965-372
Number of titles published annually: 25 Print
Total Titles: 348 Print
Imprints: ESH (English for Speakers of Hebrew)

**Urim Publications+**
9 Hauman St, 2nd floor, 91521 Jerusalem
Mailing Address: PO Box 52287, 91521 Jerusalem
*Tel:* (02) 679-7633 *Fax:* (02) 679-7634
*E-mail:* publisher@urimpublications.com
*Web Site:* www.urimpublications.com
*Key Personnel*
Publisher: Tzvi Mauer
Children's Book Editor: Shari Dash Greenspan
  *E-mail:* children@urimpublications.com
Founded: 1997
Also worldwide distributor of new & classic books with Jewish content.
Subjects: Biblical Studies, Biography, Ethnicity, Fiction, Human Relations, Literature, Literary Criticism, Essays, Religion - Jewish, Women's Studies
ISBN Prefix(es): 965-7108
Number of titles published annually: 8 Print
Total Titles: 22 Print; 1 CD-ROM
*U.S. Office(s):* Lambda Publishers, 3709 13 Ave, Brooklyn, NY 11218, United States *Tel:* 718-972-5449 *Fax:* 718-972-6307
Distributed by Ingram (North America)
Distributor for Lambda Publishers, Inc (Jewish bookstores in North America)
*Distribution Center:* Lambda Publishers, 3709 13 Ave, Brooklyn, NY 11218, United States *Tel:* 718-972-5449 *Fax:* 718-972-6307

**The Van Leer Jerusalem Institute**
43 Jabotinsky St, 91040 Jerusalem
Mailing Address: PO Box 4070, 91040 Jerusalem
*Tel:* (02) 5605222 *Fax:* (02) 5619293
*E-mail:* values@vanleer.org.il
*Web Site:* www.vanleer.org.il
*Key Personnel*
Executive Editor: Esther Shashar
Founded: 1959
Subjects: Foreign Countries, Government, Political Science, Psychology, Psychiatry, Science (General), Social Sciences, Sociology
ISBN Prefix(es): 965-271

**Yachdav, United Publishers Co Ltd**
29 Carlebach St, 67132 Tel Aviv
Mailing Address: POB 20123, 61201 Tel Aviv
*Tel:* (03) 5614121 *Fax:* (03) 5611996
*E-mail:* maalot@tbpai.co.il
*Web Site:* www.tbpai.co.il
*Key Personnel*
Man Dir: Amnon Ben-Shmuel
Founded: 1960
Established by the Book Publishers' Association of Israel as a jointly-owned publishing house in which most of the members of the Association are shareholders.

Subjects: Philosophy, Psychology, Psychiatry, Public Administration, Social Sciences, Sociology
*Parent Company:* Book Publishers Association of Israel

**Yad Eliahu Kitov**
PO Box 894, 91008 Jerusalem
*Tel:* (02) 6248868 *Fax:* (02) 6248838
*E-mail:* benarza@netvision.net.il
*Key Personnel*
Man Dir: Chanoch Ben Arza *E-mail:* benarza@netvision.net.il
Subjects: Religion - Jewish
ISBN Prefix(es): 965-252

**Yad Izhak Ben-Zvi Press+**
Ben-Zvi Institute, 12 Abrabanel St, Gan Hakuzari, 91076 Jerusalem
Mailing Address: PO Box 7660, 91076 Jerusalem
*Tel:* (02) 5398887; (02) 5398888 *Fax:* (02) 5638310
*E-mail:* ybz@ybz.org.il
*Web Site:* ybz.org.il
*Key Personnel*
Dir: Dr Zvi Zameret
Chairman, Public Governing Council: Dr Shimshon Shoshani
English Publications Coordinator: Yohai Goell *Tel:* (02) 5398825
Founded: 1966
Specialize in the history of Palestine/Israel & the Oriental Jewish Communities.
Subjects: Geography, Geology, History, Regional Interests, Religion - Jewish
ISBN Prefix(es): 965-235; 965-217
Total Titles: 320 Print

**Yad Tabenkin**
52960 Ramat Efal
*Tel:* (03) 5346268 *Fax:* (03) 5346376
*E-mail:* yadtab@inter.net.il
*Web Site:* www.ic.org
Founded: 1976 (Research Institute)
ISBN Prefix(es): 965-282
Number of titles published annually: 4 Print

**Yad Vashem - The Holocaust Martyrs' & Heroes' Remembrance Authority+**
PO Box 3477, Jerusalem 91034
*Tel:* (02) 6443400 *Fax:* (02) 6443443
*E-mail:* general.information@yadvashem.org.il
*Web Site:* www.yad-vashem.org.il *Cable:* YADVASHEM JERUSALEM
*Key Personnel*
Chairman: Avner Shalev
Vice Chairman: Johanan Bein
Editorial: Prof Israel Gutman
Yad Vashem Studies: David Silberklang
Secretary-General: Ishai Amrami
Administrative Dir: Vashem Yad
Publications: Esther Aran
Founded: 1953
Subjects: Biography, Education, History, Nonfiction (General), Holocaust Research
ISBN Prefix(es): 965-308
*Branch Office(s)*
Heychal Wolyn, 10 Korazin St, PO Box 803, Givatayim
*U.S. Office(s):* American Society for Yad Vashem, 500 Fifth Ave, No 1600, New York, NY 10110, United States
Distributed by Rubin Mass Ltd, Publishers & Booksellers
*Bookshop(s):* Yad Vashem Distribution, PO Box 3477, Jerusalem 91034

**Yaron Golan Publishers**
3 Burla St, Tel Aviv 69364
*Tel:* (03) 6992867 *Fax:* (03) 6952664
Specializes in Hebrew books of prose & poetry.

ISBN Prefix(es): 965-395
Total Titles: 10 Print

**Yavneh Publishing House Ltd+**
4 Mazeh St, 65213 Tel Aviv
*Tel:* (03) 6297856 *Fax:* (03) 6293638
*E-mail:* publishing@yavneh.co.il
*Web Site:* www.dbook.co.il
*Key Personnel*
Man Dir: Eliav Cohen
Founded: 1932
Subjects: Fiction, Music, Dance, Religion - Jewish, Religion - Other, Science (General)
ISBN Prefix(es): 965-7305

**Yedioth Ahronoth Books+**
10 Kehilat Venezia St, 61534 Tel Aviv
Mailing Address: PO Box 53494, 61534 Tel Aviv
*Tel:* (03) 768-3333 *Fax:* (03) 768-3300
*E-mail:* info@yedbooks.co.il
*Web Site:* www.ybook.co.il
*Telex:* 33847
*Key Personnel*
Man Dir: Mr Dov Eichenwald
Editor-in-Chief: Aliza Ziegler
Founded: 1952
Subjects: Fiction, Health, Nutrition, How-to, Music, Dance, Nonfiction (General), Religion - Jewish
ISBN Prefix(es): 965-482
Number of titles published annually: 120 Print
*Parent Company:* Yedioth Ahronoth (The Evening Newspaper of Israel)
*Associate Companies:* Books in the Attaic, Amdan 5, Tel Aviv, Editor-in-Chief: Yehuda Melzer *Tel:* (03) 602-9010 *E-mail:* ilai@actcom.co.il
*Subsidiaries:* Miskal
*Warehouse:* 19 Hamerkava St, Holon

**Y L Peretz Publishing Co**
14 Brenner St, Tel Aviv 63826
*Tel:* (03) 5281751 *Fax:* (03) 5257983
*Key Personnel*
Man Dir: Israel Stein
Founded: 1956
Subjects: Art, History, Literature, Literary Criticism, Essays, Philosophy, Poetry, Religion - Jewish, Social Sciences, Sociology
ISBN Prefix(es): 965-7012

**Zakheim Publishing House+**
3 Bar Kochva St, 51263 Bney-Brak
Mailing Address: PO Box 2238, 52111 Bney-Brak
*Tel:* (03) 5708840 *Fax:* (03) 5708850
*E-mail:* zakheim@netvision.net.il
*Key Personnel*
General Manager: Eli Zakheim
Founded: 1967
Publishing house, wholesaler & distributor of educational materials & electronic kits of educational subjects. Specializes in children's books, educational equipment, encyclopedias & dictionaries for youths & children.
Total Titles: 4 Print

**The Zalman Shazar Center+**
2 Betar, 91041 Jerusalem
Mailing Address: PO Box 4179, 91041 Jerusalem
*Tel:* (02) 5650444; (02) 5650445 *Fax:* (02) 6712388
*E-mail:* shazar@shazar.org.il
*Web Site:* www.shazar.org.il
*Key Personnel*
Chairman & Editorial, Hebrew: Prof Richard I Cohen
Executive Dir & Dir, Rights & Permissions: Zvi Yekutiel
Editorial Board Secretary: Maayan Avineri-Rebhun *E-mail:* maayan@shazar.org.il

Founded: 1973
Specialize in Jewish history.
Membership(s): The Historical Society of Israel.
Subjects: History, Religion - Jewish, Collected Essays, Historical Novels for Youth, Monographs, Pictorial Albums, Textbooks
ISBN Prefix(es): 965-227
Total Titles: 250 Print

**Zmora-Bitan, Publishers Ltd**
11 Lev Pesach, 71293 N Industrial Area Lod
*Tel:* (08) 9246565 *Fax:* (08) 9251770
*E-mail:* info@zmora.co.il
*Key Personnel*
Man Dir: Ohad Zmora
Publisher & Publicity: Asher Bitan
Sales: Eran Zmora
Production: Maya Dvash
Founded: 1973
Subjects: Anthropology, Biography, Cookery, Economics, Fiction, Government, Political Science, History, Nonfiction (General), Self-Help
ISBN Prefix(es): 965-03
*Associate Companies:* Bitan; Machbarot Lesifrut
*Subsidiaries:* Alpha Publishing House; Dvir Publishing House; Erez Books; Metziuth Books; Marganit Books

# Italy

## General Information

*Capital:* Rome
*Language:* Italian. Various others according to region
*Religion:* Predominantly Roman Catholic
*Population:* 57.6 million
*Bank Hours:* 0830-1330, 1500-1600 Monday-Friday
*Shop Hours:* 0830 or 0900-1300, 1500 or 1600-1930 or 2000 Monday-Saturday; many close Monday morning
*Currency:* 100 Eurocents = 1 Euro; 1936.27 Italian lira = 1 Euro
*Export/Import Information:* Member of the European Economic Community. 4% VAT on books; advertising matter other than single copies is dutied. No import license required.
*Copyright:* UCC, Berne, Florence (see Copyright Conventions, pg xi)

**A & A+**
Via Montenapoleone, 18, 20121 Milan
*Tel:* (02) 876 999 *Fax:* (02) 877 928
Founded: 1988
Also photojournalist agent.
Subjects: Photography
ISBN Prefix(es): 88-85279

**Gruppo Abele+**
Corso Trapani, 95, 10141 Turin
*Tel:* (011) 3841066
*E-mail:* segreteria@gruppabele.it
*Web Site:* www.gruppoabele.it
*Key Personnel*
Man Dir & Editorial: Carla Martino
Sales: Doretta Graneris
Production: Pierangelo Bassignana
Publicity, Rights & Permissions: Silvia Mazza
Founded: 1983
Subjects: Child Care & Development, Communications, Education, Environmental Studies, Ethnicity, Health, Nutrition, Human Relations, Military Science
ISBN Prefix(es): 88-7670
*Warehouse:* Via Bologne 164, Turin

**Edizioni Abete+**
Via Prenestina 685, 00155 Rome
*Tel:* (06) 225821 *Fax:* (06) 2282960
*Telex:* 620370 ABETE I
*Key Personnel*
Chief Executive: Dr Luigi Abete
Editorial: Dr Giancarlo Abete
Sales: Dr Francesco Matassi; Franco Morbiducci
Founded: 1946
Subjects: Drama, Theater, Economics, Environ-
   mental Studies, Literature, Literary Criticism,
   Essays, Philosophy
ISBN Prefix(es): 88-7047
*Parent Company:* ABeTE SpA - Azienda Ben-
   eventana Tipografica Editoriale

**Editrice Abitare Segesta**
Via Ventura, 5, 20134 Milan
*Tel:* (02) 210581 *Fax:* (02) 21058316
*Web Site:* www.abitare.it
*Telex:* 315302 ABIT I
*Key Personnel*
Publisher: Renato Minetto
Founded: 1976
ISBN Prefix(es): 88-86116

**Mario Adda Editore SNC**
Via Tanzi 59, 70121 Bari
*Tel:* (080) 5539502 *Fax:* (080) 5539502
*E-mail:* info@addaeditore.it
*Web Site:* www.addaeditore.it
*Key Personnel*
Man Dir: Mario Adda
Founded: 1963
Subjects: Archaeology, Architecture & Interior
   Design, Art, Crafts, Games, Hobbies, History,
   Literature, Literary Criticism, Essays, Music,
   Dance, Philosophy, Photography, Poetry, Re-
   gional Interests, Social Sciences, Sociology
ISBN Prefix(es): 88-8082

**Adea Books**, *imprint of* Adea Edizioni

**Adea Edizioni+**
Via Lago Gerundo 31, 26100 Cremona
*Tel:* (0372) 430402 *Fax:* (0372) 43363
*E-mail:* info@adea.it
*Web Site:* www.adea.it/edizioni.html
*Key Personnel*
Editor: Mauro Maggio
Founded: 1992
Subjects: Astrology, Occult, Biography, Human
   Relations, Literature, Literary Criticism, Es-
   says, Philosophy, Physical Sciences, Religion -
   Buddhist, Theology
ISBN Prefix(es): 88-86274
Imprints: Adea Books
Subsidiaries: Adea Education; Adea Incense;
   Adea Music; Adea SRL

**Adelphi Edizioni SpA+**
Via San Giovanni sul Muro 14, 20121 Milan
*Tel:* (02) 725731 *Fax:* (02) 89010337
*E-mail:* info@adelphi.it
*Web Site:* www.adelphi.it
*Key Personnel*
Man Dir, Editorial Dir & Chairman: Roberto
   Calasso
Publicity: Matteo Codignola
Foreign Rights Manager: Simonetta Mazza
   *E-mail:* rightsdept@adelphi.it
Founded: 1962
Subjects: Anthropology, Biography, Fiction, His-
   tory, Literature, Literary Criticism, Essays,
   Mathematics, Mysteries, Philosophy, Physics,
   Poetry, Religion - Buddhist, Religion - Hindu,
   Science (General)
ISBN Prefix(es): 88-459
Foreign Rights: Ute Koerner Literary Agency
   (Spain); Nouvelle Agence (France)
*Bookshop(s):* Via Brentano 2, 20121 Milan

*Warehouse:* Via Mecenate 87/4, 20138 Milan
*Orders to:* Servizio Vendita Libri c/o RCS Libri
   & Grandi Opere SpA, Via Mecenate 91, 20138
   Milan *Tel:* (02) 50951

**AdP**, *imprint of* Segretariato Nazionale
Apostolato della Preghiera

**Adriana Gallina Editore**, *imprint of* Adriano
Gallina Editore sas

**Aesthetica**
Via Giusti 25, 90144 Palermo
*Tel:* (091) 308290 *Fax:* (091) 308290
*E-mail:* aesthetica@unipa.it
*Key Personnel*
President: Lucia Pizzo
Editorial Dir: Luigi Russo
Founded: 1985
Subjects: Art, Philosophy
ISBN Prefix(es): 88-7726

**Edizioni della Fondazione Giovanni Agnelli**
   (Giovanni Agnelli Foundation Publishing)+
Via Giacosa 38, 10125 Turin
*Tel:* (011) 6500500 *Fax:* (011) 6502777
*E-mail:* staff@fga.it
*Web Site:* www.fondazione-agnelli.it
*Key Personnel*
President: Marco Demarie
Sales Mgr: Franco Picollo
Subjects: Economics, Geography, Geology, Gov-
   ernment, Political Science, Social Sciences,
   Sociology
Number of titles published annually: 8 Print

**De Agostini Scolastica**
Via Montefeltro 6/A, 20156 Milan
*Tel:* (02) 380861 *Fax:* (02) 38086448
*Web Site:* www.scuola.com
Subjects: Education, Geography, Geology, His-
   tory, Science (General)
ISBN Prefix(es): 88-423; 88-402; 88-415

**AIB Associazione Italiana Bibliotheche** (Italian
   Library Association)+
Viale del Castro Pretorio 105, 00185 Rome
*Tel:* (06) 4463532 *Fax:* (06) 4441139
*E-mail:* aib@aib.it
*Web Site:* www.aib.it
*Key Personnel*
President: Miriam Scarabo *E-mail:* presidenza@
   aib.it
Vice President: Maria Cristina Di Martino
Secretary: Marco Cupellaro *E-mail:* cupellaro@
   aib.it
Founded: 1930
The Italian association of professional librarians
   & information specialists
Membership(s): IFLA; EBLIDA; IASL.
Subjects: Library & Information Sciences
ISBN Prefix(es): 88-7812
Number of titles published annually: 13 Print; 1
   CD-ROM; 2 Online
Total Titles: 148 Print; 1 CD-ROM; 2 Online

**L'Airone Editrice+**
Imprint of Gremese Editore
Via Virginia Agnelli, 88, 00151 Rome
*Tel:* (06) 6570758 *Fax:* (06) 65740509
*E-mail:* gremese@gremese.com
*Web Site:* www.gremese.com
*Key Personnel*
Publisher & Executive Manager: Alberto Gremese
   *Tel:* (06) 65740507 *E-mail:* alberto@gremese.
   com
Founded: 1992
Subjects: Astrology, Occult, Crafts, Games, Hob-
   bies, Humor, Mysteries, Nonfiction (General),

Parapsychology, Photography, Sports, Athletics,
   Travel
ISBN Prefix(es): 88-7944

**Alba**
Corso Porta Po 82/A, 44100 Ferrara
*Tel:* (0532) 249854 *Fax:* (0532) 249854
*E-mail:* alba_editrice@virgilio.it
*Key Personnel*
Head of Company: Flavio Puviani
Founded: 1971
Subjects: Art, Literature, Literary Criticism, Es-
   says, Poetry

**Ermanno Albertelli Editore+**
CP 395, 43100 Parma
*Tel:* (0521) 290387 *Fax:* (0521) 290387
*E-mail:* info@tuttostoria.it
*Web Site:* www.tuttostoria.it *Cable:*
   ALBERTELLI PARMA
*Key Personnel*
Chief Executive, Production: Ermanno Albertelli
Sales: Viviana de Luca
Founded: 1968
Subjects: Military Science, Transportation
ISBN Prefix(es): 88-85909; 88-87372
Subsidiaries: Tuttostoria (Azienda di dis-
   tribuzione)

**Alberti Libraio Editore**
Corso Garibaldi 74, 28921 Verbania
*Tel:* (0323) 402534 *Fax:* (0323) 401074
*E-mail:* info@albertilibraio.it
*Web Site:* www.albertilibraio.it
Founded: 1954
Subjects: History, Natural History, Regional Inter-
   ests
ISBN Prefix(es): 88-7245; 88-85004
Number of titles published annually: 5 Print; 1
   CD-ROM
Total Titles: 200 Print; 1 CD-ROM

**Alessandro Tesauro Editore**, *imprint of* Edizioni
Ripostes

**Libreria Alfani Editrice SRL**
Via Alfani 84/86R, 50121 Florence
*Tel:* (055) 2398800 *Fax:* (055) 218251
*E-mail:* info@librerialfani.it
*Web Site:* www.librerialfani.it
*Key Personnel*
Chief Executive: Umberto Panerai
Founded: 1968
ISBN Prefix(es): 88-88288
Total Titles: 40 Print
*Bookshop(s):* Libreria Alfani, Via degli Alfani 84-
   86 R, 1-50121 Florence

**Edizioni Alice**
Viale Col di Lana, 4, 20136 Milan
*Tel:* (02) 83 61 347
*E-mail:* info@hod.it
*Web Site:* www.hod.it

**Alinari Fratelli SpA Istituto di Edizioni
   Artistiche**
Largo Fratelli Alinari, 15, 50123 Florence
*Tel:* (055) 23951 *Fax:* (055) 2382857
*E-mail:* info@alinari.it
*Web Site:* www.alinari.com
*Telex:* 572123 Alidea
*Key Personnel*
Man Dir: Claudio de Polo Saibanti
Founded: 1852
Subjects: Art, Education, Photography
ISBN Prefix(es): 88-7292
*Bookshop(s):* Fratelli Alinari, Via Vigna Nuova
   48r, Florence; Fratelli Alinari, Via Alibert 16,
   Rome

**Alinea+**
Via Pl da Palestrina 17/19R, 50144 Florence
*Tel:* (055) 333428 *Fax:* (055) 331013
*E-mail:* ordini@alinea.it; info@alinea.it
*Web Site:* www.alinea.it
Founded: 1980
Specialize in architecture, art & engineering.
Subjects: Architecture & Interior Design, Art, Engineering (General)
ISBN Prefix(es): 88-8125
Distributed by Kappa-Clean
*Book Club(s):* Internazionale

**All'Insegna del Giglio**
Via Piccinni 32, 50141 Florence
*Tel:* (055) 451593 *Fax:* (055) 450030
*E-mail:* ins.giglio@dada.it
Founded: 1976
Subjects: Archaeology, History
ISBN Prefix(es): 88-7814

**Umberto Allemandi & C SRL+**
Via Mancini 8, 10131 Turin
*Tel:* (011) 8199111 *Fax:* (011) 8193090
*E-mail:* info@allemandi.com
*Web Site:* www.allemandi.com
*Key Personnel*
Contact: Dr Christiano Casassa Mont
Founded: 1982
Subjects: Antiques, Archaeology, Architecture & Interior Design, Art, House & Home, Photography, Science (General)
ISBN Prefix(es): 88-422
*Associate Companies:* Umberto Allemandi & Co Publishing Srl

**Editrice Ancora+**
Via G B Niccolini 8, 20154 Milan
*Tel:* (02) 3456081 *Fax:* (02) 34560866
*E-mail:* editrice@ancora-libri.it
*Web Site:* www.ancora-libri.it
*Key Personnel*
Man Dir: Gilberto Zini
Foreign Rights Manager: Gloria Mari
Founded: 1934
Subjects: Religion - Other, Social Sciences, Sociology
ISBN Prefix(es): 88-7610; 88-514
*Bookshop(s):* Brescia *E-mail:* libreria.brescia@ancora-libri.it; Milan *E-mail:* libreria.hp@ancora-libri.it; Rome *E-mail:* libreria.zoma@ancora-libri.it; Trento *E-mail:* libreria.trento@ancora-libri.it

**Franco Angeli SRL+**
Viale Monza 106, 20127 Milan
*Tel:* (02) 28 37 141 *Fax:* (02) 26 14 47 93
*E-mail:* redazioni@francoangeli.it
*Web Site:* www.francoangeli.it
*Key Personnel*
Man Dir: Dr Franco Angeli
Sales: Dr Stefano Angeli *Fax:* (02) 2613268
Founded: 1955
Subjects: Anthropology, Business, Economics, History, How-to, Management, Marketing, Psychology, Psychiatry, Social Sciences, Sociology
ISBN Prefix(es): 88-204; 88-464
Number of titles published annually: 600 Print
Total Titles: 9,000 Print

**Editrice Antroposofica SRL**
Via Sangallo 34, 20133 Milan
*Tel:* (02) 7491197 *Fax:* (02) 70103173
*E-mail:* libri@rudolfsteiner.it
*Web Site:* www.rudolfsteiner.it/editrice/index.htm
*Key Personnel*
Man Dir: Dr Iberto Bavastro
Founded: 1959
Subjects: Religion - Other
ISBN Prefix(es): 88-7787

*Parent Company:* Rudolf Steiner Verlag, Switzerland
Distributed by Edipromo (Emilia); Fozzi v L (Sardegna); Dino Giorgi srl (Tuscany/Umbria); Libri e Libri (Marche/Abruzzi); Il Libro (Liguria); Macrocampania (Campania/Puglia); Psiche (Piemonte); Tilopa (Lazio); Vecchi (Triveneto); Venturini (Lombardia)
Distributor for Edizioni Arcobaleno; Fenice Edizioni; Filadelfia Editore; Novalis; Psiche; Terra Biodinamica

**APE**, *imprint of* Organizzazione Didattica Editoriale Ape

**Apimondia+**
Corso Vittorio Emanuele II 101, 00186 Rome
*Tel:* (06) 6852286 *Fax:* (06) 6852287
*E-mail:* apimondia@mclink.it
*Web Site:* www.apimondia.org
*Key Personnel*
President: A S Jorgensen *Tel:* (045) 57561777 *Fax:* (045) 57561703 *E-mail:* asj@krl.dk
General Secretary: R Jannoni-Sebastianini
Founded: 1949
Subjects: Agriculture, Biological Sciences, Economics, Marketing, Technology, Veterinary Science
ISBN Prefix(es): 88-7643

**Apogeo srl - Editrice di Informatica**
Via Battaglia, 12, 20127 Milan
*Tel:* (02) 289981 *Fax:* (02) 26116334
*E-mail:* apogeo@apogeonline.com
*Web Site:* www.apogeonline.com
*Key Personnel*
Contact: Ivo Quartiroli
ISBN Prefix(es): 88-85146; 88-7303; 88-503

**Apostolato della Preghiera+**
Segretariato Nazionale Apostolato della Preghiera, Via Degli Astalli, 16, 00186 Rome
*Tel:* (06) 697 607 1 *Fax:* (06) 67 81 063
*E-mail:* adp@adp.it
*Web Site:* www.adp.it
*Key Personnel*
Dir: Massimo Taggi *E-mail:* mt@adp.it
Contact: Roberto Izzi *Tel:* (06) 697607205
Founded: 1844 (in France, 1861 in Italy)
Bibles, books & leaflets.
Subjects: Psychology, Psychiatry, Religion - Other, Bibles, spirituality, pastoral activities, & prayer
ISBN Prefix(es): 88-7357
Total Titles: 198 Print; 198 Online
*Parent Company:* ADP International
Distributed by Messaggero Distribution SRL
*Bookshop(s):* Via Degli Astalli, 17, 00186 Rome *Tel:* (06) 697 607 201

**Arcadia Edizioni Srl+**
Via Caselline, 121, 41058 Vignola MO
*Tel:* (059) 76 60 34 *Fax:* (059) 77 92 79
*E-mail:* edizioni@arcadiabooks.com
*Web Site:* www.arcadiabooks.com
*Key Personnel*
Contact: Antony Shugaar
Subjects: Architecture & Interior Design, Art, Environmental Studies, Sports, Athletics, Travel
ISBN Prefix(es): 88-85684

**Arcanta Aries Gruppo Editoriale**
Via Makelle 97/1, 35138 Padova
*Tel:* (049) 8712477 *Fax:* (049) 8713851
*Key Personnel*
Chief Executive: Dr Franco Muzzio
Production: Sergio Fardin
Publicity: Stella Longato Muzzio
Founded: 1956
Subjects: Astrology, Occult, Health, Nutrition, Psychology, Psychiatry, Sports, Athletics

ISBN Prefix(es): 88-87564
*Associate Companies:* Franco Muzzio & C Editore SpA

**Archimede Edizioni™**, *imprint of* Paravia Bruno Mondadori Editori

**Archimede Edizioni**
Imprint of Paravia Bruno Mondadori Editori
Via Archimede 23, 20129 Milan
*Tel:* (02) 748231 *Fax:* (02) 74823278
*Key Personnel*
Man Dir: Roberto Gulli
Editorial Dirs & International Rights: Paola Rosci
Sales Dir: Dario Ramilli
Editorial Dirs & International Rights: Emilio Zanette
Founded: 1990
Educational publisher.
Subjects: Biological Sciences, Earth Sciences, Education, English as a Second Language, Fiction, History, Mathematics
ISBN Prefix(es): 88-7952

**Rosellina Archinto Editore+**
Via Santa Valeria 3, 20123 Milan
*Tel:* (02) 86460237 *Fax:* (02) 86451955
*E-mail:* info@archinto.it
*Web Site:* www.archinto.it
*Key Personnel*
President: Rosellina Archinto
Founded: 1986
Subjects: Biography, Literature, Literary Criticism, Essays, Nonfiction (General), Poetry
ISBN Prefix(es): 88-7768
Number of titles published annually: 20 Print
*Shipping Address:* Vivalibri, Via Isonzo, 25, 00198 Rome, Contact: Pietro D'Amore *Tel:* (06) 84242153 *Fax:* (06) 84085679 *E-mail:* vivalibri@tin.it
*Distribution Center:* Messaggerie Libri, Via Tevere, 8, Assago-Milan 20090, Contact: Carlo Cherichi *Tel:* (02) 45774200, 45774210 *Fax:* (02) 45774230, 45774240
*Orders to:* Messaggerie Libri, Via Verdi, 8, Assago-Milan 20090 *Tel:* (02) 45774200, 45774210 *Fax:* (02) 45774230, 45774240

**Archivio Guido Izzi Edizioni**
Via Lazzarini 19, 00136 Rome
*Tel:* (06) 39735580 *Fax:* (06) 39734433
*E-mail:* agizzi@iol.it
Founded: 1984
Subjects: Art, History, Literature, Literary Criticism, Essays
ISBN Prefix(es): 88-85760; 88-88846

**L'Archivolto+**
Via Marsala 3, 20121 Milan
*Tel:* (02) 29010444; (02) 29010424 *Fax:* (02) 29001942
*E-mail:* info@archivolto.com
*Web Site:* www.archivolto.com
Founded: 1986
Specialize in architecture & interior design.
Subjects: Architecture & Interior Design, Art, Gardening, Plants, Photography
ISBN Prefix(es): 88-7685
Subsidiaries: Edizioni L'Archivolto

**Arcipelago Edizioni di Chiani Marisa+**
Via Carlo d'Adda, 21, 20143 Milan
*Tel:* (02) 36525177 *Fax:* (02) 36553002
*E-mail:* info@arcipelagoedizioni.com
*Web Site:* www.arcipelagoedizioni.com
*Key Personnel*
Owner: Marisa Chiani
Founded: 1971
Subjects: Advertising, English as a Second Language, Film, Video, Language Arts, Linguistics, Literature, Literary Criticism, Essays,

Management, Marketing, Social Sciences, Sociology, Italian as a Second Language
ISBN Prefix(es): 88-7695
Number of titles published annually: 30 Print; 1 CD-ROM; 1 Audio
Total Titles: 1 CD-ROM; 1 Audio

**Edizioni ARES+**
Via Stradivari 7, 20131 Milan
*Tel:* (02) 29514202; (02) 29526156 *Fax:* (02) 29520163
*E-mail:* aresed@tin.it; info@ares.mi.it
*Web Site:* www.ares.mi.it
*Key Personnel*
Dir: Dr Cesare Cavalleri *E-mail:* cesare.cavalleri@ares.mi.it
Assistant Dir: Andrea Beolchi *E-mail:* andrea.beolchi@ares.mi.it
Founded: 1957
Subjects: Architecture & Interior Design, Philosophy, Psychology, Psychiatry, Theology
ISBN Prefix(es): 88-8155

**Argalia**
Formerly Argalia Grafiche Editorial
Via S Donato 148/c, 61029 Urbino (Pesaro)
*Tel:* (0722) 328733 *Fax:* (0722) 328756
Founded: 1942
Also book packager.
Subjects: Drama, Theater, Economics, Education, Fiction, History, Literature, Literary Criticism, Essays, Philosophy, Poetry, Science (General)

**Argalia Grafiche Editorial**, see Argalia

**Aries**, see Arcanta Aries Gruppo Editoriale

**Edizioni Arka SRL+**
Via Sanzio, 7, 20149 Milan
*Tel:* (02) 4818230 *Fax:* (02) 4816752
*E-mail:* arka.edizioni@tin.it
*Key Personnel*
Man Dir: Ginevra Viscardi
Founded: 1984
Subjects: Animals, Pets, Art
ISBN Prefix(es): 88-8072; 88-85762
Number of titles published annually: 20 Print

**Arktos**
Via Gardezzana 57, 10022 Carmagnola TO
*Tel:* (011) 9773941 *Fax:* (011) 9715340
*E-mail:* arktos@cometacom.it
Founded: 1976
Subjects: Astrology, Occult, Philosophy, Religion - Islamic
ISBN Prefix(es): 88-7049

**Editore Armando SRL+**
Viale Trastevere, 236, 00153 Rome
*Tel:* (06) 5894525 *Fax:* (06) 5818564
*E-mail:* info@armandoeditore.com
*Web Site:* www.armando.it
*Key Personnel*
President: Enrico Iacometti
Founded: 1963
Subjects: Anthropology, Behavioral Sciences, Child Care & Development, Communications, Disability, Special Needs, Education, Health, Nutrition, Journalism, Language Arts, Linguistics, Medicine, Nursing, Dentistry, Philosophy, Psychology, Psychiatry, Radio, TV, Self-Help, Social Sciences, Sociology
ISBN Prefix(es): 88-7144
Number of titles published annually: 150 Print; 4 CD-ROM
Total Titles: 4 CD-ROM
*Parent Company:* Sovera Multimedia SRL, Via V Brunacci 55
*Associate Companies:* Sovera Multimedia, via Brunacci 55/55A, Rome, Caludia Iacometti
*Tel:* (06) 5562429 *Fax:* (06) 5580723

*Bookshop(s):* Via Vincenzo Brunacci, 53, 00146 Rome *Tel:* (06) 5587850 *Fax:* (06) 5580723
*Warehouse:* Sovera Multimedia SRL, Via V Brunacci, 55, 00146 Rome

**Gruppo Editoriale Armenia SpA+**
Via Valtellina 63, 20159 Milan
*Tel:* (02) 683911 *Fax:* (02) 6684884
*E-mail:* armenia@armenia.it
*Web Site:* www.armenia.it
*Key Personnel*
Chief Executive: Dr Giovanni Armenia
Rights & Permissions: Fabiola Marchet *E-mail:* editoriale@armenia.it
Founded: 1972
Specialize in New Age, positive thinking & fantasy.
Subjects: Animals, Pets, Astrology, Occult, Crafts, Games, Hobbies, Fiction, Health, Nutrition, How-to, Humor, Nonfiction (General), Parapsychology, Science Fiction, Fantasy, Self-Help, New Age
ISBN Prefix(es): 88-344; 88-7216
Number of titles published annually: 80 Print
Total Titles: 500 Print; 2 CD-ROM
*Warehouse:* Via Vialba 71, 20026 Novate Milanese, Milan *Tel:* (02) 38200208 *Fax:* (02) 38200208
*Distribution Center:* Massaggerie Libri SA, Via Giuseppe Verdi 8, Assago, Milan *Tel:* (02) 457741 *Fax:* (02) 45701032

**Arnaud Editore SRL+**
Via Nardi 27, 50132 Florence
*Tel:* (055) 216485 *Fax:* (055) 260466
*Key Personnel*
Chief Executive: Alfredo Meletti
Founded: 1944
Subjects: Art, Government, Political Science, History
ISBN Prefix(es): 88-8015
*Associate Companies:* Nuova Expolibro Toscana SRL, Via Ricasoli 7, I-50122 Florence
*Warehouse:* Via De' Pucci 2, 50122 Florence

**Arsenale Editrice SRL+**
Via Monte Comun, 40, 37057 Verona
*Tel:* (04) 5545166 *Fax:* (04) 5545057
*E-mail:* arsenale@arsenale.it
*Web Site:* www.arsenale.it
*Telex:* 480481 Apiver I sub 128
*Key Personnel*
Man Dir, Rights & Permissions & Production: Andrea Grandese
Editorial: Cinzia Boscolo
Sales: Giorgio Tamaro
Production: Andrea Grandese
Founded: 1984
Subjects: Architecture & Interior Design, Art
ISBN Prefix(es): 88-7743
*Parent Company:* Editoriale Bortolazzi - Stei SRL
*U.S. Office(s):* Moseley Assoc, 19 West 44 St, Suite 1200, New York, NY 10036, United States, Contact: Bert Paolucci
*Bookshop(s):* San Croce 29, 30135 Venice

**Artema**
Via Borgone 57, 10139 Turin
*Tel:* (011) 3853656 *Fax:* (011) 3853244
*E-mail:* cse@estorinese.inet.it
*Key Personnel*
President: Francesco Martiny
International Rights: Valentina Kalk
Founded: 1992
Subjects: Art
ISBN Prefix(es): 88-8052

**Edi.Artes srl+**
Viale Enrico Forlanini 65, 20134 Milan
*Tel:* (02) 70209917 *Fax:* (02) 70209919

*Key Personnel*
Man Dir: Raffaele Grandi
Founded: 1985
Subjects: Art
ISBN Prefix(es): 88-7724
*Associate Companies:* Edi.Ermes srl, Viale Enrico Forlanini 65, 20134 Milan

**Artioli Editore**
Via Emilia Ovest 669, 41100 Modena
*Tel:* (059) 827181 *Fax:* (059) 826819
*E-mail:* artiolip@pianeta.it
Founded: 1899
Subjects: Antiques, Architecture & Interior Design, Art, Drama, Theater, Photography, Regional Interests
ISBN Prefix(es): 88-7792

**Associazione Carmelo Teresiano Italiano, OCD**
Carmelitani Scalzi, Via Anagnina, 662 b, 00040 Morena (Rome)
*Tel:* (06) 7989081 *Fax:* (06) 79890840
*Web Site:* www.edizioniocd.it
*Key Personnel*
Dir: Rodolfo Girardello; Arnaldo Pigna *Tel:* (06) 79890834
Officer: Massimo Angelelli *Tel:* (06) 79890830; Fiorenzo Bugin *Tel:* (06) 79890836
Administration: Teresa Alpini *Tel:* (06) 79890823; Onelia Paoletti *Tel:* (06) 79890824; Luigia Paolitti *Tel:* (06) 79890822
ISBN Prefix(es): 88-7229
*Branch Office(s)*
Edizioni Cattoliche

**Associazione Internazionale di Archeologia Classica**
Piazza San Marco, 49, 00186 Rome
*Tel:* (06) 6798798 *Fax:* (06) 69789119
*E-mail:* info@aiac.org; segreteria@aiac.org
*Web Site:* www.aiac.org
*Key Personnel*
President: Prof Paolo Liverani
Vice President: Dr Elizabeth Fentress
Founded: 1922
Membership(s): International Association of Classical Archeology; International Association of Research Institutes in the History of Art (RIHA); International Union of the Institutes of Archeology, History & History of Art in Rome; The National Institute of Studies of the Renaissance; Associated with the National Committee of Research & The Jean Berard Centre in Naples.
Subjects: Archaeology, Art
ISBN Prefix(es): 88-7275

**Casa Editrice Astrolabio-Ubaldini Editore+**
Via Guido D'Arezzo 16, 00198 Rome
*Tel:* (06) 855 21 31 *Fax:* (06) 855 27 56
*Key Personnel*
Chief Executive: Francesco Gana *E-mail:* f.gana@astrolabio-ubaldini.com
Editorial: Francesco Cardelli
Sales, Production: Fiorenzo Bertillo
Founded: 1946
Subjects: Philosophy, Psychology, Psychiatry, Social Sciences, Sociology, Oriental studies
ISBN Prefix(es): 88-340
Number of titles published annually: 35 Print
Total Titles: 1,050 Print

**Editrice Atanor SRL+**
Via Avezzano, 16, 00182 Rome
*Tel:* (06) 7024595 *Fax:* (06) 7014422
*Key Personnel*
Man Dir: Anna Maria Papini
Editorial: Francesco Albanese
Founded: 1912
Subjects: Asian Studies, Astrology, Occult, Science (General)
ISBN Prefix(es): 88-7169

**Edizioni Dell'Ateneo Sr**, see Instituti Editoriali E Poligrafici Internazionali SRL

**Athesia Verlag Bozen+**
Portici 41, 39100 Bolzano
*Tel:* (0471) 92 72 03 *Fax:* (0471) 92 72 07
*E-mail:* buchverlag@athesia.it *Cable:* ATHESIA VERLAG, BOZEN
*Key Personnel*
Man Dir, Production: Dr Peter Silbernagl
Sales Manager: Richard Fieg
Publicity Manager: Aron Mairhofer
Founded: 1907
Subjects: Art, Cookery, Geography, Geology, History, How-to, Humor, Law, Military Science, Outdoor Recreation, Poetry, Religion - Catholic, Travel
ISBN Prefix(es): 88-7014; 88-8266
Subsidiaries: Athesiadruck GmbH
*Bookshop(s):* Bozen; Brixen; Bruneck; Meran; Schlanders; Sterzing

**Atlantica Editrice SARL**
Casella Postale 34, 71100 Foggia
Founded: 1974
Subjects: Language Arts, Linguistics, Regional Interests, Science (General)
ISBN Prefix(es): 88-7085
*Branch Office(s)*
Casella Postale 38, 71043 Manfredonia

**Automobilia srl+**
Via Mario 16, 20149 Milan
*Tel:* (02) 4802 1671 *Fax:* (02) 4819 4968
*E-mail:* automobilia@tin.it
*Key Personnel*
President: Bruno Alfieri
Editorial: Ippolito Alfieri
Sales: Luisa Alfieri
Production: Verde Alfieri
Founded: 1979
Subjects: Architecture & Interior Design, Art, Automotive, Maritime, Transportation
ISBN Prefix(es): 88-85058; 88-85880; 88-7960

**Baha'i**
Via F Turati 9, 00040 Ariccia, Rome
*Tel:* (06) 9334334 *Fax:* (06) 9334335
*E-mail:* ceb@bahai.it
*Web Site:* www.bahai.it
Founded: 1969
Subjects: Biography, Economics, Education, Religion - Other, Social Sciences, Sociology
ISBN Prefix(es): 88-7214

**Bancaria Editrice SpA**
Subsidiary of ABI Italian Banking Association
via della Cordonata, 7, 00187 Rome
*Tel:* (06) 6767222; (06) 6767475 *Fax:* (06) 6767250
*Web Site:* www.bancariaeditrice.it
*Key Personnel*
Dir: Nicola Forti
Subjects: Business, Economics, Finance, Law, Management, Marketing
ISBN Prefix(es): 88-449

**Bardi Editore srl**
Via Piave 7, 00817 Rome
*Tel:* (06) 4817656 *Fax:* (06) 48912574
*E-mail:* bardied@tin.it
*Web Site:* www.bardieditore.com
*Key Personnel*
Man Dir: Garcia Y Garcia Laurent
Founded: 1921
Specialize in Oriental studies, scientific books, subscription & mail order books.
Subjects: Antiques, Archaeology, Architecture & Interior Design, History, Music, Dance
ISBN Prefix(es): 88-85699
Total Titles: 300 Print

**Bastogi**
Via Zara, 47, 71100 Foggia FG
*Tel:* (0881) 725070 *Fax:* (0881) 728119
*E-mail:* bastogi@tiscali.it
*Web Site:* www.bastogi.it
Founded: 1979
Subjects: History, Literature, Literary Criticism, Essays, Religion - Other
ISBN Prefix(es): 88-86452; 88-8185

**Casa Editrice Luigi Battei**
Str Cavour 5/C, 43100 Parma
*Tel:* (0521) 233733 *Fax:* (0521) 231291
*Key Personnel*
Chief Executive: Antonio Battei
Founded: 1872
Subjects: Architecture & Interior Design, Literature, Literary Criticism, Essays, Regional Interests
*Showroom(s):* La Pillotta
*Bookshop(s):* La Pillotta
*Warehouse:* Borgo Serena 3, 43100 Parma
*Tel:* (0521) 234747

**Battelloavapore**, *imprint of* Edizioni Piemme SpA

**BC News**, *imprint of* Edizioni del Centro Camuno di Studi Preistorici

**BCSP**, *imprint of* Edizioni del Centro Camuno di Studi Preistorici

**BEL srl**, *imprint of* Belforte Editore Libraio srl

**Belforte Editore Libraio srl+**
Via dei Cavalieri, 8, 57123 Livorno
*Tel:* (0586) 210919 *Fax:* (0586) 210349
*E-mail:* belforte@librinformatica.it
*Web Site:* www.librinformatica.it
*Key Personnel*
International Rights: Dr Riccardo Tagliati
Founded: 1834
Subjects: Antiques, Art, Behavioral Sciences, Biography, Child Care & Development, Education, Fiction, Human Relations, Library & Information Sciences, Literature, Literary Criticism, Essays, Nonfiction (General), Philosophy, Poetry, Psychology, Psychiatry, Regional Interests, Religion - Jewish, Wine & Spirits, Women's Studies
ISBN Prefix(es): 88-7997
Imprints: BEL srl
Subsidiaries: Librinformatica SRL

**BeMa**
Via Teocrito 50, 20128 Milan
*Tel:* (02) 252071 *Fax:* (02) 27000692
*E-mail:* segreteria@bema.it
*Web Site:* www.bema.it
Founded: 1975
Subjects: Antiques, Architecture & Interior Design, Earth Sciences, Engineering (General), English as a Second Language, Geography, Geology, Technology
ISBN Prefix(es): 88-7143
Imprints: Visual Itineraries

**Bertello Edizioni**
Via Bassigiano 46, 12100 Cuneo
*Tel:* (0171) 699002 *Fax:* (0171) 697729
ISBN Prefix(es): 88-8067

**Bianco**
Via Messina, 31, 00198 Rome
*Tel:* (06) 8554962 *Fax:* (06) 8844703 *Cable:* DEL BIANCO UDINE
Founded: 1933
Subjects: Art, Engineering (General), History, Science (General)

**Editrice Bibliografica SpA**
Via Bergonzoli, 1/5, 20127 Milan
*Tel:* (02) 28315996 *Fax:* (02) 28315906
*E-mail:* bibliografica@bibliografica.it
*Web Site:* www.bibliografica.it
*Key Personnel*
Administrator: Michele Costa
Editor: Giuliano Vigini
Founded: 1974
Membership(s): Associazione Italiana Editori; Associazione Italiana per la difesa della reprografia delle opere; gestisce l'agenzia Italiana dell'ISBN.
Subjects: Library & Information Sciences
ISBN Prefix(es): 88-7075
Number of titles published annually: 40 Print
Total Titles: 300 Print; 1 CD-ROM
*Associate Companies:* Informazioni Editoriali-IE SRL, Via Bergonzoli 1/5, 20127 Milan, Contact: Mauro Zerbini *Tel:* (02) 283151 *Fax:* (02) 28315900

**Bibliopolis - Edizioni di Filosofia e Scienze Srl**
Via Arangio Ruiz 83, 80122 Naples
*Tel:* (081) 664606 *Fax:* (081) 7616273
*E-mail:* info@bibliopolis.it
*Web Site:* www.bibliopolis.it
*Key Personnel*
Man Dir: Dr Francesco del Franco
Contact: Emilia del Franco
*E-mail:* emiadelfranco@fiscolinet.it
Founded: 1976
Subjects: Archaeology, Literature, Literary Criticism, Essays, Mathematics, Philosophy, Physical Sciences, Physics, Science (General)
ISBN Prefix(es): 88-7088
Total Titles: 374 Print

**Biblioteca Elle**, *imprint of* Mondolibro Editore SNC

**Biblioteca World**, *imprint of* Mondolibro Editore SNC

**Biblos srl+**
Via delle Pezze 33, 35013 Cittadella, Padova
*Tel:* (049) 5975236 *Fax:* (049) 9409875
*E-mail:* info@biblos.it
*Web Site:* www.biblos.it
*Key Personnel*
Man Dir: Lanfranco Lionello
Subjects: Architecture & Interior Design, Art
ISBN Prefix(es): 88-86214; 88-88064
*Showroom(s):* Buchmesse Frankfurt

**Editoriale Bios+**
Via Sicilia, 5, 87100 Cosenza CS
*Tel:* (0984) 854149 *Fax:* (0984) 854038
*E-mail:* info@edibios.it
*Web Site:* www.edibios.it
*Key Personnel*
Contact: Irene Olivieri
Founded: 1981
Subjects: Engineering (General), Medicine, Nursing, Dentistry
ISBN Prefix(es): 88-7740

**Edizioni Blues Brothers**, *imprint of* Kaos Edizioni SRL

**BMG Ricordi SpA+**
Via Liguria, 4, 20098 San Giuliano Milan
*Tel:* (02) 988131 *Fax:* (02) 88812212
*E-mail:* bmgricordi@bmg.com
*Web Site:* www.bmgricordi.it
*Telex:* 310177 Ricor I
*Key Personnel*
President: Adrian Berwick

Vice President: Gianni Babini
Founded: 1808
Subjects: Art, Drama, Theater, Music, Dance
ISBN Prefix(es): 88-7592; 88-8192; 88-492; 88-87018
*Associate Companies:* Ricordi Americana SAEC, Argentina; Ricordi Brasileira S/A, Rua Conselheiro Nebias 1136, 012036 Sao Paulo SP, Brazil; Ricordi Canada, Canada; Ricordi Londra, United Kingdom; G Ricordi & Co, Paseo de la Reforma 481-A, 06500 Mexico, DF, Mexico; Ricordi Monaco, Monaco; Ricordi Parigi, France
Subsidiaries: Arti Grafiche Ricordi SpA; Dischi Ricordi SpA; Gruppo Editoriale Musica Leggera Ricordi
*Warehouse:* via Salomone 77, 20138 Milan

### Bollati Boringhieri Editore+
Corso Vittorio Emanuele II 86, 10121 Turin
*Tel:* (011) 55 91 711 *Fax:* (011) 54 30 24
*E-mail:* info@bollatiboringhieri.it
*Web Site:* www.bollatiboringhieri.it *Cable:* EDIBOR
*Key Personnel*
Man Dir, Editorial: Romilda Bollati
Foreign Rights: Christa Pardatscher
Founded: 1957
Subjects: Economics, History, Literature, Literary Criticism, Essays, Philosophy, Science (General), Social Sciences, Sociology
ISBN Prefix(es): 88-339

### Bompiani-RCS Libri+
Via Mecenate 91, 20138 Milan
*Tel:* (02) 50951 *Fax:* (02) 5065361
*Web Site:* www.rcslibri.it; www.bompiani.rcslibri.it
*Telex:* 311321 Fabbri I *Cable:* LIBRIFABBRI MILANO
*Key Personnel*
Dir: Mario Andreose
Editor-in-Chief: Elisabetta Sgarbi
  *Tel:* (02) 50952666 *Fax:* (02) 50952788
  *E-mail:* elisabetta.sgarb@res.it
Founded: 1929
Membership(s): Gruppo Editoriale Fabbri, Bompiani, Sonzogno, Etas SpA.
Subjects: Art, Drama, Theater, Fiction, Nonfiction (General), Science (General)
ISBN Prefix(es): 88-451; 88-452

### Bonacci editore+
Via Mercuri 8, 00193 Rome
*Tel:* (06) 68300004 *Fax:* (06) 68806382
*E-mail:* info@bonacci.it
*Web Site:* www.bonacci.it
*Key Personnel*
Man Dir: Alessandra Bonacci
Founded: 1942
Specialize in the production of material for the teaching of Italian as a foreign language.
Subjects: Education, Italian as a Foreign Language
ISBN Prefix(es): 88-7573
Total Titles: 4 Print; 1 Audio
Foreign Rep(s): Attica (France); Grivas (Greece); Intext Book (Australia); Klett Verlag (Germany); SGEL (Spain)
*Warehouse:* Via Pietro Cavallini 24/B *Tel:* (06) 321 57 08 *Fax:* (06) 321 57 08

### Giuseppe Bonanno Editore+
Via Vittorio Emanuele, 194, 95024 Acireale, Catania
*Tel:* (095) 601984 *Fax:* (095) 604380
*Web Site:* www.bonannoedizioni.it
*Key Personnel*
Editorial: Giuseppe Bonanno
Dir: Dr Mauro Bonanno *E-mail:* bonannomauro@tiscalinet.it
Founded: 1966

Subjects: Architecture & Interior Design, Art, Behavioral Sciences, Cookery, Economics, Fiction, Foreign Countries, Government, Political Science, History, Law, Literature, Literary Criticism, Essays
ISBN Prefix(es): 88-7796
Number of titles published annually: 30 Print
Total Titles: 250 Print
Divisions: AEB Editrice
*Branch Office(s)*
Bonanno Editore Roita, Via Torino 150, Rome
  *Tel:* (064) 740467
*Bookshop(s):* Libreria Bonanno
*Warehouse:* Via Cozzale, 36 95024 Acireale, Catania

### Casa Editrice Bonechi+
Via dei Cairoli 18B, 50131 Florence
*Tel:* (055) 576841 *Fax:* (055) 5000766
*E-mail:* redazione@bonechi.it; informazioni@bonechi.it
*Web Site:* www.bonechi.it
*Telex:* 571323 CEB
*Key Personnel*
Man Dir: Giampaolo Bonechi
Editorial: Marco Banti; Giovanna Magi
Sales Dir: Claudio Magnani
Founded: 1973
Subjects: Art, Cookery, Travel
ISBN Prefix(es): 88-7009; 88-8029; 88-476
Imprints: CEB

### Bonechi-Edizioni Il Turismo Srl
Via G Di Vittorio 31, 50145 Florence
*Tel:* (055) 375739; (055) 3424527 *Fax:* (055) 374701
*E-mail:* info@bonechionline.com
*Web Site:* www.bonechionline.com
*Key Personnel*
Editorial Dir: Barbara Bonechi *E-mail:* barbara@bonechionline.com
Contact: Piero Bonechi *E-mail:* bbonechi@dada.it
Founded: 1954
Subjects: Archaeology, Art, Travel
ISBN Prefix(es): 88-7204

### Bonsignori Editore SRL+
Viale dei Quattro Venti 47, Rome 00152
*Tel:* (06) 5881496 *Fax:* (06) 5882839
*E-mail:* redazione@bonsignori.it
*Key Personnel*
Chief Executive: Mario Bonsignori; Simona Bonsignori
Founded: 1992
Subjects: Archaeology, Architecture & Interior Design, Art, History, Specializes in archeology, architecture & history of art
ISBN Prefix(es): 88-7597
Number of titles published annually: 20 Print

### Book Editore
Via della Chiesa 49/b, 40013 Castel Maggiore, Bologna
*Tel:* (051) 71 47 20 *Fax:* (051) 71 12 16
*E-mail:* bookeditore@libero.it
*Web Site:* web.tiscali.it/bookeditore
*Key Personnel*
Dir: Massimo Scrignoli
Founded: 1987
Subjects: Language Arts, Linguistics, Literature, Literary Criticism, Essays, Philosophy, Poetry
ISBN Prefix(es): 88-7232
*Bookshop(s):* Diest, Via Cavalcanti, 11, 10132 Turin *Tel:* (011) 89 81 164 *Fax:* (011) 89 81 164

### Bookservice+
Via Maresca, 66b, 04024 Gaeta Latina
*Tel:* (0771) 744350 *Fax:* (0771) 744350
*Key Personnel*
Man Dir: Gabriele Chiusano

Founded: 1992
Subjects: History, Literature, Literary Criticism, Essays, Philosophy, Poetry, Social Sciences, Sociology
ISBN Prefix(es): 88-87106

### Edizioni Bora SNC di E Brandani & C
Via Jacopo di Paolo 42, 40128 Bologna
*Tel:* (051) 356133 *Fax:* (051) 4159651
*E-mail:* daniele.brandani@mailbox.dsnet.it
Founded: 1971
Subjects: Art, Biography
ISBN Prefix(es): 88-85638; 88-85345; 88-88600
Total Titles: 4 Print

### Edizioni Borla SRL+
Via delle Fornaci 50, 00165 Rome
*Tel:* (06) 39376728 *Fax:* (06) 39376620
*E-mail:* borla@edizioni-borla.it
*Web Site:* www.edizioni-borla.it
*Key Personnel*
Man Dir: Dr Vincenzo D'Agostino
Founded: 1863
Subjects: Anthropology, Education, Government, Political Science, History, Philosophy, Psychology, Psychiatry, Religion - Other, Social Sciences, Sociology
ISBN Prefix(es): 88-263

### Bovolenta
Via della Ginestra, 227, 44100 Ferrara
*Tel:* (0532) 259386 *Fax:* (0532) 259387
Founded: 1975
Subjects: History, Literature, Literary Criticism, Essays, Philosophy
ISBN Prefix(es): 88-369

### Edizioni Brenner+
Via Monte S Michele, 13A, 87100 Cosenza
*Tel:* (0984) 74537 *Fax:* (0984) 74537
*Key Personnel*
Man Dir, Editorial: Walter Brenner
Sales: Maria Gerbasi
Founded: 1956
Subjects: Ethnicity, History, Medicine, Nursing, Dentistry, Regional Interests

### Editore Giorgio Bretschneider
Via Crescenzio 43, 00193 Rome
Mailing Address: CP 30011, Roma 47, 00193 Rome
*Tel:* (06) 6879361 *Fax:* (06) 6864543
*E-mail:* info@bretschneider.it
*Web Site:* www.bretschneider.it *Cable:* GIOBREROM
*Key Personnel*
Man Dir: Boris Bretschneider *E-mail:* bb@bretschneider.it
Founded: 1974
Subjects: Archaeology, History, Ancient History, Greek & Roman Antiquities, Greek & Roman Archaeology
ISBN Prefix(es): 88-85007; 88-7689
Number of titles published annually: 20 Print
Total Titles: 400 Print
Distributor for Italiana Di Atene; Scuola Archaeologica; Universita di Messina; Universita di Macerata

### Edizioni Bucalo SNC
Casella Postale 51, 04100 Latina
*Tel:* (0773) 410036 *Fax:* (0773) 410036
*E-mail:* info@bucalo.it
*Web Site:* www.bucalo.it
*Key Personnel*
Chief Executive: Andrea Bucalo
Founded: 1965
Subjects: Law
ISBN Prefix(es): 88-7456
*Parent Company:* C Sopra

**Buffetti**
Via del Fosso di Santa Maura snc, 00169 Rome
*Tel:* (06) 231951 *Fax:* (06) 2389796
*Web Site:* www.buffetti.it
Founded: 1973
Subjects: Economics, Law, Management
ISBN Prefix(es): 88-19

**Bulzoni Editore SRL (Le Edizioni
Universitarie d'Italia)+**
via dei Liburni, 14, 00185 Rome
*Tel:* (06) 4455207 *Fax:* (06) 4450355
*E-mail:* bulzoni@bulzoni.it
*Web Site:* www.bulzoni.it
*Key Personnel*
Man Dir, Editorial: Anna Bulzoni
Sales: Ivana Capitani
Production: Paola Bulzoni
Publicity: Anna Catarinozzi
Founded: 1969
Subjects: Art, Drama, Theater, Engineering (General), Fiction, Film, Video, Language Arts, Linguistics, Law, Literature, Literary Criticism, Essays, Philosophy, Science (General), Social Sciences, Sociology
ISBN Prefix(es): 88-7119; 88-8319
*Bookshop(s):* Libreria Ricerche, Via Liburni 10/12, I-00185 Rome *Tel:* (06) 491851

**Cacucci Editore+**
Via Nicolai 39, 70122 Bari
*Tel:* (080) 521 42 20 *Fax:* (080) 523 47 77
*E-mail:* info@cacucci.it
*Web Site:* www.cacucci.it
*Key Personnel*
Man Dir: Dr Nicola Cacucci
Contact: Nicholas Abbatangelo
Founded: 1929
Subjects: Economics, Law, Mathematics, Public Administration
ISBN Prefix(es): 88-8422
*Showroom(s):* Salone del Libro Torino; Expolibro Bari
*Bookshop(s):* Via Cairoli 140, Bari; Via S Matarrese 2/D, Bari

**Edizioni Cadmo SRL+**
Via Benedetto da Maiano 3, 50014 Fiesole (Florence)
*Tel:* (055) 50 18 1 *Fax:* (055) 50 18 201
*E-mail:* info@casalini.it
*Web Site:* www.casalini.it
*Key Personnel*
Man Dir: Mario Casalini
Founded: 1975
Subjects: Art, History, Language Arts, Linguistics, Music, Dance, Philosophy, Social Sciences, Sociology
ISBN Prefix(es): 88-86101; 88-7923

**CADSR**, *imprint of* Centro Ambrosiano di Documentazione e Studi Religiosi

**Calosci+**
Loc Vallone 35L, 52042 Camucia-Cortona (Arezzo)
*Tel:* (0575) 678282 *Fax:* (0575) 678282
*E-mail:* info@calosci.com
*Web Site:* www.calosci.com
Founded: 1964
Subjects: Archaeology, Architecture & Interior Design, Art, History, Literature, Literary Criticism, Essays, Medicine, Nursing, Dentistry, Music, Dance, Regional Interests, Transportation
ISBN Prefix(es): 88-7785
Distributed by The Courier srl

**Camera dei Deputati Ufficio Pubblicazioni
Informazione Parlamentare+**
Palazzo Montecitorio-Piazza Montecitorio, 00186 Rome
*Tel:* (06) 67601 *Fax:* (06) 67603522; (06) 6783082
*Web Site:* www.camera.it
*Telex:* 612523
*Key Personnel*
Chief Executive: Dr Stefano Rizzo *Fax:* (06) 67602449 *E-mail:* rizzo_s@camera.it
Sales: Monica Fier *Tel:* (06) 67609909
  *E-mail:* fier_m@camera.it
Founded: 1848
Specialize in bibliographies, books, pamphlets, proceedings, reference works.
Subjects: Economics, History, Law
Number of titles published annually: 20 Print
Total Titles: 250 Print
*Bookshop(s):* Libreria della Camera dei Deputati, Via Uffici del Vicario 17, Rome *Tel:* (06) 67603715 *E-mail:* sg-pi_libreria@camera.it

**Campanotto+**
Via Marano 46, 33037 Pasian di Prato (UD)
*Tel:* (0432) 699390; (0432) 690155 *Fax:* (0432) 644728
*E-mail:* edizioni@campanottoeditore.it
*Web Site:* www.campanottoeditore.it
*Key Personnel*
President: Frank Campanotto
Publishing Dir: Carlo Marcello Conti
Contact: Inga Conti
Founded: 1976
Subjects: Archaeology, Art, Fiction, History, Literature, Literary Criticism, Essays, Music, Dance, Philosophy, Photography, Poetry, Radio, TV, Religion - Catholic, Religion - Other
ISBN Prefix(es): 88-456
Subsidiaries: Grafiche Piratello

**Canova SRL**
Libreria Canova, Via Calmaggiore 31, 31100 Treviso
*Tel:* (0422) 262397 *Fax:* (0422) 433673
*E-mail:* info@canovaedizioni.it
*Web Site:* www.canovaedizioni.it
*Key Personnel*
Man Dir: Danilo Gasparini
Sales: Luigi Facchini
Founded: 1945
Subjects: Art, History
ISBN Prefix(es): 88-85066; 88-86177; 88-8409
*Bookshop(s):* Libreria Canova, Via Cavour 6/b, 31015 Conegliano

**Edizioni Cantagalli+**
Str Massetana Romana, 12, 53100 Siena
*Tel:* (0577) 42102 *Fax:* (0577) 45363
*E-mail:* cantagalli@edizionicantagalli.com
*Web Site:* www.edizionicantagalli.com
*Key Personnel*
Chief Executive: Pietro Cantagalli
  *E-mail:* david@edizionicantagalli.com
Founded: 1927
Subjects: Biblical Studies, Disability, Special Needs, History, Music, Dance, Nonfiction (General), Philosophy, Regional Interests, Religion - Catholic, Science (General), Theology
ISBN Prefix(es): 88-8272

**Franco Cantini Editore**, see OCTAVO Produzioni Editoriali Associale

**Capone Editore SRL+**
Sp Lecce-Cavallino, Km 1, 250, 73100 Lecce
*Tel:* (0832) 612618 *Fax:* (0832) 611877
*Key Personnel*
Editorial: Lorenzo Capone
Founded: 1980

Subjects: Art, Communications, Ethnicity, History, Literature, Literary Criticism, Essays, Philosophy, Regional Interests
ISBN Prefix(es): 88-8349

**Cappelli Editore+**
Via Farini 14, 40124 Bologna
*Tel:* (051) 239060 *Fax:* (051) 239286
*E-mail:* info@cappellieditore.com
*Web Site:* www.cappellieditore.com *Cable:* CAPPELLI EDITORE BOLOGNA
*Key Personnel*
Man Dir: Mario Musso
Editorial: Massimo Manzoni
Founded: 1851
Subjects: Art, Biography, Drama, Theater, Fiction, Film, Video, Government, Political Science, History, Medicine, Nursing, Dentistry, Music, Dance, Philosophy, Poetry, Psychology, Psychiatry, Religion - Other, Science (General), Social Sciences, Sociology
ISBN Prefix(es): 88-379
*Associate Companies:* Nicola Milano Editore

**Edizioni Del Capricorno**, *imprint of* Centro Scientifico Torinese

**Edizioni del Capricorno**
Via Borgone, 37, 10139 Turin
*Tel:* (011) 386500 *Fax:* (011) 3853244
*E-mail:* cse@estorinese.inet.it
*Key Personnel*
Editor: Dr Walter Martiny
Foreign Rights Manager: Valentine Kalk
Subjects: Photography
ISBN Prefix(es): 88-7707
*Parent Company:* Centro Scientific Torinese SrL

**Edizioni Carmelitane**
Via Sforza Pallavicini, 10, 00193 Rome
*Tel:* (06) 68100886 *Fax:* (06) 68100887
*E-mail:* edizioni@ocarm.org
*Web Site:* www.carmelites.info/edizioni
*Key Personnel*
Dir: E Evaldo Xavier Gomes
Founded: 1954
Publishing house of the Carmelite Order.
Subjects: Biblical Studies, History, Religion - Catholic, Theology
ISBN Prefix(es): 88-7229; 88-7288
Number of titles published annually: 5 Print
Total Titles: 1,000 Print

**Edizioni Carroccio**
Via Alfieri, 1, 35010 Vigodarzere (Padova)
*Tel:* (049) 700568 *Fax:* (049) 700568
*Key Personnel*
Man Dir: Luciano Lincetto
Founded: 1947
Subjects: Religion - Catholic, Religion - Other

**Edizioni Cartedit SRL+**
Via Industriale 7, 26010 Monte Cremasco (Cremona)
*Tel:* (0373) 277410 *Fax:* (0373) 277405
*Key Personnel*
Editor: Sig Pigon Lavinio
Founded: 1992
ISBN Prefix(es): 88-86170; 88-8070

**Edizioni Cartografiche Milanesi+**
Via Reali 3/5, 20037 Padermo Dugnano (MI)
*Tel:* (02) 9101649 *Fax:* (02) 9101118
*E-mail:* info@ortelio-ecm.it
*Web Site:* www.ortelio-ecm.it
Subjects: Geography, Geology
ISBN Prefix(es): 88-8151
Number of titles published annually: 40 Print
Total Titles: 70 Print
Imprints: Ortelio

**Cartoonseries**, *imprint of* Stampa Alternativa - Nuovi Equilibri

**Casa Editrice Dr A Milani**, see CEDAM (Casa Editrice Dr A Milani)

**Casa Editrice Giuseppe Principato Spa+**
Via Fauche 10, 20154 Milan
*Tel:* (02) 312025; (02) 3315309 *Fax:* (02) 33104295
*E-mail:* info@principato.it
*Web Site:* www.principato.it
*Key Personnel*
Publishing Dir: Franco Menin
Founded: 1887
Subjects: Biological Sciences, Chemistry, Chemical Engineering, Earth Sciences, English as a Second Language, Geography, Geology, History, Literature, Literary Criticism, Essays, Mathematics, Philosophy, Physics
ISBN Prefix(es): 88-416
Number of titles published annually: 30 Print
Total Titles: 500 Print

**Casa Editrice Libraria Ulrico Hoepli SpA+**
Via U Hoepli 5, 20121 Milan
*Tel:* (02) 864871 *Fax:* (02) 864322
*E-mail:* hoepli@hoepli.it
*Web Site:* www.hoepli.it *Cable:* HOEPLI MILAN
*Key Personnel*
Man Dir: Gianni Hoepli; Dr Ulrico Carlo Hoepli
Rights & Permissions: Dr Susanna Schwarz Bellotti
Contact: Daniela Grazi
Founded: 1870
Subjects: Art, Engineering (General), How-to, Law, Social Sciences, Sociology, Technology
ISBN Prefix(es): 88-203
*Bookshop(s):* Hoepli Ulrico Libreria Internazionale
*Shipping Address:* Via Mameli 13, 20129 Milan

**Casa Editrice Lint Srl**
Via di Romagna 30, 34134 Trieste
*Tel:* (040) 360396 *Fax:* (040) 361354
*Web Site:* www.linteditoriale.com
*Key Personnel*
President: Prof Riccardo Maetzke
Advisor: Maria Rosa Casagrande Maetzke
Founded: 1962
Subjects: Art, Science (General)
ISBN Prefix(es): 88-86179; 88-85083; 88-8190

**Casa Musicale Edizioni Carrara SRL**
Via Calepio 2/4, 24125 Bergamo
*Tel:* (035) 243618 *Fax:* (035) 270398
*E-mail:* info@edizionicarrara.it
*Web Site:* www.edizionicarrara.it *Cable:* CARRARA MUSICA BERGAMO
*Key Personnel*
Editorial, Production: Vinicio Carrara
Sales, Publicity: Vittorio Carrara
Founded: 1912
Subjects: Music, Dance, Religion - Catholic

**Casa Musicale G Zanibon SRL+**
Via Berchet, 2, 20121 Milan
*Tel:* (02) 88811 *Fax:* (02) 88814317
*Telex:* 88814317 *Cable:* IDROCIR MILANO
*Key Personnel*
Contact: Cristiano Giovannini
Founded: 1908
Subjects: Education, Music, Dance
ISBN Prefix(es): 88-86642
Imprints: GZ; ZAN
Subsidiaries: Edizioni Drago; Edizioni Orfeo

**Casalini Libri**
Via Benedetto da Maiano, 3, 50014 Florence
*Tel:* (055) 5018 1 *Fax:* (055) 5018 201
*E-mail:* info@casalini.it

*Web Site:* www.casalini.it *Cable:* CASALINI FIESOLE
*Key Personnel*
President: Gerda von Grebmer
Man Dir: Barbara Casalini *E-mail:* barbara@casalini.it; Michele Casalini *E-mail:* michele@casalini.it
Founded: 1958
Firm's main functions are book exporter, bibliographic agent & library supplier.
ISBN Prefix(es): 88-85297
*Associate Companies:* CADMO

**Casa Editrice Castalia** (Castalia Books Limited)+
Via Principi d'Acaja 20, 10138 Turin
*Tel:* (011) 4342621 *Fax:* (011) 4342621
*Key Personnel*
Chairperson: Dr Mario Miglietti
Dir: Silvia Camodeca
Founded: 1984
Publisher of children's books.
Subjects: Fiction
ISBN Prefix(es): 88-7701
Number of titles published annually: 10 Print
Total Titles: 98 Print
Imprints: Mario Miglietti

**Il Castello srl+**
Via Scarlatti, 12, 20090 Trezzano sul Naviglio, Milan
*Tel:* (02) 48401629 *Fax:* (02) 4453617
*E-mail:* il_castello@tin.it
*Key Personnel*
Chief Executive: Luca Belloni
Editorial: Mose Menotti
Founded: 1955
Subjects: Art, Astronomy, Cookery, Crafts, Games, Hobbies, Outdoor Recreation, Photography, Fitness
ISBN Prefix(es): 88-8039; 88-88112
Number of titles published annually: 60 Print
Total Titles: 300 Print

**Editrice Il Castoro+**
Viale Abruzzi 72, 20131 Milan
*Tel:* (02) 29513529 *Fax:* (02) 29529896
*E-mail:* editrice.castoro@iol.it
*Web Site:* www.castoro-on-line.it
*Key Personnel*
Administrator & Editor: Renata Gorgani
Rights: Marta Spinelli
Editorial: Silvia Pareti
Founded: 1993
Subjects: Biography, Fiction, Film, Video
ISBN Prefix(es): 88-8033

**CCSP**, *imprint of* Edizioni del Centro Camuno di Studi Preistorici

**CEB**, *imprint of* Casa Editrice Bonechi

**CEDAM (Casa Editrice Dr A Milani)**
Via Jappelli 5/6, 35121 Padova
*Tel:* (049) 8239111 *Fax:* (049) 8752900
*E-mail:* info@cedam.com
*Web Site:* www.cedam.com
*Key Personnel*
President: Dott Antonio Milani
Administrator: Francesco Giordano; Carlo Porta
Founded: 1903
Subjects: Biological Sciences, Criminology, Economics, Finance, Government, Political Science, Law, Management, Marketing, Mathematics, Medicine, Nursing, Dentistry, Philosophy, Psychology, Psychiatry, Public Administration, Social Sciences, Sociology
ISBN Prefix(es): 88-13
*Warehouse:* Via Uruguay n 14, 35127 Camin PD

**Edizioni CELI**, *imprint of* Gruppo Editoriale Faenza Editrice SpA

**CELID**
Via Enrico Cialdini 26, 10138 Turin
*Tel:* (011) 447 47 74 *Fax:* (011) 447 47 59
*E-mail:* edizioni@celid.it
*Web Site:* www.celid.it
*Key Personnel*
Contact: Antonio Catalano; Vanda Cremona
Founded: 1974
Subjects: Architecture & Interior Design, Engineering (General), History
ISBN Prefix(es): 88-7661
*Branch Office(s)*
V Mattioli 39, 10125 Turin
Corso Duca Degli Abruzzi 24, 10129 Turin
*Bookshop(s):* Via S Ottavio 20, 10124 Turin

**Celuc Libri**
Via Santa Valeria 5, 20123 Milan
*Tel:* (02) 86 45 07 76 *Fax:* (02) 86 45 14 24
*Key Personnel*
Man Dir: Rita Barbatiello
Founded: 1969 (as CELUC), 1974 (as Celuc Libri SRL)
Subjects: Economics, Government, Political Science, History, Law, Literature, Literary Criticism, Essays, Mathematics, Philosophy, Religion - Other, Science (General), Social Sciences, Sociology
*Bookshop(s):* Libreria Celuc Libri, Via Santa Valeria 5, 20123 Milan

**CEM**, see Casa Editrice Maccari (CEM)

**Istituto Centrale per il Catalogo Unico delle Biblioteche Italiane e per le Informazioni Bibliografiche** (Central Institute of the Union Catalog of Italian Libraries & Bibliographical Information)
Viale del Castro Pretorio 105, 00185 Rome
*Tel:* (06) 4989484 *Fax:* (06) 4959302
*Web Site:* www.iccu.sbn.it
*Key Personnel*
Dir: Dr Luciano Scala
Subjects: Library & Information Sciences
ISBN Prefix(es): 88-7107

**Centro Ambrosiano di Documentazione e Studi Religiosi**
Corso di Porta Ticenese 33, 20123 Milan
*Tel:* (02) 83.75.476 *Fax:* (02) 58.10.09.49
*E-mail:* cadr@cadr.it
*Web Site:* www.cadr.it
Founded: 1972
Subjects: History, Religion - Other
ISBN Prefix(es): 88-7098
Imprints: CADSR

**Centro Biblico**
Via Domitiana, 80014 Giugliano, Naples
*Tel:* (081) 3340532 *Fax:* (081) 3340877
*Web Site:* www.centrobiblico.it
*Key Personnel*
Dir: David Freitag
Founded: 1952
Subjects: Biblical Studies, Religion - Protestant, Theology
ISBN Prefix(es): 88-7054

**Centro Di**
Lungarno Serristori, 35, 50125 Florence
*Tel:* (055) 2342668 *Fax:* (055) 2342667
*E-mail:* edizioni@centrodi.it
*Web Site:* www.centrodi.it *Cable:* Centrodi Florence
*Key Personnel*
Man Dir: Alessandra Marchi Pandolfini
Founded: 1968
Subjects: Art
ISBN Prefix(es): 88-7038

**Centro Documentazione Alpina**
Via Invorio 24a, 10146 Turin
*Tel:* (011) 7720444 *Fax:* (011) 7732170
*Web Site:* www.cda.it
*Key Personnel*
Editorial: Pietro Giglio; Mario Frasciome
Founded: 1970
Subjects: Geography, Geology
ISBN Prefix(es): 88-85504

**Centro Editoriale Valtortiano SRL+**
Viale Piscicelli 91, 03036 Isola del Liri FR
*Tel:* (0776) 807032 *Fax:* (0776) 809789
*E-mail:* cev@mariavaltorta.com
*Web Site:* www.mariavaltorta.com
*Key Personnel*
Editor: Emilio Pisani
Author: Maria Valtorta
Founded: 1985
Subjects: Religion - Catholic, Theology
ISBN Prefix(es): 88-7987
Number of titles published annually: 6 Print
Total Titles: 94 Print

**Centro Italiano di Studi Sull'Alto Medioevo,**
see CISAM

**Centro Italiano Studi Alto Medioevo**
Piazza della Liberta 12, 06049 Spoleto (Perugia)
*Tel:* (0743) 225630 *Fax:* (0743) 49902
*E-mail:* cisam@cisam.org
*Web Site:* www.cisam.org
*Key Personnel*
President: Prof Enrico Menesto
Founded: 1952
To promote meetings & scientific publications on
the high Middle Ages.
Subjects: Art, History, Literature, Literary Criticism, Essays, Philosophy
ISBN Prefix(es): 88-7988
Number of titles published annually: 24 Print
Total Titles: 500 Print
Imprints: CISAM

**Centro Programmazione Editoriale (CPE)**
Via Canaletto, 20 b, 41030 San Prospero MO
*Tel:* (059) 908065 *Fax:* (059) 908271
*Web Site:* www.cpe-oggiscuola.com
Founded: 1973
Subjects: Education, Mathematics, Psychology,
Psychiatry
ISBN Prefix(es): 88-7378

**Centro Scientifico Editore,** *imprint of* Centro
Scientifico Torinese

**Centro Scientifico Torinese+**
Via Borgone 57, 10139 Turin
*Tel:* (011) 3853656 *Fax:* (011) 3853244
*E-mail:* cse@estorinese.inet.it
*Key Personnel*
President: Francesco Martiny
Editor: Dr Walter Martiny
Administrator: Pier Luigi Massaza
Founded: 1973
Subjects: Health, Nutrition, Human Relations,
Medicine, Nursing, Dentistry, Psychology, Psychiatry
ISBN Prefix(es): 88-7640
*Associate Companies:* Artema Srl; Centro Scientifico Internazionale
Imprints: Edizioni Del Capricorno; Centro Scientifico Editore; Soleverde

**Edizioni Centro Studi Erickson+**
Loc Spini di Gardolo, 38014 Gardolo, Trento
*Tel:* (0461) 950690 *Fax:* (0461) 950698
*E-mail:* info@erickson.it
*Web Site:* www.erickson.it
*Key Personnel*
Dir: Dario Ianes; Fabio Folgheraiter

Editor: Carmen Calovi *E-mail:* calovi@erickson.
it; Francesca Cretti *E-mail:* cretti@erickson.it;
Riccardo Mazzeo *E-mail:* ric@erickson.it
Founded: 1984
Subjects: Behavioral Sciences, Child Care & Development, Education, Nonfiction (General),
Psychology, Psychiatry, Self-Help, Social Sciences, Sociology
ISBN Prefix(es): 88-7946; 88-85857
Number of titles published annually: 30 Print; 8
CD-ROM
Total Titles: 250 Print; 8 CD-ROM

**Centro Studi Terzo Mondo** (Study Center for
the Third World)+
Via GB Morgagni 39, 20129 Milan
*Tel:* (02) 29409041 *Fax:* (02) 29409041
*E-mail:* cstm@libero.it
*Key Personnel*
Chief Executive: Prof Umberto Melotti
*Tel:* (0330) 687866 *E-mail:* melotti@uniroma1.
it
Editorial, Rights & Permissions: Elena Sala
Founded: 1964
Books & journals on social sciences & on the
problems of the Third World.
Subjects: Anthropology, Economics, Ethnicity,
Geography, Geology, Government, Political
Science, History, Literature, Literary Criticism,
Essays, Poetry, Social Sciences, Sociology
Number of titles published annually: 12 Print
Total Titles: 120 Print
Imprints: CSTM; Ed La Cultura Sociologica

**il Cerchio Iniziative Editoriali+**
via Dell' Allodola n 8, 47900 Rimini
*Tel:* (0541) 21158; (0541) 708190 *Fax:* (0541)
799173
*E-mail:* info@ilcerchio.it
*Web Site:* www.ilcerchio.it
*Key Personnel*
Man Dir, Production, Rights & Permissions: Dr
Adolfo Morganti
Editorial: Dr Maurizio Mecozzi
Sales: Gloria Rubinato
Publicity: Dr Sergio de Vita
Desktop Publishing: Davide Peggi
Founded: 1978
Subjects: Anthropology, Art, Economics, Government, Political Science, History, Literature,
Literary Criticism, Essays, Nonfiction (General), Philosophy, Religion - Islamic, Religion
- Other, Science (General), Social Sciences,
Sociology, Mythology
ISBN Prefix(es): 88-86583
*Parent Company:* Cooperativa Culturale Il Cerchio, Via Gambalunga, 91, 47037 Rimini
*Bookshop(s):* Libreria Cooperativa Il Cerchio, Via
Gambalunga, 91, 47900 Rimini

**CG Ediz Medico-Scientifiche+**
Via Viberti 7, 10141 Turin
*Tel:* (011) 338507 *Fax:* (011) 3852750
*Web Site:* www.cgems.it
*Key Personnel*
Contact: Pier Paola Pratis Palazzo
Founded: 1958
Specialize in medical books.
Subjects: Biological Sciences, Medicine, Nursing,
Dentistry, Veterinary Science
ISBN Prefix(es): 88-7110

**CIC Edizioni Internazionali+**
Corso Trieste, 42, 00198 Rome
*Tel:* (06) 8412673 *Fax:* (06) 8412688; (06)
8412687
*E-mail:* info@gruppocic.it
*Web Site:* www.gruppocic.it
*Telex:* 622099 CICI
*Key Personnel*
President: Prof Andrea Salvati *E-mail:* a.salvati@
gruppocic.it

Dir General: Dr Raffaele Salvati *E-mail:* r.
salvati@gruppocic.it
Advertising Dept: Patrizia Arcangioli
*E-mail:* arcangioli@gruppocic.it
Foreign Rights Dept: Marilena Cefa
*E-mail:* cefa@gruppocic.it
Sales & Subscriptions Dept: Amelia Assi
*E-mail:* assi@gruppocic.it
Founded: 1970
Membership(s): ANES; USPI.
Subjects: Health, Nutrition, Medicine, Nursing,
Dentistry, Psychology, Psychiatry
ISBN Prefix(es): 88-7141
Number of titles published annually: 150 Print;
10 CD-ROM; 15 Audio
Total Titles: 600 Print; 10 CD-ROM; 30 Audio
Subsidiaries: Centro Italiano Congressi; Kairos;
Librerie CIC Edizioni Internazionali
*Branch Office(s)*
Centro Italiano Congress, CIC SUD, via le Escriva N° 28, 70124 Bari, Contact: Olimpia Cassano *Tel:* (080) 5043737 *Fax:* (080) 5043736
Viale E Caldara, 35/A, 20122 Milan, Contact: Antonietta Garzonio *Tel:* (02) 55187057
*Fax:* (02) 55187061
Distributor for George Thieme Verlag (Italian territory)
*Warehouse:* Circonvallazione Nomentana, 482,
00162 Rome

**Cideb Editrice SRL+**
Via Venezia 93, 16035 Rapallo (Genova)
*Tel:* (0185) 60241 *Fax:* (0185) 230100
*E-mail:* info@cideb.com
*Web Site:* www.cideb.it
*Key Personnel*
Manager: Ornella Caffo
Founded: 1992
Subjects: Literature, Literary Criticism, Essays
ISBN Prefix(es): 88-7754; 88-530
*Orders to:* Cideb SRL, Via Torre Civica 8, 16035
Rapallo (Genova)

**Il Cigno Galileo Galilei-Edizioni di Arte e
Scienza**
Piazza San Salvatore Lauro 15, 00186 Rome
*Tel:* (06) 6865493; (06) 6873842 *Fax:* (06)
6892109
*E-mail:* info@ilcigno.org
*Key Personnel*
Contact: Delfina Bergamaslhi
Founded: 1968
Also specialize in printing graphic works & publish catalogues & art volumes.
Subjects: Art, Law, Mathematics, Science (General)
ISBN Prefix(es): 88-7831
Number of titles published annually: 40 Print; 4
CD-ROM
Total Titles: 385 Print; 4 CD-ROM
*Showroom(s):* Archivi Greco, Museo Mastroianni
& Il Cigno Galileo Galilei La Stamperia
*Distribution Center:* Gaetano Amodio, Via
Francesco Battiato 24, 95039 Catania
*Tel:* (03095) 321328 (South Italy)
Pecorini Sas, Foro Buonaparte 48, 20121 Milan
*Tel:* (02) 86460660 *Fax:* (02) 72001462 (North
Italy)

**Ciranna e Ferrara**
Via Solferino, 163, 20038 Seregno (Milan)
*Tel:* (0362) 230849 *Fax:* (0362) 326213
Founded: 1976
ISBN Prefix(es): 88-8144

**Ciranna - Roma**
Via Besio 127, 143, 90145 Palermo
*Tel:* (091) 224499 *Fax:* (091) 311064
*E-mail:* info@ciranna.it
*Web Site:* www.ciranna.it

*Key Personnel*
Chief Executive, Rights & Permissions: Dr Lidia
  Fabiano
Founded: 1953
Subjects: Art, Business, Education, Geography,
  Geology, History, Language Arts, Linguistics,
  Law, Literature, Literary Criticism, Essays,
  Mathematics, Philosophy, Psychology, Psychi-
  atry, Public Administration, Science (General),
  Technology
ISBN Prefix(es): 88-8322
*Orders to:* Via Capograssa 1115

**Cisalpino**, *imprint of* Monduzzi Editore SpA

**Cisalpino**
Via Eustachi, 12, 20129 Milan
*Tel:* (02) 2040 4031 *Fax:* (02) 2040 4044
*Web Site:* www.monduzzi.com/cisalpino
Founded: 1946
Subjects: Economics, History, Language Arts,
  Linguistics, Law, Literature, Literary Criticism,
  Essays, Management
ISBN Prefix(es): 88-205; 88-323
*Parent Company:* Monduzzi Editore SpA, Via
  Ferrarese 119/2, 40128 Bologna

**CISAM**, *imprint of* Centro Italiano Studi Alto
Medioevo

**CISAM**
Palazzo Ancaiani, Piazza della Liberta 12, 06049
  Spoleto, Perugia
*Tel:* (0743) 225630 *Fax:* (0743) 49902
*E-mail:* cisam@cisam.org
*Web Site:* www.cisam.org
*Key Personnel*
Chairman: Enrico Menesio
Dir: Stefano Brufani
ISBN Prefix(es): 88-7988
*Branch Office(s)*
Palazzo Ancaiani, 06049 Spoleto, Perugia
*Orders to:* Indirizzo Sopra

**Citta Nuova Editrice+**
Via degli Scipioni 265, 00192 Rome
*Tel:* (06) 3216212 *Fax:* (06) 3207185
*E-mail:* segr.rivista@cittanuova.it
*Web Site:* www.cittanuova.it
*Key Personnel*
Man Dir: Dr Vittorio Fasciotti; Dr Giovanni Bat-
  tista Dadda
Founded: 1959
Subjects: Biblical Studies, Education, Philoso-
  phy, Psychology, Psychiatry, Religion - Other,
  Social Sciences, Sociology, Theology
ISBN Prefix(es): 88-311
Subsidiaries: Ciudad Nueva (Argentina); Unistad
  Verspreiding RV (Belgium); Cidade Nova Edi-
  tora (Brazil); Ciudad Nueva (Colombia); Nou-
  velle Cite (France); Verlag Neue Stadt GmbH
  (Germany); Nieuwe Stad (Netherlands); New
  City (Philippines); Cidade Nova (Portugal); Ed-
  itorial Ciutat Nova (Spain); Verlag Neue Stadt
  (Switzerland); New City (United Kingdom);
  New City Press (United States)
*Shipping Address:* Via V Ussani 88, 00151 Rome
*Warehouse:* Via V Ussani 88, 00151 Rome

**Cittadella Editrice+**
Imprint of Pro Civitate Christiana
Via Ancajani 3, 06081 Assisi (Perugia)
*Tel:* (075) 813595 *Fax:* (075) 813719
*E-mail:* amministrazione@cittadellaeditrice.com
*Web Site:* www.cittadellaeditrice.com *Cable:*
  CITTADELLA EDITRICE
*Key Personnel*
Trans Off: Gabriella Persico *E-mail:* redazione@
  cittadellaeditrice.com
Editorial Manager: Giuseppina Pompei
  *E-mail:* gpompei@cittadellaeditrice.com

Foreign Rights: Franco Ferrari *E-mail:* fferrari@
  cittadellaeditrice.com
Press Office Manager: Franco Ferrari *Tel:* (075)
  813231
Founded: 1939
Subjects: Biblical Studies, Biography, Psychol-
  ogy, Psychiatry, Religion - Catholic, Religion -
  Other, Social Sciences, Sociology, Theology
ISBN Prefix(es): 88-308
Number of titles published annually: 21 Print
Total Titles: 501 Print
*Bookshop(s):* Libreria Cittadella

**Claudiana Editrice+**
Via Principe Tommaso 1, 10125 Turin
*Tel:* (011) 6689804 *Fax:* (011) 6504394
*E-mail:* info@claudiana.it
*Web Site:* www.claudiana.it
*Key Personnel*
Dir: Manuel Kromer
Founded: 1855
Membership(s): AIE
Subjects: Biblical Studies, History, Religion -
  Protestant, Theology
ISBN Prefix(es): 88-7016
Distributor for Edizioni GBU (Rome)
*Bookshop(s):* Libreria Claudiana, Via Francesco
  Sforza 12A, 20122 Milan; Libreria Claudiana,
  Piazza Liberta, 10066 Torre Pellice (Turin); Via
  Pr Tommaso 1, 10125 Turin; Libreria di Cul-
  tura Religiosa, Piazza Cavour 32, 00193 Rome

**CLEUP - Cooperative Libraria Editrice dell
  'Universita di Padova+**
Via Prati 19, 35122 Padova
*Tel:* (049) 8753496 *Fax:* (049) 650261
*E-mail:* redazione@cleup.it
*Key Personnel*
President: Fulvio Ursini
Vice President: Sergio Relai
Founded: 1962
Also book packager.
Subjects: Engineering (General), Government,
  Political Science, Language Arts, Linguistics,
  Mathematics, Medicine, Nursing, Dentistry,
  Psychology, Psychiatry, Science (General)
ISBN Prefix(es): 88-7178
*Bookshop(s):* Libreria CLEUP, Via San Francesco
  64, 35100 Padua *Tel:* 049-39557

**CLUEB (Cooperativa Libraria Universitaria
  Editrice Bologna)+**
Via Marsala 31, 40126 Bologna
*Tel:* (051) 220736 *Fax:* (051) 237758
*E-mail:* clueb@clueb.com; info@clueb.com
*Web Site:* www.clueb.com
*Key Personnel*
Man Dir: Luigi Guardigli *E-mail:* gua@clueb.com
Editorial Man: Giulio Forconi *E-mail:* g.forconi@
  clueb.com
Founded: 1959
Specialize also in theatre, detective stories & crit-
  icism of D.S.
Subjects: Accounting, Agriculture, Architecture &
  Interior Design, Art, Business, Economics, Ed-
  ucation, History, Human Relations, Language
  Arts, Linguistics, Literature, Literary Criticism,
  Essays, Music, Dance, Philosophy, Psychology,
  Psychiatry, Science (General)
ISBN Prefix(es): 88-8091; 88-491
Number of titles published annually: 150 Print; 3
  CD-ROM
Total Titles: 15 Print; 1 CD-ROM
Subsidiaries: Clueb DPE
*U.S. Office(s):* Paul & Company Publishers Con-
  sortium, PO Box 442, Concord, MA 01742,
  United States
Distributor for Universita' di Trento
*Bookshop(s):* Libreria Clueb, Bologna

**CLUT Editrice+**
Corso Duca degli Abruzzi 24, 10129 Turin

*Tel:* (011) 5647980 *Fax:* (011) 542192
*E-mail:* informazioni@clut.it
*Web Site:* www.clut.it
*Key Personnel*
Man Dir: Michele Ruffino
Editorial: Toscano Donatella
Founded: 1960
Subjects: Human Relations, Science (General),
  Technology
ISBN Prefix(es): 88-7992
*Parent Company:* Cooperativa Libraria Universi-
  taria Torinese Scrl, Corso Duca degli Abruzzi
  24, 10129 Turin

**La Coccinella Editrice SRL**
Via Crispi, 77/79, 21100 Varese
*Tel:* (0332) 224690 *Fax:* (0332) 222025
*Telex:* 326169 per La Coccinella
*Key Personnel*
Editorial Dir: Domenico Caputo
Sales, Rights & Permissions: Giuliana Crespi
Production Dir: Valerio Morelli
Founded: 1977
Subjects: Crafts, Games, Hobbies, Education
ISBN Prefix(es): 88-7703
Subsidiaries: RCS Rizzoli Libri
*Warehouse:* RCS Rizzoli, Via Angelo Rizzoli 4,
  Milan

**Collana**, *imprint of* Mondolibro Editore SNC

**Colonnese Editore+**
Via San Pietro a Majella, 7, 80138 Naples
*Tel:* (081) 293900 *Fax:* (081) 455420
*E-mail:* info@colonnese.it
*Web Site:* www.colonnese.it
*Key Personnel*
Dir, Publishing & Sales: Gaetano Colonnese
Rights & Permissions: Edgar Colonnese
  *E-mail:* edgar@colonnese.it
Founded: 1965
Subjects: Archaeology, Drama, Theater, Fiction,
  History, Humor, Language Arts, Linguistics,
  Literature, Literary Criticism, Essays, Photogra-
  phy, Poetry, Women's Studies
ISBN Prefix(es): 88-87501
Number of titles published annually: 12 Print
Total Titles: 400 Print
Distributed by Zambon Verlag & Vertrieb (Ger-
  many)
Foreign Rights: Guido Lagomarsino (Italy)
*Bookshop(s):* Libreria Colonnese SAS, Via
  San Pietro a Majella 32/33, 80138 Naples
  *Tel:* (081) 459858
*Distribution Center:* PDE SRL, Via Tevere 54,
  50019 Osmannoro, Carlo Cherici
*Orders to:* Colonnese, Via S Pa Majella 32-33,
  80138 Naples *Tel:* (081) 459858

**Le Comete**, *imprint of* Passigli Editori

**Edizioni di Comunita SpA+**
Division of Mondadori
Via Biancamano 2, 10121 Turin
*Tel:* (011) 5656363 *Fax:* (011) 5656351
*E-mail:* novarese@amemail.mondadori.it
*Web Site:* www.comunita.einaudi.it
*Key Personnel*
Res Administrator: R Veglia *Tel:* (011) 5656205
  *E-mail:* veglia@amemail.mondadori.it
Founded: 1946
Subjects: Architecture & Interior Design, Art,
  Computer Science, Economics, Government,
  Political Science, History, Law, Science (Gen-
  eral), Social Sciences, Sociology
ISBN Prefix(es): 88-245
Total Titles: 70 Print
*Ultimate Parent Company:* Einaudi
*Associate Companies:* Arnoldo Mondadori Edi-
  tore SpA
Distributed by A Mondadori

**Consiglio Nazionale delle Ricerche Rep
Pubblicazioni e Informazioni Scientifiche**
(National Research Council)
P le Aldo Moro, 7, 00185 Rome
*Tel:* (06) 49932019 *Fax:* (06) 49933077
*E-mail:* pgiugni@dcire.cnr.it
*Web Site:* www.urp.cnr.it

**Continental SRL Editrice**
Via Suardi 7, 24100 Bergamo
*Tel:* (035) 237088 *Fax:* (035) 237039
*Key Personnel*
Man Dir, Rights & Permissions: Luigi Maria
    Facheris
Editorial: Ornella Crispiatico
Sales, Publicity: Paola Sala
Production: Roberto Poli
Founded: 1974
Subjects: Education

**Cooperativa Libraria Editrice dell' Universita**,
    see CLEUP - Cooperative Libraria Editrice dell
    'Universita di Padova

**Cooperativa Libraria Universitaria Editrice
Bologna**, see CLUEB (Cooperativa Libraria
    Universitaria Editrice Bologna)

**Cooperativa Libraria Universitaria Torinese**,
    see CLUT Editrice

**Edizioni Cooperative Scarl**
Via Stelvio, 1, 00141 Rome
*Tel:* (06) 844391 *Fax:* (06) 84439406
*E-mail:* info@legacoop.it
*Web Site:* www.legacoop.it
*Key Personnel*
President: Giuliano Poletti
ISBN Prefix(es): 88-7361

**Casa Editrice Corbaccio srl+**
Cso Italia 13, 20122 Milan
*Tel:* (02) 80206338 *Fax:* (02) 804067
*E-mail:* info@corbaccio.it
*Web Site:* www.corbaccio.it
*Key Personnel*
President: Mario Spagnol
Man Dir: Stefano Mauri
Editorial: Cecilia Perucci
Sales: Giuseppe Somenzi
Production: Alfredo Bonfiglio
Publicity: Valentina Fortichiari
Rights & Permissions: Cristina Foschini
Founded: 1992
ISBN Prefix(es): 88-7972
*Parent Company:* Longanesi & C
*Associate Companies:* Finarte, GdP
*U.S. Office(s):* Nina Collins Association, 584
    Broadway, Suite 607, New York, NY 10012,
    United States
*Warehouse:* Messaggerie Italiane Spa, Maggazz-
    ino Editoriale Via Bereguardina, Casarile
    20080
*Orders to:* Pro Libro, Corso Italia 13, 20122 Mi-
    lan

**Libreria Cortina Editrice SRL+**
Via Alberto Mario 10, 37121 Verona
*Tel:* (045) 594177 *Fax:* (045) 597551
*E-mail:* info@libreriacortina.it; cortinab@tin.it
*Web Site:* www.libreriacortina.it
*Key Personnel*
Chief Executive, Editorial: Cunego Pierpiorgio
Founded: 1971
Also book packager.
Subjects: Medicine, Nursing, Dentistry, Science
    (General)
ISBN Prefix(es): 88-85037; 88-7749

*Bookshop(s):* Palazzetto d'Ingresso, Policlinico
    Borgo Roma, Via delle Menegone, 1-37134
    Verona *Tel:* (065) 505270 *Fax:* (065) 584594
    *E-mail:* cortinab@tin.it

**Costa e Nolan SpA+**
Via Boscovich, 44, 20124 Milan
*Tel:* (022) 9402156 *Fax:* (022) 047922
*Key Personnel*
Man Dir, Rights & Permissions: Carla Costa
Editorial: Eugenio Buonaccorsi
Sales, Publicity: Stefano Tettamanti
Founded: 1982
Subjects: Art, Drama, Theater, Economics, Fic-
    tion, Literature, Literary Criticism, Essays
ISBN Prefix(es): 88-7648

**CPE**, see Centro Programmazione Editoriale
    (CPE)

**Edizioni Cremonese SRL+**
Borgo S Croce 17, 50122 Florence
*Tel:* (055) 2476371 *Fax:* (055) 2476372
*E-mail:* cremonese@ed-cremonese.it
*Web Site:* www.ed-cremonese.it *Cable:*
    EDIZIONI CREMONESE
*Key Personnel*
Man Dir: Alberto Stianti *E-mail:* cremonese@ed-
    cremonese.it
Founded: 1930
Subjects: Aeronautics, Aviation, Civil Engineer-
    ing, Electronics, Electrical Engineering, Engi-
    neering (General), Mathematics, Mechanical
    Engineering, Science (General), Technology
ISBN Prefix(es): 88-7083

**Crisalide+**
Via Campodivivo 43, 04020 Spigno Saturnia
    (Latina)
*Tel:* (0771) 64463 *Fax:* (0771) 639121
*E-mail:* crisalide@crisalide.com
*Web Site:* www.crisalide.com
*Key Personnel*
President & Owner: Raffaele Iandolo *Tel:* (0771)
    639121
Founded: 1988
Subjects: Astrology, Occult, Parapsychology, Psy-
    chology, Psychiatry, Religion - Buddhist
ISBN Prefix(es): 88-7183
Number of titles published annually: 20 Print
Total Titles: 150 Print
Distributed by C D A

**CSTM**, *imprint of* Centro Studi Terzo Mondo

**Edizioni Cultura della Pace+**
Via Venezia, 18b, 50121 Florence
*Tel:* (055) 576149 *Fax:* (055) 5088003
*Key Personnel*
President: Enrico Palmerini
Founded: 1986
Subjects: Anthropology, Biography, Communi-
    cations, Developing Countries, Education, En-
    vironmental Studies, Ethnicity, Foreign Coun-
    tries, Government, Political Science, History,
    Human Relations, Philosophy, Religion - Bud-
    dhist, Religion - Catholic, Religion - Hindu,
    Religion - Islamic, Religion - Jewish, Religion
    - Protestant, Religion - Other, Social Sciences,
    Sociology, Theology, Women's Studies
ISBN Prefix(es): 88-09; 88-87183
Imprints: ECP
*Orders to:* Edizioni Cultura della Pace, Via
    Brunetto Latini 49, 50131 Florence

**Ed La Cultura Sociologica**, *imprint of* Centro
    Studi Terzo Mondo

**La Cultura Sociologica+**
Via GB Morgagni 39, 20129 Milan

*Tel:* (02) 29409041 *Fax:* (02) 29409041
*Key Personnel*
Chief Executive: Prof Umberto Melotti
    *Tel:* (0330) 687866 *E-mail:* melotti@uniroma1.
    it
Editorial, Rights & Permissions: Elena Sala
Founded: 1964
Books on social sciences.
Subjects: Biological Sciences, Economics, Eth-
    nicity, Government, Political Science, History,
    Philosophy, Social Sciences, Sociology
Number of titles published annually: 8 Print
Total Titles: 100 Print
*Associate Companies:* Centro Studi Terzo Mondo

**Edizioni Curci SRL+**
Galleria del Corso 4, 20122 Milan
*Tel:* (02) 760361 *Fax:* (02) 76014504
*E-mail:* info@edizionicurci.it
*Web Site:* www.edizionicurci.it
*Key Personnel*
President & General Manager: Giuseppe Gramitto
    Ricci
Man Dir: Michele Delvecchio
Classical Dept: Laura Moro
Founded: 1860
Subjects: Music, Dance
ISBN Prefix(es): 88-485
*Associate Companies:* Edizioni Accordo SRL
*Warehouse:* Via Ripamonti, 129, 20141 Milan,
    Lina Manfra *Tel:* (02) 57410561 *Fax:* (02)
    5390043

**Damanhur Edizioni**
Via Pramarzo, 3, 10080 Baldissero Canavese
    (Turin)
*Tel:* (0124) 512213 *Fax:* (0124) 512213
*E-mail:* dhbooks@damanhurbooks.com
*Web Site:* www.damanhurbooks.com
Founded: 1978
*Membership(s):* Casa Edittice Della Comunita Di
    Damanhur.
Subjects: Astrology, Occult, Earth Sciences, Mys-
    teries, Social Sciences, Sociology
ISBN Prefix(es): 88-7012

**Dami Editore SRL+**
Via Gesu 10, 20121 Milan
*Tel:* (02) 76006533 *Fax:* (02) 784010
*E-mail:* damieditore@damieditore.it
*Web Site:* www.damieditore.it
Founded: 1972
Subjects: Animals, Pets, Fiction
ISBN Prefix(es): 88-09

**D'Anna+**
Via Dante da Castiglione, 8, 50125 Florence
*Tel:* (055) 2335513 *Fax:* (055) 225932
*E-mail:* gdanna@tin.it; gdanna@mbox.vol.it
    *Cable:* D'ANNA FLORENCE
*Key Personnel*
Man Dir, Sales, & Rights & Permissions: Al-
    bertina D'Anna
Editorial & Production: Gabriele D'Anna; Guido
    D'Anna
Founded: 1926
Subjects: Art, Chemistry, Chemical Engineering,
    Education, History, Literature, Literary Criti-
    cism, Essays
ISBN Prefix(es): 88-8104; 88-8321
Imprints: Editoriale Paradigma; G D'Anna-Sintesi
*Warehouse:* Loescher Editore, via Vajont 93,
    Cascine Vica Rivoli, Turin
*Orders to:* Loescher Editore, Via V Amedeo II,
    18-1021 Torin

**G D'Anna-Sintesi**, *imprint of* D'Anna

**Datanews+**
Via di S Erasmo, 22, 00184 Rome
*Tel:* (06) 70450318/9 *Fax:* (06) 70450320

*E-mail:* info@datanews.it
*Web Site:* www.datanews.it
*Key Personnel*
President: Corrado Perna
Man Dir: Francisco Florentano
Founded: 1985
Subjects: Economics, Environmental Studies, Ethnicity, Government, Political Science, History
ISBN Prefix(es): 88-7981

**M d'Auria Editore SAS+**
Palazzo Pignatelli, Calata Trinita Maggiore 52-53, 80134 Naples
*Tel:* (081) 5518963 *Fax:* (081) 5493827; (081) 5518963
*E-mail:* info@dauria.it
*Web Site:* www.dauria.it
*Key Personnel*
Dir: Gianni Macchiavelli
Publicity: Paola Raeli
Founded: 1837
Also acts as sales agent.
Subjects: Antiques, Archaeology, History, Literature, Literary Criticism, Essays, Religion - Other
ISBN Prefix(es): 88-7092
Number of titles published annually: 20 Print
Total Titles: 45 Print
Distributor for Edizioni Di Storia E Letteratura SRL; Instituto Universitario Orientale
*Bookshop(s):* Libreria Internazionale-International Book Center M d'Auria, Calata Trinita Maggiore 52/53, 80134 Naples

**G De Bono Editore+**
Via Masaccio, 220, 50132 Florence
*Tel:* (055) 576022 *Fax:* (055) 5001665
*Key Personnel*
Chief Executive: Giuseppe De Bono
Editorial: Prof Aldo De Bono
Founded: 1958
Subjects: Education, Fiction, Philosophy

**Giovanni De Vecchi Editore SpA+**
Via Pisani, 16, 20124 Milan
*Tel:* (02) 66984851 *Fax:* (02) 6701548
Founded: 1973
Subjects: Agriculture, Animals, Pets, Antiques, Astrology, Occult, Business, Career Development, Crafts, Games, Hobbies, Gardening, Plants, Health, Nutrition, How-to, Humor, Law, Medicine, Nursing, Dentistry, Outdoor Recreation, Sports, Athletics
ISBN Prefix(es): 88-412

**DEA**, see DEA Diffusione Edizioni Anglo-Americane

**DEA Diffusione Edizioni Anglo-Americane**
Via Lima 28, 00198 Rome
*Tel:* (06) 8551441 *Fax:* (06) 8543228
*E-mail:* info@deanet.it
*Web Site:* www.deanet.com
ISBN Prefix(es): 88-86188
*Branch Office(s)*
Massimo D'Azeglio 27, 40123 Bologna
*Tel:* (051) 236100 *Fax:* (051) 220882
Via Pascoli 56, 20133 Milan *Tel:* (02) 2364306 *Fax:* (02) 2362738
Via Domenico Cimarosa 91/c, 80127 Naples
*Tel:* (081) 5787576 *Fax:* (081) 5780739
Via G D Cassini 75/8, 10129 Turin *Tel:* (011) 503202 *Fax:* (011) 595559
Via Diaz 19/1, 34124 Trieste *Tel:* (040) 301257 *Fax:* (040) 310993

**Edizioni Dedalo SRL+**
Viale Luigi Jacobini 5, 70123 Bari
Mailing Address: CP BA/19, 70123 Bari
*Tel:* (080) 5311413; (080) 5311400; (080) 5311401 *Fax:* (080) 5311414

*E-mail:* info@edizionidedalo.it
*Web Site:* www.edizionidedalo.it
*Key Personnel*
Man Dir: Raimondo Coga
Editorial Manager: Claudia Coga
   *E-mail:* claudiacoga@edizionidedalo.it
Founded: 1965
Also acts as printing house.
Subjects: Anthropology, Architecture & Interior Design, Art, Film, Video, Government, Political Science, History, Philosophy, Physical Sciences, Physics, Psychology, Psychiatry, Science (General), Social Sciences, Sociology
ISBN Prefix(es): 88-220
Number of titles published annually: 30 Print
Total Titles: 1,000 Print
*Parent Company:* Dedalo Litostampa Srl

**Edizioni Dehoniane Bologna (EDB)+**
Via Nosadella, 6, 40123 Bologna
*Tel:* (051) 4290011 *Fax:* (051) 4290099
*E-mail:* webmaster@dehoniane.it
*Web Site:* www.dehoniane.it
*Key Personnel*
Man Dir: Alfio Filippi
Sales Dir, Rights & Permissions: Cesano Giacomo
Publicity Dir: Gabriella Zucchi
Contact: Vanda Persiani
Founded: 1965
Subjects: Biblical Studies, Education, Religion - Catholic, Religion - Other, Theology
ISBN Prefix(es): 88-10
*Associate Companies:* Data Service Center
Imprints: EDB
Distributed by Dehoniana Libri SpA
*Bookshop(s):* Dehoniana Libri, Via Nosadella, 6, 40123 Bologna
*Shipping Address:* Via Dal Ferro 4, 40138 Bologna

**Edizioni Dehoniane+**
Via Casale S Pio, 20, 00165 Rome
*Tel:* (06) 624996 *Fax:* (06) 6628326
*E-mail:* webmaster@dehoniane.it
*Web Site:* www.dehoniane.it *Cable:* EDIZIONI DEHONIANE ROME
*Key Personnel*
Chief Executive: Vitantonio Giampietro
Editorial: Luigi Cortese
Sales, Publicity: Antonio Bozza
Production: Umberto Chiarello
Founded: 1956
Subjects: Education, Philosophy, Psychology, Psychiatry, Religion - Other, Social Sciences, Sociology, Theology
ISBN Prefix(es): 88-396
*Parent Company:* Provincia Meridonale Italiana della Congregazi one dei Sacerdoti del S Cuore di Gesu', via Marechiaro, 46 Naples
*Bookshop(s):* Libreria Dehoniana, Via Depretis 60, 80133 Naples

**DEI Tipographia del Genio Civile**
Via Nomentana 16/20, 00161 Rome
*Tel:* (06) 44163792 *Fax:* (06) 4403307
*E-mail:* dei@build.it
*Web Site:* www.build.it
*Key Personnel*
Man Dir, Production: Maria Cecilia Bartoli
Editorial, Publicity, Sales: Giuseppe Rufo
Founded: 1869
Subjects: Architecture & Interior Design, Civil Engineering, Electronics, Electrical Engineering, Law, Technology
ISBN Prefix(es): 88-7722; 88-496
*Warehouse:* Via Mesula 12, 00161 Rome

**Casa Editrice Istituto della Santa**
Via dei Caccia 5, Novara 28100
*Tel:* (0321) 22371 *Cable:* Dellasanta Novara

Founded: 1956
Subjects: Business

**Edizioni Della Torre di Salvatore Fozzi & C SAS+**
Via Contivecchi 8/2, 09122 Cagliari
*Tel:* (070) 270507 *Fax:* (070) 270507
*E-mail:* info@librisardi.it
*Web Site:* www.librisardi.it
*Key Personnel*
Chief Executive: Salvatore Fozzi *Tel:* (070) 271411 *Fax:* (070) 272542
Founded: 1974
Subjects: Archaeology, Art, Geography, Geology, History, Language Arts, Linguistics, Natural History, Poetry, Regional Interests
ISBN Prefix(es): 88-7343
Total Titles: 225 Print
*Associate Companies:* Scuola Domani, via Toscana 82, 09124 Cagliari
Subsidiaries: Agenzia Libraria Fozzi
*Bookshop(s):* Libreria Fozzi, Via Dante 72, 09100 Cagliari

**Edizioni dell'Orso+**
Via Rattazzi 47, 15100 Alessandria
*Tel:* (0131) 252349 *Fax:* (0131) 257567
*E-mail:* direzione.commerciale@ediorso.it
*Web Site:* www.ediorso.it
*Key Personnel*
Man Dir: Gian Paolo Calligaris
Editorial: Lorenzo Massobrio
Founded: 1979
Subjects: History, Language Arts, Linguistics, Poetry, Regional Interests
ISBN Prefix(es): 88-7694

**Demetra SRL+**
Via Stra 167, 37030 Colognola al Colli (Verona)
*Tel:* (045) 6159711 *Fax:* (045) 6159700
*Key Personnel*
Man Dir: Silvano Pizzighella
Founded: 1983
Subjects: Agriculture, Biological Sciences, Health, Nutrition, Literature, Literary Criticism, Essays
ISBN Prefix(es): 88-7122; 88-440

**Di Baio Editore SpA+**
Via Settembrini, 11, 20124 Milan
*Tel:* (02) 6692254 *Fax:* (02) 6709257
*Web Site:* www.dibaio.com
*Key Personnel*
President: Giuseppe Maria Jonghi Lavarini
Man Dir: Fabio Alberti
Founded: 1973
Subjects: Architecture & Interior Design, Cookery, Crafts, Games, Hobbies, Gardening, Plants, House & Home, Technology
ISBN Prefix(es): 88-7080

**Organizzazione Didattica Editoriale Ape+**
Via degli Artisti, 8b, 50132 Florence
*Tel:* (055) 572584 *Fax:* (055) 578243 *Cable:* APE MURRI 565 BOLOGNA
*Key Personnel*
Chief Executive, Editorial, Production, Rights & Permissions: Gina Cesari
Sales: Giorgio Ognibene
Founded: 1964
Subjects: Fiction, Regional Interests
ISBN Prefix(es): 88-86515
Imprints: APE
*Bookshop(s):* Gottardi Concession, via Zanardi 60, IV Bologna

**Dimensione Umana**, *imprint of* Le Stelle Scuola

**Directorate of Archives**, see Direzione Generale Archivi

**Direzione Generale Archivi**
Via Gaeta 8a, 00185 Rome
*Tel:* (06) 4742177 *Fax:* (06) 4742177
*E-mail:* studi@archivi.beniculturali.it
*Web Site:* www.archivi.beniculturali.it
*Telex:* (06) 623278
*Key Personnel*
Dir: Antonio Dentoni-Litta
Publishing branch of the Italian State Archives
  Administration.
Subjects: History, Law, Library & Information
  Sciences, Public Administration
ISBN Prefix(es): 88-7125
Number of titles published annually: 20 Print
Total Titles: 450 Print
*Parent Company:* Ministero Beni e Attivita Cul-
  turali
*Orders to:* Istituto poligrafico e Zecca dello stato,
  Via Marciana Marina, No A, 00199 Rome
  *Tel:* (06) 85 081 *Fax:* (06) 85 084117
Direzione editoriale, Via Marciana Marina, No
  A, 00199 Rome *Tel:* (06) 85 081 *Fax:* (06) 85
  084117
Libreria dello Stato, Via Marciana Marina, No
  A, 00199 Rome *Tel:* (06) 85 081 *Fax:* (06) 85
  084117

**Domus Academy**
via Savona 97, 20144 Milan
*Tel:* (02) 42414001 *Fax:* (02) 4222525
*E-mail:* info@domusacademy.it
*Web Site:* www.domusacademy.com
ISBN Prefix(es): 88-7184; 88-85187

**Editoriale Domus SpA+**
Via Gianni Mazzocchi 1/3, 20089 Rozzano, Milan
*Tel:* (02) 82472 1
*E-mail:* editorialedomus@edidomus.it
*Web Site:* www.edidomus.it
*Key Personnel*
Publicity: Gabriele Vigano
Founded: 1929
Subjects: Aeronautics, Aviation, Architecture &
  Interior Design, Art, Automotive, Cookery,
  Transportation, Travel
ISBN Prefix(es): 88-7212

**Dunod**, *imprint of* Masson SpA

**Edizioni E - Elle SRL**
via S Cilino 16, 34126 Trieste
*Tel:* (040) 566821 *Fax:* (040) 566819
*Telex:* (040) 637969
*Key Personnel*
Man Dir: Giancarlo Stavro Santarosa
Editorial: Orietta Fatucci
Rights & Permissions: Sandra Goruppi
Founded: 1984
ISBN Prefix(es): 88-85326

**Edizioni E/O+**
Via Camozzi, 1, 00195 Rome
*Tel:* (06) 3722829 *Fax:* (06) 37351096
*E-mail:* info@edizionieo.it
*Web Site:* www.edizioni-eo.it
*Key Personnel*
Man Dir, Rights & Permissions: Sandro Ferri
Editorial: Sandra Ozzola
Sales: Tom Joannucci
Production: Alfredo Lavarini
Publicity: Sergio Vezzali
Founded: 1979
Subjects: Fiction
ISBN Prefix(es): 88-7641

**Edizioni EBE**
Via dei Magazzini 22, 01016 Tarquinia (Viterbo)
*Tel:* (0766) 858878 *Fax:* (0766) 858877
*Key Personnel*
Chief Executive: Giovanni Di Capua
Sales: Norma Merli

Founded: 1973
Subjects: Government, Political Science, History
ISBN Prefix(es): 88-7977
*Orders to:* Via FS Nitti 12, 00191 Rome *Tel:* (06)
  3272972

**EBF**, *imprint of* Biblioteca Francescana

**ECIG+**
Via Brignole de Ferrari 9, 16125 Genoa
*Tel:* (010) 2512399 *Fax:* (010) 2512398
*Key Personnel*
Man Dir: Dr Gian Luigi Blengino
Founded: 1971
Specialize in Sapiential essays.
Subjects: Literature, Literary Criticism, Essays,
  Philosophy, Psychology, Psychiatry
ISBN Prefix(es): 88-7545; 88-7544
*Showroom(s):* Salone Del Libro Torino, Largo
  Regio Parco, 9-10152 Torino; Frankfurt
  Buchmesse, Frankfurt, Germany
*Bookshop(s):* Piazza Santa Sabina 2 sc A/2,
  Genoa *Tel:* (010) 203788; Salita Inf della Noce
  8 rosso 16131, Genoa *Tel:* (010) 510355; Via S
  Gallo 21R, Florence *Tel:* (055) 261693; Viale
  Morgagni 31, Florence *Tel:* (055) 4361722; Via
  Ormea 90, Turin *Tel:* (011) 683527; Via Santa
  maria 7, Pisa *Tel:* (050) 501426; Via dei Mille
  32, Pisa *Tel:* 050 35310; Via De Amicis 60,
  Naples *Tel:* (081) 5469304
*Orders to:* CLU - Salita Inferiore, Della NOCE
  10 R, IDEM, 16143 Genoa

**Ecole Francaise de Rome+**
Piazza Farnese, 67, 00186 Rome
*Tel:* (06) 68 60 11 *Fax:* (06) 687 48 34
*E-mail:* publ@ecole-francaise.it
*Web Site:* www.ecole-francaise.it
*Key Personnel*
Publisher: Francois-Charles Uginet *Tel:* (06)
  68885305
Founded: 1881
Subjects: Archaeology, Art, History, Law
ISBN Prefix(es): 2-7283
Number of titles published annually: 30 Print
Total Titles: 400 Print

**ECP**, *imprint of* Edizioni Cultura della Pace

**Edagricole - Edizioni Agricole+**
Via Goito, 13, 40126 Bologna
*Tel:* (051) 65751 *Fax:* (051) 6575800
*E-mail:* sede@gce.it
*Web Site:* www.edagricole.it
*Key Personnel*
Man Dir & Editorial: Alberto Perdisa
Sales: Luigi Perdisa, Jr *Tel:* (051) 6226849
  *Fax:* (051) 540000
Publicity: Franco Metri *Tel:* (051) 6226818
  *E-mail:* stampa@calderini.agriline.it
Founded: 1935
Subjects: Agriculture, Animals, Pets, Biological
  Sciences, Gardening, Plants, Health, Nutrition,
  Science (General), Veterinary Science
ISBN Prefix(es): 88-206
Total Titles: 5,000 Print
*Parent Company:* Calderini SRL, Via Emilia Lev-
  ante N 31/2, 40139 Bologna
*Associate Companies:* Edizioni Calderini;
  Calderini Industrie Grafiche ed Editoriali SRL;
  Edagricole Periodici SpA
*Bookshop(s):* Via Zamboni 18, Bologna; Via
  Bronzino 14, Milan; Via Boncompagni 73,
  Rome

**EDAS**
Via Bosco, 17, 98122 Messina
*Tel:* (090) 675653 *Fax:* (090) 675653
*E-mail:* info@edas.it
*Web Site:* www.edas.it
Founded: 1975

Subjects: History, Science (General)
ISBN Prefix(es): 88-7820
Number of titles published annually: 10 Print
Total Titles: 100 Print

**EDB**, *imprint of* Edizioni Dehoniane Bologna
  (EDB)

**EDB**, see Edizioni Dehoniane Bologna (EDB)

**Ediart Editrice**
Imprint of Livro Grai
Loc Montelupino, 82/13, 06059 Todi (PG)
*Tel:* (075) 8943594 *Fax:* (075) 8942411
*E-mail:* ediart@ediart.it
*Web Site:* www.ediart.it
*Key Personnel*
Editor: Leonilde Dominici
Founded: 1983
Specialize in the history of art & architecture.
Subjects: Architecture & Interior Design, Art
ISBN Prefix(es): 88-85311
Number of titles published annually: 4 Print
Total Titles: 70 Print

**Edicart**
Via Jucker, 28, 20025 Legnano, Milan
*Tel:* (0331) 74291 *Fax:* (0331) 74292
*E-mail:* info@edicart.it
*Web Site:* www.edicart.it
Founded: 1986
ISBN Prefix(es): 88-474; 88-7774

**Ediciclo Editore SRL+**
Via Cesar Beccaria, 13/15, 30026 Portogruaro
  (Venezia)
*Tel:* (0421) 74475 *Fax:* (0421) 282070
*E-mail:* posta@ediciclo.it
*Web Site:* www.ediciclo.it
*Key Personnel*
Administrative Dir: Vittorio Anastasia
Founded: 1992
Subjects: Economics, Environmental Studies, His-
  tory, Outdoor Recreation, Science (General),
  Social Sciences, Sociology, Sports, Athletics,
  Travel
ISBN Prefix(es): 88-85327; 88-85318; 88-88829
Imprints: Nuova Dimensione

**EDIFIR SRL+**
Edizioni Firenze, Via Fiume, 8, 50123 Florence
*Tel:* (055) 289639 *Fax:* (055) 289478
*E-mail:* edizioni-firenze@edifir.it
*Web Site:* www.edifir.it
*Key Personnel*
President: Wanda Miletti Ferragamo
Administrator: Dr Pierfrancesco Pacini
International Rights: Dr Fabio Tongiorgi
Founded: 1985
Specialized in publications on fashion, custom.
Subjects: Architecture & Interior Design, History
ISBN Prefix(es): 88-7970

**Edipuglia+**
Via Dalmazia 22/b, 70050 S Spirito (Bari)
*Tel:* (080) 5333056 *Fax:* (080) 5333057
*E-mail:* edipuglia@tin.it
*Web Site:* www.edipuglia.it
*Key Personnel*
Administrator: Ceglie Oronzo
Founded: 1979
Subjects: Antiques, Archaeology, History
ISBN Prefix(es): 88-7228
Number of titles published annually: 10 Print
Total Titles: 150 Print

**Editrice Edisco+**
Via Pastrengo 28, 10128 Turin
*Tel:* (011) 54 78 80 *Fax:* (011) 51 75 396
*E-mail:* info@edisco.it
*Web Site:* www.edisco.it

*Key Personnel*
General Manager: Corrado Jaria
Founded: 1952
Subjects: Chemistry, Chemical Engineering, Education, Electronics, Electrical Engineering, English as a Second Language, Literature, Literary Criticism, Essays, Mechanical Engineering, Physics, Science (General)
ISBN Prefix(es): 88-441
Number of titles published annually: 25 Print
Total Titles: 300 Print
*Shipping Address:* Via Barletta 124, 10136 Turin
*Warehouse:* Via Barletta 124, 10136 Turin

**Edisport Editoriale SpA**
Via Gradisca 11, 20151 Milan
*Tel:* (02) 380851 *Fax:* (02) 38010393
*E-mail:* edisport@edisport.it
*Web Site:* www.edisport.it
*Telex:* 353629 EDISP I
*Key Personnel*
Marketing: Donatella Tardini

**Edistudio+**
Via Bruno, 6/8, 56125 Pisa
*Tel:* (050) 48670; (050) 2208745 *Fax:* (050) 500585
*E-mail:* edistudio@edistudio.it *Cable:* Edistudio CP 213 Pisa
*Key Personnel*
Chief Executive: Brunetto Casini
Founded: 1977
Also specialize in local culture & local magazines.
Subjects: Drama, Theater, Education, Fiction, Geography, Geology, Language Arts, Linguistics, Literature, Literary Criticism, Essays, Music, Dance, Poetry, Science (General), Sports, Athletics
ISBN Prefix(es): 88-7036
Total Titles: 70 Print
Subsidiaries: Composit (Fotocomposizione elaborazione grafica)

**Editalia (Edizioni d'Italia)**
Via Marine Marciana 28, 00138 Rome
*Tel:* (06) 85081 *Toll Free Tel:* 800 01 4858 *Fax:* (06) 85085165
*Web Site:* www.editalia.it
*Key Personnel*
Man Dir: Lidio Bozzini
Rights & Permissions: Arrigo Pecchioli
Founded: 1952
Subjects: Art, Ethnicity, History
ISBN Prefix(es): 88-7060

**Editori Laterza+**
Via di Villa Sacchetti, 17, 00197 Rome
*Tel:* (06) 3218393 *Fax:* (06) 3223853
*E-mail:* laterza@laterza.it
*Web Site:* www.laterza.it
*Key Personnel*
President: Dr Giuseppe Laterza
Founded: 1901
Subjects: Anthropology, Archaeology, Communications, History, Law, Philosophy, Religion - Other
Number of titles published annually: 120 Print
Foreign Rep(s): Alice Chambers; Eulama Literary Agency

**Edizioni Associate/Editrice Internazionale Srl+**
Viale Ippocrate 156, 00161 Rome
*Tel:* (06) 44704513 *Fax:* (06) 44704513
*E-mail:* easso@tin.it
*Key Personnel*
President: Livio Fabjan
Administrative Delegate & Editorial Dir: Rean Mazzone
Founded: 1992

Subjects: Government, Political Science, Literature, Literary Criticism, Essays
ISBN Prefix(es): 88-267
*Associate Companies:* Editrice Ila Palma, Tea Nova Srl
*Showroom(s):* Torino e Francoforte
*Bookshop(s):* Distribuzione Libraria PDE
*Warehouse:* c/o Tea Nova Srl, Via Isidoro la Lumia 5/7, 90139 Palermo
*Orders to:* c/o Sede V Le, Via Casini 8, 00153 Rome

**Edizioni d'Arte Antica e Moderna EDAM+**
Via di Monte Oliveto, 2, 50124 Florence
*Tel:* (055) 2298578 *Fax:* (055) 220837
Founded: 1962
Subjects: Antiques, Architecture & Interior Design, Art
ISBN Prefix(es): 88-7244

**Edizioni del Centro Camuno di Studi Preistorici+**
Division of Centro Camuno di Studi Preistoric
Via Marconi, 7, 25044 Capo di Ponte (Brescia)
*Tel:* (0364) 42091 *Fax:* (0364) 42572
*E-mail:* ccspreist@tin.it
*Web Site:* www.rockart-ccsp.com *Cable:* CENTROSTUDI CAPODIPONTE
*Key Personnel*
Chief Executive: Prof Emmanuel Anati
Production: Ariela Fradkin
Founded: 1964
Publishing division of a research institution.
Subjects: Anthropology, Antiques, Archaeology, Art, Biblical Studies, Ethnicity, History, Religion - Other
ISBN Prefix(es): 88-86621
Number of titles published annually: 3 Print
Total Titles: 90 Print
*Associate Companies:* Arts & Crafts International; IDAPEE (Institut des Arts Prehistoriques et Ethnologique), Paris, France
Imprints: BCSP; BC News; CCSP
Subsidiaries: WARA: World Archives of Rock Art

**Edizioni del Delfino,** *imprint of* Adriano Gallina Editore sas

**Edizioni di Storia e Letteratura**
Via delle Fornaci, 24, 00165 Rome
*Tel:* (06) 39670307 *Fax:* (06) 39671250
*E-mail:* info@storiaeletteratura.it
*Web Site:* www.storiaeletterature.it
*Key Personnel*
Chief Executive: Lodovico Steide
Founded: 1943
Subjects: History, Literature, Literary Criticism, Essays, Philosophy
ISBN Prefix(es): 88-900138; 88-87114; 88-8498
Number of titles published annually: 120 Print; 10 Online
Total Titles: 1,000 Print; 10 Online

**Edizioni di Torino,** see EDT Edizioni di Torino

**Edizioni Giuridiche Economiche Aziendali,** see EGEA (Edizioni Giuridiche Economiche Aziendali)

**Edizioni Gruppo Abele,** see Gruppo Abele

**Edizioni Il Punto d'Incontro SAS**
Via Zamenhof 685, 36100 Vicenza
*Tel:* (0444) 239189 *Fax:* (0444) 239266
*E-mail:* ordini@edizionilpuntocontro.it
*Web Site:* www.edizionilpuntodincontro.it
Subjects: Astrology, Occult, Ethnicity, Health, Nutrition, Philosophy, Religion - Buddhist, Re-

ligion - Catholic, Religion - Hindu, Religion - Islamic, Religion - Other
ISBN Prefix(es): 88-8093

**Edizioni la Scala**
Abbazia Madonna Della Scala, Zona B 58, 70015 Noci (Bari)
*Tel:* (080) 4975838 *Fax:* (080) 4975839
*E-mail:* lascala@abbazialascala.com
*Web Site:* www.abbazialascala.com *Cable:* BENEDETTINI NOCI
*Key Personnel*
Chief Executive, Editorial: Padre Giuseppe Quirino Poggi
Founded: 1947
Subjects: Biography, Music, Dance, Philosophy, Religion - Catholic

**Edizioni l'Arciere SRL+**
Viale Sarrea, 7, 12025 Dronero, Cuneo
*Tel:* (0171) 905566 *Fax:* (0171) 905730
*E-mail:* info@arciere.com
*Web Site:* www.arciere.com *Cable:* ARCIERE EDIZIONI CUNEO
*Key Personnel*
Chief Executive, Sales, Rights & Permissions: Aldo Sacchetti
Editorial, Production & Publicity: Mario Donadei
Founded: 1973
Subjects: Art, Biography, Fiction, Geography, Geology, History, Literature, Literary Criticism, Essays, Military Science, Poetry, Regional Interests, Travel
ISBN Prefix(es): 88-86398

**Edizioni L'Eta Dell'Acqua Rio,** *imprint of* Lindau

**Edizioni Qiqajon+**
Comunita monastica di Bose, 13887 Magnano (Biella)
*Tel:* (015) 679115 *Fax:* (015) 6794949
*E-mail:* acquisti@qiqajon.it
*Web Site:* www.qiqajon.it
*Key Personnel*
President: Enzo Bianchi
International Rights: Guido Dotti *E-mail:* guido.dotti@qiqajon.it
Founded: 1983
Subjects: Religion - Catholic, Religion - Jewish, Religion - Protestant, Theology
ISBN Prefix(es): 88-85227; 88-8227
Number of titles published annually: 20 Print
Total Titles: 220 Print

**Edizioni Realizzazioni Grafiche - Artigiana,** see ERGA SNC di Carla Ottino Merli & C (Edizioni Realizzazioni Grafiche - Artigiana)

**Edizioni Studio Domenicano (ESD)+**
Via Dell' Osservanza 72, 40136 Bologna
*Tel:* (051) 582034 *Fax:* (051) 331583
*E-mail:* esd@alinet.it
*Web Site:* www.esd-domenicani.it
*Key Personnel*
Dir: Benetollo Ottorino *E-mail:* esd.benetollo@tiscalinet.it
Founded: 1985
Subjects: Philosophy, Religion - Catholic, Social Sciences, Sociology, Theology, Works of St Thomas Aquinas (Latin & Italian)
ISBN Prefix(es): 88-7094
Number of titles published annually: 60 Print
Total Titles: 500 Print

**Edizioni Universitarie di Lettere Economia Diritto,** see LED - Edizioni Universitarie di Lettere Economia Diritto

**EDT Edizioni di Torino+**
Via Alfieri, 19, 10121 Turin
*Tel:* (011) 5591816 *Fax:* (011) 2307034
*E-mail:* edt@edt.it
*Web Site:* www.edt.it
*Key Personnel*
Chief Executive: Enzo Peruccio
Founded: 1976
Subjects: Music, Dance, Travel
ISBN Prefix(es): 88-7063
Distributor for Instituto di Studi Verdiani; Lonely
Planet Inc


**EE**, *imprint of* Edi.Ermes srl


**EE**, *imprint of* Editrice Eraclea


**Effata Editrice+**
Via Tre Denti 1, Cantalupa, Turin
*Tel:* (0121) 353452 *Fax:* (0121) 353839
*E-mail:* info@effata.it
*Web Site:* www.effata.it
*Key Personnel*
Dir: Paolo Pellegrino
Founded: 1994
A publishing house that is engaged to spread sig-
nificant words to answer the deepest questions
of the human soul.
Subjects: Drama, Theater, Education, Fiction, Hu-
man Relations, Psychology, Psychiatry, Reli-
gion - Catholic, Self-Help, Words for helping
& giving joy
ISBN Prefix(es): 88-86617; 88-7402
Number of titles published annually: 20 Print
Total Titles: 80 Print
*Orders to:* Mescat, Viale Bacchiglione 20/A,
20139 Milan, Contact: Francesco Crespi
*Tel:* (02) 55210800 *Fax:* (02) 55211315


**EFR**, *imprint of* EFR-Editrici Francescane


**EFR-Editrici Francescane**
Via Orto Botanico, 11, 35123 Padova
*Tel:* (049) 8225702 *Fax:* (049) 8225713
*E-mail:* info@bibliotecafrancescana.it
*Web Site:* www.biblia.it
*Key Personnel*
President & International Rights: Aristide Cabassi
*Tel:* (02) 29002736
Founded: 1995
Subjects: Religion - Catholic
ISBN Prefix(es): 88-8135
*Associate Companies:* Edizioni Bibliotea Frances-
cana Milano, Piazza S Angelo, 2, 20121 Mi-
lan; Edizioni Messaggero Padova, Via Orto
Botanico, 11, 35123 Padova; Edizioni Porz-
iuncola Assisi, Piazza Porziuncola, 1, 06088
Santa Maria Degli Angeli (PG); Libreria Inter-
nazionale Edizioni Francescane, Borgo S Lucia
38/40, 36100 Vicenza
Imprints: EFR
Distributor for Messaggero Distribuzione


**EGEA (Edizioni Giuridiche Economiche
Aziendali)+**
Via Sarfatti, 25, 20136 Milan
Mailing Address: Via Calatafimi, 10, 20122 Milan
*Tel:* (02) 58365751 *Fax:* (02) 58365753
*E-mail:* egea.edizioni@egea.uni-bocconi.it
*Key Personnel*
President: Prof Alberto Bertoni
Editor: Adriana Macchi
Founded: 1988
Subjects: Advertising, Career Development, Eco-
nomics, Finance, History, Law, Management,
Marketing, Philosophy, Public Administration
ISBN Prefix(es): 88-238
*Associate Companies:* Giuffre Editore SpA, Via
Busto Arsizio 40, 20151 Milan

*Bookshop(s):* EGEA SpA, Via Sarfatti 25, 20136
Milan
*Orders to:* Messaggerie Libri SpA, Via G Car-
cano 32, 20141 Milan


**EGGM**, *imprint of* EuroGeoGrafiche Mencattini


**International EILES**, see Edizioni Internazionali
di Letteratura e Scienze


**Giulio Einaudi Editore SpA+**
Via Biancamano, 2, 10121 Turin
*Tel:* (011) 56561 *Fax:* (011) 542903
*Web Site:* www.einaudi.it
*Key Personnel*
President: Giulio Einaudi
Vice President: Leonardo Mondadori
Editor: Vittorio Bo
Founded: 1933
Subjects: Art, Fiction, History, Music, Dance,
Philosophy, Poetry, Psychology, Psychiatry, So-
cial Sciences, Sociology
ISBN Prefix(es): 88-06
*Parent Company:* A Mondadori Editore SpA
*Associate Companies:* Elemond SpA/ Edizioni E
Elle SpA
*Bookshop(s):* Libreria Einaudi, Via Manzoni 40,
20121 Milan
*Warehouse:* Arnoldo Mondadori, Via Montelun,
37131 Verona
*Orders to:* Ufficio Commerciale, Via Biancamano
2, 10121 Turin


**EL**, *imprint of* Editrice Liguria SNC di Norberto
Sabatelli & C


**EL**, *imprint of* Edizioni Lavoro SRL


**Electa**
Via Trentacoste, 7, 20134 Milan
*Tel:* (02) 21563426 (ext 406) *Fax:* (02) 21563350
*Web Site:* www.electaweb.it
*Telex:* 350523 Eleper I
*Key Personnel*
Dir: Giorgio Fantoni; Massimo Vitta Zelman
Editorial: Carlo Pirovano
Rights & Permissions: Marisa Inzaghi; Mirella
Tenderini
Founded: 1948
Subjects: Architecture & Interior Design, Art,
Photography
ISBN Prefix(es): 88-435; 88-370
Subsidiaries: Alfieri Edizioni d'Arte; Giulio Ein-
audi Editore SpA; Electa Firenze; Electa Edi-
tori Umbri Associati; Electa Napoli; Fantoni-
grafica; Electa Moniteu


**Edizioni dell'Elefante+**
Via de Bossi, 37, 00161 Rome
*Tel:* (06) 4423 4315; (06) 9784 0709 *Fax:* (06)
9784 0052
*E-mail:* info@edelefante.it
*Web Site:* www.edelefante.it
*Key Personnel*
Chief Executive: Dr Enzo Crea
Editorial: Benedetta Origo Crea
Founded: 1964
Subjects: Art
ISBN Prefix(es): 88-7176


**Eliseo**, *imprint of* Loescher Editore SRL


**Elle Di Ci - Libreria Dottrina Cristiana**
C So Francia, 214, 10090 Cascine Vica-Rivoli
Turin
*Tel:* (011) 9552111 *Fax:* (011) 9574048
*E-mail:* editoriale@elledici.org
*Web Site:* www.elledici.org
Founded: 1941

Subjects: Biblical Studies, Child Care & Devel-
opment, Education, Music, Dance, Religion -
Catholic, Theology
ISBN Prefix(es): 88-01
*Branch Office(s)*
Corso C Alberto 77, 60127 Ancona *Tel:* (071)
2810306 *Fax:* (071) 2810306
Via Martiri d'Otranto, 69, 70123 Bari *Tel:* (080)
5740059 *Fax:* (080) 5797054
Via G Matteotti, 23/D, 40129 Bologna *Tel:* (051)
355242 *Fax:* (051) 355242
Viale M Rapisardi, 95124 Catania *Tel:* (095)
441379 *Fax:* (095) 441379
Via S Giovanni Bosco, 98122 Messina *Tel:* (090)
718874 *Fax:* (090) 718874
Via M Gioia, 62, 20124 Milan *Tel:* (02)
67072085 *Fax:* (02) 67071776
Via Donnaregina, 7, 80138 Naples *Tel:* (081)
449167 *Fax:* (081) 291862
Via G Jappelli, 6, 35121 Padova *Tel:* (049)
875138 *Fax:* (049) 875138
Corso Francia, 214, 10090 Rivoli *Tel:* (011)
9552333
Via Marsala, 40, 00185 Rome *Tel:* (06) 491400
*Fax:* (06) 4450370
Via Conciliazione, 26/28, 00193 Rome *Tel:* (06)
68806735 *Fax:* (06) 6874559
Via C Rolando, 63/r, 16151 GE Sampierdarena
*Tel:* (010) 6459306 *Fax:* (010) 6459306
Via M Ausiliatrice, 10152 Turin *Tel:* (011)
5211925 *Fax:* (011) 5211925


**Ellissi**, *imprint of* Esselibri


**Elmedi™**, *imprint of* Paravia Bruno Mondadori
Editori


**ELS**, *imprint of* Edizioni Librarie Siciliane


**EMI**, see Editrice Missionaria Italiana (EMI)


**EMP**, see Messaggero di San Antonio


**Enna**
Via S Agata 90, 94100 Enna
*Tel:* (0935) 500368 *Fax:* (0935) 500568
ISBN Prefix(es): 88-7154


**Enne+**
Via Monforte, 7, 86100 Campobasso
*Tel:* (0874) 412357 *Fax:* (0874) 412357
*E-mail:* ed.enne@virgilio.it
Founded: 1965
ISBN Prefix(es): 88-7213


**EQ**, *imprint of* Edizioni Quasar di Severino
Tognon SRL


**ER**, *imprint of* Editori Riuniti


**Editrice Eraclea**
Imprint of Compagnia Delle Cinque Vie SRL
Via del Bollo 8, 20123 Milan
*Tel:* (02) 8693633 *Fax:* (02) 86453613
*E-mail:* cinquevie@libero.it
*Key Personnel*
Man Dir: Mario Calori
Founded: 1974
Number of titles published annually: 10 Print
Total Titles: 85 Print
Imprints: EE


**ERGA SNC di Carla Ottino Merli & C
(Edizioni Realizzazioni Grafiche -
Artigiana)+**
Via Biga 52r, 16144 Genoa
*Tel:* (010) 8328441 *Fax:* (010) 8328799
*Web Site:* www.erga.it

*Key Personnel*
Chief Executive: Marcello Merli
Editorial: Marco Merli
Founded: 1964
Subjects: Art, Cookery, Ethnicity, History, Law, Literature, Literary Criticism, Essays, Music, Dance, Poetry, Regional Interests, Religion - Other, Romance, Science (General), Self-Help, Sports, Athletics
ISBN Prefix(es): 88-8163

**L'Erma di Bretschneider SRL+**
Via Cassiodoro 19, 00193 Rome
*Tel:* (06) 6874127 *Fax:* (06) 6874129
*E-mail:* edizioni@lerma.it
*Web Site:* www.lerma.it
*Key Personnel*
Chief Executive & Editorial: Dr Roberto Marcucci *E-mail:* roberto.marcucci@lerma.it
Founded: 1946
Subjects: Archaeology, Architecture & Interior Design, Art, History, Language Arts, Linguistics, Religion - Other
ISBN Prefix(es): 88-7062; 88-8265
Number of titles published annually: 65 Print
Total Titles: 2,000 Print
*Bookshop(s):* Libreria L'Erma

**Edi.Ermes srl+**
Viale Enrico Forlanini 65, 20134 Milan
*Tel:* (02) 7021121 *Fax:* (02) 70211283
*E-mail:* eeinfo@eenet.it
*Key Personnel*
Chief Executive: Raffaele Grandi
Founded: 1973
Also book packager.
Subjects: Art, Biological Sciences, Economics, Medicine, Nursing, Dentistry, Sports, Athletics, Veterinary Science
ISBN Prefix(es): 88-85019; 88-7051
*Associate Companies:* Edi.Artes srl, Viale Enrico Forlanini 65, 20134 Milan
Imprints: EE

**ES**, *imprint of* Editoriale Scienza

**ESI SpA**, see Edizioni Scientifiche Italiane

**Essegi+**
Via Faentina 362, 48010 Ravenna RA
*Tel:* (0544) 499203 *Fax:* (0544) 499076
*E-mail:* essegi_libri@libero.it
*Key Personnel*
President: Dal Re Patrizia
Editorial Dir: Rieel Matteo
Founded: 1982
Specialize in contemporary art.
Subjects: Anthropology, Antiques, Archaeology, Architecture & Interior Design, Art, Astronomy, Drama, Theater, Fashion, History, Language Arts, Linguistics, Literature, Literary Criticism, Essays, Photography
ISBN Prefix(es): 88-7189
Divisions: Spazio Espositivo Essegi
*Showroom(s):* Spazio Espositivo Essegi

**Esselibri+**
Via Russo, 33, 80123 Naples
*Tel:* (081) 5757255 *Fax:* (081) 5757944
*E-mail:* info@simone.it
*Web Site:* www.simone.it
Founded: 1989
Publish academic, technical & professional books.
Subjects: Architecture & Interior Design, Business, Communications, Computer Science, Economics, Government, Political Science, Labor, Industrial Relations, Law, Psychology, Psychiatry, Public Administration, Securities, Technology
ISBN Prefix(es): 88-244

Number of titles published annually: 450 Print
Imprints: Ellissi; Finanze & Lavoro; Nissolino; Sigma; Edizioni Giuridiche Simone; Simone per la Scuola; Sistemi Editorali

**Etas Libri+**
Division of RCS Libri Spa
Via Mecenate, 91, 20138 Milan
*Tel:* (02) 50951 *Fax:* (02) 50952309
*E-mail:* etaslab@rcs.it
*Web Site:* www.etaslab.it
*Key Personnel*
Contact: Lorena Ferrari *E-mail:* lorena.ferrari@rcs.it
Professor: Dr Direttore Divisione
Founded: 1963
Subjects: Business, Economics, Engineering (General), Management, Mathematics
ISBN Prefix(es): 88-453
*Orders to:* RCS Libri Spa *Tel:* (050) 952333 *Fax:* (050 952300

**ETR (Editrice Trasporti su Rotaie)** (Rail Transport Publishing)+
Member of FerPress
Piazza Vittorio Emanuele 42, 25087 Salo (BS)
*Tel:* (03) 6541092 *Fax:* (03) 6541092
*E-mail:* etr@itreni.com
*Web Site:* www.itreni.com
*Key Personnel*
President: Hans Juergen Rosenberger
Founded: 1980
Publish the monthly illustrative magazine *TRENI*.
Subjects: Crafts, Games, Hobbies, Transportation, Travel
ISBN Prefix(es): 88-85068
Number of titles published annually: 2 Print

**EUR**, *imprint of* Edizioni Universitarie Romane

**Eura Press**, *imprint of* Todariana Editrice

**EuroGeoGrafiche Mencattini+**
Via Po, 45, 52100 Arezzo
*Tel:* (0575) 900010 *Fax:* (0575) 911161
*E-mail:* eurogeo@egm.it
*Web Site:* www.egm.it
*Key Personnel*
President: Dr Silvano Mencattini
Vice President: Daniel Mencattini
Founded: 1974
Specialize in tourist guides & cartography.
Membership(s): USPI; AIE; AIPE.
Subjects: Geography, Geology, Travel
ISBN Prefix(es): 88-86263
Imprints: EGGM

**Edizioni Europa**
Via G Martini, 6, 00198 Rome
*Tel:* (06) 8419124
Founded: 1944
Subjects: Art, Economics, Government, Political Science, History, Music, Dance
Subsidiaries: Le Edigioni del Lavors

**Fanucci**
Via delle Fornaci, 66, 00165 Rome
*Tel:* (06) 639366384 *Fax:* (06) 6382998
*E-mail:* info@fanucci.it
*Web Site:* www.fanucci.it
*Key Personnel*
Editor: Sergio Fanucci
Founded: 1972
Subjects: Science Fiction, Fantasy
ISBN Prefix(es): 88-347
Imprints: FE

**Fatatrac+**
Via Ricorboli 28, 50126 Florence
*Tel:* (055) 6810124 *Fax:* (055) 6810260

*E-mail:* info@fatatrac.com
*Web Site:* www.fatatrac.com/
*Key Personnel*
Publisher: Nicoletta Codignola *E-mail:* n.codignola@fatatrac.com
Founded: 1978
Subjects: Animals, Pets, Art, Child Care & Development, Developing Countries, Education, Literature, Literary Criticism, Essays, Photography, Science Fiction, Fantasy
ISBN Prefix(es): 88-85089; 88-86228; 88-8222
Number of titles published annually: 18 Print
Foreign Rep(s): Nicoletta Codignola

**FE**, *imprint of* Fanucci

**Federico Motta Editore SpA+**
Via Branda Castiglioni, 7, 20156 Milan
*Tel:* (02) 300761; (02) 30076231 *Fax:* (02) 38010046; (02) 33403275
*E-mail:* info@mottaeditore.it
*Web Site:* www.mottaeditore.it
*Telex:* 350397 Motta I
*Key Personnel*
Chief Executive Officer & Publisher: Federico Motta
Dir, Financial & Administration: Massimo Fumagalli
Sales, Encyclopaedia Dept: Patrizia Ruffo
Press & Advertising Relations: Natalina Costra
Dir, Sales, Book Dept: Lorena Vazzola
Founded: 1929
Subjects: Architecture & Interior Design, Art, Photography
ISBN Prefix(es): 88-7179

**Feguagiskia' Studios+**
Via Crosa di Vergagni, 3 r, 16124 Genoa
*Tel:* (010) 2757544 *Fax:* (010) 2510838
*Key Personnel*
Publisher: Gualtiero Schiaffino
Founded: 1982
Subjects: Child Care & Development, Literature, Literary Criticism, Essays

**Giangiacomo Feltrinelli SpA**
Via Andegari, 6, 20121 Milan
*Tel:* (02) 725721 *Fax:* (02) 72572500
*Web Site:* www.feltrinelli.it *Cable:* Fedit Milan
Founded: 1954
Subjects: Art, Fiction, History, Philosophy, Poetry, Science (General)
ISBN Prefix(es): 88-07

**Fenice 2000+**
Via della Maggiolina, 24, 20125 Milan
*Tel:* (02) 66984638; (02) 67075155 *Fax:* (02) 67074283
*Key Personnel*
President: Dr Enzo Angelucci
Man Dir: Dr Pierluigi Bozzia
Founded: 1986
Subjects: Aeronautics, Aviation, Animals, Pets, Art, Cookery, Crafts, Games, Hobbies, Gardening, Plants, Photography
ISBN Prefix(es): 88-8017

**Festina Lente Edizioni+**
via della Croce, 11, 50023 Impruneta, Florence
*Tel:* (055) 292612 *Fax:* (055) 292612
*Key Personnel*
Contact: Paolo Gori Savellini; Andrea del Sere
Founded: 1989
Subjects: Architecture & Interior Design, Art, History, Literature, Literary Criticism, Essays, Medicine, Nursing, Dentistry, Psychology, Psychiatry
ISBN Prefix(es): 88-85171

**Fiabesca**, *imprint of* Stampa Alternativa - Nuovi Equilibri

**Finanze & Lavoro**, *imprint of* Esselibri

**Flaccovio Dario+**
Via E Oliveri Mandala 35, 90146 Palermo
*Tel:* (091) 202533 *Fax:* (091) 227702
*E-mail:* press@darioflaccovio.com
*Web Site:* www.darioflaccovio.com
*Key Personnel*
Contact: Marisa Flaccovio
Founded: 1980
ISBN Prefix(es): 88-7758
*Bookshop(s):* Via Ausonia, 70-90144 Palermo

**Flaccovio Editore**
Via Ruggiero Settimo, 37, 90139 Palermo
*Tel:* (091) 589442 *Fax:* (091) 331992
*E-mail:* info@flaccovio.com
*Web Site:* www.flaccovio.com
Founded: 1939
Membership(s): AIE.
Subjects: Archaeology, Architecture & Interior Design, Art, History, Regional Interests, Science (General)
ISBN Prefix(es): 88-7804
*Parent Company:* S F Flaccovio sas
*Bookshop(s):* Libreria SF Flaccovio, Via Ruggiero Settimo, 34, 90139 Palermo

**FMR**, see Franco Maria Ricci Editore (FMR)

**Fogola Editore+**
Piazza Carlo Felice, 19, 10123 Turin
*Tel:* (011) 535897 *Fax:* (011) 530305
*E-mail:* info@fogola.com
*Web Site:* www.fogola.com
Founded: 1965
Subjects: Fiction, History, Literature, Literary Criticism, Essays
ISBN Prefix(es): 88-7406
Total Titles: 115 Print
*Showroom(s):* Paztecipozione al Salone Del Libro Ditorino
*Bookshop(s):* Libreria Dante Alighieri, Piazza Carlo Felice 19, 10123 Turin

**Editoriale Fernando Folini**, *imprint of* Editoriale Fernando Folini

**Editoriale Fernando Folini+**
Il Battaglino, 15052 Casalnoceto, Alessandria
*Tel:* (0131) 807001 *Fax:* (0131) 807001
*E-mail:* edifolini@edifolini.com
*Web Site:* www.edifolini.com
*Key Personnel*
President: Dr Fernando Folini *E-mail:* folinif@edifolini.com
Founded: 1986
Membership(s): Associazione Italiana Editori.
Subjects: Biological Sciences, Cookery, Environmental Studies, Health, Nutrition, Medicine, Nursing, Dentistry, Self-Help
ISBN Prefix(es): 88-7266
Imprints: Editoriale Fernando Folini

**Arnaldo Forni Editore SRL**
Via Gramsci 164, 40010 Sala Bolognese (Bologna)
*Tel:* (051) 6814142; (051) 6814198 *Fax:* (051) 6814672
*E-mail:* info@fornieditore.com
*Web Site:* www.fornieditore.com
*Key Personnel*
Man Dir: Aurelia Forni
Founded: 1973
Subjects: Antiques, Archaeology, Architecture & Interior Design, Art, Astrology, Occult, Astronomy, Biography, Cookery, Drama, Theater, Earth Sciences, Economics, Gardening, Plants, Genealogy, Geography, Geology, History, Language Arts, Linguistics, Law, Literature, Literary Criticism, Essays, Mathematics, Medicine,

Nursing, Dentistry, Music, Dance, Philosophy, Psychology, Psychiatry, Regional Interests, Religion - Catholic, Religion - Other
ISBN Prefix(es): 88-271
Number of titles published annually: 20 Print
Total Titles: 3,200 Print
*Bookshop(s):* Via Galliera 15, 40121 Bologna
*Tel:* (051) 221417 *Fax:* (051) 6814672
*E-mail:* rarebooks@fornieditore.com

**Biblioteca Francescana+**
Piazza S Angelo, 2, 20121 Milan
*Tel:* (02) 29002736 *Fax:* (02) 29002736
*E-mail:* info@bibliotecafrancescana.it
*Web Site:* www.bibliotecafrancescana.it
*Key Personnel*
International Rights: Cabassi Aristide
Founded: 1977
Specialize in Francescanesimo.
Subjects: History, Religion - Catholic, Theology
ISBN Prefix(es): 88-7962
Imprints: EBF
Distributor for Messaggero Distributione (Italy)

**Edizioni Frassinelli SRL+**
Via Durazzo 4, 20134 Milan
*Tel:* (02) 217211 *Fax:* (02) 21721277
*E-mail:* cosmaro@sperling.it
*Web Site:* www.sperling.it
*Key Personnel*
President & Publisher: Valerio Anna Patrizia
Editorial Dir: Carla Tanzi
Marketing Dir: Giuseppe Baroffio
Rights & Permissions: Laura Casonato
Scout: Linda Clark
Contracts: Marica Fioroni
Founded: 1932
Subjects: Art, Biography, Fiction, Nonfiction (General)
ISBN Prefix(es): 88-7684; 88-7824; 88-8274; 88-88320
*Parent Company:* Sperling e Kupfer Editori SpA
*U.S. Office(s):* 225 Lafayette St, Suite 602, New York, NY 10012, United States (Scout Office)

**Fratelli Conte Editori SRL+**
Via Luigi Carluccio 3, 73100 Lecce
*Tel:* (0832) 228827 *Fax:* (0832) 220280
*E-mail:* casaeditrice@conteditore.it
*Web Site:* www.conteditore.it
*Key Personnel*
Man Dir: Ferdinando Conte; Mario Conte
Founded: 1967
Subjects: Fiction

**Frati Editori di Quaracchi**
Via Vecchia per Marino 28-30, 00046 Grottaferrata (Rome)
*Tel:* (06) 94551259 *Fax:* (06) 94551267
*E-mail:* quaracchi@ofm.org
*Web Site:* www.quaracchi.ofm.org
Founded: 1877
Subjects: History, Religion - Other, Theology
ISBN Prefix(es): 88-7013
*Parent Company:* Fondazione Collegio San Bonaventura Grottaferrata

**Edizioni Futuro SRL**
Via Cesiolo, 10, 37126 Verona
*Tel:* (045) 915622 *Fax:* (045) 8300261
*Telex:* 480833
*Key Personnel*
Chief Executive: Vinicio de Lorentiis
Editorial: Francesca Pomini
Sales: Marta de Lorentiis
Rights & Permissions: Elena Zoccatelli
Founded: 1979
Subjects: Art, Biography, Environmental Studies, How-to
ISBN Prefix(es): 88-7650
*Subsidiaries:* Edizioni Vinicio de Lorentiis; Moderna International

**Adriano Gallina Editore sas+**
Salita Tarsia, 143, 80135 Naples
*Tel:* (081) 5496730 *Fax:* (081) 5448747
*Key Personnel*
Man Dir: Rossana Gallina
Editorial: Maria Gallina
Sales: Giuseppe Gallina
Founded: 1968
Subjects: Archaeology, Art, Cookery, Ethnicity, Music, Dance, Poetry, Regional Interests, Travel
ISBN Prefix(es): 88-87350
Imprints: Adriana Gallina Editore; Edizioni del Delfino
Divisions: Edizioni del Delfino

**Galzerano Editore+**
84040 Casalvelino Scalo, Salerno
*Tel:* (0974) 62028 *Fax:* (0974) 62028 *Cable:* GALZERANO CASALVELINO SCALO (SA)
*Key Personnel*
Chief Executive: Giuseppe Galzerano
Founded: 1975
Subjects: Biography, Ethnicity, Fiction, Government, Political Science, History, Poetry
Number of titles published annually: 10 Print

**Gamberetti Editrice SRL+**
Via del Casaletto 186, 00151 Rome
*Tel:* (06) 3728394 *Fax:* (06) 3728394
*E-mail:* gamberetti@gamberetti.it
*Web Site:* www.gamberetti.it
*Key Personnel*
Contact: Stefano Chiarini *E-mail:* schiarin@tiscali.it
Founded: 1992
Specializes in the conflicts of the "New World Order," Middle East, Former Yugoslavia, Ireland, Italy, Latin America, Armenia, Polisario & North-South relationship.
Subjects: Fiction, Literature, Literary Criticism, Essays
ISBN Prefix(es): 88-7990
Total Titles: 32 Print
Distributed by PDE Distribuzione (Firenze)

**Gammalibri-Rock Books**, *imprint of* Kaos Edizioni SRL

**Gangemi Editore spa+**
Piazza S Pantaleo 4, 00186 Rome
*Tel:* (06) 6872774; (06) 68806189 (orders) *Fax:* (06) 68806189
*E-mail:* info@gangemieditore.it
*Web Site:* www.gangemieditore.it
*Key Personnel*
Chief Executive: Giuseppe Gangemi
Marketing Executive Manager: Emilia Gangemi
Publishing Editor Manager: Fabio Gangemi
Founded: 1962
Subjects: Agriculture, Anthropology, Archaeology, Architecture & Interior Design, Art, Disability, Special Needs, History, Literature, Literary Criticism, Essays, Medicine, Nursing, Dentistry, Philosophy, Romance, Social Sciences, Sociology
ISBN Prefix(es): 88-492; 88-7448
Number of titles published annually: 100 Print
Total Titles: 2,500 Print
Distributed by Accorn Aviante; Arobaleno; CDM; Licosa; Messaggerie Libri; Plymbridge
Distributor for Iter Mundi
*Bookshop(s):* Corso Garibaldi, 168, 89100 Reggio Calabria *Tel:* (0965) 894844 *Fax:* (0965) 894845; Via Cavour, 255, 00184 Rome *Tel:* (06) 4821661

**Editrice Garigliano SRL+**
Via Aligerno, 91/93, 03043 Cassino (Frosinone)

*Tel:* (0776) 21869 *Fax:* (0776) 21869 *Cable:* Editrice Garigliano Cassino
*Key Personnel*
Chief Executive: Marisa Canzano; Stefano Vitale
Editorial: Rodolfo Vitale
Sales: Brunella Martucci
Production: Antonio Violo
Publicity: Giovanni Violo
Rights & Permissions: Elena Vettese
Founded: 1968
Subjects: Education, Literature, Literary Criticism, Essays, Philosophy, Psychology, Psychiatry
ISBN Prefix(es): 88-7103
*Bookshop(s):* Libreria Universitaria

**Garolla**
Via Guido d'Arezzo 4, 20145 Milan
*Tel:* (02) 48005574 *Fax:* (02) 48003915
*Key Personnel*
Contact: Federico Garolla
Subjects: Archaeology, Art
ISBN Prefix(es): 88-7682

**Garzanti Libri+**
Via Gasparotto 1, 20124 Milan
*Tel:* (02) 674171 *Fax:* (02) 67417323
*Web Site:* www.garzanti.it
*Telex:* 325218 Gared *Cable:* Garzantieditore
*Key Personnel*
Publisher: Dr Livio Garzanti
Editorial: Dr Giananarea Piccioli
Sales Manager: Francesco Rampini
Rights & Permissions: Marie Louise Zarmanian
Founded: 1861
Subjects: Art, Biography, Fiction, Government, Political Science, History, Literature, Literary Criticism, Essays, Poetry
ISBN Prefix(es): 88-11
*Associate Companies:* A Vallardi, Via Newton, 18A, 20148 Milan
*Bookshop(s):* Libreria Garzanti, Galleria Vittorio Emanuele 66-68, 20121 Milan; Libreria Garzanti, Palazzo Dell' Universita, Pavia; Libreria della Spiga, Via della Spiga 30, 20121 Milan

**Edizioni GB+**
Via Callegari, 33, 35133 Padova
*Tel:* (049) 8647834 *Fax:* (049) 8647834
Founded: 1985
Membership(s): WWF.
Subjects: Alternative, Anthropology, Architecture & Interior Design, Biological Sciences, Environmental Studies, Government, Political Science, Library & Information Sciences, Medicine, Nursing, Dentistry, Philosophy, Physical Sciences, Science (General), Social Sciences, Sociology, Sports, Athletics, Travel
ISBN Prefix(es): 88-86272
Subsidiaries: Edizioni GB - Brasile

**Istituto Geografico de Agostini SpA**
Via Giovanni da Verrazzano 15, 28100 Novara
*Tel:* (0321) 4241 *Fax:* (0321) 471286
*E-mail:* info@deagostini.it
*Web Site:* www.deagostini.it
*Telex:* 200290 Edidea I *Cable:* GEOGRAFICO NOVARA
*Key Personnel*
Contact: Chiara Boroli
Founded: 1901
Subjects: Art, Gardening, Plants, Geography, Geology, History, Literature, Literary Criticism, Essays, Regional Interests, Religion - Other
ISBN Prefix(es): 88-402; 88-415; 88-410; 88-418; 88-406
*Branch Office(s)*
Uffici di Milano, Via Montefeltro 6/A, 20156 Milan *Tel:* (02) 380861 *Fax:* (02) 38086324

**Gereria Cortina Editrice SRL**, see Libreria Cortina Editrice SRL

**Bruno Ghigi Editore+**
Via Pleiadi, 6, 47900 Rimini
*Tel:* (0541) 791727 *Fax:* (0541) 791727
*Key Personnel*
All offices: Bruno Ghigi
Founded: 1955
Subjects: Geography, Geology, History
ISBN Prefix(es): 88-85640

**Ghisetti e Corvi Editori**
Corso Concordia 7, 20129 Milan
*Tel:* (02) 76006232 *Fax:* (02) 76009468
*E-mail:* sedes.spa@gpa.it
*Web Site:* www.ghisetticorvi.it
Founded: 1937
Subjects: Art, Literature, Literary Criticism, Essays, Mathematics, Physics, Science (General)
ISBN Prefix(es): 88-8013

**Giancarlo Politi Editore**
Via Carlo Farini 68, 20159 Milan
*Tel:* (02) 6887341 *Fax:* (02) 66801290
*E-mail:* politi@interbusiness.it
*Web Site:* politi.undo.net
*Key Personnel*
Publisher: Giancarlo Politi
Editor: Helena Kontova
Subjects: Art
ISBN Prefix(es): 88-7816
*U.S. Office(s):* 799 Broadway, Room 226, New York, NY 10003, United States

**G Giappichelli Editore SRL+**
Via Po, 21, 10124 Turin
*Tel:* (011) 8153111 *Fax:* (011) 8125100
*E-mail:* spedizioni@giappichelli.com
*Web Site:* www.giappichelli.it
Founded: 1921
Subjects: Economics, Government, Political Science, Law, Philosophy, Social Sciences, Sociology
ISBN Prefix(es): 88-348
*Bookshop(s):* Libreria Editrice Scientifica di G Giappichelli, Via Vasco 2, 1-10124 Turin

**Giovanni Tranchida Editore**, *imprint of* Giovanni Tranchida Editore

**Edizioni del Girasole srl**
Via P Costa, 10, 48100 Ravenna
*Tel:* (0544) 212830 *Fax:* (0544) 38432
*E-mail:* info@europart.it
*Key Personnel*
President: Lapucci Egle
Publishing Dir: Ivan Simonini
Founded: 1965
Subjects: Archaeology, Art, History, Photography, Poetry, Romance
ISBN Prefix(es): 88-7567

**A Giuffre Editore SpA+**
Via Busto Arsizio, 40, 20151 Milan
*Tel:* (02) 380891 *Fax:* (02) 38009582
*E-mail:* giuffre@giuffre.it
*Web Site:* www.giuffre.it
*Key Personnel*
Man Dir: Giuseppe Giuffre
Chief Editor: Gaetano Giuffre
Founded: 1931
Subjects: Economics, Government, Political Science, History, Law, Social Sciences, Sociology
ISBN Prefix(es): 88-14
*Branch Office(s)*
Via V Colonna 40, I-00193 Rome *Tel:* (06) 659938; (06) 6569792
*Bookshop(s):* Giuffre Libreria, Pza S Stefano, 5, 20122 Milan

**Giunti Gruppo Editoriale** (Giunti Publishing Group)+
Via Bolognese 165, 50139 Florence
*Tel:* (055) 5062376 *Fax:* (055) 5062397
*E-mail:* informazioni@giunti.it
*Web Site:* www.giunti.it
*Telex:* 571438 Giunti *Cable:* MARZOLIB FLORENCE
*Key Personnel*
Dir: Dr Sergio Giunti
Rights & Permissions: Roberto Borrani
Founded: 1840
Group comprises: Giunti Marzocco, ME/DI Sviluppo, OS (Organizzazioni Speciali SRL), Lisciani e Giunti Editori, Edizioni Primavera.
Subjects: Art, Chemistry, Chemical Engineering, Education, Fiction, History, How-to, Language Arts, Linguistics, Literature, Literary Criticism, Essays, Mathematics, Psychology, Psychiatry, Science (General)
ISBN Prefix(es): 88-09
Imprints: Giunti Marzocco
Subsidiaries: Edizioni Primavera; Giunti Industrie Grafiche; Giunti Multimedia; Lisciani & Giunti; ME/DI Sviluppo; OS Org Speciali
*Branch Office(s)*
Ancona
Bari
Cagliari
Catania
Genoa
Lamezia Terme
Milan
Naples
Padua
Palermo
Rome

**Editrice la Giuntina**
Via Ricasoli 26, 50122 Florence
*Tel:* (055) 268684 *Fax:* (055) 219718
*E-mail:* giuntina@fol.it
*Web Site:* www.giuntina.it
*Key Personnel*
Contact: Daniel Vogelmann
Founded: 1980
Specialize in Jewish subjects.
Subjects: Religion - Jewish
ISBN Prefix(es): 88-85943; 88-8057
Total Titles: 240 Print

**Edizioni Giuridico Scientifiche (SRL)+**
Via Donizetti, 37, 20122 Milan
*Tel:* (02) 55192219 *Fax:* (02) 76009444
*Key Personnel*
Editor: Ennio Alessio Mizzau
ISBN Prefix(es): 88-85874

**Gius Laterza e Figli SpA+**
Piazza Umberto I, 54, 70121 Bari
*Tel:* (080) 5281211 *Fax:* (080) 5243461
*E-mail:* laterza@laterza.it
*Web Site:* www.laterza.it
*Telex:* 623168
*Key Personnel*
Man Dir, Rome: Vito Laterza
Editorial Dir, Rome: Alessandro Laterza; Giuseppe Laterza
Production: Claudio Lodoli
Press, Publicity & Advertising (Rome): Karina Laterza
Rights & Permissions: Antonia Sollecito
Sales Dir, Bari: Caterina D'Ambrosio
Founded: 1885
Subjects: Archaeology, Architecture & Interior Design, Art, Biography, Economics, History, Philosophy, Psychology, Psychiatry, Religion - Other, Science (General), Social Sciences, Sociology
ISBN Prefix(es): 88-420

*Bookshop(s):* Libreria Internazionale Laterza, Via Sparano 134, 1-70121 Bari
*Shipping Address:* Via F Zippitelli 3, Zona Industriale, 70123 Bari

**Giuseppe Laterza Editore+**
Via Suppa 16, 70122 Bari
*Tel:* (080) 5237936 *Fax:* (080) 5237360
*Web Site:* www.giuseppelaterza.it
*Key Personnel*
Editor: Giuseppe Laterza
Founded: 1980
Subjects: Computer Science, Electronics, Electrical Engineering, Government, Political Science, Law, Literature, Literary Criticism, Essays, Poetry, Psychology, Psychiatry, Veterinary Science
ISBN Prefix(es): 88-86243; 88-8231
Imprints: Edizioni Fratelli Laterza
Subsidiaries: Laterza Litostampa; Libreria Fratelli Laterza; Cartoleria Fratelli Laterza

**Glossa+**
Piazza Paolovi, 6, 20121 Milan
*Tel:* (02) 877609 *Fax:* (02) 72003162
*E-mail:* informazioni@glossaeditrice.it
*Web Site:* www.glossaeditrice.it
Founded: 1987
Subjects: Theology
ISBN Prefix(es): 88-7105
Number of titles published annually: 12 Print
Total Titles: 165 Print
*Distribution Center:* Dehoniana Libri Spa, Via Scipione dal Ferro 4, Bologna

**GM**, *imprint of* Giorgio Mondadori & Associati

**Gozzini**, see Libreria Gozzini di Pietro e Francesco Chellini (SNC)

**Grafica e Arte srl+**
Via Francesco Coghetti 108, 24128 Bergamo
*Tel:* (035) 255014 *Fax:* (035) 250164
*E-mail:* info@graficaearte.it
*Web Site:* www.graficaearte.it
*Key Personnel*
Man Dir: Emilio Agazzi
Founded: 1975
Subjects: Art, Ethnicity, History, Photography
Number of titles published annually: 10 Print
Total Titles: 250 Print
Distributed by Dehoniana Libri Sp
*Showroom(s):* Via Francesco Coghetti, 90, 24128 Bergamo

**Marchesi Grafiche Editoriali SpA**
Via Bomarzo 32, 00191 Rome
*Tel:* (06) 331359 *Fax:* (06) 3336505
*Web Site:* www.vol.it/marchesi.index.htm
Founded: 1927
Specialize in publishing & printing for other firms.
ISBN Prefix(es): 88-86248

**Grafo**
Via Maiera 27, 25123 Brescia
*Tel:* (030) 393221 *Fax:* (030) 3701411
*Web Site:* www.grafo.it
*Key Personnel*
Chief Executive: Matteo Montagnoli
Sales: Franco Agnelli
Founded: 1973
Subjects: Anthropology, Archaeology, Art, Ethnicity, History, Regional Interests
ISBN Prefix(es): 88-7385

**Libreria Editrice Gregoriana**
Via Roma 82, 35122 Padova
*Tel:* (049) 657493 *Fax:* (049) 659777
*Key Personnel*
Man Dir: Don Giancarlo Minozzi

Contact: Claudio Zanetto
Founded: 1922
Subjects: Philosophy, Psychology, Psychiatry, Religion - Other, Social Sciences, Sociology
ISBN Prefix(es): 88-7706
*Parent Company:* Euganea Editoriale Comunicazion SRL, Via Roma 82, 35122 Padova
*Bookshop(s):* Via Roma 37, Padova; Via Vescovado 33, Padova; Piazza Duomo 5, Padova

**Ernesto Gremese Editore srl+**
Via Virginia Agnelli 88, V Le Dei Colli Portuensi 537, 00151 Rome
*Tel:* (06) 65740507 *Fax:* (06) 65740509
*E-mail:* gremese@gremese.com
*Web Site:* www.gremese.com
*Key Personnel*
Chief Executive: Alberto Gremese
*E-mail:* alberto@gremese.com
Founded: 1954
Subjects: Art, Astrology, Occult, Cookery, Crafts, Games, Hobbies, Drama, Theater, Erotica, Fashion, Fiction, Film, Video, Health, Nutrition, House & Home, How-to, Literature, Literary Criticism, Essays, Music, Dance, Radio, TV, Sports, Athletics, Travel, Wine & Spirits
ISBN Prefix(es): 88-7605; 88-7742; 88-8440
Number of titles published annually: 80 Print
Total Titles: 700 Print
Imprints: L'Airone Editrice
*Bookshop(s):* Libreria Internazionale Ernesto Gremese SNC, Via Cola di Rienzo 136, 00192 Rome *Tel:* (06) 3235367 *Fax:* (06) 3235374 *E-mail:* info@liberia.gremese.it *Web Site:* www.liberiagremese.it

**Gremese International srl+**
Via Virginia Agnelli, 88, 00151 Rome
*Tel:* (06) 65740507 *Fax:* (06) 65740509
*E-mail:* gremese@gremese.com
*Web Site:* www.gremese.com
*Key Personnel*
Chief Executive: Alberto Gremese
Founded: 1991
Subjects: Art, Astrology, Occult, Cookery, Crafts, Games, Hobbies, Film, Video, History, Music, Dance, Nonfiction (General), Photography, Travel
ISBN Prefix(es): 88-7301
*Parent Company:* Ernest Gremese Editore rrl
Subsidiaries: Gremese Editore
*Distribution Center:* National Book Network, 4720 Boston Way, Lanham, MD 20706, United States

**Piero Gribaudi Editore+**
Via C Baroni, 190, 20141 Milan
*Tel:* (02) 89302244 *Fax:* (02) 89302376
*E-mail:* info@gribaudi.it
*Web Site:* www.gribaudi.it
*Key Personnel*
Publisher: Cesare Crespi; Maurizio Sola
Foreign Rights: Sandra Zerilli *E-mail:* szerilli@gribaudi.it
Founded: 1966
Subjects: Behavioral Sciences, Biblical Studies, Biography, Education, Human Relations, Humor, Religion - Catholic, Religion - Jewish, Self-Help, Theology
ISBN Prefix(es): 88-7152
Number of titles published annually: 50 Print
Total Titles: 750 Print
Imprints: PGE

**Gruppo Editoriale Faenza Editrice SpA+**
Via pier de Crescenzi, 44, 48018 Faenza (Ravenna)
*Tel:* (0546) 670411 *Fax:* (0546) 660440
*E-mail:* info@faenza.com
*Web Site:* www.faenza.com
*Key Personnel*
Man Dir: Franco Rossi

Sales: Luisa Teston *E-mail:* lteston@faenza.com
Founded: 1965
Subjects: Architecture & Interior Design, Art, Engineering (General), Medicine, Nursing, Dentistry, Science (General)
ISBN Prefix(es): 88-8138
Number of titles published annually: 98 Print
Imprints: Edizioni CELI

**Gruppo Editoriale Internazionale SRL (GEI)**, see Instituti Editoriali E Poligrafici Internazionali SRL

**Gruppo Editorialeil Saggiatore+**
Via Melzo, 9, 20129 Milan
*Tel:* (02) 202301 *Fax:* (02) 29513061
*Web Site:* www.saggiatore.it
*Key Personnel*
Chief Executive: Vittorio Bo
Editorial, Production, Publicity, Rights & Permissions: Susanna Boschi
Founded: 1976
Subjects: Drama, Theater, History, Philosophy
ISBN Prefix(es): 88-7380

**Ugo Guanda Editore+**
Corso Italia 13, 20122 Milan
*Tel:* (02) 80206322 *Fax:* (02) 72000306
*E-mail:* info@guanda.it
*Web Site:* www.guanda.it
*Telex:* 353273 LONG I
*Key Personnel*
President: Mario Spagnol
Man Dir: Stefano Mauri
Editorial: Luigi Brioschi
Sales: Giuseppe Somenzi
Production: Alfredo Bonfiglio
Publicity: Valentina Fortichiari
Rights & Permissions: Cristina Foschini
Founded: 1932
Subjects: Art, Poetry
ISBN Prefix(es): 88-7746; 88-235; 88-8246
*Parent Company:* Longanesi & C
Subsidiaries: Gdp
*U.S. Office(s):* Nina Collins Association, 584 Broadway, Suite 607, New York, NY 10012, United States
*Warehouse:* Messaggerie Italiane Spa, Magazzino Editoriale, Via Bereguardina, 20080 Casarile (Mi)
*Orders to:* Pro Libro, Strada della Repubblica 56, 43100 Parma

**Edizioni Guerini e Associati SpA+**
Viale Filippetti 28, 20122 Milan
*Tel:* (02) 582980 *Fax:* (02) 58298030
*E-mail:* info@guerini.it
*Web Site:* www.guerini.it
*Key Personnel*
President: Angelo Guerini
Printing Office: Federico Gagliardo *Tel:* (02) 58298017
Foreign Rights Manager: Claudia Premoli *Tel:* (02) 58298016
Founded: 1987
Essays, Books & Reviews.
Subjects: Anthropology, Management, Philosophy, Psychology, Psychiatry, Social Sciences, Sociology, Literary Criticism, Architecture & Gardens, Media Studies & Geopolitics
ISBN Prefix(es): 88-7802; 88-8107 (Guerini scientifica); 88-8335; 88-8195 (contiere italia)
Total Titles: 1,000 Print
*Bookshop(s):* Libreria Guerini, Piazza Soldini 5, 21053 Castellanza *Tel:* (0331) 508918 *Fax:* (0331) 508972 *E-mail:* libreria@liuc.it
*Shipping Address:* Pea Italia, Via Spallanzani 16, 20129 Milan

**Guerra Edizioni GURU srl**
Via A Manna, 25/27, 06132 Perugia
*Tel:* (075) 5289090 *Fax:* (075) 5288244

*E-mail:* geinfo@guerra-edizioni.com
*Web Site:* www.guerra-edizioni.com
*Telex:* Cuper I Rux
*Key Personnel*
Publicity Manager: Chellini Gastone
Founded: 1883
Subjects: Education, Language Arts, Linguistics
ISBN Prefix(es): 88-7715
*Orders to:* RUX edel, Via E Fermi 26, 06100 Perugia *Tel:* (075) 751324

**Guide del Cuore**, *imprint of* Passigli Editori

**Guide del Sole**, *imprint of* Passigli Editori

**GZ**, *imprint of* Casa Musicale G Zanibon SRL

**Herbita Editrice di Leonardo Palermo+**
Via Errante, 44, 90127 Palermo
*Tel:* (091) 6167732 *Fax:* (091) 6167716
*Web Site:* www.herbitaeditrice.it *Cable:*
  HERBITA PALERMO
*Key Personnel*
Chief Executive: Leonardo Palermo
Founded: 1973
Subjects: Archaeology, Art, Computer Science, Economics, Geography, Geology, Government, Political Science, Law, Literature, Literary Criticism, Essays, Mathematics, Philosophy, Religion - Catholic
ISBN Prefix(es): 88-7994

**Herder Editrice e Libreria**
Piazza Montecitorio, 120, 00186 Rome
*Tel:* (06) 679 53 04; (06) 679 46 28 *Fax:* (06) 678 47 51
*E-mail:* distr@herder.it
*Web Site:* www.herder.it
*Key Personnel*
Man Dir: Oriol Schaedel
Founded: 1925
Subjects: Archaeology, Asian Studies, History, Language Arts, Linguistics, Philosophy, Religion - Other, Theology, Classical Philology, Languages & Oriental studies
ISBN Prefix(es): 88-85876
*Associate Companies:* Verlag Herder & Co, Austria (Austria); Verlag Herder GmbH & Co KG, Germany (Germany); Herder und Herder GmbH, Germany (Germany); Verlag A G Ploetz GmbH & Co KG, Germany (Germany); Editorial Herder SA, Spain (Spain); Herder AG, Switzerland (Switzerland)
Distributor for Academia Latinitati Fovendae (Rome); Academy Cardinalis Bessarionis (Rome); Center Studies "Girolamo Baruffaldi" (Hundreds); Center Studies Varroniani (Rieti); Church Abbaziale di Montecassino (Cassino); Department of Linguistica, University (Florence); Editions Universitaires Fribourg (Switzerland) (Italy); European Comunity (Rome); Faculty of Mastery University (Messina); Institute for East "C to Nallino" (Rome); Institute for the Ecclesiastical History Padovana (Padova); Institute of Indologia University (Turin); Instituto Espanol de Historia Eclesiastica (Rome); Institutum Historicum Polonicum (Rome); Italian Institute for the Mean & Far East (IsMEO) (Rome); Italian Institute of Germanic Studies (Rome); OECD, Paris (Rome); Properziana Academy of the Subasio (Assisi); Sargon Publishing limited liability company (Padova); University Institute Orients Them (Naples); University of the Studies of Rome "the Wisdom"; World Bank (Rome)

**Hermes Edizioni SRL+**
Subsidiary of Edizioni Mediterranee SRL
Via Flaminia 109, 00196 Rome
*Tel:* (06) 3235433 *Fax:* (06) 3236277

*E-mail:* info@ediz-mediterranee.com
*Web Site:* www.ediz-mediterranee.com
*Key Personnel*
General Manager: Giovanni Canonico
Editorial: Paola Maria Canonico
Sales: Maria Satulli
Rights & Permissions: Canonico Assia
Contact: Eleasa Canonico
Founded: 1979
Subjects: Anthropology, Health, Nutrition, How-to, Medicine, Nursing, Dentistry, Parapsychology, Psychology, Psychiatry, Religion - Buddhist, Religion - Hindu, Religion - Other, Sports, Athletics
ISBN Prefix(es): 88-7938
Total Titles: 300 Print

**Institutum Historicum Societatis Iesu** (Jesuit Historical Institute)
Via dei Penitenzieri, 20, 00193 Rome
*Tel:* (06) 689 77673 *Fax:* (06) 686 1342; (06) 689 77663
*E-mail:* ihsiroma@tin.it
*Web Site:* space.tin.it/scuola/mmorales/ihsi.html
*Key Personnel*
Dir: Rev Martin M Morales
Editor: Rev Thomas M McCoog
Founded: 1932
Subjects: History
Total Titles: 50 Print

**Hopeful Monster Editore**
Via Santa Chiara, 30, 10122 Turin
*Tel:* (011) 4367197; (011) 4358519 *Fax:* (011) 4369025
*E-mail:* info@hopefulmonster.net
*Web Site:* www.hopefulmonster.net
*Key Personnel*
Publisher: Beatrice Merz *E-mail:* beatricemerz@hopefulmonster.net
Founded: 1986
Specialize in art books & catalogues concerning contemporary art.
Subjects: Art, History, Philosophy, Photography, Science (General), Travel
ISBN Prefix(es): 88-7757
Number of titles published annually: 15 Print
Distributed by Albolibro (Italy); Angelo Vecchi & C (Italy); Art Books International (UK & Eire); Campania Libri; Centro Di (Europe, Giappone & USA); Centro Distribuzione Editoriale (CDE) (Italy); Distribook (Italy); Distributed Art Publishers (DAP) (USA, Canada, South America & Asia); Erre Libri (Italy); Italia Libri SRL (Italy); Joker Art Diffusion (France & Belgium); L'Aquilone (Italy); Licosa (Europe (except UK, Eire)); Serena Libri (Italy)

**Hora+**
Milano 2, Res Tre Fili, 421, 20090 Segrate Milan
*Tel:* (02) 26412203 *Fax:* (02) 26412203
*Web Site:* www.hora.it
*Key Personnel*
President: Giuseppe Brusa
Founded: 1989
Subjects: English as a Second Language
ISBN Prefix(es): 88-85144

**Ibis+**
Via Crispi 8, 22100 Como
*Tel:* (031) 3371367; (031) 306836 *Fax:* (031) 306829
*E-mail:* info@ibisedizioni.it
*Web Site:* www.ibisedizioni.it
*Key Personnel*
President: Giulio Veronesi
Editorial Dir: Paolo M Veronesi
Founded: 1989
Subjects: Anthropology, Biological Sciences, Fiction, History, Literature, Literary Criticism, Essays, Philosophy, Social Sciences, Sociology, Travel

ISBN Prefix(es): 88-7164
Number of titles published annually: 15 Print
Total Titles: 130 Print

**Idea Books+**
Via Regia, 53, 55049 Viareggio LU
*Tel:* (0584) 425410 *Fax:* (178) 609 8685
*E-mail:* info@ideabooks.com
*Web Site:* www.ideabooks.com *Cable:* (178) 609 8685
*Key Personnel*
Dir: Filippo Passigli
Founded: 1979
Subjects: Architecture & Interior Design, Art, Fashion, Photography
ISBN Prefix(es): 88-7017; 88-88033
Number of titles published annually: 8 Print

**Casa Editrice Libraria Idelson di G Gnocchi+**
Via Michele Pietravalle, 85, 80131 Naples
*Tel:* (081) 5453443 *Fax:* (081) 5464991
*E-mail:* info@idelson-gnocchi.com
*Web Site:* www.idelson-gnocchi.com *Cable:*
  IDELSON NAPLES
*Key Personnel*
Chief Executive: Guido Gnocchi
Founded: 1908
Subjects: Biological Sciences, Medicine, Nursing, Dentistry
ISBN Prefix(es): 88-7069

**Idelson-Gnocchi Edizioni Scientifiche**
Via Michele Pietravalle, 85, 80131 Naples
*Tel:* (081) 5453443 *Fax:* (081) 5464991
*E-mail:* ordini@idelson-gnocchi.com
*Web Site:* www.idelson-gnocchi.com
*Key Personnel*
Contact: Guido Gnocchi
Founded: 1993
Subjects: Medicine, Nursing, Dentistry
ISBN Prefix(es): 88-7947
*U.S. Office(s):* Idelson Gnocchi Scientific Publications, 12255 NW Highway 225A, Reddick, FL 32686, United States *Tel:* 352-591-1136 *Fax:* 352-591-1189

**Istituto Idrografico della Marina**
Passo dell'Osservatorio 4, 16134 Genoa
*Tel:* (010) 24431 *Fax:* (010) 261400
*E-mail:* iim.sre@marina.difesa.it
*Web Site:* www.marina.difesa.it
*Telex:* 270435; 275521 Maridr I *Cable:*
  MARIDROGRAFICO
*Key Personnel*
Dir: Corrado Fiori
Vice Dir: Giuseppe Borsa
Production: Antonio Sfregola
Public Relations: Antonio Cairo
Map Division: Raffaele Gargiulo
Founded: 1872
Subjects: Maritime

**IHT Gruppo Editoriale SRL**
Via Monte Napoleone 9, 20121 Milan
*Tel:* (02) 794181 *Fax:* (02) 784021
*E-mail:* info@iht.it
*Web Site:* www.iht.it
*Key Personnel*
Founder, President & Publisher: Lisa Massimiliano
Founded: 1985
Subjects: Art, Film, Video, Microcomputers, Military Science, Science (General), Technology
ISBN Prefix(es): 88-7803
Imprints: IHT Video
Distributed by Messaggerie Periodic
*Orders to:* IHT Publishing Group, Via Monte Napoleone 9, 20121 Milan

**IHT Video**, *imprint of* IHT Gruppo Editoriale SRL

**Ila - Palma, Tea Nova+**
Via Puglisi 63, 90143 Palermo
*Tel:* (091) 6124415 *Fax:* (091) 6259260
*Key Personnel*
Editor: Rean Mazzone
Founded: 1960
Subjects: Archaeology, Art, Economics, History, Literature, Literary Criticism, Essays, Management, Philosophy
ISBN Prefix(es): 88-7704
Subsidiaries: Nef; Tea; Tea Nova
*Orders to:* Via Benedetto Castiglia 6, 90141 Palermo

**In Dialogo+**
Via S Antonio 5, 20122 Milan
*Tel:* (02) 58391342 *Fax:* (02) 58391345
*E-mail:* indial@tin.it
Founded: 1980
Subjects: Biblical Studies, Child Care & Development, Communications, Education, Government, Political Science, Human Relations, Religion - Catholic, Theology
ISBN Prefix(es): 88-8123; 88-85985
*Shipping Address:* Via Andolfato 3, 20126 Milan
*Warehouse:* Via Andolfato 3, 20126 Milan
*Orders to:* Dehoniana Libri SRL

**Iniziative Culturali SRL**, see Servitium

**Editrice Innocenti SNC+**
Via Zara 40, 38100 Trento
*Tel:* (0461) 236521 *Fax:* (0461) 230115
*Cable:* EDITRICE INNOCENTI TRENTO
*Key Personnel*
Chief Executive: Luciano Innocenti
Publicity: Silvia Nones
Founded: 1972
Subjects: Language Arts, Linguistics
*Associate Companies:* Casa Editrice Bulgarini, Via Petrolin, 8-50137 Florence; Casa Editrice Principato, Via Fauche, Milan

**Instituti Editoriali E Poligrafici Internazionali SRL+**
Via Giosue Carducci, 60, 56010 Ghezzano (Pisa)
*Tel:* (050) 878066 *Fax:* (050) 878732
*E-mail:* iepi@iepi.it
*Web Site:* www.iepi.it
*Key Personnel*
Man Dir: Lucia Carmignani
Founded: 1995
Specialize in philosophy, archaeology, history, sociology, anthropology & Italian.
Subjects: Anthropology, Archaeology, History, Language Arts, Linguistics, Philosophy, Social Sciences, Sociology, Transportation
ISBN Prefix(es): 88-8147
*Shipping Address:* The Courier srl, viel A DeBasis 25, 50165 Florence *Tel:* (055) 300443 *Fax:* (055) 300036
*Warehouse:* The Courier srl, viel A DeBasis 25, 50165 Florence *Tel:* (055) 300443 *Fax:* (055) 300036
*Orders to:* The Courier srl, Viel A DeBasis 25, 50165 Florence *Tel:* (055) 300443 *Fax:* (055) 300036

**International Ediemme**
Via Innocenzo XI, 41, 00165 Rome
*Tel:* (06) 39378788 *Fax:* (06) 6380839
*E-mail:* iscd@colosseum.it
*Key Personnel*
Editor-in-Chief: Pierfrancesco Morganti
ISBN Prefix(es): 88-7821

**International Federation of Beekeepers' Associations**, see Apimondia

**International University Press Srl+**
Via Monte della Gioie 22, 00199 Rome

*Tel:* (06) 8380067 *Fax:* (06) 8380064
*Key Personnel*
President: Felice Alivernini
Founded: 1987
Membership(s): USPI.
Subjects: Medicine, Nursing, Dentistry
ISBN Prefix(es): 88-85314
*U.S. Office(s):* Little, Brown & Company, 24 Beacon St, Boston, MA 02108, United States

**Edizioni Internazionali di Letteratura e Scienze+**
Via Casal Selce, 264, 00166 Rome
*Tel:* (06) 61905463 *Fax:* (06) 61905463
Founded: 1972
Also specialize in historical experimentation of dynamic physiology comparison.
Subjects: History, Language Arts, Linguistics, Literature, Literary Criticism, Essays, Romance, Science Fiction, Fantasy, Social Sciences, Sociology
ISBN Prefix(es): 88-7130

**Iperborea**
Via Palestro 22, 20121 Milan
*Tel:* (02) 781458 *Fax:* (02) 798919
*E-mail:* iperborea@iol.it
*Key Personnel*
President & Editorial Dir: Emilia Lodigiani
Founded: 1987
Subjects: Literature, Literary Criticism, Essays
ISBN Prefix(es): 88-7091

**ISAL (Istituto Storia dell'Arte Lombarda)**
Via Garibaldi, 20, 20031 Milan
*Tel:* (03) 62528118 *Fax:* (03) 62659417
*E-mail:* isalbibl@tin.it
*Key Personnel*
Editor: Maria Luisa Gatti Perer
Founded: 1955
Subjects: Archaeology, Art
ISBN Prefix(es): 88-85153

**ISMEO**, see Istituto Italiano Per Il Medio Ed Estremo Oriente (ISMEO)

**Isper SRL+**
Corso Dante 122, 10126 Turin
*Tel:* (011) 66 47 803 *Fax:* (011) 66 70 829
*E-mail:* isper@isper.org
*Web Site:* www.isper.org
*Key Personnel*
Chief Executive: Dr Carlo Actis Grosso
Contact: Paola Riccardi
Founded: 1965
Subjects: Business, Management
*Branch Office(s)*
Via Lambro 4, 20129 Milan
Via N Porpora 12, 00198 Rome
Corso del Popolo 46, 30172 Venice
*Book Club(s):* Isper Club

**Ist Patristico Augustinianum**
Via Paolo VI 25, 00193 Rome
*Tel:* (06) 680 069 *Fax:* (06) 680 06 298
*E-mail:* segr_ipa@aug.org
*Key Personnel*
President: Angelo Di Berardino
Founded: 1969
Subjects: Antiques, Literature, Literary Criticism, Essays, Religion - Catholic
ISBN Prefix(es): 88-7961
Imprints: SEA

**Istituto della Enciclopedia Italiana+**
Piazza Paganica, 4, 00186 Rome
*Tel:* (06) 68981 *Fax:* (06) 68982294
*E-mail:* dir.edit@treccani.it
*Web Site:* www.treccani.it *Cable:* ENCICLOPEDIA

*Key Personnel*
Dir: Francesco Schino
Editorial Dir: Bray Massimo
Founded: 1925
Subjects: Art
ISBN Prefix(es): 88-12

**Istituto Storia dell'Arte Lombarda**, see ISAL (Istituto Storia dell'Arte Lombarda)

**Itaca+**
Piazza De Angeli, 1, 20146 Milan
*Tel:* (02) 48009484 *Fax:* (02) 48009493
*E-mail:* info@editoriale-itaca.it
*Web Site:* www.editoriale-itaca.it
*Key Personnel*
Communications: Barbara Crepaldi
Administrator: Girolamo Frisina
Founded: 1985
Specialize in total quality management.
Subjects: Business, Communications, Management, Marketing
ISBN Prefix(es): 88-7206

**Edizioni Italiane**, *imprint of* Todariana Editrice

**Istituto Italiano Edizioni Atlas+**
Via Crescenzi 88, 24123 Bergamo
*Tel:* (035) 249711 *Fax:* (035) 216047
*E-mail:* edizioniatlas@edatlas.it
*Web Site:* www.edatlas.it
*Key Personnel*
Contact: Dr Marco Carreri
ISBN Prefix(es): 88-268

**Istituto Italiano Per Il Medio Ed Estremo Oriente (ISMEO)**
Via Merulana 248, 00185 Rome
*Tel:* (06) 732741; (06) 732742; (06) 732743
*E-mail:* iias@let.leidenuniv.nl
*Web Site:* www.iias.nl
*Telex:* 624163
Founded: 1933

**Editoriale Jaca Book SpA+**
Via Gioberti, 7, 20123 Milan
*Tel:* (02) 48561520-29 *Fax:* (02) 48193361
*E-mail:* jacabook@jacabook.it
*Web Site:* www.jacabook.it
*Key Personnel*
President & Publisher: Sante Bagnoli
Editorial Dir: Maretta Campi
Administrative Dir: Guido Orsi *E-mail:* admin@jacabook.it
Academic Dep: Massimo Guidetti
Co-editions: Silvia Vassena *E-mail:* coeditions@jacabook.it
Rights: Ida Bonali *E-mail:* produzione@jacabook.it
Founded: 1978
Subjects: Anthropology, Archaeology, Architecture & Interior Design, Art, Asian Studies, Earth Sciences, Economics, Fiction, Geography, Geology, Government, Political Science, History, Human Relations, Literature, Literary Criticism, Essays, Music, Dance, Native American Studies, Natural History, Nonfiction (General), Philosophy, Photography, Physics, Poetry, Religion - Catholic, Religion - Other, Science (General), Social Sciences, Sociology, Theology
ISBN Prefix(es): 88-16
Total Titles: 130 Print
Subsidiaries: Jaca/Edizioni Universitarie

**Gruppo Editoriale Jackson SpA**
Via XXV Aprile, 39, 20091 Bresso (Milan)
*Tel:* (02) 665261 *Fax:* (02) 66526222
*E-mail:* ordini@futura-ge.it
*Telex:* 316213
*Key Personnel*
Man Dir, President: Paolo Reina

Marketing Manager: Filippo Canavese
Dir, Periodicals: Pierantonio Palerma
Dir, Book Shops: Roberto Pancaldi
Administrative Dir: Luigi Gadola
Dir, Production & Aquisitions: Luigi Beccaria
International: Stefania Scroglieri
Founded: 1975
ISBN Prefix(es): 88-7056; 88-256
Subsidiaries: Jackson Hispania SA; GEJ Publishing Group Inc
*Warehouse:* Piazza Amendola 45, Paderno Dugnano, Milan

**Jandi-Sapi Editori**
Via Crescenzio 62, 00193 Rome
*Tel:* (06) 68805515; (06) 6876054 *Fax:* (06) 68218203
*E-mail:* info@jandisapi.com
*Web Site:* www.jandisapi.com
Founded: 1941
Subjects: Art, Law
ISBN Prefix(es): 88-7142
Imprints: JSE
Divisions: Archivi Arte Antica

**Editrice Janus SpA+**
Via dei Capodiferro 12, 24121 Bergamo
*Tel:* (035) 24 71 80 *Fax:* (035) 24 70 92
*Key Personnel*
Sales, Production: Marcello Riva
Founded: 1956
Subjects: Literature, Literary Criticism, Essays

**L Japadre Editore+**
Corso Federico 11, 49, 67100 l'Aquila
*Tel:* (0862) 26025 *Fax:* (0862) 25587
*Key Personnel*
Man Dir: Leandro Ugo Japadre
Founded: 1966
Subjects: Art, Economics, Ethnicity, Fiction, History, Language Arts, Linguistics, Literature, Literary Criticism, Essays, Philosophy, Poetry, Psychology, Psychiatry, Religion - Other, Science (General), Social Sciences, Sociology, Technology
ISBN Prefix(es): 88-7006
*Branch Office(s)*
Via G Boni 20, 00162 Rome *Tel:* (06) 44291182
Distributor for DASP (Deputazione Abruzzese Di Storia Patria)
*Warehouse:* Contrada Cappelli
Pal Prosperini

**Jazz People**, *imprint of* Stampa Alternativa - Nuovi Equilibri

**Jouvence+**
Via Monte Zebio 24, 00195 Rome
*Tel:* (06) 3211500 *Fax:* (06) 3202897
*E-mail:* jouvence@flashnet.it
*Web Site:* www.jouvence-ed.com
*Key Personnel*
Editorial Dir: Alessandro Gallo
Administrator: Claudia Pozzessere
Founded: 1979
Subjects: Archaeology, Asian Studies, History, Literature, Literary Criticism, Essays, Philosophy, Religion - Islamic
ISBN Prefix(es): 88-7801
*Warehouse:* Via Cassia, 1081-00189 Rome

**Casa Editrice Dott Eugenio Jovene SpA**
Via Mezzocannone, 109, 80134 Naples
*Tel:* (081) 5521019; (081) 5521274; (081) 5523471 *Fax:* (081) 5520687
*E-mail:* info@jovene.it
*Web Site:* www.jovene.it *Cable:* JOVENE
*Key Personnel*
Man Dir: Dr Alessandro Rossi
Founded: 1854

Subjects: Economics, Law
ISBN Prefix(es): 88-243

**JSE**, *imprint of* Jandi-Sapi Editori

**Kaos Edizioni SRL+**
Via Catone, 3, 20158 Milan
*Tel:* (02) 39310296 *Fax:* (02) 39325749
*E-mail:* kaosedizioni@kaosedizioni.com
*Web Site:* www.kaosedizioni.com
*Key Personnel*
Man Dir: Lorenzo Ruggiero
Founded: 1985
Subjects: Biography, Drama, Theater, Film, Video, Government, Political Science, History, Music, Dance, Nonfiction (General), Social Sciences, Sociology
ISBN Prefix(es): 88-7953
Imprints: Edizioni Blues Brothers; Gammalibri-Rock Books

**Kompass Fleischmann**
Localita Ghiaie 166/d, 38014 Gardolo (Trento)
*Tel:* (0461) 961240 *Fax:* (0461) 961203
*Key Personnel*
Dir: Mario Cont
Administrator: Dr Petra Fleischmann
Founded: 1973
Subjects: Animals, Pets, Geography, Geology, Natural History, Travel
ISBN Prefix(es): 88-431

**L'Airone Editrice**, *imprint of* Ernesto Gremese Editore srl

**Edizioni L' Eta dell'Acquario**, *imprint of* Edizioni Lindau

**LAC - Litografia Artistica Cartografica Srl**
Via del Romito 11/13 R, 50134 Florence
*Tel:* (055) 483 557 *Fax:* (055) 483 690
*E-mail:* info@lac-cartografia.it
*Web Site:* www.lac-cartografia.it
*Key Personnel*
President: Maria G Garbarino
Contact: Mrs Cinzia Cassai
Founded: 1949
Subjects: Geography, Geology, Travel
ISBN Prefix(es): 88-7914

**Lalli Editore SRL+**
Via Fiume, 60, 53036 Poggibonsi (Siena)
*Tel:* (0577) 933305 *Fax:* (0577) 983308
*E-mail:* lalli@lallieditore.it
*Web Site:* www.lallieditore.it *Cable:* LALLIEDIT POGGIBONSI
*Key Personnel*
Chief Executive: Antonio Lalli
Editorial: Fioranna Casamenti
Founded: 1966
Subjects: Art, Biography, Drama, Theater, Education, Ethnicity, Fiction, Film, Video, Government, Political Science, Humor, Philosophy, Poetry, Regional Interests, Religion - Other, Science (General), Social Sciences, Sociology
*Warehouse:* Via Modena 12, 53036 Poggibonsi SI

**Lanfranchi**
Via Madonnina 10, 20121 Milan
*Tel:* (02) 86465210 *Fax:* (02) 8056083
*E-mail:* info@lanfranchieditore.com
*Web Site:* www.lanfranchieditore.com
ISBN Prefix(es): 88-363

**Lang Edizioni™**, *imprint of* Paravia Bruno Mondadori Editori

**Laruffa Editore SRL+**
Via dei Tre Mulini, 14, 89124 Reggio, Calabria

*Tel:* (0965) 814948 *Fax:* (0965) 814954
*E-mail:* laruffa@laruffaeditore.com
*Web Site:* www.laruffaeditore.com
Founded: 1980
Subjects: Agriculture, Archaeology, Architecture & Interior Design, Education, History, Religion - Catholic, Social Sciences, Sociology, Travel
ISBN Prefix(es): 88-7221

**Editrice LAS+**
Piazza dell'Ateneo Salesiano 1, 00139 Rome
*Tel:* (06) 87290626
*E-mail:* las@ups.urbe.it
*Web Site:* www.las.ups.urbe.it
Founded: 1974
Subjects: Biblical Studies, Education, Philosophy, Psychology, Psychiatry, Religion - Catholic, Social Sciences, Sociology, Theology
ISBN Prefix(es): 88-213
Number of titles published annually: 20 Print
Total Titles: 300 Print; 2 CD-ROM

**Edizioni Fratelli Laterza**, *imprint of* Giuseppe Laterza Editore

**Edizioni Lavoro SRL+**
Via Lancisi 25, 00161 Rome
*Tel:* (06) 44251174 *Fax:* (06) 44251177
*E-mail:* info@edizionilavoro.it
*Web Site:* www.edizionilavoro.it
*Key Personnel*
President: Peter Gelardi
Editorial: Alessandra Belardelli
Founded: 1982
Subjects: Economics, Government, Political Science, History, Labor, Industrial Relations, Philosophy, Religion - Islamic, Romance, Social Sciences, Sociology
ISBN Prefix(es): 88-7910; 88-7313
Number of titles published annually: 40 Print
Imprints: EL
Foreign Rights: Eulama Literary Agency (Worldwide)

**Il Lavoro Editoriale+**
Division of Progetti Editoriale SRL
Via de Bosis 8, 60100 Ancona
Mailing Address: CP 297, 60100 Ancona
*Tel:* (071) 2072210 *Fax:* (071) 2083058
*E-mail:* ilepro@tin.it
*Web Site:* www.illavoroeditoriale.com
*Key Personnel*
Editorial Board Chief: Giorgio Mangani
Founded: 1980
Subjects: Art, History, Human Relations, Literature, Literary Criticism, Essays, Marche Region, Italy
ISBN Prefix(es): 88-7663
Number of titles published annually: 15 Print

**LED - Edizioni Universitarie di Lettere Economia Diritto** (LED - University Press)+
Via Cervignano 4, 20137 Milan
*Tel:* (02) 59902055 *Fax:* (02) 55193636
*E-mail:* led@lededizioni.it
*Web Site:* www.lededizioni.it
*Key Personnel*
Man Dir: Maria Grazia Gelo
International Rights: Valeria Passerini
Founded: 1991
Subjects: Economics, History, Law, Literature, Literary Criticism, Essays, Philosophy, Psychology, Psychiatry, Social Sciences, Sociology
ISBN Prefix(es): 88-7916
Number of titles published annually: 20 Print; 7 Online; 4 E-Book
Total Titles: 240 Print; 16 Online; 9 E-Book

**L'Editrice Scientifica**, see Nagard

**LEF**, *imprint of* Libreria Editrice Fiorentina

**LER**, see Libreria Editrice Rogate (LER)

**L'eta D'oro Dell Illustrazione**, *imprint of* Stampa Alternativa - Nuovi Equilibri

**Casa Editrice Le Lettere SRL**
Costa S Giorgio 28, 50125 Florence
*Tel:* (055) 2342710; (055) 2476319 *Fax:* (055) 2346010
*E-mail:* staff@lelettere.it
*Web Site:* www.lelettere.it
*Key Personnel*
Chief Executive: Dr Giovanni Gentile
Publishing Dir: Nicoletta Pescarolo
Sales, Administration: Carlo De Simone
Founded: 1956
Subjects: History, Language Arts, Linguistics, Literature, Literary Criticism, Essays, Philosophy
ISBN Prefix(es): 88-7166
*Associate Companies:* Progedi Srl, Viale Gramsci, 18, 50132 Florence
*Shipping Address:* Licosa Spa, Via Duca Di Calabria 1/1, 50125 Florence
*Warehouse:* Via Francesco Gioli 5-11, 50018 Scandicci

**Levante Editori+**
Via Napoli 35, 70123 Bari
*Tel:* (080) 5213778 *Fax:* (080) 5213778
*E-mail:* levanted@tin.it
*Web Site:* www.levantebari.com
*Key Personnel*
Contact: Sara Cavalli
Founded: 1967
Subjects: Criminology, Drama, Theater, Mysteries, Philosophy, Psychology, Psychiatry, Travel
ISBN Prefix(es): 88-7949
Number of titles published annually: 20 Print

**Levrotto e Bella Libreria Editrice Universitaria SAS+**
Corso Vittorio Emanuele 26f, 10123 Turin
*Tel:* (011) 8121205 *Fax:* (011) 8124025
*E-mail:* levrotto@ipsnet.it
*Key Personnel*
Sales: Carmela Bueti; Giampiero Garnero
Founded: 1942
Also book packager.
Subjects: Science (General), Technology
ISBN Prefix(es): 88-8218
*Bookshop(s):* Libreria del Politecnico, Corso Einaudi 57, 10129 Turin

**Libreria Editrice Fiorentina+**
Via Giambologna, 5, 50132 Florence
*Tel:* (055) 579921 *Fax:* (055) 579921
*Key Personnel*
Editorial: Vittorio Zani
Founded: 1902
Subjects: Education, Regional Interests, Religion - Other, Social Sciences, Sociology
Imprints: LEF

**Librex**
Via Bellezza 15, 20136 Milan
*Tel:* (02) 58302006
*Telex:* 320208 *Cable:* Librex Milan
*Key Personnel*
General Manager: Antonio Mancia
Export: M Luisa Franceschini
Production: Luciano Baroni
Founded: 1966

**Liguori Editore SRL+**
Via Posillipo 394, 80123 Naples
*Tel:* (081) 7206111; (081) 7206202 (orders) *Fax:* (081) 7206244
*E-mail:* liguori@liguori.it
*Web Site:* www.liguori.it *Cable:* LIGUORI NAPOLI

*Key Personnel*
Man Dir, Editorial, Rights & Permissions: Guido Liguori
Sales: Franco Liguori
Publicity: Maria Liguori
Founded: 1949
Subjects: Anthropology, Economics, History, Language Arts, Linguistics, Law, Literature, Literary Criticism, Essays, Mathematics, Medicine, Nursing, Dentistry, Philosophy, Science (General), Social Sciences, Sociology, Theology
ISBN Prefix(es): 88-207
Number of titles published annually: 150 Print; 3 E-Book
Total Titles: 3,500 Print; 10 CD-ROM
*Bookshop(s):* Librerie Commissionarie Liguori SRL, Via Mezzocannone 21-23, 80134 Naples *Tel:* (081) 5527702; Via Cinthia 36/B, 80126 Naples *Tel:* (081) 7675228
*Warehouse:* Via Ciccarelli 16G, 80167 Naples

**Editrice Liguria SNC di Norberto Sabatelli & C**
Via De Mari 4r, 17100 Savona
*Tel:* (019) 829917 *Fax:* (019) 8387798
*Key Personnel*
Chief Executive: Norberto Sabatelli
Founded: 1934
Subjects: Art, Drama, Theater, Fiction, History, Literature, Literary Criticism, Essays, Poetry, Technology, Travel
ISBN Prefix(es): 88-8055
Imprints: EL

**LIM**, *imprint of* LIM Editrice SRL

**LIM Editrice SRL+**
Via di Arsina 296f, 55100 Lucca
Mailing Address: PO Box 198, 55100 Lucca
*Tel:* (0583) 394464 *Fax:* (0583) 394469
*E-mail:* lim@lim.it
*Web Site:* www.lim.it
*Key Personnel*
Contact: Paola Borriero *E-mail:* p.borriero@lim.it
Founded: 1988
Membership(s): AIE.
Subjects: Music, Dance
ISBN Prefix(es): 88-7096
*Associate Companies:* Akademos, LIM Antiquaria, Una Cosa Rara
Imprints: LIM
Distributor for Adeva; Alamire; Broude Brothers; Garland; Fondazione Locatelli; Pendragon Press; Fondazione Rossini
*Orders to:* PO Box 198, 55100 Lucca

**L'immaginazion**, *imprint of* Piero Manni srl

**Lindau**, *imprint of* Lindau

**Lindau+**
Via Galliari, 15b, 10125 Turin
*Tel:* (011) 6693910; (011) 6693924 *Fax:* (011) 6693929
*E-mail:* info@lindau.it
*Web Site:* www.lindau.it
*Key Personnel*
Executive & Editorial Dir: Ezio Quarantelli *E-mail:* quarantelli@lindau.it
Founded: 1989
Subjects: Fiction, Film, Video
ISBN Prefix(es): 88-7180
Number of titles published annually: 80 Print
Total Titles: 450 Print
Imprints: Lindau; Edizioni L'Eta Dell'Acqua Rio

**Edizioni Lindau+**
Via Galliari, 15b, 10125 Turin
*Tel:* (011) 6693910; (011) 6693924 *Fax:* (011) 6693929
*E-mail:* lindau@lindau.it

*Web Site:* www.lindau.it
*Key Personnel*
Dir: Ezio Quarantelli
Founded: 1971
Membership(s): New York Academy of Science.
Subjects: Nonfiction (General), Parapsychology, Religion - Other
ISBN Prefix(es): 88-7136
Imprints: Edizioni L' Eta dell'Acquario
*Showroom(s):* c/o Lingotto, Salone del Libro Di Torino, Turin

**Linea d'Ombra Libri** (Linea D'Ombra Books)
Via della Madonna, 9, 31015 Conegliano (TV)
*Tel:* (0438) 412647 *Fax:* (0438) 412690
*E-mail:* info@lineadombra.it
*Web Site:* www.lineadombra.it
Founded: 1996
Publisher of art books & exhibition catalogues.
Subjects: Art, Photography, Poetry
ISBN Prefix(es): 88-09
Number of titles published annually: 20 Print
*Parent Company:* Linea D'Ombra

**Linea Verde**, *imprint of* Le Stelle Scuola

**Lisciani e Giunti Editori**, see Giunti Gruppo Editoriale

**Litografia Artistica Cartografia Srl - LAC**, see LAC - Litografia Artistica Cartografica Srl

**Vincenzo Lo Faro Editore**
Via S Giovanni Laterano 276, 00184 Rome
*Tel:* (06) 70451187 *Fax:* (06) 70451641
*Key Personnel*
Chief Executive: Vincenzo Lo Faro
Editorial: Letizia Carile
Founded: 1967
Subjects: Art, Drama, Theater, Education, Environmental Studies, Fiction, Law, Medicine, Nursing, Dentistry, Philosophy, Poetry, Religion - Other, Social Sciences, Sociology
ISBN Prefix(es): 88-87428

**Editrice la Locusta**
Via del Castello 20, 36100 Vicenza
*Tel:* (0444) 324051
*E-mail:* la_locusta@yahoo.com
*Web Site:* space.tin.it/io/pibeltra/lalocust.htm
*Key Personnel*
Chief Executive & Publishing Dir: Rienzo Colla
Founded: 1954
Subjects: History, Literature, Literary Criticism, Essays, Poetry

**Loescher Editore SRL+**
Via Vittorio Amedeo II 18, 10121 Turin
*Tel:* (011) 5654111 *Fax:* (011) 56 25822
*E-mail:* mail@loescher.it
*Web Site:* www.loescher.it
*Key Personnel*
President: Lorenzo Enriques
Vice President: Federico Enriques
Dir General: Riccardo Botrini
Editorial Head: Aron Buttarelli
Commerical Dir: Giorgio Sacco
Founded: 1867
Subjects: Chemistry, Chemical Engineering, English as a Second Language, Geography, Geology, History, Language Arts, Linguistics, Literature, Literary Criticism, Essays, Philosophy
ISBN Prefix(es): 88-201; 88-7608; 88-8094; 88-7159
*Parent Company:* Zanichelli Editore SpA
Imprints: The Ma; Eliseo
Distributed by Cambridge (Italy); Klett Edition Deutsch (Italy)

**Loffredo Editore Napoli SpA®**
Via Consalvo 99 h, Parco S Luigi isolato D,
  80126 Naples
*Tel:* (081) 5937073 *Fax:* (081) 5936953
*E-mail:* info@loffredo.it
*Web Site:* www.loffredo.it
*Key Personnel*
Chief Executive: Mario Loffredo
Editorial, Sales, Rights & Permissions: Alfredo
  Loffredo
Production: Alfredo Loffredo, Jr
Publicity: Enzo Loffredo
Founded: 1880
Subjects: History, Language Arts, Linguistics, Lit-
  erature, Literary Criticism, Essays, Philosophy,
  Religion - Other, Science (General)
ISBN Prefix(es): 88-8096
*Bookshop(s):* Libreria Luigi Loffredo, Via Ker-
  baker 19/21, 1-80129 Naples

**Longanesi & C+**
Corso Italia 13, 20122 Milan
*Tel:* (02) 80206310 *Fax:* (02) 72000306
*E-mail:* info@longanesi.it
*Web Site:* www.longanesi.it
*Key Personnel*
President: Stefano Passigli
Sales: Giuseppe Somenzi
Production: Alfredo Bonfiglio
Publicity: Valentina Fortichiari
Rights & Permissions: Cristina Foschini
  *E-mail:* christina.foschini@longanesi.it
Editorial Dir: Luigi Brioschi
Founded: 1946
Subjects: Art, Biography, Fiction, History, How-
  to, Medicine, Nursing, Dentistry, Music, Dance,
  Philosophy, Psychology, Psychiatry, Religion
  - Other, Science (General), Social Sciences,
  Sociology
ISBN Prefix(es): 88-304
Number of titles published annually: 100 Print
Total Titles: 5 Print
*Parent Company:* Messaggerie Italiane
*Associate Companies:* Guanda, Cristina Fos-
  chini; Corbaccio, Cristina Foschini; Neri Pozza,
  Cristina Foschini; Ponte alle Grazie, Cristina
  Foschini
Subsidiaries: Finarte
*Orders to:* Pro Libro, Corso Italia 13, 20122 Mi-
  lan

**Longman Italia srl**
Via G Fara, 28, 20124 Milan
*Tel:* (02) 6739761 *Fax:* (02) 673976501
*E-mail:* longman-italia@pearsoned-ema.com
*Web Site:* www.longman-elt.com
*Key Personnel*
Man Dir, ELT: David Evans
Finance Manager, ELT: Lucia Donatellis
Publishing Manager, ELT: Barbara Cunsolo
Sales & Marketing Manager, ELT: Alan Osman
ISBN Prefix(es): 88-8339

**Angelo Longo Editore+**
Via Paolo Costa 33, 48100 Ravenna
*Tel:* (0544) 217026 *Fax:* (0544) 217554
*E-mail:* longo-ra@linknet.it
*Web Site:* www.longo-editore.it
*Key Personnel*
General Manager: Alfio Longo
Founded: 1965
Subjects: Archaeology, Art, Drama, Theater, Fic-
  tion, Film, Video, History, Language Arts, Lin-
  guistics, Literature, Literary Criticism, Essays,
  Music, Dance, Philosophy, Photography, Poetry,
  Women's Studies
ISBN Prefix(es): 88-8063
Number of titles published annually: 60 Print; 30
  Online
Total Titles: 1,180 Print; 68 Online
*Bookshop(s):* Libreria Dante di A M Longo, Via
  Diaz 39, 48100 Ravenna, Contact: Roberta
  Plazzi *Tel:* (0544) 33500

**Carlo Lorenzini Editore+**
Via Cavour 9, 33037 Pasiandi Prato (Ud)
*Tel:* (0432) 691412 *Fax:* (0432) 691412
Founded: 1981
ISBN Prefix(es): 88-7093

**Lorenzo Editore+**
Via Monza, 6, 10152 Turin
Mailing Address: CP 23, 10100 Turin
*Tel:* (011) 2485387 *Fax:* (011) 2485387
*E-mail:* info@loredi.it
*Web Site:* www.loredi.it *Cable:* ITALSCAMBI CP
  23 TURIN
*Key Personnel*
Chief Executive: Lorenzo Masetta
Founded: 1975
Specialize in poetry.
Subjects: Fiction, Literature, Literary Criticism,
  Essays, Poetry
ISBN Prefix(es): 88-85199; 88-87362
Subsidiaries: 'Talento' (current events periodical)

**LPE**, *imprint of* Luigi Pellegrini Editore

**Lubrina+**
Via Cesare Correnti, N 50, 24124 Bergamo
*Tel:* (035) 3470139396 *Fax:* (035) 241547
*E-mail:* editorelubrina@lubrina.it
*Web Site:* www.lubrina.it
*Key Personnel*
Man Dir: Ornella Bramani Mastropietro
  *E-mail:* obramas@lubrina.it
Founded: 1995
Membership(s): EQ Consorzio di Editor di
  Qualita.
Subjects: Biblical Studies, Biography, Literature,
  Literary Criticism, Essays, Philosophy, Psy-
  chology, Psychiatry
ISBN Prefix(es): 88-7766

**Edizioni de Luca SRL**
Via Visconti, 11, 00193 Rome
*Tel:* (06) 32650712 *Fax:* (06) 32650715
Founded: 1935
Subjects: Archaeology, Art, History
ISBN Prefix(es): 88-8016

**La Luna+**
Via DiGiovanni, 14, 90144 Palermo
*Tel:* (091) 345799 *Fax:* (091) 301650
*E-mail:* laluna@arcidonna.it
*Key Personnel*
President: Valeria Ajovalasit
Vice President: Roberta Messina
Founded: 1986
Membership(s): Arcidonna.
Subjects: Anthropology, Art, Fiction, Journalism,
  Literature, Literary Criticism, Essays, Nonfic-
  tion (General), Romance, Women's Studies
ISBN Prefix(es): 88-7823
Distributed by PDE

**Luni**
Via Procaccini, 11, 20154 Milan
*Tel:* (02) 89693000 *Fax:* (02) 89693011
*E-mail:* luni.editrice@fastwebnet.it
*Key Personnel*
Prof: Matteo Luteriani; Laura Niccolini
Founded: 1992
Subjects: Literature, Literary Criticism, Essays,
  Philosophy, Religion - Buddhist, Religion - Is-
  lamic, Religion - Other, Sports, Athletics
ISBN Prefix(es): 88-7984; 88-7435

**Lusva Editrice**
Via Roncaglia, 27, 20146 Milan
*Tel:* (02) 4985386
*Key Personnel*
Chief Executive: Luca Maria Vizzotto
Founded: 1977
Subjects: Education, Fiction, Poetry

**Lybra Immagine+**
Via Vincenzo Monti 6, 20123 Milan
*Tel:* (02) 48000818 *Fax:* (02) 48012748
*E-mail:* lybra@lybra.it
*Web Site:* www.lybra.it
*Key Personnel*
Editor: Mario Mastropietro
Founded: 1984
Subjects: Architecture & Interior Design, Fashion,
  Marketing, Photography
ISBN Prefix(es): 88-8223

**Lyra Libri**
Via Polidoro daCaravaggio, 37, 20156 Milan
*Tel:* (02) 30 241 311 *Fax:* (02) 30 241 333
*E-mail:* info@red-edizioni.it
*Key Personnel*
Chief Executive, Editorial: Maurizio Rosenberg
  Colorni
Founded: 1986
Subjects: Health, Nutrition, Psychology, Psychia-
  try, Self-Help, Women's Studies
ISBN Prefix(es): 88-7733

**The Ma**, *imprint of* Loescher Editore SRL

**Casa Editrice Maccari (CEM)+**
Via Trento 53, 43100 Parma
*Tel:* (0521) 771268 *Fax:* (0521) 771268
  *Cable:* CEMPARMA
*Key Personnel*
Man Dir: Cesare Maccari, Jr
Production: Camilla Albera
Founded: 1946
Subjects: Biological Sciences, Literature, Literary
  Criticism, Essays, Medicine, Nursing, Dentistry
ISBN Prefix(es): 88-7532
Number of titles published annually: 12 Print
Total Titles: 4 Print
Subsidiaries: Editrice La Pilotta

**Macro Edizioni+**
Via Savona 66, 47023 Diegaro di Cesena
*Tel:* (0547) 346290; (0547) 346317 *Fax:* (0547)
  345091; (0547) 345141
*E-mail:* ordini@macroedizioni.it
*Web Site:* www.macroedizioni.it
*Key Personnel*
President & Editor: Giorgio Gustavo Rosso
  *E-mail:* dizezione@macroedizione.it
Founded: 1987
Membership(s): AIE (Association Itaugna Edi-
  tori).
Subjects: Alternative, Archaeology, Biblical Stud-
  ies, Cookery, Education, Environmental Stud-
  ies, Health, Nutrition, House & Home, How-to,
  Philosophy, Psychology, Psychiatry, Religion -
  Other, Science (General)
ISBN Prefix(es): 88-7507
Total Titles: 300 Print
*Associate Companies:* Macro/Post
Distributor for Edizioni Essere Felici
*Showroom(s):* Salone Del Libro, Turin
*Book Club(s):* Il Giardino Dei Libri; Macro Li-
  brarsi, Via Savona 66-Diagaro, 47023 Cesena
  (Forli)
*Orders to:* Macro/Post, Via San Mauro 55,
  47041 Bellaria *Tel:* (0541) 344820 *Fax:* (0541)
  344824

**Magnus Edizioni SpA+**
Via dei Fabrizio, 57, 33034 Fagagna (Udine)
*Tel:* (0432) 800081 *Fax:* (0432) 810071
*E-mail:* info@magnusedizioni.it
*Web Site:* www.magnusedizioni.it
*Key Personnel*
Chief Executive & Editorial: Rene Leonarduzzi
Sales & Publicity: Antonio Stella

Founded: 1977
Subjects: Architecture & Interior Design, Art,
   Photography
ISBN Prefix(es): 88-7057
Subsidiaries: Grafiche Lema SpA

**Giuseppe Maimone Editore+**
Via A di Sangiuliano, 278, 95124 Catania
*Tel:* (095) 310315 *Fax:* (095) 310315
*E-mail:* maimone@maimone.it
*Web Site:* www.maimone.it
*Key Personnel*
Administrator: Guiseppe Maimone
Founded: 1985
Subjects: Architecture & Interior Design, Art,
   Biography, Film, Video, History, Literature,
   Literary Criticism, Essays, Regional Interests
ISBN Prefix(es): 88-7751
Subsidiaries: Maimone & Associati; SAS di Mai-
   mone Giuseppe
*Showroom(s):* Salone Del Libro Torino, 19-24
   Maggio, c/o Palazzo Lingotto, 10152 Torino;
   Mostra Parole Nel Tempo, 25-26 Settembre,
   c/o Castello Di Belgioioso, via Garibaldi 1, Bel-
   gioioso (Pavia); Il Libro, Salone Della Editoria
   Siciliana, 24 27 Marzo, c/o Ente Autonomo
   Fiera Di Messina Campionaria Internazionale,
   Viale Della Liberta, 98121 Messina

**Manfrini Editori**
SS del Brennero, 2, 38060 Calliano (TN)
*Tel:* (0464) 839111 *Fax:* (0464) 835086
*E-mail:* manfrini@tin.it
*Telex:* 400581 Manfri I *Cable:* Grafiche Manfrini
*Key Personnel*
Man Dir: Edoardo Manfrini
Founded: 1919
Subjects: Art, History, Literature, Literary Crit-
   icism, Essays, Nonfiction (General), Science
   (General), Travel
ISBN Prefix(es): 88-7024
*Parent Company:* R Manfrini SpA Vallagarina
   Arti Grafiche, SS del Brennero, 2, 38060 Cal-
   liano (Trento)
*Branch Office(s)*
Via Virgilio 6, 39100 Bolzano

**Manif,** see Manifestolibri

**Manifestolibri+**
Member of Il Manifesto Daily Newspaper
Via Tomacelli, 146, 00186 Rome
*Tel:* (06) 588 1496 *Fax:* (06) 588 2839
*E-mail:* redazione@manifestolibri.it; book@
   manifestolibri.it
*Web Site:* www.manifestolibri.it
*Key Personnel*
Chief Editor: Marco Bascetta
General Manager: Simona Bonsignori
   *E-mail:* bons@bonsignori.it
Founded: 1990
Publishing house in the group of "il Manifesto"
   daily newspaper. Carries books, online services,
   audio & CD-ROMs.
Subjects: Government, Political Science, Philos-
   ophy, Social Sciences, Sociology, Socio eco-
   nomic issues & affairs
ISBN Prefix(es): 88-7285
Total Titles: 400 Print; 2 CD-ROM; 10 Audio
*Branch Office(s)*
Manifestolibri, Viale Dei 4, Venti 47, 00152
   Rome, Contact: Simona Bonsignori

**Manni/Lupetti,** *imprint of* Piero Manni srl

**Marchese Grafiche Editoriali SpA,** see
   Marchesi Grafiche Editoriali SpA

**Casa Editrice Marietti SpA+**
Via Pisani 31, 20124 Milan
*Tel:* (02) 67101053 *Fax:* (02) 67389081

*E-mail:* marietti1820@split.it
*Key Personnel*
President: Flavio Repetto
Editor: Carla Villata
Foreign Rights: Carla Palazzesi
Founded: 1820
Subjects: Biblical Studies, History, Literature, Lit-
   erary Criticism, Essays, Philosophy, Religion -
   Catholic, Religion - Islamic, Religion - Jewish,
   Theology
ISBN Prefix(es): 88-211
Number of titles published annually: 30 Print
Total Titles: 550 Print

**Tommaso Marotta Editore Srl+**
Via dei Mille 78/82, Naples
*Tel:* (081) 5758060 *Fax:* (081) 418411
*Key Personnel*
Man Dir: Thomas F Marianos
Editorial: Teresa Nuzzo
Founded: 1979
Subjects: Art, Biography, Fiction, History, Music,
   Dance, Poetry, Regional Interests

**Marsilio Editori SpA+**
Marittima Fabbricato 205, 30135 Venice
*Tel:* (041) 2406511 *Fax:* (041) 5238352
*E-mail:* info@marsilioeditori.it
*Web Site:* www.marsilioeditori.it
*Key Personnel*
President & Sales Dir: Prof Cesare De Michelis
Editorial Dir: Emanuela Bassetti
Rights & Permissions & Acquisitions: Rita Vivian
Founded: 1961
Subjects: Art, Computer Science, Fiction, Film,
   Video, Literature, Literary Criticism, Essays,
   Nonfiction (General), Psychology, Psychiatry,
   Social Sciences, Sociology
ISBN Prefix(es): 88-317; 88-7693
*U.S. Office(s):* Marsilio Publishers, 853 Broad-
   way, Suite 1509, New York, NY 10003, United
   States *Tel:* 212-473-5300 *Fax:* 212-473-7865
Distributor for Giovanni Tranchida Editore

**Giunti Marzocco,** *imprint of* Giunti Gruppo
   Editoriale

**Marzorati Editore SRL+**
Via Tirso, 26, 00198 Rome
*Tel:* (06) 8546146 *Fax:* (06) 8411225
*Key Personnel*
Man Dir & Editorial: Antonio Marzorati
Sales: Carlo Marzorati
Production: Franco Faglioni
Publicity: Patrizia Fatigati
Rights & Permissions: Francesca Marzorati
Founded: 1942
Subjects: Geography, Geology, History, Literature,
   Literary Criticism, Essays, Philosophy
ISBN Prefix(es): 88-280
*Warehouse:* Via Galilei 1/5, 20010 Cornaredo

**Editrice Massimo SAS di Crespi Cesare e C+**
Viale Bacchiglione 20A, 20139 Milan
*Tel:* (02) 55 21 08 00 *Fax:* (02) 55 21 13 15
*Key Personnel*
Man Dir: Dr Cesare Crespi
Founded: 1951
Subjects: Astronomy, Biblical Studies, Biogra-
   phy, Drama, Theater, Fiction, History, Liter-
   ature, Literary Criticism, Essays, Philosophy,
   Psychology, Psychiatry, Religion - Catholic,
   Religion - Other, Romance, Science (General),
   Social Sciences, Sociology, Theology
ISBN Prefix(es): 88-7030
Total Titles: 400 Print
*Bookshop(s):* Agenzia Mescat, Milan

**Masson,** *imprint of* Masson SpA

**Masson SpA+**
Via Attendolo, 7/9, 20141 Milan
*Tel:* (02) 574952315 *Fax:* (02) 574952-371
*E-mail:* info@masson.it
*Web Site:* www.masson.it
*Key Personnel*
Man Dir: Jean-Paul Baudouin
Publicity: Gianluigi Cervi
Rights & Permissions: Lidia Lupi
Founded: 1976
Subjects: Chemistry, Chemical Engineering,
   Medicine, Nursing, Dentistry, Physics, Science
   (General), Technology
ISBN Prefix(es): 88-214
*Parent Company:* Masson, France
Imprints: Dunod; Masson; Massonscoula

**Massonscoula,** *imprint of* Masson SpA

**Edizioni Gabriele Mazzotta SRL+**
Foro Buonaparte, 52, 20121 Milan
*Tel:* (02) 8055803 *Fax:* (02) 8693046
*E-mail:* ufficiopromozione@mazzotta.it
*Web Site:* www.mazzotta.it
*Key Personnel*
Rights & Permissions & Man Dir: Gabriele Maz-
   zotta
Sales Dir: Antonio Vitagliano
Publicity Dir: Cristiana Rota
Founded: 1966
Subjects: Architecture & Interior Design, Art,
   Film, Video, Photography
ISBN Prefix(es): 88-202

**McGraw-Hill Libri Italia SRL**
Via Ripamonti 89, 20139 Milan
*Tel:* (02) 5357181 *Fax:* (02) 5398775
*E-mail:* editor@mcgraw-hill.it
*Key Personnel*
International Rights Contact: Italo Raimondi
ISBN Prefix(es): 88-386; 88-7700
*Parent Company:* The McGraw-Hill Companies,
   1221 Avenue of the Americas, New York, NY
   10020, United States
*Associate Companies:* McGraw-Hill Book Co Eu-
   rope
*Warehouse:* McGraw-Hill Magazzine Editoriale,
   Via Milano 6/2, 20068 Peschiera Borroreo, Mi-
   lan

**McRae Books+**
Via dei Rustici 5, Florence 50122
*Tel:* (055) 264384 *Fax:* (055) 212573
*Key Personnel*
Publisher: Anne McRae *E-mail:* mcrae@tin.it
Packagers of children's & adults illustrated non-
   fiction books for the international co-edition
   market.
Subjects: Art, Cookery, Geography, Geology, His-
   tory, Nonfiction (General), Religion - Other,
   Science (General)
ISBN Prefix(es): 88-88166; 88-900126; 88-
   900466

**Edizioni Medicea SRL+**
via della Villa Lorenzi, 8, 50139 Florence
*Tel:* (055) 416048 *Fax:* (055) 416048
*E-mail:* edizionimedicea@tiscalinet.it
*Web Site:* www.edizionimedicea.it
Founded: 1975
Subjects: Architecture & Interior Design, Gov-
   ernment, Political Science, Radio, TV, Science
   (General), Social Sciences, Sociology
ISBN Prefix(es): 88-900171

**Mediserve SRL+**
Via G Quagliariello 35/E, 80131 Naples
*Tel:* (081) 5452717 *Fax:* (081) 5462026
*E-mail:* contact@mediserve.it
*Web Site:* www.mediserve.it
*Key Personnel*
Man Dir, Editorial: Luigi Martinucci

Sales: Giuseppe Cerasuolo
Rights & Permissions: Ivonne Carbonaro
Founded: 1978
Subjects: Medicine, Nursing, Dentistry, Science (General)
ISBN Prefix(es): 88-8204
*Bookshop(s):* Libreria Scienze Mediche Martinucci, Via T de Amicis 60, 80145 Naples

**Edizioni Mediterranee SRL+**
Via Flaminia 109, 00196 Rome
*Tel:* (06) 3235433 *Fax:* (06) 3236277
*E-mail:* info@ediz-mediterranee.com
*Web Site:* www.ediz-mediterranee.com *Cable:* 0039-6
*Key Personnel*
General Manager: Giovanni Canonico *Tel:* (06) 3222797
Editorial: Paola Maria Canonico
Sales: Maria Satulli
Rights & Permissions: Assia Canonico; Eleasa Canonico
Founded: 1953
Subjects: Alternative, Archaeology, Art, Astrology, Occult, Biography, Gardening, Plants, Health, Nutrition, How-to, Medicine, Nursing, Dentistry, Military Science, Parapsychology, Philosophy, Psychology, Psychiatry, Religion - Other, Sports, Athletics, Alchemy, Esoterism, Magic, Martial Arts, Meditation, New Age, UFO, Yoga
ISBN Prefix(es): 88-272
Total Titles: 1,500 Print
Subsidiaries: Hermes Edizioni SRL; Edizioni Studio Tesi

**Memorie Domenicane**
Piazza San Domenico 1, 51100 Pistoia
*Tel:* (0573) 22056; (0573) 28158 *Fax:* (0573) 975808
*E-mail:* centroriviste@tiscalinet.it
*Key Personnel*
Editorial: Eugenio Marino; Armando F Verde
   *E-mail:* armando.verde@tin.it
Founded: 1884
Subjects: History, Theology
*Parent Company:* Centro Riviste della Provincia Romana dei Frati Predicatori
*Shipping Address:* Centro Riviste della Provincia Romana dei Frati Predicatori
*Warehouse:* Centro Riviste della Provincia Romana dei Frati Predicatori
*Orders to:* Centro Riviste della Provincia Romana dei Frati Predicatori

**Casa Editrice Menna di Sinisgalli Menna Giuseppina+**
Via Scandone 16, 83100 Avellino
*Tel:* (0825) 24080 *Fax:* (0825) 24080
*Key Personnel*
Chief Executive: Nunzio Menna
Founded: 1976
Subjects: Drama, Theater, History, Law, Literature, Literary Criticism, Essays, Poetry
Imprints: Verso il Futuro
*Warehouse:* CE MENNA, CP 80 Avellino

**Meravigli, Libreria Milanese**
Via Plezzo 36, 20132 Milan
*Tel:* (02) 2157240 *Fax:* (02) 2157833
ISBN Prefix(es): 88-7954; 88-7955

**Messaggero di San Antonio+**
Via Orto Botanico 11, 35123 Padova
*Tel:* (049) 8225000 *Fax:* (049) 8225688
*E-mail:* info@mess-s-antonio.it
*Web Site:* www.mess-s-antonio.it
*Telex:* 430855 Msa I *Cable:* Messaggero Padova
*Key Personnel*
Chief Executive: P Luciano Marini
Editorial: P Giacomo Panteghini

Sales, Production, Publicity, Rights & Permissions: P Agostino Varotto
Subjects: Biography, History, Journalism, Religion - Other
ISBN Prefix(es): 88-7026; 88-250
*Bookshop(s):* Libreria Messaggero, Piazza del Santo 17, 35123 Padova

**Mario Miglietti**, *imprint of* Casa Editrice Castalia

**Milano Libri**
Via Mecenate, 91, 20138 Milan
*Tel:* (02) 50951 *Fax:* (02) 5065361
Subjects: Fiction, Literature, Literary Criticism, Essays
ISBN Prefix(es): 88-318; 88-7811; 88-17
*Associate Companies:* RCS Rizzoli Libri SpA

**Nicola Milano Editore+**
Via Farini 14, 40124 Bologna
*Tel:* (051) 239060 *Fax:* (051) 239286
*E-mail:* scuola@nicolamilano.com
*Web Site:* www.nicolamilano.com
*Key Personnel*
Chief Executive: Mario Musso
Founded: 1969
ISBN Prefix(es): 88-419

**Milella di Lecce Spazio Vivo srl+**
Via Palmieri 30, 73100 Lecce
*Tel:* (0832) 241131 *Fax:* (0832) 303057
*E-mail:* leccespaziovivo@tiscalinet.it
*Key Personnel*
President: Antonio Pati
Professor: Gaetano Quarta
Founded: 1945
Subjects: Disability, Special Needs, Education, English as a Second Language, History, Human Relations, Literature, Literary Criticism, Essays, Philosophy, Psychology, Psychiatry, Social Sciences, Sociology
ISBN Prefix(es): 88-7048
*Bookshop(s):* Via M DePietro, Via Palmieri 30, 73100 Lecce; Via G Palmieri, Viale dell'UniVersite, 1, 30-73100 Lecce *Tel:* (0832) 308885 *Fax:* (0832) 308885
*Warehouse:* Via M DePietro, Via Palmieri, 30, 9-73100 Leece *Tel:* (0832) 308885
*Orders to:* Via M DePietro, Viale dell'UniVersite, 1, 9-73100 Lecce *Tel:* (0832) 308885

**Minerva Italica SpA**
Via Durazzo 4, 20134 Milan
*Tel:* (02) 21213643 *Fax:* (02) 21213698
*E-mail:* info@minervaitalica.it
*Web Site:* www.minervaitalica.it
*Key Personnel*
Man Dir: Arnoldi Gianni
Founded: 1951
Subjects: Art, Education, Fiction
ISBN Prefix(es): 88-298
*Branch Office(s)*
Via Lattanzio 90-94, 70126 Bari
Via Alfani 68, 50121 Florence
Via S Sebastiano is 247a, 98100 Messina
Via Petrella 6, 20124 Milan
Via A Emo 162-168, 00136 Rome

**Il Minotauro+**
Via Quirino Majorana 221, 00152 Rome
*Tel:* (06) 5591864 *Fax:* (06) 5592337
*E-mail:* ilminotauro@tin.it
*Web Site:* www.ilminotauroeditore.it
*Key Personnel*
Contact: Dr Giorgio Ferrari
Founded: 1993
Subjects: Fiction, Government, Political Science, Literature, Literary Criticism, Essays, Philosophy, Travel
ISBN Prefix(es): 88-8073
Distributed by PDE Milano

**Editrice Missionaria Italiana (EMI)+**
Via di Corticella 181, 40128 Bologna
*Tel:* (051) 326027 *Fax:* (051) 327552
*E-mail:* sermis@emi.it
*Web Site:* www.emi.it
*Key Personnel*
Man Dir, Editorial, Production: Francesco Grasselli
Sales: Father Noe Cereda
Administrator: Father Giuseppe Mariani
Founded: 1977
Subjects: Anthropology, Religion - Other, Social Sciences, Sociology
ISBN Prefix(es): 88-307
*Bookshop(s):* Libreria Comboniana, Galleria Mazzini, 37121 Verona

**mnemes - Alfieri & Ranieri Publishing+**
Via F Bentivegna, 38, 90139 Palermo
*Tel:* (091) 588813 *Fax:* (091) 588813
*E-mail:* info@mnemes.com
*Web Site:* www.mnemes.com
Founded: 1995
Subjects: Music, Dance
ISBN Prefix(es): 88-8161

**Arnoldo Mondadori Editore SpA+**
Via Mondadori, 1, 20090 Segrate (Milan)
*Tel:* (02) 75421 *Fax:* (02) 75422302
*Web Site:* www.mondadori.it
*Telex:* 320457 Mondmi I *Cable:* MONDADORI SEGRATE (MI)
*Key Personnel*
Vice President & Deputy Chairman: Luca Formenton
Chief Executive Officer: Maurizio Costa
Corporate Communications & Advertising Dir: Andrea Zagami
Press Relations Officer: Angelo Allegri *Tel:* (02) 75422729 *E-mail:* aallegri@mondadori.it
Founded: 1907
*Legal Headquarters:* Via Bianca di Savoia 12, 20122 Milan
*Representative Office:* Via Sicilia, 136, 00187 Rome
*Foreign Offices:* Artes Graficas Toledo SA (officine grafiche): Carretera Toledo Ocono km 8, Poligono Industriale SIN/N, Toledo, and Calle Principe De Vergara, 13, 28016 Madrid (both Spain); Mondadori UK Ltd, 43-45 Charlotte St, London W1P 1HA, UK; A Mondadori Deutschland GmbH, Tal 21, 80331 Munich, Germany; A Mondadori Editore, c/o Mondgraph, 9/11 Ave F Roosevelt, 75008 Paris, France; AME Publishing Ltd, 740 Broadway, New York, NY 10003, USA; Random House Mondori, Arago, 385, 08013 Barcelona.
Subjects: Art, Biography, Education, Fiction, History, How-to, Medicine, Nursing, Dentistry, Music, Dance, Mysteries, Philosophy, Poetry, Psychology, Psychiatry, Religion - Other, Romance, Science (General)
ISBN Prefix(es): 88-04
*Parent Company:* Fininvest
*Associate Companies:* Agenzia Lombarda Distribuzione, Via Stamira d'Ancona 30, 20127 Milan *Tel:* (02) 26113470 *Fax:* (02) 26113351; Gruner & Jahr Mondadori SpA, Corso Monforte 54, 20122 Milan *Tel:* (02) 762101 *Fax:* (02) 76013439; Harlequin Mondadori SpA, Corso Concordia, 7, 20129 Milan *Tel:* (02) 760381 *Fax:* (02) 780397; Mach 2 Libri SpA, Via B Quaranta, 40, 20139 Milan *Tel:* (02) 55210585 *Fax:* (02) 5396931; SIES Societa Italiana Editrice Stampatrice SpA *Fax:* (02) 66724360; Societa Europea di Edizioni SpA, Via Negri 4, 20123 Milan *Tel:* (02) 85661 *Fax:* (02) 73023880
Subsidiaries: Cemit Direct Media SpA; Club delgi Editori Sp; Edizioni di Comunita Srl; Edizioni Frassinelli Srl; Elemond SpA; Ellemme Srl; Giulio Einaudi Editore SpA; Random House Mondadori S A; Leonardo Arte Srl; Mondadori

Franchising SpA; Mondadori Informatica SpA; Mondadori Pubblicita SpA; Riccardo Ricciardi Editore SpA; Sperling & Kupfer Editori SpA
*Branch Office(s)*
Corso Europa 5/7, 20122 Milan *Tel:* (02) 77941 *Fax:* (02) 7794359
Via Sicilia 136, 00187 Rome *Tel:* (06) 474971 *Fax:* (06) 47497336
Via Virgilio 8, 00195 Rome *Tel:* (06) 6838899 *Fax:* (06) 6874107
Via Mondadori 15, 37131 Verona *Tel:* (045) 934111 *Fax:* (045) 934697
*Foreign Rights:* AME Publishing Ltd (US); Continental Printing Ltd (UK); E-M Livres (France); Mondadori (Spain); Arnoldo Mondadori Deutschland GmbH (Germany); Mondgraph (France); Tuttle Mori Agency Inc (Japan)
*Bookshop(s):* Via Vittorio Emanuele 36, 22100 Como *Tel:* (031) 273424 *Fax:* (031) 273314; Via XX Settembre 210/R, 16121 Genova *Tel:* (010) 585743 *Fax:* (010) 5704810; Largo Corsia de Servi 11, 20122 Milan *Tel:* (02) 76005832 *Fax:* (02) 76014902; Piazza Cola Di Rienzo 81/83, 00192 Rome *Tel:* (06) 3220188 *Fax:* (06) 3210323; Via Appia Vuova 51, 00183 Rome *Tel:* (06) 7003690 *Fax:* (06) 7003450

**Bruno Mondadori™**, *imprint of* Paravia Bruno Mondadori Editori

**Edizioni Scolastiche Bruno Mondadori™**, *imprint of* Paravia Bruno Mondadori Editori

**Giorgio Mondadori & Associati+**
Corso Magenta 55, 20123 Milan
*Tel:* (02) 433 131 *Fax:* (02) 89125880
*E-mail:* edgmonai@tin.it
*Telex:* GIOMON 1 314369
*Key Personnel*
President: Giorgio Mondadori
Dir General, Administration & Finance: Vito Leovino
Founded: 1978
Subjects: Antiques, Architecture & Interior Design, Art, Foreign Countries, Gardening, Plants, House & Home
ISBN Prefix(es): 88-374
Imprints: GM
Subsidiaries: Gardenia srl; Giorgio Mondadori Periodici/Airone di Giorgio Mondadori & Associati; Editoriale Giorgio Mondadori; Giorgio Mondadori Editore; Giorgio Mondadori srl

**Edizioni del Mondo Giudiziario**
Viale Angelico 90, 00195 Rome
*Tel:* (06) 3721071 *Fax:* (06) 35350961
*E-mail:* info@mguidiziario.it
*Web Site:* www.mgiudiziario.it
*Key Personnel*
Man Dir: Augusto Brusca
Editorial, Sales: Anna Tabili Brusca; Federico Carlo Brusca
Founded: 1946
Subjects: Law

**Mondolibro Editore SNC+**
Via Sillano 11a, 50022 Greve in Chianti (FI)
*Tel:* (055) 2658269 *Fax:* (055) 2679522
*E-mail:* info@mondolibroeditore.com
*Web Site:* www.mondolibroeditore.com
*Key Personnel*
Contact: Dr Ettore de Parentela
*E-mail:* eparentela@yahoo.it
Founded: 1987
Bookshops located in major cities throughout Italy, as well as New York, Los Angeles, London, Paris, Frankfurt & Tokyo.
Subjects: Art, Drama, Theater, Fiction, Film, Video, Literature, Literary Criticism, Essays, Nonfiction (General), Travel

ISBN Prefix(es): 88-85143
Imprints: Biblioteca Elle; Biblioteca World; Collana
Subsidiaries: Coloristi
Distributed by Albolibro SrL; Casalini Libri SpA; Cosma Libraria snc; DEM Libri SrL; L'Acquilone; Medialibri SrL; Midilibri SrL; Rossano Libri SrL

**Monduzzi Editore SpA**
Via Ferrarese 119/2, 40128 Bologna
*Tel:* (051) 4151123 *Fax:* (051) 4151125
*Web Site:* www.monduzzi.com
*Telex:* 512654 Mondbo I
*Key Personnel*
President: Dr Gianni Monduzzi
Man Dir: Dr Mauro Bettocchi
Founded: 1978
Subjects: Biological Sciences, Chemistry, Chemical Engineering, Economics, Engineering (General), Law, Literature, Literary Criticism, Essays, Medicine, Nursing, Dentistry, Physics, Psychology, Psychiatry, Social Sciences, Sociology
ISBN Prefix(es): 88-323
Imprints: Cisalpino
Divisions: International Proceedings Division

**Le Monnier**, *imprint of* Edumond Le Monnier

**Edumond Le Monnier+**
Via Bianca di Savoia 12, 20122 Milan
*Tel:* (055) 64910 *Fax:* (055) 6491200
*E-mail:* monnier@tin.it
*Key Personnel*
President: Giuseppe De Rita
Vice President: Dr Enrico Paoletti
Publishing Dir: Dr Guglielmo Paoletti
Man Dir: Dr Vanni Paoletti
Office Prints: Dr Simone Paoletti
Founded: 1836
Subjects: Biography, Education, History, Language Arts, Linguistics, Philosophy, Religion - Catholic
ISBN Prefix(es): 88-00
Imprints: Le Monnier

**Editrice Morcelliana SpA+**
Via Gabriele Rosa 71, 25121 Brescia
*Tel:* (030) 46451 *Fax:* (030) 2400605
*E-mail:* redazione@morcelliana.it
*Web Site:* www.morcelliana.it
*Key Personnel*
Man Dir: Stefano Minelli
Founded: 1925
Subjects: History, Philosophy, Religion - Other, Social Sciences, Sociology
ISBN Prefix(es): 88-372
*Associate Companies:* Editrice La Scuola SpA

**Moretti & Vitali Editori srl+**
Via Segantini 6a, 24128 Bergamo
*Tel:* (035) 251300 *Fax:* (035) 4329409
*E-mail:* info@morettievitali.it
*Web Site:* www.morettievitali.it
*Key Personnel*
President & Publishing Dir: Enrico Moretti
*E-mail:* direzione@morettievitali.it
Administration: Fanny Honegger
*E-mail:* administrazione@morettievitali.it
Editor-in-Chief: Salvatore Zingale
*E-mail:* redozione@morettievitali.it
Founded: 1989
Subjects: Architecture & Interior Design, Art, Biography, Human Relations, Literature, Literary Criticism, Essays, Psychology, Psychiatry
ISBN Prefix(es): 88-7186

**Federico Motta Editore**
Via Branda Castiglioni, 7, 20156 Milan

*Tel:* (02) 300761; (02) 30076231 *Fax:* (02) 38010046; (02) 33403275
*E-mail:* info@mottaeditore.it
*Web Site:* www.mottaeditore.it
ISBN Prefix(es): 88-7179

**Motta Junior Srl**
Via Branda Castiglioni, 7, 20156 Milan
*Tel:* (02) 300761; (02) 30076231 *Fax:* (02) 38010046; (02) 33403275
*E-mail:* info@mottaeditore.it
*Web Site:* www.mottaeditore.it
*Key Personnel*
Dir, Sales Books Department: Lorena Vazzola
Pres: Massimo Fumagalli
Edit Dir: Madeleine Thoby
ISBN Prefix(es): 88-8279

**Mucchi Editore SRL**
Via Emilia Est 1527, 41100 Modena
*Tel:* (059) 374094 *Fax:* (059) 282628
*E-mail:* info@mucchieditore.it
*Web Site:* www.mucchieditore.it
Founded: 1646
Subjects: Crafts, Games, Hobbies, Education, History, Language Arts, Linguistics, Law, Literature, Literary Criticism, Essays, Philosophy, Science (General)
ISBN Prefix(es): 88-7000

**Societa Editrice Il Mulino+**
Str Maggiore 37, 40125 Bologna
*Tel:* (051) 256011 *Fax:* (051) 256034
*E-mail:* info@mulino.it
*Web Site:* www.mulino.it
*Key Personnel*
Man Dir: Giuliano Bassani
Sales Dir: Maria Selleri
Publicity Dir: Ida Meneghello
Rights & Permissions: Paola Pecchioli
*E-mail:* paola.pecchioli@mulino.it
Editorial Dir: Giovanni Evangelisti
Founded: 1954
Subjects: Economics, Government, Political Science, History, Language Arts, Linguistics, Law, Philosophy, Psychology, Psychiatry, Social Sciences, Sociology
ISBN Prefix(es): 88-15

**Ass Italiana Sclerosi Multipla**
Vico Chiuso Paggi, 3, 16128 Genova
*Tel:* (010) 27131 *Fax:* (010) 2470226
*E-mail:* genesi@genesi.org
*Web Site:* www.aism.org
ISBN Prefix(es): 88-7148

**Mundici - Zanetti**
Via dei Lapidari, 10, 40129 Bologna
*Tel:* (051) 325347 *Fax:* (051) 326109
*E-mail:* info@zanetti.co.it
Founded: 1977
Subjects: Astrology, Occult, Cookery, House & Home, Humor
ISBN Prefix(es): 88-7410

**Gruppo Ugo Mursia Editore SpA+**
Via Melchiorre Gioia 45, 20124 Milan
*Tel:* (02) 67378500 *Fax:* (02) 67378605
*E-mail:* info@mursia.com
*Web Site:* www.mursia.com
*Key Personnel*
President & Publisher: Fiorenza Mursia
Publicity: Lorenza Sala
Rights & Permissions: Milena Molinari
Founded: 1922
Subjects: Art, Biography, Education, Fiction, History, Maritime, Philosophy, Poetry, Religion - Other, Science (General), Social Sciences, Sociology, Sports, Athletics
ISBN Prefix(es): 88-425
*Warehouse:* Via Cassanese antica, 20060 Vignate, Milan

**Museo storico in Trento+**
Via Torre d'Augusto, 41, 38100 Trento
*Tel:* (0461) 230482 *Fax:* (0461) 237418
*E-mail:* info@museostorico.tn.it
*Web Site:* www.museostorico.tn.it/editoria_ricerca
*Key Personnel*
Editorial Coordinator: Rodolfo Taiani *Tel:* (0461)
264660 *E-mail:* rtaiani@museostorico.tn.it
Founded: 1923
Subjects: History, Literature, Literary Criticism,
Essays, Social Sciences, Sociology
ISBN Prefix(es): 88-7197
Number of titles published annually: 5 Print
Total Titles: 110 Print

**Musumeci SpA+**
Localita Amerique 99, 11020 Quart (Acosta)
*Tel:* (0165) 761216 *Fax:* (0165) 761296
*Key Personnel*
Dir: Piero Minuzzo
ISBN Prefix(es): 88-7032

**Franco Muzzio Editore+**
Via Riccardo Grazioli Lante, 5, 00195 Rome
*Tel:* (06) 3725748 *Fax:* (06) 6868696
*E-mail:* franco@muzzioeditore.it
*Web Site:* www.muzzioeditore.it
*Telex:* 432005 Muzzio
*Key Personnel*
Chief Executive & Publicity: Franco Muzzio
Editorial: Riccardo Degli Innocenti
Sales: Ennio Pengo
Production: Massi Miliano Muzzio
Rights & Permissions & Editorial: Stella Longato
Founded: 1973
Subjects: Computer Science, Electronics, Electri-
cal Engineering, Energy, Music, Dance, Nonfic-
tion (General), Science (General)
ISBN Prefix(es): 88-7021; 88-7413
*Associate Companies:* Arcana Editrice SRL, Viale
Sondrio 7, 20124 Milan; Casa Editice MEB
SRL
*Warehouse:* Via Makalle 73, 35138 Padua

**N**, *imprint of* Pizzicato Edizioni Musicali

**Giorgio Nada Editore SRL+**
Via Treves 15/17, 20090 Vimodrone MI
Mailing Address: Via Claudio Treves 15/17,
20090 Vimodrone MI
*Tel:* (02) 27301126 *Fax:* (02) 27301454
*E-mail:* info@giorgionadaeditore.it
*Web Site:* www.giorgionadaeditore.it
*Key Personnel*
Chairman: Giorgio Nada *E-mail:* giorgio.nada@
giorgioeditore.it
Founded: 1988
Specialize in books on history of Italian cars &
motorcycle makes (Ferrari, Ducati, etc.)
Subjects: Automotive, History, Transportation
ISBN Prefix(es): 88-7911
Number of titles published annually: 15 Print
Total Titles: 200 Print
Subsidiaries: Libreria dell'Automobile
Distributed by Haynes Publishing-Sparkford
Yeovil (England); MBI Publishing Company
(US)
*Book Club(s):* Corso Venezia, 43, 20121 Milan

**Nagard**
Via Larga 9, 20122 Milan
*Tel:* (02) 58371400 *Fax:* (02) 58304790
*E-mail:* fondazionedragan@libero.it
Founded: 1977
Subjects: Chemistry, Chemical Engineering, Edu-
cation
ISBN Prefix(es): 88-85010

**Casa Editrice Roberto Napoleone**
Via Antonio Chinotto, 16, 00195 Rome
*Tel:* (06) 3729096 *Fax:* (06) 3729103

*Key Personnel*
Chief Executive: Roberto Napoleone
Founded: 1974
ISBN Prefix(es): 88-7124

**Accademia Naz dei Lincei**
Via della Lungara 10, 00165 Rome
*Tel:* (06) 680271 *Fax:* (06) 6893616
*E-mail:* pugwash@iol.it
Founded: 1847
Subjects: Archaeology, Art, Biological Sciences,
Economics, History, Management, Mathematics
ISBN Prefix(es): 88-218; 88-7052

**Istituto Nazionale di Studi Romani**
Piazza dei Cavalieri di Malta, 2, 00153 Rome
*Tel:* (06) 5743442; (06) 5743445 *Fax:* (06)
5743447
*E-mail:* studiromani@studiromani.it
*Web Site:* www.studiromani.it
*Key Personnel*
President: Prof Mario Mazza
Vice President: Prof Letizia Ermini Pani
Dir: Dr Fernanda Roscetti
Founded: 1925
Subjects: Architecture & Interior Design, Art,
History, Literature, Literary Criticism, Essays
ISBN Prefix(es): 88-7311
Number of titles published annually: 7 Print
Total Titles: 848 Print

**New Magazine Edizioni+**
Via dei Mille 69, 38100 Trento
*Tel:* (0461) 925007 *Fax:* (0461) 925007
*E-mail:* newmagazine@tin.it
*Web Site:* www.newmagazine.it; www.
rivistamedica.it
*Key Personnel*
International Rights: Bruno Zanotti
Founded: 1982
Specialize in medicine.
Subjects: Civil Engineering, Literature, Literary
Criticism, Essays, Medicine, Nursing, Dentistry
ISBN Prefix(es): 88-8041
Distributed by Del Porto SpA (Worldwide)

**Newton & Compton Editori**
Via Portuense 1415, 00050 Rome
*Tel:* (06) 65002553 *Fax:* (06) 65002892
*E-mail:* info@newtoncompton.com
*Web Site:* www.newtoncompton.com
Founded: 1969
Subjects: Anthropology, Archaeology, Fiction,
Government, Political Science, History, How-
to, Mathematics, Philosophy, Poetry, Psychol-
ogy, Psychiatry, Science (General), Social Sci-
ences, Sociology
ISBN Prefix(es): 88-7983; 88-8183; 88-8289

**NIE**, *imprint of* La Nuova Italia Editrice SpA

**Nissolino**, *imprint of* Esselibri

**Nistri - Lischi Editori+**
Via XXIV Maggio 28, 56123 Pisa
*Tel:* (050) 563371 *Fax:* (050) 562726
*Web Site:* www.nistri-lischi.it *Cable:* LISCHI
PISA
*Key Personnel*
Man Dir: Luciano Lischi
Sales: Lucia Lischi
Founded: 1780
Subjects: Literature, Literary Criticism, Essays
*Warehouse:* Via Carducci, La Fontina, Pisa

**NodoLibri+**
Via Volta, 38, 22100 Como
*Tel:* (031) 243113 *Fax:* (031) 3306370
*E-mail:* nodo.como@libero.it
Founded: 1989

Subjects: Art, History, Photography, Regional Interests
ISBN Prefix(es): 88-7185

**Nord**, *imprint of* Casa Editrice Nord SRL

**Casa Editrice Nord SRL**
Via Rubens, 25, 20148 Milan
*Tel:* (02) 405708 *Fax:* (02) 4042207
*E-mail:* nord@fantascienza.it
*Web Site:* www.nord.fantascienza.it
*Key Personnel*
President: Gianfranco Viviani
Vice President: Marco Viviani
Editorial: Alex Voglino; Piergiorgio Nicolazzini
Founded: 1964
Subjects: Science Fiction, Fantasy
ISBN Prefix(es): 88-429
Imprints: Nord

**Novecento Editrice Srl+**
Via Siracusa, 16, 90141 Palermo
*Tel:* (091) 587417 *Fax:* (091) 585702
*E-mail:* novedi@mbox.vol.it
*Key Personnel*
Administrator: Alessi Maria Caterina Domitilla
Founded: 1980
Subjects: Art, Literature, Literary Criticism, Es-
says, Photography
ISBN Prefix(es): 88-373
*Bookshop(s):* Libreria Novelento, via Siracusa 7/
A, 90141 Palermo *Tel:* (091) 6256814
*Warehouse:* Via Agrigento 15, 90141 Palermo

**Nugae, Interli Nee, Libri Di Bron, Cuccioli**,
*imprint of* Pagano Editore

**Nuova Alfa Editoriale+**
Via Trentacoste, 7, 20134 Milan
*Tel:* (02) 215631 *Fax:* (02) 26413121
*Key Personnel*
Man Dir, Production: Maurizio Armaroli
Editorial, Publicity: Emanuela Spinsanti
Sales: Piera Raimondi
Founded: 1954
Subjects: Art, Literature, Literary Criticism, Es-
says
ISBN Prefix(es): 88-7779

**Nuova Coletti Editore Roma**
Via Clitunno 24/f, 00198 Rome
*Tel:* (06) 8557981 *Fax:* (06) 8557981
*E-mail:* materiale.web@futura-ge.com
Founded: 1987
Subjects: Biblical Studies, Education, History,
Literature, Literary Criticism, Essays, Philoso-
phy, Religion - Catholic, Theology
ISBN Prefix(es): 88-7826
*Warehouse:* Borgo Pio 105, 00193 Rome

**Nuova Dimensione**, *imprint of* Ediciclo Editore
SRL

**Nuova Ipsa Editore srl**
Via G Crispi 50, 90145 Palermo
*Tel:* (091) 6819025 *Fax:* (091) 6816399
*E-mail:* info@nuovaipsa.it
*Web Site:* www.nuovaipsa.it
*Key Personnel*
Editorial Dir: Claudio Mazza
Founded: 1982
ISBN Prefix(es): 88-7676

**La Nuova Italia Editrice SpA**
Via Mecenate, 91, 20138 Milan
*Tel:* (02) 50951 *Fax:* (02) 50952309
*Key Personnel*
Man Dir: Federico Codignola; Sergio Colleoni;
Mario Ermini; Carmelo Sambugar
Founded: 1926

Subjects: Art, Biography, History, Philosophy, Psychology, Psychiatry, Social Sciences, Sociology
ISBN Prefix(es): 88-221
Imprints: NIE
*Branch Office(s)*
Via Sacco Vantetti 8, 60131 Ancona
Via E Bernardi 14, 40133 Bologna
Via Del Fangario 25, 09122 Cagliari
Via Degli Stan 28, 87100 Cosenza
Via B Lupi 1, 50129 Florence
Via di Serretto 41/2, 16131 Genoa
Via Negroli 12, 20133 Milan
Ste St Le 98 Km 79,400 (Complesso Big Center), 70026 Modugno-Bari
Via S Alfonso Maria de'Liguori 3, 80141 Naples
Via Altichiero da Zevio 3, 35100 Padua
Via Olanda 15, 90146 Palermo
Viale Carso 46, 00195 Rome
Via Bassano 16, 10136 Turin
Arbizzano- Negrar, Via L da Vinci, 37020 Verona

**Editrice Nuovi Autori**
Via Gaudenzio Ferrari 14, 20123 Milan
*Tel:* (02) 89409338 *Fax:* (02) 58107048
*E-mail:* faglier@tin.it
*Web Site:* www.paginegialle.it/ednuoviaut
*Key Personnel*
Man Dir: Fulvio Aglieri
Editorial & Publicity: Alessandra Aglieri
Sales: Graziella Mosconi
Founded: 1980
Also acts as book packager.
Subjects: Biography, History, Literature, Literary Criticism, Essays, Poetry
ISBN Prefix(es): 88-7230

**Nuovi Sentieri Editore**
Via Ripa 2, 32100 Belluno
*Tel:* (0437) 590308
*Key Personnel*
Man Dir: Bepi Pellegrinon
Editorial: Loris Santomaso
Sales: Antonio Zullo
Founded: 1971
Subjects: Art, History, Literature, Literary Criticism, Essays, Photography, Poetry, Regional Interests
ISBN Prefix(es): 88-85510

**Il Nuovo Melangolo+**
Via di Porta Soprana 3/1, 16123 Genoa
*Tel:* (010) 2514002 *Fax:* (010) 2514037
*E-mail:* info@ilmelangolo.com
*Web Site:* www.ilmelangolo.com
Founded: 1976
Subjects: Fiction, Literature, Literary Criticism, Essays, Philosophy, Poetry, Religion - Buddhist, Religion - Catholic, Religion - Jewish, Religion - Other, Theology
ISBN Prefix(es): 88-7018

**OCTAVO Produzioni Editoriali Associale+**
Borgo Santa Croce 8, 50122 Florence
*Tel:* (055) 2346022 *Fax:* (055) 2346109
*Web Site:* www.octavo.it
*Key Personnel*
Man Dir: Franco Cantini
Founded: 1993
Specialize in art.
Subjects: Antiques, Archaeology, Architecture & Interior Design, Art, Education, Fiction, History, Photography
ISBN Prefix(es): 88-8030

**OEMF**, see OEMF srl International

**OEMF srl International+**
Via Muzio Attendolo detto Sforza 7/9, 20141 Milan
*Tel:* (02) 5749521 *Fax:* (02) 33210200

*E-mail:* info@mason.it
*Web Site:* www.oemf.it
*Key Personnel*
Dir: Carlo Marini
Founded: 1940
Subjects: Medicine, Nursing, Dentistry, Veterinary Science
ISBN Prefix(es): 88-7076

**Officina Edizioni di Aldo Quinti+**
Via Nicola Ricciotti 11, 00195 Rome
*Tel:* (06) 316336 *Fax:* (06) 65740514
*E-mail:* officinaedizioni@yahoo.com
*Key Personnel*
Chief Executive: Aldo Quinti
Publicity: Jolanda Ridolfi
Founded: 1966
Subjects: Architecture & Interior Design, Art, Drama, Theater, Ethnicity, Film, Video, Language Arts, Linguistics, Social Sciences, Sociology
*Warehouse:* Via Virginia Agnelli, 52, 00151 Rome

**Editoriale Olimpia SpA+**
Via E Ferni, 24, 50019 Fiorentino, Florence
*Tel:* (055) 30321 *Fax:* (055) 3032280
*E-mail:* editore@edolimpia.it; moie@edolimpia.it
*Web Site:* www.edolimpia.it
*Telex:* 573084 Edol I
*Key Personnel*
Man Dir, Editorial, Rights & Permissions: Renato Cacciaputi
Founded: 1939
Specialize in publications on hunting, fishing, dogs, scuba diving, weapons, handgliding-paragliding, tourism, digital photography, etc.
Subjects: Aeronautics, Aviation, Animals, Pets, Biological Sciences, Outdoor Recreation, Sports, Athletics, Technology
ISBN Prefix(es): 88-253
Number of titles published annually: 220 Print
Subsidiaries: Editoriale Olimpia

**Edizioni Olivares**
Via Pietro Mascagni, 7, 20122 Milan
*Tel:* (02) 76001753 *Fax:* (02) 76002579
*E-mail:* olivares@edizioniolivares.com
*Web Site:* www.edizioniolivares.com
Founded: 1986
Membership(s): AIPE (Associazione Italiano Piccoli Editori) & AIE.
Subjects: Business, Management, Women's Studies
ISBN Prefix(es): 88-85982
*Parent Company:* Redifin SpA, Via P Mascagni, 7, 20122 Milan
*Showroom(s):* Parole In Tasca-Salone del libro tascabile, c/o Castello di Belgioso, Via Garibaldi 1, 27011 Belgioso (Paira)
*Warehouse:* M ED Via dei Mille 20, Carugate (MI)

**Leo S Olschki**
Viuzzo del Pozzetto, 8, 50126 Florence
*Tel:* (055) 6530684 *Fax:* (055) 6530214
*E-mail:* celso@olschki.it
*Web Site:* www.olschki.it
Founded: 1886
Subjects: Anthropology, Archaeology, Architecture & Interior Design, Art, Astronomy, Biblical Studies, Geography, Geology, Government, Political Science, History, Language Arts, Linguistics, Library & Information Sciences, Literature, Literary Criticism, Essays, Music, Dance, Natural History, Philosophy, Physical Sciences, Religion - Catholic, Religion - Jewish, Science (General), Social Sciences, Sociology, Theology
ISBN Prefix(es): 88-222
Number of titles published annually: 150 Print
Total Titles: 3,000 Print

**Organizzazioni Speciali SRL**, see OS (Organizzazioni Speciali SRL)

**Edizioni Orientalia Christiana**, see Pontificio Istituto Orientale

**Ortelio**, *imprint of* Edizioni Cartografiche Milanesi

**OS (Organizzazioni Speciali SRL)+**
Via Sarpi, 7a, 50136 Florence
*Tel:* (055) 6236501 *Fax:* (055) 669446
*Telex:* 571438
Founded: 1950
Membership(s): Giunti Publishing Group.
Subjects: Psychology, Psychiatry
ISBN Prefix(es): 88-09
*Associate Companies:* O S Consulting
*Branch Office(s)*
Milan
Ripa Porta Ticinese
*Showroom(s):* Via Campo nell'Elba, 27 Rome

**Osanna Venosa+**
Via Appia 3 a, 85029 Venosa, Potenza
*Tel:* (0972) 35952 *Fax:* (0972) 35723
*E-mail:* osanna@osannaedizioni.it
*Web Site:* www.osannaedizioni.it
*Key Personnel*
Editorial Dir: Antonio Vaccaro
Subjects: Archaeology, History, Literature, Literary Criticism, Essays
ISBN Prefix(es): 88-8167

**Maria Pacini Fazzi Editore**
Via dell'Angelo Custode, 33, 55100 Lucca
Mailing Address: CP 394, 55100 Lucca
*Tel:* (0583) 440188 *Fax:* (0583) 464656
*E-mail:* mpf@pacinifazzi.it
*Web Site:* www.pacinifazzi.it
*Key Personnel*
President: Maria Pacini Fazzi
Vice President: Giovan Pio Moretti
Editorial Dir: Francesca Fazzi
Founded: 1966
Subjects: Art, Cookery, Drama, Theater, History, Literature, Literary Criticism, Essays, Philosophy, Social Sciences, Sociology
ISBN Prefix(es): 88-7246

**Pagano Editore+**
Piazza San Domenico Maggiore 9, 80134 Naples
*Tel:* (081) 5642968 *Fax:* (081) 5646694
*E-mail:* redazione@paganoeditore.com
*Key Personnel*
Man Dir: Flavio Pagano
Founded: 1985
Subjects: History, Literature, Literary Criticism, Essays, Music, Dance
ISBN Prefix(es): 88-85228
*Parent Company:* Edipica
Imprints: Nugae, Interli Nee, Libri Di Bron, Cuccioli
Subsidiaries: Vox Neapolis
Divisions: Scompaginate

**Paideia Editrice+**
Via A Manzoni 20, 25020 Flero (Brescia)
*Tel:* (030) 3582434 *Fax:* (030) 3582691
*E-mail:* paideiaeditrice@tin.it
*Key Personnel*
Man Dir: Prof Giuseppe Scarpat, PhD
Editorial: Dr Marco Scarpat
Founded: 1945
Subjects: Art, Asian Studies, Biblical Studies, Music, Dance, Philosophy, Poetry, Religion - Catholic, Religion - Jewish, Religion - Protestant, Religion - Other
ISBN Prefix(es): 88-394

**Palatina Editrice**
Borgo Tommasini 9/A, 43100 Parma
*Tel:* (0521) 282388 *Fax:* (0521) 282388
*Web Site:* culturitalia.uibk.ac.at
*Key Personnel*
Chief Executive: Carlotta Capacchi
Editorial: Guglielmo Capacchi
Founded: 1965
Subjects: Art, Genealogy, History, Language Arts,
Linguistics, Literature, Literary Criticism, Es-
says, Music, Dance, Regional Interests, Reli-
gion - Other, Travel
Number of titles published annually: 9 Print
Total Titles: 37 Print
*Bookshop(s):* Libreria Palatina Editrice, Borgo
Tommasini 9/A, Parma 43100 *Tel:* (0521)
282388 *Fax:* (0521) 282388

**Fratelli Palombi SRL**
Via dei Gracchi 181-185, 00192 Rome
*Tel:* (06) 3214150 *Fax:* (06) 3214752
*E-mail:* flli.palombi@mail.stm.it
*Key Personnel*
Man Dir: Dr Mario Palombi
Founded: 1914
Subjects: Art, History, Regional Interests
ISBN Prefix(es): 88-7621
Subsidiaries: Organizzazione Rab (sales)

**G B Palumbo & C Editore SpA+**
Via Ricasoli 59, 90139 Palermo
*Tel:* (091) 588850 *Fax:* (091) 6111848
*E-mail:* redazione@palumboeditore.it
*Web Site:* www.palumboeditore.it
*Key Personnel*
President: Giorgio Palumbo
Founded: 1939
Subjects: Language Arts, Linguistics, Literature,
Literary Criticism, Essays
ISBN Prefix(es): 88-8020
*Warehouse:* Via Maggiore G Galliano 17,
Palermo

**Franco Cosimo Panini Editore**
Viale Corassori, 24, 41100 Modena
*Tel:* (059) 343572 *Fax:* (059 )344274
*E-mail:* info@fcp.it
*Web Site:* www.fcp.it; www.francopanini.com
*Key Personnel*
Chairman: Franco Panini
Man Dir: Dr Enrico Berardi
Editorial Dir: Dr Ermanno Mammarella
Founded: 1960 ((1st book published in 1978))
Subjects: Archaeology, Architecture & Interior
Design, Art, Crafts, Games, Hobbies, Educa-
tion, History, Literature, Literary Criticism,
Essays, Poetry, Regional Interests, Sports, Ath-
letics
ISBN Prefix(es): 88-7686; 88-248; 88-8290

**Editoriale Paradigma**, *imprint of* D'Anna

**Paramond™**, *imprint of* Paravia Bruno
Mondadori Editori

**Paravia™**, *imprint of* Paravia Bruno Mondadori
Editori

**Paravia Bruno Mondadori Editori+**
Subsidiary of Edizioni Bruno Mondadori
Via Archimede 10/23/27/51, Corso Trapani 16
10139 Torino, 20129 Milan
*Tel:* (02) 748231 *Fax:* (02) 74823362
*Web Site:* www.paravia.it; www.
paramond.it; langedizoni.it;
edizioniscolastichebrunomondadori.it
*Key Personnel*
Chairman: Marco Galateri
General Manager: Agostino Cattaneo
Man Dir: Roberto Gulli; T U Paravia

Editorial Dir: R Formento; A Fresco; M Garena;
Paola Rosci; Emilio Zanette
Founded: 1998
Membership(s): AIE member Publisher Educa-
tional.
Subjects: Biological Sciences, Earth Sciences,
Education, English as a Second Language, Ge-
ography, Geology, History, Literature, Literary
Criticism, Essays, Mathematics, Philosophy
ISBN Prefix(es): 88-424
Total Titles: 200 Print
*Associate Companies:* Edizioni Electa-Bruno
Mondadori
Imprints: Archimede Edizioni™; Elmedi™; Lang
Edizioni™; Bruno Mondadori™; Edizioni Sco-
lastiche Bruno Mondadori™; Paramond™; Par-
avia™
Distributor for Edizioni Electa-Bruno Mondadori

**G B Paravia & C SpA**
Corso Trapani 16, 10139 Turin
*Tel:* (011) 7502111 *Fax:* (011) 75021510
*E-mail:* master@paravia.it
*Web Site:* www.paravia.it
*Telex:* 221652 Edito I
*Key Personnel*
Editorial: Dr Guido Gay
Founded: 1700
ISBN Prefix(es): 88-395

**Passigli Editori+**
Via Chiantigiana, 62, 50011 Antella (Florence)
*Tel:* (055) 640265 *Fax:* (055) 644627
*E-mail:* info@passiglieditori.it
*Web Site:* www.passiglieditori.it
*Key Personnel*
Man Dir: Prof Stefano Passigli
Editorial: Dr Fabrizio Dall'Aglio; Dr Luca Mer-
lini
Sales: Dr Alvise Passigli
Rights: Domitilla Baldeschi
Founded: 1981
Subjects: Biography, History, Literature, Literary
Criticism, Essays, Music, Dance, Poetry, Travel
ISBN Prefix(es): 88-368; 88-86161
Imprints: Guide del Sole; Guide del Cuore; Le
Comete
Subsidiaries: Scala, Instituto Fotografico Editori-
ale

**Patron Editore SrL+**
Via Badini 12, 40050 Quarto Inferiore (Bologna)
*Tel:* (051) 767003 *Fax:* (051) 768252
*E-mail:* info@patroneditore.com
*Web Site:* www.patroneditore.com
*Key Personnel*
General Dir: Riccardo Patron
Founded: 1925
Subjects: Agriculture, Art, Engineering (General),
History, Language Arts, Linguistics, Law, Lit-
erature, Literary Criticism, Essays, Medicine,
Nursing, Dentistry, Philosophy, Psychology,
Psychiatry, Social Sciences, Sociology
ISBN Prefix(es): 88-555
*Bookshop(s):* Libreria Internazionale Patron, Via
Zamboni 26, 40121 Bologna

**PE**, *imprint of* Pizzicato Edizioni Musicali

**Editoriale PEG**
Via Vittoria Colonna 4, 20149 Milan
*Tel:* (02) 4859181 *Fax:* (02) 485918220
*E-mail:* info@millerfreeman.it
*Telex:* 323088
*Key Personnel*
President: Solly Cohen
Administrator: Giancarlo Meani
Founded: 1950
ISBN Prefix(es): 88-7067

**Luigi Pellegrini Editore+**
Via de Rada, 67, 87100 Cosenza
*Tel:* (0984) 795065 *Fax:* (0984) 792672
*E-mail:* info@pellegrinieditore.it
*Web Site:* www.pellegrinieditore.it *Cable:*
PELLEGRINI EDITORE COSENZA
*Key Personnel*
Chief Executive, Rights & Permissions: Luigi
Pellegrini
Editorial, Sales: Walter Pellegrini
Publicity: Erminia Petramala
Founded: 1952
Subjects: Drama, Theater, Fiction, History, Litera-
ture, Literary Criticism, Essays, Poetry
ISBN Prefix(es): 88-8101
Imprints: LPE
*Branch Office(s)*
Via Rendano, 25, 87040 Castrolibero

**Il Pensiero Scientifico Editore SRL+**
Via Bradano, 3/C, 00199 Rome
*Tel:* (06) 862821 *Fax:* (06) 86282250
*E-mail:* pensiero@pensiero.it
*Web Site:* www.pensiero.it
*Key Personnel*
President: Annamaria De Feo
General Manager: Francesco De Fiore
Publicity Manager: Luciano De Fiore
Marketing & Sales Manager: Luca De Fiore
Foreign Rights: Andres De Fiore; Silvana Guida
Founded: 1946
The publishing mission is the statement of the hu-
man values as the basis of medical research &
the development of all evidence based clinical
practice.
Subjects: Education, Health, Nutrition, Psychol-
ogy, Psychiatry, Medicine, Nursing & Oncol-
ogy
ISBN Prefix(es): 88-7002
Number of titles published annually: 50 Print

**PGE**, *imprint of* Piero Gribaudi Editore

**Pheljna Edizioni d'Arte e Suggestione**
Stradale Torino 11, 10018 Pavone Canavese
(Turin)
*Tel:* (0125) 234114 *Fax:* (0125) 230085
*Key Personnel*
Editor: Ljdia Priuli
Founded: 1982
Subjects: Art, Cookery, Photography

**PIAC**, *imprint of* Pontificio Istituto di
Archeologia Cristiana

**Daniela Piazza Editore+**
Via Sanfront 13, 10138 Turin
*Tel:* (011) 434 27 06 *Fax:* (011) 434 24 71
*E-mail:* daniela.piazza@tiscalinet.it
*Web Site:* www.danielapiazzaeditore.com
*Key Personnel*
Publisher: Daniela Piazza
Founded: 1972
Subjects: Art, Biography, Cookery, History, Po-
etry, Regional Interests, Travel
ISBN Prefix(es): 88-7889

**Piccin Nuova Libraria SpA+**
Via Altinate 107, 35121 Padua
*Tel:* (049) 655566 *Fax:* (049) 8750693
*E-mail:* info@piccinonline.com
*Web Site:* www.piccinonline.com
*Key Personnel*
Man Dir, Production: Dr Massimo Piccin
Editorial & Sales: Dr Antonella Noventa
*E-mail:* a.noventa@piccinonline.com
Founded: 1980
Subjects: Biological Sciences, Law, Literature,
Literary Criticism, Essays, Medicine, Nursing,
Dentistry, Science (General)

ISBN Prefix(es): 88-299
Foreign Rep(s): Scholium International Inc
(Canada, Mexico, US)

**Piemme Junior**, *imprint of* Edizioni Piemme
SpA

**Edizioni Piemme SpA+**
Via del Carmine 5, 15033 Casale Monferrato
(AL)
*Tel:* (0142) 3361 *Fax:* (0142) 74223
*E-mail:* info@edizpiemme.it
*Web Site:* www.edizpiemme.it
*Key Personnel*
Man Dir: Pietro Marietti
Piemme Editorial: Francesca Cristoffanini
Rights & Permissions: Valeria Casonato
Press Officer: Valerie Caprioglio
Piemme Junior Editorial: Elisabetta Dami
Founded: 1982
Subjects: Biblical Studies, Cookery, Fiction, Gar-
dening, Plants, Nonfiction (General), Religion -
Catholic, Romance, Self-Help, Theology
ISBN Prefix(es): 88-384
Imprints: Battelloavapore; Piemme Junior

**Piero Lacaita Editore+**
Vico degli Albanesi, 4, 74024 Manduria (Taranto)
*Tel:* (099) 9711124 *Fax:* (099) 9711124
*Key Personnel*
Editorial Dir: Piero Lacaita
Founded: 1987
Subjects: History, Literature, Literary Criticism,
Essays
ISBN Prefix(es): 88-87280; 88-88546

**Piero Manni srl+**
Via Bixio, 11b, 73100 Lecce
*Tel:* (0832) 387057 *Fax:* (0832) 387057
*E-mail:* pieromannisrl@clio.it
*Key Personnel*
Contact: Grazia Manni; Piero Manni; Anna
Grazia D'Oria
Founded: 1983
Subjects: Human Relations, Literature, Literary
Criticism, Essays, Poetry, Social Sciences, So-
ciology
ISBN Prefix(es): 88-8176
Imprints: Manni/Lupetti; L'immaginazion

**Libreria Gozzini di Pietro e Francesco Chellini
(SNC)**
V Ricasoli 49, 50122 Florence
*Tel:* (055) 212433 *Fax:* (055) 211105
*E-mail:* gozzini@gozzini.it; info@gozzini.com
*Web Site:* www.gozzini.com
Founded: 1850
Membership(s): Socio ALAI-LILA.
Total Titles: 200 E-Book

**La Pilotta Editrice Coop RL+**
Str Universtia, 11, Via Palermo, 44, 43100 Parma
*Tel:* (0521) 771268 *Fax:* (0521) 771268
*Key Personnel*
President: Maria Pia Luchini
Editorial: Cesare Maccari
Founded: 1978
Subjects: Fiction, Literature, Literary Criticism,
Essays, Poetry
*Parent Company:* Cemcasa Editrice Maccari

**Francesco Pirella Editore+**
Via Casaregis 51, 16129 Genoa
*Tel:* (010) 363628 *Fax:* (010) 1782281081
*Web Site:* www.pirella.net
*Key Personnel*
Man Dir: Francesco Pirella
Founded: 1972
ISBN Prefix(es): 88-85514
*Orders to:* Serena Libri, Via Monte Zovetto 23 R,
16145 Genoa

**Pitagora Editrice SRL+**
Via del Legatore 3, 40138 Bologna
*Tel:* (051) 530003 *Fax:* (051) 535301
*E-mail:* pited@pitagoragroup.it
*Web Site:* www.pitagoragroup.it
*Key Personnel*
Chief Executive: Franco Stignani
Editorial: Mauro Bovini
Sales: Adolfo Francioni
Publicity: Antonella Valzania
Founded: 1958
Subjects: Engineering (General), Environmental
Studies, Geography, Geology, Language Arts,
Linguistics, Mathematics, Technology
ISBN Prefix(es): 88-371
Number of titles published annually: 60 Print
Total Titles: 900 Print
*Associate Companies:* Tecnoprint S N C, Via del
Legatore 3, 40138 Bologna *Tel:* (051) 531159
*Fax:* (051) 535301
*Bookshop(s):* Via Saragozza 112, 40136 Bologna;
Via Zamboni 57, 40126 Bologna

**Amilcare Pizzi SpA+**
Via Pizzi, 14, 20092 Cinisello Balsamo, Milan
*Tel:* (02) 618361 *Fax:* (02) 61836283
*Key Personnel*
Chief Executive: Massimo Pizzi *E-mail:* massimo.
pizzi@amilcarepizzi.it
Founded: 1914
Subjects: Art
*Associate Companies:* American Pizzi Offset Co,
370 Lexington Ave, Suite 505, New York, NY
10017, United States
Subsidiaries: Silvana Editoriale SpA

**Pizzicato Edizioni Musicali**
Via del Padule 23/E, 50018 Scandicci
*Tel:* (0432) 45288 *Fax:* (0432) 45288
*Web Site:* www.pizzicato.ch
*Key Personnel*
President: Anna Maria Fasano
Editor: Bruno Rossi
Founded: 1985
Subjects: Biography, Ethnicity, Music, Dance
ISBN Prefix(es): 88-7736; 88-7636
Imprints: N; PE; PVH

**Plurigraf SPA**
Via Cairoli, 18a, 50131 Florence
*Tel:* (05) 5576841 *Fax:* (05) 55000766
*E-mail:* plurigraf@tiscalinet.it
*Key Personnel*
President: Mr Mario Previsani
Founded: 1972
Subjects: Travel
ISBN Prefix(es): 88-7280

**Il Polifilo**
Via Borgonuovo, 2, 20121 Milan
*Tel:* (02) 6551549 *Fax:* (02) 6598045
ISBN Prefix(es): 88-7050

**Istituto Poligrafico e Zecca dello Stato+**
Piazza Verdi, 10, 00198 Rome
*Tel:* (06) 85081 *Toll Free Tel:* 800-864035
*Fax:* (06) 85082517
*E-mail:* infoipzs@ipzs.it
*Web Site:* www.ipzs.it
*Telex:* 611008 IPZSRO
*Key Personnel*
Dir: Salvatore Ficaio
Founded: 1928
State Publishing House & Italian State Stationery
Office.
Subjects: Art, Government, Political Science,
Language Arts, Linguistics, Law, Literature,
Literary Criticism, Essays
ISBN Prefix(es): 88-240
Subsidiaries: Editalia SpA

**Il Poligrafo**
Turazza 19, 35128 Padova
*Tel:* (049) 776986 *Fax:* (049) 775328
*Key Personnel*
Contact: Chiara Finesso
Founded: 1987
Subjects: History, Literature, Literary Criticism,
Essays, Philosophy, Psychology, Psychiatry,
Regional Interests, Science (General)
ISBN Prefix(es): 88-7115

**Il Pomerio**
Via Della Costa N, 4, 26900 Lodi
*Tel:* (0371) 420381 *Fax:* (0371) 422080
*Web Site:* www.ilpomerio.com
*Key Personnel*
Contact: Andrea Schiavi
Founded: 1994
Subjects: Architecture & Interior Design, Art,
History
ISBN Prefix(es): 88-7121

**Pontificio Istituto di Archeologia Cristiana**
Via Napoleone III 1, 00185 Rome
*Tel:* (06) 4465574; (06) 4453169 *Fax:* (06)
4469197
*E-mail:* piac@piac.it
*Web Site:* www.piac.it
*Key Personnel*
Rector: Prof Philippe Pergola
Library Dir: Dr Giorgio Nestori
Founded: 1925
Subjects: Archaeology, History, Religion - Other,
Christianity-last Roman painting, sculpture,
mosaics; epigraphy
ISBN Prefix(es): 88-85991
Imprints: PIAC

**Pontificio Istituto Orientale** (Pontifical Oriental
Institute)
Piazza Santa Maria Maggiore 7, 00185 Rome
*Tel:* (06) 447417104 *Fax:* (06) 4465576
*Web Site:* www.pio.urbe.it
*Key Personnel*
General Dir: Jaroslaw Dziewicki
*E-mail:* jdziewi@tin.it
Founded: 1923
Subjects: Antiques, Archaeology, Art, Asian Stud-
ies, Biblical Studies, Religion - Catholic, Reli-
gion - Other
ISBN Prefix(es): 88-7210

**Neri Pozza Editore+**
Contra Oratorio dei Servi, 21, 36100 Vicenza
*Tel:* (0444) 320787; (0444) 323036 *Fax:* (0444)
324613
*Web Site:* www.neripozza.it
*Key Personnel*
President: Vittorio Mincato
Man Dir: Alexander Zelger
Founded: 1946
Subjects: Art, History, Literature, Literary Criti-
cism, Essays
ISBN Prefix(es): 88-7305
*Parent Company:* Longanesi & C
Subsidiaries: Athesis, Longanesi, GdP

**Edizioni Luigi Pozzi SRL+**
Via Panama, 68, 00198 Rome
*Tel:* (06) 8553548 *Fax:* (06) 8554105
*E-mail:* edizioni_pozzi@tin.it
*Key Personnel*
Chief Executive: Luigi Pozzi
Editorial: Maurizio Pozzi
Founded: 1893
Subjects: Medicine, Nursing, Dentistry
ISBN Prefix(es): 88-7025
Number of titles published annually: 15 Print

**Primavera**, see Giunti Gruppo Editoriale

**Edizioni Primavera SRL+**
Via Bolognese, 165, 50139 Florence
*Tel:* (055) 50621 *Fax:* (055) 5062298
*E-mail:* d.bascialfarei@giunti.it
*Key Personnel*
President: Bruno Piazzesi
Editor: Roberto Cappello
Founded: 1981
Subjects: Travel
ISBN Prefix(es): 88-09
Imprints: Edizioni Quadrifoglio
*Orders to:* Giunti Marzocco, Via V Gioberti 34,
    50121 Florence

**Principato+**
Via Fauche 10, 20154 Milan
*Tel:* (02) 312025 *Fax:* (02) 33104295
*E-mail:* princi.red@comm2000.it
*Key Personnel*
Advisory Delegate: G Potesta
Publishing & Editorial Dir: Franco Menin
Founded: 1926
Subjects: Chemistry, Chemical Engineering, Earth
    Sciences, English as a Second Language, Ge-
    ography, Geology, History, Literature, Literary
    Criticism, Essays, Mathematics, Physics
ISBN Prefix(es): 88-416

**Prismi - Editrice Politecnica**
Via Caracciolo, 13, 80122 Naples
*Tel:* (081) 7612884 *Fax:* (081) 668339
ISBN Prefix(es): 88-7065

**Priuli e Verlucca, Editori+**
Stradale Torino, 11, 10018 Pavone Canavese
    (Turin)
*Tel:* (0125) 23 99 29 *Fax:* (0125) 23 00 85
*E-mail:* info@priulieverlucca.it
*Web Site:* www.priulieverlucca.it
*Key Personnel*
Chairman: Gherardo Priuli
Founded: 1971
Subjects: Anthropology, Antiques, Art, Cookery,
    Environmental Studies, Ethnicity, Photography,
    Regional Interests, Travel
ISBN Prefix(es): 88-8068

**Psicologica Editrice+**
Viale dele Medaglie, d'Oro, 428, 00136 Rome
*Tel:* (06) 35453558 *Fax:* (06) 35341466
*E-mail:* ontonet@tin.it
Subjects: Art, Economics, Education, Philoso-
    phy, Psychology, Psychiatry, Science (General),
    Women's Studies, Ontopsychology
ISBN Prefix(es): 88-86766
Number of titles published annually: 5 Print
Total Titles: 60 Print

**Il Punto D Incontro+**
Via Zamenhof, 685, 36100 Vicenza
*Tel:* (0444) 239189 *Fax:* (0444) 239266
*E-mail:* ordini@edizionilpuntodincontro.it
*Web Site:* www.edizionilpuntodincontro.it
*Key Personnel*
International Rights: Christina Levi; Patrizia
    Saterini
Contact: Sergio Peterlini
Specialize in books intended to sustain life's
    deepest foundations.
Subjects: Alternative, Astrology, Occult, Health,
    Nutrition, Philosophy, Religion - Buddhist, Re-
    ligion - Hindu, Self-Help
ISBN Prefix(es): 88-8093

**PVH**, *imprint of* Pizzicato Edizioni Musicali

**Il Quadrante SRL**
Via Morgioni, 48, 80077 Ischia (Na)
*Tel:* (081) 991433 *Fax:* (081) 981672
*E-mail:* info@ilquadrante.com
*Web Site:* www.ilquadrante.com

*Key Personnel*
Man Dir: Franco Di Costanzo
    *E-mail:* fdicostanzo@ilquadrante.com; Michele
    Lacono *E-mail:* miacono@ilquadrante.com
Sales: Grazia Angelini
Publicity: Marcella Longo
Rights & Permissions: Simonetta Violi
Founded: 1980
Subjects: Art, Biography, Fiction, Literature, Lit-
    erary Criticism, Essays
ISBN Prefix(es): 88-381
*Associate Companies:* Edizioni Studio Tesi SRL
Subsidiaries: Mostre e Musei SRL

**Edizioni Quadrifoglio,** *imprint of* Edizioni
    Primavera SRL

**Edizioni Quasar di Severino Tognon SRL+**
Via Ajaccio 43, 00198 Rome
*Tel:* (06) 84241993; (06) 85358444 *Fax:* (06)
    85833591
*E-mail:* qn@edizioniquasar.it
*Web Site:* www.edizioniquasar.it
*Key Personnel*
Contact: Stesso Indirizzo
Founded: 1972
Subjects: Archaeology, Art, History, Poetry,
    Travel
ISBN Prefix(es): 88-7097; 88-7140; 88-85086
Imprints: EQ
*Bookshop(s):* Libreria Archeologica Srl, Via
    Palermo 23, 00184 Rome *Tel:* (06) 4828504

**Edizioni Quattroventi SNC+**
Piazza Rinascimento 4, 61029 Urbino PU
*Tel:* (0722) 2588 *Fax:* (0722) 320998
*E-mail:* info@edizioniquattroventi.it
*Web Site:* www.edizioniquattroventi.it
*Key Personnel*
Man Dir, Editorial: Anna Veronesi
Sales, Production: Giorgio Balestrieri
Founded: 1981
Subjects: Archaeology, Art, History, Literature,
    Literary Criticism, Essays, Philosophy, Sports,
    Athletics
ISBN Prefix(es): 88-392
*Bookshop(s):* Libreria La Goliardica, Piazza Ri-
    nascimento 7, 61029 Urbino PS

**Editrice Queriniana+**
Via Ferri, 75, 25123 Brescia
*Tel:* (030) 2306925 *Fax:* (030) 2306932
*E-mail:* direzione@queriniana.it; redazione@
    queriniana.it
*Web Site:* www.queriniana.it
*Key Personnel*
Man Dir: Rosino Gibellini
Sales & Advertising: Mario de Risio
Rights & Permissions: Giordana Maranesi
Founded: 1965
Subjects: Biblical Studies, Philosophy, Religion -
    Catholic, Religion - Other, Theology
ISBN Prefix(es): 88-399

**Quesire SRL**
Via Ovidio 20, 00192 Rome
*Tel:* (06) 68136068 *Fax:* (06) 68134167
*E-mail:* ristucciad@quesire.it
*Web Site:* www.ristucciaadvisors.com
*Key Personnel*
President: Sergio Ristuccia
ISBN Prefix(es): 88-391

**Queste Istituzioni Ricerche,** see Quesire SRL

**Aldo Quinti,** see Officina Edizioni di Aldo
    Quinti

**Edition Raetia Srl-GmbH+**
23 Via Grappoli, 39100 Bolzano

*Tel:* (0471) 976904 *Fax:* (0471) 976908
*E-mail:* info@raetia.com
*Web Site:* www.raetia.com
Subjects: Art, Government, Political Science, His-
    tory, Humor, Photography, Regional Interests
ISBN Prefix(es): 88-7283

**RAI-ERI+**
Viale Mazzini 14, 00195 Rome
*Tel:* (06) 36864418 *Fax:* (06) 36822071
*E-mail:* rai-eri@rai.it
*Web Site:* www.eri.rai.it *Cable:* EDRAD TURIN
    06/37513749
*Key Personnel*
Dir General: Dr Guiseppe Marchetti Tricamo
    *Fax:* (06) 36822072
Founded: 1949
Membership(s): AIE-FEIG.
Subjects: Art, Communications, Fiction, Film,
    Video, Journalism, Nonfiction (General), Radio,
    TV, Social Sciences, Sociology
ISBN Prefix(es): 88-397
*Parent Company:* RAI Radiotelevisione Italiana
*Associate Companies:* Raitrade, Via U Novaro
    18, 00195 Rome; Sipra, Via Bertola 34, Turin;
    Telespazio, Via Alberto Bergamini 50, Rome

**Edizioni RAI Radiotelevisione Italiano SpA,**
    see RAI-ERI

**Rara Istituto Editoriale di Bibliofilia e
    Reprints**
Via Monti, 8, 20123 Milan
*Tel:* (02) 4983264 *Fax:* (02) 4814676
Founded: 1990
Subjects: Cookery, History, Literature, Literary
    Criticism, Essays, Medicine, Nursing, Den-
    tistry, Technology
ISBN Prefix(es): 88-7270

**RCS Libri SpA+**
Via Mecenate 91, 20138 Milan
*Tel:* (02) 50951 *Fax:* (02) 5065361
*Web Site:* www.rcslibri.it
*Telex:* 311321 Fabbri I *Cable:* LIBRIFABBRI
    MILAN
*Key Personnel*
Man Dir: Gianni Vallardi
International Dir of Coeditions: Massimo
    Rondinelli *Tel:* (02) 50952420 *Fax:* (02)
    50952311 *E-mail:* massimo.rondinelli@rcs.it
Rights: Giovanna Canton *Tel:* (02) 50952288
    *Fax:* (02) 50952288 *E-mail:* giovanna.canton@
    zcs.it
Founded: 1945
Other members of the group are Rizzoli, Bom-
    piani, Fabbri, Sonzogno.
Subjects: Art, Business, Crafts, Games, Hobbies,
    History, Medicine, Nursing, Dentistry, Music,
    Dance, Outdoor Recreation, Science (General)
ISBN Prefix(es): 88-17; 88-451; 88-452; 88-318;
    88-7811; 88-486
*Parent Company:* RCS Editori

**RCS Rizzoli Libri SpA**
Via Mecenate 91, 20138 Milan
*Tel:* (02) 50951 *Fax:* (02) 5065361
*Web Site:* www.rcslibri.it
*Telex:* Rizzoli 333543 *Cable:* RCS EDITORI
    SPA, MILAN
*Key Personnel*
Chairman: Dr Giorgio Fattori
Dir General: Giovanni Ungarelli
Editorial: Rosaria Carpinelli; Evaldo Violo
Marketing: Bruno Appelius
Founded: 1909
Also literary agent.
Subjects: Art, Biography, Crafts, Games, Hobbies,
    Economics, Fiction, History, Medicine, Nurs-
    ing, Dentistry, Music, Dance, Religion - Other,
    Social Sciences, Sociology

ISBN Prefix(es): 88-17; 88-451; 88-452; 88-318; 88-7811; 88-486
*Associate Companies:* Milano Libri; Sansoni Editore Nuova
Subsidiaries: Rizzoli International Publications
*Bookshop(s):* Libreria Rizzoli, Bologna, Milan, Rome, Turin

**RE**, *imprint of* Rugginenti Editore

**Red Ezizioni**, *imprint of* Red/Studio Redazionale

**Red/Studio Redazionale+**
Via Polidoro daCaravaggio, 37, 20156 Milan
*Tel:* (02) 30 241 311 *Fax:* (02) 30 241 333
*E-mail:* info@red-edizioni.it
*Web Site:* www.red-edizioni.it
*Key Personnel*
Chief Executive, Editorial: Maurizio Rosenberg Colorni
Manager Foreign Rights: Mrs Meriem Peillet
Founded: 1977
Subjects: Agriculture, Child Care & Development, Earth Sciences, Environmental Studies, Health, Nutrition, Medicine, Nursing, Dentistry, Psychology, Psychiatry, Technology
ISBN Prefix(es): 88-7031
Imprints: Red Ezizioni

**Reverdito Edizioni+**
Via G Catoni, 49, Mattarello, Trento TN 38060
*Tel:* (0461) 942285 *Fax:* (0461) 946563
*E-mail:* reverditoedizioni@virgilio.it
*Web Site:* www.culturitalia.uibk.ac.at
*Key Personnel*
Contact: Luigi Reverdito
Founded: 1990
Subjects: Cookery, Health, Nutrition, History, Literature, Literary Criticism, Essays, Parapsychology, Poetry, Religion - Catholic
ISBN Prefix(es): 88-7978
Number of titles published annually: 4 Print
Total Titles: 130 Print

**Franco Maria Ricci Editore (FMR)**
Via Montecuccoli 32, 20147 Milan
*Tel:* (02) 414101 *Fax:* (02) 48301473
*E-mail:* ricci@fmrmagazine.it
*Web Site:* www.fmrspa.it
*Key Personnel*
Publisher: Franco Maria Ricci
Contact: Pietro Ruffini *Tel:* (02) 41410354
    *E-mail:* ruffini@frmmagazine.it
Founded: 1965
Subjects: Art
ISBN Prefix(es): 88-216
Number of titles published annually: 30 Print
*Bookshop(s):* Librerie Ricci
*Book Club(s):* Club dei Bibliofili; Collectors Club of Franco Maria Ricci

**Riccardo Ricciardi Editore SpA**
Via Biancamano, 2, 10121 Turin
*Tel:* (01) 156561
*Web Site:* www.mondadori.it
*Key Personnel*
President: Prof Gian Arturo Ferrari
Founded: 1907
Subjects: History, Language Arts, Linguistics, Literature, Literary Criticism, Essays, Philosophy, Poetry
ISBN Prefix(es): 88-7817
*Parent Company:* Arnoldo Mondadori Editore SpA
Distributed by Arnoldo Mondadori Editore SpA

**Edizioni del Riccio SAS di G Bernardi+**
Via Lungagnana 30, 50025 Montespertoli (Florence)
*Tel:* (0571) 609338 *Fax:* (055) 716362

*Key Personnel*
Chief Executive: Giuliano Bernardi
Founded: 1977
Subjects: Cookery, Medicine, Nursing, Dentistry, Psychology, Psychiatry, Travel
ISBN Prefix(es): 88-7099
Number of titles published annually: 8 Print

**Edizioni Ripostes+**
Via Lungomare Colombo, 225, 84129 Salerno
*Tel:* (089) 336049 *Fax:* (089) 336049
*Web Site:* web.tiscali.it/ripostes
*Key Personnel*
Man Dir, Sales: Alessandro Tesauro
Editorial: Marco Amendolara; Serafina Bartoli; Elvira Spena
Founded: 1981
Subjects: Architecture & Interior Design, Art, History, Literature, Literary Criticism, Essays, Philosophy, Photography, Poetry, Psychology, Psychiatry
ISBN Prefix(es): 88-86819
Imprints: Alessandro Tesauro Editore
*Branch Office(s)*
Viale delle Tamerici 4, 84100 Salerno
*Warehouse:* Viale delle Tamerici, 4-89100 Salerno

**RIREA**, *imprint of* Rirea Casa Editrice della Rivista Italiana di Ragioneria e di Economia Aziendale

**Rirea Casa Editrice della Rivista Italiana di Ragioneria e di Economia Aziendale+**
Via delle Isole 30, 00198 Rome
*Tel:* (06) 8417690 *Fax:* (06) 8845732
*E-mail:* rirea_@infinito.it
*Key Personnel*
Dir: Dr Giovanna Nobile
Founded: 1901
Subjects: Accounting, Economics, Management
ISBN Prefix(es): 88-85333
Number of titles published annually: 20 Print
Imprints: RIREA

**Editori Riuniti+**
Via Alberico II, 33, 00193 Rome
*Tel:* (06) 68801021 *Fax:* (06) 68392028
*E-mail:* ufficio.stampa@editoririuniti.it
*Web Site:* www.editoririuniti.it
*Key Personnel*
Man Dir: Motarianni Michelangelo
Sales Dir, Publicity: Claudio Capotosti
Rights & Permissions: Ombretta Borgia
Founded: 1953
Subjects: Art, Economics, Education, Fiction, Government, Political Science, History, Language Arts, Linguistics, Law, Literature, Literary Criticism, Essays, Philosophy, Psychology, Psychiatry, Science (General), Social Sciences, Sociology
ISBN Prefix(es): 88-359
Imprints: ER

**Laurus Robuffo Edizioni**
Via della Macchiarella 146, 00119 Rome
*Tel:* (06) 5651492 *Fax:* (06) 5651233
*E-mail:* post@laurusrobuffo.it
*Web Site:* www.laurusrobuffo.it
*Key Personnel*
Chief Executive: Mario Robuffo
Founded: 1973
Subjects: Law
ISBN Prefix(es): 88-8087
*Associate Companies:* Edizioni FAG Srl, Via Garibaldi 5, 20090 Assago MI; NDM SRL, Via E Toti, 69/be, 70125 Bari; Epidromo SRL, Via Selva di Pescarola 6/6, 40131 Bologna; Giampaolo Fornasiero, Via Guido Rossa 2, 60020 Candia AN; Tecnolibri srl, Via Pratesi 217, 50145 Florence; Libraria Ligure, Via Luigi Conepa, 11, 1, 16165 Geneva; Alfe snc, Via

Stefano Breda 24/26, 35010 Limena PD; DLC snc, Via Nazionale Delle Puglie 200/a 105, 80026 Napoli Arpino Casoria; Libraria Distribuzioni snc, Via Olbia 33, 08100 Nuoro; M M Distribuzione Libraria Di C Marinaci & C snc, 90145 Palermo; Distributrice; Libraria Laziales srl, Via di Tor Florence, 27 00199 Roma
*Bookshop(s):* Libreria Laurus Robuffo, Via S Martino delle Battaglia 35, 00185 Rome

**Libreria Editrice Rogate (LER)+**
Via dei Rogazionisti 8, 00182 Rome
*Tel:* (06) 7023430 *Fax:* (06) 7020767 *Cable:* ROGATE ROGAZIONISTI ROME
*Key Personnel*
Editorial: Vito Magno
Publicity: Nunzio Spinelli
Founded: 1976
Subjects: Religion - Other, Theology
ISBN Prefix(es): 88-8075

**Edizioni Universitarie Romane**
Via Michelangelo Poggioli 3, 00161 Rome
*Tel:* (06) 491503; (06) 4940658 *Fax:* (06) 4453438
*E-mail:* eur@eurom.it
*Web Site:* www.eurom.it
*Key Personnel*
Contact: Gian Vittorio Pallai
Founded: 1974
Subjects: Biological Sciences, Business, Chemistry, Chemical Engineering, Human Relations, Mathematics, Medicine, Nursing, Dentistry, Psychology, Psychiatry, Science (General), Social Sciences, Sociology
ISBN Prefix(es): 88-7730
Imprints: EUR

**Rosenberg e Sellier Editori in Torino**
Via Doria 14, 10123 Turin
*Tel:* (011) 8127820 *Fax:* (011) 8127808
*E-mail:* info@rosenbergesellier.it
*Web Site:* www.rosenbergesellier.it *Cable:* ROSENBERG SELLIER
*Key Personnel*
Man Dir: Katie Roggero
Sales, Marketing: Teresa Silletti
Production: Ada Lanteri
Founded: 1883
Subjects: Language Arts, Linguistics, Philosophy, Social Sciences, Sociology, Women's Studies
ISBN Prefix(es): 88-7011
*Associate Companies:* Rosenberg e Sellier Libreria Pera Documentazione Scientifica

**Rossato+**
Via Bella Venezia, 13/C, 36074 Novale di Valdagno (Vicenza)
*Tel:* (0455) 411000 *Fax:* (0455) 411550
*E-mail:* grossato@didanet.it
*Key Personnel*
Contact: Gino Rossato; Vania Rossato
Membership(s): AIE.
Subjects: History, Military Science, Travel
ISBN Prefix(es): 88-8130

**Rubbettino Editore+**
Viale Rosario Rubbettino, 8, 88049 Soveria Mannelli (CZ)
*Tel:* (0968) 662034 *Fax:* (0968) 662035
*E-mail:* info@rubbettino.it
*Web Site:* www.rubbettino.it *Cable:* RUBBETTINO SOVERIA MANNELLI
*Key Personnel*
President: Florindo Rubbettino
Editorial Dir: Giacinto Marra
Editorial: Angela Cimino; Gabriella Grandinetti
Sales: Antonio Colosino
Founded: 1972
Subjects: Anthropology, Art, Drama, Theater, Economics, Government, Political Science, History, Law, Literature, Literary Criticism, Es-

says, Philosophy, Poetry, Public Administration, Religion - Other, Romance, Social Sciences, Sociology, Theology, Women's Studies
ISBN Prefix(es): 88-7284; 88-498
*Parent Company:* Rubbettino SRL
*Associate Companies:* Calabria Letteraria Editrice
E-mail: cle@rubbettino.it

**Rugginenti Editore+**
Via Dei Fontanili 3, 20141 Milan
*Tel:* (02) 89501283 *Fax:* (02) 89531273
*E-mail:* info@rugginenti.com
*Web Site:* www.rugginenti.com
*Key Personnel*
Editor: Gianni Rugginenti
Founded: 1968
Subjects: Music, Dance
ISBN Prefix(es): 88-7665
Total Titles: 40 Audio
Imprints: RE

**Rusconi Libri Srl+**
via del Progresso, 21, 47822 Santarcangelo di Romagna
*Tel:* (05) 41326306 *Fax:* (05) 41392344
*E-mail:* relazioniesterne@rusconi.it
*Telex:* 312233 *Cable:* RUSCONI EDITORE MILANO
*Key Personnel*
Editorial Dir: Alberto Conforti
Chief Editor: Pieranna Pagan
Sales: Marco Mattio
Foreign Rights: Olivia Olivieri
Founded: 1968
Subjects: Biography, History, Literature, Literary Criticism, Essays, Music, Dance, Nonfiction (General), Philosophy, Psychology, Psychiatry, Religion - Other
ISBN Prefix(es): 88-18
*Parent Company:* Rusconi Editore
*Associate Companies:* Eurolibri
*U.S. Office(s):* Rusconi Inc, 375 Park Ave, Suite 3307, New York, NY 10152, United States
*Warehouse:* Via Pacinotti, 16-20092 Cinisello Balsamo
*Orders to:* Eurolibri

**Norberto Sabatelli & C**, see Editrice Liguria SNC di Norberto Sabatelli & C

**SAGEP Libri & Comunicazione Srl**
Galleria Mazzini 1/8, 16121 Genoa
*Tel:* (010) 593355 *Fax:* (010) 581713
*E-mail:* info@sagep.it
*Web Site:* www.sagep.it
*Telex:* 281343 SAGEP I
*Key Personnel*
Publisher: Eugenio de Andreis
Sales Manager: Carla Bisacchi
Founded: 1965
Subjects: Architecture & Interior Design, Art, Economics, Ethnicity, History, Science (General), Travel
ISBN Prefix(es): 88-7058

**Il Saggiatore+**
Via Melzo 9, 20129 Milan
*Tel:* (02) 202301 *Fax:* (02) 29513061
*E-mail:* stampa@saggiatore.it
*Web Site:* www.saggiatore.it
*Key Personnel*
President: Luca Formenton
Editorial Dir: Marco Tropea
Founded: 1958
Subjects: Anthropology, Art, Asian Studies, Fiction, History, Literature, Literary Criticism, Essays, Music, Dance, Nonfiction (General), Philosophy, Poetry, Romance, Science (General), Social Sciences, Sociology
ISBN Prefix(es): 88-428; 88-515
*Associate Companies:* Marco Tropea Editore; Nuova Practiche Editrice

**Adriano Salani Editore srl+**
Corso Italia, 13, 20122 Milan
*Tel:* (028) 0206624 *Fax:* (027) 2018806
*E-mail:* info@salani.it
*Telex:* 353273 LONG I
*Key Personnel*
President: Mario Spagnol
Man Dir: Luigi Spagnol
General Manager: Stefano Maure
Editorial: Maria Grazia Mazzitelli
Sales: Giuseppe Somenzi
Production: Alfredo Bonfiglio
Publicity: Allessandra Gnecchi
Rights & Permissions: Cristina Foschini
Founded: 1862
Subjects: Fiction
ISBN Prefix(es): 88-7782; 88-8451
*Parent Company:* Longanesi & C
*Subsidiaries:* Messaggerie Italiane
*U.S. Office(s):* Nina Collins Association, 584 Broadway, Suite 607, New York 10012, United States
*Warehouse:* Messaggerie Italiane, Magazzino Editoriale, Via Bereguardina, 20080 Casarile (Mi)
*Orders to:* Pro Libro, Florence

**Salerno Editrice SRL+**
Via Valadier 52, 00193 Rome
*Tel:* (06) 3608201 *Fax:* (06) 3223132
*E-mail:* info@salernoeditrice.it
*Web Site:* www.salernoeditrice.it
*Key Personnel*
Chief Executive: Prof Enrico Malato
Founded: 1972
Subjects: Biography, Fiction, History, Language Arts, Linguistics, Literature, Literary Criticism, Essays, Social Sciences, Sociology, Italian Literature & Historic Studies
ISBN Prefix(es): 88-85026; 88-8402
Number of titles published annually: 40 Print
*Warehouse:* Viale dei Colli Portuensi, 591, Rome 00151 *Tel:* (06) 55266684

**Samaya SRL**
Localita Lu Cupuneddu, 07028 Teresa di Gallura (Sassari)
*Tel:* (0789) 750039 *Fax:* (0789) 750081
*E-mail:* info@benesseresardegna.com
*Key Personnel*
President: Milvia Pagan
Founded: 1980
Subjects: Child Care & Development, Health, Nutrition
ISBN Prefix(es): 88-85302

**Editoriale San Giusto SRL Edizioni Parnaso**
Via Coroneo 5, 34133 Trieste
*Tel:* (040) 370200 *Fax:* (040) 3728970
*E-mail:* info@edizioniparnaso.it
*Web Site:* www.edizioniparnaso.it
Subjects: Literature, Literary Criticism, Essays, Philosophy
ISBN Prefix(es): 88-86474
Number of titles published annually: 10 Print
Total Titles: 90 Print

**Edizioni San Lorenzo**
Via Gandhi 24, 42100 Reggio Emilia
*Tel:* (0522) 323140 *Fax:* (0522) 323140
*E-mail:* redazione@edizioni-sanlorenzo.it
*Web Site:* www.edizioni-sanlorenzo.it
Founded: 1985
ISBN Prefix(es): 88-8071

**Editrice San Marco SRL+**
Via Abbadia 13, 24069 Trescore Balneario (Bergamo)
*Tel:* (035) 940178 *Fax:* (035) 944385
*E-mail:* info@editricesanmarco.it
*Web Site:* www.editricesanmarco.it

*Key Personnel*
Man Dir: Giulio Belotti
Founded: 1955
Subjects: Agriculture, Biological Sciences, Education, Energy, Government, Political Science, Labor, Industrial Relations, Marketing, Technology
ISBN Prefix(es): 88-86285

**Edizioni San Paolo SRL+**
Piazza Soncino 5, 20092 Cinisello Balsamo (Milan)
*Tel:* (02) 660751 *Fax:* (02) 66075211
*E-mail:* sanpaoloedizioni@stpauls.it
*Key Personnel*
Man Dir: Emilio Bettati
General Manager: Vincenzo Santarcangelo
Editorial: Elio Sala
Production: Angelo Zenzalari
Founded: 1914
Subjects: Art, Biography, Fiction, History, How-to, Medicine, Nursing, Dentistry, Music, Dance, Philosophy, Psychology, Psychiatry, Religion - Other
ISBN Prefix(es): 88-215
*Parent Company:* Societa San Paolo, Rome
*Subsidiaries:* DISP SRL; Multimedia San Paolo SRL; Periodici San Paolo SRL; SAIE Editrice SRL
*Warehouse:* DISP SRL, Piazza San Paolo 14, I-12051 Alba *Tel:* (0173) 361040 (Cuneo)

**Sansoni-RCS Libri+**
Division of RCS Libri Spa
Via Mecenate, 91, 20138 Milan
*Tel:* (02) 50951 *Fax:* (02) 5065361
*E-mail:* sansoni@rcs.it
Founded: 1873
Subjects: Fiction
ISBN Prefix(es): 88-383
*Associate Companies:* RCS Rizzoli Libri SpA
*Warehouse:* RCS Libri Spa, Via Mecanate 91, 20138 Milan

**Sapere 2000 SRL**
Piazza Fanti 42, 00185 Rome
*Tel:* (06) 4465363 *Fax:* (06) 4465363
*E-mail:* sapere2000@flshnet.it
*Key Personnel*
Man Dir: Angelo Ruggieri
Founded: 1976
Subjects: Architecture & Interior Design, Ethnicity, Government, Political Science, Religion - Other, Social Sciences, Sociology
ISBN Prefix(es): 88-7673

**Sardini Editrice+**
Via della Pace 37, 25046 Bornato in Franciacorta (BS)
*Tel:* (030) 7750430 *Fax:* (030) 7254348
*E-mail:* sardini@intelligenza.it
*Web Site:* www.sardini.it *Cable:* Fausto Sardini-Editore-Bornato
*Key Personnel*
Chief Executive: Fausto Sardini
Editorial: Davide Sardini
Founded: 1969
Subjects: Art, Fiction, History, Poetry, Regional Interests, Religion - Catholic, Science (General), Theology
ISBN Prefix(es): 88-7506
*Subsidiaries:* Intelligenza e Informatica SRL
*Divisions:* Informatica

**Scala Group spa**
Via Chiantigiana 62, 50011 Antella, Florence
*Tel:* (055) 623311 *Fax:* (055) 6233280
*E-mail:* info@scalagroup.com
*Web Site:* scalagroup.it
*Key Personnel*
President: Dr Alberto Milla

Vice President & Chief Executive Officer: Alvise
Passigli *E-mail:* a.passigli@scalagroup.com
Man Dir: Gianni Mancassola
Founded: 1953
Also book packager & broadband files.
Subjects: Archaeology, Art, Education, Film,
Video, Photography, Travel, Museums & Art
Guides
ISBN Prefix(es): 88-8117; 88-87090
Number of titles published annually: 10 Print; 20
CD-ROM; 5 Online
Total Titles: 100 Print; 200 CD-ROM
Subsidiaries: E-ducation.it
Distributed by Hazan (Francophone countries);
Riverside (US & Canada); Slovo (Russia)

**Lo Scarabeo Srl+**
Via Varese 15C, 10152 Turin
*Tel:* (011) 283793; (011) 283978 *Fax:* (011)
280756
*E-mail:* info@loscarabeo.com
*Web Site:* www.loscarabeo.com
*Key Personnel*
President: Pietro Alligo
Founded: 1987
Subjects: Art
ISBN Prefix(es): 88-86131

**Schena Editore+**
Viale Stazione 177, 72015 Fasano (Brindisi)
*Tel:* (080) 4414681 *Fax:* (080) 4426690
*E-mail:* info@schenaeditore.com
*Web Site:* www.schenaeditore.it
*Key Personnel*
Editor: Nunzio Schena
Founded: 1972
Subjects: Archaeology, Architecture & Interior
Design, Art, Language Arts, Linguistics, Litera-
ture, Literary Criticism, Essays
ISBN Prefix(es): 88-7514; 88-8229

**Salvatore Sciascia Editore**
Corso Umberto Iº, 111, 93100 Caltanissetta
*Tel:* (0934) 551509 *Fax:* (0934) 551366
*E-mail:* sciasciaeditore@virgilio.it *Cable:*
SCIASCIA EDITORE
*Key Personnel*
Man Dir: Quiseppe Sciascia
Editor: Salvatore Sciascia
Founded: 1946
Subjects: Art, History, Literature, Literary Criti-
cism, Essays, Poetry
ISBN Prefix(es): 88-8241
*Warehouse:* Via Pietro Leone SN, 93100 Caltanis-
setta

**Libreria Scientifica Cortina**, see Libreria
Cortina Editrice SRL

**Edizioni Scientifiche Italiane+**
Via Chiatamone 7, 80121 Naples
*Tel:* (081) 7645443 *Fax:* (081) 7646477
*E-mail:* info@esispa.com
*Key Personnel*
President: Pietro Perlingieri
Administration: Francesco De Simone
Editorial Dir: Giovanna Delfino
Founded: 1945
Subjects: Architecture & Interior Design, Art,
Cookery, Drama, Theater, Economics, Geogra-
phy, Geology, History, Law, Literature, Literary
Criticism, Essays, Medicine, Nursing, Den-
tistry, Music, Dance, Philosophy, Psychology,
Psychiatry, Science (General), Social Sciences,
Sociology, Technology
ISBN Prefix(es): 88-7104; 88-8114; 88-495
*Branch Office(s)*
Via Porta Rettori, 19, 82100 Benevento
*Tel:* (0824) 43752 *Fax:* (0824) 43666

Via F lli Bronzetti, 11, 20129 Milan *Tel:* (02)
730846 *Fax:* (02) 730849
Via dei Taurini, 27, 00185 Rome *Tel:* (06)
4462664 *Fax:* (06) 4461308

**Editoriale Scienza** (Science Publishing)+
Via Romagna 30, 34134 Trieste
*Tel:* (040) 364810 *Fax:* (040) 364909
*E-mail:* info@editscienza.it
*Web Site:* www.editscienza.it
Founded: 1990
Specialize in science books for children.
Membership(s): Associazione Aie.
Subjects: Animals, Pets, Astronomy, Biological
Sciences, Computer Science, Crafts, Games,
Hobbies, Earth Sciences, Geography, Geol-
ogy, Health, Nutrition, Mathematics, Nonfiction
(General), Physical Sciences, Science (Gen-
eral), Science Fiction, Fantasy, Technology
ISBN Prefix(es): 88-7307
Number of titles published annually: 20 Print
Imprints: ES
Distributed by Messaggerie Libri

**Casa Editrice Marietti Scuola SpA**
Str del Portone 179, 10095 Grugliasco, Turin
*Tel:* (011) 2098741; (011) 2098720 *Fax:* (011)
2098765
*E-mail:* redazione@mariettiscuola.it
*Web Site:* www.mariettiscuola.it
*Key Personnel*
Man Dir: Dr Federico Franchi
ISBN Prefix(es): 88-393

**Editrice la Scuola SpA+**
Via L Cadorna, 11, 25186 Brescia
*Tel:* (030) 29931 *Fax:* (030) 2993299
*Web Site:* www.lascuola.it *Cable:* SCUOLA
BRESCIA
*Key Personnel*
President: Dr Ing Luciano Silveri
Man Dir: Dr Ing Adolfo Lombardi
General Manager: Giuseppe Covone
Founded: 1904
Subjects: Education, Philosophy, Psychology, Psy-
chiatry, Religion - Other
ISBN Prefix(es): 88-350
*Associate Companies:* Editrice Morcelliana SpA
*Branch Office(s)*
Bari
Bologna
Milan
Naples
Padua
Pescara
Rome

**SEA**, *imprint of* Ist Patristico Augustinianum

**Edizioni Segno SRL+**
Via E Fermi, 80, 33010 Tavagnacco Udine
*Tel:* (0432) 575179 *Fax:* (0432) 575589
*E-mail:* info@edizionisegno.it
*Web Site:* www.edizionisegno.it
*Key Personnel*
Dir: Pietro Mantero *E-mail:* collaboratori@
edizionisegno.it
Founded: 1988
Subjects: Biblical Studies, Fiction, Myster-
ies, Nonfiction (General), Poetry, Religion -
Catholic, Theology, Private Revelations, Signs
of the Times Based on a Catholic Background,
Supernatural
ISBN Prefix(es): 88-7282
Number of titles published annually: 70 Print; 1
Audio
Total Titles: 400 Print; 1 Audio

**Segretariato Nazionale Apostolato della
Preghiera+**
Via degli Astalli 16, 00186 Rome

*Tel:* (06) 6976071 *Fax:* (06) 6781063
*E-mail:* adp@adp.it
*Web Site:* www.adp.it
*Key Personnel*
Administrative Dir: Massimo Taggi *Tel:* (06)
697607 Ext 202 *E-mail:* mt@adp.it
Founded: 1844
Subjects: Religion - Catholic
ISBN Prefix(es): 88-7357
Imprints: AdP

**SEI**, see Societa Editrice Internazionale (SEI)

**Sellerio Editore**
Via Siracusa, 50/2, 90141 Palermo
*Tel:* (091) 6254110 *Fax:* (091) 6258802
Founded: 1969
Subjects: Anthropology, Archaeology, Art, His-
tory, Literature, Literary Criticism, Essays,
Photography, Social Sciences, Sociology
ISBN Prefix(es): 88-7681

**Servitium**
Priorato S Egidio, 24039 Sotto il Monte (Berg-
amo)
*Tel:* (035) 4398011 *Fax:* (035) 792030
*E-mail:* servitium@spm.it
Subjects: Anthropology, Religion - Catholic, Ro-
mance, Theology, Spiritual
ISBN Prefix(es): 88-8166
Distributed by Dehoniana Libri SpA (Italy only)

**Servizio Italiano Pubblicazioni Internazionali
Srl**, see SIPI (Servizio Italiano Pubblicazioni
Internazionali) Srl

**Edizioni Dr Antonino Sfameni**, see EDAS

**Sicania+**
Via Catania 62, 98124 Messina
*Tel:* (090) 2936373 *Fax:* (090) 2932461
*Web Site:* www.sicania.me.it
*Key Personnel*
Publisher: Ugo Magno
Editorial Dir: Gianvito Resta
Editor: Giovanni Molonia
Public Relations: Caterina Pastura
Founded: 1986
Subjects: Art, Drama, Theater, History, Language
Arts, Linguistics, Literature, Literary Criticism,
Essays, Philosophy, Photography, Regional In-
terests
ISBN Prefix(es): 88-7268
Subsidiaries: Edizioni GBM

**Edizioni Librarie Siciliane+**
Via da Portella Rebuttone, 90030 Santa Cristina
Gela, Palermo
*Tel:* (091) 8570221 *Fax:* (091) 342670
*Key Personnel*
Dir General: Gaetano Mantovani
Founded: 1978
Subjects: Anthropology, Antiques, Archaeology,
Architecture & Interior Design, Art, History,
Human Relations, Natural History, Philosophy
Imprints: ELS

**Sigma**, *imprint of* Esselibri

**Silva**
Via Nazionale, 23, 43044 Collecchio (Parma)
*Tel:* (0521) 804106 *Fax:* (0521) 804406
ISBN Prefix(es): 88-7765

**Silvana Editoriale SpA+**
Via Margherita de Vizzi 86, 20092 Cinisello Bal-
samo Milan
*Tel:* (02) 618361 *Fax:* (02) 6172464
*E-mail:* international@silvanaeditoriale.it

*Web Site:* www.silvanaeditoriale.it
*Telex:* 330006 Ampiz I
*Key Personnel*
Chief Executive: Massimo Pizzi
Founded: 1953
Subjects: Architecture & Interior Design, Art, Photography
ISBN Prefix(es): 88-366; 88-8215
*Parent Company:* Amilcare Pizzi SpA
*Associate Companies:* American Pizzi Offset Co, 141 E 44 St, New York, NY 10017, United States

**Edizioni Giuridiche Simone**, *imprint of* Esselibri

**Simone per la Scuola**, *imprint of* Esselibri

**SIPI**, *imprint of* SIPI (Servizio Italiano Pubblicazioni Internazionali) Srl

**SIPI (Servizio Italiano Pubblicazioni Internazionali) Srl**
Viale Pasteur 6, 00144 Rome
*Tel:* (06) 5920509 *Fax:* (06) 5924819
*Web Site:* www.sipi.it
Founded: 1951
Subjects: Economics, Government, Political Science, Labor, Industrial Relations, Regional Interests
ISBN Prefix(es): 88-7153
Imprints: SIPI

**Sistemi Editorali**, *imprint of* Esselibri

**Societa Editrice Internazionale (SEI)+**
Corso Regina Margherita 176, 10152 Turin
*Tel:* (011) 52271 *Fax:* (011) 5211320
*Web Site:* www.seieditrice.com
*Telex:* 216216 SEI TO I *Cable:* SEI TORINO
*Key Personnel*
President: Alessandro Braja
Man Dir & General Manager: Gian Nicola Pivano
Dir, Editorial Management, Marketing & Public Relations: Alessandro Rangaioli
Founded: 1908
Subjects: Education, Geography, Geology, History, Literature, Literary Criticism, Essays, Mathematics, Philosophy, Physics, Psychology, Psychiatry, Religion - Catholic
ISBN Prefix(es): 88-05

**Societa Editrice la Goliardica Pavese SRL+**
Viale Golgi, 6, 27100 Pavia
*Tel:* (0382) 529570 *Fax:* (0382) 423140
*E-mail:* info@lagoliardicapavese.it
*Web Site:* www.lagoliardicapavese.it
*Key Personnel*
Chief Executive: Dario De Bona
Founded: 1977
Subjects: Biological Sciences, Chemistry, Chemical Engineering, Medicine, Nursing, Dentistry, Physical Sciences, Physics, Science (General)
ISBN Prefix(es): 88-7830
*Branch Office(s)*
Via Lombroso 21, Pavia *Tel:* (0382) 525709
*Bookshop(s):* Via Lombroso u 21, 27100 Pavia

**Societa Napoletana Storia Patria Napoli**
Via Marina 33, 80133 Naples
*Tel:* (081) 2536340 *Fax:* (081) 2536509
*E-mail:* snsp@unina.it
*Web Site:* www.storia.unina.it
*Key Personnel*
Dir: Prof Giovanni Muto
Subjects: History, Monographies, diplomatics & history of art
ISBN Prefix(es): 88-8044

**Societa Stampa Sportiva+**
Via Guinizelli 56, 00152 Rome

*Tel:* (06) 5817311 *Fax:* (06) 5806526
*E-mail:* segreteria@stampasportiva.com
*Web Site:* www.stampasportiva.com
*Key Personnel*
President: Francesco Paolo Palumbo
Founded: 1967
Subjects: Physical Sciences, Sports, Athletics
ISBN Prefix(es): 88-8313
Number of titles published annually: 20 Print
Total Titles: 532 Print
*Warehouse:* Via Di Villa Pamphili 33/F, 00152 Rome

**Societa Storica Catanese**
Via Etnea 248, 95131 Catania
*Tel:* (095) 434782
*Key Personnel*
Man Dir: Dr Michele D'Agata
Editorial: Giuseppe Trovato Pennisi
Sales: Francesco Romeo Giuzzetta
Production: Giovanni Assaro
Publicity: Dr Davide D'Agata
Rights & Permissions: Prof Rita Siciliano
Founded: 1955
Subjects: History, Law, Literature, Literary Criticism, Essays, Poetry, Regional Interests, Social Sciences, Sociology
Imprints: SSC

**Edizioni Rosminiane Sodalitas**
Corso Umberto I, 15, 28838 Stresa (Verbania)
*Tel:* (0323) 30091 *Fax:* (0323) 31623
*E-mail:* edizioni@rosmini.it
*Web Site:* www.rosmini.it/EdRosminiane.htm
*Key Personnel*
Publicity: Muratore Umberto
Founded: 1906
Subjects: Philosophy, Theology

**Il Sole 24 Ore Libri**
Via Lomazzo 51, 20154 Milan
*Tel:* (02) 30223944 *Fax:* (02) 3022405
*E-mail:* servizioclienti.libri@ilsole24ore.com
*Web Site:* www.ilsole24ore.com
*Telex:* 331325 I 24 Ore
*Key Personnel*
Dir General: Gianni Rizzoni
Editorial: Francesco Bogliari
Founded: 1983
Subjects: Economics, Law, Management
ISBN Prefix(es): 88-7187; 88-8363

**Il Sole 24 Ore Pirola**
Via Castellanza, 11, 20151 Milan
*Tel:* (02) 30226651 *Fax:* (02) 38011205
*E-mail:* servizio.abbonamenti@ilsole24ore.com
*Web Site:* www.ilsole24ore.com
Founded: 1781
Subjects: Architecture & Interior Design, Business, Economics, Engineering (General), Law, Management, Social Sciences, Sociology
ISBN Prefix(es): 88-324

**Soleverde**, *imprint of* Centro Scientifico Torinese

**Edizioni Sonda+**
Corso Indipendenza, 63, 15033 Casale Monferrato (Al)
*Tel:* (0142) 461516 *Fax:* (0142) 461523
*E-mail:* sonda@sonda.it
*Web Site:* www.sonda.it
*Key Personnel*
Contact: Antonio Monaco
Founded: 1988
ISBN Prefix(es): 88-7106
*Associate Companies:* Consorzio "Leonardo"; Consorzio "Omniatech"; Il Tappeto Volante srl

**Sonzogno**
Via Mecenate 91, 20138 Milan
*Tel:* (02) 50951 *Fax:* (02) 5065361

*Web Site:* www.sonzogno.rcslibri.it
*Telex:* 311321 Fabbri I *Cable:* Librifabbri Milan
*Key Personnel*
Dir: Mario Andreose
Rights & Permissions: Carla Tanzi
Founded: 1818
Membership(s): Gruppo Editoriale Fabbri, Bompiani, Sonzogno, Etas SpA.
Subjects: Fiction, Mysteries, Nonfiction (General)
ISBN Prefix(es): 88-451; 88-452; 88-454

**Sorbona+**
Via Pietravalle, 85, 80131 Naples
*Tel:* (08) 15453443 *Fax:* (08) 15464991
*Key Personnel*
Contact: Dr F Bonadei
Founded: 1981
Subjects: Chemistry, Chemical Engineering, Medicine, Nursing, Dentistry, Physics, Science (General)
ISBN Prefix(es): 88-7150

**Sperling e Kupfer Editori SpA+**
Via Durazzo, 4, 20134 Milan
*Tel:* (02) 217211 *Fax:* (02) 21721277
*Web Site:* www.sperling.it
*Key Personnel*
Chief Executive Officer: Roberto Avanzo
President: Valerio Anna Patrizia
Editorial Dir: Carla Tanzi
Rights & Permissions & Contract: Stefania Klein De Pasquale *E-mail:* sdepas@mondadori.it
Scout (US): Linda Clark
Scout (France): Zeline Guena
Scout (UK): Ros Ramsay
Founded: 1899
Subjects: Biography, Economics, Fiction, Health, Nutrition, How-to, Management, Nonfiction (General), Science (General), Sports, Athletics, Travel
ISBN Prefix(es): 88-200; 88-86845; 88-87592; 88-7339
*Parent Company:* Mondadori
*Subsidiaries:* Edizioni Frassinelli SRL
*U.S. Office(s):* 28 E 57 St, 7th Floor, New York, NY 10022, United States (scout office)

**Spirali Edizioni+**
Via Fratelli Gabba 3, 20121 Milan
*Tel:* (02) 8054417; (02) 8053602 *Fax:* (02) 8692631
*E-mail:* redazione@spirali.com
*Web Site:* www.spirali.it; www.spirali.com
*Key Personnel*
President: Armando Verdiglione
Man Dir: Cristina Frua De Angeli
Editorial: Annalisa Scallo
Founded: 1978
Subjects: Art, Law, Literature, Literary Criticism, Essays, Music, Dance, Philosophy, Poetry, Psychology, Psychiatry
ISBN Prefix(es): 88-7770
Number of titles published annually: 10 Print

**SSC**, *imprint of* Societa Storica Catanese

**Stampa Alternativa - Nuovi Equilibri+**
Strada Tuscanese Km 4, 800, 01100 Viterbo
*Tel:* (0761) 352277; (0761) 353485 *Fax:* (0761) 352751
*E-mail:* nuovi.equilibri@agora.it
*Web Site:* www.stampalternativa.it
*Key Personnel*
Man Dir, Editorial: Marcello Baraghini
Sales: Angelo Leone
Founded: 1971
Subjects: Art, Health, Nutrition, Literature, Literary Criticism, Essays, Medicine, Nursing, Dentistry, Music, Dance
ISBN Prefix(es): 88-7226

Imprints: Cartoonseries; Fiabesca; Jazz People; L'eta D'oro Dell Illustrazione
*Orders to:* Nuovi Equilibri, PO Box 97, 01100 Viterbo *Tel:* (0761) 352277 *Fax:* (0761) 352751

**Edizoni Le Stelle**, *imprint of* Le Stelle Scuola

**Le Stelle Scuola**
Via Vasari 15, 20135 Milan
*Tel:* (02) 55181460 *Fax:* (02) 5400017
Founded: 1954
Subjects: Education, Fiction, Geography, Geology, History, Music, Dance, Religion - Other, Science (General)
Imprints: Dimensione Umana; Linea Verde; Edizoni Le Stelle

**Istituto Storico Italiano per l'Eta Moderna e Contemporanea**
Via Caetani 32, 00186 Rome
*Tel:* (06) 68806922 *Fax:* (06) 6875127
*E-mail:* iststor@libero.it
*Key Personnel*
Man Dir: Prof Luigi Lotti
Editorial: Dr Marina Maura
Founded: 1934
Subjects: History

**Studio Bibliografico Adelmo Polla+**
Via Prato 2, 67044 Cerchio
*Tel:* (0863) 78522 *Fax:* (0863) 78522
*Key Personnel*
Man Dir: Adelmo Polla
Editorial: Maria G Romanelli
Founded: 1974
Subjects: Archaeology, History, Language Arts, Linguistics, Literature, Literary Criticism, Essays, Travel

**Studio Editoriale Programma**
Via S Eufemia, 5, 35121 Padova
*Tel:* (049) 8753110 *Fax:* (049) 8755870
Founded: 1981
Subjects: Art, History, Literature, Literary Criticism, Essays, Travel
ISBN Prefix(es): 88-7123

**Edizioni Studio Tesi SRL**
Subsidiary of Edizioni Mediterranee SRL
Via Flaminia, 109, 00196 Rome
*Tel:* (06) 3235433 *Fax:* (06) 3236277
*E-mail:* info@ediz-mediterranee.com
*Web Site:* www.ediz-mediterranee.com *Cable:* EST
*Key Personnel*
Chief Executive & Editorial: Giovanni Canonico
Founded: 1977
Subjects: Economics, Fiction, History, Literature, Literary Criticism, Essays, Music, Dance, Science (General)
ISBN Prefix(es): 88-7692
Subsidiaries: Edizioni dello Zibaldone

**Edizioni Studium SRL+**
Via Cassiodoro 14, 00193 Rome
*Tel:* (06) 68 65 846 *Fax:* (06) 68 75 456
*E-mail:* edizionistudium@libero.it *Cable:* STUDIUM ROME
Founded: 1927
Periodicals.
Subjects: History, Literature, Literary Criticism, Essays, Philosophy, Religion - Other, Science (General), Social Sciences, Sociology
ISBN Prefix(es): 88-382
Number of titles published annually: 30 Print
Total Titles: 600 Print
*Associate Companies:* Editrice La Scuola SpA
Distributed by Editrice Le Seulo - Buscie

**Sugarco Edizioni SRL**
Via Gnocchi 4, 20148 Milan
*Tel:* (02) 4078370 *Fax:* (02) 4078493
*E-mail:* info@sugarcoedizioni.it
*Web Site:* www.sugarcoedizioni.it
*Key Personnel*
Man Dir: Dr Oliviero Cigada
Founded: 1956
Subjects: Biography, Fiction, History, How-to, Philosophy
ISBN Prefix(es): 88-7198

**ME/DI Sviluppo**, see Giunti Gruppo Editoriale

**Tappeiner**
Zona Industriale, 6, 39011 Lana d'Adige (Bolzano)
*Tel:* (0473) 563666 *Fax:* (0473) 563689
*E-mail:* tappeiner@pass.dnet.it
Subjects: Archaeology, Architecture & Interior Design, Art, Cookery, Geography, Geology, History, Outdoor Recreation
ISBN Prefix(es): 88-7073

**La Tartaruga Edizioni SAS**
Via Crocefisso 21, 20122 Milan
*Tel:* (02) 584501 *Fax:* (02) 58307512
Founded: 1975
Subjects: Cookery, Drama, Theater, Literature, Literary Criticism, Essays, Women's Studies
ISBN Prefix(es): 88-7738; 88-85678

**Tassotti Editore**
Via San F Lazzaro 103, 36061 Bassano del Grappa (Vicenza)
*Tel:* (0424) 566105 *Fax:* (0424) 566205
*E-mail:* info@tassotti.it
*Web Site:* www.tassotti.it
Founded: 1984
Subjects: Art, History, Travel
ISBN Prefix(es): 88-7691
Divisions: Grafiche Tassotti SRL

**TEA Tascabili degli Editori Associati SpA+**
Corso Italia 13, 20122 Milan
*Tel:* (02) 80206625 *Fax:* (02) 8900844
*Web Site:* www.tealibri.it
*Key Personnel*
President: Stefano Mauri
Man Dir: Marco Taro
Editorial Dir: Stefano Res *E-mail:* stefano.res@tealibri.it
Sales: Giuseppe Somenzi
Production: Alfredo Bonfiglio
Publicity: Elena Cristiano; Valentina Fortichiari
Rights & Permissions: Sabine Schultz
Founded: 1987
Subjects: Art, Cookery, Fiction, Health, Nutrition, History, How-to, Humor, Nonfiction (General), Philosophy, Poetry, Psychology, Psychiatry, Science Fiction, Fantasy, Self-Help
ISBN Prefix(es): 88-7818; 88-502; 88-7819
Number of titles published annually: 180 Print
Total Titles: 1,500 Print
Subsidiaries: Longanesi

**Tecniche Nuove SpA+**
Via Eritrea, 21, 20157 Milan
*Tel:* (02) 390901 *Fax:* (02) 7610351
*E-mail:* info@tecnichenuove.com; vendite-libri@tecnichenuove.com
*Web Site:* www.tecnichenuove.com
*Key Personnel*
Man Dir: Giuseppe Nardella
Editorial: E Guaglione
Publicity: S Savona
Founded: 1960
Subjects: Business, Computer Science, Electronics, Electrical Engineering, Energy, Health, Nutrition, Technology
ISBN Prefix(es): 88-7081; 88-85009; 88-481

Number of titles published annually: 150 Print; 15 CD-ROM; 20 E-Book
Total Titles: 700 Print; 30 CD-ROM; 30 E-Book
Subsidiaries: Grafica Quadrifoglio
*U.S. Office(s):* Tecniche Nuove USA, 844 Gage Drive, San Diego, CA 92106, United States
*Warehouse:* Via Castel Morrone 15

**Tema Celeste**
10 Piazza Borromeo, 20123 Milan
*Tel:* (02) 8065171; (02) 80651732 (subscriptions) *Fax:* (02) 80651743
*E-mail:* editorial@temaceleste.com; subscriptions@temaceleste.com
*Web Site:* www.gabrius.com/default_tc.htm
*Key Personnel*
Publisher: Alberico Cetti Serbelloni
Editor: Simona Vendrame *E-mail:* vendrame@temaceleste.com
Man Editor: Daniele Perra *E-mail:* perra@temaceleste.com
Advertising: Roberta Pollio *E-mail:* ad@temaceleste.com
Founded: 1983
Subjects: Art
ISBN Prefix(es): 88-85265; 88-7304

**Edizioni del Teresianum**
Piazza San Pancrazio 5/A, 00152 Rome
*Tel:* (06) 585401 *Fax:* (06) 58540300
*Key Personnel*
Chief Executive: Cumer Dario
Sales, Publicity: Piergiorgio Mantovani
Founded: 1966
Subjects: Biblical Studies, Biography, History, Religion - Catholic, Theology
ISBN Prefix(es): 88-85317
*Parent Company:* Edizioni dei Padri Carmelitani Scalzi, Corso d'Italia 38, 00198 Rome

**Nicola Teti e C Editore SRL**
Via Rezia, 4, 20135 Milan
*Tel:* (02) 55015584 *Fax:* (02) 55015595
*E-mail:* teti@teti.it
*Web Site:* www.teti.it
*Key Personnel*
Man Dir: Nicola Teti
Editorial: Piero Lavatelli
Sales: Vincenzo Fracchiolla
Rights & Permissions & Production: Rita Vaccari
Production: Vanna Guzzi
Publicity: Nino Oppo
Founded: 1971
Subjects: Education, Government, Political Science, History, Natural History, Social Sciences, Sociology
ISBN Prefix(es): 88-7039

**Edizioni Thyrus SRL+**
Via della Rinascita 12, 05031 Arrone (Terni)
*Tel:* (0744) 389496 *Fax:* (0744) 388700
*E-mail:* thyrus@bellaumbria.net
*Web Site:* www.bellaumbria.net/thyrus *Cable:* UFFICIO POSTALE ARRONE
*Key Personnel*
Man Dir, Production, Rights & Permissions: Dr Osvaldo Panfili
Editorial: Prof Lido Pirro
Sales: Nobili Nevia
Founded: 1956
Subjects: Education, Fiction, History, Literature, Literary Criticism, Essays, Psychology, Psychiatry, Regional Interests, Social Sciences, Sociology, Theology
ISBN Prefix(es): 88-87675
*Book Club(s):* Circolo Astrolabio

**Tilgher-Genova sas**
Via Assarotti 31/15, 16122 Genoa
*Tel:* (010) 839 11 40 *Fax:* (010) 870653
*E-mail:* tilgher@tilgher.it

*Web Site:* www.tilgher.it
*Key Personnel*
Chief Executive: Lucio Bozzi
Founded: 1971
Subjects: Biological Sciences, Literature, Literary Criticism, Essays, Philosophy

**Editrice Tirrenia Stampatori SAS**
Via Ferrari 5, 10124 Turin
*Tel:* (011) 8177010 *Fax:* (011) 8177010
*E-mail:* info@tirreniastampatori.it
*Web Site:* www.tirreniastampatori.it
*Key Personnel*
Editorial & Publicity: Anna Maria Bertolina
Founded: 1977
Specialize in University publishing.
Subjects: Geography, Geology, History, Language Arts, Linguistics, Literature, Literary Criticism, Essays, Mathematics, Philosophy, Psychology, Psychiatry, Social Sciences, Sociology
ISBN Prefix(es): 88-7763
*Orders to:* The Courier SRL, Distibozione Libr, VLA Debosis, 25-27, 80145 Florence

**Todariana Editrice+**
Via Gardone, 29, 20139 Milan
*Tel:* (02) 56812953 *Fax:* (02) 55213405
*E-mail:* toeurs@tin.it
*Key Personnel*
Chief Executive: Teodoro Giuttari
Founded: 1967
Subjects: Fiction, Language Arts, Linguistics, Literature, Literary Criticism, Essays, Poetry, Psychology, Psychiatry, Science Fiction, Fantasy, Social Sciences, Sociology, Travel
ISBN Prefix(es): 88-7015
Number of titles published annually: 12 Print
Imprints: Eura Press; Edizioni Italiane

**Tomo Edizioni srl+**
Via Pienza, 255, 00138 Rome
*Tel:* (081) 00920 *Fax:* (081) 00920
*E-mail:* tomoedizioni@libero.it
Founded: 1989
Subjects: Art, Photography
ISBN Prefix(es): 88-7151

**Trainer International Editore-I Libri del Bargello+**
Corso Italia 29, 50123 Florence
*Tel:* (055) 288162 *Fax:* (055) 218951
*Telex:* 571136
*Key Personnel*
Editorial Dir: Enrico Bosi
Coordinator: Enrica Fuligni Nannelli
Founded: 1990
Subjects: Art, History, Travel, Wine & Spirits
ISBN Prefix(es): 88-85271
*Warehouse:* V Baldanzese, 118-50041 Calenzano Firenze

**Giovanni Tranchida Editore+**
Via Giuseppe Frua 18, 20146 Milan
*Tel:* (02) 66802270 *Fax:* (02) 69003425
*E-mail:* tranchida@infinito.it
*Web Site:* www.tranchida.it
*Key Personnel*
Man Dir: Giovanni Tranchida
Founded: 1983
Membership(s): AIE.
Subjects: Architecture & Interior Design, Fiction, Literature, Literary Criticism, Essays, Philosophy, Psychology, Psychiatry
ISBN Prefix(es): 88-8003; 88-85685
Imprints: Giovanni Tranchida Editore
Distributor for Nessaggerie Libri Spa

**Transeuropa+**
Via Boscovich 44, 20124 Milan
*Tel:* (02) 29 402156 *Fax:* (02) 20 47922

*Key Personnel*
Man Dir: Massimo Canalini
Founded: 1988
Subjects: Architecture & Interior Design, Biological Sciences, Fiction, Film, Video, History, Literature, Literary Criticism, Essays, Medicine, Nursing, Dentistry, Philosophy, Women's Studies
ISBN Prefix(es): 88-7828
*Orders to:* PO Box 118, Ancona

**Editrice Trasporti su Rotaie,** see ETR (Editrice Trasporti su Rotaie)

**Casa Editrice Luigi Trevisini**
Via Tito Livio 12, 20137 Milan
*Tel:* (02) 5450704 *Fax:* (02) 55195782
*E-mail:* trevisini@trevisini.it
*Web Site:* www.trevisini.it *Cable:* TREVISINI-MILANO
*Key Personnel*
Chief Executive: Luigi Trevisini
Editorial: Dr Giusi Trevisini
Founded: 1859
ISBN Prefix(es): 88-292

**Marco Tropea Editore+**
Via Melzo 9, 20129 Milan
*Tel:* (02) 202301 *Fax:* (02) 29513061
*E-mail:* stampa@saggiatore.it
*Web Site:* www.saggiatore.it
*Key Personnel*
President: Luca Formenton
Editor: Marco Tropea
Founded: 1995
Subjects: Fiction, Nonfiction (General)
ISBN Prefix(es): 88-438
*Associate Companies:* Il Saggiatore SpA e Nuova Pratiche Editrice

**Turris+**
Corso Garibaldi, 215, 26100 Cremona
*Tel:* (0372) 23845 *Fax:* (0372) 23845
Founded: 1981
Subjects: Art, Music, Dance
ISBN Prefix(es): 88-85635; 88-7929

**Edizioni Ubulibri SAS+**
Via Ramazzini 8, 20129 Milan
*Tel:* (02) 20241604 *Fax:* (02) 29510265
*E-mail:* edizioni@ubulibri.it
*Key Personnel*
Man Dir, Editorial: Franco Quadri
General Manager & Publicity: Tania Rainini
Founded: 1979
Subjects: Drama, Theater, Film, Video, Music, Dance
ISBN Prefix(es): 88-7748
Number of titles published annually: 12 Print
Total Titles: 160 Print
*Warehouse:* Messaggerie Libri SPA, Via Verdi 8, 20090 Assago *Tel:* (02) 457741

**Editoriale Umbra SAS di Carnevali e**
Via Pignattara, 34, 06034 Foligno (Perugia)
*Tel:* (0742) 357541 *Fax:* (0742) 351156
*E-mail:* editumbra@libero.it
*Web Site:* www.italand.com/eu *Cable:* EDITORIALE UMBRA FOLIGNO
*Key Personnel*
Man Dir, Editorial, Rights & Permissions, Sales: Giovanni Carnevali
Publicity: M Lise Burget
Founded: 1982
Subjects: Art, History, Literature, Literary Criticism, Essays, Regional Interests
ISBN Prefix(es): 88-85659

**Edizioni Unicopli SpA+**
Via Rosalba Carriera, 11, 20146 Milan
*Tel:* (02) 42299666 *Fax:* (02) 76021612

*E-mail:* info@edizioniunicopli.it
*Web Site:* www.edizioniunicopli.it
*Key Personnel*
Chief Executive: Michele Salvatore
Chief Editor: Marzio Zanantoni
Editorial, Psychology, Psychiatry: Stefano Nutini
Publicity: Roselle Savari
Founded: 1985
Subjects: Literature, Literary Criticism, Essays
ISBN Prefix(es): 88-7061; 88-400; 88-7090

**Unipress+**
Via Battisti, 231, 35121 Padova
*Tel:* (049) 8752542 *Fax:* (049) 8752542
*Key Personnel*
Editorial Dir: Gian Luigi Borgato
Founded: 1987
Subjects: Agriculture, Biological Sciences, Chemistry, Chemical Engineering, Language Arts, Linguistics, Literature, Literary Criticism, Essays, Philosophy, Psychology, Psychiatry
ISBN Prefix(es): 88-8098

**Editrice Uomini Nuovi**
Via Mazzini 73, 21030 Marchirolo (Varese)
*Tel:* (0332) 723007 *Fax:* (0332) 723264
*E-mail:* libreria@eun.ch; eunitaly@eun.ch
*Web Site:* www.eun.ch
*Key Personnel*
Chief Executive, Editorial: Dr Giuseppe E Laiso
Sales: Ruth Laiso
Publicity: Anna Rossinelli
Founded: 1964
Subjects: Biblical Studies, Biography, Human Relations, Psychology, Psychiatry, Religion - Other, Self-Help
ISBN Prefix(es): 88-8077
Subsidiaries: Radio Uomini Nuovi (Radio Cristiana Internazionale)
*Bookshop(s):* EUN

**Urbaniana University Press+**
Division of Pontificia Universitas Urbaniana
Via Urbano VIII, 16, 00120 Citta del Vaticano
*Tel:* (06) 6988 2182 *Fax:* (06) 6988 2182
*E-mail:* uupamm@urbaniana.edu
*Web Site:* www.urbaniana.edu/uup
*Key Personnel*
Dir: Gaspare Mura, PhD *Tel:* (06) 6988 9651
*E-mail:* uupdir@urbaniana.edu
Administration: Giuseppe de Summa
*E-mail:* uupamm@tiscali.it
Editorial: Sandro Scalabrin *Tel:* (06) 6988 1745
*E-mail:* uupdir@urbaniana.edu
Founded: 1968
Specialize in periodicals & essays.
Subjects: Anthropology, Biblical Studies, Law, Philosophy, Psychology, Psychiatry, Religion - Catholic, Theology, Missiology
ISBN Prefix(es): 88-401
Number of titles published annually: 14 Print
Total Titles: 500 Print
Imprints: UUP
Distributed by Dehoniana Libri
*Showroom(s):* Franfurt Book Messe
*Bookshop(s):* Libreria Bookshop, Pontificia Universita Urbaniana, 00120 Citta Del Vaticano; Libreria Vaticana
*Orders to:* Dehoniana Libri, Via Delle Fornaci, 47-51, 00165 Rome *Tel:* (06) 6382607 *Fax:* (06) 6390402

**UT Orpheus Edizioni Srl+**
Piazza di Porta Ravegnana, 1, 40126 Bologna
*Tel:* (051) 226468 *Fax:* (051) 263720
*E-mail:* mail@utorpheus.com
*Web Site:* www.utorpheus.com
*Key Personnel*
Contact: Roberto De Caro; Dr Antonello Lombardi
Sales Manager: Prof Valeria Tarsetti
*E-mail:* vtarsetti@utorpheus.com
Founded: 1994

Italian publisher specializing in the publication of books on different music subjects, classical music.
Subjects: Music, Dance, Classical Music Editions
ISBN Prefix(es): 88-8109
Number of titles published annually: 100 Print
Total Titles: 820 Print
Distributor for Forni (Facsimiles); Spes (Facsimiles)
Foreign Rep(s): MKT (Italy)
Bookshop(s): Ut Orpheus Libreria Musicale, Via Marsala 31/E, 40126 Bologna Fax: (051) 239295
Warehouse: Via Aldina 26/A Calderara Di Reno, Elisabetta Pistolozzi Tel: (051) 726138
Distribution Center: MKT Musikit, Via Sardegna 7, 25124 Brescia Fax: (030) 222067
Orders to: Ut Orpheus Libreria Musicale, Via Marsala 31/E, 40126 Bologna Fax: (051) 239295

**UTET Periodici Scientifici**
Viale Tunisia, 37, 20124 Milan
Tel: (02) 6241171 Fax: (02) 62411720
E-mail: utet@utet.it
Web Site: www.utetperiodici.it
Key Personnel
General Manager: Corrado Trevisan
International Rights: Grazia Raccolli
Founded: 1987
Subjects: Medicine, Nursing, Dentistry
ISBN Prefix(es): 88-7933; 88-85647
Parent Company: UTET SpA

**UTET (Unione Tipografico-Editrice Torinese)**
Corso Raffaello 28, 10125 Turin
Tel: (011) 2099111 Fax: (011) 2099394
E-mail: utet@utet.it
Web Site: www.utet.it Cable: UTET Turin
Founded: 1791
Subjects: Architecture & Interior Design, Art, History, Law, Music, Dance, Philosophy, Psychology, Psychiatry, Religion - Other, Science (General), Social Sciences, Sociology, Veterinary Science
ISBN Prefix(es): 88-02

**UUP**, imprint of Urbaniana University Press

**Vaccari SRL**
Via M Buonarroti 46, 41058 Vignola Modena
Tel: (059) 764106; (059) 771251 Fax: (059) 760157
E-mail: info@vaccari.it
Web Site: www.vaccari.it
Key Personnel
Book Manager: Valeria Vaccari
Founded: 1989
Subjects: Crafts, Games, Hobbies, Collecting, Philately, Postal History
ISBN Prefix(es): 88-85335
Number of titles published annually: 10 Print; 10 Online
Total Titles: 80 Print; 80 Online

**Valdonega SRL**
Division of Stamperia Valdomega
Via Genova 17, 37020 Arbizzano, Verona
Tel: (045) 6020444 Fax: (045) 6020334
E-mail: valdonega@valdonega.it
Specialize in books on books, limited art editions & quality productions.
ISBN Prefix(es): 88-85033
Number of titles published annually: 3 Print
Total Titles: 15 Print

**Vallardi & Assoc**
Via Galilei 6, 20124 Milan
Tel: (02) 6555545 Fax: (02) 6555640
Telex: 330326 GECVAL I
ISBN Prefix(es): 88-85202

**Vallardi Industrie Grafiche+**
Via Trieste 20, 20020 Lainate, Milan
Tel: (02) 9370284 Fax: (02) 93570442
Web Site: www.vallardi.com
Key Personnel
Publisher: Giuseppe Vallardi
Editorial: Emanuela Vallardi
Founded: 1969
ISBN Prefix(es): 88-7696

**Valmartina Editore SRL+**
Stra del Portone 179, 10095 Grugliasco, Turin
Tel: (011) 2098741; (011) 2098720 Fax: (011) 2098765
E-mail: redazione@valmartina.it
Web Site: www.valmartina.it
Key Personnel
President: Luigi Vecchia
Editorial: Carlo Pasquinelli
Production: Giorgio Raccis
Rights & Permissions: Michela Melchiori
Founded: 1951
Subjects: Language Arts, Linguistics, Travel
ISBN Prefix(es): 88-494
Orders to: Via L Dottesio 1, 35138 Padua Tel: (049) 8710099

**Societa Editrice Vannini**
Via Mandolossa, 117/A, 25064 Gussago
Tel: (030) 313374 Fax: (030) 314078
E-mail: info@vanniieditrice.it
Web Site: www.vannieditrice.it Cable: VANNINI BRESCIA
Founded: 1950
ISBN Prefix(es): 88-86430; 88-7436

**Libreria Editrice Vaticana**
Via della Tipografia, 00120 Citta del Vaticano
Tel: (06) 69885003 Fax: (06) 69884716
E-mail: lev@publish.va
Web Site: www.libreriaeditricevaticana.com
ISBN Prefix(es): 88-209

**Verso il Futuro**, imprint of Casa Editrice Menna di Sinisgalli Menna Giuseppina

**Vianello Libri+**
Via Postioma 85, 31050 Ponzano (Treviso)
Tel: (0422) 440666 Fax: (0422) 440645
E-mail: info@vianellolibri.it
Web Site: www.vianellolibri.it
Key Personnel
Contact: Giancarlo Buscaini; Andrea Montagnani; Livio Scibilia
Subjects: Architecture & Interior Design, Photography
ISBN Prefix(es): 88-7200
Orders to: Grafiche Vianello

**Vinciana Editrice sas+**
Via V Foppa, 14, 20144 Milan
Tel: (02) 4982306 Fax: (02) 48003275
E-mail: info@vinciana.com
Web Site: www.vinciana.com
Founded: 1976
Specialize in fine art.
Subjects: Art, Crafts, Games, Hobbies, How-to
ISBN Prefix(es): 88-86256
Total Titles: 42 Print

**Vision Srl**
Via Livorno, 20, 00161 Rome
Tel: (06) 44292688 Fax: (06) 44292688
E-mail: info@visionpubl.com
Web Site: www.visionpubl.com
Founded: 1959

**Visual Itineraries**, imprint of BeMa

**Vita e Pensiero+**
L go A Gemelli, 1, 20123 Milan
Tel: (02) 72342335; (02) 72342259 Fax: (02) 72342260
E-mail: editvep@mi.unicatt.it
Web Site: www.vitaepensiero.it
Telex: 321033 Ucatmi I
Key Personnel
President: Prof Sergio Zaninelli
Editorial Dir: Dr Aurelio Mottola Fax: (02) 72342660 E-mail: aurelio.mottola@unicatt.it
Founded: 1918
Membership(s): Associazione Italiana Editori, Unione Editori Cattolici Italiani, Unione Stampa Periodica Italiana, Associazione Librai Italiani.
Subjects: History, Literature, Literary Criticism, Essays, Mathematics, Medicine, Nursing, Dentistry, Philosophy, Psychology, Psychiatry, Religion - Other
ISBN Prefix(es): 88-343
Number of titles published annually: 100 Print
Bookshop(s): Libreria Vita e Pensiero, L go A Gemelli, 1, 20123 Milan E-mail: eibreria.vp@mi.umicatt.it

**Edizioni La Vita Felice**
Via Tadino 52, 20129 Milan
Tel: (02) 29 52 46 00 Fax: (02) 29 40 18 96
E-mail: lavitafelice@iol.it
Web Site: www.lavitafelice.it
Key Personnel
Publishing Dir: Gerardo Mastrullo
Public Relations: Chicca Gagliardo Marina Mauri
Editorial Dir: Cesare Salami
Editor: Paola Gerevini
Founded: 1993
Subjects: Fiction, Literature, Literary Criticism, Essays, Poetry
ISBN Prefix(es): 88-86314; 88-7799
Number of titles published annually: 24 Print
Total Titles: 80 Print

**Vivalda Editori SRL+**
Via Invorio 24 a, 10146 Turin
Tel: (011) 7720444 Fax: (011) 7732170
E-mail: cdavivalda@cdavivalda.it
Web Site: www.cdavivalda.it
Key Personnel
President: Silvio Colombino
Founded: 1972
Subjects: Sports, Athletics
ISBN Prefix(es): 88-7808
Divisions: CDA

**Vivere In SRL**
Contrada Piangevio, 224a, 70043 Bari
Tel: (08) 06907030 Fax: (08) 06907026
E-mail: edizioniviverein@tint.it
Web Site: www.viverein.it
Subjects: Biblical Studies, Biography, Philosophy, Poetry, Regional Interests, Religion - Catholic, Social Sciences, Sociology, Theology, Essays
ISBN Prefix(es): 88-7263
Number of titles published annually: 15 Print
Total Titles: 350 Print
Distributed by Agenzia Libraria GALL SRL; Agenzia Libraria S Fozzi; Citta Nuova Centro; DEM Libri SRL; Distrimedia SRL; Ditta Restivo SRL; L'Editoriale SRL; Ferrari Libri SRL

**Viviani Editore srl+**
Piazza della Maddalena 6, 00186 Rome
Tel: (06) 6872855 Fax: (06) 6872856
Web Site: www.vivianeditore.net
Key Personnel
Contact: Lia Viviani
Founded: 1992
Membership(s): AIE.

Subjects: Art, Biography, Drama, Theater, Literature, Literary Criticism, Essays
ISBN Prefix(es): 88-7993

**Voce della Bibbia**
Via Cavallotti 14, 41043 Formigine (Modena)
*Tel:* (059) 55 63 03; (059) 55 79 10 *Fax:* (059) 57 31 05
*E-mail:* bbbitaly@tin.it
*Web Site:* www.vocedellabibbia.org
*Key Personnel*
General Dir: Ettore Calanchi
Founded: 1961
Subjects: Biblical Studies, Health, Nutrition, Music, Dance
*Parent Company:* Back to the Bible Broadcast, Box 82808, Lincoln, NE 68501, United States

**Who's Who In Italy srl**
Via E De Amicis 2, 20091 Bresso Milan
*Tel:* (02) 66503753; (02) 6101627 *Fax:* (02) 6105587
*E-mail:* whoswhogc@attglobal.net
*Web Site:* www.whoswho-sutter.com
*Key Personnel*
Man Dir: Giancarlo Colombo
Founded: 1977
Specialize in reference books, International publishers of Who's Who titles in 6 different nations in the English language & of particular interest to the world of business, politics, culture, art, science, education, etc, with cross-references between biographies & profiles of companies & institutions.
Membership(s): Associazione Italiana Editori (Italian Publishers' Association).
Subjects: Biography, Business, Management
ISBN Prefix(es): 88-85246
Number of titles published annually: 3 Print; 3 Online
*Parent Company:* Who's Who Sutters International Red Series Verlag AG, Seestr 357, 8038 Zurich, Switzerland
Subsidiaries: Who's Who in Spain; Who's Who Strategic Area
Distributed by The Eurospan Group (England); Independent Publishers Group (USA & Canada); United Publishers Services Ltd (Japan)

**Silvio Zamorani editore**
Saint Course Maurizio 25, 10124 Turin
*Tel:* (011) 8125700 *Fax:* (011) 8126144
*E-mail:* szamora@tin.it
*Web Site:* www.zamorani.com
Founded: 1984
ISBN Prefix(es): 88-7158

**ZAN**, *imprint of* Casa Musicale G Zanibon SRL

**Zanfi-Logos+**
Via Curtatona 5/2, 41100 Modena
Mailing Address: PO Box 70, 41100 Modena
*Tel:* (059) 418810 *Fax:* (059) 418747
*Telex:* 522272
*Key Personnel*
Contact: Celestino Zanfi
Founded: 1979
Membership(s): Distripress.
Subjects: Cookery, Fashion, Gardening, Plants, Health, Nutrition, Outdoor Recreation, Religion - Buddhist, Travel
ISBN Prefix(es): 88-85168; 88-86169; 88-8169

**Zanichelli Editore SpA+**
Via Irnerio 34, 40126 Bologna
*Tel:* (051) 293111; (051) 245024 *Fax:* (051) 249782
*E-mail:* zanichelli@zanichelli.it
*Web Site:* www.zanichelli.it

*Key Personnel*
Chairman: Lorenzo Enriques
Dir General & Vice President: Federico Enriques
Founded: 1859
Subjects: Anthropology, Architecture & Interior Design, Biological Sciences, Chemistry, Chemical Engineering, Computer Science, Earth Sciences, Economics, Education, Electronics, Electrical Engineering, Engineering (General), English as a Second Language, Geography, Geology, History, Language Arts, Linguistics, Law, Literature, Literary Criticism, Essays, Mechanical Engineering, Medicine, Nursing, Dentistry, Philosophy, Photography, Physics, Psychology, Psychiatry, Science (General), Social Sciences, Sociology
ISBN Prefix(es): 88-08
Subsidiaries: CEA Casa Editrice Ambrosiana srl; ESAC Edizioni Scientifiche A Cremonese srl; Loescher Editore srl
Distributor for Bovolenta; Decibel; Lucisano; Signorelli
*Warehouse:* Via Del Lavoro 15, 40050 Quarto Inferiore (BO)

**Edizioni Zara**
Via Toscana 80, 43100 Parma
*Tel:* (0521) 45945 *Fax:* (0521) 241750
*Key Personnel*
Chief Executive: Isabella Marchesi
Editorial: Giancarlo Zarattini
Founded: 1979
Also acts as distributor for Edizioni Artegrafica Silva, Parma.
Subjects: Drama, Theater, Environmental Studies, Geography, Geology, Language Arts, Linguistics, Literature, Literary Criticism, Essays, Natural History, Philosophy, Religion - Catholic
Distributor for Parita; Silva Editore

# Jamaica

## General Information

*Capital:* Kingston
*Language:* English
*Religion:* Predominantly Protestant
*Population:* 2.5 million
*Bank Hours:* 0900-1400 Monday-Thursday; 0900-1200, 1430-1700 Friday
*Shop Hours:* Downtown Kingston: 0900-1600 Monday and Tuesday, Thursday-Saturday; 0900-1200 Wednesday. Other areas: 0900-1700, with early closing Thursday
*Currency:* 100 cents = 1 Jamaican dollar
*Export/Import Information:* No tariff on books, but advertising matter dutied. No import license required for books; no obscene literature permitted. No exchange restrictions.
*Copyright:* Berne (see Copyright Conventions, pg xi)

**American Chamber of Commerce of Jamaica+**
81 Knutsford Blvd, Kingston 5
*Tel:* 876-929-7866 *Fax:* 876-929-8597
*E-mail:* info@amchamjamaica.org
*Web Site:* www.amchamjamaica.org
*Key Personnel*
Chief Executive Officer: Dr Ofe S Dudley
Editor: Becky Stockhausen
Membership(s): Chamber of Commerce of The USA.
Subjects: Environmental Studies, Management, Marketing
ISBN Prefix(es): 976-8113
*Parent Company:* Chamber of Commerce of The USA (COCUSA)
Divisions: Association of American Chamber of Commerce of Latin America (AACCLA)

**Association of Development Agencies**
14 South Ave, Kingston 10
*Tel:* 876-960-2319; 876-968-3605 *Fax:* 876-929-8773
Founded: 1985
Forum for collective analysis, discussion, planning & collaboration.
Subjects: Communications, Developing Countries, House & Home, Regional Interests, Self-Help, Women's Studies
ISBN Prefix(es): 976-8112

**Canoe Press**, *imprint of* University of the West Indies Press

**Canoe Press+**
Imprint of The University of the West Indies Press
One A Aqueduct Flats, Mona, Kingston 7
*Tel:* 876-935-8432; 876-935-8470; 876-977-2659 *Fax:* 876-977-2660
*E-mail:* uwipress_marketing@cwjamaica.com; cuserv@cwjamaica.com (customer service & orders)
*Web Site:* www.uwipress.com
*Key Personnel*
General Manager: Linda Speth *E-mail:* lspeth@cwjamaica.com
Founded: 1992
Primarily publishes scholarly discourse such as conference papers & textbooks.
ISBN Prefix(es): 976-640
Distributor for UWI Publications

**Carib Publishing Ltd+**
78 Slipe Rd, Kingston 5
*Tel:* 876-960-2602 *Fax:* 876-960-2602
*E-mail:* carib@toj.com
*Key Personnel*
Chairman: Patrick H O Rousseau
Man Dir: D Andrew Rousseau
Publishing Manager: Diane Browne
Production & Communications Manager: Gina Harrison
Founded: 1976
Subjects: Cookery, Education, Fiction, Geography, Geology, History, Mathematics, Science (General)
ISBN Prefix(es): 976-605
Subsidiaries: The Book Shop Ltd; Book Traders (Caribbean) Ltd
Distributor for Heinemann UK (Northern Caribbean)
*Bookshop(s):* The Springs, 15-17 Constant Spring Rd, Kingston 10; LOJ Shopping Centre, Shop No 12, 28-48 Barbados Ave, Kingston 5; LOJ Shopping Centre, Shop No 17, 28-48 Barbados Ave, Kingston 5; Lane Plaza, 36 Manchester Rd, Manchester; 17 Burke Rd, Spanish Town; Montego Bay Shopping Centre, Shops 12 & 13, Howard Cooke Blvd, Montego Bay, St James
*Orders to:* Book Traders (Caribbean) Ltd, Kingston

**Caribbean Authors Publishing**
12 Brentford Rd, Kingston 5
*Tel:* 876-929-6163 *Fax:* 876-929-1226
*Key Personnel*
Dir: Peter D Clarke
ISBN Prefix(es): 976-8037
*Associate Companies:* Multi Sector Consultants Ltd

**Caribbean Food & Nutrition Institute**
University of the West Indies, Mona, Kingston 7
Mailing Address: PO Box 140, Kingston 7
*Tel:* 876-927-1540; 876-927-1927 *Fax:* 876-927-2657
*E-mail:* e-mail@cfni.paho.org *Cable:* CAJANUS
*Key Personnel*
Dir: Dr Henry Fitzroy

Founded: 1967
Subjects: Health, Nutrition
ISBN Prefix(es): 976-626
*Parent Company:* Pan American Health Organization/World Health Organization

**Caribbean Law Publishing Co**, *imprint of* Ian Randle Publishers Ltd

**Carlong Publishers (Caribbean) Ltd+**
33 Second St, Newport West, Kingston 10
Mailing Address: PO Box 489, Kingston 10
*Tel:* (876) 923-7008 *Fax:* (876) 923-7003
*E-mail:* sales@carlpub.com *Cable:* CARLONG KINGSTON
*Key Personnel*
Publisher: Jenni Anderson *E-mail:* janderson@carlongpublishers.com
Publishing Manager, Rights & Permissions: Dorothy Noel *E-mail:* dnoel@carlongpublishers.com
Man Dir: Shirley Carby
Sales & Distribution: Lorna Allen
Editor: Benedicta Nakawuki *E-mail:* bnakawuki@carlongpublishers.com; Stacy Ramanand-Howard *E-mail:* showard@carlongpublishers.com; Sasha Robins *E-mail:* srobins@carlongpublishers.com
Founded: 1990
Subjects: Business, Drama, Theater, Foreign Countries, Geography, Geology, History, Human Relations, Language Arts, Linguistics, Literature, Literary Criticism, Essays, Mathematics, Science (General), Social Sciences, Sociology
ISBN Prefix(es): 976-8010; 976-638
Total Titles: 92 Print
Distributor for Pearson Education (Restrictions: Publishing); Penguin Books Ltd (N B Now own the right to publish some titles formerly belonging to Carib Publishing Limited)
Foreign Rights: Lloyd Austin (Guyana); Louis Forde (Barbados); Ken Jaikaransingh (Trinidad & Tobago); Franklyn Laws (Saint Kitts & Nevis); Henry Nathaniel (Saint Lucia)
*Showroom(s):* 17 Ruthven Rd, Bldg 3, Kingston 10, Contact: Mrs Dorothy Noel
*Tel:* (876) 960 9364-6 *Fax:* (876) 968 1353
*E-mail:* commissioning@carlpub.com (Publishing)

**CFM Publications+**
University of the West Indies, Mona Campus, Kingston 7
*Tel:* 876-927-1660; 876-927-1669 *Fax:* 876-927-0997
*E-mail:* helpdesk@uwimona.edu.jm
*Web Site:* www.uwimona.edu.jm
*Key Personnel*
International Rights: Margaret Mendes
Founded: 1987
Specialize in Caribbean accounting texts.
Subjects: Accounting, Management
ISBN Prefix(es): 976-8053
Distributed by The Press; University of the West Indies

**Eureka Press Ltd**
5 1/2 Caledonia Rd, Mandeville
Mailing Address: PO Box 628, Mandeville
*Tel:* 876-962-3947 *Fax:* 876-961-5383
*E-mail:* eurekapr@cwjamaica.com
Subjects: Biography, Education, Religion - Other, Theology
ISBN Prefix(es): 976-8029

**Gleaner Co Ltd**
7 North St, Kingston
Mailing Address: PO Box 40, Kingston
*Tel:* 876-922-3400 *Fax:* 876-922-2319; 876-922-6297; 876-922-6223

*Telex:* 2319
ISBN Prefix(es): 976-612

**Institute of Jamaica Publications+**
2A Suthermere Rd, Kingston 10
*Tel:* 876-929-4785; 876-929-4786 *Fax:* 876-926-8817
*Key Personnel*
Man Dir: Patricia V Stevens
Founded: 1967
Subjects: Ethnicity, Fiction, History, Natural History, Nonfiction (General), Science (General), Social Sciences, Sociology
ISBN Prefix(es): 976-8017

**The Jamaica Bauxite Institute**
PO Box 355, Kingston 6
*Tel:* (876) 927-2073; (876) 927-2079 *Fax:* (876) 927-1159
*E-mail:* info@jbi.org.jm
*Telex:* 2309 *Cable:* JAMBAUX JA
*Key Personnel*
Chairman: Carlton E Davis
General Manager: Mr Parris A Lyew-Ayee
Public Relations Officer: Hilary Coulton
Founded: 1975
Subjects: Earth Sciences, Economics
ISBN Prefix(es): 976-8072

**Jamaica Bureau of Standards**
6 Winchester Rd, Kingston 10
Mailing Address: PO Box 113, Kingston 10
*Tel:* (876) 926-3140; (876) 926-3145 *Fax:* (876) 929-4736
*E-mail:* info@jbs.org.jm
*Web Site:* www.jbs.org.jm/
*Telex:* 2291 Stanbur Ja *Cable:* STANBUREAU
*Key Personnel*
Executive Dir: Omer S Lloyd Thomas
Librarian: Andrea Robins
Founded: 1968
Formulate, promote & implement standards for products, processes & practices.
Membership(s): the International Organization for Standardization.
ISBN Prefix(es): 976-604

**Jamaica Information Service**
58A Half Way Tree Rd, Kingston 10
*Tel:* (876) 926-3740; (876) 926-3749 *Fax:* (876) 926-6715
*E-mail:* jis@jis.gov.jm; research@jis.gov.jm
*Web Site:* www.jis.gov.jm
ISBN Prefix(es): 976-633
*Ultimate Parent Company:* Office of the Prime Minister
*U.S. Office(s):* 1520 New Hampshire Ave NW, Washington, DC 20036, United States *Tel:* 202-452-0660 *Fax:* 202-986-0184
Jamaica Consulate General, 842 Ingraham Bldg, 25 SE Second Ave, Miami, FL 33131, United States *Tel:* 305-374-8385 *Fax:* 305-374-9674 *E-mail:* jismiami@bellsouth.net
767 Third Ave, 3rd floor, New York, NY 10017, United States *Tel:* 212-935-9000 *Fax:* 212-935-7507 (ext 7) *E-mail:* jis_nyc@yahoo.com

**Jamaica Printing Services**
77 1/2 Duke St, Kingston
*Tel:* 876-967-2250; 876-967-2253; 876-967-2279; 876-967-2280; 876-922-3957 *Fax:* 876-967-2225
*E-mail:* info@jps1992.com; sales@jps1992.com
*Web Site:* www.jps1992.com/
Subjects: Law

**Jamaica Publishing House Ltd+**
97 Church St, Kingston
*Tel:* (876) 922-1385; (876) 967-3866 *Fax:* (876) 922-5412
*E-mail:* jph@jol.com.jm *Cable:* JAPUB

*Key Personnel*
Chairman: Woodburn Miller
Manager: Elaine R Stennett
Founded: 1969
Subjects: Biography, Education, Geography, Geology, History, House & Home, Language Arts, Linguistics, Literature, Literary Criticism, Essays, Mathematics, Psychology, Psychiatry, Social Sciences, Sociology
ISBN Prefix(es): 976-606
*Parent Company:* Jamaica Teachers' Association
Distributor for A & C Black; Schofield & Sims

**Jamrite Publications+**
Suite 22, Spanish Court, One Lucia Ave, Kingston 5
*Tel:* (876) 926-1180; (876) 926-1181 *Fax:* (876) 968-4519
*E-mail:* blackolive@cwjamaica.com
*Key Personnel*
Contact: Christopher Issa *Tel:* (876) 968 9939
Founded: 1981
Subjects: Books on Jamaican Culture
*Parent Company:* Richard James & Associates Ltd

**LMH Publishing Ltd**
LOJ Industrial Complex, 7 Norman Rd, Suite 10, Kingston CSO
Mailing Address: PO Box 8296, Kingston CSO
*Tel:* (876) 938-0005 *Fax:* (876) 759-8752
*E-mail:* lmhbookpublishing@cwjamaica.com
*Web Site:* www.lmhpublishingjamaica.com
*Telex:* Fitzgram 2293 *Cable:* KINGBOOKS
*Key Personnel*
Chairman & Publisher: Mike Henry
Managing/Marketing Dir, Overseas: Dawn Chambers-Henry
Editor: Kevin Harris; Charles Moore
Subjects: Cookery, Fiction, Music, Dance, Nonfiction (General), Romance, Travel
Foreign Rep(s): Turnaround Publisher Services Ltd (UK, Europe)
*Shipping Address:* Caribtrans Inc, 12600 NW 107th Ave, Miami, FL 33178, United States
*Tel:* 305-696-1200 *Fax:* 305-691-3786
*E-mail:* miaterminal@caribtrans.com

**Packer-Evans & Associates Ltd+**
13 Stevenson Ave, Kingston 8
Mailing Address: PO Box 525, Kingston 8
*Tel:* 876-929-0531 *Fax:* 876-926-3487
*Key Personnel*
Chairman, Rights & Permissions & Sales: Omri I Evans
Man Dir & Sales: Dr Claude Packer
Sales & Publicity: Norma Evans
Production: Gloria Foresythe; Carol Anglin
Publicity: Lisa Packer
Founded: 1984
Subjects: Mathematics
ISBN Prefix(es): 976-8022

**The Press**, *imprint of* University of the West Indies Press

**The Press+**
Imprint of University of the West Indies
One A Aqueduct Flats, Mona, Kingston 7
*Tel:* (876) 977-2659 *Fax:* (876) 977-2660
*E-mail:* uwipress_marketing@cwjamaica.com; cuserv@cwjamaica.com (customer service & orders)
*Web Site:* www.uwipress.com
*Key Personnel*
General Manager: Linda Speth *E-mail:* lspeth@cwjamaica.com
Marketing & Sales Manager: Donna Muirhead
Founded: 1992
Also acts as marketer & distributor for departments of the University of the West Indies.
Membership(s): Book Industry Association of Jamaica.

Subjects: Ethnicity, Government, Political Science, History
ISBN Prefix(es): 976-640

**Ian Randle Publishers Ltd+**
11 Cunningham Ave, Kingston 6
Mailing Address: PO Box 686, Kingston 6
*Tel:* (876) 978-0739; (876) 978-0745
    *Toll Free Tel:* 866-330-5469 (orders) *Fax:* (876)
    978-1156
*E-mail:* info@ianrandlepublishers.com
*Web Site:* www.ianrandlepublishers.com
*Key Personnel*
Chairman & Publisher: Ian Randle *Tel:* (876)
    978-3587 *E-mail:* ian@ianrandlepublishers.com
Man Dir: Christine Randle *E-mail:* clp@
    ianrandlepublishers.com
Business Manager: Carlene Randle
Founded: 1990
Specializes in Caribbean Studies including Law,
    as well as trade & general books.
Membership(s): Caribbean Publishers Network;
    Caribbean Studies Association; Society for
    Caribbean Studies (UK).
Subjects: Art, Biography, Cookery, History, Law,
    Literature, Literary Criticism, Essays, Music,
    Dance, Poetry, Sports, Athletics, Women &
    Gender Studies
ISBN Prefix(es): 976-8100; 976-8123; 976-8167
Number of titles published annually: 50 Print
Total Titles: 250 Print
Imprints: Caribbean Law Publishing Co (law
    books & journals)
Foreign Rep(s): Global Book Marketing (UK, Europe)

**Scientific Research Council**
Hope Gardens, Kingston 6
Mailing Address: PO Box 350, Kingston 6
*Tel:* 876-927-1771; 876-927-1774 *Fax:* 876-927-
    1990
*E-mail:* prinfo@src-jamaica.org
*Web Site:* www.src-jamaica.org
*Telex:* 3631 SRCSTIN *Cable:* SCIENTIST
Founded: 1960
The National center for the transformation, acquisition, conversion & application of knowledge
    to run the engine of growth & development.
ISBN Prefix(es): 976-8126
Subsidiaries: Marketech Ltd

**Twin Guinep Ltd+**
Seymour Park, Suite 21, 2 Seymour Ave,
    Kingston 10
*Tel:* 876-927-5390; 876-944-4324 *Fax:* 876-944-
    4324
*E-mail:* info@twinguinep.com; sales@twinguinep.
    com
*Web Site:* www.twinguinep.com
*Key Personnel*
International Rights: Dennis Ranston
    *E-mail:* ranston@kasnet.com; Jacqueline
    Ranston
Founded: 1974
ISBN Prefix(es): 976-8007

**University of the West Indies Press+**
One A Aqueduct Flats, Mona, Kingston 7
*Tel:* (876) 977-2659 *Fax:* (876) 977-2660
*E-mail:* cuserv@cwjamaica.com (customer service
    & orders); uwipress_marketing@cwjamaica.
    com
*Web Site:* www.uwipress.com
*Key Personnel*
General Manager: Linda E Speth *E-mail:* lspeth@
    cwjamaica.com
Finance Manager: Nadine Buckland
    *E-mail:* nbuckland@cwjamaica.com
Administrative Officer: Dionne Williams
    *E-mail:* d_wills@cwjamaica.com
Marketing & Sales Manager: Donna Muirhead

Man Editor: Shivaum Hearne *E-mail:* hearnes@
    cwjamaica.com
Sales & Distribution Coordinator: Karen Smith
Founded: 1992
Academic book publisher.
Subjects: Anthropology, Environmental Studies,
    Ethnicity, History, Literature, Literary Criticism, Essays, Natural History, Social Sciences,
    Sociology, Women's Studies
ISBN Prefix(es): 976-8125; 976-640; 976-41
Number of titles published annually: 25 Print
Total Titles: 160 Print
Imprints: Canoe Press; The Press
Distributed by University of Oklahoma Press
Distributor for The Mill Press; Sir Arthur Lewis
    Institute
Foreign Rep(s): Eurospan (Middle East, UK &
    the continent); EWEB (Australia, Asia, New
    Zealand, The Pacific); Lexicon (Trinidad & Tobago); University of Oklahoma Press (Canada,
    North America)
*Distribution Center:* The University of Oklahoma
    Press, 4100 28 Ave NW, Norman, OK 73069,
    United States
Eurospan, 3 Henrietta St, Covent Garden, London
    WC2E 8LU, United Kingdom *Tel:* (020) 7240-
    0856 *Fax:* (020) 7379-0609

**UWI Publishers' Association**
University of West Indies, Mona Campus,
    Kingston 7
Mailing Address: PO Box 42, Kingston
*Tel:* 876-927-1660; 876-927-1669 *Fax:* 876-977-
    2660
*E-mail:* helpdesk@uwimona.edu.jm
*Key Personnel*
Publication Officer: Annie Paul
Subjects: Literature, Literary Criticism, Essays
ISBN Prefix(es): 976-43

# Japan

## General Information

*Capital:* Tokyo
*Language:* Japanese
*Religion:* Shinto and Buddhism
*Population:* 125 million
*Bank Hours:* 0900-1500 Monday-Friday; 0900-
    1200 Saturday
*Shop Hours:* Same as bank hours
*Currency:* 100 yen = 1 dollar
*Export/Import Information:* 3% consumption; tax
    on books.
*Copyright:* UCC, Berne, Florence, Rome (see
    Copyright Conventions, pg xi)

**ACCJ,** *imprint of* The American Chamber of
    Commerce in Japan

**ADA Edita Tokyo Co Ltd**
12-14 Sendagaya chome, Shibuya-ku, Tokyo 151-
    0051
*Tel:* (03) 3403-1581 *Fax:* (03) 3497-0649
*E-mail:* info@ga-ada.co.jp
*Web Site:* www.ga-ada.co.jp
*Key Personnel*
Dir: Yukio Futagawa
Sales Manager: Tatsuo Futagawa
Founded: 1972
Subjects: Architecture & Interior Design
ISBN Prefix(es): 4-87140
*U.S. Office(s):* G A International/Co Ltd, 180 Varick St, 4th Floor, New York, NY 10014, United
    States *Tel:* 212-741-6329 *Fax:* 212-741-6283

**Aiki News**
14-17-103 Matsugae-cho, Sagamihara-shi, Kanagawa 228-0813
*Tel:* (042) 748-1240 *Fax:* (042) 748-2421
*Web Site:* aikinews.com
*Key Personnel*
Editor-in-Chief: Stanley A Pranin
    *E-mail:* editor@aikidojournal.com
English Editor: Diane Skoss
Founded: 1988
Membership(s): COSMEP.
Subjects: Sports, Athletics
ISBN Prefix(es): 4-900586

**Akita Shoten Publishing Co Ltd**
2-10-8 Iidabashi, Chioyoda-ku, Tokyo 102-8101
*Tel:* (03) 3264-7011 *Fax:* (03) 3265-5906
*E-mail:* license@akitashoten.co.jp
*Web Site:* www.akitashoten.co.jp
*Key Personnel*
President: Sadami Akita
Editorial: Nobumichi Akutsu; Taizo Kabemura
Sales: Toshimichi Okubo
Foreign Rights: Noriyoshi Oda
Foreign Rights & Trade: Hirokazu Takahashi
Founded: 1948
Subjects: Fiction, History, Literature, Literary
    Criticism, Essays, Social Sciences, Sociology
ISBN Prefix(es): 4-253

**Alice-Kan+**
2-2 Kanda-ogawa-machi, Tokyo 101
*Tel:* (03) 3293 9755 *Fax:* (03) 3293 9756
*Key Personnel*
President: Yu Kobayashi
Founded: 1981
Subjects: Child Care & Development
ISBN Prefix(es): 4-7520
*Parent Company:* Rodojunposh

**The American Chamber of Commerce in
    Japan+**
Mesonick 39 MT Bldg 10f, 2-4-5 Azabudai,
    Minato-ku, Tokyo 106-0041
*Tel:* (03) 3433-5381 *Fax:* (03) 3433-8454
*E-mail:* info@accj.or.jp
*Web Site:* www.accj.or.jp
*Key Personnel*
Dir, Publications: Jeanmarie Todd
Founded: 1948
Specialize in helping US business expand in
    Japan.
Subjects: Business, Foreign Countries, Marketing,
    Travel
ISBN Prefix(es): 4-915682
Imprints: ACCJ
*U.S. Office(s):* ACCJ, c/o US Chamber of Commerce, International Division, 1615 "H" St
    NW, Washington, DC 20062, United States
    *Tel:* 202-463-5460 *Fax:* 202-463-3114
Distributed by Charles E Tuttle Co (Japan &
    USA)

**Aoki Shoten Co Ltd**
60, Kanda-Jimbocho 1 chome, Chiyoda-ku, Tokyo
    101-0051
*Tel:* (03) 3219 2341 *Fax:* (03) 3219 2585
*Web Site:* www.aokishoten.co.jp
*Key Personnel*
President, Foreign Rights & Trade: Masato Aoki
Founded: 1948
Subjects: Economics, Education, History, Philosophy, Social Sciences, Sociology
ISBN Prefix(es): 4-250

**Asahiya Shuppan**
Seisen-Ichigaya Bldg, 4 Ichigaya-Sadowara-cho-3
    chome, Tokyo 162-8402
*Tel:* (03) 3267-0861 *Fax:* (03) 3267-0875
*Key Personnel*
President: Takeshi Hayashima
ISBN Prefix(es): 4-7511

**Asakura Publishing Co Ltd+**
6-29 Shin-Ogawa machi, Shinjuku-ku, Tokyo
162-8707
*Tel:* (03) 3260 0141 *Fax:* (03) 3260 0180
*E-mail:* edit@asakura.co.jp
*Web Site:* www.asakura.co.jp
*Key Personnel*
President: Kunizo Asakura
Foreign Trade: Hideo Shirahara
Foreign Rights: Haruo Obata
Founded: 1929
ISBN Prefix(es): 4-254

**Aspect+**
Kinsan Bldg, 3-18-3, Kanda Nishikicho, Chiyoda-
ku, Tokyo 101-0054
*Tel:* (03) 5281-2550 *Fax:* (03) 5281-2552
*E-mail:* takahira@aspect.co.jp
*Web Site:* www.aspect.co.jp
*Key Personnel*
President & Publisher: Kosei Takahira
    *E-mail:* takahira@aspect.co.jp
Founded: 1978
Subjects: Business, History, Mysteries, Nonfic-
tion (General), Psychology, Psychiatry, Science
(General), Science Fiction, Fantasy
*Parent Company:* Aspect Corporation
Foreign Rights: Altair Book Scouts (US)

**Atelier Publishing Co Ltd**
Shinichi Bldg, 8 Yotsuya 2 chome, Shinjuku-ku,
Tokyo 160-0004
*Tel:* (03) 3357-2741 *Fax:* (03) 3357-2194
*Key Personnel*
President: Taisuke Hirabayashi
ISBN Prefix(es): 4-7518

**Baberu Inc+**
3-1 Ariake, TFT Bldg, Koutou-ju, Tokyo 135-
8071
*Tel:* (03) 5530-2205 *Fax:* (03) 5530-2204
*E-mail:* buc@babel.co.jp
*Web Site:* www.babel.co.jp
*Key Personnel*
President: Miyoko Yuasa
Dir, Planning & Editing Dept: Mr Maruhama Tet-
suro
Founded: 1974
ISBN Prefix(es): 4-931049; 4-89449
*U.S. Office(s):* San Francisco, CA, United States

**Baifukan Co Ltd**
4-3-12 Kudan-Minami, Chyoda-ku, Tokyo 102-
0074
*Tel:* (03) 3262-5270 *Fax:* (03) 3262-5276
*E-mail:* bfkeigyo@mx7.mesh.ne.jp
*Web Site:* www.baifukan.co.jp/
*Key Personnel*
Chairman: Kenji Yamamoto
President & Foreign Rights & Trade: Itaru Ya-
mamoto
Editorial: Masayuki Gotou; Kazunori Matsumoto;
Takashi Murayama
Production: Fumio Shigematu
Editorial, Rights & Permissions: Tsuyoshi Nohara
Founded: 1924
Subjects: Biological Sciences, Chemistry, Chem-
ical Engineering, Computer Science, Engineer-
ing (General), Mathematics, Physics, Psychol-
ogy, Psychiatry, Social Sciences, Sociology
ISBN Prefix(es): 4-563

**Baseball Magazine-Sha Co Ltd+**
10-10 Misakicho 3 chome, Chiyoda-ku, Toyko
101-8381
*Tel:* (03) 3238-0081 *Fax:* (03) 3238-0106
*Web Site:* www.bbm-japan.com
*Key Personnel*
President: Tetsuo Ikeda
Founded: 1946

Subjects: History, Psychology, Psychiatry, Sports,
Athletics, Travel
ISBN Prefix(es): 4-583
Subsidiaries: Kobunsha Co Ltd
*Branch Office(s)*
Doujma TSS Bldg, 6F 2-5-3 Sonezaki-Shinchi,
Kita-ku, Osaka-shi, Osaka 530-0002 *Tel:* (06)
3418825

**Bijutsu Shuppan-Sha, Ltd**
Inaokakudan Bldg, 2-38 Kanda Jinbo-cho,
Chiyoda-ku, Tokyo 101-8417
*Tel:* (03) 32342159 *Fax:* (03) 32349451
*E-mail:* shoseki@bijutsu.co.jp; artmedia@bijutsu.
co.jp
*Web Site:* www.bijutsu.co.jp *Cable:* FINEART
BOOK TOKYO
*Key Personnel*
Chairman: Atsushi Oshita
President: Kentaro Oshita
Sales Manager: Hiroshi Mizukoshi
Founded: 1905
Subjects: Architecture & Interior Design, Art,
Crafts, Games, Hobbies, How-to
ISBN Prefix(es): 4-568

**Bun-ichi Sogo Shuppan**
Kawakami Bldg, 2-5 Nishi-Gokencho, Shinjuku-
ku, Tokyo 162-0812
*Tel:* (03) 3235-7341 *Fax:* (03) 3269-1402
*E-mail:* bunichi@bun-ichi.co.jp
*Web Site:* www.bun-ichi.co.jp/
*Key Personnel*
President: Hiroshi Saito
Founded: 1959
Subjects: Biological Sciences, Electronics, Elec-
trical Engineering, Engineering (General), En-
vironmental Studies, Natural History, Photogra-
phy, Science (General), Bird watching
ISBN Prefix(es): 4-8299

**Bunkasha Publishing Co Ltd+**
29-6, Ichibancho, Chiyoda-ku, Tokyo 102-8405
*Tel:* (03) 3222-5111 *Fax:* (03) 3222-3672
*E-mail:* fukai@bunkasha.co.jp
*Web Site:* www.bunkasha.co.jp
*Key Personnel*
President: Kenichi Kai
Founded: 1948
Membership(s): Japan Book Publishers Associa-
tion; Japan Magazine Fair Trade Council for
the Promotion of Book Reading; Japan Maga-
zine Publishers Association; Japan Publishers
Club; National Council to Promote Ethics of
Mass Media; Publishers Association for Cul-
tural Exchange.
Subjects: Fashion, Fiction, Film, Video, History,
Humor, Literature, Literary Criticism, Essays,
Social Sciences, Sociology, Sports, Athletics

**Bunkashobo-Hakubun-Sha**
9-9 Mejirodai 1 chome, Bunkyo-ku, Tokyo 112-
0015
*Tel:* (03) 3947-2034 *Fax:* (03) 3947-4976
*Web Site:* www.user.net-web.ne.jp/bunka
*Key Personnel*
President: Sadayoshi Suzuki
Foreign Rights & Trade: Yoshio Amano
Founded: 1957
Subjects: Education, History, Literature, Literary
Criticism, Essays, Social Sciences, Sociology
ISBN Prefix(es): 4-8301

**Business Center for Academic Societies Japan**
C-21 Gakkai Center, 5-16-9 Honkomagome,
Bunkyo-ku, Tokyo 113-8622
*Tel:* (03) 5814-5800 *Fax:* (03) 5814-5823
*E-mail:* nuehara@bcasj.or.jp; haraki@bcasj.or.jp
*Web Site:* www.bcasj.or.jp
*Key Personnel*
Dir General: Mitsuoka Tomotari, PhD

Man Dir, Rights & Permissions: Konno Shozo
Production: B Todoroki
Founded: 1971
Subjects: Science (General)
ISBN Prefix(es): 4-930813; 4-89114
*Associate Companies:* Japan Scientific Societies
Press, 2-10 Hongo 6-chome, Bunkyo-ku, Tokyo
113; Center for Academic Publications Japan,
4-16, Yayoi 2-chome, Bunkyo-ku, Tokyo 113

**Chijin Shokan Co Ltd+**
15, Naka-machi, Shinjuku-ku, Tokyo 162-0835
*Tel:* (03) 3235-4422 *Fax:* (03) 3235-8984
*E-mail:* chijinshokan@nifty.com
*Web Site:* www.chijinshokan.co.jp
*Key Personnel*
President: Osamu Kamijo
Editorial Manager: Akira Tsuda
Man Dir: Tomoaki Ogawa
Founded: 1930
Membership(s): Japan Book Publishers Associa-
tion.
Subjects: Engineering (General), Medicine, Nurs-
ing, Dentistry, Physical Sciences, Science
(General), Technology
ISBN Prefix(es): 4-8052
Total Titles: 450 Print
Foreign Rep(s): Asano Agency (Worldwide);
English Agency (Japan); Japan Uni Agency
(Japan); Orion Press (Worldwide); Tuttle-Mori
Agency (Japan)

**Chikuma Shobo Publishing Co Ltd+**
5-3 Kuramae, Komuro Bldg, 2 Chome, Taito-ku,
Tokyo 111-8755
*Tel:* (048) 651-0053 *Fax:* (048) 666-4648
*Web Site:* www.chikumashobo.co.jp
*Key Personnel*
President: Akio Kikuchi *E-mail:* kikuchia@
chikumashobo.co.jp
Editorial, Rights & Permissions: Tetsuo Matsuda
Sales, Publicity: Tatsuji Tanaka
Production: Isao Miyazono
Founded: 1940
Subjects: Biography, Communications, Eco-
nomics, Education, Fiction, History, Human
Relations, Nonfiction (General), Philosophy,
Religion - Buddhist, Social Sciences, Sociol-
ogy, Women's Studies
ISBN Prefix(es): 4-480

**Chikyu-sha Co Ltd**
3-5 Akasaka 4 chome, Minato-ku, Tokyo 107-
0052
*Tel:* (03) 3585-0087 *Fax:* (03) 3589-2902
*Key Personnel*
President: Minoru Toda
Foreign Rights & Trade: Yutaka Toda
Founded: 1946
Subjects: Agriculture, Civil Engineering, Educa-
tion, Forestry; Home economics
ISBN Prefix(es): 4-8049

**Child Honsha Co Ltd+**
24-21 Koishikawa 5 chome, Bunkyo-ku, Tokyo
112-8512
*Tel:* (03) 3813-3781 *Fax:* (03) 3818-3765
*E-mail:* ehon@childbook.co.jp
*Web Site:* www.childbook.co.jp
*Key Personnel*
President: Yoshiaki Shimazaki
Foreign Rights & Trade: Kazuhisa Uemura
Sales, Publicity & Foreign Trade: Katsuharu
Mibu
Production: Shunzi Asaka
Rights & Permissions: Kotaro Ohashi
Founded: 1930
Subjects: Education
ISBN Prefix(es): 4-8054
*Associate Companies:* Kyodo Printing Co Ltd
Subsidiaries: Basic Inc; Hisakata Child Co Ltd

**Chuo-Tosho Co Ltd+**
Aburakoji-dori, Motoseiganji-sagaru, Kamigyo-ku,
Kyoto 602-0952
*Tel:* (075) 441-2174 *Fax:* (075) 441-3300
*Key Personnel*
President: Yuji Kamioka
Editorial, Publicity, Rights & Permissions:
Takanori Ikeda
Sales: Tetsuo Hattori
Production: Tsuneo Takeuchi
Founded: 1950
Subjects: Education
ISBN Prefix(es): 4-482

**Chuokoron-Shinsha Inc**
2-8-7 Kyobashi, Yomiuri-Chuko Bldg, Chuo-ku,
Tokyo 104-8320
*Tel:* (03) 3563-1431 *Fax:* (03) 3561-5922
*E-mail:* honyaku-irie@chuko.co.jp
*Web Site:* www.chuko.co.jp
*Telex:* J32505 Chuokor *Cable:* Chuokoron Tokyo
*Key Personnel*
President: Jin Nakamura
Foreign Rights & Trade: Norio Irie
Founded: 1886
Subjects: Art, Economics, Government, Political
Science, History, Literature, Literary Criticism,
Essays, Philosophy, Religion - Other, Science
(General), Social Sciences, Sociology
ISBN Prefix(es): 4-12

**CMC Publishing Co Ltd+**
5-4 Uchi-Kanda 1 chome, Miyako Bldg, Chiyoda-
ku, Tokyo 101-0047
*Tel:* (03) 3293-2065 *Fax:* (03) 3293-2069
*E-mail:* info@cmcbooks.co.jp
*Web Site:* www.cmcbooks.co.jp
*Key Personnel*
President: Kentaro Shima
Foreign Rights & Trade: Takashi Fukuda
Founded: 1961
Subjects: Biological Sciences, Business, Electron-
ics, Electrical Engineering, Science (General),
Technology
ISBN Prefix(es): 4-88231
*Branch Office(s)*
Osaka

**Contex Corporation+**
Suzuki Bldg 1-13-14, Akebono-cho, Tachikawa,
Tokyo 190-0012
*Tel:* (03) 42-522-0051 *Fax:* (03) 42-526-2345;
(03) 42-548-2400
*E-mail:* contex@jade.dt.ne.jp
*Web Site:* contex.co.jp/
*Key Personnel*
President: Shigeru Tsukakoshi
Contact: Yuko Tsukakoshi
Founded: 1982
Restaurant menu guide consisting of ten language
interpretations. English, Chinese, Korean,
Japanese, French, Spanish, German, Italian
& Portuguese cookery books & travel guides.
Chinese, Korean & Japanese foods.
Subjects: Cookery, Travel
ISBN Prefix(es): 4-907653
Total Titles: 1 Print
Foreign Rep(s): Value Supply Inc

**Corona Publishing Co Ltd**
46-10 Sengoku 4 chome, Bunkyo-ku, Tokyo 112-
0011
*Tel:* (03) 3941-3131 *Fax:* (03) 3941-3137
*E-mail:* info@coronasha.co.jp
*Web Site:* www.coronasha.co.jp
*Key Personnel*
President: Tatsumi Gorai
Editorial Dir: Sumio Hatano; Hiroshi Nakamata
Foreign Rights & Trade: Masaya Gorai
Founded: 1927
Subjects: Civil Engineering, Computer Science,
Electronics, Electrical Engineering, Mechanical
Engineering, Science (General), Technology,
Metallurgy
ISBN Prefix(es): 4-339

**Daiichi Shuppan Co Ltd**
39, Kanda-Jimbocho, Chiyoda-ku, Tokyo 101-
0051
*Tel:* (03) 3291-4576 *Fax:* (03) 3291-4579
*Web Site:* www.daiichi-shuppan.co.jp
*Key Personnel*
President & Foreign Rights & Trade: Hideji
Ishikawa *E-mail:* ishikawa@japan.email.ne.jp
Founded: 1944
Subjects: Economics, Health, Nutrition, House &
Home, Medicine, Nursing, Dentistry
ISBN Prefix(es): 4-8041
Number of titles published annually: 10 Print; 1
CD-ROM
Total Titles: 150 Print; 5 CD-ROM

**Dainippon Tosho Publishing Co, Ltd+**
9-10 Ginza 1 chome, Chuo-ku, Tokyo 104-0061
*Tel:* (03) 3561-8672 *Fax:* (03) 3563-5596
*Web Site:* www.dainippon-tosho.co.jp
Founded: 1890
Subjects: Chemistry, Chemical Engineering, Edu-
cation, Fiction, Psychology, Psychiatry, Science
(General)
ISBN Prefix(es): 4-477

**Diamond Inc+**
6-12-17 Jingumae, Shibuya-ku, Tokyo 150-8409
*Tel:* (03) 5778-7232 *Fax:* (03) 5778-6612
*Web Site:* www.diamond.co.jp
*Key Personnel*
President: Norio Tamura
Foreign Rights & Trade: Eiji Mitachi
Founded: 1913
Subjects: Business, Career Development, Eco-
nomics, Environmental Studies, Management,
Marketing, Nonfiction (General), Psychology,
Psychiatry, Science (General), Self-Help, Fore-
casting, Industrial, Research & Development
ISBN Prefix(es): 4-478
Subsidiaries: Diamond Agency; Diamond Big;
Diamond Fund; Diamond Graphics; Diamond
Service
*Branch Office(s)*
Osaka, India

**Dobunshoin Publishers Co**
24-3 Koishikawa 5 chome, Bunkyo-ku, Tokyo
112-0002
*Tel:* (03) 3812-7777 *Fax:* (03) 3812-7792
*E-mail:* dobun@dobun.co.jp
*Web Site:* www.dobun.co.jp
*Key Personnel*
President: Fumihiro Uno
Foreign Rights & Trade: Sawako Shimaya
Founded: 1928
Subjects: Business, Computer Science, How-to,
Medicine, Nursing, Dentistry, Microcomputers,
Nonfiction (General), Science (General), Social
Sciences, Sociology, Sports, Athletics
ISBN Prefix(es): 4-8103

**Dogakusha Inc**
10-7 Suido 1 chome, Bunkyo-ku, Tokyo 112-
0005
*Tel:* (03) 3816-7011 *Fax:* (03) 3816-7044
*E-mail:* eigyoubu@dogakusha.co.jp
*Web Site:* www.dogakusha.co.jp
*Key Personnel*
President: Kusuji Kondo
Founded: 1950
All publications in German.
ISBN Prefix(es): 4-8102

**Dohosha Publishing Co Ltd+**
Tas Bldg, 2-5-2 Nishi-Kanda, Chiyoda-ku, Tokyo
101-0065

*Tel:* (03) 5276 0831 *Fax:* (03) 5276 0840
*Key Personnel*
President: Satoru Imada
Foreign Rights: Takuya Kosaka
Founded: 1918
Subjects: Architecture & Interior Design, Art,
Asian Studies, Cookery, History, How-to,
Medicine, Nursing, Dentistry, Religion - Bud-
dhist
ISBN Prefix(es): 4-8104
*Associate Companies:* DDP Digital Publishing
Inc; Ochanomizu Management Laboratory;
OML Information Service Center
Subsidiaries:
*Warehouse:* 34-1, Shironokoshi-cho, Shimotoba,
Fushimi-ku, Kyoto 612

**Eichosha Company Ltd**
Kusaka Bldg, 28 Kanda Jimbocho 2 chome,
Chiyoda-ku, Tokyo 101-0051
*Tel:* (03) 3263-1641 *Fax:* (03) 3263-6174
*E-mail:* info@eichosha.co.jp
*Web Site:* www.eichosha.co.jp
*Key Personnel*
President: Shozo Doki
Subjects: English as a Second Language, Lan-
guage Arts, Linguistics, Literature, Literary
Criticism, Essays
ISBN Prefix(es): 4-268

**The Eihosha Ltd**
21 Sanaicho, Ichigaya, Shinjuku-ku, Tokyo 162-
8691
*Tel:* (03) 5206-6020 *Fax:* (03) 5206-6022
*E-mail:* e@eihosha.co.jp
*Web Site:* www.eihosha.co.jp
*Key Personnel*
President: Gen Sasaki
Contact: Masao Uji
Founded: 1949
Subjects: Literature, Literary Criticism, Essays
ISBN Prefix(es): 4-269

**Elsevier Science**
9-15 Higashi-Azabu 1 chome, Minato-ku, Tokyo
106-0044
*Tel:* (03) 5561-5033 *Toll Free Tel:* (0120) 383-
608 (within Japan) *Fax:* (03) 5561-5047
*E-mail:* info@elsevier.co.jp
*Web Site:* www.elsevier.co.jp
*Key Personnel*
Man Dir: Ryoji Fukada
Sales & editorial services office of Elsevier Sci-
ence BV, Netherlands.
ISBN Prefix(es): 4-86034
*Parent Company:* Elsevier Science BV, Nether-
lands

**Froebel - kan Co Ltd+**
14-9 Honkomagome 6 chome, Bunkyo-ku, Tokyo
113-8611
*Tel:* (03) 5395-6600 *Fax:* (03) 5395-6627
*E-mail:* info-e@froebel-kan.co.jp
*Web Site:* www.froebel-kan.co.jp
*Telex:* J24907
*Key Personnel*
President: Kennosuke Arai *E-mail:* arai-k@
froebel.kan.co.jp
Dir: Mitsuhiro Tada *E-mail:* tada-m@froebel-kan.
co.jp
Founded: 1907
Subjects: Animals, Pets, Education, Anpanman
ISBN Prefix(es): 4-577
Number of titles published annually: 120 Print
Total Titles: 1,000 Print; 1 CD-ROM
*Parent Company:* Toppan Printing Co Ltd

**Fuji Keizai Company Ltd**
FK Bldg, 2-5 Nihombashi Kodemma-cho, Chou-
ku, Tokyo 103-0001
*Tel:* (03) 3644-5811 *Fax:* (03) 3661-0165
*Web Site:* www.fuji-keizai.co.jp

*Key Personnel*
President: Hideo Abe
Founded: 1962
Subjects: Electronics, Electrical Engineering
ISBN Prefix(es): 4-89225; 4-8349
Subsidiaries: Fuji Khimera Institute
*U.S. Office(s):* Fuji Keizai, 141 E 55 St, Suite 3F, New York, NY, United States

**Fukuinkan Shoten Publishers Inc+**
6-6-3, Honkomagome, Bunkyo-ku, Tokyo 113-8686
*Tel:* (03) 39420032 *Fax:* (03) 39421401
*Web Site:* www.fukuinkan.co.jp *Cable:* FUKUINKANSHOTEN TOKYO
*Key Personnel*
Chairman: Katsumi Sato
President: Shiro Tokita
Sales Dir: Noboru Ogura
Dir (International Dept): Mariko Ogawa
Founded: 1952
Specialize in children's books, including illustrated books.
Subjects: Fiction, Literature, Literary Criticism, Essays, Nonfiction (General), Science (General), Science Fiction, Fantasy
ISBN Prefix(es): 4-8340
Number of titles published annually: 150 Print
Total Titles: 1,000 Print

**Fukumura Shuppan Inc**
2-30-7 Hongo, Bunkyo-ku, Tokyo 113-0033
*Tel:* (03) 3813-3981 *Fax:* (03) 3818-2786
*Web Site:* www.fukumura.co.jp
*Key Personnel*
President: Junichi Fukumura
Founded: 1939
Subjects: Education, History, Philosophy, Psychology, Psychiatry, Social Sciences, Sociology
ISBN Prefix(es): 4-571

**Fumaido Publishing Company Ltd+**
14-9 Otsuka 2 chome, Bunkyo-ku, Tokyo 112-0012
*Tel:* (03) 3946-2345 *Fax:* (03) 3947-0110
*E-mail:* fumaido@tkd.att.ne.jp
*Key Personnel*
President: Michio Miyawaki
Founded: 1960
Subjects: Education, Health, Nutrition, Sports, Athletics, Physical education, recreation
ISBN Prefix(es): 4-8293

**Fuzambo Publishing Co+**
1-3, Kanda-Jimbocho, Chiyoda-ku, Toyko 101-0051
*Tel:* (03) 3291-2171 *Fax:* (03) 3291-2179
*Key Personnel*
President: Yoshihiro Sakamoto
Founded: 1886
Subjects: Art, Geography, Geology, History, Language Arts, Linguistics, Law, Literature, Literary Criticism, Essays, Philosophy, Religion - Other, Social Sciences, Sociology
ISBN Prefix(es): 4-572

**Gakken Co Ltd+**
4-40-5 Kamiikedai, Ohta, Tokyo 145-8502
*Tel:* (03) 3726-8111 *Fax:* (03) 3493-3338
*Web Site:* www.gakken.co.jp
*Key Personnel*
President: Yoichiro Endo
Foreign Rights & Trade: Takeshi Kubodera
Founded: 1946
Subjects: Art, Astrology, Occult, Automotive, Business, Child Care & Development, Computer Science, Education, Electronics, Electrical Engineering, Environmental Studies, Gardening, Plants, House & Home, Nonfiction (General), Outdoor Recreation, Radio, TV, Comic Books
ISBN Prefix(es): 4-05

**GakuseiSha Publishing Co Ltd**
2-2-4 Kudan-minami, Chiyoda-ku, Tokyo 102-0074
*Tel:* (03) 3857-3031 *Fax:* (03) 3857-3037
*E-mail:* info@gakusei.co.jp
*Web Site:* www.gakusei.co.jp
*Key Personnel*
President: Ichiro Tsuruoka
Foreign Rights Executive: Shigeru Ohas
Founded: 1952
Subjects: Archaeology, Business, Geography, Geology, History, Language Arts, Linguistics, Law, Literature, Literary Criticism, Essays, Philosophy, Religion - Other, Social Sciences, Sociology
ISBN Prefix(es): 4-311

**Genko-Sha**
1-5 Iidabashi 4 chome, Chiyoda-ku, Tokyo 102-8716
*Tel:* (03) 3263-3515 *Fax:* (03) 3239-5886
*E-mail:* gks@genkosha.co.jp
*Web Site:* www.genkosha.co.jp
*Key Personnel*
President: Morio Kitahara *Tel:* (03) 3263 3511 *Fax:* (03) 3263 3830
Dir: Chuichi Kaneko *E-mail:* kaneko@genkosha.co.jp
Founded: 1931
Membership(s): JBPA.
Subjects: Art, Film, Video, How-to, Photography
ISBN Prefix(es): 4-7683
Subsidiaries: Salon Agency Co Ltd (advertising agency)
*Warehouse:* Ono Poking Co Ltd, Inari Souka City *Tel:* (0489) 32 2911 *Fax:* (0489) 36 5333
*Orders to:* Nippan IPS Co Ltd, 11-6, 3 Cho-Me, Iidabashi, Chiyoda-Ku, Toyko 102 *Tel:* (03) 3238 0700 *Fax:* (03) 3238 0707
*E-mail:* ips05@nippan-ips.co.jp

**Gyosei Corporation**
30-16, Ogikubo 4 chome, Suginami-ku, Tokyo 167-8088
*Tel:* (03) 5349-6666 *Fax:* (03) 5349-6655
*E-mail:* eigyo1@gyosei.co.jp
*Web Site:* www.gyosei.co.jp
ISBN Prefix(es): 4-324

**Hakubunkan-Shinsha Publishers Ltd**
14-6, Koishikawa, 2 chome, Bunkyo-ku, Tokyo 112-0002
*Tel:* (03) 3811-4721; (03) 3811-6693 *Fax:* (03) 3818-1431
*Web Site:* www.hakubunkan.co.jp
*Key Personnel*
President: Kazuhiro Ohashi
ISBN Prefix(es): 4-89177; 4-86115
*Parent Company:* Hakuyusha Publishing Co Ltd

**Hakusui-Sha Co Ltd**
3-24, Kanda-Ogawa-cho, Chiyoda-ku, Tokyo 101-0052
*Tel:* (03) 3291-7811 *Fax:* (03) 3291-8448
*E-mail:* hpmaster@hakusuisha.co.jp
*Web Site:* www.hakusuisha.co.jp *Cable:* Hakusuisha Tokyo
*Key Personnel*
President: Masayuki Kawamura
Foreign Rights & Trade: Motofumi Ibuki
Founded: 1915
Subjects: Art, Drama, Theater, Fiction, History, Language Arts, Linguistics, Literature, Literary Criticism, Essays, Music, Dance, Nonfiction (General), Philosophy
ISBN Prefix(es): 4-560

**Hakutei-Sha+**
65-1, Ikebukuro 2 chome, Toshima-ku, Tokyo 171-0014
*Tel:* (03) 3986-3271 *Fax:* (03) 3986-3272

*E-mail:* LDX00227@nifty.ne.jp
*Key Personnel*
President: Yasuo Sato
Foreign Rights & Trade: Takako Sato
Founded: 1977
Subjects: Health, Nutrition, Language Arts, Linguistics, Literature, Literary Criticism, Essays, Religion - Buddhist, Sports, Athletics
ISBN Prefix(es): 4-89174

**Hakuyo-Sha**
3F Hakuyo Dai 2 Bldg, 7-7 Kandasurugadai, One Chome, Chiyoda-ku, Tokyo 101-0062
*Tel:* (03) 5281-9772 *Fax:* (03) 5281-9886
*E-mail:* hakuyo@mars.dti.ne.jp
*Web Site:* www.hakuyo-sha.co.jp
*Key Personnel*
President: Hiroshi Nakamura
Founded: 1920
Subjects: Animals, Pets, Nonfiction (General), Psychology, Psychiatry, Science (General)
ISBN Prefix(es): 4-8269

**Hakuyu-Sha**
2-27, Agebacho, Shinjuku-ku, Tokyo 162-0824
*Tel:* (03) 3268-8271 *Fax:* (03) 3268-8273
*Web Site:* www.hakubunkan.co.jp
*Key Personnel*
President: Kazuhiro Ohashi
Foreign Trade Executive: Montaro Ono
Publicity & Advertising: Kazuya Baba
Foreign Rights: Eiji Takamori
Founded: 1948
Subjects: Agriculture, Labor, Industrial Relations, Science (General), Haiku
ISBN Prefix(es): 4-8268

**Hara Shobo**
2-3 Kanda Jimbocho, Chiyoda-ku, Tokyo 101-0051
*Tel:* (03) 5212-7801 *Fax:* (03) 3230-1158
*E-mail:* toshi@harashobo.com
*Web Site:* www.harashobo.com
*Key Personnel*
President: Kyo Naruse
Handle wide variety of ukiyo-e prints, paintings, illustrated books from 17th century to 20th century, & shin-hanga (modern prints) as well as reproductions, catalogues & reference books.
Membership(s): Ukiyo-e Dealers Association of Japan; board member of International Ukiyo-e Society; founding member of Japan Print of Art Auction (JPAA).
ISBN Prefix(es): 4-562

**Hayakawa Publishing Inc**
2 Kanda-Tacho 2 chome, Chiyoda-ku, Tokyo 101-0046
*Tel:* (03) 3254-3111 *Fax:* (03) 3254-1550
*Telex:* 02222331 Books J *Cable:* Hayakawa Tokyo
*Key Personnel*
President: Hiroshi Hayakawa
Founded: 1945
Subjects: Art, Biography, Business, Drama, Theater, Fiction, Government, Political Science, History, Literature, Literary Criticism, Essays, Management, Mysteries, Nonfiction (General), Philosophy, Religion - Other, Science (General), Science Fiction, Fantasy, Social Sciences, Sociology
ISBN Prefix(es): 4-15

**Heibonsha Ltd, Publishers+**
2-29-4 Hakusan, Izumi Hakusan Bldg, Bunkyo Ku, Tokyo 112-0001
*Tel:* (03) 3818-0873; (03) 3818-0874 (sales) *Fax:* (03) 3818-0857
*E-mail:* shop@heibonsha.co.jp
*Web Site:* www.heibonsha.co.jp *Cable:* BOOKSHEIBONSHA

*Key Personnel*
President: Naoto Shimonaka
Foreign Rights & Trade: Hidenori Sekiguchi
Founded: 1914
Subjects: Art, Education, History, Nonfiction (General), Philosophy, Science (General), Social Sciences, Sociology
ISBN Prefix(es): 4-582; 4-256

**Hikarinokuni Ltd**
3-2-14 Uehonmachi, Tennoji-ku, Osaka 543-0001
*Tel:* (06) 6768-1151 *Fax:* (06) 6768-6795
*E-mail:* hikari@skyblue.ocn.ne.jp
*Web Site:* www.hikarinokuni.co.jp
*Key Personnel*
President: Takeshi Okamoto
Man Dir: Yotaro Matsumoto
Editorial & Export Dir: Masaaki Tsuchiya
Founded: 1945
Subjects: Economics, Education, House & Home
ISBN Prefix(es): 4-564

**Hinoki Publishing Co Ltd**
One Kanda-Ogawa-machi, 2 chome, Chiyoda-ku, Tokyo 101-0052
*Tel:* (03) 32912488 *Fax:* (03) 32953554
*E-mail:* info@hinoki-shoten.co.jp
*Web Site:* www.hinoki-shoten.co.jp
*Key Personnel*
Chairman: Hisako Suginomori
President: Tsunemasa Hinoki
Founded: 1659
Publisher of Noh & Kyogen Books.
ISBN Prefix(es): 4-8279

**Hirokawa Publishing Co+**
3-27-14 Hongo, Bunkyo-ku, Tokyo 113-0033
*Tel:* (03) 3815 3651 *Fax:* (03) 5684 7030 *Cable:* HIGESEHI TOKYO
*Key Personnel*
President: Setsuo Hirokawa
Vice President: Hideo Hirokawa
Dir: Haruo Hirokawa
Founded: 1926
Subjects: Biological Sciences, Chemistry, Chemical Engineering, Medicine, Nursing, Dentistry, Science (General)
ISBN Prefix(es): 4-567
Total Titles: 50 Print

**Hoikusha Publishing Co Ltd**
4-8-6 Tsurumi ku Tsurumi, Osaka City, Osaka 538
*Tel:* (06) 932-6601 *Fax:* (06) 933-8577
*Web Site:* www.hoikusha.co.jp *Cable:* Hoikusha
*Key Personnel*
President: Yuki Imai
Man Dir: Osamu Yoshino
Editorial: Hiroshi Murakami
Founded: 1947
Subjects: Art, Biography, Crafts, Games, Hobbies, Geography, Geology, History, How-to, Music, Dance, Natural History, Poetry, Science (General)
ISBN Prefix(es): 4-586
*Branch Office(s)*
1-1 Minami-Otsuka, Toshima-ku, Tokyo 170

**Hokkaido University Press**
Kito-9-Jo, Nishi 8-chome, Kita-Kujo Sapporo-shi, Hokkaido 060-0809
*Tel:* (011) 747-2308 *Fax:* (011) 736-8605
*E-mail:* hupress_6@hup.gr.jp
*Web Site:* www.hup.gr.jp
*Key Personnel*
President: Hiroshi Saeki
Vice President: Mutsuo Nakamura
Foreign Rights & Trade: Hideki Kudanami
Founded: 1970

Subjects: Science (General), Social Sciences, Sociology, Technology, Humanities, natural science
ISBN Prefix(es): 4-8329

**Hokuryukan Co Ltd+**
8-14, Takanawa 3 chome, Minato-ku, Tokyo 108-0074
*Tel:* (03) 5449-4591 *Fax:* (03) 5449-4950
*E-mail:* hk-ns@mk1.mqcnet.or.jp
*Key Personnel*
President: Hisako Fukuda
Foreign Rights & Trade: Masako Kamase
Founded: 1891
Subjects: Agriculture, Biological Sciences, Education, Medicine, Nursing, Dentistry, Science (General)
ISBN Prefix(es): 4-8326
Subsidiaries: New Science Publishing Co

**The Hokuseido Press**
32-4 Honkomagome, 3 Chome, Bunkyo-ku, Tokyo 113-0021
*Tel:* (03) 38270511 *Fax:* (03) 38270567
*E-mail:* info@hokuseido.com *Cable:* HOKSEDPRES TOKYO
*Key Personnel*
Dir: Masazo Yamamoto
Sales, Advertising, Rights & Permissions: Keisuke Yamamoto
Founded: 1914
Subjects: Biography, Philosophy, Poetry, Religion - Other
ISBN Prefix(es): 4-590
*Orders to:* Book East, PO Box 13352, Portland, OR 97213, United States *Tel:* 503-287-0974 *Fax:* 503-281-3693 *E-mail:* kwakiyama@aol.com

**Holp Book Co Ltd**
Shinhana Bldg, 19-7 Shinjuku 1 chome, Shinjuku-ku, Tokyo 160
*Tel:* (03) 5285-5011 *Fax:* (03) 3225-1663
*E-mail:* holp@holp.co.jp
*Web Site:* www.holp.co.jp
*Key Personnel*
President: Mr Seiji Ohyabu
Founded: 1964
Subjects: Art, Education, Geography, Geology, Literature, Literary Criticism, Essays, Mathematics, Science (General)
ISBN Prefix(es): 4-89427
Subsidiaries: Holp Shuppan Publishers

**Horitsu Bunka-Sha**
71, Iwagakakiuchicho, Kamigamo, Kita-ku, Kyoto 603-8053
*Tel:* (075) 791-7131 *Fax:* (075) 721-8400
*E-mail:* eigy@hou-bun.co.jp
*Web Site:* web.kyoto-inet.or.jp/org/houritu
*Key Personnel*
President: Tsutomu Okamura
Founded: 1947
Subjects: Economics, Law, Philosophy, Public Administration, Social Sciences, Sociology, Politics
ISBN Prefix(es): 4-589

**Hyoronsha Publishing Co Ltd**
2-21 TsukudoHachimancho, Shinjuku-ku, Tokyo 162-0815
*Tel:* (03) 3260-9401 *Fax:* (03) 3260-9408
*Web Site:* www.hyoronsha.co.jp
*Key Personnel*
President: Harunobu Takeshita
Chief Editor: Kunio Hitomi
Sales Manager: Zenzo Uchida
Founded: 1948
Subjects: Education, History, Language Arts, Linguistics, Law, Philosophy, Religion - Buddhist, Religion - Other, Social Sciences, Sociology
ISBN Prefix(es): 4-566

**IBC Publishing Inc+**
Akasaka Community Bldg, 1-1-8 Moto-Akasaka, Minato-ku, Tokyo 107-0051
*Tel:* (03) 5770-2438 *Fax:* (03) 5786-7419
*E-mail:* ibc@ibcpub.co.jp
*Web Site:* www.ibcpub.co.jp
*Key Personnel*
President: Hiroshi Kagawa
Editor-in-Chief: Kuniaki Ura
Founded: 2003
Subjects: Art, Asian Studies, English as a Second Language, Language Arts, Linguistics
ISBN Prefix(es): 4-89684; 4-925080
*Parent Company:* Yohan Inc

**Ichiryu-Sha**
5-18 Yanaka 2 chome, Taito-ku, Tokyo 110-0001
*Tel:* (03) 3822-0585 *Fax:* (03) 3821-3964
*Key Personnel*
President: Tsuguo Hikosaka
Founded: 1951
Subjects: Law, Social Sciences, Sociology
ISBN Prefix(es): 4-7527

**Ie-No-Hikari Association+**
11 Ichigaya-Funagawaracho, Shinjuku-ku, Tokyo 162-8448
*Tel:* (03) 3266-9029 *Fax:* (03) 3266-9053
*E-mail:* hikari@mxd.meshnet.or.jp
*Web Site:* www.ienohikari.or.jp
*Key Personnel*
President: Masahiko Takada
Man Dir: Masaya Kakunaka
Executive Dir: Katsuro Kawaguchi; Kazuyuki Morishita
Book Publication: Kenji Yokoyama
Foreign Rights & Trade: Satoshi Sekiguchi
Founded: 1925
Subjects: Agriculture, Economics, House & Home, Social Sciences, Sociology, Cooperatives
ISBN Prefix(es): 4-259

**Igaku-Shoin Ltd+**
24-3 Hongo, 5 Chome, Bunkyo-ku, Tokyo 113-8719
*Tel:* (03) 38175600 *Fax:* (03) 38157791
*E-mail:* info@igaku-shoin.co.jp
*Web Site:* www.igaku-shoin.co.jp
*Key Personnel*
President: Yu Kanehara
Vice President, Medical Publications: Hideho Nakamura
Vice President, Sales: Kensaku Kobayashi
Senior Manager, Foreign Books & Journals: Kazuo Kuwabara *Tel:* (03) 3817 5676
*E-mail:* k-kuwabara@igaku-shoin.co.jp
Founded: 1944
Subjects: Medicine, Nursing, Dentistry
ISBN Prefix(es): 4-260
Subsidiaries: Medical Sciences International Ltd; LWW Igaku-Shoin Ltd; Igaku-Shoin Medical Publishers Inc

**Institute for Financial Affairs Inc-KINZAI**
Kinyu-Zaisei-Kaikan, 19 Minami-motomachi, Shinjuku-ku, Tokyo 160-8520
*Tel:* (03) 3355-2355 *Fax:* (03) 3358-2069
*Web Site:* www.kinzai.or.jp
*Key Personnel*
President: Mr Akira Kanai
General Manager: Mr Hiroyuki Nishino
Founded: 1950
Subjects: Accounting, Finance
ISBN Prefix(es): 4-322
Subsidiaries: KINZAI Corporation
*Branch Office(s)*
Fukuoka
Nagoya
Osaka
*U.S. Office(s):* 600 Third Ave, 23rd floor, New York, NY 10016, United States *Tel:* 212-687-8316 *Fax:* 212-687-8317

**International Society for Educational Information (ISEI)**
Affiliate of Ministry of Foreign Affairs, Japan
Shinko Ofisomu 502, 20-3 San'ei-cho, Shinjuku-ku, Tokyo 160-0008
*Tel:* (03) 33581138 *Fax:* (03) 33597188
*E-mail:* kaya@isei.or.jp
*Web Site:* www.isei.or.jp
*Key Personnel*
Chair, Board of Directors: Michiko Kaya
  *E-mail:* kaya@isei.or.jp
Founded: 1958
Specialize in publications about Japan.
Subjects: Art, Crafts, Games, Hobbies, Economics, Geography, Geology, History, Culture, Japan
Number of titles published annually: 10 Print
Total Titles: 48 Print

**Ishihara Publishing Co Ltd**
13-2, Nishi-Sengokucho, Kagoshima City, Kagoshima 892-0847
*Tel:* (0992) 391200 *Fax:* (0992) 391202
*E-mail:* info@isihara-kk.co.jp
*Web Site:* www.isihara-kk.co.jp
*Key Personnel*
President: Kanichiro Ishihara
Foreign Rights/Trade: Tetsu Nakahata
Founded: 1990
ISBN Prefix(es): 4-900611
Imprints: Ishihara's Decade Diary
Distributed by Japan Publication & Selling Co Ltd; Mail Order House Catalog House Co Ltd; Tokyo Book Seller's Co Ltd

**Ishihara's Decade Diary**, *imprint of* Ishihara Publishing Co Ltd

**Ishiyaku Publishers Inc**
1-7-10, Honkomagome, Bunkyo-ku, Tokyo 113-8612
*Tel:* (03) 5395-7600 *Fax:* (03) 5395-7603
*E-mail:* dev-mdp@nna.so-net.ne.jp
*Telex:* 2723298 Mdp J *Cable:* MEPHARMA TOKYO
*Key Personnel*
President: Katsuji Fujita
Publisher, Dental Books: Yukuhide Yonekawa
Publisher, Medical: Akio Fukushima
Publisher, Dental Journals: Takao Suda
Marketing Dir: Akira Iwase; Tai Watanabe
Foreign Rights/Trade: Ms Shoko Ishimura
Founded: 1921
Subjects: Health, Nutrition, Medicine, Nursing, Dentistry, Veterinary Science, Natural Science
ISBN Prefix(es): 4-263; 4-281
*Branch Office(s)*
c/o Manden Bldg, 11-23 Nishi-Tenma 4-Chome, Kita-ku, Osaka-shi
*Orders to:* Tokyo Mail Service Co Ltd, 1-30-6 Sugamo, Toshimaku, Tokyo 170

**Itaria Shobo Ltd**
2-23, Kanda-Jimbocho, Chiyoda-ku, Tokyo 101-0051
*Tel:* (03) 3262-1656 *Fax:* (03) 3234-6469
*E-mail:* HQM01271@nifty.ne.jp *Cable:* ITALIASHOBO
*Key Personnel*
President: Motomichi Ito
Foreign Rights/Trade: Doichi Ito
Founded: 1958
Specialize in Italian, Spanish & Portuguese imported books.
ISBN Prefix(es): 4-900143

**Iwanami Shoten, Publishers+**
2-5-5, Hitotsubashi, Chiyoda-ku, Tokyo 101-0003
*Tel:* (03) 5210-4115 *Fax:* (03) 3239-9619
*Web Site:* www.iwanami.co.jp

*Key Personnel*
President: Nobukazu Otsuka
Editorial Dir: Suzuki Minoru
Foreign Rights Manager: Sachiko Kagaya
Foreign Rights: Rika Ito *E-mail:* rika-ito@iwanami.co.jp; Noa Shimizu
Founded: 1913
Subjects: Art, Biography, Economics, Electronics, Electrical Engineering, History, Literature, Literary Criticism, Essays, Philosophy, Photography, Psychology, Psychiatry, Science (General), Social Sciences, Sociology
ISBN Prefix(es): 4-00
Number of titles published annually: 700 Print; 10 CD-ROM
Total Titles: 5,000 Print; 30 CD-ROM; 10 Audio
*Orders to:* Japan Publications Trading Co, Ltd, 1-2-1 Sarugakucho, Chiyoda-ku, Tokyo *Tel:* (03) 32923751 *Fax:* (03) 32920410

**Iwasaki Shoten Publishing Co Ltd**
1-9-2 Suido, Bunkyo-ku, Tokyo 112-0005
*Tel:* (03) 3812-9131 *Fax:* (03) 3816-6033
*E-mail:* ask@iwasakishoten.co.jp
*Web Site:* www.iwasakishoten.co.jp
*Key Personnel*
President: Hiro Iwasaki
Sales Manager: Tutomu Yasuda
Editorial: Toshio Iino
Founded: 1934
Membership(s): Japan Children's Books Association.
Subjects: Art
ISBN Prefix(es): 4-265
*Associate Companies:* Iwasaki Gakujutsu Publishing Co
Subsidiaries: Iwasaki Art Publishing Co

**Japan Bible Society**
4-5-1 Ginza, Chuo-ku, Tokyo 104-0061
Mailing Address: PO Box 6, Kyobashi
*Tel:* (03) 3567-1990; (03) 3567-1987 (distribution) *Fax:* (03) 3567-4436 (administration)
*E-mail:* info@bible.or.jp
*Web Site:* www.bible.or.jp
*Key Personnel*
President: Hiroshi Omiya
Foreign Rights/Trade: Rev Makoto Watabe
  *E-mail:* makoto-w@bible.or.jp
Founded: 1875
Membership(s): United Bible Societies.
ISBN Prefix(es): 4-8202

**Japan Broadcast Publishing Co Ltd+**
41-1, Udagawacho, Shibuya-ku, Tokyo 150-8081
*Tel:* (03) 3780-3356 *Fax:* (03) 3780-3348
*E-mail:* webmaster@npb.nhk-grp.co.jp
*Key Personnel*
President: Takeshi Matsuo
Contact: Chieako Ishizuka
Foreign Rights/Trade: Masahiro Kizaki
Founded: 1931
Subjects: Art, Crafts, Games, Hobbies, Education, Fiction, Geography, Geology, History, How-to, Language Arts, Linguistics, Literature, Literary Criticism, Essays, Nonfiction (General), Science (General), Social Sciences, Sociology
ISBN Prefix(es): 4-14
*Parent Company:* NHK (Japan Broadcasting Corporation)

**Japan Educational Publishing Co Ltd**, see Nihon-Bunkyo Shuppan (Japan Educational Publishing Co Ltd)

**Japan Industrial Publishing Co Ltd+**
Suzuki Bldg, 10-1 Azabu-10-Ban 3 chome, Minato-ku, Tokyo 106-0045
*Tel:* (03) 3456-1827 *Fax:* (03) 3944-6826
*E-mail:* info@nikko-pb.co.jp; yktech@mx.nikko-pb.co.jp

*Web Site:* www.nikko-pb.co.jp
*Key Personnel*
President: Sakutarou Kobayashi
Founded: 1953
Subjects: Construction Machinery & Equipment, Hydraulics & Pneumatics
ISBN Prefix(es): 4-88045
Subsidiaries: Nikkoh Techno Research Co Ltd

**Japan Publications Inc+**
5F Nichibo Bldg, 1-2-2 Sarugaku-cho, Chiyoda-ku, Tokyo 101-0064
*Tel:* (03) 3295 8411 *Fax:* (03) 3295 8416
*E-mail:* jpub@nichibou.co.jp
*Web Site:* www.nichibou.co.jp
*Telex:* J27161 *Cable:* NICHIBOSHUPPAN TOKYO
*Key Personnel*
President: Toshihiro Kuwahara
Vice President: Yoshiro Fujiwara
Editor-in-Chief: Yukishige Takahashi
Rights & Permissions: Masatoshi Sato
Founded: 1942
Subjects: Agriculture, Asian Studies, Child Care & Development, Cookery, Crafts, Games, Hobbies, Health, Nutrition
ISBN Prefix(es): 4-8170
*Parent Company:* Japan Publications Trading Co Ltd (Import & Export)
*Orders to:* Oxford University Press, 198 Madison Ave, New York, NY 10016, United States

**Japan Scientific Societies Press**, see Business Center for Academic Societies Japan

**The Japan Times Ltd**
4-5-4 Shibaura, Minato-ku, Tokyo 108-0023
*Tel:* (03) 3453-2013 *Fax:* (03) 3453-8023
*E-mail:* books@japantimes.co.jp
*Web Site:* bookclub.japantimes.co.jp
*Key Personnel*
President: Toshiaki Ogasawara
Foreign Rights/Trade: Junichi Saito
Founded: 1897
Subjects: Asian Studies, Nonfiction (General)
ISBN Prefix(es): 4-7890

**Japan Travel Bureau Inc**
JTB 6F-7F, 2-3-11, Higashi, Shinagwa-ku, Tokyo 140-8603
*Tel:* (03) 5796-5525 *Fax:* (03) 5796-5529
*Web Site:* www.jtb.co.jp
*Telex:* 2228020 Jtb Bok J *Cable:* Jtbbook Tokyo
*Key Personnel*
Vice President, Publishing: Mitsumasa Iwada
Man Dir: Reiji Aoki
Editor-in-Chief, Books in English: Teruo Saito
Foreign Rights/Trade: Hiroshi Miyazaki
Founded: 1947
Subjects: Geography, Geology, History, Language Arts, Linguistics, Travel, Fine Arts
ISBN Prefix(es): 4-533
Subsidiaries: Densan Process Co; Kotsu Print Co; Kotsu Seihon Co; Toyo Books Co
*Branch Office(s)*
The Royal Exchange Bldg, 56 Pitt St, Sydney, Australia
20 rue Quentin Bauchart, Paris 75008, France
c/o Guam Hilton Hotel, Ipao Beach, Guam
Hotel Miramar, Rm 2123, Nathan Rd, Kowloon, Hong Kong
Via Emilia 47, Rome, Italy
5 Rue Chantepoulet, Geneva, Switzerland
50-51 Russell Sq, London WC1B 4JQ, United Kingdom
*U.S. Office(s):* 624 S Grand Ave, Suite 1410, Los Angeles, CA 90014, United States
402 Qantas Bldg, Union Sq, 360 Post St, San Francisco, CA 94018, United States
Waikiki Business Plaza, 2270 Kalakaua Ave, Honolulu, HI 96815, United States
The International Bldg, 45 Rockfeller Plaza, New York, NY 10020, United States

**Jiho**
Hitotsbashi Bldg, 2-6-3 Hitotsubashi 5F, Chiyoda-ku, Tokyo 101-8421
*Tel:* (03) 3265-8853 *Fax:* (03) 3265-7752
*E-mail:* pj@jiho.co.jp
*Web Site:* www.jiho.co.jp
*Key Personnel*
President: Shozo Takeda
Specialize in pharmaceutical industry & regulation, & pharmaceutical sciences.
ISBN Prefix(es): 4-8407

**Journey Editions**, *imprint of* Charles E Tuttle Publishing Co Inc

**JUSE Press Ltd**, see Nikkagiren Shuppan-Sha (JUSE Press Ltd)

**Kadokawa Shoten Publishing Co Ltd**
2-13-3 Fujimi, Chiyoda-ku, Tokyo 102-8177
*Tel:* (03) 32388431 *Fax:* (03) 32627733
*E-mail:* K-master@kadokawa.co.jp
*Web Site:* www.kadokawa.co.jp
*Key Personnel*
Man Dir: Ohora Kunimitsu
Editorial: Kichinosuke Sato
President, Sales: Tsuguuhiko Kadokawa
Production: Yukio Hashimoto
Publicity: Masatoshi Tojo
Rights & Permissions: Hiroshi Tagami
Founded: 1945
Subjects: Art, Fiction, History, Literature, Literary Criticism, Essays, Religion - Other
ISBN Prefix(es): 4-04

**Kaibundo Shuppan**
5-4 Suido 2 chome, Bunkyo-ku, Tokyo 112-0005
*Tel:* (03) 3815-3291 *Fax:* (03) 3815-3953
*E-mail:* LED04737@nifty.ne.jp
*Key Personnel*
President: Yoshihiro Okada
Editorial Dir & Foreign Rights/Trade: Yuhji Tamura
Founded: 1914
Subjects: Business, Engineering (General), Maritime, Microcomputers, Technology, Navigation, Ship-building
ISBN Prefix(es): 4-303

**Kaisei-Sha Publishing Co Ltd+**
3-5 Ichigaya Sadohara-cho, Shinjuku-ku, Tokyo 162-8450
*Tel:* (03) 32603229 *Fax:* (03) 32603540
*E-mail:* foreign@kaiseisha.co.jp
*Web Site:* www.kaiseisha.co.jp
*Key Personnel*
President: Masaki Imamura
Editorial Dir: Kimiko Matsukura
Editor, Foreign Rights: Hiroshi Konno
Founded: 1936
Subjects: Animals, Pets, Art, Biography, Crafts, Games, Hobbies, Disability, Special Needs, Environmental Studies, Foreign Countries, History
ISBN Prefix(es): 4-03
Number of titles published annually: 150 Print
Total Titles: 4,000 Print

**Kaitakusha+**
2-5-4, Kanda-Jinbocho, Chiyoda-ku, Tokyo 101-0051
*Tel:* (03) 5842-8900 *Fax:* (03) 5842-5560
*E-mail:* webmaster@kaitakusha.co.jp
*Web Site:* www.kaitakusha.co.jp
*Key Personnel*
President: Yoshiko Naganuma
Foreign Trade: Kenichi Naganuma
Foreign Rights: Yasuhiko Yamamoto
Founded: 1927
Subjects: Education, English as a Second Language, Language Arts, Linguistics, Literature, Literary Criticism, Essays

ISBN Prefix(es): 4-7589
Number of titles published annually: 30 Print; 3 CD-ROM; 3 Audio
Total Titles: 300 Print; 10 CD-ROM; 50 Audio

**Kajima Institute Publishing Co Ltd**
6-5-13 Akasaka, Minato-ku, Tokyo 107-8345
*Tel:* (03) 5561-2550 *Fax:* (03) 5561 2560
*E-mail:* info@kajima-publishing.co.jp
*Web Site:* www.kajima-publishing.co.jp
*Telex:* 02422467 Kajima J attn Kajima Inst Pub Co
*Key Personnel*
President: Takaaki Ida
Foreign Rights/Trade: Humio Odagiri
Founded: 1963
Subjects: Architecture & Interior Design, Civil Engineering, Engineering (General), Social Sciences, Sociology, Fine Arts, Urban Problems
ISBN Prefix(es): 4-306
*Bookshop(s):* Kasumigaseki Bookstore, 3-2-5 Kasumigaseki, Chiyoda-ku, Tokyo; Shinjuku Mitsui Building Bookstore, 2-1 Nishishinjuku, Shinjuku-ku, Tokyo; Shibuya Tohoseimei Building Bookstore, 2-15 Shibuya, Shibuya-ku, Tokyo

**Kanehara & Co Ltd**
31-14, 2-chome Yushima, Bunkyo-ku, Tokyo 113-8687
*Tel:* (03) 3811-7185; (03) 3811-7184 (sales) *Fax:* (03) 3813-0288
*Web Site:* www.kanehara-shuppan.co.jp *Cable:* Kaneharaco Tokyo
*Key Personnel*
President: Hiromitsu Kawai
Founded: 1875
Subjects: Medicine, Nursing, Dentistry
ISBN Prefix(es): 4-307

**Kansai University Press**
3-3-35, Yamatecho, Suita-Shi, Osaka 564-8680
*Tel:* (06) 6368-1121 *Fax:* (06) 6389-5162
*Web Site:* www.kansai-u.ac.jp/index.html
*Key Personnel*
Chairman, Board of Trustees: Heian Hazama
Founded: 1947
Subjects: Social Sciences, Sociology, Natural Science
ISBN Prefix(es): 4-87354

**Kawade Shobo Shinsha Publishers**
2-32-2 Sendagaya, Shibuya-ku, Tokyo 151-0051
*Tel:* (03) 3404-1201 *Fax:* (03) 3404-6386
*E-mail:* info@kawade.co.jp
*Web Site:* www.kawade.co.jp
*Key Personnel*
President: Shigeo Wakamori
Founded: 1886
Subjects: Art, Fiction, History, Nonfiction (General), Philosophy, Science (General), Social Sciences, Sociology
ISBN Prefix(es): 4-309

**Kazamashobo Co Ltd+**
1-34 Kanda Jimbocho, Chiyoda-ku, Tokyo 101-0051
*Tel:* (03) 3291-5729 *Fax:* (03) 3291-5757
*E-mail:* kazama@wd6.so-net.ne.jp
*Web Site:* www.kazamashobo.co.jp
*Key Personnel*
President: Tsutomu Kazama
Founded: 1933
Membership(s): Japan Book Publishers Association.
Subjects: Education, History, Literature, Literary Criticism, Essays, Philosophy, Psychology, Psychiatry, Social Sciences, Sociology
ISBN Prefix(es): 4-7599

**Keigaku Publishing Co Ltd+**
1-46 Kanda-Jimbo-cho 1 chome, Chiyoda-ku, Tokyo 101-0051
*Tel:* (03) 3233-3733 *Fax:* (03) 3233-3730
*Key Personnel*
Publisher: Kazumi Mitsui
Editorial Dir, Foreign Rights Manager: Kiyoshi Yoshizaki
Sales Manager: Yoshiaki Tokunaga
Production Manager: Isoyoshi Yamamoto
Foreign Rights Associate: Naoko Sakaki
Founded: 1969
Subjects: Computer Science, Electronics, Electrical Engineering, Science (General)
ISBN Prefix(es): 4-7665
*Associate Companies:* Yugaku-sha Ltd

**Keisuisha Publishing Company Ltd**
1-4 Komachi, Naka-ku, Hiroshima 733-0041
*Tel:* (082) 2467909 *Fax:* (082) 2467876
*E-mail:* info@keisui.co.jp
*Web Site:* www.keisui.co.jp
*Key Personnel*
President: Itsushi Kimura *E-mail:* kimura@keisui.co.jp
Founded: 1975
Subjects: Asian Studies, Economics, Education, History, Language Arts, Linguistics, Literature, Literary Criticism, Essays, Philosophy, Social Sciences, Sociology
ISBN Prefix(es): 4-87440
Number of titles published annually: 40 Print
Total Titles: 710 Print

**Kenkyusha Ltd**
2-11-3, Fujimi, Chiyoda-ku, Tokyo 102-8152
*Tel:* (03) 3288-7777; (03) 3288-7856 *Fax:* (03) 3288-7799
*Web Site:* www.kenkyusha.co.jp
*Key Personnel*
President: Kunikatsu Araki
Foreign Trade Executive: Hiroji Yamazaki
Foreign Rights Executive: Josuke Okada
Founded: 1907
Subjects: Language Arts, Linguistics
ISBN Prefix(es): 4-327; 4-7674

**Kin-No-Hoshi Sha Co Ltd**
4-3 Kojima 1 chome, Taito-ku, Tokyo 111-0056
*Tel:* (03) 3861-1861 *Fax:* (03) 3861-1507
*E-mail:* gonta@kinnohoshi.co.jp
*Web Site:* www.kinnohoshi.co.jp
*Key Personnel*
President: Masakazu Saito
Vice President: Matsuo Ishibashi
Editor: Masao Okohira
Foreign Rights: Yuko Saito
Founded: 1919
Subjects: Education
ISBN Prefix(es): 4-323
*Warehouse:* 1997-1 Hizaore 3-chome, Asaka-City, Saitama

**Kindai Kagaku Sha Co Ltd+**
Kindai Kagaku-Sha Bldg, 2-7-15 Ichigaya-Tamachi, Shinjuku City, Tokyo 162-0843
*Tel:* (03) 3260-6101 *Fax:* (03) 3260-6102
*Web Site:* www.kindaikagaku.co.jp
*Key Personnel*
Chief Executive Officer: Ryohji Sakurai
Founded: 1959
Membership(s): Kohgakusho Kyokai (Association of Engineering Book Publishers); Shokyoh (Japan Book Publishers Association.
Subjects: Computer Science, Electronics, Electrical Engineering, Mathematics, Physics
ISBN Prefix(es): 4-7649

**Kinokuniya Co Ltd (Publishing Department)+**
3-13-11 Higashi, Shibuya-ku, Tokyo 150-0011
*Tel:* (03) 5469-5919 *Fax:* (03) 5469-5958
*E-mail:* publish@kinokuniya.co.jp; info@kinokuniya.co.jp

*Web Site:* www.kinokuniya.co.jp *Cable:* KINOKUNI
*Key Personnel*
General Manager: Shinjiro Kuroda
Sales: Yoshichika Ogasawara
Founded: 1926
Subjects: Art, Biography, History, Literature, Literary Criticism, Essays, Philosophy, Psychology, Psychiatry, Science (General), Social Sciences, Sociology
ISBN Prefix(es): 4-314
*Associate Companies:* Kinokuniya Bookstores of America Co Ltd, 1581 Webster St, San Francisco, CA 94115, United States; Kinokuniya Publications Service of New York Co Ltd, 10 W 49 St, New York, NY 10020, United States; Kinokuniya Publications Service of London Co Ltd, Radnor House, 93-97 Regent St, London W1R 7TG, United Kingdom

**Kinpodo**
34, Nishi-Teramaecho, Shishigatani, Sakyo-ku, Kyoto 606-8425
*Tel:* (075) 751-1111 *Fax:* (075) 751-6858
*E-mail:* kkinpodo@kb3.so-net.ne.jp
*Key Personnel*
President: Katsusuke Shibata
Foreign Rights/Trade: Terukazu Ichii
Founded: 1948
Subjects: Medicine, Nursing, Dentistry
ISBN Prefix(es): 4-7653

**KINZAI Corporation+**
19, Minami-Motomachi, Shinjuku-ku, Tokyo 160-8520
*Tel:* (03) 33580011 *Fax:* (03) 33580036
*Web Site:* www.kinzai.or.jp
*Key Personnel*
President: Akira Kanai
General Manager: Shigeru Abe *E-mail:* s.abe@kinzai.or.jp
Founded: 1971
Subjects: Finance, Banking, Security Business
ISBN Prefix(es): 4-322
*Parent Company:* Institute for Financial Affairs Inc
*Branch Office(s)*
Fukuoka Cities
Nagoya
Osaka

**Kodansha International Ltd+**
Subsidiary of Kodansha Ltd
1-17-14 Otowa, Bunkyo-ku, Tokyo 112-8652
*Tel:* (03) 39446491 *Fax:* (03) 39446394
*E-mail:* sales@kodansha-intl.co.jp
*Web Site:* www.thejapanpage.com; www.kodansha-intl.co.jp
*Key Personnel*
President: Fumio Hatano
Editorial Vice President: Kazuichi Ohmura
Sales Vice President: Kazuhide Sainowaki
Editorial Dir: Stephen Shaw *Tel:* (03) 3944-6493 *E-mail:* shaw@kodansha-intl.co.jp
International Rights: Ayako Akaogi
Founded: 1963
Specialize in Japan & Asia.
Subjects: Art, Cookery, Crafts, Games, Hobbies, Fiction, History, How-to, Language Arts, Linguistics, Philosophy, Sports, Athletics, Martial arts
ISBN Prefix(es): 4-7700
*Branch Office(s)*
Kodansha Europe, 95 Aldwych, London WC2B 4JF, United Kingdom *Tel:* (020) 7304 4095 *Fax:* (020) 7304 4096
*U.S. Office(s):* Kodansha America, 575 Lexington Ave, New York, NY 10022, United States *Tel:* 917-322-6200 *Fax:* 212-935-6929

**Kodansha Ltd+**
1-17-14 Otowa, Bunkyo-ku, Tokyo 112-8652

*Tel:* (03) 3944-6493
*E-mail:* sales@kodansha-intl.com
*Web Site:* www.kodansha.co.jp
*Telex:* J34509 Kodansha *Cable:* KODANSHAPUBLISH TOKYO
*Key Personnel*
President: Mitsuru Tomita
Editorial: Akira Higashiura
Sales: Hironobu Hamada
Rights & Permissions: Takashi Kasahara *E-mail:* t-kasahara@kodansha.co.jp
Founded: 1909
Subjects: Art, Economics, Education, Fiction, Geography, Geology, History, House & Home, Humor, Language Arts, Linguistics, Literature, Literary Criticism, Essays, Medicine, Nursing, Dentistry, Nonfiction (General), Philosophy, Religion - Other, Social Sciences, Sociology
ISBN Prefix(es): 4-06
Subsidiaries: Kodansha Europe Ltd (London, UK); Kodansha International Ltd (Tokyo, Japan)
*Branch Office(s)*
Osaka
*U.S. Office(s):* Kodansha America, 575 Lexington Ave, New York, NY 10022, United States *Tel:* (917) 322-6200 *Fax:* (212) 935-6929
*Book Club(s):* Kodansha Disney Children's Book Club

**Kogyo Chosakai Publishing Co Ltd**
2-14-7, Hongo, Bunkyo-ku, Tokyo 113-8466
*Tel:* (03) 3817-4701 *Fax:* (03) 3817-4748
*E-mail:* m-order@po.iijnet.or.jp; rtb87919@mtd.biglobe.ne.jp
*Web Site:* www.iijnet.or.jp/kocho
*Key Personnel*
President: Yukio Shimura
Foreign Rights/Trade: Shigeki Shintani
Founded: 1954
Subjects: Architecture & Interior Design, Engineering (General), Science (General), Technology

**Kokudo-Sha Co Ltd**
1-16-7, Kamiochiai, Shinjuku-Ku, Tokyo 161-8510
*Tel:* (03) 53483710 *Fax:* (03) 53483765
*Web Site:* www.koutoku.co.jp/kokudosha/index.html
*Key Personnel*
President: Michiaki Suzuki
Founded: 1948
Subjects: Biography, Child Care & Development, Education, Literature, Literary Criticism, Essays, Psychology, Psychiatry, Social Sciences, Sociology
ISBN Prefix(es): 4-337

**Kokushokankokai Co Ltd**
2-10-5, Shimura, Itabashi-ku, Tokyo 174-0056
*Tel:* (03) 5970-7421 *Fax:* (03) 5970-7427
*E-mail:* info@kokusho.co.jp
*Web Site:* www.kokusho.co.jp
*Key Personnel*
President: Kesao Sato
Chief Editor: Junichi Isozaki
Editor: Reiko Iwamoto
Founded: 1971
Subjects: Asian Studies, Education, Fiction, History, Language Arts, Linguistics, Literature, Literary Criticism, Essays, Military Science, Religion - Buddhist, Western Fiction
ISBN Prefix(es): 4-336
*Warehouse:* 3-11-26 Vchiya, Vrawa-sh, Saitama Prefecture 336

**Komine Shoten Co Ltd**
4-11, Ichigaya-Daimachi, Shinjuku-ku, Tokyo 162-0066
*Tel:* (03) 3357-3521 *Fax:* (03) 3357-1027
*E-mail:* info@komineshoten.co.jp

*Web Site:* www.komineshoten.co.jp
*Key Personnel*
President: Norio Komine
Foreign Rights/Trade: Noriko Kojima
Founded: 1947
Subjects: Education, Science (General)
ISBN Prefix(es): 4-338

**Kosei Publishing Co Ltd**
Affiliate of Rissho Kosei-kai
7-1 Wada, 2 Chome, Suginami-ku, Tokyo 166-8535
*Tel:* (03) 5385-2319 *Fax:* (03) 5385-2331
*Web Site:* www.kosei-shuppan.co.jp/english/
*Key Personnel*
President: Yukio Yokota
Foreign Trade, Foreign Rights Executive: Toru Nakagawa
Dir, International Publishing Section: Koichiro Yoshida *E-mail:* yoshida@kosei-shuppan.co.jp
Founded: 1966
Membership(s): Japan Book Publishers Association.
Subjects: Art, Child Care & Development, Education, History, Human Relations, Literature, Literary Criticism, Essays, Music, Dance, Nonfiction (General), Philosophy, Psychology, Psychiatry, Religion - Buddhist, Self-Help, Travel
ISBN Prefix(es): 4-333
Number of titles published annually: 50 Print; 5 Audio
Total Titles: 1,072 Print; 1 CD-ROM; 133 Audio
Distributed by Charles E Tuttle Co Inc

**Koseisha-Koseikaku Co Ltd**
8, San'eicho, Shinjuku-ku, Tokyo 160-0008
*Tel:* (03) 3359-7371 *Fax:* (03) 3359-7375
*E-mail:* koseisha@po.iijnet.or.jp
*Web Site:* www.vinet.or.jp/~koseisha; www.kouseisha.com
*Key Personnel*
President: Hisao Satake
Editorial: Fukase Simao
Publishing: Hajime Torizuka
Founded: 1922
Subjects: Astrology, Occult, Astronomy, Education, Labor, Industrial Relations, Philosophy, Science (General), Social Sciences, Sociology, Technology, Fishery
ISBN Prefix(es): 4-7699

**Koyo Shobo+**
7 Kita-Yakakecho, Saiin, Ukyo-ku, Kyoto 615-0026
*Tel:* (075) 312-0788 *Fax:* (075) 312-7447
*Key Personnel*
President: Yoshiki Ueda
Foreign Rights/Trade: Tatsuo Murata
Founded: 1960
Subjects: Archaeology, Art, Business, Developing Countries, Drama, Theater, Economics, Education, Environmental Studies, Ethnicity, Government, Political Science, History, Law, Management, Marketing, Philosophy, Psychology, Psychiatry, Social Sciences, Sociology
ISBN Prefix(es): 4-7710

**Kyodo-Isho Shuppan Co Ltd+**
3-21-10 Hongo, Bunkyo-ku, Tokyo 113-0033
*Tel:* (03) 3818-2361 *Fax:* (03) 3818-2368
*E-mail:* kyodo-ed@fd5.so-net.ne.jp
*Web Site:* www.kyodo-isho.co.jp
*Key Personnel*
President & Foreign Rights/Trade: Setsu Kinoshita
Founded: 1947
Subjects: Medicine, Nursing, Dentistry
ISBN Prefix(es): 4-7639

**Kyoritsu Shuppan Co Ltd**
4-6-19, Kohinata, Bunkyo-ku, Tokyo 112-8700
*Tel:* (03) 3947-2511 *Fax:* (03) 3944-8182

*E-mail:* general@kyoritsu-pub.co.jp
*Web Site:* www.kyoritsu-pub.co.jp
*Key Personnel*
President, Editorial Dir & Foreign Rights/Trade:
  Mitsuaki Nanjo
Sales Dir: Hiroshi Todoroki
Founded: 1926
Subjects: Biological Sciences, Chemistry, Chemical Engineering, Computer Science, Engineering (General), Mathematics, Medicine, Nursing, Dentistry, Natural History, Physics, Technology, Information Science, Natural Science
ISBN Prefix(es): 4-320

**Library & Information Science,** *imprint of*
Riso-Sha

**Maruzen Co Ltd**
2-3-10, Nihombashi, Chuo-ku, Tokyo 103-8245
Mailing Address: PO Box 5050, Tokyo International 100-3191
*Tel:* (03) 3272-0514 *Fax:* (03) 3272-0527
*E-mail:* webmaster@maruzen.co.jp
*Web Site:* www.maruzen.co.jp; www.maruzen.co.jp/home-eng/index.html
*Telex:* J26516; J26517 *Cable:* MARUYA TOKYO
*Key Personnel*
Chairman: Kumao Ebihara
President: Nobuo Suzuki
Executive Dir: Ryozo Fujiwara
Man Dir: Isamu Tanahashi; Hiroshi Muko
Senior General Manager: Tsuneo Miyama
Founded: 1869
Subjects: Architecture & Interior Design, Biological Sciences, Chemistry, Chemical Engineering, Civil Engineering, Computer Science, Electronics, Electrical Engineering, Mechanical Engineering, Physics, Science (General)
ISBN Prefix(es): 4-621
*Associate Companies:* Maruzen Planet Co Lt, Tokyo
Subsidiaries: Maruzen Asia (Pte) Ltd; Maruzen International Co Ltd
*Branch Office(s)*
Fukuoka
Hiroshima
Kanazawa
Kobe
Kyoto
Nagoya
Okayama
Osaka
Sendai
Tsukuba
Yokohama
*Warehouse:* 5-7-1, Heiwajima, Ohta-ku, Tokyo 143

**Medical Sciences International Ltd+**
1-28-36 Hongo, Bunkyo-ku, Tokyo 113-0033
*Tel:* (03) 5804-6050 *Fax:* (03) 5804-6055
*E-mail:* info@medsi.co.jp
*Web Site:* www.medsi.co.jp *Cable:* MEDSIJAPAN TOKYO
*Key Personnel*
President: Hiroshi Wakamatsu
Founded: 1979
Subjects: Medicine, Nursing, Dentistry
ISBN Prefix(es): 4-89592; 4-943921
Imprints: MEDSI

**MEDSI,** *imprint of* Medical Sciences
International Ltd

**Meiji Shoin Co Ltd**
1-1-7 Okubo, Shinjuku-ku, Tokyo 169-0072
*Tel:* (03) 5292-0117 *Fax:* (03) 5292-6182
*E-mail:* nihongol@oak.ocn.ne.jp
*Web Site:* www.meijishoin.co.jp
*Key Personnel*
President: Yuzuru Miki

Editorial: Kunio Kawami
Sales: Harunori Saito
Foreign Rights/Trade: Kazuo Kitsuuchi
Founded: 1896
Subjects: History, Literature, Literary Criticism, Essays, Philosophy, Poetry, Chinese Philosophy & Literature, Haiku & Tanka Poetry, Japanese & Chinese Classic Literature, Japanese & Kanji Dictionaries, Japanese Textbooks
ISBN Prefix(es): 4-625
*Branch Office(s)*
Fukuoka
Osaka

**Mejikaru Furendo-sha** (Medical Friend)+
2-4 Kudan Kita 3 Chome, Chiyoda-ku, Tokyo 102-0073
*Tel:* (03) 32646611 *Fax:* (03) 32616602 (distribution); (03) 32640704 (editorial affairs)
*E-mail:* mfhensyu@mb.infoweb.ne.jp; mfeigyou@mb.infoweb.ne.jp; mfsoumu@mb.infoweb.ne.jp
*Key Personnel*
President, Rights & Permissions: Yoshihiro Ogura
Foreign Rights: Hiromi Ikoma
Founded: 1947
Subjects: Art, Health, Nutrition, Medicine, Nursing, Dentistry
ISBN Prefix(es): 4-8392
*Associate Companies:* The International Nursing Foundation of Japan (INFJ)
*Warehouse:* 36-1 Hiraoka-cho, Hachioji, Tokyo 192

**Minerva Shobo Co Ltd+**
One Tsutsumidani-cho, Hinooka, Yamashina-ku, Kyoto 607-8494
*Tel:* (075) 581-5191 *Fax:* (075) 581-0589
*E-mail:* info@minervashobo.co.jp
*Web Site:* www.minervashoboco.jp
*Key Personnel*
President: Nobuo Sugita *Tel:* (075) 581 5191 93
Foreign Trade: Keizo Sugita
Editorial Dir: Kiyoshi Igarashi
Foreign Rights: Hiroshi Inui
Founded: 1948
Membership(s): Japan Book Publishers Association.
Subjects: Child Care & Development, Disability, Special Needs, Economics, Education, Government, Political Science, History, Medicine, Nursing, Dentistry, Philosophy, Psychology, Psychiatry, Social Sciences, Sociology
ISBN Prefix(es): 4-623
Total Titles: 4,000 Print
Imprints: Tohan-Nippan
*Branch Office(s)*
3-6 Nishiki-cho, Kanda, Chiyoda-Ku, Tokyo 101-0034 *Tel:* (03) 8296-1615 *Fax:* (03) 3396-1620
Distributed by Nihon Shuppan Hanbai Co
Foreign Rights: The Asano Agency Inc

**Mirai-Sha**
7-2, Koishikawa, Bunkyo-ku, Tokyo 112-0002
*Tel:* (03) 3814-5521 *Fax:* (03) 3814-8600
*Key Personnel*
President & Foreign Rights/Trade: Yoshihide Nishitani *E-mail:* nishitani@sjk.mag.ne.jp
Founded: 1951
Subjects: History, Human Relations, Literature, Literary Criticism, Essays, Philosophy, Religion - Other, Social Sciences, Sociology, Politics, Theatre
ISBN Prefix(es): 4-624

**Misuzu Shobo Ltd+**
5-32-21 Hongo, Bunkyo-ku, Tokyo 113-0033
*Tel:* (03) 3815-9181 *Fax:* (03) 3818-8497
*E-mail:* nakagawa@msz.co.jp
*Web Site:* www.msz.co.jp
*Key Personnel*
President: Takashi Arai
Editorial Dir: Shogo Morita

Foreign Rights: Ms Misako Nakagawa
Founded: 1946
Subjects: Art, Human Relations, Literature, Literary Criticism, Essays, Psychology, Psychiatry, Science (General), Social Sciences, Sociology
ISBN Prefix(es): 4-622

**Mita Press, Mita Industrial Co Ltd+**
Ochanomizu Center Bldg, 2-12 Hongo 3 chome, Bunkyo-ku, Tokyo 113
*Tel:* (03) 3817-7200 *Fax:* (03) 3817-7207
*Key Personnel*
President: Yoshihiro Mita
Man Dir: Akio Etori
International Relations Manager: Atsushi Mifune
Founded: 1988 (originally founded 1934 as Mita Industrial Co, Ltd)
Subjects: Astronomy, Biological Sciences, Medicine, Nursing, Dentistry, Nonfiction (General), Physical Sciences, Physics, Psychology, Psychiatry, Science (General), Technology
ISBN Prefix(es): 4-89583

**Morikita Shuppan Co Ltd**
1-4-11, Fujimi, Chiyoda-ku, Tokyo 102-0071
*Tel:* (03) 3265-8341 *Fax:* (03) 3264-8709
*E-mail:* hiro@morikita.co.jp
*Web Site:* www.morikita.co.jp
*Key Personnel*
President: Hajime Morikita
Foreign Trade Executive: Kazuo Mori
Foreign Rights: Hiroshi Morikita
Founded: 1950
Subjects: Earth Sciences, Geography, Geology, Mathematics, Physics, Science (General), Technology, Botany, Natural Science
ISBN Prefix(es): 4-627

**Myrtos Inc+**
Kudan-Sakura Bldg, 1-10-5, Kudan-Kita, Chiyoda-ku, Tokyo 102-0073
*Tel:* (03) 3288-2200 *Fax:* (03) 3288-2225
*E-mail:* pub@myrtos.co.jp
*Web Site:* www.myrtos.co.jp
*Key Personnel*
President: Kazumitsu Kawai
Founded: 1985
Subjects: Archaeology, Education, History, Literature, Literary Criticism, Essays, Philosophy, Religion - Jewish, Religion - Protestant
ISBN Prefix(es): 4-89586
*Branch Office(s)*
Jerusalem, Israel

**Nagai Shoten Co Ltd**
21-15, Fukushima, 8 Chome, Fukushima-ku, Osaka 553-0003
*Tel:* (06) 6452-1881 *Fax:* (06) 6452-1882
*E-mail:* nagai05@gold.ocn.ne.jp
*Key Personnel*
President: Tadao Nagai
Founded: 1946
Subjects: Medicine, Nursing, Dentistry
ISBN Prefix(es): 4-8159

**Nagaoka Shoten Co Ltd+**
1-7-14, Toyotama-Kami, Nerima-ku, Tokyo 176-8515
*Tel:* (03) 3992-5155 *Fax:* (03) 3948-3021
*E-mail:* info@nagaokashoten.co.jp
*Key Personnel*
President: Shuichi Nagaoka
Foreign Rights/Trade: Yoji Tamaki
Founded: 1963
Subjects: Animals, Pets, Cookery, Crafts, Games, Hobbies, Gardening, Plants, Health, Nutrition, House & Home, How-to, Law, Sports, Athletics, Travel
ISBN Prefix(es): 4-522
Subsidiaries: Cosumo Shuppan Company Ltd; Lesson Company Ltd; Okaichi Company Ltd

**Nakayama Shoten Co Ltd+**
1-25-14 Hakusan, Bunkyo-ku, Tokyo 113-8666
*Tel:* (03) 3813-1100 *Fax:* (03) 3816-1015
*Web Site:* www.nakayamashoten.co.jp
*Key Personnel*
President: Kurohiko Nakayama
Founded: 1948
Membership(s): Japan Book Publishers Association; Japan Medical Publishers Association.
Subjects: Biological Sciences, Medicine, Nursing, Dentistry, Science (General)
ISBN Prefix(es): 4-521
Number of titles published annually: 70 Print; 5 CD-ROM
Total Titles: 3,850 Print; 5 CD-ROM
Distributor for American Heart Association

**Nankodo Co Ltd+**
42-6, Hongo 3-Chome, Bunkyo-ku, Tokyo 113-8410
*Tel:* (03) 3811-7239 *Fax:* (03) 3811-7230
*E-mail:* info@nankodo.co.jp
*Web Site:* www.nankodo.co.jp
*Telex:* 2722203 Nankod J *Cable:* Booknankodo
*Key Personnel*
President: Nobuhiko Hongo
Dir, Publications: Makoto Ueda
Foreign Rights/Trade: Masao Takahashi
Sales Dir: Makoto Sagwara
Manager, Planning, Publicity: Shun Takahashi
Manager, Imports: Iwao Tojo
Founded: 1879
Subjects: Language Arts, Linguistics, Medicine, Nursing, Dentistry, Science (General), Technology, Pharmacology
ISBN Prefix(es): 4-524
*Branch Office(s)*
Oike-minami Teramachi dori, Nakakyo-ku, Kyoto 604

**Nan'un-Do Co Ltd+**
361, Yamabukicho, Shinjuku-ku, Tokyo 162-0801
*Tel:* (03) 3268-2311 *Fax:* (03) 3268-2650
*E-mail:* nanundo@post.e-mail.ne.jp
*Web Site:* www.nanun-do.co.jp
*Key Personnel*
President: Kazunori Nagumo
Foreign Rights/Trade: Goro Saso
Founded: 1950
Membership(s): J P A.
Subjects: Education, Language Arts, Linguistics, Literature, Literary Criticism, Essays
ISBN Prefix(es): 4-523
Subsidiaries: Nan'un-Do Phoenix Co Ltd

**Nanzando Co Ltd**
1-11 Yushima 4 chome, Bunkyo-ku, Tokyo 113-0034
*Tel:* (03) 56897868 *Fax:* (03) 56897857
*E-mail:* info@nanzando.com
*Web Site:* www.nanzando.com
*Key Personnel*
Man Dir: Hajime Suzuki
Founded: 1901
Subjects: Medicine, Nursing, Dentistry, Pharmaceutical
ISBN Prefix(es): 4-525

**Nensho-Sha**
3-5, Kitayamacho, Tennoji-ku, Osaka 543-0035
*Tel:* (06) 6771-9223 *Fax:* (06) 6771-9424
*E-mail:* fujinami@nenshosha.co.jp
*Web Site:* www.nenshosha.co.jp
*Key Personnel*
President: Masaru Fujinami
Founded: 1934
Subjects: History, Science (General), Technology, Secretarial Science
ISBN Prefix(es): 4-88978

**NHK Publishing**, *imprint of* Nippon Hoso Shuppan Kyokai (NHK Publishing)

**Nigensha Publishing Co Ltd+**
2-2, Kanda-Jimbocho, Chiyoda-ku, Tokyo 101-8419
*Tel:* (03) 5210-4703 *Fax:* (03) 5210-4704
*E-mail:* sales@nigensha.co.jp
*Web Site:* www.nigensha.co.jp
*Key Personnel*
President: Mr Takao Watanabe
Marketing Manager, Overseas: Yuji Nagai
Foreign Rights/Trade: Yukiko Kurosu
Founded: 1955
Membership(s): Azusakai Publishers Association; Japan Book Publishers Association.
Subjects: Art, Automotive, History, Art Reproduction, Calligraphy
ISBN Prefix(es): 4-544

**Nihon Bunka Kagakusha Co Ltd**
6-15-17 Honkomagome, 6 Chome, Bunkyo-ku, Tokyo 113-0021
*Tel:* (03) 39463137 *Fax:* (03) 39450908
*Cable:* Nihonbunkamm Tokyo
*Key Personnel*
President: Hideyuki Motegi
Foreign Trade Executive: Yoshihiro Hoshi
*E-mail:* y_hoshi@nichibun.co.jp
Founded: 1948
Subjects: Education, Medicine, Nursing, Dentistry, Social Sciences, Sociology
ISBN Prefix(es): 4-8210

**Nihon-Bunkyo Shuppan (Japan Educational Publishing Co Ltd)**
7-5, Minami-Sumiyoshi 4 chome, Sumiyoshi-ku, Osaka 558-0041
*Tel:* (06) 6692-1261 *Fax:* (06) 6606-5172; (06) 6692-8927
*E-mail:* webadmin@nichibun-g.co.jp
*Web Site:* www.nichibun-g.co.jp
*Key Personnel*
President: Rituro Shimono
Founded: 1951
Subjects: Art, Education, English as a Second Language, Social Sciences, Sociology, Sports, Athletics
ISBN Prefix(es): 4-536
Subsidiaries: Kiroku Eigasha Production Co Ltd; Shugakusha Co Ltd

**Nihon Hoso Shuppan Kyokai**, see Japan Broadcast Publishing Co Ltd

**Nihon Keizai Shimbun Inc Publications Bureau**
1-9-5, Otemachi, Chiyoda-ku, Tokyo 100-8066
*Tel:* (03) 3270-0251 *Fax:* (03) 5201-7505
*Web Site:* www.nikkei.co.jp/pub
*Key Personnel*
President: Toyohiko Kobayashi
General Manager: Takeshi Higuchi
Foreign Rights/Trade: Katsuharu Uchida
Founded: 1946
Subjects: Business, Economics, Science (General), Social Sciences, Sociology, Fine Arts
ISBN Prefix(es): 4-532
*Associate Companies:* Nikkei Science Inc
Subsidiaries: Nikkei Publications Services Inc

**Nihon Rodo Kenkyu Kiko** (The Japan Institute for Labour Policy & Training)
4-8-23 Kami Shakujii, Nerima-Ku, Tokyo 177-8502
*Tel:* (03) 5903-6111 *Fax:* (03) 3594-1113
*E-mail:* jil@jil.go.jp
*Web Site:* www.jil.go.jp
*Key Personnel*
Dir, Publishing Dept: Ms Atsuko Hojo
Subjects: Labor, Industrial Relations
ISBN Prefix(es): 4-538
Divisions: Research Institute

**Nihon Tosho Center Co Ltd**
3-8-2 Otsuka, Bunkyo-ku, Tokyo 112-0012
*Tel:* (03) 3945-6448 *Fax:* (03) 3945-4515
*E-mail:* info@nihontosho.co.jp
*Web Site:* www.nihontosho.co.jp
*Key Personnel*
President: Yoshio Takano
Editorial Dir: Yochisada Kyuma
Sales Dir: Minami Nonaka
Founded: 1975
Subjects: Education, History, Literature, Literary Criticism, Essays, Social Sciences, Sociology, Autobiography, Social Welfare
ISBN Prefix(es): 4-8205
*Branch Office(s)*
Osaka

**Nihon Vogue Co Ltd+**
3-23 Ichigaya-Honmuracho, Shinjuku-ku, Tokyo 162-8705
*Tel:* (03) 5261-5081 *Fax:* (03) 3269-8760
*E-mail:* nvsales@giganet.net
*Web Site:* www.tezukuritown.com
*Key Personnel*
President: Nobuaki Seto *Tel:* (03) 5261 5089 *Fax:* (03) 3269 7874 *E-mail:* seto@tezukuritown.com
Manager, Overseas Department: Takuya Wada
Founded: 1954
Specialize in publication of handicrafts books.
Subjects: Cookery, Crafts, Games, Hobbies, Gardening, Plants, Health, Nutrition, Sports, Athletics
ISBN Prefix(es): 4-529
Subsidiaries: NV Planing Co Ltd

**Nikkagiren Shuppan-Sha (JUSE Press Ltd)**
Nikka-Giren-3-Gokan, 5-4-2, Sendagaya, Shibuya-ku, Tokyo 151-0051
*Tel:* (03) 5379-1238 *Fax:* (03) 3356-3419
*E-mail:* sales@juse-p.co.jp
*Web Site:* www.juse-p.co.jp
*Key Personnel*
President: Teruhide Haga
Foreign Rights/Trade: Goro Fukushima
Founded: 1955
Subjects: Business, Computer Science, Education, Finance, Human Relations, Library & Information Sciences, Management, Mathematics, Science (General), Self-Help, Technology
ISBN Prefix(es): 4-8171

**The Nikkan Kogyo Shimbun Ltd**
1-8-10, Kudan-Kita, Chiyoda-ku, Tokyo 102-8181
*Tel:* (03) 3222-7131 *Fax:* (03) 3234-8504
*Web Site:* www.nikkan.co.jp
*Telex:* NIKKANKO J29687 *Cable:* DAILYKOGYO TOKYO
*Key Personnel*
President: Taihei Kanno
President, Osaka: Kiyosi Muramoto
President, Tohoku: Tatsuo Uchida
Bureau Chief, New York: Joji Ito
Bureau Chief, Los Angeles: Etsuji Nakamura
Bureau Chief, London: Hidemasa Naka
Bureau Chief, SE Asia: Yasushi Abe
Editor, Chu-Shikoku: Keijyu Moriwaki
Editor, Osaka: Toshiyuki Takakura
Editor, Nagoya: Koichi Ota
Editor, Seibu: Tsutomu Sasaki
Editor, Tohoku: Susuma Suzuki
Foreign Rights/Trade: Toru Suzuki
Founded: 1945
Subjects: Business, Engineering (General), Technology, Information Management
ISBN Prefix(es): 4-526
*Branch Office(s)*
1-17-18 Uesugi, Aoba-ku, Sendai
2-16 Kitahama-higashi, Chuo-ku, Osaka
2-21-28 Izumi, Higashi-ku, Nagoya
1-1 Furumonndo-Cho, Hakata-ku, Fukuoka

10 Anson Rd, No 27-04, International Plaza, Singapore 0207, Singapore
No 44 Ludgate House, 107/111 Fleet St, London EC4, United Kingdom
*U.S. Office(s):* 611 W Sixth St, No 3201, Los Angeles, CA 90017, United States
60 E 42 St, No 1411, New York, NY 10165, United States

**Nippon Hoso Shuppan Kyokai (NHK Publishing)+**
41-1, Udagawacho, Shibuya-ku, Tokyo 150-8081
*Tel:* (03) 3780-3356 *Fax:* (03) 3780-3348
*E-mail:* webmaster@npb.nhk-grp.co.jp
*Web Site:* www.nhk-grp.co.jp *Cable:* NHPUBLISHCO TOKYO
*Key Personnel*
President: Takeshi Matsuo
Man Dir: Fumihiko Inatsugu
Project Development Editor & Foreign Rights/Trade: Masahiro Kizaki
Founded: 1931
Subjects: Art, Astronomy, Biological Sciences, Business, Chemistry, Chemical Engineering, Communications, Cookery, Crafts, Games, Hobbies, Drama, Theater, Earth Sciences, Economics, Education, Electronics, Electrical Engineering, English as a Second Language, Environmental Studies, Fashion, Fiction, Foreign Countries, Gardening, Plants, Geography, Geology, Government, Political Science, Health, Nutrition, History, Language Arts, Linguistics, Law, Literature, Literary Criticism, Essays, Management, Mathematics, Mechanical Engineering, Music, Dance, Mysteries, Nonfiction (General), Regional Interests, Religion - Buddhist, Religion - Catholic, Religion - Hindu, Religion - Islamic, Religion - Jewish, Religion - Protestant, Religion - Other, Science (General), Social Sciences, Sociology, Sports, Athletics, Technology, Travel, Western Fiction
ISBN Prefix(es): 4-14
*Parent Company:* NHK (Japan Broadcasting Corporation)
Imprints: NHK Publishing
Subsidiaries: Hoso-Shuppan Circulation Center; Hoso-Shuppan Production; Niiza-Biso
*Branch Office(s)*
Fukuoka
Hiroshima
Matsuyama
Nagoya
Osaka
Sapporo
Sendai
Distributed by Weatherhill Inc
*Warehouse:* Hoso-Shuppan Circulation Center, 1-7-7 Hatanaka, Niiza-City, Saitama 352
*Orders to:* Japan Broadcast Publishing Co, Ltd, Shibuya-ku, Tokyo

**Nippon Jitsugyo Publishing Co Ltd+**
3-2-12, Hongo, Bunkyo-ku, Tokyo 113-0033
*Tel:* (03) 3814-5161 *Fax:* (03) 3818-1881
*E-mail:* int@njg.co.jp
*Web Site:* www.njg.co.jp
*Key Personnel*
Chairman: Yoichiro Nakamura
Founded: 1950
Subjects: Accounting, Business, Computer Science, Economics, Management, Marketing, Psychology, Psychiatry, Science (General)
ISBN Prefix(es): 4-534
*Associate Companies:* Four U (Publishing) Co Ltd

**Nishimura Co Ltd+**
1-754-39, Asahi-cho-dori, Asahimachi-dori, Niigata 951-8122
*Tel:* (025) 223-2388 *Fax:* (025) 224-7165
*E-mail:* office@nishimurashoten.co.jp
*Web Site:* www.nishimurashoten.co.jp

*Key Personnel*
President: Masanori Nishimura
General Dir: Masanobu Nishiyama
Sales Manager: Masaru Gotoh; Kenji Sakai
Production & Publicity Manager: Tsutomu Maeda; Keiichi Ninomiya
Foreign Rights/Trade: Azumi Nishimura
Founded: 1916
Subjects: Art, Medicine, Nursing, Dentistry, Veterinary Science
ISBN Prefix(es): 4-89013
*Associate Companies:* West Village Co Ltd
   *Fax:* (025) 2235750
*Branch Office(s)*
Akita
Toyko
*Bookshop(s):* 68-2 Aza-Hasunuma, Hiroomote, Akita-shi 010; 1-754-39, Asahi-cho-dori, Asahimachi-dori, Niigata 951-8122

**Nosangyoson Bunka Kyokai**
7-6-1 Akasaka, Minato-ku, Tokyo 107-0052
*Tel:* (03) 35851141 *Fax:* (03) 35891387
*E-mail:* mbk@mail.ruralnet.or.jp
*Key Personnel*
Chief Dir: Takashi Sakamoto
Founded: 1940
Subjects: Agriculture, Education, Environmental Studies, Health, Nutrition, Medicine, Nursing, Dentistry
ISBN Prefix(es): 4-540
*Bookshop(s):* Nobunkyo Otemachi Branch, JA Bldg, Basement floor, 1-8-3 Otemachi, Chiyoda-ku, Tokyo 100

**Obunsha Co Ltd**
78, Yaraicho, Shinjuku-ku, Tokyo 162-8680
*Tel:* (03) 3266-6487; (03) 3266-6000 *Fax:* (03) 3266-6478
*Web Site:* www.obunsha.co.jp *Cable:* OBUNSHA TOKYO
*Key Personnel*
Chief Executive Officer: Fumio Akao
Advertising Manager: Masaru Wakabayashi
Foreign Rights/Trade: Hong Sung Keun
Founded: 1931
Subjects: Computer Science, Education, History, Language Arts, Linguistics, Science (General), Sports, Athletics
ISBN Prefix(es): 4-01
*Associate Companies:* The Asahi National Broadcasting Co Ltd, 1-1-1 Roppong, Minato-ku, Toyko 106; English Educational Foundation of Japan, 55 Yokodera-cho, Shinjuku-ku, Toyko 162; Japan LL Education Center, Tokyo; Nippon Cultural Broadcasting Inc, 1-5 Wakabacho, Shinjuku-ku, Toyko 160; The Society for Testing English Proficiency, 1 Yarai-cho, Shinjuku-ku, Tokyo 162
*Branch Office(s)*
Fukuoka
Hiroshima
Nagoya
Osaka
Sapporo
Sendai

**Ohmsha Ltd+**
3-1 Kanda-Nishiki-cho, Chiyoda-ku, Tokyo 101-8460
*Tel:* (03) 3233-0641 *Fax:* (03) 3233-2426
*E-mail:* kaigaika@ohmsha.co.jp
*Web Site:* www.ohmsha.co.jp
*Key Personnel*
President: Seiji Sato
Dir, Foreign Rights & International Business: Osami Takeo *Tel:* (03) 3233-2425 *E-mail:* takeo@ohmsha.co.jp
Founded: 1914
Subjects: Engineering (General), Science (General)
ISBN Prefix(es): 4-274

Number of titles published annually: 300 Print
Total Titles: 3,000 Print
Distributed by IOS Press
Distributor for IOS Press

**Ondorisha Publishers Ltd**
4 Tsukiji-machi, Shinjuku-ku, Tokyo 162-8708
*Tel:* (03) 3268-3101 *Fax:* (03) 3235-3530
*Key Personnel*
President: Hideaki Takeuchi
Editor: Hideaki Sanada
Sales: Yoshihiro Ikuta
Foreign Rights/Trade: Hiroshi Morozumi
Founded: 1945
Subjects: Crafts, Games, Hobbies, Crochet, Embroidery, Knitting, Lacework
ISBN Prefix(es): 4-277

**Ongaku No Tomo Sha Corporation+**
6-30, Kagurazaka, Shinjuku-ku, Tokyo 162-8716
*Tel:* (03) 3235-2091 *Fax:* (03) 3235-2148
*E-mail:* home@ongakunotomo.co.jp
*Web Site:* www.ongakunotomo.co.jp
*Key Personnel*
President: Hiroshi Okabe
Copyright Dept: Kazuyuki Nabeshima
Foreign Rights/Trade: Tetsuo Morita
Founded: 1941
Subjects: Education, Music, Dance
ISBN Prefix(es): 4-276
Subsidiaries: Musica Nova Co (at above main address); Suiseisha Music Publishers; T O A Music International Co; Tomo Music Enterprise Co (at above main address)
*Branch Office(s)*
Osaka
Distributed by Theodore Presser Co
Distributor for Theodore Presser Co

**The Oriental Economist,** see Toyo Keizai Shinpo-Sha

**Otsuki Shoten Publishers+**
2-11-9, Hongo, Bunkyo-ku, Tokyo 113-0033
*Tel:* (03) 3813-4651 *Fax:* (03) 3813-4656
*E-mail:* otsuki@meibun.or.jp
*Key Personnel*
President, Production & Foreign Rights/Trade: Sadamu Nakagawa
Editorial: Kunio Shuto
Sales: Atsuo Harada
Founded: 1946
Subjects: Economics, History, Literature, Literary Criticism, Essays, Philosophy, Social Sciences, Sociology, Politics
ISBN Prefix(es): 4-272

**Oxford University Press KK**
Edomizaka Mori Bldg 6F, 4-1-40 Toranomon, Minato-ku 105-8529
*Tel:* (03) 3459 6489 *Fax:* (03) 3459 8661
*Web Site:* www.oupjapan.co.jp
*Key Personnel*
Man Dir: Sumio Takiguchi
General Manager, Academic & General Books Dept: Fumiha Ito
General Manager, English Language Teaching Dept: Paul Riley
ISBN Prefix(es): 4-7552
*Parent Company:* Oxford University Press, United Kingdom

**Pacifica Ltd,** see Seibu Time Co Ltd

**Pearson Education Japan+**
Nishi-Shinjuku KF Bldg 101, 8-14-24 Nishi Shinjuku, Shinjuku-ku, Tokyo 160-0023
*Tel:* (03) 3365 9001 *Fax:* (03) 3365 9009
*E-mail:* firstname.lastname@pearsoned.co.jp; elt@pearsoned.co.jp
*Web Site:* www.pearsoned.co.jp

*Key Personnel*
Man Dir: Naoto Ono
Business Development Dir: Katsuhiro Kawahara
General Manager, Local Publishing: Yukio Miwa
General Manager, ELT: Mieko Otaka
Founded: 1978
Subjects: Business, Computer Science, Economics, English as a Second Language, Medicine, Nursing, Dentistry, Microcomputers
ISBN Prefix(es): 4-938712; 4-88735; 4-87471; 4-89471; 4-931356
Number of titles published annually: 100 Print
Total Titles: 400 Print
*Parent Company:* Pearson Education, One Lake St, Upper Saddle River, NJ 07458, United States
*Branch Office(s)*
1-13-19 Sekiguchi, Bunkyo-ku, Tokyo 112-0014
  *Tel:* (03) 3266 0404 *Fax:* (03) 3266 0326
Distributed by Hachette (France); SGEL (Spain)
Distributor for Chambers Harrap (UK); Hachette (France); SGEL (Spain)
Foreign Rights: Fumi Nishijima

**Periplus Editions**, *imprint of* Charles E Tuttle Publishing Co Inc

**PHP Institute Inc**
3-10 Sanban-cho, Chiyoda-ku, Tokyo 102-8331
*Tel:* (03) 3239-6233 *Fax:* (03) 3239-6263
*Web Site:* www.php.co.jp
*Telex:* J5422 402 PHPJ
*Key Personnel*
President: Masaharu Matsushita
Man Dir: Katsuhiko Eguchi
Founded: 1946
Subjects: Business, Social Sciences, Sociology
ISBN Prefix(es): 4-569
Subsidiaries: PHP Editors Group Inc; PHP Institute of America Inc; PHP International (Singapore) Pte Ltd
*Branch Office(s)*
Kizu
Kyushu
Nagoya
Tokyo

**Poplar Publishing Co Ltd+**
5, Sugacho, Shinjuku-ku, Tokyo 160-8565
*Tel:* (03) 3357-2211 *Fax:* (03) 3359-2359
*E-mail:* henshu@poplar.co.jp
*Web Site:* www.poplar.co.jp *Cable:* POPLARPUB
*Key Personnel*
President: Hiroyuki Sakai
Foreign Rights/Trade: Kiyoshi Fukushima
Foreign Rights: Mari Sasaki
Founded: 1948
Subjects: Biography, Fiction, Geography, Geology, History, Science (General)
ISBN Prefix(es): 4-591

**President Inc+**
Bridge Stone Hirakawa-cho Bldg, 13-12 Hirakawa-cho, 2 Chome, Chiyoda-ku, Tokyo 102-0093
*Tel:* (03) 32373734 *Fax:* (03) 32373746
*E-mail:* matu-pre@po.iijnet.or.jp
*Web Site:* www.president.co.jp; www.president.co.jp/pre/english.html
*Key Personnel*
President: Yoshio Watabiki
International Rights: Keijiro Amano
Founded: 1963
Subjects: Business, Cookery, Economics, Finance, Government, Political Science, Management, Marketing, Philosophy
ISBN Prefix(es): 4-8334
*Parent Company:* Time Warner Publishing BV
*Branch Office(s)*
2-3-18 Nakanoshima, Kita-ku, Osaka

**Reimei-Shobo Co Ltd+**
EBS-Bldg, 3-6-27 Marunouchi, Naka-ku, Nagoya 460-0002
*Tel:* (052) 9623045 *Fax:* (052) 9519065
*E-mail:* reimei@mui.biglobe.ne.jp
*Web Site:* wwwl.biz.biglobe.ne.jp/~reimei/
*Key Personnel*
President: Kunihiro Buma
International Rights: Masako Yoshikawa
Founded: 1947
Membership(s): Japan Book Publishers Association.
Subjects: Child Care & Development, Disability, Special Needs, Education, Psychology, Psychiatry
ISBN Prefix(es): 4-654
Number of titles published annually: 50 Print
Total Titles: 1,700 Print
*Warehouse:* 374 Sangen-cho, Kita-ku, Nagoya 462-0004

**Rinsen Book Co Ltd+**
No 8, Tanaka-Shimoyanagi-Cho, Sakyo-Ku, Kyoto 606-8204
*Tel:* (075) 721-7111 *Fax:* (075) 781-6168
*E-mail:* kyoto@rinsen.com
*Web Site:* www.rinsen.com *Cable:* RINSEN KYOTO
*Key Personnel*
President: Eizo Kataoka
Foreign Rights/Trade: Satoko Matsumura
Founded: 1932
Publisher & Antiquarian Bookseller.
Membership(s): Antiquarian Booksellers' Association of Japan; International League of Antiquarian Booksellers.
Subjects: Archaeology, Asian Studies, History, Literature, Literary Criticism, Essays, Religion - Buddhist, Fine Arts, Japanology, Orientalism
ISBN Prefix(es): 4-653
*Branch Office(s)*
Saikachizaka Bldg, 2-11-16 Kanda-Surugadai, Chiyoda-Ku, Tokyo 101-0062 *Tel:* (03) 3293-5021 *Fax:* (03) 3293-5023 *E-mail:* tokyo@rinsen.com

**Riso-Sha**
614-17, Minoridai, Matsudo City, Chiba 270-2231
*Tel:* (047) 366-8003 *Fax:* (047) 360-7301
*E-mail:* risosha@risosha.co.jp
*Web Site:* www.risosha.co.jp
*Key Personnel*
President: Sumio Miyamoto
Founded: 1927
Subjects: Education, Library & Information Sciences, Philosophy, Psychology, Psychiatry, Religion - Buddhist, Religion - Catholic, Social Sciences, Sociology
ISBN Prefix(es): 4-650
*Parent Company:* Iwao-Syobou
Imprints: Library & Information Science

**Ryosho-Fukyu-Kai Co Ltd**
8-2 Kasuga 1 chome, Bunkyo-ku, Tokyo 112-0003
*Tel:* (03) 3813-1251 *Fax:* (03) 3811-6490
*E-mail:* ryosho@po.iijnet.or.jp
*Key Personnel*
President: Ichigaku Kawanaka
Foreign Trade Executive: Isao Hiramatsu
Foreign Rights Executive: Fumio Kimura
Man Dir: Kiyoshi Funakoshi
Founded: 1914
Subjects: Economics, Government, Political Science, Law, Public Administration, Social Sciences, Sociology, Local administration & politics
ISBN Prefix(es): 4-656

**Saela Shobo (Librairie Ca et La)+**
3-1, Ichigaya-Sadowaracho, Shinjuku-ku, Tokyo 162-0842

*Tel:* (03) 3268-4261 *Fax:* (03) 3268-4264
*E-mail:* info@saela.co.jp
*Web Site:* www.saela.co.jp
*Key Personnel*
President: Toshiichi Uraki *E-mail:* uraki@saela.co.jp
Founded: 1948
Subjects: Education, Fiction, Language Arts, Linguistics, Mathematics, Science (General), Technology
ISBN Prefix(es): 4-378
Number of titles published annually: 24 Print
Total Titles: 450 Print
Imprints: Toshiichi Uraki

**Sagano Shoin**
39 Ushigase-Minami-No-Kuchi-Cho, Nishikyo-ku Kyoto-shi, Kyoto 615-8045
*Tel:* (075) 391-7686 *Fax:* (075) 391-7321
*E-mail:* sagano@mbox.kyoto-inet.or.jp
*Web Site:* www.saganoshoin.co.jp
*Key Personnel*
President: Tadayoshi Nakamura
Contact: Takayo Shito
Founded: 1968
Subjects: Business, Computer Science, Economics, Education, Ethnicity, Law, Literature, Literary Criticism, Essays, Marketing, Sports, Athletics, Women's Studies
ISBN Prefix(es): 4-7823

**Saiensu-Sha Co Ltd**
1-3-25 Sendagaya, Shibuya-ku, Tokyo 151-0051
*Tel:* (03) 5474-8500 *Fax:* (03) 5474-8900
*E-mail:* rikei@saiensu.co.jp
*Key Personnel*
President: Yuzo Morihira
Contact: Nobuhiko Tajima
Founded: 1969
ISBN Prefix(es): 4-7819
Subsidiaries: Shinsei-sha Co Ltd; Suurikougaku-sha Co Ltd

**The Sailor Publishing Co, Ltd**
OCM Bldg, 10-18 Mouri 2 chome, Koutou-ku, Tokyo 135-0001
*Tel:* (03) 3846-2955 *Fax:* (03) 3846-0452
*Key Personnel*
President & Foreign Rights & Trade: Etsu Ogawa
Founded: 1985
ISBN Prefix(es): 4-88330; 4-915632
*Parent Company:* The Sailor Fountain Pen Co Ltd

**Salesian Press/Don Bosco Sha+**
9-7 Yotsuya 1 Chome, Shinjuku-ku, Tokyo 160
*Tel:* (03) 3351-7041 *Fax:* (03) 3351-5430
*Key Personnel*
President: Aldo Cipriani
Founded: 1930
Subjects: Religion - Catholic
ISBN Prefix(es): 4-88626
*Warehouse:* 1-22-12 Wakaba Cho, Shinjuku-ku, Tokyo

**Sangyo-Tosho Publishing Co Ltd**
11-3, Iidabashi 2 chome, Chiyoda-ku, Tokyo 102-0072
*Tel:* (03) 3261-7821 *Fax:* (03) 3239-2178
*E-mail:* info@san-to.co.jp
*Web Site:* www.san-to.co.jp
*Key Personnel*
President & Foreign Rights & Trade: Takehiko Ezura
Sales: Koji Nara
Founded: 1925
Subjects: Biological Sciences, Chemistry, Chemical Engineering, Computer Science, Electronics, Electrical Engineering, Engineering (General), Mathematics, Mechanical Engineering, Philosophy, Physical Sciences, Physics, Psychology, Psychiatry, Religion - Other, Science (General), Technology, Natural science, industry

ISBN Prefix(es): 4-7828
Total Titles: 500 Print

**Sankyo Publishing Company Ltd**
2, Kanda-Jimbocho 3 chome, Chiyoda-ku, Tokyo 101-0051
*Tel:* (03) 3264-5711 *Fax:* (03) 3264-5149
*Web Site:* www.sankyoshuppan.co.jp
*Key Personnel*
President: Sachiko Hagiwara
Founded: 1948
Subjects: Chemistry, Chemical Engineering, Economics, House & Home, Physics, Science (General)
ISBN Prefix(es): 4-7827

**Sanseido Co Ltd**
22-14, Misakicho 2 chome, Chiyoda-ku, Tokyo 101-8371
*Tel:* (03) 3230-9404 *Fax:* (03) 3230-9569
*Web Site:* www.sanseido-publ.co.jp/
*Key Personnel*
Chairman: Hisanori Ueno
President: Toshio Gomi
Man Dir: Masaaki Moriya
Editorial, Publicity: Eiichi Tsunoda
Production: Akihiko Ejima
Foreign Rights & Trade: Yasuaki Horiuchi
Founded: 1881
Subjects: Earth Sciences, Education, History, Language Arts, Linguistics, Law, Literature, Literary Criticism, Essays, Science (General), Social Sciences, Sociology
ISBN Prefix(es): 4-385

**Sanshusha Publishing Co, Ltd+**
5-34, Shitaya 1 chome, Taito-ku, Tokyo 110-0004
*Tel:* (03) 3842-1711 *Fax:* (03) 3845-3965
*E-mail:* info@sanshusha.co.jp
*Web Site:* www.sanshusha.co.jp
*Telex:* Oisco J33380
*Key Personnel*
President: Kanji Maeda *E-mail:* maeda-k@ sanshusha.co.jp
Foreign Rights & Trade: Toshihide Maeda
Founded: 1938
Specialize in lectronic publishing.
Membership(s): Asian Pacific Publishers Association (APPA); Japan Book Publishers Association (JBPA); Multimedia & Electronic Book International Committee (MEBIC).
Subjects: Education, English as a Second Language, Language Arts, Linguistics, Literature, Literary Criticism, Essays, Philosophy, Religion - Buddhist, Science (General), Social Sciences, Sociology, Travel
ISBN Prefix(es): 4-384

**Sanyo Shuppan Boeki Co Inc+**
No 2 Taiko Bldg, 3F 3-11-16 Nishi-Shinjuku, Shiniuku-ku, Tokyo 160-0023
*Tel:* (03) 5351-3021 *Fax:* (03) 5351-3028
*E-mail:* ssb01@mx1.alpha-web.ne.jp
*Telex:* 2524435 Sanyob *Cable:* Sanyobook Tokyo
*Key Personnel*
President: Hisatoshi Hattori
Foreign Trade: Koichi Ohnishi
Founded: 1956
Also importers & booksellers.
Subjects: Chemistry, Chemical Engineering, Cookery, Science (General)
ISBN Prefix(es): 4-87930
*Associate Companies:* ITO-Sanyo SA
*Branch Office(s)*
Niihama
Osaka

**Seibido+**
22, Kanda-Ogawamachi 3 chome, Chiyoda-ku, Tokyo 101-0052
*Tel:* (03) 3291-2261 *Fax:* (03) 3293-5490

*E-mail:* seibido@mua.biglobe.ne.jp
*Web Site:* www.seibido.co.jp
*Key Personnel*
President: Yoshimitsu Sano
Foreign Rights & Trade: Eiichiro Sano
Editor: Toshiko Kobayashi; Mark Brown
Founded: 1955
Publisher of ESL textbooks for the university market.
Subjects: English as a Second Language, Language Arts, Linguistics, Literature, Literary Criticism, Essays
ISBN Prefix(es): 4-7919

**Seibido Shuppan Company Ltd**
8-2 Suido 1 chome, Bunkyo-ku, Tokyo 112-8533
*Tel:* (03) 3814-4351 *Fax:* (03) 3814-4355
*Web Site:* www.seibidoshuppan.co.jp
*Key Personnel*
President & Man Dir: Etsuji Fukami
Founded: 1966
Subjects: Agriculture, Animals, Pets, Astrology, Occult, Automotive, Business, Career Development, Child Care & Development, Computer Science, Cookery, Crafts, Games, Hobbies, Gardening, Plants, Health, Nutrition, House & Home, How-to, Medicine, Nursing, Dentistry, Music, Dance, Outdoor Recreation, Photography, Sports, Athletics, Travel
ISBN Prefix(es): 4-415
Number of titles published annually: 300 Print; 5 CD-ROM
Total Titles: 1,200 Print; 10 CD-ROM

**Seibu Time Co Ltd**
SSC, Kinzan Bldg, 3-18-3 Kanda-nishiki-cho, Chiyoda-ku, Tokyo 101-8467
*Tel:* (03) 5283-0270 *Fax:* (03) 5283-0234
*Key Personnel*
Publisher: Sueaki Takaoka
Editor-in-Chief: Masatoshi Takeuchi
Founded: 1983
Subjects: Fiction, Nonfiction (General)
ISBN Prefix(es): 4-8275
*Parent Company:* S S Communications

**Seibundo**
514, Waseda-Tsurumakicho, Shinjuku-ku, Tokyo 162-0041
*Tel:* (03) 3203-9201 *Fax:* (03) 3203-9206
*E-mail:* eigyobu@seibundoh.co.jp
*Web Site:* www.seibundoh.co.jp
*Key Personnel*
President: Koichi Abe
Founded: 1947
Subjects: Business, Economics, Law, Social Sciences, Sociology, Politics
ISBN Prefix(es): 4-7923

**Seibundo Publishing Co Ltd+**
2-8-5, Shimanouchi, Chuo-ku, Osaka 542-0082
*Tel:* (06) 6211-6265 *Fax:* (06) 6211-6492
*Key Personnel*
President: Shigeo Maeda
Foreign Rights & Trade: Hiroo Maeda
Founded: 1963
Subjects: History, Language Arts, Linguistics, Literature, Literary Criticism, Essays, Regional Interests
ISBN Prefix(es): 4-7924
Distributed by Japan Publication Trading Co Ltd
Distributor for Tohan Co LTD

**Seibundo Shinkosha Publishing Co Ltd**
IPB Ochanomizu Bldg, 3-3-1, Honogo, Bunkyo-ku, Tokyo 113-0033
*Tel:* (03) 5800-5780 *Fax:* (03) 5800-5781
*Web Site:* www.seibundo.net
*Key Personnel*
President: Yuichi Ogawa
Editorial: Hajime Hishikawa

Foreign Rights & Trade: Kiyoshi Motoki
Founded: 1912
Subjects: Business, Crafts, Games, Hobbies, Electronics, Electrical Engineering, Gardening, Plants, Management, Science (General), Technology, Graphic design
ISBN Prefix(es): 4-416

**Seishin Shobo**
20-6, Otsuka 3 chome, Bunkyo-ku, Tokyo 112-0012
*Tel:* (03) 3946-5666 *Fax:* (03) 3945-8880
*Web Site:* www.seishinshobo.co.jp
*Key Personnel*
President: Shukuko Shibata
Founded: 1955
Subjects: Psychology, Psychiatry, Social Sciences, Sociology, Psychoanalysis, social work & welfare, Zen
ISBN Prefix(es): 4-414

**Seiun-Sha+**
3-21-10 Otsuka, Bunkyo-ku, Toyko 112 0012
*Tel:* (03) 3947-1021 *Fax:* (03) 3947-1617
*E-mail:* greatobe@yo.rim.ur.jp
*Key Personnel*
President: Keiko Moritani
Foreign Rights & Trade: Mineo Moritani
Founded: 1982
Publicize Christian Truth.
Membership(s): Japan Book Publishers Association.
Subjects: All fields of learning helpful to Christian purpose
ISBN Prefix(es): 4-7952; 4-434
Total Titles: 1,000 Print
*Parent Company:* The Zion Press Corporation

**Seiwa Shoten Co Ltd**
2-5 Kamitakaido, 1-chome, Suginami-ku, Tokyo 168-0074
*Tel:* (03) 3329-0033 *Fax:* (03) 5374-7186
*E-mail:* sales@seiwa-pb.co.jp
*Web Site:* www.seiwa-pb.co.jp *Cable:* Seiwapublishers
*Key Personnel*
President: Youji Ishizawa
Editor-in-Chief: Yoshinori Asanuma
Sales Manager: Masaharu Fujiwara
System Manager: Yukio Shimura
Foreign Books Manager: Yumi Matsuzawa
Founded: 1976
Subjects: Language Arts, Linguistics, Medicine, Nursing, Dentistry, Psychology, Psychiatry
ISBN Prefix(es): 4-7911
*Bookshop(s):* 1-11 Kamitakaido, 1-chome, Suginamiku, Tokyo 168
*Book Club(s):* Bookclub Psyche

**Seizando-Shoten Publishing Co Ltd**
Seizando Bldg, 4-51, Minami-Motomachi, Shinjuku-ku, Tokyo 160-0012
*Tel:* (03) 3357-5861 *Fax:* (03) 3357-5867
*E-mail:* publisher@seizando.co.jp
*Web Site:* www.seizando.co.jp
*Key Personnel*
President: Minoru Ogawa
Foreign Rights & Trade: Yoshihiro Munekata
Sales: Yoshio Kimura
Production: Yuhei Shibuya
Publicity: Masayuki Toyama
Rights & Permissions: Kokichi Shioji
Founded: 1954
Subjects: Economics, Law, Maritime, Technology, Transportation, Aviation, Fishery
ISBN Prefix(es): 4-425

**Sekai Bunka-Sha**
2-29, Kudan-Kita 4 chome, Chiyoda-ku, Tokyo 102-8187
*Tel:* (03) 3262-5111 *Fax:* (03) 3237-8446
*Web Site:* www.sekaibunka.com *Cable:* Sebunpub

*Key Personnel*
President: Tsutomu Suzuki
Foreign Rights & Trade: Kosei Kobayashi
Founded: 1946
Subjects: Art, Education, Geography, Geology,
    History
ISBN Prefix(es): 4-418
*U.S. Office(s):* 501 Fifth Ave, Suite 2102, New
    York, NY 10017, United States

**Shakai Hoken Shuppan-Sha**
Hikida Bldg, 9 Kanda-Surugadai 2 chome,
    Chiyoda-ku, Tokyo 101-0062
*Tel:* (03) 3291-9841 *Fax:* (03) 3291-9847
*Key Personnel*
President: Hidefumi Sano
ISBN Prefix(es): 4-7846

**Shakai Shiso-Sha**
25-13, Hongo 3 chome, Bunkyo-ku, Tokyo 113-
    0033
*Tel:* (03) 3813-8101 *Fax:* (03) 3813-9061
*Key Personnel*
President: Yasuo Miyakawa
Sales: Tadashi Kamatsuka
Founded: 1947
Subjects: Architecture & Interior Design, Art,
    Drama, Theater, Fiction, History, Music,
    Dance, Poetry, Social Sciences, Sociology,
    Travel
ISBN Prefix(es): 4-390

**Shibun-Do**
4-2, Nishi Goken-cho, Shinjuku-ku, Tokyo 162-
    0812
*Tel:* (03) 3268-2441 *Fax:* (03) 3268-3550
*E-mail:* eigy@imail.plala.or.jp
*Key Personnel*
President: Jun Kawakami
Foreign Rights & Trade: Hiroshi Kurosawa
Founded: 1915
Subjects: Art, Asian Studies, History, Literature,
    Literary Criticism, Essays, Philosophy, Re-
    gional Interests
ISBN Prefix(es): 4-7843

**Shiko-Sha Co Ltd**
10-12 Hiroo 2 chome, Shibuya-ku, Tokyo 150-
    0012
*Tel:* (03) 3400-7151 *Fax:* (03) 3400-7294
*Telex:* J24903 *Cable:* Lmdecw Tokyo
*Key Personnel*
Man Dir: Yasoo Takeichi
Founded: 1950
Subjects: Religion - Catholic, Religion - Protes-
    tant
ISBN Prefix(es): 4-7834

**Shimizu-Shoin**
1-11, Higashi-Gokencho, Shinjuku-ku, Tokyo
    162-0813
*Tel:* (03) 3260-5261 *Fax:* (03) 3260-5270
*Web Site:* www.shimizushoin.co.jp
*Key Personnel*
President: Kyuya Nomura
Founded: 1946
Subjects: Biography, History, Nonfiction (Gen-
    eral), Philosophy, School aids
ISBN Prefix(es): 4-389

**Shincho-Sha Co Ltd+**
71 Yaraicho, Shinjuku-ku, Tokyo 162-8711
*Tel:* (03) 3266 5411 *Fax:* (03) 3266 5534
*E-mail:* matsuie@shinchosha.co.jp
*Web Site:* www.shinchosha.co.jp
*Telex:* G27433 Shincho *Cable:* SHINCHOSHA
*Key Personnel*
President: Takanobu Sato
Sales: Tadahiko Arai
Publishing Dept: Masaya Kurihara
Foreign Rights: Masashi Matsuye

Founded: 1896
Subjects: Biography, Business, Fiction, Film,
    Video, Literature, Literary Criticism, Essays,
    Mysteries, Nonfiction (General), Photography,
    Romance, Science (General), Science Fiction,
    Fantasy
ISBN Prefix(es): 4-10

**Shingakusha Co Ltd+**
11-39 Higashino-Naka-Inove-cho, Yamashina-ku
    Kyoto-shi, Kyoto 607-8501
*Tel:* (075) 581-6111 *Fax:* (075) 501-0514
*E-mail:* info@sing.co.jp
*Web Site:* www.sing.co.jp
*Key Personnel*
President: Miki Iwasaki
Executive Dir: Toshihiro Ueda; Takeshi
    Yoshikawa
Foreign Rights & Trade: Mikio Yamamoto
Founded: 1957
Subjects: Education
ISBN Prefix(es): 4-7868
*Branch Office(s)*
Fukuoka
Sapporo
Tokushima
Tokyo

**Shinkenchiku-Sha Co Ltd+**
31-2, Yushima 2 chome, Bunkyo-ku, Tokyo 113-
    8501
*Tel:* (03) 38117101 *Fax:* (03) 38128229
    *Cable:* JAPANARCH TOKYO
*Key Personnel*
President: Yoshio Yoshida
Man Dir: Nobuyuki Yoshida
General Manager, Foreign Rights Executive:
    Ryugo Maru
Founded: 1925
Subjects: Architecture & Interior Design
ISBN Prefix(es): 4-7869
*Associate Companies:* A&U Publishing Co, Ltd

**Akane Shobo Co Ltd+**
2-1, Nishi-Kanda 3 chome, Chiyoda-ku, Tokyo
    101-0065
*Tel:* (03) 3263-0641 *Fax:* (03) 3263-5440
*E-mail:* mail@akaneshobo.co.jp
*Web Site:* www.akaneshobo.co.jp/
*Key Personnel*
President: Masaharu Okamoto
Foreign Rights & Trade: Tadao Sudo *Tel:* (03)
    3263-0644 *Fax:* (03) 3263-2094
Founded: 1949
Subjects: Fiction, Literature, Literary Criticism,
    Essays, Nonfiction (General), Science (General)
ISBN Prefix(es): 4-251

**Shobunsha Publications Inc+**
3-1, Kojimachi, Chiyoda-ku, Tokyo 102-8238
*Tel:* (03) 3556-8154 *Fax:* (03) 3556-5973
*E-mail:* LEH05353@niftyserve.or.jp
*Web Site:* www.mapple.co.jp
*Key Personnel*
President: Eiji Aoyagi
Foreign Rights & Trade: Kesayuki Tsunoda
Founded: 1960
Membership(s): Japan Book Publishers Associ-
    ation; Japan Digital Road Map Association;
    Mapping Enterprises Association of Japan.
Subjects: Travel
ISBN Prefix(es): 4-398
Total Titles: 300 Print
Subsidiaries: Shobunsha Map Research Center

**Shogakukan Inc+**
2-3-1 Hitotsubashi, Chiyoda-ku, Tokyo 101-8001
*Tel:* (03) 3230-5211 *Fax:* (03) 3234-5660
*E-mail:* info@shogakukan.co.jp
*Web Site:* skygarden.shogakukan.co.jp

*Key Personnel*
President: Masahiro Ohga
Dir: Tetsuo Takaishi
Senior Manager, Foreign Rights: Toshiki Ishii
Founded: 1922
Subjects: Art, Earth Sciences, Economics, Edu-
    cation, Geography, Geology, History, Comics,
    Japanese Manga, Magazines
ISBN Prefix(es): 4-09

**Mitsumura Suiko Shoin+**
Higashi-iru, Kitayama-dori, Kita-ku, Kyoto-shi
    603-8115
*Tel:* (075) 493-8244 *Fax:* (075) 493-6011
*E-mail:* mitsumur@mbox.kyoto-inet.or.jp
*Web Site:* www.mitsumura-suiko.co.jp
*Key Personnel*
President: Kozo Nagasawa
Editor: Ueda Keiichiro
Founded: 1958
Subjects: Architecture & Interior Design, Art,
    Philosophy, Religion - Buddhist
ISBN Prefix(es): 4-8381

**Shokabo Publishing Co Ltd**
8-1, Yombancho, Chiyoda-ku, Tokyo 102-0081
*Tel:* (03) 3262-9166 *Fax:* (03) 3262-9130
*E-mail:* shkb-01@cb3.so-net.ne.jp
*Web Site:* www.shokabo.co.jp/
*Key Personnel*
President: Tatsuji Yoshino
Foreign Rights & Trade: Saneatsu Makiya
Founded: 1716
Subjects: Mathematics, Science (General), Tech-
    nology
ISBN Prefix(es): 4-7853

**Shokokusha Publishing Co Ltd**
25, Sakamachi, Shinjuku-ku, Tokyo 160-0002
*Tel:* (03) 3359-3231 *Fax:* (03) 3357-3961
*Web Site:* www.shokokusha.co.jp
*Key Personnel*
President: Takeshi Goto
Sales Dir: Mineharu Matsuba
Founded: 1932
Subjects: Architecture & Interior Design, Art, Ed-
    ucation, Engineering (General), Science (Gen-
    eral), Technical
ISBN Prefix(es): 4-395

**Shorin-Sha Co ltd+**
Kasuga-syougaku Bldg, 3-23 Koishikawa 2
    chome, Bunkyo-ku, Tokyo 112-0002
*Tel:* (03)3815 4921 *Fax:* (03) 3815 4923
*Key Personnel*
President: Shuichi Takahashi
Founded: 1985
Subjects: Medicine, Nursing, Dentistry
ISBN Prefix(es): 4-7965

**Shueisha Inc**
5-10 Hitotsubashi 2 chome, Chiyoda-ku, Tokyo
    101-8050
*Tel:* (03) 3230-6111 *Fax:* (03) 3238 9239
*Web Site:* www.shueisha.co.jp
*Key Personnel*
President & Chief Executive Officer: Naoyoshi
    Taniyama
Editorial: Toshio Kawaguchi
Sales & Foreign Trade: Katsunori Kawaziri
Foreign Rights: Norifumi Sunou; Takaaki Ike
Foreign Rights & Trade: Takaaki Nanao
Founded: 1926
Specialize in comics, magazines & smaller-sized
    paperbacks
Subjects: Art, Fiction, Language Arts, Linguistics,
    Literature, Literary Criticism, Essays, Nonfic-
    tion (General)
ISBN Prefix(es): 4-08
*Associate Companies:* Shogakukan Inc

**Shufu-to-Seikatsu Sha Ltd**
3-5-7, Kyobashi, Chuo-ku, Tokyo 104-8357
*Tel:* (03) 3563-5120 *Fax:* (03) 3563-2073
*Web Site:* www.shufu.co.jp
*Key Personnel*
President: Hideo Kikuchi
Editor-in-Chief: Miss Miyako Kiyohara
Publishing Dept, Foreign Rights: Shujiro Murakawa
Founded: 1935
Subjects: Art, Cookery, Crafts, Games, Hobbies, Economics, Fashion, Fiction, History, House & Home, Literature, Literary Criticism, Essays, Medicine, Nursing, Dentistry, Philosophy, Religion - Other, Technology, Comics, Fishing, Interior, Recreation
ISBN Prefix(es): 4-391

**Shufunotomo Co Ltd+**
9, Kanda-Surugadai 2 chome, Chiyoda-ku, Tokyo 101-8911
*Tel:* (03) 5280-7539 *Fax:* (03) 5280-7587
*E-mail:* international@shufunotomo.co.jp
*Web Site:* www.shufunotomo.co.jp
*Key Personnel*
President: Kunihiko Muramatsu
Foreign Rights & Trade: Shunichi Kamiya
Founded: 1916
Subjects: Architecture & Interior Design, Career Development, Child Care & Development, Cookery, Crafts, Games, Hobbies, Education, Fashion, Fiction, Gardening, Plants, Health, Nutrition, House & Home, How-to, Medicine, Nursing, Dentistry, Nonfiction (General), Photography, Religion - Buddhist, Travel
ISBN Prefix(es): 4-07
Total Titles: 1,200 Print; 10 CD-ROM; 3 E-Book

**Shunjusha**
18-6, Soto-Kanda 2 chome, Chiyoda-ku, Tokyo 101-0021
*Tel:* (03) 3255-9614 *Fax:* (03) 3253-9370
*E-mail:* main@shunjusha.co.jp
*Web Site:* www.shunjusha.co.jp
*Key Personnel*
President: Akira Kanda
Founded: 1918
Subjects: Economics, History, Literature, Literary Criticism, Essays, Music, Dance, Psychology, Psychiatry, Religion - Other, Social Sciences, Sociology
ISBN Prefix(es): 4-393

**Shuppan News Co Ltd**
40-7 Kanda-Jimbo-cho 2 chome, Chiyoda-ku, Tokyo 101-0051
*Tel:* (03) 3262-2076 *Fax:* (03) 3261-6817
*E-mail:* snews@snews.net
*Web Site:* www.snews.net
*Key Personnel*
Editorial: Takeo Yoshizawa
Sales: Keiji Kinoshita
Rights & Permissions: Tetsuzo Suzuki
Founded: 1949
ISBN Prefix(es): 4-7852

**Oru Shuppan+**
2-4 Kudan-Kita 3 chome, Chiyoda-ku, Tokyo 102-0073
*Tel:* (03) 3234-0971 *Fax:* (03) 3261-6602
*Key Personnel*
Contact: Mika Hirano
ISBN Prefix(es): 4-279

**The Simul Press Inc**
13-9 Araki-cho, Shinjuku-ku, Tokyo 160-0007
*Tel:* (03) 3226-2861 *Fax:* (03) 3226-2860
*Key Personnel*
President: Katsuo Tamura
Senior Man Dir: Eiko Ikuta
Dir, Overseas Affairs: Masumi Muramatsu

Senior Editor: Daitaro Suwabe
Founded: 1967
Subjects: Business, Economics, Education, History, Language Arts, Linguistics, Literature, Literary Criticism, Essays, Philosophy, Regional Interests, Religion - Other, Social Sciences, Sociology
ISBN Prefix(es): 4-377
*Associate Companies:* Simul International Inc

**Sobun-Sha**
6-7, Kojimachi 2 chome, Chiyoda-ku, Tokyo 102-0083
*Tel:* (03) 3263-7101 *Fax:* (03) 3263-6789
*E-mail:* info@sobunsha.co.jp
*Web Site:* www.sobunsha.co.jp
*Key Personnel*
President: Hirotoshi Kuboi
Vice President: Masaaki Kuboi
Founded: 1951
Academic Publishers.
Subjects: Asian Studies, Biblical Studies, Business, Developing Countries, Economics, Education, Ethnicity, Finance, Foreign Countries, History, Law, Philosophy, Religion - Other, Humanities
ISBN Prefix(es): 4-423

**Sogensha Publishing Co Ltd+**
3-6 Awaji-machi 4 chome, Chuo-ku Osaka-shi Osaka 541-0047
*Tel:* (06) 62319011 *Fax:* (06) 62333112
*E-mail:* sgse@email.msn.com
*Web Site:* www.sogensha.co.jp
*Key Personnel*
President: Keiichi Yabe
Founded: 1925
Subjects: Art, Education, History, Medicine, Nursing, Dentistry, Philosophy, Psychology, Psychiatry, Religion - Other
ISBN Prefix(es): 4-422
*Associate Companies:* Tokyo Sogensha Co Ltd

**Sony Magazines Inc+**
5-1, Gobancho, Chiyoda-ku, Tokyo 102-8679
*Tel:* (03) 3234-5811 *Fax:* (03) 3234-5842
*Web Site:* www.sonymagazines.jp
*Key Personnel*
President: Koichi Hase
Foreign Rights & Trade: Kenichi Shigematsu
Founded: 1979
Subjects: Literature, Literary Criticism, Essays, Music, Dance
ISBN Prefix(es): 4-7897
*Parent Company:* Sony Music Entertainment Inc

**Soryusha**
5 Koji-machi 3 chome, Chiyoda-ku, Tokyo 102
*Tel:* (03) 32631471 *Fax:* (03) 32632943
*Key Personnel*
President & Manager: Kotaro Tanaka
Subjects: How-to, Mathematics
ISBN Prefix(es): 4-88176
*Parent Company:* Tokyo Hyoujun
*Associate Companies:* Kougakusha; Tokyo Souken
*Book Club(s):* Japan Book Publishers Association

**Soshisha Co Ltd+**
2-33-8, Sendagaya, Shibuya-ku, Tokyo 151-0051
*Tel:* (03) 3476-6565 *Fax:* (03) 3470-2640
*E-mail:* soshisha@magical.egg.or.jp
*Key Personnel*
President: Masao Kase
Editor-in-Chief: Haruo Kitani
Sales Manager: Tomio Kobayashi
Founded: 1966
Subjects: Literature, Literary Criticism, Essays, Nonfiction (General), Science (General)
ISBN Prefix(es): 4-7942

**Springer-Verlag Tokyo+**
3-3-13 Hongo, Bunkyo-ku, Tokyo 113-0033
*Tel:* (03) 3812-0757 *Fax:* (03) 3812-0719
*Web Site:* www.springer-tokyo.co.jp/
Founded: 1983
Subjects: Economics, Mathematics, Medicine, Nursing, Dentistry, Science (General)
ISBN Prefix(es): 4-431
Total Titles: 300 Print; 15 CD-ROM
*Parent Company:* Springer-Verlag GmbH & Co KG, Heidelberger Platz 3, 14197 Berlin, Germany

**Surugadai-Shuppan Sha**
Surugadai Bldg, 7, Kanda-Surugadai 3 chome, Chiyoda-ku, Tokyo 101-0062
*Tel:* (03) 3291-1676 *Fax:* (03) 3291-1675
*E-mail:* edit@surugadai.com
*Web Site:* www.e-surugadai.com
*Key Personnel*
President: Yoji Ida
Founded: 1954
Subjects: Economics, Law, Literature, Literary Criticism, Essays, Philosophy
ISBN Prefix(es): 4-411

**Taimeido Publishing Co Ltd**
3-22, Kanda-Ogawamachi, Chiyoda-ku, Tokyo 101-0052
*Tel:* (03) 3291-2374 *Fax:* (03) 3291-2376
*E-mail:* taimei1@ibm.net
*Key Personnel*
President: Yuzo Kanbe
Founded: 1918
Subjects: Agriculture, Economics, Geography, Geology, History, Philosophy, Religion - Other, Population
ISBN Prefix(es): 4-470

**Takahashi Shoten Co Ltd**
22-13, Otowa 1 chome, Bunkyo-ku, Tokyo 112-0013
*Tel:* (03) 3943-4525 *Fax:* (03) 3943-4288
*Web Site:* www.takahashishoten.co.jp
*Key Personnel*
President: Hideo Takahashi
Foreign Rights & Trade: Takashi Okubo
Founded: 1952 (as Kowado Co Ltd)
Guidebooks, juvenile, picture books.
Subjects: Education, Language Arts, Linguistics, Law, Medicine, Nursing, Dentistry, Technology
ISBN Prefix(es): 4-471

**Tamagawa University Press+**
1-1, Tamagawa-Gakuen 6 chome, Machida-shi, Tokyo 194-8610
*Tel:* (042) 739-8935 *Fax:* (042) 739-8940
*E-mail:* tup@tamagawa.ac.jp
*Web Site:* www.tamagawa.ac.jp/sisetu/up
*Key Personnel*
President: Yoshiaki Obara
Dir & Editor: Mikio Shionoya
Foreign Rights & Trade: Takamasa Narita
Founded: 1929
Membership(s): The Association of Japanese University Press (AJUP); International Association of Scholarly Publishers (IASP).
Subjects: Art, Education, Philosophy, Regional Interests, Religion - Other, Social Sciences, Sociology
ISBN Prefix(es): 4-472

**Tankosha Publishing Co Ltd**
19-1, Murasakino miya-Nishi-machi, Kita-ku, Kyoto-shi 603-8158
*Tel:* (075) 432 5151 *Fax:* (075) 432 0275
*E-mail:* info@tankosha.co.jp
*Web Site:* tankosha.topica.ne.jp
*Key Personnel*
President: Yoshito Naya
Founded: 1949
Subjects: Antiques, Architecture & Interior Design, Art, Cookery, Crafts, Games, Hobbies,

Ethnicity, Gardening, Plants, History, Philosophy, Photography, Religion - Other
ISBN Prefix(es): 4-473
Total Titles: 4,000 Print
*Branch Office(s)*
Sugaya Bldg, 39-1 Ichigaya Yanagi-cho, Shinjuku-ku, Tokyo 162-0061

**TBS-Britannica Co Ltd**
Itochu Nenryo Bldg, 24-12, Meguro 1 chome, Meguro-ku, Tokyo 153-8940
*Tel:* (03) 5436-5701 *Fax:* (03) 5436-5746
*Key Personnel*
President: Shinichi Hamanaka
Foreign Rights & Trade: Hiroshi Ishikawa
Founded: 1969
Subjects: Art, Literature, Literary Criticism, Essays, Social Sciences, Sociology
ISBN Prefix(es): 4-484

**Teikoku-Shoin Co Ltd**
29 Kanda Jimbo-cho 3 chome, Chiyoda-ku, Tokyo 101-0051
*Tel:* (03) 32620834 *Fax:* (03) 32627770
*E-mail:* kenkyu@teikokushoin.co.jp
*Web Site:* www.teikokushoin.co.jp
*Key Personnel*
President: Misao Moriya
Manager, Research Section: Jun Hirayama
Founded: 1926
Subjects: Geography, Geology, Government, Political Science, History
ISBN Prefix(es): 4-8071

**Thomson Learning Japan+**
3F Hirakawacho Kyowa Bldg, 2-1 Hirakawa-cho 2 chome, Chiyoda-ku, Tokyo 102
*Tel:* (03) 3221-1385 *Fax:* (03) 3237-1459
*E-mail:* elt@tlj.co.jp
*Web Site:* www.tlj.co.jp
*Key Personnel*
General Manager: Yuko Matsuoka
*E-mail:* yuko@tlj.co.jp
Founded: 1989
Publisher for ELT & academic texts
Also acts as importing agent for Thompson affiliated companies.
Subjects: Communications, English as a Second Language, Language Arts, Linguistics
ISBN Prefix(es): 4-900718; 4-931321
*Parent Company:* The Thomson Corporation
Distributor for Boyd & Fraser; Brooks/Coe; Chapman & Hall/Blackie & Son Academic; Course Technology Inc; Delmar; Gale Research/St James; Heinle & Heinle/Newbury House; Little, Brown/Legal (Japan); MacMillan (ELT only-USA); Thomas Nelson & Sons Ltd (UK); Onword; PWS-Kent; South-Western; Van Nostrand Reinhold; Wadsworth

**3A Corporation**
Shoei Bldg, 6-3, Sarugaku-cho 2 chome, Chiyoda-ku, Tokyo 1010064
*Tel:* (03) 32925751 *Fax:* (03) 32925754
*E-mail:* 3ac@mail.at-m.or.jp
*Web Site:* www.at-m.or.jpl~3ac
*Key Personnel*
President: Michihiro Takai
Founded: 1973
Subjects: Language Arts, Linguistics, Management
ISBN Prefix(es): 4-88319; 4-906224
Distributed by Chapman & Hall, London (except USA & Japan); Quality Resources, New York (USA)

**Tohan-Nippan**, *imprint of* Minerva Shobo Co Ltd

**Toho Book Store+**
1-9-4F Kanda-Jinbo-cho, Chiyoda-ku, Tokyo 101-0051

*Tel:* (03) 32331001 *Fax:* (03) 32950800
*Key Personnel*
President: Masakazu Fukushima
Founded: 1951
Specialize in China.
Membership(s): Japan Book Publisher's Association.
Subjects: Archaeology, Art, Asian Studies, Crafts, Games, Hobbies, Economics, Geography, Geology, History, Language Arts, Linguistics, Literature, Literary Criticism, Essays, Medicine, Nursing, Dentistry, Nonfiction (General), Philosophy, Regional Interests, Religion - Other
ISBN Prefix(es): 4-497
*Branch Office(s)*
Osaka
*Bookshop(s):* 1-10-2 Takashimadaira, Itabashi-Ku, Tokyo 175
*Warehouse:* 1-10-2 Takashimadaira, Itabashi-Ku, Tokyo 175
*Orders to:* 1-10-2 Takashimadaira, Itabashi-ku, Tokyo 175

**Toho Shuppan+**
Yasuda Seimei Tennouji Bldg, 1-8-15, Oomichi, Tennoji-ku, Osaka 543-0052
*Tel:* (06) 6779-9571 *Fax:* (06) 6779-9573
*E-mail:* info@tohoshuppan.co.jp
*Web Site:* www.tohoshuppan.co.jp
*Key Personnel*
President: Shigeto Imahigashi
Founded: 1978
Subjects: Art, Asian Studies, Crafts, Games, Hobbies, History, Philosophy, Photography, Religion - Buddhist
ISBN Prefix(es): 4-88591

**Tokai University Press**
Tokai University Alumni Hall, 3-10-35 Miramiyana, Hadano-shi, Kanagawa 257-0003
*Tel:* (0463) 79-3921 (Sales); (0463) 79-3921 (Editorial) *Fax:* (0463) 69-5087
*E-mail:* webmaster@press.tokai.ac.jp
*Web Site:* www.press.tokai.ac.jp
*Key Personnel*
President: Tatsuro Matsumae
Dir: Sumio Semizu
Editor-in-Chief, Foreign Rights & Trade: Yoshihiro Miura
Founded: 1962
Subjects: Art, Biological Sciences, Earth Sciences, History, Language Arts, Linguistics, Literature, Literary Criticism, Essays, Philosophy, Religion - Other, Social Sciences, Sociology, Technology
ISBN Prefix(es): 4-486

**Tokuma Shoten Publishing Co Ltd+**
2-2-1 Shiba-daimon, Minato-ku, Tokyo 105-8055
*Tel:* (03) 5403-4300 *Fax:* (03) 3573-8771
*E-mail:* iwabuchi@shoten.tokuma.com
*Web Site:* www.tokuma.jp
*Key Personnel*
President: Takeyoshi Matsushita
Foreign Rights & Trade: Kyoko Aoyama
Founded: 1954
Specialize in classics.
Subjects: Art, Crafts, Games, Hobbies, Economics, Fiction, History, House & Home, How-to, Literature, Literary Criticism, Essays, Nonfiction (General), Social Sciences, Sociology, Sports, Athletics
ISBN Prefix(es): 4-19
*U.S. Office(s):* 150 Skyline Tower, 10900 NE Fourth, Bellevue, WA 98004, United States

**Tokyo Kagaku Dojin Co Ltd+**
36-7, Sengoku 3 chome, Bunkyo-ku, Tokyo 112-0011
*Tel:* (03) 3946-5311 *Fax:* (03) 3946-5316
*E-mail:* tokyokagakudozin@a.email.ne.jp

*Key Personnel*
President: Minako Ozawa
Foreign Rights & Trade: Mutsure Sumita
Founded: 1961
Subjects: Biological Sciences, Chemistry, Chemical Engineering, Engineering (General), Medicine, Nursing, Dentistry, Science (General)
ISBN Prefix(es): 4-8079

**Tokyo Shoseki Co Ltd+**
17-1 Horifune 2 chome, Kita-ku, Tokyo 114-0004
*Tel:* (03) 5390-7531 *Fax:* (03) 5390-7409
*E-mail:* home@tokyo-shoseki.co.jp
*Web Site:* www.tokyo-shoseki.co.jp
*Key Personnel*
President & Chief Executive Officer: Yoshikatsu Kawauchi
Foreign Rights & Trade: Shigeki Oyama
*E-mail:* shoseki@tokyo-shoseki.co.jp
Founded: 1909
Associated with Toppan International Group.
Subjects: Art, Disability, Special Needs, Education, English as a Second Language, Fiction, History, Mathematics, Religion - Buddhist, Science (General), Travel
ISBN Prefix(es): 4-487
Total Titles: 1,000 Print; 100 CD-ROM
Subsidiaries: Astro Publishing Co Ltd (Domestic Only); Froebel-Kan Co Ltd
*Branch Office(s)*
Chubu (domestic only)
Chugoku (domestic only)
Hokkaido (domestic only)
Kansai (domestic only)
Kyushu (domestic only)
Tohoku (domestic only)

**Tokyo Sogensha Co Ltd**
1-5, Shin-Ogawamachi, Shinjuku-ku, Tokyo 162-0814
*Tel:* (03) 3268-8201 *Fax:* (03) 3268-8230
*Web Site:* www.tsogen.co.jp
*Key Personnel*
Chairman: Takao Akiyama
President: Shinichi Hasegawa
Sales: Haruo Hashimoto
Foreign Rights & Trade: Mari Igaki
Founded: 1954
Subjects: Art, Criminology, History, Literature, Literary Criticism, Essays, Music, Dance, Mysteries, Philosophy, Science Fiction, Fantasy, Social Sciences, Sociology
ISBN Prefix(es): 4-488
*Associate Companies:* Sogensha Publishing Co Ltd

**Tokyo Tosho Co Ltd**
5-22, Suido 2 chome, Bunkyo-ku, Tokyo 112-0005
*Tel:* (03) 3814-7818 *Fax:* (03) 3815-7330
*Web Site:* www.tokyo-tosho.co.jp
*Key Personnel*
President: Tooru Katayama
Foreign Rights & Trade: Shizuo Sudo
Founded: 1954
Subjects: Biography, Mathematics, Physics, Science (General), Technical
ISBN Prefix(es): 4-489

**Toppan Co Ltd+**
1-11-1 Shimura, Itabashi-ku, Tokyo 174-8558
*Tel:* (03) 3968-5111 *Fax:* (03) 5418-2529
*E-mail:* kouhou@toppan.co.jp
*Web Site:* www.toppan.co.jp
*Key Personnel*
Chief Executive: Hiroshi Yuri *Tel:* (03) 5418-253
*E-mail:* yuri@top.co.jp
Man Dir: Naomi Yoshikawa
Founded: 1963
Membership(s): Japan Book Association of International Publications.

Subjects: Biological Sciences, Computer Science, Environmental Studies, Library & Information Sciences
ISBN Prefix(es): 4-8101
Total Titles: 350 Print
*Parent Company:* Toppan Printing Co Ltd
*Associate Companies:* Tokyo Shoseki Co Ltd
Distributor for Prentice Hall Japan Ltd (Japan)

**Tosui Shobo Publishers**
Touho Gakki Honkan, 4-1, Nishi-Kanda 2 chome, Chiyoda-ku, Tokyo 101-0065
*Tel:* (03) 3261-6190 *Fax:* (03) 3261-2234
*E-mail:* tousuishobou@nifty.com
*Key Personnel*
President: Michiya Kuwabara
Foreign Rights & Trade: Fumie Nakamura
Founded: 1978
Subjects: Anthropology, Archaeology, History, Comparative study of civilizations, folklore
ISBN Prefix(es): 4-88708

**Toyo Keizai Shinpo-Sha+**
2-1, Nihombashi-Hongokucho 1 chome, Chuo-ku, Tokyo 103-8345
*Tel:* (03) 3246-5467 *Fax:* (03) 3270-4127
*E-mail:* tk@toyokeizai.co.jp
*Web Site:* www.toyokeizai.co.jp/
*Key Personnel*
President: Junji Asano
Rights Manager: Kurono Yukiharu
Foreign Rights & Trade: Mahito Fujii
Founded: 1895
Subjects: Business, Economics, Finance, Labor, Industrial Relations, Nonfiction (General), Social Sciences, Sociology
ISBN Prefix(es): 4-492
*U.S. Office(s):* Toyo Keizai America Inc, 380 Lexington Ave, Room 4505, New York, NY 10168, United States *Tel:* 212-949-6737

**Tsukiji Shokan Publishing Co**
7-4-4-201, Tsukiji, Chuo-ku, Tokyo 104-0045
*Tel:* (03) 3542-3731 *Fax:* (03) 3541-5799
*E-mail:* doi@tsukiji-shokan.co.jp
*Web Site:* www.tsukiji-shokan.co.jp
*Key Personnel*
President & Foreign Rights & Trade: Jiro Doi
  *E-mail:* JDHO7647@niftyserve.or.jp
Founded: 1953
Subjects: Anthropology, Archaeology, Biological Sciences, Child Care & Development, Earth Sciences, Environmental Studies, Social Sciences, Sociology, Sports, Athletics
ISBN Prefix(es): 4-8067

**Tutbooks**, *imprint of* Charles E Tuttle Publishing Co Inc

**Charles E Tuttle Publishing Co Inc+**
RK Bldg, 2nd floor, 2-12-10 Shimo-Meguro, Meguro-ku, Tokyo 153
*Tel:* (03) 5437-0171 *Fax:* (03) 5437-0755
*E-mail:* info@tuttlepublishing.com
*Web Site:* www.tuttlepublishing.com
*Key Personnel*
President, Singapore: Eric Oey
Man Dir, Tokyo Office: John Moore
Rights & Permissions & International Right, Boston Office: Penny Probst
Founded: 1948
Subjects: Art, Asian Studies, Cookery, Crafts, Games, Hobbies, Fiction, Language Arts, Linguistics, Literature, Literary Criticism, Essays, Poetry, Public Administration, Social Sciences, Sociology, Sports, Athletics, Travel
ISBN Prefix(es): 4-8053
Imprints: Journey Editions; Periplus Editions; Tutbooks; Yenbooks
Subsidiaries: Periplus Editions (HK) Ltd
Divisions: Berkeley Books Pte Ltd

*U.S. Office(s):* Charles E Tuttle Publishing Co Inc, 153 Milk St, Boston, MA 02109-4809, United States *Tel:* 617-951-4080 *Fax:* 617-951-4045
Airport Industrial Park, 364 Innovation Dr, North Clarendon, VT 05759-9436, United States
*Tel:* 802-773-8930 *Fax:* 802-773-6993

**United Nations University Press+**
53-70, Jingumae 5-chome, Shibuya-ku, Tokyo 150-8925
*Tel:* (03) 3499-2811 *Fax:* (03) 3406-7345
*E-mail:* mbox@hq.unu.edu
*Web Site:* www.unu.edu/unupress
*Telex:* 25442 unat unix *Cable:* UNATUNIV TOKYO
*Key Personnel*
Marketing Manager: Marc Benger
Publications Officer: Scott McQuade
Founded: 1975
Specialize in books in the social sciences, humanities & pure & applied natural sciences related to the University's research into the pressing global problems of human survival, development & welfare.
Subjects: Asian Studies, Developing Countries, Economics, Environmental Studies, Ethnicity, Geography, Geology, Health, Nutrition, Social Sciences, Sociology
ISBN Prefix(es): 92-808
Number of titles published annually: 17 Print; 17 Online
Total Titles: 300 Print; 150 Online
Imprints: UNU-INTECH Publications; UNU/WIDER Publications
*Branch Office(s)*
UNU Office in North America, 2 UN Plaza, DC2-2062, New York, NY 10017, United States
Foreign Rep(s): Brookings Institution Press (UK, US)
*Warehouse:* Brookings Institution Press, c/o Tasco, 9 Jay Gould Court, Waldorf, MA 20601, United States

**Universal Academy Press, Inc+**
BR-Hongo-5 Bldg, 6-16-2, Hongo, Bunkyo-ku, Tokyo 113-0033
*Tel:* (03) 3813-7232 *Fax:* (03) 3813-5932
*E-mail:* general@uap.co.jp
*Web Site:* www.uap.co.jp
*Key Personnel*
President: Masahito Sakui
Founded: 1986
Specialize in publishing Japanese research in English.
Subjects: Engineering (General), Medicine, Nursing, Dentistry, Science (General), Technology
ISBN Prefix(es): 4-946443
*Orders to:* CPO, Box 235, Tokyo 100-8691

**The University of Nagoya Press**
Furo-cho, Chikusa-ku, Nagoya City, Aichi Prefecture 464-8601
*Tel:* (052) 781-5353 *Fax:* (052) 781-0697
*E-mail:* info@unp.nagoya-u.ac.jp
*Web Site:* www.unp.or.jp
*Key Personnel*
President: Shin-ichi Hirano
ISBN Prefix(es): 4-8158
*Orders to:* Japan Publications Trading Co Ltd, 1-2-1 Sarugaku-cho 1 chome, PO Box 5030, Chiyoda-ku, Tokyo 101-0064 *Tel:* (03) 3292-3751 *Fax:* (03) 3292-0410

**University of Tokyo Press+**
7-3-1 Hongo, Bunkyo-ku, Tokyo 113-8756
*Tel:* (03) 3815-7789 *Fax:* (03) 3812-6958
*Web Site:* www.u-tokyo.ac.jp *Cable:* UNIVERSITYPRESS
*Key Personnel*
Man Dir: Tadashi Yamashita

Associate Dir: Isao Watanabe
Manager, International Publications: Etsuko Hamao
Founded: 1951
Membership(s): AAUP, STM, AJUP.
Subjects: Engineering (General), History, Medicine, Nursing, Dentistry, Philosophy, Psychology, Psychiatry, Religion - Other, Science (General), Social Sciences, Sociology
ISBN Prefix(es): 4-13
*U.S. Office(s):* Columbia University Press, 136 S Broadway, Irvington, NY 10533, United States

**UNU-INTECH Publications**, *imprint of* United Nations University Press

**UNU/WIDER Publications**, *imprint of* United Nations University Press

**Toshiichi Uraki**, *imprint of* Saela Shobo (Librairie Ca et La)

**Waseda University Press**
1-104-25 Totsukamachi, Shinjuku-ku, Tokyo 169-0071
*Tel:* (03) 32031551; (03) 32031570 *Fax:* (03) 32070406; (03) 32031570
*E-mail:* info@waseda-up.co.jp
*Web Site:* www.waseda-up.co.jp
*Key Personnel*
President: Shigenor Watabe
Foreign Rights & Trade: Koji Terayama
Founded: 1886
Subjects: Anthropology, Archaeology, Economics, Education, Film, Video, Finance, Government, Political Science, History, Law, Literature, Literary Criticism, Essays, Philosophy, Psychology, Psychiatry, Social Sciences, Sociology, Sports, Athletics
ISBN Prefix(es): 4-657
Number of titles published annually: 35 Print
Total Titles: 550 Print

**Yakuji Nippo Ltd**
One Kanda-Izumicho, Chiyoda-ku, Tokyo 101-8648
*Tel:* (03) 3862-2141 *Fax:* (03) 3866-8495
*E-mail:* shuppan@yakuji.co.jp
*Web Site:* www.yakuji.co.jp/
*Key Personnel*
President: Osamu Tanemura
Foreign Rights & Trade: Terue Hasshu
Founded: 1948
Subjects: Medicine, Nursing, Dentistry, Pharmacy
ISBN Prefix(es): 4-8408

**Yama-Kei Publishers Co Ltd+**
1-1-33 Shiba-Daimon, Minato-ku, Tokyo 105-8503
*Tel:* (03) 3436-4055 *Fax:* (03) 34334057
*E-mail:* info@yamakei.co.jp
*Key Personnel*
General Manager, International Division: Tony S Endo
President: Yoshimitsu Kawasaki
Founded: 1930
Subjects: Earth Sciences, Geography, Geology, Sports, Athletics, Travel
ISBN Prefix(es): 4-635
*Branch Office(s)*
1-12-12 Esaka-cho, Fukita-Shi, Osaka

**Yamaguchi Shoten+**
72, Ichijoji-Tsukudacho, Sakyo-ku, Kyoto 606-8175
*Tel:* (075) 781-6121 *Fax:* (075) 705-2003
*Key Personnel*
President: Kanya Yamaguchi
Founded: 1949
Subjects: Education, English as a Second Language, Language Arts, Linguistics, Literature, Literary Criticism, Essays

ISBN Prefix(es): 4-8411
*Branch Office(s)*
Fukuoka
Hiroshima
Nagoya
Tokyo

**Yenbooks**, *imprint of* Charles E Tuttle Publishing Co Inc

**Yokendo Ltd**
30-15, Hongo 5 chome, Bunkyo-ku, Tokyo 113-0033
*Tel:* (03) 3814-0911 *Fax:* (03) 3812-2615
*E-mail:* yokendo@gol.com
*Key Personnel*
President: Kiyoshi Oikawa
Foreign Rights: Akira Suzuki
Founded: 1914
Subjects: Agriculture, Engineering (General), Physical Sciences, Science (General)
ISBN Prefix(es): 4-8425

**Yoshioka Shoten**
87, Tanaka-Monzencho, Sakyo-ku, Kyoto 606-8225
*Tel:* (075) 781-4747 *Fax:* (075) 701-9075
*Web Site:* www3.ocn.ne.jp/~yoshioka
*Key Personnel*
President: Makoto Yoshioka
Foreign Rights & Trade: Shigeho Maeda
Founded: 1964
Subjects: Science (General), Technical
ISBN Prefix(es): 4-8427

**Yugaku-sha Ltd+**
46 Kanda Jinbo-cho 1 chome, Chiyoda-ku, Tokyo 101-0051
*Tel:* (03) 32333731 *Fax:* (03) 32333730
*Key Personnel*
Publisher: Kazumi Mitsui
Editorial, Sales Manager: Yoshiaki Tokunaga
Production Manager: Isoyoshi Yamamoto
Foreign Rights Associate: Naoko Sakaki
Founded: 1969
ISBN Prefix(es): 4-8416
*Associate Companies:* Keigaku Publishing Co Ltd

**Yuhikaku Publishing Co Ltd**
2-17, Kanda Jimbocho, Chiyoda-ku, Tokyo 101-0051
*Tel:* (03) 3264-1319 *Fax:* (03) 3264-5030
*E-mail:* soumu@yuhikaku.co.jp *Cable:* Yuhikakubook
*Key Personnel*
Chairman: Shiro Egusa
President: Tadataka Egusa
Foreign Trade & Rights: Osamu Nomura
Foreign Rights & Trade: Susumu Ito
Founded: 1877
Subjects: Economics, Education, History, Law, Management, Psychology, Psychiatry, Social Sciences, Sociology
ISBN Prefix(es): 4-641

**Yuki Shobo**
39-12, Sekiguchi 1 chome, Bunkyo-ku, Tokyo 112-0014
*Tel:* (03) 3203-0151 *Fax:* (03) 3203-0157
*Key Personnel*
President: Setsuko Takahashi
Foreign Rights & Trade: Hideo Oku
Founded: 1957
Subjects: Social Sciences, Sociology, Sports, Athletics, Home economics; recreation
ISBN Prefix(es): 4-638

**Yushodo Shuppan+**
29, San-ei-cho, Shinjuku-ku, Tokyo 160-0008
*Tel:* (03) 3943-5791 *Fax:* (03) 3351-5855; (03) 3943-6024

*E-mail:* intl@yushodo.co.jp
*Web Site:* www.yushodo.co.jp
*Key Personnel*
Chief Executive Officer: Mitsuo Nitta
President: Tamio Kawashima
Contact: R Carpenter
Founded: 1932
Specialize in antiquarian books, periodicals, new books & microforms. Also wholesaler & book dealer.
Subjects: Asian Studies, Economics, Regional Interests
ISBN Prefix(es): 4-8419
*Associate Companies:* JCC-Culture Japan; Newfield Building Co Ltd
Subsidiaries: Yushodo Fantas Corp; Yushodo Press Co Ltd
*Branch Office(s)*
Kansai
Kyoto
Ohtsuka
*Warehouse:* Yushodo Operation Center, 1542 Nakagawa, Isawa-cho, Higashiyatsushiro-gun, Yamanashi-Ken 406

**Zeikei insatsu**, *imprint of* Zeimukeiri-Kyokai

**Zeimukeiri-Kyokai+**
5-13 Simo-Ochiai 2 chome, Shinjuku-ku, Toyko 161-0033
*Tel:* (03) 3953 3325 *Fax:* (03) 3565 3391
*E-mail:* katsu@zeikei.co.jp
*Web Site:* www.zeikei.co.jp
*Key Personnel*
President: Yoshiharu Otsubo
Founded: 1945
Subjects: Accounting, Behavioral Sciences, Business, Economics, Human Relations, Law, Management, Marketing
ISBN Prefix(es): 4-419
Number of titles published annually: 100 Print
Total Titles: 1,700 Print
Imprints: Zeikei insatsu
Subsidiaries: Senbundo (Japan)

**Zenkoku Kyodo Shuppan**
10-32, Wakaba 1 chome, Shinjuku-ku, Tokyo 160-0011
*Tel:* (03) 3359-4811 *Fax:* (03) 3358-6174
*Key Personnel*
President: Takao Onaka
Founded: 1946
Subjects: Agriculture, Economics, Law, Management, Social Sciences, Sociology, Co-operatives
ISBN Prefix(es): 4-7934

**Zoshindo JukenKenkyusha**
2-19-15, Shinmachi, Nishi-ku, Osaka 550-0013
*Tel:* (06) 6532-1581 *Fax:* (06) 6532-1588
*E-mail:* jzoshindo@ybb.ne.jp
*Web Site:* www.zoshindo.co.jp
*Key Personnel*
President: Akitaka Okamoto
Foreign Rights & Trade: Masataka Sakamoto
Founded: 1890
Subjects: Education, Bookkeeping
ISBN Prefix(es): 4-424

# Jordan

## General Information

*Capital:* Amman
*Language:* Arabic. English widely used by business people
*Religion:* Predominantly Sunni Muslim
*Population:* 3.6 million
*Bank Hours:* 0830-1230 Saturday-Thursday

*Shop Hours:* 0900-1300, 1500-1900 Saturday-Thursday
*Currency:* 1000 fils = 1 dinar; 10 fils is known as a piastre
*Export/Import Information:* No tariffs on books and advertising matter, but tax applies. Import licenses required but granted freely. Air freight must be by Jordanian national airline. Transportation insurance must be arranged in Jordan.
*Copyright:* No copyright conventions signed

**Al-Tanwir Al Ilmi (Scientific Enlightenment Publishing House)+**
PO Box 4237, al-Mahatta, Amman 11131
*Tel:* (026) 4899619 *Fax:* (026) 4899619
*Key Personnel*
Owner: Dr Taisir Subhi Mahmoud
*E-mail:* taisir@yahoo.com
Founded: 1990
Subjects: Education, Electronics, Electrical Engineering, Philosophy, Science (General), Social Sciences, Sociology
Total Titles: 55 Print

**JBC**, *imprint of* Jordan Book Centre Co Ltd

**Jordan Book Centre Co Ltd+**
PO Box 301 (Al-Jubeiha), Amman 11941
*Tel:* (06) 676-882 *Fax:* (06) 5152016
*E-mail:* jbc@nets.com.jo
*Telex:* 21153 *Cable:* JORDAN BOOK CENTRE/ AMMAN
*Key Personnel*
President: I Sharbain
Founded: 1982
Subjects: Business, Computer Science, Economics, Engineering (General), Fiction, Medicine, Nursing, Dentistry, Nonfiction (General)
Imprints: JBC
*Showroom(s):* University St, Amman

**Jordan Distribution Agency Co Ltd**
PO Box 375, Amman 11118
*Tel:* (06) 4630191; (02) 4648949 *Fax:* (06) 4635152
*E-mail:* jda@go.com.jo
*Telex:* 22083 Distag Jo *Cable:* JODISTAG AMMAN
*Key Personnel*
Chairman & General Manager: Raja Elissa
Deputy Chairman, Dir: Nadia Elissa
Founded: 1951
Subjects: History

**Jordan House for Publication**
Basman St, Amman
Mailing Address: PO Box 1121, Amman
*Tel:* (06) 24224 *Fax:* (06) 51062
*Telex:* 22056 bestours jo
*Key Personnel*
Man Dir: Mursi El-Ashkar
Editorial: Dr Mohamad Takrouri
Founded: 1952
Subjects: Medicine, Nursing, Dentistry
*Bookshop(s):* 2 Basman St; Jabal Amman St, Amman

# Kazakstan

## General Information

*Capital:* Almaty
*Language:* Kazakh
*Religion:* Islamic (mostly Sunni Muslim)
*Population:* 17.1 million
*Bank Hours:* Generally open for short hours between 0930-1230 Monday-Friday

*Shop Hours:* Generally 0900-1800 Monday-
Friday; often open weekends
*Currency:* 100 kopeks = 1 rubl
*Export/Import Information:* According to
Ukrainian quotas and customs duties, companies engaged in trade should register with
the Ukraine Ministry of Foreign Relations. Licenses for export and import are also required
for trade with Russia.
*Copyright:* UCC (see Copyright Conventions, pg
xi)

**Gylym, Izd-Vo**
Ul Puskina 111/113, 480100 Almaty
*Tel:* (03272) 618005; (03272) 618845
 *Fax:* (03272) 618845; (03272) 618005
*Telex:* 251232 PTB Su
*Key Personnel*
Contact: Sagin-Girey Baimenov
Founded: 1946
Subjects: Biological Sciences, Chemistry, Chem-
ical Engineering, Earth Sciences, Economics,
Engineering (General), Mathematics, Physical
Sciences, Science (General), Social Sciences,
Sociology
ISBN Prefix(es): 5-628; 9965-07

**Al-Farabi Kazakh National University+**
Al-Farabi Ave 71, Almaty 480078
*Tel:* (03272) 471691 *Fax:* (03272) 472609
*E-mail:* anurmag@kazsu.kz
*Web Site:* www.kazsu.kz
Founded: 1934
Subjects: Archaeology, Asian Studies, Biologi-
cal Sciences, Business, Chemistry, Chemical
Engineering, Computer Science, Criminology,
Economics, Environmental Studies, Foreign
Countries, Geography, Geology, Government,
Political Science, History, Journalism, Law,
Management, Mathematics, Mechanical En-
gineering, Philosophy, Physics, Psychology,
Psychiatry, Social Sciences, Sociology

**Kazakhstan, Izd-Vo**
Prospect Abaja 143, Dom Izdatel'stv, Almaty
480009
*Tel:* (03272) 422929; (03272) 428562
 *Fax:* (03272) 422929
*Key Personnel*
Dir: E H Syzdykov
Editor-in-Chief: M A Rashev; M D Sit'ko
Founded: 1920
Subjects: Economics, Government, Political Sci-
ence, Medicine, Nursing, Dentistry, Science
(General), Social Sciences, Sociology
ISBN Prefix(es): 5-615; 9965-10

**Kramds-reklama Publishing & Advertising+**
Ul Mira 115, Almaty 480091
*Tel:* (03272) 453968 *Fax:* (03272) 696753
*Telex:* 251233 RPAMS SU *Cable:* 251103 Y
CNEX
*Key Personnel*
Dir: Lubov Shabykina
Chief Editor & Producer: Olga Tolanova
Chief Designer: Hasan Baimuratov
Manager: Tatyana Shah
Journalist: Rakip Nasyrow
Photographer: Oleg Belyalov; Vladimir Morozov
Founded: 1990
Subjects: Photography
ISBN Prefix(es): 5-86636
*Parent Company:* Kramds Corporation

**Respublikanskij izdatel skij Kabinet**
Ul Dzambula 25, Almaty 48000
*Tel:* (03272) 910703; (03272) 910333
 *Fax:* (03272) 631207
ISBN Prefix(es): 5-8380; 9965-08; 9965-518

**Zazusy, Izd-Vo+**
Prospect Abaya 143, Almaty 480009
*Tel:* (03272) 422849
*Key Personnel*
Dir: D I Isabekov
Editor-in-Chief: A T Saraev
Founded: 1934
Subjects: Literature, Literary Criticism, Essays,
Poetry
ISBN Prefix(es): 5-605

# Kenya

## General Information

*Capital:* Nairobi
*Language:* Kiswahili (officially); English, Kikuyu
& Luo also spoken
*Religion:* Most follow traditional beliefs; some
Christian and Muslim also
*Population:* 26.2 million
*Bank Hours:* 0900-1400 Monday-Friday; 0900-
1100 first and last Saturday of each month (ex-
cept on coast, where banks open and close half
an hour earlier)
*Shop Hours:* 0830-1230, 1400-1630 Monday-
Friday; 0830-1200 or 1230 Saturday
*Currency:* 100 cents = 1 Kenya shilling
*Export/Import Information:* No tariff on books
or advertising matter. Import licenses and ex-
change controls.
*Copyright:* UCC, Berne (see Copyright Conven-
tions, pg xi)

**AALAE,** see African Association for Literacy &
Adult Education (AALAE)

**Academy Science Publishers+**
Miotoni Rd, Off Miotoni Lane, Karen, Nairobi
Mailing Address: PO Box 24916-00502, Nairobi
*Tel:* (020) 884401; (020) 884405 *Fax:* (020)
884406
*E-mail:* aas@africaonline.co.ke; asp@africaonline.
co.ke
*Web Site:* www.aasciences.org
*Key Personnel*
Founder: Prof Thomas R Odhiambo
Editor-in-Chief: Prof Keno E Mshigani
Publishing Manager: Prof Samuel O Okatch
Founded: 1989
Membership(s): African Book Collectives Ltd
London; APNET; KPA; African Academy of
Sciences; Third World Academy of Sciences.
Subjects: Developing Countries, Environmental
Studies, Science (General), Technology
ISBN Prefix(es): 9966-831
Number of titles published annually: 4 Print
Total Titles: 23 Print
*Parent Company:* The African Academy of Sci-
ences
Subsidiaries: Third World Academy of Sciences
*Showroom(s):* African Books Collective, The Jam
Factory, 27 Park End St, Oxford OX1 1KU,
United Kingdom
*Bookshop(s):* Prestige Bookshop, Nairobi; Text-
book Centre Nairobi

**Action Publishers+**
PO Box 74419, Nairobi
*Tel:* (020) 608-810 *Fax:* (020) 753-227
*E-mail:* actonpublishersinfo@acton.co.ke
*Web Site:* www.acton.co.ke
*Key Personnel*
Man Dir & Publisher: Dr J N K Mugambi
Founded: 1992

Subjects: Career Development, Developing Countries, Education, How-to, Music, Dance, Philosophy, Religion - Other, Self-Help, Theology
ISBN Prefix(es): 9966-888

**ACTS,** see African Centre for Technology
Studies (ACTS)

**AFER (African Ecclesial Review),** *imprint of*
Gaba Publications Amecea, Pastoral Institute

**Africa Book Services (EA) Ltd+**
Rattansi Educational Trust Bldg, Koinange St,
Nairobi
Mailing Address: PO Box 45245, Nairobi
*Tel:* (020) 223641 *Fax:* (020) 330272
*E-mail:* abs@mref.co.ke
*Key Personnel*
Dir: Talat Lone
Founded: 1955
Membership(s): Kenya Publishers Association &
Kenya Book Sellers Association.
Subjects: Accounting, Library & Information Sci-
ences, Nonfiction (General)
ISBN Prefix(es): 9966-914
*U.S. Office(s):* Dars, 919 Blair Ave, Neenah, WI
54956-2000, United States
Distributor for IMF; UNESCO; World Bank

**African Association for Literacy & Adult
Education (AALAE)**
PO Box 50768, Nairobi
*Tel:* (020) 222-391; (020) 331-512 *Fax:* (02) 340-
849
*Telex:* 22096
ISBN Prefix(es): 9966-9901

**African Centre for Technology Studies
(ACTS)+**
PO Box 45917, Nairobi 00100
*Tel:* (020) 7224700; (020) 7224000 *Fax:* (020)
7224701; (020) 7224001
*E-mail:* acts@cgiar.org
*Web Site:* www.acts.or.ke
*Key Personnel*
Communications & Publications Officer: Harri-
son Maganga *Tel:* (020) 7224705 *E-mail:* h.
maganga@cgiar.org
Founded: 1988
Conducts policy research for sustainable develop-
ment, publication of research findings.
Subjects: Agriculture, Developing Countries, En-
vironmental Studies, Health, Nutrition, Science
(General), Technology
ISBN Prefix(es): 9966-41
Divisions: Acts Press, Policy Outreach
Distributed by Zed Books (UK)

**African Council for Communication Education**
PO Box 47495, Nairobi
*Tel:* (020) 215270-33424 (ext 2068, 2328); (020)
227043 *Fax:* (020) 216135; (020) 750329;
(020) 229168
*E-mail:* acceb@arcc.or.ke; acceb@form-net.com
*Key Personnel*
President: Francis Wete
Documentalist: Lydiah Gachung
Founded: 1976
ISBN Prefix(es): 9966-45

**Book Sales (K) Ltd**
PO Box 20377, Nairobi
*Key Personnel*
Chief Executive: Adrian Louis
Founded: 1976
Also bookseller.
ISBN Prefix(es): 9966-840
Subsidiaries: Kesho Book Centre

**Bookman Consultants Ltd+**
PO Box 31191, Nairobi
*Tel:* (020) 245146 *Fax:* (020) 336771
*E-mail:* bookman@wananchi.com
*Key Personnel*
Man Dir: Stanley Irura
Founded: 1988
Organizers of the Nairobi Book Fair.
Membership(s): Kenya Publishers Association, Afro-Asian Book Council; also acts as Publishing Consultant & Publisher of the Kenya Bookseller.
Subjects: Publishing & Book Trade Reference
ISBN Prefix(es): 9966-867

**British Institute in Eastern Africa**
Nairobi
Mailing Address: PO Box 30710, Nairobi
*Tel:* (02) 4343190; (02) 4343330 *Fax:* (02) 43365
*E-mail:* britinst@insightkenya.com
*Web Site:* www.britac.ac.uk/institutes/eafrica
*Key Personnel*
Dir: Dr Paul Lane
Secretary: Elizabeth Kiarie
Founded: 1962
Subjects: Archaeology, Ethnicity, History, Language Arts, Linguistics
Number of titles published annually: 1 Print
*Branch Office(s)*
10 Carlton House Terrace, London SW1Y5AH, United Kingdom *Tel:* (020) 7969 5201 *Fax:* (020) 7969-5401 *E-mail:* biea@britac. ac.uk
Distributed by Oxbow Books (UK); Oxbow Books (USA)

**Camerapix Publishers International Ltd+**
3rd Floor, ABC Place, Waiyaki Way, Nairobi
Mailing Address: PO Box 45048, Nairobi
*Tel:* (02) 4448923; (02) 4448924; (02) 4448925 *Fax:* (02) 4448818
*E-mail:* info@camerapix.com; camerapix@ iconnect.co.ke
*Web Site:* www.camerapix.com
*Telex:* 22576 *Cable:* MOVIETONE NAIROBI
*Key Personnel*
Chief Executive Officer, Operations & Business Development Dir: Salim Amin
Man Dir: Rukhsana Haq; Rand Pearson
Founded: 1960
Subjects: Art, Regional Interests, Travel
ISBN Prefix(es): 1-874041
Imprints: CPI
Subsidiaries: Camerapix Daares Salaam; Camerapix Karachi
*Branch Office(s)*
Camerapix London, 8 Ruston Mews, London W11 1RB, United Kingdom *Tel:* (020) 7221 0077 *Fax:* (020) 7792 8105 *E-mail:* camerapixuk@btinternet.com
Distributor for Hunter & Struik

**Cosmopolitan Publishers Ltd+**
PO Box 18470, Nairobi
*Tel:* (020) 333448 *Fax:* (020) 333448
*Telex:* 22143
*Key Personnel*
Chairman: Dr Afrifa K Gitonga
Dir: Mr Murithi K Micheu
Marketing & Operations Dir: Boniface Wangaine
Founded: 1991
Subjects: Government, Political Science, Management, Mathematics, Psychology, Psychiatry
ISBN Prefix(es): 9966-881

**CPI,** *imprint of* Camerapix Publishers International Ltd

**Danmar Publishers+**
PO Box 75493, Nairobi
*Tel:* (020) 600431; (020) 600432

*Key Personnel*
President: Daniel Irungu
Vice President & Author: Mary Irungu
Editor: Robert Irungu
Founded: 1990
Specialize in reading & spelling guides for beginners.
Subjects: English as a Second Language
ISBN Prefix(es): 9966-863
*Parent Company:* Danmar Publishers Printers & Stationer
*Showroom(s):* Chania Bookshop, PO Box 32413, Nairobi; Savanis Book Centre, PO Box 42157, Nairobi
*Bookshop(s):* Chania Bookshop, PO Box 32413, Nairobi; Savanis Book Centre, PO Box 42157, Nairobi

**Dhillon Publishers Ltd+**
PO Box 32197, Nairobi
*Tel:* (020) 552566; (020) 537533 *Fax:* (020) 537553
*E-mail:* dhillon@wananchi.com
Founded: 1992
Subjects: English as a Second Language
ISBN Prefix(es): 9966-890

**Egerton University**
PO Box 536, Njoro
*Tel:* (051) 61620; (051) 61031; (051) 61032 *Fax:* (051) 62527
*Web Site:* www.egerton.ac.ke
*Telex:* 33075
ISBN Prefix(es): 9966-838

**Evangel Publishing House+**
Lumumba Drive, Roysambu, Off Thika Rd, Nairobi
Mailing Address: Private Bag 28963, Nairobi 00200
*Tel:* (020) 8560839; (020) 8562047 *Fax:* (020) 8562050
*E-mail:* evanglit@maf.or.ke; publisher@ evangelpublishing.org
*Web Site:* www.evangelpublishing.org *Cable:* EVANGELIT NAIROBI
*Key Personnel*
Man Dir: Barine A Kirimi *Tel:* (0733) 613896 *E-mail:* kirimi.barine@juno.com
Man Editor, Rights & Permissions: Paul Kimani *E-mail:* pkimani@evangelpublishing.org
Founded: 1952
Christian Publishing.
Subjects: Religion - Protestant, Religion - Other, Theology
ISBN Prefix(es): 9966-850; 9966-20
Number of titles published annually: 12 Print
Total Titles: 265 Print

**Focus Publishers Ltd+**
Siwaka Estate, Hse 125, Opp, Strathmore University, Ole Sangale Rd, 00200 Nairobi
Mailing Address: PO Box 28176, 00200 Nairobi
*Tel:* (020) 600737
*E-mail:* focus@africaonline.co.ke
*Key Personnel*
Man Dir: Serah T K Mwangi
Founded: 1991
Subjects: Accounting, Business, Economics, Education, English as a Second Language, Fiction, Finance, Geography, Geology, Law, Literature, Literary Criticism, Essays, Mathematics, Philosophy, Religion - Catholic, Catechism
ISBN Prefix(es): 9966-882
Number of titles published annually: 20 Print
Total Titles: 120 Print
Distributor for Scepter Ltd (UK); Sinag-Tala (Philippines)

**Foundation Books Ltd**
PO Box 73435, Nairobi

*Tel:* (020) 765485
*Key Personnel*
Man Dir: F O Okwanya
Editorial: C O Ojienda
Sales Promotion: Moses Gondi
Production: Sophia Wanjiku Ojienda
Founded: 1974
Sub-regional Co-ordinator, Regional Centre for Book Promotion in Africa; Co-publishing program Eastern Africa Region.
Subjects: Biography, Poetry
ISBN Prefix(es): 9966-849

**Gaba Publications Amecea, Pastoral Institute+**
PO Box 4002, 30100 Eldoret
*Tel:* (0321) 61218; (0321) 62153 *Fax:* (0321) 62570
*E-mail:* gabapubs@africaonline.co.ke
*Web Site:* www.amecea.org
*Key Personnel*
Dir & Editor: Fr Eugene Ngoma
Assistant Dir & Editor: Sr Justin Nabushawo
Founded: 1959
Subjects: Anthropology, Biblical Studies, Religion - Catholic, Religion - Other, Theology
ISBN Prefix(es): 9966-836
Imprints: AFER (African Ecclesial Review); Spearhead

**Government Press**
PO Box 30128, Nairobi
*Tel:* (020) 334075
ISBN Prefix(es): 9966-26

**Guru Publishers Ltd+**
PO Box 32542, Nairobi
*Tel:* (020) 764146
*Key Personnel*
Man Dir, Proprietor & International Rights: Krishan Kumar Prabhakar
Founded: 1989
Specialize in secondary math & mathematical tables.
Membership(s): Kenya Publishers Association.
Subjects: Mathematics
ISBN Prefix(es): 9966-9878
Distributed by Book Distributors Ltd-NBI (Kenya)

**Heinemann Kenya Ltd (EAEP)+**
PO Box 45314, Nairobi
Mailing Address: PO Box 45314, Nairobi
*Tel:* (020) 4445700; (020) 4445200 *Fax:* (020) 448753; (020) 226286 *Cable:* EDPUBS NAIROBI
*Key Personnel*
Man Dir, Chief Executive & Rights & Permissions: Henry Chakava
Publishing Dir: Jimmi Makotsi
Sales & Marketing Dir: Winston Mutua Nzioki
Finance Dir: Fabian Murugu
Warehouse Dir: Charles Oduor Munjal
Publicity Manager: James Ogola
Publishing Manager, English Language Teaching: B O Muluka
Editor, Kiswahili: G Lilian Dhahabu
Editorial, Secondary: Anne Mithamo
Off Manager: Onyango Ogutu
Accountant: Mark Abonyo
Founded: 1965
Co-publishers with James Currey Africa Books Collective Publishers (UK), Ohio University Press (USA), African Publishing Network (AP-NET) (Zimbabwe).
Membership(s): Kenya Publishers Association.
Subjects: Accounting, Agriculture, Art, Automotive, Biological Sciences, Business, Cookery, Drama, Theater, Economics, Education, Fashion, Fiction, Finance, Geography, Geology, Government, Political Science, History, Literature, Literary Criticism, Essays, Management, Music, Dance, Nonfiction (General), Philosophy, Physical Sciences, Physics, Poetry, Public

Administration, Religion - Other, Social Sciences, Sociology, Theology
ISBN Prefix(es): 9966-46; 9966-9953
*Associate Companies:* East African Educational Publishers (Uganda Branch) Ltd, Pioneer House, Suite 9, Plot 28, Jinja Rd, PO Box 11542, Kampala, Uganda
Imprints: Spear Books, EAEP Kenya Writers Series; Wandishi wa Kiafricka
Subsidiaries: Kenway Publications
Distributor for James Currey Publishers (UK); Heinemann International (UK)
*Warehouse:* East African Book Distributors Ltd, PO Box 10324, Nairobi *Tel:* (02) 220520 *Fax:* (02) 226286 (EABD)
*Orders to:* East African Book Distributors Ltd (EABD), PO Box 10324, Nairobi *Tel:* (02) 220520 *Fax:* (02) 226286

**Horizon Books**, *imprint of* Space Sellers Ltd

**ICRAF**, see International Centre for Research in Agroforestry (ICRAF)

**International Centre for Research in Agroforestry (ICRAF)**
United Nations Ave, Gigiri, Nairobi
Mailing Address: PO Box 30677, Nairobi
*Tel:* (02) 524000 *Fax:* (02) 524001
*E-mail:* icraf@cgiar.org
*Web Site:* www.worldagroforestrycentre.org
*Key Personnel*
Dir General: Dr Dennis P Garrity
Assistant Dir General: Bruce Scott
Founded: 1977
International not-for-profit organization.
Subjects: Agriculture, Environmental Studies
ISBN Prefix(es): 92-9059

**Jacaranda Designs Ltd+**
PO Box 76691, Nairobi
*Tel:* (020) 569736; (020) 568353 *Fax:* (020) 740524
*Key Personnel*
Man Dir & International Rights: Susan Scull-Carvalho
Marketing Manager: Brown Onduso
Man Editor: Bridget King
Founded: 1991
Membership(s): Association of International Schools in Africa (AISA); Kenya Publishers Association; Multi-Cultural Publishers Exchange Association.
Subjects: Fiction, Nonfiction (General)
ISBN Prefix(es): 9966-884
*U.S. Office(s):* Jacaranda Designs Ltd USA, PO Box 7936, Boulder, CO 80306, United States
Distributed by Southern Book Publishers (South Africa)

**JKF**, *imprint of* The Jomo Kenyatta Foundation

**KEMRI**, see Kenya Medical Research Institute (KEMRI)

**Kenway Publications Ltd+**
Woodvale Grove, Westlands, Brick Court, Nairobi
Mailing Address: PO Box 45314-00100 GPO, Nairobi
*Tel:* (02) 444700; (02) 445260; (02) 445261 *Fax:* (02) 448753
*E-mail:* eaep@africaonline.co.ke
*Web Site:* www.eastafricanpublishers.com
*Telex:* EDPUBS
*Key Personnel*
Chairman & Chief Executive Officer: Henry Chakava
Man Dir: Barrack O Muluka
Sales & Marketing Dir: Winston Mutua Nzioki *Tel:* (02) 544295
Publicity Manager: Rebecca Wabwoba

Founded: 1981
Specialize in tourism books, city maps.
Membership(s): African Publishing Network; Kenya Publishers Association.
Subjects: Animals, Pets, Anthropology, Biography, Cookery, Government, Political Science, History, Humor, Language Arts, Linguistics, Music, Dance, Natural History, Nonfiction (General), Regional Interests, Sports, Athletics, Travel
ISBN Prefix(es): 9966-46; 9966-848; 9966-25
Number of titles published annually: 4 Print
Total Titles: 56 Print
*Parent Company:* East African Educational Publishers Ltd, Nairobi, Man Dir: Barrack Muluka
*Associate Companies:* Transmedia Uganda, Plot 51/53, Nkrumah Rd, PO Box 28104, Kampala, Uganda, Ignatius Tumwesigye *Tel:* (041) 235860 *Fax:* (041) 347235 *E-mail:* transmed@swiftuganda.com *Web Site:* www.eastafricanpublishers.com
Distributed by African Books Collective (UK)
Foreign Rep(s): African Books Collective (UK, Europe)
*Shipping Address:* East African Book Distributors Ltd, PO Box 10324, Nairobi
*Warehouse:* East African Book Distributors Ltd, PO Box 10324, Nairobi, Warehouse Manager: Charles Munjal *Tel:* (02) 544321, (02) 545903, (02) 534020 *Fax:* (02) 532095 *E-mail:* eaep@nbnet.co.ke *Web Site:* www.eastafricanpublishers.com
*Orders to:* East African Book Distributors Ltd, PO Box 10324, Nairobi, Warehouse Manager: Charles O Munjal *Tel:* (02) 534020, (020) 544321, (020) 545903 *Fax:* (02) 532095 *E-mail:* eaep@nbnet.co.ke *Web Site:* www.eastafricanpublishers.com

**Kenya Energy & Environment Organisation, Kengo**
PO Box 48197, Nairobi
*Tel:* (020) 749747; (020) 748281 *Fax:* (020) 749382
*Telex:* 25222 *Cable:* KENGO KE
*Key Personnel*
Executive Dir: Mr Achoka Awori
Assistant Marketing Officer: Julie Kariuki
Founded: 1981
Subjects: Agriculture, Energy, Environmental Studies
ISBN Prefix(es): 9966-841

**Kenya Literature Bureau**
Bellevue Area, Off Mombasa Rd, Nairobi
Mailing Address: PO Box 30022, Nairobi
*Tel:* (02) 608305; (02) 608806; (02) 605595; (02) 351196; (02) 351197; (02) 506158 *Fax:* (02) 605600 *Fax on Demand:* 601474
*E-mail:* klb@onlinekenya.com *Cable:* Literature Nairobi
*Key Personnel*
Man Dir: M A Karauri
Publishes, prints & distributes affordable books & other reading materials. Also encourages Kenyan authors through financial incentives, advice on how to write, etc.
Subjects: Agriculture, Animals, Pets, Education, Health, Nutrition, Law, Mathematics, Medicine, Nursing, Dentistry, Science (General), Science Fiction, Fantasy, Veterinary Science
ISBN Prefix(es): 9966-44
Total Titles: 700 Print

**Kenya Medical Research Institute (KEMRI)**
PO Box 54840, Nairobi
*Tel:* (02) 722541; (02) 722672; (02) 722532 *Fax:* (02) 720030
*E-mail:* kemrilib@ken.healthnet.org
*Web Site:* www.kemri.org
*Key Personnel*
Dir: Dr Davy Koech

Subjects: Biological Sciences, Environmental Studies, Health, Nutrition, Medicine, Nursing, Dentistry
ISBN Prefix(es): 9966-869

**Kenya Meteorological Department**
PO Box 30259, Nairobi
*Tel:* (02) 567880 *Fax:* (02) 576955
*E-mail:* director@lion.meteo.go.ke; imtr@lion.meteo.go.ke
*Web Site:* www.meteo.go.ke
*Telex:* 22208 Weather *Cable:* WEATHER NAIROBI
*Key Personnel*
Dir: Dr Joseph Romanus Mukabana
Subjects: Electronics, Electrical Engineering, Environmental Studies
ISBN Prefix(es): 9966-830

**Kenya Quality & Productivity Institute+**
PO Box 57225, Nairobi
*Key Personnel*
Contact: Silas Gachanja Maina
Founded: 1992
Subjects: Developing Countries, Economics, Management, Mathematics, Self-Help
ISBN Prefix(es): 9966-894

**The Jomo Kenyatta Foundation+**
Industrial Area, Enterprise Rd, Nairobi
Mailing Address: PO Box 30533, Nairobi
*Tel:* (02) 557222; (02) 531965 *Fax:* (02) 531966
*E-mail:* publish@jomokenyattaf.com
*Web Site:* www.kenyaweb.com/education/klb.html *Cable:* Foundation
Founded: 1966
Membership(s): Kenya Publishers Association.
ISBN Prefix(es): 9966-22
*Parent Company:* Ministry of Education, PO Box 30040, Nairobi
Imprints: JKF
*Warehouse:* Kijabe St, PO Box 30533, Nairobi
*Orders to:* c/o Sales & Marketing Manager, Industrial Area, Enterprise Rd, PO Box 30533, Nairobi

**Lake Publishers & Enterprises Ltd+**
PO Box 1743, Kisumu
*Tel:* (057) 42750; (057) 2153
*Key Personnel*
President: James C Odaga
Dir: Mrs Asenath Bole Odaga
Editor: Aol Ohito
Founded: 1982
Membership(s): African Publishing Network (APNET); Kenya Booksellers Association; Kenya Publishers Association.
Subjects: Biological Sciences, Drama, Theater, Education, Fiction, Government, Political Science, Labor, Industrial Relations, Literature, Literary Criticism, Essays, Mathematics, Music, Dance, Poetry, Religion - Protestant
ISBN Prefix(es): 9966-847
*Associate Companies:* Thu Tinda Book Distribution Ltd; Thu Tinda Bookshop
Subsidiaries: Innervision Communication
Distributor for ABC (outside Africa)
*Showroom(s):* Kenya Industrial Estate, Airport Rd, Kisumu

**Life Challenge AFRICA**
PO Box 50770, Nairobi
*Tel:* (02) 561121; (02) 722314 *Fax:* (02) 564030
*E-mail:* lca@umsg.org
*Key Personnel*
Contact: Eric Walter
Subjects: Religion - Islamic, Religion - Other
ISBN Prefix(es): 9966-895
*U.S. Office(s):* SIM Int, Box 7900, Charlotte, NC 28241, United States

**Macmillan Kenya Publishers Ltd+**
Kijabe St, Nairobi
Mailing Address: PO Box 30797, Nairobi
*Tel:* (02) 220 012; (02) 224 485 *Fax:* (02) 212 179
*Web Site:* www.macmillan-africa.com
*Key Personnel*
Man Dir: David Muita *E-mail:* dmuita@macken.co.ke
Founded: 1970
ISBN Prefix(es): 9966-885; 9966-945
*Parent Company:* Macmillan Publishers Ltd, United Kingdom

**Midi Teki Publishers+**
PO Box 52906, Nairobi
*Tel:* (02) 506993
Founded: 1977
Subjects: Accounting, Business, Developing Countries, Government, Political Science, Public Administration, Social Sciences, Sociology
ISBN Prefix(es): 9966-861
*Bookshop(s):* Mihuti Bookshop, Box 31, Kangema, Muringo *Tel:* 0157-22164

**Nairobi University Press+**
Jomo Kenyatta Memorial Library Bldg, PO Box 30197, Nairobi
*Tel:* (02) 334244 (ext 28581) *Fax:* (02) 336885
*E-mail:* nup@uonbi.ac.ke
*Web Site:* www.uonbi.ac.ke
*Telex:* 22095 Varsity KE
*Key Personnel*
Secretary: Omari E Gichobi *Tel:* (02) 334244, ext 222235 *E-mail:* gichobi@uonbi.ac.ke
Founded: 1984
Subjects: Accounting, African American Studies, Behavioral Sciences, Developing Countries, Geography, Geology, Government, Political Science, History, Law, Mathematics, Philosophy, Physical Sciences, Physics, Real Estate, Religion - Protestant, Social Sciences, Sociology, Veterinary Science
ISBN Prefix(es): 9966-846
*Parent Company:* University of Nairobi (Company fully-owned by University of Nairobi)
Distributed by African Books Collective (Europe, USA)

**Paulines Publications-Africa+**
PO Box 49026, Nairobi
*Tel:* (020) 4447202; (020) 4447203 *Fax:* (020) 4442097
*E-mail:* publications@paulinesafrica.org
*Web Site:* www.paulinesafrica.org
*Key Personnel*
President: Sr Samuela Gironi
Dir: Sr Teresa Marcazzan
Editor: Silvano Borruso; Peter Onyango-Ajus
Founded: 1985
Subjects: Biblical Studies, Biography, Child Care & Development, Communications, Education, History, Nonfiction (General), Psychology, Psychiatry, Religion - Catholic, Religion - Other, Theology, Women's Studies
ISBN Prefix(es): 9966-21
Number of titles published annually: 70 Print
Total Titles: 800 Print
*Parent Company:* Paulines Publications, Ring Rd Riverside, Nairobi 00100 GPO
*Ultimate Parent Company:* Daughters of St. Paul, 6 Amore Str off Toyin Str, IKEJA, PMB 21243, Lagos, Nigeria
*Branch Office(s)*
Catholic Book Centre, PO Box 2454, Addis Ababa, Ethiopia
Catholic Book Centre, PO Box CY738, Causway, Harare, Zimbabwe
Livraria Edicoes Paulistas, CP 3659, Maputo, Mozambique *Tel:* (01) 303397 *Fax:* (01) 304257 *E-mail:* paulines@virconn.com

Paulines Book & Media Centre, PMP 21243, Lagos State, Nigeria *Tel:* (01) 7741636 *Fax:* (01) 4932128 *E-mail:* paulines@infoweb.com.ng
San Paolo Multimedia, Via del Mascherino 94, 00193 Rome, Italy *Tel:* (06) 6872354 *Fax:* (06) 68308093 *E-mail:* pmultimedia@pcn.net
*Bookshop(s):* Cathedral Bookshop, PO Box 2381, Dar Es Salaam, United Republic of Tanzania, Contact: Sister Carmel *Tel:* (022) 2113204 *Fax:* (022) 2113204 *E-mail:* cathbshop@cats-net.com; Catholic Bookshop, PO Box 30249, Nairobi *Tel:* (020) 3338514 *Fax:* (020) 4442144 *E-mail:* cbsn@bidii.com; Paulines Book & Media Centre, PO Box 4392, Kampala, Kampala, Uganda *Tel:* (041) 256346 *Fax:* (041) 349135 *E-mail:* paulines@africaonline.co.ug; Paulines Catholic Bookshop, PO Box 36291, Lusaka, Zambia *Tel:* (01) 220264 *Fax:* (01) 250134 *E-mail:* paulines@zamnet.zm; Paulines Multimedia Centre, PO Box 641, Bruma, Johannesburg 2026, South Africa *Tel:* (011) 6220488; (011) 6220489 *Fax:* (011) 6220490 *E-mail:* paulines@iafrica.com

**Phoenix Publishers Ltd+**
PO Box 18650, Nairobi 00500
*Tel:* (020) 223262; (020) 222309 *Fax:* (020) 339875
*E-mail:* phoenix@insightkenya.com
*Web Site:* www.phoenixpublishers.co.ke
*Key Personnel*
Secretary: Ann Wanjiru
Contact: G Woruingi
Founded: 1988
Membership(s): Kenya Publishers' Association.
Subjects: Education, Environmental Studies, Geography, Geology, History, Mathematics, Physical Sciences, Poetry, Social Sciences, Sociology, Women's Studies
ISBN Prefix(es): 9966-47
Distributed by MK Publishers (Uganda); Taasisi ya Uchunguzi wa Kiswahili (TUKI) (Tanzania)
Distributor for MK Publishers (Uganda); Taasisi ya Uchunguzi wa Kiswahili (TUKI) (Tanzania)
Foreign Rep(s): MK Publishers (Uganda)
Foreign Rights: Taasisi ya Uchunguzi wa Kiswahili (TUKI) (Tanzania)
*Distribution Center:* Kijabe St, Nairobi

**Sasa Sema Publications Ltd+**
South Gate Centre, Suite 6, South B, Nairobi
Mailing Address: PO Box 13956, Nairobi 00800
*Tel:* (020) 550400; 722-200544; 734-600887
*E-mail:* sasasema@wananchi.com
*Web Site:* www.sasasema.com
*Key Personnel*
Man Dir: Lila Luce *E-mail:* lucelila@yahoo.fr
Publishing Manager: Silas Okutoyi
Marketing Manager: Simon Mwangi
Founded: 1996
Publisher of Kenyan children's books, especially comic books (graphic novels; bandes dessinees) in Swahili & English; children's biographies of great African women & men in English; short literature in English & Swahili. Also publish editorial cartoons, study guides & pre-school activity books.
Membership(s): Kenya Publishers Association.
Subjects: African American Studies, Biography, Developing Countries, Fiction, Foreign Countries, History, Humor, Poetry, Religion - Islamic, Religion - Protestant, Science Fiction, Fantasy
ISBN Prefix(es): 9966-9609; 9966-951
Number of titles published annually: 6 Print
Total Titles: 35 Print
Distributed by Peppercorn Books & Press (Canada & USA)
Distributor for Readit Books (Kenya, Uganda, USA & Canada)

*Orders to:* Peppercorn Books & Press, PO Box 693, Snow Camp, NC 27349, United States, Contact: Andrew Pates *E-mail:* post@peppercornbooks.com

**Shirikon Publishers+**
PO Box 46154, Nairobi
*Key Personnel*
Dir: Sylvester J Ouma
Subjects: Accounting, Anthropology, Biblical Studies, Business, Developing Countries, Economics, Education, History, Literature, Literary Criticism, Essays, Management, Philosophy, Religion - Catholic, Religion - Protestant, Social Sciences, Sociology, Theology, Women's Studies
ISBN Prefix(es): 9966-870; 9966-9842

**Space Sellers Ltd+**
PO Box 47186, Nairobi
*Tel:* (02) 555811; (02) 557517; (02) 557863 *Fax:* (02) 557815; (02) 558847
*E-mail:* sstms@africaonline.co.ke *Cable:* salespower
*Key Personnel*
Contact: Sylvia King *Tel:* (02) 530598
Founded: 1975
Membership(s): NPA.
Subjects: Automotive, Business, Career Development, Gardening, Plants, How-to, Self-Help, Travel
ISBN Prefix(es): 9968-68
Number of titles published annually: 6 Print
Total Titles: 23 Print
*Associate Companies:* Target Mail Services, PO Box 30759, Nairobi, Contact: Ann Thieth *Tel:* (02) 556916 *Fax:* (02) 558847 *E-mail:* sstms@africaonline.co.ke
Imprints: Horizon Books

**Spear Books, EAEP Kenya Writers Series**, *imprint of* Heinemann Kenya Ltd (EAEP)

**Spearhead**, *imprint of* Gaba Publications Amecea, Pastoral Institute

**Sudan Literature Centre**
Lenana Rd, PO Box 44838, Nairobi 00100 GPO
*Tel:* (020) 565641 *Fax:* (020) 564141
*E-mail:* across@across-sudan.com
*Web Site:* www.across-sudan.org
*Key Personnel*
Coordinator: Rev Anthony Poggo
Founded: 1988
Producer of church books for Sudan.
Subjects: Health, Nutrition, Religion - Protestant
ISBN Prefix(es): 9966-876; 9966-32
Number of titles published annually: 20 Print
Total Titles: 20,000 Print
*Parent Company:* Across

**Transafrica Press**
PO Box 48239, Nairobi
*Tel:* (020) 244724
*Key Personnel*
Man Dir: John Nottingham
Founded: 1976
Subjects: Biography, Education, Fiction, History, How-to, Nonfiction (General), Poetry, Regional Interests, Religion - Other, Social Sciences, Sociology
ISBN Prefix(es): 9966-940

**Tree Shade Technical Services**
PO Box 71222, Nairobi
*Tel:* (02) 225798; (02) 220712
*Key Personnel*
Dir: Timothy Gathirimu
Founded: 1992
Subjects: Environmental Studies
ISBN Prefix(es): 9966-892

Uzima, *imprint of* Uzima Press Ltd

**Uzima Press Ltd+**
PO Box 48127, Nairobi
*Tel:* (020) 21239
*E-mail:* uzima@wananchi.com
*Key Personnel*
General Manager: Kiraka James
Founded: 1974
Membership(s): Christian Booksellers Association
  (CBA); Kenya Publishers Association (KPA).
Subjects: Fiction, Nonfiction (General), Religion
  - Protestant, Religion - Other, Social Sciences,
  Sociology, Theology
ISBN Prefix(es): 9966-855
Imprints: Uzima

**Vipopremo Agencies**
PO Box 47717, Nairobi
*Tel:* (02) 227189; (02) 333882
Subjects: Education, How-to
ISBN Prefix(es): 9966-845

**Wandishi wa Kiafricka**, *imprint of* Heinemann
  Kenya Ltd (EAEP)

**Gideon S Were Press+**
PO Box 10622, Nairobi
*Tel:* (020) 331135
*E-mail:* gswere@nbnet.co.ke
Founded: 1983
Home science; Christian religious education.
Subjects: Anthropology, Government, Political
  Science, History, Social Sciences, Sociology,
  Women's Studies
ISBN Prefix(es): 9966-852
Total Titles: 68 Print
*Associate Companies:* Star Academy

# Democratic People's Republic of Korea

## General Information

*Capital:* Pyongyang
*Language:* Korean
*Religion:* Buddhism, Christian & Chundo Kyo
*Population:* 22.2 million
*Currency:* 100 chon = 1 won
*Export/Import Information:* No tariff informa-
  tion; all importation and exportation must go
  through Korea Publications Export & Import
  Corporation, Pyongyang.

**Academy of Sciences Publishing House**
Nammundung, Dir Choe Kwan Sik, Pyongyang
*Tel:* (02) 51956
Founded: 1953
Subjects: Biological Sciences, Chemistry, Chemi-
  cal Engineering, Economics, Education, Geog-
  raphy, Geology, History, Philosophy, Physics,
  Science (General)

**Educational Books Publishing House**
Pyongyang
Subjects: Education

**The Foreign Language Press Group**
Pyongyang Publishing Trade Association,
  Sochon-dong, Sosong District, Pyongyang

*Tel:* (02) 841342 *Fax:* (02) 812100
*Telex:* 37021 PP KP
*Key Personnel*
President: Sun Myong Hwang
Subjects: Archaeology, Art, Biography, Child
  Care & Development, Cookery, Education, His-
  tory, Philosophy

**Foreign Languages Publishing House**
Sosong District, Pyongyang
*Tel:* (02) 51-863
*Key Personnel*
Dir: Hwang Sun Myong
Subjects: Asian Studies

**Grand People's Study House**
PO Box 200, Pyongyang
*Tel:* (02) 34 40 66 *Fax:* (02) 381-4427; (02) 381-
  2100
Subjects: Alternative, Asian Studies, Biblical
  Studies, Biography, Child Care & Develop-
  ment, Communications, Education, Electronics,
  Electrical Engineering

**Guahak Baikkwa Sajon Chulpansa**, see Korea
  Science & Encyclopedia Publishing House

**Industrial Publishing House** (Gongpop
  Chulpansa)
Botonggang District, Pyongyang
Mailing Address: PO Box 73, Pyongyang
*Fax:* 3814410; 3814427
*Key Personnel*
Dir: Kim Tong Su
Subjects: Business
ISBN Prefix(es): 9946-25

**Korea Science & Encyclopedia Publishing
  House** (Guahak Baikkwa Sajon Chulpansa)+
Jangyongdong, Sosong District, Pyongyang
Mailing Address: PO Box 73, Pyongyang
*Tel:* (02) 381 8091 (Call between 18 & 21 hours
  Pyongyang local time, Mon, Wed & Fri only)
  *Fax:* (02) 381 4550 (24 hours); (02) 381 4410;
  (02) 381 4427
*Key Personnel*
President & Dir General: Kim Yong Il
Contact: Mr Jean Bahng
Founded: 1953
Editing & publishing dictionaries, encyclopedias,
  various books & periodicals (magazines).
Subjects: Agriculture, Animals, Pets, Architecture
  & Interior Design, Art, Biological Sciences,
  Chemistry, Chemical Engineering, Civil En-
  gineering, Communications, Economics, Ed-
  ucation, Electronics, Electrical Engineering,
  Engineering (General), Geography, Geology,
  Government, Political Science, History, Law,
  Literature, Literary Criticism, Essays, Math-
  ematics, Mechanical Engineering, Medicine,
  Nursing, Dentistry, Natural History, Philosophy,
  Physical Sciences, Physics, Science (General),
  Social Sciences, Sociology, Technology, Veteri-
  nary Science
ISBN Prefix(es): 9946-1

**Literature and Art Publishing House**
Pyongyang
*Key Personnel*
President: Jong So Chon
Subjects: Art, Fiction

**Transportation Publishing House**
Namgyo-dong, Hyongjaesan District, Pyongyang
*Key Personnel*
Editor: Paek Jong Han
Subjects: Travel

**Working People's Organization Publishing
  House**
Pyongyang
*Key Personnel*
Dir: Pak Se Hyok
Subjects: Fiction, Government, Political Science

# Republic of Korea

## General Information

*Capital:* Seoul
*Language:* Korean (English also spoken in busi-
  ness)
*Religion:* Predominantly Mahayana Buddhist and
  Christian
*Population:* 44.1 million
*Bank Hours:* 0930-1600 Monday-Friday; 0930-
  1300 Saturday
*Shop Hours:* 1000-1900 Monday-Saturday
*Currency:* 100 chun = 10 hwan = 1 won
*Export/Import Information:* No tariffs on books
  and advertising matter. Authorizations for im-
  port of books and publications are reviewed
  annually by the Korean government. Import li-
  censes are required. Exchange controls; prior
  deposits required at present.
*Copyright:* UCC (see Copyright Conventions, pg
  xi)

**Ahn Graphics+**
260-88 Songbuk 2-dong Seongbug, Songbuk-gu,
  Seoul 136-823
*Tel:* (02) 743 8065; (02) 743 8066; (02) 743
  4154; (02) 743 3353 *Fax:* (02) 743 3352
*E-mail:* ask@ag.co.kr
*Web Site:* www.ag.co.kr
*Key Personnel*
President: Ok-Chul Kim
Founded: 1985
Specialize in art books.
Membership(s): Korean Publishers Association.
Subjects: Art, Computer Science
ISBN Prefix(es): 89-7059

**Anam Publishing Co+**
386-125, Sindang2-dong, Jung-gu, Seoul 100-452
*Tel:* (02) 22380491 *Fax:* (02) 22524334
*Key Personnel*
President: Lee Chang-Sik
Founded: 1978
Subjects: Career Development
ISBN Prefix(es): 89-7235

**Ario Company Ltd+**
5-36 Hyochang-dong, Yongsan-gu, Seoul 140-120
*Tel:* (02) 7122001; (02) 7122003 *Fax:* (02)
  7023156
*Key Personnel*
Publisher: Yoong-Yeoup Lee
Founded: 1970
Subjects: Career Development
ISBN Prefix(es): 89-86063
*Associate Companies:* ARIO JSC Ltd, 5-36
  Hyoch'ang-dong, Yongsan-gu, Seoul 140-120

**B & B+**
4F Yureka Bldg, 15-12, Nonhyeon-dong,
  Gangnam-gu, Seoul 135-811
*Tel:* (02) 540-4425 *Fax:* (02) 517-8793
*E-mail:* bbpress-98@hanmail.net
*Key Personnel*
Planning Dir: Jae-Woo Lee
Founded: 1996
Subjects: Computer Science
ISBN Prefix(es): 89-86929

## Ba-reunsa Publishing Co
355-8, Misa-dong, Hanam-si Gyeonggi-do 465-140
*Tel:* (031) 792-0185
*Key Personnel*
International Rights: Joung-Ouk Park
Founded: 1987
Subjects: History, Poetry, Science (General)
ISBN Prefix(es): 89-7109

## Bakyoung Publishing Co
Jungam Bldg, 13-31 Pyeong-Dong, Jongroo-gu Seoul 110-102
*Tel:* (02) 7336771 *Fax:* (02) 7364818
*E-mail:* psy@pakyoungsa.co.kr
*Key Personnel*
President: Jong-man Ahn
Founded: 1952
Subjects: Language Arts, Linguistics, Literature, Literary Criticism, Essays, Philosophy, Science (General), Social Sciences, Sociology
ISBN Prefix(es): 89-10

## Bal-eon+
2F, 238-66 Yongdu-dong, Dongdaemun-gu, Seoul 130-070
*Tel:* (02) 293546; (02) 293547 *Fax:* (02) 293548
Subjects: Architecture & Interior Design, Art
ISBN Prefix(es): 89-7763

## BCM Media Inc+
10 F Dongil Bldg, 1305-7 Seocho-dong, Seocho-gu, Seoul 137-070
*Tel:* (02) 567-0644; (02) 533-0089 *Fax:* (02) 552-9169
*E-mail:* bcmpub@nuri.net
*Web Site:* www.bcm.co.kr
*Key Personnel*
Chairman: Dr Byoung-Chul Min
Also distributes language educational materials.
Subjects: Education, Language Arts, Linguistics, English, Japanese & Chinese educational publications
ISBN Prefix(es): 89-7512
Distributor for Child's Play; Houghton Mifflin; Steck-Vaughn
*Shipping Address:* 752-27 Yuksam-Dong, B1 Jeil Bldg, Gangnam-gu, Seoul 135-080
*Warehouse:* 752-27 Yuksam-Dong, B1 Jeil Bldg, Gangnam-gu, Seoul 135-080
*Returns:* 752-27 Yuksam-Dong, B1 Jeil Bldg, Gangnam-gu, Seoul 135-080

## Bi-bong Publishing Co
3F Milinae Bldg, 480-10, Seogyo-dong, Mapa-gu, Seoul 121-842
*Tel:* (02) 3142-6555 *Fax:* (02) 3142-6556
*E-mail:* beebook@hitel.net
*Key Personnel*
Publisher: Kie-Bong Park
Founded: 1980
Subjects: Business, Economics, Management
ISBN Prefix(es): 89-376

## Big Tree Publishing+
62209 Saengmyeong gonghaggwan Seong-gyungwan University, 300 Cheoncheon-dong, Janguan-gu, Suwon-si, Gyeonggi-do 440-746
*Tel:* (031) 290-7802 *Fax:* (031) 290-7891
*E-mail:* khkang@skku.ac.kr
*Key Personnel*
Contact: Ik-Su Han
Founded: 1993
Subjects: Fiction, Nonfiction (General), Romance
ISBN Prefix(es): 89-954729

## BIR Publishing Co, *imprint of* Min-eumsa Publishing Co Ltd

## BIR Publishing Co+
5F Gangnam Publishing Culture Center, 506 Sinsa-dong, Gangnam-Gu, Seoul 135-887
*Tel:* (02) 3443-4318; (02) 3443-4319 *Fax:* (02) 3442-4661
*Web Site:* www.bir.co.kr
*Key Personnel*
President: Park Sang Hee *Tel:* (02) 515 2003
Foreign Rights Manager: Ms Jungha Song *Fax:* (02) 3444-5185 *E-mail:* ha@minumsa.com
Founded: 1996
Picture & story books for young children.
ISBN Prefix(es): 89-491
Number of titles published annually: 130 Print
*Parent Company:* Minumsa Publishing Co Ltd

## Bo-jinjae Printing Co Ltd
8, Dangsandong 5-ga, Yeongdeungpo-gu, Seoul 150-045
*Tel:* (02) 6792351; (02) 6792355 *Fax:* (02) 6762821
*Key Personnel*
President: Dai-Hoon Lee
Founded: 1912
ISBN Prefix(es): 89-7197

## Bo Moon Dang+
448-6 Sinsoo-Dong, Mapo-Ku, Seoul 121-110
*Tel:* (02) 7047025 *Fax:* (02) 7042324
*Key Personnel*
President: Byung-Gye Kim
Subjects: Architecture & Interior Design, Chemistry, Chemical Engineering, Civil Engineering, Computer Science, Electronics, Electrical Engineering, Engineering (General), Mechanical Engineering, Science (General)

## Bo Ri Publishing Co Ltd+
480-26 Seogyo-dong, Mapo-gu Seoul 121-842
*Tel:* (02) 3233676 *Fax:* (02) 3240285
*Key Personnel*
Contact: Kwang-Ju Cha
International Rights: Ri Bo
Founded: 1991
Specialize in books for children.
Subjects: Child Care & Development, Education, Labor, Industrial Relations, Literature, Literary Criticism, Essays
ISBN Prefix(es): 89-85494; 89-8428
*Associate Companies:* Dotori Publishing Co; Jakenchak Publishing Co

## Borim Publishing Co+
Geumsan Bldg, 4th floor, 364-22 Seogyo-Dong, Mapo-gu, Seoul 121-210
*Tel:* (02) 3141-2222 *Fax:* (02) 3141-8474
*E-mail:* namu@borimplc.co.kr
*Web Site:* www.borimplc.co.kr
*Key Personnel*
President: Kwon Jong-Taek
Executive Dir: Park Sang-Yong
Founded: 1976
Subjects: Animals, Pets, Fiction, History, Nonfiction (General), Science (General), Picture Book
ISBN Prefix(es): 89-433
*Distribution Center:* Network International Inc, PO Box 1081, Northbrook, IL 60065-1081, United States (exclusive distribution for US & Canada)

## Bum-Woo Publishing Co
21-1 Gusu-dong, Mapo-gu, Seoul 121-130
*Tel:* (02) 7172121; (02) 7172122 *Fax:* (02) 7170429
*E-mail:* yhd@bumwoos.co.kr
*Key Personnel*
Chief Executive: Hyung-Doo Yoon
Founded: 1966
Subjects: Communications, Drama, Theater, Fiction, History, Literature, Literary Criticism, Essays, Philosophy, Publishing & Book Trade Reference, Social Sciences, Sociology
ISBN Prefix(es): 89-08
*Associate Companies:* Yoon Communications

## Cham Kae, *imprint of* O Neul Publishing Co

## Chang-josa Publishing Co
20-1, Shinmunro 2-ga, Jongro-gu, Seoul 110-062
*Tel:* (02) 7380393
*Key Personnel*
President: Duk-kyo Choi
Founded: 1963
Subjects: History, Language Arts, Linguistics, Literature, Literary Criticism, Essays
ISBN Prefix(es): 89-85139

## Cheong-mun-gag Publishing Co+
Cheongmun Bldg, 486-9 Gileum 3-Dong, Seongbug-gu, Seoul 136-113
*Tel:* (02) 9851451; (02) 9897423; (02) 9897421 *Fax:* (02) 9828679
*E-mail:* CMGbook@hitel.kol.co.kr
*Key Personnel*
Chief Executive: Hong-Seok Kim
International Rights: Han-Seung Kim
Founded: 1975
Subjects: Science (General), Technology
ISBN Prefix(es): 89-7088
Subsidiaries: Ham Seung Publishing Co
Divisions: Trade Books

## Cheong-rim Publishing Co Ltd
Yeong Bldg 63, Nonhyeon-dong, Gangnam-gu, Seoul 135-010
*Tel:* (02) 546-4341 *Fax:* (02) 546-8053
*Key Personnel*
Contact: Koh Young-Soo
Founded: 1971
Also acts as Director of Korea Publication Association.
Subjects: Accounting, Advertising, Art, Behavioral Sciences, Biography, Business, Career Development, Child Care & Development, Communications, Computer Science, Crafts, Games, Hobbies, Economics, Education, Electronics, Electrical Engineering, English as a Second Language, Fiction, Finance, History, How-to, Human Relations, Humor, Journalism, Labor, Industrial Relations, Law, Literature, Literary Criticism, Essays, Management, Marketing, Music, Dance, Nonfiction (General), Philosophy, Psychology, Psychiatry, Real Estate, Religion - Protestant, Romance, Science (General), Science Fiction, Fantasy, Social Sciences, Sociology, Technology, Travel, Women's Studies
ISBN Prefix(es): 89-352
Number of titles published annually: 80 Print; 3 CD-ROM; 6 Online; 6 E-Book
Total Titles: 1,300 Print; 3 CD-ROM; 6 Online; 6 E-Book
*Associate Companies:* Kolis Co Ltd; Pan Rae Wolbo SA; Woo Jin Publishing Co

## Chong No Books Publishing Co Ltd
45-1 Gwancheol-Dong, Jongro-gu, Seoul 110-111
*Tel:* (02) 7325381 *Fax:* (02) 7326202
*Key Personnel*
Chief Executive: Ha-Gu Chang
Founded: 1954
Subjects: History, Language Arts, Linguistics, Literature, Literary Criticism, Essays, Philosophy, Religion - Other
ISBN Prefix(es): 89-305

## The Chosun Ilbo Co, Ltd
61 Taepyongro 1-ga, Jung-gu, Seoul 100-756
*Tel:* (02) 724-5114 *Fax:* (02) 724-6199
*Key Personnel*
Contact: Sang-Hun Bang
ISBN Prefix(es): 89-7365

**The Christian Literature Society of Korea**
169-1 Samsung-Dong, Gangnam-gu, Seoul 135-090
*Tel:* (02) 553-0870 *Fax:* (02) 555-7721
*Key Personnel*
President: So Young Kim
Founded: 1890
ISBN Prefix(es): 89-511
*Bookshop(s):* CLS Bookstore, 136-46, Yonjidong, Chongro-ku, Seoul

**Dae Won Sa Co Ltd+**
358-17 Huam-Dong, Yongsan-gu, Seoul 140-190
*Tel:* (02) 7576717 *Fax:* (02) 7758043
*Key Personnel*
Vice President: S W Chang
Contact: Min-Do Cha
Founded: 1986
Subjects: Antiques, Architecture & Interior Design, Art, Crafts, Games, Hobbies, Environmental Studies, Philosophy, Science (General), Travel
ISBN Prefix(es): 89-369

**Daehan Printing & Publishing Co Ltd**
41-10, Jamwon-dong, Seacho-gu, Seoul
*Tel:* (031) 730-3850 *Fax:* (031) 735-8104
*E-mail:* mschung@daehane.com; james@daehane.com; sabrachili@daehane.com
*Web Site:* www.daehane.com
*Key Personnel*
President: Lee Hae-Dong
Subjects: Advertising, Agriculture, Antiques, Architecture & Interior Design, Art
ISBN Prefix(es): 89-378
*U.S. Office(s):* 3271 Sawtelle Blvd, No 104, Los Angeles, CA 90066, United States *Tel:* 310-737-0058 *Fax:* 310-737-9213

**Daeyoung Munhwasa+**
200 Jeil Bldg, 178-2 Cheongpa-Dong 1-Ga, Yongsan-Gu, Seoul 140-131
*Tel:* (02) 716-3883 *Fax:* (02) 703-3839
*E-mail:* spotto29@hotmail.com
*Key Personnel*
Contact: Choon-Hwan Rim
Subjects: Public Administration, Philosophy of Administration
ISBN Prefix(es): 89-7644
*Book Club(s):* Korean Publish Association

**Dai Hak Publishing Co**
420-5 Ahyon 1- Dong, Mapo-ku, Seoul 121-011
*Tel:* (02) 364-9788 *Fax:* (02) 393-9045
*Key Personnel*
President: Jin Young Yoon
Subjects: Technology

**DanKook University Press**
San 8 Hannam-dong, Yongsan-ku, Seoul 140-714
*Tel:* (02) 793-5034 *Fax:* (02) 709-5814
*E-mail:* omslit@dankook.ac.kr; pencil58@yahoo.com
*Web Site:* www.dankook.ac.kr
*Key Personnel*
President: Seung-Kook Kim
Subjects: History, Literature, Literary Criticism, Essays
ISBN Prefix(es): 89-7092

**Dong-A Publishing & Printing Co Ltd**
295-15 Toksan-Dong, Seoul 140-100
*Tel:* (02) 866-8800 *Fax:* (02) 862-0410
*Key Personnel*
Chief Executive: Hyun-Shik Kim
Founded: 1980
ISBN Prefix(es): 89-00

**Dong Hwa Publishing Co**
130-4 Weonhyoro 1-ga, Yongsan-gu, Seoul 140-111

*Tel:* (02) 7135411; (02) 7135415 *Fax:* (02) 7017041
*Key Personnel*
President: In-Kyu Lim
Editorial Dir: Kyoung-Sik Roh
Sales Dir: Byong-Don Ann
Production Dir: Chong-Choon Seo
Publicity Dir: Kun-Han Park
Founded: 1968
Subjects: Art, History, Literature, Literary Criticism, Essays, Philosophy
ISBN Prefix(es): 89-431

**Eulyu Publishing Co Ltd+**
46-1 Susong-Dong, Jongro-Ju, Seoul 110-603
*Tel:* (02) 7338151; (02) 7338152; (02) 7338153 *Fax:* (02) 7329154 *Cable:* EULYOO SEOUL
*Key Personnel*
President: Chin Sook Chung
Man Dir: Pil Young Choung
Editorial & Production: Ko Jung Gi
Sales: Sam Taek Huh
Founded: 1945
Subjects: History, Language Arts, Linguistics, Literature, Literary Criticism, Essays, Philosophy
ISBN Prefix(es): 89-324
Distributor for UN Publications

**Ewha Womans University Press**
11-1 Daehyun-Dong, Seodaemun-gu, Seoul 120-170
*Tel:* (02) 3277-2114 *Fax:* (02) 393-5903
*Web Site:* www.ewha.ac.kr/
*Key Personnel*
President: Li Sook Cheung
Dir: Young-Il Kim
Founded: 1949
Subjects: Art, Education, Human Relations, Language Arts, Linguistics, Music, Dance, Philosophy, Religion - Other, Science (General), Social Sciences, Sociology
ISBN Prefix(es): 89-7300

**Gim-Yeong Co+**
170-4 Gahoe-dong, Jongro-gu, Seoul 110260
*Tel:* (02) 7454823; (02) 7454825 *Fax:* (02) 7454826
*Key Personnel*
President: Jung Sup Gimm
International Rights Contact: Mee Sung Kim
Founded: 1976
Subjects: Business, Environmental Studies, Fiction, How-to, Management, Marketing, Mysteries, Philosophy, Religion - Other, Science (General), Self-Help
ISBN Prefix(es): 89-349

**Golden Bough Publishing Co**, *imprint of* Min-eumsa Publishing Co Ltd

**Gomdori**, *imprint of* Woongjin Media Corporation

**Gyeom-jisa**
375-13 Seokyo-Dong, Mapo-gu Seoul 121-210
*Tel:* (02) 3351985 *Fax:* (02) 3351986
*Key Personnel*
Publisher: Chung Hae-Sang
Founded: 1964
Subjects: Science (General)
ISBN Prefix(es): 89-7169
Distributed by Min Jung Book Distribution Co

**Haedong+**
15-4 Namyeong-dong, Yongsan-gu, Seoul 140-160
*Tel:* (02) 953707 *Fax:* (02) 953707
*Key Personnel*
President & Author: B Ryong Chung
Founded: 1993
Subjects: Poetry

ISBN Prefix(es): 89-86861
Distributed by Bomoon-Dang; Han-yang Distributor

**Hainaim Publishing Co Ltd**
5-6F Hainaim Bldg, 368-4 Seokyo-dong, Mapo-gu, Seoul 121-210
*Tel:* (02) 326-1600 *Fax:* (02) 326-1625
*Web Site:* www.hainaim.com
*Key Personnel*
President: Young-Seok Song
Rights Dir: Duran Kim *E-mail:* durankim@hainaim.com
Rights Manager: Karen Lee *E-mail:* karenlee@hainaim.com
Founded: 1982
Subjects: Education, Fiction, History, Nonfiction (General), Science (General), Comics
ISBN Prefix(es): 89-7337

**Hak Won Publishing Co**
25-36, Chungsin-Dong, Jongro-gu, Seoul 110-490
*Tel:* (02) 741-4621; (02) 741-4623 *Fax:* (02) 765-1877
*E-mail:* ccnstar@hanmail.net
*Key Personnel*
President: Young-Su Kim
Founded: 1945
Subjects: Art, Child Care & Development, Cookery, Literature, Literary Criticism, Essays, Social Sciences, Sociology
ISBN Prefix(es): 89-16

**Hakgojae Publishing Inc+**
77 Sogyeog-Dong, Jongro-gu, Seoul 110-200
*Tel:* (02) 7361713 *Fax:* (02) 7398592
*E-mail:* hkjass@hitel.kol.co.kr
*Key Personnel*
Contact: Chan-Kyu Woo
International Rights: Hyun-ki Park
Founded: 1991
Subjects: Archaeology, Architecture & Interior Design, Art, Asian Studies, Foreign Countries, History, Literature, Literary Criticism, Essays, Photography, Korean Studies
ISBN Prefix(es): 89-85846
*Book Club(s):* Kyobo Book Club

**Hakmunsa Publishing Co+**
6F Sahaghoegwan, 7-2, Sajik-dong, Jongro-gu Seoul 110-054
*Tel:* (02) 738-5118 *Fax:* (02) 733-8998
*E-mail:* hakmun@hakmun.co.kr
*Web Site:* www.hakmun.co.kr
*Key Personnel*
President: Young Chul Kim
Internal Dept: Ki-Hyoung Kim
Founded: 1963
Subjects: Business, Child Care & Development, Computer Science, Education, Engineering (General), English as a Second Language, Science (General), Social Sciences, Sociology
ISBN Prefix(es): 89-467; 89-87510
*Branch Office(s)*
Pusan *Tel:* (051) 502-8104
Taegu *Tel:* (053) 422-5000

**Hanjin Publishing Co**
4f, 40-21, Munbae-dong, Yongsan-gu, Seoul 140-100
*Tel:* (02) 7137453 *Fax:* (02) 7135510
*Key Personnel*
President: Gab Han Jin
Subjects: Art, Literature, Literary Criticism, Essays, Religion - Other
ISBN Prefix(es): 89-86412

**Hangil Art Vision**
402 Gangnamculpanmunhwa Center, 506, Sinsa-dong, Gangnam-gu, Seoul 135-120

*Tel:* (02) 5154811; (02) 5154813 *Fax:* (02)
5154816
*Key Personnel*
Chief Executive: Euon-Ho Kim
Founded: 1976
Subjects: History, Literature, Literary Criticism,
Essays, Philosophy, Social Sciences, Sociology
ISBN Prefix(es): 89-436

**Hanul Publishing Co+**
501 Hyuam Bldg, 503-24 Changcheon-dong,
Seodaemun-gu, Seoul 120-180
*Tel:* (02) 3260095; (02) 3366183 *Fax:* (02)
3337543
*E-mail:* newhanul@nuri.net
*Key Personnel*
Publisher: Kim Chong-Soo
Dir: Ms Lim Hee-Kun *Tel:* (02) 336-6183
Founded: 1980
Subjects: Asian Studies, Economics, Geography,
Geology, Health, Nutrition, History, Journal-
ism, Law, Literature, Literary Criticism, Es-
says, Medicine, Nursing, Dentistry, Philosophy,
Social Sciences, Sociology, Theology, Women's
Studies
ISBN Prefix(es): 89-460; 89-7058
Number of titles published annually: 150 Print
Total Titles: 1,200 Print
*Associate Companies:* Seoul Media Co; Siinsa
Publishing Co

**Haseo Publishing Co+**
370-27, Shindang-Dong, Jung-gu, Seoul 100-454
*Tel:* (02) 2378161; (02) 2378165 *Fax:* (02)
2376575
*E-mail:* haseo@haseo.co.kr
*Web Site:* www.haseo.co.kr
*Key Personnel*
Chief Executive: Sang-Wook Kim
Founded: 1964
Subjects: Art, Literature, Literary Criticism, Es-
says, Social Sciences, Sociology
ISBN Prefix(es): 89-7330
Subsidiaries: Jigyung Publishing Co

**Hollym Corporation**
13-13 Gwancheol-dong, Jongno-gu, Seoul 110-
111
*Tel:* (02) 735-7551 *Fax:* (02) 730-5149; (02) 730-
8192
*E-mail:* hollym@chollian.net; info@hollym.co.kr
*Web Site:* www.hollym.co.kr
*Key Personnel*
President: Kim-Man Ham
Sales Dir: Ki Lee
Founded: 1963
Subjects: Art, Cookery, Economics, Fiction, His-
tory, Poetry, Travel
ISBN Prefix(es): 0-930878; 1-56591; 89-7094
*U.S. Office(s):* Hollym International Corp, 18
Donald Pl, Elizabeth, NJ 07208, United States
*Tel:* 908-353-1655 *Fax:* 908-353-0255

**Hongik Media Plus Ltd**, see Hongikdong

**Hongikdong+**
Formerly Hongik Media Plus Ltd
4F Suseog Bldg, 4-13 Singongdeok-dong, Mapo-
gu, Seoul 121-711
*Tel:* (02) 704-7500 *Fax:* (02) 703-5695
*E-mail:* hongikcb@soback.kornet.nm.kr
Subjects: Biography, Career Development, Com-
puter Science, Education, English as a Second
Language
ISBN Prefix(es): 89-89815
Subsidiaries: Hongik Media CNC Ltd

**Hw Moon Publishing Co**
30 Kyunji-dong, Chongno-ku, Seoul 110
*Tel:* (02) 724897

*Key Personnel*
Man Dir: Myong Hui Yi
Founded: 1961
Subjects: Biography, Fiction, History, Philosophy,
Poetry, Religion - Other

**Hyangmunsa Publishing Co**
201 Jiseong Bldg, 645-20, Yeogsam-Dong,
Gangnam-gu, Seoul 135-080
*Tel:* (02) 5385671; (02) 5385672 *Fax:* (02)
5385673
*Key Personnel*
President: Joong Ryol Nah
Founded: 1957
Subjects: Agriculture, Economics, Engineering
(General), History, Science (General)
ISBN Prefix(es): 89-7187

**Hyein Publishing House**
Usin Bldg, Suite 202, 11-2 Gusan-Dong,
Eunpyeoung-Gu, Seoul 122-060
*Tel:* (02) 3836928 *Fax:* (02) 3836929
*E-mail:* vvh103@chollian
*Web Site:* www.hyeinbooks.co.kr
*Key Personnel*
Contact: Choon-Won Cho
Founded: 1993
Subjects: Education, Health, Nutrition, Science
(General), Travel
ISBN Prefix(es): 89-7853

**Hyun Am Publishing Co**
1660-15, 7-dong Bongceon, Gwanag, gu, Seoul
151-057
*Tel:* (02) 877-2565 *Fax:* (02) 877-2566
*Key Personnel*
Man Dir: Keun-Tae Cho
Publicity: Sang-Won Cho
Founded: 1951
Subjects: Literature, Literary Criticism, Essays,
Philosophy, Religion - Other
ISBN Prefix(es): 89-87969

**Iljisa Publishing House**
46-1 Junghag-Dong, Jongro-gu, Seoul 110-150
*Tel:* (02) 7329320 *Fax:* (02) 7222807
*Key Personnel*
Man Dir: Sung-Jae Kim
Publicity Dir: Byungki Yoo; Donhong Cho
Founded: 1956
Subjects: Archaeology, Fiction, History, Language
Arts, Linguistics, Philosophy, Poetry, Social
Sciences, Sociology
ISBN Prefix(es): 89-312

**Iljo-gag Publishers+**
9 Gongpyeuung-Dong, Jongro-gu, Seoul 110-160
Mailing Address: KPO Box 279, Seoul 110-160
*Tel:* (02) 7335430; (02) 7335431 *Fax:* (02)
7385857
*E-mail:* ilchokak@hitel.kol.co.kr; ilchokak@
chollian.dacom.co.kr *Cable:* ICHOPUBLICO
SEOUL
*Key Personnel*
President: Man-Nyun Han
Sales Dir: J Y Chot
Publicity Dir: J Y Choi
Founded: 1953
Subjects: Anthropology, Education, Engineer-
ing (General), History, Law, Medicine, Nurs-
ing, Dentistry, Psychology, Psychiatry, Science
(General), Social Sciences, Sociology
ISBN Prefix(es): 89-337

**Jeong-eum Munhwasa**
203, 182-22, Nonhyeon-dong, Gangnam-gu, Seoul
135-010
*Tel:* (02) 5680070 *Fax:* (02) 5650352 *Cable:*
Jeongeumsa
*Key Personnel*
President: Tong-Seek Chair

Sales Dir: Choong-tae Kim
Publicity & Advertising: Joo Park
Founded: 1928
Subjects: Fiction, Philosophy, Social Sciences,
Sociology
ISBN Prefix(es): 89-7158

**Jigyungsa Ltd+**
790-14, Yeoksam-Dong, Kangnam, Seoul 135-080
*Tel:* (02) 557-6351 *Fax:* (02) 557-6352
*E-mail:* jigyung@uriel.net
*Web Site:* www.jigyung.co.kr
*Key Personnel*
President: Byung-Joon Kim
Dir, International & Planning Dept: Hyosik Kim
Dir, Marketing: Seong-Ho Lee
Dir, Production: Byung-Sik Kim
Founded: 1978
Subjects: Fiction, Nonfiction (General)
Subsidiaries: Miraejungbosa
Divisions: Walt Disney Books & Magazines

**Jung-ang Media**, see Jung-ang Munhwa Sa

**Jung-ang Munhwa Sa**
172-11 Yeomri-dong, Mapo-gu, Seoul 121-090
*Tel:* (02) 717-2114 *Fax:* (02) 716-1369
*Key Personnel*
Chief Executive: Duck-Ke Kim
Founded: 1972
ISBN Prefix(es): 89-7511

**Ke Mong Sa Publishing Co Ltd+**
772 Yoksam-dong, Kangnam-gu, Seoul 135-080
*Tel:* (02) 531-5535 *Fax:* (02) 531-5550
*Key Personnel*
President: Choon-sik Kim
Man Dir: Jong-uk Lee
Assistant Manager, Foreign Rights: Park Yeon
Founded: 1947
Specialize in children's books.
Subjects: Biography, English as a Second Lan-
guage, Fiction, Geography, Geology, Nonfiction
(General), Science (General)
ISBN Prefix(es): 89-06
Subsidiaries: Young Printing Co, Ltd; Kemong
Enterprise Co Ltd; EMI - Kemongsa Co Ltd

**Ki Moon Dang**
286-20 Haengdang-dong, Sungdong-gu, Seoul
133-070
*Tel:* (02) 2295-6171 *Fax:* (02) 296-8188
*E-mail:* kimoon2@chollian.net
*Key Personnel*
Chief Executive: Hae-Jak Kang
Founded: 1976
Subjects: Art, Engineering (General)

**Korea Britannica Corp**
701 Jeilsangho B/D 7th Floor, 117 Jangchung-
dong 1-ga, Jung-gu Seoul 100-391
*Tel:* (02) 2272-9731; (02) 2264-0924 (sales)
*Fax:* (02) 2278-9983
*E-mail:* corporate@britannica.co.kr
*Web Site:* www.britannica.co.kr
*Key Personnel*
President: Hosang Jang
Founded: 1968
Subjects: Education
ISBN Prefix(es): 89-7544
*Parent Company:* Encyclopaedia Britannica Inc,
Britannica Centre, 310 South Michigan Ave,
Chicago, IL 60604, United States

**Korea Local Authorities Foundation for
International Relations**
Royal Bldg 720, 5 Dangju-dong, Jongro-gu,
Seoul 110-721
*Tel:* (02) 730 2711; (02) 2170-6098 *Fax:* (02) 737
8970; (02) 737-7903
*E-mail:* others@klafir.or.kr
*Web Site:* www.klafir.or.kr/

Subjects: Public Administration
ISBN Prefix(es): 89-86815

**Korea Psychological Testing Institute+**
501 Sambohojeong Bldg, 14-24, Yeoyidodong
    Yeongdeunpogu, Seoul 150-010
*Tel:* (02) 784-0990 *Fax:* (02) 784-0993
*E-mail:* KPIT@unitel.co.kr
*Web Site:* www.kpti.com
*Key Personnel*
Contact: Myung-Joon Kim
Founded: 1972
Subjects: Psychology, Psychiatry
*Associate Companies:* Consulting Psychologists
    Press

**Korea Textbook Co**, see Kwangmyong
    Publishing Co

**Korea Textbook Co Ltd**
3F, 299-2, Seongsu 2-ga 3-dong, Seongdong-gu,
    Seoul 133-833
*Tel:* (02) 465-1341 *Fax:* (02) 464-1318
*E-mail:* kpp0114@hanmail.net
*Key Personnel*
President: Keun-Woo Lee
Subjects: Art, Education, Government, Political
    Science
ISBN Prefix(es): 89-85182
*Parent Company:* Kwangmyong Printing & Pub-
    lishing Co Ltd

**Korea University Press**
1-2 Anam-dong 5-ga, Seongbug-gu, Seoul 136-
    701
*Tel:* (02) 3290 4231 *Fax:* (02) 923 6311
*Key Personnel*
President: Sung Gi Jon
Founded: 1956
Subjects: Agriculture, Earth Sciences, Education,
    Engineering (General), History, Language Arts,
    Linguistics, Literature, Literary Criticism, Es-
    says, Philosophy, Psychology, Psychiatry, So-
    cial Sciences, Sociology
ISBN Prefix(es): 89-7641

**Korean Publishers Association+**
105-2 Sagan-Dong, Chongno-Gu, Seoul 110-190
*Tel:* (02) 735-2701; (02) 735-2704 *Fax:* (02) 738-
    5414
*E-mail:* kpa@kpa21.or.kr
*Web Site:* www.kpa21.or.kr
*Key Personnel*
President: Jung Il Lee
Secretary General: Jong Jin Jung
Founded: 1947
Subjects: Publishing & Book Trade Reference
ISBN Prefix(es): 89-85231

**Koreaone Press Inc+**
9F Gyeongun Bldg, 70 Gyeongun-dong, Jongho-
    gu, Seoul 100-310
*Tel:* (02) 739-1156 *Fax:* (02) 734-3512
*Key Personnel*
Chief Executive: Nark-Cheon Kim
Man Dir: Cho Il-Kwan
Founded: 1978
Subjects: Biography, Business, Career Develop-
    ment, Economics, Education, English as a Sec-
    ond Language, Environmental Studies, Fiction,
    Language Arts, Linguistics, Literature, Liter-
    ary Criticism, Essays, Management, Mysteries,
    Nonfiction (General), Philosophy, Religion -
    Buddhist, Romance, Science (General), Science
    Fiction, Fantasy, Social Sciences, Sociology,
    Western Fiction
ISBN Prefix(es): 89-12
*Associate Companies:* Koreaone Media Inc; Kore-
    aone Chest Inc

Divisions: Foreign Rights Department
*U.S. Office(s):* Koreaone International, 520 W
    Eighth St, Los Angeles, CA 90005, United
    States

**Kukmin Doseo Publishing Co Ltd+**
822, Guro-dong, Guro-gu, Seoul 152-050
*Tel:* (02) 858-2461; (02) 858-2463 *Fax:* (02) 858-
    2464
*E-mail:* younhlee@chollian.net
*Key Personnel*
President: Young-Hoon Lee
Founded: 1978
Specializes in religious books.
Subjects: Religion - Protestant, Theology
ISBN Prefix(es): 89-401
*Associate Companies:* Kookmin Daily News Press
Subsidiaries: Yae-In Publishing Co
Distributor for Koonmin Daily News Press

**Kukminseokwan Publishing Co Ltd**
257-3 Gongdeog-dong Bldg, Mapo-gu, Seoul
    121-804
*Tel:* (02) 7107722; (02) 7107724 *Fax:* (02)
    7155771
*Key Personnel*
Chief Executive: Yoo-Kwang Lee
Founded: 1961
Subjects: Social Sciences, Sociology
ISBN Prefix(es): 89-11

**Kumsung Publishing Co Ltd+**
242-63 Gongdeok-Dong, Mapo-gu, Seoul 121-803
*Tel:* (02) 713-9651 *Fax:* (02) 704-1979; (02) 718-
    4362
*E-mail:* webmaster@kumsungpub.co.kr
*Web Site:* www.kumsungpub.com
*Key Personnel*
Chairman: Moo-Sang Kim
Editorial Dir: Sung-Chul Kang
Man Dir: Lee Jeong-Sam
Manager: Dae-Shik Kim
Assistant Manager: Chae-Hyung Lee; Gwang-So
    Lee
Founded: 1965
Subjects: Fiction, Nonfiction (General)
ISBN Prefix(es): 89-07
*Associate Companies:* Shin Won Editorial Center,
    250-4 Towha-dong, Mapo-ku, Seoul; Shinwon
    Agency Co, 372-6 Seogyo-dong, Mapo-gu,
    Seoul 121-022
Subsidiaries: Kumsung Textbook Co Ltd; Kum-
    sung Artcom
*Branch Office(s)*
Kaiserstr 42, 60329 Frankfurt am Main, Germany

**Kwangmyong Publishing Co**
5F Gyeongbok Bldg, 40, Euljiro 6-ga, Jung-gu,
    Seoul 100-196
*Tel:* (02) 2274-1552 *Fax:* (02) 2264-3309
*E-mail:* kwangmgl@hanmail.net
*Telex:* K27229 Kortuna *Cable:* Kwangmyong,
    Seoul
*Key Personnel*
President: Keun-Woo Lee
Dir: Yun Bai Yoon
Founded: 1951
Subjects: Art, Regional Interests
ISBN Prefix(es): 89-90022; 89-952319
Subsidiaries: Korea Textbook Co; Kwangmyong
    Toppan Moore Printing Co

**Kyobo Book Centre Co Ltd**
Gyobosaengmyeong Bldg, 1, Jongnol-ga, Jongro-
    gu, Seoul 110-714
Mailing Address: PO Box 1685, Kwangwhamun,
    Seoul 110-121
*Tel:* (02) 3973508; (02) 3973509 *Fax:* (02)
    7350030
*E-mail:* eslee@kyobobook.co.kr
*Web Site:* www.kyobobook.co.kr

Subjects: Government, Political Science, Law,
    Literature, Literary Criticism, Essays
ISBN Prefix(es): 89-7085

**Kyohaksa Publishing Co Ltd+**
150-67 Gongdeok-Dong, Mapo-Ku, Seoul 152-
    020
*Tel:* (02) 7174561; (02) 8592017 *Fax:* (02)
    7183976
*Key Personnel*
President: Cheol-Woo Yang
Subjects: Business, Nonfiction (General)

**Kyungnam University Press**
449 Wolyong-dong, Masan, Kyungnam 631-701
*Tel:* (055) 245-5000 *Fax:* (055) 246-6184
*Web Site:* www.kyungnam.ac.kr
*Key Personnel*
President: Dr Jae Kyu Park
Subjects: Philosophy, Social Sciences, Sociology
ISBN Prefix(es): 89-8421; 89-86696

**Literature Academy Publishing**
133 Iwha-Dong, Jongro-Gu, Seoul 110-500
*Tel:* (02) 7645057 *Fax:* (02) 7458516
*E-mail:* webmaster@munhakac.co.kr
*Web Site:* www.munhakac.co.kr
*Key Personnel*
Contact: Je-Chun Park
Founded: 1988
Subjects: Art, Language Arts, Linguistics, Litera-
    ture, Literary Criticism, Essays, Poetry
ISBN Prefix(es): 89-400
Total Titles: 280 Print

**Maeil Gyeongje**
51-9, Phil-Dong 1-ga, Jung-gu, Seoul 100-728
*Tel:* (02) 276-0210; (02) 2760211; (02) 2760212;
    (02) 2760213; (02) 2760214; (02) 2760215
    *Fax:* (02) 271-0463
*E-mail:* mpd@unitel.co.kv
*Key Personnel*
President & Publisher: Dae-Whan Chang, PhD
Subjects: Business, Economics

**Min-eumsa Publishing Co Ltd+**
5F Kangnam Publishing Culture Center, 506
    Sinsa-Dong, Gangnam-gu, Seoul 135-120
*Tel:* (02) 515-2000; (02) 515-2005; (02) 515-9108
    *Fax:* (02) 515-2007; (02) 3444-5185
*Web Site:* www.minumsa.com
*Key Personnel*
President: Park Maeng-ho
Vice President: Park Geun-sup
Editorial: Park Sang Soon
Sales: Jung Dae Yong
Foreign Rights Manager: Michelle Nam *Tel:* (02)
    515-2003, ext 206 *E-mail:* michellenam@
    minumsa.com
Founded: 1966
Publishes a literary magazine, *World Literature*.
Subjects: Fiction, History, Literature, Literary
    Criticism, Essays, Nonfiction (General), Phi-
    losophy, Science (General), Social Sciences,
    Sociology
ISBN Prefix(es): 89-374
Total Titles: 200 Print
Imprints: BIR Publishing Co; Golden Bough Pub-
    lishing Co; Science Books Ltd
Subsidiaries: BIR Publishing Co Ltd; Golden-
    Bough Publishing Co Ltd

**Min Jung Seo Rim Publishing Co**
161-7 Yeomni Dong, 4F Hancheong-Sireob Bldg,
    Mapo-gu, Seoul 121-090
*Tel:* (02) 7036541; (02) 7036547 *Fax:* (02)
    7036549
*E-mail:* editmin@minjungdic.co.kr
*Web Site:* www.minjungdic.co.kr
*Key Personnel*
President: Chul Hwan Kim

Editorial: Cha Hyun Yun
Founded: 1979
ISBN Prefix(es): 89-387
*Parent Company:* Beupmun Sa Publishing Co

**Minjisa Publishing Co+**
673-3 Mia-Dong, Gangbug-gu, Seoul 132-105
*Tel:* (02) 9806382 *Fax:* (02) 9861531
*E-mail:* minjisa@nownuri.net
*Web Site:* www.minjisa.co.kr
*Key Personnel*
President: Tai-Seung Ri *Tel:* (02) 9434385; (02)
   9858035 *E-mail:* tsri201@yahoo.co.kr
Founded: 1982
Subjects: Child Care & Development, Education,
   Health, Nutrition, History, Literature, Literary
   Criticism, Essays, Psychology, Psychiatry
ISBN Prefix(es): 89-7362
Number of titles published annually: 8 Print
Total Titles: 136 Print

**Mirinae+**
1011 Singeong Sangaa, 192-30, Inhyeondong 2
   ga, Junggu, Seol 100-282
*Tel:* (02) 2279-2669 *Fax:* (02) 2279-2665
*E-mail:* mrn@lycos.co.kr
*Key Personnel*
Publisher: Kim Jin-Shik
Subjects: Literature, Literary Criticism, Essays,
   Poetry
ISBN Prefix(es): 89-7082

**The Monthly Magazine for Ceramics Co, Ltd**
130-27, Nonhyeon-dong, Gangnam-gu, Seoul
   135-010
*Tel:* (02) 583-2747 *Fax:* (02) 597-8639
Founded: 1988
ISBN Prefix(es): 89-86742
*Parent Company:* Daeho Yoeop Co Ltd

**Moon Jin Media Co Ltd**
6F, Seojeong Bldg, 1308-14 Seocho-4dong,
   Seocho-ku, Seoul 137-074
*Tel:* (02) 3453-9800 *Fax:* (02) 3453-4001
*E-mail:* mjmedia@hitel.kol.co.kr
*Key Personnel*
President: Sang Chuu Lee
International Rights: Jong Yeon Park
Subjects: English as a Second Language
*Bookshop(s):* Kim & Johnson, 4F, Seojeong B1
   1308-14, Seocho-4-dong, Seocho-ku, Seoul
   137-074

**Mun Un Dang**
45-3 Myeongryundong 1-ga, Jongro-gu, Seoul
   110-521
*Tel:* (02) 7433504; (02) 7433505 *Fax:* (02)
   7450265
*Key Personnel*
President: Seoung-Beum Lee
Founded: 1962
Subjects: Engineering (General), Science (Gen-
   eral)
ISBN Prefix(es): 89-7393

**Munhag-gwan**
34-22, Sinsu-dong, Mapo-gu, Seoul 121-130
*Tel:* (02) 7186810 *Fax:* (02) 7062225
*Key Personnel*
Chief Executive: Byong-Ik Kim
Founded: 1975
Subjects: Art, History, Literature, Literary Criti-
   cism, Essays, Philosophy, Social Sciences, So-
   ciology
ISBN Prefix(es): 89-7077

**Munye Publishing Co+**
32-11 Chungjeongro 3-ga, Seodaemun-gu, Seoul
   120-013
*Tel:* (02) 3935681; (02) 3935684 *Fax:* (02)
   3935685

*Key Personnel*
Chief Executive: Byung-Suk Chun
Founded: 1966
Subjects: Art, Fiction, History, Literature, Literary
   Criticism, Essays, Nonfiction (General), Phi-
   losophy, Social Sciences, Sociology, Women's
   Studies
ISBN Prefix(es): 89-310

**Nanam Publications Co+**
501 Jihun Bldg, 1364-39 Seocho-dong, Seocho-
   gu, Seoul 137-070
*Tel:* (02) 552-8535; (02) 552-8537 *Fax:* (02) 552-
   0711
*E-mail:* nanamcom@soback.kornet21.net; edit@
   nanamcom.co.kr; post@nanamcom.co.kr
*Web Site:* www.nanamcom.co.kr
*Key Personnel*
Chief Executive: Sang-Ho Cho
Founded: 1979
Subjects: Advertising, Art, Communications, Jour-
   nalism, Literature, Literary Criticism, Essays,
   Poetry, Social Sciences, Sociology
ISBN Prefix(es): 89-300
*Parent Company:* Korea Society Review

**O Neul Publishing Co+**
458 Yonggang-dong, Mapo-gu, Seoul 121-070
*Tel:* (02) 716-2811 *Fax:* (02) 712-7392
*Key Personnel*
Editor: Yoon-Seon Park
Contact: Jong-Chun Lee
Founded: 1980
Subjects: Child Care & Development, Fiction,
   History, House & Home, Mysteries, Nonfiction
   (General), Poetry, Women's Studies
ISBN Prefix(es): 89-355
Imprints: Cham Kae

**Ohmsa+**
Sekee Bldg, 17 Kalweol-Dong, Yongsan-Ku,
   Seoul
*Tel:* (02) 776-4868-9 *Fax:* (02) 779-6757
*E-mail:* ohm@ohm.co.kr
*Web Site:* www.ohm.co.kr
*Key Personnel*
Contact: Jong-Hak Kwak
Founded: 1975
Subjects: Computer Science, Microcomputers,
   Telecommunication
Subsidiaries: Robot & Computer Company (R&C
   Sha)

**Omun Gak**
Madang Bldg, 3rd Floor, Yeoksam-Dong,
   Kangnam-Ku, Seoul 135-080
*Tel:* (02) 3453-8278 *Fax:* (02) 508-5210
*Key Personnel*
President: Sun-Ki Jeon
Editorial: Kyun Hee Kim
Publicity: Jai Yung You
Sales: Jai Yong Kim
Production: In Soo Kim
Rights & Permissions: Kae Choong Chang
Founded: 1959
Subjects: Literature, Literary Criticism, Essays,
   Social Sciences, Sociology
*Associate Companies:* Yueil Publishing and Mar-
   keting Cooperation, Room 509, Jungeun Bldg,
   22-5 Chungmu-ro Fifth Avenue, Chung-ku,
   Seoul 100

**The Organizing Committee of the 11th
   International Zeolite Conference**
Hwahaggonghaggwa KAIST, 373-1 Guseong-
   dong, Yuseong-gu, Daejeon 305-701
*Tel:* (042) 69-8161 *Fax:* (042) 69-8170
*E-mail:* skihm@sorak.kaist.ac.kr
*Key Personnel*
International Rights: Prof Son-Ki Ihm
ISBN Prefix(es): 89-950030

**Oriental Books**
375-5 Seogyo-Dong, Mapo-gu, Seoul 121-210
*Tel:* (02) 334-9404 *Fax:* (02) 334-6624
*Key Personnel*
Contact: Tae-Woong Kim
Founded: 1993
ISBN Prefix(es): 89-8300; 89-85705

**Oruem Publishing House+**
1420-6, 1-dong Seoco, Seoco-gu, Seoul 137-070
*Tel:* (02) 5859122; (02) 5859123 *Fax:* (02)
   5847952
*Key Personnel*
President: Seong-Ok Boo
Founded: 1993
Subjects: Asian Studies, Business, Communi-
   cations, Economics, Education, Government,
   Political Science, Public Administration, Social
   Sciences, Sociology
ISBN Prefix(es): 89-7778

**Pan Korea Book Corporation**
1-222, 2-Ga, Shinmun-Ro, Chongno-Ku, Seoul
   110-601
*Tel:* (02) 733-2011; (02) 733-2018 *Fax:* (02) 736-
   8696
*E-mail:* info@bumhanbook.co.kr
*Web Site:* www.bumhanbook.co.kr
*Telex:* Pkbook K24149 *Cable:* Pankorbooks Seoul
*Key Personnel*
President: Mr Yoon-Sun Kim
Founded: 1956
Also book importer & distributor.
Subjects: Language Arts, Linguistics, Literature,
   Literary Criticism, Essays, Technology
ISBN Prefix(es): 89-7129

**Panmun Book Co Ltd+**
No 41-34 Anam-Dong 4Ka, 136-074 Sungbuk-ku,
   Seoul
Mailing Address: CPO Box 1016, 136-074
   Sungbuk-ku, Seoul
*Tel:* (02) 953-2451 (ext 5) *Fax:* (02) 953-2456
   (ext 7)
*E-mail:* pmbtrd2@chollian.net; pmbimp@unitel.
   co.kr
*Telex:* K27546 Panmuse *Cable:* PANMUSE
   SEOUL
*Key Personnel*
Chairman & Chief Executive Officer: S K Liu
Man Dir: I H Liu
Sales Dir: S H Kim
Founded: 1955
Subjects: Medicine, Nursing, Dentistry, Science
   (General), Social Sciences, Sociology
*Associate Companies:* International Publications
   Service Inc
Subsidiaries: The STM Books & Journals Inc
*Branch Office(s)*
Kwangju
Pusan
Taegu
Taejon
*Bookshop(s):* 16 Kwangbok-dong 1-ka, Pusan; 40
   Chongno 1-ga, Chongno-gu, Seoul
*Warehouse:* 15-7 Anam-dong 4-Ka, Sungbuk-ku,
   Seoul

**Pearson Education Korea Ltd+**
No 402 Sin La 2 Bldg, 137-5 Yeonhee-Dong,
   Seodaemun-ku, Seoul 120-111
*Tel:* (02) 353 0422 *Fax:* (02) 335 0092
*E-mail:* elt@pearsoned.co.kr
*Key Personnel*
General Manager: Yong-Jin Oh *E-mail:* yongjin.
   oh@pearsoned.co.kr
Senior Sales Manager, HE: Pock-Man Hur
   *Tel:* (02) 335 7987 *Fax:* (02) 335 7988
   *E-mail:* pockman.hur@pearsoned.co.kr

Finance/Administration Manager: Eun-Ja Lee
*Tel:* (02) 335 0267 *Fax:* (02) 335 7988
*E-mail:* eunja.lee@pearsoned.co.kr
Sales Manager: Bong- Jo Choi *Tel:* (02) 335
7987 *Fax:* (02) 335 7988 *E-mail:* bongjo.
choi@pearsoned.co.kr; Chong-Dae Chung
*E-mail:* chongdae.chung@pearsoned.co.kr
Rights/Publishing Manager: Yeon-Jung Lee
*Tel:* (02) 3142 5776 *Fax:* (02) 335 7988
*E-mail:* yeonjung.lee@pearsoned.co.kr
Founded: 1997
Subjects: Computer Science, Engineering (General)
ISBN Prefix(es): 89-450
Number of titles published annually: 30 Print
Total Titles: 500 Print
*Parent Company:* Pearson Education, One Lake
Street, Upper Saddle River, NJ 01867, United
States
*Ultimate Parent Company:* Pearson Plc
*Holding Company:* Pearson Education Korea
*Branch Office(s)*
PEK Daegu Office, 1160-12 Jisan-Dong, Susung-
Ku, 3rd floor, Daegu 706-090

**PoChinChai Printing Co Ltd**
514-2, PajuBookCity, Munbal-ri, Gyoha-eub,
Paju-Si, Gyeonggi-do 413-832
*Tel:* (031) 955-1150; (031) 955-1151 *Fax:* (031)
943-3234
*Web Site:* www.pochinchai.com
*Telex:* Pochcha K33448
*Key Personnel*
Chairman: Kim Joon-Ki
President: Kim Jung-Sun
Chief Executive: Dal-Hoon Lee
Editorial: Kang Hurh
Founded: 1912
Subjects: Art, History, Social Sciences, Sociology,
Technology

**Prompter Publications+**
PO Box 167, Chongnyangni, Tongdaemoon-gu,
Seoul 130-650
SAN: 297-4584
*Tel:* (02) 82 2214 1794
*Key Personnel*
President & International Rights: Myungkark Park
Founded: 1989
US publisher.
Subjects: Chemistry, Chemical Engineering, Computer Science, Crafts, Games, Hobbies, Library
& Information Sciences, Mathematics, Philosophy, Physics, Science (General)
ISBN Prefix(es): 1-877974
Number of titles published annually: 5 Print
Total Titles: 35 Print

**Pyeong-hwa Chulpansa+**
150 Palpan-Dong, Jongro-gu, Seoul 110-220
Mailing Address: CPO Box 5066, Seoul 121-110
*Tel:* (02) 7343341; (02) 7343343 *Fax:* (02)
7392129
*Key Personnel*
Publisher: Chang-Sung Huh
Founded: 1963
Subjects: Crafts, Games, Hobbies, English as a
Second Language, Gardening, Plants, How-to,
Literature, Literary Criticism, Essays, Outdoor
Recreation, Sports, Athletics, Travel
ISBN Prefix(es): 89-367
Subsidiaries: Jinsun Publishers
Distributed by Seoul Publication Distribution Co
Ltd

**St Pauls+**
103-36 Mia 9-Dong, Kangbug-gu, Seoul 142-109
*Tel:* (02) 9861361; (02) 9861364 *Fax:* (02) 984-
4622
*E-mail:* miari@paolo.net; felix@paolo.net;
stpaul@paolo.net
*Web Site:* www.paolo.net

*Key Personnel*
General & Editiorial Dir: Chang-Ouk Lee
*Tel:* (02) 986-1361-4 *Fax:* (02) 986-1365
*E-mail:* felix@paolo.net
Founded: 1991
Publication of literary, children's books, theology
& philosophy books, religious books. Publishes
*My Friends,* monthly comic magazine.
Subjects: Biblical Studies, Fiction, Human Relations, Philosophy, Poetry, Religion - Catholic,
Theology
Total Titles: 150 Print; 30 Audio
*Book Club(s):* St Pauls Book Club *Tel:* (02) 986-
1361; (02) 986-1365 *E-mail:* bookclub@paolo.
net

**Samho Music Publishing Co Ltd**
718-8, Banpo 1-Dong, Seocho-gu, Seoul 137-041
*Tel:* (02) 512-3578 *Fax:* (02) 512-3594
*E-mail:* webmaster@samhomusic.com
*Web Site:* www.samhomusic.com
*Key Personnel*
President: Jung-Tae Kim
International Rights: Sang-min Lee
Founded: 1977
Subjects: Art, Crafts, Games, Hobbies, Music,
Dance, Outdoor Recreation, Publishing & Book
Trade Reference, Sports, Athletics
ISBN Prefix(es): 89-326
Subsidiaries: Samho Media Co

**Samhwa Publishing Co Ltd**
15, 2-ga Eulijiro, Jung-gu, Seoul 110-192
*Tel:* (02) 7766687 *Fax:* (02) 7732993
*Key Personnel*
President: Kon Su Yu
Founded: 1962
Subjects: Art, Language Arts, Linguistics, Social
Sciences, Sociology
ISBN Prefix(es): 89-87846

**Samkwang Publishing Co**
499-39 Seokyo-Dong, Mapo-Ku, Seoul
*Tel:* (02) 3237275 *Fax:* (02) 3251153
*Key Personnel*
Contact: Myung-Woo Lee
Founded: 1978
Subjects: Social Sciences, Sociology

**Samseong Publishing Co Ltd+**
1516-2, Seocodong, Seoco-gu, Seoul 137-070
*Tel:* (02) 3470-6852 *Fax:* (02) 3452-2907
*Key Personnel*
President: Bong-Kyu Kim
Planning & Coordination Dir: Seok Hyun Cho
Founded: 1952
Subjects: Art, Business, History, Literature, Literary Criticism, Essays, Women's Studies
ISBN Prefix(es): 89-15
*Orders to:* 60-32 Garibong-dong, Guro-gu, Seoul

**Science Books Ltd,** *imprint of* Min-eumsa
Publishing Co Ltd

**Se-Kwang Music Publishing Co+**
232-32 Seogye-Dong, Yongsan-gu, Seoul 140-140
*Tel:* (02) 714-0046 *Fax:* (02) 719-2191
*Key Personnel*
President & Chairman: Shin-Joon Park
Sales Dir: Moon-Suk Kang
Publicity & Publication Manager: Nam-Jae Kang
Copyright Manager: Kichul Han
Founded: 1953
Subjects: Music, Dance
ISBN Prefix(es): 89-03
*U.S. Office(s):* Park Soon Tai, 3170 W Olympic
Blvd, No E, Los Angeles, CA 90006, United
States

**Sejong Daewang Kinyom Saophoe**
1-57 Chongryangli-dong, San, Iongno-ku, Seoul

*Key Personnel*
President: Gwan Ku Yi
Subjects: History, Religion - Other

**Seogwangsa+**
119-46 Yongdu 2-Dong, Dongdaemun-gu, Seoul
130-072
*Tel:* (02) 9246161; (02) 9246165 *Fax:* (02)
9224993
*Key Personnel*
President: Shin-Hyeok Kim
Editor: Min-Sook Bae
Founded: 1974
Subjects: Anthropology, Asian Studies, Education, Philosophy, Religion - Buddhist, Religion
- Catholic, Religion - Hindu, Religion - Other
ISBN Prefix(es): 89-306

**Seoul International Publishing House**
94-60 Hwayang-dong, Seongdong-gu, Seoul 133-
130
*Tel:* (02) 4698326; (02) 4698327
*Key Personnel*
President: Chung-Gil Shim
Founded: 1977
Subjects: Art, Cookery, History, Language Arts,
Linguistics, Photography, Regional Interests,
Travel
ISBN Prefix(es): 89-85113
*Orders to:* European Book Service, Flevolaan 36-
38, Postbus 124, 1380 AC Weesp, Netherlands
Charles E Tuttle Co Inc, PO Box 410, Rutland,
VT 05701, United States

**Seoul National University Press**
San 56-1, Sinrim-dong, Kwanak-gu, Seoul 151-
742
*Tel:* (02) 880-5114 *Fax:* (02) 885-5272
*Web Site:* www.snu.ac.kr
*Key Personnel*
President: Un-Chan Chung
Dir: Prof Soon Jong Lee *Tel:* (02) 880-5217
*Fax:* (02) 881-4148
Founded: 1961
Subjects: Art, Earth Sciences, History, Language
Arts, Linguistics, Literature, Literary Criticism,
Essays, Medicine, Nursing, Dentistry, Philosophy, Science (General), Social Sciences, Sociology
ISBN Prefix(es): 89-7096; 89-521

**Shinkwang Publishing Co**
278-1 Bomun-Dong 6-ka, Sungbuk-ku, Seoul
136-086
*Tel:* (02) 9255051; (02) 9255053 *Fax:* (02)
9255054
*Key Personnel*
Chief Executive: Yong-Ha Lee
Founded: 1972
Subjects: Cookery, Medicine, Nursing, Dentistry,
Science (General)

**Sogang University Press**
CPO Box 1142, Seoul 100-611
*Tel:* (02) 705-8213 *Fax:* (02) 705-0797
*E-mail:* chisook@ccs.sogang.ac.kr
*Web Site:* www.sogang.ac.kr
*Key Personnel*
Contact: Ku Jae Sung
Founded: 1978
Subjects: History, Language Arts, Linguistics,
Literature, Literary Criticism, Essays, Science
(General), Social Sciences, Sociology
ISBN Prefix(es): 89-7273

**Sohaksa+**
10-1 Namyeong-dong, Yongsan-gu, Seoul 140-
160
*Tel:* (02) 7967600 *Fax:* (02) 7968700
*Key Personnel*
Contact: Young-Whan Suhl

Founded: 1988
Subjects: Anthropology, Archaeology, English
as a Second Language, History, Management,
Philosophy, Psychology, Psychiatry, Social Sciences, Sociology

**Suhagsa**
1586-4 Seocho 3-Dong, Seocho-Ku, Seoul 137-
073
*Tel:* (02) 584-4642 *Fax:* (02) 521 1458
*Key Personnel*
President: Young-Ho Lee *Tel:* (02) 584-4642
Founded: 1953
Subjects: Fashion, Health, Nutrition, House &
Home
ISBN Prefix(es): 89-7140
Total Titles: 143 Print
*Book Club(s):* KPA

**Twenty-First Century Publishers, Inc+**
5 FIil Bldg, 315-3, 1 dong, Ganseog, Namdong-
gu, Inceon 405-231
*Tel:* (032) 429-9411 *Fax:* (032) 429-9418
*Key Personnel*
President: Mr Y D Ahn
Editor: Ms Youngmi Kwon
Founded: 1988
Subjects: Business, Economics, Management
ISBN Prefix(es): 89-87457

**Universal Publications Agency Press**
54, Gyeonji-dong, Jongro-gu, Seoul 110-170
*Tel:* (02) 32-8175 *Fax:* (02) 32-8176
*E-mail:* upa@upa.co.kr
*Web Site:* www.upa.co.kr
*Telex:* K28504 Unipub *Cable:* CHANGHOSHIN
SEOUL
*Key Personnel*
Manager: Il Chung Ha
ISBN Prefix(es): 89-7613

**Woongjin Media Corporation+**
Ungjinmedia Bldg, 343-7, Gasandong, Geum-
ceongu, Seoul 153-023
*Tel:* 3281-6471 *Fax:* 3281-6473
*E-mail:* wjmhky@woongjin.co.kr
*Web Site:* www.woongjin.com
*Key Personnel*
Chairman: Suck-keum Yoon
President: Hwan-kee Ryu
Man Dir: Heungsung Lee
Founded: 1987
Specialize in multi-media packages, educational
& home videos, CAI-software, compact discs.
Subjects: Business, Fiction, History, Nonfiction
(General), Science (General)
ISBN Prefix(es): 89-02
*Parent Company:* Woongjin Publishing Co Ltd
Imprints: Gomdori
Subsidiaries: Woongjin (USA) Inc

**Woongjin.com Co Ltd+**
112-2 Inyi-dong, Jongno-gu, Seoul 110-717
*Tel:* (02) 3670-1064 *Fax:* (02) 3670-1474
*E-mail:* wjmap@chollian.dacom.co.kr
*Key Personnel*
Foreign Rights Manager: Seang-Ju Hong
Founded: 1980
Subjects: Business, Education, English as a Sec-
ond Language, How-to, Literature, Literary
Criticism, Essays, Mysteries, Nonfiction (Gen-
eral), Romance, Travel
ISBN Prefix(es): 89-01; 89-345
Subsidiaries: Woong Nin Media Co Ltd

**Word of Life Press+**
Division of TEAM Mission Korea
32-43 Songwol Dong, Jongro-ku, Seoul 110-101
Mailing Address: PO Box 680, Kwanghwamoon,
Seoul 110-062
*Tel:* (02) 738 6555 *Fax:* (02) 739 3824

*Key Personnel*
President & International Rights: Jay-Kwon Kim
*E-mail:* jaykkim@chollian.net
Founded: 1953
Specialize in Christian book publishing.
Subjects: Religion - Protestant, Missionary Work
ISBN Prefix(es): 89-04
Number of titles published annually: 510 Print
Total Titles: 2,000 Print
Divisions: World of Life Books in USA
*U.S. Office(s):* Los Angeles, CA, United States
Washington, DC, United States
Chicago, IL, United States

**YBM/Si-sa+**
YBM Bldg, Editorial Dept, 10th floor, 55-1
Chongno 2-ga, Chongno-gu, Seoul 110-122
*Tel:* (02) 2000-0501; (02) 2000-0330 (orders)
*Fax:* (02) 2265-7573
*E-mail:* suite@ybmsisa.co.kr
*Web Site:* www.ybm.co.kr; www.ybmsisa.co.kr
*Key Personnel*
Chairman: Young-Bin Min
President: Sun-Shik Min
Editorial Dir: Hye-Ryoung Kim *E-mail:* hrkim@
ybmsisa.com
Sales Dir: Jong-Chul Kim
Founded: 1961
Book & Magazine Publishing, Language Schools,
Testing Activities, Music Company, IT Busi-
ness, ELT Materials, Multi-media Publications,
On-line Publishing, English Language Study
Materials, TOETL & TOEIC Prep Books.
Membership(s): IPA; FIPP; ABC.
Subjects: Economics, English as a Second Lan-
guage, Literature, Literary Criticism, Essays,
Photography, Travel
ISBN Prefix(es): 89-17
Number of titles published annually: 1,000 Print;
24 CD-ROM; 48 Online; 100 E-Book; 600 Au-
dio
Total Titles: 13,000 Print; 50 CD-ROM; 89 On-
line; 199 E-Book; 6,500 Audio
*Branch Office(s)*
Beijing City Chaoyang District Waisi Language
Training Center, America School of English,
China Merchants Onward Center, 4th floor, No
118, Chaoyang District Jianguo Rd, Beijing
100022, China *Tel:* (010) 6566 0786
YBM/ELS Language Centers, 549 Howe St, 6th
floor, Vancouver, BC V6C 2C2, Canada, Dir:
Mike Walkey *Tel:* 604-684-9577 *Fax:* 604-
684-9588 *E-mail:* info@elscanada.com *Web
Site:* www.elscanada.com
YBM/ELS Language Centers, 36 Victoria St,
Toronto, ON M5C 1H3, Canada, Dir: Zbig-
niew Andrzejcuk *Tel:* 416-203-6466 *Fax:* 416-
203-6766 *E-mail:* info@elscanada.com *Web
Site:* www.elscanada.com
*U.S. Office(s):* Young & Son Global, 3250
Wilshire Blvd, Suite 2007, Los Angeles,
CA 90010, United States *E-mail:* hylee58@
ybmsisa.com
Distributor for Barron's; ETS/Chauncey; McGraw
Hill; McMillan; National Geographic Society;
Newsweek International; Pearson; Peterson's;
Reader's Digest; Simon & Schuster

**Yearimdang Publishing Co**
Yearim Bldg, 153-3, Samseong-dong, Gangnam-
gu, Seoul 135-878
*Tel:* (02) 5661004 *Fax:* (02) 5679660
*E-mail:* webmaster@yearim.co.kr
*Web Site:* www.yearim.co.kr
*Key Personnel*
Chief Executive: Choon Na
Founded: 1973
Subjects: Cookery, Education, Fiction, Nonfiction
(General)
ISBN Prefix(es): 89-507; 89-302; 89-87941

**Yeha Publishing Co+**
736-37, Yeogsam-dong, Gangnam-gu, Seoul 135-
080
*Tel:* (02) 5535933; (02) 5535936 *Fax:* (02)
5525149
*Key Personnel*
Contact: Khil-Boo Park
Founded: 1987
Membership(s): Korean Publishers Association.
Subjects: Business, Literature, Literary Criticism,
Essays, Music, Dance
ISBN Prefix(es): 89-7359

**Yonsei University Press**
134 Sinchon-dong, Seodaemun-gu, Seoul 120-749
*Tel:* (02) 3926201 *Fax:* (02) 3931421
*E-mail:* ysup@bubble.yonsei.ac.kr
*Web Site:* www.yonsei.ac.kr
*Key Personnel*
President: Byung-Soo Kim
Dir: Suk-Hyun Kim
Business Manager: Ho-Sun Choi
Founded: 1955
Subjects: Art, History, Medicine, Nursing, Den-
tistry, Philosophy, Religion - Other, Science
(General), Social Sciences, Sociology, Technol-
ogy
ISBN Prefix(es): 89-7141

**Youlhwadang Publisher+**
520-10, Paju Book City, Munbal-Ri, Gyoha-Eup,
Paju-Si, Gyeonggi-Do
*Tel:* (031) 955-7000-5; (02) 5153143; (02)
5153142 *Fax:* (031) 955-7010
*E-mail:* yhdp@hitel.net; horang2@unitel.co.kr;
webmaster@youlhwadang.co.kr
*Web Site:* www.youlhwadang.co.kr
*Key Personnel*
President: Ki-Ung Yi
Editor & Foreign Rights: Ji-Hong Park
Founded: 1971
Specialize in Korean traditional art.
Subjects: Antiques, Architecture & Interior De-
sign, Art, Crafts, Games, Hobbies, Film, Video,
Music, Dance, Photography, Korean Art
ISBN Prefix(es): 89-301
Number of titles published annually: 20 Print
Total Titles: 500 Print

# Kuwait

## General Information

*Capital:* Kuwait
*Language:* Arabic. English also used commercially
*Religion:* Muslim
*Population:* 1.58 million
*Bank Hours:* 0800-1200 (0830-1230 during Ramadan) Saturday-Thursday
*Shop Hours:* 0800-1200 or 1230, 1530 or 16-
2030 Saturday-Thursday; 0800-1200 Friday
(markets and shopping centers also open 1530-
2030); during Ramadan: 0830 or 0900-1230,
1930-1030 or 0200 Saturday-Thursday. Some
shopping centers open 1600-2100 Friday
*Currency:* 1000 fils = approximately 3 US dollars
*Export/Import Information:* No tariffs on books or
advertising in reasonable quantity; all immoral
and seditious publications prohibited. Import
license required. No exchange permit required.
*Copyright:* No copyright conventions signed

**Kuwait Publishing House**
PO Box 5209, 13053 Safat, Kuwait City
*Tel:* 2414697
*Key Personnel*
Dir: Amin Hamadeh

**Ministry of Information**
Ministry of Communication, Bldg 2, Shuwaikh,
13008 Safat, Kuwait City
Mailing Address: PO Box 748, 13008 Safat,
Kuwait City
*Tel:* 245-1566 *Fax:* 245-9530
*E-mail:* admin@media.gov.kw
*Web Site:* www.moinfo.gov.kw
*Telex:* Mi 22030 Kt, Mi 46151 Kt *Cable:*
ALIRSHAD
Subjects: Art, Education, Geography, Geology,
History, Language Arts, Linguistics, Litera-
ture, Literary Criticism, Essays, Mathematics,
Physics, Social Sciences, Sociology

**Press Agency+**
PO Box 1019, 13011 Safat
*Tel:* 432269; 417732 *Fax:* 411495
*Telex:* Matboat 46046 Kt; Matboat 46246 Kt
*Cable:* MATBOAT
*Key Personnel*
Man Dir: Abdullah M N Harami
Editorial: K A Harami; Ibrahim M Hadi
Founded: 1954
*Bookshop(s):* in Kuwait & Salmaiy

# Laos People's Democratic Republic

## General Information

*Capital:* Vientiane
*Language:* Lao (official), French, English and
Tribal dialects
*Religion:* Theravada Buddhist
*Population:* 4.47 million
*Bank Hours:* 0800-1700 Monday-Friday
*Shop Hours:* 0800-2200 Monday-Friday, seven
days a week for Vietnamese Morning Market
*Export/Import Information:* Import license re-
quired. Exchange controls.
*Copyright:* UCC (see Copyright Conventions, pg
xi)

**Lao-phanit**
Vientiane Ministere de l'Education nationale, Bu-
reau des manuels, scolaires, Vientiane
Subjects: Art, Cookery, Economics, Education,
Fiction, Geography, Geology, History, Music,
Dance, Physics, Social Sciences, Sociology

**Pakpassak Kanphin**
9-11 quai Fa-Hguun, Vientiane

# Latvia

## General Information

*Capital:* Riga
*Language:* Latvian (Lettish)
*Religion:* Predominantly Christian (mostly
Lutheran)
*Population:* 2.7 million
*Bank Hours:* Generally open for short hours be-
tween 0930-1230 Monday-Friday
*Shop Hours:* Generally 0900-1800 Monday-
Friday; often open weekends
*Currency:* 100 kopeks = 1 rubl
*Copyright:* Berne (see Copyright Conventions, pg
xi)

**Alberts XII+**
Katolu 22, Riga 1003
*Tel:* (02) 7205286 *Fax:* (02) 7205284
*E-mail:* alberts@internet.lv
*Key Personnel*
Man Dir: Karlis Skruzis
Membership(s): Latvian Publishers' Association
(LPA).
Subjects: Astrology, Occult, Cookery, Crafts,
Games, Hobbies, Health, Nutrition, Nonfiction
(General), Romance, Science Fiction, Fantasy
ISBN Prefix(es): 9984-557; 9984-645

**Artava Ltd+**
Bezdeligu 12, 1007 Riga
*Tel:* (02) 7222472 *Fax:* (02) 7830254
*E-mail:* arta@com.latnet.lv
*Key Personnel*
Dir: Vladis Spare
Foreign Rights: Elfrida Melbarzde
Founded: 1991
Membership(s): Latvian Publishers' Association
(LPA).
Subjects: Biography, Fiction, How-to, Poetry, Ro-
mance, Science Fiction, Fantasy, Self-Help
ISBN Prefix(es): 9984-12; 9984-529

**Avots+**
Puskina 1a, Riga LV-1050
*Tel:* (02) 7211394 *Fax:* (02) 7225824
*E-mail:* avots@apollo.lv
*Web Site:* www.vardnicas.lv
*Key Personnel*
Man Dir: Janis Leja
Contact: Dzintra Kalnina
Founded: 1980
Membership(s): Latvian Publishers' Association
(LPA).
Subjects: English as a Second Language, Garden-
ing, Plants, House & Home, How-to, Language
Arts, Linguistics, Nonfiction (General)
ISBN Prefix(es): 9984-757

**Bibliography Institute of the National Library
of Latvia**
K Barona 14, Riga LV-1423
*Tel:* (02) 7289874 *Fax:* (02) 7280851
*E-mail:* lnb@com.latnet.lv; lnb@lbi.lnb.lv
*Web Site:* www.lnb.lv
*Key Personnel*
Deputy Dir, NLL: Anita Goldberga
*E-mail:* anitag@lnb.lv
Founded: 1940
Statistical information & analysis of publishing
activities & national bibliography.
Membership(s): Latvian Publishers' Association
(LPA).
Subjects: Publishing & Book Trade Reference,
Publishing/reference library & information sci-
ences
ISBN Prefix(es): 9984-607; 9984-9006; 9984-
9007
Total Titles: 3 Print; 2 Online
*Parent Company:* The National Library of Latvia

**Egmont Latvia SIA+**
Balasta dambis 3, LV-1081 Riga
Mailing Address: PO Box 30, LV-1081 Riga
*Tel:* (07) 244066; (07) 467931; (07) 468671
*Fax:* (07) 860049
*E-mail:* egmont@egmont.lv
*Web Site:* www.egmont.lv
*Key Personnel*
Man Dir: Roman Filippov
General Manager: Janis Blums *E-mail:* janis@
egmont.lv
Editor-in-Chief: Antra Chigure
Founded: 1991

Subjects: Advertising, Fiction, Film, Video, Non-
fiction (General), Sports, Athletics, Western
Fiction, Comics, Cartoons
*Parent Company:* International Egmont Holding
A/S

**Finland-Lestvian**, *imprint of* S/A Tiesiskas
informacijas cerfus

**Hermess Ltd+**
Maskavas iela 150, Riga 1058
*Tel:* (02) 7112743 *Fax:* (02) 7313130
*E-mail:* hermess@binet.lv
*Key Personnel*
Executive Dir: Juris Zablovskis
Dir: Natalija Sazenova
Founded: 1993
Subjects: Science Fiction, Fantasy
ISBN Prefix(es): 9984-580; 9984-9036

**Lielvards Ltd+**
Skolas Iela 5, 5070 Lielvarde Ogresraj
*Tel:* (050) 71860 *Fax:* (050) 71861
*E-mail:* lielvards@lielvards.lv
*Web Site:* www.lielvards.lv *Cable:* 030
Founded: 1992
Membership(s): Latvian Publishers' Association
(LPA).
Subjects: Biological Sciences, Chemistry, Chemi-
cal Engineering, Computer Science, Geography,
Geology, Health, Nutrition, History, Physics,
Social Sciences, Sociology
ISBN Prefix(es): 9984-11; 9984-513
*Showroom(s):* Araisu iela 37, Riga LV-1039, Riga

**Madonas Poligrafistr Ltd**, *imprint of* S/A
Tiesiskas informacijas cerfus

**Madris+**
Tallinas iela 36a, Riga LV-1001
*Tel:* 7374000; 7374700 *Fax:* 7374000
*E-mail:* madris@latnet.lv
*Key Personnel*
General Manager: Skaidrite Naumova
Founded: 1996
Subjects: Fiction, Poetry, Science (General),
Travel
Number of titles published annually: 20 Print

**Nordik/Tapals Publishers Ltd+**
Daugavgrivas 36-9, Riga LV-1007
*Tel:* (02) 7602672; (02) 7602816 *Fax:* (02)
7602818
*E-mail:* nordik@nordik.lv
*Web Site:* www.nordik.lv
*Key Personnel*
Dir: Janis Juska *E-mail:* janis@tapals.lv
Editor-in-Chief: Ieva Janaite
Founded: 1991
Membership(s): Latvian Publishers Association.
Subjects: Animals, Pets, Astrology, Occult, Biog-
raphy, Communications, Crafts, Games, Hob-
bies, Criminology, Earth Sciences, Environmen-
tal Studies, Fiction, History, Human Relations,
Law, Nonfiction (General), Poetry
ISBN Prefix(es): 9984-510
Number of titles published annually: 85 Print
*Warehouse:* Elijas 17, 1st floor, Riga LV-1007
*Tel:* (02) 7225667

**Patmos, izdevnieciba**
Baznicas iela 12a, Riga 1050
*Tel:* (02) 7289674 *Fax:* (02) 7820437
*E-mail:* bauc@mail.bkc.lv
*Key Personnel*
Publishing Dir: Zigurds Laudurgs
Editor: Dace Morica
Subjects: Biblical Studies, Health, Nutrition, Reli-
gion - Protestant, Theology

## Preses Nams+

Division of Preses Nams Corp
3, Balasta Dambis, Riga LV-1081
*Tel:* (02) 7062270 *Fax:* (02) 7062344
*E-mail:* presesnams@presesnams.lv
*Web Site:* www.presesnams.lv
*Key Personnel*
Dir, Publishing House: Mara Caune
Founded: 1990
Publisher of books, calendars, etc.
Membership(s): Latvian Publishers' Association (LPA).
Subjects: Agriculture, Animals, Pets, Art, Astrology, Occult, Behavioral Sciences, Biography, Biological Sciences, Business, Child Care & Development, Civil Engineering, Crafts, Games, Hobbies, Disability, Special Needs, Drama, Theater, Education, Environmental Studies, Fiction, Film, Video, Gardening, Plants, Health, Nutrition, History, House & Home, Human Relations, Humor, Literature, Literary Criticism, Essays, Music, Dance, Philosophy, Photography, Poetry, Psychology, Psychiatry, Sports, Athletics, Travel, Women's Studies
ISBN Prefix(es): 9980-0
Total Titles: 600 Print
*Ultimate Parent Company:* AS Ventspils Nafta

## S/A Tiesiskas informacijas cerfus

Baznicas icla 27/29, Riga 1010
*Tel:* (02) 7220422 *Fax:* (02) 7213854
*E-mail:* mariss@date.lv
*Key Personnel*
Dir: Signe Terihova
Founded: 1991
Subjects: Law
*Parent Company:* a/s SWHIS Kemerccentas
Imprints: Madonas Poligrafistr Ltd; Finland-Lestvian
Subsidiaries: LR Tieslictuministrijas A/S Dati
*Book Club(s):* Association of Latvian Book's publishers

## Spriditis Publishers+

Kaleju iela 51, Riga 1050
*Tel:* (02) 7286516 *Fax:* (02) 7286818
Founded: 1990
Subjects: Biblical Studies, Fiction, History, Religion - Catholic, Religion - Protestant, Travel
ISBN Prefix(es): 5-7960; 9984-699
*Bookshop(s):* Kaleju St 51, Riga LV-1050

## Vaidelote, SIA+

Gaismas iela, Kekava 17-19, Kekavas Pag, 2123 Rigas Rajons
*Tel:* 7937943; 9561812 *Fax:* 7542649
Founded: 1993
Subjects: Animals, Pets, Fiction
ISBN Prefix(es): 9984-507

## Vieda, SIA+

Lubanas 6-4, Riga 1019
*Tel:* 7140680 *Fax:* 7140680
*Key Personnel*
Dir General: Aivars Garda
Founded: 1989
Subjects: Astrology, Occult, History, Parapsychology, Philosophy
ISBN Prefix(es): 5-85745; 9984-701

## Zvaigzne ABC Publishers Ltd+

K Valdemara 6, Riga 1010
*Tel:* (0371) 7508799 *Fax:* (0371) 7508798
*E-mail:* foreign.rights@zvaigzne.lv
*Web Site:* www.zvaigzne.lv
*Key Personnel*
President: Vija Kilbloka
Editorial Dir: Ilze Brige *Tel:* (02) 7372112
Foreign Rights & Sales Manager: Ruta Keisa *Tel:* (02) 7372358

Foreign Rights & Sales Executive: Vija Birnbauma *Tel:* (02) 7372358
Founded: 1965
Specialize in educational literature for the needs of Latvia.
Subjects: Animals, Pets, Astrology, Occult, Child Care & Development, Education, English as a Second Language, Fiction, Literature, Literary Criticism, Essays, Nonfiction (General), Psychology, Psychiatry, Romance, Science Fiction, Fantasy, Travel, Adventure, Classics, Estoerics/New Age, Fairy Tales
ISBN Prefix(es): 5-405; 9984-04; 9984-17; 9984-560
Total Titles: 1,700 Print
Foreign Rights: Zvaigzne ABC Publishers

# Lebanon

## General Information

*Capital:* Beirut
*Language:* Arabic (French widely used)
*Religion:* 43% Christian (mostly Roman Catholic, predominantly Maronite), 57% Muslim (mostly Sunni & Shiite)
*Population:* 3.4 million
*Bank Hours:* 0830-1230 Monday-Friday; 0830-1200 Saturday
*Shop Hours:* Vary. Generally 0900-1900 in winter, 0800-1500 in summer
*Currency:* 100 piastres = 1 Lebanese pound
*Copyright:* UCC, Berne (see Copyright Conventions, pg xi)

## Arab Scientific Publishers BP+

Ayn Al-Tenah Reem Bldg, POB 13 5574, Beirut
*Tel:* (01) 785107; (01) 785108; (01) 786607 *Fax:* (01) 786230; (01) 860138
*E-mail:* asp@asp.com.lb
*Web Site:* www.asp.com.lb
*Key Personnel*
President: Bassam Chebaro *E-mail:* bchebaro@asp.com.lb
Founded: 1986
Subjects: Automotive, Biological Sciences, Computer Science, Cookery, Travel
ISBN Prefix(es): 2-84409; 9953-29
Number of titles published annually: 300 Print; 10 CD-ROM; 15 E-Book
*Associate Companies:* Abjad Graphics; Mediterranean Press, Arabization & Software Center
*Bookshop(s):* Book Maze, Marriott Square

**Editions Arabes**, *imprint of* Naufal Group Sarl

## Dar Al-Kitab Al-Loubnani

BP13-5352, Beirut
Mailing Address: PO Box 11, 8330 Beirut
*Tel:* 861563; (01) 735732 *Fax:* (01) 351433
*E-mail:* info@daralkitab-online.com
*Telex:* 22865 Ktl *Cable:* DAKALBAN-BEIRUT-LEBANON
*Key Personnel*
Man Dir: Dr Hasan El-Zein
Founded: 1929
Specialize in educational publications & textbooks for many countries worldwide.
*Associate Companies:* Dar Al-Kitab Al-Masri, 33 Kasr El Nile St, PO Box 156, Cairo 11511, Egypt (Arab Republic of Egypt) *Tel:* (02) 3922168; (02) 3924614 *Fax:* (02) 3924657
*Branch Office(s)*
Paris, France
Casablanca, Morocco
Madrid, Spain
Geneva, Switzerland

## Dar Al-Maaref-Liban Sarl

BP 11-232, Beirut
*Tel:* (01) 931243 *Cable:* Damaref Beirut
*Key Personnel*
Man Dir: Dr Fouad Ibrahim
General Manager: Joseph Nachou
Sales: Joseph Ibrahim
Founded: 1959
*Parent Company:* Dar Al-Maaref, Egypt (Arab Republic of Egypt)

## Dar Al-raed Al-Loubani

Kamel Al Assad Bldgs, Hazmieh St, Beirut
Mailing Address: BP 93, Beirut
*Tel:* (01) 450757; (01) 451581
*Telex:* 43499 leraed *Cable:* Kassammoury
*Key Personnel*
Chief Executive: Raed Sammouri
Editorial: Fadia Khoury
Sales: Ola Ramadan
Production: George Jabro
Publicity: Rima Khoury
Rights & Permissions: Hussein Ibrahim
Founded: 1971
*Branch Office(s)*
Dar Al Raed Al Rabi, Rawchi Blvd, Al Istiklal

## Dar An-Nahar Sal

36, rue Andraos Achrafieh, Beirut
Mailing Address: PO Box 11-226, Beirut
*Tel:* (01) 561 687 *Fax:* (01) 561 693
*Key Personnel*
President: Mohamed Ali Hamade
Founded: 1967
ISBN Prefix(es): 2-84289; 9953-10

## Dar El Ilm Lilmalayin

Center Metco, 2nd Floor, Mar Elias St, Beirut 2045-8402
Mailing Address: PO Box 1085, 1085 Beirut
*Tel:* (09611) 306666 *Fax:* (09611) 701657
*E-mail:* info@malayin.com
*Web Site:* www.malayin.com
Subjects: Business, Cookery, Education, Literature, Literary Criticism, Essays, Science (General)

**EDIFRAMO**, see Edition Francaise pour le Monde Arabe (EDIFRAMO)

**Editions de la Revue d'Etudes Palestiniennes**, see Institute for Palestine Studies

## Dar-El-Machreq Sarl+

Rue de l'Universite Saint-Joseph, Beirut 1100 2150
Mailing Address: BP 166778, Achrafie, Beirut 1100 2150
*Tel:* (01) 202423; (01) 202424 *Fax:* (01) 329348
*E-mail:* machreq@cyberia.net.lb
*Web Site:* www.darelmachreq.com
*Key Personnel*
Man Dir, Rights & Permissions: Camille Hechaime
Founded: 1853
Subjects: Biblical Studies, History, Language Arts, Linguistics, Literature, Literary Criticism, Essays, Philosophy, Religion - Catholic, Religion - Islamic, Theology
ISBN Prefix(es): 2-7214
Number of titles published annually: 25 Print
Total Titles: 600 Print
*Orders to:* Librairie Orientale, PO Box 1986, Beirut, Contact: M Maroun Nehme *Tel:* (01) 485793; (01) 492112 *Fax:* (01) 485793; (01) 485794; (01) 485795 *E-mail:* libor@cyberia.net.lb

## Edition Francaise pour le Monde Arabe (EDIFRAMO)

Immeuble Elissar, Rue Bliss, Beirut
Mailing Address: BP 113, 6140 Beirut

*Tel:* (01) 862437; (01) 341650; (01) 341614
*Telex:* 42530 LE
*Key Personnel*
Manager: Tahseen S Khayat
*Branch Office(s)*
Julie Hse, 3 Themistocles Dervis St, PO Box
   1612, Nicosia, Cyprus
22 blvd Poissonnieer, 75009 Paris, France

### GEOprojects Sarl
Al-Wahad Bldg, Rue Jeane D'Arc, Beirut
Mailing Address: PO Box 8375, Beirut
*Tel:* (01) 350721 *Fax:* (01) 353000
*Telex:* 22661 Eltoup le
*Key Personnel*
Man Dir: Tahseen Khayat
Founded: 1978
Subjects: Regional Interests, Travel
*Branch Office(s)*
GEOprojects Ltd, Newtown Rd, Henley-on-
   Thomas, Oxon R69 1HG, United Kingdom
*Tel:* (049) 122175

### Institute for Palestine Studies
Anis Nsouli St Verdun, 1107 2230 Beirut
Mailing Address: PO Box 11-7164, 1107 2230
   Beirut
*Tel:* (01) 868387; (01) 814175; (01) 804959
   *Fax:* (01) 814193; (01) 868387
*E-mail:* ipsbrt@palestine-studies.org
*Web Site:* www.palestine-studies.org
*Key Personnel*
Dir: Mr Mahmoud Soueid
Chairperson: Dr Hisham Nashabe
Executive Secretary: Prof Walid Khalidi
Founded: 1963
Independent nonprofit research & publication cen-
   ter, not affiliated with any political organization
   or government.
Subjects: Government, Political Science, Social
   Sciences, Sociology
ISBN Prefix(es): 2-905448
*Branch Office(s)*
c/o Les Editions de Minuit, 7 Rue Bernard -
   Palissy, 75006 Paris, France, Dir: Elias San-
   bar *Tel:* (01) 44393920 *Fax:* (01) 45448236
   *E-mail:* ipsfr@palestine-studies.org
Institute of Jerusalem Studies, Tarifi Boldg,
   nr Jordanian Trade Center, 4th floor, No
   6, Yafa St, Ramallah, Israel, Dir: Dr Salim
   Tamari *Tel:* (02) 581 9777 *Fax:* (02) 582 8543
   *E-mail:* ipsquds@palestine-studies.org
*U.S. Office(s):* 3501 "M" St NW, Washington,
   DC 20007, United States, Dir: Linda But-
   ler *Tel:* 202-342-3990 *Fax:* 202-342-3927
   *E-mail:* ipsdc@palestine-studies.org
*Orders to:* IPS Marketing Dept, 3501 "M" St
   NW, Washington, DC 20007, United States
   *Tel:* 202-342-3990

### The International Documentary Centre of Arab Manuscripts
Immeuble Hanna, Beirut
Mailing Address: PO Box 2668
*Key Personnel*
Proprietor: Zouhair Baalbaki
Founded: 1965

### Khayat Book and Publishing Co Sarl
90-94 rue Bliss, Beirut
*Key Personnel*
Man Dir: Paul Khayat
Subjects: Art, Crafts, Games, Hobbies, Education,
   Fiction, History, Medicine, Nursing, Dentistry,
   Religion - Other, Social Sciences, Sociology,
   Sports, Athletics

### Librairie du Liban Publishers (Sal)+
Sayegh Bldg, Zouk Mosbeh, Kesrouwan
Mailing Address: PO Box 11-9232, Beirut

*Tel:* (09) 217 944; (09) 217945; (09) 217 946;
   (09) 217 735 *Fax:* (09) 217734; (09) 217 434
*E-mail:* info@ldlp.com
*Web Site:* www.ldlp.com
*Telex:* 21037-45297 libsayle *Cable:* LIBRARIE
   DU LIBAN, BEIRUT
*Key Personnel*
Man Dir, Rights & Permissions: Khalil Sayegh
Man Dir, Publicity: George S Trad
Editorial: Ahmad Khatib; George Abdel Massih
Sales: Suheil Berjawi
Production: Wafic Mizhir
Founded: 1944
Subjects: Animals, Pets, Astronomy, Child Care
   & Development, Computer Science, Cookery,
   Education, Fiction, Health, Nutrition, Language
   Arts, Linguistics, Literature, Literary Criticism,
   Essays, Mysteries, Physics, Science (General),
   Science Fiction, Fantasy, Technology, Travel,
   Adventure, Nature, Thriller
*Showroom(s):* Longman Arab World Centres, PO
   Box 11-945, Beirut; Amir Mohamed St, Al
   Houjairi Bldg, PO Box 6587, Amman *Tel:* (06)
   637871; (06) 624216; 15 St, Central Khartoum,
   PO Box 1391, Sudan *Tel:* 80344
*Bookshop(s):* Lebanon Bookshop; Sayegh Book-
   shop, Diab Bldg, Al Salhieh, in Front of the
   Parliament, PO Box 784, Damascus, Syrian
   Arab Republic *Tel:* (011) 218456
*Distribution Center:* Sayegh Bldg, Zokak el Blat,
   PO Box 11-945, Beirut *Tel:* (01) 376 821;
   (01) 376 822; (01) 376 823 *Fax:* (01) 376 818
   *E-mail:* sberjaoui@ldlp.com

### Librairie Orientale sal+
Sin el-Fil, Jisr el-Wati, Immeuble Librairie, Ori-
   entale, Beirut
Mailing Address: PO Box 55-206, Orientale,
   Beirut
*Tel:* (01) 485793; (01) 485794; (01) 485795
   *Fax:* (01) 485796; (01) 216021
*E-mail:* libor@cyberia.net.lb
*Key Personnel*
Chief Executive Officer: M Maroun Nehme
Founded: 1948
Specialize in dictionaries, research, philosophy,
   literature, children books & text books in Ara-
   bic, French & English.
Subjects: Accounting, Animals, Pets, Archae-
   ology, Child Care & Development, Cookery,
   Education, English as a Second Language, His-
   tory, How-to, Language Arts, Linguistics, Lit-
   erature, Literary Criticism, Essays, Nonfiction
   (General), Philosophy, Regional Interests, Reli-
   gion - Catholic, Theology
Number of titles published annually: 200 Print
Total Titles: 1,000 Print
*Branch Office(s)*
Ashrafieh-Park Bldg, Beirut, Contact: Mrs Achou
   *Tel:* (01) 200875; (01) 216364 *Fax:* (01)
   216021
Distributor for Dar el-Majani; Dar el-Mashreq
Foreign Rep(s): Aladdin Books UK (Middle
   East, North Africa); DTV Germany (Middle
   East, North Africa); Edicart-Italy (Middle East,
   North Africa)

**Macdonald**, *imprint of* Naufal Group Sarl

**Naufal**, *imprint of* Naufal Group Sarl

### Naufal Group Sarl+
99, Sourati St, Beirut
Mailing Address: BP 11-2161, Beirut
*Tel:* 354394 *Fax:* 354898
*Key Personnel*
Man Dir, Editorial & Rights & Permissions: Tony
   P Naufal
Editorial: Kamal Khauli
Sales, Production: Khaled Shamaa
General Manager (Paris): Sami Naufal
Founded: 1970

Subjects: Fiction, History, Law, Literature, Liter-
   ary Criticism, Essays
ISBN Prefix(es): 2-906958
Imprints: Editions Arabes; Macdonald; Naufal
Subsidiaries: Les Editions Arabes SA; Macdonald
   Middle East Sarl
*Bookshop(s):* Librairies Antoine, Hamra, PO Box
   656, Beirut (five shops)

### Publitec Publications+
BP 166142, Jisr Bacha, Beirut
*Tel:* (01) 495401; (01) 495403 *Fax:* (01) 493330
*Telex:* 44828
*Key Personnel*
President: Charles Gedeon
Manager: B Calfa
Assistant Manager: Ms M Sarkissian
Founded: 1953
ISBN Prefix(es): 2-903188
Subsidiaries: Publitec Publications
Distributed by Gale Research Inc (USA)

### The Rihani House Estate
Formerly Rihani Printing & Publishing House
Abdallah Mashnouk St, Beirut
Mailing Address: PO Box 13-5378, Beirut
*Tel:* (01) 868384 *Fax:* (01) 868384
*Key Personnel*
Proprietor: Albert Rihani
Manager: Daoud Stephan
Founded: 1963
ISBN Prefix(es): 9953-433

**Rihani Printing & Publishing House**, see The
   Rihani House Estate

### World Book Publishing+
Sanayeh, 282 Emile Edee St, Beirut
Mailing Address: PO Box 11-3176, Beirut
*Tel:* (01) 349370; (01) 743357; (01) 743358
   *Fax:* (01) 351226
*E-mail:* info@wbpbooks.com
*Web Site:* www.arabook.com *Cable:* KITALIBAN
*Key Personnel*
Dir-General: El Zein Said-Mohamed
   *E-mail:* editor@wbpbooks.com
Vice President: Toufic El Zein *E-mail:* toufic@
   wbpbooks.com
Vice President & Man Dir: Rafic El Zein
   *E-mail:* rafic@wbpbooks.com
Founded: 1929
Subjects: Education, Literature, Literary Criti-
   cism, Essays, Philosophy, Poetry, Religion -
   Islamic
ISBN Prefix(es): 1-55206
Total Titles: 3,000 Print; 1,000 Online
*Associate Companies:* Editions Africaines/Dar Al
   Kitab Al-Alami
Subsidiaries: Librairie De L'ecole
Divisions: Livre Scolaire
*Showroom(s):* Hawd Al-Wilaga, Basta, Beirut
*Bookshop(s):* Librairie de l'Ecole, Rue Emile
   Edde, Beirut

# Lesotho

## General Information

*Capital:* Maseru
*Language:* English, Sesotho (a Bantu language)
*Religion:* Roman Catholic, Lesotho, Evangelical
   and Anglican
*Population:* 1.8 million
*Bank Hours:* 0830-1300 Monday-Friday; 0830-
   1100 Saturday
*Shop Hours:* Winter: 0830-1630 Monday-Friday;
   0830-1300 Saturday; Summer: 0800-1630
   Monday-Friday; 0800-1300 Saturday. Usually
   closed weekdays 1300-1400

*Currency:* 100 lisente = 1 loti South African currency is also legal tender
*Export/Import Information:* No tariffs on books or advertising matter. No import license required; no obscene literature permitted. Exchange controls being relaxed.
*Copyright:* Berne (see Copyright Conventions, pg xi)

**Government Printer**
PO Box 527, Maseru 100
*Tel:* 313023
ISBN Prefix(es): 99911-10

**Mazenod Book Centre**
PO Box 39, Mazenod 160
*Tel:* 35 0224 *Fax:* 35 0010
*Telex:* 427KO
*Key Personnel*
Manager: Fr B Mohlalisi
Founded: 1933
Subjects: History, Literature, Literary Criticism, Essays, Regional Interests, Religion - Other
ISBN Prefix(es): 99911-24

**Saint Michael's Mission Social Centre**
PO Box 25, Roma
*Key Personnel*
Man Dir: Rev Fr M Ferrange
Production: Peter Ntsaoana
Founded: 1968
Subjects: Anthropology, Biography, History, Regional Interests, Religion - Other, Social Sciences, Sociology

# Libyan Arab Jamahiriya

## General Information

*Capital:* Tripoli
*Language:* Arabic (official), also English and Italian
*Religion:* Muslim
*Population:* 4.5 million
*Bank Hours:* Generally Winter: 0830-1230; Summer: 0800-1200 Saturday-Thursday
*Shop Hours:* Vary greatly. Friday is weekly holiday but some Christian shops closed Sunday. Many are open 0830-1230, 1500-1730 Saturday-Thursday (slightly earlier hours in summer months)
*Currency:* 1,000 dirhams = 1 Libyan dinar
*Export/Import Information:* No tariff on books; advertising dutied. Charity Tax and Municipal Tax levied on dutiable goods. Open General License for books. Exchange permit, liberally granted, is required. Import and export of books is handled by the General Company for Publishing, Advertising and Distribution, Tripoli.
*Copyright:* Berne (see Copyright Conventions, pg xi)

**Al-Fateh University**
PO Box 13040, Tripoli
*Tel:* (02133) 621988
*Telex:* 20629 TP Univ Ly
Founded: 1955
ISBN Prefix(es): 9959-816
*Bookshop(s):* University Bookshop, PO Box 13113, Tripoli

# Liechtenstein

## General Information

*Capital:* Vaduz
*Language:* German
*Religion:* Predominantly Roman Catholic
*Population:* 28,642
*Bank Hours:* 0800-1200, 1330-1630 Monday-Friday
*Shop Hours:* 0800-1200, 1330-1830 Monday-Friday; 0800-1600 Saturday
*Currency:* 100 rapen = 1 francen (swiss franc)
*Export/Import Information:* 2% VAT on books. Most books exempt from Turnover Tax. Advertising matter usually dutiable, some exempt from Turnover Tax. No import licenses required. No exchange controls. Swiss regulations to a Customs Treaty.
*Copyright:* UCC, Berne, Florence (see Copyright Conventions, pg xi)

**Bonafides Verlags-Anstalt**
Austr 50, 9490 Vaduz
*Tel:* (075) 82510
Founded: 1991
Subjects: Accounting, Finance, Government, Political Science, Nonfiction (General)
ISBN Prefix(es): 3-905193

**Botanisch-Zoologische Gesellschaft**
Liechtenstein-Sargans-Werdenberg, Heiligkreuz 52, 9490 Vaduz
*Tel:* (00423) 2324819 *Fax:* (00423) 2332819
*E-mail:* renat@pingnet.li
*Key Personnel*
Contact: Georg Willi
Founded: 1970
Subjects: Animals, Pets, Earth Sciences, Gardening, Plants, Physical Sciences
ISBN Prefix(es): 3-905195

**Buchervertriebsanstalt**
Postfach 461, 9490 Vaduz
ISBN Prefix(es): 3-905238

**A R Gantner Verlag KG**
Industriestr 105A, 9491 Ruggell
Mailing Address: Postfach 131, 9491 Ruggell
*Tel:* 377 1808 *Fax:* 377 1802
*E-mail:* bgc@adon.li
*Web Site:* www.gantner-verlag.com *Cable:* GANTR FL
*Key Personnel*
Manager: Mrs Bruni Gantner-Caplan
ISBN Prefix(es): 3-7182
*Associate Companies:* Litag Anstalt

**Verlag HP Gassner AG**
Austr 7, 9494 Vaduz
*Tel:* (075) 2327253 *Fax:* (075) 2323720
*Key Personnel*
Publisher: Hans Peter Gassner; Traugott Schneidtinger
Founded: 1979
Subjects: Art, History, Literature, Literary Criticism, Essays
ISBN Prefix(es): 3-906250

**Historischer Verein fur das Furstentum Liechtenstein** (Historical Society for the Principality of Liechtenstein)
Messinastr 5, 9495 Triesen
Mailing Address: Postfach 626, 9495 Triesen
*Tel:* 392 17 47 *Fax:* 392 17 05
*E-mail:* info@hvfl.li
*Web Site:* www.hvfl.li
*Key Personnel*
Man Dir: Klaus Biedermann *E-mail:* kgb@adon.li
Founded: 1901

Historical research.
Subjects: Archaeology, History
ISBN Prefix(es): 3-906393
Number of titles published annually: 1 Print

**Kliemand Verlag**
Sonnblickstr 6, 9490 Vaduz
*Tel:* 2321048
*Key Personnel*
Contact: Mrs Evi Klicmand
Subjects: Art, Poetry
ISBN Prefix(es): 3-906603

**Kunstmuseum Liechtenstein Vaduz**
Staedtle 32, 9490 Vaduz
Mailing Address: Postfach 370, 9490 Vaduz
*Tel:* 235 03 00 *Fax:* 235 03 29
*E-mail:* mail@kunstmuseum.li
*Web Site:* www.kunstmuseum.li
Specialize in 19th Century to Contemporary Art.
Number of titles published annually: 5 Print
Total Titles: 40 Print

**Liechtenstein Verlag AG+**
Herrengasse 21, 9490 Vaduz
Mailing Address: PO Box 339, 9490 Vaduz
*Tel:* 2396010 *Fax:* 2396019
*E-mail:* flbooks@verlag-ag.lol.li
*Web Site:* www.lol.li/verlag_ag
*Key Personnel*
Man Dir: Albart Piet Schiks
Founded: 1945
Also acts as Literary Agent.
Subjects: Finance, Government, Political Science, History, Law
ISBN Prefix(es): 3-85789

**Verlag der Liechtensteinischen Akademischen Gesellschaft**
Bahnhofstr 15a, 9494 Schaan
Mailing Address: Postfach 829, 9494 Schaan
*Tel:* 232 30 28 *Fax:* 233 14 49
*Key Personnel*
Dir: Norbert Jansen *E-mail:* jansen@mediateam.li
Founded: 1972
Subjects: Economics, Government, Political Science, Law
ISBN Prefix(es): 3-7211
Number of titles published annually: 3 Print

**Litag Anstalt- Literarische, Medien und Kuenstler Agentur**
Industriestr 105A, 9491 Ruggell
Mailing Address: Postfach 131, 9491 Ruggell
*Tel:* (0423) 3771809 *Fax:* (0423) 3771802
*Key Personnel*
Dir: Mrs B Gantner-Caplan
Founded: 1956
ISBN Prefix(es): 3-7211
*Parent Company:* Verlag der Liechtensteinischen Akademischeen Gesellschaft, Am Schragenluegz, 9490 Vaduz

**Megatrade AG+**
Aeulestrasse 45, 9490 Vaduz, Fuerstentum
*Tel:* 237 5252 *Fax:* 237 5253
*E-mail:* info@wanger.net
*Web Site:* www.wanger.net *Cable:* JURT FL
*Key Personnel*
Managing Partner: Markus Wille
Senior Partner: Dr Markus Wanger
Subjects: Art, Business, Economics, Law
ISBN Prefix(es): 3-9520331
*Parent Company:* Wanger Group

**Rheintal Handelsgesellschaft Anstalt**
Industiestr Postfach 444, 9495 Triesen
*Tel:* (075) 3921882; (01) 8442786 *Fax:* (075) 3923646; (01) 8442806
*E-mail:* vetsch.p@bluewin.ch
*Key Personnel*
International Rights: Nick U Schweinfurth

Founded: 1889
Subjects: Career Development, Education, Interactive Audio Courses on CD-ROM
ISBN Prefix(es): 3-9520574
*Orders to:* Rheintal Hondelsgesellschaft Niederlassung ZH/Huttikon, Birkenweg 3, 8115 Huttikon, Switzerland

**Saendig Reprint Verlag, Hans-Rainer Wohlwend**
Am Schraegen Weg 12, 9490 Vaduz
*Tel:* 232 36 27 *Fax:* 232 36 49
*E-mail:* saendig@adon.li
*Web Site:* www.saendig.com
*Key Personnel*
Manager: Christian Wohlwend
Founded: 1981
Subjects: Art, History, Language Arts, Linguistics, Mathematics, Music, Dance, Physical Sciences, Religion - Other, Science (General)
ISBN Prefix(es): 3-253

**Topos Verlag AG**
Industriestr 105A, 9491 Ruggell
Mailing Address: Postfach 551, 9491 Ruggell
*Tel:* 3771111 *Fax:* 3771119
*E-mail:* topos@supra.net
*Web Site:* www.topos.li *Cable:* TOPOS
*Key Personnel*
Man Dir: Graham A P Smith
Founded: 1977
Subjects: Economics, Education, Law, Social Sciences, Sociology
ISBN Prefix(es): 3-289

**Frank P van Eck Publishers+**
Haldenweg 9, 9495 Triesen
Mailing Address: Postfach 565, 9495 Triesen
*Tel:* (075) 3923000 *Fax:* (075) 3922277
*E-mail:* vaneck@datacomm.ch
*Telex:* 77030
*Key Personnel*
Manager: Elisabeth van Eck-Schaedler
Editor: Frank P van Eck
Founded: 1982
Subjects: Art, Sports, Athletics
ISBN Prefix(es): 3-905501
*Associate Companies:* Saentis Verlag
Subsidiaries: Edition Fuchs & Hase
*Shipping Address:* Schweizer Buchzertrum, Industrie Ost, 4614 Magendorf
*Warehouse:* Schweizer Buchzertrum, Industrie Ost, 4614 Magendorf
*Orders to:* Schweizer Buchzertrum, Industrie Ost, 4614 Magendorf

# Lithuania

## General Information

*Capital:* Vilnius
*Language:* Lithuanian
*Religion:* Predominantly Roman Catholic
*Population:* 3.8 million
*Bank Hours:* 0900-1200/1300 Monday-Friday
*Shop Hours:* 0900-1300 and 1400-1800 Monday-Friday
*Currency:* 100 cents = 1 litas
*Export/Import Information:* There are no customs duties and very few export restrictions.
*Copyright:* Berne (see Copyright Conventions, pg xi)

**Academia**, see Lietuvos Mokslu Akademijos Leidykla

**Algarve+**
Rinktines 3/11, 2600 Vilnius

*Tel:* (02) 725910; (02) 721635 *Fax:* (02) 721462
*Key Personnel*
Publisher: Algimantas Matulevicius
Founded: 1995
Joint stock company.
Subjects: Advertising, Fiction, Health, Nutrition, Science (General), esoteric, applied health education literature
ISBN Prefix(es): 9986-856
Total Titles: 40 Print

**Alma Littera+**
A Juozapavieiaus g 6/2, 09310 Vilnius
*Tel:* (05) 263 88 77 *Fax:* (05) 272 80 26
*E-mail:* post@almali.lt
*Web Site:* www.almalittera.lt
*Key Personnel*
Dir: Arvydas Andrijauskas
Founded: 1990
Membership(s): EEPG.
Subjects: English as a Second Language, Fiction
Number of titles published annually: 260 Print; 2 CD-ROM
Total Titles: 3,000 Print; 8 Audio

**Andrena Publishers+**
Pasilaiciu 8-13, 2022 Vilnius
*Tel:* (02) 703834; (02) 627015
*E-mail:* andrena@takas.lt
*Key Personnel*
Contact: Nijole Petrosiene
Founded: 1995
Subjects: Poetry, Psychology, Psychiatry, Religion - Catholic, Romance
ISBN Prefix(es): 9986-37
Total Titles: 27 Print

**AS Narbuto Leidykla (AS Narbutas' Publishers)+**
Klevu 9, 76335 Siauliai
*Tel:* (041) 429335
*Key Personnel*
Contact: Amalijus S Narbutas *E-mail:* amalijus@takas.lt
Founded: 1990
Subjects: Art, Astrology, Occult, Humor, Language Arts, Linguistics, Literature, Literary Criticism, Essays, Medicine, Nursing, Dentistry, Parapsychology, Philosophy, Psychology, Psychiatry
ISBN Prefix(es): 9986-552

**Baltos Lankos+**
Laisves pr 115a-54, 2022 Vilnius
*Tel:* (05) 240 86 73; (05) 240 79 06 *Fax:* (05) 240 74 46
*E-mail:* leidykla@baltoslankos.lt
*Web Site:* www.baltoslankos.lt
*Key Personnel*
Dir: Saulius Zukas
Foreign Rights: Daiva Cibutaviciene
Founded: 1992
A humanities & social sciences publisher.
Subjects: Art, Biography, Cookery, Education, Fiction, History, Language Arts, Linguistics, Literature, Literary Criticism, Essays, Mysteries, Nonfiction (General), Philosophy, Photography, Poetry, Romance, Social Sciences, Sociology, Classics
*U.S. Office(s):* 2016 W Huron, No 2F, Chicago, IL, United States, Contact: Jura Avizienis *Tel:* 312-243-0799

**Centre of Legal Information**
Gedimino pr 30/1, 2695 Vilnius
*Tel:* (02) 61 75 29; (02) 62 36 50 *Fax:* (02) 62 15 23
*E-mail:* webadm@utic.tm.lt
Subjects: Law
ISBN Prefix(es): 9986-452

**Dargenis Publishers+**
PO Box 2090, 44 009 Kaunas
*Tel:* (037) 205241 *Fax:* (037) 205241
*E-mail:* dargenis@kaunas.omnitel.net
*Key Personnel*
Dir: Dalia Celiesiute
Founded: 1997
Subjects: Child Care & Development, English as a Second Language, Human Relations, Psychology, Psychiatry, Self-Help
ISBN Prefix(es): 9986-9196; 9955-403

**Egmont Lietuva+**
Algirdo 51A, 2006 Vilnius
*Tel:* (02) 231265; (02) 231266; (02) 231267 *Fax:* (02) 231269
*E-mail:* egmont@egmont.com
*Web Site:* www.egmont.com
*Key Personnel*
Dir: Irina Glagoleva
Founded: 1993
Subjects: Fiction, Nonfiction (General), Comics & Cartoons
ISBN Prefix(es): 9986-22
*Parent Company:* Egmont International Holding A/S

**Eugrimas+**
Silutes 42A, 2042 Vilnius
*Tel:* 52 733 955; 52 754 754 *Fax:* 52 733 955
*E-mail:* info@eugrimas.lt
*Web Site:* www.eugrimas.lt
*Key Personnel*
Dir: Eugenija Petruliene
Founded: 1995
Subjects: Criminology, Economics, Education, Government, Political Science, History, Law, Philosophy
ISBN Prefix(es): 9986-752

**Klaipedos Universiteto Leidykla+**
H Manto 84, 92294 Klaipeda
*Tel:* (06) 398890 *Fax:* (06) 398999
*E-mail:* leidykla@ku.lt
*Web Site:* www.ku.lt
*Key Personnel*
Manager: Lolita Zemliene *Tel:* (06) 398891 *E-mail:* lolita.zemliene@ku.lt
Founded: 1992
Subjects: Agriculture, Archaeology, Art, Biological Sciences, Chemistry, Chemical Engineering, Computer Science, Drama, Theater, Economics, Education, Geography, Geology, History, Library & Information Sciences, Literature, Literary Criticism, Essays, Management, Maritime, Marketing, Mathematics, Mechanical Engineering, Music, Dance, Philosophy, Physical Sciences, Poetry, Psychology, Psychiatry, Public Administration, Religion - Catholic, Religion - Protestant, Science (General), Social Sciences, Sociology, Technology, Theology
Number of titles published annually: 100 Print
Total Titles: 800 Print
*Parent Company:* Klaipeda University

**Lietus Ltd+**
A Jakto 8/10, 2600 Vilnius
*Tel:* (02) 312298; (02) 8299 35423; (02) 745720 *Fax:* (02) 312298
*Key Personnel*
President: Liudas Pilius
International Rights: Agne Kudirkaite
Founded: 1991
Membership(s): Lithuanian Publisher's Association.
Subjects: Education, Fiction, Nonfiction (General)
ISBN Prefix(es): 9986-431
Total Titles: 70 Print
*Warehouse:* Musu Knyga Ltd, Vilkpedes 20, Vilnius *Tel:* (02) 632921

**Lietuvos Mokslu Akademijos Leidykla**
Formerly Academia
A Gostauto 12, 2600 Vilnius
*Tel:* (02) 626851 *Fax:* (02) 226351
*Key Personnel*
Dir: A Garliauskas *Tel:* (02) 626861
Founded: 1990
Subjects: Agriculture, Art, Biological Sciences, Chemistry, Chemical Engineering, Energy, Geography, Geology, Language Arts, Linguistics, Medicine, Nursing, Dentistry, Philosophy, Social Sciences, Sociology

**Lietuvos Rasytoju Sajungos Leidykla**
(Lithuanian Writers' Union Publishers)+
K Sirvydo 6, 01101 Vilnius
*Tel:* (05) 2628945; (05) 2628643 *Fax:* (05) 2628945
*E-mail:* info@rsleidykla.lt
*Web Site:* www.rsleidykla.lt
*Key Personnel*
Dir: Giedre Soriene
Editor-in-Chief: Valentinas Sventickas
Editor: Saulius Repecka *Tel:* (02) 628643
Founded: 1990
Membership(s): Lithuanian Publishers Association.
Subjects: Fiction, Literature, Literary Criticism, Essays, Poetry
ISBN Prefix(es): 9-986
Number of titles published annually: 45 Print
*Bookshop(s):* Atzalynas, Antakalnio g 97, 2040 Vilnius; Fabijoniskiy, Stanevic’s g 24, 2029 Vilnius

**Lithuanian National Museum Publishing House**
Division of National Museum of Lithuania
Arsenalo g 1, 01100 Vilnius
*Tel:* (05) 262 77 74 *Fax:* (05) 261 10 23
*E-mail:* info@lnm.lt; muziejus@lnm.lt
*Web Site:* www.lnm.lt
*Key Personnel*
Dir: Birute Kulnyte
Subjects: Archaeology, History, Photography, Ethnography, Iconography, Numismatics
ISBN Prefix(es): 9955-415
Number of titles published annually: 10 Print
Total Titles: 105 Print

**Lithuanian Publishers' Association**
K Sirbydo, 2600 Vilnius
*Tel:* (02) 617740 *Fax:* (02) 617740
*E-mail:* lla@centras.lt
*Web Site:* www.lla.lt
*Key Personnel*
Dir: Aleksandras Krasnovas
Founded: 1990
Membership(s): International Publishers Association.

**Martynas Mazvydas National Library of Lithuania** (Lietuvos Nacionaline Martyno Mazvydo Biblioteka)+
Gedimino pr 51, 01504 Vilnius
*Tel:* 52398687 *Fax:* 52639111
*E-mail:* leidyba@lnb.lt
*Web Site:* www.lnb.lt
*Key Personnel*
Acting Dir: Vytautas Gudaitis *Tel:* 52497023 *Fax:* 52496129 *E-mail:* gudaitis@lnb.lt
Founded: 1919
Subjects: Library & Information Sciences
ISBN Prefix(es): 9986-530

**Mokslo ir enciklopediju leidybos institutas**
(Science & Encyclopedia Publishing Institute)+
L Asanaviciutes g 23, 2050 Vilnius
*Tel:* (02) 45 85 26; (02) 457980; (02) 458528 *Fax:* (02) 45 85 37
*E-mail:* meli@meli.lt

*Web Site:* www.meli.lt
*Key Personnel*
Dir: Rimantas Kareckas *Tel:* 02 458525
Chief Editor: Jonas Varnauskas
Founded: 1992
Membership(s): the Lithuanian Publishers' Association.
Subjects: Agriculture, Biological Sciences, History, Language Arts, Linguistics, Literature, Literary Criticism, Essays, Mathematics, Medicine, Nursing, Dentistry, Physics, Science (General)
Imprints: Vilnius

**Margi Rastai Publishers+**
Laisves pr 60, 2056 Vilnius
*Tel:* (02) 429526; (02) 427909; (02) 429527; (02) 426705 *Fax:* (02) 426705
*E-mail:* margirastai@takas.lt
Subjects: Agriculture, Economics, Fiction, History, Sports, Athletics
ISBN Prefix(es): 9986-09

**Scena+**
Tuskulenu 13-14, 2051 Vilnius
*Tel:* (02) 751 828; (02) 614 145 *Fax:* (02) 610 814
*Key Personnel*
Dir: Rasa Andrasiunaite
Founded: 1992
Specialize in books about theater.
Subjects: Art, Drama, Theater
ISBN Prefix(es): 9986-412

**Sviesa Publishers+**
Vytauto Ave 25, 3000 Kaunas
*Tel:* (0837) 409126 *Fax:* (0837) 342032
*E-mail:* mail@sviesa.lt
*Web Site:* www.sviesa.lt
*Key Personnel*
Dir: Vaidotas Gadliauskas *Tel:* (0837) 341834 *E-mail:* v.gadliauskas@sviesa.lt
Founded: 1945
Subjects: Career Development, Child Care & Development, Crafts, Games, Hobbies, Education, English as a Second Language, House & Home, Sports, Athletics, Travel
ISBN Prefix(es): 5-430

**Teisines Informacijos Centras**, see Centre of Legal Information

**TEV Leidykla+**
Akademijos 4, 2021 Vilnius
*Tel:* (02) 729318; (02) 729803 *Fax:* (02) 729804
*E-mail:* tev@tev.lt
*Web Site:* www.tev.lt
*Key Personnel*
Contact: Elmundas Zalys
Founded: 1991
Subjects: Computer Science, Education, Engineering (General), Mathematics, Physics, Science (General)
ISBN Prefix(es): 9986-546
Distributed by VSP International Publications; Zeist
Distributor for VSP International Publications; Zeist

**Tyto Alba Publishers+**
J Jasinskio 10, 2600 Vilnius
*Tel:* (02) 498 602; (02) 497 453; (02) 497 597 *Fax:* (02) 498 602
*E-mail:* tytoalba@taide.lt
*Web Site:* www.tytoalba.lt
*Key Personnel*
Dir: Lolita Varanaviciene
Rights Manager: Ausra Viliuniene
Founded: 1993 (joint-stock company)

Subjects: Art, Biography, Business, Education, Fiction, How-to, Human Relations, Nonfiction (General), Philosophy, Self-Help
ISBN Prefix(es): 9986-16
Number of titles published annually: 50 Print
Total Titles: 300 Print

**Vaga Ltd+**
Gedimino str 50, 2600 Vilnius
*Tel:* (02) 49 81 21 *Fax:* (02) 49 81 22
*E-mail:* info@vaga.lt
*Web Site:* www.vaga.lt
*Key Personnel*
Dir: Arturas Mickevicius
Dir General: Kornelijus Platelis
Founded: 1945
Subjects: Art, Biography, Ethnicity, Fiction, Government, Political Science, Literature, Literary Criticism, Essays, Nonfiction (General), Philosophy, Photography, Poetry, Religion - Catholic, Religion - Jewish, Self-Help, Social Sciences, Sociology, Theology
ISBN Prefix(es): 5-415
*Associate Companies:* Vaga Trading Ltd; Vaga Publishers Ltd
*Bookshop(s):* M K Ciurlionio St 75, Druskininkai *Tel:* (0233) 5 15 25; Gedimino St 25/2, Kaisedorys *Tel:* (0256) 6 03 91; Smilgos St 2, Kedainiai *Tel:* (0257) 5 26 61; Aitvaras, Taikos pr 39, Klaipeda *Tel:* (026) 41 06 64; Centras, Turgaus aikste 2, Klaipeda *Tel:* (026) 41 15 90; Taikos pr 97, Klaipeda *Tel:* (026) 34 59 69; H Manto St, Klaipeda *Tel:* (026) 41 15 93; Lyros St 13, Siauliai *Tel:* (021) 55 26 05; Tauragnu St 2, Utena *Tel:* (0239) 5 96 79; Draugyste, Gedimino pr 2, Vilnius *Tel:* (02) 61 18 23; Versme, Didzioji St 27, Vilnius *Tel:* (02) 62 64 10; Ateities St 20, Vilnius *Tel:* (02) 71 46 88; Darbininku St 16, Vilnius *Tel:* (02) 26 49 48; Gedvydziu St 17, Vilnius *Tel:* (02) 47 86 56; Pergales St 13/2, Vilnius *Tel:* (02) 67 49 03; Ukmerges St 25, Vilnius, Luxembourg

**Victoria Publishers+**
Sviesos 4-6, Grigskes, 4058 Traku rajonas
*Tel:* (02) 221915; (02) 632632; (02) 221914 *Fax:* (02) 630797
*Key Personnel*
Contact: Natalija Stagiene
Founded: 1991
Subjects: Animals, Pets, Child Care & Development, Crafts, Games, Hobbies, Geography, Geology, Romance, Women's Studies

**Vilnius**, *imprint of* Mokslo ir enciklopediju leidybos institutas

**Vilnius Art Academy Publishing House**
The Old House, 3rd floor, Maironio St 6, 2600 Vilnius
*Tel:* (02) 22 30 63 *Fax:* (02) 61 99 66
*E-mail:* muziejus@vda.lt
*Web Site:* vdamuziejus.mch.mii.lt
*Key Personnel*
Chief Curator: Valentas Cibulskas

**Vyturys Vyturio leidykla, UAB**
J Tumo, Vaiganto 2, 2600 Vilnius
*Tel:* (02122) 027404; (02122) 622542 *Fax:* (02122) 629407
*E-mail:* vyturys@vyturys.lt
*Web Site:* www.vyturys.lt
Founded: 1985
Subjects: Education, Fiction, Literature, Literary Criticism, Essays, Poetry, Romance, Comics & Cartoons
ISBN Prefix(es): 5-7900

**Magazyn Wilenski**
Laisves pr 60, 2056 Vilnius
*Tel:* (05) 242 77 18

*E-mail:* magazyn@magwil.lt
*Web Site:* www.magwil.lt
*Key Personnel*
Editor: Michal Mackiewicz *Tel:* (05) 242 60 76
*Fax:* (05) 242 90 65
ISBN Prefix(es): 9986-542

# Luxembourg

## General Information

*Capital:* Luxembourg
*Language:* Luxembourgian, German, French, English
*Religion:* Predominantly Roman Catholic (about 97%)
*Population:* 437,389
*Bank Hours:* Vary. Generally 0830-1200, 1330-1630 Monday-Friday
*Shop Hours:* 0830-1200, 1330-1800 Monday-Saturday. Most close Monday morning. Some have late night shopping until 2000
*Currency:* 100 Eurocents = 1 Euro; 40.3399 Luxembourg francs = 1 Euro
*Export/Import Information:* Member of the European Union. In economic and monetary union with Belgium and Netherlands. No Tariff on books except children's picture books from non-EU; advertising other than single copied dutied. VAT on books and advertising. No import license required. No exchange controls.
*Copyright:* UCC, Berne, Florence (see Copyright Conventions, pg xi)

### Editions APESS ASBL
17, rue Muller-Fromes, Diekirch, 9261 Luxembourg
*Tel:* 80 8358 *Fax:* 80 2813
*E-mail:* apess@ci.edu.lu
*Web Site:* www.restena.lu/apess
*Key Personnel*
Contact: Carlo Felten
Founded: 1982
Subjects: Art, Education, History, Literature, Literary Criticism, Essays, Philosophy, Poetry, Science (General)
ISBN Prefix(es): 2-87979
Total Titles: 35 Print

### ARA International
58, Domaine Mehlstrachen, 6942 Niederanven
*Tel:* 34 85 91 *Fax:* 34 85 91
*E-mail:* amisrelart@pt.lu
*Web Site:* www.ara-international.lu
*Key Personnel*
International President: Emile van der Vekene *E-mail:* evekene@pt.lu
Founded: 1996
*Associate Companies:* ARA-Belgique, Ave de Messidor 184, bte 1, 1180 Brussels, Belgium, Contact: Marianne Delvaulx *Tel:* (02) 346 10 02 *Fax:* (02) 346 10 02 *E-mail:* marianne.delvaulx@belgacom.net; ARA-Canada, 1275, chemin Sainte-Foy, Quebec, QC G1S 4W8, Canada, President: Jonathan Tremblay *Tel:* 416-843-2238 *E-mail:* ara-canada@oricom.ca *Web Site:* www.aracanada.org; ARA-Catalunya, Carrer Camprodon, 17 baixos, 08021 Barcelona, Spain, President: Germana Cavalcanti *Tel:* (093) 200 18 68 *E-mail:* germanacavalcanti@yahoo.com; ARA-France, 122, blvd Murat, 75016 Paris, France, President: Annick Terrasson *E-mail:* fc.terrasson@wanadoo.fr; ARA-Grece, 19 rue Didotou, 106 80 Athens, Greece, President: Sotirios K Koutsiaftis *Tel:* 2108020316 *Fax:* 2103620188 *E-mail:* sotkoutsiaftis@yahoo.gr; ARA-Italia, Fondazione Querini

Stampalia, Castello 5252, 30122 Venice, Italy, President: Gabriele Giannini *Tel:* (041) 522 52 35 *Fax:* (041) 522 49 54 *E-mail:* info.ara@libero.it *Web Site:* www.amicirilegaturadarte.com; ARA-Suisse, 31 Beausejour, 1762 Givisiez, Switzerland, President: Gian-Andri Barblan *E-mail:* g-a.barblan@bluemail.ch *Web Site:* www.arasuisse.com
Foreign Rep(s): Pedro de Azevedo (Portugal); Joel Benarrous (Israel); Marisa Garcia de Souza (Brazil); Paula Maria Gourley (US); Fred Kroon (Netherlands); Sabine Pierard (Australia); Ivan Piskov (Russia); Emile van der Vekene (Luxembourg); Reuko Yamanue (Japan)

### Guy Binsfeld & Co Sarl+
14, pl du Parc, 2313 Luxembourg
*Tel:* 49 68 68-1 *Fax:* 40 76 09; 48 87 70
*E-mail:* editions@binsfeld.lu
*Web Site:* www.editionsguybinsfeld.lu
*Key Personnel*
Man Dir, Production, Publicity, Rights & Permissions: Guy Binsfeld *E-mail:* gbinsfeld@binsfeld.lu
Founded: 1979
Subjects: Biography, Cookery, Fiction, Gardening, Plants, How-to, Law, Nonfiction (General), Photography
ISBN Prefix(es): 3-88957; 2-87954
Total Titles: 204 Print
Divisions: Binsfeld-Conseils Communications Agency
Distributed by Altera Diffusion (Belgium); Fausto Gardini (US); Gollenstein Verlag (Germany, Austria & Switzerland); Lanaguages de Luxe (Great Britain); Messageries du Livre (Luxembourg & other countries); Editions Serpenoise (France); Willems Adventure (Netherlands)

### Editions Emile Borschette
21 Fielserstrooss, 7640 Christnach
*Tel:* 87177 *Fax:* 879599
Founded: 1987
Subjects: Accounting, Career Development, Cookery, Drama, Theater, Education, Gardening, Plants, History, How-to, Humor, Language Arts, Linguistics, Literature, Literary Criticism, Essays, Mathematics, Music, Dance, Photography, Poetry, Regional Interests
ISBN Prefix(es): 2-87982
Subsidiaries: Atelier de Reliures

### Cahiers Luxembourgeois
67, rue Roger Barthel, 7212 Bereldingen
*Tel:* 338885 *Fax:* 336513
*Key Personnel*
Publisher: Nic Weber
Founded: 1993
Subjects: Biography, History, Literature, Literary Criticism, Essays, Poetry, Regional Interests
ISBN Prefix(es): 2-919976
Divisions: Edition Raymon Mehlen

### Centre Culturel De Differdange
69 rue Prinzenberg, 4650 Niederkorn
*Tel:* 587045 *Fax:* 580295
*Key Personnel*
President & Editor: Cornel Meder *E-mail:* cornel.meder@ci.culture.lu
Founded: 1982
Subjects: Ethnicity, Literature, Literary Criticism, Essays
ISBN Prefix(es): 2-87991

### Chambre des Employes Prives
13, rue de Bragance, 1255 Luxembourg
*Tel:* 44 40 91-1 *Fax:* 44 40 91-250
*E-mail:* info@cepl.lu
*Web Site:* www.cepl.lu

*Key Personnel*
President: Jos Kratochwil
Dir: Theo Wiltgen

### Editpress
44, rue du Canal, 4050 Esch/Alzette
*Tel:* 547131 *Fax:* 547130
*E-mail:* tageblatt@tageblatt.lu

### Eiffes Romain
293, Avenue de Luxembourg, L-4940 Bascharage
*Tel:* 23651052
*E-mail:* rend@pt.lu
*Key Personnel*
Contact: Mr Romain Eiffes
Founded: 1995
Membership(s): SACEM/Paris (Societe des Auteurs Compositeurs et Editeurs de Musique Paris).
Subjects: English as a Second Language, Music, Dance, Poetry
ISBN Prefix(es): 2-9599899

### Essay und Zeitgeist Verlag
c/o Patrick Kontz, BP 2116, 1021 Luxembourg
*Fax:* 425227
Founded: 1994
Subjects: Literature, Literary Criticism, Essays, Philosophy, Social Sciences, Sociology
ISBN Prefix(es): 2-9599981
*Orders to:* BP 2767, L-1207 Luxembourg

### Galerie Editions Kutter
BP 319, 2013 Luxembourg
*Tel:* 22 35 71 *Fax:* 47 18 84
*E-mail:* kuttered@pt.lu
*Web Site:* www.kutter.lu
Founded: 1960
Subjects: Art, Photography, Regional Interests
ISBN Prefix(es): 2-87952

### Grande Loge de Luxembourg
5, rue de la Loge, 2018 Luxembourg
Mailing Address: BP 851, 2018 Luxembourg
*Tel:* 463-566 *Fax:* 463566
ISBN Prefix(es): 2-9599875

### Hubsch
24, rue des Genets, 3482 Dudelange
*E-mail:* 101755.3213@compuserve.com
Subjects: Humor, Romance, Science Fiction, Fantasy
ISBN Prefix(es): 2-9599996

### Keyware sarl+
11, rue de la Montagne, 5460 Trintange
*Tel:* 358660
*E-mail:* texthaus@webcom.com
Founded: 1996
Subjects: Education
ISBN Prefix(es): 2-919891

### Ministere de la Culture
20 Montee de la Pe'trusse, 2327 Luxembourg
*Tel:* 478-1 *Fax:* 40-24-27
ISBN Prefix(es): 2-87984

### Edition Objectif Lune+
One rue de Schoenfels, 8151 Bridel
*Tel:* 335230 *Fax:* 335230
*E-mail:* objectif.lune@cmdnet.lu
*Key Personnel*
President: Jean-Paul Kieffer
Specialize in photographic stills.
Subjects: Drama, Theater, Film, Video, Photography
ISBN Prefix(es): 2-9599934

**Office des Publications Officielles des Communautes Europeennes** (Office for Official Publications of the European Communities)
2 rue Mercier, 2985 Luxembourg
*Tel:* 292942001 *Fax:* 292942700
Founded: 1969
*U.S. Office(s):* Bernan Associates, 4611-F Assembly Drive, Lanham, MD 20706-4391, United States *Tel:* 800-274-4447 *Fax:* 800-865-3450 *E-mail:* query@bernan.com *Web Site:* www. bernan.com

**Op der Lay+**
19, rue d'Eschdorf, 9650 Esch-sur-Sure
*Tel:* 83 97 42 *Fax:* 89 93 50
*E-mail:* opderlay@pt.lu
*Web Site:* webplaza.pt.lu/public/opderlay; www. phi.lu
*Key Personnel*
Contact: Robert Gollo Steffen; Renee Weber
Founded: 1987
Specialize in compact disc & music cassettes, literature & music from Luxembourg.
Also music publisher.
Subjects: Music, Dance, Poetry, Travel
ISBN Prefix(es): 2-87967
Total Titles: 7 Audio

**Passerelle Editions**, *imprint of* Editions Promoculture

**Editions Phi+**
PO Box 321, 4004 Esch, Alzette
*Tel:* 541382-220 *Fax:* 541387
*E-mail:* editions.phi@editpress.lu; phi@phi.lu
*Web Site:* www.phi.lu
*Key Personnel*
Dir: Angelika Thome
Editorial: Jean Portante
Founded: 1980
Subjects: Art, Drama, Theater, Literature, Literary Criticism, Essays
ISBN Prefix(es): 3-88865; 2-87962

**Editions Promoculture+**
14 rue Duchscher, 1424 Luxembourg
Mailing Address: BP 1142, 1011 Luxembourg
*Tel:* 480691 *Fax:* 400950
*E-mail:* promocul@pt.lu
*Web Site:* www.promoculture.lu
*Key Personnel*
Dir: Albert Daming *E-mail:* daming@pt.lu
Founded: 1989
Law & fiscal publisher.
Also major book dealer.
Subjects: Accounting, Economics, Finance, Law
ISBN Prefix(es): 2-87974
Number of titles published annually: 15 Print; 1 CD-ROM; 2 E-Book
Total Titles: 120 Print; 2 CD-ROM; 2 E-Book
Imprints: Passerelle Editions
*Warehouse:* One rue Duchscher, 1424 Luxembourg *E-mail:* info@promoculture.lu

**Editions Saint-Paul+**
5 rue Christophe Plantin, 2988 Luxembourg
*Tel:* 4993-275 *Fax:* 4993-580
*E-mail:* info@biblioservice.lu
*Web Site:* www.biblioservice.lu; www.libo.lu (orders)
*Telex:* Wortlu 3471; 275256
*Key Personnel*
Man Dir: Paul Zimmer
Production: Jean Breser
Publicity: Patrick Ludovicy
Publishing Manager: Dirk Sumkoetter
   *Tel:* 4993256 *E-mail:* dirk.sumkoetter@editions.lu
Founded: 1886

Subjects: History, Literature, Literary Criticism, Essays
ISBN Prefix(es): 2-87963
*Parent Company:* Group Saint-Paul SA
*Bookshop(s):* Librarie Beaumont, 24 rue Beaumont, 1249; Librairie Bourbon, rue du Fort Bourbon, 1249; Librairie du Sud, 74 rue de l'Alzette, 4010 Eschlalzette; Librairie Daman, 4 rue de Brabant, 9213 Diekirch

**Service Central de la Statistique et des Etudes Economiques (STATEC)**
Les bureaux du Statec se trouvent au centre de Luxembourg-Ville, Centre Administratif Pierre Werner, 13, rue Erasme, 1468 Luxembourg-Kirchberg
Mailing Address: BP 304, 2013 Luxembourg
*Tel:* 478-4384 *Fax:* 464289
*E-mail:* info@statec.etat.lu
*Web Site:* www.statec.lu; www.statec.public.lu
*Key Personnel*
Dir: Serge Allegrezza
Principal Inspector & Head of Information: Guy Zacharias *Tel:* 478-4281 *E-mail:* guy. zacharias@statec.etat.lu
Founded: 1962
National Statistical Institute of Luxembourg, under the authority of the Minister of the Economy.
Subjects: Agriculture, Business, Economics, Finance, Labor, Industrial Relations, Library & Information Sciences, Public Administration, Social Sciences, Sociology
ISBN Prefix(es): 2-87988
Number of titles published annually: 100 Print

**Service Central des Imprimes et des Fournitures de Bureau de l'Etat**
22, rue des Bruyeres, 1274 Howald
Mailing Address: BP 1302, 1013 Howald
*Tel:* 4988111 *Fax:* 400881
*E-mail:* hotline@scie.etat.lu
*Web Site:* www.scie.etat.lu
*Key Personnel*
Contact: Claude Schaber *Tel:* 498811-901 *E-mail:* claude.schaber@scie.etat.lu
Founded: 1969
Specialize in textbooks.
Subjects: Archaeology, Art, Law, Natural History, Public Administration
ISBN Prefix(es): 2-495
Number of titles published annually: 70 Print
Total Titles: 1,023 Print

**STATEC**, see Service Central de la Statistique et des Etudes Economiques (STATEC)

**Thesen Verlag Vowinckel**
Place de la Gare, 3, 6674 Mertert
Mailing Address: Postfach 3570, 54225 Trier, Germany
*Tel:* 748715 *Fax:* 26740429
*Key Personnel*
Man Dir: Dr Ilse Schirmer-Vowinckel
   *E-mail:* schirm.vow@pt.lu
Founded: 1969 (in Germany, since 1992 resident in the Grand-Duche of Luxembourg)
Specialize in scholarly books, book review "Kritikon Litterarum" literary criticism.
Membership(s): Borsenverein des Deutschen Buchhandels.
ISBN Prefix(es): 3-7677

**Editions Tousch+**
8 rue Ernest Koch, 1864 Luxembourg
*Tel:* 452977 *Fax:* 458743
Subjects: Art, History, Humor, Photography, Poetry
ISBN Prefix(es): 2-919971

**Varkki Verghese+**
Maison 23A, 9769 Roder
*Tel:* 923121 *Fax:* 929076
Founded: 1993
Membership(s): GEMA.
Subjects: Alternative, Asian Studies, Economics, Government, Political Science, Music, Dance, Poetry, Theology, Women's Studies
ISBN Prefix(es): 2-9599891
*Associate Companies:* Whitelion Ltd, United Kingdom
Divisions: Acanthus Records
Distributed by Oyster (India only)

# Macau

## General Information

*Capital:* Macau
*Language:* Portuguese and Chinese (Cantonese dialect) both official. English also widely spoken
*Religion:* Roman Catholic, Chinese Buddhist, Daoism, & Confucianism
*Population:* 373,904
*Bank Hours:* 0930-1700 Monday-Friday; 0930-1200 Saturday
*Shop Hours:* 0900-1730 Monday-Saturday
*Currency:* 100 avos = 1 pataca. Hong Kong currency is also widely used but there is no fixed exchange rate.
*Export/Import Information:* Macau is a free port.
*Copyright:* Berne (see Copyright Conventions, pg xi)

**Livros Do Oriente+**
Edificio Marina Gardens, Av Amizade, 876, 15 E Macau
*Tel:* 700320; 700421 *Fax:* 700423
*E-mail:* livros.macau@loriente.com
*Web Site:* www.loriente.com
*Key Personnel*
General Manager: Rogerio Beltrao Coelho
Executive Manager: Cecilia Jorge
Founded: 1990
Subjects: Anthropology, Biography, Photography, Romance, Social Sciences, Sociology, Travel
ISBN Prefix(es): 972-9418
*Branch Office(s)*
Rua da Fonte Santa, 91, 2050-112 Aveiras de Cima, Portugal, Contact: Chacara Lilau *Fax:* (0263) 476890 *E-mail:* chacara@mail. telepac.pt

**Museu Maritimo** (Maritime Museum)
Largo do Pagode da Barra, n 1, Sul da China
*Tel:* 595481; 595483 *Fax:* 512160
*E-mail:* museumaritimo@marine.gov.mo
*Web Site:* www.museumaritimo.gov.mo
*Key Personnel*
Dir: Wu Chu Pang
Subjects: Asian Studies, History, Maritime, Technology, Transportation
ISBN Prefix(es): 972-96755; 972-97714
Number of titles published annually: 3 Print
Total Titles: 58 Print

**Instituto Portugues Oriente**
Rua Pedro Nolasco da Silva, n° 45, 1° andar, Macau
*Tel:* 530227; 530243 *Fax:* 530277
*E-mail:* info@ipor.org
*Web Site:* www.ipor.org
*Key Personnel*
President: Prof Antonio Vasconcelos de Saldanha *E-mail:* presidente@ipor.org
Founded: 1989

Subjects: Asian Studies, History, Language Arts, Linguistics, Literature, Literary Criticism, Essays
ISBN Prefix(es): 972-8013
*Bookshop(s):* Livraria Portuguesa, Rua de Sao Domingos, No 16-18, Contact: Manuel Almeida *Tel:* (0853) 566442; (0853) 356235 *Fax:* (0853) 378014 *E-mail:* malmeida. livraria@ipor.org

# The Former Yugoslav Republic of Macedonia

## General Information

*Capital:* Skopje
*Language:* Macedonian
*Religion:* Predominantly Eastern Orthodox, some Muslim
*Population:* 2.1 million
*Copyright:* UCC, Berne (see Copyright Conventions, pg xi)

### Detska radost+
Mito Hadzivasilev bb, 91000 Skopje
*Tel:* (091) 112394; (091) 213059 *Fax:* (091) 225830; (091) 213059
*E-mail:* detskaradost@yahoo.com
*Web Site:* www.detskaradost.com
*Telex:* YUNOVMAK 51154
*Key Personnel*
International Rights: Kiril Donev
Editor-in-Chief: Aleksandar Cvetkovski
Founded: 1945
Specialize in children's books.
Subjects: Fiction, Literature, Literary Criticism, Essays, Nonfiction (General), Poetry, Science Fiction, Fantasy
*Associate Companies:* NIP, Nova Makedonija, Skopje

### Gjurgja Journalistic & Publishing Firm
11 Oktomvri 2/6-2, 1000 Skopje
*Tel:* (02) 228076
*Key Personnel*
Dir: Olga Kosteska
ISBN Prefix(es): 9989-676; 9989-920
Subsidiaries: Literary-Painting Salon

### Ktitor+
Engelsova 8/18, 2000 Stip
*Tel:* (092) 21903; (092) 34746 *Fax:* (092) 34746
*Telex:* 53618 MAK.YU
Subjects: Drama, Theater, Literature, Literary Criticism, Essays, Music, Dance, Philosophy, Poetry, Religion - Other, Science (General)
ISBN Prefix(es): 9989-608

### Macedonia Prima Publishing House+
ul Krste Misirkov 8, 6000 Ohrid
*Tel:* (096) 37-109 *Fax:* (096) 23-172
*Key Personnel*
Editor-in-Chief: Pasko Kuzman
Dir: Nikola Bozdoganov
Editor: Slave Banar
Artistic Designer: Slavko Upevce
Founded: 1993
Membership(s): Association of Macedonian Publishers.
Subjects: Archaeology, Art, History, Literature, Literary Criticism, Essays, Photography, Po-

etry, Science Fiction, Fantasy, Social Sciences, Sociology
ISBN Prefix(es): 9989-619

### Makedonska kniga (Knigoizdatelstvo)
11-ti Oktomvri, 1000 Skopje
*Tel:* (02) 116 473; (02) 3 1610; (02) 235 524 *Fax:* (02) 1212 77
*Telex:* 51637 *Cable:* MAKEDONSKA KNIGA
*Key Personnel*
Dir: Ms Nada Miloshevska-Ristovska
Founded: 1947
Subjects: Art, Fiction
ISBN Prefix(es): 9989-46

### Medis Informatika+
ul Mito Hadzi Vasilev-Jasiminstr 36/1-2, 1000 Skopje
*Tel:* (091) 222253 *Fax:* (091) 222235
*E-mail:* medis@informa.mk
*Key Personnel*
President: Dr Mirko Spiroski
Founded: 1991
Specialize in medicine & computer science.
Subjects: Biological Sciences, Communications, Computer Science, Education, Electronics, Electrical Engineering, Mathematics, Medicine, Nursing, Dentistry, Microcomputers
ISBN Prefix(es): 9989-620
Total Titles: 10 E-Book

### Menora Publishing House
bul Jane Sandanski 36-4/13, 1000 Skopje
*Tel:* (02) 458447 *Fax:* (02) 418872
*E-mail:* menora@lotus.mpt.com.mk
*Key Personnel*
Dir: Jordan Pop-Atanasov
Specialize in literature with scientific & scholarly contents.
Subjects: Science (General)
ISBN Prefix(es): 9989-632
*Bookshop(s):* Porta Bunjakovec, A-2, Dijadema, Lam I, BR 12-I, 91000 Skopje

### Mi-An Knigoizdatelstvo
vl Ivan Agouski 1/I, 91000 Skopje
*Tel:* (091) 252565
*E-mail:* mtimes@soros.org.mk
*Key Personnel*
President: Vanja Tosevski
Vice President: Mishel Pavlovski
Editor-in-Chief: Jovan Pavlovski
Assistant Editor-in-Chief: Boshko Nacevski
Founded: 1991
Subjects: Journalism, Literature, Literary Criticism, Essays, Poetry, Publishing & Book Trade Reference
ISBN Prefix(es): 9989-613
*Branch Office(s)*
American Information Centre, str, Nikola Vaptsarov 8 *Tel:* 116-623

### Murgorski Zoze+
ul Budimpestanska 37B, 1000 Skopje
*Tel:* (091) 241340
Founded: 1991
Subjects: Education, English as a Second Language, Language Arts, Linguistics
ISBN Prefix(es): 9989-651
Distributed by Kultura (Macedonia)

### Narodna i univerzitetska biblioteka, see St Clement of Ohrid National & University Library

### Nov svet (New World)+
Briselska 1, 1000 Skopje
*Tel:* (02) 3078-662
*Key Personnel*
Academic Poet: Dr Jozo T Boskovski Jon
Founded: 1966

Specialize in translations. The company "Nov svet" (New World) was an illegal editorial of the Desidents Writers. Now it is a regular publishing house, with programs sponsored by the Government of the Republic of Macedonia.
Also acts as wholesaler & publishing house for books, newspapers & periodicals.
Subjects: Art, Journalism, Literature, Literary Criticism, Essays, Philosophy, Poetry, Science (General)
Total Titles: 2,000 Print
*Associate Companies:* Cross-Cultural Communications, 239 Wynsum Ave, Merrick, NY 11566-4725, United States

### Prosvetno Delo Publishing House
Dimitie Cupovski 15, 1000 Skopje
*Tel:* (02) 117 255; (02) 2 225 434 *Fax:* (02) 129 402; (02) 225 434
*E-mail:* prodelo@nic.mpt.com.mk
*Web Site:* www.prodelo.com.mk
*Key Personnel*
General Manager: Pavle Petrov
Editor-in-Chief: Jelica Makazlieva
Contact: Nadica Mihajlovska
Founded: 1945
Specialize in school textbooks, pedagogical materials & teaching aids.
Subjects: Education
ISBN Prefix(es): 86-351
Number of titles published annually: 400 Print
Total Titles: 8,000 Print
*Bookshop(s):* Dame Gruev BB, 91000 Skopje *Tel:* (02) 2 222 621 *Fax:* (02) 2 222 621
*Warehouse:* Aco Sopov, 6 91000 Skopje

### St Clement of Ohrid National & University Library+
Bul Goce Delcev 6, 91000 Skopje
*Tel:* (02) 3115 177; (02) 3133 418 *Fax:* (02) 3226 846
*E-mail:* kliment@nubsk.edu.mk
*Web Site:* www.nubsk.edu.mk
*Key Personnel*
Dir & Chief Executive: Vera Kalajlievska
Contact: Veljan Ristevski
Founded: 1944
Scholarly & scientific works collections, including monograph titles, periodicals, newspapers & other printed materials (patents, standards, etc). Specialized collections include: old Slavonic manuscripts, printed & rare books & periodicals, oriental manuscripts, archive copies of Macedonia publications (1944 to present), prints & drawings, cartographic items, microfilms, doctoral dissertations, Master's theses, scientific & scholarly research projects. Online catalogue available.
Subjects: Library & Information Sciences
ISBN Prefix(es): 9989-652
Membership(s): International Federation of Library Associations & Institutions

### Seizmoloska Opservatorija+
PO Box 422, 91000 Skopje
*Tel:* (091) 231953 *Fax:* (091) 114042
*E-mail:* ljupco@iunona.pmf.ukim.edu.mk
*Key Personnel*
Editor & International Rights: Vera Cejkovska; Dragana Cernih
Membership(s): International Association of Seismology & Physics of the Earth's Interior - (IASPEI); International Union of Geodesy & Geophysics (IUGG).
Subjects: Computer Science, Earth Sciences, Electronics, Electrical Engineering, Geography, Geology
ISBN Prefix(es): 9989-631

### STRK Publishing House+
ul Jurij Gagarin Br 17-2-17, 1000 Skopje
*Tel:* (091) 20 53 93 *Fax:* (091) 20 53 93

*Key Personnel*
Dir: Nikola Strkovski
Editor: Snezana Strkovska
Founded: 1992
Also acts as importer/exporter of office supplies & paper; wholesale & retail.
Subjects: Astrology, Occult, Behavioral Sciences, Biography, Economics, History, Literature, Literary Criticism, Essays, Poetry, Romance
ISBN Prefix(es): 9989-662

**Zumpres Publishing Firm+**
ul Vanjamin Madukovski 6, P fah 363, 1000 Skopje
*Tel:* (091) 163-539; (091) 425-175 *Fax:* (091) 429-196; (091) 425-175
*E-mail:* zumpres@yahoo.com
*Key Personnel*
Dir & Editor-in-Chief: Vinka Sazdova
Founded: 1994
Subjects: Anthropology, Archaeology, Architecture & Interior Design, Art, Astrology, Occult, Astronomy, Behavioral Sciences, Biblical Studies, Biography, Computer Science, Fiction, History, Human Relations, Language Arts, Linguistics, Literature, Literary Criticism, Essays, Mysteries, Parapsychology, Philosophy, Poetry, Psychology, Psychiatry
ISBN Prefix(es): 9989-42

# Madagascar

## General Information

*Capital:* Antananarivo
*Language:* French and Malagasy
*Religion:* Most follow traditional beliefs, about 43% Christian and some Islamic
*Population:* 12.6 million
*Bank Hours:* 0800-1100, 1400-1600 Monday-Friday. Closed afternoon preceding a holiday
*Shop Hours:* 0800-1200, 1400-1800 Monday-Saturday
*Currency:* 100 centimes = 1 franc malgache (Malagasy franc)
*Export/Import Information:* For books and advertising matter, customs and import duties, also unique tax. Import license required.
*Copyright:* Berne, Florence (see Copyright Conventions, pg xi)

**Editions Ambozontany**
c/o Librairie St Paul Ambatomena, BP 1170, Fianarantsoa 301
*Tel:* (07) 50027; (07) 51441
*Key Personnel*
Man Dir: Justin Bethaz
Editorial: Nicola Giambrone
Sales: Jose Minien
Founded: 1962
Subjects: Ethnicity, History, Religion - Other, Social Sciences, Sociology

**Librairie Ambozontany**
BP 1170, 301 Fianarantsoa
*Tel:* (07) 50027; (07) 51441

**Maison d'Edition Protestante ANTSO+**
19 Lalana Venance Manifatra, Tananrive 101
Mailing Address: BP 660, Imarivolanitra Tananrive 101
*Tel:* (022) 20886 *Fax:* (022) 26372
*E-mail:* fjkm@dts.mg *Cable:* FIJEKRIMA ANTSO
*Key Personnel*
Man Dir: Hans Andriamampianina
Founded: 1966

Subjects: Biblical Studies, Developing Countries, Education, Journalism, Literature, Literary Criticism, Essays, Religion - Protestant
Number of titles published annually: 6 Print
Total Titles: 13 Print
*Bookshop(s):* Bookshop Antso, Lot IIB 18, Totohabato Ranavalona 1, Tananarive 101 *Tel:* (022) 347 10; Librairie ANTSO, rue Bertho Anjoma, Toamasina 501 *Tel:* 33944

**Centre National de Production de Materiel Didactique (CNAPMAD)**
BP 665, Ankorondrano, Antananarivo 101
*Tel:* (02) 289-54 *Fax:* (02) 200-53
*Key Personnel*
Manager: Mr Jersin Manjato Razafimahefa

**CNAPMAD**, see Centre National de Production de Materiel Didactique (CNAPMAD)

**Foibe Filan-Kevitry NY Mpampianatra (FOFIPA)**
BP 202, Antananarivo 101
Mailing Address: rue Jean Andriamady Faravohitra, Antananarivo
*Tel:* (02) 27500 *Fax:* (02) 35788
Subjects: Accounting, Agriculture, Cookery, English as a Second Language
Distributed by Les Libraries de Madagascar

**Government Printer (Imprimerie Nationale)**
BP 38, Ambatomena, Tananrive 101
*Tel:* (02) 23675

**JEAG**
120 rue Rainandriamampandry, 101 Antananarivo
*Tel:* (02022) 24141 *Fax:* (02022) 20397
*Key Personnel*
Director: Harilala Adrianarimanana
ISBN Prefix(es): 2-910885
*Parent Company:* Jureco SA
Distributor for Foi & Justice

**Librarie Mixte**
37 rue 26 Jona 1960 Analakely, 101 Tananrive
Mailing Address: BP 3204, 101 Tananrive
*Tel:* (02) 25130 *Fax:* (02) 25130

**Madagascar Print & Press Company+**
rue Rabesahala - Antsakaviro, Tananrive 101
Mailing Address: BP 953, Tananrive 101
*Tel:* (02) 22526 *Fax:* (02) 2234534
*E-mail:* roi@dts.mg
*Key Personnel*
Man Dir, Editorial: Georges Ranaivosoa
Founded: 1969
*Sales, Publicity:* Societe CEMOI.
Subjects: History, Literature, Literary Criticism, Essays
Imprints: Editions Revue de l'Ocean Indien
Subsidiaries: Communication et Media - Ocean Indien (Societe CEMOI)
*Sales Office(s):* Societe CEMOI

**MADPRINT**, see Madagascar Print & Press Company

**Societe Malgache d'Edition+**
Route des Hydrocarbures, Ankorondrano, 101 Tananrive
Mailing Address: BP 659, 101 Tananrive
*Tel:* (02) 2222635 *Fax:* (02) 2222254
*E-mail:* tribune@bow.dts.mg
*Telex:* 22340 RAMEX MG TANANARIVE
*Key Personnel*
Man Dir: Rahaga Ramaholimihaso
Founded: 1943
Subjects: Communications, Economics, Education, Finance, Journalism, Law
Imprints: SME

**Musee d'Art et d'Archaeologie**
Universite de Madagascar, 17 rue Dr Villette, Isoraka, Tananrive 101
Mailing Address: BP 564, Tananrive 101
*Tel:* (02) 21047 *Fax:* (02) 28218
*E-mail:* musedar@syfed.refer.mg
*Key Personnel*
Dir: Dr J A Rakotoarisoa
Subjects: Travel

**Editions Revue de l'Ocean Indien**, *imprint of* Madagascar Print & Press Company

**SME**, *imprint of* Societe Malgache d'Edition

**Imprimerie Takariva**
rue Radley Antanimena, Tananrive 101
Mailing Address: BP 1029, Tananrive
*Tel:* (02) 23856
*Key Personnel*
Man Dir: Paul Rapatsalahy
Founded: 1933
Subjects: Fiction

**Trano Printy Fiangonana Loterana Malagasy (TPFLM)-(Imprimerie Lutherienne)**
Imprint of Fiangonana Loterana Malagasy
9 ave Grandidier Isoraka, 101 Tananrive
Mailing Address: BP 538, Tananrive 101
*Tel:* (020) 223340 *Fax:* (020) 262643
*E-mail:* impluth@dts.mg
*Key Personnel*
Man Dir: Raymond Randrianatoandro *Tel:* 2224569
Editorial: Pastor Samoela Georges
Founded: 1877
Membership(s): F L M, Union Professionnelle Des Imprimeurs De Madagascar.
Subjects: Fiction, Religion - Other
Number of titles published annually: 100 Print
*Associate Companies:* Fiangonana Loterana Malagasy, BP 1741, 101 Tananrive, Contact: Raymond Randrianatoandro *Tel:* 022 24569
*Bookshop(s):* Analakely & Antsahamanitra
*Distribution Center:* BP 533, 101 Tananrive

**Tsileondriaka Edition**
Lot II M 79 Andravoahangy, Tananrive 101
Mailing Address: BP 1239, Tananrive 101
*Tel:* (02) 31033; (02) 30659 *Fax:* (02) 31033

**Tsipika Edition**
48 rue Ny Havana-Antsahabe, Tananrive 101
*Tel:* (02) 24595
*Key Personnel*
Manager: Claude Rabenoro
Founded: 1990
Subjects: Environmental Studies, History
Distributed by Harmattan (France)

# Malawi

## General Information

*Capital:* Lilongwe
*Language:* English and Chichewa
*Religion:* About 50% Christian (Roman Catholic and Presbyterian), some Islamic and Hindu, remainder traditional beliefs
*Population:* 9.6 million
*Bank Hours:* 0800-1300 Monday-Friday; Saturday closed
*Shop Hours:* 0730 or 0800-1600 or 1700 Monday-Friday (with some closing for lunch); until midday Saturday
*Currency:* 100 tambala = 1 Malawi kwacha

*Export/Import Information:* No tariff on books; some advertising matter subject to duty. Import license required on certain category of goods. Exchange controls.
*Copyright:* UCC, Berne (see Copyright Conventions, pg xi)

**Central Africana Ltd+**
PO Box 631, Blantyre
*Tel:* 631509; 243595 *Fax:* 622236
*E-mail:* africana@sdwp.org.mw
*Key Personnel*
Chairman & Publisher: Frank M I Johnston
  *Tel:* 821316
Founded: 1989
Subjects: History, Travel
ISBN Prefix(es): 99908-14
Number of titles published annually: 3 Print
Total Titles: 15 Print
*Branch Office(s)*
A231 St Martini Gardens, Queen Victoria St, Cape Town 8000, South Africa
  *Tel:* (021) 4243595 *Fax:* (021) 4243595
  *E-mail:* africana@iafrica.com
Foreign Rep(s): Struik & Southern Book Publishers (South Africa)

**Christian Literature Association in Malawi**
PO Box 503, Blantyre
*Tel:* 620839; 673091
*Key Personnel*
General Manager: J T Matenje
Sales Manager: E C Mtumbati
Founded: 1968
Subjects: Biography, Fiction, History, Poetry, Regional Interests, Religion - Other
ISBN Prefix(es): 99908-16

**Dzuka Publishing Co Ltd** (Rise Publishing Co Ltd)
Private Bag 39, Blantyre
*Tel:* (01) 672548; (01) 670637 *Fax:* (01) 671114; (01) 670021
*E-mail:* dzuka@malawi.net
*Telex:* 44112 AFNEWSMI
*Key Personnel*
General Manager: Iness Malemia
Founded: 1975
Publisher of educational & other materials.
Subjects: Agriculture, Biography, Business, Education, Fiction, Geography, Geology, History, Mathematics
ISBN Prefix(es): 99908-17
Total Titles: 150 Print
*Parent Company:* Blantyre Printing & Publishing Co Ltd

**Government Printer (Imprimerie Nationale)**
PO Box 37, Zomba
*Tel:* (050) 525155 *Fax:* (050) 52230133
*Telex:* 45162 Geoprint MI
ISBN Prefix(es): 99908-20

**Popular Publications+**
PO Box 5592, Limbe
*Tel:* 651 833 *Fax:* 651 17133
*E-mail:* mpp@malawi.net
*Telex:* 44814 Montfort Ml
*Key Personnel*
General Manager, Publisher, Rights & Permissions: Vales Machila
Editorial: Prince C Shonga
Sales: M Kapelewera
Production: H Chinawa
Founded: 1976
Subjects: Biblical Studies, Fiction
ISBN Prefix(es): 99908-29
*Parent Company:* Montfort Press, PO Box 5592, Limbe
*Bookshop(s):* Moni Bookshop, PO Box 5592, Limbe

# Malaysia

## General Information

*Capital:* Kuala Lumpur
*Language:* Bahasa Malaysia (based on Malay) is official language; English widely used; Chinese, Tamil and Iban also spoken
*Religion:* Islam predominates, there is a large Buddhist group among the Chinese, Hindu among the Indians
*Population:* 18.4 million
*Bank Hours:* West Malaysia (some states observe Muslim weekly holiday): 1000-1500 Monday-Friday; 0930-1130 Saturday. Sabah: 0800-1200, 1400-1500 Monday-Friday; 0900-1100 Saturday. Sarawak: 1000-1500 Monday-Friday; 0930-1130 Saturday
*Shop Hours:* West Malaysia varies; average 0830-1830 Monday-Saturday. Sabah: 0800-1830 Monday-Saturday. Sarawak: 0900-1800 Monday-Friday; 0900-1300 Saturday
*Currency:* 100 sen = 1 ringgit or Malaysian dollar
*Export/Import Information:* No tariff on books. Advertising matter dutied per lb, subject to CIF surtax. No obscene literature allowed. Import licenses required only in Sabah, for books not having the name, printer and publisher on first or last printed page. No exchange controls.
*Copyright:* Berne (see Copyright Conventions, pg xi)

**S Abdul Majeed & Co+**
7 Jalan 3/82B, Bangsar Utama, Off Jalan Bangsar, 59000 Kuala Lumpur
*Tel:* (03) 283-2230 *Fax:* (03) 282-5670
*Key Personnel*
Man Partner: Peer Mohamed Majid
  *E-mail:* peer@pc.jaring.my
Founded: 1952
Subjects: Asian Studies, Child Care & Development, Cookery, English as a Second Language, Health, Nutrition, Management, Marketing, Religion - Islamic, Travel
ISBN Prefix(es): 983-9629; 983-9550; 983-136; 983-899
Imprints: Malaysia Heritage Series
*Branch Office(s)*
35, Jalan Sekerat Off Tranofer Rd, 10050 Pinang
*Showroom(s):* 107c, Jalan Rajalaut, 50350 Kuala Lumpur

**Academia Publications P Ltd**
22, Jalan Bukit Bintang, 55100 Kuala Lumpur
*Tel:* (03) 572455
ISBN Prefix(es): 967-9925

**Pustaka Aman Press Sdn Bhd**
4200A, Jalan Sultan Yahya Putra, Simpang Tiga Tellpot, 15150 Kota Bahru, Kelantan
*Tel:* (09) 7443681 *Fax:* (09) 7487064
ISBN Prefix(es): 983-867

**Amiza Associate Malaysia Sdn Bhd+**
71 Jalan SS 6/12, Kelana Jaya, 47301 Petaling Jaya, Selangor Darul Ehsan
*Tel:* (03) 78036100 *Fax:* (03) 78036100
*Key Personnel*
Marketing Manager: Jeremy Thor
Founded: 1982
Membership(s): Malaysian Book Publishers Association.
Subjects: Business, Education
ISBN Prefix(es): 967-966
*Parent Company:* Johor State Economic Development Corporation, Johor Bahru

**AMK Interaksi Sdn Bhd+**
NO7, Jalan 3/82 B Bangsar Utama, Off Jalan Bangsar, 59200 Kuala Lumpur

*Tel:* (03) 215306 *Fax:* (03) 718067
*Telex:* MA 30226 MAHIR
*Key Personnel*
President: Miss Chin Choo Yuen
Founded: 1988
ISBN Prefix(es): 983-9617; 983-99555
*Parent Company:* Mahir Holdings Sdn Bhd
*Shipping Address:* Master Agencies Sdn Bhd, 110 Jl 27, Kawasan 16, Sungei Rasa, 41300 Kelang
*Warehouse:* 28, Jl SS26/13 Taman Mayang Jaya, 47301 Petaling Jaya

**Pustaka Antara**
UG 10-13, Kompleks Wilayah, Jl Munshi Abdullah, 50100 Kuala Lumpur
*Tel:* (03) 26980044 *Fax:* (03) 26917997
*Telex:* MA 28140 *Cable:* Antara
ISBN Prefix(es): 967-937

**Associated Educational Distributors (M) Sdn Bhd+**
550 Taman Melaka Raya, 75000 Melaka
*Tel:* (06) 2844786 *Fax:* (06) 2844697
Subjects: Fiction
ISBN Prefix(es): 967-948

**Berita Publishing Sdn Bhd**
Desa Business Park, Taman Desa, 16-20 Jalan 4/109E, 59100 Kuala Lumpur
*Tel:* (03) 7620 8111 *Fax:* (03) 7620 8026
*Web Site:* www.beritapublishing.com.my
*Telex:* MA 30259
*Key Personnel*
Senior General Manager: Swaminathan Mv
  *E-mail:* swami@beritapub.com.my
Editor-in-Chief: Datuk A Kadir Jasin
  *E-mail:* akadirjasin@beritapub.com.my
Senior Editor: Ibrahim Yahaya *E-mail:* tiger@beritapub.com.my
Senior Manager, Ads & Promotions: Vs Ganesan
  *E-mail:* ganesan@beritapub.com.my
Senior Manager, Circulation: Mohd Azizi Bin Puteh *E-mail:* azizi@beritapub.com.my
Founded: 1973
Subjects: Business, Cookery, Education, Fiction
ISBN Prefix(es): 967-969; 983-99124
*Parent Company:* The New Straits Times Press (Malaysia) Berhad Balai Berita, 31 Jalan Riong, Kuala Lumpur 22-03
Subsidiaries: Berita Book Centre Sdn Bhd; Berita Distributors Sdn Bhd

**Biro Penyediaan Teks Itm (Biroteks)+**
Institut Teknologi Mara, 40450 Shah Alam, Selangor Darul Ehsan
*Tel:* (03) 55164548 *Fax:* (03) 55163453
Founded: 1981
ISBN Prefix(es): 967-958

**Butterworths**, *imprint of* Malayan Law Journal Sdn Bhd

**Castle**, *imprint of* Glad Sounds Sdn Bhd

**Darulfikir+**
329-B Jl Abd Rahman Idris off Jl Raja Muda, 50300 Kuala Lumpur
*Tel:* (03) 2981636; (03) 26913892 *Fax:* (03) 26928757
*E-mail:* e-mel@darulfikir.com.my
*Web Site:* www.darulfikir.com.my
*Telex:* MA 31533 Action
*Key Personnel*
Man Dir: Mohamad Ahmad
Founded: 1984
Subjects: Education, Language Arts, Linguistics, Religion - Islamic
ISBN Prefix(es): 983-99583; 983-9668

Number of titles published annually: 40 Print
Total Titles: 1,700 Print

**Pustaka Delta Pelajaran Sdn Bhd+**
Member of Delta Publishing Group
Lot 18 Jl 51A/223, Wisma Delta, 46100 Petaling
Jaya, Selangor Darul Ehsan
*Tel:* (03) 7570000 *Fax:* (03) 7570001
*Telex:* MA20382 AB Delta
*Key Personnel*
Executive Dir: Ms Lee Yuet Yee
Man Dir: Mr Lim Swee Sing; Mr Lim Kim Wah
Group General Manager: Mr Phang Sang Choy;
Mr Phang Sang Moi
Founded: 1979
Subjects: Economics, English as a Second Lan-
guage, Environmental Studies, Geography,
Geology, History, Mathematics, Religion - Is-
lamic, Science (General)
ISBN Prefix(es): 967-67
Subsidiaries: Baron Production Sdn Bhd; Delta
Editions Sdn Bhd; Delta Distributors Sdn Bhd;
Delta Publishing Sdn Bhd; Gedung Ilum Sdn
Bhd; Gunung Mutiara Sdn Bhd; Penerbit Jayat-
inta Sdn Bhd; Tempo Publishing (M) Sdn Bhd
*Branch Office(s)*
No 174 Jalan Pasar, 41400 Kelang, Selangor
Darul Ehsan

**Dewan Bahasa dan Pustaka+**
Jl Dewan Bahasa, 50460 Kuala Lumpur
*Tel:* (03) 21481011 *Fax:* (03) 21447248
*Web Site:* www.dbp.gov.my *Cable:* Bahasa
*Key Personnel*
Dir General: Dato Haji A Aziz Deraman *Tel:* (03)
2486785; (03) 21485656 *E-mail:* aziz@dbp.
gov.my
Dir, Publishing: Dato Anuar Rethwan *Tel:* (03)
2488136; (03) 21482230 *Fax:* (03) 2449614
*E-mail:* anuar@dbp.gov.my
Rights & Licensing: Othman Ismail
*E-mail:* othman@dbp.gov.my
Founded: 1956
Specialize in Malay language & linguistics,
Malay literature & Malay culture.
ISBN Prefix(es): 983-62
Number of titles published annually: 300 Print
*Branch Office(s)*
Dewan Bahasa dan Pustaka Cawangan Sabah, PO
Box 149, Teluk Likas, 88999 Kota Kinabalu,
Sabah, Contact: Hamzah Hamdani *Tel:* (088)
439217; (088) 439316 *Fax:* (088) 439732;
(088) 439314
Dewan Bahasa dan Pustaka Cawangan Sarawak,
PO Box 1390, 93728 Kuching, Sarawak,
Contact: Zaini Oje *Tel:* (082) 444706; (082)
444711 *Fax:* (082) 444707
Dewan Bahasa dan Pustaka Wilayah Sela-
tan, Larkin Perdana Business Park, No 1-3,
Jalan Susur Dewata I, Johor Bharu, Johor,
Zubaidi Abas *Tel:* (07) 2361616; (07) 2358686
*Fax:* (07) 2358686
Dewan Bahasa dan Pustaka Wilayah Timur, Jalan
Abdul Kadir Adabi, Lot PT 107-109, Kota
Bharu, Kelantan, Contact: Sallehuddin Abang
Shokeran *Tel:* (09) 7475656 *Fax:* (09) 7475252
Dewan Bahasa dan Pustaka Wilayah Utara, No
31, Lorong PS 2, Bandar Perda, 14000 Bukit
Mertajam, Pulau Pinang, Contact: Mohamad
Yussop Ishak *Tel:* (04) 6211011 *Fax:* (04)
6211013; (04) 621914

**Dewan Pustaka Islam+**
10-2-1, Jln 14/22, 46100 Petaling Jaya, Selangor
Darul Ehsan
*Tel:* (03) 755 7225 *Fax:* (03) 755 7871
*Key Personnel*
Executive Chairman: Mohd Anuar Tahir
Man Dir: Ahmad Azam Abdul Rahman
Founded: 1971
Membership(s): Book Contractor Association of
Malaysia.

Subjects: Religion - Islamic
ISBN Prefix(es): 983-66
*Associate Companies:* Blue-T Sdn Bhd
Subsidiaries: Budaya Ilmu Sdn Bhd; Tradisi Ilmu
Sdn Bhd
Distributed by Cekap Edar; Hizbi
Distributor for Institut Kajan Dasar; Institute of
Strategic & International Studies (ISIS); Juta &
Co (South Africa); Universiti Malaya Publica-
tion
*Bookshop(s):* Tradisi Ilmu Sdn Bhd, 10-2 Corner
Jln 14/22, 46100 Petaling Jaya, Selangor Darul
Ehsan
*Warehouse:* Lot 1032, Jln Cempaka, Kg Sg Kayu
Ara, 47400 Damansara Utama

**Earlybird**, *imprint of* Federal Publications Sdn
Bhd

**Eastview Malaysiana Library**, *imprint of*
Eastview Productions Sdn Bhd

**Eastview Productions Sdn Bhd**
No 7, Jl BS 7/15, Kawasan, Perindustrian Bukit
Serdang, 43300 Seri Kembangan Selangor
*Tel:* (03) 89438866 *Fax:* (03) 89435675
*Key Personnel*
Man Dir: Johnny Ong
Founded: 1980
ISBN Prefix(es): 967-60
*Associate Companies:* Anthonian Store Sdn Bhd;
Pacific Book Centre, Singapore; Pan Pacific
Publications Pte Ltd, Singapore
Imprints: Eastview Malaysiana Library; Eastview
Visual Library

**Eastview Visual Library**, *imprint of* Eastview
Productions Sdn Bhd

**Fairy Tales**, *imprint of* Mecron Sdn Bhd

**Federal**, *imprint of* Federal Publications Sdn Bhd

**Federal Publications Sdn Bhd+**
Tingkat 1, Bangunan Times Publishing, Lot 46,
Subang Hi-Tech Industrial Park, Batu Tiga,
40000 Shah Alam, Selangor Darul Ehsan
*Tel:* (03) 7351511 *Fax:* (03) 73 64620
*E-mail:* kesoon@pc.jaring.my
*Key Personnel*
Vice President & General Manager: Stephen Lim
*Tel:* (03) 7364621
Founded: 1957
Subjects: Astronomy, Career Development, Child
Care & Development, Computer Science, Ed-
ucation, English as a Second Language, Gar-
dening, Plants, Mathematics, Science (General),
Self-Help, Sports, Athletics
Total Titles: 500 Print
*Parent Company:* Times Publishing Limited
*Associate Companies:* Federal Publications (HK)
Ltd, Hong Kong; Federal Publications (S) (Pte)
Ltd, Singapore
Imprints: Earlybird; Federal; Times
Divisions: Times Trade Direcories
*Shipping Address:* Federal Publications (HK) Ltd,
Hong Kong
*Warehouse:* Federal Publications (HK) Ltd, Hong
Kong
*Orders to:* Federal Publications (S) (Pte) Ltd, Sin-
gapore
Federal Publications (HK) Ltd, Hong Kong

**FEP International Sdn Bhd**
6 Jalan SS 4C/5, 47301 Petaling Jaya, Selangor
Darul Ehsan
Mailing Address: PO Box 1091, Petaling Jaya,
Selangor Darul Ehsan
*Tel:* (03) 7036150; (03) 7036152; (03) 7036154
*Fax:* (03) 7036989 *Cable:* BOOKMARK

*Key Personnel*
Man Dir: Mok Hai Lim
ISBN Prefix(es): 967-63
*Associate Companies:* FEP International Pvt Ltd,
Singapore

**Forum Publications+**
11 Jalan 11-4E, 46200 Petaling Jaya, Selangor
Darul Ehsan
*Tel:* (03) 7554007 *Fax:* (03) 7561879
*E-mail:* g2jomo@umcsd.um.edu.my
*Key Personnel*
President: Abdul Karim Hassan
Marketing Dir: Tong-Sin Chong
Founded: 1978
Subjects: Anthropology, Developing Countries,
Economics, Government, Political Science,
History, Labor, Industrial Relations, Regional
Interests, Religion - Islamic
ISBN Prefix(es): 983-876
*Parent Company:* Institute of Social Analysis (IN-
SAN)
*Associate Companies:* Malaysian Social Science
Association
Subsidiaries: Ikraq

**Geetha Publishers Sdn Bhd**
13A Jalan Kovil Hilir, 51100 Kuala Lumpur
*Tel:* (03) 40417073 *Fax:* (03) 40417073
*Key Personnel*
Man Dir: Soma Narayanan
Subjects: Education, History, How-to, Publishing
& Book Trade Reference
ISBN Prefix(es): 983-9594

**Glad Sounds Sdn Bhd+**
20 Jalan SS 21/35, Damansara Utama, 47400
Petaling Jaya, Selangor Darul Ehsan
*Tel:* (03) 7562901; (03) 7556442 *Fax:* (03)
7560528
*E-mail:* gladsnd@po.jaring.my
*Key Personnel*
General Manager: Peter Khong
Founded: 1976
Subjects: Management, Religion - Other, Self-
Help
ISBN Prefix(es): 983-897
Imprints: Castle
*Branch Office(s)*
Jaya Shopping Centre
Kota Raya Complex
Yik Foong Complex

**Holograms (M) Sdn Bhd+**
6, Jorong Bukit Pantai Satu, 59100 Kuala Lumpur
*Tel:* (03) 2824002 *Fax:* (03) 2822751
*Key Personnel*
International Rights: Chuah Guat Eng
Founded: 1994
Subjects: Developing Countries, Ethnicity, Fiction
ISBN Prefix(es): 983-9132

**IBS Buku Sdn Bhd**
24 20/16A-06, PJ Industrial Park, Jalan Ken-
najuan, 46300 Petaling Jaya, Selangor Darul
Ehsan
*Tel:* (03) 7751763; (03) 775-1566; (03) 7760514
*Fax:* (03) 79576026; (03) 776-8551
*E-mail:* ibsbuku@po.jaring.my
*Key Personnel*
Man Dir, Production, Rights & Permissions: M N
Meera
Editorial: Miss Chong
Dir, Sales & Publicity: Mohamed Mustafa
Founded: 1972
Subjects: Career Development
ISBN Prefix(es): 967-950
Subsidiaries: Pelanduk Publications (M) Sdn Bhd

**International Book Service**, see IBS Buku Sdn
Bhd

**International Law Book Services+**
10 Jalan PJU 8/5G, Damansara Perdana, 47820
Petaling Jaya, Selangor
Mailing Address: PO Box 11664, 50752 Kuala
Lumpur
*Tel:* (03) 7727 4121; (03) 7727 4122; (03) 7727
3890; (03) 7728-3890 *Fax:* (03) 7727 3884
*E-mail:* gbc@pc.jaring.my
*Web Site:* www.malaysialawbooks.com
*Key Personnel*
Sole Proprietor: Syed Ibrahim
Founded: 1981
Publishes the *Malaysian Law Statutes* & other
general titles pertaining to law.
Membership(s): Malaysian Book Publishers Asso-
ciation.
Subjects: Law
ISBN Prefix(es): 967-89; 967-9960
Number of titles published annually: 75 Print
Total Titles: 950 Print; 1 CD-ROM

**Jabatan Penerbitan Universiti Malaya**, see
University of Malaya, Department of
Publications

**K Publishing & Distributors Sdn Bhd+**
Stadium Shah Alam, Aras 1, Quadron B, Seksyen
13, 40000 Shah Alam, Selangor
*Tel:* (03) 5501755; (03) 5501442 *Fax:* (03)
5501826
*Telex:* MA 30226 MAHIR
*Key Personnel*
President: En Ahmad Mahir Kamaruddin
Founded: 1985
Subjects: Fiction
ISBN Prefix(es): 967-9906; 983-852
*Parent Company:* Mahir Holdings Sdn Bhd
*Shipping Address:* Master Agencies Sdn Bhd, 110
Jl 27, Kawasan 16, Sungei Rasa, 41300 Kelang
*Warehouse:* 28, Jl SS26/13 Taman Mayang Jaya,
47301 Petaling Jaya, Selangor

**Kharisma Publications Sdn Bhd**
22 Jl USJ 9/5P, Subang Business Centre, 47620
Subang Jaya
*Tel:* (03) 724660 *Fax:* (03) 724602
ISBN Prefix(es): 983-050
*Parent Company:* Moy Publications Sdn Bhd

**Lamina Series**, *imprint of* Mecron Sdn Bhd

**Little Board Books**, *imprint of* Mecron Sdn Bhd

**Mahir Publications Sdn Bhd+**
39 Jln Nilam, 1/2 Taman Teknologi Tinggi
Swoang, 40000 Shah Alam, Selangor
*Tel:* (03) 56379044 *Fax:* (03) 56379048
*Telex:* MA30226MAHIR
*Key Personnel*
Man Dir: Ahmad Mahir Kamaruddin
Publishing Manager: Choo Yuen Chin
Founded: 1990
Specialize in school titles.
Subjects: Education, English as a Second Lan-
guage
ISBN Prefix(es): 983-70
*Parent Company:* Mahir Holdings Sdn Bhd
Subsidiaries: Quill Publishers
*Shipping Address:* Master Agencies Sdn Bhd, 110
Jalan 27, Kawasan 16, Sungai Rasa, 41300 Ke-
lang
*Warehouse:* Taman Mayang Jaya, 28 Jalan SS 26/
16, 47310 Petaling Jaya

**Malaya Books Suppliers Co**
272-E Jalan Air Itam, 11400 Ayer Itam Penang
*Tel:* (04) 8284430
*Key Personnel*
Manager: Tony Lau
ISBN Prefix(es): 983-835

**Malaya Educational Supplies Sdn Bhd**
306, Block C, Glomac Business Centre, 10, JISS
6/1 Kelana Jaya, 47301 Petaling Jaya, Selangor
*Tel:* (03) 7046628 *Fax:* (03) 7046629
Subjects: Education
ISBN Prefix(es): 967-9923

**The Malaya Press Sdn Bhd**
6 Jalan TPK 1/4, Taman Perindustrian Kinrara,
58200 Kuala Lumpur
*Tel:* (03) 5755890; (03) 5757817 *Fax:* (03)
5757194
*Key Personnel*
Man Dir: Lai Wing Chun
Editorial: Yiu Hong
Sales: Chong Tim Seng
Founded: 1958
Subjects: Education
ISBN Prefix(es): 967-934
*Parent Company:* Union Cultural Organization
Sdn Bhd, 10 Jalan 217, Petaling Jaya
*Associate Companies:* Hong Kong Cultural Press
Ltd, 9 College Rd, Kowloon, Hong Kong; Sin-
gapore Press (Pte) Ltd, 303 North Bridge Rd,
Singapore 7, Singapore
*Bookshop(s):* Ipoh Book Co, 75 Market St, Ipoh,
Perak; Malaya Book Co, 22-24 Jalan Bukit
Bintang, Kuala Lumpur

**Malayan Law Journal Sdn Bhd**
Member of The LexisNexis Group
Unit A5-1, 5th floor, Wisma HB, Megan II
Ave, 12 Jalan Yap Kwan Seng, 50450 Kuala
Lumpur
*Tel:* (03) 2162 2822 *Fax:* (03) 2162 3811
*Web Site:* www.mlj.com.my
*Key Personnel*
Managing Editor, New Product Development:
Julie Anne Thomas
Commissioning Editor: Prema Arumugam
Sales Dir: Ronald Tan
Area Sales Manager: Lawrence Tan
Commercial Dir: Pook Li Ping
Fulfillment Manager: Chow Wai Leng
Founded: 1932
Subjects: Law
ISBN Prefix(es): 967-962
*Associate Companies:* Butterworths Hong Kong,
12/F, Hennessy Centre, 500 Hennessy Rd,
Causeway Bay, Hong Kong, Commission-
ing Editor: Anisha Sakhrani *Tel:* 2965 1400
*Fax:* 2976 0840 *Web Site:* www.butterworths-
hk.com; Butterworths India, Vijaya Bldg,
14th floor, 17, Barakhamba Rd, New Delhi
110001, India, Publishing Manager: Ambika
Nair *Tel:* (011) 373 9614 *Fax:* (011) 332 6456
*Web Site:* www.butterworths-india.com; But-
terworths Singapore, No 1 Temasek Ave, 17-
01 Millenia Tower, Singapore 039192, Singapore, Regional Publishing Dir: Conita Leung
*Tel:* 336 9661 *Fax:* 336 9662 *Web Site:* www.
butterworths.com.sg
Imprints: MLJ; Butterworths
*Shipping Address:* No 3, Jalan PJS 11/20, Bandar Sunway, 46150 Petaling Jaya, Selangor
*Tel:* (03) 733 1893 *Fax:* (03) 733 1823
*Warehouse:* No 4, Lot 752, Jalan Subang 3,
Taman Perindustrian Subang, 47610 Subang
Jaya, Selangor Darul Ehsan, Warehouse Manager: Patrick Lee *Tel:* (03) 5636 1740
*Orders to:* No 3, Jalan PJS 11/20, Bandar Sun-
way, 46150 Petaling Jaya, Selangor *Tel:* (03)
733 1893 *Fax:* (03) 733 1823

**Malaysia Heritage Series**, *imprint of* S Abdul
Majeed & Co

**The Malaysian Current Law Journal Sdn
Bhd+**
Jalan Selaman 1/2, E1-2, 2nd floor, Dataran
Palma, 68000 Ampang
*Tel:* (03) 42705400 *Fax:* (03) 42705402

*E-mail:* rahim@cljlaw.com
*Web Site:* www.cljlaw.com
*Key Personnel*
Chief Editor: Gan Peng Chiang
Man Dir: Abdul Latiff Ibrahim
Founded: 1981
Subjects: Law
ISBN Prefix(es): 983-9680

**MDC Publishers Printers Sdn Bhd+**
2717 & 2718, Wisma MDC, Jalan Permata Em-
pat, Taman Permata, Ulu Kelang, 53300 Kuala
Lumpur
*Tel:* (03) 41086600 *Fax:* (03) 41081506
*E-mail:* mdcpp@mdcpp.com.my
*Web Site:* www.mdcpp.com.my
*Key Personnel*
Dir: Tajuddin Husain
Marketing Executive: Ameer Hussain; Ahmed
Hussain
Founded: 1976
Reprinting & translation of foreign publications &
co-publishing with foreign publishers.
Membership(s): Malaysian Book Publishers As-
sociation; Malaysian Booksellers Association;
Malaysian Book Importers Association.
Subjects: Business, Economics, Law, Manage-
ment
Number of titles published annually: 300 Print
*Branch Office(s)*
L3-04, 3rd floor, Shaw Parade, Changkat Thambi
Dollah, Kuala Lumpur *Tel:* (03) 2457745
Distributor for International Labour Organiza-
tion (ILO); Japan External Trade Organization
(JETRO); UNESCO; United Nations; World
Bank; World Intellectual Property Organization
(WIPO); World Trade Organization

**Mecron Sdn Bhd+**
No B5-3 Binova Ind Center, No 1 Jalan 2/57 B,
51200 Kuala Lumpur
*Tel:* (016) 280 8772 *Fax:* (03) 6251 9869
*Web Site:* www.mecronbooks.com *Cable:*
MECROMAN KUALA LUMPUR
*Key Personnel*
Chief Executive: Dr Y Mansoor Marican
*E-mail:* nmansoor@tm.net.my
Dir: Zaliha B Samsudeen
Founded: 1984
Specialize in children's books; also act as pack-
ager.
ISBN Prefix(es): 983-9072; 983-9556; 983-9387
Imprints: Fairy Tales; Lamina Series; Little Board
Books; See & Read Series; Well Loved Tales
*Warehouse:* Binova No B5-3, No 1, Jalan 2/57B
(Segambut), 51200 Kuala Lumpur

**Pustaka Melayu Baru**
U0213 Jl Bahasa, PO Box 107, 87008 Labuan
Wilayan Persekutuan
*Tel:* (03) 087-413615 *Fax:* (03) 087-412184
ISBN Prefix(es): 967-9931

**Minerva Publications**
96 Jalan Dato' Bandar, Tunggal, 70000 Serem-
ban, Negeri Sembilan
*Tel:* (06) 734439 *Fax:* (06) 734439
*Key Personnel*
Man Dir: Haji Tajuddin MS
Founded: 1964
Subjects: Business, Career Development, English
as a Second Language, Religion - Islamic, Self-
Help
ISBN Prefix(es): 983-68
*Parent Company:* News & Periodicals Store

**MLJ**, *imprint of* Malayan Law Journal Sdn Bhd

**Oscar Book International+**
37A Jl 20-16, Paramount Garden, 46300 Petaling
Jaya, Selangor Darul Ehsan

*Tel:* (03) 7753515; (03) 7762797 *Fax:* (03) 7762797
*Key Personnel*
Proprietor: Windfred Chee Moon Hock
Founded: 1980
Specialize in English & Malay.
Subjects: Language Arts, Linguistics
ISBN Prefix(es): 967-941
Total Titles: 120 Print

**Pan Malayan Publishing Co Sdn Bhd**
72C, Jalan Sungai Besi, 57100 Kuala Lumpur
*Tel:* (603) 7910420 *Fax:* (603) 92214333
*Key Personnel*
Contact: Yeoh Suh Shyun
ISBN Prefix(es): 967-922

**Panther Publishing**
130-1 Jalan Thamby Abdullah, 50470 Kuala Lumpur
*Tel:* (03) 2749854
*Key Personnel*
Chief Executive, Publicity: R Vijesurier
Editorial, Production: Bella Mary Peters
Sales: Mary Rajam
Founded: 1972
Subjects: Travel
ISBN Prefix(es): 983-99627
*Branch Office(s)*
Block 151, No 650-K, Lorong 4, Toa Payoh, Singapore 1231, Singapore

**Parry's Press**
60 Jalan Negara, Taman Melawati, 58100 Kuala Lumpur
*Tel:* (03) 4079179 *Fax:* (03) 4079180
*E-mail:* haja@pop.3.jaring.my
*Telex:* Parry's MA 33243 *Cable:* PABOKCENT
ISBN Prefix(es): 983-9342
Subsidiaries: Parry's Book Center Pte Ltd (Singapore)
*Orders to:* 528-A MacPherson Rd, Singapore 368217, Singapore

**Pearson Education Malaysia Sdn Bhd+**
Lot 2, Jalan 215, Off Jalan Templer, 46050 Petaling Jaya, Selangor Darul Ehsan
*Tel:* (03) 7782 0466; (03) 7782 0659; (03) 7782 0702 *Fax:* (03) 7781 8005
*E-mail:* inquiry@pearsoned.com.my
*Web Site:* www.pearson.com
*Telex:* 37600
*Key Personnel*
General Manager/Dir, School Pub: Wong Mei Mei
General Manager/HE: Edward Teoh Swee Ong
Publishing Manager: Poh Swee Hiang
Finance Dir: Mok Chek Khek
Founded: 1961
Subjects: Literature, Literary Criticism, Essays, Mathematics, Physics, Science (General)
ISBN Prefix(es): 967-976
Number of titles published annually: 300 Print
Total Titles: 2,000 Print
*Parent Company:* Pearson Education
*Holding Company:* Addison Wesley

**Pelanduk Publications (M) Sdn Bhd+**
Subang Jaya Industrial Estate, 12, Jalan SS13/3E, 47500 Subang Jaya, Selangor Darul Ehsan
Mailing Address: PO Box 8265, 46785 Kelana Jaya, Selangor Darul Ehsan
*Tel:* (03) 56386573; (03) 56386885 *Fax:* (03) 56386577; (03) 56386575
*E-mail:* pelpub@tm.net.my
*Web Site:* www.pelanduk.com
*Key Personnel*
Man Dir, Production: Ng Tieh Chuan
Editorial: Chong Meow Lian
Sales & Publicity: Jackson Tan
Editorial: Woo Kum Wah

Contact: Ms M H Chong
Founded: 1984
Subjects: Biography, Business, Economics, Language Arts, Linguistics, Management, Religion - Islamic, Social Sciences, Sociology
ISBN Prefix(es): 967-978
Distributed by China Books (Australia); IBS Buku Sdn Bhd (Malaysia); National Book Store (Philippines); Peace Book Co Ltd (Hong Kong); Recreaids Pte Ltd (Singapore); Weatherhill Inc (US)
*Distribution Center:* Asia Books, Bahnhofstr 132, 69151 Neckargemund, Germany *Tel:* (06223) 6849 *Fax:* (06223) 72466 *E-mail:* chris.rieger@t-online.de
Asia Books Co Ltd, 5 Sukhumuit Rd, Soi 61, Bangkok 10110, Thailand *Tel:* (02) 3912680 *Fax:* (02) 3811621 *E-mail:* asiabook@comnet2.ksc.net.th
Australian Book Exports, 9/30 Pitt St, Parramatta, NSW 2150, Australia *Tel:* (02) 9687 8286 *Fax:* (02) 9687 8286 *E-mail:* dsoh@enternet.com.au
Combined Book Services, Units 1/K, Paddock Wood Dist. Centre, Paddock Wood, Tonbridge, Kent TN12 6UU, United Kingdom *Tel:* (01892) 837171 *Fax:* (01892) 837272 *E-mail:* orders@combook.co.uk
Ming Ya Books & Trade Co, PO Box 803, 1000 AV Amsterdam, Netherlands *Tel:* (070) 3651887 *Fax:* (070) 3652146
Pacific Century Distribution, G/F 2-, Lower Kai Yuen Lane, North Point, Hong Kong, Hong Kong *Tel:* 2811 5505 *Fax:* 2565 8624 *E-mail:* pcdltd@hknet.com
PT Gramedia Asri Media, Jl Gajah Mada 109, Jakarta 11140, Indonesia *Tel:* (021) 2601234 *Fax:* (021) 6337268
I J Sangun Enterprises, PO Box 4322, CPO Manilla 1099, Philippines *Tel:* (02) 6651946 *Fax:* (02) 6588466
United Publishers Services Ltd, Kenkyu-sha Bldg, 9 Kanda Surugadai 2-chome, Chiyoda-ku Tokyo, Japan *Tel:* (03) 3291-4541 *Fax:* (03) 3292-8610

**Pelangi Publishing Pte Ltd**, see Penerbitan Pelangi Sdn Bhd

**Penerbit Fajar Bakti Sdn Bhd+**
4 Jl Pemaju U1/15, Seksyen U1, Hicom Glenmarie Industrial Park, 40150 Shah Alam, Selangor
*Tel:* (03) 7047011 *Fax:* (03) 7047024
*Key Personnel*
Man Dir: M Sockalingam
Founded: 1969
ISBN Prefix(es): 967-65; 967-933
*Parent Company:* Oxford University Press, United Kingdom
Subsidiaries: South-East Asian Publishing Unit

**Penerbit Jayatinta Sdn Bhd+**
Member of Delta Publishing Group
No 18 Jalan 51A/223, 46100 Petaling Jaya, Selangor Darul Ehsan
*Tel:* (03) 7764036
*Telex:* MA20382 AB Delta
*Key Personnel*
Man Dir: Mr Lim Swee Sing; Mr Lim Kim Wah
Executive Dir: Ms Lee Yuet Yee
Group General Manager: Mr Phang Sang Choy; Mr Phang Sang Moi
Founded: 1988
Subjects: Economics, English as a Second Language, Environmental Studies, Geography, Geology, History, Philosophy, Religion - Islamic, Science (General)
ISBN Prefix(es): 983-883
Subsidiaries: Baron Production Sdn Bhd; Delta Distributors Sdn Bhd; Delta Editions Sdn Bh; Delta Publishing Sdn Bhd; Gedung Ilmu Sdn

Bhd; Gunung Mutiara Sdn Bhd; Pustaka Delta Pelajaran Sdn Bhd; Tempo Publishing (M) Sdn Bhd
*Branch Office(s)*
No 174 Jalan Pasar, 41400 Kelang, Selangor Darul Ehsan (factory)

**Penerbit Prisma Sdn Bhd+**
10 Jalan PJS 7/17 Bandar Sunway, 46150 Petaling Jaya, Selangor Darul Ehsan
*Tel:* (03) 56380541 *Fax:* (03) 56347250
*Key Personnel*
Man Dir: Wong Peng Khuen
Founded: 1986
ISBN Prefix(es): 983-9665; 983-99556; 983-823; 983-877

**Penerbit Universiti Sains Malaysia+**
d/a Perpustakaan Universiti Sains Malaysia, Minden, 11800 Pulau Pinang
*Tel:* (04) 6533888 *Fax:* (04) 6575714
*E-mail:* penerbitusm@notes.usm.my
*Web Site:* www.lib.usm.my/press
*Telex:* MA40254 *Cable:* UNISAINS
*Key Personnel*
Chairman: Prof Jamjan Rajikan
Secretary: Ms Rashidah Begum
*E-mail:* rashidah@usm.my
Chief Editor: Mr Akhiar Salleh *Tel:* (04) 6534422
*E-mail:* akhiar@notes.usm.my
Founded: 1974
Subjects: Biological Sciences, Chemistry, Chemical Engineering, Computer Science, Education, Electronics, Electrical Engineering, Management, Mathematics, Social Sciences, Sociology
*Bookshop(s):* Co-operative Bookshop Ltd, Universiti Sains Malaysia, d/a Perpustakaan Universiti Sains Malaysia, 11800 Pulau Pinang

**Penerbitan Jaya Bakti+**
No 28 & 30 Wisma Jaya Bakti, Jalan Cenderuh 2, Baut 4, Jalan Ipoh, 51200 Kuala Lumpur
*Tel:* (03) 62519399 *Fax:* (03) 62519585
*Key Personnel*
Man Dir: Silvaraju A L Kunjupillai
Founded: 1980
Membership(s): Malaysian Book Publishers Association.
ISBN Prefix(es): 967-900
*Showroom(s):* 30, Wisma Jaya Bakti, Jalan Cenderuh 2, Batu 4, Jalan Ipoh, 51200 Kuala Lumpur

**Penerbitan Pelangi Sdn Bhd+**
Jalan Pingai, Taman Pelangi, Johor Bahru, 80400 Johor Darul Takzim
*E-mail:* info@pelangibooks.com; ppsb@po.jaring.my
*Web Site:* www.pelangibooks.com
*Key Personnel*
Chief Executive Officer & Man Dir: Mr Sum Kown Cheek
Founded: 1979
Subjects: Art, English as a Second Language, Photography
ISBN Prefix(es): 967-951; 983-50; 983-878
Number of titles published annually: 200 Print
Total Titles: 8,000 Print
*Branch Office(s)*
Bangi, Selangor

**Institut Penyelidikan Minyak Kelapa Sawit Malaysia**
PO Box 10620, 50720 Kuala Lumpur
*Tel:* (03) 8335155; (03) 8259775 *Fax:* (03) 8259446
*E-mail:* pub@porim.gov.my
*Telex:* MA 31609
*Key Personnel*
Dir-General: Dr Yusof bin Basiron
ISBN Prefix(es): 967-961

**Perfect Frontier Sdn Bhd**
B201, Block B, No 11, Jalan Sepadu, Taman
United, Off Jalan Klang Lama, 58200 Kuala
Lumpur
*Tel:* (03) 7832926 *Fax:* (03) 7816448
ISBN Prefix(es): 983-865

**Preston Corporation Sdn Bhd**
18 Jalan 19/3, 46300 Petaling Jaya, Selangor
Darul Ehsan
*Tel:* (03) 7563734 *Fax:* (03) 7573607
*Telex:* Prest MA 37433
Subjects: Education
ISBN Prefix(es): 967-917; 983-158
*Associate Companies:* Preston Corporation (Pte)
Ltd, 9 Irving Pl, Singapore 1336, Singapore;
Times Educational Co Sdn Bhd; Vista Produc-
tions Ltd, A7/F Melbourne Industrial Bldg, 16
Westlands Rd, Quarry Bay, Hong Kong

**Pustaka Cipta Sdn Bhd+**
58 C Jalan Kampung Attap, 50460 Kuala Lumpur
*Tel:* (03) 2744593 *Fax:* (03) 2749588
*E-mail:* rrapc@pc.jaring.my
*Key Personnel*
President: Baharuddin Zainal
Publication Dir: Rosihan Juara Baharuddin
Founded: 1985
Membership(s): IKATAN, Malaysian Burriputra
Publishers Association.
Subjects: Art, Biography, Communications, Com-
puter Science, Education, English as a Second
Language, Fiction, Journalism, Literature, Lit-
erary Criticism, Essays, Nonfiction (General),
Poetry, Publishing & Book Trade Reference,
Religion - Islamic, Science (General), Science
Fiction, Fantasy, Technology, Travel, Women's
Studies
ISBN Prefix(es): 967-9974; 967-99962; 983-101
*Associate Companies:* Essential Mark (M) Sdn
Bhd; Puncak Indah Sdn Bhd
Subsidiaries: Dasar Buku Sdn Bhd; Dasar Cetak
Sdn Bhd; Dasar Padu Sdn Bhd

**Pustaka Sistem Pelajaran Sdn Bhd+**
17-22 Jl Satu, Ber Satu Industrial Park, Cheras
Jaya, 43200 Balakong, Selangor
*Tel:* (03) 904-7558; (03) 904-7017; (03) 904-7018
*Fax:* (03) 90747573
*Key Personnel*
Man Dir: Michael Ong
Founded: 1973
ISBN Prefix(es): 967-902
Subsidiaries: Pustaka Yakin Pelajar Sdn Bhd; B H
S Book Printing Sdn Bhd
*Bookshop(s):* The Bintang Store, 251 Jl Tun Sam-
banthan, 50470 Kuala Lumpur

**SBT Professional Publications**
Menara Summit, 10th floor, 14-20, Jl Hang Lekir,
47600 Persiaran Kewajipan
*Tel:* (03) 80265811; (03) 80235663 *Fax:* (03)
8023566; (03) 80265999
*E-mail:* admin@sbtpp.com
*Web Site:* www.sbtpp.com
*Key Personnel*
Editor: Vivien Khoo
Manager: Ah Tu Yeoh
Founded: 1985
Membership(s): Malaysian Book Publishers Asso-
ciation.
Subjects: Accounting
ISBN Prefix(es): 967-9924

**See & Read Series**, *imprint of* Mecron Sdn Bhd

**Syarikat Cultural Supplies Sdn Bhd+**
306 Block C Glomac Business Centre, 10 Jalan
556/1, Kelana Jaya, 47301 Selangor Darul
Ehsan

*Tel:* (03) 7046628; (03) 7554103; (03) 7915728
*Fax:* (03) 7046629
*E-mail:* malian@po.jaring.my
*Key Personnel*
Dir: Kow Ching Chuan
Founded: 1977
Subjects: Education
ISBN Prefix(es): 967-9917

**Tempo Publishing (M) Sdn Bhd+**
Member of Delta Publishing Group
Bilik 118, Wisma Delta 18, Jalan 51A/223, 46100
Petaling Jaya, Selangor Darul Ehsan
*Tel:* (03) 7570000 *Fax:* (03) 7576688; (03)
7587001
*Telex:* MA20382 AB Delta
*Key Personnel*
Man Dir: Mr Lim Swee Sing; Mr Lim Kim Wah
Executive Dir: Ms Lee Yuet Yee
Group General Manager: Mr Phang Sang Choy;
Mr Phang Sang Moi
Founded: 1990
Subjects: Fiction, Literature, Literary Criticism,
Essays, Nonfiction (General)
ISBN Prefix(es): 983-888
Subsidiaries: Baron Production Sdn Bhd; Delta
Distributors Sdn Bhd; Delta Editions Sdn Bhd;
Delta Publishing Sdn Bhd; Gedung Ilmu Sdn
Bhd; Gunung Mutiara Sdn Bhd; Penerbit Jay-
atinta Sdn Bhd; Pustaka Delta Pelajaran Sdn
Bhd
*Branch Office(s)*
No 174 Jalan Pasar, 41400 Kelang, Selangor
Darul Ehsan

**Text Books Malaysia Sdn Bhd**
39 Jalan Buluh Kesap, 85007 Segamat, Johor D
Ta'Zim
Mailing Address: PO Box 30, 85007 Segamat,
Johor D Ta'Zim
*Tel:* (074) 911181 *Fax:* (074) 911181
*E-mail:* textbook@tm.net.my
Founded: 1969
ISBN Prefix(es): 967-9929
*Bookshop(s):* Tai Kuang & Co, 41 Jalan Awang,
85000 Segamat, Johor D Ta'Zim

**Time Track (M) Sdn Bhd**
69, Medan Gopeng 5, Jalan Lapangan Terbang,
31350 Ipoh, Perak
*Tel:* (05) 3124329; (05) 3127541 *Fax:* (05)
2630305
ISBN Prefix(es): 983-069

**Times**, *imprint of* Federal Publications Sdn Bhd

**Times Educational Co Sdn Bhd**
22 Jalan 19/3, 46300 Petaling Jaya, Selangor
*Tel:* (03) 7571766 *Fax:* (03) 7573607
*Telex:* MA 37433 *Cable:* Timesbooks
Subjects: Cookery
ISBN Prefix(es): 967-919
*Parent Company:* Times Educational Co Ltd,
Hong Kong
*Associate Companies:* Preston Corporation (Pri-
vate) Ltd, Singapore; Preston Corporation Sdn
Bhd; Preston-Times Printing & Publishing, Se-
langor
*Orders to:* Preston Corporation Sdn Bhd, 18 Jalan
19/3, Petaling Jaya, Selangor

**Penerbitan Tinta+**
32-B, Jalan Cemur, Off Jalan Tun Razak, 50400
Kuala Lumpur
*Tel:* (03) 4424163 *Fax:* (03) 4424640
*Key Personnel*
Dir: Mohd Haneefa
Founded: 1974
Subjects: Business, Education, English as a Sec-
ond Language, Management, Marketing
ISBN Prefix(es): 983-9588; 983-044

*Associate Companies:* Fargoes Books Sdn Bhd
Subsidiaries: Penerbitan Fargoes Sdn Bhd

**Trix Corporation Sdn Bhd+**
Pusat Bandar Damansara, Damansara Heights,
Block G, Room 2 level 6, 50490 Kuala
Lumpur
*Tel:* (03) 253 2019 *Fax:* (03) 255 1068
*E-mail:* cpd@trix.po.my
*Key Personnel*
Man Dir: Mr B S Neoh
Subjects: Career Development, Education, Securi-
ties
ISBN Prefix(es): 983-9102

**Tropical Press Sdn Bhd+**
56-1 Jalan Maarof, Bangsar Baru, 59100 Kuala
Lumpur
*Tel:* (03) 22825138; (03) 22825338 *Fax:* (03)
22823526
*E-mail:* feedback@tpress.po.my
*Key Personnel*
Man Dir: Winston Ee
Founded: 1975
Membership(s): Malaysian Book Publishers Asso-
ciation.
Subjects: Child Care & Development, Mathemat-
ics, Natural History, Physical Sciences, Science
(General), Technology
ISBN Prefix(es): 967-73
*Associate Companies:* Art Printing Works Sdn
Bhd

**Uni-Text Book Co**
42B Jl SS 20/10, Damansara Kim, 47400 Petaling
Jaya, Selangor Darul Ehsan
*Tel:* (03) 7185426
*Key Personnel*
Man Dir: Bob E S Lim
Editorial: E S Lim
Production: E H Lim
Sales: Theresa Chung
Subjects: Education, History, Literature, Literary
Criticism, Essays, Regional Interests, Religion -
Other
ISBN Prefix(es): 967-935
*Associate Companies:* Uni-Text Distributors Pri-
vate Ltd, 42B Jl SS 20/10, Damansara Kim,
47400 Petaling Jaya, Selangor Darul Ehsan

**Penerbit Universiti Teknologi Malaysia**
(Universiti Teknologi Malaysia Press)+
34-38 JLN Kebudayaan 1, Taman Universiti,
81300 Skudai, Johor
*Tel:* (07) 521 8131; (07) 521 8180; (07) 521 8166
*Fax:* (07) 521 8174
*E-mail:* penerbit@utm.my
*Web Site:* www.penerbit.utm.my
*Telex:* MA60205
*Key Personnel*
Dir: Dr Ummul Khair Ahmad
Marketing & Sales: Yosman Mohd Bain
Founded: 1986
Subjects: Aeronautics, Aviation, Behavioral Sci-
ences, Chemistry, Chemical Engineering, Civil
Engineering, Computer Science, Education,
Electronics, Electrical Engineering, Engineer-
ing (General), Mathematics, Mechanical Engi-
neering, Physical Sciences, Physics, Regional
Interests, Religion - Islamic, Science (General),
Social Sciences, Sociology, Technology
ISBN Prefix(es): 983-52
Number of titles published annually: 30 Print
Total Titles: 350 Print
*Ultimate Parent Company:* Universiti Teknologi
Malaysia, Skudai, Johor

**University of Malaya, Department of
Publications+**
Lembah Pantai, 50603 Kuala Lumpur
*Tel:* (03) 79574361 *Fax:* (03) 79574473
*E-mail:* terbit@um.edu.my
*Web Site:* www.um.edu.my/umpress

*Telex:* MA 39845 *Cable:* VARSITIPRESS
 KUALA LUMPUR
*Key Personnel*
Head of Dept, Publicity, Rights & Permis-
 sions, Editorial: Dr Hamedi Mohd Adnan
 *E-mail:* hamedi@um.edu.my
Founded: 1954
Subjects: Biography, Economics, Fiction, For-
 eign Countries, Government, Political Science,
 History, Medicine, Nursing, Dentistry, Poetry,
 Science (General), Social Sciences, Sociology
ISBN Prefix(es): 967-9940; 983-9705; 983-100
Number of titles published annually: 30 Print
Total Titles: 250 Print

**Utusan Publications & Distributors Sdn Bhd+**
Level 7, Menara PGRM, No 8 Jalan Pudu Ulu,
 Cheras, 56100 Kuala Lumpur
*Tel:* (03) 9287 7777 *Fax:* (03) 9282 7751
*E-mail:* corporate@utusan.com.my
*Web Site:* www.utusangroup.com.my
*Key Personnel*
Group Editor-in-Chief: Khalid Mohd
 *E-mail:* khalidm@utusan.com.my
Group Manager, Publishing: Roselina Johari
 *E-mail:* rose@utusan.com.my
Subjects: Business, Economics, Education, Man-
 agement, Religion - Other, Technology
ISBN Prefix(es): 967-61

**Vinpress Sdn Bhd+**
5 & 7 Lorong Datuk Sulaiman 7, Taman Tun Dr
 Ismail, 60000 Kuala Lumpur
*Tel:* (03) 7173333; (03) 7188877 *Fax:* (03)
 7192942
*E-mail:* vinsoh@pc.jaring.my
*Key Personnel*
Man Dir: Thomas Soh
Founded: 1985
Membership(s): Malaysian Book Publishers Asso-
 ciation.
Subjects: Ethnicity, Health, Nutrition, Philosophy,
 Regional Interests, Religion - Other
ISBN Prefix(es): 967-81
*Associate Companies:* Vintrade Sdn Bhd

**Well Loved Tales,** *imprint of* Mecron Sdn Bhd

# Maldive Islands

## General Information

*Capital:* Male
*Language:* Dhivehi (Maldivian)
*Religion:* Islam is the state religion (most Sunni
 Muslim)
*Population:* 226,000
*Currency:* 100 laari (larees) = 1 rufiyaa (maldi-
 vian rupee)

**Non-Formal Education Centre**
Salahuddeen Bldg, Male 20-03
*Tel:* 324622 *Fax:* 322231
*Key Personnel*
Deputy Dir: Abdul Raheem Hasan
Founded: 1986
Subjects: Agriculture, Child Care & Develop-
 ment, Education, English as a Second Lan-
 guage, Environmental Studies, Health, Nu-
 trition, Religion - Islamic, Science (General),
 Social Sciences, Sociology, Sports, Athletics
ISBN Prefix(es): 99915-50; 99915-58
*Parent Company:* Ministry of Education

**Novelty Printers & Publishers+**
Maafannu, Vaarey Villa, Izzudhdheen Magu, Male
 20317
*Tel:* 318844 *Fax:* 327039

*E-mail:* novelty@dhivehinet.net.mv
*Key Personnel*
Chairman: Ali Hussain
Man Dir: Asad Ali
Founded: 1965
Subjects: Animals, Pets, Foreign Countries, Re-
 gional Interests, Travel
ISBN Prefix(es): 99915-3
Subsidiaries: Novelty Bookshop

# Mali

## General Information

*Capital:* Bamako
*Language:* French
*Religion:* Predominantly Islamic
*Population:* 10 million
*Currency:* 100 centimes = 1 CFA franc
*Export/Import Information:* Member of the West
 African Economic Community. No tariff on
 books but subject to VAT at varying rates. Ad-
 vertising matter (more than single copy) subject
 to tariff, import tax and VAT. All goods subject
 to local tax of percentage of customs value.
 Import license required. Importation is either
 by private importers or state enterprises. Ex-
 change controls for non-franc zone.
*Copyright:* Berne (see Copyright Conventions, pg
 xi)

**EDIM SA+**
642 av Mardiagne, Bamako
Mailing Address: BP 2412, Bamako
*Tel:* 225522 *Fax:* 238503
*Key Personnel*
Man Dir: Aliou Tomota
Editor: Hr E Alain Kone
Founded: 1972
Subjects: Biography, Fiction, History, Nonfiction
 (General), Poetry, Religion - Other, Social Sci-
 ences, Sociology
ISBN Prefix(es): 2-913213
Subsidiaries: Editions populaires; Imprimerie
 Kasse Keita; Imprimerie nationale
*Bookshop(s):* Librairie Papeterie du Sondan, BP
 21, Bamako

# Malta

## General Information

*Capital:* Valletta
*Language:* Maltese and English (official), Italian
 widely spoken
*Religion:* Predominantly Roman Catholic
*Population:* 365,000
*Bank Hours:* 0830-1230 Monday-Thursday; 0830-
 1230, 1700-1900 Friday; 0830-1200 Saturday
*Shop Hours:* 0900-1300, 1530-1900 Monday-
 Saturday
*Currency:* 1,000 mils = 100 cents = 1 Maltese
 lira
*Export/Import Information:* No tariff on books
 or advertising. No import license required. Ex-
 change control by Central Bank. Trade Associ-
 ation agreement with the European Economic
 Community states all Malta made goods that
 enter the European Economic Community are
 duty and quota free. Different rates of duty
 apply for imports with special preference for
 European Economic Community countries.
*Copyright:* Berne, UCC (see Copyright Conventions, pg xi)

**Fondazzjoni Patrimonju Malti+**
115 Triq it-Teatru l-Qadim, Valletta VLT 09
*Tel:* 21231515 *Fax:* 21250118
*E-mail:* patrimonju@keyworld.net
*Web Site:* www.patrimonju.org.mt
*Key Personnel*
Administration Executive: Peter Calascione
 *Tel:* 21244777
Founded: 1996
Specialize in catalogues raisonne, collections of
 essays, art quality of Maltese history & cul-
 tural heritage subjects (known collectively as
 "Melitensia").
Subjects: Antiques, Archaeology, Art, Biography
ISBN Prefix(es): 9932-10
Number of titles published annually: 5 Print
Total Titles: 54 Print

**Gaulitana**
2, Triq Gedrin, Rabat - Gozo VCT 104
*Tel:* 2155-4212 *Fax:* 2155-4598
*E-mail:* joseph.bezzina@um.edu.mt
Founded: 1985
Subjects: History, Religion - Catholic, Travel
ISBN Prefix(es): 99909-57
Number of titles published annually: 6 Print

**Gozo Press**
Mgarr Rd, Gh'sielem, Gozo GSM 102
Mailing Address: Str 1 Main Gate St, 1st floor,
 Str 2 Victoria, Gozo VCT 103
*Tel:* 551534; 564395 *Fax:* 560857
*E-mail:* gozopress@orbit.net.mt
*Key Personnel*
Dir: Achilles F Cauchi
Manager: Carmel Mizzi
Membership(s): The Periodical & Book Publish-
 ers Association.
Subjects: Crafts, Games, Hobbies, History, Lit-
 erature, Literary Criticism, Essays, Religion -
 Other
*Orders to:* Gozo Press Office, Main Gate St, Vic-
 toria, Gozo

**Media Centre+**
Media Centre Complex, National Rd, Blata I-
 Bajda HMR 02
*Tel:* 21249005; 21223047; 21244913;
 21247460; 25699113; 25699114; 25699115
 *Fax:* 25699128
*Key Personnel*
Man Dir: Jeffrey Calafato
Manager, Publications: George Fava
Manager, Marketing: Sylvana Magro
Founded: 1981
Subjects: Biblical Studies, Communications, Ed-
 ucation, Religion - Catholic, Social Sciences,
 Sociology
ISBN Prefix(es): 99909-2
*Book Club(s):* Klaab Qari Nisrani (Maltese lan-
 guage publications)

**Merlin Library Ltd**
Mountbatten Str, Blata 1-Badja
*Tel:* 221205; 234438 *Fax:* 221135
*E-mail:* mail@merlinlibrary.com
*Web Site:* www.merlinlibrary.com
*Key Personnel*
Dir: Arthur J Gruppetta
Founded: 1964
ISBN Prefix(es): 99909-1

**PEG Ltd,** see Publishers' Enterprises Group
 (PEG) Ltd

**Progress Press Co Ltd+**
Strickland House, 341 St Paul St, Valletta VLT
 01
*Tel:* 21241464; 21241469; 21241411; 21241412
 *Fax:* 21241171
*Telex:* Mw 341 *Cable:* PROGRESS

*Key Personnel*
Man Dir: Dr Austin Bencini
Publication Manager: Joseph Tortell
   *E-mail:* jtortell@timesofmalta.com
Founded: 1957
Also wholesaler.
Subjects: Literature, Literary Criticism, Essays
ISBN Prefix(es): 99909-3
Number of titles published annually: 10 Print
Total Titles: 63 Print
*Parent Company:* The Allied Newspapers Ltd
Distributed by Bay Foreign Language Books
Distributor for Apple; Brimax; Brown Watson;
   Carlton; David & Charles; Egmont; Hodder
   Headline; New Holland; The Octopus Group;
   Orion; Osprey; Piatkus; Time Warner
*Bookshop(s):* 4 Castille Pl, Valletta VLT 01

**Publishers' Enterprises Group (PEG) Ltd**
PEG Bldg, UB7 Industrial Estate, San Gwann
   SGN 09
*Tel:* 21440083; 21448539; 21490540
   *Fax:* 21488908
*E-mail:* contact@peg.com.mt
*Web Site:* www.peg.com.mt
*Key Personnel*
Man Dir, Editorial, Rights & Permissions:
   Emanuel Debattista
Sales: Victor Mifsud
Production & Publicity: Gaetan Cilia
Founded: 1983
Subjects: Cookery, Crafts, Games, Hobbies, Edu-
   cation, Outdoor Recreation, Travel
ISBN Prefix(es): 99909-0

**The University of Malta Publications Section**
The University of Malta, Administration Bldg,
   Msida MSD 06
*Tel:* 21333903-6 *Fax:* 21336450
*Web Site:* www.um.edu.mt
*Telex:* Mw 407 Hieduc *Cable:* University Malta
Founded: 1953
Subjects: Ethnicity, Language Arts, Linguistics,
   Law, Natural History, Regional Interests
ISBN Prefix(es): 99909-46

# Martinique

## General Information

*Capital:* Fort-de-France
*Language:* French and Creole
*Religion:* Predominantly Roman Catholic
*Population:* 359,579
*Currency:* 100 Eurocents = 1 Euro
*Export/Import Information:* Tariff same as France.
   Overseas tax and reduced VAT on books. Small
   quantity of advertising free. No import licenses
   required. Exchange restrictions as in France.
*Copyright:* Berne (see Copyright Conventions, pg
   xi)

**Editions Gondwana+**
Morne Pavillon Tartane, 97220 Trinite
*Tel:* 580676; 580014 *Fax:* 580014
*Key Personnel*
Contact: Eric Leroy
Founded: 1987
Subjects: Agriculture, Archaeology, Gardening,
   Plants
ISBN Prefix(es): 2-908490
Distributed by Distique (Metropolitan France &
   Europe)

**George Lise-Huyghes des Etages**
108 rue de la Republique, 97200 Fort-de-France
*Tel:* 736819

Subjects: Behavioral Sciences, Education, Human
   Relations, Psychology, Psychiatry
ISBN Prefix(es): 2-909260

**Virlogeux Francoise-COMEDIT**
Rue de la Reine-Hortense, 97229 Les Trois Ilets
*Tel:* 683985 *Fax:* 683423
Founded: 1994
ISBN Prefix(es): 2-910746

# Mauritania

## General Information

*Capital:* Nouakchott
*Language:* Arabic (official and national), Poular,
   Wolof and Solinke (national)
*Religion:* Islamic
*Population:* 2.1 million
*Bank Hours:* 0800-1115, 1430-1630 Monday-
   Friday
*Shop Hours:* Vary. Generally 0800-1200, 0730-
   1500 Saturday-Thursday. Some closed Monday
   morning, some open Sunday morning
*Currency:* 5 khoums = 1 ouguiya
*Export/Import Information:* Member of the West
   African Economic Community. No tariff on
   books. Advertising matter (other than single
   copies) subject to fiscal, customs duty and
   added tax. Import licenses and exchange con-
   trols apply to imports outside of EEC and franc
   zone.
*Copyright:* Berne (see Copyright Conventions, pg
   xi)

**Imprimerie Commerciale et Administrative de**
   **Mauritanie**
BP 164, Nouakchott
Subjects: Education

# Mauritius

## General Information

*Capital:* Port Louis
*Language:* English (official) and Creole
*Religion:* Hindu, Christian and Muslim
*Population:* 1.1 million
*Bank Hours:* 1000-1400 Monday-Friday, 0930-
   1130 Saturday
*Shop Hours:* 0800-1600 or later Monday-Saturday
*Currency:* 100 cents = 1 Mauritian rupee
*Export/Import Information:* No tariff on books
   and advertising but there is a special levy. No
   import license required.
*Copyright:* UCC, Berne (see Copyright Conven-
   tions, pg xi)

**African Cultural Centre,** see Nelson Mandela
   Centre for African Culture

**Mauritius Bhojpuri Institute**
15 Menagerie Rd, Cassis, Port Louis
*Tel:* 2082956 *Fax:* 4643445
ISBN Prefix(es): 99903-902
Distributed by Editions de l'Ocean Indien Ltd;
   Editions Le Printemps; Mauritius Reading As-
   sociation

**De l'edition Bukie Banane**
5 Lari Edwin Ythier, Rose Hill
*Tel:* 4542327
*E-mail:* limem@intnet.mu
*Web Site:* pages.intnet.mu/develog/

*Key Personnel*
Man Dir: Dev Virahsawmy
Founded: 1979
Subjects: Drama, Theater, Poetry, Regional Inter-
   ests
*Orders to:* Librairie le Cygne, Royal Rd, Rose
   Hill

**Editions Capucines**
20 Ave des Capucines, Quatre Bornes
*Tel:* 4641563 *Fax:* 4641563
*E-mail:* edcapsee@intnet.mu
*Key Personnel*
Manager: S Seewoochurn
Founded: 1994
Subjects: Asian Studies, Education, History, Reli-
   gion - Hindu, Religion - Other
Number of titles published annually: 5 Print
Total Titles: 8 Print
Distributed by Editions de l'Ocean Indien; Edi-
   tions Le Printemps
Distributor for Editions de l'Ocean Indien

**EOI Ltd,** see Editions de l'Ocean Indien Ltd

**Golden Publications**
4 Cite Pere Laval St, Port Louis
*Tel:* 2416640
ISBN Prefix(es): 99903-44

**Government Printer (Imprimerie Nationale)**
La Tour Koenig, Pointe-aux-Sables
*Tel:* 2345284; 2345295
ISBN Prefix(es): 99903-1

**Hemco Publications**
7 Virgil Naz St, Rose Hill
*Tel:* 4643141
*Key Personnel*
Editor: Dr H Gyaram
Founded: 1993
Subjects: Education, Medicine, Nursing, Den-
   tistry, Religion - Buddhist, Religion - Catholic,
   Religion - Hindu, Religion - Islamic, Religion -
   Other
ISBN Prefix(es): 99903-27

**Imprimerie et Papeterie Commerciale, IPC**
23 Menagerie Rd, Cassis
*Tel:* 2124190; 2127701; 2127702 *Fax:* 2083523
ISBN Prefix(es): 99903-38

**Nelson Mandela Centre for African Culture**
Formerly African Cultural Centre
4th floor Astor Court, Lislet Geoffroy St, Port
   Louis
*Tel:* 212-4131; 208-6851 *Fax:* 208-8620
*E-mail:* acc1086@intnet.mu
*Web Site:* mandelacentre.gov.mu
Founded: 1985
ISBN Prefix(es): 99903-904

**Editions de l'Ocean Indien Ltd+**
Stanley, Rose Hill
*Tel:* 4646761 *Fax:* 4643445
*E-mail:* eoibooks@intnet.mu
*Telex:* MESYND 4739 IW
*Key Personnel*
Gen Mgr: A Beeharry Panray
Founded: 1977
Subjects: Accounting, Agriculture, Art, Biogra-
   phy, Business, Career Development, Computer
   Science, Cookery, Economics, Education, Fic-
   tion, Geography, Geology, Health, Nutrition,
   Literature, Literary Criticism, Essays, Manage-
   ment, Marketing, Philosophy, Poetry, Science
   (General), Travel
ISBN Prefix(es): 2-7410
Number of titles published annually: 89 Print
Total Titles: 365 Print
Subsidiaries: Mauritius Printing Specialists Ltd

*Branch Office(s)*
Gound floor, Manhattan, Curepipe *Tel:* 6749065
Vel Plaza, Royal Rd, Goodlands *Tel:* 2838729
1st floor, NPF Bldg, Jules Koeing St, Port-Louis
  *Tel:* 2111310
Kung Hing Mall Bldg, 30, Joseph Riviere St,
  Port-Louis *Tel:* 2423738
Student Complex, University of Mauritius, Reduit
  *Tel:* 4542258
Arcades Rond Point, Rose-Hill *Tel:* 4646391
Virginie Commercial Centre, Centre de Flacq
  *Tel:* 4132273
Distributed by Librarie L' Harmattan; African
  Books Collective Ltd (UK)
Distributor for Librarie L' Harmattan

**Editions Le Printemps+**
4 Club Rd, Vacoas
*Tel:* 6961017 *Fax:* 6867302
*E-mail:* elp@intnet.mu
*Key Personnel*
Man Dir: Ahmud Islam Sulliman
Subjects: Biography
ISBN Prefix(es): 99903-23
Subsidiaries: AIS Marketing

**Vizavi Editions+**
29, rue Saint Georges St, Port Louis
*Tel:* 2112435 *Fax:* 2113047
*E-mail:* vizavi@intnet.mu
*Key Personnel*
Dir: Mrs P M Siew
Founded: 1993
Membership(s): Association of Mauritian Publish-
  ers.
Subjects: Biography, Cookery, Government, Polit-
  ical Science, History, Literature, Literary Criti-
  cism, Essays, Nonfiction (General)
ISBN Prefix(es): 99908-37
Number of titles published annually: 3 Print

# Mexico

## General Information

*Capital:* Mexico City
*Language:* Spanish
*Religion:* Predominantly Roman Catholic
*Population:* 92.4 million
*Bank Hours:* 0900-1330 Monday-Friday
*Shop Hours:* 1000-1900 Monday, Tuesday, Thurs-
  day, Friday; 1100-2000 Wednesday and Saturday
*Currency:* 100 centavos = 1 Mexican peso
*Export/Import Information:* Member of the Latin
  American Free Trade Association. Foreign language books and textbooks generally dutied
  per kg legal weight, children's picture books
  ad valorem or per kg, whichever greater, and
  require import license. Three copies of non-
  Spanish advertising catalogs free but all others
  require license and dutied ad valorem. Customs
  request from Bank of Mexico all necessary information to decide cases of tariff.
*Copyright:* UCC, Berne, Buenos Aires (see Copyright Conventions, pg xi)

**Aconcagua Ediciones y Publicaciones SA**
Pino Suarez, Col Centro, 06020 Mexico, DF
*Tel:* (05) 555223120 *Fax:* (05) 5432280
*Key Personnel*
Dir: Julio Sanz Crespo
Subjects: Education, History, How-to, Literature,
  Literary Criticism, Essays, Religion - Other,
  Technology
ISBN Prefix(es): 968-6000

*Associate Companies:* Editorial Timun Mas SA,
  Spain
*Branch Office(s)*
Ediciones Ceac SA, Spain

**Addison Wesley,** *imprint of* Pearson Educacion
  de Mexico, SA de CV

**Adivinar y Multiplicar, SA de CV** (Guess &
  Multiply)+
Av Cuauhtemoc 1129-202, Col Letran-Valle,
  03650 Mexico, DF
*Tel:* (055) 91164450; (055) 11349065 *Fax:* (055)
  5604-1583
*E-mail:* multiplimx@msn.com
*Key Personnel*
Dir General: Jesus E Rodriguez y Rodriguez
Founded: 1985
Publisher of didactic books for children.
Subjects: Education, Mathematics
ISBN Prefix(es): 968-7458

**Editorial AGATA SA de CV+**
Pino Suares No 169, Col Sector Hidalgo, 44100
  Guadalajara Jalisco
*Tel:* (033) 614-4902; (03) 614-4909 *Fax:* (033)
  613-8429
*Key Personnel*
Editor: Jaime Alvarez G Alvarez del Castillo
Founded: 1986
Membership(s): National Art Graphics Associa-
  tion; National Commerce Association; Publish-
  ers Association.
Subjects: Drama, Theater, Journalism, Literature,
  Literary Criticism, Essays, Poetry, Regional
  Interests, Travel
ISBN Prefix(es): 968-7310; 970-657

**AGT Editor SA**
Au Progreso No 202 PA Escandon, Col Escan-
  don, 11800 Mexico, DF
*Tel:* (05) 273-9228 *Fax:* (05) 2771696
*Key Personnel*
Contact: Roger Grasa Soler
Founded: 1978
Subjects: Agriculture, Biological Sciences, Veteri-
  nary Science
ISBN Prefix(es): 968-463
Imprints: Rustica

**Aguilar Altea Taurus Alfaguara SA de CV**
Member of Grupo Santillana
Av Universidad 767, Colonia Del Valle, 03100
  Mexico, DF
*Tel:* (05) 688 89 66; (05) 688 82 77; (05) 688 75
  66 *Fax:* (05) 6042304; (05) 6886538
*E-mail:* info@editorialaguilar.com
*Web Site:* www.alfaguara.com.mx
*Key Personnel*
Dir: Miguel Angel Cayuela
Subjects: Advertising, Biography, Drama, Theater,
  Education, Fiction, Language Arts, Linguistics,
  Literature, Literary Criticism, Essays, Music,
  Dance, Philosophy, Photography, Poetry, Psy-
  chology, Psychiatry, Self-Help, Social Sciences,
  Sociology
ISBN Prefix(es): 968-19

**Alfaomega Grupo Editor SA de CV+**
Pitagoras 1139, Colonia Del Valle, 03100 Mex-
  ico, DF
*Tel:* (05) 5755022 (ext 126); (05) 5755022 (ext
  222) *Fax:* (052) 5752490
*E-mail:* universitaria@alfaomega.com.mx
*Web Site:* www.alfaomega.com.mx
*Key Personnel*
Dir: Benito Juarez
Dir de Edicione: Ferreyrs C Gonzalo
  *E-mail:* gferreyrs@spin.com.mx
Founded: 1965

Subjects: Computer Science, Electronics, Electri-
  cal Engineering, Engineering (General), Man-
  agement, Microcomputers, Technology
ISBN Prefix(es): 968-6062; 968-6223
*Associate Companies:* Publicaciones Marcombo
  SA

**Alianza Editorial Mexicana, SA de CV**
San Lorenzo No 160, lztapalapa, 09860 Mexico,
  DF
*Tel:* (05) 5670-4887; (05) 5670-4712 *Fax:* (05)
  5619797
*Key Personnel*
Man Dir: Alberto E Diaz
ISBN Prefix(es): 968-6001; 968-6354; 968-6423
*Associate Companies:* Alianza Editorial SA,
  Spain

**Allyn & Bacon,** *imprint of* Pearson Educacion de
  Mexico, SA de CV

**Ediciones Alpe+**
Rio de la Plata 14-2 Entre Panuco y Lerma, Col
  Cuahutemoc, 06500 Mexico, DF
*Tel:* (05) 2114523
Founded: 1991
Subjects: Cookery, Fiction, Health, Nutrition, Hu-
  mor, Poetry, Radio, TV, Religion - Hindu, Ro-
  mance, Self-Help
ISBN Prefix(es): 968-6426

**Arbol Editorial SA de CV+**
Ave Cuauhtemoc, No 1434, Col Santa Cruz
  Atoyac, 03310 Mexico, DF
*Tel:* (05) 6884828; (05) 6886458
*Key Personnel*
Man Dir, Production: Gerardo Gally
Rights & Permissions: Gilda Moreno
Founded: 1979
Subjects: Drama, Theater, Environmental Studies,
  Health, Nutrition, Religion - Other
ISBN Prefix(es): 968-461

**Ariel,** see Editorial Planeta Mexicana SA

**Grupo Editorial Armonia+**
Rio Balsas 101, Colonia Cuauhtemoc, 06500
  Mexico, DF
*Tel:* 54 42 96 00
*E-mail:* corporativo@grupoarmonia.com.mx
*Web Site:* www.grupoarmonia.com.mx
*Key Personnel*
Founder: Maria Eugenia Moreno
General Dir: Liliana Moreno
International Development Dir: Ileana Ramirez
Planning & Development Dir: Javier Pina
Founded: 1977
Membership(s): Mexican Association of Publish-
  ers.
Subjects: Cookery, Fashion, Health, Nutrition,
  House & Home
ISBN Prefix(es): 968-6598

**Artes de Mexico y del Mundo SA de CV+**
Plaza Rio de Janeiro 52, Colonia Roma, 06700
  Mexico, DF
*Tel:* (05) 208 3684; (05) 525 4036; (05) 525 5905
  *Fax:* (05) 525 5925
*E-mail:* artesmex@internet.com.mx;
  artesdemexico@artesdemexico.com
*Web Site:* www.artesdemexico.com
*Key Personnel*
Contact: Alberto Ruy Sanchez Lacy
Founded: 1953
Subjects: Architecture & Interior Design, Art, Po-
  etry

**Editores Asociados Mexicanos SA de CV (EDAMEX)+**
Heriberto Frias No 1104, Col Del Valle, 03100 Mexico, DF
*Tel:* (05) 5598588 *Fax:* (05) 5757035; (05) 5750555
*Web Site:* www.edamex.com
*Key Personnel*
Executive President: Octavio V Colmenares
Man Dir: Manuel G Colmenares
Sales: Irene Fohri
Production: Antonio Escamilla
Founded: 1963
Also acts as literary agent for authors.
Subjects: Economics, Government, Political Science, Humor, Literature, Literary Criticism, Essays, Social Sciences, Sociology
ISBN Prefix(es): 968-409; 970-661
*Associate Companies:* Colmenares Editores SA; Editorial Meridiano SA
Divisions: Noroeste
*Bookshop(s):* Centro Cultural Edamex, Mexico, DF

**Editorial Avante SA de Cv**
Luis Gonzalez Obregon No 9, Col Centro, 06020 Mexico, DF
*Tel:* (05) 5214548; (05) 5217563; (05) 5127634; (05) 5127563 *Fax:* (05) 5215245
*E-mail:* editorialavante@infosel.net.mx
*Web Site:* www.editorialavante.com.mx
*Key Personnel*
Man Dir: Mario Alberto Hinojosa Saenz
Production: Ana Luisa Quiros Esteban
Sales, Publicity: Luis Quiros Esteban
Founded: 1950
Subjects: Biography, Drama, Theater, Education, Language Arts, Linguistics, Poetry, Social Sciences, Sociology
ISBN Prefix(es): 968-6006
Imprints: Impresora Galve SA; Heidel Impresos SA de CV; Impresora Multiple SA

**Grupo Azabache Sa de CV+**
Formerly Servicios Especiales Maciel SA de CV
Dallas 85-4 Piso, Col Napoles, 03810 Mexico, DF
*Tel:* (05) 543-2786 *Fax:* (05) 543-2949
*Key Personnel*
General Dir: Maria Luisa Sabau Garcia
Foreign Rights Manager: Jorge Ruiz Esparza
Founded: 1987
Membership(s): National Association of the Publishing Industry.
Subjects: Architecture & Interior Design, Art, Cookery, Photography
ISBN Prefix(es): 968-6084; 968-6963; 970-678

**Azteca**, *imprint of* Fondo de Cultura Economica

**Editorial Azteca SA+**
Calle de la Luna No 225, Col Guerrero, 06300 Mexico, DF
*Tel:* (05) 5261157 *Cable:* Edasa
*Key Personnel*
Man Dir: Alfonso Alemon Jalomo
Sales Dir: Juan Alemon Jalomo
Founded: 1956
Subjects: Literature, Literary Criticism, Essays, Science (General)
ISBN Prefix(es): 968-6008

**Editorial Banca y Comercio SA de CV**
Liverpool No 5, Col Juarez CP, 06600 Mexico, DF
*Tel:* (05) 2089692; (05) 2081785; (05) 2081705 *Fax:* (05) 2081803
*E-mail:* ventas@edbyc.com.mx
*Web Site:* www.edbyc.com.mx
*Key Personnel*
Man Dir: Carlos Prieto Sierra

Assistant Manager: Amparo Quintanar
Founded: 1934
Subjects: Business, Law, Mathematics
ISBN Prefix(es): 968-6010

**Biblioteca Interamericana Bilingue**, *imprint of* Ediciones Euroamericanas

**Libreria y Ediciones Botas SA**
Sierra No 52, Col Centro, 06020 Mexico, DF
*Tel:* (05) 5702-4083; (05) 5702-5403 *Fax:* (02) 55101788
*E-mail:* botas@mail.nextgeninter.net.mx
*Key Personnel*
Man Dir: Andres Botas Herandez
Sales Dir: Laura Botas Herandez
Founded: 1910
Subjects: Art, Economics, Fiction, History, Law, Medicine, Nursing, Dentistry, Philosophy, Science (General)
ISBN Prefix(es): 970-92521

**Ediciones el Caballito SA**
Tlazopilli, No 7, Col Nuevo Renacimento de Axalco, 14406 Mexico, DF
*Tel:* (05) 5849-2533; (05) 5963400
*Key Personnel*
Rights & Permissions & Man Dir, Editorial: Manuel Lopez Gallo
Sales: Alfonso Garcia Espino
Production & Rights & Permissions: Teresa Dey
Founded: 1967
Subjects: Economics, History, Nonfiction (General), Regional Interests, Social Sciences, Sociology
ISBN Prefix(es): 968-6125; 968-5674
*Associate Companies:* Impoli SA, Isabel la Catolica 922, Col Postal, 03140 Mexico, DF
Subsidiaries: Presencia Latinoamerica
*Bookshop(s):* Libreria del Soltano SA, Ave Juarez 64, Satano Centro, Mexico, DF 1

**Camion Escolar y Limusa**, *imprint of* Editorial Limusa SA de CV

**Casa & Gente**, *imprint of* Cuernavaca Editorial S A

**Editorial la Cebra**
Av Revolucion 528-700, Col San Pedro de Los Pinos, 03800 Mexico, DF
*Tel:* (05) 2779529; (05) 2779797; (05) 2737717; (05) 2737888 *Fax:* (05) 2737866
*E-mail:* info@adcebra.com
*Key Personnel*
Dir General & Administrator: Andrzej Rattinger Aranda
Editor: Alejandro Ayala; Selene Monforte; Diana Penagos
Founded: 1992
Publishers of Adcebra, Mexico's marketing & advertising magazine.

**CEMCA**, see Centro de Estudios Mexicanos y Centroamericanos

**CEMLA**, see Centro de Estudios Monetarios Latinoamericanos (CEMLA)

**CEMO SA**, see Centro Editorial Mexicano Osiris SA

**Centro de Estudios Mexicanos y Centroamericanos+**
Sierra Leona No 330, Lomas de Chapultepec, 11000 Mexico, DF
Mailing Address: Apdo 41-879, 11000 Mexico, DF

*Tel:* (05) 5 40 59 21; (05) 5 40 59 22 *Fax:* (05) 2 02 77 94
*E-mail:* cemca.lib@francia.org.mx
*Web Site:* www.francia.org.mx/cemca
*Key Personnel*
Dir: Joelle Gaillac *E-mail:* cemca.pub@francia.org.mx
Head of Publications: Catherine Marielle
Founded: 1982
Edition De Boccard (Europe).
Subjects: Anthropology, Archaeology, Biological Sciences, Earth Sciences, Economics, Environmental Studies, Ethnicity, Foreign Countries, Government, Political Science, History, Music, Dance, Science (General), Social Sciences, Sociology
ISBN Prefix(es): 968-6029
Subsidiaries: Ministere des Affaires Etrangeres
Distributed by INAH

**Centro Editorial Mexicano Osiris SA**
Sierra Ventana No 545, Col Lomas de Chapultepec, 11000 Mexico, DF
*Tel:* (05) 5406902; (05) 2027185 *Fax:* (05) 2027185
*Key Personnel*
Contact: Thania Nicolopulos Joannides
Founded: 1976
Subjects: Astrology, Occult, Cookery, Literature, Literary Criticism, Essays, Parapsychology, Poetry
ISBN Prefix(es): 968-6225

**Editora Cientifica Medica Latinoamerican SA de CV**
Pennsylvania No 109, Col Napoles, 03810 Mexico, DF
*Tel:* (05) 5206135; (05) 5405600 *Fax:* (05) 52020926
*Key Personnel*
Contact: Pedro Vera Cerera
Founded: 1986
Subjects: Computer Science, Medicine, Nursing, Dentistry
ISBN Prefix(es): 968-6166

**El Coleccionista, Centro Historico**, *imprint of* Cuernavaca Editorial S A

**El Colegio de Mexico AC**
Camino al Ajusco No 20, Col Pedregal de Santa Teresa, 10740 Mexico, DF
Mailing Address: Apdo Postal 20671, 01000 Mexico, DF
*Tel:* (05) 54953080 *Fax:* (05) 54493083
*E-mail:* fgomez@colmex.mx
*Web Site:* www.colmex.mx
*Telex:* 1777585 Colme *Cable:* COLMEX
*Key Personnel*
Publications Coordinator: Marta Lilia Prieto
Founded: 1940
Subjects: Anthropology, Asian Studies, Business, Economics, Environmental Studies, Government, Political Science, History, Language Arts, Linguistics, Library & Information Sciences, Literature, Literary Criticism, Essays, Nonfiction (General), Philosophy, Science (General), Social Sciences, Sociology, Women's Studies
ISBN Prefix(es): 968-12

**Colegio de Postgraduados en Ciencias Agricolas**
Km 36.5 Carretera Mex-Texcoco, Montecillo, 56230 Mexico, DF
*Tel:* (0595) 95 2 02 00; (055) 58 04 59 00
*E-mail:* seia@colpos.mx
*Web Site:* www.colpos.mx
*Key Personnel*
Secretary: Dr Alfonso Larque Saavedra
Founded: 1959
Membership(s): Mexican National Association of Publishers.

Subjects: Agriculture, Biological Sciences, Economics, Education, Mathematics, Science (General), Social Sciences, Sociology, Technology, Veterinary Science
ISBN Prefix(es): 968-839
*Bookshop(s):* LIC Enrique Moreno Sanchez, Carr, Mexico-Texcoco KM, 35.5 Montecillo, 56230 Chapingo Edo
*Orders to:* LIC Enrique Moreno

**Comision Nacional Forestal**
Periferico Pte Int 5° Piso, 45019 Zapopan Jalisco
*Tel:* (05) 5349707; (05) 5247862
Subjects: Government, Political Science, History, Medicine, Nursing, Dentistry, Social Sciences, Sociology
ISBN Prefix(es): 968-6021

**Compania Editorial Continental SA de CV+**
Calzada de Tiapan 4620, Col Barrio del Nino Jesus, 14000 Mexico, DF
*Tel:* (05) 5732300 *Fax:* (05) 5618155
*Key Personnel*
President: Carlos Frigolet Lerma
Dir General, Editorial, Production & Sales: Victorico Albores Santiago
Rights & Permissions: Demetrio Garmendia Guerrero
Production: Mario Munoz Rodriguez
Founded: 1954
Subjects: Engineering (General), Management, Mathematics, Science (General), Technology
ISBN Prefix(es): 968-26; 968-7249

**Compania General de Ediciones SA de CV**, see Selector SA de CV

**Ediciones Contables y Administrativas SA**
Heriberto Frias 1451-101, Col Del Valle, 03100 Mexico, DF
*Tel:* (05) 6040140; (05) 6041998; (05) 6040260 *Fax:* (05) 6056730
*Key Personnel*
Man Dir: Pedro Gasca Rocha
Sales Dir: Gustavo Gasca Breton
Founded: 1967
Subjects: Accounting, Business
ISBN Prefix(es): 968-6014; 968-6317; 970-617; 968-5323
*Branch Office(s)*
Zaragoza 39-106, Guadalajara, Jalisco

**Ediciones Corunda SA de CV+**
Oaxaca No 1, Con Periferico, Col Magdalena Contreras, 10700 Mexico, DF
*Tel:* (05) 6525511; (05) 6525581 *Fax:* (05) 6525211
*Key Personnel*
Contact: Silvia Molina
Founded: 1988
Subjects: Literature, Literary Criticism, Essays, Science Fiction, Fantasy
ISBN Prefix(es): 968-6044; 968-7444

**Publicaciones Cruz O SA**
Patriotismo No 875-D, Colonia Mixcoac, Delegacion Benito Juarez, 03910 Mexico, DF
*Tel:* (055) 56-80-61-22 *Fax:* (055) 56-80-61-22
*E-mail:* infolibros@libros.com.mx; atencionaclienteslibros@libros.com.mx
*Web Site:* www.libros.com.mx
*Telex:* 01776232
*Key Personnel*
General Dir: Oscar Rene Cruz
Founded: 1977
Cultural divulgation.
Membership(s): National Association of Publishers.
Subjects: Biography, Economics, Law, Philosophy, Psychology, Psychiatry, Religion - Bud-

dhist, Religion - Catholic, Religion - Jewish, Social Sciences, Sociology
ISBN Prefix(es): 968-20
Total Titles: 285 Print
Subsidiaries: Libreria Cruz O SA
Divisions: Publicaciones Cruz O SA de Guatemala CA

**Cuernavaca Editorial S A+**
Oxford No 23, Col Juarez, 06600 Mexico, DF
*Tel:* (05) 5113619; (05) 5142529; (05) 2867794 *Fax:* (05) 2117112
*Telex:* 1771422 PROME
*Key Personnel*
Editor: Nicolas H Sanchez-Osorio; Elia Cordova; Anne de Sanchez Osorio
Founded: 1985
Membership(s): De Camara Nal Industria Editorial.
Subjects: Art
ISBN Prefix(es): 968-6188
*Parent Company:* Ediarte SA de CV
Imprints: Casa & Gente; El Coleccionista, Centro Historico

**Ediciones Culturales Internacionales SA de CV Edicion Compra y Venta de Libros, Casetes, Videos+**
Lago mask No 393, Col Granada, 11520 Mexico, DF
*Tel:* (05) 2508099 (ext 200) *Fax:* (05) 55311597
*Key Personnel*
General Dir: Mireya Cuentas Montejo
Editorial Manager: Ma Aurora Aguilar Chavez
Founded: 1983
Subjects: Art, Child Care & Development, Ethnicity
ISBN Prefix(es): 968-418

**Ediciones CUPSA, Centro de Comunicacion Cultural CUPSA, AC**
Heroes No 83, Guerrero, 06300 Mexico, DF
*Tel:* (05) 5925252; (05) 5662307; (05) 5462100
*Key Personnel*
Dir: Moises Valderrama
Founded: 1958
Subjects: Astrology, Occult, Biblical Studies, Poetry, Religion - Protestant, Religion - Other, Theology
ISBN Prefix(es): 968-7011

**Ediciones Dabar, SA de CV+**
Calzada del Acueducto 165-D, San Lorenzo Huipulco, 14370 Mexico, DF
*Tel:* (05) 6550396 *Fax:* (05) 6033674
*E-mail:* dabar@data.net.mx
*Key Personnel*
Contact: Jose Vaderrey Falagan
Founded: 1991
Also distributors of religious books in Spanish; theological, Bibles, spiritual & catechisms.
Subjects: Religion - Other
ISBN Prefix(es): 968-6768; 968-7506

**Maria Esther De Fleischmann**
Atlaltunco No 57, Colonia San Miguel Techmacalco, 53970 Mexico
Mailing Address: San Francisco 109, Colonia Rancho San Francisco, 01800 Nayarit
*Tel:* (05) 5852698 *Fax:* (05) 5854296
*E-mail:* fleischmann1@compuserve.com.mx
*Key Personnel*
Contact: Maria Esther Serafin Garcia
Subjects: Disability, Special Needs
ISBN Prefix(es): 968-499; 970-91523

**Del Verbo Emprender SA de CV+**
Fuente de Piramides No 20, Planta Baja Local B, Tecamachalco, 53950 Huxquilucan, Edo de Mexico

*Tel:* (05) 294-1160; (05) 294-8633 *Fax:* (05) 294-8633
*Key Personnel*
Founder & Dir: Salo Grabinsky *E-mail:* gsalo@mail.internet.com.mx
Founded: 1989
Subjects: Child Care & Development, Human Relations, Management, Self-Help
ISBN Prefix(es): 968-6427

**Editorial Diana SA de CV+**
Arenal No 24, Edif Norte, Ex Hacienda Guadalupe Chimalistac, Delegacion Alvaro Obregon, 01050 Mexico, DF
*Tel:* (05) 5089-1220 *Fax:* (052) 5089-1230
*E-mail:* 4sales@diana.com.mx; editors@diana.com.mx
*Web Site:* www.diana.com.mx *Cable:* EDISA
*Key Personnel*
President: Jose Luis Ramirez C
Vice President: Jose Luis Ramirez M
Literature Editor: Fausto Rosales *E-mail:* faustoro@diana.com.mx
General Interest Editor: Doris Bravo V
Technical Books Editor: V Manuel Fernandez *E-mail:* manfer@diana.com.mx
Sales: Vincente Perez *E-mail:* vincenteperez@diana.com.mx
Founded: 1946
Membership(s): National Association of the Mexican Publishing Industry.
Subjects: Advertising, Animals, Pets, Archaeology, Astrology, Occult, Biography, Career Development, Child Care & Development, Cookery, Economics, Education, Fiction, Health, Nutrition, History, Human Relations, Journalism, Literature, Literary Criticism, Essays, Management, Nonfiction (General), Parapsychology, Philosophy, Religion - Catholic, Self-Help, Sports, Athletics
ISBN Prefix(es): 968-13
Imprints: Edivision Cia, Editorial, SA de CV
*Branch Office(s)*
Buenos Aires, Argentina
Santafe de Bogota, Colombia
Barcelona, Spain
Caracas, Venezuela
*Shipping Address:* Roberto Cayol 1323, Col del Valle, 03100 Mexico, DF

**Direccion General de Publicaciones CNCA Coordinacion Juridica**
Av Mexico Coyocan 371 col xoco, 03330 Mexico, DF
*Tel:* (05) 605-85-89 (ext 5127-149) *Fax:* (05) 605-87-31
*Key Personnel*
Dir General: Felipe Garrido Reyes *Tel:* (05) 601-02-60; (05) 601-02-85 *E-mail:* dpg01@conaculta.gob.mx
Production Dir: Miguel Angel Echegaray Zuniga
ISBN Prefix(es): 968-29; 970-18
*Parent Company:* Educal, SA de CV, Av Ceylan 450, 02660 Col Euzkadi

**Directorio,** *imprint of* Medios y Medios, Sa de CV

**Ediciones Don Bosco SA de C**
Moneda, No 24, Delegagion Cuauhtemoc, 06060 Mexico, DF
*Tel:* (05) 3963349
*Key Personnel*
Dir: Argeo Corona Thelian Cortes
Deputy Dir, Rights & Permissions: Milagros Magana del Campo
Sales: Jorge Rangel
Founded: 1958
Subjects: Religion - Other
ISBN Prefix(es): 968-6662; 968-6969
*Associate Companies:* Central Catequista Salesiana, Madrid Alcala 164, Madrid, Spain; Li-

breria Dectrina Cristiana, Corzo Francia 214,
10096 Leuman (Turin), Italy
*Bookshop(s):* 5 de Mayo 23, 06000 Mexico, DF;
Ignacio Mariscal 8, Col revolucion, 06030
Mexico, DF

**Ediciones Eca SA de CV+**
Member of Cachoy Balcarcel, SA
Calle B Manzana 11 No 20, Col Educacion,
04400 Mexico, DF
*Tel:* (055) 5787325; (055) 5549-3477; (055)
5689-1244; (055) 5689-3074 *Fax:* (055) 5689-
9935
*Web Site:* www.centroescolareca.edu.mx
*Key Personnel*
Contact: Gracia Ma Cacho
Founded: 1950
Subjects: Accounting, Business
ISBN Prefix(es): 968-14

**Edamex SA de CV+**
Heriberto Frias No 1104, Col Del Valle, Del Ben-
ito Juarez, 03100 Mexico, DF
*Tel:* (05) 55598588 *Toll Free Tel:* 800 024 8588
*Fax:* (05) 55750555; (05) 55757035
*E-mail:* info@edamex.com
*Web Site:* www.edamex.com
*Key Personnel*
President: Octavio Colmenares Vargas
Dir General: Monica Colmenares
Foreign Sales: Valeria Bastarrachea
Founded: 1963
Membership(s): Camara Nacional de la Industria
Editorial Socio No 40.
Subjects: Architecture & Interior Design, Art,
Biography, Journalism, Management, Parapsy-
chology, Public Administration, Self-Help, So-
cial Sciences, Sociology, Sports, Athletics
ISBN Prefix(es): 968-409; 970-409
Number of titles published annually: 120 Print;
120 E-Book
Total Titles: 60 Print; 420 Online; 420 E-Book
*Parent Company:* Edamex
Foreign Rep(s): Books Information & Ser-
vices (Puerto Rico); Distribuidora Lewis, SA
(Panama); Giron Spanish Books; Internacional
Libros; Libreria Alexandria (Costa Rica); Li-
breria Cientifica (Ecuador); Philobliblia, SA
(Dominican Republic); Presa Peyran Editores,
CA (Venezuela)

**Editorial Edicol SA**
esq Actipan No 45, Murcia No 2, Col Mixcoac
Insurgentes, 03920 Mexico, DF
*Tel:* (05) 5636990 *Fax:* (05) 5981512
*Key Personnel*
Man Dir: Jorge Silva Escamilla
Founded: 1970
Subjects: Architecture & Interior Design, Com-
munications, Education, History, Language
Arts, Linguistics, Social Sciences, Sociology
ISBN Prefix(es): 968-408

**Edivision Cia, Editorial, SA de CV**, *imprint of*
Editorial Diana SA de CV

**Education Pabla**, see Direccion General de
Publicaciones CNCA Coordinacion Juridica

**El Colegio de Michoacan AC**
Martinez de Navarete 505, Las Fuentes, Apdo
207, 59699 Zamora, Michoacan CP
*Tel:* (0351) 515 71 00 *Fax:* (0351) 5157100 (ext
1742)
*E-mail:* publica@colmich.cmich.udg.mx;
publica@colmich.edu.mx
*Web Site:* www.colmich.edu.mx
*Key Personnel*
President: Rafael Diego-Fernandez
Publications: Patricia Delgado Gonzalez
  *E-mail:* pdelgado@colmich.edu.mx

Founded: 1979
Subjects: Americana, Regional, Anthropology,
Archaeology, Behavioral Sciences, Develop-
ing Countries, Education, Environmental Stud-
ies, Government, Political Science, History,
Language Arts, Linguistics, Native American
Studies, Philosophy, Religion - Catholic, Social
Sciences, Sociology, Theology
ISBN Prefix(es): 968-6959; 968-7230
Number of titles published annually: 30 Print

**Editorial El Manual Moderno SA de CV+**
Av Sonora 206, Hipodromo, 06100 Mexico, DF
*Tel:* (055) 2651100; (055) 2651124; (055)
2651121 *Fax:* (055) 2651175
*E-mail:* mmoderno@compuserve.com.ux
*Web Site:* www.manualmoderno.com.mx
*Key Personnel*
Chairman: Dr Gustavo Setzer
President: Ing Hugo Setzer
Vice President: C P Hector Morales
Editorial: lug Felipe Gerua
Marketing & Sales: Jose Pesez
Founded: 1958
Membership(s): The International Association
of Scientific, Technical & Medical Publishers
(STM).
Subjects: Biological Sciences, Health, Nutrition,
Medicine, Nursing, Dentistry, Psychology, Psy-
chiatry, Self-Help, Veterinary Science
ISBN Prefix(es): 968-426
Subsidiaries: Editorial El Manual Moderno
(Colombia), Ltda
Distributed by Editorial Atlante Argentina
SRL (Argentina); H F Martinez de Murguia
SA (Spain); Ediciones Nueva Vision CA
(Venezuela); Ediciones Tecnicas Paraguayas
(Paraguay); Ediciones Trecho SA (Uruguay)
Distributor for Appleton & Lange (Mexico); At-
lante Argenti (Mexico); Celsus (Mexico); Edi-
ciones Diaz de Santos, Medicina (Latin Amer-
ica); Harcourt Brace/Mosby-Doyma Libros
(Mexico); Springer Verlag Iberica (Latin Amer-
ica)

**Empresas Editoriales SA**
Praga No 56, Planta Baja Col Juarez, 06600 Mex-
ico, DF
*Tel:* (05) 5288979; (05) 5288417 *Fax:* (05)
5288417
Founded: 1944
Subjects: Fiction
ISBN Prefix(es): 968-7035

**Entretenlibro SA de CV**
Washington No 1127-Altos, 64007 Monterrey,
Nuevo Leon
*Tel:* (09183) 425570
*Key Personnel*
Contact: Jesus Rendon Contreras
Founded: 1983
Subjects: Education
ISBN Prefix(es): 968-462

**Ediciones Era SA de CV+**
Calle del Trabajo 31, Col La Fama Del Tlalpan,
14269 Mexico, DF
*Tel:* (055) 55 28 1221 *Fax:* (055) 56 06 2904
*E-mail:* edicionesera@edicionesera.com.mx
*Web Site:* www.edicionesera.com.mx
*Key Personnel*
Man Dir: Mrs Nieves Espresate Xirau
Founded: 1960
Subjects: Art, Economics, Fiction, Government,
Political Science, History, Literature, Literary
Criticism, Essays, Social Sciences, Sociology
ISBN Prefix(es): 968-411
Number of titles published annually: 25 Print
Total Titles: 300 Print

**Revista Mensual Escuela**, *imprint of* Fernandez
Editores SA de CV

**Editorial Esfinge SA de CV**
Member of Grupo Cultural Esfinge SA de CV
Esfuerzo 18-A Fracc Industrial Atoto, Naucalpan,
CP 53510 Mexico
*Tel:* (05) 3591313; (05) 3591111; (05) 3591515
*Fax:* (05) 5761343
*E-mail:* editorial@esfinge.com.mx
*Web Site:* www.esfinge.com.mx
Founded: 1957
Specialize in textbooks.
Membership(s): National Chamber of the Indus-
trial Editorial.
Subjects: Accounting, Chemistry, Chemical En-
gineering, Geography, Geology, History, Law,
Literature, Literary Criticism, Essays, Mathe-
matics, Physics
ISBN Prefix(es): 968-412
*Associate Companies:* Altadir SA de CV; Distr
Imagen Esfinge SA de CV; Inmobiliaria
Acribia SA de CV
Distributor for Addison-Wesley Iberoamericana
Mexico

**Espasa-Calpe Mexicana SA**
Insurgentes Sur N 1162, Col Del Valle, 03100
Mexico, DF
*Tel:* (05) 5758585 *Fax:* (05) 5758980
ISBN Prefix(es): 968-413
*Branch Office(s)*
Editorial Espasa-Calpe SA, Spain

**Centro de Estudios Monetarios
Latinoamericanos (CEMLA)+**
Durango 54, 06700 Mexico, DF
*Tel:* (05) 533-0300 *Fax:* (05) 525-4432
*E-mail:* cemlasub@mail.internet.com.mx
*Web Site:* www.cemla.org
*Key Personnel*
Man Dir: Lic Sergio Ghigliazza
Editorial, Rights & Permissions & Production:
Juan Manuel Rodriguez *Tel:* (05) 5114020
*Fax:* (05) 2077024
Sales: Claudio Antonovich
Founded: 1952
Subjects: Computer Science, Economics, Finance
ISBN Prefix(es): 968-6154

**Ediciones Euroamericanas+**
Apdo 69-774, 04461 Mexico, DF
*Tel:* (05) 56 10 01 33 *Fax:* (05) 56 10 01 33
*E-mail:* thielemedina@prodigy.net.mx
*Key Personnel*
Man Dir: Klaus Thiele
Founded: 1971
Direct sales only to booksellers worldwide.
Subjects: Anthropology, Archaeology, History,
Regional Interests
ISBN Prefix(es): 968-414
Number of titles published annually: 2 Print
Total Titles: 16 Print
Imprints: Biblioteca Interamericana Bilingue; Pag-
inas Mesoamericanas

**Ediciones Exclusivas SA+**
Monrovia 1105, Apdo 21-148, Mexico, DF
*Tel:* (05) 815878
*Key Personnel*
Contact: Jose Figueroa Marti
Founded: 1973
Membership(s): La Camara Nacional de la Indus-
tria Editorial.
Subjects: Health, Nutrition, Human Relations,
Medicine, Nursing, Dentistry, Psychology, Psy-
chiatry
ISBN Prefix(es): 968-7039
*U.S. Office(s):* Latin Trading Corp, 539 "H" St,
Suite B, Chula Vista, CA 91911, United States
*Tel:* 619-427-7867

**Editorial Extemporaneos SA**
Poniente 126-A-400, Col Nueva Vallejo, 07750
   Mexico, DF
*Tel:* (05) 5875424 *Fax:* (05) 5878785 *Cable:*
   EDIEXTEMPO MEXICO
*Key Personnel*
Dir-General, Editorial: Lautaro Gondalez Porcel
Sales, Publicity & Production: Romeo Medina
Rights & Permissions: Eva Somlo
Founded: 1975
Subjects: Anthropology, Architecture & Interior
   Design, Art, Drama, Theater, Economics, Edu-
   cation, Government, Political Science, Humor,
   Literature, Literary Criticism, Essays, Philoso-
   phy, Social Sciences, Sociology
ISBN Prefix(es): 968-415
*Bookshop(s):* Librerias Extemporaneos SA, Ham-
   burgo 260, Mexico 6, DF
*Book Club(s):* Club de Lectores Extemporaneos

**Editorial Fata Morgana SA de CV+**
Virgilio No 7-12, Col Polanco, 11560 Mexico,
   DF
Mailing Address: Monte Elbruz 164-13, Lomas
   Chapultepec, 11000 Mexico, DF
*Tel:* (055) 52 80 08 29 *Fax:* (055) 52 80 81 37
*E-mail:* editorial@fatamorgana.com.mx
*Web Site:* www.fatamorgana.com.mx
*Key Personnel*
Contact: Maria Abac Klemm
Founded: 1990
Subjects: Psychology, Psychiatry
ISBN Prefix(es): 968-6757
Number of titles published annually: 1 Print
Total Titles: 8 Print
*Orders to:* Virgilio No 7, Dept 12, Col Polanco,
   11560 Mexico, DF

**Fernandez Editores SA de CV+**
Eje 1 Poniente Mexico Coyoacan 321, Col Xoco,
   03330 Mexico, DF
*Tel:* (05) 6056557 *Fax:* (05) 6889173
*Web Site:* www.fernandezeditores.com.mx
*Key Personnel*
President: Gonzalez Luis Fernandez
Man Dir: Luis Gerardo Fernandez
Production Manager: Luis Benjamin Fernandez
Commercial Manager: Luis Miguel Fernandez
Founded: 1943
Manufacturer of game tables & materials.
Membership(s): Camara Editorial of Mexico.
Subjects: Animals, Pets, Child Care & Devel-
   opment, Education, Environmental Studies,
   History, Literature, Literary Criticism, Essays,
   Mathematics, Nonfiction (General), Physics,
   Religion - Catholic, Science (General), Science
   Fiction, Fantasy, Social Sciences, Sociology
ISBN Prefix(es): 970-03; 968-416
Imprints: Revista Mensual Escuela

**Fondo de Cultura Economica+**
Carretera Picacho-Ajusco 227-1, Heroes de
   Padierna, 14200 Mexico, DF
*Tel:* (05) 2274672 *Fax:* (05) 2274640
*E-mail:* adiezc@fce.com.mx (editorial)
*Web Site:* www.fondodeculturaeconomica.com
*Key Personnel*
Man Dir: Miguel de la Madrid
Senior Editor: Adolfo Castanon
Production: Alejandro Ramirez
Sales: David Turner y Barragan
Publicity: Maria Luisa Armendariz
Foreign Rights: Socorro Cano
Founded: 1934
Specialize in editorial materials.
Subjects: Advertising, Agriculture, Anthropol-
   ogy, Archaeology, Architecture & Interior De-
   sign, Art, Behavioral Sciences, Biological Sci-
   ences, Communications, Developing Countries,
   Drama, Theater, Earth Sciences, Economics,
   Education, Energy, Ethnicity, Fiction, Gov-
   ernment, Political Science, History, Literature,

Literary Criticism, Essays, Nonfiction (Gen-
   eral), Philosophy, Photography, Poetry, Psy-
   chology, Psychiatry, Public Administration, Sci-
   ence (General), Science Fiction, Fantasy, Social
   Sciences, Sociology, Women's Studies
ISBN Prefix(es): 968-16
Imprints: Azteca; La Gaceta; Galeras; El
   Trimestre Economico
*Branch Office(s)*
Fondo de Cultura Economica de Argentina SA,
   El Salvador 5665, C1414BQE Capital Federal,
   Buenos Aires, Argentina, Contact: Alejandro
   Katz *Tel:* (01) 14-777-1547; (01) 14-777-1934;
   (01) 14-777-1219 *Fax:* (01) 14-771-8977 (ext
   19) *E-mail:* info@fce.com.ar
Fondo de Cultura Economica Brasil Ltda, Rua
   Bartira 351, Perdizes, Sao Paulo CEP 05009-
   000, Brazil, Contact: Isac Vinic *Tel:* (011)
   3672-3397; (011) 3672-3864; (011) 3672-1496
   *Fax:* (011) 3862-1803 *E-mail:* aztecafondo@
   uol.com.br
Fondo de Cultura Economica Chila SA, Paseo
   Bulnes 152, Santiago, Chile, Contact: Julio Sau
   Aguayo *Tel:* (02) 697-2644; (02) 695-4843;
   (02) 699-0189; (01) 688-1630 *Fax:* (02) 696-
   2329 *E-mail:* fcechile@ctcinternet.cl
Fondo de Cultura Economica Ltda, Carrera 16
   No 80-18, Barrio el Lago, Bogota, Colombia,
   Contact: Juan Camilo Sierra *Tel:* (01) 531-2288
   *Fax:* (01) 531-1322 *E-mail:* fondoc@cable.net.
   co *Web Site:* www.fce.com.co
Fondo de Cultura Economica de Guatemala
   SA, 6a Ave 8-65, Zona 9, Guatemala, Con-
   tact: Sagrario Castellanos *Tel:* 334-3351; 362-
   6563; 362-6539; 334-3354 *Fax:* 332-4216
   *E-mail:* fceguate@gold.guate.net
Fondo de Cultura Economica del Peru SA, Jiron
   Berlin No 238, Miraflores, Lima 18, Peru, Con-
   tact: German Carnero Roque *Tel:* (01) 242-
   0559; (01) 242-9448; (01) 447-2848 *Fax:* (01)
   447-0760 *E-mail:* fce-peru@terra.com.pe *Web
   Site:* www.fceperu.com.pe
Fondo de Cultura Economica de Espana SL,
   C/Fernando El Catolico No 86, Conjunto Resi-
   dencial Galaxia, Madrid 28015, Spain, Contact:
   Maria Luisa Capella *Tel:* (091) 543-2904; (091)
   543-2960; (091) 549-2884 *Fax:* (091) 549-8652
   *E-mail:* capella@terra.es
Fondo de Cultura Economica Venezuela SA, Edif
   Torre Polar, PB Local E, Plaza Venezuela,
   Caracas, Venezuela, Contact: Pedro Juan Tucat
   Zunino *Tel:* (02) 574-4753 *Fax:* (02) 574-7442
   *E-mail:* salonofc@cantv.net
*U.S. Office(s):* Fondo de Cultura Economica
   EUA Inc, 2293 Verus St, San Diego, CA
   92154, United States, Contact: Benjamin Mire-
   les *Tel:* 619-429-0455 *Fax:* 619-429-0827
   *E-mail:* info@fceusa.com *Web Site:* www.
   fecusa.com
*Bookshop(s):* Carret Picacho Ajusco, No 227, CP
   14200 Mexico, DF
*Shipping Address:* Jose Maria Joaristi 205, Paraje
   San Juan, San Lorenzo, Iztapalapa 09830

**Fondo Editorial de la Plastica Mexicana+**
Cda de Malitzin No 28, 04100 Mexico, DF
*Tel:* (05) 5549-4291 *Fax:* (05) 5688-1168
Founded: 1961
Subjects: Art, Regional Interests
ISBN Prefix(es): 968-6658
Number of titles published annually: 3 Print
Total Titles: 20 Print

**La Gaceta**, *imprint of* Fondo de Cultura
   Economica

**Galeras**, *imprint of* Fondo de Cultura Economica

**Impresora Galve SA**, *imprint of* Editorial Avante
   SA de Cv

**Ediciones Gili SA de CV**
Valle de Bravo No 21, Fracc-el Mirador, Naucal-
   pan, 53050 Mexico
*Tel:* (05) 373-1744; (05) 5606011 *Fax:* (05)
   3601453
*Telex:* 1772918 Gilime *Cable:* GUSTO MEXICO
ISBN Prefix(es): 968-887; 968-6085
*Associate Companies:* Editorial Gustavo Gili SA,
   Spain

**Gomez Gomez Hermanos Editores S de RL
   Edicion de Libros y Revistas+**
Moneda 19-B, Col Centro, 06060 Mexico, DF
*Tel:* (05) 55225903; (05) 6123906 *Fax:* (05)
   633786
*Key Personnel*
Contact: Victor J Gomez
ISBN Prefix(es): 968-7030
Subsidiaries: El Mejor Regalo un Libro SRL

**Editorial Grijalbo SA de CV+**
Homero No 544, Chapultepec Morales, 11570
   Mexico, DF
*Tel:* (05) 5545 1620
*Web Site:* www.randomhousemondadori.com.mx
*Key Personnel*
Editorial: Rogelio Carvajal Davila; Ariel Rosales
   Ortiz
Sales: Rodolfo Munguia Calderon; Irma P
   Chavarria
Publicity: Oscar Davalos; Alicia Velazquez
Founded: 1936
Membership(s): Camara Espanola de Comercio
   & Mexico y Camara Italiana de Comercio en
   Mexico.
Subjects: Fiction, Nonfiction (General), Poetry,
   Self-Help, Mythology
ISBN Prefix(es): 968-419; 970-05
*Parent Company:* Grijalbo Mondadori, Spain
*Ultimate Parent Company:* Random House Mon-
   dadori
*Associate Companies:* Arnoldo Mondadori Edi-
   tore

**Grupo Editorial Iberoamerica, SA de CV+**
Rio Ganges No 64, Col Cuauhtemoc, 06500 Mex-
   ico, DF
*Tel:* (05) 5111267; (05) 5116760
*Key Personnel*
President: Nicolas Grepe Philp
Founded: 1983
Book publisher & distributor to Latin America.
Subjects: Agriculture, Career Development,
   Chemistry, Chemical Engineering, Computer
   Science, Economics, Engineering (General),
   Environmental Studies, Finance, Management,
   Mathematics, Mechanical Engineering
ISBN Prefix(es): 968-7270; 970-625
*Branch Office(s)*
Grupo Editorial Iberoamerica de Colombia, SA,
   Carrera 23 No 49-30, Barrio Palermo, Santa
   Fe de Bogota, Colombia *Tel:* (0571) 3202010
   *Fax:* (0571) 3106553

**Grupo Editorial Z Zeta SA de CV**
Oculistas No 43, Col Sifon, 09400 Mexico, DF
*Tel:* (05) 6705627; (05) 5817929 *Fax:* (05)
   5758280
*Key Personnel*
Contact: Francisco Campos Fontanet
ISBN Prefix(es): 970-610
*Warehouse:* Ignacio Manuel Aaltamirano, 212 B
   Col Hank Gonzalez, 09750 Mexico, DF

**Heidel Impresos SA de CV**, *imprint of* Editorial
   Avante SA de Cv

**Editorial Hermes SA+**
Calz Ermita Iztapalapa No 266, Col Sinatel,
   09470 Mexico, DF

*Tel:* (05) 6741425 (ext 171); (05) 6741894; (05) 6744385 *Fax:* (05) 6743949 *Cable:* EDITERMES
*Key Personnel*
Man Dir: Sergio Sanchez Davila
Sales: Adolfo de la Becerril
Production, Rights & Permissions: Virginia Garcia Fiesco
Founded: 1944
Subjects: Art, Fiction, History
ISBN Prefix(es): 968-446
*Associate Companies:* Editorial Albastros SA ci, Buenos Aires, Argentina; Tercer Mundo Distribuidores, Santa Fe de Bogota, Colombia

**Editorial Herrero SA**
Rio Amazonas No 44, Col Cuauhtemoc, 06500 Mexico, DF
*Tel:* (05) 5664900 *Fax:* (05) 5664900
*Key Personnel*
General Dir: Donato Elias Herrero
Manager: Ricardo Arancon L
Founded: 1945
Subjects: Art
ISBN Prefix(es): 968-420

**Hoja Casa Editorial SA de CV+**
Av Cuauhtemoc No 1430, Col Santa Cruz Atoyac, 03310 Mexico, DF
*Tel:* (055) 688-4828; (055) 688-6458; (055) 605-7677; (055) 604-0843 *Fax:* (055) 605-7677
*E-mail:* editorialpax@editorialpax.com
*Web Site:* www.editorialpax.com
*Key Personnel*
General Dir: Gerardo Gally
General Manager: Consuelo Saizar
Rights & Permissions: Gilda Moreno
Founded: 1990
Subjects: Astrology, Occult, Fiction, Literature, Literary Criticism, Essays, Self-Help
ISBN Prefix(es): 968-6565

**Ibcon SA+**
Gutenberg 224, Col Anzures, 11590 Mexico, DF
*Tel:* (055) 52 55 45 77 *Fax:* (055) 52 55 45 77
*E-mail:* ibcon@ibcon.com.mx; ibcon@infosel.net.mx
*Web Site:* www.ibcon.com.mx
*Key Personnel*
Editor: Gabriel Zaid *E-mail:* ibcon1@ibcon.com.mx
Founded: 1954
Specialized directories (print, CD, online).
Subjects: Business, Government, Political Science, Health, Nutrition, Law, Library & Information Sciences, Marketing, Microcomputers, Women's Studies
ISBN Prefix(es): 968-5097; 970-760
Number of titles published annually: 18 Print; 3 CD-ROM; 1 Online
Total Titles: 21 Print; 2 CD-ROM; 1 Online
Foreign Rep(s): Netlibrary (US)

**Instituto Indigenista Interamericano**
(Inter-American Indian Institute)
Av de las Fuentes 106, Col Jardines del Pedregal, Delegacion Alvaro, 01900 Mexico, DF
Mailing Address: Apdo 20315, 01001 Mexico, DF
*Tel:* (05) 5595 8410; (05) 5595 4324 *Fax:* (05) 595 8410
*E-mail:* ininin@data.net.mx *Cable:* INDIGENI
*Key Personnel*
Man Dir, Rights & Permissions: Dr Jose Matos Mar
Founded: 1940
Specialize in the development of the Pueblo Indian in America.
Membership(s): OEA.
Subjects: Anthropology, History
ISBN Prefix(es): 968-6020
Number of titles published annually: 600 Print

**INEGI**, see Instituto Nacional de Estadistica, Geographia e Informatica

**Informatica Cosmos SA de CV+**
Calzado del Hueso 122-A12, Col Ex-Hacienda Coapa, 14300 Mexico, DF
*Tel:* (05) 6774868; (05) 6776043 *Fax:* (05) 6793575
*E-mail:* online@cosmos.com.mx
*Web Site:* www.cosmos.com.mx
*Key Personnel*
Man Dir: Raul Macazaga *E-mail:* macazaga@cosmos.com.mx
Dir, International Sales: Mary Christen *E-mail:* christen@cosmos.com.mx
Founded: 1956
Specialize in industry guides, products, producers, suppliers of industry, chemicals, food & feed, container & packaging, rubber, plastics & resins & equipment.
*U.S. Office(s):* Schnell Publishing Co Inc, 2 Rector St, 26th floor, New York, NY 10006-1819, United States, Contact: Stacey Davis *Tel:* 212-791-4251 *Fax:* 212-791-4311 *E-mail:* sdavis@chemepo.com

**Editorial Institucional y Desarrollo Humanistico SA de CV Edicion de Libros** (IDH Ediciones)+
Av Juarez No 14-7 Piso, 11560 Mexico, DF
*Tel:* (05) 5215060; (05) 5215009
*Key Personnel*
Contacts: Ms Alicia Sosa; Enrique Martinez Cruz
Founded: 1982
ISBN Prefix(es): 968-883
*Parent Company:* Grupo IDH

**Intersistemas SA de CV+**
Pennsylvania 109, Colonia Napoles, 03810 Mexico, DF
*Tel:* (055) 1107-1903 *Fax:* (055) 1107-0196
*E-mail:* ventas@medikatalogo.com
*Web Site:* www.medikatalogo.com
*Telex:* 5403764
*Key Personnel*
Man Dir: Pedro Vera-Cervera
Editorial: Elvia Espino-Barros
Sales: Miguel Alberto Gonzalez
Founded: 1970
Subjects: Medicine, Nursing, Dentistry
ISBN Prefix(es): 970-655
*Associate Companies:* Vier Lista Anexa, EMC Colombia Federal Buenos Aires, Buenos Aires, Argentina; Graficas Enar SA, Pedro Muguruza 3-1, Madrid 16, Spain; Intermedica Inc, 322 West Port Ave, Norwalk, CT 06851, United States

**El Inversionista Mexicano SA de CV**
Felix Cuevas 301-204, Col Del Valle, Deleg Benito Juarez, CP 03100 Mexico, DF
*Tel:* (05) 5245396; (05) 5349297 *Fax:* (05) 5243794
*E-mail:* elimmbi@iserve.net.mx
*Key Personnel*
Contact: Evangelina Astorga Dorantes
Founded: 1969

**Editorial Iztaccihuatl SA+**
Miguel E Schultz No 21, Col San Rafael, 06470 Mexico, DF
*Tel:* (05) 7050938; (05) 7051063 *Fax:* (05) 5352321 *Cable:* EIZTAMEXA
*Key Personnel*
President: Orlando Vieyra Legorreta
Founded: 1946
Subjects: Cookery, Literature, Literary Criticism, Essays, Wine & Spirits
ISBN Prefix(es): 968-421

**Janibi Editores SA de CV**
Matias Romero 1221-3, Col Del Valle, Del Benito Juarez, 03100 Mexico, DF
*Tel:* (05) 6046160 *Fax:* (05) 6882848
*Key Personnel*
Contact: Victor Munoz Polit
Founded: 1975
Subjects: Fashion, Music, Dance

**Editorial Jilguero, SA de CV**
Administracion de Correos 10, 11000 Mexico, DF
*Tel:* (05) 2590939; (05) 2590814 *Fax:* (05) 5401771
*E-mail:* mexdesco@compuserve.com.mx
*Web Site:* www.mexicodesconocido.com.mx
Subjects: Animals, Pets, Anthropology, Antiques, Archaeology, Architecture & Interior Design, Cookery, Crafts, Games, Hobbies, History, Music, Dance, Outdoor Recreation, Travel

**Editorial Joaquin Mortiz SA de CV+**
Member of Grupo Editorial Planeta
Avda Insurgentes Sur No 1898-11, Col Florida, 01030 Mexico, DF
*Tel:* (055) 5322-3610 *Fax:* (055) 5322-3636
*Telex:* 1764458 EDARME
*Key Personnel*
Man Dir, Production, Rights & Permissions: Joaquin Diez-Canedo
Founded: 1962
Subjects: Fiction, History, Literature, Literary Criticism, Essays, Nonfiction (General), Philosophy, Poetry, Psychology, Psychiatry, Social Sciences, Sociology
ISBN Prefix(es): 968-27
*Associate Companies:* Editorial Planeta SA, Spain
*Warehouse:* Ave Gavilan 3, Bodega 1 & 2, Col Guadalupe del Mora, Delegacion Iztapalapa, 09360 Mexico, DF
*Orders to:* Editorial Planeta Mexicana, Ave Insurgentes Sur No 1162-3, Col Del Valle, 03100 Mexico, DF

**Editorial Jus SA de CV+**
Plaza de Abasolo 14, Col Guerrero, 06300 Mexico, DF
*Tel:* (05) 5260538; (05) 5260540 *Fax:* (05) 5290951
*E-mail:* editjus@data.net.mx
*Key Personnel*
President: Juan Landerreche
Man Dir: Tomas Reynoso
Sales Manager: Jorge Espinosa
Founded: 1941
Subjects: Biblical Studies, Economics, Education, Government, Political Science, History, Law, Literature, Literary Criticism, Essays, Philosophy, Religion - Catholic, Self-Help, Social Sciences, Sociology, Theology
ISBN Prefix(es): 968-423
Subsidiaries: Distribuidora Editorial Jus SA

**Ediciones Larousse SA de CV+**
Dinamarca No 81 B1, Colonia Juarez, 06600 Mexico, DF
*Tel:* (05) 52082005; (05) 2085677 *Fax:* (05) 2086225
*Web Site:* www.larousse.com.mx
*Key Personnel*
President: Dominique Bertin *E-mail:* dbertin@larousse.com.mx
Founded: 1965
Subjects: English as a Second Language
ISBN Prefix(es): 970-607; 968-6042; 968-6147; 968-6347
*Parent Company:* Havas Publications Edition, France
*Warehouse:* Acalotenco 94-1, Mexico, DF

**Lasser Press Mexicana SA de CV**
Praga 56 - Piso 4, Col Juarez, 06600 Mexico, DF

*Tel:* (05) 5112312; (05) 5142705 *Fax:* (05)
5112576
*Telex:* 1777529 Coseme *Cable:* LASPRESA
*Key Personnel*
President: Guillermo Menendez Castro
Editorial Dir: Elisa Tovar
Founded: 1972
Subjects: Biography, Literature, Literary Criti-
cism, Essays, Nonfiction (General)
ISBN Prefix(es): 968-458; 968-7063

**Libra Editorial SA de CV+**
Melesio Morales No 16, Colonia Guadalupe Inn,
01020 Mexico, DF
*Tel:* (05) 6641454; (05) 6514156 *Fax:* (05)
6641454
*Key Personnel*
President: Georgina Greco y Herrera
Editor: Gabriela Escalante de Figueroa
Founded: 1984
Subjects: Astrology, Occult, Child Care & De-
velopment, Cookery, Education, Gay & Les-
bian, How-to, Humor, Language Arts, Linguis-
tics, Nonfiction (General), Self-Help, Women's
Studies
ISBN Prefix(es): 970-606; 968-6636
*Warehouse:* Av Centenario 514, Letra A

**Ediciones Libra, SA de CV**
Melesio Morales, No 16, Col Guadalupe Inn,
01020 Mexico, DF
*Tel:* (05) 5651-4156 *Fax:* (05) 5664-1454
*Key Personnel*
Contact: Victor Munoz Polit
Founded: 1986
Subjects: Crafts, Games, Hobbies, Fashion, Mu-
sic, Dance
ISBN Prefix(es): 970-606; 968-6636

**Libreria Parroquial de Claveria SA Edicion
   Compra y Venta de Libros+**
Floresta No 79, Col Claveria, 02080 Mexico, DF
*Tel:* (05) 3967027; (05) 3967718 *Fax:* (05)
3991243
*Key Personnel*
Contact: Padre Basilio Nunez Garcia
Founded: 1964
ISBN Prefix(es): 968-442

**Libros y Revistas SA de CV**
Mier y Pesado 130, Col del Valle, 03100 Mexico,
DF
*Tel:* (05) 5437295 *Fax:* (05) 5364622
*Telex:* 01771403 dsayme
*Key Personnel*
General Dir, Editorial, Rights & Permissions:
Marcial Frigolet Lerma
General Manager, Commercial Dir: Joaquin Roca
Romero
Production: Miguel Montano
Founded: 1925
Subjects: Crafts, Games, Hobbies, Education,
Fashion, Health, Nutrition
ISBN Prefix(es): 968-7066
*Parent Company:* Publicaciones Sayrols SA de
CV
*Associate Companies:* Metropolitana de Publica-
ciones SA

**Editorial Limusa SA de CV+**
Balderas No 95, Col Centro, 06040 Mexico, DF
*Tel:* (05) 5128503; (05) 5128050 *Fax:* (05) 512
2903
*E-mail:* limusa@noriega.com.mx
*Web Site:* www.noriega.com.mx
*Key Personnel*
Chairman of the Board: Carlos Noriega Milera
Chairman & Chief Executive Officer: Carlos Nor-
iega Arias
Vice President & Editorial Dir: Miguel Noriega
Arias

Founded: 1962
Subjects: Accounting, Advertising, Aeronautics,
Aviation, Agriculture, Architecture & Interior
Design, Art, Astronomy, Automotive, Behavioral Sciences, Biological Sciences, Business,
Career Development, Chemistry, Chemical Engineering, Child Care & Development, Civil
Engineering, Communications, Computer Science, Cookery, Crafts, Games, Hobbies, Criminology, Drama, Theater, Earth Sciences, Economics, Education, Electronics, Electrical En-
gineering, Energy, Engineering (General), Finance, Geography, Geology, Government, Polit-
ical Science, Health, Nutrition, House & Home,
Human Relations, Journalism, Labor, Industrial
Relations, Law, Management, Marketing, Math-
ematics, Mechanical Engineering, Medicine,
Nursing, Dentistry, Microcomputers, Physi-
cal Sciences, Physics, Psychology, Psychiatry,
Public Administration, Radio, TV, Real Estate,
Religion - Catholic, Science (General), Social
Sciences, Sociology, Sports, Athletics, Technol-
ogy, Transportation, Veterinary Science
ISBN Prefix(es): 968-18
Total Titles: 2,500 Print
*Parent Company:* Grupo Noriega Editores
Imprints: Camion Escolar y Limusa; Nori; Nor-
iega Editores; Uteha
Subsidiaries: Alamex; Grupo Noriega Editores de
Colombia Ltda; Limex
Divisions: Uteha; Nori; Limusa; Noriega Editores;
Camion Escolar
*Branch Office(s)*
E Robles Gil No 437, Col Americana SJ,
Guadalajara, Contact: Francisco Haro *Tel:* (03)
269 032 *Fax:* (03) 268 899 *E-mail:* limusa@
noriega.com.mx
M M Del Llano 417 Ote, Monterrey, NL, Con-
tact: Sra Agustin Medina *Tel:* (08) 345 7505
*Fax:* (08) 345 7505 *E-mail:* limusa@noriega.
com.mx
Distributed by Anisa (Puerto Rico); Cuspide CIA
(Argentina); Dimaxi (Ecuador); Ediciones Tec-
nicas Paraguayas (Paraguay); Hispania SRL;
Fundacion Del Libro Universitario Libun (Peru)
Distributor for Meditor (America Latina); V Vives
(Mexico)
*Showroom(s):* Ayuntamiento 112, Centro 06040
*Bookshop(s):* Integra Escolar, Felix Berenguer
106, Lomas Virreyes *Tel:* (05) 520 6592; Li-
breria Bellas Artes, Av Juarez, No 18-D, 6770
Mexico, DF *Tel:* (05) 518 2917
*Book Club(s):* Librerias de Cristal, Tehuantepec
170, Roma Sur, 06770 Mexico, DF *Tel:* (05)
564 4677
*Warehouse:* Oriente 171 No 108, Col Aragon In-
guaran, Contact: Sra Carlos Sanchez *Tel:* (057)
81 61 57 *Fax:* (057) 81 08 74

**Logos Consorcio Editorial SA+**
General Molinos del Capo 64, Col San Miguel
Chapultepec, 11850 Mexico, DF
*Tel:* (055) 515-16-33
*Key Personnel*
Man Dir: Enrico Garcia Alonso S
ISBN Prefix(es): 968-425

**Longman,** *imprint of* Pearson Educacion de
Mexico, SA de CV

**Macmillan Editores SA de CV**
Av Prolongacion San Antonio 170, Col Carola,
CP 01180 Mexico, DF
*Tel:* (05) 482 2200 *Fax:* (05) 482 2203
*E-mail:* elt@macmillan.com.mx
*Web Site:* www.macmillan.com.mx/
*Key Personnel*
Chief Executive: Christopher West
*E-mail:* cwest@macmillan.com.mx
Man Dir: Helen Melia *E-mail:* hmelia@
macmillan.com.mx
Founded: 1982

*Parent Company:* Macmillan Publishers Ltd,
United Kingdom
*Associate Companies:* Editorial Macmillan de
Mexico SA de CV

**Editorial Macmillan de Mexico SA de CV**
Av Prolongacion San Antonio 170, Col Carola,
01180 Mexico, DF
*Tel:* (05) 482 2200 *Fax:* (05) 482 2202
*Toll Free Fax:* 800-00-64-100; 800-71-22-363
*Web Site:* www.macmillan.com.mx
*Key Personnel*
Chief Executive: Christopher West
*E-mail:* cwest@macmillan.com.mx
Man Dir: Helen Melia *E-mail:* hmelia@
macmillan.com.mx
Founded: 1982
English language teaching publishers.
ISBN Prefix(es): 968-6589; 968-7188; 968-7380;
970-650; 970-662
*Parent Company:* Macmillan Publishers Ltd,
United Kingdom
*Associate Companies:* Macmillan Editores SA de
CV

**Mass + Medios,** *imprint of* Medios y Medios, Sa
de CV

**Masson Editores**
Dakota No 383, Col Napoles, 03810 Mexico, DF
*Tel:* (05) 6870933
*Telex:* 1777604
*Key Personnel*
President: Dr Jerome Talamon
Man Dir: Bruno Vanneuville
Founded: 1978
ISBN Prefix(es): 968-6099
*Parent Company:* Masson Editeur, France
*Associate Companies:* Editora Masson do Brasil
Ltda, Brazil; Masson italia editori - ETM, via
Pascoli 55, I-20133 Milan, Italy; Masson SA,
Spain; Masson Publishing USA Inc, 211 E 43
St, Rm 1306, New York, NY 10017, United
States

**McGraw-Hill Interamericana Editores, SA de
   CV+**
Atlacomulco 499, San Andres Atoto, Naucalpan,
53500 Mexico, DF
*Tel:* 576-73-04; 576-90-44 (ext 156)
*E-mail:* mcgraw-hill@infosel.net.mx
*Web Site:* www.mcgraw-hill.com.mx
*Telex:* 01774284 LMCHME
*Key Personnel*
Man Dir: Carlos Rios
Controller & Business Manager: Hugo Solis
Production Manager: Miguel Palafox
EDP Manager: Javier Carranza
Human Resources Manager: Rocio Gonzalez
Publisher, Professional Division: David Mejia
Publisher, College Division, BCV: Javier Neyra
Publisher, High School Division, BCV: Enrique
Pereda
Publisher, Elementary-Junior High School Divi-
sion, K-9: Joaquin Esponda
Distributor & Bookstore Sales Manager, Mexico:
Rodolfo Munguia
Export Division Manager, Central America,
Caribbean & South America: Lynette Kew
Sales Manager, Central America: Nathaniel
Maxwell *Tel:* (02) 437667 (Ecuador) *Fax:* (02)
436553 (Ecuador)
Sales Manager, College (Chile, Ecuador & Peru):
Gilberto Capellan
Founded: 1966
Subjects: Business, Engineering (General), Mathe-
matics, Public Administration, Social Sciences,
Sociology
ISBN Prefix(es): 968-25; 968-451; 968-422; 970-
10

*Parent Company:* The McGraw-Hill Companies, 1221 Avenue of the Americas, New York, NY 10020, United States
*Sales Office(s):* 13 Calle "A" 31-76, Zona 7, Apdo 1477, Colonia Tika III, Guatemala, Guatemala *Tel:* (02) 914793 *Fax:* (02) 519598

## McGraw-Hill Mexico
Division of The McGraw-Hill Companies
Prolong Paseo de la Reforma, No 1015 Torre A Piso 17 Del Alvaro Obregon, 01376 Punta Santa Fe
*Tel:* (055) 1500-5000 *Toll Free Tel:* 800 713-4540 *Fax:* (055) 1500-5127
*E-mail:* tele_marketing@mcgraw-hill.com
*Web Site:* www.mcgraw-hill.com.mx
*Key Personnel*
Group Vice President: Francisco Albisua
Regional offices in Mexico, Venezuela, Colombia, Chile, Puerto Rico.
ISBN Prefix(es): 968-25; 968-451; 968-422; 970-10

## Medios Publicitarios Mexicanos SA de CV
### Editora de Directorios de Medios
Av Eugenia No 811, Col Del Valle, Mexico, DF CP 03100
*Tel:* (05) 523-3346; (05) 523-3342 *Fax:* (05) 523-3379
*E-mail:* suscrip@mpm.com.mx; editorial@mpm.com.mx
*Web Site:* www.mpm.com.mx
*Key Personnel*
Contact: A Fernando Villamil
Founded: 1958
Subjects: Advertising
*Associate Companies:* SRDS LP, 1700 Higgins Rd, Des Plaines, IL 60018, United States

## Medios y Medios, Sa de CV
Av Universidad 783-4, Col Del Valle, Del Benito Juarez, 03100 Mexico, DF
*Tel:* (05) 56-01-85-11 *Fax:* (05) 56-88-59-85
*E-mail:* mass+medios@camoapa.com.mx
*Key Personnel*
Dir: David Ramirez-Solis
Founded: 1993
Subjects: Advertising, Radio, TV
Imprints: Directorio; Mass + Medios

## Mercametrica Ediciones SA Edicion de Libros
Av Universidad 1621, piso 3, Col Hacienda de Guadalupe Chimalistac, 01050 Mexico, DF
*Tel:* (055) 56-61-62-93; (055) 56-61-92-86 *Fax:* (055) 56-62-33-08
*E-mail:* mercametrica@mercametrica.com
*Web Site:* www.mercametrica.com.mx
*Key Personnel*
President: Ignacio Gomez
Founded: 1976
Subjects: Economics, Management, Marketing
ISBN Prefix(es): 968-7267

## Editores Mexicanos Unidos SA
Luis Gonzalez Obregon, No 5, Colonia Centro, 06020 Mexico, DF
*Tel:* (05) 5218870 al 74 *Fax:* (05) 5218516
*E-mail:* editmusa@mail.internet.com.mx
*Web Site:* www.editmusa.com.mx
*Key Personnel*
Man Dir, Editorial: Fidel Miro Solanes
Dir: Sonia Miro de Laclau
Manager: Roque Laclau Gaona
Founded: 1954
Subjects: Fiction, Nonfiction (General)
ISBN Prefix(es): 968-15
*Bookshop(s):* Libro-Mex Editores Srl, Argentina 23, Mexico 1, DF

## Editorial Minutiae Mexicana SA
Insurgentes Centro No 114-210, Col Revolucion, 06030 Mexico, DF
*Tel:* 55-5535-9488 *Fax:* (052) 722-232-0662
*Key Personnel*
Publisher: Virginia V De Barrios
*E-mail:* barriosb@prodigy.net.mx
Founded: 1963
Specialize in books in English only.
Subjects: Anthropology, Archaeology, Biological Sciences, Cookery, Crafts, Games, Hobbies, History, Natural History, Religion - Catholic, Travel
ISBN Prefix(es): 968-7074
*U.S. Office(s):* MEX/ICS, 124 Cota Ave, San Clemente, CA 92672, United States, Contact: Jean Stenzel *Tel:* 949-492-1257 *Fax:* 949-492-1257

## Galeria de Arte Misrachi SA
Genova No 20-A, Col Juarez, 06600 Mexico, DF
*Tel:* (05) 5334551 *Fax:* (05) 55257187
*E-mail:* misrachi@acnet.net
*Key Personnel*
Manager: Enrique Beraha Misrachi
Editorial, Sales, Production, Rights & Permissions, Publicity: Beraha Carlos Cohen
Founded: 1961
Subjects: Art
ISBN Prefix(es): 968-7047
Subsidiaries: Galeria Misrachi SA de CV

## Impresora Multiple SA, *imprint of* Editorial Avante SA de Cv

## Mundo Medico SA de CV Edicion y Distribucion de Revistas Medicas
Ejercito Nacional No 381, Col Granada, 11520 Mexico, DF
*Tel:* (05) 5203-8111 *Fax:* (05) 5601-0815
*E-mail:* info@grupomundomedico.com
*Web Site:* www.grupomundomedico.com
*Key Personnel*
Contact: Julieta Cano Garcia
Founded: 1973
Subjects: Medicine, Nursing, Dentistry
ISBN Prefix(es): 968-7204
*U.S. Office(s):* Mundo Medico, 600 B Lake St, Ramsey, NJ 07446, United States

## Instituto Nacional de Antropologia e Historia
(National Institute of Anthropology & History)+
Cordoba 45, Col Roma, 06700 Mexico, DF
Mailing Address: Editor Coord Nat Difusion/Alvaro Obregon, No 151-3 Col Roma, CP 06700 Mexico, DF
*Tel:* (055) 5335246; (055) 5332272; (055) 2074559; (055) 2074584 *Fax:* (055) 2074633
*E-mail:* difusion.cdifus@inah.gob.mx
*Web Site:* www.inah.gob.mx
*Key Personnel*
International Rights: Gerardo Jaramillo
Founded: 1822
Governmental Institution devoted to the preservation, research & promotion of Mexican historical heritage.
Subjects: Americana, Regional, Anthropology, Antiques, Archaeology, Art, History, Language Arts, Linguistics, Music, Dance, Native American Studies, Photography, Social Sciences, Sociology
ISBN Prefix(es): 968-6038; 968-6068; 968-6487
Total Titles: 120 Print
Distributed by Educal Libros y Arte
*Orders to:* Coord Control y Promocion, Calle Frontera, No 53, Col San Angel, CP 01000 Mexico, DF, Contact: Laura Hernandez *Tel:* (055) 550-9714; (055) 550-9676; (055) 550-8631 *Fax:* (055) 550-3503
*E-mail:* coordinacion.cncpbs@inah.gob.mx *Web Site:* www.tiendadelmuseo.com.mx

## Instituto Nacional de Estadistica, Geographia e Informatica (National Institute of Statistics, Geography & Informatics)
Av Heroe de Nacozari Sur No 2301, Jardines del Parque, 20270 Aguascalientes Ags CP
*Tel:* 449 910 5300 (ext 5021) *Fax:* 449 918 2232
*E-mail:* ventas@dgd.inegi.gob.mx
*Web Site:* www.inegi.gob.mx
*Key Personnel*
Contact: Daniel de Lira Luna
Subjects: Developing Countries, Earth Sciences, Economics, Geography, Geology, Social Sciences, Sociology
ISBN Prefix(es): 970-13; 968-892

## Naves Internacional de Ediciones SA+
Amores No 135, Col Del Valle, Del Benito Juarez, 03100 Mexico, DF
*Tel:* (05) 6690595; (05) 9180055595 *Fax:* (05) 6823728
*E-mail:* niesa@mpsnet.com.mx
*Key Personnel*
Contact: Pablo Llaca
Founded: 1981
Subjects: Advertising, Architecture & Interior Design, Art, Cookery, Photography
*Associate Companies:* Ramon Llaca y Cia SA
Distributor for Celeste; Folio; Idea Books; Juventud; Naturart; Tursen
*Book Club(s):* Club de Editores, AC

## Nori, *imprint of* Editorial Limusa SA de CV

## Noriega Editores, *imprint of* Editorial Limusa SA de CV

## Nova Grupo Editorial SA de CV+
Panama 820-3, Portales, 03300 Mexico, DF
*Tel:* (05) 5320946 *Fax:* (05) 6050879
*Key Personnel*
Contact: Oscar Pruneda Portilla
Founded: 1987
Subjects: Communications, Education, Health, Nutrition, Language Arts, Linguistics, Mathematics, Nonfiction (General), Science (General), Self-Help
ISBN Prefix(es): 968-6197
*Associate Companies:* Oscar Edwin Pruneda Alvarez
Distributor for Oscar Edwin Pruneda Alvarez
*Orders to:* Zacahuitzco 165, 09440 Mexico, DF
*Tel:* (05) 5397678 *Fax:* (05) 5497666

## Editorial Nova, SA de CV
Goldsmith 37-401, Col Polanco, CP 11550 Mexico, DF
*Tel:* (05) 2 80 60 80 *Fax:* (05) 2 80 31 94
*E-mail:* bolind@viernes.iwm.com.mx
*Key Personnel*
Dir: Valades Humberto *E-mail:* hvaldes@iwm.com.mx
Subjects: Advertising

## Editorial Nuestro Tiempo SA+
Av Copilco 300 Locales 6 y 7, 04360 Mexico, DF
*Tel:* (05) 5503165; (05) 5503170
*Key Personnel*
Man Dir: Esperanza Nacif Barquet
Founded: 1966
Subjects: Social Sciences, Sociology
ISBN Prefix(es): 968-427
*Branch Office(s)*
Agencia Guadalajara, Federalismo 958 Sur, Sol Moderna, 44100 Guadalajara, Jalisco *Tel:* (036) 126037

## Editorial Nueva Imagen SA
Blvd Adolfo Lopez Mateos 202 50 Piso, Col San Pedro de los Pinos, 03800 Mexico, DF
*Tel:* (05) 2711980; (05) 2714524
*Telex:* 1771427 Eni Me

*Key Personnel*
Administrative Dir: Enrique Sealtiel Alatriste L
Editorial Dir: Guillermo J Schavelzon
Founded: 1976
Subjects: Anthropology, Art, Economics, Fiction, Health, Nutrition, History, Humor, Language Arts, Linguistics, Regional Interests, Science (General), Social Sciences, Sociology
ISBN Prefix(es): 968-429

**Organizacion Cultural LP SA de CV+**
Praga No 56 - 40° Piso, Col Juarez, 06600 Mexico, DF
*Tel:* (05) 55112312; (05) 147608
*E-mail:* orgcult@mail.internet.com.mx
*Key Personnel*
Contact: Joaquin Martin Gamero Castillo
Subjects: Accounting, Astronomy, Biological Sciences, Child Care & Development, Computer Science, Cookery, Management, Sports, Athletics
ISBN Prefix(es): 968-6007; 970-01

**Origen Editorial SA**
c/o Roberto Gayol 1219-A, Col del Valle, 03100 Mexico, DF
*Tel:* (055) 575-07-11 (ext 30); (055) 575-07-11 (ext 31)
ISBN Prefix(es): 968-847

**Editorial Orion**
Sierra Mojada No 325, Col Lomas de Chapultepec, CP 11000 Mexico DF
*Tel:* (05) 5200224 *Fax:* (05) 5200224
*Key Personnel*
Man Dir: Silvia Hernandez Vda de Cardenas
Sales Dir, Rights & Permissions: Laura Hernandez Baltazar
Publicity Dir: Silvia Hernandez Baltazar
Founded: 1942
Subjects: Astrology, Occult, Literature, Literary Criticism, Essays, Parapsychology, Philosophy, Psychology, Psychiatry, Religion - Other
ISBN Prefix(es): 968-6053; 968-6957
Subsidiaries: Edit Cuzamil SA

**Paginas Mesoamericanas**, *imprint of* Ediciones Euroamericanas

**Editorial Paidos Mexicana, SA**
Ruben Dario 118, Colonia Moderna, 03510 Mexico, DF
*Tel:* (05) 5795922; (05) 5795113 *Fax:* (05) 5904361
*E-mail:* epaidos@paidos.com.mx
*Web Site:* www.paidos.com
*Key Personnel*
International Rights: Mauricio M Morlett
Founded: 1945
ISBN Prefix(es): 968-853

**Palabra Ediciones SA de CV**
Triunfo de la Libertad No 5-2, Col Tlalpan, 14000 Tlalpan
*Tel:* (05) 5730985 *Fax:* (05) 5730985
*Key Personnel*
Contact: Henry C Bergonzi Braconi
Subjects: Religion - Catholic
ISBN Prefix(es): 968-6460; 968-7515
*Associate Companies:* Cosmos Libros Srl, Av Callao 737, 1023 Buenos Aires, Argentina

**Instituto Panamericano de Geografia e Historia**
Ex-Arzobispado 29, Col Observatorio, 11800 Mexico, DF
*Tel:* (05) 2775888; (05) 5151910; (05) 2775791 *Fax:* (05) 2716172
*E-mail:* cvasi@ipgh.spin.com.mx *Cable:* IPAGHIS
*Key Personnel*
Secretary-General: Carlos Carvallo Yanez

Founded: 1928
Specialized organization of the OEA.
Subjects: Anthropology, Archaeology, Ethnicity, Geography, Geology, History, Regional Interests
ISBN Prefix(es): 968-6384; 84-8420

**Pangea Editores, Sa de CV+**
Arenal 2553-4, Santa Ursula Xitla, 14420 Mexico, DF
*Tel:* (05) 5738684 *Fax:* (05) 5130638
*E-mail:* pangea@data.net.mx
Founded: 1986
Subjects: Anthropology, Archaeology, Astrology, Occult, Astronomy, Biography, Biological Sciences, Science Fiction, Fantasy, Self-Help
ISBN Prefix(es): 968-6177

**Panorama Editorial, SA+**
Manuel Maria Contreras, No 45 B, Col San Rafael, 06470 Mexico, DF
*Tel:* (05) 5359348; (05) 5359074; (05) 5350377 *Fax:* (05) 5359202; (05) 5351217
*E-mail:* panorama@iserve.net.mx
*Web Site:* www.panoramaed.com.mx
*Key Personnel*
Dir General: Luis Castaneda
Commercial Dir: Pilar Marquez
Founded: 1979
Subjects: Business, Health, Nutrition, History, Human Relations, Humor, Management, Regional Interests, Self-Help, Travel
ISBN Prefix(es): 968-38

**Editorial Libreria Parroquial de Claveria SA de CV+**
Floresta 79, Col Claveria, 02080 Mexico, DF
*Tel:* (05) 396-7027; (05) 396-7718 *Fax:* (05) 399-1243
ISBN Prefix(es): 968-442

**Editorial Patria SA de CV+**
Av San Lorenzo No 160, Col Esther Zuno de Echeverria-1, 09860 Mexico, DF
*Tel:* (05) 6704712; (05) 6704887 *Fax:* (05) 5613218
*Telex:* 1764172
*Key Personnel*
Man Dir: Rene Solis
Deputy Manager & Administrator, Rights & Permissions: Isabel Lasa
Sales & Publicity Dir: Rogelio Villarreal
Founded: 1933
Subjects: Biography, History, How-to, Literature, Literary Criticism, Essays, Philosophy
ISBN Prefix(es): 968-6054; 968-39
Divisions: Alianza; Nueva Imagen; Promexa

**Editorial Pax Mexico+**
Av Cuauhtemoc 1430, Col Santa Cruz Atoyac, 03310 Mexico, DF
*Tel:* 5688-4828; 5604-0843 *Fax:* 5605-7677
*E-mail:* editorialpax@editorialpax.com
*Web Site:* www.editorialpax.com
*Key Personnel*
Man Dir: Gerardo Gally *E-mail:* gerardogally@editorialpax.com
Founded: 1936
Subjects: Business, Career Development, Education, Health, Nutrition, How-to, Psychology, Psychiatry
ISBN Prefix(es): 968-860
*Associate Companies:* Hoja Casa Editorial SA
Subsidiaries: Arbol Editorial SA

**Pearson Educacion de Mexico, SA de CV+**
Atlacomulco No 500, 4to, Piso Industrial Atoto Naucalpah, Estado de Mexico 53370
*Toll Free Tel:* 800 005 4276 *Fax:* (05) 387-0700
*E-mail:* firstname.lastname@pearsoned.com
*Web Site:* www.pearson.com.mx

*Key Personnel*
President, Mexico, Central America & Caribbean: Steve Marban
Dir, Finance & Operations: Sven Boes
Dir, ELT & School USP Division: Juan M Abarca
Dir, Edition & Manufacturing: Juan A Rodriguez
Founded: 1984
Subjects: Art, Biological Sciences, Business, Chemistry, Chemical Engineering, Computer Science, Economics, Education, History, Language Arts, Linguistics, Management, Mathematics, Microcomputers, Physics, Psychology, Psychiatry, Science (General), Securities, Sports, Athletics, Technology
ISBN Prefix(es): 968-444; 968-880; 970-17
Total Titles: 76 Print
*Parent Company:* Pearson Plc
Imprints: Addison Wesley; Allyn & Bacon; Longman; Penguin Readers; Prentice Hall Hispanoamericana; Scott Foresman; Silver Burdette Ginn
*Branch Office(s)*
Barrio La Guaria Moravia, 75 M Norte del Porton Norte del Club la Guaria, Casa con Reja Blanca, San Jose, Costa Rica, Regional Manager: Luis Diego Barrientos *Tel:* 382-3931 *Fax:* 280-6569
El Monte Mall-Suite 21-B, Ave Munoz Rivera, Hato Rey 00918-4621, Puerto Rico, Regional Manager: Jose Javier Rivera *Tel:* (787) 751-4830 *Fax:* (787) 751-1677
*Warehouse:* Calle Negra Modelo No 12 & 12B, Fracc Industrial Alce Blanco, Naucalpan de Juarez, Estado de Mexico 53770 *Tel:* (05) 363 0842 *Fax:* (05) 363 4579

**Penguin Readers**, *imprint of* Pearson Educacion de Mexico, SA de CV

**Publicaciones Piramide, SA de CV+**
3ra Cerrada del Lago Silverio, No 30, Col Anahuac, 11320 Mexico, DF
*Tel:* (05) 5313215 *Fax:* (05) 2725883
*Key Personnel*
Dir General: Clive Alexander Bayne
Founded: 1983
ISBN Prefix(es): 968-6070

**Editorial Planeta Mexicana SA**
Member of Grupo Planeta
Insurgentes Sur No 1898-11, Col Florida, 01030 Mexico, DF
*Tel:* (05) 5322-3610 *Fax:* (05) 5322-3636
*Web Site:* www.editorialplaneta.com.mx
*Key Personnel*
Man Dir, Editorial: Joaquin Diez-Canedo
Production, Rights & Permissions: Francisco Campos
Founded: 1977
Subjects: Fiction, History, Nonfiction (General), Psychology, Psychiatry, Social Sciences, Sociology
ISBN Prefix(es): 968-6640; 970-9031
*Branch Office(s)*
Editoriales Ariel, Planeta, Seix Barral, Joaquin Planeta

**Plaza y Valdes SA de CV+**
Cedro No 299, Col Sta Maria La Rivera, 06400 Mexico, DF
*Tel:* (05) 5359851; (05) 5664055
*E-mail:* editorial@plazayvaldes.com.mx
*Key Personnel*
Dir General: Fernando Valdes
Founded: 1987
Membership(s): Mexican Publishing Association.
Subjects: Agriculture, Anthropology, Archaeology, Communications, Public Administration, Religion - Buddhist, Science (General), Science Fiction, Fantasy, Social Sciences, Sociology
ISBN Prefix(es): 968-856

*Associate Companies:* Libermex SA-de-CV Libreria Bunuel
*U.S. Office(s):* Libros Sin Fronteras, PO Box 2085, Olympia, WA 98507-2085, United States
*Tel:* 206-357-4332 *Fax:* 206-357-4332
*Bookshop(s):* Insurgentes sur 32 Col Juarez, 06600 Mexico, DF

## Editorial Porrua SA

Ave Republica, Argentina No 15, Centro, 06020 Mexico, DF
*Tel:* (05) 7025467 *Fax:* (05) 7024574 *Cable:* PORRUAS MEXICO
*Key Personnel*
Dir General & President: Jose Antonio Perez Porrua
Founded: 1900
Subjects: Literature, Literary Criticism, Essays
ISBN Prefix(es): 968-432; 968-452; 970-07
*Orders to:* Libreria de Porrua Hnos y Cia SA, Apdo M-7990, Argentina 15

## Ediciones Cientificas La Prensa Medica Mexicana SA de CV+

Paseo de las Facultades 26, Col Copilco Universidad Coyoacan, 04360 Mexico, DF
*Tel:* (05) 5504500 *Fax:* (05) 6589193 *Cable:* LAPREMEMEX
*Key Personnel*
Man Dir, Rights & Permissions: Carlos A Fournier Amor
Administration & Assistant Manager: Abel Zavaleta
Sales & Promotion: Angelica Ruiz
Founded: 1945
Membership(s): National Chamber of the Mexican Editorial Industry.
Subjects: Biological Sciences, Education, Medicine, Nursing, Dentistry, Social Sciences, Sociology, Veterinary Science
ISBN Prefix(es): 968-435

## Prentice Hall Hispanoamericana, *imprint of* Pearson Educacion de Mexico, SA de CV

## Editorial Progreso SA de CV

Sabino 275, Col Santa Maria La Ribera, 06400 Mexico, DF
*Tel:* (05) 547-1780 *Fax:* (05) 541-1189
*E-mail:* editprogresosav@infosel.net.mx
*Key Personnel*
Dir: Joaquin Flores Segura *E-mail:* progdir@webtelmex.net.mx
Founded: 1952
Subjects: Education, Religion - Catholic
ISBN Prefix(es): 968-436; 970-641
Number of titles published annually: 300 Print

## Ediciones Promesa, SA de CV+

Justo Sierra, 53-A, Circuito Educadores, Ciudad Satelite, Edo de
Mailing Address: Apdo P97 CP 53140 Boulevares, Edo de Mexico, Mexico
*Tel:* (05) 5623174; (05) 3938707 *Fax:* (05) 5623174
*E-mail:* promesa@mati.net.mx; riveraluisa@hotmail.com
*Key Personnel*
Contact: Fernando B Rivera
Founded: 1979
Subjects: Anthropology, Architecture & Interior Design, Biography, Child Care & Development, Education, Fashion, Fiction, Film, Video, Human Relations, Language Arts, Linguistics, Music, Dance, Philosophy, Poetry, Psychology, Psychiatry, Religion - Catholic, Theology, Women's Studies
ISBN Prefix(es): 968-7224

## Promociones de Mercados Turisticos SA de CV

Gral Juan Cano No 68, Col San Miguel Chapultepec, Del Miguel Hidalgo, 11850 Mexico, DF
Mailing Address: Apartado 6-1007, 06600 Mexico, DF
*Tel:* (05) 2771480; (05) 5160162; (05) 2714736 *Fax:* (05) 2725942
*E-mail:* tm@mail.internet.com.mx
*Web Site:* www.travelguidemexico.com
*Key Personnel*
Dir: Chris A Luhnow
Specialize in publishing & editing. Publishes the most complete & best selling guide book to Mexico.
Subjects: Travel
Total Titles: 3 Print

## Publicaciones Cultural SA de CV

Renacimiento 180, Col San Juan Tlihuaca, Azcapotzalco, 02400 Mexico, DF
*Tel:* (05) 55618333; (05) 55619299 *Fax:* (05) 5615231; (05) 55614063
*E-mail:* info@patriacultural.com.mx
*Web Site:* www.patriacultural.com.mx
*Key Personnel*
President: Carlos Frigolet Lerma
General Dir, Editorial, Production & Sales: Victorico Albores Santiago
Rights & Permissions: Ofelia Garcia Martinez
Production: Mario Munoz Rodriguez
Founded: 1965
ISBN Prefix(es): 968-439; 970-16

## Publicaciones Importantes SA

Bolivar No 8-601, Col Centro, CP 06000 Mexico 1, DF
*Tel:* (05) 5101884; (05) 5109489 *Fax:* (05) 5129411
*Key Personnel*
Contact: Alfredo Farrugia Reed

## Editorial Quehacer Politico SA

Manuael Gonzales No 545, Col Atlampa, CP 06450 Mexico, DF
*Tel:* (05) 5414245 *Fax:* (05) 5384855
*Key Personnel*
General Dir: Miguel Canton Zetina
Editorial Dir: Jorge Luis Sierra Guzman
ISBN Prefix(es): 968-6553; 968-7320

## Red Editorial Iberoamericana Mexico SA de CV+

Lago Mayor No 186, Col Anahuac, 11320 Mexico, DF
*Tel:* (05) 5456860; (05) 5456861 *Fax:* (05) 5619112
*Key Personnel*
President: Carlos Frigolet Lerma
Rights & Permissions: Victorico Albores Santiago
Production: Mario Munoz Rodriguez
Founded: 1986
ISBN Prefix(es): 968-456

## Ediciones Roca, SA+

Insurgentes Sur 1162, Col Del Valle, 03100 Mexico, DF
*Tel:* (05) 5758585; (05) 2770946
*Fax on Demand:* (05) 5758980
*Telex:* 1772155
*Key Personnel*
General Manager: Victor Lemus Dominquez
Founded: 1972
Subjects: Education, Environmental Studies, Fiction, History, Literature, Literary Criticism, Essays, Religion - Other
ISBN Prefix(es): 968-21

## Rustica, *imprint of* AGT Editor SA

## Salvat Editores de Mexico+

Presidente Mazarik No 101-5 Piso, Col Chapultepec Morales, 11560 Mexico, DF
*Tel:* (05) 2034813; (05) 2034393 *Fax:* (05) 5318773
*E-mail:* hachettemex@hachette.ex.com.mx
*Key Personnel*
President, Editorial, Rights & Permissions: Jean Claude Lhomme
Sales (Encyclopedias): Jacobo Jimenez Parker
Production: Teresa Ponce
Subjects: Cookery, Fiction, Geography, Geology, History, Medicine, Nursing, Dentistry
ISBN Prefix(es): 968-32
*Parent Company:* Salvat Editores SA, Spain
Subsidiaries: Promotora Editorial SA De C V
*Bookshop(s):* Libreria de Cd Universitatia, Odontologia 69, Local 9; Libreria Satelite, Plaza Satelite, Local D-155, Cd Satelite; Libreri de Morelia, Ave Francisco I Madero Pte 533, Centro, Mrelia, Mich

## Editorial Santillana SA de CV

Av Universidad No 767, Col Del Valle, 03100 Mexico, DF
*Tel:* (05) 6887566; (05) 6888227; (05) 6888966 *Fax:* (05) 6042304
*E-mail:* mexico@santillana.com.mx
*Web Site:* www.gruposantillana.com
*Key Personnel*
Dir, Publications: Fernando Garcia Cortes
ISBN Prefix(es): 968-430; 970-642
*Parent Company:* Grupo Santillana

## Grupo Santillana

Av Universidad No 767, Col Del Valle, 03100 Mexico, DF
*Tel:* (05) 6888966; (05) 6887566; (05) 6888227 *Fax:* (05) 6042304
*E-mail:* mexico@santillana.com.mx
*Web Site:* www.gruposantillana.com
*Key Personnel*
Dir General: Jorge Delkader Teig
Contact: Manuel Sabido Duran
ISBN Prefix(es): 968-430; 970-642
Divisions: Actea; Aguilar; Distribuidora Aguilar; Aguilar Mexicana de Ediciones; Alfaquara SA de CV; Altea Taurus; Editorial Santillana SA de CV; Taurus

## Sayrols Editorial SA de CV+

Mier y Pesado No 128, Col Del Valle, 03100 Mexico, DF
*Tel:* (05) 660-3535 *Fax:* (05) 687-4699
*E-mail:* ventas@sayrols.com.mx
*Web Site:* www.sayrols.com.mx
*Key Personnel*
General Dir: Roberto Davo *E-mail:* rodavo@sayrols.com.mx
Corporate Sales Dir: Federico Falkner *E-mail:* ffalkner@sayrols.com.mx
Business & Technology Sales Manager: Beatriz Coria *Tel:* (0525) 536-4115 *E-mail:* beatrizc@sayrols.com.mx
Administrative Dir: Lourdes Noriega *E-mail:* lnoriega@sayrols.com.mx
Finance Manager: Raul Saryols *E-mail:* rauls@saryols.com.mx
Circulation Manager: Luis Sayrols *E-mail:* luiss@sayrols.com.mx
Founded: 1925
Specialize in information technology & business titles. Provides editorial, printing & distribution services.
Subjects: Astrology, Occult, Automotive, Business, Computer Science, Cookery, Crafts, Games, Hobbies, Education, Fashion, Sports, Athletics, Women's Studies
ISBN Prefix(es): 968-6117
Total Titles: 30 Print
*Associate Companies:* Mystic Impresiones SA (Printing); Publicaciones Sayrols SA

Subsidiaries: Servicios Editoriales Sayrols SA de CV

Distributor for AIE (Italy); Grupo Editorial Ideas SA (Mexico); Hymsa Edipress (Spain); Ediciones Pleyades (Spain); Servicios de Edicion Mexico SA (editorial); Servicios Editoriales Sayrols SA (editorial); Servicios Graficos Sayrols SA (design & prepress services)

**Scott Foresman**, *imprint of* Pearson Educacion de Mexico, SA de CV

**SCRIPTA - Distribucion y Servicios Editoriales SA de CV+**
Copilco 178 Edif 21-501, Col Copilco Universidad, 04340 Mexico, DF
Mailing Address: Apdo Postal 70 649, 140000 Mexico, DF
*Tel:* (05) 5481716 *Fax:* (05) 6161496
*E-mail:* dyse@data.net.mx
*Key Personnel*
Contact: Bertha R Alavez Magana
Founded: 1986
Also acts as exporter & distributor.
Subjects: Art, Business, Film, Video, History
ISBN Prefix(es): 968-6269
*U.S. Office(s):* Scripta, 4011 Creek Rd, Youngstown, NY 14174, United States
*Tel:* 716-754-8145 *Fax:* 716-754-2707

**Selector SA de CV+**
Dr Erazo 120 Colonia Doctores, 06720 Mexico, DF
*Tel:* (055) 588-7272 *Fax:* (055) 761-5716
*E-mail:* info@selector.com.mx
*Web Site:* www.selector.com.mx
*Key Personnel*
President: Gonzalo Araico Montes de Oca
Sales Dir: Francisco Merino Nieto
Publisher: Ma del Carmen Leal
Editorial Assistant: Rocio Flores
Management Dir: Maricruz Vazquez Ruiz
Production Dir: Victor Becerra Rodriguez
Founded: 1949
Subjects: Child Care & Development, Crafts, Games, Hobbies, English as a Second Language, Health, Nutrition, Human Relations, Humor, Nonfiction (General), Science Fiction, Fantasy, Self-Help
ISBN Prefix(es): 968-403; 970-643
Number of titles published annually: 77 Print
*Branch Office(s)*
Prisciliano Sanchez 579, Col Centr, 44100 Guadalajara, Jalisco
Sucursal Monterrey, Washington 112 B, Altos, Col Centro, Monterrey, NL, Contact: Francisco Mendoza Salazar *Tel:* (08) 340 3260
Distributed by Ediciones Oceano Argentina SA; Editorial Diana Colombia Ltda; Carlos Federspiel y Co SA; Editorial Diana Chilena Ltd; Editorial Oceano Ecuatorian SA; Almacenes Siman SA; Distribuciones Alfaomega SA; Publicaciones Yuquivo; Central De Libros C POR A; Giron Spanish Book; Lectorum Publications Inc; Editorial Oceno Peruana SA; Vendiana Editorial AC; Editorial Oceano De Venezuela SA
Foreign Rep(s): Almacenes Siman (El Salvador); Central de Libros C Por A (Dominican Republic); Editorial Diana Chilena Ltda (Chile); Editorial Diana Colombiana Ltda (Colombia); Distribuciones Alfaomega SA (Spain); Carlos Federspiel y Co SA (Costa Rica); Giron Spanish Book Distributors Inc (US); Lectorum Publications Inc (US); Libreria Lehmann SA (Costa Rica); Ediciones Oceano Argentina SA (Argentina); Editorial Oceano Ecuatoriana SA (Ecuador); Publicaciones Yuquiyu (Puerto Rico); Santa Maria Representaciones Editoriales (Central America); Venediana Editorial AC (Venezuela)
*Bookshop(s):* Lectorum, SA de CV, Calzada Del Hueso 809, Locales 8 y 9, Col Mirador Coapa,

Mexico, DF *Tel:* (055) 6030790; Un Paseo Por Libros, Pasaje Zocalo-Pino Suarez, Local 21, Mexico, DF *Tel:* (055) 522 3578; (055) 522 3486

**Servicios Especiales Maciel SA de CV**, see Grupo Azabache Sa de CV

**Siglo XXI Editores SA de CV+**
Av Cerro del Agua, No 248, Col Romero de Terreros, 04310 Mexico, DF
*Tel:* (05) 6587999; (05) 6587588 *Fax:* (05) 6587599
*E-mail:* sigloxxi@inetcorp.net.mx
*Web Site:* www.sigloxxi-editores.com.mx *Cable:* SIGLOEDIT
*Key Personnel*
Man Dir, Editorial: Arnaldo Orfila; Jaime Labastida
General Manager, Rights & Permissions & Publicity: Guadalupe Ortiz
Sales & Contact: Marta De la Rosa
Production: Maria Oscos
Founded: 1966
Subjects: Anthropology, Architecture & Interior Design, Art, Criminology, Economics, Education, Government, Political Science, Health, Nutrition, History, Language Arts, Linguistics, Law, Literature, Literary Criticism, Essays, Philosophy, Psychology, Psychiatry, Regional Interests, Science (General), Social Sciences, Sociology
ISBN Prefix(es): 968-23

**Silver Burdette Ginn**, *imprint of* Pearson Educacion de Mexico, SA de CV

**Sistemas Tecnicos de Edicion SA de CV+**
San Marcos No 102, Col Tlalpan, 14000 Mexico, DF
*Tel:* (05) 6559144; (05) 6845220 *Fax:* (05) 5739412
*Telex:* 1771410 *Cable:* SITEME
*Key Personnel*
President: Jose Ignacio Echeverria
Editor: Marsella Cruz
International Operations: Emma Moreno
Founded: 1985
Subjects: Animals, Pets, Behavioral Sciences, Biological Sciences, Cookery, Earth Sciences, History, Language Arts, Linguistics, Management, Mathematics, Self-Help
ISBN Prefix(es): 968-6579; 970-629; 968-6048; 968-6394; 968-6135

**Sistemas Universales, SA+**
Insurgentes Centro 123, Col San Rafael, 06470 Mexico, DF
Mailing Address: Apdo Postal 61-178, 06470 Mexico, DF
*Tel:* (05) 705-4568; (05) 705-5937 *Fax:* (05) 705-3421
*Key Personnel*
Contact: Arturo Delgado
Founded: 1970
Specialize in post secondary technical books for distance education.
Subjects: Accounting, Automotive, Electronics, Electrical Engineering, English as a Second Language, Microcomputers
ISBN Prefix(es): 968-6064
Total Titles: 290 Print
Distributed by Hemphill California Corporation

**Ediciones Suromex SA+**
General Francisco Murguia No 7, Col Hipodromo de la Condesa, 06170 Mexico, DF
*Tel:* (055) 2770744; (055) 2723570; (055) 2723630; (055) 2734989 *Fax:* (055) 2710470; (055) 2719378
*E-mail:* suromex@mail.internet.com.mx

*Web Site:* www.intralector.com/suromex/
*Key Personnel*
General Manager: Victor Lemus Dominguez
Founded: 1982
Subjects: Animals, Pets, Art, Astrology, Occult, Astronomy, Biography, Cookery, Earth Sciences, Gardening, Plants, House & Home, Religion - Other, Self-Help, Sports, Athletics
ISBN Prefix(es): 968-855
Number of titles published annually: 70 Print
Total Titles: 350 Print
*Parent Company:* Susaeta Ediciones SA

**Time-Life Internacional de Mexico**
Paseo de la Reforma 195, 10° Decimo Piso, Col Cuauhtemoc, 06500 Mexico, DF
*Tel:* (055) 5469000 *Fax:* (055) 5159764
*Web Site:* www.timelife.com
*Key Personnel*
General Manager: Koos H Siewers
Founded: 1962
Subjects: Nonfiction (General)
ISBN Prefix(es): 968-7123

**Travelers Guide to Mexico**, see Promociones de Mercados Turisticos SA de CV

**Editorial Trillas SA de CV+**
Av Rio Churubusco 385, Pedro Maria Anaya, 03340 Mexico, DF
*Tel:* (055) 6330612; (055) 6331112 *Fax:* (055) 6330870; (055) 6342221
*E-mail:* laviga@trillas.com.mx; Trillasenvios@att.net.mx
*Web Site:* www.trillas.com.mx
*Telex:* 1762109 Etrime *Cable:* ETRILLASA
*Key Personnel*
Man Dir: Francisco Trillas
Editorial: Carlos Trillas
Sales: Jesus Galera
Production: Alfonso Duran
Publicity: Sergio Shinji
Founded: 1953
Subjects: Architecture & Interior Design, Business, Child Care & Development, Crafts, Games, Hobbies, Education, English as a Second Language, House & Home, Law, Mathematics, Medicine, Nursing, Dentistry, Psychology, Psychiatry, Science (General), Social Sciences, Sociology, Veterinary Science
ISBN Prefix(es): 968-24
*Associate Companies:* Cia Editorial Carmex SA, Venezuela 1962, Buenos Aires, Argentina; Cia Editorial Atlante; Limex Venezolana CA, Ave Lima Quinta Lourdes, Los Caobos, Caracas, Venezuela; Trillas Colombia, Carreroi 15 No 33-71 Apdo, Aereo 15-151, Santa Fe de Boqota, Colombia, Contact: Joslyne Reyno; Biblouex SA, Raigizas 10.28026, Madrid, Spain
*Branch Office(s)*
Calzada de la Viga 1132, Col Apatlaco, Delegacon Iztapalapa, 09439 Mexico, DF *Tel:* (055) 6579188 *Fax:* (055) 6579235
*Orders to:* Calzada de la Viga 1132, Col Apatlaco, Delegacon Iztapalapa, 09439 Mexico, DF *Tel:* (055) 6579188 *Fax:* (055) 6579235

**El Trimestre Economico**, *imprint of* Fondo de Cultura Economica

**Editorial Turner de Mexico**
Edificio Condesa, Cda de Matehuala 1-6, Colonia Condesa, 06140 Mexico, DF
*Tel:* (055) 5553 1183 *Fax:* (055) 5211 2070
*Web Site:* www.turnerlibros.com
*Key Personnel*
Rights: Alexandra Garcia *E-mail:* alexgarcia@turnermexico.com
Founded: 2003
General nonfiction in the fields of history, literary criticism, art philosophy, music & bullfighting.

Subjects: Art, Business, Economics, Finance, Literature, Literary Criticism, Essays, Music, Dance, Photography, Bullfighting
Number of titles published annually: 120 Print
Total Titles: 400 Print
*Parent Company:* Turner Publicaciones
*Branch Office(s)*
Turner Publicaciones SL, C/Rafael Calvo, 42, esc izda, 2a planta, 28010 Madrid, Spain, Contact: Juan Garcia de Oteyza *Tel:* (091) 308 33 36 *Fax:* (091) 319 39 30 *E-mail:* turner@turnerlibros.com
Distributed by Distributed Art Publishers (DAP) (USA); Editorial Oceano SA de CV (Latin America)

**Universidad Nacional Autonoma de Mexico Centro (National University of Mexico)+**
Zona Cultural s/n Edificio B 3° Piso, Col Ciudad Universitaria, 04510 Mexico, DF
*Tel:* (05) 6226329; (05) 6226330 *Fax:* (05) 6226328
*E-mail:* libros@bibliounam.unam.mx
*Key Personnel*
Dir: Mario Mendoza Castaneda
Assistant Dir: Leonardo Duenas Garcia
Founded: 1935
Subjects: Anthropology, Archaeology, Architecture & Interior Design, Chemistry, Chemical Engineering, Drama, Theater, Economics, Education, Engineering (General), Ethnicity, Geography, Geology, History, Journalism, Language Arts, Linguistics, Law, Literature, Literary Criticism, Essays, Mathematics, Medicine, Nursing, Dentistry, Music, Dance, Philosophy, Physics, Psychology, Psychiatry, Science (General), Social Sciences, Sociology, Technology, Veterinary Science
ISBN Prefix(es): 968-36
*U.S. Office(s):* Hemisfair Plaza, PO Box 830426, San Antonio, TX 78283-0426, United States
*Bookshop(s):* Libreria Central, Corredor de Zona Comercial, Ciudad Universitaria, 04510 Mexico, DF; Libreria del Palacio de Mineria, Tacuba 5, 06000 Mexico, DF; Casa Universitaria del Libro, Orizaba y Puebla, Col Roma, 06710 Mexico, DF; Libreria Julio Torri, Zona Cultura, Cuidad Universitaria, 04510 Mexico, DF

**Universidad Veracruzana Direccion General Editorial y de Publicaciones**
Lomas del Estadio s/n, Col Centro, 91000 Jalapa, Veracruz
*Tel:* (029) 71316
*E-mail:* direditaspeedy@coacade.uv.mx
*Web Site:* www.uv.mx
*Key Personnel*
Sales & Subscriptions: Jaime Pasquel Brash
Founded: 1957
Subjects: Anthropology, Art, Drama, Theater, Education, Fiction, History, Music, Dance, Philosophy, Psychology, Psychiatry, Social Sciences, Sociology
ISBN Prefix(es): 968-834
Total Titles: 15 Print
*Parent Company:* Universidad Veracruzana
Distributed by Direccion Editorial Universidad Veracruzana (Mexico)

**Editorial Universo SA de CV**
Roberto Gayol No 1219, Col Del Valle, 03100 Mexico, DF
*Tel:* (05) 5750711 ext 30; (05) 5750711 ext 31
*Key Personnel*
Man Dir, Rights & Permissions: Enrique Ivan H Garcia
Editorial: Fausto Rosales
Sales: Manuel Valdez Islas
Production: Enrique Escamilla
Publicity: Maria del Refugio Salinas
Founded: 1979

Subjects: Fiction, Nonfiction (General)
ISBN Prefix(es): 968-35
*Parent Company:* Editorial Diana SA
*Associate Companies:* Editorial Origen SA; Edivision Cia Editorial SA
*Branch Office(s)*
Buenos Aires, Argentina
Guadalajara
Monterrey
Caracas, Venezuela

**Universo Editorial SA de CV Edicion de Libros Revistas y Periodicos+**
c/o Arco Iris Editorial, Emelia Carranza No 105, 78290 San Luis Potosi
*Tel:* (048) 21593
*Key Personnel*
Contact: Edmundo Llamas
Founded: 1991
Subjects: Biological Sciences, Fiction, Journalism, Literature, Literary Criticism, Essays, Medicine, Nursing, Dentistry, Poetry
ISBN Prefix(es): 968-6504

**Uteha,** *imprint of* Editorial Limusa SA de CV

**Editorial Varazen SA+**
Herodoto No 42, Col Anzures, 11590 Mexico, DF
*Tel:* (05) 5459230; (05) 5335274 *Fax:* (05) 2555172
*Key Personnel*
Man Dir: Luis Maria Molachino Agostena
Founded: 1968
Subjects: Education, Ethnicity
ISBN Prefix(es): 968-7128
*Associate Companies:* Editorial Juventud, SA, Barcelona, Spain

**Ventura Ediciones, SA de CV**
Rio Ganges No 64, Col Cuauhtemoc, 06500 Mexico, DF
*Tel:* (05) 2087681; (05) 5530798 *Fax:* (05) 5431173
*Key Personnel*
General Dir: Nicolas Grepe
Founded: 1988
Subjects: Computer Science, Microcomputers
ISBN Prefix(es): 968-6346; 968-7393

**Javier Vergara Editor SA de CV**
Av Cuauhtemoc 1100, Col Vertiz Navarte, 03600 Mexico, DF
*Tel:* (05) 6053374; (05) 6048283
*Key Personnel*
General Manager: Elsa Marino
Founded: 1978
Subjects: Biography, Business, Fiction, History, Music, Dance, Nonfiction (General), Psychology, Psychiatry, Self-Help
ISBN Prefix(es): 968-497
*Parent Company:* Javier Vergara Editor Argentina

**Editorial Vuelta, SA de CV+**
Av Contreras 516, Col San Jeronimo Lidice, 10200 Mexico, DF
*Tel:* (05) 6835633 *Fax:* (05) 6580074
*Key Personnel*
President: Octavio Paz
Manager: Patricia Rodriguez Ochoa
Secretary: Enrique Krauze
ISBN Prefix(es): 968-6229; 968-7656

**Martha Zamora Edicion de Libros**
Bosque del Castillo 35, La Herradura, Huixquilucan Edo, 53920 Mexico, DF
*Tel:* (05) 2940231 *Fax:* (05) 2943856
*Key Personnel*
Contact: Martha Zamora
ISBN Prefix(es): 970-91616

**Zona Ediciones y Publications SA de CV**
Beta No 97 Col Romero de Terreros-Coyoacan, 04310 Mexico, DF
*Tel:* (05) 5547438
*Key Personnel*
Contact: Francisco Campos Fontanet
ISBN Prefix(es): 968-6174
*Warehouse:* Ignacio Manuel Altamirano, 212 B Col Hank Gonzalez, 09750 Mexico, DF

# Republic of Moldova

## General Information

*Capital:* Kishinev
*Language:* Romanian
*Religion:* Predominantly Christian (mostly Eastern Orthodox)
*Population:* 4.5 million
*Bank Hours:* Generally open for short hours between 0930-1230 Monday-Friday
*Shop Hours:* Generally 0900-1800 Monday-Friday; often open weekends
*Currency:* 100 kopeks = 1 rubl
*Export/Import Information:* According to Ukrainian quotas & customs duties, companies engaged in trade should register with the Ukraine Ministry of Foreign Economic Relations. Licenses for export & import are also required for trade with Russia.
*Copyright:* UCC (see Copyright Conventions, pg xi)

**Editura Cartea Moldovei**
bd Stefan Cel Mare 180, 2004 Chisinau
*Tel:* (02) 244022 *Fax:* (02) 246411
*Key Personnel*
Dir: N N Mumzhi
Editor-in-Chief: I A Tsurkanu
Founded: 1927
Subjects: Agriculture, Economics, Fiction, Government, Political Science, Human Relations, Literature, Literary Criticism, Essays, Social Sciences, Sociology, Scientific Research Literature
ISBN Prefix(es): 5-362

**Editura Hyperion**
Bdl Stefan cel Mare 180, 2004 Chisinau
*Tel:* (02) 244259
*Key Personnel*
Dir: Valeriu Matei
Founded: 1976
Subjects: Art, Fiction, Literature, Literary Criticism, Essays, Music, Dance
ISBN Prefix(es): 5-368

**Editura Lumina**
bd Stefan cel Mare, 180, et 5, 505, 2004 Chisinau
*Tel:* (02) 246397; (02) 246398 *Fax:* (02) 246395
*E-mail:* lumina@mdl.net
*Key Personnel*
Manager: Vladimir Chistruga
Editor-in-Chief: Chiril Vaculovschi
Founded: 1966
Specialize in Textbooks, University Presses, Scholarly Books.
Subjects: Biological Sciences, Chemistry, Chemical Engineering, Child Care & Development, Geography, Geology, History, Language Arts, Linguistics, Literature, Literary Criticism, Essays, Mathematics, Medicine, Nursing, Dentistry, Physics, Psychology, Psychiatry, Training Manuals & Literature
ISBN Prefix(es): 5-372; 9975-65

# Monaco

## General Information

*Capital:* Monaco
*Language:* French. Monegasque, Italian and English also spoken
*Religion:* Roman Catholic
*Population:* 29,712
*Bank Hours:* 0830-1730 Monday-Friday
*Shop Hours:* 0830-1300, 1600-1930 Monday-Friday
*Currency:* 100 centimes = 1 franc
*Copyright:* Berne, UCC (see Copyright Conventions, pg xi)

**Editions Alphee+**
28 rue Comte-Felix-Gastaldi, 98015 Monaco Cedex
Mailing Address: BP 524, 98015 Monaco Cedex
*Tel:* (093) 30-40-06 *Fax:* (099) 99-67-18
ISBN Prefix(es): 2-907573
*Associate Companies:* Editions du Rocher
  *Tel:* (099) 99-67-17 *E-mail:* info@ editionsdurocher.net

**Editions EGC+**
9 Av du Prince Hereditair Albert, BP 438, 98011 Monaco Cedex
*Tel:* (093) 97984006 *Fax:* (093) 92052422
*E-mail:* multip@webstore.mc
*Key Personnel*
Administrator: M Gerard Comman
Subjects: Economics, History, Literature, Literary Criticism, Essays
ISBN Prefix(es): 2-911469

**Editions Victor Gadoury**
57, rue Grimaldi, 98000 Monaco
*Tel:* (093) 251296 *Fax:* (093) 501339
*E-mail:* contact@gadoury.com
*Web Site:* www.gadoury.com
Founded: 1967
ISBN Prefix(es): 2-906602

**Marsu Productions SAM**
9, Ave des Castelans, 98000 Monte-Carlo
*Tel:* (093) 92056111 *Fax:* (093) 92057660
*E-mail:* info@marsupilami.com
  marsuproductions@compuserve.com
*Web Site:* www.marsupilami.com
ISBN Prefix(es): 2-9502211

**Editions de l'Oiseau-Lyre SAM**
Les Remparts, MC 98015 Monaco, Cedex
Mailing Address: BP 515, MC 98015 Monaco, Cedex
*Tel:* (093) 300944 *Fax:* (093) 301915
*E-mail:* oiseaulyre@monaco377.com
*Web Site:* www.oiseaulyre.com
*Key Personnel*
Man Dir: Moroney Davitt
Founded: 1932
Subjects: Music, Dance
ISBN Prefix(es): 2-87855

**Publications du Palais de Monaco**
Archives du Palais Princier, BP 518, 98015 Monaco Cedex
*Tel:* 093 251831
ISBN Prefix(es): 2-903147

**Les Editions du Rocher+**
28 rue Comte Felix Gastaldi, 98015 Monaco, Cedex
*Tel:* (093) 40465400 *Fax:* (093) 43293506
*E-mail:* jpb.droits@wanadoo.fr
Founded: 1943

Subjects: Antiques, Astrology, Occult, Biography, Crafts, Games, Hobbies, Drama, Theater, Fiction, Health, Nutrition, History, How-to, Humor, Literature, Literary Criticism, Essays, Military Science, Mysteries, Philosophy, Psychology, Psychiatry, Religion - Other, Romance, Science Fiction, Fantasy, Self-Help, Sports, Athletics, Western Fiction
ISBN Prefix(es): 2-268
Subsidiaries: Jean-Paul Bertrand Editeur
*Shipping Address:* 6 Place Saint, Sulpice, 75279 Paris, France *Tel:* (01) 40465400 *Fax:* (01) 40469136

**Rondeau Giannipiero a Monaco+**
4 rue Langl e, 98000 Monaco
*Tel:* (093) 303075 *Fax:* (093) 257047
*Key Personnel*
President: S Roudeau
International Rights: G Roudeau
Founded: 1993
Subjects: Art, Fiction, History, Humor, Literature, Literary Criticism, Essays
ISBN Prefix(es): 2-910305

**Editions Andre Sauret SA**
One blvd Suisse, 98000 Monaco
*Tel:* (093) 506794 *Fax:* (093) 307104
Subjects: Art, Fiction, Library & Information Sciences
ISBN Prefix(es): 2-85051

# Mongolia

## General Information

*Capital:* Ulaanbaatar
*Language:* Mongolian
*Religion:* Buddhist Lamaism, Islamic, Christian
*Population:* 2.6 million
*Bank Hours:* 0900-1200, 1400-1700 Monday-Saturday
*Shop Hours:* 0900-1900 Monday-Saturday
*Currency:* 100 mongo = 1 togrog (tughrik)

**Mongol Knigotorg**
41 Ul Lenina, Ulan-Bator
Also functions as distributor.

**State Press**
Ulan-Bator
Subjects: Geography, Geology, Government, Political Science, Law

# Morocco

## General Information

*Capital:* Rabat
*Language:* Arabic (official), Berber, French, Spanish (northern regions)
*Religion:* Islamic
*Population:* 27 million
*Bank Hours:* Summer: 0830-1130, 1500-1700 Monday-Friday; rest of year: 0815-1130, 1415-1630 Monday-Friday
*Shop Hours:* Tangiers: 0900-1200, 1600-2000; rest: 0900-1200, 1500-1800 or 1900
*Currency:* 100 centimes = 1 Moroccan dirham
*Export/Import Information:* No tariff on books; most advertising dutiable. Special Tax, and Stamp Duty of percentage of import duty. No

import licenses required. Exchange controls but permission liberally granted.
*Copyright:* UCC, Berne (see Copyright Conventions, pg xi)

**Access International Services+**
80 Blvd de La Resistance, Casablanca
*Tel:* (02) 316068 *Fax:* (02) 304685
*Key Personnel*
President: Rachid Bennis
Founded: 1985
Also acts as editor & exporter of Moroccan publications.
Subjects: Advertising, Art, Business, Communications, Economics, How-to, Human Relations, Law, Publishing & Book Trade Reference, Religion - Islamic
ISBN Prefix(es): 9981-9756
Imprints: Le Repere
*Branch Office(s)*
African Imprint Library Services, 236 Main St, Falmouth, MA 02540, United States

**Editions Al-Fourkane+**
8, rue Ibn Habbous, Av Yacoub El Mansour, App No 2, Hay Salam, Casablanca
Mailing Address: BP 20362, Hay Salam, Casablanca
*Tel:* (02) 983351 *Fax:* (02) 983351
*Key Personnel*
Dir: Dr El Otmani Saad-Dine
Subjects: Biography, Government, Political Science, Religion - Islamic, Social Sciences, Sociology
ISBN Prefix(es): 9981-811
*Parent Company:* Al Fouruane

**Annuaine Fax Telex**, *imprint of* Office Marocain D'Annonces-OMA

**Association de la Recherche Historique et Sociale+**
BP 57, Ksar El Kebir 92-150
*Tel:* 918239
*Key Personnel*
Contact: Mohamed Akhrif
Subjects: Antiques, Archaeology, Art, Biography, History, Natural History, Poetry
ISBN Prefix(es): 9981-9778
Distributed by Editeurs Particuliers
Distributor for Imprimerie de Tanger SA

**Cabinet Conseil CCMLA**
44 rue Oued Ziz, Agdal, 10000 Rabat
*Tel:* (07) 770229; (07) 770264 *Fax:* (07) 770264
*Key Personnel*
Manager: Michele Malaval
Founded: 1992
Subjects: Accounting, Developing Countries, Economics
ISBN Prefix(es): 9981-9699

**Dar El Kitab**
Place de la Mosquee, 4018, Habous, Casablanca
*Tel:* (02) 304581; (02) 305419 *Fax:* (02) 304581
*Telex:* 26630 Darki
*Key Personnel*
President: Boutaleb Abdou Abdelhay
Manager: Mrs Soad Kadiri
Publicity Manager: Mounjedine Abdel-Ghani
Production: Ferhat Mohamed
Founded: 1948
Subjects: History, Philosophy, Regional Interests, Science (General), Social Sciences, Sociology
ISBN Prefix(es): 9981-133

**Dar Nachr Al Maarifa Pour L'Edition et La Distribution+**
Cite Yacoub El-Mansour, Rue Errakha, Quartier Industriel, BP 1213, Rabat
Mailing Address: 10, Ave Fadela, QI CYM Rabat

*Tel:* (07) 795702; (07) 796914 *Fax:* (07) 790343
*Key Personnel*
Contact: Mr Zhiri M'Hamed
Founded: 1988
Also acts as distributor.
Membership(s): Moroccan Association of Publishers; International Publishers Association.
Subjects: Economics, Education, History, Law, Literature, Literary Criticism, Essays, Mathematics, Science (General), Social Sciences, Sociology
ISBN Prefix(es): 9981-808
Number of titles published annually: 10 Print
Total Titles: 3 Print
Distributor for APREJ
*Bookshop(s):* Librairie EL Maarif, SA, Rue Bab Chellah, BP 239, Rabat *Tel:* (07) 726524; 730701

**Edition Diffusion de Livre au Maroc+**
71 ave des Forces armees royales, 21000 Casablanca
Mailing Address: BP 7537, Casablanca
*Tel:* (02) 442375; (02) 442376; (02) 445986 *Fax:* (02) 313565
*E-mail:* info@eddif.net.ma
*Telex:* 23793M
*Key Personnel*
Chairman: Abdelkader Retnani
Dir: Fadwa Akkor
Founded: 1979
Membership(s): Moroccan Association of Profession of Books (AMPL).
Subjects: Archaeology, Art, Drama, Theater, Education, Fiction, History, How-to, Humor, Law, Literature, Literary Criticism, Essays, Medicine, Nursing, Dentistry, Music, Dance, Philosophy, Psychology, Psychiatry, Religion - Other, Social Sciences, Sociology, Travel, Women's Studies
ISBN Prefix(es): 2-908801; 9981-09
Total Titles: 300 Print
*Associate Companies:* Comptoir Marocain du Livre, Angles rues des Landes et Vignemale, Casablanca 20000 *Tel:* (022) 258781
*Branch Office(s)*
La Croisee Des Chemins
Distributor for Ceres Production (Tunisia)
*Bookshop(s):* Carrefour Des Arts, Rue Essanaani, Quartier Boorgogne, 20000 Casablanca *Tel:* (022) 26 05 01 05 *Fax:* (022) 29 43 64 *E-mail:* mrctruni@caromail.com; Carrerour Des Livres, Angle rues des landes et Vignemale, Maarif Casablanca 20000 *Tel:* (022) 258781; Librairie 11 Janview, 53 av de madagascar, Rabat *Tel:* (07) 704580

**Europages,** *imprint of* Office Marocain D'Annonces-OMA

**Editions Le Fennec+**
193 av Hassan II, 01 Casablanca
*Tel:* (02) 220519; (02) 268008; (02) 264380 *Fax:* (02) 264941
*E-mail:* fennec@techno.net.ma
*Telex:* 45468
*Key Personnel*
President, Editor: Laila Chaouni
Author: Fatima Mernissi
Founded: 1987
Subjects: Drama, Theater, Economics, Fiction, Health, Nutrition, Language Arts, Linguistics, Literature, Literary Criticism, Essays, Mysteries, Poetry, Psychology, Psychiatry, Religion - Islamic, Social Sciences, Sociology, Women's Studies
ISBN Prefix(es): 9981-838
Distributed by Vilo-Diffusion-Paris (Europe & Canada)

**Formation Entreprises,** *imprint of* Office Marocain D'Annonces-OMA

**Le Gourmand,** *imprint of* Office Marocain D'Annonces-OMA

**Government Printer (Imprimerie Officielle)**
Ave Jean Mermoz, Rabat-Chellah
*Tel:* (077) 65024

**Les Editions du Journal L' Unite Maghrebine+**
2, Lotissement El Menzah, Bettana, Sale
*Tel:* 780169 *Fax:* 780169
*Telex:* 780169
*Key Personnel*
Founder: Mohamed El Alami
Dir: Buthayma Ebrahim
Founded: 1988
Subjects: Economics, Ethnicity, Government, Political Science, Science (General), Sports, Athletics
*Parent Company:* Agence Afro-Asiatique de Press et d'Information (API)

**Les Editions Maghrebines, EDIMA**
Blvd E, N 15, Ain Sebaa, Quartier Industriel, 05 Casablanca
*Tel:* (02) 353230; (02) 353249; (02) 351797 *Fax:* (02) 355541
*Telex:* 26954
ISBN Prefix(es): 9981-24
*Bookshop(s):* Librairie EDIMA-5, Place de la Mosquee Mohammadi, Habous, Casablanca

**Office Marocain D'Annonces-OMA**
332 Blvd Brahim Roudani, Casablanca
*Tel:* (02) 234891; (02) 232342 *Fax:* (02) 234892
*Key Personnel*
Contact: Assya Djellab
Membership(s): Satellite de l' AEEA & de l'ATC Paris.
Subjects: Career Development
ISBN Prefix(es): 9981-9854
Imprints: Annuaine Fax Telex; Europages; Formation Entreprises; Le Gourmand; Les Pages Jannes Maroc
Distributor for Euredit pour le Maroc

**Editions Okad+**
4, Ave Hassan II-Quartier Industrial, Route de Casablanca, Rabat
*Tel:* (07) 796970; (07) 796971; (07) 796973 *Fax:* (07) 798556
*E-mail:* okad@wanadoo.net.ma
*Telex:* 32687
*Key Personnel*
Dir General: El Hadi Lasmer
Founded: 1981
Subjects: Economics, History, Language Arts, Linguistics, Poetry
ISBN Prefix(es): 9981-806

**Editions Oum+**
25 rue Ibn Battouta, 20000 Casablanca
*Tel:* (02) 274972; (02) 220454 *Fax:* (02) 208882; (02) 950963
*Key Personnel*
PDG: M Sijelmassi
Founded: 1992
Subjects: Art, How-to, Medicine, Nursing, Dentistry, Photography
ISBN Prefix(es): 9981-9506
Distributor for ACR; Flammarion; Gallimand

**Les Pages Jannes Maroc,** *imprint of* Office Marocain D'Annonces-OMA

**Editions La Porte+**
281 Ave Mohammed-V, Rabat
Mailing Address: BP 331, Rabat
*Tel:* (07) 709958; (07) 706476 *Fax:* (07) 709958; (07) 706478

*Key Personnel*
Man Dir: Mohamed Rafii Doukkali
Subjects: Economics, Government, Political Science, Language Arts, Linguistics, Law, Religion - Islamic, Religion - Other, Travel
ISBN Prefix(es): 9981-889
Subsidiaries: Librairie aux Belles Images (bookshop)

**Le Repere,** *imprint of* Access International Services

**Editions Services et Informations pour Etudiants+**
Cite Al Inara 1, No 155 Ave Dakhla, 02 Casablanca
Mailing Address: BP 156691 CASA-PrP, 20001 Casablanca
*Tel:* (02) 210163
*Key Personnel*
Dir: Mr Aitcaid Mustapma
Subjects: How-to

**Societe Ennewrasse Service Librairie et Imprimerie**
70 Ave Okba Bnou Nafie, Agdal, 10000 Rabat
*Tel:* (077) 6413 *Fax:* (077) 6413
*Key Personnel*
Contact: Mohamed Ali Omar
Subjects: Anthropology, Antiques, Business, Communications, Criminology, History, Human Relations, Law, Literature, Literary Criticism, Essays, Religion - Islamic, Women's Studies
ISBN Prefix(es): 9981-9645
*Parent Company:* Annawrasse (Sarl)

# Mozambique

## General Information

*Capital:* Maputo
*Language:* Portuguese
*Religion:* Catholic, Protestant & Islamic
*Population:* 16.6 million
*Bank Hours:* 0800-1200 Monday - Friday
*Shop Hours:* 0800-1230, 1400-1700 Monday-Saturday
*Currency:* One US dollar = 11,251 meticais
*Export/Import Information:* Children's picture books dutied per kg net weight, otherwise books and advertising matter duty-free. No additional taxes apply. Import licenses and strict exchange controls; authorities have classified books and advertising as List 3 in priorities.

**Associacao dos Escritores Mocambicanos (AEMO)**
Av 24 de Julho, 1420 Maputo
Mailing Address: CP 4187, 1420 Maputo
*Tel:* (01) 420727
*Key Personnel*
Man Dir: Pedro Chissano

**Empresa Moderna Lda**
Avda 25 de Setembro, Maputo CP 473
*Tel:* (01) 424594
*Key Personnel*
Man Dir: Louis Galloti
Founded: 1937
Subjects: Education, Fiction, History, Regional Interests

**Centro De Estudos Africanos+**
Universidade Eduardo Mondlane, CP 1993, Maputo
*Tel:* (01) 490828; (01) 499876 *Fax:* (01) 491896
*E-mail:* ceadid@zebra.uem.mz

*Web Site:* www.cea.uem.mz
*Telex:* 6-740 CEA MO
*Key Personnel*
Dir: Coronel Sergio Vieira
Founded: 1976
Specializes in Social Science.
Subjects: Economics, Foreign Countries, Government, Political Science, History, Regional Interests

**Editora Minerva Central**
Rua Consiglieri Pedroso, 66/84, Maputo
*Tel:* (01) 420198 *Fax:* (01) 423677
*E-mail:* minerva@sortmoz.com
*Telex:* 6-561 Miner Mo
*Key Personnel*
Man Dir: J F Carvalho
Founded: 1908
Subjects: Medicine, Nursing, Dentistry, Science (General)
Subsidiaries: J A Carvalho & Co Ltd

# Myanmar

## General Information

*Capital:* Yangon
*Language:* Burmese (English used for foreign correspondence)
*Religion:* Buddhism
*Population:* 42.6 million
*Bank Hours:* 1000-1400 Monday-Friday; 1000-1200 Saturday
*Shop Hours:* Generally 0800-1700 Monday-Saturday
*Currency:* 100 pyas = 1 kyat
*Export/Import Information:* Myanmar has own complex tariff system, but duties are paid by State Trading Corporation No 9, 550-552 Merchant St, Rangoon, and Printing and Publishing Corporation, 228 Theinbyu St, Rangoon, principally. No tariffs on advertising. Books exempt from sales tax. Import license required. Exchange controls; priorities apply.
*Copyright:* No copyright conventions signed

**Hanthawaddy Book House**
157 Bo Aung Gyaw St, Rangoon
*Bookshop(s):* Hanthawaddy Bookshop

**Knowledge Press & Bookhouse**
130, Bogyoke Aung San St, Pazundaung Tsp
*Tel:* (01) 290927
Subjects: Art, Education, Government, Political Science, Religion - Other, Social Sciences, Sociology
*Bookshop(s):* Knowledge Book House

**Kyi-Pwar-Ye Book House**
84 St, Letse-gan Mandalay
*Tel:* (02) 21003 *Cable:* LUDU
Subjects: Art, Religion - Other, Travel

**Sarpay Beikman Public Library**
529-531 Merchant St, Kyauktada Tsp, Rangoon
*Tel:* (01) 283277 *Cable:* Sarbeikman
*Key Personnel*
Chairman: Aung Htay
Secretary: Lt-Col Mg MgLay
Sales, Publicity & Advertising: U Tin Gyi
Editorial: Myo Thant
Founded: 1947
Subjects: Agriculture, Biography, Ethnicity, History, Law, Literature, Literary Criticism, Essays, Science (General)
*Bookshop(s):* Sarpay Beikman Bookshop
*Book Club(s):* Sarpay Beikman Book Club

**Shumawa Publishing House**
146 Bogyoke Aung San Market, Rangoon
Subjects: Mechanical Engineering
*Bookshop(s):* Shumawa Book House

**Shwepyidan Printing & Publishing House**
12 A Hninban, Yegwaw Quarter, Rangoon
Subjects: Government, Political Science, Law, Religion - Other

**Smart & Mookerdum**
221 Sule Pagoda Rd, Rangoon
Subjects: Art, Cookery, Science (General)

**Thudhammawaddy Press**
55-56 Moung Khine St, Rangoon
Mailing Address: PO Box 419, 55-56, Rangoon
Subjects: Religion - Other

**Universities Administration Office**
Prome Rd, University Post Office, Rangoon
*Key Personnel*
Chief Editor, Translations & Publications Department: U Wun

# Namibia

## General Information

*Capital:* Windhoek
*Language:* English (official), Afrikaans and German widely used
*Religion:* Predominantly Christian
*Population:* 1.6 million
*Bank Hours:* 0900-1530 Monday-Friday
*Shop Hours:* 0830-1700 Monday-Friday, 0800-1300 Saturday
*Currency:* 100 cents = 1 Namibian dollar
*Export/Import Information:* Part of the Southern African Customs Union (SACU). Import licenses required. Payment of hard currency or any other currency for trade transactions strictly against documentation. Strict foreign exchange controls and regulations. No exchange control applicable to non-residents. Gradual easing exchange control of residents.
*Copyright:* Berne (see Copyright Conventions, pg xi)

**Agrivet Publishers+**
PO Box 3134, Windhoek
*Tel:* (061) 228909 *Fax:* (061) 230619
*E-mail:* agrivet@iafrica.com.na
Founded: 1992
Subjects: Foreign Countries, Travel, Veterinary Science

**Bible Society of Namibia**
PO Box 13294, Windhoek 9000
*Tel:* (061) 235090 *Fax:* (061) 228663
*E-mail:* bsn@nambible.org.na
*Web Site:* www.biblesociety.org
Founded: 1986
ISBN Prefix(es): 99916-713

**Desert Research Foundation of Namibia (DRFN)**
7 Rossini St, Windhoek
Mailing Address: PO Box 202 32, Windhoek
*Tel:* (061) 229855 *Fax:* (061) 228286
*E-mail:* info@drfn.org.na
*Web Site:* www.drfn.org.na
*Key Personnel*
Dir: Mary Seely *Fax:* (061) 230770
   *E-mail:* mseely@drfn.org.na
Founded: 1963

Subjects: Agriculture, Behavioral Sciences, Biological Sciences, Developing Countries, Earth Sciences, Education, Energy, Environmental Studies, Geography, Geology, Natural History, Physical Sciences, Regional Interests, Science (General), Botany, Zoology, Desertification Issues, Environmental Training, Water Management
ISBN Prefix(es): 99916-709
*U.S. Office(s):* Friends of Gobabeb, c/o Prof C S Crawford, Dept of Biology, University of New Mexico, Albuquerque, NM 87131, United States

**DRFN**, see Desert Research Foundation of Namibia (DRFN)

**Gamsberg Macmillan Publishers (Pty) Ltd**
19 Faraday St, Windhoek
Mailing Address: PO Box 22830, Windhoek
*Tel:* (061) 232165 *Fax:* (061) 233538
*E-mail:* gmp@iafrica.com.na
*Web Site:* www.macmillan-africa.com
*Key Personnel*
Man Dir, Editorial, Rights & Permissions: Herman van Wyk
Publishing: Peter Reiner *E-mail:* gmpubl@iafrica.com.na
Production: Ingrid van Graan
Sales, Publicity: Kotie van der Merwe
Orders & Prices: Cecelia Blom *Fax:* (061) 234830
Founded: 1977
Subjects: Literature, Literary Criticism, Essays
ISBN Prefix(es): 0-86848; 99916-0

**Kuiseb-Verlag**
PO Box 67, Windhoek
*Tel:* (061) 225372 *Fax:* (061) 226846
*E-mail:* nwg@iafrica.com.na
*Key Personnel*
Contact: Ingrid Demasius
Founded: 1925
ISBN Prefix(es): 99916-703

**McGregor Publishers**
PO Box 9338, Windhoek
*Tel:* (061) 62155 *Fax:* (061) 63059
*E-mail:* gmcgregor@unam.na
*Key Personnel*
Contact: Gordon McGregor
Founded: 1990
Specialize in German occupied Southwest Africa.
Subjects: Military Science
ISBN Prefix(es): 99916-700

**Media Institute of Southern Africa (MISA)**
PMB 13386, Windhoek
*Tel:* (061) 232975 *Fax:* (061) 248016
*E-mail:* postmaster@ingrid.misa.org.na
*Web Site:* www.misanet.org
*Key Personnel*
Regional Dir: Luckson Chipare *E-mail:* director@misa.org.na

**Multi-Disciplinary Research Centre Library**
340 Mundume Ndemufayo Ave, Pioneers Park, Windhoek
Mailing Address: PMB 13301, Windhoek
*Tel:* (061) 206 3909; (061) 206 3051 *Fax:* (061) 206 3050; (061) 206 3684
*E-mail:* tgases@unam.na
*Web Site:* www.unam.na
*Key Personnel*
Head: Dr L Hangula
Contact: Dr Ben Fuller
Coordinator: Selma Nangulah
   *E-mail:* snangulah@unam.na
Founded: 1989
Subjects: Agriculture, Developing Countries, Economics, Environmental Studies, Geography,

Geology, Government, Political Science, Science (General), Social Sciences, Sociology, Gender Issues, Life Sciences
*Parent Company:* University of Namibia
Divisions: Life Sciences Division; Science & Technology Division; Social Sciences Division
*U.S. Office(s):* J Diescho, University of Namibia Office, Africa/American Institute, 833 United Nations Plaza, New York, NY 10017, United States

# Nepal

## General Information

*Capital:* Kathmandu
*Language:* Nepali (official), also Maithir & Bhojpuri
*Religion:* Predominantly Hindu, also some Buddhist and Muslim
*Population:* 20.1 million
*Bank Hours:* 1000-1430 Sunday-Thursday; 1000-1230 Friday
*Shop Hours:* 1000-2000 Sunday-Friday
*Currency:* 100 paisa = 1 Nepalese rupee
*Export/Import Information:* No tariff on books and advertising. Import licenses required. Exchange controls.

**International Standards Books & Periodicals (P) Ltd+**
Kamabakshee Tole, Gha 3-333, Chowk Bhitra, Kathmandu 44601
Mailing Address: PO Box 3000-ISB-NFSLA Kathmandu-3-30-15B, Kathmandu 44601
*Tel:* (01) 212289; (01) 224005; (01) 223036
*Fax:* (01) 223036
*Telex:* 3000 ISB-ASS-NP *Cable:* ANTERRASHTRIYASTARKOSAPHOOPASA, KATHMANDU
*Key Personnel*
Chairman: Sugat Dass Tuladhar
Chief Executive Man Dir: Ganesh Lall Chhipa
Chief Man Dir: Suindra Lall Chhipa
Senior Man Dir: Yogendra Lall Chhipa
Junior Man Dir: Bijendra Lall Upasak
Man Dir: Ganesh Dass Chhipa
Company Secretary: Udhdab Lall Chhipa
Editorial Dir: Dharma Ratna Ranjit
Marketing Dir: Chandra Lexmee Ranjit
General Sales Dir: Pawan Ratna Tuladhar
General Order Dir: Bhawanyshowr Ranjit
Production Dir: Bhumaheshwor Ranjit
Promotion Dir: Suneeta Shobha Ranjit
Subscription Dir: Aneeta Shobha Ranjit
Distribution Dir: Miss Nanee Shobha Tuladhar
Customer Dir: Miss Bheem Shobha Tuladhar
Publishing Dir: Mrs Rameeta Shobha Tuladhar
Foreign Rights Dir: Rajendra K Ranjit
Supplies Dir: Shant Shobha Ranjit
Sales Manager: Basant Bahadur Basnet
Business Manager: Bijendra Man Tuladhar
General Trade Dir: Amrit Lall Ranjit
Circulation Dir: Surya Man Ranjit
Reference Dir: Ms Saraswati Shrestha
Acquisition Dir: Mrs Subarna Laxmi Chhipa
Export Dir: Jaya Ram Ranjit
Import Dir: Mrs Saroja Ranjit
Rights & Permission Dir: Shanta Dass Ranjit
Information Dir: Shanta Lall Ranjit
Publicity Manager: Mona Ranjit
Foreign Order Manager: Jambu Ranta Ranjitkar
Subsidiary Rights Manager: Ms Babee Shobha Ranjit
Marketing Manager: Jambu Ranta Ranjit
Founded: 1965
Centre for Central General Selling, Distribution & Wholesales, Order Supplies, Subscription & Publication.

Subjects: Agriculture, Anthropology, Archaeology, Architecture & Interior Design, Art, Business, Career Development, Chemistry, Chemical Engineering, Earth Sciences, Economics, Education, Engineering (General), Gardening, Plants, Geography, Geology, Government, Political Science, History, Human Relations, Language Arts, Linguistics, Law, Literature, Literary Criticism, Essays, Mathematics, Medicine, Nursing, Dentistry, Music, Dance, Natural History, Philosophy, Physics, Psychology, Psychiatry, Social Sciences, Sociology
*Branch Office(s)*
Arniko Main, Arniko Barhabise - 9, Ariko Rajmarg 87 KM
Ason Kamabakshee Tole, Kathmandu City
Bhotahity Tole, Kathmandu Valley
*Showroom(s):* Ason Kamabakshee Tole, Cha 1/112, Chowk Bhitra, Kathmandu 3
*Bookshop(s):* A R N I K O, Barhabise-9, Arniko Rajmarg-87 KM, Bagmati Anchal, Barhabise, Kathmandu 45303; S A A R C Books & Periodicals Shop, 09-53-01 Bhindyo Tole, Purano Bazar, Kathmandu
*Shipping Address:* Naradevee Tole, Gha 3/460, Nyata Twa, Chowk Bhitra, PO Box 3000-ISB, Kathmandu City 44601-3000
*Warehouse:* Bhurungkhel Tole, Cha 4/394, Ikhapokhary, Kshetrapaty, PO Box 5000-ISB, Kathmandu City 44601-5000
*Orders to:* Bhotahity Tole, Cha 1/333, Chowk Bhitra, 5th floor, PO Box 5000-ISB, Kathmandu City 44601-5000
Maroohity Tole, Chha 3/333, Chowk Bhitra, 1st Floor, PO Box 3000-ISB, Kathmandu City 44601-3000

**Royal Nepal Academy**
Khumaltar, Lalitpur 178 MEMS
Mailing Address: PO Box 3323, Katmandu
*Tel:* (01) 547714; (01) 547715; (01) 547716; (01) 547717; (01) 547718 *Fax:* (01) 547713
*E-mail:* info@ronast.org.np; ronast@mos.com.np
*Web Site:* www.ronast.org.np
*Key Personnel*
President: Prof Dayanand Bajracharya
Library Chief: T D Bhandari
Founded: 1957
Subjects: Art, History, Literature, Literary Criticism, Essays, Science (General), Social Sciences, Sociology

**Sajha Prakashan, Co-operative Publishing Organization**
Pulchowk, Lalitpur, Kathmandu
*Tel:* (01) 5521118
*Key Personnel*
Chairman: Deepak Baskota
General Manager: Narayan S Gajurel
Marketing Manager: Ram Krishna Bhandari
Founded: 1966
Subjects: Literature, Literary Criticism, Essays

**Worldwide Publishings Systems**, see International Standards Books & Periodicals (P) Ltd

# Netherlands

## General Information

*Capital:* Amsterdam
*Language:* Dutch; Frisian in Friesland (though all speakers of Frisian also speak Dutch). English is common second language
*Religion:* Mainly Roman Catholic and Protestant
*Population:* 15.9 million

*Bank Hours:* 0900-1600 Monday-Friday; some open Saturday morning and on late night shopping evenings
*Shop Hours:* 0900-1730 or 1800 Monday-Saturday. Many close Monday morning
*Currency:* 100 Eurocents = 1 Euro; 2.20371 Dutch guilders = 1 Euro
*Export/Import Information:* Member of the European Economic Community. No tariff on books except children's picture books from non-EEC; advertising other than single copies is dutied; 6% VAT on books. Import licenses required for certain countries (not USA or UK).
*Copyright:* UCC, Berne, Florence (see Copyright Conventions, pg xi)

**Academic Publishers Associated**, see APA (Academic Publishers Associated)

**Agathon**, *imprint of* Unieboek BV

**Agon**, *imprint of* Uitgeverij de Arbeiderspers

**Uitgeversmaatschappij Agon B V+**
Herengracht 376, 1016 CH Amsterdam
*Tel:* (020) 521 97 77 *Fax:* (020) 622 49 37
*E-mail:* info@boekboek.nl
*Web Site:* www.boekboek.nl
*Key Personnel*
Publisher: R J W Dietz
Founded: 1987
Subjects: History, Regional Interests, Travel
ISBN Prefix(es): 90-5157
*Parent Company:* Weekblad pers groep

**Agora**, *imprint of* Uitgeverij J H Kok BV

**Allert de Lange BV**
Damrak 62, 1012 LM Amsterdam
*Tel:* (020) 6246744 *Fax:* (020) 6384975
*Key Personnel*
Man Dir: W J van Loon
Founded: 1880
ISBN Prefix(es): 2-90-6133; 2-90-5336
*Parent Company:* Allert de Lange Beheer BV
*Associate Companies:* Nilsson & Lamm BV
*Bookshop(s):* Robert Premsela, Van Baerlestraat 78, 1071 BB Amsterdam; Ala Carte, Utrechtsestraat 110-112, 1017 VS Amsterdam

**Altamira-Becht**, *imprint of* Gottmer Uitgevers Groep

**Uitgeverij Ambo BV+**
Keizersgracht 630, 1017 ER Amsterdam
*Tel:* (020) 5245411 *Fax:* (020) 4200422
*E-mail:* info@amboanthos.nl
*Web Site:* www.amboanthos.nl
*Telex:* 43272
*Key Personnel*
Publisher: Ms Eva Cossee
Founded: 1963
Membership(s): Combo Group, Netherlands.
Subjects: Biography, Fiction, History, Literature, Literary Criticism, Essays, Music, Dance, Nonfiction (General), Philosophy, Photography, Psychology, Psychiatry, Religion - Other, Social Sciences, Sociology, Theology
ISBN Prefix(es): 90-263; 90-6074; 90-414
*Warehouse:* Combo Nijkerk, Gezellestraat 16, 3861 RD Nijkerk
*Orders to:* Combo, Postbus 1, 3740 AA Baarn

**Ankh-Hermes BV+**
Smyrnastr 5, 7413 BA Deventer
Mailing Address: Postbus 125, 7400 AC Deventer
*Tel:* (0570) 678911 *Fax:* (0570) 624632
*E-mail:* info@ankh-hermes.nl
*Web Site:* www.ankh-hermes.com
*Key Personnel*
Dir: Nicole de Haas
Financial Dir: Mr A L Steenbergen

Founded: 1949
Subjects: Astrology, Occult, Education, Gardening, Plants, Health, Nutrition, Management, Parapsychology, Philosophy, Religion - Buddhist, Religion - Protestant
ISBN Prefix(es): 90-202

**Uitgeverij Anthos+**
Keizersgracht 630, 1017 ER Amsterdam
*Tel:* (020) 5245411 *Fax:* (020) 4200422
*E-mail:* info@amboanthos.nl
*Web Site:* www.amboanthos.nl
*Key Personnel*
Man Dir: Robbert Ammerlaan
Membership(s): the Combo Group.
Subjects: Biography, Fiction, Science (General)
ISBN Prefix(es): 90-6074

**AO**, *imprint of* Stichting IVIO

**APA (Academic Publishers Associated)**
Postbus 806, 1000 AV Amsterdam
*Tel:* (020) 626 5544 *Fax:* (020) 528 5298
*E-mail:* info@apa-publishers.com
*Web Site:* www.apa-publishers.com
*Key Personnel*
Man Dir: G van Heusden
Founded: 1966
Subjects: Art, Asian Studies, Biblical Studies, History, Human Relations, Language Arts, Linguistics, Law, Library & Information Sciences, Philosophy, Religion - Other, Science (General), Social Sciences, Sociology, Theology
ISBN Prefix(es): 90-6037; 90-6023; 90-302; 90-6039; 90-6022; 90-6024; 90-6025; 90-6042
Subsidiaries: Fontes Pers; Gerard Th van Heusden; Hissink & Co; Holland University Press BV; Oriental Press BV; Philo Press CV

**Aramith**, *imprint of* Gottmer Uitgevers Groep

**Uitgeverij de Arbeiderspers+**
Herengracht 370-372, 1016 CH Amsterdam
*Tel:* (020) 5247500
*E-mail:* info@arbeiderspers.nl
*Web Site:* www.ap-archipel.nl
*Key Personnel*
Man Dir: R J W Dietz
Subjects: Biography, Criminology, Fiction, History, Literature, Literary Criticism, Essays, Nonfiction (General), Philosophy, Poetry, Romance, Travel
ISBN Prefix(es): 90-295
*Parent Company:* Weekbladpers Group
Imprints: Agon

**Uitgeverij Arbor+**
Member of The Combo Group
Postbus 1, 3740 AA Baarn
*Tel:* (035) 5422141 *Fax:* (035) 15433
*Key Personnel*
Man Dir: Robbert Ammerlaan
Subjects: Religion - Other
ISBN Prefix(es): 90-5158

**Architectura & Natura**
Leliegracht 22, 1015 DG Amsterdam
*Tel:* (020) 6236186 *Fax:* (020) 6382303
*E-mail:* info@architectura.nl
*Web Site:* www.architectura.nl
*Key Personnel*
Contact: G Kemme *E-mail:* kemme@architectura.nl
Founded: 1939
Specialize in Architecture & Landscape Architecture.
Subjects: Architecture & Interior Design
ISBN Prefix(es): 90-71570
Number of titles published annually: 6 Print
Total Titles: 96 Print

Imprints: Goose Press
Subsidiaries: Goose Press

**Arena**, *imprint of* J M Meulenhoff bv

**Uitgeverij Arena BV+**
Subsidiary of J M Meulenhoff BV
Herengracht 505, 1017 BV Amsterdam
Mailing Address: PO Box 100, 1000 AC Amsterdam
*Tel:* (020) 55 40 500 *Fax:* (020) 42 16 868
*E-mail:* info@boekenarena.nl
*Web Site:* www.meulenhoff.nl; www.boekenarena.nl
*Key Personnel*
Man Dir: Anne Rube
Publisher: Tanja Hendriks
Editorial: Ingrid Meurs; Maaike Le Noble
Production: Bregitta Kramer
Publicity: Piet van Riele
Founded: 1989
Subjects: Biography, Fiction, Literature, Literary Criticism, Essays, Nonfiction (General), Travel
ISBN Prefix(es): 90-6974
Total Titles: 50 Print
*Ultimate Parent Company:* PCM Algemene boeken

**Uitgevirj Aristos+**
Provenierssingel 73a, 3033 EJ Rotterdam
*Tel:* (010) 243 73 70 *Fax:* (010) 243 76 00
*E-mail:* aristos@xs4all.nl
*Web Site:* www.xs4all.nl/~feico/aristos
*Key Personnel*
Publisher: Gerrit Bussinh
Founded: 1997
Subjects: Fiction, Literature, Literary Criticism, Essays, Management, Nonfiction (General)
ISBN Prefix(es): 90-6935
Total Titles: 27 Print
*Warehouse:* Centraal Boehh, Erasmusweg 19, 4101 AK Culemberg *Tel:* (0345) 475911

**Ark Boeken+**
Donauweg 4, 1043 AJ Amsterdam
*Tel:* (020) 6114847 *Fax:* (020) 6114864
*E-mail:* arkboeken@wxs.nl
*Key Personnel*
General Dir: J Kor *Tel:* (020) 4802981
Publishing Dir: P Foget
Founded: 1913
Ark Boeken Publishing House combines the activities of Vereniging tot Verspreiding der Heilige Schrift (Association for Distribution of the Holy Scripture) & Bijbel Kiosk Vereniging (Bible Kiosk Society).
Subjects: Religion - Protestant
ISBN Prefix(es): 90-338
Total Titles: 500 Print; 1 Audio
*Bookshop(s):* BKV-Lektuurcentrum, Hoofdstraat 55, 3971 KB Driebergen

**Uitgeverij Jan van Arkel+**
A Numankd 17, 3572 KP Utrecht
*Tel:* (030) 2731840 *Fax:* (030) 2733614
*E-mail:* i-books@antenna.nl
*Web Site:* www.antenna.bl/i-books
*Key Personnel*
Chief Executive: Jan van Arkel
Founded: 1974
Specialize in books on the environment & development, in books in the Dutch & English languages.
Subjects: Economics, Environmental Studies, Geography, Geology, Government, Political Science, Social Sciences, Sociology, Women's Studies
ISBN Prefix(es): 90-6224; 90-5727 (International Books)
Total Titles: 150 Print
Imprints: International Books

Distributed by Bushbooks; Jon Carpenter Publishing (UK); International Books (Netherlands); Paul & Company, Publishers Consortium Inc (US)
*Shipping Address:* Central Books, 99 Wallis Rd, London E9 5LN, United Kingdom *Tel:* (020) 986 4854 *Fax:* (020) 533 5821
*Orders to:* c/o A Weitsel, 2 Home Farm Cottages, Sandy Lane, St Paul's Cray, Kent BR5 3HZ, United Kingdom *Tel:* (01689) 870437
Independent Publishers Group - IPG, 814 N Franklin St, Chicago, IL 60610, United States *Tel:* 312-337-0747; 800-888-4741 *Fax:* 312-337-5985 *E-mail:* frontdesk@ipgbook.com

**Ars Scribendi bv Uitgeverij+**
Productieweg 5, 3481 MH Harmelen
Mailing Address: PO Box 65, 3480 DB Harmelen
*Tel:* (0348) 443998 *Fax:* (0348) 444076
*E-mail:* info@arsscribendi.com
*Web Site:* www.arsscribendi.com
*Key Personnel*
President: R E C Richter
Founded: 1988
Membership(s): KVB. Also acts as publishers' agents.
ISBN Prefix(es): 90-72718; 90-5495; 90-74777; 90-5566
Number of titles published annually: 20 Print
Total Titles: 300 Print
*Parent Company:* Richter's Alg Boek Centrale bv
*Associate Companies:* Intertext PvbA
Imprints: Corona; Fantom; Flash; Magnum
Subsidiaries: Handelsonderneming Dykhof bv; De Laude Scriptorum bv
Distributed by Agora bvba

**Athenaeum-Polak & Van Gennep**, *imprint of* Em Querido's Uitgeverij BV

**B M Israel BV**
Lamoraalweg 73, 1934 CC Egmond aan den Hoef, 1012 WL Amsterdam
*Tel:* (020) 624 70 40 *Fax:* (020) 507 20 32
*E-mail:* bmisrael@xs4all.nl
*Web Site:* www.nvva.nl/israelbm
*Key Personnel*
General Manager: M Israel
Subjects: Art, Medicine, Nursing, Dentistry, Science (General), Technology, Travel
ISBN Prefix(es): 90-6078
*Bookshop(s):* B M Israel Boekhandel en Antiquariaat BV

**Backhuys Publishers BV+**
Warmonderweg 80, 2341 KZ Oegstgeest
Mailing Address: PO Box 321, 2300 AH Leiden
*Tel:* (071) 5170208 *Fax:* (071) 5171856
*E-mail:* info@backhuys.com
*Web Site:* www.backhuys.com
*Key Personnel*
President: Dr W Backhuys
Editor: Mike Ruijsenaars *E-mail:* mike@backhuys.com
Publisher: Wil R Peters *Tel:* (071) 5170927 *E-mail:* peters@backhuys.com
Founded: 1989
Publish & distribute scholarly books in the natural sciences (botany, zoology, geology)
Also acts as distributor of Museum Publications, University Presses & sells antiquarian books in the same subjects.
Subjects: Biological Sciences, Earth Sciences, Geography, Geology, Natural History
ISBN Prefix(es): 90-73348; 90-73239; 90-220; 90-327; 90-5103; 2-85653; 90-5782; 2-86515
Number of titles published annually: 40 Print
Total Titles: 400 Print
Subsidiaries: Seashell Treasure Books
*U.S. Office(s):* Balogh Scientific Books, Champaign, IL 61822, United States, Contact: Pamela Burns *Tel:* 217-355-9331 *Fax:* 217-355-9413

Distributed by Balogh Scientific Books (North America)

Distributor for Editions Boubee (France); Israel Academy of Sciences & Humanities (Zoology & Botany titles only); Museum national d'Histoire naturelle (France); Naturalis (Netherlands); Service du Patrimoine Naturel (France)

Foreign Rep(s): Balogh Scientific Books

**Uitgeverij Balans+**
Herengracht 370/372, 1016 CH Amsterdam
Mailing Address: Postbus 2877, 1000 CW Amsterdam
*Tel:* (020) 524 75 80 *Fax:* (020) 524 75 89
*E-mail:* balans@uitgeverijbalans.nl
*Web Site:* www.uitgeverijbalans.nl
*Key Personnel*
Publisher: Jan G Gaarlandt
Rights & Permissions: Francoise Gaarlandt-Kist
Founded: 1986
Subjects: Biography, Fiction, History, Journalism, Literature, Literary Criticism, Essays, Nonfiction (General), Regional Interests, Religion - Other
ISBN Prefix(es): 90-5018
Total Titles: 40 Print
*Orders to:* Centraal Boekhuis, Postbus 100, 4100 BA Culemborg *Tel:* (0345) 475896

**A A Balkema Uitgevers BV+**
Member of Taylor & Francis Group
PO Box 825, 2160 SZ Lisse
*Tel:* (0252) 435111 *Fax:* (0252) 435447
*E-mail:* orders@swets.nl
*Web Site:* www.balkema.nl
*Key Personnel*
Man Dir: Martin Scrivener *Tel:* (0252) 435101 *E-mail:* scrivy@swets.nl
Rights & Permissions: Rosemarie Daal
Sales Promotion: Ms Deet van Toledo
Founded: 1972
Specialize in Engineering.
Subjects: Archaeology, Biological Sciences, Civil Engineering, Earth Sciences, Engineering (General), Environmental Studies, Geography, Geology, Mechanical Engineering, Natural History, Physics
ISBN Prefix(es): 90-6191 (90-5809); 90-5410
Total Titles: 1,000 Print; 10 CD-ROM
*U.S. Office(s):* A A Balkema Publishers, 2252 Ridge Rd, Brookfield, VT 05036-9704, United States *Tel:* 802-276-3162 *Fax:* 802-276-3837 *E-mail:* info@ashgate.com

**Benjamin & Partners Art Books,** *imprint of* BoekWerk

**John Benjamins BV+**
Klaprozenweg 105, 1033 NN Amsterdam
Mailing Address: PO Box 36224, 1020 ME Amsterdam
*Tel:* (020) 6304747 *Fax:* (020) 6739773
*E-mail:* customer.services@benjamins.nl
*Web Site:* www.benjamins.com
*Key Personnel*
Editorial: Isja Conen *E-mail:* isja.conen@benjamins.nl; Bertie Kaal *E-mail:* bertie.kaal@benjamins.nl; Anke de Looper *E-mail:* anke.delooper@benjamins.nl; Kees Vaes *E-mail:* kees.vaes@benjamins.nl
Marketing & Promotion: Karin Plijnaar
Production: Ian Spoelstra *E-mail:* ian.spoelstra@benjamins.nl
Founded: 1964
Subjects: Art, Education, Language Arts, Linguistics, Literature, Literary Criticism, Essays, Philosophy, Psychology, Psychiatry, Social Sciences, Sociology, Applied Linguistics, Pragmatics, Translation Cognition, Historical Linguistics
ISBN Prefix(es): 90-272
Imprints: B R Gruener Publishing Co

*Branch Office(s)*
John Benjamins North America Inc, 821 Bethlehem Pike, Philadelphia, PA 19038, United States *Tel:* 215-836-1200 *Fax:* 215-836-1204

**Bertollucci,** *imprint of* J M Meulenhoff bv

**Bertollucci,** *imprint of* Uitgeverij Vassallucci bv

**De Bezige Bij B V Uitgeverij**
Van Miereveldstr 1, 1071 DW Amsterdam
Mailing Address: PO Box 75184, 1070 AD Amsterdam
*Tel:* (020) 3059810 *Fax:* (020) 3059824
*E-mail:* info@debezigebij.nl
*Web Site:* www.debezigebij.nl *Cable:* BEEBOOK
*Key Personnel*
President & Publisher: Robbert Ammerlaau
Founded: 1944
Subjects: Fiction, Literature, Literary Criticism, Essays, Nonfiction (General), Poetry
ISBN Prefix(es): 90-234

**Big Balloon BV+**
Fonteinlaan 5, 2012 JG Haarlem
Mailing Address: Postbus 701, 2003 RS Haarlem
*Tel:* (023) 5176620 *Fax:* (023) 5176630
*E-mail:* info@bigballoon.nl
*Web Site:* www.bigballoon.nl
*Key Personnel*
Man Dir: Cees de Groot *E-mail:* degroot@bigballoon.nl
Marketing Manager: Kees Kooijman *E-mail:* kooijman@bigballoon.nl
Marketing: Willemijn Roselaar *E-mail:* roselaar@bigballoon.nl
Licensing: Corinne van Roozendaal *E-mail:* vanroozendaal@bigballoon.nl
Editorial: Annerieke Bijeman *E-mail:* bijeman@bigballoon.nl; Rikky Schrever *E-mail:* schrever@bigballoon.nl
Founded: 1990
ISBN Prefix(es): 90-320; 90-5425

**Erven J Bijleveld+**
Janskerkhof 7, 3512 BK Utrecht
*Tel:* (030) 2310800 *Fax:* (030) 2311774
*E-mail:* info@bijleveldbooks.nl
*Web Site:* www.bijleveldbooks.nl
*Key Personnel*
Man Dir: J B Bommelje, Sr
Founded: 1865
Subjects: Child Care & Development, Computer Science, History, Microcomputers, Philosophy, Psychology, Psychiatry, Religion - Jewish, Religion - Other, Social Sciences, Sociology, Theology
ISBN Prefix(es): 90-72019; 90-5548; 90-6131
Imprints: Bijleveld Press

**Bijleveld Press,** *imprint of* Erven J Bijleveld

**BIS Publishers**
Herengracht 370-372, 1016 CH Amsterdam
Mailing Address: Postbox 323, 1000 AH Amsterdam
*Tel:* (020) 524 75 60 *Fax:* (020) 524 75 57
*E-mail:* bis@bispublishers.nl
*Web Site:* www.bispublishers.nl
*Key Personnel*
Owner & Dir: Rudolf van Wezel
Founded: 1986
Subjects: Architecture & Interior Design, Communications
ISBN Prefix(es): 90-72007
Distributed by Hearst Books International

**H W Blok Uitgeverij BV**
Division of Nieuws Tribune Publishing BV
Postbus 1, 1000 AA Amsterdam

*Tel:* (020) 5159222 *Fax:* (020) 5159100
ISBN Prefix(es): 90-70008; 90-72763

**Boekencentrum BV+**
Goudstr 50, 2700 AA Zoetermeer
Mailing Address: Postbus 29, 2700 AA Zoetermeer
*Tel:* (079) 3615481; (079) 3628282 (sales) *Fax:* (079) 3615489
*E-mail:* info@boekencentrum.nl
*Web Site:* www.boekencentrum.nl
*Key Personnel*
General Dir: N A de Waal
Founded: 1948
Subjects: Education, Religion - Protestant, Theology
ISBN Prefix(es): 90-239; 90-211
Imprints: Meinema

**De Boekerij BV+**
Herengracht 540, 1017 CG Amsterdam
*Tel:* (020) 535 31 35 *Fax:* (020) 535 31 30
*E-mail:* info@boekerij.nl
*Web Site:* www.boekerij.nl
*Key Personnel*
Editorial Dir: Marijke Bartels
Man Dir & Sales: R C M Hogenes
Editorial, Children's: Dorine Louwerens
Publicity: Marc Van Biezen
Production: Hans Van den Broek
Contracts & Rights: Frederike Leffelaar
Founded: 1986
Subjects: Biography, Child Care & Development, Criminology, Fiction, Health, Nutrition, History, Mysteries, Nonfiction (General), Romance, Science Fiction, Fantasy
ISBN Prefix(es): 90-225
*Ultimate Parent Company:* PCM Algemene Boeken
*Associate Companies:* Bruna; T M Meulenhoff; Prometherus/Bert Bakker; Standaard; Unieboek/Van Reemst
Imprints: Forum; Parel Pockets; Piccolo; Van Goor

**BoekWerk+**
Waldeck Pyrmontstr 2, 9722 GM Groningen
*Tel:* (050) 5265559 *Fax:* (050) 5268198
*Key Personnel*
Dir: G M Nuis
Founded: 1988
Subjects: Art, Business, Computer Science, Management, Marketing, Microcomputers
ISBN Prefix(es): 90-5402; 90-71677
Imprints: Benjamin & Partners Art Books

**Bohn Scheltema en Holkema,** see Uitgeverij Bohn Stafleu Van Loghum BV

**Uitgeverij Bohn Stafleu Van Loghum BV**
Het Spoor 2, 3994 AK Houten
Mailing Address: Postbus 246, 3990 GA Houten
*Tel:* (030) 63 83 830 *Fax:* (030) 63 83 839
*Web Site:* www.bsl.nl
*Key Personnel*
Man Dir: H J Demoet
Founded: 1752
Part of Wolters Kluwer Business Publishing.
Subjects: Biography, Human Relations, Medicine, Nursing, Dentistry, Social Sciences, Sociology
ISBN Prefix(es): 90-313; 90-368; 90-6016; 90-6065; 90-311; 90-6001; 90-6014; 90-6051; 90-6060; 90-6502; 90-940013

**Boom Uitgeverij** (Boom Publishers)+
Affiliate of Boom Law Publishers
Prinsengracht 747-751, 1017 JX Amsterdam
*Tel:* (020) 625 33 27 *Fax:* (020) 625 33 27
*E-mail:* info@uitgeverijboom.nl
*Web Site:* www.uitgeverijboom.nl

*Key Personnel*
President: Dries van Ingen *Tel:* (020) 5200 131
  *E-mail:* vaningen@uitgeverijboom.nl
Deputy Manager: Sjef van de Wiel *Tel:* (020)
  5200 134 *E-mail:* s.vandewiel@uitgeverijboom.
  nl
Product Coordinator: Katrien Buising *Tel:* (020)
  622 61 07 *E-mail:* kbuising@uitgeverijboom.nl
Publicity: Margreet Flink *Tel:* (020) 5218 145
  *E-mail:* m.flink@uitgeverijboom.nl
Marketing Coordinator: Marieke Hoogwout
  *Tel:* (020) 5200 123 *E-mail:* hoogwout@
  uitgeverijboom.nl
Founded: 1842
Subjects: Behavioral Sciences, Child Care & De-
  velopment, Communications, Education, Envi-
  ronmental Studies, Government, Political Sci-
  ence, History, Language Arts, Linguistics, Law,
  Philosophy, Psychology, Psychiatry, Social Sci-
  ences, Sociology, Statistics
ISBN Prefix(es): 90-6009; 90-5352
*Parent Company:* Royal Boom Publishers, Post-
  bus 1058, 7940 KB Meppel (directie@boom.nl)
Distributor for Institute for Politics; Netherlands
  Institute for Banking; Royal Institute of the
  Tropes; TMC Asser Institute
*Orders to:* Boom Distributiecentrum, Postbus 400,
  7940 AK Meppel

**Brill Academic Publishers+**
Plantijnstr 2, 2321 JC Leiden
Mailing Address: Postbus 9000, 2300 PA Leiden
*Tel:* (071) 53 53 500 *Fax:* (071) 53 17 532
*E-mail:* cs@brill.nl
*Web Site:* www.brill.nl
*Telex:* 39296 *Cable:* BRILL LEIDEN
*Key Personnel*
Manager: R J Kasteleijn *E-mail:* kasteleijn@brill.
  nl
International Sales Manager: L Empringham
  *E-mail:* empringham@brill.nl
Marketing Manager: Alexander Dek
  *E-mail:* dek@brill.nl
Founded: 1683
Subjects: Archaeology, Asian Studies, Behavioral
  Sciences, Biological Sciences, History, Religion
  - Islamic, Religion - Jewish, Religion - Other,
  Science (General), Social Sciences, Sociology,
  Theology
ISBN Prefix(es): 90-04
Total Titles: 2,700 Print
Imprints: Leiden University Press
Subsidiaries: Brill Academic Publishers Inc
*Branch Office(s)*
VSP BV, International Science Publishers, God-
  fried van Seijstlaan 47, 3700 BR Zeist, Market-
  ing Manager: Els van Egmond *Tel:* (060) 693
  2081 *Fax:* (060) 692 5790 *E-mail:* vsppub@
  compuserve.com
*U.S. Office(s):* Brill Academic Publishers Inc,
  112 Water St, Suite 601, Boston, MA 02109,
  United States, Contact: Patrick Alexan-
  der *Tel:* 617-263-2323 *Fax:* 617-263-2324
  *E-mail:* cs@brillusa.com
*Distribution Center:* PO Box 605, Herndon,
  VA 20172, United States *Tel:* 703-661-1585
  *Fax:* 703-661-1501 *E-mail:* cs@brillusa.com
  (USA, Canada & Mexico orders, shipping &
  returns)

**D van Brummen**, *imprint of* Buijten en
  Schipperheijn BV Drukkerij en
  Uitgeversmaatschappij

**A W Bruna Uitgevers BV+**
Kobaltweg 23-25, 3504 AA Utrecht
Mailing Address: Postbus 40203, 3504 AA
  Utrecht
*Tel:* (030) 2470411 *Fax:* (030) 2410018
*E-mail:* a.w.bruna@awbruna.nl
*Web Site:* www.awbruna.nl

*Key Personnel*
Dir: Joop Boezeman
Acquiring Editor, Fiction & Nonfiction: Steven
  Maat
Founded: 1868
Subjects: Computer Science, Fiction, History,
  Mysteries, Nonfiction (General), Philosophy,
  Psychology, Psychiatry, Science (General), So-
  cial Sciences, Sociology, Thrillers, Suspense
ISBN Prefix(es): 90-229; 90-449; 90-5672
*Parent Company:* PCM Algemene Boeken bv,
  Utrecht
Imprints: Zwarte Beertjes; A W Bruna Informat-
  ica; Signature
*Branch Office(s)*
Standaard Uitgeverij, Belgium
*U.S. Office(s):* Mary Anne Thompson Associates,
  80 E 11 St, Suite 441, New York, NY, United
  States

**A W Bruna Informatica**, *imprint of* A W Bruna
  Uitgevers BV

**BSL**, see Uitgeverij Bohn Stafleu Van Loghum
  BV

**Buijten en Schipperheijn BV Drukkerij en
Uitgeversmaatschappij+**
Paasheuvelweg 44, 1105 BJ Amsterdam
Mailing Address: PO Box 22708, 1011 DE Ams-
  terdam
*Tel:* (020) 5241010 *Fax:* (020) 5241011
*E-mail:* info@bijten.nl
*Key Personnel*
Man Dir: G Sneep
Founded: 1902
Subjects: Biblical Studies, Human Relations, Phi-
  losophy, Poetry, Psychology, Psychiatry, Reli-
  gion - Other, Theology, Travel
ISBN Prefix(es): 90-6064; 90-5881
Imprints: D van Brummen; Buijten en Schipper-
  heijn Motief; Buijten en Schipperheijn Recre-
  atief

**Buijten en Schipperheijn Motief**, *imprint of*
  Buijten en Schipperheijn BV Drukkerij en
  Uitgeversmaatschappij

**Buijten en Schipperheijn Recreatief**, *imprint of*
  Buijten en Schipperheijn BV Drukkerij en
  Uitgeversmaatschappij

**Business Contact BV+**
Subsidiary of Veen, Bosch & Keuning Uitgevers
  NV
Herengracht 481, 1017 BT Amsterdam
Mailing Address: Postbus 13, 1000 AA Amster-
  dam
*Tel:* (020) 5249800 *Fax:* (020) 6276851
*E-mail:* info@contact-bv.nl
*Web Site:* www.boekenwereld.com
*Key Personnel*
Dir: Marij Bertram
Publisher: Mizzi van der Pluijm
Marketing: Anne Schroen *E-mail:* aschroen@
  contact-bv.nl
Publicity: Anne Kramer; May Meurs
  *E-mail:* mmeurs@contact-bv.nl
Sales: Thea Bon; Ingrid Kee; Petra Wildvank
Subjects: Accounting, Business, Career Develop-
  ment, Economics, Finance, How-to, Manage-
  ment, Marketing
ISBN Prefix(es): 90-254
Number of titles published annually: 30 Print
Total Titles: 400 Print

**BV Uitgevery NZV (Nederlandse
Zondagsschool Vereniging)+**
Van Hogendorplaan 10, 3800 BL Amersfoort
Mailing Address: Postbus 1492, 3800 BL Amers-
  foort

*Tel:* (033) 460 60 11 *Fax:* (035) 460 60 20
*E-mail:* info@nzv.nl
*Web Site:* www.nzv.nl
*Key Personnel*
Manager: Sir E K van de Plassche
International Rights & Publisher: Sir J Graafland
Subjects: Crafts, Games, Hobbies, Religion -
  Other, Affectionate Development, Nature &
  Environment
ISBN Prefix(es): 90-6986
*Parent Company:* NZV
Imprints: Kwintessens
Distributor for Ark Boeken; Boekencentrum; Cal-
  lenbach; Christofoor; Clavis; Groen/Jongbloed;
  Kok; NBG; Piramide

**BZZTOH Publishers+**
Laan van Meerdervoort 10, 2517 AJ The Hague
*Tel:* (070) 3632934 *Fax:* (070) 3631932
*E-mail:* info@bzztoh.nl
*Web Site:* www.bzztoh.nl
*Key Personnel*
Dir: Phil Muysson
Financial Dir: Arend Meijboom
Foreign Rights Manager: Karin Hasselo
  *E-mail:* karin@bzztoh.nl
Founded: 1970
Subjects: Animals, Pets, Astrology, Occult, Biog-
  raphy, Cookery, Fiction, Finance, Health, Nu-
  trition, Humor, Literature, Literary Criticism,
  Essays, Music, Dance, Mysteries, Nonfiction
  (General), Philosophy, Real Estate, Religion -
  Buddhist, Religion - Hindu, Religion - Jewish,
  Romance, Self-Help, Sports, Athletics, Travel,
  Women's Studies
ISBN Prefix(es): 90-6291; 90-5501; 90-453
Number of titles published annually: 130 Print

**Cadans**, *imprint of* Sjaloom Uitgeverijen

**Cadans+**
Imprint of Sjaloom Uitgeverij
Postbus 1895, 1000 BW Amsterdam
*Tel:* (020) 6206263 *Fax:* (020) 4288540
*E-mail:* post@sjaloom.nl
*Web Site:* www.sjaloom.com
Founded: 1992
Subjects: Criminology, Erotica, Fiction, History,
  Literature, Literary Criticism, Essays, Mys-
  teries, Nonfiction (General), Poetry, Regional
  Interests, Travel
ISBN Prefix(es): 90-5132

**Callenbach BV+**
Ijsseldijk 31, 8266 AD Kampen
Mailing Address: Postbus 5019, 8260 GA Kam-
  pen
*Tel:* (038) 3392555 *Fax:* (038) 3311776
*E-mail:* algemeen@kok.nl
*Key Personnel*
Man Dir: G F Callenbach
Foreign Rights: Lia van Essen
Founded: 1854
Membership(s): Combo Group, Netherlands.
Subjects: Animals, Pets, Biblical Studies, Fiction,
  History, Mysteries, Poetry, Religion - Protes-
  tant, Religion - Other, Theology
ISBN Prefix(es): 90-266

**Uitgeverij Cantecleer BV+**
Subsidiary of Veen Bosch & Keuning Uitgevers
  NV
Julianalaan 11, 3743 JG Baarn
Mailing Address: Postbus 309, 3740 AH Baarn
*Tel:* (035) 5486600 *Fax:* (035) 5486615
*E-mail:* cancleer@worldonline.nl
*Key Personnel*
Man Dir & Editor: J Van Beusekom
Editor: J Junge; E Neele; L Uyterlinde
Founded: 1948
Subjects: Art, Crafts, Games, Hobbies, Film,
  Video, House & Home, Nonfiction (General),
  Photography, Wine & Spirits

ISBN Prefix(es): 90-246; 90-213
*Shipping Address:* Magazyn Centraal Boekhuis, Evasmusweg 10, Culemborg

**Castrum Peregrini Presse+**
Herengracht 401, 1017 BP Amsterdam
Mailing Address: PO Box 645, 1000 AP Amsterdam
*Tel:* (020) 235287 *Fax:* (020) 6247096
*E-mail:* mail@castrumperegrini.nl
*Web Site:* castrumperegrini.nl
*Key Personnel*
Man Dir & International Rights: M Defuster
Contact: Andrea Korte *E-mail:* a.korte@castrumperegrini.nl
Founded: 1951
Subjects: Antiques, Biography, Literature, Literary Criticism, Essays, Poetry
ISBN Prefix(es): 90-6034
Total Titles: 100 Print
*Orders to:* Hermannstr 61, 53225 Bonn, Germany

**De Centaur**, *imprint of* Omega Boek BV

**Uitgeverij Christofoor**
Steniaweg 32, 3702 AG Zeist
Mailing Address: Postbus 234, 3700 AE Zeist
*Tel:* (030) 692 39 74 *Fax:* (030) 691 48 34
*E-mail:* info@christofoor.nl
*Key Personnel*
Contact: Dhr E Hezemans
Subjects: Animals, Pets, Biblical Studies, Biography, Child Care & Development, Cookery, Crafts, Games, Hobbies, Education, Fiction, History, How-to, Philosophy, Psychology, Psychiatry, Science Fiction, Fantasy
ISBN Prefix(es): 90-6238

**de Cocon**, *imprint of* Unieboek BV

**Uitgeverij Conserve+**
Tureluur 12, 1873 JW Groet Schoorl
Mailing Address: Postbus 74, 1870 AB Schoorl
*Tel:* (072) 5093693 *Fax:* (072) 5094370
*E-mail:* info@conserve.nl
*Web Site:* www.conserve.nl
*Key Personnel*
President: Kees De Bakker
Founded: 1983
Subjects: Biography, Fiction, History, Literature, Literary Criticism, Essays, Mysteries, Caribbean, Surinam, World War II
ISBN Prefix(es): 90-71380; 90-5429
Total Titles: 250 Print

**Corona**, *imprint of* Ars Scribendi bv Uitgeverij

**Uitgeverij Coutinho BV** (Coutinho Publishing)+
Slochterenlaan 7, 1405 AL Bussum
Mailing Address: Postbus 333, 1400 AH Bussum
*Tel:* (035) 6949991 *Fax:* (035) 6947165
*E-mail:* info@coutinho.nl
*Web Site:* www.coutinho.nl
*Key Personnel*
Man Dir, Editorial: Dick Coutinho
 *E-mail:* coutinho@coutinho.ul; Marleen Klein
 *E-mail:* kleijn@coutinho.nl
Marketing: Carlijn Leijen *E-mail:* leijen@coutinho.nl
Founded: 1976
Specialize in Dutch as a second language.
Membership(s): NUW.
Subjects: Communications, Economics, Education, English as a Second Language, History, Human Relations, Language Arts, Linguistics, Literature, Literary Criticism, Essays, Philosophy
ISBN Prefix(es): 90-6283
Distributed by EPO (Belgium)

**Otto Cramwinckel Uitgever**
Herengracht 416, 1017 BZ Amsterdam
*Tel:* (020) 627 66 09 *Fax:* (020) 638 38 17
*E-mail:* info@cram.nl
*Web Site:* www.cram.nl
Founded: 1985
Subjects: Communications, Radio, TV
ISBN Prefix(es): 90-71894; 90-75727

**Davaco Publishers**
Beukenlaan 3, 8085 RK Doornspijk
*Tel:* (0525) 661823 *Fax:* (0525) 662153
*E-mail:* main@davaco.com
*Web Site:* www.davaco.com
Founded: 1969
Specialize in 16th & 17th century Dutch painting & Flemish art.
Subjects: Art
ISBN Prefix(es): 90-70288

**De Brink (adult books)**, *imprint of* Uitgeverij Ploegsma BV

**De Graaf Publishers**
Zuideinde 40, 2420 AK Nieuwkoop
Mailing Address: Postbus 6, 2420 AA Nieuwkoop
*Tel:* (0172) 57 1461 *Fax:* (0172) 57 2231
*E-mail:* degraaf.books@wxs.nl
*Web Site:* www.antiqbook.nl/degraafbooks
*Key Personnel*
Man Dir: Maria Emilie de Graaf
Founded: 1959
Subjects: Religion - Other
ISBN Prefix(es): 90-6004
Total Titles: 350 Print
Subsidiaries: Miland Publishers

**De Ruiter**, *imprint of* Educatieve Partners Nederland bv

**De Toorts**, *imprint of* Uitgeverij De Toorts

**De Vier Windstreken**, *imprint of* Meander Uitgeverij BV

**De Walburg Pers**
Zaadmarkt 86, 7201 DE Zutphen
Mailing Address: Postbus 4159, 7200 BD Zutphen
*Tel:* (0575) 510522 *Fax:* (0575) 542289
*E-mail:* info@walburgpers.nl
*Web Site:* www.walburgpers.nl
*Key Personnel*
Man Dir, Publicity, Rights & Permissions: Dr C F Schriks; J Smal; J van't Leven
Founded: 1961
Subjects: Architecture & Interior Design, Drama, Theater, Ethnicity, History
ISBN Prefix(es): 90-6011; 90-5730

**Delft University Press+**
Prometheusplein 1, 2628 ZC Delft
Mailing Address: PO Box 98, 2600 MG Delft
*Tel:* (015) 2785706 *Fax:* (015) 2785678
*E-mail:* info@library.tudelft.nl
*Web Site:* www.library.tudelft.nl
*Key Personnel*
Dir: Pam Maas
Dir of Publishing: Lydia M ter Horst-ten Wolde
 *Tel:* (015) 2781616 *E-mail:* l.m.terhorst@library.tudelft.nl
Dir of Electronic Publications: Dr Nicole Potters
 *Tel:* (015) 2783254 *E-mail:* n.potters@library.tudelft.nl
Founded: 1972
Subjects: Architecture & Interior Design, Chemistry, Chemical Engineering, Civil Engineering, Electronics, Electrical Engineering, Engineering (General), Mechanical Engineering, Physics, Science (General), Technology

ISBN Prefix(es): 90-6275; 90-407
*Parent Company:* Delft University of Technolog

**van Dishoeck**, *imprint of* Unieboek BV

**Uitgeversmaatschappij Ad Donker BV+**
Kon Emmaplein 1, 3016 AA Rotterdam
Mailing Address: Postbus 23096, 3001 KB Rotterdam
*Tel:* (010) 4363009 *Fax:* (010) 4362963
*E-mail:* donker@bart.nl
*Web Site:* www.uitgeverijdonker.nl
*Key Personnel*
Dir & Publisher: Willem A Donker
 *E-mail:* donker@bart.nl
Founded: 1938
Subjects: Biography, Education, Fiction, History, Psychology, Psychiatry, Social Sciences, Sociology
ISBN Prefix(es): 90-6100
Number of titles published annually: 25 Print
Total Titles: 150 Print
Imprints: Wilkerdon

**De Driehoek BV, Uitgeverij+**
Keizersgracht 756, 1017 EZ Amsterdam
*Tel:* (020) 624 64 26 *Fax:* (020) 638 71 55
*E-mail:* driehoek.uitgeverij@planet.nl
*Key Personnel*
Dir: H J Heule; Dr W Heule
Founded: 1933
Subjects: Asian Studies, Health, Nutrition, Medicine, Nursing, Dentistry, Religion - Buddhist
ISBN Prefix(es): 90-6030

**Uitgeverij Dwarsstap**, *imprint of* Uitgeverij SUN

**East-West Publications Fonds BV+**
Anna Paulownastr 78, 2518 BJ The Hague
Mailing Address: Postbus 85617, 2508 CH The Hague
*Tel:* (70) 364 45 90 *Fax:* (70) 361 48 64
*E-mail:* epublica@packardbell.org
*Key Personnel*
Chief Executive: L W Carp
Sales: A Neuvel
Founded: 1966
Subjects: Music, Dance, Regional Interests, Religion - Other, Esoteric/spiritual
ISBN Prefix(es): 90-70104; 90-5340
Number of titles published annually: 8 Print
Total Titles: 10 Print
*Associate Companies:* East-West Publications (UK) Ltd
*Orders to:* 8 Caledonia St, London N1 9DZ, United Kingdom *Tel:* (020) 7837 5061 *Fax:* (020) 7278 4429

**ECI voor Boeken en platen BV+**
Laanakkerweg 14-16, 4131 PB Vianen Zh
Mailing Address: Postbus 400, 4130 EK Vianen Zh
*Tel:* (0347) 379214 *Fax:* (0347) 379380
*E-mail:* service@eci.nl
*Web Site:* www.eci.nl
*Telex:* 47449 ecihk nl
*Key Personnel*
Man Dir: Mr B M Tromp
Editorial, Nonfiction: Mrs B Eggels
Editorial, Fiction: Mr J Boezeman
Rights & Permissions: Mrs R Swaalf
Founded: 1967
Subjects: Fiction, Nonfiction (General)
ISBN Prefix(es): 90-70038; 90-5108
*Parent Company:* Bertelsmann AG, Munich, Germany
*Book Club(s):* ECI voor Boeken en Platen BV

**Educatieve Uitgeverij Edu'Actief BV+**
Zomerdijk 9-e, 7942 JR Meppel
Mailing Address: Postbus 1056, 7940 KB Meppel

*Tel:* (0522) 235235 *Fax:* (0522) 235222
*E-mail:* info@edu-actief.nl
*Web Site:* www.edu-actief.nl
*Key Personnel*
Man Dir: I Buwalda
Founded: 1848
Membership(s): GEU.
Subjects: Communications, Economics, Education, Foreign Countries, Geography, Geology, Management, Marketing, Nonfiction (General)
ISBN Prefix(es): 90-5117; 90-372; 90-5766
*Parent Company:* Koninklyke Boom Pers BV

**Educaboek,** *imprint of* Educatieve Partners Nederland bv

**Educatieve Partners Nederland bv+**
Het Spoor 2, 3994 DB Houten
Mailing Address: Postbus 666, 3990 Dr Houten
*Tel:* (030) 6383001 *Fax:* (030) 6383004
*E-mail:* info@epn.nl
*Web Site:* www.epn.nl
*Key Personnel*
Man Dir: J H van Vloten
Founded: 1970
Part of Wolters Kluwer Educational Activities.
Subjects: Science (General)
ISBN Prefix(es): 90-11; 90-05; 90-207
*Parent Company:* Wolters Kluwer NV
Imprints: Stam Techniek; Stenfert Kroese; Schoolpers; De Ruiter; Robyns; Educaboek

**Eekhoorn BV Uitgeverij+**
Alexander Bellstr 11, 3261 LX Oud-Beijerland
*Tel:* (036) 610577 *Fax:* (036) 620982
*E-mail:* info@weton-wesgram.nl
*Web Site:* www.eekhoorn.com
*Key Personnel*
President: M G Stenvert
Editor: E H Kolk
Producer: F H A Kanters
Founded: 1920
Membership(s): GAU.
ISBN Prefix(es): 90-6056
*Showroom(s):* Sutton 10, 7327 AB Apeldoorn, New Zealand
*Warehouse:* Sutton 10, 7327 AB Apeldoorn, New Zealand

**Elektor,** *imprint of* Segment BV

**Elektuur,** *imprint of* Segment BV

**Element Uitgevers+**
Oude Haven 32, 1411 WB Naarden
*Tel:* (035) 6941750 *Fax:* (035) 6945824
*E-mail:* element@wxs.nl
*Key Personnel*
Publisher: Jan van Willegen
Founded: 1995
ISBN Prefix(es): 90-5689
Total Titles: 50 Print

**Elmar BV+**
Delftweg 147, 2289 BD Delft
*Tel:* (015) 215 32 32 *Fax:* (015) 215 32 30
*E-mail:* elmar@elmar.nl
*Web Site:* 212.83.197.79
*Key Personnel*
Man Dir: H Masthoff; M Roodnat
Founded: 1961
Subjects: Biography, Health, Nutrition, History, How-to, Humor, Nonfiction (General), Sports, Athletics, Travel
ISBN Prefix(es): 90-6120; 90-389; 90-5814

**Elsevier,** *imprint of* Elsevier Science BV

**Elsevier Science BV**
Sara Burgerhartstr 25, 1055 KV Amsterdam
*Tel:* (020) 5862560 *Fax:* (020) 4852457
*E-mail:* nlinfo-f@elsevier.nl
*Telex:* 10704
*Key Personnel*
Chairman & Chief Executive Officer: H P Spruijt
Dir: C J Blake; G P Joebsis; R C White; Frans H J Visscher; P Nientker; K J Leeflang; N Farmer; P Shepherd; R Dietz; H Gerbrandy; R Van Charldorp
Founded: 1946
Subjects: Biological Sciences, Chemistry, Chemical Engineering, Computer Science, Earth Sciences, Economics, Engineering (General), Mathematics, Medicine, Nursing, Dentistry, Physics, Science (General), Technology
ISBN Prefix(es): 0-444; 90-444
*Parent Company:* Reed Elsevier, Van de Sande Bakhuyzenstr 4, Postbus 470, 1000 AL Amsterdam
*Associate Companies:* Editora Campus, Brazil; Elsevier Science Ireland Ltd, Ireland; Elsevier Science SA, Switzerland; Elsevier Science Ltd, United Kingdom; Elsevier Science Inc
Imprints: Elsevier; Excerpta Medica; North Holland; Pergamon
Subsidiaries: Elsevier Geo Abstracts
Divisions: Secondary Publishing Division; Elsevier Science NL
*U.S. Office(s):* Elsevier Scientific Inc, 655 Ave of the Americas, New York, NY 10010, United States
*Orders to:* Elsevier Science BV, PO Box 211, Amsterdam *Tel:* (020) 4853753 *Fax:* (020) 4853705

**Uitgeverij Elzenga**
Division of Zwijsen Algemeen B V Uitgeverij
Postbus 805, 5000 AV Tilburg
*Tel:* (020) 55 11 262
*Key Personnel*
Man Dir: Hans Elzenga
Founded: 1982
Subjects: Fiction, Mysteries
ISBN Prefix(es): 90-6692; 90-276

**Johan Enschede Amsterdam BV**
Donauweg 6, 1043 AJ Amsterdam
Mailing Address: Postbus 8023, 1005 AA Amsterdam
*Tel:* (020) 585 86 00 *Fax:* (020) 585 86 01
*E-mail:* info@jea.nl
*Web Site:* www.jea.nl
*Telex:* 41049
*Key Personnel*
Manager, Sales & Marketing: Henk Reuter *E-mail:* h.reuter@jea.nl
ISBN Prefix(es): 90-70024

**ENTERBOOKS,** *imprint of* Uitgeverij De Toorts

**Excerpta Medica,** *imprint of* Elsevier Science BV

**Fantom,** *imprint of* Ars Scribendi bv Uitgeverij

**Frank Fehmers Productions+**
Singel 512, 1017 AX Amsterdam
*Tel:* (020) 6238766 *Fax:* (020) 6246262
*Web Site:* www.fbg.nl/34927
*Telex:* 16740 fepro nl *Cable:* Intpubcon
*Key Personnel*
Man Dir: Frank Fehmers
International Co-productions: Meghan Ferrill
Subjects: Business, Film, Video, Publishing & Book Trade Reference, Radio, TV
ISBN Prefix(es): 90-6151
*Associate Companies:* Frank Fehmers Productions Inc, 300 E 59 St, New York, NY 10022, United States; Frank Fehmers Productions Ltda, Estrada do Tombo 401, Bloco N Apt

102, 22450 Rio de Janeiro RJ, Brazil; Frank Fehmers Publishing BV, Groot Davelaarweg 20, Curacao, Netherlands Antilles

**Fibula,** *imprint of* Unieboek BV

**Flash,** *imprint of* Ars Scribendi bv Uitgeverij

**Uitgeverij De Fontein BV**
Subsidiary of Veen, Bosch & Keuning Uitgevers NV
Prinses Marielaan 8, 3743 JA Baarn
*Tel:* (035) 5486311 *Fax:* (035) 5423855
*E-mail:* info@defonteinbaarn.nl
*Web Site:* www.veenboschenkeuning.nl/pages/fontein.htm
*Key Personnel*
Dir: Toine Akveld
Head of Sales & Marketing: Theo van der Voort *Tel:* (035) 5486337 *E-mail:* tvoort@defonteinbaarn.nl
Promotion & Publicity: Ruth ter Voort *Tel:* (035) 5486335 *E-mail:* rtervoort@defonteinbaarn.nl
Founded: 1946
Membership(s): The Combo Group.
Subjects: Cookery, Fiction, History, Humor, Mysteries, Nonfiction (General), Science (General), Technology, Women's Studies
ISBN Prefix(es): 90-325; 90-261
*Associate Companies:* De Prom Uitgeverij
Imprints: De Fontein jeugd; De Kern; Piramide; Sesam Junior

**De Fontein jeugd,** *imprint of* Uitgeverij De Fontein BV

**Fontes Pers,** *imprint of* Holland University Press BV (APA)

**Forum,** *imprint of* De Boekerij BV

**W Gaade,** *imprint of* Unieboek BV

**Gaberbocchus Press+**
PO Box 3547, 1001 AH Amsterdam
*Tel:* (020) 6245181 *Fax:* (020) 6230672
*E-mail:* info@deharmonie.nl
*Web Site:* www.gaberbocchus.nl
Subjects: Literature, Literary Criticism, Essays
ISBN Prefix(es): 90-6169
Total Titles: 26 Print
*Parent Company:* De Harmonie Publishers, Spuistraat 272, 1012 VW Amsterdam

**Uitgeverij en boekhandel Van Gennep BV+**
Niuwezijds Voorburgwal 330, 1012 RW Amsterdam
*Tel:* (20) 6247033 *Fax:* (20) 6247035
*E-mail:* vangennep@wxs.nl
*Key Personnel*
Man Dir: BIM Kat
Founded: 1969
Subjects: Art, Fiction, Foreign Countries, Government, Political Science, History, Literature, Literary Criticism, Essays, Philosophy, Psychology, Psychiatry, Religion - Buddhist, Religion - Catholic, Religion - Hindu, Religion - Islamic, Religion - Jewish, Religion - Protestant, Religion - Other, Social Sciences, Sociology
ISBN Prefix(es): 90-6012; 90-5515
Imprints: Sara

**Uitgeverij De Geus BV**
Oude Vest 9, 4811 HR Breda
Mailing Address: Postbus 1878, 4801 BW Breda
*Tel:* (076) 522 81 51 *Fax:* (076) 522 25 99
*E-mail:* email@degeus.nl
*Web Site:* www.degeus.nl
*Key Personnel*
President: E Visser

Rights: Marie-Lou Huijts *E-mail:* m.huijts@
 degeus.nl
Founded: 1983
Subjects: Fiction, Nonfiction (General)
ISBN Prefix(es): 90-5226; 90-6222; 90-70610;
 90-445
Number of titles published annually: 100 Print

**BV Uitgeversbedryf Het Goede Boek+**
Koningin Wilhelminastr 8, 1271 PH Huizen
Mailing Address: Postbus 122, 1270 AC Huizen
*Tel:* (35) 525 35 08 *Fax:* (35) 525 40 13
*Key Personnel*
Dir: F Rikmans
Founded: 1932
Also acts as distributor.
Subjects: Aeronautics, Aviation, Maritime, Sports,
 Athletics
ISBN Prefix(es): 90-240
Number of titles published annually: 3 Print
Total Titles: 48 Print

**Gooi & Sticht**, *imprint of* Uitgeverij J H Kok BV

**Van Goor BV+**
Herengracht 406, 1017 BX Amsterdam
*Tel:* (020) 5353135 *Fax:* (020) 5353130
*E-mail:* boekerij@boekery.nl
*Web Site:* www.van-goor.nl
*Key Personnel*
Editorial Dir: Mrs Henny Bodenkamp; Mrs
 Dorine Louwerens
Publicity: Marc Van Biezen
Production: Hans van den Broek
International Rights Contact: Geri Brandjes
*Parent Company:* De Boekery BV
*Ultimate Parent Company:* Meulenhoff & Co BV
*Associate Companies:* Bruna; T M Meulen-
 hoff; Prometheus/Bert Bakker; Standaard;
 Unieboek/Van Reemst
Imprints: Piccolo
Subsidiaries: De Boekeryij bv

**Goose Press**, *imprint of* Architectura & Natura

**Uitgeverij CJ Goossens BV+**
Delftweg 147, 2289 BD Rijswijkzh Zn
*Tel:* (015) 2123623 *Fax:* (015) 2124295
Founded: 1980
Subjects: Literature, Literary Criticism, Essays
ISBN Prefix(es): 90-6551

**Gottmer Uitgevers Groep** (Gottmer Publishing
 Group)+
Wilhelminapark 6, 2012 KA Haarlem
Mailing Address: Postbus 317, 2000 AH Haarlem
*Tel:* (023) 541 11 90 *Fax:* (023) 527 44 04
*E-mail:* info@gottmer.nl
*Web Site:* www.gottmer.nl
*Telex:* 41856
*Key Personnel*
Man Dir: Mr Cees van Wijk
Founded: 1937
Subjects: Crafts, Games, Hobbies, Fiction, House
 & Home, Nonfiction (General), Religion -
 Other, Science (General), Travel, Body-Mind-
 Spirit, Lifestyle, Nautical
ISBN Prefix(es): 90-257; 90-230; 90-6834
Imprints: Altamira-Becht; Aramith; Hollandia

**Griffioen Paperbacks**, *imprint of* Em Querido's
 Uitgeverij BV

**De Groot Goudriaan**, *imprint of* Uitgeverij J H
 Kok BV

**B R Gruener Publishing Co**, *imprint of* John
 Benjamins BV

**de Haan**, *imprint of* Unieboek BV

**Hagen & Stam Uitgeverij Ten**
Postbus 34, 2501 AG The Hague
*Tel:* (070) 3045700 *Fax:* (070) 3045800
Membership(s): the Wolters Kluwer Group.
Subjects: Architecture & Interior Design, Biologi-
 cal Sciences, Chemistry, Chemical Engineering,
 Civil Engineering, Computer Science, Electron-
 ics, Electrical Engineering, Energy, Engineering
 (General), Environmental Studies, Labor, In-
 dustrial Relations, Management, Mechanical
 Engineering, Microcomputers, Real Estate, Sci-
 ence (General), Technology, Transportation
ISBN Prefix(es): 90-70011; 90-71694; 90-76304;
 90-76383; 90-440

**De Harmonie Uitgeverij** (De Harmonie
 Publishers)+
Spuistr 272, 1012 VW Amsterdam
Mailing Address: PO Box 3547, 1001 AH Ams-
 terdam
*Tel:* (020) 6245181 *Fax:* (020) 6230672
*E-mail:* info@deharmonie.nl
*Web Site:* www.deharmonie.nl
*Key Personnel*
Man Dir: Jaco Groot
Rights & Permissions: Elsbeth Louis
Founded: 1972
Subjects: Fiction, Humor, Literature, Literary
 Criticism, Essays, Poetry
ISBN Prefix(es): 90-6169; 90-803481
Number of titles published annually: 35 Print
Total Titles: 1,200 Print; 6 Audio
Subsidiaries: Gaberbocchus Press

**Uitgeverij Ten Have+**
Division of Bosch en Keuning NV
Member of Bosch & Keuning Group
Ijsseldijk 31, 8266 AD Kampen
Mailing Address: Postbus 260, 3740 AG Baam
*Tel:* (038) 3392555 *Fax:* (038) 3311776
*Key Personnel*
Man Dir: C Sbiti
Managing Editor: P de Boer
Founded: 1831
Subjects: Biblical Studies, Philosophy, Religion -
 Jewish, Religion - Protestant, Religion - Other,
 Theology
ISBN Prefix(es): 90-259
Total Titles: 300 Print

**Hemma Holland BV**
Willemsparkweg 94, 1701 HM Amsterdam
*Tel:* (020) 675 53 26 *Fax:* (020) 679 62 54

**HES & De Graaf Publishers BV+**
Tuurdijk 16, 3997 MS 'tGoy-Houten, Utrecht
*Tel:* (030) 6011955 *Fax:* (030) 6011813
*E-mail:* info@hesdegraaf.com
*Web Site:* www.hesdegraaf.com
*Key Personnel*
Chief Executive, Editorial & Publicity: S S Hes-
 selink *E-mail:* hesselink@forum-hes.nl
Contact: E Kempers
Founded: 1971
Subjects: History, Language Arts, Linguistics, Lit-
 erature, Literary Criticism, Essays, Philosophy,
 Theology
ISBN Prefix(es): 90-6194

**Heuff Amsterdam Uitgever**
Lauriehof 8, 1016 MA Amsterdam
*Tel:* (020) 620 46 25 *Fax:* (020) 620 46 25
*Cable:* Heuff/Nieuwkoop
*Key Personnel*
Man Dir: H Heuff
Founded: 1970
Subjects: Art, Fiction, History, Music, Dance
ISBN Prefix(es): 90-6141

**Uitgeverij Heureka**
Hooqstr 20, 1381 VS Weesp
*Tel:* (0294) 480 000 *Fax:* (0294) 415 183
*E-mail:* heureka@belboek.com
*Web Site:* www.belboek.com/heureka; www.
 belboek.com/index.html
*Key Personnel*
Man Dir: F H B Cladder
Founded: 1976
Subjects: History
ISBN Prefix(es): 90-6262
*Bookshop(s):* Belboek - Int order Bookshop,
 Weesp *Tel:* (0294) 80000

**Historische Uitgeverij+**
Westersingel 37, 9718 CC Groningen
*Tel:* (050) 3181700; (050) 3135258 *Fax:* (050)
 3146383
*E-mail:* info@histuitg.nl
*Web Site:* www.histuitg.nl
*Key Personnel*
Publisher: Patrick M Th Everard *E-mail:* p.
 everard@histuitg.nl
Founded: 1986
Subjects: History, Journalism, Literature, Literary
 Criticism, Essays, Nonfiction (General), Philos-
 ophy, Poetry, Psychology, Psychiatry
ISBN Prefix(es): 90-6554
Number of titles published annually: 20 Print
Total Titles: 150 Print

**van Holkema**, *imprint of* Unieboek BV

**Waren Holkema**, *imprint of* Unieboek BV

**Uitgeverij Holland**
Spaarne 110, 2011 CM Haarlem
*Tel:* (023) 5323061 *Fax:* (023) 5342908
*E-mail:* info@uitgeverijholland.nl
*Web Site:* www.uitgeverijholland.nl
*Key Personnel*
Man Dir: Rolf van Ulzen
Sales Dir, Permissions: Ruurt van Ulzen
Founded: 1921
Subjects: Fiction, Poetry, Science (General)
ISBN Prefix(es): 90-251

**Holland University Press BV (APA)**
Subsidiary of APA (Academic Publishers Associ-
 ated)
Postbus 806, 1000 AV Amsterdam
*Tel:* (020) 626 5544 *Fax:* (020) 528 5298
*E-mail:* info@apa-publishers.com
*Web Site:* www.apa-publishers.com
Subjects: History, Human Relations, Language
 Arts, Linguistics, Law, Theology
ISBN Prefix(es): 90-6037; 90-302; 90-6039; 90-
 6042
Imprints: Fontes Pers

**Hollandia**, *imprint of* Gottmer Uitgevers Groep

**Uitgeverij Hollandia BV+**
Professor van Vlotenweg 1-A, 2061 EB Bloemen-
 daal
Mailing Address: Postbus 160, 2060 AD Bloe-
 mendaal
*Tel:* (023) 5257150 *Fax:* (023) 52574404
*E-mail:* gottmer@x54all.nl
*Web Site:* www.hiswa.nl
*Key Personnel*
Man Dir: Tonnis Muntinga
Founded: 1899
Subjects: Fiction, Maritime, Sports, Athletics,
 Transportation, Travel
ISBN Prefix(es): 90-6410; 90-6045

**Uitgeverij Homeovisie BV+**
Postbus 9292, 1800 GG Alkmaar
*Tel:* (072) 566 1133 *Fax:* (072) 566 1295
*E-mail:* info@vsm.nl

*Web Site:* www2.vsminfo.nl
*Key Personnel*
President: Mr F Bech
Editor: Marianne Meijer
Founded: 1976
Specialize in homeopathy.
Subjects: Health, Nutrition, Medicine, Nursing, Dentistry
ISBN Prefix(es): 90-71669

**Hotei Publishing**, *imprint of* KIT - Royal Tropical Institute Publishers

**Hotei Publishing+**
Imprint of KIT Publishers - Royal Tropical Institute
Mauritskade 63, 1092 AD Amsterdam
Mailing Address: PO Box 95001, 1090 HA Amsterdam
*Tel:* (020) 568 8330 *Fax:* (020) 568 8286
*Web Site:* www.kit.nl/hotei
*Key Personnel*
Man Dir: Ron Smit *E-mail:* r.smit@kit.nl
Publisher: Arlette Kouwenhoven *E-mail:* a.kouwenhoven@kit.nl
Manager Marketing & Sales: Erik Rasmussen *E-mail:* e.rasmussen@kit.nl
Finance Dir: Stefan van Goor *E-mail:* s.v.goor@kit.nl
Founded: 1999
Membership(s): Dutch Publishers Association.
Subjects: Art, Asian Studies, Gardening, Plants, History, Photography, Religion - Buddhist, Japan
ISBN Prefix(es): 90-74822
Number of titles published annually: 15 Print
Total Titles: 40 Print; 1 CD-ROM
Foreign Rep(s): Bookwise Asia (Southeast Asia); Bookwise International (Australia, New Zealand); Durnell Marketing (UK, Europe); Premier Book Marketing (UK); Yagi Shoten (Japan); Stylus Publishing, LLC (Canada, US); Yohan (Japan)

**ICG Publications BV+**
Dr H P Bremmerstr 20, 2552 MJ The Hague
*Tel:* (070) 4480203 *Fax:* (070) 4480177
*Cable:* INTERGRAPH DORDRECHT
*Key Personnel*
Man Dir: Henk J La Porte
Founded: 1978
Subjects: Language Arts, Linguistics, Medicine, Nursing, Dentistry
ISBN Prefix(es): 90-5569; 90-6765; 90-70176
*Parent Company:* Holland Academic Graphics
Subsidiaries: I C G Printing BV

**International Books**, *imprint of* Uitgeverij Jan van Arkel

**Uitgevery International Theatre & Film Books+**
Nieuwpoortkade 2A, 1055 RX Amsterdam
*Tel:* (020) 60 60 911 *Fax:* (020) 60 60 914
*E-mail:* info@itfb.nl
*Web Site:* www.itfb.nl
*Key Personnel*
President: Mrs M Oele
Founded: 1975
Specialize in theatre & film books.
Subjects: Drama, Theater, Film, Video, Music, Dance
ISBN Prefix(es): 90-6403
Number of titles published annually: 25 Print
Total Titles: 500 Print

**Uitgeverij Intertaal BV**
Transistorstr 80, 1322 CH Amsterdam
Mailing Address: PO Box 60081, 1320 AB Almere
*Tel:* (036) 5471650 *Fax:* (036) 5471582

*E-mail:* int@intertaal.nl
*Web Site:* www.intertaal.nl
Founded: 1963
Subjects: Language Arts, Linguistics
ISBN Prefix(es): 90-70885; 90-5451; 90-800002
*Showroom(s):* Inter L, Schuttershofstr 43, 2000 Antwerp
*Warehouse:* Lemelerbergweg 21-22, 1101 AJ Amsterdam Z O

**IOS Press BV+**
Nieuwe Hemweg 6B, 1013 BG Amsterdam
*Tel:* (020) 688 33 55 *Fax:* (020) 620 3419
*E-mail:* info@iospress.nl
*Web Site:* www.iospress.nl
*Key Personnel*
Dir: Dr E H Fredriksson
Founded: 1987
Subjects: Biological Sciences, Chemistry, Chemical Engineering, Computer Science, Electronics, Electrical Engineering, Environmental Studies, Health, Nutrition, Language Arts, Linguistics, Management, Mathematics, Mechanical Engineering, Medicine, Nursing, Dentistry, Physics, Technology
ISBN Prefix(es): 90-5199; 1-58603
Number of titles published annually: 90 Print
Total Titles: 500 Print
Subsidiaries: IOS Press Inc
*Branch Office(s)*
IOS Press/Lavis Marketing, 73 Lime Walk, Oxford OX3 7AD, United Kingdom *Tel:* (01865) 76 7575 *Fax:* (01865) 75 0079
IOS Press, Akademische Verlagsgesellschaft aka GmbH, Neue Promenade 6, 10178 Berlin, Germany *Tel:* (030) 2472 9840 *Fax:* (030) 2839 4100
Distributor for OHMSHA Ltd (Japan)

**JeugdSalamander Paperbacks**, *imprint of* Em Querido's Uitgeverij BV

**Kartoen**
Salland 231, 9405 GL Assen
*Tel:* (050) 3110505 *Fax:* (050) 3112299
*E-mail:* mondria@worldonline.nl
Subjects: Humor, Self-Help

**Katholieke Bijbelstichting** (Catholic Bible Center Netherlands)+
Orthenstr 290, 5211 SX Hertogenbosch
Mailing Address: Postbus 1274, 5200 BH 's-Hertogenbosch
*Tel:* (073) 6133220 *Fax:* (073) 6910140
*Web Site:* www.willibrordbijbel.nl/kbs
*Key Personnel*
Manager: Ph L van Heusden *E-mail:* p.v.heusden@rkbijbel.nl
Founded: 1961
Subjects: Biblical Studies, Religion - Catholic
ISBN Prefix(es): 90-6173
Number of titles published annually: 10 Print; 2 CD-ROM; 1 Online; 1 Audio
Total Titles: 100 Print; 2 CD-ROM; 1 Online; 1 Audio

**De Kern**, *imprint of* Uitgeverij De Fontein BV

**Kimio Uitgeverij bv+**
Postbus 1117, 1400 BC Bussum
*Tel:* (035) 6950760 *Fax:* (035) 6951548
*E-mail:* info@kimio.nl
*Web Site:* www.kimio.nl
*Key Personnel*
Publishing & Man Dir: J van den Boom
Founded: 1985
ISBN Prefix(es): 90-71368

**KIT - Royal Tropical Institute Publishers**
Mauritskade 63, 1092 AD Amsterdam

Mailing Address: PO Box 95001, 1090 HA Amsterdam
*Tel:* (020) 5688 272 *Fax:* (020) 5688 286
*E-mail:* publishers@kit.nl
*Web Site:* www.kit.nl/publishers
*Key Personnel*
Man Dir: Ron Smit
Subjects: Agriculture, Anthropology, Art, Developing Countries, Health, Nutrition
ISBN Prefix(es): 90-6832
Imprints: Hotei Publishing
Distributed by Bookwise Asia (Southeast Asia); Bookwise International (Australia & New Zealand); Marston Book Services (UK & Europe (except Holland)); Media Logistics (Netherlands); Stylus Publishing LLC (USA & Canada)
Foreign Rep(s): Bookwise Asia (Southeast Asia); Bookwise International (Australia, New Zealand); Durnell Marketing (UK, Europe); Premier Book Marketing (UK); Stylus Publishing LLC (Canada, US)

**KITLV Press Royal Institute of Linguistics & Anthropology+**
Division of Royal Institute of Linguistics & Anthropology
Reuvensplaats 2, 2311 BE Leiden
Mailing Address: PO Box 9515, 2300 RA Leiden
*Tel:* (071) 5272295 *Fax:* (071) 5272638
*E-mail:* kitlvpress@kitlv.nl
*Web Site:* www.iias.leidenuniv.nl/institutes/kitlv
*Key Personnel*
Dir: Prof W A L Stokhof
Founded: 1851
Subjects: Anthropology, Asian Studies, Economics, Environmental Studies, History, Language Arts, Linguistics, Social Sciences, Sociology, Women's Studies, Caribbean Studies
ISBN Prefix(es): 90-6718
Number of titles published annually: 15 Print
Total Titles: 250 Print
Distributed by The Asian Experts (Australia & the South Pacific); United Publishers Services Ltd (Japan); University of Washington Press
Distributor for Monash Asia Institute; Research School of Pacific & Asian Studies

**Uitgeverij Kluitman Alkmaar BV**
Jan Ligthartstr 11, 1817 MR Alkmaar
Mailing Address: Postbus 9000, 1800 GR Alkmaar
*Tel:* (072) 52 75 075 *Fax:* (072) 52 09 400
*E-mail:* webmaster@kluitman.nl
*Web Site:* www.kluitman.nl
*Key Personnel*
Dir: Dr P F A Stanco; Mrs H Stanco-Gerla
Founded: 1864
ISBN Prefix(es): 90-206

**Kluwer Bedrijfswetenschappen**
Division of Kluwer Transpua
Leeuwenbrug 99-103, 7411 TH Deventer
Mailing Address: PO Box 23, 7400 GA Deventer
*Tel:* (0570) 647111 *Fax:* (0570) 638040
*Telex:* 49774
*Key Personnel*
Publisher: P J A Snakkers
Chief Executive: A Langevoort
Subjects: Business, Economics, Technology
ISBN Prefix(es): 90-267; 90-6500; 90-5576; 90-5577; 90-13; 90-14; 90-201; 90-6501
*Parent Company:* Wolters Kluwer NV
*Warehouse:* Intermedia bv, PO Box 4, 2400 MA Alphen 4d Ryn

**Kluwer Law International+**
PO Box 85889, The Hague 2508 CN
*Tel:* (070) 308 1500 *Fax:* (070) 308 1515
*Key Personnel*
Man Dir: Mr A Fillingham
Dir of Sales & Marketing: Ms A Timmers
Marketing Manager: Ms Joyce M Rivers

Founded: 1995
Subjects: Law, Specialize in International Law & International Relations
ISBN Prefix(es): 90-411
*Parent Company:* Wolters Kluwer NV
*U.S. Office(s):* Aspen Publishers, 11015 Avenue of the Americas, 37th fl, New York, NY 10036, United States
*Warehouse:* Extenza Turpin
*Orders to:* Extenza Turpin, Stratton Business Park, Pegasus Dr, Biggleswade, SG18 8QB Bedforshire *Tel:* 01767 604853 *Fax:* 01767 604948 *E-mail:* sales@kluwerlaw.com *Web Site:* www.kluwerlaw.com

**Kluwer Technische Boeken BV+**
Leeuwenbrug 99-103, 7411 TH Deventer
Mailing Address: PO Box 23, 7400 GA Deventer
*Tel:* (0570) 647111 *Fax:* (0570) 638040
*Telex:* 49560 KLUTB NL
*Key Personnel*
Man Dir & Chief Executive: N H L van Herk
Editorial: Benno van Lochem; Rob van Berkel; Jan Schukking
Sales: Hans Ulenberg
Production: Dick Laus
Part of Wolters Kluwer Trade Publishing.
Subjects: Management, Mechanical Engineering, Science (General), Technology
ISBN Prefix(es): 90-267; 90-201; 90-5576; 90-5577
*Parent Company:* Wolters Kluwer NV
Subsidiaries: Kluwer Technische Boeken Belgie
*Warehouse:* Intermedia bv, PO Box 4, 2400 MA Alphen 4d Ryn

**Koenen,** *imprint of* Van Dale Lexicografie BV

**Uitgeverij J H Kok BV+**
Subsidiary of Veen Bosch & Keuning Uitgevers NV
Ijsseldijk 31, 8266 AD Kampen
Mailing Address: Postbus 5019, 8260 GA Kampen
*Tel:* (038) 3392555 *Fax:* (038) 3311776
*E-mail:* algemeen@kok.nl
*Web Site:* www.kok.nl
*Key Personnel*
Man Dir: B A Endedijk
Publisher: P de Boer; F J Jonkers; C Verboom
Executive Secretary: Tineke Bouma *Tel:* (038) 3392528 *E-mail:* tbouma@kok.nl
Founded: 1894
Subjects: Fiction, History, Poetry, Religion - Other, Science (General), Social Sciences, Sociology
ISBN Prefix(es): 90-266; 90-242; 90-6140; 90-297; 90-435; 90-205; 90-391; 90-304
Imprints: Agora; Gooi & Sticht; De Groot Goudriaan; VCL (series of novels)/Westfriesland; Voorhoeve
Subsidiaries: Callenbach; Kok; Ten Have

**Koninklijke Vermande bv+**
Postbus 20025, 2500 EA The Hague
*Tel:* (070) 3789880 *Fax:* (070) 3789783
*E-mail:* sdu@sdu.nl
*Web Site:* www.sdu.nl/uitg/vermande
*Key Personnel*
President: Dr J Emeis
Founded: 1750
Subjects: Accounting, Criminology, Environmental Studies, Law, Management, Science (General)
ISBN Prefix(es): 90-6040; 90-5458
Divisions: Kugler Publications BV
*Orders to:* SDU Service Centrum, PO Box 20014, 2500 EA The Hague *Tel:* (070) 3789880

**Kugler Publications+**
Imprint of SPB Academic Publishing bv

Prinsegracht 59A, 2512 EX The Hague
Mailing Address: PO Box 97747, 2509 GC The Hague
*Tel:* (070) 33-00253 *Fax:* (070) 33-00254
*E-mail:* kuglerspb@wxs.nl
*Web Site:* www.kuglerpublications.com
*Key Personnel*
President & International Rights: S P Bakker
Founded: 1974
Subjects: Criminology, Medicine, Nursing, Dentistry, Specializes in ophthalmology, otorhinolaryngolgy, neurology & neurosciences
ISBN Prefix(es): 90-6299
Number of titles published annually: 10 Print
Total Titles: 115 Print

**Kwintessens,** *imprint of* BV Uitgevery NZV (Nederlandse Zondagsschool Vereniging)

**LCG Malmberg BV**
Leeghwaterlaan 16, 5223 BA Hertogenbosch
Mailing Address: Postbus 233, 5201 AE's, Hertogenbosch
*Tel:* (073) 6288811 *Fax:* (073) 6210512
*Web Site:* www.malmberg.nl *Cable:* MALMBERG'S-HERTOGENBOSCH
*Key Personnel*
General Manager: Dr J V Nelthoven
Publisher: Dr J J Mathigssen
Founded: 1885
Firm is a part of Educational Publishing division of VNU BV.
Subjects: Biological Sciences, Chemistry, Chemical Engineering, Education, Physics
ISBN Prefix(es): 90-208; 90-345

**Leiden University Press,** *imprint of* Brill Academic Publishers

**Uitgeverij Lemma BV+**
Furkaplateau 15, 3524 ZH Utrecht
Mailing Address: Postbus 3320, 3502 GH Utrecht
*Tel:* (030) 2545652 *Fax:* (030) 2512496
*E-mail:* infodesk@lemma.nl
*Web Site:* www.lemma.nl
*Key Personnel*
Dir: Ruud K Veen *E-mail:* rveen@lemma.nl
Publisher: Stephanie Harmon *E-mail:* stephanie.harmon@lemma.nl; Karin Vlug *E-mail:* karin.vlug@lemma.nl
Founded: 1988
Independent educational & scientific publishing company.
Subjects: Business, Communications, Economics, Education, Health, Nutrition, Labor, Industrial Relations, Law, Management, Marketing, Physical Sciences, Psychology, Psychiatry, Social Sciences, Sociology, Technology
ISBN Prefix(es): 90-5189
Total Titles: 400 Print

**Lemniscaat+**
Vyverlaan 48, 3062 HL Rotterdam
Mailing Address: Postbus 4066, 3006 AB Rotterdam
*Tel:* (010) 2062929 *Fax:* (010) 4141560
*E-mail:* info@lemniscaat.nl
*Web Site:* www.lemniscaat.nl *Cable:* LEMNISCAAT ROTTERDAM
*Key Personnel*
Dir: J C Boele van Hensbroek *Tel:* (010) 2062920 *E-mail:* jcboele@lemniscaat.nl
Editor: Monique Postma *Tel:* (010) 2062925 *E-mail:* monique@lemniscaat.nl
Rights & Permissions: Susanne Padberg *Tel:* (010) 2062924 *E-mail:* susanne@lemniscaat.nl
Contact: F M van den Hoek *Tel:* (010) 2062927
Founded: 1963
Subjects: Psychology, Psychiatry, Social Sciences, Sociology

ISBN Prefix(es): 90-6069; 90-5637
Total Titles: 380 Print

**Uitgeverij Leopold BV**
Singel 262, 1016 AC Amsterdam
Mailing Address: Postbus 3879, 1001 AR Amsterdam
*Tel:* (020) 5511250 *Fax:* (020) 4204699
*E-mail:* verkoop@leopold.nl
*Web Site:* www.leopold.nl
*Key Personnel*
Man Dir: Liesbeth ten Houten
Permissions: Jacolien Kingmans
Founded: 1923
Subjects: Fiction, History
ISBN Prefix(es): 90-258
*Parent Company:* Nijgh en Van Ditmar NV
*Associate Companies:* BV Uitgeverij de Arbeiderspers

**Van Loghum Slaterus,** see Uitgeverij Bohn Stafleu Van Loghum BV

**Magnum,** *imprint of* Ars Scribendi bv Uitgeverij

**Meander Uitgeverij BV+**
Industrieweg 7, 2254 AE Voorschoten
*Tel:* (071) 5601040 *Fax:* (071) 5619741
*E-mail:* info@vierwindstreken.com
*Web Site:* www.vierwindstreken.com
*Key Personnel*
Contact: Bob Markus
Founded: 1996
ISBN Prefix(es): 90-5579; 90-5116
Number of titles published annually: 50 Print
Imprints: De Vier Windstreken

**Stichting Evangelische Uitgeverij H Medema**
Emsterweg 96, 8171 PK Vaassen
Mailing Address: Postbus 113, 8170 AC Vaassen
*Tel:* (0578) 574995 *Fax:* (0578) 573099
*E-mail:* info@medema.nl
*Web Site:* www.medema.nl
*Key Personnel*
Contact: H P Medema
Founded: 1951
ISBN Prefix(es): 90-6353

**Meinema,** *imprint of* Boekencentrum BV

**Uitgeverij Meinema+**
Postbus 29, 2700 AA Zoetermeer
*Tel:* (079) 3615481 *Fax:* (079) 3615489
*E-mail:* info@boekencentrum.nl
*Web Site:* www.boekencentrum.nl
*Key Personnel*
Editor: C Korenhof *E-mail:* korenhof@boekencentrum.nl
Subjects: Religion - Catholic, Religion - Protestant, Theology
ISBN Prefix(es): 90-211
Number of titles published annually: 40 Print
Total Titles: 220 Print
*Parent Company:* Boekencentrum, Goudstr 50, 2718 RC Zoetermeer
Distributed by Denis

**Mets & Schilt Uitgevers en Distributeurs+**
Westeinde 16, 1017 ZP Amsterdam
*Tel:* (020) 6256087 *Fax:* (020) 6270242
*E-mail:* info@metsenschilt.com
*Web Site:* www.metsenschilt.com
*Key Personnel*
Dir: J Mets; M J Schilt
Founded: 1981
Subjects: Art, Biography, Business, Cookery, Developing Countries, Foreign Countries, History, Journalism, Nonfiction (General), Social Sciences, Sociology, Travel
ISBN Prefix(es): 90-5330

Distributed by Van Halewyck (Belgium); Transaction Publishers (USA) (Africa, Asia, Australia, Ireland, New Zealand, North America, South America, UK)

**J M Meulenhoff bv+**
Herengracht 505, 1017 BV Amsterdam
Mailing Address: PO Box 100, 1000 AC Amsterdam
*Tel:* (020) 55 33 500 *Fax:* (020) 62 58 511
*E-mail:* info@meulenhoff.nl
*Web Site:* www.meulenhoff.nl
*Key Personnel*
Man Dir: Anne Rube
Publisher: Annette Portegies
Editorial: Leonoor Broeder; Reinjan Mulder; Pieter Swinkels
Production: Breditta Kramer
Publicity: Piet van Riele
Founded: 1895
Subjects: Biography, Fiction, History, Literature, Literary Criticism, Essays, Nonfiction (General), Poetry, Travel, Also specializing in commercial & Dutch language books
ISBN Prefix(es): 90-290
Total Titles: 1,000 Print
*Parent Company:* Meulenhoff & Co BV
*Ultimate Parent Company:* PCM Algemene boeken
Imprints: Arena; Bertollucci; Meulenhoff/Manteau; Vassallucci
Subsidiaries: Meulenhoff International

**Meulenhoff/Manteau**, *imprint of* J M Meulenhoff bv

**Miland Publishers**
Zuideinde 40, 2421 AK Nieuwkoop
Mailing Address: Postbus 6, 2420 AA Nieuwkoop
*Tel:* (0172) 57 1461 *Fax:* (0172) 57 2231
*E-mail:* degraaf.books@wxs.nl
*Web Site:* www.antiqbook.nl/degraafbooks
Founded: 1969
ISBN Prefix(es): 90-6003
*Parent Company:* De Graaf Publishers

**Uitgeverij Mingus+**
Meidoornalaan 12, 3461 ET Linschoten
Mailing Address: Postbus 242, 3440 AE Woerden
*Tel:* (0348) 42 55 07 *Fax:* (0348) 42 55 07
*E-mail:* mingus-vk@planet.nl
*Key Personnel*
Contact: Teus Verweij
Founded: 1981
Subjects: Fiction, Nonfiction (General)
ISBN Prefix(es): 90-6564

**Ministerie van Verkeer en Waterstaat**
(Information & Documentation Division)
Plesmanweg 1-6, 2597 JG The Hague
Mailing Address: Postbus 20901, 2500 EX The Hague
*Tel:* (070) 3517086 *Fax:* (070) 3516430
*E-mail:* venwinfo@postbus51.nl
*Web Site:* www.minvenw.nl
*Telex:* 32562 minvwnl
Subjects: Transportation
ISBN Prefix(es): 90-369

**Mirananda Publishers BV+**
Postbus 85749, 2508 CK The Hague
*Tel:* (070) 358 59 43 *Fax:* (070) 358 68 43
*E-mail:* info@mirananda.nl
*Web Site:* www.mirananda.nl
*Key Personnel*
Man Dir: Jan-Carel Diecken
Contact: Reinoud Douwes
Founded: 1976
Subjects: Art, Astrology, Occult, Education, Language Arts, Linguistics, Philosophy, Psychol-

ogy, Psychiatry, Religion - Other, Science (General)
ISBN Prefix(es): 90-6271
Number of titles published annually: 25 Print
Total Titles: 250 Print
Imprints: Moon Press (children's)
*Orders to:* Centraal Boekhuis, Erasmusweg 10, Culemborg

**Mirran+**
Oude Trambaan 23, 5085 NH Esbeek
*Tel:* (013) 5169534 *Fax:* (013) 4684764
*E-mail:* info@mirran.com
*Web Site:* www.mirran.com
*Key Personnel*
Director: Mieke de Jonge
Founded: 1996
Specialize in Danish children's books in Dutch translations.
Membership(s): GAU.
ISBN Prefix(es): 90-75837
Total Titles: 11 Print
Foreign Rep(s): Denis & Co (Belgium)
*Shipping Address:* Centraal Boekhuirs, PO Box 125, Culemborg

**Mondria Publishers+**
Westerkade 13a, 9718 AR Groningen
*Tel:* (050) 3110505 *Fax:* (050) 3112299
*E-mail:* post@mondria.nl
*Key Personnel*
Chief Executive, Sales & Publicity: E Vos
Founded: 1980
Subjects: Humor
ISBN Prefix(es): 90-6555; 90-432

**Moon Press (children's)**, *imprint of* Mirananda Publishers BV

**Uitgeverij Maarten Muntinga+**
Nieuwezijds Voorburgwal 292, 1012 RT Amsterdam
Mailing Address: Postbus 2465, 1000 CL Amsterdam
*Tel:* (020) 521 67 67 *Fax:* (020) 626 05 96
*E-mail:* info@rainbow.nl
*Web Site:* www.rainbow.nl
*Key Personnel*
President: Maarten Muntinga
Publisher: Hilbrand Gringhuis
Founded: 1983
Subjects: Biography, Fiction, History, Humor, Literature, Literary Criticism, Essays, Nonfiction (General), Self-Help
ISBN Prefix(es): 90-6766; 90-417
Imprints: Rainbow Crime; Rainbow Pocketboeken

**Nai Publishers**
Mauritsweg 23, 3012 JR Rotterdam
*Tel:* (010) 2010133 *Fax:* (010) 2010130
*E-mail:* info@naipublishers.nl
*Web Site:* www.naipublishers.nl
*Key Personnel*
Publisher & Director: Simon Franke
Editor & Production: Caroline Gautier; Barbera van Kooij
Office Manager: Marion Pot
Finance: Peter Pols
Founded: 1994
Publisher of books about architecture, art & urban design.
Subjects: Architecture & Interior Design, Art, Urban Design
Foreign Rep(s): Art Data (UK, Ireland); Coen Sligting Bookimport (Austria, Belgium, Germany, Switzerland); DAP (Central America, North America, South America); Le Funambule (France); Modern Journal (Australia, New Zealand); Penny Padovani (Gibraltar, Greece, Italy, Portugal, Slovenia, Spain); Roger Ward International Book Marketing (Asia)

**Narratio Theologische Uitgeverij+**
Kwakernaat 10, 4205 PK Gorinchem
Mailing Address: Postbus 1006, 4200 CA Gorinchem
*Tel:* (0183) 62 81 88 *Fax:* (0183) 64 04 96
*E-mail:* lvdherik@narratio.nl
*Web Site:* www.narratio.nl
*Key Personnel*
International Rights: L van den Herik
Founded: 1989
Subjects: Biblical Studies, History, Religion - Catholic, Religion - Protestant, Theology, Women's Studies
ISBN Prefix(es): 90-5263
Total Titles: 220 Print; 7 Audio

**Nederlands Literair Produktie-en Vertalingen Fonds (NLPVF)** (Foundation for the Production & Translation of Dutch Literature)
Singel 464, 1017 AW Amsterdam
*Tel:* (020) 620 62 61 *Fax:* (020) 620 71 79
*E-mail:* office@nlpvf.nl
*Web Site:* www.nlpvf.nl
*Key Personnel*
Man Dir: Henk Propper
Subjects: Fiction, Nonfiction (General), Poetry
ISBN Prefix(es): 90-803223

**Uitgeverij H Nelissen BV**
Birkstr 95-97, 3768 HD Soest
Mailing Address: Postbus 3167, 3760 DD Soest
*Tel:* (035) 5412386 *Fax:* (035) 5423877
*E-mail:* info@nelissen.nl
*Web Site:* www.nelissen.nl
*Key Personnel*
Man Dir, Editorial, Permissions: Dick Boer
*E-mail:* dickboer@nelissen.nl
Sales & Publicity: Pieter Zwart
Founded: 1922
Subjects: Business, Communications, Economics, Education, Government, Political Science, Labor, Industrial Relations, Management, Philosophy, Psychology, Psychiatry, Religion - Other, Social Sciences, Sociology
ISBN Prefix(es): 90-244

**Nieuwe Stad Stichting**
Utrechtseweg 171, 3818ED Amersfoort
*Tel:* (033) 4614615 *Fax:* (033) 4635885
Founded: 1960
ISBN Prefix(es): 90-71734
*Parent Company:* Citta Nuova Editrice, Italy

**Nieuwe Wieken**, *imprint of* Omega Boek BV

**Nijgh & Van Ditmar Amsterdam+**
Singel 262, 1016 AC Amsterdam
Mailing Address: Postbus 3879, 1001 AR Amsterdam
*Tel:* (020) 55 11 262 *Fax:* (020) 6203509
*E-mail:* verkoop@querido.nl; info@querido.nl
*Web Site:* www.querido.nl
*Key Personnel*
President: Ary Langbroek
Vice President: Vic va de Reijt
Editor: Lidewijde Paris
Founded: 1837
Publisher of Zoetermeer: young/young debut writers' upmarket literary fiction & nonfiction.
Subjects: Fiction, Humor, Literature, Literary Criticism, Essays, Mysteries, Nonfiction (General), Poetry, Social Sciences, Sociology
ISBN Prefix(es): 90-388
*Parent Company:* Em Querido bv
Imprints: Zoetermeer
Divisions: Dedalus (for Belgium)

**NLPVF**, see Nederlands Literair Produktie-en Vertalingen Fonds (NLPVF)

**North Holland**, *imprint of* Elsevier Science BV

**Omega Boek BV+**
Fregat 35, 1113 EE Diemen
*Tel:* (020) 690 59 97 *Fax:* (020) 695 74 28
*E-mail:* info@omegaboek.nl
Founded: 1968
Subjects: Art, Fiction, Management, Military Science, Nonfiction (General)
ISBN Prefix(es): 90-6057; 90-6142
Imprints: De Centaur; Nieuwe Wieken; Omega Jeugdboekerij; Triton Pers
*Book Club(s):* ECI voor boeken en platen BV
*Orders to:* Centraal Boekhuis, Erasmusweg 10, Culemborg

**Omega Jeugdboekerij,** *imprint of* Omega Boek BV

**Ooievaar+**
Herengracht 507, 1017 BV Amsterdam
Mailing Address: Postbus 1662, 1000 BR Amsterdam
*Tel:* (020) 624 19 34 *Fax:* (020) 622 54 61
*E-mail:* pbo@pbo.nl
*Web Site:* www.pbo.nl
*Key Personnel*
Man Dir & Publisher: Plien van Albada
Editor: Josje Kraamer; Job Lisman; Bertram Mourits; Maaike le Noble
Foreign Rights: Hedda Sanders *Fax:* (020) 427 93 81 *E-mail:* rights@pbo.nl
*Associate Companies:* Bert Bakker; Prometheus

**Oriental Press BV (APA)**
Subsidiary of APA (Academic Publishers Associated)
Postbus 806, 1000 AV Amsterdam
*Tel:* (020) 626 5544 *Fax:* (020) 528 5298
*E-mail:* info@apa-publishers.com
*Web Site:* www.apa-publishers.com
Subjects: Asian Studies, Religion - Islamic
ISBN Prefix(es): 90-6023

**Parel Pockets,** *imprint of* De Boekerij BV

**Partners Training & Innovatie**
Dwerggras 30, 3068 PC Rotterdam-Ommoord
*Tel:* (010) 4071599 *Fax:* (010) 4202227
*E-mail:* info@ced.nl
*Web Site:* www.ced-groep.nl
*Key Personnel*
Publisher: Mr C A van Dongen
Founded: 1992
Subjects: Education
ISBN Prefix(es): 90-5819; 90-75074
Total Titles: 104 Print; 11 Audio
*Parent Company:* LED

**Passage, Uitgeverij+**
Camphuysenstr 58, 9721 KH Groningen
Mailing Address: Postbus 216, 9700 AE Groningen
*Tel:* (050) 5271332
*E-mail:* info@uitgeverijpassage.nl
*Web Site:* www.uitgeverijpassage.nl
*Key Personnel*
Publisher: Anton Scheepstra
Founded: 1991
Specialize in Dutch literature.
Membership(s): KVB; NUV (GAU).
Subjects: Dutch Literature
ISBN Prefix(es): 90-5452
Total Titles: 60 Print
Distributed by Maklu
Foreign Rep(s): Maklu (Belgium)

**Pearson Education Benelux**
Concertgebouwplein 25, 1071 LM Amsterdam
Mailing Address: Postbus 75598, 1070 AM, Amsterdam
*Tel:* (020) 575-5800 *Fax:* (020) 664-5334

*E-mail:* firstname.lastname@mail.aw.nl; amsterdam@pearsoned-ema.com
*Web Site:* www.pearsoneducation.nl
*Key Personnel*
President: Rita Snaddon
Finance & P&O: Hennie Haverkort
Marketing Manager, Professional Education: Sue Young
Publishing Manager: Arianne Strating
Founded: 1942
Subjects: Business, Computer Science, Economics, Education, Management, Technology
ISBN Prefix(es): 0-201
*Parent Company:* Pearson Plc

**Penguin Books Netherlands BV**
Postbus 3507, 1001 AH Amsterdam
*Tel:* (020) 6259566 *Fax:* (020) 6258676
ISBN Prefix(es): 90-75320

**The Pepin Press+**
PO Box 10349, 1001 EH Amsterdam
*Tel:* (020) 420 20 21 *Fax:* (020) 420 11 52
*E-mail:* mail@pepinpress.com
*Web Site:* www.pepinpress.com
*Key Personnel*
Publisher & International Rights: Mr Pepin Van Roojen
Founded: 1995
Specialize in high quality art publications.
Subjects: Antiques, Archaeology, Architecture & Interior Design, Art, Asian Studies, Fashion, History
ISBN Prefix(es): 90-5496

**Pergamon,** *imprint of* Elsevier Science BV

**Philo Press (APA)**
Subsidiary of APA (Academic Publishers Associated) (Netherlands)
Postbus 806, 1000 AV Amsterdam
*Tel:* (020) 626 5544 *Fax:* (020) 528 5298
*E-mail:* info@apa-publishers.com
*Web Site:* www.apa-publishers.com
Founded: 1963
Firm incorporates Gerard Th Van Heusden (APA) & G W Hissink & Co (APA).
Subjects: Art, Asian Studies, Biblical Studies, History, Human Relations, Religion - Islamic, Religion - Jewish, Science (General), Theology
ISBN Prefix(es): 90-6022; 90-6024; 90-6025

**Picaron Editions+**
Postbus 8024, 6710 AA Ede Gid
*Tel:* (020) 6201484
Founded: 1987
Subjects: Art, Philosophy
ISBN Prefix(es): 90-71466

**Piccolo,** *imprint of* De Boekerij BV

**Piccolo,** *imprint of* Van Goor BV

**Piramide,** *imprint of* Uitgeverij De Fontein BV

**Plateau,** *imprint of* Uitgeverij De Vuurbaak BV

**Uitgeverij Ploegsma BV+**
Singel 262, 1016 AC Amsterdam
*Tel:* (020) 5511250 *Fax:* (020) 6203504
*E-mail:* info@ploegsma.nl
*Web Site:* www.ploegsma.nl
*Key Personnel*
President: Peter Frohlich
Founded: 1901
Subjects: Child Care & Development, Fiction, How-to, Nonfiction (General), Science (General)

ISBN Prefix(es): 90-216
Imprints: Ploegsma (children's books); De Brink (adult books)

**Ploegsma (children's books),** *imprint of* Uitgeverij Ploegsma BV

**Podium Uitgeverij+**
Singel 450, 1017 AV Amsterdam
*Tel:* (020) 421 38 30 *Fax:* (020) 421 37 76
*E-mail:* post@uitgeverijpodium.nl
*Web Site:* www.uitgeverijpodium.nl
*Key Personnel*
Dir: Joost Nijsen *Fax:* (020) 421 37 76
    *E-mail:* jn@uitgeverijpodium.nl
Founded: 1997
Specializes in Dutch literature.
Subjects: Anthropology, Fiction, History, Literature, Literary Criticism, Essays, Nonfiction (General), Social Sciences, Sociology
ISBN Prefix(es): 90-5759
Number of titles published annually: 25 Print
Total Titles: 100 Print

**De Prom**
Subsidiary of Veen Bosch & Keuning Uitgevers NV
Prinses Marielaan 8, 3743 JA Baarn
Mailing Address: Postbus 1, 3740 AA Baarn
*Tel:* (035) 5482403 *Fax:* (035) 5418221
*E-mail:* info.fontein@defonteinbaarn.nl
*Key Personnel*
Man Dir: U Hazeu
Subjects: Art, Biography, History, Literature, Literary Criticism, Essays, Music, Dance, Photography, Religion - Catholic, Religion - Protestant, Theology
ISBN Prefix(es): 90-6801

**Prometheus**
Herengracht 507, 1017 BV Amsterdam
*Tel:* (020) 624 19 34 *Fax:* (020) 622 54 61
*E-mail:* pbo@pbo.nl
*Web Site:* www.pbo.nl
*Key Personnel*
Man Dir & Publisher: Ms Plien van Albada
Editor: Josje Kraamer; Job Lisman; Bertram Mourits; Maaike le Noble
Foreign Rights: Hedda Sanders *Tel:* (020) 427 93 81 *E-mail:* rights@pbo.nl
Founded: 1893
Subjects: Gay & Lesbian, History, Language Arts, Linguistics, Literature, Literary Criticism, Essays, Nonfiction (General), Philosophy, Poetry, Psychology, Psychiatry, Science (General)
ISBN Prefix(es): 90-6019; 90-5333; 90-351
Number of titles published annually: 300 Print
*Associate Companies:* Ooievaar
*Orders to:* Ivec, Postbus 154, 1380 AD Weesp

**Publitronic,** *imprint of* Segment BV

**Em Querido's Uitgeverij BV**
Singel 262, 1016 AC Amsterdam
Mailing Address: Postbus 3879, 1001 AG Amsterdam
*Tel:* (020) 55 11 200 *Fax:* (020) 55 11 256
*E-mail:* info@querido.nl
*Web Site:* www.querido.nl
*Key Personnel*
Editor-in-Chief: Jacques Dohmen *E-mail:* j.dohmen@querido.nl
President: Ary T Langbroek *E-mail:* b.langbroek@querido.nl
Foreign Rights: Lucienne van der Leije *E-mail:* l.van.der.leije@querido.nl
Publisher: Baerbel Dorweiler *E-mail:* b.dorweiler@querido.nl
Founded: 1915
Subjects: Art, Biography, Drama, Theater, Fiction, History, Mathematics, Poetry, Romance

ISBN Prefix(es): 90-214; 90-253
Imprints: Athenaeum-Polak & Van Gennep; Griffioen Paperbacks; JeugdSalamander Paperbacks; Salamander Paperbacks; De Viergang

**Rainbow Crime**, *imprint of* Uitgeverij Maarten
Muntinga

**Rainbow Pocketboeken**, *imprint of* Uitgeverij
Maarten Muntinga

**Rebo Productions BV+**
le Poellaan 6, 2161 LB Lisse
Mailing Address: PO Box 314, 2160 AH Lisse
*Tel:* (0252) 431 556 *Fax:* (0252) 431 557
*E-mail:* info@rebo-publishers.com
*Web Site:* www.rebo-publishers.com
*Key Personnel*
President: Henk Wagner *E-mail:* h.wagner@rebo-
publishers.com
Commercial Dir: E P A Veltman
International Rights: J A M Wagner
Founded: 1983
Subjects: Animals, Pets, Crafts, Games, Hobbies,
Gardening, Plants
ISBN Prefix(es): 90-366
*Associate Companies:* Zuid Boekprodukties BV
Subsidiaries: Rebo Productions SRO; Celetna ii

**Reed Elsevier Nederland BV+**
Radarwg 29, 1043 NX Amsterdam
*Tel:* (020) 485 2222 *Fax:* (020) 618 0325
*Web Site:* www.elsevier.com
*Key Personnel*
Chief Executive: Derk Haank
Legal Dir: Erik Ekker
*Operating Companies:* Argus; Bonaventura; Dag-
bladunie; Elsevier Opleidingen; Krips Repro;
Misset; Pan European Publishing Company
*Divisions, Subsidiaries & Branches:* Elsevier
Training NV, Brussels, International Equipment
News Europe NV, Brussels (both Belgium);
Editions Elsevier Thomas SA, Boulogne Bil-
lancourt, France; Elsevier Thomas Fachverlag
GmbH, Mainz, Germany; Audet Tijdschriften,
Arnheim, De Dordtenaar BV, Dordrecht, To-
eristiek BV, Oostwoud, Dagblad van Rijn en
Gouwe BV, Alphen aan den Rijn, Brabants
Niewsblad BV, Roosendaal, Rotterdams Dag-
blad CV, Rotterdam, Nederlands Studiecen-
trum, Vlaardingen, CBBM BV, Zwijndrecht (all
Netherlands); Elsevier Prensa SA, Barcelona,
Arte y Cemento Bilbao (Both Spain).
Subjects: Science (General)

**La Riviere Creatief**
Postbus 309, 3740 AH Baarn
*Tel:* (035) 5486600 *Fax:* (035) 5486675

**Robyns**, *imprint of* Educatieve Partners
Nederland bv

**Rodopi**
Tijnmuiden 7, 1046 AK Amsterdam
*Tel:* (020) 6114821 *Fax:* (020) 4472979
*E-mail:* info@rodopi.nl
*Web Site:* www.rodopi.nl
*Key Personnel*
Dir: Fred van der Zee *E-mail:* f.van.der.zee@
rodopi.nl
Founded: 1966
Subjects: Human Relations
ISBN Prefix(es): 90-6203; 90-5183; 90-420
Number of titles published annually: 3 CD-ROM;
50 Online
Total Titles: 4,000 Print; 100 Online
*U.S. Office(s):* One Rockefeller Plaza, Suite 1420,
New York, NY 10020, United States *Tel:* 212-
265-6360 *Fax:* 212-265-6402 *E-mail:* info@
rodopi.nl *Web Site:* www.rodopi.nl

**Rothschild & Bach+**
Kleine Garmanplantsoen 21 VII, 1017 RP Ams-
terdam
*Tel:* (020) 6389329
ISBN Prefix(es): 90-5371
*Associate Companies:* International Theatre &
Film Books

**Salamander Paperbacks**, *imprint of* Em
Querido's Uitgeverij BV

**Samsom BedrijfsInformatie BV**
Alphen 22n den Rijn, 2400 MA Amsterdam
Mailing Address: Prinses Margrietlaanz, 2404 HA
Alphenaanden Rijn
*Tel:* 0172 466633 *Fax:* 0172 475933
*E-mail:* info@kluwer.nl
*Web Site:* www.kluwer.nl
*Key Personnel*
Man Dir: C J Steur
Founded: 1882
Part of Wolters Kluwer Business Publishing.
Subjects: Advertising, Business, Finance, Labor,
Industrial Relations, Management, Marketing,
Public Administration, Social Sciences, Sociol-
ogy, Technology
ISBN Prefix(es): 90-6500
*Parent Company:* Wolters Kluwer NV
Divisions: Hofstad Vakpers

**Samsom Stafleu**, see Uitgeverij Bohn Stafleu Van
Loghum BV

**Sara**, *imprint of* Uitgeverij en boekhandel Van
Gennep BV

**Schoolpers**, *imprint of* Educatieve Partners
Nederland bv

**Scriptum+**
Postbus 293, 3100 AG Schiedam
*Tel:* (010) 4271022 *Fax:* (010) 4736625
*E-mail:* info@scriptum.nl
*Web Site:* www.scriptum.nl
*Key Personnel*
Publisher: Hans Ritman *E-mail:* ritman@
scriptum.nl
Founded: 1985
Subjects: Antiques, Art, Business, Management,
Marketing
ISBN Prefix(es): 90-71542; 90-5594
Number of titles published annually: 25 Print
Total Titles: 200 Print
Imprints: Scriptum Art; Scriptum Management;
Scriptum Topography

**Scriptum Art**, *imprint of* Scriptum

**Scriptum Management**, *imprint of* Scriptum

**Scriptum Topography**, *imprint of* Scriptum

**SDU Juridische & Fiscale Uitgeverij**
Christoffel Plantijnstr 2, 2515 TZ The Hague
Mailing Address: Postbus 20024, 2500 EA The
Hague
*Tel:* (070) 3789880; (070) 3789911 *Fax:* (070)
3854321; (070) 3789783; (070) 3458068
*E-mail:* sdu@sdu.nl
*Web Site:* www.sdu.nl
*Key Personnel*
Marketing Manager: Mrs M J Geevers
Founded: 1991
Subjects: Finance, Law
ISBN Prefix(es): 90-5409

**Sdu Uitgevers bv**
Christoffel Plantijnstr 2, 2515 TZ The Hague

Mailing Address: Postbus 20014, 2500 EA The
Hague
*Tel:* (070) 378 99 11; (070) 378 98 80 *Fax:* (070)
385 43 21; (070) 378 97 83
*E-mail:* sdu@sdu.nl
*Web Site:* www.sdu.nl
*Telex:* 32486
Subjects: Government, Political Science
ISBN Prefix(es): 90-12; 90-399; 90-5332

**Segment BV+**
Peter Treckpoelstr 2, 6191 VK Beek Lb
Mailing Address: PO Box 75, 6190 AB Beek Lb
*Tel:* (046) 43894444 *Fax:* (046) 4389401; (046)
4370161
*E-mail:* secretariant@segment.nl
*Web Site:* www.segment.nl
*Key Personnel*
Man Dir: Menno M J Landman
Founded: 1961
Part of Wolters Kluwer Trade Publishing.
Subjects: Electronics, Electrical Engineering, Phi-
losophy, Science (General)
ISBN Prefix(es): 90-5381; 90-70160; 90-73035;
0-905705
*Parent Company:* Wolters Kluwer NV
Imprints: Elektuur; Elektor; Publitronic
Subsidiaries: Elektor (Germany, France & UK)

**SEMAR Publishers SRL+**
Nachtegaallaan, 1, 2566 JJ The Hague
SAN: 136-5967
*Tel:* (070) 356 04 03; (070) 345 90 38 *Fax:* (070)
360 24 71
*E-mail:* info@semar.org
*Web Site:* www.semar.org *Cable:* SEMAR
*Key Personnel*
President & Chief Executive Officer: Luciano
Sahlan Momo, PhD *E-mail:* momo@semar.org
Founded: 1986
Specialize in editions with sustainable conserva-
tion criteria.
Membership(s): AIE; NUV.
Subjects: Anthropology, Archaeology, Art, Asian
Studies, Drama, Theater, Education, Environ-
mental Studies, Human Relations, Language
Arts, Linguistics, Literature, Literary Criticism,
Essays, Philosophy, Photography, Poetry, Psy-
chology, Psychiatry, Religion - Buddhist, Re-
ligion - Hindu, Religion - Islamic, Religion -
Jewish, Social Sciences, Sociology, Theology
ISBN Prefix(es): 88-7778
Number of titles published annually: 15 Print; 2
CD-ROM; 2 Online; 5 E-Book; 2 Audio
Total Titles: 206 Print; 8 CD-ROM; 43 Online; 5
E-Book; 5 Audio
Imprints: SPANDA
*Distribution Center:* Gazelle Book Services,
White Cross Mill, Lancaster LA1 4XS, United
Kingdom *Tel:* (01524) 68765 *Fax:* (01524)
63232 *E-mail:* sales@gazellebooks.co.uk *Web
Site:* www.gazellebooks.co.uk

**Semic Junior Press**
Zwarteweg 6c, 1412 GD Naarden
*Tel:* (035) 6944914 *Fax:* (035) 6944909
*Telex:* 4473114 cacjp nl
*Key Personnel*
Man Dir: Guillermo Hierro
Subjects: Astrology, Occult
ISBN Prefix(es): 90-305; 90-72073; 90-6236; 90-
940020; 90-940022; 90-940054; 90-940058;
90-940060; 90-940061; 90-940067; 90-940077;
90-940137
*Parent Company:* Semic International AB, Swe-
den

**Sesam Junior**, *imprint of* Uitgeverij De Fontein
BV

**Signature**, *imprint of* A W Bruna Uitgevers BV

**Sjaloom Uitgeverijen+**
Postbus 1895, 1000 BW Amsterdam
*Tel:* (020) 6206263 *Fax:* (020) 4288540
*E-mail:* post@sjaloom.nl
*Web Site:* www.sjaloom.nl
Founded: 1982
Subjects: Criminology, Erotica, Fiction, Health, Nutrition, History, Literature, Literary Criticism, Essays, Mysteries, Nonfiction (General), Regional Interests
ISBN Prefix(es): 90-6249
Imprints: Cadans

**Koninklijke Smeets Offset** (Royal Smeets Offset)+
Molenveldstr 90, 6001 HL Weert
Mailing Address: Koninklijke Smeets Offset BV, Postbus 17, 6000 AA Weert
*Tel:* (0495) 57 09 11 *Fax:* (0495) 54 29 05
*E-mail:* rswinfo@rotosmeets.com
*Telex:* 37550
*Key Personnel*
Manager: V Pokorny
Subjects: Art
ISBN Prefix(es): 90-6220
*Associate Companies:* VBI/Smeets

**Sociaal en Cultureel Planbureau+**
Postbus 16164, 2500 BD The Hague
*Tel:* (070) 3407000 *Fax:* (070) 3407044
*E-mail:* info@scp.ul
*Web Site:* www.scp.nl
*Key Personnel*
Dir: Prof Paul Schnabel
Founded: 1973
Subjects: Child Care & Development, Criminology, Education, Ethnicity, Government, Political Science, Health, Nutrition, Radio, TV, Real Estate, Social Sciences, Sociology, Women's Studies
ISBN Prefix(es): 90-377

**SPANDA**, *imprint of* SEMAR Publishers SRL

**Uitgeverij Het Spectrum BV**
Postbus 2073, 3500 GB Utrecht
*Tel:* (030) 2650650 *Fax:* (030) 2620850
*E-mail:* het@spectrum.nl
*Web Site:* www.spectrum.nl
*Key Personnel*
Dir: Joost C Bloemsma
Vice Dir, Sales Publicity: Yvonne Koolen
Editorial: Marjon Aardema; Bart Drubbel; Mechteld Jansen; George Pape; Renee Swaalf; Henk ter Borg
Production: Ludger van Zwetszelaar
Publisher, Multimedia: Ton von Bladel
Rights & Permissions: Jane Baird; Anry van Esch
*Tel:* (030) 2650656 *E-mail:* anry@spectrum.nl
Sales: Caroline Clasen *Tel:* (030) 2650683 *Fax:* (030) 2627045 *E-mail:* verkoop@spectrum.nl
Marketing: Aukje van den Berg *Tel:* (030) 2650697 *E-mail:* a.vandenberg@spectrum.nl; Mariska Hoksbergen *Tel:* (030) 2650671 *E-mail:* m.hoksbergen@spectrum.nl; Francoise Parlevliet *Tel:* (030) 2650618 *E-mail:* francoise@spectrum.nl
Founded: 1935
Subjects: Astrology, Occult, Computer Science, Criminology, Environmental Studies, History, Literature, Literary Criticism, Essays, Management, Mysteries, Nonfiction (General), Science Fiction, Fantasy, Travel
ISBN Prefix(es): 90-315; 90-274
Total Titles: 800 Print; 100 CD-ROM

**Spunk**, *imprint of* Uitgeverij Vassallucci bv

**Stam Techniek**, *imprint of* Educatieve Partners Nederland bv

**Stedelijk Van Abbemuseum**
Bilderdijklaan 10, 5600 AE Eindhoven
Mailing Address: Postbus 235, 5600 AE Eindhoven
*Tel:* (040) 2381000 *Fax:* (040) 2460680
*E-mail:* info@vanabbemuseum.nl
*Web Site:* www.vanabbemuseum.nl
*Key Personnel*
Dir: J Debbaut
Founded: 1936
Subjects: Art, Library & Information Sciences
ISBN Prefix(es): 90-70149

**Steltman Editions**
Teniersstr 6, Johannes Vermeerstr, 1071 DX Amsterdam
*Tel:* (020) 622 8683 *Fax:* (020) 620 7588
*E-mail:* steltman@steltman.com
*Web Site:* www.steltman.com
*Key Personnel*
President: Gerrit Steltman
Founded: 1982
Specialize in art design, Michael Parkes exclusive.
Subjects: Art
ISBN Prefix(es): 90-71867
*U.S. Office(s):* Steltman, 41 E 57 St, New York, NY 10022, United States

**Stenfert Kroese**, *imprint of* Educatieve Partners Nederland bv

**Stenvert Systems & Service BV**
Postbus 593, 3800 AN Amersfoort
*Tel:* (033) 457 0199 *Fax:* (033) 457 0198
*E-mail:* info@stenvert.nl
*Web Site:* www.stenvert.nl
*Key Personnel*
President: M G Stenvert
Editor: E H Kolk
Producer: F H A Kanters
Founded: 1925
Membership(s): GEU.
ISBN Prefix(es): 90-281
*Showroom(s):* Sutton 10, 7327 AB Apeldoorn
*Warehouse:* Sutton 10, 7327 AB Apeldoorn

**Stichting IVIO+**
Pascallaan 70c, 8218 NJ Lelystad
Mailing Address: Postbus 37, 8200 AA Lelystad
*Tel:* (0320) 229900 *Fax:* (0320) 229999
*E-mail:* info@ivio.nl
*Web Site:* www.ivio.nl
*Key Personnel*
Manager: A L Greiner *Tel:* (0320) 229912 *E-mail:* jmoes@ivio.nl
Founded: 1936
Subjects: Education
ISBN Prefix(es): 90-6121
Total Titles: 200 Print
Imprints: AO; Wereldschool

**Uitgeverij SUN**
Prinsengracht 747-751, 1017 JX Amsterdam
*Tel:* (020) 622 61 07 *Fax:* (020) 625 33 27
*E-mail:* info@uitgeverijboom.nl
*Web Site:* www.uitgeverijboom.nl
*Key Personnel*
Publisher: Sjef van de Wiel *Tel:* (020) 5200 134 *E-mail:* s.vandewiel@uitgeverijsun.nl
Editor: Mayke van Dieten *Tel:* (020) 5218 148 *E-mail:* m.vandieten@uitgeverijsun.nl; Henk Hoeks *Tel:* (020) 5200 133 *E-mail:* h.hoeks@uitgeverijsun.nl; Lucy Klaasen *Tel:* (020) 5218 147 *E-mail:* l.klaasen@uitgeverijsun.nl
Founded: 1969
Subjects: Architecture & Interior Design, Ethnicity, History, Philosophy
ISBN Prefix(es): 90-6168
*Parent Company:* Royal Boom Publishers, PO Box 1058, 7940 KB Meppel
Imprints: Uitgeverij Dwarsstap

**Swets & Zeitlinger Publishers+**
Member of Taylor & Francis Group plc
Heereweg 347 B, 2161 CA Lisse
Mailing Address: Postbus 800, 2160 SZ Lisse
*Tel:* (0252) 435111 *Fax:* (0252) 415888
*E-mail:* info@nl.swets.com
*Web Site:* www.swets.nl
*Telex:* 41325 szlis nl *Cable:* SWEZEIT-LISSE
*Key Personnel*
Chief Executive Officer: Eric van Amerongen
Founded: 1901
Also subscription agent.
Subjects: Education, Engineering (General), Health, Nutrition, Labor, Industrial Relations, Language Arts, Linguistics, Medicine, Nursing, Dentistry, Music, Dance, Psychiatry, Science (General), Technology
ISBN Prefix(es): 90-70430; 90-265
*U.S. Office(s):* PO Box 582, Downingtown, PA 19335-9998, United States

**SWP, BV Uitgeverij+**
Plantage Middenlaan 2-H, 1018 DD Amsterdam
Mailing Address: PO Box 257, 1000 AG Amsterdam
*Tel:* (020) 3307200 *Fax:* (020) 3308040
*E-mail:* swp@wxs.nl
*Web Site:* www.swpbook.com
*Key Personnel*
Publisher: Paul E Roosenstein
Founded: 1982
Specialize in early childhood education, health issues & social welfare.
Subjects: Child Care & Development, Criminology, Management, Psychology, Psychiatry
ISBN Prefix(es): 90-6665
Number of titles published annually: 40 Print; 1 CD-ROM
Total Titles: 300 Print; 2 CD-ROM

**Syntax Publishers**, *imprint of* Tilburg University Press

**Synthese-Miranda**, see Mirananda Publishers BV

**Telos Boeken+**
c/o Buyten en Schipperheijn, PO Box 22708, 1000 Amsterdam
*Tel:* (020) 5241010 *Fax:* (020) 5241011
*E-mail:* info@buijten.nl
*Web Site:* www.buijten.nl
*Key Personnel*
International Rights: Guido Sneep
Founded: 1902
Subjects: Human Relations, Philosophy, Religion - Protestant, Theology, Travel
ISBN Prefix(es): 90-6064; 90-6353 (Medema); 90-324; 90-5560 (De Vuurbaak); 90-5881

**Uitgeverij Terra bv+**
Postbus 1080, 7230 AB Warnsveld
*Tel:* (0575) 58 13 10 *Fax:* (0575) 52 52 42
*E-mail:* terra@terraboek.nl
*Web Site:* www.terraboek.nl
*Key Personnel*
President: H Weesjes
Man Dir: T van Lexmond
Founded: 1971
Subjects: Architecture & Interior Design, Cookery, Crafts, Games, Hobbies, Gardening, Plants, Health, Nutrition
ISBN Prefix(es): 90-6255
*Warehouse:* Terra Magazijn, Distrimedia NV, Meulenbeeksesteenweg 20, 8700 Tielt

**ThiemeMeulenhoff+**
Postbus 19240, 3501 DE, Utrecht
*Tel:* (030) 239 2 111 *Fax:* (030) 239 2 270
*E-mail:* info.bao@thiememeulenhoff.nl

*Web Site:* www.thiememeulenhoff.nl
*Key Personnel*
Man Dir: C J J van Steijn
Publishing Dir: P A Stadhouders
Subjects: Education
ISBN Prefix(es): 90-03; 90-238; 90-06; 90-433
*Parent Company:* Meulenhoff & Co BV
Subsidiaries: NIB-Software

**Thoth Publishers+**
Prins Hendriklaan 13, 1405 AK Bussum
*Tel:* (035) 6944144 *Fax:* (035) 6943266
*E-mail:* thoth@euronet.nl
*Key Personnel*
Publisher: Kees van den Hoek
Founded: 1985
Subjects: Architecture & Interior Design, Art, Literature, Literary Criticism, Essays, Nonfiction (General)
ISBN Prefix(es): 90-6868

**Uitgeverij de Tijdstroom BV+**
Asschatterweg 44, 3831 JW Leusden
*Tel:* (0342) 450867 *Fax:* (0342) 450365
*E-mail:* info@tijdstroom.nl
*Web Site:* www.tijdstroom.nl
Founded: 1924
Subjects: Health, Nutrition, Management, Medicine, Nursing, Dentistry, Physics, Psychology, Psychiatry, Social Sciences, Sociology
ISBN Prefix(es): 90-5898

**Tilburg University Press**
Warandelaan 2, Bldg L, 5037 AB Tilburg
Mailing Address: PO Box 90153, 5000 LE Tilburg
*Tel:* (013) 466 2124 *Fax:* (013) 466 2996
*E-mail:* library@kub.nl
*Web Site:* www.tilburguniversity.nl
*Key Personnel*
Librarian: Hans Geleijnse
Subjects: Behavioral Sciences, Biblical Studies, Economics, Language Arts, Linguistics, Library & Information Sciences, Philosophy, Psychology, Psychiatry, Theology
ISBN Prefix(es): 90-361
Imprints: Syntax Publishers

**Tirion Uitgevers BV+**
Subsidiary of Veen Bosch & Keuning Uitgevers NV
Julianalaan 11, 3743 JG Baarn
Mailing Address: PO Box 309, 3704 AH Baarn
*Tel:* (035) 5486600 *Fax:* (035) 5486675
*E-mail:* info@tirionuitgevers.nl
*Web Site:* www.tirionuitgevers.nl
*Key Personnel*
Dir: Aernoud Oosterholt
Marketing: Joanneke van Zadelhoff *Tel:* (035) 5486609 *E-mail:* jvzadelhoff@tirionuitgevers.nl
Founded: 1987
Subjects: Animals, Pets, Archaeology, Biography, Child Care & Development, Computer Science, Crafts, Games, Hobbies, Film, Video, Health, Nutrition, History, Humor, Medicine, Nursing, Dentistry, Music, Dance, Philosophy, Photography, Psychology, Psychiatry, Religion - Protestant, Social Sciences, Sociology, Sports, Athletics, Theology, Travel, Veterinary Science
ISBN Prefix(es): 90-5121; 90-5210; 90-439
Distributed by Agora
Distributor for Davidsfonds (Belgium)

**Ton Bolland**, *imprint of* Uitgeverij De Vuurbaak BV

**Uitgeverij De Toorts+**
Conradkade 6, 2031 CL Haarlem
Mailing Address: Postbus 9585, 2003 LN Haarlem
*Tel:* (023) 5532920 *Fax:* (023) 5320635

*E-mail:* uitgeverij@toorts.nl
*Web Site:* www.toorts.nl
*Key Personnel*
Man Dir & Production: J Hesseling
Sales, Editorial, Publicity, Rights & Permissions: Mrs M Klis
Founded: 1936
Subjects: Behavioral Sciences, Child Care & Development, Cookery, Health, Nutrition, Human Relations, Music, Dance, Psychology, Psychiatry, Self-Help, Wine & Spirits
ISBN Prefix(es): 90-6020
Imprints: De Toorts; ENTERBOOKS

**Triton Pers**, *imprint of* Omega Boek BV

**Twente University Press**
Unit of University of Twente
Postbus 217, 7500 AE Enschede
*Tel:* (053) 4899111 *Fax:* (053) 4892000
*E-mail:* info@utwente.nl
*Web Site:* www.utwente.nl/tupress
*Key Personnel*
Coordinator: Henny Leferink
Editing: Hans van Eerden
Founded: 1995
Subjects: Career Development, Computer Science, Education, Environmental Studies, Management, Mechanical Engineering, Medicine, Nursing, Dentistry, Public Administration, Regional Interests, Social Sciences, Sociology, Technology
ISBN Prefix(es): 90-365
Total Titles: 60 Print

**Uitgeverij Altamira-Becht BV+**
Postbus 317, 2000 AH Haarlem
*Tel:* (023) 54 11 190 *Fax:* (023) 52 74 404
*E-mail:* post@gottmer.nl
*Web Site:* www.altamira-becht.nl
Founded: 1985
Subjects: Literature, Literary Criticism, Essays
ISBN Prefix(es): 90-6963
*Parent Company:* Gottmer Uitgevers Groep

**Uitgeverij Contact** (Contact Publishers)
Subsidiary of Veen, Bosch & Keuning Uitgevers NV
Herengracht 481, 1017 BT Amsterdam
Mailing Address: PO Box 13, 1000 AA Amsterdam
*Tel:* (020) 5249800 *Fax:* (020) 6276851
*E-mail:* businesscontact@contact-bv.nl
*Web Site:* www.boekenwereld.com
*Key Personnel*
Dir: Marij Bertram
Marketing: Anne Schroen *E-mail:* aschroen@contact-bv.nl
Publicity: Anne Kramer; May Meurs *E-mail:* mmeurs@contact-bv.nl
Publisher: Mizzi van der Pluijm
Sales: Thea Bon; Ingrid Kee; Petra Wildvank
ISBN Prefix(es): 90-254

**Uitgeversmy Segment BV**, see Segment BV

**Unieboek BV+**
Onderdoor 7, 3995 DB Houten
Mailing Address: Postbus 97, 3990 DB Houten
*Tel:* (030) 63 77 660 *Fax:* (030) 63 77 600
*E-mail:* info@unieboek.nl
*Web Site:* www.unieboek.nl
*Telex:* 40468 Uboek nl *Cable:* UNIEBOEK
*Key Personnel*
Man Dir: Wouter van Gils
Editorial Dir: Toine Akveld
Sales Dir: Ramon Dahmen
Publisher: Riet Goes; Frank Noe; Dick Rog; Martine Schaap
Founded: 1891

Subjects: Animals, Pets, Architecture & Interior Design, Child Care & Development, Computer Science, Cookery, Crafts, Games, Hobbies, Fiction, History, How-to, Human Relations, Literature, Literary Criticism, Essays, Mysteries, Nonfiction (General), Photography, Romance, Self-Help, Travel, Women's Studies
ISBN Prefix(es): 90-226; 90-228; 90-269
*Parent Company:* Meulenhoff & Co BV
*Associate Companies:* De Boekerij BV; A W Bruna BV; M & P BV; Meulenhoff Nederland BV; Prometheus BV; Standaard Uitgeverij
Imprints: Agathon; de Cocon; van Dishoeck; Fibula; W Gaade; de Haan; van Holkema; Waren Holkema; Warendorf; het Wereldvenster

**Uniepers BV+**
Heinkuitenstr 26, 1390 AB Abcoude
Mailing Address: Postbus 69, 1390 AB Abcoude
*Tel:* (0294) 285111 *Fax:* (0294) 283013
*E-mail:* info@uniepers.nl
*Web Site:* www.uniepers.nl
*Key Personnel*
Chief Executive & Sales: Marinus H van Raalte
Dir: Marieke Bemelman
Sales Manager: Ingrid de Jong
Production: Albert van de Klashorst
Founded: 1961
Also book packagers.
Subjects: Anthropology, Antiques, Archaeology, Architecture & Interior Design, Art, Ethnicity, Health, Nutrition, History, Music, Dance, Natural History, Photography, Regional Interests, Culture, Nature
ISBN Prefix(es): 90-6825

**V S P International Science Publishers**
Subsidiary of Brill Academic Publishers
PO Box 346, 3700 AH Zeist
*Tel:* (030) 692 5790 *Fax:* (030) 693 2081
*E-mail:* vsppub@brill.nl
*Web Site:* www.vsppub.com
*Key Personnel*
Contact: Ms Els van Egmond
Founded: 1983
Specialize in STM journal & book publishing.
Membership(s): STM.
Subjects: Astronomy, Biological Sciences, Chemistry, Chemical Engineering, Earth Sciences, Mathematics, Medicine, Nursing, Dentistry, Physics, Psychology, Psychiatry, Science (General), Technology, Transportation
ISBN Prefix(es): 90-6764
*Orders to:* Books International Inc, PO Box 605, Herndon, VA 22070, United States *Tel:* 703-661-1500 *Fax:* 703-661-1501

**Van Buuren Uitgeverij BV+**
Postbus 10356, 6000 GJ Weert
*Tel:* (023) 5325440 *Fax:* (023) 5327017
*Key Personnel*
Publisher: Gerrit van Buuren; Jenny van Buuren; Patrick van Buuren
Founded: 1995
Membership(s): Royal Dutch Booktrade Organization.
Subjects: Fiction, History, Mysteries, Nonfiction (General)
ISBN Prefix(es): 90-5695; 90-76680
Total Titles: 50 Print
Distributed by Standaard Uitgeverij NV (Dutch speaking part of Belgium)

**De Grote Van Dale**, *imprint of* Van Dale Lexicografie BV

**Van Dale Grote Woordenboeken voor hedendaags taalgebruik**, *imprint of* Van Dale Lexicografie BV

**Van Dale Handbibliotheek**, *imprint of* Van Dale Lexicografie BV

**Van Dale Handwoordenboeken**, *imprint of* Van Dale Lexicografie BV

**Van Dale Kinderwoordenboeken**, *imprint of* Van Dale Lexicografie BV

**Van Dale Lexicografie BV**
Subsidiary of Veen Bosch & Keuning Uitgevers NV
St Jacobsstr 127, 3511 BP Utrecht
Mailing Address: Postbus 19232, 3501 DE Utrecht
*Tel:* (031) 232 47 11 *Fax:* (031) 231 68 50
*E-mail:* info@vandale.nl
*Web Site:* www.vandale.nl
*Key Personnel*
Chief Operating Officer: Jan Egas
Man Dir, Export Sales, Rights & Permissions: Bram Wolthoorn
Publisher: Marcel Jansen; Margreet Moerland; Rick Schutz
Sales Dir: Tanja Nijhuis
Production: J Butterfield
Founded: 1976
ISBN Prefix(es): 90-6648
Imprints: De Grote Van Dale; Van Dale Grote Woordenboeken voor hedendaags taalgebruik; Van Dale Handwoordenboeken; Koenen; Van Dale Kinderwoordenboeken; Van Dale Handbibliotheek
*Branch Office(s)*
Van Dale Lexicografie Belgie, Ternesselei 326, 2160 Wommelgem, Belgium *Tel:* 0032-3-3552830 *Fax:* 0032-3-3552841 (Distributor)
*Orders to:* PO Box 19232, 3501 DE Utrecht

**Van Goor**, *imprint of* De Boekerij BV

**Van Gorcum & Comp BV+**
Industrieweg 38, 9403 AB Assen
Mailing Address: Postbus 43, 9400 AA Assen
*Tel:* (0592) 37 95 55 *Fax:* (0592) 37 20 64
*E-mail:* assen@vgorcum.nl
*Web Site:* www.vangorcum.nl *Cable:* VANGORCUM
*Key Personnel*
General Dir & Publisher: Louwe Dijkema *Tel:* (0592) 379550 *Fax:* (0592) 379552 *E-mail:* l.dijkema@vangorcum.nl
Publisher, Medical Sciences: Wouter Oude Groothuis *Tel:* (0592) 379564 *Fax:* (0592) 379552 *E-mail:* w.oudegroothuis@vangorcum.nl
Publisher, Theology, History, Philosophy, Language & Literature: Theo Joppe *Tel:* (0592) 376936 *Fax:* (0592) 379552 *E-mail:* t.joppe@vangorcum.nl
Publisher, Social Sciences & Geography: Roelof Meijering *Tel:* (0592) 379566 *Fax:* (0592) 379552 *E-mail:* r.meijering@vangorcum.nl
Editor: Nathan Brinkman *Tel:* (0592) 379568 *Fax:* (0592) 379552 *E-mail:* n.brinkman@vangorcum.nl; Meta Kampen *Tel:* (0592) 379563 *Fax:* (0592) 379552 *E-mail:* m.kampen@vangorcum.nl
Production Leader: Bert Veenstra *Tel:* (0592) 379569 *Fax:* (0592) 379552 *E-mail:* l.veenstra@vangorcum.nl
Marketing: Susanne Gerritsen *Tel:* (0592) 379573 *Fax:* (0592) 379552 *E-mail:* s.gerritsen@vangorcum.nl
Head of Sales: Jan van Veen *Tel:* (0592) 379572 *Fax:* (0592) 379552 *E-mail:* j.van.veen@vangorcum.nl
Production Leader: Berta Oosterloo *Tel:* (0592) 379567 *Fax:* (0592) 372064 *E-mail:* b.oosterloo@vangorcum.nl
Founded: 1800

Subjects: Anthropology, Economics, Education, Geography, Geology, History, Language Arts, Linguistics, Law, Literature, Literary Criticism, Essays, Medicine, Nursing, Dentistry, Philosophy, Psychology, Psychiatry, Religion - Other, Social Sciences, Sociology
ISBN Prefix(es): 90-232; 90-255; 90-5693; 90-72371
Subsidiaries: Styx Publications

**Uitgeverij G A van Oorschot bv+**
Herengracht 613, 1017 CE Amsterdam
*Tel:* (020) 623 14 84 *Fax:* (020) 625 40 83
*E-mail:* verkoop@vanoorschot.nl
*Key Personnel*
President: W J van Oorschot
Vice President: Mrs G M Nefkens
Founded: 1945
Membership(s): KNUB.
Subjects: Literature, Literary Criticism, Essays, Nonfiction (General), Poetry
ISBN Prefix(es): 90-282

**Uitgeverij Van Walraven BV**
Imprint of Nijgh Versluys
Ericastr 18, 3742 SG Baarn
Mailing Address: Postbus 225, 3740 AE Baarn
*Tel:* (035) 5482421 *Fax:* (035) 5421672
Membership(s): the Combo Group.
ISBN Prefix(es): 90-6049

**Uitgeverij Van Wijnen+**
Zilverstr 4, 8801 KC Franeker
Mailing Address: Postbus 172, 8800 AD Franeker
*Tel:* (0517) 394588 *Fax:* (0517) 397179
*E-mail:* info@uitgeverijvanwijnen.nl
*Web Site:* www.uitgeverijvanwijnen.nl
*Key Personnel*
Dir: D van Wijnen
Founded: 1988
Subjects: Government, Political Science, History, Philosophy, Religion - Other, Theology
ISBN Prefix(es): 90-5194

**Vassallucci**, *imprint of* J M Meulenhoff bv

**Uitgeverij Vassallucci bv+**
Subsidiary of J M Meulenhoff bv
Herengracht 505, 1017 BV Amsterdam
Mailing Address: PO Box 100, 1000 AC Amsterdam
*Tel:* (020) 521 8322 *Fax:* (020) 623 6761
*E-mail:* info@vassallucci.nl
*Web Site:* www.vassallucci.nl
*Key Personnel*
Man Dir: Anne Rube
Dir & Publisher: Oscar van Gelderen
Publicity: Joni Zwart
Founded: 1995
Specialize in literary fiction.
Subjects: Fiction, Literature, Literary Criticism, Essays, Nonfiction (General)
ISBN Prefix(es): 90-5000
Total Titles: 80 Print
*Ultimate Parent Company:* PCM Algemene boeken
Imprints: Bertollucci; Spunk
Foreign Rep(s): Laura Susijn (London)
*Shipping Address:* Central Boekhuis, Culemborg

**VCL (series of novels)/Westfriesland**, *imprint of* Uitgeverij J H Kok BV

**Veen Bosch & Keuning Uitgevers NV+**
St Jacobsstr 125, 3511 BP Utrecht
Mailing Address: Postbus 8049, 3503 RA Utrecht
*Tel:* (030) 2349311 *Fax:* (030) 2349208
*E-mail:* algemeen@veenboschenkeuning.nl
*Web Site:* www.veenboschenkeuning.nl
*Key Personnel*
Man Dir: A de Groot *Fax:* (030) 2300145

An independent trade publisher of books, magazines, dictionaries & CD-ROMs.
ISBN Prefix(es): 90-246; 90-263; 90-266; 90-213; 90-259; 90-204; 90-245; 90-218; 90-215; 90-254
Number of titles published annually: 500 Print; 30 CD-ROM; 10 E-Book
Total Titles: 4,000 Print; 100 CD-ROM; 1 Online; 20 E-Book
Subsidiaries: Ambo-Anthos bv; Atlas; Augustus; Bekadidact bv; Uitgeverij Cantecleer BV; Contact bv; Uitgeverij Contact bv; Uitgeverij De Fontein BV; HBuitgevers bv; Uitgeverij Houtekiet; J H Kok bv; Kosmos-Z&K Uitgevers; Uitgeverij Luitingh-Sijthoff; Nijgh Versluys bv; Poema Pandora; De Prom; Tirion Uitgevers bv; Van Dale Lexicografie; Veen Algemene Boeken; Veen Magazines; Veen Uitgevers Groep Belgie

**Uitgeverij Verloren** (Verloren Publishers)+
Torenlaan 25, 1211 JA Hilversum
Mailing Address: PO Box 1741, 1200 BS Hilversum
*Tel:* (035) 6859856 *Fax:* (035) 6836557
*E-mail:* info@verloren.nl
*Web Site:* www.verloren.nl
*Key Personnel*
President: Mr L M VerLoren van Themaat
Founded: 1979
Subjects: Biography, Genealogy, History
ISBN Prefix(es): 90-6550
Number of titles published annually: 70 Print
Total Titles: 900 Print

**De Viergang**, *imprint of* Em Querido's Uitgeverij BV

**VNU Business Press Group BV+**
Division of Intermediair
PO Box 4020, 2003 EA Haarlem
*Tel:* (023) 546 3396 *Fax:* (023) 546 5541
*Web Site:* www.vnubp.nl
*Key Personnel*
Man Dir: F X I Koot
Subjects: Business, Career Development, Computer Science, Library & Information Sciences, Marketing
ISBN Prefix(es): 90-72802; 90-6434

**VNU Business Publications BV**
Division of Intermediair
Postbus 4020, 2003 EA Haarlem
*Tel:* (023) 546 3396 *Fax:* (023) 546 5541
*E-mail:* klatenservice@bp.vnu.com; info@bp.vnu.com
*Web Site:* www.vnubp.nl
*Telex:* 41549
ISBN Prefix(es): 90-72802; 90-6434
*Parent Company:* VNU - Verenigde Nederlandse Uitgeversbedrijven BV
Subsidiaries: Educational Publishing (comprising LCG Malmberg BV qv); Uitgeverij Het Spectrum; Uitgeverij J van In; WNU Business Information Services; VNU Business Press Group BV; VNU Magazine Group; VNU Newspaper Group; VNU Printing Group; VNU Sales Group

**Voorhoeve**, *imprint of* Uitgeverij J H Kok BV

**VU Boekhandel/Uitgeverij BV+**
De Boelelaan 1105, 1081 HV Amsterdam
*Tel:* (020) 64 443 55 *Fax:* (020) 646 27 19
*E-mail:* info@vuboekhandel.nl
*Web Site:* www.vuboekhandel.nl
*Key Personnel*
Man Dir & Editorial: M Rienks; P R Rienks
Production: Karin Sinnema
Sales: M Zitman
Founded: 1980

Subjects: Biological Sciences, Economics, History, Language Arts, Linguistics, Law, Medicine, Nursing, Dentistry, Philosophy, Psychology, Psychiatry, Public Administration, Science (General), Social Sciences, Sociology, Theology
ISBN Prefix(es): 90-6256; 90-5383
Imprints: VU Uitgeverij; VU University Press

**VU Uitgeverij**, *imprint of* VU Boekhandel/Uitgeverij BV

**VU University Press**, *imprint of* VU Boekhandel/Uitgeverij BV

**Uitgeverij De Vuurbaak BV** (The Lighthouse)+
Hermesweg 20, 3771 ND Barneveld
Mailing Address: Postbus 257, 3770 AG Barneveld
*Tel:* (0342) 411731 *Fax:* (0342) 411731
*E-mail:* vuurbaak@nd.nl; plateau@nd.nl
*Web Site:* www.vuurbaak.nl
*Key Personnel*
President & International Rights: B M van Hulst
Founded: 1965
Subjects: Religion - Protestant, Theology
ISBN Prefix(es): 90-6015; 90-5560; 90-5804
Number of titles published annually: 60 Print; 2 CD-ROM
Total Titles: 300 Print; 4 CD-ROM
*Parent Company:* Nedag Holding bv
*Associate Companies:* Telos; Uitgeverij
Imprints: Plateau; Ton Bolland
Divisions: Nedag Beheer

**Uitgeverij Waanders BV+**
Faradaystr 17, 8013 PH Zwolle
Mailing Address: Postbus 1129, 8001 BC Zwolle
*Tel:* (038) 4658628 *Fax:* (038) 4655989
*E-mail:* info@waanders.nl
*Web Site:* www.waanders.nl
*Key Personnel*
President: W J G M Waanders
Man Dir: H van de Wal
Deputy Director: M L M Waanders
Founded: 1836
Subjects: Antiques, Art, Ethnicity, History
ISBN Prefix(es): 90-6630; 90-400; 90-70072
*Parent Company:* Waanders Printers
*Bookshop(s):* Eiland 9, Zwolle

**Wageningen Academic Publishers+**
Bldg 304, Dreijenlaan 2, 6703 HA Wageningen
Mailing Address: PO Box 220, 6700 AE Wageningen
*Tel:* (0317) 47 65 16 *Fax:* (0317) 45 34 17
*E-mail:* info@wageningenacademic.com
*Web Site:* www.wageningenacademic.com
*Key Personnel*
Man Dir: Mike Jacobs *E-mail:* jacobs@wageningenacademic.com
Marketing & Sales: Dineke van den Biezenbos *E-mail:* biezenbos@wageningenacademic.com
Technical Dir: Enrico Kunst *E-mail:* kunst@wageningenacademic.com
Founded: 2002
Publisher of scientific & technical books. Specialize in animal science & agriculture
Textbooks, Proceedings & Monographs.
Subjects: Agriculture, Animals, Pets
ISBN Prefix(es): 90-74134
Total Titles: 80 Print

**Warendorf**, *imprint of* Unieboek BV

**Wegener Falkplan BV**
Battesakker 19-21, 5625 TC Eindhoven
Mailing Address: Postbus 9510, 5602 LM Eindhoven
*Tel:* (040) 2 642 111 *Fax:* (040) 2 410 955
*E-mail:* info@suurland.nl

*Web Site:* www.suurland.nl
*Telex:* 51874 svehv
*Key Personnel*
Man Dir: D R A Suurland; J A Suurland
Sales: Agnes Roag *Tel:* (040) 2 645 680
*E-mail:* a.roag@falk.nl
ISBN Prefix(es): 90-287
*Associate Companies:* Suurland Holding BV

**Wereldbibliotheek+**
Spuistr 283, 1012 VR Amsterdam
*Tel:* (020) 638 18 99 *Fax:* (020) 638 44 91
*E-mail:* info@wereldbibliotheek.nl
*Web Site:* www.wereldbibliotheek.nl
*Key Personnel*
Man Dir: J B I M Kat
Publisher: Koen van Gulik; Joos Kat
Editor: Gerda Scheltes
Founded: 1905
Subjects: Fiction, History, Nonfiction (General), Philosophy, Public Administration
ISBN Prefix(es): 90-284
Total Titles: 200 Print

**Wereldschool**, *imprint of* Stichting IVIO

**het Wereldvenster**, *imprint of* Unieboek BV

**Uitgeverij Westers**
Hammarskjoeldhof 35, 3527 HD Utrecht
*Tel:* (030) 2931043 *Fax:* (030) 2944586
*E-mail:* boekhandel@westers-utrecht.nl *Cable:* WESTERS UTRECHT
*Key Personnel*
Man Dir: R J N M Westers, Sr
Founded: 1967
Subjects: Fiction
ISBN Prefix(es): 90-6107

**Wilkerdon**, *imprint of* Uitgeversmaatschappij Ad Donker BV

**Wolters Kluwer B.V. Juridische Boekenen Tijschriften**
Division of Tjeenk Willink WEJ BV
Staverenstr 15, 7418 CJ Deventer
Mailing Address: PO Box 23, 7400 GA Deventer
*Tel:* (0570) 647111 *Fax:* (0570) 636683
*Key Personnel*
Contact: A E van Arkel
Founded: 1972
Subjects: Law
ISBN Prefix(es): 90-271; 90-268
*Parent Company:* Wolters Kluwer Rechtswetenschappen BV
*Ultimate Parent Company:* Wolters Kluwer NV

**Wolters-Noordhoff BV+**
Damsport 157, 9728 PS Groningen
Mailing Address: PO Box 58, 9700 MB Groningen
*Tel:* (050) 5226922 *Fax:* (050) 5277599
*E-mail:* info@wolters.nl
*Web Site:* www.wolters.nl
*Key Personnel*
Acting Manager: Dr M J van Dalen
Founded: 1836
Part of Wolters Kluwer Nederland.
ISBN Prefix(es): 90-01
*Parent Company:* Wolters-Kluwer
Subsidiaries: Martinus Nijhoff; Wolters-Noordhoff

**Uitgeverij 010+**
Watertorenweg 180, 3063 HA Rotterdam
*Tel:* (010) 4333509 *Fax:* (010) 4529825
*E-mail:* office@010publishers.nl
*Web Site:* www.010publishers.nl
*Key Personnel*
Publisher: Hans Oldewarris; Peter de Winter
Founded: 1983

Subjects: Architecture & Interior Design, Art, History, Photography
ISBN Prefix(es): 90-6450

**Zoetermeer**, *imprint of* Nijgh & Van Ditmar Amsterdam

**Zuid Boekprodukties BV+**
PO Box 314, 2160 AH Lisse
*Tel:* (0252) 431565 *Fax:* (0252) 431567
*E-mail:* info@rebo-publishers.com
*Web Site:* www.rebo-publishers.com
*Key Personnel*
Dir: F Voerman
Founded: 1983
Subjects: Animals, Pets, Cookery, Crafts, Games, Hobbies, Gardening, Plants
ISBN Prefix(es): 90-6248
*Associate Companies:* REBO Productions BV
Imprints: Zuidboek

**Zuidboek**, *imprint of* Zuid Boekprodukties BV

**Zwarte Beertjes**, *imprint of* A W Bruna Uitgevers BV

**Uitgeverij Zwijsen BV**
Gasthuisring 58, 5041 DT Tilburg
Mailing Address: Postbus 805, 5000 AV Tilburg
*Tel:* (013) 5838800 *Fax:* (013) 5838880
*E-mail:* klantenservice@zwijsen.nl
*Web Site:* www.zwijsen.nl
*Key Personnel*
Man Dir: Robert Francissen
Publisher & Rights Manager: Jan Plooij; Agnes Starmans
Publicity Manager: Miranda de Jong
Founded: 1846
ISBN Prefix(es): 90-276

# Netherlands Antilles

## General Information

*Capital:* Willemstad
*Language:* Dutch and Papiamento. English and Spanish widely spoken
*Religion:* Roman Catholic and Protestant
*Population:* 184,000
*Bank Hours:* 0830-1130, 1400-1600 Monday-Friday. St Maarten: 0800-1300 Monday-Friday (also 1600-1700 on Friday)
*Shop Hours:* 0800-1200, 1400-1800 Monday-Saturday
*Currency:* 100 cents = 1 Netherlands Antilles gulden or florin
*Export/Import Information:* No tariff on books or advertising. No import licenses. No exchange controls.
*Copyright:* UCC, Berne (see Copyright Conventions, pg xi)

**De Wit Stores NV**
L G Smith Blvd 110, Oranjestad, Aruba
*Tel:* (0297) 823500 *Fax:* (0297) 821575
*E-mail:* dewitstores@sctarnet.aw *Cable:* Dewitstores
*Key Personnel*
Man Dir: R de Zwart
Founded: 1948
Subjects: Gardening, Plants, Health, Nutrition, Regional Interests, Self-Help, Travel, Women's Studies

ISBN Prefix(es): 90-6163; 99904-81
*Bookshop(s):* De Wit Book & Gift Store, Aruba; Aruba Post, Aruba; Boulevard Book and Drugstore, Aruba

**Drukkerij Scherpenheuvel Haseth**
Scherpenhuevel 1, Curacao
*Tel:* (09) 7671134
*Key Personnel*
Dir: Ronald Yrausquin
Subjects: Law
ISBN Prefix(es): 99904-915

# New Caledonia

## General Information

*Capital:* Noumea
*Language:* French
*Religion:* Predominantly Roman Catholic and Protestant
*Population:* 145,368
*Currency:* 100 centimes = CFP or Pacific franc
*Export/Import Information:* No tariff on books except luxury bindings and children's picture books. Advertising matter generally dutiable. Special Tax on all. No import licenses required.

**Editions du Santal**
BP 3072, 98800 Noumea
*Tel:* (0687) 262533 *Fax:* (0687) 262533
*E-mail:* santal@offratel.nc
*Key Personnel*
Director: Paul-Jean Stahl
Subjects: History, Travel
ISBN Prefix(es): 2-9508739

**Savannah Editions SARL**
49 rue de la Boudeuse magenta Que mo, 98846 Noumea
*Tel:* (0687) 252919 *Fax:* (0687) 282470
Founded: 1994
Subjects: How-to, Maritime, Outdoor Recreation, Sports, Athletics, Travel
ISBN Prefix(es): 2-9508530
Distributed by Editions Vilo Paris

# New Zealand

## General Information

*Capital:* Wellington
*Language:* English
*Religion:* Predominantly Christian (mostly Anglican & Roman Catholic)
*Population:* 3.3 million
*Bank Hours:* 0930-1600 Monday-Friday
*Shop Hours:* Vary. Most open 6-7 days a week
*Currency:* 100 cents = 1 New Zealand dollar
*Export/Import Information:* No tariffs on books and advertising. No import licenses, but literature which is indecent, advocates violence, lawlessness, disorder or seditiousness is prohibited. No special exchange controls.
*Copyright:* UCC, Berne, Florence (see Copyright Conventions, pg xi)

**ABA Books**
2d/6 Brooklyn Rd, Claudelands, Hamilton
Mailing Address: PO Box 11-099, Hamilton
*Tel:* (07) 8549360 *Fax:* (07) 8549361
*Web Site:* www.ababooks.co.nz
*Key Personnel*
Dir: Elizabeth Maree Abbott

Man Dir: Graeme Hamilton Abbott
*E-mail:* graeme@ababooks.co.nz
Founded: 1986
Educational book publishers.
Subjects: Chemistry, Chemical Engineering, Cookery, Language Arts, Linguistics, Mathematics, Physical Sciences, Physics, Science (General)
ISBN Prefix(es): 0-908866

**Aoraki Press Ltd**
PO Box 11-699, Wellington 6034
*Tel:* (04) 3858528 *Fax:* (03) 3858528
*E-mail:* aoraki@actrix.gen.nz
*Key Personnel*
Editor: Dr Maarire Goodall
Founded: 1990
Subjects: Drama, Theater, Foreign Countries, History, Law, Music, Dance, Regional Interests, Social Sciences, Sociology
ISBN Prefix(es): 0-908925
Distributor for Aoraki Productions; Otago Heritage Press
*Orders to:* PO Box 25-029, Christchurch *Tel:* (03) 3524001 *Fax:* (03) 3524001

**Aspect Press**
Subsidiary of Association of Handcraft Printers (AHP)
13 Kinross, St Levin
*Tel:* (06) 368-2887
*Key Personnel*
Editor & Author: P J Parr
Founded: 1971
Specialize in private press booklets.
Subjects: History, Religion - Buddhist
ISBN Prefix(es): 0-908779
Total Titles: 48 Print
*Book Club(s):* TSP

**Auckland University Press+**
University of Auckland, 1-11 Short St, Auckland
Mailing Address: University of Auckland, Private Bag 92019, Auckland
*Tel:* (09) 373 7528 *Fax:* (09) 373 7465
*E-mail:* aup@auckland.ac.nz
*Web Site:* www.auckland.ac.nz/aup/
*Key Personnel*
Dir: Elizabeth P Caffin *E-mail:* e.caffin@auckland.ac.nz
Office Manager: Annie Irving *E-mail:* a.irving@auckland.ac.nz
Marketing Manager: Christine O'Brien *E-mail:* c.obrien@auckland.ac.nz
Production Editor: Katrina Duncan *E-mail:* k.duncan@auckland.ac.nz
Founded: 1966
Subjects: Archaeology, Art, Biography, Government, Political Science, History, Literature, Literary Criticism, Essays, Poetry, Social Sciences, Sociology, Women's Studies
ISBN Prefix(es): 1-86940
Distributed by HarperCollins (New Zealand)
*Shipping Address:* Anzac Ave entrance, 1-11 Short St, Auckland
*Warehouse:* HarperCollins, 31 View Rd, Glenfield, Auckland
*Orders to:* Eurospan, 3 Henrietta St, London WC2E 8LU, United Kingdom *Tel:* (020) 7240 0856 *Fax:* (020) 7379 0609 *E-mail:* info@eurospan.co.uk *Web Site:* www.eurospan.co.uk
HarperCollins, PO Box 1, Auckland
Independent Publishers Group (IPG), 814 N Franklin St, Chicago, IL 60610, United States *Tel:* 312-337-0747 *Fax:* 312-337-5985 *E-mail:* frontdesk@ipgbook.com *Web Site:* www.ipgbook.com
Unireps, University of New South Wales, Sydney, NSW 2034, Australia *Tel:* (02) 9664 0999 *Fax:* (02) 9664 5420 *E-mail:* info.press@unsw.edu.au *Web Site:* www.unswpress.com.au

**Barkfire Press+**
Newton, Auckland 1032
Mailing Address: PO Box 68582, Newton, Auckland 1032
*Tel:* (09) 3031039 *Fax:* (09) 3031059
*E-mail:* info@barkfire.com
*Web Site:* www.barkfire.com
*Key Personnel*
Man Dir: Ralph Talmont *E-mail:* ralph@barkfire.com
Founded: 1996
Packager, contract publisher, book producer.
Subjects: Americana, Regional, Architecture & Interior Design, Art, Asian Studies, Cookery, Ethnicity, Geography, Geology, Health, Nutrition, House & Home, How-to, Journalism, Music, Dance, Native American Studies, Natural History, Outdoor Recreation, Photography, Religion - Jewish, Travel, Wine & Spirits, Women's Studies, Yachting & Mythology
ISBN Prefix(es): 0-9583668
*Parent Company:* Mandragora Productions Ltd

**David Bateman Ltd+**
30 Tarndale Grove, Albany, Auckland
*Tel:* (09) 415 7664 *Fax:* (09) 415 8892
*E-mail:* bateman@bateman.co.nz
*Web Site:* www.bateman.co.nz
*Key Personnel*
Chairman & Publisher: David L Bateman
Man Dir, Sales & Distribution: Paul C Parkinson *Tel:* (09) 415 5922
Man Dir, Publishing, Rights & Permissions: Paul Bateman
Secretary: Maureen Robinson
Founded: 1979
Membership(s): Booksellers New Zealand & Book Publishers Association of New Zealand.
Also acts as agent for overseas publishers.
Subjects: Art, Business, Cookery, Gardening, Plants, Natural History, Travel
ISBN Prefix(es): 1-86953
Total Titles: 250 Print

**Brick Row Publishing Co Ltd+**
POB 100-05 7, North Shore Mail Centre, Auckland 10
*Tel:* (09) 4106993 *Fax:* (09) 4106993
*Key Personnel*
Man Dir, Editorial: Oswald L Kraus
Sales, Publicity: Ruth Kraus
Founded: 1978
Subjects: Biography, Fiction, Literature, Literary Criticism, Essays, Nonfiction (General), Poetry, Science (General)
ISBN Prefix(es): 0-908595
Total Titles: 30 Print
Imprints: Southern Lights
*U.S. Office(s):* 1040 E Paseo El Mirador, Palm Springs, CA 92262, United States, Contact: O L Kraus *Tel:* 760-322-4342 *Fax:* 760-322-4342
Distributor for John Calder (UK); Excalibur (USA); Free Spirit (USA)

**Brookers Ltd**
Level 1, Guardian Trust House, 15 Willeston St, Wellington
Mailing Address: PO Box 43, Wellington
*Tel:* (04) 4998178 *Fax:* (04) 4998173
*E-mail:* service@brookers.co.nz
*Web Site:* www.brookers.co.nz
*Key Personnel*
Man Dir: Neil Story
GM Publishing & Marketing: Nigel Royfee
GM Market Development: Geoff Adlam
GM Technology & Business Development: Carl Olson
Founded: 1910
Specialize in looseleaf & electronic legal, tax & professional information.
Subjects: Accounting, Business, Law
ISBN Prefix(es): 0-86472
*Parent Company:* The Thomson Corporation

Distributed by Carswell; Lawbook Co; Sweet & Maxwell; Westlaw
Distributor for Carswell; Lawbook Co; Sweet & Maxwell; Westlaw

**Brookfield Press**
22 Marriott Rd, Pakuranga, Auckland
*Tel:* (09) 576 5438 *Fax:* (09) 529 0938
*E-mail:* esp@psychic.co.nz
*Key Personnel*
Man Dir, Editorial: Richard Webster
Sales, Publicity: Don Kaye
Founded: 1971
Subjects: Astrology, Occult, Philosophy
ISBN Prefix(es): 0-86467
*Parent Company:* Brookings Bookshop 1971 Ltd
Distributed by Peaceful Living Publications (New Zealand)

**Bush Press Communications Ltd**
4 Bayview Rd, Hauraki Corner, Takapuna, Auckland 1309
Mailing Address: PO Box 33029, Takapuna, Auckland 1309
*Tel:* (09) 486 2667 *Fax:* (09) 486 2667
*E-mail:* bush.press@clear.net.nz
*Key Personnel*
Man Dir: Gordon Ell
Founded: 1979
Also television production & publishing services.
Subjects: Archaeology, Art, Cookery, Crafts, Games, Hobbies, Earth Sciences, Gardening, Plants, Genealogy, Geography, Geology, History, How-to, Natural History, Nonfiction (General), Outdoor Recreation, Photography, Regional Interests
ISBN Prefix(es): 0-908608
Number of titles published annually: 6 Print
Total Titles: 24 Print
Imprints: The Bush Press of New Zealand
Divisions: Bush Films; The Bush Press
Distributor for Geological Society of New Zealand
*Warehouse:* Forrester Books (NZ) Ltd, 10 Tarndale Dr, Albany, Auckland 1310 *Tel:* (09) 415 2080 *Fax:* (09) 415 2083 *E-mail:* forr@forrester.co.nz

**The Bush Press of New Zealand,** *imprint of* Bush Press Communications Ltd

**Business Bureau Christchurch Ltd+**
PO Box 8226, Christchurch
*Tel:* (03) 3585287
*Key Personnel*
Contact: Geoff McDonnell
Founded: 1981
Subjects: Finance, Gardening, Plants
ISBN Prefix(es): 0-908852

**Butterworths New Zealand Ltd**
205-207 Victoria St, Wellington 1
Mailing Address: PO Box 472, Wellington 1
*Tel:* (04) 385 1479 *Fax:* (04) 385 1598
*E-mail:* Customer.Relations@butterworths.co.nz
*Web Site:* www.butterworths.co.nz; www.lexisnexis.com/au/nz
*Key Personnel*
Man Dir: Philip G Kirk
Legal Publishing Dir: Hellen Papadopoulos
National Sales Manager: Lara Stewart
*E-mail:* Lara.Stewart@butterworths.co.nz
Founded: 1914
Subjects: Law
ISBN Prefix(es): 0-409; 0-407; 0-408; 0-406
*Parent Company:* Reed Elsevier plc, 25 Victoria St, London SW1H 0EX, United Kingdom
*Associate Companies:* Butterworths Australia Ltd, Reed Elsevier Bldg, Tower 2, 475-495 Victoria Ave, Chatswood, NSW 2067, Australia *Tel:* (02) 9422 2222 *Fax:* (02) 9422 2444 *Web*

*Site:* www.butterworths.com.au; Butterworths Canada Ltd, 75 Clegg Rd, Markham, ON L6G 1A1, Canada *Tel:* 905-479-2665 *Fax:* 905-479-2826 *Web Site:* www.butterworths.ca; Butterworths Asia, 3/F Baskerville House, 13 Duddell St, Central, Hong Kong, Hong Kong *Tel:* 537 6662 *Fax:* 537 6672; Butterworth India, C71-A Malviya Nagar, New Delhi 100 017, India *Tel:* (011) 623 6124 *Fax:* (011) 621 3861; Butterworth (Ireland) Ltd, 16 Upper Ormand Quay, Dublin 7, Ireland *Tel:* (031) 731 555 *Fax:* (031) 873 1876; Butterworths, C/- Shin Nichibo Bldg, 2-1 Sarugaku-cho, 1 Chome, Chiyoda-Ku, Tokyo 101, Japan *Tel:* (03) 3291 3970 *Fax:* (03) 3219 5260; Malayan Law Journal Sdn Bhd, No 18, Jalan Tuanku Abdul Rahman, 50100 Kuala Lumpur, Malaysia *Tel:* (03) 291 7273 *Fax:* (03) 291 6440; Butterworth & Co Publishers Ltd, 7 Jahangir St, Islamia Park, Poonch Rd, Lahore, Pakistan *Tel:* (042) 41 5226; Butterworths Asia/Malayan Law Journal, 10 Anson Rd, No 32-01 International Plaza, Singapore 0207, Singapore *Tel:* 220 3684 *Fax:* 225 5026; Butterworth Publishers Pty Ltd, 8 Walter Place, Waterval Park, Mayville, Durban 4001, South Africa *Tel:* (03) 1268 3111 *Fax:* (03) 1268 3108 *Web Site:* www.butterworths.co.za; Butterworth & Co (Publishers) Ltd, Halsbury House, 35 Chancery Lane, London, United Kingdom *Tel:* (020) 7400 2500 *Fax:* (020) 7400 2842 *Web Site:* www.butterworth.co.uk; LEXIS Law Publishing, 701 E Water St, Charlottesville, VA 22906-7587, United States *Tel:* 804-972-7600 *Fax:* 804-972-7666 *Web Site:* www.michie.com

**C&S Publications**
121 Taupo Rd, Taumarunui
Mailing Address: PO Box 148, Taumarunui
*Tel:* (0812) 56807 *Fax:* (0812) 8966583
*Key Personnel*
Contact: Ron Cooke
Founded: 1980
Subjects: History
ISBN Prefix(es): 0-908724

**Canterbury University Press+**
University of Canterbury, Private Bag 4800, Christchurch
*Tel:* (03) 364-2914 *Fax:* (03) 364-2044
*E-mail:* mail@cup.canterbury.ac.nz
*Web Site:* www.cup.canterbury.ac.nz
*Key Personnel*
Dir: Jeff Field
Editor: Richard King
Office Manager: Kaye Godfrey
Founded: 1964
Specialize in botany, marine science, history, Maori & Pacific studies.
Subjects: Biography, Biological Sciences, History, Natural History, Nonfiction (General)
ISBN Prefix(es): 0-900392; 0-908812
Distributed by Book Representation & Distribution Ltd (UK & Europe); HarperCollins (NZ) Ltd (New Zealand); UNIREPS (Australia); University of New South Wales Press

**Cape Catley Ltd+**
83 Ngataringa Rd, Devonport, Auckland
Mailing Address: PO Box 32-622, Devonport, Auckland
*Tel:* (09) 445-9668 *Fax:* (09) 445-9668
*E-mail:* cape.catley@xtra.co.nz
*Web Site:* www.capecatleybooks.co.nz
*Key Personnel*
Man Dir: Christine Cole Catley
Founded: 1973
Subjects: Biography, Fiction, History, Literature, Literary Criticism, Essays, Mysteries, Nonfiction (General), Poetry
Number of titles published annually: 5 Print

Total Titles: 100 Print
Distributed by HarperCollins NZ Ltd (New Zealand)

**The Caxton Press**
113 Victoria St, Christchurch
*Tel:* (03) 366 8516 *Fax:* (03) 365 7840
*E-mail:* print.design@caxton.co.nz
*Web Site:* www.caxton.co.nz
*Key Personnel*
Man Dir: Bruce Bascand *Tel:* (03) 353 0731
General Manager: Peter Watson *Tel:* (03) 353 0734
Customer Services: Lorene Soli
Founded: 1935
Subjects: Biography, Gardening, Plants, Nonfiction (General)
ISBN Prefix(es): 0-908563

**CCEAM,** see Commonwealth Council for Educational Administration & Management

**CCH New Zealand Ltd**
24 The Warehouse Way, Northcote, Auckland
Mailing Address: PO Box 2378, Auckland 1
*Tel:* (09) 488 2760 *Toll Free Tel:* 800 500224 (New Zealand only) *Fax:* (09) 488 6911
*E-mail:* nzsales@cch.co.nz
*Web Site:* www.cch.co.nz
Founded: 1973
Subjects: Accounting, Law
ISBN Prefix(es): 0-86475; 0-86903
*Parent Company:* Walters Kluwer NV
*U.S. Office(s):* Walters Kluwer USA, 161 N Clark, 48th floor, Chicago, IL 60601, United States

**Church Mouse Press**
38 Joseph St, Palmerston North
*Tel:* (063) 357-2445 *Fax:* (063) 357-2445
*Key Personnel*
Proprietor: Anne De Roo
Founded: 1989
Direct sales & through bookshops & churches, books for adults & children.
Subjects: Biblical Studies, Fiction, Theology
ISBN Prefix(es): 0-908949
Total Titles: 16 Print

**Cicada Press+**
PO Box 34509, Birkenhead South, Auckland 10
*Tel:* (09) 4180890 *Fax:* (09) 4181142
*Key Personnel*
Man Dir: R K St Cartmail
Founded: 1978
Subjects: Art, Fiction, Poetry, Religion - Other
ISBN Prefix(es): 0-908599

**Clerestory Press+**
PO Box 21-120, Christchurch 8001
*Tel:* (03) 3553588 *Fax:* (03) 3553588
*E-mail:* young.writers@xtra.co.nz
*Key Personnel*
International Rights: Dr Glyn Strange; Francine Bills
Founded: 1994
Membership(s): BPANZ.
Subjects: Archaeology, Biography, Drama, Theater, Education, Genealogy, History, Law, Literature, Literary Criticism, Essays, Regional Interests, Women's Studies
ISBN Prefix(es): 0-9583706; 0-9582201
*Shipping Address:* 31 Mersey St, Christchurch

**Commonwealth Council for Educational Administration & Management**
AUT Technology Park, PO Box 12397, Penrose, Auckland 1135
*Tel:* (09) 917 9568 *Fax:* (09) 917 9501
*Web Site:* www.cceam.org

*Key Personnel*
President: Mrs Jo Howse *E-mail:* jo.howse@
cceam.org
Founded: 1970
Publisher of International Studies in Educational
Administration.
Subjects: Education, Management
Distributed by The Education Publishing Co Ltd
(UK)

**Concept Publishing Ltd+**
30 Tiri Rd, Auckland
*Tel:* (09) 489 1121; (021) 804-480 *Fax:* (09) 489
5335
*E-mail:* info@concept-publishing.co.nz
*Key Personnel*
Man Dir: Richard Beckett
Founded: 1997
Subjects: Cookery
ISBN Prefix(es): 1-877193
Total Titles: 32 Print
Foreign Rights: Peter Elek & Associates

**Craig Potton Publishing+**
98 Vickerman St, Nelson
Mailing Address: PO Box 555, Nelson
*Tel:* (03) 5489009 *Fax:* (03) 5489009
*E-mail:* info@cpp.co.nz
*Web Site:* www.cpp.co.nz
*Key Personnel*
Man Dir & Publisher: Robbie Burton
  *E-mail:* robbie@cpp.co.nz
Founded: 1987
Specialize in wilderness photography & writing
  & high-quality, illustrated nonfiction; also acts
  as book packagers, produce calendars, posters,
  postcards.
Subjects: Architecture & Interior Design, Art,
  Biological Sciences, Crafts, Games, Hobbies,
  Natural History, Nonfiction (General), Outdoor
  Recreation, Photography
ISBN Prefix(es): 0-908802

**Craig Printing Co Ltd**
122 Yarrow St, Invercargill
Mailing Address: PO Box 99, Invercargill
*Tel:* (03) 211-0393 *Fax:* (03) 214-9930
*E-mail:* sales@craigsatlas.co.nz
*Web Site:* www.craigprint.co.nz
*Key Personnel*
Chief Executive Officer: Rodger Wills
General Manager: Neil Jackson
Founded: 1876
Subjects: Aeronautics, Aviation, History, Nonfic-
  tion (General), Regional Interests, Travel
ISBN Prefix(es): 0-9597554
*Branch Office(s)*
5 Athol St, Queenstown *Tel:* (03) 441 3367
  *Fax:* (03) 441 3368 *E-mail:* qtown@
  craigprintco.nz

**Wendy Crane Books**
53 Wilford St, Lower Hutt
*Tel:* (04) 5664228
*Key Personnel*
Contact: Wendy Crane
Subjects: Biological Sciences, Earth Sciences,
  Geography, Geology, Physical Sciences
ISBN Prefix(es): 0-908895

**Curly Tales**, *imprint of* Magari Publishing

**Current Pacific Ltd+**
7 La Roche Pl, Northcote, Auckland 1309
Mailing Address: PO Box 36-536 Northcote,
  Auckland 1330
*Tel:* (09) 480-1388 *Fax:* (09) 480-1387
*E-mail:* info@cplnz.com
*Web Site:* www.cplnz.com
*Key Personnel*
Editor: Amy M Yeung

Founded: 1992
Publisher of *New Zealand Trade Directory*, a
  business/trade directory containing more than
  6000 firms including manufacturers, importers,
  exporters, distributors, food processors, banks
  & financial firms, tourism services, trade promotion organizations, government departments,
  tertiary & secondary education institutions, professional institutions, libraries, etc.
Subjects: Business
Total Titles: 2 Print

**David's Marine Books**
121 Beaumont St, Westhaven, Auckland
Mailing Address: PO Box 1874, Auckland
*Tel:* (09) 303 1459 *Toll Free Tel:* 508 242 787;
  800 422 427 *Fax:* (09) 307 8170
*E-mail:* sales@transpacific.co.nz
*Web Site:* www.transpacific.co.nz
Founded: 1963
Subjects: Crafts, Games, Hobbies, Electronics,
  Electrical Engineering, Fiction, How-to, Sports,
  Athletics, Travel, Marine
*Parent Company:* Trans Pacific Marine
Distributor for Adlard Coles; Fernhurst; Sheridan
  House; Stationery Office

**Doubleday New Zealand Ltd+**
One Parkway Dr, Mairangi Bay Industrial Estate,
  Auckland 10
Mailing Address: Private Bag 102947, North
  Shore Mail Centre, Auckland 1333
*Tel:* (09) 4782846; (09) 4792200 (member service
  hotline)
*E-mail:* membercare@doubledayclubs.co.nz
*Telex:* NZ60589
*Key Personnel*
Contact: Petrus van der Schaaf

**Dunmore Press Ltd+**
PO Box 5115, Palmerston North
*Tel:* (06) 3579242 *Fax:* (06) 3579242
*E-mail:* books@dunmore.co.nz
*Web Site:* www.dunmore.co.nz
*Key Personnel*
Dir & Editorial: Murray Gatenby
Dir & Marketing & Editorial, Rights & Per-
  missions: Sharmian Firth *E-mail:* sharmian@
  dunmore.co.nz
Founded: 1975
Independent publishing house specializing in aca-
  demic & nonfiction titles.
Subjects: Accounting, Business, Economics, Edu-
  cation, Ethnicity, History, Nonfiction (General)
ISBN Prefix(es): 0-908564; 0-86469
Number of titles published annually: 25 Print
Total Titles: 180 Print
Subsidiaries: Dunmore Printing Company Ltd
Foreign Rep(s): Federation Press (Australia)

**Educational Distributors Ltd**
1/1 Akatea Rd, Glendene, Auckland 7
*Tel:* (09) 818 4473 *Fax:* (09) 836 2399
*E-mail:* ed.nz@xtra.co.nz
*Key Personnel*
Manager: Ron Simpson
Founded: 1976
Specialize in distribution of educational & library
  lists within New Zealand.
Membership(s): BPANZ.
*Parent Company:* School Supplies Ltd

**ESA Publications (NZ) Ltd+**
Unit G, 665 Great South Rd, Penrose, Auckland
Mailing Address: Box 9453, Newmarket, Auck-
  land
*Tel:* (09) 579 3126 *Toll Free Tel:* (0800) 372-266
  *Fax:* (09) 579 4713 *Toll Free Fax:* (0800) 329-
  372
*E-mail:* info@esa.co.nz
*Web Site:* www.esa.co.nz

*Key Personnel*
Publisher & Man Dir: Mark Sayes
  *E-mail:* mark@esa.co.nz
Sales & Administration: Andrea Tihore
  *E-mail:* andrea@esa.co.nz
Founded: 1985
Publisher of educational books.
Membership(s): Book Publishers Association of
  New Zealand (BPANZ).
Subjects: Accounting, Biological Sciences, Chem-
  istry, Chemical Engineering, Computer Science,
  Economics, English as a Second Language, Ge-
  ography, Geology, Health, Nutrition, History,
  Mathematics, Physics, Science (General), So-
  cial Sciences, Sociology
ISBN Prefix(es): 0-908756; 0-9597692; 1-877234;
  1-877291
Number of titles published annually: 30 Print
Total Titles: 95 Print
*Parent Company:* Sayes Corp Ltd

**Eton Press (Auckland) Ltd**
35 Enterprise St, Unit N, Birkenhead, Auckland
  1310
*Tel:* (09) 4183635 *Fax:* (09) 4806488
*E-mail:* info@eton.co.nz
*Web Site:* www.eton.co.nz
*Key Personnel*
Dir: Anthony Matthews
Founded: 1968
Also acts for Tarquin & Dime Publications,
  Haese & Harris.
Membership(s): Book Publishers Association of
  New Zealand (BPANZ).
Subjects: Mathematics

**Evagean Publishing+**
205A Whittaker St, Te Aroha, Auckland
Mailing Address: PO Box 199, Te Aroha, Auck-
  land
*Tel:* (07) 884-8783 *Fax:* (07) 884-8783
*E-mail:* alison.honeyfield@clear.net.nz
*Web Site:* www.evagean.co.nz
*Key Personnel*
Owner: Andrew Honeyfield; Alison Jane Hunter
Founded: 1990
Specialize in compiling, publishing & marketing
  family histories & genealogies.
Subjects: Genealogy
*Branch Office(s)*
18 Waygrove Ave, Earlwood, NSW 2206, Aus-
  tralia *Tel:* (02) 9789-4550 *Fax:* (02) 9789-4550
PO Box 1167, South Perth, WA 6951, Australia
  *Tel:* (08) 3676578 *Fax:* (08) 3676578
PO Box 288, Warragul, Victoria 3820, Australia
  *Tel:* (03) 56236887 *Fax:* (03) 56236882
14 Kaweka St, Havelock North, Hawkes Bay
  *Tel:* (06) 877 1210

**Exisle Publishing Ltd+**
PO Box 60-490, Titirangi, Auckland 1230
*Tel:* (09) 817 9192 *Fax:* (09) 817 2295
*E-mail:* admin@exisle.co.nz
*Web Site:* www.exisle.co.nz
*Key Personnel*
Chief Executive: Gareth St John Thomas
  *E-mail:* gareth@exisle.co.nz
International Rights: Benny Thomas
  *E-mail:* benny@exisle.co.nz
Administrative Manager: Carole Doesburg
  *E-mail:* carole@exisle.co.nz
Founded: 1993
Membership(s): Book Publishers of New Zealand.
Subjects: Biography, Business, Maritime, Natural
  History, Nonfiction (General), Outdoor Recre-
  ation, Pacific Studies
ISBN Prefix(es): 0-908988
Number of titles published annually: 4 Print
Total Titles: 12 Print
*Parent Company:* Exisle Holdings Ltd
*Branch Office(s)*
Moonrising, Narrone Creek Rd, Wollombi, NSW
  2325, Australia, Administrative Manager: Ja-

neen Greig *Tel:* (02) 4998 3327 *Fax:* (02) 4998 3347 *E-mail:* janeen@exislepublishing.com
Distributed by Berkeley Books (Singapore/SE Asia); Celebrity Books Ltd; Kirby Books Ltd
*Distribution Center:* Pacific Island Books, 2802 E 132 Circle, Thornton, CO 80241, United States, Contact: Kathy Tundermann *Tel:* (303) 457 9795 *E-mail:* pacificbks@aol.com

**Flamingo**, *imprint of* HarperCollinsPublishers (New Zealand) Ltd

**Fraser Books**
Ranginui, Chamberlain Rd, RD 8, Masterton
*Tel:* (06) 3771359 *Fax:* (06) 3771359
*Key Personnel*
Partner: Diane Grant *E-mail:* degrant@xtra.co.nz; Ian F Grant *E-mail:* ifgrant@xtra.co.nz
Founded: 1980
Specialize in book packaging.
Subjects: Agriculture, Biography, Economics, Government, Political Science, History, Regional Interests, Social Sciences, Sociology
ISBN Prefix(es): 0-9582052
Number of titles published annually: 10 Print
Total Titles: 100 Print
*Shipping Address:* Nationwide Book Distributors, PO Box 4176, Christchurch
*Warehouse:* Nationwide Book Distributors, PO Box 4176, Christchurch
*Distribution Center:* Nationwide Book Distributors, PO Box 4176, Christchurch
*Orders to:* Nationwide Book Distributors, PO Box 4176, Christchurch
*Returns:* Nationwide Book Distributors, PO Box 4176, Christchurch

**Gauntlet Press**, *imprint of* Hazard Press Ltd

**GCL Publishing (1997) Ltd+**
Level 1, 15 Bath St, Parnell, Auckland
Mailing Address: PO Box 37745, Parnell, Auckland
*Tel:* (09) 3092444 *Fax:* (09) 3092449
*E-mail:* info@gcl.co.nz
*Web Site:* www.gcl.co.nz; www.auto.co.nz
*Key Personnel*
Publisher: Mr Vern Whitehead *E-mail:* vern@gcl.co.nz
Founded: 1972
Publishers for the auto industry including newsletters, manuals, stock lists & pricing guides.
Subjects: Automotive
ISBN Prefix(es): 0-9598007
Number of titles published annually: 2 Print
Total Titles: 6 Print

**Gnostic Press Ltd**
100 Riverland Rd, Kumeu, Auckland
Mailing Address: RD 2, Kumeu, Auckland
*Tel:* (09) 4838619 *Fax:* (09) 4190319
*E-mail:* gnostic.press@ihug.co.nz
*Web Site:* homepages.ihug.co.nz/~gnosticpress
*Key Personnel*
Dir: John Searle
Founded: 1978
Created for the dispersment of the works of Abdullah Dougan (Sufi teacher).
Subjects: Philosophy, Religion - Buddhist, Religion - Hindu, Religion - Islamic, Religion - Other, Self-Help
ISBN Prefix(es): 0-473; 0-9597566; 0-477; 0-478; 0-475

**Godwit Publishing Ltd+**
PO Box 34-683, Birkenhead, Auckland
*Tel:* (09) 4805410 *Fax:* (09) 4805930
Founded: 1990
Subjects: Art, Gardening, Plants, Genealogy, Natural History, Nonfiction (General)

ISBN Prefix(es): 0-908877; 1-86962
*Orders to:* Reed Publishing, Birkenhead, Auckland 1310

**Gondwanaland Press**
24 Glasgow St, Kelburn, Wellington 6005
*Tel:* (04) 4758092 *Fax:* (04) 4756194
*Key Personnel*
Manager: Hugh Price *E-mail:* randellprice@xtra.co.nz
Founded: 1992
Small private book publisher.
Subjects: Education, Government, Political Science, History, Public Administration, Chiefly education
ISBN Prefix(es): 0-9597766; 0-9582083
Number of titles published annually: 3 Print
Total Titles: 20 Print

**GP Publications**, see Legislation Direct

**Grantham House Publishing+**
6/9 Wilkinson St, Oriental Bay, Wellington
*Tel:* (04) 3813071 *Fax:* (04) 3813067
*E-mail:* gstewart@iconz.co.nz
*Key Personnel*
Chief Executive: Graham Stewart
Founded: 1985
Membership(s): Booksellers New Zealand; Specialize in Railways, Tramways, Aviation, Shipping, Naval, Air Force, New Zealand history.
Subjects: History, Regional Interests, Transportation
ISBN Prefix(es): 1-86934
Total Titles: 40 Print
*Parent Company:* Bookprint Consultants Ltd
*Shipping Address:* PO Box 17256, Karosi, Wellington 6005
*Warehouse:* PO Box 17256, Karosi, Wellington 6005

**Graphic Educational Publications**
514 Dominion Rd, Auckland 3
*Tel:* (09) 6300488 *Fax:* (09) 6234196
*Key Personnel*
President, Editor & International Rights: Tom Newnham *E-mail:* tom@pl.net
Founded: 1963
Subjects: Asian Studies, Biography, Genealogy
ISBN Prefix(es): 0-9597819
Number of titles published annually: 3 Print
Total Titles: 10 Print

**Halcyon Publishing Ltd+**
PO Box 360, Auckland 1
*Tel:* (09) 4895337 *Fax:* (09) 4442399
*E-mail:* info@halcyonpublishing.co.nz
*Key Personnel*
Man Dir, Sales: Graham Gurr *E-mail:* gurr@halcyonpublishing.co.nz
Editorial Consultant: Antony Entwistle
Founded: 1984
Membership(s): BPANZ & BSNZ.
Subjects: Cookery, Crafts, Games, Hobbies, Maritime, Outdoor Recreation, Sports, Athletics
ISBN Prefix(es): 0-908685; 0-908689; 1-877256
Imprints: Halcyon Sporting Heritage
Subsidiaries: Halcyon Books; The Halcyon Press; Hole in the Bank Books
*Warehouse:* Unit 11 Diana Court, 101-111 Diana Dr, Glenfield Auckland

**Halcyon Sporting Heritage**, *imprint of* Halcyon Publishing Ltd

**Harlen Books**, *imprint of* R P L Books

**Harper Sports**, *imprint of* HarperCollinsPublishers (New Zealand) Ltd

**HarperCollins New Zealand**, *imprint of* HarperCollinsPublishers (New Zealand) Ltd

**HarperCollinsPublishers (New Zealand) Ltd+**
31 View Rd, Glenfield, Auckland
Mailing Address: PO Box 1, Auckland
*Tel:* (09) 443 9400 *Fax:* (09) 443 9403
*E-mail:* editors@harpercollins.co.nz
*Web Site:* www.harpercollins.co.nz *Cable:* Folio
*Key Personnel*
Chief Executive Officer: Brian Murray
Man Dir: Tony Fisk
Sales Manager: Chris Casey
Marketing Manager, Trade Fiction & Nonfiction: Anne Simpson
Marketing Manager, Childrens;, Lifestyle & Reference: Dawn Allan
Publicity Manager: Lorraine Steele
Financial Controller: Graham Mitchell
Operations Manager: Michelle Enoka
Commissioning Editor: Lorain Day
Founded: 1888
Subjects: Art, Biography, Cookery, Fiction, Gardening, Plants, History, Humor, Natural History, Regional Interests, Self-Help, Sports, Athletics, Travel
ISBN Prefix(es): 1-86950
Total Titles: 100 Print
*Parent Company:* HarperCollins Publishers, 10 E 53 St, New York, NY 10022, United States
*Ultimate Parent Company:* News Corporation
Imprints: Flamingo; Harper Sports; HarperCollins New Zealand
Distributor for Auckland University Press; David Bennett/Big Fish; Cape Catley; Collins & Brown; In Tune Books; Innovative Kids; Institute of Policy Studies; Paper Tiger; Pavilion Books; Pease Training; Simon & Schuster; University of Otago Press; Usborne

**Hazard Press Ltd+**
202 Hereford St, Christchurch 8000
Mailing Address: PO Box 2151, Christchurch
*Tel:* (03) 3770370 *Fax:* (03) 3770390
*E-mail:* info@hazard.co.nz
*Web Site:* www.hazardpress.com
*Key Personnel*
Publisher & Man Dir: Quentin Wilson *E-mail:* quentin@hazard.co.nz
Founded: 1987
Membership(s): Booksellers Association of New Zealand & Book Publishers Association of New Zealand.
Subjects: Art, Biography, Cookery, Drama, Theater, Fiction, Gardening, Plants, Government, Political Science, History, Humor, Literature, Literary Criticism, Essays, Nonfiction (General), Poetry, Travel
ISBN Prefix(es): 0-908790; 1-877161; 1-877270
Number of titles published annually: 30 Print
Total Titles: 320 Print; 2 E-Book
Imprints: Gauntlet Press

**Heinemann Education**, *imprint of* Reed Publishing (NZ) Ltd

**Heritage Press Ltd**
9B Pounamu Ave, Greenhithe, Auckland 1450
*Tel:* (09) 4137503; (09) 4139343 *Fax:* (09) 4137503; (09) 4139343
*E-mail:* heritagepressltd@xtra.co.nz
*Web Site:* www.heritagepress.co.nz
*Key Personnel*
Managing Editor: Alyson B Cresswell
Founded: 1984
Subjects: Biography, Genealogy, History, Regional Interests
ISBN Prefix(es): 0-908708

**Hodder Moa Beckett Publishers Ltd+**
4 Whetu Pl, Mairangi Bay 1330

Mailing Address: PO Box 100-749, North Shore Mail Centre, Auckland 1330
*Tel:* (09) 4781000 *Fax:* (09) 4781010
*E-mail:* admin@hoddermoa.co.nz
*Key Personnel*
Man Dir: Neil Aston Aston
Publisher: Sarah Beresford
Founded: 1971
Publishes & distributes a broad range of titles in New Zealand.
Subjects: Architecture & Interior Design, Biography, Business, Cookery, Fiction, Humor, Nonfiction (General), Sports, Athletics, Transportation
ISBN Prefix(es): 1-86958; 1-86957; 1-86947; 0-908570; 0-908676; 0-9597562
*Parent Company:* Hodder Headline Ltd, United Kingdom

**Huia Publishers+**
39 Pipitea St, Wellington, Aotearoa
Mailing Address: PO Box 17335, Aotearoa, Wellington
*Tel:* (04) 473-9262 *Fax:* (04) 473-9265
*E-mail:* customer.services@huia.co.nz
*Web Site:* www.huia.co.nz
*Key Personnel*
International Rights: Robyn Bargh
Books Manager: Brian Bargh *E-mail:* brian.b@huia.co.nz
Founded: 1991
Specializes in books about & by Maori; educational resources in Maori language; children's books in English & Maori; histories of colonization in New Zealand.
Subjects: Art, Biography, Drama, Theater, Education, Erotica, Ethnicity, Fiction, History, Bi-cultural, Indigenous Studies, Maori, Maori English Language
ISBN Prefix(es): 0-908975
Number of titles published annually: 30 Print
Total Titles: 100 Print
*Parent Company:* Huia (NZ) Ltd
Divisions: Huia Communications
Foreign Rep(s): South Pacific Books (US)
*Distribution Center:* Reed Publishing (NZ)
South Pacific Books (United States)

**IPL Publishing Group+**
Transpress House, 8 Chisbury St, Wellington
Mailing Address: PO Box 10-215, Wellington
*Tel:* (04) 477 3032 *Fax:* (04) 477 3035
*E-mail:* transpress@paradise.net.nz
*Web Site:* www.transpressnz.com
*Key Personnel*
Contact: G Churchman
Founded: 1985
Membership(s): BPANZ.
Subjects: History, Transportation, Technical & Practical
ISBN Prefix(es): 0-908876
Number of titles published annually: 10 Print
Total Titles: 5 Print
*Parent Company:* Transpress New Zealand
Subsidiaries: IPL Books (Australia) Pty Ltd; IPL Wordprint
Divisions: IPL Books; IPL Video; IPL Publishing Services
Distributed by Gary Allen Pty Ltd (Australia); Pacific Island Books (USA)
*Warehouse:* 10 Tarndale Grove, Auckland

**Kahurangi Cooperative+**
43 Landscape Rd, Papatoetoe
*Tel:* (09) 2782731
*Key Personnel*
Publisher & Editor: Bernard Gadd
Founded: 1983
Non-profit educational project.
Specialize in Learn-to-read books for ages 10 & over, novels & short stories for teenagers.

Subjects: Literature, Literary Criticism, Essays, Regional Interests
ISBN Prefix(es): 0-86477
Subsidiaries: Hallard Press
*Showroom(s):* Brick Row, 11 Cockayne Crescent, Sunnynook, Auckland 10

**Knowing Science**, *imprint of* Magari Publishing

**Kotuku Media Ltd+**
Box 54/234, Plimmerton, Wellington
*Tel:* (04) 2331842
*E-mail:* kotuku.media@xtra.co.nz
*Key Personnel*
Contact: Ross Miller
Founded: 1991
Subjects: Regional Interests
ISBN Prefix(es): 0-908967

**Kowhai Publishing Ltd**
10 Peacock St, Auckland 5
Mailing Address: PO Box 25-325, St Heliers
*Tel:* (09) 5759126 *Fax:* (09) 5753178
*Key Personnel*
Contact: Bruce Campbell
Specialize in photographic books of New Zealand scenery.
Subjects: Travel
ISBN Prefix(es): 0-908598

**Landcare Research NZ**
Canterbury Agricultural & Science Center, Gerald St, Lincoln 8152
Mailing Address: PO Box 40, Lincoln 8152
*Tel:* (03) 3256700 *Fax:* (03) 3252127
*E-mail:* mwpress@landcare.cri.nz
*Web Site:* www.landcare.cri.nz/mwpress/
*Key Personnel*
Manager: Greg Comfort
Sales: Catherine Montgomery
Founded: 1992
Specialize in scientific publications.
Subjects: Biological Sciences, Earth Sciences, Natural History, Science (General)
ISBN Prefix(es): 0-477; 0-478
Imprints: Manaaki Whenua Press
*U.S. Office(s):* Balogh Scientific Books, 1911 N Duncan Rd, Champaign, IL 61821, United States
Distributor for Csiro Publishing (Australia)

**Learning Guides (Writers & Publishers Ltd)+**
PO Box 48-147, Upper Hut
*Tel:* (04) 239 9400 *Fax:* (04) 239 9400
*E-mail:* learning.guides@xtra.co.nz
*Key Personnel*
Manager: Lynda Litchfield
Founded: 1996
Subjects: Business, Computer Science, How-to, Management, Science (General)
ISBN Prefix(es): 0-9583643
*Parent Company:* Ecological Research Associates of New Zealand Inc, Upper Hutt

**Learning Media Ltd+**
State Services Commission Bldg, 100 Molesworth St, Level 3, Wellington 6001
Mailing Address: Box 3293, Wellington 6001
*Tel:* (04) 472 5522 *Fax:* (04) 472 6444
*E-mail:* info@learningmedia.co.nz
*Web Site:* www.learningmedia.co.nz; www.learningmedia.com
*Key Personnel*
Chief Executive: Neale Pitches
Founded: 1993
Membership(s): NZ Book Publishers Association.
Subjects: Education
ISBN Prefix(es): 0-478
Total Titles: 2 CD-ROM

*U.S. Office(s):* Learning Media, 1235 Indiana Court, Suite 108, Redlands, CA 92374, United States
Distributed by Celebration Press (USA); Learning Media (New Zealand); Madeleine Lindley Ltd (UK); Thomas Nelson (UK)
Distributor for ITP Nelson (Canada); Lioncrest Pty Ltd (Australia); Pacific Stores Pty Ltd (Singapore)
*Orders to:* SSC Bldg, Level 3, Private Bag 3293, Wellington 6015

**Legislation Direct+**
Division of Blue Star Print Group
PO Box 12-418, Wellington
*Tel:* (04) 495 2882 *Fax:* (04) 495 2880
*E-mail:* ldorders@legislationdirect.co.nz
*Web Site:* gplegislation.co.nz
*Key Personnel*
General Manager: Chris Eales
Administration Manager: Wendy Gaylor
*E-mail:* wendy@legislationdirect.co.nz
Subjects: Career Development, Finance, Government, Political Science, Law, Nonfiction (General)
ISBN Prefix(es): 0-86956
*Associate Companies:* Bennetts Government London Bookshops, London, United Kingdom; Whitcoulls (retail)
*U.S. Office(s):* Aubrey Books, 721 Ellsworth Dr, Suite 203A, Silver Spring, MD 20910-4436, United States
Distributor for Business Round Table; Ministry for the Environment; Ministry of Justice; NZ Statistics; Parliamentary Commission for the Environment
*Bookshop(s):* 47 Stephenson St, Birmingham B2 4DH, United Kingdom

**Lincoln College Centre for Resource Management+**
Lincoln University, Ellesmere Junction Rd/ Springs Rd, Lincoln, Canterbury
Mailing Address: Lincoln University, PO Box 56, Canterbury 8150
*Tel:* (03) 3252811 *Fax:* (03) 325156
*Web Site:* www.lincoln.ac.nz
*Telex:* 4200 NZ
*Key Personnel*
Dir, Rights & Permissions: Dr John Hayward
Founded: 1960
Subjects: Environmental Studies
ISBN Prefix(es): 0-908584; 1-86931

**Lincoln University Press+**
8 Glenbervie Terrace, Thorndon, Wellington
Mailing Address: PO Box 12-214, Thorndon, Wellington
*Tel:* (04) 4710601 *Fax:* (04) 4710489
*E-mail:* learn@lincoln.ac.nz
*Web Site:* learn.lincoln.ac.nz
*Key Personnel*
Man Dir & Publisher: Daphne Brasell
*E-mail:* daphne@brasell.co.nz
International Rights: Maureen Marshall
*E-mail:* dba@clear.net.nz
Founded: 1987
Membership(s): Book Publishers Association of New Zealand; Booksellers New Zealand.
Subjects: Fiction, Gay & Lesbian, Literature, Literary Criticism, Essays, Women's Studies, Resource Management
ISBN Prefix(es): 0-9597837; 0-908896
*Parent Company:* Daphne Brasell Associates Ltd & Lincoln University
*Ultimate Parent Company:* Daphne Brasell Associates Ltd
Imprints: Whitireia Publishing
Subsidiaries: Lincoln University Press; Whitireia Publishing
*Branch Office(s)*
Orchard Hall, Lincoln University, PO Box

195, Lincoln, Canterbury, Contact: Daphne
Brasell *Tel:* (03) 325 3873 *Fax:* (03) 325 3890
*E-mail:* braselld@lincoln.ac.nz
Distributed by Unireps (Australia)
Foreign Rep(s): Hemisphere (East Asia, The Pacific); Unireps (Australia)


**David Ling Publishing+**
67 Hinemoa St, Birkenhead, Auckland 10
Mailing Address: PO Box 34-601, Birkenhead,
Auckland 10
*Tel:* (09) 4182785 *Fax:* (09) 4182785
*E-mail:* davidling@xtra.co.nz
*Web Site:* www.davidling.co.nz
*Key Personnel*
Man Dir & International Rights: David Ling
Founded: 1992
Publisher & packager.
Membership(s): Booksellers New Zealand; Book
Publishers Association of New Zealand.
Subjects: Aeronautics, Aviation, Art, Biography,
Fiction, History, Maritime
ISBN Prefix(es): 0-908990; 1-877378
Number of titles published annually: 10 Print
Total Titles: 80 Print
Distributed by David Bateman Ltd


**Longacre Press+**
9 Dowling St, Dunedin
Mailing Address: PO Box 5340, Dunedin
*Tel:* (03) 4772911 *Fax:* (03) 4772911
*E-mail:* longacre.press@clear.net.nz
*Key Personnel*
Managing Editor: Barbara Larson
Publicity Manager: Annette Riley
Founded: 1994
Subjects: Biography, Gardening, Plants, Gay &
Lesbian, Natural History, Nonfiction (General),
Sports, Athletics
ISBN Prefix(es): 0-9583405; 0-9583465; 1-
877135
Number of titles published annually: 10 Print
Total Titles: 75 Print
Distributed by Dennis Jones & Associates
(Australia); Reed Publishing (NZ) Ltd (New
Zealand)


**Longman**, *imprint of* Pearson Education (PENZ)


**Macmillan Publishers New Zealand Ltd+**
6 Ride Way, Albany, Auckland
*Tel:* (09) 414 0350; (09) 414 0356 (customer service); (09) 414 0352 (trade sales); (09) 415
6672 *Fax:* (09) 414 0351
*Web Site:* www.macmillan.co.nz *Cable:*
Macpublish
*Key Personnel*
Man Dir: David Joel *E-mail:* david@macmillan.
co.nz
Trade Sales: Chris Baty *E-mail:* chris@
macmillan.co.nz
School Sales: Robyn Garvan *E-mail:* robyn@
macmillan.co.nz
Academic Sales: Victoria Johnson *E-mail:* vicki@
macmillan.co.nz
Customer Service: Lyn O'Connor *E-mail:* lyn@
macmillan.co.nz
Founded: 1843
ISBN Prefix(es): 0-908923; 1-86965
*Parent Company:* Macmillan Publishers Ltd,
United Kingdom
*Associate Companies:* Macmillan Education Australia; Pan Macmillan Australia


**Magari Publishing+**
Imprint of Natural Expressions Ltd
PO Box 104, Taupo 2730
*Tel:* (07) 3770169 *Fax:* (07) 3773134
*E-mail:* frontdesk@magari.co.nz
*Web Site:* www.magari.co.nz

*Key Personnel*
Publisher: Margaret Woodhouse
*E-mail:* margaret@magari.co.nz
Marketing Dir: Jack Gower
Founded: 1987
Subjects: Education, Humor, Self-Help, Cat books
& Fun books
ISBN Prefix(es): 0-908801
Imprints: Curly Tales; Knowing Science
*Warehouse:* 3/29 Manuka St, Taupo


**Mallinson Rendel Publishers Ltd+**
15 Courtenay Pl, Level 5, Wellington
Mailing Address: PO Box 9409, Wellington
*Tel:* (04) 802 5012 *Fax:* (04) 802 5013
*E-mail:* publisher@mallinsonrendel.co.nz
*Web Site:* www.mallinsonrendel.co.nz
*Key Personnel*
Man Dir: E A Mallinson
Account: J D Harper
Publisher: Ann Mallinson *E-mail:* ann@
mallinsonrendel.co.nz
Founded: 1980
ISBN Prefix(es): 0-908783; 0-908606
Number of titles published annually: 6 Print
Total Titles: 180 Print


**Manaaki Whenua Press**, *imprint of* Landcare
Research NZ


**Maori Publications Unit**
PO Box 2061, Kopeopeo, Whakatane
*Tel:* (07) 3087254 *Fax:* (07) 3085098
*Key Personnel*
Contact: Dir
Subjects: English as a Second Language
ISBN Prefix(es): 1-877152; 0-908771
*Showroom(s):* Cor Domain Rd & McAlister St,
Whakatane


**Mills Group+**
PO Box 30818, Lower Hutt
*Tel:* (04) 5696744 *Fax:* (04) 5697464
*Web Site:* www.millsonline.com
*Key Personnel*
Chief Executive: Harry Mills *E-mail:* harry.
mills@millsonline.com
Founded: 1982
Subjects: Nonfiction (General)
ISBN Prefix(es): 0-908722


**Millwood Press Ltd**
291B Tinakori Rd, Wellington
*Tel:* (04) 4735176 *Fax:* (04) 4735177
*Telex:* 31255 *Cable:* Siersprod
*Key Personnel*
Dir: Jim Siers; Judy Siers
Founded: 1972
Subjects: Foreign Countries
ISBN Prefix(es): 0-908582


**Moss Associates Ltd+**
7 Dorset Way, Wilton, Wellington 6005
*Tel:* (04) 4728226 *Fax:* (04) 4728226
*E-mail:* moss@xtra.co.nz
*Web Site:* www.mossassociates.co.nz
*Key Personnel*
Dir: Geoffrey R Moss
Founded: 1986
Subjects: Business, Career Development, Communications, Human Relations, Management
ISBN Prefix(es): 0-9583538
Distributed by Ane Books (India); Bagolyvar
Publishing House (Hungary); Best Literary
& Rights Agency (Korea); CCH (Australia);
DPB Publications (India); Dragon's Eye Communications (Korea); Federal Publications (S)
Pte Ltd (Singapore); Francolin Publishers (Pty)
Ltd (South Africa); Joint Publishing (China);
Kogan Page (UK); LDI Training (Indonesia);
McGraw-Hill (USA); McGraw-Hill Book Co

Australia Pty Ltd (Australia); Moss Associates
Ltd (New Zealand); Prommociones Jumerca
(Spain); Qingdao Publishing House (China);
SE-Education Public Co Ltd (Thailand); Shanghai People's Publishing House (China); Singapore Institute of Management (Singapore &
Malaysia); Tech Publications Pty Ltd (Singapore); Thomson Learning (India); Times Media
Pvt Ltd (Singapore); UBS Publishers' Distributors Ltd (India); Vijay Nicole Imprints (India);
Vikas Publishing House Pvt Ltd (India); Yale
International Publishing House (Taiwan)


**Nagare Press+**
PO Box 934, Palmerston North
*Tel:* (06) 3572531
*Key Personnel*
Editor & International Rights: Dr Wilhelmina
Drummond
Subjects: Child Care & Development, Education, Fiction, Human Relations, Poetry, Wine
& Spirits, Adolescence, Human Development
ISBN Prefix(es): 0-908822


**Nahanni Publishing Ltd+**
PO Box 34-179, Birkenhead, Auckland 10
*Tel:* (09) 419 0681 *Fax:* (09) 419 0695
*E-mail:* info@nahanni-publishing.com; sales@
nahanni.co.nz (for orders)
*Web Site:* www.nahanni-publishing.com
*Key Personnel*
Man Dir: Dr Ian Brooks *E-mail:* brooks@
nahanni.co.nz
Founded: 1995
Subjects: Business
ISBN Prefix(es): 0-9583506; 0-9582036


**Nelson Price Milburn Ltd+**
One Te Puni St, Petone, Wellington
Mailing Address: PO Box 38-945, Wellington
Mail Centre, Petone, Wellington
*Tel:* (04) 5687179 *Toll Free Tel:* 0508635766
*Fax:* (04) 5682115
*Web Site:* www.thomsonlearning.com.au/primary
*Key Personnel*
General & Publishing Manager: Greg Browne
Secretary: John Heffernan
Customer Service Rep: Jacqui Rivera
*E-mail:* jacqui.rivera@thomson.com
Founded: 1957
Distributor for Thomas Nelson UK & Thomas
Nelson Australia.
Subjects: Accounting, Biological Sciences, Business, Chemistry, Chemical Engineering, Child
Care & Development, Communications, Computer Science, Drama, Theater, Economics,
Education, Electronics, Electrical Engineering,
Finance, Geography, Geology, Health, Nutrition, History, Language Arts, Linguistics, Law,
Management, Marketing, Mathematics, Outdoor
Recreation, Physical Sciences, Physics, Poetry,
Science (General), Social Sciences, Sociology,
Sports, Athletics, Technology
ISBN Prefix(es): 0-7055; 1-86955; 1-86961; 0-
86871
*Parent Company:* Thomas Nelson Australia, Australia
*Ultimate Parent Company:* The Thomson Corp,
Suite 2706, Toronto Dominion Bank Tower, PO
Box 24, Toronto Dominion Centre, Toronto,
ON M5K 1A1, Canada
*Associate Companies:* 102 Dodds St, South Melbourne, Victoria 3205, Australia


**Nestegg Books+**
46 Owhiro Bay Pde, Wellington 6002
*Tel:* (04) 3836645
*Key Personnel*
Author, Editor & Publisher: Sheila Natusch
Founded: 1991
Subjects: Biography, History, Natural History, Regional Interests
ISBN Prefix(es): 0-9582007; 0-9582140

**New House Publishers Ltd+**
31 Castor Bay Rd, Takapuna, Auckland
Mailing Address: PO Box 33376, Takapuna,
Auckland
*Tel:* (09) 4106517 *Fax:* (09) 4106329
*E-mail:* service@newhouse.co.nz
*Web Site:* www.newhouse.co.nz
*Key Personnel*
Dir: David Heap *E-mail:* david@newhouse.co.nz
Founded: 1988
Specialize in educational textbooks & materials.
Subjects: Accounting, Chemistry, Chemical Engi-
neering, Earth Sciences, Economics, English as
a Second Language, Geography, Geology, Lan-
guage Arts, Linguistics, Mathematics, Physics,
Science (General), Technology
ISBN Prefix(es): 1-86946
Number of titles published annually: 25 Print
Total Titles: 300 Print

**New Women's Press Ltd+**
PO Box 47339, Auckland
*Tel:* (09) 3767150 *Fax:* (09) 3767150
*Key Personnel*
Man Dir: Wendy Harrex
Founded: 1982
Subjects: Women's Studies
ISBN Prefix(es): 0-908652
*Warehouse:* HarperCollins Publishers, PO Box 1,
Auckland

**New Zealand Council for Educational
Research+**
10th floor, West Block, Education House, 178-
182 Willis St, Wellington
Mailing Address: PO Box 3237, Wellington
*Tel:* (04) 384 7939 *Fax:* (04) 384 7933
*Web Site:* www.nzcer.org.nz
*Key Personnel*
Dir: Robyn Baker *E-mail:* robyn.baker@nzcer.
org.nz
Publicity Dir, Rights & Permissions: Bev Webber
*E-mail:* bev.webber@nzcer.org.nz
Founded: 1934
Subjects: Education
ISBN Prefix(es): 0-908567; 0-908916; 1-877140
Imprints: NZCER
Distributor for ACER; NFER; SCRE
*Showroom(s):* Education House, 178 Willis St,
Wellington
*Bookshop(s):* Education House, 178 Willis St,
Wellington
*Shipping Address:* Education House, 178 Willis
St, Wellington
*Warehouse:* Education House, 178 Willis St,
Wellington
*Orders to:* Education House, 178-182 Willis St,
Wellington 6000 (Distribution Services)

**Nielsen BookData Asia Pacific**
PO Box 46-018, Herne Bay, Auckland 1030
*Tel:* (09) 360 3294 *Fax:* (09) 360 8853
*E-mail:* info@nielsenbookdata.co.nz
*Web Site:* www.nielsenbookdata.co.nz
*Key Personnel*
Man Dir: Ka Meechan *E-mail:* ka.meechan@
nielsenbookdata.co.nz
Founded: 1987
Specialize in a range of computer-based bibli-
ographic information services for the inter-
national book trade; bibliographic CD-ROM
database & online services.
*Parent Company:* VNU Media Measurement &
Information

**Northland Historical Publications Society**
PO Box 285, Kerikeri, Northland
*Tel:* (09) 4028244 *Fax:* (09) 4028296
Founded: 1989
Subjects: History
ISBN Prefix(es): 0-9583705; 0-9597926

**NZCER**, *imprint of* New Zealand Council for
Educational Research

**Orca Publishing, Certes Press**, *imprint of* Orca
Publishing Services Ltd

**Orca Publishing Services Ltd**
202 Hereford St, Christchurch
Mailing Address: PO Box 2151, Christchurch
*Tel:* (03) 377-0370 *Fax:* (03) 377-0390
*E-mail:* info@hazard.co.nz
*Web Site:* www.hazardonline.com
*Key Personnel*
Man Dir & Publisher: Quentin Wilson
*E-mail:* quentin@hazard.co.nz
Editor: Antoinette Wilson *E-mail:* antoinette@
orcapublishing.co.nz
Founded: 1986
Membership(s): Book Publishers Association of
NZ.
Subjects: Fiction, Nonfiction (General), Poetry
ISBN Prefix(es): 1-877162
*Associate Companies:* Hazard Press Ltd
Imprints: Orca Publishing, Certes Press
Distributed by Mosaic Press

**Otago Heritage Books**
PO Box 6318, Dunedin
*Tel:* (03) 477 1500 *Fax:* (03) 477 1500
*E-mail:* otagoheritagebooks@clear.net.nz
*Key Personnel*
Editorial: G J Griffiths
Rights & Permissions: J A Cox
Founded: 1977
Specialize in regional books; also acts as retailer.
Subjects: History, Natural History, Regional Inter-
ests
ISBN Prefix(es): 0-908774; 0-9597723
Total Titles: 55 Print

**Outrigger Publishers**
PO Box 1198, Hamilton
*Tel:* (07) 856 6981
*Key Personnel*
Man Dir, Editorial: Norman Simms
*E-mail:* nsimms@waikato.ac.nz
Founded: 1973
Publishes small magazines.
Subjects: Anthropology, Archaeology, Biblical
Studies, History, Language Arts, Linguistics,
Literature, Literary Criticism, Essays, Psychol-
ogy, Psychiatry, Religion - Jewish
ISBN Prefix(es): 0-908571
Number of titles published annually: 2 Print

**Oxford University Press**
Wellesley St, Auckland
Mailing Address: GPO Box 2784Y, Melbourne
3001, Australia
*Tel:* (03) 9934 9123 *Toll Free Tel:* 1300 650 616
(Australia); 0800 442 502 (New Zealand)
*Fax:* (03) 9934 9100 *Toll Free Fax:* 0800-442-
503
*E-mail:* cs@oup.com.au
*Web Site:* www.oup.com.au
*Key Personnel*
Publisher: Linda Cassells
Subjects: Agriculture, Art, Biography, Economics,
History, Law, Literature, Literary Criticism,
Essays, Natural History, Poetry
ISBN Prefix(es): 0-19
*Parent Company:* Oxford University Press, United
Kingdom

**Paerangi Books**
PO Box 13-320, Johnsonville, Wellington 6004
*Tel:* (04) 4787789
*Key Personnel*
Contact: Trevor M Cobeldick
Founded: 1979

Subjects: Regional Interests
ISBN Prefix(es): 0-908965

**Pasifika Press+**
Formerly Polynesian Press
PO Box 68 446, Newton, Auckland
*Tel:* (09) 377-6068 *Fax:* (09) 377-6069
*E-mail:* press@pasifika.co.nz
*Web Site:* www.pasifika.co.nz
*Key Personnel*
Contact: Robert Holding
Founded: 1976
ISBN Prefix(es): 0-908597
Distributed by University of Hawaii Press
Distributor for University of Hawaii Press

**Pearson Education (PENZ)+**
46 Hillside Rd, Glenfield, Auckland 10
Mailing Address: Private Bag 102908, North
Shore Mail Centre, Auckland 10
*Tel:* (09) 444 4968 *Fax:* (09) 444 4957
*E-mail:* firstname.lastname@pearsoned.co.nz
*Web Site:* www.pearsoned.co.nz
*Key Personnel*
Man Dir: Rosemary Stagg *E-mail:* rosemary.
stagg@pearsoned.co.nz
Publisher, Schools: Ken Harrop
Marketing Manager Schools: Pat Fisk
Publisher, Tertiary: Bronwen Nicholson
Tertiary Sales Manager: Adrian Keane
Trade National Accounts Manager: John Cum-
merfield
Design/Production Manager: Polly Faulks
Administration Manager: Vera Bainbridge
Operations Manager: Ingeborg Van Elburg
Assistant to Man Dir: Sheila Jenkins
Founded: 1968
All New Zealand curriculum subjects in schools,
higher education focus on business, economics
& the social sciences.
ISBN Prefix(es): 0-582
Number of titles published annually: 60 Print
Total Titles: 600 Print
*Parent Company:* Pearson Education
*Ultimate Parent Company:* Pearson Plc
Imprints: Longman; Prentice Hall
Distributor for Sybex (New Zealand); WW Nor-
ton (New Zealand)

**Penguin Books (NZ) Ltd**
Corner Rosedale & Airborne Rds, Auckland
Mailing Address: PMB 102902, North Shore
Mall, Auckland 10
*Tel:* (09) 415-4700; (09) 415-4702 (orders)
*Fax:* (09) 415-4701; (09) 415-4703 (orders)
*E-mail:* marketing@penguin.co.nz
*Web Site:* www.penguin.co.nz
*Key Personnel*
Man Dir: Tony Harkins
Sales Dir: Colin Cox
Publishing Dir: Geoff Walker
Marketing Dir: Karen Ferns
Founded: 1973
ISBN Prefix(es): 0-14
*Parent Company:* Penguin Publishing Co Ltd,
United Kingdom

**Polynesian Press**, see Pasifika Press

**Prentice Hall**, *imprint of* Pearson Education
(PENZ)

**Profile Publishing Ltd**
Suite 2.1, 72 Dominion Rd, Mt Eden, Auckland
Mailing Address: PO Box 5544, Auckland
*Tel:* (09) 6308940; (09) 3585455 *Fax:* (09)
6302307; (09) 6301046; (09) 3585462
*E-mail:* info@profile.co.nz
*Web Site:* www.profile.co.nz
*Key Personnel*
Publisher & Editor: Reg Birchfield
*E-mail:* editor@management.co.nz

General Manager: Kevin Lawrence
E-mail: kevin@profile.co.nz
ISBN Prefix(es): 0-9582045

**Publishing Solutions Ltd**
86-90 Lambton Quay, 9th floor, Wellington
Tel: (04) 4710582 Fax: (04) 4710717
E-mail: gen@pubsol.co.nz
Founded: 1992
Specialize in technical publishing.
Subjects: Maritime, Veterinary Science
ISBN Prefix(es): 0-9582063

**Pursuit Publishing+**
22 Second Ave, Whangarei
Mailing Address: PO Box 984, Whangarei
Tel: (09) 4385725 Fax: (09) 4382543
Web Site: www.pursuit.co.nz
Key Personnel
Author & President: Frank Newman
E-mail: frank@newman.co.nz
Founded: 1988
Subjects: Business
ISBN Prefix(es): 0-9597904
Distributed by Reed (NZ) Ltd (New Zealand)

**R P L Books+**
10 Rozella Pl, Murrays Bay, Auckland
Mailing Address: North Shore Mail Center, PO
Box 100 243, Auckland 1330
Tel: (09) 4437448 Fax: (09) 4430147
E-mail: rplbooks@rplbooks.co.nz
Key Personnel
Man Dir: Duncan Sutherland E-mail: duncan@
rplbooks.co.nz
Founded: 1970
Subjects: Biography, Sports, Athletics
ISBN Prefix(es): 0-908630; 0-908757; 0-9583371;
0-9597553; 0-9597884
Total Titles: 20 Print; 3 E-Book
Parent Company: Medialine Holdings Ltd
Imprints: Harlen Books; The Sporting Press
Subsidiaries: Harlen Publishing Company Ltd;
The Sporting Press Ltd
Distribution Center: Forrester Books NZ Ltd, 10
Tarndale Grove, Auckland, Contact: David For-
rester Tel: (09) 4152080 Fax: (09) 4152083
E-mail: forr@forrester.co.nz
Orders to: Forrester Books NZ Ltd, Private Bag
102907, NSMC, Auckland, Contact: David For-
rester Tel: (09) 4152080 Fax: (09) 4152083

**Reach Publications+**
PO Box 10-010, Dominion Rd, Auckland
Tel: (09) 376 3235 Fax: (09) 376 3250
E-mail: giftedednz@xtra.co.nz
Key Personnel
Managing Editor: Rory Cathcart
Founded: 1994
Subjects: Child Care & Development, Disability,
Special Needs, Education
ISBN Prefix(es): 0-473
Parent Company: George Parkyn Centre for
Gifted Education

**Reed Books**, imprint of Reed Publishing (NZ)
Ltd

**Reed Children's Books**, imprint of Reed
Publishing (NZ) Ltd

**Reed Publishing (NZ) Ltd+**
Division of Harcourt Education International
39 Rawene Rd, Birkenhead, Auckland 10
Mailing Address: PO B0x 34901, Birkenhead,
Auckland 10
Tel: (09) 441 2960 Fax: (09) 480 4999
E-mail: info@reed.co.nz
Web Site: www.reedpublishing.co.nz
Key Personnel
Man Dir: Alan Smith E-mail: asmith@reed.co.nz

Founded: 1907
Subjects: Biography, Cookery, Fiction, History,
Natural History, Nonfiction (General), Outdoor
Recreation, Regional Interests, Travel
ISBN Prefix(es): 0-589; 0-7900; 0-86863; 1-
86948; 0-474; 1-86944
Number of titles published annually: 100 Print
Total Titles: 280 Print; 2 Audio
Imprints: Reed Books; Heinemann Education;
Reed Children's Books
Divisions: Reed Exports; Heinemann Educational;
Book Circle
Distributor for BBC Books; Octopus Publishing
Group; Virgin Books

**Resource Books Ltd+**
37 Pembroke Crescent, Glendowie, Auckland
1005
Mailing Address: PO Box 25-598, St Heliers,
Auckland 1130
Tel: (09) 5758030 Fax: (09) 5758055
E-mail: sales@resourcebooks.co.nz
Web Site: www.resourcebooks.co.nz
Key Personnel
Manager: Peter Biggs E-mail: pbiggs@
resourcebooks.co.nz
Founded: 1984
Subjects: Art, Education, Medicine, Nursing,
Dentistry
ISBN Prefix(es): 0-908618

**RIMU Publishing Co Ltd**
49 Casey Ave Fairfield, Hamilton
Tel: (07) 8555536 Fax: (07) 8555536
Key Personnel
Man Dir: Theola Wyllie
Founded: 1984
Subjects: Nonfiction (General)
ISBN Prefix(es): 0-908703

**River Press**
41 York St, Picton
Mailing Address: PO Box 10, Picton
Tel: (03) 5738383 Fax: (03) 5738383
Key Personnel
Contact: Carol Dawber E-mail: carol.dawber@
xtra.co.nz
Founded: 1992
Also acts a book packager.
Subjects: History, Maritime, Mysteries, Nonfiction
(General), Romance, Travel
ISBN Prefix(es): 0-9598041
Subsidiaries: Best Books

**RSVP Publishing Co Ltd+**
24 Tiri Rd, Oneroa, Waiheke Island, Auckland
Mailing Address: PO Box 47166, Ponsonby,
Auckland
Tel: (09) 3723480 Fax: (09) 3728480
E-mail: rsvppub@iconz.co.nz
Web Site: www.rsvp-publishing.co.nz
Key Personnel
Publisher: Stephen Picard
Editorial Manager: Rosie Parkes
Founded: 1990
Membership(s): BPANZ.
Subjects: Alternative, Astrology, Occult, Envi-
ronmental Studies, Fiction, Law, Nonfiction
(General), Photography, Social Sciences, So-
ciology, Travel, Also specializes in eclectic &
metaphysical books, illustrated books
ISBN Prefix(es): 0-9597948; 0-9582182
Number of titles published annually: 3 Print
Total Titles: 12 Print; 9 Online; 9 E-Book
Distributed by Banyan Tree Book Distributors
Foreign Rep(s): Banyan Tree (Australia)

**Saint Publishing+**
11 Akepiro St, Mt Eden, Auckland
Mailing Address: PO Box 8157, Symonds St,
Auckland

Tel: (09) 623-2510 Fax: (09) 623-2890
E-mail: info@saintpublish.co.nz
Key Personnel
Man Dir: Selwyn Jacobson
Editor: Tom Hepburn
Founded: 1979
Specialize in calendars & lifestyle/coffee table
books.
Subjects: Art, Humor, Sports, Athletics
ISBN Prefix(es): 1-877186; 1-877247
Number of titles published annually: 2 CD-ROM
Total Titles: 6 Print
Distributor for Avalanche Publishing (New
Zealand)

**Seagull Press**
2/226 Marine Parade, New Brighton, Christchurch
Tel: (03) 3899338
Key Personnel
Author: R B Mehlhopt
Subjects: Poetry
ISBN Prefix(es): 0-908738; 0-9597686; 1-877278

**Shearwater Associates Ltd+**
108 Mana Esplanade, Paremata, Wellington
Mailing Address: PO Box 54-224, Plimmerton
Tel: (04) 2399024 Fax: (04) 2399024
Key Personnel
Contact: Michael Keith
Founded: 1990
Specialize in children's & educational publishing.
Subjects: Education, Fiction, History, Natural His-
tory, Nonfiction (General)
ISBN Prefix(es): 0-908864
Imprints: Shearwater Books; Titi Tuhiwai

**Shearwater Books**, imprint of Shearwater
Associates Ltd

**Shoal Bay Press Ltd+**
4 Cliff St, Moncks Bay, Christchurch
Mailing Address: PO Box 17661, Christchurch
Tel: (03) 384 6057 Fax: (03) 384 6087
E-mail: ros@shoalbay.co.nz
Key Personnel
Contact: David Elworthy E-mail: david@
shoalbay.co.nz
Founded: 1984
Subjects: Business, Child Care & Development,
Crafts, Games, Hobbies, Finance, Gardening,
Plants, History, Management, Marketing, Nat-
ural History, Nonfiction (General), Outdoor
Recreation, Photography, Sports, Athletics,
Travel
ISBN Prefix(es): 0-908704; 1-877251
Warehouse: Macmillan Publishers, 6 Ridge Way,
Albany, Auckland
Orders to: Macmillan Publishers, 6 Ridge Way,
Albany, Auckland

**Shortland Publications Ltd**
PO Box 11-904, Auckland 5
Tel: (09) 687128 Fax: (09) 6230143
E-mail: heather_peach@mcgraw-hill.com Cable:
NEWSPRESS
Key Personnel
Man Dir: Avelyn Davidson
Sales Manager: Jenny Boyd
Founded: 1977
Subjects: Sports, Athletics
ISBN Prefix(es): 0-7901; 0-86867
Parent Company: Wilson & Horton Ltd, 46 Al-
bert St, PO Box 32, Auckland

**SIR Publishing+**
Science House, 11 Turnbull St, Thorndon,
Wellington
Mailing Address: PO Box 399, Wellington
Tel: (04) 472 7421 Fax: (04) 473 1841
E-mail: sirp@rsnz.govt.nz
Web Site: www.rsnz.govt.nz/publ Cable: SIDSIR

*Key Personnel*
Manager: Robert Lynch
Founded: 1991
Publishers of scientific research journals, focusing on New Zealand, Australia, SW Pacific & Antarctica, Scientific Proceedings of Symposia & Workshops; Scientific Treatises; Science Education Resources. Incorporated within The Royal Society of New Zealand.
Subjects: Agriculture, Biological Sciences, Earth Sciences, Environmental Studies, Science (General)
ISBN Prefix(es): 0-477; 0-908654
*Parent Company:* The Royal Society of New Zealand, 4 Halswell St, Thorndon, PO Box 598, Wellington
*Branch Office(s)*
Eurospan Ltd, 3 Henrietta St, Covent Garden, London WC2E 8LU, United Kingdom *Tel:* (020) 7240 0856 *Fax:* (020) 7379 0609
*U.S. Office(s):* Allen Press Inc, PO Box 1897, Lawrence, KS 66044-8897, United States *Tel:* 913-843-1234 *Fax:* 913-843-1274

**Southern Lights**, *imprint of* Brick Row Publishing Co Ltd

**Southern Press Ltd**
PO Box 50-134, Porirua
*Tel:* (04) 233-1899
*Key Personnel*
Man Dir, Editorial: R H Stott
Publicity: J Stott
Founded: 1971
Subjects: Aeronautics, Aviation, Archaeology, Civil Engineering, Maritime, Mechanical Engineering, Technology, Transportation
ISBN Prefix(es): 0-908616
Distributed by ARHS, NSW Division
Distributor for Australian Railway Historical Society, NSW Division
*Shipping Address:* High Ridge, Paekakariki Hill Rd, Pauatahanui, R D 1, Porirua Wellington

**Spinal Publications New Zealand Ltd+**
8 Parata St, Waikanae
Mailing Address: PO Box 93, Waikanae
*Tel:* (04) 2937020 *Fax:* (04) 2932897
*E-mail:* enquiries@spinalpublications.co.nz
*Web Site:* www.spinalpublications.co.nz
*Key Personnel*
General Manager: Jan McKenzie
Founded: 1980
Membership(s): BPANZ.
Subjects: Health, Nutrition, Self-Help, Diagnosis & Treatment of Lumbar & Cervical Spine
ISBN Prefix(es): 0-9583647; 0-9598049; 0-9597446; 0-9597746
Distributed by Esaki Medical Instrument Co (Japan); Spinal Publications Italia (Italy)

**The Sporting Press**, *imprint of* R P L Books

**Statistics New Zealand**
Aorangi House, 85 Molesworth St, Wellington
Mailing Address: PO Box 2922, Wellington
*Tel:* (04) 931 4600 *Fax:* (04) 931 4610
*E-mail:* info@stats.govt.nz
*Web Site:* www.stats.govt.nz
Subjects: Agriculture, Business, Economics, Education, Finance, Mathematics, Women's Studies
ISBN Prefix(es): 0-478

**Sunshine Books International Ltd+**
PO Box 74543, Auckland 1130
*Tel:* (09) 5203049 *Toll Free Fax:* 0800 85 1000
*E-mail:* orders@my-dictionary.com
*Web Site:* www.my-dictionary.com

*Key Personnel*
Co-Dir: Jenny Aston *E-mail:* jenny@my-dictionary.com
ISBN Prefix(es): 0-9597734

**Sunshine Multi Media Ltd, Wendy Pye Ltd**
413 Great South Rd, Penrose, Auckland 1005
*Tel:* (09) 525-3575 *Fax:* (09) 525-4205
*E-mail:* admin@sunshine.co.nz
*Web Site:* www.sunshine.co.nz
Founded: 1986
ISBN Prefix(es): 1-877190
*Branch Office(s)*
433 Wellington St, Clifton Hill, Melbourne, Victoria 3068, Australia *Tel:* (0613) 9489-3968 *Fax:* (0613) 9482-2416
Maaholm Publishing House, Almevej 12, 2900 Hellerup, Denmark *Tel:* (0453) 9627 892 *Fax:* (0453) 9627 891
20 Heathbridge, Brooklands Rd, Weybridge, Surrey KT13 OUN, United Kingdom *Tel:* (044-1932) *Fax:* 850062

**Tandem Press+**
2 Rugby Rd, Birkenhead, Auckland 10
Mailing Address: PO Box 34-272, Birkenhead, Auckland
*Tel:* (09) 480-1452 *Fax:* (09) 480-1455
*E-mail:* customers@tandempress.co.nz
*Web Site:* www.tandempress.co.nz
*Key Personnel*
Man Dir, Editorial: Robert M Ross *E-mail:* bobross@tandempress.co.nz
Dir, Marketing: Helen E Benton *E-mail:* helenb@tandempress.co.nz
Founded: 1990
Subjects: Business, Cookery, Ethnicity, Fiction, Health, Nutrition, Nonfiction (General), Outdoor Recreation, Photography, Psychology, Psychiatry, Self-Help, Travel, Women's Studies
ISBN Prefix(es): 1-877178; 0-908884; 9-781877
Total Titles: 135 Print
Distributed by Forrester Books
Distributor for New Women's Press (NZ)
*Distribution Center:* Australian Book Group, PO Box 214, Gembrook, Victoria 3783, Australia, Contact: Morgan Blackthorne *Tel:* (03) 5967 7009

**Taylor Books+**
51 Sixth Ave, Tauranga
*Tel:* (07) 5786024
*Key Personnel*
Head: Peter Rotherham
Founded: 1994
Subjects: English as a Second Language, Self-Help

**Te Waihora Press**
PO Box 512, Christchurch
*Tel:* (03) 304-8555 *Fax:* (03) 355-9706
*Key Personnel*
Managing Editor: Dr John Wilson *E-mail:* johnwilson56@xtra.co.nz
Founded: 1984
Subjects: Architecture & Interior Design, History
ISBN Prefix(es): 0-908714
Total Titles: 2 Print

**Titi Tuhiwai**, *imprint of* Shearwater Associates Ltd

**Transworld Publishers (NZ) Ltd**
3 William Pickering Dr, Albany, Auckland
*Tel:* (09) 4156210 *Fax:* (09) 4156221
*Key Personnel*
Contact: Jacqui Dimes
ISBN Prefix(es): 0-908821
*Parent Company:* Bertelsmann AG, Germany

*Associate Companies:* Transworld Publishers, Australia; Bantam Doubleday Dell Inc, 1540 Broadway, New York, NY 10036, United States; Transworld Publishers, United Kingdom
Distributor for Avon; Dover (US); Langenscheidt; David Ling Publishing; Lonely Planet Publications; Workman; Trail Blazer; de Roos

**Universal Business Directories, Australia Pty Ltd**
2 Robert St, Ellerslie, Auckland
Mailing Address: PO Box 11-264, Ellerslie, Auckland
*Tel:* (09) 526-6300 *Toll Free Tel:* 800 823-225 (New Zealand only) *Fax:* (09) 526-6313 *Toll Free Fax:* 800 329 823 (New Zealand only)
*E-mail:* sales@ubd.co.nz
*Web Site:* www.ubd.co.nz
*Key Personnel*
General Manager: Allan Parker
Founded: 1932
Subjects: Business
ISBN Prefix(es): 0-7261
*Parent Company:* Wilson & Horton Ltd
*Associate Companies:* New Zealand Herald
Subsidiaries: Wises Mapping

**University of Otago Press+**
398 Cumberland St, Level 1, Dunedin
Mailing Address: PO Box 56, Dunedin
*Tel:* (03) 479 8807 *Fax:* (03) 479 8385
*E-mail:* university.press@otago.ac.nz
*Web Site:* www.otago.ac.nz
*Key Personnel*
Managing Editor & International Rights: Wendy Harrex *E-mail:* wendy.harrex@stonebow.otago.ac.nz
Publicist: Amanda Smith *Tel:* (03) 479 9094 *E-mail:* amanda.smith@stonebow.otago.ac.nz
Founded: 1958
Membership(s): Book Publishers Association of New Zealand (BPANZ); International Association of Scholarly Publishers (IASP).
Subjects: Anthropology, Art, Biography, Education, Environmental Studies, Ethnicity, Fiction, Government, Political Science, History, Literature, Literary Criticism, Essays, Natural History, Photography, Poetry, Psychology, Psychiatry, Social Sciences, Sociology
ISBN Prefix(es): 0-908569; 1-877133; 1-877276
Number of titles published annually: 24 Print
Total Titles: 130 Print
Foreign Rep(s): International Specialized Book Services (ISBS) (North America); UniReps (Australia)
*Orders to:* HarperCollins, 31 View Rd, Glenfield, Auckland 10 *Tel:* (09) 4439400 *Fax:* (09) 4439402

**Victoria University Press+**
49 Rawhiti Terrace, Kelburn, Wellington 6001
Mailing Address: PO Box 600, Wellington
*Tel:* (04) 463 6580 *Fax:* (04) 463 6581
*E-mail:* victoria-press@vuw.ac.nz
*Web Site:* www.vuw.ac.nz
*Key Personnel*
Publisher: Fergus Barrowman
Editor: Rachel Lawson *E-mail:* rachel.lawson@vuw.ac.nz
Founded: 1979
Membership(s): Booksellers New Zealand.
Subjects: Anthropology, Architecture & Interior Design, Drama, Theater, Government, Political Science, History, Language Arts, Linguistics, Law, Literature, Literary Criticism, Essays, Poetry, Social Sciences, Sociology
ISBN Prefix(es): 0-86473
Total Titles: 180 Print
Distributed by Random House (New Zealand)

*Warehouse:* Random House NZ Ltd, 18 Poland Rd, Glenfield, Auckland
*Orders to:* Archetype Book Agents, PO Box 105, Auckland 200 *Tel:* (09) 3773800 *Fax:* (09) 3773811

**Viking Sevenseas Ltd**, *imprint of* Viking Sevenseas NZ Ltd

**Viking Sevenseas NZ Ltd**
23B Ihakara St, Paraparaumu, Wellington
Mailing Address: PO Box 152, Paraparaumu 6150, Wellington
*Tel:* (04) 902-8240 *Fax:* (04) 902-8240
*E-mail:* vikings@paradise.net.nz *Cable:* VIKSEVEN
*Key Personnel*
Man Dir: Murdoch Riley
Founded: 1957
Subjects: Ethnicity, Natural History
ISBN Prefix(es): 0-85467
Imprints: Viking Sevenseas Ltd

**Wellington Orchid Society Publications**
14 Putnam St, Northland, Wellington
*Tel:* (04) 4758765
*Key Personnel*
Manager: N D Neilson
Subjects: Culture Guides-Cymbidium, Lycaste/Anguloa, Oncidium, Paphiopedilum, Cattleya
ISBN Prefix(es): 0-908684

**Whitireia Publishing**, *imprint of* Lincoln University Press

**Bridget Williams Books Ltd+**
Level 2, 262 Thorndon Quay, Thorndon, Wellington 6001
Mailing Address: PO Box 5482, Wellington 6040
*Tel:* (04) 4946054 *Fax:* (04) 4998942
*E-mail:* info@bwb.co.nz
*Web Site:* www.bwb.co.nz
*Key Personnel*
Dir: Bridget Williams
Business Manager: John Schiff
Founded: 1990
An independent publishing company focusing on New Zealand subjects, including Maori history & politics.
Subjects: Biography, Government, Political Science, History, Nonfiction (General), Women's Studies
ISBN Prefix(es): 0-908912
Number of titles published annually: 10 Print
Total Titles: 30 Print
Distributed by Independent Publishing Group (IPG)
Distributor for NIL
*Distribution Center:* Craig Potton Publishing Ltd, PO Box 555, Nelson

**Wilson & Horton Publications Ltd**
318 Richmond Rd, Grey Lynn, Auckland 1002
Mailing Address: PO Box 90-119, Auckland Mail Centre, Auckland
*Tel:* (09) 6388105; (09) 3603820 *Fax:* (09) 3603831
*E-mail:* whpubs@listener.co.nz
*Web Site:* www.apn.com.au
*Telex:* NZ 2325 *Cable:* HERALD
*Key Personnel*
Man Dir: H M Horton
Managing Editor: Terry Snow
Sales Manager: B Morgan
ISBN Prefix(es): 0-86864; 0-9583614; 1-877214
*Parent Company:* APN News & Media
*Branch Office(s)*
NZ1 Bldg, Hamilton
22 Panama St, Wellington

**Words Work**
31 Robertson St, Rotorua
Mailing Address: PO Box 604, Rotorua 3201
*Tel:* (07) 3482953 *Fax:* (07) 3482953
*E-mail:* wordswrk@clear.net.nz
*Key Personnel*
Dir: Philippa Harrison *E-mail:* philippa@wordswo-k.co.nz; philippa@nzbike.co.nz
Founded: 1996
Prepress, graphic design, editing. Publish New Zealand's only cycling magazine
50% partner in Phoenix Publishing.
Subjects: Child Care & Development, Fiction, How-to, Poetry, Religion - Protestant

# Nicaragua

## General Information

*Capital:* Managua
*Language:* Spanish
*Religion:* Predominantly Roman Catholic
*Population:* 3.8 million
*Bank Hours:* 0830-1500 Monday-Friday; 0830-1130 Saturday
*Shop Hours:* 0800-1200, 1430-1730 or longer Monday-Saturday
*Currency:* 100 centavos = 1 new cordoba
*Export/Import Information:* Catalogues dutied per gross kilo Compensatory tax on advertising. No import licenses or exchange controls.
*Copyright:* UCC, Buenos Aires, Florence (see Copyright Conventions, pg xi)

**Academia Nicaraguense de la Lengua**
(Nicaraguan Academy of Letters)
Ave del Campo No 42, Las Colinas, Apdo 2711, Managua
*Tel:* 2495389 *Fax:* 2495389
Subjects: Language Arts, Linguistics
ISBN Prefix(es): 99924-0

**ENN**, see Editorial Nueva Nicaragua

**Editorial Nueva Nicaragua**
Paseo Salvador Allende, Km 3 1/2 Carretera Sur, Apdo RP-073, Managua
*Tel:* (02) 666520
*Key Personnel*
Dir Gen: Roberto Diaz Castillo
President: Sergio Ramirez Mercado
Production Dir: Irene Menocal Bravo
Financial: Mayra Rivera Juarez
Sales: Maria Jose Bermudez Moreno
Founded: 1981
Also acts as co-productions.
Subjects: Ethnicity, Fiction, Government, Political Science, Literature, Literary Criticism, Essays, Nonfiction (General), Poetry, Religion - Other, Social Sciences, Sociology

# Niger

## General Information

*Capital:* Niamey
*Language:* French (official) and 10 other national languages
*Religion:* 85% Islamic, most of remainder traditional beliefs
*Population:* 8.1 million
*Bank Hours:* 0800-1100, 1600-1700 (cool season 1530-1700) Monday-Friday

*Currency:* 100 centimes = 1 CFA franc
*Export/Import Information:* Member of West African Economic Community. No tariff on books; advertising matter subject to fiscal and customs duties (EEC members pay percentage of customs duty). Also statistical tax.
*Copyright:* UCC, Berne (see Copyright Conventions, pg xi)

**Government Printer (Societe De L'Imprimerie Nationale Du Niger)**
BP 61, Niamey
*Tel:* 734798
*Telex:* 5313

# Nigeria

## General Information

*Capital:* Abuja
*Language:* English (official), also Hausa, Yoruba, Ibo & Fulani
*Religion:* Islamic (mainly in north), Christian, and traditional beliefs
*Population:* 88.5 million
*Bank Hours:* 0800-1500 Monday; 0800-1300 Tuesday-Friday
*Shop Hours:* Vary locally. 0800-1230, 1400-1630 Monday-Friday; 0800-1230 Saturday
*Currency:* 100 kobo = 1 naira
*Export/Import Information:* No tariffs on books or advertising matter. Open general license. Obscene literature prohibited. Exchange controls.
*Copyright:* UCC, Berne, Florence (see Copyright Conventions, pg xi)

**ABIC Books & Equipment Ltd+**
18 Kenyatta St, Nsukka Enugu
Mailing Address: PO Box 13740, Nsukka Enugu
*Tel:* (042) 331827 *Fax:* (042) 334811
*Key Personnel*
President: C N C Asomugha
Founded: 1987
Membership(s): Nigerian Publishers Assoc. Specializes in Reference Books & Children's Books; also participates in Book Selling & as a Literary Agent.
Subjects: History, Poetry
ISBN Prefix(es): 978-2269
*Branch Office(s)*
PO Box 71391, Victoria Island, Lagos

**Abisega Publishers (Nigeria) Ltd+**
Isolak Bldg, 9 Queen Elizabeth Rd, Mokola, Rounabout
Mailing Address: PO Box 14398 UI, Ibadan
*Tel:* (022) 415802
*Key Personnel*
Man Dir: Adedeji Muyiwa
Membership(s): Nigerian Publishers Association.
Subjects: Accounting
ISBN Prefix(es): 978-30339
Imprints: Opatoki Press

**Adebara Publishers Ltd**
PO Box 1970, Ibadan
*Telex:* 20311
*Key Personnel*
Man Dir, Editorial: Dele Adebara
Sales, Publicity: Bisi Oke
Production: Layi Bankole
Rights & Permissions: Kayode Ayeni
Founded: 1979
Subjects: Biography, Business, Education, Ethnicity, Fiction, Foreign Countries, Religion - Other
ISBN Prefix(es): 978-147

Imprints: Awoko; Gangan; Kakaki
*Book Club(s):* Amebo Book Club


**African Books Collective Ltd**, *imprint of*
Nigerian Institute of International Affairs


**African Universities Press+**
305 Herbert Macaulay St, Yaba, Lagos
Mailing Address: PO Box 3560, Yaba, Lagos
*Tel:* (022) 317218
*Telex:* 20311 Box 078 *Cable:* PILGRIM
    IBADAN
*Key Personnel*
Executive Dir: Dr E A M Leigh
Founded: 1963
ISBN Prefix(es): 978-148
*Parent Company:* Pilgrim Books Ltd
Subsidiaries: Aureol Publishers Ltd (West Africa)
*Branch Office(s)*
Klm 8 Zaria/Kaduna Rd, Nr Wasasa Junction,
    PMB 146 Kaduna State
187 Awka Rd, Onitsha, Anambra State


**Africana-FEP Publishers Ltd+**
13B Oguta Rd, Onitsha Anambra State
Mailing Address: PMB 1639, Onitsha Anambra
    State
*Tel:* (046) 210669 *Cable:* AFRIBOOK,
    ONITSHA, NIGERIA
*Key Personnel*
Man Dir: Ralph O Ekpeh *Tel:* (080) 33125 705
Founded: 1971
Subjects: How-to, Science (General)
ISBN Prefix(es): 978-175
*Branch Office(s)*
3 Main St, Gidan Juma
9 Old Lagos Rd, PMB 5632 Ibadan *Tel:* (022)
    311383
53 Barracks Rd Uyo, Presbook BP 13 Limbe,
    Cameroon


**Ahmadu Bello University Press Ltd+**
PMB 1094, Zaria, Kaduna State
*Tel:* (069) 550054
*E-mail:* abupl@abu.edu.ng
*Telex:* 57241 ZARABU NIG *Cable:* Unibello
    Press Zaria
*Key Personnel*
Man Dir, Editorial, Rights & Permissions: Saidu
    H Adamu
Editorial: George Ibrahim
Production: Oko Sunday
Marketing: Onwuaha I Sunday
Founded: 1974
Publishing & printing.
Subjects: Biography, Education, Environmental
    Studies, Government, Political Science, History,
    Law, Literature, Literary Criticism, Essays, Sci-
    ence (General), Social Sciences, Sociology,
    Sports, Athletics, Technology, Veterinary Sci-
    ence
ISBN Prefix(es): 978-125


**Albah Publishers+**
PO Box 6177, Bompai, Kano
*Cable:* Albah Kano
*Key Personnel*
Chairman, Editorial: Bashari F Roukbah
Sales & Publicity Manager: Idris A Muhammad
Production: Basiru Ahmad
Founded: 1978
Subjects: Education
ISBN Prefix(es): 978-2380
*Parent Company:* Elbash Limited
*Associate Companies:* Brunswick Publishing Co,
    PO Box 555, Lawrenceville, VA 23868, United
    States
Subsidiaries: Albah Research Centre
*Bookshop(s):* Baban Layi, Gyadi-Gyadi, Zariya
    Rd, Kano


**Alliance West African Publishers & Co**
Orindingbin Estate, New Aketan Layout, Oyo
Mailing Address: PMB 1039, Oyo
*Tel:* (085) 230798
*Key Personnel*
Chairman, Man Dir: Chief M O Ogunmola
Sales: L Oyeniji
Publicity & Permissions: Kehinde Ogunmola
Founded: 1971
Subjects: Biography, Ethnicity, Foreign Countries,
    History, How-to, Science (General)


**Aromolaran Publishing Co Ltd+**
Ibadan, Oyo State
Mailing Address: PO Box 1800, Ibadan, Oyo
    State
*Tel:* (02) 24392
*Telex:* 31158NG
*Key Personnel*
Man Dir: Dr Gabriel Adekunle Aromolaran
Sales: Mrs V M Aromolaran
Founded: 1970
Subjects: Art, Biography, How-to, Poetry, Reli-
    gion - Other, Science (General)
ISBN Prefix(es): 978-127


**Awoko**, *imprint of* Adebara Publishers Ltd


**Black Academy Press+**
Owerri, Imo State
Mailing Address: PO Box 255, Owerri, Imo State
*Tel:* (083) 230606; (083) 232606 *Cable:*
    BAPRESS
*Key Personnel*
Man Dir: Dr S Okechukwu Mezu
Founded: 1970
Subjects: Biography, History, Nonfiction (Gen-
    eral), Poetry
ISBN Prefix(es): 978-150
*Parent Company:* Mezu International Ltd, 6 Mezu
    Lane, Owerri, Imo State
*Associate Companies:* Black Academy Press Inc
*Orders to:* PO Box 66142, Baltimore, MD 21239,
    United States


**Book Representation & Publishing Co Ltd**
Agodi/Loyola College Rd, PMB 5349, Ibadan
    Oyo State
*Tel:* (022) 710242
*Key Personnel*
Executive Chairman, Dir: Chief B A Ajayi
Dirs: Chief M A Ajasin; Chief R F Fasoranti;
    Chief Funso Afelumo; Chief 'Bola Ige
General Manager: 'Bisi Taiwo
Administrative Manager: A L Salawu
Founded: 1973
Subjects: Education
ISBN Prefix(es): 978-172
*Associate Companies:* Circle Books Ltd, Ibadan


**CEM Publishers Ltd**
4 Yemi Ogunniyi St, Ajao Estate, Anthony Vil-
    lage, Lagos
Mailing Address: PO Box 4267, Lagos
ISBN Prefix(es): 978-176


**Cross Continent Press Ltd+**
PO Box 282, Yaba, Lagos State
*Tel:* (01) 862437 *Fax:* (01) 685679 *Cable:*
    Croconpres Yaba, Lagos
*Key Personnel*
Man Dir: Dr T C Nwosu
Editorial: Prof Theo Vincent
Production: Kess Nwagwu
Publicity: Miss A A Ikeme
Marketing: Miss P N Ikekwem
Sales Coordinator: Dr J O Enwerem
General Consultant: Prof E J Nwosu
Founded: 1974
Subjects: Biography, Fiction, How-to, Nonfiction
    (General), Poetry


ISBN Prefix(es): 978-134
*Parent Company:* Tanhigh Holdings Ltd
*Associate Companies:* Vista Books Ltd
Subsidiaries: Editorial Consultancy & Agency
    Services
*Branch Office(s)*
Senator E P Echeruo, Executive Director, PO Box
    2273, Owerri, Imo State
*Showroom(s):* 59 Awolowo Rd, SW Ikoyi, Lagos,
    Nigeria
*Orders to:* 59 Awolowo Rd, SW Ikoyi, Lago


**CSS Bookshops+**
Division of CSS Limited
19 Broad St, Lagos
Mailing Address: PO Box 174, Lagos
*Tel:* (01) 2633081; (01) 2637009; (01) 2637023;
    (01) 2633010 *Fax:* (01) 2637089
*E-mail:* cssbookshops@skannet.com.ng *Cable:*
    BOOKSHOPS
*Key Personnel*
Chief Executive: Kola Olaitan
Secretary: Dotun Adegboyega
Subjects: Biography, Ethnicity, Foreign Countries,
    History, Law, Medicine, Nursing, Dentistry,
    Nonfiction (General), Religion - Other, Science
    (General)
ISBN Prefix(es): 978-143; 978-2951; 978-32292


**Daily Times of Nigeria Ltd (Publication
    Division)**
3, 5 & 7 Kakawa St, Marina, Lagos
Mailing Address: Lateef Jakande Rd, Agidingbi,
    PMB, 21340 Ikeja, Lagos
*Tel:* (01) 4977280 *Fax:* (01) 4977284
*Web Site:* www.dailytimesofnigeria.com
*Telex:* 21333 Times Ng *Cable:* Daily Times
    Lagos
*Key Personnel*
Chief Executive: Segun Osoba
Editorial: Faruk Mohammed
Sales: Funsho Akindele
Production: J M Teshola
Founded: 1925
Subjects: Foreign Countries
ISBN Prefix(es): 978-144; 978-2171
Subsidiaries: Times Press Ltd; Newsstand Agen-
    cies Limited
*Book Club(s):* Times Book Club


**Daystar Press (Publishers)+**
Daystar House, Ibadan, Oyo State
Mailing Address: PO Box 1261, Ibadan, Oyo
    State
*Tel:* (022) 412670
*Telex:* 31176
*Key Personnel*
Man Dir, Editorial, Rights & Permissions & Pub-
    licity: Phillip Adelakun Ladokun
Trade: James Akinboye
Marketing: Tunde Felix
Founded: 1962
Subjects: Ethnicity, Health, Nutrition, House &
    Home, Religion - Other
ISBN Prefix(es): 978-122


**Delta Publications (Nigeria) Ltd+**
172 Ogui Rd, Enugu, Enugu State
Mailing Address: PO Box 3606, Lagos
*Tel:* (042) 3606
*Key Personnel*
Man Dir, Rights & Permissions: C D E Onyeama
Editorial Dir: Mrs E O Onyeama
Sales: Nicholas Ohaekweiro; Ebere Nwadigbo
Production, Publicity: Miss Nwanneka Okwu
Founded: 1982
Subjects: Biography, Fiction
ISBN Prefix(es): 978-2335
*Bookshop(s):* Enugu Airport Bookshop
*Book Club(s):* The Delta Book Club

**ECWA Productions Ltd**
10 Kano Rd, Jos Plateau State
Mailing Address: PMB 2010, Jos Plateau State
*Tel:* (073) 53897; (073) 52230
*Telex:* 81120 Ecwap Ng
*Key Personnel*
Man Dir: Dr Philip S Usman
General Manager, Publications: Jonathan A Bab-
stunde
Challenge Publications is Publishing Division of
ECWA Productions Ltd.
Subjects: Education, Religion - Other
ISBN Prefix(es): 978-137
*Bookshop(s):* Challenge Bookshops

**Educational Research & Study Group**
c/o Professor Pai Obanya, Institute of Education,
University of Ibadan, Ibadan
*Key Personnel*
Man Dir: Areoye Oyebola
Founded: 1970
Subjects: Biography, Ethnicity, Foreign Countries,
History, How-to, Nonfiction (General), Religion
- Other, Science (General), Social Sciences,
Sociology
ISBN Prefix(es): 978-30054

**Egret Books**, *imprint of* Paperback Publishers Ltd

**Egret Stars Series**, *imprint of* Paperback
Publishers Ltd

**Ethiope Publishing Corporation+**
34 Murtala Mohammed St, Benin City, Bendel
State
Mailing Address: PMB 1192, Benin City, Bendel
State
*Tel:* (052) 253036
*Telex:* 41110NG *Cable:* Ethiope
*Key Personnel*
Sole Administrator: Rev P O Ross-Imienwanrin
Founded: 1970
Subjects: Fiction, Foreign Countries, History,
Law, Social Sciences, Sociology
ISBN Prefix(es): 978-123
Total Titles: 55 Print

**Evans Brothers (Nigeria Publishers) Ltd**
Jericho Rd, Ibadan, Oyo State
Mailing Address: PMB 5164, Ibadan, Oyo State
*Tel:* (022) 417570; (022) 417601; (022) 407626
*Telex:* 31104 Edbook *Cable:* EDBOOKS
IBADAN
*Key Personnel*
Man Dir: B O Bolodeoku
Sales Dir: S A Oke
General Manager: V A Aladejana
Founded: 1966
Membership(s): Nigerian Publishers Association
(NPA).
Subjects: Accounting, Agriculture, Child Care
& Development, Civil Engineering, Drama,
Theater, Economics, Education, Electronics,
Electrical Engineering, Environmental Stud-
ies, Fiction, Geography, Geology, Government,
Political Science, History, Journalism, Law,
Literature, Literary Criticism, Essays, Manage-
ment, Mathematics, Medicine, Nursing, Den-
tistry, Philosophy, Romance, Science (General),
Self-Help, Social Sciences, Sociology, Sports,
Athletics, Technology
ISBN Prefix(es): 978-167; 978-020
*Associate Companies:* Evans Brothers Ltd, UK,
United Kingdom
*Branch Office(s)*
Kaduna
Lagos
Owerri

**Olaiya Fagbamigbe Ltd (Publishers)**
11 Methodist Church Rd, POB 14, Akure

Mailing Address: PO Box 1176, Agodi Gate,
Ibadan
*Tel:* (034) 2075 *Cable:* Fagbamigbe Akure
*Key Personnel*
Man Dir: Mrs M E Fagbamigbe
Editor: Yemi Fagbamigbe
Publicity: Gbenga Fagbamigbe
Rights & Permissions: Yetunde Fagbamigbe
Founded: 1976
Specialize in children's books, novels & text-
books.
Subjects: Education
ISBN Prefix(es): 978-164
*Warehouse:* New Ife Rd, PO Box 1176, Agodi
Gate, Ibadan

**Fountain Series**, *imprint of* Paperback Publishers
Ltd

**Fourth-Dimension Publishers**, *imprint of* Fourth
Dimension Publishing Co Ltd

**Fourth Dimension Publishing Co Ltd+**
Fourth Dimension Plaza, 16 Fifth Ave, City Lay-
out, PMB 01164, Enugu 400001
*Tel:* (042) 459969 *Fax:* (042) 456904
*E-mail:* info@fdpbooks.com; fdpbook@aol.com
*Web Site:* www.fdpbooks.com
*Key Personnel*
Chief Executive & Rights & Permissions: Mrs
Oby Nwankwo
General Manager: Jeremiah O Udochu
*E-mail:* jerryudochu@yahoo.com
Publishing & Editorial: Eva Igwilo
Production: Carolene Okorafor
Founded: 1976
Membership(s): Nigerian Publishers' Association
(NPA); African Publishers' Network (APNET);
Nigerian Book Foundation (NBF); International
Publishers' Association (IPA).
Subjects: Biography, Business, Cookery, Educa-
tion, Fiction, Government, Political Science,
Law, Social Sciences, Sociology
ISBN Prefix(es): 978-156
Number of titles published annually: 100 Print
Total Titles: 1,555 Print
Imprints: Fourth-Dimension Publishers
Foreign Rep(s): African Books Collective Ltd
(Europe, US)
Foreign Rights: African Books Collective Ltd
(Europe, US)
*Showroom(s):* ABC Ltd, 27 Park End St, Oxford
OX1 1HU, United Kingdom, Contact: Justin
Cox
*Warehouse:* ABC Ltd, Unite 3, Off Pytts Lane,
Burford, Oxon OX18 4SJ, United Kingdom,
Contact: Mary Jay
*Distribution Center:* World Bank Publishers, Mar-
keting Division (Nigeria)
*Orders to:* ABC Ltd, 27 Park End St, Oxford
OX1 1HU, United Kingdom

**Gangan**, *imprint of* Adebara Publishers Ltd

**Gbabeks Publishers Ltd**
L16 Ibadan St, Kaduna
Mailing Address: PO Box 3538, Kaduna, Kaduna
State
*Tel:* (062) 217976
*Key Personnel*
Man Dir: Tayo Ogunbekun
Founded: 1982
Membership(s): National Publishers Association.
Subjects: Education, Language Arts, Linguistics,
Science (General), Social Sciences, Sociology
ISBN Prefix(es): 978-2416

**Goldland Business Co Ltd+**
85 Saint Finbarrs College Rd, Akoka, Lagos
Mailing Address: PO Box 2541, Yaba, Lagos
*Tel:* (01) 8023179087; (01) 821203

*E-mail:* goldland@consultant.com
*Key Personnel*
Author & International Rights Contact: Dr
Jonathan A O Ifechukwu
Founded: 1982
Business consultants, researchers, trainers & pub-
lishers
Specialize in publishing books in business & re-
lated fields.
Subjects: Business, Finance, Government, Politi-
cal Science, How-to, Management, Marketing,
Technology
ISBN Prefix(es): 978-30035
Number of titles published annually: 1 Print
Total Titles: 8 Print

**Heritage Books+**
2-8 Calcutta Crescent, Gate 1, 101251 Apapa,
Lagos
Mailing Address: PO Box 610, 101251 Apapa,
Lagos
*Tel:* (01) 5871333; (01) 5871333
*E-mail:* obw@infoweb.abs.net
*Key Personnel*
Editor: Naiwu Osahon
Senior Editor, Rights & Permissions: Bakin Ku-
nama
Publicity: Edia Apolo
Founded: 1971
Subjects: Ethnicity, Fiction, Nonfiction (General),
Poetry, Pan-Africanism
ISBN Prefix(es): 978-2358
*Associate Companies:* Third World First Publica-
tions
Imprints: Heritage Series; Obobo Series; Oyoyo
Series
Subsidiaries: Obobo Books
*Bookshop(s):* Heritage (The Bookshop), PO Box
930, 101251 Apapa, Lagos *Tel:* (01) 5871 333
*E-mail:* obw@infoweb.abs.net

**Heritage Series**, *imprint of* Heritage Books

**Hudanuda Publishing Co Ltd+**
PO Box 984, Zaria, Kaduna State
*Tel:* (069) 5141
*Key Personnel*
Man Dir: Abdullahi Khalil
Founded: 1981
Membership(s): Nigerian Publishers Association
(NPA).
Subjects: Literature, Literary Criticism, Essays
ISBN Prefix(es): 978-2368
*Associate Companies:* Hodder & Stoughton Pub-
lishers, Mill Rd, Dunton Green, Sevenoaks,
Kent TN13 2YA, United Kingdom
*Branch Office(s)*
Islamic Publsihing Co, Kukuru Byepass, Jos
Dal Arabia Publishing Co Ltd, Kano
*Showroom(s):* Zangon Shanu, Samaru, Zaria
*Bookshop(s):* No 28 Sobon Gari, Zaria
*Warehouse:* Zangon Shanu, PO Box 984, Zaria,
Kaduna State

**Ibadan University Press+**
PMB 16, University of Ibadan Post Office,
Ibadan, Oyo State
*Tel:* (022) 400550; (022) 400614 (ext 1244, 1042,
1032, 1093) *Cable:* Univpress Ibadan
*Key Personnel*
Head of Marketing: Bisi Ogunleye
Founded: 1952
Subjects: Agriculture, Ethnicity, Foreign Coun-
tries, History, Law, Medicine, Nursing, Den-
tistry, Philosophy, Psychology, Psychiatry, Sci-
ence (General), Social Sciences, Sociology,
Technology
ISBN Prefix(es): 978-121

**Institute of African Studies, Onyeka, A**
University of Nigeria, Nsukka
*Tel:* (022) 400550; (022) 400614 (ext 12444)

*Key Personnel*
Dir, Editorial, Rights & Permissions: Prof Bolanle
  Awe
Editorial, Sales & Production: Dele Layiwola
Founded: 1962
Subjects: Ethnicity
ISBN Prefix(es): 978-2450; 978-31426

## International Publishing & Research
### Company+
PO Box 1210, Festac Town, Lagos
*Tel:* (080) 2317-5915 *Fax:* (080) 4213 2351
*Key Personnel*
Executive Chairman: Dr M J A Iginla
Founded: 1990
Subjects: Developing Countries, Government, Po-
  litical Science, Philosophy, Publishing & Book
  Trade Reference, Social Sciences, Sociology,
  Women's Studies
ISBN Prefix(es): 978-30855; 978-2438
*Parent Company:* Ipreco Group of Companies
Subsidiaries: Unity Publishing & Research Co
  Ltd
*Shipping Address:* 711 Road B Close, H 33 Fes-
  tac Town, Lagos

## JAD Publishers Ltd+
40 Adamson St, Keta, Victoria Island, Lagos
Mailing Address: PO Box 72320, Victoria Island,
  Lagos
Founded: 1989
Subjects: Behavioral Sciences, Biography, Bio-
  logical Sciences, Developing Countries, Eco-
  nomics, Environmental Studies, Government,
  Political Science, History, Law, Mathematics,
  Social Sciences, Sociology
ISBN Prefix(es): 978-2863

**Kakaki**, *imprint of* Adebara Publishers Ltd

## Kola Sanya Publishing Enterprise
2 Epe Rd, Oke-Owa, Ijebu-Ode
Mailing Address: PMB 2099, Ijebu-Ode
*Tel:* (037) 432638
*Key Personnel*
Man Dir: Chief K Osunsanya
Subjects: How-to, Nonfiction (General), Science
  (General)
ISBN Prefix(es): 978-171

**Lantern Books**, *imprint of* Literamed
  Publications Nigeria Ltd

## Literamed Publications Nigeria Ltd+
Plot 45, Alausa Bus Stop, Oregun Rd, PMB
  1068, Ikeja
*Tel:* (01) 4962512; (01) 4935258 *Fax:* (01)
  4972217
*E-mail:* information@lanternbooks.com
*Web Site:* www.lantern-books.com
*Key Personnel*
Production Manager: M O Dawodu
Publishing Dir: L A Aladesuyi
Finance Dir: S O Ayorinde
Founded: 1969
Membership(s): the Nigeria Publishers Associa-
  tion (NPA).
Subjects: Education, Government, Political Sci-
  ence, Social Sciences, Sociology
ISBN Prefix(es): 978-142
Number of titles published annually: 25 Print
Total Titles: 120 Print
Imprints: Lantern Books

## Longman Nigeria Plc
52 Oba Akran Ave, PMB 21036, Ikeja, Lagos
  State
*Tel:* (01) 497 89259 *Fax:* (01) 496 4370
*E-mail:* longman@infoweb.abs.net
*Telex:* 26639 longman ng *Cable:* Longman Ikeja

*Key Personnel*
Man Dir & Chief Executive: Abiodun Olowoniyi
Executive Dir (Northern Area Operations): Alhaji
  Musa Halliru
Deputy Chief Executive: Azed Echebiri
Marketing Dir: Dan Obidiegwu
Founded: 1961
Subjects: Biography, Ethnicity, Fiction, History,
  Nonfiction (General), Poetry, Psychology, Psy-
  chiatry, Religion - Other, Science (General),
  Social Sciences, Sociology, Technology
ISBN Prefix(es): 978-139

**Merryland**, *imprint of* Joe-Tolalu & Associates

## Thomas Nelson (Nigeria) Ltd+
2 Kofo Abayomi Ave, Apapa, Lagos
Mailing Address: PO Box 336, Apapa, Lagos
*Tel:* (01) 961452
*Telex:* 26736 *Cable:* NELPITMAN IKEJA
*Key Personnel*
Executive Chairman Chief: C O Taiwo
General Manager: A Fasemore
Marketing Dir: L Solarin
Editor, Science: M O Omotoye
Editor, Humanities: F O Bada
Founded: 1965
Also acts as publishers for (NERDC) Nigerian
  Education Research & Development Council &
  the University of Lagos Press.
Subjects: Fiction, Nonfiction (General), Science
  (General), Social Sciences, Sociology
ISBN Prefix(es): 978-126
*Parent Company:* The Thomson Corp, Toronto
  Dominion Bank Tower, Suite 2706, PO Box
  24, Toronto Dominion Centre, Toronto, ON
  M5K 1A1, Canada
*Associate Companies:* University Publishing Co
*Branch Office(s)*
Edo Textile Mills Rd, Benin City, Edo State
120, Orlu Rd, Owerri 3

## New Africa Publishing Company Ltd
PO Box 1178, Owerri, Imo State
*Tel:* (083) 231891
*Key Personnel*
Chairman & Man Dir: H K Offonry
Dir: S O Igwe; B E Ogbuagu
Founded: 1981
Subjects: Art, Biography, Business, Education,
  Finance, Human Relations, Humor, Law, Man-
  agement
ISBN Prefix(es): 978-2357

## New Era Publishers+
PO Box 27720, Agodi, Ibadan
*Tel:* (022) 715706
*Key Personnel*
Executive Chairman: Prof O Imoagene
Founded: 1991
Also acts as consultants.
Subjects: Fiction, Science (General)
ISBN Prefix(es): 978-2853
*Parent Company:* New-Era Holdings Ltd
*Associate Companies:* New-Era Equippers; Petro-
  Allied Services Ltd
Subsidiaries: New-Era Consultants Ltd
Distributed by Africa Book Centre (UK)

## New Horn Press Ltd
PO Box 4138, Agodi Gate, Ibadan
*Tel:* (02) 41 29 72
*Key Personnel*
Chairman: Dr Abiola Irele
Senior Editor, Rights & Permissions: Mrs Bassey
  Irele
Founded: 1974
Subjects: Fiction, How-to, Nonfiction (General),
  Poetry
ISBN Prefix(es): 978-2266

## Nigerian Environmental Study Team
Oluokun St, Bodija, Ibadan
Mailing Address: University of Ibadan, PO Box
  5297, Ibadan
*Tel:* (02) 8102644; (02) 8105167 *Fax:* (02)
  8102644
*E-mail:* nesting@nest.org.ng
ISBN Prefix(es): 978-31203

## Nigerian Institute of Advanced Legal Studies
University of Lagos Campus, Akoka, PMB
  12820, Lagos
*Tel:* (01) 821752; (01) 821711; (01) 821753
  *Fax:* (01) 497 6076; (01) 825558; (09) 234
  6505
*Telex:* 27506
Subjects: Law
ISBN Prefix(es): 978-31963

## Nigerian Institute of International Affairs
13/15 Kofo Abayomi Rd, Victoria Island, Lagos
Mailing Address: GPO Box 1727, Lagos
*Tel:* (01) 61 56 06; (01) 61 56 07; (01) 61 56 09;
  (01) 61 56 10 *Fax:* (01) 61 64 04; (01) 61 63
  60
*E-mail:* niia@ric.nig.com
*Telex:* 22638 *Cable:* INTERNATIONS LAGOS
*Key Personnel*
Ag Dir-General Editorial: Prof R A Akindele
Editorial: Dr Bola Akinterinwa; Prof Bassey Ate;
  Dr Cyril Obi; Dr R O Olaniyan
Marketing & Sales: E A Ude
Founded: 1961
Established as an independent, nonofficial, non-
  political & nonprofit making organization. In
  August 1991, the Institute was taken over by
  the Nigerian government.
Encourage & facilitate the understanding of in-
  ternational affairs; circumstances, conditions
  & attitudes of foreign countries & their peo-
  ple. Provide & disseminate information upon
  international questions, as we also promote
  the study & investigation of such international
  questions through such fora as conferences,
  lectures, discussions, to compliment our publications, journals & records.
Subjects: Economics, Law
ISBN Prefix(es): 978-2276
Imprints: African Books Collective Ltd

## Nigerian Trade Review
10, Makinde St, Alausa, Ikeja, Lagos State
Mailing Address: PO Box 427, Ikeja, Lagos State
*Tel:* (01) 961147
*Key Personnel*
Man Dir: Chief P A Dawodu
Founded: 1958
ISBN Prefix(es): 978-2242

## Northern Nigerian Publishing Co Ltd+
Gaskiya Bldg, Zaria, Kaduna State
Mailing Address: PO Box 412, Zaria, Kaduna
  State
*Tel:* (069) 32087
*Telex:* 75243
*Key Personnel*
Man Dir: Hussain Hayat
Man Editor: Muhammad Abubakar
Marketing Manager: Aliyu Haruna
Sales Manager: Johanna Madaki
Founded: 1966
Membership(s): Nigerian Publishers Association.
Subjects: Nonfiction (General), Poetry, Regional
  Interests, Religion - Other
ISBN Prefix(es): 978-169
*Parent Company:* Gaskiya Corp Ltd
*Branch Office(s)*
Kano, Kaduna & Jos

## NPS Educational Publishers Ltd (Nigeria
### Publishers Services)+
South West Ring Rd, off Akinyemi Way, Ibadan
Mailing Address: PO Box 62, Ibadan

*Tel:* (02) 2316006; (803) 370-0838
*Key Personnel*
Chairman & Man Dir: Chief Duro Otesanya
General Manager: Dr Isaac Muyiwa-Ojo
Also distributors.
Membership(s): Nigeria Publishers Association.
Subjects: Mathematics, Science (General)
ISBN Prefix(es): 978-2556
Number of titles published annually: 13 Print
Total Titles: 32 Print
*Branch Office(s)*
37A Omeagana St, off Modebe Ave, PO Box 4073, Onitsha *Tel:* (046) 413774
BB2 Old Jos Rd, PO Box 722, Zaria *Tel:* (069) 34170

**Nwamife Publishers Ltd+**
10, Ibiam St, Uwani, Enugu, Anambra State
Mailing Address: POB 480, Enugu, Anambra State
*Tel:* (042) 338454 *Cable:* Nwamife Enugu
*Key Personnel*
Chairman: Dr Felix C Adi
Sales, Production, Publicity: Samuel Umesike
Editorial, Rights & Permissions: Dr Nina Mba
Founded: 1970
Subjects: Biography, Education, Ethnicity, Fiction, History, How-to, Law, Nonfiction (General), Poetry, Science (General)
ISBN Prefix(es): 978-124

**Obafemi Awolowo University Press Ltd+**
Obafemi Awolowo University, Ile-Ife, Oyo State
Mailing Address: PMB 004, OAU Post Office, Ile-Ife
*Tel:* (036) 230290-9; (036) 230284
*Telex:* AVPL *Cable:* PRESS AWOVARSITY
*Key Personnel*
General Manager: Akin Fatokun
Editorial: Stephen Eyeh
Production: Isola Akinremi
Marketing: T A Kudoro
Founded: 1968
Specializes in professional texts.
Membership(s): International Publishers Association; National Publishers Association.
Subjects: Biography, Education, Ethnicity, History, Law, Medicine, Nursing, Dentistry, Philosophy, Religion - Other, Social Sciences, Sociology
ISBN Prefix(es): 987-136
Number of titles published annually: 6 Print
Total Titles: 100 Print
Foreign Rep(s): ABC London (Europe, US)

**Obobo Books+**
2/8 Calcutta Crescent, Gate 4, Apapa, 101251 Lagos
Mailing Address: PO Box 610, Apapa, 101251 Lagos
*Tel:* (01) 871333; (01) 875389
*E-mail:* obw@infoweb.abs.net
*Key Personnel*
Chief Executive: Ms Osahon Obobo
Editorial: Bakin Kunama
Sales, Publicity: Edia Apolo
Production: Edun Osahon
Founded: 1981
Also produce the television program *Obobo Playhouse.*
Subjects: Biography, Fiction, History, Coloring books
ISBN Prefix(es): 978-186
Number of titles published annually: 3 Print
Total Titles: 106 Print
*Parent Company:* Heritage Books, 2, Culcutta Crescent, Gate 4, PO Box 610 Apapa, 101251 Lagos
*Associate Companies:* Third World First Publications
*Bookshop(s):* Heritage, PO Box 930, 2-8 Calcutta Crescent, Gate 1, Apapa, 101251 Lagos

**Obobo Series,** *imprint of* Heritage Books

**Ogunsanya Press, Publishers and Bookstores Ltd**
64, Agbeni St, Ibadan, Oyo State
Mailing Address: PO Box 95, Ibadan, Oyo State
*Tel:* (022) 310924 *Cable:* Pombapress
*Key Personnel*
Man Dir, Editorial, Rights & Permissions: Chief Lucas Justus Popo-Ola Ogunsanya
Sales & Publicity: E A Faleke
Production: A S Banjo
Founded: 1970
Subjects: Geography, Geology, History, Language Arts, Linguistics, Mathematics, Science (General), Social Sciences, Sociology
ISBN Prefix(es): 978-170
*Branch Office(s)*
Popo-Ola Jubilee Lodge, Oke Imoru, PO Box 155, Ijebu Ode, Ogun State

**Onibon-Oje Publishers**
Felele Layout, Molete, Ibadan
Mailing Address: PO Box 3109, Ibadan
*Tel:* (022) 313956
*Telex:* 31657 Bonoje NG
*Key Personnel*
Chairman: Gabriel Onibonoje
Man Dir: J Olu Onibonoje
Founded: 1958
Subjects: Biography, Ethnicity, Fiction, Foreign Countries, History, How-to, Nonfiction (General), Poetry, Religion - Other, Science (General), Social Sciences, Sociology
ISBN Prefix(es): 978-145
*Branch Office(s)*
Benin City
Ikot Ekpene
Jos
Kano
Lagos
Onitsha
Sokoto
Zaria
*Bookshop(s):* SW8/77 Oke-Ado, Ibadan

**Opatoki Press,** *imprint of* Abisega Publishers (Nigeria) Ltd

**Oyoyo Series,** *imprint of* Heritage Books

**Paperback Publishers Ltd+**
Alafin Ave, Plot 7, Block 10, Oluyole Estate, SW, Ring Rd, Ibadan
Mailing Address: UI PO Box 14470, Ibadan
*Tel:* (022) 317363
*Key Personnel*
Man Dir: Agbo Areo
Sales Dir: S G Oyetunde
Founded: 1985
Membership(s): the Nigerian Publishers Association.
Subjects: Education, Fiction
ISBN Prefix(es): 978-2432
Imprints: Egret Books; Fountain Series; Egret Stars Series
*Branch Office(s)*
Dayspring House, 15 Ogunsefunmi Str, Anifowose IKEJA

**Riverside Communications+**
100C Elelenwo, GRA Phase 1, Port Harcourt, Rivers State
Mailing Address: PO Box 7390, Port Harcourt, Rivers State
*Tel:* (084) 334042 *Fax:* (084) 334042
*E-mail:* isoun@aol.com; rvsdcom@aol.com
*Key Personnel*
President: Prof T T Isoun
Executive Dir: Miriam Isoun
Founded: 1987

Subjects: Anthropology, Biological Sciences, Chemistry, Chemical Engineering, Cookery, Developing Countries, Environmental Studies, History, Language Arts, Linguistics, Mathematics, Medicine, Nursing, Dentistry, Nonfiction (General), Religion - Catholic, Religion - Protestant, Science (General), Veterinary Science
ISBN Prefix(es): 978-31226; 978-30333
*Parent Company:* Riverside Biotech Nigeria Limited 100
*U.S. Office(s):* Riverside Communications, 5575 Seminary Rd, No 104, Falls Church, VA 22041, United States, Contact: Miriam Isoun
*E-mail:* isoun@aol.com

**Saros International Publishers**
24, Aggrey Rd, Port-Harcourt
Mailing Address: PO Box 193, Port-Harcourt
*Tel:* (084) 331763 *Fax:* (084) 331763
*Key Personnel*
Publisher: Ken Saro-Wiwa
Founded: 1985
Subjects: Drama, Theater, Fiction, Literature, Literary Criticism, Essays, Poetry
ISBN Prefix(es): 978-2460
*Orders to:* African Books Collective Ltd, The Jam Factory, 27 Park End St, Oxford OX1 1KU, United Kingdom

**Spectrum Books Ltd+**
Ring Rd, Spectrum House, Ibadan
Mailing Address: PO Box 1319, Ibadan
*Tel:* (02) 2310058; (02) 2311215; (02) 2312705 *Fax:* (02) 2312705; (02) 2318502
*E-mail:* admin1@spectrumbooksonline.com
*Web Site:* www.spectrumbooksonline.com
*Key Personnel*
Chief Executive: Joop Berkhout
Editorial: Tony Igboekwe
Sales & Publicity: Edgman Igbinosun
Founded: 1978
Subjects: Education, Fiction
ISBN Prefix(es): 978-029
*Associate Companies:* Safari Books (Export) Ltd, 17 Bond St, 1st Floor, St Helier, Jersey, Channel Islands, United Kingdom
Distributed by ABC Oxford

**Tabansi Press Ltd+**
135 Awka Rd, Onitsha, Anambra State
Mailing Address: PO Box 243, Onitsha, Anambra State
*Tel:* (046) 211661; 08033243783; 08033418218
*Key Personnel*
Chief Executive: F N Tabansi
Deputy Chief Executive: P O Tabansi
Editor: Angus Abalum
Author: M O Odiaka
Founded: 1955
Printer & publisher. Specialize in educational book publishing.
Subjects: Government, Political Science, Religion - Other, Science (General), Social Sciences, Sociology
Number of titles published annually: 50,000 Print
Total Titles: 2,500,000 Print

**Tana Press Ltd & Flora Nwapa Books Ltd+**
2A, Menkiti Lane, Ogui, Enugu
Mailing Address: PO Box 62, Enugu
*Tel:* (042) 338857
*Telex:* 51164 Lake NG *Cable:* TANA
*Key Personnel*
Man Dir, nee Nwapa: Flora Nwakuche
Editorial: Dipl Ing Nina Mba
Production: E N Benyeogo; M A Ubah
Founded: 1979
*Rights & Permissions:* Tana Press, Ltd, Books Ltd.
Subjects: Fiction
ISBN Prefix(es): 978-2272

*Branch Office(s)*
PO Box 2, Oguta, Imo State
*Warehouse:* 22 Mbanugo, St Ogbete, Enugu
*Orders to:* Nigerian Publishers Services Ltd,
Trusthouse, PO Box 62, Ibadan
Three Continents Press, 1346 Connecticut Ave
NW, Washington, DC 20036, United States

**Joe-Tolalu & Associates+**
PO Box 3333, Mapo Post Office, Ibadan, Oyo
State
*Tel:* (01) 4925078
*Key Personnel*
Man Dir: Tosin Awolalu
Founded: 1983
Also acts as literary agent & publishing consultant.
Subjects: Biography, Humor, Religion - Other,
Travel
ISBN Prefix(es): 978-2415
Imprints: Merryland
Subsidiaries: Interprint Services
Divisions: Booktrust
Distributor for Delphi Publications; New Pen
Publishing; Pelins Ltd

**University of Lagos Press+**
PO Box 132, Unilag PO, Akoka, Lagos
*Tel:* (01) 825048 *Fax:* (01) 825048
*Telex:* 21210 *Cable:* UNILAG PRESS, LAGOS
*Key Personnel*
Dir: Mrs B A Awere
Editor: Bukola Olugasa *E-mail:* bukiolu@yahoo.
com
Founded: 1980
Europe & UK.
Subjects: Biography, Education, Ethnicity, Foreign
Countries, Human Relations, Law, Medicine,
Nursing, Dentistry, Social Sciences, Sociology
ISBN Prefix(es): 978-2264; 978-017
Distributed by African Books Collective
*Showroom(s):* Marketing Unit, Commercial Rd,
Unilag Akoka, Yaba, Lagos

**University Publishing Co+**
11, Central School Rd, Onitsha
Mailing Address: PO Box 386, Onitsha
*Tel:* (046) 230013 *Cable:* Varsity Box 386
Onitsha
*Key Personnel*
Dir: F C Ogbalu; W C Ifezue
Editorial: J Oranyeludike
Sales: D O Dandy
Production: I Nweke
Publicity: Christian Ogbalu
Permissions: Cecilia Ogbalu
Founded: 1959
Subjects: Biography, Ethnicity, Foreign Countries,
History, Nonfiction (General), Philosophy, Po-
etry, Religion - Other
ISBN Prefix(es): 978-160
*Associate Companies:* Cynako International Press,
Aba; Thomas Nelson (Nigeria) Ltd; African
Literature Bureau, Aba
*Branch Office(s)*
Azikiwe Rd, Aba
Varsity Bookshop/Press, Oye Agu Junction, Aba-
gana, Njikoka LGA
Afor Igwe, Ogidi
Oye Olisa Ogbunike, Onitsha-Enugu Rd, Awka
Eke-Amawbia, Awka
64 New Market Rd, Onitsha
*Bookshop(s):* Varsity Bookshop/Press at: Oye-
Agu, Abagana, Njikoka LGA; Eke-Amawbia,
Amawbia, Awka LGA; Aba; Abiriba, Ohafia
LGA
*Orders to:* Varsity Bookshop, 64 New Market Rd,
Onitsha

**Vantage Publishers International Ltd+**
98A Samonda, Old Airport Area, Ibadan, Oyo
State

Mailing Address: PO Box 7669 Secretariat PO,
Ibadan
*Tel:* (022) 415341
*Key Personnel*
Chairman & Publisher: Mr 'Poju Amori
Executive Dir: Mr Adewale Abiodun Amori
Founded: 1983
Membership(s): International Scholary Publishers;
Specialize in scholarly journals for Research
Institutes & Faculty of Law & Publishing (edi-
torial & production consulting).
Subjects: Biblical Studies, Biography, Biological
Sciences, Business, Drama, Theater, Education,
English as a Second Language, Fiction, Gov-
ernment, Political Science, Language Arts, Lin-
guistics, Literature, Literary Criticism, Essays,
Nonfiction (General), Poetry, Public Adminis-
tration, Religion - Protestant, Social Sciences,
Sociology
ISBN Prefix(es): 978-2458
Subsidiaries: Vantage Paper & Stationeries
Divisions: Vantage Productions
*Bookshop(s):* 98A Airport Area, Ibadan, Oyo
State

**West African Book Publishers Ltd+**
One Babalola St, Mushin, Lagos
Mailing Address: Ilupeju Industrial Estate, PO
Box 3445, Lagos
*Tel:* (01) 960760; (01) 960764; (01) 825020; (01)
526616 *Fax:* (01) 619835
*Telex:* 26144 *Cable:* ACADPRESS
*Key Personnel*
Chairman: B A Idris Animashaun
Dir: Mrs A O Obadagbonyi
Editor: H O Mazi
Founded: 1967
Subjects: Advertising, Agriculture, Chemistry,
Chemical Engineering, Child Care & Develop-
ment, Economics, Geography, Geology, Gov-
ernment, Political Science, Human Relations,
Mathematics, Science (General)
ISBN Prefix(es): 978-153; 978-31973
*Associate Companies:* Academy Computers LTD;
Academy Press PLC; Lithotec LTD; Richware
Pottery LTD

**John West Publications Co Ltd+**
Acme Rd, Lagos
Mailing Address: PO Box 2416, Lagos
*Tel:* (01) 932011
*Telex:* 26446 wepal ng *Cable:* JAKPRESS
Founded: 1962
Subjects: Biography, How-to, Nonfiction (Gen-
eral)
ISBN Prefix(es): 978-163

# Norway

## General Information

*Capital:* Oslo
*Language:* Norwegian. There are two distinct
forms, Bokmal (sometimes called Riksmal) and
Nynorsk (formerly called Landsmal) whose rel-
ative importance has changed in recent years.
About 90% of Norwegian books are now pub-
lished in Bokmal and it is the medium of in-
struction in most schools. Danish and Swedish
are usually intelligible to speakers of Norwe-
gian
*Religion:* Predominantly Evangelical Lutheran
*Population:* 4.3 million
*Bank Hours:* 0830-1530 Monday-Friday; 0830-
1500 (summer)
*Shop Hours:* 0830 or 0900-1700 or 1800
Monday-Friday; 0830 or 0900-1400 or 1600
Saturday

*Currency:* 100 ore = 1 Norwegian krone
*Export/Import Information:* Member of the European Free Trade Association. No tariff on
books except children's picture books. Books
exempt from VAT. No duty on advertising.
No import license required. Nominal exchange
controls.
*Copyright:* UCC, Berne, Florence (see Copyright
Conventions, pg xi)

**Altera Forlag A/S**
Postboks 2657, St Hanshaugen, 0131 Oslo
*Tel:* 22569590 *Fax:* 22565088
ISBN Prefix(es): 82-7608; 82-90494; 82-990826

**Andresen & Butenschon AS+**
Tollbugt 3, 0107 Sentrum, Oslo
Mailing Address: PO Box 1153, 0107 Sentrum,
Oslo
*Tel:* (047) 23139240 *Fax:* (047) 22335805
*E-mail:* abforlag@abforlag.no
*Key Personnel*
Man Dir: Sverre Morkhagen
Publisher: Hans B Butenschon *E-mail:* hb@
abforlag.no
Founded: 1992
Subjects: Antiques, Architecture & Interior De-
sign, Art, Biography, History, How-to, Cultural
Heritage
ISBN Prefix(es): 82-7694; 82-91004
Number of titles published annually: 25 Print
Total Titles: 150 Print
*Distribution Center:* Sentraldistribusjon ANS, O
Aker vei 61, 0581 Oslo

**Ansgarboker**, *imprint of* Atheneum Forlag A/S

**Ariel Lydbokforlag+**
Postboks 1546 Vika, 0117 Oslo
*Tel:* 64943510 *Fax:* 64943510
*Key Personnel*
Chief Editor: Inger Schjoldager
Founded: 1988
Subjects: Education, Fiction, Poetry
ISBN Prefix(es): 82-7509

**Aschehoug Forlag**
Sehestedsgate 3, 0102 Oslo
Mailing Address: PO Box 363 Sentrum, 0102
Oslo
*Tel:* 22400400 *Fax:* 22206395
*E-mail:* epost@aschehoug.no
*Web Site:* www.aschehoug.no
Subjects: Antiques, Architecture & Interior De-
sign, Art, Business, Child Care & Develop-
ment, Economics, Education, Fiction, Garden-
ing, Plants, Health, Nutrition, History, How-to,
Language Arts, Linguistics, Law, Mathematics,
Philosophy, Poetry, Science (General), Self-
Help, Social Sciences, Sociology, Travel
*Parent Company:* H Aschehoug & Co (W Ny-
gaard) A/S

**H Aschehoug & Co (W Nygaard) A/S**
Sehestedsgate 3, 0164 Oslo
Mailing Address: PO Box 363, Sentrum, 0102
Oslo
*Tel:* 22400400 *Fax:* 22206395
*E-mail:* epost@aschehoug.no
*Web Site:* www.aschehoug.no *Cable:* ACO OSLO
*Key Personnel*
Man Dir & Publr: William Nygaard
Dir: Erik Holst
Dir, School Book Dept: Kari-Anne Haugen
Editorial: Marit Notaker; Irja Thorenfeldt
Rights & Permissions: Ivar Havnevik
Founded: 1872
Subjects: Antiques, Architecture & Interior De-
sign, Art, Business, Child Care & Develop-
ment, Economics, Education, Fiction, Garden-
ing, Plants, Health, Nutrition, How-to, Lan-
guage Arts, Linguistics, Law, Mathematics,

Philosophy, Poetry, Science (General), Science Fiction, Fantasy, Self-Help, Social Sciences, Sociology, Travel
ISBN Prefix(es): 82-03
Subsidiaries: Kunnskapsforlaget I/S (jointly owned with Gyldendal Norsk Forlag); Olaf Norlis Bokhandel A/S (jointly owned with Norake Skog A/S); Tano A/S Forlaget; Kirkelig Kulturverksted A/S; Universitetsforlaget A/S; Yrkesopplaring ANS; Oktober Forlag A/S; Lydbokforlaget A/S
*Book Club(s):* Den Norske Bokklubben A/S (with three other Norwegian publishers)

**Atheneum Forlag A/S+**
Mollerveien 4, 0182 Oslo
*Tel:* 23292072; 23291900 *Fax:* 23291901
*Key Personnel*
Executive Dir, Publisher, Rights & Permissions: Svenn Otto Brechan
Founded: 1934
Subjects: Art, Biography, Fiction, Poetry, Psychology, Psychiatry, Religion - Other
ISBN Prefix(es): 82-503; 82-7334
*Associate Companies:* Ansgarboker
Imprints: Ansgarboker
*Warehouse:* Ansgar/Atheneum, Nesset, 1433 Vinterbro

**Bladkompaniet A/S+**
Apotedergaten 12, 0180 Oslo
Mailing Address: Postboks 6974, St Olavs plass, 0130 Oslo
*Tel:* 24 14 68 00 *Fax:* 24 14 68 01
*E-mail:* bladkompaniet@bladkompaniet.no
*Web Site:* www.bladkompaniet.no
*Key Personnel*
Man Dir: Tor Erik Solberg
Administration Coordinator: Gro Gundersen
Secretary: Inger Lise Lovasen
Founded: 1915
Subjects: Fiction
ISBN Prefix(es): 82-509

**F Bruns Bokhandel og Forlag A/S**
Kongensgate 10, 7484 Trondheim
*Tel:* 73510022; 73509320 *Fax:* 73509320
*E-mail:* brunslb@online.no
*Key Personnel*
Dir: Fridthjov Brun
Founded: 1873
Subjects: Science (General), Technology
ISBN Prefix(es): 82-7028

**Cappelen akademisk forlag**
Postboks 9047, Groenland, 0133 Oslo
*Tel:* 22985800 *Fax:* 22985841
*Web Site:* www.cappelen.no/main/info.asp
*Key Personnel*
Man Dir: Kai Solheim
Subjects: Economics, Management, Nonfiction (General)
ISBN Prefix(es): 82-7037; 82-456

**J W Cappelens Forlag A/S**
Mariboesgt 13, 0183 Oslo
Mailing Address: Postboks 350, Sentrum, 0101 Oslo
*Tel:* (022) 365000 *Fax:* (022) 365040
*E-mail:* web@cappelen.no
*Web Site:* www.cappelen.no *Cable:* CAPPELEN
*Key Personnel*
Chairman: Sigmund Stromme
Man Dir: Sindre Guldvog
Editor-in-Chief: Per Glad
Publisher: Anders Heger
Editorial: Jan O Bruvik; Aase Gjerdrum; Ola Haugen; Tove Storsveel
Sales: Kirsti Soegstad
Production: Kjell Nordahl
Rights & Permissions: Kirsten Lier

Founded: 1829
Subjects: Fiction, Nonfiction (General), Religion - Other
ISBN Prefix(es): 82-02
*Parent Company:* Albert Bonniers Foerlag AB, Sweden
Subsidiaries: Bedriftsoekonomens Forlag A/S; Boksenteret A/S; Aventura Forlag A/S; Chr Grondahls Forlag A/S; Sentraldistribusson ANS
*Book Club(s):* Den Norske Bokklubben A/S (with three other Norwegian publishers)

**Credo,** *imprint of* Genesis Forlag

**N W Damm og Son A/S**
Fridtjof Nansens vei 14, 0055 Oslo
*Tel:* 24 05 10 00 *Fax:* 24 05 10 99
*E-mail:* post@egmont.no
*Web Site:* www.damm.no
*Key Personnel*
Man Dir: Tom H Jenssen *E-mail:* tom.harald.jenssen@damm.no
Founded: 1845
Subjects: Fiction, Nonfiction (General)
ISBN Prefix(es): 82-517
*Parent Company:* Egmont Group, Copenhagen, Denmark

**Det Norske Samlaget+**
JensBjelkes gate 12, 0506 Oslo
*Tel:* (022) 70 78 00 *Fax:* (022) 68 75 02
*E-mail:* det.norske@samlaget.no
*Web Site:* www.samlaget.no
*Key Personnel*
Man Dir: Audun Heskestad
Editorial, Rights & Permissions: Nina Refseth
Sales: Sjur Mossige
Production: Olav Stokkmo
Founded: 1868
Membership(s): Den norske Forleggerforening.
Subjects: Biography, Cookery, Education, Fiction, History, Humor, Literature, Literary Criticism, Essays, Nonfiction (General), Philosophy, Poetry, Religion - Other
ISBN Prefix(es): 82-521
Number of titles published annually: 200 Print
*Associate Companies:* Noregs Boklag L/L

**J W Eides Forlag A/S+**
Postboks 4081, Dreggen 5835 Bergen
Mailing Address: Sandbrugaten 11, Dreggen 5835 Bergen
*Tel:* (05) 32 90 40 *Fax:* (05) 31 90 18
*Web Site:* www.eideforlag.no
*Key Personnel*
Man Dir: Trine Kolderup Flaten
Subjects: Art, Education, Film, Video, History, Music, Dance, Radio, TV
ISBN Prefix(es): 82-514

**Elanders Publishing AS**
Brobekkvn 80, Sentrum, 0107 Oslo
Mailing Address: Postboks 1156, Sentrum, 0107 Oslo
*Tel:* 22636400 *Fax:* 22636594
*Key Personnel*
Publisher: Aina Thorstensen *Tel:* 22636281 *E-mail:* aina.thorstensen@elanders.no
Founded: 1844 (AS Fabritius)
Subjects: Chemistry, Chemical Engineering, Law, Maritime, Medicine, Nursing, Dentistry, Transportation
ISBN Prefix(es): 82-90545; 82-07; 82-7180
*Parent Company:* Elanders Norge AS
*Ultimate Parent Company:* Elanders AB

**Ex Libris Forlag A/S+**
Tordenskioldsgt 6B, 0055 Oslo
*Tel:* (022) 47 11 00 *Fax:* (022) 47 11 49
*E-mail:* nwd@egmont.no

*Key Personnel*
Publisher: Hagen Oyvind
Editor: Toruun Andersen
Founded: 1982
Subjects: Alternative, Cookery, Health, Nutrition, Human Relations, Humor, Publishing & Book Trade Reference
ISBN Prefix(es): 82-7384; 82-474; 82-90473

**Forlaget Fag og Kultur**
Biskop Jens Nilssons gate 5A, 0659 Oslo
Mailing Address: Postbox 6633 Etterstad, 0607 Oslo
*Tel:* (022) 23 30 24 00 *Fax:* (022) 23 30 24 04
*E-mail:* firmapost@fagogkultur.no
*Web Site:* www.fagogkultur.no
*Key Personnel*
Publisher: Mari Ettre Olsen
Founded: 1987
Subjects: Gardening, Plants, Language Arts, Linguistics, Science (General), Technology
ISBN Prefix(es): 82-11

**Fonna Forlag L/L**
St Olavs Plass 3, 0130 Oslo
Mailing Address: Postboks 6912, St Olavs Plass, 0130 Oslo
*Tel:* 22201303 *Fax:* 22201201
Founded: 1940
Subjects: Biography, Fiction, Poetry
ISBN Prefix(es): 82-513

**Fono Forlag+**
Postboks 169, 1361 Billingsted
*Tel:* 66846490 *Fax:* 66847507
*E-mail:* mail@fonoforlag.no
*Web Site:* www.fonoforlag.no
*Key Personnel*
General Manager: Halvor Haneborg *E-mail:* h.haneborg@fonoforlag.no
Membership(s): Norsk Forleggerforening.
Subjects: Education, Fiction, Humor, Literature, Literary Criticism, Essays, Mysteries, Nonfiction (General)
ISBN Prefix(es): 82-7844; 82-91171

**Genesis Forlag+**
Kongens gt 22, 0153 Oslo
Mailing Address: Postboks 1180 Sentrum, 0107 Oslo
*Tel:* (022) 31 02 40 *Fax:* (022) 31 02 05
*E-mail:* genesis@genesis.no
*Web Site:* www.genesis.no
*Key Personnel*
Publisher: Magne Lero
International Rights: Anne Mant Jordahl
Founded: 1996
Subjects: Biography, Health, Nutrition, Human Relations, Nonfiction (General), Psychology, Psychiatry, Religion - Protestant, Theology
ISBN Prefix(es): 82-476
*Parent Company:* Vaart Land
Imprints: Credo

**Glydendal Akademisk+**
Subsidiary of Gyldendal Norsk Forlag
Kristian IVs g 13, 0164 Oslo
Mailing Address: PO Box 6730, St Olavs Pl, 0130 Oslo
*Tel:* (022) 034300 *Fax:* (022) 034305
*E-mail:* akademisk@gyldendal.no
*Web Site:* www.gyldendal.no/akademisk
*Key Personnel*
Man Dir: Fredrik Nissen *E-mail:* fredrik.nissen@gyldendal.no
Founded: 1988
Subjects: Accounting, Business, Economics, Education, Finance, Government, Political Science, Health, Nutrition, Law, Medicine, Nursing, Dentistry, Philosophy, Psychology, Psychiatry, Social Sciences, Sociology
ISBN Prefix(es): 82-05
Number of titles published annually: 100 Print

**John Grieg Forlag AS**
Valkendorfs gt 1a, 5012 Bergen
Mailing Address: Postboks 248, 5001 Bergen
*Tel:* 55213181 *Fax:* 55218180 *Cable:* Bokgrieg
*Key Personnel*
Man Dir: Hermond J Berg Lindersen
Founded: 1721
Subjects: Fiction, Nonfiction (General), Sports,
   Athletics
ISBN Prefix(es): 82-533; 82-7129

**Gyldendal Norsk Forlag A/S+**
Sehestedsgt 4, 0130 Oslo
Mailing Address: Postboks 6860, St Olavs plass,
   0130 Oslo
*Tel:* 22034100 *Fax:* 22034105
*E-mail:* gnf@gyldendal.no
*Web Site:* www.gyldendal.no
*Telex:* 72880 Gyldn n *Cable:* Gyldendal
*Key Personnel*
Man Dir: Bjorgun Hysing
Dir, Marketing: Jorgen Klafstad
Dir, Educational: Paul Hedlund
Dir, Fiction: Bjarne Buset
Dir, Nonfiction & Children: Unni Fjesme
Dir, Legal: Torger Andersen
Dir, University Press: Fredrik Nissen
Rights & Permissions: Eva Lie-Nielsen
Founded: 1925
Subjects: Art, Biography, Fiction, Government,
   Political Science, History, How-to, Music,
   Dance, Philosophy, Poetry, Psychology, Psychi-
   atry, Religion - Other, Science Fiction, Fantasy,
   Social Sciences, Sociology
ISBN Prefix(es): 82-05
Subsidiaries: Kunnskapsforlaget I/S (jointly
   owned with H Aschehoug & Co A/S)
*Book Club(s):* Den Norske Bokklubben A/S (with
   three other Norwegian publishers)

**Hilt & Hansteen A/S+**
Fossveien 24b, 0554 Oslo
Mailing Address: Postboks 2062 G, 0505 Oslo
*Tel:* (022) 38 40 10 *Fax:* (022) 37 40 15
*Web Site:* hilt-hansteen.no
*Telex:* 72400 fotex n att: hiltoslo *Cable:*
   HILTOSLO
*Key Personnel*
Publisher: Bjorn Hansteen Fossum; Torstein Hilt
   *E-mail:* torstein.hilt@genrica.no
Founded: 1983
Subjects: Alternative, Health, Nutrition, Human
   Relations, Mysteries, Parapsychology, Self-
   Help
ISBN Prefix(es): 82-7413
*Book Club(s):* Bokklubben Energica A/S
*Orders to:* Forlagsentralen 1/S, Postboks 1, 1010
   Oslo

**Hjemmenes Forlag**
Postboks 25 Holmenkollen, 0324 Oslo
*Tel:* 22143151 *Fax:* 22920738
*Key Personnel*
Publisher: Yngve Woxholth
Subjects: Ethnicity, History
ISBN Prefix(es): 82-7006

**Kolibri Forlag A/S**
Postboks 33, Bygdoy, 0211 Oslo
*Tel:* (022) 438778 *Fax:* (022) 447740
*E-mail:* post@kolibriforlag.no
*Web Site:* www.kolibriforlag.no
ISBN Prefix(es): 82-7917; 82-90478

**Kunnskapsforlaget ANS**
Kristian Augustsgate 10, 0130 Oslo
Mailing Address: Postboks 6736 St Olvas plass,
   N 0130 Oslo
*Tel:* (022) 03 66 00 *Fax:* (022) 03 66 05
*E-mail:* kundeservice@kunnskapsforlaget.no
*Web Site:* www.kunnskapsforlaget.no

*Key Personnel*
Man Dir: Harald S Stromme
Sales Dir: Tor Hallaraker
Chief Editor: Petter Henricksen
Multimedia Man: Finn Jorgen Solberg
Production: Svein F Heige
Founded: 1975
ISBN Prefix(es): 82-573
*Parent Company:* H Aschehoug & Co A/S,
   Gyldendal Norsk Forlag; Gyldendal Norah For-
   lag ASA

**Libretto Forlag+**
Eilert Sundts Gate 32, 0259 Oslo
*Tel:* (022) 443011 *Fax:* (022) 443012
*Key Personnel*
Publisher: Tom Thorsteinsen *E-mail:* tomthor@
   online.no
Founded: 1991
ISBN Prefix(es): 82-91091; 82-7886

**Lunde Forlag AS+**
Sinsenveien 25, 0572 Oslo
*Tel:* (022) 00 73 50 *Fax:* (022) 00 73 73
*E-mail:* lunde@nlm.no
*Web Site:* www.lunde-forlag.no
*Key Personnel*
President & Publisher: Asbjorn Kvalbein
Production & International Rights: Reidun Lind-
   heim
Editor: Ingeborg Eidsvaag
Founded: 1905
Subjects: Biography, Education, Fiction, Poetry,
   Religion - Other, Theology
ISBN Prefix(es): 82-520
Number of titles published annually: 90 Print
Total Titles: 250 Print
*Book Club(s):* Perspektiv, 4604 Kristiansand
   *Tel:* 38 02 10 06

**Luther Forlag A/S**
Grensen 15, 0129 Oslo
Mailing Address: Postboks 6640, St Olavs Pl,
   0129 Oslo
*Tel:* (022) 33 06 08 *Fax:* (022) 42 10 00
*E-mail:* postkasse@lutherforlag.no
*Web Site:* www.lutherforlag.no
*Key Personnel*
Man Dir: Kurt Hjemdal; Asle Dingstad
   *E-mail:* asle.dingstad@lutherforlag.no
Founded: 1868
Subjects: Biography, Fiction, Religion - Protes-
   tant, Religion - Other
ISBN Prefix(es): 82-531
Number of titles published annually: 40 Print
Total Titles: 250 Print

**Ernst G Mortensens Forlag A/S+**
Kr Augustsgt 14, Majorstua, Oslo
Mailing Address: PO Box 5461, 0305 Majorstua
*Tel:* 22941000 *Fax:* 22113040
*Telex:* 77626 *Cable:* Pressmort
*Key Personnel*
Man Dir: Per Stokken
Editorial: Knut Enger; Solveig Hoysaeter
Sales: Egil Storaas
Information: Knut-Jorgen Erichsen
Advertising: R Marthinsen
Rights & Permissions: Per R Mortensen
Founded: 1933
ISBN Prefix(es): 82-527
Subsidiaries: NPS (Norsk Presseservice A/S);
   Forenede Trykkerier A/S

**NKI Forlaget**
Hans Burums vei 30, 1357 Bekkestua
Mailing Address: Postboks 111, 1319 Bekkestua
*Tel:* (067) 58 88 00 *Fax:* (067) 53 05 00
*E-mail:* post-fj@nki.no
*Web Site:* www.nki.no

*Key Personnel*
Publisher: Marit Anmarkrud
Sales & Marketing Manager: Randi Flugstad
Founded: 1967
Subjects: Chemistry, Chemical Engineering, Elec-
   tronics, Electrical Engineering, English as a
   Second Language, Environmental Studies,
   Mathematics, Mechanical Engineering, Physics,
   Transportation
ISBN Prefix(es): 82-562

**Norsk Bokreidingslag L/L**
Postboks 684, 5807 Bergen
*Tel:* 55301899 *Fax:* 55320356
*E-mail:* post@bodonihus.no
*Key Personnel*
Manager: Froydis Lehmann *Tel:* 55136942
   *E-mail:* fr-lehm@online.no
Founded: 1939
Subjects: Fiction, History, Language Arts, Lin-
   guistics, Poetry
ISBN Prefix(es): 82-90186; 82-7834
Number of titles published annually: 4 Print

**Novus Forlag+**
Herman Foss' Gate 19, 0171 Oslo
*Tel:* 2271 7450 *Fax:* 2271 8107
*E-mail:* novus@novus.no
*Web Site:* www.novus.no
*Key Personnel*
Publisher: Olav Rosset
Founded: 1972
Subjects: Education, Science (General)
ISBN Prefix(es): 82-7099
Total Titles: 300 Print

**Forlaget Oktober A/S**
Kristian Augusts gate 11, 0130 Oslo
Mailing Address: PO Box 6848, St Olavs plass,
   0130 Oslo
*Tel:* (022) 23 35 46 20 *Fax:* (022) 23 35 46 21
*E-mail:* oktober@oktober.no
*Web Site:* www.oktober.no
*Key Personnel*
Publisher: Geir Berdahl *Tel:* (022) 23 35 46 25
   *E-mail:* geir.berdahl@oktober.no
ISBN Prefix(es): 82-7094

**Omnipax,** *imprint of* Pax Forlag A/S

**Origo Forlag**
Postboks 28, 0905 Grorud, Oslo
*Tel:* 22160769 *Fax:* 22164837
*Key Personnel*
President: Leif-Runa R Forsth
Editor: Bodil Nordvik
ISBN Prefix(es): 82-597

**Pax Forlag A/S+**
Huitfeldtsgt 15, 0201 Oslo
Mailing Address: Postboks 2336 Solli, 0201 Oslo
*Tel:* (023) 136900 *Fax:* (023) 136919
*Key Personnel*
Man Dir: Bjorn Smith Simonsen
Editorial & Rights & Permissions: Birgit Bjerck
Founded: 1964
Subjects: Fiction, Nonfiction (General), Philoso-
   phy, Psychology, Psychiatry, Social Sciences,
   Sociology, Women's Studies
ISBN Prefix(es): 82-530
Imprints: Omnipax (children's books)

**Sambandet Forlag+**
Vestlandskes bokhandel, Vetrisalm, 1, 5014
   Bergen
*Tel:* 55317963 *Fax:* 55310944
*E-mail:* vestlandskes.bokhandel@c2i.net
*Key Personnel*
Publishing Dir: Ingar Hjelset
Founded: 1945
Subjects: Religion - Other
ISBN Prefix(es): 82-7752

**Erik Sandberg+**
Kongensgt 14, 0153 Oslo
*Tel:* 22335555 *Fax:* 22413562
*Telex:* 17580
*Key Personnel*
Chief Executive, Rights & Permissions: Trond
  Wikborg
Editorial: Arild Ronsen; Per Martinsen
Sales: Tor Nilsen
Production: Iril Kolle
Publicity: Solveig Thime
Founded: 1973
Subjects: Fiction, Nonfiction (General)
ISBN Prefix(es): 82-7316; 82-90160

**Sandviks Bokforlag+**
Strandsvingen 14, 4032 Stavanger
*Tel:* (051) 44 00 00 *Fax:* (051) 44 00 99
*Web Site:* www.sandviks.com
*Key Personnel*
President & Publisher: Marius Sandvik
Editorial Dir: Kitt Sandvik
Marketing Dir: Eli A Cantillon
Art Dir: Ingvild Forberg
Founded: 1965
Subjects: Health, Nutrition, Maritime, Medicine,
  Nursing, Dentistry
ISBN Prefix(es): 82-7106
Subsidiaries: Baby's First Book Club; Go'boken
  Book Club, Helsingborg, Sweden & Stavanger;
  The International Log Book, Bath (UK & Sta-
  vanger)
*U.S. Office(s):* Sandvik Publishing Ltd, 460 E
  Swedesford Rd, Suite 2030, Wayne, PA 19087,
  United States
*Warehouse:* DFU-huset, Figgjo

**Scandinavian University Press**, see
  Universitetsforlaget

**Schibsted Forlagene A/S+**
Subsidiary of Schibsted ASA
Apotekergt 12, 0180 Oslo
Mailing Address: Postboks 6974 St Olavs plass,
  0130 Sentrum, Oslo
*Tel:* 24 14 68 00 *Fax:* 24 14 68 01
*E-mail:* schibstedforlagene@schibstedforlagene.no
*Web Site:* www.schibstedforlagene.no
*Telex:* 71230 aft n
*Key Personnel*
Publisher: Vebjorn Rogne; Liv Rosjo Sande; Dag
  Lonsjo
Publishing Dir: Tor Erik Solberg
Founded: 1843
Subjects: Biography, Earth Sciences, How-to,
  Nonfiction (General), Travel
ISBN Prefix(es): 82-516
*Warehouse:* Forlagssentralen, Postboks 1 Furuset,
  1001 Oslo
*Orders to:* Forlagssentralen, Postboks 1 Furuset,
  1001 Oslo

**Snofugl Forlag+**
Radhusvegen 3, Melhus
Mailing Address: Postboks 95, 7221 Melhus
*Tel:* 72872411 *Fax:* 72871013
*E-mail:* snofugl@online.no
*Key Personnel*
Manager: Asmund Snofugl
Founded: 1972
Membership(s): Den Norske Forleggerforening.
Subjects: Biography, Fiction, Government, Politi-
  cal Science, History, Literature, Literary Criti-
  cism, Essays, Nonfiction (General), Poetry
ISBN Prefix(es): 82-7083
Total Titles: 150 Print
*Associate Companies:* A/S Bygdetrykk, 7084
  Melhus
*Warehouse:* Melhus skysstasjon, 7221 Melhus

**Solum Forlag A/S+**
Postboks 140 Skoyen, 0212 Oslo

*Tel:* (022) 50 04 00 *Fax:* (022) 50 14 53
*E-mail:* solumfor@online.no
*Web Site:* www.solumforlag.no
*Key Personnel*
Man Dir: Knut Endre Solum
Founded: 1974
Subjects: Disability, Special Needs, Fiction, Po-
  etry, Science (General), Educational materials,
  Humanities
ISBN Prefix(es): 82-560
Distributed by International Specialized Book
  Service (USA)

**Stabenfeldt A/S+**
NorSea Dusavik, Bygg 19, 4068 Stavanger
Mailing Address: Postboks 8054, 4068 Stavanger
*Tel:* (051) 84 54 00 *Fax:* (051) 84 54 91
*E-mail:* int.post@stabenfeldt.no
*Web Site:* www.stabenfeldt.no *Cable:* BOKORM
*Key Personnel*
Man Dir: Tor Tjeldflat
Marketing Dir: J O Skara Hansen
Founded: 1920
Subjects: Fiction, Nonfiction (General)
ISBN Prefix(es): 82-532
*Parent Company:* Bongs AB, Sweden
Divisions: Stabenfeldt AB

**Teknologisk Forlag**
Tordenskioldsgt 6B, 0055 Oslo
*Tel:* 22471100 *Fax:* 22471149
*Key Personnel*
Man Dir, Rights & Permissions: Rudolf Jenssen
Assistant Dir: Tom Harald Jenssen
Editorial Dir: Tore Egeberg
Sales Dir: Karl H Ormen
Founded: 1958
Subjects: Engineering (General), How-to, Philoso-
  phy, Science (General)
ISBN Prefix(es): 82-512

**Tell Forlag+**
Nilsemarka 5c, 1390 Vollen
Mailing Address: Postboks 62, 1390 Vollen
*Tel:* 66780918 *Fax:* 66900572
*E-mail:* tell@online.no
*Web Site:* www.tell.no
*Key Personnel*
Publisher: Tell-Chr Wagle
Founded: 1987
Subjects: Art, Crafts, Games, Hobbies, Dance,
  Educational Books, Textbooks, Theatre
ISBN Prefix(es): 82-7522
Number of titles published annually: 25 Print

**Tiden Norsk Forlag**
Kristian Augusts gt 12, Oslo
Mailing Address: Postboks 6704, St Olavs plass,
  0130 Oslo
*Tel:* (022) 23 32 76 60 *Fax:* (022) 23 32 76 97
*E-mail:* tiden@tiden.no
*Web Site:* www.tiden.no *Cable:* TIDEN
*Key Personnel*
Dir: Liv Lysaker
Editorial, Rights & Permissions: Per Bangsund;
  Bjorn Willadssen
Production: Torgeir Aass
Editor-in-Chief: Sindre Hovdenakk *Tel:* 23 32
  7674 *E-mail:* sindre.hovdenakk@tiden.no
Founded: 1933
Subjects: Fiction, Literature, Literary Criticism,
  Essays, Management, Nonfiction (General),
  Science Fiction, Fantasy
ISBN Prefix(es): 82-10; 82-990075
*Book Club(s):* Den Norske Bokklubben A/S (with
  three other Norwegian publishers)

**Universitetsforlaget+**
Sehesteds gt 3, 0105 Oslo
Mailing Address: Postboks 508, 0105 Oslo
*Tel:* (022) 24147500 *Fax:* (022) 24147501

*E-mail:* post@universitetsforlaget.no
*Web Site:* www.universitetsforlaget.no
*Telex:* 11896 Ufor N
  *Cable:* UNIVERSITYPRESS, OSLO
*Key Personnel*
Man Dir: Ms Siri Hatlen *Fax:* (022) 575354
  *E-mail:* sha@scup.no
Publishing Dir, Books: Ms Inger M Tellefsen
  *Tel:* 22575496 *Fax:* 22575352 *E-mail:* ite@
  scup.no
Publishing Dir, Journals: Mr Arne Henrik Frogh
  *Tel:* 22575349 *Fax:* 22575454 *E-mail:* afr@
  scup.no
Personnel Dir: Ms Randi Bauer *Tel:* 22575386
  *Fax:* 22575352 *E-mail:* rba@scup.no
Head of Marketing, Books: Ms Anne Borch-
  Nielson *Tel:* 22575490 *E-mail:* ani@scup.no
Head of Marketing, Journals: Ms Claire
  Sharp-Sundt *Tel:* 22575414 *Fax:* 22575454
  *E-mail:* csu@scup.no
Rights Manager: Mr Lars Allden *Tel:* 22575401
  *Fax:* 22575499 *E-mail:* lal@scup.no
Founded: 1950
Publishers for Scandinavian Universities & other
  institutions of higher learning, learned societies
  of Scandinavia.
Membership(s): European Educational Publish-
  ers Group (EEPG); European Union Publishers
  Forum; International Association of Scientific,
  Technical & Medical Publishers (STM); Nor-
  wegian Publishers' Association.
Subjects: Behavioral Sciences, Biological Sci-
  ences, Business, Education, Language Arts,
  Linguistics, Law, Mathematics, Mechanical En-
  gineering, Medicine, Nursing, Dentistry, Philos-
  ophy, Science (General), Health Care & Mod-
  ern Language
ISBN Prefix(es): 82-00
Total Titles: 2,000 Print; 10 CD-ROM; 35 Online;
  20 Audio
Subsidiaries: Scandinavian University Press
*Branch Office(s)*
Scandinavian University Press United Kingdom,
  60 St Aldates, Oxford OX1 1ST, United King-
  dom, Mr George Drennan *Tel:* (01865) 791 891
  *Fax:* (01865) 791 891
Copenhagen, Denmark
Stockholm, Sweden
*U.S. Office(s):* Scandinavian University Press
  North America, 875 Massachusetts Ave, Suite
  84, Cambridge, MA 02139, United States,
  Contact: Charles Germain *Tel:* 617-497-6515
  *Fax:* 617-354-6875 *E-mail:* 75201.571@
  compuserve.com
Membership(s): American Association of Univer-
  sity Presses

**Verbum Forlag**
Underhaugsvn 15, 0306 Oslo
Mailing Address: Postboks 7062 Majorstua, 0306
  Oslo
*Tel:* (022) 93 27 00 *Fax:* (022) 93 27 27
*E-mail:* verbumforlag@verbumforlag.no
*Web Site:* www.verbumforlag.no
*Key Personnel*
Editor: Turid Barth Pettersen *Tel:* (022) 93 27 20
  *E-mail:* tbp@verbumforlag.no

**Vett & Viten AS+**
Vakaas vn 7, Hvalstad, Asker
Mailing Address: Postboks 203, 1379 Nesbru
*Tel:* 66849040 *Fax:* 66845590
*E-mail:* vv@vettviten.no
*Web Site:* www.vettviten.no
*Key Personnel*
Publisher: Jan Lien *Tel:* 66983984 *E-mail:* jan.
  lien@vettviten.no
Marketing & Sales: Tormod Tvinnereim
  *E-mail:* tormod.tvinnereim@vettviten.no
Finance: Jan Kveine *Tel:* 66983982 *E-mail:* jan.
  kveine@vettviten.no
Founded: 1987

Subjects: Computer Science, Earth Sciences, Electronics, Electrical Engineering, Engineering (General), Environmental Studies, Film, Video, Geography, Geology, Medicine, Nursing, Dentistry, Radio, TV, Technology, Dance
ISBN Prefix(es): 82-412
Number of titles published annually: 50 Print; 20 E-Book
Total Titles: 350 Print
Divisions: Norsk Bokdistribusjon (computer ooks)
*Branch Office(s)*
Vett & Viten Toensberg, Fjordgaten 13, N-3125 Toensberg, Contact: Ragnar Kihle
  *Tel:* 33381900 *Fax:* 33381901 *E-mail:* ragnar.kihle@vettviten.no
*Sales Office(s):* J A Sisson, 8713 Prudence Dr, Annadale, VA 22003, United States

# Oman

## General Information

*Capital:* Muscat
*Language:* Arabic, English in business
*Religion:* Predominantly Muslim (mostly Ibadi, some Sunni)
*Population:* 1.6 million
*Currency:* 1,000 baiza = 1 rial Omani

**Apex Press & Publishing**
PO Box 2616, Ruwi 112, Muscat
*Tel:* 799388 *Fax:* 793316
*E-mail:* apexoman@gto.net.om
*Web Site:* www.apexstuff.com
*Key Personnel*
President: Saleh M Talib
Editor: Anju Visen-Singh
Founded: 1980
Specialize in Oman.
Subjects: Art, Business, Gardening, Plants, History, Outdoor Recreation, Travel

# Pakistan

## General Information

*Capital:* Islamabad
*Language:* Urdu is national language but English is used extensively. Other principal languages are Punjabi, Pushto, Sindhi and Saraiki
*Religion:* Predominantly Islamic
*Population:* 121.7 million
*Bank Hours:* 0900-1300 Saturday-Wednesday; 0900-1100 Thursday
*Shop Hours:* 0930-1300, 1500-2000 Saturday-Thursday
*Currency:* 100 paisa = 1 Pakistan rupee
*Export/Import Information:* No tariff on books, magazines and advertising matter. Import license issued freely if required. Anti-Islamic and obscene literature prohibited. Exchange controls.
*Copyright:* UCC, Berne, Buenos Aires, Florence (see Copyright Conventions, pg xi)

**SMP**, *imprint of* Sang-e-Meel Publications

**Academy of Education Planning & Management (AEPAM)**
Taleemi chowk, G-8/1, Islamabad 44000
*Tel:* (051) 926-1096 *Fax:* (051) 926-1353; (051) 926-1359
*E-mail:* webinfo@aepam.gov.pk
*Web Site:* www.aepam.gov.pk *Cable:* AEPAM

*Key Personnel*
Chief Documentation Officer: M H Shabab
Founded: 1982
Subjects: Economics, Education, English as a Second Language, Library & Information Sciences, Management, Microcomputers
ISBN Prefix(es): 969-444
*Parent Company:* Ministry of Education

**Admission Times International**, *imprint of* International Educational Services

**AEPAM**, see Academy of Education Planning & Management (AEPAM)

**Aina-e-Adab**
Chowk Minar Anarkali, Lahore 1
*Tel:* (042) 54069
*Key Personnel*
Proprietor: Sh Abdul Salam
ISBN Prefix(es): 969-430

**Sheikh Shaukat Ali & Sons+**
MA Jinnah Urdu Bazar, Karachi 74200
*Tel:* (021) 214585; (021) 212289 *Fax:* (021) 2637877
*Key Personnel*
Marketing Executive: Mohammad Ali
  *E-mail:* m_ali_sheikh@hotmail.com
Subjects: Poetry, Religion - Islamic
ISBN Prefix(es): 969-440
*Branch Office(s)*
Mian Market, Ghazni St, Lahore

**Sheikh Muhammad Ashraf Publishers**
7 Aibak Rd, New Anarkali, Lahore 7
*Tel:* (042) 353171; (042) 353489 *Fax:* (042) 353489 *Cable:* ISLAMICLIT LAHORE
*Key Personnel*
Publisher: Sh Muhammad Ashraf
Man Dir: Sh Shahzad Riaz
Home Sales: Muhammad Hamayun
Export Sales: Muhammad Amin
Literary Adviser: A Hassan
Founded: 1923
Subjects: Biography, Geography, Geology, Government, Political Science, History, Law, Religion - Other
ISBN Prefix(es): 969-432
*U.S. Office(s):* Halalco Books, 108 E Fairfax St, Falls Churchs, VA 20046, United States
  Specialty Promotions Co Inc, 6841 S Cregier Ave, Chicago, IL 60649, United States
*Bookshop(s):* Urdu Bazar, Ghazni St; Kashmiri Bazar
*Warehouse:* 9 Aibak Rd, New Anarkali, Lahore 7

**ASR Publications+**
Flat 8, 2nd floor, Sheraz Plaza, Main Market Gulberg II, Lahore
Mailing Address: PO Box 3154, Lahore
*Tel:* (042) 877613; (042) 877496 *Fax:* (042) 5711575 *Cable:* SOCFEM
*Key Personnel*
International Rights: Nighat Said Khan
Subjects: Women's Studies
ISBN Prefix(es): 969-8217
Distributed by Mr Books; Saeed Book Bank

**The Book House+**
8 Malik Jala Trust Bldg, Urdu Bazar, Lahore 2
Mailing Address: PO Box 734, Urdu Bazar, Lahore 54000
*Tel:* (042) 61212; (042) 232415 *Fax:* (042) 6360955 *Cable:* BOOKHOUSE
*Key Personnel*
Proprietor: Muhammad Saeed
General Manager: Muhammad Sheikh Saeed
Founded: 1951
Exporters of English & Urdu books & Textbooks.

Subjects: Antiques, Education
ISBN Prefix(es): 969-437

**Centre for South Asian Studies**
Quaid-i-Azam Campus, University of the Punjab, Lahore 54590
*Tel:* (042) 864014 *Fax:* (042) 5867206 *Cable:* SASCUP
*Key Personnel*
Dir: Dr Rafique Ahmed
Dir & Editor: Dr Sarfaraz Hussain Mirza
Publication Officer: Ovais Nizaini
  *E-mail:* ovaisn@hotmail.com
Founded: 1973
Subjects: Asian Studies, Economics, Ethnicity, Government, Political Science, Social Sciences, Sociology, Foreign Affairs, South Asia
ISBN Prefix(es): 969-471

**Classic+**
42 The Mall, Lahore 54000
*Tel:* (042) 323963; (042) 312977 *Fax:* (042) 7238236 *Cable:* CLASSIC LAHORE
*Key Personnel*
Man Dir, Editorial, Production, Permissions: Agha Amir Hussain
Sales, Publicity: S Rashid Hussain Agha
Founded: 1956
Subjects: Art, Fiction
ISBN Prefix(es): 969-28; 969-8136
*Parent Company:* Classic Publishers & Booksellers
*Associate Companies:* Menarva Publications, Lahore
Subsidiaries: Shish Mahal Kitab Ghar; Classic Bookshop

**East & West Publishing Co+**
22-Corner Chambers, I I Chundrigar Rd, Karachi 74200
*Tel:* (021) 212036 *Fax:* (021) 7784362 *Cable:* GOODBOOKS
*Key Personnel*
Publisher: Rafique Akhtar
Man Dir: Dr Nasir Rafique
Founded: 1971
Subjects: Biography, Regional Interests
ISBN Prefix(es): 969-8017

**Fazlee Sons (Pvt) Ltd+**
Temple Rd, Urdu Bazar, 74200 Karachi
*Tel:* (021) 214585; (021) 212289 *Fax:* (021) 6640522
*E-mail:* fazlee@tarique.khi.sdnpk.undp.org
Founded: 1948
Membership(s): Association of Pakistan Printing & Graphic Arts Industry (PAPGAI); Pakistan Booksellers & Publishers Association (PBSPA).
Subjects: Literature, Literary Criticism, Essays, Religion - Other
ISBN Prefix(es): 969-441
*Associate Companies:* Printing Services (Pvt) Ltd
Subsidiaries: IS Asia
*Bookshop(s):* Fazlee Book Supermarket, 4 Mama Parsi Bldg, Temple Rd, Urdu Bazar, Karachi 74200
*Orders to:* 1-K-5/A, Commercial Area, Nazimabad No 1, Karachi *Tel:* 6622212-5

**Ferozsons (Pvt) Ltd**
60, Shahrah-e-Quaid-e-Azam, Lahore
*Tel:* (042) 6301196; (042) 6301197; (042) 6301198 *Fax:* (042) 6369204
*E-mail:* ferozsons@showroom.edunet.sdnpk.undp.org
*Telex:* 44382 Feroz PK *Cable:* FEROZSONS
*Key Personnel*
Man Dir & Publicity: A Salam
Editorial & Sales Dir: Mr Zaheer Salam
Founded: 1894
Subjects: Regional Interests, Religion - Islamic

ISBN Prefix(es): 969-0
*Branch Office(s)*
33/C-6, Karachi 29

**Hamdard Foundation Pakistan**
Hamdard Centre, No 3, Nazimabad, Karachi
74600
*Tel:* (021) 6616001; (021) 6616002; (021)
6616003; (021) 6616004; (021) 6620945
*Fax:* (021) 6611755
*E-mail:* hamdard@khi.paknet.com.pk
*Web Site:* www.hamdard.com.pk
*Key Personnel*
President: Mrs Sadia Rashid
Founded: 1953
Also education & philanthropy.
Subjects: Biography, Education, Health, Nutrition,
History, Literature, Literary Criticism, Essays,
Religion - Islamic
ISBN Prefix(es): 969-412
*Parent Company:* Hamdard Laboratories (Waqf)
Pakistan
*Branch Office(s)*
Karachi
Lahore
Peshawar
Rawalpindi
*Bookshop(s):* Hamdard Kitabistan, Seva Kunj
Bldg, Shahrah-e-Liaquat, Karachi *Tel:* (021)
3371

**HMR Publishing Co+**
725, Shadman House, Main Bullavard Shadmad
Colony, Lahore
*Tel:* (042) 7588972; (042) 7588967 *Fax:* (042)
7581212
*Key Personnel*
Man Dir: M Akhter *E-mail:* makhter@1hr.
comsats.net.lk
Founded: 1986
Subjects: Biological Sciences, Health, Nutrition,
Medicine, Nursing, Dentistry, Religion - Is-
lamic, Science (General)
ISBN Prefix(es): 969-8019

**Idara-e-Tehqiqat-e-Islami**
Shah Faisal Masjid, Islamabad
Mailing Address: PO Box 1035, Islamabad
*Tel:* (051) 850751-5; (051) 850755
*Telex:* 54068 IIU Pak *Cable:* ISLAMSERCH
*Key Personnel*
Contact: Mr Zafar Ishaque Ansary
ISBN Prefix(es): 969-408

**Idara Siqafat-e-Islamia**
Club Rd, Lahore 3
*Tel:* (042) 53908
ISBN Prefix(es): 969-429

**Institute of Islamic Culture**
2 Club Rd, Lahore
*Tel:* (042) 6305920; (042) 6363127 *Cable:*
ICULT
*Key Personnel*
Chairman of the Board: Sayyid Wajid Ali Shah
Founded: 1951
Subjects: Religion - Islamic
ISBN Prefix(es): 969-469

**International Educational Services+**
617 Husain Centre, Shahrah-e-Iraq, Saddar,
Karachi 74400
Mailing Address: PO Box 10505, Saddar, Karachi
*Tel:* (021) 732-6602 *Fax:* (021) 813-1919
*Key Personnel*
Dir: Mohammad S Mirza
Founded: 1980
Subjects: Advertising, Business, Education, En-
glish as a Second Language, Language Arts,
Linguistics, Management, Marketing, Publish-
ing & Book Trade Reference

ISBN Prefix(es): 969-33
Imprints: Admission Times International

**International Institute of Islamic Thought+**
28, Main Double Rd, F-10/2, Islamabad
Mailing Address: PO Box 1959, Islamabad
*Tel:* (051) 229-3734 *Fax:* (051) 228-0489
*E-mail:* ziansari@iiitpak.sdnpk.undp.org
*Web Site:* www.iiit.org
*Key Personnel*
Man Dir, Editorial, Publicity, Rights & Permis-
sions: Muhammad Jamil
Production: Zeb Alam
Founded: 1981
Subjects: Ethnicity, Religion - Islamic
ISBN Prefix(es): 969-462

**Islamabad**, *imprint of* Pakistan Institute of
Development Economics (PIDE)

**Islamic Book Centre+**
25B Masson Rd, Lahore 54000
Mailing Address: PO Box 1625, Lahore 54000
*Tel:* (042) 6316803 *Fax:* (042) 6360955
*Cable:* ISLAMIBOOK
*Key Personnel*
Man & Publicity Dir: Muhammad Sajid Saeed
Sales, Advertising Dir & Proprietor: Muhammad
Hamid Saeed
Founded: 1961
Subjects: Religion - Other
ISBN Prefix(es): 969-436
Subsidiaries: Book House
*Branch Office(s)*
26 Paisa Akhbar (Anarkali), Lahore 2 *Tel:* (042)
61212
Malik, Jal-al Bldg, Urdu Bazar, Lahore 54000

**Islamic Publications (Pvt) Ltd**
13-E Shah Alam Market, Lahore 54000
*Tel:* (042) 325243; (042) 3664504 *Fax:* (042)
7248676 *Cable:* ALILM
*Key Personnel*
Man Dir: Prof Muhammad Aminv Javed
General Manager: Muhammad Munir Afzal
*Tel:* (042) 7669546
Finance Manager: Abdul Ghaffar
Founded: 1960
Specialize in literature on Islam.
Membership(s): Lahore Chamber of Commerce
& Industry; Pakistan Publishers & Booksellers
Association.
Subjects: Religion - Islamic
ISBN Prefix(es): 969-423
Number of titles published annually: 20 Print
Total Titles: 700 Print
*Parent Company:* Corporate Law Authority (Pak-
istan)
*Showroom(s):* Islamic Publications, 10-Chaterjee
Rd, Urdu Bazar, Lahore
*Bookshop(s):* Islamic Publications, 10-Chaterjee
Rd, Urdu Bazar, Lahore

**Islamic Research Institute**
International Islamic University, Faisal Masjid,
PO Box 1035, Islamabad
*Tel:* (051) 850751; (051) 850755 *Fax:* (051)
853360
*E-mail:* dg-iri@iri-iiu.sdnpd.undp.org
*Telex:* 54068 IIU Pak *Cable:* Islamserch
*Key Personnel*
Dir-General: Dr Zafar Ishaque Ansari
Sales: Mumtaz Liaqat
Founded: 1960
The Institute is part of the International Islamic
University, Islamabad.
Subjects: History, Law, Religion - Other
ISBN Prefix(es): 969-462

**H I Jaffari & Co Publishers+**
Tahir Plaza 37/B, Blue Area, Islamabad 44000

*Tel:* (051) 811153 *Cable:* AMBOOKCO
*Key Personnel*
President: Hasan I Jaffri
Vice President: Raza I Jaffri
Contact: Muneer Hussain
Founded: 1959
Membership(s): Pakistan Publishers & Book-
sellers Association (Federal Zone) Islamabad.
Subjects: History, Poetry, Religion - Islamic,
Sports, Athletics
ISBN Prefix(es): 969-467
Subsidiaries: American Book Co

**Kazi Publications**
121-Zulqarnain Chambers, Ganpat Rd, Lahore
*Tel:* (042) 7311359; (042) 7350805 *Fax:* (042)
7117606; (042) 7324003
*E-mail:* kazip@brain.net.pk; kazipublications@
hotmail.com
*Web Site:* www.brain.net.pk/~kazip
*Key Personnel*
Proprietor: Muhammad Ikram Siddiqi
Founded: 1978
Subjects: Islam

**Library Promotion Bureau+**
Karachi University Campus, Dastagir Society,
Federal B Area, Karachi 75270
Mailing Address: PO Box 8421, Karachi 75270
*Tel:* (021) 6321959 *Fax:* (021) 6321959
*Key Personnel*
President: Dr Ghaniul Akram Sabzwari
*E-mail:* gsabzwari@hotmail.com
Secretary General: Nasim Fatima
Man Editor: R A Samdani
Founded: 1966
Subjects: Library & Information Sciences
ISBN Prefix(es): 969-459
Distributed by M S Royal Book Co

**Maktaba-i-Danial**, *imprint of* Pakistan Publishing
House

**Malik Sirajuddin & Sons+**
Kashmiri Bazar, Lahore 8
*Tel:* (042) 7657527 *Fax:* (042) 7657490
*E-mail:* sirajco@brain.net.pk
*Telex:* 44942 CTOLH PK *Cable:* TAJIRKUTUB;
LAHORE
*Key Personnel*
Man Dir: A R Malik *Tel:* (042) 7225809
Editorial, Publicity: S A Malik *Tel:* (042)
5867839 *Fax:* (042) 5861620
Sales: A A Malik *Tel:* (042) 7225812 *Fax:* (042)
7224586
Founded: 1934
Subjects: Biography, Fiction, How-to, Psychology,
Psychiatry, Religion - Islamic
ISBN Prefix(es): 969-29
*Associate Companies:* Gul I Khandan, Urdu
Monthly, Kashmiri Baza, Lahore 8; Islamic
Juntri, Kashmiri Baza, Lahore 8
Subsidiaries: Siraj Mohammadi Press; Ayaz Book
Binding Works
*Branch Office(s)*
Chowk Urdu Bazar, Lahore *Tel:* (042) 7666226;
(042) 7669062 *Fax:* (042) 7224586
18-19 M J Hospital (WAQF), O/S Mori Gate, Cir-
cular Rd, Lahore
*Shipping Address:* 48C Lower Mall Rd, PO Box
2250, Lahore, Contact: Ayaz Ahmad Malik
*Tel:* (042) 7225809, (042) 7225812 *Fax:* (042)
7224586

**Maqbool Academy+**
199 Circular Rd, Chowk Anarkali, Lahore 2
*Tel:* (042) 7233165 *Fax:* (042) 7324164
*Key Personnel*
Proprietor: Maqbool Ahmed Malik *Tel:* (042)
7324164 *Fax:* (042) 7324164
Chief Executive: Dr Zafar Maqbool
*E-mail:* zmaqbool@yahoo.com

Founded: 1954
Membership(s): Lahore Chamber of Commerce & Industries.
Subjects: Asian Studies, Cookery, Drama, Theater, Education, Fashion, Fiction, Gardening, Plants, Government, Political Science, History, Humor, Literature, Literary Criticism, Essays, Poetry, Religion - Islamic, Religion - Other, Romance, Science (General)
ISBN Prefix(es): 969-442; 969-510
Total Titles: 100 Print
*Associate Companies:* Maqbool Books, Abuzar Lentre Modeltown Link Rd, Lahore *Tel:* (042) 5169923; (042) 5169924
Subsidiaries: Bustan-E-Adab
*Branch Office(s)*
Good Books, 3 Iqra Center, Ghazni St, Urdu Bazar, Lahore 2 *Tel:* (042) 7121966
Distributed by Book Centre
*Showroom(s):* 10 Dayalsingh Mansion, The Mall, Lahore *Tel:* (042) 7357058; (042) 7238241 *Fax:* (042) 7238241
*Bookshop(s):* Igraa Centre, Ghazni St, Urdu Bazar, Lahore *Tel:* (042) 7121966

**Nafees Academy**
Tirath Das Rd, Karachi
Mailing Address: PO Box 91, Urdu Bazaar
*Key Personnel*
Proprietor: Tariq Iqbal Gahandri
Subjects: Education, History
ISBN Prefix(es): 969-421

**Nashiran-e-Quran Pvt Ltd+**
38-Urdu Bazar, Lahore
*Tel:* (042) 58581; (042) 58581
*Key Personnel*
Chairman: Abdul Hamid Khan
Man Dir: Adbul Rashid Khan
Dir: Khan Abdul Khaliq
Founded: 1967
Subjects: Literature, Literary Criticism, Essays, Religion - Islamic
ISBN Prefix(es): 969-431
*Parent Company:* Kitabistan Publishing Co 38-Urdu Bazar, Lahore
*Warehouse:* 4C Mela Ram Darbar Market, Lahore

**National Book Foundation+**
6-Mauve Area, G-8/4, PO Box 1169 & 1610, Taleemi Chowk, Islamabad
*Tel:* (051) 9261533; (051) 255572 *Fax:* (051) 2264283; (051) 2264283
*E-mail:* nbf@paknet2.ptc.pk
*Web Site:* nbf.org.pk *Cable:* BOOKFOUND ISLAMABAD PAKISTAN
*Key Personnel*
Man Dir: Dr Ahmad Faraz *Tel:* (051) 2255572
Secretary: Muhammad Aslam Rao
Deputy Dir Sales: Abdul Hafeez Tauqir *Tel:* (051) 9261535
Assistant Dir, Production: Maqbool Ahmad *Tel:* (051) 9261036
Founded: 1972
Specialize in publishing & provision of books at low prices, book development & promotion, promotion of reading habit.
Membership(s): Asia/Pacific Publishers Association.
Subjects: Accounting, Agriculture, Behavioral Sciences, Biological Sciences, Business, Career Development, Chemistry, Chemical Engineering, Civil Engineering, Religion - Islamic
ISBN Prefix(es): 969-37
Number of titles published annually: 135 Print
Total Titles: 320 Print
*Branch Office(s)*
First floor, Public Library, Jalal Baba Auditorium, Abbottabad *Tel:* (0992) 9310291
Quaid-i-Azam Medical College, Near Library, Bahawalpur

GOR Colony, Latifabad No 1, Hyderabad, Contact: Mr Lutuf Ali Narejo *Tel:* (0221) 28219 *Fax:* (0221) 783859
Liaquat Memorial Library Premises, Ground Floor, Stadium Rd, Karachi, Contact: Mr Muhammad Yaqub *Tel:* (021) 4934969 *Fax:* (021) 4936724
56-57 Tufail Market, Shadman Colony, Lahore, Contact: Mr Muhammad Nasim *Tel:* (042) 7587735; (042) 7530329; (042) 7550161 *Fax:* (042) 7587735
Chandka Medical College, Main Gate, Larkana, Contact: Mr Lutuf Ali Narejo *Tel:* (0741) 458215 *Fax:* (0741) 458215
A-1, Gulgasht Colony, Bosan Rd, Near UBL College Chowk, Multan, Contact: Mr Ghulam Murtaza *Tel:* (061) 9210119 *Fax:* (061) 9210119
48/D, Jamrud Rd, University Town, Peshawar, Contact: Mr Nazir Ahmad Yousufzai *Tel:* (091) 844340 *Fax:* (091) 844340
3-9/15, Natha Singh St, Quetta, Contact: Mr Muhammad Idrees *Tel:* (081) 9201570; (081) 9201869 *Fax:* (081) 9201570
178-B Sarwar Rd, Rawalpindi, Contact: Kanwar Tariq Mahmood *Tel:* (051) 5568242 *Fax:* (051) 5568242
Public Library, Sukkur, Contact: Mr Jahan Khan Jamro *Tel:* (071) 25103
*Bookshop(s):* New Kitab Markaz, Bhawana Bazar, Faisalabad

**National Institute of Historical & Cultural Research**
102 Rauf Centre, Fazlul Haq Rd, Blue Area, Islamabad
*Tel:* (051) 218535
*Key Personnel*
Dir: Dr S M Zaman
Founded: 1973
Specialize in history & culture of South Asia with special emphasis on Pakistan.
Subjects: Biography, Ethnicity, History, Regional Interests
ISBN Prefix(es): 969-415

**Pak American Commercial (Pvt) Ltd**
53/2 Kashmir Rd, Rawalpindi
Mailing Address: PO Box 294, Rawalpindi
*Tel:* (051) 563709 *Fax:* (051) 565190 *Cable:* PAKACINC KARACHI
*Key Personnel*
Dir: Agha M Jaffri
Editorial, Production: M Younus Shaikh
Sales, Publicity: Ahsan Jaffri
Rights & Permissions: Abbas Jaffri
Founded: 1949
Subjects: Government, Political Science, History
ISBN Prefix(es): 969-8152
*Branch Office(s)*
1st floor, Pak Chambers, 5 Temple Rd, Lahore

**Pakistan Institute of Development Economics (PIDE)**
Quaid-e-Azam University Campus, Islamabad
Mailing Address: PO Box 1091, Islamabad
*Tel:* (051) 9206610-27 *Fax:* (051) 9210886
*E-mail:* pide@apollo.net.pk
*Web Site:* www.pide.org.pk *Cable:* PIDE
*Key Personnel*
Dir: Dr A R Kemal
Literary Editor & Chief, Publications Division: Prof Aurangzeb A Hashmi
Founded: 1957
Focal points of the following organizations: World Bank; International Labor Organization; Asian Development Bank; International Development Research Centre; South Asia Network of Economic Research Institutes.
Subjects: Agriculture, Anthropology, Developing Countries, Economics, Environmental Studies, Labor, Industrial Relations, Library & In-

formation Sciences, Religion - Islamic, Social Sciences, Sociology, Women's Studies, Demography
ISBN Prefix(es): 969-461
Total Titles: 50 Print
*Parent Company:* Government of Pakistan Planning & Development Division
Imprints: PIDE; Islamabad

**Pakistan Publishing House+**
Victoria Chambers, Abdullah Haroon Rd, Saddar Karachi 74400
*Tel:* (021) 5681457
*Telex:* 23259 HONEY Pk Attn Noorani *Cable:* PRILECT
*Key Personnel*
Dir: Ms Hoori Noorani
Sales Manager: Aamir Hussain
Production Manager: Mohammad Yusuf
Rights & Permissions: Mohammad Iqbal
Founded: 1966
Subjects: History, Law, Literature, Literary Criticism, Essays
ISBN Prefix(es): 969-419
*Associate Companies:* Pakistan Law House, Pakistan Chowk, PO Box 90, Karachi 1
Imprints: PPH; Maktaba-i-Danial

**PIDE**, *imprint of* Pakistan Institute of Development Economics (PIDE)

**PPH**, *imprint of* Pakistan Publishing House

**Publishers United Pvt Ltd+**
176, Anarkali, Lahore 54000
*Tel:* (042) 7352238 *Fax:* (042) 6316015
*E-mail:* smalipub2@hotmail.com; smalipub@wol.net.pk *Cable:* PUBUN
*Key Personnel*
Man Dir: Ahmad Ali Sheikh
Founded: 1942
Subjects: Accounting, Agriculture, Anthropology, Antiques, Archaeology, Art, Asian Studies, Biography, Biological Sciences, Chemistry, Chemical Engineering, Economics, Geography, Geology, History, Library & Information Sciences, Mathematics, Philosophy, Physics, Psychology, Psychiatry, Religion - Islamic, Theology
ISBN Prefix(es): 969-433
*Book Club(s):* National Book Foundation of Pakistan
*Warehouse:* 9 Rattigan Rd, Lahore *Tel:* (042) 353423

**Quaid-i-Azam University Department of Biological Sciences**
Quaid-i-Azam University, Islamabad
*Tel:* (051) 2482513 *Fax:* (051) 2482513
*E-mail:* qau@gmx.net; daud@gmx.net
*Web Site:* members.tripod.com/qau *Cable:* Quaid-i-Azam University Islamabad
*Key Personnel*
Manager: Rashid Ahmed Khan
Founded: 1973
Subjects: Chemistry, Chemical Engineering, Social Sciences, Sociology
ISBN Prefix(es): 969-8329

**Research Society of Pakistan**
University of the Punjab, Old Campus, Lahore 3
*Tel:* (042) 322542
ISBN Prefix(es): 969-425

**Royal Book Co+**
232 Saddar Co-operative Market, Abdullah Haroon Rd, Karachi 74400
Mailing Address: PO Box 7737, Karachi 74400
*Tel:* (021) 5684244 *Fax:* (021) 5683706
*Key Personnel*
Proprietor: Jamshed Mirza
Founded: 1963

Subjects: Economics, Finance, Government, Political Science, History
ISBN Prefix(es): 969-407
*Showroom(s):* 402 Rehman Centre, Zaibunisa St, Karachi 74400
*Warehouse:* 402 Rehman Centre, Zaibunisa St, Karachi 74400

**Sang-e-Meel Publications+**
25 Lower Mall, Lahore 54000
*Tel:* (042) 7220100; (042) 7228143 *Fax:* (042) 7245101
*E-mail:* smp@sang-e-meel.com
*Web Site:* www.sang-e-meel.com
*Key Personnel*
Chief Executive: Niaz Ahmad *E-mail:* nahmad@sang-e-meel.com
Production Dir: Afzaal Ahmad *E-mail:* aahmad@sang-e-meel.com
Founded: 1964
Membership(s): Lahore Chamber of Commerce & Industry; Pakistan Publishers & Booksellers Association.
Subjects: Agriculture, Anthropology, Art, Asian Studies, Criminology, Drama, Theater, Fiction, Health, Nutrition, History, Journalism, Literature, Literary Criticism, Essays, Poetry, Travel
ISBN Prefix(es): 969-35
Imprints: SMP

**Sh Ghulam Ali & Sons (Pvt) Ltd+**
Ashrafia Park, Ferozepur Rd, Lahore
*Tel:* (042) 7588979; (042) 7501664 *Fax:* (042) 7583611
*Key Personnel*
Dir: Sh Bashir Ahmad; Sh Niaz Ahmed; Mr Arshad Niaz
Subjects: Education, Religion - Islamic
ISBN Prefix(es): 969-31
*Branch Office(s)*
Chotki Ghitti, Hyderabad *Tel:* (0221) 24431
M A Jinnah Rd, Karachi *Tel:* (0221) 722254
Yadkar Line, Chotki Ghitti, Hyderabad *Tel:* (0221) 24431

**Shibil Publications (Pvt) Ltd**
2nd floor, Uzma Arcade, Main Clifton Rd, Karachi 75600
*Tel:* (021) 533414; (021) 539570; (021) 571488 *Cable:* SHAMAILS KARACHI
*Key Personnel*
Author: Jawaid A Siddiqi
Founded: 1985
Membership(s): Pakistan Publishers & Booksellers Association.
Subjects: Government, Political Science
ISBN Prefix(es): 969-451
*Parent Company:* Messrs Shamail Traders (Pvt) Ltd
Imprints: Urdu

**Urdu**, *imprint of* Shibil Publications (Pvt) Ltd

**Urdu Academy Sind+**
16-Bahadur Shah Market, M A Jinah Rd, Karachi 2
*Tel:* (021) 2631485 *Cable:* LITERATURE
*Key Personnel*
Dir & International Rights: Aziz Khalid
Also acts as printer.
Membership(s): Pakistan Publishers & Booksellers Association.
Subjects: Education, Literature, Literary Criticism, Essays, Science (General)
ISBN Prefix(es): 969-30
*Associate Companies:* Falak Publishers, Karachi
Subsidiaries: Kitab Agency
*Branch Office(s)*
Urdu Markaz, Ganpat Rd, Lahore
*Showroom(s):* Rahmat Bldg, M A Jinnah Rd

*Bookshop(s):* Rahmat Bldg, M A Jinnah Rd
*Shipping Address:* Westwharf, Karachi

**Vanguard Books Ltd+**
45 The Mall, Lahore
*Tel:* (042) 7243779; (042) 7120776; (042) 7120781; (042) 7243783; (042) 7235767 *Fax:* (042) 7245097; (042) 73551978
*Web Site:* www.vanguardbooks.com
*Key Personnel*
Chief Executive Officer & International Rights: Najam Sethi *E-mail:* nasethi@lhr.comsats.net.pk
Chief Accountant: Aleem Ansari
Founded: 1978
Membership(s): Pakistan Publishers & Booksellers Association.
Subjects: Asian Studies, Economics, Regional Interests, Religion - Islamic
ISBN Prefix(es): 969-402
Number of titles published annually: 30 Print
Total Titles: 325 Print
*Branch Office(s)*
Vanguard Books, Mashriq Centre, Shah Suleman Rd, Gulshan Iqbal, Karachi
Vanguard Books, 3 Commercial St, Karachi
Vanguard Books, Jinnah Super Market, Islamabad
Vanguard Books, 5-L Commercial, Lahore
Vanguard Books, Mussee Road, Rawalpindi
Distributor for Blackwell; Macmillan Press; Penguin Books (UK); Pluto Press; Routledge; I B Tauris; Zed Press
Foreign Rep(s): Curzon Press (UK); Zed Press (UK)
*Bookshop(s):* Vanguard Books, Ejaz Center, Main Blvd, Gulberg, Lahore; Vanguard Books, Lok Virsa Bldg, Super Market, Islamabad; Vanguard Books, Mashriq Centre, Shah Suleman Rd, Gulshan Iqbal, Karachi

**West Pakistan Publishing Co (Pvt) Ltd**
17 Urdu Bazar, Lahore
Mailing Address: GPO Box No 374, Lahore
*Tel:* (042) 52427 *Cable:* WESPUBLISH LAHORE
*Key Personnel*
Chief Executive: Syed Mahmud Shah
Founded: 1932
Also government printers.
Subjects: Religion - Islamic
ISBN Prefix(es): 969-434

# Panama

## General Information

*Capital:* Panama
*Language:* Spanish (English widely used)
*Religion:* Roman Catholic
*Population:* 2.7 million
*Bank Hours:* 0800-1600 Monday-Friday; 0900-1200 Saturday
*Shop Hours:* 0900-1800 Monday-Saturday
*Currency:* 100 centimos = 1 balboa. US currency also used
*Export/Import Information:* No tariffs on books and advertising matter. No import licenses or exchange controls.
*Copyright:* UCC, Buenos Aires (see Copyright Conventions, pg xi)

**Focus Publications International SA**
Ave Justo Arosemena y Calle 42, Apdo Aereo 6-3287, Bella Vista
Mailing Address: 6-3287, El Dorado, Panama
*Tel:* 225 6638 *Fax:* 225 0466
*E-mail:* focusint@sinfo.net
*Web Site:* focuspublicationsint.com

*Key Personnel*
Publisher: Kenneth Jones
Founded: 1970
Subjects: Marketing, Travel
ISBN Prefix(es): 958-95276

**Fondo Educativo Interamericano**
Edificio Eastern 6, Avda Federico Boyd y Calle 51, Apdo 6-3099, Panama
*Tel:* 2691511; 2230210
*Telex:* 2481
*Key Personnel*
Dir: Alicia Chavarria
President: Juan J Fernandez
Vice President: J Rose
Marketing Manager: C Merodio
Founded: 1985

**Editorial Universitaria**
Urb El Cangrejo Calle Jose, Apdo Aereo Estafeta Universitaria, Panama 4
*Tel:* 264-2087 *Fax:* 269-2684 *Cable:* Cuidad Universitaria
*Key Personnel*
Man Dir, Editorial: Dr Carlos M Gasteazoro
Sales: Eduvigis Vergara
Production: Prof Carlos N Ho
Publicity: Mary R de Natera
Founded: 1969
Subjects: Architecture & Interior Design, Art, Education, Geography, Geology, History, Law, Literature, Literary Criticism, Essays, Philosophy, Science (General), Social Sciences, Sociology
*Bookshop(s):* University Bookshop

# Papua New Guinea

## General Information

*Capital:* Port Moresby
*Language:* Pidgin, English and Motu (all official) as well as approximately 742 native languages
*Religion:* Predominantly Christian
*Population:* 4 million
*Bank Hours:* 0900-1400 Monday-Thursday; 0900-1700 Friday
*Shop Hours:* 0900-1800 Monday-Friday; 0900-1200 Saturday
*Currency:* 100 teoa = 1 kina
*Export/Import Information:* No tariff on books and advertising but import tax on non-educational books. No import license for books, but no obscene literature permitted.
*Copyright:* No copyright law

**Assemblies of God Mission**
PO Box 34, Maprik, East Sepik Province
*Tel:* 881256
Subjects: Religion - Other
ISBN Prefix(es): 9980-85
*Parent Company:* Assemblies Publications
*Orders to:* PO Box 254, Mitcham, Victoria 3132, Australia

**The Christian Book Centre**
PO Box 712, Madang
*Tel:* 852 2043 *Fax:* 852 3376
*Key Personnel*
Manager: Rex Bangs
Subjects: Literature, Literary Criticism, Essays, Religion - Other
ISBN Prefix(es): 9980-74; 0-85804
*Parent Company:* Kristen Press

**Coffee Industry Corporation**
PO Box 137, Goroka, Eastern Highlands Province
441
*Tel:* 732 1266; 732 2466 *Fax:* 732 1431
*E-mail:* cicgka@daltron.com.pg
*Web Site:* www.coffeecorp.org.pg
*Telex:* NE 72647 COFFEE
ISBN Prefix(es): 9980-85

**IMPS Research Ltd**
PO Box 986, Port Moresby, National Capital District 121
*Tel:* 3213283 *Fax:* 3217360
*E-mail:* imps@online.net.pg
*Key Personnel*
Man Dir: Steve Landon
Founded: 1989
Information services.
Subjects: Economics, Government, Political Science, Mining/Petroleum
ISBN Prefix(es): 9980-916; 9980-920
Number of titles published annually: 3 Print
Distributor for Focus Economics; Insights PNL

**KPI**, *imprint of* Kristen Press

**Kristen Press+**
PO Box 712, Madang 511
*Tel:* 8522988 *Fax:* 823313
*Key Personnel*
Executive Dir: Dennis T Brown
Publishing Manager & International Rights: Rev Kasek Kautil
Founded: 1969
Also act as printers & stationers.
Subjects: Agriculture, Biblical Studies, Biography, Business, Education, Fiction, Health, Nutrition, Religion - Protestant, Theology, Women's Studies
ISBN Prefix(es): 9980-74; 0-85804
Imprints: KPI; Yangpela Didiman
*Bookshop(s):* Christian Book Centre, PO Box 3098, Lae; Christian Book Centre, PO Box 712, Madang Province

**Melanesian Institute**
PO Box 571, Goroko, Eastern Highlands Province
*Tel:* 732 1777 *Fax:* 732 1214
Subjects: Anthropology, Religion - Catholic, Religion - Protestant, Religion - Other, Social Sciences, Sociology, Theology
ISBN Prefix(es): 9980-65

**National Research Institute of Papua New Guinea**
PO Box 5854, Boroko, National Capital District
*Tel:* 326 0061; 326 0079; 326 0083 *Fax:* 326 0213
*E-mail:* nri@global.net.pg
*Web Site:* www.nri.org.pg
*Key Personnel*
Assistant Dir: Dr Richard Guy
Publishing Manager: James Robins
Founded: 1975
Applied research & policy making.
Subjects: Anthropology, Criminology, Developing Countries, Economics, Education, Environmental Studies, Government, Political Science, Social Sciences, Sociology
ISBN Prefix(es): 9980-75

**Office of Libraries & Archives, Papua New Guinea**
PO Box 734, Waigani, National Capital District
*Tel:* 325-6200 *Fax:* 325-1331
*E-mail:* ola@datec.com.pg
*Key Personnel*
Dir General: Daniel Paraide
Founded: 1975
Also acts as country's ISBN Agency.
ISBN Prefix(es): 9980-69

**Papua New Guinea Institute of Medical Research (PNGIMR)**
PO Box 60, Goroka, Eastern Highlands Province
*Tel:* 732-2800 *Fax:* 732-1998
*E-mail:* general@pngimr.org.pg
*Web Site:* www.pngimr.org.pg
*Key Personnel*
Dir: Prof John Reeder *Tel:* 732-1469
  *E-mail:* jreeder@pngimr.org.pg
Produces *PNG Bibliography on Medicine.*
Subjects: Anthropology, Medicine, Nursing, Dentistry, Social Sciences, Sociology
ISBN Prefix(es): 0-909531; 9980-71
Number of titles published annually: 1 Print

**Summer Institute of Linguistics+**
PO Box 413, Ukarumpa vie Lae, Eastern Highlands Province
*Tel:* 7373544 *Fax:* 7374111
*E-mail:* png@sil.org
Founded: 1957
Subjects: Anthropology, Language Arts, Linguistics, Papua New Guinea Studies
ISBN Prefix(es): 9980-0; 0-909456; 0-7263
Total Titles: 24,000 Print

**University of Goroka**
PO Box 1078, Goroka, Eastern Highlands Province
*Tel:* 731 1700 *Fax:* 732 2620
*E-mail:* infouog@uog.ac.pg
*Web Site:* www.uog.ac.pg
*Key Personnel*
Librarian: N Amarasinghe
ISBN Prefix(es): 9980-85; 0-9599993; 9980-915

**University of Papua New Guinea Press**
PO Box 320 University Post Office, Boroko
*Tel:* 3267654 *Fax:* 3260127
*Key Personnel*
Development Manager: John Evans *Tel:* 3267260
  *Fax:* 367187 *E-mail:* john.evans@upng.ac.pg
Founded: 1995
Books on & about Papua New Guinea in any subject area.
ISBN Prefix(es): 9980-84
Total Titles: 30 Print

**Victory Books**
PO Box 376, Mount Hagen, Western Highlands Province
*Tel:* 5421081 *Fax:* 5423030
*E-mail:* bcbes@datec.com.pg
*Key Personnel*
Publications Dir: Brian Bett
Subjects: Religion - Protestant, Theology
ISBN Prefix(es): 9980-67
Number of titles published annually: 7 Print
*Bookshop(s):* Nazarene Book Store, PO Box 456, Mount Hagen, Western Highlands Province

**Yangpela Didiman**, *imprint of* Kristen Press

# Paraguay

## General Information

*Capital:* Asuncion
*Language:* Spanish & Guarani (both official)
*Religion:* Predominantly Roman Catholic
*Population:* 5.6 million
*Bank Hours:* 0930-1145 Monday-Friday
*Shop Hours:* 0900-2000 Monday-Saturday
*Currency:* $1.00 US = 2000 Guarani
*Export/Import Information:* Member of MERCOSUR; ALADI; GATT & WTO. Children's picture books and atlases are dutied, plus added

tax and compensatory tax. Advertising catalogs subject to added tax compensatory tax. Additional taxes on all goods; also Consular fee. No import licenses required. Exchange controls; foreign exchange surcharge.
*Copyright:* UCC, Berne, Buenos Aires (see Copyright Conventions, pg xi)

**Instituto de Ciencias de la Computacion (NCR)+**
EE UU 961 c/ Tte Farina, 4 to piso, Asuncion
*Tel:* (021) 490076 *Fax:* (021) 497849
*Key Personnel*
Dir: Javier Cosp *E-mail:* jcosp@ecsalink.com.py
Founded: 1969
Entrenamiento en Computacioi.
Subjects: Computer Science, Microcomputers, Technology, Computation
*Branch Office(s)*
Mcal Estigarribia 134, Fernando de la Mora
Distributed by Rafael Peroni Editor

**Intercontinental Editora+**
Caballero 270, Asuncion
*Tel:* (021) 496991; (021) 449738 *Fax:* (021) 448721
*Web Site:* www.libreriaintercontinental.com.py
*Key Personnel*
Dir: Alejandro Gatti *E-mail:* agatti@pla.net.py
Subjects: Computer Science, Government, Political Science, History, Law, Literature, Literary Criticism, Essays, Parapsychology, Poetry, Self-Help, Economy, Languages, Software

**NCR**, see Instituto de Ciencias de la Computacion (NCR)

# Peru

## General Information

*Capital:* Lima
*Language:* Spanish, Quechua & Aymara (all official)
*Religion:* Predominantly Roman Catholic
*Population:* 22.8 million
*Bank Hours:* January-December 0900-1500 Monday-Friday
*Shop Hours:* 1000-1500 Monday- Friday
*Currency:* 100 centisimos = 1 new sol
*Export/Import Information:* Children's picture books and advertising matter dutied per kg plus VAT, sales tax applies on advertising matter. No freight tax on books, but there is a wholesaler's tax. No import licenses required. No exhange controls.
*Copyright:* UCC, Berne, Buenos Aires (see Copyright Conventions, pg xi)

**Librerias ABC SA**
Avda Paseo de la Republica 3440, Local B-32, Lima
*Tel:* (054) 422900; (054) 422902 *Fax:* (054) 422901
*Key Personnel*
Man Dir: Herbert H Moll
Founded: 1956
Subjects: Archaeology, Art, History

**American Bookstore Center SA**, see Librerias ABC SA

**Biblioteca Nacional**
Av Abancay 4ta cuadra, Lima
*Tel:* (01) 4287690; (01) 4287696 *Fax:* (01) 4277331
*E-mail:* dn@binape.gob.pe

*Web Site:* www.binape.gob.pe
ISBN Prefix(es): 9972-601

**Ediciones Brown SA+**
Av Arequipa No 4455, Miraflores, Lima 18
*Tel:* (01) 4462753 *Fax:* (01) 4462753
*Key Personnel*
Dir: Brown P Fortunato
Founded: 1985
Subjects: Communications, English as a Second Language, How-to, Language Arts, Linguistics, Nonfiction (General)
ISBN Prefix(es): 9972-9030

**Asociacion Editorial Bruno+**
Av Arica 751, Brena
Mailing Address: Apdo 1759, Lima 5
*Tel:* (01) 4244134; (01) 4251248 *Fax:* (01) 4251248
*Key Personnel*
Dir: Maximo Segredo
Manager: Federico Diaz Pineo
Founded: 1950
Subjects: Education, Religion - Catholic
ISBN Prefix(es): 9972-1

**Bulletin de l'Institut Francais d'Etudes Andines**, *imprint of* Instituto Frances de Estudios Andinos, IFEA

**Carvajal SA**
Av Jorge Basadre 990 San Isidro, Lima 27
*Tel:* (01) 440 9685; (01) 440 9618 *Fax:* (01) 440 5871
*E-mail:* carvajal@correo.dnet.com.pe
*Web Site:* www.carvajal.com.co
*Telex:* 055555; 055650 *Cable:* Carvajales Cali
ISBN Prefix(es): 9972-745
Subsidiaries: Editorial Norma SA

**Catalogo**, *imprint of* Ediciones Peisa (Promocion Editorial Inca SA)

**Centro de la Mujer Peruana Flora Tristan**
(Peruvian Women's Centre Flora Tristan)
Parque Hernan Velarde 42, Lima 1
*Tel:* (01) 433-2765; (01) 433-1457; (01) 433-9060 *Fax:* (01) 433-9500
*E-mail:* postmast@flora.org.pe
*Web Site:* www.flora.org.pe
*Key Personnel*
Executive Dir: Blanca Fernandez
Editor: Gaby Cevasco *E-mail:* gaby@flora.org.pe
Founded: 1979
NGO & Feminist
Specialize in issues on communication, development, feminism, gender, health, library, research, tell-stories, violence, women's rights, history, literature & poetry.
Subjects: Government, Political Science, Health, Nutrition, History, Literature, Literary Criticism, Essays, Poetry, Science (General), Social Sciences, Sociology
ISBN Prefix(es): 9972-610
Number of titles published annually: 10 Print; 5 Online
Total Titles: 50 Print

**Editorial Desarrollo SA+**
Ica 242, Of 106-716, Lima 1
*Tel:* (01) 428-5380 *Fax:* (01) 428-6628
*Key Personnel*
Man Dir: Luis Sosa Nunez
Assistant Manager: Bertha de Berrospi
Founded: 1965
Subjects: Accounting, Business

**Instituto de Estudios Peruanos+**
Horacio Urteaga 694, Jesus Maria, Lima

*Tel:* (01) 332-6194; (01) 332-2156; (01) 332-6173; (01) 431-3167 *Fax:* (01) 432-4981
*E-mail:* libreria@iep.org.pe
*Web Site:* iep.perucultural.org.pe *Cable:* IEPERU
*Key Personnel*
Dir: Carolina Trivelli
Publications Dir: Carlos Contreras
Founded: 1964
Subjects: Anthropology, Archaeology, Developing Countries, Economics, Education, Ethnicity, Government, Political Science, Health, Nutrition, History, Social Sciences, Sociology, Technology, Women's Studies
ISBN Prefix(es): 9972-51

**Fondo Editorial de la Pontificia Universidad Catolica del Peru**
Avda Universitaria cdra 18, San Miguel, Apdo 1761, Lima 100
*Tel:* (01) 4602870 *Fax:* (01) 4626390
*Web Site:* www.pucp.edu.pe
*Key Personnel*
Executive Dir: Agueero Gonzalex
Man Dir: Jose Enrique
Subjects: Anthropology, Archaeology, Computer Science, Economics, Education, Ethnicity, History, Language Arts, Linguistics, Law, Literature, Literary Criticism, Essays, Philosophy, Physical Sciences, Psychology, Psychiatry, Science (General), Social Sciences, Sociology, Theology
ISBN Prefix(es): 84-8390; 84-89309; 9972-42; 84-89292

**Instituto Frances de Estudios Andinos, IFEA**
Av Arequipa 4595-2° piso, Miraflores, Lima 18
*Tel:* (01) 447-6070 *Fax:* (01) 445-7650
*E-mail:* postmaster@ifea.org.pe
*Web Site:* www.ifeanet.org
*Key Personnel*
Dir: Henri Godard
Founded: 1948
Research institution.
Subjects: Agriculture, Anthropology, Archaeology, Earth Sciences, Geography, Geology, History, Language Arts, Linguistics, Social Sciences, Sociology
ISBN Prefix(es): 84-89302; 9972-623
Number of titles published annually: 7 Print
Imprints: Bulletin de l'Institut Francais d'Etudes Andines; Travaux de l'Institut Francais d'Etudes Andines

**Editorial Horizonte**
Av Nicolas de Pierola 995, Lima 1
*Tel:* (01) 427-9364 *Fax:* (01) 427-4341
*Key Personnel*
Manager: Humberto Damonte
Production Manager: Eduardo Collazos
Sales Manager: Fernando Damonte
Founded: 1968
Subjects: Anthropology, Art, Economics, Education, History, Language Arts, Linguistics, Literature, Literary Criticism, Essays, Philosophy, Social Sciences, Sociology
ISBN Prefix(es): 84-89307
*Associate Companies:* Codice Ediciones, Casilla 2118, Lima 100

**Editorial Lima 2000 SA**
Av Arquipa 2625, Lince, Lima 14
*Tel:* (01) 440-3486 *Fax:* (01) 440-3480
*E-mail:* informes@lima2000.com.pe
*Web Site:* www.lima2000.com.pe
*Key Personnel*
Dir: Doris C Lopez
Subjects: Cartography
ISBN Prefix(es): 9972-654

**Lluvia Editores Srl+**
Av Inca Garcilaso de la Vega 1976, Lima 1

*Tel:* (01) 3326641 *Fax:* (01) 4320732
*E-mail:* lluviaeditores2002@yahoo.com
*Key Personnel*
Contact: Esteban Quiroz Cisneros
Founded: 1978
Subjects: Literature, Literary Criticism, Essays
ISBN Prefix(es): 9972-627

**Ediciones Peisa (Promocion Editorial Inca SA)**
Av Dos de Mayo 1285, San Isidro, Lima 27
*Tel:* (01) 4404603; (01) 4410473 *Fax:* (01) 4425906
*E-mail:* peisa@terro.com.pe
*Key Personnel*
Man Dir: German Coronado Vallenas
Editor: Martha Munoz de Coronado
Founded: 1969
Subjects: Foreign Countries
ISBN Prefix(es): 9972-40
Imprints: Catalogo
Distributor for Aranco (Spain); Concorcio Natuzart (Spain); Folio (Spain); Tres Torres (Spain)

**Libreria Studium SA+**
Pl Francia 1164, Lima 1
Mailing Address: PO Box 2139, Lima 1
*Tel:* (01) 326278; (01) 275960; (01) 325528 *Fax:* (01) 4325354
*Key Personnel*
Manager: Enrique Remy V
Purchasing & Exporting Manager: Sergio Costa B
Founded: 1936
Subjects: Ethnicity

**Sur Casa de Estudios del Socialismo**
Av Brasil 1329-201, Lima 11
*Tel:* (01) 4235431 *Fax:* (01) 4235431
*E-mail:* casasur@terra.com.pe
*Web Site:* www.casasur.org
*Key Personnel*
Dir: Cecilia Rivera Orams
Founded: 1986
Membership(s): The Camara Peruana del Libro.
Subjects: Anthropology, Developing Countries, Economics, History, Literature, Literary Criticism, Essays, Philosophy, Social Sciences, Sociology
ISBN Prefix(es): 9972-619

**Tarea Asociacion de Publicaciones Educativas+**
Parque Oseres 161, Pueblo Libre, Lima 21
*Tel:* (01) 424-0997 *Fax:* (01) 332-7404
*E-mail:* postmaster@tarea.org.pe
*Web Site:* www.tarea.org.pe
*Key Personnel*
President: Luisa Pinto
Dir: Julio del Valle Ramos
Founded: 1974
Subjects: Education
ISBN Prefix(es): 84-89296; 9972-618

**Tassorello SA**
Ave Flora Tristan 547, Magdalena del Mar, Lima 17
*Tel:* (01) 460-2040; (01) 460-0255 *Fax:* (01) 461-5714
*E-mail:* tassorello@terra.com.pe
*Key Personnel*
Contact: Andres Carbone
Founded: 1992
Subjects: Accounting, Education, Human Relations
ISBN Prefix(es): 9972-609

**Travaux de l'Institut Francais d'Etudes Andines**, *imprint of* Instituto Frances de Estudios Andinos, IFEA

**Universidad de Lima-Fondo de Desarollo Editorial+**
Av Manuel Olguin 125, Urb Los Granados, Surco, Lima 33
*Tel:* (01) 437-6767 *Fax:* (01) 437-8066; (01) 435-3396
*E-mail:* fondo_ed@lima.edu.pe
*Web Site:* www.ulima.edu.pe
*Key Personnel*
Executive Dir: Jose Valdizan Ayala
Founded: 1962
Subjects: Communications, Computer Science, Economics, Engineering (General), Film, Video, Finance, Journalism, Law, Management, Marketing, Photography, Psychology, Psychiatry, Radio, TV, Science (General)
ISBN Prefix(es): 84-89358; 9972-45
Number of titles published annually: 40 Print
Total Titles: 500 Print

**Universidad Nacional Mayor de San Marcos**
Ciudad Universitaria, Av German Amezaga, Lima
*Tel:* (01) 428-9272; (01) 433-5922 *Fax:* (01) 428-5210
*Web Site:* www.unmsm.edu.pe
*Key Personnel*
Man Dir: Dr Wilson Reateggui Chavez
Founded: 1952
Subjects: Engineering (General), Law, Literature, Literary Criticism, Essays, Medicine, Nursing, Dentistry, Science (General)
*Bookshop(s):* Av Nicolas de Pierola 1222, Lima 1

**Editorial Universo SA**
Ave Nicolas Arriola 2285, Urb Apolo, La Victoria, Apdo 241, Lima 30
*Tel:* (014) 241639; (014) 233190
*Key Personnel*
Man Dir: Jose Antonio Aquino Benavides
Executive Manager: Salvador Lau Barraza
Founded: 1967
Subjects: Social Sciences, Sociology

# Philippines

## General Information

*Capital:* Quezon City
*Language:* Filipino (based on Tagalog) is the native national language. English widely used. Nine other major languages of the Malayo-Polynesian group, and about 60 other languages, are also spoken
*Religion:* Predominantly Roman Catholic and some Islamic
*Population:* 67.1 million
*Bank Hours:* 0900-1600 Monday-Friday
*Shop Hours:* Vary. Many open 0900-1200, 1400-1930 Monday-Saturday (some close 1730; some open Sunday)
*Currency:* 100 centavos = 1 Philippine peso
*Export/Import Information:* Duty on books except those which are philosophical, historical, economic, scientific, technical or vocational, approved by Department of Education for use of certain institutions (not exceeding 10 copies for an institution, or two for an individual) or for encouragement of sciences or fine arts; no tariffs on Bibles and similar religious books. No duty on advertising matter. No import licenses, but no obscene or immoral literature permitted. Release certificate issued on behalf of Central Bank required to clear goods. Imports subject to sales tax. No formal exchange controls but most imports need Letter of Credit (over $100 in any month, for example).
*Copyright:* UCC (see Copyright Conventions, pg xi)

**Abiva Publishing House Inc+**
851-881 Gregorio Araneta Ave, 1113 Quezon City
*Tel:* (02) 7120245 *Fax:* (02) 7320308
*E-mail:* info@abiva.com.ph
*Web Site:* www.abiva.com.ph
*Key Personnel*
President: Luis Q Abiva Jr
Executive Vice President: Nena A Garcia
Vice President, International Rights: Jorge Abiva Garcia
Founded: 1936
Subjects: Education, History, Religion - Other, Science (General)
ISBN Prefix(es): 971-553
Total Titles: 1 CD-ROM; 1 Audio
Subsidiaries: ACG Asian Tradelinks Inc; Hiyas Press
*Branch Office(s)*
2/F, Cebu Holdings Cente, Cebu Business Park, Cebu City
Matina Highway, Davao City

**Anvil Publishing Inc+**
Team Pacific Bldg, 2nd floor, Jose Cruz St, Bo Ugong, Pasig City
*Tel:* (02) 671888 *Fax:* (02) 6719235
*E-mail:* anvil@fc.emc.com.ph; pubdept@anvil.com.ph
*Key Personnel*
General Manager: Cecilia R Licauco
Publishing Manager: Karina A Bolasco
Marketing Consultant: Gwenn Jessica A Galvez
Founded: 1990
Also acts as wholesaler & distributor of paperbacks & tradebooks from the US & UK.
Subjects: Cookery, Crafts, Games, Hobbies, Fiction, Gardening, Plants, Health, Nutrition, How-to, Humor, Language Arts, Linguistics, Literature, Literary Criticism, Essays, Mysteries, Religion - Catholic, Romance, Science Fiction, Fantasy, Western Fiction, Women's Studies
ISBN Prefix(es): 971-27
Number of titles published annually: 150 Print
Total Titles: 600 Print
*Parent Company:* National Bookstore, 125 Pioneer St, Mandaluyong City, Metro Manila
*Associate Companies:* Megastrat Inc
*Shipping Address:* 8007-B Pioneer St, Brgy, Kapitolyo, 1600 Pasig City *Tel:* (02) 637-5692; (02) 637-3621 *Fax:* (02) 637-6084
*E-mail:* anvilsales@eudoramail.com
*Warehouse:* 8007-B Pioneer St, Brgy, Kapitolyo, 1600 Pasig City *Tel:* (02) 637-5692; (02) 637-3621 *Fax:* (02) 637-6084 *E-mail:* anvilsales@eudoramail.com

**Ateneo de Manila University Press+**
Katipunan Rd, Loyola Heights, 1108 Quezon City
*Tel:* (02) 4265984; (02) 4261238 *Fax:* (02) 4265909
*E-mail:* unipress@pusit.admu.edu.ph (business/operations)
*Web Site:* www.admu.edu.ph
*Key Personnel*
Dir: Esther M Pacheco *E-mail:* empachec@pusit.admu.edu.ph
Founded: 1972
Membership(s): Book Development Association of the Philippines; International Association of Scholarly Publishers.
Subjects: Anthropology, Architecture & Interior Design, Asian Studies, Behavioral Sciences, Drama, Theater, Economics, Education, Environmental Studies, Fiction, Government, Political Science, History, Literature, Literary Criticism, Essays, Poetry, Psychology, Psychiatry, Religion - Catholic, Social Sciences, Sociology, Theology, Women's Studies, Social Sciences
ISBN Prefix(es): 971-550
Number of titles published annually: 25 Print
Total Titles: 150 Print

*Parent Company:* Ateneo de Manila University
Distributed by University of Hawaii Press

**BFP Super Romance**, *imprint of* Books for Pleasure Inc

**Bookman Printing & Publishing House Inc+**
2/F Bookman Bldg, 373 Quezon Ave, 1114 Quezon City
*Tel:* (02) 712-4813; (02) 712-4818; (02) 712-4843; (02) 740-8108; (02) 740-8107; (02) 712-3587 *Fax:* (02) 712-4843
*E-mail:* bookman@info.com.ph *Cable:* BOOKMAN
*Key Personnel*
President: Lina P Enriquez
Vice President: Marietta P Martinez
Editorial Dir: Ursula G Picache
Founded: 1945
Subjects: Education, English as a Second Language, Mathematics, Nonfiction (General), Science (General)
ISBN Prefix(es): 971-712

**Bookmark Inc+**
264-A Pablo Ocampo Sr Ave, Makati City
*Tel:* (02) 8958061; (02) 8958062; (02) 8958063; (02) 8958064; (02) 8958065 *Fax:* (02) 8970824; (02) 8994248
*E-mail:* bookmark@info.com.ph; bookmktg@info.com.ph
*Web Site:* www.bookmark.com.ph
*Telex:* Bookmark Manila
*Key Personnel*
President: Amb Bienvenido A Tan, Jr
Vice President: Florencia D Reyes
General Manager: Jose Maria Lorenzo Tan
Founded: 1945
Membership(s): Association of Philippine Booksellers.
Subjects: Child Care & Development, Cookery, Gardening, Plants, History, Religion - Other, Travel
ISBN Prefix(es): 971-569
*Branch Office(s)*
Taft Ave, Makati, Metro Manila
Delta Arcade Bldg, Makati, Metro Manila
*Showroom(s):* 357 T Pinpin Escolta, Manila; Delta Arcade Bldg, Makati, Metro Manila
*Bookshop(s):* Delta Arcade Bldg, Makati, Metro Manila; 357 T Pinpin Escolta, Manila

**Books for Pleasure Inc+**
FORC Bldg, Room 302, N Domingo Cor F Roman St, 1500 San Juan, Metro Manila
*Tel:* (02) 771807 *Fax:* (02) 7275240
*E-mail:* vromance@compass.com.ph
*Key Personnel*
Vice President: Ramon A Fabella
Founded: 1976
Subjects: Cookery, Mysteries, Romance
ISBN Prefix(es): 971-502
Imprints: BFP Super Romance; Hiwaga Mystery Novels; Valentine Romance; Young Love

**Bright Concepts Printing House+**
095 Santiago, 2022 Sta Ana, Pampanga
*Tel:* (0917) 627-3803
*E-mail:* dawnphilatelics@yahoo.com
*Key Personnel*
Author, Publisher: Jorge Henson Cuyugan *Tel:* (0917) 647-3803
Founded: 1992
Subjects: Business, Crafts, Games, Hobbies
ISBN Prefix(es): 971-607
*Orders to:* Booklore Publishing Corp, Blk 2, Lot 13, Ridgemont Village, Cainta, Rizal *Tel:* 252-4280, 251-0771 *Fax:* 563-7629

**Cacho Publishing House, Inc+**
Pines Cor Union St, 1501 Mandaluyong City,
Metro Manila
*Tel:* (02) 783011-13 *Fax:* (02) 6315244
*E-mail:* cacho@s.com.ph
*Key Personnel*
President: Herbert T Veloso
General Manager: Ramon C Sunico
Founded: 1880
ISBN Prefix(es): 971-19
*Parent Company:* National Bookstore Inc
*Associate Companies:* Anvil Publishing Inc; Ca-
cho Hermanos Inc *Tel:* (02) 6318361 *Fax:* (02)
6315244 *E-mail:* cacho@mozcom.com
Distributed by Impex (Japan)

**Claretian Communications Inc+**
UPPO Box 4, 1101 Diliman, Quezon City
*Tel:* (02) 9213984 *Fax:* (02) 9217429
*E-mail:* cci@claret.org; claret@info.com.ph
*Web Site:* www.bible.claret.org
*Key Personnel*
Executive Dir, Rights & Permissions: Fr Alberto
Rossa *Fax:* (02) 9219429
Founded: 1983
Subjects: Biblical Studies, Environmental Studies,
Law, Theology, Women's Studies
ISBN Prefix(es): 971-501
*Bookshop(s):* Claretian Publications (CP) Book-
store, Fr Alberto Rossa

**Communication Foundation for Asia Media
Group (CFAMG)**
4427 Second Old Sta Mesa, Manila
Mailing Address: PO Box SM434, Manila
*Tel:* (02) 607411; (02) 607412; (02) 607413;
(02) 607414; (02) 607415; (02) 607416; (02)
7132981 *Fax:* (02) 612504; (02) 7132974
*E-mail:* cfa@mozcom.com
*Telex:* 27854 Cfa Ph *Cable:* SOCOMTER
MANILA
*Key Personnel*
Moderator: Filoteo C Pelingon
Founded: 1965
Membership(s): The People in Communication
Network (BOARD); The Association of Foun-
dations; Philippine Partnership for the Devel-
opment of Human Resources in Rural Areas
(PHILDHRRA); OCICUNDA.
Subjects: Agriculture, Biblical Studies, Biography,
Communications, Environmental Studies, Film,
Video, Philosophy, Religion - Other, Theol-
ogy, AV Productions, Communication Training,
Communication Research & Planning, Devel-
opment Communication, Print Media & Publi-
cations
ISBN Prefix(es): 971-577
*Branch Office(s)*
Communication Training Center (Sanggar Bina
Tama), Suddirman no 3, Surayaba 60136, In-
donesia, Contact: Dr John Tondowidjojo

**De La Salle University+**
DBB-B Dasmarinas, De La Salle University, 4115
Cavite
*Tel:* (02) 741-9271; (046) 416-0338; (046) 416-
3878 *Fax:* (02) 5264237
*E-mail:* mcovatg@dlsu.edu.ph
*Web Site:* www.dasma.dlsu.edu.ph
*Key Personnel*
Contact: Mr Anthon Garcia
Founded: 1983
Membership(s): International Association of
Scholarly Publishers.
Subjects: Asian Studies, Business, Education, Fic-
tion, Literature, Literary Criticism, Essays, Phi-
losophy, Poetry, Religion - Catholic
ISBN Prefix(es): 971-92082

**Estrella Publishing+**
66 Niog St, Bacoor, 4102 Cavite

*Key Personnel*
Author & Publisher: Ervie Nangca-Antonio
Founded: 1993
Pocket books.
Subjects: Fiction, Romance
ISBN Prefix(es): 971-645
*Book Club(s):* Kapisanan Ng Mga Manunulat Ng
Nobelang Popular

**Galleon Publications+**
National Federation of Womens Club Bldg, 962
Josefa Escoda St, 1000 Emrita, Manila
*Tel:* (02) 592-519; (02) 523-1825 *Fax:* (02) 525-
6129
*Key Personnel*
President & Publisher: Alfonso J Aluit
Founded: 1968
Publish guidebooks to Philippine destinations &
works on topical Philippine history.
Subjects: Biography, History, Travel
ISBN Prefix(es): 971-8521
Total Titles: 30 Print
Distributed by Bookmark Inc
Membership(s): SATW

**Garotech**
903 Quezon Ave, 4332 Quezon City, Metro
Manila
*Tel:* (02) 993286 *Cable:* Romgar Manila
*Key Personnel*
Man Dir, Sales, Publicity: Rolando M Garcia
Editorial: Maridel Garcia
Founded: 1951
Subjects: Business, Education, Ethnicity, Foreign
Countries, Government, Political Science, His-
tory
ISBN Prefix(es): 971-8711
*Parent Company:* Garcia Publishing House Inc
*Orders to:* PO Box 1860, Manila

**Hiwaga Mystery Novels**, *imprint of* Books for
Pleasure Inc

**International Rice Research Institute (IRRI)**
Los Banos, Laguna
Mailing Address: PO Box 7777, Metro Manila
*Tel:* (02) 845-0563; (02) 845-0569 *Fax:* (02) 845-
0606
*E-mail:* irri@cgiar.org
*Web Site:* www.irri.org
*Telex:* (IIT) 45365 RICE INST PM
*Key Personnel*
Dir General: Ronald P Cantrell
Founded: 1960
A nonprofit agricultural research & training insti-
tute established to improve the well-being of
present & generations of rice farmers & con-
sumers, particularly with low incomes.
Membership(s): Consultative Group on Interna-
tional Agricultural Research.
Subjects: Agriculture
ISBN Prefix(es): 971-22
*Parent Company:* CGIAR: Consultative Group on
International Research
Imprints: IRRI
*Bookshop(s):* Harvest Farm Magazine, 14 Wen-
chow St, Taipei, Taiwan, Province of China;
S Toeche-Mittler Verlag, Hindenburgstr 33,
6100 Darmstadt, Germany; Haryana Scientific
Corporation, Gandhi Chowk, Hisar, Haryana
125001, India; Oxford Book & Stationery Co,
Scindia House, New Delhi 11001, India; Amer-
ican Overseas Company, 550 Walnut St, Nor-
wood, NJ 07648, United States; Agribookstore
IADS Inc, 1611 North Kent St, Arlington, VA
22209, United States

**IRRI**, *imprint of* International Rice Research
Institute (IRRI)

**J C Palabay Enterprises+**
67 Gen Ordonez St, Marikina Heights, 1800
Marikina City
*Tel:* (02) 9424512 *Fax:* (02) 9424513
*Telex:* 29001 PXO PH; 23322 PXO PH
*Key Personnel*
President: Jescie L Palabay
Vice President: Jemellie P Gonzales
Author: Concepcion Javier; Servillano Marquez,
Jr
Editor: Lourdes Arellano; Erlinda Valientes
Founded: 1974
Also importer of science laboratory equipment &
globes.
Subjects: History
ISBN Prefix(es): 971-13
*Parent Company:* J C Palabay Enterprises Inc
*Associate Companies:* Four J Arts; Instructional
Material Council, Meralco Ave, Pasig City;
Mhelle L Publications

**Kadena Press+**
2 Mayumi St, Up Village, Dilman, 1101 Quezon
City, Metro Manila
*Tel:* (02) 9217429; (02) 9213984
*Key Personnel*
Executive Dir: Fr Alberto Rossa
Founded: 1991
Subjects: Fiction
ISBN Prefix(es): 971-32
*Parent Company:* Claretian Communications Inc

**Logos (Divine Word) Publications Inc+**
1916 Oroquieta St, Sta Cruz, Manila
*Tel:* (02) 7111323 *Fax:* (02) 7322736
*E-mail:* dwpsvd@rp1.net
*Key Personnel*
Dir: Fr Gerry del Pinado SVD
Founded: 1987
Subjects: Business, Communications, Education,
Religion - Other
ISBN Prefix(es): 971-510
Total Titles: 5 Audio
*Parent Company:* Society of the Divine Word

**Marren Publishing House, Inc**
851 Oroquieta St, 1003 Santa Cruz, Manila
*Tel:* (02) 7115829 *Fax:* (02) 7115830
*Key Personnel*
Sales & Marketing Manager: Joan Elena B Cel-
lona
Subjects: Cookery, Fiction
ISBN Prefix(es): 971-649
Subsidiaries: MRE Trading Inc

**Sonny A Mendoza+**
Unit 31, Parian Commercial Center, Common-
wealth Ave, Dilman, 1100 Quezon City, Metro
Manila
*Tel:* (02) 8691111
*Key Personnel*
Publisher: Sonny Mendoza
Marketing Manager: Ramon N Orbeta
Production Manager: Armando S Peralta
Founded: 1991
Specialize in Filipino/Tagalog crosswords puzzles;
also acts as distributor of Tagalog romance
novels.
Subjects: Crafts, Games, Hobbies, Humor, Ro-
mance
ISBN Prefix(es): 971-599
*Orders to:* Apt 2, No 59 Paseo de Roxas, Ur-
baneta Village, Makati, Metro Manila

**Mindanao State University - Mamitua Saber
Research Center**
Andres Bonifacio Ave, 9200 Iligan City
*Tel:* (063) 2214050; (063) 3516151; (063)
3516152; (063) 3516172; (063) 3516174; (063)
3516153; (063) 3516154; (063) 3516155; (063)
3516156 *Fax:* (063) 221405

*Web Site:* www.msumain.edu.ph/units/msrc/
*Key Personnel*
Dir, Research: Federico V Magdalena, PhD
Managing Editor: Khayruddin M Tawano
ISBN Prefix(es): 971-8708

**Mutual Book Inc+**
425 Shaw Blvd, Mandaluyong City
*Tel:* (02) 796050 *Cable:* MUBINC
*Key Personnel*
President: Alfredo S Nicdao, Jr
Founded: 1959
Subjects: Accounting, Business, Computer Science, Economics, Management, Mathematics
ISBN Prefix(es): 971-587
*Associate Companies:* Alfredo S Nicdao Jr Inc
*Shipping Address:* PO Box 245, Greenhills, San Juan, 1502 Metro Manila

**National Book Store Inc**
Quad Alpha Centrum, 125 Pioneer St, 1550 Mandaluyong City
*Tel:* (02) 6318061; (02) 6318062; (02) 6318063; (02) 6318064; (02) 6318065; (02) 6318066
*Fax:* (02) 6318079
*E-mail:* info@nationalbookstore.com.ph
*Web Site:* www.nationalbookstore.com.ph
*Telex:* 27890 NBS-PH; 41144 NBS-PM
*Cable:* Nabost Manila
*Key Personnel*
Man Dir: Mr Benjamin C Ramos
Sales Dir: Mitto Licauco
Publicity, Advertising: Mrs Socorro C Ramos
Rights & Permissions: Mr Alfredo C Ramos
Founded: 1945
Firm reprints over 300 titles annually for foreign publishers.
Subjects: Art, Fiction, How-to, Music, Dance, Nonfiction (General)
ISBN Prefix(es): 971-08

**National Historical Institute**
Affiliate of National Commission on Culture & the Arts
TM Kalaw St, 4th floor, Ermita, Manila
*Tel:* (02) 590646; (02) 572644 *Fax:* (02) 5250144
*Key Personnel*
Curator: Teresita L Pagulayan
ISBN Prefix(es): 971-538

**National Museum of the Philippines**
P Burgos St, 1000 Manila
*Tel:* (02) 5271215 *Fax:* (02) 5270306
*E-mail:* nmuseum@i-next.net
*Web Site:* members.tripod.com/philmuseum/index; nmuseum.tripod.com/index.htm
*Key Personnel*
Dir & Proprietor: Gabriel S Casal
Curator: Rosario B Tantoco
Founded: 1901
The National Museum collects, identifies, preserves & exhibits the country's rich cultural heritage.
Subjects: Anthropology, Archaeology, Art, Biological Sciences, Geography, Geology, Natural History, Botanical, Ethnological, Zoological collections
ISBN Prefix(es): 971-567
Total Titles: 50 Print; 4 CD-ROM; 1 Online; 1 E-Book
*Bookshop(s):* National Museum Souvenir Shop, P Burgos St, Manila, Contact: Elenita D V Alba *Tel:* (02) 5270278 *Fax:* (02) 5270306 *E-mail:* nmuseum@i-next.net *Web Site:* nmuseumi-next.net

**New Day Publishers+**
11 Lands St, VASRA, 1100 Quezon City
Mailing Address: PO Box 1167, 1100 Quezon City

*Tel:* (02) 9988046; (02) 9275982 *Fax:* (02) 9246544
*E-mail:* newday@pworld.net.ph; newdayorders@edsamail.com.ph
*Key Personnel*
Executive Dir, Rights/Permissions & Manuscript Submissions: Ms Bezalie Bautista Uc-Kung
*Tel:* (02) 9268049
Publicity, Marketing & Promotions: Mr Jesus Bacolores
Founded: 1969
Membership(s): World Association for Christian Communication; Book Development Association of the Philippines; National Book Development Board.
Subjects: Anthropology, Asian Studies, Behavioral Sciences, Biblical Studies, Biography, Business, Career Development, Communications, Cookery, Economics, Education, Ethnicity, Fiction, History, How-to, Human Relations, Humor, Labor, Industrial Relations, Literature, Literary Criticism, Essays, Management, Marketing, Nonfiction (General), Philosophy, Poetry, Religion - Catholic, Religion - Protestant, Romance, Science Fiction, Fantasy, Self-Help, Theology
ISBN Prefix(es): 971-10
Number of titles published annually: 20 Print
Total Titles: 500 Print

**Newark International Enterprises+**
Room 507, FUBC Bldg, Escolta, Manila
*Tel:* (02) 2432077 *Fax:* (02) 2414893
*Key Personnel*
General Manager & Publisher: Mabini D Castillo
ISBN Prefix(es): 971-9071
Distributed by Goodwill Bookstore/Goodwill Trading Co Inc; Merriam & Webster Inc

**Our Lady of Manaoag Publisher+**
3078-B Reposo Ext, Sta Mesa, Manila
*Tel:* (02) 610214; (02) 610219 *Fax:* (06) 610219
*Key Personnel*
President: Dr Tomas Q D Andres
Marketing Dir: Pilar Corazon I Andres
Circulation Manager: Pilar Philamer I Andres; Thomas Philamer Andres
Founded: 1980
Also acts as a training centre that conducts Philippine based managment in Filipino language.
Subjects: Anthropology, Art, Asian Studies, Behavioral Sciences, Biblical Studies, Business, Career Development, Child Care & Development, Communications, Developing Countries, Education, Ethnicity, Film, Video, History, Humor, Management, Philosophy, Religion - Catholic
ISBN Prefix(es): 971-26; 971-91093
*Parent Company:* Values & Technologies Management Centre
Subsidiaries: Management Business Achievers Inc
Divisions: Philippine Institute of Management
*Warehouse:* 2004 C Arellano St, Sta Mesa, Manila

**Pearson Education Asia**
2/F J-L Bldg, 23 Matalino St, Bgy. Central, Dillman, 11011 Quezon City
*Tel:* (02) 434 5501 *Fax:* (02) 433466
*E-mail:* custserv@pearsoned.com.ph
*Web Site:* www.pearsoned.com
*Key Personnel*
Marketing Executive: Mary Antonette Tucit
*E-mail:* dovie@pearsoned.com.ph; Ariel Pagdanganan *E-mail:* arielp@pearson.com.ph; Mary Ann Gonzalez *E-mail:* gonzalez@pearson.com.ph
Sales Manager: Dennis Elmer Lazo
*E-mail:* denlazo@pearsoned.com.ph
Number of titles published annually: 30 Print

Total Titles: 60 Print
*Parent Company:* Pearson Education

**Philippine Baptist Mission SBC FMB Church Growth International**
2444 Taft Av, Malate, Metro Manila
*Tel:* (02) 526-0264; (02) 526-0265; (02) 526-0266; (02) 526-0267; (02) 599256; (02) 599257
*Fax:* (02) 522-4639
*E-mail:* csm@i-manila.com.ph
*Web Site:* www.fsbc.org.ph
*Key Personnel*
Mission Administrative Officer: J Allen Hill
*E-mail:* pbml-maoffice@netasia.net
Dir, Business Services: David "Chip" Clary
*E-mail:* pbml-bservices@netasia.net
Dir, Field Services: Phillip Brewster
*E-mail:* brewster@skyinet.net
Subjects: Biblical Studies, History, Religion - Protestant, Theology
ISBN Prefix(es): 971-512
*Shipping Address:* Church Strengthening Ministry, 4796 Mercado St, Makati, Metro Manila
*Orders to:* Church Strengthening Ministry, 4796 Mercado St, Makati, Metro Manila

**Philippine Education Co Inc**
140 Amorsolo St, 7th floor, Legaspi Village, Metro Manila
*Tel:* (02) 487215; (02) 487317
*E-mail:* publications@pidsnet.pids.gov.ph
*Web Site:* www.pids.gov.ph
*Telex:* 7222321 *Cable:* Pecoi Manila
*Key Personnel*
General Manager: Antero L Soriano
Subjects: Art, Education, Fiction, Social Sciences, Sociology
ISBN Prefix(es): 971-09

**Rex Bookstores & Publishers+**
84 P Florentino St, Sta Mesa Heights, 1008 Quezon City, Metro Manila
*Tel:* (02) 7437688; (02) 4143512; (02) 4146774
*Fax:* (02) 7437687
*E-mail:* rex@usinc.net
*Key Personnel*
President: Dominador D Buhain
International Sales & Foreign Rights Coordinator: Sonia A Santiago *E-mail:* sasantiago@rexpublishing.com.ph
Founded: 1950
Membership(s): Asia/Pacific Publishers Association; International Publishers Association.
Subjects: Accounting, Agriculture, Anthropology, Archaeology, Behavioral Sciences, Biological Sciences, Business, Child Care & Development, Cookery, Criminology, Economics, Education, Environmental Studies, Finance, History, Human Relations, Labor, Industrial Relations, Law, Maritime, Marketing, Mathematics, Parapsychology, Physics, Psychology, Psychiatry, Science (General), Social Sciences, Sociology, Theology, Travel
ISBN Prefix(es): 971-23
Number of titles published annually: 100 Print
*Ultimate Parent Company:* Rex Group of Companies
*Branch Office(s)*
1906 Cecile Bldg, Mac-Arthur H-way, Balibago, Angeles City, Acting Officer In Charge: Almira Manaloto *Tel:* (045) 892-17-21
Ateneo Professional School, 1st floor, Rockwell Center, Bel-Air Makati, Officer In Charge: Helen Riosa *Tel:* 729-20-75
Duran Bldg, del Pilar Ext (crossing) Sangitan E, Cabanatuan, Officer In Charge: Gigi Yatco *Fax:* (044) 600-56-84
Cor J Serina St, Valmenta Blvd, Carmen, Cagayan de Oro, Officer In Charge: Lourdes Dicipulo *Tel:* (088) 858-67-75

11 Sanciangko St, Cebu City, Officer In Charge:
Mabel Quijano *Tel:* (032) 254-67-73; (032)
254-67-74 *Fax:* (032) 254-64-66
Rustan's Superstore Bldg, Unit 4-A, Cubao, Officer In Charge: Luisa Lagat *Fax:* 911-10-70
156 CM Recto St, Davao City, Officer In Charge:
Lourdes Dicipulo *Tel:* (082) 225-31-67, (082)
221-78-40 *Fax:* (088) 221-02-72
Aparente St, Dadiangas Heights, General San-
tos City, Officer In Charge: Hilda Malayao
*Tel:* (083) 554-71-02
75 Brgy San Isidro Lopez-Jaena Jaro, Iloilo, Of-
ficer In Charge: Mabel Quijano *Tel:* (033) 329-
03-32 *Fax:* (033) 329-03-36
Magallanes cor Alonzo St, Legaspi City, Officer
In Charge: Ben Pring *Tel:* (052) 820-22-70
Star Centrum Bldg, Unit UG-2, Sen Gil Puyat
Ave, Makati, Officer In Charge: Helen Riosa
*Tel:* 893-37-44; 818-53-63
Facilities Center Bldg, 548 Shaw Blvd, Man-
daluyong, Officer In Charge: Tina de la Cruz
*Tel:* 531-13-06 *Fax:* 531-13-39
Zone 6 Pinmaludpod Urdaneta, Pangasinan, Offi-
cer In Charge: Che che Agcamaran *Fax:* (075)
568-39-75
856 Nicanor Reyes St, Samp, Manila, Officer
In Charge: Fatima Yumiaco *Tel:* 736-05-67
*Fax:* 736-41-91
1977 CM Recto Ave, Sampaloc, Manila, Officer
In Charge: Teodora Anastacio *Tel:* 735-55-27
*Fax:* 735-55-34
Lot 6, Blk 5 Cityview IV Brgy Tanauan, Tanza
Cavity, Officer In Charge: Easter Rapada
*Book Club(s):* Phil Educational Publishers Associ-
ation, Contact: Dominador D Buhain
*Warehouse:* 84 P Florentino Av, 1008 Quezon
City *Tel:* (02) 712 4101 (ext 128) *Fax:* (02)
740 2702 *E-mail:* sasantiago@rexpublishing.
com.ph

**Saint Mary's Publishing Corp+**
3/F VCC Bldg, 1308 P Guevarra St, Sta Cruz,
Manila
*Tel:* (02) 7119730; (02) 7119743 *Fax:* (02)
7350955
*Key Personnel*
Contact: Jerry Vicente S Catabijan
Founded: 1995
Membership(s): PEPA; BDAP; CLAPI.
Subjects: Economics, Education, English as a
Second Language, Geography, Geology, His-
tory, Language Arts, Linguistics, Mathematics,
Science (General), Social Sciences, Sociology
ISBN Prefix(es): 971-509

**Salesiana Publishers Inc+**
Pasay Rd cor Pasong Tamo, Makati City, Manila
*Tel:* (02) 8161506; (02) 889234 *Fax:* (02)
8922154 *Cable:* SALESIANA PUBLISHERS
MANILA
*Key Personnel*
Rector, Editor-in-Chief & all other offices: Fr
Demetrio M Carmona
Founded: 1979
Subjects: Communications, Computer Science,
Earth Sciences, Human Relations, Language
Arts, Linguistics, Literature, Literary Criti-
cism, Essays, Mathematics, Physics, Religion
- Catholic, Science (General), Social Sciences,
Sociology, Technology
ISBN Prefix(es): 971-8532; 971-522
*Branch Office(s)*
Salesiana-Bacolod, c/o RU Commercial Center,
North Drive, Bacolod City (in front of River-
side Hospital)
Salesiana-Baguio, UB Commercial Complex, Gen
Luuna St, Baguio City
*Book Club(s):* Philippine Bookfair Association

**San Carlos Publications**
University of San Carlos, 6000 Cebu City

Mailing Address: P Del Rosario St, 6000 Cebu
City
*Tel:* (032) 253-1000 *Fax:* (032) 255-4341
*E-mail:* uscjournals@lycos.com
*Key Personnel*
Editor: Harold Olofson
Founded: 1973
Membership(s): International Association of
Scholarly Publishers & Council of Editors of
Learned Journals.
Subjects: Anthropology, Archaeology, Biological
Sciences, History, Social Sciences, Sociology
ISBN Prefix(es): 971-539

**SIBS Publishing House Inc**
8/F Globe Telecom Plaza II, Pioneer Highlands,
Pioneer Corner Madison Streets, 1552 Man-
daluyong City
*Tel:* 687-6164 *Fax:* 687-1716
*E-mail:* sibsbook@info.com.ph; sibs@eyp.ph
*Web Site:* www.sibs.com.ph
*Key Personnel*
President: Carmen Mimette M Sibal
Vice President, Operations: Anita S Mangalindan
Head, Research & Development: Dr Juanita S
Guerrero
Editor-in-Chief: Rogelio Mangahas
Managing Editor: Mamel Teh
Art Dir: Antonio M Concepcion
Head, Promotions Department: Cora A Sapo
Project Coordinator: Agnes S Apostol *Tel:* (062)
372-7313
Founded: 1996
Membership(s): International Publishers Associa-
tion; Philippine Educational Publishers Associ-
ation.
Subjects: Art, Biological Sciences, Economics,
Education, English as a Second Language,
Environmental Studies, History, Journalism,
Language Arts, Linguistics, Literature, Liter-
ary Criticism, Essays, Mathematics, Nonfiction
(General), Religion - Other, Science (General),
Social Sciences, Sociology, Christian Living
Education, Civics & Culture, English, Filipino,
Preschool books - reading, language, math &
art, Values Education
ISBN Prefix(es): 971-791
*Branch Office(s)*
Mayor Maximo V Patalinghug Ave, Barangay
Pajo, 6015 Lapu-Lapu City, Cebu
*Tel:* (032) 340-6809 *Fax:* (032) 340-6808
*E-mail:* vismin@sibs.com.ph

**Silsilah Publication**
Edificio Ciudad, San Jose Rd, Zamboanga City
*Tel:* (02) 5663
ISBN Prefix(es): 971-31

**Sinag-Tala Publishers Inc+**
4th floor, Regina Bldg, cor Trasierra St, Legaspi
Village, Makati City, Manila
*Tel:* (02) 8192681 *Fax:* (02) 8192563
*Key Personnel*
Man Dir, Rights & Permissions: L A Uson
Marketing Dir: V A Tur
Founded: 1969
Subjects: Business, Economics, Religion -
Catholic
ISBN Prefix(es): 971-554

**Solidaridad Publishing House**
531 Padre Faura, Ermita, Manila
*Tel:* (02) 586581; (02) 591241 *Fax:* (02) 525-
5038 *Cable:* SOLDAD MANILA
*Key Personnel*
General Manager: F Sionil Jose
Founded: 1965
Subjects: Biography, Fiction, History
ISBN Prefix(es): 971-8845

**University of the Philippines Press+**
Unit of University of the Philippines System

E de los Santos St, Diliman, 1101 Quezon City
*Tel:* (02) 9205301; (02) 9205302; (02) 9205303;
(02) 9205304; (02) 9205305; (02) 9266642;
(02) 9253243; (02) 9253244 *Fax:* (02) 9282558
*E-mail:* press@nicole.upd.edu.ph; uppress@
uppress.org
*Web Site:* www.upd.edu.ph
*Key Personnel*
Dir, Rights & Permissions: Cristina Pantoja Hi-
dalgo
Sales, Publicity: Mabi David Balangue
Production: Conrado Calma
Editorial: Gerardo Los Banos
Founded: 1965
Subjects: Art, Business, Education, Fiction,
Government, Political Science, How-to, Law,
Medicine, Nursing, Dentistry, Music, Dance,
Philosophy, Psychology, Psychiatry, Religion
- Other, Science (General), Social Sciences,
Sociology, Technology
ISBN Prefix(es): 971-542
Number of titles published annually: 40 Print
Total Titles: 300 Print

**UST Publishing House+**
Beato Angelico Bldg, Espana St, Sampaloc, 1008
Manila
*Tel:* (02) 7313101 *Fax:* (02) 7811473
*E-mail:* qui_test@ust.edu.ph
*Web Site:* www.ust.edu.ph
*Key Personnel*
Contact: Joselito B Zulueta
Founded: 1593
Subjects: Architecture & Interior Design, Asian
Studies, Biblical Studies, Biological Sciences,
Business, Chemistry, Chemical Engineering,
Economics, Education, English as a Second
Language, Health, Nutrition, History, Liter-
ature, Literary Criticism, Essays, Medicine,
Nursing, Dentistry, Philosophy, Poetry, Religion
- Catholic, Social Sciences, Sociology, Theol-
ogy
ISBN Prefix(es): 971-506
*Parent Company:* University of Santo Tomas
Distributor for Bookmark; Heritage; Rarebook;
Solidaridad
*Book Club(s):* Book Development Association of
the Phillipines; Asian Catholic Publishers

**Valentine Romance,** *imprint of* Books for
Pleasure Inc

**Vera-Reyes Inc+**
4th floor, Mariwasa Bldg, 77 Aurora Blvd, Que-
zon City 1112
*Tel:* (02) 7218792 *Fax:* (02) 7218782
*Telex:* 63740 Vri pn *Cable:* Verareyes Manila
*Key Personnel*
Man Dir: L O Reyes
Publishing Dir: Gerardo P Legaspi
Dir, Medical Books: Gia Reyes
Founded: 1964
Subjects: Art, History, Medicine, Nursing, Den-
tistry, Philosophy, Religion - Other
ISBN Prefix(es): 971-575
Subsidiaries: International Typesetting Services;
Vera-Reyes Medical Books
*Bookshop(s):* Vera-Reyes Medical Books

**Vibal Publishing House Inc (VPHI)**
1253 G Araneta Ave, Quezon City
*Tel:* (02) 712-9156; (02) 712-2722; (02) 712-
9157; (02) 712-9158; (02) 712-9159 *Fax:* (02)
711-8852
*E-mail:* sales@vibalpublishing.com
*Web Site:* www.vibalpublishing.com
*Telex:* ITT 40404 *Cable:* VIBAL INC, MANILA
*Key Personnel*
Chief Executive: Esther A Vibal
Editorial: Rhodora S Yatco
Sales: Dina C Tapang
Production: Rolando S Mata

Publicity, Rights & Permissions: Carian M Espino
Founded: 1955
Subjects: Ethnicity, Foreign Countries, Language
Arts, Linguistics, Mathematics, Religion -
Other, Science (General), Social Sciences, So-
ciology
ISBN Prefix(es): 971-07
Parent Company: Nasionale Boekhandel Ltd
Subsidiaries: ASN Graphics; SD Publications
Branch Office(s)
VPHI Cebu Branch, 0290 Nivel Hills, Lahug,
Cebu City Tel: (032) 2330173; (032)
2330176; (032) 2332568 Fax: (032) 2332983
E-mail: vpcebu@vibalpublishing.com
Kalamansi St, Juna Subdivision, First St, Matina,
Davao City Tel: (082) 2975226 Fax: (082)
2978550 E-mail: vpdavao@vibalpublishing.
com

**VPHI**, see Vibal Publishing House Inc (VPHI)

**Young Love**, *imprint of* Books for Pleasure Inc

# Poland

## General Information

*Capital:* Warsaw
*Language:* Polish and some German. English also
used, especially among young people
*Religion:* Predominantly Roman Catholic
*Population:* 38.4 million
*Bank Hours:* 0800-1900 Monday-Friday, 0800-
1600 Saturday
*Shop Hours:* 1100-1900 Monday-Friday; 0900-
1300 Saturday
*Currency:* 100 groszy = 1 zloty
*Export/Import Information:* Import of books and
newspapers, duty free, no tax. Individual private importers allowed to act. Advertising may
be placed through AGPOL Foreign Trade Advertising agency, ul Kierbedzia 4, 7, 00-957
Warsaw. No import licenses as such required.
All overseas trade is conducted in foreign currency. Small quantities of advertising materials
duty free.
*Copyright:* UCC, Berne (see Copyright Conventions, pg xi)

### Albatros
Kazury 2/12, 02-795 Warsaw
*Tel:* (022) 842-9867 *Fax:* (022) 842-9867
*Key Personnel*
Owner & Editor-in-Chief: Andrzej Kurylowicz
E-mail: akurylowicz@wp.pl
Subjects: Fiction, Nonfiction (General)
Number of titles published annually: 80 Print
Total Titles: 110 Print

**Alfa**, *imprint of* Wydawnictwa Normalizacyjne
Alfa-Wero

### Aritbus et Historiae, Rivista Internationale di arti visive ecinema, Institut IRSA - Verlagsanstatt+
ul Szczepanska 9, 31-011 Krakow
*Tel:* (012) 421 90 30; (012) 421 91 55 *Fax:* (012)
421 48 07
*E-mail:* irsa@irsa.com.pl
*Web Site:* www.irsa.com.pl
*Key Personnel*
Publisher: Dr Jozef Grabski
Founded: 1979
Specialize in the history of art.
Subjects: Architecture & Interior Design, Art,
History
ISBN Prefix(es): 3-900731

### Wydawnictwo Arkady+
ul Dobra 28, skrytka pocztowa 137, 00-344 War-
saw
*Tel:* (022) 8268980; (022) 8267079; (022)
8269316; (022) 635 83 44 *Fax:* (022) 827 41
94
*E-mail:* arkady@arkady.com.pl
*Web Site:* arkady.com.pl
*Key Personnel*
President & Dir: Janina Krysiak *Tel:* (022) 826
93 16
Editor-in-Chief: Elzbieta Leszczynska *Tel:* (022)
826 22 57
Production Dir: Wieslaw Pyszka *Tel:* (022) 828
38 17; (022) 826 75 80
International Rights: Jadwiga Marek *Tel:* (022)
826 75 80
Founded: 1957
Subjects: Antiques, Architecture & Interior De-
sign, Art, Crafts, Games, Hobbies, Environ-
mental Studies, Photography
ISBN Prefix(es): 83-213

### Arlekin-Wydawnictwo Harlequin Enterprises sp zoo
Ul Rakowiecka 4, 00-975 Warsaw
Mailing Address: PO Box 11, 02-600 Warsaw 13
*Tel:* (022) 8499557; (022) 8499498; (022)
8498630 *Fax:* (022) 8499557
*Key Personnel*
Man Dir: Barbara Jozwiak
Founded: 1991
Subjects: Romance
ISBN Prefix(es): 83-7149; 83-7070

### Wydawnictwa Artystyczne i Filmowe
ul Pulawska 61, 02-595 Warsaw
*Tel:* (022) 8455301; (022) 8455584; (022)
8455465; (022) 8453936 *Fax:* (022) 8455584;
(022) 8455465; (022) 8453936
*Key Personnel*
Man Dir: Janusz Fogler
Editorial: Edward Rylukowski
Editorial, Publicity: Andrzej Dulewicz
Founded: 1959
Subjects: Art, Drama, Theater, Film, Video, Pho-
tography
ISBN Prefix(es): 83-221

### Atena
Ul Warszawska 13, 85-959 Bydgoszcz
*Tel:* (061) 228685 *Fax:* (061) 524082
*E-mail:* atena@poz1.commet.pl
ISBN Prefix(es): 83-902443

### Wydawnictwo Baturo (Baturo Publishers)+
ul Drobniewicza 26, 43-309 Bielsko-Biala
*Tel:* (033) 81 25 086; (033) 81 40 955;
(033) 81 62 703 *Fax:* (033) 81 40 955
*Fax on Demand:* (033) 8140955
*E-mail:* baturo@baturo.com.pl
*Web Site:* www.baturo.com.pl
*Key Personnel*
Contact: Andrzej Baturo; Inez Baturo
Founded: 1991
Membership(s): PTWK; PIK; Polish Book Cham-
ber; Polish Association of Book Publishers.
Subjects: Animals, Pets, Architecture & Interior
Design, Gardening, Plants, How-to, Photogra-
phy
ISBN Prefix(es): 83-900564; 83-905021
Number of titles published annually: 5 Print

**Beta Books**, *imprint of* Wydawnictwa
Normalizacyjne Alfa-Wero

**Beta Comics**, *imprint of* Wydawnictwa
Normalizacyjne Alfa-Wero

### Biblioteka Narodowa w Warszawie (The National Library in Warsaw)
ul Niepodleglosci 213, 02-086 Warsaw
*Tel:* (022) 608-2999; (022) 452-2999 *Fax:* (022)
825-7751
*E-mail:* biblnar@bn.org.pl
*Web Site:* www.bn.org.pl
*Telex:* 816761
*Key Personnel*
Head, Conservation Division: Ms Maria A Woz-
niak
Founded: 1928
Membership(s): IFLA; FID; IAM; AIB; ASLIB.
Subjects: Library & Information Sciences
ISBN Prefix(es): 83-7009

### BOSZ scp+
Olszania 311, 38-722 Olszanica
*Tel:* (013) 469 90 00 *Fax:* (013) 469 61 88
*E-mail:* biuro@ks.onet.pl
*Web Site:* www.bosz.com.pl
Subjects: Architecture & Interior Design, Art,
Photography, Travel

### Spoldzielnia Wydawnicza 'Czytelnik'+
ul Wiejska 12a, 00-490 Warsaw
*Tel:* (022) 6281441 *Fax:* (022) 6283178
*E-mail:* sekretariat@czytelnik.pl
*Web Site:* www.czytelnik.pl *Cable:* CZYTELNIK
WARSAW
*Key Personnel*
Man Dir, Chairman: Zakowski Marek
Foreign Rights: Anna Mencwel *Tel:* (022)
6289508 *E-mail:* am@czytelnik.pl
Founded: 1944
Subjects: Biography, Fiction, Journalism, Poetry,
Social Sciences, Sociology
ISBN Prefix(es): 83-07
Number of titles published annually: 90 Print

### Wydawnictwo DiG (DiG Publishing)+
Aleja Wojska Polskiego 4, 01-524 Warsaw
*Tel:* (022) 839 0838 *Fax:* (022) 828-00-96
*E-mail:* biuro@dig.com.pl
*Web Site:* www.dig.com.pl
*Key Personnel*
Man Dir: Slawomir Gorzynski
Dir: Krzysztof Dabrowski *E-mail:* kjd@dig.com.
pl
Founded: 1991
Independent publishing company specializing in
history & humanities.
Membership(s): Polska Izba Ksiazki (Polish Book
Chamber).
Subjects: Antiques, Archaeology, Art, Biography,
Genealogy, History, Language Arts, Linguistics,
Library & Information Sciences, Literature,
Literary Criticism, Essays
ISBN Prefix(es): 83-7181; 83-85490
Number of titles published annually: 80 Print; 2
CD-ROM; 2 Online; 2 E-Book
Total Titles: 250 Print
Distributed by Polnische Buchhandlung; Orbis
Book Ltd
*Bookshop(s):* Al Niepodlegosci 213, 02-086 War-
saw

### Wydawnictwo Dolnoslaskie+
ul Straznicza 1-3, 50-206 Warsaw
*Tel:* (071) 328 89 54; (071) 328 89 52; (071) 328
89 51; (071) 328 82 06 *Fax:* (071) 328 89 54
*E-mail:* sekretariat@wd.wroc.pl; wyd-dol@
mikrozet.wroc.pl
*Key Personnel*
President: Andrzej Adamus
Vice President & Editorial Manager: Jan Stolar-
czyk
Executive Secretary: Barbara Kocowska
E-mail: kocowska@wd.wvoc.pl
Production: Jacek Sajdak
Founded: 1986
Membership(s): the Polish Book Chamber.

Subjects: Art, Fiction, History, Literature, Literary Criticism, Essays, Mysteries, Poetry
ISBN Prefix(es): 83-7023; 83-7384
Number of titles published annually: 70 Print
Orders to: Ars Polona SAV, Krakowskie Przedmiescie 7, 00-950 Warsaw

**Dom Wydawniczy Bellona**
ul Grzybowska 77, 00-844 Warsaw
Tel: (022) 620 42 71; (022) 652 2765; (022) 45 70 306 Fax: (022) 620 42 71; (022) 652 2765; (022) 45 70 306
E-mail: handel@bellona.pl
Web Site: ksiegarnia.bellona.pl
Key Personnel
Dir: Jozef Skrzypiec

**Drukarnia I Ksiegarnia Swietego Wojciecha, Dziat Wydawniczy**
pl Wolnosci 1, 61-738 Poznan
Tel: (061) 8529186 Fax: (061) 8523746
E-mail: wydawnictwo.ksw@archpoznan.org.pl
Telex: 0414220 Kmp Cable: Albertinum Poznan
Key Personnel
Man Dir: Bogdan Reformat
Founded: 1895
Subjects: Biblical Studies, Religion - Catholic, Theology
ISBN Prefix(es): 83-7015
Branch Office(s)
ul Freta 48, 00-227 Warsaw
ul Krolewska 15, 20-109 Lubin
Bookshop(s): St Adalbert's Bookshop, pl Wolnosci 1, 61-738 Poznan

**Polskie Wydawnictwo Ekonomiczne PWE SA+**
ul Canaletta 4, Warsaw 00-099
Tel: (022) 827 80 01 Fax: (022) 827 55 67
E-mail: pwe@pwe.com.pl
Web Site: www.pwe.com.pl
Key Personnel
President & Editor-in-Chief: Alicja Rutkowska Tel: (022) 826 41 82 E-mail: arutko@pwe.com.pl
Dir: Blandyna Chmiel Tel: (022) 827 74 87 E-mail: chmiel@pwe.com.pl; Mariola Rozmus Tel: (022) 826 41 82 E-mail: mrozmus@pwe.com.pl
Founded: 1949
Polish economics publishers.
Membership(s): Polish Chamber of Books.
Subjects: Accounting, Advertising, Business, Economics, Environmental Studies, Finance, Management, Marketing
ISBN Prefix(es): 83-208
Number of titles published annually: 70 Print
Total Titles: 5,000 Print

**Energeia sp zoo Wydawnictwo**
ul Szturmowa 1, 02-678 Warsaw
Mailing Address: Skr Poczt 43, 00-976 Warsaw
Tel: (022) 847 00 53 Fax: (022) 847-00-53
Key Personnel
Man Dir: Jan E Okuniewski
Founded: 1991
Subjects: Drama, Theater, English as a Second Language, Language Arts, Linguistics, Literature, Literary Criticism, Essays
ISBN Prefix(es): 83-85118; 83-88236
Distributor for Julius Groos Verlag Heidelberg (Germany)

**Gdanskie Wydawnictwo Psychologiczne SC**
(Gdansk Psychology Publishing Company)+
ul Bema 4/1a, 81-753 Sopot
Tel: (058) 551-61-04; (058) 550-16-04; (058) 551-11-01 Fax: (058) 551-61-04; (058) 550-16-04
Web Site: www.gwp.pl
Key Personnel
General Manager: Magdalena Zylicz E-mail: magdaz@gwp.gda.pl

Founded: 1991
Publishes exclusively psychology books: academic textbooks, counselling books for psychotherapists & practical psychology for the general market.
Subjects: Psychology, Psychiatry, Self-Help
ISBN Prefix(es): 83-85416; 83-87957; 93-89120
Number of titles published annually: 20 Print
Total Titles: 100 Print

**Wydawnictwa Geologiczne**
ul Rakowiecka 4, 02-517 Warsaw
Tel: (022) 495351 (ext 518)
Key Personnel
Dir: Dr Marian Soldan
Founded: 1953
Subjects: Geography, Geology, Mathematics
ISBN Prefix(es): 83-220

**Instytut Historii Nauki PAN+**
Unit of Polish Academy of Sciences
ul Nowy Swiat 72, Pok 9, 00-330 Warsaw
Tel: (022) 826 87 54; (022) 65 72 746 Fax: (022) 826 61 37
E-mail: ihn@ihnpan.waw.pl
Web Site: www.ihnpan.waw.pl
Key Personnel
Editorial Manager: Anna Zawadzka
International Rights: Prof Andrzej Srodka
Subjects: Astronomy, Biography, Biological Sciences, Chemistry, Chemical Engineering, Earth Sciences, Education, Geography, Geology, History
ISBN Prefix(es): 83-900065; 83-900482; 83-900891; 83-86062
Total Titles: 10 Print

**Wydawnictwo Harcerskie 'Horyzonty'**, see Spotdzielna Anagram

**Impuls+**
31-559 Krakow ul, Grzegorzecka, 69-107 Krakow
Tel: (012) 422-41-80 Fax: (012) 422-59-47
E-mail: impuls@impulsoficyna.com.pl
Web Site: www.impulsoficyna.com.pl
Key Personnel
Dir: Wojciech Sliwerski
Editor-in-Chief: Piotr Niwinski
Founded: 1989
Membership(s): Polish Book Chamber.
Subjects: Education, Environmental Studies, Literature, Literary Criticism, Essays, Philosophy, Religion - Catholic, Social Sciences, Sociology
ISBN Prefix(es): 83-86994; 83-85543; 83-88030

**Instytut Meteorologii i Gospodarki Wodnej**
(Institute of Meteorology & Water Management)
ul Podlesna 61, 01-673 Warsaw
Tel: (022) 56-94-100 Fax: (022) 834-54-66
E-mail: sekretariat@imgw.pl
Web Site: www.imgw.pl
Key Personnel
Dir: Prof Jan Zielinski
Founded: 1945
Subjects: Earth Sciences, Environmental Studies, Foreign Countries, Geography, Geology, Library & Information Sciences, Physical Sciences, Meteorology, Hydrology, Oceanology, Water Management, Water Engineering, Water Quality
ISBN Prefix(es): 83-88887
Number of titles published annually: 20 Print
Parent Company: Ministry of Environment
Branch Office(s)
Gdynia
Katowice
Krakow
Poznan
Wroclaw

**Instytut Wydawniczy Pax, Inco-Veritas+**
Wybrzeze Kosciuszkowskie 21a, 00390 Warsaw
Tel: (022) 625 23 01 Fax: (022) 625 68 86
E-mail: iwpax@com.pl
Web Site: www.iwpax.com.pl
Key Personnel
Chief Editor: Amelia Szafranska
Founded: 1949
Subjects: Biblical Studies, Education, History, Literature, Literary Criticism, Essays, Philosophy, Poetry, Religion - Catholic, Theology
ISBN Prefix(es): 83-211
Bookshop(s): Piekna 16b, 00-449 Warsaw
Warehouse: Biuro Sprzedazy IW Pax, Wybrzeze Kosciuszkowskie 21a, 00390 Warsaw
Orders to: Biuro Handlu Zagranicznego Inco-Veritas, ul Wspolna 25, 00-159 Warsaw Tel: (022) 293216 Fax: (022) 295202

**Interpress+**
ul Bagatela 12, 00-585 Warsaw
Tel: (022) 6214876; (022) 6289331; (022) 6289202; (022) 6282818; (022) 6291060; (022) 6282225 Fax: (022) 6289331; (022) 6289202; (022) 6226850
E-mail: paiwydaw@pol.pl
Telex: 816336 pai pL Cable: INTERPRESS WARSZAWA
Key Personnel
Editor-in-Chief, Publicity: Bohdan Gawronski
Publicity, Rights & Permissions: Zofia Lewandowska
Production, Sales: Jawusz Malinowski
Founded: 1967
Subjects: History, Regional Interests, Science (General)
ISBN Prefix(es): 83-223
Branch Office(s)
Buero der Polnischen Informationen Agentur (PAI), Vinohradska 1616, Praha 2, Czech Republic Tel: 236117
Orders to: Dzial Handlowy, Wydawnictwo Interpress, ul Bagatela 12, 00-585 Warsaw

**Iskry - Publishing House Ltd spotka zoo+**
ul Smolna 11, 00-375 Warsaw
Tel: (022) 827 94 15 Fax: (022) 827 94 15
E-mail: iskry@iskry.com.pl
Web Site: www.iskry.com.pl
Key Personnel
President: Wieslaw Uchanski
Dir: Krzysztof Oblucki Tel: (022) 827 94 24; Marek Rosiecki Tel: (022) 827 87 79
Founded: 1952
Subjects: Aeronautics, Aviation, Biography, Cookery, History, Literature, Literary Criticism, Essays, Maritime, Mysteries, Parapsychology, Philosophy, Regional Interests, Science Fiction, Fantasy, Self-Help, Travel
ISBN Prefix(es): 83-207

**ITB**, imprint of Instytut Techniki Budowlanej, Dzial Wydawniczo- Poligraficzny

**Katolicki Uniwersytet Wydawniczo -Redakcja+**
ul Konstatynow 1, 20-708 Lublin
Tel: (081) 5257151 Fax: (081) 541246
E-mail: sekret@kul.lublin.pl
Key Personnel
Dir: Edward Pudelko E-mail: pudelko@kul.lublin.pl
Founded: 1957
Subjects: Biblical Studies, History, Law, Philosophy, Psychology, Psychiatry, Religion - Catholic, Social Sciences, Sociology, Theology
ISBN Prefix(es): 83-228
Imprints: RW-KUL
Divisions: Redakcja Wydawnictw KUL; Zaklad Malej Poligrafii KUL

*Orders to:* Kolportaz Dzialu Wydawniczo-Poligraficznego KUL, ul Konstatynow 1, 20-708 Lublin *Tel:* (081) 5257166 *Fax:* (081) 5241246 *E-mail:* kolprw@kul.lublin.pl

**KAW Krajowa Agencja Wydawnicza**
ul Smolna 12, 00-375 Warsaw
*Tel:* (022) 6578886 *Fax:* (022) 6578887
*E-mail:* kaw@univcomp.waw.pl
*Web Site:* www.polska2000.pl
*Telex:* 813487 Kaw Pl
*Key Personnel*
Man Dir & Editor-in-Chief: Dobroslaw Kobielski
Editorial: Jedrzej Bednarowicz
Deputy Editor: Tadeusz Kaczmarek; Zbigniew Zlotnicki
Production: Wladyslaw Szeszko
Sales: Jozef Maka
Founded: 1974
Membership(s): RSW.
Subjects: Education, Ethnicity, Government, Political Science, Science (General), Travel
ISBN Prefix(es): 83-03; 83-88072
*Branch Office(s)*
ul Podedwornego 12a, 15-269 Bialystok
ul sw Ducha 111/113, 80-801 Gdansk
ul 3 Maja 36, 40-097 Katowice
ul Florianska 33, 31-019 Krakow
ul Sienkiewicza 3/5, 90-113 Lodz
ul Buczka 28, 20-076 Lublin
ul Slowackiego 22, 60-823 Poznan
ul Komunistow 10, 35-030 Rzeszow
ul Orla Bialego 5, 70-562 Szczecin
pl Solny 14, 50-062 Wroclaw

**Komputerowa Oficyna Wydawnicza Help+**
Dworcowa 8, 05-816 Michalowice
*Tel:* (022) 723 89 21 *Fax:* (022) 723 87 64
*E-mail:* kowhelp@pol.pl
*Web Site:* www.besthelp.pl
*Key Personnel*
Man Dir: Piotr Gomolinski *E-mail:* piotr@besthelp.pl
Founded: 1989
Specialize in computer books.
Subjects: Computer Science
ISBN Prefix(es): 83-87211
Number of titles published annually: 15 Print
Total Titles: 200 Print

**Wydawnictwa Komunikacji i Lacznosci Co Ltd+**
ul Kazimierzowska 52, 02-546 Warsaw 12
*Tel:* (022) 849 27 51 *Fax:* (022) 849 23 22
*E-mail:* wkl@wkl.com.pl
*Web Site:* www.wkl.com.pl
*Key Personnel*
Dir: Jerzy Kozlowski
Editor-in-Chief: Bogumil Zielinski
Sales & Marketing Dir: Ewa Berus
Founded: 1949
Transport & Communications Publishers.
Subjects: Aeronautics, Aviation, Communications, Electronics, Electrical Engineering, Mechanical Engineering, Radio, TV, Transportation
ISBN Prefix(es): 83-206
*Bookshop(s):* ul Kazimierzowska 52, 02-546 Warsaw 12 *Tel:* (022) 8492032
*Warehouse:* ul Kazimierzowska 52, 02-546 Warsaw 12 *Tel:* (022) 8492304

**Krajowa Agencja Wydawnicza**, see KAW Krajowa Agencja Wydawnicza

**'Ksiazka i Wiedza' Spotdzielnia Wydawniczo-Handlowa+**
ul Smolna 13, 00-375 Warsaw
*Tel:* (022) 8275401; (022) 8279416 *Fax:* (022) 8279416; (022) 8279423
*E-mail:* publisher@kiw.com.pl
*Web Site:* www.kiw.com.pl

*Telex:* 817630 Kiw Pl *Cable:* KIW WARSZAWA
*Key Personnel*
Dir & Editor-in-Chief: Stanistan Soltus; Marta Stuhr
Editor: Jaroslaw Ladosz; Tadeusz Tarnogrodzki
Production: Andrzej Gierkowski
Founded: 1918
Membership(s): RSW.
Subjects: Animals, Pets, Biography, Government, Political Science, History, Philosophy, Social Sciences, Sociology, Travel
ISBN Prefix(es): 83-05

**Ksiaznica Publishing Ltd+**
ul Powstancow 30/401, 40-039 Katowice
*Tel:* (032) 257 22 16 *Fax:* (032) 257 22 17
*E-mail:* ksiaznica@domnet.com.pl
*Key Personnel*
President: Mariusz Morga
Vice President: Bozena Sek
International Rights: Joanna Ociepka
Specialize in encyclopedic thematic dictionaries.
Membership(s): Polish Chamber of Books.
Subjects: Fiction, Health, Nutrition, Nonfiction (General), Romance
ISBN Prefix(es): 83-85348; 83-7132

**Laumann-Polska+**
ul Zymierskiego 53A/4, 58-573 Piechowice
*Tel:* (075) 7617182 *Fax:* (075) 7617192
*Key Personnel*
President: Maria Iburg
Subjects: Regional Interests, Travel
ISBN Prefix(es): 83-85716
*Book Club(s):* Polska Izba Ksiazki

**Wydawnictwo Literackie+**
ul Dluga 1, 31-147 Krakow
*Tel:* (012) 4225423; (012) 4232254; (012) 4231251 *Fax:* (012) 4225423
*E-mail:* redakcja@wl.interkom.pl; handel@wl.net.pl; promocja@wl.net.pl
*Web Site:* www.wl.net.pl
*Key Personnel*
Dir: Janusz Adamczyk
Finance Dir: Halina Ofiarska
Editorial Staff: Krzysztof Lisowski
Sales & Marketing: Barbara Leszczynska
Publicity: Boguslawa Stanowska-Cichon
Founded: 1953
Subjects: Art, Biography, Drama, Theater, Film, Video, History, Literature, Literary Criticism, Essays
ISBN Prefix(es): 83-08

**Wydawnictwo Lodzkie+**
ul Piotrkowska 171, Skr Poczt 372, 90-447 Lodz
*Tel:* (042) 6360331; (042) 6366189 *Fax:* (042) 6368524
*Key Personnel*
Editorial Dir: Jacek Zaorski
Sales & Publicity: Janina Sobczak
Production: Grazyna Bis-Stepniak
Rights & Permissions: Alfreda Gorzkiewicz
Founded: 1957
Subjects: Biography, Human Relations
ISBN Prefix(es): 83-218

**Wydawnictwo Lubelskie**
ul Droga Meczennikow Majdanka 67, 20-325 Lublin
*Tel:* (081) 7442667
*Key Personnel*
Dir & Editor-in-Chief: Ireneusz Caban
Deputy Editor: Ludwik Zabielski
Founded: 1957
Subjects: Government, Political Science, Human Relations, Poetry, Science (General), Social Sciences, Sociology
ISBN Prefix(es): 83-87399

**Ludowa Spoldzielnia Wydawnicza+**
ul Grzybowska 4, 00-131 Warsaw
*Tel:* (022) 6205718; (022) 6205719 *Fax:* (022) 6207277 *Cable:* LSW, WARSZAWA
*Key Personnel*
Chairman & Editor-in-Chief: Rajewski Krzysztof
Editorial: Jerzy Dobrzanski
Founded: 1946
People's publishing cooperative.
Subjects: Agriculture, Biography, History, Literature, Literary Criticism, Essays, Poetry
ISBN Prefix(es): 83-205

**Magnum Publishing House Ltd+**
ul Narbutta 25A, 02-536 Warsaw
*Tel:* (022) 6460085; (022) 8485505 *Fax:* (022) 8485505
*E-mail:* magnum@it.com.pl
*Key Personnel*
President: Jolanta Woloszanska
Vice President: Marcin Jarek
Founded: 1994
Membership(s): Polish Chamber of Books.
Subjects: Biography, Government, Political Science, History
ISBN Prefix(es): 83-85852

**Wydawnictwo Medyczne Urban & Partner+**
ul M Sklodowskiej-Curie 55/61, 50-950 Wroclaw
*Tel:* (071) 328 54 87; (071) 328 30 68 *Fax:* (071) 328 43 91
*E-mail:* info@urbanpartner.pl
*Web Site:* www.urbanpartner.pl
*Key Personnel*
President: Wieslawa Hombek
President & International Rights: Miroslaw Gornicki
Founded: 1992
Subjects: Medicine, Nursing, Dentistry
ISBN Prefix(es): 83-85842; 83-87944
*Parent Company:* Urban & Schwarzenberg, Munich, Germany

**Muza SA+**
ul Marszalkowska 8 IIp, 00-590 Warsaw
*Tel:* (022) 621-17-75; (022) 621-50-58; (022) 629-50-83 *Fax:* (022) 629-23-49
*E-mail:* muza@muza.com.pl
*Web Site:* www.muza.com.pl
*Key Personnel*
President: Marcin Garlinski
International Rights: Agata Radkiewicz *E-mail:* a.radkiewicz@muza.com.pl
Founded: 1991
Subjects: Art, Cookery, Education, Fiction, House & Home, Nonfiction (General), Social Sciences, Sociology, Travel
ISBN Prefix(es): 83-7079; 83-7200; 83-85325; 83-7319
Imprints: Sport I Turystyka; Warszawskie Wydawnictwo Literackie
*Book Club(s):* Klub Czytelnikow Muza SA
*Warehouse:* ul Cybernetyki 9, 00-677 Warsaw

**Polskie Wydawnictwo Muzyczne+**
ul Krasijskiego 11a, 31-111 Krakow
*Tel:* (012) 4227171; (012) 4227044 *Fax:* (012) 4227171
*E-mail:* pwm@pwm.com.pl
*Web Site:* www.pwm.com.pl
*Telex:* 813370 *Cable:* PWM
*Key Personnel*
Editor-in-Chief: Andrzej Kosowski
Head, Copyright: Janina Warzecha
Editorial: Ewa Nyozek
Production: Grazyna Adamczyk
Founded: 1945
Polish music publishers.
Subjects: Music, Dance
ISBN Prefix(es): 83-224
Imprints: Poligrafia PWM
Subsidiaries: Centralnaa Biblioteka Muzyczna-Nutowa (PWM Hire Department)

*U.S. Office(s):* Theodore Presser, One Presser Place, Bryn Mawr, PA 19010-3490, United States *Fax:* 610-527-7841
Distributed by Kalmvs (Great Britain Commonwealth & Australia); Leduc (France); Schott (Germany & Switzerland); Universal (Austria)

**Wydawnictwo Nasza Ksiegarnia Sp zoo** (Nasza Ksiegarnia Publishing House)+
ul Sarabandy 24c, 02-868 Warsaw
*Tel:* (022) 643 93 89 *Fax:* (022) 643 70 28
*Cable:* NASZA KSIEGARNIA
*Key Personnel*
President: Agnieszka Tokarczyk
Editor-in-Chief: Jolanta Sztuczynska
Founded: 1921
Subjects: Education, Fiction, Science (General)
ISBN Prefix(es): 83-10

**Wydawnictwo Naukowe PWN**, see Polish Scientific Publishers PWN

**Wydawnictwa Naukowo-Techniczne+**
ul Mazowiecka 2/4, 00-048 Warsaw
*Tel:* (022) 826-72-71 *Fax:* (022) 826-86-20
*E-mail:* wnt@pol.pl
*Web Site:* www.wnt.com.pl *Cable:* ENTE WARSZAWA
*Key Personnel*
General Manager: Dr Aniela Topulos
Rights & Permissions: Agnieszka Koztowska
*Tel:* (022) 8272833
Founded: 1949
Subjects: Chemistry, Chemical Engineering, Computer Science, Electronics, Electrical Engineering, Mathematics, Mechanical Engineering, Microcomputers, Physics, Technology
ISBN Prefix(es): 83-204
Imprints: WNT

**Norbertinum+**
ul Ksiezycowa 15, 20-060 Lublin
*Tel:* (081) 5333895 *Fax:* (081) 5341243
*E-mail:* norbertinum@norbertinum.com.pl
*Web Site:* www.norbertinum.com.pl
*Key Personnel*
President & International Rights: Norbert Wojciechowski
Founded: 1989
Subjects: Biography, Fiction, History, Literature, Literary Criticism, Essays, Poetry, Religion - Catholic, Science (General), Social Sciences, Sociology, Theology
ISBN Prefix(es): 83-85131; 83-86837; 83-7222

**Wydawnictwa Normalizacyjne**, see Wydawnictwa Normalizacyjne Alfa-Wero

**Wydawnictwa Normalizacyjne Alfa-Wero+**
Ul Nowogrodzka 22, 00-511 Warsaw
*Tel:* (02) 6218750 *Fax:* (02) 6218750
*Telex:* 812374 Wuen Pl
*Key Personnel*
Editor-in-Chief: Jerzy Wysokinski
Production Dir: Zdzislaw Adamski
Sales Manager: Malgorzata Lukaszczuk
Foreign Rights Manager: Wiktor Bukato
Founded: 1956
Subjects: Crafts, Games, Hobbies, Fiction, Science (General), Science Fiction, Fantasy
ISBN Prefix(es): 83-7001; 83-7179
Imprints: Alfa; Beta Books; Beta Comics
*Bookshop(s):* ul Sienna 63, Warsaw

**Ossolineum Zaklad Narodowy im Ossolinskich - Wydawnictwo+**
pl Solny 14a, 50-062 Wroclaw
*Tel:* (071) 3436961 *Fax:* (071) 3448103
*E-mail:* wydawnictwo@ossolineum.pl
*Telex:* 0712771

*Key Personnel*
Man Dir: Wojciech Karwacki
Editor-in-Chief: Stanislaw Roscicki
Founded: 1817
Subjects: Archaeology, Architecture & Interior Design, Art, Biography, Biological Sciences, Environmental Studies, History, Language Arts, Linguistics, Literature, Literary Criticism, Essays, Medicine, Nursing, Dentistry, Philosophy, Poetry, Science (General), Social Sciences, Sociology
ISBN Prefix(es): 83-04
*Bookshop(s):* Sw Marka 12, 31-018 Krakow; ul Marcinkowskiego 30, 61-745 Poznam; Jaworzynska 4, 00-634 Warsaw; Rynek 6, 50-106 Wroclaw
*Orders to:* Export Dept c/o Ossolineum, Plac Solny 14a, 50-062 Wroclaw

**P P H Penta**
ul Bogumila ZUGA 27/1, 01-806 Warsaw
*Tel:* (022) 834 08 43 *Fax:* (022) 8641854; (022) 8340843
*E-mail:* penta@pol.pl
*Web Site:* www.penta.pl
Founded: 1988
Membership(s): Polish Book Charitex.
ISBN Prefix(es): 83-85440; 83-900031

**Pallottinum Wydawnictwo Stowarzyszenia Apostolstwa Katolickiego+**
al Przybyszewskiego 30 skr poczt 23, 60-959 Poznan
*Tel:* (061) 867-52-33 *Fax:* (061) 867-52-38
*E-mail:* pallottinum@pallottinum.pl
*Web Site:* www.pallottinum.pl
*Key Personnel*
Dir: Stefan Dusza *Tel:* (061) 8672118
*E-mail:* dusza@pallottinum.pl
Deputy Dir: Stanislaw Gawrylo
Editorial: Kazimierz Jacaszek
Founded: 1948
Publishers of the Catholic Apostolate Association.
Subjects: Biblical Studies, Philosophy, Religion - Catholic, Theology
ISBN Prefix(es): 83-7014

**Panstwowe Przedsiebiorstwo Wydawnictw Kartograficznych**
ul Solec 18, 00-410 Warsaw
*Tel:* (022) 6283251; (022) 6214850 *Fax:* (022) 6280236; (022) 6214850
*E-mail:* ppwk@pdsox.com *Cable:* PEPEWUKA WARSZAWA
*Key Personnel*
Dir: Alina Meljon
Founded: 1951
ISBN Prefix(es): 83-7000

**Panstwowe Wydawnictwo Rolnicze i Lesne+**
Al Jerozolimskie 28, poczt 374, 00-950 Warsaw
*Tel:* (022) 8276338 *Fax:* (022) 8276338
*Telex:* 817509 Pl Pwril *Cable:* Pewril Warszawa
*Key Personnel*
Dir & Chief Editor: Mr Marian Bajorek
Deputy Editor: Halina Gutowski
Deputy Editor, Periodicals: Jan Czajka
Production: Danuta Kozlowska
Founded: 1947
State agricultural & forestry publishers.
Subjects: Agriculture, Environmental Studies, Health, Nutrition, Veterinary Science
ISBN Prefix(es): 83-09
*Branch Office(s)*
ul Ratajczaka 33, 61-816 Poznan

**Panstwowy Instytut Wydawniczy (PIW)**
(National Publishing Institute)+
ul Foksal 17, 00-372 Warsaw
Mailing Address: skr poczt 377, 00-372 Warsaw

*Tel:* (022) 8260201; (022) 8260202; (022) 8260203; (022) 8260204; (022) 826-02-05
*Fax:* (022) 826-15-36
*E-mail:* piw@piw.pl
*Web Site:* www.piw.pl
*Telex:* 8261536 *Cable:* PIW
*Key Personnel*
Dir: Radoslaw J Utnik *Tel:* (022) 8264879
*E-mail:* dyrektor@piw.pl
Sales: Malgorzata Stawida
Production: Irena Rzepkowska
Rights: Stanislawa Lewicka
Founded: 1946
State publishing institute.
Subjects: Biography, Drama, Theater, Ethnicity, Fiction, History, Literature, Literary Criticism, Essays, Poetry, Science (General)
ISBN Prefix(es): 83-06
Number of titles published annually: 60 Print

**Pearson Education Polska Sp z oo**
ul Jana Olbrachta 94, 01-102 Warsaw
*Tel:* (022) 533 1533 *Toll Free Tel:* 0800 1200 76
*Fax:* (022) 533 1534
*E-mail:* office@longman.com.pl
*Web Site:* www.longman.com.pl
*Key Personnel*
Man Dir: Ms Danuta A Lapkiewicz *Tel:* (022) 533 1555 *Fax:* (022) 533 1556
Finance & Operations Dir: Marcin Rudnik
*Tel:* (022) 533 1551 *Fax:* (022) 533 1556
Commercial Dir: Rajmund Sawka *Tel:* (022) 553 1565
Marketing Manager: Anna Dadej *Tel:* (022) 533 1571
PA Marketing Dir: Katarzyna Glowinska
*Tel:* (022) 533 1557 *Fax:* (022) 533 1556
Founded: 1991
ISBN Prefix(es): 83-88291

**PIW**, see Panstwowy Instytut Wydawniczy (PIW)

**Wydawnictwo Podsiedlik-Raniowski i Spolka+**
ul Zmigrodzka 41/49, 60-171 Poznan
*Tel:* (061) 867 95 46 *Fax:* (061) 867 68 50
*E-mail:* office@priska.com.pl
*Key Personnel*
Dir: Michal Stecki *E-mail:* michals@priska.com.pl
Founded: 1990
Specialize also in read-alongs & popular-scientific.
Subjects: Crafts, Games, Hobbies, Education, History, How-to, Poetry
ISBN Prefix(es): 83-85165; 83-7083

**Poligrafia PWM**, *imprint of* Polskie Wydawnictwo Muzyczne

**Polish Scientific Publishers PWN+**
ul Miodowa 10, 00-251 Warsaw
*Tel:* (022) 6954321; (022) 6954181
*Fax:* (022) 8267163; (022) 6954288
*Fax on Demand:* 080020145
*E-mail:* pwn@pwn.com.pl
*Web Site:* www.pwn.pl *Cable:* PEWUEN WARSZAWA
*Key Personnel*
Manager International Dept Rights & Contracts: Anna Raiter-Rosinska *E-mail:* anna.rosinska@pwn.com.pl
President: Richard Knauff *E-mail:* richard.knauff@pwn.com.pl
Editorial Dir: Anna Szemberg
Founded: 1951
Reference & academic publisher. Cooperates with foreign publishers.
Membership(s): STM-Scientific, Technical & Medical Publishers Association.
Subjects: Agriculture, Art, Behavioral Sciences, Biological Sciences, Business, Chemistry,

Chemical Engineering, Civil Engineering, Computer Science, Earth Sciences, Economics, Education, Electronics, Electrical Engineering, Engineering (General), English as a Second Language, Environmental Studies, Finance, Geography, Geology, History, Language Arts, Linguistics, Management, Marketing, Mathematics, Mechanical Engineering, Philosophy, Physical Sciences, Physics, Psychology, Psychiatry, Science (General), Social Sciences, Sociology, Technology
ISBN Prefix(es): 83-01
Subsidiaries: All-Poland Distribution System-AZYMUT; School Publishers PWN; Wydawnictwo Lekarskie PZWL (medical & health)
*Bookshop(s):* Ksiegarnia PWN, ul Miodowa 10, 00-251 Warsaw; ul SW Tomasza 30, 31-027 Krakow; ul Wieckowskiego 13, 90-721 Lodz; ul Kuznicza 56, 50-138 Wroclaw
*Book Club(s):* Biblioteka PWN

## Oficyna Wydawnicza Politechniki Wroclawskiej
Wybrzeze Wyspianskiego 27, 50-370 Wroclaw
*Tel:* (071) 320 29 94; (071) 320 38 23; (071) 328 29 40 *Fax:* (071) 328 29 40
*E-mail:* oficwyd@pwr.wroc.pl
*Web Site:* wsww.pwr.wroc.pl
*Telex:* 712254
*Key Personnel*
Dir: Halina Dudek
Founded: 1968
Subjects: Architecture & Interior Design, Engineering (General), Environmental Studies, Microcomputers, Physical Sciences, Physics, Science (General), Technology
ISBN Prefix(es): 83-7085
*Bookshop(s):* Pl Grunwaldzki 13, PL 50-370 Wroclaw

## Wydawnictwo Polskiego Towarzystwa Wydawcow Ksiazek
Mazowiecka 2/4, 00048 Warsaw
*Tel:* (022) 826 72 71, Ext 345; (022) 826 07 35 *Fax:* (022) 826 07 35
*Key Personnel*
President: Janusz Fogler
Contact: Jacek Gdaniec
Founded: 1921
ISBN Prefix(es): 83-7029; 83-85000

## POMORZE-Pomorskie Wydawnictwo Prasowe
ul Paderewskiego 26, 85-075 Bydgoszcz
*Tel:* (052) 220237; (052) 211396; (052) 210452
Membership(s): RSW.
ISBN Prefix(es): 83-7003

## Pomorze Wydawnictwo Spoldzielnia Pracy
ul Paderewskiego 26, 85-075 Bydgoszcz
*Tel:* (052) 220237; (052) 211396; (052) 210452
*Telex:* 0562845
*Key Personnel*
Chief Executive: Zbigniew Cieslinski
Editorial: Dr Ryszard Zietek
Sales, Production, Publicity, Rights & Permissions: Ewa Grinberg
Founded: 1982
ISBN Prefix(es): 83-7003
*Bookshop(s):* Ksiegarnia Domu Ksiazki, ul Marii Konopnickiej 30, 85-124 Bydgoszcz

## Wydawnictwo Prawnicze Co
ul gen K Sosnkowskiego 1, 02-495 Warsaw
*Tel:* (022) 5729500; (022) 5729507 *Fax:* (022) 5729509
*E-mail:* biuro@lexisnexis.pl
*Web Site:* sklep.lexpolonica.pl
*Key Personnel*
President, Dir & Editor-in-Chief: Dr Jerzy Kowalski

Founded: 1952
Subjects: Criminology, Law, Marketing, Public Administration, Securities
ISBN Prefix(es): 83-219; 83-7334
*Shipping Address:* ul Sosnkowskiego 1, 02-495 Warsaw-Ursus
*Warehouse:* ul Sosnkowskiego 1, 02-495 Warsaw-Ursus

## Przedsiebiorstwo Wydawniczo-Handlowe Wydawnictwo Siedmiorog+
ul Swiatnicka 7, 52-018 Wroclaw
*Tel:* (071) 341 68 71 *Fax:* (071) 341 68 87
*E-mail:* siedmiorog@siedmiorog.com.pl
*Web Site:* www.siedmiorog.pl
*Key Personnel*
Man Dir: Tomasz Michalowski
Subjects: Philosophy, Science Fiction, Fantasy
ISBN Prefix(es): 83-7162
Number of titles published annually: 100 Print
Total Titles: 570 Print
*Showroom(s):* ul Swiatniche 7, Wroclaw
*Bookshop(s):* ul Ch Toohue 39, Warsaw

## Wydawnictwa Przemyslowe WEMA+
ul Danilowiczowska 18, 00-950 Warsaw
*Tel:* (022) 8275456; (022) 8272117 *Fax:* (022) 6355779
*Telex:* 814548
*Key Personnel*
Chief Executive: Andrzej Januszewicz
Founded: 1967
Also specialize in printing.
Subjects: Electronics, Electrical Engineering, Mechanical Engineering
ISBN Prefix(es): 83-85250

**PWE**, see Polskie Wydawnictwo Ekonomiczne PWE SA

## PZWL Wydawnictwo Lekarskie Ltd+
Unit of PWN Publishers Group
ul Miodowa 10, 00-251 Warsaw
Mailing Address: Skr poczt 379, 00-950 Warsaw
*Tel:* (022) 6954033; (022) 6954497 *Fax:* (022) 6954032; (022) 6954497
*E-mail:* promocja@pzwl.pl
*Web Site:* www.pzwl.pl *Cable:* WYDLEK WARSZAWA
*Key Personnel*
President: Krystyna Regulska
Foreign Rights Manager: Anna Czyzewska
*Tel:* (022) 8314345 *Fax:* (022) 8314345
*E-mail:* anna.czyzewska@pzwl.pl
Founded: 1945
Medical Publishers Company Ltd.
Subjects: Biological Sciences, Chemistry, Chemical Engineering, Child Care & Development, Health, Nutrition, Medicine, Nursing, Dentistry, Psychology, Psychiatry, Veterinary Science
ISBN Prefix(es): 83-200
Total Titles: 400 Print; 2 CD-ROM
*Parent Company:* Scientific Publishers
Distributed by Scientific Publishers PWN
Distributor for Harcourt Brace & Co Ltd
*Warehouse:* ul Rolnicza 11, 05-092 Dziekanow Polski *Tel:* (022) 7511334 *Fax:* (022) 7511334

## Wydawnictwa Radia i Telewizji
ul Chelmska 9, 00-724 Warsaw
*Tel:* (022) 412264
*Key Personnel*
Dir & Editor-in-Chief: Teresa Bartoszek
Production: Maciej Pcion
Founded: 1968
Subjects: Education, Fiction, Radio, TV, Science (General)
ISBN Prefix(es): 83-212

## Oficyna Wydawnicza Read Me (Read Me Publishing House)+
Skr Poczt 144, 00-987 Warsaw 4
*Tel:* (022) 8706024 (ext 130) *Fax:* (022) 6771425
*E-mail:* readme@rm.com.pl
*Web Site:* www.rm.com.pl
*Key Personnel*
Man Dir: Wlodzimierz Binczyk
Licensing Coordinator & International Rights: Joanna Kopanczyk *E-mail:* joanna@rm.com.pl
Contact: Janusz Fajfer; Tomasz Zajbt
Founded: 1991
Subjects: Computer Science, Economics, Education, Health, Nutrition, Microcomputers, Outdoor Recreation, Self-Help, Travel
ISBN Prefix(es): 83-85769; 83-7147; 83-87216; 83-900451
Number of titles published annually: 100 Print
*Associate Companies:* Wydawnictwo Eremis; Wydawnictwo RM

## Res Polona+
ul Gdanska 80, 90-613 Lodz
*Tel:* (042) 6363634; (042) 6374587; (042) 6374607 *Fax:* (042) 6373010
*E-mail:* info@res-polona.com.pl
*Web Site:* www.res-polona.com.pl
*Key Personnel*
President: Jozef Fraszczynski
Founded: 1989
Subjects: Education
ISBN Prefix(es): 83-85063; 83-7071
Subsidiaries: Res Polona

## Rosikon Press+
Aleja Debow 4, 05-080 Izabelin Warsaw
*Tel:* (022) 7226101; (022) 7226102; (022) 7226666 *Fax:* (022) 7226667
*E-mail:* biuro@rosikonpress.com; office@ rosikompress.com
*Web Site:* www.rosikonpress.com
*Key Personnel*
Man Dir: Grazyna Kasprzycka-Rosikon *Tel:* (022) 7226666 *E-mail:* g.kasprzycka@rosikonpress. com
Founded: 1990
Membership(s): Polish Chamber of Books.
Subjects: Art, History, Photography, Religion - Catholic
ISBN Prefix(es): 83-900695
Number of titles published annually: 5 Print
Total Titles: 3 Print
Distributed by Azymut (Poland)

## Wydawnictwo RTW+
ul Broniewskiego 9a, 01-780 Warsaw
*Tel:* (022) 633 70 10; (022) 663 74 74 *Fax:* (022) 633 70 10; (022) 39120123
*E-mail:* rtw@wydawrtw.media.pl
*Key Personnel*
Rights Manager: Anna Wisniewska
Foreign Relations Assistant: Dorota Trusiak
Founded: 1992
Independent individual company.
Subjects: Animals, Pets, Education, Geography, Geology, History, Science (General), Atlases
ISBN Prefix(es): 83-86822; 83-7294; 83-85493; 83-87974
Number of titles published annually: 50 Print; 20 Audio
Total Titles: 80 Print; 25 Audio
*Warehouse:* ul Koleyowa 19/21, Warsaw, Contact: Dorota Trusiak

**RW-KUL**, *imprint of* Katolicki Uniwersytet Wydawniczo -Redakcja

## Wydawnictwo SIC+
ul Chelmska 27/23, 00-724 Warsaw
*Tel:* (022) 8400753 *Fax:* (022) 8400753
*E-mail:* sic@sic.ksiazka.pl

*Key Personnel*
Man Dir: Elzbieta Czerwirlska
Editor-in-Chief: Ranata Lis
Founded: 1993
Subjects: Human Relations, Self-Help
ISBN Prefix(es): 83-86056; 83-88807
Total Titles: 50 Print
*Orders to:* Hydawnictwo Siel, ul Tucka 2/4/6 m 21, 00-845 Warsaw, Contact: Katarzyna Jaskiewicz *Fax:* (022) 6546784 *E-mail:* sic@sic.ksiazka.pl

**'Slask' Ltd+**
Al W Korfantego 51, 40-161 Katowice
*Tel:* (032) 258 07 56; (032) 2581812; (032) 2583222; (032) 2581910 *Fax:* (032) 2583229
*E-mail:* biuro@slaskwn.com.pl
*Web Site:* www.slaskwn.com.pl
*Key Personnel*
President: Tadeusz Sierny
Manager: Grzegorz Bociek; Bogumila Cyron
Founded: 1954
Membership(s): The Polish Chamber of the Book.
Subjects: Advertising, English as a Second Language, History, Literature, Literary Criticism, Essays, Nonfiction (General), Poetry, Regional Interests, Science (General)
ISBN Prefix(es): 83-900705; 83-900814; 83-85831; 83-7164

**Spoleczny Instytut Wydawniczy Znak+**
ul Kosciuszki 37, 30-105 Krakow
*Tel:* (012) 4291469; (012) 4219776 *Fax:* (012) 4219814
*E-mail:* rucinska@znak.com.pl
*Web Site:* www.znak.com.pl *Cable:* KOSCIUSZKI 37
*Key Personnel*
Contact: Jolanta Wlodarczyk
Founded: 1959
Subjects: History, Philosophy, Religion - Other
ISBN Prefix(es): 83-7006
*Bookshop(s):* ul Slawkowska 1, 31-007 Krakow

**Sport I Turystyka**, *imprint of* Muza SA

**Spotdzielna Anagram**
al 3 Maja 2 Pok, 4, 00-391 Warsaw
*Tel:* (022) 6229324; (022) 6229326
*Key Personnel*
Agency Editor-in-Chief: Zygmunt Konopka
Editorial: Andrzej Murawski
Sales: Halina Popiolek
Production: Wieslaw Felczak
Founded: 1974
Youth publishing agency & publishing co-operative.
This organization replaces the former Wydawnictwo Harcerskie 'Horyzonty'. It is also a workers' publishing co-operative, allied to RSW. Mlodziezowa acts as both agency & publisher for Polish youth.
Subjects: Ethnicity, Government, Political Science, Science (General), Social Sciences, Sociology
ISBN Prefix(es): 83-203; 83-86086

**Wydawnictwa Szkolne i Pedagogiczne** (Polish Educational Publishers)+
Al Jerozolimskie, 136, 02-305 Warsaw
Mailing Address: skr poczt 480, 00-959 Warsaw
*Tel:* (022) 8265451; (022) 8265452; (022) 8265453; (022) 8265454; (022) 8265455; (022) 5762500; (022) 5762501 *Toll Free Tel:* 800-220555 *Fax:* (022) 8279280
*E-mail:* wsip@wsip.com.pl
*Web Site:* www.wsip.com.pl
*Telex:* 816132 *Cable:* WUESIPE WARSZAWA
*Key Personnel*
Man Dir: Andrzej Chrzanowski
Rights & Permissions: Maciej Lipko

Advertising: Wojciech Krasuski
Contact: Maria Bogobowicz
Founded: 1945
Membership(s): EEPG, Polish Chamber of the Book.
Subjects: Education, Psychology, Psychiatry
ISBN Prefix(es): 83-02
*Branch Office(s)*
Delegatura WSiP, Basztowa 15, 31-143 Krakow
*Orders to:* Ars Polona, PO Box 1001, 00-068 Warsaw

**Oficyna Wydawnicza Szkoly Glownej Handlowej w Warszawie Oficyna Wydawnicza SGH+**
ul Rakowiecka 24, Budynek "A" 6, 13, 14 & 17, 02-554 Warsaw
*Tel:* (022) 337 92 13; (022) 337 92 17; (022) 337 97 61; (022) 337 97 69 *Fax:* (022) 646 61 03
*E-mail:* dwz@sgh.waw.pl
*Web Site:* www.sgh.waw.pl
*Telex:* 816031sgh
*Key Personnel*
Dir: Dr Bogdan Radomski *E-mail:* bradomski@sgh.waw.pl
Deputy Dir: Elzbieta Fonberg-Stokluska *E-mail:* estokl@sgh.waw.pl
Founded: 1917
Subjects: Economics, English as a Second Language, Finance, History, Law, Mathematics, Philosophy, Public Administration, Social Sciences, Sociology
ISBN Prefix(es): 83-86689; 83-7225; 83-7378

**Instytut Techniki Budowlanej, Dzial Wydawniczo- Poligraficzny**
ul Ksawerow 21, 02-656 Warsaw
*Tel:* (022) 8431471 *Fax:* (022) 8432931
*E-mail:* wydawnictwa_itb@pro.onet.pl
*Web Site:* www.itb.pl
*Key Personnel*
Man Dir: Stanislaw Wierzbicki
Founded: 1945
Subjects: Civil Engineering
ISBN Prefix(es): 83-7130; 83-7226; 83-7290; 83-7321; 83-7370
Imprints: ITB
*Bookshop(s):* ul Filtrowa 1, 00-611 Warsaw *Tel:* (022) 825 52 29 *Fax:* (022) 57 96 295

**Towarzystwo Naukowe w Toruniu**
ul Wysoka 16, 87-100 Torun
*Tel:* (056) 6223941 (ext 8)
*Key Personnel*
Editorial Manager: Bozena Soltys
Founded: 1875
Specialize in humanities.
Subjects: Archaeology, Art, Biological Sciences, Geography, Geology, History, Language Arts, Linguistics, Law, Medicine, Nursing, Dentistry, Physical Sciences, Regional Interests
ISBN Prefix(es): 83-85196; 83-87639

**Wydawnictwo TPPR Wspolpraca+**
ul Marszalkowska 115, 00-932 Warsaw
*Tel:* (022) 200301 (ext 227)
*Key Personnel*
Chief Executive: Ryszard Pogonowski
Production: Kazimierz Andruk
Founded: 1984
Subjects: Government, Political Science, Literature, Literary Criticism, Essays
ISBN Prefix(es): 83-7018

**Wydawnictwa Uniwersytetu Warszawskiego+**
Imprint of Wydawnictwa Uniwersytetu Warszawskiego
ul Nowy Swiat 4, 00-497 Warsaw
*Tel:* (022) 5531318 *Fax:* (022) 5531318
*E-mail:* wuw@uw.edu.pl

*Key Personnel*
Dir: Michal Szewielow
Rights & Permissions: Ryszard Burek
Assistant Marketing Manager: Monika Glowacz
Founded: 1956
A predominant share in our offer is taken by the publications of the Polish Faculty (theory & history of literature, linguistics) & books on culture written from the point of view of various humanistic disciplines.
Subjects: African American Studies, Agriculture, Americana, Regional, Anthropology, Archaeology, Asian Studies, Behavioral Sciences, Biography, Biological Sciences, Chemistry, Chemical Engineering, Economics, Education, English as a Second Language, Environmental Studies, Ethnicity, Genealogy, Geography, Geology, Government, Political Science, History, Social Sciences, Sociology
ISBN Prefix(es): 83-230; 83-235
Number of titles published annually: 38 Print
Total Titles: 2,319 Print
*Orders to:* Centrala Handlu Zagranicznego, Ars Polona SA, ul Obroncow 25, 00-933 Warsaw *Tel:* (022) 5098638 *Fax:* (022) 5098637 *E-mail:* arspolona@arspolona.com.pl

**Wydawnictwo Uniwersytetu Wroclawskiego SP ZOO**
pl Uniwersytecki 15, 50-137 Wroclaw
*Tel:* (071) 3752809 *Fax:* (071) 3752735
*E-mail:* marketing@wuwr.com.pl
*Web Site:* www.wuwr.com.pl
*Key Personnel*
President: Marek Gorny
Founded: 1996
Scientific handbooks for students of Wroclawskiego University.
ISBN Prefix(es): 83-229

**Verbinum Wydawnictwo Ksiezy Werbistow+**
ul Ostrobramska 98, 04-118 Warsaw
*Tel:* (022) 6107878; (022) 8703286 *Fax:* (022) 6107775
*Key Personnel*
Editor: P Antoni Koszorz
Founded: 1983
Subjects: Developing Countries, Religion - Other
ISBN Prefix(es): 83-85009; 83-85762; 83-7192
*Parent Company:* Verbinum
Subsidiaries: Verbinum, Dzial Kolportazu

**Videograf II Sp z o o Zaklad Poracy Chronionej**
al W Korfantego 191, 40-153 Katowice
*Tel:* (03) 2036558; (03) 2036559; (03) 2036560 *Fax:* (03) 2036558; (03) 2036559; (03) 2036560
*E-mail:* videograf@videograf.dnd.com.pl
*Key Personnel*
Editor-in-Chief & International Rights: Jacek Illg
Man Dir: Franciszek Leki
Founded: 1996
Subjects: Biography, Education, Fiction, Film, Video, Gardening, Plants, Mysteries, Photography
ISBN Prefix(es): 83-7183; 83-86831

**Vocatio Publishing House+**
Skr Poczt 41, Polnej Rozy 1, PL-02792 Warsaw 78
*Tel:* (022) 648-5450 *Fax:* (022) 648-6382
*E-mail:* vocatio@vocatio.com.pl
*Web Site:* www.vocatio.com.pl
*Key Personnel*
President & Chief Executive Officer: Piotr Waclawik *E-mail:* wydawca@vocatio.com.pl
Founded: 1991
Membership(s): ECPA, ICCC.
Subjects: Biblical Studies, Religion - Catholic, Religion - Protestant, Theology, Bible reference books; children's books, video books, music
ISBN Prefix(es): 83-85435; 83-7146

**Wydawnictwo WAB** (WAB Publishers)+
Lowicka 31 Str, 02-502 Warsaw
*Tel:* (022) 646 05 10; (022) 646 05 11; (022) 646
01 74; (022) 646 01 75 *Fax:* (022) 646 05 10;
(022) 646 05 11; (022) 646 01 74; (022) 646
01 75
*E-mail:* wab@wab.com.pl
*Web Site:* www.wab.com.pl
*Key Personnel*
Editor: Beata Stasinska
Founded: 1991
Specialize in promoting & publishing Polish con-
temporary literary fiction, as well as transla-
tions.
Subjects: Fiction, Health, Nutrition, Human Rela-
tions, Nonfiction (General)
ISBN Prefix(es): 83-87021; 83-88221; 83-85554
Number of titles published annually: 40 Print
Total Titles: 450 Print

**Warszawskie Wydawnictwo Literackie**, *imprint
of* Muza SA

**'Wiedza Powszechna' Panstwowe
Wydawnictwo+**
ul Jasna 26, 00-054 Warsaw
*Tel:* (022) 8277651 *Fax:* (022) 8269592; (022)
8268594
*Key Personnel*
Dir: Teresa Korsak
Deputy: Tadeusz Mazurek
Founded: 1952
Subjects: Language Arts, Linguistics, Science
(General)
ISBN Prefix(es): 83-214

**Wydawnictwo Wilga sp zoo** (Wilga Publishing
Ltd)+
ul Smulikowskiego 1/3, 00-389 Warsaw
*Tel:* (022) 826-08-82; (022) 827-90-11 (ext 282)
*Fax:* (022) 826-06-43
*E-mail:* wilga@wilga.com.pl
*Key Personnel*
President & Foreign Rights: Jan Wojnilko
Vice President: Anna Sikorska-Michalak
Editor-in-Chief: Olga Wojnilko
Founded: 1993
Subjects: Education, Fiction
ISBN Prefix(es): 83-7156; 83-86664; 83-901029;
83-903028
Number of titles published annually: 300 Print
Total Titles: 1,200 Print
Subsidiaries: Wilga Marketing
*Warehouse:* Panstwowe Magazyny Ustugowe,
Przejazdowa 25, 05-800 Pruszkow

**WNT**, *imprint of* Wydawnictwa
Naukowo-Techniczne

**WOSI "Wspolna Sprawa" Warsaw**, *imprint of*
Wydawn Na Sprawa' Wydawniczo-Oswiatowa
Spotdzielnia Inwalidow

**WUW**, see Wydawnictwa Uniwersytetu
Warszawskiego

**Wydawn Na Sprawa' Wydawniczo-Oswiatowa
Spotdzielnia Inwalidow+**
ul Zelazna 40, 00-832 Warsaw
*Tel:* (022) 6209071 (ext 26) *Fax:* (022) 6209197
*Key Personnel*
President: Zdzislaw Kozanecki
Vice President, Publishing Manager: Marianna
Malejko
Founded: 1956
Educational Publishing Co-operative of the Dis-
abled.
Subjects: Crafts, Games, Hobbies
ISBN Prefix(es): 83-85048
Imprints: WOSI "Wspolna Sprawa" Warsaw
*Showroom(s):* Al Solidarnosci, 82

**Zaklad Wydawnictw Statystycznych**
al Niepodleglosci 208, 00-925 Warsaw
*Tel:* (022) 6083223; (022) 608-32-10 (orders);
(022) 608-38-10 (orders) *Fax:* (022) 625-9078;
(022) 608-38-67 (orders)
*Telex:* 814581a *Cable:* GUS 12WS
*Key Personnel*
Man Dir: Andrzej Stasiun
Marketing: Christo Cwetkow
Founded: 1966
Statistical Publications Board of the Central Sta-
tistical Office.
Subjects: Economics, Mathematics, Social Sci-
ences, Sociology
ISBN Prefix(es): 83-7027
Divisions: Zaklad Wydawnictwo

**Instytut Wydawniczy Zwiazkow Zawodowych**
ul Jaracza 5, 00-378 Warsaw
*Tel:* 6250765
*Key Personnel*
Dir: Andrzej Wacowski
Founded: 1950
Publishing house of trade unions.
Subjects: Labor, Industrial Relations
ISBN Prefix(es): 83-202
*Bookshop(s):* Ksiegarnia Skladowa, Mariensztat 8,
00-302 Warsaw

# Portugal

## General Information

*Capital:* Libson
*Language:* Portuguese
*Religion:* Predominately Roman Catholic, some
Protestant
*Population:* 10 million
*Bank Hours:* 0830-1500 Monday-Friday
*Shop Hours:* 0900-1300, 1500-1900 Monday-
Friday (some do not close midday); 0900-1300
Saturday. Generally closed Monday morning
October-November
*Currency:* 100 Eurocents = 1 Euro; 200.482 Por-
tuguese escudos = 1 Euro
*Export/Import Information:* Member of European
Economic Community. Foreign language books
from most countries dutied per kg (free from
UK and reduced from EEC); atlases and chil-
dren's picture books have higher tariff rate and
children's picture books have an import surcharge. 5% VAT on books. Small quantity of
advertising duty-free. No import license required for goods not exceeding a certain value,
otherwise license including permission to transfer foreign exchange required.
*Copyright:* UCC, Berne (see Copyright Conventions, pg xi)

**Academia das Ciencias de Lisboa**
R Academia das Ciencias 19-1, 1200 Lisbon
*Tel:* (021) 346-3866 *Fax:* (021) 342-0395
*Key Personnel*
President: Prof J M Toscano Rico
ISBN Prefix(es): 972-623

**Africa Literatura Arte Cultura - ALAC**
Av D Pedro V 11-2° D, 2795 Linda-A-Velha
*Tel:* (021) 4192274
ISBN Prefix(es): 972-9041

**Edicoes Afrontamento+**
Rua Costa Cabral 859, 4200-225 Porto
*Tel:* (02) 507 42 20 *Fax:* (02) 507 42 29
*E-mail:* afrontamento@mail.telepac.pt

*Key Personnel*
Man Dir, Editorial, Production: Jose Sousa
Ribeiro
Sales, Publicity, Rights & Permissions: Andrea
Peniche
Founded: 1963
Subjects: Film, Video, Government, Political Sci-
ence, Literature, Literary Criticism, Essays,
Social Sciences, Sociology
ISBN Prefix(es): 972-36
Number of titles published annually: 40 Print
Total Titles: 900 Print

**ALAC**, see Africa Literatura Arte Cultura -
ALAC

**Publicacoes Alfa SA+**
Rua Luis Pastor de Macedo, 1-B, 1700 Lisbon
*Tel:* (021) 7587320
*Key Personnel*
Administrator: Francisco Lyon de Castro
Founded: 1973
Subjects: History
ISBN Prefix(es): 972-626
*Parent Company:* Publicacoes Europa-America
*Branch Office(s)*
Commercial & Editorial Departments, Estrada
Lisboa-Sintra, Km 14, Edificio CETOP, 2725-
377 Mem Martins
*Bookshop(s):* Livraria Alfa, Avenida Antonio Au-
gusto de Aguiar 150-A, 1050 Lisbon; Livraria
Alfa, Rua Luis Pastor de Macedo, 1-B, 1750
Lisbon

**Livraria Almedina**
Arco de Almedina 15, 3000 509 Coimbra
*Tel:* 239 851 903
*E-mail:* editora@almedina.net
*Web Site:* www.almedina.net
*Telex:* 52207 acic p
*Key Personnel*
Man Dir: Joaquim Machado
Founded: 1955
Subjects: Education, Law
ISBN Prefix(es): 972-40
*Associate Companies:* Edicoes Globo Ltda, Rua
S Filipe Nery 37A, 1250; Porto Ltda, Rua de
Ceuta 79, 4050 Oporto
*Bookshop(s):* Arco de Almedina 15, Rua Ferreira
Borges 121, 3049 Coimbra, Codex

**Armenio Amado Editora de Simoes, Beirao &
Ca Lda+**
Rua Estrela 2-2°, 3000 Coimbra
*Tel:* (039) 92150 *Fax:* (039) 851901
*Key Personnel*
Man Dir: Joaquim Machado
Founded: 1929
Subjects: Architecture & Interior Design, Gov-
ernment, Political Science, History, Language
Arts, Linguistics, Law, Philosophy, Psychology,
Psychiatry, Religion - Other, Social Sciences,
Sociology
ISBN Prefix(es): 972-628

**Edicoes Antigona**
Rua Jorge Barradas, 212-4° D, 1500 Lisbon
*Tel:* (021) 749483 *Fax:* (021) 749483
*Key Personnel*
Editorial, Sales: Manuel Luis de Oliveira
Founded: 1979
Subjects: Fiction, Government, Political Science,
History, Literature, Literary Criticism, Essays,
Social Sciences, Sociology
ISBN Prefix(es): 972-608

**Apaginastantas - Cooperativa de Servicos
Culturais**
Apdo 4254, 1507 Lisbon Codex
*Tel:* (021) 668987

*Key Personnel*
Man Dir: Anabela Mendes
Editorial: Joao Barrento
Founded: 1982
Subjects: Literature, Literary Criticism, Essays,
   Social Sciences, Sociology
ISBN Prefix(es): 972-607

**Apostolado da Oracao Secretariado Nacional**
Largo das Teresinhas 5, 4719-504 Braga Codex
*Tel:* (053) 22485 *Fax:* (053) 201221
*Key Personnel*
Man Dir, Editorial: Manuel Morujao; Americo
   Nunes
Founded: 1874
Subjects: Biography, Poetry, Religion - Other,
   Theology
ISBN Prefix(es): 972-39

**Livraria Arnado Lda**
Rua Joao Machado 9-11, 3007 Coimbra Codex
*Tel:* (0239) 27573 *Fax:* (0239) 22598
*Key Personnel*
Man Dir: Vasco Antunes Domingos
Founded: 1966
Subjects: Law, Literature, Literary Criticism, Es-
   says, Mathematics
ISBN Prefix(es): 972-701
*Parent Company:* Porto Editora Lda
*Associate Companies:* Empresa Literaria Flumi-
   nense, Lda

**Arquivo Universidade de Coimbra**
Rua S Pedro 11-2, 3000 Coimbra
*Tel:* (0239) 25422 *Fax:* (0239) 25841
*Web Site:* www.uc.pt
*Telex:* 52273
*Key Personnel*
Contact: Manuel Augusto Rodrigues
ISBN Prefix(es): 972-594

**Arvore Coop de Actividades Artisticas, CRL**
Pr Azevedo Albuquerque 1, 4000 Porto
*Tel:* (02) 383867 *Fax:* (02) 2002684
*Key Personnel*
President: Jose Rodrigues
Founded: 1963
Subjects: Architecture & Interior Design, Art
ISBN Prefix(es): 972-9089

**Assirio & Alvim**
R Passos Manuel 67B, 1100 Lisbon
*Tel:* (021) 555580 *Fax:* (021) 3152935
*Key Personnel*
Editor: Herminio Monteiro
Subjects: Art, History, Literature, Literary Criti-
   cism, Essays, Photography
ISBN Prefix(es): 972-37

**Atica, SA Editores e Livreiros**
Rua Alvaro Coutinho, 2-3º D, 1100 Lisbon
*Tel:* (021) 8153220 *Fax:* (021) 8153219
*Key Personnel*
Man Dir: Vasco Silva; Jose Rodrigues
Editorial, Rights & Permissions: Vasco Silva
Founded: 1935
Subjects: Drama, Theater, Literature, Literary
   Criticism, Essays, Poetry, Social Sciences, So-
   ciology
ISBN Prefix(es): 972-617

**Basica Editora**
Rua de Entrecampos 36 - r/c E, 1700 Lisbon
*Tel:* (021) 779273
*Key Personnel*
Man Dir, Rights & Permissions: Francisco Prata
   Ginja
Editorial: Rui Ferreira Lopes da Costa
Production, Publicity: Maria Jorge Lopes da
   Costa
Founded: 1974

Subjects: Education
ISBN Prefix(es): 972-631
Imprints: BE
*Sales Office(s):* Platano Editora SARL
*Bookshop(s):* Livraria Basica, Ave Elias Garcia
   49-B, 1000 Lisbon


**BE**, *imprint of* Basica Editora


**Bertrand Editora Lda+**
Rua Anchieta 29 1ro, 1200 Lisbon
*Tel:* (021) 320084 *Fax:* (021) 3468286
*Telex:* 42748
*Key Personnel*
Man Dir: Joao Carlos Alvim
Sales, Rights & Permissions: Teresa Mendonca
Production: Mario Correia
Publicity: Laura Pinheiro
Founded: 1727
Subjects: Art, Literature, Literary Criticism, Es-
   says, Social Sciences, Sociology
ISBN Prefix(es): 972-25
*Bookshop(s):* Sociedades Livreiras Bertrand


**Bezerr-Editorae e Distribuidora de Abel
   Antonio Bezerra**
Bairro Duarte Pacheco, Rua do Rosmaninho 110,
   4703 Braga Codex
Mailing Address: Apdo 313, Braga Codex
*Tel:* (0253) 22604 *Fax:* (0253) 617105
*Key Personnel*
Man Dir: Abel Antonio Bezerra
Founded: 1996
Subjects: Drama, Theater, Education, Ethnicity,
   Fiction, History, Poetry, Travel
ISBN Prefix(es): 972-97378


**Biblioteca Geral da Universidade de Coimbra**
   (University of Coimbra General Library)
Division of Universidade de Coimbra
Largo da Porta Ferrea, 3000-447 Coimbra
*Tel:* (0239) 859800; (0239) 859900 *Fax:* (0239)
   827135
*E-mail:* bguc@uc.pt
*Web Site:* www.uc.pt
*Key Personnel*
Dir: Prof Carlos Fiolhais
Contact: Paula Fernandes Martins
Subjects: Education, History, Library & Informa-
   tion Sciences, Literature, Literary Criticism,
   Essays, Music, Dance, Religion - Catholic, Re-
   ligion - Other
ISBN Prefix(es): 972-616
*Parent Company:* Universidade de Coimbra


**Biblioteca Publica Municipal do Porto**
Rua D Joao IV, 4049 017 Porto
*Tel:* (022) 5193480 *Fax:* (022) 5193488
*E-mail:* bpmp@em-porto.pt
Founded: 1833
ISBN Prefix(es): 972-634


**Brasilia Editora (J Carvalho Branco)+**
Rua Jose Falcao 173, 4000 Porto
*Tel:* (02) 315854 *Fax:* (02) 2055854 *Cable:*
   BRASILIAEDITORA
*Key Personnel*
Man Dir: J Carvalho Branco *Tel:* 02 2001896
   *Fax:* 02 2001904
Editorial, Rights & Permissions: Dr Zulmira C
   Branco
Sales, Publicity: Dr Isabel C Branco
Production: Joana Carvalho Branco
Founded: 1961
Subjects: Astrology, Occult, Biography, Fiction,
   Government, Political Science, Health, Nutri-
   tion, How-to, Philosophy, Poetry, Psychology,
   Psychiatry, Religion - Other, Social Sciences,
   Sociology
ISBN Prefix(es): 972-557

*Parent Company:* Livraria Leitura - Fernandes e
   Branco Lda, Rua de Ceuta 88, 4050
*Associate Companies:* Livraria Leitura - Fer-
   nandes e Branco Lda, Rua de Ceuta 88, 4050
   Porto
Subsidiaries: Livraria Brasilia Editora
*Bookshop(s):* Livraria Brasilia Editora, Ave Almi-
   rante Reis 256B, 1000 Lisbon


**Broteria Associacao Cultural e Cientifica**
Rua Maestro Antonio Taborda, 14, 1293 Lisbon
   Codex
*Tel:* (021) 3961660 *Fax:* (021) 3956629
ISBN Prefix(es): 972-9076


**Camara Municipal de Castelo**
R Candido Reis-Viana Castelo, 4901-887 Viana
   do Castelo
*Tel:* (058) 809300 *Fax:* (058) 809347
*Telex:* 32582
Subjects: Antiques, Archaeology, Architecture &
   Interior Design, Art, History, Poetry
ISBN Prefix(es): 972-588
*Associate Companies:* Biblioteca Municipal,
   Museo Municipal
Subsidiaries: Livraria Municipal


**Editorial Caminho SARL+**
Al Santo Antonio dos Capuchos, 6 B, 1100 Lis-
   bon
*Tel:* (021) 3152683 *Fax:* (021) 534346
*E-mail:* caminho@mail.telepac.pt
*Telex:* 65792
*Key Personnel*
Man Dir: Zeferino Antas de Coelho
Founded: 1977
Subjects: Fiction, Government, Political Science
ISBN Prefix(es): 972-21


**CAPU**
Av Almirante Gago Coutinho, 158, 1700 Lisbon
*Tel:* (021) 8429190 *Fax:* (021) 8409361
*E-mail:* capu@capu.pt
*Web Site:* www.capu.pt
*Key Personnel*
President: Torcato Lopes
ISBN Prefix(es): 972-580


**Editora Caravela+**
Rua General Morais Sarmento 9 c/v, 1500 Lisbon
*Tel:* (01) 7155848 *Fax:* (021) 155848
*Key Personnel*
Man Dir & International Rights: Jose Chaves Fer-
   reira
Founded: 1986
ISBN Prefix(es): 972-639


**Casa Publicadora da Convencao das
   Assembleias de Deus em Portugall**, see
   CAPU


**Celta Editora, Lda**
Rua Vera Cruz 2B, 2780-305 Oeiras
*Tel:* (021) 4417433 *Fax:* (021) 4467304
*E-mail:* mail@celtaeditora.pt; celtaeditora@mail.
   telepac.pt
*Web Site:* www.celtaeditora.pt
*Key Personnel*
Editorial: Carla Pinheiro
ISBN Prefix(es): 972-8027; 972-774


**Centro Estudos Geraficos**
Faculdade de Letras Cidade Universitaria, 1699
   Lisbon Codex
*Tel:* (021) 778883 *Fax:* (021) 7938690
*E-mail:* ceg@mail.telepac.pt
*Key Personnel*
President: Dr Diogo de Abreu
Founded: 1944
Subjects: Geography, Geology, Social Sciences,
   Sociology
ISBN Prefix(es): 972-636

**Centro Psicologia Clinica+**
Via Lucania 42, 65121 Pescara
*Tel:* (085) 4211986 *Fax:* (085) 4211986
*E-mail:* cdibera@tin.it
*Web Site:* www.centro-psicologia.it
*Key Personnel*
President: Dr Carlo Di Berardino
ISBN Prefix(es): 972-725

**Edicoes Cetop+**
PO Box 7, 2726 Mem Martins Codex
*Tel:* (021) 926 3222 *Fax:* (021) 921 7940
*Telex:* 42255 pea p
*Key Personnel*
Man Dir: Tito Lyon de Castro
Editorial Dir, Rights & Production: Jose Antonio
  Rosa *E-mail:* jose.rosa@oninet.pt
Founded: 1965
Membership(s): Euro-Business Publishing Net-
  work.
Subjects: Advertising, Business, Career Devel-
  opment, Computer Science, Finance, Manage-
  ment, Microcomputers, Technology, Travel
ISBN Prefix(es): 972-641
Subsidiaries: Lyon Multimedia Edicoes
*Orders to:* Publicacoes Europa America, Apdo 8,
  2726 Mem Martins Codex

**Cidade Nova Editora**
Rua Dr Camilo Dionisio Alvares, 233, 2775
  Parede
*Tel:* (01) 2478734 *Fax:* (01) 2476369
*Web Site:* perola.net-rubi.com.br
ISBN Prefix(es): 972-9159

**Publicacoes Ciencia e Vida Lda+**
Rua Victor Cordon 24-1° D, 1200 Lisbon
*Tel:* (021) 3427989 *Fax:* (021) 3460224
*Key Personnel*
Man Dir, Editorial: Jeronimo Simoes
Founded: 1979
Subjects: Agriculture, Animals, Pets, Environmen-
  tal Studies, Medicine, Nursing, Dentistry
ISBN Prefix(es): 972-590

**Livraria Civilizacao (Americo Fraga Lamares
  & Ca Lda)+**
R Dr Alberto Aires de Gouveia, 27, 4000 Porto
*Tel:* (022) 20002286 *Fax:* (022) 312382
  *Cable:* Alamares
*Key Personnel*
Man Dir: Arquitecto Moura Bessa
Rights & Permissions: Maria Alice Moura Bessa
Founded: 1921
Subjects: Art, Economics, Fiction, Government,
  Political Science, History, Social Sciences, So-
  ciology
ISBN Prefix(es): 972-26
*Branch Office(s)*
Ave Almirante Reis 102 r/c-Dto, Lisbon 1
  *Tel:* (021) 823389 *Fax:* (021) 823389

**Editora Classica+**
R da Gloria, 10 - R/C, 1298 Lisbon Codex
*Tel:* (021) 372386 *Fax:* (021) 3474729
*Telex:* 18570 escoli p.
*Key Personnel*
Editorial: Francisco Paulo
Subjects: Behavioral Sciences, Business, Com-
  munications, Drama, Theater, Fiction, History,
  Management, Science Fiction, Fantasy, Social
  Sciences, Sociology, Wine & Spirits
ISBN Prefix(es): 972-561
*Bookshop(s):* Cascais Shopping, Loja 12B, 2675
  Cascais; Shopping dos Clerigos, 4000 Porto
*Orders to:* Distribuidora Internacional de Livros
  Lda, Rua Vale Formoso 37, 1900 Lisbon
  *Tel:* (021) 8681183 *Fax:* (021) 8581257

**Coimbra Editora Lda+**
Rua do Arnado, 3001-951 Coimbra

Mailing Address: Apdo 101, 3001-951 Coimbra
*Tel:* (0239) 85 2650 *Fax:* (0239) 85 2651
*E-mail:* sede@mail.coimbraeditora.pt; revistas@
  mail.coimbraeditora.pt
*Web Site:* www.coimbraeditora.pt
*Key Personnel*
Man Dir: Antonio Frederico Araujo Serpa
Founded: 1920 (5)
Subjects: Education, Language Arts, Linguistics,
  Law, Literature, Literary Criticism, Essays,
  Psychology, Psychiatry
ISBN Prefix(es): 972-32; 972-96761
*Bookshop(s):* Faculdade de Direito da Uni-
  versidade do Porto, Praca Coronel Pacheco
  15, 4050-453 Porto *Tel:* (022) 339 0587
  *Fax:* (022) 339 0588 *E-mail:* liv_FDP@mail.
  coimbraeditora.pt; Livraria AAC, Rua Padre
  Antonio Vieira, Edificio AAC, 3000-315
  Coimbra *Tel:* (0239) 83 4123 *Fax:* (0239) 85
  2651 *E-mail:* liv_AAC@mail.coimbraeditora.
  pt; Livraria Chiado, Rua Nova do Almada,
  90, 1200-290 Lisbon *Tel:* (021) 342 4917
  *Fax:* (021) 347 1464 *E-mail:* liv_chiado@mail.
  coimbraeditora.pt; Livraria FDL, Faculdade de
  Direito da Universidade de Lisboa, 1649-014
  Lisbon *Tel:* (021) 796 3122 *Fax:* (021) 780
  0763 *E-mail:* liv_FDL@mail.coimbraeditora.pt;
  Livraria Ferreira Borges, Rua Ferreira Borges
  77-79, 3000-180 Coimbra *Tel:* (0239) 85 2650
  *Fax:* (0239) 85 2651 *E-mail:* liv_fborges@
  mail.coimbraeditora.pt; Livraria Juridica -
  Centro Comercial Arco-Iris, Av Julio Di-
  nis, 6 A-Lj 30, 36, 37 & 38, 1069-215 Lisbon *Tel:* (021) 780 0468 *Fax:* (021) 780 0469
  *E-mail:* liv_jurarcoiris@mail.coimbraeditora.pt

**Edicoes Colibri+**
Apdo 42 001, Telheiras, 1601-801 Lisbon Codex
*Tel:* (021) 7964038 *Fax:* (021) 7964038
*E-mail:* colibri@edi-colibri.pt
*Web Site:* www.edi-colibri.pt
*Key Personnel*
Man Dir: Fernando Mao de Ferro
Founded: 1991
Membership(s): Associacao Portuguesa de Edi-
  tores e Livreiros (APEL).
Subjects: Archaeology, Environmental Studies,
  Geography, Geology, History, Literature, Liter-
  ary Criticism, Essays, Philosophy, Social Sci-
  ences, Sociology, Political science
ISBN Prefix(es): 972-772; 972-8047; 972-8288
Number of titles published annually: 50 Print
Total Titles: 400 Print; 400 Online
Distributed by Dinapress; Sodilivros (Only in Por-
  tugal); Sodiexpor
*Bookshop(s):* Livraria Colibri-Faculdade de Ciencias Sociais e Humanas da Universidade Nova
  de Lisboa, Av de Berna, 26-C, 1069-061 Lisbon

**Comissao para a Igualdade e Direitos das
  Mulheres+**
Av Republica 32-1 E, 1050-193 Lisbon
*Tel:* (021) 7983000 *Fax:* (021) 7983099
*E-mail:* cidm@mail.telepac.pt
*Key Personnel*
President: Maria Amelia Paiva
Editor: Madalena Barbosa
Founded: 1977
Subjects: Women's Studies
ISBN Prefix(es): 972-597

**Editorial Confluencia Lda+**
Calcada do Combro 99, 1116 Lisbon Codex
*Tel:* (021) 663853 *Fax:* (021) 326921
*E-mail:* livroshorizonte@mail.telepac.pt
*Key Personnel*
Man Dir & Editorial: Rogerio Mendes de Moura;
  Eduardo Loureiro de Moura
Sales, Rights & Permissions: Manuela Duarte
Production: Paulo Caracas
Publicity: M Conceicao Silva

Founded: 1945
ISBN Prefix(es): 972-9014

**Constancia Editores, SA**
Estrada da Outurela, 118, 2794-084 Carnaxide
*Tel:* (021) 4246901; (021) 4246902
*E-mail:* info@constancia-editores.pt; prosa@
  santillana.pt
*Web Site:* www.constancia-editores.pt; www.
  santillana.pt
Founded: 1989
Subjects: Art, Astronomy, Biological Sciences,
  Chemistry, Chemical Engineering, Earth Sci-
  ences, Economics, Education, Energy, English
  as a Second Language, Geography, Geology,
  History, Language Arts, Linguistics, Mathemat-
  ics, Music, Dance, Natural History, Philosophy,
  Physical Sciences, Social Sciences, Sociology,
  Technology
ISBN Prefix(es): 972-761; 972-8150; 972-9444
*Branch Office(s)*
Rua da Venezuela, 177, 4150-744 Porto
  *Tel:* (022) 6099195 *Fax:* (022) 6007277

**Contexto Editora+**
Rua Rosa 105-2° Dto, 1200 Lisbon
*Tel:* (021) 347 97 69 *Fax:* (021) 347 97 70
*E-mail:* context-editora@clix.pt
*Key Personnel*
Dir: Manuel de Brito
Founded: 1979
Subjects: Fiction, Poetry
ISBN Prefix(es): 972-575

**Edicoes Cosmos+**
Rua Emenda, 111-1°, 1200 Lisbon
*Tel:* (021) 3468201 *Fax:* (021) 799 99 79
*E-mail:* cosmos@liv-arcoiris.pt *Cable:* COSMOS
  LISBOA
*Key Personnel*
Man Dir: Mario de Couceicas dos Reis
Founded: 1938
Subjects: Anthropology, Economics, Geography,
  Geology, History, Language Arts, Linguistics,
  Law, Literature, Literary Criticism, Essays,
  Music, Dance, Philosophy, Public Administra-
  tion, Social Sciences, Sociology
ISBN Prefix(es): 972-762

**Didactica Editora**
Av Ilha da Madeira, 26-A, 1400 Lisbon
*Tel:* (021) 301 17 31 *Fax:* (021) 273 04 23
*E-mail:* didacticaeditora@mail.telepac.pt; info@
  didactica.pt
*Web Site:* viriato.viatecla.pt/didactica
*Key Personnel*
President: Francisco Prata Ginja
Founded: 1944
Membership(s): APEL (Portuguese Association of
  Publishers & Booksellers).
Subjects: Mathematics, Physical Sciences, Science
  (General)
ISBN Prefix(es): 972-650
*Bookshop(s):* Av da Ilha da Madeira, 22-A, 1400
  Lisbon

**DIFEL - Difusao Editorial SA+**
Rua D Estefania, 46B, 1000 Lisbon
*Tel:* (021) 537677 *Fax:* (021) 545886
*E-mail:* difel.as@mail.telepac.pt
*Telex:* 64030
*Key Personnel*
Man Dir & Editorial: Rita Fezas Vital
General Dir: Francisco Vicente
Founded: 1983
Subjects: Fiction, Nonfiction (General)
ISBN Prefix(es): 972-29

**Difusao Cultural+**
Rua Luis Freitas Branco, 3A/B, 1000 Lisbon
*Tel:* (021) 7599364 *Fax:* (021) 7594418
*Telex:* 60380

*Key Personnel*
General Manager: Dr Eduardo Martins Soares
Editorial Dir: Paulo Ramos
Founded: 1989
Subjects: Art, Behavioral Sciences, Child Care &
Development, Cookery, Economics, Environ-
mental Studies, Fiction, Management
ISBN Prefix(es): 972-709
Number of titles published annually: 40 Audio
Total Titles: 180 Print

**Dinalivro+**
Travessa Convento de Jesus, 15-r/c, 1200 Lisbon
*Tel:* (021) 670 348 *Fax:* (021) 60 84 89
*E-mail:* dinalivro@ip.pt
*Key Personnel*
President: Silverio Amaro
Founded: 1969
Subjects: Accounting, Aeronautics, Aviation, Ar-
chitecture & Interior Design, Art, Astronomy,
Biological Sciences, Computer Science, Edu-
cation, Electronics, Electrical Engineering, En-
gineering (General), Gardening, Plants, Health,
Nutrition, History, Literature, Literary Criti-
cism, Essays, Medicine, Nursing, Dentistry,
Photography, Physics, Psychology, Psychiatry,
Science (General), Social Sciences, Sociology
ISBN Prefix(es): 972-576
Subsidiaries: Dinapress
*Bookshop(s):* Centro Cultural Brasileiro, Largo
Dr Antonio de Sousa de Macedo, 5, 1200 Lis-
bon; Nova Fronteira-Shopping Center Brasilia,
5 Piso-Loja 505-A, 4000 Porto
*Shipping Address:* Travessa do Convento de Je-
sus, 14, 1200 Lisbon
*Warehouse:* Travessa do Convento de Jesus, 14,
1200 Lisbon

**Direccao Geral Familia**
Praca Londres 2-5º, 1091 Lisbon Codex
*Tel:* (021) 8470430 *Fax:* (021) 8491516
Subjects: Child Care & Development, Social Sci-
ences, Sociology
ISBN Prefix(es): 972-718

**Distri Cultural Lda**
R Vasco da Gamma, 4-4 A, 2685 Sacavem
*Tel:* (021) 942 53 94 *Fax:* (021) 941 98 93; (021)
942 52 14
*Telex:* 15094
*Key Personnel*
Man Dir: Karl-Heinz Petzler
Sales Dir: Carlos Alberto
Editorial: Jose Maria Rogagels
Founded: 1980
Subjects: Architecture & Interior Design, Art,
Nonfiction (General), Travel
ISBN Prefix(es): 972-9472; 972-655
*Parent Company:* Grupo Distri
*Bookshop(s):* Internation Book Centre, Cenrto
Comercial de Amoreiras, P-1000 Lisbon

**Elo**, *imprint of* Perspectivas e Realidades, Artes
Graficas, Lda

**Edicoes ELO+**
Rua Almirante Gago Coutinho, 2640 Mafra
*Tel:* (061) 812 143; (061) 812 344 *Fax:* (061) 81
28 20
*E-mail:* eloag@elografica.pt
*Web Site:* www.elografica.pt
*Key Personnel*
Man Dir: Joao Osorio de Castro
Founded: 1962
Subjects: Art, Education, History, House &
Home, Travel
ISBN Prefix(es): 972-9181

**Editorial Estampa, Lda+**
Rua da Escola do Exercito, 9 R/C, Dto, 1150 Lisbon

*Tel:* (021) 355 56 63 *Fax:* (021) 314 19 11
*E-mail:* estampa@mail.telepac.pt
*Web Site:* www.browser.pt/estampa
*Telex:* 66012 estampp
*Key Personnel*
Contact: Antonio Carlos Pinheiro
Founded: 1960
Subjects: Anthropology, Antiques, Architecture &
Interior Design, Art, Astrology, Occult, Cook-
ery, Drama, Theater, Economics, Education,
Fiction, Geography, Geology, Health, Nutri-
tion, History, Law, Literature, Literary Crit-
icism, Essays, Medicine, Nursing, Dentistry,
Nonfiction (General), Parapsychology, Philoso-
phy, Psychology, Psychiatry, Religion - Other,
Romance, Social Sciences, Sociology, Sports,
Athletics
ISBN Prefix(es): 972-33
*Warehouse:* Travessa da Escola Araujo, 34 C,
1150 Lisbon

**Publicacoes Europa-America Lda**
Estr Lisbon-Sintra Km 14, 2725 Mem Martins
*Tel:* (01) 9211461; (01) 9211462 *Fax:* (01)
9217846
*Telex:* 42255 peap *Cable:* EUROPAMERICA
*Key Personnel*
Man Dir: Francisco Lyon de Castro
Sales Dir: Eduardo Lyon de Castro
Manager: Tito Lyon de Castro
Founded: 1945
Subjects: Art, Biography, Education, Engineering
(General), Fiction, History, How-to, Medicine,
Nursing, Dentistry, Music, Dance, Philosophy,
Poetry, Psychology, Psychiatry, Science (Gen-
eral), Social Sciences, Sociology, Technology
ISBN Prefix(es): 972-1
Subsidiaries: Editorial Inquerito Lda; Grafica Eu-
ropam Lda; Publicacoes Forum Lda; Publica-
coes Trevo Lda; Edicoes Cetop
*Branch Office(s)*
Delegacao de Lisboa, Rua das Flores, 45 - 2 Lis-
bon
Delegacao do Porto, Rua 31 de Janeiro, 221
Oporto
*Bookshop(s):* Lojas Europa-America, Ave Mar-
ques de Tomar 1-B; Ave 28 de Maio 61,
Castelo Branco; Pr Ferreira de Almeida 21-22,
Faro; Ave 25 de Abril 48, Almada; Rua Jose
Relvas, 15 B-C Parede; Arcadas do Parque, Es-
toril; 225 Estrada Nacional 6-25, Cascais (Cen-
tro Comercial Pao de Acucar, Lojas 6, 7); Ave
dos Bons Amigos 27-A, Cacem; Ave Antonio
Enes 14-B; Ave Elias Garcia 104-B, Queluz

**Europress Editores e Distribuidores de
Publicacoes Lda+**
Praceta da Republica, Loja A Iote A-1, 2675
Povoa de Santo Adriao
*Tel:* (01) 9387180; (01) 9387190; (01) 9387317;
(01) 9877560; (01) 9381450 *Fax:* (01)
9381452; (01) 9877560
*E-mail:* europress@mail.telepac.pt
*Key Personnel*
Publisher, Man Dir, Editorial: Antonio Bento Vin-
tem
Editor: Dulia Maia Rebocho
Sales: Carlos Vladimiro Ricardo Vintem
Production: Victor M Pinto Pedro
Publicity: Ana Christina Amaro
Founded: 1982
Also acts as national & international distributor,
exporter & printer.
Membership(s): APEL; APIGT.
Subjects: Chemistry, Chemical Engineering,
Drama, Theater, Fiction, Health, Nutrition,
History, Humor, Law, Literature, Literary Crit-
icism, Essays, Medicine, Nursing, Dentistry,
Nonfiction (General), Poetry, Religion - Other,
Romance, Science (General), Sports, Athletics,
Western Fiction
ISBN Prefix(es): 972-559

*Associate Companies:* Pentaedro-Publicidade e
Artes Graficas Lda, Praceta da Republica, Lote
A-1, Loja B, Povoa Sto Adriao, 2675 Odivelas;
Revista de Biotecnologia e Bioquimica Apli-
cada, Rua D Luisa de Gusmao 6 - 1 Esq, 1600
Lisbon
Subsidiaries: Heuris; Lua Viajante, Ed Com de
Livros e Material Audiovisual, Lda
*Branch Office(s)*
Maputo, Mozambique
Cidade Da Praia, Cabo Verde
Distributor for Ed-Maputo (Mozambique);
Livraria LEIA; Sintra Editora
*Bookshop(s):* Bolsonoite I-Livraria Bar Lda,
Avenida Rainha D Leonor 25-A, 1600 Lisbon;
Bolsonoite II, Rua Augusto Gil 6-A, 2675 Odi-
velas
*Warehouse:* Rua Augusto Gil 6-A, 2675 Odivelas
*Tel:* 9347366; 9347367 *Fax:* 9347368

**Everest Editora**
Parque Industrial - Edificio Meramar II - Ar-
mazem 1 - Cabra Figa, 2635 047 Rio de
Mouro
*Tel:* (021) 9152483; (021) 9152510 *Fax:* (021)
9152525
*E-mail:* everesteditora@mail.telepac.pt
*Web Site:* www.everest.pt
*Key Personnel*
Publisher: Carla Pires
Founded: 1994
Subjects: Cookery, Travel
ISBN Prefix(es): 972-750

**FCA Editora de Informatica**
Rua D Estefania 183, 1º E-Lisbon, 1096 Lisbon
Codex
*Tel:* (021) 3151218 *Fax:* (021) 577827
*Telex:* 15432
Founded: 1991
Subjects: Computer Science
ISBN Prefix(es): 972-722

**Fenda Edicoes+**
Affiliate of APEL
Apdo 21334, 1131 Lisbon, Codex
*Tel:* (021) 8823650 *Fax:* (021) 8823659
*E-mail:* info@fenda.pt
*Key Personnel*
Editor: Mr Vasco Santos *E-mail:* vasco.santos@
fenda.pt
Public Relations: Elsa Sertorio *E-mail:* elsa.
sertorio@fenda.pt
Founded: 1979
Specialize in edition of books.
Subjects: Literature, Literary Criticism, Essays,
Poetry, Psychology, Psychiatry
ISBN Prefix(es): 972-9184
Total Titles: 93 Print
Distributed by Sodilivros
Foreign Rights: Capra Press (USA); Carmen Bal-
cells (Europe); Gallimard (France); Rowohlt
(Denmark)

**Chaves Ferreira Publicacoes SA**
Rua D Carlos Mascarenhas, 16A Porta-A, 1000
Lisbon
*Tel:* (021) 3871373 *Fax:* (021) 7161396
*E-mail:* chavesferreira@mail.telepac.pt
*Key Personnel*
Man Dir: Fernando Duval Chaves Ferreira
Founded: 1989
Subjects: Art, History, Technology
ISBN Prefix(es): 972-9402

**Livraria Editora Figueirinhas Lda**
Praca Liberdade, 68, 4000 Porto
*Tel:* (022) 324985 *Fax:* (022) 3325907
*E-mail:* correio@liv-figueirinhas.pt
*Key Personnel*
Editorial, Rights & Permissions: Francisco Pi-
menta
Founded: 1944

Subjects: Literature, Literary Criticism, Essays
ISBN Prefix(es): 972-661

**Empresa Literaria Fluminense, Lda**
Rua S Joao Nepomuceno, 8A, 1200 Lisbon
*Tel:* (021) 601138 *Fax:* (021) 3963371
*Key Personnel*
Man Dir: Antonio Nobre
Founded: 1905
ISBN Prefix(es): 972-555
*Parent Company:* Porto Editora Lda
*Associate Companies:* Livraria Arnado Lda

**Editorial Franciscana+**
Areal de Cima - Montariol, 4710 Braga Codex
Mailing Address: Apdo 1217, 4711-856 Braga
  Codex
*Tel:* (0253) 22490 *Fax:* (0253) 619735
*Key Personnel*
Man Dir: Antonio Pedro da Anunciacao
Founded: 1922
Membership(s): Filiada na APEL - Lisbon.
Subjects: Art, Biography, History, Music, Dance,
  Philosophy, Religion - Other, Theology
ISBN Prefix(es): 972-9190; 972-784
Subsidiaries: Delegacao da Editorial Franciscana
*Bookshop(s):* Livraria Editorial Franciscana, Rua
  de Cedofeita 350, Oporto

**Editorial Futura+**
Rua Gen Morais Sarmento, 9 C/V, 1600 Lisbon
*Tel:* (021) 7155848 *Fax:* (021) 155848
*Key Personnel*
Man Dir: Jose Chaves Ferreira
Founded: 1970
Subjects: Humor, Literature, Literary Criticism,
  Essays
ISBN Prefix(es): 972-587

**Gabinete de Especializcao e Cooperacao
  Tecnica Internacional**, see GECTI (Gabinete
  de Especializacao e Cooperacao Tecnica
  Internacional L)

**GECTI (Gabinete de Especializacao e
  Cooperacao Tecnica Internacional L)+**
Ave Republica 47-6 Dt, 1050 Lisbon
*Tel:* (021) 7968877; (021) 7971940; (021)
  7972154 *Fax:* (021) 7963465
*E-mail:* gecti@mail.telepac.pt
*Web Site:* www.inedita.com/gecti
*Key Personnel*
Man Dir, Editorial: A Almeida Teixeira
Founded: 1963
Subjects: Business, Marketing, Public Administra-
  tion
ISBN Prefix(es): 972-9012

**Girassol Edicoes, LDA+**
Affiliate of Susaeta Ediciones
Rua Actriz Adelina Fernandes, 19-A, 2795 Linda
  a Velha
*Tel:* (021) 41 43942 *Fax:* (021) 41 43518
*E-mail:* girassol@mail.telepac.pt
*Key Personnel*
General Manager: Fernando Sarmento
Founded: 1994
ISBN Prefix(es): 972-756
Number of titles published annually: 120 Print
Total Titles: 775,000 Print
Imprints: Multinova; Susaeta Ediciones
*Branch Office(s)*
Banco Espirito Santo *Tel:* (021) 4185367
Banco Santander *Tel:* (021) 4588390

**Gradiva-Publicacnoes Lda+**
Rua Almeida & Sousa 21, R/C Esq, 1399-041
  Lisbon
*Tel:* (021) 397 40 67; (021) 397 40 68; (021) 397
  13 57 *Fax:* (021) 395 34 71
*E-mail:* geral@ip.pt

*Web Site:* www.gradiva.pt
*Key Personnel*
Man Dir: Deolinda Valente
Editor: Guilherme de Carvalho Negrnao Valente
Foreign Rights Department: Joana Gongalves
Vice Dir, Sales & Rights & Permissions: Rodolfo
  Miguel D S B Begonha
Production: Fernando Guerreiro
Sales Manager: Carlos Rosa
Founded: 1981
Specialize in science books.
Subjects: Anthropology, Asian Studies, Astron-
  omy, Behavioral Sciences, Biological Sciences,
  Communications, Computer Science, Crafts,
  Games, Hobbies, Earth Sciences, Economics,
  Education, Engineering (General), Environ-
  mental Studies, Fiction, Geography, Geology,
  Government, Political Science, History, Hu-
  man Relations, Humor, Journalism, Literature,
  Literary Criticism, Essays, Management, Math-
  ematics, Natural History, Nonfiction (General),
  Philosophy, Physics, Psychology, Psychiatry,
  Romance, Science (General), Science Fiction,
  Fantasy, Self-Help, Social Sciences, Sociology
ISBN Prefix(es): 972-662
Number of titles published annually: 80 Print
Total Titles: 700 Print
Distributor for Sinais de Fogo

**Guimaraes Editores, Lda+**
Rua da Misericordia, 68-70, 1200-273 Lisbon
*Tel:* (021) 324 3120 *Fax:* (021) 324 3129
*E-mail:* guimaraes.ed@mail.telepac.pt
*Web Site:* www.guimaraes-ed.pt
*Telex:* 16337
*Key Personnel*
Man Dir: Isabel Leao
Man Dir, Editorial: Francisco da Cunha Leao
Founded: 1899
Subjects: Drama, Theater, Fiction, History, Phi-
  losophy, Poetry, Social Sciences, Sociology
ISBN Prefix(es): 972-665
*Bookshop(s):* Livraria Guimaraes, Rua da Miseri-
  cordia 68, 1200-273 Lisbon
*Shipping Address:* Rua Conceiccao da Gloria 75,
  1250-080 Lisbon
*Warehouse:* Rua Conceiccao da Gloria 75, Lisbon
*Orders to:* Rua Conceiccao da Gloria 75, 1250-
  080 Lisbon

**Impala**
Rua Cristino da Silva, 1 B, Monte Abraao, 2745
  Queluz
*Tel:* (021) 4364401 *Fax:* (021) 4366572
*Telex:* 16088 cendi p
Founded: 1983
Membership(s): APCT; AIND.
Subjects: Astronomy, Biography, Career Develop-
  ment, Child Care & Development, Economics,
  Education, Fashion, Gardening, Plants, Geog-
  raphy, Geology, How-to, Humor, Literature,
  Literary Criticism, Essays, Microcomputers,
  Music, Dance, Photography, Radio, TV, Sports,
  Athletics, Women's Studies
ISBN Prefix(es): 972-574; 972-766
Imprints: Lisgrafica
*Book Club(s):* AIND

**Imprensa Nacional-Casa da Moeda**
Av Antonio Jose de Almeida, 1000 042 Lisbon
*Tel:* (021) 781 07 00 *Fax:* (021) 781 07 54
*Web Site:* www.incm.pt
*Telex:* 15328 incmp *Cable:* INCM
*Key Personnel*
President: Antonio Braz Teixeira
Editorial Dir: Dr Margarida Santos
  *E-mail:* margarida.santos@incm.pt
Founded: 1768
Subjects: Anthropology, Archaeology, Art, Bi-
  ography, Economics, Ethnicity, Government,
  Political Science, History, Language Arts, Lin-
  guistics, Law, Literature, Literary Criticism, Es-

says, Medicine, Nursing, Dentistry, Philosophy,
  Poetry, Public Administration, Social Sciences,
  Sociology
ISBN Prefix(es): 972-27
*Branch Office(s)*
Coimbra
Lisbon
Porto
*Bookshop(s):* Rua de D Francisco Manuel de
  Melo, 5, 1070 002 Lisbon *Tel:* (021) 383 58 00
  *Fax:* (021) 383 58 34 *E-mail:* livraria.m.melo@
  incm.pt; Rua do Marques de Sa da Bandeira,
  16-A e 16-B, Lisbon 1050 148 *Tel:* (021) 330
  17 00 *Fax:* (021) 330 17 07 *E-mail:* livraria.
  s.bandeira@incm.pt; Rua da Escola Politecnica, Lisbon 1250 100 *Tel:* (021) 394 57
  00 *Fax:* (021) 394 57 33 *E-mail:* livraria.r.
  escola@incm.pt; Ave de Fernao de Magalhaes, 486, 3000 173 Coimbra *Tel:* (023) 985
  64 00 *Fax:* (023) 985 64 16 *E-mail:* livraria.
  coimbra@incm.pt; Praca de Guilherme Gomes
  Fernandes, 84, 4050 294 Porto *Tel:* (022) 339
  58 20 *Fax:* (022) 339 58 23 *E-mail:* livraria.
  porto@incm.pt; Livraria Camoes, Rua Bitten-
  court da Silva nº 12 Loja C, Rio de Janeiro
  RJ, Brazil *Tel:* (021) 2624776 *E-mail:* livraria.
  camoes@incm.com.br; Rua des Portas de
  Santo Antao nº 2-2A, (Palacio da Independencia), 1150 320 Lisbon *Tel:* (021) 324 04
  07 *Fax:* (021) 324 04 09 *E-mail:* livraria.
  s.antao@incm.pt; Rua D Filipa de Vilhena
  12, 12A, 1000 136 Lisbon *Fax:* (021) 781
  07 95 *E-mail:* livraria.f.vilhena@incm.pt; Av
  Roma, 1000 260 Lisbon *Tel:* (021) 840 10 23
  *Fax:* (021) 840 09 61 *E-mail:* livraria.roma@
  incm.pt

**INCM**, see Imprensa Nacional-Casa da Moeda

**Editorial Inquerito Lda+**
Apdo 8, 2726 Mem Martins Codex
*Tel:* (021) 9211 460 *Fax:* (021) 9217 940
*E-mail:* publicidade@iol.pt
*Telex:* 42255
*Key Personnel*
Man Dir: Francisco Lyon de Castro
Founded: 1938
Subjects: Economics, History, Law, Philosophy,
  Social Sciences, Sociology
ISBN Prefix(es): 972-670
*Parent Company:* Publicacoes Europa-America
  Lda
*Associate Companies:* Publicacoes Europa-
  America
Distributed by Publicacoes Europe-America
*Distribution Center:* Publicacoes Europe-America
*Orders to:* Publicacoes Europa-America Lda,
  Estrada Lisboa-Sintra, Km 14, Apartado 8,
  2726-901 Mem Martins

**Instituto Tecnico de Alimentacao Humana**, see
  Edicoes ITAU (Instituto Tecnico de
  Alimentacao Humana) Lda

**Instituto de Investigacao Cientifica Tropical**
  (Tropical Sciences Research Institute)
Rua da Junqueira, nº 86-1º, 1300-344 Lisbon
*Tel:* (021) 361 63 40 *Fax:* (021) 363 14 60
*E-mail:* iict@iict.pt
*Web Site:* www.iict.pt
*Telex:* IICT 66932
*Key Personnel*
Contact: Maria Virginia Aires Magrio
Founded: 1883
Specialize in tropical areas.
Subjects: Agriculture, Anthropology, Archaeol-
  ogy, Biological Sciences, Earth Sciences, En-
  vironmental Studies, Ethnicity, Geography,
  Geology, History, Social Sciences, Sociology,
  Veterinary Science
ISBN Prefix(es): 972-672
Number of titles published annually: 23 Print

*Bookshop(s):* Imprensa Nacional-Casa da Moeda, Rua D Francisco Manuel de Melo, 5-D, 1000 Lisbon; Livraria Portugal, Rua do Carmo, 70, 1200-094 Lisbon *Tel:* (021) 347 49 82 *Fax:* (021) 347 02 64 *E-mail:* liv.portugal@mail.telepac.pt; Sodilivros, Sociedade Distribuidora de Livros e Publicacoes, SA, Rua de Campolide, N° 783-B, 1070-029 Lisbon *Tel:* (021) 381 56 00 *Fax:* (021) 387 62 81 *E-mail:* sodilivros@mail.telepac.pt
*Warehouse:* Travessa Paulo Martins, N° 31-A, 1300 Lisbon *Tel:* (021) 363 59 38 *Fax:* (021) 363 59 38
*Orders to:* Centro de Documentacao e Informacao, IICT, Rua General Joao de Almeida, Palacio do Conde da Calheta, 1300-266 Lisbon *Tel:* (021) 361 97 30 *Fax:* (021) 362 82 18 *E-mail:* cdi@iict.pt

**Edicoes ITAU (Instituto Tecnico de Alimentacao Humana) Lda**
Rua Dr Oliveira Salazar 2, 2665 Malveira
*Tel:* (01) 9661603 *Fax:* (01) 9661227
*Key Personnel*
Man Dir: Julio Roberto
Editorial, Sales, Production, Publicity: Jose Maria Paula
Founded: 1969
Subjects: Education, Health, Nutrition, Literature, Literary Criticism, Essays, Poetry, Social Sciences, Sociology
ISBN Prefix(es): 972-9055
*Parent Company:* Instituto Tecnico de Alimentacao Humana Lda
*Orders to:* Ave Elias Garcia 87-A, Lisbon 1

**Americo Fraga Lamares & Ca Lda**, see Livraria Civilizacao (Americo Fraga Lamares & Ca Lda)

**Latina Livraria Editora**
Rua de Santa Catarina 2-10, 4000-441 Porto
*Tel:* (02) 2001294 *Fax:* (02) 2086053
*Key Personnel*
President: Henrique Fonseca Perdigao
Vice President: Maria Luisa Fonseca Perdigao
Founded: 1941
Subjects: Aeronautics, Aviation, Architecture & Interior Design, Art, History, House & Home, Literature, Literary Criticism, Essays, Music, Dance, Photography, Romance, Travel, Wine & Spirits
ISBN Prefix(es): 972-95647; 972-95657

**Edicoes Manuel Lencastre+**
Vale de Vigueira, 22, 2300, Tomar
*Tel:* 4688328
Founded: 1988
Subjects: Asian Studies, Astrology, Occult, Health, Nutrition, Philosophy, Religion - Buddhist, Religion - Catholic, Religion - Hindu, Religion - Islamic, Religion - Other
ISBN Prefix(es): 972-9054

**Lidel Edicoes Tecnicas, Lda+**
Rua D Estefania 183 r/c Dto, 1096 Lisbon Codex
*Tel:* (021) 571288 *Fax:* (021) 577827
*Telex:* 15432
*Key Personnel*
Man Dir: Engo Frederico Annes
Editorial Dir: Jose Jomem de Mello
Founded: 1963
Membership(s): Publishers & Booksellers Portuguese Association.
Subjects: Computer Science, Labor, Industrial Relations, Language Arts, Linguistics
ISBN Prefix(es): 972-9018

**Lisgrafica**, *imprint of* Impala

**Livraria Apostolado da Imprensa+**
Largo das Teresinhas, 5, 4719 Braga Codex
*Tel:* (0253) 22485 *Fax:* (0253) 201221
*Key Personnel*
Man Dir, Editorial: Manuel Morujao; Americo Nunes
Founded: 1922
Subjects: Biography, Philosophy
ISBN Prefix(es): 972-571
*Branch Office(s)*
Rua da Lapa 111, 1200 Lisbon

**Livraria Luzo-Espanhola Lda**
Rua Nova do Almada 86, 1200 Lisbon
*Tel:* (021) 3424917 *Cable:* LIVRALUSO
*Key Personnel*
Man Dir: Inocencio Casimiro Araujo; Joao Pinto Soares
Founded: 1941
Subjects: Economics, Medicine, Nursing, Dentistry
ISBN Prefix(es): 972-9465
*Bookshop(s):* Livraria Luzo-Espanhola e Brasileira Lda, Ave 13 Maio 23 - 4, Rio de Janerio, Brazil; Livraria Luzo-Espanhola Lda, Rua da Sofia 121 - 1, Coimbra; Livraria Cientifico Medico do Porto, Rua do Carmo 14, Oporto

**Livraria Minerva+**
Rua dos Gatos 10, 3000 Coimbra
*Tel:* (0239) 26259 *Fax:* (0239) 717267
*E-mail:* livrariaminerva@mail.telepac.pt
*Key Personnel*
Manager: Isabel Garcia; Jose Alberto Garcia
Founded: 1985
Subjects: Computer Science, Drama, Theater, Finance, Literature, Literary Criticism, Essays, Medicine, Nursing, Dentistry, Philosophy, Poetry, Romance
ISBN Prefix(es): 972-9316; 972-9318
Distributed by Faculdade de Letras da Universidade de Coimbra
*Showroom(s):* Rua Carlos Seixas, 74-P, 3000 Coimbra
*Bookshop(s):* Rua de Macau, 52, 3030 Coimbra

**Editora Livros do Brasil Sarl**
Rua Caetanos, 22, 1200 Lisbon
*Tel:* (021) 3426113 *Fax:* (021) 342 84 87
*E-mail:* livbrasil@clix.pt *Cable:* Librasil
*Key Personnel*
Man Dir, Rights & Permissions: Antonio de Souza-Pinto
Editorial, Publicity: Joao Palma-Ferreira
Sales: Jose Manuel Lopes Filipe
Founded: 1944
Subjects: Biography, Government, Political Science, History, Philosophy, Science (General), Science Fiction, Fantasy
ISBN Prefix(es): 972-38
*Associate Companies:* Editores Associados Lda
*Branch Office(s)*
Rua de Ceuta 80, Oporto

**Livros Horizonte Lda+**
Rua Chagas 17-1° D, 1200 Lisbon
*Tel:* (021) 346 69 17 *Fax:* (021) 326921
*E-mail:* livroshorizonte@mail.telepac.pt *Cable:* LIVROSHORIZONTE
*Key Personnel*
Man Dir & Editorial: Rogerio de Mendes Moura; Eduardo de Loureiro Moura
Sales, Rights & Permissions: Manuela Duarte
Production: Paulo Caracas
Publicity: M Conceicao Silva
Founded: 1953
Subjects: Art, Education, History, Psychology, Psychiatry, Social Sciences, Sociology
ISBN Prefix(es): 972-24

**Livraria Lopes Da Silva-Editora de M Moreira Soares Rocha Lda**
Rua Cha 101-103, 4000 Porto
*Tel:* (02) 21678 *Fax:* (02) 2006017
*Key Personnel*
Man Dir: Adelino Silva
Founded: 1870
Subjects: Medicine, Nursing, Dentistry, Science (General), Technology
ISBN Prefix(es): 972-682

**Lua Viajante-Edicao e Distribuicao de Livros e Material Audiovisual, Lda**
Praceta Republica Ioja A, 2675 Povoa de Santo Adriao
*Tel:* (01) 9376180 *Fax:* (01) 9381452; (01) 9377560
*E-mail:* europress@mail.telepac.pt
*Key Personnel*
Publisher & Man Dir, Editorial: Antonio Bento Vintem
Editor: Dulia Maria Rebocho
Sales: Carlos Vladimiro Ricardo Vintem
Production: Victor M Pinto Pedro
Publicity: Ana Christina Amaro
Founded: 1992
Subjects: Computer Science
ISBN Prefix(es): 972-8038
*Associate Companies:* Europress-Editores & Distribuidores de Publicacoes Lda, Praceta Republica Ioja A, 2675 Povoa de Santo Adriao; Pentaedro-Publicidade e Artes Graficas Lda, Praceta Republica Loja A, 2675 Povoa de Santo Adriao
Distributed by Europress Editores & Distribuidores
*Warehouse:* Rua Augusto Gil 6-A, Odivelas
*Tel:* (01) 9347366; (01) 9347367 *Fax:* (01) 9347368

**Mafra**, *imprint of* Perspectivas e Realidades, Artes Graficas, Lda

**Livraria Tavares Martins+**
Rua Clerigos, 14, 4000 Porto
*Tel:* (022) 23459
*Key Personnel*
Man Dir: Jorge de Amorim
Founded: 1911
Subjects: Art, Biography, Drama, Theater, History, Law, Philosophy, Poetry, Religion - Other
ISBN Prefix(es): 972-694

**Editora McGraw-Hill de Portugal Lda**
Rua Barata Salgueiro, Ed Castilho 5 r/chao fraccao "A", Lisbon
*Tel:* (021) 355 3180 *Fax:* (021) 355 3189
*E-mail:* servico-clientes@mcgraw-hill.com
*Web Site:* www.mcgraw-hill.pt
*Telex:* 14724
*Key Personnel*
General Manager: Francisco Paes Mamede
Business Manager: Jose Temes
Sales Manager: Joao Esquivel
Editor: Hugo Xavier
Founded: 1977
Subjects: Agriculture, Architecture & Interior Design, Biological Sciences, Business, Chemistry, Chemical Engineering, Civil Engineering, Computer Science, Economics, Education, Electronics, Electrical Engineering, Engineering (General), Environmental Studies, Government, Political Science, Health, Nutrition, Human Relations, Law, Management, Marketing, Mathematics, Mechanical Engineering, Medicine, Nursing, Dentistry, Physics, Psychology, Psychiatry, Science (General), Social Sciences, Sociology
ISBN Prefix(es): 972-9241; 972-773; 972-8298
*Parent Company:* The McGraw-Hill Campanies, 1221 Avenue of the Americas, New York, NY 10020, United States

*Associate Companies:* Distribuidora Cuspide, Suipacha 764, 1008 Buenos Aires, Argentina, President: Joaquin Gil Paricio *Tel:* (01) 3228366 *Fax:* (01) 3223456; (01) 3223465; Makron Books do Brazil Editora Ltda, Rua Tabapua 1105, Itaim Bibi, CP 20689, 04533 Sao Paulo, Brazil, President: Milton Mira de Assumpcao, Filho *Tel:* (011) 8206622; (011)8208528; (011) 8296251 *Fax:* (011) 8294970

**Melhoramentos de Portugal Editora, Lda+**
Rua Embaixador Teixeira Sampaio, 4, 1300 Lisbon
*Tel:* (021) 3963225 *Fax:* (021) 678254
*Telex:* 42802 SAGRIL P
*Key Personnel*
Man Dir: Carolina Andrade
Founded: 1990
Subjects: Literature, Literary Criticism, Essays
ISBN Prefix(es): 972-713
*Associate Companies:* Companhia Melhoramentos de Sao Paulo, Brazil

**Meriberica/Liber+**
Av Duque d'Avila, 69-r/c E, 1000 Lisbon
*Tel:* (021) 8583849 *Fax:* (021) 8581536
*E-mail:* geral@meriberica.pt; bd@meriberica.pt; encomendar@meriberica.pt (orders)
*Web Site:* www.meriberica.pt
*Telex:* 14598 merlib p
*Key Personnel*
Partner: Bruno Protasio; Daniel Protasio; Marlos Protasio
Partner & Manager: Patricia Protasio
Manager: J Ribeiro Teles
Founded: 1974
Membership(s): Apel Portuguesa de Editores e Livreiros Associagao.
Subjects: Cookery, Humor, Comics
ISBN Prefix(es): 972-45
Number of titles published annually: 40 Print
Total Titles: 650 Print
Distributor for Casterman; Dargaud; Delcourt; Hachette; La Martiniere; Albin Michel; NORMA

**Editorial Minerva+**
R Luz Soriano 33, 1200-246 Lisbon
*Tel:* (021) 3220540 *Fax:* (021) 3220549
*Key Personnel*
Dir: Joao Fernandes Domingues
Founded: 1927
Subjects: Fiction
ISBN Prefix(es): 972-591

**Monitor-Projectos e Edicoes, LDA+**
R Abade Faria, 6, 2°-D-Lisbon, 1900 006 Lisbon
*Tel:* (021) 849-48-93 *Fax:* (021) 793-45-51
*E-mail:* monitor@esoterica.pt
*Key Personnel*
Prof: Victor Roldao *Tel:* (021) 7973656
Subjects: Career Development, Engineering (General), Human Relations, Management, Self-Help
ISBN Prefix(es): 972-9413; 972-95278
Total Titles: 65 Print
*Branch Office(s)*
Av Igreja, 66,3°-E-Lisbon, 1700 240 Lisbon
*Tel:* (021) 7973656 *Fax:* (021) 7934551

**Mosaico Editores, LDA**
Calcada Mestres-1-6° D, 1000 Lisbon
*Tel:* (021) 681902 *Fax:* (021) 387-10-81
*E-mail:* mosaico@mail.telepac.pt
ISBN Prefix(es): 972-95663

**Multinova**, *imprint of* Girassol Edicoes, LDA

**Multinova+**
Av Santa Joana Princesa, 12-C/E, 1700 357 Lisbon
*Tel:* (021) 8481820 *Fax:* (021) 8483436
*E-mail:* geral@multinova.pt
*Web Site:* www.multinova.pt
*Key Personnel*
Contact: Carlos Santos
Founded: 1970
Also specialize in directing commercials.
ISBN Prefix(es): 972-9035

**Musicoteca Lda**
Rua Joao Pereira da Rosa, 8, 1200 Lisbon
*Tel:* (021) 3462653 *Fax:* (021) 3476637
*E-mail:* musicoteca@mail.telepac.pt
Founded: 1990
Subjects: Music, Dance
ISBN Prefix(es): 972-9449

**Editorial Noticias+**
Rua Padre Luis Aparicio, n 10, 1°, 1150-248 Lisbon
*Tel:* (021) 3552130 *Fax:* (021) 3552168; (021) 3552169
*E-mail:* geral@editorialnoticias.pt
*Web Site:* www.editorialnoticias.pt
*Telex:* 64381
*Key Personnel*
Executive Editor: Marta Ramires *E-mail:* marta.ramires@editorialnoticias.pt
Contact: Alexandra Manuel
Founded: 1985
Also acts as editor, distributor & bookseller.
Subjects: Cookery, Fiction, History, Journalism, Law, Religion - Other, Self-Help
ISBN Prefix(es): 972-46
Total Titles: 90 Print
*Ultimate Parent Company:* Lusomundo
*Associate Companies:* Oficina Do Livro
Subsidiaries: Oficina Do Livro
*Bookshop(s):* Aveiro Forum, Rua Homem Cristo Filho, Centro Comercial Forum Loja 1, 01, 3810 Aveiro; Aveiro Glicinias, Centro Comercial Glicinias, Loja 41, 3810 Aveiro; Livraria Noticias, Centro Comercial Eborim, R do Eborim, 18, 7000-659 Evora; Livaria Noticias, Rua de Sao Francisco, n° 8 A, 9000-050 Funchal; R da Olivenca 9, 2800 Almada; Rossio, 11, 1100 Lisbon *Tel:* (021) 342 17 77 *Fax:* (021) 322 57 33; Rossio, 13, 1100-199 Lisbon; Avenida da Libserdade, 266-1250, 1250 Lisbon *Tel:* (021) 318 78 43

**Internationale Nouvelle Acropole** (New Acropolis International)+
Rua Maria, 48-3°, 1100 Lisbon
*Tel:* (021) 827097
*Web Site:* www.acropolis.org
*Key Personnel*
Contact: Paulo Loucao
Founded: 1979
Specialize in human sciences & esoterism.
Subjects: Anthropology, Archaeology, Astrology, Occult, History, Philosophy
ISBN Prefix(es): 972-9026
*Branch Office(s)*
4710 Braga
R Prof Machado Nilela, 285-3d90

**Nova Arrancada Sociedade Editora SA+**
Rua Vitor Cordon, 41-47, 1200 Lisbon
*Tel:* (021) 3468837 *Fax:* (021) 3475122
*E-mail:* novaarrancada@mail.telepac.pt
*Key Personnel*
Executive Dir: Jose Luis Henriques
Founded: 1995
Subjects: Drama, Theater, Economics, Government, Political Science, History, Literature, Literary Criticism, Essays, Religion - Catholic, Social Sciences, Sociology

ISBN Prefix(es): 972-8369
Number of titles published annually: 30 Print

**Editorial O Livro Lda**
R Maj Neutel Abreu 16-A/B/C, 1500 Lisbon
*Tel:* (021) 7783577 *Fax:* (021) 7783536
*E-mail:* prof@editorialolivro.pt
*Web Site:* www.editorialolivro.pt
*Key Personnel*
Man Dir: Carlos de Moura
ISBN Prefix(es): 972-552

**Observatorio Astronomico de Lisboa**
Tapada da Ajuda, 1349-018 Lisbon
*Tel:* (021) 361 6739; (021) 361 6730 *Fax:* (021) 362 1722
*E-mail:* info@oal.ul.pt
*Web Site:* www.oal.ul.pt
ISBN Prefix(es): 972-573

**Edicoes Ora & Labora**
Mosteiro de Singeverga, 4780 Santo Tirso
*Tel:* (0252) 94 11 76 *Fax:* (0252) 87 29 47
*E-mail:* msingeverga@net.sapo.pt
Founded: 1950
Membership(s): Society of Portuguese Publishers & Booksellers.
Subjects: Anthropology, Biography, Religion - Catholic, Theology
ISBN Prefix(es): 972-9278

**Palas Editores Lda+**
Rua Quirino da Fonseca, 4-c/v D, 1000 Lisbon
*Tel:* (021) 574903 *Fax:* (021) 795-4019
*Key Personnel*
Editor: Maria De Fatima De Sa Ressoa
Founded: 1973
Membership(s): APEL.
Subjects: Education, History
ISBN Prefix(es): 972-9000

**Paulinas+**
Rua Alexandre Rey Colaco, 1700 Lisbon
*Tel:* (021) 848 43 55 *Fax:* (021) 847 41 51
*E-mail:* paulinas@mail.telepac.pt
Founded: 1950
Subjects: Biblical Studies, Biography, Human Relations, Literature, Literary Criticism, Essays, Religion - Catholic, Romance, Science Fiction, Fantasy, Securities
ISBN Prefix(es): 972-751
*Bookshop(s):* Paulinas Multimedia, Rua Morais Soares, 56 A-1900 Lisbon *Tel:* (021) 813 90 38 *Fax:* (021) 847 41 51; Paulinas Multimedia, Rua de Cedofeita, 355-4050 Porto *Tel:* (02) 31 49 56 *Fax:* (02) 32 08 31; Paulinas Multimedia, Rua Dr Fernao de Ornelas, 379050 Funchal-Maderia *Tel:* (091) 23 56 99 *Fax:* (091) 23 36 17; Paulinas Multimedia, Rua do Municipio, 12-8000 Faro *Tel:* (089) 82 30 27 *Fax:* (089) 80 56 79; Paulinas Multimedia, Praca Teofilo Braga, 12-13, 2900 Setubal *Tel:* (065) 53 42 14 (Centro Social S Francisco Xavier)

**Paz-Editora de Multimedia, LDA+**
Rua da Bela Vista a Graca, 27-A, 1170 Lisbon
*Tel:* (021) 8101282 *Fax:* (021) 8101287
*E-mail:* paz@esoterica.pt
*Key Personnel*
Partner: Helfried Bauer
Jr Partner: Peter C Wiesenthal
Founded: 1996
Membership(s): APEL.
Subjects: Health, Nutrition, Well being & reference
ISBN Prefix(es): 972-8416
*Associate Companies:* Felecidade-Editora de Multimidia Ltda, Rio de Janeiro, Brazil

**Editora Pergaminho Lda**
Rua Tierno Galvan, torre 3, sala 607, 1200 Lisbon
*Tel:* (021) 652441 *Fax:* (021) 687543
*E-mail:* pergaminho@mail.telepac.pt
*Key Personnel*
Contact: Mario Mendes Moura
Founded: 1990
Subjects: Art, Music, Dance, Radio, TV
ISBN Prefix(es): 972-711

**Perspectivas e Realidades, Artes Graficas, Lda**
Rua Ruben A Leitao 4,2° Esq, 1200-392 Lisbon
*Tel:* (021) 3471371 *Fax:* (021) 3471372
*Telex:* 42458 Perspe P
*Key Personnel*
Man Dir: Dr Joao Soares
Executive Dir: Dr Carlos Capelas
Publicity: Rui Perdigao
Founded: 1975
Subjects: Government, Political Science, Literature, Literary Criticism, Essays, Poetry
ISBN Prefix(es): 972-620
*Associate Companies:* Diglivro Lda
Imprints: Elo; Mafra

**Petrony Livraria**
Rua Assuncao n° 90, 1100 Lisbon
*Tel:* (021) 3423911 *Fax:* (021) 3431602
Founded: 1955
Subjects: Law
ISBN Prefix(es): 972-685

**Planeta Editora, LDA+**
Trav do Noronha 21-1 F, 1200 Lisbon
*Tel:* (021) 397-87-56 *Fax:* (021) 395-10-26
*Key Personnel*
International Rights: Gloria Ribeiro
Subjects: Astrology, Occult, Astronomy, Biblical Studies, Earth Sciences, Fiction, Mysteries, Science Fiction, Fantasy
ISBN Prefix(es): 972-731

**Platano Editora SA+**
Av de Berna, 31-2° Esq, 1069 Lisbon Codex
*Tel:* (021) 7979278 *Fax:* (021) 7954019
*E-mail:* geral@platanoeditora.pt
*Web Site:* www.plantanoeditora.pt
*Key Personnel*
President: Francisco Prata Ginja
Founded: 1972
Membership(s): the Portuguese Association of Book Publishers.
Subjects: Drama, Theater, Poetry
ISBN Prefix(es): 972-621; 972-707; 972-770
Subsidiaries: Alicerce Editora Lda; Paralelo Editora Lda; Didactica Editora Lda; Platano Edicoes Tecnicas Lda; Editora de Ensino a Distancia Lda
*Branch Office(s)*
Platano Editora SA, Coimbra
*Bookshop(s):* Alicerce Editora Lda, Rua Guerra Junqueiro 456, 4100 Porto
*Warehouse:* Rua Joao Ortigao Ramos 29-B, 1500 Lisbon
Servicor Ceutrais de Preducco e Armazens Quinta dos Lagoas, Almada 2800

**Porto Editora Lda+**
Rua da Restauracao, 365, 4099 023 Porto
*Tel:* (02) 2005813 *Fax:* (02) 313072
*E-mail:* pe@portoeditora.pt
*Web Site:* www.portoeditora.pt
*Telex:* 27205 ported p
*Key Personnel*
Man Dir: Graciete Teixeira; Jose A Teixeira; Rosalia G Teixeira; Vasco F Teixeira
Founded: 1944
Subjects: Education, Language Arts, Linguistics, Nonfiction (General)
ISBN Prefix(es): 972-0

*Associate Companies:* Empresa Literaria Fluminense Lda, Av Almirante Gago Coutinho 57 A, 1700 Lisbon *Tel:* (021) 8430900 *Fax:* (021) 8430901
Subsidiaries: Livraria Arnado Lda
*Bookshop(s):* Rua da Fabrica 90, Oporto *Tel:* (02) 2087669 *Fax:* (02) 2087669; Praca D Filipa de Lencastre 42, Oporto *Tel:* (02) 2087681 *Fax:* (02) 2087681

**Portugalmundo+**
Rua Graca, 28, 1100 Lisbon
*Tel:* (021) 877611 *Fax:* (021) 8144746
*Key Personnel*
Dir: Maria Jose Palmela Pinto
Founded: 1976
Membership(s): APEL.
Subjects: Law
ISBN Prefix(es): 972-9288

**Editorial Presenca+**
Estrada das Palmeiras, 59, Queluz de Baixo, 2745-578 Barcarena
*Tel:* (021) 4347000 *Fax:* (021) 4346502
*E-mail:* info@editpresenca.pt
*Web Site:* www.editpresenca.pt
*Telex:* 62596 *Cable:* PRESENCA LISBOA
*Key Personnel*
President: Francisco Espadinha
Executive Dir: Manuel Aquino
Production: Maria Eugenia Queiroz
Rights & Permissions: Manuela Cardoso
Administration: Joao Espadinha
Finance Executive: Hugo Moura
Founded: 1960
Subjects: Animals, Pets, Architecture & Interior Design, Art, Astrology, Occult, Biography, Business, Child Care & Development, Computer Science, Cookery, Crafts, Games, Hobbies, Education, Fiction, Gardening, Plants, Government, Political Science, Health, Nutrition, History, How-to, Human Relations, Language Arts, Linguistics, Management, Marketing, Mysteries, Nonfiction (General), Philosophy, Poetry, Psychology, Psychiatry, Religion - Buddhist, Science (General), Self-Help, Social Sciences, Sociology, Sports, Athletics, Travel, Travel Guides, Art Techniques, Esoterics, Lesiure Books
ISBN Prefix(es): 972-23
Divisions: Marketing Department
*Warehouse:* Estrada das Palmeiras, 59, 2745-663 Barcarena *Tel:* (021) 4357544 *Fax:* (021) 4357540

**Publicacoes Dom Quixote Lda+**
Member of Grupo Planeta
Rua Luciano Cordeiro 116-2, 1098 Lisbon
*Tel:* (021) 538079 *Fax:* (021) 574595
*Telex:* 14331 quixot p *Cable:* QUIXOTE
*Key Personnel*
Man Dir: Nelson de Matos; Isabel Dionisio
Production: Gina Martins
Publicity: Cecilia Andrade
Rights & Permissions: Cecilia Andrade
Founded: 1965
Subjects: Education, Fiction, History, Philosophy, Poetry, Science (General), Social Sciences, Sociology
ISBN Prefix(es): 972-20

**Puma Editora Lda**
Rua Vasco da Gama, 4-4 A, 2685 Sacavem
*Tel:* (021) 9425394 *Fax:* (021) 9425214
*Key Personnel*
Man Dir: Karl-Heinz Petzler
Editorial, Rights & Permissions: Adriano Lopes
Founded: 1990
Subjects: Fiction, Nonfiction (General)
ISBN Prefix(es): 972-9469
*Parent Company:* Grupo Distri
*Sales Office(s):* Distri Cultural

**Quatro Elementos Editores+**
Rua Arneiros, 54-lote F-2° F, 1500 Lisbon
*Tel:* (021) 703695
Founded: 1978
Subjects: Art, Fiction, Literature, Literary Criticism, Essays, Photography, Poetry
ISBN Prefix(es): 972-9296

**Quetzal Editores+**
Affiliate of Livrania Bertrand, SGPS
Rua da Rosa 105, 2° Esq, 1200 Lisbon
*Tel:* (021) 3426172 *Fax:* (021) 3426173
*E-mail:* quetzal@ip.pt
*Telex:* 65732 pegest p
*Key Personnel*
Chairman: Maria Da Piedade Ferreira
Subjects: Art, Literature, Literary Criticism, Essays, Poetry, Romance, Travel
ISBN Prefix(es): 972-564
*Shipping Address:* Distribuidorz de Livnos Bertrand, Rua Terras do Vale, Amadora, Contact: Eduardo Morais *Tel:* (01) 4958787 *Fax:* (01) 4960255

**Quid Juris - Sociedade Editora+**
A Marques da Fronteira, 92-1° Dt°, 1000 Lisbon
*Tel:* (021) 651946 *Fax:* (021) 3875538
*E-mail:* quidjuris@mail.telepac.pt
*Key Personnel*
Contact: Rua Sarmento Beires
Founded: 1988
Subjects: Criminology, Economics, Journalism, Law, Social Sciences, Sociology
ISBN Prefix(es): 972-724

**Quimera Editores Lda+**
R Actor Isidoro, 17-R/C Esq, 1900-015 Lisbon
*Tel:* (021) 845 59 50 *Fax:* (021) 845 59 51
*E-mail:* quimera@quimera-editores.com
*Web Site:* www.quimera-editores.com
*Key Personnel*
Contact: Jose Alfaro
Founded: 1987
Subjects: Art, Biography, Drama, Theater, Fiction, History
ISBN Prefix(es): 972-589

**Realizacoes Artis**
Apdo 8, 2726 Mem Martins
*Tel:* (01) 363796 *Fax:* (01) 9170130
*Key Personnel*
Man Dir: Rogerio de Freitas; Ermelinda Penedo
Founded: 1950
Subjects: Art, Biography, Poetry
ISBN Prefix(es): 972-9298

**Editora Replicacao Lda+**
Ave Infante Santo 343, r/c Esq, 1300 Lisbon
*Tel:* (021) 677058 *Fax:* (021) 396 9808
*E-mail:* replic@mail.telepac.pt
*Key Personnel*
Dir: J C Anaia Cristo; Luisa Galhardo
Founded: 1982
La Spiga Language representative.
Subjects: Astrology, Occult, Biological Sciences, English as a Second Language, Health, Nutrition, Humor, Mathematics, Science (General), Sports, Athletics, Study of Foreign Languages
ISBN Prefix(es): 972-570
*Associate Companies:* Leianaia-Livreiros, Editores e Importadores Anaia, Idc

**Revista Penteado**
Rua Bacalhoeiros 99, 2° E, 1100 Lisbon
*Tel:* (021) 862963 *Fax:* (021) 870972
*E-mail:* rromano@mail.telepac.pt
*Telex:* 64904
*Key Personnel*
International Rights: Leonor Veiga De Macedo
*Parent Company:* Rui Romano Lda

**M Moreira Soares Rocha Lda**, see Livraria Lopes Da Silva-Editora de M Moreira Soares Rocha Lda

**Edicoes Rolim Lda**
Rua Fialho de Almeida, 38-2º D, 1000 Lisbon
*Tel:* (021) 526375
*Key Personnel*
Man Dir: Maria Rolim Ramos
Founded: 1976
Subjects: Government, Political Science, History, Language Arts, Linguistics, Literature, Literary Criticism, Essays, Social Sciences, Sociology
ISBN Prefix(es): 972-687

**Ediciões Joao Sa da Costa Lda+**
Av Brasil, 118-3 3/4 E, 1700 Lisbon
Mailing Address: Av 5 Outubro, 10-7 3/4 /4, 1000 Lisbon
*Tel:* (021) 8400428; (021) 571118; (021) 563603 *Fax:* (021) 534194
*Telex:* 43534 fundis p
*Key Personnel*
Man Dir: Joao Sa da Costa
Executive Dir: Idalina Sa da Costa
Founded: 1984
ISBN Prefix(es): 972-9230

**Sa da Costa Livraria**
Praca Luis de Camoes, 22-4º, 1200 Lisbon
*Tel:* (021) 346 07 21; (021) 346 07 23; (021) 346 07 24; (021) 346 07 25 *Fax:* (021) 346 07 22
*Telex:* Sacost 15574 P *Cable:* Livrosacosta
Founded: 1913
Subjects: History, Literature, Literary Criticism, Essays, Philosophy
ISBN Prefix(es): 972-562
*Bookshop(s):* Livraria Sa da Costa

**Edicoes Salesianas**
Rua Dr Alves da Veiga 124, 4022 Porto Codex
*Tel:* (022) 565750 *Fax:* (022) 536 58 00
*E-mail:* edisal@clix.pt
*Key Personnel*
Man Dir: Jose Santos
Editorial, Production & Publicity: Jose Pedrosa Ferreira
Founded: 1947
Subjects: Biography, Education, Humor, Psychology, Psychiatry, Religion - Other
ISBN Prefix(es): 972-690
*Branch Office(s)*
Rua Saraiva de Carvalho 275, Lisbon *Tel:* (021) 3964142
*Bookshop(s):* Livraria Salesiana, Largo Luis de Camoes 7-9, 7000 Evora *Tel:* (066) 24570; Rua Saraiva de Carvalho 275, 1300 Lisbon *Tel:* (021) 609065

**Edicoes 70 Lda+**
Rua Luciano, Cordeiro, 123-2 Esq, 1069-157 Lisbon
*Tel:* (021) 319 02 40 *Fax:* (021) 319 02 49
*E-mail:* edi.70@mail.telepac.pt
*Web Site:* www.edicoes70.pt
Founded: 1970
Subjects: Animals, Pets, Anthropology, Architecture & Interior Design, Art, Astrology, Occult, Education, History, Language Arts, Linguistics, Literature, Literary Criticism, Essays, Music, Dance, Nonfiction (General), Parapsychology, Philosophy, Photography, Social Sciences, Sociology
ISBN Prefix(es): 972-44
Number of titles published annually: 24 Print
Total Titles: 1,000 Print

**Edicoes Silabo+**
Rua Cidade de Manchester, 2, 1170 100 Lisbon
*Tel:* (021) 525880 *Fax:* (021) 314 58 80
*E-mail:* silabo@mail.telepac.pt

*Key Personnel*
Marketing Dir: Manuel Robalo
*E-mail:* manuelrobalo@silabo.pt
Founded: 1983
Membership(s): APEL.
Subjects: Computer Science, Economics, Management, Mathematics, Philosophy, Physics, Science (General)
ISBN Prefix(es): 972-618

**SocTip SA**
Estrada Nacional 10, Km 10813 Porto Alto, 2135-114 Samora Correia
*Tel:* (021) 263 00 99 00 *Fax:* (021) 263 00 99 99
*E-mail:* soctip@soctip.pt
*Web Site:* www.soctip.pt
*Telex:* 65517 SOCTIP P
*Key Personnel*
Dir: Cristina Ferreira *E-mail:* cristinaferreira@soctip.pt
Founded: 1936
Subjects: Art
ISBN Prefix(es): 972-9435

**Solivros+**
Alto do Castelo, Villa de Trofa, 4780 Santo Tirso
*Tel:* (0252) 42385
*Key Personnel*
President & Editor: David Jorge Pereira
Founded: 1974
Specialize in publications of art works.
Subjects: Art, English as a Second Language, Literature, Literary Criticism, Essays, Poetry, Regional Interests, Religion - Catholic
ISBN Prefix(es): 972-693

**Sousa & Almeida Livraria**
Rua da Fabrica 42, 4050 245 Porto
*Tel:* (022) 2050073 *Fax:* (022) 2050073
*E-mail:* sousaealmeida@net.sapo.pt; geral@sousaealmeida.com
*Web Site:* www.sousaealmeida.com
*Key Personnel*
Contact: Sousa Almeida
ISBN Prefix(es): 972-9329

**Susaeta Ediciones**, *imprint of* Girassol Edicoes, LDA

**Edicoes Talento+**
Av Gomes Pereira, 41-1º E, 1500 Lisbon
*Tel:* (021) 7154281 *Fax:* (021) 7154257
*Key Personnel*
Dir: Francisco Santos
Financial Dir: Francisco Neves Ferro
Editorial Manager: Patricia Samos
Founded: 1988
Subjects: Biography, Music, Dance, Sports, Athletics
ISBN Prefix(es): 972-8065
*Branch Office(s)*
Edipromo-Edicoes e Promocoes Ltda, 143 Vila Mariana, 0415 San Paulo SP, Brazil
*Book Club(s):* Club Mania Show

**Almerinda Teixeira**
Av 25 de Abril, 5-16 E, 2800 Almada
*Tel:* (021) 2762352 *Cable:* Classica
*Key Personnel*
Editorial, Rights & Permissions: Francisco Paulo
Production, Publicity: Jose Ramos
Founded: 1903
Subjects: Agriculture, Economics, Electronics, Electrical Engineering, Fiction, History, Language Arts, Linguistics, Management, Poetry, Psychology, Psychiatry, Religion - Other, Science (General), Social Sciences, Sociology
ISBN Prefix(es): 972-95393

**Tempus Editores**
Rua Viana do Castelo, 8 Cave Esq, Bairro Sao Joao, 2775 Carcavelos
*Tel:* (021) 4535000 *Fax:* (021) 4426482
*Key Personnel*
Contact: Paula Santos
Founded: 1994
Subjects: Law, Literature, Literary Criticism, Essays, Romance
ISBN Prefix(es): 972-8198

**Teorema+**
Rua Padre Luis Aparicio 9-1º F, 1100 Lisbon
*Tel:* (021) 529988 *Fax:* (021) 352 14 80
*E-mail:* editorial.teorema@netc.pt
*Key Personnel*
President: Dr Carlos Da Veiga Ferreira
Founded: 1973
Subjects: Anthropology, Economics, Fiction, History, Literature, Literary Criticism, Essays, Nonfiction (General), Philosophy, Psychology, Psychiatry, Romance, Science (General), Social Sciences, Sociology
ISBN Prefix(es): 972-695

**Texto Editores+**
Estrada de Paco de Arcos, 66, 66-A, 2735-336 Cacem
*Tel:* (021) 427 22 00 *Fax:* (021) 427 22 01
*E-mail:* info@textoeditores.com
*Web Site:* www.textoeditores.com
*Key Personnel*
Man Dir: Manuel Jose Ferrao; Carlos Santiago; Luis Carlos Veloso
Founded: 1977
Subjects: Cookery, Education, Fiction, Health, Nutrition, Humor, Management, Romance, Self-Help
ISBN Prefix(es): 972-47
*Associate Companies:* Publilivro - Editora e Distribuidora de Publicacoes Lda
*Branch Office(s)*
Beco Veloso Salgado, 31, 4450-808 Ceca da Palmeira
*Bookshop(s):* Livraria Texto Editores, Rua Joaquim Paco d'Arcos, 13, 1500-365 Lisbon; Livraria Texto Editores, Rua Damiao de Gois, 45, 4050-225 Porto

**Sociedade Tipografica SA**, see SocTip SA

**Publicacoes Trevo Lda**
Apdo 50, 2726 Mem Martins Codex
*Tel:* (021) 9211461 *Fax:* (021) 9217940
*Telex:* 42255 pea p
*Key Personnel*
Man Dir, Editorial: Tito de Lyon Castro
Sales: Eduardo de Lyon Castro
Founded: 1976
ISBN Prefix(es): 972-696
*Parent Company:* Publicacoes Europa-America Lda

**Turinta-Turismo Internacional**
Rua Marques de Pombal, 347, Murches, 2755 247 Alcabideche Cascais
*Tel:* (021) 487 9420 *Fax:* (021) 487 2099
*E-mail:* info@turinta.pt
*Web Site:* www.turinta.pt
*Key Personnel*
General Dir: Hilario Sanches
International Rights: Eva Sanches
Founded: 1975
Membership(s): IMTA.
ISBN Prefix(es): 972-8134; 989-556
Distributed by Map Link (USA)

**Editora Ulisseia Lda+**
Av August Antonio de Aguiar, 148, 1069-019 Lisbon
*Tel:* (021) 380 1100 *Fax:* (021) 386 5397

*Web Site:* www.editorialverbo.pt
*Telex:* 15177 Verbo P
*Key Personnel*
Man Dir: Fernando Guedes
Editorial, Production: Martins de Oliveira
Sales: Jose Luis Fonseca
Publicity: Carlos Castro
Founded: 1950
Subjects: Literature, Literary Criticism, Essays
ISBN Prefix(es): 972-568
*Parent Company:* Editorial Verbo SA
*Warehouse:* Alto da Bela Vista, Calem 2735
*Orders to:* Rua Carlos Testa 1 - 2, 1000 Lisbon

**Usus Editora+**
Rua Viana do Castelo, 8 c/v Esq, 2775 Carcavelos
*Tel:* (021) 4535000 *Fax:* (021) 4426482
*Key Personnel*
Contact: Josi Caselas
Subjects: Law, Literature, Literary Criticism, Essays, Philosophy, Poetry, Theology
ISBN Prefix(es): 972-8070

**Vega-Publicacao e Distribuicao de Livros e Revistas, Lda+**
Alto dos Moinhos, 6A, 1500 Lisbon
*Tel:* (021) 789414 *Fax:* (021) 786395
*Key Personnel*
Contact: Dr Assirio Bacelar
Founded: 1975
Subjects: Anthropology, Architecture & Interior Design, Art, Astrology, Occult, Behavioral Sciences, Biography, Child Care & Development, Communications, Computer Science, Cookery, Drama, Theater, Economics, Education, Fashion, Fiction, Gay & Lesbian, History, Humor, Law, Literature, Literary Criticism, Essays, Philosophy, Photography, Poetry, Religion - Buddhist, Religion - Other, Romance, Science Fiction, Fantasy, Social Sciences, Sociology
ISBN Prefix(es): 972-699

**Editorial Verbo SA+**
Av Antonio Augusto de Aguiar, 148-6°, 1069-019 Lisbon
*Tel:* (021) 380 21 31; (021) 380 11 00 *Fax:* (021) 386 11 22; (021) 386 53 97
*Web Site:* www.editorialverbo.pt
*Telex:* 15177 Verbo P *Cable:* VERBO
*Key Personnel*
Man Dir: Fernando Guedes
Dir, Commercial: Dr Jose Luis Fonseca
Founded: 1959
Door-to-door sales by EDC-Empresa de Divulgacao Cultural Sarl, Ave Duque de Avila 193, Lisbon; direct mail sales by Verbo Postal.
Subjects: Education, History, Science (General)
ISBN Prefix(es): 972-22
Subsidiaries: Editora Verbo, S Paulo; Editora Ulisseia Lda; Verbo Publicacoes Periodicas; Litecnica, Luanda

**Livraria Verdade e Vida Editora**
Rua Santa Isabel, 16, 2495 Fatima
*Tel:* (0249) 531417 *Fax:* (0249) 531417
Founded: 1945
Subjects: Biography, Education, Fiction, History, Philosophy, Psychology, Psychiatry, Religion - Other, Theology
ISBN Prefix(es): 972-96166

# Puerto Rico

## General Information

*Capital:* San Juan
*Language:* Spanish and English

*Religion:* Predominantly Roman Catholic
*Population:* 3.6 million
*Bank Hours:* 0900-1430 Monday-Friday
*Shop Hours:* 0900-1730 or 1800 Monday-Saturday
*Currency:* US currency: 100 cents = 1 US dollar
*Export/Import Information:* No tariff on books and advertising matter. No import licenses required.
*Copyright:* UCC (see Copyright Conventions, pg xi)

**Editorial Antillana,** *imprint of* Editorial Cultural Inc

**Editorial Cordillera Inc**
Calle Mexico 17, Oficina 1-A, Hato Rey 00917
Mailing Address: PO Box 192363, San Juan 00919-2363
*Tel:* 787-767-6188 *Fax:* 787-767-8646
*E-mail:* info@editorialcordillera.com
*Web Site:* www.editorialcordillera.com
*Key Personnel*
President & Editorial: Hector E Serrano
Sales & Publicity: Isaac Serrano
Founded: 1962
Subjects: Literature, Literary Criticism, Essays, Social Sciences, Sociology
ISBN Prefix(es): 0-88495

**Instituto de Cultura Puertorriquena** (Institute of Puerto Rican Culture)
Apdo 9024184, San Juan 00902-4184
*Tel:* 787-724-0700 *Fax:* 787-724-8393
*E-mail:* www@icp.gobierno.pr
*Web Site:* www.icp.gobierno.pr
*Telex:* 3859686
*Key Personnel*
Dir: Carmelo Degardo Cintron
Editorial Dir: Marta Aponte Alsina
Sales: Ileana Colon de Barreto
Founded: 1955
Subjects: Anthropology, History, Literature, Literary Criticism, Essays, Music, Dance, Poetry
ISBN Prefix(es): 0-86581
*Bookshop(s):* Libreria del Instituto de Cultura Puertorriquena, San Francisco 305, San Juan 00901
*Orders to:* San Francisco 305, San Juan 00901

**Editorial Cultural Inc**
Calle El Roble No 51, Rio Piedras 00925
Mailing Address: Apdo 21056, Rio Piedras 00928
*Tel:* 787-765-9767 *Fax:* 787-765-9767
*E-mail:* cultural@coqui.net
*Web Site:* www.editorialcultural.com
*Key Personnel*
Man Dir: Francisco M Vazquez
   *E-mail:* francesco@editorialcultural.com
Administrator: Thin Sonia
Founded: 1949
Subjects: Biography, History, Literature, Literary Criticism, Essays
ISBN Prefix(es): 1-56758; 84-399
Imprints: Editorial Antillana
*Bookshop(s):* Libreria Cultural

**EDUPR,** see University of Puerto Rico Press (EDUPR)

**Libros-Ediciones Homines+**
PO Box 190374, Hato Rey, San Juan 00919
*Tel:* (787) 250-1912 (ext 2347)
*Key Personnel*
International Rights: Dr Aline Frambes-Buxeda
   *E-mail:* a.frambes@inter.edu
Founded: 1977
Subjects: Behavioral Sciences, Government, Political Science, Regional Interests, Social Sciences, Sociology, Women's Studies
ISBN Prefix(es): 0-9623590

Number of titles published annually: 2 CD-ROM
Total Titles: 45 Print; 7 CD-ROM
*Ultimate Parent Company:* Universidad Interamericana de Puerto Rico

**Ediciones Huracan Inc+**
874 Baldorioty de Castro, Rio Piedras 00925
*Tel:* (787) 763-7407 *Fax:* (787) 753-1486
*Key Personnel*
Dir: Carmen Rivera-Izcoa
Founded: 1975
Subjects: History, Literature, Literary Criticism, Essays, Social Sciences, Sociology
ISBN Prefix(es): 0-940238; 0-929157

**McGraw-Hill Intermericana del Caribe, Inc**
1121 Ave Munoz Rivera, Rio Piedras 00925
*Tel:* (787) 751-2451; (787) 751-3451 *Fax:* (787) 764-1890
*Web Site:* www.mhschool.com/contactus/international.html
*Key Personnel*
Regional Manager: Carlos Davila
   *E-mail:* carlos_davila@mcgrawhill.com
Subjects: Architecture & Interior Design, Business, Education, Engineering (General), English as a Second Language, Medicine, Nursing, Dentistry, Nonfiction (General), Technology

**Modern Guides Company+**
804 Calle Marti, San Juan 00907-3324
Mailing Address: PO Box 9021340, San Juan 00902-1340
*Tel:* (787) 723-9105 *Fax:* (787) 723-4380
*E-mail:* avc1941@attglobal.net
*Key Personnel*
President: Cristina Banac
Founded: 1985
Also provides marketing support & distribution
Subjects: Fiction, Travel
ISBN Prefix(es): 0-940788
Number of titles published annually: 2 Print; 2 Online
Total Titles: 3 Print; 2 Online
Distributed by Spanish Periodicals (USA)

**Piedras Press, Inc**
Carr 173, Km 4 6, Int Bo Hato Nuevo, Guaynabo 00931
Mailing Address: PO Box 21735, San Juan 00931-1735
*Tel:* (809) 731-9215
*Key Personnel*
President: Marc Schnitzer *Tel:* (787) 789-8928
Vice President & Treasurer: Emily Krasinski
Subjects: How-to, Language Arts, Linguistics, Self-Help
ISBN Prefix(es): 0-9630685
Number of titles published annually: 1 Print
Total Titles: 2 Print

**Publishing Resources Inc**
373 San Jorge St, 2nd floor, Santurce 00912
Mailing Address: PO Box 41307, Santurce 00940
*Tel:* (787) 268-8080 *Fax:* 787-774-5781
*E-mail:* publishingresources@att.net
*Key Personnel*
Owner & President: Ronald J Chevako
Owner & Editor-in-Chief: Anne W Chevako
Retail Manager: Terry C Burns
Publishes magazines including *San Juan, Puerto Rico's City Magazine;* Bienestar (environmental) & *Dimension* (engineering).
Subjects: Ethnicity, Regional Interests, Science (General), Travel
ISBN Prefix(es): 0-89825

**Ediciones Puerto+**
Edif Olimpic Mills, Guaynabo
Mailing Address: PO Box 3309, Old San Juan Station, San Juan 00902
*Tel:* 787-721-0844 *Fax:* 787-725-0861

*E-mail:* feriapr@caribe.net
*Key Personnel*
President: Jose Carvajal
Founded: 1971
Subjects: Poetry, Social Sciences, Sociology
ISBN Prefix(es): 0-942347

**University of Puerto Rico Press (EDUPR)+**
University of Puerto Rico Sta, Rio Piedras 00931-3322
Mailing Address: PO Box 23322
*Tel:* (787) 758-6932; (787) 758-8345 (sales)
    *Fax:* (787) 753-9116
*Telex:* 9573 *Cable:* EDUPR
*Key Personnel*
Dir: Marta Aponte-Alsina
Manager: Dalidia Colon-Pieretti
Production Manager: Juan Abascal
Editor-in-Chief: Gloria Madrazo-Vicens
Editor: Ana Garcia San Inocencio; Jesus Tome
Founded: 1932
Subjects: Art, Education, History, Nonfiction (General), Philosophy, Poetry, Psychology, Psychiatry, Social Sciences, Sociology
ISBN Prefix(es): 0-8477
*Branch Office(s)*
Edificio Vick Center-D Ave, Munoz Rivera No 867, Ofic 304, Rio Piedras 00925
*Warehouse:* Planta Piloto de Ron, Rd No 1 to Caguas, Rio Piedras

**Publicaciones Voz de Gracia**
PO Box 50581, Levittown 00950
*Tel:* 809-784-4366 *Fax:* 809-261-5401
*E-mail:* vozdegra@caribe.net
*Web Site:* www.cristo.org
Founded: 1994
Subjects: Biblical Studies, Music, Dance
ISBN Prefix(es): 0-9633439
Divisions: Ministerios Alabanza y Adoracion

# Reunion

## General Information

*Capital:* Saint-Denis
*Language:* French
*Religion:* Predominantly Roman Catholic
*Population:* 626,000
*Bank Hours:* 0800-1500
*Currency:* 100 centimes = 1 French franc
*Export/Import Information:* No tariff on books and advertising. Books have reduced VAT. No import license. Nominal exchange control over certain value.
*Copyright:* Berne (see Copyright Conventions, pg xi)

**ADER**, see Association des Ecrivains Reunionnais (ADER)

**Association des Ecrivains Reunionnais (ADER)**
36, rue de Gaulle, 97400 Saint-Denis de La Reunion
*Tel:* (0262) 213317 *Fax:* (0262) 431601
*Key Personnel*
President: Alain Gili *E-mail:* agili@guetali.fr
Founded: 1975
Books, little review.
ISBN Prefix(es): 2-9507282
Number of titles published annually: 3 Print
Total Titles: 7 Audio

**Editions Ocean**
305, rue de la Communaute, 97440 Saint Andre
*Tel:* 588400 *Fax:* 588410
*E-mail:* ocean@guetali.fr

*Key Personnel*
Contact: Jean-Pierre Boyer
Founded: 1987
Subjects: Crafts, Games, Hobbies, History, Social Sciences, Sociology
ISBN Prefix(es): 2-907064
Distributor for ARS-Terres Creoles; CNH; CRI

# Romania

## General Information

*Capital:* Bucharest
*Language:* Romanian
*Religion:* Predominantly Romanian Orthodox
*Population:* 23.2 million
*Bank Hours:* 0900-1200, 1300-1500 Monday-Friday; 0900-1200 Saturday
*Shop Hours:* 0900-1900 Monday-Friday; early closing Saturday
*Currency:* 100 bani = 1 leu
*Export/Import Information:* Book import and export coordinated by Centrala Editoriala, Piata Sciinteii 1, R-79715 Bucharest. The commercial operations are carried out by Artexim-Foreign Trade Co, 33-16, R-70055 Bucharest. Import licenses required. Exchange controls: terms of payment established in the sales contract.
*Copyright:* Berne (see Copyright Conventions, pg xi)

**Editura Academiei Romane** (Publishing House of the Romanian Academy)
Str 13 Septembrie, nr 13, Bucuresti, sector 5, 791717 Bucharest
*Tel:* (0410) 411 90 08; (0410) 410 32 00
    *Fax:* (0410) 410 39 83
*E-mail:* edacad@ear.ro
*Web Site:* www.ear.ro *Cable:* EDACAD
*Key Personnel*
General Manager: Prof Gheorghe Mihaila
Executive Manager: Dr Ing Ioan Ganea
Executive Manager Technical Dept: Elena Popescu
Executive Manager Economic, Commercial Dept: Liliana Ionescu
Founded: 1948
Publishing House of the Academy of Romania.
Subjects: Anthropology, Archaeology, Art, Astronomy, Biological Sciences, Chemistry, Chemical Engineering, Computer Science, Earth Sciences, Electronics, Electrical Engineering, Energy, Foreign Countries, History, Language Arts, Linguistics, Law, Mathematics, Medicine, Nursing, Dentistry, Philosophy, Physical Sciences, Physics, Psychology, Psychiatry, Social Sciences, Sociology
ISBN Prefix(es): 973-27
*Orders to:* Orion Srl, Press International, Sos Oltenitei 35-37, Sect 4, PO Box 61-170, Bucharest *Tel:* (01) 534 63 45 *Fax:* (01) 312 51 09

**Aion Verlag+**
Str Cantacuzino No 8F, bl PB 18, et 1, ap 7, Oradea
*Tel:* (059) 147595
*Key Personnel*
President & Editor: Nicolae Olteanu
Founded: 1994
Subjects: Anthropology, Communications, How-to, Human Relations, Journalism, Philosophy, Psychology, Psychiatry, Religion - Other, Social Sciences, Sociology
ISBN Prefix(es): 973-97662
*Parent Company:* S C Varsatorul Impex SRL
*Bookshop(s):* Varsatorul Company

**Editura Aius+**
Str Nicolae Titulescu, bl 46, et 1, ap 7, Craiova 1100
*Tel:* (051) 196136 *Fax:* (051) 196135
*E-mail:* aius@euroweb.ro
*Key Personnel*
Executive Manager: George Sorin Singer
Founded: 1991
Subjects: Economics, History, Literature, Literary Criticism, Essays, Medicine, Nursing, Dentistry
ISBN Prefix(es): 973-9251; 973-95229; 973-96340; 973-96913; 973-97385
Total Titles: 3 Print

**Editura Albatros**
Piata Presei Libere 1, 79718 Bucharest
*Tel:* (01) 2228493 *Fax:* (01) 2228493
*Key Personnel*
Man Dir: Dan Petrescu
Chief Publisher: Georgetta Dimisianu
Founded: 1969
Subjects: History, Literature, Literary Criticism, Essays, Religion - Other
ISBN Prefix(es): 973-24

**Alcor-Edimpex (Verlag) Ltd+**
Bd 1 Mihalache 45, bl 16B+C, SC D, ap 116, sector 1, Bucurest
*Tel:* (01) 665-34-40 *Fax:* (01) 665 34 40
*E-mail:* ed_alcor@yahoo.com
*Web Site:* www.rotravel.com/alcor
*Key Personnel*
General Manager: Corina Firuta
Founded: 1994
Subjects: Art, Crafts, Games, Hobbies, History, Religion - Other, Travel
ISBN Prefix(es): 973-96752; 973-97200; 973-97901; 973-98341; 973-95673; 973-96304; 973-98935; 973-8160
Number of titles published annually: 10 Print
Imprints: Arta Grafica Printing House, ao; Editura CNI Coresi

**Editora All+**
B-dul Timisoara 58, 76548 Bucharest
*Tel:* (01) 402 26 00 *Fax:* (01) 402 26 10
*E-mail:* info@all.ro
*Web Site:* www.all.ro
*Key Personnel*
President: Mihail Penescu
Rights Manager: Carmen Penescu
Founded: 1992
Subjects: Computer Science, Education, Fiction, History, Medicine, Nursing, Dentistry, Nonfiction (General), Science (General)
ISBN Prefix(es): 973-96090; 973-9156; 973-571; 973-684; 973-8171
Number of titles published annually: 300 Print
Total Titles: 1,800 Print
*Parent Company:* Bic All

**Alternative Editura+**
Piata Presei Libere nr 1, corp B, et 4, sector 1, 71341 Bucharest
*Tel:* (021) 2234966; (021) 2229468 *Fax:* (021) 6756074; (021) 2234971
*Key Personnel*
Contact: Nicolae Lotreanu
ISBN Prefix(es): 973-9216; 973-9461; 973-95550; 973-96300; 973-96996

**Ararat -Tiped, Editura+**
Bdul Carlo I nr 45, Sector 2, Bucharest
*Tel:* (01) 3111425; (01) 6134050 *Fax:* (01) 3111420
*Key Personnel*
General Manager: Sirun Terzian
Dir: Stefan Agopian
Founded: 1994
Also book manufacturer.

Subjects: History, Literature, Literary Criticism, Essays, Philosophy, Social Sciences, Sociology
ISBN Prefix(es): 973-9310; 973-97869; 973-97127; 973-96682
Distributed by Humanitas (Romania)

**Ars Longa Publishing House+**
Str Elena Doamna 2, 700398 Iasi
*Tel:* (0232) 215078 *Fax:* (0232) 215078
*E-mail:* arslonga@mail.dntis.ro
*Key Personnel*
President: Christian Tamas
International Rights: Mrs Brandusa Tamas
Founded: 1994
Subjects: Fiction, History, Language Arts, Linguistics, Literature, Literary Criticism, Essays, Philosophy, Poetry, Religion - Catholic, Theology
ISBN Prefix(es): 973-96681; 973-97252; 973-9325
Number of titles published annually: 55 Print
Total Titles: 260 Print

**Arta Grafica Printing House, ao**, *imprint of* Alcor-Edimpex (Verlag) Ltd

**Artemis Verlag**
Piata Presei Libere nr 1, sector 1, Bucharest 71341
*Tel:* (01) 2226661
*Key Personnel*
Contact: Mirella Acsente
Founded: 1991
Subjects: Art, Biography, History, Nonfiction (General), Religion - Other
ISBN Prefix(es): 973-566

**Editura Cartea Romaneasca**
Calea Victoriei nr 115, Sector 1, 79721 Bucharest
*Tel:* (01) 3123733; (01) 6148802 *Fax:* (01) 3110025
*Key Personnel*
Dir: George Balaita
Founded: 1969
Subjects: Drama, Theater, Fiction, Literature, Literary Criticism, Essays, Poetry
ISBN Prefix(es): 973-23

**Casa Editoriala Independenta Europa+**
Str Brazda lui Novac, Bl nr 6/III/7, Craiova
*Tel:* (051) 153487; (051) 425801 *Fax:* (051) 153487
*Key Personnel*
Dir: Ion Deaconescu
Founded: 1990
Subjects: Art, History, Literature, Literary Criticism, Essays, Science (General)
ISBN Prefix(es): 973-9013; 973-95780; 973-99118
*Associate Companies:* Editura Libertatea, Serbia and Montenegro; Editura Hyperion, Republica Moldova
Subsidiaries: Brasov
*Branch Office(s)*
Brasov
Bucharest
*Showroom(s):* rue A I Cuza nr 10, Craiova
*Warehouse:* Calea Bucuresti, bl M5, Craiova

**The Center for Romanian Studies+**
Oficiul Postal 1, Casuta Postala 108, Str Poligon nr 11a, 6600 Iasi
*Tel:* (032) 219000 *Fax:* (032) 219010
*Key Personnel*
Dir: Dr Kurt W Treptow
Office Manager: Petronela Postolache
Editor-in-Chief: Viorica Rusu
Founded: 1996
Membership(s): Romanian Publishers Association.

Subjects: Biography, Foreign Countries, History, Language Arts, Linguistics, Literature, Literary Criticism, Essays, Poetry, Sports, Athletics
ISBN Prefix(es): 973-9432; 973-98391; 973-98091; 973-9155
Number of titles published annually: 12 Print
Total Titles: 60 Print; 2 CD-ROM
Imprints: Iasi; Oxford; Portland
*Branch Office(s)*
40 Drake International Services, Market Moose, Market Place, Deddington 0X15 OSE, United Kingdom, Contact: Norman Drake *Tel:* (01869) 338240 *Fax:* (01869) 338310 *E-mail:* romcen@drakeint.co.uk
*U.S. Office(s):* c/o ISBS, 5804 NE Hassalo St, Portland, OR 97213-3644, United States, Contact: Tamma Greenfield *Tel:* 503-287-3093 *Fax:* 503-280-8832 *E-mail:* tamma@isbs.com
Distributed by International Specialized Book Services (North America)

**Editura Ceres**
Piata Presei Libere nr 1, 79722 Bucharest
*Tel:* (01) 2224836
*Key Personnel*
Man Dir: Ecaterina Mosu
Founded: 1953
Subjects: Agriculture, Animals, Pets, Environmental Studies, Veterinary Science
ISBN Prefix(es): 973-40

**Editura Clusium+**
Piata Unirii nr 1, 3400 Cluj
*Tel:* (064) 196940 *Fax:* (064) 196940
*E-mail:* clusium@codec.ro
*Key Personnel*
Man Dir: Valentin Tascu
Chief Editor: Corina Tascu
Copyright/Foreign Rights: Nicolae Mocanu
Founded: 1990
Subjects: Art, Biography, Computer Science, Engineering (General), Fiction, History, Humor, Literature, Literary Criticism, Essays, Medicine, Nursing, Dentistry, Nonfiction (General), Philosophy, Poetry, Religion - Other, Science (General), Social Sciences, Sociology, Technology
ISBN Prefix(es): 973-555

**Editura CNI Coresi**, *imprint of* Alcor-Edimpex (Verlag) Ltd

**Coresi SRL+**
Str Dem I. Dobrescu 4-6, Sector 1, Bucharest 78302
*Tel:* (01) 6386045; (01) 6386158; (01) 6386164; (00) 3127115; (00) 6154781 *Fax:* (01) 2230177
*Key Personnel*
Executive Manager: Michiela Gaga
General Manager: Vasile Poenaru
Founded: 1989
Specialize in children's literature & educational publications.
Subjects: Career Development, English as a Second Language, Language Arts, Linguistics
ISBN Prefix(es): 973-608
Number of titles published annually: 50 Print
Total Titles: 300 Print

**Corint Publishing Group+**
54A Mihal Eminescu St, Bucharest 010517
*Tel:* (0212) 11 97 66 *Fax:* (0212) 10 70 86
*E-mail:* corint@dnt.ro
*Key Personnel*
President: Cristian Gresanu
Vice President: Daniel Penescu
International Rights: Andreea Riess
Foreign Rights: Raluca Popescu
Founded: 1994
Specialize in scholarly books.

Subjects: Education, Fiction, Geography, Geology, History, Mathematics, Outdoor Recreation, Physics, Social Sciences, Sociology, Travel
ISBN Prefix(es): 973-6536; 973-7785; 973-7786; 973-7789; 973-86877; 973-86878; 973-86879; 973-86887
Number of titles published annually: 250 Print
Total Titles: 1,200 Print
*Book Club(s):* Corint

**Editure Ion Creanga**
P-ta Presei Libere 1, 79725 Bucharest
*Tel:* (01) 2231112
*Key Personnel*
Deputy Dir: Daniela Crasnaru
Editor-in-Chief: Gheorghe Zarafu
Founded: 1969
Subjects: Art, Biography, Fiction, History, Literature, Literary Criticism, Essays, Music, Dance, Poetry
ISBN Prefix(es): 973-25

**Editura Cronos SRL**
Str Progresului bl 39, ap 6, 70700 Baicoi, Prahova
*Tel:* (044) 262245; (044) 7690952 *Fax:* (01) 2231025
*E-mail:* cronos@dial.kappa.ro
*Key Personnel*
Manager: Florin Chita
Founded: 1990
Cronos Publishing House by Cronos Foreign Service offers at request encyclopedic materials, informations & statistical data regarding Romania, also provides illustrations & maps of Romania, & proofs or actualizes different materials concerning Romania for foreign publishing houses, including encyclopedic articles.
Subjects: Advertising, Business, Travel
ISBN Prefix(es): 973-9000

**Editura Dacia**
Str Dorobantilor nr 3, Ap 13, 3400 Judetul Cluj
*Tel:* (0264) 452178 *Fax:* (0264) 452178
*E-mail:* office@edituradacia.ro
*Web Site:* www.edituradacia.ro; www.cjnet.ro
*Telex:* 31347
*Key Personnel*
Dir General: Ion Vadan
Founded: 1969
Subjects: Astrology, Occult, Biological Sciences, Chemistry, Chemical Engineering, Electronics, Electrical Engineering, Fiction, Finance, Geography, Geology
ISBN Prefix(es): 973-35

**Editura Didactica si Pedagogica+**
12 Spiru Haret St, 70738 Bucharest
*Tel:* (01) 3150043 *Fax:* (01) 3122885
*E-mail:* edpdirector@mail.codecnet.ro
*Key Personnel*
General Manager: Adrian-Paul Iliescu
Founded: 1951
ISBN Prefix(es): 973-30
Number of titles published annually: 300 Print

**Editura DOINA SRL**
Plaiul Unirii nr 39, Bl m12, sc B35, Bucharest
*Tel:* (01) 3228107 *Fax:* (01) 3227541
*Key Personnel*
Dir: Jenica Panaitescu
Founded: 1992
Subjects: Biography, Literature, Literary Criticism, Essays
ISBN Prefix(es): 973-95318; 973-95859; 973-96301; 973-9193

**Editura Eminescu**
One, Piata Presei Libere, Bucharest 1
*Tel:* (01) 2228540

*Key Personnel*
Man Dir: Valerin Rapeanu
Subjects: History, Poetry
ISBN Prefix(es): 973-22

**Editura Enciclopedia RAO**, *imprint of* Grupul Editorial RAO

**Enzyklopadie Verlag+**
Piata Presei Libere nr 1, Bucharest 79737
*Tel:* (01) 2243667; (01) 2244014 *Fax:* (01) 2243667
*Key Personnel*
Dir: Marcel Popa
International Rights: Irina Popa
Founded: 1968
Subjects: Antiques, Archaeology, Biography, Biological Sciences, Economics, History, Religion - Other
ISBN Prefix(es): 973-45
Total Titles: 24 Print

**Euro Print Verlag**
Str Dunitru Petrescu nr 73, block 8L, sc 1, et 2, ap 63, sector 4, Bucharest 77314
*Tel:* (021) 0781-3716
*Key Personnel*
Contact: Neculai Bratu
Founded: 1994
Editing & distribution. Specializes in stories, fairy tales, coloring & painting books for children.
Limited company.
ISBN Prefix(es): 973-95419

**Editura Excelsior Art** (Excelsior Verlag - Publishing House)+
Affiliate of The Association of the Romanian Publishers
Cam 24A, Nr 5, Proclamatia de la Timisoara, 300054 Timisoara
Mailing Address: CP 262, OP 1, 1900 Timisoara
*Tel:* (0256) 201078 *Fax:* (0256) 201078
*E-mail:* edituraelcelsior@rdslink.ro
*Key Personnel*
Dir: Corina Victoria Badulescu
Founded: 1990
Membership(s): Writers Union of Romenien.
Subjects: Anthropology, Archaeology, Biblical Studies, Biography, Business, Communications, Cookery, Crafts, Games, Hobbies, Drama, Theater, Economics, Education, Ethnicity, Fiction, Health, Nutrition, History, Human Relations, Humor, Journalism, Language Arts, Linguistics, Library & Information Sciences, Literature, Literary Criticism, Essays, Mechanical Engineering, Medicine, Nursing, Dentistry, Mysteries, Nonfiction (General), Parapsychology, Philosophy, Poetry, Psychology, Psychiatry, Publishing & Book Trade Reference, Regional Interests, Religion - Other, Science (General), Science Fiction, Fantasy, Social Sciences, Sociology, Technology, Western Fiction, Science & fiction
ISBN Prefix(es): 973-9015; 973-592
Number of titles published annually: 50 Print
Total Titles: 680 Print
Distributor for Aletheia-Bistrita; Compact-Brasov; Dacia Traina-Sibiu; Libraria Eminescu; Librarii-TG Mures; Libris-Galati; Novus-Craiova; Prolibris-Ramnicu Valcea; Sedcomlibris-Iasi; Sedcomlibris-Suceava; Timlibris Timisoara

**Editura Fahrenheit**, *imprint of* Grupul Editorial RAO

**FF Press**
Calea Mosilor 209, sc A et 7, ap 26, Sector 2, Bucharest
*Tel:* (01) 6191544 *Fax:* (01) 3129694
*Key Personnel*
President: Serban Florea

Editor: Ion Covaci
Contact: Dr Florea Doina
Founded: 1992
Subjects: Finance, History, Literature, Literary Criticism, Essays, Poetry, Science (General)
ISBN Prefix(es): 973-96089; 973-96745; 973-96837

**Casa de editura Globus+**
Piata Presei Libere 1, et 8, cam 853, Sector 1, Bucharest 78202
*Tel:* (01) 2231510; (01) 2231530 *Fax:* (01) 6664265
*Key Personnel*
President: Tudor Stoica
Publisher: Petre Barbulescu
Author: Mihai Ungheanu
Founded: 1990
Subjects: Economics, Government, Political Science, History
ISBN Prefix(es): 973-49

**Editura Gryphon+**
Division of Gryphon Ltd
Str IL Caragiale, No 6, 500413 Brasov
*Tel:* (0268) 313 642; (0268) 312 888 *Fax:* (0268) 312 888
*E-mail:* gryphon@gryphon.ro
*Web Site:* www.gryphon.ro
*Key Personnel*
President & General Manager: Eugen Ioan Popa
*Tel:* (0722) 609 253
Founded: 1990
Specialize in importing books, provider for libraries & universities publishing house.
Subjects: Art, Civil Engineering, Earth Sciences, Health, Nutrition, Medicine, Nursing, Dentistry, Science (General), Technology, Veterinary Science
ISBN Prefix(es): 973-604
Number of titles published annually: 6 Print
Total Titles: 17 Print
Distributor for Grolier Inc USA

**Gryphon Publishing Ltd**, see Editura Gryphon

**Hasefer**
Bd I C Bratianu 35, et 2, ap 9, sector 3, 970478 Bucharest
*Tel:* (021) 312 22 84 *Fax:* (021) 312 22 84
*E-mail:* hasefer@fx.ro
*Key Personnel*
Dir: Sandu Singer
Subjects: Biblical Studies, Education, History, Literature, Literary Criticism, Essays, Religion - Other
ISBN Prefix(es): 973-8056
Number of titles published annually: 30 Print
*Parent Company:* Romanian Federation of Jewish Communities

**Humanitas Publishing House+**
One, Piata Presei Libere, 013701 Bucharest
*Tel:* (021) 3-17-18-19 *Fax:* (021) 3-17-18-24
*E-mail:* editors@humanitas.ro
*Web Site:* www.humanitas.ro
*Key Personnel*
General Dir: Gabriel Liiceanu
*E-mail:* secretariat@humanitas.ro
Editorial Dir: Anca Dumitru *Tel:* (021) 3-17-18-25 *E-mail:* anca.dumitru@humanitas.ro
Foreign Rights Executive: Gabriela Niculae *Tel:* (021) 3-17-18-25 *E-mail:* gabriela.niculae@humanitas.ro
Founded: 1990
Specialize in humanities & fiction.
Subjects: Biography, Fiction, Government, Political Science, History, Literature, Literary Criticism, Essays, Philosophy, Psychology, Psychiatry, Religion - Buddhist, Religion - Catholic, Religion - Hindu, Religion - Islamic, Religion

- Jewish, Science (General), Social Sciences, Sociology, Theology
ISBN Prefix(es): 973-28; 973-50
*Associate Companies:* Societatea Comerciala Librariile Humanitas
Subsidiaries: Societatea Comerciala Librariile Humanitas; Societate franco romana de difuzare a cartii SA
*Bookshop(s):* Libraria din fundul curtii, Cl Victoriei nr 120, Bucharest; Libraria Humanitas, Pasajul Kretzulescu CI Victoriei nr 45, Bucharest

**Iasi**, *imprint of* The Center for Romanian Studies

**Editura Institutul European+**
17, Cronicar Mustea St, 6600 Iasi
*Tel:* (032) 230197; (032) 233731; (032) 233800 *Fax:* (032) 230-197
*E-mail:* rtvnova@mail.cccis.ro; euroedit@mail.dntis.ro
*Key Personnel*
President: Anca Untu-Dumitrescu
Editor-in-Chief: Sorin Parvu
Public Relations: Liliana Buruiana-Popovici
Founded: 1991
Membership(s): The Association of Romaniau Editors.
Subjects: Education, English as a Second Language, Government, Political Science, History, Literature, Literary Criticism, Essays, Medicine, Nursing, Dentistry, Philosophy, Religion - Other, Theology
ISBN Prefix(es): 973-9148; 973-95528; 973-586; 973-95671; 973-611; 973-95870
Distributed by Humanitas
Distributor for Ceu Press (Budapest)

**Editura Junimea+**
Bd Carol 1 nr 3-5, 6600 Isai
*Tel:* (032) 117290
*Key Personnel*
Dir: Nicolae Cretu
Administrative Dir: Constantin Ursache
Foreign Rights: Christian Tamas
Founded: 1969
Subjects: Literature, Literary Criticism, Essays, Technology
ISBN Prefix(es): 973-37

**Editura Kriterion SA+**
Str Justitiei 41-43, Ap 4, Sector 4, 70529 Bucharest
*Tel:* (01) 3366509 *Fax:* (01) 313 11 07
*E-mail:* krit@dnt.ro; kriterion@mail.dnt.cj.ro
*Key Personnel*
Manager & Dir: H Szabo Gyula *Tel:* (095) 1634377 *E-mail:* szabogyula@yahoo.com
Founded: 1969
Subjects: Art, Ethnicity, Fiction, History, Literature, Literary Criticism, Essays, Poetry
ISBN Prefix(es): 973-26
Number of titles published annually: 40 Print
Total Titles: 200 Print
*Branch Office(s)*
Kriterion Cluj, Str S Mict, MNr 12A Cluj
*Tel:* (064) 197450 *Fax:* (064) 197450
*E-mail:* kriterion@mail.dntej.ro

**Lider Verlag+**
Bd Libertati No 4, bl 117, et 111, ap7, sector 4, Bucharest 761061
*Tel:* (01) 337-33-067; (01) 3374881 *Fax:* (01) 337-48-22
*Key Personnel*
President & International Rights: Casandra Enescu
Founded: 1994
Subjects: Art, History, Language Arts, Linguistics, Literature, Literary Criticism, Essays, Medicine, Nursing, Dentistry, Philosophy, Romance
ISBN Prefix(es): 973-8117; 973-97836

**Litera Publishing House**
Piata Presei Libere nr 1, Bucharest
*Tel:* (01) 2331349; (01) 2332749 *Fax:* (01)
2231873
*E-mail:* info@litera.ro
*Web Site:* www.litera-publishing.com
*Key Personnel*
Manager: Gheorghe Buzatu
Subjects: Literature, Literary Criticism, Essays
ISBN Prefix(es): 973-43

**MAST Verlag+**
Str Craesti 2, bl A47, ap 10, Bucharest 77418
*Tel:* (01) 7786950 *Fax:* (01) 4104588
*Key Personnel*
Contact: Florin Mateescu
Founded: 1994
Subjects: Agriculture, Animals, Pets, Antiques,
Astrology, Occult, Gardening, Plants, Medicine,
Nursing, Dentistry, Veterinary Science
ISBN Prefix(es): 973-97297; 973-97867; 973-
97868; 973-8011

**Editura Medicala** (Medical Publishing House)+
Bulevardul Pache Protopopescu, nr 131, sectoe 2,
131 Bucharest
*Tel:* (01) 25 25 186 *Fax:* (01) 25 25 189
*E-mail:* edmedicala@fx.ro
*Web Site:* www.ed-medicala.ro
*Key Personnel*
Man Dir: Alexandru Oproiu *E-mail:* oproiu@fx.ro
Founded: 1954
Medical Publishing House.
Subjects: Medicine, Nursing, Dentistry
ISBN Prefix(es): 973-39
Number of titles published annually: 30 Print

**Mentor Kiado+**
Member of Hungarian Book Guild From Romania
Str Paltinis nr 4, cod 4300, Targu-Mure, Mure
*Tel:* (0265) 256975 *Fax:* (0265) 256975
*Key Personnel*
Ed-in-Chief: Istvan Kiraly
Editor: Gyorgy Galfvi *Tel:* (065) 167091
*Fax:* (065) 167087; Andras Ferenc Kovacs
*Tel:* (065) 167091 *Fax:* (065) 167087; Zsolt
Lang *Tel:* (065) 167091 *Fax:* (065) 167087
Founded: 1993
Main mission is the publication of works of liv-
ing Hungarian literature, particularly those of
Transylvanian (province of Romania) writers.
Special focus is the patronage of new writers &
the Minomtates Mundi series, which presents
the literary traditions of minority peoples.
Subjects: Art, Drama, Theater, Ethnicity, History,
Literature, Literary Criticism, Essays, Philoso-
phy, Poetry, Romance, Social Sciences, Sociol-
ogy
ISBN Prefix(es): 973-95943; 973-96650; 973-
97072; 973-9263
Total Titles: 5 Print

**Editura Meridiane+**
P-ta Presei Libere 1, corp D, et 8, sector 1, 71341
Bucharest
Mailing Address: PO Box 33-47, 79729
Bucharest
*Tel:* (021) 222-33-93 *Fax:* (021) 222-30-37
*E-mail:* meridiane@fx.ro
*Key Personnel*
Dir: Elena Victoria Jiquidi
Senior Editor, Acquisitions & Foreign Rights:
Livia Szasz Campeanu; Andrei Niculescu
Founded: 1952
Subjects: Anthropology, Archaeology, Architec-
ture & Interior Design, Art, Biography, Drama,
Theater, Fashion, Film, Video, History, Lan-
guage Arts, Linguistics, Literature, Literary
Criticism, Essays, Medicine, Nursing, Den-
tistry, Music, Dance, Nonfiction (General),
Religion - Other, Social Sciences, Sociology,

Travel, Art History, Design, Cultural studies,
Media
ISBN Prefix(es): 973-33
Number of titles published annually: 25 Print
Total Titles: 65 Print

**Editura Militara+**
Str Gen, Cristescu nr 5, 79735 Bucharest
*Tel:* (01) 3112191; (01) 6133601 *Fax:* (01)
3237822
*Key Personnel*
Dir: Cornel Barbulescu
Founded: 1950
Subjects: Education, Electronics, Electrical Engi-
neering, Engineering (General), History, Mili-
tary Science, Mysteries, Social Sciences, Soci-
ology
ISBN Prefix(es): 973-32
*Bookshop(s):* Libraria Militara (Military Book-
shop), Piate Natiunilor Unite nr 3, Bucharest

**Editura Minerva+**
Bdul Metalurgiei nr 32-34, sector 4, Bucharest
*Tel:* (01) 3308808; (01) 3308840 *Fax:* (01)
3308808; (01) 3308840
*E-mail:* desfacere@edituraaramis.ro
Founded: 1969
Subjects: Astrology, Occult, Biography, Computer
Science, Education, Film, Video, Finance, Li-
brary & Information Sciences
ISBN Prefix(es): 973-21
*Parent Company:* Editura Minerva
Subsidiaries: Series Biblioteca Pentru Toti

**Monitorul Oficial, Editura+**
Palace of Parliament, 2-4 Izvor St, Sector 5
Bucharest
*Tel:* (01) 402-2173; (01) 402-2176; (01) 411-5833
*Fax:* (01) 312-0901; (01) 312-4703; (01) 410-
7736
*E-mail:* ramomrk@bx.logicnet.ro
*Key Personnel*
Manager: Eugenia Clubancan
Founded: 1832
Subjects: Law
ISBN Prefix(es): 973-567
Distributed by Kubon & Sagner (Germany)
*Bookshop(s):* Str Blanduziei nr 1, sector 1,
Bucharest

**Editura Muzicala**
Str Calea Victoriei nr 141, 79733 Bucharest
*Tel:* (01) 3129867 *Fax:* (01) 3129867
*E-mail:* editura_muzicala@hotmail.com
*Key Personnel*
Man Dir: Vlad Ulpiu; Marius Vasileanu
Founded: 1958
Books, musical scores, compact discs & CD-
ROM's.
Subjects: Biography, Music, Dance
ISBN Prefix(es): 973-42
*Orders to:* Bucharest

**Nemira Verlag+**
Bdul Ion Mihalache nr 125, sector 1, Casa Presei
Libere, corp D, etj 3, sector 1, Bucharest
*Tel:* (01) 2242156 *Fax:* (01) 2241600
*E-mail:* editura@nemira.ro
*Key Personnel*
Editorial Dir: Vlad T Popescu
International Rights: Iulia Stoica
Founded: 1991
Subjects: Accounting, Advertising, Economics,
Education, Government, Political Science, Lit-
erature, Literary Criticism, Essays, Marketing,
Science Fiction, Fantasy
ISBN Prefix(es): 973-569; 973-9301; 973-9144;
973-99576; 973-95169; 973-9177; 973-96255
*Associate Companies:* Nemira & Co; Nemira
Multimedia

*Bookshop(s):* Edutura Nemira, PO Box 33-22,
71341 Bucharest
*Book Club(s):* Clubul cartii
*Shipping Address:* Edutura Nemira, PO Box 33-
22, 71341 Bucharest
*Warehouse:* Edutura Nemira, PO Box 33-22,
71341 Bucharest
*Orders to:* Edutura Nemira, PO Box 33-22,
71341 Bucharest

**Editura Niculescu+**
Str Octav Cocarascu 79, Sector 1, 781821
Bucharest
*Tel:* (01) 2242898; (01) 2220372 *Fax:* (01)
2242898; (01) 2220372
*E-mail:* edit@niculescu.ro
*Web Site:* www.niculescu.ro
*Key Personnel*
President: Dr Christian Niculescu *Tel:* (09)
2342900
Marketing & Distribution: Lavona George
Founded: 1993
Subjects: Accounting, Biography, Biological Sci-
ences, Business, Career Development, Child
Care & Development, Cookery, Economics,
Education, Engineering (General), English
as a Second Language, Fiction, Film, Video,
Gardening, Plants, Geography, Geology, Gov-
ernment, Political Science, Health, Nutrition,
History, House & Home, Humor, Language
Arts, Linguistics, Law, Management, Market-
ing, Mathematics, Mysteries, Natural History,
Nonfiction (General), Outdoor Recreation, Phi-
losophy, Physics, Science (General), Self-Help,
Social Sciences, Sociology, Wine & Spirits,
Reference Work
ISBN Prefix(es): 973-568
Number of titles published annually: 180 Print;
18 CD-ROM
Total Titles: 70 Print; 12 CD-ROM
*Associate Companies:* Clubul de Carte Niculescu,
Str Octav Cocarascu 79, 78182 Bucharest
*Tel:* (01) 224-24-80

**Editura Orion+**
Str Ion Brezoianu 51B, 70711 Bucharest
*Tel:* (01) 3125250 *Fax:* (01) 2104636
*Key Personnel*
President: Cristian Corneliu Bigica
Editor: Florin Lupescu
ISBN Prefix(es): 973-95052; 973-95532; 973-
97273; 973-98353; 973-8020
*Parent Company:* Orion Enterprises Ltd

**Oxford,** *imprint of* The Center for Romanian
Studies

**Editura Paideia+**
Str Tudor Arghezi nr 15, sector 2, Bucharest
*Tel:* (01) 2115804; (01) 2120347 *Fax:* (01)
2120348
*E-mail:* paideia@fx.ro
*Key Personnel*
President: Ion Bansoiu *Tel:* (01) 2529850
Founded: 1990
Non-profit organization.
Subjects: Literature, Literary Criticism, Essays,
Philosophy, Religion - Other, Social Sciences,
Sociology
ISBN Prefix(es): 973-9131; 973-95306; 973-9368;
973-9393; 973-8064; 973-596
Number of titles published annually: 60 Print; 10
CD-ROM
Total Titles: 30 Print; 6 CD-ROM; 4 Audio
Foreign Rep(s): Anca Chelaru (US)
Foreign Rights: Radu Lungu (France)

**Pallas-Akademia Editura**
Str Petofi nr4, CP140 Miercurea-Ciuc
*Tel:* (066) 171036 *Fax:* (066) 171036
*E-mail:* pallas@nextra.ro

*Key Personnel*
Man Dir: Josef Gyula Tozser
Chief Editor: Maria Kozma
Copyright/Foreign Rights: Eva Herta
Founded: 1993
Subjects: Biography, Computer Science, Engineering (General), Ethnicity, Fiction, Journalism, Literature, Literary Criticism, Essays, Regional Interests, Religion - Catholic, Science (General), Social Sciences, Sociology, Technology, Art History
ISBN Prefix(es): 973-96702
Number of titles published annually: 30 Print
Distributed by Aligator kft Koenyvkereskedes (Cluj-Napoca, Romania); Babits Kiado (Szekszard, Hungary); Carthographia Kiado (Budapest, Hungary); Casa de Presa (Bucarest, Romania); Custos Koenyvkereskedes (Bucarest, Romania); Editura Humanitas (Bucarest, Romania); Editura Lyra (Targu-Mures, Romania); Sc Bon Ami (Stantu-Gheorghe, Romania); Sc Cartimpex Koenyvkeseskedes (Cluj-Napoca, Romania); Sc Libris srl (Satu-Mare, Romania); Sc Samlibris (Satu-Mare, Romania); Sc Zalanta Prest (Salonta, Romania)
Distributor for Akademiai Kiado (Budapest, Hungary); Babits Kiado (Szekszard, Hungary); Bagolyvar Kiado (Budapest, Hungary); Carthogrphia Kiado (Budapest, Hungary); Editura Dacia (Cluj-Napoca, Romania); Editura Humanita (Bucharest, Romania); Editura Ion Creanga (Bucharest, Romania); Editura Komp-Press (Cluj-Napoca, Romania); Editura Rao (Bucarest, Romania); Euro pa Kiado (Budapest, Hungary); Kossuth Kiado (Budapest, Hungary); Magveto Kiado (Budapest, Hungary); Magyar Koenyvklubb (Budapest, Hungary); Mentor Kiado (Targu-Mures, Romania); Mora Ferenc Kiado (Budapest, Hungary); Osiris Kiado (Budapest, Hungary); Park Kiado (Budapest, Hungary); Polis Kiado (Cluj-Napoca, Romania); Sprinter Koenyvkereskedes (Budapest, Hungary); Szent Istvan Tarsulat (Budapest, Hungary); Szukits Kiado (Szeged, Hungary)
*Bookshop(s):* str Petofi nr 4, Miercurea Ciuc 4100; P-ta Libertatii 5/A, Gheorgheni 4200; P-ta Marton Aron nr 2, Odorheiu-Secuiesc 4150; Str Koroesi Csoma Sandor nr 2, SPantu Gheorghe 4000; P-ta Trandafirilor nr 57, Targu-Mures 4300; Str M Sadoveanu nr 3, Brasov 2200; Str Universitatii nr 1, Cluj-Napoca 3400; Str Horea nr 6, Satu-Mare; Sindicatelor nr 7, Salonta 3650; Libraria Eminescu, Bul Elisabeta nr 5, Sector 5, Bucharest

**Pandora Publishing House+**
B-dulLacul Tei nr 123, bloc 4, Apt 177, Bucharest 020383
*Tel:* (021) 243 3739
*Key Personnel*
Dir: Ion Monafu *E-mail:* ionmonafu@yahoo.com
Founded: 1991
Specialize in fiction, nonfiction, translation from contemporary foreign authors, science & children's books.
Subjects: Biography, Fiction, Humor, Literature, Literary Criticism, Essays, Nonfiction (General), Poetry, Science (General), Science Fiction, Fantasy
ISBN Prefix(es): 973-96336; 973-96932; 973-95148; 973-8147
Number of titles published annually: 15 Print
Total Titles: 120 Print
Foreign Rep(s): Dan Monafu (Canada); Valer Monafu (US)

**Petrion Verlag+**
Calea Plevnei 124, sector 6, Bucharest 70700
*Tel:* (01) 3103407; (01) 3152641 *Fax:* (01) 3124525; (01) 3152641
*E-mail:* petrion@stranets.ro
Founded: 1990

Subjects: Education, Mathematics, Microcomputers, Physics
ISBN Prefix(es): 973-9116

**Polirom Verlag+**
4, Copou Blvd, PO Box 266, 6600 Iasi
*Tel:* (032) 214-100; (032) 214-111; (032) 217-440 *Fax:* (032) 214-100; (032) 214-111; (032) 217-440
*E-mail:* office@polirom.ro
*Web Site:* www.polirom.ro
*Key Personnel*
Manager: Silviu Lupescu
Founded: 1995
Subjects: Anthropology, Communications, History, Journalism, Literature, Literary Criticism, Essays, Management, Marketing, Medicine, Nursing, Dentistry, Philosophy, Psychology, Psychiatry, Social Sciences, Sociology
ISBN Prefix(es): 973-9248; 973-97108; 973-97410; 973-97522; 973-683

**Portland**, *imprint of* The Center for Romanian Studies

**Editura RAO Bucuresti**, *imprint of* Grupul Editorial RAO

**Grupul Editorial RAO** (RAO Publishing Group)+
Str Turda, Nr 117-119, Bl 6, parter, 78219 Bucharest
*Tel:* (01) 224-12-31; (01) 224-14-72; (01) 224-18-47; (01) 224-21-36 *Fax:* (01) 224-12-31; (01) 224-14-72; (01) 224-18-47; (01) 224-21-36
*E-mail:* office@raobooks.com; club@raobooks.com
*Web Site:* www.raobooks.com
*Key Personnel*
President: Anca Enculescu
Editorial Dir: Ondine Dascalita
Contact: Ovidiu Enculescu
Founded: 1993
Membership(s): AER; IBBY.
Subjects: Biography, Education, Fiction, History, Nonfiction (General), Science Fiction, Fantasy, Self-Help, Classic & Contemporary Fiction, Textbooks
ISBN Prefix(es): 973-576; 973-98762; 973-98626
Total Titles: 280 Print
Imprints: Editura Enciclopedia RAO; Editura Fahrenheit; Editura RAO Bucuresti; RAO International Publishing Co
*Warehouse:* Str Tiate Mics 4, Sibiu *Fax:* (069) 215605 *E-mail:* rao.sb@bx.logicnet.ro
*Orders to:* RAO International Publishing Co, PO Box 2-124, Bucharest, Contact: Catalina Manolache

**RAO International Publishing Co**, *imprint of* Grupul Editorial RAO

**RAO International Publishing Co+**
Imprint of Grupul Editorial RAO
125 Ion Mihalache Blvd, Bl 7, sc A, sector 1, Bucharest
*Tel:* (01) 224-1002; (01) 224-1704 *Fax:* (01) 222-8059
*E-mail:* rao.b@bx.logicnet.ro
*Key Personnel*
Dir: Ondine Dascalita
Subjects: Biography, Fiction, Literature, Literary Criticism, Essays, Mysteries, Nonfiction (General), Religion - Other, Romance, Science Fiction, Fantasy
ISBN Prefix(es): 973-576; 973-9164; 973-96203; 973-96204
Subsidiaries: Rao Educational
*Book Club(s):* Rao Buchklub

**Realitatea Casa de Edituri Productie Audio-Video Film+**
B-dul Dacia nr 126, 70267 Bucharest
*Tel:* (01) 6117105; (01) 6517105; (01) 6332468; (01) 6143793 *Fax:* (01) 2105411
*E-mail:* leu@dnt.ro
*Key Personnel*
President: Corneliu Leu
Editor: George Atanasiu; Leu Vlad
Founded: 1990
Specialize in film production & video cassettes.
Membership(s): Romanian Copyright Society.
Subjects: Education, Government, Political Science, Literature, Literary Criticism, Essays, Nonfiction (General), Philosophy, Romance
ISBN Prefix(es): 973-9025
*Parent Company:* Realitatea-Publishers & Producers Ltd
*U.S. Office(s):* Monolith Corporation, 37 4181 St, Suite A2, Jackson Heights, NY 11372, United States *Tel:* 718-507-2870
*Bookshop(s):* Bucharest, Timisoara, Iassi, Busteni (Romania)

**Rentrop & Straton Verlagsgruppe und Wirtschaftsconsulting+**
4, Natiunile Unite Blvd, Bloc 107A, sector 5, Bucharest 050122
*Tel:* (021) 337.4146 *Fax:* (021) 337.2211
*E-mail:* rs@rs.ro; office@rs.ro
*Web Site:* www.rs.ro
*Key Personnel*
General Editor: George Straton
International Rights: Violeta Carutasu
Founded: 1995
Subjects: Accounting, Advertising, Business, Career Development, Child Care & Development, Communications, Computer Science, Economics, Finance, How-to, Law, Management, Marketing, Nonfiction (General), Self-Help, Travel
ISBN Prefix(es): 973-97748; 973-98033; 973-8154
*Associate Companies:* VNR Verlag fur die Deutsche Wirtschaft AG, Bonn, Germany
*Bookshop(s):* Libraria Rentrop & Straton, 22-24, Cantemir Blvd, Bucharest, sector 4; Libraria Rentrop & Straton, ROMEXPO, pavilion35, 53-57, Marasti Blvd, Bucharest, sector 1

**Saeculum IO+**
Teodosie Rudeanu, 29, 011257 Bucharest
*Tel:* (021) 2228597 *Fax:* (021) 3452827; (021) 2228597
*E-mail:* saeculum@tcnet.ro
*Web Site:* www.saeculum.ro
*Key Personnel*
Proprietor: Prof Ionel Oprisan, PhD
Founded: 1994
Membership(s): SER (Publishers' Society of Romania).
Subjects: Anthropology, Art, Biography, Fiction, History, Literature, Literary Criticism, Essays, Mysteries, Parapsychology, Philosophy, Poetry, Romance, Theology
ISBN Prefix(es): 973-9211; 973-9399; 973-642
*Parent Company:* Saeculum IO
*Associate Companies:* Saeculum Vizual; Vestala, Ciucea, 5, bloc L19, Ap 216, 032522 Bucharest

**Editura 'Scrisul Romanesc'**
Str Mihai Viteazul 4, 1100 Craiova
*Tel:* (051) 419506
*Key Personnel*
Dir: Ilarie Hinoveanu
Founded: 1972
'Romanian Writing' Publishing House.
Subjects: Government, Political Science, Literature, Literary Criticism, Essays, Social Sciences, Sociology
ISBN Prefix(es): 973-38

**Editura Signata+**
Str Chiriac nr 26, 1900 Timisoara
*Tel:* (056) 153081
*Key Personnel*
Dir: Ioan Iancu
Founded: 1990
Membership(s): Romanian Writers' Association.
Subjects: Technology
ISBN Prefix(es): 973-551

**Editura Stiintifica SA** (Scientific Publishing House)+
Piata Presei Libere nr 1, 79737 Bucharest
*Tel:* (01) 3351654; (01) 3367442 *Fax:* (01) 3356499
*Key Personnel*
Man Dir: Dinu Grama
Founded: 1990
Subjects: Biological Sciences, Geography, Geology, History, Mathematics, Nonfiction (General), Philosophy, Psychology, Psychiatry, Science (General)
ISBN Prefix(es): 973-44

**Editura Stiintifica si Enciclopedica** (Scientific & Encyclopedia Publishing House)
Piata Presei Libere nr 1, 78737 Bucharest
*Tel:* (01) 175168
*Key Personnel*
Manager: Dinu Grama
Production Manager, Sales Dir: Alexandru Banciu
Founded: 1975 (by amalgamation of Romanian Encyclopaedic Publishing House & Scientific Publishing House)
The Foreign Encyclopedias Office supplies any encyclopedic materials, information, data, statistics, maps & illustrations concerning Romania required by foreign publishing houses.
Subjects: Language Arts, Linguistics, Literature, Literary Criticism, Essays, Science (General), Social Sciences, Sociology
ISBN Prefix(es): 973-29

**Est-Samuel Tastet Verlag+**
Bdul Uverturii nr 57-69, Bl 10, sc C, et 1, ap 87, sector 6, Bucharest
Mailing Address: ap 24, sector 1, Bucharest
*Tel:* (01) 6386250 *Fax:* (01) 3122012
*Key Personnel*
Contact: Samuel Tastet
Founded: 1995
Subjects: Art, Biography, Drama, Theater, Fiction, Literature, Literary Criticism, Essays, Poetry
ISBN Prefix(es): 973-96902; 973-98094

**Editura Tehnica**
Piata presei libere 1, 79738 Bucharest
*Tel:* (01) 222-33-21 *Fax:* (01) 222-37-76
Founded: 1950
Also book packager.
Subjects: Engineering (General), Science (General), Technology
ISBN Prefix(es): 973-31

**Editura Teora+**
Calea Mosilor 211, sector 2, Bucharest 70325
*Tel:* (021) 2106204 *Fax:* (021) 2103828
*E-mail:* mesaj@teora.ro
*Web Site:* www.teora.ro
*Key Personnel*
Dir: Teodor Raducanu
Founded: 1990
Subjects: Computer Science, Economics, Electronics, Electrical Engineering, Law, Medicine, Nursing, Dentistry, Philosophy, Psychology, Psychiatry, Science Fiction, Fantasy, Sports, Athletics, Technology
ISBN Prefix(es): 973-601; 973-609

**Editura Top Suspans**
Aleea Terasei, Nr 6, Bl R2, Ap 5, Sect 4, Bucharest 75582
*Tel:* (021) 6830924; (021) 6103359
*Key Personnel*
Dir: Nicolae Carp
ISBN Prefix(es): 973-9060

**Editura Univers SA+**
Str Ionel Perlea nr 9, et 2, ap 4, int 24C, 79739 Bucharest
*Tel:* (01) 2244640; (01) 3104510 *Fax:* (01) 3104510
*E-mail:* univers@rnc.ro *Cable:* 1 PIATA PRESEI LIBERE, 79739 BUCHAREST
*Key Personnel*
General Dir: Prof Martin Mircea
Editor: Denisa Comanescu
Foreign Rights Editor: Adrian Mihaltianu
Founded: 1961
Subjects: Biography, Education, Fiction, Literature, Literary Criticism, Essays, Philosophy, Poetry, Romance, Science Fiction, Fantasy
ISBN Prefix(es): 973-34
Subsidiaries: Univers Informatic

**Universal Dalsi+**
Piata Presei Libere, corp b1, et 4, cam 379-380, sector 1, Bucharest
*Tel:* (01) 3355354; (01) 3371682 *Fax:* (01) 3373566; (01) 3129709
*E-mail:* marian@kappa.ro
*Key Personnel*
Dir: Maria Marian *Tel:* (01) 650 6091 *Fax:* (01) 312 9709
Founded: 1992
Private publishing house specialized in belles lettres in Romanian & other languages.
Subjects: Education, Fiction, Literature, Literary Criticism, Essays, Philosophy, Poetry, Science (General), Social Sciences, Sociology, Theology
ISBN Prefix(es): 973-9166; 973-8157; 973-95690; 973-96039; 973-9409
Total Titles: 10 Print
Distributor for Letos Mimai, Balasion

**Editura Valahia SRL**
Str Trivale, bloc 61, sc B, ap 9, Pitesti, Jud Arges
*Tel:* (097) 680948
*Key Personnel*
Dir: George Nitu
Founded: 1990
ISBN Prefix(es): 973-95049

**Editura de Vest+**
Piata Sf Gheorghe nr 3, 1900 Timisoara
*Tel:* (056) 191959 *Fax:* (056) 14212
*Key Personnel*
Dir: Vasile Popovici
Founded: 1972
Subjects: Art, Fiction, Science (General), Technology
ISBN Prefix(es): 973-36

**Vestala Verlag+**
Str Teodosie Rudeanu nr 29, 74696 Bucharest
*Tel:* (01) 222-8596 *Fax:* (01) 222-8596
*E-mail:* saeculum@pcnet.ro
*Key Personnel*
Contact: Dr Ionel Oprisan
Founded: 1993
Membership(s): Publishers' Association of Romania (Asociatia Editorilor din Romania).
Subjects: Art, Biography, History, Literature, Literary Criticism, Essays, Mysteries, Parapsychology, Philosophy
ISBN Prefix(es): 973-9200; 973-96063; 973-96421; 973-96817; 973-9418
Number of titles published annually: 30 Print
Total Titles: 120 Print

*Parent Company:* Saeculum Verlag, 74696 Bucharest
*Associate Companies:* Saeculum i o Verlag

**Vox Editura+**
Str Petru Maior nr 32, sec 1, Bucharest 781232
*Tel:* (01) 2220213; (01) 2220214 *Fax:* (01) 2220213
*E-mail:* edituravox@hotmail.com
*Key Personnel*
General Manager: Lucia Ovezea
Founded: 1994
Subjects: Gardening, Plants
ISBN Prefix(es): 973-96922; 973-97848; 973-98159; 973-9381

**Vremea Publishers Ltd+**
Str Constantin Daniel 14, sect 1, 71121 Bucharest
*Tel:* (01) 3358131 *Fax:* (01) 3110219
*E-mail:* vremea@fx.ro
*Key Personnel*
President: Nicolae Henegariu
Vice President: Cristina Cantacuzino
Man Dir & Chief Editor: Silvia Colfescu
  *Tel:* (092) 226088
Copyright/Foreign Rights: Maria Giugariu
Founded: 1990
Membership(s): AER Romanian Publishers Association.
Subjects: Art, Astrology, Occult, Biography, Child Care & Development, Education, Fiction, Health, Nutrition, History, Literature, Literary Criticism, Essays, Medicine, Nursing, Dentistry, Parapsychology, Philosophy, Poetry, Religion - Other, Science Fiction, Fantasy, Social Sciences, Sociology
ISBN Prefix(es): 973-9162; 973-95063; 973-95581
Number of titles published annually: 45 Print
Total Titles: 250 Print

# Russian Federation

## General Information

*Capital:* Moscow
*Language:* Russian
*Religion:* Predominantly Christian (mostly Russian Orthodox), also Islam and Buddhist
*Population:* 149.5 million
*Bank Hours:* Generally open for short hours between 0930-1230 Monday-Friday
*Shop Hours:* Generally 0900-1800 Monday-Friday; often open weekends
*Currency:* 100 kopeks = 1 rubl
*Export/Import Information:* According to Ukrainian quotas and customs duties, companies engaged in trade should register with the Ukraine Ministry of Foreign Economic Relations. Licenses for export and import are also required for trade with Russia.
*Copyright:* UCC, Berne, Florence (see Copyright Conventions, pg xi)

**Agni Publishing House**
23 Michurin St, 443110 Samara
*Tel:* (08462) 70-32-87; (08462) 70-23-87 (ext 445 - Orders) *Fax:* (08462) 70-23-85
*E-mail:* cdk@transit.samara.ru
*Web Site:* www.agni.samara.ru
*Key Personnel*
Manager: Gennady Karev
Also producers of fine art reproductions of paintings by Russian artists, photo-landscapes, framing & art albums.

Subjects: History, Philosophy
ISBN Prefix(es): 5-94650

**Airis Press+**
106 Prospekt Mira, Office 555, 129626 Moscow
*Tel:* (095) 9561684; (095) 7852925 *Fax:* (095)
9561684; (095) 7852925
*E-mail:* rolf@airis.ru
*Web Site:* www.airis.ru
*Key Personnel*
Marketing Dir: Igor Chesnokov *E-mail:* iches@
airis.ru
Founded: 1993
Specialize in educational literature, books help-
ing school-leavers & students to prepare for the
exams, handbooks & textbooks in foreign lan-
guages, popular educational books, reference
books.
Subjects: Business, Career Development, Child
Care & Development, Cookery, Crafts, Games,
Hobbies, Education, English as a Second Lan-
guage, Gardening, Plants, Health, Nutrition,
How-to, Language Arts, Linguistics, Medicine,
Nursing, Dentistry
ISBN Prefix(es): 5-7836; 5-8112
Number of titles published annually: 70 Print; 3
Audio
Total Titles: 180 Print; 3 Audio
Distributor for Foulsham; New Market Press; Par-
enting Press

**ARGO-RISK Publisher**
ul Staryj Gaj 6-1-419, 111402 Moscow
*Tel:* (095) 4768538 *Fax:* (095) 2926511
*E-mail:* zayats@glas.apc.org
*Key Personnel*
Dir: Vladislav Artsatbanov
Editor-in-Chief: Dmitri Kuz'min
Founded: 1993
Subjects: Gay & Lesbian, Literature, Literary
Criticism, Essays, Poetry
ISBN Prefix(es): 5-900506

**Armada Publishing House+**
Kronshtadtskii Blvd, 37b, 125499 Moscow
*Tel:* (095) 4544301; (095) 45431526 *Fax:* (095)
4542481
*E-mail:* riv@armada.msk.ru
*Key Personnel*
President: Dmitri Adamov
Editor: Anton Rybin
Foreign Rights: Olga Zasetskaya
Founded: 1992
Subjects: Animals, Pets, Fiction, Mysteries, Ro-
mance, Science Fiction, Fantasy
ISBN Prefix(es): 5-7632

**Aspect Press Ltd+**
ul Plehanova 23, corpus 3, 111398 Moscow
*Tel:* (095) 3094062 *Fax:* (095) 3091166
*E-mail:* info@aspectpress.ru
*Web Site:* www.aspectpress.ru
*Key Personnel*
Dir & Owner: Leonid Shipov *E-mail:* shipov@
aspectpress.ru
Founded: 1992
Specialize in university textbooks in humanities;
Russian biographical dictionary in 33 vols.
Subjects: Economics, Government, Political Sci-
ence, History, Philosophy, Social Sciences, So-
ciology
ISBN Prefix(es): 5-7567
Number of titles published annually: 50 Print
Total Titles: 110 Print
Distributed by Nauka Ltd (Japan)

**Aurora Art Publishers+**
7/9 Nevsky Prospect, 191065 St Petersburg
*Tel:* (0812) 312-3753 *Fax:* (0812) 312-5460
*Telex:* 121562 *Cable:* FOREIGN TRADE FIRM
AURORA LENINGRAD

*Key Personnel*
President, Rights & Permissions: Boris Pidemsky
Commercial Dir: Zenobius Spetchinsky
Production: Faina Timofeeva
Founded: 1969
Publishes in foreign languages (English, French
& German).
Subjects: Art
ISBN Prefix(es): 5-7300
*Associate Companies:* Aurora Design

**N E Bauman Moscow State Technical
University Publishers+**
5, 2nd Baumanskaya, 107005 Moscow
*Tel:* (095) 263-67-98; (095) 263-60-45; (095)
265-37-97 *Fax:* (095) 265-42-98
*E-mail:* press@bmstu.ru
*Web Site:* www.bmstu.ru
*Key Personnel*
Dir: Tatyana I Popenchenko
Founded: 1989
Subjects: Biblical Studies, Business, Commu-
nications, Computer Science, Earth Sciences,
Economics, Education, Electronics, Electrical
Engineering, Energy, Engineering (General),
Law, Management, Mathematics, Mechanical
Engineering, Microcomputers, Physical Sci-
ences, Science (General), Technology
ISBN Prefix(es): 5-7038
*Parent Company:* Moscow State Technical Uni-
versity

**Beta-Service ZAO,** see Mir Knigi Ltd

**BLIC, russko-Baltijskij informaciionnyj centr,
AO+**
ul krasnogo flota 4, 190000 St Petersburg
*Tel:* (0812) 3112252 *Fax:* (0812) 3112252; (0812)
1135896
*E-mail:* blitz@blitz.spb.ru
*Key Personnel*
Press-Attache: Natalya Mikhailova *Tel:* (0812)
3121440
Founded: 1992
Specializes in various archival references, cata-
logs, historical books & monographies.
Subjects: Biography, Drama, Theater, Fiction,
History, Maritime, Nonfiction (General), Poetry,
Religion - Other, Romance, Science (General),
Science Fiction, Fantasy, Sports, Athletics
ISBN Prefix(es): 5-86789
Total Titles: 70 Print
*Branch Office(s)*
Blumenstrape 126, 47798 Kreferd, Germany,
Contact: Marina Potapova *Tel:* (0215) 1608453
*Fax:* (0215) 1608453
*U.S. Office(s):* 307 Mission Ave, San Rafael,
CA 34901, United States, Contact: W Edward
Nute *Tel:* 415-453-3579 *Fax:* 415-453-0343
*E-mail:* enute@igc.apc.org

**Izdatelstvo Bolshaya Rossiyskaya Entsiklopedia**
Pokrovskij bul'var' 8, 109817 Moscow
*Tel:* (095) 9177582; (095) 9179009 *Fax:* (095)
9177139
*Key Personnel*
Dir: Dr A Gorkin
Founded: 1925
The Great Encyclopedia of Russia Publishing
House.
ISBN Prefix(es): 5-85270

**CentrePolygraph Traders & Publishers Co+**
18 Oktyabrskaya St, 127018 Moscow
*Tel:* (095) 2817411 *Fax:* (095) 2844074
*Key Personnel*
Editorial Dir: Igor Lazarev
Founded: 1991
Subjects: Astrology, Occult, Fiction, Mysteries,
Science Fiction, Fantasy, Western Fiction
ISBN Prefix(es): 5-7001

*Showroom(s):* 20/1 Decabristov ul, Moscow
*Bookshop(s):* ul 32 Raspletina, Moscow
*Warehouse:* 70/1 Nizhegordoskaya ul, Moscow

**Izdatel'stovo Dal'nevostonogo
Gosudarstvennogo Universite** (Far-East State
University Press)+
Oktjabrskaja ul 27, 690600 Vladivostok
*Fax:* 257200
*Telex:* 213218 FESU SU
*Key Personnel*
Dir: Tatyana V Prudkoglyad *Tel:* 57779
Founded: 1982
Subjects: Human Relations, Mathematics
ISBN Prefix(es): 5-7444
*Bookshop(s):* Fesupress Bookshop, Oktjabrskaja
ul 27, 690600 Vladivostok

**Izdatelstvo Detskaya Literatura** (Children's
Literature Publishing)+
Malyi Cherkasskij pereulok 1, 103720 Moscow
*Tel:* (095) 9280803 *Fax:* (095) 9213007
*Key Personnel*
Dir: Tamara M Shatunova
Foreign Rights, Sales: Tatyana P Vladimirskaya
*Tel:* (095) 9213007
Founded: 1933
Children's Literature Publishing.
Subjects: Art, Fiction, History, Literature, Literary
Criticism, Essays, Poetry
ISBN Prefix(es): 5-08
Subsidiaries: Detskaya Literatura Publishers
*Branch Office(s)*
Dom Detskoy Knigi, I Tverskaya-Yamskaya 13,
Moscow

**Dobraya Kniga Publishers+**
11 Petrovsky blvr, 127051 Moscow
*Tel:* (095) 200 2078; (095) 200 1681 *Fax:* (095)
200 2094
*E-mail:* mail@dkniga.ru
*Web Site:* www.dkniga.ru
*Key Personnel*
Publisher & Chief Executive Officer: Roman
Kozyrev *Tel:* (095) 761 5632
Editor-in-Chief: Irina Andreeva
*E-mail:* andreeva@dkniga.ru
Rights Manager: Ulyana Bednarskaya
*E-mail:* yana@dkniga.ru
Founded: 2001
Books for highly effective life to help people
and communities achieve worthwhile pur-
poses through continuous learning and self-
development.
Subjects: Advertising, Animals, Pets, Anthropol-
ogy, Behavioral Sciences, Business, Career De-
velopment, Economics, English as
a Second Language, Human Relations, Humor,
Management, Marketing, Psychology, Psychia-
try, Self-Help, Social Sciences, Sociology
ISBN Prefix(es): 5-98124
Number of titles published annually: 120 Print
Total Titles: 200 Print
Foreign Rep(s): Akonit (Ukraine); Janus (Latvia);
Vertan (Belarus)

**Dom, Izdatel'stvo sovetskogo deskkogo fonda
im & I Lenina+**
Armjanskij per, 11/2a, 101963 Moscow
*Tel:* (095) 9236661 *Fax:* (095) 9285322
*Key Personnel*
Editor-in-Chief: A Likhanov
Founded: 1989
Subjects: Child Care & Development, Cookery,
Crafts, Games, Hobbies, Education, Fiction,
House & Home, How-to, Women's Studies
ISBN Prefix(es): 5-85201

**Druzhba Narodov+**
ul Petrovka 26, 101409 Moscow
*Tel:* (095) 9258671
*Key Personnel*
Dir: Gennady S Gots

Editor-in-Chief: Leonid A Teracopyan
Commercial Manager: Mikhail A Malygin
Founded: 1990
Membership(s): the Association of Soviet Publishers.
Subjects: Crafts, Games, Hobbies, Theology
ISBN Prefix(es): 5-285
*Parent Company:* Ministry of Printing of Russian Federation
*Associate Companies:* Publishing houses of Russian Federation & other Soviet Republic All-Union Society "Book"; All-Union Culture Fund; Pushkin Fund

**Izdatelstvo Ekologija**
ul Kirova 40, 101000 Moscow
*Tel:* (095) 9287860
*Key Personnel*
Dir: L P Tizensgauzen
Editor-in-Chief: G P Dolgovykh
Founded: 1963
Forest Industry Publishing House.
Subjects: Environmental Studies
ISBN Prefix(es): 5-7120

**Izdatelstvo 'Ekonomika'**
Berezhkovskaia naberezhnaya 6, 123995 Moscow
*Tel:* (095) 240-4877; (095) 240-4848 *Fax:* (095) 240-4817
*E-mail:* info@economizdat.ru
*Web Site:* www.economizdat.ru
*Key Personnel*
Dir: E V Polievktova
Founded: 2000
Economics publishing house.
Subjects: Accounting, Agriculture, Business, Cookery, Economics, Education, Finance, Law, Literature, Literary Criticism, Essays, Management, Natural History, Science (General)
ISBN Prefix(es): 5-282

**Nalchik Book Publishing House Elbrus,** *imprint of* Kabardino-Balkarskoye knizhnoye izdatelstvo

**Energoatomizdat**
ul Rozdestvenka 5/7, 103031 Moscow
*Tel:* (095) 9259993 *Fax:* (095) 2356585
*Key Personnel*
Dir: A P Aleshkin
Editor-in-Chief: G G Malkin
Founded: 1963
Publishing House for Atomic Literature.
Subjects: Computer Science, Electronics, Electrical Engineering, Environmental Studies, Literature, Literary Criticism, Essays, Physics, Science (General), Technology
ISBN Prefix(es): 5-283

**FGUP Izdatelstvo Mashinostroenie**
(Mashinostroenie Publishers)+
Stromynskij pereulok 4, 107076 Moscow
*Tel:* (095) 2683858 *Fax:* (095) 2694897
*E-mail:* mashpubl@mashin.ru
*Web Site:* www.mashin.ru
*Key Personnel*
Dir: Olga N Rumyantseva
Deputy Dir: Liubov I Kouzovkina *Tel:* (095) 268-4968 *E-mail:* kouzovkina@umail.ru
Founded: 1931
Publishing House for Mechanical Engineering.
Subjects: Aeronautics, Aviation, Automotive, Biography, Computer Science, Economics, Engineering (General), Environmental Studies, Mathematics, Mechanical Engineering, Technology
ISBN Prefix(es): 5-217
*Associate Companies:* Aspect

**Finansy i Statistika Publishing House** (Finance & Statistics Publishing House)+
ul Pokrovka 7, 101000 Moscow
*Tel:* (095) 925-47-08; (095) 925-35-02 *Fax:* (095) 925-09-57
*E-mail:* mail@finstat.ru
*Web Site:* www.finstat.ru
*Key Personnel*
Man Dir & Editor-in-Chief: Alevtina N Zvonova
Translator: Margarita Ter-Oganian *Tel:* (095) 923 0483
Founded: 1924
Finance & Statistics Publishing House.
Membership(s): Russian Association of Book Publishers; Russian Association of Book Sellers; Guild of Russian Financiers.
Subjects: Accounting, Business, Career Development, Computer Science, Economics, Environmental Studies, Finance, Human Relations, Law, Library & Information Sciences, Management, Marketing, Mathematics, Microcomputers, Public Administration, Real Estate, Securities, Self-Help
ISBN Prefix(es): 5-279
Total Titles: 25 Print
Distributed by KnoRus
Distributor for KnoRus

**Izdatelstvo Fizkultura i Sport+**
ul Kaljaevskajastr 27, 101421 Moscow
*Tel:* (095) 2582690 *Fax:* (095) 2001217
*Key Personnel*
Dir: Valery L Shteinbakh
Editor-in-Chief: V I Vinokurov
Founded: 1923
Subjects: Outdoor Recreation, Sports, Athletics
ISBN Prefix(es): 5-278

**Fizmatlit Publishing Co+**
ul Profsojuznaja 90, 117997 Moscow
*Tel:* (095) 3347151 *Fax:* (095) 3360666
*Key Personnel*
Dir: L I Gladneva
Deputy Dir: A N Zotov
Founded: 1931
Subjects: Astronomy, Communications, Computer Science, Mathematics, Mechanical Engineering, Microcomputers, Physical Sciences, Physics
ISBN Prefix(es): 5-02
*Parent Company:* Nauka Publishers

**Izdatelstvo Galart**
ul Cernjahovskogo 4a, 125319 Moscow
*Tel:* (095) 1512502; (095) 1514513 *Fax:* (095) 1513761
*Key Personnel*
Dir: V V Goryainov
Chief Editor: B Z Yashchina
Founded: 1969
Subjects: Art
ISBN Prefix(es): 5-269

**Gidrometeoizdat+**
ul Beringa 38, 199226 St Petersburg
*Tel:* (0812) 3520815 *Fax:* (0812) 3522688 *Cable:* LENINGRAD B-115 GIMIZ
*Key Personnel*
Dir: A I Ugriumov
Editor-in-Chief: Antonina S Andreeva
Publicity, Promotion: Sergey A Smoliakov
Founded: 1934
Subjects: Agriculture, Animals, Pets, Earth Sciences, Environmental Studies, Geography, Geology, Science (General)
ISBN Prefix(es): 5-286

**Glas New Russian Writing+**
PO Box 47, 119517 Moscow
*Tel:* (095) 441 9157 *Fax:* (095) 441 9157
*Web Site:* www.russianpress.com/glas/

*Key Personnel*
Publisher & Editor: Natasha Perova
*E-mail:* perova@glas.msk.su
Founded: 1992
Specialize in contemporary Russian literature in English translation, bringing publishers & interested readers up to date on the latest hits in Russian literary fiction. Features various literary trends with a view to show the entire literary map of Russia today. More than 100 authors in 23 issues have come out to date.
Subjects: Fiction, Literature, Literary Criticism, Essays
ISBN Prefix(es): 5-7172
Number of titles published annually: 4 Print
Total Titles: 28 Print
*Branch Office(s)*
University of Birmigham, Russian Dept, Birmigham B15 TT, United Kingdom, Contact: Dr Arch Tait *Tel:* (0121) 414 6047 *Fax:* (0121) 414 6047 *E-mail:* a.l.tait@bham.ac.uk *Web Site:* www.bham.ac.uk/glas
*U.S. Office(s):* 1332 N Halsted St, Chicago, IL 60622-2694, United States, Contact: Ivan Dee *Tel:* (312) 787-6262 *Fax:* (312) 787-6269 *E-mail:* elephant@ivanrdee.com
Foreign Rep(s): Arch Tait (Worldwide); Ivan R Dee (USA) (Worldwide)
*Shipping Address:* National Book Network, 4720 Boston Way, Lanham, MD, United States *Tel:* (301) 459-3366 *Fax:* (301) 459-1705 *E-mail:* rfreese@nbnbooks.com
*Warehouse:* 15200 NBN Way, Blue Ridge Summit, PA 17214, United States
*Distribution Center:* Ivan R Dee, 1332 N Halsted St, Chicago, IL 60622-2694, United States, Contact: Alexander Dee *Tel:* (312) 787-6262 *Fax:* (312) 787-6269 *E-mail:* elephant@ivanrdee.com
*Orders to:* Central Books Ltd, 99 Wallis Rd, London E9 5LN, United Kingdom, Contact: Bill Norris *Tel:* (020) 8986 4854 *Fax:* (020) 8533 5821 *E-mail:* orders@centralbooks.com (only UK & Europe)
Northwestern University Press, Chicago Distribution Center, 11030 South Langley Ave, Chicago, IL 60628, United States *Tel:* (773) 568-1550 *Fax:* (773) 660-2235 (USA & Canada)

**INFRA-M Izdatel 'skij dom+**
107 Dmitrovskoye Shosse, 127214 Moscow
*Tel:* (095) 4857077; (095) 4855918 *Fax:* (095) 4855318
*E-mail:* books@infra-m.ru
*Web Site:* www.infra-m.ru
*Key Personnel*
Dir General: Helen Valentinovn's Mel'chuk *Tel:* (095) 485-7077 *E-mail:* offiche@infra-m.ru
Editor-in-Chief: Prudnikov Vladmiir Mikhaylovich *Tel:* (095) 485-5779 *E-mail:* prudnik@orch.ru
Sales Manager: Ilyukhin Vyacheslav Yevgen'evich *Tel:* (095) 485-7400
Head of Sales: Anna Mikhaylonv's Tokmadzhyan *Tel:* (095) 485-7177
Foreign Rights Manager: Regina Bouglo *Tel:* (095) 4855918 *E-mail:* regina@orc.ru
Founded: 1992
Publisher of business books in accounting, management, law, public sector & produces audio & video courses of foreign languages.
Subjects: Accounting, Business, Computer Science, Economics, Education, Film, Video, Finance, Government, Political Science, Language Arts, Linguistics, Law, Management, Marketing, Technology
ISBN Prefix(es): 5-86225; 5-16
Distributed by Infra M Kniga

**Interbook-Business AO**
Spiridonevsky per 12/9, App 11, 103104 Moscow

*Tel:* (095) 2006462; (095) 956-37-52 *Fax:* (095) 956-37-52
*E-mail:* interbook@msk.tsi.ru
*Key Personnel*
Dir: Gennadi Popov
Founded: 1992
Subjects: Art, Cookery, Crafts, Games, Hobbies, Gardening, Plants, Health, Nutrition, History, Regional Interests, Sports, Athletics
ISBN Prefix(es): 5-89164

**Izdatelstvo Iskusstvo+**
Sobinovskij per 3, 103009 Moscow
*Tel:* (095) 2035872 *Fax:* (095) 2918882
*Key Personnel*
Dir: O A Makarov
Deputy Dir: Bodnarouk Tatyana; Yamshchikov Anatoly
Founded: 1938 (as Izogiz & Iskusstvo)
Publishing house for art literature.
Specialize in Art.
Subjects: Architecture & Interior Design, Art, Drama, Theater, Film, Video, History, Philosophy
ISBN Prefix(es): 5-210
Distributed by Calmann & King (UK)
Distributor for Booth-Clibborn Editions; Giunti (Italy); Jaca Book (Italy)

**Izvestia Sovetov Narodnyh Deputatov Russian Federation (RF)**
Pukinskaja pl 5, 103798 Moscow
*Tel:* (095) 2093738 *Fax:* (095) 2095394
*Telex:* 411121 Vesti SU
*Key Personnel*
Dir: Y F Yefremov
Subjects: Agriculture, Business, Economics, Government, Political Science, Law, Public Administration, Social Sciences, Sociology, Sports, Athletics
ISBN Prefix(es): 5-206

**Kabardino-Balkarskoye knizhnoye izdatelstvo+**
ul Malo-Kabardinskaja 1, 360000 Nalchik Kabardino Balkarskoye respublika
*Tel:* 54184
*Key Personnel*
Dir: Ibragim Matgerievich Gadiev
Chief Editor: Anatoly Muratovich Bitsuev
Founded: 1928
Subjects: Ethnicity
ISBN Prefix(es): 5-86778
*Parent Company:* Ministry of Press & Mass Informatio
Imprints: Nalchik Book Publishing House Elbrus

**Kavkazskaya Biblioteka Publishing House+**
prosp Karl Marksa 78, 355045 Stavropol'
*Tel:* (8652) 32314
*Key Personnel*
Dir: Eugen Panasko
Founded: 1990
Subjects: Fiction, Human Relations, Literature, Literary Criticism, Essays, Poetry, Science Fiction, Fantasy
ISBN Prefix(es): 5-8436
Distributor for Samarskiy Dom Pechaty & Sovremennic

**Izdatelstvo Kazanskago Universiteta+**
ul Lenina 18, 420008 Kazan Respublika Tatarstan
*Tel:* 325363
*E-mail:* kacimov@niimm.kazan.su
*Key Personnel*
Dir: Andrei Vatrushkin
Founded: 1957
Subjects: Chemistry, Chemical Engineering, Criminology, Economics, Environmental Studies, Mathematics
ISBN Prefix(es): 5-7464

**Izdatelstvo Khudozhestvennaya Literatura+**
Nov Basmannaya ul 19, 107882 Moscow
*Tel:* (095) 261-85-41 *Fax:* (095) 261-83-00
*Key Personnel*
Editor-in-Chief: V S Modestov *Tel:* (095) 261-38-64
Dir: A N Petzov *Tel:* (095) 261-88-65
Founded: 1930 (as The State Publishers of Fiction)
Publishing house for fiction, poetry & literary biography.
Subjects: Biography, Fiction, Literature, Literary Criticism, Essays, Music, Dance, Poetry
ISBN Prefix(es): 5-280

**Izdatelstvo Kniga+**
ul Tverskaja 50, 125047 Moscow
*Tel:* (095) 2516003 *Fax:* (095) 2500489
*Telex:* 411871
*Key Personnel*
Vice President: Vladimar Y Shvedov
Chairman of the Board, Dir: Viktor N Adamov
Editor-in-Chief: Ivan A Prokhorov
Founded: 1964
Subjects: Library & Information Sciences, Publishing & Book Trade Reference
ISBN Prefix(es): 5-212
Subsidiaries: Kniga Printshop (owned jointly-Kniga Publishers, Russia & Fargo Group, Toronto, Ontario, Canada); The Culture Center at Bol shaya Polianka (owned jointly-USSR & USA); Business Week- Russian Language Edition (jointly by McGraw-Hill Corp, USA Publishers & Kniga Publishers, Russia)

**Izdatelstvo Knizhnaya Palata**
ul. Oktjabr'skaja 4, 103009 Moscow
*Tel:* (095) 2889247 *Fax:* (095) 1635827
*Key Personnel*
Dir: Alexey F Kurilko
Editor-in-Chief: V T Kabanov
Founded: 1987
Publishing House "Book Chamber".
Subjects: Fiction, Publishing & Book Trade Reference
ISBN Prefix(es): 5-7000

**Izdatelskii Dom Kompozitor** (Kompozitor Publishing House)
ul Sadovaja-Triumfalnaja, 12/14, 127006 Moscow
*Tel:* (095) 2092380; (095) 2094105 *Fax:* (095) 2095498
*E-mail:* music@sumail.ru
*Key Personnel*
Dir: G Voronov
Founded: 1957
Subjects: Biography, Education, Music, Dance
ISBN Prefix(es): 5-85285

**KUbK Publishing House+**
ul Gurjanova 5-134, 109548 Moscow
*Tel:* (095) 1640910; (095) 3679473 *Fax:* (095) 1528689
*Key Personnel*
President: Viktor Oubeiko
International Rights: Natalia Oubeiko
Founded: 1992
Subjects: Animals, Pets, Computer Science, Cookery, Romance
ISBN Prefix(es): 5-85554

**Kul'tura redakcionno-izdatel skij kompleks**
ul 35 Arbat, 121835 Moscow
*Tel:* (095) 2481151 *Fax:* (095) 2302180
ISBN Prefix(es): 5-8334
*Branch Office(s)*
Nevsky Pz, 15, St Petersburg

**Ladomir Publishing House+**
K-617, Korp 1435, 103617 Moscow

*Tel:* (095) 530-9833; (095) 530-8477 *Fax:* (095) 537-4742-7870
*Key Personnel*
Editor-in-Chief: Yu Mirhailov
Founded: 1990
Subjects: Antiques, Asian Studies, Fiction, Government, Political Science, History, Philosophy, Religion - Buddhist, Religion - Hindu, Religion - Islamic, Science Fiction, Fantasy, Sports, Athletics
ISBN Prefix(es): 5-86218

**Legprombytizdat**
1-J Kadashevskii pereulok 12, 113035 Moscow
*Tel:* (095) 2330947
*Key Personnel*
Dir: T G Gromova
Editor-in-Chief: T P Drozdova
Founded: 1932
Light Industry & the Services Publishing House.
Subjects: Business, Labor, Industrial Relations, Social Sciences, Sociology
ISBN Prefix(es): 5-7088

**Izdatelstvo Lenizdat+**
ul Fontanka 59, 191023 St Petersburg
*Tel:* (0812) 3111451 *Fax:* (0812) 3151295
*Telex:* I22-693 IZDAT
*Key Personnel*
Gen Dir: V N Nabirukhin
Editor-in-Chief: V N Bunin
Founded: 1917
St Petersburg Publishing House.
Membership(s): the Association of Bookpublishers of Russia. Founder of Russian International Book Exchange.
Subjects: Agriculture, Art, Fiction, Government, Political Science, Science (General), Science Fiction, Fantasy, Technology
ISBN Prefix(es): 5-289
*Parent Company:* Ministry of the Press & Mass Media of the Russian Federation

**Publishing House Limbus Press+**
Izmailovsky pr , 14, 198005 St Petersburg
*Tel:* (0812) 1126547 *Fax:* (0812) 1126706
*E-mail:* limbus.press@ru.net; limbus@limbuspress.ru
*Web Site:* www.limbuspress.ru
*Key Personnel*
Publisher: Konstantin Tublin
Editor-in-Chief: Victor Toporov
Foreign Rights: Julia Goumen
Subjects: Biography, Fiction, Nonfiction (General)
ISBN Prefix(es): 5-8370
Number of titles published annually: 60 Print
*Branch Office(s)*
Moscow
Foreign Rep(s): Anna Benn (England); Catherine Fzagou (Greece); Anastasia Lester (France); Christian Marti-Menzel (Spain)

**Izdatelstvo Malysh**
ul Davydkovskaja 5, 121352 Moscow
*Tel:* (095) 4430654 *Fax:* (095) 4430655
*Key Personnel*
Dir: V M Maiiboroda
Editor-in-Chief: V A Rybin
Founded: 1957
Children's World Publishing House.
ISBN Prefix(es): 5-213

**Izdatelstvo Medicina+**
Petroverigskij pereulok 6/8, 103000 Moscow
*Tel:* (095) 9248785 *Fax:* (095) 9286003
*Telex:* 412282 MEDIZ SU
*Key Personnel*
Dir: A M Stochik *Tel:* (095) 9288648
Editor-in-Chief: N R Paleev *Tel:* (095) 9248785
Foreign Rights Manager: O H Sheshukova
  *Tel:* (095) 9239368
Founded: 1918
Publishing house for medicine.

Subjects: Health, Nutrition, Medicine, Nursing, Dentistry, Psychology, Psychiatry, Science (General)
ISBN Prefix(es): 5-225
*Associate Companies:* Association for Medical Literature
*Bookshop(s):* Komsomolski pr 25, Moscow; Begovaya, 11, Moscow

**Izdatelstvo Metallurgiya+**
2j Obydenskij pereulok 14, 119857 Moscow
*Tel:* (095) 2025532 *Fax:* (095) 2025752
*Key Personnel*
Dir: A G Belikov
Editor-in-Chief: N N Marchenko
Founded: 1939
Publishing house for metallurgy.
Subjects: Earth Sciences, Engineering (General), Technology
ISBN Prefix(es): 5-229

**Izdatelstvo Mezdunarodnye Otnoshenia+**
ul Sadovaja-Spasskaja 20, 107078 Moscow
*Tel:* (095) 2076793 *Fax:* (095) 2002204
*Key Personnel*
Chief Executive: B P Likhachev
Production: M Rodin
Founded: 1957
International relations publishing house.
Subjects: Biography, Government, Political Science
ISBN Prefix(es): 5-7133
*Parent Company:* Goscomizdat, Strastnoi bul 5, 101409 Moscow

**Middle Urals Publishing House**, see
Sredne-Uralskoye knizhnoye izatelstve (Middle Urals Publishing House)

**Ministerstvo Kul 'tury RF+**
Kitaijskij pr d 7, 103693 Moscow
*Tel:* 220 4560
*E-mail:* rnb@q1as.apc.org
Membership(s): IFLA.
Subjects: Genealogy, History, Library & Information Sciences, Social Sciences, Sociology
ISBN Prefix(es): 5-7196
Distributed by Kubon & Sagner

**Izdatelstvo Mir** (Mir Publishers)+
1-j Rizskij per 2, 129820 Moscow
*Tel:* (095) 286-17-83 *Fax:* (095) 288-95-22
*Web Site:* www.mir-pubs.dol.ru
*Key Personnel*
Dir: Dr Kh P Abdullaev *E-mail:* khpa@mir.msk.ru
Editor-in-Chief: Dr V I Propoi *Tel:* (095) 286 43 00 *E-mail:* vivp@mir.msk.ru
International Relations Supervisor: V V Gerasimovsky *Tel:* (095) 286 17 00 *E-mail:* vvg@mir.msk.ru
Founded: 1946 (under name Mir since 1964)
Translation & publication of scientific & technical books.
Membership(s): ASKI (Book Publishers Association of Russia), Association "Task Force Against Piracy".
Subjects: Aeronautics, Aviation, Animals, Pets, Astronomy, Biological Sciences, Chemistry, Chemical Engineering, Communications, Computer Science, Earth Sciences, Electronics, Electrical Engineering, Engineering (General), Environmental Studies, Fiction, Geography, Geology, Health, Nutrition, Mathematics, Mechanical Engineering, Microcomputers, Physical Sciences, Physics, Psychology, Psychiatry, Science (General), Science Fiction, Fantasy, Self-Help, Technology
ISBN Prefix(es): 5-03
Number of titles published annually: 50 Print
Total Titles: 170 Print

**Mir Knigi Ltd+**
ul Sadovaja-Spasskaja 6, 107045 Moscow
*Tel:* (095) 2083879 *Fax:* (095) 7428579
*Key Personnel*
Media Project Dir: Slovovieva Rimma
*E-mail:* rimma@beta.ru
Founded: 1999
Publisher of *Mir Knigi* magazine.
Subjects: Fiction, Nonfiction (General)
ISBN Prefix(es): 5-7043
*Owned by:* Beta-Service

**Izdatelstvo Molodaya Gvardia**
ul Suscevskaja 21, 103030 Moscow
*Tel:* (095) 9722288 *Fax:* (095) 9720582
*Key Personnel*
General Dir: Valentin Yurkin
Founded: 1922
Young Guard Publishing House of the Young Communist League Central Committee.
Subjects: Art, Biography, Government, Political Science, History, Literature, Literary Criticism, Essays, Poetry, Social Sciences, Sociology, Sports, Athletics
ISBN Prefix(es): 5-235

**Izdatelstvo Mordovskogo gosudar stvennogo**
Sovetskaja 24, 430000 Saransk, Mordovskaja resp
*Tel:* 74771 *Fax:* 74771
*Telex:* teletype srn87aelita
*Key Personnel*
Dir: Aleksander N Zernov
Founded: 1990
Specialize in scientific & educational publications for high school.
Subjects: Agriculture, Civil Engineering, Economics, Education, Engineering (General), Geography, Geology, History, Language Arts, Linguistics, Literature, Literary Criticism, Essays, Mathematics, Medicine, Nursing, Dentistry, Philosophy, Social Sciences, Sociology
ISBN Prefix(es): 5-7103
Total Titles: 1,098 Print
*Parent Company:* Mordovian State University
*Bookshop(s):* ul Bolshevitskya 68, 430000 Saransk

**Moscow University Press+**
5/7, Bolshaya Nikitskaya St, 103009 Moscow
*Tel:* (095) 229-50-91; (095) 229-75-41 *Fax:* (095) 203-66-71; (095) 229-75-41
*E-mail:* kd_mgu@df.ru
*Telex:* 411483 MGUSU
*Key Personnel*
Dir: N S Timofeyev
Founded: 1756
Membership(s): University Press Council.
Subjects: Education, Mathematics, Medicine, Nursing, Dentistry, Science (General), Sports, Athletics
ISBN Prefix(es): 5-211
*Branch Office(s)*
Rights & Permissions: VAAP, Bolshaya Bronnaya 6a, 103670 Moscow

**Izdatelstvo Moskovskii Rabochii+**
Cistoprudnyj bul'var' 8, 101854 Moscow
*Tel:* (095) 2210735 *Fax:* (095) 9254274
*Key Personnel*
President, All Moscow, Dir, Moskovskii Rabochiy: Dmitri V Evdokimov
General Dir, All Moscow: Ferdinand V Kaploun
Vice President: Oleg P Benukh; Alexei Vengerov
Editor-in-Chief: G I Broido
Founded: 1922
Moscow Worker Publishing House.
Subjects: Fiction, Nonfiction (General)
ISBN Prefix(es): 5-239; 5-7110
*Branch Office(s)*
Konstatin Evdokimov Bosmsco, 131 Beverly St, Boston, MA 02114, United States *Tel:* 617-248-3988 *Fax:* 617-248-3885

**Izdatelstvo Muzyka+**
14 Neglinnaya St, 103031 Moscow
*Tel:* (095) 923-04-97 *Fax:* (095) 928-33-04
*Key Personnel*
Dir: I Savintsen
Chief Distributor: Aleksey Grebennikov
Founded: 1861
State Music Publishing House.
Subjects: Education, Music, Dance
ISBN Prefix(es): 5-7140; 5-87356
Number of titles published annually: 150 Print
Subsidiaries:
Distributor for Schott
*Showroom(s):* ul Petrovka 26, 103031 Moscow
*Bookshop(s):* Music World, ul B.Nikitskaya, 13, 103871 Moscow
*Warehouse:* Ul Petrovka 26, 103031 Moscow
*Orders to:* ul Petrovka 26, 103031 Moscow

**Izdatelstvo Mysl+**
Leninskj Prospect 15, II907I Moscow
*Tel:* (095) 2324248; (095) 952-5065; (095) 955-0458
*Key Personnel*
Dir: Timofeyev Yevgeny Alexeyevich
Founded: 1963
Subjects: Economics, Geography, Geology, History, Philosophy, Science (General)
ISBN Prefix(es): 5-244

**Nauka Publishers+**
ul Profsoyuznaya 90, 117997 Moscow
*Tel:* (095) 334 71 51 *Fax:* (095) 420 22 20
*E-mail:* secret@naukaran.ru
*Web Site:* www.maik.rssi.ru; www.naukaran.ru
*Telex:* 411612 IZAN *Cable:* Moscow-485
*Key Personnel*
Dir: V Vasiliev
Editor-in-Chief: T Filippova *Tel:* (095) 336 1022
Head of International Dept: Vitali Anishchenko *Tel:* (095) 336 0266
Sales: V Bogomolov *Tel:* (095) 334 7479 *Fax:* (095) 334 7479
Founded: 1727
Scientific books & journals in all fields of knowledge, university textbooks, popular science, academic monographs.
There are six self-supporting branches of Nauka in Moscow, two divisions in Novosibirsk & St Petersburg, Akademkniga Book selling firm & four printshops. The firm's other business activities include direct mail & advertising.
Subjects: Aeronautics, Aviation, Archaeology, Art, Asian Studies, Astronomy, Biological Sciences, Chemistry, Chemical Engineering, Communications, Computer Science, Earth Sciences, Economics, Education, Electronics, Electrical Engineering, Energy, Engineering (General), Environmental Studies, Geography, Geology, Government, Political Science, Health, Nutrition, History, Language Arts, Linguistics, Law, Library & Information Sciences, Literature, Literary Criticism, Essays, Management, Marketing, Mathematics, Mechanical Engineering, Medicine, Nursing, Dentistry, Microcomputers, Natural History, Physics, Psychology, Psychiatry, Radio, TV, Science (General), Social Sciences, Sociology, Technology
ISBN Prefix(es): 5-02
Number of titles published annually: 1,000 Print
Total Titles: 80 Print
Subsidiaries: Akademkniga Booktrading Co; Oriental Literature Publishing Co Nauka; Physical & Mathematical Literature Publishing Co Nauka
Divisions: Printshops Nauka
*Branch Office(s)*
Siberian Publishing Co Nauka, Sovetskaya Ul 18, 63009 Novosibirsk, Dir: Ye A Lazarchuk *Tel:* (03832) 225 181 *Fax:* (03832) 233 502

St Petersburg Publishing Co Nauka,
Mendeleevskaya Liniya 1, 199034 St Petersburg, Dir: S V Valchuk *Tel:* (0812) 328 3912
*Fax:* (0812) 328 0051
Ural Publishing Co Nauka, Ul Amundsena 100,
620016 Yekaterinburg, Dir: Yu Ye Kezhun
*Tel:* (03432) 288 149 *Fax:* (03432) 678 872
*Bookshop(s):* Shubinsky Per 6, 121009 Moscow,
GSP *Tel:* (095) 241 0309 *Fax:* (095) 241 0277
*E-mail:* akademkniga@g23.relcom.ru *Web
Site:* www.ak-book.naukaran.ru
*Shipping Address:* Nauka-Export Booktrading Co,
Profsoyuznaya Ul 90, 117997 Moscow, Dir:
V V Bogomolov *Tel:* (095) 334 7479; (095)
334 7140 *Fax:* (095) 334 7479; (095) 334 7140
*E-mail:* nauka@naukae.msk.ru

**Izdatelstvo Nedra+**
Tverskaja Zastava 3, 125047 Moscow
*Tel:* (095) 2505255 *Fax:* (095) 2502772
*Key Personnel*
Dir: V D Menshicov
Founded: 1963
Natural Resources Publishing House.
Subjects: Earth Sciences, Energy, Geography, Geology
ISBN Prefix(es): 5-247

**Izdatel'stvo Nizhegorodskogo
Gosudarstvennogo Univ**
prosp Gagarina 23, kpmn 230, 603600 Nizhniy
Novgorod
*Tel:* (08312) 657825 *Fax:* (08312) 658592
*E-mail:* rector@nnucnit.unn.ac.ru
*Web Site:* www.unn.ac.ru
Founded: 1990
Subjects: Archaeology, Biological Sciences,
Chemistry, Chemical Engineering, Computer
Science, Economics, Education, Electronics,
Electrical Engineering, Engineering (General),
English as a Second Language, Environmental
Studies, Government, Political Science, History,
Law, Marketing, Mathematics, Mechanical Engineering, Microcomputers, Philosophy, Physical Sciences, Physics, Psychology, Psychiatry,
Social Sciences, Sociology
ISBN Prefix(es): 5-680; 5-85746

**Novosti Izdatelstvo+**
7 Bolsyuaya Of pochyutovaya st, 107082
Moscow
*Tel:* (095) 265-5008 *Fax:* (095) 975-2065; (095)
230-2119; (095) 230-2667
*E-mail:* novosty@df.ru
*Web Site:* www.novosty.ru
*Telex:* 7581; 7582
*Key Personnel*
Dir: Alexander Eidinov *Tel:* (095) 265-6335
Man Dir: Alexander Proskurin
Rights Dept: Alexei Triumfov *Tel:* (095) 265-
5135
Founded: 1963
Subjects: Art, Economics, Fiction, Government,
Political Science, History, Nonfiction (General),
Philosophy, Social Sciences, Sociology
ISBN Prefix(es): 5-7020

**Obdeestro Znanie+**
Lubjanskij poezed 4, 101835 Moscow
*Tel:* (095) 9281531
*Key Personnel*
Dir & Editor-in-Chief: V C Beliakov
Founded: 1951
The Knowledge.
Subjects: Business, Child Care & Development,
Fiction, Science (General), Science Fiction,
Fantasy, Self-Help
ISBN Prefix(es): 5-07

**Okoshko Ltd Publishers (Izdatelstvo)+**
Zubovskij Blvd 17, 119859 Moskva

*Tel:* (095) 2450998 *Fax:* (095) 2053424
*Key Personnel*
Dir: Ivan A Logashin
Founded: 1993
Russian - Belgian Joint Publishing Venture
Also acts as an exclusive Zuidnederlandse Uitgeverij's representative in CIS & Baltic countries.
Subjects: Education, English as a Second Language, Language Arts, Linguistics
ISBN Prefix(es): 5-7400
Total Titles: 23 Print
*Parent Company:* Zuidnederlandse Uitgeverij NV,
Belgium

**Panorama Publishing House+**
Bol Tishinskoj per 38, 123557 Moscow
*Tel:* (095) 2053707 *Fax:* (095) 2053708
*Key Personnel*
Dir: Valery S Buyanov
Founded: 1974
Subjects: Art, Child Care & Development, Fiction, Health, Nutrition, History, House & Home
ISBN Prefix(es): 5-85220

**Izdatel'stvo Patriot**
Olimpijskij prospekt 22, 129110 Moscow
*Tel:* (095) 2844904
Founded: 1951
Voluntary Society for the Promotion of the Army,
Air Force & Navy.
Subjects: Military Science
ISBN Prefix(es): 5-7030

**Pedagogika Press**
Smolenskij Bulvar 4, 119034 Moscow
*Tel:* (095) 2465969 *Fax:* (095) 2465969
*Key Personnel*
Dir: V S Khelemendik
Founded: 1969
Subjects: Education, Science (General)
ISBN Prefix(es): 5-7155

**Permskaja Kniga**
ul K Marksa 30, 614000 Perm
*Tel:* (03422) 324245
*Key Personnel*
Editor-in-Chief: Almira G Zebzeeva
Subjects: Cookery, Crafts, Games, Hobbies, Fiction, Gardening, Plants, House & Home, Poetry, Romance
ISBN Prefix(es): 5-7625

**Planeta Publishers+**
ul Petrovka 8/11, 103031 Moscow
*Tel:* (095) 9230470 *Fax:* (095) 2005246
*Telex:* 411733 *Cable:* PETROVKA 8/11
MOSCOW
*Key Personnel*
Dir: Vladimir Seredin
Editor-in-Chief: Gennadiy Alifanov
Founded: 1969
Subjects: Architecture & Interior Design
ISBN Prefix(es): 5-85250
*Associate Companies:* Interprint
Subsidiaries: Jupiter

**Pressa Publishing House**
ul Pravdy 24, 125867 Moscow
*Tel:* (095) 2573482 *Fax:* (095) 2505205
*Key Personnel*
Dir: VP Leontiev
Subjects: Earth Sciences, Fiction, Literature, Literary Criticism, Essays
ISBN Prefix(es): 5-253

**Profizdat+**
ul Kirova 13, 101000 Moscow
*Tel:* (095) 924-5740; (095) 924-8225 (books);
(095) 924-4637 (periodicals) *Fax:* (095) 975-
2329
*E-mail:* profizdat@profizdat.ru

*Web Site:* www.profizdat.ru
*Key Personnel*
Dir: Vladimir N Soloviev
Founded: 1930
Information & publishing house.
Subjects: Art, Cookery, Fiction, Gardening,
Plants, Labor, Industrial Relations, Nonfiction
(General), Poetry, Sports, Athletics
ISBN Prefix(es): 5-255

**Progress Publishers**
17 Zubovskij Blvd, 119847 Moscow
*Tel:* (095) 2469032 *Fax:* (095) 2302403
*Telex:* 411800 Kegl
*Key Personnel*
Dir: A K Avelitchev
Editor-in-Chief: V N Loskutov; B V Oreshkin
Production: Mikhail Pavlovich Kryakovkin
Founded: 1931
Subjects: Biography, Economics, Fiction, Government, Political Science, History, Language
Arts, Linguistics, Law, Literature, Literary Criticism, Essays, Philosophy, Social Sciences, Sociology
ISBN Prefix(es): 5-01

**Prometej Izdatelstvo**
ul Usacheva 64, 119048 Moscow
*Tel:* (095) 2454495
*Key Personnel*
Dir: V N Bukreev
Founded: 1987
ISBN Prefix(es): 5-7042; 5-8300

**Izdatelstvo Prosveshchenie** (Prosveshcheniye
Publishers)+
3-j proezd Marinoi Roshchi 41, 129846 Moscow
*Tel:* (095) 789-30-29; (095) 789-30-40 *Fax:* (095)
200-42-66; (095) 289-33-98
*E-mail:* msamodwrova@prosv.ru
*Web Site:* www.prosv.ru
*Telex:* 111999 Park
*Key Personnel*
Dir General: Mr Alexander M Kondakov
Commercial Dir: Mr Mikhail Yu Kozhevnikov
Founded: 1930
Educational books & products.
Membership(s): EEPG.
Subjects: Astronomy, Biological Sciences, Chemistry, Chemical Engineering, Computer Science,
Cookery, Crafts, Games, Hobbies, Earth Sciences, Education, Geography, Geology, History,
Literature, Literary Criticism, Essays, Mathematics, Music, Dance, Physical Sciences,
Physics, Poetry
ISBN Prefix(es): 5-09
Number of titles published annually: 700 Print;
10 CD-ROM; 20 Audio
Total Titles: 80,000 Print; 15 CD-ROM; 60 Audio
*Associate Companies:* Prosveshchenie Media

**Izdatelstvo Radio i Svyaz+**
Poctant, a/ja 693, 101000 Moscow
Mailing Address: ul Myasnizkaya 40, 101000
Moscow
*Tel:* (095) 2585351
*Key Personnel*
Dir: E N Salnikov
Founded: 1981
Communications publishing house.
Subjects: Communications, Computer Science,
Electronics, Electrical Engineering, Radio, TV
ISBN Prefix(es): 5-256

**Raduga Publishers+**
4, Aptekarsky Per, 105005 Moscow
*Tel:* (095) 265-55-28 *Fax:* (095) 265-55-28
*E-mail:* raduga@pol.ru *Cable:* MOSCOW TITUL
*Key Personnel*
Dir: Nina S Litvinets
Marketing Dir: Nikolai P Iamskoi
Founded: 1982

Subjects: Art, Biography, Cookery, Education, Fiction, History, Literature, Literary Criticism, Essays, Philosophy, Poetry, Romance, Science Fiction, Fantasy
ISBN Prefix(es): 5-05

**Respublika**
Politizdat lzd, Miusskaja pl 7, 125811 Moscow
*Tel:* (095) 251-7956
*Key Personnel*
Dir: A P Poliakov
Editor-in-Chief: E P Loshkariev
Founded: 1918
Publishers of political literature.
Subjects: Government, Political Science, History
ISBN Prefix(es): 5-250

**Russkaya Kniga Izdatelstvo (Publishers)**
(Russian Book State Publishing House)+
Bolshoy Tishinsky pereulock, h 38, 123557 Moscow
*Tel:* (095) 2053377 *Fax:* (095) 2053424
*Key Personnel*
Dir: M F Nenashev
Founded: 1957
Russian Book State Publishing House.
Subjects: Art, Cookery, Fiction, Government, Political Science, Health, Nutrition, History
ISBN Prefix(es): 5-268

**Russkij Jazyk+**
Staropanskij pereulok 1/5, 103012 Moscow
*Tel:* (095) 9239705 *Fax:* (095) 9288906
*Web Site:* www.russyaz.ru
*Key Personnel*
Dir: V I Nazarov
Chief Editor: A A Alexeeva
Founded: 1974
Russian language publishers.
Subjects: English as a Second Language
ISBN Prefix(es): 5-200

**St Andrew's Biblical Theological College+**
Jerusalem St 3, 109316 Moscow
*Tel:* (095) 2702200 *Fax:* (095) 2707644
*E-mail:* standrews@standrews.ru
*Web Site:* www.standrews.ru
*Key Personnel*
Contact: Dr Alexei Bodrov *E-mail:* abodrov@ standrews.ru
Sales & Marketing Manager: German Utenov
Founded: 1990
Independent theological college publishing house. Textbooks on Biblical studies & themes & two journals. High quality religious & theological literature.
Subjects: Archaeology, Art, Biblical Studies, Child Care & Development, Education, History, Philosophy, Publishing & Book Trade Reference, Religion - Other, Theology
ISBN Prefix(es): 5-89647
Number of titles published annually: 25 Print
Total Titles: 100 Print

**Scorpion Publishers+**
Mozajskoe 9-41, 121471 Moscow
*Tel:* (095) 4436991
*Key Personnel*
President: Tatjana Piljajena
Founded: 1990
Membership(s): the Association of Pubishers; specialize in publishing & trade; also acts as agent of buying or selling international rights & editions.
Subjects: Animals, Pets, Crafts, Games, Hobbies, Health, Nutrition, Philosophy, Theology, Veterinary Science
ISBN Prefix(es): 5-86408
Distributed by Solutions Ltd (West Europe)

**Izdatelstvo Sovetskii Pisatel**
ul Sadovay Triumfalnaya 14-12, 103006 Moscow
*Tel:* (095) 209 2384; (095) 209 4105; (095) 209 1942 *Fax:* (095) 2023200
*Key Personnel*
Director: A N Zhukov
Chief Editor: V I Mussalitin
Founded: 1935
USSR Writer's Union Publishing House
Publishes monthly magazine *Soviet Motherland* in Yiddish.
Subjects: Art, Literature, Literary Criticism, Essays, Poetry
ISBN Prefix(es): 5-265

**Sovremennik Publishers Too**
Horosevskoe sosse 62, 123007 Moscow
*Tel:* (095) 9412992 *Fax:* (095) 9413544
*Key Personnel*
Dir: L A Frolov
Chief Editor: A P Karelin
Founded: 1970
Subjects: Drama, Theater, Fiction, Literature, Literary Criticism, Essays
ISBN Prefix(es): 5-270

**SP Interbuk, Russian-Slovenien jv**
ul Petrovka 26, 101409 Moscow
*Tel:* (095) 9245081 *Fax:* (095) 2002281; (095) 2302403
*Key Personnel*
Dir General: Alexander M Pershin
Editor-in-Chief: Sergei V Goncharenko
Commercial Dir: Mr Juri G Ivanov
15 in various cities of the former USSR.
Membership(s): the Board of All-Russian Publishers' Association, All-Russian Books Distributors Association, All-Russia Publishers Club, Board of Izdatbank, All-Russia Union of Independent Publishers, Advisory Board of the Ministry of Information.
ISBN Prefix(es): 5-7664
Subsidiaries: Alma-Ata; Donetsk; Drozdy; Ekaterinograd; Forest; Kiev; Logos; Sibir; Slavia; Slavutich; St Petersburg; Tjumen
Divisions: Commercial Centre; Interbook Business; Printing Centre; Advertising Centre
*Showroom(s):* Starosadsky per 7/10, str 5, 101000 Moscow
*Shipping Address:* Interbuk Transport & Depots, Russian-Slovenien jv ul Petrovka 26, 101409 Moscow *Tel:* (095) 9245081 *Fax:* (095) 2002281

**Sredne-Uralskoye knizhnoye izatelstve (Middle Urals Publishing House)+**
Malysheva 24, GSP-351, 620219 Sverdlovsk
*Tel:* (03432) 514162 *Fax:* (03432) 512859
*Key Personnel*
Dir: Victor J Selivanov
Founded: 1920
Subjects: Fiction, Literature, Literary Criticism, Essays
ISBN Prefix(es): 5-7529
Subsidiaries:
*Warehouse:* Artinskaya St 23B, 620046 Ekaterinburg

**Izdatelstvo Standartov+**
Novo presnenskij per 3, 123557 Moscow
*Tel:* (095) 252 0348 *Fax:* (095) 268-4724
*E-mail:* standard@online.ru
*Key Personnel*
Dir: N V Zen'kovich
Editor-in-Chief: V P Videneyev
Founded: 1926
Official publications of the state service on standard data.
Subjects: Advertising, Law
ISBN Prefix(es): 5-7050

**Stroyizdat Publishing House**
Dolgorukovskaya u 23 a, 101442 Moscow
*Tel:* (095) 2516967
*Key Personnel*
Dir: Vladimir A Kasatkin
Chief Editor: G A Zhigatcheva
Founded: 1932
Subjects: Architecture & Interior Design, Geography, Geology, Mechanical Engineering, Social Sciences, Sociology
ISBN Prefix(es): 5-274

**Izdatelstvo Sudostroenie+**
ul Gogolja 8, 191065 St Petersburg
*Tel:* (0812) 3124479 *Fax:* (0812) 3120821
*Key Personnel*
Man Dir & Editor-in-Chief: Anatoly A Andreev
Founded: 1940
Publishing House for Shipbuilding.
Subjects: Advertising, Education, Engineering (General), History, Maritime, Mechanical Engineering, Military Science, Science (General), Technology, Transportation
ISBN Prefix(es): 5-7355
*Bookshop(s):* Varag, Malaja Morskaja 8, 191186 St Petersburg

**Teorija Verojatnostej i ee Primenenija+**
ul Vavilova, 42, 117966 Moscow
*Tel:* (095) 1352380; (095) 3324410 *Fax:* (095) 1135125
*E-mail:* tvp@caravan.ru
*Key Personnel*
Dir & Partner: V I Khokhlov
Editor-in-Chief: Yu V Prokhorov
Founded: 1990
Worldwide except the territory of the former USSR.
Specialize in mathematical applied sciences; also acts as research laboratories & as a distribution center for Western Scientific & Professional Editions & Software.
Subjects: Communications, Economics, Mathematics, Military Science, Physics, Securities
ISBN Prefix(es): 5-85484
Subsidiaries: TEV PLC; TBIMC; TVP-Interkniga
Distributed by SIAM USA; VSP (Netherlands)
Distributor for Academic Press; Blackwell; Cambridge University Press; Chapman & Hall; Harcourt Brace; O'Reilly; Pitman; Prentice Hall; John Wiley & Sons (all Russia)
*Showroom(s):* TVP, 1921 Nakhimovskii prosp 47, 117418 Moscow
*Orders to:* TVP, 1921, Nakhimovskii props 47, 117418 Moscow

**Text Publishers Ltd Too+**
7 Cosmonavta Volkova St, 125299 Moscow
*Tel:* (095) 150-04-72; (095) 150-04-82 *Fax:* (095) 150-04-72; (095) 150-04-82
*E-mail:* textpubl@mtu-net.ru
*Web Site:* www.mtu-net.ru/textpubl/
*Key Personnel*
Editor-in-Chief: Mikhail Chernenko
President: Vitaly Babenko
Dir: Olgert Libkin
Commercial Dir: Valery Genkin
Art Dir: Vladimir Lubarov
Founded: 1988
Membership(s): Association of Russian Publishers.
ISBN Prefix(es): 5-7516; 5-87106
*Shipping Address:* 56 Proezd Cherepanovykh, 125183 Moscow
*Warehouse:* 56 Proezd Cherepanovykh, 125183 Moscow
*Orders to:* 56 Proezd Cherepanovykh, 125183 Moscow

**Top Secret Collection Publishers**
ul B Nikitzkaya 22 of 12, 103009 Moscow

*Tel:* (095) 2022011; (095) 2024531 *Fax:* (095) 2913885
*E-mail:* topsec@glasnet.ru
*Key Personnel*
Rts Mgr: Elena Pavlova
Founded: 1993
Subjects: Biography, Fiction, Nonfiction (General), Travel
ISBN Prefix(es): 5-85275

**Izdatelstvo Transport**
Basmannyj Tupik 6a, 103064 Moscow
*Tel:* (095) 2625964 *Fax:* (095) 2611322
*Key Personnel*
Dir: V G Peshkov
Founded: 1923
Subjects: Aeronautics, Aviation, Automotive, Maritime, Transportation
ISBN Prefix(es): 5-277

**Izdatelstvo Ural' skogo+**
Prosp Lenina 135, 620219 Ekaterinburg
*Tel:* (03432) 515448 *Fax:* (03432) 51-54-48
*E-mail:* info@idc.e-burg-ru
*Key Personnel*
Dir: Victor Kochkin
Chief Editor: Fiodor Eremeyev
Founded: 1986
Specialize in monographs & handbooks.
Subjects: Literature, Literary Criticism, Essays, Mathematics, Philosophy
ISBN Prefix(es): 5-7525

**Voronezh State University Publishers**
ul Engelsa 8, 394000 Voronezh
*Tel:* (0732) 560481
*Key Personnel*
Dir: Olga D Tekutyeva
Founded: 1958
Subjects: Biological Sciences, Chemistry, Chemical Engineering, Economics, Geography, Geology, Language Arts, Linguistics, Literature, Literary Criticism, Essays, Mathematics, Social Sciences, Sociology
ISBN Prefix(es): 5-7455
Total Titles: 540 Print

**Voyenizdat+**
ul Zorge 1, 103160 Moscow
*Tel:* (095) 1950154 *Fax:* (095) 1952454
*Key Personnel*
Dir: U J Stadnyuk
Chief Editor: S P Kulichkin; N P Sinitzin
Founded: 1919
Publishing House, Ministry of Defence
ASCI publishing.
Subjects: Biography, Fiction, Government, Political Science, History, Military Science
ISBN Prefix(es): 5-203

**Vsesoyuznii Molodejnii Knizhnii Centre**
Petrovka 26, 101409 Moscow
*Tel:* (095) 924 7879
*Key Personnel*
Gen Dir: A D Tchavchanidze
Founded: 1989
All-Union Youth Book Centre.
Subjects: Fiction, Literature, Literary Criticism, Essays, Science (General)
ISBN Prefix(es): 5-7012

**Vsesoyuznoe Obyedineniye Vneshtorgizdat**
ul Fadeeva 1, 125047 Moscow
*Tel:* (095) 2505162 *Fax:* (095) 2539794
*Telex:* 411238 *Cable:* VNESHTORGIZDAT MOSCOW
*Key Personnel*
Dir-General: Vladimir I Prokopov
Chief Editor: Nickolai I Romanenko
Sales: Valentin A Sirotkin
Production: Vladimir A Melnichenko

Founded: 1925
Foreign Trade Publishing House
Publish Catalogs, Prospectuses & Advertising Material in Russian & Foreign Languages on Soviet exports. Execute foreign firms' orders for printing services, translation & publishing in Russian of maintenance & other documents.
Subjects: Business
ISBN Prefix(es): 5-85025

**Izdatelstvo Vysshaya Shkola** (Higher School Publishing House)+
ul Neglinnaja 29/14, 101439 Moscow
*Tel:* (095) 2000456 *Fax:* (095) 2090350
*Cable:* 101430 GSP-4
*Key Personnel*
Dir: M I Kiselev
Chief Editor: A M Trubitsin
Founded: 1939
Membership(s): Publishers' Association of the Russian Federation.
Subjects: Biological Sciences, Chemistry, Chemical Engineering, Economics, History, Language Arts, Linguistics, Literature, Literary Criticism, Essays, Philosophy, Physics, Technology
ISBN Prefix(es): 5-06

# Rwanda

## General Information

*Capital:* Kigali
*Language:* Kinyarwanda (a Bantu tongue) and French (both official) and Kiswahili
*Religion:* Traditional beliefs (about 50%), most of rest Roman Catholic
*Bank Hours:* 0800-1800 Monday-Friday; 0800-1300 Saturday
*Shop Hours:* 0800-1900 Monday-Saturday
*Currency:* 100 centimes = 1 Rwanda franc
*Export/Import Information:* No tariff on books and advertising, but Statistical tax. Import license, for statistical purposes, and Foreign Exchange License required. Application to National Bank, through authorized bank.
*Copyright:* UCC, Berne (see Copyright Conventions, pg xi)

**Diocese de Kabjayi**, see Imprimerie de Kabgayi

**Government Printer (Imprimerie National du Rwanda)**
BP 351, Kigali
*Tel:* 75350 *Fax:* 75820

**Imprimerie de Kabgayi+**
BP 66, Gitarama
*Tel:* 62252; 62877 *Fax:* 62345
*Key Personnel*
Man Dir: Thomas Habimana
Founded: 1932
*Associate Companies:* Diocese de Kabgayi ASBL, BP 66, Gitarama; Editions Bibliques et Liturgiques, BP 66, Gitarama

**INADES (Institut Africain pour le Developpment Economique et Social)**
15, rue Jean-Mermoz, Cocody, Abidjam 08
Mailing Address: BP 2088, Abidjan 08
*Tel:* (0225) 22404720; (0225) 2244 20 59
*Fax:* (0225) 44 84 38
*E-mail:* inades@africaonline.co.ci; inades@ci.refer.org
*Web Site:* www.inades.ci.refer.org
*Key Personnel*
Sales: Michel Guery

Founded: 1975
Subjects: Literature, Literary Criticism, Essays, Regional Interests, Religion - Other, Social Sciences, Sociology

# Samoa

## General Information

*Capital:* Apia
*Language:* Samoan, English
*Religion:* Predominantly Christian (Congregational, Roman Catholic & Methodist)
*Population:* 165,000
*Bank Hours:* 0930-1500 Monday-Friday
*Shop Hours:* 0800-1200, 1330-1630 Monday-Friday; 0800-1230 Saturday
*Currency:* 100 sene = 1 tala (western Samoan dollar)
*Export/Import Information:* No tariff on most books, printed advertising generally free but some subject to duty. No import license or exchange controls.

**Institute for Research Extension and Training in Agriculture (IRETA)**
The University of the South Pacific, Alafua Campus, PMB, Apia
*Tel:* (0685) 22372; (0685) 21882; (0685) 21671
*Fax:* (0685) 22347; (0685) 22933
*E-mail:* uspireta@samoa.usp.ac.fj
*Telex:* 251 USP SX
*Key Personnel*
Dir: Mohammed Umar *E-mail:* umar_m@samoa.usp.ac.fj
*Parent Company:* The University of the South Pacific

**IRETA**, see Institute for Research Extension and Training in Agriculture (IRETA)

# Saudi Arabia

## General Information

*Capital:* Riyadh
*Language:* Arabic (English widely understood)
*Religion:* Islamic (officially) with about 85% of the Sunni sect
*Population:* 16.9 million
*Bank Hours:* 0830-1200, 1700-1900 Saturday-Wednesday; 0830-1130 Thursday. During Ramadan: 1000-1330 Saturday-Thursday
*Shop Hours:* 0900-1200, 1600-2100 Saturday-Thursday. During Ramadan closed until sunset, then open until 0200
*Currency:* 100 halalahs = 20 qurush = 1 Saudi riyal
*Export/Import Information:* No tariffs on books; advertising matter subject to ad valorem duty but if total duty on one consignment is less than 50 riyals, matter can enter free. Catalogues distributed gratis, usually admitted free. All printed matter except textbooks subject to censorship. No import licenses required.
*Copyright:* UCC (see Copyright Conventions, pg xi)

**Asam Establishment for Publishing & Distribution**
PO Box 87782, Riyadh 11652
*Tel:* (01) 4453732 *Fax:* (01) 4412583
*Key Personnel*
General Manager, Owner: Fahed M Abo Rdoun

Subjects: Religion - Islamic
ISBN Prefix(es): 9960-714

**Dar Al-Mirrikh (Mars Publishing House)**
PO Box 10720, Riyadh 11443
*Tel:* (01) 464 7531; (01) 465 7939; (01) 4658523
  *Fax:* (01) 465 7939
*Telex:* 403129
*Key Personnel*
President: Abdullah Majid
Vice President: Shams Zakaria
Contact: Mr Abdul Hameed Noor Mohd
ISBN Prefix(es): 9960-24

**Dar Al-Rayah for Publishing & Distribution**
PO Box 40124, Riyadh 11499
*Tel:* (01) 4931869 *Fax:* (01) 4911985
ISBN Prefix(es): 9960-661

**Dar Al-Shareff for Publishing & Distribution+**
PO Box 2479, Riyadh 11563
*Tel:* (01) 4779491
*Key Personnel*
President: Ibrahim Al-Hazemi
Founded: 1992
Subjects: Animals, Pets, Astronomy, Behavioral
  Sciences, Biography, Drama, Theater, History,
  Humor, Literature, Literary Criticism, Essays,
  Medicine, Nursing, Dentistry, Nonfiction (Gen-
  eral), Philosophy, Religion - Islamic, Romance,
  Sports, Athletics, Veterinary Science, Women's
  Studies
ISBN Prefix(es): 9960-640; 9960-741

**International Publications Agency (IPA)**
PO Box 70, Dhahran Airport
*Tel:* (03) 8954925
*Telex:* 871229
*Key Personnel*
Manager: Said Salah
Subjects: Regional Interests

**Al Jazirah Organization for Press, Printing,
  Publishing**
Al-Nassiriah St, Riyadh 11411
Mailing Address: PO Box 354, Riyadh
*Tel:* (01) 4419999 *Fax:* (01) 4412536
*Key Personnel*
Dir General: Saleh Al-Ajroush
Editor-in-Chief: Khalid el Malek
Founded: 1964
Subjects: Government, Political Science, Law
ISBN Prefix(es): 9960-9190

**King Saud University+**
PO Box 2254, Riyadh 11451
*Tel:* (01) 4672832 *Fax:* (01) 4672894
*Web Site:* www.ksu.edu.sa
*Telex:* 461019 KSU SJ
*Key Personnel*
President: Prof Abdullah Al-Faisal
Vice President: Prof Ibrahim Al-Mish'Al
Vice President, Research & Higher Studies: Prof
  Khalid Al Hamoudi
Dir, Translation Center: Prof Ahmed A Almohan-
  dis
Dean, University Libraries: Dr Sulaiman S Al
  Ugla
Founded: 1957
Subjects: Agriculture, Behavioral Sciences, Bi-
  ological Sciences, Chemistry, Chemical Engi-
  neering, Geography, Geology, Language Arts,
  Linguistics, Mathematics, Medicine, Nursing,
  Dentistry, Technology
ISBN Prefix(es): 9960-05

**Saudi Publishing & Distributing House+**
3rd Floor, Al-Jawhara Bldg No 1, Medina Rd,
  Baghdadiah, Jeddah 21451
Mailing Address: PO Box 899, Dammam
*Tel:* (03) 8334158 *Fax:* (03) 8335520

*E-mail:* info@spdh-sa.com
*Web Site:* www.spdh-sa.com *Cable:*
  NASHRADAR
*Key Personnel*
Chairman & Man Dir: Mohammed Salahuddin
Founded: 1966
Also act as importers & distributors of English &
  Arabic books (academic, reference & general).
Subjects: Literature, Literary Criticism, Essays,
  Religion - Other, Science (General)
ISBN Prefix(es): 9960-26
*Branch Office(s)*
PO Box 899, Riyadh *Tel:* (01) 464 7894
*Bookshop(s):* Hyat Plaza Complex, King Saud
  St, Dammam Dhahran St Near Governorate,
  Dannan *Tel:* (03) 8323515; Zouman Shopping
  Centre, opposite S Fakhee Hospital, Jeddah
  *Tel:* (02) 6608964

# Senegal

## General Information

*Capital:* Dakar
*Language:* French
*Religion:* About 90% Islamic, 5% Christian
  (mostly Roman Catholic), the rest follow tra-
  ditional beliefs
*Population:* 8.2 million
*Bank Hours:* Generally 0800-1115, 1430-1630
  Monday-Friday
*Shop Hours:* Vary, and some open Sunday morn-
  ing, some close Monday morning. Generally
  are 0800-1200, 1430-1800 Monday-Saturday
*Currency:* 100 centimes = 1 CFA franc
*Export/Import Information:* Member of West
  African Economic Community. No tariff on
  books except atlases. Added taxes apply to atlases. Advertising matter (more than one copy)
  subject to fiscal and customs duty plus added
  taxes. Import licenses and exchange controls
  apply for imports from outside EEC, Franc
  Zone, USA and Canada.
*Copyright:* Berne, UCC (see Copyright Conventions, pg xi)

**Nouvelles Editions Africaines du Senegal
  (NEAS)+**
10, Rue El Hadj Amadou Assane-Ndoye, Dakar
Mailing Address: BP 260, Dakar
*Tel:* 8211381; 8221580 *Fax:* 8223604
*Key Personnel*
President: Souleymane Bachir Diagne
Dir General: Mr Doudou Ndiaye
Founded: 1989
Subjects: Literature, Literary Criticism, Essays,
  Social Sciences, Sociology
ISBN Prefix(es): 2-7236
Distributed by African Imprint Library Services

**Agence de Distribution de Presse (ADP)**
BP 374, Dakar
*Tel:* (08) 310052 *Fax:* (08) 324915
*E-mail:* adpresse@sentoo.sn
*Key Personnel*
Man Dir: Philipe Schorp
Founded: 1943
Affiliated to NMPP, Paris.
*Parent Company:* NMPP, Paris, France

**CAEC**, see Centre Africain d'Animation et
  d'Echanges Culturels Editions Khoudia (CAEC)

**Centre Africain d'Animation et d'Echanges
  Culturels Editions Khoudia (CAEC)+**
HLM Fass-Paillote, Immeuble 7, Dakar

*Tel:* 211023 *Fax:* 215109
*Key Personnel*
Production Dir: Ms Aissatou Dia
Founded: 1989
Subjects: Anthropology, Drama, Theater, Edu-
  cation, Ethnicity, Fiction, Literature, Literary
  Criticism, Essays, Poetry
ISBN Prefix(es): 2-87895
Distributed by Edilis (Ivory Coast); Presence
  Africaine (France)
Distributor for Edilis (Ivory Coast); Haho (Togo)

**Centre de Linguistique Appliquee**
Universite de Dakar, Faculte des Lettres et Sci-
  ences Humaines, Fann Parc, Dakar
*Tel:* 230126
Subjects: Language Arts, Linguistics, Literature,
  Literary Criticism, Essays

**CODESRIA (Council for the Development of
  Social Science Research in Africa)+**
PO Box 3304, Dakar, Avenue Cheikh Anta Diop
  X Canal IV, Dakar
*Tel:* 8259814; 8259822 *Fax:* 8241289; 8640143
*E-mail:* codesria@sonatel.senet.net
*Web Site:* www.cordesria.org
*Telex:* 61339 Codes SG
*Key Personnel*
Head of Publications & Communications: Felicia
  Oyekanmi *E-mail:* felicia.oyekanmi@codesria.
  sn
Founded: 1973
Publish in four languages: English, French, Por-
  tuguese & Arab. Specialize in social sciences.
  Also acts as a coordinator of social science re-
  search in Africa.
Membership(s): International Research Councils.
Subjects: Behavioral Sciences, Developing Coun-
  tries, Economics, Education, Environmental
  Studies, Ethnicity, Government, Political Sci-
  ence, History, Labor, Industrial Relations, So-
  cial Sciences, Sociology, Women's Studies
ISBN Prefix(es): 1-870784; 2-86978
Number of titles published annually: 10 Print
Total Titles: 186 Print
*Warehouse:* African Books Collective Ltd,
  The Jam Factory, 27 Park End St, Oxford
  0X1 1KU, United Kingdom *E-mail:* abc@
  africanbookscollective.com
Karthala, Edition Diffusion, 22-24 Blvd Arago,
  75013 Paris, France

**Council for the Development of Social Science
  Research in Africa**, see CODESRIA (Council
  for the Development of Social Science
  Research in Africa)

**Enda Tiers Monde**
4 & 5 rue Kleber, Dakar
Mailing Address: BP 3370, Dakar
*Tel:* (0221) 821-60-27; (0221) 822-42-29
  *Fax:* (0221) 822-26-95
*E-mail:* enda@enda.sn
*Web Site:* www.enda.sn
*Telex:* 51456SG
*Key Personnel*
President: Cheikh Hamidou Kane
Founded: 1972

**Environment & Development Action in the
  Third World**, see Enda Tiers Monde

**Institut Fondamental d'Afrique Noire (IFAN)**
  (Fundamental Institute of Black Africa, Sheik
  Anta Diop)
Universite Cheikh Anta DIOP, Dakar
Mailing Address: BP 206, Dakar
*Tel:* 825 00 90; 825 98 90; 825 71 24 *Fax:* 24 49
  18
*E-mail:* bifan@telecomplus.sn
*Web Site:* www.refer.sn/ifan

*Key Personnel*
Dir: Prof Samb Djibril
Founded: 1936
*Branch Office(s)*
Musee de la Mer, Campus universitaire, BP 206
    Dakar-Fann
Musee historique, Campus universitaire, BP 206
    Dakar-Fann
Musees d'Art africain, Campus universitaire, BP
    206 Dakar-Fann


**IFAN**, see Institut Fondamental d'Afrique Noire
    (IFAN)


**NEAS**, see Nouvelles Editions Africaines du
    Senegal (NEAS)


**Les Nouvelles Editions Africaines du Senegal
NEAS+**
BP 260, 10 rue El Hadj Amadou Assane, Ndoye,
    Dakar
*Tel:* (08) 211381; (08) 221580 *Fax:* (08) 223604
*E-mail:* neas@sentoo.sn
*Key Personnel*
Dir General: Francois Boirot
Commercial Dir: Mamadou Kasse
Founded: 1972
Subjects: Biography, Education, Ethnicity, Fiction,
    History, Nonfiction (General), Philosophy, Po-
    etry, Psychology, Psychiatry, Religion - Other,
    Science (General), Social Sciences, Sociology
ISBN Prefix(es): 2-7236
Number of titles published annually: 15 Print
Total Titles: 800 Print
Distributed by CEDA; Editions Donniya; Editions
    Jamana; Ganndal; NEI
Distributor for CEDA; Editions Donniya; Editions
    Jamana; Ganndal; NEI


**Edition Sahel+**
9 rue Thiong, BP 3683, Dakar
*Tel:* 212164
*Telex:* 469 teranga sg
*Key Personnel*
Contact: Niane Idrissa
Founded: 1982
ISBN Prefix(es): 2-906993


**Societe Africaine d'Edition**
14 Rue Jules Ferry, BP 1877, Dakar
*Tel:* 217977; 220284
*Key Personnel*
Man Dir: Pierre Biarnes
Founded: 1961
Subjects: Economics, Foreign Countries, Govern-
    ment, Political Science
*Branch Office(s)*
32 rue de l'Echiquier, 75010 Paris, France
    *Tel:* 5230233


**Societe d'Edition d'Afrique Nouvelle**
10 rue El Hadj Amadou Assane Ndoye, BP 260,
    Dakar
*Tel:* (08) 211381; (08) 221580 *Fax:* (08) 223604
*Telex:* 21 450 NEA SG
*Key Personnel*
Man Dir: Athanase Ndong
Senior Editor, Rights & Permissions: Rene Odou
Subjects: Foreign Countries, Religion - Other
ISBN Prefix(es): 2-7236

# Serbia and Montenegro

## General Information

*Capital:* Belgrade
*Language:* Serbian, Albanian, Croation and
    Bosnian
*Religion:* Predominately Eastern Orthodox (65%),
    also Islamic, Roman Catholic and Protestant
*Population:* 10.8 million
*Bank Hours:* 0800-1500 Monday-Friday
*Shop Hours:* 0800-2000 Monday-Friday; 0800-
    1500 Saturday. Some open weekdays continu-
    ously and early Sunday morning
*Currency:* 100 paras = 1 Yugoslav New Dinar
*Export/Import Information:* No tariffs on books
    except on publications by publishers from Ser-
    bia and Montenegro printed abroad. Advertis-
    ing catalogs for such books dutied, otherwise
    free; non-Serbian language advertising mate-
    rials dutied. Special equalization tax, customs
    clearance charge and import surcharge when
    goods are subject to duty. No import licenses
    required. Exchange controls. The basic com-
    mercial unit is known as an enterprise but there
    are no state monopolies.
*Copyright:* UCC, Berne (see Copyright Conven-
    tions, pg xi)


**AGAPE+**
Cara Dusana 4, 21000 Novi Sad
*Tel:* (021) 469-474 *Fax:* (021) 469-382
*E-mail:* agape@eunet.yu
*Web Site:* www.agape.yu
*Key Personnel*
President & International Rights: Karoly Harmath
    *E-mail:* harmath@eunet.yu
Founded: 1977
Membership(s): ELCE; Association of Hungarian
    Catholic Publishers; International Association
    of Franciscan Publishers, UCIP.
Subjects: Religion - Catholic, Theology
ISBN Prefix(es): 86-463
Number of titles published annually: 50 Print
*Parent Company:* AGAPE Kft, Hu-Szeged,
    Matyas ter 26, 6725 Szeged, Hungary, Eva
    Balogh


**Alfa-Narodna Knjiga**
Safarikova 11, PO Box 247, 11000 Belgrade
*Tel:* (011) 3221-484; (011) 3227-426; (011) 3223-
    910 *Fax:* (011) 3227-946
*E-mail:* alfankkl@eunet.yu
*Web Site:* www.narodnaknjiga.co.yu
*Key Personnel*
Editor-in-Chief: Milicko Mijovic
Foreign Rights Mgr: Tea Jovanovic *Tel:* (011)
    3227-426 *Fax:* (011) 3227-946 *E-mail:* tea@
    eunet.yu
Subjects: Art, Astrology, Occult, Child Care &
    Development, Cookery, Criminology, Fiction,
    Government, Political Science, Health, Nutri-
    tion, History, How-to, Journalism, Language
    Arts, Linguistics, Literature, Literary Criticism,
    Essays, Medicine, Nursing, Dentistry, Myster-
    ies, Nonfiction (General), Philosophy, Poetry,
    Psychology, Psychiatry, Religion - Other, Sci-
    ence (General), Self-Help
ISBN Prefix(es): 86-331
Number of titles published annually: 300 Print
Total Titles: 1,000 Print


**Association of Serbia & Montenegro
Publishers & Booksellers**
Kneza Milosa 25, 11000 Belgrade
Mailing Address: POB 570, 11000 Belgrade
*Tel:* (011) 2642-533; (011) 2642-248 *Fax:* (011)
    2686-539; (011) 2646-339

*E-mail:* uikj@eunet.yu
*Web Site:* www.beobookfair.co.yu
*Key Personnel*
General Dir: Mr Zivadin Mitrovic
Book Fairs, Department Manager: Marina Radoji-
    cic
Founded: 1954
Organizer of the International Book Fair in Bel-
    grade.
Membership(s): IPA, Geneve.
ISBN Prefix(es): 86-7115


**Beogradski Izdavacko-Graficki Zavod**
Bulevar Vojvode Misica 17/VI, 11000 Belgrade
*Tel:* (011) 650-235; (011) 651-666 *Fax:* (011)
    651-841
*Web Site:* www.suc.org/biz/BIGZ/
*Telex:* 11855 Yu Bigz *Cable:* BEOGRAF
*Key Personnel*
Man Dir: Gojko Zecar
Editorial Dir, Permissions: Vidosav Stevanovic
Founded: 1831
Subjects: Philosophy, Poetry, Social Sciences, So-
    ciology
ISBN Prefix(es): 86-13
Imprints: BIGZ
*Book Club(s):* Book Lovers' Club


**BIGZ**, *imprint of* Beogradski Izdavacko-Graficki
    Zavod


**Borba**
Trg Marksa I Engelsa 7, Belgrade 11000
*Tel:* (011) 3243-437 *Fax:* (011) 3244-913
*Web Site:* www.borba.co.yu
*Key Personnel*
Dir: Novica Dukic
Founded: 1922
ISBN Prefix(es): 86-80105


**Decje Novine**, see Niro Decje Novine


**Forum**
Vojvode Misica 1, 22100 Novi Sad
*Tel:* (021) 57 286 *Fax:* (021) 57 691
*Telex:* yu-14199
*Key Personnel*
Dir: Kalman Petkovics
Subjects: Fiction, Government, Political Science
ISBN Prefix(es): 86-323


**Gradevinska Knjiga**
Trg Nikole Pasica 8/11, 11000 Belgrade
*Tel:* (011) 323 35 65; (011) 324 76 62 *Fax:* (011)
    323 32 34
*Key Personnel*
Man Dir: Milan Visnic
Editor & Chief: Milica Dodic
Commercial Manager: Jovo Karadzic
Founded: 1948
Subjects: Architecture & Interior Design, Engi-
    neering (General)
ISBN Prefix(es): 86-395
*Bookshop(s):* Narodnog fronta 14, Belgrade; Stu-
    dent, 27 marta 78, Belgrade


**Izdavacka preduzece Gradina+**
Pobede 38, 18000 Nis
*Tel:* (018) 25 864; (018) 25 456 *Fax:* (018) 25
    456
*E-mail:* gradinar@bankerinter.net
*Key Personnel*
Dir: Gordana Jovanovic
Subjects: Art, Science (General)
ISBN Prefix(es): 86-7129
*Bookshop(s):* ul pobede 113Y, Nis; Veljka Vla-
    hovica 2, Nis; Dimitrija Tucovica bb, Nis


**Jugoslavijapublik+**
Knez Mihailova 10, 11000 Belgrade

*Tel:* (011) 633 266 *Fax:* (011) 622 858
*Telex:* 11125
*Key Personnel*
General Manager: Slobodan Zaric
Founded: 1962
Subjects: History, Philosophy, Religion - Other
ISBN Prefix(es): 86-7121

**Jugoslovenska Revija**
Karatordeva 41, 11000 Belgrade
*Tel:* (011) 625-829
*Telex:* 12954 Yurew
*Key Personnel*
Dir: Rajko Bobot
Permissions: Milovan Ignjatovic
Subjects: Art, Travel
ISBN Prefix(es): 86-7413

**Tehnicka Knjiga** (Technical Book)+
Vojvode Stepe 89, 11000 Belgrade
*Tel:* (011) 468 596 *Fax:* (011) 473 442
*E-mail:* tknjiga@eunet.yu
*Web Site:* www.tehknjiga.co.yu
*Key Personnel*
Editor-in-Chief: Mrdjenovic Dragi
Man Dir: Grbovic Radivoje
Sales Manager: Cosovic Llida
Subjects: Computer Science, Electronics, Electrical Engineering, Engineering (General), How-to, Science (General)
ISBN Prefix(es): 86-325

**Kultura**
XIV VUSB 4-6, 21470 Backi Petrovac
*Tel:* (021) 780-144 *Fax:* (021) 780-291 *Cable:* Obzor Novi Sad
*Key Personnel*
Dir: Anna Makanova
ISBN Prefix(es): 86-7103
*Bookshop(s):* Backi Petrovac Bodvis Jan

**Libertatea**
Zarka Zrenjanina 7, 26000 Pancevo
*Tel:* (013) 33-51; 13 346 447 *Fax:* (013) 46-447
*Cable:* Libertatea Pancevo
*Key Personnel*
Dir: Todor Gilezan
ISBN Prefix(es): 86-7001

**Minerva**
Trg 29 novembra 3, 24000 Subotica
*Tel:* (024) 28834; (024) 25712 *Fax:* (024) 23-208
*Cable:* Minerva Subotica
*Key Personnel*
Dir: Josip Prcic
Subjects: Science (General)
ISBN Prefix(es): 86-7099
*Bookshop(s):* ul oktobra 4, 24000 Subotica; Maksima Gorkog 20, 24000 Subotica; Put M Pijade 25, 24000 Subotica

**MiS Sport IGP**
Radnicka 24, 11030 Belgrade
*Tel:* (011) 3220226; (011) 3225361 *Cable:* Sportska Knjiga
*Key Personnel*
Dir: Dragoslav Bajic
Editor: Sava Bjelajac
Founded: 1949
Subjects: Sports, Athletics
ISBN Prefix(es): 86-7107

**Narodna Biblioteka Srbije** (National Library of Serbia)
Skerliceva 1, 11000 Belgrade
*Tel:* (011) 451 2429 *Fax:* (011) 451 289
*E-mail:* kovacevic@nbsbg.nbs.bg.ac.yu
*Web Site:* www.nbs.bg.ac.yu
*Telex:* NBS 12208
*Key Personnel*
Dir: Svetislav Duric

Founded: 1832
Subjects: History
ISBN Prefix(es): 86-7035

**Naucna Knjiga+**
Uzun Mirkova 5/1, 11000 Belgrade
*Tel:* (011) 635 819; (011) 637 868; (011) 637 230
*Fax:* (011) 638 070 *Cable:* NAUCNA KNJIGA
*Key Personnel*
Man Dir: Dr Blazo Perovic
Founded: 1947
Subjects: Education, Engineering (General), Medicine, Nursing, Dentistry, Science (General)
ISBN Prefix(es): 86-23; 86-321
*Bookshop(s):* Znanje, Gracanicka br 16, Belgrade; Naucna Knjiga, Knez Mihailova gr 19 & 40, Belgrade; Naucna knjiga, Jug Bogdanova 68, Prokuplje

**Nio Pobjeda - Oour Izdavacko-Publicisticka Djelatnost**
Bulevar revolucije 11, 81000 Podgorica
*Tel:* (081) 45955; (081) 44433; (081) 44474
*Fax:* (081) 52803
*Telex:* 61243 YU pob
*Key Personnel*
Dir: Ljubo Buric
Publishing Dir: Mileta Radovanovic
Editor: Branko Banjevic; Djerdj Djokaj; Ratko Vujosevic; Vojislav Minic
Sales, Trade Dir: Miodrag Raonic
Founded: 1962
Subjects: Science (General)
ISBN Prefix(es): 86-309
*Branch Office(s)*
Safarikova 15, 21000 Novi Sad *Tel:* (021) 51086
Miladin Popovica bb, 38000 Pristina *Tel:* (038) 24062
Karadordev trg 7, 11080 Zemun *Tel:* (011) 600652

**Niro Decje Novine**
pf 24, Tihomira Matijevica 4, 32300 Gornji Milanovac
*Tel:* (032) 712246; (032) 712247; (032) 714970; (032) 711256; (032) 711248; (011) 3221476; (011) 342010 *Fax:* (032) 711248
*Telex:* 13731 GM, 12206 BGB
Subjects: Education
ISBN Prefix(es): 86-367

**Nolit Publishing House+**
Terazije 27/II, 11000 Belgrade
*Tel:* (011) 345 017; (011) 355 510 *Fax:* (011) 627285 *Cable:* NOLIT BGD
*Key Personnel*
Man Dir: Radivoje Nesie
Editorial: Radivoje Mikic
Dir: Branko Nikezic
Founded: 1928
Subjects: Agriculture, Art, Fiction, History, Philosophy, Psychology, Psychiatry, Social Sciences, Sociology
ISBN Prefix(es): 86-19

**Obod**
Njegoseva 3, 81250 Cetinje
*Tel:* (086) 233-331 *Fax:* (086) 233-951
*E-mail:* ipobod@cg.ju *Cable:* OBOD CETINJE
*Key Personnel*
Dir: Vasko Jankovic
Founded: 1946
Membership(s): Association of Yugoslav Publishers & Booksellers.
Subjects: Education, Fiction, Language Arts, Linguistics, Nonfiction (General), Poetry, Science (General)
ISBN Prefix(es): 86-305
Number of titles published annually: 30 Print

*Branch Office(s)*
Dobracina 32, 11000 Belgrade *Tel:* (011) 626-553
*Bookshop(s):* Njegoseva 11, 11000 Belgrade

**Izdavacka Organizacija Rad**
Mose Pijade 12, 11000 Belgrade
*Tel:* (011) 3239-758; (011) 3239-998 *Fax:* (011) 3230-923
*Key Personnel*
Man Dir: Bravislav Milosevic
Sales Dir: Milovan Vlahovic
21 bookshops throughout Serbia and Montenegro.
Subjects: Biography, Economics, Engineering (General), Government, Political Science, Philosophy, Poetry, Social Sciences, Sociology
ISBN Prefix(es): 86-09
*Bookshop(s):* Papirus, Terazije 26, Belgrade; Frankopanska 5, Zagreb

**Panorama NIJP/ID Grigorije Bozovic**
Dom Stampe BB, 38000 Pristina
*Tel:* (038) 29 090; (038) 21 156; (038) 29 866
*Fax:* (038) 29 809 *Cable:* Jedinstvo Pristina
*Key Personnel*
Dir: Milan Seslija
Subjects: Government, Political Science, History, Medicine, Nursing, Dentistry, Philosophy, Social Sciences, Sociology
ISBN Prefix(es): 86-7019

**Partenon MAM Sistem+**
Simina 9a/1, 11000 Belgrade
*Tel:* (011) 632535; (011) 625942; (011) 633465
*Fax:* (011) 632535; (011) 2623980
*E-mail:* partenon@infosky.net
*Key Personnel*
Dir: Momcilo Mitrovic
Subjects: Agriculture, Fiction, Science (General), Linguistics
ISBN Prefix(es): 86-7157
Number of titles published annually: 30 Print

**Izdavacko Preduzece Matice Srpske+**
Ulica Matice srpske 1, 21000 Novi Sad
*Tel:* (021) 420 199; (021) 420 198 *Fax:* (021) 28 574; (021) 25 859
*E-mail:* bms@bms.ns.ac.yu
*Web Site:* www.bms.ns.ac.yu
*Key Personnel*
Dir: Milorad Grujic *E-mail:* m.grujic@sezampro.yu
Editor: Ivan Negrisorac; Milica Micic Dimovski; Dragan Mojovic
Founded: 1826
Subjects: History, Human Relations, Literature, Literary Criticism, Essays
ISBN Prefix(es): 86-363
*Bookshop(s):* Zmaj Jovina 4, Novi Sad, Milenko Ranin *Tel:* 29-436; Trg Toz Markovica 24, Novi Sad, Zdravko Gaseric *Tel:* 29-307

**Privredni Pregled**
Marsala Birjuzova 3, 11000 Belgrade
*Tel:* (011) 625522; (011) 628477 *Fax:* (011) 3281473; (011) 3281912
*E-mail:* novinska@hotmail.com; desk@grmec.co.yu
*Web Site:* www.grmec.co.yu
*Telex:* 11509 Yu Pp *Cable:* Privredni Pregled Bgd
*Key Personnel*
Dir: Toma Markovic
Contact: Dusan Jugovic; Stana Sehalic
Editor-in-Chief: Slobodan Kljajic
Subjects: Economics, Law, Management
ISBN Prefix(es): 86-315
*Branch Office(s)*
Orce Nikolova 79, Skopje
Mose Pijade, 21 Zagreb
Hala 'Tivoli', Ljubljana
Marsala Tita 86, Sarajevo

**Prosveta**
Cika Ljubina 1, 11000 Belgrade
*Tel:* (011) 629 843; (011) 631 566 *Fax:* (011) 182 581
*Telex:* 11609 Yu
*Key Personnel*
General Dir: Vidosav Stevanovic
Editor-in-Chief: Milisav Savic
Export Manager: Milutin Trifunovic
Rights & Permissions: Branka Simic
Founded: 1945
Subjects: Human Relations
ISBN Prefix(es): 86-07
*Book Club(s):* Prosveta

**Radnicka Stampa**
Trg Nikole Pasica 5/V, 11000 Belgrade
Mailing Address: Postanski fah 995, 11000 Belgrade
*Tel:* (011) 3230-927; (011) 3230-921; (011) 3236-259
*E-mail:* radstamp@sezampro.yu
*Web Site:* www.radnickastampa.co.yu/
*Telex:* RSNIRO YU 72638 *Cable:* Radnicka stampa Belgrade
*Key Personnel*
Dir: Radoslav Roso
Sales Manager: Cedo Males
Subjects: Economics, Government, Political Science, Social Sciences, Sociology
ISBN Prefix(es): 86-7073

**Republicki Zavod za Unapredivanje Vaspitanja i Obrazovanja**
Kneza Milosa 101, 11000 Belgrade
*Tel:* (011) 659322
*Key Personnel*
Chief Executive: Milivoje Brajove
Editor-in-Chief: Krsto Lekovie
Sales Manager: Radmila Miranovie
Founded: 1973
Republic Institution for the Improvement of Education.
Subjects: Education
ISBN Prefix(es): 86-80871
*Bookshop(s):* Knjizara Zavoda, Kneza Milosa 101, 11000 Belgrade

**Savez Inzenjera i Tehnicara Jugoslavije** (Union of Engineers & Technicians of Yugoslavia)+
Kneza Milosa 9, 11000 Belgrade
*Tel:* (011) 3243653; (011) 3243652 *Fax:* (011) 3243652
*E-mail:* internet@eunet.yu *Cable:* SITJ BEOGRAD
*Key Personnel*
President: Mihailo Milojevic, PhD
Vice President: Budimir Cetkovic; Radomir Simic, PhD
General Secretary: Milorad Terzic, PhD
Founded: 1919
Membership(s): World Federation of Engineering Organizations; World Federation of Scientific Workers; Regional Council of Coordination of Central & East-European Engineering Organizations.
Subjects: Civil Engineering, Communications, Economics, Electronics, Electrical Engineering, Engineering (General), Mechanical Engineering, Science (General), Technology
ISBN Prefix(es): 86-80067

**Savremena Administracija**
Crnotravska 7-9, 11000 Belgrade
*Tel:* (011) 668567; (011) 661913; (011) 667436 *Fax:* (011) 667436
*Telex:* 12233 Yu Sa
*Key Personnel*
Dir: Vojin Moraca
Contact: Miroslav Spasojevic
Founded: 1954

Subjects: Economics, Law
ISBN Prefix(es): 86-387

**Sluzbeni List**
Jovana Ristica 1, 11000 Belgrade
*Tel:* (011) 3060333; (011) 3060310 *Fax:* (011) 3060393
*Telex:* 11756 Yu Slist
*Key Personnel*
Dir: Dusan Masovic
Contact: Blagoje Nikolic
Subjects: Law
ISBN Prefix(es): 86-355
*Bookshop(s):* Prodavnica 1, Brankova 16, Belgrade, Croatia; Prodavnica 2, 9 Novembra 1a

**Srpska Knjizevna Zadruga** (Serbian Literary Association)
Srpskih vladara 19/I, 11000 Belgrade
*Tel:* (011) 330 305 *Fax:* (011) 626-224
Founded: 1892
Subjects: History
ISBN Prefix(es): 86-379

**Svetovi** (The Worlds)+
Arse Teodorovica 11, 21000 Novi Sad
*Tel:* (021) 28032; (021) 28036 *Fax:* (021) 28036; (021) 28032
*E-mail:* aum.mar@eunet.yu
*Key Personnel*
Dir: Jovan Zivlak
Founded: 1951
Subjects: Anthropology, Art, Fiction, Philosophy, Poetry
ISBN Prefix(es): 86-7047
Number of titles published annually: 40 Print
Total Titles: 2,000 Print
*Bookshop(s):* Pasiceva 32, Novi Sad *Tel:* (021) 23-071

**Tehnika**, see Savez Inzenjera i Tehnicara Jugoslavije

**Turisticka Stampa+**
Dure Dakovica 100, 11000 Belgrade
*Tel:* (011) 750-740; (011) 759 076 *Fax:* (011) 762-236
*Key Personnel*
Man Dir & Editorial: Dragan Kankaras
Founded: 1953
Subjects: Art
ISBN Prefix(es): 86-7041

**Vesti**
Ljube Stojanovica 5, 31000 Uzice
*Tel:* (031) 513261; (031) 514263 *Fax:* (031) 511941
*E-mail:* redakcija@vesti.co.yu
*Web Site:* www.vesti.co.yu/onama.htm
*Key Personnel*
Dir: Zoran Lazic
ISBN Prefix(es): 86-7319

**VINC**, *imprint of* Vojnoizdavacki i novinski centar

**Vojnoizdavacki i novinski centar+**
Bircaninova 5, 11000 Belgrade
*Tel:* (011) 644 188; (011) 641 159 *Fax:* (011) 645 020
*Key Personnel*
President: Dr Nikola Popovic
Editor-in-Chief: Milisav Djordjevic
Editor, Foreign Writers' Edition: Novica Stevanovic
Founded: 1945
Subjects: Military Science
ISBN Prefix(es): 86-335; 86-80641

Imprints: VINC
*Bookshop(s):* Poslovni biro "Vojna Knjiga", Vase Carapica 22, 11000 Belgrade

**Vuk Karadzic+**
Bulevar Revolucije 77A, 11000 Belgrade
*Tel:* (011) 423-290; (011) 424-558; (011) 424-560 *Fax:* (011) 422-012 *Cable:* VUK KARADZIC BELGRADE
*Key Personnel*
Man Dir: Ancic Vojin
Founded: 1956
Subjects: Art, History, Philosophy, Psychology, Psychiatry, Science (General), Social Sciences, Sociology
ISBN Prefix(es): 86-307
*Branch Office(s)*
Dure Dakovica 5, Banja Luka *Tel:* (078) 60080
Bul 23, oktobra 35, Novi Sad *Tel:* (021) 611763
Francuska 10, Smederevska Palanka
Novosadska bb, Svetozarevo *Tel:* (035) 223313

**Zavod za Izdavanje Udzbenika**
Sremska 7, 21000 Novi Sad
*Tel:* (021) 22068 *Fax:* (021) 22069
*Key Personnel*
Man Dir: Vasilije Lalatovic
Contact: Slobodan Babic
Founded: 1965
Subjects: Education
ISBN Prefix(es): 86-413

**Zavod za udzbenike i nastavna sredstva** (Publishing House for Textbooks & Teaching Aids)
Obilicev venac 5, 11000 Belgrade
*Tel:* (011) 635-142; (011) 3051-900 (sales) *Fax:* (011) 2390-072 (sales)
*E-mail:* prodaja@zavod.co.yu (sales)
*Web Site:* www.zavod.co.yu
*Key Personnel*
Manager: Dr Rados Ljusic *Tel:* (011) 638-463 *E-mail:* direktor@zavod.co.yu
Founded: 1957
Subjects: Education
ISBN Prefix(es): 86-17
*Bookshop(s):* Kosovska 45, 11000 Belgrade; Vukasoviceva 50, 11090 Belgrade

# Sierra Leone

## General Information

*Capital:* Freetown
*Language:* English
*Religion:* Predominantly traditional beliefs, also some Islamic and Christian
*Population:* 4.5 million
*Bank Hours:* 0800-1330 Monday-Thursday; 0800-1400 Friday
*Shop Hours:* 0800-1300, 1400-1830 Monday-Saturday
*Currency:* 100 cents = 1 leone
*Export/Import Information:* No tariff on books except children's picture books and advertising matter. Open general license. Exchange controls.

**Macmillan Education**
34-36 Rawdon St, Private Mail Bag 904, Freetown
*Tel:* (022) 225683 *Fax:* (022) 229186
*E-mail:* macmillan@sierratel.sl
*Web Site:* www.macmillan-africa.com
*Key Personnel*
General Manager: Kai Fomba
*Parent Company:* Macmillan Publishers Ltd, United Kingdom

**Njala Educational Publishing Centre**
Njala University PMB, Freetown
*Tel:* (022) 228788
*E-mail:* nuc@sierratel.sl; nuclib@sierratel.sl
*Web Site:* www.nuc-online.com
*Key Personnel*
Principal: Prof A M Alghali

**United Christian Council Literature Bureau**
Bunumbu Press, Bo
Mailing Address: PO Box 28, Bo
*Tel:* 032462
*Key Personnel*
Man Dir: Joseph E Tucker

# Singapore

## General Information

*Capital:* Singapore
*Language:* Malay (national and official), also Chinese (Mandarin), Tamil and English (all official)
*Religion:* Daoism, Buddhist, Islamic, Christian, Hindu and Taoism
*Population:* 2.8 million
*Bank Hours:* 1000-1500 Monday-Friday; 930-1130 Saturday
*Shop Hours:* 0900-1800 Monday-Saturday
*Currency:* 100 cents = 1 Singapore dollar
*Export/Import Information:* No tariffs on books and advertising. Import licenses; no seditious publications permitted. Normal exchange control.
*Copyright:* Florence (see Copyright Conventions, pg xi)

**K C Ang Publishing Pte Ltd+**
Imprint of Bunny Books
93 Hitam Manis, Chip Bee Garden, Singapore 278503
*Tel:* 4741680 *Fax:* 2542002
*Key Personnel*
Man Dir: K C Ang
Founded: 1985
Specialize in children's books.
ISBN Prefix(es): 9971-974

**APA Production Pte Ltd+**
38 Joo Koon Rd, Singapore 628990
*Tel:* 8651600; 8651601 *Fax:* 8616438
*E-mail:* apasin@singnet.com.sg
*Telex:* RS 36201APASIN
*Key Personnel*
Man Dir: Hans Hoefer; Yinglock Chan
Founded: 1971
Subjects: Travel
ISBN Prefix(es): 9971-925; 9971-982; 981-234
*Parent Company:* Langenscheidt KG
*Associate Companies:* APA Publications (HK), Hong Kong
Imprints: Insight Guides; Insight Pocket Guides; Insight Topics
*U.S. Office(s):* Langenscheidt Publishers, Inc, 46-35 54 Rd, Maspeth, NY 11378, United States
Distributor for Langenscheidt (Asia)

**APAC Publishers Services Pte Ltd+**
05-03 Hiap Huat House, 70 Bedemeer Rd, Singapore 339940
*Tel:* 6844 7333 *Fax:* 6747 8916
*E-mail:* service@apacmedia.com.sg
*Key Personnel*
Man Dir: Steven Goh *E-mail:* sgohapac@singnet.com.sg
Founded: 1990

Subjects: Architecture & Interior Design, Business, Chemistry, Chemical Engineering, Civil Engineering, Computer Science, Economics, Engineering (General), Environmental Studies, Management, Medicine, Nursing, Dentistry, Science (General), Social Sciences, Sociology, Technology
ISBN Prefix(es): 981-3045
Total Titles: 6 Print
Distributor for American Medical Assn; American Society of Microbiology; Berg Publishers; Berghahn Publishers; Blackwell Publishing; CAB International; Columbia University Press; Haworth Press; Health Press; Hong Kong University Press; Humana Press; Industrial Press; Institute of Chemical Engineers; John Hopkins University Press; S Karger; Lippincott Williams & Wilkins; Marcel Decker; New York University Press; W W Norton; Quality Medical Publishing; Lynne Rienner Publishers; Royal Society of Chemistry; Schattauer; M E Sharpe; Springer Publishing; Teachers College Press; Thomas Telford; UNSW Press; Woodhead Publishing

**Aquanut Agencies Pte Ltd**
305 Clementi Avenue 4, No 08-427, Singapore S 120305
*Tel:* 7753614 *Fax:* 7753614
*E-mail:* aquanut@singnet.com.sg
*Web Site:* www.aquanut.com.sg
*Key Personnel*
Dir: Mr Leslie Lung
Founded: 1998
To carry on the business of publisher, book & print sellers. Also consultant for print, publishing & publicity.
Subjects: Asian Studies, Behavioral Sciences, How-to, Human Relations, Humor, Nonfiction (General), Self-Help, Social Sciences, Sociology
Number of titles published annually: 12 Print
Total Titles: 3 Print
Distributed by Horizon Books Pte Ltd

**Archipelago Press+**
26 Bukit Pasoh Rd, Singapore 089840
*Tel:* 2248044 *Fax:* 2247400
*E-mail:* edm@pacific.net.sg
*Key Personnel*
Chairman: Didier Millet
Man Dir: Charles Orwin
Editorial Dir: Timothy Auger
Founded: 1989
Subjects: Architecture & Interior Design, Art, Asian Studies, Cookery, Crafts, Games, Hobbies, History, Natural History, Photography, Travel
ISBN Prefix(es): 981-3018
Imprints: Archipelago Press, Les Editions du Pacifique

**Archipelago Press, Les Editions du Pacifique**, *imprint of* Archipelago Press

**Asiapac Books Pte Ltd+**
996 Bendemeer Rd, No 06-08, Singapore 339944
*Tel:* 63928455 *Fax:* 63926455
*E-mail:* asiapacbooks@pacific.net.sg
*Web Site:* www.asiapacbooks.com
*Key Personnel*
President: Chong Shin-Kian
Publisher: Lim Li-Kok
Publishing Dir: Lydia Lum
Founded: 1982
Membership(s): Singapore Book Publishers Association; specialize in publishing & distribution.
Subjects: Asian Studies, History, Humor, Philosophy
ISBN Prefix(es): 9971-985; 981-3029; 981-3068; 981-229
Number of titles published annually: 50 Print

Total Titles: 400 Print; 4 Audio
Distributed by Asia Books Co Ltd (Thailand); Caves Books Ltd (Taiwan); China Book Import Centre (China); China Books (Australia); China Books & Periodicals Inc (US); China National Publications (China); Eastwind Books & Arts Inc (US); Eastwind Books of Berkeley (US); Eslite Bookstore (Taiwan); Eslite Corporation (Taiwan); Goodwill Trading Co Inc (Philippines); Kinokuniya Bookstores of Taiwan Co Ltd (Taiwan); Kyobo Book Centre Co Ltd (Korea); Marketing Services for Publishers (Philippines); National Bookstore Inc (Philippines); Peace Books Company Ltd (Hong Kong); P T Gramedia Asri Media (Indonesia)
Distributor for China Books & Periodicals Inc (US); Chinese Literature Press (SE Asia); CNPIEC (China); Foreign Languages Press (China); Millbank Books Ltd (UK); National Textbook Co (USA); Oriental Publications (Australia); Penton Overseas, Inc (USA); Sterling Publishing Co, Inc (USA)

**Cannon International+**
Legal Deposit Section, Singapore Resource Library, National Library Board, Stamford Rd, Singapore 178896
*Tel:* 6546 7271 *Fax:* 6546 7262
*E-mail:* legaldep@nlb.gov.sq
*Web Site:* www.nlb.gov.sg
*Key Personnel*
Chief Executive, Rights & Permissions: Wu Cheng Tan
Sales: Amirudin Bin Marzuki
Publicity: Pearlyn Peh
Founded: 1975
Subjects: Education, Language Arts, Linguistics, Literature, Literary Criticism, Essays
ISBN Prefix(es): 9971-84; 9971-83; 981-00; 9971-941; 9971-943
Imprints: Kingsway Publishers
Subsidiaries: Kingsway Publisher
Distributor for Robert Gibson (Singapore)

**Marshall Cavendish Books**, *imprint of* Times Media Pte Ltd

**Marshall Cavendish Books**
One New Industrial Rd, Singapore 536196
*Tel:* (065) 2848844 *Fax:* (065) 2854871
*E-mail:* te@corp.tpl.com.sg
*Web Site:* www.timesone.com.sg/te
*Parent Company:* Times Publishing Ltd

**Marshall Cavendish Continuity Sets**, *imprint of* Times Media Pte Ltd

**Celebrity Educational Publishers**
Block 474 Tampines St 43, No 01-108, Singapore 520474
*Tel:* 6785 7274 *Fax:* 6748 9108
*Key Personnel*
Man Dir, Editorial: Christopher S C Tan
Sales: Henry K H Ng
Production, Publicity: Lily Tay
Founded: 1983
Subjects: Language Arts, Linguistics, Science (General)
ISBN Prefix(es): 981-201
Subsidiaries: Willet Children's Books Australia

**China Knowledge Press+**
2 Tan Quee Lan St, 05 01 Primero Place, Singapore 188091
*Tel:* 6310 8737 *Fax:* 6310 8738
*E-mail:* info@chinaknowledge-press.com
*Web Site:* www.chinaknowledge-press.com
*Key Personnel*
Contact: Sharon Tang *E-mail:* sharon@chinaknowledge-press.com
Founded: 2000

Provides independent insight, analysis & information to foreign investors to help them explore opportunities & determine values in the China market.

Specializes in translation projects, investment & consultancy services for the China market.

Subjects: Business

ISBN Prefix(es): 981-04

Number of titles published annually: 6 Print

Total Titles: 3 Print; 2 Online

*Branch Office(s)*

20 Millstream Close, Hitchin, Herts SG4 0D4, United Kingdom, Contact: Ms Weai-Hunt Yap *Tel:* (0146) 442230 *E-mail:* ywhunt@ chinaknowledge.com

**Chopsons Pte Ltd+**
Siglap PO Box 264, Singapore 914503
*Tel:* 64483634 *Fax:* 64481071
*E-mail:* chopsons@singnet.com.sg
*Key Personnel*
Man Dir: Mr N T S Chopra
Founded: 1969
Supplies publications from Southeast Asia to the libraries all over the world - monographs & journals/serials
Also acts as Literary Agent.
Subjects: Asian Studies, Education, Fiction, Government, Political Science, Poetry, Religion - Other, Science (General), Social Sciences, Sociology
ISBN Prefix(es): 9971-68
Distributor for Centre for Advanced Studies; Institute of Southeast Asian Studies; Singapore University Press; Sociology Department, National University of Singapore; World Scientific Publishing

**Daiichi Media Pte Ltd**
21 Kim Keat Rd, No 04-01, Singapore 328805
*Tel:* 6849 8666 *Fax:* 6256 5922
*E-mail:* info@daiichimedia.com.sg; sales@ daiichimedia.com.sg
*Web Site:* www.daiichimedia.com
*Key Personnel*
Business Development Manager: Edward Poon *E-mail:* edward@daiichimedia.com
Founded: 1993
Subjects: Art, Geography, Geology, Health, Nutrition, History, Mathematics, Science (General)
Total Titles: 15 CD-ROM

**Earlybird Books**, *imprint of* Federal Publications (S) Pte Ltd

**les editions du Pacifique**, *imprint of* Times Media Pte Ltd

**EPB**, *imprint of* SNP Panpac Pacific Publishing Pte Ltd

**EPB Publishers Pte Ltd+**
Block 162, Bukit Merah Central, 04-3545, Singapore 150162
*Tel:* 278 0881 *Fax:* 278 2456
*E-mail:* epb@sbg.com.sg
*Telex:* EPB RS 56289 *Cable:* EDUPUBS
*Key Personnel*
General Manager: Au Pui Chuan
Marketing: Kenny Koh
Production: Steven Tan
Founded: 1967
Membership(s): Singapore Book Publishers' Association.
Subjects: Education
ISBN Prefix(es): 9971-0
*Parent Company:* Singapore National Printers Ltd, 303 Upper Serangoon Rd, Singapore 1334
*Bookshop(s):* EPB Bedok, North Street 1, 01-423 1646 *Tel:* 4437980; EPB Bukit Batok, 376 Bukit Batok St 31, 01-110

650376 *Tel:* 5624023; EPB Bukit Merah, 161 Bukit Merah Central, 01-3719 150161 *Tel:* 2730092; EPB Clementi Ave 3, 01-297 0512 *Tel:* 7770052; EPB Clementi West, 725 Clementi West St 2, 01-206 0521 *Tel:* 7788923; EPB Jurong West St 51, 01-213 2264 *Tel:* 5624106; 20 Outram Park, 02-187/213 0316 *Tel:* 2202377; EPB Tampine, 138 Tampines St 11, 01-132 1852 *Tel:* 7831939
*Warehouse:* PSA Multi Storey Complex, Blk 22 Pasir Pahjang Rd, No 06-29 Singapore

**Europhone Language Institute (Pte) Ltd+**
3 Coleman St No 04-33, Singapore 179803
*Tel:* 3373617; 3363992 *Fax:* 3374506 *Cable:* LANGUAGE SINGAPORE
*Key Personnel*
Chief Executive: K P Sivam
Founded: 1970
ISBN Prefix(es): 981-3019; 9971-9910; 9971-9912
*Branch Office(s)*
122 Campbell Complex, Kuala Lumpur, Malaysia

**Federal Publications (S) Pte Ltd+**
Times Centre, One New Industrial Rd, Singapore 536196
*Tel:* 62139288 *Fax:* 62844733
*E-mail:* tpl@tpl.com.sg
*Web Site:* www.tpl.com.sg
*Telex:* 35846 *Cable:* FEDPUBS, SINGAPORE
*Key Personnel*
General Manager: June Oei *E-mail:* juneoei@tpl. com.sg
Publisher & Editorial Manager: Joy Tan
Sales Manager: Marina Ooi
Founded: 1957
Subjects: Education
ISBN Prefix(es): 981-01; 9971-4
*Parent Company:* Times Publishing Ltd, Times Centre, One New Industrial Rd 536196
*Associate Companies:* Federal Publications (HK) Ltd, Hong Kong; Federal Publications Sdn Bhd, Malaysia
Imprints: Earlybird Books; Times Academic Press
Distributor for Chambers Harrap Publishers Ltd

**FEP International Pvt Ltd**
108 Pasir Panjand Rd, No 05-01A, Singapore 118535
*Tel:* 4743135 *Fax:* 4752389
*Telex:* Fep rs 25601 *Cable:* Bookmark
*Key Personnel*
Publishing Manager, Rights & Permissions: Wong Sek Ohn
Publishing, Science & Math: Dr S Ramalingam
Publishing, Language & Arts: Ms Goh Bee Choo
Founded: 1960
Firm is also a large offset printer specializing in color work.
ISBN Prefix(es): 9971-1
*Branch Office(s)*
Australia
Egypt (Arab Republic of Egypt)
Ghana
Hong Kong
India
Jamaica
Kenya
Lesotho
Malaysia
Nigeria
Pakistan
Philippines
Swaziland
Trinidad & Tobago
United Kingdom
Zimbabwe

**Global Educational Services Pte Ltd+**
4 Jalan Mata Ayer, Irving Industrial Bldg, Singapore 759147

Mailing Address: Blk 844 Sims Ave, No 01-706, Singapore 400844
*Tel:* 7585086 *Fax:* 7586172
*E-mail:* global@signet.com.sg
*Key Personnel*
Man Dir: Yoke Yin Ong
Founded: 1986
Joint projects with education institutions in design & publishing of educational materials; exclusive distributor for National University of Singapore on a series of operations research/management software for universities & management programs.
Specialize in pre-school books design, education software, OEM publishing projects, operations research software.
Subjects: Language Arts, Linguistics, Mathematics, Science (General)
ISBN Prefix(es): 981-3006; 981-3032; 981-3059; 981-3098; 981-4106
*Associate Companies:* Global Educational Services Sdn Bhd, Malaysia
Subsidiaries: Global Educational Services Inc
*Orders to:* 222 Fourteenth St, Unit 5, Charlottesville, VA 22903, United States *Fax:* 434-979-0823

**Gordon & Breach**, *imprint of* International Publishers Distributor (S) Pte Ltd

**Graham Brash Pte Ltd**
Block 1, Level 2, 45 Kian Teck Dr, Singapore 628859
Mailing Address: Jurong Point Post Office, PO Box 884, Singapore 916430
*Tel:* 6262 4843 *Fax:* 6262 1519
*E-mail:* graham_brash@giro.com.sg
*Web Site:* www.grahambrash.com.sg
*Telex:* rs 23718 Feenix GB
*Key Personnel*
Chief Executive Officer: Chuan Campbell
Dir: Helene Campbell
General Manager: Evelyn Lee
Founded: 1926
Subjects: Business, Education, Ethnicity, Government, Political Science, Religion - Other, Self-Help
ISBN Prefix(es): 9971-947; 981-218; 9971-9901; 981-4115
Distributed by Asia Books Co Ltd (Taiwan); Bookazine (Thailand); Booker International (Brunei); Bookmark Inc (Philippines); Caves Books Ltd (Taiwan); China Books (Australia); The Commercial Press (HK) Ltd (Hong Kong); Dymocks Franchise Systems (Singapore); Far East Media (HK) Ltd (Singapore); Gazelle Book Services Ltd (UK); Goodwill Trading Co Inc (Philippines); Heian International Inc (US); Hong Kong Book Centre (Singapore); Hushion House (Canada); Java Books (Indonesia); Kelly & Walsh Ltd (Singapore); National Book Store Inc (Philippines); PageOne The Bookshop (Hong Kong & Philippines); Pansing Distribution Sdn Bhd (Singapore); Peace Book Co Ltd (Singapore); Editions le Printemps Ltd (Mauritius); SAP Group (Indonesia); W H Smith (Singapore); Swindon Book Co (Hong Kong); Times/Federal Publication (Singapore)

**Harwood Academic Publishers**, *imprint of* International Publishers Distributor (S) Pte Ltd

**Hillview Publications Pte Ltd+**
Blk 231 Bain St No 04-59, Bras Basah Complex, Singapore 3348996
*Tel:* 334 8996 *Fax:* 334 8997
*Key Personnel*
Man Dir: L M Ng
Contact: Ms Ng Lai Mien
Founded: 1984
Membership(s): Spore Book Publishers Association.

Subjects: Accounting, Economics, Education, English as a Second Language, Geography, Geology, Mathematics, Physics, Social Sciences, Sociology
ISBN Prefix(es): 981-202; 981-3052; 981-4013; 981-4041; 981-4073; 981-4099

**Insight Guides**, *imprint of* APA Production Pte Ltd

**Insight Pocket Guides**, *imprint of* APA Production Pte Ltd

**Insight Topics**, *imprint of* APA Production Pte Ltd

**Institute of Southeast Asian Studies+**
30 Heng Mui Keng Terrace, Pasir Panjang, Singapore 119614
*Tel:* 6778 0955 *Fax:* 6775 6259
*E-mail:* pubsunit@iseas.edu.sg
*Web Site:* bookshop.iseas.edu.sg
*Key Personnel*
Dir: K Kesavapany *Tel:* 6870 2405
Man Editor: Triena Ong *Tel:* 6870 2448
    *E-mail:* triena@iseas.edu.sg
Book Promotions & Secretary: Celina Kiong
    *E-mail:* celina@iseas.edu.sg
Founded: 1968
Scholarly publishers
Conduct post-doctoral research on politics, economics & social issues pertaining to the Asia-Pacific.
Subjects: Asian Studies, Economics, Energy, Environmental Studies, Finance, Foreign Countries, Government, Political Science, Social Sciences, Sociology
ISBN Prefix(es): 9971-902; 981-3035; 981-230
Number of titles published annually: 40 Print; 40 Online; 40 E-Book
Total Titles: 1,000 Print; 1 CD-ROM; 27 Online; 890 E-Book
Imprints: ISEAS
Distributed by Asia Books; James Bennett Library Services; Eurospan; Taylor & Francis Asia Pacific; United Publishers Services Ltd

**Intellectual Publishing Co**
113 Eunos Ave 3 04-08, Gordon Industrial Bldg, Singapore 409838
*Tel:* 7466025 *Fax:* 7489108
*Telex:* RS 55708 Ipccp *Cable:* IPC INTELLE
*Key Personnel*
Manager: B C Poh
Editorial, Rights & Permissions: B L Poh
Sales, Publicity: B S Poh
Founded: 1971
Subjects: Language Arts, Linguistics
ISBN Prefix(es): 9971-907; 9971-960; 981-200
*Associate Companies:* Intellectual Publishing Sdn Bhd, 29A 1st floor, Jalan Selimang, Taman Tenaga, Cheras 3 1/2 ms, Kuala Lumpur, Malaysia
Subsidiaries: Intellectual Publishing Co Ltd

**International Publishers Distributor (S) Pte Ltd+**
Kent Ridge, Singapore 911106
Mailing Address: PO Box 1180, 911106 Singapore
*Tel:* 741 6933 *Fax:* 741 6922
*E-mail:* ipdmktg@sg.gbhap.com
*Key Personnel*
Man Dir: K C Ang *E-mail:* kcang@singnet.com
Founded: 1989
Subjects: Art, STM
Total Titles: 3,000 Print
*Parent Company:* Gordon & Breach Publishing Group

Imprints: Gordon & Breach; Harwood Academic Publishers
*U.S. Office(s):* PO Box 20029, River Front Plaza Station, Newark, NJ 07102-0301, United States

**IPD**, see International Publishers Distributor (S) Pte Ltd

**ISEAS**, *imprint of* Institute of Southeast Asian Studies

**Kingsway Publishers**, *imprint of* Cannon International

**LexisNexis**
3 Killiney Rd, No 08-08 Winsland House One, Singapore 239519
*Tel:* 6733 1380 *Fax:* 6773 1719
*Web Site:* www.lexisnexis.com.sg
*Key Personnel*
Man Dir: Michael Evans *Tel:* 6434 3800
    *Fax:* 6339 0163
Regional Publishing Dir: Conita Leung *Tel:* 6434 3830
Publishing Manager: Balasakher Shunmugam
    *Tel:* 6434 3838
Man Editor: Zabrina Hamid *Tel:* 6434 3841; Andrew Yeoh *Tel:* 6434 3842
Senior Editor: Sharon Kaur *Tel:* 6434 3847; Yee See Mun *Tel:* 6434 3809
Regional Sales Dir: Bryan Barrington *Tel:* 6434 3850
Founded: 1982
Subjects: Law
*Parent Company:* Reed Elsevier
*Associate Companies:* 12/F, Hennessy Centre, 500 Hennessy Rd, Causeway Bay, Hong Kong, Business Development Manager: Anisha Sakhrani *Tel:* 2965 1400 *Fax:* 2976 0840 *Web Site:* www.lexisnexis.com.hk; Vijaya Bldg, 14th floor, 17, Barakhamba Rd, New Delhi 110001, India, Publishing Manager: Ambika Nair *Tel:* (011) 373 9614 *Fax:* (011) 332 6456 *Web Site:* www.lexisnexis.co.in; Malayan Law Journal Sdn Bhd, Wisma HB, Unit A-5-1, 5th floor, Megan Phileo Ave, 12 Jalan Yap Kwan Seng, 50450 Kuala Lumpur, Malaysia, Managing Editor, New Business Development: Julie Anne Thomas *Tel:* (03) 2162 2833 *Fax:* (03) 2162 3811 *Web Site:* www.mjl.com.my

**Maruzen Asia (Pte) Ltd**
391A Orchard Rd No 04-08, Singapore 238872
*Tel:* 7751577 *Fax:* 7351678
*Telex:* Mapore rs 26521 *Cable:* Maruzen Singapore
*Key Personnel*
Dir: Tadao Nireki
Man Dir, Editorial: Yuki Hatori
Marketing: David Tan
Founded: 1689
Subjects: Asian Studies, Medicine, Nursing, Dentistry, Social Sciences, Sociology, Technology
ISBN Prefix(es): 9971-954
*Parent Company:* Maruzen Co Ltd, Japan
*Associate Companies:* Maruzen International Co Ltd, NY, United States

**Masagung Books Pte Ltd**
41 Sixth Ave, Off Bukit Timah Rd, Singapore 276483
*Tel:* 4683276 *Fax:* 345000
*Telex:* rs 34500 A; B Gasing *Cable:* Gasing Singapore
*Key Personnel*
Chairman: Haji Masagung
Manager: Tan Tho Quek
Founded: 1980
Subjects: Foreign Countries
ISBN Prefix(es): 9971-927
*Parent Company:* CV Haji Masagung, Indonesia

**McGallen & Bolden Associates+**
Subsidiary of McGallen & Bolden PR Corporation
20 Maxwell Rd, No 04-01F, Suite F, Maxwell House, Singapore 069113
*Tel:* 63246588 *Fax:* 63246966
*E-mail:* sales@mcgallen.com
*Web Site:* www.mcgallen.net
*Key Personnel*
Agent & Publicist: Ms Hui Peng Ter
    *Tel:* 63246588 *Fax:* 63246966 *E-mail:* sales@mcgallen.com
Founded: 1991
Subjects: Advertising, Art, Biography, Biological Sciences, Business, Chemistry, Chemical Engineering, Child Care & Development, Communications, Computer Science, Economics, Education, Fiction, Geography, Geology, History, Language Arts, Linguistics, Medicine, Nursing, Dentistry, Philosophy, Psychology, Psychiatry, Religion - Other, Social Sciences, Sociology
Number of titles published annually: 2 Print; 2 CD-ROM; 10 Online; 2 Audio
Total Titles: 10 Print; 6 CD-ROM; 13 Online; 5 Audio
*U.S. Office(s):* McGallen & Bolden PR Corp, 1901 60th Place, Suite L1029, Bradenton, FL 34203-5076, United States, Editor: Dr Seamus Phan *E-mail:* sales@mcgallen.com

**McGraw-Hill Asia/India Group**
Division of The McGraw-Hill Companies
60 Tuas Basin Link, Jurong 638775
*Tel:* 6863-1580 *Fax:* 6861-9296
*E-mail:* mghasia@mcgraw-hill.com.sg
*Web Site:* www.asia-mcgraw-hill.com.sg
*Key Personnel*
Group Vice President & Man Dir Asian Group: Gunawan Hadi *E-mail:* gunawan_hadi@mcgraw-hill.com
Regional offices in Singapore, Hong Kong, Taiwan, Korea, Malaysia, Thailand, India, Philippines, Japan, China.

**Newscom Pte Ltd+**
Blk 105, Boon Keng Rd, No 04-17, Singapore 339776
*Tel:* 6291 9861 *Fax:* 6293 1445
*E-mail:* circulation@newscom-mail.com
*Web Site:* www.newscomonline.com
*Key Personnel*
Chairman: Austin Morais
Circulation Manager: Dinesh Charles
    *E-mail:* dineshcharles@newscom-mail.com
Founded: 1987
Acts as media representative.
Membership(s): the BPA & ABC (UK).
Subjects: Publishing & Book Trade Reference, Technology
*Parent Company:* NewSources Investments Ltd, Unit B, 19th floor, 133 Wanchai Rd, Wanchai, Hong Kong
*Associate Companies:* Newsteam SDN BHD, 87-89 Jalan Ipoh, 3rd floor, 51200 Kuala Lumpur, Malaysia *Tel:* (03) 4044-8599 *Fax:* (03) 4044-9599

**Pan Pacific Publications (S) Pte Ltd+**
16 Fan Yoong Rd, Singapore 629793
*Tel:* 2616288 *Fax:* 2616088
*E-mail:* ppps@pacific.net.sg
*Telex:* 36496
*Key Personnel*
Chairman: Steve Seow Kui Lim
General Manager: Catherine Ngien
Man Editor: Margaret Tan
Operations Manager: Brenda Goh
Founded: 1971
Membership(s): Publishers' Association (Singapore).
Subjects: Education
ISBN Prefix(es): 981-208; 9971-63
*Parent Company:* Pan Pacific Public Co Ltd

*Associate Companies:* Eastview Publications Sdn
Bhd, Malaysia
Subsidiaries: Manhattan Press (HK) Ltd; Manhattan Press (S) Pte Ltd

**Panpac,** *imprint of* SNP Panpac Pacific
Publishing Pte Ltd

**Pearson Education Asia Pte Ltd**
23/25 First Lok Yang Rd, Jurong 629734
*Tel:* 3199388 *Fax:* 3199175
*E-mail:* asia@pearsoned.com.sg
*Web Site:* www.pearsoned-asia.com
*Key Personnel*
Publishing Manager, Higher Education: Yew Kee
Chiang
Dir, Singapore Education: Andrew Yeo
Founded: 1998
Subjects: Education
ISBN Prefix(es): 981-247; 981-4063; 981-4069;
981-4075; 981-4079; 981-4080; 981-4083; 981-
4085; 981-4087; 981-4088; 981-4093; 981-
4096; 981-4098; 981-4105; 981-4110; 981-
4114; 981-4119
*Parent Company:* Pearson Education, One Lake
St, Upper Saddle River, NJ 07458, United
States

**PG Medical Books+**
6A Napier Rd, Gleneagles Annexe, Block No 02-
38 Gleneagles Hospital, Singapore 258500
*Tel:* 4726339 *Fax:* 4728279
*Telex:* rs 39967 *Cable:* PG PUB
*Key Personnel*
Chief Executive, Rights & Permissions: Ms
Chiam Soo Lee
Editorial & Production: Mrs Sook-Cheng Lim
International Marketing: Lew Kok Liat
Production: Mary Cho
Founded: 1982
Subjects: Medicine, Nursing, Dentistry
ISBN Prefix(es): 9971-909; 9971-973; 981-3096;
981-206
*Bookshop(s):* PG Lucky Plaza Medical Books

**Printworld Services Pte Ltd**
80 Genting Lane Na 09-07, Genting Blk, Ruby
Industrial Complex, Singapore 349565
*Tel:* 7442166 *Fax:* 7460845
*E-mail:* printw@mbox2.singnet.com.sg
*Telex:* 28990 (print)
*Key Personnel*
Man Dir: N T Nair
ISBN Prefix(es): 981-3093

**Pustaka Nasional Pte Ltd**
Joo Chiat Complex, Blk 2 Joo Chiat Rd No 05-
1125, Singapore 420002
*Tel:* 67454321; 67454649 *Fax:* 67452417
*E-mail:* sales@pustaka.com.sg; mohamed@
pustaka.com.sg
*Web Site:* www.pustaka.com.sg
*Telex:* rs 26746 Smcc Pn *Cable:* HUDAYA
*Key Personnel*
Manager: Mr Syed Ali Bin Syed Zain
Founded: 1965
Subjects: Foreign Countries, Religion - Islamic
ISBN Prefix(es): 9971-77
*Associate Companies:* Pustaka Islamiyah SDN
BHD
Distributor for Dewan Bahasa Dan Pustaka
(Malaysia)
*Showroom(s):* Blk 1, Jalan Pasar Baru, No 01-41,
Singapore 402001

**Reed Elsevier, South East Asia+**
51 Changi Business Park, Central 2, No 07-01,
The Signature, Singapore 486066
*Tel:* 6789 9900 *Fax:* 6789 9966
*Web Site:* www.reed-elsevier.com

*Key Personnel*
Executive Dir: Paul Beh
Founded: 1986
Membership(s): Singapore Book Publishers Association & Afro Asian Book Council.
Subjects: Biological Sciences, Chemistry, Chemical Engineering, Electronics, Electrical Engineering, Law, Physical Sciences, Physics,
Science (General), Social Sciences, Sociology,
Technology, Travel
ISBN Prefix(es): 9971-64
*Parent Company:* Reed Elsevier plc, 25 Victoria
St, London SW1H 0EX, United Kingdom

**Ridge Books,** *imprint of* Singapore University
Press Pte Ltd

**Select Publishing Pte Ltd+**
19 Tanglin Rd No 03-15, Tanglin Shopping Centre, Singapore 247909
*Tel:* 6732 1515 *Fax:* 6736 0855
*E-mail:* info@selectbooks.com.sg
*Web Site:* www.selectbooks.com.sg
*Key Personnel*
Man Dir: Lena U Wen Lim
Founded: 2000
Specialize in books on Southeast Asia.
Membership(s): Publishers Association (Singapore).
Subjects: Alternative, Architecture & Interior Design, Art, Asian Studies, Developing Countries,
Drama, Theater, Fiction
ISBN Prefix(es): 981-4022
Total Titles: 30 Print
Distributed by Asia Books (Thailand)

**The Shanghai Book Co (Pte) Ltd**
81 Victoria St, Singapore 188013
*Tel:* 336 0144 *Fax:* 336 0490
*E-mail:* shanghaibooks@sbg.com.sg
*Key Personnel*
Man Dir: Mong Hock Chen
*E-mail:* chenmonghock@pacific.net.sg
Founded: 1925
ISBN Prefix(es): 9971-906
*Associate Companies:* Shanghai Book Co (KL)
SDN BHD, No 63C Jalan Sultan, 50000 Kuala
Lumpur, Malaysia *Tel:* (03) 2384642 *Fax:* (03)
2320700

**Shing Lee Group Publishers+**
120 Hillview Ave 05-06/07, Kewalran Hillview,
Singapore 669594
*Tel:* 7601388 *Fax:* 7651506
*E-mail:* kongjing@shinglee.com.sg
*Telex:* rs 39255 Bai *Cable:* SHINGBOOK
*Key Personnel*
Marketing Dir: Mr Peh Chin Thye
Executive Dir: Soh-Ngoh Peh
Founded: 1985
Subjects: Cookery
ISBN Prefix(es): 9971-61
Subsidiaries: Booktree; Concorde Publishers
Pte Ltd; Dragon Investment PL; Dragon Link
Granite PL; First Dragon Development PL;
Second Dragon Development PL; Shing Lee
Bookstore Pte Ltd; Shing Lee Investment Pte
Ltd; Shing Lee Publishers Pte Ltd; Shing Lee
Realty Pte Ltd; Super Food Investment International PL; Tech Media; Third Dragon Development PL; Third Dragon Holdings PL; Qingdao
Huashan International Country Club

**Singapore University Press,** *imprint of*
Singapore University Press Pte Ltd

**Singapore University Press Pte Ltd**
National University of Singapore, AS3-01-02. 3,
Arts Link, Singapore 117569
*Tel:* 67761148; 68742382 *Fax:* 67740652
*E-mail:* nusbooks@nus.edu.sg

*Web Site:* www.nus.edu.sg/npu
*Telex:* rs 51112 NUSBUR *Cable:* SINGPRESS
*Key Personnel*
Man Dir: Peter Schoppert
*E-mail:* peter_schoppert@nus.edu.sg
Founded: 1971
Publishing house of the National University of
Singapore.
Specialize in Southeast Asian & Asia-Pacific titles (scholarly & academic).
Membership(s): IASP; Singapore Book Publishers
Association (SBPA).
Subjects: Asian Studies, Economics, Environmental Studies, Finance, Government, Political Science, History, Language Arts, Linguistics, Law,
Literature, Literary Criticism, Essays, Management, Maritime, Psychology, Psychiatry,
Science (General), Social Sciences, Sociology,
Architecture, Medicine
ISBN Prefix(es): 9971-69
Number of titles published annually: 30 Print
Total Titles: 1 CD-ROM; 1 Online
*Ultimate Parent Company:* National University of
Singapore
Imprints: Ridge Books; Singapore University
Press
Distributed by APD Singapore Pte Ltd (Southeast
Asia only)
Foreign Rep(s): Europsan Ltd (Africa, Europe,
Middle East); UNIREPS (Australia, New
Zealand); United Publishers Services (Japan);
University of Hawaii Press (Latin America,
North America, South America)
Foreign Rights: B K Norton (China, Korea, Taiwan)

**SNP Panpac Pacific Publishing Pte Ltd+**
Jurong Bldg, No 04-00 CPF, 21 Jurong East St,
13, Singapore 609646
*Tel:* 6261 6288 *Fax:* 6261 6088
*Web Site:* www.snp.com/sg
*Key Personnel*
General Manager: Rick Ang *E-mail:* rickang@
snp.com.sg
Publisher & Sales: Lim Geok Leng
Sales & Marketing Manager: Kelvyn Chong
Customer Service Manager: Agnes Sim Hwee Bin
Man Editor: Zuraidah Jaffar
Subjects: Education
ISBN Prefix(es): 981-3001; 981-208
*Associate Companies:* SNP Eastview Publications
Sdn Bhd, Lot 3, Jalan Saham, 23/3, Kawasan
MIEL, Phase 8, 40675 Shah Alam, Selangor Darul Ehsan, Malaysia *Tel:* 5548 1088
*Fax:* 5548 1080 *E-mail:* yhchia@snpo.com.
my; SNP Manhattan Press (Hong Kong) Ltd,
Eastern Sea Industrial Bldg, 48-56 Tai Lin
Pai Rd, Kwai Chung, Hong Kong *Tel:* 2481
1930 *Fax:* 2481 3379 *E-mail:* shumjeff@
manhattanpress.com.hk
Imprints: EPB; Panpac
*Bookshop(s):* SNP Bookstores Pte Limited, Suntec City Mall, 3 Temasek Blvd, B1-025, Singapore 038983 *Tel:* 6 333 5976 *Fax:* 6 333 9236
*E-mail:* ashleyb@snp.com.sg

**Stamford College
Publishers/Authors-Publishers+**
Legal Deposit Section, Singapore Resource Library, National Library Board, Stamford Rd,
Singapore 178896
*Tel:* 65467271 *Fax:* 65467262
*E-mail:* legaldep@nlb.gov.sq.hdtsdnl@technet.sq
*Web Site:* www.nlb.gov.sg
*Key Personnel*
Man Dir, Publicity: L P Nicol
Editorial: L Thomas
Sales: J Dennis
Production: Mr Arangasamy
Founded: 1970

Subjects: Education
*Branch Office(s)*
Stamford Executive Bookshop, Petaling Jaya,
Malaysia

**Success Publications Pte Ltd+**
Blk 3013 Bedok Industrial Park E, No 04-2102,
Bedok North Av 4, Singapore 489979
*Tel:* 4432003; 4430512 *Fax:* 4453156
*E-mail:* succpub@signet.com.sg
Distributing, importing, exporting & publishing
of educational books & materials; reading pro-
gram; assessment books; Chinese.
Subjects: Education, English as a Second Lan-
guage, Mathematics, Science (General)
ISBN Prefix(es): 981-216; 981-3017; 981-3088;
981-4030; 981-4117; 981-4124; 981-4135
Subsidiaries: Steven Tuition Centre
*Orders to:* Rest of the World, Bowker-Saur Ltd,
Windsor Court, E Grinstead House, E Grin-
stead, West Sussex RH19 1XA, United King-
dom *Tel:* (01342) 326972 *Fax:* (01342) 336198

**Taylor & Francis Asia Pacific+**
Member of Taylor & Francis Group
240 Macpherson Rd, No 08-01 Pines Industrial
Bldg, Singapore 348574
*Tel:* 67415166 *Fax:* 67429356
*E-mail:* info@tandf.com.sg
*Web Site:* www.tandf.co.uk
*Key Personnel*
Man Dir: Barry D Clarke *E-mail:* barry.clarke@
tandf.com.sg
Founded: 1998
Subjects: Architecture & Interior Design, Art,
Asian Studies, Biological Sciences, Business,
Child Care & Development, Criminology, Eco-
nomics, Education, Engineering (General), En-
vironmental Studies, Ethnicity, Government,
Political Science, History, Library & Informa-
tion Sciences, Management, Medicine, Nursing,
Dentistry, Philosophy, Physical Sciences, Psy-
chology, Psychiatry, Religion - Other, Science
(General), Social Sciences, Sociology, Spe-
cialize in book distribution, publisher services,
confrences & author support
Distributor for American Psychological Associa-
tion (USA); Aslib (UK); Brookings Institution
(USA); Earthscan (UK); Edinburgh University
Press (UK); Edward Elgar (UK); Lawrence Erl-
baum & Associates (USA); Free Press (USA);
David Fulton (UK); Guilford Press (USA); Idea
Group (UK); Information Age (USA); Insti-
tute International Economics (USA); Library
Association (UK); Pluto Press (UK); Transac-
tion Publishers (USA); Westview Press (USA);
World Bank (USA)

**Tech Publications Pte Ltd+**
No B1-39 Sim Lim Tower, 10 Jalan Besar, Singa-
pore 0820
*Tel:* 7449113; 7428782 *Fax:* 7449835
*E-mail:* techpub@pacific.net.sg
*Telex:* 7449835
*Key Personnel*
President: Gyan Jain
Vice President & Marketing Manager: Rajiv Jain
Founded: 1984
Subjects: Computer Science, Electronics, Electri-
cal Engineering
ISBN Prefix(es): 981-214; 981-3005; 981-3091
*Associate Companies:* Micro Tech Publications,
Dubai, United Arab Emirates
*Bookshop(s):* 04-35 Funan Centre 179097
*Warehouse:* 211 Henderson Rd, Henderson Bldg
No 02-11 159552

**Tecman**, *imprint of* Tecman Bible House

**Tecman Bible House+**
No 04-47 Bras Basah Complex, 231 Bain St, Singapore 180231

*Tel:* 6338-6764 *Fax:* 6338-8236
*E-mail:* tecman@tecman.com.sg
*Web Site:* www.tecman.com.sg
*Key Personnel*
President: Jane Tan
Founded: 1971
Import, export, retail & wholesale of Christian
publications & products.
Subjects: Biblical Studies, Religion - Protestant,
Theology
Imprints: Tecman

**Times Academic Press**, *imprint of* Federal
Publications (S) Pte Ltd

**Times Books International**, *imprint of* Times
Media Pte Ltd

**Times Editions**, *imprint of* Times Media Pte Ltd

**Times Media Pte Ltd+**
Times Centre, One New Industrial Rd, Singapore
536196
*Tel:* 62848844 *Fax:* 62771186
*E-mail:* tedcsd@tpl.com.sg
*Web Site:* www.timesone.com.sg/te
*Telex:* RS25713 *Cable:* TIMES
*Key Personnel*
Deputy Publisher: David Yip *E-mail:* davidyip@
tpl.com.sg
International Sales & Rights: Angeline Lim
*Tel:* 62139404 *E-mail:* angelinelim@tpl.com.sg
Founded: 1979
Subjects: Art, Cookery, Gardening, Plants, Gov-
ernment, Political Science, Health, Nutrition,
Literature, Literary Criticism, Essays, Travel,
Culture, Heritage, International Interests, Par-
enting
ISBN Prefix(es): 981-204; 2-85700; 981-232
*Parent Company:* Times Publishing Group, One
New Industrial Rd 536196
*Associate Companies:* Marshall Cavendish Books
Ltd
Imprints: Marshall Cavendish Books; Marshall
Cavendish Continuity Sets; les editions du
Pacifique; Times Books International; Times
Editions
*Branch Office(s)*
Bangunan Times Publishing, Lot 46, Subang In-
dustrial Park, Bahu riga, 60000 Shah Alam,
Malaysia, Contact: Christine Chong *Fax:* (03)
7354620
Times Books International, Malaysia

**John Wiley & Sons (Asia) Pte Ltd+**
2 Clementi Loop, No 02-01, Singapore 129809
*Tel:* 64632400 *Fax:* 64634605; 64634604
*E-mail:* enquiry@wiley.com.sg
*Web Site:* www.wiley.co.uk
*Key Personnel*
Vice President, Asia: Steven Miron
Publisher: Nick Wallwork
Foreign Rights Executive: Ira Tan
Number of titles published annually: 20 Print
*Parent Company:* John Wiley & Sons Inc, 111
River St, Hoboken, NJ 07030, United States
*Associate Companies:* John Wiley & Sons, Ltd,
United Kingdom; Jacaranda Wiley, Ltd, Aus-
tralia

**World Scientific Publishing Co Pte Ltd+**
5 Toh Tuck Link, Singapore 596224
*Tel:* 6467-5775 *Fax:* 6467-7667
*E-mail:* wspc@wspc.com.sg
*Web Site:* www.worldscientific.com
*Key Personnel*
Man Dir: Doreen Liu
Dir & Publisher: Mrs Sook Cheng Lim
Assistant Dir: Miss G K Tan
Manager, Sales: Ms Siew Lan Tan
Founded: 1980

Membership(s): STM; Pub Assoc (Spore).
Subjects: Asian Studies, Biological Sciences,
Chemistry, Chemical Engineering, Civil En-
gineering, Computer Science, Economics, Elec-
tronics, Electrical Science, Engineering
(General), Environmental Studies, Finance,
Management, Mathematics, Mechanical Engi-
neering, Medicine, Nursing, Dentistry, Physics,
Technology
ISBN Prefix(es): 1-86094; 981-02; 9971-950;
9971-966; 9971-978; 981-238; 981-256
Number of titles published annually: 400 Print
Total Titles: 6,000 Print
Subsidiaries: Imperial College Press
*Branch Office(s)*
World Scientific Publishing (HK) Co Ltd,
PO Box 72482, Kowloon Central Post Of-
fice, Kowloon, Hong Kong *Tel:* 2771-8791
*Fax:* 2771-8155 *E-mail:* wsped@pacific.net.hk
No 16 SW Boag Rd, T Nagar, Chennai 600 017,
India *Tel:* (044) 520 71164 *E-mail:* sales-ind@
wspc.com
5F-6, No 88, Sec 3, Hsin-Sheng S Rd, Taipei,
Taiwan, Province of China *Tel:* (02) 2369-1366
*Fax:* (02) 2369-0460 *E-mail:* wsptw@ms13.
hinet.net
World Scientific Publishing Co Ltd, 57 Shelton
St, London WC2H 9HE, United Kingdom
*Tel:* (020) 7836-0888 *Fax:* (020) 7836-2020
*E-mail:* sales@wspc.co.uk
*U.S. Office(s):* World Scientific Publishing Co
Inc, 1060 Main St, Suite 202, River Edge,
NJ 07661, United States *Tel:* 201-487-9655
*Fax:* 201-487-9656 *E-mail:* wspc@wspc.com
*Web Site:* www.worldscientific.com
Distributor for Imperial College Press (UK); The
National Academy Press, USA (Asia-Pacific
except Japan, Australia, New Zealand)

# Slovakia

## General Information

*Capital:* Bratislava
*Language:* Slovak
*Religion:* Predominantly Roman Catholic, some
Lutheran
*Population:* 5.3 million
*Currency:* 100 Halerue = 1 koruna
*Export/Import Information:* There are plans to
establish custom-free zones to stimulate foreign
investment. 6% VAT on books.
*Copyright:* UCC, Berne (see Copyright Conven-
tions, pg xi)

**ARCHA sro Vydavatel'stro+**
Staromestska 6, 813 36 Bratislava
*Tel:* (02) 54415609 *Fax:* (02) 5441586
*E-mail:* archa@internet.sk
*Key Personnel*
Editor-in-Chief: Marian Sapak
International Rights: Petra Bombikova
Subjects: Government, Political Science, History,
Law, Philosophy, Science (General), Social Sci-
ences, Sociology
ISBN Prefix(es): 80-7115

**AV Studio Reklamno-vydavatel'ska agentura**
Lykovcova 7, 841 04 Bratislava
*Tel:* (02) 65426297 *Fax:* (02) 65429750
Founded: 1993
Subjects: Health, Nutrition, Religion - Other
ISBN Prefix(es): 80-88779

**Bakalar spol sro** (Bachelor Ltd)+
Skladova 1, 917 01 Trnava
*Tel:* (019) 36258105
*Key Personnel*
Dir & President: Katerina Rubasova

Founded: 1991
ISBN Prefix(es): 80-901213

**Danubiaprint**
Fucikova 22, 81580 Bratislava
*Tel:* (02) 309167 *Fax:* (02) 362613
*Key Personnel*
Dir: Viliam Kacer
Firm is the publishing house of the Central Committee of the Communist Party of Slovakia.
Subjects: Biography, Economics, Fiction, Government, Political Science, History, Law, Philosophy, Social Sciences, Sociology
ISBN Prefix(es): 80-218; 80-85444
*Book Club(s):* CKP (Clenska kniznica Pravdy)

**Dennik Smena**
Dostojevskeho rad 1, 81924 Bratislava
*Tel:* (02) 491455; (02) 497171
*Telex:* 09341 *Cable:* BRATISLAVA SMENA
*Key Personnel*
Dir: Jaroslav Sisolak
Editor-in-Chief: Marie Caganova
Founded: 1949
Publishing House of Slovak.
Subjects: Biography, Crafts, Games, Hobbies, Fiction, Fiction, History, Philosophy, Poetry, Psychology, Psychiatry, Social Sciences, Sociology
ISBN Prefix(es): 80-85686
*Book Club(s):* Maj

**Dom Techniky Zvazu Slovenskych Vedeckotechnickych Spolocnosti Ltd**
Nabrezie Mladeze 1, 94901 Nitra
*Tel:* (037) 7721102; (037) 7721103 *Fax:* (037) 7721102
*E-mail:* zsvts@rainside.sk
*Key Personnel*
Dir: Dipl Ing Lubomir Mravec
Manager: Dipl Ing Anna Kamasova
Founded: 1974
Subjects: Business, Finance, Management, Marketing, Mechanical Engineering
ISBN Prefix(es): 80-230; 80-233; 80-236

**Egmont, SRO+**
Nevadzova 8, Box 20, 827 99 Bratislava 27
*Tel:* (02) 4333 8064; (02) 4333 3933 *Fax:* (02) 43338755
*E-mail:* egmont@netlab.sk
*Key Personnel*
Man Dir: Stanislar Valko
Founded: 1990
Subjects: Humor
ISBN Prefix(es): 80-7134; 80-550
*Parent Company:* Egmont Holding International, Denmark

**Vydavatelstvo Junior sro Slovart Print+**
Pekna cesta c 6, 83403 Bratislava
*Tel:* (02) 44872378; (02) 44872379 *Fax:* (02) 44872133
*E-mail:* obchod@junior.sk
*Web Site:* www.junior.sk
*Key Personnel*
Commercial Dir: Marta Horakova
Contact: Jaroslav Pijak *E-mail:* pijak@junior.sk
Founded: 1994
ISBN Prefix(es): 80-7146
*Associate Companies:* Nakladatelstvi Junior, Prague, Czech Republic
Distributor for Slowakei

**Kalligram spol sro** (Kalligram Ltd)+
Staromestska 6/d, 811 03 Bratislava
*Tel:* (02) 54415028 *Fax:* (02) 54410809
*Web Site:* www.kalligram.sk
*Key Personnel*
Dir: Laszlo Szigeti *E-mail:* szig@kalligram.sk
Contact: Attila Agoston *E-mail:* kiado@kalligram.sk

Founded: 1991
Subjects: Art, Fiction, Philosophy, Social Sciences, Sociology, Politics
ISBN Prefix(es): 80-7149
Number of titles published annually: 70 Print
Total Titles: 600 Print
*Branch Office(s)*
Pesti Kalligram Kft, Tuzolto utca 8, fe 2, 1094 Budapest, Hungary *Tel:* (01) 2157954 *Fax:* (01) 2166875 *E-mail:* kalligram@interware.hu
*Orders to:* Kalligram Publishers

**Svet Kridel+**
Sustekova 8, 851 04 Bratislava-Petrzalka
*Tel:* (0267) 201921; (0267) 201922 *Fax:* (0267) 201910
*E-mail:* casiopisv@press.sk
*Web Site:* www.svetkridel.cz
*Key Personnel*
Contact: Dr Zdenek Usela
Subjects: Aeronautics, Aviation
ISBN Prefix(es): 80-86808
*Associate Companies:* Magnet Press

**Luc vydavatelske druzstvo+**
Kozicova 2, 841 10 Bratislava
*Tel:* (02) 65730331 *Fax:* (02) 65730331
*Key Personnel*
International Rights: Anna Kolkova
Founded: 1989
Membership(s): Association of Slovak Catholic Publishers; Publishers of Catholic Libraries of Europe.
Subjects: Biography, Education, History, Philosophy, Poetry, Religion - Catholic, Theology
ISBN Prefix(es): 80-7114

**Mlade leta Spd sro**
Sasinkova 5, 815 19 Bratislava 1
*Tel:* (02) 55 56 45 12; (02) 55 56 62 82 *Fax:* (02) 21 57 14
*Web Site:* www.mlade-leta.sk
*Telex:* 093421
*Key Personnel*
Man Dir: Oldrich Polak
Editorial: Magda Baloghova
Sales Dir: Jana Misikova
Production: Jozef Sipos
Publicity: Eva Hornisova
Founded: 1950
Young Years: Slovak Publishing House of Children's Literature.
ISBN Prefix(es): 80-06
Distributed by Distribucna agentura Valko (Bratislava & Western Slovakia); Knizna distribucia Pezolt (Eastern Slovakia); Knizne Centrum spol sro (Central Slovakia); Marcan spol sro (Bratislava & Western Slovakia); Modul spol sro (Bratislava & Western Slovakia); Sabol Marek - Marsab (Eastern Slovakia); Slovart - Store spol sro (Bratislava & Western Slovakia)
*Bookshop(s):* Detska Kniha, Hurbanovo nam 7, Bratislava (The Child's Book); Klincova 35, Bratislava, Slovenia *Tel:* (07) 55 56 65 08
*Book Club(s):* Club of Young Readers

**Vydavatelstvo Obzor+**
Spitalska 35, 81585 Bratislava
*Tel:* (02) 368395 *Fax:* (02) 368395 *Cable:* VYDAVATELSTVO OBZOR BRATISLAVA
*Key Personnel*
Acting Dir: Ing Richard Dame
Founded: 1953
Horizon: Slovak Book & Periodical Publishing House for People's Education.
Subjects: Archaeology, Art, Law, Literature, Literary Criticism, Essays, Mysteries, Parapsychology
ISBN Prefix(es): 80-215

**Opus Records & Publishing House+**
Mlynske Nivy 73, 827 99 Bratislava

*Tel:* (02) 222680
*E-mail:* opus@ba.profinet.sk
*Key Personnel*
Man Dir: Prof Milos Jurkovic
Commercial Dir: Emilia Suta
Editorial: Slavka Dzadikova
Publicity: Dr Alena Jarosova
Founded: 1971
Membership(s): IFPI & Sound Carriers.
Subjects: Music, Dance
ISBN Prefix(es): 80-7093
*Parent Company:* Bonton Slovagcia
*Associate Companies:* Music-Video-Express

**Vydavatel'stvo Osveta (Verlag Osveta)+**
Osloboditelov 21, 036 01 Martin
*Fax:* (043) 413 5036; (043) 413 5060
*Key Personnel*
Proprietor: Martin Farkas
Founded: 1953
Subjects: Education, Fiction, Medicine, Nursing, Dentistry, Nonfiction (General), Science (General), Travel
ISBN Prefix(es): 80-217; 80-88824; 80-967377; 80-8063
*Bookshop(s):* Spitalska 18, 811 08 Bratislava; Knihkupectvi Klaty Klas, Osveta Exact Service, Lannova 6, 370 01 Ceske Budejovice, Czech Republic; M R Stefanika, 075 01 Trebisov
*Warehouse:* Expedicny Sklad Vydavatelstva Osveta, 038 41 Kost'any nad Turcom

**Vydavatel'stvo SFVU Pallas**
Trnavska 112, 82633 Bratislava
Mailing Address: PO Box 224, 82633 Bratislava
*Tel:* (02) 296627 *Fax:* (02) 294229; (02) 292820
Publishing House of the Slovak Fund of Fine Arts.
Subjects: Art, Biography, Literature, Literary Criticism, Essays
ISBN Prefix(es): 80-7095

**Polygraf Print sro**
Espajevova 44, 08001 Presov
*Tel:* (051) 74 60 111 *Fax:* (051) 77 13 270
*E-mail:* polygrafprint@polygrafprint.sk
*Web Site:* www.polygrafprint.sk
Founded: 1996

**Priroda Publishing+**
Kocelova 17, 82108 Bratislava
*Tel:* (02) 5556 4672 *Fax:* (02) 5556 4669
*E-mail:* priroda@priroda.sk
*Web Site:* www.priroda.sk
*Key Personnel*
Dir: Emilia Jankovitsova
Editorial: Jela Fellegiova
Founded: 1949
Publishing House.
Subjects: Business, Gardening, Plants, House & Home, How-to, Management, Outdoor Recreation, Self-Help, Travel, Veterinary Science, Nature
ISBN Prefix(es): 80-07
Number of titles published annually: 100 Print
Total Titles: 8,000 Print
Distributed by Aktis (Czech Republic); EUROMEDIA; Bertlesmann Group in Czech Republic
*Warehouse:* Plynarenska 6, 82109 Bratislava

**Serafin+**
Frantiskanska 2, 811 01 Bratislava
*Tel:* (02) 54432159 *Fax:* (02) 54434342
*E-mail:* vydserafin@orangemail.sk
*Web Site:* www.serafin.sk
*Key Personnel*
Contact: Adriana Alexyova; P Stefan Bankovic
Founded: 1990
Membership(s): Zdruzenie katolickych vydavatelstiev Slovenska.

Subjects: Foreign Countries, Poetry, Religion -
Catholic, Medicine
ISBN Prefix(es): 80-85310; 80-88944
Number of titles published annually: 15 Print
Total Titles: 125 Print
*Parent Company:* Zdruzenie katolickych vydava-
telstiev Slovenska
*Bookshop(s):* Frantisek

**Slo Viet**
Palarikova 21, 811 04 Bratislava
*Tel:* (02) 52494886
Founded: 1990
Membership(s): SSPOL & SSPUL.
Subjects: Asian Studies, Ethnicity, History, Lan-
guage Arts, Linguistics, Poetry
ISBN Prefix(es): 80-900500; 80-89071; 80-
968193
Number of titles published annually: 3 Print

**Slovenska Narodna Kniznica, Martin** (Slovak
National Library, Martin)+
Mudronova 26, 03652 Martin
*Tel:* (0842) 31861 *Fax:* (0842) 32993
*E-mail:* vms@esix.matica.sk
*Key Personnel*
Publicity Manager: Tomas Winkler
Founded: 1863
Subjects: Biography, Ethnicity
ISBN Prefix(es): 80-7090

**Slovenske pedagogicke nakladateistvo** (Slovak
Pedagogical Publishing House)+
Sasinkova 5, 81560 Bratislava
*Tel:* (02) 55423892 *Fax:* (02) 55571894
*E-mail:* spn@spn.sk
*Web Site:* www.spn.sk *Cable:* SPN BRATISLAVA
*Key Personnel*
General Dir: Maria Sedlakova
Sales Manager: Eva Sarandiova *Tel:* (02)
55563229
Founded: 1920
Slovak Publishing House for Educational Litera-
ture.
Subjects: Education, English as a Second Lan-
guage, Ethnicity, History, Language Arts, Lin-
guistics, Literature, Literary Criticism, Essays,
Mathematics, Music, Dance, Physics, Psychol-
ogy, Psychiatry, Social Sciences, Sociology,
Sports, Athletics, Travel, Specializes in lan-
guages
ISBN Prefix(es): 80-08
Number of titles published annually: 160 Print; 1
CD-ROM
Total Titles: 1 CD-ROM
*Parent Company:* Media Trade sro, Krizna 28,
Bratislava 1 81107
*Bookshop(s):* Krizna 47, Wagnerova, Contact: An-
drej Martinka *Tel:* (02) 55425504
*Orders to:* Media Trade sro - SPN, Sasinkova 5,
Bratislava *Tel:* (02) 55563229 *E-mail:* spn@
spn.sk

**Vydavatel'stvo Slovenskej akademie vied**, see
VEDA (Vydavatel'stvo Slovenskej akademie
vied)

**Slovensky Spisovatel Ltd as+**
Andreja Plavku 12, 813 67 Bratislava
*Tel:* (02) 399790; (02) 399736 *Fax:* (02) 399736
*Key Personnel*
Dir: Martin Chovanec *E-mail:* martin.ch@
slovspis.sk
Editor-in-Chief: Stefan Strazay
Founded: 1951
Subjects: Fiction, Literature, Literary Criticism,
Essays, Poetry
ISBN Prefix(es): 80-220
*Bookshop(s):* Laurinska 2, 81367 Bratislava
*Book Club(s):* KMP (Kruh milovnikov poezie);
SPKK (Spolocnost'priatel'ov krasnych knih)
*Warehouse:* Vajnorska 128, 83292 Bratislava

**Vydavatelstvo Slovensky Tatran spol sro**
Michalska 9, 815 82 Bratislava
*Tel:* (02) 54435849 *Fax:* (02) 54435777
*Key Personnel*
Man Dir: Eva Mladekova
Founded: 1947
Slovak Publishing House of Belles Lettres.
Rights & Permissions: LITA, Slovak Literary
Agency, Partizanska 21, 811 03 Bratislava.
Subjects: Art, Drama, Theater, Literature, Literary
Criticism, Essays, Nonfiction (General), Poetry,
Regional Interests
ISBN Prefix(es): 80-222

**Sofa+**
Vazska 11, 82107 Bratislava 211
*Tel:* (02) 55422508 *Fax:* (02) 55422508
*E-mail:* sofa@ba.sknet.sk
Founded: 1992
Subjects: Child Care & Development, Economics,
Health, Nutrition, Human Relations, Library &
Information Sciences, Philosophy, Physics, Psy-
chology, Psychiatry, Publishing & Book Trade
Reference, Social Sciences, Sociology
ISBN Prefix(es): 80-85752; 80-89033

**Sport Publishing House Ltd+**
Vajnorska ulica 100/A, 83258 Bratislava
*Tel:* (02) 69674; (02) 69223; (02) 69235; (02)
69240 *Fax:* (02) 6919 560324
*Key Personnel*
Man Dir: Ludovit Svenk
Founded: 1957
Founded as publishing house of Slovak Central
Committee of Czechoslovak Physical Culture
Organization, 1992 transformed to Sport Pub-
lishing House Ltd.
Specializes in sports, travel & Western fiction.
Subjects: Fiction, Science Fiction, Fantasy,
Sports, Athletics, Travel, Western Fiction
ISBN Prefix(es): 80-7096
Number of titles published annually: 6 Print
Total Titles: 2 Print

**Svepomoc**
Hurbanovo nam 9, 811 03 Bratislava
*Tel:* (02) 333208 *Fax:* (02) 24223439
Publishing House of the Central Cooperative
Council.
ISBN Prefix(es): 80-85168

**Technicka Univerzita**
T G Masaryka 2117/24, 960 53 Zvolen
*Tel:* (045) 63545 *Fax:* (045) 20027
*Telex:* 72267 VSLDC
Founded: 1997
Subjects: Agriculture, Animals, Pets, Architecture
& Interior Design, Economics, Education, En-
vironmental Studies, Science (General), Tech-
nology
ISBN Prefix(es): 80-228

**Trade Leas Spol Sro+**
Odborarske nam 3, 815 70 Bratislava 1
*Tel:* (02) 50239248; (02) 50239250 *Fax:* (02)
55571690
*Key Personnel*
Dir: Miroslav Bernath
Founded: 1946
Praca Publishing House.
Subjects: Cookery, Crafts, Games, Hobbies, Fi-
nance, Law, Outdoor Recreation, Romance
ISBN Prefix(es): 80-7094
Divisions: Nakladatelstvo
*Bookshop(s):* Knizna predajna Praca, 81271
Bratislava, nam SNP 20

**Ustav informacii a prognoz skolstva mladeze a
telovychovy+**
Stare Grunty 52, 842 44 Bratislava

*Tel:* (02) 6542 5166; (02) 6542 6182 *Fax:* (02)
6542 6180
*E-mail:* hrab@uip.sanet.sk
Founded: 1975
Subjects: Career Development, Computer Science,
Education, Labor, Industrial Relations, Library
& Information Sciences, Management, Micro-
computers, Outdoor Recreation, Psychology,
Psychiatry, Social Sciences, Sociology
ISBN Prefix(es): 80-7098
*Associate Companies:* Slovenska pedagogicka
kniznica

**VEDA (Vydavatel'stvo Slovenskej akademie
vied)**
Dubravska Cesta 9, 852 86 Bratislava
*Tel:* (02) 5477 4253 *Fax:* (02) 5477 2682
*Web Site:* www.veda-sav.sk
*Telex:* 93464 UKSAV *Cable:* VEDA
BRATISLAVA
*Key Personnel*
Dir: Dr Milan Brnak
Editor-in-Chief: Emil Borcin
Sales & Marketing Manager: Anna Markova
*E-mail:* markova@centrum.sk
Founded: 1953
Publishing House of the Slovak Academy of Sci-
ences.
Subjects: Archaeology, Earth Sciences, History,
Language Arts, Linguistics, Literature, Liter-
ary Criticism, Essays, Nonfiction (General),
Philosophy, Psychology, Psychiatry, Regional
Interests, Social Sciences, Sociology, Technol-
ogy
ISBN Prefix(es): 80-224
*Bookshop(s):* Knihkupectvo VEDY, Stefanikova 3,
81106 Bratislava *Tel:* (02) 5249 8095

**Vysoka Vojenska Skola Letecka**
Rampova 7, 041 21 Kosice
Mailing Address: PO Box 26, 041 21 Kosice
*Tel:* (055) 6512183; (055) 6333851 *Fax:* (055)
333851
*Key Personnel*
Contact: Frantisek Olejnik
ISBN Prefix(es): 80-7166

**Vydavatelstvo Wist sro+**
Kozmonautov 35, 03601 Martin
*Tel:* (043) 4289652 *Fax:* (043) 4289652
*E-mail:* wist@enelux.sk
*Key Personnel*
President: Robert Schwandner
Editor-in-Chief: Tomasz Trancygier
*E-mail:* ttran@enelux.sk
International Rights: Prava I Prevodi
Founded: 1993
Subjects: Fiction, Romance
ISBN Prefix(es): 80-8049; 80-85516; 80-88756
Number of titles published annually: 50 Print

**Zilinska Univerzita**
Moyzesova 20, 010 26 Zilina
*Tel:* (089) 625919; (089) 621247 *Fax:* (089)
620023
*Web Site:* www.utc.sk
*Key Personnel*
Manager: Miroslav Kopecky
Dir: Milan Dado; Pavol Kostial; Frantisek
Schlosser
Founded: 1953
ISBN Prefix(es): 80-7100; 80-8070

**ZSVTS**, see Dom Techniky Zvazu Slovenskych
Vedeckotechnickych Spolocnosti Ltd

# Slovenia

## General Information

*Capital:* Ljubljana
*Language:* Slovenian and Serbo-Croat
*Religion:* Predominantly Roman Catholic
*Population:* 2 million
*Bank Hours:* 0730-1800 Monday-Friday and
  0730-1200 Saturday
*Shop Hours:* 0800-1900 Monday-Friday; 0800-
  1300 Saturday, some open Saturday afternoon
*Currency:* Tolar
*Export/Import Information:* 3% VAT on books.
*Copyright:* UCC, Berne (see Copyright Conventions, pg xi)

**Cankarjeva Zalozba+**
Kopitarjeva ul 2, 1512 Ljubljana
*Tel:* (01) 2312 287 *Fax:* (01) 2318 782
*E-mail:* knjigarna.oxford@cankarjeva-z.si
*Web Site:* www.cankarjeva-z.si
*Telex:* 31821 Yu Cankar
*Key Personnel*
Man Dir: Dr Martin Znidersic
Editor: Janez Stanic
Rights & Permissions: Dagmar Dolinar
Subjects: Biography, Cookery, Education, Fiction,
  History, How-to, Law, Philosophy, Poetry, Psychology, Psychiatry, Social Sciences, Sociology
ISBN Prefix(es): 86-361; 961-231

**East West Operation (EWO) Ltd+**
Cankarjeva 1, 1000 Ljubljana
*Tel:* (01) 4256 272 *Fax:* (01) 2517 348
*E-mail:* ewo-arkadna@siol.net
*Key Personnel*
General Manager: Slavko Pregl
Foreign Rights: Irene Motaln-Sezun
Founded: 1991
Subjects: Art, Economics, Gardening, Plants,
  Health, Nutrition, History, Wine & Spirits
ISBN Prefix(es): 961-207
Subsidiaries: EWO Buechhandel GmbH

**Franc-Franc podjetje za promocijo kulture
  Murska Sobota d o o+**
Trg Zmage 8, 9000 Murska Sobota
Mailing Address: PP 27, 9000 Murska Sobota
*Tel:* (02) 5141 841 *Fax:* (02) 5141 841
*E-mail:* franc.franc@siol.net
*Key Personnel*
Owner, Dir & International Rights: Franci Just
Owner: Feri Lainscek
Founded: 1992
Membership(s): Verbandes der Veleger und Buchhaendler Sloweniens. Specialize in Literature.
Subjects: Fiction, Journalism, Language Arts,
  Linguistics, Literature, Literary Criticism, Essays, Poetry, Regional Interests
ISBN Prefix(es): 961-219

**Javno Podjetje Uradni list Republike Slovenije
  d o o**
Slovenska cesta 9, 1000 Ljubljana
*Tel:* (01) 4251 419 *Fax:* (01) 4250 199
*E-mail:* info@uradni-list.si
*Web Site:* www.uradni-list.si
*Key Personnel*
Chief Executive: Polutnik Marko
Editorial: Leskovic Alenka; Kurt Marija
Founded: 1946
Subjects: Law, Legislation
ISBN Prefix(es): 86-7085; 961-204

**Mladinska Knjiga International+**
Slovenska cesta 29, 1000 Ljubljana
*Tel:* (01) 2413 284; (01) 2413 288 *Fax:* (01) 4252
  294
*E-mail:* intsales@mkz-lj.si

*Web Site:* www.emka.si
*Key Personnel*
Man Dir: Majda Sikosek
Editor: Vasja Krasevec
Subjects: Art, Astrology, Occult, Biblical Studies, Biography, Biological Sciences, Chemistry,
  Chemical Engineering, Child Care & Development, Cookery, Crafts, Games, Hobbies,
  Drama, Theater, Education, Fiction, Gardening, Plants, Health, Nutrition, History, House
  & Home, How-to, Language Arts, Linguistics,
  Literature, Literary Criticism, Essays, Mathematics, Military Science, Mysteries, Nonfiction
  (General), Physics, Poetry, Psychology, Psychiatry, Regional Interests, Romance, Science
  (General), Science Fiction, Fantasy, Self-Help,
  Travel, Women's Studies
ISBN Prefix(es): 86-11

**Moderna galerija Ljubljana/Museum of
  Modern Art+**
Tomsiceva 14, 1000 Ljubljana
*Tel:* (01) 2416 800 *Fax:* (01) 2514 120
*E-mail:* info@mg-li.si
*Web Site:* www.mg-lj.si
*Key Personnel*
Dir: Ms Zdenka Badovinac
Founded: 1948
Subjects: Art
ISBN Prefix(es): 86-81787; 961-206
Total Titles: 5 Print

**Pomurska zalozba**
Lendavska 1, 9000 Murska Sobota
*Tel:* (02) 5361-422 *Fax:* (02) 5311-086
*Telex:* 35-229 Yu Zgpmsb
*Key Personnel*
Dir: Ludvik Socic
Editor-in-Chief: Joze Hradil
Subjects: Fiction, Literature, Literary Criticism,
  Essays, Poetry
ISBN Prefix(es): 86-7195
*Bookshop(s):* Dobra knjiga, Titova c, 69000
  Murska Sobota; Knjigarna Gornja Radgona
  69250, Serbia and Montenegro; Knjigarna Lendava 69220, Serbia and Montenegro; Knjigarna
  Ljutomer 69240, Serbia and Montenegro

**Slovenska matica**
Kongresni trg 8, 1001 Ljubljana
*Tel:* (01) 2514 200; (01) 2514 227; (01) 4263 190
  *Fax:* (01) 2514 200
*Key Personnel*
President: Dr Joza Mahnic
Vice President: Peter Vodopivec
Publisher: Drago Jancar
Founded: 1864
Subjects: Literature, Literary Criticism, Essays,
  Philosophy
ISBN Prefix(es): 86-80933; 961-213

**Univerza v Ljubljani Ekonomska Fakulteta+**
Kardeljeva pl 17, 1000 Ljubljana
*Tel:* (01) 5892-400 *Fax:* (01) 5892-698
*Web Site:* www.ef.uni-lj.si
*Key Personnel*
Dir: Prof Maks Tajnikar
Founded: 1946
Subjects: Accounting, Advertising, Business, Economics, Finance, Government, Political Science, Language Arts, Linguistics, Law, Management, Marketing, Mathematics, Securities
ISBN Prefix(es): 86-398; 961-6081; 961-6273;
  961-6343; 961-6430

**Zalozba Mihelac d o o+**
Slomkova 15, 1000 Ljubljana
*Tel:* (01) 4344 431 *Fax:* (01) 4344 431
*Key Personnel*
Contact: Mihelac Spela
Founded: 1990

Subjects: Art, Astrology, Occult, Astronomy,
  Biblical Studies, Child Care & Development,
  Communications, Drama, Theater, English as a
  Second Language, Fiction, Foreign Countries,
  Government, Political Science, History, Journalism, Language Arts, Linguistics, Literature,
  Literary Criticism, Essays, Medicine, Nursing,
  Dentistry, Parapsychology, Philosophy, Photography, Psychology, Psychiatry, Regional Interests, Religion - Buddhist, Religion - Catholic,
  Self-Help, Social Sciences, Sociology, Theology, Travel
ISBN Prefix(es): 961-6271
*Showroom(s):* Dunajska 23, 1000 Ljubljana
*Bookshop(s):* Dunajska 23, 1000 Ljubljana
*Book Club(s):* MOLJ
*Orders to:* Dunajska 23, 1000 Ljubljana

**Zalozba Obzorja d d Maribor+**
Partizanska 3-5, 2000 Maribor
*Tel:* (02) 2348100 *Fax:* (02) 2348135
*E-mail:* info@zalozba-obzorja.si
*Web Site:* www.zalozba-obzorja.si
*Key Personnel*
Chief Executive: Pavla Pece
Editor: Bojan Osterc
Founded: 1950
Subjects: Animals, Pets, Anthropology, Biography, Biological Sciences, Business, Chemistry,
  Chemical Engineering, Child Care & Development, Cookery, Crafts, Games, Hobbies,
  Criminology, Drama, Theater, Earth Sciences,
  Economics, Education, English as a Second
  Language, Environmental Studies, Fiction, Gardening, Plants, Gay & Lesbian, Health, Nutrition, History, Journalism, Language Arts,
  Linguistics, Law, Literature, Literary Criticism,
  Essays, Management, Marketing, Mathematics,
  Medicine, Nursing, Dentistry, Music, Dance,
  Nonfiction (General), Philosophy, Photography, Physics, Poetry, Psychology, Psychiatry,
  Regional Interests, Religion - Other, Science
  (General), Self-Help, Social Sciences, Sociology, Travel
ISBN Prefix(es): 86-377; 961-230
Divisions: Zalozba Obzorja p.o. Maribor
*Bookshop(s):* Zalozba Obzorja-Knjigarna,
  Gosposka 24 SLO, 2000 Maribor
*Warehouse:* Turnerjeva 17, SLO, 2000 Maribor

# South Africa

## General Information

*Capital:* Pretoria
*Language:* Afrikaans and English (both official)
  11 other official languages exist
*Religion:* Predominantly Christian. Politically
  most important is the Dutch Reformed Church
  (about 30% of the white population). Also
  many Methodist, Anglican and African Independent Churches among African Christians
*Population:* 41.25 million
*Bank Hours:* 0900-1530 Monday-Friday
*Shop Hours:* Vary province to province. Often
  0900-1700 Monday-Friday
*Currency:* 1 rand = 4.32 USDL (June 1996)
*Export/Import Information:* Printed books,
  brochures, leaflets and similar matter (tariff
  heading 49.01) are free of duty and surcharge
  with the exception of directories, guide books,
  year books, Christmas annuals and hand-books
  relating to South Africa which attract duty at
  a rate of 20% or 11c/Kg. No objectionable or
  undesirable literature permitted. No import permit required. Trade advertising matter, commercial catalogues and the like (tariff heading 4911.10.10 to 4911.10.30) are free of duty

(otherwise 25% and 20% duty respectively). 5% surcharge is payable in all instances. 14% VAT on books. No import permit is required.

**AA The Motorist Publications**, *imprint of* Reader's Digest Southern Africa

**Acacia Books**, *imprint of* Nasou Via Afrika

**Acorn Books+**
PO Box 4845, Randburg 2125
*Tel:* (011) 8805768 *Fax:* (011) 8805768
*E-mail:* acorbook@iafrica.com
*Key Personnel*
Publisher: Eleanor-Mary Cadell
Founded: 1985
Specialize in natural history & African wildlife.
Subjects: Natural History, Travel, African Wildlife
ISBN Prefix(es): 1-874802
Total Titles: 6 Print

**Addison Wesley**, *imprint of* Maskew Miller Longman

**Addison Wesley Longman**, *imprint of* Pearson Education (Prentice Hall)

**Africasouth Paperbacks**, *imprint of* New Africa Books (Pty) Ltd

**Afritech**, *imprint of* Nasou Via Afrika

**Afro**, *imprint of* Nasou Via Afrika

**Allyn & Bacon**, *imprint of* Maskew Miller Longman

**Anansi Publishers/Uitgewers+**
PO Box 559, Durbanville 7551
*Tel:* (021) 968411 *Fax:* (021) 969698
*E-mail:* anansi@global.co.za
*Key Personnel*
Man Dir, Editorial: Dr Lydia Snyman
Man Dir, Financial: Andre Conradie
Founded: 1989
ISBN Prefix(es): 1-86843; 0-947454; 1-874885
*Warehouse:* c/o Newman and Swart Street, Durbanville

**Appleton Lange**, *imprint of* Pearson Education (Prentice Hall)

**Ashanti Publishing+**
PO Box 5091, Rivonia 2128
*Tel:* (011) 8032506 *Fax:* (011) 8035094
*Key Personnel*
Man Dir: Nicholas Combrinck
Founded: 1987
Subjects: Environmental Studies, Foreign Countries, Government, Political Science, Military Science, Sports, Athletics
ISBN Prefix(es): 1-874800; 1-919686
*Parent Company:* Ashanti International Films Ltd, Gibraltar
Subsidiaries: Gibraltar
*U.S. Office(s):* Daring Publishing Group, 913 Tuscarawas St W, Canton, OH 44702, United States

**Atlas**, *imprint of* Nasou Via Afrika

**Jonathan Ball Publishers**
PO Box 33977, Jeppestown, Johannesburg 2043
*Tel:* (011) 622-2900 *Fax:* (011) 622-7610
*Key Personnel*
Publishing & Rights: Francine Blum
Marketing: Eugene Ashton
Sales: Alastair Steyn

Founded: 1977
Subjects: Biography, Government, Political Science, History, Literature, Literary Criticism, Essays, Sports, Athletics
ISBN Prefix(es): 1-86842; 1-874959; 0-86850; 0-947464; 0-9583751
*Parent Company:* Nasionale Boekhandel
*Ultimate Parent Company:* Nasionale Pers
Imprints: Delta Books; Ad Donker Publications

**Jossey Bass**, *imprint of* Pearson Education (Prentice Hall)

**Bateleur**, *imprint of* Nasou Via Afrika

**Benjamin Cummings**, *imprint of* Maskew Miller Longman

**Bible Society of South Africa**
15 Anton Anreith Arcade, Cape Town 8001
Mailing Address: PO Box 6215, Roggebay, Cape Town 8012
*Tel:* (021) 421-2040 *Fax:* (021) 419-4846
*E-mail:* biblia@biblesociety.co.za
*Web Site:* www.biblesociety.co.za
*Telex:* 527964 *Cable:* Testaments Cape Town
*Key Personnel*
General Secretary: Rev Gerrit Kritzinger
Chief Executive, General Secretary, Rights & Permissions: Dr D Tolmie
Sales, Production: Rev A C Human
Publicity: N Turley
Founded: 1820 (as auxiliary of British & Foreign Bible Society, 1965 as autonomous body)
Subjects: Biblical Studies, Religion - Other
ISBN Prefix(es): 0-7982
Imprints: Bybelgenootskap
*Branch Office(s)*
220 Kimberley Rd, Bloemfontein 9301, PO Box 12149, Brandhof 9324, Regional Secretary: Rev Jan de Wet *Tel:* (051) 448-9451 *Fax:* (051) 448-9455 *E-mail:* bibbfn@biblesociety.co.za
J1776 Zinhlamvu St, PO Box 160, Esikhawini 3887, Regional Secretary: Dr Josiah Mazibuko *Tel:* (035) 796-1181 *Fax:* (035) 796-2028 *E-mail:* bibkwaz@biblesociety.co.za
Stand 5080 Zone 5, Pimbille, Private Bag X05, Kliptown 1812, Regional Secretary: Rev Sello Maboea *Tel:* (011) 938-1453 *Fax:* (011) 938-1561 *E-mail:* bibsow@biblesociety.co.za
18 Central Ave, PO Box 2002, Kempton Park 1620, Regional Secretary: Rev Kobie Krige *Tel:* (011) 970-4010 *Fax:* (011) 970-2506 *E-mail:* bibjhg@biblesociety.co.za
70-76 Ramsay Ave, PO Box 30801, Mayville 4058, Regional Secretary: Dr Andries Boshoff *Tel:* (031) 207-4933 *Fax:* (031) 207-1058 *E-mail:* bibdbn@biblesociety.co.za
31 Cotswold Ave, Cotswold, PO Box 7579, Newton Park 6055, Regional Secretary: Rev Ben Fourie *Tel:* (041) 364-1138 *Fax:* (041) 365-2634 *E-mail:* bibpe@biblesociety.co.za
15 Anton Anreith Arcade, Cape Town 8001, PO Box 6446, Roggebaai 8012, Regional Secretary: Rev Eugene Louw *Tel:* (021) 421-2040 *Fax:* (021) 419-4846 *E-mail:* bibcpt@biblesociety.co.za

**Brabys Brochures**
Publishing House, 34 Kings Rd, Pinetown 3610
Mailing Address: PO Box 1426, Pinetown 3600
*Tel:* (031) 717 4000 *Fax:* (031) 717 4001
*E-mail:* brabys@brabys.com
*Web Site:* www.brabys.com
*Key Personnel*
Product Manager: P M Dahn *E-mail:* pam@brabys.co.za
Founded: 1904
Business directory publisher, maps, brochures, media sales & online advertising.
Subjects: Business

ISBN Prefix(es): 0-620; 1-86833; 1-874834
*Parent Company:* Brabys AC (Pty) Ltd, 12 Caversham Rd, Pinetown, 3600 KwaZulu-Natal

**The Brenthurst Press (Pty) Ltd**
PO Box 87184, Houghton, Johannesburg 2041
*Tel:* (011) 6466024 *Fax:* (011) 4861651
*E-mail:* orders@brenthurst.co.az
*Web Site:* www.brenthurst.org.za
*Key Personnel*
Sales Manager: Sally MacRoberts
*E-mail:* sallymac@brenthurst.co.za
Founded: 1974
Subjects: History, Natural History, Regional Interests
ISBN Prefix(es): 0-909079

**Bybelgenootskap**, *imprint of* Bible Society of South Africa

**Killie Campbell Africana Library**, *imprint of* University of KwaZulu-Natal Press

**Cape Provincial Library Service**
PO Box 2108, Cape Town 8000
*Tel:* (021) 4832234 *Fax:* (021) 4197541
*Web Site:* www.capegateway.gov.za
*Key Personnel*
Contact: Mrs Liesel de Villiers *E-mail:* lieseldu@cpls.wcapc.gov.za
Founded: 1950
Subjects: Library & Information Sciences
ISBN Prefix(es): 0-7984

**Centre for Conflict Resolution**
University of Cape Town, Private Bag, Rondebosch 7701
*Tel:* (021) 6502503; (021) 6502750 *Fax:* (021) 6852142; (021) 6504053
*E-mail:* ccr@uctvax.uct.ac.za
*Web Site:* www.uct.ac.za
*Telex:* 5-21439
*Key Personnel*
Executive Dir: Mr Laurie Nathan *Tel:* (021) 4222512 *Fax:* (021) 4222622 *E-mail:* lnathan@ccr.uct.ac.za
Founded: 1968
Specialize in conflict management.
Subjects: Human Relations, Social Sciences, Sociology
ISBN Prefix(es): 0-7992
Number of titles published annually: 10 Print
Total Titles: 24 Print

**Charles Merrill**, *imprint of* Maskew Miller Longman

**Clever Books+**
PO Box 13816, Pretoria, Hatfield 0005
*Tel:* (012) 3424715 *Fax:* (012) 4302376
*E-mail:* inl0631@mweb.co.za
*Key Personnel*
Owner: J Steenhuisen
Founded: 1981
Specialize in educational books & worksheets.
Membership(s): S A Publishers Association & S A Book Dealers Association; also specialize in Study Guides.
Subjects: Biological Sciences, Education, English as a Second Language, Language Arts, Linguistics, Mathematics, Physical Sciences, Science (General)
ISBN Prefix(es): 0-947056; 1-86817
Total Titles: 1,200 Print; 12 CD-ROM
*Book Club(s):* Clever Book Club

**CMP Reprints**, *imprint of* Sasavona Publishers & Booksellers

**Conflict Management; Africa; Peacemaking; Peacebuilding**, see Centre for Conflict Resolution

**CUM Books (Pty) Ltd**, see Digma Publications

**Benjamin Cummings**, *imprint of* Pearson Education (Prentice Hall)

**Daan Retief**, *imprint of* HAUM - Daan Retief Publishers (Pty) Ltd

**Daan Retief**, *imprint of* Jacklin Enterprises (Pty) Ltd

**De Jager Haum**, *imprint of* Maskew Miller Longman

**De Jager Publishers**, see HAUM - De Jager Publishers

**Delta Books**, *imprint of* Jonathan Ball Publishers

**Digma Publications**
Division of Butterworth Publishers
PO Box 65042, Benmore 2010
*Tel:* (011) 8834854 *Fax:* (011) 8836540
*Telex:* 425847 *Cable:* Chrispub
*Key Personnel*
Chairman: J J M Jacobs
Publisher: Freddie Crous; Koos van Niekerk
Founded: 1939
Subjects: Law, Religion - Other
ISBN Prefix(es): 0-86984; 1-86829; 1-86832

**Ad Donker (Pty) Ltd+**
Imprint of Jonathan Ball Publishers (Pty) Ltd
PO Box 33977, Jeppestown 2043
*Tel:* (011) 622-2900 *Fax:* (011) 622-7610
*Key Personnel*
Publishing & Permissions: Francine Blum
   *E-mail:* fplum@jonathanball.co.za
Marketing: Eugene Ashton
Sales: Alastair Steyn
Founded: 1973
Subjects: Nonfiction (General), General South African
ISBN Prefix(es): 0-86852; 0-949937
*Parent Company:* Nasionale Boekhandel
*Ultimate Parent Company:* Nasionale Pers
*Associate Companies:* Delta Books (Pty) Ltd
*Warehouse:* Jonathan Ball Publishers (Pty) Ltd, 10-14 Watkins St, Denver Ext 4, Johannesburg 2094

**Ad Donker Publications**, *imprint of* Jonathan Ball Publishers

**Educum**, *imprint of* Maskew Miller Longman

**Educum Publishers Ltd**
PO Box 396, Capetown 8000
*Key Personnel*
Group Man Dir: P Greyling
Senior General Manager: W Struik
General Manager: W C De Wet
Sales: C Mahlaba
Founded: 1947
Subjects: Accounting, Agriculture, Art, Biblical Studies, Biological Sciences, Business, Chemistry, Chemical Engineering, Computer Science, Cookery, Economics, Education, Engineering (General), Geography, Geology, Government, Political Science, History, Literature, Literary Criticism, Essays, Mathematics, Music, Dance, Natural History, Physical Sciences, Physics, Poetry, Religion - Protestant, Science (General), Social Sciences, Sociology, Technology

ISBN Prefix(es): 0-7980
*Parent Company:* Perskor Books (Pty) Ltd
*Associate Companies:* Varia Publishers, PO Box 3068, Halfway House, 1685; Lex Patria Publishers, PO Box 845, Johannesburg 2000

**Casselt Elt**, *imprint of* Pearson Education (Prentice Hall)

**Woodhead Faulkner**, *imprint of* Pearson Education (Prentice Hall)

**Fernwood Press (Pty) Ltd+**
PO Box 15344, Vlaeberg, Capetown 8018
*Tel:* (021) 7948686 *Fax:* (021) 7948339
*E-mail:* ferpress@iafrica.com
*Web Site:* www.fernwoodpress.co.za
*Key Personnel*
Man Dir & International Rights: Pieter Struik
Founded: 1991
Subjects: Art, History, Natural History, Nonfiction (General), Regional Interests, Travel, Wine & Spirits
ISBN Prefix(es): 1-874950; 0-9583154
Number of titles published annually: 5 Print
Distributed by Central Books Ltd/Global Book Marketing

**Financial Times**, *imprint of* Maskew Miller Longman

**Financial Times-Pitman**, *imprint of* Pearson Education (Prentice Hall)

**Flesch WJ & Partners+**
PO Box 3473, Cape Town 8001
*Tel:* (021) 4617472 *Fax:* (021) 4613758
*E-mail:* sflesch@iafrica.com
*Key Personnel*
Man Dir: S Flesch *E-mail:* sflesch@iafrica.com
Editorial: M G K Maher
Sales Manager: Peter Duncan
Founded: 1966
Membership(s): Publishers Association of South Africa.
Subjects: Aeronautics, Aviation, Animals, Pets, Business, Maritime
ISBN Prefix(es): 0-949989
Total Titles: 3 Print; 1 CD-ROM
*Associate Companies:* W J Flesch & Partners (Pty) Ltd
*Branch Office(s)*
104 Greenway, Greenside 2193

**Folio**, *imprint of* Juventus/Femina Publishers

**Russel Friedman Books**
PO Box 73, Halfway House 1685
*Tel:* (011) 702-2300 *Fax:* (011) 702-1403
*E-mail:* rfbooks@iafrica.com
*Web Site:* www.rfbooks.co.za
*Key Personnel*
Contact: Russel Friedman
Founded: 1982
Subjects: Natural History
ISBN Prefix(es): 0-9583223; 1-875091
*U.S. Office(s):* 4651 Glenshire Pl, Atlanta, GA 30338, United States

**Galago**, *imprint of* Galago Publishing Pty Ltd

**Galago Publishing Pty Ltd+**
8 First Ave, Alberton North
Mailing Address: PO Box 1645, 1450 Alberton
*Tel:* (011) 9072029 *Fax:* (011) 8690890
*E-mail:* lemur@mweb.co.za
*Web Site:* www.galago.co.za
*Key Personnel*
Man Dir: Francis Stiff

Founded: 1982
Specialize in general nonfiction, military, hunting & Africa.
Membership(s): Publishers' Association South Africa.
Subjects: Aeronautics, Aviation, African American Studies, Biography, Foreign Countries, History, Military Science, Nonfiction (General), Hunting & Africa
Number of titles published annually: 6 Print
Total Titles: 20 Print
*Parent Company:* Lemur Books Pty Ltd
Imprints: Galago

**Gecko Poetry**, *imprint of* University of KwaZulu-Natal Press

**GK Hall**, *imprint of* Maskew Miller Longman

**Government Printer**
Private Bag X85, Pretoria 0001
*Tel:* (012) 3344500 *Fax:* (012) 3239574
   *Cable:* QUAD
Subjects: Education, Geography, Geology
ISBN Prefix(es): 0-621
*Branch Office(s)*
Cape Town *Tel:* (021) 465-7531

**Hadeda Books**, *imprint of* University of KwaZulu-Natal Press

**G K Hall**, *imprint of* Pearson Education (Prentice Hall)

**Harvester Wheatsheaf**, *imprint of* Maskew Miller Longman

**Harvester Wheatsheaf**, *imprint of* Pearson Education (Prentice Hall)

**HAUM - Daan Retief Publishers (Pty) Ltd+**
PO Box 629, Pretoria 0001
*Tel:* (012) 3228474 *Fax:* (012) 3222424
*Key Personnel*
Man Dir, Production: M A C Jacklin
Editorial, Sales, Publicity, Rights & Permissions: Dr H J M Retief
Founded: 1973
Subjects: Education, Regional Interests
*Parent Company:* HAUM (Hollandsch Afrikaansche Uitgevers Maatschapplij)
*Associate Companies:* HAUM-De Jager Publishers
Imprints: Daan Retief
*Book Club(s):* Kinderklub; Young People's Book Club

**De Jager Haum**, *imprint of* Pearson Education (Prentice Hall)

**HAUM - De Jager Publishers**
PO Box 629, Pretoria 0001
*Tel:* (012) 3284620 *Fax:* (012) 3284706; (012) 3283809
*Key Personnel*
Man Dir: Chris Richter
General Manager, Publishing: Lena Kohler
General Manager, Marketing: Johann Verreynne
Founded: 1894 (as HAUM)
Subjects: Literature, Literary Criticism, Essays, Religion - Other
ISBN Prefix(es): 0-7986
*Parent Company:* HAUM (Hollandsch Afrikaansche Uitgevers Maatschappij)
*Associate Companies:* HAUM-Daan Retief Publishers (Pty) Ltd
*Branch Office(s)*
Blomfontein
Cape Town
Durban
King William's Town

Pietersburg
Pretoria
Vereeniging
Witwatersrand
*Orders to:* PO Box 12635, Clubview 0014

**HAUM (Hollandsch Afrikaansche Uitgevers Maatschappij)+**
PO Box 629, Pretoria 0001
*Tel:* (012) 32284620 *Fax:* (012) 3284706; (012) 3283809
*Key Personnel*
Manager, Publisher: Chris Richter
Subjects: Biography, Education, Ethnicity, Fiction, History, Nonfiction (General), Poetry
ISBN Prefix(es): 0-7986
Subsidiaries: HAUM-Daan Retief Publishers (Pty) Ltd; HAUM-De Jager Publishers; HAUM Educational Publishers; IKUT; Juventus/Femina Publishers; Rostrum
*Bookshop(s):* HAUM Academic Bookshop; HAUM Booksellers

**Heinemann Educational Publishers Southern Africa+**
Division of Harcourt Education International
Heinemann House, Bldg 3, Grayston Office Park, 128 Peter Rd, Sandton 2146
Mailing Address: PO Box 781940, 2146 Sandton
*Tel:* (011) 322 8600 *Fax:* (011) 322 8716
*E-mail:* customerliaison@heinemann.co.za
*Web Site:* www.heinemann.co.za
*Key Personnel*
Publishing Dir: Saul Molobi
Founded: 1986
Branch offices located in Botswana, Cape Town, Eastern Cape, Free State, Lesotho, Mpumalanga, Namibia, North West, Pietermaritzburg, & Limpopo. Warehouse located in Isando.
Membership(s): South African Publishers Association.
Subjects: Economics, Education, English as a Second Language, Mathematics, Mechanical Engineering
ISBN Prefix(es): 0-435; 0-620

**Heinemann Publishers (Pty) Ltd+**
PO Box 781940, Sandton 2146
*Tel:* (011) 3228621 *Fax:* (011) 3228717
*E-mail:* customerliaison@heinemann.co.za
*Web Site:* www.heinemann.co.za
*Key Personnel*
Man Dir, Rights & Permissions: Kevin Kroeger
Publishing: Robert Sulley
Production: Angela Tuck
Publicity: Andrew Meyer
Founded: 1966
Subjects: Computer Science, Medicine, Nursing, Dentistry, Nonfiction (General), Science (General), Technology
ISBN Prefix(es): 1-86813; 0-908379; 0-947034; 0-947472; 1-86834; 1-86853; 1-874820; 1-874914

**The Hippogriff Press CC+**
PO Box 191, Parklands, Johannesburg 2121
*Tel:* (011) 6464229 *Fax:* (011) 6464229
*Key Personnel*
Contact: E M MacPhail
Founded: 1989
Membership(s): IPASA (Independent Publishers Association of South Africa).
Subjects: Fiction, Poetry
ISBN Prefix(es): 0-9583122

**Homeros**, *imprint of* Tafelberg Publishers Ltd

**Ellis Horwood**, *imprint of* Pearson Education (Prentice Hall)

**Human & Rousseau (Pty) Ltd+**
Naspers, 12th floor, 40 Heerengracht, Roggebai 8012
Mailing Address: PO Box 5050, Cape Town 8000
*Tel:* (021) 406 3033 *Fax:* (021) 406 3812
*E-mail:* humanhk@humanrousseau.com
*Web Site:* www.humanrousseau.com
*Key Personnel*
General Manager: Kerneels Breytenbach
Operations Manager: Riel Hauman
Marketing Manager: Elsa Wolfaard
Founded: 1959
Subjects: Anthropology, Architecture & Interior Design, Art, Biography, Business, Child Care & Development, Communications, Cookery, Crafts, Games, Hobbies, Drama, Theater, Economics, Fiction, Gardening, Plants, History, House & Home, How-to, Language Arts, Linguistics, Literature, Literary Criticism, Essays, Management, Marketing, Music, Dance, Natural History, Nonfiction (General), Philosophy, Poetry, Religion - Protestant, Romance, Self-Help, Sports, Athletics
ISBN Prefix(es): 0-7981
*Parent Company:* Nasionale Boekhandel Ltd
*Branch Office(s)*
Johannesburg
Pretoria
*Orders to:* Nasionale Boekhandel, PO Box 487, Bellville 7535 *Tel:* (021) 918 8500 *Fax:* (021) 951 4903

**Human Sciences Research Council+**
134 Pretouris St, Pretoria 0002
Mailing Address: Private Bag X41, Pretoria 0001
*Tel:* (012) 302 2999 *Fax:* (012) 326 5362
*Web Site:* www.hsrc.ac.za
*Key Personnel*
Publisher: Mrs R Keet *E-mail:* rkeet@beauty.hsrc.ac.za
Founded: 1965
Research Institution, Human Sciences only. Publish own research, selected external authors & co-publish with one UK publisher.
Subjects: Behavioral Sciences, Career Development, Criminology, Education, Government, Political Science, Human Relations, Philosophy, Psychology, Psychiatry, Regional Interests, Social Sciences, Sociology, Women's Studies
ISBN Prefix(es): 0-7969; 0-86965
Total Titles: 274 Print
*Branch Office(s)*
CSIR Bldg, 359 King George V Ave, 4th Floor, Private Bag X07, Durban 4014 *Tel:* (031) 273 1400 *Fax:* (031) 273 1403
Plein Park Bldg, 69-83 Plein St, 14th Floor, Private Bag X9182, Cape Town 8000 *Tel:* (021) 467 4420 *Fax:* (021) 467 4424
Distributor for Zed Books (London)
*Bookshop(s):* HSRC Publishers, PO Box 5556, Petoria 0001, Contact: J Moagi *Tel:* (012) 3022004 *Fax:* (012) 3022933 *E-mail:* jels@beauty.hsrc.ac.za
*Orders to:* PO Box 5556, Pretoria 0001, Contact: J Moagi *Tel:* (012) 3022330 *Fax:* (012) 2022442 *E-mail:* jels@beauty.hsrc.ac.za

**Institute for Reformational Studies CHE+**
c/o Potchefstroom University for Christian Higher Education, Private Bag X6001, Potchefstroom 2520
*Tel:* (018) 299-1111 *Fax:* (018) 299-2799
*E-mail:* navrae@puk.ac.za
*Web Site:* www.puk.ac.za
*Telex:* 346019 *Cable:* PUK
*Key Personnel*
Dir: Prof B J van der Walt
Editorial: Rita Swanepoel
Administration: Dr A J van der Walt
Founded: 1962
Subjects: Anthropology, Art, Biblical Studies, Developing Countries, Education, Government,

Political Science, Religion - Protestant, Theology, Women's Studies
ISBN Prefix(es): 0-86990; 1-86822
*Parent Company:* Potchefstroom University for Christian Higher Education

**Ithemba! Publishing+**
PO Box 1048, Auckland Park 2006
*Tel:* (011) 726 6529 *Fax:* (011) 726 6529
*E-mail:* firechildren@icon.co.za
*Web Site:* www.icon.co.za/~firechildren/ithemba/ithemba.htm
*Key Personnel*
Man Dir: Bronwen Jones
Founded: 1994
Membership(s): Publishers Association of South Africa & Children's Book Forum. Publisher of South African produced books only.
Subjects: Biography, Fiction, Regional Interests
ISBN Prefix(es): 0-9583900; 0-9584107; 0-9584412
*U.S. Office(s):* Lucretia Humphrey, 3026 Fifth Ave N, Great Falls, MT 59401, United States
Distributed by Africa Book Centre; Lucretia Humphrey (USA); National Book Trust of India (Asia)

**Ivy Publications+**
PO Box 397, Pretoria 0001
*Tel:* (012) 218931 *Fax:* (012) 3255984
*E-mail:* therese@statelib-pww.gov.za
*Key Personnel*
Contact: Ian Bruton-Simmonds
Founded: 1989
Subjects: Education, English as a Second Language, Journalism, Language Arts, Linguistics, Literature, Literary Criticism, Essays, Management, Nonfiction (General), Romance
ISBN Prefix(es): 0-620

**Jacana Education+**
5 Saint Peter Rd, Bellevue, Gauteng 2198
Mailing Address: PO Box 2004, Houghton, Gauteng 2041
*Tel:* (011) 648 1157 *Fax:* (011) 648 5516
*E-mail:* marketing@jacana.co.za; accounts@jacana.co.za
*Web Site:* www.jacana.co.za
Founded: 1991
Independent publisher specializing in books, maps & guides.
Subjects: Child Care & Development, Education, English as a Second Language, Environmental Studies, Gardening, Plants, Health, Nutrition, Medicine, Nursing, Dentistry, Travel
ISBN Prefix(es): 1-874955; 1-919777; 1-919931

**Jacklin Enterprises (Pty) Ltd+**
PO Box 521, Parklands 2121
*Tel:* (011) 265 4200 *Fax:* (011) 314 2984
*E-mail:* mjacklin@jacklin.co.za
*Web Site:* www.jacklin.co.za
*Key Personnel*
Man Dir: Mike Jacklin *Tel:* (011) 265 4299
Editorial, Rights & Permissions: Daleen Malan
Production: Shiraaz Abdoola
Sales: Drienie Kemp
Founded: 1992
Specialize in children's book clubs (5); mail order fulfillment for books, magazines & partworks.
Subjects: Fiction, Romance, Technology, Transportation
ISBN Prefix(es): 1-86839; 1-874927; 1-86914; 1-86904
Total Titles: 2,000 Print; 2 Audio
Imprints: Daan Retief; Mike Jacklin; Kennis Onbeperk
Divisions: Daan Retief Book Clubs; Disney Book Club; Partworks Subscriptions; Read & Learn Programme
Distributor for De Agostini (all South Africa only); BBC; Eaglemoss; Fabbri; Marshall Cavendish

**Mike Jacklin**, *imprint of* Jacklin Enterprises (Pty) Ltd

**Janssen Publishers CC**
PO Box 404, Simon's Town 7995
*Tel:* (021) 7861548 *Fax:* (021) 7862468
*E-mail:* janssenp@iafrica.com
*Web Site:* www.janssenbooks.co.za
Founded: 1981
Specialize in photo & art books of the male nude.
Subjects: Art, Erotica, Gay & Lesbian, Photography
ISBN Prefix(es): 1-919901
Number of titles published annually: 10 Print
Total Titles: 120 Print
*Distribution Center:* SOVA-Sozialistische Verlagsauslieferung GmbH, Friesstr 20-24, 60388 Frankfurt, Germany *Tel:* (069) 410 211 *Fax:* (069) 410 280 *E-mail:* sovaffm@t-online.de
Weatherhill, Inc, 41 Monroe Turnpike, Trumbull, CT 06611, United States *Tel:* 203-459-5090 *Fax:* 203-459-5095

**Jasmyn**, *imprint of* Tafelberg Publishers Ltd

**Johannesburg Art Gallery**
PO Box 23561, Joubert Park, Johannesburg 2044
*Tel:* (011) 7253130; (011) 7253180 *Fax:* (011) 7206000
*Web Site:* www.saevents.co.za/gallery.htm
*Key Personnel*
Dir: Rochelle Keene
Curator of Publications: Sandy Shoolman
Founded: 1910
Membership(s): AAM, SAMA & ICOM.
Subjects: Art, Education, Photography
ISBN Prefix(es): 1-874836
Total Titles: 20 Print

**Juta & Co+**
Mercury Crescent, Hillstar Industria, Wetton, Cape Town 7779
Mailing Address: PO Box 14373, Lansdown 7779
*Fax:* (021) 797 5569 (orders only)
*E-mail:* books@juta.co.za
*Web Site:* www.juta.co.za *Cable:* JUTA
*Key Personnel*
Chief Executive Officer: Rory Wilson
*Tel:* (021) 797 5101 *Fax:* (021) 797 0121 *E-mail:* rwilson@juta.co.za
Founded: 1853
*Overseas Agents:* Blackstone Press Ltd, 1st Floor, 104 Ebley St, Bondi Junction, Sydney, NSW 2022, Australia; BRAD, 244A London Rd, Hadleigh, Essex SS7 2DE, UK. Tel: (0702) 552912 Fax: (0702) 556095 (academic, medical & technical titles); Hammick's Law Bookshop, 191-192 Fleet St, London EC4A 2AH, UK (law titles).
Membership(s): ABSA & SAPA.
Subjects: Accounting, Business, Education, Law, Medicine, Nursing, Dentistry
ISBN Prefix(es): 0-7021; 1-874859
Number of titles published annually: 500 Print; 10 CD-ROM
Total Titles: 44 CD-ROM
*Parent Company:* Juta Holdings (Pty) Ltd
*Associate Companies:* Juta (UK) Ltd, The Kidlington Centre, Suite E, Oxford OX52DL, United Kingdom; Jutastat (Pty) Ltd
*Branch Office(s)*
Mercury Crescent Kenwyn, Cape Town 7790
*Tel:* (021) 7975101 *Fax:* (021) 7627424
PO Box 1010, Johannesburg 2000
*Showroom(s):* Madeira St, Umtata, Transkei *Tel:* (0471) 23634

*Shipping Address:* Hillstar Industrial Township, Wetton Cape, Jenny Newby *E-mail:* jnewby@juja.co.za
*Warehouse:* Hillstar Industrial Township, Wetton Cape, Winston Bell *Fax:* (021) 7616267 *E-mail:* wbell@juta.co.za

**Juventus/Femina Publishers+**
PO Box 629, Pretoria 0001
*Tel:* (012) 3284620 *Fax:* (012) 3283809
*Telex:* 30435
*Key Personnel*
Man Dir: Piet Scholtz
Manager, Editorial: Lena Kohler
Chief Publisher: Kobie Gouws
Sales: Robbie Goossen
Production: Manus Oberholzer
Publicity: Sas Klopper
Rights & Permissions: Hettie Scholtz
Founded: 1980
Subjects: Fiction, Nonfiction (General), Social Sciences, Sociology, Women's Studies
ISBN Prefix(es): 0-86816; 0-907996
*Parent Company:* HAUM (Hollandsch Afrikaansche Uitgevers Maatschappij)
Imprints: Folio

**Kagiso**, *imprint of* Maskew Miller Longman

**Kagiso**, *imprint of* Pearson Education (Prentice Hall)

**Kennis Onbeperk**, *imprint of* Jacklin Enterprises (Pty) Ltd

**Kima Global Publishers+**
Kima Global House, 11 Columbine Rd, Rondebosch, Cape Town 7700
Mailing Address: PO Box 374, Rondebosch 7701
*Tel:* (021) 686-7154 *Fax:* (021) 686-9066
*E-mail:* info@kimaglobal.co.za
*Web Site:* www.kimaglobal.co.za
*Key Personnel*
Founder, Publisher & Man Dir: Mr Robin Beck *E-mail:* robin@kimaglobal.co.za
Founded: 1993
Independent company specializing in personal growth books.
Membership(s): PMA.
Subjects: Alternative, Astrology, Occult, Behavioral Sciences, How-to, Human Relations, Psychology, Psychiatry, Religion - Other, Self-Help
ISBN Prefix(es): 0-9584261; 0-9584359; 0-958693; 0-9584
Number of titles published annually: 6 Print
Total Titles: 40 Print
*U.S. Office(s):* c/o Holistic Marketing Cooperative, 705-B SE Melody Lane, Suite 329, Lee's Summit, MO 64063, United States, Contact: Diana Trott *Tel:* 816-525-1802 *Fax:* 816-471-7091
Distributor for Summit University Press
Foreign Rights: David Hiatt (US)
*Warehouse:* Packaging Dynamics, 8800 NE Undergroud Dr, Kansas City, MO 64108, United States
*Distribution Center:* Banyan Tree, 13 College Rd, Kent Town 5067, Australia, Contact: Susan van der Heiden *Tel:* (08) 8363 4244 *Fax:* (08) 8363 4255 *Web Site:* www.banyantreebooks.com
New Leaf Distributing, 401, Thornton Rd, Lithia Springs, GA 30122-1557, United States, Contact: Judith Hawkins-Tillerson *Tel:* 770-948-7845 *Fax:* 770-944-2313 *Web Site:* www.newleaf-dist.com
*Orders to:* Holistic Marketing Cooperative, 705B SE Melody Lane, Suite 329, Lee's Summit, MO 64063, United States, Contact: Diana Trott *Tel:* 816-525-1802 *E-mail:* diana@holisticmarketing.com

**KZN Books**, *imprint of* Nasou Via Afrika

**Ladybird Books**, *imprint of* Maskew Miller Longman

**LAPA Publishers (Pty) Ltd+**
380 Bosman St, Pretoria 0002
Mailing Address: PO Box 123, Pretoria 0001
*Tel:* (012) 401 0700 *Fax:* (012) 3255498
*E-mail:* lapa@atkv.org.za
*Key Personnel*
Publication & Administrative Officer: Esme Smith *E-mail:* esmes@atkv.org.za
Founded: 1943
Publisher & bookseller.
Subjects: Fiction, Law, Nonfiction (General), Philosophy, Religion - Other
ISBN Prefix(es): 0-7993
Number of titles published annually: 140 Print
*Ultimate Parent Company:* ATKV, Dover St, Randburg 2194
Imprints: Symbol Books
*Book Club(s):* Eike-Boekklub; Keurbiblioteek; President Boekklub; Romankeur; Symbol; Treffer-Boekklub

**LexisNexis Butterworths South Africa**
215 North Ridge Rd, Morningside, 4001 Durban
Mailing Address: PO Box 792, 4000 Durban
*Tel:* (031) 268 3111; (031) 268 3007 (customer service) *Fax:* (031) 268 3108; (021) 268 3109 *Toll Free Fax:* (031) 268 3102 (Marketing)
*Web Site:* www.lexisnexis.co.za
*Key Personnel*
Chief Executive Officer: Billy Last *Tel:* (031) 268 3253 *Fax:* (031) 29 8686
Sales & Marketing Dir: James Martens *Tel:* (031) 268 3246 *Fax:* (031) 268 3114
Electronic Publishing Dir: Chris Uniacke *Tel:* (031) 268 3256 *Fax:* (031) 268 3114
Publishing Dir: Theuns Viljoen *Tel:* (031) 268 3247 *Fax:* (031) 268 3114
National Sales Executive: Wendy de Sornay *Tel:* (031) 268 3261 *Fax:* (031) 268 3271
Marketing Manager: Shannon MacLennan *Tel:* (031) 268 3251
Marketing Coordinator: Tracy Naicker *Tel:* (031) 268 3243
Subjects: Economics, Education, Law
ISBN Prefix(es): 0-409
*Parent Company:* LexisNexis Butterworth & Co (Publishers) Ltd, United States
*Ultimate Parent Company:* Reed Elsevier plc, 25 Victoria St, London SW1H 0EX, United Kingdom
*Branch Office(s)*
F10 Centurion Business, Bosmansdam Rd, Milnerton, 7441 Capetown *Tel:* (021) 551 8900 *Fax:* (021) 551 5121
Grayston 66, 2 Norwich Close, Sandton, 2196 Johannesburg *Tel:* (011) 784 8009 *Fax:* (011) 883 6540
Distributor for Butterworth-Heinemann

**Longman**, *imprint of* Maskew Miller Longman

**Longman**, *imprint of* Pearson Education (Prentice Hall)

**Maskew Miller Longman**, *imprint of* Pearson Education (Prentice Hall)

**Lux Verbi (Pty) Ltd+**
33 Waterkant St, Cape Town 8000
Mailing Address: PO Box 5, Wellington 7654
*Tel:* (021) 8733851 *Fax:* (021) 8730069
*E-mail:* luxverbi.publ@kinglsey.co.za
*Telex:* 526922
*Key Personnel*
Executive Chairman: Willem J van Zijl
Publishing: Hester Venter

Marketing: Maryna Volschenk
Founded: 1956
Subjects: Religion - Other, Theology
ISBN Prefix(es): 0-86997; 0-7963
Subsidiaries: Waterkant-Uitgewers (Edms) Bpk
*Bookshop(s):* OK Centre Shop, 404 Murchison St,
   Ladysmith; Central Square 37, Union St, Lon-
   don; The Mall, c/o Malanand Sauer St, Vander-
   bijlpark
*Book Club(s):* New Day Readers Circle

**MacMillan**, *imprint of* Maskew Miller Longman

**MacMillan Books**, *imprint of* Maskew Miller
   Longman

**MacMillan College**, *imprint of* Maskew Miller
   Longman

**MacMillan ELT**, *imprint of* Maskew Miller
   Longman

**MacMillan Reference**, *imprint of* Maskew Miller
   Longman

**Maskew Miller Longman+**
Howard Drive, Pinelands, Cape Town 7405
Mailing Address: PO Box 396, Cape Town 8000
*Tel:* (021) 531 7750 *Fax:* (021) 531 4877
*E-mail:* firstname@mml.co.za
*Web Site:* www.mml.com
*Telex:* 526053 SA
*Key Personnel*
Chief Executive: Fathima Dada *E-mail:* fathima@
   mml.co.za
Publishing Dir: Japie Pienaar *E-mail:* japie@mmi.
   co.za
Dir, Trade & Adult: Orenna Krut
   *E-mail:* orenna@mml.co.za
Dir MML International: Graham van der Vyver
   *E-mail:* graham@mmo.co.za
Financial Dir: Ms Cornelius Vamvadelis
Dir, Publishing Services, Editorial & Production:
   Jeremy Boraine
Founded: 1893
Subjects: Education, Language Arts, Linguistics,
   Literature, Literary Criticism, Essays
ISBN Prefix(es): 0-623; 0-636
*Parent Company:* Pearson Education
*Ultimate Parent Company:* Pearson Plc
Imprints: Unibook; De Jager Haum; Educum;
   Kagiso; Longman; Pearson Education South
   Africa; Perskor; Phumelela; Sached; Vlae-
   berg; Addison Wesley; Allyn & Bacon; Ben-
   jamin Cummings; Charles Merrill; Financial
   Times; GK Hall; Harvester Wheatsheaf; La-
   dybird Books; MacMillan; MacMillan Books;
   MacMillan College; MacMillan ELT; MacMil-
   lan Reference; Prentice Hall; Prentice Hall
   Australia; Prentice Hall Europe; Prentice Hall
   South Africa; QUE College; Regents Prentice
   Hall; Scribner; Woodhead Faulkner
*Branch Office(s)*
Private Bag X08, Amethyst St, Bertsham, 2013
   Johannesburg *Tel:* (011) 4961730 *Fax:* (011)
   4961117

**Mayibuye Books+**
Private Bag X 17, Belville, 7535 Cape Town
*Tel:* (021) 9592529; (021) 9592954 *Fax:* (021)
   9593411
*E-mail:* mayibuye@mweb.co.za
*Key Personnel*
Head, Marketing/Distribution: Lavona George
   *E-mail:* lavona@intekom.co.za
Dir: B Feinberg *E-mail:* bfeinberg@uwc.ac.za
Founded: 1992
A pioneering project helping to recover areas of
   South African history that have been neglected.
Subjects: Biography, History, Literature, Literary
   Criticism, Essays

ISBN Prefix(es): 1-86808
Total Titles: 94 Print; 1 CD-ROM

**Media House Publications+**
PO Box 782395, Sandton 2146
*Tel:* (011) 8826237 *Fax:* (011) 8829652
*Key Personnel*
Contact: K Everingham
Founded: 1983
Subjects: Humor, Nonfiction (General)

**Charles Merrill**, *imprint of* Pearson Education
   (Prentice Hall)

**The Methodist Publishing House**
Unit of The Methodist Church of Southern Africa
PO Box 708, Capetown 8000
*Tel:* (021) 4483640 *Fax:* (021) 4483716
*Key Personnel*
General Manager: D R Leverton *E-mail:* dave@
   methbooks.co.za
Founded: 1894
Christian Booktrade.
Subjects: Religion - Protestant
ISBN Prefix(es): 0-949942; 0-947450; 1-919883
Total Titles: 10 Print
Distributor for Abingdon (South Africa); Eagle
   (South Africa); Highland (South Africa); Up-
   per Room Books (South Africa); WCC (South
   Africa); Westminster/John Knox (South Africa)
*Bookshop(s):* PO Box 1452, Benoni 1500
   *E-mail:* benoni@methbooks.co.za; PO Box
   130430, Bryanston 2074 *E-mail:* vicky@
   methbooks.co.za; PO Box 708, Cape Town
   8000 *E-mail:* arnette@methbooks.co.za; PO
   Box 108, Durban 4000 *E-mail:* jackie@
   methbooks.co.za; PO Box 8508, Johannesburg 2000 *E-mail:* jhb@methbooks.co.za; PO
   Box 1042, Kimberley 8300 *E-mail:* leahanne@
   methbooks.co.za; 164 Chapel St, Pietermaritzburg 3200 *E-mail:* roland@methbooks.co.za

**Nasionale Boekhandel Ltd**
386 Voortekker Rd, Parow 7500
Mailing Address: PO Box 150, 7500 Parow
*Tel:* (021) 5911131
*Telex:* 526951 SA *Cable:* Nasboek
*Key Personnel*
Group Man Dir: P J Botha
Founded: 1950
Subjects: Education, Medicine, Nursing, Dentistry
Subsidiaries: Cape Booksellers Ltd; Human &
   Rousseau (Pty) Ltd; Nasboek (Natal) Ltd; Na-
   sionale Boekwinkels Bpk; Nasou Ltd; Nasou
   Oudiovista; Natal Booksellers Ltd; J L van
   Schaik (Pty) Ltd; Van Schaik's Bookstore (Pty)
   Ltd; Tafelberg Publishers Ltd; Via Afrika Ltd;
   Via Afrika (Bophuthatswana) Ltd; Via Afrika
   (Ciskei) Ltd; Via Afrika (OFS) Ltd; Via Afrika
   (Transkei) Ltd, Umtata; Via Afrika (Lebowa)
   Ltd; Rygill's Educational Suppliers; Heer Print-
   ers (Pty) Ltd, Pretoria (all in Republic of South
   Africa); Nasionale Boekhandel (SWA) (Pty)
   Ltd
*Book Club(s):* Leserskring (Leisure Books)

**Nasou Via Afrika+**
40 Heerengracht, Cape Town 8001
Mailing Address: PO Box 5197, Cape Town 8000
*Tel:* (021) 406-3314; (021) 406-3005 (customer
   service) *Fax:* (021) 406-2922; (021) 406-3086
*E-mail:* mdewitt@nasou.com (customer service)
*Web Site:* www.nasou-viaafrika.com *Cable:* Via
   Afrika
*Key Personnel*
General Manager: D H Schroeder
   *E-mail:* dschroed@nasou.com
Senior Manager, Publishing: G Niebuhr
   *E-mail:* gniebuhr@nasou.com
Marketing Manager: T Priem *E-mail:* tpriem@
   nasou.com

Founded: 1970
Subjects: Fiction, Poetry, Science (General), So-
   cial Sciences, Sociology, Technology
ISBN Prefix(es): 0-77004; 0-625; 0-7994
Total Titles: 1,500 Print
*Parent Company:* Via Afrika
*Ultimate Parent Company:* NASPERS
Imprints: Acacia Books; Afritech; Afro; Atlas;
   Bateleur; KZN Books
*Bookshop(s):* PO Box 1058, Bloemfontein 9300
   *Tel:* (051) 448-2345 *Fax:* (051) 448-4544
   *E-mail:* bfn@afribooks.com; 15 Kraal St,
   East End, PO Box 1097, Bloemfontein 9300
   *Tel:* (051) 447-5295 *Fax:* (051) 447-1754; PO
   Box 5485, Cape Town 8000 *Tel:* (021) 406-
   3880; (021) 406-3992 *Fax:* (021) 406-3371
   *E-mail:* bvl@afribooks.com; 40 Heerengracht,
   PO Box 2834, Cape Town 8000 *Tel:* (021) 406-
   3313 *Fax:* (021) 406-2932; Loxford House,
   Hill St, 3rd floor, PO Box 1163, East Lon-
   don 5200 *Tel:* (043) 722-2464; (043) 742-0722
   *Fax:* (043) 743-9914; PO Box 279, East Lon-
   don 5200 *Tel:* (043) 735-3888 *Fax:* (043) 735-
   4200 *E-mail:* el@afribooks.com; PO Box 82,
   George 6530 *Tel:* (044) 873-2812 *Fax:* (044)
   873-2811 *E-mail:* grg@afribooks.com; In-
   vestec House, Hatfield Sq, 1st/2nd floor, 1115
   Burnette St, PO Box 11943, Hatfield 0028
   *Tel:* (012) 362-1141 *Fax:* (012) 362-4658 (Publishing); (012) 362-8671 (Marketing); Private
   Bag X5022, Kimberley 8300 *Fax:* (053) 832-
   9475; Tarentaal Trading Post, Cor Kaapse-
   hoop Rd & N4, PO Box 2400, Nelspruit 1200
   *Tel:* (013) 741-1936 *Fax:* (013) 741-3086; PO
   Box 556, Pinetown 3600 *Tel:* (031) 705-2417
   *Fax:* (031) 701-8300 *E-mail:* ptn@afribooks.
   com; Ground floor, Charter House, Crompton
   St, PO Box 2505, Pinetown 3600 *Tel:* (031)
   702-6184 *Fax:* (031) 702-6189; Nedbank Bldg,
   10th floor, Office No 1001, 59-60 Landros
   Mare St, Polokwane 0699 *Tel:* (015) 291-4978;
   (015) 291-5328 *Fax:* (015) 291-5250; PO Box
   95, Port Elizabeth 6000 *Tel:* (041) 363-1163
   *Fax:* (041) 363-1183 *E-mail:* pe@afribooks.
   com; PO Box 3626, Randburg 2125 *Tel:* (011)
   792-2213 *Fax:* (011) 792-2239 *E-mail:* rbg@
   afribooks.com; 49 Steen St, Room No 10, PO
   Box 9749, Rustenburg 0300 *Tel:* (014) 594-
   0514 *Fax:* (014) 594-0337

**National Botanical Institute**
Private Bag X7, Claremont 7735
*Tel:* (021) 799 8800 *Fax:* (021) 761 4687
*E-mail:* rpub@nbipre.nbi.ac.za
*Web Site:* www.nbi.ac.za
*Key Personnel*
Head Research, Support Services & Publications:
   M Joubert *E-mail:* mf@nbipre.nbi.ac.za
Directed toward research & conservation in the
   botanical field.
Subjects: Biological Sciences, Environmental
   Studies, Gardening, Plants, Natural History,
   Science (General)
ISBN Prefix(es): 0-9583205; 1-874907; 1-919684
Total Titles: 100 Print
Distributor for Briza Publications (South Africa)

**New Africa Books (Pty) Ltd+**
99 Garfield Rd, Claremont, Cape Town 7700
Mailing Address: PO Box 23317, Claremont,
   Cape Town 7735
*Tel:* (021) 67441387 *Fax:* (021) 6742920
*Web Site:* www.newafricabooks.co.za
*Key Personnel*
Man Dir: Brian Wafawarowa
Founded: 1971
Membership(s): PASA.
Subjects: Agriculture, Anthropology, Archaeol-
   ogy, Architecture & Interior Design, Biography,
   Child Care & Development, Cookery, Develop-
   ing Countries, Drama, Theater, Economics, Ed-
   ucation, English as a Second Language, Envi-
   ronmental Studies, Fiction, Government, Polit-

ical Science, History, Humor, Literature, Literary Criticism, Essays, Natural History, Nonfiction (General), Photography, Poetry, Publishing & Book Trade Reference, Regional Interests, Women's Studies
ISBN Prefix(es): 1-919876; 1-86928
*Ultimate Parent Company:* New Africa Investments Ltd
Imprints: Africasouth Paperbacks; David Philip; New Africa Education; Spearhead
*Branch Office(s)*
PO Box 32328, Braamfontein 2017 *Tel:* (011) 727 7062 *Fax:* (011) 727 7063
526 16 Rd, Constantia Sq, Halfway House, Midrand, Johannesburg, Contact: Gillian Temple *Tel:* (011) 805-6096 *Fax:* (011) 805-1622 *E-mail:* patience.tsotetsi@jhb.dpp.co.za
Distributed by Africa Book Centre
Distributor for James Currey (Johannesburg); Christopher Hurst; Oneworld Publications; Zed Books

**New Africa Education**, *imprint of* New Africa Books (Pty) Ltd

**Oceanographic Research Institute (ORI)**
Division of South African Association of Marine Biological Research (SAAMBR)
PO Box 10712, Marine Parade, Durban 4056
*Tel:* (031) 3288222; (031) 3288238 *Fax:* (031) 3288188
*E-mail:* ori@saambr.org.za
*Web Site:* www.ori.org.za
*Key Personnel*
Dir: Prof R P van der Elst
Deputy Dir: Prof M H Schleyer
Librarian: Mrs A B Kleu
Founded: 1958
Library services, exchange of scientific publications.
Subjects: Biological Sciences, Environmental Studies, Natural History, Science (General), Marine Biology, Conservation, Fisheries, Coastal Management, Pollution Studies
ISBN Prefix(es): 0-86989
Total Titles: 1 Print
*Associate Companies:* Sea World, Durban *Tel:* (031) 3288222 *Fax:* (031) 3288188

**Peachpit Press**, *imprint of* Pearson Education (Prentice Hall)

**Pearson Education (Prentice Hall)**
Mill St, 8010 Cape Town
Mailing Address: PO Box 12122, Cape Town 7700
*Tel:* (021) 686 6356 *Fax:* (021) 686 4590
*E-mail:* firstname@mml.co.za
*Web Site:* www.pearsoned.com
*Key Personnel*
Man Dir: Marian DeWet
Publisher, Higher Education: Hanli Venter
Founded: 1994
Distributes Prentice Hall titles in South Africa. Publish & distribute our subsidiaries. Specialize in higher education.
Subjects: Education
*Parent Company:* Pearson Plc
*Associate Companies:* Maskew Miller Longman (Pty) Ltd, Howard Dr, PO Box 96, Cape Town 8000, Man Dir: Fathima Dada *Tel:* (021) 5137750 *Fax:* (021) 5314049
Imprints: Addison Wesley Longman; Appleton Lange; Benjamin Cummings; Casselt Elt; Charles Merrill; De Jager Haum; Ellis Horwood; G K Hall; Harvester Wheatsheaf; Jossey Bass; Kagiso; Longman; Maskew Miller Longman; Peachpit Press; PH Macmillan ELT; PH Macmillan College; PH Macmillan Reference; Prentice Hall; Prentice Hall (Australia); Prentice Hall (Canada); Prentice Hall (Europe); Prentice Hall International; Prentice Hall

(South Africa); Que College; Regents Prentice Hall; Schirmer; Scribner Reference; Woodhead Faulkner; Financial Times-Pitman
*Showroom(s):* Maskew Miller Longman (Midrand)

**Pearson Education South Africa**, *imprint of* Maskew Miller Longman

**Perskor**, *imprint of* Maskew Miller Longman

**Perskor Books (Pty) Ltd**
Postbus 3068, Halfway House 1685
*Tel:* (011) 315-3647 *Fax:* (011) 315-2757
*E-mail:* vlaeberg@icon.co.za
*Telex:* 83561; 87483 *Cable:* Vaderland
*Key Personnel*
Man Dir: F Wessels
Editorial, Rights & Permissions: P V Heerden
Sales: S J Fourie
Production: A Bothma
Publicity: S Kloppers
Founded: 1940
Subjects: Education, Law
ISBN Prefix(es): 0-628
Subsidiaries: Educum Publishers Ltd; Perskor Publishers
*Bookshop(s):* Johannesburgse Boekwinkel; Perskor Bookshop
*Book Club(s):* Klub-Dagbreek; Klub 707; Klub Saffier
*Orders to:* Perskor-Boekwinkel, 4 Banfield Rd, Industrial North, Maraisburg 1700

**PH Macmillan College**, *imprint of* Pearson Education (Prentice Hall)

**PH Macmillan ELT**, *imprint of* Pearson Education (Prentice Hall)

**PH Macmillan Reference**, *imprint of* Pearson Education (Prentice Hall)

**David Philip**, *imprint of* New Africa Books (Pty) Ltd

**Phumelela**, *imprint of* Maskew Miller Longman

**Prentice Hall**, *imprint of* Maskew Miller Longman

**Prentice Hall**, *imprint of* Pearson Education (Prentice Hall)

**Prentice Hall (Australia)**, *imprint of* Pearson Education (Prentice Hall)

**Prentice Hall Australia**, *imprint of* Maskew Miller Longman

**Prentice Hall (Canada)**, *imprint of* Pearson Education (Prentice Hall)

**Prentice Hall (Europe)**, *imprint of* Pearson Education (Prentice Hall)

**Prentice Hall Europe**, *imprint of* Maskew Miller Longman

**Prentice Hall International**, *imprint of* Pearson Education (Prentice Hall)

**Prentice Hall (South Africa)**, *imprint of* Pearson Education (Prentice Hall)

**Prentice Hall South Africa**, *imprint of* Maskew Miller Longman

**Publitoria Publishers+**
PO Box 23334, Innesdale, Pretoria 0031
*Tel:* (012) 3790279 *Fax:* (012) 3793464
*Key Personnel*
Man Dir: L S van der Walt
Founded: 1982
Subjects: Education, Poetry
ISBN Prefix(es): 0-86880; 1-874991

**QUE College**, *imprint of* Maskew Miller Longman

**Que College**, *imprint of* Pearson Education (Prentice Hall)

**Queillerie Publishers+**
PO Box 879, Cape Town 8000
*Tel:* (021) 4232677 *Fax:* (021) 4242510
*E-mail:* rbarnard@quellerie.com
*Key Personnel*
Manager: Frederik de Jager
Founded: 1992
Membership(s): Publishers Association of South Africa (PASA).
Subjects: Biography, Business, Cookery, Fiction, Gay & Lesbian, Human Relations, Labor, Industrial Relations, Nonfiction (General)
ISBN Prefix(es): 0-7958; 1-919710
*Parent Company:* Nasionale Boekhandel
*Associate Companies:* Jonathan Ball Publishers; Human & Rousseau Publishers; Kwela Books; Leisure Hour; Leo Books; Nasou Via Afrika; Tafelberg Publishers; Van Schaik Bookstore; J L Van Schaik
*Shipping Address:* Nasionale Boekhandel, PO Box 487, Bellville 7535
*Warehouse:* Nasionale Boekhandel, PO Box 487, Bellville 7535
*Orders to:* Nasionale Boekhandel, PO Box 487, Bellville 7535 *Tel:* (021) 918-8607 *Fax:* (021) 951-4903 *E-mail:* rdoman@naspers.com

**Ravan Press (Pty) Ltd+**
PO Box 32484, Braamfontein, Johannesburg 2017
*Tel:* (011) 4840916 *Fax:* (011) 4842631
*Key Personnel*
General Manager: Monica Seeber
Sales, Publicity & Rights: Ipuseng Kotsokoane
Book Design, Production: Matthew Seal
Founded: 1972
Membership(s): the Publishers Association of South Africa.
Subjects: Anthropology, Biography, Business, Economics, Education, Environmental Studies, Ethnicity, Fiction, Government, Political Science, History, Labor, Industrial Relations, Management, Music, Dance, Nonfiction (General), Social Sciences, Sociology, Women's Studies
ISBN Prefix(es): 0-86975; 1-86917
*Parent Company:* Hodder & Stoughton Educational Southern Africa
Distributed by Hodder & Stoughton Educationa (Europe & UK); Ohio University Press (USA)
*Warehouse:* PSD, PO Box 15016, Hurlyvale 1611

**Reader's Digest Southern Africa+**
21 Dreyer St, 1st fl, Sanclare Bldg, Claremont, 8000 Cape Town
Mailing Address: Private Bag 15, 8003 Capemail
*Tel:* (021) 670 6100 *Fax:* (021) 670 6200
*E-mail:* customer.sa@readersdigest.com
*Web Site:* www.readersdigest.co.za
*Key Personnel*
Man Dir: Barry Lloyd *Fax:* (021) 6706204 *E-mail:* barry@heritage.co.za
Editorial, Books & Rights & Permissions: D O Oakes *Tel:* (021) 6706252 *Fax:* (021) 6706203 *E-mail:* dongie.oakes@readersdigest.com

Editorial, Magazines: A Spencer-Smith *Tel:* (021) 6706182 *E-mail:* tony.spencer-smith@ readersdigest.com
Financial Dir: Jeff Mann *Tel:* (021) 6702789 *Fax:* (021) 6706209 *E-mail:* jeff.mann@ readersdigest.com
Marketing, Publicity, Dir: Philip Bateman *Tel:* (021) 6702690 *Fax:* (021) 618763 *E-mail:* philip@heritage.co.za
Sr Project Editor: Sandy Shepherd *Tel:* (021) 6706255 *E-mail:* sandy.shepherd@ readersdigest.com
Direct mail books & catalogs.
Subjects: Computer Science, Cookery, Gardening, Plants, Health, Nutrition, Medicine, Nursing, Dentistry, Nonfiction (General), Travel
ISBN Prefix(es): 1-874912; 1-919750
Number of titles published annually: 5 Print
Total Titles: 53 Print
*Parent Company:* Reader's Digest Association, PO Box 235, Pleasantville, NY 10570, United States
*Ultimate Parent Company:* Heritage Collection Holdings Ltd
Imprints: AA The Motorist Publications
*Branch Office(s)*
Johannesburg Advertising Office, John Annandale *Tel:* (011) 799 2907 *Fax:* (011) 799 2999
Distributed by R D Vainons
Foreign Rights: Leigh Rautenbach (Southern Africa)
*Warehouse:* 8 Moorsom Ave, Epping 2 7475, Contact: Omar Kahaar *Fax:* (021) 548446 *E-mail:* omar-wdmkahaar@heritage.co.za

**Regents Prentice Hall**, *imprint of* Maskew Miller Longman

**Regents Prentice Hall**, *imprint of* Pearson Education (Prentice Hall)

**Renaissance**, *imprint of* Tafelberg Publishers Ltd

**Rostrum**, see HAUM (Hollandsch Afrikaansche Uitgevers Maatschappij)

**Sable Media**, see Struik Publishers (Pty) Ltd

**Sached**, *imprint of* Maskew Miller Longman

**Sasavona Books**, *imprint of* Sasavona Publishers & Booksellers

**Sasavona Publishers & Booksellers**
Private Bag X8, Braamfontein, Johannesburg 2017
*Tel:* (011) 4032502; (011) 4034150 *Fax:* (011) 3397274
*Key Personnel*
Manager: A E Kalteurider
Founded: 1974 (1875 as Swiss Mission Publishing)
Subjects: Education, Literature, Literary Criticism, Essays, Religion - Other
ISBN Prefix(es): 0-907985; 0-949985; 0-949981
*Parent Company:* Evangelical Presbyterian Church - Swiss Mission in SA, Private Bag X8, Braamfontein, Johannesburg 2017
Imprints: CMP Reprints; Sasavona Books; Swiss Mission Publications

**Schirmer**, *imprint of* Pearson Education (Prentice Hall)

**Scribner**, *imprint of* Maskew Miller Longman

**Scribner Reference**, *imprint of* Pearson Education (Prentice Hall)

**Shuter & Shooter Publishers (Pty) Ltd**
PO Box 109, Pietermaritzburg 3200
*Tel:* (033) 394 8881 *Fax:* (033) 342 7419
*Web Site:* www.shuter.co.za *Cable:* SHUSHOO
*Key Personnel*
Man Dir: Dave Ryder *E-mail:* dryder@shuter.co.za
Editorial, Rights & Permissions: J Inglis
Publicity: T Hepworth
Production: J Sharpe
Founded: 1925
Also major book dealer.
Subjects: Biography, Ethnicity, History, Nonfiction (General), Science (General), Social Sciences, Sociology, Technology
ISBN Prefix(es): 0-947476; 0-7960; 0-86985; 0-947475; 1-919778
*Parent Company:* The Natal Witness (Pty) Ltd
*Associate Companies:* Ikhwezi Publishers, PO Box 648, Umtata 5100 *Tel:* (0471) 23988 *Fax:* (0471) 22786; Reach Out Publishers (at above address)
Subsidiaries: Shuter & Shooter (Gazankulu) (Pty) Ltd; Shuter & Shooter (Transkei) (Pty) Ltd
*Branch Office(s)*
219 Werdmuller Centre, Main Rd, Claremont, Cape Town 7700
Pharmacy House, 2nd floor, 26 Juta St, Braamfontein 2017
O & S Building, Shop 18E, 18 Witklip St, Ladanna 0704
19 Fifth Avenue, Walmer 6070

**South African Institute of International Affairs+**
University of the Witwatersrand, Jan Smuts House, East Campus, 2017 Johannesburg
Mailing Address: PO Box 31596, Braamfontein, Johannesburg 2017
*Tel:* (011) 339 2021 *Fax:* (011) 339 2154
*E-mail:* saiiagen@global.co.za
*Web Site:* www.wits.ac.za/saiia
*Key Personnel*
National Dir: Dr Greg Mills
Founded: 1934
Subjects: Economics, Foreign Countries, Government, Political Science, Military Science
ISBN Prefix(es): 0-908371; 0-909239; 1-874890; 1-919810; 1-919969
*Branch Office(s)*
Cape Town, Contact: Alan Harvey *Tel:* (021) 788-9295 *Fax:* (021) 788-9261
Durban, Contact: John Dickson *Tel:* (031) 201-4877 *Fax:* (031) 201-4914
Grahamstown
Pietermaritzburg
Port Elizabeth, Contact: Peter Warmington *Tel:* (0331) 940381 *Fax:* (0331) 942332
Pretoria, Contact: Roland Henwood *Tel:* (012) 420-2687 *Fax:* (012) 420-3886
Witwatersrand, Contact: Philip Clayton *Tel:* (011) 636-2904 *Fax:* (011) 636-0512

**South African Institute of Race Relations**
PO Box 31044, Braamfontein, Johannesburg 2017
*Tel:* (011) 403-3600 *Fax:* (011) 403-3671; (011) 339-2061
*E-mail:* sairr@sairr.org.za
*Web Site:* www.sairr.org.za
*Key Personnel*
Dir: J S Kane-Berman
Marketing Manager: Joe Mpye
Founded: 1929
Specialize in human rights.
Subjects: Agriculture, Business, Ethnicity, Government, Political Science, Human Relations, Law, Public Administration, Social Sciences, Sociology, Human Rights
ISBN Prefix(es): 0-86982

**Southern Book Publishers (Pty) Ltd+**
PO Box 5563, Johannesburg 2128

*Tel:* (011) 8072292 *Fax:* (011) 8070506
*E-mail:* reneef@struik.co.za
*Key Personnel*
Man Dir: C F B Van Rooyen
Editorial, Rights & Permissions: Louise Grantham
Local Sales, Publicity: Jane Winters
Production: Renee Ferreira
Office Manager: Bernice Janse Van Rensburg *E-mail:* bernicejvr@struik.co.za
Founded: 1987
Subjects: Animals, Pets, Gardening, Plants, Health, Nutrition, How-to, Natural History, Nonfiction (General), Travel
ISBN Prefix(es): 1-86812; 0-86954
Distributed by New Holland Publishers
*Warehouse:* SDC, PO Box 193, Maitland
*Orders to:* SDC, PO Box 193, Maitland

**Spearhead**, *imprint of* New Africa Books (Pty) Ltd

**Struik Publishers (Pty) Ltd+**
Cornelis Struik House, 80 McKenzie St, Cape Town 8001
*Tel:* (021) 4624360 *Fax:* (021) 462-4379; (021) 461-9378
*E-mail:* admin@struik.co.za
*Web Site:* www.struik.co.za *Cable:* DEKENA CAPETOWN
*Key Personnel*
Man Dir: Steve Connolly
Sales Dir: Deone Maasch
Founded: 1962
Subjects: Business, Child Care & Development, Cookery, Environmental Studies, Fiction, Gardening, Plants, Humor, Natural History, Nonfiction (General), Travel, African Countries/Interests, Lifestyle, Women's Interest
ISBN Prefix(es): 0-86977; 0-947458
*Parent Company:* New Holland Publishing (South Africa) (Pty) Ltd, PO Box 1144, Cape Town 8000
*Ultimate Parent Company:* Johnnie Communications
*Associate Companies:* Struik Christian Books, PO Box 1144, Cape Town 8000
Imprints: Timmins Publishers (Pty) Ltd
Subsidiaries: Timmins; Struik-Winchester
Distributed by National Book Distributors; New Holland Publishers
*Warehouse:* Booksite Afrika, Graph Ave, Montague Gardens 7441 *Tel:* (021) 5295900 *Fax:* (021) 5511124 *Web Site:* www.booksite. co.za

**Struik-Winchester**, see Struik Publishers (Pty) Ltd

**Swiss Mission Publications**, *imprint of* Sasavona Publishers & Booksellers

**Symbol Books**, *imprint of* LAPA Publishers (Pty) Ltd

**Tafelberg Publishers Ltd+**
PO Box 879, Cape Town 8000
*Tel:* (021) 406 3033 *Fax:* (021) 406 3812
*E-mail:* tafelbrg@tafelberg.com
*Web Site:* www.nb.co.za/tafelberg *Cable:* BOEKNUUS CAPE TOWN
*Key Personnel*
General Manager: Harres Van Zyl
Founded: 1950
Publishes forms in African literature, author & political publications, books for young children & young readers in all the official languages & a wide variety of illustrated nonfiction.
Subjects: Cookery, Crafts, Games, Hobbies, Fiction, Gardening, Plants, Literature, Literary Criticism, Essays, Nonfiction (General), Romance
ISBN Prefix(es): 0-624

Number of titles published annually: 100 Print; 1
CD-ROM
Total Titles: 1,200 Print; 1 CD-ROM
*Parent Company:* Nasionale Boekhandel Ltd
*Ultimate Parent Company:* Nasionale Publisher
Imprints: Homeros; Jasmyn; Renaissance
*Orders to:* Nasionale Boekhandel, PO Box 487,
Bellville 7535 *Tel:* (021) 918-8500 *Fax:* (021)
951-4903 *E-mail:* rdoman@naspers.com

**Target Publishers (Edms) Bpk**
PO Box 2688, Klerksdorp 2570
*Tel:* (018) 4627556 *Fax:* (018) 4627557
ISBN Prefix(es): 0-9583132

**Taurus+**
PO Box 39400, Bramley 2018
*Tel:* 7860018
*Key Personnel*
Chief Executive: Tienie du Plessis; Hans Pienaar;
Gerrit Olivier; John Miles; Ampie Coetzee
Founded: 1975
ISBN Prefix(es): 0-947046
*Parent Company:* Licomil Co (Pty) Ltd

**Timmins Publishers (Pty) Ltd**, *imprint of* Struik
Publishers (Pty) Ltd

**TML Trade Publishing**
PO Box 182, Pinegowrie 2123
*Tel:* (011) 7892144 *Fax:* (011) 7893196
ISBN Prefix(es): 0-9583086; 0-9583865
*Parent Company:* Times Media Ltd

**Unibook**, *imprint of* Maskew Miller Longman

**Unisa Press+**
University of South Africa, PO Box 392, Pretoria
0003
*Tel:* (012) 42931111 *Fax:* (012) 4293221
*Web Site:* www.unisa.ac.za/dept/press/index.html
*Cable:* UNISA
*Key Personnel*
Head, Unisa Press: Mrs P Van Der Walt
*Tel:* (012) 429 3051 *E-mail:* vdwp@alpha.
unisa.ac.za
Head, Publishing & Secretary, International
Rights: Ms S J Moolman *Tel:* (012) 429 3023
*E-mail:* moolms@alpha.unisa.ac.za
Founded: 1957
Specialize in academic publications.
Subjects: Economics, Education, History, Lan-
guage Arts, Linguistics, Law, Nonfiction (Gen-
eral), Psychology, Psychiatry, Theology
ISBN Prefix(es): 0-86981; 1-86888
Total Titles: 128 Print
*Parent Company:* University of South Africa Pre-
tonia
*Orders to:* The Business Section, Unisa Press, PO
Box 392, Pretoria 0002

**United Protestant Publishers (Pty) Ltd**, see Lux
Verbi (Pty) Ltd

**University of Durban-Westville Library**
PB X54001, Durban 4000
*Tel:* (031) 8202640 *Fax:* (031) 821873
*E-mail:* mmoodley@pixie.udw.ac.za
*Telex:* 623228
*Key Personnel*
Chief Librarian: Mr M M Moodley
*E-mail:* mmoodley@pixie.udw.ac.za
Founded: 1961
Subjects: Drama, Theater, Music, Dance
ISBN Prefix(es): 0-949947; 0-947445

**University of KwaZulu-Natal Press+**
Gate M14, Ridge Rd, Scottsville, Pietermaritzburg, KwaZulu-Natal 3201

Mailing Address: Private Bag X01, Scottsville,
KwaZulu-Natal 3209
*Tel:* (033) 260 5226; (033) 260 5225 *Fax:* (033)
260 5801
*E-mail:* books@ukzn.ac.za
*Web Site:* www.ukznpress.co.za
*Key Personnel*
Publisher: Glenn Cowley
Founded: 1947
Membership(s): PASA (Publishers Association of
South Africa).
Subjects: Biography, Biological Sciences, Educa-
tion, Genealogy, Government, Political Science,
Health, Nutrition, History, Literature, Literary
Criticism, Essays, Poetry, Psychology, Psychia-
try, Regional Interests, Social Sciences, Sociol-
ogy, Women's Studies, Natural Science
ISBN Prefix(es): 0-86980; 1-86914
Number of titles published annually: 20 Print
Imprints: Killie Campbell Africana Library;
Gecko Poetry; Hadeda Books
Distributed by Africa Book Centre (London); In-
ternational Specialist Book Services (USA)

**Van Schaik Publishers+**
1064 Arcadia St, 1st floor, Hatfield 0083
Mailing Address: PO Box 12681, Hatfield 0028
*Tel:* (012) 342-2765 *Fax:* (012) 430-3563
*E-mail:* vanschaik@vanschaiknet.com
*Web Site:* www.vanschaiknet.com
*Key Personnel*
Chief Executive Officer: Leanne Martini
*E-mail:* lmartini@vanschaiknet.com
Founded: 1914
Specialize in publishing high-quality academic
texts at affordable prices. Aim to provide aca-
demic content in any form, combination or for-
mat.
Subjects: Business, Economics, Education, Gov-
ernment, Political Science, History, Labor, In-
dustrial Relations, Language Arts, Linguistics,
Management, Medicine, Nursing, Dentistry,
Public Administration, Social Sciences, Sociol-
ogy, Natural Sciences
ISBN Prefix(es): 0-627; 0-86874
Number of titles published annually: 20 Print; 3
CD-ROM; 1 Online
Total Titles: 800 Print; 3 CD-ROM; 1 Online; 6
Audio
*Parent Company:* Via Afrika
*Ultimate Parent Company:* NASPERS
Imprints: Van Schaik Publishers Academica
Distributor for Jacana
*Warehouse:* On the Dot Distribution, PO Box
487, Bellville, Contact: Marietha Van Wyk
*Tel:* (021) 918 8500 *Fax:* (021) 951 4903
*E-mail:* mjvanwy@naspers.com
*Orders to:* PO Box 487, Bellville 7535, Contact:
Cathleen Cloete *Tel:* (021) 918 8584 *Fax:* (021)
951 4903 *E-mail:* ccloete@naspers.com

**Van Schaik Publishers Academica**, *imprint of*
Van Schaik Publishers

**Vivlia Publishers & Booksellers+**
One Amanda Ave, Lea Glen, Florida 1716
Mailing Address: PO Box 1040, Florida Hills
1716
*Tel:* (011) 472-3912 *Fax:* (011) 472-4904
*E-mail:* vivlia@icon.co.ta
*Key Personnel*
Man Dir: Albert N Nemukula
National Sales & Marketing: S Mota
Editorial Service Manager: G Nose
Founded: 1990 (To serve the disadvantaged group
& publish mainly South African, 11 official
languages)
Services schools & libraries.
Subjects: Education, Literature, Literary Criti-
cism, Essays, Mathematics, Science (General)
ISBN Prefix(es): 0-9583125; 1-86867; 1-874868;
1-919799

Total Titles: 15 Print
*Branch Office(s)*
PO Box 4180, Randburg 1716
Distributor for Africa World Press Inc (US)
*Showroom(s):* Africa Book Centre, 38 King St,
London, United Kingdom, Contact: A W Zur-
burg *Tel:* (020) 7497 0309

**Vlaeberg**, *imprint of* Maskew Miller Longman

**Waterkant-Uitgewers (Edms) Bpk**
33 Waterkant St, Posbus 4539, Cape Town 8000
*Tel:* (021) 215540 *Fax:* (021) 4191865
*E-mail:* luxverbi.publ@kingsley.co.za
*Key Personnel*
Man Dir: W J van Zijl
Publicity: Mrs E M Volschenk
Founded: 1980
Subjects: Religion - Other
ISBN Prefix(es): 0-907992; 1-875081
*Parent Company:* Lux Verbi (Pty) Ltd
*Associate Companies:* Waterkant Publishers

**Who's Who of Southern Africa**
PO Box 411697, Craighall, Johannesburg 2024
*Tel:* (011) 263 4970
*Web Site:* www.whoswhosa.info/southafrica.asp
*Key Personnel*
Publisher: Gail van Zyl-Webber
Founded: 1907
Total Titles: 1 Print
*Parent Company:* Jonathan Ball Publishers SA

**Witwatersrand University Press+**
23 Junction Ave, Parktown, Johannesburg
Mailing Address: PO Wits, Johannesburg 2050
*Tel:* (011) 717 1000 *Fax:* (011) 717 1065
*Web Site:* www.wits.ac.za/wup.html
*Key Personnel*
Publisher: Veronica Klipp *Tel:* (011) 4845910
Commissioning Editor: Maggie Mostert
Founded: 1922
Scholarly publisher specializing in the Humani-
ties.
Membership(s): Publisher's Association of South
Africa.
Subjects: Anthropology, Archaeology, Biogra-
phy, Business, Crafts, Games, Hobbies, Drama,
Theater, Economics, Education, Ethnicity, Fi-
nance, Government, Political Science, History,
Language Arts, Linguistics, Law, Literature,
Literary Criticism, Essays, Medicine, Nursing,
Dentistry, Natural History, Religion - Jewish,
Science (General)
ISBN Prefix(es): 1-86814
Number of titles published annually: 20 Print
Total Titles: 160 Print
Distributed by Africa Book Centre (UK & Eu-
rope); Transaction Publishers
*Orders to:* Book Promotions, PO Box 5, Plum-
stead 7800, Contact: Rose Meny-Gibert
*Tel:* (021) 706 0949 *Fax:* (021) 706 0941
*E-mail:* orders@bookpro.ca.za

**Woodhead Faulkner**, *imprint of* Maskew Miller
Longman

**Zebra Press**, see Struik Publishers (Pty) Ltd

# Spain

## General Information

*Capital:* Madrid
*Language:* Castilian Spanish (official) is the most
widely used. Also Basque in the north, Catalan
in the northeast, Galician in the northwest
*Religion:* Roman Catholic

*Population:* 40 million
*Bank Hours:* 0900-1400 Monday-Friday; 0900-1300 Saturday
*Shop Hours:* 0900-1300, 1700-2000 Monday-Saturday
*Currency:* 100 Eurocents = 1 Euro; 166.386 Spanish pesetas = 1 Euro
*Export/Import Information:* Member of European Economic Community. Tariffs on books same as other EEC members. 4% VAT on books. Import license not required; foreign books subject to censorship. No exchange controls.
*Copyright:* UCC, Berne, Florence (see Copyright Conventions, pg xi)

**Aache Ediciones**
Avda Constitucion, 33 bajo B, 19003 Guadalajara
SAN: 000-006X
*Tel:* (0949) 220 438 *Fax:* (0949) 220 438
*E-mail:* ediciones@aache.com
*Web Site:* aache.iberlibro.net
*Key Personnel*
Dir: Antonio Herrera Casado
Founded: 1990
Specialize in Guadalajara (Spain) books.
ISBN Prefix(es): 84-87743; 84-95179

**Publicacions de l'Abadia de Montserrat**
Ausias March, 92-98, Interior C, 08013 Barcelona
SAN: 004-668X
*Tel:* (093) 2450303; (093) 2314001 *Fax:* (093) 2473594
*E-mail:* pamsa@pamsa.com
*Web Site:* www.pamsa.com
*Key Personnel*
Administrator: Jordi Ubeda i Baulo
Dir: Josep Massot i Muntaner
Founded: 1914
Subjects: Biography, Fiction, History, Language Arts, Linguistics, Literature, Literary Criticism, Essays, Music, Dance, Philosophy, Religion - Catholic, Theology
ISBN Prefix(es): 84-7202; 84-7826; 84-8415

**Academia de la Llingua Asturiana**
C/Marques de Santa Cruz 6-2, Apartau de Correos 574, 33080 Uvieu/Oviedo Asturias
SAN: 000-0205
*Tel:* (0985) 211837 *Fax:* (0985) 226816
*E-mail:* alla@asturnet.es
*Web Site:* www.asturnet.es/alla
*Key Personnel*
President: Ana Maria Cano Gonzalez
Founded: 1981
Subjects: Anthropology, Language Arts, Linguistics, Literature, Literary Criticism, Essays
ISBN Prefix(es): 84-8168; 84-9750; 84-86936
*Orders to:* Albora Llibros, Pz Romualdo Alvargonzalez 5, 33202 Xixon *Tel:* 85354213 *Fax:* 85354213

**Acantilado+**
Subsidiary of Quaderns Crema
Muntaner, 462 3 1, 08006 Barcelona
*Tel:* (093) 4144906 *Fax:* (093) 4147107
*E-mail:* correo@elacantilado.com
*Web Site:* www.elacantilado.com
*Key Personnel*
Man Dir: Jaume Vallcorba
Founded: 1999
Subjects: History, Literature, Literary Criticism, Essays, Poetry, Narratives
ISBN Prefix(es): 84-95359; 84-930657
Number of titles published annually: 50 Print
Total Titles: 100 Print

**Editorial Acanto SA**
Bertran, 113, 08023 Barcelona
SAN: 022-2322
*Tel:* (093) 4189093 *Fax:* (093) 4189088
*E-mail:* acantocb@dtinf.net

*Key Personnel*
Editor: Silvia Blume
Founded: 1987
Subjects: Cookery, Crafts, Games, Hobbies, Gardening, Plants, Health, Nutrition, Sports, Athletics
ISBN Prefix(es): 84-86673; 84-95376

**Acento Editorial+**
Joaquin Turina 39, 28004 Madrid
SAN: 000-0361
*Tel:* (091) 5088996; (091) 5085145; (091) 4228976 *Fax:* (091) 5089927; (091) 5084974
*E-mail:* informa@acento-editorial.com
*Key Personnel*
Contact: MaPaz Serrano
Founded: 1993
Subjects: Fiction, How-to, Music, Dance, Nonfiction (General), Science (General), Self-Help, Travel
ISBN Prefix(es): 84-483

**Editorial Acervo SL+**
Ronda General Mitre 200, 08006 Barcelona
SAN: 022-2349
*Tel:* (093) 2122664 *Fax:* (093) 4174425
*E-mail:* acervo25@hotmail.com
*Key Personnel*
Man Dir: Ana Perales
Founded: 1954
Subjects: History, Law, Literature, Literary Criticism, Essays, Science Fiction, Fantasy
ISBN Prefix(es): 84-7002
Total Titles: 1 Print

**Editorial Acribia SA+**
Royo Urieta 23, 50006 Zaragoza
SAN: 022-2357
Mailing Address: PO Box 466, 50080 Zaragoza
*Tel:* (0976) 232089 *Fax:* (0976) 219212
*E-mail:* acribia@editorialacribia.com
*Web Site:* www.editorialacribia.com
*Key Personnel*
Man Dir & other offices: Pascual Lopez Lorenzo
Founded: 1957
Subjects: Agriculture, Medicine, Nursing, Dentistry, Natural History, Science (General), Veterinary Science
ISBN Prefix(es): 84-200; 84-370
Number of titles published annually: 30 Print
Total Titles: 980 Print

**Centro de Estudios Adams-Ediciones Valbuena SA**
Alcala, 135, 28009 Barcelona
SAN: 002-046X
*Tel:* (093) 4465000; (0902) 333 543 *Fax:* (093) 4465004
*E-mail:* info@adams.es
*Web Site:* www.adams.es
*Key Personnel*
Dir General: Felix Perez Ruiz de Valbuena
Founded: 1957
Subjects: Accounting, Career Development, Computer Science, Labor, Industrial Relations, Psychology, Psychiatry, Public Administration, Transportation
ISBN Prefix(es): 84-7357; 84-8303; 84-9731

**Editorial AEDOS SA+**
Consell de Cent, 391, 08009 Barcelona
SAN: 022-2373
*Tel:* (093) 488 34 92 *Fax:* (093) 487 76 59
*Web Site:* www.mundiprensa.es
*Key Personnel*
Manager: Cristina Concellon
Founded: 1939
Subjects: Agriculture, Animals, Pets, Biological Sciences, Developing Countries, Earth Sciences, Economics, Energy, Environmental Studies, Foreign Countries, Human Relations,

Labor, Industrial Relations, Management, Veterinary Science
ISBN Prefix(es): 84-7003
*Parent Company:* Mundiprensa Libros

**AENOR (Asociacion Espanola de Normalizacion y Certificacion)+**
Genova, 6, 28004 Madrid
*Tel:* (091) 4 32 60 00; (0902) 102 201 *Fax:* (091) 3 10 36 95
*E-mail:* info@aenor.es
*Web Site:* www.aenor.es
*Key Personnel*
President: Manual Lopez Cachero
General Dir: Ramon Naz Pajares
Dir, Operations: Avelino Brito Marquinas
*Fax:* (01) 913 10 31 72
Head, Publishing Dept: Silvia Sevilla
*E-mail:* ssevilla@aenor.es
Founded: 1986
Membership(s): ISO; IEC; CEN; CENELEC; ETSI, COPANT, IQNET; GENE.
Subjects: Standardization & Certification
ISBN Prefix(es): 84-8143

**Editorial Afers, SL+**
La Llibertat, 12, Apartat de Correus 267, 46470 Catarroja, Valencia
*Tel:* (0961) 26 86 54 *Fax:* (0961) 27 25 82
*E-mail:* afers@provicom.com
*Web Site:* www.provicom.com/afers
*Key Personnel*
Dir: Rafael Aracil i Marti i Josep Termes i Ardevol
Editorial Dir: Vicent S Olmos i Tamarit
*E-mail:* vicent.olmos@provicom.com
Promotion & Rights: Tremedal Ortiz
Founded: 1985
Subjects: History, Regional Interests, Social Sciences, Sociology
ISBN Prefix(es): 84-86574
Foreign Rep(s): Agusti Colomines

**Agata**, *imprint of* Libsa Editorial SA

**Agencia Espanola de Cooperacion**
Ave de los Reyes Catolicos, 4, 28040 Madrid
SAN: 001-6446
*Tel:* (091) 5838100; (091) 5838254; (091) 5838101; (091) 5838102 *Fax:* (091) 5838310; (091) 5838311; (091) 5838313
*Web Site:* www.aeci.es
*Key Personnel*
Publishing Dir: Antonio Papell Cervera
Subjects: Art, Biography, Drama, Theater, Economics, Education, History, Law, Literature, Literary Criticism, Essays, Poetry, Social Sciences, Sociology
ISBN Prefix(es): 84-7232

**Agora Editorial+**
Carreteria 92, 29008 Malaga
SAN: 003-9683
*Tel:* (095) 2228699; (095) 2221847 *Fax:* (095) 2226411
*Key Personnel*
Publicity Dir: Antonio Gonzalez Alcalde
Commercial Dir: Jose Conzado Mora
Founded: 1979
Subjects: Literature, Literary Criticism, Essays, Mathematics
ISBN Prefix(es): 84-85698; 84-8160

**Ediciones Agrotecnicas, SL**
Plaza de Espana 10 5° Izq, 28008 Madrid
*Tel:* (091) 5473515 *Fax:* (091) 5474506
*E-mail:* agrotecnicas@agrotecnica.com
*Web Site:* www.agrotecnica.com
Subjects: Agriculture, Civil Engineering
ISBN Prefix(es): 84-87480
Subsidiaries: ISLA Agricola, SA

**Editorial Aguaclara+**
C/Rosello, 55, 03010 Alacant
SAN: 002-242X
*Tel:* 965 240064 *Fax:* 965 259302
*E-mail:* edit.aguaclara@natural.es
*Key Personnel*
Dir: Luis T Bonmati Gutierrez
Founded: 1982
Subjects: Fiction, Literature, Literary Criticism,
Essays, Poetry, Religion - Catholic
ISBN Prefix(es): 84-86234

**Aguilar SA de Ediciones**
Torrelaguna, 60, 28043 Madrid
SAN: 000-0779
*Tel:* (091) 7449060 *Fax:* (091) 7449224
*E-mail:* limarquezes@santillana.es
*Web Site:* www.gruposantillana.com
*Telex:* 47137 Agata *Cable:* GUILARDITOR
*Key Personnel*
President: Jesus de Polanco Gutierrez
Vice President: Francisco Perez Gonzalez
Dir General: Ambrosio Maria Ochoa Vazquez
Editorial Dir: Jaime Salinas Bonmati; Mauricio
Santos Arrabal
Dir, Children's Books: Miguel Azaola
Sales Dir: Miguel Lendinez
Founded: 1960
Publisher of nonfiction books in Spanish.
Subjects: Art, Fiction, Geography, Geology, His-
tory, How-to, Humor, Journalism, Language
Arts, Linguistics, Medicine, Nursing, Dentistry,
Nonfiction (General), Philosophy, Religion -
Other, Science (General), Self-Help, Travel
ISBN Prefix(es): 84-03
*Branch Office(s)*
Aguilar SA, Argentina
Isla Negra SA, Chile
Libreria Cientifica, Colombia
Edidac, Ecuador
Aguilar SA, Mexico
La Familia y Studium, Peru
Itaca SA
Editemas y Dilae SA, Venezuela

**AITIM (Asociacion de Investigacion Tecnica de
las industrias de la Madera y Corcho)+**
Flora 3-2, 28013 Madrid
*Tel:* (091) 5425864 *Fax:* (091) 5590512
*E-mail:* informame@aitim.es
*Web Site:* www.aitim.es
*Key Personnel*
Dir: Fernando Peraza Sanchez; J Enrique Peraza
Sanchez *E-mail:* e.peraza@aitim.es
Founded: 1964

**Ediciones Akal SA+**
Sector Foresta, 1, 28760 Tres Cantos, Madrid
SAN: 001-5326
*Tel:* (091) 8061996 *Fax:* (091) 6564911; (091)
8044028
*E-mail:* pedidos.akal@akal.com (orders);
edicion@akal.com; universidad@akal.com;
educacion@akal.com; prensa@akal.com
*Web Site:* www.akal.com
*Key Personnel*
Editor: Ramon Acal
International Rights: Juan Barja
Founded: 1973
Subjects: Anthropology, Archaeology, Architec-
ture & Interior Design, Art, Asian Studies,
Behavioral Sciences, Economics, Education,
English as a Second Language, Film, Video,
Law, Philosophy, Psychology, Psychiatry, So-
cial Sciences, Sociology
ISBN Prefix(es): 84-460; 84-406; 84-7339; 84-
7600
*Associate Companies:* Ediciones Istmo

**Editorial 'Alas'+**
C/Villarroel N° 124, 08011 Barcelona
SAN: 002-2446

Mailing Address: Apdo 36.274, 08080 Barcelona
*Tel:* (093) 4537506; (093) 3233445 *Fax:* (093)
4537506
*E-mail:* sala@editorial-alas.com
*Web Site:* www.editorial-alas.com
*Key Personnel*
Contact: Jordi Sala
Founded: 1923
Specialize in sports subjects with emphasis on
martial arts.
Subjects: Health, Nutrition, Parapsychology, Reli-
gion - Buddhist, Sports, Athletics, Martial arts
ISBN Prefix(es): 84-203

**Alba,** *imprint of* Libsa Editorial SA

**Alberdania SL+**
Istillaga Plaza, 2 Behea C, 20304 Irun, Gipuzkoa
SAN: 000-1201
*Tel:* (0943) 63 28 14 *Fax:* (0943) 63 80 55
*E-mail:* alberdania@ctv.es
*Key Personnel*
Contact: Jorge Gimenez Bech
Founded: 1993
Subjects: Anthropology, Art, Literature, Literary
Criticism, Essays
ISBN Prefix(es): 84-88669; 84-95589

**El Aleph Editores,** *imprint of* Grup 62

**El Aleph Editores**
Imprint of Grup 62
Peu de la Creu, 4, 08001 Barcelona
*Tel:* (093) 443 71 00 *Fax:* (093) 443 71 30
*E-mail:* correu@grup62.com
*Web Site:* www.grup62.com
*Key Personnel*
Rights Manager: Laura Pujol
ISBN Prefix(es): 84-931977

**Alfaguara Ediciones SA - Grupo Santillana+**
Torrelaguna, 60, 28043 Madrid
SAN: 001-5431
*Tel:* (091) 744 90 60 *Fax:* (091) 744 92 24
*E-mail:* loboan@santillana.es
*Web Site:* www.santillana.es
*Telex:* 47137 Agata *Cable:* GUARA MADRID
*Key Personnel*
Man Dir: Guillermo Schavelzon
Editor: Amaya Elezcano
Editor Assistant: Asun Lasaosa
Rights & Permissions: Rosa Arrizabalaga
Founded: 1960
Subjects: Fiction, Literature, Literary Criticism,
Essays, Travel
ISBN Prefix(es): 84-204
Subsidiaries: Alfaguara; Aguilar; Attea; El Pais-
Aguilar; Taurus
*U.S. Office(s):* Santillana Publishing Co, 901
W Walnut St, Bldg A, Compton, CA 90220,
United States

**Ediciones Alfar SA**
Centro Andaluz del Libro, Pol Ind La Chaparrilla,
parcela 34-36, Carretera Sevilla-Malaga, KM 3,
41016 Sevilla
SAN: 001-544X
*Tel:* (095) 4406100; (095) 4406366; (095)
4406614 *Fax:* (05) 4402580
*Key Personnel*
President: Manuel Angel Vazquez Medel
Dir General: Manuel Diaz Vargas
Founded: 1982
Subjects: Anthropology, Archaeology, Behavioral
Sciences, Fiction, History, Literature, Liter-
ary Criticism, Essays, Mathematics, Medicine,
Nursing, Dentistry, Philosophy, Social Sciences,
Sociology
ISBN Prefix(es): 84-7898; 84-8248; 84-86256

**Edicions Alfons el Magnanim, Institucio
Valenciana d'Estudis i Investigacio+**
Quevedo 10, 46001 Valencia
SAN: 002-0923
*Tel:* (096) 3883756 *Fax:* (096) 3883751
*Web Site:* www.alfonselmagnanim.com
*Key Personnel*
President: Fernando Giner Giner
Vice President: Vicente Ferrer Rosello
Dir: Ricardo Belleveser Icardo *Tel:* (0963)
883 168 *E-mail:* ricardbellveser@
alfonselmagnanim.com
Subjects: Ethnicity, Government, Political Sci-
ence, History, Social Sciences, Sociology
ISBN Prefix(es): 84-7822; 84-500; 84-398; 84-
505; 84-600
*Warehouse:* Corona, 36, 46002 Valencia *Tel:* (06)
3912561; 3912562
*Orders to:* LLIG, Pl Manises, 3, 46003 Valencia
*Tel:* (06) 3866170

**Editorial Algazara+**
Lisboa, 48, 29006 Malaga
SAN: 002-2519
*Tel:* (095) 2358284 *Fax:* (095) 2333175
Founded: 1991
Membership(s): Editors Association of Andalucia.
Subjects: History, Literature, Literary Criticism,
Essays
ISBN Prefix(es): 84-87999

**Alianza Editorial SA+**
Division of General Edition
Juan Ignacio Luca de Tena, 15, 28027 Madrid
SAN: 000-1570
*Tel:* (091) 3938888 *Fax:* (091) 3207480
*E-mail:* alianza@anaya.es; mmorales@anaya.es
*Web Site:* www.alianzaeditorial.es
*Key Personnel*
Man Dir: Luis Sunen Garcia
Marketing: Ruth Zauner
Rights & Permissions: Laura Malejakis
Founded: 1966
Specialize in books for adults.
Subjects: Art, Fiction, Government, Political Sci-
ence, History, Mathematics, Music, Dance,
Philosophy, Poetry, Science (General), Social
Sciences, Sociology
ISBN Prefix(es): 84-206
*Parent Company:* Grupo Anaya
*Associate Companies:* Alianza Editorial Ar-
gentina, Av Belgrano 355-Piso 10, Buenos
Aires 1092, Argentina, Jorge Lafforgue
*Tel:* (1) 4342 4426; Alianza Editorial Mex-
icana, 180 Remacimiento, Col San Juan Tli-
huaca, Azcapotzalco 02400 DF, Mexico, Juan
Carlos Arguelles *Tel:* (05) 561 8333 *Fax:* (05)
561 5231

**Alinco SA - Aura Comunicacio**
Placa Lesseps, 33, 08023 Barcelona
SAN: 000-5339
*Tel:* (093) 2172054 *Fax:* (093) 2373469
ISBN Prefix(es): 84-87711

**Alta Fulla Editorial**
Passatge d'Alio, 10, 08037 Barcelona
SAN: 000-1694
*Tel:* (093) 4590708 *Fax:* (093) 2075203
*E-mail:* altafulla@altafulla.com
*Web Site:* www.altafulla.com
*Key Personnel*
Editor & Dir: Josep J Moli Cambray
Founded: 1977
Specialize in linguistics & paperback books.
Subjects: Anthropology, Architecture & Interior
Design, Cookery, Crafts, Games, Hobbies, Eco-
nomics, Social Sciences, Sociology, Antropolo-
gia, Artes y Oficios, Cultura Popular, Etno-
grafia, Facsimiles de Libros Antiguos, Folklore,
Mythology
ISBN Prefix(es): 84-85403; 84-86556; 84-7900

**Altea, Taurus, Alfaguara SA**
Torrelaguna, 60, 28043 Madrid
SAN: 005-0881
*Tel:* (091) 744 90 60 *Fax:* (091) 744 92 24
*E-mail:* clientes@santillana.es
*Web Site:* www.alfaguara.santillana.es
*Key Personnel*
Man Dir: Ambrosio Ochoa
Editorial: Jose Antonio Millan; Luis Sunen
Publicity & Promotion: Maria de Calonje
Rights & Permissions: Rosa Arrizabalaga
Founded: 1956
Subjects: Anthropology, Art, Biography, Educa-
    tion, Government, Political Science, History,
    Language Arts, Linguistics, Literature, Literary
    Criticism, Essays, Music, Dance, Philosophy
ISBN Prefix(es): 84-306; 84-372; 84-204

**Ediciones Altera SL+**
Comte d'Urgell, 64 1r 1a, 08011 Barcelona
SAN: 006-3428
*Tel:* (093) 4519537 *Fax:* (093) 4517441
*E-mail:* editorial@altera.net
*Key Personnel*
Commerical Manager: Mr Guillermo Losada
Founded: 1995
Subjects: Literature, Literary Criticism, Essays
ISBN Prefix(es): 84-920659; 84-89779
Number of titles published annually: 8 Print
Total Titles: 34 Print
*Orders to:* Prologo Distribuciones, Mascado 35,
    Bajas, 08032 Barcelona

**Ambit Serveis Editorials, SA+**
Consell de Cent, 282 baixos, 08007 Barcelona
SAN: 000-183X
*Tel:* (093) 4881342 *Fax:* (093) 4874772
*Key Personnel*
Dir: Josep M A Benach Olivella
Founded: 1981
Subjects: Art, Cookery, Geography, Geology,
    Photography, Craftsmanship, Fine Arts, Nature
ISBN Prefix(es): 84-89681; 84-87342; 84-86147

**Amnistia Internacional Editorial SL**
Palmera, 15, 28029 Madrid
SAN: 002-2608
*Tel:* (091) 315 2851 *Fax:* (091) 323 2158
*E-mail:* amnistia.internacional@a-i.es
*Key Personnel*
Dir: Cristina Martinez
Founded: 1987
Subjects: Developing Countries, Education, For-
    eign Countries, Government, Political Science,
    Law, Nonfiction (General), Regional Interests,
    Social Sciences, Sociology
ISBN Prefix(es): 84-86874
*U.S. Office(s):* AI-USA, 304 Pennsylvania Ave
    SE, Washington, DC, DC 20003, United States
Distributed by La Catarata; El Pais Aguilar

**AMV Ediciones**, see Ediciones A Madrid
    Vicente

**AMV Ediciones+**
Calle Almansa, 94, 28040 Madrid
*Tel:* (091) 5336926; (091) 5349368 *Fax:* (091)
    5530286
*Web Site:* www.amvediciones.com
*Key Personnel*
Manager: Antonio Madrid Vicente
    *E-mail:* amadrid@acta.es
Founded: 1986
Specialize also in cooling, heating & construction.
Subjects: Agriculture, Electronics, Electrical En-
    gineering, Engineering (General), Gardening,
    Plants, Health, Nutrition, Medicine, Nursing,
    Dentistry, Science (General), Technology, Wine
    & Spirits, Food Technology
ISBN Prefix(es): 84-89922

Number of titles published annually: 15 Print;
    110 Online; 1 E-Book
Total Titles: 110 Print; 10 CD-ROM; 110 Online;
    1 E-Book

**Editorial Anagrama SA**
Pedro de la Creu, 58, 08034 Barcelona
SAN: 022-2616
*Tel:* 93 203 76 52 *Fax:* 93 203 77 38
*E-mail:* anagrama@anagrama-ed.es
*Web Site:* www.anagrama-ed.es
*Telex:* 98753 Agram E
*Key Personnel*
Publisher: Jorge Herralde
Founded: 1968
Subjects: Anthropology, Literature, Literary Criti-
    cism, Essays, Philosophy, Psychology, Psychia-
    try, Social Sciences, Sociology
ISBN Prefix(es): 84-339

**Ediciones Anaya SA+**
Juan Ignacio Luca de Tena, 15, 28027 Madrid
*Tel:* (091) 393 86 00 *Fax:* (091) 320 91 29; (091)
    742 66 31
*E-mail:* cga@anaya.es
*Web Site:* www.anaya.es
*Telex:* 22039 Anaya E *Cable:* Edinaya
*Key Personnel*
Chairman: Maria Isabel Andres Bravo
Vice President: Juan Jose Losada
Man Dir: Enrique Coque
Editorial, Rights & Permissions: Ramiro Sanchez
Sales: Antonio Gutierrez
Founded: 1959
Subjects: Education
ISBN Prefix(es): 84-207
*Parent Company:* Grupo Anaya, Juan Ignacio,
    Luca de Tena 15, 28027 Madrid
*Associate Companies:* Credsa, Calabria 108,
    08015 Barcelona; Algaida Editores SA, Avda
    de San Francisco Javier s/n, Edificio Hermes,
    41005 Seville, Juan Ignacio, Luca de Tena 15,
    28027 Madrid; Ediciones Generales Anaya,
    Anaya Multimedia, Juan Ignacio, Luca de Tena
    15, 28027 Madrid; Edicions Xerais de Galicia,
    Doctor Maranon 10, 36211 Vigo; Ediciones
    Catedra SA; Ediciones Piramide SA; Ediciones
    Versal SA; Editorial Barcanova SA; Editorial
    Biblograf SA; Editorial Tecnos SA

**Anaya Educacion**
Juan Ignacio Luca de Tena, 15, 28027 Madrid
*Tel:* (091) 393 86 00 *Fax:* (091) 320 91 29; (091)
    742 66 31
*E-mail:* cga@anaya.es
*Web Site:* www.anaya.es
*Key Personnel*
Marketing Dir: Alejandro Sanchez
    *E-mail:* asanchez@anaya.es
ISBN Prefix(es): 84-207

**Anaya-Touring Club+**
Unit of Grufo Anaya SA
Juan Ignacio Luca de Tena, 15, 28027 Madrid
*Tel:* (091) 393 86 00 *Fax:* (091) 742 66 31; (091)
    320 91 29
*E-mail:* cga@anaya.es
*Web Site:* www.anaya.es
*Key Personnel*
Publisher: Pedro Pardo *Tel:* (01) 3938935
    *Fax:* (01) 3207022 *E-mail:* ppardo@anaya.es
International Rights: Luis Bartolome
Founded: 1989
Specialize in travel books, guides, phrase books.
Subjects: Travel
ISBN Prefix(es): 84-8165
Number of titles published annually: 30 Print
Total Titles: 280 Print
Imprints: Guia Viva; Guiarama; Guiatotal

**Anglo-Didactica, SL Editorial+**
Santiago de Compostela, 16, BAJO-B, 28034
    Madrid
SAN: 002-2667
*Tel:* (091) 3780188 *Fax:* (091) 3780188
*E-mail:* anglodidac@aregen.net
*Key Personnel*
Chief Executive Officer & Administration:
    Ana Merino Olmos *E-mail:* anamerino@
    worldonline.es
Founded: 1986
Specialize in bilingual books (Spanish-English)
    for learning or teaching both English & Span-
    ish.
Subjects: Education, English as a Second Lan-
    guage, Language Arts, Linguistics
ISBN Prefix(es): 84-86623
Number of titles published annually: 4 Print
Total Titles: 60 Print
Distributed by Bilingual Publications Co

**Editorial Anthropos del Hombre+**
Poligono Industrial Can Roses, nave 22, 08191
    Rubi Barcelona
SAN: 000-2313
*Tel:* (093) 6972296 *Fax:* (093) 6972296
*Key Personnel*
Editorial Dir: Esteban Mate
Founded: 1981
ISBN Prefix(es): 84-7658; 84-85887
*Distribution Center:* Literal Book Distributors,
    PO Box 713, Adelphi, MD 20783, United
    States (USA), Contact: Jose Valencia

**Arambol, SL+**
Garcia de Paredes, 86, 28010 Madrid
SAN: 002-2713
*Tel:* (091) 3194057 *Fax:* (091) 3194057
*E-mail:* arambolsl@hotmail.com
*Key Personnel*
Administrator: Monica Guijarro
Founded: 1988
Subjects: Music, Dance
ISBN Prefix(es): 84-88128
Distributed by Piles; Seemsa
Distributor for Schell Music

**Editorial Aranzadi SA**
Ctra de Aoiz, Km 3, 5, 31486 Elcano
SAN: 002-273X
*Tel:* (0902) 444 144 *Fax:* (0948) 297 200
*E-mail:* clientes@aranzadi.es
*Web Site:* www.aranzadi.es
*Key Personnel*
President: Mariae de Aranzadi
General Dir: Jose Ruiz Cerrillo; Fernando Lopez
    Lorente
Sales & Marketing Dir: Rafael Rodriguez Galobart
Information Dir: Luis De La Guardia
Personnel Dir: Herminio De Vicente Medina
Publications Dir: Alberto Larrondo Ilondain
Sales Administrative Dir: Edurne Goni
Finance Dir: Pello Irujo Amezaga
Founded: 1929
Loose leaf publications, books & online products.
Subjects: Finance, Law, Management
ISBN Prefix(es): 84-7016; 84-8193; 84-9767; 84-
    8410
Total Titles: 25 CD-ROM; 15 Online
*Branch Office(s)*
Elcano Navarra
Geova
Madrid
Editorial Aranzadi Madrid, C/Genova 25, Madrid,
    Contact: Inigo Mosloso *Tel:* (091) 3080835
    *Fax:* (091) 3101071 *E-mail:* clientes@aranzadi.
    es

**Editorial Franciscana Aranzazu**
Santuario de Aranzazu, 20567 Onati
SAN: 000-2682

*Tel:* (043) 780797; (043) 780951 *Fax:* (043) 783370
*Key Personnel*
Dir: Juan Ignacio Larrea
ISBN Prefix(es): 84-7240; 84-404; 84-398

**Arco Libros SL+**
Juan Bautista de Toledo, 28, 28002 Madrid
*Tel:* (091) 4153687; (091) 4161371 *Fax:* (091) 4135907
*E-mail:* arcolibros@arcomuralla.com
*Web Site:* www.arcomuralla.com
*Key Personnel*
Man Dir: Lidio Nieto Jimenez *Tel:* (091) 4161371
Founded: 1985
Subjects: History, Language Arts, Linguistics, Library & Information Sciences, Literature, Literary Criticism, Essays, Philology
ISBN Prefix(es): 84-7635

**Arguval Editorial SA+**
Heroes de Sostoa, 122, 29002 Malaga
SAN: 002-2780
*Tel:* (095) 2318784; (095) 2360213 *Fax:* (095) 2323715
*E-mail:* editorial@arguval.com
*Web Site:* www.arguval.com
*Key Personnel*
Dir: Francisco Arguelles
Founded: 1983
ISBN Prefix(es): 84-86167; 84-89672; 84-95948

**Editorial Ariel SA+**
Member of Grupo Planeta
Diagonal 662-664, 7a planta B, 08008 Barcelona
*Tel:* (093) 496 70 30 *Fax:* (093) 496 70 32
*E-mail:* editorial@ariel.es
*Web Site:* www.ariel.es
*Key Personnel*
General Manager: Jose Luis Castillejo
    *E-mail:* castillejo@ariel.es
Publisher, Foreign Rights: Asuncion Hernandez
    *E-mail:* ahernandez@ariel.es
Founded: 1941
Subjects: Economics, Geography, Geology, History, Literature, Literary Criticism, Essays, Philosophy, Psychology, Psychiatry, Science (General), Social Sciences, Sociology
ISBN Prefix(es): 84-344
Number of titles published annually: 80 Print; 80 Online; 80 E-Book
Total Titles: 700 Online; 700 E-Book
*Associate Companies:* Editorial Seix Barral SA
*U.S. Office(s):* Planeta Publishing Corp, 939 Crandon Blvd, Unidades 18 & 19, Key Biscayne, FL 33149, United States, Contact: Eugeni Roca *Tel:* 305-361-0053 *Fax:* 305-361-0054 *E-mail:* eroca@netrox.net

**Asociacion de Investigacion Tecnica de las industrias de la Madera y Corcho**, see AITIM (Asociacion de Investigacion Tecnica de las industrias de la Madera y Corcho)

**Asociacion para el Progreso de la Direccion (APD)**
Jose Maria Olabarri, 2, 48001 Bilbao
SAN: 000-3662
*Tel:* (094) 423 22 50 *Fax:* (094) 423 62 49
*E-mail:* apd@bil.apd.es
*Web Site:* www.apd.es
*Key Personnel*
Dir, Publications: Vidal Perez Herrero
Subjects: Business
ISBN Prefix(es): 84-7019

**Editorial Astri SA+**
Riera Can Pahissa, 14-18 Nave 11, Poligono Industrial CL PLA, 08750 Molins de Rei Barcelona
SAN: 002-2829

*Tel:* (034) 936 801 207 *Fax:* (034) 936 803 194
*E-mail:* astri@astri.es
*Web Site:* www.astri.es *Cable:* ASTRI
*Key Personnel*
Manager: Joaquin Minano
Founded: 1983
Subjects: Art, Astrology, Occult, Cookery, Crafts, Games, Hobbies, Fashion, Film, Video, Gardening, Plants, Health, Nutrition, House & Home, How-to, Nonfiction (General), Science Fiction, Fantasy, Self-Help, Western Fiction
ISBN Prefix(es): 84-7590; 84-469
Number of titles published annually: 80 Print
*Bookshop(s):* Passatje del Libre, Torret del Olla, 166, 08023 Barcelona

**Sociedad de Educacion Atenas SA+**
Mayor 81, 28013 Madrid
SAN: 004-9646
*Tel:* (091) 5480127 *Fax:* (091) 5591771
*Key Personnel*
Man Dir, Editorial: Santiago L de Vega
Founded: 1935
Subjects: Biography, Education, Psychology, Psychiatry, Religion - Other
ISBN Prefix(es): 84-7020

**Atrium Books**, *imprint of* Atrium Group

**Atrium Group+**
Ganduxer, 112, 1st floor, 08022 Barcelona
SAN: 000-2801
*Tel:* (093) 2540099 *Fax:* (093) 2118139
*E-mail:* atrium@atriumgroup.org
*Web Site:* www.atriumbooks.com
Founded: 1993
Subjects: Architecture & Interior Design
ISBN Prefix(es): 84-8185
Imprints: Atrium Books
Distributed by CDS Inc

**Augustinus Editorial**, see Avgvstinvs

**Biblioteca de Autores Cristianos+**
Don Ramon de la Cruz, 57, 1° A-B, 28001 Madrid
SAN: 003-9004
*Tel:* (091) 3090862; (091) 3090973 *Fax:* (091) 3091980
*E-mail:* bac@planalfa.es
*Key Personnel*
Dir: D Bernardo Herradez Rubio
Sales: Manuel Garcia Hernandez
Publicity: Bartolome Parera Galmes
Founded: 1945
Subjects: Astrology, Occult, History, Philosophy, Religion - Other, Theology
ISBN Prefix(es): 84-7914; 84-220
*Warehouse:* Aragoneses, No 8, Poligono Industrial, 28100 Alcobendas

**Avgvstinvs**
General Davila 5, bajo D, 28003 Madrid
SAN: 000-443X
*Tel:* (091) 5342070 *Fax:* (091) 5544801
*E-mail:* revista@avgvstinvs.org
*Web Site:* www.avgvstinvs.org
*Key Personnel*
Dir: John J Oldfield *E-mail:* oar.sezeq@terra.es
Subjects: Theology
ISBN Prefix(es): 84-85096; 84-604; 84-605; 84-400; 84-300

**Editorial Ayuso**
San Bernardo 48, 28015 Madrid
SAN: 000-5193
*Tel:* (091) 2228080
Subjects: Social Sciences, Sociology
ISBN Prefix(es): 84-336

**Ediciones B, SA+**
Bailen, 84, 08009 Barcelona
SAN: 001-5911
*Tel:* (093) 484 66 00 *Fax:* (093) 232 46 60
*Web Site:* www.edicionesb.es; www.edicionesb.com
*Telex:* 53183
*Key Personnel*
Man Dir: Blanca Rosa Roca
Assistant Dir: Carlos Ramos
Production Dir: Jordi Omella
Head of Production: Jordi Aspa
Public Relations: Silvia Fernandez
Rights: Alejandra Segrelles
Founded: 1986
Subjects: Biography, Fiction, Humor, Nonfiction (General)
ISBN Prefix(es): 84-406; 84-7735

**BAC**, see Biblioteca de Autores Cristianos

**Baile del Sol, Colectivo Cultural+**
Apdo de Correos 133, 38280 Tegueste, Santa Cruz de Tenerife
SAN: 001-0103
*Tel:* 676438253; 922570196
*E-mail:* baile@idecnet.com
*Web Site:* www.bailedelsol.com
*Key Personnel*
General Coordinator: Tito Exposito
Founded: 1992
Subjects: Alternative, History, Poetry, Self-Help
ISBN Prefix(es): 84-88671; 84-95309

**Editorial Barath SA+**
Blasco de Garay 15, 28015 Madrid
SAN: 002-2977
*Tel:* (091) 4496049
*Key Personnel*
Man Dir: Victorino del Pozo
Sales: Cinta Barrobes
Production: Jorge Vines
Founded: 1980
Subjects: Astrology, Occult, Human Relations
ISBN Prefix(es): 84-85799
*Associate Companies:* Distribuciones Alfaomega SA, Calle Calvo Asensio 13, 28015 Madrid

**Editorial Barcanova SA+**
Placa Lesseps, 33 entl, 08023 Barcelona
SAN: 022-2985
*Tel:* (093) 2172054 *Fax:* (093) 2373469
*E-mail:* barcanova@barcanova.es
*Web Site:* www.barcanova.es
*Key Personnel*
Dir General: Ramon Besora Oliva
Editorial: Jordi Galofre
Production: Enric Canut
Founded: 1981
Subjects: Education
ISBN Prefix(es): 84-7533; 84-489; 84-85923; 84-485; 84-95103; 84-95184
*Parent Company:* Grupo Anaya, Madrid
*Associate Companies:* Ediciones Anaya SA

**Editorial Barcino SA+**
Montseny, 9 baixos, 08012 Barcelona
SAN: 002-3000
*Tel:* (093) 2186888 *Fax:* (093) 2186888
*E-mail:* ebarcino@editorialbarcino.com
*Web Site:* www.editorialbarcino.com
*Key Personnel*
Literary Dir: Amadeu J Soberanas i Lleo
Founded: 1924
Subjects: Literature, Literary Criticism, Essays
ISBN Prefix(es): 84-7226

**Beascoa SA Ediciones**
Travessera de Gracia 47-49, 08021 Barcelona
SAN: 001-5997
*Tel:* (093) 3660300 *Fax:* (093) 3660449
*E-mail:* info@beascoa.com

*Web Site:* www.plaza.es
*Key Personnel*
President: Francisco Beascoa-Anton
ISBN Prefix(es): 84-488; 84-7546
*Associate Companies:* Sol-Jouem, Lisbon, Portugal
Subsidiaries: Beascoa Internacional

**Ediciones Bellaterra SA**
Navas de Tolosa, 289b, 08027 Barcelona
SAN: 001-6004
*Tel:* (093) 3499786 *Fax:* (093) 3520851
*E-mail:* bellaterra@retermail.es
*Key Personnel*
Man Dir: Felio Riera Domenech
Editorial: Jeannine Rochefort
Sales: Angeles Galan Gallego
Founded: 1972
Subjects: Science (General), Social Sciences, Sociology, Technology
ISBN Prefix(es): 84-7290; 84-300

**Beta Editorial SA**
Roux 67, 08017 Barcelona
SAN: 000-5746
*Tel:* (093) 2804640 *Fax:* (093) 2806320
Founded: 1943
ISBN Prefix(es): 84-7091

**Biblioteca 'NT'**, *imprint of* EUNSA (Ediciones Universidad de Navarra SA)

**Editorial Biblioteca Nueva SL**
Almagro, 38, 28010 Madrid
SAN: 002-3086
*Tel:* (091) 3100436 *Fax:* (091) 3198235
*E-mail:* editorial@bibliotecanueva.com
*Web Site:* www.bibliotecanueva.es
*Key Personnel*
Man Dir: Antonio Roche
Sales Dir: Paz Casas Ruiz-Castillo
Founded: 1920
Subjects: Biography, Economics, History, Poetry, Psychology, Psychiatry
ISBN Prefix(es): 84-7030; 84-9742
Number of titles published annually: 140 Print
Total Titles: 3,895 Print

**Biografia Joven**, *imprint of* Editorial Casals SA

**Boletin Oficial del Estado**
Ave de Manoteras, 54, 28050 Madrid
SAN: 000-6254
*Tel:* (091) 902 365 303 *Fax:* (091) 5382349
*E-mail:* info@docu.boe.es
*Web Site:* www.boe.es
*Key Personnel*
Dir General: Beatriz Martin
Founded: 1661
Subjects: Law, Public Administration
ISBN Prefix(es): 84-340

**Bookbank SL Agencia Literaria+**
San Martin de Porres 14, 28035 Madrid
*Tel:* (091) 3733539 *Fax:* (091) 3165591
*E-mail:* bookbank@nexo.es
*Key Personnel*
Dir: Alicia Gonzalez Sterling
Founded: 1983
Specialize in representing foreign publishers & agents in Spain & Latin America & Spanish authors worldwide.

**Antoni Bosch Editor SA+**
Manuel Girona, 61, 08034 Barcelona
*Tel:* (093) 206 07 30 *Fax:* (093) 206 07 31
*E-mail:* info@antonibosch.com
*Web Site:* www.antonibosch.com
*Key Personnel*
President: Antoni Bosch-Domenech

Production, Rights & Permissions & Man Dir: Isabel Cruz Saez *E-mail:* icruz@antonibosch.com
Founded: 1978
Subjects: Economics, Music, Dance, Science (General)
ISBN Prefix(es): 84-85855; 84-95348
*Associate Companies:* Bon Ton
Distributor for Bon Ton

**Bosch Casa Editorial SA+**
Comte d'Urgell, 51 bis, 08011 Barcelona
SAN: 000-6297
*Tel:* (093) 4548437; (093) 4544629; (093) 4521050 *Fax:* (093) 3236736
*E-mail:* bosch@boschce.es
*Web Site:* www.boschce.es
*Key Personnel*
President: Agustin Bosch Domenech
Man Dir: J Manuel Ianez
Marketing Manager: Albert Ferre
Founded: 1934
Focus is on law books & legal matters.
Membership(s): Publishers Association of Catalonia.
Subjects: Criminology, Journalism, Language Arts, Linguistics, Law, Literature, Literary Criticism, Essays, Public Administration, Radio, TV
ISBN Prefix(es): 84-7162; 84-7676

**J M Bosch Editor+**
Ronda Universidad, 11, 08029 Barcelona
*Tel:* (093) 2654466 *Fax:* (093) 2659031
*E-mail:* info@nexica.com
*Web Site:* www.libreriabosch.es/jmb
*Key Personnel*
Dir: Javier Bosch *E-mail:* direccion@libreriabosch.es
Founded: 1889
Subjects: Law
ISBN Prefix(es): 84-7698
Number of titles published annually: 35 Print
Total Titles: 530 Print
*Parent Company:* Libreria Bosch

**Editorial Maria Jesus Bosch SL**
Villarroel, 39-3r.3a, 08011 Barcelona
SAN: 006-6435
*Tel:* (093) 4539717
*E-mail:* mjbosch@colon.net
*Key Personnel*
Dir: Maria Jesus Bosch
Subjects: Criminology, Law
ISBN Prefix(es): 84-89591

**Edicions Bromera SL+**
Poligon Industrial I, Ronda Tintorers 117, Apartat de correus 147, 46600 Alzira
SAN: 002-0974
*Tel:* (096) 2402254 *Fax:* (096) 2403191
*E-mail:* illa@bromera.com; bromera@bromera.com
*Web Site:* www.bromera.com
Founded: 1986
Membership(s): the Valencia Publisher's Association.
Subjects: Literature, Literary Criticism, Essays
ISBN Prefix(es): 84-7660

**Editorial Bruno+**
Maestro Alonso, 21, 28028 Madrid
SAN: 002-3175
*Tel:* (091) 724 48 00 *Fax:* (091) 361 31 33
*E-mail:* informacion@editorial-bruno.es
*Web Site:* www.editorial-bruno.es
*Key Personnel*
Man Dir: Francisco Fernandez Cilleruelo
Founded: 1897
Subjects: Communications, Education, Religion - Catholic

ISBN Prefix(es): 84-216
*Warehouse:* Av Castilla, 15-17, Pol Ind S Fernando 1, 28850 Torrejon de Ardoz (Madrid)

**Cabildo Insular de Gran Canaria Departamento de Ediciones**
Calle Bravo Murillo 21, 35002 Las Palmas de Gran Canaria
SAN: 000-6793
*Tel:* (0928) 219421 *Fax:* (0928) 381627
*E-mail:* webadmin@grancanaria.com
*Web Site:* www.grancanaria.com
*Key Personnel*
Dept Head: Jesus Bombin Quintana
President: Jose Manuel Soria Lopez
Subjects: Geography, Geology, History, Natural History, Regional Interests
ISBN Prefix(es): 84-8103; 84-86127; 84-500; 84-505; 84-600

**Caja de Ahorros del Mediterraneo-Obras Sociales**
San Fernando, 40, 03001 Alicante
SAN: 000-6290
*Tel:* (06) 5906363; (06) 5905785 *Fax:* (06) 5905828
*E-mail:* cam@cam.es
*Web Site:* www.cam.es
ISBN Prefix(es): 84-7599; 84-88440

**Calambur Editorial, SL+**
Maria Teresa, 17-1° C, 28028 Madrid
*Tel:* (091) 913553033 *Fax:* (091) 913553033
*E-mail:* calambur@calumbureditorial.com
*Web Site:* www.calambureditorial.com
*Key Personnel*
Man Dir: Fernando Saenz *E-mail:* fsaenz@calumbureditorial.com
Founded: 1998
Subjects: Fiction, Humor, Poetry
ISBN Prefix(es): 84-88015
Number of titles published annually: 12 Print
Total Titles: 86 Print

**Calamo Editorial**
C/Pintor Aparicio, 13, 03003 Alicante
SAN: 002-3213
*Tel:* (096) 5130581 *Fax:* (096) 5115345
*E-mail:* calamo@lobocom.es
*Web Site:* www.lobocom.es/~calamo
*Key Personnel*
Dir: Ana Cristina Baidal Lopez *E-mail:* anacris@lobocom.es
Founded: 1990
Subjects: Fiction, Human Relations, Literature, Literary Criticism, Essays, Religion - Islamic, Travel, Arab & Mediterranean Culture
ISBN Prefix(es): 84-87839

**Calesa SA Editorial La+**
Camino Viejo de Zaratan, km 1,5, 47610 Zaratan (Valladolid)
SAN: 002-5119
Mailing Address: Parque Tecnologico de Boecillo, Parcela 134, 47151 Boecillo (Valladolid)
*Tel:* (0983) 548 102 *Fax:* (0983) 548 024
*E-mail:* editorial@la-calesa.com
*Web Site:* www.la-calesa.com
*Key Personnel*
Manager: Jacinto Altes-Bustelo
Founded: 1989
Subjects: Language Arts, Linguistics, Mathematics
ISBN Prefix(es): 84-8105; 84-87463
Subsidiaries: Boecillo Editora Multimedia, SA

**Edicions Camacuc+**
Arquebisbe Olaetxea, 18-baux esq, Apdo de Correos 11007, 46080 Valencia
SAN: 002-0990
*Tel:* (096) 357 28 56 *Fax:* (096) 357 28 56

*Key Personnel*
Pastor: Amparo Sospedra
Founded: 1987
Subjects: History, Literature, Literary Criticism,
Essays, Science Fiction, Fantasy
ISBN Prefix(es): 84-86970; 84-89938

**Editorial Cantabrica SA+**
Nervion 3-6, 48001 Bilbao
SAN: 002-3280
*Tel:* (04) 4245307 *Fax:* (04) 4231984
*Key Personnel*
Man Dir: Begona Grijelmo Mattern
Founded: 1960
Subjects: Cookery, Humor, Language Arts, Lin-
guistics, Sports, Athletics
ISBN Prefix(es): 84-221
*Warehouse:* Andres Isasi, 11-3, 48012 Bilbao Viz-
caya

**Carroggio SA de Ediciones+**
C Pelai, 28-30, 08001 Barcelona
SAN: 000-7439
*Tel:* (093) 4949922 *Fax:* (093) 4949923
*E-mail:* carroggio@carroggio.com
*Web Site:* www.carroggio.es
*Key Personnel*
General Administrator: Santiago Carroggio
Founded: 1911
Specialize in art & educational books.
Subjects: Art, History, Literature, Literary Criti-
cism, Essays, Natural History
ISBN Prefix(es): 84-7254
*Branch Office(s)*
San Ignacio de Loyola, 4, 46006 Valencia
*Tel:* (096) 3854377 *Fax:* (096) 3820159

**Instituto Cartografico Latino**, *imprint of*
Editorial Vicens-Vives

**Casa de Velazquez+**
C/de Paul Guinard, Ciudad Universitaria, 28040
Madrid
SAN: 000-7471
*Tel:* (091) 5433605 *Fax:* (091) 5446870
*E-mail:* bcv@bibli.cvz.es
*Key Personnel*
Dir: Gerard Chastagnaret
Head of Publishing: Vincent Lautie
Founded: 1928
Subjects: Archaeology, Geography, Geology, His-
tory, Language Arts, Linguistics, Literature,
Literary Criticism, Essays, Social Sciences, So-
ciology
ISBN Prefix(es): 84-86839; 84-9750; 84-404; 84-
500; 84-398; 84-300; 2-87634; 84-95555

**Editorial Casals SA+**
Casp 79, 08013 Barcelona
*Tel:* (093) 2449550 *Fax:* (093) 2656895
*E-mail:* casals@editorialcasals.com
*Web Site:* www.editorialcasals.com
*Key Personnel*
Man Dir: Ramon Casals *E-mail:* export@
editorialcasals.com
Rights & Permissions: Angelica Regidor
Founded: 1870
Subjects: Art, Education, Literature, Literary Crit-
icism, Essays, Mathematics, Music, Dance,
Philosophy, Religion - Catholic, Science (Gen-
eral), Social Sciences, Sociology
ISBN Prefix(es): 84-218; 84-7552
Number of titles published annually: 200 Print
Total Titles: 1,800 Print
*Associate Companies:* Combel Editorial, SA; Edi-
torial Magisterio Espanol, SA
Imprints: Biografia Joven; Punto Juvenil; Novelas
y Cuentos
*Warehouse:* Juli Galve i Brusons 72-74, 08912
Badalona

**Editorial Casariego+**
c/Cristobal Bordiu, 3, 28003 Madrid
SAN: 002-3329
*Tel:* (091) 4424339; (091) 4425178; (091)
4411330; (091) 4416829 *Fax:* (091) 4426224
*E-mail:* casariego@infonegocio.com
*Web Site:* www.casariego.com
*Key Personnel*
Man Dir, Production, Rights & Permissions: Car-
men Diaz-Casariego
Editorial, Sales: Isabel Rodriguez
Founded: 1959
Subjects: Art
ISBN Prefix(es): 84-86760
*Bookshop(s):* Libreria Facsimilia y Arte, Calle
Cristobal Bordiu 36, 28003 Madrid

**Casset Ediciones SL+**
Pez Austral, 9, 28007 Madrid
SAN: 001-6225
*Tel:* (091) 5043584 *Fax:* (091) 2508841
*Key Personnel*
Editorial Dir: Javier Parra Alvarez
Founded: 1990
Subjects: Humor, Parapsychology
ISBN Prefix(es): 84-87859

**Editorial Castalia**
Zurbano, 39, 28010 Madrid
SAN: 002-3345
*Tel:* (091) 3195857 *Fax:* (091) 3102442
*E-mail:* castalia@infornet.es
*Web Site:* www.castalia.es
*Key Personnel*
Man Dir: Amparo Soler
Sales Dir: Federico Ibanez
Founded: 1941
Specialize in editions of the classics.
Subjects: Education, Literature, Literary Criti-
cism, Essays
ISBN Prefix(es): 84-7039; 84-9740

**Edicios do Castro**
O Castro de Samoedo, 15168 Sada (A Coruna)
SAN: 001-4605
*Tel:* (0981) 621494; (0981) 620937; (0981)
620200 *Fax:* (0981) 623804
*E-mail:* edicios.ocastro@sargadelos.com
*Web Site:* www.sargadelos.com
*Key Personnel*
Dir: Isaac Diaz Pardo
Founded: 1963
Subjects: Art, Drama, Theater, Economics, Ge-
ography, Geology, History, Literature, Literary
Criticism, Essays, Poetry, Science (General),
Social Sciences, Sociology
ISBN Prefix(es): 84-7492; 84-8485; 84-85134
Imprints: Graficas do Castro/Moret

**Graficas do Castro/Moret**, *imprint of* Edicios do
Castro

**Catalogo**, *imprint of* Ediciones Maeva

**Biblioteca de Catalunya** (National Library of
Catalonia)
Carrer de l'Hospital, 56, 08001 Barcelona
*Tel:* (093) 270 23 00 *Fax:* (093) 270 23 04
*E-mail:* infocat@gencat.net
*Web Site:* www.gencat.es/bc
*Key Personnel*
Dir: Mrs Vinyet Panyella *E-mail:* vinyetp@bnc.es
Chief of Difussion Area: Montserrat Fonoll
*E-mail:* mfonoll@bnc.es
Founded: 1914
Subjects: Art, History, Library & Information Sci-
ences, Literature, Literary Criticism, Essays,
Music, Dance
ISBN Prefix(es): 84-7845; 84-500; 84-505; 84-
600
Number of titles published annually: 6 Print

*Parent Company:* Department of Culture
*Ultimate Parent Company:* Generalitat De
Catalunya
*Distribution Center:* Les Punxes Distribuidora S
L, Sardenya 75 81, 08018 Barcelona *Tel:* (093)
485-63-10 *Fax:* (093) 300-90-91

**Ediciones Catedra SA+**
Juan Ignacio Luca de Tena, nº 15, 28027 Madrid
SAN: 001-6144
*Tel:* (091) 3200119; (091) 3938800; (091)
3938787 *Fax:* (091) 7426631; (091) 7412118
*E-mail:* catedra@catedra.com
*Web Site:* www.catedra.com
*Telex:* 41071 MAEG
*Key Personnel*
Man Dir: Gustavo Dominguez Leon
Rights & Permissions: Marisa Barreno; Josune
Garcia
Founded: 1973
Subjects: Art, Film, Video, History, Human Re-
lations, Language Arts, Linguistics, Literature,
Literary Criticism, Essays, Music, Dance, Phi-
losophy, Poetry, Women's Studies
ISBN Prefix(es): 84-376
*Parent Company:* Grupo Anaya, Juan Ignacio,
Luca de Tena 15, 28027 Madrid
*Associate Companies:* Ediciones Anaya SA; Tec-
nos; Piramide; Algaida
*Bookshop(s):* Iriarte 4, 28028 Madrid
*Warehouse:* Avda Ferrocarril s/n, 28346 Madrid
*Orders to:* Comercial Grupo Anaya, SA Calle
Iriaste, 4, 28028 Madrid *Tel:* (01) 3597600
*Fax:* (01) 3559403

**CCG**, see Consello da Cultura Galega - CCG

**Editorial CCS**, see Central Catequistica
Salesiana (CCS)

**Ediciones CEAC+**
Peru, 164, 08020 Barcelona
SAN: 003-3634
*Tel:* (093) 2545300 *Fax:* (093) 2545315
*E-mail:* edicionesceac@e-deusto.com; info@
ceacedit.com
*Web Site:* www.editorialceac.com
*Key Personnel*
Man Dir: Santiago Pintanel
International Rights & Permissions Dir: Julia Es-
teve
Technical, Literary Dir: Norma Fenoglio
Founded: 1947
Membership(s): Publishers Association of Spain.
Subjects: Architecture & Interior Design, Educa-
tion, Electronics, Electrical Engineering, Engi-
neering (General), Fiction, Health, Nutrition,
Photography, Science Fiction, Fantasy
ISBN Prefix(es): 84-329
*Parent Company:* Grupo Planeta
*Associate Companies:* Grupo Ceac SA
Subsidiaries: Editorial Timun Mas SA; Ediciones
Vidorama SA
*Branch Office(s)*
Aconcagua Ediciones y Publicaciones SA, Xochi-
calco, 352 Col Narvarte, 03020 Mexico, DF,
Mexico
*Warehouse:* Poligono Can Magarola calle, 08100
Mollet del Valles

**Cedel, Ediciones Jose O Avila Monteso ES+**
Rossend Arus 6, 08014 Barcelona
SAN: 001-625X
*Tel:* (093) 4211880 *Fax:* (093) 4228971
*E-mail:* cedel@kadex.com
*Web Site:* www.kadex.com/cedel
*Key Personnel*
President: Sr Oriol Avila i Monteso, Sr
Man Dir, Rights & Permissions: Jose Avila
Founded: 1956

Subjects: Agriculture, Biological Sciences, Environmental Studies, Health, Nutrition
ISBN Prefix(es): 84-352

**CEIC Alfons El Vell**
Pza Rei en Jaume, 10, 46700 Gandia, Valencia
*Tel:* (06) 2876551 *Fax:* (06) 2875286
*Key Personnel*
Dir: Gabriel Garcia Frasquet

**Celeste Ediciones+**
Cobre, 1, 28850 Torrejon de Ardoz
SAN: 000-7722
*Tel:* (091) 6749221 *Fax:* (091) 6557101
*E-mail:* info@celesteediciones.com
*Key Personnel*
Manager: Miguel Angel San Jose
Dir of Export: Jesus Miranda
Rights: Cristina Fernandez Calderon
Founded: 1980
Subjects: Advertising, Architecture & Interior Design, Art, Economics, History, Mathematics, Music, Dance, Photography, Science (General), Travel
ISBN Prefix(es): 84-87553; 84-8211

**Central Catequistica Salesiana (CCS)**
Alcala, 166, 28028 Madrid
SAN: 002-3701
*Tel:* (091) 7252000 *Fax:* (091) 7262570
*E-mail:* apedidos@editorialccs.com; sei@editorialccs.com
*Web Site:* www.editorialccs.com
Founded: 1944
Subjects: Biblical Studies, Biography, Crafts, Games, Hobbies, Drama, Theater, Education, Religion - Catholic
ISBN Prefix(es): 84-7043; 84-8316

**Centro de Cultura Tradicional**
Plaza de Colon, 4, 37001 Salamanca
SAN: 000-7951
*Tel:* (0923) 293255 *Fax:* (0923) 293256
*E-mail:* cultura@lasalina.es; cctl@lasalina.es
*Web Site:* www.dipsanet.es/cultura/culturatradicional
ISBN Prefix(es): 84-87339; 84-505

**Centro de Estudios Avanzados en Ciencias Sociales (CEACS) del Instituto Juan March de Estudios e Investigaciones**
Castello, 77, 28006 Madrid
*Tel:* (091) 4354240 *Fax:* (091) 5763420
*E-mail:* webmast@mail.march.es
*Web Site:* www.march.es
*Key Personnel*
President: Juan March
Vice-President: Carlos March
Man Dir: Jose Luis Yuste Grijalba
Dir: Jose Maria Maravall

**Centro de Estudios Politicos Y Constitucionales+**
Plaza de la Marina Espanola, 9, 28071 Madrid
SAN: 000-8109
*Tel:* (091) 5401950 *Fax:* (091) 5419574
*E-mail:* cepc@cepc.es
*Web Site:* www.cepc.es
*Key Personnel*
Dir: Carmen Iglesias Cano
Assistant Dir: Feliciano Barrios Pintado
Founded: 1939
Subjects: Government, Political Science, History, Law, Philosophy, Social Sciences, Sociology
ISBN Prefix(es): 84-259

**Centro UNESCO de San Sebastian**
Urbieta, 11-1°, 20006 San Sebastian
*Tel:* (0943) 427003 *Fax:* (0943) 427003
*E-mail:* unescoeskola@retemail.es
*Web Site:* www.servicom.es/unesco

*Key Personnel*
Executive Dir: Juan Ignacio Martinez de Morentin de Goni
Founded: 1992
Specialize in Unesco training courses, manuals & student books.
Subjects: Education
Total Titles: 107 Print; 7 Online; 5 E-Book; 310 Audio
*Parent Company:* Unesco

**Circe Ediciones, SA+**
Milanesat, 25-27, 08017 Barcelona
SAN: 000-9865
*Tel:* (093) 2040990 *Fax:* (093) 2041183
*E-mail:* circe@oceano.com
*Telex:* 51735 Exit-E
*Key Personnel*
Editor: Silvia Lluis
Founded: 1986
Subjects: Biography, Fiction, Literature, Literary Criticism, Essays, Nonfiction (General)
ISBN Prefix(es): 84-7765

**Cisneros**
Joaquin Costa, 36, 28002 Madrid
SAN: 003-9799
*Tel:* (091) 5619900 *Fax:* (091) 5613990
*Key Personnel*
Contact: A Enrique Chacon
Founded: 1914
ISBN Prefix(es): 84-7047

**Editorial Ciudad Nueva**
Jose Picon 28, 28028 Madrid
*Tel:* (091) 725 95 30; (091) 356 96 12 *Fax:* (091) 713 04 52
*E-mail:* editorial@ciudadnueva.com
*Web Site:* www.ciudadnueva.com
*Key Personnel*
Editorial Dir: Jose Luis Romero
Founded: 1964
Subjects: Religion - Other
ISBN Prefix(es): 84-86987; 84-85159; 84-89651; 84-9715
*Parent Company:* Citta Nuova Editrice, Italy
Subsidiaries: Ciutat Nova (Publicaciones en lengua Catalana)
*U.S. Office(s):* Living City Office, 99-28 64 Rd, Rego Park, NY 10465, United States

**Civitas SA Editorial**
Barbara de Braganza, 10, 28004 Madrid
SAN: 002-3205
*Tel:* (091) 902 011 787 *Fax:* (091) 725 26 73
*E-mail:* clientes@civitas.es
*Web Site:* www.civitas.es
*Key Personnel*
President & Counselor: Eduardo Garcia de Enterria
Founded: 1970
Subjects: Economics, Law, Public Administration
ISBN Prefix(es): 84-470; 84-7398
*Bookshop(s):* General Pardinas, 24, 28001 Madrid

**Editorial Claret SA+**
Roger de Lluria, 5, 08010 Barcelona
*Tel:* (093) 3010887 *Fax:* (093) 3174830
*E-mail:* editorial@claret.es; admin@claret.es
*Web Site:* www.claret.es
*Key Personnel*
Man Dir & Production: Pere Codina Mas
Editorial Manager: Marcel-Li Lopez Rodriguez
Sales: Carlos Delgado Martinez
Publicity: Luis Vinoles del val
Founded: 1926
Subjects: Religion - Other
ISBN Prefix(es): 84-7263; 84-8297

**Editorial Clie+**
Editorial Clie Galvani 113, 08224 Terrassa, Barcelona
SAN: 004-0010
*Tel:* (093) 7884262; (093) 7885722 *Fax:* (093) 7800514
*E-mail:* libros@clie.es
*Web Site:* www.clie.es
*Key Personnel*
Sales Manager: Alfonso Trivino *E-mail:* ventas@clie.es
Founded: 1924
Subjects: Biblical Studies, History, Religion - Catholic, Religion - Protestant, Theology
ISBN Prefix(es): 84-7645; 84-7228; 84-8267; 84-300

**Climent, Eliseau Editor+**
Perez Bayer 11, 46002 Valencia
SAN: 002-7936
*Tel:* (06) 3516492 *Fax:* (06) 3529872
*E-mail:* 3i4@arrakis.es
*Key Personnel*
Editor: Elisen Climent Corbera
Founded: 1968
ISBN Prefix(es): 84-85211; 84-7502

**Cofas SA**, *imprint of* Vinaches Lopez, Luisa

**Ediciones Colegio De Espana (ECE)+**
Compania, 65, 37008 Salamanca
*Tel:* (023) 21 47 88 *Fax:* (023) 21 87 91
*E-mail:* info@colesp.eurart.es
*Web Site:* www.eurart.es/emp/colesp
*Key Personnel*
Executive: Jose Luis de Celis
Founded: 1987
Subjects: Art, Language Arts, Linguistics, Literature, Literary Criticism, Essays
ISBN Prefix(es): 84-86408; 84-9750; 84-404; 84-604; 84-300
Number of titles published annually: 20 Print
Total Titles: 50 Print

**COLEX**, see Editorial Constitucion y Leyes SA - COLEX

**Columna Edicions, Libres i Comunicacio, SA+**
Member of Grupo Planeta
Diagonal 6626E, 08034 Barcelona
SAN: 001-0391
*Tel:* (093) 4967061 *Fax:* (093) 4967065
*E-mail:* rmaymo@grupcolumna.com
*Web Site:* www.columnaedicions.com
Founded: 1985
Subjects: Fiction, Poetry
ISBN Prefix(es): 84-7809; 84-8300; 84-86433; 84-606; 84-664; 84-8330
Subsidiaries: Aea

**Combel**, *imprint of* Editorial Esin, SA

**Combel Editorial SA+**
Affiliate of Editorial Casals SA
c/Casp 79, 08013 Barcelona
*Tel:* (093) 2449550 *Fax:* (093) 2656895
*E-mail:* casals@editorialcasals.com
*Key Personnel*
Man Dir: Ramon Casals
Rights: Angelica Regidar
Founded: 1989
ISBN Prefix(es): 84-7864
Number of titles published annually: 50 Print
Total Titles: 500 Print
Foreign Rep(s): Independent Publishers Group-Chicago (US)

**Los Libros del Comienzo+**
Arriaza, 14, 28008 Madrid
SAN: 004-0487

*Tel:* (091) 5481079 *Fax:* (091) 5400378
*E-mail:* buzon@libroscomienzo.com
*Web Site:* www.libroscomienzo.com
*Key Personnel*
Publisher: Eduardo Rosello
Founded: 1990
Subjects: Self-Help
ISBN Prefix(es): 84-87598

**Compania Literaria+**
Padilla, 56, 28006 Madrid
SAN: 001-0693
*Tel:* (091) 4015312 *Fax:* (091) 4015312
*Key Personnel*
Dir: Juan Bercelo
Founded: 1994
Subjects: Anthropology, Biography, History, Journalism, Literature, Literary Criticism, Essays, Nonfiction (General), Social Sciences, Sociology, Travel
ISBN Prefix(es): 84-8213

**Ediciones de la Universidad Complutense de Madrid+**
Donoso Cortes, 63-3 planta, 28015 Madrid
*Tel:* (091) 394 64 60; (091) 394 64 61 *Fax:* (091) 394 64 58
*E-mail:* ecsa@rect.ucm.es
*Web Site:* www.ucm.es/info/ecsa
*Key Personnel*
Dir General: D Juan Diego Perez Gonzalez
Founded: 1986
Subjects: Anthropology, Biological Sciences, Economics, History, Psychology, Psychiatry, Social Sciences, Sociology
ISBN Prefix(es): 84-7754
*Parent Company:* Grupo Anaya
*Orders to:* Grupo Distribuidor ED, Ferrer del Rio 35, 28028 Madrid

**Editorial Complutense SA+**
Donoso Cortes, 63-3 planta, 28015 Madrid
*Tel:* (091) 3946460; (091) 3946461 *Fax:* (091) 3946458
*E-mail:* ecsa@rect.ucm.es
*Web Site:* www.ucm.es/info/ecsa
*Key Personnel*
Council Delegate: Antonio de Juan Abad
Dir General: Miguel Saugar
Dir Editorial: Isabel Merino Pella
   *E-mail:* imerino@eucmos.sim.ucm.cs
Founded: 1995
Specialize in biographies, dictionaries, medicine & nursing.
Subjects: Anthropology, Art, Biography, History, Medicine, Nursing, Dentistry, Philosophy, Science (General), Social Sciences, Sociology, Women's Studies
ISBN Prefix(es): 84-89784; 84-89365; 84-7491; 84-600
Number of titles published annually: 50 Print
*Bookshop(s):* Libreria Complutense, c/Donoso Lortes 65, 28015 Madrid *Tel:* (091) 5437558 *Fax:* (091) 5437476 *E-mail:* ecsa3@interbook.net

**Comunica Press SA+**
c/Real 33, portal 15, 1° A, 28250 Madrid
SAN: 001-074X
*Tel:* (091) 8591604 *Fax:* (091) 8595269
*E-mail:* info@comunica.es
*Web Site:* www.comunica.es
*Key Personnel*
Dir General: Tito Drago
Founded: 1989
ISBN Prefix(es): 84-88817
*Associate Companies:* Inter Press Service
Subsidiaries: Comunica Press

**Comunidad Autonoma de Madrid, Servicio de Documentacion y Publicaciones**
Fortuny, 51, 28010 Madrid

SAN: 001-0820
*Tel:* (091) 702 76 21 *Fax:* (091) 319 85 68
*Key Personnel*
Contact: Gomez Garcia
Founded: 1983
Subjects: Agriculture, Animals, Pets, Archaeology, Architecture & Interior Design, Art, Biological Sciences, Business, Communications, Cookery, Crafts, Games, Hobbies, Economics, Education, Film, Video, Gardening, Plants, History, Law, Management, Medicine, Nursing, Dentistry, Music, Dance, Natural History, Poetry, Science (General), Sports, Athletics, Transportation, Travel, Wine & Spirits
ISBN Prefix(es): 84-451; 84-500; 84-505; 84-606

**Consejo Superior de Investigaciones Cientificas+**
Vitruvio, 8, 28006 Madrid
SAN: 001-1347
*Tel:* (091) 561-2833; (091) 5629633 *Fax:* (091) 5629634
*E-mail:* publ@orgc.csic.es
*Web Site:* www.csic.es/publica
*Key Personnel*
Contact: Teodoro Sacristan *E-mail:* t.sacristan@orgc.csic.es
Founded: 1911
Subjects: Science (General)
ISBN Prefix(es): 84-00

**Consello da Cultura Galega - CCG**
Pazo de Raxoi 2° Andar, 15705 Santiago de Compostela
SAN: 001-141X
*Tel:* (0981) 957202 *Fax:* (0981) 957205
*E-mail:* consello.cultura.galega@xunta.es
*Web Site:* www.consellodacultura.org
*Key Personnel*
President: Carlos Otero Diaz
Subjects: Anthropology, Architecture & Interior Design, Art, Biological Sciences, Journalism, Law, Photography
ISBN Prefix(es): 84-87172; 84-505

**Editorial Constitucion y Leyes SA - COLEX**
Sor Angela de la Cruz, n° 6-7a Pl, 28020 Madrid
*Tel:* (091) 5813485 *Fax:* (091) 5813490
*E-mail:* colexeditor@interbook.net
*Web Site:* www.colex.es
*Key Personnel*
Dir: Rosario Fonseca-Herrero Raimundo
Founded: 1981
Subjects: Economics, Government, Political Science, Law, Management
ISBN Prefix(es): 84-7879; 84-86123

**Costaisa SA+**
Pau Alcover, 33, 08017 Barcelona
*Tel:* (093) 536 100 *Fax:* (093) 057 917
*E-mail:* costaisa@costaisa.com
*Web Site:* www.costaisa.com
*Key Personnel*
Computer Science: Jordi Bisbe
Founded: 1968
Specialize in Multimedia, CD-ROM & the Internet.

**Creaciones Monar Editorial**
Rec Molinar, Isla C, Nave 2, 08024 Barcelona
SAN: 001-1894
*Tel:* (093) 5 686 960; (093) 616 952 594
   *Fax:* (093) 5 683 311
*E-mail:* creaciones@monar.com
*Web Site:* www.monar.com
*Key Personnel*
Contact: Vicente Monar Puerto
Founded: 1956
Subjects: Biblical Studies
ISBN Prefix(es): 84-85131; 84-89068

**Ediciones Cristiandad+**
Serrano 51-1 Izquierda, 28006 Madrid
*Tel:* (091) 781 99 70 *Fax:* (091) 781 99 77
*E-mail:* info@kgm.es
*Web Site:* www.edicionescristiandad.com
Subjects: Biblical Studies, History, Philosophy, Religion - Catholic, Social Sciences, Sociology
ISBN Prefix(es): 84-7057

**Ediciones Cruilla SA+**
Subsidiary of Ediciones SM
Balmes 245-4, 08006 Barcelona
*Tel:* (093) 2376344; (093) 2922172 *Fax:* (093) 2380116
*Web Site:* www.cruilla.com
*Key Personnel*
Man Dir: Josep Herrero Casanovas
Founded: 1984
Publishes only in the Catalan language.
ISBN Prefix(es): 84-7629; 84-8286; 84-661
Total Titles: 1,152 Print

**CSIC,** see Consejo Superior de Investigaciones Cientificas

**CTE-Centro de Tecnologia Educativa SA+**
Via Augusta, 4 6a Planta, 08006 Barcelona
SAN: 000-9040
*Tel:* (093) 217 74 00 *Fax:* (093) 217 62 53
*Web Site:* www.centrocte.com
*Key Personnel*
Manager: Diego De Herrera Gimenez; Jose Luis Baron Sese
Founded: 1983
Specialize in technical books.
Membership(s): ANCED.
Subjects: Business, Education
ISBN Prefix(es): 84-7608; 84-404
*Warehouse:* Puig-gari, 21, 08014 Barcelona

**Ediciones la Cupula SL+**
Plaza de las Beates, 3, 08003 Barcelona
SAN: 001-8066
*Tel:* (093) 268 28 05 *Fax:* (093) 268 07 65
*E-mail:* lacupula@eix.intercom.es
*Web Site:* www.lacupula.com
*Key Personnel*
Manager: Jose M Berenguer Sanchez
Founded: 1979
Subjects: Humor, Young & Adult Comics (Humor & Sex)
ISBN Prefix(es): 84-7833; 84-85733

**Curial Edicions Catalanes SA**
Bruc 144, 08037 Barcelona
SAN: 001-2181
*Tel:* (093) 4588101 *Fax:* (093) 2077427
*E-mail:* curial@lix.intercom.es
*Key Personnel*
Administrator: Carmina Garcia I Roca
Subjects: Art, Ethnicity, Geography, Geology, History, Literature, Literary Criticism, Essays
ISBN Prefix(es): 84-7256

**Rafael Dalmau, Editor**
Carrer del Pi, 13-1-1, 08002 Barcelona
SAN: 004-7295
*Tel:* (093) 3173338 *Fax:* (093) 3173338
Founded: 1959
Subjects: Anthropology, Biography, Ethnicity, Geography, Geology, History
ISBN Prefix(es): 84-232
Distributor for Garsineu

**Ediciones Daly S L** (Daly Technical Books Publishers)+
Cordoba 11 - 2 F, 29640 Fuengirola, Malaga
SAN: 001-6527
*Tel:* (095) 2582569 *Fax:* (095) 2583619
*E-mail:* daly@edicionesdaly.com
*Web Site:* edicionesdaly.com

Key Personnel
Dir: David Fernandez Garcia
Manager: Hugo Armando Quiroga Capovilla
Founded: 1986
Membership(s): Association of Andalusia Publishers.
Subjects: Architecture & Interior Design, Art, Cookery, Crafts, Games, Hobbies, Education, Engineering (General), Gardening, Plants, Technology, Carpentry, Wrought Iron
ISBN Prefix(es): 84-86584
Total Titles: 200 Print
Showroom(s): Tokyo, Japan
Warehouse: Poligono Industrial La Vega, Mijas, Malaga

**Editorial Deimos, SL**
Glorieta del Puente de Segovia, 3, 28011 Madrid
Tel: (091) 479-23-42 Fax: (091) 5438214
E-mail: editorial@deimos-es.com
Web Site: www.deimos-es.com
Key Personnel
Administrator: Paulina Pardo Castaneda
Subjects: History, Mathematics, Religion - Catholic
ISBN Prefix(es): 84-86379
Number of titles published annually: 6 Print
Total Titles: 46 Print

**Editorial Revista de Derecho Privado Editorial de Derecho Financiero**, imprint of EDERSA (Editoriales de Derecho Reunidas SA)

**Espanola Desclee De Brouwer SA+**
Henao, 6-3º Dcha, Apartado de Correos, 277, 48009 Bilbao
SAN: 002-4090
Tel: (094) 4233045; (094) 4246843 Fax: (094) 4237594
E-mail: info@desclee.com
Web Site: www.desclee.com
Key Personnel
Manager: Javier Gogeascoechea Arrien
Founded: 1958
Subjects: Biblical Studies, Management, Psychology, Psychiatry, Religion - Other
ISBN Prefix(es): 84-330

**Ediciones Desnivel, SL**
Calle San Victorino, 8, 28025 Madrid
SAN: 001-2858
Tel: (091) 3602242 Fax: (091) 3602264
E-mail: edicionesdesnivel@desnivel.com
Web Site: www.desnivel.com
Key Personnel
Coordinator: Ana Fernandez Soto
Editorial Dir: Dario Rodriguez
Editor: Hector del Campo; Jordi Pastor
Dir, Publicity: Ana Vinuesa
ISBN Prefix(es): 84-87746; 84-89969; 84-95760
Bookshop(s): Librerio Desnivel, c/Dmore de Dios, 11, 28011 Madrid

**Ediciones Destino SA+**
Member of Grupo Planeta
Provenza nº 260, 5a Planta, 08008 Barcelona
SAN: 001-6586
Tel: (093) 496 70 01 Fax: (093) 496 70 02
E-mail: edicionesdestino@stl.logiccontrol.es
Web Site: www.edestino.es
Key Personnel
President: Joaquin Palau Fau
Founded: 1942
Subjects: Architecture & Interior Design, Art, Fiction, History, Literature, Literary Criticism, Essays, Nonfiction (General)
ISBN Prefix(es): 84-233

**Ediciones Deusto SA**
Alda Recalde, 27-7º, 48009 Bilbao Bizkaia
SAN: 001-6594

Tel: (094) 4356177 Fax: (094) 4356173
E-mail: edicio01@sarenet.es
Web Site: www.e-deusto.com
Key Personnel
General Dir: Xavier Arrufat
Founded: 1960
Subjects: Accounting, Finance, Management
ISBN Prefix(es): 84-234

**Editorial Diagonal del grup 62+**
Peu de la Creu 4, 08001 Barcelona
Tel: (093) 4437100 Fax: (093) 4437129
Key Personnel
President: Josep Maria Fortia Vinolas
General Dir: Jaime Igea Noguera
Founded: 1962
Specialize in literary work consultations.
Subjects: Geography, Geology, History
ISBN Prefix(es): 84-87254; 84-95808; 84-9762
Divisions: Catalana d'Ediciones SA
Warehouse: Joan d'Austria 57-59, 08005 Barcelona

**Editorial Diagonal**, imprint of Grup 62

**Ediciones Diaz de Santos SA+**
Dona Juana I de Castilla 22, Urb Quinta de los Molinos, 28027 Madrid
SAN: 001-6519
Tel: (091) 7434890 Fax: (091) 7434023
E-mail: librerias@diazdesantos.es
Web Site: www.diazdesantos.es
Telex: 45141 Dsan E ref Ediciones
Key Personnel
Man Dir: Joaquin Vioque Lozano
Sales: Antonio Vila Fernandez
Founded: 1983
Subjects: Business, Computer Science, Economics, Management, Medicine, Nursing, Dentistry, Science (General)
ISBN Prefix(es): 84-87189; 84-86251; 84-7978
Distributed by Grupo Editorial Iberoamerica (Mexico)
Bookshop(s): Diaz de Santos SA - Libreria Cientifico-Tecnica, Lagasca, 95, 28006 Madrid

**Didaco Comunicacion y Didactica, SA+**
Regas, 3 bajos, 08006 Barcelona
Tel: (093) 237 64 00 Fax: (093) 218 92 77
E-mail: didaco@cambrabcn.es
Web Site: www.didaco.es
Key Personnel
Manager: Lin Balague E-mail: lin@didaco.es
Administrator: Manuel Pastor E-mail: pastor@didaco.es
Publicity: Charo Latorre E-mail: charolatorre@didaco.es
International Sales: Victor Mesalles E-mail: vmesalles@didaco.es
National Sales: Alfonso R Salmeron E-mail: mail@didaco.es
Founded: 1986
Producers of multimedia English courses.
Subjects: Biological Sciences, English as a Second Language, Health, Nutrition, Language Arts, Linguistics, Nonfiction (General)
ISBN Prefix(es): 84-86983; 84-89712
Total Titles: 9 CD-ROM
Showroom(s): Bologna Children's Book Fair, Frankfurt Buchmesse, Liber, Barcelona

**Dilagro SA**
Comerc 48, 25007 Lleida
Tel: (0973) 24 51 00; (0973) 23 34 80 Fax: (0973) 23 64 13
Web Site: www.dilagro.com
Key Personnel
Man Dir: Jorge Marimon
Subjects: Agriculture, Ethnicity, History, Regional Interests

ISBN Prefix(es): 84-7234
Bookshop(s): Libreria Tenica, Comercio 48, 25007 leida

**Dinsic Publicacions Musicals**
Santa Anna 10, E 3a, 08002 Barcelona
Tel: (093) 318 06 05 Fax: (093) 412 05 01
E-mail: dinsic@dinsic.com
Web Site: www.dinsic.com/
Key Personnel
International Rights: Francesca Galofre Mora
Founded: 1988
Subjects: Music, Dance
ISBN Prefix(es): 84-86949; 84-95055

**Ediciones Diputacion de Salamanca**
Division of Diputacion de Salamanca
Felipe Espino 1, 37002 Salamanca
SAN: 001-348X
Tel: (0923) 29 31 00 Fax: (0923) 29 31 29
E-mail: informacion@dipsanet.es
Web Site: www.dipsanet.es
Key Personnel
President: Isabel Jimenez Garcia
Founded: 1982
Subjects: Geography, Geology, History, Regional Interests
ISBN Prefix(es): 84-7797; 84-500; 84-505
Distributed by Distribuciones Breogan

**Diputacion Provincial de Cordoba**
Avda del Mediterraneo, s/n, 14011 Cordoba
SAN: 001-3307
Tel: (0957) 211392; (0957) 211323 Fax: (0957) 211387
Key Personnel
Administration: Delores Martinez Coca
ISBN Prefix(es): 84-8154; 84-87034; 84-500; 84-505

**Diputacion Provincial de Malaga**
Av de los Guindos, 48, 29004 Malaga
Tel: (0952) 069 207 Fax: (0952) 069 215
E-mail: cedma@cedma.com
Web Site: cedma.com
Key Personnel
Publication Dir: Victoria Rosado E-mail: vrosado@cedma.com
Founded: 1973
Subjects: Anthropology, Archaeology, Art, Drama, Theater, Geography, Geology, History, Literature, Literary Criticism, Essays, Poetry
ISBN Prefix(es): 84-7785; 84-505
Number of titles published annually: 1 CD-ROM; 1 Online
Total Titles: 50 Print; 2 CD-ROM; 1 Online
Distributed by Atenea; Bitacora; Breogan
Warehouse: Avda-Guindos, 48, 29004 Malaga

**Diputacion Provincial de Sevilla, Servicio de Publicaciones**
Av Menendez y Pelayo, 32, 41004 Sevilla
SAN: 001-3501
Tel: (095) 4550029 Fax: (095) 4550050
E-mail: caba174@dipusevilla.es
Web Site: www.dipusevilla.es
Key Personnel
Dir: Carmen Barriga Guillen
Founded: 1967
Subjects: History, Literature, Literary Criticism, Essays, Social Sciences, Sociology
ISBN Prefix(es): 84-7798; 84-500; 84-505

**Diseno Editorial SA**
Estudiantes, 5, 28040 El Escorial, Madrid
Tel: (091) 5533168
Key Personnel
Dir: Ramon Nieto Alvarez-Uria
Founded: 1985
Books in Castellano & Catalan.

Subjects: Education, Literature, Literary Criticism, Essays
ISBN Prefix(es): 84-87666
Number of titles published annually: 4 Print
Total Titles: 2 Print
*Warehouse:* Colonia Guell, 08690 Sta Coloma De Cervello, Barcelona
*Orders to:* Exclusivas Escolares, Carretera Nacional II, km 593-4, 08740 Sant Andreu de la Barca, Barcelona *Tel:* (093) 635 1300

**DOC 6, SA**
Mallorca. 272, Planta 3a, 08037 Barcelona
*Tel:* (093) 215 43 13 *Fax:* (093) 488 36 21
*E-mail:* mail@doc6.es
*Web Site:* www.doc6.es

**Ediciones Doce Calles SL**
De La Ribera 36, 28300 Aranjuez (Madrid)
SAN: 001-6659
*Tel:* (091) 8924201; (091) 8924218 *Fax:* (091) 925 137 060
*E-mail:* docecalles@infonegocio.com
*Key Personnel*
Dir General: Pedro Miguel Sanchez Moreno
Dir, Marketing: Isabel Santos Esteras
    *E-mail:* isantos@infonegocio.com
Founded: 1987
Subjects: Aeronautics, Aviation, African American Studies, Anthropology, Architecture & Interior Design, Civil Engineering, Health, Nutrition, History, Medicine, Nursing, Dentistry, Natural History
ISBN Prefix(es): 84-87111; 84-89796; 84-9744
Number of titles published annually: 6 Print
Total Titles: 105 Print
Foreign Rep(s): Puvill Libros SA

**Editorial Donostiarra SA+**
Pokopandegi, 4, Pabellon Igaralde Barrio de Igara, Apdo 671, 20018 San Sebastian Guipuzcoa
SAN: 002-3825
*Tel:* (0943) 215 737; (0943) 213 011 *Fax:* (0943) 219 521
*E-mail:* info@donostiarra.com
*Web Site:* www.donostiarra.com
*Key Personnel*
President: Francisco Javier Rodriguez de Abajo
Marketing Dir: Jacobo Vidal Luzuriaga
Founded: 1965
Subjects: Accounting, Engineering (General), Film, Video, Finance, Health, Nutrition, Technology
ISBN Prefix(es): 84-7063
Distributor for EGA-Donostiarra-Profesores-Editores, SA; Larrauri Editorial SA
*Book Club(s):* Anele

**Dorleta SA+**
Avda JA Zunzunegi, 3, 48013 Bilbao
SAN: 001-4133
*Tel:* (094) 427 3880 *Fax:* (094) 427 4512
*E-mail:* dorletoi@sarenet.es
*Key Personnel*
Editor: Angel Tona
Dir: Jose Gondra
Dir, Commercial: Yolanda Domingo
Founded: 1985
Subjects: Sports, Athletics
ISBN Prefix(es): 84-87812; 84-404

**Editorial Dossat SA**
Plaza de Santa Ana 9, 28012 Madrid
SAN: 002-3833
*Tel:* (091) 3694011 *Fax:* (091) 3691398
*Key Personnel*
Man Dir: Barrera San Martin Eugeniano
Subjects: Architecture & Interior Design, Automotive, Civil Engineering, Disability, Special Needs, Electronics, Electrical Engineering,

Engineering (General), Journalism, Medicine, Nursing, Dentistry, Science (General)
ISBN Prefix(es): 84-237

**Ediciones Doyma SA+**
Travesera de Gracia, 17-21, 08021 Barcelona
SAN: 001-6675
*Tel:* (093) 2000 711 *Fax:* (093) 2091 136
*Web Site:* www.doyma.es
*Telex:* 51964 Ink E
*Key Personnel*
Man Dir: Jose A Dotu
Journal Division Manager: Edgar Dotu
Book Division Manager: German Covas
Editorial Manager: Dr Oscar Vilarroya
Foreign Rights: Pilar Aparicio
Manager: Lorenzo Matas; Jose Latorre
Founded: 1971
Subjects: Medicine, Nursing, Dentistry
ISBN Prefix(es): 84-85285; 84-7592
Subsidiaries: AP (Americana de Publicaciones); Doyma Argentina SA; Doyma Andina SA; Doyma Mexicana SA CV; Ediciones Doyma de Venezuela CA

**Durvan SA de Ediciones+**
Subsidiary of Club Internacional Del Libro
Colon de Larreategui 13-3 izda, 48001 Bilbao, Vizcaya
SAN: 001-4214
*Tel:* (094) 4230777 *Fax:* (094) 4243832
*E-mail:* editorial@durvan.com
*Web Site:* www.durvan.com
*Key Personnel*
Man Dir: Lorenzo Portillo Sisniega *Tel:* (090) 2104020
Founded: 1960
ISBN Prefix(es): 84-85001; 84-7677
Number of titles published annually: 2 Print; 1 CD-ROM; 1 Online
Total Titles: 42 Print; 3 CD-ROM; 1 Online
*Associate Companies:* Durclub, SA de Ediciones
Distributor for Carroggio, SA de Ediciones; Club Internacional del Libro; Ediciones Rueda JM, SA; Urmo, SA
*Warehouse:* C/Nervion, 3-3, 48001 Bilbao

**Dykinson SL+**
Melendez Valdes 61, 28015 Madrid
*Tel:* (091) 544 28 46; (091) 544 28 69 *Fax:* (091) 544 60 40
*E-mail:* info@dykinson.com
*Web Site:* www.dykinson.es; www.dykinson.com
*Key Personnel*
Contact: Rafael Tigeras Sanchez
Founded: 1973
Subjects: Economics, Education, Law, Psychology, Psychiatry
ISBN Prefix(es): 84-88030; 84-8155; 84-86133; 84-88038; 84-9772
Total Titles: 850 Print

**Ediciones Ebenezer+**
Camelies 19, 08024 Barcelona
SAN: 001-6713
*Tel:* (093) 2133515 *Fax:* (093) 2131684
*E-mail:* 101745.1635@compuserve.com
*Key Personnel*
Manager: Carlos A Piedad
Libreria & Distribution.
Subjects: Film, Video, Music, Dance
ISBN Prefix(es): 84-87498; 84-404
*Associate Companies:* Libreria Biblica ALFA & OMEGA, Apdo 20159, 08080 Barcelona
Distributor for Broadman & Holman; Clie; Ed Carribe; Spanish House

**ECE**, see Ediciones Colegio De Espana (ECE)

**Editorial EDAF SA+**
Jorge Juan 30, 28001 Madrid

SAN: 002-3884
*Tel:* (091) 435 82 60 *Fax:* (091) 431 52 81
*E-mail:* edaf@edaf.net
*Web Site:* www.edaf.es
*Key Personnel*
President: Luciano Fossati
Dir: Jose Antonio Fossati
Publicity: Gerardo Fossati
Founded: 1959
Subjects: Astrology, Occult, Health, Nutrition, History, Literature, Literary Criticism, Essays, Self-Help
ISBN Prefix(es): 84-414; 84-7166; 84-7640
Total Titles: 1,000 Print
*Branch Office(s)*
Edaf del Plata, Lavalle, 1646-piso 7°, oficina, 21, 1048 Buenos Aires, Argentina, Contact: Alfonso Barredo *Tel:* (011) 11 43 75 55 00 *Fax:* (011) 11 43 75 55 00 *E-mail:* edafall@ interar.com.ar
Edaf Y Morales, SA, Oriente 180 n 279, Col Moctezuma 2a Sec, Delg Venustiano Carranza 15530, Mexico, Contact: Gildardo Morales *Tel:* (05) 55 785 19 51 *Fax:* (05) 55 785 27 51 *E-mail:* edaf@edaf-y-morales.com.mx
*Warehouse:* Poligno Azque, Ctra de Daganzo KM, 3400 Naves 2Y3-Alcala de Henares, Madrid, Contact: Horacio Mallo *Tel:* (091) 8809514 *Fax:* (091) 8893851

**Edebe**
Passeig Sant Joan Bosco 62, 08017 Barcelona
SAN: 001-4435
*Tel:* (093) 2037408 *Fax:* (093) 2054670
*E-mail:* informacion@edebe.com
*Web Site:* www.edebe.com
*Key Personnel*
Dir: Antonio Garrido Gonzalez
Publication Dir: Jose Luis Gomez Cutillas
Specialize in education & literature.
Subjects: Education, Fiction, Literature, Literary Criticism, Essays, Technology
ISBN Prefix(es): 84-236
*Associate Companies:* Editorial Don Bosco SA, Mexico; Editorial Edebe, Argentina

**Edelsa Group Didascalia SA**
Pza Ciudad de Salta 3, 28043 Madrid
SAN: 001-4443
*Tel:* (091) 4165511; (091) 4165218 *Fax:* (091) 4165411
*E-mail:* edelsa@edelsa.es
*Web Site:* www.edelsa.es
*Telex:* 47088 Edse E
*Key Personnel*
Man Dir: Miguel Angel Garcia Cuesta
Founded: 1986
Subjects: Language Arts, Linguistics
ISBN Prefix(es): 84-85786; 84-7711; 84-389
*Branch Office(s)*
Ediseis SA, Rosellon 55, 08029 Barcelona
*Bookshop(s):* The English Bookshop, Calaf 52, 08021 Barcelona

**EDERSA (Editoriales de Derecho Reunidas SA)**
Leganitos, 15 5°-1, 28013 Madrid
SAN: 001-4451
*Tel:* (091) 5477961 *Fax:* (091) 5478001
*E-mail:* dijusa@dijusa.es *Cable:* REVIPRIV
*Key Personnel*
Man Dir: Narciso Amoros Dorda
Marketing Dir: Narciso Amoros Koehler
Founded: 1913
Subjects: Biography, History, Law, Philosophy, Social Sciences, Sociology
ISBN Prefix(es): 84-7130; 84-400; 84-8494
Imprints: Ediciones Pegaso; Editorial Revista de Derecho Privado Editorial de Derecho Financiero

**Edex, Centro de Recursos Comunitarios+**
Indautxu n° 9, 48011 Bilboa, Vizcaya

*Tel:* (094) 442 57 84 *Fax:* (094) 441-7512
*E-mail:* edex@edex.es
*Web Site:* www.edex.es
*Key Personnel*
Editor: Claudia Alcepay
Subjects: Child Care & Development, Education

**EDHASA (Editora y Distribuidora Hispano-Americana SA)+**
Av Diagonal, 519-521, 2° piso, 08029 Barcelona
*Tel:* (093) 4949720 *Fax:* (093) 4194584
*E-mail:* info@edhasa.es
*Web Site:* www.edhasa.es
*Key Personnel*
Editorial Dir: Daniel Fernandez *E-mail:* d.fdez@edhasa.es
General Manager: Anna Ardid *E-mail:* a.ardid@edhasa.es
Rights Department: Esther Lopez *E-mail:* e.lopez@edhasa.es
Publisher's Assistant: Cecilia Asker *E-mail:* c.asker@edhasa.es
Founded: 1946
Subjects: Fiction, History, Literature, Literary Criticism, Essays
ISBN Prefix(es): 84-350
Number of titles published annually: 60 Print
Total Titles: 600 Print

**Edi-Liber Irlan SA+**
Corsega 314, 08037 Barcelona
SAN: 001-4516
*Tel:* (093) 4160641 *Fax:* (093) 4160774
*E-mail:* ediliber@mx3.redestb.es
*Key Personnel*
Editor & International Rights: Monica Bertran
Founded: 1983
Membership(s): Associacio D'Escriptors en Llengua Catalana.
Subjects: Cookery, Drama, Theater, Fiction, Literature, Literary Criticism, Essays, Poetry
ISBN Prefix(es): 84-7589
Distributor for L'arc de Bera'
*Book Club(s):* Club De Lectors Dels Paisos Catalans-Cercle De Lectors

**EDICEP+**
Almirante Cadarso, 11, 46005 Valencia
SAN: 001-0480
*Tel:* (096) 395 20 45; (096) 395 72 93 *Fax:* (096) 395 22 97
*E-mail:* edicep@edicep.com
*Web Site:* www.edicep.com
*Key Personnel*
Man Dir: Mora Pilar Taroncher
Founded: 1979
Subjects: Biblical Studies, History, Law, Philosophy, Religion - Catholic
ISBN Prefix(es): 84-7050

**Ediciones Ceac**, *imprint of* Grupo Editorial CEAC SA

**Ediciones El Almendro de Cordoba SL+**
El Almendro 6, bajo, 14006 Cordoba
SAN: 001-6810
*Tel:* (0957) 082 789; (0957) 274 692 *Fax:* (0957) 274 692
*E-mail:* ediciones@elalmendro.org
*Web Site:* www.elalmendro.org
*Key Personnel*
Man Dir, Editorial: Jesus Pelaez del Rosal
Founded: 1982
Also book packager.
Subjects: Biblical Studies, Religion - Catholic, Religion - Jewish, Religion & Judaism
ISBN Prefix(es): 84-8005; 84-86077
Subsidiaries: PI El Guijar
Distributed by Alma Roma (Italy); Asoc Libreria Editorial Salesiana (Peru); Casa de la Biblia (Mexico); Disliber Spes Mejico (Mexico);

Distal Libros (Argentina); Distribuciones Libreria de Habla Hispana (USA); Distribuidora Loyola (Brasil); Editorial Claretiana (Argentina); Editorial Letraviva (Brasil); Editorial Verbo Divino (Bolivia & Ecuador); Estados Unidos de America (USA); Fundacion Verbo Divino (Colombia); Hijas de San Pablo (El Salvador, Nicaragua, Paraguay, Peru, Puerto Rico, Uruguay, Portugal & Venezuela); Libreria Agape (Argentina); Libreria Catolica (Panama); Libreria Catolica Ave Maria (Puerto Rico); Libreria Hispanoamericana (Nicaragua); Libreria Juan Pablo II (Honduras & Dominican Republic); Libreria Manantial (Italy); Libreria Parroquial (Mexico); Libreria Pontificia Universita Gregoriana (Italy); Libreria Proa Ltda (Chile); Libreria Salesiana (El Salvador); Libreria San Pablo (Colombia, Panama & USA); Libreria Sole (Italy); Libreria Sorgente (Italy); Libreria Verbum (Mexico); Libreria Verdade E Vida (Portugal); Livro Ibero Americano Ltda (Brasil); Manantial, Libraria Loyola (Guatemala); Nueva Libreria Parroquial (Mexico); Paulinas (Brasil, Colombia, Ecuador, USA & Italy); Paulinos (Venezuela); Rubaisen S EN CS (Argentina); San Pablo (Costa Rica & Italy); Verdad Y Vida - Libreria Diocesana (Paraguay)
*Distribution Center:* America Ediexport, Vereda de los Barros, 77, 28925 Alcorcon
*Tel:* (091) 632 32 88 *Fax:* (091) 633 48 21
*E-mail:* ediexport@teleline.es
Distribuidora Azteca de Publicaciones SL, Marquesa de Argueso, 36, 28019 Madrid
*Tel:* (091) 560 43 60 *Fax:* (091) 565 29 22
*E-mail:* azteca@infornet.es *Web Site:* www.aztecadist.es

**Ediciones l'Isard, S L+**
Affiliate of Gremi D'Editors de Catalunya
Corsega, 663-665, entl A, 08026 Barcelona
*Tel:* (093) 436 81 18 *Fax:* (093) 436 03 41
*E-mail:* isard@isard.net
*Web Site:* www.isard.net
*Key Personnel*
Dir: Jordi Marti i Canellas
Founded: 1995
Subjects: Architecture & Interior Design, Art, Cookery, Health, Nutrition, Wine & Spirits
ISBN Prefix(es): 84-921314; 84-89931
Number of titles published annually: 4 Print
Total Titles: 20 Print

**Institut d'Edicions de la Diputacio de Barcelona**
Londres, 55, 1r bis, 08036 Barcelona
SAN: 001-3188
*Tel:* (093) 4022116
*E-mail:* diputacio@diba.es
*Web Site:* www.diba.es
*Key Personnel*
Dir: Josep Montanyes
Founded: 1991
ISBN Prefix(es): 84-7794; 84-500; 84-505

**Edicola-62**, *imprint of* Grup 62

**Edicomunicacion SA+**
Las Torres, 75-77, 08042 Barcelona
SAN: 002-1350
*Tel:* (093) 3590866 *Fax:* (093) 3590004
*Web Site:* www.edicomunicacion.com
*Key Personnel*
Dir: Jose Luis Salgado
Subjects: Astrology, Occult, Humor, Nonfiction (General), Parapsychology, Poetry
ISBN Prefix(es): 84-7672; 84-8461

**Edigol Ediciones SA+**
Sant Gabriel, 50, 08950 Esplugues de Llobregat, Barcelona

SAN: 002-144X
*Tel:* (093) 372 63 04 *Fax:* (093) 371 76 32
*E-mail:* info@edigol.com
*Web Site:* www.edigol.com
*Telex:* Cllc E
*Key Personnel*
Man Dir: Jorge Onrubia
Sales: Joana Rius; Carmentxu Aparicio
Founded: 1976 (as Edigol Ediciones Cartograficas)
General service on Educational Cartography. Wall charts on drugs, anatomy, children's letters & numbers charts.
Subjects: Education, Geography, Geology, Educational Cartography, School Maps
ISBN Prefix(es): 84-85406
*Parent Company:* Industria Grafica Offset Lito SA, Sant Gabriel, 50, Esplugues de Llobregat, 08950 Barcelona

**Edika-Med, SA+**
Josep Tarradellas, 52, 08029 Barcelona
SAN: 002-1490
*Tel:* (093) 454 96 00 *Fax:* (093) 323 48 03
*E-mail:* info@edikamed.com
*Web Site:* www.edikamed.com
*Key Personnel*
Manager: Dolores Gandia
Founded: 1988
Membership(s): Grenio Publications; Specialize in Medical Literature.
Subjects: Medicine, Nursing, Dentistry, Psychology, Psychiatry
ISBN Prefix(es): 84-7877

**Edilesa-Ediciones Leonesas SA+**
Camino Cuesta Luzar, S/N, 24010 Trobajo del Camino, Leon
SAN: 001-8198
*Tel:* (0987) 80 11 16 *Fax:* (0987) 84 00 28
*E-mail:* edilesa@edilesa.es
*Web Site:* www.edilesa.es
*Key Personnel*
Dir: Jesus Vincente Pastor Benavides
Founded: 1981
Subjects: Architecture & Interior Design, Art, Cookery, Literature, Literary Criticism, Essays, Photography, Travel
ISBN Prefix(es): 84-8012; 84-86013
Distributor for Hullera Vasco-Leonesa y Fundacion Hullera Vasco-Leonesa
*Book Club(s):* Club Bibliofilo Leones

**Edilux+**
c/Juncos n° 7-bajo, 18006 Granada
SAN: 003-8245
*Tel:* (0958) 08 20 00; (0958) 184056 *Fax:* (0958) 184056; (0958) 082472
*E-mail:* ediluxsl@supercable.es
Founded: 1984
Subjects: Art, Photography, Travel
ISBN Prefix(es): 84-87282; 84-95856

**EDIMSA - Editores Medicos SA+**
Gabriela Mistral, 2, 28035 Madrid
SAN: 002-1601
*Tel:* (091) 376 81 40 *Fax:* (091) 373 99 07
*E-mail:* edimsa@edimsa.es
*Web Site:* www.edimsa.es
*Key Personnel*
General Dir: Carlos Gimenez Antolin
ISBN Prefix(es): 84-87054; 84-95076; 84-7714

**Ediciones Edinford SA+**
Marmolistas, 3 y 5, 29013 Malaga
SAN: 001-6748
*Fax:* (095) 254689
*Key Personnel*
Contact: Jose Luis Gonzalez Sodis
Founded: 1989
Subjects: College & Local Textbooks
ISBN Prefix(es): 84-87555; 84-404

**Editorial Editex SA+**
Complejo Empresarial Atica 7 Edificio 3, Planta
3a, Oficina B via dos Castillas 33 Pozuelo de
Alarcon, 28224 Madrid
SAN: 002-3914
*Tel:* (091) 7992040 *Fax:* (091) 7150444
*E-mail:* correo@editex.es
*Web Site:* www.editex.es
*Key Personnel*
Dir General: Severino Basarrate Elorrieta
Founded: 1946
Subjects: Child Care & Development, Health, Nu-
trition, Management
ISBN Prefix(es): 84-7131

**Editora y Distribuidora Hispano Americana
SA (EDHASA)**, see EDHASA (Editora y
Distribuidora Hispano-Americana SA)

**Editorial Everest SA+**
Ctra Leon-La Coruna, Km 5, Apdo 339, 24080
Leon
*Tel:* (0987) 844200 *Fax:* (0987) 844202
*E-mail:* publicaciones@everest.es
*Web Site:* www.everest.es
*Telex:* 89916 *Cable:* EVEREST LEON
*Key Personnel*
Man Dir: Jose Antonio Lopez Martinez
Publication Dir: Raquel Lopez Varela
Export Dir: Severino Fernandez
Marketing Manager: Fernando Rodriguez Pereyra
Founded: 1958
Subjects: Animals, Pets, Astrology, Occult, Cook-
ery, Crafts, Games, Hobbies, Gardening, Plants,
History, Physics, Religion - Catholic
ISBN Prefix(es): 84-241
*Associate Companies:* Lectorum Publications Inc,
137 W 14th St, New York, NY 10011, United
States (US Distributor)
Subsidiaries: Ediciones Gaviota SL
*Orders to:* Everest de Ediciones & Distribucion
SL, Carretera Leon-Coruna, Km 5, Apdo 339,
24080 Leon, Manager: Javier Atienza

**EDUNSA**, see Tres Torres Ediciones SA

**Ediciones Ega+**
Juan de Garay, 15, 48003 Bilbao
SAN: 001-7124
*Tel:* (04) 4216787 *Fax:* (04) 4213010
*Key Personnel*
Dir & Editor: Jose Maria Gogeascoechea Arrien
Founded: 1988
Subjects: Religion - Other
ISBN Prefix(es): 84-7726

**Egales (Editorial Gai y Lesbiana)+**
Cervantes, 2, 08002 Barcelona
*Tel:* (093) 4127283 *Fax:* (093) 4127283
*E-mail:* egales@auna.com
*Web Site:* www.editorialegales.com
*Key Personnel*
Dir: Helle Bruun
International Rights: Connie Dagas
Founded: 1995
Subjects: Gay & Lesbian
ISBN Prefix(es): 84-95346
Total Titles: 84 Print
Distributed by Alamo Square Distributors (Only
USA)

**Publicaciones de El Ciervo, S.A.**, see EL Ciervo
96

**EL Ciervo 96**
Calvet 56, 08021 Barcelona
SAN: 004-6345
*Tel:* (093) 200 51 45; (093) 201 00 96 *Fax:* (093)
201 10 15
*E-mail:* redaccion@elciervo.es
*Web Site:* www.elciervo.es

*Key Personnel*
Dir: Lorenzo Gomis
ISBN Prefix(es): 84-87178

**El Hogar y la Moda SA**
Muntaner, 40-42, 08011 Barcelona
SAN: 002-7715
*Tel:* (093) 508 70 00 *Fax:* (093) 454 87 72
*E-mail:* hymsa@hymsa.com
*Web Site:* www.hymsa.com
*Telex:* 50482
*Key Personnel*
Man Dir: Xavier Elies
Editorial: Josep Sarret
Sales, Rights & Permissions: Carlos Elies
Production: Jordi Balmana
Founded: 1909
Subjects: Women's Studies
ISBN Prefix(es): 84-7183
*Parent Company:* Editorial Everest, SA,
Muntaner, 40-42, 08011 Barcelona
*Associate Companies:* Sociedad General de Pub-
licaciones, Carretera Montcada s/n, Poligono
Industrial, Barcelona; ASMI SA, Calle Aribau
20 pral, Barcelona
Subsidiaries: Servicios Editoriales SA; Publiventa
SA
*Bookshop(s):* Libreria Hogar y Moda, Muntaner,
40-42, 08011 Barcelona

**El Viso, SA Ediciones**
Lopez de Hoyos, 350, 28043 Madrid
SAN: 001-690X
*Tel:* (091) 5196576; (091) 5196583 *Fax:* (091)
5196583
*E-mail:* lvisoh@anexo.es
*Key Personnel*
Contact: Custodia Caballero
Founded: 1981
Subjects: Art, Photography
ISBN Prefix(es): 84-86022; 84-95241
Distributed by Les Punxes, SL; Visor Distibu-
ciones, SL

**Ediciones Elfos SL** (Publishing Company
ELFS)+
Alberes, 34, 08017 Barcelona
*Tel:* (093) 4069479 *Fax:* (093) 4069006
*E-mail:* eltos-ed@teleline.es
*Web Site:* www.edicioneselfos.com
*Key Personnel*
Man Dir: Rita Schnitzer
Founded: 1980
Subjects: Cookery, Health, Nutrition, Humor,
Decorative Art
ISBN Prefix(es): 84-85791; 84-87251; 84-88990;
84-8423
Number of titles published annually: 18 Print
*Orders to:* Naturart, SA, Avda Mare de Deu de
Lorda, 20, 08034 Barcelona *Tel:* (093) 2054000
*Fax:* (093) 2051441

**Elkar, Euskal Liburu eta Kantuen
Argitaldaria, SL+**
Igara Bidea, 88 bis, 20003 San Sebastian
*Tel:* (943) 310327 *Fax:* (943) 310345
*Key Personnel*
Administrator: Jose Maria Sors
Founded: 1972
Specialize in student languages.
Subjects: Education
ISBN Prefix(es): 84-7529; 89-7917; 84-85485
*Warehouse:* Zabaltzen, Igarabidea, 88 bis, Donos-
tia *Tel:* (043) 2122144/212033 *Fax:* (043)
212192

**EmpresaActiva**, *imprint of* Ediciones Urano, SA

**Editorial Empuries**, *imprint of* Grup 62

**Editorial Empuries**
Imprint of Grup 62
Provenca 278, 08008 Barcelona
*Tel:* (093) 4870062 *Fax:* (093) 4874147
*Key Personnel*
Rights Manager: Laura Pujol
Founded: 1983
ISBN Prefix(es): 84-7596

**Enciclopedia Catalana, SA+**
Diputacio, 250, 08007 Barcelona
*Tel:* (093) 412 0030 *Fax:* (093) 301 4863
*Web Site:* www.enciclopedia-catalana.com
*Key Personnel*
Foreign Rights Manager: Iolanda Bethencourt
    *E-mail:* ibethencourt@grec.com
Founded: 1965
Subjects: Art, Cookery, Education, Fiction, Ge-
ography, Geology, Health, Nutrition, History,
Literature, Literary Criticism, Essays, Poetry,
Publishing & Book Trade Reference, Religion -
Catholic, Romance, Travel
ISBN Prefix(es): 84-412

**Ediciones Encuentro SA+**
Cedaceros, 3, 2°, 28014 Madrid
*Tel:* (091) 532 26 07 *Fax:* (091) 532 23 46
*E-mail:* encuentro@ediciones-encuentro.es
*Web Site:* www.ediciones-encuentro.es
*Key Personnel*
President: Jose Miguel Oriol
Man Dir: Carmina Salgado
Sales: Joan R De la Serna
Production: Norberto Moreno
Editorial, Rights & Permissions: Gabriel Lanzas
Founded: 1978
Subjects: Anthropology, Art, Economics, History,
Literature, Literary Criticism, Essays, Philoso-
phy, Social Sciences, Sociology, Theology
ISBN Prefix(es): 84-7490
Number of titles published annually: 50 Print
Total Titles: 700 Print
Foreign Rep(s): Bookstore Banquet Jose Cubas
(Argentina); Bookstore Juan Pablo II (Do-
minican Republic); Bookstore Miraflores Time
Shred of Union (Peru); Bookstore Prow Mac
Iver (Chile); Bookstore Stadium (Ecuador);
Bookstore the Apdo Internationa (Costa Rica);
Byblos Editorial Eduardo (Uruguay); Catholic
Bookstore (Panama); Catholic University of
Puerto Rico Bookstore (Puerto Rico); Cost
Hispamer This of the UCA (South America);
Disliber-Spec-Mexico SA of CU (Mexico);
Distributing Paulinas (US); Distritexto Ltda
(Colombia); El Libro (Ecuador); Interservice
Distribution SA of CU Col Copilco University
(Mexico); Paulinas Jr (Peru); Warp Editions
(Venezuela); World Book Centre (Chile)

**Ediciones Endymion**
Marques deSanta Ana, 4, 28004 Madrid
SAN: 001-6977
*Tel:* (01) 5223668; (01) 5222210
*Key Personnel*
President: Jesus Moya Andrinal
Founded: 1986
Subjects: Poetry
ISBN Prefix(es): 84-7731

**EOS Gabinete de Orientacion Psicologica**
Avda Reina Victoria, 8, 2a Planta, 28003 Madrid
*Tel:* (091) 554 12 04 *Fax:* (091) 554 12 03
*E-mail:* eos@eos.es
*Web Site:* www.eos.es
Founded: 1971
Subjects: Psychology, Psychiatry
ISBN Prefix(es): 84-85851; 84-9727; 84-89967

**Erein+**
Tolosa Etorbidea 107, 20018 Donostia
SAN: 002-8436
*Tel:* (0943) 218300; (0943) 218211 *Fax:* (0943)
218311

*E-mail:* erein@erein.com
*Web Site:* www.erein.com
*Key Personnel*
Man Dir, Production, Rights & Permissions: Aramaio Julen Lizundia
Editorial: Beitia Inaki Aldecoa
Sales, Publicity: Arzamendi Pello Elzaburu
Founded: 1976
Subjects: Education, Literature, Literary Criticism, Essays, Poetry
ISBN Prefix(es): 84-7568; 84-85324; 84-400; 84-9746

**Ediciones Eseuve SA**
Batalla del Salado, 34, 28045 Madrid
SAN: 001-7027
*Tel:* (091) 539-01-03 *Fax:* (091) 528-87-59
*Key Personnel*
Contact: Angel Sabat Gomez
Founded: 1987
ISBN Prefix(es): 84-87301; 84-404
*Parent Company:* Ediciones Rialp SA
Subsidiaries: Esmon Publicidad SA

**Esic Editorial**
Avda de Valdenigrales, s/n, 28223 Pozuelo de Alarcon, Madrid
*Tel:* (091) 3527716 *Fax:* (091) 3528534
*E-mail:* editorial.mad@esic.es
*Web Site:* www.esic.es
*Key Personnel*
Contact: Maria Jesus Merino Sanz
    *E-mail:* mariajesusmerino@esic.es
Founded: 1970
Specializes in economy, marketing & enterprise.
Subjects: Accounting, Economics
ISBN Prefix(es): 84-7356

**ESIN**, *imprint of* Editorial Esin, SA

**Editorial Esin, SA+**
Casp, 79, 08013 Barcelona
*Tel:* (093) 244 95 50 *Fax:* (093) 265 68 95
*E-mail:* combel@editorialcasals.com
*Web Site:* www.editorialcasals.com
*Key Personnel*
Man Dir: Casals Ramon
Founded: 1987
Subjects: Education, Fiction, Religion - Catholic
ISBN Prefix(es): 84-7864; 84-88017
Number of titles published annually: 50 Print
Total Titles: 400 Print
*Associate Companies:* Editorial Casals, SA
Imprints: Combel; ESIN
*Warehouse:* Juli Galve i Brussons, 72, 08912 Badalona

**Editorial Espasa-Calpe SA+**
Member of Grupo Planeta
Carreterade Irun, Km 12, 200, Apdo de correos, 547, 28049 Madrid
*Tel:* (091) 3589689 *Fax:* (091) 3589364; (091) 3589505
*E-mail:* sagerencias@espasa.es
*Web Site:* www.espasa.com
*Telex:* 48850 Espac E *Cable:* ESPACALPE
*Key Personnel*
General Manager: Jorge Hernandez
Editorial Dir: Rafael Gonzalez Cortes
Rights & Permissions: Carlos Ezponda Ibanez
Founded: 1925
Membership(s): Planeta Group (Spain).
Subjects: Art, Biography, Child Care & Development, Cookery, English as a Second Language, Fiction, History, Literature, Literary Criticism, Essays, Nonfiction (General), Science Fiction, Fantasy, Self-Help, Social Sciences, Sociology
ISBN Prefix(es): 84-339; 84-239; 84-670; 84-8326
*Branch Office(s)*
Roger de Lluria 33, 08009 Barcelona

Balbino Marron s/n, Edf Viapol portal A 5a, 41008 Sevilla
Simon Bolivar, 27 - dpto 34-35, 48013 Bilbao
Hebreista Perez Bayer, 9-10A, 46002 Valencia
Distributed by Planeta International S A (Restrictions Latin America)
*Bookshop(s):* Libreria Austral, Roger de Lluria 33, 08009 Barcelona; Casa del Libro Espasa-Calpe SA, Gran Via, 29, 28013 Madrid; Casa del Libro, Maestro Victoria 3, 28013 Madrid; Casa del Libro, Colon de Larreategui 41, 48009 Bilbao; Casa del Libro, Paseo de Gracia 62, 08007 Barcelona

**Editorial Espaxs SA**
Rossello, 132, 08036 Barcelona
*Tel:* (093) 253 0706 *Fax:* (093) 4510149
*E-mail:* espax-adm@stl.logiccontrol.es
*Telex:* 50679 Espx E
Subjects: Medicine, Nursing, Dentistry
ISBN Prefix(es): 84-7179
*Bookshop(s):* Libreria Espaxs, Rosellon 132, 08036 Barcelona; Facultad de Medicina, 28804 Alcala de Henares, Madrid; Calle Zaragoza 5, 11003 Cadiz; Cami de Riudoms 6, local 2, 43201 Reus (Tarragona); Calle Fernando el Catolico 57, 50006 Zaragoza

**Espiritualidad**
Triana, 9, 28016 Madrid
*Tel:* (091) 350-49-22 *Fax:* (091) 350-49-22
*E-mail:* ede@edespiritualidad.org
*Web Site:* www.edespiritualidad.org
Founded: 1948
ISBN Prefix(es): 84-7068

**Estudio de Bioinformacion, S L+**
Embajador Vich, 22-4°-8a, 46002 Valencia
*Tel:* (096) 351 46 27 *Fax:* (096) 394 37 27
*E-mail:* bioinformacion@bioinformacion.com
*Web Site:* www.bioinformacion.com
*Key Personnel*
Dir: Ernesto Hanquet
Subjects: Psychology, Psychiatry
ISBN Prefix(es): 84-86772; 84-921862

**Instituto de Estudios Fiscales+**
Alcala 9, 1a planta, 28014 Madrid
*Tel:* (091) 5063740 (ext 51307) *Fax:* (091) 5273951
*E-mail:* ventas.campillo@minhac.es
*Web Site:* www.minhac.es/ief
*Key Personnel*
Coordinator, Editorial Production: Alberto Romero Martin
Subjects: Accounting, Economics, Law, Public Administration
ISBN Prefix(es): 84-476
*Parent Company:* Ministerio de Economia y Hacienda
*Warehouse:* Centro de Publicaciones del Ministerio de Economia y Hacienda, Pza Campillo del Mundo Nuevo, 3-28005 Madrid
*Orders to:* Centro de Publicaciones del Ministerio de Economia y Hacienda Pza, Campillo del Mundo Nuevo, 3-28005 Madrid

**Instituto de Estudios Riojanos**
Muro de la Mata, 8 Principal, 26071 Logrono La Rioja
*Tel:* (0941) 262064; (0941) 262065 *Fax:* (0941) 246667
*Key Personnel*
Dir: Jose Miguel Delgado Idarreta
Founded: 1946
Membership(s): CECEL (Confederacioon Espanola de Centros de Estudios Locales).
Subjects: Archaeology, Art, Biological Sciences, Chemistry, Chemical Engineering, Earth Sciences, Geography, Geology, History, Language Arts, Linguistics, Literature, Literary Criticism,

Essays, Mathematics, Physical Sciences, Regional Interests, Social Sciences, Sociology
ISBN Prefix(es): 84-87252; 84-89362; 84-89747

**Institut d'Estudis Metropolitans de Barcelona**
Bellaterra, 08193 Barcelona
*Tel:* (093) 691 83 61; (093) 691 97 97; (093) 691 91 82 *Fax:* (093) 580 65 72
*E-mail:* iermb@uab.es
*Web Site:* www.uab.es/iemb/
*Key Personnel*
Dir: Oriol Nel lo i Colom

**Publicaciones Etea** (ETEA Publishing)
Escritor Castilla Aguayo, 4, 14004 Cordoba
SAN: 002-8724
*Tel:* (0957) 222100 *Fax:* (0957) 222182
*E-mail:* comunica@etea.com
*Web Site:* www.etea.com
*Key Personnel*
Dir: Jesus N Ramirez Sobrino *E-mail:* jramirez@etea.com
Founded: 1963
University education.
Subjects: Business, Economics, Labor, Industrial Relations
ISBN Prefix(es): 84-86785; 84-9750
Number of titles published annually: 20 Print
*Parent Company:* ETEA - Institucion Universitaria de la Compenia de Jesus
Distributed by Desclee de Brouwer
Foreign Rights: Desclee de Brouwer (Spain)

**Etu Ediciones SL+**
Grau de Sant Andreu 415, 08030 Barcelona
*Tel:* (093) 2741671 *Fax:* (093) 2741671
*E-mail:* etu@arrakis.es
*Key Personnel*
Dir General: Tristan Llop
Founded: 1996 (Founded by Kabaleb's son)
Courses of occult sciences.
Subjects: Astrology, Occult, Religion - Other, Angels
Total Titles: 7 Print
Distributed by Indigo (Spain & South America)
Distributor for Alfaomega S L (Spain)

**Eumo Editorial+**
P de Miquel de Clariana, 3, 08500 Vic, Barcelona
SAN: 002-9351
*Tel:* (093) 889 28 18; (093) 889 29 61 *Fax:* (093) 889 35 41
*E-mail:* eumoeditorial@eumoeditorial.com
*Web Site:* www.eumoeditorial.com
*Key Personnel*
Dir General: Montse Ayats
Founded: 1979
Subjects: Archaeology, Education, Health, Nutrition, History, Library & Information Sciences, Literature, Literary Criticism, Essays, Nonfiction (General), Poetry, Women's Studies
ISBN Prefix(es): 84-7602; 84-9750; 84-300; 84-9766
Number of titles published annually: 25 Print
Total Titles: 1,100 Print
*Distribution Center:* Arc De Bera, C de Belgica 47-49, Poligon Montigala, 08911 Badalona, Contact: Pep Vila *Tel:* (093) 465 30 08 *Fax:* (093) 465 87 90

**EUNSA (Ediciones Universidad de Navarra SA)+**
Plaza de los Sauces, 1-2, 31010 Baranain Navarra
*Tel:* (0948) 256850 *Fax:* (0948) 256854
*E-mail:* eunsa@ibernet.com
*Web Site:* www.eunsa.es
*Key Personnel*
Editorial Dir: Jose Martinez Echalar
Production: Abel del Rio
Chairman: Damaso Rico
Founded: 1967
Subjects: Architecture & Interior Design, Biological Sciences, Business, Economics, Education,

Engineering (General), History, Journalism, Language Arts, Linguistics, Law, Library & Information Sciences, Literature, Literary Criticism, Essays, Medicine, Nursing, Dentistry, Philosophy, Religion - Other, Theology
ISBN Prefix(es): 84-313
Imprints: Biblioteca 'NT' (number of paperback series covering the arts & sciences, current affairs, religion & philosophy, etc)

**Fondo de Cultura Economica de Espana SL+**
Via de los Poblados, s/n, Edif Indubuilding-Goico, 4-15, 28033 Madrid
SAN: 003-0562
*Tel:* (091) 7632800; (091) 7632766 *Fax:* (091) 7635133
*E-mail:* fcevent@interbook.es
*Key Personnel*
Man Dir: Arturo Azuela
Founded: 1934
Subjects: Anthropology, Economics, Government, Political Science, History, Language Arts, Linguistics, Law, Literature, Literary Criticism, Essays, Philosophy, Psychology, Psychiatry, Science (General), Social Sciences, Sociology, Technology
ISBN Prefix(es): 84-375
*Parent Company:* Fondo de Cultura Economica, Mexico
*U.S. Office(s):* Fondo de Cultura Economica, 2293 Verus St, San Diego, CA 92154, United States
*Bookshop(s):* Libreria Mexico, c/Fernando el Catolico, 86, 28015 Madrid

**Miguel Font Editor**
Pedro Ripoll Palov, 20, Apdo 128, E-07008 Palma de Mallorca, Baleares
SAN: 004-2196
*Tel:* (071) 477300 *Fax:* (071) 476805
*E-mail:* miquel@globalnet.es
*Key Personnel*
Manager: Miguel Font i Cirer
Founded: 1984
ISBN Prefix(es): 84-86366; 84-7967

**Forum Artis, SA+**
Serrano, 7-1 izda, 28001 Madrid
SAN: 003-0805
*Tel:* (091) 4353180; (091) 4350548 *Fax:* (091) 4355124
*E-mail:* forum@adenet.es
*Key Personnel*
Dir: Mario Antolin Paz
Founded: 1991
Subjects: Art
ISBN Prefix(es): 84-88836

**Naipes Heraclio Fournier SA**
Poligono Industrial de Gojain, Avda San Blas, 19, 01171 Legutiano
SAN: 004-3400
Mailing Address: PO Box 94, 01006 Vitoria
*Tel:* (0945) 465525 *Fax:* (0945) 465543
*E-mail:* fournier@nhfournier.es
*Web Site:* www.nhfournier.es
*Telex:* 35510 *Cable:* FOURNIER
ISBN Prefix(es): 84-85074; 84-88928

**Fragua Editorial**
Andres Mellado, 64, 28015 Madrid
*Tel:* (091) 544 22 97; (091) 549 18 06 *Fax:* (091) 549 18 06
*E-mail:* fragua@fragua.com
*Web Site:* www.fragua.com
*Key Personnel*
Man Dir: Mariano Munoz Alonso
Founded: 1972
Subjects: Advertising, Communications, Journalism, Language Arts, Linguistics, Library &

Information Sciences, Philosophy, Photography, Radio, TV, Technology
ISBN Prefix(es): 84-7074; 84-7974

**Fundacio La Caixa**
Avda Diagonal, 621-629 Torre II, pl 12, 08028 Barcelona
SAN: 003-1240
*Tel:* (093) 404 6079 *Fax:* (093) 3395703
*E-mail:* info@lacaixa.es
*Web Site:* portal1.lacaixa.es
*Key Personnel*
Vice President: Alejandro Plasencia
ISBN Prefix(es): 84-7664; 84-604; 84-500; 84-505

**Fundacion Biblioteca Alemana Gorres**
Subsidiary of Fundacion Deutsche Stiftung
San Buenaventura, 9, 28005 Madrid
*Tel:* (091) 3668508; (091)3668509
*Key Personnel*
Dir: Hans Juretschke
Librarian: Jutta Ploss
Founded: 1955

**Fundacion Coleccion Thyssen-Bornemisza**
Paseo del Prado, 8, 28014 Madrid
*Tel:* (091) 420 39 44 *Fax:* (091) 4202780
*E-mail:* umseo.thyssen-bornemisza@offcampus.es
*Key Personnel*
Contact: Laura Estevez Couras *E-mail:* lestevez@umseothyssen.org
Subjects: Art
ISBN Prefix(es): 84-88474
Distributed by Lunwerg SA

**Fundacion de Estudios Libertarios Anselmo Lorenzo**
Paseo de Alberto Palacios, 2, 28021 Madrid
*Tel:* (091) 7970424 *Fax:* (091) 5052183
*E-mail:* fal@cnt.es
*Web Site:* www.cnt.es/fal
*Key Personnel*
President: Ignacio Soriano
Librarian: Manuel Carlos Garcia
Founded: 1986
Subjects: Biography, Economics, History, Labor, Industrial Relations, Literature, Literary Criticism, Essays, Social Sciences, Sociology, Anarchism, Trade Unionism
ISBN Prefix(es): 84-86864
Number of titles published annually: 4 Print
Distributed by Taluzma (Barcelona)
Distributor for Lucina; Nossa y Jara Editores

**Fundacion de los Ferrocarriles Espanoles**
Santa Isabel, 44, 28012 Madrid
*Tel:* (091) 1511 071 *Fax:* (091) 5284822; (091) 5391415
*E-mail:* fuccu20@ffe.es
*Web Site:* www.ffe.es
*Key Personnel*
Dir: Carlos Zapatero
Specialize in railways.
Subjects: Transportation, Railways
ISBN Prefix(es): 84-404; 84-604; 84-398; 84-88675; 84-505

**Fundacion Gratis Date**
Apdo 2154, 31080 Pamplona
*Tel:* (0948) 123612 *Fax:* (0948) 123612
*E-mail:* fundacion@gratisdate.org
*Web Site:* www.gratisdate.org
*Key Personnel*
Dir: Jose Maria Iraburu
ISBN Prefix(es): 84-87903; 84-404

**Fundacion Juan March**
Castello, 77, 28006 Madrid
*Tel:* (091) 435 42 40 *Fax:* (091) 576 34 20
*E-mail:* webmast@mail.march.es

*Web Site:* www.march.es
*Key Personnel*
Dir General: Jose Luis Yuste
ISBN Prefix(es): 84-7075; 84-500; 84-400

**Fundacion Marcelino Botin**
Pedrueca, 1, 39003 Santander, Cantabria
*Tel:* (0942) 226072 *Fax:* (0942) 226045
*E-mail:* fmabotin@fundacionmbotin.org
*Web Site:* www.fundacionmbotin.org
*Key Personnel*
Dir: Rafael Benjumea Cabeza De Saca
Contact: Isabel Cubria *E-mail:* prensa@fundacionmbotin.org
Founded: 1990
Subjects: Archaeology, Art, Environmental Studies, History, Human Relations, Science (General)
ISBN Prefix(es): 84-87678; 84-95516; 84-404; 84-500; 84-398
Number of titles published annually: 12 Print
Distributed by Emiliano Garcia de la Torre (Spain)

**Fundacion Rosacruz+**
Apdo de Correos, 1219, 50080 Zaragoza
*Tel:* (076) 589100 *Fax:* (076) 589161
*E-mail:* correo@fundacionrosacruz.org
*Web Site:* www.fundacionrosacruz.org
Founded: 1993
Subjects: Literature, Literary Criticism, Essays, Mysteries, Philosophy, Religion - Other
ISBN Prefix(es): 84-87055
*Parent Company:* Stichting Rozkruis Pers, Netherlands
*Associate Companies:* Rozekruis Pers, France
Distributed by Totem (Balears Islands); Unicornio (Canary Islands)
*Showroom(s):* 49 bajos, Alicante *Tel:* (01) 5144805; del Oro, 23, Barcelona *Tel:* (093) 2184368; Porvenir, 12, entlo, Gerona; Tabares, 10 transversal izda. no2, La Cuesta (Tenerife); Santa Ana, 69, Leon *Tel:* (087) 213767; Francisco de Ricci, 7, Madrid *Tel:* (091) 5595992; Ladron de Guevara, 12, Malaga *Tel:* (05) 2253949; Goethe, 15 A, Palma De Mallorca *Tel:* (071) 285629; Po de la Pechina, 6 bajo, Valencia *Tel:* (06) 3910267; Santa Cruz, 8, Zaragoza *Tel:* (076) 574268

**Editorial Fundamentos+**
Caracas, 15-3 ctro dcha, 28010 Madrid
*Tel:* (091) 319 96 19 *Fax:* (091) 319 55 84
*E-mail:* fundamentos@editorialfundamentos.es
*Web Site:* www.editorialfundamentos.es
*Key Personnel*
Man Dir: Juan Serraller Ibanez
Editorial: Cristina Vizcaino
Founded: 1970
Subjects: Alternative, Crafts, Games, Hobbies, Drama, Theater, Fiction, Film, Video, Government, Political Science, Literature, Literary Criticism, Essays, Music, Dance, Philosophy, Psychology, Psychiatry, Social Sciences, Sociology
ISBN Prefix(es): 84-245

**Galaxia SA Editorial+**
Reconquista, 1, 36201 Vigo Pontevedra
*Tel:* (0986) 432100; (0986) 433238 *Fax:* (0986) 223205
*E-mail:* galaxia@editorialgalaxia.es
*Web Site:* www.editorialgalaxia.es
*Key Personnel*
Dir General: Carlos Casares
Founded: 1950
Subjects: Art, History, Literature, Literary Criticism, Essays, Philosophy, Poetry, Social Sciences, Sociology, Travel
ISBN Prefix(es): 84-7154; 84-8288; 84-400
*Warehouse:* Trav Vigo, 71 (Sotano), 36206 Vigo Pontevedra

**La Galera, SA Editorial+**
Diputacio, 250, 08007 Barcelona
*Tel:* (093) 4120030 *Fax:* (093) 3014863
*Web Site:* www.enciclopedia-catalana.com
*Key Personnel*
Man Dir: Roma Doria Forcada
Founded: 1963
Subjects: Education
ISBN Prefix(es): 84-246

**Vicent Garcia Editores, SA**
Guardia Civil, 22 Torre 3a, piso 1º, 3a, 46020
Valencia
SAN: 005-318X
*Tel:* (096) 361 9559; (096) 3691589; (096) 369
3246 *Fax:* (096) 393 00 57
*E-mail:* vgesa@combios.es
*Web Site:* www.vgesa.com
*Key Personnel*
Dir General: Ricardo J Vicent
Founded: 1974
Specialize in facsimiles of manuscripts, incunab-
ula & ancient books.
Subjects: Antiques, Art, Gardening, Plants, His-
tory, Language Arts, Linguistics, Law, Religion
- Catholic, Travel
ISBN Prefix(es): 84-85094; 84-87988; 84-400
*Book Club(s):* Club Konrad Haebler

**Ediciones Gaviota SA+**
Subsidiary of Editorial Everest SA
Manuel Tovar, 8, 28034 Madrid
*Tel:* (091) 358 01 08 *Fax:* (091) 729 38 58
*E-mail:* publicaciones@ediciones-gaviota.es
*Web Site:* www.everest.es
*Key Personnel*
Man Dir: Jose Antonio Lopez Martinez
Publication Dir: Matthew Todd Borgens
Export Dir: Severino Fernandez
Founded: 1980
Specialize in Children's & Juvenile Books.
ISBN Prefix(es): 84-392
*Associate Companies:* Lectorum Publications Inc,
137 West 14 St, New York, NY 10011, United
States (US Distributor)
Subsidiaries: Everset de Ediciones y Distribucion
*Orders to:* Everset de Ediciones y Distribucion

**Editorial Gedisa SA+**
Bonanova Stroll, 9 1º 1a, 08022 Barcelona
*Tel:* (093) 253 09 04 *Fax:* (093) 253 09 05
*E-mail:* gedisa@gedisa.com
*Web Site:* www.gedisa.com
*Key Personnel*
Publisher: Victor Landman
Founded: 1977
Subjects: Biography, Education, Human Rela-
tions, Nonfiction (General), Philosophy, Psy-
chology, Psychiatry, Social Sciences, Sociology,
Sports, Athletics
ISBN Prefix(es): 84-7432
Subsidiaries: Editorial Celtia SA; Editorial Gedisa
Mexicana SA

**Generalitat de Catalunya Diari Oficial de la
Generalitat vern**
Carrer Rocafort, 120, 08015 Barcelona
*Tel:* (093) 302 64 62 *Fax:* (093) 318 62 21
*E-mail:* llibrcn@gencat.net
*Web Site:* www.gencat.net/diari
*Key Personnel*
General Dir: Ricard Lobo
Founded: 1977
Subjects: Art, Education, Health, Nutrition, His-
tory, Law, Public Administration, Regional In-
terests
ISBN Prefix(es): 84-393
*Bookshop(s):* Llibreria de la Generalitat de
Catalunya, Rambla dels Estudis 118, 08002
Barcelona *E-mail:* llibrgi@gencat.net; Llibre-
ria de la Generalitat de Catalunya, Gran Via
de Jaume 1, 38, 17001 Girona *Tel:* (0972)

22 72 67 *E-mail:* llibrgi@gencat.net; Llibreria de la Generalitat de Catalunya, Rambla
d'Arago, 43, 25003 Lleida *Tel:* (0973) 28 19
30 *E-mail:* llibrlle@gencat.net
*Orders to:* Llibreria de la Generalitat de
Catalunya, Rambla dels Estudis 118, 08002
Barcelona *E-mail:* llibrcn@gencat.net

**Ediciones Gestio 2000 SA+**
Comte Borrell, 241, 08029 Barcelona
*Tel:* (093) 4106767 *Fax:* (093) 4109645
*E-mail:* bustia@gestion2000.com
*Web Site:* www.gestion2000.com
*Key Personnel*
Dir: Alexandre Amat *E-mail:* aamat@
gestion2000.com
Founded: 1986
Specialize in business management.
Subjects: Accounting, Advertising, Business, Ca-
reer Development, Computer Science, Eco-
nomics, Finance, Human Relations, Manage-
ment, Marketing, Technology
ISBN Prefix(es): 84-86703; 84-8088; 84-86582
Total Titles: 400 Print; 10 CD-ROM
*Bookshop(s):* Libreria de la Empresa c/Muntaner,
90 08011 Barcelona *E-mail:* libreria.empresa@
gestion2000.com

**Instituto de Cultura Juan Gil-Albert+**
Avda Estacion, 6, 03005 Alicante
*Tel:* (096) 5121 214 *Fax:* (096) 5921 824
*E-mail:* galbert@dip-alicante.es
*Web Site:* www.dip-alicante.es/galbert/
*Key Personnel*
President: Antonio Mira Perceval
Dir: Emilio La Parra Lopez
Founded: 1983
Also acts as Council for scientific research.
Subjects: Art, Poetry, Social Sciences, Sociology
ISBN Prefix(es): 84-7784; 84-500; 84-398; 84-
505; 84-600

**Editorial Gustavo Gili SA+**
Rossello, 87-89, 08029 Barcelona
*Tel:* (093) 3228161 *Fax:* (093) 3229205
*E-mail:* info@ggili.com
*Web Site:* www.ggili.com
*Key Personnel*
President: Gustavo Gili
Editor-in-Chief & Man Dir: Monica Gili
Man Dir & Sales General Manager: Gabriel Gili
Sales Export: Saskia Adriaensen; Pepita Sanchez
Production: Andreas Schweiger
Foreign Rights: Elena Llobera
Founded: 1902
Publisher specializing in architectural books &
magazines
Also subscription & periodical publications.
Subjects: Architecture & Interior Design, Art,
Communications, Photography, Technology,
Travel
ISBN Prefix(es): 84-252
Number of titles published annually: 50 Print
Total Titles: 1,200 Print
*Associate Companies:* Ediciones G Gili, SA de
CV, Avda Valle de Bravo, 21-53050, Mexico
(ISBN: 968-887)
Distributor for Colegio De Arquitectos de Alme-
ria; Collegi D'Arquitectes de Catalunya
*Distribution Center:* Trucatriche, 3800 Main St,
Suite 8, Chula Vista, CA 91911, United States,
Contact: Pedro Alonzo *Tel:* 619-426-2690
*Fax:* 619-426-2695 *E-mail:* info@trucatriche.
com (international orders, attn Gustavo Gili)

**Gran Enciclopedia-Asturiana Silverio Canada**
Menendez Valdes, 33-1, 33201 Gijon, Asturias
SAN: 004-9476
*Tel:* (0985) 170921; (0985) 349684 *Fax:* (0985)
349542
*E-mail:* gea.edi@teleline.es; gea_edi@yahoo.es
*Web Site:* www.enciclopediaasturiana.com

*Telex:* 89736 Edju E
*Key Personnel*
Man Dir, Editorial: Silverio Canada
Sales: Fernando Alvarez Conde
Production: Manuel Cardenas
Founded: 1970
Subjects: Regional Interests
ISBN Prefix(es): 84-7286
*Orders to:* Alto Atocha 7, Gijon

**Grao Editorial+**
Francesc Tarrega, 32-34, 08027 Barcelona
*Tel:* (093) 4080464 *Fax:* (093) 3524337
*E-mail:* grao@grao.com
*Web Site:* www.grao.com
*Key Personnel*
Manager: Joaquim Mart
Editorial Dir: Cinta Vidal
Founded: 1977
Subjects: Education
ISBN Prefix(es): 84-7827; 84-85729
Number of titles published annually: 25 Print
Total Titles: 250 Print
*Parent Company:* Institut de Recursos I Investiga-
cio per a la Foirmacio, SK (IRIF)

**Grao Editorial+**
Francesc Tarrega, 32-34, 08027 Barcelona
*Tel:* (093) 4080464; (093) 4050455 *Fax:* (093)
3524337
*E-mail:* grao@grao.com
*Web Site:* www.grao.com
*Key Personnel*
Delegated Counselor: Antoni Zabala i Vidiella
Founded: 1977
Subjects: Education
ISBN Prefix(es): 84-7827
Number of titles published annually: 50 Print
Total Titles: 300 Print
Divisions: Grao Editorial; Interactiva

**Editorial Gredos SA+**
Sanchez Pacheco, 85, Apdo 2076, 28002 Madrid
*Tel:* (091) 7444920 *Fax:* (091) 5192033
*E-mail:* comercial@editorialgredos.com
*Web Site:* www.editorialgredos.com
Founded: 1944
Subjects: Economics, Education, History, Liter-
ature, Literary Criticism, Essays, Philosophy,
Psychology, Psychiatry
ISBN Prefix(es): 84-249

**Grijalbo Mondadon SA Junior+**
Arago 385, 08013 Barcelona
*Tel:* (093) 4767100 *Fax:* (093) 4767121
*Web Site:* www.grijalbo.com
*Key Personnel*
President: Juan Grijalbo
Council Delegate: Jose Maria Vives
Assistant Council Delegate: Gonzalo Ponton
Manager: Josep Maria Pujol
Founded: 1974
Membership(s): Grupo & Grijalbo-Mondadori
Publications in Barcelona.
Subjects: Humor
ISBN Prefix(es): 84-7419; 84-478
*Warehouse:* Grijalbo Comercial, SA, Progreso,
274, Badelona (Barcelona)

**Grijalbo Mondadori SA+**
Arago 385, 08013 Barcelona
*Tel:* (093) 4767100 *Fax:* (093) 4767121
*E-mail:* marketing@grijalbo.com
*Web Site:* www.grijalbo.com
*Key Personnel*
General Manager: Riccardo Cavallero
*Tel:* (093) 476 71 23 *Fax:* (093) 476 71 21
*E-mail:* ricky@grijalbo.com
General Editor: Claudio Lopez de Lamadrid
*Tel:* (093) 476 71 03 *E-mail:* claudio@grijalbo.
com

Editor: Cristina Arminana *Tel:* (093) 476 71 00
*E-mail:* cristina@grijalbo.com; Silvia Querini
*Tel:* (093) 476 71 05 *E-mail:* silviaq@grijalbo.
com
Rights: Isabelle Bordallo *Tel:* (093) 476 71 03
*E-mail:* bordallo@grijalbo.com; Dora Hernando
*E-mail:* dora@grijalbo.com
Contact: Carmen Garrido Montero
*E-mail:* carmen@grijalbo.com
Founded: 1962
Subjects: Architecture & Interior Design, Fiction,
Gardening, Plants, Human Relations, Humor,
Literature, Literary Criticism, Essays, Nonfic-
tion (General), Poetry
ISBN Prefix(es): 84-253; 84-397; 84-7515; 84-
8441; 84-85297
Number of titles published annually: 400 Print
*Branch Office(s)*
Grijalbo SA, Av Belgrano, 1256/64, 1093 Buenos
Aires, Argentina *Tel:* (0383) 74 03, 49 40
*Fax:* (0381) 27 26 *E-mail:* info@grijalbo.com.
ar
Distribuidora Exclusiva Grijalbo SA, Centro In-
dustiral Eldorado, Calle 64, 88 A-06, inte-
rior 1-2, Bogota D E, Colombia *Tel:* (0224)
74 28; (0252) 26 75 *Fax:* (0252) 95 97
*E-mail:* grijalbo@cdl.telecom.com.co
Editorial Grijalbo SA, Almirante Barroso, 27,
Santiago De Chile, Chile *Tel:* (0672) 30
27 *Fax:* (0672) 18 50 *E-mail:* mondador@
entelchile.net
Editorial Grijalbo SA DE C V, Av Homero, No
544, Col Chapultepec-Morales, 11570 Mexico
D F, Mexico *Tel:* (05) 2030660; (05) 2030955
*Fax:* (05) 2547683
Ap Correos, 106-62260 Chacao, Av Principal
Diego Cisnero, Edificio colegial Bolivari-
ana, piso 2, local 2-2 Los Ruices, Caracas,
Venezuela *Tel:* (0238) 13 22 *Fax:* (0239) 03
08 *E-mail:* griven@etheron.net
Distributor for Dedicersa De Cervantes Ediciones
SA; Editorial Amazonas SA; Electa Espana
SA; Forza Editores Inc
Foreign Rights: Ros Ramsay (UK); Mary Anne
Thompson

**Editorial Grupo Cero**
Duque de Osuna Nº 4 Locales, 28015 Madrid
*Tel:* (091) 758 19 40; (091) 542 33 49 *Fax:* (091)
758 19 41
*E-mail:* pedidos@editorialgrupocero.com
*Web Site:* www.editorialgrupocero.com
*Key Personnel*
Dir: Miguel Oscar Menassa
Founded: 1976
Subjects: Literature, Literary Criticism, Essays,
Medicine, Nursing, Dentistry, Poetry, Psychol-
ogy, Psychiatry, Social Sciences, Sociology
ISBN Prefix(es): 84-85498

**Grupo Comunicar**
Apdo Correos 527, 21080 Huelva
*Tel:* (0959) 248380 *Fax:* (0959) 248380
*E-mail:* info@grupocomunicar.com
*Web Site:* www.grupo-comunicar.com
*Key Personnel*
President: Jose Ignacio Aguaded Gomez
Vice President: Enrique Martinez-Salanova
Sanchez
Founded: 1989
Subjects: Communications, Education
Number of titles published annually: 4 Print; 3
CD-ROM; 4 Online; 2 E-Book
Total Titles: 40 Print; 5 CD-ROM; 4 Online; 5 E-
Book
Distributor for Abis & Books; Amares; A-Z Dis-
libros; Carrer de Llibres; Centro Andaluz del
Libro; Andres Garcia; Grial; Ikuska; Lemus

**Grupo Editorial**, see Ediciones SM

**Grupo Editorial CEAC SA+**
Paseig Manel Girona, 71 Baixos, 08034
Barcelona
SAN: 003-357X
*Tel:* (093) 2472424 *Fax:* (093) 2315115
*E-mail:* atencioncliente@ceacedit.com
*Web Site:* www.ceacedit.com; www.editorialceac.
com
*Key Personnel*
President: Guillermo Menal, Sr
Executive Manager: Jaume Pintanel
Dir, International: Esteve Julia
Editorial Dir: Isabel Marti *E-mail:* imarti@
ceacedit.com; Jose Lopez Jara *Tel:* (093) 307
52 59 *E-mail:* jljara@caecedit.com
Subjects: Education, Science Fiction, Fantasy,
Technology
Imprints: Ediciones Ceac; Timun Mas; Libros
Cupula

**Grupo Santillana de Ediciones SA+**
Torrelaguna, 60, 28043 Madrid
*Tel:* (091) 7449060 *Fax:* (091) 3224475
*E-mail:* grupo@santillana.es
*Web Site:* www.gruposantillana.com
*Key Personnel*
President: Emiliano Martinez
Vice President: Francisco Perez Gonzalez; Ri-
cardo Diez Hochleitner
Man Dir: Isabel de Polanco Moreno
Founded: 1960
Subjects: Education
ISBN Prefix(es): 84-294; 84-668
*Associate Companies:* Editorial Santillana, Ar-
gentina; Editorial Santillana, Bolivia; Editorial
Santillana, Chile; Editorial Santillana, Colom-
bia; Editorial Santillana, Costa Rica; Edito-
rial Santillana, Dominican Republic; Editorial
Santillana, Ecuador; Editorial Santillana, El
Salvador; Editorial Santillana, Guatemala; Ed-
itorial Santillana, Mexico; Editorial Santillana,
Paraguay; Editorial Santillana, Peru; Editorial
Santillana, Puerto Rico; Editorial Santillana,
Uruguay; Editorial Santillana, Venezuela
Divisions: Aguilar; Alfaguara; Altea; Richmond;
Taurus
*U.S. Office(s):* Santillana Publishing Co, 2105
NW 86 Ave, Miami, FL 33112, United States

**Guadalquivir SL Ediciones**
Asuncion, 61, 41011 Sevilla
SAN: 003-3863
*Tel:* (095) 422 19 76; (095) 422 19 17 *Fax:* (095)
421 33 20
*E-mail:* guadalquivir.ed@svq.servicom.es
*Web Site:* www.guadalquivirediciones.com
Founded: 1979
Subjects: Art, History, Literature, Literary Criti-
cism, Essays
ISBN Prefix(es): 84-8093; 84-86080
Subsidiaries: Varflora
*Orders to:* Varflora, 17 Bajo, 41001 Seville

**Guia Viva**, *imprint of* Anaya-Touring Club

**Guiarama**, *imprint of* Anaya-Touring Club

**Guiatotal**, *imprint of* Anaya-Touring Club

**Editorial Gulaab**
Alquima, 6 (P 1 Los Rosales), 28933 Mostoles
*Tel:* (091) 6170867 *Fax:* (091) 6170867
*E-mail:* alfaomega@sew.es
*Key Personnel*
Editor: J M Beltran Alorda
Subjects: Human Relations, Philosophy, Religion
- Buddhist, Religion - Hindu, Religion - Other,
Women's Studies
ISBN Prefix(es): 84-86797

Distributed by Alfa Omego (Spain); Ed Cerro
Manupuehue (Chile); Ed luz de Luna (Ar-
gentina); Ed Moderna (Colombia); Unicornio
(Spain)

**Harlequin Iberica SA**
Hermosilla, 21, 28001 Madrid
SAN: 003-407X
*Tel:* (091) 4358623 *Fax:* (091) 4310484
*E-mail:* atencionalcliente@harlequiniberica.com
*Web Site:* www.harlequiniberica.com
*Key Personnel*
General Dir: Maria Teresa Villar
Founded: 1982
Subjects: Romance
ISBN Prefix(es): 84-396
*Parent Company:* Harlequin Enterprises Ltd,
Toronto, ON, Canada

**Heinemann Iberia SA**, see Macmillan
Heinemann ELT

**Hercules de Ediciones, SA**
Comandonte fontenes 6-1 AB, 15003 A Coruna
La Coruna
*Tel:* (0981) 220585; (0981) 226443 *Fax:* (0981)
220717
*E-mail:* empg05052@empresas-galicia.com
*Key Personnel*
President: Francisco Rodriguez Iglesias
Manager: Nicolas Salvador Egido
Subjects: Anthropology, Child Care & Develop-
ment, Education
ISBN Prefix(es): 84-87244; 84-89468
*Branch Office(s)*
Hercules Astur
*Warehouse:* Rua Chinto Crespo, 2, A Gandara,
San Pedro, L A Coruna

**Editorial Herder SA+**
Provenca, 388, 08025 Barcelona
*Tel:* (093) 476 26 26 *Fax:* (093) 207 34 48
*E-mail:* herder@herdereditorial.com
*Web Site:* www.herder-sa.com
*Telex:* 54120 Hegr E *Cable:* HERDER
*Key Personnel*
Man Dir: Friedl Antonio Valtl
Publicity: Carlos Rey
Founded: 1943
Subjects: Economics, Education, Language Arts,
Linguistics, Medicine, Nursing, Dentistry, Phi-
losophy, Psychology, Psychiatry, Religion -
Other, Social Sciences, Sociology, Theology
ISBN Prefix(es): 84-254
*Associate Companies:* Verlag Herder & Co, Aus-
tria; Verlag Herder GmbH & Co KG, Ger-
many; Herder und Herder GmbH, Germany;
Herder Editrice e Libreria, Italy; Herder AG,
Switzerland
*Branch Office(s)*
Herder Editorial y Livreria, Calle 12, No 6/89,
Apdo Aereo, 6855 Bogota, Colombia (Delega-
cione de Venta)
Hesperia SA Editorial y Libreria, Ave Callao
565, Buenos Aires, Argentina (Delegacione
de Venta)
*Bookshop(s):* Libreria Herder

**Ediciones Hiperion SL+**
Salustiano Olozaga, 14, 28001 Madrid
*Tel:* (091) 577 60 15; (091) 577 60 16 *Fax:* (091)
435 86 90
*E-mail:* info@hiperion.com
*Web Site:* www.hiperion.com
*Key Personnel*
Man Dir, Editorial: Jesus Munarriz
Sales: Maite Merodio
Founded: 1976
Subjects: Language Arts, Linguistics, Literature,
Literary Criticism, Essays, Poetry, Religion -
Islamic, Religion - Jewish
ISBN Prefix(es): 84-7517; 84-85272
Number of titles published annually: 30 Print

Total Titles: 600 Print
*Bookshop(s):* Libreria Hiperion, Calle Salustiano Olozaga 14, 28001 Madrid *Tel:* (091) 577 60 15

## Editorial Hispano Europea SA+
Bori i Fontesta, 6-8, 08021 Barcelona
*Tel:* (093) 2013709; (093) 2018500 *Fax:* (093) 4142635
*E-mail:* hispaneuropea@mx3.redestb.es
*Telex:* 98772 cllcE
*Key Personnel*
Man Dir, Editorial & Publicity: Jorge J Prat
Sales: Xavier Campillo
Production: Jose Madueno
Founded: 1956
Subjects: Animals, Pets, Business, Gardening, Plants, Health, Nutrition, Sports, Athletics
ISBN Prefix(es): 84-255
Number of titles published annually: 50 Print
Total Titles: 536 Print

## Editorial Horsori SL
Rambla de Fabra i Puig 10-12 1 1a, 08030 Barcelona
*Tel:* (093) 3461997 *Fax:* (093) 3118498
*E-mail:* horsori@retemail.net
*Web Site:* www.horsori.es
*Key Personnel*
Contact: Francisco Segu
Subjects: Education, Philosophy
ISBN Prefix(es): 84-85840
*Warehouse:* MADE Av Catalonya sln Pol Ind Can Coll, 08185, Lliga de Vall Barcelona

## Ibaizabal Edelvives SA
Barrio San Miguel, s/n, 48340 Amorebieta-Etxano, Vizcaya
*Tel:* (094) 6308036 *Fax:* (094) 6308028
*E-mail:* ibaizabal@ibaizabal.biz
*Key Personnel*
Dir: Jose Iraolagoitia Mendibe
Contact: Itziar Osa
Founded: 1990
Materials for school teaching literary editions.
Subjects: Education, Literature, Literary Criticism, Essays, Religion - Catholic
ISBN Prefix(es): 84-8325; 84-7992
Number of titles published annually: 123 Print
Total Titles: 1,436 Print
*Warehouse:* Edelvives, Barrio San Miguel S/A, 48340 Amorebieta-Etxano, Vizcaya *Tel:* (04) 4532009; (04) 4532174 *Fax:* (04) 4532091
*Orders to:* Edelvives, Barrio San Miguel S/A, 48340 Amorebieta-Etxano, Vizcaya *Tel:* (04) 4532009; (04) 4532174 *Fax:* (04) 4532091

## Editorial Iberia, SA+
Plato, 26, 08006 Barcelona
*Tel:* (093) 2010599; (093) 2013807 *Fax:* (093) 2097362
*E-mail:* omega@ediciones-omega.es
*Web Site:* www.ediciones-omega.es
*Telex:* 98095
*Key Personnel*
Administrator: Antonio Paricio Larrea
Founded: 1945
Subjects: Art, Biography, Education, Fiction, Health, Nutrition, Literature, Literary Criticism, Essays, Physics, Psychology, Psychiatry, Science (General), Self-Help, Travel
ISBN Prefix(es): 84-7082
*Parent Company:* Ediciones Omega, SA
*Associate Companies:* Ediciones Medici, SL

## Iberico Europea de Ediciones SA
Serrano, 44, 28001 Madrid
SAN: 003-4762
*Tel:* (091) 4357243
Founded: 1966

Subjects: Art, Biography, Business, How-to, Music, Dance, Social Sciences, Sociology
ISBN Prefix(es): 84-256

## Icaria Editorial SA+
Ausias Marc, 16, 3r, 2a, 08010 Barcelona
*Tel:* (093) 3011723 *Fax:* (093) 3178242
*E-mail:* icario@icariaeditorial.com
*Web Site:* www.icariaeditorial.com
*Key Personnel*
Man Dir, Editorial, Rights & Permissions: Anna Monjo Omedes
Founded: 1977
Subjects: Anthropology, Cookery, Developing Countries, Economics, Energy, Environmental Studies, Literature, Literary Criticism, Essays, Poetry, Social Sciences, Sociology, Women's Studies, Analysis of International Politics, Critical Economy, Ecology, Relations of the North-South, Social Sciences, Voices & Proposals
ISBN Prefix(es): 84-7426; 84-400
*Warehouse:* Lepanto, 135-7, 08013 Barcelona

## Publicaciones ICCE (Calasanz Institute for Educational Sciences)+
Eraso 3, Madrid 28028
SAN: 003-6277
*Tel:* (091) 725 72 00 *Fax:* (091) 361 10 52
*E-mail:* info@ciberaula.net
*Web Site:* www.ciberaula.net
*Key Personnel*
Dir: Juan Yzuel *E-mail:* direccion@ciberaula.net
Publishing Dept Dir: Luis M Bandres
    *E-mail:* editorial@ciberaula.net
Founded: 1967
Subjects: Education, History, Psychology, Psychiatry, Religion - Other, Social Sciences, Sociology
ISBN Prefix(es): 84-7278
Number of titles published annually: 10 Print
Total Titles: 85 Print
*Parent Company:* Calasanzian Fathers

## Icono Perpetuo Socorro, *imprint of* Editorial El Perpetuo Socorro

## Idea Books, SA+
c/ Huelva 10, 08940 Cornella de Llobregat, Barcelona
*Tel:* (093) 4533002 *Fax:* (093) 4541895
*E-mail:* ideabooks@ideabooks.es
*Web Site:* www.ideabooks.es
*Key Personnel*
Co-owner & International Rights & Permissions: Jorge Fernandez
Founded: 1990
Publisher of nonfiction books for professionals, students & children. Specialize in woodworking, furniture, iron & construction.
Membership(s): Society of Editors.
Subjects: Agriculture, Biological Sciences, Child Care & Development, Crafts, Games, Hobbies, Earth Sciences, Education, Geography, Geology, Human Relations, Music, Dance, Philosophy, Physics, Religion - Other, Science (General)
ISBN Prefix(es): 84-8236; 84-87624
Number of titles published annually: 35 Print; 2 Audio
Imprints: Idea Musica; Idea Universitaria

## Idea Musica, *imprint of* Idea Books, SA

## Idea Universitaria, *imprint of* Idea Books, SA

## Editorial Pablo Iglesias
Monte Esquinza, 30-3-D, 28010 Madrid
*Tel:* (091) 104 313 *Fax:* (091) 194 585
*E-mail:* administracion@fpi.es
*Web Site:* www.fpabloiglesias.es

*Key Personnel*
Dir: Manuel Ortuno Armas
ISBN Prefix(es): 84-85691

## Imagen y Deporte, SL+
Marte, 1 bajo, 50012 Zaragoza
*Tel:* (0976) 75 40 00 *Fax:* (0976) 75 40 00
*E-mail:* imadepor@encomix.es
*Web Site:* www.imagenydeporte.com
*Key Personnel*
Man Dir: Carlos Torres *E-mail:* produccion@ imagenydeporte.com
International Manager: Elena Rodrigo
    *E-mail:* internacional@imagenydeporte.com
National Sales: Elisa de Pedro *E-mail:* editorial@ imagenydeporte.com
Production Manager: Jose Torres
    *E-mail:* imagenydeporte@imagenydeporte.com
Founded: 1988
Production & distribution company of educational products, domentines & books.
Subjects: Education, Sports, Athletics
ISBN Prefix(es): 84-89117; 84-605

## Impredisur, SL+
Cuesta Molinos, 7 bajo, 18008 Granada
*Tel:* (0958) 202955; (0958) 290577
*Key Personnel*
President: Ignacio Llamas Labella
Founded: 1990
Subjects: Law, Regional Interests
ISBN Prefix(es): 84-7933
*Bookshop(s):* Libros Adaiz, Colegios 3, 18001 Granada
*Orders to:* Apdo de Correos 878, 18080 Granada

## Incafo Archivo Fotografico Editorial, SL
Castello, 59, 28001 Madrid
SAN: 002-4864
*Tel:* (091) 4313460; (091) 5780961 *Fax:* (091) 4313589
*Telex:* 42459 Icf E
*Key Personnel*
Man Dir, Editorial: Luis Blas Aritio
Production: Javier Echevarri
Rights & Permissions: Margarita Mendez de Vigo
Founded: 1973
Subjects: Art, Environmental Studies, Natural History
ISBN Prefix(es): 84-85389; 84-8089
*Book Club(s):* Club del Libro de la Naturaleza

## INEF Madrid, see Instituto Nacional del Educacion Fisica Madrid (INEF-Madrid)

## Institucion Fernando el Catolico de la Excma Diputacion de Zaragoza
Plaza de Espana, 2, 50071 Zaragoza
*Tel:* (0976) 28 88 78; (0976) 28 88 79
    *Fax:* (0976) 28 88 69
*E-mail:* info@ifc.dpz.es
*Web Site:* www.dpz.es
*Key Personnel*
President: D Javier Lamban
Dir: Dr Gonzalo Borras
Secretary: D Jose Barranco
Founded: 1943
Subjects: Agriculture, Archaeology, Art, Geography, Geology, History, Law, Literature, Literary Criticism, Essays, Music, Dance
ISBN Prefix(es): 84-7820; 84-600
*Branch Office(s)*
Centro de Estudios Borjanos, Casa de Aguilar, Borja
Centro de Estudios Bibilitanos, Puerta de Terrer, Calatayud
Grupo Cultural Caspolino, Palacio Barberan, 50700 Caspe
Centro de Estudios Darocenses, Puerta Baja, 50360 Daroca

Centro de Estudios Cinco Villas, Ramon y Caja, 17, 50600 Ejea Caballeros

Centro de Estudios Turiasonenses, Apdo 39, 50500 Tarazona

**Instituto de Estudios Economicos** (Institute for Economic Studies)
Castello, 128, 6a planta, 28006 Madrid
*Tel:* (091) 782 05 80 *Fax:* (091) 562 36 13
*E-mail:* iee@ieemadrid.com
*Web Site:* www.ieemadrid.com
*Key Personnel*
Administrator: D Jose Maria Goizueta Besga
Founded: 1979
Subjects: Economics, Social Sciences, Sociology
ISBN Prefix(es): 84-85719

**Instituto Nacional de Administracion Publica**
Calla Atocha, 106, 28012 Madrid
*Tel:* (091) 3493115; (091) 3493241 *Fax:* (091) 3493287
*E-mail:* cati.fuente@inap.map.es
*Web Site:* www.inap.map.es
ISBN Prefix(es): 84-7088; 84-500; 84-505
*Branch Office(s)*
Plaza de San Diego s/n, 28801 Alcala de Henares (Madrid) *Tel:* (091) 888 22 00 *Fax:* (091) 880 28 61
Calle de Jose Maranon, 12, 28010 Madrid
*Tel:* (091) 594 97 00 *Fax:* (091) 445 08 39
Avenida del Doctor Marcelino Roca s/n, Peniscola (Casellon de la Plana) *Tel:* (0964) 48 08 25 *Fax:* (0964) 48 06 49

**Instituto Nacional del Educacion Fisica Madrid (INEF-Madrid)**
Martin Fierro, s/n, 28040 Madrid
*Tel:* (091) 336 4000 *Fax:* (091) 336 4032
*E-mail:* info@inef.upm.es
*Web Site:* www.inef.upm.es
*Key Personnel*
Subdirector INEF: Teresa Gonzales Aja
Founded: 1961

**Instituto Nacional de Estadistica**
Paseo de la Castellana, 183, 28071 Madrid
*Tel:* (091) 583 91 00 *Fax:* (091) 583 91 58
*E-mail:* info@ine.es
*Web Site:* www.ine.es
*Key Personnel*
President: Jose Ouevedo
Subjects: Mathematics
ISBN Prefix(es): 84-260
Distributed by Libreria Lines-Chiel; Mundi-Prensa Libros, SA

**Instituto Nacional de la Salud**
P° del Prado 18-20 (planta baja), 28014 Madrid
*Tel:* (0901) 400-100 *Fax:* (091) 5964480
*E-mail:* oiac@msc.es
*Web Site:* www.msc.es
*Key Personnel*
Dir General: Josep Bonet Bertomeu
Head of Documentation & Publications: Carmen Limon Mendizabal
Subjects: Health, Nutrition
ISBN Prefix(es): 84-351; 84-500; 84-505

**Instituto Vasco de Criminologia**
Villa Soroa Ategorrieta, 22, 20013 Donostia-San Sebastian
*Tel:* (0943) 321411; (0943) 321412 *Fax:* (0943) 321272
*Web Site:* www.sc.ehu.es
*Key Personnel*
Dir: Antonio Beristain
Founded: 1976
Subjects: Criminology, Human Rights
ISBN Prefix(es): 84-920328

**Ediciones Internacionales Universitarias SA+**
Pantoja 14, 28002 Madrid
*Tel:* (091) 5193907 *Fax:* (091) 4136808
*E-mail:* eiunsa@ibernet.com
*Web Site:* www.eunsa.es
*Key Personnel*
Contact: Damaso Rico
Founded: 1967
Subjects: Biography, Economics, Journalism, Nonfiction (General), Philosophy, Theology
ISBN Prefix(es): 84-87155; 84-8469; 84-89893
*Holding Company:* Plaza de los Sauces, 1-2, 31010 Baranain (Navarra) *Tel:* (0948) 256850 *Fax:* (0948) 256854 *E-mail:* eunsa@cin.es
*Branch Office(s)*
Pantoja 14, 28002 Madrid *Tel:* (091) 5193907 *Fax:* (091) 4136808 *E-mail:* eiunsa@inbernet.com

**Intress,** see Institut de Treball Social - Serveis Socials

**IR Indo Edicions**
Av Florida 30, 36210 Vigo, Galicia
*Tel:* (0986) 21 48 34 *Fax:* (0986) 21 11 33
*E-mail:* correo@irindo.com
*Web Site:* www.irindo.com; irindo.net
*Key Personnel*
Contact: Bieito Ledo
Founded: 1985
ISBN Prefix(es): 84-7680

**Iralka Editorial SL+**
Ametzagana, 21-Local 10, 20012 San Sebastian
*Tel:* (0943) 32 30 14 *Fax:* (0943) 32 30 22
*E-mail:* iralka@euskalnet.net
*Web Site:* www.euskalnet.net/iralka
*Key Personnel*
Editor: Manuel Muner Sorazu
Founded: 1993
Subjects: Anthropology, Literature, Literary Criticism, Essays, Philosophy, Poetry, Social Sciences, Sociology
ISBN Prefix(es): 84-89806; 84-605; 84-920202; 84-920963
Number of titles published annually: 5 Print
Total Titles: 40 Print
Distributed by Andalucia Rodriguez Santos; Bibliotecas y Exportacion Purvill Libros, S A; Catalunya Virus Editorial; Delegacion Granada; Euskal Herria Bitarte

**IRIF,** see Grao Editorial

**Iru Editorial SA+**
Roger de Flor, 91, 08013 Barcelona
*Tel:* (093) 2318032 *Fax:* (093) 2653670
*Key Personnel*
Contact: Xabier Etxarri
Founded: 1982
Subjects: Cookery, Humor
ISBN Prefix(es): 84-8065; 84-86819

**Editorial Isidoriana, Libreria**
Plaza de San Isidoro, 4, 24003 Leon
Mailing Address: Apdo 126, 24080 Leon
*Tel:* (0987) 876161 *Fax:* (0987) 876162
*E-mail:* sanisidoro@infonegocio.com
*Key Personnel*
Dir: Antonio Vinayo Gonzalez *Tel:* (0987) 876070 *Fax:* (0987) 876061

**Ediciones Istmo SA+**
Sector Foresta, 1, 28760 Tres Contos
SAN: 001-7817
*Tel:* (091) 8061996 *Fax:* (091) 8044028
*Key Personnel*
Man Dir: Eduardo Casado Martindela Camara
Founded: 1969

Subjects: Anthropology, Art, History, Language Arts, Linguistics, Literature, Literary Criticism, Essays, Philosophy, Social Sciences, Sociology
ISBN Prefix(es): 84-7090

**Ediciones JJB**
Perez Galdos 12, 4, Apdo 1084, 26002 Logrono, La Rioja
*Tel:* (041) 236928 *Fax:* (041) 226127
*Key Personnel*
Dir: Julian de Juan Berzosa
Founded: 1977
ISBN Prefix(es): 84-85305

**Ediciones JLA+**
PO Box 54122, 2080 Madrid
SAN: 001-8007
*Tel:* (091) 3158577 *Fax:* (091) 7336239
*Key Personnel*
Dir: Jose Luis Alvarez *Tel:* (091) 3864292 *Fax:* (091) 3161882 *E-mail:* vinilos@vinilos.com
Founded: 1975
Subjects: Radio, TV
ISBN Prefix(es): 84-7872; 84-86570
*Warehouse:* c/o Valdesahgil, 26-Local, 28039 Madrid

**Joyas Bibliograficas SA**
Fomento, 5, 28013 Madrid
SAN: 003-8210
*Tel:* (091) 5470220
*Key Personnel*
Administrator: Carlos Romero de Lecea
Subjects: History, Literature, Literary Criticism, Essays, Poetry
ISBN Prefix(es): 84-7094

**Ediciones Jucar+**
Menendez Valdes, 33-1, 33201 Gijon Asturias
*Tel:* (098) 5170921; (098) 5349684 *Fax:* (098) 55349545
*Telex:* 89736 Edju E
*Key Personnel*
Man Dir: Silverio Canada Acebal
Editorial: Maria de Calonje
Production: Manuel Cardenas
Founded: 1974
Subjects: Fiction, Government, Political Science, Literature, Literary Criticism, Essays, Music, Dance, Poetry
ISBN Prefix(es): 84-334
*Orders to:* Honesto Batalon 7, Gijon *Tel:* (985) 355790

**Junta de Castilla y Leon Consejeria de Educacion y Cultura**
Avda de Soria, 15, 47071 La Disterniga (Valladolid)
*Tel:* (0983) 411587 *Fax:* (0983) 411527
*E-mail:* publicaciones.cec@pop-in.jcyl.es
*Web Site:* www.jcyl.es
*Key Personnel*
Dir: Agustin Garcia Simon *E-mail:* agustin.garcia@cec.jcyl.es
Founded: 1984
Subjects: Archaeology, Art, Biography, History, Literature, Literary Criticism, Essays, Poetry, Regional Interests, Science (General), Travel
ISBN Prefix(es): 84-7846; 84-9718; 84-500; 84-505
Distributor for Lidiza; Siglo

**Editorial Juventud SA+**
Provenza, 101, 08029 Barcelona
*Tel:* (093) 444 18 00 *Fax:* (093) 439 83 83
*E-mail:* info@editorialjuventud.es
*Web Site:* www.editorialjuventud.es *Cable:* JUVENTUD
*Key Personnel*
Dir General: Luis Zendrera Duniau

Founded: 1923
Subjects: Accounting, Aeronautics, Aviation, Animals, Pets, Architecture & Interior Design, Art, Biography, Fiction, History, Language Arts, Linguistics, Sports, Athletics, Travel
ISBN Prefix(es): 84-261
*Associate Companies:* Editorial Juventud SA, Mexico
Subsidiaries: Editorial Juventud de Espana Ltd
Distributed by Editorial Corimbo; Editorial Parsifal

**Editorial Kairos SA+**
Numancia, 117-121, Edificio Centro Planta 2a, puerta 3a, 08029 Barcelona
*Tel:* (093) 494 9490 *Fax:* (093) 410 5166
*E-mail:* kairos@sendanet.es *Cable:* KAIROS
*Key Personnel*
Man Dir: Salvador Paniker
Editorial, Rights & Permissions, Sales: Agustin Paniker
Production, Publicity: Pilar Tomas
Founded: 1966
Publishes a growing range of new consciousness titles.
Subjects: Philosophy, Psychology, Psychiatry, Religion - Other, Social Sciences, Sociology
ISBN Prefix(es): 84-7245

**Laertes SA de Ediciones+**
Virtud, 8, 08012 Barcelona
*Tel:* (093) 2187020; (093) 2185558 *Fax:* (093) 2174751
*E-mail:* laertes@jet.es
*Key Personnel*
Man Dir & Editorial: Eduardo Suarez Alonso
Sales, Publicity: Carmen Miret
Founded: 1975
Subjects: Anthropology, Archaeology, Biography, Education, Fiction, Film, Video, Gay & Lesbian, Literature, Literary Criticism, Essays, Philosophy, Travel, Medicine & Nursing
ISBN Prefix(es): 84-85346; 84-7584; 84-400
Total Titles: 525 Print
Foreign Rep(s): Ediciones Del Aguazul (Argentina); Ediciones Del Aguazul (Mexico)

**Editorin Laiovento SL+**
Rua do Horreo, 60, Apdo 1 072, 15072 Santiago de Compostela Galiza
*Tel:* (0981) 887570 *Fax:* (0981) 572239
*E-mail:* laiovento@laiovento.com
*Web Site:* www.laiovento.com
*Key Personnel*
President: Afonso Ribas Fraga
Founded: 1989
Subjects: Economics, Education, History, Literature, Literary Criticism, Essays, Poetry, Science (General), Science Fiction, Fantasy, Social Sciences, Sociology, Technology, Humanities & Social Sciences
ISBN Prefix(es): 84-87847; 84-89896
Imprints: Lengua Gallega Y Portuguesa
Distributor for Ninguna

**Leandro Lara Editor+**
Ave Antonio Gaudi, 76-126 NAVE 1 bis Pol Ind Rubi Sud, 08191 Rubi
*Tel:* (093) 6970036; (093) 6970364
*E-mail:* leandro@covnet.com
*Key Personnel*
Contact: Leandro Lara Merino
ISBN Prefix(es): 84-7699

**Larousse Editorial SA+**
Avda Diagonal 407 bis 10, 08008 Barcelona
*Tel:* (093) 2922666 *Fax:* (093) 2922162; (093) 2922163
*E-mail:* larousse@larousse.es
*Key Personnel*
Contact: Yolanda Portillo Jimenez

Founded: 1991
ISBN Prefix(es): 84-8016
Subsidiaries: Grandes De La Cite International

**Las Ediciones de Arte (LEDA)**, see LEDA (Las Ediciones de Arte)

**LEDA (Las Ediciones de Arte)+**
Riera Sant Miguel 37 entl, 08006 Barcelona
*Tel:* (093) 2379389; (093) 2155273
*Key Personnel*
Man Dir: Daniel Basilio Bonet
Founded: 1942
Subjects: Advertising, Architecture & Interior Design, Art, Child Care & Development, Crafts, Games, Hobbies
ISBN Prefix(es): 84-7095

**Edicions de l'Eixample, SA+**
Mallorca 297, pral, 08037 Barcelona
*Tel:* (093) 4584600 *Fax:* (093) 2076248
*Key Personnel*
Council Delegates: Salvador Saura; Ramon Torrente
Dir: Isabel Segura
Founded: 1983
Subjects: Fiction
ISBN Prefix(es): 84-86279

**Lengua Gallega Y Portuguesa**, *imprint of* Editorin Laiovento SL

**Liber Ediciones, SA**
Travesia Bayona, 1, 31011 Pamplona
*Tel:* (0902) 300 307 *Fax:* (0948) 176 667
*E-mail:* info@arsliber.com
*Web Site:* www.arsliber.com
*Key Personnel*
Contact: Juan Jose Izquierdo Broncano
Founded: 1989
Subjects: Art
ISBN Prefix(es): 84-89339

**Ediciones Libertarias/Prodhufi SA+**
C Bravo Murillo, 37-1 Dcha, 28015 Madrid
*Tel:* (091) 593 33 93 *Fax:* (091) 594 16 96
*E-mail:* libertarias@libertarias.com
*Web Site:* www.libertarias.com
*Key Personnel*
Publisher: Carmelo Martinez Garcia
Communication Dir: Annamaria Duran
Founded: 1979
Subjects: Cookery, Government, Political Science, Health, Nutrition, History, Literature, Literary Criticism, Essays, Poetry, Psychology, Psychiatry, Science Fiction, Fantasy, Social Sciences, Sociology
ISBN Prefix(es): 84-7954; 84-87095; 84-85641; 84-7683; 84-86943
Distributed by Conty SA de CV (Central America); Libertarias Prodhufi, SA

**Libros Cupula**, *imprint of* Grupo Editorial CEAC SA

**Libsa**, *imprint of* Libsa Editorial SA

**Libsa Editorial SA+**
San Rafael, 4, 28108 Alcobendas Madrid
*Tel:* (091) 657 25 80 *Fax:* (091) 657 25 83
*E-mail:* libsa@libsa.es
*Web Site:* www.libsa.es
*Key Personnel*
President: Amado Sanchez *E-mail:* rocio@libsa.redestb.es
Foreign Rights: Alberto Boix
Foreign Rights Manager: Francisco Saavedra
Founded: 1980
Subjects: Art, Cookery, Crafts, Games, Hobbies, Gardening, Plants, Health, Nutrition, House &

Home, Language Arts, Linguistics, Literature, Literary Criticism, Essays, Nonfiction (General), Self-Help, Children/Adult lists, Leisure & Practical Guides
ISBN Prefix(es): 84-7630; 84-662
Imprints: Agata; Alba; Libsa

**LID Editorial Empresarial, SL** (LID Business Publisher)+
Sopelana, 22, 28023 Madrid
SAN: 004-010X
*Tel:* (091) 372 90 03 *Fax:* (091) 372 85 14
*E-mail:* info@lideditorial.com
*Web Site:* www.lideditorial.com
*Key Personnel*
President: Marcelino Elosua
Editor: Isabel Saavedra; Mercedes Vidaurrazaga
Founded: 1993
Membership(s): Gremio de Editores de Madrid.
Subjects: Biography, Business, Career Development, Economics, Finance, Language Arts, Linguistics, Marketing, Self-Help, Economics & Business, Spanish Business History, Specialized Business Dictionaries
ISBN Prefix(es): 84-88717
Number of titles published annually: 12 Print; 1 CD-ROM
Total Titles: 50 Print; 2 CD-ROM
*Distribution Center:* LOGISTA (Spain)

**Llibres del Segle+**
La Rectoria, 17466 Gaueses Girona
*Tel:* (093) 795079; (093) 794023 *Fax:* (093) 210354
*E-mail:* costapau@releline.es
*Key Personnel*
Production: Rosa M Tries
Subjects: Art, Education, History, Literature, Literary Criticism, Essays, Nonfiction (General), Poetry, Social Sciences, Sociology
ISBN Prefix(es): 84-89885; 84-920952; 84-8128
Total Titles: 12 Print
Distributor for L'Arc de Bera

**Loguez Ediciones+**
Carretera de Madrid 90, Apdo 1, 37900 Santa Marta de Tormes (Salamanca)
SAN: 003-8849
*Tel:* (0923) 138541 *Fax:* (0923) 138586
*E-mail:* loguezediciones@eresmas.com
*Key Personnel*
Man Dir, Sales: L Rodriguez Lopez
Editorial, Publicity: Maribel G Martinez
Founded: 1978
Specialize in children's literature & musical books.
Subjects: Art, Earth Sciences, Education, Fiction, Gay & Lesbian, Literature, Literary Criticism, Essays, Music, Dance, Religion - Catholic, Religion - Other, Self-Help, Theology
ISBN Prefix(es): 84-85334; 84-89804
Number of titles published annually: 12 Print; 3 CD-ROM

**Ediciones Luciernaga**, *imprint of* Grup 62

**Ediciones Luciernaga**
Peu de la Creu 4, 08001 Barcelona
*Tel:* (093) 443 71 00 *Fax:* (093) 443 71 30
*E-mail:* correu@grup62.com
*Web Site:* www.grup62.com
*Key Personnel*
Rights Manager: Laura Pujol
Founded: 1963
ISBN Prefix(es): 84-87232; 84-89957

**Editorial Luis Vives (Edelvives)+**
63a Feria del Libro, 28034 Madrid
*Tel:* (091) 334 48 83 *Fax:* (091) 334 48 93
*E-mail:* jmarketing@edelvives.es
*Web Site:* www.grupoeditorialluisvives.com
    *Cable:* EDELVIVES

*Key Personnel*
Man Dir: Antonio Gimenez de Baguees
Editorial Dir: Jose Manuel Gomez Luque
Production Dir: Jesus Agudo
Commercial Dir: Jose Luis Illana
Founded: 1890
Subjects: Education
ISBN Prefix(es): 84-263
Number of titles published annually: 200 Print
Total Titles: 35,000 Print; 6 CD-ROM; 3 Audio
*Associate Companies:* Editorial Ibaizabal, Barrio
de San Miguel s/n Euba-Amorebieta, 48290
Vizcaya *Tel:* (046) 308036 *Fax:* (046) 308028
*E-mail:* ibaizabal@euskalnet.net
Subsidiaries: Edicions Baula
*Branch Office(s)*
Poligono de Cranda s/n, 33199 Asturias
*Tel:* (098) 579 46 16 *E-mail:* asturias@
edelvives.es
Passeo Valldaura, 184, 08042 Barcelona
*Tel:* (093) 354 03 99 *E-mail:* barcelona@
endelvives.es
Ayagaures 8 Nave D, Urb Ind Lomo Blanco-
Las Torres, 35010 Las Palmas de Gran Ca-
naria 9 *Tel:* (0928) 48 12 47 *E-mail:* canarias@
edelvives.es
Manuel Tovar, esq. Estrada, 28034 Madrid
*Tel:* (091) 344 48 84 *E-mail:* madrid@
edelvives.es
Veracruz, 32 (Pol. San Luis), 29006 Malaga
*Tel:* (095) 236 3409 *E-mail:* malaga@
edelvives.es
Via Apia, 32, (Pol. Ind. Fuentequintillo), 41089
Montequintille (Sevilla) *Tel:* (095) 4 129 180
*E-mail:* sevilla@edelvives.es
Avda Txori-Erri, 46 No, Modulo 4, Letra E,
48150 Sondika (Vizcaya) *Tel:* (094) 453 20
09 *E-mail:* bilbao@edelvives.es
Poligono 1-2 (Tafaea) Parcela 28, 45600 Talav-
era de la Reina (Toledo) *Tel:* (0925) 81 74 34
*E-mail:* toledo@edelvives.es
Avda Ausias March 222, Pista de Silla,
46026 Valencia *Tel:* (096) 375 98 11
*E-mail:* valencia@edelvives.es
Acero 4, (Pol San Cristobal), 47012 Valladolid
*Tel:* (0983) 21 30 38 *E-mail:* valladolid@
edelvives.es
Severino Cobas 142 (Lavadores), 36214 Vigo
*Tel:* (0986) 27 20 13 *E-mail:* vigo@edelvives.
es
Ctra de Madrid, km 315 700, 50012 Zaragoza
*Tel:* (0976) 30 40 30 *E-mail:* zaragoza@
edelvives.es
*Distribution Center:* Editorial Luis vives, Ctra de
Madrid km 315 700, 50012 Zaragoza, Fran-
cisco Calleja *Tel:* (0976) 304030 *Fax:* (0976)
340630 *E-mail:* zaragoza@edelvives.es

**Editorial Lumen SA+**
Travessera de Gracia 47-5°-pl, 08021 Barcelona
*Tel:* (093) 3660300 *Fax:* (093) 3660013
*E-mail:* lumen@editoriallumen.com
*Key Personnel*
Man Dir: Esther Tusquets
Founded: 1939
Subjects: Art, Fiction, Humor, Literature, Liter-
ary Criticism, Essays, Poetry, Social Sciences,
Sociology
ISBN Prefix(es): 84-264

**Lunwerg Editores, SA+**
Beethoven, 12, 08021 Barcelona
SAN: 004-072X
*Tel:* (093) 2015933 *Fax:* (093) 2011587
*E-mail:* lunwerg.mad@retemail.es
*Key Personnel*
Man Dir: Juan Carlos Luna
Rights & Permissions: Carmen Garcia
Founded: 1980
Subjects: Archaeology, Architecture & Interior
Design, Art, Cookery, Drama, Theater, History,
Maritime, Photography, Transportation, Travel,
Wine & Spirits

ISBN Prefix(es): 84-7782; 84-85983; 84-9785
Number of titles published annually: 60 Print

**Lynx Edicions**
Montseny, 8, E-08193 Bellaterra, Barcelona
*Tel:* (093) 594 77 10 *Fax:* (093) 592 09 69
*E-mail:* pruizolalla@hbw.com
*Web Site:* www.hbw.com
*Key Personnel*
Contact: Pilar Ruiz-Olalla
Founded: 1989
Subjects: Animals, Pets, Natural History
ISBN Prefix(es): 84-87334
*U.S. Office(s):* Lynx Edicions, c/o Mail Manage-
ment Group Inc, 81 N Forest Ave, Rockville
Centre, NY 11570, United States

**Antonio Machado, SA**
Tomas Breton, 55, 28045 Madrid
*Tel:* (091) 4681398 *Fax:* (091) 4681098
*E-mail:* editorial@visordis.es
*Key Personnel*
Dir: Jose Miguel Garcia Sanchez
Books, Magazines, Journals, Newspapers.
Subjects: Architecture & Interior Design, Art,
Drama, Theater, Education, Government, Po-
litical Science, History, Language Arts, Lin-
guistics, Literature, Literary Criticism, Essays,
Music, Dance, Philosophy, Psychology, Psy-
chiatry, Publishing & Book Trade Reference,
Regional Interests, Self-Help, Social Sciences,
Sociology, Cultural History, Performing Arts
ISBN Prefix(es): 84-7644

**Macmillan Heinemann ELT**
Martin de Vargas 5, Esc C 1, 28005 Madrid
*Tel:* (091) 517 85 40 *Fax:* (091) 517 85 54
*E-mail:* madrid@mad.heinemann.es
*Web Site:* www.heinemann.es
*Parent Company:* Macmillan Publishers Ltd
Distributor for Language Teaching Publica-
tions (LTP); Max Hueber Verlag/Verlag Fuer
Deutsch

**Mad SL Editorial+**
Polig Merka C/B, naves 1-3, 41500 Alcala de
Guadaira Sevilla
*Tel:* (095) 5635900 *Fax:* (095) 5630713
*E-mail:* info@mad.es
*Web Site:* www.mad.es
*Key Personnel*
Administrator: Dolores Lopez-Jurado
Dir: Luis Abril Mula *E-mail:* luis@mad.es
Gen Dir: Narciso Sanchez-Valdenaura
*E-mail:* nsv@mad.es
Founded: 1983
Subjects: Law
ISBN Prefix(es): 84-86526; 84-665; 84-8311; 84-
88834; 84-89464

**Ediciones Maeva+**
Benito de Castro 6, 28028 Madrid
*Tel:* (091) 355 95 69 *Fax:* (091) 355 19 47
*E-mail:* maeva@infornet.es
*Web Site:* www.maeva.es
*Key Personnel*
Contact: Cuadros Lopez Maite
Founded: 1985
Subjects: Anthropology, Biography, Foreign
Countries, History, Literature, Literary Criti-
cism, Essays, Nonfiction (General), Regional
Interests, Travel
ISBN Prefix(es): 84-86478; 84-95354
Imprints: Catalogo
Subsidiaries: Editoriales Exclusivas
*Orders to:* SGEL, c/o Avda Valdelaparda, 29,
Poligono Industrial, 28108 Alcobendas-Madrid
*Tel:* (091) 6576955 *Fax:* (091) 6576958

**Editorial Magisterio Espanol SA+**
Casp 79, 08013 Barcelona

*Tel:* (093) 902107007 *Fax:* (093) 6420086
*Web Site:* www.editorialcasals.com
*Key Personnel*
General Manager: Ramon Casals
Founded: 1866
Subjects: Education, Fiction, Literature, Liter-
ary Criticism, Essays, Philosophy, Religion -
Catholic
ISBN Prefix(es): 84-265
*Parent Company:* Editorial Casals, SA

**Magoria,** *imprint of* Obelisco Ediciones S

**Edicions de la Magrana SA+**
Santa Perpetua, 10-12, 08012 Barcelona
*Tel:* (093) 2170088 *Fax:* (093) 2171174
*E-mail:* magrana@rba.es
*Web Site:* www.rbalibros.com
*Key Personnel*
Man Dir: Carles-Jordi Guardiola
Production: Lluis Baselga
Assistant Dir: Eva Eduardo
Founded: 1975
Subjects: Biography, Cookery, Fiction, Literature,
Literary Criticism, Essays, Philosophy, Science
(General), Social Sciences, Sociology
ISBN Prefix(es): 84-7410

**Mandala Ediciones+**
Escalinata, 9, 28013 Madrid
SAN: 004-1114
*Tel:* (091) 5840954 *Fax:* (091) 5480326
*Key Personnel*
Man Dir: Fernando Cabal *Tel:* (091) 5480954
Editorial: Gonzalo Rivero
Founded: 1980
Subjects: Architecture & Interior Design, Astrol-
ogy, Occult, Behavioral Sciences, Cookery,
Earth Sciences, Environmental Studies, Film,
Video, Health, Nutrition, Medicine, Nursing,
Dentistry, Music, Dance, Psychology, Psychi-
atry, Religion - Buddhist, Religion - Hindu,
Religion - Islamic, Biological Agriculture, Bi-
ological Medicine, Chinese Medicine, Dietetic
Natural, Ecological Architecture, Ecology, Fi-
toterapia, Homeopatia, Manual Medicine, Mas-
sage, Relaxation
ISBN Prefix(es): 84-86961; 84-88769; 84-95052
Total Titles: 210 Print

**Editorial Mapfre SA**
Paseo de Recoletos, 25, 28004 Madrid
*Tel:* (091) 581 53 60 *Fax:* (091) 581 18 83
*E-mail:* edimap@mapfre.com
*Web Site:* www2.mapfre.com
*Key Personnel*
Man Dir: Miguel Angel Gimeno
Subjects: Financial Security & Services, Insur-
ances
ISBN Prefix(es): 84-7100

**Marcial Pons Ediciones Juridicas SA**
San Sotero, 6, 28037 Madrid
*Tel:* (091) 304 33 03 *Fax:* (091) 327 23 67; (091)
7541218
*E-mail:* librerias@marcialpons.es; ediciones@
marcialpons.es
*Web Site:* www.marcialpons.es
Founded: 1990
Subjects: Economics, Law, Public Administration
ISBN Prefix(es): 84-7248; 84-9768
Number of titles published annually: 80 Print
Total Titles: 1,500 Print

**Marcombo SA+**
Gran Via de les Corts Catalanes, 594, 08007
Barcelona
*Tel:* (093) 3180079 (Editor) *Fax:* (093) 3189339
*E-mail:* marcombo.boixareu@marcombo.es
*Web Site:* www.marcombo.es
*Key Personnel*
Man Dir: Josep M Boixareu Vilaplana

Marketing & Sales Manager: Jose Romero Gonzalez
Founded: 1945
Subjects: Anthropology, Automotive, Business, Civil Engineering, Communications, Computer Science, Economics, Electronics, Electrical Engineering, Energy, Finance, Management, Marketing, Mathematics, Microcomputers, Radio, TV
ISBN Prefix(es): 84-267
*Branch Office(s)*
Marcombo SA, Plaza de la Villa 1, 28005 Madrid
Distributed by Distribuciones Alba, S.A.; Alfaomego Grupo Editor (Colombia, Mexico, Guatemala, Costa Rica, Ecuador, Nicaragua, Honduras, El Salvador); Asturlibros, Poligono Silvota; Be Nvil, S.A. Llibres; Carrasco Libros, S.L.; Contemporanea de Ediciones (Venezuela); Distribuidora Cuspide, S.R.L. (Argentina); Galileo Libros, Ltd (Chile); Andres Libreros - Libro Tecnico; Lidiza, S.A.; Losa Libros Ltda (Uruguay); Marcombo, S.A.; Odon Molina, Distribuidor de Libros; Palma Distribucions, S.L.; Pato Libros; Distribuidora Del Sur; UNBE, S.A.; Unidisa, Demetrio Sillero; Viuber, S.L.Delegacion de Edit
*Bookshop(s):* Libreria Hispano Americana

**Editorial Marfil SA+**
Sant Eloi 17, 03804 Alcoi
*Tel:* (096) 5523311 *Fax:* (096) 5523496
*E-mail:* editorialmarfil@editorialmarfil.com
*Web Site:* www.editorialmarfil.com *Cable:* MARFIL
*Key Personnel*
Contact: Veronica Canto Domenych
Founded: 1947
Subjects: Education, Literature, Literary Criticism, Essays, Psychology, Psychiatry
ISBN Prefix(es): 84-268; 84-7816

**Editorial Marin SA+**
Avda San Julian, 234, Poligono Industrial El Congost, 08400 Granollers Barcelona
*Tel:* (093) 8468101 *Fax:* (093) 8468107
*Cable:* MARINEDI
*Key Personnel*
Administrator: Manuel Marin
Man Dir: Jorge Fernandez
Founded: 1900
Subjects: Art, Medicine, Nursing, Dentistry, Nonfiction (General)
ISBN Prefix(es): 84-7102
*Branch Office(s)*
Editorial Marin SA, Anaxagoras 1400, Colonia Santa Cruz Atoyac, 03310 Mexico, DF, Mexico
*Warehouse:* Calle Industria 5/n, Polzono Industrial, El Papiol

**Ediciones Marova SL+**
Cedaceros, 3, 28014 Madrid
SAN: 004-1610
*Tel:* (091) 5322606 *Fax:* (091) 5225123
*E-mail:* glanzas@infornet.es
*Key Personnel*
Man Dir: Jose Miguel Oriol
Founded: 1956
Subjects: Education, Psychology, Psychiatry, Religion - Other, Social Sciences, Sociology, Theology
ISBN Prefix(es): 84-269

**Ediciones Martinez Roca SA+**
Member of Grupo Planeta
Paseo de Recoletos, 4, 3a planta, 28001 Madrid
*Tel:* (091) 423 0314 *Fax:* (091) 423 0306
*E-mail:* info@ediciones-martinez-roca.com
*Web Site:* www.edicionesmartinezroca.com
*Key Personnel*
Man Dir: Fernando Calvo Aparicio
Founded: 1965

Subjects: Animals, Pets, Astrology, Occult, Biography, Crafts, Games, Hobbies, Fiction, Health, Nutrition, How-to, Literature, Literary Criticism, Essays, Nonfiction (General), Psychology, Psychiatry, Romance, Science Fiction, Fantasy, Self-Help, Sports, Athletics
ISBN Prefix(es): 84-270

**Masbytes+**
Pablo Sarasate, 9 Bajo, 31500 Tudela, Navarra
*Tel:* (0948) 848031 *Fax:* (0948) 848158
*E-mail:* mb@masbytes.es
*Web Site:* www.masbytes.es
*Key Personnel*
Dir General: Pedro Llorente Apat
Founded: 1987
ISBN Prefix(es): 84-7768

**La Mascara, SL Editorial+**
Pza Juan Pablo II 5-B izda, 46015 Valencia
SAN: 002-5127
*Tel:* (096) 3486500 *Fax:* (096) 3487440
*E-mail:* lamascara@arrakis.es
*Key Personnel*
Commercial Dir: Celso Andres
Founded: 1991
Subjects: Biography, Music, Dance, Poetry
ISBN Prefix(es): 84-7974
Subsidiaries: La Mascara France, Sarl

**McGraw-Hill/Interamericana de Espana SAU+**
Basauri 17, Edificio Valrealty, Planta 1, 28023 Aravaca, Madrid
*Tel:* (091) 1803000
*Web Site:* www.mcgraw-hill.es
*Telex:* 43817 DIE
*Key Personnel*
Group Man Dir: Antonio Garcia-Maroto
  *E-mail:* agmaroto@attmail.com
Publisher, Business & Professional Division: Eduardo Susanna
Publisher, High School Vocational Technical Division: Wenceslao Ortega
Distributor & Book Store Sales Manager: Fernando Serrano
Controller & Business Manager: Jose Castellano
Production Manager: Jose Martinez Alaminos
EDP Manager: Miguel Angel de Dios
Founded: 1974
Iberian/Mercosur Peninsula Group. Markets served: Spain, Portugal, Argentina, Uruguay, Paraguay.
Subjects: Biological Sciences, Education, Health, Nutrition, Medicine, Nursing, Dentistry, Science (General), Technology
ISBN Prefix(es): 84-7615; 84-85240; 84-481; 84-486
*Parent Company:* The McGraw-Hill Companies, 1221 Avenue of the Americas, New York, NY 10020, United States
*Branch Office(s)*
Mercosur, Argentina, Suipacha 764, 1008 Buenos Aires, Argentina *Tel:* (011) 3228868 *Fax:* (011) 3223456 (Distribudora Cuspide)
Mercosur, Paraguay, Suipacha 764, 1008 Buenos Aires, Argentina *Tel:* (011) 3228868 *Fax:* (011) 3223456 (Distribudora Cuspide)
Mercosur, Uruguay, Suipacha 764, 1008 Buenos Aires, Argentina *Tel:* (011) 3228868 *Fax:* (011) 3223456 (Distribudora Cuspide)

**ME Editores, SL+**
Marcelina, 23, 28029 Madrid
SAN: 004-0908
*Tel:* (091) 3151008 *Fax:* (091) 3230844
Founded: 1992
ISBN Prefix(es): 84-495

**Editorial Medica JIMS, SL**
Balmes, 266, 08006 Barcelona

*Tel:* (093) 2188800 *Fax:* (093) 2188928
  *Cable:* EDITOJIMS
*Key Personnel*
Man Dir, Editorial, Publicity: Antonio Jimenez Sanchez
Sales: Teresa Jimenez Sayo
Production: Luis Jimenez Sayo
Founded: 1956
Subjects: Medicine, Nursing, Dentistry
ISBN Prefix(es): 84-7092

**Ediciones Medici SA+**
Plato, 26, 08006 Barcelona
*Tel:* (093) 2 010 599; (093) 2 013 807; (093) 2 012 144 *Fax:* (093) 2 097 362
*E-mail:* omega@ediciones-omega.es
*Web Site:* www.ediciones-medici.es; www.ediciones-omega.es
*Key Personnel*
Man Dir: Ana Dexeus; Antonio Paricio; Gabriel Paricio
Founded: 1983
Subjects: Child Care & Development, Cookery, Education, Health, Nutrition, Human Relations, Medicine, Nursing, Dentistry, Nonfiction (General)
ISBN Prefix(es): 84-86193
*Parent Company:* Ediciones Omega SA
*Orders to:* Ediciones Omega/Medici, Plato, 26, 08006 Barcelona

**Editorial Mediterrania SL+**
Guillem Tell 15 - 17 entlo, 08006 Barcelona
*Tel:* (093) 218 34 58; (093) 237 86 65 *Fax:* (093) 237 22 10
*E-mail:* edit.med@retemail.es
*Key Personnel*
Man Dir & Sales: Eduard Fornes
Editorial, Rights & Permissions: Josep Abril
Production: Nuria Carpena
Publicity: Monica Estrich
Founded: 1980
Membership(s): Association of Editors in the Catalan Language & Editors Guild of Catalunya.
Subjects: Art, Health, Nutrition, History, Literature, Literary Criticism, Essays, Outdoor Recreation, Photography, Religion - Catholic, Sports, Athletics, Travel
ISBN Prefix(es): 84-8334

**Ediciones Mensajero+**
Sancho de Azpeitia, 2, Apdo 73, 48014 Bilbao
SAN: 001-852X
*Tel:* (094) 4 470 358 *Fax:* (094) 4 472 630
*E-mail:* mensajero@mensajero.com
*Web Site:* www.mensajero.com *Cable:* MENSAJERO
*Key Personnel*
Man Dir: Angel Antonio Perez
Editorial, Production: Josu Leguina
  *E-mail:* josuleguina@mensajero.com
Publicity & Sales: Jose Manuel Diaz
Founded: 1915
Subjects: Education, How-to, Philosophy, Psychology, Psychiatry, Religion - Other, Social Sciences, Sociology
ISBN Prefix(es): 84-271

**Editorial Milenio Arts Grafiques Bobala, SL+**
Sant Salvador 8, 25005 Lleida
*Tel:* (0973) 236 611 *Fax:* (0973) 240 795
*E-mail:* editorial.milenio@cambrescat.es
*Web Site:* www.edmilenio.com
*Key Personnel*
Dir: Lluis Pages i Marigot *Fax:* (0973) 740 795
Founded: 1996
Specialize in Spanish & Latin American books.
ISBN Prefix(es): 84-89790
Total Titles: 20 Print
*Associate Companies:* Pages Editors, SL
Distributed by Espana y America
*Book Club(s):* Eventualmente

**Ministerio de Economia y Hacienda Secretario General Tecnica Centro de Publicaciones**
Plaza Campillo del Mundo Nuevo, 3, 28005 Madrid
SAN: 004-2315
*Tel:* (091) 5063740 (ext 51307) *Fax:* (091) 5273951
*E-mail:* ventas.campillo@sgt.meh.es
*Web Site:* www.minhac.es
*Key Personnel*
Technical General Secretary: Rosa Rodriguez-Moreno
ISBN Prefix(es): 84-460; 84-476; 84-7196; 84-85482; 84-500; 84-505

**Ministerio de Educacion y Culture Centro de Publicaciones**
Ciudad Universitaria, 28071 Madrid
*Tel:* (091) 453 98 00 *Fax:* (091) 453 98 00
*Web Site:* www.mec.es/mec
*Key Personnel*
Editorial Control Head: Antonio Arenas Carrera
ISBN Prefix(es): 84-369

**Ministerio de Justicia e Interior, Centro de Publicaciones**
San Bernardo, 62 Planta baja, 28071 Madrid
*Tel:* (091) 390 20 87; (091) 390 20 82; (091) 390 20 97 *Fax:* (091) 390 20 92
*E-mail:* publicaciones@sb.mju.es
*Web Site:* www.mju.es
*Key Personnel*
General Assistant Dir of Documentation & Publications: Gonzalo Puebla De Diego
Founded: 1947
Subjects: Law
ISBN Prefix(es): 84-7787; 84-500; 84-505
Distributed by BOE; DIJUSA; Diputacion de Barcelona; Edisofer, S.L.; Marcial Pons; Reydis Libros, Lazaro Pascual Yague S.L.; Tapia Libros, S.A.
*Warehouse:* C/Ocana, 151-28047 Madrid

**Ministerio de Trabajo y Asuntos Sociales**
Torrelaguna 73, 28027 Madrid
*Tel:* (091) 4037000 *Fax:* (091) 4030050
*E-mail:* sugerir@sta.mtas.es
*Web Site:* www.mtas.es/insht/index.htm
*Key Personnel*
Dir: Javier Gomez-Hortiguela Amillo
ISBN Prefix(es): 84-7425; 84-500; 84-400; 84-505

**Ediciones Minotauro+**
Member of Grupo Planeta
Adva Diagonal 662, 08034 Barcelona
*Tel:* (093) 492 8869 *Fax:* (093) 496 7041
*E-mail:* edicionesminotauro@arrakis.es
*Web Site:* www.edicionesminotauro.com
*Key Personnel*
Man Dir: Francisco Porrua
Founded: 1955
Subjects: Biography, Fiction, Literature, Literary Criticism, Essays, Science Fiction, Fantasy
ISBN Prefix(es): 84-450
Total Titles: 150 Print

**Editores Mira, SA**
Dalia 11, 50012 Zaragoza
*Tel:* (0976) 460505 *Fax:* (0976) 460446
*E-mail:* miraeditores@ctv.es
*Web Site:* www.miraeditores.com
ISBN Prefix(es): 84-86778; 84-88688; 84-89859; 84-8465

**MK Ediciones y Publicaciones**
Castello 30, 28001 Madrid
SAN: 004-3311
*Tel:* (091) 4316305 *Fax:* (091) 5754978
*Key Personnel*
Editorial Dir: Marta Ferre Pich

Founded: 1975
Specialize in theater.
Subjects: Drama, Theater
ISBN Prefix(es): 84-7389

**M Moleiro Editor, SA+**
Travesera de Gracia, 17-21, 08021 Barcelona
*Tel:* (093) 414 20 10 *Fax:* (093) 201 50 62
*E-mail:* mmoleiro@moleiro.com
*Web Site:* www.moleiro.com
*Key Personnel*
President: Manuel Moleiro
International Rights: Ms Monica Miro
Founded: 1992
Specialize in facsimile editions of medieval illuminated manuscripts & maps.
Subjects: Art, Biblical Studies, Medicine, Nursing, Dentistry
ISBN Prefix(es): 84-88526

**Editorial Molino+**
Calabria, 166, 08015 Barcelona
*Tel:* (093) 226 06 25 *Fax:* (093) 226 69 98
*E-mail:* molino@menta.net
*Web Site:* www.editorialmolino.es *Cable:* MOLINO BARCELONA
*Key Personnel*
Man Dir: Luis A del Molino
Founded: 1933
Subjects: Education, Fiction, Mysteries, Sports, Athletics
ISBN Prefix(es): 84-272
Number of titles published annually: 100 Print
Total Titles: 1,345 Print

**Editorial Moll SL+**
Can Valero, 25, Poligon Can Valero, 07011 Palma de Mallorca, Balearic Islands
*Tel:* (0971) 72 41 76 *Fax:* (0971) 72 62 52
*E-mail:* info@editorialmoll.es
*Web Site:* www.editorialmoll.es
*Key Personnel*
Man Dir: Francesc de B Moll
Founded: 1934
Also acts as book distributor to the Balearic Islands.
Subjects: Art, Biography, Fiction, History, Language Arts, Linguistics, Literature, Literary Criticism, Essays, Natural History, Poetry, Regional Interests, Social Sciences, Sociology, Travel
ISBN Prefix(es): 84-273
Number of titles published annually: 60 Print
Total Titles: 950 Print
*Bookshop(s):* Llibres Mallorca, Esglesia de Sta Eulalia, 11, 07001 Palma de Mallorca, Contact: Victor Moll *Tel:* (0971) 728453 *Fax:* (0971) 728453

**Monograma Ediciones**
Padre Bartolome Pou, 24, 07003 Palma de Mallorca, Baleares
SAN: 004-2617
*Tel:* (071) 754124; (071) 712593 *Fax:* (071) 712593
*E-mail:* totem@atlas-iap.es
*Key Personnel*
Dir General: Leonardo Sainz Fernandez
ISBN Prefix(es): 84-88777
*Orders to:* Palau Reial, No 3, 07001 Palma de Mallorca, Baleares

**Editorial Monte Carmelo**
Padre Silverio, 2, Apdo, 19, 09001 Burgos
*Tel:* (0947) 25 60 61 *Fax:* (0947) 25 60 62; (0947) 27 32 65
*E-mail:* editorial@montecarmelo.com
*Web Site:* www.montecarmelo.com
*Key Personnel*
Dir: Alberto Pacho Polvorinos

Subjects: Religion - Catholic
ISBN Prefix(es): 84-7239

**Ediciones Morata SL+**
Mejia Lequerica, 12, 28004 Madrid
*Tel:* (091) 448 09 26 *Fax:* (091) 448 09 25
*E-mail:* morata@edmorata.es
*Web Site:* www.edmorata.es
*Key Personnel*
Man Dir: Florentina Gomez Morata
Founded: 1920
Subjects: Behavioral Sciences, Child Care & Development, Disability, Special Needs, Education, Human Relations, Philosophy, Psychology, Psychiatry, Self-Help, Social Sciences, Sociology, Women's Studies
ISBN Prefix(es): 84-7112
Total Titles: 300 Print
Distributed by Berriak - Comercial de Edit. S.L.; Cerezo Libros; Distriforma, S.A.; EA Libros; Andres Garcia Libros, S.L.; Gea Llibres, S.L.; Lemus, Distribuciones, CB; Modesto Alonso Estravis, Distribuciones; Nogara Libros, SA; Norte, Promociones y Distrib. S.L.; Les Punxes Distribuidora, S.L.; Serrano Libros; La Tierra Libros, SL

**Anaya & Mario Muchnik+**
Juan Ignacio Luca de Tena, 15, 28027 Madrid
*Tel:* (091) 393 86 00 *Fax:* (091) 320 91 29; (091) 742 66 31
*E-mail:* cga@anaya.es
*Web Site:* www.anaya.es
*Key Personnel*
General Dir: Victor Freixanes
Founded: 1990
Subjects: Literature, Literary Criticism, Essays
ISBN Prefix(es): 84-7979
*Parent Company:* Grupo Anaya SA
Distributor for America Latina

**Instituto de la Mujer (Miniterio de Trabajo y Asuntos Sociales)**
Condesa de Venadito, n° 34, 28027 Madrid
*Tel:* (091) 363 80 00
*E-mail:* inmujer@mtas.es
*Web Site:* www.mtas.es/mujer
*Key Personnel*
Dir General: Pilar Davila del Cerro
ISBN Prefix(es): 84-7799; 84-500; 84-505

**Mundi-Prensa Libros SA+**
Castello, 37, 28001 Madrid
*Tel:* (091) 4 36 37 00 *Fax:* (091) 5 75 39 98
*E-mail:* liberia@mundiprensa.es
*Web Site:* www.mundiprensa.es *Cable:* MUNDIPREN
*Key Personnel*
Man Dir: Jose Maria Hernandez
   *E-mail:* hernandez@mundiprensa.es
Manager: Ramon Reverte *E-mail:* resavbp@data.net.mx
Editorial & Publicity: Maria Isabel Hernandez
   *E-mail:* liberia@mundiprensa.es
Associate to Commercial Dir: Jose Chai
   *E-mail:* jchai@mundiprensa.es
International Agency of Subscriptions: Pilar Garcia Gil *E-mail:* pilargarcia@mundiprensa.es
Administration: Ana Lopez *E-mail:* lopez@mundiprensa.es
Sales Mgr: Mariano Estaban *E-mail:* barcelona@mundiprensa.es
Information: Joaquin Alcaniz
   *E-mail:* informatica@mundiprensa.es
Accounting: Agustin de las Heras
   *E-mail:* delasheras@mundiprensa.es
Founded: 1948
Subjects: Agriculture, Animals, Pets, Biological Sciences, Economics, Gardening, Plants, Mechanical Engineering, Technology, Veterinary Science
ISBN Prefix(es): 84-7114; 84-8476

Subsidiaries: Mundi-Prensa Mexico, SA de CV; Libreria Agricola; Editorial Aedos, SA
Divisions: Mundi-Prensa Barcelona
*Bookshop(s):* Libreria Mundi-Prensa; Libreria Agricola; Editorial Aedos, SA; Libreria Internacional, Aedos-Consejo de ciento 391, 08009 Barcelona

**Mundo Negro Editorial+**
Arturo Soria, 101, 28043 Madrid
SAN: 002-5690
*Tel:* (091) 4158115; (091) 4152412 *Fax:* (091) 5192550
*E-mail:* 100623.1651@compuserve.com
*Key Personnel*
Dir: Antonio Villarino
Founded: 1960
Subjects: Anthropology, Art, Biography, Developing Countries, Ethnicity, Foreign Countries, History, Religion - Catholic, Religion - Other, Theology
ISBN Prefix(es): 84-7295

**Munoz Moya Editor+**
28 de Febrero 8, 41310 Brenes
*Tel:* (05) 5653058
*E-mail:* editorial@mmoya.com; ediextre@mmoya.com
*Web Site:* www.mmoya.com
*Key Personnel*
Contact: Miguel Angel Munoz Moya
Founded: 1984
Specialize in Biblioteca Americana.
Subjects: Anthropology, Astrology, Occult, History, Literature, Literary Criticism, Essays, Mysteries, Poetry, Religion - Buddhist, Religion - Catholic, Religion - Jewish
ISBN Prefix(es): 84-8010; 84-86335; 84-931192
Number of titles published annually: 24 Online; 24 E-Book
Total Titles: 45 Online; 45 E-Book

**Editorial la Muralla SA+**
Constancia 33, 28002 Madrid
SAN: 002-5143
*Tel:* (091) 415 36 87; (091) 416 13 71 *Fax:* (091) 413 59 07
*E-mail:* arcolibros@arcomuralla.com
*Web Site:* www.arcomuralla.com
*Key Personnel*
Man Dir: Lidio Nieto
Publicity, Rights & Permissions: Nuria Nieto
Production: Julio Sanchez
Founded: 1968
Subjects: Art, Biological Sciences, Education, Geography, Geology, History, Language Arts, Linguistics, Literature, Literary Criticism, Essays, Mathematics, Music, Dance, Physical Sciences, Physics, Technology
ISBN Prefix(es): 84-7133; 84-404
Distributed by Distribudora Malaguena Atenea; Distribuciones Cimadevilla SA; Egatorre; Andres Garcia Libros; Grial; Carmen Fernandez Lappi; Libregus SL; LOGI; Lyra; Marcelino Perich Rasclosa; Odon Molina; Palma Distribucion SL; Pedidos; PROLOGO; La Tierra Libros; UNIDISA

**Editorial Musica Moderna**
Garcia Luna, 1 y 3, Apdo 2401, 28080 Madrid
SAN: 002-5356
*Tel:* (091) 416 91 81; (091) 415 37 78
*Key Personnel*
Editor, Dir: Francisco Carmona
Founded: 1935
Subjects: Music, Dance
ISBN Prefix(es): 84-86292

**Naque Editora+**
Pasaje Gutierrez Ortega, 1, 13001 Ciudad Real
*Tel:* (0926) 216714 *Fax:* (0926) 216714

*E-mail:* naque@naque.es
*Web Site:* www.naque.es
*Key Personnel*
Editor: Cristina Ruiz Perez
Founded: 1995
Specialize in bimonthly magazines & translations.
Subjects: Art, Drama, Theater, Education, Literature, Literary Criticism, Essays, Cultural Management, Pedagogy
ISBN Prefix(es): 84-89987
Number of titles published annually: 10 Print
Total Titles: 69 Print
Distributor for Arbole Marionetas; IGDEM

**Narcea SA de Ediciones+**
Av Dr Federico Rubio y Gali, 9, 28039 Madrid
*Tel:* (091) 554 64 84; (091) 554 61 02 *Fax:* (091) 554 64 87
*E-mail:* narcea@narceaediciones.es
*Web Site:* www.narceaediciones.es
*Key Personnel*
Editorial Dir: A de Miguel
Sales: N Nacher
Production: P Pazos
Rights & Permissions: C Vegas
Founded: 1968
Subjects: Education, Psychology, Psychiatry, Religion - Other, Social Sciences, Sociology
ISBN Prefix(es): 84-277

**Ediciones Nauta Credito SA+**
Loreto, 16, 08029 Barcelona
*Tel:* (093) 4392204 *Fax:* (093) 4107314
*Telex:* 54495 sele e *Cable:* EDINAUTA
*Key Personnel*
President: Jose Luis Ruiz de Villa Macho
Founded: 1962
Also book packager.
Subjects: Art, Nonfiction (General)
ISBN Prefix(es): 84-278
*Warehouse:* N Sra Montserrat 84-86, 08020 Barcelona

**Navarra, Comunidad Autonoma, Servicio de Prensa, Publica Pamplona**
Calle de las Navas de Tolosa, 21, 31002 Pamplona, Navarra
*Tel:* (0848) 427121 *Fax:* (0848) 427123
*E-mail:* fondo.publicaciones@cfnavarra.es
*Web Site:* www.cfnavarra.es/publicaciones
*Key Personnel*
Press Dir: Felix Carmona Salinas
ISBN Prefix(es): 84-235
*Orders to:* Fondo de Publicaciones Gobierno de Navarra

**NER,** *imprint of* Editorial El Perpetuo Socorro

**Editorial Nerea SA+**
San Bartolome, 2-5° dcha, 20007 San Sebastian (Guipuzcoa)
*Tel:* (0943) 432227 *Fax:* (0943) 433379
*E-mail:* nerea@nerea.net
*Key Personnel*
Editor: Nerea Atxega
Contact: Marta Casares
Founded: 1987
Subjects: Architecture & Interior Design, Art, History, Women's Studies, Art History
ISBN Prefix(es): 84-86763; 84-89569

**Noguer y Caralt Editores SA+**
Santa Amelia, 22 bajos, 08034 Barcelona
SAN: 004-0568
*Tel:* (093) 280 13 99 *Fax:* (093) 280 19 93
*E-mail:* noguer-caralt@mx2.redestb.es
*Key Personnel*
President: Emilio Ardevol
Founded: 1942
Subjects: Art, Astrology, Occult, Biography, Cookery, Fiction, Geography, Geology, History,

Literature, Literary Criticism, Essays, Nonfiction (General), Outdoor Recreation
ISBN Prefix(es): 84-279; 84-217
*Associate Companies:* Editorial Noguer SA

**Editorial Noray+**
Cardenal Vives i Tuto, 59, bajos, 08034 Barcelona
*Tel:* (093) 280 59 66 *Fax:* (093) 280 61 90
*E-mail:* info@noray.es
*Web Site:* www.noray.es
*Key Personnel*
Man Dir: Pablo Zendrera Zariquiey
Editorial: Panxo Pi-Suner Canellas
Founded: 1978
Subjects: Crafts, Games, Hobbies, Fiction, Maritime, Sports, Athletics
ISBN Prefix(es): 84-7486
Number of titles published annually: 20 Print
*Bookshop(s):* Libreria Maritima Noray

**Ediciones Norma SA+**
Parque Europolis, C/V, nave 16B, Apto Postal 116, 28230 Las Rozas de Madrid
*Tel:* (091) 6370760; (091) 6377414 *Fax:* (091) 5470133; (091) 6370760
*E-mail:* norma-capitel@normacapitel.com
*Web Site:* www.norma-capitel.com
*Key Personnel*
Man Dir, Editorial, Rights & Permissions: Alonso Rafael Perez *E-mail:* rpa@norma-capitel.com
Founded: 1978
Subjects: Alternative, Career Development, Child Care & Development, Cookery, How-to, Medicine, Nursing, Dentistry, Self-Help
ISBN Prefix(es): 84-7487
*Associate Companies:* Ediciones Eilea SA
Subsidiaries: Eilea SA; Libros Gamma
*Showroom(s):* Ronda de la Plazuela 8, 28230 Las Rozas, Madrid
*Bookshop(s):* Ronda de la Plazuela 8, 28230 Las Rozas, Madrid
*Shipping Address:* Ronda de la Plazuela 8, 28230 Las Rozas, Madrid
*Warehouse:* Ronda de la Plazuela 8, 28230 Las Rozas, Madrid
*Orders to:* Ronda de la Plazuela 8, 28230 Las Rozas, Madrid

**Novelas y Cuentos,** *imprint of* Editorial Casals SA

**Nuer Ediciones**
Plaza Conde de Miranda 4 1° 4a, 28005 Madrid
*Tel:* (091) 674 92 21; (091) 902 118 298 *Fax:* (091) 655 71 01
*E-mail:* nuer@pasadizo.com; correo@pasadizo.com
*Web Site:* www.pasadizo.com
*Key Personnel*
Dir: Carlos Diaz Maroto *E-mail:* cdmaroto@pasadizo.com; Miguel San Jose Romano *E-mail:* miguel@pasadizo.com
ISBN Prefix(es): 84-8068

**Nueva Acropolis+**
Pizarro 19, Bajo dcha, 28004 Madrid
*Tel:* (091) 5228730 *Fax:* (091) 5312952
*E-mail:* oinaes@jet.es
*Web Site:* www.acropolis.org
Founded: 1957
Membership(s): the School of Philosophy.
Subjects: Anthropology, Archaeology, Astrology, Occult, Astronomy, History, Parapsychology, Philosophy, Religion - Other
ISBN Prefix(es): 84-85982; 84-400; 84-300

**OASIS, Producciones Generales de Comunicacion+**
Perez Galdos, 36, Barcelona 08012
*Tel:* (093) 2372020 *Fax:* (093) 2177378

*Key Personnel*
Contact: Tomas Mata; Ua Matthiasdottir
Founded: 1978
Subjects: Alternative, Cookery, Earth Sciences, Environmental Studies, Ethnicity, Health, Nutrition, Outdoor Recreation, Psychology, Psychiatry, Self-Help, Sports, Athletics
ISBN Prefix(es): 84-7901

**Obelisco Ediciones S (Obelisco Publishing)+**
Pedro IV, 78, 3°, 5, 08005 Barcelona
*Tel:* (093) 3098525 *Fax:* (093) 3098523
*E-mail:* comercial@edicionesobelisco.com; obelisco@edicionesobelisco.com
*Web Site:* www.edicionesobelisco.com
*Key Personnel*
Manager: Julio Peradejordi Salazar
Founded: 1981
Subjects: Alternative, Astrology, Occult, Biblical Studies, Crafts, Games, Hobbies, Health, Nutrition, How-to, Human Relations, Medicine, Nursing, Dentistry, Nonfiction (General), Parapsychology, Psychology, Psychiatry, Religion - Buddhist, Religion - Catholic, Religion - Hindu, Religion - Islamic, Religion - Jewish, Religion - Protestant, Religion - Other, Self-Help, Astrology, New Age, Occult, Spiritualism, Alternative psychology, Judaica
ISBN Prefix(es): 84-7720; 84-86000
Number of titles published annually: 60 Print
Total Titles: 900 Print
Imprints: Magoria
*U.S. Office(s):* Obelisco Publishing, 8871 SW 129 Terrace, Miami, FL 33176, United States *Tel:* 305-233-3365 *E-mail:* miami@edicionesurano.com
Distributed by Libreria Artemis Edinter SA (Guatemala); Ediciones Cruz Del Sur (Panama); Dellare (Guatemala); Distribuciones del Futuro (Argentina); Forsa Editions Inc (Puerto Rico); Endiciones Gaviota (Colombia); Gussi Libros (Uruguay); Lectorum Sa De CV (US); Los Andes (Costa Rica); Mr Books (Ecuador); Pomaire (Venezuela); Ediciones Urano (Chile); Corporacion Yupanqui SA (Peru)

**Ediciones Oceano Grupo SA+**
Milanesado, 21-23, 08017 Barcelona
*Tel:* (093) 280 20 20 *Fax:* (093) 203 17 91
*E-mail:* info@oceano.com
*Telex:* 51735 Exit E
*Key Personnel*
Man Dir: Jose Lluis Monreal
Editorial: Carlos Gispert
Sales: Roberto Niubo
Production: Jose Gay
Rights & Permissions: Marta Bueno
Founded: 1950
Subjects: Art, Education, Fiction, Geography, Geology, History, Literature, Literary Criticism, Essays, Management, Science (General)
ISBN Prefix(es): 84-7069
*Associate Companies:* Ediciones Centrum Tecnicas y Cientificas SA, Milanesat, 21-23, 08017 Barcelona; Circe Ediciones SA, Milanesat, 21-23, 08017 Barcelona; Ediciones Manfer SA, Milanesat, 21-23, 08017 Barcelona
*Subsidiaries:* Instituto Gallach de Libreria y Ediciones SL
*Orders to:* Ediciones Oceano, SA, Paseo de Gracia, 26, 08007 Barcelona

**Ediciones Offo, SA**
Los Mesejo 23, 28007 Madrid
SAN: 001-8929
*Tel:* (091) 5514214 *Fax:* (091) 5010699
*Key Personnel*
Council Delegate: Joaquin Zuazo Martinez
Founded: 1957
ISBN Prefix(es): 84-7117

**Oikos-Tau SA Ediciones+**
Montserrat 12-14, 08340 Vilassar de Mar, Barcelona
*Tel:* (093) 7590791 *Fax:* (093) 7506825
*Key Personnel*
Man Dir, Editorial: Jordi Garcia-Bosch
Sales: Climent Garcia-Bosch
Founded: 1963
Membership(s): Editors Guild of Cataluna & Federation of Editors of Spain.
Subjects: Agriculture, Anthropology, Architecture & Interior Design, Behavioral Sciences, Biography, Biological Sciences, Earth Sciences, Economics, Education, Geography, Geology, History, Language Arts, Linguistics, Literature, Literary Criticism, Essays, Marketing, Medicine, Nursing, Dentistry, Poetry, Psychology, Psychiatry, Social Sciences, Sociology
ISBN Prefix(es): 84-281

**Ediciones Ojeda**
c/Seneca, 12 bajos izquierda, 08006 Barcelona
Mailing Address: PO Box 34055, E-08080 Barcelona
*Tel:* (093) 2370009 *Fax:* (093) 4159845
*E-mail:* lib.europa@mx3.redestb.es
*Key Personnel*
International Rights: Angel Garcia Fuente de la Oyeda
ISBN Prefix(es): 84-920591; 84-931390

**Ediciones Olimpic, SL+**
Placa de Lessaps, 33, 08023 Barcelona
*Tel:* (093) 2382864
*E-mail:* edolimpic@worldonline.es
*Key Personnel*
Administrator: Rafael Barberan
Contact: Angels Gimeno *E-mail:* angelsgimeno@hotmail.com
Founded: 1987
Specialize in legal books for universities.
Subjects: Fiction, Science Fiction, Fantasy, Social Sciences, Sociology, Western Fiction
ISBN Prefix(es): 84-7750

**Ediciones Omega SA+**
Plato 26, 08006 Barcelona
*Tel:* (093) 2010599; (093) 2013807; (093) 2012144 *Fax:* (093) 2097362
*E-mail:* omega@ediciones-omega.es
*Web Site:* www.ediciones-omega.es
*Key Personnel*
Man Dir: Gabriel Paricio; Antonio Paricio
Founded: 1948
Also specialize in field guides.
Subjects: Agriculture, Biological Sciences, Chemistry, Chemical Engineering, Film, Video, Geography, Geology, Natural History, Photography, Science (General), Technology
ISBN Prefix(es): 84-282

**Omnicon, SA+**
Mendez Alvaro, 66-A - 5° C, 28045 Madrid
*Tel:* (091) 527 82 49 *Fax:* (091) 528 13 48
*E-mail:* omnicon@skios.es
*Web Site:* www.omnicon.es
*Key Personnel*
Dir & International Rights: Juan M Varela
Founded: 1988
Subjects: Photography, Photography & Imaging Technical Books
ISBN Prefix(es): 84-88914; 84-404; 84-604

**Opera Tres Ediciones Musicales+**
Cuesta de Santo Domingo, 11, 28013 Madrid
SAN: 004-4210
*Tel:* (091) 542 4320 *Fax:* (091) 541 0580; (091) 680 76 26
*Key Personnel*
Contact: Blanca R Garcia

Subjects: Music, Dance
ISBN Prefix(es): 84-7893

**Ediciones Orbis SA**
Av Diagonal, 652 Edif A, 6, 08034 Barcelona
*Tel:* (093) 2800512 *Fax:* (093) 2801472
*E-mail:* orbis@edorbis.es
*Key Personnel*
Dir: Monica Casetti
ISBN Prefix(es): 84-402; 84-7530; 84-7634

**Ediciones del Oriente y del Mediterraneo**
Prado Luis, 11, 28440 Guadarrama (Madrid)
*Tel:* (091) 854 34 28 *Fax:* (091) 854 83 52
*E-mail:* sicamor@teleline.es
*Web Site:* www.webdoce.com/orienteymediterraneo
*Key Personnel*
Dir: Fernando Garcia Burillo
Subjects: Asian Studies, Biography, Developing Countries, Education, Ethnicity, Fiction, Foreign Countries, History, Literature, Literary Criticism, Essays, Nonfiction (General), Philosophy, Poetry, Religion - Islamic, Social Sciences, Sociology, Women's Studies
ISBN Prefix(es): 84-87198
Number of titles published annually: 12 Print
Total Titles: 74 Print
Distributed by Distribuciones Gracia Alvarez, SL; Arcadia Libros, SL; Distribuciones Cimadevilla, SA; Comercial Kalandraka, SL; Gaia Libros, SL; Gea Llibres, SL; Icaro Distribuidora, SL; Ikuska Libros, SL; Antonio Machado Libros, SA; Marketing i Distribucio Editorial, SL; Nadales Libros, SL; Odon Molina Distribuidor de Libros, SL; Palma Distribucions, SL; Puvill Libros, SA
*Distribution Center:* L' Alebrije, c/Gosol, 39, 08017 Barcelona

**Editorial Alfredo Ortells SL**
Sagunto, n° 5, 46009 Valencia
SAN: 002-2500
*Tel:* (096) 347 10 00 *Fax:* (096) 347 39 10
*E-mail:* editorial@ortells.com
*Web Site:* www.ortells.com
*Key Personnel*
Man Dir: Alfredo Ortells
Founded: 1952
ISBN Prefix(es): 84-7189; 84-9748

**Oxford University Press Espana SA+**
c/o Parque Empresarial San Fernando, Edificio Atenas 1, 28831 San Fernando de Henares, Madrid
*Tel:* (091) 6602600 *Fax:* (091) 6602626; (091) 6602629
*Key Personnel*
Man Dir: Jesus Lezcano
Founded: 1991
Subjects: Education, Language Arts, Linguistics
ISBN Prefix(es): 84-8104
Total Titles: 93 Print
*Parent Company:* Oxford University Press, United Kingdom
*Subsidiaries:* Parque Empresarial San Fernando; Girona; Mayor; Plaza de los Alfeceres; Pintor Rodriguez Acosta; Linares Rivas; Don Cristian; Uria; Doctor Manuel Candela; Paseo de Zorrilla; Reina Fabiola; Marques De Nervion

**Pages Editors, SL+**
Sant Salvador, 8, 25005 Lleida
*Tel:* (0973) 23 66 11 *Fax:* (0973) 24 07 95
*E-mail:* ed.pages.editors@cambrescat.es; editorial.milenio@cambrescat.es
*Key Personnel*
Dir: Lluis Pages i Marigot
Editor: Ramon Badia
Founded: 1991
Specialize in Catalan & Spanish books.
Subjects: Agriculture, Anthropology, Drama, Theater, Ethnicity, Fiction, History, Nonfiction

(General), Philosophy, Psychology, Psychiatry, Religion - Catholic, Social Sciences, Sociology
ISBN Prefix(es): 84-7935
*Associate Companies:* Editorial Milenio Arts Grafiques Bobala, SL *E-mail:* editorial. milenio@cambrescat.es

**Ediciones Paidos Iberica SA+**
Mariano Cubi, 92, 08021 Barcelona
*Tel:* (093) 241 92 50 *Fax:* (093) 202 29 54
*E-mail:* paidos@paidos.com
*Web Site:* www.paidos.com
*Key Personnel*
Man Dir: Javier Colomo
Production: Rosa Hurtado
Founded: 1945
Specialize in social sciences.
Subjects: Communications, Psychology, Psychiatry, Self-Help, Social Sciences, Sociology
ISBN Prefix(es): 84-7509
*Parent Company:* Editorial Paidos, Argentina
*Associate Companies:* Editorial Paidos Mexicana SA, Ruben Dario 118, Colonia Moderna, 03510 Mexico DF, Mexico

**Editorial Paidotribo SL+**
Consejo de Ciento, 245 bis 1° 1a, 08011 Barcelona
*Tel:* (093) 3233311 *Fax:* (093) 4535033
*E-mail:* paidotribo@paidotribo.com
*Web Site:* www.paidotribo.com
*Key Personnel*
Editor: Emilio Ortega Gomez
Founded: 1985
Subjects: Education, Health, Nutrition, Sports, Athletics, Anatomy
ISBN Prefix(es): 84-8019; 84-86475

**Ediciones El Pais SA**
Gran via 32-6 planta, 28013 Madrid
SAN: 001-6888
*Tel:* (091) 3301015 *Fax:* (091) 7449093
*E-mail:* elpaisaguilar@santillana.es
*Key Personnel*
Dir: Guillermo Schauelzon
Founded: 1976
Subjects: How-to, Journalism, Language Arts, Linguistics, Nonfiction (General), Self-Help, Travel, travel
ISBN Prefix(es): 84-86459; 84-95595

**Pais Vasco Servicio Central de Publicaciones**
Division of Gobierno VASCO
Libreria Donostia 1, 01010 Vitoria-Gazteiz
SAN: 003-2964
*Tel:* (0945) 01 68 66 *Fax:* (0945) 01 87 09
*E-mail:* hac-sabd@ej-gv.es
*Web Site:* www.ej-gv.net/publicaciones/cpa0/SCP. htm
*Key Personnel*
Contact: Pedro Castro Uribarren
Founded: 1980
Subjects: Agriculture, Art, Business, Education, Health, Nutrition, History, Law, Public Administration, Social Sciences, Sociology
ISBN Prefix(es): 84-457; 84-500; 84-7542
Number of titles published annually: 200 Print; 10 CD-ROM
Total Titles: 3,450 Print; 30 CD-ROM
Distributed by Bidea 2000 SL
*Bookshop(s):* Gobierno Vasco Dto de Hacienda y Administracion Publica Libreria, Duque de Wellington 2, Vitoria 01010 *Tel:* (0945) 018557 *Fax:* (0945) 078709 *E-mail:* hac-sabd@ej-gv.es
*Orders to:* Bidea 2000 SL, N Salcedo, 9, 48012 Bilbao *Tel:* (094) 4278177 *Fax:* (094) 4273745
Egartorre, Mirlo, 23, Madrid *Tel:* (01) 7116008 *Fax:* (01) 7116763
Zabaltzen, Portuetxe Kalea 88, 20009 San Sebastian *Tel:* (0943) 310301 *Fax:* (0943) 310452

**El Paisaje Editorial+**
Arrangoiti 8, Aranguren 48850
*Tel:* (04) 6390774
*Key Personnel*
Dir General: Agustin Garcia Alonso
Founded: 1981
Subjects: Biography, Drama, Theater, Fiction, Literature, Literary Criticism, Essays, Music, Dance, Poetry
ISBN Prefix(es): 84-7697; 84-7541; 84-85956
*Parent Company:* El Paisaje, Urazurrutia, 37 Bajo 1: Centro, 48003 Bilbao
*Branch Office(s)*
Apdo 88, Cordoba
*Bookshop(s):* Centro Comercial del Libro, SA, Urbanizduion Torres de San Lamberto 3, 50011 Zaragoza

**Ediciones Palabra SA+**
Paseo de la Castellana, 210-2, 28046 Madrid
*Tel:* (091) 350 1179; (091) 350 7720 *Fax:* (091) 359 02 30
*E-mail:* ayuda@edicionespalabra.es
*Web Site:* www.edicionespalabra.es
*Key Personnel*
Chief Executive Officer: Belen Martin
*E-mail:* belenmartin@edicionespalabra.es
Manager: Ricardo Regidor
*E-mail:* ricardoregidor@edicionespalabra.es
Founded: 1963
Subjects: Biography, Education, History, Religion - Other, family & leisure time
ISBN Prefix(es): 84-7118; 84-8239
Number of titles published annually: 80 Print; 1 CD-ROM
Total Titles: 500 Print; 1 CD-ROM

**Ediciones Paraiso, SL+**
Munoz Degrain, 15, 33007 Oviedo
*Tel:* (0985) 203 789
*E-mail:* paraiso@seteas.com
*Key Personnel*
Owner, Dir: Maria Emilia Fernandez Garcia
ISBN Prefix(es): 84-88472; 84-604

**Editorial Paraninfo SA+**
Magallanes, 25, 28015 Madrid
*Tel:* (091) 4463350 *Fax:* (091) 4456218; (091) 4478892
*E-mail:* info@paraninfo.es
*Web Site:* www.paraninfo.es
*Key Personnel*
Man Dir: Alfonso Mangada Sanz
Sales Dir: Miguel Mangada Ferber; Manuel Montalban Velasco
Founded: 1948
Subjects: Biological Sciences, Business, Computer Science, How-to, Management, Physical Sciences, Science (General), Technology
ISBN Prefix(es): 84-283
*Bookshop(s):* Melendez Valdes 65, Madrid 28015

**Parlamento Vasco**
Becerro de Bengoa, s/n, 01005 Vitoria-Gasteiz, Alava
*Tel:* (0945) 004 000 *Fax:* (0945) 146 016
*E-mail:* legebiltzarra@parlam.euskadi.net
*Web Site:* parlamento.euskadi.net
*Key Personnel*
Dir: Juan Carols da Silva Ochoa
Subjects: History, Law, Social Sciences, Sociology
ISBN Prefix(es): 84-87122; 84-500; 84-505

**Parramon Ediciones SA+**
Ronda de Sant Pere, 5 4th Fl, 08010 Barcelona
*Tel:* (093) 289 27 20 *Fax:* (093) 426 37 30
*E-mail:* sales@parramon.com
*Web Site:* www.parramon.com
*Key Personnel*
Man Dir: Fernando Penuela

Foreign Rights Dir: Remei Piqueras
*E-mail:* remei@parramon.es
Foreign Rights: Gemma Isus; Esther Serra
*E-mail:* eserra@parramon.es
International Relations: Montse Soriano
Founded: 1958
Subjects: Art, Crafts, Games, Hobbies, Education, Health, Nutrition, How-to, Practical Art, Fiction & Non-Fiction Children & Juvenile Illustrated Books, Human Body, Parenting & Reference Books
ISBN Prefix(es): 84-342
*Parent Company:* Carvajal, SA
*Warehouse:* Parramon Ediciones, Pedrosa B, 29-31, Poligono Pedrosa, 08908 L'Hospitalet del LLobregat, Barcelona

**Ediciones Partenon+**
Paseo de la Habana 56, 28036 Madrid
SAN: 004-4903
*Tel:* (091) 5634450 *Fax:* (091) 5628405
*Key Personnel*
Man Dir: Rafael Torres Gorriz
Founded: 1969
Subjects: Language Arts, Linguistics, Literature, Literary Criticism, Essays, Social Sciences, Sociology
ISBN Prefix(es): 84-7119
*U.S. Office(s):* Ave Domenech 284, 00918 San Juan, Puerto Rico *Tel:* 787-753-8879 *Fax:* 787-754-8265 *E-mail:* proex@icepr.com

**Editorial Parthenon Communication, SL+**
Cami Del Pla de Can Sans No 24, Sant Andreu de Llavaneres, 08392 Barcelona
*Tel:* (093) 7952008 *Fax:* (093) 7952008
Founded: 1991
Specialize in graphics design.
Subjects: Architecture & Interior Design, Biography, Environmental Studies
ISBN Prefix(es): 84-88251

**Centre de Pastoral Liturgica+**
Rivadeneyra 6, 7, 08002 Barcelona
*Tel:* (093) 3022235 *Fax:* (093) 3184218
*E-mail:* cpl@tsai.es
*Web Site:* www.cpl.es/
*Key Personnel*
President: Josep Urdeix
Founded: 1966
Subjects: Literature, Literary Criticism, Essays, Religion - Other, Theology
ISBN Prefix(es): 84-7467
*Warehouse:* Pujudes, 77-79, Barcelona

**Pearson Educacion SA+**
Nunez de Balboa, 120, 28006 Madrid
SAN: 002-2527
*Tel:* (091) 5903432 *Fax:* (091) 5903448
*E-mail:* firstname.lastname@pearsoned-ema.com
*Telex:* 47688 Wxyz E *Cable:* EDIMBRASA
*Key Personnel*
President: Bill Anderson
Man Dir, Higher Education Division: Luis Collado
Man Dir, School Division & VP: Luisa Crespo
Editorial Dir, School Division: Concho Ordonez
Man Dir, Professional & Trade Division: Ricardo Mendiola
VP, Finance/Operations: Robert Meek
Founded: 1942
Subjects: Art, Education, History, Language Arts, Linguistics, Medicine, Nursing, Dentistry, Philosophy, Psychology, Psychiatry, Science (General)
ISBN Prefix(es): 84-205
*Parent Company:* Pearson Plc
*Branch Office(s)*
Enrique Granados 46, 08008 Barcelona
Iruna 12, 48014 Bilbao
Saturnino Calleja 1, 28002 Madrid

Calle Amores 2027 Editorial Alhambra Mexicana SA de CV, Colonia del Valle, 03100 Mexico, DF, Mexico
Plaza de las Descalzas 2, 18009 Granada
Pasadizo de Pernas 13, 15005 La Coruna
Tomas Morales 48, 35003 Las Palmas
General Porlier 14, 38004 Santa Cruz de Tenerife
Reina Mercedes 35, 41012 Seville
Cabillers 5, 46003 Valencia
Julio Ruiz de Alda 12, 47013 Valladolid
Concepcion Arenal 25, 50005 Zaragoza
*Bookshop(s):* Nunez de Balboa, 120, 28006 Madrid SAN: 002-2527

**Ediciones Pegaso**, *imprint of* EDERSA (Editoriales de Derecho Reunidas SA)

**Ediciones Peninsula**, *imprint of* Grup 62

**Ediciones Peninsula**
Imprint of Grup 62
Peu de la Creu, 4, 08001 Barcelona
*Tel:* (093) 443 71 00 *Fax:* (093) 443 71 30
*E-mail:* correu@grup62.com
*Web Site:* www.grup62.com
*Key Personnel*
Rights Manager: Laura Pujol
Founded: 1963

**Pentalfa Ediciones+**
Division of Grupo Helicon SA
Apdo de Correos 360, 33080 Oviedo
*Tel:* (034) 985 985 386 *Fax:* (034) 985 985 512
*E-mail:* pentalfa@helicon.es
*Web Site:* www.helicon.es/pentalfa.htm
*Key Personnel*
Dir: Gustavo Bueno Sanchez *E-mail:* gbs@fgbueno.es
Founded: 1974
Subjects: Anthropology, Philosophy
ISBN Prefix(es): 84-85422; 84-7848
Total Titles: 3 Print; 2 CD-ROM

**Perea Ediciones+**
Velazquez, 31, 13620 Pedro Munoz, Ciudad Real
*Tel:* (026) 568261 *Fax:* (026) 586386
*Key Personnel*
Manager: Jose Perea Ramirez
Founded: 1987
Subjects: Astrology, Occult, Literature, Literary Criticism, Essays
ISBN Prefix(es): 84-7729

**Editorial Peregrino SL** (Pilgrim Publications)+
Ctra CM-412, km 65, Apdo 19, 13350 Moral de Calatrava, Ciudad Real
*Tel:* (0926) 338 245 *Fax:* (0926) 338 042
*E-mail:* editorialperegrino@mac.com
*Web Site:* www.editorialperegrino.net
*Key Personnel*
Manager: Demetrio Canovas
Founded: 1979
Editing & distributing religious literature.
Subjects: Biblical Studies, Biography, Religion - Protestant
ISBN Prefix(es): 84-86589
Number of titles published annually: 10 Print
Total Titles: 60 Print
*Parent Company:* Evangelical Press
Distributed by Cristianismo Historico (USA); Distribuidora Bereana (USA)
Distributor for El Estandarte de la Verdad (Spain)
*Book Club(s):* Club Peregrino, Apdo 19, 13350 Moral de Calatrava, Ciudad Real

**Editorial Perfils**
Del Bages, 7, 25006 Lleida
Mailing Address: PO Box 794, 25080 Lleida
*Tel:* (0973) 242160 *Fax:* (0973) 221670
*E-mail:* perfils@arrakis.es

*Key Personnel*
Dir: Mario Arque Domingo *Tel:* (973) 234453
ISBN Prefix(es): 84-87695

**Permanyer Publications+**
Mallorca 310, 08037 Barcelona
*Tel:* (093) 207 59 20 *Fax:* (093) 457 66 42
*E-mail:* permanyer@permanyer.com
*Web Site:* www.dolor.es; www.aidsreviews.com
*Key Personnel*
Dir General & Editor: Ricard Permanyer
Founded: 1973
Publishes journals & books.
Subjects: Medicine, Nursing, Dentistry, Veterinary Science
*Associate Companies:* Permanyer Portugal, Av Duque d'Avila 92, Lisbon, Portugal

**Editorial Perpetuo Socorro+**
C/ Covarrubias, 19, 28010 Madrid
*Tel:* (091) 445 51 26 *Fax:* (091) 445 51 27
*E-mail:* perso@pseditorial.com
*Web Site:* www.pseditorial.com
*Key Personnel*
Dir: Antonio Manuel C Baptista
Founded: 1946
Subjects: Education, Religion - Other, Theology
ISBN Prefix(es): 972-563

**Editorial El Perpetuo Socorro**
Covarrubias 19, 28010 Madrid
SAN: 002-399X
*Tel:* (091) 445 51 26 *Fax:* (091) 445 51 27
*E-mail:* ed-ps@planalfa.es
*Key Personnel*
Dir: Vidal Ayala Sacristan
Founded: 1943
Membership(s): AECE (Catholic Association of Publishers of Spain), Coedit Lit (Liturgical Coeditors of Spanish Episcopal Conference).
Subjects: Behavioral Sciences, Biblical Studies, Biography, Music, Dance, Religion - Catholic, Theology
ISBN Prefix(es): 84-284
Imprints: Icono Perpetuo Socorro; NER
Distributed by PPC
Distributor for Perpetuo Socorro (Mexico)

**Ediciones Piramide SA+**
Juan Ignacio Luca de Tena 15, 28007 Madrid
*Tel:* (091) 393 89 89 *Fax:* (091) 742 36 61
*E-mail:* piramide@anaya.es
*Web Site:* www.edicionespiramide.es
*Telex:* 41071 Maeg E
*Key Personnel*
Chairman: Maria Isabel Andres Bravo
Dir: Guillermo de Toca
Rights & Permissions: Paloma Rivero; Guillermo de Toca
Founded: 1973
Subjects: Business, Economics, Law, Psychology, Psychiatry, Science (General), Technology
ISBN Prefix(es): 84-368; 84-369
*Parent Company:* Grupo Anaya, Juan Ignacio, Luca de Tena 15, 28027 Madrid
*Associate Companies:* Ediciones Anaya

**Pirene Editorial, sal+**
Ausias March, 16, 3r. la., 08010 Barcelona
*Tel:* (093) 3178682 *Fax:* (093) 3178242
*Key Personnel*
Literary Dir: Francesc Boada
Founded: 1987
Editions in Spanish & Catalan.
Specialize in infant's & children's books.
Subjects: Biography, Education, Fiction, Humor
ISBN Prefix(es): 84-7766

**Editorial Planeta SA+**
Member of Grupo Planeta

Edifici Planeta Diagonal 662-664, 08034 Barcelona
*Tel:* (093) 2285800 *Fax:* (093) 2177140; (093) 2177748
*E-mail:* marketing@planeta.es
*Web Site:* www.editorial.planeta.es
*Telex:* 93458 Edtp *Cable:* EDIPLAN
*Key Personnel*
Chairman: Jose Manuel Lara Hernandez
General Manager: Jose Manuel Lara Bosch
Publishing General Manager: Ymelda Navajo
Founded: 1952
Subjects: Fiction, Nonfiction (General)
ISBN Prefix(es): 84-320; 84-395; 84-08
*Associate Companies:* Planeta/Agostini (Forum y Fasciculos Planeta), Aribau 185, 08021 Barcelona; Sudamericana/Planeta SA (Editores), Argentina; Lord Cochrane SA, Ave Providencia 727, Santiago, Chile; Editorial Artemisa SA, Ave Cuauhtemoc 1236 - 4, Colonia Vertiz Narvarte, Delegacion Benito Juarez, 03600 Mexico, DF, Mexico; Editorial Joaquin Mortiz SA, Mexico

**Plawerg Editores SA**
Member of Grupo Planeta
Beethoven, 10, 1°, 2a, 08021 Barcelona
*Tel:* (093) 414 72 26 *Fax:* (093) 209 50 01
*E-mail:* info@plawerg.es
*Web Site:* www.plawerg.com
*Key Personnel*
Man Dir: Juan Carlos Brinardeli
Founded: 1994
Specialize in multimedia editions.
ISBN Prefix(es): 84-89351

**Editorial Playor SA+**
Alberto Boch, 10-2 dcha, 28014 Madrid
SAN: 002-6239
*Tel:* (091) 3690652 *Fax:* (091) 3694441
*E-mail:* playor@attglobal.net
*Key Personnel*
Man Dir: Carlos A Montaner
Manager: Linda Periut
Founded: 1971
Subjects: Education, History, Language Arts, Linguistics, Literature, Literary Criticism, Essays, Mathematics, Science (General)
ISBN Prefix(es): 84-359

**Plaza y Janes Editores SA+**
Travessera de Gracia 47-49, 08021 Barcelona
*Tel:* (093) 3660340 *Fax:* (093) 3660105
*Web Site:* www.plaza.es
*Key Personnel*
Man Dir: Manfred Grebe
Dir Sales Division: Juan Pascual
Editorial Dir: Nuria Tey
Founded: 1959
Subjects: Biography, Fiction, History, Nonfiction (General)
ISBN Prefix(es): 84-01
Number of titles published annually: 100 Print
Total Titles: 500 Print
*Parent Company:* Verlagsgruppe Bertelsmann International GmbH, Munich, Germany

**Pleniluni Edicions+**
Roger de Lluria, 5, 08010 Barcelona
*Tel:* (093) 301 08 87 *Fax:* (093) 3174830
Founded: 1979
Membership(s): Association of Editors in Llengua, Catalana & Gremi.
Subjects: Crafts, Games, Hobbies, Science Fiction, Fantasy, Sports, Athletics
ISBN Prefix(es): 84-85752

**Editorial Pliegos+**
Gobernador 29 4A, 28014 Madrid
SAN: 002-6247
*Tel:* (091) 4291545 *Fax:* (091) 4291545

*Key Personnel*
Dir: Cesar E Leante
Founded: 1983
Subjects: Drama, Theater, Fiction, Journalism, Literature, Literary Criticism, Essays, Poetry
ISBN Prefix(es): 84-88435; 84-86214; 84-96045

**Polifemo, Ediciones**
Avda de Bruselas, 44, 28028 Madrid
*Tel:* (091) 7257101 *Fax:* (091) 3556811
*E-mail:* libros@polifemo.com
*Web Site:* www.polifemo.com
Founded: 1985
Subjects: Anthropology, Archaeology, Asian Studies, History, Travel
ISBN Prefix(es): 84-86547
Total Titles: 45 Print

**Editorial Popular SA+**
Dr Esquerdo, 173 6 Izda, 28007 Madrid
SAN: 002-6263
*Tel:* (091) 409 35 73 *Fax:* (091) 573 41 73
*E-mail:* epopular@infornet.es
*Web Site:* www.editorialpopular.com
*Key Personnel*
Man Dir: Ricardo Herrero-Velarde
Dir: Mercedes Calero
Founded: 1972
Subjects: Education, Government, Political Science, Literature, Literary Criticism, Essays, Social Sciences, Sociology
ISBN Prefix(es): 84-85016; 84-86524; 84-7884

**Editorial Portic SA+**
Imprint of Enciclopedia Catalana, SA
Diputacio, 250, 08007 Barcelona
*Tel:* (093) 412 00 30 *Fax:* (093) 301 48 63
*E-mail:* hiperenciclopedia@grec.com
*Web Site:* www.enciclopedia-catalana.com
*Key Personnel*
Rights Department: Monica Rocamora
Founded: 1963
Subjects: Biography, Journalism, Literature, Literary Criticism, Essays
ISBN Prefix(es): 84-7306

**PPC Editorial y Distribuidora, SA+**
Impresores, 15, Urbanizacion Prado del Espino, 28660 Boadilla del Monte (Madrid)
*Tel:* (091) 4228800 *Fax:* (091) 4226117
*E-mail:* buzonppc@ppc-editorial.com
*Web Site:* www.ppc-editorial.com *Cable:* PEPECE
*Key Personnel*
President: Antonio Montero
Man Dir: Angel Alos
Sales Dir: Ignacio Martin
Rights & Permissions: Javier Cortes
Publicity: Monica Hernandez
Founded: 1955
Subjects: Education, Philosophy, Religion - Other
ISBN Prefix(es): 84-288; 84-400
*Bookshop(s):* Librerias PPC

**Pre-Textos+**
Luis Santangel, 10, 46005 Valencia
SAN: 001-4354
*Tel:* (096) 333 32 26 *Fax:* (096) 395 54 77
*E-mail:* info@pre-textos.com
*Web Site:* www.pre-textos.com
*Key Personnel*
Man Dir: D Manuel Borras Arana
Production Manager: Manuel Ramirez
Founded: 1976
Subjects: Biography, Fiction, Language Arts, Linguistics, Literature, Literary Criticism, Essays, Music, Dance, Nonfiction (General), Philosophy, Poetry
ISBN Prefix(es): 84-85081; 84-87101; 84-8191
Number of titles published annually: 50 Print
Total Titles: 600 Print
*Warehouse:* CELESA, Moratines 22, 28005 Madrid

**Editorial Prensa Espanola**
Padilla 6, 28006 Madrid
SAN: 002-6328
*Tel:* (091) 4462616
*Key Personnel*
Dir: Rogelio Gonzalez-Ubeda
Founded: 1905
Subjects: Fiction, Nonfiction (General)
ISBN Prefix(es): 84-287; 84-487

**Prensas Universitarias de Zaragoza+**
Edificio de Ciencias Geologicas Pedro Cerbuna, 12, 50009 Zaragoza
*Tel:* (0976) 761330 *Fax:* (0976) 761063
*E-mail:* spublica@posta.unizar.es
*Web Site:* wzar.unizar.es/spub/
*Key Personnel*
Editorial Dir: D Guillermo Perez Sarrion
    *E-mail:* gperez@posta.unizar.es
Founded: 1542
Subjects: History, Literature, Literary Criticism, Essays, Science (General), Social Sciences, Sociology, Academic
ISBN Prefix(es): 84-7733; 84-600
Distributed by Bitacora

**Editorial Presencia Gitana**
Valderrodrigo 76 y 78, bajos A, 28039 Madrid
*Tel:* (091) 373 62 07 *Fax:* (091) 373 44 62
*E-mail:* anpregit@teleline.es
*Key Personnel*
Responsable Legal: Manuel Martin Ramirez
Founded: 1987
Membership(s): the European's Net Interface; specialize in gypsies.
Subjects: Anthropology, Biography, Education, Ethnicity, History, Humor, Social Sciences, Sociology, Antiracism, Gipsies (culture, language, story)
ISBN Prefix(es): 84-87347

**Edicions Proa, SA+**
Diputacio 250-1, 08007 Barcelona
*Tel:* (093) 4120030 *Fax:* (093) 3014863
*E-mail:* enciclo.catalan@bcn.servicom.es
*Key Personnel*
Literary Dir: Oriol Izquierdo Llopis
Founded: 1928
Subjects: Fiction, Literature, Literary Criticism, Essays, Poetry, Social Sciences, Sociology
ISBN Prefix(es): 84-8256
*Parent Company:* Enciclopedia Catalana, SA
*Bookshop(s):* Proa Espais, Diputacio 250, 08007 Barcelona

**Progensa Editorial+**
Parque Industrial PISA, c/Comercio 12, 41927 Mairena del Aljarafe, Sevilla
*Tel:* (0954) 186 200 *Fax:* (0954) 186 111
*E-mail:* progensa@progensa.com
*Web Site:* www.progensa.es
*Key Personnel*
Manager: Francisco Chica Gonzalez
Founded: 1980
Publishers of technical books.
Subjects: Electronics, Electrical Engineering, Energy, How-to, Technology
ISBN Prefix(es): 84-86505; 84-398; 84-95693
Total Titles: 2 Print; 1 CD-ROM

**Promocion Popular Cristiana**, see PPC Editorial y Distribuidora, SA

**Pronaos, SA Ediciones+**
Mayor, 58-6, 28013 Madrid
SAN: 001-9364
*Tel:* (091) 5418199; (091) 5412766 *Fax:* (091) 4203429; (091) 5412766
*E-mail:* pronaos@teleline.es; jaire@teleline.es
*Key Personnel*
International Rights: Rosario Alberdi

Subjects: Architecture & Interior Design, Art, Gardening, Plants
ISBN Prefix(es): 84-85941
Total Titles: 2 CD-ROM
*Bookshop(s):* Naos-Libros, Quintana-12, 28013 Madrid *Tel:* (091) 5473916

**Instituto Provincial de Investigaciones y Estudios Toledanos (IPIET)+**
Pza de la Merced, 4, 45002 Toledo
SAN: 003-536X
*Tel:* (0925) 259367 *Fax:* (0925) 259348
*E-mail:* diputolepu@diputoledo.es
*Key Personnel*
President: Miguel A Ruiz Ayucar Alonso
Dir: Julio Porres de Mateo
Founded: 1963
Subjects: Archaeology, Art, Biological Sciences, Cookery, Drama, Theater, Ethnicity, Geography, Geology, History, Poetry, Social Sciences, Sociology
ISBN Prefix(es): 84-87103; 84-9750; 84-500; 84-505
Distributed by Pedro Alcantarilla (Spain)

**Publicaciones de la Universidad de Alicante**
Apdo de correos 99, 03080 Alicante
*Tel:* (0965) 909 576 *Fax:* (0965) 909 445
*E-mail:* publicaciones.ventas@ua.es
*Web Site:* publicaciones.ua.es
*Key Personnel*
Publication Dir: Jose Ramon Giner Mallol
    *Tel:* (0965) 90 34 80 *Fax:* (0965) 90 94 45
    *E-mail:* JRamon.Giner@ua.es
Subjects: Agriculture, Chemistry, Chemical Engineering, Economics, Literature, Literary Criticism, Essays, Medicine, Nursing, Dentistry, Regional Interests, Science (General), Social Sciences, Sociology
ISBN Prefix(es): 84-7908; 84-600; 84-86809
Distributed by Distribuciones de Enlace SA; Resto del mundo; Servei del Llibre l'Estaquirot; Sudamerica
*Orders to:* L'Estaquirot, Mare de Deu del Coll, 53, 08023 Barcelona

**Publicaciones de la Universidad Pontificia Comillas-Madrid**
Alberto Aguilera 23, 28015 Madrid
*Tel:* (091) 542 28 00 *Fax:* (091) 734 45 70
*E-mail:* edit@pub.upco.es
*Web Site:* www.upco.es
*Key Personnel*
Dir: Eusebio Gil Coria
Founded: 1975
Subjects: Economics, History, Law, Medicine, Nursing, Dentistry, Philosophy, Social Sciences, Sociology, Theology, Women's Studies
ISBN Prefix(es): 84-87840; 84-89708; 84-600; 84-8468
Distributed by Edisofer; Ikuska Libros; Melisa; Odon Molina; Sal Terrae; Sendra Marco

**Publicaciones y Ediciones Salamandra SA+**
Mallorca, 237-Entlo, 1, 08008 Barcelona
*Tel:* (093) 2151199 *Fax:* (093) 2154636
*E-mail:* derechos@salamandra-info.com
*Key Personnel*
Contact: Sigrid Kraus de Carril
Founded: 1989
Subjects: Child Care & Development, Fiction, History, Romance
ISBN Prefix(es): 84-7888
*Parent Company:* Emece Editores, Argentina
Distributed by Emece Editores Argentina SA; Emece Editores Mexico SA

**Pulso Ediciones, SL+**
Rambla del Celler, 117-119, 08190 Sant Cugat del Valles, Barcelona

*Tel:* (0935) 896 264 *Fax:* (0935) 895 077
*E-mail:* pulso@pulso.com
*Web Site:* www.pulso.com
*Key Personnel*
Manager: Gloria Pasias Lomelino
Founded: 1978
Subjects: Animals, Pets, Architecture & Interior Design, Behavioral Sciences, Computer Science, Health, Nutrition, Medicine, Nursing, Dentistry, Psychology, Psychiatry, Science (General), Veterinary Science
ISBN Prefix(es): 84-86671

**Punto Juvenil**, *imprint of* Editorial Casals SA

**Quaderns Crema SA+**
Muntaner, 462 3° 1a, 08006 Barcelona
*Tel:* (093) 4144906 *Fax:* (093) 4147107
*E-mail:* correo@acantilado.es
*Web Site:* www.quadernscrema.com
*Key Personnel*
Man Dir: Jaume Vallcorba
Founded: 1979
Subjects: History, Literature, Literary Criticism, Essays, Poetry, Narratives
ISBN Prefix(es): 84-85704; 84-7727
Number of titles published annually: 32 Print
Total Titles: 325 Print
Subsidiaries: Acantilado

**RA-MA, Libreria y Editorial
    Microinformatica+**
Jarama 3A, Poligno Industrial lgarsa, 28860 Paracuellos de Jarama, Madrid
*Tel:* (091) 658 42 80 *Fax:* (091) 662 81 39
*E-mail:* editorial@ra-ma.com
*Web Site:* www.ra-ma.com
*Key Personnel*
Contact: Jose L Ramirez *E-mail:* joselrc@ra-ma.com
Founded: 1984
Subjects: Computer Science, Microcomputers
ISBN Prefix(es): 84-86381; 84-7897

**RACC-62**, *imprint of* Grup 62

**RACC-62**
Imprint of Grup 62
Peu de la Creu, 4, 08001 Barcelona
*Tel:* (093) 443 71 00 *Fax:* (093) 443 71 30
*E-mail:* correu@grup62.com
*Web Site:* www.grup62.com
*Key Personnel*
Rights Manager: Laura Pujol

**Editora Regional de Murcia - ERM**
Isaac Albeniz, 4, 30009 Murcia
*Tel:* (068) 280246 *Fax:* (068) 298293
*E-mail:* editora.regional@carm.es
*Web Site:* www.carm.es
*Key Personnel*
President: Ramon Luis Valcarcel Siso
Founded: 1980
Subjects: Anthropology, Archaeology, Architecture & Interior Design, Art, Cookery, Crafts, Games, Hobbies, Economics, Education, Environmental Studies, Gardening, Plants, Geography, Geology, History, Literature, Literary Criticism, Essays, Music, Dance, Outdoor Recreation, Philosophy, Poetry, Regional Interests, Religion - Islamic
ISBN Prefix(es): 84-7564; 84-500; 84-505;
Distributed by Distribuidora M Atenea, SL; Carisma Libros; Distribuciones Cimadevilla; M Alonso Estravis Distribuidora; Herro Ediciones; Icaro Distribuidora, SL; Lidiza; Servei del Llibre; Distribuidora Literaria de Editorial Siglo XXI; Miguel Sanchez Libros; La Tierra Libros; Troquel; Viuber
*Orders to:* Siglo XXI, c/Plaza 5, 28043 Madrid *Tel:* (091) 7591809

**Editorial Reus SA**
Calle Preciados, 23-2, 28013 Madrid
*Tel:* (091) 2213619; (091) 2223054 *Fax:* (091) 5312408
*E-mail:* reus@editorialreus.es
*Web Site:* www.editorialreus.es
*Key Personnel*
President: Jose Luis Allende y Garcia-Baxter
Founded: 1852
Subjects: Law
ISBN Prefix(es): 84-290
Distributed by Edisofer
*Warehouse:* Avda Democracia, Nave 305, 7-28031 Madrid

**Ediciones Luis Revenga**
Travesia de Andres Mellado, 9, 28015 Madrid
SAN: 001-8317
*Tel:* (091) 5434646 *Fax:* (091) 5434706
*E-mail:* cuadcerv@elr.es
*Key Personnel*
Dir: Oscar Berdugo
ISBN Prefix(es): 84-87607; 84-398

**Editorial Reverte SA+**
Loreto 13-15 Local B, 08029 Barcelona
Mailing Address: Apdo de Correos 1237, 08029 Barcelona
*Tel:* (093) 419 33 36; (093) 419 32 76 *Fax:* (093) 419 51 89
*E-mail:* istz0125@tsai.es; prom.reverte@teleline.es
*Web Site:* www.ludosoft.net/reverte/present.htm
    *Cable:* EDIREVER
*Key Personnel*
Dir: Felipe Reverte
Editorial: Amado J Sala
Sales: Pablo Reverte
Rights & Permissions: Marta Sala
Founded: 1947
Subjects: Engineering (General), Science (General)
ISBN Prefix(es): 84-291
*Associate Companies:* Marsala, SA, Ave Angel Gallardo 613, 1405 Buenos Aires, Argentina; Salvatore Conforti, SL, Calle 37, No 22-72, (Barrio La Soledad), Bogota DE, Colombia; REPLA SA, de CV, Rio Panuco, 141-A, 06500 Mexico DF, Mexico; Editorial Miro CA, Venezuela

**Editorial Revista Agustiniana**
Ramonet 3, 28033 Madrid
*Tel:* (091) 550-5000 *Fax:* (091) 550-5225
*E-mail:* revista@agustiniana.com
*Web Site:* www.agustiniana.com
*Key Personnel*
Dir: Rafael Lazcano
Founded: 1960
Subjects: Biblical Studies, Philosophy, Religion - Catholic
ISBN Prefix(es): 84-86898; 84-95745
Distributed by Ediciones Y Distribuciones Isla

**Ediciones Rialp SA+**
Alcala 290, 28027 Madrid
*Tel:* (091) 3260504 *Fax:* (091) 3261321
*E-mail:* ediciones@rialp.com
*Web Site:* www.rialp.com/
*Telex:* 43229 Coim E (abonado 701) *Cable:* RIALPSA
*Key Personnel*
President: Jaime Vicens
Vice President: Jesus Domingo Garcia
Editorial: Miguel Arango
Children's Editorial: Carmen Gomez de Agueero
Public Relations: Teresa Arregui; Alfonso Rascon
Rights & Permissions: Eva Rubira
Membership(s): Editors Association of Spain & Commerce Association of Spain.
Subjects: Cookery, Economics, Education, Gardening, Plants, Health, Nutrition, History, Lit-

erature, Literary Criticism, Essays, Military Science, Music, Dance, Philosophy, Poetry, Religion - Other, Science (General)
ISBN Prefix(es): 84-321
*Branch Office(s)*
Via Augusta, No 6, pral la 08006 Barcelona
*Warehouse:* Logistica de Ediciones, SA, Bembibre, 28-30, Polg Cobo Calleja, (28940 Fuenlabrada, Madrid *Tel:* (091) 6420086 *Fax:* (091) 6421696
*Orders to:* Cauce, Distribuidora de Ediciones SA, Sebastian Elcano, 30, 28012 Madrid *Tel:* (091) 4672666 *Fax:* (091) 5302537

**Riquelme y Vargas Ediciones SL+**
Avda de Andalucia 29, 23006 Jaen
*Tel:* (053) 270066 *Fax:* (053) 270066
*Key Personnel*
Contact: Elias Riquelme Ibanez
Founded: 1982
Subjects: Agriculture, Art, History, Law, Literature, Literary Criticism, Essays
ISBN Prefix(es): 84-86216; 84-300

**Editorial Roasa SL**
Carretera de Huetor Vega, Edif Roma, 5-1A, 18008 Granada
*Tel:* (058) 0227846 *Fax:* (058) 132530 *Cable:* APDO 2069
*Key Personnel*
Man Dir, Sales: Felix J Rodriguez
Editorial: Jorge Alonso
Production: Manuel Alonso
Founded: 1982
Membership(s): Association of Editions of Andalucia (AEA).
Subjects: Art, History
ISBN Prefix(es): 84-86043; 84-8042; 84-300

**Ediciones Joaquin Rodrigo**
General Yague 11, 28020 Madrid
*Tel:* (091) 555 2728 *Fax:* (091) 556 4334
*E-mail:* ediciones@joaquin-rodrigo.com
*Web Site:* www.joaquin-rodrigo.com
*Key Personnel*
General Manager: Cecilia Rodrigo
Specialize in classical music.
Subjects: Music, Dance
ISBN Prefix(es): 84-88558; 84-604

**Ediciones ROL SA+**
San Elias, 29 bajos, 08006 Barcelona
*Tel:* (093) 200 80 33 *Fax:* (093) 200 27 62
*E-mail:* rol@e-rol.es
*Web Site:* www.e-rol.es
*Key Personnel*
Man Dir: Julia Martinez Saavedra
Founded: 1977
Membership(s): The Spanish Association of Technical Press.
Subjects: Health, Nutrition, Human Relations, Medicine, Nursing, Dentistry, Psychology, Psychiatry, Science (General), Social Sciences, Sociology
ISBN Prefix(es): 84-85535

**Josep Ruaix Editor**
Av de la Vila 18, 08180 Moia, Barcelona
*Tel:* (093) 820 81 36; (093) 830 02 33
*Web Site:* www.ruaix.com/
*Key Personnel*
Contact: J Ruaix
Founded: 1976
Subjects: Language Arts, Linguistics
ISBN Prefix(es): 84-920619; 84-404; 84-604; 84-398; 84-400; 84-300; 84-89812
Number of titles published annually: 3 Print
Total Titles: 62 Print
Distributed by Gran Via Llibres; L'Arc de Bera, SA

**Rueda, SL Editorial+**
Fisicas 5, Pol Urtinsa II, 28923 Alcorcon, Madrid
*Tel:* (091) 619 27 79; (091) 619 25 64 *Fax:* (091)
610 28 55
*E-mail:* ed_rueda@infornet.es
*Web Site:* www.editorialrueda.es
*Key Personnel*
International Rights: Sanchez Rafael Rueda
Founded: 1970
Subjects: Agriculture, Architecture & Interior De-
sign, Biological Sciences, Civil Engineering,
Earth Sciences, Environmental Studies, Garden-
ing, Plants, Geography, Geology
ISBN Prefix(es): 84-7207

**Salvat Editores SA+**
45, Calle Mallorca, 08029 Barcelona
*Tel:* (090) 2117547 *Fax:* (093) 4955710
*E-mail:* infosalvat@salvat.com
*Web Site:* www.salvat.es
*Key Personnel*
Financial Dir: Jean Paul Dupoizat
ISBN Prefix(es): 84-345
*Parent Company:* Hachette Livre SA, Paris,
France
Divisions: Venta Directa; Fasciculos; Literatura

**Editorial Miguel A Salvatella SA**
Sant Domenec, 5, 08012 Barcelona
*Tel:* (093) 2189026 *Fax:* (093) 2177437
*E-mail:* editorial@salvatella.com
*Web Site:* www.salvatella.com
Founded: 1922
Subjects: Education, Origami
ISBN Prefix(es): 84-7210; 84-8412

**Editorial San Martin+**
Arenal 23, 28013 Madrid
SAN: 002-6654
*Tel:* (091) 8599964 *Fax:* (091) 8599964
*Key Personnel*
Man Dir: Jorge Tarazona
Founded: 1854
Subjects: Aeronautics, Aviation, History, Military
Science
ISBN Prefix(es): 84-7140
*Bookshop(s):* Libreria San Martin, Puerta del Sol
6, 28013 Madrid
*Warehouse:* Libreria San Martin, Puerta del Sol, 6
28013 Madrid

**San Pablo Ediciones+**
Protasio Gomez 15, 28027 Madrid
SAN: 001-9739
*Tel:* (091) 917 425 113 *Fax:* (091) 917 425 723
*E-mail:* dir.editorial@sanpablo-ssp.es
*Web Site:* www.sanpablo-ssp.es
*Key Personnel*
President: Antonio Marono Pena *Fax:* (091) 305
2050 *E-mail:* ventao@sanpablo-ssp.es
Publication Dir: Ezequiel Varona
Administration: Antonio Diaz Martinez
Sales: Cecilio Ortiz
Production: Jose Maria Fernandez
Founded: 1936
Editorial.
Subjects: Biography, Education, Religion - Other,
Theology
ISBN Prefix(es): 84-285
Number of titles published annually: 100 Print
Total Titles: 1,500 Print
*Parent Company:* Sociedad de San Pablo
*Bookshop(s):* Eight in Spain
*Warehouse:* Resina 1, 28021 Madrid
*Orders to:* Resina 1, 28021 Madrid

**Ediciones San Pio X+**
M de Mondejar, 32, 28028 Madrid
SAN: 001-9720
*Tel:* (091) 726.28.17; (091) 355 2727 *Fax:* (091)
726.28.17

*E-mail:* espx@planalfa.es
*Key Personnel*
Dir: Cesar Pallares Munoz
Founded: 1967
Subjects: Biblical Studies, Education, Philosophy,
Religion - Catholic, Social Sciences, Sociology,
Theology
ISBN Prefix(es): 84-7221
Number of titles published annually: 25 Print
Total Titles: 315 Print
*Associate Companies:* Bruno, Maestro Alonso,
21, 28028 Madrid *Tel:* (091) 3610448
*Fax:* (091) 3613133 *E-mail:* info@editorial.
bruno.es
*U.S. Office(s):* 170-23 83 Ave, Jamaica, NY
11432, United States *Tel:* 212-291 9891
*Fax:* 212-291 9830

**Universidad de Santiago de Compostela+**
Campus Universitario Sur, 15782 Santiago de
Compostela
SAN: 005-2728
*Tel:* (0981) 593 500 *Fax:* (0981) 593 963
*E-mail:* spublic@usc.es
*Key Personnel*
Technical Dir: Marisa Melon-Rodriguez
Technical Coordinator: Juan L Blanco Valdes
Founded: 1945
Membership(s): Association of Spanish Editorial
University.
Subjects: Art, Education, Electronics, Electrical
Engineering, Geography, Geology, History,
Language Arts, Linguistics, Law, Philosophy,
Physics, Science (General), Social Sciences,
Sociology
ISBN Prefix(es): 84-7191; 84-8121; 84-9750
Number of titles published annually: 50 Print; 3
CD-ROM
Total Titles: 1,500 Print; 7 CD-ROM
Distributed by Klaus Dieter Vervuert (Europe)
Distributor for Breogan Distribuciones (Spain,
Center); Editorial Galaxia (Galicia); L'Alebrije
(South America); Libraria Couceiro (Portugal);
Puvill Libros (Europe & America); Bitacora
(Catalonia)

**SARPE,** see Axel Springer Publicaciones

**Ediciones Scriba SA+**
Affiliate of Libreria Martinez Perez
Valencia, 246, 08007 Barcelona
*Tel:* (093) 215 20 89; (093) 215 19 33 *Fax:* (093)
487 37 66
*Telex:* 98772 Cllc E (Scriba)
*Key Personnel*
Man Dir: Manuel Martinez Bravo *E-mail:* mmb@
scriba.jazztel.es
Founded: 1890
Subjects: Art, Medicine, Nursing, Dentistry, Sci-
ence (General)
ISBN Prefix(es): 84-85835
*Bookshop(s):* Libreria Martinez Perez, Valencia,
246, 08007 Barcelona *E-mail:* lmp@scriba.
jazztel.es

**Secretariado Trinitario+**
Av Filiberto Villalobos 80, 37007 Salamanca
*Tel:* (0923) 23 56 02 *Fax:* (0923) 23 56 02
*E-mail:* editorialst@secretariadotrinitario.org
*Web Site:* www.aecae.es/secretrinitario
*Key Personnel*
Man Dir: Nereo Silanes
Rights & Permissions: Laurentino Silanes
Founded: 1967
Subjects: Religion - Catholic, Religion - Other,
Theology
ISBN Prefix(es): 84-88643; 84-85376; 84-500;
84-400
*Parent Company:* Orden de la Santisima Trinidad

**Editorial Seix Barral SA+**
Member of Grupo Planeta

Avda Diagonal 662-664 7a, 08034 Barcelona
*Tel:* (093) 496 7003 *Fax:* (093) 496 7004
*E-mail:* editorial@seix-barral.es
*Web Site:* www.seix-barral.es
*Telex:* 98255 Sxbl E
*Key Personnel*
Editorial Dir: Adolfo Garcia Ortega
*E-mail:* agarcia@seix-barral.es
Editorial: Pere Gimferrer
General Manager: Julian Leon *E-mail:* jleon@
planeta.es
Founded: 1911
Specialize in foreign language, drama, essay.
Membership(s): the Planeta Group (see Editorial
Planeta SA).
Subjects: Fiction, Poetry
ISBN Prefix(es): 84-322
Number of titles published annually: 60 Print
*Orders to:* Editorial Planeta SA, Corcega 273,
08008 Barcelona

**Selecta-Catalonia Ed**
Ronda de Sant Pere, 3 pral, 08010 Barcelona
*Tel:* (093) 3172331; (093) 3185183 *Fax:* (093)
3024793
*Key Personnel*
Delegate, Advisor: Sebastia Borras i Tey
Founded: 1943
Publications in Catalonian language.
Subjects: Ethnicity, Literature, Literary Criticism,
Essays, Regional Interests
ISBN Prefix(es): 84-7667
*Bookshop(s):* Libreria Catalonia SA, Ronda de
Sant Pere, 3 pral, 08010 Barcelona

**Ediciones del Serbal SA+**
Francesc Tarrega, 32, 08027 Barcelona
Mailing Address: Apartado de Correos 1386,
08080 Barcelona
*Tel:* (093) 408 08 34 *Fax:* (093) 408 07 92
*E-mail:* serbal@ed-serbal.es
*Web Site:* www.ed-serbal.es
*Key Personnel*
Man Dir, Editorial, Production: Jose Maria Riano
de Castro
Publicity: Noelia Riano
Sales: Rafael Alvarez Luque
Founded: 1980
ISBN Prefix(es): 84-85800; 84-7628

**Servicio de Publicaciones Universidad de
Cadiz+**
Dr Maranon, 3, 11002 Cadiz
Mailing Address: Apdo de Correos 439, 11080
Cadiz
*Tel:* (0956) 015268 *Fax:* (0956) 015634
*E-mail:* publicaciones@uca.es
*Web Site:* www.uca.es/serv/publicaciones
*Key Personnel*
Dir: Antonio Serrano Cueto *Tel:* (0956) 015 267
*E-mail:* antonio.serrano@uca.es
Founded: 1980
Subjects: Chemistry, Chemical Engineering, En-
gineering (General), History, Law, Literature,
Literary Criticism, Essays, Medicine, Nursing,
Dentistry, Science (General)
ISBN Prefix(es): 84-7786; 84-398; 84-505; 84-
300; 84-600
Distributed by Libreria Telmatica Espanola
Distributor for L'Alebrije (For America)
*Distribution Center:* Breogan Distribuciones,
c/Lanuza, 11 Local Derecha, 28028 Madrid,
Contact: Jose Miguel Ramos *Tel:* (01) 7130631
*Fax:* (01) 7130631

**Servicio de Publicaciones Universidad de
Cordoba+**
Avda Menendez Pidal s/n, 14071 Cordoba
*Tel:* (0957) 21 81 25 *Fax:* (0957) 21 81 96; (057)
218666 (Director)
*E-mail:* publicaciones@uco.es; pal1gocag@
lucano.uco.es (Director)

*Web Site:* www.uco.es/organiza/servicios/publica/
  presenta.htm
*Key Personnel*
Dir: Gustavo Gomez Castro
Founded: 1976
Subjects: Agriculture, Archaeology, Biological
  Sciences, Computer Science, Economics, Geogra-
  phy, Geology, Law, Veterinary Science
ISBN Prefix(es): 84-7801
Distributed by DOR SA; Francisco Baena SL

**Servicio de Publicaciones y Produccion
  Documental de la Universidad de Las
  Palmas de Gran Canaria**
Juan de Quesada, nº 30, 35001 Las Palmas de
  Gran Canaria
*Tel:* (0928) 451000; (0928) 451023 *Fax:* (0928)
  451022
*E-mail:* universidad@ulpgc.es
*Web Site:* www.ulpgc.es
*Key Personnel*
Coordinator: German Santana Henriquez
ISBN Prefix(es): 84-89728; 84-88412; 84-606;
  84-600; 84-95792; 84-95286

**Ediciones Seyer+**
Canizares 23, 29002 Malaga
SAN: 001-9798
*Tel:* (095) 2320887 *Fax:* (095) 2325511
*Key Personnel*
Dir: Antonio Abad
Founded: 1979
Subjects: Art, Literature, Literary Criticism, Es-
  says, Maritime, Music, Dance, Poetry, Science
  Fiction, Fantasy, Sports, Athletics
ISBN Prefix(es): 84-86975
*Warehouse:* San Millan, 15 29013 Malaga

**SGEL**, see Sociedad General Espanola de
  Libreria SA - SGEL

**Siglo XXI de Espana Editores SA+**
Principe de Vergara 78, 28006 Madrid
*Tel:* (091) 562 37 23; (091) 561 77 48 *Fax:* (091)
  561 58 19
*E-mail:* sigloxxi@sigloxxieditores.com
*Web Site:* www.sigloxxieditores.com *Cable:*
  SIGLOEDIT
*Key Personnel*
Man Dir, Production: Joaquin Garcia Ballestero
Sales: Eduardo Rivas
Man Dir: Javier Abasolo Fernandez
Founded: 1967
Subjects: Anthropology, Government, Political
  Science, History, Literature, Literary Criticism,
  Essays, Philosophy, Psychology, Psychiatry,
  Social Sciences, Sociology
ISBN Prefix(es): 84-323
Subsidiaries: Siglo XXI Editores SA de CV
Distributed by Distribuidora Literaria De Editorial
  Siglo XXI, SA

**Signament I Comunicacio, SL Signament
  Edicions+**
Enric Granados 11 entresol 1a, 08007 Barcelona
*Tel:* (093) 4516888 *Fax:* (093) 3234417
*Key Personnel*
Editor & Author: Xavier Escura-Dalmau
Founded: 1993
Subjects: History, Medicine, Nursing, Dentistry
ISBN Prefix(es): 84-604; 84-605; 84-921381; 84-
  931634

**Ediciones Sigueme SA+**
C/Garcia Tejado 23-27, Salamanca 37007
*Tel:* (0923) 21 82 03 *Fax:* (0923) 27 05 63
*E-mail:* sigueme@ctv.es *Cable:* SIGUEME
  SALAMANCA
*Key Personnel*
Man Dir, Editorial: Santiago L de Vega
Sales: Jose Maria Hernandez

Production: Jesus Pulido
Publicity: Jorge Sans Vila
Founded: 1958
Subjects: Biblical Studies, Biography, History,
  Philosophy, Religion - Catholic, Religion -
  Protestant, Theology
ISBN Prefix(es): 84-301
*Bookshop(s):* Libreria Sigueme, Francisco Garcia
  Tejado 23-27, 37007 Salamanca

**Silex Ediciones+**
Alcala 202, 28028 Madrid
*Tel:* (091) 356.69.09 *Fax:* (091) 361.00.75
*E-mail:* pedidosweb@silexediciones.com
*Web Site:* www.silexediciones.com
*Key Personnel*
President: D Eleonor Dominguez Ramirez
Founded: 1972
Subjects: Aeronautics, Aviation, Archaeology,
  Art, Biography, History, Maritime, Photogra-
  phy, Travel
ISBN Prefix(es): 84-85041; 84-7737

**Editorial Sintes SA**
Ronda Universitat 4, 08007 Barcelona
*Tel:* (093) 3182838
*Key Personnel*
Man Dir, Editorial: Luis Sintes Pros; Jorge Sintes
  Pros
Founded: 1968
Subjects: Health, Nutrition, Sports, Athletics
ISBN Prefix(es): 84-302
*Bookshop(s):* Libreria Sintes, Ronda Universitat
  4, 08007 Barcelona

**Editorial Sintesis, SA+**
Vallehermoso, 34, 28015 Madrid
*Tel:* (091) 593 20 98 *Fax:* (091) 445 86 96
*E-mail:* sintesis@sintesis.com
*Web Site:* www.sintesis.com
*Key Personnel*
President: Felisa Cedenilla Lorente
Contact: Francisco Belloso Cruzado
Founded: 1986 (Editorial Sintesis was founded in
  1986 to provide high quality scientific & aca-
  demic texts for University students in all areas
  of study)
Subjects: Biography, Biological Sciences, Chem-
  istry, Chemical Engineering, Communications,
  Computer Science, Earth Sciences, Economics,
  Education, Engineering (General), Geography,
  Geology, History, Journalism, Language Arts,
  Linguistics, Library & Information Sciences,
  Literature, Literary Criticism, Essays, Manage-
  ment, Mathematics, Mechanical Engineering,
  Nonfiction (General), Philosophy, Physical Sci-
  ences, Psychology, Psychiatry, Science (Gen-
  eral), Social Sciences, Sociology, Travel
ISBN Prefix(es): 84-7738; 84-9756
Number of titles published annually: 100 Print
Foreign Rep(s): Colofon (Mexico); Proeme (Latin
  America, US)

**Equipo Sirius SA+**
Avda Rafael Finat, 34, 28044 Madrid
*Tel:* (091) 710 73 49 *Fax:* (091) 705 43 04
*E-mail:* sirius@equiposirius.com
*Web Site:* www.equiposirius.com
*Key Personnel*
Contact: Carmen de Pablo Urcelay
Founded: 1985
Subjects: Archaeology, Astronomy, Crafts,
  Games, Hobbies, Education, Photography,
  Physical Sciences, Science (General)
ISBN Prefix(es): 84-86639; 84-95495
Distributed by Editorial Hispano Andina Ltda
  (Colombia); Cuspide Libros SA (Argentina);
  Libreria Escolar Editora (Portugal); Reverte
  Ediciones SA de CV (Mexico); Sousa, So-
  brinho y Freixo (Portugal)

**Sirmio+**
Ferrar Valls i Taberner 8, 08006 Barcelona
*Tel:* (093) 2123808 *Fax:* (093) 4182317
*E-mail:* qcrema@mito.ibernet.com
*Key Personnel*
Man Dir: Jaume Vallcorba
Founded: 1989
Subjects: Art, Fiction, History, Literature, Literary
  Criticism, Essays, Philosophy, Poetry
ISBN Prefix(es): 84-7769
*Parent Company:* Quaderns Crema

**Ediciones Siruela SA+**
Plaza de Manuel Becerra 15, 28028 Madrid
*Tel:* (091) 3555720; (091) 3554605; (091)
  3552202 *Fax:* (091) 3552201
*E-mail:* atencionlector@siruela.com
*Web Site:* www.siruela.com
*Key Personnel*
Dir: Jacobo F J Stuart
Founded: 1982
Subjects: Animals, Pets, Art, Biography, Fic-
  tion, Humor, Literature, Literary Criticism,
  Essays, Mysteries, Nonfiction (General), Phi-
  losophy, Poetry, Religion - Buddhist, Religion -
  Catholic, Religion - Hindu, Religion - Islamic,
  Religion - Jewish, Religion - Other, Social Sci-
  ences, Sociology, Theology
ISBN Prefix(es): 84-7844; 84-85876

**Edicions 62**, *imprint of* Grup 62

**Edicions 62+**
Imprint of Grup 62
Peu de la Creu, 4, 08001 Barcelona
*Tel:* (093) 4437100 *Fax:* (093) 4437130
*E-mail:* correu@grup62.com
*Web Site:* www.grup62.com
*Key Personnel*
Man Dir: Juan Capdevila
Editorial Dir: Oriol Castanys
Sales & Publicity: Joaquim Sabria
Rights Manager: Laura Pujol
General Secretary: Josefina Revilla
Founded: 1962
Subjects: Art, Biography, Drama, Theater, Fiction,
  History, Literature, Literary Criticism, Essays,
  Music, Dance, Nonfiction (General), Philoso-
  phy, Poetry, Social Sciences, Sociology, Travel
ISBN Prefix(es): 84-297

**Grup 62+**
Peu de la Creu, 4, 08001 Barcelona
*Tel:* (093) 443 71 00 *Fax:* (093) 443 71 30
*E-mail:* correu@grup62.com
*Web Site:* www.grup62.com
*Key Personnel*
Man Dir: Pere Sureda Vinolas
Editorial Dir: Martina Ros
Literary Dir: Xavier Folch
Sales & Publicity: Sergi Martinez
Rights Manager: Laura Pujol
Subjects: Biography, Drama, Theater, Fiction,
  History, Language Arts, Linguistics, Literature,
  Literary Criticism, Essays, Nonfiction (Gen-
  eral), Parapsychology, Philosophy, Poetry, Psy-
  chology, Psychiatry, Science (General), Travel
ISBN Prefix(es): 84-297 (Peninsula Edicions); 84-
  89999 (Difusio Editorial S L)
Imprints: El Aleph Editores; Editorial Diago-
  nal; Edicola-62; Editorial Empuries; Ediciones
  Luciernaga; Ediciones Peninsula; RACC-62;
  Edicions 62
Foreign Rep(s): Grupo Editorial Norma (South
  America, US)

**Ediciones SM+**
Joaquin Turina 39, 28044 Madrid
*Tel:* (091) 4228800 *Fax:* (091) 5089927
*E-mail:* jcabrerap@ediciones-sm.com
*Telex:* 44710 Edsm E
*Key Personnel*
Dir General: Jorge Delkader Teig

Production Dir: Ignacio Fernandez
Publication Dir, Scholarly: Fernando Lopez-Aranguren
Publication Dir, General: Jose A Camacho
Rights: NcPaz Serrano
Communications & Public Relations: Juan A Cabrera
Founded: 1950
Specialize in publication of children's, juveniles, young adults & textbooks.
Subjects: Biography, Education, Humor, Literature, Literary Criticism, Essays, Philosophy, Religion - Other, Social Sciences, Sociology, Theology
ISBN Prefix(es): 84-348
Parent Company: Editions SM
Associate Companies: Cruilla, Calle Balmes 245 - 4, pta 3, 08006 Barcelona
Subsidiaries: Acento Editorial; Cesma; Ediciones SM; Editorial Crvilla; PPC
Orders to: CESMA SA, Aguacate 25, 28044 Madrid

**Sociedad General Espanola de Libreria SA - SGEL**
Avda Valdelaparra 29, 28108 Alcobendas, Madrid
Tel: (091) 657 69 00 Fax: (091) 657 69 28
Web Site: www.sgel.es
Key Personnel
Dir General: Enrique Valles
Founded: 1914
Subjects: English as a Second Language
ISBN Prefix(es): 84-7143
Parent Company: HDS

**Ramon Sopena SA+**
Corcega, 60 bajos, 08029 Barcelona
Tel: (093) 3220035 Fax: (093) 3223703
E-mail: edsopena@teleline.es
Key Personnel
Man Dir, Rights & Permissions: Ramon Sopena Rimblas
Production: Ramon Sopena, Jr
Founded: 1894
Subjects: Art, History, Language Arts, Linguistics, Science (General)
ISBN Prefix(es): 84-303
Total Titles: 200 Print

**SPES Editorial SL+**
C/Aribau 197-199, 3a, 08021 Barcelona
SAN: 000-5975
Tel: (093) 2413505 Fax: (093) 2413511
E-mail: vox@vox.es
Web Site: www.vox.es
Telex: 54155 Cvox E Cable: Biblograf
Key Personnel
Man Dir: Alberto Cliarlau
Founded: 1952
Subjects: Language Arts, Linguistics
ISBN Prefix(es): 84-7153; 84-8332
Parent Company: Grupo Anaya, Juan Ignacio Luca de Terra 15, 28027 Madrid
Associate Companies: Ediciones Anaya SA

**Axel Springer Publicaciones+**
Pedro Teixeira 8, 8 planta, 28020 Madrid
SAN: 000-4448
Tel: (091) 5140600 Fax: (091) 5140624
Telex: 46148 Srpe
Key Personnel
Man Dir: Alfredo Marron Gomez
Editorial: Marisa Perez Bodegas
Sales: Jose Aguilera Morena
Production: Andres Salcedo Pena
Publicity: Javier Jaen
Founded: 1952
Subjects: Art, Cookery, Crafts, Games, Hobbies, Gardening, Plants, History, Language Arts, Linguistics, Medicine, Nursing, Dentistry, Mili-

tary Science, Music, Dance, Science (General), Sports, Athletics, Transportation
ISBN Prefix(es): 84-7291; 84-7700

**Springer-Verlag Iberica, SA**
Provenca, 388, 1 planta, 08025 Barcelona
Tel: (093) 4570227; (093) 4570759 Fax: (093) 4571502
E-mail: springer.bcn@springer.es
Key Personnel
Man Dir: Stephanie Van Duin
Founded: 1990
ISBN Prefix(es): 84-07
Parent Company: Springer-Verlag GmbH & Co KG, Heidelberger Platz 3, 14197 Berlin, Germany

**Stanley Editorial+**
Mendelu 15, 28280 Hondarribia
Tel: (0943) 64 04 12 Fax: (0943) 64 38 63
Web Site: www.libross.com
Key Personnel
Manager: Edward R Rosset E-mail: erossetc.stanley@nexo.es
Contact: Richard S Rosset E-mail: rrossety.stanley@nexo.es
Founded: 1998
Specialize in languages.
Subjects: History, Language Arts, Linguistics
ISBN Prefix(es): 84-7873; 84-86859
Total Titles: 100 Print
Subsidiaries: Cosmos (Mexico)
Distributor for ELI; Express Publishing
Warehouse: Popigono Olivares, c/o Sierra de Albarracin 3, Arganda del Rey, Madrid 28500
Tel: (091) 195928 Fax: (091) 195551

**Editorial Rudolf Steiner+**
Guipuzcoa 11-1 izda, 28020 Madrid
SAN: 002-6603
Tel: (091) 5 531 481 Fax: (091) 5 531 481
E-mail: rudolfsteiner@teleline.es
Key Personnel
President: Isabel Novillo Gavin
Founded: 1977
Subjects: Agriculture, Education, Philosophy, Psychology, Psychiatry, Religion - Other
ISBN Prefix(es): 84-89197; 84-85370
Number of titles published annually: 12 Print

**Suaver, Javier Presa Suarez**
Gran Via, 8, 36203 Vigo, Pontevedra
SAN: 005-0288
Mailing Address: Apdo Postal n 427, 36280 Vigo
Tel: (086) 439507
Key Personnel
Dir: Javier Presa Suarez
Founded: 1990
Subjects: Poetry
ISBN Prefix(es): 84-88446; 84-604
Distributed by Puvill Libros SA

**Ediciones Susaeta SA**
Campezo 13, 28022 Madrid
SAN: 005-0431
Tel: (091) 3009100 Fax: (091) 3009110
E-mail: ediciones.susaeta@nexo.es
Telex: 22148 Ssta e
Key Personnel
Sales Dir: Jose Ignacio Susaeta Erburu
Subjects: Biblical Studies, Cookery, Crafts, Games, Hobbies, Fiction, Gardening, Plants, Travel
ISBN Prefix(es): 84-305

**T F Editores+**
Aragoneses 2, Acceso 11, Poligono Industrial de Alcobendas, 28108 Alcobendas, Madrid
Tel: (091) 484 1870; (091) 484 1878 Fax: (091) 661 3594
E-mail: editorial@tfeditores.com

Web Site: www.tfeditores.com
Key Personnel
Dir General: Alfredo Carrilero
Founded: 1994
Publisher & printer.
Subjects: Architecture & Interior Design, Art, Literature, Literary Criticism, Essays, Photography
ISBN Prefix(es): 84-89162; 84-95183
Number of titles published annually: 40 Print
Total Titles: 215 Print
Parent Company: Tf Artes Grafices

**Ediciones Tabapress, SA+**
Barquillo, 7, 28004 Madrid
SAN: 005-0644
Tel: (01) 5320876 Fax: (01) 5325890
E-mail: ediciones.tabapress@tsai.es
Key Personnel
Dir: Jesus Campos
Founded: 1988
Subjects: Art, History
ISBN Prefix(es): 84-7952; 84-86938; 84-500; 84-398

**Ediciones Tarraco**
San Francisco, 10, 43003 Tarragona
SAN: 002-0001
Tel: (077) 233813 Fax: (077) 233851
Key Personnel
Man Dir: Javier Elias
Founded: 1976
Subjects: Art, Education
ISBN Prefix(es): 84-7320
Parent Company: F Sugranes Editors SA, San Francisco, 10, 43003 Tarragona

**TEA Ediciones SA+**
Calle Fray Bernardino de Sahagun 24, 28036 Madrid
Tel: (091) 912 705 000 Fax: (091) 913 458 608
E-mail: madrid@teaediciones.com
Web Site: www.teaediciones.com
Telex: 22135 Cable: TEACEGOS
Key Personnel
Man Dir: Jaime Perena Brand
Sales: Milagros Anton
Production: Carlos Segura
Founded: 1957
Subjects: Psychology, Psychiatry
ISBN Prefix(es): 84-7174
Number of titles published annually: 15 Print
Total Titles: 300 Print
Parent Company: TEA-Cegos SA, Calle Fray Bernardino de Sahagun 24, 28036 Madrid
Branch Office(s)
Calle Paris, 211, 08008 Barcelona
Avda S Francisco Savier 21, 41005 Sevilla
Bidebarrieta 12, 48008 Bilbao
Bookshop(s): Paris 211, 08008 Barcelona

**Ediciones Tecnicas Rede, SA**
Ecuador, 91, 08029 Barcelona
Tel: (093) 4103097 Fax: (093) 4392813
Key Personnel
Founding Editor: Pascual Gomez Aparicio
Subjects: Electronics, Electrical Engineering
ISBN Prefix(es): 84-247

**Editores Tecnicos Asociados SA**
Loreto, 13-15, Local B, 08029 Barcelona
Tel: (093) 4193336
Key Personnel
Man Dir: Carlos Palomar
Founded: 1963
Subjects: Architecture & Interior Design, Computer Science, Engineering (General), How-to
ISBN Prefix(es): 84-7146

**Instituto Tecnologico de Galicia, ITG**
Pocomaco, Sector 1, Portal 5, 15190 A Coruna
Tel: (0981) 17 32 06 Fax: (0981) 17 32 23

E-mail: itg@itg.es
Web Site: www.itg.es
Key Personnel
Manager: Carlos Bald Orosa
Founded: 1991
ISBN Prefix(es): 84-89473

**Editorial Tecnos SA+**
Juan Ignacio Luca de Tena 15, 28027 Madrid
Tel: (091) 393 86 88; (091) 393 86 86 Fax: (091) 7426631
Web Site: www.tecnos.es
Telex: Maeg 41071
Key Personnel
Man Dir, Editorial: Alejandro Sierra Benayas
Production: Mariano Moreno
Publicity, Rights & Permissions: Pilar Lagarma
Founded: 1947
Subjects: Art, Business, Economics, Education, History, Law, Literature, Literary Criticism, Essays, Philosophy, Psychology, Psychiatry, Science (General), Social Sciences, Sociology, Technology
ISBN Prefix(es): 84-309
Parent Company: Grupo Anaya, Ferrer del Rio 35, 28028 Madrid
Associate Companies: Ediciones Anaya SA
Sales Office(s): Grupo Distribuidor Editorial SA, D Ramon de la Cruz 67, 28001 Madrid

**Editorial Teide SA**
Viladomat 291, 08029 Barcelona
Tel: (093) 4398009 Fax: (093) 3224192
E-mail: info@editorialteide.es
Web Site: www.editorialteide.es
Key Personnel
Man Dir, Publicity, Rights & Permissions, Editorial, Sales: Federico Rahola
Founded: 1942
Subjects: Education
ISBN Prefix(es): 84-307
Branch Office(s)
Calle Hierbabuena 50, 28039 Madrid Tel: (091) 5707920
Warehouse: Tambor del Bruch 8, 08970 San Juan Despi

**Editorial Augusto E Pila Telena SL+**
Pozo Nuevo 12 bajos, 28430 Alpedrete, Madrid
Tel: (091) 857 28 88; (607) 25 20 82 Fax: (091) 857 28 80
E-mail: pilatena@arrakis.es
Web Site: www.arrakis.es/~pilatena
Key Personnel
Man Dir: Augusto E Pila Telena
Editorial: Augusto Pila
Sales: Raquel Laviste
Founded: 1972
Specialize in physical education.
Subjects: Sports, Athletics
ISBN Prefix(es): 84-85514; 84-400; 84-922803; 84-922838; 84-923778; 84-95353

**Ediciones Temas de Hoy, SA+**
Member of Grupo Planeta
Paseo de Recoletos, 4 planta, 28001 Madrid
Tel: (091) 4230318 Fax: (091) 4230309
E-mail: info@temasdehoy.es
Web Site: www.temasdehoy.es
Key Personnel
Council Delegate: Ymelda Navajo Lazaro
Founded: 1987
Subjects: Biography, History, How-to, Humor, Literature, Literary Criticism, Essays, Self-Help
ISBN Prefix(es): 84-7880; 84-86675; 84-8460

**Editorial Sal Terrae+**
Poligolo de Raos, Parcela 14-1, 39600 Maliano (Cantabria)
Mailing Address: Section 77, 39080 Santander (Cantabria)

Tel: (0942) 369 198 Fax: (0942) 369 201
E-mail: salterrae@salterrae.es
Web Site: www.salterrae.es
Key Personnel
Man Dir: Jesus Garcia-Abril
Founded: 1919
Subjects: Anthropology, Biography, History, Literature, Literary Criticism, Essays, Philosophy, Psychology, Psychiatry, Religion - Other, Theology, Autobiography, memoirs, letters, bible, family & relationships, nursing, love & sexuality
ISBN Prefix(es): 84-293

**Tesitex, SL**
Melchor Cano 15, 37007 Salamanca
Tel: (0923) 255115 Fax: (0923) 258703
E-mail: tesitex@tesitex.es
Web Site: www.tesitex.es
Key Personnel
Dir General: Jose Antonio Romero
Founded: 1988
Specialize in Electronic Book & Congress.
Subjects: Nonfiction (General), Publishing & Book Trade Reference
ISBN Prefix(es): 84-89609; 84-920313

**Thales Sociedad Andaluza de Educacion Matematica**
Facultad de Matematicas, Apdo 1160, 41080 Sevilla
Tel: (095) 4623658 Fax: (095) 4236378
E-mail: thales@cica.es
Web Site: thales.cica.es
Key Personnel
President: D Salvador Guerrero Hidalgo
Vice President: Vicenta Serrano Gil
Founded: 1981
Subjects: Education, Mathematics
ISBN Prefix(es): 84-920056; 84-404; 84-604

**Editorial Thassalia, SA**
muntaner, 48-50-3, 08011 Barcelona
Tel: (093) 4511298 Fax: (093) 4511283
Key Personnel
Dir General: Joan Agut
Founded: 1994
Subjects: Fiction, History, Nonfiction (General), Religion - Buddhist, Religion - Hindu, Religion - Islamic, Spirituality
ISBN Prefix(es): 84-8237
Orders to: Distribuciones Prologo, Mascaro 35, 08032 Barcelona Tel: (093) 347 25 11 Fax: (093) 459 95 06

**Timun Mas**, imprint of Grupo Editorial CEAC SA

**Tirant lo Blanch SL Libreriaa+**
Artes Graficas 14, Bajo dcha, 46010 Valencia
SAN: 002-6964
Tel: (096) 3610048 Fax: (096) 3694151
E-mail: tlb@tirant.es
Web Site: www.tirant.es
Key Personnel
Manager: Candelaria Lopez-Quiles
Founded: 1976
Subjects: Criminology, Education, Labor, Industrial Relations, Law, Management, Social Sciences, Sociology
ISBN Prefix(es): 84-8002; 84-86558; 84-8442
Branch Office(s)
Campus Universitario Borrio, 12071 Castellon
Gravador Esteve, 5, 46021 Valencia Tel: (0034) 963749840 Fax: (0034) 963341835
Warehouse: Calle Mendez Nunez, 34, 46024 Valencia

**Titania**, imprint of Ediciones Urano, SA

**Ediciones de la Torre+**
Espronceda 20, 28003 Madrid
Tel: (091) 692 20 34 Fax: (091) 692 20 34
E-mail: info@edicionesdelatorre.com
Web Site: www.edicionesdelatorre.com
Key Personnel
Manager: Jose Maria Gutierrez
Editorial: Rosa Perez
Founded: 1976
Subjects: Advertising, Child Care & Development, Communications, Drama, Theater, Education, Geography, Geology, History, Human Relations, Journalism, Literature, Literary Criticism, Essays, Nonfiction (General), Philosophy, Physics, Poetry, Radio, TV, Science (General), Social Sciences, Sociology
ISBN Prefix(es): 84-7960; 84-85866; 84-85277; 84-86587
Warehouse: C/Sorgo, 45, 28029 Madrid
Orders to: C/Sorgo, 454, 28029 Madrid

**Torremozas SL Ediciones**
Apdo de Correos 19032, 28080 Madrid
Tel: (091) 359 03 15 Fax: (091) 345 85 32
E-mail: ediciones@torremozas.com
Web Site: www.torremozas.com
Founded: 1982
Specialize in Poetry.
Subjects: Literature, Literary Criticism, Essays, Poetry, Women's Studies
ISBN Prefix(es): 84-7839; 84-86072
Distributed by Maidhisa SL

**Trea Ediciones, SL+**
Maria Gonzalez La Pondala, 98, Nave D Polig Indl de Somonte, 33393 Gijon, Asturias
Tel: (098) 5303801 Fax: (098) 5303717; (098) 5303712
E-mail: trea@trea.es
Key Personnel
Manager: Miguel A Blanco Vazquez
Editor: Alvaro Diaz Huici
International Rights: Ferwanda Poblet
Founded: 1990
Subjects: Art, Biological Sciences, Cookery, Education, Fiction, Geography, Geology, History, Library & Information Sciences, Literature, Literary Criticism, Essays, Nonfiction (General), Photography, Poetry, Public Administration, Travel
ISBN Prefix(es): 84-87733; 84-89427; 84-9704; 84-95178

**Institut de Treball Social - Serveis Socials**
Avda Diagonal, 482, 20, tercera, 08006 Barcelona
Tel: (093) 217 26 64 Fax: (093) 237 36 34
E-mail: intressbar@intress.org
Web Site: www.intress.org
Key Personnel
President: Rosa Domenech Ferrer
Founded: 1984
ISBN Prefix(es): 84-87400

**Tres Torres Ediciones SA+**
Viladomat, 247-249 1º-4a, 08029 Barcelona
SAN: 001-5091
Tel: (093) 3637450 Fax: (093) 3637452
Telex: 98772 CLLCE
Key Personnel
Administration Manager: Rufino Torres Castineira
Editorial Dir: Albert Ferre Cardona
Founded: 1985
Subjects: Art, Chemistry, Chemical Engineering, Language Arts, Linguistics, Marketing, Mathematics
ISBN Prefix(es): 84-7747; 84-85257

**Trito Edicions, SL**
Av de la Catedral 3, 08002 Barcelona
Mailing Address: Apartat de Correus, 2254, 08080 Barcelona
Tel: (093) 342 61 75 Fax: (093) 302 26 70
E-mail: info@trito.es

*Web Site:* www.trito.es
Founded: 1993
Subjects: Music, Dance
ISBN Prefix(es): 84-88955

**Editorial Trivium, SA+**
Molina, 20, 28029 Madrid
SAN: 002-7006
*Tel:* (091) 3147495 *Fax:* (091) 3153236
*Key Personnel*
President: Carlos Tapia Navarro
Founded: 1982
Subjects: Economics, Law
ISBN Prefix(es): 84-7855; 84-86440
*Bookshop(s):* Libreria Trivium, SA
*Warehouse:* Pintores, 30 (Polig Urtinsa II), 28925 Alcorcon Madrid

**Trotta SA Editorial+**
Ferraz, 55, 28008 Madrid
*Tel:* (091) 5430361 *Fax:* (091) 5431488
*E-mail:* editorial@trotta.es
*Web Site:* www.trotta.es
*Key Personnel*
President: Alejandro Sierra Benayas
General Secretary: Christiane Schwamborn
Founded: 1990
Hardcover & Paperback.
Subjects: History, Law, Literature, Literary Criticism, Essays, Philosophy, Psychology, Psychiatry, Religion - Catholic, Religion - Islamic, Religion - Jewish, Religion - Other, Social Sciences, Sociology, Theology
ISBN Prefix(es): 84-87699; 81-8164
Number of titles published annually: 60 Print
Total Titles: 700 Print

**Ediciones Turner**, see Turner Publicaciones

**Turner Publicaciones+**
Rafael Calvo 42-2 esc izda, 28010 Madrid
SAN: 002-029X
*Tel:* (091) 308 33 36 *Fax:* (091) 319 39 30
*E-mail:* turner@turnerlibros.com
*Web Site:* www.turnerlibros.com
*Key Personnel*
President: Andrea Nasi
Publisher: Manuel Arroyo
Chief Executive Officer: Santiago F de Cayela
    *E-mail:* sfcayela@turnerlibros.com
Editorial Dir: Juan G de Oteyza
    *E-mail:* jgoteyza@turnerlibros.com
Founded: 1973
Specialize in production of catalogues & illustrated books; publishes general nonfiction.
Subjects: Architecture & Interior Design, Art, History, Literature, Literary Criticism, Essays, Nonfiction (General), Philosophy, Photography, Poetry, Regional Interests, Museum Catalogues
ISBN Prefix(es): 84-7506; 84-85137
Number of titles published annually: 120 Print
Total Titles: 400 Print; 5 Audio
Subsidiaries: Editorial Turner de Mexico SA

**Tursen, SA**
Mazarredo, 4-5 B, 28005 Madrid
*Tel:* (091) 3667148 *Fax:* (091) 3653148
*Key Personnel*
Contact: Alicia Parrilla
Founded: 1990
Membership(s): la Camara, federacion y gremio de Editores; also acts as book illustrator.
Subjects: Advertising, Architecture & Interior Design, Art, Child Care & Development, Cookery, Crafts, Games, Hobbies, Disability, Special Needs, Environmental Studies, Gardening, Plants, Outdoor Recreation, Photography, Self-Help, Sports, Athletics, Travel
ISBN Prefix(es): 84-87756
*Book Club(s):* Circulo des Lectores
*Warehouse:* Poligono Industrial Las Monjas C/Invierno S/N Naves 14-15, Torrejon, Madrid

**Tusquets Editores+**
Cesare Cantu 8, 08017 Barcelona
*Tel:* (093) 2530400 *Fax:* (093) 4176703; (093) 4188698 (Rights & Editing)
*E-mail:* general@tusquets-editores.es
*Web Site:* www.tusquets-editores.com
*Key Personnel*
Man Dir: Beatriz de Moura; Antonio Lopez Lamadrid
Sales: Rosa Maria Segala
Publicity: Natalia Gil
Production: Orencio Sales
Foreign Rights & Permissions: Patricia Sanchez
    *E-mail:* rightspat@tusquets-editores.es
Foreign Rights Acquisitions: Carmen Corral
Founded: 1969
Subjects: Biography, Fiction, History, Literature, Literary Criticism, Essays, Science (General)
ISBN Prefix(es): 84-7223
*Branch Office(s)*
Tusquets Editores SA, Venezuela 1664, 1096 Buenos Aires, Argentina *Tel:* (011) 43814520 *Fax:* (011) 43811760 *E-mail:* tusquets@interar.com.ar
Tusquets Editores Mexico, SA de CV, Edgar Allan Poe 91, Col Polanco 11560, Mexico *Tel:* (055) 281 50 40; (055) 281 53 44 *Fax:* (055) 281 55 92 *E-mail:* tusquets@mail.nextgeninter.net.mx
*Warehouse:* Carretera del Prat 39, Poligono Industrial Almeda nave n 5, 08940 Cornella, Barcelona

**Ediciones Tutor SA+**
Marques de Urquijo, 34-2 izq, 28008 Madrid
SAN: 002-0303
*Tel:* (091) 5599832 *Fax:* (091) 5410235
*E-mail:* tutor@autovia.com
*Key Personnel*
President: Jesus Domingo Garcia
Editorial Dir & Rights & Permissions: David Domingo Yanes
Marketing, Public Relations: Vivas Francisco Rubira
Founded: 1989
Subjects: Animals, Pets, Career Development, Cookery, Crafts, Games, Hobbies, Gardening, Plants, Health, Nutrition, Humor, Outdoor Recreation, Sports, Athletics
ISBN Prefix(es): 84-7902
*Associate Companies:* Editorial El Drac SL
*Warehouse:* ADT, c/o Pelaya ue4, Poligono Industrial Rio de Janeiro, 28110 algete, Madrid *Tel:* (091) 6280606
*Orders to:* I Taca SA Distribuciones Editoriales, Lopez de Hoyos, 141, 28002 Madrid *Tel:* (091) 3224400 *Fax:* (091) 3224370

**Ediciones 29 - Libros Rio Nuevo+**
Francesc Vila, Nave 14, Poligono Industrial Can Magi, 08190 Sant Cugat del Valles, Barcelona
*Tel:* (093) 675 41 35 *Fax:* (093) 590 04 40
*E-mail:* ediciones29@comunired.com
*Web Site:* www.ediciones29.com
*Key Personnel*
Man Dir: Alfredo Llorente Diez
Founded: 1968
Subjects: Astrology, Occult, Cookery, Erotica, Literature, Literary Criticism, Essays, Poetry, Religion - Catholic, Self-Help
ISBN Prefix(es): 84-7175
Total Titles: 200 Print

**Editorial Txertoa+**
Plz de Olaeta (Ferrerias) s/n-bajo, 20011 San Sebastian
SAN: 002-7022
*Tel:* (0943) 45 97 57 *Fax:* (0943) 46 09 41
*E-mail:* txertoa@nexo.es
*Key Personnel*
Man Dir: Luis Aberasturi
Founded: 1968

Subjects: Anthropology, Art, Biography, Ethnicity, Geography, Geology, Language Arts, Linguistics, Literature, Literary Criticism, Essays, Regional Interests, Religion - Other, Science (General), Social Sciences, Sociology
ISBN Prefix(es): 84-7148
Number of titles published annually: 12 Print
Total Titles: 250 Print

**Ultramar Editores SA**
San Andres, 505, 08030 Barcelona
*Tel:* (093) 3460612 *Fax:* (093) 8412334
*E-mail:* ultramar@javajan.com
*Telex:* 53132 Saedi E
*Key Personnel*
Man Dir: Emilio Teixidor
Founded: 1973
Subjects: Biography, Fiction, Film, Video, Literature, Literary Criticism, Essays, Science Fiction, Fantasy
ISBN Prefix(es): 84-7386

**Umbriel**, *imprint of* Ediciones Urano, SA

**Universidad de Granada**
Antiguo Colegio Maximo, Campus Universitario de Cartuja, Universidad de Granada, 18015 Granada
*Tel:* (0958) 243025 *Fax:* (0958) 243066
*Web Site:* www.ugr.es
*Key Personnel*
Dir: Rafael G Peinado Santaella
Deputy Dir: Antonio Martin
Subjects: Anthropology, Archaeology, Art, Biological Sciences, Education, Geography, Geology, History, Law, Literature, Literary Criticism, Essays, Medicine, Nursing, Dentistry, Music, Dance, Philosophy, Science (General), Social Sciences, Sociology
ISBN Prefix(es): 84-338; 84-600

**Universidad de Las Palmas de Gran Canaria, Escuela Universitaria de Informatica (ULPGC)**
Campus Universitario de Tafira, 35017 Las Palmas de Gran Canaria
*Tel:* (0928) 45-87-81; (0928) 45-87-00
    *Fax:* (0928) 45-87-11
*E-mail:* organizacion@sinf.ulpgc.es
*Key Personnel*
Dir: Eugenia Rua-Figueroa
ISBN Prefix(es): 84-8098

**Universidad de Malaga+**
Campus de Teatinos, Blvd Louis Pasteur 30, 29071 Malaga
SAN: 005-2310
*Tel:* (095) 213 29 17 *Fax:* (095) 213 29 18
*E-mail:* buzon@uma.es
*Web Site:* www.uma.es
*Key Personnel*
Dir: Adelaida de la Calle
Founded: 1978
Subjects: Agriculture, Art, Earth Sciences, Economics, Education, History, Law, Medicine, Nursing, Dentistry, Philosophy, Social Sciences, Sociology
ISBN Prefix(es): 84-7496; 84-9750
Distributed by Distribuciones de Enlace SA

**Ediciones Universidad de Navarra SA**, see EUNSA (Ediciones Universidad de Navarra SA)

**Universidad de Navarra, Ediciones SA+**
Plaza de los Sauces 1-2, 31010 Baranain, Navarra
*Tel:* (0948) 256850 *Fax:* (0948) 256854
*E-mail:* eunsa@ibernet.com
*Web Site:* www.eunsa.es

*Key Personnel*
President: Manuel de Muga
Sales: Juan de Muga
Founded: 1967
Subjects: Art
ISBN Prefix(es): 84-313

**Universidad de Oviedo Servicio de Publicaciones**
Arguelles 19, 33003 Oviedo
*Tel:* (0985) 210160; (0985) 222428 *Fax:* (0985) 218352
*Web Site:* www.uniovi.es
*Key Personnel*
Dir: Ubaldo Gomez
Subjects: Behavioral Sciences, Language Arts, Linguistics, Physical Sciences, Science (General), Social Sciences, Sociology
ISBN Prefix(es): 84-7468; 84-9750; 84-8317

**Ediciones Universidad de Salamanca+**
Plaza de San Benito, 23, Salamanca 37008
*Tel:* (0923) 294598 *Fax:* (0923) 262579
*E-mail:* eus@usal.es
*Web Site:* www3.usal.es
*Key Personnel*
Man Dir: Jose Manuel Bustos Gisbert
 *E-mail:* jbustos@gugu.usal.es
Founded: 1486
Subjects: Education, History, Literature, Literary Criticism, Essays, Philosophy, Science (General)
ISBN Prefix(es): 84-7880; 84-7481; 84-500; 84-400; 84-600; 84-7800
Number of titles published annually: 100 Print
*Bookshop(s):* Salamanca

**Universidad de Sevilla Secretariado de Publicaciones**
Porvenir 27, 41013 Sevilla
*Tel:* (095) 487444; (095) 487442 *Fax:* (095) 487 7443
*E-mail:* secpub@pop.us.es
*Web Site:* publius.cica.es
*Key Personnel*
Dir: Enrique Valdivieso Gonzalez
ISBN Prefix(es): 84-472; 84-7405; 84-500; 84-600
Distributed by Distribuciones de Enlace SA; L'Alebrije; L'Estaquirot

**Universidad de Valladolid Secretariado de Publicaciones e Intercambio Editorial+**
c/Juan Mambrilla, 14, 47003 Valladolid
*Tel:* (0983) 187810 *Fax:* (0983) 187812
*E-mail:* spic@uva.es
*Web Site:* www.uva.es
*Key Personnel*
Dir: Palacio Zuniga
Founded: 1949
Subjects: Accounting, Archaeology, Architecture & Interior Design, Art, Business, Chemistry, Chemical Engineering, Computer Science, Economics, Education, Electronics, Electrical Engineering, Engineering (General), Geography, Geology, Government, Political Science, History, Law, Literature, Literary Criticism, Essays, Medicine, Nursing, Dentistry, Philosophy, Physics, Psychology, Psychiatry, Science (General), Social Sciences, Sociology
ISBN Prefix(es): 84-7762; 84-8448; 84-500; 84-600; 84-86192

**Publicacions de la Universitat de Barcelona+**
Gran Via de les Corts Catalanes 585, 08007 Barcelona
*Tel:* (093) 402 11 00 *Fax:* (093) 403 54 46
*E-mail:* srodon@pu.ges.ub.es
*Web Site:* www.ub.es
*Key Personnel*
Dir: Joan Duran i Fontanals

Editorial: Carmen Garcia Gonzalez
Founded: 1935
Membership(s): de Gremi d'Editors de Catalunya & de Asociacion Editoriales Universitarias Espanoles.
Subjects: Art, Economics, Education, History, Law, Mathematics, Science (General), Social Sciences, Sociology
ISBN Prefix(es): 84-475
*Bookshop(s):* Balmes-21, 08071 Barcelona
*Warehouse:* Baldiri I Reixac, s/n 08028 Barcelona

**Universitat de Valencia Servei de Publicacions**
Avda Blasco Ibanez, 46010 Valencia
*Tel:* (0963) 86 41 00
*E-mail:* publicacions@uv.es
*Web Site:* www.uv.es
*Key Personnel*
Editor: Maite Simon Mendez
Technical Editorial: Immaculada Mesa Ballester
Subjects: Biological Sciences, Economics, Education, History, Literature, Literary Criticism, Essays, Medicine, Nursing, Dentistry, Philosophy
ISBN Prefix(es): 84-370; 84-604; 84-500; 84-398; 84-600

**Edicions de la Universitat Politecnica de Catalunya SL**
Jordi Girona, 31, 08034 Barcelona
*Tel:* (093) 4016 883 *Fax:* (093) 4015 885
*E-mail:* edicions-upc@upc.es
*Web Site:* www.edicionsupc.es
*Key Personnel*
Publisher: Josep Maria Serra-Munoz
 *E-mail:* josep.maria.serra@upc.es
Founded: 1994
Subjects: Architecture & Interior Design, Chemistry, Chemical Engineering, Civil Engineering, Computer Science, Electronics, Electrical Engineering, Engineering (General), Science (General)
ISBN Prefix(es): 84-7653

**Urano,** *imprint of* Ediciones Urano, SA

**Ediciones Urano, SA+**
Aribau 142, pral, 08036 Barcelona
*Tel:* (902) 131 315; (093) 2375 564 *Fax:* (093) 4153 796
*E-mail:* info@edicionesurano.com; atencion@edicionesurano.com
*Web Site:* www.edicionesurano.com
*Key Personnel*
Manager: Joaquin Sabate
Literary Dir & International Rights: Gregorio Vlastelica *E-mail:* edit@edicionesurano.com
Fiction Editor: Aranzazu Sumalla
Founded: 1983
Subjects: Alternative, Astrology, Occult, Business, Fiction, Health, Nutrition, How-to, Management, Mysteries, Psychology, Psychiatry, Romance, Self-Help
ISBN Prefix(es): 84-7953; 84-86344; 84-95618; 84-95752
Number of titles published annually: 74 Print
Total Titles: 561 Print
Imprints: EmpresaActiva; Titania; Umbriel; Urano
*Branch Office(s)*
Castillo 540, 1414 Buenos Aires, Argentina
 *Tel:* (011) 477 143 82 *Fax:* (011) 477 143 82
 *E-mail:* argentina@edicionesurano.com
Av Francisco Bilbao, 2809 Providencia, Santiago, Chile *Tel:* (02) 341 67 31 *Fax:* (02) 225 38 96
 *E-mail:* chile@edicionesurano.com
Transversal 43, No 97-75, Santafe de Bogota DC, Colombia *Tel:* (01) 253 24 88 *Fax:* (01) 226 24 73 *E-mail:* colombia@edicionesurano.com
Vito Alessio Robles, No 140, Col Florida, 01030 Alvaro Obregon, Mexico *Tel:* (05) 661 0774 *Fax:* (05) 661 7590 *E-mail:* mexico@edicionesurano.com

Avda Luis Roche-Edif Santa Clara, PB Altamira Sur, 1062 Caracas, Venezuela *Tel:* (02) 264 03 73 *Fax:* (02) 261 69 62 *E-mail:* venezuela@edicionesurano.com

**Urmo SA de Ediciones+**
Nervion 3-6, 48001 Bilbao
*Tel:* (094) 424 53 07 *Fax:* (094) 423 19 84
*E-mail:* urmo@infonegocio.com
*Web Site:* www.urmo.com
*Key Personnel*
Chairman: Federico Guillermo Grijelmo Ribechnin
Contact: Begona Grijelmo Mattern
Founded: 1963
Subjects: Engineering (General), Microcomputers, Science (General)
ISBN Prefix(es): 84-314
Total Titles: 210 Print

**Editorial De Vecchi SA**
Balmes, 114, 1º, 08008 Barcelona
*Tel:* (093) 272 46 70 *Fax:* (093) 487 74 94
Founded: 1967
Subjects: Agriculture, Animals, Pets, Cookery, Crafts, Games, Hobbies, Sports, Athletics
ISBN Prefix(es): 84-315

**Editorial Verbo Divino+**
Ave de Pamplona 41, 31200 Estella Navarra
*Tel:* (0948) 55 65 05; (0948) 55 65 11
 *Fax:* (0948) 55 45 06
*E-mail:* ventas@verbodivino.es; evd@verbodivino.es
*Web Site:* www.verbodivino.es *Cable:* VERBODIVINO
*Key Personnel*
Man Dir: Father Tomas Langarica
Sales Dir: Martin Esparza
Advertising, Rights & Permissions: Maria Puy Larramendi
Founded: 1957
Subjects: Biblical Studies, Religion - Catholic, Social Sciences, Sociology, Theology
ISBN Prefix(es): 84-7151; 84-8169
Distributed by Alpa Libros (Spain); Bidea 2000 (Spain); Centro Biblico Verbo Divino (Ecuador); Centro Paulino (Venezuela); Claret Libreria (Spain); Comercial Gravi - Libros (Spain); Departamento Pastoral Biblica (Mexico); Distribucion Buho Azul (Spain); Distribucion Icaro (Spain); Distribucion Vilas Duran (Spain); Distribuciones Edit Lyra (Spain); Distriforma SA (Spain); Editorial Guadalupe (Argentina); Editorial Verbo Divino (Bolivia); Emaus Libros SL (Spain); Empresa Periodistica Mundo (Chile); Fundacion Editores Verbo Divino (Colombia); Libreria Catolica Gethesemani (United States); Libreria Centro Biblico Verbo Divino (Paraguay); Libreria Hispamer SA (Nicaragua); Libreria San Pablo (Venezuela); Libreria Verbum (Mexico); Libros D&D Unidisa (Spain); Manantial Cultura - Lib Loyola (Guatemala); Paulinas Distribuidora (United States); PPC Edit y Distribuidora SA (Spain); PPC Editorial y Distribuidora (Spain); Spanish Speaking Bookstore Distrib (United States)

**Editorial Verbum SL+**
Equilaz 6, 2º Derecha, 28010 Madrid
*Tel:* (091) 446 88 41 *Fax:* (091) 594 45 59
*E-mail:* verbum@globalnet.es
*Key Personnel*
Dir: Pio E Serrano
Administrator: Aurora Calvino
Founded: 1991
Specialize in Spanish for foreigners.
Subjects: Drama, Theater, Fiction, Language Arts, Linguistics, Literature, Literary Criticism, Essays, Music, Dance, Philosophy, Poetry
ISBN Prefix(es): 84-7962; 84-7926
Total Titles: 136 Print; 1 Audio

Foreign Rep(s): Sara Grecco Editoriales (Puerto Rico); Interlogos (Italy)
*Warehouse:* Calle del Pez 21, 28004 Madrid

**Javier Vergara Editor SA**
Fernando III 1-1E, 28670 Villaviciosa de Odon
SAN: 003-7613
*Tel:* 6163600 *Fax:* 6163708
*Key Personnel*
General Manager: Rodolfo Blanco
Publicity Manager: Maria Eugenia Delso
Founded: 1987
Subjects: Biography, Business, Fiction, History, Music, Dance, Nonfiction (General), Psychology, Psychiatry, Self-Help
ISBN Prefix(es): 84-7417
*Parent Company:* Javier Vergara Editor Argentina

**Veron Editor+**
Calle de la Torre, 17 local 1, 08006 Barcelona
*Tel:* (093) 4161643 *Fax:* (093) 4161433
*E-mail:* veron@veroneditor.com
*Key Personnel*
Man Dir, Sales, Rights & Permissions: Lluis Veron Jane
Founded: 1965
Subjects: Literature, Literary Criticism, Essays, Nonfiction (General)
ISBN Prefix(es): 84-7255

**Ediciones Versal SA**
Rosello, 41-45, 08029 Barcelona
*Tel:* (093) 494 85 90 *Fax:* (093) 419 02 97
*E-mail:* cga.barcelona@cga.es
*Web Site:* www.anaya.es
*Telex:* 54155 CVOX E
*Key Personnel*
Dir General & Editorial: Antoni Munne
Production: Blanca Marques
Founded: 1984
Subjects: Biography, Literature, Literary Criticism, Essays, Nonfiction (General)
ISBN Prefix(es): 84-86311; 84-86717; 84-7876
*Parent Company:* Grupo Anaya, Juan Ignacio Luca de Tena, 15, 28027 Madrid
*Associate Companies:* Ediciones Anaya SA
*Orders to:* Grupo Distribuidor Editorial SA, Ferrer del Rio, 35, 28028 Madrid

**Gobierno de Canarias - Viceconsejeria de Cultura y Deportes**
Comodoro Rolin, 1 casa de cultura, planta 5, 38007 Santa Cruz de Tenerife
SAN: 005-3171
*Tel:* (0922) 202202 *Fax:* (092) 2474165
*Key Personnel*
Director General: Horacio Umpierrez Sanchez
ISBN Prefix(es): 84-7947; 84-87137; 84-505; 84-87317
Distributed by Bitacora Servicios Editoriales (Spain); Dist Edit Breogan SL (Spain); Distribuciones Lemus (Spain); Rafael Roca Suarez E Hijos (Spain); Servei Del Llibre (Spain)

**Vicens Basica,** *imprint of* Editorial Vicens-Vives

**Vicens Universidad,** *imprint of* Editorial Vicens-Vives

**Editorial Vicens-Vives+**
Av de Sarria 130-132, 08017 Barcelona
*Tel:* (093) 2523700; (093) 2523703 *Fax:* (093) 2523710
*E-mail:* e@vicensvives.es
*Web Site:* www.vicensvives.es
*Telex:* 51425 Live E
*Key Personnel*
President: Roser Rahola; Pere Vicens
Dir: Albert Vicens; Anna Vicens
Founded: 1942

Subjects: Education, Ethnicity, Fiction, History, Mathematics, Science (General)
ISBN Prefix(es): 84-316
Imprints: Instituto Cartografico Latino; Vicens Basica; Vicens Universidad

**Ediciones A Madrid Vicente+**
Almansa, 94, 28040 Madrid
SAN: 000-2437
*Tel:* (091) 5336926; (091) 5349368 *Fax:* (091) 5330286
*E-mail:* amadrid@acta.es
*Web Site:* www.amvediciones.com
*Key Personnel*
Dir: Antonio Madrid Vicente
Founded: 1986
Subjects: Agriculture, Electronics, Electrical Engineering, Technology, Specialize in books about food technology, refrigeration, air conditioning, electricity, construction, coatings & pharmacy
ISBN Prefix(es): 84-89922; 84-87440; 84-398
Total Titles: 100 Print
Foreign Rep(s): Mundi Prensa Calle Castello 37 (Latin America, Portugal, Spain, US)

**Vinaches Lopez, Luisa+**
Cervantes 34, 03570 Villajoyasa
*Tel:* (01) 3694488 *Fax:* (01) 3694488
*Key Personnel*
Dir: Lidia Falcon
International Rights: Elvira Siurana
Founded: 1976 (Vindicacion, 1997 Kira Edit)
Membership(s): Spanish Feminist party.
Subjects: Anthropology, Biography, Drama, Theater, Fiction, Literature, Literary Criticism, Essays, Nonfiction (General), Poetry, Women's Studies, Feminism
ISBN Prefix(es): 84-922067; 84-404; 84-604; 84-605
*Parent Company:* Vindicacion Feminista Publicaciones
Imprints: Cofas SA
Divisions: Aconcagua Publishing
Distributed by Aconcagia Publishing; Editorial Hacer; Kira Edit

**Visor Distribuciones, SA+**
Tomas Breton, 55, 28045 Madrid
*Tel:* (091) 4681248; (091) 4681011; (091) 4681102 *Fax:* (091) 4681098
*E-mail:* editorial@visordis.es
*Web Site:* www.visordis.es
*Key Personnel*
Dir: Jose Miguel Garcia Sanchez
Founded: 1987
Subjects: Art, Education, Literature, Literary Criticism, Essays, Philosophy, Psychology, Psychiatry
ISBN Prefix(es): 84-7774

**Visor Libros+**
Isacc Peral, 18, 28015 Madrid
*Tel:* (091) 5492655 *Fax:* (091) 544 86 95
*E-mail:* visor-libros@visor-libros.com
*Web Site:* www.visor-libros.com
*Key Personnel*
Contact: Jesus Garcia Sanchez
Founded: 1970
Subjects: Language Arts, Linguistics, Literature, Literary Criticism, Essays, Poetry
ISBN Prefix(es): 84-7522; 84-398

**VOSA, SL Ediciones**
Hermosilla, 132-bajo, 28028 Madrid
*Tel:* (091) 7259430 *Fax:* (091) 7259430
*E-mail:* mauosa@terra.es
Founded: 1983
Subjects: Government, Political Science, History
ISBN Prefix(es): 84-8218; 84-86293
Number of titles published annually: 6 Print
Total Titles: 150 Print

**Ediciones Vulcano+**
Matilde Hernandez, 71, 28025 Madrid
SAN: 003-3812
*Tel:* (091) 500 16 49 *Fax:* (091) 461 44 58
*E-mail:* vulcano@vulcanoediciones.com
*Web Site:* www.vulcanoediciones.com
*Key Personnel*
Editor: Isidoro Correa
Founded: 1980
Subjects: Literature, Literary Criticism, Essays, Poetry, Technology, Travel
ISBN Prefix(es): 84-7828

**Wolters Kluwer Espana SA**
Collado Mediano 9, 28230 Lass Rozas Madrid
*Tel:* (091) 6020023 *Fax:* (091) 6020021
*E-mail:* pilarg@wke.es
*Telex:* 99020 EPWS
*Key Personnel*
Resident Dir: P C Minderhout
ISBN Prefix(es): 84-87670
*Parent Company:* Wolters Kluwer NV, Netherlands

**Ediciones Xandro+**
Apdo 40 020, Avda del Mediterraneo, 18, 28007 Madrid
SAN: 002-0591
*Tel:* (091) 5520261 *Fax:* (091) 5014145
*Key Personnel*
Contact: Belda German
Founded: 1987
Subjects: Psychology, Psychiatry
ISBN Prefix(es): 84-88665; 84-404; 84-604; 84-398; 84-400; 84-300

**Edicions Xerais de Galicia**
Doctor Maranon, 12, 36211 Vigo
SAN: 001-4591
*Tel:* (0986) 214888 *Fax:* (0986) 201366
*E-mail:* xerais@xerais.es
*Web Site:* www.xerais.es
*Key Personnel*
Contact: Manuel Bragado Rodriguez
Founded: 1976
Subjects: Education, Fiction, History, Language Arts, Linguistics, Poetry, Social Sciences, Sociology
ISBN Prefix(es): 84-7507; 84-8302

**Xunta de Galicia**
Conselleria de Cultura Comunicacion Social e Turismo, San Caetano s-n, 15771 Santiago de Compostela
*Tel:* (081) 544816 *Fax:* (081) 544887
*Key Personnel*
Subdirector Xeral of Culture: Xabier Senin Fernandez
Conselleria de Cultura e Xuventude, Ed San Caetano, s/n.
Subjects: Agriculture, Animals, Pets, Art, Biological Sciences, Business, Economics, Education, Fiction, Finance, Geography, Geology, Health, Nutrition, History, Law, Literature, Literary Criticism, Essays, Management, Maritime, Marketing, Military Science, Public Administration, Science (General), Sports, Athletics, Design, graphic arts
ISBN Prefix(es): 84-453

**Editorial Zendrera Zariquiey, SA+**
Cardenal Vivesi Tuto 59 bajos, 08034 Barcelona
*Tel:* (093) 280 12 34 *Fax:* (093) 280 61 90
*E-mail:* info@editorialzendrera.com
*Web Site:* www.editorialzendrera.com
*Key Personnel*
Man Dir: Zendrera Zariquiey
International Rights: Ms Fabregat
Founded: 1997
Subjects: Computer Science, Cookery, Travel
ISBN Prefix(es): 84-8418; 84-89675

Total Titles: 120 Print
*Associate Companies:* Editorial Sirpus, SL

# Sri Lanka

## General Information

*Capital:* Colombo
*Language:* Sinhala & Tamila (official & national) & English (national)
*Religion:* Predominantly Buddhism
*Population:* 17.6 million
*Bank Hours:* 0900-1300 Monday-Friday
*Shop Hours:* 0800-1730 Monday-Friday
*Currency:* 100 cents = 1 Sri Lanka rupee
*Export/Import Information:* No tariff on books or advertising. Import license required for most book importation. Exchange controls.
*Copyright:* UCC, Berne, Florence (see Copyright Conventions, pg xi)

**Buddhist Publication Society Inc**
54 Sangharaja Mawatha, Kandy
Mailing Address: PO Box 61, Kandy
*Tel:* (08) 223679; (08) 237283 *Fax:* (08) 223679
*E-mail:* bps@metta.lk
*Web Site:* www.metta.lk
*Key Personnel*
President, Editor: Bhikkhu Bodhi
  *E-mail:* venbodhi@metta.lk
Administrative Secretary: L B W Seneviratne
Founded: 1958
Subjects: Religion - Buddhist
ISBN Prefix(es): 955-24
Foreign Rep(s): Vipassana Research Publications of America (US)
Foreign Rights: Dhamma Books (India); Wisdom Books (UK)

**Business Directory of Lanka Ltd+**
Ward Place, No 49, Colombo 07
*Tel:* (011) 2695095; (011) 4721560; (011) 4721561; (011) 4712659 *Fax:* (011) 4721560
*E-mail:* info@lanka.com
*Web Site:* www.lanka.com
*Key Personnel*
Man Dir: Mangala Wickramarachchi
  *E-mail:* kompass@itmin.com
Founded: 1994
Membership(s): Ceylon Chamber of Commerce.
ISBN Prefix(es): 955-9405
Subsidiaries: Kompass Lanka (Pvt) Ltd; Raffles Lanka (Pvt) Ltd

**Calvary Press+**
123 Highlevel Rd, Kirillapone, Colombo 6
*Tel:* (01) 553110
Subjects: Religion - Protestant
ISBN Prefix(es): 955-587

**Department of Census & Statistics**
PO Box 563, Colombo 7
*Tel:* (01) 324348
*E-mail:* colombo@statistics.gov.lk
*Web Site:* www.statistics.gov.lk
*Key Personnel*
Dir General: Mr A G W Nanayakkara
ISBN Prefix(es): 955-577

**The Ceylon Chamber of Commerce**
50 Navam Mawatha, Colombo 02
*Tel:* (01) 2452183; (01) 2421745; (01) 2329143
  *Fax:* (01) 2437477; (01) 2449352
*E-mail:* info@chamber.lk
*Web Site:* www.chamber.lk
*Key Personnel*
Chairman: Mr Tilak De Zoysa
Vice Chairman: Mr P D Rodrigo

Founded: 1839
ISBN Prefix(es): 955-604

**Colombo Book Association+**
PO Box 1946, Colombo
*Tel:* (01) 686878; (01) 072270652 *Fax:* (01) 696578
*Key Personnel*
President: Dhammadesha Ambalampitiya
Founded: 1983
Successful UNESCO project devoted to developing literacy.
Subjects: Education, English as a Second Language
ISBN Prefix(es): 955-588
Imprints: Denuma

**Danuma**, *imprint of* Danuma Prakashakayo

**Danuma Prakashakayo+**
84 Serpentine Rd, Borella, Colombo 8
*Tel:* (01) 686878 *Fax:* (01) 696578
Founded: 1983
Subjects: Literature, Literary Criticism, Essays, Poetry, Science Fiction, Fantasy
ISBN Prefix(es): 955-556
Imprints: Danuma
Subsidiaries: Colombo Children's Book Society
*Orders to:* 84 Leslie, Ranagala Mawatha, Colombo 8

**Denuma**, *imprint of* Colombo Book Association

**Edirisooriya & Company**
68, Elie House Rd, Colombo 15
*Tel:* (01) 522555; (01) 523216 *Fax:* (01) 446380; (01) 074618905
*Telex:* 21701 GLOBAL CE *Cable:* UNIMER
*Key Personnel*
Printing Manager: Lindwal Peiris *Tel:* (01) 074618905
Founded: 1985
Printing & binding of local circulation school books, web offset machines, etc.
Subjects: *Specialize in stickers, labels, diaries & calendars*
ISBN Prefix(es): 955-9228
*Parent Company:* S P Samy & Co (Pvt) Ltd
Subsidiaries: United Merchants Ltd
*Branch Office(s)*
Edirisooriya & Co, 30 Prince St, Colombo 11, Contact: Mr Ganesh *Tel:* (01) 441560; (01) 446380 *Fax:* (01) 446380

**Gihan Book Shop**
144C Hill St, Dehiwala
*Key Personnel*
Author: W O T Fernando
Founded: 1980
Subjects: Mathematics
ISBN Prefix(es): 955-593
Imprints: Sanjana Offset

**M D Gunasena & Co Ltd**
217 Olcott Mawatha, Colombo 11
Mailing Address: PO Box 246, Colombo 11
*Tel:* (01) 323981; (01) 323982; (01) 323983; (01) 323984 *Fax:* (01) 323336
*E-mail:* mdgunasena@mail.ewisl.net
*Web Site:* mdgunasena.com
Founded: 1913
Associated imprints include Ananda Books Ltd, Sirisara Vidyalaya.
ISBN Prefix(es): 955-21

**Inter-Cultural Book Promoters+**
21 G4 Peramuna Mawatha, Eldeniya, Kadawatha
*Tel:* 525359 *Fax:* 525359
*E-mail:* inculture@eureka.lk
Founded: 1985

Subjects: Language Arts, Linguistics, Philosophy, Religion - Buddhist, Religion - Catholic, Religion - Hindu, Religion - Islamic, Religion - Jewish, Religion - Protestant, Religion - Other
ISBN Prefix(es): 955-9036
*Parent Company:* Inter-cultural Research Center

**International Centre for Ethnic Studies+**
554/1 Peradeniya Rd, Kandy
*Tel:* (08) 234892 *Fax:* (08) 234892
*E-mail:* ices@slt.lk
*Web Site:* www.icescolombo.org
*Key Personnel*
Executive Dir: Dr Radhika Coomaraswamy
Librarian: Mr Ponudurai Thambirajah
Founded: 1982
A social science & policy research institute.
Subjects: Ethnicity, Women's Studies
ISBN Prefix(es): 955-580
Total Titles: 20 Print
*Branch Office(s)*
Kynsey Terrace, Colombo 8
Distributed by St Martin's Press
Distributor for Frances Pinter (UK)

**J K Publications**
J K 50, Katuwawala, Borelasgamuwa
*Tel:* (01) 518954
*Key Personnel*
Author: Jayasena Kottegoda
Subjects: Music, Dance
ISBN Prefix(es): 955-9438
Total Titles: 7 Print
Distributed by Godage; Gunasena; Lake House

**Dayawansa Jayakody & Co+**
101 Ven S Mahinda, Thero Mawatha, Colombo 10
*Tel:* (011) 2695773 *Fax:* (011) 2696653
*E-mail:* dayawansa@slt.lk
*Key Personnel*
Chairman: Dayawansa Jayakody
Man Dir: Veronica Damayanthi Jayakody
Founded: 1960
Membership(s): IPA; APPA; Sri Lanka Association of Publishers.
Subjects: Drama, Theater, Fiction, Literature, Literary Criticism, Essays, Poetry
ISBN Prefix(es): 955-551
Number of titles published annually: 84 Print
Total Titles: 4,200 Print
*Associate Companies:* Helabima Publishers
*U.S. Office(s):* Dayawansa Jayakody & Company (USA), 131 Banwell Lane, Mount Laurel, NJ 08054, United States *Tel:* 856-234-8001; 502-212-9154 *Fax:* 856-234-8001; 502-212-9154
  *E-mail:* dayawanska@eureka.lk (US Sales)
Distributor for Helabima Publishers
Foreign Rep(s): Uditha Daminda Jayakody (US)
*Warehouse:* 163/4, Siri Dhamma Mawatha, Colombo 10

**Karunaratne & Sons Ltd+**
647, Kuluratne Mawatha, Colombo 10
*Tel:* (071) 229 9860 *Fax:* (071) 229 9860
*E-mail:* info@calcey.com
*Web Site:* www.calcey.com
*Key Personnel*
Chief Executive Officer: Mangala Karunaratne
Founded: 1971
Membership(s): Sri Lanka Association of Publishers.
Subjects: Archaeology, Economics, Education, Ethnicity, History, Philosophy, Religion - Buddhist, Social Sciences, Sociology, Women's Studies
ISBN Prefix(es): 955-9098

**KVG de Silva & Sons+**
415 Galle Rd, Colombo 4
*Tel:* (01) 84146 *Fax:* (01) 586598

*Key Personnel*
Managing Partner: Mrs Devini Dias; K V N
  Silva; Mrs Veena Silva
Founded: 1898
Subjects: History, Regional Interests, Religion -
  Other
ISBN Prefix(es): 955-9112
*Bookshop(s):* Fort, Colombo & YMBA Shopping
  Complex, 44/9 YMBA Bldg, Borella, Colombo

**Lake House Investments Ltd+**
41 W A D Ramanayake Mawatha, Colombo 2
*Tel:* (01) 35175; (01) 33271 *Fax:* (01) 44 7848;
  (01) 44 9504
*E-mail:* lhl@srilanka.net
*Telex:* 21266 Lakexpo CE *Cable:* COLOMBO 2
  SRI LANKA
*Key Personnel*
Chairman: R S Wijewardene
Manager: S M Aziz
Founded: 1965
Specialize in text books on science & law, both in
  Sinhala & English.
Membership(s): The Book Publishers' Association
  of Sri Lanka.
Subjects: Education, Fiction, History, Law,
  Medicine, Nursing, Dentistry, Music, Dance,
  Science (General), Sports, Athletics
ISBN Prefix(es): 955-552
*Associate Companies:* Lake House Printers &
  Publishers Ltd
Divisions: Chitrafoto; Lake House Bookshop;
  Lakexpo
*Bookshop(s):* Columbo University Bookshop,
  Columbo University, Cumarathuga Munidasa
  Mawatha, Columbo; Lake House Book-
  shop, 100 Chittampalam Gardinar Mawatha,
  Colombo 2

**Law Publishers Association+**
21 Sownders Court, Colombo 2
*Tel:* (01) 330363 *Fax:* (01) 436629
Founded: 1990
Subjects: Biography, Law
ISBN Prefix(es): 955-9210
Divisions: FAMYS
*Orders to:* FAMYS, 21 Sownders Court,
  Colombo 2

**Ministry of Cultural Affairs**
8th floor Sethsiripaya, Battaramulla
*Tel:* (01) 872001; (01) 876586 *Fax:* (01) 872020
*E-mail:* mcasec@sltnet.lk
*Web Site:* www.mca.gov.lk *Cable:* Sunlay
*Key Personnel*
Dir, Publications: R L Wimaladharma
Deputy Dir, Publications: K G Amaradasa
Editorial: Prof J D Dheerasekera; Prof D E Het-
  tiaratchi; D P Ponnamperuma
Founded: 1971
Subjects: Art, Ethnicity, Literature, Literary Criti-
  cism, Essays, Religion - Other
ISBN Prefix(es): 955-9117
*Bookshop(s):* Jayanti Bookshop, 135 Dharmapala
  Mawatha, Colombo 7
*Book Club(s):* Book Club of the Ministry of Cul-
  tural Affairs of Sri Lanka

**Ministry of Education+**
Isurupaya, Sri Jayawardenapura Kotte, Battara-
  mulla
*Tel:* 565141-5150
*Key Personnel*
Contact: Richard Pathirana
Subjects: Accounting, Agriculture, Chemistry,
  Chemical Engineering, Computer Science, Ge-
  ography, Geology, Mathematics, Physics, Sci-
  ence (General)
ISBN Prefix(es): 955-28
Subsidiaries: Educational Publications Dept

**National Children's Educational Foundation+**
International Headquarters, Mulleriyawa New
  Town
*Tel:* 578090 *Fax:* 578090
ISBN Prefix(es): 955-9104

**National Library & Documentation Centre**
No 14, Independence Ave, Colombo 07
Mailing Address: PO Box 1764, Colombo 07
*Tel:* (01) 685198; (01) 685199; (01) 698847; (01)
  685199 *Fax:* (011) 2685201
*E-mail:* natlib@sltnet.lk
*Web Site:* www.natlib.lk
*Key Personnel*
Chairman: Ms Tissa Kariyawasam
Dir General: Mr M S U Amarasiri *Tel:* (011)
  2687581 *E-mail:* dg@mail.natlib.lk
Deputy Dir: M A Nalani
Founded: 1970
Membership(s): IFLA; COMLA; CDNLAO;
  ACCU; AMIC.
Subjects: Communications, Computer Science,
  Ethnicity, Human Relations, Library & Infor-
  mation Sciences, Literature, Literary Criticism,
  Essays, Regional Interests, Social Sciences, So-
  ciology
ISBN Prefix(es): 955-9011
Total Titles: 2 CD-ROM

**Department of National Museums**
PO Box 854, Colombo 7
*Tel:* (01) 595366 *Fax:* (01) 595366
*Key Personnel*
Contact: W T T P Gunawardane
Subjects: Anthropology, Antiques, Natural History
ISBN Prefix(es): 955-578
Subsidiaries: National Museum (Galle); National
  Museum (Kandy); National Museum (Ratna-
  pura); Folk Museum; Dutch Period Museum;
  National Museum of Natural History; School
  Science Museum; School Science Museum;
  School Science Museum; School Science Mu-
  seum; Puppetry & Children's Museum; Na-
  tional Maritime Museum

**Pradeepa Publishers+**
34/34 Lawyers Off Complex, St Sebastian Hill,
  Colombo 12
*Tel:* (094) 435074; (094) 863261; (071) 735532
  *Fax:* (094) 863261
*Key Personnel*
Author & Editor: K Jayatilake *E-mail:* kjayatie@
  hotmail.com
Founded: 1968
Membership(s): the Writers Association, Sri
  Lanka Book Publishers Association.
Subjects: Fiction, Literature, Literary Criticism,
  Essays, Religion - Buddhist
ISBN Prefix(es): 955-554

**Saara Buddhi Publication**
19/1, Haltotawatta Lane, Avissawella 10700
ISBN Prefix(es): 955-9415

**Saman Saha Madara Publishers**
194 Sri Jayawardenapura Mawatha, Welikada,
  Rajagiriya
*Tel:* (01) 2862055 *Fax:* (01) 2868071
*E-mail:* prince@eureka.lk
*Key Personnel*
President: Mahinda Ralapanawe
  *E-mail:* ralapanawe@sltnet.lk
Founded: 1970
Subjects: Fiction, Literature, Literary Criticism,
  Essays
ISBN Prefix(es): 955-563
Total Titles: 2 Print

**Samayawardena Printers Publishers &
  Booksellers+**
53 Maligakanda Rd, Maradana, Colombo 10

*Tel:* (01) 694682 *Fax:* (01) 698977; (01) 683525
*E-mail:* samaya@applestr.lk
Founded: 1960
Membership(s): Sri Lanka Book Publishers Asso-
  ciation & Asia Pacific Book Publishers Associ-
  ation.
Subjects: Education, English as a Second Lan-
  guage, Nonfiction (General), Philosophy, Reli-
  gion - Buddhist
ISBN Prefix(es): 955-570
*Bookshop(s):* Samayawardhana Book Shop, 61
  Maligakanda Rd, Colombo 10 *Tel:* (01) 677539
  *Fax:* (01) 683986

**Sanjana Offset**, *imprint of* Gihan Book Shop

**Somawathi Hewavitharana Fund**
Mahabodhi Mandiraya, 130 Maligakanda Rd,
  Colombo 10
Mailing Address: 36/6 Rosmead Pl, Colombo 7
*Tel:* (01) 698079
*Key Personnel*
Trustee: Noel Wijenaike; Nanda Amerasinghe
  *Tel:* (01) 694026; Parinda Ranasinghe
Tripitaka Publications.
Subjects: Religion - Buddhist
ISBN Prefix(es): 955-616
Number of titles published annually: 6 Print
Total Titles: 80 Print

**Sri Lanka Jama'ath-e-Islami**
77, Dematagoda Rd, Colombo 9
*Tel:* (01) 687091 *Fax:* (01) 686030
ISBN Prefix(es): 955-608
*Bookshop(s):* Sri Lanka Jama'ath-e-Islami Book
  Stall, 77, Dematagoda Rd, Colombo 9

**State Printing Corp+**
95 Sir Chittampalam Gardiner Mawatha,
  Colombo 2
*Tel:* (01) 503694 *Fax:* (01) 503694
*Key Personnel*
Marketing Manager: Jagath Gamanayake
ISBN Prefix(es): 955-610

**Sunera Publishers+**
64, Devala Rd, Nugegoda
*Tel:* 511527
Founded: 1989
Subjects: Career Development, Economics, Law,
  Management
ISBN Prefix(es): 955-9128

**Swarna Hansa Foundation+**
9 Windsor Ave, Dehiwala
Mailing Address: PO Box 16, Dehiwala
*Tel:* (01) 712566 *Fax:* (01) 733649
*Key Personnel*
Program Executive: Gallege Punyawardana
Founded: 1978
Branch Offices: Hasalaka; Hiniduma; Kalawana;
  Nikaweratiya; Regional Centres at Kandy.
Subjects: Agriculture, Education, Environmental
  Studies, Health, Nutrition, History, Journalism,
  Literature, Literary Criticism, Essays, Poetry,
  Religion - Buddhist, Social Sciences, Sociol-
  ogy, Women's Studies
ISBN Prefix(es): 955-560
*Branch Office(s)*
Hiniduma

**Trumpet Publishers (Pvt) Ltd+**
A-4, Perahera Mawatha, Colombo 3
*Tel:* (01) 447622
*Web Site:* www.lankawebdirectory.com
Specialize in printing.
ISBN Prefix(es): 955-565
*Parent Company:* T F & I Printers
*Associate Companies:* Tanatha Finance & Invest-
  ment Co Ltd

**Unigraphics (Pte) Ltd**
732, Maradana Rd, Colombo 10
*Tel:* (01) 694538 *Fax:* (01) 693731
*E-mail:* uni.graphics@lanka.ccom.lk
ISBN Prefix(es): 955-619

**Vidura Science Publishers**
55/A First Lane, Medawelikada Rd, Rajagiriya
*Tel:* (091) 564713
Subjects: Science (General)
ISBN Prefix(es): 955-567
Subsidiaries: Anura C Printers

**Warna Publishers+**
Aluth Rd, Wennappuwa
Subjects: Chemistry, Chemical Engineering, Government, Political Science, Mathematics, Science (General), Science Fiction, Fantasy
ISBN Prefix(es): 955-9375
*Branch Office(s)*
New Rd, Wennappuwa
Distributed by Godage Bookshop; Gunasena Book Shop; Lake House Book Shop

**Waruni Publishers+**
72/15 A Second Lane, Pushpanada Mawatha, Kandy
*Tel:* (08) 24370 *Fax:* (08) 32343
*Telex:* 22787 Matsui CE
*Key Personnel*
Man Dir: K P Vimala Jharma
Subjects: Agriculture, Biography, Genealogy
ISBN Prefix(es): 955-566

# Sudan

## General Information

*Capital:* Khartoum
*Language:* Arabic (official), English also used
*Religion:* Muslims (north), Animists or Christians (south)
*Population:* 28.3 million
*Bank Hours:* 0830-1200 Sunday-Thursday
*Shop Hours:* 0800-1300, 1700-2000 Saturday-Thursday
*Currency:* 1,000 milliemes = 100 piastres = 1 Sudanese pound
*Export/Import Information:* No tariff on books; some advertising matter may be dutied. Import licenses required. Exchange controls; annual foreign exchange budget.

**ACADI**, see Arab Organization for Agricultural Development

**AOAD**, see Arab Organization for Agricultural Development

**Arab Center for Agricultural Documentation**, see Arab Organization for Agricultural Development

**Arab Organization for Agricultural Development**
St No 7 Amarat, Khartoum 11111
Mailing Address: PO Box 474, Khartoum
*Tel:* (011) 78760; (011) 78761; (011) 78762; (011) 78763 *Fax:* (011) 471402
*E-mail:* inquiry@aoad.org; info@aoad.org
*Web Site:* www.aoad.org
*Telex:* 22554SD *Cable:* AOAD
Founded: 1970
*Parent Company:* Arab League

**Al-Ayam Press Co Ltd**
Aboul Ela Bldgs, United Nations Sq, Khartoum
Mailing Address: PO Box 363, Khartoum
*E-mail:* kalhashmi@alayam.com
*Web Site:* www.alayam.com
*Key Personnel*
Man Dir: Beshir Muhammad Said
Founded: 1953
Subjects: Fiction, Nonfiction (General), Poetry

**Khartoum University Press**
Elbarlaman St, Khartoum
Mailing Address: PO Box 321, Khartoum
*Tel:* (011) 80558; (011) 81806 *Fax:* (011) 870558
*Web Site:* www.khartoumuniversity.edu
*Key Personnel*
Man Dir, General Editor: Ali El-Mak
Sales Manager: Abdel Raham Ibrahim
Editorial, Rights & Permissions: Jamal Abdel Malik; Judy El-Nagar
Founded: 1968
Subjects: Biography, Ethnicity, Fiction, History, Nonfiction (General), Philosophy, Poetry, Religion - Other, Science (General), Social Sciences, Sociology, Technology
*Bookshop(s):* University of Khartoum Bookshop

# Suriname

## General Information

*Capital:* Paramaribo
*Language:* Dutch. Hindustani and Javanese also spoken
*Religion:* Christian, Hindu & Islamic
*Population:* 410,000
*Bank Hours:* 0730-1400 Monday-Friday
*Shop Hours:* 0730-1630 Monday-Friday; 0730-1300 Saturday
*Currency:* 100 cents = 1 Suriname gulden or florin
*Export/Import Information:* No tariff on books except children's picture books; none on small quantities of advertising matter. Added taxes charged. Import licenses liberally granted. Exchange controls.
*Copyright:* Berne (see Copyright Conventions, pg xi)

**Apollo's Reklame en Uitgeversburo**
Toreniastraat 3, Paramaribo
Mailing Address: PO Box 574, Paramaribo
ISBN Prefix(es): 99914-908

**NV Drukkerij Eldorado**
Eldoradolaan 1, Paramaribo
*Tel:* 472362
ISBN Prefix(es): 99914-51

**Groto Publikasi**
Moengostr 75, Paramaribo
*Tel:* 493569
Specialize in Dutch & Suriname language publications.
ISBN Prefix(es): 99914-914

**R Ishaak**
Oranje Nassaustr 72, Nieuw Nickerie
*Tel:* 031917 *Fax:* 031917
ISBN Prefix(es): 99914-924

**C Kersten & Co**
Steenbakkerijstraat 27, Paramaribo
*Tel:* 471150 *Fax:* 472320
*E-mail:* kersten@sr.net
*Web Site:* www.kersten.sr

*Telex:* 142
ISBN Prefix(es): 99914-52

**Lutchman, Drs LFS+**
Elizelaan 10, Paramaribo
*Tel:* 465558; 453419
*Key Personnel*
Editor & Author: Sylvia Singh
Specialize in Poetry.
Subjects: Fiction, Poetry
ISBN Prefix(es): 99914-918
*Associate Companies:* Buitenweg; Handelsdrukkery; dr S Redmondstr 70
*Bookshop(s):* Vaco NV, Domineestr 26-32, Paramaribo; C Kersten & Co, NV-Steenbakkerij str 27

**Mavis A Noordwijk**
Regentessestr 3, Paramaribo
Mailing Address: PO Box 2653, Paramaribo
*Tel:* 479402
ISBN Prefix(es): 99914-907

**Dr C D Ooft**
Dr H D Benjaminstr 28, Paramaribo
*Tel:* 499139
ISBN Prefix(es): 99914-910

**Orchid Press**
PO Box 28, Paramaribo
ISBN Prefix(es): 99914-904

**Pro Media Productions**
Domineestr 12 boven, Paramaribo
*Tel:* 479355
ISBN Prefix(es): 99914-912

**Publishing Services Suriname** (Gowtu Stari Publishing)+
Van Idsingastraat 133, Paramaribo
*Tel:* 472746; 455792 *Fax:* 410366
*E-mail:* pssmoniz@sr.net
*Web Site:* www.parbo.com
*Key Personnel*
Author, Publisher: I Krishnadath
Illustration, Publisher: A Slyngard
Founded: 1992
Specialize in children's books, educational matters, Surinamese literature.
Subjects: Education, Literature, Literary Criticism, Essays
ISBN Prefix(es): 99914-915; 99914-920; 99914-928
Total Titles: 20 Print
*Associate Companies:* Uitgeverij Lees Mee

**Educatieve Uitgeverij Sorava**
Latourweg 10, Paramaribo
*Tel:* 483879
*Web Site:* www.icpcredit.com
ISBN Prefix(es): 99914-906; 99914-57

**Stichting Kinderkrant Suriname**
PO Box 3013, Paramaribo
ISBN Prefix(es): 99914-53

**Stichting Volksboekwinkel**
Keizerstr 197, Paramaribo
Mailing Address: PO Box 3040, Paramaribo
*Tel:* 472469
ISBN Prefix(es): 99914-901; 99914-4

**Stichting Wetenschappelijke Informatie+**
Prins Hendrikstr 38, Paramaribo
*Tel:* 475232 *Fax:* 422195
*E-mail:* swin@sr.net
*Key Personnel*
Man Dir, Editorial, Production, Publicity: J K Menke

Sales: W Boedhoe
Founded: 1977
Subjects: Anthropology, Developing Countries, Ethnicity, Government, Political Science, History, Labor, Industrial Relations, Literature, Literary Criticism, Essays, Science (General), Social Sciences, Sociology, Women's Studies
ISBN Prefix(es): 99914-900
Distributor for Local Surinamese Publications

**Vaco**, *imprint of* Vaco NV Uitgeversmij

**Vaco NV Uitgeversmij+**
Domineestr 32 Boven, Paramaribo
Mailing Address: PO Box 1841, Paramaribo
*Tel:* 472545
*E-mail:* interf@sr.net
*Telex:* 123 INCO SN
*Key Personnel*
Man Dir: E Hogenboom
Publisher: J Trotman
Founded: 1952
Subjects: History, Regional Interests
ISBN Prefix(es): 99914-0
*Parent Company:* Interfund NV
Imprints: Vaco

**Drs F H R Oedayrajsingh Varma+**
PO Box 9192, Paramaribo
*Key Personnel*
Dir: Dr Ferdinand H Varma
Subjects: Regional Interests
ISBN Prefix(es): 99914-903
*Branch Office(s)*
Postbus 70225, 1007 KE Amsterdam, Netherlands
  *Tel:* (020) 628163

**M Waagmeester-Verkuyl**
Naarstr 4, Paramaribo
Mailing Address: PO Box 9166, Paramaribo
*Tel:* 498356
ISBN Prefix(es): 99914-905; 99914-88

# Swaziland

## General Information

*Capital:* Mbabane
*Language:* Siswati, English used in business
*Religion:* Christian (about 60%), most others follow traditional beliefs
*Population:* 913,000
*Bank Hours:* Until 1100 Saturday
*Shop Hours:* 0700-1800
*Currency:* 100 cents = 1 lilangeni = 1 South African rand
*Export/Import Information:* Same as South Africa.

**Boleswa**, *imprint of* Macmillan Boleswa Publishers (Pty) Ltd

**Macmillan Boleswa Publishers (Pty) Ltd**
Plot 230/231, First Ave, Matsapa Industrial Estate, Manzini
Mailing Address: PO Box 1235, Manzini
*Tel:* 84533 *Fax:* 85247
*E-mail:* macmillan@iafrica.sz
*Web Site:* www.macmillansa.co.za; www.macmillan-africa.com
*Telex:* 2221 MACSW WD
*Key Personnel*
Man Dir: Elias Nwandwe
Founded: 1978
Subjects: Education
ISBN Prefix(es): 0-333; 0-7978

*Parent Company:* Macmillan Publishers Ltd, United Kingdom
Imprints: Boleswa
Subsidiaries: Macmillan Swaziland National Publishing Co; Macmillan Botswana Publishing Co
*Branch Office(s)*
Matsapa

# Sweden

## General Information

*Capital:* Stockholm
*Language:* Swedish. Some Finnish and Lapp also spoken
*Religion:* Evangelical Lutheran Church of Sweden
*Population:* 8.8 million
*Bank Hours:* 0930-1500 Monday-Friday
*Shop Hours:* 0900-1800 Monday-Friday (later Friday); 0900-1400 or 1600 Saturday
*Currency:* 100 oere = 1 Swedish korona
*Export/Import Information:* Member of the European Free Trade Association. No tariff on books. Advertising tax. 25% VAT on books. No import licenses. No exchange controls.
*Copyright:* UCC, Berne, Florence (see Copyright Conventions, pg xi)

**Acta Universitatis Gothoburgensis**
Renstroemsgatan 4, 405 30 Gothenburg
Mailing Address: Box 222, Gothenburg 405 30
*Tel:* (031) 7731000 *Fax:* (031) 163797
*E-mail:* library@ub.gu.se
*Web Site:* www.ub.gu.se
*Key Personnel*
Man Dir: Jon Erik Norstrand
Publishes only works produced at or connected with Goteborg University.
Subjects: Art, Education, Language Arts, Linguistics, Literature, Literary Criticism, Essays, Social Sciences, Sociology, Women's Studies
ISBN Prefix(es): 91-7346
*Parent Company:* Goeteborgs Universitetsbibliotek

**Akademiforlaget Corona AB**
Box 5, 201 20 Malmo
*Tel:* (040) 286161 *Fax:* (040) 286162
*E-mail:* kundservice@cor.se
*Web Site:* www.cor.se
*Key Personnel*
Man Dir: Lars Welinder *E-mail:* lars.welinder@cor.se
Founded: 1961
Subjects: Education, Fiction, Nonfiction (General)
ISBN Prefix(es): 91-564; 91-7034

**Alfabeta Bokforlag AB+**
Svartensgatan 6, Stockholm
Mailing Address: PO Box 4284, 102 66 Stockholm
*Tel:* (08) 714 36 30 *Fax:* (08) 643 24 31
*E-mail:* info@alfamedia.se
*Web Site:* www.alfamedia.se *Cable:* ALFABETA STOCKHOLM
*Key Personnel*
Man Dir, Rights & Permissions: Dag Hernried
Sales & Production: Lena Spaulding
  *E-mail:* lena@alfamedia.se
Founded: 1976
Subjects: Art, Ethnicity, Fiction, Film, Video, Music, Dance, Nonfiction (General), Psychology, Psychiatry, Travel
ISBN Prefix(es): 91-7712; 91-85328
Subsidiaries: Gammafon AB (audio cassettes)

**Allt om Hobby AB+**
Box 90133, 120 21 Stockholm
*Tel:* (08) 99 93 33 *Fax:* (08) 99 88 66
*E-mail:* order@hobby.se
*Web Site:* www.hobby.se
*Key Personnel*
Publisher: Freddy Stenbom *E-mail:* freddy.stenbom@hobby.se
Founded: 1966
Subjects: Aeronautics, Aviation, Communications, Crafts, Games, Hobbies, Electronics, Electrical Engineering, History, Maritime, Military Science, Photography, Transportation
ISBN Prefix(es): 91-85496; 91-7243
*Book Club(s):* Allt om Hobbys Bokklubb; Flygboklubben

**Almquist & Wiksell**, *imprint of* Liber AB

**Almqvist och Wiksell International**
PO Box 7634, 10394 Stockholm
*Tel:* (08) 613 61 00 *Fax:* (08) 24 25 43
*E-mail:* scand.mongr@awi.se
*Web Site:* www.akademibokhandeln.se
*Key Personnel*
Dir: Mats Thomasson
Sales Manager: Hans Linder
Affiliated to the Akademibokhandeln Group & publishers to the universities of Stockholm, Uppsala & Lund.
Subjects: Science (General)
ISBN Prefix(es): 91-22

**Apotekarsocietetens Forlag**
PO Box 1136, 111 81 Stockholm
*Tel:* (08) 7235000 *Fax:* (08) 205511
*Key Personnel*
Man Dir: Yvonne Andersson *E-mail:* andersson.y@swepharm.se

**AB Arcanum+**
Tollestorpsvagen 2H, S-443 03 Stenkullen
*Tel:* (0302) 242 70 *Fax:* (0302) 242 73
*E-mail:* info@arcanum-utbildning.se
*Web Site:* www.arcanum-utbildning.se
*Key Personnel*
Man Dir: Bo Ramme
Founded: 1970
Subjects: Medicine, Nursing, Dentistry
ISBN Prefix(es): 91-85690

**Arkitektur Forlag AB**
Fishargatan 8, 10266 Stockholm
Mailing Address: PO Box 4296, 10266 Stockholm
*Tel:* (08) 7027850 *Fax:* (08) 6115270
*E-mail:* redaktionen@arkitektur.se
*Web Site:* www.arkitektur.se
*Key Personnel*
Contact: Marianne Lundqvist *E-mail:* marianne.lundqvist@arkitektur.se
Founded: 1901
Subjects: Architecture & Interior Design
ISBN Prefix(es): 91-86050
Number of titles published annually: 4 Print

**Bokforlaget Atlantis AB+**
Sturegatan 24, 11436 Stockholm
*Tel:* (08) 7830440 *Fax:* (08) 6617285
*E-mail:* mail@atlantis-publishers.se *Cable:* ATLANTISBOOKS
*Key Personnel*
Man Dir: Kjell Peterson
Production: Lennart Rolf
Marketing Dir & Rights & Permissions: Hans Bjornell
Founded: 1977
Subjects: Art, Cookery, Fiction, Health, Nutrition, History, Nonfiction (General)
ISBN Prefix(es): 91-7486
*Associate Companies:* Clio History Book Club
*Book Club(s):* Clio History Book Club

**Bokforlaget Axplock+**
Eskilsgatan 12B, 645 30 Strangnas
Mailing Address: Box 100, 645 22 Strangnas
*Tel:* (0152) 150 60 *Fax:* (0152) 151 40
*E-mail:* post@axplock.se
*Web Site:* www.axplock.se
*Key Personnel*
Publisher: Hans Richter
Founded: 1985
Subjects: Drama, Theater, Fiction, Gardening,
  Plants, History, How-to, Humor, Language
  Arts, Linguistics, Music, Dance, Mysteries,
  Nonfiction (General), Poetry, Self-Help
ISBN Prefix(es): 91-86436
Number of titles published annually: 10 Print
Total Titles: 90 Print

**BBB Bokklubben Bra Bocker**, *imprint of*
Bokforlaget Bra Bocker AB

**Berghs**
PO Box 45084, 104 30 Stockholm
*Tel:* (08) 31 65 59 *Fax:* (08) 32 77 45
*E-mail:* info@berghsforlag.se
*Web Site:* www.berghsforlag.se
*Key Personnel*
Chairman: Anders Oehman
Man Dir: Carl Hafstroem
Editorial Dir: Eva Vider
Founded: 1954
Subjects: Crafts, Games, Hobbies, Nonfiction
  (General)
ISBN Prefix(es): 91-502
*Orders to:* Foerlagssystem, PO Box 30195, 10425
  Stockholm *Tel:* (08) 6574510

**BBT Bhaktivedanta Book Trust**
c/o ISKCON, Korsnas gard, 147 92 Grodinge
*Tel:* (08) 530 257 72
*E-mail:* p.huy@t-online.de
Subjects: Cookery, Music, Dance, Philosophy,
  Religion - Hindu, Religion - Other
ISBN Prefix(es): 91-7149; 91-85580
*U.S. Office(s):* BBT, 3764 Watseka Ave, Los An-
  geles, CA 90034, United States *Tel:* 310-836-
  2676

**Bibliotekstjaenst AB**
Traktorvaegen 11, 221 82 Lund
Mailing Address: PO Box 200, 221 82 Lund
*Tel:* (046) 18 00 00 *Fax:* (046) 18 01 25
*E-mail:* btj@btj.se
*Web Site:* www.btj.se
*Telex:* 32200 btjlund s
*Key Personnel*
Press Contact: Martin Petri
Founded: 1951
Subjects: Library & Information Sciences
ISBN Prefix(es): 91-7018
*Associate Companies:* BTJ Europe, Belgium; BTJ
  Inc, United States; BTJ Norge, Norway
Subsidiaries: BTJ Tryck AB
Divisions: BTJ Database; BTJ Media

**Bonnier Audio+**
Box 3159, 103 63 Stockholm
*Tel:* (08) 6968700 *Fax:* (08) 6968757
*E-mail:* info@bonnieraudio.se
*Web Site:* www.bonnieraudio.se
*Key Personnel*
President & Publisher: Christina Andersson
  *E-mail:* christina.andersson@bonnieraudio.se
Founded: 1986
Specialize in audio books.
Subjects: Fiction
ISBN Prefix(es): 91-7950
Number of titles published annually: 35 Print
Total Titles: 350 Print
*Parent Company:* Bonnierfoerlagen

**Bonnier Carlsen Bokforlag AB**
Drottninggatan 82, 11183 Stockholm
*Tel:* (08) 59895500 *Fax:* (08) 59895545
*Key Personnel*
Man Dir: Pentti Molander
Sales: Johnny Gustafsson
Founded: 1968
Subjects: Animals, Pets, Erotica, Fiction, History,
  Mysteries, Romance, Science Fiction, Fantasy,
  Social Sciences, Sociology, Sports, Athletics,
  Cartoons, Child care, Comics, Fantasy, Fairy
  tales, Adventure, Classics, Health, Holidays,
  Horror & Ghost, Love & Sexuality, Social Sit-
  uations
ISBN Prefix(es): 91-510; 91-48; 91-638
*Parent Company:* Bonnierforlagen AB

**Bonnier Utbildning AB**
Sveavagen 56, 103 63 Stockholm
Mailing Address: PO Box 3159, 103 63 Stock-
  holm
*Tel:* (08) 696 85 90 *Fax:* (08) 696 86 55
*E-mail:* info@bonnierutbildning.se
*Web Site:* www.bonnierutbildning.se
*Key Personnel*
Publisher: Lars Malmius
Founded: 1987
Specialize in schoolbooks.
ISBN Prefix(es): 91-622
*Parent Company:* Bonnierforlagen AB

**Albert Bonniers Forlag+**
Division of The Bonnier Group
Box 3159, 103 63 Stockholm
*Tel:* (08) 696 86 20 *Fax:* (08) 696 8369; (08) 696
  8347
*E-mail:* info@abforlag.bonnier.se
*Web Site:* www.albertbonniersforlag.com
*Key Personnel*
Publisher: Eva Bonnier
Man Dir: Kerstin Angelin
Rights & Permissions: Teresa Carlstrom
Founded: 1837
Subjects: Fiction, Nonfiction (General)
ISBN Prefix(es): 91-7458; 91-0; 91-34; 91-85015

**Albert Bonniers Forlag AB**
PO Box 3159, 103 63 Stockholm
*Tel:* (08) 696 86 20 *Fax:* (08) 696 83 61
*E-mail:* info@abforlag.bonnier.se
*Web Site:* www.albertbonniersforlag.se *Cable:*
  BONNIERS
*Key Personnel*
Man Dir: Kerstin Angelin
Publishing Dir: Eva Bonnier
Publisher: Karl Otto Bonnier
Rights & Permissions & Production: Arne Bjo-
  erkman
Rights & Permissions: Teresa Carlstroem
Production: Robert Hedberg
Publicity: Ingela Palmquist; Carina Soederman
Subjects: Art, Cookery, Fiction, Nonfiction (Gen-
  eral)
ISBN Prefix(es): 91-7458; 91-0; 91-34; 91-85015
*Parent Company:* Bonnierfoerlagen AB
*Warehouse:* Samdistribution, PO Box 449, S-
  19104 Sollentuna

**Bokforlaget Bra Bocker AB**
Box 890, 201 80 Malmo
*Tel:* (040) 665 46 00 *Fax:* (040) 665 46 22
*E-mail:* kundservice@bbb.se
*Web Site:* www.bbb.se
*Key Personnel*
President & Marketing: Rolf Nilstam
Vice President, Production: Janson Anders
Editorial, Encyclopedia: Christer Engstoem
Editorial, Nonfiction: Lillemor Eagle
Editorial, Fiction: Goeran Green Claes
Founded: 1965
Subjects: Fiction, Geography, Geology, History
ISBN Prefix(es): 91-7024; 91-7119; 91-7133

*Parent Company:* International Masters Publishers
  AB, PO Box 814, 201 80 Malmoe
Imprints: BBB Bokklubben Bra Bocker

**Brombergs Bokforlag AB+**
Hantverkargatan 26, 112 98 Stockholm
Mailing Address: Box 12 886, 112 98 Stockholm
*Tel:* (08) 562 62 080 *Fax:* (08) 562 62 085
*E-mail:* info@brombergs.se
*Web Site:* www.brombergs.se
*Telex:* 12442 Fotex Bropublish S
*Key Personnel*
Man Dir, Publicity: Dorotea Bromberg
Production, Rights & Permissions: Ylva Aaberg
  *E-mail:* ylva.aberg@brombergs.se
Founded: 1973
Subjects: Fiction, Nonfiction (General)
ISBN Prefix(es): 91-7608
Number of titles published annually: 25 Print

**Forlaget By och Bygd**
PO Box 22087, 104 22 Stockholm
*Tel:* (08) 652 09 55
*Key Personnel*
Man Dir: Asa-Britt Karlsson
Subjects: Government, Political Science, Social
  Sciences, Sociology
ISBN Prefix(es): 91-85354

**Byggforlaget+**
Narvavaegen 19, 114 81 Stockholm
Mailing Address: PO Box 5456, 114 81 Stock-
  holm
*Tel:* (08) 665 36 50 *Fax:* (08) 667 39 49
*Web Site:* www.byggforlaget.se
*Key Personnel*
Man Dir: Claes Dymling *Tel:* (08) 6653670
  *E-mail:* claes@byggforlaget.se
Founded: 1948
Subjects: Architecture & Interior Design
ISBN Prefix(es): 91-85194; 91-7988

**Calago Foerlag**, *imprint of* Ordfront Foerlag AB

**Carlsson Bokfoerlag AB+**
Stora Nygatan 31, 111 27 Stockholm
*Tel:* (08) 411 23 49 *Fax:* (08) 796 84 57
*Key Personnel*
Man Dir: Trygve Carlsson
Founded: 1983
Subjects: Anthropology, Art, Government, Polit-
  ical Science, History, Journalism, Literature,
  Literary Criticism, Essays, Travel, Women's
  Studies, Ethnology
ISBN Prefix(es): 91-7798; 91-7203
*Warehouse:* Foerlagssystem, Loevasvagen 26, 791
  45 Falun

**Citadell**, *imprint of* Raben och Sjoegren
Bokforlag

**Rene Coeckelberghs Bokfoerlag AB**
PO Box 45059, 104 30 Stockholm
*Tel:* (08) 7230880 *Fax:* (08) 7230311
*Telex:* 14277 reco S
*Key Personnel*
Man Dir: Rene Coeckelberghs
Subjects: Fiction, Nonfiction (General), Poetry
ISBN Prefix(es): 91-7250; 91-7103; 91-7212; 91-
  7640

**Combi International AB**, see Forlagshuset
  Norden AB

**Bokforlaget Cordia AB+**
Box 1723, 701 17 Orebro
*Tel:* (019) 333850 *Fax:* (019) 333859
*E-mail:* forlaget@cordia.se
*Web Site:* www.cordia.se
*Key Personnel*
President: Lars-G Stahl
Publisher: Goran Rask *E-mail:* g.rask@verbum.se

Founded: 1995
Subjects: History, Human Relations, Nonfiction
(General), Spirituality
ISBN Prefix(es): 91-7085; 91-86082; 91-7080
*Parent Company:* Verbum AB
*Associate Companies:* Foerlagshuset Gothia;
Gleerups Foerlag; Verbum Foerlag

**Dahlia Books, International Publishers &
Booksellers**
Box 1025, 751 40 Uppsala
*Tel:* (018) 133511
*E-mail:* dahlia@comhem.se
Founded: 1973
Major function of this company is bookselling
(antiquarian & new).
ISBN Prefix(es): 91-974094; 91-972293

**Egmont Serieforlaget**
Oestra Foerstadsgatan 34, 20508 Malmo
*Tel:* (040) 6939400 *Fax:* (040) 6939498
*E-mail:* info@egmont.com
*Web Site:* www.egmont.com
*Telex:* 32449 Hemmet S
Founded: 1920
Subjects: Fiction, Human Relations, Cartoons,
Comics
ISBN Prefix(es): 91-7300; 91-7674; 91-7912
*Parent Company:* Gutenberghus Group, Denmark
*Associate Companies:* Ehapa-Verlag GmbH, Germany; Gutenberghus Publishing Service A/S,
Denmark; NW Damm og Son A/S, Norway
*Book Club(s):* Part-owner of Kalle Ankas Pocket

**Ekelunds Forlag AB+**
Rasundav 160, 169 02 Solna
Mailing Address: PO Box 2050, 169 02 Solna
*Tel:* (08) 821320 *Fax:* (08) 832956
*E-mail:* education@ekelunds.se
*Key Personnel*
Contact: Marit Ekelund
Founded: 1981
Subjects: Education, English as a Second Language
ISBN Prefix(es): 91-7724; 91-646

**Liber Ekonomi**, *imprint of* Liber AB

**Ekonomibok Forlag AB**
Groentevaegen 5, 254 84 Helsingborg
*Tel:* (042) 929 50 *Fax:* (042) 929 50
*Key Personnel*
Man Dir: Maj-Britt Hallgren *E-mail:* hallgren@
ekonomibok.se
Founded: 1973
Subjects: Business, Fiction, Finance
ISBN Prefix(es): 91-86406

**Ellerstroms+**
Fredsgatan 6, 222 20 Lund
*Tel:* (046) 323295 *Fax:* (046) 323295
*E-mail:* info@ellerstroms.se
*Web Site:* www.ellerstroms.se
*Key Personnel*
Editor: Vilhelm Ekelund
Founded: 1983
Publisher of fiction, prose & poetry. Swedish &
translations.
Subjects: Fiction, Literature, Literary Criticism,
Essays, Poetry
ISBN Prefix(es): 91-7247; 91-86488; 91-86489
Number of titles published annually: 20 Print
Total Titles: 220 Print
*Distribution Center:* Postservice *Tel:* (411) 45400
*Fax:* (411) 45401

**Energica Foerlags AB/Halsabocker+**
PO Box 8, 794 93 Orsa
*Tel:* (0250) 55 20 00 *Fax:* (0250) 43191
*Web Site:* www.energica.com

*Key Personnel*
Man Dir: Monica Katarina Frisk
*E-mail:* monica@energica.se
Founded: 1985
Subjects: Health, Nutrition, Psychology, Psychiatry
ISBN Prefix(es): 91-87056
Total Titles: 50 Print
*Parent Company:* Energica Foerlags AB

**Eriksson & Lindgren Bokforlag+**
St Eriksgatan 14, 102 23 Stockholm
Mailing Address: PO Box 12085, 102 23 Stockholm
*Tel:* (08) 6523226; (08) 6523227 *Fax:* (08)
6523223
*E-mail:* info@eriksson-lindgren.se
*Key Personnel*
Publisher & Man Dir: Claes Eriksson
Publisher: Marianne Eriksson
Founded: 1989
Subjects: Child Care & Development
ISBN Prefix(es): 91-87804; 91-87805; 91-87803;
91-85199
Number of titles published annually: 30 Print

**Bokforlaget Fingraf AB+**
PO Box 4084, 151 04 Soedertaelje
*Tel:* (08) 550 300 23 *Fax:* (08) 550 695 70
*Key Personnel*
Man Dir: Ossi Nikula
Editorial: Eivor Nikula
Founded: 1979
Subjects: Fiction, Humor, Medicine, Nursing,
Dentistry
ISBN Prefix(es): 91-85964; 91-88556
*Associate Companies:* Fingraf Bookprinters AB,
Forradsvagen 8, Box 4084, S-151 04 Soedertalje

**Fischer & Co+**
Norrlandsgatan 15, 111 43 Stockholm
*Tel:* (08) 242160 *Fax:* (08) 247825
*E-mail:* bokforlaget@fischer-co.se
*Web Site:* www.fischer-co.se
*Key Personnel*
Man Dir: Sara Nillson *E-mail:* sara@fischer-co.se
Founded: 1969
Subjects: Biography, Fiction, History, Nonfiction
(General)
ISBN Prefix(es): 91-7054
Total Titles: 1 Audio
*Book Club(s):* Bockernas Klubb

**Forlagshuset Norden AB+**
PO Box 305, 201 23 Malmoe
*Tel:* (040) 93 42 50 *Fax:* (040) 93 01 56
Founded: 1931
ISBN Prefix(es): 91-86442
Subsidiaries: Combi International AB

**Folkuniversitetets foerlag+**
Magle Lilla Kyrkogata 4, 223 51 Lund
*Tel:* (046) 148720 *Fax:* (046) 132904
*E-mail:* info@folkuniversitetsforlag.se
*Web Site:* www.folkuniversitetsforlag.se
*Key Personnel*
Man Dir: Goran Fasth
Editorial, Production, Rights & Permissions:
Kristin Nilsson
Sales, Publicity, Editor: Annalisa Mikaelsson
Founded: 1971
Subjects: Education, Language Arts, Linguistics
ISBN Prefix(es): 91-7434
Number of titles published annually: 10 Print
Total Titles: 140 Print

**Foreningen Svenska Laromedelsproducenter
(The Swedish Association of Educational
Publishers)**
Drottninggatan 97, 2tr, 113 60 Stockholm

*Tel:* (08) 736 19 40 *Fax:* (08) 736 19 44
*E-mail:* fsl@fsl.se
*Web Site:* www.fsl.se
*Key Personnel*
Man Dir: Lena Westerberg *Tel:* (08) 7361943
*E-mail:* lena.westerberg@forlagskansli.se
Founded: 1974
ISBN Prefix(es): 91-85386

**Bengt Forsbergs Foerlag AB+**
Soedra Tullgatan 4, 211 40 Malmoe
*Tel:* (040) 763 20 *Fax:* (040) 303939
*E-mail:* info@forsbergsforlag.se
*Web Site:* www.forsbergsforlag.se *Cable:*
GODBOK
*Key Personnel*
Man Dir: Joergen Forsberg
Rights: Claes Forsberg
Sales Dir: Matts Forsberg
Founded: 1944
Specialize in telephone sales.
Subjects: Animals, Pets, Art, History, Medicine,
Nursing, Dentistry, Photography
ISBN Prefix(es): 91-7046
Subsidiaries: Editions Corniche

**Bokforlaget Forum AB+**
Gamla Brogatan 26, 107 23 Stockholm
Mailing Address: PO Box 70321, 107 23 Stockholm
*Tel:* (08) 696 84 40; (08) 6968410 (Orders)
*Fax:* (08) 696 83 67
*Key Personnel*
Publisher & Man Dir: Karin Leijon
Publisher, Editorial: Viveca Peterson
Information: Anneli Eldh
Marketing: Irene Westin Ahlgren
Rights & Permissions: Birgitta Lindgren
Production: Bengt Permatz
Senior Editor: Kerstin Bergfors; Karin Linge
Nordh
Founded: 1944
Subjects: Fiction, Nonfiction (General)
ISBN Prefix(es): 91-37
*Parent Company:* Bonnierforlagen

**C E Fritzes AB**
10647 Stockholm
*Tel:* (08) 6909190 *Fax:* (08) 6909191
*E-mail:* order.fritzes@liber.se
*Web Site:* www.fritzes.se
*Key Personnel*
Man Dir: Christer Bunge-Meyer *E-mail:* christer.
bunge-meyer@liber.se
Founded: 1837
Official publications from Swedish government &
authorities.
ISBN Prefix(es): 91-38
*Parent Company:* Wolters Kluwer Scandinavia
*Orders to:* Kundtjaenst, S-10647 Stockholm

**Gedins Forlag+**
Tysta Gatan 10, 115 20 Stockholm
*Tel:* (08) 662 15 51 *Fax:* (08) 6637073
*E-mail:* gedins@perigab.se
*Key Personnel*
Publisher: Per I Gedin
Founded: 1987
Subjects: Fiction, Nonfiction (General)
ISBN Prefix(es): 91-7964
*Book Club(s):* Part-owner of Manadens Bok
*Orders to:* Sam Distribution, PO Box 449,
19124 Sollentuna *Tel:* (08) 6968400 *Fax:* (08)
6968358

**SK-Gehrmans Musikforlag AB+**
Vastberga alle 5, 12630 Hagersten
Mailing Address: PO Box 42026, 12612 Stockholm
*Tel:* (08) 6100610 *Fax:* (08) 6100627
*E-mail:* sales@gehrmans.se
*Web Site:* www.sk-gehrmans.se

*Key Personnel*
Man Dir: Magnus Filipsson
Founded: 1999
Music publisher
Orchestral parts rental.
Subjects: Music, Dance, Folk music & ballads,
music with Christian lyrics accordion music,
orchestral music for brass & woodwinds, contemporary music, classical music, music for
choirs, educational publications, sheet music
publications & compilations, sheet whole sale
distributions & printing plant
ISBN Prefix(es): 91-7748

**Gidlunds Bokforlag**
PO Box 123, 776 23 Hedemora
*Tel:* (0225) 77 11 55 *Fax:* (0255) 77 11 65
*E-mail:* hedemora@gidlunds.se
*Web Site:* www.gidlunds.se
*Key Personnel*
Man Dir: Krister Gidlund
Founded: 1984
Subjects: Art, Biography, History, Philosophy,
Social Sciences, Sociology
ISBN Prefix(es): 91-7844

**Foerlagshuset Gothia** (Gothia Publishing
House)+
Box 15169, 104 65 Stockholm
*Tel:* (08) 4622660 *Fax:* (08) 4620322
*E-mail:* info.gothia@verbum.se
*Web Site:* www.gothia.nu
*Key Personnel*
President, Publisher & Man Dir: Olle Sundling
*E-mail:* olle.sundling@verbum.se
Rights & Permissions: Agneta Lundin
Founded: 1985
Subjects: Child Care & Development, Education,
Health, Nutrition, Medicine, Nursing, Dentistry,
Regional Interests, Social Care
ISBN Prefix(es): 91-526; 91-7205; 91-85174; 91-
86028; 91-7728; 91-85232; 91-85660

**Gothia Publishing House**, see Foerlagshuset
Gothia

**Hagaberg AB+**
PO Box 6471, 113 82 Stockholm
*Tel:* (08) 690 90 00 *Fax:* (08) 7021940
*Key Personnel*
Man Dir: Ingrid Olausson
Editorial: Rune Olausson
Founded: 1983
Subjects: Gardening, Plants, Philosophy, Psychol-
ogy, Psychiatry, Theology
ISBN Prefix(es): 91-86584

**Hallgren och Fallgren Studieforlag AB**
Skolgatan 3, 753 12 Uppsala
*Tel:* (018) 50 71 00 *Fax:* (018) 12 72 70
*E-mail:* info@hallgren-fallgren.se
*Web Site:* www.hallgren-fallgren.se
*Key Personnel*
Man Dir, Editorial, Rights & Permissions: Daniel
Aberg; Karin Hallgren
Founded: 1973
Subjects: Education, Science (General)
ISBN Prefix(es): 91-7382

**Hanseproduktion AB** (Hanse Production AB)
Tranhusgatan 29, 621 55 Visby
*Tel:* (0498) 24 93 18 *Fax:* (0498) 24 93 18
*Key Personnel*
Chief Executive: Thorbjoern Oedin
Founded: 1978
Subjects: Art, Regional Interests
ISBN Prefix(es): 91-85716

**Bokforlaget Hegas AB**
Box 201, 263 21 Hoeganaes
*Tel:* (042) 330 340 *Fax:* (042) 330 141

*E-mail:* kom.litt@helsingborg.se
*Key Personnel*
Contact: Lena Hultberg
ISBN Prefix(es): 91-86650; 91-86651; 91-973287;
91-973620; 91-973621

**Liber Hermods**, *imprint of* Liber AB

**Hillelforlaget** (Hillel Publishing House)+
Wahreudorfksgutau 3B, 11147 Stockholm
Mailing Address: Box 7427, 10391 Stockholm
*Tel:* (08) 587 858 04 *Fax:* (08) 587 858 58
*Key Personnel*
Man Dir: Marina Burstein *E-mail:* marina.
burstein@hillel.nu
Founded: 1969
Subjects: Regional Interests, Religion - Jewish
ISBN Prefix(es): 91-85164
Number of titles published annually: 3 Print
Total Titles: 20 Print

**Lars Hoekerbergs Bokfoerlag**
Fleminggatan 21, 112 26 Stockholm
*Tel:* (08) 244360 *Fax:* (08) 6503984
*E-mail:* hokerbook@ebox.tninet.se
*Key Personnel*
Man Dir: Jan Hoekerberg
Founded: 1882
Subjects: Fiction, Nonfiction (General)
ISBN Prefix(es): 91-7084; 91-7157
Number of titles published annually: 1 Print
Total Titles: 3 Print

**Hundskolan i Solleftea AB**
Overgard Pl 7015, SE-881 93 Solleftea
*Tel:* (0620) 832 00 *Fax:* (0620) 832 29
*E-mail:* gundvald@hundskolan.se
*Web Site:* www.humanitydog.se
*Key Personnel*
Contact: Gunvald Andersen
ISBN Prefix(es): 91-971825

**ICA bokforlag+**
Stora gatan 41, 721 85 Vasteras
*Tel:* (021) 194000 *Fax:* (021) 194283
*E-mail:* bok@forlaget.ica.se
*Web Site:* www.forlaget.ica.se/bok
*Telex:* 40486 ica s *Cable:* ICAFOeRLAGET
*Key Personnel*
Publisher: Goran Sunehag *Tel:* (021) 192470
*E-mail:* goran.sunehag@forlaget.ica.se
Rights Manager: Ulla Joneby *E-mail:* ulla.
joneby@forlaget.ica.se
Founded: 1945
Subjects: Animals, Pets, Cookery, Crafts, Games,
Hobbies, Gardening, Plants, Health, Nutrition,
House & Home, How-to, Self-Help
ISBN Prefix(es): 91-534
Number of titles published annually: 70 Print
Total Titles: 450 Print

**Idrottsantikvariatet**, *imprint of* Stroemberg B&T
Forlag AB

**Industrilitteratur Vindex, Forlags AB**
PO Box 5513, 114 85 Stockholm
*Tel:* (08) 783 81 00 *Fax:* (08) 660 59 11
*E-mail:* aestan.orstadius@industrilitteratur.se
Founded: 1887
Subjects: Ethnicity, Marketing, Public Administra-
tion
ISBN Prefix(es): 91-7548
*Parent Company:* Swedish Trade Council; Federa-
tion of Swedish Industry

**Informationsfoerlaget AB**
Sveavaegen 61, S-113 86 Stockholm
Mailing Address: PO Box 6884, 113 86 Stock-
holm
*Tel:* (08) 34 09 15 *Fax:* (08) 31 39 03

*E-mail:* red@informationsforlaget.se
*Web Site:* www.informationsforlaget.se
*Key Personnel*
Man Dir: Ulf Heimdahl
Senior Editor: Ylva Aberg
Founded: 1979
Specialize in sponsored books in cooperation with
Swedish industry and authorities.
Subjects: Cookery, How-to, Wine & Spirits
ISBN Prefix(es): 91-7736

**Ingenjoersforlaget AB+**
106 12 Stockholm
*Tel:* (08) 796 66 90 *Fax:* (08) 22 77 44
*E-mail:* redaktionen@miljorapporten.se
*Telex:* 17191 Tecnews S *Cable:* Ingforlag
*Key Personnel*
Man Dir: Hakan Ryden
Founded: 1970
Subjects: Science (General)
ISBN Prefix(es): 91-7284; 91-85804; 91-973810

**Interculture+**
Box 4160, 102 62 Stockholm
*Tel:* (08) 642 78 04 *Fax:* (08) 642 35 91
*Telex:* 909 Teleopr S attn Intconswed *Cable:*
INTCONSWED
*Key Personnel*
Man Dir: Jan Valdelin
Founded: 1983
Subjects: Fiction, Film, Video
ISBN Prefix(es): 91-86608
*Parent Company:* ICS Interconsult Sweden A

**International Bible Society**
Box 205, 524 23 Herrljunga
*Tel:* (0513) 219 30 *Fax:* (0513) 215 01
*Key Personnel*
Executive Dir: Hans-Lennart Raask
ISBN Prefix(es): 91-7165; 91-87412
*Parent Company:* Colorado Springs, CO, United
States
Subsidiaries: IBS

**Internationella bibelsaellskapet**, see
International Bible Society

**Interskol Forlag AB**
Schaktugnsgatan 2, 216 16 Malmoe
*Tel:* (040) 51 01 95 *Fax:* (040) 15 06 25
*E-mail:* info@interskol.se
*Web Site:* www.interskol.se
*Key Personnel*
Dir: Kenneth Arvidsson
Founded: 1975
Specialize in school books.
ISBN Prefix(es): 91-7306

**Invandrarfoerlaget+**
Katrinedalsgatan 43, 504 51 Boras
*Tel:* (033) 13 60 70 *Fax:* (033) 13 60 75
*E-mail:* migrant@immi.se
*Web Site:* www.immi.se
*Key Personnel*
Editor: Miguel Benito
Founded: 1973
Subjects: Education, Ethnicity
ISBN Prefix(es): 91-85242; 91-7906
Number of titles published annually: 4 Print
Total Titles: 140 Print
*Parent Company:* Immigrant-institute, Ka-
trinedalsgatan 43, 50451 Boras

**ITK Laromedel AB**, see Lars Hokerbergs
Bokverlag

**Iustus Forlag AB**
Ostra Agatan 9, 753 22 Uppsala
*Tel:* (018) 693091 *Fax:* (018) 693099
*E-mail:* iustus@iustus.se
*Web Site:* www.iustus.se

*Key Personnel*
Man Dir: Eva Thorell *Tel:* (018) 693068
 *E-mail:* eva.thorell@iustus.se
Marketing: Ewa Waites *Tel:* (018) 693063
 *E-mail:* ewaw@iustus.se
Founded: 1973
Specialize in law books, aimed at both university level & practicing lawyers, judges, civil servants.
Subjects: Business, Economics, Finance, Government, Political Science, Law, Management, Public Administration
ISBN Prefix(es): 91-7678
Number of titles published annually: 40 Print
Total Titles: 200 Print

**IVA,** see Kungl Ingenjoersvetenskapsakademien (IVA)

**Jannersten Forlag AB+**
774 27 Avesta
*Tel:* (0226) 619 00 *Fax:* (0226) 10927
*E-mail:* bridge@jannersten.se
*Web Site:* www.jannersten.com
*Key Personnel*
Dir: Per Jannersten
Founded: 1939
Subjects: Crafts, Games, Hobbies
ISBN Prefix(es): 91-85024

**Johnston & Streiffert Editions+**
Soedermalmsgatan 35, 431 69 Moelndal
*Tel:* (031) 826160 *Fax:* (031) 825150
*Key Personnel*
President: Turlough Johnston *E-mail:* turlough. johnston@swipnet.se
Contact: Eleonore Wagner
Founded: 1985
Also acts as print broker & agent.
Subjects: Animals, Pets, Automotive, Crafts, Games, Hobbies, How-to, Maritime, Sports, Athletics
ISBN Prefix(es): 91-87036
Number of titles published annually: 3 Print
Total Titles: 10 Print
*Associate Companies:* Streiffert Foerlag, Stockholm
Subsidiaries: Johnston Print Consultants

**Liber Kartor,** *imprint of* Liber AB

**Klassikerforlaget**
PO Box 45022, 104 30 Stockholm
*Tel:* (08) 457 03 00 *Fax:* (08) 457 03 34
*E-mail:* klassikerforlaget@raben.se
*Key Personnel*
Editor: Anders Stroem
Founded: 1953
Subjects: Literature, Literary Criticism, Essays
ISBN Prefix(es): 91-7102; 91-88680
*Parent Company:* P A Norstrdt & Soner AB

**Konsultforlaget AB**
PO Box 2070, 750 02 Uppsala
*Tel:* (018) 55 50 80 *Fax:* (018) 55 50 81
*E-mail:* info@uppsala-publishing.se
*Web Site:* www.uppsala-publishing.se
*Key Personnel*
Man Dir: Mats Josephson
Founded: 1986
ISBN Prefix(es): 91-7005

**Kungl Ingenjoersvetenskapsakademien (IVA)**
 (Royal Swedish Academy of Engineering Sciences)
Grev Turegatan 14, 102 42 Stockholm SE
Mailing Address: PO Box 5073, 102 42 Stockholm
*Tel:* (08) 7912900 *Fax:* (08) 6115623
*E-mail:* info@iva.se
*Web Site:* www.iva.se *Cable:* Ivacademi

*Key Personnel*
President: Lena Torell
Editorial: Cissi Billgren Askwall
Editor: Eva Reinholdren *E-mail:* er@iva.se
Founded: 1919
Royal Swedish Academy of Engineering Sciences.
Subjects: Management, Science (General), Technology
ISBN Prefix(es): 91-7082

**Hans Richter Laromedel+**
Box 100, 645 22 Straengnaes
SAN: 105-0893
*Tel:* (0152) 150 60; (0200) 11 55 30 (orders)
 *Fax:* (0152) 151 40; (0200) 11 55 31 (orders)
*E-mail:* info@richter.d.se
*Web Site:* www.richter.d.se
*Key Personnel*
Dir: Hans Richter *E-mail:* post@richter.d.se
Founded: 1982
Also acts as agent, mail order distribution & direct marketing to businesses & schools.
Membership(s): Swedish Publishers Association; FSL.
Subjects: Education, English as a Second Language, Language Arts, Linguistics, Music, Dance
ISBN Prefix(es): 91-7884
Imprints: Nyforlaget
Subsidiaries: Bokforlaget Axplock
Distributor for Bokforlaget Axplock; Nyforlaget

**Lars Hokerbergs Bokverlag+**
Formerly ITK Laromedel AB
Box 8071, 10420 Stockholm
*Tel:* (08) 24 43 60 *Fax:* (08) 650 39 84
*Key Personnel*
Man Dir: Jan Hoekerberg
Contact: Annika Thiam
Founded: 1923
Subjects: Science (General), Technology
ISBN Prefix(es): 91-7084; 91-7157

**Bokforlaget Robert Larson AB+**
Box 6074, 121 06 Johanneshov
*Tel:* (08) 732 84 60 *Fax:* (08) 732 71 76
*E-mail:* info@larsonforlag.se
*Web Site:* www.larsonforlag.se *Cable:* LARSONBOOKS
*Key Personnel*
Dir: Birgitta Larson; Joakim Larson; Robert Larson
Founded: 1971
Subjects: Nonfiction (General)
ISBN Prefix(es): 91-514

**Legenda,** *imprint of* Bokfoerlaget Natur och Kultur

**Liber AB+**
Rasundavagen 18i Solna, 11398 Stockholm
*Tel:* (08) 6909200 *Fax:* (08) 6909458
*E-mail:* export@liber.se; infomaster@liber.se
*Web Site:* www.liber.se
*Key Personnel*
President: Jan Thurfell *E-mail:* hedwig. hermanson@liber.se
Subjects: Business, English as a Second Language, Geography, Geology, Health, Nutrition, History, Language Arts, Linguistics, Mathematics, Medicine, Nursing, Dentistry, Science (General), Social Sciences, Sociology, Technology
ISBN Prefix(es): 91-21; 91-40
*Parent Company:* Wolters Kluwer Scandinavia
Imprints: Almquist & Wiksell; Liber Ekonomi; Liber Hermods; Liber Kartor
Subsidiaries: Liber Distribution; Norstedts Tuvidik

**Liber Hermods AB+**
Besoksadress Norra Vallgatan 100, 205 10 Malmo
*Tel:* (040) 258600 *Fax:* (040) 304600
*Web Site:* www.liberhermods.se
*Key Personnel*
President: Per Bergknut
Founded: 1898
Specialize in educational & business publishing & distance education.
Membership(s): Euro Business Publishing Network.
ISBN Prefix(es): 91-21; 91-23

**Libris Bokforlaget+**
PO Box 1213, 701 12 Oerebro
*Tel:* (019) 208400 *Fax:* (019) 208430
*E-mail:* info@libris.se
*Web Site:* www.libris.se
*Key Personnel*
Man Dir: Soren Liljedahl *E-mail:* soren. liljedahl@libris.se
Publicity Dir: Anna Stenlund
Rights & Permissions: Inger Lundin
Founded: 1916
Subjects: Fiction, Theology
ISBN Prefix(es): 91-7194; 91-7195; 91-7218; 91-85796
*Parent Company:* Libris Media AB
*Book Club(s):* Libris Bok & Musikklubb

**Lidman Production AB+**
Vaertavaegen 8, 115 24 Stockholm
Mailing Address: PO Box 5098, 102 42 Stockholm
*Tel:* (08) 6633615 *Fax:* (08) 6633590
*E-mail:* lidman@canit.se
*Key Personnel*
Publisher: Sven Lidman *E-mail:* lidman@canit.se
Founded: 1973
Subjects: Education

**Metodistkyrkans Foerlag,** see Forlaget Sanctus (Metodistkyrkans Forlag)

**Mezopotamya Publishing & Distribution+**
Box 4036, 141 04 Huddinge
*Tel:* (08) 774 73 54 *Fax:* (08) 7110836
*Key Personnel*
Editor: Nedim Dagdeviren
Specialize in publishing & distribution of Kurdish books, children's books & musical productions.
Subjects: Asian Studies, Ethnicity, History, Language Arts, Linguistics
ISBN Prefix(es): 91-971307

**Bokfoerlaget Natur och Kultur+**
Karlavaegen 31, 102 54 Stockholm
Mailing Address: PO Box 27323, 102 54 Stockholm
*Tel:* (08) 4538600 *Fax:* (08) 4538790
*E-mail:* info@nok.se
*Web Site:* www.nok.se
*Key Personnel*
Man Dir & Chief Executive Officer: Lars Grahn
Editorial Dir, Academic Books, Fiction & Nonfiction: Christian Reimers
Editorial Dir, Textbooks: Lars Kaellquist
Rights & Permissions, Children's Books: Johanna Ringertz *E-mail:* johanna.ringertz@nok.se
Rights & Permissions, General Nonfiction & Fiction: Katarina Grip *E-mail:* katarina.grip@nok.se
Information Technology & New Media: Christina Forsberg
Founded: 1922
Subjects: Biography, Fiction, History, Nonfiction (General), Psychology, Psychiatry, Science (General), Social Sciences, Sociology
ISBN Prefix(es): 91-27; 91-582
Number of titles published annually: 350 Print
Total Titles: 5,000 Print; 12 CD-ROM; 60 Audio

Imprints: Legenda (commercial fiction & suspense novels)
Subsidiaries: Natur och Kultur/Fakta etc
*Book Club(s):* Boeckernas Klubb, Box 3317, 103 66 Stockholm; Natur och Kultur Direkt
*Warehouse:* Foerlagsdistribution, Skarpraettarvaegen 1, PO Box 706, Jaerfaella 176 27

**Natur och Kultur Fakta etc+**
Ostermalmsgatan 45, 11426 Stockholm
Mailing Address: Box 27323, 10254 Stockholm
*Tel:* (08) 4538725 *Fax:* (08) 4538798
*E-mail:* info@nok.se
*Web Site:* www.nok.se
*Key Personnel*
Man Dir: Rolf Ellnebrand *Tel:* (08) 4538729 *E-mail:* rolf.ellnebrand@nok.se
Production Manager: Torbjorn Tesch *Tel:* (08) 4538728 *E-mail:* torbjorn.tesch@nok.se
Permissions: Viveka Pettersson *Tel:* (08) 4538733 *E-mail:* viveka.pettersson@nok.se
Founded: 1935
Subjects: Agriculture, Animals, Pets, Cookery, Crafts, Games, Hobbies, Gardening, Plants, Health, Nutrition, House & Home, Photography, Science (General)
ISBN Prefix(es): 91-27
Number of titles published annually: 30 Print
Total Titles: 300 Print; 300 Online
*Parent Company:* Bokfoerlaget Natur och Kultur

**Nautiska Foerlaget AB** (The Nautical Publishing Co Ltd)+
Box 15410, 104 65 Stockholm
*Tel:* (08) 677 00 00 *Fax:* (08) 677 00 10
*E-mail:* nautiska.ab@nautiskamf.se *Cable:* Namco
*Key Personnel*
Manager: H Hultkrantz
Subjects: Maritime
ISBN Prefix(es): 91-970094; 91-89564; 91-973537

**Nordiska Bokhandelns**
Broetvaegen 32, 161 39 Bromma
*Tel:* (08) 26 98 09 *Fax:* (08) 25 42 46 *Cable:* NORDBOK
*Key Personnel*
Man Dir: Hans Molander
Founded: 1851
ISBN Prefix(es): 91-516
*Bookshop(s):* AB Nordiska Bokhandeln

**P A Norstedt & Soener AB**
PO Box 2052, 103 12 Stockholm
*Tel:* (08) 769 87 00 *Fax:* (08) 21 40 06
*Key Personnel*
Chief Executive: Kjell Bohlund
Contact: Lise-Lott Olofsson *Tel:* (08) 769 87 11 *E-mail:* lise-lott.olofsson@norstedts.se
Founded: 1823
Subsidiaries: Norstedts Akademiska Forlag; Norstedts Forlag; Bokforlaget Prisma; Raben & Sjoegren; Tiden
Foreign Rights: Pan Agency
*Book Club(s):* Barnens Bokklubb (Partially owned); Boeckernas Klubb (Partially owned); Clio (Partially owned); Hem & Tradgard; Manadens Bok (Partially owned); Mat & Njutning

**Norstedts Akademiska Forlag** (Norstedts Academic Publishers)
Subsidiary of P A Norstedt & Soener AB
PO Box 2052, 103 12 Stockholm
*Tel:* (08) 769 89 50 *Fax:* (08) 769 89 62
*E-mail:* info@norstedtsakademiska.se
*Web Site:* www.norstedtsakademiska.se
*Key Personnel*
Publishing Dir: Erik Liedberg
Market Coordinator: Amelie Bennet; Lovisa Boberg

Head of Production: Bjorn Westberg
*Ultimate Parent Company:* KF Media

**Norstedts Forlag+**
Subsidiary of P A Norstedt & Soener AB
PO Box 2052, 103 12 Stockholm
*Tel:* (08) 769 88 50 *Fax:* (08) 769 88 64
*E-mail:* info.norstedts@liber.se
*Web Site:* www.norstedts.se
*Key Personnel*
Man Dir: Svante Weyler *E-mail:* svante.weyler@norstedts.se
Rights & Permissions: Agneta Markas *E-mail:* agneta.markas@norstedts.se
Secretary: Gerd Ronnberg *E-mail:* gerd.ronnberg@norstedts.se
Founded: 1823
Subjects: Fiction, Nonfiction (General)
ISBN Prefix(es): 91-1
Number of titles published annually: 100 Print

**Norstedts Juridik AB**
Halsingegatan 49, 113 82 Stockholm
Mailing Address: PO Box 6472, 113 82 Stockholm
*Tel:* (08) 690 9100 *Fax:* (08) 690 9033
*E-mail:* kundservice.njab@liber.se
*Web Site:* www.nj.se
Subjects: Law
ISBN Prefix(es): 91-38; 91-7598; 91-87364; 91-39; 91-88134; 91-970450; 91-970756
*Parent Company:* Wolters Kluwer

**Bokforlaget Nya Doxa AB+**
Kungsgatan 5, 713 23 Nora
Mailing Address: Box 113, 713 23 Nora
*Tel:* (0587) 104 16 *Fax:* (0587) 142 57
*E-mail:* info@nya-doxa.se
*Web Site:* www.nya-doxa.se
*Key Personnel*
Publisher: Dr David Stansvik *E-mail:* david.stansvik@nya-doxa.se
International Rights: Karina Klok Madsen
Founded: 1991 (1974 as Bokfoerlaget Doxa AB)
Also distribution & sales for Bokfoerlaget Thales, Sweden.
Subjects: Art, Biblical Studies, Communications, Ethnicity, History, Literature, Literary Criticism, Essays, Nonfiction (General), Philosophy, Science (General), Social Sciences, Sociology, Theology, Women's Studies
ISBN Prefix(es): 91-88248; 91-578
Number of titles published annually: 30 Print
Total Titles: 200 Print

**Nyforlaget,** *imprint of* Hans Richter Laromedel

**Bokforlaget Opal AB**
Tegelbergsvaegen 31, 161 02 Bromma
Mailing Address: PO Box 20 113, 161 02 Bromma
*Tel:* (08) 6571990 *Fax:* (08) 6183470
*E-mail:* opal@opal.se
*Web Site:* www.opal.se
*Key Personnel*
Man Dir: Bengt Christell
Joint Publisher: Valborg Segerhjelm
Founded: 1973
Subjects: Animals, Pets, Fiction, Humor, Literature, Literary Criticism, Essays, Social Sciences, Sociology, Sports, Athletics, Adventure, Classics, Horror & Ghost, Nature
ISBN Prefix(es): 91-7270; 91-7299
*Book Club(s):* Barnens Bokklub (jointly owned)

**Ordfront Foerlag AB** (Ordfront Publishing House)+
PO Box 17506, 118 91 Stockholm
*Tel:* (08) 462 44 00 *Fax:* (08) 4624490
*E-mail:* forlaget@ordfront.se; info@ordfront.se

*Web Site:* www.ordfront.se *Cable:* ORDFRONT STOCKHOLM
*Key Personnel*
Man Dir: Leif Ericsson
Editorial, Rights & Permissions: Eva Stenberg *E-mail:* eva@ordfront.se
Vice President & Publishing Dir: Jan-Erik Pettersson
Founded: 1969
Membership(s): Swedish Publishers Association; Specialize in history, politics, journalism & fiction.
Subjects: Fiction, History, Journalism, Publishing & Book Trade Reference, Social Sciences, Sociology
ISBN Prefix(es): 91-7324; 91-7037
Total Titles: 50 Print
Imprints: Calago Foerlag
*Book Club(s):* Ordfront Bookclub
*Distribution Center:* Foerlagssystem AB, PO Box 30195, S-10425 Stockholm

**Pagina Forlags AB+**
PO Box 2103, 174 02 Sundbyberg
*Tel:* (08) 564 218 00 *Fax:* (08) 564 218 19
*E-mail:* info@pagina.se
*Web Site:* www.pagina.se
*Key Personnel*
President: Lauri Pappinen
Founded: 1979
Subjects: Computer Science
ISBN Prefix(es): 91-86200; 91-86201; 91-636
*Parent Company:* Pagina AB
Subsidiaries: Pagina Oy
*Orders to:* FoerlagsSystem AB, Box 13195, 104 25 Stockholm *Tel:* (08) 657 19 90 *Fax:* (08) 657 19 95 *E-mail:* order@fsys.se

**Pandang,** *imprint of* Raben och Sjoegren Bokforlag

**Bokforlaget Plus AB**
Sankt Eriksgatan 48, 112 34 Stockholm
*Tel:* (08) 654 74 08
*Key Personnel*
Man Dir: Bengt Svensson
Founded: 1976
Subjects: Fiction, Nonfiction (General)
ISBN Prefix(es): 91-7406

**Bokforlaget Prisma+**
Subsidiary of P A Norstedt & Soener AB
Tryckerigatan 4, 103 12 Stockholm
Mailing Address: PO Box 2052, 103 12 Stockholm
*Tel:* (08) 7698900; (08) 7698700 (international rights) *Fax:* (08) 241276; (08) 7698804 (international rights)
*E-mail:* prisma@prismabok.se
*Web Site:* www.prismabok.se
*Key Personnel*
Man Dir: Viveca Ekelund *E-mail:* viveca.ekelund@prismabok.se
Secretary: Gunnel Nordsater *E-mail:* gunnel.nordsater@prismabok.se
Founded: 1963
Subjects: Animals, Pets, Child Care & Development, Cookery, Fiction, Gardening, Plants, Health, Nutrition, History, House & Home, Natural History
ISBN Prefix(es): 91-518
Foreign Rights: Pan Agency

**Psykologifoerlaget AB+**
Arstaangsvagen 1C, Box 47054, 100 74 Stockholm
*Tel:* (08) 775 09 00; (08) 775 09 10 (orders) *Fax:* (08) 775 09 20
*E-mail:* info@psykologiforlaget.se
*Web Site:* www.psykologiforlaget.se

*Key Personnel*
Man Dir: Catharina Mabon
Founded: 1957
Subjects: Education, Psychology, Psychiatry
ISBN Prefix(es): 91-7418


**R & S Books**, *imprint of* Raben och Sjoegren
Bokforlag


**Raben och Sjoegren Bokforlag+**
Subsidiary of P A Norstedt & Soener AB
Tryckerigatan 4, 103 12 Stockholm
Mailing Address: PO Box 2052, 103 12 Stockholm
*Tel:* (08) 7698800 *Fax:* (08) 7698813
*E-mail:* raben-sjogren@raben.se
*Web Site:* www.raben.se
*Key Personnel*
Publishing Dir: Suzanne Ohman-Sunden
 *E-mail:* suzanne.ohman-sunden@raben.se
Publisher: Birgitta Westin *E-mail:* birgitta.
 westin@raben.se
Secretary: Alva Settepassi *E-mail:* alva.
 settepassi@raben.se
Founded: 1942
Subjects: Nonfiction (General)
ISBN Prefix(es): 91-29
Imprints: Citadell; Pandang; R & S Books; Tiden
*Book Club(s):* Barnens Bokklubb (jointly owned)


**Bokforlaget Rediviva, Facsimileforlaget**
PO Box 15148, 161 15 Bromma
*Tel:* (08) 25 70 07
*Key Personnel*
Man Dir: Karin Skrutkowska
Founded: 1968
Subjects: Geography, Geology
ISBN Prefix(es): 91-7120


**Richters Egmont**
Sallerupsvaegen 9, 205 75 Malmoe
*Tel:* (040) 38 06 00 *Fax:* (040) 933708
*E-mail:* egmont@egmont.com
*Web Site:* www.egmont.com
*Telex:* 33180 richt S
*Key Personnel*
Man Dir, Rights & Permissions: Lars G Gustafsson
Editorial: Ia Atterholm; Annika Bladh
Sales: Lena Oeman; Ulf Ottosson
Production: Anders Enquist
Founded: 1942
Subjects: Fiction, Nonfiction (General), Comics/
 Cartoons
ISBN Prefix(es): 91-7705; 91-7706; 91-7707; 91-
 7709; 91-7711; 91-7715
*Parent Company:* Gutenberghus Group, Copenhagen, Denmark
*Book Club(s):* Kalle Ankas Bokklubb; Kokboksklubben God Mat; Laeslandet; Richters Bokklubb; Richters Ungdomsbokklub; Skoenhet och Haelsa; Spaenningsbokklubben


**Samsprak Forlags AB**
PO Box 247, 701 44 Oerebro
*Tel:* (019) 13 24 45 *Fax:* (019) 18 72 55
*E-mail:* info@samsprak.se
*Web Site:* www.samsprak.se
*Key Personnel*
Contact: Sven Olov Stalfelt
Founded: 1980
Subjects: Communications, Education
ISBN Prefix(es): 91-86020; 91-88052
Total Titles: 10 Print; 1 CD-ROM; 14 Audio


**Forlaget Sanctus (Metodistkyrkans Forlag)**
PO Box 45130, 104 30 Stockholm
*Tel:* (08) 31 55 70 *Fax:* (08) 31 55 79
*Telex:* 909 Teleopr S
Founded: 1873

The Publishing House of the United Methodist
 Church in Sweden.
Subjects: Religion - Protestant, Theology
ISBN Prefix(es): 91-7214


**Schultz Forlag AB**
Asogatan 164, 116 32 Stockholm
*Fax:* (08) 641 35 36
*Key Personnel*
Dir: Barbro Schultz-Lundestam *Tel:* (01)
 43298392 *E-mail:* Lundest@attglobal.net
Founded: 1982
Specializes in film/video production & novels,
 artbooks & poetry.
Subjects: Art, Film, Video, Literature, Literary
 Criticism, Essays, Photography, Poetry
ISBN Prefix(es): 91-87370
Number of titles published annually: 4 Print
Total Titles: 30 Print
*Associate Companies:* Schultz Forlag SARL
Distributed by Printed Matter (New York)
*Distribution Center:* Amigo Musik AB, Fredrik
 Boquist *Tel:* (08) 5566970 *Fax:* (08) 55696979
 *Web Site:* www.amigo.se


**Bokforlaget Semic AB**
Landsvaegen 57, 172 25 Sundbyberg
Mailing Address: Box 1243, 172 25 Sundbyberg
*Tel:* (08) 799 30 50 *Fax:* (08) 799 30 64
*E-mail:* info@semic.se
*Web Site:* www.semic.se
*Key Personnel*
Publisher: Mans Gahrton *E-mail:* mans.gahrton@
 semic.se
Founded: 1945
Subjects: Animals, Pets, Architecture & Interior
 Design, Cookery, Crafts, Games, Hobbies, Gardening, Plants, House & Home, Sports, Athletics
ISBN Prefix(es): 91-552
*Parent Company:* Semic International AB


**Semic Bokforlaget International AB+**
Landsvaegen 57, 172 25 Sundbyberg
Mailing Address: Box 1243, 172 25 Sundbyberg
*Tel:* (08) 779 30 50 *Fax:* (08) 799 30 64
*E-mail:* info@semic.se
*Web Site:* www.semic.se *Cable:* SEMICPRESS S
*Key Personnel*
Man Dir: Richard Ekstroem
Founded: 1950
Subjects: Cookery, Crafts, Games, Hobbies, Humor, Sports, Athletics
ISBN Prefix(es): 91-552
*Parent Company:* Bonnierforetagen, Torsgatan 21,
 113 90 Stockholm
Subsidiaries: Bokfoerlaget Semic AB; Jultidningsfoerlaget AB; Kustannus Oy Semic; Semic
 Press AB


**Bokforlaget Settern AB+**
Florshult, 286 92 Oerkelljunga
*Tel:* (0435) 80070 *Fax:* (0435) 80400
*E-mail:* info@settern.se
*Web Site:* www.settern.se
*Key Personnel*
Man Dir: Magdalena Roenneholm
 *E-mail:* magdalena@settern.se
Sales, Publicity, Advertising Dir: Joergen Wahlen;
 Tomas Wahlen
Founded: 1974
Specialize in hunting & fishing books.
Membership(s): Svenska Forlaggare foreningen,
 NOFF.
Subjects: Nonfiction (General), Hunting & Fishing
ISBN Prefix(es): 91-7586; 91-85274
Number of titles published annually: 15 Print
Total Titles: 600 Print
*Distribution Center:* BTj Seelig & direct Bokforlaget Settern

**Sjoestrands Foerlag**
Box 1305, 172 26 Sundbyberg
*Tel:* (08) 29 99 32 *Fax:* (08) 98 46 45
*Key Personnel*
Man Dir: Ulla-Britt Sjoestrand
Editor: Mr Stellan Forsman
Founded: 1978
Subjects: Astrology, Occult, Fiction, Nonfiction
 (General), Science Fiction, Fantasy
ISBN Prefix(es): 91-7574


**SNS Foerlag+**
Skoeldungagatan 1-2, 114 27 Stockholm
Mailing Address: Box 5629, 114 86 Stockholm
*Tel:* (08) 507 025 00 *Fax:* (08) 507 025 15
*E-mail:* info@sns.se
*Web Site:* www.sns.se
*Key Personnel*
Man Dir: Torgny Wadensjoe
Founded: 1948
Subjects: Economics, Social Sciences, Sociology
ISBN Prefix(es): 91-7150


**Sober Foerlags AB**
10536 Stockholm
*Tel:* (08) 672 6000 *Fax:* (08) 672 6001
*Key Personnel*
Man Dir: Kjell E Johanson
Editorial: Ann-Marie Tjaernkvist
Founded: 1972
Subjects: Health, Nutrition, Social Sciences, Sociology
ISBN Prefix(es): 91-7296
*Orders to:* Sober Forlags AB, Metallvagen 4, 435
 83 Molnlycke


**Bokforlaget Spektra AB+**
PO Box 7024, 300 07 Halmstad
*Tel:* (035) 360 30 *Fax:* (035) 361 77
*Key Personnel*
Man Dir: Ake Hallberg; Solveig Hallberg
Founded: 1965
Subjects: Computer Science, Crafts, Games, Hobbies, Fiction, How-to, Publishing & Book
 Trade Reference, Science (General)
ISBN Prefix(es): 91-7136
*Associate Companies:* Grafisk Kompetens, Spektra Studio AB, Box 7039, 300 07 Halmstad


**Stenstroems Bokfoerlag AB+**
PO Box 24086, 104 50 Stockholm
*Tel:* (08) 6637601; (08) 662078028 *Fax:* (08)
 6632201
*Key Personnel*
Publisher: Bengt Stenstroem
Founded: 1976
Specialize in reference books.
ISBN Prefix(es): 91-86448; 91-86600; 91-88970;
 91-970221; 91-970393
*Associate Companies:* Interpublishing AB Stenstroem


**Frank Stenvalls Forlag+**
Foereningsgatan 67, 211 52 Malmoe
Mailing Address: Box 17111, 200 10 Malmoe
*Tel:* (040) 127703 *Fax:* (040) 127700
*E-mail:* fstenval@algonet.se
*Key Personnel*
Man Dir: Frank Stenvall
Founded: 1966
Subjects: Aeronautics, Aviation, Maritime, Transportation
ISBN Prefix(es): 91-7266
Number of titles published annually: 5 Print
Total Titles: 60 Print
*Bookshop(s):* Stenvalls
*Book Club(s):* Swedish Military Bookclub


**Stiftelsen Kursverksamhetens Foerlag**, see
 Folkuniversitetets foerlag

**Streiffert Forlag AB**
Karlavaegen 71, 102 47 Stockholm
Mailing Address: PO Box 5334, 102 47 Stockholm
*Tel:* (08) 661 58 80 *Fax:* (08) 783 04 33
*E-mail:* info@streiffert.se
*Web Site:* www.streiffert.se
*Key Personnel*
Man Dir: Bo Streiffert *E-mail:* bo@streiffert.se
Founded: 1985
Subjects: Travel
ISBN Prefix(es): 91-7886
Number of titles published annually: 8 Print
Total Titles: 41 Print

**Stroemberg B&T Forlag AB+**
Box 65, 162 11 Vallingby
*Tel:* (08) 6201900 *Fax:* (08) 7399836
*E-mail:* marcus@stromberg.se
*Web Site:* www.stromberg.se
*Key Personnel*
Publisher: Hanserik Tonnheim
Founded: 1990
Subjects: Art, History, Religion - Other, Sports,
  Athletics
ISBN Prefix(es): 91-7151; 91-7148; 91-7198; 91-
  85110; 91-86184
Imprints: Idrottsantikvariatet; Stroembergs Bok-
  forlag
*Warehouse:* Johnson & Johnsonhuset, Staffausvag
  2, 19184 Sollentuna

**Stroembergs Bokforlag**, *imprint of* Stroemberg
  B&T Forlag AB

**Stromberg+**
Box 65, 162 11 Vaellingby
*Tel:* (08) 6201900 *Fax:* (08) 7399836
*E-mail:* marcus@stromberg.se
*Web Site:* www.stromberg.se
*Key Personnel*
Publisher: Hanserik Tonnheim
Man Dir: Thomas Bjorklund
Founded: 1991
Subjects: Cookery, Economics, Education, Law,
  Nonfiction (General), Regional Interests
ISBN Prefix(es): 91-7151; 91-7148
*Warehouse:* Seelig & Co, Box 1308, Solna
*Orders to:* Seelig & Co, Box 1308, Solna

**Studentlitteratur AB+**
Akergraenden 1, 221 00 Lund
Mailing Address: PO Box 141, 221 00 Lund
*Tel:* (046) 312000 *Fax:* (046) 305338
*E-mail:* info@studentlitteratur.se
*Web Site:* www.studentlitteratur.se
*Key Personnel*
President: Stefan Persson
Publishing Dir: Robert Kipowski; Sven-Ake
  Lennung
Rights Manager: Kristina Karlssol
  *E-mail:* kristina.karlssol@studentlitteratur.se;
  Susanne Worning *E-mail:* susanne.worning@
  studentlitteratur.se
Production: Thomas Lundgren
Founded: 1963
Subjects: Accounting, Behavioral Sciences, Bio-
  logical Sciences, Business, Chemistry, Chem-
  ical Engineering, Computer Science, Educa-
  tion, Engineering (General), Language Arts,
  Linguistics, Law, Management, Mathemat-
  ics, Medicine, Nursing, Dentistry, Philosophy,
  Physical Sciences, Psychology, Psychiatry, So-
  cial Sciences, Sociology, Technology
ISBN Prefix(es): 91-44; 91-88618; 91-971791
Number of titles published annually: 200 Print
Total Titles: 2,500 Print
*Parent Company:* Bratt International A/B, Lund

**Studieforlaget i Goteborg Stiftelsen
  Kursverksamhetens Forlag**
Box 2542, 403 17 Gothenburg

*Tel:* (031) 106580 *Fax:* (031) 135359
*E-mail:* kursbokhandeln@folkuniversitetet.se
*Key Personnel*
Contact: Bo Nordell
ISBN Prefix(es): 91-7602

**Svenska alliansmissionens (SAM) foerlage**
Box 11054, 551 11 Joenkoeping
*Tel:* (036) 71 98 70 *Fax:* (036) 71 98 20
*E-mail:* info@sam.f.se
*Web Site:* www.sam.f.se *Cable:* SAM
*Key Personnel*
Man Dir: Torbjoern Wetteroe
Subjects: Religion - Other
ISBN Prefix(es): 91-7484

**Svenska Arbetsgivareforeningens forlag**
114 82 Stockholm
*Tel:* (08) 553 430 00 *Fax:* (08) 553 430 99
  *Cable:* EMPLOYERS
*Key Personnel*
Manager: Kjell Frykhammar
ISBN Prefix(es): 91-7152

**Svenska Foerlaget liv & ledarskap ab+**
Box 3313, 103 66 Stockholm
*Tel:* (08) 412 27 00 *Fax:* (08) 411 41 30
*E-mail:* kundservice@svenskaforlaget.com
*Web Site:* www.svenskaforlaget.com
*Key Personnel*
President: Lena Kjellgren
Publisher: Peter Stenson
Founded: 1982
Subjects: Animals, Pets, Biography, Business, Ca-
  reer Development, History, Human Relations,
  Management, Nonfiction (General), Philosophy,
  Psychology, Psychiatry, Self-Help
ISBN Prefix(es): 91-7738
*Parent Company:* Schibsted ASA
*Book Club(s):* Bokklubben Liv & Ledarskap

**Svenska Institutet+**
Skeppsbron 2, Box 7434, 103 91 Stockholm
*Tel:* (08) 453 78 00 *Fax:* (08) 20 72 48
*E-mail:* si@si.se
*Web Site:* www.si.se
Founded: 1945
Specialize in information about Sweden-culture &
  society in many languages.
ISBN Prefix(es): 91-520

**The Swedish Association of Educational
  Publishers (Foreningen Svenska
  Laromedelsproducenter)**, see Foreningen
  Svenska Laromedelsproducenter (The Swedish
  Association of Educational Publishers)

**Teknografiska Institutet AB**
PO Box 1243, 171 24 Solna
*Tel:* (08) 83 42 85 *Fax:* (08) 73 04 13
*Key Personnel*
Production: Ingrid Karpebaeck
Founded: 1946
ISBN Prefix(es): 91-7172

**Tiden**, *imprint of* Raben och Sjoegren Bokforlag

**Timbro+**
Grev Turegatan 19, 102 45 Stockholm
Mailing Address: PO Box 5234, 102 45 Stock-
  holm
*Tel:* (08) 587 898 00 *Fax:* (08) 587 898 55
*E-mail:* info@timbro.se
*Web Site:* www.timbro.se
*Key Personnel*
President: Mattias Bengtsson
Production: Barbro Bengtson
Permissions & International Rights: Kristina von
  Unge *Tel:* (08) 587 898 34 *E-mail:* kristinau@
  timbro.se

Founded: 1978
Publishes a periodical for culture, politics & eco-
  nomics (Smedjan-www.smedjan.com).
Subjects: Economics, Government, Political Sci-
  ence, Nonfiction (General), Social Sciences,
  Sociology, Free Enterprise
ISBN Prefix(es): 91-7566
*Parent Company:* Stiftelsen Fritt Naringsliv

**Tryckeriforlaget AB+**
PO Box 7093, 183 07 Taby
*Tel:* (08) 756 74 45 *Fax:* (08) 756 03 95
*E-mail:* tidkort@tidkort.se
*Key Personnel*
Dir: Leif Lindberg
Subjects: Antiques, Business, Wine & Spirits
ISBN Prefix(es): 91-970081; 91-971201; 91-
  972765

**Var Skola Foerlag AB+**
Riddargatan 17, 114 57 Stockholm
*Tel:* (08) 662 33 51 *Fax:* (08) 6621843
*E-mail:* var.skola@pi.se
*Key Personnel*
Man Dir: Gunnel Radahl; Stig Radahl
Subjects: Nonfiction (General)
ISBN Prefix(es): 91-7396

**Verbum Forlag AB+**
Goetgatan 22 A, Stockholm
Mailing Address: Box 15169, 104 65 Stockholm
*Tel:* (08) 743 65 00 *Fax:* (08) 641 45 85
*E-mail:* info.forlag@verbum.se
*Web Site:* www.verbum.se
*Key Personnel*
Man Dir: Johan F Dalman
Founded: 1911
Membership(s): FSL, SBF, IPA & Worlddidac.
Subjects: Music, Dance, Religion - Other, Theol-
  ogy
ISBN Prefix(es): 91-526
*Parent Company:* Verbum AB
*Associate Companies:* Gleerups Foerlag; Foer-
  lagshuset Gothia
Subsidiaries: Libraria Konsthantverk AB
Divisions: Publishing, Stationery
*Bookshop(s):* V Hamngatan 21, Gothenburg

**AB Wahlstroem & Widstrand+**
Sturegatan 32, 114 85 Stockholm
Mailing Address: Box 5587, 114 85 Stockholm
*Tel:* (08) 696 84 80 *Fax:* (08) 696 83 80
*E-mail:* info@wwd.se
*Web Site:* www.wwd.se *Cable:* WAHLWID S
*Key Personnel*
Publisher & Man Dir: Unn Palm
Sales Dir: Bengt Hennings
Rights & Permissions: Marina Kosjanov
  *E-mail:* marina.kosjanov@wwd.se
Founded: 1884
Specialize in novels, poetry, illustrated nature
  books, travel guides, health, psychology.
Subjects: Fiction, Health, Nutrition, Nonfiction
  (General), Poetry, Psychology, Psychiatry
ISBN Prefix(es): 91-46
*Parent Company:* Bonnierforlagen AB

**Wahlstrom & Widstrand**
Sturegatan 32, 114 85 Stockholm
Mailing Address: PO Box 5587, 114 85 Stock-
  holm
*Tel:* (08) 696 84 80 *Fax:* (08) 696 83 80
*E-mail:* info@wwd.se
*Web Site:* www.wwd.se *Cable:* Bebolag
*Key Personnel*
Man Dir: Unn Palm *Tel:* (08) 696 84 81
  *E-mail:* unn.palm@wwd.se
Subjects: Art, Biography, Cookery, Fiction, His-
  tory, Nonfiction (General)
ISBN Prefix(es): 91-46; 91-500

**B Wahlstroms**
Warfvinges vaeg 30, 104 25 Stockholm
Mailing Address: PO Box 30022, 104 25 Stockholm
*Tel:* (08) 619 86 00 *Fax:* (08) 618 97 61
*E-mail:* info@wahlstroms.se
*Web Site:* www.wahlstroms.se
*Key Personnel*
Chairman & Man Dir: Bertil Wahlstroem
Editor-in-Chief & Permissions: Brit-Marie Johansson
Founded: 1911
Subjects: Fiction, Nonfiction (General)
ISBN Prefix(es): 91-32
*Parent Company:* J A Lindblads Bokfoerlag AB
*Bookshop(s):* Kungsholmens Bokhandel AB, PO Box 49014, 100 28 Stockholm
*Warehouse:* Loevasvaegen 26, 791 29 Falun

**Zindermans AB**
1a Langgatan 6, 413 03 Gothenburg
Mailing Address: Box 31029, 400 32 Gothenburg
*Tel:* (031) 775 04 00 *Fax:* (031) 12 06 60 *Cable:* ZINDERMANS
*Key Personnel*
Man Dir: Leif Stigsjoeoe
Founded: 1960
Subjects: Biography, Fiction, Government, Political Science, History, How-to, Nonfiction (General), Psychology, Psychiatry, Social Sciences, Sociology
ISBN Prefix(es): 91-528

# Switzerland

## General Information

*Capital:* Berne
*Language:* 3 official: German, French and Italian
*Religion:* Protestant and Roman Catholic
*Population:* 6.8 million
*Bank Hours:* 0800 or 0830-1200 or 1230, 1300 or 1330-1630 Monday-Friday
*Shop Hours:* 0800-1200, 1330-1830 Monday-Friday; in most cities, closed Monday morning; 0800-1200, 1330-1600 or 1700 Saturday
*Currency:* 100 rappen (centimes) = 1 Swiss franc
*Export/Import Information:* Member of the European Free Trade Association. No tariff on books. Most books exempt from Turnover Tax. Advertising matter usually dutiable, some exempt from Turnover Tax. 2% VAT on books. No import licenses required. No exchange controls.
*Copyright:* UCC, Berne, Florence (see Copyright Conventions, pg xi)

**Aare-Verlag+**
Ausserfeldstr 9, 5036 Oberentfelden
*Tel:* (062) 836 86 86 *Fax:* (062) 836 86 20
*E-mail:* bildung@sauerlaender.ch
*Web Site:* www.sauerlaender.ch
*Key Personnel*
Publishing Manager: Hans Christof Saueriaender
Editor: Barbara Kueper
International Rights: Claudia Kukla
Founded: 1953
Subjects: Education
ISBN Prefix(es): 3-7260
Subsidiaries: Verlag Sauerlaende
*Orders to:* Koch, Neff & Oetringer, Schockenriedstr 39, 70565 Stuttgart, Germany

**AD**, *imprint of* Editions Andre Delcourt & Cie

**Editions Ad Solem**
2, rue des Voisins, 1211 Geneva 12
Mailing Address: Postfach 479, 1211 Geneva 12
*Tel:* (022) 321 19 30 *Fax:* (022) 321 19 31
*E-mail:* office@adsolem.ch
*Web Site:* www.ad-solem.com
Subjects: Christian literature

**ADIRA+**
29, rue du Rhone, Geneve 1204
*Tel:* (022) 312 25 43 *Fax:* (022) 312 26 13
*E-mail:* adira@adira.net
*Web Site:* www.adira.net
*Key Personnel*
President: Dominique Mottas
Author: Michel Potay
Founded: 1974
Also acts as distributor.
Subjects: Philosophy, Religion - Other, Spirituality
ISBN Prefix(es): 2-901821
Number of titles published annually: 2 Print
Total Titles: 12 Print
*Parent Company:* Editions Michel Potay
*Ultimate Parent Company:* Maison de la Revelation
*U.S. Office(s):* ADIRA New York, 590 Madison Ave, 21st Floor, New York, NY 10022, United States
Distributed by Hervey's; Pathways

**Adonia-Verlag+**
Postfach 3060, 8800 Thalwil
*Tel:* (01) 7207712 *Fax:* (01) 9800622
*Web Site:* www.libroplus.ch
Founded: 1986
Membership(s): SBVV, SSV, Pen.
Subjects: Poetry, Women's Studies
ISBN Prefix(es): 3-905009

**Editions L'Age d'Homme - La Cite**
Rue de Geneve 10, 1000 Lausanne 9
Mailing Address: CP 32, 1000 Lausanne
*Tel:* (021) 312 00 95 *Fax:* (021) 320 84 40
*E-mail:* agedhomme@iprolink.ch
*Key Personnel*
Man Dir: Vladimir Dimitrijevic
Founded: 1966
Subjects: Art, Biography, Drama, Theater, Fiction, Film, Video, Literature, Literary Criticism, Essays, Music, Dance, Philosophy, Poetry, Psychology, Psychiatry, Regional Interests, Religion - Other, Science Fiction, Fantasy, Social Sciences, Sociology
ISBN Prefix(es): 2-8251
*Branch Office(s)*
5 rue Ferou, 75006 Paris, France *Tel:* (01) 46 34 18 51 *Fax:* (01) 40 51 71 02
*Bookshop(s):* Librairie la Proue, Escaliers du Marche 17, 1000 Lausanne; Librairie Le Rameau d'Or, 19 blvd Georges Favon, 1200 Geneva

**J H Goehre Albanus Verlag**
Hulfteggstr 10, 8401 Winterthur 1
*Tel:* (052) 293503
*Key Personnel*
Contact: J H Goehre
Founded: 1946
Membership(s): SBVV/VVDS
ISBN Prefix(es): 3-85510

**Amboss-Verlag E Widmer+**
Industriestr 25, Postfach 364, 9434 Au SG
*Tel:* (071) 711236; (071) 7444590 *Fax:* (071) 714590
*Key Personnel*
Contact: Charlotte Knoepfli-Widmer
Founded: 1968
ISBN Prefix(es): 3-85517

**Ammann Verlag & Co+**
Neptunstr 20, 8032 Zurich
*Tel:* (01) 268 10 40 *Fax:* (01) 268 10 50
*E-mail:* info@ammann.ch
*Web Site:* www.ammann.ch
*Key Personnel*
Publisher: Egon Ammann; Marie-Luise Flammersfeld
Sales, Marketing & Press: Patrik Zeller
Production: Beate Becker
Editor: Stephanie von Harrach
Editor, Rights & Permissions: Laurenz Bolliger
Founded: 1981
Subjects: Art, Biography, Fiction, History, Literature, Literary Criticism, Essays, Nonfiction (General), Poetry, Religion - Islamic, Science (General), Travel
ISBN Prefix(es): 3-250
Number of titles published annually: 20 Print
*Orders to:* Ammann Verlag, Buchzentrum AG, B2, 4601 Olten

**Antonius-Verlag**
Gaertnerstr 7, 4500 Solothurn
*Tel:* (032) 6253742
*Key Personnel*
Contact: Maria Gasser
Subjects: Education, Medicine, Nursing, Dentistry, Psychology, Psychiatry
ISBN Prefix(es): 3-85520
*Branch Office(s)*
Testzentrale der Deutschen Psychologen, Robert-Bosch-Breite 25, 37079 Gottingen, Germany
Testzentrale der Schweizer Psychologen, Laenggassstr 76, Bern 9, Germany
Universitaetsverlag, Perolles 42, 1700 Fribourg

**Arche Verlag AG+**
Niederdorfstr 90, 8001 Zurich
*Tel:* (01) 252 24 10 *Fax:* (01) 261 11 15
*E-mail:* info@arche-verlag.com
*Web Site:* www.arche-verlag.com
*Telex:* 815239
*Key Personnel*
Owner: Elisabeth Raabe; Regina Vitali
Founded: 1944
Subjects: Biography, Fiction, Literature, Literary Criticism, Essays, Music, Dance, Poetry, Travel
ISBN Prefix(es): 3-7160
Divisions: Arche Verlag GmbH

**Archivio Storico Ticinese**
Via del Bramantino 3, 6500 Bellinzona
*Tel:* (091) 820 0101 *Fax:* (091) 825 1874
*E-mail:* casagrande@casagrande-online.ch
*Web Site:* www.casagrande-online.ch
*Telex:* 846266
*Key Personnel*
Man Dir: Virgilio Gilardoni
Sales, Production: Libero Casagrande
Founded: 1960
Subjects: Art, Economics, History, Literature, Literary Criticism, Essays
ISBN Prefix(es): 88-7714
*Parent Company:* Edizioni Casagrande SA

**Ariston Editions+**
Imprint of Heinrich Hegendubel Verlag AG
Villa Bellevue, Hauptstr 14, Kreuzlingen 8280
Mailing Address: Postfach 1066, 1211 Geneve 6
*Tel:* (071) 6771190 *Fax:* (071) 6771191
*E-mail:* 106420.3235@compuserve.com
*Telex:* 413428 arve ch *Cable:* ARISTON
*Key Personnel*
Man Dir, Editorial & Sales: Dr Monika Roell
Founded: 1964
Subjects: How-to, Medicine, Nursing, Dentistry, Nonfiction (General), Parapsychology, Psychology, Psychiatry, Self-Help
ISBN Prefix(es): 3-7205; 3-7162; 2-8267
*Branch Office(s)*
Ariston Verlag GmbH und Co Verlagsservice,

Boschetsriederstr 12, 81379 Munich, Germany
*Tel:* (089) 7241034 *Fax:* (089) 7241718
Ariston-P R Presse, Hauptrasse 14, 8280 Kreu-
zlingen

**Armenia Editions+**
PO Box 2621, 1260 Nyon
*Tel:* (022) 794474593
*Key Personnel*
Contact: Elisabeth Tavitian
Founded: 1991
Membership(s): American Booksellers Associa-
tion.
Subjects: Architecture & Interior Design, Art,
Biography, Cookery, History, Language Arts,
Linguistics, Literature, Literary Criticism, Es-
says, Music, Dance, Poetry, Regional Interests,
Religion - Other, Romance, Theology, Travel,
Armenian Art, Armenian History, Armenian
Literature, Religion-Apostolic
ISBN Prefix(es): 2-88421

**Collection Artou,** *imprint of* Editions Olizane

**Ascona Presse**
Passaggio San Pietro 7, 6612 Ascona
*Tel:* (091) 791 13 34 *Fax:* (091) 791 13 34
*E-mail:* info@rmeuter.ch
*Web Site:* www.rmeuter.ch
Founded: 1986
Subjects: Art

**ASELF,** see Association Suisse des Editeurs de
Langue Francaise

**Association pour la Diffusion Internationale de
la Revelation d'Ares,** see ADIRA

**Association Suisse des Editeurs de Langue
Francaise** (Swiss Publishers' Association
(French Language))
2, Av Agassit, 1001 Lausanne
*Tel:* (021) 3197111 *Fax:* (021) 7963311
*E-mail:* pschibli@centrepatronal.ch
*Key Personnel*
President: Francine Bouchet
Subjects: Architecture & Interior Design, Busi-
ness, Earth Sciences, Economics, Environmen-
tal Studies, Fiction, History, How-to, Law,
Medicine, Nursing, Dentistry, Physics, Sci-
ence (General), Self-Help, Coffee Table Books,
Ecology, Environmental Science, Picture Books
ISBN Prefix(es): 2-88303

**Astrodata AG+**
Albisriederstr 232, 8047 Zurich
*Tel:* (043) 343 33 33 *Fax:* (043) 343 33 43
*E-mail:* info@astrodata.ch
*Web Site:* www.astrodata.ch
*Key Personnel*
President: Claude Weiss
Founded: 1978
Subjects: Astrology, Occult, Psychology, Psychia-
try
ISBN Prefix(es): 3-907029
Distributor for Edition Astroterra

**AT Verlag+**
Division of AZ Fachverlage AG
Stadtturmstr 19, 5401 Baden
*Tel:* (062) 836 6666 *Fax:* (062) 836 6667
*E-mail:* at-verlag@azag.ch
*Web Site:* www.at-verlag.ch
*Key Personnel*
Editorial Dir: Urs Hunziker *E-mail:* urs.
hunziker@azag.ch
Editorial: Monika Schmidhofer *E-mail:* monika.
schmidhofer@azag.ch

Production: Edith Guenter *E-mail:* edith.guenter@
azag.ch; Adrian Pabst *E-mail:* adrian.pabst@
azag.ch
Sales: Karin Asti *E-mail:* karin.asti@azag.
ch; Christine Gutknecht *E-mail:* christine.
gutknecht@azag.ch
Marketing: Eugen Jung *E-mail:* eugen.jung@
azag.ch
Foreign Rights: Danielle Schwab
*E-mail:* danielle.schwab@azag.ch
Founded: 1967
This is the book publishing section of the Aar-
gauer Zeitung AG.
Subjects: Cookery, Health, Nutrition, How-to,
Mysteries, Regional Interests
ISBN Prefix(es): 3-905214; 3-85502; 3-03800
*Warehouse:* Grafische Betriebe Aargauer Zeitung
AG, Neumattstr 1/Betrieb Telli, 5004 Aarau

**Athenaeum Verlag AG**
Via Miravalle 23, 6900 Lugano-Massagno
*Tel:* (091) 571536 *Cable:* athenag
*Key Personnel*
Man Dir: J-E Nussbaumer
Administration: J Wuest-Wolfensberger
Editorial: J Steiner
Founded: 1972
Subjects: Art, Biography, Government, Political
Science, History, Literature, Literary Criticism,
Essays, Nonfiction (General), Science (General)
ISBN Prefix(es): 3-85532
*Branch Office(s)*
Buchauslieferung, Schweizer Buchzentrum, Olten

**Atlantis Musikbuch+**
Imprint of Schott Musik International
Jungholzstr 28, 8059 Zurich
*Tel:* (01) 305 7068 *Fax:* (01) 305 7069
Founded: 1976
Subjects: Music, Dance
ISBN Prefix(es): 3-254

**Atlantis-Verlag AG**
Kreuzstr 39, 8008 Zurich
*Tel:* (01) 2622717 *Fax:* (01) 2512615
*Telex:* 815987
Founded: 1930
Subjects: Art, Geography, Geology
ISBN Prefix(es): 3-7611
*Branch Office(s)*
Atlantis-Verlag GmbH & Co KG, Germany

**Atrium Verlag AG+**
Obere Bahnhofstra 10A, 8910 Affoltern am Albis
Mailing Address: Post Box 262, 8030 Zurich
*Tel:* (01) 7603171 *Fax:* (01) 7603171
*Key Personnel*
Contact: Uwe Weitendorf
Founded: 1936
Subjects: Fiction, Literature, Literary Criticism,
Essays
ISBN Prefix(es): 3-85535

**Augustin-Verlag**
Druckerel, 8240 Thayngen
*Tel:* (052) 649 31 31 *Fax:* (052) 649 31 94
*E-mail:* info@augustin.ch
*Web Site:* www.augustin.ch
*Key Personnel*
Dir: Kurt Sigg *E-mail:* sigg.kurt@augustin.ch
Founded: 1911
Publish journals (weekly newspapers for village
people named Heimatblatt).
Subjects: Geography, Geology, History, Regional
Interests
ISBN Prefix(es): 3-85540; 3-905116; 3-9521861

**Editions de la Baconniere SA+**
Division of Medecine et Hygiene
46, chemin de la Mousse, 1225 Chene-Bourg
*Tel:* (022) 8690029 *Fax:* (022) 8690015

*E-mail:* DEB@medecinehygiene.ch
*Key Personnel*
Contact: Denis Bertholet
Founded: 1927
Subjects: Art, Biography, History, Music, Dance,
Philosophy, Poetry, Social Sciences, Sociology
ISBN Prefix(es): 2-8252

**U Baer Verlag+**
Mainaustr 35, 8008 Zurich
*Tel:* (01) 3835500 *Fax:* (01) 3836883
*Key Personnel*
Man Dir: Dr Ulrich Baer
Editorial, Production: Marianne Widmer
Founded: 1971
Subjects: Art, Photography
ISBN Prefix(es): 3-905137

**Barenreiter Verlag Basel AG+**
Heinrich-Schuetz-Allee 35, 34131 Kassel
*Tel:* (061) 3105-0 *Fax:* (061) 3105-176
*E-mail:* info@baerenreiter.com
*Web Site:* www.baerenreiter.com
*Key Personnel*
President: Leonard Scheuch
Member Board: Peter G Isler
Founded: 1923
Membership(s): Swiss Society of Music Publish-
ers.
Subjects: Music, Dance
ISBN Prefix(es): 3-7618; 3-87618
*Parent Company:* Baerenreiter Praha
*Associate Companies:* Baerenreiter Verlag GmbH
& KO KG, Heinrich-Schutz-Allee 35, 34131
Kassel-Wilhelmshohe, Germany, Barbara
Scheuch *Tel:* (0561) 3105-0 *Fax:* (0561) 3105-
240 *E-mail:* info@baerenreiter.com

**Buchhandlung Baeschlin+**
Hauptstr 32, 8750 Glarus
*Tel:* (055) 6401125 *Fax:* (055) 6406594
*E-mail:* office@baeschlin.ch
*Web Site:* www.baeschlin.ch
Founded: 1853
ISBN Prefix(es): 3-85546

**H R Balmer AG Verlag**
Neugasse 12, 6301 Zug
*Tel:* (041) 726 9797 *Fax:* (041) 726 9798
*E-mail:* info@buecher-balmer.ch
*Web Site:* www.buecher-balmer.ch
*Telex:* 868812 buch ch
*Key Personnel*
Man Dir: Christoph Balmer
Founded: 1974
Subjects: History, Literature, Literary Criticism,
Essays, Psychology, Psychiatry
ISBN Prefix(es): 3-85548
*Warehouse:* Boesch 41, 6331 Huenenberg

**Bargezzi-Verlag AG+**
Wasserwerksgasse 19, 3011 Bern
Mailing Address: Postfach 28, 3000 Berne 13
*Tel:* (031) 221380; (031) 211434 *Cable:* Bargezzi
Berne
*Key Personnel*
Man Dir, Editorial, Sales, Publicity, Rights & Per-
missions: Josef Gruebel
Production: Werner F Waegli
Founded: 1948
Subjects: Literature, Literary Criticism, Essays,
Religion - Other
ISBN Prefix(es): 3-85550

**Bartschi Publishing**
Sternenstr 20b, 8903 Birmensdorf ZH
Mailing Address: Postfach 80, 8903 Birmensdorf
*Tel:* (01) 7372518 *Fax:* (01) 7372556
*Key Personnel*
Dir: Helen Bartschi
Founded: 1989

Subjects: Literature, Literary Criticism, Essays,
Poetry, Psychology, Psychiatry
ISBN Prefix(es): 3-9520020

**Basileia Verlag und Basler
Missionsbuchhandlung**
Missionsstr 21, 4003 Basel
*Tel:* (061) 251766 *Fax:* (061) 2688321; (061)
232523
*Key Personnel*
Man Dir: Rudolf Kellenberger
Subjects: Religion - Other, Social Sciences, Soci-
ology
ISBN Prefix(es): 3-85555

**Basilius Presse AG+**
Gueterstr 86, 4002 Basel
*Tel:* (061) 228004; (061) 228005 *Fax:* (061)
232523 *Cable:* BASILIUS VERLAG
*Key Personnel*
Man Dir: P Weibel
Founded: 1957
Subjects: Art, Nonfiction (General), Science
(General)
ISBN Prefix(es): 3-85560

**Baumgartner Blicher**, *imprint of* Terra
Grischuna Verlag Buch-und Zeitschriftenverlag

**Editions Belle Riviere**
La Fontanelle, 1882 Gruyon
*Tel:* (024) 498 40 49 *Fax:* (024) 498 40 46
*Key Personnel*
Man Dir: Eugene Chave
Founded: 1974
ISBN Prefix(es): 2-88121

**Benteli Verlag+**
Seftigenstr, 310, 3084 Wabern-Bern
*Tel:* (031) 9608484 *Fax:* (031) 9617
*E-mail:* info@benteliverlag.ch
*Web Site:* www.benteliverlag.ch
*Key Personnel*
Man Dir: Till Schapp
Founded: 1899
High quality books.
Subjects: Art, Photography
ISBN Prefix(es): 3-7165
Number of titles published annually: 35 Print
Total Titles: 350 Print

**Benziger Verlag AG+**
Bellerivstr 3, 8008 Zurich
*Tel:* (01) 2527050 *Fax:* (01) 2624792
*Key Personnel*
Contact: Christian Machalet
Founded: 1792
Subjects: Art, Music, Dance, Religion - Catholic,
Religion - Protestant, Theology
ISBN Prefix(es): 3-545
*Parent Company:* Patmos Verlag

**Beobachter Buchverlag**
Foerrlibuckstr 70, Postfach, 8021 Zurich
*Tel:* (01) 043 444 53 07 *Fax:* (01) 043 444 53 09
*E-mail:* buchverlag@beobachter.ch
*Web Site:* www.beobachter.ch
*Key Personnel*
Contact: H Hausherr *Tel:* (01) 4488984
*E-mail:* hhausherr@beobachter.ch
ISBN Prefix(es): 3-85569
Total Titles: 60 Print
*Branch Office(s)*
Industriestr 54, Postfach 8152, Glattbrugg-Zurich

**Berchtold Haller Verlag+**
Nageligasse 9, 3000 Bern 7
Mailing Address: Postfach 15, 3000 Bern 7
*Tel:* (031) 3111145 *Fax:* (031) 3112583
*Web Site:* www.egw.ch

*Key Personnel*
Contact: Peter Schranz *E-mail:* schranz@theol-
buch.ch
Founded: 1848
Subjects: Religion - Protestant, Romance
ISBN Prefix(es): 3-85570
Number of titles published annually: 3 Print
Total Titles: 40 Print; 13 Audio
*Parent Company:* Evangelisches Geweinschafhw-
erth EGW

**Bergli Books AG+**
Ruemelinplatz 19, 4001 Basel
*Tel:* (061) 373 27 77 *Fax:* (061) 373 27 78
*E-mail:* info@bergli.ch
*Web Site:* www.bergli.ch
*Key Personnel*
Man Dir: Dianne Dicks
Founded: 1990
Specialize in books in English that focus on
Switzerland, in intercultural books on crossing
cultures, emigration, intercultural marriages,
bi-lingualism, short story anthologies.
Subjects: Behavioral Sciences, Ethnicity, Foreign
Countries, Human Relations, Literature, Lit-
erary Criticism, Essays, Nonfiction (General),
Travel, Women's Studies
ISBN Prefix(es): 3-9520002; 3-905252; 2-88407
Distributor for Survival Books; Travelers' Tales

**Berichthaus Verlag, Dr Conrad Ulrich**
Voltastr 43, 8044 Zurich
*Tel:* (01) 2526349 *Fax:* (01) 2526426
Subjects: History, History of Zurich & Switzer-
land
ISBN Prefix(es): 3-85572
*Orders to:* Schweiz Buchzentrum, 4601 Olten

**Beroa-Verlag**
Zellerstr 61, 8038 Zurich
*Tel:* (01) 4801313 *Fax:* (01) 4801312
Founded: 1957
Subjects: Biblical Studies
ISBN Prefix(es): 3-905335; 3-905336; 3-909337

**Editions Medicales Roland Bettex**
78 rue de la Roseraie, 1211 Geneva 13
Mailing Address: CP 456, 1211 Geneva 13
*Tel:* (022) 7029311 *Fax:* (022) 7029355
ISBN Prefix(es): 2-88113
*Branch Office(s)*
3, rue des Fontenalilles CP 193, 1000 Lausanne
13
Street 8, rue Copernic, 75116 Paris, France
*Tel:* (0147) 271559

**Editions Beyeler**
Baeumleingasse 9, 4001 Basel
*Tel:* (061) 235412 *Fax:* (061) 229691
*Key Personnel*
Owner: Ernst Beyeler
Founded: 1967
Subjects: Art
ISBN Prefix(es): 3-85575; 3-9520156

**Bibellesbund Verlag+**
Flugplatzstr 5, Postfach, 8404 Winterthur
*Tel:* (052) 245 14 45 *Fax:* (052) 245 14 46
*E-mail:* info@bibellesebund.ch
*Web Site:* www.bibellesebund.ch
*Key Personnel*
Secretary-General, Switzerland: Andreas Zimmer-
mann
Secretary-General, Germany: Reinhold Frey
Man Dir, Sales, Production, Publicity, Switzer-
land: Martin Wassmer
Man Dir, Sales, Production, Publicity, Germany:
Karl-Martin Gunther
Founded: 1930
Scripture Union of Switzerland & Germany.
Subjects: Religion - Protestant

ISBN Prefix(es): 3-87982
*Associate Companies:* Bibellesebund eV Indus-
triestr 2, Postfach, 51703 Marienheide-Roth,
Germany *Tel:* (02264) 7045 *Fax:* (02264) 7155
*E-mail:* info@bibellesebund.de
Distributed by Haenssler Verlag; Brunnen Verlag

**Bibliographisches Institut & F A Brockhaus
AG**
Gubelstr 11, 6304 Zug
Mailing Address: Postfach 4531, 6304 Zug
*Tel:* (041) 7108375 *Fax:* (041) 7108325
*Web Site:* www.bifab.de
*Key Personnel*
Man Dir: Dr Ernst Grab
Founded: 1967
Subjects: Biological Sciences, Business, Chem-
istry, Chemical Engineering, Computer Sci-
ence, Earth Sciences, Economics, Education,
Environmental Studies, Geography, Geology,
Health, Nutrition, History, Language Arts, Lin-
guistics, Mathematics, Music, Dance, Nonfic-
tion (General), Philosophy, Physics, Religion -
Other, Science (General)
ISBN Prefix(es): 3-411; 3-7653
*Parent Company:* Bibliographisches Institut und F
A Brockhaus AG, Germany

**Verlag Bibliophile Drucke von Josef Stocker
AG**
Hasenbergstr 7, 8953 Dietikon
Mailing Address: PO Box 66, 8953 Dietikon
*Tel:* (01) 7404444
*Key Personnel*
Man Dir: Mr Stocker
Subjects: Poetry
ISBN Prefix(es): 3-85577; 3-7276
*Parent Company:* Verlag Stocker-Schmid AG
*Bookshop(s):* Buchhandlung Stocker-Schmid,
Hasenbergstr 7, PO Box 66, 8953 Dietikon

**La Bibliotheque des Arts+**
55, Ave de Rumine, 1005 Lausanne
*Tel:* (021) 3123667 *Fax:* (021) 3123615
*E-mail:* archinf@archinform.de
*Web Site:* www.archinform.net
*Key Personnel*
Dir: Mr Francois Daulte
Founded: 1952
Subjects: Art
ISBN Prefix(es): 2-85047; 2-88453
Subsidiaries: La Bibliotheque des Arts
*Branch Office(s)*
Archer Fields Inc, 636 Broadway, New York, NY
10012, United States

**Birkhauser Verlag AG+**
Viaduktstr 42, 4051 Basel
Mailing Address: PO Box 133, 4010 Basel
*Tel:* (061) 2050707 *Fax:* (061) 2050799
*E-mail:* info@birkhauser.ch; sales@birkhauser.ch
*Web Site:* www.birkhauser.ch *Cable:* EDITA
*Key Personnel*
General & Editorial Manager: Edward Mazenauer
Marketing Manager: Sven Steiner; Patrick
Schneebeli
Rights & Licences: Liv Etienne *Tel:* (061)
2050707 *E-mail:* etienne@birkhauser.ch
Founded: 1879
Subjects: Architecture & Interior Design, Biolog-
ical Sciences, Engineering (General), Environ-
mental Studies, Mathematics, Physics
ISBN Prefix(es): 3-7643
Total Titles: 200 Print
*Parent Company:* Springer Science+Business Me-
dia, Tiergartenstrasse A7, Heidelberg 69121,
Germany
Imprints: Birkhauser Verlag fuer Architektur
Subsidiaries: Birkhauser Boston Inc
*U.S. Office(s):* Birkhauser Boston Inc, c/o
Springer-Verlag New York Inc, 175 Fifth Ave,
New York, NY 10010, United States *Web
Site:* www.birkhauser.com

Distributor for Princeton Architectural Press (USA, UK)
*Warehouse:* Springer Auslieferungs Gesellschaft, Haberstrasse 7, Heidelberg 69121, Germany
*Tel:* (049) 6221345-0

**Birkhauser Verlag fuer Architektur**, *imprint of* Birkhauser Verlag AG

**Blaukreuz-Verlag Bern+**
Lindenrain 5a, 3001 Bern
Mailing Address: Postfach 6813, 3001 Bern
*Tel:* (031) 300 58 60 *Fax:* (031) 300 58 69
*E-mail:* ifbc.bern@bluewin.ch
*Web Site:* www.blaueskreuz.ch *Cable:* BLAUKREUZVERLAG
*Key Personnel*
Man Dir: Ernst Zuercher
Founded: 1884
Publishes for the Blue Cross health & religious movement.
Subjects: Biography, Health, Nutrition, Religion - Protestant, Religion - Other
ISBN Prefix(es): 3-85580
*Parent Company:* Blaues Kreuz der deutschen Schweiz

**Les Editions de la Fondation Martin Bodmer**
Case Postale 7, 1223 Cologny
*Tel:* (022) 7362370 *Fax:* (022) 7001540
*Key Personnel*
Contact: Dr Martin Bircher
Founded: 1971
Subjects: Language Arts, Linguistics
ISBN Prefix(es): 3-85682

**Bohem Press Kinderbuchverlag+**
Hardturmstr 122, 8005 Zurich
*Tel:* (01) 440 7000 *Fax:* (01) 440 7001
*E-mail:* art@bohem.ch
*Web Site:* www.bohem.ch
*Key Personnel*
Dir: O Bozejovsky v Rawennoff *Tel:* (01) 4407004
Publisher: Susanne Zeller
Founded: 1973
Subjects: Animals, Pets, Child Care & Development, Fiction
ISBN Prefix(es): 3-85581

**Brunnen-Verlag Basel+**
Wallstr 6, 4002 Basel
*Tel:* (061) 2956000 *Fax:* (061) 2956068
*E-mail:* brunnen-verlag@bluewin.ch
*Key Personnel*
Man Dir: Hans-Peter Zueblin
Founded: 1921
Subjects: Biography, Child Care & Development, Fiction, How-to, Religion - Other, Self-Help
ISBN Prefix(es): 3-7655
*Bookshop(s):* Buchhandlung Pilgermission, Spalenberg 20, 4002 Basel; Brunnen-Buchhandlung, Marktgasse 31, 8180 Buelach; Brunnen-Buchhandlung, St Gallerstr 6, 8500 Frauenfeld; Libreria La Fonte, Viale Stazione 1, 6512 Giubiasco; Buechegge AG, Loewengasse 37, 8810 Horgen; Christlicher Buecherladen zur Arche, Amtshausgasse 10, 4410 Liestal; Evangelische Buchhandlung, Haupstr 25, 5734 Reinach AG; Christliche Buchhandlung, Ave Mercier de Molin 1, 3960 Sierre; Christliche Buchhandlung, Bahnhofstr 42, 6210 Sursee; Christliche Buchhandlung, Susann-Muellerstr 14, 9630 Wattwil; Christliche Buchhandlung "Brunne-Stube", Schmidstr 3, 8570 Weinfelden; Brunnen-Buchhandlung, untere Bahnofstr 20, 9500 Wil; Christliche Buchhandlung, HERTI-Zentrum, 6300 Zug; Sunnaewirbel, Buecher & Geschenke, Olympstr 4, 6440 Brunnen; Senfkorn-Laden, Haupstr 33, 5262 Frick

**Verlag Bucheli+**
Baarerstr 43, 6304 Zug
Mailing Address: Postfach 4161, 6304 Zug
*Tel:* (041) 741 77 55 *Fax:* (041) 741 71 15
*E-mail:* info@bucheli-verlag.ch
*Web Site:* www.mueller-rueschlikon.ch/bucheli.htm
*Key Personnel*
Contact: Hans-Joerg Degen
Subjects: Automotive
ISBN Prefix(es): 3-7168

**Buchhaus AG**, see Office du Livre SA (Buchhaus AG)

**Buchverlag Basler Zeitung**
Missionstr 36, 4012 Basel
Mailing Address: Postfach 393, 4012 Basel
*Tel:* (061) 2646450 *Fax:* (061) 2646488
*E-mail:* order@reinhardt.ch
*Web Site:* www.opinio.ch
*Key Personnel*
Marketing: Jasmine Gasser
ISBN Prefix(es): 3-85815
*Book Club(s):* SBVV

**Bugra Suisse Burchler Grafino AG+**
Seftigenstr 310, 3084 Wabern
*Tel:* (031) 548111 *Fax:* (031) 544562
*Telex:* 911934
*Key Personnel*
Man Dir, Rights & Permissions: Dr Rudolf Gysi
Marketing: Erich Hirschi
Editorial: Peter Wyss
Founded: 1886
Subjects: Art, Education, Regional Interests
ISBN Prefix(es): 3-7170

**Cahiers de la Renaissance Vaudoise**
One Place Grand-Saint-Jean, 1002 Lausanne
Mailing Address: Postfach 3414, 1002 Lausanne
*Tel:* (021) 3121914 *Fax:* (021) 3126714
*E-mail:* courrier@ligue-vaudoise.ch
*Web Site:* www.ligue-vaudoise.ch
*Key Personnel*
President: Olivier Delacretaz
Subjects: Government, Political Science, History
ISBN Prefix(es): 2-88017

**Les Editions Camphill**
Fondation Perceval, 1211 Saint-Prex
*Tel:* (021) 8062269 *Fax:* (021) 8061897
*Key Personnel*
Contact: John Byrde
Founded: 1979
Subjects: Anthropology, Education, Social Sciences, Sociology
ISBN Prefix(es): 2-8299

**Carre d'Art Edition Archigraphie+**
c/o NLDA, One Pl de l'Ile, 1204 Geneva
*Tel:* (022) 311 57 50 *Fax:* (022) 312 21 21
Founded: 1989
Subjects: Architecture & Interior Design
ISBN Prefix(es): 2-88287
*Branch Office(s)*
3 ruede Fribourg, 1201 Geneva

**Edizioni Casagrande SA+**
Via del Bramantino, 3, 6500 Bellinzona
*Tel:* (091) 820 0101 *Fax:* (091) 825 1874
*E-mail:* casagrande@casagrande-online.ch
*Web Site:* www.casagrande-online.ch
*Telex:* 846266
*Key Personnel*
Man Dir, Editorial: Libero Casagrande
Founded: 1972
Subjects: Art, History, Literature, Literary Criticism, Essays
ISBN Prefix(es): 88-7713

Subsidiaries: Archivio Storico Ticinese; Istituto Editoriale Ticinese (IET) SA; Istituto Grafico Casagrande SA
*Bookshop(s):* Libreria Casagrande, Viale Stazione, 6500 Bellinzona

**Castle Publications SA**
22, rue Centrale, 1248 Hermance
*Tel:* (022) 511036 *Fax:* (022) 7511111; (022) 7884240
*Key Personnel*
Man Dir: Nicolas Ferguson
Founded: 1972
Subjects: Communications, Language Arts, Linguistics
ISBN Prefix(es): 2-88344
*Associate Companies:* CEEL (Centre Experimental pour l'Enseignement des Langues)
Imprints: SAPL
Subsidiaries: Castle Mexico; Didasko (Castle Japan) 6-7-31-611 Itashibori; SAOL Publications, Canada; Castle France

**Causa Verlag GmbH**, see Tobler Verlag

**Caux Books**
Rue du Panorama, 1824 Caux
*Tel:* (021) 9629469 *Fax:* (021) 9629465
*E-mail:* info@caux.ch
*Web Site:* www.caux.ch
Subjects: Biography, Religion - Other, Social Sciences, Sociology
ISBN Prefix(es): 3-85601; 2-88037; 2-85233
Subsidiaries: Caux Edition SA

**Caux Edition SA**
Rue de Panorama, 1824 Caux
*Tel:* (021) 963 94 69 *Fax:* (021) 962 94 65
*E-mail:* info@caux.ch
*Web Site:* www.caux.ch
*Key Personnel*
Man Dir, Editorial: Chas Piguet
Founded: 1965
Subjects: Biography, Drama, Theater, Religion - Other, Social Sciences, Sociology
ISBN Prefix(es): 2-88037
*Parent Company:* Caux Verlag AG
*Branch Office(s)*
22, av Robert-Schuman, 92100 Boulogne-Billancourt, France *Tel:* (01) 41104050 *Fax:* (01) 41108067
*Bookshop(s):* Librairie de Caux, Rue de Panorama, 1824 Caux

**Verlag Bo Cavefors**
c/o Mardatropa AG, 8001 Zurich
Mailing Address: Postfach 5837, 8001 Zurich
*Tel:* (01) 2017200
*Key Personnel*
Man Dir: Bo Cavefors
Subjects: Fiction, Poetry, Religion - Catholic
ISBN Prefix(es): 3-85593

**CEC-Cosmic Energy Connections+**
Belsitostr 12, 8044 Zurich
*Tel:* (0761) 7059 632 *Fax:* (0761) 7059 633
Founded: 1985
Subjects: Education, Human Relations, Philosophy, Psychology, Psychiatry, Self-Help, Sports, Athletics
ISBN Prefix(es): 3-905276
*Warehouse:* Bailey Distribution Ltd, Lea Royd Rd, Mountfield Industrial Estate, New Romney, Kent TN28 8XU, United Kingdom *Tel:* (0679) 66905 *Fax:* (0679) 66638
*Orders to:* Bailey Distribution Ltd, Lea Royd Rd, Mountfield Industrial Estate, New Romney, Kent TN28 8XU, United Kingdom *Tel:* (0679) 66905 *Fax:* (0679) 66638

**Cedilivre SA**, see Editions Foma SA

**Centre Experimental pour l'Enseignement des Langues**, see Castle Publications SA

**Chamaeleon Verlag AG**
Weinbergstr 11, 8001 Zurich
*Tel:* (01) 2525497 *Fax:* (01) 2725282
*Key Personnel*
Manager: Mrs Andree Mathis
Founded: 1985
ISBN Prefix(es): 3-905274

**Christiana-Verlag+**
Postfach 174, 8260 Stein am Rhein
*Tel:* (052) 741 41 31 *Fax:* (052) 741 20 92
*E-mail:* orders@christiana.ch
*Web Site:* www.christiana.ch
*Key Personnel*
Man Dir & International Rights: Arnold Guillet
　*Tel:* (052) 7414131
Founded: 1948
Subjects: Biological Sciences, Education, Philosophy, Religion - Catholic, Demonology, Angeology, Hagiographic
ISBN Prefix(es): 3-7171
Number of titles published annually: 12 Print
*Branch Office(s)*
Postfach 110, 78201 Singen, Germany *Tel:* (052) 741 41 31 *Fax:* (052) 741 20 92
*Distribution Center:* Ennstaler GesmbH & Co KG, Stadtplatz 26, 4402 Steyr, Austria *Tel:* (07252) 5205320 *Fax:* (07252) 5205322
Marianne Pattloch, Lindenhof 3, Postfach 1254, 63825 Westerngrund, Germany *Tel:* (06024) 24 75 *Fax:* (06024) 26 07 (Germany)
*Orders to:* Postfach 110, 78201 Singen, Germany

**Christoph Merian Verlag+**
St Alban-Vorstadt 5, 4002 Basel
*Tel:* (061) 226 33 25 *Fax:* (061) 226 33 45
*E-mail:* verlag@merianstiftung.ch
*Web Site:* www.christoph-merian-verlag.ch
*Key Personnel*
Chief Executive, Editorial: Dr Beat von Wartburg
Chief Executive: Claus Donau
Marketing: Franzijka Nyffenegger
　*E-mail:* fnyffenegger@cmsbas.ch
Founded: 1976
Subjects: Art, History, Literature, Literary Criticism, Essays, Photography, Regional Interests
ISBN Prefix(es): 3-85616
Total Titles: 80 Print
*Shipping Address:* Schweizer Bridezentrum SBZ, Postbach, 4601 Olten, Contact: Yvonne Sardoz *Tel:* (062) 209 2704 *Fax:* (062) 209 2788

**Chronos Verlag+**
Eisengasse 9, 8008 Zurich
*Tel:* (01) 265 4343 *Fax:* (01) 265 4344
*E-mail:* info@chronos-verlag.ch
*Web Site:* www.chronos-verlag.ch
Founded: 1985
Specialize in gender studies, media & theatre studies.
Subjects: Drama, Theater, Fiction, Film, Video, History, Nonfiction (General), Social Sciences, Sociology, Women's Studies
ISBN Prefix(es): 3-905312; 3-905314; 3-905315; 3-905313; 3-905311; 3-905310; 3-905278
Number of titles published annually: 50 Print
Total Titles: 350 Print
*Orders to:* AVA, Centralweg 16, Postfach 27, 8910 *Tel:* (01) 762 4260 *Fax:* (01) 762 4210 (Switzerland/Liechtenstein)
GVA, Postfach 2021, Goettingen, Germany *Tel:* (0551) 48 71 77 *Fax:* (0551) 4 13 92 (Germany/European Union)

**Clairefontaine, Editions**
14 av de Florimont, 1006 Lausanne
*Tel:* (021) 323 08 79
*Key Personnel*
Contact: Albert Mermoud

**Werner Classen Verlag**
Im waidlilo, 8142 Uitikon Waldegg
*Tel:* (01) 4916362 *Fax:* (01) 4916362 *Cable:* CLASSENVERLAG ZURICH
*Key Personnel*
Dir: Werner Classen
Founded: 1945
Subjects: Humor, Music, Dance, Poetry, Psychology, Psychiatry
ISBN Prefix(es): 3-7172

**De Clivo Press**
Usterstr 126, 8600 Duebendorf
*Tel:* (01) 8201124
*Telex:* CH 55256 Serco *Cable:* Declivopress Duebendorf
*Key Personnel*
Proprietor: Dr Walter Amstutz
ISBN Prefix(es): 3-85634

**Cockatoo Press (Schweiz), Thailand-Publikationen** (Cockatoo Press (Switzerland) Thailand Publications)+
Im Leeacher 30, 8123 Hinteregg bei Zuerich
*Tel:* (044) 984 17 25 *Fax:* (044) 984 34 20
*E-mail:* books@thailine.com
Founded: 1991
Specialize in publishing & promotion, information service.
Subjects: Antiques, Archaeology, Asian Studies, Business, Cookery, Foreign Countries, Language Arts, Linguistics, Mysteries, Religion - Buddhist, Social Sciences, Sociology, Travel
ISBN Prefix(es): 3-905302
*Parent Company:* Thailine R Mueller
*Associate Companies:* Chiang Saen Internet Ltd Part, 299 Moo 2, Tambon Wieng, A. Chiangsaen Chiangrai 57150, Thailand, Mrs.: Ratanaporn Kaewdam *E-mail:* info@ chiangsaen.biz *Web Site:* www.chiangsaen.co.th
*Subsidiaries:* Thailand Publications Switzerland
Distributor for Editions Duang Kamol; Pilot Publishing; Suriwong Books; White Lotus Press

**Rene Coeckelberghs Editions**
Museggstr 7, 6004 Lucerne
*Tel:* (041) 515060 *Fax:* (041) 516645
Packagers.
Subjects: Nonfiction (General)
ISBN Prefix(es): 2-8310; 3-905285

**Conseil oecumenique de Eglises**, see World Council of Churches (WCC Publications)

**Consejo Mundial de Iglesias**, see World Council of Churches (WCC Publications)

**Cosa Verlag+**
Giusep Condrau SA, 7180 Disentis
*Tel:* (081) 947 64 64 *Fax:* (081) 947 63 52
*E-mail:* condrau@cosa.ch
*Web Site:* www.cosa.ch *Cable:* DESERTINA DISENTIS
*Key Personnel*
Man Dir, Rights & Editorial: Pius Condrau
Founded: 1953
Subjects: Art
ISBN Prefix(es): 3-9521636

**Cosmic Energy Connections-CEC**, see CEC-Cosmic Energy Connections

**Cosmos-Verlag AG**
Krayigenweg 2, CP 425, 3074 Muri BE
Mailing Address: PO Box 5776, 3001 Bern
*Tel:* (31) 9506464 *Fax:* (31) 9506460
*E-mail:* info@cosmosverlag.ch
*Key Personnel*
Contact: Regina Haener *E-mail:* haener@ cosmosverlag.ch

Founded: 1923
Subjects: Accounting, Business, Fiction, Finance, Management, Regional Interests
ISBN Prefix(es): 3-85621; 2-8296; 3-305
Number of titles published annually: 12 Print

**Comite international de la Croix-Rouge** (International Committee of the Red Cross)
19 Ave de la Paix, 1202 Geneva
*Tel:* (022) 734 60 01 *Fax:* (022) 733 20 57; (022) 730 27 68
*Web Site:* www.icrc.org
*Telex:* CICR 414226
*Key Personnel*
Head of Publishing Unit: Charles Pierrat *Fax:* (022) 73 8768
Founded: 1863
Subjects: Law
ISBN Prefix(es): 2-88145; 2-88077
Total Titles: 4 Print; 2,000 Online
*U.S. Office(s):* International Committee of the Red Cross, 780 Third Ave, 28th Floor, New York, NY 10017, United States

**Cultur Prospectiv, Edition**
Muehlebachstr 35, 8008 Zurich
*Tel:* (01) 260 69 29 *Fax:* (01) 260 69 29
*E-mail:* cpinstitut@smile.ch
*Web Site:* www.culturprospectiv.ch
*Key Personnel*
Contact: Dr Hans-Peter Meier
Founded: 1990
Subjects: Social Sciences, Sociology
ISBN Prefix(es): 3-905345

**Edizioni Armando Dado, Tipografia Stazione**
Via Orelli 29, 6600 Locarno
*Tel:* (091) 751 48 02 *Fax:* (091) 752 10 26
*Key Personnel*
Man Dir: Armando Dado
Subjects: Art, History, Literature, Literary Criticism, Essays, Photography
ISBN Prefix(es): 88-85115; 88-86315; 88-8281

**Daimon Verlag AG+**
Hauptstr 85, 8840 Einsiedeln
*Tel:* (055) 412 2266 *Fax:* (055) 412 2231
*E-mail:* daimon@compuserve.com
*Web Site:* www.daimon.ch
*Key Personnel*
Publisher: Dr Robert Hinshaw *E-mail:* r@daimon. ch
Founded: 1979
Specialize in Dream Interpretation.
Membership(s): SBVV.
Subjects: Environmental Studies, History, Poetry, Psychology, Psychiatry
ISBN Prefix(es): 3-85630
Distributor for Chiron; Eranos; Parabola; Sounds True Rec; Spring Publication & Spring Audio/ Journal
*Orders to:* Bookworld Companies, 1941 Whitfield Park Loop, Sarasota, FL 34243, United States

**Daphnis-Verlag**
Kappelistr 15, 8002 Zurich
*Tel:* (01) 202 52 71 *Fax:* (01) 201 42 31
*Key Personnel*
Man Dir: J Fischlin
Founded: 1959
Subjects: Poetry
ISBN Prefix(es): 3-85631

**De Vier Winstreken**, *imprint of* Nord-Sued Verlag

**Marcel Dekker AG+**
Hutgasse 4, 4001 Basel
Mailing Address: Postfach 812, 4001 Basel
*Tel:* (061) 260 63 00 *Fax:* (061) 260 63 33

*E-mail:* intlcustserv@dekker.com
*Web Site:* www.dekker.com
*Key Personnel*
President: Bruno Baumgartner
Founded: 1975
Subjects: Business, Chemistry, Chemical Engineering, Civil Engineering, Earth Sciences, Electronics, Electrical Engineering, Mathematics, Medicine, Nursing, Dentistry
ISBN Prefix(es): 0-8247
*Parent Company:* Marcel Dekker Inc, 270 Madison Ave, New York, NY 10016, United States

**Editions Delachaux et Niestle SA+**
2, rue de l Etrat, 1027 Lonay 21
*Tel:* (021) 8110711 *Fax:* (021) 8110712
*E-mail:* contact@delachaux-niestle.com
*Key Personnel*
Man Dir: David Perret
Sales, Permissions: Yvette Perret
Founded: 1861
Subjects: Earth Sciences, Education, Medicine, Nursing, Dentistry, Psychology, Psychiatry, Science (General), Social Sciences, Sociology
ISBN Prefix(es): 2-603; 2-8255; 2-242
Subsidiaries: Delachaux Niestle, France SA
*Branch Office(s)*
4 rue Laferriere, 75009 Paris, France
82 rue de Courcelles, 75008 Paris, France
    *Tel:* (01) 48881239 *Fax:* (01) 48881277

**Editions Andre Delcourt & Cie+**
27, rue de la Borde, 1017 Lausanne
Mailing Address: CP 584, 1017 Lausanne
*Tel:* (021) 6479772 *Fax:* (021) 6478831
*Key Personnel*
Publisher: Andre Delcourt
Founded: 1986
Subjects: Architecture & Interior Design, Art, Literature, Literary Criticism, Essays, Medicine, Nursing, Dentistry, Photography
ISBN Prefix(es): 2-88161; 2-88253
Imprints: AD; Delta; Delta et Spes; Spes

**Delta**, *imprint of* Editions Andre Delcourt & Cie

**Delta et Spes**, *imprint of* Editions Andre Delcourt & Cie

**Verlag Harri Deutsch+**
Riedstr 2, 3600 Thun
*Tel:* (033) 2223975 *Fax:* (033) 2223950
*E-mail:* verlag@harri-deutsch.de
*Web Site:* www.harri-deutsch.de
*Key Personnel*
Man Dir: Harri Deutsch
Editor: Bernd Mueller
Founded: 1971
Subjects: Astronomy, Biological Sciences, Chemistry, Chemical Engineering, Computer Science, Economics, Electronics, Electrical Engineering, Mathematics, Physics, Science (General), Sports, Athletics, Technology
ISBN Prefix(es): 3-87144; 3-8171
Total Titles: 900 Print; 7 CD-ROM; 5 Online; 5 E-Book
*Parent Company:* Verlag Harri Deutsch, Germany
*Bookshop(s):* Naturwiss Fachbuchhandlung an der Universitaet, Graefstr 47, 60486 Frankfurt, Germany *Tel:* (069) 775021 *Fax:* (069) 7073739
*Web Site:* www.harri-deutsch.de
*Orders to:* Brockhaus Commission, Postfach 1220, 70806 Kornwestheim, Germany *Tel:* (07) 154-132720 *Fax:* (07) 154-132710

**Didax**, *imprint of* Editions Foma SA

**Diogenes Verlag AG+**
Sprecherstr 8, 8032 Zurich
*Tel:* (01) 2548511 *Fax:* (01) 2528407
*E-mail:* info@diogenes.ch

*Web Site:* www.diogenes.ch *Cable:* DIOGENESVERLAG ZURICH
*Key Personnel*
Man Dir & Owner, Publisher: Daniel Keel
Man Dir & Owner, Administration & Finance: Rudolf C Bettschart
Man Dir, Organization & Marketing: Stefan Fritsch
Editorial Dir: Winfried Stephan
Publicity & Promotion: Ruth Geiger
Sales & Marketing: Ulrich Richter
Production: Res Schenk
Foreign Rights & Permissions: Susanne Bauknecht
Corporate Finance: Martha Pfyl
Founded: 1952
Subjects: Art, Drama, Theater, Fiction, Literature, Literary Criticism, Essays, Mysteries, Philosophy, Children's Books
ISBN Prefix(es): 3-257

**Drei-D-World und Foto-World Verlag und Vertrieb+**
Postfach 339, 4003 Basel
*Tel:* (061) 3013081 *Fax:* (094) 3133862
*E-mail:* gah@swissonline.ch
*Key Personnel*
International Rights: David Haisch
Founded: 1982
Subjects: Art, Business, Communications, Ethnicity, Foreign Countries, How-to, Marketing, Photography, Real Estate, Travel
ISBN Prefix(es): 3-905450
*Associate Companies:* Pamelart
Subsidiaries: Icebear Group Branch
*Branch Office(s)*
Icebear Group, 103-2 Lewis Pl, CL-11500 Negoubo, Sri Lanka *Fax:* (031) 33862
Distributor for Pamelart

**Librairie Droz SA+**
11 rue Massot, 1211 Geneva 12
Mailing Address: PO Box 389, 1211 Geneva 12
*Tel:* (022) 3466666 *Fax:* (022) 3472391
*E-mail:* droz@droz.org
*Web Site:* www.droz.org
*Key Personnel*
Man Dir, Rights & Permissions: Max Engammare
Sales Dir: Mrs Burquier
Founded: 1924
Subjects: Antiques, History, Literature, Literary Criticism, Essays, Social Sciences, Sociology
ISBN Prefix(es): 2-600
Number of titles published annually: 80 Print; 2 CD-ROM; 2 E-Book
Total Titles: 80 Print; 4 CD-ROM; 2 E-Book

**Duboux Editions SA+**
Frutigenstr 6, 3600 Thun
*Tel:* (033) 2256060 *Fax:* (033) 2256066
*E-mail:* duboux@duboux.ch
*Web Site:* www.duboux.ch
*Key Personnel*
President & Publisher: Jean-Pierre Duboux
Founded: 1988
Subjects: Cookery, Travel
ISBN Prefix(es): 3-907950
Distributed by Verlag Handwerk & Technik

**Gottlieb Duttweiler Institute for Trends & Futures**
Langhaldenstr 21, 8803 Rueschlikon, Zurich
Mailing Address: Postfach 531, 8803 Rueschlikon, Zurich
*Tel:* (01) 7246111 *Fax:* (01) 7246262
*E-mail:* info@gdi.ch
*Web Site:* www.gdi.ch *Cable:* GREEN MEADOW
*Key Personnel*
Chief Executive Officer: David Bosshart
Marketing: Karin Hartmann
Founded: 1963

Subjects: Economics, Management, Marketing, Social Sciences, Sociology
ISBN Prefix(es): 3-7184
*Parent Company:* Migros-Genossenschafts-Bund, Zurich
Imprints: GDI

**Editions l'Eau Vive**
13 rue de Monthoux, 1201 Geneva
*Tel:* (022) 7329847 *Fax:* (022) 7410482
*Key Personnel*
Man Dir: Rolande Gloor
Founded: 1960
Subjects: Biography, Religion - Other
ISBN Prefix(es): 2-88035

**Eboris-Coda-Bompiani+**
11 rue Maunoir, 167 Geneva
*Tel:* (022) 7188820 *Fax:* (022) 7079199
*Key Personnel*
President: Isabella Coda-Bompiani
Founded: 1994
Subjects: History, Literature, Literary Criticism, Essays, Photography
ISBN Prefix(es): 2-940121
Number of titles published annually: 30 Print; 35 E-Book
Total Titles: 130 Print; 140 E-Book

**Editions Eboris SA**, see Eboris-Coda-Bompiani

**Eco Verlags AG+**
Langstr 187, 8005 Zurich
*Tel:* (01) 440400
*Key Personnel*
Man Dir: Verena Stettler
Founded: 1976
Subjects: Literature, Literary Criticism, Essays, Nonfiction (General)
ISBN Prefix(es): 3-85647
Imprints: Literatheke; Neue Szene

**Verlag ED Emmentaler Druck AG**
Dorfstr, 3550 Langnau im Emmental
*Tel:* (035) 21911 *Fax:* (035) 0524642
*Key Personnel*
Man Dir, Sales: Paul Hartmann
Editorial & Publicity: Markus F Rubli
Founded: 1845
Subjects: Fiction, Photography, Regional Interests
ISBN Prefix(es): 3-85654

**Editions Edita+**
Route de Geneve, CP 85, 1000 Lausanne 9
*Tel:* (021) 6251392 *Fax:* (021) 6254291
*Telex:* 450296
*Key Personnel*
Contact: Michel Ferloni; Francois Mukundi
Founded: 1953
Subjects: Art, History
ISBN Prefix(es): 2-88001
Subsidiaries: Editions Office du Livre
*Orders to:* Office du Livre Distribution, 101 Route de Villars, 1701 Fribourg

**Editeurs et Libraires Catholiques d'Europe ELCE**
Hans-Walter Luthi, Wattstr 6, 9012 Saint Gallen
*Tel:* (071) 279580 *Fax:* (071) 279580
*E-mail:* hawas@mhs.ch
*Key Personnel*
Contact: Hans-Walter Luthi
ISBN Prefix(es): 3-905559

**Edition Epoca+**
Werdstr 128, 8003 Zurich
*Tel:* (01) 4511717 *Fax:* (01) 4511717
*E-mail:* info@epoca.ch
*Web Site:* www.epoca.ch
*Key Personnel*
Contact: Urs Kummer; Adrian Stokar
Founded: 1995

Subjects: Fiction, Literature, Literary Criticism, Essays, Philosophy, Social Sciences, Sociology
ISBN Prefix(es): 3-905513
Number of titles published annually: 7 Print

**eFeF-Verlag/Edition Ebersbach+**
Klosterparkgaessli 8, 5430 Wettingen
*Tel:* (056) 4260618 *Fax:* (056) 4270461
*E-mail:* info@efefverlag.ch
*Web Site:* www.efefverlag.ch
Founded: 1984
Subjects: Biography, Fiction, Women's Studies
ISBN Prefix(es): 3-9521022
*Orders to:* Buch 2000, Obfeldstr 35, 8910 Affoltern

**Drei Eidgenossen Verlag**
Huegelweg 15, 4102 Binningen
*Tel:* (061) 475166 *Fax:* (061) 475166
*Key Personnel*
Man Dir: Mr Hosch
Founded: 1936
ISBN Prefix(es): 3-85643

**Editions Eisele SA**
Av de la Confrerie 42, 1008 Prilly/Lausanne
*Tel:* (024) 4531149 *Fax:* (024) 4531901
*E-mail:* pied.du.jura@vtx.ch
*Web Site:* www.eisele.ch
*Key Personnel*
International Rights: Jean-Luc Eisele
Subjects: Education, History, Science (General)
ISBN Prefix(es): 2-88002

**Elektrowirtschaft Verlag**
Militaerstr 36, 8021 Zurich
Mailing Address: Postfach 3080, 8021 Zurich
*Tel:* (01) 2994141 *Fax:* (01) 2994140
*E-mail:* redaktion@infel.ch
*Web Site:* www.infel.ch
Subjects: Electronics, Electrical Engineering
ISBN Prefix(es): 3-85651

**Elvetica Edizioni SA+**
CP 134, 6834 Morbio Inferiore
*Tel:* (091) 6835056 *Fax:* (091) 6837605
*E-mail:* info@swissfinance.com
*Key Personnel*
General Managaer: Dr M G Grosso
Founded: 1967
Membership(s): Societa Editori Svizzera Italiana; Association Europeenne des Editeurs d'Annuaires; Schweizer Adressbuch Verleger Verband.
Subjects: Economics, Novels, Essays & Literature
ISBN Prefix(es): 88-86639
Total Titles: 1 CD-ROM; 1 E-Book

**Erker-Verlag**
Division of Erker-Galerie AG
Gallusstr 32, 9000 St Gallen
*Tel:* (071) 227979 *Fax:* (071) 227919
*Key Personnel*
Contact: Franze Larese; Juerg Janett
Founded: 1946
Subjects: Art, Literature, Literary Criticism, Essays, Philosophy, Poetry
ISBN Prefix(es): 3-905542; 3-905543; 3-905544; 3-905545; 3-905546
*Distribution Center:* Balmer Ag, Bucherlager, Bosch 41, Hunenberg (Switzerland)
Stuttgarter Verlagskontor SVK GmbH, Rotebuhlstr 77, D-70178 Stuttgart, Germany (Rest of the world)

**Edition Hans Erpf Edition+**
Postfach 6018, 3001 Bern
*Tel:* (037) 711385 *Fax:* (037) 711968 *Cable:* BUCHERPF
*Key Personnel*
Man Dir: Hans Erpf

Founded: 1966
Subjects: Humor, Literature, Literary Criticism, Essays
ISBN Prefix(es): 3-905517; 3-905520
Number of titles published annually: 20 Print

**Espaces Photographiques**, *imprint of* Editions Olizane

**Editions Esprit Ouvert+**
5, ch du Canal, 1260 Nyon
*Tel:* (022) 3639240 *Fax:* (022) 3639242
Founded: 1988
Subjects: Film, Video, Literature, Literary Criticism, Essays
ISBN Prefix(es): 2-88329

**Eular Verlag** (Eular Publishers)
Subsidiary of Friedrich Reinhardt AG
Missionsstr 36, 4012 Basel
*Tel:* (061) 251317 *Fax:* (061) 251286
*E-mail:* eular@reinhardt.ch
*Key Personnel*
Publisher & International Rights: Ruedi Reinhardt
Founded: 1977
Official publishers of The European League Against Rheumatism (EULAR).
Subjects: Health, Nutrition, Medicine, Nursing, Dentistry
ISBN Prefix(es): 3-7177
*Orders to:* Reinhardt Media-Service

**Europa Verlag AG**
Raemistr 5, 8024 Zurich
*Tel:* (01) 2611629; (01) 2516081
*Telex:* 816534 fere ch *Cable:* Europaverlag Zurich
*Key Personnel*
Man Dir: Emmie Oprecht
Founded: 1933
Distributor for UNESCO, Paris.
Subjects: Art, Government, Political Science, History, Philosophy
ISBN Prefix(es): 3-85665
*Associate Companies:* Verlag Oprecht, Zurich (Theatrical)

**Edition Exodus**
Imprint of Societe Cooperative Edition Exodus
Bederstr 76, 8027 Zurich
Mailing Address: Postfach 8027, 8027 Zurich 5
*Tel:* (01) 2041774 *Fax:* (01) 2024933
*E-mail:* editionexodus@compuserve.com
*Web Site:* www.kath.ch/exodus
*Key Personnel*
Publisher: Markus Koferli
Founded: 1982
Subjects: History, Philosophy, Religion - Catholic, Religion - Protestant, Social Sciences, Sociology, Theology
ISBN Prefix(es): 3-905575

**AZ Fachverlage AG**, see AT Verlag

**Faksimile Verlag AG**
Maihofstr 25, 6000 Lucerne 6
*Tel:* (041) 429 08 20 *Fax:* (041) 429 08 40
*E-mail:* faksimile@faksimile.ch
*Web Site:* www.faksimile.ch
Founded: 1974
Subjects: Antiques, Art, History
ISBN Prefix(es): 3-85672

**FEDA SA+**
Via Frasca 8, 6900 Lugano
*Tel:* (091) 9235677 *Fax:* (091) 9220171
Founded: 1990
Subjects: Archaeology, Architecture & Interior Design, Art, Photography
ISBN Prefix(es): 88-7269

*Associate Companies:* Edizioni Gottardo SA, Lugano, Italy; Giampiero Casagrande Editore, Lugano, Italy
Imprints: FIDIA

**Editions Francois Feij**
Pl de l'Eglise, 1166 Perroy
*Tel:* (021) 8254675
Subjects: Law
ISBN Prefix(es): 2-88030

**FIDIA**, *imprint of* FEDA SA

**Fidia Edizioni d'Arte**, see FEDA SA

**Fischer Media AG fur Verlag und Publishing**
Bahnhofplatz 1, 3110 Muensingen
*Tel:* (031) 7205111 *Fax:* (031) 7205112
*E-mail:* info@fischerprint.ch
*Web Site:* www.fischergroup.ch
*Key Personnel*
Manager: Heinrich Gasser
ISBN Prefix(es): 3-85681
*Parent Company:* Fischer Druck AG

**Maurice et Pierre Foetisch SA**
6, rue de Bourg, 1003 Lausanne
*Tel:* (021) 3239444; (021) 3239445 *Fax:* (021) 3115011
*Telex:* 524227
*Key Personnel*
Man Dir & other offices: Jean-Claude Foetisch
Founded: 1947
Subjects: Education, Music, Dance, Radio, TV
*Associate Companies:* Disco SA

**Editions Foma SA**
5, Av Longemalle, 1020 Renens-Lausanne
*Tel:* (021) 6351361 *Fax:* (021) 6351704
*Telex:* CH-Cedil 25416
*Key Personnel*
Man Dir, Editorial: J-L Peverelli
Sales: M Sculati
Publicity: Ann-Mari Mingard
Rights & Permissions: F Buhler
Founded: 1948
Subjects: Film, Video, Literature, Literary Criticism, Essays, Photography, Psychology, Psychiatry, Sports, Athletics
ISBN Prefix(es): 2-88003
Imprints: Didax
Subsidiaries: 5 Continents, Cedilivre SA
*Bookshop(s):* Didax

**Fondation de l'Encyclopedie de Geneve**
5, Place de la Taconnerie, CP 843, 1211 Geneva 3
*Fax:* (022) 3120960; (022) 3120963
*Key Personnel*
President: Catherine Santschi
Founded: 1979
Description of Geneva's past & present.
Subjects: History
ISBN Prefix(es): 2-940069
Total Titles: 11 Print

**Fortuna Finanz-Verlag AG+**
Haslerholz 7, 8123 Ebmatingen
Mailing Address: Postfach 52, 8123 Ebmatingen
*Tel:* (01) 9803622 *Fax:* (01) 9103353
*E-mail:* info@goldseiten.de
*Web Site:* www.goldseiten.de
*Key Personnel*
Man Dir: Ueli Vonau
Founded: 1953
Subjects: Finance
ISBN Prefix(es): 3-85684

**Fotorotar AG/EGG ZH**, *imprint of*
Schweizerisches Jugendschriftenwerk, SJW

**Frobenius AG**
Spalenring 31, 4012 Basel
*Tel:* (061) 7715677 *Fax:* (061) 7116218
*Key Personnel*
Publicity: Otto Rymann
Subjects: History, Law, Literature, Literary Criticism, Essays, Regional Interests
ISBN Prefix(es): 3-85695

**G+B Arts International+**
Postfach 91, 4004 Basel
*Tel:* (061) 2610138 *Fax:* (061) 2610173
*Key Personnel*
Contact: Linda Lowery-Stuart
Subjects: Architecture & Interior Design, Art, Drama, Theater, History, Photography
*Associate Companies:* Craftsman House; Fine Arts Press; Harwood Academic; Verlag der Kunst; Harvey Miller Publishers; neue bildende Kunst
*Orders to:* Marston Book Services Ltd, PO Box 269, Abingdon, Oxon OX14 4YN, United Kingdom *Tel:* (01) 2354 65500 *Fax:* (01) 2354 65555

**Verlag Gachnang & Springer, Bern-Berlin**
Muristr 16, 3006 Bern
*Tel:* (031) 351 83 83 *Fax:* (031) 351 83 85
*E-mail:* verlag@gachnang-springer.com
*Web Site:* www.gachnang-springer.com
*Key Personnel*
President: Johannes Gachnang
Editor: Constance Lotz; Christine Meyer-Thoss
Founded: 1983
Subjects: Art, Philosophy
ISBN Prefix(es): 3-906127
Distributed by buch 2000 (Switzerland); DAP Distributed Art Publishers (USA, Canada); Buchhandlung Walther Koenig (Europe, excluding Switzerland)

**Garuda-Verlag+**
Sonneggstr 10, 8953 Dietikon 1
Mailing Address: Postfach 717, 8953 Dietikon
*Tel:* (056) 6401014 *Fax:* (056) 6401012
*E-mail:* garuda@bluewin.ch
*Key Personnel*
Dir: P Eisenegger; K Eisenegger
Founded: 1985
Also acts as book distributor & agent.
Subjects: Religion - Buddhist
ISBN Prefix(es): 3-906139
Distributor for Diamant Verlag; Fabri-Verlag; GARUDA-VERLAG

**GC**, *imprint of* Giampiero Casagrande Editore

**GDI**, *imprint of* Gottlieb Duttweiler Institute for Trends & Futures

**Georg et Cie SA**, see Georg Editeur SA

**Georg Editeur SA+**
chemin de la Mousse 46, 1225 Chene-Bourg
*Tel:* (022) 8690029 *Fax:* (022) 8690015
*E-mail:* livres@medecinehygiene.ch
*Web Site:* www.medecinehygiene.ch
*Key Personnel*
Man Dir: Henri Weissenbach *E-mail:* henri. weissenbach@medecinehygiene.ch; Jean-Francois Balavoine
Founded: 1857
Subjects: Economics, Environmental Studies, Ethnicity, Government, Political Science, History, Language Arts, Linguistics, Law, Music, Dance, Philosophy, Psychology, Psychiatry, Religion - Other, Science (General), Social Sciences, Sociology
ISBN Prefix(es): 2-8257
Number of titles published annually: 35 Print
Total Titles: 450 Print; 1 CD-ROM

*Parent Company:* Medecine & Hygiene
*Associate Companies:* Editions Eshel, Paris, France
Imprints: Editions Medecine et Hygiene
*Distribution Center:* Vilo Distribution, 25 rue Ginoux, 75015 Paris, France *Tel:* (01) 45770805 *Fax:* (01) 45757553

**Giampiero Casagrande Editore+**
Via Frasca 8, 6900 Lugano
*Tel:* (091) 9235677 *Fax:* (091) 9220171
*Telex:* 030
Founded: 1982
Subjects: Architecture & Interior Design, Art, History, Photography
ISBN Prefix(es): 88-7795
Imprints: GC
Subsidiaries: Fidia Edizioni d'Arte (FEDA SA)

**Verlag Gleitschirm**
Postfach 68, 7007 Chur
*Tel:* (081) 235241 *Fax:* (081) 221452
ISBN Prefix(es): 3-906334
Divisions: Gleitschirm-Reisen

**Globi Verlag AG**
Binzstr 15, 8045 Zurich
*Tel:* (01) 4552130 *Fax:* (01) 4552188
*E-mail:* info@globi.ch
*Web Site:* www.globi.ch
*Telex:* 813282 *Cable:* GLOBIVERLAG ZURICH
*Key Personnel*
Man Dir: Emil Herzog
Founded: 1944
Subjects: Humor
ISBN Prefix(es): 3-85703
*Warehouse:* B D Buecherdienst Einsiedeln, 8840 Einsiedeln

**Goethe-Verlag, Godhard von Heydebrand**
Worbstr 20, Postfach 38, 3067 Boll
*Tel:* (031) 833248
*Key Personnel*
Manager: Godhard von Heydebrand
Founded: 1955
ISBN Prefix(es): 3-85730

**Victor Goldschmidt Verlagsbuchhandlung**
Mostackerstr 17, 4003 Basel
*Tel:* (061) 236565 *Fax:* (061) 2616123
*Key Personnel*
Contact: Salomon Goldschmidt
Founded: 1902
Membership(s): Swiss Booksellers & Publishers Association.
Subjects: Religion - Jewish, "Judaica" & "Hebraica", Hebrew, German, English, French & Yiddish
ISBN Prefix(es): 3-85705

**Pierre Gonin Editions d'Art**
Ch Du Grand-Praz 1, 1012 Lausanne-Chailly
*Tel:* (021) 7285948 *Fax:* (021) 7285948
*E-mail:* agonin@freesurf.ch
*Web Site:* www.lemeilleur.ch/editionsgonin
*Key Personnel*
Contact: Francoise Gonin
Founded: 1926
ISBN Prefix(es): 2-88016

**Gotthelf-Verlag**
Missionsstr 36, 4012 Basel
Mailing Address: Postf 393, 4012 Basel
*Tel:* (01) 2646460 *Fax:* (01) 2646488
*E-mail:* rms@reinhardt.ch
*Key Personnel*
Man Dir: Alfred Ruedisuehli
Founded: 1928
Subjects: Religion - Other
ISBN Prefix(es): 3-85706
*Associate Companies:* CVB Buch und Druck

**Govinda-Verlag** (Govinda Press)+
Postfach 257, 8212 Neuhausen 2
*Tel:* (052) 6726677 *Fax:* (052) 6726678
*E-mail:* info@govinda.ch
*Web Site:* www.govinda.ch
*Key Personnel*
Manager: Ronald Zuerrer *E-mail:* rz@govinda.ch
Founded: 1989
Subjects: Astrology, Occult, Mysteries, Parapsychology, Philosophy, Poetry, Religion - Hindu, Religion - Other
ISBN Prefix(es): 3-906347
Number of titles published annually: 5 Print
Total Titles: 50 Print

**Graduate Institute of International Studies+**
132 rue de Lausanne, 1211 Geneva 21
*Tel:* (022) 9085700 *Fax:* (022) 9085710
*E-mail:* info@hei.unige.ch
*Web Site:* www.hei.unige.ch
*Key Personnel*
Dir, Publications Department: Vera Gowlland *E-mail:* gowlland@hei.unige.ch
Founded: 1927
Publishes only works originating from the Institute.
Subjects: Economics, History, Law
*U.S. Office(s):* Columbia University Press, 61 W 62 St, New York, NY 10023, United States *Tel:* 212-459-0600 *Fax:* 212-459-3678
Distributed by Kegan Paul International (UK); Kluwer (The Hague); Presses Universitaires de France (PUF) (France)

**Editions du Grand-Pont**
2 Place Bel Air, 1003 Lausanne
*Tel:* (021) 3123222 *Fax:* (021) 3113222
Founded: 1971
ISBN Prefix(es): 2-88148

**Editions du Griffon** (Neuchatel)
Faubourg du Lac 536, 2001 Neuchatel
Mailing Address: CP 536, 2001 Neuchatel
*Tel:* (032) 7252204
Founded: 1944
Subjects: Art
ISBN Prefix(es): 2-88006

**Editions Francois Grounauer**
One rue du Belvedere, 1203 Geneva
*Tel:* (022) 447948
Founded: 1972
Subjects: Government, Political Science, History, Social Sciences, Sociology
ISBN Prefix(es): 2-88076

**GSMBA, Edition Bruno Gasser**
Kasernenstr 23, 4058 Basel
*Tel:* (061) 6811103; (061) 6816698 *Fax:* (061) 6811103
*E-mail:* gasser@dial-switch.ck
ISBN Prefix(es): 3-905504

**Guides-Olizane**, *imprint of* Editions Olizane

**Th Gut Verlag**
Seestr 86, 8712 Staefa
*Tel:* (01) 9285211 *Fax:* (01) 9285200
*Web Site:* www.gutverlag.ch/
*Telex:* 875668
*Key Personnel*
Contact, All offices: Ulrich Gut
Founded: 1943
Subjects: Ethnicity, Government, Political Science, Regional Interests
ISBN Prefix(es): 3-85717

**GVA Publishers Ltd+**
PO Box 135, Champel, 1211 Geneva 12

*Tel:* (022) 3112424 *Fax:* (022) 3112556
*Key Personnel*
Executive Vice President: Alain Nicollier
Founded: 1979
Membership(s): American Booksellers Association.
Subjects: Art, Travel
ISBN Prefix(es): 2-88115

**Haffmans Verlag AG+**
Seefeldstr 301, 8008 Zurich
*Tel:* (01) 386 4000 *Fax:* (01) 386 4001
*E-mail:* verlag@haffmans.ch *Cable:* HAFFMANS VERLAG
*Key Personnel*
Man Dir, Publisher: Gerd Haffmans
Man Dir, Finance Production: Urs Jakob
Editor: Heiko Arntz
Editor & International Rights: Sophie von Heppe
Sales: Constantin Ragusa
Founded: 1982
Subjects: Art, Fiction, Humor, Literature, Literary Criticism, Essays, Mysteries, Philosophy, Poetry, Science Fiction, Fantasy
ISBN Prefix(es): 3-251
Number of titles published annually: 60 Print; 10 Audio
Total Titles: 350 Print; 17 Audio

**Hagenbach & Bender GMBH**
Literary & Media Agency, Gutenbergstr 20, 3011 Bern
*Tel:* (031) 3816666 *Fax:* (031) 3816677
*E-mail:* rights@hagenbach-bender.com
*Web Site:* www.hagenbach-bender.com
*Key Personnel*
Contact: Dieter A Hagenbach *E-mail:* dieter@hagenbach-bender.com
Founded: 2001
Literary & media agency.

**Hallwag Kummerly & Frey AG+**
Grubenstr 109, 3322 Schoenbuehl, Bern
*Tel:* (031) 423131 *Fax:* (031) 414133
*Telex:* 912661 Hawa CH *Cable:* HALLWAG BERNE
*Key Personnel*
President: Dr Juergen Schad
Editorial, Permissions: Beat Koelliker
Sales: Juerg Burri
Founded: 1912
Subjects: Animals, Pets, Art, Cookery, History, How-to, Nonfiction (General), Science (General), Travel
ISBN Prefix(es): 3-444
*Branch Office(s)*
Hallwag Verlagsgesellschaft mbH, Germany

**Paul Haupt Bern+**
Falkenplatz 14, 3001 Bern
*Tel:* (031) 3012425 *Fax:* (031) 3014669
*E-mail:* info@haupt.ch
*Web Site:* www.haupt.ch *Cable:* HAUPTBERN
*Key Personnel*
Man Dir, Permissions: Men Haupt
Production: Erich Hauri
Sales, Publicity: Cordula Frevel
Editor, Rights: Regina Balmer
Contact: Matthias Haupt
Founded: 1906
Subjects: Art, Crafts, Games, Hobbies, Economics, Education, How-to, Science (General), Social Sciences, Sociology
ISBN Prefix(es): 3-258
Total Titles: 2,500 Print; 5 CD-ROM
Foreign Rights: Gudruu Hebel (Scandinavia)
*Bookshop(s):* Hoeheweg 11, Interlaken 3800

**Institut fuer Heilpaedagogik**
Moosmattstr 12, 6005 Lucerne
*Tel:* (041) 3170033 *Fax:* (041) 3170034

*E-mail:* info@ihpl.ch
*Web Site:* www.ihpl.ch
*Key Personnel*
President: Anton Huber
ISBN Prefix(es): 3-85745

**Max Heindel Verlag Rosenkreuzer Philosophie**
(Max Heindel Publishing House Rosicrucian Philosophy)
Suot Crastas, 7514 Sils Maria/Fex
*Tel:* (081) 834 20 03 *Fax:* (081) 834 20 04
*E-mail:* info@max-heindel.ch
*Web Site:* www.heindel-verlag.ch
*Key Personnel*
Contact: Annemarie Giovanoli-Troost *Tel:* (081) 834 2122 *Fax:* (081) 834 2124

**Heinrich Hugendubel AG**
Villa Bellevue, Hauptstr 14, 8280 Kreuzlingen
*Tel:* (071) 67711-90 *Fax:* (071) 67711-91

**Helbing und Lichtenhahn Verlag AG+**
Elisabethenstr 8, 4051 Basel
*Tel:* (061) 2289070 *Fax:* (061) 2289071
*E-mail:* info@helbing.ch
*Web Site:* www.helbing.ch
*Key Personnel*
Dir: Men Haupt *E-mail:* men.haupt@helbing.ch
Founded: 1822
Subjects: Anthropology, Economics, Environmental Studies, Government, Political Science, History, Language Arts, Linguistics, Law, Management
ISBN Prefix(es): 3-7190
*Associate Companies:* Sauerlaender AG

**Verlag Helvetica Chimica Acta**
Hofwiesenstr 26, 8042 Zurich
*Tel:* (01) 3602434 *Fax:* (01) 3602435
*E-mail:* info@wiley-vch.de; vhca@vhca.ch
*Web Site:* www.wiley-vch.de
*Key Personnel*
Man Dir: Dr M V Kisakuerek
Subjects: Chemistry, Chemical Engineering
ISBN Prefix(es): 3-85727; 3-906390

**Herder AG Basel**
Muttenzerstr 109, 4133 Pratteln 1
*Tel:* (061) 8279060 *Fax:* (061) 8279067
*E-mail:* verkauf@herder.ch
*Telex:* 64358
Subjects: Philosophy, Religion - Other, Theology
ISBN Prefix(es): 3-906371; 3-906372
*Associate Companies:* Verlag Herder & Co, Austria; Editorial Herder SA, Spain; Herder Editrice e Libreria, Italy; Verlag Herder GmbH & Co KG, Germany; Herder und Herder GmbH, Germany; Verlag A G Ploetz GmbH & Co KG, Germany

**Verlag Huber & Co AG+**
Division of Huber & Co AG
Promenadenstr 16, Postfach 382, 8500 Frauenfeld
*Tel:* (052) 723 5617 *Fax:* (052) 723 5619
*E-mail:* buchverlag@huber.ch
*Web Site:* www.huber.ch
*Key Personnel*
Man Dir & Publisher: Hansrudolf Frey *Tel:* (052) 723 5618
Production: Arthur Miserez *Tel:* (052) 723 5656 *Fax:* (052) 721 4977
Marketing: Charlotte Krahenbuehl
Founded: 1809
Subjects: Agriculture, Art, Environmental Studies, Ethnicity, Government, Political Science, History, Language Arts, Linguistics, Regional Interests
ISBN Prefix(es): 3-7193; 3-274
Total Titles: 200 Print

*Bookshop(s):* Buchhandlung Huber & Co AG, Freiestr 8, 8501 Frauenfeld *Tel:* (052) 7235858 *E-mail:* info@huberbooks.ch *Web Site:* www.huberbooks.ch

**Hug & Co+**
Grossmuenstrerplatz 7, 8001 Zurich
Mailing Address: Limmatquai 28-30, Postfach, 8022 Zurich
*Tel:* (01) 269 41 40 *Fax:* (01) 269 41 06
*E-mail:* info@hug-musikverlage.ch
*Web Site:* www.hug-musikverlage.ch
*Telex:* 829311 muvich
*Key Personnel*
Dir: Erika Hug
Founded: 1807
Subjects: Music, Dance
ISBN Prefix(es): 3-906415
*Associate Companies:* Edition Foetisch-Foetisch Freres, Case postale, 1002 Lausanne
*Warehouse:* Musica Vivam Flughofstr 61, 8152 Glattbrugg, Zurich
*Orders to:* Musica Vivam Flughofstr 61, 8152 Glattbrugg, Zurich

**Editions Charles Huguenin Pro Arte**
rue du Sapin 2a, 2114 Fleurier
*Tel:* (038) 61 27 27 *Fax:* (038) 61 37 19
*Key Personnel*
Man Dir: Jean-Charles Frochaux
*Parent Company:* Schola Cantorum-Triton
*Associate Companies:* Cantate Domino

**Idegraf SA, Editions**
route de Chancy, 28, 1213 Petit-Lancy
*Tel:* (022) 792 03 96 *Fax:* (022) 793 63 30
*E-mail:* 101512.3363@compuserve.com
ISBN Prefix(es): 2-88259

**Editions Ides et Calendes SA+**
Evole 19, 2001 Neuchatel
*Tel:* (032) 725 38 61 *Fax:* (032) 725 58 80
*E-mail:* info@idesetcalendes.com; artides@artides.com; ides@livre.net
*Web Site:* www.artides.com; www.livre.net/ides
*Key Personnel*
Chief Executive: Alain Bouret
Founded: 1941
Subjects: Art, Law, Lives d'art & peiuture; photoarchive, photogalerie
ISBN Prefix(es): 2-8258

**Verlag Industrielle Organisation+**
Dietzingerstr 3, 8036 Zurich
*Tel:* (01) 4667711 *Fax:* (01) 4667412
*E-mail:* info@ofv.ch
*Web Site:* www.ofv.ch
*Key Personnel*
Contact: Gerhard Labitzke *Tel:* (01) 466 74 76 *E-mail:* glabitzke@ofv.ch
Founded: 1931
Subjects: Electronics, Electrical Engineering, Human Relations, Management, Marketing
ISBN Prefix(es): 3-85743
*Parent Company:* Orell Fussli Verlag

**Interfrom AG Editions+**
Schaffhauserstr 466, 8052 Zurich
Mailing Address: Postfach 5005, 8022 Zurich
*Tel:* (01) 3065200 *Fax:* (01) 3065205
*Key Personnel*
Publisher: Leo V Fromm
Executive Vice President & Editorial: A Harms-Hunold
Sales Manager: Annegret Busch
Public Relations: Ursula Malzahn
Founded: 1974
Popular Science by German-speaking experts.
Subjects: Economics, Education, Environmental Studies, Ethnicity, Government, Political

Science, History, Science (General), Social Sciences, Sociology
ISBN Prefix(es): 3-7201
Imprints: Zurich
Branch Office(s)
Verlag A Fromm, Breiter Gang 10-16, 49076 Osnabrueck, Germany
U.S. Office(s): Fromm International Publishing Corporation, 560 Lexington Ave, New York, NY 10022, United States
Warehouse: Schweizer Buchzentrum, 4601 Olten
Orders to: Schweizer Buchzentrum, 4601 Olten

**Iris Verlag AG**
c/o Poly Laupen AG, Bahnweg 2, 3177 Laupen
Tel: (031) 7473300 Fax: (031) 7473301
E-mail: polyinfo@rentsch.com
Web Site: www.poly-laupen.ch
Key Personnel
Man Dir: Horst Hochrein
Deputy Man Dir: Peter Konrad
ISBN Prefix(es): 3-85751

**ISIOM Verlag fur Tondokumente, Weinreb Tonarchiv+**
CP 362, 6600 Locarno
Tel: (091) 7513524 Fax: (091) 7516154
E-mail: isiom@bluewin.ch
Key Personnel
President: Hans Haessig-Tellenbach
Author: Friedrich Weinreb; Graf Duerckneim
Founded: 1974
Specialize in audio books.
Subjects: Ethnicity, Philosophy, Religion - Jewish, Theology
ISBN Prefix(es): 88-85151

**Jordanverlag AG+**
Steffenstr 1, 8052 Zurich
Tel: (01) 3023676
Key Personnel
Contact: Peter Buff
Founded: 1984
Subjects: Biblical Studies, Religion - Catholic, Religion - Protestant
ISBN Prefix(es): 3-906561

**Editions Jouvence+**
CP 184, 1233 Bernex, Geneva
Tel: (022) 794 66 22 Fax: (022) 794 67 86
E-mail: info@editions-jouvence.com
Web Site: www.editions-jouvence.com
Key Personnel
Dir: Jacques Maire
Editorial Dir: Olivier Clerc Tel: (0450) 432862 E-mail: olivier.clerc@usa.net
Founded: 1989
Subjects: Child Care & Development, Environmental Studies, Health, Nutrition, Psychology, Psychiatry, Self-Help, Social Sciences, Sociology
ISBN Prefix(es): 2-88353
Associate Companies: BP 7, 74161 St Julien-en-Genevois, France Tel: (0450) 43 28 60 Fax: (0450) 43 29 24

**JPM Publications SA+**
12 av William Fraisse, 1006 Lausanne
Tel: (021) 6177561 Fax: (021) 6161257
E-mail: information@jpmguides.com
Web Site: www.jpmguides.com
Key Personnel
Man Dir: Mr Jean-Paul Minder Tel: (021) 617 75 66 E-mail: jeanpaul.minder@jpmguides.com
Founded: 1992
Subjects: Travel
ISBN Prefix(es): 2-88452
U.S. Office(s): 245 E 19 St, 3D, New York, NY 10003, United States, Contact: Dorsey Smith
Distributed by Hunter Publishing

**Jugend mit einer Mission Verlag+**
Poststr 14, Postfach 144, 2500 Biel 8
Tel: (032) 418988 Fax: (032) 418920
Key Personnel
Publisher: Eva Stopper
Founded: 1991
Subjects: Biblical Studies, Education, Religion - Protestant, Theology
ISBN Prefix(es): 3-906568

**Junod Nicolas**
12 rue Robert-de-Traz, 1206 Geneva
Tel: (022) 347 02 42 Fax: (022) 347 02 42
Telex: 23381 trib ch
Key Personnel
Man Dir, Rights & Permissions: Henri Heizmann
Founded: 1977
Subjects: Art, Cookery, Government, Political Science, Health, Nutrition, History, Humor, Radio, TV
ISBN Prefix(es): 2-8297
Parent Company: SA de la Tribune de Geneve

**Juris Druck & Verlag AG**
Basteiplatz 5, 8953 Dietikon 1
Mailing Address: Postfach 627, 8953 Dietikon
Tel: (01) 7409038; (01) 2117747 Fax: (01) 7409019
E-mail: juris@swissonline.ch
Key Personnel
Man Dir: Markus Christen
Founded: 1945
Membership(s): SBVV.
Subjects: History, Law
ISBN Prefix(es): 3-260

**Kalos-Verlag**
Fritz Aerni-Schaffhauserstr 446, 8052 Zurich
Tel: (01) 3022751 Fax: (01) 3022751
ISBN Prefix(es): 3-906598

**Kanisius Verlag+**
ave de Beauregard 3, 1701 Fribourg
Mailing Address: Postfach 1052, 1701 Fribourg, Germany
Tel: (026) 425 87 30 Fax: (026) 425 87 38
E-mail: info@canisius.ch
Web Site: www.canisius.ch Cable: KANISIUSWERK FRIBOURG
Key Personnel
Man Dir, Publicity: Dr Barbara Evers-Greder
Production Manager: Peter Ledergerber
Founded: 1898
Subjects: Biblical Studies, Biography, Cookery, Religion - Catholic, Self-Help, Theology
ISBN Prefix(es): 3-85764; 3-85740
Bookshop(s): Kanisiusbuchhandlung,, Bahnhofplatz 6, 1701 Fribourg Tel: (037) 221345; Kanisiusbuchhandlung, Haengebrueckstr 16, 1702 Fribourg Tel: (037) 222954; Kanisiuswerk, Blarerstr 18, 78462 Konstanz, Germany

**S Karger AG, Medical & Scientific Publishers+**
Allschwilerstr 10, 4009 Basel
Tel: (061) 3061111 Fax: (061) 3061234
E-mail: karger@karger.ch
Web Site: www.karger.com
Key Personnel
President: Dr Thomas Karger
Man Dir: Steven Karger
Dir, Sales & Marketing: Mr Moritz Thommen
Rights & Permissions: Mrs Carmen Scaglia
Founded: 1890
Anatomy Atlas.
Subjects: Biological Sciences, Medicine, Nursing, Dentistry, Psychology, Psychiatry, Veterinary Science
ISBN Prefix(es): 3-8055
Associate Companies: Karger Japan, Inc, Yushima S Bldg 3F, 4-2-3, Yushima, Bunkyo-ku, Tokyo

113-0034, Japan Tel: (03) 3815-1800 Fax: (03) 3815-1802 E-mail: publisher@karger.jp; S Karger AG, 4 Rickett St, London SW6 1RU, United Kingdom Tel: (020) 7610 3331 Fax: (020) 7610 3337 E-mail: uk@karger. ch; S Karger Publishers Inc, 26 W Avon Rd, PO Box 529, Farmington, CT 06085, United States Tel: 860-675-7834 Fax: 860-675-7302 E-mail: karger@snet.net; Panther Publishers Private Ltd, 33 First Main, Koramangala First Block, Bangalore 560 034, India Tel: (080) 5505 836, 5505 837 Fax: (080) 5505 981 E-mail: panther_publishers@vsnl.com
Branch Office(s)
DA Information Services, 648 Whitehorse Rd, PO Box 163, Mitcham, Victoria 3132, Australia Tel: (03) 92107777 Fax: (03) 92107788 E-mail: service@dadirect.com.au
Web Site: www.dadirect.com.au
Librairie Luginbuehl, 36 bd de Latour-Maubourg, 75007 Paris, France Tel: (01) 45514258 Fax: (01) 45560780 E-mail: liblug@club-internet.fr
APAC Publishers Service Pte Ltd, 70, Bendemeer Rd, 05-03 Hiap Huat House, 339940 Singapore, Singapore Tel: 6844 7333 Fax: 6747 8916 E-mail: service@apacmedia.com.sg
Bookshop(s): Karger Libri AG, Petersgraben 31, 4009 Basel Tel: (061) 306 1111 Fax: (061) 306 1516 E-mail: books@libri.karger.ch Web Site: www.libri.ch

**KBV**, see Kinderbuchverlag Luzern

**Verlag Walter Keller, Dornach**
Lehmenweg 5, 4143 Dornach 2
Tel: (061) 7015713 Fax: (061) 7015716
E-mail: info@verlag-walterkeller.ch
Web Site: www.verlag-walterkeller.ch
Key Personnel
Contact: Ingrid Bergmann E-mail: i-bergmann@ verlag-walterkeller.ch
Founded: 1969
Specialize in eurythmic.
Subjects: Art
ISBN Prefix(es): 3-906633
Distributed by Anthroposophic Press Inc

**Editions Ketty & Alexandre+**
1063 Chapelle-sur-Moudon
Tel: (021) 9051111 Fax: (021) 9056050
Key Personnel
Contact: Alexandre Gisiger
Founded: 1975
Subjects: History
ISBN Prefix(es): 2-88114

**Kinderbuchfonds Baobab**
Laufenstr 16, 4018 Basel
Tel: (061) 3332727 Fax: (061) 3332726
E-mail: info@access.ch
Web Site: www.baobabbooks.ch
Founded: 1983
Editor of children's books from Africa, Asia & Latin America.
Total Titles: 3 Print

**Kinderbuchverlag Luzern+**
Ausserfeldstr 9, 5036 Oberentfelden
Tel: (062) 836 86 86 Fax: (062) 836 86 20
E-mail: verlag@sauerlaender.ch
Web Site: www.sauerlaender.ch
Key Personnel
Publisher: Hans Uristof
Editorial & Foreign Rights Dir: Jasua Zagovc
Founded: 1979
Subjects: Animals, Pets, Art, Natural History, Nonfiction (General)
ISBN Prefix(es): 3-276

**Kindler Verlag AG**
Nelkenstr 20, 8006 Zurich

*Tel:* (01) 3633007
*Telex:* 045 57608 *Cable:* Kindlerverlag Zurich
*Key Personnel*
Publisher: Helmut Kindler; Nina Kindler
Subjects: Anthropology, Psychology, Psychiatry
ISBN Prefix(es): 3-463

**Klett und Balmer & Co Verlag**
Baarerstr 95, 6302 Zug
Mailing Address: Postfach 2357, 6302 Zug
*Tel:* (041) 726 28 00 *Fax:* (041) 726 28 01
*E-mail:* info@klett.ch
*Web Site:* www.klett.ch
*Key Personnel*
Man Dir: Christoph Balmer; Michael Klett;
   Roland Klett; Dr Thomas Klett
Manager: Hans Egli
Founded: 1967
Subjects: Education, Government, Political Science, Philosophy, Science (General)
ISBN Prefix(es): 3-264
*Parent Company:* Ernst Klett KG, Stuttgart, Germany

**Kober Verlag Bern AG**
Hildegardstr 6, 3097 Liebefeld
*Tel:* (031) 9714687
*E-mail:* koberpress@mindspring.com
*Key Personnel*
President: Harald Blum
Man Dir, Sales: Emil Zillig
Founded: 1816
Subjects: Philosophy, Religion - Other, Theology
ISBN Prefix(es): 3-85767
*Associate Companies:* The Kober Press, PO Box 2194, San Francisco, CA 94126, United States

**Kolumbus-Verlag+**
Muehlebuehlstr 10, 5737 Menziken
*Tel:* (064) 7711370 *Cable:* VDB MENZIKEN
*Key Personnel*
Man Dir: Dr G van den Bergh
Founded: 1945
Subjects: Language Arts, Linguistics, Philosophy
ISBN Prefix(es): 3-85769

**Kommissionsverlag Leobuchhandling**
Gallusstr 20, 9001 St Gallen
*Tel:* (071) 222917 *Fax:* (071) 220587
*Key Personnel*
Man Dir: Eugen Hettinger
Founded: 1918
ISBN Prefix(es): 3-85788; 3-9520218

**Galerie Kornfeld & Co**
Laupenstr 41, 3001 Bern
Mailing Address: Postfach 6265, 3001 Bern
*Tel:* (031) 381 46 73 *Fax:* (031) 382 18 91
*E-mail:* galerie@kornfeld.ch
*Web Site:* www.kornfeld.ch
*Key Personnel*
Proprietor: Eberhard W Kornfeld
Founded: 1864
Subjects: Art
ISBN Prefix(es): 3-85773

**Kossodo Verlag AG**
av Lignon 27-28, 1219 Le Lignon
*Tel:* (022) 962230
*Key Personnel*
Dir: Martha Duessel
Founded: 1956
Subjects: Art
ISBN Prefix(es): 3-7208

**Verlag Karl Kraemer & Co+**
Postfach 1209, 8034 Zurich
*Tel:* (01) 2528454 *Fax:* (0711) 784960 (Germany)
*E-mail:* info@kraemerverlag.com
*Web Site:* www.kraemerverlag.com

*Key Personnel*
Publisher, President & Man Dir: Karl H Kraemer
   *E-mail:* karl.kraemer@kraemerverlag.com
International Rights: Mrs Gudrun Kraemer
Founded: 1962
Specialize in publishing books & magazines on architecture, town planning & building construction.
Subjects: Architecture & Interior Design
ISBN Prefix(es): 3-85774
*Associate Companies:* Kark Kraemer Verlag GmbH und Co, Schulze-Delitzsch-Str 15, 70565 Stuttgart, Germany *Tel:* (0711) 78 49 60 *Fax:* (0711) 78 49 620
*Bookshop(s):* Karl Kraemer Fachbuchhandlung, Rotebuehlstr 42, 70178 Stuttgart, Germany *Tel:* (0711) 66993-0 *Fax:* (0711) 628955

**Verlag Rene Kramer AG+**
33, via del Tiglio, 6906 Lugano-Cassarate
*Tel:* (091) 518941 *Cable:* Edikramer Lugan 06
*Key Personnel*
Man Dir, Publicity: Rene Kramer
Founded: 1962
Subjects: Cookery
ISBN Prefix(es): 2-88290

**Kranich-Verlag, Dres AG & H R Bosch-Gwalter+**
Dufourstr 30, 8702 Zollikon
*Tel:* (01) 3918484 *Fax:* (01) 3920884
*E-mail:* boschag@zik.ch
Founded: 1951
Specialize in Special Editions.
Subjects: Architecture & Interior Design, Art, Biblical Studies, Biography, Business, Economics, History, Language Arts, Linguistics, Law, Literature, Literary Criticism, Essays, Philosophy, Poetry, Psychology, Psychiatry, Religion - Catholic, Religion - Protestant, Theology, Travel
ISBN Prefix(es): 3-906640; 3-909194
Number of titles published annually: 5 Print
Total Titles: 115 Print; 2 CD-ROM

**Kuemmerly & Frey (Geographischer Verlag)**
Grubenstr 109, 3322 Schoenbuehl
*Tel:* (031) 850 3131 *Fax:* (031) 850 3130
*E-mail:* info@swisstravelcenter.ch
*Web Site:* www.swisstravelcenter.ch
*Telex:* 912765 *Cable:* KUMMERLYFREY
*Key Personnel*
Public Relations: Danielle Zingg
Founded: 1852
Subjects: Geography, Geology, Travel
ISBN Prefix(es): 3-259
*Associate Companies:* Kuemmerly & Frey Verlags-GmbH, Austria; BLay-Foldex, France; Kuemmerly & Frey Verlags-GmbH, Germany

**Imprimerie A Kuendig**
49 Chemin de l'Etang, CP 26, 1219 Chatelaine/Geneva
*Tel:* (022) 966013
*Key Personnel*
Manager: Georges Naef
Founded: 1923
ISBN Prefix(es): 2-88018

**Edition Kunzelmann GmbH**
Gruetstr 28, 8134 Adliswil
*Tel:* (01) 7103681 *Fax:* (01) 7103817
*Web Site:* www.kunzelmann.ch
Founded: 1945
Subjects: Music, Dance
ISBN Prefix(es): 3-85662; 3-9521049

**Labor et Fides SA+**
One rue Beauregard, 1204 Geneva
*Tel:* (022) 311 32 69 *Fax:* (022) 781 30 51
*E-mail:* contact@laboretfides.com

*Web Site:* www.laboretfides.com
*Key Personnel*
Chairman: Gabriel de Montmollin
Founded: 1924
Subjects: Religion - Other, Social Sciences, Sociology, Theology
ISBN Prefix(es): 2-8309

**Herbert Lang & Cie AG, Buchhandlung, Antiquariat**
Muenzgraben 2, Ecke Amthausgasse, 3000 Bern 9
*Tel:* (031) 3108484 *Fax:* (031) 3108494
*Telex:* 912867 lang ch *Cable:* Librilang
*Key Personnel*
President: Christoph H Lang
Founded: 1813 (re-formed 1921)
Agents for libraries throughout the world.
Subjects: Science (General)
ISBN Prefix(es): 3-261

**Peter Lang AG+**
Hochfeldstr 32, 3000 Bern 9
Mailing Address: PO Box 746, 3000 Bern 9
*Tel:* (031) 306 17 17 *Fax:* (031) 306 17 27
*E-mail:* info@peterlang.com
*Web Site:* www.peterlang.com
*Key Personnel*
Editorial: Tony Albala de Rivas
Founded: 1977
Specialize in academic publications.
Subjects: Art, History, Language Arts, Linguistics, Law, Literature, Literary Criticism, Essays, Philosophy, Social Sciences, Sociology, Theology
ISBN Prefix(es): 0-8204; 3-631; 3-906750; 3-906751; 3-906752; 3-906753; 3-906754; 3-906755; 3-906757; 3-906758; 3-906759; 3-906756; 3-906760; 3-906761; 3-906762; 3-906763; 3-906764; 3-906765; 3-906766; 3-906767; 3-906768; 3-906769
Subsidiaries: Peter Lang GmbH; Peter Lang Publishing, Inc; PIE-Peter Lang SA
*Orders to:* Moosstr 1, PO Box 350, 2542 Pieterlen *Tel:* (032) 376 17 17 *Fax:* (032) 376 17 27

**Langenscheidt AG Zuerich-Zug**
Gratis-Anrufumleitung n Zur, 8001 Zurich
Mailing Address: Postfach 326, 8021 Zurich
*Tel:* (01) 2115000 *Fax:* (01) 2122149
*Key Personnel*
Administration: Doctor Ernst Grub
Membership(s): the Langenscheidt Group, Germany.
Subjects: Language Arts, Linguistics
ISBN Prefix(es): 3-269; 3-906725
*Parent Company:* Langenscheidt KG, Germany

**Franz Larese und Juerg Janett**, see
   Erker-Verlag

**Larousse (Suisse) SA**
c/o Acces-Direct, 3 Route du Grand-Mont, 1052 Le Mont-sur-Lausanne
*Tel:* (021) 335336
*Telex:* 24797
*Key Personnel*
Man Dir: Jean-Claude Viatte
ISBN Prefix(es): 2-8276
*Parent Company:* Librairie Larousse, France

**Lehrmittelverlag des Kantons Zurich+**
Unit of State of Kanton Zurich
Raeffelstr 32, 8045 Zurich
*Tel:* (01) 465 85 85 *Fax:* (01) 465 85 89
*E-mail:* lehrmittelverlag@lmv.zh.ch
*Web Site:* www.lehrmittelverlag.com
*Key Personnel*
Assistant Dir: Robert Fuchs *Tel:* (01) 4658507
Sales Manager: Engemann Beat *Tel:* (01) 4658540 *E-mail:* beat.engemann@lmv.ch

Founded: 1851
Subjects: Film, Video, Radio, TV

**Lenos Verlag+**
Spalentorweg 12, 4051 Basel
*Tel:* (061) 261 34 14 *Fax:* (061) 261 35 18
*E-mail:* lenos@lenos.ch
*Web Site:* www.lenos.ch
*Key Personnel*
Program Dir, Publicity: Heidi Sommerer
Sales: Tom Forrer
Founded: 1970
Subjects: Government, Political Science, Journalism, Nonfiction (General)
ISBN Prefix(es): 3-85787

**Leonis Verlag+**
Tufweg 1, Postf 513, 8044 Zurich
*Tel:* (01) 821 4055 *Fax:* (01) 821 4065 *Cable:* LEONISVERLAG ZURICH
*Key Personnel*
Proprietor, Man Dir: Dr Wolfgang M Metz
Founded: 1976
Subjects: How-to, Religion - Other, Self-Help
ISBN Prefix(es): 3-7210; 3-85627
*Associate Companies:* Doulos Verlag

**Bernard Letu Editeur+**
2 rue Calvin, 1204 Geneva
*Tel:* (022) 204757 *Fax:* (022) 208492
Founded: 1973
Subjects: Art, Photography
ISBN Prefix(es): 2-88051

**Lia rumantscha**
Obere Plessurstr 47, 7001 Chur
*Tel:* (081) 258 3222 *Fax:* (081) 258 3223
*E-mail:* liarumantscha@rumantsch.ch
*Web Site:* www.liarumantscha.ch
*Key Personnel*
Dir: Gion A Derungs
Founded: 1919
Company also gives financial support to other publications in Romansh in the Romansh-speaking area.
Subjects: History, Language Arts, Linguistics, Literature, Literary Criticism, Essays, Music, Dance, Poetry, Regional Interests, Religion - Other
ISBN Prefix(es): 3-906680

**Die Libelle Verlag Ag Libellen Haus**
Sternengarten 6, 8574 Lengwil
*Tel:* (071) 688 35 55 *Fax:* (071) 688 35 65
*E-mail:* info@libelle.ch
*Web Site:* www.libelle.ch
ISBN Prefix(es): 3-909081

**Limmat Verlag**
Quellenstr 25, 8031 Zurich
*Tel:* (044) 445 80 80 *Fax:* (044) 445 80 88
*E-mail:* presse@limmatverlag.ch
*Web Site:* www.limmatverlag.ch
*Key Personnel*
Sales: Juerg Zimmerli *Tel:* (044) 445 80 81
    *E-mail:* zimmerli@limmatverlag.ch
Founded: 1975
Subjects: Art, Biography, Fiction, Film, Video, Government, Political Science, Literature, Literary Criticism, Essays, Poetry, Social Sciences, Sociology, Women's Studies
ISBN Prefix(es): 3-85791
Number of titles published annually: 30 Online
Total Titles: 500 Print

**Literatheke**, *imprint of* Eco Verlags AG

**E Lopfe-Benz AG Rorschach, Graphische Anstalt und Verlag**
Pestalozzistr 5, 9401 Rorschach

*Tel:* (071) 8440444 *Fax:* (071) 8440445
*Key Personnel*
Dir: Emil Enderle; Dieter Mildenberger
Editorial: Werner Meier
Sales: Peter Kruijsen
Advertising: Hans Schoebi; Peter Bick; Daniel Anderegg
Founded: 1875
Graphical Institute & Publisher.
Subjects: History, Humor, Poetry
ISBN Prefix(es): 3-85819; 3-906785; 3-9521222
Subsidiaries: Nebelspalter Verlag

**Maihof Verlag**
Sihlbruggstr 105A, 6341 Baar
*Tel:* (041) 767 76 76 *Fax:* (041) 767 76 77
*E-mail:* info@maihofverlag.ch
*Web Site:* www.maihofdruck.ch
*Key Personnel*
Publisher: Margrit Boschung
Founded: 1959
Subjects: Biography, History, Maritime
ISBN Prefix(es): 3-9520027; 3-9520756; 3-906970; 3-9522033

**La Maison de la Bible+**
Chemin de Praz-Roussy 4bis, 1032 Romanel-sur-Lausanne
*Tel:* (021) 867 10 10 *Fax:* (021) 867 10 15
*E-mail:* info@bible.ch
*Web Site:* www.bible.ch
*Key Personnel*
Chief Executive Dir & International Rights: Paul-Andre Eicher *Tel:* (021) 811 40 50
    *E-mail:* pae@bible.ch
Contact: Vivian Andre; Olivia Festal; Stefan Waldmann
Founded: 1917
Specialize in publishing & translating bibles, books, audio & CD-ROM.
Membership(s): CBA & ECPA.
Subjects: Biblical Studies, Biography, Human Relations, Religion - Protestant, Theology, Family
ISBN Prefix(es): 2-8260; 2-608
Number of titles published annually: 25 Print
Total Titles: 340 Print; 4 CD-ROM; 47 Audio
*Parent Company:* Geneva Bible Society
Imprints: Editions OURANIA
Divisions:
Distributed by Haenssler/Bolanz/C L Verlag (Germany); Service d'Orientation Biblique (Canada); Servidis (Switzerland)
Distributor for Crossway; Focus on the Family; Harvest House; Lion, OM; Moody (US); STL; Thomas Nelson (US); Zondervan (US)
Foreign Rep(s): Stephan Waldmann (Worldwide)
Foreign Rights: Olivia Festal (Worldwide)

**Manesse Verlag GmbH**
Badergasse 9, 8001 Zurich
*Tel:* (01) 2525551 *Fax:* (01) 2625347
*E-mail:* buch@dva.de
*Web Site:* www.manesse.ch
*Key Personnel*
Man Dir: Anne Marie Wells
International Rights: Angelika Rachor
Founded: 1944
Subjects: Fiction, History, Literature, Literary Criticism, Essays, Philosophy, Poetry
ISBN Prefix(es): 3-7175
Total Titles: 350 Print
*Parent Company:* Deutsche Verlags-Anstalt GmbH (DVA), Germany

**Manus Verlag**
Bergstr 90, 8708 Maennedorf
*Tel:* (01) 920 27 27 *Fax:* (01) 920 27 40
*E-mail:* manart@bluewin.ch
*Web Site:* www.manus.ch
*Key Personnel*
Manager: Kurt Borer

Founded: 1970
ISBN Prefix(es): 3-907003; 3-906982; 3-906956; 3-907956

**Librairie-Editions J Marguerat+**
2 pl St Francois, 1002 Lausanne
*Tel:* (021) 3237717 *Fax:* (021) 3126732
*Key Personnel*
Dir: Jean Bakker
Founded: 1940
Subjects: Ethnicity, Geography, Geology, History, Music, Dance, Travel
ISBN Prefix(es): 2-88008

**MARKT & TECHNIK AG**, see Pearson Education

**MARP**, see Muslim Architecture Research Program (MARP)

**Viktoria-Verlag Peter Marti**, see Viktoria-Verlag Peter Marti

**Les Editions la Matze**
One rue du Mont, 1951 Sion
*Tel:* (027) 3231652 *Fax:* (027) 3231652
*Key Personnel*
Man Dir, Sales: Guy Gessler
Founded: 1975
Subjects: Archaeology, Art, Fiction, History, Military Science
ISBN Prefix(es): 2-88025

**Meandre**
14 Stalden, 1700 Fribourg
*Tel:* (026) 322174 *Fax:* (026) 323287
*Key Personnel*
Contact: Gerard Bourgarel
ISBN Prefix(es): 2-88359

**Medecine et Hygiene**
78 ave de la Roseraie, 1205 Geneva
*Tel:* (022) 702 93 11 *Fax:* (022) 702 93 55
*E-mail:* direction@medecinehygiene.dr
*Web Site:* www.medhyg.ch
*Key Personnel*
Man Dir, Sales: P Y Balavoine
Publicity & Advertising Dir: G Antonietti
Editor-in-Chief: Dr B Kiefer
Founded: 1943
Subjects: Medicine, Nursing, Dentistry, Psychology, Psychiatry, Science (General)
ISBN Prefix(es): 3-88049

**Editions Medecine et Hygiene**, *imprint of* Georg Editeur SA

**Peter Meili & Co, Buchhandlung**
Fronwagplatz 13, 8200 Schaffhausen
*Tel:* (053) 254144 *Fax:* (053) 254746
*Telex:* 76777 meibuch
Founded: 1838
Subjects: Government, Political Science, History, Language Arts, Linguistics, Regional Interests
ISBN Prefix(es): 3-85805
*Bookshop(s):* Buchhandlung Meili & Co

**Memory/Cage Editions**
Edenstr 12, 8045 Zurich
*Tel:* (01) 281 35 65 *Fax:* (01) 281 35 66
*E-mail:* mail@memorycage.com
*Web Site:* www.memorycage.com
*Key Personnel*
Publisher: Daniel Kurjakovic
    *E-mail:* kurjakovic@memorycage.com
Founded: 1994
Subjects: Art, Literature, Literary Criticism, Essays, Photography

ISBN Prefix(es): 3-907053
*Orders to:* DAP, 155 Sixth Ave, New York, NY 10013, United States, Contact: Amy Lozada
*Tel:* 212-627-1999 *Fax:* 212-627-9484

## Editions H Messeiller SA
11 St Nicolas, 2006 Neuchatel
*Tel:* (032) 7251296 *Fax:* (032) 7241937
*Key Personnel*
Dir: Cl-H Messeiller
Founded: 1887
Subjects: Art, Education, Law, Psychology, Psychiatry, Public Administration, Religion - Other
ISBN Prefix(es): 2-8261

## Minervaverlag Bern+
Seftigenstr 25, 3001 Bern
Mailing Address: PO Box 6849, 3001 Bern
*Tel:* (031) 3726223 *Fax:* (031) 3726223
*Key Personnel*
Contact: Louis R Jenzer
Founded: 1991
Membership(s): Swiss Bookseller & Editera Association.
ISBN Prefix(es): 3-9520216
Total Titles: 2 Print; 8 Audio
Distributor for Prodest SA Lugano; WerdtVerlag Zuerich

## Editions Minkoff
8 rue Eynard, 1211 Geneva 12
Mailing Address: CP 377, 1211 Geneva 12
*Tel:* (022) 310 46 60 *Fax:* (022) 310 28 57
*E-mail:* minkoff@minkoff-editions.com
*Web Site:* www.minkoff-editions.com
*Key Personnel*
Dir: Sylvie Minkoff *E-mail:* minkoff@ipzolink.ch
Founded: 1970 (in France, 1989)
Specialize in fac-similes
Also acts as agents for: Editions des Abbesses; Centre de Music Baroque de Versailles; Patrimoine Musical Regional francais; Editions Universite-Conservatrioe de Musique de Geneve; Editions EBL-La Borie en Limousin; New Grove Dictionary of Music & Musicians, London; Editions de l'Oiseau-Lyre, Monaco; Bibliotheque Nationale music publications, Claude Debussy Documentation Centre, CNRS music publications & the French Musicological Society, Paris.
Subjects: Art, Drama, Theater, History, Music, Dance
ISBN Prefix(es): 2-8266
Number of titles published annually: 50 Print
Total Titles: 1,200 Print
*Parent Company:* Minkoff France Editeur
*Bookshop(s):* A La Regle d'Or, Librairie Musicale, Minkoff France Editeur, 23 rue de Fleurus, 75006 Paris, France *Tel:* (01) 45449433 *Fax:* (01) 45449430

## Mondo SA (Editions-Verlag-Edizioni)
St Antoine 7, 1800 Vevey
*Tel:* (021) 924 12 40 *Fax:* (021) 924 46 62
*E-mail:* info@mondo.ch
*Web Site:* www.mondo.ch
*Telex:* 452100 Spn Ch
*Key Personnel*
Dir: Arslan Alamir
ISBN Prefix(es): 2-88168

## Motovun Book GmbH+
Grendelstr 15, 6004 Lucerne
*Tel:* (041) 4109515 *Fax:* (041) 4109516
*E-mail:* motovun@bluewin.ch
*Web Site:* www.motovun-group-association.org
*Key Personnel*
Man Dir & Publisher: Juergen Braunschweiger
Rights & Permissions: Brigitte Abeida
Founded: 1999
Also acts as publisher & packager.

Membership(s): Motovun Group Association; Swiss Publishers Association.
Subjects: Archaeology, Art, Crafts, Games, Hobbies, Geography, Geology, History, Religion - Other, Travel
Subsidiaries: Motovun Productions & Trade

## Verlag Rudolf Muehlemann
Haus zu Lagerstr 6, 8570 Weinfelden
*Tel:* (071) 622 53 53 *Fax:* (071) 622 30 04
*E-mail:* wolfau-druck@bluewin.ch
Founded: 1949
ISBN Prefix(es): 3-85809

## Lars Mueller Publishers+
PO Box 912, 5401 Baden
*Tel:* (056) 430-17-40 *Fax:* (056) 430-17-41
*E-mail:* info@lars-mueller-publishers.com
*Web Site:* www.lars-mueller-publishers.com
*Key Personnel*
Manager: Lars Mueller
Founded: 1983
Subjects: Architecture & Interior Design, Art, Photography, Graphic design & typography
ISBN Prefix(es): 3-906700; 3-907044; 3-907078; 3-03778
Number of titles published annually: 20 Print
*U.S. Office(s):* Distributed Art Publishers Inc, 155 Sixth Ave, 2nd floor, New York, NY 10013-1507, United States, Contact: Donna Wingate *Tel:* 212-627-1999 *E-mail:* dwingate@dapinc.com

## Mueller Rueschlikon Verlags AG+
Gewerbestr 10, 6330 Cham
Mailing Address: Postfach 4561, 6304 Zug
*Tel:* (041) 443040-42 *Fax:* (041) 417115
*Key Personnel*
Rights & Licenses: Monika Hess
Publicity: Roland Dietschi
Founded: 1938
Subjects: Animals, Pets, Cookery, Crafts, Games, Hobbies, Fiction, How-to, Outdoor Recreation, Wine & Spirits
ISBN Prefix(es): 3-275

## Editions Musicales De La Schola Cantorum
Epinassey, 1890 St-Maurice
*Tel:* (024) 485 24 80 *Fax:* (024) 485 34 60
*E-mail:* frochaux-schola@bluewin.ch; labatiaz@bluewin.ch
*Key Personnel*
Contact: Roulin Blaise
Founded: 1896
Specializes in choral music, organ & choral methods.
Membership(s): ASMEM.
Subjects: Music, Dance
*Parent Company:* Labatiaz
*Associate Companies:* Cantate Domino
Distributor for Chorus (Pierre Kaelin); Gesseney; Henn; Labatiaz; Musique Abbe Bovet; Tales

## Muslim Architecture Research Program (MARP)+
Postfach 207, 8061 Zurich 4
*Tel:* (02) 4711228 *Fax:* (02) 4711228
*Key Personnel*
Contact: Alena Norod
Founded: 1973
Publisher of the first encyclopedia of architecture
Also acts as Archaeological Institute & Architectural Office.
Subjects: Archaeology, Architecture & Interior Design, Art
ISBN Prefix(es): 3-906995
*Warehouse:* Muenchenbuchsea
Ostrov, Czech Republic

## Edito Georges Naef SA+
33 quai Wilson, 1211 Geneva 21

Mailing Address: CP 256, 1211 Geneva 21
*Tel:* (022) 7315000 *Fax:* (022) 7384224
*E-mail:* naef@kister.ch
*Web Site:* www.kister.ch
*Key Personnel*
Contact: Georges Naef
Founded: 1986
Specialize in internet development.
ISBN Prefix(es): 2-8313
Total Titles: 24 CD-ROM
*Parent Company:* Kister SA
Subsidiaries: Naef Diffusion

## Verlag Nagel & Kimche AG, Zurich+
Imprint of Sanssouci
Nordstr 9, Postfach, 8035 Zurich
*Tel:* (01) 366 66 80 *Fax:* (01) 366 66 88
*E-mail:* info@nagel-kimche.ch
*Web Site:* www.nagel-kimche.ch
*Telex:* 897522 naki
*Key Personnel*
International Rights: Monika Kemptner
Contact: Dr Dirk Vaihinger *E-mail:* vaihinger@nagel-kimche.ch
Founded: 1983
Subjects: Fiction
ISBN Prefix(es): 3-312
*Ultimate Parent Company:* Carl Hanser Verlag, Munich, Germany
*Associate Companies:* Zsolnay Verlag

## Les Editions Nagel SA (Paris)
Staffelistr 6, 8409 Winterthur 7
Mailing Address: Postfach 59, 8409 Winterthur
*Tel:* (052) 242 4816 *Fax:* (052) 242 4827
*E-mail:* info@nagel.ch
*Web Site:* www.nagel.ch
*Key Personnel*
Man Dir: Guillaume Briquet
Founded: 1928
Subjects: Archaeology, Art, Government, Political Science, Philosophy, Travel
ISBN Prefix(es): 2-8263

## Natura-Verlag Arlesheim
Pfeffingerweg 1, 4144 Arlesheim
*Tel:* (061) 717111 *Fax:* (061) 7064201
Subjects: Astrology, Occult, Education, Philosophy
ISBN Prefix(es): 3-85817

## Nebelspalter-Verlag
Pestalozzistr 5, 9401 Rorschach
*Tel:* (071) 8440444 *Fax:* (071) 8440445
*Key Personnel*
Dir: E Enderle; D Mildenberger
Founded: 1875
Subjects: Humor
ISBN Prefix(es): 3-85819; 3-906785; 3-9521222
*Parent Company:* E Loepfe-Benz AG

## Neptun-Verlag
Erlenstr 2, 8280 Kreuzlingen
Mailing Address: Postfach 1220, 8280 Kreuzlingen
*Tel:* (071) 677 96 55 *Fax:* (071) 677 96 50
*E-mail:* neptun@bluewin.ch
*Web Site:* www.neptunart.ch
*Telex:* 882221 nept ch
*Key Personnel*
Manager: Herbert Berchtold
Founded: 1946
Subjects: History, Travel
ISBN Prefix(es): 3-85820

**Neue Szene,** *imprint of* Eco Verlags AG

## Neue Zuercher Zeitung AG Buchverlag+
Falkenstr 11, 8021 Zurich
*Tel:* (01) 2581505 *Fax:* (01) 2581399
*E-mail:* buch.verlag@nzz.ch
*Web Site:* www.nzz-buchverlag.ch

*Key Personnel*
Publicity Manager: Walter Koepfli *E-mail:* buch.
verlag@nzz.ch
Book publishing division of Zurich daily newspaper.
ISBN Prefix(es): 3-85823; 3-03823; 3-907092
Total Titles: 200 Print; 10 CD-ROM

**Verlag Arthur Niggli AG**
Steinackerstr 8, 8583 Sulgen
*Tel:* (071) 6449111 *Fax:* (071) 6449190
*E-mail:* info@niggli.ch
*Web Site:* www.niggli.ch
*Key Personnel*
Man Dir: Bruno Waldburger
Founded: 1950
Subjects: Architecture & Interior Design, Art, Typography
ISBN Prefix(es): 3-7212

**Les Editions Noir sur Blanc+**
Le Motta, 1147 Montricher
*Tel:* (021) 8645931 *Fax:* (021) 8644026
*E-mail:* noirsurblanc@bluewin.ch *Cable:*
EDINOBL
*Key Personnel*
Contact: Vera Michalski-Hoffmann
Founded: 1986
Subjects: Biography, Cookery, Drama, Theater,
Fiction, History, Humor, Literature, Literary
Criticism, Essays
ISBN Prefix(es): 2-88250
*Branch Office(s)*
123 blvd Saint Germain, 75006 Paris, France
*Tel:* (01) 43269846 *Fax:* (01) 40518792
ul Frascati 18, 00483 Warsaw, Poland

**Editions Nord-Sud**, *imprint of* Nord-Sued Verlag

**Nord-Sud Edizioni**, *imprint of* Nord-Sued Verlag

**Nord-Sued Verlag**
Industriestr 8, 8625 Gossau, Zurich
*Tel:* (01) 9366868 *Fax:* (01) 9366800
*E-mail:* info@nord-sued.com *Cable:*
NORDSUED
*Key Personnel*
Dir: Davy Sidjanski
Editorial: Brigitte Hanhart Sidjanski; Jurgen Lassig
Public Relations: Sabine Reiner
Production: Ulrich Gaebler
Rights & Permissions: Monika Giuliani
Founded: 1961
ISBN Prefix(es): 3-85825; 3-314; 2-8311; 3-03733
Imprints: De Vier Winstreken; Editions Nord-Sud;
North-South Books; Nord-Sud Edizioni
Divisions: Michael Neugebauer Verlag

**North-South Books**, *imprint of* Nord-Sued Verlag

**Novalis Media AG**
PO Box 1021, 8201 Schaffhausen
*Tel:* (052) 6201490 *Fax:* (052) 6201491
*E-mail:* info@novalis.ch
*Web Site:* www.novalis.ch *Cable:* Novalis
Schaffhausen
*Key Personnel*
Contact: Eva Frensch *Tel:* (052) 932780
*Fax:* (052) 932784; Mr M Frensch *Tel:* 052
6201490
Founded: 1946
Subjects: Anthropology, Art, Education, History,
Language Arts, Linguistics, Philosophy, Psychology, Psychiatry, Religion - Other, Social
Sciences, Sociology, Theology
Number of titles published annually: 6 Print
Total Titles: 44 Print

*Branch Office(s)*
PO Box 600, 78266 Buesingen, Contact: Mr
Bracker *Tel:* (07734) 932780 *Fax:* (07734)
932781

**NZN Buchverlag AG+**
Hirschengraben 66, 8001 Zurich
*Tel:* (01) 266 12 92 *Fax:* (01) 266 12 93
*E-mail:* nzn@nzn.ch
*Web Site:* www.nzn.ch
*Key Personnel*
Editor-in-Chief: Magdalena Eberhard
Founded: 1946
Subjects: Religion - Catholic
ISBN Prefix(es): 3-85827
Number of titles published annually: 4 Print

**NZZ Buchverlag**, see Neue Zuercher Zeitung
AG Buchverlag

**Objectif Terre**, *imprint of* Editions Olizane

**Octopus Verlag**
Vazerolgasse 1, 7000 Chur
*Tel:* (081) 252 10 29 *Fax:* (081) 252 94 66
ISBN Prefix(es): 3-279

**Oekumenischer Rat der Kirchen**, see World
Council of Churches (WCC Publications)

**Oesch Verlag AG+**
Jungholzstr 28, 8050 Zurich
*Tel:* (01) 305 70 60 *Fax:* (01) 305 70 66
*E-mail:* info@oeschverlag.ch
*Web Site:* www.oeschverlag.ch *Cable:* OESCH
*Key Personnel*
Dir: Martin Brugger
Editorial: Natasha Fischer *E-mail:* lektorat@
oeschverlag.ch
Rights & Permissions: Anne Brugger
Founded: 1935
Subjects: Career Development, Fiction, Health,
Nutrition, Management, Marketing, Nonfiction
(General), Self-Help
ISBN Prefix(es): 3-85833; 3-0350
Number of titles published annually: 40 Print
Total Titles: 2 Audio
*Associate Companies:* Conzett Verlag
*E-mail:* info@oeschverlag.ch *Web Site:* www.
finanzbuch.ch; Jopp Verlag *E-mail:* info@
oeschverlag.ch *Web Site:* www.joppverlag.ch

**Office du Livre SA (Buchhaus AG)**
ZI3, Corminboeuf, 1701 Fribourg
Mailing Address: PO Box 1152, 1701 Fribourg
*Tel:* (026) 4675111 *Fax:* (026) 4675466
*E-mail:* information@olf.ch
*Web Site:* www.olf.ch
*Telex:* 942291 Olf CH *Cable:* Livreoffice
*Key Personnel*
Dir: Jean-Marc Rod
Founded: 1947
Subjects: Antiques, Architecture & Interior Design, Art, Asian Studies, Crafts, Games, Hobbies, Sports, Athletics
ISBN Prefix(es): 3-7215; 2-8264

**Editions Olizane+**
11 rue des Vieux-Grenadiers, 1205 Geneva
*Tel:* (022) 328 52 52 *Fax:* (022) 328 57 96
*E-mail:* guides@olizane.ch
*Web Site:* www.olizane.ch
*Key Personnel*
Man Dir: Matthias Huber
Founded: 1981
Subjects: Ethnicity, Photography, Travel
ISBN Prefix(es): 2-88086

Imprints: Objectif Terre; Collection Artou; Espaces Photographiques; Guides-Olizane; Etudes
Orientales
Foreign Rights: Gaia Media Basel (Germany)

**Edition Olms AG+**
Breitlenstr 11, 8634 Hombrechtikon/Zurich
Mailing Address: Postfach 233, 8634 Hombrechtikon/Zurich
*Tel:* (01) 2445030 *Fax:* (01) 2445031
*E-mail:* info@edition-olms.com
*Web Site:* www.edition-olms.com
*Key Personnel*
Man Dir & other offices: Manfred Olms
Founded: 1977
Subjects: Art, Film, Video, Humor, Music, Dance,
Photography
ISBN Prefix(es): 3-283
*Warehouse:* VVA/Bertelsmann, DFA/B, attn: Mrs
Pia Brenne, PO Box 7600, 33310 Guetersloh,
Germany

**Opinio Verlag AG+**
Formerly Wiese Verlag AG
Missionsstr 36, 4012 Basel
Mailing Address: PO Box 393, 4012 Basel
*Tel:* (061) 2646450 *Fax:* (061) 2646488
*E-mail:* opinio@reinhardt.ch
*Web Site:* www.opinio.ch
*Key Personnel*
Publisher: Peter Zwicky
Founded: 1988
Subjects: Architecture & Interior Design, Art,
Crafts, Games, Hobbies
ISBN Prefix(es): 3-85815; 3-85504; 3-909158;
3-909164; 3-85975; 3-9520932; 3-03999; 3-905352
*Parent Company:* Basler Zeitung
*Book Club(s):* SBVV

**Orell Fuessli Buchhandlungs AG+**
Dietzingerstr 3, 8036 Zurich
*Tel:* (01) 466 77 11 *Fax:* (01) 466 74 12
*E-mail:* info@ofv.ch
*Web Site:* www.ofv.ch
*Telex:* 813021 orla ch *Cable:* ORELLVERLAG
ZURICH
*Key Personnel*
Man Dir & Sales, Marketing: Dr Manfred Hiefner
Rights & Permissions: Pia Hiefner-Hug
Founded: 1519
Subjects: Accounting, Art, Biography, Business,
Economics, Education, Geography, Geology,
History, How-to, Law
ISBN Prefix(es): 3-280; 3-7249
*Parent Company:* Orell Fuessli Graphische Betriebe AG
Imprints: Eugen Rentsch Verlag AG
*Bookshop(s):* Orell Fuessli Buchhandlung, Pelikanstr 10, 8022 Zurich

**Verlag Organisator AG**
Molkenstr 21, 8026 Zurich
*Tel:* (01) 2961030 *Fax:* (01) 2961031
*E-mail:* redaktion@organisator.ch
*Web Site:* www.organisator.ch
*Telex:* 813834 *Cable:* orga/ch
*Key Personnel*
Man Dir, Editorial: F Borner
Sales, Publicity, Production: Bruno Waldburger
Founded: 1919
Subjects: Accounting, Government, Political Science, Labor, Industrial Relations
ISBN Prefix(es): 3-7220
*Parent Company:* Rudolf Haufe Verlag GmbH &
Co KG, Germany
*Bookshop(s):* Basel; Lucerne; St Gallen;
Schaffhausen; Winterthur; Zurich; others
throughout Switzerland

**Etudes Orientales**, *imprint of* Editions Olizane

**Origo Verlag+**
Rathausgasse 30, 3011 Bern
*Tel:* (031) 3114480 *Fax:* (031) 3114470
*Key Personnel*
Proprietor & Man Dir: Alexander Wild
Founded: 1947
Subjects: Mysteries, Parapsychology, Philosophy,
   Psychology, Psychiatry, Religion - Buddhist,
   Religion - Jewish, Religion - Other, Theology
ISBN Prefix(es): 3-282; 3-85835
*Associate Companies:* Verlag Alexander Wild

**Orte-Verlag**
Wirtschaft Kreuz, 9427 Wolfhalden
*Tel:* (01) 888 1556
*E-mail:* info@orteverlag.ch
*Web Site:* www.orteverlag.ch
*Key Personnel*
Man Dir: Werner Bucher
Publicity: Ruth Good-Ramp
Subjects: Poetry
ISBN Prefix(es): 3-85830

**Ostschweiz Druck und Verlag**
Hofstetstr 14, 9303 Wittenbach
*Tel:* (071) 2922929 *Fax:* (071) 2922938
*Telex:* 77393
*Key Personnel*
Man Dir, Sales: Dr Emil Daehler
Founded: 1892
Subjects: Art, History, Music, Dance, Poetry, So-
   cial Sciences, Sociology
ISBN Prefix(es): 3-85837; 3-9521313

**Ott Verlag Thun** (Ott Publishers Inc)+
Laenggasse 57, 3607 Thun 7
Mailing Address: Postfach 802, 3607 Thun 7
*Tel:* (033) 225 39 39 *Fax:* (033) 225 39 33
*E-mail:* info@ott-verlag.ch
*Web Site:* www.ott-verlag.ch *Cable:* OTTPUBL
   THUN
*Key Personnel*
Man Dir: Hans M Ott
Founded: 1923
Specialize in printers & editors.
Subjects: Business, Earth Sciences, Economics,
   Gardening, Plants, Geography, Geology, Man-
   agement, Military Science, Nonfiction (Gen-
   eral), Sports, Athletics
ISBN Prefix(es): 3-7225
*Associate Companies:* Translegal Ltd (publishers
   of dictionaries)

**Editions OURANIA,** *imprint of* La Maison de la
   Bible

**Editions du Panorama**
CP 3511, 2500 Bielefeld 3
*Tel:* (032) 3581665 *Fax:* (032) 3581665
*Key Personnel*
Man Dir: Paul Thierrin
Founded: 1951
Subjects: Business, Fiction
ISBN Prefix(es): 2-88019

**Panorama Verlag,** see Tobler Verlag

**Parkett Publishers Inc+**
Quellenstr 27, 8031 Zurich
*Tel:* (01) 2718140 *Fax:* (01) 2724301
*E-mail:* info@parkettart.com
*Web Site:* www.parkettart.com
*Key Personnel*
Man Dir: Dieter von Graffenried; Bice Curiger
Founded: 1984
Subjects: Art
ISBN Prefix(es): 3-907509
*U.S. Office(s):* Parkett Publishers, 155 Avenue of
   the Americas, Spring St, New York, NY 10013,
   United States *Tel:* 212-673-2660 *Fax:* 212-271-
   0704 *E-mail:* info@parkettart.com

**Editions Parole et Silence+**
Le Muveran, 1888 Les Plans
*Tel:* (024) 6982301 *Fax:* (024) 6982311
*Key Personnel*
Contact: Sabine Larive
ISBN Prefix(es): 2-84573

**Editions du Parvis**
1648 Hauteville
*Tel:* (026) 915 93 93 *Fax:* (026) 915 93 99
*E-mail:* book@parvis.ch
*Web Site:* www.parvis.ch
*Key Personnel*
Executive: Jean-Marie Castella
Founded: 1970
Subjects: Health, Nutrition, Religion - Catholic
ISBN Prefix(es): 2-88022; 3-907523; 3-907525
Number of titles published annually: 20 Print
Distributed by Gallus (Austria)
Distributor for Centro Editoriale Valtortiano (Eu-
   rope)

**Foundation Simon I Patino,** see Editions Patino

**Editions Patino+**
8, rue Giovanni Gambini, 1211 Geneva 25
Mailing Address: CP 182, 1211 Geneva 25
*Tel:* (022) 3470211 *Fax:* (022) 7891829
*Key Personnel*
Contact: John Dubouchet; Roger Guggisberg
Founded: 1986
Subjects: Fiction, Philosophy
ISBN Prefix(es): 2-88213
*Orders to:* Vilo L'Amateur, 25 rue Ginoux, 75015
   Paris, France *Fax:* (1) 45757553

**Paulus Verlag,** see Editions Saint-Paul

**Editions Payot Lausanne+**
18 ave de la Gare, 1001 Lausanne
Mailing Address: CP 529, 1001 Lausanne
*Tel:* (021) 3290264 *Fax:* (021) 3290266
*E-mail:* ed.payot.nadir@bluewin.ch
*Key Personnel*
Publisher: Jacques Scherrer
Founded: 1875
Membership(s): ASELF.
Subjects: Anthropology, Archaeology, Architec-
   ture & Interior Design, History, Law, Liter-
   ature, Literary Criticism, Essays, Medicine,
   Nursing, Dentistry, Music, Dance, Nonfiction
   (General), Philosophy, Regional Interests, Sci-
   ence (General), Social Sciences, Sociology
ISBN Prefix(es): 2-601
Total Titles: 490 Print
*Parent Company:* Nadir SA/Jacques Scherrer Edi-
   teur, Lausanne
Distributed by Doin Editeurs, Paris (for medical
   books in France, Belgium & Canada)
Distributor for Olympic Museum Publications
   (France & Belgium)
*Orders to:* Olf, ZI-3 Corminboeuf, 1701 Fribourg

**Pearson Education+**
Chollerstr 37, 6300 Zug
*Tel:* 747 4747 *Fax:* 747 4777
*E-mail:* firstname.lastname@pearson.ch;
   mailbox@pearson.ch
*Web Site:* www.pearson.ch
*Key Personnel*
Business Manager: Tobias Eberhart
Chairman: Gunther Frank *Tel:* (089) 46003 121
   *Fax:* (089) 46003 120
Vice Chairman: Josef Grand
Member of the Board: Martin Frey *Tel:* (01) 384
   1414 *Fax:* (01) 384 1284
Founded: 1983
Other business activities: distribution of M&T
   Books & Software; Sub-distribution of Mi-
   crosoft, Lotus, Novell & others.
Subjects: Computer Science

*Parent Company:* Pearson Plc
Distributor for Adobe Press; BradyGAMES; Hay-
   den Books; M&T Books & Software; New
   Riders; Que; Sams; Sams.net; Waite Group
   Press; Ziff-Davis Press
*Distribution Center:* Pearson Education Schweiz
   AG, Chollerstrasse 37, CH-6301 Zug

**Pedrazzini Tipografia**
Via Varenna, 7, 6600 Locarno
*Tel:* (091) 751 7734 *Fax:* (091) 751 5118
*E-mail:* tipedra@webshuttle.ch
*Key Personnel*
Man Dir & other offices: Benedetto Pedrazzini
Founded: 1880
Subjects: Education, History, Literature, Literary
   Criticism, Essays, Publishing & Book Trade
   Reference, Religion - Other
ISBN Prefix(es): 88-7408

**Pendo Verlag GmbH+**
Forchstr 40, 8032 Zurich
Mailing Address: Postfach, 8032 Zurich
*Tel:* (01) 3897030 *Fax:* (01) 3897035
*E-mail:* info@pendo.ch
*Web Site:* www.pendo.ch
*Key Personnel*
Publisher: Ernst Piper *Tel:* (089) 13999252
   *Fax:* (089) 13999170 *E-mail:* ernst.piper@t-
   online.de
Editor: Katrin Eckert *Tel:* (01) 3897032 *Fax:* (01)
   3897035
Founded: 1971
Specialize in literature, contemporary history &
   essays.
Subjects: Government, Political Science, History,
   Literature, Literary Criticism, Essays, Poetry,
   Religion - Other
ISBN Prefix(es): 3-85842
Number of titles published annually: 35 Print
Total Titles: 200 Print
Imprints: Politics
*Branch Office(s)*
Volkarstr 13, 80634 Munich, Germany *Tel:* (089)
   13999252 *Fax:* (089) 13999170 *E-mail:* ernst.
   piper@online.de *Web Site:* www.ernst-piper.de

**Perret Edition**
Blutzwis 14, 8604 Volketswil
*Tel:* (01) 9972717 *Fax:* (01) 9972718
Founded: 1995
Subjects: Art, Photography
ISBN Prefix(es): 3-9520910

**Verlag Die Pforte im Rudolf Steiner Verlag**
Huegelweg 34, 4143 Dornach 1
Mailing Address: Postfach 135, 4143 Dornach
*Tel:* (061) 706 91 30 *Fax:* (061) 706 91 49
*E-mail:* verlag@rudolf-steiner.com
*Web Site:* www.rudolf-steiner.com
*Key Personnel*
International Rights: Benedikt Marzahn
Founded: 1960
Subjects: Anthropology, Philosophy
ISBN Prefix(es): 3-85636
Total Titles: 70 Print

**Pharos-Verlag, Hansrudolf Schwabe AG**
Therwilestr 5, 4011 Basel
Mailing Address: Postfach 68, 4011 Basel
*Tel:* (061) 541021 *Fax:* (061) 2797972
*Key Personnel*
Man Dir: Alexander Schwabe
Advertising Dir: Myrte Schwabe
Founded: 1958
Subjects: Transportation, Wine & Spirits
ISBN Prefix(es): 3-7230

**Philosophisch-Anthroposophischer Verlag am Goetheanum+**
Hugelweg 59, 4143 Dornach 1
Mailing Address: Postfach 131, 4143 Dornach
*Tel:* (061) 706 42 00 *Fax:* (061) 706 42 01
*E-mail:* info@vamg.ch
*Web Site:* www.vamg.ch
*Key Personnel*
General Secretary: Otfried Doerfler
Founded: 1908
Subjects: Art, Education, Literature, Literary Criticism, Essays, Mathematics, Medicine, Nursing, Dentistry, Philosophy, Religion - Other, Science (General), Theology
ISBN Prefix(es): 3-7235
Subsidiaries: Rudolf Geering Verlag

**Politics**, *imprint of* Pendo Verlag GmbH

**Editions Pourquoi Pas+**
CP 60, 1247 Anieres, Geneve
*Tel:* (022) 7511031
*Key Personnel*
Contact: Astrid Mirabaud
Founded: 1981
Subjects: Literature, Literary Criticism, Essays
ISBN Prefix(es): 2-88173

**Presses Polytechniques et Universitaires Romandes, PPUR+**
EPFL-Ecublens, Centre Midi, 1015 Lausanne
*Tel:* (021) 693 41 31 *Fax:* (021) 693 40 27
*E-mail:* ppur@epfl.ch
*Web Site:* www.ppur.org
*Telex:* 450 456 attn. PPUR
*Key Personnel*
President: Pierre-Francois Pittet
Man Dir, Editorial: Olivier Babel
Production: Christophe Borlat
Promotion: Sylvain Collette
International Rights: Yasmine Babel-Sraih
    *Tel:* (021) 693 60 44 *E-mail:* yasmine.babel@epfl.ch
Founded: 1980
Also acts as book packager.
Subjects: Architecture & Interior Design, Biological Sciences, Chemistry, Chemical Engineering, Civil Engineering, Computer Science, Earth Sciences, Electronics, Electrical Engineering, Engineering (General), Management, Mathematics, Mechanical Engineering, Physics, Science (General), Technology
ISBN Prefix(es): 2-88074; 2-940222
Number of titles published annually: 30 Print
Distributed by Eyrolles-Geodif (France & Maroc); Patrimoine for Belgium (Benelux); PIP (Canada & USA)

**Pro Juventute Verlag+**
Seehofstr 15, 8032 Zurich
*Tel:* (01) 2567777 *Fax:* (01) 2567778
*E-mail:* info@projuventute.ch
*Web Site:* www.projuventute.ch
ISBN Prefix(es): 3-7152

**Editions Pro Schola**
3 Place Chauderon, 1003 Lausanne
*Tel:* (021) 323 66 55 *Fax:* (021) 323 67 77
*E-mail:* benedict@benedict-schools.com
*Web Site:* www.benedict-international.com
*Key Personnel*
Man Dir: Dr Jean J Benedict
Founded: 1928
Official distributor of the Benedict Method.
Membership(s): ASDEL.
Subjects: Education, English as a Second Language, Language Arts, Linguistics
ISBN Prefix(es): 2-88009
Total Titles: 85 Print
Distributed by Buchimport Peter Reimer
*Warehouse:* 24 Rue de Geneve, 1003 Lausanne

**Promoedition SA+**
35, rue des Bains, 1211 Geneva
Mailing Address: CP 5615, 1211 Geneva
*Tel:* (022) 8099460 *Fax:* (022) 7811414
*Key Personnel*
International Rights Contact: Thierry B Opplkofer
Founded: 1972
Subjects: Business, Communications, Film, Video, Finance
ISBN Prefix(es): 2-88129

**Psychosophische Gesellschaft**
Schedlern, 9063 Stein
*Tel:* (071) 59 13 01 *Fax:* (071) 3672301
Subjects: Astrology, Occult, Education, Philosophy, Psychology, Psychiatry, Theology
ISBN Prefix(es): 3-85846

**Punktum AG, Buchredaktion und Bildarchiv+**
Klusstr 50, 8032 Zurich
*Tel:* (01) 422 45 40 *Fax:* (01) 422 48 13
*Key Personnel*
Contact: Dr Niklaus Flueeler; Marianne Flueeler-Grauwiter
Specialize in Swiss Topics.
Subjects: Art, Ethnicity, History, Travel
ISBN Prefix(es): 3-907577
Divisions: Punktum Buchredoktion (Packaging), Punktum Bildarchiv (Picture Library)

**Rabe Verlag AG Zuerich**
Frankengasse 6, 8001 Zurich
*Tel:* (01) 261 85 40 *Fax:* (01) 261 85 41 *Cable:* RABEVERLAG ZURICH
*Key Personnel*
Man Dir, Sales: Dr J Kanitz
Editorial, Rights & Permissions: Dr Elsa Kanitz
Production: Dr P Portmann
Founded: 1962
Subjects: Art
ISBN Prefix(es): 3-85852
*U.S. Office(s):* PAPYRUS Franchise Corp, 954 16 St, Oakland, CA 94608, United States
*Warehouse:* CH-8608 Bubikon Zurich/Dorfstr. 15-15a *Tel:* (055) 243 23 83

**Robert Raeber, Buchhandlung am Schweizerhof**
Schweizerhofquai 2, 6002 Lucerne
Mailing Address: Postfach 4170, 6002 Lucerne
*Tel:* (041) 512371
*Key Personnel*
Man Dir: Robert Raeber-Huber
Founded: 1973
Subjects: Fiction, Travel
ISBN Prefix(es): 3-7239
*Bookshop(s):* Raeber Buchhandlung, Schweizerhofquai 2, 6002 Lucerne

**Raphael, Editions+**
CP 1, 1801 Le Mont-Pelerin
*Tel:* (021) 9215230 *Fax:* (021) 9215237
*Key Personnel*
Dir: Mr Denis Ducatel *E-mail:* denis.ducatel@dplanet.ch
Founded: 1990
Subjects: Literature, Literary Criticism, Essays, Psychology, Psychiatry, Religion - Protestant
ISBN Prefix(es): 2-88417
Total Titles: 24 Print
Distributed by Editions Empreinte; Interlivres (Canada); Jeunesse en Mission Belgique (Belgium); Olbis

**Rauhreif Verlag**
Titlisstr 3, 4313 Moehlin
*Tel:* (061) 851 53 63
Subjects: Literature, Literary Criticism, Essays
ISBN Prefix(es): 3-907764

**Verlag fuer Recht und Gesellschaft AG**
Ringstr 75, 4106 Therwil
*Tel:* (061) 726 26 26 *Fax:* (061) 726 26 27
*E-mail:* info@vrg-verlag.ch
*Web Site:* www.vrg-verlag.ch *Cable:* REGES VERLAG
*Key Personnel*
Man Dir: Dr Peter J Amuer
Founded: 1933
Subjects: Accounting, Law
ISBN Prefix(es): 3-7242
*Associate Companies:* Sciamed Verlag AG, Ringstr 75, Postfach, 4106 Therwil

**Recom**, *imprint of* RECOM Verlag

**RECOM Verlag**
Industriestral 3, 34308 Bad Emstal
*Tel:* (056) 249224-0; (0700) 20055555 (service) *Fax:* (056) 249224-18
*E-mail:* info@recom-verlag.de
*Web Site:* www.recom-verlag.de
*Telex:* 63755 rein ch
*Key Personnel*
Man Dir, Sales, Production, Publicity: Alfred Ruedisuehli
Founded: 1971 (1985)
Subjects: Medicine, Nursing, Dentistry
ISBN Prefix(es): 3-7245; 3-497
*Parent Company:* Friedrich Reinhardt AG
Imprints: Recom

**Regenbogen Verlag+**
Gertrudstr 46, 8003 Zurich
*Tel:* (01) 454 3033 *Fax:* (01) 454 3035
*E-mail:* info@regenbogen-verlag.ch
*Web Site:* www.regenbogen-verlag.ch
*Key Personnel*
General Manager: Theo Ruff
Subjects: Art, Travel
ISBN Prefix(es): 3-85862
*Orders to:* Prolit Buchvertrieb GmbH, Siemensstr 18a, 35394 Giessen, Germany *Tel:* (0641) 77053

**Reich Verlag AG+**
Museggstr 12, 6004 Lucerne
*Tel:* (041) 4103721 *Fax:* (041) 4103227
*Web Site:* www.terramagica.de
*Key Personnel*
Man Dir: Alfons Wueest
Founded: 1974
Specialize in books of plates.
Subjects: Photography
ISBN Prefix(es): 3-7243
Number of titles published annually: 8 Print
Total Titles: 60 Print
Imprints: Terra Magica

**Verlag Friedrich Reinhardt AG**
Missionsstr 36, 4012 Basel
Mailing Address: Postfach 393, 4012 Basel
*Tel:* (061) 264 64 50 *Fax:* (061) 264 64 88
*E-mail:* verlag@reinhardt.ch
*Web Site:* www.reinhardt.ch *Cable:* Freinhardt Basle
*Key Personnel*
Man Dir, Rights & Permissions: Dr Ernst Reinhardt
Founded: 1900
Subjects: Art, Biography, Environmental Studies, Fiction, History, How-to, Religion - Other, Theology
ISBN Prefix(es): 3-7245; 3-497
Subsidiaries: Eular Verlag; Reinhardt Communications

**Eugen Rentsch Verlag AG**, *imprint of* Orell Fuessli Buchhandlungs AG

**Rex Verlag**
St Karliquai 12, 6000 Lucerne 5
Mailing Address: Postfach 5266, 6000 Lucerne
*Tel:* (041) 4194719 *Fax:* (041) 4194711
*E-mail:* info@rex-freizyt.ch
*Web Site:* www.rex-freizyt.ch
*Key Personnel*
Man Dir: Markus Kappeler
Founded: 1931
Subjects: Education, Fiction, Religion - Catholic
ISBN Prefix(es): 3-7252
*Bookshop(s):* Rex Buchladen, St Karliquair 12, Postfach 5266, 6000 Lucerne

**Rhein-Trio, Edition/Editions du Fou+**
Drahtzugstr 10, 4057 Basel
*Tel:* (061) 6831635 *Fax:* (061) 6831635
*E-mail:* rhein-trio@usa.net
Founded: 1993
Specialize in comics.
Subjects: Art, Astrology, Occult, Humor, Mysteries, Poetry
ISBN Prefix(es): 3-9520470
Distributed by Comics Virt (Austria)
Distributor for Comicwelt

**Editiones Roche**
c/o F Hoffmann-La Roche Ltd, Grenzacherstr 124, 4070 Basel
*Tel:* (061) 688 3611 *Fax:* (061) 688 2775
*Web Site:* www.roche.com
*Key Personnel*
Publications Manager: Edith E Troxler
 *E-mail:* basel.editiones_roche@roche.com
Founded: 1971
Subjects: Art, Health, Nutrition, Natural History, Science (General)
ISBN Prefix(es): 3-907046; 3-907770

**Rodana Verlag AG**, see Schweizer Spiegel Verlag Mit

**Rodera-Verlag der Cardun AG+**
Unterer Deutweg 17, Winterthur
Mailing Address: Postfach 8411, Winterthur
*Tel:* (052) 292442 *Fax:* (052) 292592
*E-mail:* info@cardun.ch
*Web Site:* www.cardun.ch
*Key Personnel*
Contact: Franz H Duebi
Founded: 1991
Subjects: Biography, History, Literature, Literary Criticism, Essays, Theology
ISBN Prefix(es): 3-907803

**Hans Rohr Verlag**
Moehrlistr 130, 8006 Zurich 1
*Tel:* (01) 3614846 *Fax:* (01) 3639513
*E-mail:* buchhandlung.hans.rohr@dm.krinfo.ch
*Key Personnel*
Man Dir: Hans R Rohr
Founded: 1921
Subjects: Antiques, Film, Video, Language Arts, Linguistics, Regional Interests, Travel
ISBN Prefix(es): 3-85865

**Rondo Verlag**
Hittenbergstr 1, 8636 Wald
*Tel:* (055) 246 39 37 *Fax:* (055) 246 42 93
*E-mail:* info1@rondo-verlag.ch
*Web Site:* www.rondo-verlag.ch
*Key Personnel*
Contact: Elisabeth Wild
ISBN Prefix(es): 3-907935

**Roth et Sauter SA**
La Pale, 1026 Denges-Lausanne
*Tel:* (021) 801 75 61 *Fax:* (021) 802 32 79
*Telex:* 458179 rsd ch
*Key Personnel*
Man Dir: Michel Logoz; Pierre Sauter

Founded: 1890
Subjects: Art
ISBN Prefix(es): 2-88075
Imprints: Editions du Verseau

**Rotpunktverlag+**
Freyastr 20, 8004 Zurich
Mailing Address: Postfach 2134, 8026 Zurich
*Tel:* (01) 2418434 *Fax:* (01) 2418474
*E-mail:* info@rotpunktverlag.ch
*Web Site:* www.rotpunktverlag.ch
*Key Personnel*
International Rights: Thomas Heilmann
Founded: 1977
Membership(s): SBVV.
Subjects: Alternative, Developing Countries, Fiction, Government, Political Science, History, Nonfiction (General), Outdoor Recreation, Travel
ISBN Prefix(es): 3-85869
*Orders to:* AS Verlagsservice Holler, Schaldorferstr 16, 8641 St Marien im Murzrtal, Austria
 *Tel:* (03864) 67 77 *Fax:* (03864) 38 88
Buch 2000/AVA, Postfach 27, 8910 Affoltern
 *Tel:* (01) 762 42 60 *Fax:* (01) 762 60 65
Prolit Verlagsauslieferung, Postfach 9, 35461 Fernwald, Germany *Tel:* (0641) 9439325 *Fax:* (0641) 9439329

**Rotten-Verlags AG**
Terbinerstr 2, 3930 Visp
*Tel:* (027) 948 30 32 *Fax:* (027) 948 30 33
*E-mail:* rottenverlag@mengis.ch
ISBN Prefix(es): 3-907816; 3-907624

**Ruegger Verlag+**
Division of Sudostschweiz Presse AG
Albisriederstr 80A, 8040 Zurich
Mailing Address: Postfach 1470, 8040 Zurich
*Tel:* (01) 4912130 *Fax:* (01) 4931176
*E-mail:* info@rueggerverlag.ch
*Web Site:* www.rueggerverlag.ch
*Key Personnel*
Secretary: Marianne Pearson *E-mail:* mpearson@rueggerverlag.ch
Publisher: Myriam Engler
Subjects: Business, Criminology, Economics, Education, Environmental Studies, Government, Political Science, Management, Psychology, Psychiatry, Social Sciences, Sociology, Women's Studies, Specialize in economics, politics, sociology, ecology & educational research
ISBN Prefix(es): 3-7253
Number of titles published annually: 30 Print
*Distribution Center:* Buendner Buchvertrieb, Postfach, Rossbodenstr 33, 7004 Chur

**SAB Schweiz Arbeitsgemeinschaft fuer die Berggebiete+**
Seilerstr 4, 3001 Bern
Mailing Address: Postfach 7836, 3001 Bern
*Tel:* (031) 382 1010 *Fax:* (031) 382 1016
*E-mail:* info@sab.ch
*Web Site:* www.sab.ch
Subjects: Agriculture, Architecture & Interior Design, Economics, Energy, Environmental Studies, Labor, Industrial Relations, Regional Interests, Social Sciences, Sociology
ISBN Prefix(es): 3-85873

**Sabe AG Verlagsinstitut+**
Laurenzenvorstadt 89, 5001 Aarau
*Tel:* (062) 8368690 *Fax:* (062) 8368695
*E-mail:* verlag@sabe.ch
*Key Personnel*
Dir: Heinrich M Zweifel
Founded: 1969
Specialize in educational material of all kinds including software.
Membership(s): Worlddidac & Swissdidac.

Subjects: Biological Sciences, Education, Geography, Geology, History, Language Arts, Linguistics, Mathematics, Natural History
ISBN Prefix(es): 3-252
Distributed by Heinevetter Verlag
Distributor for Verlag fuer Paedagogische Medien; Verlag an der Ruhr; Veritas Verlag

**Editions Saint-Augustin+**
4, rue Simplon, 1890 St-Maurice
*Tel:* (024) 486 05 04 *Fax:* (024) 486 05 23
*E-mail:* editions@staugustin.ch
*Key Personnel*
General Dir: Marc Larive
Founded: 1934
Subjects: Religion - Catholic, Theology
ISBN Prefix(es): 2-88011
*Bookshop(s):* Librairie La Procure-Le Passage, Rue de Carouge 53, 1205 Geneve; Librairie Saint-Augustin, 88 rue de Lausanne, 1700 Fribourg; Librairie Saint-Augustin, ave du Simplon 4, 1890 St-Maurice

**Editions Saint-Paul**
Perolles 42, 1705 Fribourg
*Tel:* (026) 4264331 *Fax:* (026) 4264330
*E-mail:* druckerei@st-paul.ch
*Web Site:* www.st-paul.ch
*Key Personnel*
Marketing Dir: Anton Scherer
Founded: 1873
Subjects: Education, Philosophy, Psychology, Psychiatry
ISBN Prefix(es): 3-7228; 2-88355
*Parent Company:* Imprimerie et Librairies Saint-Paul SA, 42, blvd Perolles, Case Postale 150, 1705 Fribourg
*Associate Companies:* Editions de la Sarine, 42, blvd Perolles, Case Postale 150, 1705 Fribourg; Editions Universitaires SA
*Bookshop(s):* Librairie Saint-Paul, Perolles 38, 1700 Fribourg; Librairie du Vieux Comte, rue de Vevey, 1630 Bulle

**Salvioni arti grafiche SA**
Via Ghiringhelli 9, 6500 Bellinzona
*Tel:* (091) 8211111 *Fax:* (091) 8211112
ISBN Prefix(es): 88-7967

**SAPL,** *imprint of* Castle Publications SA

**Satyr-Verlag Dr Humbel+**
Mainaustr 32, 8023 Zurich
Mailing Address: Postfach 6411, 8023 Zurich
*Tel:* (01) 380 3351 *Fax:* (01) 380 3352
*Key Personnel*
Manager: Dr Humbel
Founded: 1985
Subjects: Humor, Literature, Literary Criticism, Essays
ISBN Prefix(es): 3-906420
*Parent Company:* Satyr-Verlag Dr Humbel, 12 rue du Chateau, F-90200 Grosmagny, France

**Sauerlaender AG+**
Ausserfeldstr 9, 5036 Oberentfelden
*Tel:* (062) 836 86 86 *Fax:* (062) 836 86 20
*E-mail:* verlag@sauerlaender.ch
*Web Site:* www.sauerlaender.ch
*Telex:* 981195 SAG CH
*Key Personnel*
Publisher & Man Dir: Hans Christof Sauerlaender
Editorial: Hansten Doornkaat; Peter Egger; Paula Peretti
Man Dir, Sales & Marketing: Klaus Wilberg
Sales: Monika Roesler
Advertising Manager: Heike Ossenkop
Rights & Permissions: Kerstin Michaelis
Founded: 1807
Subjects: Education, Nonfiction (General)
ISBN Prefix(es): 3-7941; 3-0252; 3-0345
Total Titles: 600 Print; 6 CD-ROM

*Associate Companies:* SABE Verlag AG, Todis-
trasse 23, 8002 Zurich *Tel:* (01) 202-1932
*E-mail:* verlag@sabe.ch
Subsidiaries: Verlag Sauerlaender GmbH


**Scherz Verlag AG+**
Member of Verlagsgruppe Droemer Weltbild
Theaterplatz 4-6, 3000 Bern 7
Mailing Address: Postfach 850, 3000 Bern 7
*Tel:* (031) 3277117 *Fax:* (031) 3277171; (031)
3277169
*E-mail:* scherz@scherzverlag.ch *Cable:*
SCHERZEDIT
*Key Personnel*
Editoral Dir: Peter Lohmann
Man Dir: Fuerg Zurlinden
Editorial Dept: Dorthe Binkert; Rachel Gratzfeld
Rights & Permissions: Barbara Frankhauser
Marketing Dir: Thomas Reisch
Contact: Isabella Milan *E-mail:* i.milan@
scherzverlag.ch
Founded: 1938
Specialize in hardcover fiction & nonfiction.
Subjects: Biography, Fiction, History, Nonfiction
(General), Parapsychology, Philosophy, Psy-
chology, Psychiatry
ISBN Prefix(es): 3-502
Total Titles: 1,200 Print
Subsidiaries: Otto Wilhelm Barth-Verlag KG


**Schlaepfer & Co AG**
Kasernenstr 64, 9100 Herisau
Mailing Address: Postfach 219, 9100 Herisau
*Tel:* (071) 354 64 64 *Fax:* (071) 354 64 65
*E-mail:* appenzellerverlag@appon.ch
*Web Site:* www.appenzellerverlag.ch
*Key Personnel*
Man Dir: P Schlaepfer
Founded: 1974
ISBN Prefix(es): 3-85882
*Orders to:* Schlapfer & Co AG Buchverlag, CH-
9100 Herisau


**Schnellmann-Verlag+**
Rotackerstr 49, 8645 Jona-Kempraten
*Tel:* (055) 2111472 *Fax:* (055) 2111477
*Web Site:* www.dictionaries.ch
*Key Personnel*
Dir: Hans Schnellmann
Founded: 1973
ISBN Prefix(es): 3-85542


**Verlag fuer Schoene Wissenschaften**
Unterer Zielweg 36, Postfach, 4143 Dornach 2
*Tel:* (061) 7013911 *Fax:* (061) 7011417
*E-mail:* schoene_wissenschaften@bluewin.ch
*Key Personnel*
Chief Executive: Dr Heinz Matile
Founded: 1928
*Belles Lettres Publishing Co* - Albert Steffen
Foundation.
Subjects: Art, Fiction, Literature, Literary Criti-
cism, Essays, Poetry
ISBN Prefix(es): 3-85889


**A Schudel & Co AG Verlag**
Schopfgaesschen 8, 4125 Riehen 1
Mailing Address: Postfach 198, 4125 Riehen 1
*Tel:* (061) 645 1011 *Fax:* (061) 645 1045
*Web Site:* www.schudeldruck.ch
*Key Personnel*
Manager: Ch Schudel
ISBN Prefix(es): 3-85895


**Schulthess Polygraphischer Verlag AG**
Zwingliplatz 2, 8022 Zurich
*Tel:* (01) 44200 2999 *Fax:* (01) 44200 2998
*Web Site:* www.schulthess.com *Cable:* 2
*Key Personnel*
Dir, Advertising, Permissions: Werner Stocker
Founded: 1791

Firm has incorporated the former Leemann AG
Druckerei/Verlag since 1978.
Subjects: Business, Law, Social Sciences, Sociol-
ogy
ISBN Prefix(es): 3-7255


**Schwabe & Co AG**
Steinentorstr 13, 4010 Basel
*Tel:* (061) 278 95 65 *Fax:* (061) 272 95 66
*E-mail:* verlag@schwabe.ch
*Web Site:* www.schwabe.ch *Cable:*
SCHWABECO BASEL
*Key Personnel*
Man Dir: Hans-Rudolf Bienz; Dr Urs Breitenstein
Founded: 1488
Subjects: Archaeology, Art, History, Literature,
Literary Criticism, Essays, Medicine, Nursing,
Dentistry, Philosophy, Photography, Psychol-
ogy, Psychiatry, Theology
ISBN Prefix(es): 3-7965
*Orders to:* Verlag, 4132 Muttenz


**Hansrudolf Schwabe AG**, see Pharos-Verlag,
Hansrudolf Schwabe AG


**Verkehrshaus der Schweiz**, see Verkehrshaus der
Schweiz


**Schweizer Spiegel Verlag Mit+**
Raemistr 18, 8024 Zurich
*Tel:* (01) 472195 *Fax:* (01) 7502943
*Key Personnel*
Contact: Allan Guggenbuhl
Subjects: Education, Psychology, Psychiatry
ISBN Prefix(es): 3-7270; 3-85863


**Schweizerische Stiftung fuer Alpine Forschung**
(Swiss Foundation for Alpine Research)
Stadelhoferstr 42, 8001 Zurich
*Tel:* (044) 253 12 00 *Fax:* (044) 253 12 01
*E-mail:* mail@alpinfo.ch; alpineresearch@access.
ch
*Web Site:* www.alpineresearch.ch; www.alpinfo.ch
*Key Personnel*
President: Etienne Gross
Secretary: Thomas Weber-Wegst
Founded: 1939
Subjects: Biological Sciences, Environmental
Studies, Geography, Geology, Sports, Athlet-
ics
ISBN Prefix(es): 3-85515


**Schweizerischen Gesellschaft fuer Volkskunde**
(Swiss Folklore Society), *imprint of*
Verlagsbuchhandlung AG


**Schweizerischer Verein fuer Schweisstechnik**
St Alban-Rheinweg 222, 4006 Basel
Mailing Address: Postfach 136, 4006 Basel
*Tel:* (061) 3178484 *Fax:* (061) 3178480
*E-mail:* gl@svsxass.ch
ISBN Prefix(es): 3-85896


**Schweizerisches Jugendschriftenwerk, SJW+**
Uetlibergstr 20, 8045 Zurich
*Tel:* (01) 462 49 40 *Fax:* (01) 462 69 13
*E-mail:* office@sjw.ch
*Web Site:* www.sjw.ch
*Key Personnel*
Dir: Tsultrin Shabga *E-mail:* t.shabga@sjw.ch
Art Dir: Hanna Burkard
Sales: Emilienne Eberia
Founded: 1956
ISBN Prefix(es): 3-7269
Number of titles published annually: 30 Print
Total Titles: 300 Print
*Parent Company:* Edition Fondation
Imprints: Fotorotar AG/EGG ZH
*Orders to:* BD Bucherdienst/Einsiel

**Verlag Schweizerisches Katholisches Bibelwerk**
Rue de l'hopital, 1700 Fribourg
*Key Personnel*
Dir: Othmar Keel
Membership(s): AMB.
Subjects: Religion - Catholic
ISBN Prefix(es): 3-7203


**Schweizerisches Ost-Institut**, see Verlag SOI
(Schweizerisches Ost-Institut)


**Editions Scriptar SA+**
Creux de Corsy, 25, 1093 La Conversion-
Lausanne
*Tel:* (021) 7960096 *Fax:* (021) 7914084
*E-mail:* info@jsh.ch
*Key Personnel*
Publicity Manager: F Mugnier *Tel:* (021) 7960097
Founded: 1946
Publisher of Swiss Watch & Jewelry Journal In-
ternational Edition.
Subjects: Specializes in Watches & Jewelry
ISBN Prefix(es): 2-88012


**Editions Du Signal Rene Gaillard**
2-4, rue de Geneve, 1003 Lausanne
*Tel:* (021) 3290194 *Fax:* (021) 3290194
*Key Personnel*
Proprietor: Rene Gaillard
Founded: 1972
Subjects: Human Relations
ISBN Prefix(es): 2-88023


**Sinwel-Buchhandlung Verlag**
Lorrainestr 10, 3000 Bern 11
Mailing Address: Postfach 240, 3000 Bern 11
*Tel:* (031) 3325205 *Fax:* (031) 3331376
*E-mail:* sinwel@sinwel.ch
*Web Site:* www.sinwel.ch
*Telex:* 911469
Founded: 1978
Subjects: Crafts, Games, Hobbies, Outdoor Recre-
ation
ISBN Prefix(es): 3-85911


**SJW**, see Schweizerisches Jugendschriftenwerk,
SJW


**SKAT (Swiss Centre for Development
Cooperation in Technology & Management)**
Vadianstr 42, 9000 St Gallen
*Tel:* (071) 2285454 *Fax:* (071) 2285455
*E-mail:* info@skat.ch
*Web Site:* www.skat.ch
*Key Personnel*
Head of Information: Silvia Ndiaye
*E-mail:* silvia.ndiaye@skat.ch
Founded: 1978
Consulting, documentation, & project implemen-
tation of water supply, sanitation & urban de-
velopment.
Subjects: Manuals & reports
ISBN Prefix(es): 3-908001
Number of titles published annually: 10 Print
Total Titles: 66 Print
Distributed by IT Publications Ltd


**Editions D'Art Albert Skira SA**
Rue Quai des Bergues, 29, 1201 Geneva
*Tel:* (022) 906 80 00 *Fax:* (022) 3495535 *Cable:*
Edart Geneva
*Key Personnel*
Man Dir, Editorial: Mrs R Skira
Sales, Production & Publicity: Jean-Michel Skira
Founded: 1928
Subjects: Art, Education
ISBN Prefix(es): 2-605


**Slatkine Reprints**
5, rue des Chaudronniers, 1211 Geneva 3
*Tel:* (022) 3100476 *Fax:* (022) 3107101

*E-mail:* librarie@slatkine.ch
*Web Site:* www.slatkine.ch
*Key Personnel*
Man Dir: Michel E Slatkine
Founded: 1918
ISBN Prefix(es): 2-05

**Verlag SOI (Schweizerisches Ost-Institut)**
Jubilaeumsstr 41, Postfach, 3000 Bern
*Tel:* (031) 431212 *Fax:* (031) 3513801
*Telex:* 32728 *Cable:* Schweizost
*Key Personnel*
Man Dir: Peter Sager
Sales Manager: Peter Burgunder
Production Manager: Peter Dolder
Founded: 1958
Subjects: Government, Political Science, History,
Social Sciences, Sociology
ISBN Prefix(es): 3-85913
*Bookshop(s):* Buchhandlung SOI, Jubilaeumsstr
41, 3000 Berne

**Speer -Verlag**
Limmattalstr 130, 8049 Zurich
Mailing Address: Postfach 3283, 8049 Zurich
*Tel:* (01) 341 42 56; (01) 262 33 91 *Fax:* (01)
342 45 31 *Cable:* SPERVERLAG
*Key Personnel*
Man Dir: R Roemer
Founded: 1944
Subjects: Fiction, Mysteries, Philosophy, Poetry
ISBN Prefix(es): 3-85916

**Spes**, *imprint of* Editions Andre Delcourt & Cie

**Sphinx Verlag AG**
Andreaspl 12, 4051 Basel
*Tel:* (061) 2619292 *Fax:* (061) 2629221
*E-mail:* sphinx@sphinx-book.ch
*Web Site:* www.sphinx-book.ch
*Key Personnel*
Dir: H C Sauerlaender
Founded: 1975
Subjects: Astrology, Occult, Fiction, Health, Nu-
trition, Philosophy, Psychology, Psychiatry, Sci-
ence (General)
ISBN Prefix(es): 3-85914
*Associate Companies:* Sauerlaender AG

**Staatskunde Verlag E Krattiger AG**, see Tobler
Verlag

**Staempfli Verlag AG+**
Wolflistr 1, 3001 Bern
Mailing Address: PO Box 8326, 3001 Bern
*Tel:* (031) 3006311 *Fax:* (031) 3006688
*E-mail:* verlag@staempfli.com
*Web Site:* www.staempfli.com
*Key Personnel*
President, Editor, Rights & Permissions: Dr
Rudolf Staempfli
Editor, Sales & Advertising Dir: Ursula Merz
Editor: Stephan Grieb
Marketing: Susanne Farner
Founded: 1799
Membership(s): Law Books in Europe.
Subjects: Government, Political Science, Law
ISBN Prefix(es): 3-7272
*Parent Company:* Staempfli Holding AG
*Bookshop(s):* Buchstaempfli, Versandbuch-
handlung, PO Box 560, 3000 Bern 9
*Tel:* (031) 3006677 *Fax:* (031) 3006688
*E-mail:* buchstaempfli@staempfli.com

**Stahlbau Zentrum Schweiz** (Swiss Institute of
Steel Construction)
Seefeldstr 25, 8034 Zurich
Mailing Address: Postfach 1075, 8034 Zurich
*Tel:* (01) 261 89 80 *Fax:* (01) 262 09 62
*E-mail:* info@szs.ch
*Web Site:* www.szs.ch

*Key Personnel*
Man Dir: Urs Wyss
Swiss Institute of Steel Construction.
ISBN Prefix(es): 3-85920

**Rudolf Steiner Verlag**, see Verlag Die Pforte im
Rudolf Steiner Verlag

**Rudolf Steiner Verlag**
Hugelweg 34, 4143 Dornach 1
Mailing Address: Postfach 135, 4143 Dornach 1
*Tel:* (061) 706 91 30 *Fax:* (061) 706 91 49
*E-mail:* verlag@rudolf-steiner.com
*Web Site:* www.rudolf-steiner.com
*Key Personnel*
Man Dir, Editorial: Benedikt Marzahn
Publicity, Sales: Winfried Altmann
Production: Carlo Frigeri; B Marzahn
Contact: Sabine Scherrer *Tel:* (061) 7069137
Founded: 1949
Administrators of the Rudolf Steiner Literary Es-
tate.
Subjects: Philosophy
ISBN Prefix(es): 3-7274
Total Titles: 700 Print
Subsidiaries: Editrice Antroposofica SRL
*Bookshop(s):* Buchhandlung Duldeck, Haus
Duldeck, Postfach 135, 4143 Dornach 1

**Edition Stemmle AG+**
Im Fischer, Seestr 16, 8800 Zurich
Mailing Address: Postfach 365, 8201
Schaffhausen
*Tel:* (01) 7235050 *Fax:* (01) 7235059
*E-mail:* info@editionstemmle.ch
*Key Personnel*
Publisher & President: Dr Thomas N Stemmle
Vice President & General Manager: Robert Zue-
blin
Vice President & Editorial Dir: Mirjam Ghisleni-
Stemmle
Founded: 1993
Subjects: Architecture & Interior Design, Art,
Photography
ISBN Prefix(es): 3-905514

**Verlag Stocker-Schmid AG**
Hasenbergstr 7, 8953 Dietikon
Mailing Address: Postfach 66, 8953 Dietikon
*Tel:* (01) 7404444
Subjects: Library & Information Sciences, Mili-
tary Science, Regional Interests
ISBN Prefix(es): 3-85577; 3-7276
Subsidiaries: Verlag Bibliophile Drucke von Josef
Stocker AG
*Bookshop(s):* Buchhandlung Stocker-Schmid

**Strom-Verlag Luzern+**
Postfach 1461, 6000 Luzern 15
*Tel:* (041) 4408845 *Fax:* (041) 4408844
*E-mail:* pegasusbuecher@tic.ch
*Key Personnel*
Man Dir: Roland Grueter
Founded: 1956
Subjects: Ethnicity, Fiction, Natural History, Pho-
tography, Science (General), Travel
ISBN Prefix(es): 3-85921

**Swedenborg - Verlag+**
Apollostr 2, 8032 Zurich
*Tel:* (01) 3835944 *Fax:* (01) 3822944
*E-mail:* info@swedenborg.ch
*Web Site:* www.swedenborg.ch
*Key Personnel*
President: Helen Guedemann
Editor: Dr Friedemann Horn
Man Dir: Heinz Grob
Founded: 1952
Subjects: Theology
ISBN Prefix(es): 3-85927
*Orders to:* Schweizer Buchzentrum, Olten

**Swiss Centre for Development Cooperation in
Technology & Management**, see SKAT (Swiss
Centre for Development Cooperation in
Technology & Management)

**Tages-Anzeiger**
Werdstr 21, Postfach, 8021 Zurich
*Tel:* (01) 248 44 11 *Fax:* (01) 248 44 71
*E-mail:* verlag@tages-anzeiger.ch
*Web Site:* www.tamedia.ch
ISBN Prefix(es): 3-85932

**Terra Grischuna Verlag Buch-und
Zeitschriftenverlag+**
Felsenaustr 5, 7004 Chur
Mailing Address: Postfach 147, 7004 Chur
*Tel:* (081) 2867050 *Fax:* (081) 2867057
*E-mail:* info@terra-grischuna.ch
*Web Site:* www.terra-grischuna.ch
*Key Personnel*
Owner: Reto Fetz
Founded: 1942
Subjects: Geography, Geology, Natural History,
Regional Interests, Romance, Travel
ISBN Prefix(es): 3-7298
Imprints: Baumgartner Blicher
Distributed by Herold Verlags ausli efering

**Terra Magica**, *imprint of* Reich Verlag AG

**Thailand Press**, see Cockatoo Press (Schweiz),
Thailand-Publikationen

**Theologischer Verlag und Buchhandlungen
AG+**
Badenerstr 73, Postfach, 8026 Zurich
*Tel:* (01) 299 33 55 *Fax:* (01) 299 33 58
*E-mail:* tvz@ref.ch
*Web Site:* www.tvz.ref.ch
*Key Personnel*
Dir, Editorial: Werner Blum
Rights & Permissions: Mrs E Frick
Publicity: Reinhold Jost
Founded: 1934
Subjects: Biblical Studies, History, Religion -
Other, Theology
ISBN Prefix(es): 3-290
*Bookshop(s):* Theologische Buchhandlung, Raef-
felstr 20, 8045 Zurich (antiquarian bookshop)

**Theseus - Verlag AG+**
Im Eigeli 6A, 8700 Kystnacht
*Tel:* (01) 9109294 *Fax:* (01) 9108019
Founded: 1973
Subjects: Art, Fiction, Philosophy, Religion -
Buddhist
ISBN Prefix(es): 3-85936
Subsidiaries: Theseus Verlag GmbH

**3-D-World**, see 3 Dimension World (3-D-World)

**3 Dimension World (3-D-World)+**
Postfach 339, 4003 Basel
*Tel:* (061) 3013081 *Fax:* (094) 3133862
*Key Personnel*
Publishing Dir: Gerd A Haisch *E-mail:* gah@
swissonline.ch
Founded: 1982
Membership(s): SBVV/SGS.
Subjects: Art, Biography, Film, Video, Geogra-
phy, Geology, Marketing, Travel
ISBN Prefix(es): 3-905450
*Parent Company:* Pamelart/Icebear-Group Inc

**Istituto Editoriale Ticinese (IET) SA**
Via del Bramantino, 3, 6500 Bellinzona
*Tel:* (091) 8200101 *Fax:* (091) 8251874
*Telex:* 846266

*Key Personnel*
Man Dir: Libero Casagrande
Founded: 1900
Subjects: Fiction, Literature, Literary Criticism,
    Essays, Poetry
ISBN Prefix(es): 88-7713
*Parent Company:* Edizioni Casagrande SA


**Tipografia Stazione**, see Edizioni Armando
    Dado, Tipografia Stazione


**Tobler Verlag+**
Trogenerstr 80, 9450 Altstaetten
*Tel:* (071) 755 6060 *Fax:* (071) 755 1254
*E-mail:* books@tobler-verlag.ch
*Web Site:* www.tobler-verlag.ch
*Key Personnel*
Publication Manager: Hans Joerg Tobler
Tobler Verlag has merged with Causa Verlag, He-
    lion Verlag, Panorama Verlag & Staatskunde-
    Verlag E Krattiger AG.
Subjects: Health, Nutrition, Law, Management,
    Marketing, Nonfiction (General), Parapsychol-
    ogy, Philosophy, Photography, Psychology, Psy-
    chiatry
ISBN Prefix(es): 3-907506; 3-85612


**Trachsel - Verlag AG+**
Alpenblickweg 7, 3714 Frutigen
Mailing Address: Postfach 60, 3714 Frutigen
*Tel:* (33) 6711407 *Fax:* (33) 6712449
*Key Personnel*
Man Dir: Ernst Trachsel-Neukom
Founded: 1946
Subjects: Religion - Other
ISBN Prefix(es): 3-7271
Imprints: TVF


**Trans Tech Publications SA**
Brandrain 6, 8707 Zurich-uetikon
*Tel:* (01) 9221022 *Fax:* (01) 9221033
*E-mail:* info@ttp.net
*Web Site:* www.ttp.net
*Key Personnel*
Dir: T Wohlbier *E-mail:* t.wohlbier@ttp.net
Founded: 1967
Subjects: Chemistry, Chemical Engineering, Me-
    chanical Engineering, Physics
ISBN Prefix(es): 0-87849; 3-908158
Number of titles published annually: 30 Print
Total Titles: 412 Print
*Branch Office(s)*
c/o Enfield P & D Co, Inc, PO Box 699, Enfield
    *Tel:* 603-632-7377 *Fax:* 603-632-5611


**Translegal AG**
Laenggasse 57, 3607 Thun
*Tel:* (033) 2253939 *Fax:* (033) 2253933
*E-mail:* info@ott-verlag.ch
*Key Personnel*
Contact: Hans Ott
ISBN Prefix(es): 3-85942
Subsidiaries: Ott Verlag & Druck AG


**Editions du Tricorne+**
14, rue Lissignol, 1201 Geneva
*Tel:* (022) 7388366 *Fax:* (022) 7319749
*E-mail:* tricorne@tricorne.org
*Web Site:* www.tricorne.org
*Key Personnel*
Man Dir: Serge Kaplun
Founded: 1976
Essays.
Subjects: Art, Crafts, Games, Hobbies, Eco-
    nomics, Management, Mathematics, Philoso-
    phy, Poetry, Psychology, Psychiatry, Regional
    Interests, Religion - Other, Social Sciences, So-
    ciology
ISBN Prefix(es): 2-8293
Number of titles published annually: 12 Print
Total Titles: 234 Print

*Parent Company:* ASK
Distributed by Presses Universitaires de France
    (PUF)


**Editions des Trois Collines Francois Lachenal**
Sezegnin, 1285 Geneva
*Tel:* (022) 7561309 *Fax:* (022) 7561302
*Key Personnel*
Dir: Francois Lachenal
Founded: 1935
Subjects: Art, Government, Political Science, Phi-
    losophy, Psychology, Psychiatry
ISBN Prefix(es): 3-88013


**TVF**, *imprint of* Trachsel - Verlag AG


**Editions 24 Heures**
33, ave de la Gare, 1001 Lausanne
Mailing Address: CP 13898, 1001 Lausanne
*Tel:* (021) 3494500 *Fax:* (021) 3494224
*Telex:* 455745 Vgh Ch
*Key Personnel*
Man Dir: P Lamuniere
Founded: 1969
Subjects: Aeronautics, Aviation, Animals, Pets,
    Art, Automotive, Education, History, Military
    Science, Music, Dance, Transportation
ISBN Prefix(es): 2-8265; 2-88260


**Werner Ulmer & Co**
Mittlere Haltenstr 1, 3625 Heiligenschwendi
*Tel:* (033) 432220 *Fax:* (033) 434848
*Key Personnel*
Contact: Werner Ulmer
ISBN Prefix(es): 3-7222


**Der Universitatsverlag Fribourg** (University
    Editions of Fribourg)+
Perolles 42, 1705 Fribourg
*Tel:* (026) 426 43 11 *Fax:* (026) 426 43 00
*E-mail:* eduni@st-paul.ch
*Key Personnel*
Dir: Anton Scherer
Production Manager: Adolf Muller
Promotion Manager: Maurice Greder
Sales Manager & Subscriptions: Bernadette Meis-
    ter
Founded: 1953
Subjects: Art, Economics, Ethnicity, Government,
    Political Science, History, Law, Literature, Lit-
    erary Criticism, Essays, Medicine, Nursing,
    Dentistry, Music, Dance, Philosophy, Psychol-
    ogy, Psychiatry, Religion - Other, Theology
ISBN Prefix(es): 3-7278; 2-8271
*Parent Company:* Imprimerie et Librairies Saint-
    Paul SA, 42, blvd de Perolles, 1705 Fribourg
*Associate Companies:* Editions Saint-Paul; Edi-
    tions de la Sarine, 42, blvd de Perolles, 1705
    Fribourg
*Bookshop(s):* Librairie et Edition de la Suisse Ro-
    mande


**Uranium Verlag Zug**
Postfach 42, 6317 Oberwil b Zug
*Tel:* (042) 217744
*Telex:* Topaz 58280
*Key Personnel*
Man Dir, Sales: L Young
Editorial: Mrs Young
Founded: 1976
Subjects: Nonfiction (General)
ISBN Prefix(es): 3-294
*Branch Office(s)*
Atzelbergstr 22, 60389 Frankfurt am Main, Ger-
    many


**VCH Verlags-AG**
Hofwiesenstr 36, 8042 Zurich
Mailing Address: Postfach 465, 8042 Zurich
*Tel:* (01) 3602438 *Fax:* (01) 3602439
*E-mail:* info@wiley-vch.de

*Web Site:* www.wiley-vch.de
*Telex:* 911527 DMS CH
ISBN Prefix(es): 3-527
*Parent Company:* Wiley-VCH Verlag GmbH,
    Pappelallee 3, 69469 Weinheim, Germany


**Vdf Hochschulverlag AG an der ETH Zurich**
Voltastr 24, 8044 Zurich
Mailing Address: ETH Zentrum, 8092 Zurich
*Tel:* (01) 632 42 42 *Fax:* (01) 632 12 32
*E-mail:* verlag@vdf.ethz.ch
*Web Site:* www.vdf.ethz.ch
*Key Personnel*
Marketing: Claudia Signer *Tel:* (01) 632 77 72
    *E-mail:* signer@vdf.ethz.ch
International Rights: Ernst Schaerer
Founded: 1992
Subjects: Agriculture, Architecture & Interior De-
    sign, Civil Engineering, Computer Science,
    Economics, Engineering (General), Environ-
    mental Studies, Management, Mathematics,
    Physics, Science (General)
ISBN Prefix(es): 3-7281
Number of titles published annually: 70 Print; 3
    CD-ROM
Total Titles: 11 CD-ROM
*Orders to:* Brockhaus Kommissionsgeschaeft,
    Postfach 1220, 70806 Kornwestheim, Germany


**Verbandsdruckerei AG**
Laupenstr 7a, 3000 Bern
*Tel:* (031) 252911
*Telex:* 32255
*Key Personnel*
Man Dir: Markus Rubli
Founded: 1919
Book publishing branch of Grafino Grafische Be-
    triebe AG (Grafino Printing House).
Subjects: Agriculture, Nonfiction (General), Re-
    gional Interests
ISBN Prefix(es): 3-7280


**Verkehrshaus der Schweiz** (Swiss Museum of
    Transport)
Lidostr 5, 6006 Lucerne
*Tel:* (041) 370444 *Fax:* (041) 3706168
*E-mail:* mail@verkehrshaus.org
*Web Site:* www.verkehrshaus.ch
*Key Personnel*
Dir: Fredy Rey
Subjects: Communications, Transportation
ISBN Prefix(es): 3-85954
*Branch Office(s)*
Museum of Transportation & Communication


**Verlagsbuchhandling AG**
St Alban-Vorstadt 56, 4006 Basel
*Tel:* (061) 239723
*Key Personnel*
Dir: Franz Kaeser; Willy Kohler
Manager: Andre Horisberger
Founded: 1897
Subjects: Crafts, Games, Hobbies, Ethnicity, Mu-
    sic, Dance, Regional Interests
ISBN Prefix(es): 3-85775
Imprints: Schweizerischen Gesellschaft fuer Volk-
    skunde (Swiss Folklore Society)
*Orders to:* Gesellschaft fuer Volkskunde, St
    Alban-Vorstadt 56, 4006 Basel


**Editions Eliane Vernay+**
79, rue des Eaux-Vives, 1207 Geneva
*Tel:* (022) 7350460 *Fax:* (022) 7350460
*Key Personnel*
Man Dir: Eliane Vernay
Founded: 1977
Subjects: Poetry
ISBN Prefix(es): 2-88291


**Editions du Verseau**, *imprint of* Roth et Sauter
    SA

**Versus Verlag AG+**
Merkurstr 45, 8032 Zurich
*Tel:* (044) 2510892 *Fax:* (044) 2626738
*E-mail:* info@versus.ch
*Web Site:* www.versus.ch
*Key Personnel*
Contact: Anne Buechi
Founded: 1993
Subjects: Accounting, Art, Business, Economics, Finance, Human Relations, Labor, Industrial Relations, Law, Management, Marketing, Public Administration
ISBN Prefix(es): 3-908143; 3-909066; 3-03909
*Distribution Center:* AVA Buch 2000 Affoltern

**Verlag Alfred Vetter**
Gartenstr 15, 8002 Zurich
*Tel:* (01) 2011184
ISBN Prefix(es): 3-85956

**Vexer Verlag+**
Bleichestr 3, 9000 Saint Gallen
*Tel:* (071) 220986
*E-mail:* vexer@freesurf.ch
*Key Personnel*
Contact: Josef Felix Mueller
Founded: 1985
Subjects: Art, Film, Video, Literature, Literary Criticism, Essays
ISBN Prefix(es): 3-909090
Total Titles: 80 Print
Distributed by Buchhandlung Walther Konig

**Viktoria-Verlag Peter Marti**
Burgdorfstr 10, 3510 Konolfingen BE
*Tel:* (031) 7911932 *Fax:* (031) 7912564
Subjects: Humor, Regional Interests
ISBN Prefix(es): 3-85958

**Editions Vivez Soleil SA+**
15 rue Francois-Jacquier, Case Postale 313, 1225 Chene-Bourg, Geneva
Mailing Address: BP 18, 74103 Annemasse Cedex, France
*Tel:* (04) 50 87 27 09 *Fax:* (04) 50 87 27 13
*Key Personnel*
President: Dr Christian Tal Schaller
Dir: Mr Marcel-Diedier, VRAC
Founded: 1987
Subjects: Health, Nutrition, Human Relations, Parapsychology, Psychology, Psychiatry
ISBN Prefix(es): 2-88058
*Orders to:* 21, rue des Tournelles, 74100 Ville-La-Grand

**Verlag A Vogel**
Postfach 63, Haetschen, 9053 Teufen
*Tel:* (071) 335 66 66 *Fax:* (071) 335 66 88
*E-mail:* info@verlag-avogel.ch
*Web Site:* www.verlag-avogel.ch
*Key Personnel*
Contact: Silvia Loher *Tel:* (071) 335 66 70
ISBN Prefix(es): 3-906404
Number of titles published annually: 1 Print

**Vogt-Schild Ag, Druck und Verlag+**
Zuchwilerstr 21, 4501 Solothurn
Mailing Address: Postfach 748, 4501 Solothurn
*Tel:* (032) 6247111 *Fax:* (032) 6247444
*E-mail:* info@vsonline.ch
*Web Site:* www.vsonline.ch
*Telex:* 934646 *Cable:* PRINTERS SOLEURE
*Key Personnel*
Dir: Dr Markus H Haefely
Public Relations: Hans A Roelli
Founded: 1906
Specialize in periodicals.
Subjects: Architecture & Interior Design, Chemistry, Chemical Engineering, Electronics, Electrical Engineering, Technology, Transportation
ISBN Prefix(es): 3-85962

Subsidiaries: Jeger Moll Druck und Verlag AG
*Orders to:* Vogt-Schild Ag

**Verlag Die Waage+**
Dorfstr 90, 8802 Kilchberg
*Tel:* (01) 7155569; (01) 7241969 *Fax:* (01) 7153380
*Key Personnel*
Publisher & International Rights: Felix M Wiesner
Founded: 1951
Subjects: Erotica, Fiction, History, Literature, Literary Criticism, Essays, Mysteries, Philosophy, Poetry, Religion - Jewish, Religion - Other, Romance, Social Sciences, Sociology, Theology, Women's Studies
ISBN Prefix(es): 3-85966

**Verlag im Waldgut AG+**
Eisenwerk Industriestr 21, 8500 Frauenfeld
*Tel:* (052) 728 89 28 *Fax:* (052) 728 89 27
*E-mail:* waldgut.bodoni@bluewin.ch
*Web Site:* www.waldgut.ch
*Key Personnel*
President & Chief Editor: Beat Brechbuehl
Founded: 1980
Founded by Beat Brechbuehl, writer & publisher, in Wald near Zurich. In 1987 the publishing house moved to Frauenfeld & expanded its program.
Subjects: Developing Countries, Education, Ethnicity, Foreign Countries, Poetry
ISBN Prefix(es): 3-7294

**Walter Verlag AG+**
Dorfstr 81, 8706 Meilen
Mailing Address: PO Box 121, 8706 Meilen
*Tel:* (062) 341188 *Fax:* (062) 321184
*E-mail:* info@walter-verlag.ch
*Web Site:* www.walter-verlag.ch
*Key Personnel*
Dir: Machalet Chnshan
Publicity: Charlotte Kraehenbuehl
Rights & Permissions: Erika Straumann
Founded: 1924
Subjects: Psychology, Psychiatry, Regional Interests, Religion - Other
ISBN Prefix(es): 3-530

**WCC Publications**, see World Council of Churches (WCC Publications)

**Weber SA d'Editions**
CP 109, 1224 Chene-Dorugeries
*Tel:* (07) 93104541
*Key Personnel*
Man Dir: Marcel Weber
Founded: 1951
Subjects: Architecture & Interior Design, Art, Health, Nutrition, Library & Information Sciences, Photography
ISBN Prefix(es): 2-7190; 2-88301; 3-295

**Weka Informations Schriften Verlag AG+**
Hermetschloostr 77, 8010 Zurich
*Tel:* (01) 4348888 *Fax:* (01) 4348999
*Key Personnel*
Man Dir: Robert Boss
Founded: 1978
Specialize in loose-leaf publications.
Subjects: Computer Science, Law, Management
ISBN Prefix(es): 3-297
*Parent Company:* WEKA Firmengruppe GmbH, Roemerstr 4, 86438 Kissing, Germany

**Weltrundschau Verlag AG+**
Obermeuhofstr 1, 6341 Baar
*Tel:* (041) 761 54 31 *Fax:* (041) 761 44 04
*E-mail:* wrs@bluewin.ch
*Web Site:* www.wrs.ch *Cable:* WORLDREVIEW

*Key Personnel*
Man Dir: Franz Truniger
Editorial: E Gysling
Founded: 1959
Subjects: Government, Political Science, Sports, Athletics
ISBN Prefix(es): 3-7283
*Associate Companies:* Jeunesse Verlagsanstal, Kirchstr 1, Vaduz, Liechtenstein (Rights & Permissions)

**Weltwoche ABC-Verlag+**
Missionsstre 36, 4012 Basel
Mailing Address: Postfach 393, 4012 Basel
*Tel:* (061) 2646450 *Fax:* (061) 2646488
*Key Personnel*
President: Rudolf Baechtold
Man Dir: Peter Zwicky
Founded: 1937
Subjects: Art, Nonfiction (General)
ISBN Prefix(es): 3-85504; 3-85975; 3-9520932
*Book Club(s):* SBVV

**Wepf & Co AG**
Eisengasse 5, 4001 Basel
Mailing Address: Postfach 2064, 4001 Basel
*Tel:* (061) 2698515 *Fax:* (061) 253597
*E-mail:* wepf@dial.eunet.ch
*Web Site:* www.wepf.ch *Cable:* WEPFCO BASEL
*Key Personnel*
Dir: H Herrmann; M Weber
Manager: Hans Jo Pfeiffer
Founded: 1902
Subjects: Architecture & Interior Design, Earth Sciences, Ethnicity, Geography, Geology
ISBN Prefix(es): 3-85977
Number of titles published annually: 5 Print

**Werner Druck AG**
Kanonengasse 32, 4051 Basel
*Tel:* (061) 2701515 *Fax:* (061) 2701516
*E-mail:* werner@wernerdruck.ch
*Web Site:* www.wernerdruck.ch
*Key Personnel*
President & Co-Dir: Dr H G Hinderling
Co-Dir: N Werner
Founded: 1862
Subjects: Art
ISBN Prefix(es): 3-85979

**Buchverlag der Druckerei Wetzikon AG**
Rapperswilerstr 1, Postf, 8620 Wetzikon 1
*Tel:* (01) 9333111 *Fax:* (01) 9333258
*E-mail:* buchverlag@zol.ch
*Web Site:* www.zo-buchverlag.ch
*Telex:* 875547
Subjects: Environmental Studies
ISBN Prefix(es): 3-85981

**Wiese Verlag AG**, see Opinio Verlag AG

**Verlag Alexander Wild+**
Rathausgasse 30, 3011 Bern
*Tel:* (031) 3114480 *Fax:* (031) 3114470
*Key Personnel*
Man Dir, Owner: Alexander Wild
Founded: 1977
Subjects: Literature, Literary Criticism, Essays
ISBN Prefix(es): 3-7284; 3-85982
*Associate Companies:* Origo-Verlag
Distributor for Origo-Verlag

**WMO**, see World Meteorological Organization

**J E Wolfensberger AG**
Bederstr 109, 8027 Zurich
*Tel:* (01) 2857878 *Fax:* (01) 2857879
*E-mail:* office@wolfensberger-ag.ch
*Web Site:* www.wolfensberger-ag.ch
*Key Personnel*
Dir: Ulla Wolfensberger
Founded: 1905

Subjects: Art, Lithographs, Limited editions, signed & numbered
ISBN Prefix(es): 3-85987

**World Council of Churches (WCC Publications)+**
150 Route de Ferney, 1211 Geneva 2
Mailing Address: PO Box 2100, 1211 Geneva 2
*Tel:* (022) 7916111 *Fax:* (022) 7910361
*E-mail:* hs@wcc-coe.org
*Web Site:* www.wcc-coe.org
*Telex:* 415730 OIK CH *Cable:* OIKOUMENE, GENEVA
*Key Personnel*
General Secretary: Konrad Raiser
Dir & Publisher: Jan H Kok
International Rights: Heather Stunt *Tel:* (022) 7916379 *E-mail:* hs@wcc-coe.org
Founded: 1948
Subjects: Religion - Other, Theology
ISBN Prefix(es): 2-8254
Total Titles: 15 Print
*U.S. Office(s):* World Council of Churches, Room 915, 475 Riverside Dr, New York, NY 10015-0050, United States
Distributed by Asian Trading Co (India); Christian Literature Society of Korea; Conference of Churches in Aotearoa-New Zealand; Ecumenical Council of Denmark; Intercultural Publications (India); ISPCK (India); Korea Christian Book Service; Methodist Publishing House (South Africa); National Council of Churches in Australia; United Church Distribution Center (Canada)
*Bookshop(s):* Examiner Bookshop, Mumbai, India; Epworth Bookshop, Wellington, New Zealand
*Shipping Address:* Distribution Center, PO Box 348, Route 222 & Sharadin Rd, Kutztown, PA 19530-0348, United States *Fax:* (610) 683-5616

**World Meteorological Organization**
7 bis Ave de la Paix, CP 2300, 1211 Geneva 2
Mailing Address: CP 2300, 1211 Geneva 2
*Tel:* (022) 730 8111 *Fax:* (022) 730 8181
*E-mail:* wmo@wmo.int; ipa@www.wmo.ch
*Web Site:* www.wmo.int
*Telex:* 414199 OMM CH; 23260 *Cable:* METEOMOND GENEVE
Subjects: Science (General), Technology
ISBN Prefix(es): 92-63

**World Wild Life Films (Pty) Ltd**
Eduard Zingg, Postfach 2942, 8023 Zurich
*Tel:* (01) 4331444 *Fax:* (01) 4331460
*Key Personnel*
Man Dir: Eduard Zingg
ISBN Prefix(es): 3-85986

**WOZ Die Wochenzeitung** (WOZ The Weekly Paper)
Hardturmstr 66, 8031 Zurich
*Tel:* (01) 448 14 14 *Fax:* (01) 448 14 15
*E-mail:* woz@woz.ch
*Web Site:* www.woz.ch

**Wyss Verlag AG Bern**
Effingerstr 17, 3008 Bern
Mailing Address: Postfach 5860, 3008 Bern
*Tel:* (031) 253715; (031) 381 4425 *Fax:* (031) 381 4821; (031) 254821
*Key Personnel*
Dir: Christoph Wyss *E-mail:* chr.wyss@advobern.ch
Founded: 1849
Subjects: Art, History, Law
ISBN Prefix(es): 3-7285

**Zbinden Druck und Verlag AG**
St Alban-Vostadt 16, Postfach, 4006 Basel

*Tel:* (061) 2722105; (061) 2722104 *Fax:* (061) 2726722
*Key Personnel*
Man Dir: Kurt Krause
Subjects: Anthropology, Biography, Education, Poetry
ISBN Prefix(es): 3-85989

**Ziegler Druck- und Verlags-AG, Gemsberg-Verlag, Foto & Schmalfilm-Verlag**
Postfach 778, Garnmarkt 10, 8401 Winterthur
*Tel:* (052) 266 99 00 *Fax:* (052) 266 99 10
*E-mail:* info@zieglerdruck.ch
*Web Site:* www.zieglerdruck.ch
*Key Personnel*
Manager: Alfons Rueede
ISBN Prefix(es): 3-85701

**Editions Zoe**
11, rue des Moraines, 1227 Carouge, Geneva
*Tel:* (022) 309 36 06 *Fax:* (022) 309 36 03
*E-mail:* edzoe@iprolink.ch
*Web Site:* www.editionszoe.ch
*Key Personnel*
Man Dir: Marlyse Pietri-Bachmann
Founded: 1975
Subjects: History, Literature, Literary Criticism, Essays, Social Sciences, Sociology
ISBN Prefix(es): 2-88182

**Zumstein & Cie**
Zeughausgasse 24, 3000 Bern 7
*Tel:* (031) 312 00 55 *Fax:* (031) 312 23 26
*E-mail:* post_zumstein@briefmarken.ch
*Web Site:* www.briefmarken.ch
Founded: 1905
Subjects: Crafts, Games, Hobbies
ISBN Prefix(es): 3-909278; 3-85994

**Zurich**, *imprint of* Interfrom AG Editions

# Syrian Arab Republic

## General Information

*Capital:* Damascus
*Language:* Arabic and some Kurdish.
*Religion:* Islamic (mostly of the Sunni sect) and Christian
*Population:* 13.7 million
*Bank Hours:* 0800-1400 Saturday-Thursday
*Shop Hours:* 1000-1900. Closed Friday. Generally long closing at lunchtime
*Currency:* 100 piastres = 1 Syrian pound
*Export/Import Information:* No tariffs on books except children's picture books, with additional taxes; most advertising matter is dutied. State organization for control and execution of publicity and advertising within Syria is Arab Advertising Organization, Damascus. The General Advertising Institute, 2842, must get samples of commercial advertising and promotional materials before distribution permitted. Import license must be submitted to Commercial Bank of Syria in order to obtain exchange license.
*Copyright:* No copyright conventions signed

**Damascus University Press**
Damascus University Library, Damascus, Baramkah
*Tel:* (011) 2215104; (011) 2215101 *Fax:* (011) 2236010
*E-mail:* info@damascus-online.com
*Web Site:* www.damascus-online/university.htm
*Telex:* 411971

*Key Personnel*
Dir: Dr Hussain Omran
Subjects: Accounting, Agriculture, Anthropology, Archaeology, Architecture & Interior Design, Art, Behavioral Sciences, Business, Chemistry, Chemical Engineering, Civil Engineering, Communications, Computer Science, Earth Sciences, Economics, Education, Electronics, Electrical Engineering, Engineering (General), English as a Second Language, Environmental Studies, Finance, Geography, Geology, Government, Political Science, Health, Nutrition, History, Journalism, Language Arts, Linguistics, Law, Library & Information Sciences, Marketing, Mathematics, Mechanical Engineering, Medicine, Nursing, Dentistry, Natural History, Philosophy, Physics, Poetry, Psychology, Psychiatry, Public Administration, Religion - Islamic, Science (General), Social Sciences, Sociology, Transportation
Publication(s): *Arab Journal for Pharmaceutics*; *Arab Universities Journal for Medical Research and Studies*; *Damascas University Journal for Engineering Sciences*; *Damascus University Journal*; *Damascus University Journal for Agricultural Sciences*; *Damascus University Journal for Arts and Human and Educational Sciences*; *Damascus University Journal for Medical Sciences*; *Damascus University Journal for the Basic Sciences*; *Damascus University Journal for the Economic Sciences*; *Damascus University Journal for the New in the Medical Sciences*

**Dar Al Maarifah** (House of Knowledge)
29 Ayar St, Damascus
Mailing Address: PO Box 30268, Damascus
*Tel:* (011) 44670278 *Fax:* (011) 2241615
*E-mail:* info@easyquran.com
*Web Site:* www.dar-al-maarifah.com; www.easyquran.com
Founded: 1986
Also printer & distributor.
Membership(s): Arab Publishers Association.
Number of titles published annually: 1 CD-ROM
Total Titles: 240 Print; 5 CD-ROM

**Institut Francais d'Etudes Arabes de Damas**
BP 344, Damascus
*Tel:* (011) 3330214; (011) 3331692 *Fax:* (011) 3327887
*E-mail:* ifead@net.sy
*Web Site:* www.lb.refer.org/ifead
*Telex:* 412.272 IFEAD SY
*Key Personnel*
Dir: Dominique Mallet
Founded: 1922
Specialize in academic publications.
Subjects: Anthropology, Archaeology, Geography, Geology, History, Language Arts, Linguistics, Literature, Literary Criticism, Essays, Philosophy, Religion - Islamic, Social Sciences, Sociology
ISBN Prefix(es): 2-901315; 2-84128
Number of titles published annually: 8 Print
Total Titles: 4 Print
*Parent Company:* Direction Generale des Relations Culturelles Scientifiques et Techniques, Ministere des affaires Etrangeres, Paris, France
Distributed by Al-Jaffan et al Jabi (Middle East)
*Distribution Center:* Leila Books, 39 Kasr El-Nil St, 2nd floor, Daher 11271 Cairo, Egypt (Arab Republic of Egypt) *E-mail:* leilabks@intouch.com
Librairie-Boutique de l'ima, One rue des Fosses, Saint-Bernard 75236 Cedex 05, Paris, France *E-mail:* bookshop@imarabe.org
*Orders to:* Librairie d'Amerique et d'Orient (Adrien Maisonneuve), 11, rue St-Sulpice, F-75006 Paris, France *Tel:* (01) 43268635 *Fax:* (01) 43545954

# Taiwan, Province of China

## General Information

*Capital:* Taipei
*Language:* Northern Chinese (Mandarin)
*Religion:* Predominantly Buddhist, also Muslim, Daoist, & Christian
*Population:* 20.9 million
*Bank Hours:* 0900-1530 Monday-Friday; 0900-1200 Saturday
*Shop Hours:* 1000-2130 Monday-Saturday
*Currency:* 100 cents = 1 new Taiwan dollar
*Export/Import Information:* No tariffs on books and advertising. Import licenses required; exchange available when license is presented at authorized bank. Publications approved for import will not violate the Republic of China's basic national policy, undermine public morality or contravene special regulations.
*Copyright:* No copyright conventions signed. Copyright is protected by the Copyright Law. Companies and individuals, including foreigners, can register their works with the Ministry of the Interior for portection. An amendment broading the scope of the Republic of China's Copyright Law was passed 28 June 1985 by the Legislative Yuan and put into effect on 12 July 1985. The amendment, aimed at curbing pirating activities, sharply increases the maximum sentence for violating copyrights from three to five years and the maximum fine from US $75 to US $11,250, and brings computer software and video tapes under the scope of the law. Publications printed in Taiwan must acquire approval from the copyright holder before export.

**Ai Chih Book Co Ltd**
235 Chienfu St, Kaohsiung 806
*Tel:* (07) 8121571 *Fax:* (07) 8121534
*Key Personnel*
Contact: Yang Baong Min
Subjects: Child Care & Development, Literature, Literary Criticism, Essays
ISBN Prefix(es): 957-608

**Arsorigo Co Ltd+**
5D-24, No 5, Sec 5, Hsing Yi Rd, Taipei
*Tel:* (02) 2735-1274 *Fax:* (02) 2725-2387
*Key Personnel*
Chief Executive: Yuan ChiiShen

**Art Book Co Ltd+**
4F, 18, Lane 283, Roosevelt Rd, Section 3, Taipei
*Tel:* (02) 23620578 *Fax:* (02) 23623594
*E-mail:* artbook@ms43.hinet.net
*Key Personnel*
Publisher: Kung-shang Ho
Founded: 1972
Specialize in fine arts.
Subjects: Antiques, Art, History, How-to
ISBN Prefix(es): 957-672; 957-9045

**The Artist Publishing Co**
6F, 147, Chungching S Rd, Sec 1, 100 Taipei
*Tel:* (02) 23932780 *Fax:* (02) 23932012
*E-mail:* artvenue@tpts6.seed.net.tw
*Key Personnel*
Chief Executive: Ho Cheng-Kuang
Founded: 1975
Subjects: Art
ISBN Prefix(es): 957-9500; 957-8273; 957-9530

**Asian Culture Co Ltd+**
6F, No 21, Nanking E Rd, Sec 3, 104 Taipei
*Tel:* (02) 2507-2606 *Fax:* (02) 2507-4260
*E-mail:* cas@seed.net.tw
*Web Site:* www.asianculture.com.tw
*Key Personnel*
President: Eric Tong-sheng Wu
International Rights: Mr Yuan-chun Ting
Designer: Cheng Fong-Pin
Founded: 1982
Subjects: Archaeology, Art, Asian Studies, Biography, Business, Fiction, Health, Nutrition, History, Law, Literature, Literary Criticism, Essays, Military Science, Philosophy, Photography, Romance, Self-Help, Women's Studies, Dance, Autobiography
ISBN Prefix(es): 957-8983; 957-9027; 957-9449

**Bookman Books Ltd+**
2nd Fl-5, 88 Hsinsheng S Rd, Sec 3, 106 Taipei
*Tel:* (02) 2368-7226; (02) 2365-8617 *Fax:* (02) 2363-6630; (02) 2365-3548
*E-mail:* bk@bookman.com.tw
*Web Site:* www.bookman.com.tw
*Key Personnel*
Man Dir: Jerome (Cheng-lung) Su
Founded: 1977
Also acts as exclusive agents in Taiwan for W W Norton, USA, & Faber & Faber, UK.
Subjects: Literature, Literary Criticism, Essays, Social Sciences, Sociology
ISBN Prefix(es): 957-586

**Campus Evangelical Fellowship, Literature Department+**
22, Sec 4, Roosevelt Rd, Taipei 100
*Tel:* (02) 2368-2361 *Fax:* (02) 2367-2139
*E-mail:* info@cef.org.tw
*Web Site:* www.cef.org.tw
*Key Personnel*
Dir: Hui-Ping Peng
Vice Dir: Ruth Cha
Editor: Stephen Wu
Founded: 1965
Subjects: Biblical Studies, Biography, Child Care & Development, Human Relations, Religion - Protestant
ISBN Prefix(es): 957-587
*U.S. Office(s):* Overseas Campus Magazine, PO Box 638, Lomita, CA 90717-0638, United States

**Cheng Chung Book Co, Ltd**
20 Hengyang Rd, Taipei
*Tel:* (02) 2382-2815 *Fax:* (02) 2389-3571
*Web Site:* www.ccbc.com.tw
Subjects: Education
ISBN Prefix(es): 957-09

**Cheng Wen Publishing Company**
3F, No 227, Sec 3, Roosevelt Rd, Taipei 106
*Tel:* (02) 2362-8032 *Fax:* (02) 2366-0806
*E-mail:* ccicncwp@ms17.hinet.net
*Key Personnel*
Chief Executive & Publisher: Larry C Huang
Founded: 1964
Subjects: History, Literature, Literary Criticism, Essays, Philosophy
ISBN Prefix(es): 957-07

**Cheng Yun Publishing Company Ltd+**
Rm 612F, No 601, Chung Cheng Rd, Taipei 111
*Tel:* (02) 28117798 *Fax:* (02) 28123041
*E-mail:* toybook@ms34.hinet.net
*Web Site:* www.toybook.com.tw
*Key Personnel*
Chief Executive: Lai Yen-Ping
Founded: 1991
ISBN Prefix(es): 957-9241
*Associate Companies:* Seven Brocades Products Inc

**Chien Chen Bookstore Publishing Company Ltd+**
80, Liming Rd, Kaohsiung 807
*Tel:* (07) 3820363 *Fax:* (07) 3892816
*Key Personnel*
Chief Executive: Mu-Shiung Chang
Founded: 1977
Subjects: Accounting, Agriculture, Animals, Pets, Behavioral Sciences, Biological Sciences, Business, Career Development
ISBN Prefix(es): 957-9574; 957-704

**Chin Chin Publications Ltd**
4F, 125, Suhg Chinng Rd, Taipei 104
*Tel:* (02) 25084331 *Fax:* (02) 25074902
*E-mail:* wcfl768@giga.net.tw
*Web Site:* www.weichuan.org.tw
ISBN Prefix(es): 957-9427

**China Law Magazine Ltd**
130 Ch'ungch'ing S Rd Sec 1, Taipei
*Tel:* (02) 231 46871 *Fax:* (02) 23814211
*E-mail:* chinals@hk.china.com
ISBN Prefix(es): 957-99166
*Parent Company:* China Legal Service (UK) Ltd, United Kingdom

**China Times Publishing Co+**
4F, 240, Hoping West Rd Sec 3, Taipei
*Tel:* (02) 23087111 *Fax:* (02) 23027844
*Web Site:* www.chinatimes.com.tw
Founded: 1975
ISBN Prefix(es): 957-13

**Chinese Christian Literature Council Taiwan Ltd**
2F, 277, Hoping E Rd, Sec 2, Taipei
*Tel:* (02) 86676796 *Fax:* (02) 86676795
*Key Personnel*
Chief Executive: Lien-Hwa Chow
ISBN Prefix(es): 957-9186

**Chu Liu Book Company+**
1F, 5 Lane, 48 Wenchou St, Taipei 100
*Tel:* (02) 236 95 250 *Fax:* (02) 836 913 93
*E-mail:* chuliu@ms13.hinet.net
*Key Personnel*
Off Manager: Paul Hsiung
Founded: 1973
Subjects: Art, Child Care & Development, Education, History, Human Relations, Literature, Literary Criticism, Essays, Philosophy, Psychology, Psychiatry, Social Sciences, Sociology
ISBN Prefix(es): 957-732; 957-9464

**Chung Hwa Book Co Ltd+**
5F, 8, Lane 181, Chiutsung Rd, Sec 2, Taipei 114
*Tel:* (02) 8797 8669 *Fax:* (02) 8797 8909 *Cable:* 2821 TAIPEI
*Key Personnel*
Man Dir: James C Hsiung
Vice President: Erica Hsiung
Founded: 1912
Subjects: Art, Biography, Education, Engineering (General), Fiction, History, Literature, Literary Criticism, Essays, Medicine, Nursing, Dentistry, Music, Dance, Philosophy, Poetry, Psychology, Psychiatry, Religion - Other, Science (General), Social Sciences, Sociology
ISBN Prefix(es): 957-43

**Commonwealth Publishing Company Ltd+**
2F, 1, Lane 93, Sung Chiang Rd, Taipei 104
*Tel:* (02) 2517-3688 *Fax:* (02) 2517-3685
*Web Site:* www.bookzone.com.tw
*Key Personnel*
President: Charles Kao
Publisher: Cora Wang
Founded: 1982
General trade & translated titles.

Subjects: Biography, Business, Child Care & Development, Economics, Fiction, Health, Nutrition, Management, Nonfiction (General), Science (General), Self-Help
ISBN Prefix(es): 957-621
Number of titles published annually: 150 Print
*Associate Companies:* CommonWealth Magazine, 4F, No 87, Sung Chiang Rd, Taipei 104
*Tel:* (02) 2507 8627; Global Views Monthly Magazine

**Cynosure Publishing Inc+**
3FL, No 26, Alley 91, Sec 1, Nei Fo Rd, Taipei
*Tel:* 8862 2657 3275 *Fax:* (02) 2657 5300
*E-mail:* cynobook@tpts4.seed.net.tw
*Web Site:* www.books.com.tw
*Key Personnel*
Exec Dir: Jimmy C C Chen *Tel:* (02) 2657 3275
Founded: 1989
Also acts as packager.
ISBN Prefix(es): 957-9158; 957-9430
*Parent Company:* Long Ken Corp Ltd
*Book Club(s):* Hello! Book Club Inc, 5F, No 203, Chung Hsiao E Rd, Sec 3, Taipei, ROC
*Tel:* (02) 27401281 *Fax:* (02) 27401545
*E-mail:* heloclub@ms22.hinet.net *Web Site:* www.hellobookclub.com

**Dayi Information Co**
1F, 8-1, Jeikuang Rd, Taipei 114
*Tel:* (02) 8792 4088 *Fax:* (02) 8792 4089
*Web Site:* www.dayi.com
*Key Personnel*
Contact: Jeff Wang
Founded: 1992
Subjects: Business
ISBN Prefix(es): 957-99775

**Designer Publisher Inc**
7F, 159-2, Shita Rd, Taipei 100
*Tel:* (02) 236 56268 *Fax:* (02) 236 76500
*E-mail:* dpgcmg@ms18.hinet.net
*Key Personnel*
Chief Executive: Wang Su-Chao
Founded: 1992
Subjects: Advertising, Communications, Graphics, Typography
ISBN Prefix(es): 957-9570
Imprints: Wang Su-Chao
Subsidiaries: Graphic Communications Monthly

**Echo Publishing Company Ltd+**
3F, 5-2, Alley 16, Lane 72 Pateh Rd, Sec 4, Taipei 105
*Tel:* (02) 763-1452 *Fax:* (02) 27568712
*E-mail:* hrmdh@mail.echogroup.com.tw
*Web Site:* www.chinesebooks.net
*Key Personnel*
Chief Executive: Ms Linda Wu
Founded: 1970
Subjects: Anthropology, Antiques, Archaeology, Architecture & Interior Design, Art, Asian Studies, Child Care & Development, Crafts, Games, Hobbies
ISBN Prefix(es): 957-588
*Associate Companies:* Echo Communications Co Ltd
Distributed by Charles E Tuttle Co (USA & UK)

**Far East Book Co Ltd**
66, Chungking S Rd, Sec 1, Taipei
*Tel:* (02) 2311 8740 *Fax:* (02) 2311 4184
*E-mail:* service@mail.fareast.com.tw
*Web Site:* www.fareast.com.tw *Cable:* 1418 TAIPEI
*Key Personnel*
Manager: Jonathan Riverbank
Founded: 1950
Subjects: Art, Education, History, Literature, Literary Criticism, Essays, Physics, Poetry

ISBN Prefix(es): 957-9666; 957-612
Distributed by U.S. International Inc.

**Farseeing Publishing Company Ltd+**
4F, 50-1, Hsinsheng S Rd, Section 1, Taipei 100
*Tel:* (02) 23921167 *Fax:* (02) 23567448
*E-mail:* fars@msb.hinet.net
*Web Site:* www.farseeing.com.tw
*Key Personnel*
Chief Executive: Hsiao Feng-Fu
Founded: 1983
Subjects: English as a Second Language, Health, Nutrition, Medicine, Nursing, Dentistry
ISBN Prefix(es): 957-640; 957-9506; 957-99215; 957-99266
*Associate Companies:* Weyfar Books Co Ltd
Subsidiaries: Farseeing Nursing Press
Divisions: Fayfar Publishing Co Ltd

**Fuh-Wen Book Co+**
63, Linsen Rd, Sec 2, Tainan
*Tel:* (06) 2370003 *Fax:* (06) 2386937
*E-mail:* fwbook@m525.hinet.net
*Key Personnel*
President: Mr Chu Ho Wu
Vice President: James Chin
Editor: Shih Shu-Yen
Subjects: Accounting, Agriculture, Automotive, Chemistry, Chemical Engineering, Civil Engineering, Computer Science, Economics, Electronics, Electrical Engineering, Engineering (General), Environmental Studies, Finance, Marketing, Mathematics, Mechanical Engineering, Physical Sciences, Physics, Science (General)
ISBN Prefix(es): 957-536
Subsidiaries: Taiwan Fuh-Wen Sin-Yah Co Ltd
*Branch Office(s)*
985 Papen Rd, Bridgewater, NJ 08807, United States
*Book Club(s):* ABA
*Shipping Address:* The Kaohsiung Port
*Warehouse:* No 18 Alley 88 Lane 71, Fuh-Sin Rd, Yung-Kang Village, Tainan County

**Grand East Enterprise**, *imprint of* San Min Book Co Ltd

**Great China Book Company**
4F-2, 150, Chion First Rd, Chungho 235 Taipei
*Tel:* (02) 822 63341 *Fax:* (02) 822 65906
ISBN Prefix(es): 957-521

**Grimm Press Ltd+**
11F, 213, Hsinyi Rd, Sec 2, Taipei 106
*Tel:* (02) 23965698 *Fax:* (02) 23570954
*E-mail:* ishbel@cite.com.tw
*Web Site:* www.cite.com.tw
*Key Personnel*
Publisher: K T Hao
Editor: Joy Chao
Marketing Dir: Annie Lin
Rights Manager: Bruce Ishbel
International Rights: Catherine Van Hale
Publishes classic stories & modern tales from East & West.
Subjects: Animals, Pets, Biography, Fiction, History, Humor, Science (General), Technology
ISBN Prefix(es): 957-745

**Chu Hai Publishing (Taiwan) Co Ltd**
2F-1, 65, Anho Rd, Sec 2, Taipei 106
*Tel:* (02) 7080290 *Fax:* (02) 7084804
*Key Personnel*
International Rights: Gee H Luk
Subjects: Agriculture, Architecture & Interior Design, Art, Business, Civil Engineering, Computer Science, Engineering (General), Environmental Studies, Gardening, Plants, Health,

Nutrition, Medicine, Nursing, Dentistry, Social Sciences, Sociology, Travel
ISBN Prefix(es): 957-657

**Heavenly Lotus Publishing Co, Ltd**
2F, 168, Chungch'eng Rd, Sec 2, 111 Taipei
*Tel:* (02) 2873-6629 *Fax:* (02) 8736709
*Key Personnel*
President: Yun-Pen Lee
Founded: 1975
Subjects: Religion - Buddhist
ISBN Prefix(es): 957-665; 957-9397

**Hilit Publishing Co Ltd+**
11F, No 28, Roosevelt Rd, Sec 3, Taipei 100
*Tel:* (02) 2362-6602 *Fax:* (02) 2365-2552
*E-mail:* hilit.publish@msa.hinet.net
*Web Site:* www.hilit.com.tw
*Key Personnel*
Chairman: Dixson Sung
Dir: Bob Wang
Representative: Joyce Wang
Founded: 1980
Subjects: Agriculture, Antiques, Art, Asian Studies, Cookery, Crafts, Games, Hobbies, Fiction, Gardening, Plants, How-to, Photography, Travel, diet
ISBN Prefix(es): 957-629
*Associate Companies:* Highlight International Co Ltd
*Warehouse:* 35, Lanc 142, Kun Yang St, Taipei

**Ho-Chi Book Publishing Co+**
No 322-2 An Kun Rd, Nei-Hu Area, Taipei 114
*Tel:* (02) 2974-0168 *Fax:* (02) 2792-4702
*E-mail:* hochi@ms12.hinet.net; hochi@email.gcn.net.tw
*Key Personnel*
Contact: Wu Kuei-tsung
Founded: 1956
Subjects: Behavioral Sciences, Biological Sciences, Child Care & Development, Health, Nutrition, Medicine, Nursing, Dentistry, Psychology, Psychiatry, Technology, Veterinary Science, Life Science
ISBN Prefix(es): 957-666; 957-9097
Distributor for Churchill Livingstone; Lippincott-Raven; McGraw-Hill; W B Saunders; Williams & Wilkins
*Bookshop(s):* Ho-Chi Book Store (Bei-yi Branch), Suite 249, Wu-Hsing St., Taipei 110 *Tel:* (02) 2723-9404 *Fax:* (02) 2723-0997; Tai-da Branch, Suite 7, Lane 12, Roosevelt Rd., Sec 4, Taipei 100 *Tel:* (02) 2365-1544 *Fax:* (02) 2367-1266; Rong-Zong Branch, Suite 120, Shih-Pai Rd, Sec 2, Taipei 112 *Tel:* (02) 2826-5375 *Fax:* (02) 2823-9604; Taichung Branch, Suite 24, Yu-Der Rd, Taichung *Tel:* (04) 203-0795 *Fax:* (04) 202-5093; Kaohsiung Branch, Suite 1, Pei-Peng 1st St, Kaohsiung 800 *Tel:* (07) 322-6177 *Fax:* (07) 323-5118

**Hsiao Yuan Publication Co, Ltd+**
20, Lane 333, Roosevelt Rd, Sec 3, Taipei 106
*Tel:* (02) 23676789 *Fax:* (02) 23628429
*E-mail:* ufaf0130@ms5.hinet.net
*Key Personnel*
Vice President: Feng Chu Huang-Yu
Subjects: Business, Chemistry, Chemical Engineering, Computer Science, Electronics, Electrical Engineering, English as a Second Language, Literature, Literary Criticism, Essays, Mathematics, Physical Sciences, Technology
ISBN Prefix(es): 957-12
*Bookshop(s):* No 96-3, Sec 3, Hsin Sheng S Rd, Taipei

**Hsin Yi Publications+**
5F 75, Chung-Chung S Rd, Sec 2, 100 Taipei
*Tel:* (02) 23965303 *Fax:* (02) 23965015
*Web Site:* www.hsin-yi.org.tw

*Key Personnel*
Publisher: Show Chung Ho
Executive Director: Sing-ju Chang
Chief Editor: Sin-Ju Ho
Founded: 1978
Distributed by Shen's Books & Supplies, 8625
Hubbard Rd, Auburn, CA 95602.
ISBN Prefix(es): 957-642; 957-9526
Total Titles: 1,000 Print
*Parent Company:* Hsin Yi Foundation
*Associate Companies:* Hsinex International Corporation, 75 Sec 2, Chung-Chung S Rd, Taipei,
Contact: Santee Wen *Tel:* (02) 23913384
*Fax:* (02) 23913384 *E-mail:* santee@hsin-hi.
org.tw

**Hu Yu She Culture Co Ltd**, see HYS Culture
Co Ltd

**HYS Culture Co Ltd+**
2, Alley 3, Lane 130, Paoan Rd, 828 Yungan,
Kaohsiung
*Tel:* (07) 6914310 *Fax:* (02) 6914311
*E-mail:* hysccl@msl.hinet.net
*Web Site:* www.hysbook.com.tw
*Key Personnel*
General Manager: Mr G L Hsu
Subjects: Animals, Pets
ISBN Prefix(es): 957-9561

**Jillion Publishing Co+**
2F, No 9, Lane 12, Nanking W Rd, Taipei 104
*Tel:* (02) 2571-0558 *Fax:* (02) 5231891
*E-mail:* lanbri@tpts.5.seed.net.tw
*Key Personnel*
Chief Executive: Ai Tien-Shi
Founded: 1985
Subjects: Career Development, English as a Second Language, How-to, Language Arts, Linguistics
ISBN Prefix(es): 957-9415; 957-786

**Kuei Kuan Book Co Ltd**, see Laureate Book Co
Ltd

**Kwang Fu Book Co Ltd+**
6F, No 38, Fushing N Rd, Taipei
*Tel:* (02) 558 15 678 *Fax:* (02) 558 15 141
*E-mail:* lolatiao@kfgroup.com.tw
*Key Personnel*
President: Mr C H Lin
Foreign Affairs Executive: Mr Hong-Long Lin
Foreign Rights & Manager: Ming-Yen Tiao
*Tel:* (02) 2741-0415
Founded: 1962
Also specializing in distance learning.
Subjects: Art, Education, Fiction, Health, Nutrition, History, Literature, Literary Criticism,
Essays, Medicine, Nursing, Dentistry, Science
(General)
ISBN Prefix(es): 957-42
Total Titles: 2,000 Print; 80 CD-ROM
Imprints: Kwang Fu Book Enterprises Co, Ltd
Subsidiaries: Kwang Toong Book Department
Store Co Ltd
*U.S. Office(s):* Tron Link Enterprises Co, Ltd,
9401 De Vry Dr, Irvine, CA, United States,
Contact: Mr Hong-tien Lin *Tel:* 949-856-
9769; 949-854-1569 *Fax:* 949-856-9769
*E-mail:* hongtien@aol.com
*Book Club(s):* New Reader's Book Club,
Contact: Lola Tiao *Tel:* (02) 2771-6622
*E-mail:* bookclub@kfgroup.com.tw

**Kwang Fu Book Enterprises Co, Ltd,** *imprint*
*of* Kwang Fu Book Co Ltd

**Laureate Book Co Ltd+**
2F, No 542-3, Chung Cheng Rd, Hsien tien 231,
Taipei 105
*Tel:* 8862 2219 3338 *Fax:* (02) 2218-2860

*E-mail:* laureate@laureate.com.tw
*Web Site:* www.laureate.com.tw
*Key Personnel*
Manager: A-Shen Lai
Founded: 1975
Subjects: Anthropology, Behavioral Sciences,
Business, Child Care & Development, Education, Government, Political Science, History,
Literature, Literary Criticism, Essays, Management, Philosophy, Psychology, Psychiatry,
Social Sciences, Sociology, Women's Studies
ISBN Prefix(es): 957-551

**Lead Wave Publishing Company Ltd+**
2F-4, 110, Chungshan Rd, Sec 3, Chungho 23
235
*Tel:* (02) 82281288 *Fax:* (02) 82281207
*E-mail:* customer@liwil.com.tw
*Web Site:* www.liwil.com.tw
Subjects: Computer Science, Microcomputers
ISBN Prefix(es): 957-9252
*Parent Company:* Liwei Publishing Co Ltd

**Lee & Lee Communications+**
14F, No 125, Keelung Rd, Sec 2, 100 Taipei
*Tel:* (02) 237 83373 *Fax:* (02) 237 82803
*E-mail:* service@leelee.com; culture@leelee.com
*Web Site:* www.leelee.com
*Key Personnel*
Distribution Manager: Shumin Huang
Founded: 1988
Membership(s): Association of Multimedia, International.
Subjects: Antiques, Art
ISBN Prefix(es): 957-99049

**Lien Ho Wen Hsueh Press Co Ltd**, see
UNITAS Publishing Co Ltd

**Liming Cultural Enterprise Co Ltd**
3F 49, Chungching S Rd Sec 1, Taipei 100
*Tel:* (02) 23821152 *Fax:* (02) 23821244
*E-mail:* liming03@ms57.hinet.net
*Web Site:* www.limingco.com.tw
ISBN Prefix(es): 957-16
Subsidiaries: Tai-Chung Kaohsiung/Two Cities
*Bookshop(s):* 49 Chung-King S Rd, Section 1,
Taipei 100
*Warehouse:* 19 Lane 482 Chung-Shan Rd, Section
2, Chung-Ho, Hsieh

**Lin Pai Press Company Ltd+**
1F, 15, Lane 71, Lungchiang Rd, Taipei 104
*Tel:* (02) 7765889 *Fax:* (02) 7712568
*E-mail:* master@doghouse.com.tw
*Web Site:* www.doghouse.com.tw
Membership(s): Republic of China Publisher's
Association.
Subjects: Fiction, Journalism, Literature, Literary
Criticism, Essays, Mysteries, Romance
ISBN Prefix(es): 957-593; 957-812
*Parent Company:* Lin Pai Publishing Co Ltd
*Shipping Address:* 271 Chungyang Rd, Nan
Gang, Taipei
*Warehouse:* 6F3 Lane 327, Sec 2, Jongshan Rd,
Jongher, Taipei Shiang

**Linking Publishing Company Ltd+**
555 Chunghsiao East Rd, Sec 4, Taipei 110
*Tel:* (02) 27634300 (ext 5040) *Fax:* (02)
27567668
*E-mail:* linkingp@udngroup.com.tw
*Web Site:* www.udngroup.com.tw/linkingp
*Key Personnel*
Editorial Dir: Linden T C Lin *E-mail:* linden@
udngroup.com.tw
Founded: 1974
Subjects: Art, Asian Studies, Biography, Business, Career Development, Child Care & Development, Cookery, Economics, English as a
Second Language, Fiction, Health, Nutrition,

History, Human Relations, Literature, Literary Criticism, Essays, Management, Nonfiction
(General), Self-Help, Travel, Wine & Spirits,
Women's Studies
ISBN Prefix(es): 957-08

**Liwil Publishing Co Ltd**, see Lead Wave
Publishing Company Ltd

**Morning Star Publisher Inc+**
No 1, 30th Road Industry District, Taichung 407
*Tel:* (04) 23595820 *Fax:* (04) 23597123
*E-mail:* morning@tcts.seed.net.tw
*Key Personnel*
President: Ming-Min Chen
Founded: 1980
Subjects: Environmental Studies, Fiction, Health,
Nutrition, How-to, Human Relations, Management, Regional Interests, Romance, Self-Help
ISBN Prefix(es): 957-583
*U.S. Office(s):* 21311 Espada Pl, Diamond Bar
City, CA 91765, United States *Tel:* 909-396-
7811 *Fax:* 909-396-9511
*Book Club(s):* A B A

**National Museum of History**
49 Nanhai Rd, Taipei 10728
*Tel:* (02) 3610270-514 *Fax:* (02) 3610171
Subjects: Antiques, Art, Asian Studies, History

**National Palace Museum**
Publications Division, 221, Chihshan Rd, Sec 2,
Taipei
*Tel:* (02) 2881-2021 *Fax:* (02) 2882-1440
*E-mail:* service01@npm.gov.tw
*Web Site:* www.npm.gov.tw
*Key Personnel*
Director: Shou-chien Shien
Deputy Dir: Mun-lee Lin; Po-ting Lin
Head of Publications Division: Ms Sai-lan Hu
Founded: 1983
Subjects: Antiques, Archaeology, Art, History
ISBN Prefix(es): 957-562
*Bookshop(s):* World Journal Book Store, 379
Broadway, New York, NY 10013, United
States; Paragon Books, 1507 S Michigan Ave,
Chicago, IL 60605, United States

**Newton Publishing Company Ltd+**
No 9, Alley 44, Shu Wei Rd, Taipei 106
*Tel:* (02) 2706-0336 *Fax:* (02) 2707 3759
*E-mail:* newton00@m517.hinet.net
*Web Site:* www.newton.com.tw
*Key Personnel*
Chairman: Kao Yuan Chin
President: Chun-Tus Liu
Dir, International Rights Dept: Kao Yung Hsin
Subjects: Biography, Management, Marketing,
Mathematics, Medicine, Nursing, Dentistry,
Nonfiction (General), Physical Sciences, Science (General), Social Sciences, Sociology
ISBN Prefix(es): 957-627
Subsidiaries: Little Newton Co; Newton Culture
Viedeo Co
Distributed by Leader Books Co (Hong Kong);
Transforma (Malaysia)

**Pearson Education**
5F, No 147, Chung-Ching S Rd, Sec 1, Taipei
100
*Tel:* (02) 2370 8168 *Fax:* (02) 2370 8169
*E-mail:* firstname@pearsoned.com.tw
*Web Site:* www.pearsoned.com.tw
*Key Personnel*
General Manager: Angela Yang
Sales Manager/HED: Anderson Ho
Finance/Administration Manager: Chris Chen
Sales Manager/ELT: Jeff Huang
Publishing Manager/TRSL: Stella Chou

*Parent Company:* Pearson Plc
*Branch Office(s)*
7F, No 245, Roosevelt Rd, Sec 3, Taipei
*Tel:* 2368 3904 *Fax:* 2367 3994

**Petroleum Information Publishing Co**
4F-16 12 Lane 609, Chunghsin Rd Sec 5,
Sanchung 241
*Tel:* (02) 29996909 *Fax:* (02) 29996746
*E-mail:* pip@oil.net.tw
*Web Site:* www.oil.net.tw
*Key Personnel*
Chief Executive: Hong Tse-Wen
Subjects: Chemistry, Chemical Engineering, Environmental Studies, Science (General), Technology
ISBN Prefix(es): 957-9694
Subsidiaries: Petroleum Information Magazine

**San Min Book Co Ltd+**
386 Fushing N Rd, Taipei 104
*Tel:* (02) 25006600 *Fax:* (02) 25064000
*E-mail:* editor@sanmin.com.tw
*Web Site:* www.sanmin.com.tw
*Key Personnel*
Publicity Manager: Chen-Chiang Liu
International Rights: Wang Yun-Fen
Editor: Allie Hwang
Founded: 1953
Also acts as Bookseller.
Subjects: Accounting, Advertising, Agriculture, Anthropology, Art, Computer Science, Economics, Education, Government, Political Science, Law, Literature, Literary Criticism, Essays, Mathematics, Music, Dance, Philosophy, Religion - Buddhist, Religion - Other, Science (General), Technology
ISBN Prefix(es): 957-14; 957-19
Number of titles published annually: 300 Print
Total Titles: 5,000 Print
Imprints: Grand East Enterprise
*Branch Office(s)*
No 61, Section 1, Chungking S Rd, Taipei 100

**Senate Books Co Ltd+**
6F-2, No 98, Jen Rd, Sec 2, Taipei 100
*Tel:* (02) 23213054 *Fax:* (02) 23214041
*Key Personnel*
General Manager: Tiffany Lo *E-mail:* senate@ficnet.net
International Rights: James Peiscy
Founded: 1985
Subjects: Law
ISBN Prefix(es): 957-789
Distributor for Matthew Bender

**Shuttle Multimedia Inc**
1F, 8-1 Jei Kuang Rd, Taipei 114
*Tel:* (02) 87924088 *Fax:* (02) 87924089
*E-mail:* school@dayi.com
*Web Site:* www.eduplus.com
*Key Personnel*
Contact: Jeff Wang
Founded: 1993
Develop & sell software, CD-title mainly.
Subjects: Education, English as a Second Language
ISBN Prefix(es): 957-99430

**Shy Mau & Shy Chaur Publishing Co Ltd+**
5F1, No 19, Ming-Sheng Rd, Hsien 231
*Tel:* (02) 2218-3277 *Fax:* (02) 2218-3239
*E-mail:* chien218@ms5.hinet.net
*Key Personnel*
President: Chien Tai-Hsiung
Assistant Dir: Chien Yu Shan
International Rights: Lin Cheng-Tsung
Founded: 1982
Subjects: Biological Sciences, Business, Child Care & Development, Computer Science, Gardening, Plants, Health, Nutrition, History, How-

to, Journalism, Law, Management, Psychology, Psychiatry, Real Estate, Science (General), Self-Help, Social Sciences, Sociology, Travel, zoology, entertainment
ISBN Prefix(es): 957-776; 957-529

**Sinorama Magazine Co+**
5F, No 54, Chunghsiao, East Rd Sec 1, Taipei 100
*Tel:* (02) 2392-2256 *Fax:* (02) 2397-0655
*E-mail:* service@mail.sinorama.com.tw
*Web Site:* www.sinorama.com.tw
*Key Personnel*
Publisher: Jason Hu
Editor-in-Chief: Wang Jia-fong
Deputy Editor-in-Chief: Anna Y Wang
Founded: 1976
Subjects: English as a Second Language, Environmental Studies, History, Medicine, Nursing, Dentistry, cultural studies
ISBN Prefix(es): 957-9188
*U.S. Office(s):* Kwan Hwa Publishing (USA), Inc, 300 Wilshire Blvd, Suite 1510 A, Los Angeles, CA 90048, United States *Tel:* 213-782-8770 *Fax:* 213-782-8761

**SMC Publishing Inc+**
No 14, Alley 14, Lane 283, Roosevelt Rd, Sec 3, 106 Taipei
*Tel:* (02) 2362-0190 *Fax:* (02) 3623834
*Web Site:* www.smcbook.com.tw
*Key Personnel*
Manager: Wei Te-wen
Founded: 1976
Publish in English & Chinese.
Subjects: Anthropology, Art, Asian Studies, Biological Sciences, History, Medicine, Nursing, Dentistry, Religion - Buddhist
ISBN Prefix(es): 957-638; 957-9482

**The Third Wave Enterprise Co Ltd**
B1 18, Hsinyi Rd, Sec 5, Taipei 110
*Tel:* (02) 87803636 *Fax:* (02) 87805656
*E-mail:* AIWebmaster@acer.com.tw
*Web Site:* www.acertwp.com.tw
*Key Personnel*
International Information Dept Manager: David Tsai
Founded: 1981
ISBN Prefix(es): 957-23
*Parent Company:* Acer Inc
*Associate Companies:* Acer Advanced Inc; Acer Peripheral; Sertek
Distributor for Data Communication; LAN Times

**Torch of Wisdom+**
10, Lane 270, Chienkuo S Rd, Sec 1, 106 Taipei
*Tel:* (02) 7075802 *Fax:* (02) 7085054
*E-mail:* tow@ms2.hinet.net
*Key Personnel*
Contact: Pro Cheng Chen-Huang
Founded: 1951
Subjects: Asian Studies, Health, Nutrition, Religion - Buddhist
ISBN Prefix(es): 957-518

**UNITAS Publishing Co Ltd+**
10F 180 Chilung Rd Section 1, Taipei 110
*Tel:* (02) 27634300 *Fax:* (02) 27491208
*E-mail:* unitas@udngroup.com.tw
*Web Site:* www.udngroup.com.tw
*Key Personnel*
Chief Editor: Mr Ann-Ming Tsu
International Rights: Paula C Wang
Founded: 1984
Subjects: Fiction, Journalism, Literature, Literary Criticism, Essays, Nonfiction (General), Poetry, Romance, Women's Studies
ISBN Prefix(es): 957-522

**Wang Su-Chao**, *imprint of* Designer Publisher Inc

**Wei-Chuan Publishing Company Ltd+**
2F, 28 Jenai Rd, Sec 4, 106 Taipei
*Tel:* (02) 27021148 *Fax:* (02) 27042729
*Key Personnel*
Chief Executive: Huang Su-Huei
Founded: 1971
Subjects: Child Care & Development, Cookery, Crafts, Games, Hobbies, How-to
ISBN Prefix(es): 957-9285
Subsidiaries: Wei-Chuan's Publishing

**World Book Co Ltd+**
7F, 99 Chung Ching S Rd, Sec 1, Taipei 100
*Tel:* (02) 2311-3834 *Fax:* (02) 2331-7963
*E-mail:* wbc@ms2.hinet.net
*Web Site:* www.worldbook.com.tw
*Key Personnel*
President: Angela Chu Yen
Founded: 1921
Subjects: Art, Drama, Theater, History, Language Arts, Linguistics, Literature, Literary Criticism, Essays, Medicine, Nursing, Dentistry, Philosophy, Poetry, Social Sciences, Sociology, Chinese Classics
ISBN Prefix(es): 957-06

**Wu Nan Book Co Ltd+**
4F, No 339, Sec 2, Ho-Ping E Rd, 106 Taipei
*Tel:* (02) 2705-5066 *Fax:* (02) 2706-6100
*E-mail:* wunan@wunan.com.tw
*Web Site:* www.wunan.com.tw
*Key Personnel*
Manager of Planning Dept: Thomas Chen
Subjects: Anthropology, Biography, Biological Sciences, Business, Computer Science, Crafts, Games, Hobbies, Engineering (General), Environmental Studies, Finance, History, Language Arts, Linguistics, Law, Literature, Literary Criticism, Essays, Military Science, Religion - Other, Science (General), Technology, Geology, Games, Esoteric, Entertainment, Dance, Administration
ISBN Prefix(es): 957-11

**Yee Wen Publishing Co Ltd+**
4F-3, No 253, Sec 3, Roosevelt Rd, Taipei
*Tel:* (02) 2362-6012 *Fax:* (02) 2366-0977
*E-mail:* yeewen_us@yahoo.com
*Key Personnel*
Chief Executive: Feng-Chiao Yen
Sales Manager: Ming-Fang Tsai
Editorial Manager: Jammy Yen *Tel:* 650-367-5020 *Fax:* 650-364-0960
Founded: 1953
Subjects: Archaeology, Art, Asian Studies, Ethnicity, Geography, Geology, History, Literature, Literary Criticism, Essays, Philosophy, Regional Interests, Religion - Other, Science (General)
ISBN Prefix(es): 0-88691; 957-520
Number of titles published annually: 12 Print
Total Titles: 3,000 Print
*U.S. Office(s):* 518 Oak Park Way, Redwood City, CA 94062-4038, United States, Contact: Jammy Yen *Tel:* 650-367-5020 *Fax:* 650-364-0960 *E-mail:* yeewen_us@yahoo.com

**Yi Hsien Publishing Co Ltd+**
5F, No 1, Lane 7, Baugau Rd, Hsintien, Taipei
*Tel:* (02) 2918-2288 *Fax:* (02) 2917-2266
*E-mail:* yihsient@ms17.hinet.net
*Web Site:* www.yihsient.com.tw
*Key Personnel*
President & International Rights: Ed Tung
Founded: 1975
Subjects: Agriculture, Animals, Pets, Biological Sciences, Chemistry, Chemical Engineering, Earth Sciences, Health, Nutrition, Medicine,

Nursing, Dentistry, Psychology, Psychiatry, Publishing & Book Trade Reference, Science (General), Veterinary Science
ISBN Prefix(es): 957-616
*Bookshop(s):* No 3, Lane 316, Roosevelt Rd, Sec 3, Taipei; No 178, Wu-ch'ang St, Taichung

**Youth Cultural Publishing Co+**
3F, 66-1 Chungking S Rd, Sec 1, 100 Taipei
*Tel:* (02) 231 46001 *Fax:* (02) 236 12239
*E-mail:* youth@ms2.hinet.net
*Web Site:* www.youth.com.tw
*Key Personnel*
Chief Executive: Tchong-Koei Li
Contact: Ho Wei
Founded: 1958
Subjects: Cookery, Crafts, Games, Hobbies, Education, Fashion, Language Arts, Linguistics, Literature, Literary Criticism, Essays, Psychology, Psychiatry, Science (General), Travel, Entertainment, Food/Drink
ISBN Prefix(es): 957-530; 957-574
*Parent Company:* China Youth Corps
*Showroom(s):* No 219, Sung Chiang Rd, Taipei
*Bookshop(s):* No 6, Heng Yang Rd, Taipei; No 2-1, Feng Chia Rd, Taichung; No 157, Fu Hsing 2 Rd, Kaohsiung
*Warehouse:* No 21, Lane 111, Chung Ying St, Su Lin Town, Taipei

**Yuan Liou Publishing Co, Ltd+**
7F-5, No 184, Tingchow Rd, Sec 3, Taipei 100
*Tel:* (02) 2392 6899 *Fax:* (02) 2392 6658
*E-mail:* ylib@ylib.com.tw
*Web Site:* www.ylib.com.tw
*Key Personnel*
Publisher: Wang Jung-Wen
Founded: 1975
Subjects: Art, Business, Fiction, Health, Nutrition, History, How-to, Psychology, Psychiatry, Self-Help
ISBN Prefix(es): 957-32
*Associate Companies:* Meta Media International Co

**Zen Now Press**
3F, 6-2, Huaite St, Taipei 112
*Tel:* (02) 28278500 *Fax:* (02) 28236849
*E-mail:* zen@zenow.org.tw
*Key Personnel*
President: Mr Su Chun-Jung
Subjects: Religion - Buddhist
ISBN Prefix(es): 957-9622
Distributed by Hsu Sheng Book Ltd

# Tajikistan

## General Information

*Capital:* Dushanbe
*Language:* Tajik
*Population:* 5.7 million
*Bank Hours:* Generally open for short hours between 0930-1230 Monday-Friday
*Shop Hours:* Generally 0900-1800 Monday-Friday; often open weekends
*Currency:* 100 kopeks = 1 rubl
*Export/Import Information:* According to Ukrainian quotas and customs duties, companies engaged in trade should register with the Ukraine Ministry of Foreign Economic Relations. Licenses for export and import are also required for trade with Russia.
*Copyright:* UCC (see Copyright Conventions, pg xi)

**Irfon** (Knowledge)
ul N Karabayeva 17, 734018 Dushanbe

*Tel:* (03772) 33-39-06; (03772) 33-62-54
*Key Personnel*
Dir: J Sharifov
Editor-in-Chief: A Olimov
Founded: 1925
Subjects: Agriculture, Economics, Fiction, Government, Political Science, Medicine, Nursing, Dentistry, Philosophy, Social Sciences, Sociology, Technology
ISBN Prefix(es): 5-667

# United Republic of Tanzania

## General Information

*Capital:* Dar es Salem
*Language:* Swahili and English are both official languages
*Religion:* Islamic, Christian (mostly Roman Catholic), Hindu, the rest follow traditional beliefs
*Population:* 27.8 million
*Bank Hours:* Mainland Tanzania: 0900-1200 Monday-Friday; 0900-1100 Saturday. Zanzibar: 0830-1130 Monday-Friday; 0830-1000 Saturday
*Shop Hours:* 0800-1200, 1400-1715 or 1800 Monday-Saturday
*Currency:* 100 cents = 1 Tanzanian shilling
*Export/Import Information:* No tariff on books or advertising matter. Import license and exchange controls.
*Copyright:* Berne, Florence (see Copyright Conventions, pg xi)

**Africa Inland Church Literature Department,** see Inland Publishers

**Akajase Enterprises+**
PO Box 7187, Dar Es Salaam
*Tel:* (051) 26121
*Key Personnel*
Dir: R A Akwilombe
Founded: 1988
Also bookseller.
Subjects: Fiction
ISBN Prefix(es): 9987-551

**Ben & Company Ltd+**
Samora Machel Ave, PO Box 3164, Plot 3, Dar Es Salaam
*Tel:* (051) 67407 *Fax:* (511) 12440
*E-mail:* siggers@pearsoned.ema.com
*Telex:* 41816
*Key Personnel*
Man Dir & Publicity: Ian Ben Moshi
Man Editor: James Odongo Ocholla
Senior Editor: Salim Kigenda
Sales & Marketing: Sadallah Sungura Alli
Founded: 1981
Specialize in Kiswahili, arts & crafts (life skills).
Membership(s): Publishers Association of Tanzania (PATA)
Subjects: English as a Second Language, Mathematics, Science (General)
ISBN Prefix(es): 9976-920
Total Titles: 72 Print

**Benedictine Publications Ndanda,** *imprint of* Ndanda Mission Press

**Bilal Muslim Mission of Tanzania+**
PO Box 20033, Dar Es Salaam

*Tel:* (051) 30345; (051) 50924 *Fax:* 2116550
*E-mail:* bilal@raha.com
*Telex:* 41518 Geomic *Cable:* TABLIGH
*Key Personnel*
Chairman: Pyarali M Shivji *Tel:* (051) 114113
Editor: F H Abdullah
Chief Missionary: Sayid Saeed Akhtar Rizvi *Tel:* (051) 130345
Founded: 1968
An autonomous subsidiary of Shia Ithnaashery Supreme Council of Africa.
Subjects: Literature, Literary Criticism, Essays
ISBN Prefix(es): 9976-956

**Bureau of Statistics+**
PO Box 796, Dar Es Salaam
*Tel:* (051) 111634; (051) 111635 *Fax:* (051) 112352
*E-mail:* kento@raha.com
*Telex:* 41576 TASTAT TZ *Cable:* STATISTICS
*Key Personnel*
Publishing Officer: Eliab J C Chiduo
Founded: 1961
Subjects: Agriculture, Economics, Education

**Central Tanganyika Press+**
PO Box 15, Dodoma
*Tel:* (061) 22140 *Fax:* (061) 324565
*Telex:* 53328 TZ
*Key Personnel*
General Manager: James Lifa Chipaka
Marketing Sales Manager: David Tuppa
Founded: 1954
Subjects: Biblical Studies, Biography, Child Care & Development, Religion - Protestant
ISBN Prefix(es): 9976-66

**DUP (1996) Ltd+**
PO Box 35182, Dar Es Salaam
*Tel:* (051) 410300 *Fax:* (051) 410137
*E-mail:* director@dup.udsm.ac.tz
*Telex:* 41327 Uniscie *Cable:* UNIVERSITY DAR ES SALAAM
*Key Personnel*
Dir: N G Mwitta
Marketing Manager: L D T Minzi
Founded: 1979
Membership(s): Tanzania Publishers Association; also book packager.
Subjects: Accounting, Biological Sciences, Chemistry, Chemical Engineering, Civil Engineering, Developing Countries, Drama, Theater, Electronics, Electrical Engineering, History, Language Arts, Linguistics, Mathematics, Mechanical Engineering, Medicine, Nursing, Dentistry, Physical Sciences, Physics, Women's Studies
ISBN Prefix(es): 9976-60

**East African Publishing House**
PO Box 3209, Dar Es Salaam
*Tel:* (02) 557417; (02) 557788 *Cable:* Afrobooks Nairobi
*Key Personnel*
Man Dir: E N Wainaina
Chief Editor, Rights & Permissions: Gacheche Waruingi
Marketing, Publicity, Sales, Distribution: James K Muraya
Production: John Mwazo
Founded: 1965
Subjects: Biography, Education, Fiction, How-to, Nonfiction (General), Poetry, Regional Interests, Religion - Other, Science (General), Social Sciences, Sociology
ISBN Prefix(es): 9976-5
*Parent Company:* E A Cultural Trust
*Associate Companies:* Afropress Ltd, PO Box 30502, Nairobi

**Eastern Africa Publications Ltd**
PO Box 1002, Arusha
*Tel:* (057) 3176; (057) 26708

*Telex:* 42121 Concentre *Cable:* EAPL ARUSHA
*Key Personnel*
General Manager: Abdullah Saiwaad
Sales, Marketing: J J Kimpinga
Production: S M S Payowela
Founded: 1979
Subjects: Biography, Geography, Geology, Government, Political Science, History, Nonfiction (General), Poetry, Science (General)
ISBN Prefix(es): 9976-2
*Parent Company:* Tanzania Karatasi Associated Industries, PO Box 2418, Dar es Salaam
*Branch Office(s)*
PO Box 1408, Dar Es Salaam

**Emmaus Bible School**
PO Box 9322, Dar es Salaam
*Tel:* (061) 354500 *Fax:* (061) 350911
*E-mail:* CMML-Dodoma@maf.org
*Key Personnel*
Dir: Hansjoerg Schaerer
Contact: Anna Guttke
Specialize in correspondence courses.
Membership(s): TELM.
Subjects: Biblical Studies
ISBN Prefix(es): 9976-80
*Associate Companies:* Kanisa la Biblia (KLB) Publishers
Imprints: Emmaus Shule ya Biblia
*Branch Office(s)*
Emmaus Bible School, PO Box 9322, Dar es salaam *Tel:* (022) 2115920 *Fax:* (022) 2128767
Distributor for Everyday Publications Inc (Canada)

**Emmaus Shule ya Biblia**, *imprint of* Emmaus Bible School

**General Publications Ltd+**
PO Box 6804, Dar Es Salaam
*Tel:* (0741) 6195 85; (0741) 6231 82
*Key Personnel*
Man Dir: A A Macha
Founded: 1985
Specialize in primary level educational books for Tanzania schools & stationery sales.
Subjects: Education
ISBN Prefix(es): 9976-925
Number of titles published annually: 1 Print
Total Titles: 20 Print

**Government Printer**
PO Box 9124, Dar Es Salaam

**Inland Publishers**
PO Box 125, Mwanza
*Tel:* (068) 40064
*Key Personnel*
Dir: Rev S M Magesa
A publishing division of Africa Inland Church Literature Department.
Subjects: Nonfiction (General), Religion - Other
ISBN Prefix(es): 9976-906; 9976-70

**Institute of Kiswahili Research**
PO Box 35075, Dar Es Salaam
*Tel:* (051) 410376
*E-mail:* IKR@udsm.ac.tz
*Web Site:* www.uib.no/udsm/ucb/instiofkiswahili.html
*Key Personnel*
Dir: Prof David P B Massamba
Founded: 1930
Subjects: Language Arts, Linguistics, Literature, Literary Criticism, Essays
ISBN Prefix(es): 9976-911

**Kajura Publications**
PO Box 8692, Dar Es Salaam
*Tel:* (051) 866181

Subjects: Astrology, Occult, Government, Political Science, Science Fiction, Fantasy
ISBN Prefix(es): 9987-8855

**Kanisa la Biblia Publishers (KLB)**
Ipagala, Dodoma
Mailing Address: PO Box 1424, Dodoma
*Tel:* (026) 2354500 *Fax:* (026) 2350911
*Key Personnel*
Editor: Helmut Graef
Manager: Miss Inge Danzeisen
   *E-mail:* inge_danzeisen@yahoo.com
Founded: 1979
Specialize in Bible teaching books for lay people in Swahili.
Membership(s): TELM (Tanzania Evangelical Literature Ministry); BSAT (Booksellers Association of Tanzania).
Subjects: Biblical Studies, Religion - Protestant, Theology
ISBN Prefix(es): 9976-74
Number of titles published annually: 2 Print
Total Titles: 33 Print; 2 Audio
*Associate Companies:* Emmaus Bible School, Box 1424, Dodoma
Distributor for Emmaus Bible School

**Kisambo Publishers Ltd**
PO Box 6542, Dar Es Salaam
*Tel:* (051) 114876; (051) 131382 *Fax:* (051) 112351
Founded: 1985
Subjects: Social Sciences, Sociology, Theology
ISBN Prefix(es): 9976-978
Imprints: Kiwavi; Tuitional Structures
Distributed by Diamond Publishers (Tepusa)
Distributor for Ben Co; CBP; Readit Books

**Kiswahili**, *imprint of* Press & Publicity Centre Ltd

**Kiwavi**, *imprint of* Kisambo Publishers Ltd

**Ndanda Mission Press**
PO Box 1004, Ndana, Mtwara
*Fax:* (682) 623 730; (059) 510 410
*Key Personnel*
Manager: Fr S Hoibeck
Founded: 1934
Subjects: Fiction, History, Medicine, Nursing, Dentistry, Religion - Catholic, Religion - Other, Social Sciences, Sociology, Theology
ISBN Prefix(es): 9976-63
Imprints: Benedictine Publications Ndanda; Peramiho, Tanzania
Distributed by Peramiko Publications; Tabora Mission Press

**Northwestern Publishers+**
PO Box 277, Bukoba
Founded: 1990
Subjects: Language Arts, Linguistics, Religion - Protestant, Theology
ISBN Prefix(es): 9987-569
*Parent Company:* Evangelical Lutheran Church in Tanzania, Northwestern Diocese
Distributor for Ben & Co (Oxford); Central Tanganyika Press; Dar University; Tanzania Publishing House
*Bookshop(s):* ELCT Church Bookshop

**Nyota Publishers Ltd+**
PO Box 3574, Dar Es Salaam
*Tel:* (051) 25547; (051) 25549
*Key Personnel*
Dir & Author: P A Mcharo
Dir: E B Wilson; J E Kishada; Mrs P E McHaro
Subjects: Accounting, Business, Education, English as a Second Language, Fiction, Medicine, Nursing, Dentistry

ISBN Prefix(es): 9987-556
*Associate Companies:* Nyota Consultancy Co Ltd

**Oxford University Press**
PO Box 5299, Dar Es Salaam
*Tel:* (051) 222 116389; (051) 222 113704
   *Fax:* (051) 222 116614
*E-mail:* oxford@raha.com
*Web Site:* www.oup.com
*Key Personnel*
Manager: Salim Shaaban Salim
Founded: 1969
Subjects: Literature, Literary Criticism, Essays, Poetry
ISBN Prefix(es): 9976-4
*Parent Company:* Oxford University Press, United Kingdom

**Peramiho Publications**
PO Box 41, Peramiho
*Tel:* (054) 2730 *Fax:* (054) 2917
*Key Personnel*
Chief Executive: Fr Gerold Rupper
Contact: Bro Dominicus Weis; Bro Polycarr Stich
Founded: 1937
Local topics, printed mostly in Swahili.
Subjects: Agriculture, Religion - Other
ISBN Prefix(es): 9976-67
*Associate Companies:* Peramiho Printing Press
Subsidiaries: Benedictine Publication Ndanda/Peramiho
Divisions: Ndanda Mission Press
*U.S. Office(s):* Benedictine Priory, PO Box 528, Schuyler, NE 68661, United States *Tel:* 402-352-2127
Distributed by Ndanda Mission Press; TMP Tabora
*Bookshop(s):* Ndanda and Peramiho

**Peramiho, Tanzania**, *imprint of* Ndanda Mission Press

**Press & Publicity Centre Ltd+**
PO Box 20910, Dar Es Salaam
*Tel:* (051) 127765; (051) 122881; (051) 131078
   *Fax:* (051) 113619; (051) 116749
*Key Personnel*
International Rights: Akberali Manji
Founded: 1981
Membership(s): Publishers Association of Tanzania (PATA).
Subjects: Agriculture, Astrology, Occult, Computer Science, Education, Environmental Studies, Fiction, Geography, Geology, Health, Nutrition, Language Arts, Linguistics, Literature, Literary Criticism, Essays, Science (General)
ISBN Prefix(es): 9976-916
Total Titles: 30 Print
Imprints: Kiswahili
Distributed by Tepusa
Distributor for Africa Book Collective Ltd (UK)
*Bookshop(s):* Aggrey Street Shop, Nkrumah St, Dar Es Salaam

**Readit Books+**
NK Bldg, 5th floor, Msimbazi St/Sikukuu St, Dar es Salaam
Mailing Address: PO Box 20986, Dar es Salaam
*Tel:* (022) 2184077 *Fax:* (022) 2181077
*E-mail:* readit@raha.com
*Key Personnel*
Man Dir: Abdullah Saiwaad
Marketing Dir: Khalfan Abdallah
Founded: 1993
Subjects: Astronomy, Economics, Fiction, Science (General)
ISBN Prefix(es): 9987-21

**South African Extension Unit**
PO Box 70074, Dar Es Salaam

*Tel:* (051) 150314; (051) 150346 *Fax:* (051) 150346
*E-mail:* saeu@intafrica.com
*Web Site:* www.saide.org.za/worldbank/countries/ tanzania/saeu.htm
*Key Personnel*
Dir: Elizabeth Ligate
Founded: 1984
ISBN Prefix(es): 9976-73
Subsidiaries: South African Extension Uni


**Tanzania Library Services Board**
Unit of Ministry of Education & Culture
PO Box 9283, Dar es Salaam
*Tel:* (022) 215 09 23; (022) 215 00 48
*E-mail:* tlsb@africaonline.co.tz *Cable:* TANLIS
*Key Personnel*
Dir General: E A Mwinyimvua
Founded: 1963
Subjects: Library & Information Sciences
ISBN Prefix(es): 9976-65
*Branch Office(s)*
PO Box 1273, Arusha, Contact: Sophia M Labokhe *Tel:* (057) 502642
PO Box 321, Bukuoba, Contact: Mr Vedastus Muijage *Tel:* (066) 20460
PO Box 1900, Do Doma, Contact: John Mwelemi *Tel:* (061) 22063
PO Box 172, Iringa, Contact: Mr Metola Msusa Kanduru *Tel:* (061) 702421
PO Box 933, Kigoma, Contact: Rhoda Z Zamuye *Tel:* (0695) 3168
PO Box 443, Lindi, Contact: Geofrey Mushi *Tel:* (0525) 2156
PO Box 872, Mara/Musoma, Contact: Mr Hippolite Amin Latonge *Tel:* (068) 622183
PO Box 842, Mbeya, Contact: Emmanuel Luvands *Tel:* (065) 502589
PO Box 858, Mo Rogord, Contact: Leonard Ngowo *Tel:* (056) 602160
PO Box 863, Moshi, Contact: Mr Mariam Mundeme *Tel:* (055) 52432
PO Box 37, Mtwara, Contact: Emmanuel Herbert *Tel:* (059) 333352
PO Box 1363, Mwanza, Contact: Charles Katale *Tel:* (068) 41895
PO Box 804, Shinyanga, Contact: William Melale *Tel:* (08) 762151
PO Box 179, Songea, Contact: Mr Hezekia Chawe *Tel:* (065) 602041
PO Box 332, Sumbawanga, Contact: Peter Nkaki *Tel:* (065) 802259
PO Box 432, Tabora, Contact: Mr Carmilius C Nyigu *Tel:* (062) 3099
PO Box 5000, Tanga, Contact: Joseph Maginge *Tel:* (053) 43127


**Tanzania Publishing House+**
47 Samora Machel Ave, Dar Es Salaam
Mailing Address: PO Box 2138, Dar Es Salaam
*Tel:* (051) 32164 *Cable:* PUBLISH DAR ES SALAAM
*Key Personnel*
General Manager & International Rights: Primus Isidor Karugendo
Founded: 1966
Membership(s): Publishers Association of Tanzania-African Books Collective.
Subjects: Accounting, Agriculture, Animals, Pets, Art, Child Care & Development, Drama, Theater, English as a Second Language, Fiction, Gardening, Plants, Geography, Geology, Government, Political Science, Health, Nutrition, History, Journalism, Labor, Industrial Relations, Language Arts, Linguistics, Law, Management, Mathematics, Nonfiction (General), Photography, Physics, Poetry, Public Administration, Science (General), Sports, Athletics
ISBN Prefix(es): 9976-1
*Parent Company:* Tanzania Karatasi Associated Industries, Box 2418 DSM

**Tema Publishers Ltd+**
PO Box 63115, Dar es Salaam
*Tel:* (051) 113608 *Fax:* (051) 75422
*Key Personnel*
Chief Executive: T Maliyamkono
Founded: 1994
Membership(s): Publishers' Association of Tanzania (PATA).
Subjects: Education, Environmental Studies, Fiction, Nonfiction (General), Women's Studies
ISBN Prefix(es): 9987-25
Distributed by Tanzania Publishing House


**Tuitional Structures**, *imprint of* Kisambo Publishers Ltd


# Thailand

## General Information

*Capital:* Bangkok
*Language:* Thai is official language. English is widely used in government and commercial circles
*Religion:* Predominantly Buddhist of the Hinaya form
*Population:* 57.6 million
*Bank Hours:* 0830-1500 Monday-Friday
*Shop Hours:* Vary. Those catering to tourists generally open 0830-1800 or later
*Currency:* 100 satangs = 1 baht
*Export/Import Information:* No tariff on books but Standard Profit Tax and Business Tax apply (also a Municipal Tax of percentage of Business Tax). Advertising subject to same taxes and ad valorem percentage of import duty. No import licenses for books, but special permit required by importer for orders over a certain sum. Certificate of payment (from Exchange Control Authority) required.
*Copyright:* Berne, Florence (see Copyright Conventions, pg xi)

**Akson Charerntat (S/B Akson)**
142 Phraeng Sapphasat Tanao Rd, Bangkok 10200
*Tel:* (02) 2214587 *Fax:* (02) 2255356
*Key Personnel*
Executive Dir: Surapon Dheva-Aksorn
ISBN Prefix(es): 974-405; 974-406


**Bandansan**
136-138 Nakhon Sawan Rd, Bangkok 10100
*Tel:* (02) 825511
ISBN Prefix(es): 974-225


**Bannakhan**
236 Woeng Nakhon Khasem, Bangkok 10100
*Tel:* (02) 227796
ISBN Prefix(es): 974-350


**Bannakit Trading**
34-42 Thanon Nakhonsawan Rd, Bangkok 10100
*Tel:* (02) 2825520; (02) 2827537; (02) 2814213 *Fax:* (02) 2820076
Subjects: Agriculture, Biography, Fiction
ISBN Prefix(es): 974-220


**Chiang Mai University Library**
239 Huay Kaew Rd, Muang District, Chiang Mai 50200
*Tel:* (053) 944501 *Fax:* (053) 222766
*E-mail:* prasit@lib.cmunet.edu
*Web Site:* www.lib.cmu.ac.th

*Key Personnel*
Dir: Mr Prasit Malumpong
ISBN Prefix(es): 974-565; 974-656; 974-657; 974-658


**Chokechai Theues Shop+**
59 Tithong Rd, Bangkok 10200
*Tel:* (02) 2226660
*Key Personnel*
Man Dir: Wichai Rojjanaprapayon
Marketing Executive: Dr Wiwat Rojjanaprapayon
Founded: 1963
Subjects: Fiction, Romance, Science Fiction, Fantasy
ISBN Prefix(es): 974-420


**Office of Christian Education and Literature**, *imprint of* Suriyaban Publishers


**DK Book House Co Ltd**
904 Gp 6 Srinakarin Nong Bon Prawet, Bangkok 10260
*Tel:* (02) 721-9190 *Fax:* (02) 247-1033
*Telex:* 81198 Frtmast Th
ISBN Prefix(es): 974-210
*Parent Company:* Duang Kamon Co, Ltd
*Associate Companies:* D K Today Co, Ltd
Subsidiaries: D K Mah Boon Krong Co Ltd
Divisions: Technical Books
*Bookshop(s):* Mah Boon Krong Centre, 3rd floor, Prathumwan, Bangkok


**Duang Kamon Co Ltd**
244-246 Siam Sq, Soi 2 Pathumwan, Bangkok 10500
*Tel:* (02) 251-6335; (02) 253-1766
ISBN Prefix(es): 974-210


**Graphic Art (28) Co Ltd**
105/19-21 Nares Si Phaya Bang Rak, Bangkok 10500
*Tel:* (02) 2330302
*Telex:* 20657 Graphic Th
*Key Personnel*
Chief Executive: Mrs Angkana Sajjaraktrakul
Export Manager: H J Weber
Founded: 1972
Subjects: Biological Sciences, Chemistry, Chemical Engineering, Electronics, Electrical Engineering, Language Arts, Linguistics, Philosophy, Photography, Physics, Regional Interests, Science Fiction, Fantasy
ISBN Prefix(es): 974-295
Subsidiaries: Pandora Publishing
*Book Club(s):* Science Fiction Magazine Club


**Klang Withaya Publisher**
724-6 Mahachai Rd, Bangkok 10200
*Tel:* (02) 2224546; (02) 2219331
*Key Personnel*
Manager: Prachark Chaovanabutvilai
ISBN Prefix(es): 974-205


**New Generation Publishing Co Ltd+**
Soi Pechaburi 14, Pechaburi Rd, Rachathevee, Bangkok 10400
*Tel:* (02) 215 06747; (02) 215 0677 *Fax:* (02) 611 0400
*Key Personnel*
Chief Executive: Kiatchai Prasertsrisak
Founded: 1990
Subjects: Animals, Pets, Art, English as a Second Language, Fiction, History, Natural History, Science (General)
ISBN Prefix(es): 974-7642
*Parent Company:* The Manager Media Group Public Co Ltd


**Niyom Witthaya**
192 Thanon Bamrungmuang Rd, Bangkok 10200
*Tel:* (02) 217661
ISBN Prefix(es): 974-7278

**Non**
901 Soi Songpinong, Samrong Nua, Samutprakarn, Bangkok
*Tel:* (02) 90130
ISBN Prefix(es): 974-395

**Odeon Store LP**
860-2 Wangburapa, Phra Nakhon, Bangkok 10500
*Tel:* (02) 2210742 *Fax:* (02) 2253300 *Cable:*
Odeonstore
*Key Personnel*
Man Dir: Vichai Praepanich
Founded: 1947
Subjects: Nonfiction (General)
ISBN Prefix(es): 974-275
*Branch Office(s)*
218/10-2 Siam Sq, Soi 1 Pathum Wan, Bangkok
10330 *Tel:* (02) 2514476

**Orchid Press**
Formerly White Orchid Press
PO Box 19, Yuttitham Post Office, Bangkok
10907
Mailing Address: PO Box 31669, Causeway Bay,
Hong Kong
*Tel:* (02) 939-0973; (02) 930-0149 *Fax:* (02) 930-
5646
*E-mail:* wop@inet.co.th
*Web Site:* d30021575.purehost.com
ISBN Prefix(es): 974-8299

**Pearson Education Indochina, Ltd**
Rama 9, Suanluang, Bangkok 10250
*Tel:* (02) 731-7156-57; (02) 731-7150-51 (Hot-
line) *Fax:* (02) 731-7158
*E-mail:* cserv@pearson-indochina.com
*Web Site:* www.pearson-indochina.com
*Key Personnel*
President: Wong Wee Woon
Regional Manager: Narerat Ancharepirat *Tel:* (02)
722 7996
ELT Manager: Thansinee Thammapojsathid
ELT Marketing Executive: Udom Sathawara;
Wanida Yingsiri
Publishing Manager: Sopis Rungruangvoratus
Founded: 1998
Formed through the merger of Simon & Schuster
& Addison Wesley Longman.
*Parent Company:* Pearson Plc

**Pikkhanet Kanphim**
97-9 Soi Phrangsapasat, Tanao Rd, Bangkok
10200
*Tel:* (02) 222850
ISBN Prefix(es): 974-476

**Pracha Chang & Co Ltd**
87 Phaholyothin Rd, Bangkok 10100
Subjects: Education
ISBN Prefix(es): 974-7655

**Prasan Mit**
3382 New Phet Buri Rd, Bangkok 10310
*Tel:* (02) 3915287; (02) 3925230
ISBN Prefix(es): 974-467

**Ruamsarn (1977) Co Ltd+**
864 Burabha Palace, Mahachai Rd, Bangkok
10200
*Tel:* (02) 221-6483 *Fax:* (02) 222-2038
*Key Personnel*
Manager: Piya Taweevatanasarn
Founded: 1951
Subjects: Fiction, History
ISBN Prefix(es): 974-245

**Sangdad Publishing Company Ltd+**
320 Srivara Rd, Wangthonglang, Bangkok 10310
*Tel:* (02) 5385553; (02) 5387576 *Fax:* (02) 559-
2643; (02) 5381499

*E-mail:* sangdad@asianet.co.th
*Key Personnel*
Chief Executive: Nidda Hongwiwat *Tel:* (02) 538
5553
President: Mr Thavitong Hongvivatana
Founded: 1984
Largest cookery book publisher in Thailand.
Subjects: Art, Child Care & Development, Cook-
ery, History, Travel
Total Titles: 250 Print

**Silkworm Books+**
104/105 Chiang Mai, M 7, T Suthep, Muang,
Chiang Mai 50200
Mailing Address: POB 217, Ratchadammoen Rd,
Bangkok 10200
*Tel:* (053) 271889 *Fax:* (053) 275178
*E-mail:* silkworm@loxinfo.co.th
*Web Site:* www.silkwormbooks.info
*Key Personnel*
Publisher & Dir: Trasvin Jittidecharaks
Founded: 1991
Registered as Trasvin Publications Ltd, 54/1-5
Sridonchai Rd, Chiang Mai, Thailand.
Subjects: Asian Studies
ISBN Prefix(es): 974-7047
Distributed by University of Washington Press
(North America)

**Soemwit Bannakhan**
222 Woeng Nakhonkasemm, Bangkok 10100
*Tel:* (02) 214541
ISBN Prefix(es): 974-270

**Suksapan Panit (Business Organization of
Teachers Council of Thailand)**
Mansion 9, Rajdamnern Ave, Bangkok
*Tel:* (02) 514-4033 *Fax:* (02) 933-0182
*Web Site:* www.suksapan.or.th
*Telex:* 72031 Suksapa Th
*Key Personnel*
Dir: Kamthon Sathirakul
Founded: 1950
ISBN Prefix(es): 974-8101

**Suksit Siam Co Ltd**
113-115 Fuang Nakhon Rd, Bangkok 10200
*Tel:* (02) 2511630 *Fax:* (02) 222-5188
*E-mail:* sop@ffc.inet.co.th
*Key Personnel*
Manager, Publicity: Nilchawee Sivaraksa
Subjects: Government, Political Science, Social
Sciences, Sociology
ISBN Prefix(es): 974-260

**Suriyaban Publishers**
14 Pramuan Rd, Bangkok 10500
*Tel:* (02) 2347991; (02) 2347992 *Cable:* CCT
Office
*Key Personnel*
Man Dir: Pisnu Arkkapin
Founded: 1953
Subjects: Ethnicity, Literature, Literary Criticism,
Essays, Religion - Other
ISBN Prefix(es): 974-500
*Parent Company:* Department of Christian Educa-
tion and Literature, Church of Christ in Thai-
land
Imprints: Office of Christian Education and Liter-
ature
*Bookshop(s):* The Christian Bookstore

**Sut Phaisan**
683/8 Phra Chao Taksin Rd, Samre, Bangkok
10600
*Tel:* (02) 4682066; (02) 4675066
Subjects: Law
ISBN Prefix(es): 974-503

**Thai Watana Panich Co, Ltd+**
891 Rama One Rd, Bangkok 10330

*Tel:* (02) 215-0060-3 *Fax:* (02) 215-1360
*E-mail:* twpp@loxinfo.co.th
*Web Site:* www.twppress.com
*Key Personnel*
Man Dir: Thira T Suwan
Founded: 1935
Also acts as Distributor.
Subjects: Agriculture, Art, Biography, Educa-
tion, Government, Political Science, Health,
Nutrition, History, Language Arts, Linguistics,
Management, Marketing, Mathematics, Mu-
sic, Dance, Philosophy, Psychology, Psychiatry,
Religion - Buddhist, Science (General), Social
Sciences, Sociology
ISBN Prefix(es): 974-07
Distributor for Falcon; Kernerman; McGraw-
Hills; Oxford; Pearson Education; Wendy Pye;
Thomson Learning

**Unesco Regional Office, Asia & the Pacific**
PO Box 967, Prakhanong Post Office, Bangkok
10110
*Tel:* (02) 3910577 *Fax:* (02) 3910866
*E-mail:* bangkok@unescobkk.org
*Web Site:* www.unescobkk.org
*Telex:* 20591 *Cable:* UNESCO BANGKOK
Founded: 1961
Subjects: Communications, Education, Human
Relations, Social Sciences, Sociology
ISBN Prefix(es): 974-680

**Viratham**
141 St Louis South Sathon Rd, Bangkok 10120
*Tel:* (02) 866848
ISBN Prefix(es): 974-380

**Watthana Phanit**
216-220 Bamrung Muang, Bangkok 10200
*Tel:* (02) 2217225
ISBN Prefix(es): 974-250; 974-02

**White Lotus Co Ltd+**
GPO Box 1141, Bangkok 10501
*Tel:* (02) 332-4915; (02) 741-6288; (02) 741-6289
*Fax:* (02) 311-4575; (02) 741-6287; (02) 741-
6607
*Web Site:* www.thailine.com/lotus
*Key Personnel*
Chief Executive: D Ande *E-mail:* ande@loxinfo.
ch.th
Founded: 1972
Out-of-print, new.
Specialize in books on Asia (Southeast).
Subjects: Art, Ethnicity, Natural History, Phi-
losophy, Regional Interests, Religion - Other,
Ceramics, ecology, flora & fauna, linguistics,
performing arts, textiles
ISBN Prefix(es): 974-8495; 974-8496; 974-4800;
974-8434; 974-7534
Number of titles published annually: 30 Print

**White Orchid Press**, see Orchid Press

# Togo

## General Information

*Capital:* Lome
*Language:* French, Kabiye and Ewe are official
languages
*Religion:* About half follow traditional beliefs,
Christian (about 35%) and Muslim (about
15%).
*Population:* 4 million
*Bank Hours:* 0730-1130, 1430-1600 Monday-
Friday

*Shop Hours:* 0800-1200, 1430 or 1500-1730 or 1800 Monday-Friday; 0730-1230 Saturday
*Currency:* 100 centimes = 1 CFA franc
*Export/Import Information:* No tariff on books; advertising catalogs dutied. Additional taxes: Tax Forfaitaire, Statistical Tax, and Customs Stamp Tax of percentage of duties and added taxes; Small Wharfage Tax. Import license required for goods from non-franc zones above a certain value; from franc zone, need authorization of Togolese Government Office. Exchange controls on non-franc zone.
*Copyright:* Berne (see Copyright Conventions, pg xi)

### Editions Akpagnon+
BP 3531, Lome
*Tel:* 220244 *Fax:* 220244
*Key Personnel*
Man Dir: Yves-Emmanuel Dogbe
 *E-mail:* yedogbe@yahoo.fr
Founded: 1979
Subjects: Biography, Developing Countries, Education, Literature, Literary Criticism, Essays, Parapsychology, Philosophy, Poetry, Self-Help, Social Sciences, Sociology
ISBN Prefix(es): 2-86427
Number of titles published annually: 10 Print
Total Titles: 5 Print
*Orders to:* CMD Claude M Diffusion Ltee, 1544 rue Villeray, Montreal, QC H2E 1H1, Canada
L'Harmattan, 7 rue de l'Ecole Polytechnique, 75005 Paris, France
Nord-Sud Diffusion, 150 rue Berthelot, 1190 Brussels, Belgium
Presence Africaine, 25 bis, rue des Ecoles, 75005 Paris, France

### Editogo
BP 891, Lome
*Tel:* (08) 21-37-18 *Fax:* (08) 21-14-89
*Key Personnel*
Man Dir: Kokou Amedegnato
Founded: 1962
Subjects: Education

### Editions Haho, *imprint of* Maison d'Edition de la Librairie-Imprimerie Evangelique du Togo

### Maison d'Edition de la Librairie-Imprimerie Evangelique du Togo
One rue du Commerce, BP 378, Lome
*Tel:* (08) 214582 *Fax:* (08) 216967
*E-mail:* ctce@cafe.tg
*Key Personnel*
Dir General: F K Agbobli
Editorial: W Y Aladji; J C van de Werk
ISBN Prefix(es): 2-906718
Imprints: Editions Haho
*Bookshop(s):* Librairie Evangelique, One Rue du Commerce, Lome *Tel:* (08) 212967

### Les Nouvelles Editions Africaines du TOGO (NEA-TOGO)+
239 Bd du 13 Janvier, Lome
Mailing Address: BP 4862, Lome
*Tel:* (228) 21 67 61 *Fax:* (228) 22 10 03
*E-mail:* ctce@cafe.tg
*Telex:* 5393 NEAOM
*Key Personnel*
Dir: Yawo Agbeko Tsolenyanou; Mdme Christiane Tchotcho Ekue
Founded: 1990
Subjects: Fiction, Poetry
ISBN Prefix(es): 2-7236; 2-7412
*Parent Company:* Les Nouvelles Editions Africaines, Senegal
*Associate Companies:* Les Nouvelles Editions Africaines, Ivory Coast

### Presses de l'Universite du Benin
BP 1515, Lome
*Tel:* (228) 21 30 27 *Fax:* (228) 21 85 95
*E-mail:* cafmicro@ub.tg
*Web Site:* www.ub.tg
Subjects: Medicine, Nursing, Dentistry, Science (General)
ISBN Prefix(es): 2-909886

# Trinidad & Tobago

## General Information

*Capital:* Port-of-Spain
*Language:* English (officially). French, Spanish, Hindi and Chinese also spoken
*Religion:* Roman Catholic and Anglican, also Hindu and Muslim
*Population:* 1.3 million
*Bank Hours:* 0800-1400 Monday-Thursday; 0800-1200, 1500-1700 Friday
*Shop Hours:* 0800-1630 Monday-Friday; 0800-1200 Saturday
*Currency:* 100 cents = 1 Trinidad and Tobago dollar
*Export/Import Information:* No tariff on books; duty and postal fee on advertising matter. No import license required for books; no obscene literature permitted. Exchange controls.
*Copyright:* UCC, Berne (see Copyright Conventions, pg xi)

### Joan Bacchus-Xavier+
37 Tragarete Rd, Port-of-Spain
*Tel:* (868) 6420244 *Fax:* (868) 6251330
Founded: 1988
Subjects: Anthropology, History, Outdoor Recreation, Travel
ISBN Prefix(es): 976-8074

### Caribbean Epidemiology Centre
16-18 Jamaica Blvd, Federation Park, Port-of-Spain
Mailing Address: PO Box 164, Port-of-Spain
*Tel:* (868) 622-4261; (868) 622-4262 *Fax:* (868) 622-2792
*E-mail:* postmaster@carec.paho.org
*Web Site:* www.carec.org
*Telex:* 22308
ISBN Prefix(es): 976-8114

### Caribbean Telecommunications Union
Victoria Park Suites, 3rd floor, 14-17 Victoria Sq, Port-of-Spain
*Tel:* (868) 627-0281; (868) 627-0347 *Fax:* (868) 623-1523
*E-mail:* ctunion@c-t-u.org; secgen@c-t-u.org
*Web Site:* www.c-t-u.org
Founded: 1989
Governmental Agency responsible for telecommunications policy formulation for the Caribbean.
Subjects: Electronics, Electrical Engineering, Public Administration, Technology
ISBN Prefix(es): 976-8121

### Charran's Educational Publishers+
58 Western Main Rd, St James
*Tel:* (868) 622-3832 *Fax:* (868) 623-5829
*Telex:* 3000 Postlx Wg
*Key Personnel*
President: Mr Reginald Charran
Dir: Reginald Charran; Betty Charran
Sales: Terry R Ram
Founded: 1986
ISBN Prefix(es): 976-613

*Bookshop(s):* Charran's Arcade Book Shop, 12 Main Rd, Chaguanas *Tel:* (868) 671-1244; Charran's Bookshop, 76 Henry St, Port-of-Spain; Charran's Bookshop (1978) Ltd, 58 Western Main Rd, St James; Charran's Book Stores, 53 Eastern Main Rd, Tunapuna *Tel:* (868) 663-1884; Charran's Wholesale Center, 58 Western Main Rd, St James; Muir Marshall Ltd, 64a Independence Sq, Port-of-Spain

### Economic & Business Research
10 Flament St, Port-of-Spain
Mailing Address: PO Box 708, Port-of-Spain
*Tel:* (868) 624-5064 *Fax:* (868) 623-4137
*E-mail:* maxifill@opus.co.tt
*Web Site:* www.opus.co.tt./maxifill
ISBN Prefix(es): 976-8008

### Inprint Caribbean Ltd
35-37 Independence Sq, Port-of-Spain
*Tel:* (868) 6271569; (868) 6231711 *Fax:* (868) 6271451
*Telex:* 22661 *Cable:* EXPRESS
*Key Personnel*
Manager: Kim Morton
Founded: 1975
Subjects: Economics, Education, Government, Political Science, History, Social Sciences, Sociology
ISBN Prefix(es): 976-608
*Parent Company:* Caribbean Communications Network (CCN)
*Associate Companies:* Prime Radio 106.1 FM; CCN TV6
Subsidiaries: Trinidad Express Newspapers Ltd

### Jett Samm Publishing Ltd+
37 Newbury Hill, Glencoe
*Tel:* (868) 637-9548
*Key Personnel*
Editor-in-Chief: Nigel A Campbell
Founded: 1991
Subjects: Music, Dance, Travel
ISBN Prefix(es): 976-8106
*Parent Company:* Jett Samm Communications

### MacLean Art+
No 3 Breezy Hill Ave, Cascade, Port of Spain
*Tel:* (868) 622 8679 *Fax:* (868) 622 7583
*E-mail:* gml@wow.net
*Key Personnel*
Manager: Geoffrey MacLean
Founded: 1984
Also acts as Dealers in Fine Art.
ISBN Prefix(es): 976-8066
*Parent Company:* Geoffrey MacLean Ltd
*Associate Companies:* MacLean Publishing Ltd

### Moksha Institute of Caribbean Arts & Letters
One Sapphire Dr, Diego Martin
Mailing Address: PO Box 3254, Diego Martin
*Tel:* (868) 6374516
*Key Personnel*
Editor & President: Anson Gonzalez
Founded: 1991
ISBN Prefix(es): 976-609
Imprints: New Voices

### Multi-Media Ltd
4 Christina Court, Diego Martin
Mailing Address: PO Box 3290, Diego Martin
*Tel:* (868) 6288637; (868) 6226774 *Fax:* (868) 6281903
ISBN Prefix(es): 976-8098

### New Voices, *imprint of* Moksha Institute of Caribbean Arts & Letters

**Systematics Studies Ltd**
St Augustine Shopping Centre, Eastern Main Rd,
St Augustine
*Tel:* (868) 645-8466 *Fax:* (868) 645-8467
*E-mail:* tobe@trinidad.net
*Key Personnel*
Manager: Shirley Dookeran
ISBN Prefix(es): 976-8034
Distributor for The Brookings Institution; Inter-
American Development Bank; International
Center for Economic Growth/Institute for Con-
temporary Studies; International Monetary
Fund; Organization for Economic Co-operation
& Development; United Nations; The World
Bank; World Trade Organization

**University of the West Indies (Trinidad &
Tobago)**
St Augustine
*Tel:* (868) 662 2002; (868) 662 3232 (ext 2132)
*Fax:* (868) 663 9684
*E-mail:* infocentre@library.uwi.tt
*Web Site:* www.uwi.tt
*Telex:* (24520) (UWI-Wg) *Cable:* STOMATA
ISBN Prefix(es): 976-620

# Tunisia

## General Information

*Capital:* Tunis
*Language:* Arabic. French widely used
*Religion:* Islam
*Population:* 8.4 million
*Bank Hours:* 0800-1200/1400-1800 Monday-
Friday
*Shop Hours:* 0800-1300/1500-1900 Monday-
Saturday
*Currency:* 1,000 millimes = 1 Tunisian dinar
*Export/Import Information:* Tunisia had preferred
tariffs and EEC agreement but most books are
dutied. Advertising matter free. Custom formal-
ities tax per 1,000 kg or less gross weight, with
minimum rate. Consumption tax on and duty
tax paid of percentage of duty and tax paid.
Imports liberalized but in practice licenses
granted dependent on foreign exchange position.
*Copyright:* UCC, Berne (see Copyright Conventions, pg xi)

**Ben Abdallah Editions**
Rue 8601 ZI Charguia, 2035 Tunis
*Tel:* 71237011 *Fax:* 71786290
*Telex:* 18 074 *Cable:* KARIM TN
*Key Personnel*
General Dir: M Mohamed Sellami
ISBN Prefix(es): 9973-707

**Academie Tunisienne des Sciences, des Lettres
et des Arts Beit El Hekma** (Tunisian
Academy of Sciences, Letters & Arts)+
25, Av de la Republique Carthage, Hanibal 2016
*Tel:* 71277275; 71731696; (71) 731 824
*Fax:* 71731204
*Key Personnel*
President: Abdelwaheb Bouhdiba
Founded: 1983
Subjects: Art, Biography, Drama, Theater, Geog-
raphy, Geology, History, Journalism, Language
Arts, Linguistics, Law, Literature, Literary Crit-
icism, Essays, Mathematics, Medicine, Nursing,
Dentistry, Music, Dance, Philosophy, Physics,
Poetry, Religion - Islamic, Social Sciences, So-
ciology, Veterinary Science
ISBN Prefix(es): 9973-929; 9973-911
Distributed by Afrique Culture; Dar Souhnoun;
Demeter

**Alyssa Editions**
Rue Habib Thameur, 2026 Sidi Bou Saiid
*Tel:* 740989 *Fax:* 733659
*Key Personnel*
Dir Marketing: Sabria Beu Youssef
Founded: 1993
Subjects: Archaeology, Fiction, History, Myster-
ies, Regional Interests
ISBN Prefix(es): 9973-758

**Les Editions de l'Arbre**
17 rue 7112, El Manar II, 2092 Tunis
*Tel:* 71753209 *Fax:* 71887927
*Key Personnel*
Contact: A Beji
Founded: 1993
Subjects: Animals, Pets, Archaeology, Garden-
ing, Plants, History, House & Home, Humor,
Language Arts, Linguistics, Literature, Liter-
ary Criticism, Essays, Natural History, Outdoor
Recreation, Poetry, Publishing & Book Trade
Reference, Self-Help
ISBN Prefix(es): 9973-772

**Arcs Editions+**
32 Rue Charles de Gaulle, 1000 RP Tunis
*Tel:* 71351617
*Key Personnel*
Dir: Sihem Bensedrine
Assistant Dir: Afaf Bensedrine
Founded: 1988
Subjects: History
ISBN Prefix(es): 9973-740

**Editions Bouslama+**
15 Av de France, 1000 Tunis
*Tel:* 71245612 *Fax:* 71381100
*Telex:* 14230 *Cable:* Editions Bouslama
*Key Personnel*
Man Dir, Rights & Permissions: Ali Bouslama
Sales: Hichem Bouslama
Production: Riadh Bouslama
Publicity: Hatem Bouslama
Founded: 1960
Subjects: History
ISBN Prefix(es): 9973-714
*Branch Office(s)*
15 bis rue Lamine el Abassi, Tunis

**CAEU,** *imprint of* Maison d'Edition Mohamed
Ali Hammi

**Dar Arabia Lil Kitab**
Maison Arabe du Livre, Rue 7101, El-Manar 2
El-Menzah, 1004 Tunis
*Tel:* 71888255
*Telex:* 14966 Kitab
*Key Personnel*
Man Dir: Mahdi Ben Youssef
Founded: 1975
Subjects: Biography, Economics, Education, His-
tory, Language Arts, Linguistics, Literature,
Literary Criticism, Essays, Religion - Other
ISBN Prefix(es): 9973-10
*Parent Company:* Dar Arabia Lil Kitab, ave
Ghouma Mahmoud, BP 3185, Tripoli, Libyan
Arab Jamahiriya

**Dar El Afaq+**
4, rue Ahmed Bayram, 1006 Tunis
*Tel:* 71265904 *Fax:* 71569035
*Key Personnel*
President: Nabil Rebai
Founded: 1989
Subjects: Government, Political Science, Liter-
ature, Literary Criticism, Essays, Religion -
Islamic
ISBN Prefix(es): 9973-743
*Showroom(s):* 8, Rue Francoi, Boucher, 1006 Tu-
nis

*Bookshop(s):* 8, Rue Francoi, Boucher, Tunis
1006
*Shipping Address:* 8, Rue Francoi,, Boucher, 1006
Tunis
*Warehouse:* 8, Rue Francoi, Boucher, 1006 Tunis

**Demeter**
36 av F Bourguiba, 2036 Sidi Frej Soukra
*Tel:* 71 94 52 42; 71 94 52 46 *Fax:* 71 94 51 99
ISBN Prefix(es): 9973-706

**Faculte des Sciences Humaines et Sociales de
Tunis**
Blvd du 9 avril 1938, 1008 Tunis
*Tel:* 71560950; 71560840 *Fax:* 71567551
*Key Personnel*
Dir: Mr Habib Dlala
Founded: 1956
Arabic & Latin languages.
Subjects: Archaeology, Ethnicity, Geography, Ge-
ology, History, Language Arts, Linguistics, Lit-
erature, Literary Criticism, Essays, Philosophy,
Psychology, Psychiatry, Social Sciences, Soci-
ology
ISBN Prefix(es): 9973-922

**FTERSI,** see Publications de la Fondation
Temimi pour la Recherche Scientifique et
L'Information

**Government Printer (Imprimerie Officielle de
la Republique Tunisienne - IORT)**
Route de Rades, KM 2 Ave Farhat Hached, 2040
Rades
*Tel:* 71299914
*Telex:* 14939 TN
ISBN Prefix(es): 9973-906; 9973-946

**Maison d'Edition Mohamed Ali Hammi+**
Mohamed Chabouni, Immeuble Yamama, 3027
Nouvelle
*Tel:* 74407440 *Fax:* 74407441
*E-mail:* caeu@gnet.tn
*Key Personnel*
President: Abid Nouri
Founded: 1983
Subjects: History, Language Arts, Linguistics,
Literature, Literary Criticism, Essays, Mathe-
matics, Philosophy
ISBN Prefix(es): 9973-727
Imprints: CAEU
Distributor for Centre Culturel Arabic (Liban); El
Farabi (Liban)

**IORT (Imprimerie Officielle de la Republique
Tunisienne),** see Government Printer
(Imprimerie Officielle de la Republique
Tunisienne - IORT)

**El-M'aaref Editions**
7 rue Tunis, KM 131, 4000 Sousse
Mailing Address: PO Box 215, Sousse 4000
*Tel:* 73256235 *Fax:* 73256530
ISBN Prefix(es): 9973-16; 9973-712
*Parent Company:* Dar El Maaref

**Maison Tunisienne de l'Edition+**
36, rue Babel Khadra, Bab Souika, 1006 Tunis
*Tel:* 71345333 *Fax:* 71353992
*Telex:* Mac 12032
*Key Personnel*
Man Dir: Larbi Azouz
Founded: 1966
Subjects: Agriculture, Anthropology, Archaeol-
ogy, Biography, Drama, Theater, Education,
History, Literature, Literary Criticism, Essays,
Philosophy, Poetry, Public Administration, Re-
ligion - Islamic
ISBN Prefix(es): 9973-12

## Publications de la Fondation Temimi pour la Recherche Scientifique et L'Information
BP 50, 1118 Zaghouan
*Tel:* 72676446; 72680110 *Fax:* 72676710
*E-mail:* temimi.fond.@gnet.tn
*Web Site:* temimi.org (in Arabic); refer.org/6 (in French)
*Key Personnel*
Pres: Prof Abdeljelil Temimi
Founded: 1989
Subjects: Archaeology, History, Library & Information Sciences, Social Sciences, Sociology
ISBN Prefix(es): 9973-719
Number of titles published annually: 15 Print
Distributed by Geulhner & Rorin

**Scientifique et l'Information-TRSI**, see Publications de la Fondation Temimi pour la Recherche Scientifique et L'Information

## Sud Editions
lter, rc Bernard, Tunis 1002
*Tel:* 71798064 *Fax:* 71795260
*Telex:* 12363 TN
*Key Personnel*
Man Dir: M Masmoudi
Editorial Dir: Nabil Asswad
Founded: 1976
Subjects: Art, Literature, Literary Criticism, Essays
ISBN Prefix(es): 9973-703
*Warehouse:* La Soukra, Km 15, 2036 Tunis

## Editions Techniques Specialisees
2 bis, Rue du Reservoir Bab Menara, 1008 Tunis
*Tel:* 71262155; 71747004 *Fax:* 71746160
*E-mail:* info@pagesjaunes.com.tn
*Key Personnel*
International Rights: Hajer Djilani
Founded: 1978
ISBN Prefix(es): 9973-711
Subsidiaries: Redaction

## Societe Tunisienne de Diffusion
5, av de Carthage, 1000 RP Tunis
*Tel:* 71255000; 71261799 *Cable:* Studiffusion
ISBN Prefix(es): 9973-11

# Turkey

## General Information

*Capital:* Ankara
*Language:* Turkish
*Religion:* Predominantly Sunni Moslem
*Population:* 63.9 million
*Bank Hours:* 0900-1730 Monday-Friday
*Shop Hours:* 0800-1900 Monday-Saturday
*Currency:* Turkish lira
*Export/Import Information:* Books, magazines and similar publications are freely imported. International copyright laws enforced. 1% VAT on books.
*Copyright:* Berne, Florence (see Copyright Conventions, pg xi)

## ABC Kitabevi AS
Tunel Meydani 1, 80030 Beyoglu, Istanbul
*Tel:* (0212) 27 62 404; (0212) 28 51 860
*Telex:* 24094 Abck Tr
*Key Personnel*
Man Dir: Artun Altiparmak
Editorial: Oender Renkliyildirim
Sales: K Karakush
Production: Hasan Guenaydin
Publicity: Ferit Guersu
Rights & Permissions: Necip Inselel

Founded: 1976
Subjects: Education
ISBN Prefix(es): 975-09

## Ada Press Publishers+
Istiklal Cd, 475/479 Kat 3, Beyoglu, Istanbul
*Tel:* (0212) 243 1778; (0212) 243 1779
*Fax:* (0212) 249 3545
*Key Personnel*
Editor: Mr Ferit Edgue
Founded: 1976
ISBN Prefix(es): 975-438

## Afa Yayincilik Sanayi Tic AS+
Istiklal Cad. Bekar Sk No 17, Taksim, Istanbul
*Tel:* (0212) 276 27 67 *Fax:* (0212) 2444362
*Key Personnel*
President: Atil Ant
International Rights: Dilek Basak
Founded: 1985
Subjects: Biography, Child Care & Development, Drama, Theater, Film, Video, Government, Political Science, Nonfiction (General)
ISBN Prefix(es): 975-414
Distributed by DaDa Ltd
*Bookshop(s):* AFA Kitabevi, Istiklal Cad, Bekar Sok No 17, Beyoglu/Istanbul

## Akdeniz Yayincilik+
100 y1 Mah Matbaacilar Ve Ambarcilar Sitesi No 83, Bagcilar, Istanbul
*Tel:* (0212) 629-0026 *Fax:* (0212) 629-0027
*Key Personnel*
President: H Mursit Ul
Editor: Filiztekin Ferhan
Founded: 1995
Specialize in geographical atlases, school books & dictionaries.
ISBN Prefix(es): 975-6780
*Parent Company:* Altin Kitaplar Yayinevi Ve Ticaret As

## Alkim Kitapcilik-Yayimcilik+
Za Zafer Carsisi 14, Kizilay/Ankara
Membership(s): Basar Arslan.
Subjects: Astrology, Occult, Business, Child Care & Development, Computer Science, Cookery, Crafts, Games, Hobbies, Drama, Theater, Economics, Finance, How-to, Law, Management, Marketing, Microcomputers, Nonfiction (General), Psychology, Psychiatry, Sports, Athletics
ISBN Prefix(es): 975-337

## Altin Kitaplar Yayinevi
Celal Ferdi G Sk Nebioglu Han No 7/1, 34440 Cagaloglu, Istanbul
*Tel:* (0212) 5206246; (0212) 5201588; (0212) 5268010 *Fax:* (0212) 5120266
*E-mail:* info@altinkitaplar.com.tr
*Web Site:* www.altinkitaplar.com.tr
*Key Personnel*
Vice President: Mursit Ul
Publisher: Batu Bozkurt
Production: Erden Heper
Editorial: Alpar Oya
Founded: 1959
Subjects: Criminology, Economics, Fiction, History, Nonfiction (General), Philosophy, Psychology, Psychiatry, Regional Interests, Science Fiction, Fantasy
ISBN Prefix(es): 975-7620
*Showroom(s):* Celal ferdi Goekcay SK, Nebio Is Hani, Istanbul

## Arkadas Ltd+
Mithatpasa Cad No 28, Yenisehir, Ankara
*Tel:* (0312) 434 46 24 *Fax:* (0312) 435 60 57
*Key Personnel*
Chairman & Owner: Cumhur Ozdemir
*E-mail:* cumhuro@arkadas.com.tr

Editor: Meltem Ozdemir *E-mail:* meltemo@arkadas.com.tr
Founded: 1979
Specialize in computer books, textbooks; also acts as Book Distributors, Bookshop. Authorized software replicator of Microsoft Co In MENA (Middle East & North Africa).
Subjects: Animals, Pets, Computer Science, Cookery, English as a Second Language, Environmental Studies, Mathematics, Music, Dance, Physics
ISBN Prefix(es): 975-509
Number of titles published annually: 100 Print
Total Titles: 300 Print
Distributor for Microsoft Press
Foreign Rep(s): Microsoft Press (Turkey)
*Bookshop(s):* ODTUU Alisveris Merkezi, Ankara

## Arkeoloji Ve Sanat Yayinlari (Archaeology & Art Publications)+
Hayriye Cad, Corlu Apt 3/4, 80060 Galatasaray, Istanbul
*Tel:* (212) 293 0378 *Fax:* (212) 245 6877
*E-mail:* info@arkeolojisanat.com
*Web Site:* www.arkeolojisanat.com
*Key Personnel*
Publisher: Nezih Basgelen
*E-mail:* nezihbasgelen@superonline.com
Senior Editor: Brian Johnson
*E-mail:* brianjohnson@superonline.com
Founded: 1978
Since 1978 Arkeoloji ve Sanat Yayinlari (Archaeology & Art Publications) has been publishing books on archaeology, history, & art history of Turkey. With titles in Turkish, English, German & French, the company's list includes publications ranging from specialized scholarly monographs to popular guides to Turkey's famed tourist sites. Besides books, the press publishes a bimonthly journal, Arkeoloji ve Sanat, presenting the academic contributions of the world's leading scholars of Anatolian archaeology & art.
Subjects: Anthropology, Antiques, Archaeology, Architecture & Interior Design, Art, History, Photography, Travel
ISBN Prefix(es): 975-7538; 975-6899
Number of titles published annually: 20 Print
Total Titles: 100 Print

## Arkin Kitabevi
Ankara Cad No 60, 34410 Sirkeci, Istanbul
*Tel:* (0212) 522 92 24; (0212) 541 36 20
*Fax:* (0212) 512 19 01
*Telex:* 28362 Rga Tr *Cable:* BIRARKINLAR ISTANBUL
*Key Personnel*
Owner: Ramazan Goikalp Arkin; Mefra Arkin
Dir: Tarik Kinali
Founded: 1942
Subjects: Education, Science (General)
ISBN Prefix(es): 975-402

## Ataturk Kultur, Dil ve Tarih, Yusek Kurumu Baskanligi
Ataturk Bulvan No 217, 06680 Kavaklidere, Ankara
*Tel:* (0312) 428 61 00 *Fax:* (0312) 428 52 88
*E-mail:* bim@tdk.gov.tr
*Web Site:* www.tdk.gov.tr
*Key Personnel*
President: Prof Utkan Kocatuerk, PhD
Subjects: Archaeology, Ethnicity, History, Language Arts, Linguistics
ISBN Prefix(es): 975-16
*Branch Office(s)*
Atatuerk Research Ce
Turkish Culture Center
Turkish Historical Society
Turkish Language Society

**Ataturk Universitesi+**
25240 Erzurum
*Tel:* (0442) 231 11 11 *Fax:* (0442) 236 10 14
*E-mail:* ata@atauni.edu.tr
*Web Site:* www.atauni.edu.tr/
*Key Personnel*
Foreign Relations Coordinator: Dr Erol Cakmak
Founded: 1957
ISBN Prefix(es): 975-442

**Aydin Yayincilik+**
Nasuhi Akar Mahallesi, 1 Cad 25 SK No 12 A,
   Balgat/Ankara
*Tel:* (0312) 2873402; (0312) 2873403 *Fax:* (0312)
   2873402
Subjects: Mathematics, Science (General)
ISBN Prefix(es): 975-7948
Subsidiaries: Aydin Web Tesisleri (printing)
*Book Club(s):* Yayincilar Birligi
*Warehouse:* 100 yil Bolvari, Gl sok, No 29, Os-
   tim

**Bilden Bilgisayar** (Bilden Computer,
   Programming, Digital Publishing Ltd)
Ziverbey Kasap Ismail Sok, Sadikoglu Ys
   Merkezi No 13 Buro No 41, 81040 Kadikoy/Is-
   tanbul
*Tel:* (0216) 449 52 50 *Fax:* (0216) 449 52 51
*E-mail:* bilden@bilden.com.tr
*Web Site:* www.bilden.com.tr
*Key Personnel*
General Manager: Sukru Korman
Specializes in the development of educational
   software on CD-ROM for ages 3-18.
Subjects: Education, Language Arts, Linguistics,
   Mathematics, Science (General), Social Sci-
   ences, Sociology
Distributor for Encyclopedia Britannica Co; Lang-
   Master

**Birsen Yayinevi+**
Cagaloglu Yokusu Evren Carsisi No 29/13, 34440
   Cagaloglu, Istanbul
*Tel:* (0212) 5278578; (0212) 5220829 *Fax:* (0212)
   5270895
*Web Site:* www.geocities.com/birsen2us; www.
   birsenyayin.com
*Key Personnel*
President: Mr Cengiz Algin
Vice President: Mr Bahadir Algin
Founded: 1973
ISBN Prefix(es): 975-511

**Caglayan Kitabevi+**
Istiklal Cad 166, Tokatlyyan Yp hany Kat 1 No
   7-8-9-21 Beyoglu, Istanbul
*Tel:* (0212) 2454433 *Fax:* (0212) 1491794
*E-mail:* info@caglayan.com
*Key Personnel*
President: Tuncay Caglayan
Founded: 1962 (Publishing since 1952)
Subjects: Chemistry, Chemical Engineering,
   Civil Engineering, Electronics, Electrical En-
   gineering, Engineering (General), Management,
   Mathematics, Mechanical Engineering, Physics,
   Technology, Technical Books
ISBN Prefix(es): 975-436
*Associate Companies:* Caglayan Basimevi, Catal-
   cesme Sokak 26, Cagaloglu, Istanbul; Caglayan
   Yayinev, PK 517, Beyoglu, Istanbul

**CEP Kitaplari AS**, *imprint of* Varlik Yayinlari
   AS

**Cep Kitaplari AS+**
Imprint of Varlik Yayinlari AS
Piyerloti Cad Ayberk Ap 7-9, Cemberlitas, 34400
   Istanbul
*Tel:* (0212) 516 20 04 *Fax:* (0212) 516 20 05
*Web Site:* www.varlik.com.tr

*Key Personnel*
Editor-in-Chief: Osman Cetin Deniztekin
   *Tel:* (0212) 516 20 04 (ext 13) *E-mail:* varlik@
   isbank.net.tr
Founded: 1982
Membership(s): Turkish Publishers Association.
Subjects: Fiction, Nonfiction (General), Religion
   - Islamic, Science (General), Science Fiction,
   Fantasy, Women's Studies
ISBN Prefix(es): 975-480
Number of titles published annually: 5 Print
Total Titles: 60 Print
Distributed by Varlik Yayinlari AS

**Dergah Yayinlari AS**, see Ezel Erverdi (Dergah
   Yayinlari AS) Muessese Muduru

**Dokuz Eylul Universitesi**
Cumhuriyet Buluari No 144, Alsancak, 35210
   Izmir
*Tel:* (0232) 498 5050-51 *Fax:* (0232) 464 8135
*E-mail:* hukuk@deu.edu.tr
*Web Site:* www.deu.edu.tr
Founded: 1982
ISBN Prefix(es): 975-441

**Dost Kitabevi Yayinlari+**
Karanfil Sokak 29/4, 06650 Kizilay Ankara
*Tel:* (0312) 418 8772 *Fax:* (0312) 419 9397
*Key Personnel*
Chief Executive Officer: Erdal Akalin *Tel:* (0312)
   4252464 *Fax:* (0312) 4180355
Gen Mgr: Gunay Okumus *Tel:* (0312) 4188327
   *Fax:* (0312) 4180355
Dir: Raul Mansur *E-mail:* raulman@domi.net.tr
Editor-in-Chief: Levent Yilmaz *E-mail:* levent@
   easynet.fr
Founded: 1979
Chain of bookshops. Started publishing books
   in 1997. Co-editions with Dorling Kindersley,
   Franco Maria Ricci.
Membership(s): Turkish Publishers Association.
Subjects: History, Social Sciences, Sociology,
   Travel, Translated fiction
ISBN Prefix(es): 975-7501
Number of titles published annually: 60 Print
Total Titles: 80 Print
*Branch Office(s)*
105 Rue de l'Ouest, Paris, France, Mr Levent
   Yilmaz *Tel:* (01) 45410907 *E-mail:* levent@
   easynet.fr
*Orders to:* Dost Dagitim, Bayindir sokak 40/
   B, Kizilay Ankara 06650, Murat Duman
   *Tel:* (0312) 4324868 *Fax:* (0312) 4357596

**Dost Yayinlari**
Tunel Gecidi Ishanib Blok 9/210, Beyoglu, Istan-
   bul 80050
*Tel:* (0212) 245 31 41 *Fax:* (0212) 243 02 78
*Key Personnel*
Dir: Salim Sengil
Marketing Manager: Asli Sengil Cansever
Founded: 1947
Subjects: Art, Humor, Literature, Literary Criti-
   cism, Essays
ISBN Prefix(es): 975-95481; 975-7499

**Eren Yayincilik ve Kitapcilik Ltd Sti+**
Tunel, Istiklal Cad, Sofyali Sok No 34, 80050
   Beyoglu-Istanbul
*Tel:* (0212) 251-2858; (0212) 252-0560
   *Fax:* (0212) 243-3016
*E-mail:* eren@turk.net
Founded: 1983
Subjects: Engineering (General)
ISBN Prefix(es): 975-7622
*Associate Companies:* Ottomania
*Branch Office(s)*
Istanbul

**Ezel Erverdi (Dergah Yayinlari AS) Muessese
   Muduru**
Ankara Cd Pamir Han 54/3, 34410 Sirkeci, Istan-
   bul
*Tel:* (0212) 519 04 21; (0212) 516 00 47
   *Fax:* (0212) 519 04 21
*E-mail:* bilgi@dergahyayinlari.com
*Web Site:* www.dergahyayinlari.com
*Key Personnel*
Man Dir: Ezel Erverdi
Editorial: Mustafa Kutlu
Sales: Fatih Gokdag
Production: Kara Ismail
Publicity: Ashihan Erverdi
Founded: 1977
Subjects: Education, Ethnicity, Government, Polit-
   ical Science, History, Literature, Literary Criti-
   cism, Essays, Philosophy
ISBN Prefix(es): 975-7462; 975-7032
Subsidiaries: Ulke Yayin Haber Tic Ltd Sti; Emek
   matbaacilik ve ilancilik Ltd Sti
*Bookshop(s):* Ulke Yayin Haber Tic Ltd Sti,
   Ankara cad No 41/A Uygurhan Sirheci list

**Iki Nokta Arastirma Basin Yayin Sanayi ve
   Ticaret Ltd Sti**, *imprint of* IKI Nokta Research
   Press & Publications Industry & Trade Ltd

**IKI Nokta Research Press & Publications
   Industry & Trade Ltd+**
Moda Cad Usakligil Apt No 180/10, 81300
   Kadikoy, Istanbul
*Tel:* (0216) 349 01 41 *Fax:* (0216) 337 67 56
*E-mail:* ikinokta@superonline.com; ikinokta@
   turkinfo.com; ikinokta@gisoturkey.com;
   ikinokta @turkgis.com; ikinokta@infoturk.com
*Web Site:* www.ikinokta.com
*Key Personnel*
President: Yuecel Yaman
International Rights: Kerem Ahmet
Founded: 1986
Specialize in database updating.
Subjects: Archaeology, Communications, Geogra-
   phy, Geology, History
ISBN Prefix(es): 975-340
Number of titles published annually: 130 Print; 5
   CD-ROM; 1 Online; 1 E-Book
Imprints: Iki Nokta Arastirma Basin Yayin Sanayi
   ve Ticaret Ltd Sti

**Iletisim Yayinlari+**
Klodfarer Cad Iletisim Han Cagaloglu, 34122 Is-
   tanbul
*Tel:* (0212) 516 22 60 *Fax:* (0212) 516 12 58
*E-mail:* iletisim@iletisim.com.tr
*Web Site:* www.iletisim.com.tr
*Key Personnel*
Contact: Nihat Tuna; Osman Yener
Founded: 1984
Subjects: Ethnicity, Fiction, Government, Political
   Science, History, Literature, Literary Criticism,
   Essays, Nonfiction (General), Philosophy, Sci-
   ence Fiction, Fantasy, Social Sciences, Sociol-
   ogy
ISBN Prefix(es): 975-470
*Associate Companies:* Birikim Yayinlari
*Branch Office(s)*
Selanik Cad 64/11 Yenisehir, 06640 Ankara
Bodrum
Ismir

**Imge Kitabevi**
Konur Sokak No 17/12, 06650 Kizilay, Ankara
*Tel:* (0312) 419 46 10; (0312) 419 46 11
   *Fax:* (0312) 425 65 32
*E-mail:* imge@www.imge.com.tr
*Web Site:* www.imgekitabevi.com
*Key Personnel*
Contact: Refik Tabakci
ISBN Prefix(es): 975-533
*Parent Company:* IImge Kitabevi Ltd
Divisions: IImge Kitabevi Yayinlari

**Inkilap Publishers Ltd+**
Ankara Cad No 99 Kat 1, 34410 Sirkeci, Istanbul
*Tel:* (0212) 5140611; (0212) 5140610 *Fax:* (0212) 5140612
*E-mail:* info@inkilap.com
*Web Site:* www.inkilap.com
*Key Personnel*
Man Dir: Nazar Fikri; Julia Fikri; Errol Fikri
Foreign Rights: Sema Diker *E-mail:* sdiker@inkilap.com
Founded: 1935
Subjects: Animals, Pets, Archaeology, Art, Business, Child Care & Development, Cookery, Drama, Theater, Economics, Electronics, Electrical Engineering, Fiction, Gardening, Plants, Humor, Management, Mathematics, Music, Dance, Philosophy, Photography, Physics, Poetry, Psychology, Psychiatry, Religion - Islamic
ISBN Prefix(es): 975-10
*Parent Company:* Anka Offset AS, Teknografik Matbaacilik AS, Ankara Cad 95, Sirkeci, Istanbul
*Associate Companies:* Inkas, Ingilizce Nesriyat Kitapcilik AS, Ankara Cad 95, Sirkeci, Istanbul
*Branch Office(s)*
Yeni Zaman Kitabevi, Ankara Cad 155, Sirkeci, Istanbul (correspondence to Inkilap)
*Bookshop(s):* Koerfez Mah Carrefour Ticaret Merkezi B-36, Ismit *Tel:* (0262) 335 31 91 *Fax:* (0262) 335 40 25; Yeni Havaalani Cad No 40 Kipa Alisveris Merkezi Cigli, Izmir *Tel:* (0232) 386 50 70 *Fax:* (0232) 386 50 70; Inkilap Mah B061 Carrefour Ticaret merkezi Uemraniye, Istanbul *Tel:* (0216) 525 12 95 *Fax:* (0216) 525 12 97; 100 Yil Mah 100 Evler Mevkii Carrefour Ticaret Merkezi B-51, Adana *Tel:* (0322) 256 54 65 *Fax:* (0322) 256 53 82

**Isis Yayin Tic ve San Ltd+**
Semsibey Sok 10, Beylerbeyi, 81210 Beylerbeyi/Istanbul
*Tel:* (0216) 3213851; (0216) 3213847; (0216) 3213847 *Fax:* (0216) 3218666
*E-mail:* isis@turk.net
*Key Personnel*
Dir: Sinan Kuneralp
Publishing: S Helvacioglu
Founded: 1983
Subjects: History, Social Sciences, Sociology
ISBN Prefix(es): 975-428

**Kiyi Yayinlari+**
Koca Aga Sokak No 6/1, 80060 Beyoglu, Istanbul
*Tel:* (0212) 245 58 45 *Fax:* (0212) 245 40 09
*E-mail:* sbeygu@ibm.net
*Key Personnel*
Editor & Founder: Sahin Beygu *E-mail:* sbeygu@ibm.net
Founded: 1989
Membership(s): T Yay-Bir (Turkish Publishers Association).
Subjects: Fiction, Literature, Literary Criticism, Essays, Nonfiction (General), Poetry
ISBN Prefix(es): 975-444

**Kok Yayincilik+**
Incesu Cad, No 67, 06670 Kolej/Ankara
*Tel:* (0312) 434472 *Fax:* (0312) 4350497
*E-mail:* kokbilgi@kokyayincilik.com.tr
*Web Site:* www.kokyayincilik.com.tr
*Key Personnel*
International Rights: Celal Musaoglu
Founded: 1987
Subjects: Animals, Pets, Child Care & Development, Education, Health, Nutrition, House & Home, Human Relations, Mathematics, Music, Dance
ISBN Prefix(es): 975-499
Imprints: Offset

**Kubbealti Akademisi Kultur ve Sasat Vakfi+**
Peykhane Sk No 3, 34400 Cemberlitas, Istanbul

*Tel:* (0212) 516 23 56; (0212) 518 92 09 *Fax:* (0212) 517 14 60
*Key Personnel*
International Rights: Mrs Semahat Yuksel
Founded: 1978
Subjects: Architecture & Interior Design, Art, Biography, Environmental Studies, History, Literature, Literary Criticism, Essays, Music, Dance, Religion - Islamic, Culture
ISBN Prefix(es): 975-7663
Distributor for Istanbul Fetih Cemiyeti's Editions
*Bookshop(s):* Yeniceriler Cad No 43, 34490 Carsikapi, Istanbul

**Metis Yayinlari** (Metis Publishers)+
Ipek Sk No 9, 34433 Beyoglu, Istanbul
*Tel:* (0212) 245 45 19; (0212) 2454696 *Fax:* (0212) 2454519
*E-mail:* bilgi@metiskitap.com
*Web Site:* www.metisbooks.com
*Key Personnel*
International, Foreign Rights: Ms Muege Guersoy Soekmen
Founded: 1982
Membership(s): Turkish Publishers' Association. Publisher of Psychiatry, Literature, Politics & Philosophy. Also acts as Verso agent in Turkey.
Subjects: Literature, Literary Criticism, Essays, Nonfiction (General), Philosophy, Poetry, Psychology, Psychiatry, Science Fiction, Fantasy, Social Sciences, Sociology, Western Fiction, Women's Studies, Political Studies
ISBN Prefix(es): 975-342; 975-7650
Number of titles published annually: 40 Print
Total Titles: 540 Print

**Nurdan YayinlariSanayi ve Ticaret Ltd Sti+**
Prof Kazim Ysmail Guerkan Cad No 13 Kat 1, Cagaloglu-Istanbul
*Tel:* (0212) 522 55 04; (0212) 513 86 53 *Fax:* (0212) 512 51 86
*E-mail:* nurdan@nurdan.com.tr
*Web Site:* www.nurdan.com.tr
*Key Personnel*
Owner: Cetin Tuezuener
Dir: Nurdan Tuezuener
Editor: Cigdem Tuzuner
Founded: 1980
Membership(s): Turkish Publishers' Association.
Subjects: Regional Interests
ISBN Prefix(es): 975-527
Subsidiaries: Meydan Larousse Co; Nu-Do Publishing Distribution Co

**Offset**, *imprint of* Kok Yayincilik

**Oguz Yayinlari**
Babiali Cad 30/7, 34410 Cagaloglu, Istanbul
*Tel:* (0212) 5264745; (0212) 5113418 *Fax:* (0212) 5114695
*Key Personnel*
Editor: Sevgili Turan
Subjects: Religion - Islamic, Theology
ISBN Prefix(es): 975-538

**Pan Yayincilik+**
Barbaros Bulvari, 74/4, Besiktas, 80700 Istanbul
*Tel:* (0212) 2618072; (0212) 2275675 *Fax:* (0212) 2275674
*E-mail:* pan@pankitap.com
*Web Site:* www.pankitap.com
*Key Personnel*
Contact: Ferruh Gencer
Founded: 1986
Subjects: Fiction, Music, Dance, Science (General)
ISBN Prefix(es): 975-7652

**Parantez Yayinlari Ltd+**
Istiklal Cad 212, Alt Kat no 8, Beyoglu, Istanbul
*Tel:* (0212) 252 85 67 *Fax:* (0212) 252 85 67

*E-mail:* parantez@parantez.net
*Web Site:* www.geocities.com/parantez
*Key Personnel*
International Rights: Metin Zeynioglu
Founded: 1991
Membership(s): Turkish Publishers Association & Turkish Pen Club.
Subjects: Biography, Fiction, Film, Video, Gay & Lesbian, Humor
ISBN Prefix(es): 975-7939

**Payel Yayinevi+**
Cagaloglu Yokusu Evren Han Kat 4 No 63, Cagaloglu, Istanbul
*Tel:* (0212) 511 82 33; (0212) 512 43 53
*E-mail:* shemsa@ttnet.net.tr *Cable:* PAYEL YAYINEVI-CAGALOGLU-ISTANBUL
*Key Personnel*
Editor & Owner: Ahmet Ozturk
Founded: 1966
Membership(s): Publishers Association of Turkey; Cumhuriyet Book Club.
Subjects: Archaeology, Film, Video, History, Literature, Literary Criticism, Essays, Psychology, Psychiatry, Science (General), Social Sciences, Sociology, Women's Studies
ISBN Prefix(es): 975-388
*Book Club(s):* Cumhuriyet Book Club

**Pearson Education Turkey+**
Koza Is Merkezi, "B" Blok Kat 4, Murbasan Sok Balmumcu, Istanbul
*Tel:* (0212) 288 6941 *Fax:* (0212) 267 1851
*E-mail:* firstname.lastname@pearsoned-ema.com
*Web Site:* www.pearsoneduc.com
*Key Personnel*
Regional Dir, East Med/Arab World: Christine Ozden
Sales Dir, East Med/Arab World: Necip Inselel
Founded: 1995
Branch offices in Adana, Ankara, Antalya, Bursa, & Izmir.
Subjects: English as a Second Language
ISBN Prefix(es): 975-7015
*Parent Company:* Pearson Education
*Ultimate Parent Company:* Pearson Plc
*Branch Office(s)*
Ankara
Adana
Antalya
Bursa
Izmir
Distributor for Langenscheidt

**Redhouse Press+**
SEV Matbaacilik ve Yayincilik AS, Rizapasa Yokusu No 50 Mercan, 34450 Istanbul
*Tel:* (0212) 520 7778; (0212) 520 2960; (0212) 520 0090 *Fax:* (0212) 522 1909
*E-mail:* info@redhouse.com.tr; sales@redhouse.com.tr
*Web Site:* www.redhouse.com.tr
*Telex:* 23554 Peettr
*Key Personnel*
Co-Dir: Cerina Logico Blakney; Richard Blakney
Editor: Charles Brown; Serap Bezmez
Sales: Sait Sermet
Founded: 1822
Subjects: Education
ISBN Prefix(es): 975-413
*Bookshop(s):* Redhouse Boolesbave

**Remzi Kitabevi+**
Selvili Mescit Sok No 3, 34440 Cagaloglu, Istanbul
*Tel:* (0212) 522 05 83; (0212) 519 09 81; (0212) 513 94 74; (0212) 513 94 75 *Fax:* (0212) 522 90 55
*E-mail:* post@remzi.com.tr
*Web Site:* www.remzi.com.tr *Cable:* REMZI KITABEVI ISTANBUL
*Key Personnel*
Man Dir: Erol Erduran

Dir: Ahmet Erduran
Production Manager: Oemer Erduran
Founded: 1927
Subjects: Art, Biography, Education, Fiction, History, Nonfiction (General), Philosophy, Psychology, Psychiatry, Science (General), Social Sciences, Sociology
ISBN Prefix(es): 975-14
Subsidiaries: Evrim Matbaacilik Ltd
*Bookshop(s):* Etiler Istanbul *Tel:* (0212) 282 2575 76 *Fax:* (0212) 282 2577; 44 Rumeli Caddesi, Nisantasi, Istanbul *Tel:* (0212) 234 5475-76 *Fax:* (0212) 232 5934; Erenkoy, Istanbul *Tel:* (0212) 448 0373-74 *Fax:* (0212) 448 0375; Akatlar, Istanbul *Tel:* (0212) 352 3355 *Fax:* (0212) 352 3356; Mecidiyekoy, Istanbul *Tel:* (0212) 217 1225 *Fax:* (0212) 216 8288; 452 Bagdat Cad, Suadiye, Istanbul *Tel:* (0212) 368 1491-92 *Fax:* (0212) 368 1467

**Ruh ve Madde Yayinlari ve Saglik Hizmetleri AS** (Spirit & Matter Publications)+
4/8 80060, Hasnun Galip Sok Pembe Cikmazi, Beyoglu, Istanbul
*Tel:* (0212) 2431814 *Fax:* (0212) 2520718
*E-mail:* bilyay@bilyay.org.tr
*Web Site:* www.ruhvemadde.com
*Key Personnel*
Foreign Rights: Yasemin Tokatli
Founded: 1994
Subjects: Alternative, Astrology, Occult, Earth Sciences, Nonfiction (General), Parapsychology, Philosophy, Religion - Islamic, Religion - Other, Self-Help
ISBN Prefix(es): 975-8007
Number of titles published annually: 25 Print
Total Titles: 300 Print
*Parent Company:* Foundation for Spreading the Knowledge to Unify Humanity
*Associate Companies:* Society for Research on the Nature of the Human Individual
Distributed by EGE META
Distributor for EGE META, META

**Sabah Kitaplari**+
Istiklal Cad No 192, Beyoglu, Istanbul
*Tel:* (0212) 5028410; (0212) 5028319
*Key Personnel*
Contact: Serpil Demirtas *E-mail:* sdemirtas@sabah.com.tr
Founded: 1974
Subjects: Biography, Business, Criminology, History, Management, Nonfiction (General)
ISBN Prefix(es): 975-579
*Associate Companies:* Suereli Yayinlar AS, Bueyuekdere Cad, Levent, Istanbul *Tel:* (01) 692420 (Periodical Press Inc)

**Saray Medikal Yayin Tic Ltd Sti**+
168 Sok No 5-7, Bornova, Izmir
*Tel:* (0232) 3394969 *Fax:* (0232) 3733700
*E-mail:* eozkarahan@novell.cs.eng.dev.edu.tr
*Key Personnel*
Contact: Cetin Gultekin
Founded: 1993
Membership(s): Turkish Publishers Association.
Subjects: Behavioral Sciences, Child Care & Development, Computer Science, Engineering (General), Medicine, Nursing, Dentistry, Philosophy, Self-Help, Social Sciences, Sociology
ISBN Prefix(es): 975-7816; 975-7074
*Parent Company:* Saray Medikal Yayin Sar ve Tic Ltd Sti
Subsidiaries: Bassaray Printing

**Seckin Yayinevi**+
Saglik Sok 19-B, 06410 Sihhiye, Ankara
*Tel:* (0312) 4353030 *Fax:* (0312) 4352472
*E-mail:* satis@seckin.com.tr
*Web Site:* www.seckin.com.tr
*Key Personnel*
International Rights: Koray Seckin

Founded: 1959
Membership(s): Turkish Publishers Association.
Subjects: Accounting, Computer Science, Economics, Law
ISBN Prefix(es): 975-347
Number of titles published annually: 70 Print
Total Titles: 233 Print

**Soez Yayin/Oyunajans**+
4 Gazeteciler Sitesi, C-2 D 9 Levent, 80630 Istanbul
Mailing Address: P K 7 Levent, 80622 Istanbul
*Tel:* (0212) 2806701 *Fax:* (0212) 2806803
*Web Site:* www.oyunajans.com
*Key Personnel*
Contact: Mr Hueseyin Nevzat Erkmen
*E-mail:* nerkmen@turk.net; Mr Ali Erkmen
*E-mail:* aerkmen.@turk.net
Founded: 1983
Specialize in translations of Turkish literature into English.
Subjects: Advertising, Alternative, Art, Business, Career Development, Crafts, Games, Hobbies, Fiction, Film, Video, Finance, Health, Nutrition, How-to, Management, Psychology, Psychiatry, Self-Help
ISBN Prefix(es): 975-7190; 975-95491
Total Titles: 50 Print

**Toker Yayinlari**+
Ankara cad 46/14, 34420 Sirkeci, Istanbul
*Tel:* (0212) 5223309
*Key Personnel*
President: Mr Yalcin Toker
Founded: 1962
Membership(s): Turkish Publishers Association.
Subjects: Ethnicity, History, Literature, Literary Criticism, Essays
ISBN Prefix(es): 975-445
*U.S. Office(s):* C E M Toker, PO Box 39652, Phoenix, AZ 85069, United States

**Toros Yayinlari Ltd Co**
Yenicarsi Cad Luks Apt 33/1, 80050 Galatasaray, Istanbul
*Tel:* (0212) 2444155 *Fax:* (0212) 2452858; (0212) 2444155
*Key Personnel*
Author: Ali Neyzi
Editor: Rasit Goekceli *E-mail:* rgokceli@escortnet.com; Sahin Beygu
Founded: 1981
Subjects: Literature, Literary Criticism, Essays
ISBN Prefix(es): 975-433

**Turkish Republic - Ministry of Culture**+
Ataturk Bulvari No 29, 06050 Opera Ankara-Turkiye
*Tel:* (0312) 309 08 50 *Fax:* (0312) 312-4359
*E-mail:* yayimlar@kutuphanelergm.gov.tr
*Web Site:* www.kultur.gov.tr
*Key Personnel*
Dir, Publications Dept: Ali Osman Guzel
Founded: 1973
Subjects: Archaeology, Art, Drama, Theater, History, Literature, Literary Criticism, Essays
ISBN Prefix(es): 975-17
Distributed by Dosimm

**Varlik Yayinlari AS**+
Piyerloti Cad Ayerberk Ap 7-9, Cemberlitas, 34400 Istanbul
*Tel:* (0212) 5162004 *Fax:* (0212) 5162005
*E-mail:* varlik@varlik.com.tr; varlik@isbank.net.tr
*Web Site:* www.varlik.com.tr
*Key Personnel*
Publisher: Osman Deniztekin *Tel:* (0212) 5162004 (ext 13) *E-mail:* osmand@netscape.net
Founded: 1946
Membership(s): Turkish Publishers Association.

Subjects: Fiction, Nonfiction (General), Poetry, Science (General), Self-Help, Social Sciences, Sociology, Women's Studies
ISBN Prefix(es): 975-434
Number of titles published annually: 20 Print
Total Titles: 200 Print
Imprints: CEP Kitaplari AS
Distributor for CEP Kitaplari AS

**Yapi-Endustri Merkezi Yayinlari-Yem Yayin**+
Cumhuriyet Cad 329, 34367 Harbiye, Istanbul
*Tel:* (0212) 2193939 *Fax:* (0212) 2256623
*E-mail:* yem-od@yunus.mam.tubitak.gov.tr; yem@yem.net
*Web Site:* www.yem.net
*Key Personnel*
President: Dogan Hasol
Deputy General Manager: Bulent Kumral
*E-mail:* bulent_kumral@yem.net
Founded: 1968
Also acts as bookshop & book importer.
Membership(s): UICB.
Subjects: Architecture & Interior Design, Art, Civil Engineering
ISBN Prefix(es): 975-7438; 975-8599
Distributor for Melissa (Greece)

**Kabalci Yayinevi**
Himaye-i Etfal Sok, Kredi Han No 81B K3, Istanbul
*Tel:* (0212) 526 8586 *Fax:* (0212) 523 6305
*E-mail:* yayinevi@kabalcy.com.tr
*Web Site:* www.turkyaybir.org.tr/kabalci.html
*Key Personnel*
Owner: Sabri Kabalci
Dir: Mustafa Kuepuesodlu
Founded: 1984
Subjects: Anthropology, Archaeology, Art, Drama, Theater, Fiction, History, Literature, Literary Criticism, Essays, Nonfiction (General), Philosophy, Poetry, Science (General), Social Sciences, Sociology, ABC series; contemporary French thought
ISBN Prefix(es): 975-7942
*Bookshop(s):* Ortabahce Cad 22/4, Besiktas-Istanbul

**Alev Yayinlari**+
Ercelik Is Hani No 54/102, 34110 Eminonu, Istanbul
*Tel:* (0212) 519 5635 *Fax:* (0212) 292 1017
*E-mail:* bilgi@alevyayinlari.com; yayinlar@alevyayinlari.com
*Key Personnel*
Contact: Alev Yayinlari *E-mail:* yayinlar@alevyayinlari.com
Founded: 1989
Specialize in Alevite-Islamic Culture & Philosophy.
Subjects: Ethnicity, Government, Political Science, Literature, Literary Criticism, Essays
ISBN Prefix(es): 975-335
*Parent Company:* Genel Ajans Ltd
Distributed by Baris; Papiruea; Say; Yoen
Distributor for CAN; Pencere
*Book Club(s):* Cumhuriyet Book Club

**Yetkin Printing & Publishing Co Inc**+
Strazburg Cad No 31/A, Sihhiye/Ankara
*Tel:* (0312) 4181273; (0312) 2314234
*Fax on Demand:* (0312) 4174388
*Key Personnel*
President, Editor: Y Ziya Gwlkok
Founded: 1984
Subjects: Accounting, Computer Science, Law, Management
ISBN Prefix(es): 975-464
Divisions: Kazimkarahekir Cd (Printing)
*Bookshop(s):* Gulkok Bookstore, Kocabeyoglu Pst 74, Kizilay, Ankara

**Yuce Reklam Yay Dagt AS+**
PK 76, 34492 Beyazit, Istanbul
*Tel:* (01) 5227506 *Fax:* (01) 5163959
*Telex:* 22418 NEKTR
*Key Personnel*
Dir: Fahri Savasci; Ali Seven; Munip Oniz
Founded: 1982
Subjects: Computer Science, Electronics, Electrical Engineering, Medicine, Nursing, Dentistry
ISBN Prefix(es): 975-411
Subsidiaries: A F M Yayincilik-Tanitim
*Warehouse:* Dizdariye Cesme Sok 6 Emre Han, Kat: 1, Sultanahmet, 34400 Istanbul
*Orders to:* Yuce Yayin AS, PK 40 Beyazit, 34492 Istanbul

# Turkmenistan

## General Information

*Capital:* Ashkhabad
*Language:* Turkmen
*Religion:* Predominantly Sunni Muslim
*Population:* 3.8 million
*Bank Hours:* Generally open for short hours between 0930-1230 Monday-Friday
*Shop Hours:* Generally 0900-1800 Monday-Friday; often open weekends
*Currency:* 23 marats = 1 US dollar
*Export/Import Information:* Companies engaged in trade should register with the Turkmenistan Ministry of Foreign Affairs.

**Izdatelstvo Turkmenistan**
ul Kulieva 31, 744013 Aschabad
*Tel:* 68283
*Key Personnel*
Dir: A M Dzhanmuradov
Chief Editor: A Allanazarov
Founded: 1965
Turkmenistan Publishing House.
Subjects: Agriculture, Fiction, Government, Political Science, Science (General), Social Sciences, Sociology
ISBN Prefix(es): 5-87228

# Uganda

## General Information

*Capital:* Kampala
*Language:* English is official language
*Religion:* Predominantly Christian (about 60%) and some Muslim
*Population:* 19.4 million
*Bank Hours:* 0830-1400 Monday-Friday
*Shop Hours:* 0830-1230, 1400-1630 or longer; 0800-1230 Saturday
*Currency:* 100 cents = 1 new Uganda shilling
*Export/Import Information:* No tariff on books or advertising matter but subject to sales tax. Import license and exchange controls (granted automatically with import licenses).

**Centenary Publishing House Ltd+**
PO Box 6246, Kampala
*Tel:* (041) 241599 *Fax:* (041) 250427
*Key Personnel*
Man Dir, Editorial, Production, Rights & Permissions: Rev Sam Kakiza
Sales, Publicity: V Kagga-Senyonga
Founded: 1977
Subjects: Education, Religion - Other

ISBN Prefix(es): 9970-9004
*Parent Company:* Church of Uganda, PO Box 14123, Kampala

**Centre for Basic Research**
Affiliate of Network of Ugandan Researchers & Research Users (NURRU)
15 Baskerville Ave, Kololo
Mailing Address: PO Box 9863, Kampala
*Tel:* (041) 231228; (041) 235533; (041) 342987 *Fax:* (041) 235413
*E-mail:* cbr@cbr-ug.org
*Web Site:* www.cbr-ug.org
*Key Personnel*
Executive Dir: Dr Bazaara Nyangabyaki
Senior Assistant Librarian: Judith Akello
Founded: 1988
New publications covering topics on Civil Society, Human Rights, Foreign Investment, Taxation Federalism in Uganda, Trade Unions & Gender. Formed a partnership with ActionAid to undertake critical case studies on the Relevance, Access, Quality & Equity Dimensions of Universal Primary Education (UPE) in Uganda.
Membership(s): CODESRIA.
Subjects: Agriculture, Environmental Studies, Ethnicity, Geography, Geology, Government, Political Science, History, Labor, Industrial Relations, Law, Social Sciences, Sociology, Women's Studies, Social Sciences, Humanities
Total Titles: 121 Print

**Fountain**, *imprint of* Fountain Publishers Ltd

**Fountain Publishers Ltd+**
Fountain House, 55 Nkrumah Rd, Kampala
Mailing Address: PO Box 488, Kampala
*Tel:* (041) 259163; (041) 251112; (031) 263041; (031) 263042 *Fax:* (041) 251160
*E-mail:* fountain@starcom.co.ug
*Web Site:* www.fountainpublishers.co.ug
*Key Personnel*
Board Chairman & Man Dir: James Tumusiime
Business Manager: Moses Mugasa
Publishing Editor: Alex Bangirana
Marketing Manager: Paul Waddimba
Founded: 1988
Membership(s): Uganda Publishers & Booksellers Association (UPABA); African Publishers Network (APNET).
Subjects: Agriculture, Anthropology, Biography, Career Development, Cookery, Economics, Education, Fiction, Government, Political Science, Health, Nutrition, History, Humor, Language Arts, Linguistics, Mathematics, Nonfiction (General), Physical Sciences, Poetry, Psychology, Psychiatry, Science (General), Social Sciences, Sociology, Travel, Women's Studies
ISBN Prefix(es): 9970-02
Number of titles published annually: 30 Print
Total Titles: 400 Print
Imprints: Fountain
Distributed by African Books Collective (ABC) (Australia, Europe, UK & USA); James Currey Ltd (UK)
Distributor for James Currey Ltd (UK); Food Agricultural Organization (FAO) (Italy); Christopher Hurst (UK); Lion Publishers Plc (UK); Oxfam GB (UK); Princeton University Press; Scholastic Inc (USA); Zed Books Ltd (UK)
Foreign Rep(s): The African Books Collective (ABC) (Australia, Commonwealth, Europe, North America)
Foreign Rights: The African Books Collective (ABC) (Australia, Commonwealth, Europe, North America)
*Bookshop(s):* Bookpoint Ltd, PO Box 488, Kampala, Contact: Sara Namirembe *Tel:* (041) 346742 *Fax:* (041) 251160 *E-mail:* fountain@

starcom.co.ut; University Bookshop Makerere, Contact: Catherine Tugaineyo *Tel:* (041) 543442

**Roce (Consultants) Ltd**
PO Box 1481, Kampala
*Tel:* (041) 106010 *Fax:* (041) 321062
*Web Site:* www.rutaagi.com
*Key Personnel*
Man Dir: Mr Robert K Rutaagi
Operations Dir: Celia K Rutaagi
Consulting Dir: Prof Ben Kiregyera
Founded: 1984
General business, consultancy & publishing. Specialize in poetry & Swahili.
Membership(s): Uganda Publishers Booksellers Association.
Subjects: Business, Management, Marketing, Poetry, Epigrams, Sayings, Swahili
ISBN Prefix(es): 9970-402
Number of titles published annually: 1 Print
Total Titles: 6 Print
*Associate Companies:* Roce Textiles & General Merchandise, Luwum St, Entebbe Airport, Kampala
*Bookshop(s):* Uganda Bookshop; Mukono Bookshop

**T & E Publishers+**
PO Box 5784, Kampala
*Tel:* (041) 542207 *Fax:* (041) 542207
*Key Personnel*
Chief Executive: Tobias Karindiriza
Subjects: Natural History
ISBN Prefix(es): 9970-9001

# Ukraine

## General Information

*Capital:* Kiev
*Language:* Ukrainian
*Religion:* Predominantly Christian (mostly Ukrainian Orthodox)
*Population:* 52 million
*Bank Hours:* Generally open for short hours between 0930-1230 Monday-Friday
*Shop Hours:* Generally 0900-1800 Monday-Friday; often open weekends
*Currency:* 100 kopeks = 1 rubl
*Export/Import Information:* According to Ukrainian quotas and customs duties, companies engaged in trade should register with the Ukraine Ministry of Foreign Economic Relations. 28% VAT on books. Licenses for export and import are also required for trade with Russia.
*Copyright:* UCC (see Copyright Conventions, pg xi)

**ASK Ltd+**
3 Nesterova St, Kyiv 03057
Mailing Address: 2b Shamrylo-Str, PO Box 62, Kyiv 04112
*Tel:* (044) 241-94-96; (044) 456-72-51 *Fax:* (044) 455-58-89
*E-mail:* ask.sale@i.com.ua
*Key Personnel*
Executive Dir: Lebedyev Oleg *E-mail:* ask.main@i.com.ua
Founded: 1991 (Founded by Lebedyev Oleg, Motzny Oleg, Sologub Igor, Sythevsky Oleg & Zyporucha Anatoliy)
Subjects: Accounting, Astrology, Occult, Biblical Studies, Business, Career Development, Child Care & Development, Computer Science, Cookery, Economics, English as a Second Language, Fiction, Gardening, Plants, Law, Mar-

keting, Microcomputers, Nonfiction (General), Parapsychology, Science Fiction, Fantasy, Social Sciences, Sociology, Western Fiction
ISBN Prefix(es): 966-539
Number of titles published annually: 230 Print
Total Titles: 750 Print
*Bookshop(s):* 2 Sheljabov Str, 03057 Kyiv

**Derzhavne Naukovo-Vyrobnyche Pidpryemstro Kartografia** (State Scientific & Production Enterprise Kartographia)+
54 Popudrenka Str, Kyiv 02094
*Tel:* (044) 5524033 *Fax:* (044) 2388314
*E-mail:* admin@ukrmap.com.ua
*Web Site:* www.ukrmap.com.ua
*Key Personnel*
Dir: Rostyslav Sossa
Editor-in-Chief: Iryna Rudenko
Commercial Manager: Olexander Zacheshygryva
Founded: 1944
Development, production & realization of cartographic production.
Subjects: Geography, Geology
*Parent Company:* State Service of Geodesy, Cartography & Cadastre of Ukraine
*Ultimate Parent Company:* Ministry of Environment & Natural Resources of Ukraine
Distributed by Cartotravel (Germany); Kiwi Book Shop (Czech Republic); Omni Resources (US); Sklep Podroznika, InterMap (Poland)
Distributor for Freytag (Austria); GiziMap (Hungary); Hallwag (Switzerland); Ravenstein (Germany)

**Dnipro**
42 Volodymyrska St, Kyiv 01034
*Tel:* (044) 224-31-82 *Fax:* (044) 224-41-57
*Key Personnel*
Dir: Mr Taras I Serhiychuk
Editor-in-Chief: S K Zholob
Founded: 1919
Subjects: Fiction, Literature, Literary Criticism, Essays, Folk-lore, modern Ukranian & foreign authors, world classics
ISBN Prefix(es): 5-308; 966-578

**Kamenyar**
3 Pidvalna St, Lviv 79000
*Tel:* (0322) 72-19-49 *Fax:* (0322) 72-19-49
*Key Personnel*
Dir: Mr Dmytro I Sapiha
Brochures, "Dzvin" magazine, wholesale of printed materials.
ISBN Prefix(es): 5-7745; 966-7255; 966-607

**Lybid (University of Kyyiv Press)+**
10 Khreshchatyk St, Kyiv 01001
*Tel:* (044) 228-11-12; (044) 228-11-81 *Fax:* (044) 229-11-71
*Telex:* 131498 PTB SU
*Key Personnel*
Dir: Ms Olena O Boyko
Heritage of Ukranian people, national-cultural rebirth of independent Ukraine. Famous series: "Monuments of Historical Thought of Ukraine", "Literary Monuments of Ukraine.
Subjects: Education, Literature, Literary Criticism, Essays, Science (General)
ISBN Prefix(es): 5-325

**Mystetstvo Publishers+**
11 Zolotovoritska St, Kyiv 01034
*Tel:* (044) 235-43-13; (044) 224-91-01 *Fax:* (044) 229-05-64
*Key Personnel*
Dir: Nina D Prybyeha
Founded: 1932
Subjects: Art, Drama, Theater, Ethnicity, Film, Video, History, Literature, Literary Criticism, Essays, Travel
ISBN Prefix(es): 5-7715; 966-577

**Naukova Dumka Publishers**
Division of National Acedemy of Sciences of Ukraine
Ul Tereshchenkivska 3, Kiev 01601
*Tel:* (044) 2244068; (044) 2251042; (044) 2254170 *Fax:* (044) 2247060
*E-mail:* ndumka@ukrpost.net
*Key Personnel*
Dir & Editor-in-Chief: Alexeenko Igor
Founded: 1922
Subjects: Agriculture, Biological Sciences, Chemistry, Chemical Engineering, Computer Science, Earth Sciences, Economics, Environmental Studies, Geography, Geology, Health, Nutrition, History, Language Arts, Linguistics, Law, Literature, Literary Criticism, Essays, Mathematics, Mechanical Engineering, Medicine, Nursing, Dentistry, Natural History, Philosophy, Photography, Physical Sciences, Psychology, Psychiatry
ISBN Prefix(es): 966-00
Number of titles published annually: 60 Print
Total Titles: 12 Print
Distributed by ASK; Oberegi Publishers; Osnova

**Osnova, Kharkov State University Press+**
Ul Universitetskaya 16, Harkiv 61005
*Tel:* (057) 224647
*Key Personnel*
Man Dir: Nikolay N Sorokun *Tel:* (057) 219268
Dir: Valery K Gorbat'ko
Founded: 1949
Subjects: Aeronautics, Aviation, Agriculture, Archaeology, Architecture & Interior Design, Biological Sciences, Business, Chemistry, Chemical Engineering
ISBN Prefix(es): 5-7768

**Osnovy Publishers+**
5/18 Lykhachov Blv, Kyiv 01133
*Tel:* (044) 295 25 82; (044) 295 86 36 *Fax:* (044) 295 25 82; (044) 295 86 36
*E-mail:* osnovy@ukrnet.net
*Key Personnel*
Dir: Ms Valentyna Kyrylova
Rights Contact: Victor Ruzhitsky
Founded: 1993
Subjects: Business, Economics, Finance, Government, Political Science, History, Law, Management, Philosophy, Poetry, Public Administration, Social Sciences, Sociology, Women's Studies
ISBN Prefix(es): 966-500
Total Titles: 150 Print

**Osvita** (Education)
Prosp Chornovola 4, 1st floor, Lviv 79019
Mailing Address: PO Box 1596, Lviv 79019
*Tel:* (032) 297 1206 *Fax:* (032) 297 1794
*E-mail:* info@osvita.org
*Web Site:* www.osvita.org
*Key Personnel*
Center Dir: Andriy Hatalyak
Center Advisor: Angelina Belyakova
Founded: 1993
Membership(s): Pan Educational Publishers Club (PEP-Club).
Subjects: Biological Sciences, Chemistry, Chemical Engineering, Child Care & Development, Education, English as a Second Language, History, Literature, Literary Criticism, Essays, Mathematics, Music, Dance, Physical Sciences, Physics, German, French
ISBN Prefix(es): 966-04
Number of titles published annually: 108 Print
Total Titles: 500,000 Print

**Urozaj**
vul Uryc Kogo 45, Kiev 03035
*Tel:* (044) 2450995 *Fax:* (044) 2450995
*Key Personnel*
Dir: Vasily G Prikhodko

Subjects: Agriculture, Environmental Studies, Gardening, Plants, House & Home, Technology, Veterinary Science
ISBN Prefix(es): 5-337; 966-05

**Veselka Publishers+**
63 Melnykova St, Kyiv 04655
*Tel:* (044) 213-95-01; (044) 213-33-59 *Fax:* (044) 213-33-59
*E-mail:* veskiev@iptelecom.net.ua
*Key Personnel*
Dir: Mr Yarema P Hoyan
Founded: 1934
Subjects: Fiction, Literature, Literary Criticism, Essays
ISBN Prefix(es): 5-301; 966-01
*Bookshop(s):* Toronto, Canada; Prague, Czech Republic; Frankfurt am Main, Germany; Munich, Germany; Chicago, United States

# United Arab Emirates

## General Information

*Capital:* Abu Dhabi
*Language:* Arabic and English
*Religion:* Islamic
*Population:* 2.23 million
*Bank Hours:* 0800-1200 Saturday-Thursday (1100 Thursday in Abu Dhabi)
*Shop Hours:* Abu Dhabi: Summer: 0800-1300, 1600-dusk Saturday-Thursday; Winter: 0800-1300, 1530-1900 Saturday-Thursday. Northern Emirates: Summer: 0900-1300, 1630-2000 or 2100 Saturday-Thursday: Winter: 0900-1300, 1600-2000 or 2100 Saturday-Thursday
*Currency:* 100 fils = 1 UAE dirham
*Export/Import Information:* No tariff on books or advertising matter, except duty on imports in Dubai and ad valorem rates in Ras al Khaimah anf Sharjah. No import licenses requires except for obscene publications in Dubai.

**Arabian Heritage Books,** *imprint of* Motivate Publishing

**Department of Culture & Information Government of Sharjah**
Cultural Book Round About, Air Port Rd, Sharjah
Mailing Address: PO Box 5119, Sharjah
*Tel:* (06) 5671116; (06) 5673139 *Fax:* (06) 5662126; (06) 5660535
*E-mail:* shjbookfair@hotmail.com; cultural@emirates.net.ae
*Web Site:* shjbookfair.gov.ae
*Telex:* 68508 TOURSH *Cable:* THAQAFA
*Key Personnel*
Head: Mr Issam Bin Saqr Al Qassimi
Founded: 1982
Subjects: Poetry, Regional Interests

**Gulf Business Books,** *imprint of* Motivate Publishing

**Motivate Publishing+**
PO Box 2331, Dubai
*Tel:* (04) 282 4060 *Fax:* (04) 282 4436
*E-mail:* motivate@motivate.ae
*Web Site:* www.booksarabia.com
*Key Personnel*
Man Partner: Ian Fairservice
Founded: 1981
Subjects: Biography, Business, Cookery, Foreign Countries, History, Natural History, Travel
ISBN Prefix(es): 1-873544; 1-86063

Imprints: Arabian Heritage Books; Gulf Business Books
Subsidiaries: Stewart's Court
*Orders to:* Book Representation & Distribution Ltd, 244A London Rd, Hadleigh, Essex S57 2DE, United Kingdom *Tel:* (020) 7552912 *Fax:* (020) 7556095

# United Kingdom

## General Information

*Capital:* London
*Language:* English; Welsh in most of Wales (where it is used alongside English for official purposes). About 80,000 speak Scots Gaelic (in Highlands and Islands of Scotland). Irish is used in parts of Northern Ireland
*Religion:* Protestant (The Church of England) officially, Roman Catholic, Methodist, United Reformed and Baptist have significant numbers of adherents
*Population:* 57.8 million
*Bank Hours:* 0900-1730 Monday-Friday
*Shop Hours:* 0900-1730 Monday-Saturday
*Currency:* 100 pence = 1 pound sterling
*Export/Import Information:* Member of the European Union. No tariffs on books; advertising matter dutiable over a certain weight. No import licenses required; nominal exchange controls. Advertising in the UK is regulated by statutes and voluntary codes; for information contact The Advertising Standards Authority Ltd, Torrington Place, London, WC1E 7HW.
*Copyright:* UCC, Berne, Florence (see Copyright Conventions, pg xi)

**A A Publishing+**
Carr Ellison House, William Armstrong Dr, New Castle-upon-Tyne NE4 7YA
*Tel:* (01256) 491522 *Fax:* (0191) 235 5111
*E-mail:* aapublish@theaa.com
*Web Site:* www.theaa.com; www.aanewsroom.com
*Telex:* 858538 AA BASG
*Key Personnel*
Editorial Dir: Michael Buttler *Tel:* (01250) 491573 *E-mail:* michael.buttler@theaa.com
Man Dir: John Howard
Sales & Marketing Manager: Graham Sowerby
Founded: 1908
Subjects: Travel
ISBN Prefix(es): 0-86145; 0-7495; 0-901088
Total Titles: 530 Print
*Parent Company:* AA
*Warehouse:* T B S Ltd, Brantham, Near Manningtree, Essex CO11 1NW, Mr Colchester *Tel:* (01206) 255804 *Fax:* (01206) 255848

**A & C**, *imprint of* Helm Information Ltd

**A-Mail Academic**
City Bridge House, 57 Southwark St, London SE1 1RU
*Tel:* (020) 7871 9139 *Fax:* (020) 7871 9140
*E-mail:* a-mail@djlb.co.uk
*Web Site:* www.a-mail.co.uk
*Key Personnel*
Division Manager: Duncan Copplestone *E-mail:* dcopplestone@djlb.co.uk
Business Development Executive: Vivienne Medway *E-mail:* vmedway@djlb.co.uk

Sales Account Executive: Ian Wordsworth *E-mail:* iwordsworth@djlb.co.uk
Sales Administrator: James Murtagh *E-mail:* jmurtagh@djlb.co.uk
Supplier of targeted worldwide academic & library mailing lists & data.
*Parent Company:* Dudley Jenkins Group plc ("Your partners in academic marketing")

**Abacus**, *imprint of* Time Warner Book Group UK

**Abbotsford Publishing+**
2A Brownsfield Rd, Lichfield WS13 6BT
*Tel:* (01543) 255749; (01543) 258903
*Web Site:* www.abbotsfordpublishing.com
*Key Personnel*
Partner: Kathy Simmons *E-mail:* ka.simmons@btopenworld.com; Howard Clayton
Founded: 1992
Membership(s): Independent Publishers Guild.
Subjects: History, Maritime, Natural History, Poetry, Regional Interests, Travel, Local History, Mind/Body/Spirit
ISBN Prefix(es): 1-899596; 0-9503563
Number of titles published annually: 3 Print; 3 Online
Total Titles: 12 Print; 12 Online

**ABC-CLIO+**
35A Great Clarendon St, Oxford OX2 6AT
*Tel:* (01865) 311350 *Fax:* (01865) 311358
*E-mail:* oxford@abc-clio.ltd.uk
*Web Site:* www.abc-clio.com
*Key Personnel*
Editorial: Simon Mason; Robert G Neville *E-mail:* bneville@abc-clio.ltd.uk
Marketing Manager: Suzanne Wheatley *E-mail:* swheatley@abc-clio.ltd.uk
Sales: Deborah Porter *E-mail:* dporter@abc-clio.ltd.uk
Founded: 1971
Specialize in abstracting services & bibliographies in print & electronic formats.
Subjects: Anthropology, Foreign Countries, History, Literature, Literary Criticism, Essays, Sports, Athletics
ISBN Prefix(es): 0-87436; 1-57607; 0-903450; 1-85109
Number of titles published annually: 18 Print; 10 CD-ROM; 1 E-Book
Total Titles: 350 Print; 30 CD-ROM; 3 E-Book
*Parent Company:* ABC-CLIO, 130 Cremona Dr, PO Box 1911, Santa Barbara, CA 93117, United States
Foreign Rep(s): DA Information Services Pty Ltd (India, South Africa); Disvan Enterprises (India); Andrew Durnell (Austria, Belgium, Croatia, Cyprus, Czech Republic, Denmark, Netherlands, Estonia, Finland, France, Germany, Greece, Hungary, Iceland, Italy, Latvia, Lithuania, Luxembourg, Malta, Monaco, Norway, Poland, Russia, Serbia and Montenegro, Slovak Republic, Slovenia, Sweden, Switzerland, Bosnia and Herzegovina); Iberian Book Services (Gibraltar, Portugal, Spain); Phambili Agencies CC (South Africa); Publishers Marketing Services Ltd (Brunei, Malaysia, Singapore); Publishers International Marketing (Asia, Middle East); I J Sagun Enterprises, Inc (Guam, Micronesia, Philippines); United Publishers Services Ltd (Japan)
*Warehouse:* Plymbridge Distributors Ltd, Estover Rd, Plymouth PL6 7PZ
*Orders to:* Plymbridge Distributors Ltd, Estover Rd, Plymouth PL6 7PZ *Tel:* (01752) 202301 *Fax:* (01752) 202333 *E-mail:* orders@plymbridge.com

**Abington Publishing**, *imprint of* Woodhead Publishing Ltd

**Absolute Press+**
Scarborough House, 29 James St W, Bath BA1 2BT
*Tel:* (01225) 316 013 *Fax:* (01225) 445 836
*E-mail:* info@absolutepress.co.uk
*Web Site:* www.absolutepress.co.uk
*Key Personnel*
Man Dir, Publisher & International Rights: Jon Croft
Publicity: B Douglas
Founded: 1979
Also acts as agent in UK & Europe for Smith and Kraus & Streetwise Maps.
Subjects: Biography, Cookery, Gay & Lesbian, Travel, Wine & Spirits
ISBN Prefix(es): 0-948230; 0-9506785; 1-899791
Foreign Rep(s): Troika (UK)
*Distribution Center:* BHB International Inc, 302 West North Second St, Seneca, SC 29678, United States *Tel:* (864) 885-9444 *Fax:* (864) 885-1090 *E-mail:* bhbrackett@bellsouth.net
*Web Site:* www.bhbinternational.com (USA)
Central Books, 99 Wallis Rd, London E9 5LN *Tel:* (020) 8986 4854 *Fax:* (020) 8533 5821 *E-mail:* info@centralbooks.com
Peribo Pty Ltd, 58 Beaumont Rd, Mt Kuring-Gai, NSW 2080, Australia *Tel:* (02) 9457 0011 *Fax:* (02) 9457 0022 *E-mail:* peribomec@bigpond.com (Australia & New Zealand)

**Academic Press**, *imprint of* Elsevier Ltd

**Acair Ltd+**
7 James St, Stornoway, Isle of Lewis HS1 2QN
*Tel:* (01851) 703 020 *Fax:* (01851) 703 294
*E-mail:* enquiries@acairbooks.com
*Web Site:* www.acairbooks.com
*Key Personnel*
Chairman: Angus MacDonald
Founded: 1978
Publish a wide range of Gaelic, English & Bilingual books.
Subjects: Biography, Environmental Studies, Fiction, History, Poetry
ISBN Prefix(es): 0-86152

**Access Press**, *imprint of* HarperCollins UK

**Ace Books**, see Age Concern Books

**Acorn Editions**, *imprint of* James Clarke & Co Ltd

**Acorn Editions**, *imprint of* The Lutterworth Press

**Act 3 Publishing+**
67 Upper Berkeley St, London W1H 7QX
*Tel:* (020) 7402 5321
*Key Personnel*
Contact: R Keith Brian
Founded: 1985
Membership(s): Independent Publishers Guild.
Subjects: Alternative, Child Care & Development, Fiction, Film, Video, Human Relations, Humor, Nonfiction (General), Poetry, Psychology, Psychiatry, Self-Help
ISBN Prefix(es): 0-948068
Number of titles published annually: 1 Print
Total Titles: 1 Print

**Actinic Press**, *imprint of* Cressrelles Publishing Company Ltd

**Actinic Press Ltd+**
Imprint of Cressrelles Publishing Company Ltd
10 Station Rd, Industrial Estate, Colwall, Malvern WR13 6RN
*Tel:* (01684) 540154 *Fax:* (01684) 540154
*Key Personnel*
Man Dir: Leslie Smith
Founded: 1926
Specialize in Chiropody.

ISBN Prefix(es): 0-900024
Total Titles: 1 Print
*Parent Company:* Cressrelles Publishing Co Ltd

**ACU**, see Association of Commonwealth Universities (ACU)

**Acumen Publishing Ltd+**
15A Lewins Yard, East St, Chesham, Bucks HP5 1HQ
*Tel:* (01494) 794398 *Fax:* (01494) 784850
*Web Site:* www.acumenpublishing.co.uk
*Key Personnel*
Publisher: Steven Gerrard *E-mail:* steven. gerrard@acumenpublishing.co.uk
Founded: 1998
Independent publisher of academic books in philosophy, history & politics for students, lecturers & researchers in institutions of higher education worldwide.
Subjects: History, Philosophy
ISBN Prefix(es): 1-902683; 1-84465
Number of titles published annually: 20 Print
Total Titles: 60 Print
*Shipping Address:* Marston Book Services, 160 Milton Park, Abingdon, Oxon OX14 4YN
*Warehouse:* Marston Book Services, 160 Milton Park, Abingdon, Oxon OX14 4YN
*Distribution Center:* Marston Book Services, 160 Milton Park, Abingdon, Oxon OX14 4YN
*Orders to:* Marston Book Services, 160 Milton Park, Abingdon, Oxon OX14 4YN
*Returns:* Marston Book Services, 160 Milton Park, Abingdon, Oxon OX14 4YN

**Adam Matthew Publications**
Pelham House, London Rd, Marlborough, Wilts SN8 2AA
*Tel:* (01672) 511921 *Fax:* (01672) 511663
*E-mail:* info@ampltd.co.uk
*Web Site:* www.adam-matthew-publications.co.uk
*Key Personnel*
Dir: William Pidduck *E-mail:* adam_matthew@ msn.com; David Tyler *E-mail:* amp_david@ msn.com
Founded: 1990
Original manuscript collections, rare printed books & other primary source material in microform & electronic format.
Subjects: African American Studies, Asian Studies, Economics, Ethnicity, History, Music, Dance, Religion - Other, Science (General), Social Sciences, Sociology, Technology, Women's Studies
ISBN Prefix(es): 1-85711
Number of titles published annually: 1 CD-ROM; 1 Online
Distributed by Maruzen Co Ltd (Japan only)
Foreign Rep(s): Maruzen Co Ltd (Japan); Transmission Books Co Ltd (Taiwan)

**Adamantine Press Ltd+**
Richmond Bridge House, 417-421 Richmond Rd, Twickenham TW1 2EX
*Key Personnel*
Dir: Jeremy Geelan
Founded: 1976
Subjects: Business, Communications
ISBN Prefix(es): 0-7449
*Warehouse:* Central Books Ltd, 99 Wallis Rd, London E9 5LN
*Orders to:* Central Books Ltd, 99 Wallis Rd, London E9 5LN

**Addison-Wesley**, *imprint of* Pearson Education Europe, Mideast & Africa

**Adelphi Papers**, *imprint of* International Institute for Strategic Studies

**Adlard Coles Nautical+**
Imprint of A & C Black Publishers Ltd
37 Soho Sq, London W1D 3QZ
*Tel:* (020) 7758 0200 *Fax:* (020) 7758 0222
*E-mail:* acn@acblack.com
*Web Site:* www.adlardcoles.com
*Key Personnel*
Dir: Janet Murphy
Rights Dir: Paul Langridge
Founded: 1947
Specialize in nautical books for the leisure market.
Subjects: Outdoor Recreation, Sports, Athletics
ISBN Prefix(es): 0-7136
Number of titles published annually: 40 Print
Total Titles: 320 Print; 1 CD-ROM
*Associate Companies:* Thomas Reed Publications
Distributor for Sheridan House
*Warehouse:* Macmillan Distribution Ltd, Howard Rd, Eaton Socon, Huntingdon, Cambs PE19 8EZ *Tel:* (01480) 223131

**Adlib**, *imprint of* Scholastic Ltd

**Adobe Press**, *imprint of* Pearson Education Europe, Mideast & Africa

**Advisory Unit: Computers in Education+**
126 Great North Rd, Hatfield, Herts AL9 5JZ
*Tel:* (01707) 266714 *Fax:* (01707) 273684
*E-mail:* sales@advisory-unit.org.uk
*Web Site:* www.advisory-unit.org.uk
*Key Personnel*
Export Sales Dir: M Aston *E-mail:* mike@kcited. demon.co.uk
Founded: 1991
Specialize in educational software.
Membership(s): British Educational Suppliers Association (BESA); ESPA; Naace.
Subjects: Computer Science, Disability, Special Needs, Economics, Geography, Geology, Mathematics, Microcomputers, Technology
ISBN Prefix(es): 1-874164
Number of titles published annually: 4 Print
Total Titles: 20 Print; 8 CD-ROM; 1 E-Book
Distributed by Orfeus (Denmark & Scandinavia)
Distributor for Harvard Associates (North America)

**A4 Publications Ltd**
Hagley Chambers, Thornleigh, 35 Hagley Rd, Stourbridge DY8 1QR
*Tel:* (01384) 440591 *Fax:* (01384) 440582
*Key Personnel*
Publisher & Dir: Francesca Ash
*Tel:* (01892) 783535 *Fax:* (01892) 783848
*E-mail:* francesca.ash@a4publications.com
Advertising Sales: Julie Cruikshanks
*E-mail:* nought2twelve@a4publications.com; Jerry Wooldridge *E-mail:* jerrywooldridge@ a4publications.com
Founded: 1981
Membership(s): LIMA.
ISBN Prefix(es): 0-510; 0-946197; 0-9502363

**Age Concern Books+**
Astral House, 1268 London Rd, London SW16 4ER
*Tel:* (020) 8765 7200 *Fax:* (020) 8765 7211
*E-mail:* infodep@ace.org.uk
*Web Site:* www.ageconcern.org.uk
*Key Personnel*
Marketing Manager: Michael Addison
Publisher: Richard Holloway
Founded: 1971
Specialize in practical handbooks for older people & their careers & professionals working with older people; training packs for professional careers.
Subjects: Finance, Health, Nutrition
ISBN Prefix(es): 0-86242

Total Titles: 70 Print
*Parent Company:* Age Concern England
*Orders to:* Biblios Publishers Distribution Service Ltd, Star Rd, Partridge Green, West Sussex RH13 8LD

**Ai Interactive Ltd**
St Martins House, Spring Copse, Oxford OX1 5BJ
*Tel:* (01235) 529595 *Fax:* (01865) 736917
*E-mail:* medical@andromeda-interactive.co.uk
*Web Site:* www.andromeda-interactive.co.uk
*Key Personnel*
Editorial, Marketing: John Bradley *E-mail:* john@ andromeda-interactive.co.uk
Rights, Finance: Mark Ritchie *E-mail:* mark@ andromeda-interactive.co.uk
Sales: Clive Hetherington *E-mail:* clive@ andromeda-interactive.co.uk
Subjects: Medicine, Nursing, Dentistry, Graphic design
ISBN Prefix(es): 1-898137
*Distribution Center:* JA Majors, Texas

**Airlife Publishing Ltd+**
Imprint of Crowood Press Ltd
101 Longden Rd, Shrewsbury, Salop SY3 9EB
*Tel:* (01743) 235651 *Fax:* (01743) 232944
*E-mail:* info@airlifebooks.com
*Web Site:* www.crowoodpress.co.uk
*Key Personnel*
Rights & Permissions: Anne Walker
*E-mail:* anne@airlifebooks.com
Founded: 1976
Subjects: Aeronautics, Aviation, Military Science, Transportation
ISBN Prefix(es): 0-9504543; 0-906393; 1-85310; 1-84037
Number of titles published annually: 100 Print
Total Titles: 600 Print

**AK Press & Distribution+**
PO Box 12766, Edinburgh EH8 9YE
*Tel:* (0131) 5555165 *Fax:* (0131) 5555215
*E-mail:* ak@akedin.demon.co.uk
*Web Site:* www.akuk.com
Founded: 1991
Subjects: Fiction, Philosophy, Poetry, Social Sciences, Sociology
ISBN Prefix(es): 1-873176; 1-902593
*U.S. Office(s):* 674-A 23rd St, Oakland, CA 94612, United States *Tel:* 510-208-1700 *Fax:* 510-208-1701
Distributed by Bookspeed (UK); Counter Productions (UK); Turnaround (UK)

**Al-Shirkatul Islamiyyah**, *imprint of* Islam International Publications Ltd

**Aladdin Books Ltd+**
28 Percy St, London W1P 0LD
*Tel:* (020) 7323 3319 *Fax:* (020) 7323 4829
*E-mail:* kerry.mciver@aladdinbooks.co.uk
*Web Site:* www.aladdinbooks.co.uk
*Key Personnel*
Dir: C V Nicholas; E P Whittaker
Founded: 1980
Subjects: Nonfiction (General)

**Albyn Press**
2 Caversham St, Chelsea, London SW3 4AH
*Tel:* (020) 7351 4995 *Fax:* (020) 7351 4995

**Aldwych Press Ltd+**
3 Henrietta St, Covent Garden, London WC2E 8LU
*Tel:* (020) 7240 0856 *Fax:* (020) 7379 0609
*E-mail:* info@eurospan.co.uk
*Web Site:* www.eurospan.co.uk
*Key Personnel*
Man Dir: Michael Geelan

Dir: Danny Maher
Marketing: Imogen Adams
Founded: 1979
Subjects: Economics, Government, Political Science, Law, Library & Information Sciences, Military Science, Philosophy, Social Sciences, Sociology
ISBN Prefix(es): 0-86172

**Ian Allan Publishing+**
Member of Ian Allan Group
Riverdene Business Park, Molesey Rd, Hersham, Surrey KT12 4RG
*Tel:* (01932) 266600 *Fax:* (01932) 266601
*E-mail:* info@ianallanpub.co.uk
*Web Site:* www.ianallan.com
*Key Personnel*
Chairman: David Allan
Man Dir: Tony Saunders
Dir Publishing: Bill Lucas
Production Director: Nicholas Lerwill
Retail Sales Manager: Wendy Myers
Publishing Manager: Peter Waller
Sales & Marketing Manager: Nigel Passmore
Founded: 1945
Subjects: Aeronautics, Aviation, Architecture & Interior Design, Automotive, Cookery, Gardening, Plants, Maritime, Photography, Transportation
ISBN Prefix(es): 0-7110
*Associate Companies:* Ian Allan Motors Ltd; Ian Allan Printing Ltd; Ian Allan Travel Ltd; Chase Organics Ltd
Imprints: Dial House
Distributor for Mill Stream; Runpast; World of Transport; Yore Publications
Foreign Rep(s): Bill Bailey Publishers' Representatives (Austria, Belgium, Bulgaria, Croatia, Cyprus, Czech Republic, Netherlands, Estonia, France, Germany, Gibraltar, Greece, Hungary, Italy, Latvia, Liechtenstein, Lithuania, Luxembourg, Malta, Monaco, Poland, Portugal, Romania, Serbia and Montenegro, Slovenia, Spain, Switzerland); D Richard Bowen (Scandinavia); Combined Books (US); DLS Australia Pty Ltd (Australia, New Zealand, Papua New Guinea); Electra Media Group Pty Ltd (Brunei, China, Hong Kong, Japan, Korea, Malaysia, Philippines, Singapore, Taiwan, Thailand, Eastern Asia); PIM (India, Middle East, Pakistan); Vanwell Publishing Ltd (Canada)
*Bookshop(s):* 47 Stephenson St, Birmingham *Tel:* (0121) 643 2496 *Fax:* (0121) 643 6855; Main Terminal Bldg, 3rd Floor, Birmingham International Airport, Birmingham B26 3QJ *Tel:* (0121) 781 0921 *Fax:* (0121) 781 0928; 45-46 Lower Marsh, London SE1 7SG *Tel:* (020) 7401 2100 *Fax:* (020) 7401 2887; Unit 5, Piccadilly Station Approach, Manchester M1 2GH *Tel:* (0161) 237 9840 *Fax:* (0161) 237 9921
*Warehouse:* Littlehampton Book Services Ltd, Faraday Close, Durrington, Worthing, West Sussex BN13 3RB *Tel:* (01903) 828800 *Fax:* (01903) 721596

**Umberto Allemandi & Co Publishing+**
70 S Lambeth Rd, London SW8 1RL
*Tel:* (020) 7735 3331 *Fax:* (020) 7735 3332
*E-mail:* contact@theartnewspaper.com
*Web Site:* www.theartnewspaper.com
*Key Personnel*
Editor-in-Chief: Cristina Ruiz *E-mail:* c.ruiz@ theartnewspaper.com
Founded: 1983
Books on general culture; three newspapers.
Subjects: Architecture & Interior Design, Art, Gardening, Plants
ISBN Prefix(es): 88-422
Total Titles: 150 Print
*Branch Office(s)*
Via Mancini 8, Turin 10131, Italy, Contact: Nicole Kerr-Munslow *Tel:* (011) 8199111

*Fax:* (011) 8193090 *E-mail:* nicole.kerr. munslow@allemandi.com
Distributed by Antique Collectors Club (UK, USA & Australia only)

**J A Allen**, *imprint of* Robert Hale Ltd

**Allen Lane**, *imprint of* The Penguin Group UK

**Allen Lane**, *imprint of* Viking

**Allied Mouse Ltd+**
Mayfield, High St, Dingwall, Ross-shire IV15 9SS
*Tel:* (01349) 865400 *Fax:* (01349) 866066
*E-mail:* info@heartstone.co.uk
*Web Site:* www.heartstone.co.uk
*Key Personnel*
Dir: Sita Sidle; Nick Sidle
Founded: 1988
Membership(s): Publishers' Association.
Subjects: Fiction
ISBN Prefix(es): 0-9513492

**Allison & Busby+**
Subsidiary of Editorial Prensa Iberica
Bon Marche Centre, Ferndale Rd, London SW9 8BJ
*Tel:* (020) 7738 7888 *Fax:* (020) 7733 4244
*E-mail:* all@allisonbusby.com
*Web Site:* www.allisonandbusby.com
*Key Personnel*
Publishing Dir: David Shelley *E-mail:* davids@ allisonbusby.co.uk
Marketing: Fiona Hague
Editor: Debbie Hatfield
Founded: 1966
Subjects: Biography, Contemporary & Literary Fiction, Crime Fiction, Writers' Guides
ISBN Prefix(es): 0-7490
Number of titles published annually: 40 Print
Total Titles: 240 Print
*Shipping Address:* Turnaround Publisher Services, Olympia Trading Estate, Unit 3, Coburg Rd, London N22 6T2, Contact: Bill Godber *Tel:* (020) 8829 3000 *Fax:* (020) 8881 5088 *E-mail:* orders@turnaround-uk.com

**Allyn & Bacon**, *imprint of* Pearson Education Europe, Mideast & Africa

**Almond Press**, *imprint of* Sheffield Academic Press Ltd

**Altamira Press**, *imprint of* SAGE Publications Ltd

**Alun Books**
Imprint of Goldleaf Publishing
3 Crown St, Port Talbot, W Glam, Wales SA13 1BG
*Tel:* (01639) 886186
*E-mail:* enquiries@alunbooks.co.uk
*Web Site:* www.alunbooks.co.uk
*Key Personnel*
Editor: Sally Jones
Founded: 1977
Publish books about Wales &/or by Welsh authors.
Subjects: Biography, Fiction, History, Poetry, Travel
ISBN Prefix(es): 0-907117; 0-9505643
Total Titles: 56 Print
Imprints: Barn Owl Press (Children's Books); Goldleaf Publishing (Local History)
Distributor for Port Talbot Historical Society

**Amadeus Press**, *imprint of* Timber Press Inc

**Amber Books Ltd+**
Bradley's Close, 74-77 White Lion St, London N1 9PF
*Tel:* (020) 7520 7600 *Fax:* (020) 7520 7606; (020) 7520 7607
*E-mail:* enquiries@amberbooks.co.uk
*Web Site:* www.amberbooks.co.uk
*Key Personnel*
Rights & Operations Dir: Sara Ballard
Man Dir: Stasz Gynch
Founded: 1989
Subjects: Aeronautics, Aviation, Astronomy, Automotive, Cookery, Crafts, Games, Hobbies, Criminology, Gardening, Plants, History, How-to, Maritime, Military Science, Nonfiction (General), Sports, Athletics, Transportation
ISBN Prefix(es): 1-897884; 0-9543125
Total Titles: 120 Print

**Amber Lane Press Ltd+**
Cheorl House, Church St, Charlbury OX7 3PR
*Tel:* (01608) 810024 *Fax:* (01608) 810024
*E-mail:* info@amberlanepress.co.uk
*Web Site:* www.amberlanepress.co.uk
*Key Personnel*
Man Dir: Judith Scott
Founded: 1978
Subjects: Biography, Drama, Theater, Music, Dance
ISBN Prefix(es): 0-906399; 1-872868
Number of titles published annually: 3 Print
Total Titles: 100 Print

**Amber Waves**, *imprint of* Heartland Publishing Ltd

**Amberwood Publishing Ltd+**
Unit 4, Alpha House, Laser Quay, Culpeper Close, Medway City Estate, Rochester, Kent ME2 4HH
*Tel:* (01634) 290115 *Fax:* (01634) 290761
*E-mail:* books@amberwoodpublishing.com
*Web Site:* www.amberwoodpublishing.com
*Key Personnel*
Chairman: Henry Crisp *Fax:* (01483) 457101
Chief Executive: Victor Perfitt
Man Dir: June Crisp *Tel:* (01634) 290115 *Fax:* (01634) 290761
Sales: Bob Couchman *Tel:* (01634) 290115
Founded: 1991
Specialize in natural/health publications, herbs, vitamins, minerals & self-medication.
Subjects: Health, Nutrition, Aromatherapy, Herbal Medicine
ISBN Prefix(es): 1-899308; 0-9517723
Number of titles published annually: 3 Print
Total Titles: 32 Print

**American Technical Publishers**
27/29 Knowl Piece, Wilbury Way, Hitchin, Herts SG4 0SX
*Tel:* (01462) 437933 *Fax:* (01462) 433678
*E-mail:* atp@ameritech.co.uk
*Web Site:* www.ameritech.co.uk
Distributor for American Ceramic Society; American Concrete Institute; American Society for Civil Engineers; American Society for Mechanical Engineers; American Society for Testing & Materials; American Water Works Association; William Andrew; Asian Productivity Organisation; ASM International; Casti Publishing Inc; ICBO; Instrument Society of America; National Association of Corrosion Engineers; Noble Publishing Corporation; Pegasus Communications; Productivity Press; Quality Resources; Research Signpost/Transworld Research; Research Studies Press; Society for Mining, Metallurgy & Exploration; Society of Automotive Engineers; Society of Manufacturing Engineers; Synapse Information Resources Inc; Technical Association of the Pulp & Paper Industry; Water Environment Federation

**Amistad**, *imprint of* HarperCollins UK

**Amnesty International Publications**
99-119 Rosebery Ave, London EC1R 4RE
*Tel:* (020) 7814 6200 *Fax:* (020) 7833 1510
*E-mail:* information@amnesty.org.uk
*Web Site:* www.amnesty.org.uk *Cable:*
AMNESTY LONDON WC1
*Key Personnel*
Marketing: Guy Montgomery
Founded: 1961
Subjects: Human Rights
ISBN Prefix(es): 0-86210; 0-900058
*Branch Office(s)*
80A Stranmillis Rd, Belfast BT9 5AD
*Tel:* (02890) 666 216/666 001 *Fax:* (02890)
666 164 *E-mail:* enquiriesni@amnesty.org.uk
6 Castle St, Edinburgh EH2 3AT *Tel:* (0131) 466
6200 *Fax:* (0131) 466 6201 *E-mail:* rburnett@
edinburgh.amnesty.org.uk
*Orders to:* PO Box 4, Rugby, Warwickshire
CV21 1RU *Tel:* (01788) 545553 *Fax:* (01788)
579244

**Amsco Publications**, *imprint of* Omnibus Press

**Anchor**, *imprint of* Transworld Publishers Ltd

**Andersen Artists Greeting Cards**, *imprint of*
Andersen Press Ltd

**Andersen Giants**, *imprint of* Andersen Press Ltd

**Andersen Paperback Picture Books**, *imprint of*
Andersen Press Ltd

**Andersen Press Ltd+**
Affiliate of Random House
20 Vauxhall Bridge Rd, London SW1V 2SA
*Tel:* (020) 7840 8701 *Fax:* (020) 7233 6263
*E-mail:* andersenpress@randomhouse.co.uk
*Web Site:* www.andersenpress.co.uk
*Key Personnel*
Publisher & Man Dir: Klaus Flugge *Tel:* (020)
7840 8702 *E-mail:* kflugge@randomhouse.co.
uk
International Rights: Sarah Pakenham *Tel:* (020)
7840 8704 *E-mail:* spakenham@randomhouse.
co.uk
Publicity Manager: Rebecca Garrill *Tel:* (020)
7840 8704 *E-mail:* rgarrill@randomhouse.co.uk
Founded: 1976
Subjects: Fiction
ISBN Prefix(es): 0-86264; 0-905478
Total Titles: 396 Print
*Associate Companies:* Random House
Imprints: Andersen Artists Greeting Cards; An-
dersen Giants; Andersen Young Readers Li-
brary; Tigers; Andersen Paperback Picture
Books; Andersen Press Board Books
Distributed by General Publishing (Canada); Ran-
dom House (Australia); Random House (South
Africa); Random House (New Zealand)
Foreign Rep(s): General Publishing (Canada);
Akiko Iwamoto (Japan); Random House
(Guam, Indonesia, Malaysia, Philippines, Sin-
gapore, Thailand); Random House Australia
Pty Ltd (Australia); Random House (NZ) Ltd
(New Zealand); Random House of Canada Ltd
(Hong Kong, South Korea, Taiwan); Random
House of South Africa Pty Ltd (South Africa);
Wei Zhao (China)
*Warehouse:* The Book Service Ltd, Colchester
Rd, Frating Green, Colchester, Essex CO7
7DW *Tel:* (01206) 255678 *Fax:* (01206)
255930
*Orders to:* The Book Service Ltd, Colchester Rd,
Frating Green, Colchester, Essex CO7 7DW
*Tel:* (01206) 255678 *Fax:* (01206) 255930

**Andersen Press Board Books**, *imprint of*
Andersen Press Ltd

**Andersen Young Readers Library**, *imprint of*
Andersen Press Ltd

**Anderson Rand Ltd**
10 Willow Walk, Cambridge CB1 1LA
*Tel:* (01223) 566640 *Fax:* (01223) 316144;
(01223) 566643
*E-mail:* info@andrand.com
*Web Site:* www.andrand.com
*Key Personnel*
Man Dir: Dr R O Anderson *E-mail:* anderson.
rand@usa.net
Founded: 1989
Comprehensive data on European book related or-
ganizations, mainly publishers, libraries & book
sellers.
Subjects: Library & Information Sciences, Pub-
lishing & Book Trade Reference
ISBN Prefix(es): 1-873539
Total Titles: 4 Print; 4 CD-ROM

**Andre Deutsch**, *imprint of* Carlton Publishing
Group

**Chris Andrews Publications**
15 Curtis Yard, North Hinksey Lane, Oxford OX2
0LX
*Tel:* (01865) 723404 *Fax:* (01865) 725294
*E-mail:* enquiries@cap-ox.com
*Web Site:* www.cap-ox.com
*Key Personnel*
Contact: C M Andrews
Founded: 1982
Membership(s): BAPLA & IPG.
Subjects: Travel, Oxford, Cotswolds, Thames &
Chilterns
ISBN Prefix(es): 0-9509643

**Andromeda**, *imprint of* Andromeda Oxford Ltd

**Andromeda Oxford Ltd+**
11-13 The Vineyard, Abingdon, Oxon OX14 3PX
*Tel:* (01235) 550 296 *Fax:* (01235) 550 330
*E-mail:* mail@andromeda.co.uk
*Key Personnel*
Man Dir: David Holyoak *E-mail:* david.holyoak@
andromeda.co.uk
Publishing Dir: Graham Bateman *E-mail:* graham.
bateman@andromeda.co.uk
Production Dir: Clive Sparling *E-mail:* clive.
sparling@andromeda.co.uk
Sales & Marketing Dir (US, Canada, Germany &
Australia): Christopher Collier *E-mail:* chris.
collier@andromeda.co.uk
Sales Manager (UK, Europe & the Far East):
Anne-Marie Hansen *E-mail:* anne-marie.
hansen@andromeda.co.uk
Sales Executive: Hannah Longden
*E-mail:* hannah.longden@andromeda.co.uk
Founded: 1986
Produce color illustrated, multi-volume reference
works.
Subjects: Animals, Pets, Archaeology, Art, Be-
havioral Sciences, Earth Sciences, Gardening,
Plants, Geography, Geology, History, Human
Relations, Natural History, Religion - Islamic,
Religion - Jewish, Science (General)
ISBN Prefix(es): 1-86199; 1-871869
Total Titles: 500 Print
*Parent Company:* Mediainvest PLC
Imprints: Andromeda
Foreign Rights: D S Druck (Eastern Europe);
Jacky Spigel (France, Germany)

**Angels' Share**, *imprint of* Neil Wilson Publishing
Ltd

**Anglo-German Foundation for the Study of
Industrial Society** (Deutsch Britische Stiftung)
34 Belgrave Sq, London SW1X 8DZ
*Tel:* (020) 7823 1123 *Fax:* (020) 7823 2324
*E-mail:* info@agf.org.uk
*Web Site:* www.agf.org.uk
*Key Personnel*
Dir: Keith Dobson *E-mail:* kd@agf.org.uk
Press & Publications Officer: Annette Birkholz
*E-mail:* ab@agf.org.uk
Projects Manager: Ann Pfeiffer *E-mail:* ap@agf.
org.uk
Founded: 1973
Subjects: Economics, Environmental Studies,
Government, Political Science, Health, Nutri-
tion, Labor, Industrial Relations, Management,
Public Administration, Social Sciences, Sociol-
ogy
ISBN Prefix(es): 0-905492; 1-900834
Number of titles published annually: 8 Print; 2 E-
Book
Total Titles: 73 Print
*Branch Office(s)*
Humboldt Universitat Berlin/GBZ, Jagerstr 10/11,
10117 Berlin, Germany
Distributed by Palgrave (UK)
*Orders to:* YPS (York Publishing Services), 64
Hallfield Rd, Layerthorpe, York YO31 72Q
*Tel:* (01904) 431213 *Fax:* (01904) 430868

**Angus Hudson Ltd**, see Lion Hudson plc

**Anthem Press**, *imprint of* Wimbledon Publishing
Company Ltd

**Antique Collectors' Club Ltd+**
Sandy Lane, Old Martlesham, Woodbridge, Suf-
folk IP12 4SD
*Tel:* (01394) 389950 *Fax:* (01394) 389999
*E-mail:* peter.hawk@antique-acc.com; sales@
antique-acc.com
*Web Site:* www.antique-acc.com
*Key Personnel*
Man Dir: Diana Steel
Dir: Brian Cotton
Sales Dir: Mark Eastnent
Founded: 1966 (privately owned)
Subjects: Antiques, Architecture & Interior De-
sign, Art, Gardening, Plants
ISBN Prefix(es): 1-85149; 0-907462; 0-902028
Number of titles published annually: 30 Print
Total Titles: 200 Print
Imprints: Garden Art Press Ltd
*U.S. Office(s):* Antique Collectors' Club, Mar-
ket Street Industrial Park, Wappingers Falls,
NY 12590, United States, Contact: Dan Far-
rell *Tel:* 914-297-0003 *Fax:* 914-297-0068
*E-mail:* sales@antique-cc.com

**Antiques & Collectors Guides Ltd+**
Righolm, 40 High Barholm, Kilbarchan, John-
stone PA10 2EQ
*Tel:* (0141) 8480880 *Fax:* (0141) 8892063
*Key Personnel*
Editor & Author: Mr Loudon Temple
Founded: 1990
Subjects: Antiques
ISBN Prefix(es): 0-9514842

**Anvil Books Ltd+**
Unit 3, Olympia Trading Estate, Coburg Rd, Lon-
don N22 6TZ
*Tel:* (020) 8829-3000 *Fax:* (020) 8881-5088
*Cable:* ANVIL
*Key Personnel*
Man Dir, Sales, Production, Publicity, Rights &
Permissions: Rena Dardis
Editorial: Margaret Dardis
Founded: 1964
Subjects: Biography, History
ISBN Prefix(es): 0-900068; 0-947962; 1-901737
*Associate Companies:* The Children's Press, Ire-
land

## Anvil Press Poetry Ltd
Neptune House, 70 Royal Hill, London SE10 8RF
*Tel:* (020) 8469 3033 *Fax:* (020) 8469 3363
*E-mail:* info@anvilpresspoetry.com
*Web Site:* www.anvilpresspoetry.com
*Key Personnel*
Founder & Editorial Dir: Peter Jay
Sales, Marketing & Promotion: Hamish Ironside
Administration & Rights: Kit Yee Wong
Founded: 1968
Subjects: Poetry
ISBN Prefix(es): 0-85646; 0-900977
Imprints: Poetica
Distributed by Littlehampton Book Services Ltd; Midpoint Trade Books
*Warehouse:* Littlehampton Book Services, Columbia Bldg, Faraday Close, Durrington, Worthing BN13 3HP
*Distribution Center:* Consortium (US Office)
*Orders to:* Littlehampton Book Services, Columbia Bldg, Faraday Close, Durrington, Worthing BN13 3HP

## AP Information Services Ltd+
Marlborough House, 1st floor, 298 Regents Park Rd, London N3 2UU
*Tel:* (020) 8349 9988 *Fax:* (020) 8349 9797
*E-mail:* info@apinfo.co.uk
*Web Site:* www.apinfo.co.uk
*Key Personnel*
Man Dir: Alan Philipp *E-mail:* alan@apinfo.co.uk
Dir Finance & Personnel: Gail Philipp *E-mail:* gail@apinfo.co.uk
Editorial Manager, Business Publications: Helen Helmer *E-mail:* helen@apinfo.co.uk
Editorial Manager, Finance Directories: Debbie Robel *E-mail:* debbie@apinfo.co.uk
Head Sales & Marketing: Jacinta Tobin *E-mail:* jacinta@apinfo.co.uk
Marketing Manager: Philip Lowther *E-mail:* philip@apinfo.co.uk
Administrative Manager: Sally Rodohan *E-mail:* sally@apinfo.co.uk
Head of IT & Production: Kumar Divakaran *E-mail:* kumar@apinfo.co.uk
Founded: 1969
Membership(s): Directory Publishers Association.
Subjects: Business, Education, Finance
ISBN Prefix(es): 0-906247; 1-902202
Distributed by Money Market Directories (USA)

## Apex Publishing Ltd
PO Box 7086, Clacton on Sea, Essex CO15 5WN
*Tel:* (01255) 428500 *Fax:* (0870) 046 6536
*E-mail:* enquiry@apexpublishing.co.uk
*Web Site:* www.apexpublishing.co.uk
*Key Personnel*
Man Dir: Susan Kidby
Founded: 2002
Subsidy publishing for unknown & unpublished authors.
Subjects: Education, Fiction, Health, Nutrition, Nonfiction (General), Philosophy, Poetry, Religion - Other, Science Fiction, Fantasy, Self-Help
ISBN Prefix(es): 1-904444

**Apollos**, *imprint of* Inter-Varsity Press

## Apple Press+
Sheridan House, 112-116A Western Rd, Hove, East Sussex BN3 1DD
*Tel:* (01273) 727268 *Fax:* (01273) 727269
*E-mail:* information@quarto.com
*Web Site:* www.quarto.com
*Key Personnel*
UK Sales Manager: Marian Silvester
Key Accounts Manager: Stuart Henderson
Editorial Office Manager: Gail Norman *E-mail:* gailn@rotovision.com
Founded: 1984

Specialize in publishing illustrated nonfiction.
Subjects: Antiques, Art, Cookery, Crafts, Games, Hobbies, Fashion, Health, Nutrition, House & Home, Nonfiction (General), Photography, Transportation, Art Instruction, Beauty, Body/Mind/Spirit, Design, Diet, Fitness, Food & Drink, Lifestyle, Pets
ISBN Prefix(es): 1-85076; 1-84092
Number of titles published annually: 25 Print
Total Titles: 500 Print
*Parent Company:* Quarto Publishing PLC
Distributor for Walter Foster Publishing (UK & Europe only)
*Orders to:* Grantham Book Services, Isaac Newton Way, Alma Park Industrial Estate, Grantham, Lincs NG31 9SD *Tel:* (020) 754 1080 *Fax:* (020) 754 1061 *E-mail:* orders@gbs.tbs-ltd.co.uk

## Appletree Press Ltd+
The Old Potato Station, 14 Howard St S, Belfast BT7 1AP
*Tel:* (028) 9024 3074 *Fax:* (028) 9024 6756
*E-mail:* reception@appletree.ie
*Web Site:* www.appletree.ie
*Key Personnel*
Man Dir, Rights & Permissions: John D Murphy
Editorial: J Brown
Sales & Marketing: M Elliott
Founded: 1974
Publishers of gift & guidebooks in eight languages, including French, Russian, Japanese, Greek & Spanish
Also acts as Book Packager.
Subjects: Art, Cookery, Crafts, Games, Hobbies, History, Literature, Literary Criticism, Essays, Music, Dance, Photography, Regional Interests, Social Sciences, Sociology
ISBN Prefix(es): 0-904651; 0-86281
Total Titles: 300 Print

## Arcadia Books Ltd+
15-16 Nassau St, London W1W 7AB
*Tel:* (020) 7436 9898
*E-mail:* info@arcadiabooks.co.uk
*Web Site:* www.arcadiabooks.co.uk
*Key Personnel*
Publisher: Gary Pulsifer
Publishing Dir: Daniela de Groote
Founded: 1996
Subjects: Biography, Fiction, Gay & Lesbian, Travel, Autobiography, Crime, Gender Studies, Translated Fiction
ISBN Prefix(es): 1-900850
Number of titles published annually: 20 Print
Total Titles: 100 Print
*Distribution Center:* Independent Publishers Group, Chicago, IL, United States

## Architectural Association Publications+
36 Bedford Sq, London WC1B 3ES
*Tel:* (020) 7887 4021; (020) 7887 4000 *Fax:* (020) 7414 0783
*E-mail:* publications@aaschool.ac.uk
*Web Site:* www.aaschool.ac.uk/publications
*Key Personnel*
Chairman: Mohsen Mostafavi
Publications Coordinator: Marilyn Sparrow
Founded: 1847
Also acts as a School of Architecture.
Subjects: Architecture & Interior Design
ISBN Prefix(es): 1-870890; 0-904503; 1-902902

**Architectural Press**, *imprint of* Elsevier Ltd

## Arcturus Publishing Ltd+
26/27 Bickels Yard, 151-153 Bermondsey St, London SE1 3HA
*Tel:* (020) 7407 9400 *Fax:* (020) 7407 9444
*E-mail:* info@arcturuspublishing.com
*Web Site:* www.arcturuspublishing.com

*Key Personnel*
Man Dir: Ian McLellan
Founded: 1994
ISBN Prefix(es): 1-84193
Number of titles published annually: 70 Print
Total Titles: 300 Print; 2 Audio

**Argentum**, *imprint of* Aurum Press Ltd

## Argo+
c/o PolyGram Spoken Word, One Sussex Pl, London W6 9XS
Mailing Address: PO Box 1420, W6 9XS London
*Tel:* (020) 8910 5000 *Fax:* (020) 8910 5400
*Key Personnel*
Product Manager: Alex Mitchison *E-mail:* alexandra.mitchison@umusic.com
Founded: 1950
Subjects: Nonfiction (General), Poetry
ISBN Prefix(es): 1-85849
*Parent Company:* Decca Music Group
*Warehouse:* EMI Music Services, Hermes Close, Tatchbrook Park, Leamington Spa CU34 6RP

## Argyll Publishing
Cowlairs Industrial Estate, 32 Finlas St, Glasgow G22 5DU
*Tel:* 08702402182; (0141) 558 1366 *Fax:* (0141) 557 0189
*E-mail:* customerservices@booksource.net
*Key Personnel*
Publisher: Derek Rodger
Founded: 1992
Subjects: Biography, History, Poetry, Literature, Scottish Interest
ISBN Prefix(es): 1-874640; 1-902831
*Distribution Center:* Central Books, 99 Wallis Rd, London E9 5LN *Tel:* (020) 8986 4854 (England & Wales)
PD Meany, Box 118, Streetsville, ON L5M 2B7, Canada (North America)
Scottish Book Source, 137 Dundee St, Edinburgh EH11 1BG *Tel:* (0131) 229 6800 *E-mail:* enquiries@scottishbooks.org *Web Site:* www.scottishbooks.org (Scotland)

**Arkana**, *imprint of* Penguin Books Ltd

**Arms and Armour Press**, *imprint of* Cassell & Co

## Arms & Armour Press+
Wellington House, 125 Strand, London WC2R 0BB
*Tel:* (020) 7420 5555 *Fax:* (020) 7420 7261
*Telex:* 9413701
*Key Personnel*
Chairman & Chief Executive: Philip Sturrock
Editorial Dir & Rights: Alison Goff
Sales Dir: Michelle Gustave
Founded: 1966
Subjects: Aeronautics, Aviation, Crafts, Games, Hobbies, Government, Political Science, History, Maritime, Military Science, Transportation, Naval Warfare
ISBN Prefix(es): 0-85368; 1-85409
*Parent Company:* Continuum International Publishing Group Ltd

**Arnefold**, *imprint of* George Mann Publications

## Arnold+
338 Euston Rd, London NW1 3BH
*Tel:* (020) 7873 6000 *Fax:* (020) 7873 6325
*E-mail:* feedback.arnold@hodder.co.uk
*Web Site:* www.arnoldpublishers.com
*Key Personnel*
Chairman: Tim Hely-Hutchinson
Man Dir: Richard Stileman
Head of Marketing: Elizabeth Munn
STM Dir: Nick Dunton

Production Dir: Iain McWilliams
Foreign Rights & Permissions: Rebecca Duprey
Sales Dir: Andy White
Medical: Georgia Bentliff
Humanities: Christopher Wheeler
Marketing Assistant: Rachel Monk *Tel:* (020)
7873 6026 *E-mail:* rachel.monk@hodder.co.uk
Founded: 1890
Arnold is the academic, professional & medical
division of Hodder Headline Plc.
Subjects: Environmental Studies, Geography, Ge-
ology, History, Human Relations, Language
Arts, Linguistics, Literature, Literary Criticism,
Essays, Medicine, Nursing, Dentistry, Psychol-
ogy, Psychiatry, Social Sciences, Sociology,
Cultural & Media Studies, Statistics
ISBN Prefix(es): 0-340; 0-7131; 0-85324
*Parent Company:* Hodder Headline Plc
*Ultimate Parent Company:* W H Smith
*Branch Office(s)*
Hodder & Stroughton (Australia) Pty Ltd, 12
Strathalbyn St, Kew East, Victoria 3102, Aus-
tralia
Hodder Moa Becket, New Zealand
Hodder & Stoughton Educational, South Africa
Distributed by Bookpoint

**Arris Publishing Ltd+**
12 Main St, Adlestrop, Moreton in Marsh, Glos
GL56 0YN
*Tel:* (01608) 659328 *Fax:* (01608) 659345
*E-mail:* info@arrisbooks.com
*Web Site:* ww.arrisbooks.com
*Key Personnel*
Rights: Victoria Huxley *Tel:* (01608) 658758
*E-mail:* victoriama.huxley@btinternet.com
Man Dir: Geoffrey Smith *E-mail:* gcs@
arrisbooks.com
Founded: 2002
Specializes in politics, Middle East, travel, an-
cient mysteries & translated fiction.
Subjects: Art, Fiction, Foreign Countries, Gov-
ernment, Political Science, History, Military
Science, Mysteries, Natural History, Nonfiction
(General), Religion - Islamic, Travel, Ancient
Mysteries, Middle East, Politics, Translated
Fiction
ISBN Prefix(es): 1-84437; 1-905214
Number of titles published annually: 20 Print
Total Titles: 60 Print
Imprints: Chastleton Travel
*Warehouse:* Orca Book Distribution, Stanley
House, 3 Fleets Lane, Poole, Dorset BH15
3AJ, Contact: Jill Caldicott *Tel:* (01202)
665432 *Fax:* (01202) 666219
*Orders to:* Orca Book Distribution, Stanley
House, 3 Fleets Lane, Poole, Dorset BH15
3AJ, Contact: Jill Caldicott *Tel:* (01202)
665432 *Fax:* (01202) 666219

**Arrow,** *imprint of* Random House UK Ltd

**Art Books International Ltd+**
Unit 14 Groves Business Centre Shipton Rd,
Milton-under-Wychwood, Chipping Norton,
Oxon OX7 6JP
*Tel:* (020) 7720 1503; (020) 7578 1222
*Fax:* (020) 7720 3158
*E-mail:* sales@art-bks.com
*Web Site:* www.artbooksinternational.co.uk
*Key Personnel*
Man Dir: Stanley Kekwick *E-mail:* stanley@art-
bks.com
Founded: 1991
Specialize in distribution of art books.
Subjects: Antiques, Architecture & Interior De-
sign, Art, Crafts, Games, Hobbies, Drama, The-
ater, Fashion, Music, Dance, Photography
ISBN Prefix(es): 1-874044
Total Titles: 12 Print
*U.S. Office(s):* Strauss Consultants, 45 Main St,
Suite 611, Brooklyn, NY 11201-1021, United

States, Contact: Karen Strauss *Tel:* 718-625-
9382 *Fax:* 718-625-9386 *E-mail:* strausscon@
aol.com
Distributor for Apex Publishing; Art Books In-
ternational; BE-MA Editrice; Beaux Arts; Bib-
lioteque del l'Image; Black Dog Publishing;
Zelda Cheatle Press; Bernard Jacobson Gallery;
Cygnet Press; Design Line; Edwards; Form;
Hand Held; Kala Press; Editions Menges;
Khosla; Magnus Edizioni; Manchester City Art
Galleries; McCabe; Memory Cage; Momentum;
Museum of London; National Gallery of Ire-
land; Pallas Athene Arts; Raab Gallery; Royal
Academy; Salts Mill Estates; SPES; Station
Press; UIAH; Ziggurat

**The Art Newspaper,** see Umberto Allemandi &
Co Publishing

**Art Sales Index Ltd+**
194 Thorpe Lea Rd, Egham, Surrey TW20 8HA
*Tel:* (01784) 451145 *Fax:* (01784) 451144
*E-mail:* sales@art-sales-index.com
*Web Site:* www.art-sales-index.com
*Key Personnel*
Chairman: Richard Hislop *E-mail:* asi@art-sales-
index.com
Man Editor & Technical Dir: Duncan Hislop
Founded: 1968
Also acts as International On-Line Service-
Accessible World-Wide, 24 hours a day, 7 days
a week.
Subjects: Art
ISBN Prefix(es): 0-903872

**The Art Trade Press Ltd**
9 Brockhampton Rd, Havant PO9 1NU
*Tel:* (023) 9248 4943
*Key Personnel*
Editorial, Sales: Mrs J M Curley
Founded: 1907
Subjects: Art
ISBN Prefix(es): 0-900083

**Artech House+**
46 Gillingham St, London SW1V 1AH
*Tel:* (020) 7596 8750 *Fax:* (020) 7630 0166
*E-mail:* artech-uk@artechhouse.com
*Web Site:* www.artechhouse.com
*Key Personnel*
Chief Executive: William M Bazzy
Dir, Sales & Marketing: Sharon J Horn
Senior Commissioning Editor: Dr Julie A Lan-
cashire
Founded: 1969
Publisher of professional books for engineers &
managers.
Subjects: Communications, Computer Science,
Electronics, Electrical Engineering, Engineering
(General), Management, Radio, TV, Science
(General), Technology, Transportation
ISBN Prefix(es): 0-89006; 1-58053
Number of titles published annually: 70 Print; 5
CD-ROM
*Parent Company:* Artech House Inc, 685 Canton
St, Norwood, MA 02062, United States
*Associate Companies:* Horizon House Publica-
tions, 46 Gillingham St, London SWIV 1HH
*Warehouse:* Mercury International, Yeomans Dr,
Brickhill St, Blakelands TN9 1TD *Tel:* (01908)
218844

**Artetech Publishing Co**
54 Frome Rd, Bradford-on-Avon, Wilts BA15
1LD
*Tel:* (01225) 862482 *Fax:* (01225) 865601
*Key Personnel*
President: Dr G Terence Meaden *E-mail:* terence.
meaden@torro.org.uk
Founded: 1975

Also publishes the monthly international Journal
of Meteorology.
Subjects: Archaeology, Earth Sciences, Environ-
mental Studies
ISBN Prefix(es): 0-9510590
Total Titles: 3 Print
*Associate Companies:* Tornado & Storm Research
Organization
Imprints: Meteorology

**Arthur James Ltd+**
Imprint of John Hunt Publishing Ltd
46a West St, New Alresford, Hants S024 9AU
*Tel:* (01962) 736880 *Fax:* (01962) 736881
*E-mail:* office@johnhunt-publishing.com
*Web Site:* www.johnhunt-publishing.com
*Key Personnel*
Contact: J Hunt *E-mail:* johnhuntpublishing@
compuserve.com
Founded: 1935
Membership(s): Independent Publishers Guild.
Subjects: Philosophy, Psychology, Psychiatry,
Religion - Buddhist, Religion - Catholic, Re-
ligion - Hindu, Religion - Jewish, Religion -
Protestant, Social Sciences, Sociology, Theol-
ogy, Meditation
ISBN Prefix(es): 0-85305
Total Titles: 300 Print
*Associate Companies:* Cairns Publications
*Shipping Address:* Unit 9 Amor Way, Durhams
Lane, Letchworth, Herts SG6 1VA
*Warehouse:* Unit 9 Amor Way, Dunhams Lane,
Letchworth, Herts SG6 1VA

**Arts Council of England**
14 Great Peter St, London SW1P 3NQ
*Tel:* (020) 7333 0100 *Fax:* (020) 7973 6590
*E-mail:* enquiries@artscouncil.org.uk
*Web Site:* www.artscouncil.org.uk
*Key Personnel*
Chairman: Gerry Robinson
Chief Executive: Peter Hewitt
Executive Dir, Communications: Wendy Andrews
Dir, Information: Michael Clark
Assistant Officer, Infomation: J Lomas
*Tel:* 9736517 *E-mail:* jackie.lomas@artscouncil.
org.uk
Founded: 1946
Specialize in arts policy, arts management & re-
search.
Subjects: Art, Photography, Dance, Drama, Visual
Arts
ISBN Prefix(es): 0-7287
Distributed by Marston Book Services Ltd

**Ashgate Publishing Ltd**
Gower House, Croft Rd, Aldershot, Hants GU11
3HR
*Tel:* (01252) 331551 *Fax:* (01252) 344405
*E-mail:* info@ashgate.com
*Web Site:* www.ashgate.com
*Key Personnel*
Senior Administrator, Editorial & Production:
Jacque Cox *E-mail:* jcox@ashgatepub.co.uk
Senior Editor, Academic Business & Eco-
nomics: Brendan George *E-mail:* bgeorge@
ashgatepublishing.com
Senior Editor, International Relations & Pol-
itics: Kirstin Howgate *E-mail:* khowgate@
ashgatepublishing.com
Senior Editor, Sociology, Ethnic & Gender
Studies, Social Policy & Social Work: Car-
oline Wintersgill *E-mail:* cwintersgill@
ashgatepublishing.com
Editor, Art & Architectural History: Pamela Ed-
wardes
Editor, History: Thomas Gray *E-mail:* tgray@
ashgatepub.co.uk
Editor, Human Geography, Environmental Studies, Planning & Transport: Valerie Rose
*E-mail:* vrose@ashgatepublishing.com

Editor, Librarianship & Information Management: Suzie Duke *E-mail:* dukesuz@aol.com; Alison Kirk *E-mail:* akirk@ashgatepublishing.com
Editor, Music: Heidi May *E-mail:* hmay@ashgatepub.co.uk
Publishing Dir, Art Books: Lucy Myers *Tel:* (020) 7841 9800 *Fax:* (020) 7837 6322 *E-mail:* lmyers@ashgatepub.co.uk
Publishing Dir, Business & Management: Josephine Burges
Publisher, History & Variorum: John Smedley *E-mail:* jsmedley@ashgatepub.co.uk
Publisher, Music: Rachel Lynch
Publisher, Theology & Religious Studies: Sarah Lloyd *E-mail:* slloyd@ashgatepub.co.uk
Publisher, Training & Professional: Jonathan Norman
Consultant Publisher, Aviation: John Hindley *Tel:* (01483) 860336 *Fax:* (01483) 860336 *E-mail:* jhindley@ashgatepublishing.com
Consultant Publisher, Law & Legal Studies: John Irwin *E-mail:* jirwin@ashgatepublishing.com
Manager, International Sales Department: Richard Dowling *E-mail:* rdowling@ashgatepublishing. com
Founded: 1967
Subjects: Architecture & Interior Design, Art, Business, Criminology, Economics, Environmental Studies, Government, Political Science, History, Law, Library & Information Sciences, Literature, Literary Criticism, Essays, Management, Marketing, Music, Dance, Philosophy, Public Administration, Social Sciences, Sociology, Theology, Transportation
ISBN Prefix(es): 0-566; 1-85742; 1-85628; 0-86078; 0-85972; 0-86127; 0-85331; 0-291; 0-7546; 1-85521; 1-85928; 1-84014; 0-906909
Number of titles published annually: 750 Print
*Associate Companies:* Dartmouth Publishing Co Ltd; Gower Publishing Co Ltd
Imprints: Dartmouth (Law & Legal Studies); Gower Publishing Ltd (Business books & training resources); Lund Humphries (Art, architecture & design); Variorum (Collected studies in history)
*U.S. Office(s):* Ashgate Publishing Co, 101 Cherry St, Suite 420, Burlington, VT 05401-4405, United States *Tel:* 802-865-7641 *Fax:* 802-865-7847 *E-mail:* info@ashgate.com
Foreign Rep(s): Ashgate-Gower Asia Pacific (Australia, China, Malaysia, New Zealand, Singapore); Ashgate Publishing Co (North America, South America); Book Bird (Pakistan); ICK (Information & Culture Korea) (Korea); IMA (Africa exc North & South Africa); IPL Technologies (S) Pte Ltd (Indonesia, Philippines); Maya Publishers PVT Ltd (India); Publishers International Marketing (Middle East); United Publishers Services Ltd (Japan)
*Orders to:* Bookpoint Limited, Ashgate Gower Customer Service, 39 Milton Park, Abingdon, Oxon OX14 4TD *Tel:* (01235) 827730 *Fax:* (01235) 400454 *E-mail:* orders@bookpoint.co.uk *Web Site:* pubeasy.books.bookpoint.co.uk
2252 Ridge Rd, Brookfield, VT 05036-9704, United States *Tel:* 802-276-3162 *Fax:* 802-276-3837 *E-mail:* orders@ashgate.com (North America)

**Ashgrove Publishing+**
27 John St, London WC1N 2BX
*Tel:* (020) 7831 5013 *Fax:* (020) 7831 5011
*Web Site:* www.ashgrovepublishing.com
*Key Personnel*
Owner: Brad Thompson
Founded: 1970
Subjects: Cookery, Health, Nutrition, Mysteries, Religion - Other, Self-Help
ISBN Prefix(es): 0-906798; 1-85398
Number of titles published annually: 6 Print
Total Titles: 35 Print

*Parent Company:* Hollydata Publishers Ltd
*Distribution Center:* Bookworld Companies, 1941 Whitfield Park Loop, Sarasota, FL 34243, United States (USA)

**Ashmolean Museum Publications+**
Beaumont St, Oxford OX1 2PH
*Tel:* (01865) 278010 *Fax:* (01865) 278018
*E-mail:* publications@ashmus.ox.ac.uk
*Web Site:* www.ashmol.ox.ac.uk/ash/publications
*Key Personnel*
Sales & Marketing Officer: Declan McCarthy
Founded: 1683
Publishing & retail sales.
Subjects: Archaeology, Art, Asian Studies, Crafts, Games, Hobbies, History, Regional Interests, Travel
ISBN Prefix(es): 0-907849; 1-85444; 0-900090
Number of titles published annually: 15 Print
*Parent Company:* University of Oxford
Imprints: Griffith Institute
*Branch Office(s)*
Scholarly Book Services Inc, Canadian Distribution, 77 Mowat Ave, Suite 403, Toronto, ON M6K 3E3, Canada
*U.S. Office(s):* Arthur Schwarz & Co Inc, US Distribution, 15 Meades Mountain Rd, Woodstock, NY 12498, United States
*Warehouse:* Gazelle, Unit 2-3, Hightown, LEL Industrial Estate, Whitecross Mills, Lancaster
*Orders to:* Gazelle Book Services Ltd, Falcon House, Queen St, Lancaster LA1 1RN *Tel:* (01524) 68765 *Fax:* (01524) 63232
Woodstocker Books, Arthur Schwartz & Co Inc, 15 Meads Mountain Rd, Woodstock, NY 12498, United States *Tel:* 845-679-4024 *Fax:* 845-679-4093 *E-mail:* aschwartz@ aschwartzbooks.com *Web Site:* www. aschwartzbooks.com (US)

**Ashton & Denton Publishing Co (CI) Ltd**
3 Burlington House, Saint Savior's Rd, Saint Helier, Jersey JE2 4LA
*Tel:* (01534) 735461; (01534) 727976 *Fax:* (01534) 875805
*Key Personnel*
Man Dir & Sales: A D W Mackenzie
Editorial & Publicity: Mrs Y E Ashden *E-mail:* ashden@supanet.com
Production: M Mackenzie
Founded: 1948
Specialize in Channel Islands publications.
Subjects: Business, Finance, Regional Interests
ISBN Prefix(es): 0-85053
Number of titles published annually: 6 Print
Total Titles: 8 Print
*U.S. Office(s):* Ashton & Denton Publishing Co, PO Box 3, Cornish, UT, United States

**Aslib, The Association for Information Management+**
Temple Chambers, 3-7 Temple Ave, London EC4Y 0HP
*Tel:* (020) 7583 8900 *Fax:* (020) 7583 8401
*E-mail:* aslib@aslib.com; pubs@aslib.com
*Web Site:* www.aslib.co.uk
*Key Personnel*
Managing Editor: Diane Heath
Head of Publications: Sarah Blair
Marketing Manager: Chris Grandy
Founded: 1924
Membership(s): FID, ECIA, ALPSP, ICSTI.
Subjects: Business, Law, Library & Information Sciences, Management, Technology
ISBN Prefix(es): 0-85142
Distributed by DA Books & Journals Pty (Australia); Kinokuniyiya (Japan); Portland Press LD (Rest of World); Allied Publishers Pvt Ltd
*Orders to:* Portland Press Ltd, Commerce Way, Whitehall Industrial Estate, Colchester CO2 8HP

**Aspect**, *imprint of* Salamander Books Ltd

**Aspect Guides**, *imprint of* Peter Collin Publishing Ltd

**Associated University Presses**, *imprint of* Golden Cockerel Press Ltd

**The Association for Information Management**, see Aslib, The Association for Information Management

**Association for Scottish Literary Studies+**
c/o Dept of Scottish History, University of Glasgow, 9 University Gardens, Glasgow G12 8QH
*Tel:* (0141) 330 5309 *Fax:* (0141) 330 5309
*Web Site:* www.asls.org.uk
*Key Personnel*
President: Alan MacGillivray
Treasurer: Tom Ralph
Secretary: Lorna Smith
General Editorial: Dr Liam McIlvanney
General Manager: Duncan Jones *E-mail:* d. jones@scothist.arts.gla.ac.uk
Founded: 1970
ASLS is an educational charity supporting the study, teaching & writing of Scottish literature & language.
Subjects: Literature, Literary Criticism, Essays, Scottish Literature & Linguistics
ISBN Prefix(es): 0-948877; 0-9502629
Number of titles published annually: 6 Print
*Orders to:* Book Source, Cowlairs Estate, 32 Finlas St, Glasgow G22 5DU *Tel:* (0141) 557 0189 *E-mail:* orders@booksource.net

**Association of Commonwealth Universities (ACU)**
John Foster House, 36 Gordon Sq, London WC1H 0PF
*Tel:* (020) 7380 6700 *Fax:* (020) 7387 2655
*E-mail:* info@acu.ac.uk
*Web Site:* www.acu.ac.uk *Cable:* ACUMEN LONDON WC1
*Key Personnel*
Secretary General: Dr John Rowett
Head, Product Development: Sue Kirkland *Tel:* (020) 7380 6710 *E-mail:* s.kirkland@acu. ac.uk
Man Editor: Paul Turner
Founded: 1913
Specialize in promoting, in various practical ways, contact & cooperation between its member institutions.
Membership(s): 500 universities in 35 countries/regions in the Commonwealth; Directory & Database Publishers Association.
Subjects: Developing Countries, Education, Higher Education
ISBN Prefix(es): 0-85143
Number of titles published annually: 4 Print; 1 Online
Total Titles: 8 Print; 1 Online
Distributed by Palgrave Macmillan

**Association for Science Education+**
College Lane, Hatfield, Herts AL10 9AA
*Tel:* (01707) 283000 *Fax:* (01707) 266532
*E-mail:* info@ase.org.uk
*Web Site:* www.ase.org.uk
*Key Personnel*
Chief Executive: Dr Derek Bell
Deputy Chief Executive: John Lawrence
Publications Dir: Jane R Hanrott
Booksales Manager: Rob Oxley
Founded: 1901
Subjects: Biological Sciences, Chemistry, Chemical Engineering, Computer Science, Disability, Special Needs, Education, Energy, Physics, Science (General)
ISBN Prefix(es): 0-86357

Number of titles published annually: 12 Print; 1
  CD-ROM
Total Titles: 25 Print; 1 CD-ROM


**Astic**, *imprint of* Gwasg Gwenffrwd


**ATAPepperpot Gift**, *imprint of* Colour Library
Direct


**Atelier Books**
6 Dundas St, Edinburgh EH3 6HZ
*Tel:* (0131) 5574050 *Fax:* (0131) 5578382
*E-mail:* mail@bournefineart.co.uk
*Web Site:* www.bournefineart.co.uk/books.html
*Key Personnel*
Man Dir: Patrick Bourne *E-mail:* bournefineart@
  enterprise.net
ISBN Prefix(es): 1-873830
*Orders to:* Scottish Book Source, 137 Dundee
  St, Edinburgh EH11 1BG *Tel:* (0131) 229
  6800 *Fax:* (0131) 229 9070 *Web Site:* www.
  scottishbooks.org


**The Athlone Press Ltd+**
The Continuum International Publishing Group
  Ltd, The Tower Bldg, 11 York Rd, London
  SE1 7NX
*Tel:* (020) 7922 0880 *Fax:* (020) 7922 0881
*E-mail:* athlonepress@btinternet.com
*Web Site:* www.transcomm.ox.ac.uk/wwwroot/
  athlone_press.htm
*Key Personnel*
Chairman: Brian Southam
Man Dir: Doris Southam
Editorial Dir: Tristan Palmer *E-mail:* tpalmer.
  athlonepress@btinternet.com
Production Manager: P J Albutt
Founded: 1949
Subjects: Anthropology, Archaeology, Art, Asian
  Studies, Economics, Film, Video, History, Law,
  Philosophy, Science (General), Social Sciences,
  Sociology, Academic
*U.S. Office(s):* The Athlone Press, 390 Cam-
  pus Dr, Somerset, NJ 08873, United States
  *Tel:* 732-445-1245 *Fax:* 732-748-9801
*Warehouse:* Hoddle Doyle Meadows Ltd, Station
  Rd, Linton, Cambs CB1 69W
*Orders to:* c/o Book Systems Plus, BSP House,
  Station Rd, Linton, Cambs CB1 6NW
  *Tel:* (01223) 894870 *Fax:* (01223) 894871


**Atlantic Transport Publishers**
Trevithick House, West End, Penryn TR10 8HE
*Tel:* (01326) 373656 *Fax:* (01326) 378309;
  (01326) 373656
*Key Personnel*
Contact: David Joy *E-mail:* davjoy@aol.com
Founded: 1979
Subjects: History, Mechanical Engineering, Trans-
  portation
ISBN Prefix(es): 0-906899; 1-902827
*Orders to:* Atlantic Publishers, Trevithick House,
  West End, Penryn, Cornwall TR10 8HE


**Atlas Press+**
BCM Atlas Press, 27 Old Gloucester St, London
  WC1N 3XX
*Tel:* (020) 7490 8742 *Fax:* (021) 7490 8742
*E-mail:* enquiries@atlaspress.co.uk
*Web Site:* www.atlaspress.co.uk
*Key Personnel*
Partner: Alastair Brotchie; Malcolm Green
Partner & Rights Contact: Antony Melville
Copy Editor & Proofreader: Chris Allen
Founded: 1983
Accessible translations of key works of the Euro-
  pean avant-garde of the last 100 years. Mostly
  previously untranslated & often unobtainable
  in their original languages; where possible,
  editing done in collaboration with living au-

thors/groups/artists; concise introductions &
  annotation as necessary.
Subjects: Alternative, Art, Biography, Drama,
  Theater, Erotica, Fiction, European Avant-
  Garde Literature & Art, Art History, Limited
  Editions
ISBN Prefix(es): 0-947757; 1-900565
Number of titles published annually: 8 Print
Total Titles: 75 Print
Imprints: The Printed Head
Distributed by Exact Change (trade titles only);
  Marginal Distribution (Canada); Peribo Pty Ltd
  (Australia)
Distributor for Cymbalum Pataphysicum
Foreign Rep(s): Exact Exchange (US)
*Orders to:* Consortium Inc, 1045 Westgate Dr, St
  Paul, MN 51140-0165, United States *Tel:* 612-
  221-9035 *Fax:* 612-221-0124
Turnaround Publisher Services, Olympia Trading
  Estate, Unit 3, Coburg Rd, London N22 6TZ,
  Contact: Bill Godber *Tel:* (020) 8829 3000
  *Fax:* (020) 8881 5088


**Atom**, *imprint of* Time Warner Book Group UK


**Attack!**, *imprint of* Creation Books


**Audio-Forum - The Language Source**
POB 35488, St Johns Wood, London NW8 6WD
*Tel:* (020) 586 4499 *Fax:* (020) 722 1068
*E-mail:* microworld@ndirect.co.uk
*Web Site:* www.microworld.ndirect.co.uk
Subjects: Language Arts, Linguistics
Total Titles: 250 Print


**Audiobooks**, *imprint of* Random House UK Ltd


**Augener**, *imprint of* Stainer & Bell Ltd


**Aulis Publishers**
Imprint of David Percy Associates
25 Belsize Park, London NW3 4DU
*Tel:* (01672) 539 041 *Fax:* (01373) 452 888
*E-mail:* info@aulis.com
*Web Site:* www.aulis.com
*Key Personnel*
Director: David Percy
Founded: 1992
Specialize in videotapes on space.
Subjects: History, Physical Sciences
ISBN Prefix(es): 1-898541
Total Titles: 3 Print


**Aurora Northern Classics**, *imprint of* The
  Orkney Press Ltd


**Aurum Press Ltd+**
25 Bedford Ave, London WC1B 3AT
*Tel:* (020) 7637 3225 *Fax:* (020) 7580 2469
*Web Site:* www.aurumpress.co.uk
*Key Personnel*
Man Dir: Bill McCreadie *E-mail:* bill.
  mccreadie@aurumpress.co.uk
Editorial Dir: Piers Burnett *E-mail:* piers.
  burnett@aurumpress.co.uk
Sr Editor: Graham Coster
Sales Dir: Graham Eanes
Founded: 1976
Subjects: Art, Biography, Film, Video, Military
  Science, Nonfiction (General), Photography,
  Sports, Athletics, Travel, General adult nonfic-
  tion
ISBN Prefix(es): 1-85410; 1-903221 (Jacqui
  Small); 1-902538 (Argentum); 1-84513
Number of titles published annually: 70 Print
Total Titles: 250 Print

Imprints: Argentum (Specialist photography);
  Jacqui Small (Books on interiors, lifestyle, gar-
  dens)
*Warehouse:* Littlehampton Book Services, Fara-
  day Close, Durrington Worthing BN13 3HD
  *Tel:* (01903) 828500 *Fax:* (01903) 828625


**Authentic Lifestyle**, *imprint of* Paternoster
Publishing


**Autumn Publishing Ltd**
North Barn, Appledram Barns, Birdham Rd, Ap-
  pledram, Chichester PO20 7EQ
*Tel:* (01243) 531660 *Fax:* (01243) 774433
*E-mail:* autumn@autumnpublishing.co.uk
*Web Site:* www.autumnpublishing.co.uk
*Key Personnel*
Man Dir: Campbell Goldsmid *E-mail:* campbell@
  autumnpublishing.co.uk
Founded: 1976
ISBN Prefix(es): 0-946593; 1-85997; 1-904586
Imprints: Byeway Books


**Avero Publications Ltd+**
20 Great North Rd, Newcastle-upon-Tyne NE2
  4PS
*Tel:* (0191) 2615790 *Fax:* (0191) 2611209
*E-mail:* nstc@newcastle.ac.uk
*Key Personnel*
Man Dir: F J G Robinson
Dir: Gwen Averley
Founded: 1981
Specialize in CD-ROM.
Subjects: Biography, History
ISBN Prefix(es): 0-907977
Subsidiaries: Romulus Press Ltd


**Avon**, *imprint of* HarperCollins UK


**Award Publications Ltd+**
27 Longford St, 1st floor, London NW1 3DZ
*Tel:* (020) 7388 7800 *Fax:* (020) 7388 7887
*E-mail:* info@award.abel.co.uk
*Key Personnel*
Man Dir: R Wilkinson
Production Manager: Deborah Wadsworth
Contact: Anna Wilkinson
Founded: 1955
ISBN Prefix(es): 0-86163; 1-84135
Imprints: Horus Editions
*Warehouse:* Award Publications Ltd, The Old
  Riding School, Welbeck Estate, NR Work-
  shop, Notts S80 3LS *Tel:* (01909) 478 170
  *Fax:* (01909) 484 632
*Orders to:* Award Publications Ltd, The Old
  Riding School, Welbeck Estate, NR Work-
  shop, Notts S80 3LS *Tel:* (01909) 478 170
  *Fax:* (01909) 484 632


**Azure**, *imprint of* The Society for Promoting
  Christian Knowledge (SPCK)


**b small publishing+**
Pinewood, 3A Coombe Ridings, Kingston-Upon-
  Thames KT2 7JT
*Tel:* (020) 8974 6851 *Fax:* (020) 8974 6845
*E-mail:* info@bsmall.co.uk
*Web Site:* homepage.ntlworld.com/codework/
  welcome.htm
*Key Personnel*
Partner/Publisher: Catherine Bruzzone
  *E-mail:* cath@bsmall.co.uk
Founded: 1990
Specialize in general children's activity books &
  foreign language learning.
ISBN Prefix(es): 1-874735; 1-902915
Distributed by MacMillan Distribution Ltd (UK
  trade)

## BAAF Adoption & Fostering+
Skyline House, 200 Union St, London SE1 0LX
*Tel:* (020) 7593 2000 *Fax:* (020) 7593 2001
*E-mail:* mail@baaf.org.uk
*Web Site:* www.baaf.org.uk
*Key Personnel*
Chief Executive: Felicity Collier
Dir, Publications: Shaila Shah
Commissioning Editor of Adoption & Fostering
    (Journal): Roger Bullock
Publications Promotions Officer: Marianne
    Harper *Tel:* (020) 7593 2037 *E-mail:* marianne.
    harper@baaf.org.uk
Founded: 1980
Registered charity promoting best practice in both
    adoption & fostering services. Umbrella body
    for member agencies & all those working with
    children in the UK care system.
Subjects: Child Care & Development, Psychol-
    ogy, Psychiatry, Social Sciences, Sociology,
    Adoption, Childcare, Fostering
ISBN Prefix(es): 0-903534; 1-873868; 0-9506807;
    1-903699
Number of titles published annually: 15 Print
Total Titles: 120 Print

## Bernard Babani (Publishing) Ltd+
The Grampians, Shepherds Bush Rd, London W6
    7NF
*Tel:* (020) 7603 2581; (020) 7603 7296
    *Fax:* (020) 7603 8203
*E-mail:* enquiries@babanibooks.com
*Web Site:* www.babanibooks.com *Cable:*
    RADIOBOOKS LONDON W6
*Key Personnel*
Man Dir, Edit: M H Babani
Sales, Rights & Permissions: S Babani
Production, Publicity: P Pragnell
Founded: 1977 (Babani Press 1971, Bernards
    Publishers 1942)
Subjects: Computer Science, Electronics, Electri-
    cal Engineering, Radio, TV
ISBN Prefix(es): 0-85934; 0-900162
*Associate Companies:* Babani Press

## Babel Guides, *imprint of* Boulevard Books
UK/The Babel Guides

## Baha'i Publishing Trust+
4 Station Approach, Oakham, Rutland LE15
    6QW
*Tel:* (01572) 722780 *Fax:* (01572) 724280
*E-mail:* sales@bahaibooks.co.uk
*Web Site:* www.bahai-publishing-trust.co.uk
*Key Personnel*
General Manager: Gordon James Kerr
Editorial Dir: George Ballentyne
Founded: 1937
Membership(s): International Association of
    Baha'i Publishers.
Subjects: Government, Political Science, Human
    Relations, Philosophy, Religion - Other, Social
    Sciences, Sociology
ISBN Prefix(es): 0-900125; 1-870987
*Parent Company:* NSA Baha'is of UK
Imprints: Nightingale Books
*Shipping Address:* The Maltings, Station Rd, Ket-
    ton, Near Stamford, Kent, Lincs PE9 3RQ
*Warehouse:* The Maltings, Station Rd, Ketton,
    Near Stamford, Lincs PE9 3RQ

## Bill Bailey Publishers' Representatives
16 Devon Sq, Newton Abbot, Devon TQ12 2HR
*Tel:* (01626) 331079 *Fax:* (01626) 331080
*E-mail:* billbailey.pubrep@eclipse.co.uk
*Key Personnel*
Partner: W G Bailey; N Hammond; B J McGee;
    M J Parsons
Founded: 1981
Sales Representation in Europe
A partnership with all types of books.

Distributed by International Publishers Represen-
    tatives Ltd (Eastern Mediterranean & Middle
    East); JAMCO Distribution Inc (US); Maclen-
    nan & Petty Pty Ltd (Australia); The South
    African Medical Association (South Africa)

## Bailey Brothers & Swinfen Ltd
Units 1A/1B Learoyd Rd, Mountfield Industrial
    Estate, New Romney TN28 8XU
*Tel:* (01797) 366905 *Fax:* (01797) 366638
*Key Personnel*
Dir: R P Mortimore; H J Mortimore
Founded: 1937
ISBN Prefix(es): 0-561
*Parent Company:* Bailey & Swinfen Holdings Ltd
Subsidiaries: Bailey Distribution Ltd

## Bailliere Tindall Ltd, *imprint of* Elsevier Ltd

## The Banner of Truth Trust+
The Grey House, 3 Murrayfield Rd, Edinburgh
    EH12 6EL
*Tel:* (0131) 337 7310 *Fax:* (0131) 346 7484
*E-mail:* info@banneroftruth.co.uk
*Web Site:* www.banneroftruth.co.uk
*Key Personnel*
General Manager: John Rawlinson
Editorial Dir: Hywel Jones
Production Manager: Murdo MacLeod
Founded: 1957
Historic Christianity through literature.
Subjects: Religion - Protestant
ISBN Prefix(es): 0-85151
*U.S. Office(s):* PO Box 621, Carlisle, PA 17013,
    United States *Tel:* 717-249-5747 *Fax:* 717-249-
    0604 *E-mail:* info@banneroftruth.org
*Warehouse:* 17 Bankhead Dr, Sighthill Industrial
    Estate, Edinburgh EH11 4DW

## Banson
3 Turville St, London E27 7HX
*Tel:* (020) 7613 1388 *Fax:* (020) 7729 7870
*E-mail:* banson@ourplanet.com
*Key Personnel*
Man Dir: Mr B Ullstein
Founded: 1987
Specialize in packaging for International Organi-
    zations.
Subjects: Environmental Studies

## Bantam Paperbacks, *imprint of* Transworld
Publishers Ltd

## Bantam Press, *imprint of* Transworld Publishers
Ltd

## The Banton Press
Dippin Cottage, Kildonan, Isle of Arran KA27
    8SB
*Tel:* (01770) 820231 *Fax:* (01770) 820231
*E-mail:* bantonpress@btinternet.com
*Web Site:* www.bantonpress.co.uk
*Key Personnel*
Contact: Mark E G Brown
Founded: 1988
Subjects: Astrology, Occult, History, Mysteries,
    Religion - Other
ISBN Prefix(es): 1-85652
Number of titles published annually: 4 Print
Total Titles: 176 Print

## McCall Barbour+
28 George IV Bridge, Edinburgh EH1 1ES
*Tel:* (0131) 225-4816 *Fax:* (0131) 225-4816
*E-mail:* ashbethany43@hotmail.com
*Key Personnel*
Man Dir: Dr T C Danson-Smith
Founded: 1900
Christian Publishers.
Subjects: Religion - Protestant

ISBN Prefix(es): 0-7132
Total Titles: 2 Print

## Barefoot Books
124 Walcot St, Bath BA1 5BG
*Tel:* (01225) 322400 *Fax:* (01225) 322499
*E-mail:* info@barefootbooks.co.uk
*Web Site:* www.barefootbooks.com
Founded: 1993
*Branch Office(s)*
2067 Massachusetts Ave, Cambridge, MA 02140,
    United States

## Barmarick Publications
Enholmes Hall, Patrington, Hull, East Yorks
    HU12 0PR
*Tel:* (01964) 630033 *Fax:* (01964) 631716
*Web Site:* www.barmarick.co.uk
*Key Personnel*
Partner: Dr R Dobbins; A M Lunn; Dr B O
    Pettman *E-mail:* barrie.o.pettman@barmarick.
    co.uk
Founded: 1982
Subjects: Labor, Industrial Relations, Manage-
    ment, Social Sciences, Sociology
ISBN Prefix(es): 1-85385
Total Titles: 292 Print

## Barn Dance Publications Ltd+
62 Beechwood Rd, Croydon CR2 0AA
*Tel:* (020) 8657 2813 *Fax:* (020) 8651 6080
*E-mail:* barndance@pubs.co.uk
*Web Site:* www.barndancepublications.co.uk
*Key Personnel*
Dir: Derek L Jones
Founded: 1984
Membership(s): Book Data.
Subjects: Music, Dance, Fold Dance
ISBN Prefix(es): 0-9514275; 1-874565
Total Titles: 18 Print; 13 Audio

## Barn Owl Press (Children's Books), *imprint of*
Alun Books

## Barnabas, *imprint of* Bible Reading Fellowship

## Bartsky Legal Texts Ltd, *imprint of* CyberClub

## Basil Blackwell Ltd, see Blackwell Publishing
Ltd

## Batsford Ltd+
Division of Chrysalis Group
The Chrysalis Bldg, Bramley Rd, London W10
    6SP
*Tel:* (020) 7221 2213; (020) 7314 1469 (sales)
    *Fax:* (020) 7221 6455; (020) 7314 1594 (sales)
*E-mail:* enquiries@chrysalis.com
*Web Site:* www.chrysalisbooks.co.uk/books/
    publisher/batsford
*Key Personnel*
Group Sales & Marketing Dir: Richard Samson
    *Tel:* (020) 7314 1459 *Fax:* (020) 7314 1549
    *E-mail:* rsamson@chrysalisbooks.co.uk
Dir of Marketing: Kate Wood *Tel:* (020) 7314
    1496 *E-mail:* kwood@chrysalisbooks.co.uk
Marketing & Publicity Manager: Rachel Arm-
    strong *Tel:* (020) 7314 1605 *Fax:* (020) 7314
    1549 *E-mail:* rarmstrong@chrysalisbooks.co.uk
Foreign Rights Manager: Emma O'Grady
    *Tel:* (020) 7314 1447 *E-mail:* eogrady@
    chrysalisbooks.co.uk
Permissions: Terry Forshaw *Tel:* (020) 7314 1607
    *E-mail:* tforshaw@chrysalisbooks.co.uk
Founded: 1843
Subjects: Agriculture, Archaeology, Architecture
    & Interior Design, Art, Crafts, Games, Hob-
    bies, Fashion, Film, Video, Gardening, Plants,
    History, House & Home, Nonfiction (General),
    Outdoor Recreation, Photography, Social Sci-
    ences, Sociology
ISBN Prefix(es): 0-7134

*U.S. Office(s):* 9 East 40 St, 10th floor, New York, NY, United States

Distributor for Chilton Book Co; Lennard/Queen Anne Press; Meredith Books (Europe); Taunton Press; Storey Books

*Foreign Rights:* Emma O'Grady (Eastern Europe, Italy, Latin America, Portugal, Russia, Spain)

*Orders to:* HarperCollins Distribution, Campsie View, Westerhill Rd, Bishopbriggs, Glasgow G64 2QT *Fax:* (087) 0787 1995 (Trade only)

**Colin Baxter**, *imprint of* Colin Baxter Photography Ltd

**Colin Baxter Photography Ltd+**
The Old Dairy, Woodlands Industrial Estate, Grantown-on-Spey, Morayshire PH26 3NA
*Tel:* (01479) 873999 *Fax:* (01479) 873888
*E-mail:* sales@colinbaxter.co.uk
*Web Site:* www.colinbaxter.co.uk; www. worldlifelibrary.co.uk
*Key Personnel*
Man Dir: Colin Baxter
Marketing Dir & Rights: Colin Kirkwood
   *E-mail:* colin.kirkwood@colinbaxter.co.uk
Editorial & Production Dir: Mike Rensner
Founded: 1984
Independent private company.
Subjects: Natural History, Photography, Travel
ISBN Prefix(es): 0-948661; 0-900455; 1-84107
Number of titles published annually: 20 Print
Total Titles: 80 Print
Imprints: Colin Baxter; Worldlife Library
Distributed by Voyageur Press (US)
Foreign Rep(s): Ted Dougherty (Austria, Belgium, Netherlands, France, Germany, Greece, Italy, Luxembourg, Switzerland); Theo Philips (Brunei, Hong Kong, Malaysia, Philippines, Singapore, Thailand); Peter Prout (Spain); Voyageur Press Inc (US)
*Orders to:* Freepost, PO Box 1, Grantown-on-Spey, Moray PH26 3YA

**Bay View Books Ltd+**
The Red House, 25-26 Bridgeland St, Bideford EX39 2PZ
*Tel:* (01237) 479225; (01237) 421285
   *Fax:* (01237) 421286
*Key Personnel*
International Rights: Charles Herridge
Founded: 1986
Subjects: Automotive
ISBN Prefix(es): 1-870979; 1-901432
*Warehouse:* Bailey Distribution Ltd, Units 1A/B Learoyd Rd, Mountfield Industrial Estate, New Romney, Kent TN28 8XU
*Orders to:* Chris Lloyd Sales & Marketing, 463 Ashley Rd, Parkstone, Poole, Dorset BH14 0AX

**BBC Audiobooks+**
St James House, The Square, Lower Bristol Rd, Bath BA2 3SB
*Tel:* (01225) 325336 *Fax:* (01225) 310771
*E-mail:* bbc@covertocover.co.uk
*Web Site:* www.bbcaudiobooks.com
*Key Personnel*
Man Dir: Paul Dempsey
Publishing Dir: Jan Paterson
Production & Publicity Manager: Lesley Barnes
Sales Manager: Mary Finch *E-mail:* mary@ chivers.co.uk
Marketing Manager: Christine Graham
   *E-mail:* christine@chivers.co.uk
Founded: 1979
Specialize in large print books, audio books (complete & unabridged) & facsimile reprints.
Subjects: Biography, Fiction, Mysteries, Nonfiction (General), Romance, Western Fiction
ISBN Prefix(es): 0-7540
Number of titles published annually: 1,215 Print; 216 Audio

Total Titles: 4,300 Print; 2,500 Audio
*Parent Company:* BBC Worldwide, 80 Wood Lane, London W12 0TT
Imprints: Black Dagger; Cavalcade Story Cassettes; Camden Large Print; Chivers Children's Audio Books; Chivers Large Print; Galaxy Large Print; Gunsmoke Western; Paragon; Read-Along; Sterling Audio Books; Windsor Large Print Bestsellers; Word for Word Audio Books
*U.S. Office(s):* Chivers North America, One Lafayette Rd, Box 1450, Hampton, NH 03842-0015, United States, Contact: Jim Brannigan *Tel:* 603-926-8744 *Fax:* 603-929-3890
Foreign Rep(s): Booktalk Pty Ltd (audio books) (Southern Africa); Chivers North America (US); Hargraves Library Service (large print) (Australia); Hargraves Library Service (Southern Africa); The Library Supply Co Ltd (New Zealand); Michael O'Brien (Ireland); Vanwell Publishing Ltd (Canada)

**BBC Books**, *imprint of* BBC Worldwide Publishers

**BBC English+**
Woodlands, 80 Wood Lane, London W12 0TT
*Tel:* (020) 8576 2221 *Fax:* (020) 8576 3040
*Web Site:* www.bbcenglish.com
*Key Personnel*
Dir: Charles Hyde
Dir, International Publishing: Be Lenthall
Founded: 1943
Subjects: English as a Second Language
ISBN Prefix(es): 1-85497; 0-946675
*Parent Company:* BBC Worldwide Ltd

**BBC Worldwide Publishers+**
Woodlands, 80 Wood Lane, London W12 0TT
*Tel:* (020) 8433 2000 *Fax:* (020) 8749 0538
*E-mail:* bbcsales@bbc.co.uk
*Web Site:* www.bbcworldwide.com
*Telex:* 934678 BBCENTG *Cable:* BROADCASTS LONDON
*Key Personnel*
Head of Book Publishing: Chris Weller
Head of Sales & Marketing: Stuart Biles
Production Manager: Brian Dickson
Sales & Marketing Dir: Kevin Harrington
International Sales & Marketing Dir: Charles Hyde
International Rights & Export Manager: Richard Gay
Founded: 1925
Subjects: Cookery, Gardening, Plants, History, Language Arts, Linguistics, Natural History
ISBN Prefix(es): 0-7540
*Parent Company:* BBC Worldwide
Imprints: Network Books; BBC Books
*Bookshop(s):* 4-5 Langham Pl, Upper Regent St, London
*Orders to:* Exel-logistics Media Services, Invicta House, St Thomas Longley Rd, Medway City Industrial Estate, Rochester, Kent ME2 4DU
   *Tel:* (0634) 297123 *Fax:* (0634) 298000

**BCA - Book Club Associates+**
Greater London House, Hampstead Rd, Camden, London NW1 7TZ
*Tel:* (020) 7760 6500 *Fax:* (020) 7760 6501
*Web Site:* www.bca.co.uk
*Key Personnel*
Chief Executive: Alan Roe
Editorial Dir: Chris Holifield
Founded: 1966
Subjects: Aeronautics, Aviation, Animals, Pets, Antiques, Archaeology, Architecture & Interior Design, Art, Astrology, Occult, Automotive, Cookery, Crafts, Games, Hobbies, Fiction, Film, Video, Gardening, Plants, Geography, Geology, History, How-to, Humor, Literature, Literary Criticism, Essays, Microcomputers,

Military Science, Music, Dance, Mysteries, Natural History, Nonfiction (General), Outdoor Recreation, Photography, Poetry, Romance, Science (General), Science Fiction, Fantasy, Self-Help, Sports, Athletics, Travel, Wine & Spirits
*Ultimate Parent Company:* Bertelsmann AG, Germany
*Branch Office(s)*
Guild House, Farnsby St, Swindon, Wilts SN1 5DD *Tel:* (01793) 512100 *Fax:* (01793) 567711
*Book Club(s):* Ancient & Medieval History; Arts Guild; bol.com; Book Club of Ireland; Books Direct; Books for Children; English Book Club; Escape Fiction; Fantasy & Science Fiction; History Guild; Home Software World; Just Good Books; Mango; Military & Aviation; Mind, Body & Spirit; Mystery & Thriller Guild; Quality Paperbacks Direct; Railway Book Club; Taste; TSP; World Books

**BCP**, *imprint of* Gerald Duckworth & Co Ltd

**Beaconsfield**, *imprint of* Beaconsfield Publishers Ltd

**Beaconsfield Publishers Ltd+**
20 Chiltern Hills Rd, Beaconsfield, Bucks HP9 1PL
*Tel:* (01494) 672118 *Fax:* (01494) 672118
*E-mail:* books@beaconsfield-publishers.co.uk
*Web Site:* www.beaconsfield-publishers.co.uk
*Key Personnel*
President, Editor & Man Dir: John Churchill
Founded: 1979
Carefully developed titles in medicine, nursing, patient care & homeopathy.
Membership(s): IPG.
Subjects: Alternative, Health, Nutrition, Medicine, Nursing, Dentistry
ISBN Prefix(es): 0-906584
Number of titles published annually: 2 Print
Total Titles: 34 Print
Imprints: Beaconsfield
Foreign Rep(s): Astam Books (Australia); Viking Seven Seas (New Zealand)
*Orders to:* Jackson Distribution, 3 Gibsons Rd, Heaton Moor, Stockport SK4 4JX, Contact: Brian Jackson *Tel:* (0161) 947-9669 *Fax:* (0161) 947-9669 *E-mail:* jacksonpub@ aol.com
*Returns:* Jackson Distribution, 3 Gibsons Rd, Heaton Moor, Stockport SK4 4JX, Contact: Brian Jackson *Tel:* (0161) 947-9669 *Fax:* (0161) 947-9669 *E-mail:* jacksonpub@ aol.com

**Ruth Bean Publishers+**
Victoria Farmhouse, Carlton, Bedford MK43 7LP
*Tel:* (01234) 720356 *Fax:* (01234) 720590
*E-mail:* ruthbean@onetel.net.uk
*Key Personnel*
Dir: Nigel Bean; Ruth Bean
Founded: 1972
Specialize in needlecrafts & costume.
Membership(s): IPG.
Subjects: Anthropology, Crafts, Games, Hobbies, Drama, Theater, Fashion
ISBN Prefix(es): 0-903585

**Beano Books**, *imprint of* Geddes & Grosset

**Mitchell Beazley+**
2-4 Heron Quays, London E14 4JP
*Tel:* (020) 7531 8400; (020) 7531 8480 (UK sales); (020) 7531 8481 (special sales); (020) 7531 8479 (marketing); (020) 7531 8488 (publicity); (020) 7531 8482 (export sales); (020) 7531 8484 (foreign rights); (020) 7531 8476 (US sales) *Fax:* (020) 7531 8650
*E-mail:* enquiries@mitchell-beazley.co.uk
*Web Site:* www.mitchell-beazley.com

*Key Personnel*
Publisher & Man Dir: Jane Aspden
UK Sales & Marketing Dir: Mark Scott
International Sales & Marketing Dir: Kate Newton
Editorial Dir: Louise Dixon
Art Dir: Vivien Brar
Production Dir: Julie Young
Financial Controller: Paula Warrender
UK Sales Manager: Helen Twewus
Publicity Manager: Fiona Smith
Marketing Manager: Nicola Wright
Special Sales Executive: Clare Webb
Founded: 1969
High quality book publishers.
Subjects: Antiques, Cookery, Gardening, Plants, House & Home, Wine & Spirits
ISBN Prefix(es): 0-85533; 1-85732; 1-84000; 0-86134
*Parent Company:* Octopus Publishing Group
*Orders to:* Littlehampton Book Services Ltd, Faraday Close, Durrington, Worthing, West Sussex BN13 3RB *Tel:* (01933) 828800 *Fax:* (0193) 828802

**BECTA**, *imprint of* British Educational Communication & Technology Agency (BECTA)

**BECTA**, see British Educational Communication & Technology Agency (BECTA)

**Belitha Press Ltd+**
Division of Chrysalis Group
The Chrysalis Bldg, Bramley Rd, London W10 6SP
*Tel:* (020) 7221 2213; (020) 7314 1469 (sales) *Fax:* (020) 7221 6455; (020) 7314 1594 (sales)
*E-mail:* enquiries@chrysalis.com
*Web Site:* www.chrysalis.co.uk
*Telex:* 8950511 ONEONE
*Key Personnel*
Dir, Children's Sales & Marketing: Dennis McGuirk *Tel:* (020) 7314 1623 *E-mail:* dmcguirk@chrysalisbooks.co.uk
Marketing & Publicity Manager: Ben Cameron *Tel:* (020) 7314 1625 *E-mail:* bcameron@chrysalisbooks.co.uk
Publicity Officer: Tessa Arditti *Tel:* (020) 7314 1627 *E-mail:* tarditti@chrysalisbooks.co.uk
Foreign Rights Executive: Elisabeth Carlsson *Tel:* (020) 7314 1602 *E-mail:* ecarlsson@chrysalisbooks.co.uk
Founded: 1980
Publishers of high-quality illustrated children's books for the international market.
Subjects: Art, Biography, Crafts, Games, Hobbies, Environmental Studies, Foreign Countries, Geography, Geology, Mathematics, Music, Dance, Natural History, Nonfiction (General)
ISBN Prefix(es): 1-85561; 1-84138; 0-947553; 1-84458
*Orders to:* Littlehampton Book Services, Faraday Close, Off Columbia Dr, Durrington, West Sussex BN13 3HD *Tel:* (01903) 828800 *Fax:* (01903) 828802 *E-mail:* orders@lbsltd.co.uk (Trade only)

**Belknap**, *imprint of* Harvard University Press

**Bellew Publishing Co Ltd+**
Nightingale Centre, 8 Balham Hill, London SW12 9EA
*Tel:* (020) 8673 5611 *Fax:* (020) 8675 2142
*E-mail:* bellewsubs@hotmail.com
*Key Personnel*
Chief Executive & Man Dir: I B Bellew
Chairman: Ian Mcquordale
Founded: 1983
Also book packager.

Subjects: Architecture & Interior Design, Art, Crafts, Games, Hobbies, Environmental Studies, Fiction, History, Travel
ISBN Prefix(es): 0-947792; 1-85725
Imprints: Deirdre McDonald Ltd
*Orders to:* Plymbridge Distributors Ltd, Estover Rd, Plymouth PL6 7PZ

**Belton Books**, *imprint of* Stainer & Bell Ltd

**BEN Gunn**, *imprint of* SB Publications

**David Bennett Books+**
Division of Chrysalis Group
The Chrysalis Bldg, Bramley Rd, London W10 6SP
*Tel:* (020) 7221 2213; (020) 7314 1469 (sales) *Fax:* (020) 7221 6455; (020) 7314 1594 (sales)
*E-mail:* enquiries@chrysalis.com
*Web Site:* www.chrysalisbooks.co.uk/childrens/publisher/davidbennett
*Key Personnel*
Dir, Children's Sales & Marketing: Dennis McGuirk *Tel:* (020) 7314 1623 *E-mail:* dmcguirk@chrysalisbooks.co.uk
Marketing & Publicity Manager: Ben Cameron *Tel:* (020) 7314 1625 *E-mail:* bcameron@chrysalisbooks.co.uk
Publicity Officer: Tessa Arditti *Tel:* (020) 7314 1627 *E-mail:* tarditti@chrysalisbooks.co.uk
Foreign Rights Executive: Elisabeth Carlsson *Tel:* (020) 7314 1602 *E-mail:* ecarlsson@chrysalisbooks.co.uk
Founded: 1989
Specializes in picture books & novelties ages 0-7.
*Orders to:* Littlehampton Book Services, Faraday Close, Off Columbia Dr, Durrington, West Sussex BN13 3HD *Tel:* (01903) 828800 *Fax:* (01903) 828802 *E-mail:* orders@lbsltd.co.uk (Trade only)

**Berg Publishers+**
Imprint of Oxford International Publishers Ltd
Angel Court, 81 St Clements St, 1st floor, Oxford OX4 1AW
*Tel:* (01865) 245104 *Fax:* (01865) 791165
*E-mail:* enquiry@bergpublishers.com
*Web Site:* www.bergpublishers.com
*Key Personnel*
Man Dir: Kathryn Earle *E-mail:* kearle@bergpublishers.com
Production Manager: Ken Bruce *E-mail:* kbruce@bergpublishers.com
Founded: 1981
Academic publisher.
Subjects: Anthropology, Ethnicity, Fashion, Film, Video, Government, Political Science, History, Social Sciences, Sociology, Women's Studies
ISBN Prefix(es): 0-85496; 1-85973; 1-84520
Number of titles published annually: 60 Print; 3 Online; 30 E-Book
Total Titles: 800 Print; 3 Online; 75 E-Book
Imprints: Oswald Wolff Books
Distributed by Palgrave Macmillan (USA & Canada)
Foreign Rep(s): APAC Publishers Services PTE Ltd (Brunei, Burma, Cambodia, China, Hong Kong, Indonesia, Malaysia, Philippines, Singapore, Thailand, Vietnam); Andrew Durnell (Europe); Footprint Books Pty Ltd (Australia, Fiji, New Zealand, New Guinea); ICK (Information & Culture Korea) (Korea); IPS Middle East (Africa, Middle East); Maya Publishers (India); Troika (UK); Unifacmanu Trading Co Ltd (Taiwan); United Publishers Services Ltd (Japan)
*Shipping Address:* PSL Freight Ltd, Bathe Wharf, Station Rd, Maldon, Essex CM9 4GQ *Tel:* (01621) 854451 *Fax:* (01621) 840771
*Warehouse:* Orca Book Services, Stanley House, 3 Fleet Lane, BH15 3AJ Poole RH13 8LD

*Tel:* (01202) 665432 *Fax:* (01202) 666219
*E-mail:* orders@orcabookservices.co.uk
*Distribution Center:* VHPS Fulfillment, 16365 James Madison Hwy, Gordonsville, VA 22942, United States
*Orders to:* VHPS Fulfillment, 16365 James Madison Hwy, Gordonsville, VA 22942, United States
*Returns:* VHPS Fulfillment, 16365 James Madison Hwy, Gordonsville, VA 22942, United States

**Berghahn Books Ltd+**
3 Newtec Pl, Magdalen Rd, Oxford OX4 1RE
*Tel:* (01865) 250011 *Fax:* (01865) 250056
*E-mail:* info@berghahnbooks.com
*Web Site:* www.berghahnbooks.com
*Key Personnel*
Publisher: Dr Marion Berghahn
Editorial: Mark Stanton
Marketing Manager: Chris McVeigh
Founded: 1994
Subjects: Anthropology, Economics, Government, Political Science, History, Literature, Literary Criticism, Essays, Military Science, Religion - Jewish, Social Sciences, Sociology, Women's Studies, Gender, Humanities, Migration
ISBN Prefix(es): 1-57181
Number of titles published annually: 100 Print; 15 Online
Total Titles: 600 Print; 1 CD-ROM; 15 Online
*U.S. Office(s):* Berghahn Books Inc, 604 W 115 St, New York, NY 10025, United States, Publisher: Dr Marion Berghahn *Tel:* 212-222-6502 *Fax:* 212-222-5209
*Orders to:* Berghahn Books Inc, PO Box 605, Herndon, VA 20172, United States *Tel:* 703-661-1500 *Fax:* 703-661-1501 *E-mail:* tod@booksintl.com
Marston Book Services, PO Box 269, Abingdon OX14 4YN, Contact: Patrick Wehmeier *Tel:* (01235) 465500 *Fax:* (01235) 465555 *E-mail:* direct.order@marston.co.uk

**Berlitz (UK) Ltd+**
Lincoln House, 296-302 High Holborn, London WC1 7JH
*Tel:* (020) 7611 9640 *Fax:* (020) 7611 9656
*E-mail:* publishing@berlitz.co.uk
*Web Site:* www.berlitz.co.uk; languagecenter.berlitz.com/holborn
*Key Personnel*
Man Dir: Roger Kirkpatrick *Tel:* (020) 7518 8304 *E-mail:* roger.kirkpatrick@berlitz.ie
Operations Dir: Anthony Finn *Tel:* (020) 7518 8306 *E-mail:* anthony.finn@berlitz.ie
Founded: 1970
Specialize in phrase books, dictionaries, audio, video & childrens language products, travel guides & language reference.
ISBN Prefix(es): 0-7511
Total Titles: 375 Print
*Parent Company:* Berlitz Publishing Company Ltd
*Ultimate Parent Company:* Berlitz International Inc
Distributed by Virgin Publishing Ltd (United Kingdom)

**Bernards (Publishers) Ltd**, see Bernard Babani (Publishing) Ltd

**Betterway**, *imprint of* David & Charles Ltd

**BFBS**, *imprint of* Bible Society

**BFI Publishing+**
21 Stephen St, London W1T 1LN
*Tel:* (020) 7957 4789 *Fax:* (020) 74367950; (020) 76362516
*E-mail:* publishing@bfi.org.uk

*Web Site:* www.bfi.org.uk
*Key Personnel*
Head of Publishing: Andrew Lockett
Marketing & Sales: Rebecca Watts *Tel:* (20) 79574817 *E-mail:* rebecca.watts@bfi.org.uk
Production, Rights & Permissions: Tom Cabot
Marketing & Promotions: Sarah Prosser
Founded: 1980
Subjects: Film, Video, Radio, TV, Social Sciences, Sociology, Women's Studies
ISBN Prefix(es): 0-85170
Number of titles published annually: 30 Print
Total Titles: 280 Print
Distributed by Indiana University Press (North America)
*Warehouse:* Plymbridge Distributors Ltd, Estover Rd, Plymouth PL6 7PZ *Tel:* (01752) 202301
*Orders to:* Plymbridge Distributors Ltd, Estover Rd, Plymouth PL6 7PZ *Tel:* (01752) 202301

**Bible Distributors**, *imprint of* Chapter Two

**Bible Reading Fellowship+**
Elsfield Hall, 1st floor, 15-17 Elsfield Way, Oxford OX2 8FG
*Tel:* (01865) 319700 *Fax:* (01865) 319701
*E-mail:* enquiries@brf.org.uk
*Web Site:* www.brf.org.uk
*Key Personnel*
Chief Executive Officer: Richard Fisher *E-mail:* richardfisher@brf.org.uk
Commissioning Editor: Sue Doggett *E-mail:* suedoggett@brf.org.uk; Naomi Starkey *E-mail:* naomi.starkey@brf.org.uk
Marketing & Operations Manager: Karen Laister *E-mail:* karen.laister@brf.org.uk
Founded: 1922
Subjects: Biblical Studies, Education, Religion - Protestant, Theology
ISBN Prefix(es): 0-7459; 1-84101
Total Titles: 200 Print; 1 E-Book
Imprints: Barnabas
*Orders to:* Marston Book Services, PO Box 269, Oxford OX14 4YN *Tel:* (01235) 46550 *Fax:* (01235) 465555 *Web Site:* www.marston.co.uk

**Bible Society+**
Stonehill Green, Westlea, Swindon SN5 7DG
*Tel:* (01793) 418100 *Fax:* (01793) 418118
*E-mail:* info@bfbs.org.uk
*Web Site:* www.biblesociety.org.uk
*Telex:* 44283
*Key Personnel*
Chief Executive: N Crosbie
Commercial Dir: Ashley Scott
Export: Janet Edwards
Production: D Hill
Rights & Permissions: Miss K Luckett
Founded: 1804
Subjects: Biblical Studies
ISBN Prefix(es): 0-564
Imprints: BFBS

**Joseph Biddulph Publisher+**
32 Stryd Ebeneser, Pontypridd CF37 5PB
*Tel:* (01443) 662559
*Key Personnel*
Sole Proprietor: Joseph Biddulph
Founded: 1991
Subjects: Architecture & Interior Design, Language Arts, Linguistics, Literature, Literary Criticism, Essays, Heraldry
ISBN Prefix(es): 1-89799; 0-948565
Number of titles published annually: 4 Print
Total Titles: 54 Print
Imprints: Languages Information Centre

**Big Time**, *imprint of* Peter Haddock Ltd

**BILD Publications**
Campion House, Green St, Kidderminster, Worcs DY10 1JL
*Tel:* (01562) 723010 *Fax:* (01562) 723029
*E-mail:* enquiries@bild.org.uk
*Web Site:* www.bild.org.uk
*Key Personnel*
Chief Executive: Keith Smith *E-mail:* g.pardoe@bild.org.uk
Founded: 1972
Subjects: Behavioral Sciences, Child Care & Development, Disability, Special Needs, Health, Nutrition
ISBN Prefix(es): 1-873791; 0-906054; 1-902519; 1-904082
*Orders to:* Book Source, 32 Finlas St, Cowlairs Estate, Glasgow G22 SDU *Tel:* (08702) 402182 *Fax:* (0141) 557 0189

**Binky (Childrens)**, *imprint of* Grange Books PLC

**Bio Scientifica**, *imprint of* Society for Endocrinology

**Biocommerce Data Ltd**
Subsidiary of PJB Publications
Suffield House, 9 Paradise Rd, Richmond, Surrey TW9 1SJ
*Tel:* (020) 8332 4660 *Fax:* (020) 8332 4666
*E-mail:* biocom@pjbpubs.com; custserv@biocom.com (orders)
*Web Site:* www.pjbpubs.com/bcd
*Key Personnel*
Publisher: Sarah Walkley *E-mail:* sarah.walkley@informa.com
Database Manager: Ruth Williams *E-mail:* ruth.williams@pjbpubs.com
Founded: 1990
Publish directories of companies involved in biotechnology.
Subjects: Agriculture, Biological Sciences, Medicine, Nursing, Dentistry
ISBN Prefix(es): 1-871393
Total Titles: 2 Print; 2 CD-ROM; 1 Online
*Ultimate Parent Company:* T&F Informa

**BIOS Scientific Publishers Ltd+**
Member of Taylor & Francis Group PLC
4 Park Sq, Milton Park, Abingdon, Oxon OX14 4RN
*Tel:* (01235) 828600 *Fax:* (01235) 829011
*E-mail:* sales@bios.co.uk
*Web Site:* www.bios.co.uk
*Key Personnel*
Chairman: Derek Phillips
Man Dir & International Rights: Dr Jonathan Ray
Sales: Simon Watkins *E-mail:* simon.watkins@bios.co.uk
Founded: 1989
Publishers of Instant Notes, The Basics, Clinic Handbooks, Advanced Texts, Advanced Methods, Key Topics series, Genomes 2, Human Molecular Genetics 2, Clinic Intensive Care, Medical Mycology, Biotechnic & Histochemistry.
Membership(s): International Group of STM Publishers.
Subjects: Agriculture, Biological Sciences, Medicine, Nursing, Dentistry
ISBN Prefix(es): 1-872748; 1-85996
Distributed by Springer Verlag New York Inc (North America); University of New South Wales (Australia & New Zealand); Viva Books (India)
Distributor for Horizon Scientific Press; Experiemental Biology Reviews; Royal Microscopical Society (microscopy handbooks); Society of Experimental Biology
Foreign Rep(s): Academic Marketing Services (South Africa, Zimbabwe); APAC Publishers (Singapore, Southeast); Durnell Marketing

Ltd (Ireland, Europe, Northern Ireland); IPS (Middle East) Ltd (Middle East, North Africa); UNIREPS (Australia, New Zealand)
*Orders to:* Plymbridge Distributors Ltd, Estover Rd, Plymouth, Devon *Tel:* (01752) 202301 *Fax:* (01753) 202333 *E-mail:* orders@plymbridge.com
Springer-Verlag, PO Box 2485, Secaucus, NJ 07096-2485, United States *Fax:* 212-533-5587 *E-mail:* order@springer-ny.com

**Birlinn Ltd+**
West Newington House, 10 Newington Rd, Edinburgh EH9 1QS
*Tel:* (0131) 668 4371 *Fax:* (0131) 668 4466
*E-mail:* info@birlinn.co.uk
*Web Site:* www.birlinn.co.uk
*Key Personnel*
Man Dir & International Rights: Hugh Andrew
Office Manager: Sarah Tranter
Founded: 1992
Membership(s): Scottish Publishers Association.
Subjects: Fiction, History, Regional Interests
ISBN Prefix(es): 1-874744
Number of titles published annually: 80 Print
*Associate Companies:* Maclean Press
Imprints: Canongate Books "A" Ltd; John Donald Publishers Ltd; Polygon
Distributor for Maclean Press
Foreign Rep(s): Dufour Editions Distribution (North America)
*Warehouse:* Scottish Book Source, 32 Finlas St, Glasgow G22 5DU
*Orders to:* 137 Dundee St, Edinburgh, Scotland, Fiona Maxwell-Hoy *Tel:* (0131) 229 6800 *Fax:* (0131) 229 9070

**Birmingham Books**
Central Library, Chamberlain Sq, Birmingham B3 3HQ
*Tel:* (0121) 235 2868; (0121) 235 4511 *Fax:* (0121) 233 9702; (0121) 233 4458
ISBN Prefix(es): 0-7093

**Birmingham Library Information Services**
University of Birmingham, Edgbaston, Birmingham B15 2TT
*Tel:* (0121) 414 5817 *Fax:* (0121) 471 4691
*E-mail:* library@bham.ac.uk
*Web Site:* www.is.bham.ac.uk
ISBN Prefix(es): 0-7093; 0-901011

**Bishopsgate Press Ltd+**
Bartholomew House, 15 Tonbridge Rd, Hiddenborough, Tonbridge TN11 9BH
*Tel:* (01732) 833778 *Fax:* (01732) 833090
*Key Personnel*
Chief Executive: Ian Straker
Publishing Manager: Bob Wilson
Founded: 1800
Subjects: Biography, Crafts, Games, Hobbies, Film, Video, Finance, Religion - Other
ISBN Prefix(es): 0-900873; 1-85219
*Parent Company:* Whitstable Litho Ltd, Milstrood Rd, Whitstable, Kent CT5 3PP

**BLA Publishing Ltd+**
BIC Ling Kee House, One Christopher Rd, East Grinstead, West Sussex RH19 3BT
*Tel:* (01342) 318980 *Fax:* (01342) 410980
*Key Personnel*
Chairman: Bak Ling Au
Contact: Penny Kitchenham
Founded: 1981
Specialist packagers (Illustrated Trade & Children's).
Subjects: Aeronautics, Aviation, Antiques, Biological Sciences, Crafts, Games, Hobbies, Maritime, Religion - Other
ISBN Prefix(es): 0-907733
*Parent Company:* Ling Kee (UK) Ltd
*Associate Companies:* Ward Lock Educational Co Ltd

**A & C Black Publishers Ltd+**
Subsidiary of Bloomsbury Publishing PLC
37 Soho Sq, London W1D 3QZ
*Tel:* (020) 7758 0200 *Fax:* (020) 7758 0222
*E-mail:* enquiries@acblack.co.uk
*Web Site:* www.acblack.co.uk
*Key Personnel*
Chairman: Nigel Newton
Dir: Charles Black
Man Dir: Jill Coleman
Production: Oscar Heini
Rights Dir: Paul Langridge
Distribution Dir: Terry Rouelett
Publicity: Rosanna Bortoli
Founded: 1807
Subjects: Art, Crafts, Games, Hobbies, Drama,
    Theater, Education, Maritime, Music, Dance,
    Natural History, Nonfiction (General), Sports,
    Athletics, Ornithology, Reference
ISBN Prefix(es): 0-7136; 0-212
Total Titles: 1,300 Print
Imprints: Andrew Brodie; Adlard Coles Nauti-
    cal; Christopher Helm (Publishers) Ltd; Herbert
    Press Ltd; Pica Press; T & AD Poyser Ltd;
    Thomas Reed
Distributed by Midpoint Trade Books
Distributor for Magi Children's Books; Sheridan
    House; Sunflower Books; V&A Publications
*Warehouse:* Macmillan Distribution Ltd,
    Houndsmills, Basingstoke, Hants RG21
    6XS *Fax:* (01256) 327 961 *Web Site:* www.
    macmillandistribution.co.uk
*Orders to:* Macmillan Distribution Ltd,
    Houndsmills, Basingstoke, Hants RG21
    6XS *Fax:* (01256) 327 961 *Web Site:* www.
    macmillandistribution.co.uk

**Black Ace Books+**
PO Box 6557, Forfar DD8 2YS
*Tel:* (01307) 465096 *Fax:* (01307) 465494
*Web Site:* www.blackacebooks.com
*Key Personnel*
Dir: Hunter Steele; Boo Wood
Founded: 1991
Specialize in high quality fiction.
Subjects: Fiction, History, Philosophy
ISBN Prefix(es): 1-872988
Number of titles published annually: 5 Print
Total Titles: 30 Print
*Parent Company:* Black Ace Enterprises
*Associate Companies:* Maran Steele Music

**Black Dagger**, *imprint of* BBC Audiobooks

**Black Lace**, *imprint of* Virgin Publishing Ltd

**Black Spring Press Ltd+**
83 Curtain Rd, London EC2A 3BS
*Tel:* (020) 7613 3066 *Fax:* (020) 7613 0028
*E-mail:* blackspring@dexterhaven.demon.co.uk
*Key Personnel*
Dir: S R J Pettifar *E-mail:* bsp@blackspring.
    demon.co.uk; M Prausnitz *E-mail:* maja@
    blackspring.demon.co.uk
Founded: 1984
Subjects: Fiction, Music, Dance
ISBN Prefix(es): 0-948238; 0-931181
*Orders to:* Airlift Book Co, 8 The Arena, Mol-
    lison Ave, Enfield EN3 7NJ *Tel:* (020) 8804
    0400 *Fax:* (020) 8804 0044

**Black Swan**, *imprint of* Transworld Publishers
Ltd

**Blackbirch Press**, *imprint of* Thomson Gale

**Blackie Children's Books+**
80 Strand, London WC2R 0RL
*Tel:* (020) 7010 3000 *Fax:* (020) 7010 6060
*Telex:* 917181
ISBN Prefix(es): 0-216

*Parent Company:* The Penguin Group
*Shipping Address:* Penguin Books, Bath Rd, Har-
    mondsworth, Middx UB7 0DA
*Warehouse:* Penguin Books, Bath Rd, Har-
    mondsworth, Middx UB7 0DA
*Orders to:* Penguin Books, Bath Rd, Har-
    mondsworth, Middx UB7 0DA

**Blackstaff Press+**
Member of W & G Baird Group
Sydenham Business Park, 4C Heron Wharf,
    Belfast BT3 9LE
*Tel:* (028) 9045 5006 *Fax:* (028) 9046 6237
*E-mail:* info@blackstaffpress.com
*Web Site:* www.blackstaffpress.com
*Key Personnel*
Chairman: Roy Bailie
Man Dir: Anne Tannahill
Marketing & Publicity Manager: Bairbre Ryan
    *E-mail:* marketing@blackstaffpress.com
Managing Editor: Patricia Horton
Production: Elizabeth McBlain
Rights: Susan Dalzell
Publicity: Sarah Harding *E-mail:* marketing@
    blackstaffpress.com
Founded: 1971
Subjects: Art, Biography, Cookery, Drama, The-
    ater, Fiction, History, Humor, Literature, Liter-
    ary Criticism, Essays, Music, Dance, Natural
    History, Nonfiction (General), Photography, Po-
    etry, Regional Interests, Religion - Buddhist,
    Religion - Catholic, Religion - Hindu, Religion
    - Islamic, Religion - Jewish, Religion - Protes-
    tant, Religion - Other, Travel
ISBN Prefix(es): 0-85640
*Orders to:* Dufour Editions Inc, Byers Rd, PO
    Box 7, Chester Springs, PA 19425-0007,
    United States *Tel:* 610-458-5005 *Fax:* 610-458-
    7103 *E-mail:* info@dufoureditions.com
Gill & Macmillan Distribution, 10 Hume Ave,
    Park West, Dublin 12, Ireland *Tel:* (3531) 500
    9500 *Fax:* (3531) 500 9599 *E-mail:* sales@
    gillmacmillan.ie *Web Site:* www.gillmacmillan.
    ie
Peter Hyde Associates (PTY) Ltd, PO Box 2856,
    Cape Town 8000, South Africa *Tel:* (021) 423
    6692 *Fax:* (021) 422 0375 *E-mail:* peterhyde@
    intekom.co.za

**Blackwell Business**, *imprint of* Blackwell
Publishing Ltd

**Blackwell Finance**, *imprint of* Blackwell
Publishing Ltd

**Blackwell Publishing Ltd+**
Member of The Blackwell Group
108 Cowley Rd, Oxford OX4 1JF
*Tel:* (01865) 791100 *Fax:* (01865) 791347
*Web Site:* www.blackwellpublishers.co.uk
*Telex:* 837022 *Cable:* BOOKS OXFORD
*Key Personnel*
Publisher, Aquaculture & Fisheries, Food Science,
    Agriculture: Nigel Balmforth *E-mail:* nigel.
    balmforth@oxon.blackwellpublishing.com
Deputy Divisional Dir Engineering & Construc-
    tion: Julia Burden *E-mail:* julia.burden@oxon.
    blackwellpublishing.com
Commissioning Editor, Philosophy: Nick
    Bellorini *E-mail:* nick.bellorini@oxon.
    blackwellpublishing.com
Commissioning Editor, Literature: Emma
    Bennett *E-mail:* emma.bennett@oxon.
    blackwellpublishing.com
Senior Commissioning Editor, Literature & Clas-
    sical Studies: Al Bertrand *E-mail:* alfred.
    bertrand@oxon.blackwellpublishing.com
Commissioning Editor, Psychology & Educa-
    tion: Sarah Bird *E-mail:* sarah.bird@oxon.
    blackwellpublishing.com

Publisher, Nursing & Health Sciences: Griselda
    Campbell *E-mail:* griselda.campbell@oxon.
    blackwellpublishing.com
Academic & Science Books Director: Philip
    Carpenter *E-mail:* philip.carpenter@oxon.
    blackwellpublishing.com
Commissioning Editor, Dentistry & Health Sci-
    ences: Caroline Connelly *E-mail:* caroline.
    connelly@oxon.blackwellpublishing.com
Senior Commissioning Editor, Earth Sci-
    ences: Ian Francis *E-mail:* ian.francis@oxon.
    blackwellpublishing.com
Senior Commissioning Editor, Theology & Reli-
    gious Studies: Rebecca Harkin *E-mail:* rebecca.
    harkin@oxon.blackwellpublishing.com
Associate Editorial Dir, History: Tessa
    Harvey *E-mail:* tessa.harvey@oxon.
    blackwellpublishing.com
Commissioning Editor, Nursing: Beth Knight
    *E-mail:* beth.knight@oxon.blackwellpublishing.
    com
Commissioning Editor: Elizabeth Marchant
    *E-mail:* elizabeth.marchant@oxon.
    blackwellpublishing.com
Senior Commissioning Editor, Engineer-
    ing & Construction: Madeleine Met-
    calfe *E-mail:* madeleine.metcalfe@oxon.
    blackwellpublishing.com
Senior Commissioning Editor, Business & Man-
    agement: Rosemary Nixon *E-mail:* rosemary.
    nixon@oxon.blackwellpublishing.com
Dir of Medical Publishing: Andrew Robin-
    son *E-mail:* andrew.robinson@oxon.
    blackwellpublishing.com
Senior Commissioning Editor, Chemistry:
    Paul Sayer *E-mail:* paul.sayer@oxon.
    blackwellpublishing.com
Associate Publishing Dir, Veterinary Medicine:
    Antonia Seymour *E-mail:* antonia.seymour@
    oxon.blackwellpublishing.com
Commissioning Editor, Ecology & Evolution:
    Sarah Shannon *E-mail:* sarah.shannon@oxon.
    blackwellpublishing.com
Publisher, Human Geography, Sociology & Pol-
    itics: Justin Vaughan *E-mail:* justin.vaughan@
    oxon.blackwellpublishing.com
Publisher, Modern History: Christopher
    Wheeler *E-mail:* christopher.wheeler@oxon.
    blackwellpublishing.com
Marketing & Sales Dir: Tom Gold-
    Blyth *E-mail:* tom.gold-blyth@oxon.
    blackwellpublishing.com
Marketing Manager, History, Classics, An-
    thropology, Archaeology, Sociology: Jen-
    nifer Howell *E-mail:* jennifer.howell@oxon.
    blackwellpublishing.com
Senior Marketing Controller, Business & Man-
    agement, Economics & Finance, Psychology
    & Education: Eloise Keating *E-mail:* eloise.
    keating@oxon.blackwellpublishing.com
Nursing & Health Sciences: Sharon Ker-
    shaw *E-mail:* sharon.kershaw@oxon.
    blackwellpublishing.com
Senior Marketing Manager: Paul Mil-
    licheap *E-mail:* paul.millich@oxon.
    blackwellpublishing.com
Chemistry, Food, Aquaculture & Fisheries:
    Katie Moll *E-mail:* katie.moll@oxon.
    blackwellpublishing.com
Associate Divisional Marketing Manager,
    Literature & Philosophy: Laura Mont-
    gomery *E-mail:* laura.montgomery@oxon.
    blackwellpublishing.com
Veterinary Medicine & Agriculture: Sarah-Kate
    Powell *E-mail:* sarah-kate.powell@oxon.
    blackwellpublishing.com
Dir-Medical Marketing: Philip Saug-
    man *E-mail:* philip.saugman@oxon.
    blackwellpublishing.com
Dentistry: Jennifer Stewart *E-mail:* jennifer.
    stewart@oxon.blackwellpublishing.com
Medical Sales Manager: Darren Web-
    ster *E-mail:* darren.webster@oxon.
    blackwellpublishing.com

Marketing Manager - Science, Geography, Politics & Social Policy: Katherine Wheatley *E-mail:* katherine.wheatley@oxon. blackwellpublishing.com

Field Sales Manager - Asia, India, Middle East & Africa: Alberto Barraclough *E-mail:* alberto. barraclough@oxon.blackwellpublishing.com

Account Manager: Stephen Barrett *E-mail:* stephen.barrett@oxon. blackwellpublishing.com

Trade Marketing Controller: Neil Burling *E-mail:* neil.burling@oxon.blackwellpublishing. com

Sales Dir: Edward Crutchley *E-mail:* edward. crutchley@oxon.blackwellpublishing.com

Regional Sales Manager - UK & Europe: Gavin Lythe *E-mail:* gavin.lythe@oxon. blackwellpublishing.com

Account Manager: Simon Mawdsley *E-mail:* simon.mawdsley@oxon. blackwellpublishing.com; Alan Sedgman *E-mail:* alan.sedgman@oxon. blackwellpublishing.com

Sales Assistant: Elly Thomson *E-mail:* helena. thomson@oxon.blackwellpublishing.com

Senior Sales Administrator: Pam Todd *E-mail:* pam.todd@oxon.blackwellpublishing. com

Account Manager: Ben Townsend *E-mail:* ben. townsend@oxon.blackwellpublishing.com

Sales Assistant: Rachel Wilkinson *E-mail:* rachel. wilkinson@oxon.blackwellpublishing.com

Founded: 1922

*Allied Companies:* Blackwell Scientific Publications Ltd; Polity Press; NCC Blackwell.

Subjects: Business, Computer Science, Economics, Finance, Geography, Geology, Government, Political Science, History, Labor, Industrial Relations, Language Arts, Linguistics, Law, Literature, Literary Criticism, Essays, Philosophy, Psychology, Psychiatry, Religion - Other, Social Sciences, Sociology, Women's Studies

ISBN Prefix(es): 0-631; 0-85520; 0-86216; 0-943205

Imprints: Blackwell Finance; Blackwell Reference; Blackwell Business

*U.S. Office(s):* Blackwell Publishers Inc, 238 Main Street, Cambridge, MA 02142, United States *Tel:* 617-547-7110 *Fax:* 617-547-0789

*Warehouse:* Marston Book Services Ltd, Osney Mead, Oxford OX2 0DT *Tel:* (01865) 791155 *Fax:* (01865) 791927

**Blackwell Reference,** *imprint of* Blackwell Publishing Ltd

**Blackwell Science Ltd+**
Osney Mead, Oxford OX2 0EL
*Tel:* (01865) 206206 *Fax:* (01865) 721205
*E-mail:* shona.macdonald@blacksci.co.uk
*Telex:* 83355 MEDBOK G
*Key Personnel*
Chairman: Nigel Blackwell
Man Dir: Robert Campbell
Finance Dir: Martin Wilkinson
Editorial Dir: Peter Saugman
Production Dir: John Strange
Sales Dir: Edward Crutchley
Founded: 1939
Subjects: Architecture & Interior Design, Behavioral Sciences, Chemistry, Chemical Engineering, Child Care & Development, Earth Sciences, Fashion, Geography, Geology, Health, Nutrition, Law, Medicine, Nursing, Dentistry, Psychology, Psychiatry, Science (General), Sports, Athletics, Veterinary Science
ISBN Prefix(es): 0-86542; 0-632
Subsidiaries: Blackwell MZV; Blackwell Science (Australia) Pty Ltd; Munksgaard, International Booksellers & Publishers Ltd; Arnette Blackwell; Blackwell Science (Japan); Blackwell

Science Ltd; Blackwell Wissenschafts-Verlag GmbH; Blackwell Science Inc
*Bookshop(s):* Art & Poster Shop, Broad St, Oxford; MOMA, Pembroke St, Oxford
*Shipping Address:* Marston Book Services Ltd, Osney Mead, Oxford OX2 0DT
*Orders to:* Marston Book Services Ltd, Osney Mead, Oxford OX2 0DT

**John Blake Publishing Ltd+**
3 Bramber Court, 2 Bramber Rd, London W14 9PB
*Tel:* (020) 7381 0666 *Fax:* (020) 7381 6868
*E-mail:* words@blake.co.uk
*Web Site:* www.blake.co.uk
*Key Personnel*
Man Dir: John Blake *E-mail:* john@blake.co.uk
Deputy Man Dir: Rosie Ries *E-mail:* rosie@ blake.co.uk
Executive Editor: Adam Parfitt *E-mail:* adam@ blake.co.uk
Production Editor: Michelle Signore
Founded: 1991
Subjects: Biography, Criminology, Fiction, Non-fiction (General), Radio, TV
ISBN Prefix(es): 1-85782; 0-905846
Number of titles published annually: 60 Print
Imprints: Blake Publishing; Metro Publishing
*Sales Office(s):* Derek Searle Associates Ltd, The Coach House, Cippenham Lodge, Cippenham Lane, Slough, Berks SL1 5AN
*Tel:* (01753) 539 295 *Fax:* (01753) 551 863
*E-mail:* dsapublish@aol.com (UK & Europe)
*U.S. Office(s):* 82 Wall St, Suite 1105, New York, NY 10005, United States *Fax:* 212-968-7962
Distributed by Bookwise International (Australia); Hushion House Publishing Ltd (Canada); Forrester Books NZ Ltd (New Zealand); Peter Hyde Associates (South Africa); Seven Hills Book Distribtors (US)
*Orders to:* Little Hamptons, Faraday Close Durrington Worthing, West Sussex BN13 3RB
*Tel:* (01903) 828 500 *Fax:* (01903) 828 635
*E-mail:* lml@lbsltd.co.uk

**Blake Publishing,** *imprint of* John Blake Publishing Ltd

**Blaketon Hall Ltd**
Unit 1, 26 Marsh Green Rd, Marsh Barton, Exeter, Devon EX2 8PN
*Tel:* (01392) 210 602 *Fax:* (01392) 421 165
*E-mail:* sales@blaketonhall.co.uk
*Web Site:* www.blaketonhall.co.uk
*Key Personnel*
Man Dir: John Shillingford *E-mail:* martin@ blaketonhall.co.uk
Dir: Pat Shillingford
Founded: 1976
Also acts as remainder dealer.
Subjects: Animals, Pets, Crafts, Games, Hobbies, How-to, Nonfiction (General)
ISBN Prefix(es): 0-907854

**Blandford,** *imprint of* Cassell & Co

**Blandford Publishing Ltd+**
Orion House, 5 Upper St Martins Lane, London WC2H 9EA
*Tel:* (020) 7420 5555
*Key Personnel*
Chairman & Chief Executive: Philip Sturrock
Editorial Dir, Rights & Special Sales: Alison Goff
Sales Dir: Finbarr McCabe
Founded: 1919
Subjects: Animals, Pets, Astrology, Occult, Crafts, Games, Hobbies, Criminology, History, Music, Dance, Natural History, Outdoor Recreation, Sports, Athletics
ISBN Prefix(es): 0-7137

**Bloodaxe Books Ltd+**
Highgreen, Tarset, Northumb NE48 1RP
*Tel:* (01434) 240 500 *Fax:* (01434) 240 505
*E-mail:* editor@bloodaxebooks.demon.co.uk
*Web Site:* www.bloodaxebooks.com
*Key Personnel*
Chairman: Simon Thirsk
Editor: Neil Astley
Rights & Permissions Manager: Peg Osterman
Publicity: Christine MacGregor
Founded: 1978
Subjects: Poetry
ISBN Prefix(es): 0-906427; 1-85224
Number of titles published annually: 40 Print
*U.S. Office(s):* DuFour Editions Inc, PO Box 7, Chester Springs, PA 19425-0007, United States *Tel:* 610-458-5005 *Fax:* 610-458-7103
*E-mail:* dufour8023@aol.com
*Orders to:* Littlehampton Book Services, Centre Warehouse, Columbia Bldg, Faraday Durington Close, Worthing, West Sussex BN13 3RB
*Tel:* (01903) 828 800 *Fax:* (01903) 828 801
*E-mail:* orders@lbsltd.co.uk

**Bloomsbury Publishing PLC+**
38 Soho Sq, London W1D 3HB
*Tel:* (020) 7494 2111 *Fax:* (020) 7434 0151
*E-mail:* csm@bloomsbury.com
*Web Site:* www.bloomsburymagazine.com
*Key Personnel*
Chairman & Man Dir: Nigel Newton
Publishing Dir, Fiction: Liz Calder
Publishing Dir, Reference: Kathy Rooney
Production Dir: Penny Edwards
Publicity Dir: Katie Bond
Editor-in-Chief: Alexandra Pringle
International Rights: Ruth Logan
Sales, UK: David Ward
Marketing: Minna Fry
Founded: 1987
Subjects: Biography, Career Development, Child Care & Development, Communications, Cookery, Crafts, Games, Hobbies, Drama, Theater, Economics, Fiction, Finance, History, How-to, Humor, Literature, Literary Criticism, Essays, Management, Marketing, Medicine, Nursing, Dentistry, Nonfiction (General), Self-Help
ISBN Prefix(es): 0-7475
Number of titles published annually: 1,000 Print
Subsidiaries: A & C Black Publishing Ltd
*Orders to:* Macmillan Distribution Ltd, Houndsmill, Basingstoke, Hants RG21 6XS

**Blorenge Books+**
Blorenge Cottage, Church Lane, Llanfoist, Abergavenny NP7 9NG
*Tel:* (01873) 856114
*Key Personnel*
Proprietor: Chris Barber
Founded: 1985
Subjects: Fiction, History, Mysteries, Outdoor Recreation, Travel
Number of titles published annually: 3 Print
Total Titles: 12 Print

**Blueprint,** *imprint of* Routledge

**Blueprint+**
Leatherhead, Randalls Rd, Surrey KT22 7RU
*Tel:* (01372) 802080 *Fax:* (01372) 802079
*E-mail:* publications@pira.co.uk
*Key Personnel*
Publisher: Annabel Taylor
Subjects: Photography, Publishing & Book Trade Reference
*Parent Company:* Pira International

**BMJ Publishing Group+**
BMA House, Tavistock Sq, London WC1H 9JR
*Tel:* (020) 7387 4499; (020) 7383 6245
*Fax:* (020) 7383 6662
*E-mail:* customerservices@bmjbooks.com
*Web Site:* www.bmjpg.com

*Key Personnel*
Chief Executive & Editor: Dr Richard Smith
Business Development Dir: Maurice Long
Publisher: John Hudson *E-mail:* jhudson@
bmjbooks.com
Publishing Dir, Specialist Journals: Alexandra
Williamson
Production Executive: Nathan Harris
*E-mail:* nharris@bmjbooks.com
Sales & Marketing Executive: Clair Grant-Salmon
*E-mail:* cgrantsalmon@bmjbooks.com
Sales & Marketing Manager: Helen Robertson
*E-mail:* hrobertson@bmjbooks.com
Rights Executive: Kate Webster *E-mail:* rights@
bmjbooks.com
Books Division Manager, Rights & Permisssions:
John Hudson
Commissioning Editor: Mary Banks
*E-mail:* mbanks@bmjbooks.com
Development Editor: Christina Karaviotis
*E-mail:* ckaraviotis@bmjbooks.com
Founded: 1857
Subjects: Medicine, Nursing, Dentistry
ISBN Prefix(es): 0-7279; 0-900221
*Parent Company:* British Medical Association
Imprints: PSP
Subsidiaries: Professional & Scientific Publications
Distributed by AMA Services (WA) Pty Ltd
(Australia); American College of Physicians
(USA, Mexico); Apac Publishers Services
(Far East, excluding Japan & Taiwan); BMJ
Books (USA); Canadian Medical Association
(Canada); HWA Eng Trading Co (Taiwan);
Jaypee Brothers (India); Medical Association
of South Africa (South Africa); Nankodo Co
Ltd (Japan); Phi Shoten (Japan); F K Schat-
tauer (Germany)
Distributor for American Academy of Ophthal-
mology; American Academy of Physicians;
British Dental Journal; Schattauer
Foreign Rep(s): Associated Marketing Services
(France, Italy, Portugal, Spain); Brookside Pub-
lishing Services (Ireland); Anthony Rudkin As-
sociates (Cyprus, Greece, Middle East, North
Africa, Turkey, Iran); David Towle Interna-
tional (Baltic States, Scandinavia); Kelvin Van
Hasselt (Africa, Caribbean); John Wilde Part-
nership (Austria, Germany, Switzerland)
*Bookshop(s):* Burton St, London WC1
*Tel:* (020) 7383 6244 *Fax:* (020) 7383 6455
*E-mail:* orders@bmjbookshop.com *Web
Site:* www.bmjbookshop.com
*Shipping Address:* Unit 11c, North Orbital Trad-
ing Estate, Napsbury Lane, St Albans, Herts
AL1 1XB
*Warehouse:* Unit 11c, North Orbital Trading Es-
tate, Napsbury Lane, St Albans, Herts AL1
1XB

**Boatswain Press**, *imprint of* Kenneth Mason
Publications Ltd

**Bobcat Books**, *imprint of* Omnibus Press

**Bodley Head CHildrens**, *imprint of* Random
House UK Ltd

**Book Club Associates**, see BCA - Book Club
Associates

**The Book Guild Ltd+**
Temple House, 25 High St, Lewes, East Sussex
BN1 2LU
*Tel:* (01273) 472534 *Fax:* (01273) 476472
*E-mail:* info@bookguild.co.uk
*Web Site:* www.bookguild.co.uk
*Key Personnel*
Chairman: G M Nissen, CBE
Editorial Dir: Carol Biss
Founded: 1982

Membership(s): IPG; Publishers' Association.
Subjects: Art, Biography, Fiction, History, Lit-
erature, Literary Criticism, Essays, Military
Science, Travel
ISBN Prefix(es): 1-85776; 0-86332
Number of titles published annually: 100 Print
*Orders to:* Vine House Distribution, Walden-
bury, North Common, Chailey, East Sussex
BN8 4DR *Tel:* (01825) 723398 *Fax:* (01825)
724188 *E-mail:* sales@vinehouseuk.co.uk *Web
Site:* www.vinehouseuk.co.uk
*Returns:* Vine House Distribution, Waldenbury,
North Common, Chailey, East Sussex BN8
4DR

**Book House**, *imprint of* The Salariya Book Co
Ltd

**Book Marketing Ltd**
7 John St, London WC1N 2ES
*Tel:* (020) 7440 8930 *Fax:* (020) 7242 7485
*E-mail:* bml@bookmarketing.co.uk
*Web Site:* www.bookmarketing.co.uk
*Key Personnel*
Man Dir: Jo Henry
Founded: 1990
Market research company.
Subjects: Publishing & Book Trade Reference
ISBN Prefix(es): 1-873517
Total Titles: 15 Print

**Bookmarks Publications+**
One Bloomsbury St, London WC1B 3QE
*Tel:* (020) 7637 1848 *Fax:* (020) 7637 3416
*E-mail:* mailorder@bookmarks.uk.com
*Web Site:* www.bookmarks.uk.com
*Key Personnel*
Editorial: Emma Bircham *E-mail:* publications@
bookmarks.uk.com
Founded: 1979
Publisher for the Socialist Workers' Party (GB).
Subjects: Economics, Government, Political Sci-
ence, History, Labor, Industrial Relations
ISBN Prefix(es): 0-906224; 1-898876
*Branch Office(s)*
GPO Box 1473N, Melbourne 3001, Australia

**Books of Zimbabwe Publishing Co (Pvt) Ltd**
130A South Rd, Haywards Heath, West Sussex
RH16 4LP
*Tel:* (01444) 455549
*E-mail:* info@booksofzimbabwe.com
*Web Site:* www.booksofzimbabwe.com
*Key Personnel*
Rights & Permissions: Joan Hopcraft
Founded: 1968
Subjects: Biography, Education, Fiction, Foreign
Countries, History, Nonfiction (General)
ISBN Prefix(es): 0-86920
Total Titles: 140 Print
Subsidiaries: Africana Book Society (Pty) Ltd

**Books on Screen**, *imprint of* Butterworths Tolley

**Boosey & Hawkes Music Publishers Ltd+**
295 Regent St, London W1B 2JH
*Tel:* (020) 7580 2060 *Fax:* (020) 7291 7199
*E-mail:* information@boosey.com
*Web Site:* www.boosey.com/publishing
*Key Personnel*
Chief Executive: Richard Holland
Sales & Marketing Dir: S A Richards
Founded: 1890
Also acts as a distributor for other music compa-
nies & book publishers of musical background
books.
Subjects: Music, Dance
ISBN Prefix(es): 0-85162
*Parent Company:* Boosey & Hawkes PLC
Divisions: B & H Inc, Printed Music Division

*U.S. Office(s):* B & H Inc, 24 E 21 St, 2nd floor,
New York, NY, United States *Tel:* 212-358-
5302 *E-mail:* trade.uk@boosey.com
*Orders to:* The Hyde, Edgware Rd, London NW9
6JN *Tel:* (020) 8205 3861 *Fax:* (020) 8200
3737

**Borland Press**, *imprint of* Pearson Education
Europe, Mideast & Africa

**Borthwick Institute Publications**
University of York, Heslington, York YO10 SDD
*Tel:* (01904) 321160
*Web Site:* www.york.ac.uk/borthwick
Founded: 1950
Subjects: Archaeology, Genealogy, History
Number of titles published annually: 10 Print
Total Titles: 100 Print

**Boulevard Books UK**, *imprint of* Boulevard
Books UK/The Babel Guides

**Boulevard Books UK/The Babel Guides+**
71 Lytton Rd, Oxford OX4 3NY
*Tel:* (01865) 712931 *Fax:* (01865) 712931
*E-mail:* raybabel@dircon.co.uk
*Web Site:* www.babelguides.com
*Key Personnel*
Dir, Boulevard Books UK: Ray Keenoy
Rights & Marketing Mgr, Babel Guides to Fiction
in English Translation: Clara Corona
Founded: 1989
Publish contemporary world fiction in English
translation, popular guides to fiction in transla-
tion.
Subjects: Fiction, Literature, Literary Criticism,
Essays
ISBN Prefix(es): 1-899460
Number of titles published annually: 4 Print
Total Titles: 30 Print
Imprints: Babel Guides; Boulevard Books UK
Distributed by Gazelle Book Services; ISBS
(USA & Canada)

**Bounty Books**, *imprint of* Octopus Publishing
Group

**Bounty Books+**
Division of The Octopus Group Ltd
2-4 Heron Quays, London E14 4JP
*Tel:* (020) 7531 8600 *Fax:* (020) 7531 8607
*Web Site:* www.bounty-publishing.co.uk
*Key Personnel*
Man Dir: Alison Golt
Publishing & International Sales Dir: Polly
Manguel
UK National Accounts Manager: Tony Cartlidge
Export Sales Executive: Emma Harrison
Publisher of promotional titles.
Subjects: Animals, Pets, Antiques, Cookery,
Crafts, Games, Hobbies, Fiction, Gardening,
Plants, History, Natural History, Religion -
Other, Sports, Athletics, Transportation
*Distribution Center:* Little Hampton Book Ser-
vices *Tel:* (01903) 828800

**Bowerdean Publishing Co Ltd**
8 Abbotstone Rd, Putney, London SW15 1QR
*Tel:* (020) 8788 0938 *Fax:* (020) 8788 0938
*E-mail:* 101467.1264@compuserve.com
*Key Personnel*
Contact: Robert Dudley *E-mail:* rdudley@
btinternet.com
Founded: 1993
Subjects: Management, Social Sciences, Sociol-
ogy
ISBN Prefix(es): 0-906097
*U.S. Office(s):* c/o Kaimleen Hughes, IPM 22893
Quicksilver Dr, Dulles, VA 20166, United
States *Tel:* 703-661-1500 *Fax:* 703-661-1501
Distributed by Central Books (UK); DA Infor-
mation Services (Australia); International Pub-

lishers Marketing (USA & Canada); Phambili Agencies (South Africa)
*Warehouse:* Central Books, 99 Wallis Rd, London E95LN, Bill Wallis *Tel:* (020) 8986 4854 *Fax:* (020) 8533 5821

**Bowker**, see CSA (Cambridge Scientific Abstracts)

**Boxtree**, *imprint of* Pan Macmillan

**Boxtree Ltd+**
20 New Wharf Rd, London N1 9RR
*Tel:* (020) 7014 6000 *Fax:* (020) 7014 6001
*Web Site:* www.panmacmillan.com/imprints/boxtree.html
Founded: 1986
Subjects: Film, Video, Humor, Radio, TV, Science Fiction, Fantasy
ISBN Prefix(es): 1-85283; 0-7522
*Parent Company:* Pan Macmillan
*Ultimate Parent Company:* Macmillan Group
Distributor for Museum Quilts (UK); Piccadilly (UK); Rosendale (UK); Smith Gryphon (UK)
*Warehouse:* Little Hampton Book Services

**Marion Boyars Publishers Ltd+**
24 Lacy Rd, London SW15 1NL
*Tel:* (020) 8788 9522 *Fax:* (020) 8789 8122
*Web Site:* www.marionboyars.co.uk
*Key Personnel*
Man Dir, Rights & Permissions, Publicity, Production: Catheryn Kilgarriff *E-mail:* catheryn@marionboyars.com
Editorial Dir: Arthur Boyars
Editor: Rebecca Gillieron *E-mail:* rebecca@marionboyars.com
Founded: 1975
Independent literary trade publisher.
Please include return postage for unsolicited submissions.
Subjects: Drama, Theater, Fiction, Film, Video, Literature, Literary Criticism, Essays, Music, Dance, Philosophy
ISBN Prefix(es): 0-7145
Number of titles published annually: 20 Print
Total Titles: 527 Print
*U.S. Office(s):* Marion Boyars Publishers Inc, c/o The Feminist Press, 365 Fifth Ave, New York, NY 10016, United States, Dir, Publicity & Subsidiary Rights: Franklin Dennis *Tel:* 212-817-7928 *Fax:* 212-817-1593 *E-mail:* fdennis@gc.cuny.edu
Distributor for Peribo Pty Ltd (Australia & New Zealand); Stephan Phillips (South Africa)
Foreign Rep(s): Peribo Pty (Australia)
*Distribution Center:* Consortium Book Sales Distribution Inc, 1045 Westgate Dr, Saint Paul, MN 55114-1065, United States *Fax:* 651-917-6406 (US)
*Orders to:* Central Books, 99 Wallis Rd, London E9 5LN *Tel:* (020) 8986 4854 *Fax:* (020) 8533 5821 *E-mail:* orders@centralbooks.com

**Boydell & Brewer Ltd+**
PO Box 9, Woodbridge IP12 3DF
*Tel:* (01394) 610 600 *Fax:* (01394) 610 316
*E-mail:* boydell@boydell.co.uk
*Web Site:* www.boydell.co.uk
*Key Personnel*
Man Dir: Dr R W Barber
Head of Sales & Marketing: Michael Richards
Founded: 1969
Publish & distribute academic & trade history & literature studies. Also publish Hispanic & German studies, plus music, philosophy, film & African studies.
Subjects: African American Studies, Film, Video, History, Literature, Literary Criticism, Essays, Music, Dance, Philosophy, Travel
ISBN Prefix(es): 0-85115; 0-85993

Number of titles published annually: 200 Print; 5 CD-ROM
*U.S. Office(s):* Boydell & Brewer Inc, 668 Mount Hope Ave, Rochester, NY 14620-2731, United States *Tel:* 585-275-0419 *Fax:* 585-271-8778
Distributor for Almanach de Gotha; Burke's; Early English Text Society; Victoria County History
Foreign Rep(s): Nancy Bye (US); Duke Hill/Marsha Martin (US); Colin Flint (Baltic States, Denmark, Finland, Iceland, Norway, Sweden); Ben Greig (Baltic States, Scandinavia); Hushion House Publishing Inc (Canada); Iberian Book Services (Portugal, Spain); Inter Media Americana (Mexico, South Africa); Pat Malango (US); Flavio Marcello (France, Italy); Publishers International Marketing; Publishers International Marketing (Korea, Middle East, North Africa, Philippines, Southeast Asia); Remley & Associates (US); Roger Sauls (US); Ben Schrager (US); SHS (Austria, Germany, Switzerland); Siobhan Mullet (Ireland); TML (Pakistan)

**BPP Publishing Ltd**
Aldine Pl, London W12 8AA
*Tel:* (020) 8740 2222 *Fax:* (020) 8740 1111
*E-mail:* info@bpp.com
*Web Site:* www.bpp.com
Founded: 1976
Subjects: Accounting, Business, Economics, Marketing
ISBN Prefix(es): 0-7517; 0-86277; 1-871824

**BPS Books (British Psychological Society)+**
Division of British Psychological Society
St Andrews House, 48 Princess Rd E, Leicester LE1 7DR
*Tel:* (0116) 254 9568 *Fax:* (0116) 247 0787
*E-mail:* enquiry@bps.org.uk
*Web Site:* www.bps.org.uk
*Key Personnel*
Publisher: Joyce Collins
Senior Editor: Jon Reed
Founded: 1981
Membership(s): IPG (Independent Publishers Guild).
Subjects: Behavioral Sciences, Education, Management
ISBN Prefix(es): 0-901715; 1-85433
Total Titles: 100 Print
Imprints: BPS Multimedia
*U.S. Office(s):* Stylus Publishing Inc, 22883 Quicksilver Dr, Dulles, VA 20166, United States
Distributed by Paul H Brookes (USA)
*Warehouse:* Plymbridge Distributors Ltd, Estover, Plymouth PL6 7PZ

**BPS Multimedia**, *imprint of* BPS Books (British Psychological Society)

**Dr Barry Bracewell-Milnes**
26 Lancaster Court, Banstead, Surrey SM7 1RR
*Tel:* (01737) 350736 *Fax:* (01737) 371415
*Key Personnel*
Dir: J B Bracewell-Milnes *E-mail:* jim_1001@hotmail.com
Subjects: Economics, Finance, Taxation

**Bradford Books**, *imprint of* MIT Press Ltd

**Bradt Travel Guides Ltd+**
19 High St, Chalfont St Peter, Bucks SL9 9QE
*Tel:* (01753) 893444 *Fax:* (01753) 892333
*E-mail:* info@bradt-travelguides.com
*Web Site:* www.bradtguides.com
*Key Personnel*
President: Hilary Bradt
Editor: Patricia Hayne
Office Manager: Debbie Hunter

Sales & Marketing Manager: Peter Webb
Founded: 1972
Subjects: Outdoor Recreation, Travel
ISBN Prefix(es): 0-946983; 1-898323; 1-84162; 0-9505797
Total Titles: 59 Print
*Associate Companies:* The Globe Pequot Press, PO Box 480, 246 Goose Lane, Guilford, CT 06437-0480, United States *Tel:* 203-458-4500 *Fax:* 203-458-4601 *E-mail:* info@globe-pequot.com
Distributed by Altair (Spain); Camerapix Publishers International (East Africa); Cartotheque E G G (France); Craenen, bvba Mechelsesteenweg (Belgium); Eco Trip 2001 (Israel); Globe Pequot Press (North America); Greene Phoenix Marketing (New Zealand); InterMediaAmericana Ltd (Baltic States, West & Southern Africa, Indian Ocean, Middle East (Except Israel), South & Central America, Caribbean); Inter Orbis (Italy); Dennis Jones & Associates Pty Ltd (Australia); Nilsson & Lamm bv (Netherlands); OLF SA (Switzerland); Platypus (Sweden, Norway); Scanvik Books aps Esplanaden (Denmark, Norway); TransQuest Asia Publishers Pte Ltd (Spain); Wild Dog Press (South Africa)
Foreign Rep(s): Altair (Spain); Camerapix Publishers International (East Africa); Cartotheque E G G (France); Craenen, bvba Mechelsesteenweg (Belgium); Eco Trip 2001 (Israel); The Globe Pequot Press (Canada, US); Greene Phoenix Marketing (New Zealand); Inter Orbis (Italy); InterMediaAmericana Ltd (Baltic States, Caribbean, Central America, Middle East exc Israel, South Africa, South America); Dennis Jones & Associates Pty Ltd (Australia); Nilsson & Lamm bv (Netherlands); OLF SA (Switzerland); Platypus (Norway, Sweden); Scanvik Books aps Esplanaden (Denmark, Norway); TransQuest Asia Publishers Pte Ltd (Spain); Wild Dog Press (South Africa)
*Orders to:* Portfolio, Unit 5, Perivale Industrial Park, Horsenden Lane S, Greenford UB6 7RL *Tel:* (020) 8997 9000 *Fax:* (020) 8997 9097 *E-mail:* sales@portfoliobooks.com

**BradyGames**, *imprint of* Pearson Education Europe, Mideast & Africa

**Brassey's UK Ltd+**
Division of Chrysalis Group
The Chrysalis Bldg, Bramley Rd, London W10 6SP
*Tel:* (020) 7221 2213; (020) 7314 1469 (sales) *Fax:* (020) 7221 6455; (020) 7314 1594 (sales)
*E-mail:* enquiries@chrysalis.com
*Web Site:* www.chrysalis.co.uk
*Key Personnel*
Group Sales & Marketing Dir: Richard Samson *Tel:* (020) 7314 1459 *Fax:* (020) 7314 1549 *E-mail:* rsamson@chrysalisbooks.co.uk
Dir of Marketing: Kate Wood *Tel:* (020) 7314 1496 *E-mail:* kwood@chrysalisbooks.co.uk
Marketing & Publicity Manager: Rachel Armstrong *Tel:* (020) 7314 1605 *Fax:* (020) 7314 1549 *E-mail:* rarmstrong@chrysalisbooks.co.uk
Rights: Candida Buckley *Tel:* (01622) 863117 *Fax:* (01622) 863227 *E-mail:* candidabuckley@aol.com
Permissions: Terry Forshaw *Tel:* (020) 7314 1607 *E-mail:* tforshaw@chrysalisbooks.co.uk
Founded: 1886
Subjects: Aeronautics, Aviation, History, Maritime, Military Science
ISBN Prefix(es): 0-08; 1-85753; 0-85177; 0-904609
Subsidiaries: Brassey's Inc
Divisions: Conway Maritime Press; Putnam Aeronautical

*U.S. Office(s):* Brassey's Inc, Suite 100, 22883 Quicksilver Dr, Dulles, VA 20166, United States
*Orders to:* HarperCollins Distribution, Campsie View, Westerhill Rd, Bishopbriggs, Glasgow G64 2QT *Fax:* (087) 0787 1995 (Trade only)

**Nicholas Brealey Publishing+**
3-5 Spafield St, Clerkenwell, London EC1R 4QB
*Tel:* (020) 7239 0360 *Fax:* (020) 7239 0370
*E-mail:* sales@nbrealey-books.com
*Web Site:* www.nbrealey-books.com
*Key Personnel*
Man Dir: Nicholas Brealey
Marketing & Publicity Dir: Angie Tainsh *E-mail:* angiet@nbrealey-books.com
International Rights: Sue Coll *E-mail:* rights@ nbrealey-books.com
Founded: 1992
Membership(s): IPG.
Subjects: Business, Career Development, Economics, Finance, Foreign Countries, Management, Self-Help, Foreign Countries
ISBN Prefix(es): 1-85788
Total Titles: 100 Print
*U.S. Office(s):* Intercultural Press Inc, 374 US Route One, PO Box 700, Yarmouth, ME 04096, United States, Publicity & Marketing: Terri Welch *Tel:* 207-846-5168 *Fax:* 207-846-5181 *E-mail:* books@interculturalpress.com (non-trade sales)
Distributor for Intercultural Press Inc (outside USA)
*Warehouse:* The Book Service, Colchester Rd, Frating, Frating Green, Essex C07 7DW *Tel:* (01206) 256 000
*Orders to:* The Book Service, Colchester Rd, Frating, Frating Green, Essex C07 7DW *Tel:* (01206) 256 000
Nicholas Brealey Publishing, c/o National Book Network, 15200 NBN Way, Blue Ridge Summit, PA 17214, United States

**Breedon Books Publishing Company Ltd+**
Division of Breedon Publishing Group
Breedon House, 3 The Parker Centre, Mansfield Rd, Derby DE21 4SZ
*Tel:* (01332) 384235 *Fax:* (01332) 292755
*E-mail:* sales@breedonpublishing.co.uk
*Web Site:* www.breedonbooks.co.uk
*Key Personnel*
Chairman: Steve Caron *E-mail:* steve.caron@ breedonpublishing.co.uk
Customer Services Manager: Beverley Rushworth *E-mail:* beverley.rushworth@breedonpublishing. co.uk
Publicity Manager: Claire Lynes *E-mail:* claire. lynes@breedonpublishing.co.uk
Founded: 1980
Subjects: Biography, Genealogy, History, Sports, Athletics
ISBN Prefix(es): 0-907969; 1-873626; 1-85983
Number of titles published annually: 40 Print
Total Titles: 500 Print
*Associate Companies:* Soccer Publishing Inc, PO Box 1417, Princeton, NJ 08540, United States
Imprints: Breedon Heritage; Breedon Sport
*Sales Office(s):* Derek Searle Associates Ltd, Unit 13, Progress Business Centre, Whittle Parkway, Burnham, Berks SL1 6DQ *Tel:* (01628) 559500 *Fax:* (01628) 663876 *E-mail:* dsapublish@aol. com

**Breedon Heritage**, *imprint of* Breedon Books Publishing Company Ltd

**Breedon Sport**, *imprint of* Breedon Books Publishing Company Ltd

**Breslich & Foss Ltd+**
2a Union Court, 20-22 Union Rd, London SW4 6JP

*Tel:* (020) 7819 3990 *Fax:* (020) 7819 3998
*E-mail:* sales@breslichfoss.com
*Key Personnel*
Man Dir: Paula G Breslich
Foreign Sales: Janet Ravenscroft
Founded: 1978
Also acts as packager.
Subjects: Architecture & Interior Design, Art, Cookery, Crafts, Games, Hobbies, Gardening, Plants, Health, Nutrition, Wine & Spirits
ISBN Prefix(es): 1-85004

**Brewin Books**, *imprint of* Brewin Books Ltd

**Brewin Books Ltd+**
Doric House, 56 Alcester Rd, Studley, Warwicks B80 7LG
*Tel:* (01527) 854228 *Fax:* (01527) 852746
*E-mail:* enquiries@brewinbooks.com
*Web Site:* www.brewinbooks.com
*Key Personnel*
Dir: Alan Brewin
Founded: 1973
Subjects: Biography, Education, Fiction, Genealogy, Health, Nutrition, History, Military Science, Nonfiction (General), Regional Interests, Transportation, Travel, Publish a range of Midland Regional non-fiction titles on the regions history including hospital, health, housing, police, education, transport, local history, biographies, contemporary fiction & some military history. Distribute for several local authorities for walking guides & local history books
ISBN Prefix(es): 0-9505570; 0-947731; 1-85858
Number of titles published annually: 25 Print
Total Titles: 210 Print
*Associate Companies:* Supaprint (Redditch) Ltd, Enfield Estate, Unit 19, Redditch Worcs B97 6BZ, Manager: Mike Abbott *Tel:* (01527) 8562212 *Fax:* (01527) 8560451 *E-mail:* mike@ supaprint.com
Imprints: Brewin Books; Alton Douglas Books; History-into-Print
Distributor for City of Birmingham Libraries & Leisure; Hereford City Council; Rosmini House (Philosophy)
*Warehouse:* Supaprint (Redditch) Ltd, Enfield Estate, Unit 19, Redditch Worcs B97 6BZ, Manager: Mike Abbott *Tel:* (01527) 8562212 *Fax:* (01527) 8560451 *E-mail:* mike@ supaprint.com

**Bridge Books+**
61 Park Ave, Wrexham LL12 7AW
*Tel:* (01978) 358661 *Fax:* (01978) 262377
*Key Personnel*
Official Delegate, Partner: W A Williams *E-mail:* waw@bridgebooks.co.uk
Founded: 1983
Subjects: Aeronautics, Aviation, Ethnicity, Genealogy, History, Military Science, Regional Interests
ISBN Prefix(es): 1-872424; 0-9508285
Number of titles published annually: 12 Print
*Associate Companies:* Maelor Interactive Publishing Ltd, Wrexham
Subsidiaries: Maelor Interactive Publishing Ltd

**Brilliant Publications+**
One Church View, Sparrow Hall Farm, Edlesborough, Dunstable LU6 2ES
*Tel:* (01525) 229720 *Fax:* (01525) 229725
*E-mail:* sales@brilliantpublications.co.uk
*Web Site:* www.brilliantpublications.co.uk
*Key Personnel*
Publisher: Priscilla Hannaford *E-mail:* priscilla@ brilliantpublications.co.uk
Founded: 1993
Specialize in educational books for 3-13 year olds.
Membership(s): IPG; Publishers' Association.
Subjects: Education

ISBN Prefix(es): 1-897675; 1-903893
Number of titles published annually: 20 Print
Total Titles: 100 Print

**Brimax**, *imprint of* Brimax Books

**Brimax Books+**
Division of The Octopus Publishing Group
Appledram Barns, Birdham Rd, Chichester PO20 7EQ
*Tel:* (01243) 792 489 *Fax:* (020) 7531 8607
Pre-school publisher.
Subjects: Fiction, Nonfiction (General), Traditional board books, innovative interactive, classic stories & fairy tales, early learning, reference, new fiction
ISBN Prefix(es): 1-85854; 0-86112; 0-900195; 0-904494
Imprints: Brimax
*Orders to:* Littlehampton Book Services Ltd, Faraday Close, Durington, Worthing, West Sussex NN10 6RZ *Tel:* (01933) 828801

**Britannia Press**, *imprint of* East-West Publications (UK) Ltd

**British Academic Press**, *imprint of* I B Tauris & Co Ltd

**The British Academy+**
10 Carlton House Terrace, London SW1Y 5AH
*Tel:* (020) 7969 5200 *Fax:* (020) 7969 5300
*E-mail:* secretary@britac.ac.uk
*Web Site:* www.britac.ac.uk
*Telex:* 263194
*Key Personnel*
Publications Officer: James Rivington
Rights & Permissions: Janet English
Founded: 1902
The British Academy is a Registered Charity, No 233176.
Subjects: Archaeology, Art, History, Literature, Literary Criticism, Essays, Philosophy, Social Sciences, Sociology
ISBN Prefix(es): 0-85672; 0-902732
*Orders to:* OUP Distribution Services, Saxon Way West, Corby, Northamptonshire NN18 9ES
Oxbow Books, Park End Place, Oxford OX1 1HN

**The British & Foreign Bible Society**, see Bible Society

**British Association for Adoption & Fostering**, see BAAF Adoption & Fostering

**The British Council, Design, Publishing & Print Department**
10 Spring Gardens, London SW1A 2BN
*Tel:* (020) 7930 8466 *Fax:* (020) 7389 6347
*E-mail:* general.enquiries@britishcouncil.org
*Web Site:* www.britishcouncil.org
*Telex:* 8952201BRICONG
*Key Personnel*
Head of Dept: Christine Borell
Head of Editorial: Nichola Liu
Founded: 1934
Promotion abroad of a wider knowledge of Britain & the English language, development of closer cultural relations with other countries
Among book & journal titles published or co-published are *British Book News, Media in Education Development, English Language Teaching Journal, ELT Documents, Language Teaching, British Writers, How to Live in Britain, The British Council Collection 1938-84, TV English, Video English.*
Subjects: English as a Second Language, Human Relations, Regional Interests

ISBN Prefix(es): 0-86355; 0-900229; 0-901618
*U.S. Office(s):* The British Council, The Cultural Attache, British Embassy, 3100 Massachusetts Ave, Washington, DC 20008, United States

**British Educational Communication & Technology Agency (BECTA)**
Millburn Hill Rd, Science Park, Coventry CV4 7JJ
*Tel:* (024) 7641 6994 *Fax:* (024) 7641 1418
*E-mail:* becta@becta.org.uk
*Web Site:* www.becta.org.uk
*Key Personnel*
Chief Executive: Owen Lynch
Board Chair: Prof David Hargreaves
Press & Public Relations Officer: Nicola Newman
Founded: 1973
Subjects: Education, Government, Political Science, Technology
ISBN Prefix(es): 0-86184; 0-902204
Imprints: BECTA

**British Film Institute**, see BFI Publishing

**British Horse Society**
Stoneleigh Deer Park, Kenilworth, Warwicks CV8 2XZ
*Tel:* (08701) 202 244 *Fax:* (01926) 707 800
*E-mail:* enquiry@bhs.org.uk
*Web Site:* www.bhs.org.uk
*Key Personnel*
Chief Executive: Graham Cory
ISBN Prefix(es): 0-900226
Subsidiaries: The British Horse Society Trading Company Ltd

**The British Library**
St Pancras, 96 Euston Rd, London NW1 2DB
*Tel:* (0870) 444 1500
*E-mail:* nbs-info@bl.uk
*Web Site:* www.bl.uk
*Key Personnel*
Dir: Robert Smith *E-mail:* robert.smith@bl.uk
Founded: 1973
ISBN Prefix(es): 0-7123
Total Titles: 700 Print
*Orders to:* Extenza-Turpin Ltd, Stratton Business Park, Pegasus Drive, Biggleswade, Beds SG18 8QB *Tel:* (01767) 604955 *Fax:* (01767) 601640 *E-mail:* books@extenza-turpin.com

**British Library Document Supply Centre**
Document Supply Centre, Boston Spa, Wetherby, W Yorks LS23 7BQ
*Tel:* (01937) 546060 *Fax:* (01937) 546333
*E-mail:* dsc-customer-services@bl.uk
*Web Site:* www.bl.uk
*Key Personnel*
Publications Officer: Dorothy Drydale *E-mail:* garth.frankland@bl.uk
Founded: 1962
ISBN Prefix(es): 0-7123; 0-9532; 0-904654; 0-900220
*Parent Company:* British Library, 96 Euston Rd, London NW1 2DB
*Orders to:* Turpin Distribution Services Ltd, Blackhorse Rd, Letchworth, Herts SG6 1HN *Tel:* (0146) 672555 *Fax:* (0146) 480947

**British Library Publications+**
96 Euston Rd, London NW1 2DB
*Tel:* (020) 7412 7000 *Fax:* (020) 7412 7768
*E-mail:* enquiries@bl.uk
*Web Site:* www.bl.uk
*Key Personnel*
Publishing Manager: David Way *Tel:* (020) 7412 7532 *E-mail:* david.way@bl.uk
Founded: 1979
Publishing & book trade reference.
Subjects: Art, History
ISBN Prefix(es): 0-7123

Number of titles published annually: 50 Print; 3 CD-ROM
Total Titles: 600 Print; 10 CD-ROM
*Parent Company:* The British Library
Distributed by University of Toronto Press (Canada & USA)
*Orders to:* Extenza-Turpin Distribution Ltd, Stratton Business Park, Pegasus Drive, Biggleswade, Beds SG18 8QB

**British Museum Press+**
46 Bloomsbury St, London WC1B 3QQ
*Tel:* (020) 7637 1292 *Fax:* (020) 7436 7315
*E-mail:* customerservices@bmcompany.co.uk; information@thebritishmuseum.ac.uk
*Web Site:* www.britishmuseum.co.uk
*Telex:* 28592 BMPUBS G
*Key Personnel*
Man Dir: Andrew Thatcher
Production: Susan Walby
Head of Sales, Marketing & Rights: Alasdair MacLeod *E-mail:* a.macleod@bmcompany.co.uk
Publicity: Penelope Vogler
Managing Editor: Teresa Francis
Founded: 1973
Subjects: Archaeology, Art, Asian Studies, Crafts, Games, Hobbies, Ethnicity
ISBN Prefix(es): 0-7141
*Parent Company:* The British Museum Co Ltd
*Bookshop(s):* British Museum Shop, Great Russell St, London WC1
*Orders to:* Thames & Hudson Ltd, 44 Clockhouse Rd, Farnborough, Hants

**British Psychological Society**, see BPS Books (British Psychological Society)

**British Tourist Authority**
Thames Tower, Black's Rd, London W6 9EL
*Tel:* (020) 8846 9000 *Fax:* (020) 8846 0302
*Web Site:* www.visitbritain.com
*Key Personnel*
Chief Executive: David Quarmby
Founded: 1969
Subjects: Travel
ISBN Prefix(es): 0-7095; 0-85630; 0-900225
*Branch Office(s)*
Buenos Aires, Argentina
Sydney, Australia
Brussels, Belgium
Ontario, Canada
Copenhagen, Denmark
Paris, France
Frankfurt, Germany
Hong Kong, Hong Kong
Dublin, Ireland
Milan, Italy
Rome, Italy
Osaka, Japan
Tokyo, Japan
Amsterdam, Netherlands
Auckland, New Zealand
Oslo, Norway
Lisbon, Portugal
Seoul, Republic of Korea
Singapore, Singapore
Craighall, South Africa
Madrid, Spain
Stockholm, Sweden
Zurich, Switzerland
Taipei, Taiwan, Province of China
*U.S. Office(s):* Chicago, IL, United States
New York, NY, United States

**Andrew Brodie**, *imprint of* A & C Black Publishers Ltd

**Bronant Books**, *imprint of* Gwasg Gwenffrwd

**Brooklands Books Ltd**
PO Box 146, Cobham, Surrey KT11 1LG
*Tel:* (01932) 865051 *Fax:* (01932) 868803
*E-mail:* info@brooklands-books.com
*Web Site:* www.brooklands-books.com
*Key Personnel*
Man Dir: Ian Dowdeswell
Marketing Dir: Barbara Cleveland
Membership(s): British Motor Heritage.
Subjects: Automotive, Motorcycles, Military, Racing
ISBN Prefix(es): 0-906589; 0-907073; 0-946489; 0-948207; 1-85520
Number of titles published annually: 50 Print
Total Titles: 800 Print
*U.S. Office(s):* CarTech, 11605 Kost Dam Rd, North Branch, MN 55056, United States *Tel:* 651-583-3471; 800-551-4754 *Fax:* 651-583-2023
Distributor for Robert Bentley Inc

**The Brown Reference Group PLC+**
8 Chapel Pl, Rivington St, London EC2A 3DQ
*Tel:* (020) 7920 7500 *Fax:* (020) 7920 7501
*E-mail:* info@brownreference.com
*Web Site:* www.brownreference.com
*Key Personnel*
Chairman: Ashley Brown
Man Dir: Sharon Hutton *Tel:* (020) 7920 7508 *E-mail:* shutton@brownpartworks.co.uk
Founded: 1995
Packager of books, partworks & continuity series.
Subjects: Cookery, Crafts, Games, Hobbies, History, Music, Dance, Natural History, Science (General), Social Sciences, Sociology, Military History, Popular Culture
ISBN Prefix(es): 1-84044

**Brown, Son & Ferguson, Ltd**
4/10 Darnley St, Glasgow G41 2SD
*Tel:* (0141) 4291234 *Fax:* (0141) 4201694
*E-mail:* enquiry@skipper.co.uk
*Web Site:* www.skipper.co.uk *Cable:* SKIPPER GLASGOW
*Key Personnel*
Chief Executive, Editorial, Production: T Nigel Brown
Sales & Publicity: David H Provan
Rights & Permissions: L Ingram-Brown
Founded: 1832
Subjects: Drama, Theater, Maritime, Scottish Plays, Nautical Publications
ISBN Prefix(es): 0-85174
Number of titles published annually: 10 Print; 1 CD-ROM
Total Titles: 1 CD-ROM
Subsidiaries: James Munro & Co

**Brown Wells & Jacobs Ltd**
Foresters Hall, 25-27 Westow St, London SE19 3RY
*Tel:* (020) 8771 5115 *Fax:* (020) 8771 9994
*E-mail:* postmaster@popking.demon.co.uk
*Web Site:* www.bwj.org
*Key Personnel*
Man Dir: Graham Brown
Founded: 1978
Subjects: Nonfiction (General)
ISBN Prefix(es): 1-873829
Number of titles published annually: 15 Print
Total Titles: 35 Print
*Associate Companies:* Book Street Ltd

**Brunner-Routledge**, *imprint of* Taylor & Francis

**Bryntirion Press+**
Bryntirion, Bridgend CF31 4DX
*Tel:* (01656) 655886 *Fax:* (01656) 665919
*E-mail:* office@emw.org.uk
*Web Site:* www.evangelicalmvt-wales.org/books/bryntirionpress/default.htm
*Key Personnel*
Press Manager: Huw Kinsey

Founded: 1955
Publish books in Welsh & English
Also distribute for other publishers.
Subjects: Biblical Studies, Biography, History,
Religion - Protestant, Theology
ISBN Prefix(es): 0-900898; 0-9502680; 1-85049
Total Titles: 80 Print
*Parent Company:* Evangelical Movement of
Wales
Imprints: Evangelical Library of Wales
Distributed by Evangelical Press (English language titles)


**Buildings of England**, *imprint of* Penguin Books
Ltd


**Buildings of England**, *imprint of* The Penguin
Group UK


**Burall Floraprint Ltd**
Oldfield Lane, PO Box 29, Wisbech, Cambs
PE13 2TH
*Tel:* (0870) 728 72 22 *Fax:* (0870) 728 72 77
*E-mail:* floraprint@burall.com
*Web Site:* www.bflora.com
*Key Personnel*
Man Dir: Brian Pinker
Founded: 1986
Promotional print for horticulture.
Subjects: Gardening, Plants
ISBN Prefix(es): 0-903001
Total Titles: 8 Print
*Parent Company:* Burall Ltd
*Ultimate Parent Company:* The Burall Group Ltd
Foreign Rep(s): John Markham Associates
(Canada, US)
*Orders to:* John Markham Associates, 11210 El-
derberry Way, Rural Route 3, Sidney, BC V8L
5JD, Canada *Tel:* 604-655-1823 *Fax:* 604-655-
1826 (Canada & USA)


**Burns & Oates**, *imprint of* The Continuum
International Publishing Group Ltd


**Business Books**, *imprint of* Random House UK
Ltd


**Business Monitor International+**
Mermaid House, 2 Puddle Dock, Blackfriars,
London EC4V 3DS
*Tel:* (020) 7248 0468 *Fax:* (020) 7248 0467
*E-mail:* subs@businessmonitor.com
*Web Site:* www.businessmonitor.com
*Key Personnel*
Agencies & Business Development Man-
ager: Anne Wittman *Tel:* (020) 7557 7110
*E-mail:* awittman@businessmonitor.com
Publisher: Jonathan Feroze *Tel:* (020) 7557
7111 *E-mail:* jferoze@businessmonitor.com;
Richard Londesborough *Tel:* (020) 7557 7105
*E-mail:* rlondesborough@businessmonitor.com
Head of Marketing, Books: Sarah Bennett
*Tel:* (020) 7557 7106 *E-mail:* sbennett@
businessmonitor.com
Market Analysis: Terry Alexander
*E-mail:* talexander@businessmonitor.com
Syndication & Licensing: Andrew Leighton
*E-mail:* aleighton@businessmonitor.com
Subscriptions: Joanna Miller *E-mail:* jmiller@
businessmonitor.com
Consultant: Rob Anderson *E-mail:* randerson@
businessmonitor.com
Technical Support: David Mulvaney
*E-mail:* dmulvaney@businessmonitor.com
Macroeconomic Analysis: Matt Brooks
*E-mail:* mbrooks@businessmonitor.com
Commercial Intelligence Service: Nick Jotischky
*E-mail:* njotischky@businessmonitor.com
Founded: 1984
Specialize in essential news, data, analysis &
forecasts on economic, business & political

developments in global emerging markets coun-
tries.
Subjects: Business, Chemistry, Chemical Engi-
neering, Developing Countries, Economics, En-
ergy, Engineering (General), Finance, Foreign
Countries, Government, Political Science, Jour-
nalism, Securities, Social Sciences, Sociology
Number of titles published annually: 80 Print; 28
CD-ROM; 68 Online
Total Titles: 80 Print; 28 CD-ROM; 68 Online
*Associate Companies:* Commercial Intelligence
Service


**Buster Books**, *imprint of* Michael O'Mara Books
Ltd


**Butterworth Heinemann Ltd**, *imprint of*
Elsevier Ltd


**Butterworths Direct**, *imprint of* Butterworths
Tolley


**Butterworths Tolley+**
2 Addiscombe Rd, Croydon CR9 5AF
*Tel:* (020) 8686 9141; (020) 8662 2000 (customer
service) *Fax:* (020) 8686 3155; (020) 8662
2012 (customer service)
*E-mail:* customer-services@butterworths.com
*Key Personnel*
Man Dir: Paul Virik
Founded: 1818
Subjects: Accounting, Finance, Law
ISBN Prefix(es): 0-510; 0-406; 0-85459; 0-7545;
1-86012
Number of titles published annually: 120 Print;
10 CD-ROM
Total Titles: 1,000 Print; 50 CD-ROM; 25 E-
Book
*Parent Company:* Reed Elsevier plc, 25 Victoria
St, London SW1H 0EX
*Associate Companies:* Butterworths-Australia,
Reed Elsevier Bldg, Tower 2, 475-495 Victoria
Ave, Chatswood NSW 2067, Australia *Tel:* (02)
9422-2222 *Fax:* (02) 9422-2444; Butterworths-
Canada, 75 Clegg Rd, Markham, ON L6G
1A1, Canada *Tel:* 905-479-2665 *Fax:* 905-479-
2826; Butterworths-New Zealand, 205-207 Vic-
toria St, Wellington, New Zealand *Tel:* (04)
385 1479 *Fax:* (04) 385 1598; Butterworths-
Asia, N01 Temasek Ave, 17-01 Millenia Tower
039192, Singapore *Tel:* 336 9661 *Fax:* 336
9662; Butterworths-South Africa, 8 Walter
Place, Mayville 4091 Natal, South Africa
*Tel:* (031) 2683111 *Fax:* (031) 2683108
Imprints: Books on Screen; Butterworths Direct;
Eclipse; Tolley
*Branch Office(s)*
Butterworths, 26 Upper Ormond Quay, Dublin
7, Ireland *Tel:* (03531) 873 1268 (editorial en-
quiries)
2, Addiscombe Rd, Croyden, Surrey CR9 5AF
*Tel:* (020) 8686 9141 *Fax:* (020) 8686 3155
Butterworths LEXIS Direct, Globe House,
Victoria Way, Woking, Surrey GU21 1DD
*Tel:* (01483) 257725 (online publishing divi-
sion)
Butterworths, 4 Hill St, Edinburgh EH2 3JZ, Dir:
Philip Woods *Tel:* (0131) 225 7828 *Fax:* (0131)
220 1833 *E-mail:* sales.service@butterworths.
co.uk
*U.S. Office(s):* Reed Elsevier Inc, 2 Park Ave,
2nd floor, New York, NY 10016, United States
*Tel:* 212-448-2300 *Fax:* 212-448-2196
*Bookshop(s):* Butterworths Bookshop, 35
Chancery Lane, London WC2A 1EL *Tel:* (020)
7400 2868 *Fax:* (020) 7400 2870
*Warehouse:* Butterworths Warehouse, Unit 3, 2
Shipton Way, Express Park, Rusden, Northants
NN10 6GL *Tel:* (01933) 411682 *Fax:* (01933)
411857

*Orders to:* Butterworths Warehouse, Unit 3, 2
Shipton Way, Express Park, Rusden, Northants
NN10 6GL *Tel:* (01933) 411682 *Fax:* (01933)
411857


**Bwrdd Croeso Cymru** (Wales Tourist Board)
Brunel House, 2, Fitzalan Rd, Cardiff CF24 0UY
*Tel:* (029) 2047 5214 *Fax:* (029) 2048 5031
*E-mail:* info@visitwales.com
*Web Site:* www.visitwales.com
*Key Personnel*
Chief Executive: Jonathan Jones
Head of Production Services & Sales: Rhys Jones
Founded: 1969
Subjects: Travel
ISBN Prefix(es): 1-85013; 0-900784
*Orders to:* Jarrold Publishing, Whitefriars, Nor-
wich NR3 1TR


**Byeway Books**, *imprint of* Autumn Publishing
Ltd


**Bygone Kent**, *imprint of* Meresborough Books
Ltd


**CABI Publishing**
Division of CAB International
Wallingford, Oxon OX10 8DE
*Tel:* (01491) 832111 *Fax:* (01491) 833508
*E-mail:* publishing@cabi.org
*Web Site:* www.cabi-publishing.org
*Key Personnel*
Publishing Dir: David Nicholson *E-mail:* d.
nicholson@cabi.org
Book Publisher: Tim Hardwick *E-mail:* t.
hardwick@cabi.org
Man Dir: Tony Llewellyn *E-mail:* t.llewellyn@
cabi.org
Sales & Marketing Dir: Caroline McNamara
*E-mail:* c.mcnamara@cabi.org
Commercial Dir: Mr Kelvin Tunley *E-mail:* k.
tunley@cabi.org
Promotion Services Manager: Sarah Harris
*E-mail:* s.harris@cabi.org
Founded: 1928
A nonprofit international organization dedi-
cated to improving human welfare worldwide
through the dissemination, application & gen-
eration of scientific knowledge in support of
sustainable development.
Subjects: Agricultural Economics, Engineering &
Entomology, Animal Breeding, Genetics, Nu-
trition & Production, Biodiversity, Biological
Control, Crop Production & Protection, Dairy
Science, Ecology & Environment, Entomol-
ogy, Forestry, Horticulture, Human Nutrition,
Leisure/Tourism, Medicinal Plants, Nematol-
ogy, Parasitology & Infectious Diseases, Plant
Biotechnology, Breeding, Genetic & Pathology,
Postharvest, Rural Development, Sugar Indus-
try, Veterinary Medicine, Weed Science
ISBN Prefix(es): 0-85198; 0-85199
Total Titles: 300 Print; 20 CD-ROM; 1 Online; 6
E-Book
*U.S. Office(s):* 875 Massachusetts Ave, 7th
floor, Cambridge, MA 02139, United States
*Tel:* (617) 395-4056 *Fax:* (617) 354-6875
*E-mail:* cabi-nao@cabi.org


**Cadogan Guides+**
Network House, One Ariel Way, London W12
7SL
*Tel:* (020) 8740 2050 *Fax:* (020) 8740 2059
*E-mail:* info@cadoganguides.com; editorial@
cadoganguides.com; advertising@
cadoganguides.com; publicity@cadoganguides.
com; marketing@cadoganguides.com
*Web Site:* www.cadoganguides.com
*Key Personnel*
Editorial Dir: Vicki Ingle
Founded: 1985

Specialize in travel guides.
Subjects: Travel
ISBN Prefix(es): 0-947754; 0-946313; 1-86011
*Parent Company:* Morris Publications Ltd
*U.S. Office(s):* The Globe Pequot Press, 6 Business Park Rd, PO Box 833, Old Saybrook, CT 06475-0833, United States
Foreign Rep(s): Books for Europe (Austria, Czech Republic, France, Hungary, Poland, Switzerland); Capricorn Link (Australia) Pty Ltd (Australia); The Globe Pequot Press (Canada, US); Peter Hyde & Associates (Pty) Ltd (South Africa); Inter Media Americans (IMA) (Caribbean, South America); Pernille Larsen (Scandinavia); Nilsson & Lamm (Netherlands); Sandro Salucci (Croatia, Greece, Portugal, Slovenia, Spain); Nicky La Touche (Italy)
*Orders to:* Grantham Book Services, Isaac Newton Way, Alma Park Industrial Estate, Grantham, Lincs NG31 9SD

**Calder Publications Ltd+**
51 The Cut, London SE1 8LF
*Tel:* (020) 7633 0599
*E-mail:* info@calderpublications.com
*Web Site:* www.calderpublications.com
*Key Personnel*
Manager & Publishing Dir: John Calder
  *Tel:* (020) 76333
Production, Editorial, Design, Sales, Rights & Permissions: Toby Fenton
Founded: 1949
Publishers of international literature & books on cultural subjects
No unsol mss considered.
Subjects: Art, Biography, Drama, Theater, Fiction, Literature, Literary Criticism, Essays, Music, Dance, Nonfiction (General), Philosophy, Poetry
ISBN Prefix(es): 0-7145
Number of titles published annually: 30 Print
Total Titles: 400 Print; 200 Online; 200 E-Book
*Parent Company:* The Calder Educational Trust, 51 The Cut, London SE1 8LF, Contact: John Calder
*Associate Companies:* Riverrun Press, 1200 County Road 523, Flemington, NJ 08822, United States
Imprints: Riverrun Press
Distributed by Whitehurst & Clark
Foreign Rep(s): Whitehurst & Clarke, Raritan Industrial (Canada, US)
*Warehouse:* Combined Book Services, Units I-K Paddock, Wood Distribution Centre, Paddock Wood, Tonbridge, Kent TN12 6UU
  *Tel:* (01892) 837171 *Fax:* (01892) 837272
  *E-mail:* orders@combook.co.uk

**Cambridge Scientific Abstracts,** see CSA (Cambridge Scientific Abstracts)

**Cambridge University Press+**
The Edinburgh Bldg, Shaftesbury Rd, Cambridge CB2 2RU
*Tel:* (01223) 312393 *Fax:* (01223) 315052
*E-mail:* information@cup.cam.ac.uk; uksales@ cambridge.org (sales); editorial@cambridge.org (editorial enquiries); rights@cambridge.org (rights & permission); www@cambridge.org (web services)
*Web Site:* www.cambridge.org
*Key Personnel*
Chief Executive: S Bourne
Editorial Dir: R Barling; A M C Brown; A Gilfillan; M Y Holdsworth
International Dir: P Langworth
Production Dir: C Murray
Rights Sales Manager: Christina Roberts
Permissions: Linda Nicol
Founded: 1534

Subjects: Agriculture, Anthropology, Archaeology, Architecture & Interior Design, Art, Biblical Studies, Biography, Biological Sciences, Chemistry, Chemical Engineering, Computer Science, Drama, Theater, Earth Sciences, Economics, Education, Engineering (General), English as a Second Language, Environmental Studies, Geography, Geology, Government, Political Science, History, Language Arts, Linguistics, Law, Literature, Literary Criticism, Essays, Mathematics, Medicine, Nursing, Dentistry, Music, Dance, Philosophy, Physical Sciences, Psychology, Psychiatry, Social Sciences, Sociology, Theology
Number of titles published annually: 1,600 Print; 10 CD-ROM; 50 Audio
Imprints: Canto
*Branch Office(s)*
10 Stamford Rd, Oakleigh, Victoria 3166, Australia *Tel:* (03) 9568 0322 *Fax:* (03) 9563 1517 *E-mail:* info@cambridge.edu.au *Web Site:* www.cambridge.edu.au
Ruiz De Alarcon 13, 28014 Madrid, Spain
1 The Moorings, Portswood Ridge, Victoria & Alfred Waterfront, Capetown 8001, South Africa
*U.S. Office(s):* 40 W 20 St, New York, NY 10011-4211, United States
Distributor for The Asser Press (Worldwide)
Foreign Rights: Bardon-Chinese Media Agency (Hong Kong, Taiwan, Macao); Bestun Korea Agency (Korea)
*Showroom(s):* One & 2 Trinity St, Cambridge CB2 1SU

**Camden Large Print,** *imprint of* BBC Audiobooks

**Camden Press Ltd+**
46 Colebrooke Row, London N1 8AF
*Tel:* (020) 7226 2061 *Fax:* (020) 7226 2418
*Key Personnel*
Chairman: Robert Borzello
Founded: 1985
Subjects: Art, Biography, Health, Nutrition, Social Sciences, Sociology, Women's Studies
ISBN Prefix(es): 0-948491

**Camerapix Publishers International Ltd+**
6 Alston Rd, Barnet, Herts EN5 4ET
*Tel:* (020) 8449 5503 *Fax:* (020) 8449 8120
*E-mail:* camerapixuk@btinternet.com
*Web Site:* www.camerapix.com
*Key Personnel*
Man Dir: Mrs Rukhsana Haq
Dir: Salim Amin
Publisher of travel guides & photographic travel books.
Subjects: Travel
ISBN Prefix(es): 1-874041
Number of titles published annually: 3 Print
Total Titles: 65 Print

**Cameron & Hollis+**
Imprint of Cameron Books
PO Box 1, Moffat, Dumfries DG10 9SU
*Tel:* (01683) 220808 *Fax:* (01683) 220012
*E-mail:* editorial@cameronbooks.co.uk; sales@ cameronbooks.co.uk (orders)
*Web Site:* www.cameronbooks.co.uk
*Key Personnel*
Dir: Ian Cameron; Jill Hollis
Founded: 1976
Primarily packagers.
Subjects: Architecture & Interior Design, Art, Environmental Studies, Film, Video, Natural History
ISBN Prefix(es): 0-906506
*Associate Companies:* Movie
Subsidiaries: Edition, Cameron & Hollis

**Campbell Books,** *imprint of* Macmillan Children's Books

**Campbell Books,** *imprint of* Pan Macmillan

**Candle Books,** *imprint of* Lion Hudson plc

**Canongate Academic,** *imprint of* Tuckwell Press Ltd

**Canongate Books "A" Ltd,** *imprint of* Birlinn Ltd

**Canongate Books Ltd+**
14 High St, Edinburgh EH1 1TE
*Tel:* (0131) 557 5111 *Fax:* (0131) 557 5211
*E-mail:* info@canongate.co.uk; customerservices@canongate.co.uk
*Web Site:* www.canongate.net
*Key Personnel*
Publisher: Jamie Byng
Production Dir: Caroline Gorham
Rights Manager: Polly Hutchison
Sales Manager: David Graham
Founded: 1973
Subjects: Biography, Fiction, History, Literature, Literary Criticism, Essays, Music, Dance, Nonfiction (General), Poetry, Regional Interests, Travel
ISBN Prefix(es): 0-86241; 1-84195
Number of titles published annually: 65 Print
Total Titles: 350 Print
Imprints: Canongate Classics
Distributed by Grove Atlantic (USA)
*Orders to:* Publishers Group West, 1700 Fourth St, Berkeley, CA 96710, United States
  *Tel:* 510-528-1444

**Canongate Classics,** *imprint of* Canongate Books Ltd

**Canterbury Press,** *imprint of* SCM-Canterbury Press Ltd

**Canterbury Press Norwich,** *imprint of* Hymns Ancient & Modern Ltd

**Canto,** *imprint of* Cambridge University Press

**Capall Bann Publishing+**
Auton Farm, Milverton Somerset TA4 1NE
*Tel:* (01823) 401528 *Fax:* (01823) 401529
*E-mail:* enquiries@capallbann.co.uk
*Web Site:* www.capallbann.co.uk
*Key Personnel*
Publisher: Jon Day; Julia Day
Founded: 1993
Family owned & run company.
Subjects: Alternative, Animals, Pets, Archaeology, Astrology, Occult, Education, Environmental Studies, Gardening, Plants, Maritime, Music, Dance, Mysteries, Parapsychology, Philosophy, Psychology, Psychiatry, Religion - Other, Self-Help, Women's Studies, Alternative Healing, Mind, Body & Spirit
ISBN Prefix(es): 1-898307; 1-86163
Number of titles published annually: 40 Print
Total Titles: 290 Print
*Distribution Center:* Bacchus Books, South Africa *E-mail:* bacchus@telkomsa.net
Brumby Books, 10 Southfork Drive, Kilsyth South, Victoria 3137, Australia *Tel:* (03) 9761 5535 *Fax:* (03) 9761 7095 *E-mail:* brumby@ hotkey.net.au
Holmes Publishing Group, United States, Mr J D Holmes *E-mail:* jdh@jdholmes.com
New Leaf, United States

**Jonathan Cape,** *imprint of* Random House UK Ltd

**Jonathan Cape Childrens**, *imprint of* Random House UK Ltd

**Capstone Publishing Ltd+**
8 Newtec Pl, Magdalen Rd, Oxford OX4 1RE
*Tel:* (01865) 798623 *Fax:* (01865) 240941
*E-mail:* capstone_publishing@msn.com
*Web Site:* www.capstone.co.uk
*Key Personnel*
Dir: Mark Allin; Richard Burton
Sales & Marketing Dir: Simon Benham
    *Tel:* (0171) 6223082 *Fax:* (0171) 6223082
    *E-mail:* simonbenham@capstoneuk.fireserve.
    co.uk
Publishing Manager: Catherine Meyrick
Founded: 1996
Membership(s): IPG.
Subjects: Business, Economics, Management
ISBN Prefix(es): 1-900961; 1-84112
Number of titles published annually: 20 Print
Total Titles: 90 Print
Distributor for Bard Press
Foreign Rights: Susie Adams (UK)
*Warehouse:* Marston Book Services, PO Box 269, Abingdon, Oxon OX14 4YN *Tel:* (01235) 465600 *Fax:* (01235) 465655
LPG Group, 40 Commerce Park, Milford, CT 06460, United States *Tel:* 203-878-6417 *Fax:* 203-874-2308
*Orders to:* Marston Book Services, PO Box 269, Abingdon, Oxon OX14 4YN *Tel:* (01235) 465600 *Fax:* (01235) 465655

**Carcanet Press Ltd+**
Alliance House, 4th floor, Cross St, Manchester M2 7AP
*Tel:* (0161) 834 8730 *Fax:* (0161) 832 0084
*E-mail:* info@carcanet.u-net.com
*Web Site:* www.carcanet.co.uk
*Key Personnel*
Editorial & Man Dir: Michael Schmidt
Sales: Pamela Heaton *E-mail:* pam@carcanet.co.uk
Marketing & Publicity Manager: Angharad Jackson *E-mail:* angharad@carcanet.co.uk
Editorial & Production Manager: Judith Wilson *E-mail:* judith@carcanet.co.uk
Financial Dir: Julie Munro *E-mail:* julie@carcanet.co.uk
Founded: 1969
Independent Poetry & fiction translation publisher.
Subjects: Fiction, Literature, Literary Criticism, Essays, Poetry
ISBN Prefix(es): 0-85635; 0-902145; 1-85754; 1-903039
Number of titles published annually: 45 Print
Total Titles: 700 Print
*Parent Company:* Folio Holdings
*Associate Companies:* Folio Society
Imprints: From The Portuguese; Fyfield Books; Oxford Poets
Distributed by Littlehampton Book Services
*Orders to:* Paul & Co, PO Box 442, Concord, MA 01742, United States *Tel:* 508-369-3049 *Fax:* 508-369-2385

**Cardiff Academic Press+**
39 Rannoch Dr, Cardiff CF2 6LP
*Tel:* (029) 2076 2106 *Fax:* (029) 2055 4909
*E-mail:* drakegroup@btinternet.com
*Key Personnel*
Man Dir: Mr R G Drake
Founded: 1979
Subjects: Biography, Education, Literature, Literary Criticism, Essays, Regional Interests, Religion - Other, Social Sciences, Sociology, Women's Studies, Welsh Studies
ISBN Prefix(es): 1-899025; 1-870495
*Parent Company:* Drake Group

Imprints: Plantin Publishers
Distributor for ECW Press (Canada); ILSI Press (USA); Plantin Publishers (UK); TUNS Press (Canada)

**Careers Research & Advisory Centre Ltd**, see Hobsons

**Careers & Occupational Information Centre (COIC)**
Room W46, Moorfoot, Sheffield S1 4PQ
*Tel:* (0114) 259 4564 *Fax:* (0114) 259 3439
*Key Personnel*
Production Manager: David Baker
Founded: 1974
Subjects: Career Development
ISBN Prefix(es): 0-86110
*Parent Company:* Dept of Educational & Employment

**Carfax Publishing**, *imprint of* Taylor & Francis

**Carfax Publishing**
Member of Taylor & Francis Group
11 New Fetter Lane, London EC4P 4EE
*Tel:* (020) 7842 2001 *Fax:* (020) 7842 2298
*E-mail:* sales@carfax.co.uk
*Web Site:* www.carfax.co.uk
*Key Personnel*
Man Editor: Ian White
Contact: Stephen Entwistle
Founded: 1972
ISBN Prefix(es): 0-902879
*Branch Office(s)*
ITPS, Cheriton House, Northway, Andover SP10 5BE *Tel:* (01264) 342 926 *Fax:* (01264) 343 005 *E-mail:* book.orders@tandf.co.uk (European customer service operation for books)
*U.S. Office(s):* 325 Chestnut St, Suite 800, Philadelphia, PA 19106, United States *Fax:* 215-625-8914

**Carlton Books**, *imprint of* Carlton Publishing Group

**Carlton Publishing Group+**
20 Mortimer St, London W1T 3JW
*Tel:* (020) 7612 0400 *Fax:* (020) 7612 0401
*E-mail:* enquires@carltonbooks.co.uk; sales@carltonbooks.co.uk; editorial@carltonbooks.co.uk
*Web Site:* www.carltonint.co.uk
*Key Personnel*
Man Dir: Jonathan Goodman
Editorial Dir: Piers Murray Hill
International Sales Dir: Fiona Langdon
Founded: 1992
Publisher of illustrated books.
Subjects: Antiques, Architecture & Interior Design, Art, Biography, Criminology, Erotica, Fashion, Film, Video, Health, Nutrition, History, Humor, Music, Dance, Natural History, Radio, TV, Sports, Athletics, Wine & Spirits
ISBN Prefix(es): 0-233; 1-85868; 1-85375; 1-84222
Number of titles published annually: 100 Print
Total Titles: 700 Print
*Parent Company:* Carlton Communications PLC
*Associate Companies:* Carlton TV; Carlton International
Imprints: Andre Deutsch; Carlton Books; Granada Media; Manchester United Books; Prion

**Jon Carpenter**, *imprint of* Jon Carpenter Publishing

**Jon Carpenter Publishing+**
Alder House, Market St, Charlbury OX7 3PH
*Tel:* (01608) 811969 *Fax:* (01608) 811969

*Key Personnel*
Publisher: Jon Carpenter *E-mail:* jon@joncarpenter.co.uk
Founded: 1992
Specialize in distribution & representation of overseas publishers.
Subjects: Animals, Pets, Cookery, Developing Countries, Economics, Environmental Studies, Government, Political Science, Health, Nutrition, History, Social Sciences, Sociology
ISBN Prefix(es): 1-897766; 1-902279
Number of titles published annually: 10 Print
Total Titles: 120 Print
Imprints: Jon Carpenter; Wychwood Press
Distributed by Envirobook (Australia); I P G; New Horizons (South Africa)
Distributor for Apex Press (USA); Bootstrap Press (USA); Envirobook (Australia); International Books (Netherlands)
*Shipping Address:* Central Books, 99 Wallis Rd, London E9 5LN
*Warehouse:* Central Books, 99 Wallis Rd, London E9 5LN
*Orders to:* Central Books, 99 Wallis Rd, London E9 5LN

**Carrick Media**
66 John Finnie St, Kilmarnock KA1 1BS
*Tel:* (01563) 530830 *Fax:* (01563) 549503
*E-mail:* cm@carrickmedia.demon.co.uk
*Key Personnel*
Proprietor: Kenneth Roy
Production Editor: Fiona McDonald *E-mail:* fm@carrickmedia.demon.co.uk
Founded: 1983
Specialize in Scotland & British media.
ISBN Prefix(es): 0-946724

**Carroll & Brown Ltd+**
20 Lonsdale Rd, Queen's Park, London NW6 6RD
*Tel:* (020) 7372 0900 *Fax:* (020) 7372 0460
*E-mail:* carbro.prod@virgin.net
*Key Personnel*
Man Dir: Amy Carroll
Publisher: Denise Brown
Art Dir: Chrissie Lloyd
Senior Sales Dir: Simonne Waud
International Sales: Kate Hill; Lucy Paine; Cathy Slater
Founded: 1989
Publisher & packager of illustrated reference books for the coedition market. Provides a bespoke packaging service for other publishers.
Subjects: Alternative, Child Care & Development, Cookery, Crafts, Games, Hobbies, Gardening, Plants, Health, Nutrition, How-to, Nonfiction (General), Religion - Other
ISBN Prefix(es): 1-903258
Number of titles published annually: 20 Print
Distributed by Grantham Book Services

**The Cartoon Cave+**
One Willoughby Drive, Empingham, Oakham, Leics LE15 8PY
*Tel:* (01780) 460689; (01780) 460757 *Fax:* (01780) 460689
*Web Site:* www.cartooncave.co.uk
*Key Personnel*
Contact: Larry Harris *E-mail:* larryh@cartooncave.co.uk
Founded: 1980 (*Larry Harris Productions Ltd*)
Publishes fiction for children between the ages of seven & fifteen.
ISBN Prefix(es): 0-9526834
Total Titles: 4 Print
Distributed by Gardners Books

**Frank Cass Publishers+**
Crown House, 47 Chase Side, London N14 5BP
*Tel:* (020) 8920 2100 *Fax:* (020) 8447 8548
*E-mail:* info@frankcass.com

*Web Site:* www.frankcass.com
*Key Personnel*
Man Dir: Frank Cass
Editorial: Andrew Humphreys
Production: Mike Moran
Publicity Books: Eliza Dunlop
Publicity, Journals: Anne Kidson
Trade Manager: Joanna Legg
Rights & Permissions: Amna Whiston
Founded: 1957
Publisher of social science & humanities journals,
  monographs & edited collections.
Subjects: Developing Countries, Economics, His-
  tory, Law, Literature, Literary Criticism, Es-
  says, Military Science, British & International
  History, International Relations, Military Sci-
  ence & Development Studies, Politics, Sports
  Studies
ISBN Prefix(es): 0-7146; 0-85303
*Associate Companies:* Irish Academic Press
*Subsidiaries:* Vallentine, Mitchell & Co Ltd; The
  Littman Library of Jewish Civilization
*U.S. Office(s):* ISBS, 5824 NE Hassalo St, Port-
  land, OR 97213-3644, United States *Fax:* 503-
  280-8832 *E-mail:* cass@isbs.com (North Amer-
  ica)
*Warehouse:* Biblios Distribution, Star Rd,
  Partridge Green, West Sussex RH13 8LD
  *Tel:* (0403) 710971 *Fax:* (0403) 711143
*Orders to:* Plymbridge Distributors Ltd, Es-
  tover Rd, Plymouth PL6 7PY *Tel:* (01752)
  202301 *Fax:* (01752) 202331 *E-mail:* orders@
  plymbridge.com
ISBS, 5824 NE Hassalo St, Portland, OR 97213-
  3644, United States *Fax:* 503-280-8832
  *E-mail:* orders@isbs.com (North America)

**Cassell & Co+**
Wellington House, 125 Strand, London WC2R
  0BB
*Tel:* (020) 7420 5555 *Fax:* (020) 7240 7261;
  (020) 7240 8531
*Telex:* 9413701
*Key Personnel*
Chairman & Chief Executive: Philip Sturrock
Imprint Dir, Arms & Armour Press, Blandford,
  Ward Lock & Cassell: Alison Goff
Imprint Dir, Cassell Academic & Contemporary
  Studies: Janet Joyce
Imprint Dir, Victor Gollancz: Jane Blackstock
Imprint Dir, Religious & Professional: Ruth Mc-
  Curry
UK Trade Sales, Cassell: Finbarr McCabe
UK Trade Sales, Gollancz: Adrienne Maguire
UK Trade Sales, Academic: Georgian Brindley
Sales & Marketing Dir, Academic Division: Anne
  Godfrey
International Sales, General: Michael Goff
International Sales, Academic: Becca Seymour
Rights & Permissions, Gollancz: Jane Blackstock
Founded: 1848
*Overseas Representation:* Australia: New Hol-
  land Publishers Pty Ltd, NSW Australia;
  Canada: Books Inc, North Vancouver, Canada;
  Caribbean: HRA, London, UK; Central Eu-
  rope: European Marketing Services, London,
  UK; Southern Europe: Penny Padovani, Lon-
  don, UK; Hong Kong, China, Korea, Taiwan:
  APS Ltd, Hong Kong; Hungary, Czech Repub-
  lic, Slovakia, Croatia: CLB Marketing Services,
  Kecskemet, Hungary; India: Maya Publishers
  PVT Ltd, New Delhi, India; Japan: Ashton In-
  ternational Marketing Services, UK; Malaysia:
  APD Kuala Lumpur, Selangor Darul Ehsan,
  Malaysia; Middle East: Aston International
  Marketing Services, UK; Netherlands: Nilsson
  & Lamm, Netherlands; New Zealand: David
  Bateman, Auckland, New Zealand; Pakistan:
  Mackwin & Co, Karachi, India; Poland,
  Russia, Romania, Baltic States, Former USSR,
  Bulgaria: Bianca Katris, IMA, Greece; Sin-
  gapore, Indonesia, Thailand: APD Singapore
  Ltd, Singapore; Scandinavia: PKB, Glostrup,

Denmark; South America: HRA, London, UK;
  South Africa: Struik Book Distributors, Cape
  Town, South Africa; USA: Sterling Publishing
  Co Inc, New York, USA.
Subjects: Accounting, Advertising, Architecture &
  Interior Design, Art, Biblical Studies, Biogra-
  phy, Business, Career Development, Cookery,
  Crafts, Games, Hobbies, Developing Countries,
  Education, Environmental Studies, Fiction,
  Film, Video, Gardening, Plants, Gay & Les-
  bian, Geography, Geology, History, House &
  Home, How-to, Humor, Labor, Industrial Re-
  lations, Library & Information Sciences, Man-
  agement, Marketing, Military Science, Music,
  Dance, Natural History, Nonfiction (General),
  Outdoor Recreation, Photography, Poetry, Pub-
  lishing & Book Trade Reference, Religion -
  Catholic, Religion - Protestant, Science (Gen-
  eral), Science Fiction, Fantasy, Social Sciences,
  Sociology, Sports, Athletics, Theology
ISBN Prefix(es): 0-304; 0-7137; 0-7063; 0-289;
  1-85409; 1-85079; 0-575; 0-85493; 0-86187;
  1-84188
*Parent Company:* Hachette Livre
*Associate Companies:* Sterling Publishing, 387
  Park Ave S, New York, NY 10016-8810,
  United States *Tel:* 212-532-7160 *Fax:* 212-213-
  2495
*Imprints:* Arms and Armour Press; Blandford;
  Geoffrey Chapman; Leicester University Press;
  Mansell; Mowbray; New Orchard Editions;
  Pinter, Studio Vista; Tycooly; Victor Gollancz;
  Ward Lock; Wisley Handbooks; Witherby
*Subsidiaries:* Arms & Armour Press; Blandford
  Press; Geoffrey Chapman; Ward Lock Ltd;
  Mowbray; New Orchard Editions; Studio Vista;
  Victor Gollancz; Mansell; Pinter; Leicester
  University Press
Distributed by Sterling Publishing (USA &
  Canada only)
*Orders to:* Cassell, Stanley House, 3 Fleets Lane,
  Poole, Dorset BH15 3AJ *Tel:* (0202) 670581
  *Fax:* (0202) 666219
Sterling Publishing, 387 Park Ave S, New York,
  NY 10016-8810, United States *Tel:* 212-532-
  7160 *Fax:* 212-213-2495

**Cassell Illustrated**, *imprint of* Octopus
  Publishing Group

**Castle House Publications Ltd**
28-30 Church Rd, Tunbridge Wells, Kent TN1
  1TP
*Tel:* (01892) 39606 *Fax:* (01892) 39609
*Key Personnel*
Man Dir: Donald Reinders
Production Editor: Jo Lethaby
Founded: 1973
Specializes In: Medicine
Also run medical conferences.
Divisions: Castle House Medical Conferences

**Castlemead Publications+**
Raynham House, Broadmeads, Ware, Herts SG12
  9HY
*Tel:* (01920) 465525 *Fax:* (01920) 465545
*E-mail:* sales@castlemeadpublications.fsnet.co.uk
*Key Personnel*
Proprietor: Susan D M Lee
Founded: 1982
Publisher of pediatric growth charts.
Membership(s): Publishers Association.
Subjects: Aeronautics, Aviation, Child Care &
  Development, Medicine, Nursing, Dentistry,
  Natural History, Regional Interests, Transporta-
  tion
ISBN Prefix(es): 0-948555

**Kyle Cathie Ltd+**
122 Arlington Rd, London NW1 7HP
*Tel:* (020) 7692 7215 *Fax:* (020) 7692 7260
*E-mail:* general.enquiries@kyle-cathie.com

*Web Site:* www.kylecathie.co.uk
*Key Personnel*
Man Dir: Kyle Cathie *E-mail:* kcathie@aol.com
Editor: Caroline Taggart
Sales & Marketing Dir: Julia Barder *Tel:* (020)
  7692 7233 *E-mail:* julia.barder@kyle-cathie.
  com
Rights Dir: Melanie Gray *Tel:* (020) 7692 7256
  *E-mail:* melanie.gray@kyle-cathie.com
Founded: 1990
Subjects: Biography, Cookery, Gardening, Plants,
  Health, Nutrition, History, Natural History, Phi-
  losophy, Lifestyle, Health & Beauty, Mind,
  Body & Spirit
ISBN Prefix(es): 1-85626
Total Titles: 25 Print
Distributed by Simon & Schuster Pty Ltd (Aus-
  tralia); Whitecap (Canada); Reed Publishing
  NZ Ltd (New Zealand); Wild Dog (South
  America)
Foreign Rep(s): Frances Bucquet (Austria,
  Benelux, Eastern Europe, France, Germany,
  Italy, Switzerland); John Edgeler (Caribbean,
  Central America, Middle East, South Amer-
  ica, Southern Europe, Scandinavia); Gunnar Lie
  (Africa, Asia); Benji OCampo (Korea, Philip-
  pines); Pansing Distribution (Brunei, Malaysia,
  Singapore); Reed Publishing NZ Ltd (New
  Zealand); Simon & Schuster (Australia) Pty
  Ltd (Australia); Trafalgar Square (US); White-
  cap (Canada)
*Orders to:* Littlehampton Book Services Ltd,
  Faraday Close, Durrington, West Sussex BN13
  3RB *Tel:* (01903) 828800 *Fax:* (01903) 828801
  *E-mail:* orders@lbsltd.co.uk

**Catholic Institute for International Relations+**
Canonbury Yard, Unit 3, 190a New North Rd,
  London N1 7BJ
*Tel:* (020) 7354 0883 *Fax:* (020) 7359 0017
*E-mail:* ciir@ciir.org
*Web Site:* www.ciir.org
*Key Personnel*
Executive Dir: Christine Allen *E-mail:* christine@
  ciir.org
Production Editor: Adam Bradbury
  *E-mail:* adam@ciir.org
Press & Information Coordinator: Finola Robin-
  son *E-mail:* finola@ciir.org
Founded: 1940
Also acts as development agency.
Subjects: Developing Countries, Economics, Gov-
  ernment, Political Science, Theology
ISBN Prefix(es): 0-904393; 0-946848; 1-85287
*Orders to:* Central Books, 99 Wallis Rd, London
  E9 5LN

**The Catholic Truth Society+**
40-46 Harleyford Rd, Vauxhall, London SE11
  5AY
*Tel:* (020) 7640 0042 *Fax:* (020) 7640 0046
*E-mail:* info@cts-online.org.uk
*Web Site:* www.cts-online.org.uk *Cable:*
  APOSTOLIC LONDON
*Key Personnel*
General Secretary: Fergal Martin
Founded: 1884
Subjects: Education, Religion - Catholic
ISBN Prefix(es): 0-85183; 1-86082
Imprints: CTS Publications
Distributor for Liberia Editrice Vaticana;
  L'Osservatore Romano Newspaper
*Bookshop(s):* 25 Ashley Pl, London SW1P 1LT
*Book Club(s):* CTS Readers Club

**Catnip Publishing Ltd**, see Happy Cat Books

**Caucasus World**, *imprint of* RoutledgeCurzon

**Causeway Press Ltd+**
129 New Court Way, Ormskirk, Lancs L39 5HP
Mailing Address: PO Box 13, Ormskirk, Lancs
  L39 5HP

*Tel:* (01695) 576048; (01695) 577360
  *Fax:* (01695) 570714
*E-mail:* davidalcorn.causewaypress@btinternet.
  com
*Key Personnel*
Editorial, Publicity, Rights & Permissions, Sales
  & Production: Michael Haralambos
Company Secretary: David Gray
Founded: 1982
Subjects: Business, Economics, Geography, Ge-
  ology, Government, Political Science, Health,
  Nutrition, History, Mathematics, Psychology,
  Psychiatry, Social Sciences, Sociology, Tech-
  nology
ISBN Prefix(es): 0-946183; 1-873929; 1-902796
*Warehouse:* The Trade Counter, Mendlesham,
  Suffolk IP14 5NA

**Cavalcade Story Cassettes**, *imprint of* BBC
  Audiobooks

**Paul Cave Publications Ltd**
74 Bedford Pl, Southampton SO15 2DF
*Tel:* (01703) 223591; (01703) 333457
  *Fax:* (01703) 227190
*E-mail:* lanksmag@zone.co.uk
*Key Personnel*
Chairman & Editor: Paul Cave
Dir: Joan Cave
Founded: 1960
Membership(s): Periodical Publishers Association.
Subjects: Regional Interests
ISBN Prefix(es): 0-86146; 0-9501735

**Marshall Cavendish Partworks Ltd**
Member of Times Publishing Group
119 Wardour St, London W1F 0UW
*Tel:* (020) 7565 6000 *Fax:* (020) 7734 6221
*E-mail:* info@marshallcavendish.co.uk
*Web Site:* www.marshallcavendish.co.uk
*Telex:* 23880 *Cable:* MARCAV LONDON W1
*Key Personnel*
Acting Chief Executive: John Armour
Circulation Manager: Christopher Jenner
Subjects: Antiques, Art, Astrology, Occult, Cook-
  ery, Crafts, Games, Hobbies, Gardening, Plants,
  Health, Nutrition
ISBN Prefix(es): 0-7485
*Associate Companies:* ALP SNC, France; Mar-
  shall Cavendish Corporation, United States
*Orders to:* Circulation Department, 119 Wardour
  St, London W1V 3TD

**Cavendish Publishing Ltd+**
The Glass House, Wharton St, London WC1X
  9PX
*Tel:* (020) 7278 8000 *Fax:* (020) 7278 8080
*E-mail:* info@cavendishpublishing.com
*Web Site:* www.cavendishpublishing.com
*Key Personnel*
Man Editor: Jon Lloyd
Editor: Ruth Massey *E-mail:* ruthmassey@
  cavendishpublishing.com; Sanjeevi Perera
Commissioning Editor: Beverley Brown
  *E-mail:* beverleybrown@cavendishpublishing.
  com
Brand & Product Manager: Cathy Thornhill
  *E-mail:* cathythornhill@cavendishpublishing.
  com
Founded: 1990
Membership(s): Publishers Association of Great
  Britain.
Subjects: Criminology, Law, Medicine, Nursing,
  Dentistry, Securities, Social Sciences, Sociol-
  ogy
ISBN Prefix(es): 1-874241; 1-85941; 1-84314; 1-
  904385
Number of titles published annually: 100 Print
Total Titles: 500 Print
Subsidiaries: Cavendish Publishing (Australia) Pty
  Limited

**Caxton Publishing Group Ltd**, *imprint of*
  Verulam Publishing Ltd

**CBD Research Ltd+**
Chancery House, 15 Wickham Rd, Beckenham,
  Kent BR3 5JS
*Tel:* (020) 8650 7745 *Fax:* (020) 8650 0768
*E-mail:* cbd@cbdresearch.com
*Web Site:* www.cbdresearch.com
*Key Personnel*
Dir: Mrs S P Henderson; A J Henderson
Founded: 1961
Specialize in directory listings of associations,
  directories & official United Nations organiza-
  tions.
Membership(s): Directory Publishers Association;
  Independent Publishers Guild.
ISBN Prefix(es): 0-900246
Total Titles: 16 Print; 2 CD-ROM; 1 E-Book
Subsidiaries: Chancery House Press

**CCH Editions Ltd+**
145 London Rd, Kingston Upon Thames, Surrey
  KT2 6SR
*Tel:* (020) 8547 3333 *Fax:* (020) 8547 1124
*E-mail:* customerservices@cch.co.uk
*Web Site:* www.cch.co.uk
*Key Personnel*
Man Dir: Hans Staal
Founded: 1982
Subjects: Business, Law
ISBN Prefix(es): 0-86325
*Parent Company:* Commerce Clearing House Inc,
  PO Box 5490, Chicago, IL 60680-5490, United
  States

**Centaur Books**, *imprint of* Old Vicarage
  Publications

**Centaur Press (1954)**
51 Achilles Rd, London NW6 1DZ
*Tel:* (020) 7431 4391 *Fax:* (020) 7431 5129
*E-mail:* books@opengatepress.co.uk
*Web Site:* www.opengatepress.co.uk
*Key Personnel*
Man Dir: T J L Wynne-Tyson
Founded: 1954
Linden Press at the above address has no connec-
  tion with the Simon & Schuster imprint of the
  same name.
Subjects: Education, Environmental Studies
ISBN Prefix(es): 0-900000; 0-900001
*Parent Company:* Open Gate Press
Subsidiaries: The Linden Press
*Bookshop(s):* Keele's, Fontwell, Arundel, West
  Sussex BN18 0TA

**Center for Advanced Welsh & Celtic Studies**
National Library of Wales, Aberystwyth, Ceredi-
  gion SY23 3HH
*Tel:* (01970) 626717 *Fax:* (01970) 627066
*E-mail:* cawcs@wales.ac.uk
*Web Site:* www.aber.ac.uk/~awcwww/s/
  cyflwyniad.html
*Key Personnel*
Dir: Geraint H Jenkins *E-mail:* gcj@aber.ac.uk
Editorial Officer: Glenys Howells *E-mail:* glh@
  aber.ac.uk
Founded: 1985
Specialize in academic & celtic.
ISBN Prefix(es): 0-907158; 0-901833; 1-86225
*Parent Company:* University of Wales

**Center for Information on Language Teaching
  & Research (CILT)**, see CILT, the National
  Centre for Languages

**Centre for Alternative Technology+**
Machynlleth, Powys SY20 9AZ
*Tel:* (01654) 705980; (01654) 705959 (mail or-
  der); (01654) 705993 (CAT shop) *Fax:* (01654)

702782; (01654) 705999 (mail order); (01654)
  703605 (education & courses)
*E-mail:* pubs@cat.org.uk
*Web Site:* www.cat.org.uk
*Key Personnel*
Publisher: Caroline Oakley
Marketing Manager: Allan Shepherd
Production Manager: Graham Preston
Founded: 1974
Publisher of DIY Titles for environmentalists
Registered charity.
Subjects: Energy, Gardening, Plants, Nonfiction
  (General), Technology, Sustainable Lifestyles
Number of titles published annually: 4 Print
Distributed by New Society Publishers (USA &
  Canada)
Foreign Rep(s): New Society Publishers (Canada,
  US)
*Shipping Address:* CAT Mail Order *Tel:* (01654)
  705959 *Fax:* (01654) 705999 *E-mail:* mail.
  order@cat.org.uk (24-hour mail order)

**Century**, *imprint of* Random House UK Ltd

**Chadwyck-Healey Ltd+**
The Quorum, Barnwell Rd, Cambridge CB5 8SW
*Tel:* (01223) 215512 *Fax:* (01223) 215513
*E-mail:* marketing@proquest.co.uk
*Web Site:* www.proquest.co.uk
*Key Personnel*
Vice President of Publishing: Julie Carroll-Davis
  *E-mail:* julie.carroll-davis@proquest.co.uk
Rights & Contracts Manager: Caroline Gomm
  *E-mail:* caroline.gomm@proquest.co.uk
Founded: 1973
Specialize in electronic publishing.
Subjects: Art, Drama, Theater, Economics, Film,
  Video, History, Literature, Literary Criticism,
  Essays, Music, Dance, Radio, TV, Science
  (General), Social Sciences, Sociology, Humani-
  ties
ISBN Prefix(es): 0-85964
*Parent Company:* Proquest Information & Learn-
  ing

**Chambers Harrap Publishers Ltd+**
Division of Lagardere
7 Hopetoun Crescent, Edinburgh EH7 4AY
*Tel:* (0131) 5565929 *Fax:* (0131) 5565313
*E-mail:* admin@chambers.co.uk; webmanager@
  chambers.co.uk
*Web Site:* www.chambersharrap.co.uk
*Telex:* 727967 Words G
*Key Personnel*
Man Dir: Maurice Shepherd
Publishing Manager: Patrick White
  *E-mail:* pwhite@chambersharrap.co.uk
Sales & Marketing Manager: Jane Camillin
Sales & Rights Manager: Stephanie Divens
Reference publisher.
ISBN Prefix(es): 0-550; 0-245
Number of titles published annually: 20 Print
Distributed by Allied Publishers Ltd (India);
  David Bateman Ltd (New Zealand); Andrew
  Betsis ELT (Greece); Bohemian Ventures
  (Czech Republic); Gemcraft Books (Aus-
  tralia); Houghton Mifflin (USA & English-
  speaking Canada); Inter Logos srl. (Italy);
  Larousse-Bordas (France & French-speaking
  countries); Ediciones Larousse SA (Mexico
  & Latin America); Livraria Martins (Brazil);
  The Macmillan Press (UK); Paramount Books
  (Pvt) Ltd (Pakistan); Quartet Sales & Market-
  ing (South Africa); Readwide Bookshop Ltd
  (Ghana); Slovak Ventures (Slovakia); Spes
  SA (Spain); Times Media Private (Brunai,
  Malaysia, Singapore & Thailand)
*Orders to:* The Macmillan Press, Brunel Rd,
  Houndmills, Basingstoke, Hants RG21 6XS
  *Tel:* (01256) 406817 *Fax:* (01256) 812521

**Chancellor Publications**
32 Hatton Garden, 1st Floor, London EC1N 8DL
*Tel:* (020) 7269 9150 *Fax:* (020) 7269 9151
*E-mail:* mail@chancellorpublication.com
*Web Site:* www.chancellorpublication.com
*Key Personnel*
Man Dir: Jonathan Bloch *E-mail:* jbloch@
globalnet.co.uk
Founded: 1994
Supplier of legal & financial texts for practition-
ers & laymen.
Membership(s); IPG.
Subjects: Law
ISBN Prefix(es): 1-899217
Total Titles: 5 Print
*U.S. Office(s):* ISBS Inc, 920 NE 58 Ave,
Suite 300, Portland, OR 97213-3644, United
States *Tel:* 800-944-6190 *Fax:* 503-280-8832
*E-mail:* rod@isbs.com *Web Site:* www.isbs.com

**Channel 4 Books**, *imprint of* Pan Macmillan

**Channel View Publications**, *imprint of*
Multilingual Matters Ltd

**Chapman**
4 Broughton Pl, Edinburgh EH1 3RX
*Tel:* (0131) 5572207 *Fax:* (0131) 5569565
*E-mail:* admin@chapman-pub.co.uk
*Web Site:* www.chapman-pub.co.uk
*Key Personnel*
Editor: Joy Hendry *E-mail:* editor@chapman.co.
uk
Founded: 1970
Specialize in Scottish culture generally. Publish &
develop Scottish literature in particular, also in-
ternational writing. Quarterly magazine devoted
to Scottish literature & arts. Features mainly
poetry & plays.
Subjects: Drama, Theater, Literature, Literary
Criticism, Essays, Poetry, Women's Studies
ISBN Prefix(es): 0-906772
Number of titles published annually: 4 Print
Total Titles: 60 Print; 1 Online; 1 E-Book

**Geoffrey Chapman**, *imprint of* Cassell & Co

**Geoffrey Chapman**, *imprint of* The Continuum
International Publishing Group Ltd

**Paul Chapman Publishing**, *imprint of* SAGE
Publications Ltd

**Chapter Two**
Fountain House, Conduit Mews, London SE18
7AP
*Tel:* (020) 8316 5389 *Fax:* (020) 8854 5963
*E-mail:* chapter2UK@aol.com
*Web Site:* www.chaptertwo.org.uk
*Key Personnel*
Dir: Edwin N Cross
Founded: 1976
Publisher & bookseller
Specialize in Plymouth Brethren Literature &
their history.
Subjects: Language Arts, Linguistics, Religion -
Protestant, Theology
ISBN Prefix(es): 1-85307; 0-947588
Number of titles published annually: 20 Print
Total Titles: 190 Print
Imprints: Bible Distributors
Distributed by Beroea Verlag (Switzerland)
*Distribution Center:* Believers Bookshelf, 5205
Regional Rd 81, Unit 3, Beamsville, ON L0R
1B3, Canada
Believers Bookshelf Inc, Box 261, Sunbury, PA
17801, United States
Bible & Book Depot, Box 25119, Christchurch 5,
New Zealand
Bible, Book & Tract Depot, 23 Santa Rosa Ave,
Ryde, NSW 2112, Australia

Bible House, Gateway Mall, 35 Tudor St,
Bridgetown, Barbados
Bibles & Publications Chretiennes, 30 rue
Chateauvert, 26000 Valence, France
Bible Treasury Bookstore, 46 Queen St, Dart-
mouth, NS B2Y 1G1, Canada
The Bookshelf, 263 St Heliers Bay Rd, Auckland
5, New Zealand
Chapter Two Bookshop, 199 Plumstead Common
Rd, London SE18 2UJ
Christian Truth Bookroom, Paddisonpet, Tenali,
522 201 Andhra, Pradesh, India
CSV, An der Schlossfabrik 30, 42499 Hueck-
eswagen, Germany
Depot de Bibles et Traites Chretiens, 4 rue du
Nord, 1800 Vevey, Switzerland
Echoes of Truth, No 11 Post Office Rd, PO Box
2637, Mushin, Lagos, Nigeria
El Ekhwa Library, 3 Anga Hanem St, Shoubra,
Cairo, Egypt (Arab Republic of Egypt)
Grace & Truth Bookroom, 87 Chausee Rd, Cas-
tries, St Lucia, West Indies, Jamaica
HoldFast Bible & Tract Depot, 100 Camden Rd,
Tunbridge Wells, Kent TN1 2QP
Kristen Litteratur, Tjosvoll ost, 4270 Akrehamn,
Norway
Uit het Woord der Waarheid, Postbus 260, 7120
AG Aalten, Netherlands
Words of Life Trust, 3 Chuim, Khar Village,
Mumbai 400052, India
Words of Truth, PO Box 147, Belfast BT8 4TT

**Deborah Charles Publications+**
173 Mather Ave, Liverpool L18 6JZ
*Tel:* (0151) 724 2500 *Fax:* (0151) 729 0371
*E-mail:* dcp@legaltheory.demon.co.uk
*Web Site:* www.legaltheory.demon.co.uk
*Key Personnel*
Prof: B S Jackson
Founded: 1988
Subjects: Law, Philosophy, Social Sciences, Soci-
ology, Legal Theory
ISBN Prefix(es): 0-9513793; 0-9528938

**Charnwood Library Series**, see Ulverscroft
Large Print Books Ltd

**Chartered Institute of Bankers (CIB)**
**Publications**, *imprint of* Institute of Financial
Services

**The Chartered Institute of Building**
Englemere, Kings Ride, Ascot, Berks SL5 7TB
*Tel:* (01344) 630700 *Fax:* (01344) 630777
*E-mail:* reception@ciob.org.uk
*Web Site:* www.ciob.org.uk
*Key Personnel*
Chief Executive: Keith Banbury
Editorial, Production, Rights & Permissions:
David Petori
Bookshop: Sally Marsh *E-mail:* smarsh@
englemer.co.uk
Librarian: Katherine Bowyer
Subjects: Architecture & Interior Design, Envi-
ronmental Studies, Law, Management, Regional
Interests
ISBN Prefix(es): 0-906600; 1-85380; 0-901822
*Associate Companies:* American Institute of Con-
structors

**Chartered Institute of Library & Information**
**Professionals in Scotland**
Scottish Centre for Information & Library Ser-
vices, Brandon Gate, Bldg C, 1st floor, Leech-
lee Rd, Hamilton ML3 6AU
*Tel:* (01698) 458888 *Fax:* (01698) 283170
*E-mail:* slic@slainte.org.uk
*Web Site:* www.slainte.org.uk
*Key Personnel*
Dir: Elaine Fulton *E-mail:* e.fulton@slainte.org.uk
Founded: 1908

Membership(s): Scottish Publishers Association.
Subjects: History, Library & Information Sci-
ences, Regional Interests
ISBN Prefix(es): 0-900649; 0-9541160
Number of titles published annually: 3 Print
Total Titles: 12 Print
*Orders to:* Scottish Book Source, The Scottish
Book Centre, 137 Dundee St, Edinburgh EH11
1BG *Tel:* (0131) 2296800 *Fax:* (0131) 2299070
*E-mail:* info@booksource.net *Web Site:* www.
booksource.net

**Chartered Institute of Personnel &**
**Development+**
CIPD House, Camp Rd Wimbledon, London
SW19 4UX
*Tel:* (020) 8971 9000 *Fax:* (020) 8263 3333
*E-mail:* publish@cipd.co.uk
*Web Site:* www.cipd.co.uk
*Key Personnel*
Head of Publishing: Sarah Brown
Sales & Marketing Manager: Jim Ellis
Founded: 1913
Specialize in books & reports covering the whole
range of training, personnel & development is-
sues, from practical guides & texts for students
to books on best practice & strategic issues.
Subjects: Business, Human Relations, Manage-
ment
ISBN Prefix(es): 0-85292
Number of titles published annually: 35 Print
*Warehouse:* CIPD Distribution, c/o Plymbridge
Distributors Ltd, Estover, Plymouth PL6 7PZ
*Orders to:* CIPD Distribution, c/o Plymbridge
Distributors Ltd, Estover, Plymouth PL6 7PZ

**The Chartered Institute of Public Finance &**
**Accountancy**
3 Robert St, London WC2N 6BH
*Tel:* (020) 7543 5600 *Fax:* (020) 7543 5607
*E-mail:* publications@cipfa.org
*Web Site:* www.cipfa.org.uk/shop
*Key Personnel*
Publications Manager: Sara Hackwood
Subjects: Accounting, Finance

**Chastleton Travel**, *imprint of* Arris Publishing
Ltd

**Chatham House**, see Royal Institute of
International Affairs

**Chatham House Papers**, *imprint of* Royal
Institute of International Affairs

**Chatham Publishing+**
Park House, One Russell Gardens, London NW11
9NN
*Tel:* (020) 8458 6314 *Fax:* (020) 8905 5245
*E-mail:* info@chathampublishing.com
*Web Site:* www.chathampublishing.com
*Key Personnel*
Editorial Dir: Julian Mannering *E-mail:* julian@
chathampublishing.co.uk
Publisher: Robert Gardiner *E-mail:* robert@
chathampublishing.co.uk
Founded: 1996
Small publishing house concerned principally
with maritime history & narrative history.
Subjects: Maritime, Nonfiction (General), Nauti-
cal Archaeology, Naval or Mercantile History
& Biography, Ship Modelling
ISBN Prefix(es): 1-86176
Number of titles published annually: 30 Print
Total Titles: 150 Print
*Parent Company:* Trident Publishing Ltd
Distributed by Grantham Book Services
*Distribution Center:* Peribo Pty Limited,
58 Beaumont Rd, Mount Kuring-Gai
NSW 2080, Australia *Fax:* (02) 457 0022
*E-mail:* peribomec@bigpond.com

Publishers Marketing Services Pte Ltd, 10c
Jalan Ampas, No 07-01, Warehouse, Ho Seng
Lee Flatted 1232, Singapore *Fax:* 253 0008
*E-mail:* raymondlim@pms.com.sg
Vanwell Publishing Ltd, PO Box 2131, 1
Northrup Crescent, St Catharines L2R 7S2,
ON, Canada *Tel:* (905) 937 3100 *Fax:* (905)
937 1760 *E-mail:* sales@vanwell.com
Titles SA, PO Box 411196, Craiighall
2024, South Africa *Fax:* (01) 1497 5377
*E-mail:* prenew@iafrica.com
Publishers Marketing Services Pte Ltd, 28a Jalan
SS21/58, Damansara Utama, Petaling Jaya
47400, Malaysia *Fax:* (03) 718 7997
Stackpole Books, 5067 Ritter Rd, Mechanics-
burg, PA 17055, United States *Tel:* (717) 796
0411 *Fax:* (717) 796 0412 *E-mail:* sales@
stackpolebooks.com *Web Site:* www.
stackpolebooks.com
South Pacific Books, PO Box 68097, Newton,
Auckland 2, New Zealand *Fax:* (09) 376 2141
*E-mail:* sales@soupacbooks.co.nz

**Chatto & Windus**, *imprint of* Random House
UK Ltd

**The Chemical Society**, *see* The Royal Society of
Chemistry

**Cherrytree**, *imprint of* Evans Brothers Ltd

**Cherrytree Books+**
Imprint of Evans Brothers Ltd
2A Portman Mansions, Chiltern St, London W1U
6NR
*Tel:* (020) 7487 0920 *Fax:* (020) 7487 0921
*E-mail:* sales@evansbrothers.co.uk
*Web Site:* www.evansbooks.co.uk
*Key Personnel*
Man Dir: Julian Batson
Rights Manager: Britta Martins
Publisher: Angela Sheehan
Production Dir: Lesley Barnes
Founded: 1988
Publish illustrated information books for children
ages 5-15 years, mainly for the school library.
ISBN Prefix(es): 0-7451; 0-7540
*Associate Companies:* Chivers Press Ltd; Evans
Brothers Ltd; Zero to Ten Ltd
*U.S. Office(s):* Chivers North America Inc, One
Lafayette Rd, Hampton, NH 03842, United
States

**Child's Play (International) Ltd+**
Ashworth Rd, Bridgemead, Swindon, Wilts SN5
7YD
*Tel:* (01793) 616286 *Fax:* (01793) 512795
*E-mail:* allday@childs-play.com
*Web Site:* www.childs-play.com
*Key Personnel*
Chairman: Michael Twinn
UK Sales: Paul Gerrish
Publicity: Libby New
Editor: Sue Baker *Tel:* (01793) 616286
*E-mail:* sue@childs-play.com
Education Officer: Imogen Cooper
Chief Executive Officer (Sales & Marketing):
Richard Searle-Barnes *Tel:* (01793) 616286
*E-mail:* richard@childs-play.com
Founded: 1972
Specialize in Early Years Education.
Membership(s): BTHMA & IPG.
ISBN Prefix(es): 0-85953; 1-904550
Total Titles: 400 Print; 7 Audio
Subsidiaries: Childs Play Australia
*U.S. Office(s):* Childs Play USA, 67 Minot Ave,
Auburn, ME 04210, United States, Contact:
Laurie Reynolds *Tel:* 207-784-7252 *Fax:* 207-
784-7358 *E-mail:* cmpmaine@aol.com

**Child's World Education Ltd**
PO Box 1881, Gerrards Cross, Bucks SL9 9AN
*Tel:* (01753) 647060 *Fax:* (01753) 645522
*Key Personnel*
Contact: Susan Daughtrey
Subjects: Education
ISBN Prefix(es): 1-898696

**Chivers Children's Audio Books**, *imprint of*
BBC Audiobooks

**Chivers Large Print**, *imprint of* BBC
Audiobooks

**Chorion IP+**
Vernon House, 40 Shaftesbury Ave, London W1D
7ER
*Tel:* (020) 7434 1880 *Fax:* (020) 7434 1882
*E-mail:* info@enidblyton.co.uk
*Web Site:* www.chorion.co.uk
Founded: 1998
Crime novels.
Subjects: Fiction, Film, Video, Finance
ISBN Prefix(es): 1-903614
*Ultimate Parent Company:* Chorion PLC, Ald-
wych House, 81 Aldwych, London WC2B
4HN

**Chough Series (Educational Packs)**, *imprint of*
Lodenek Press

**Christian Education+**
1020 Bristol Rd, Selly Oak, Birmingham B29
6LB
*Tel:* (0121) 472 4242 *Fax:* (0121) 472 7575
*E-mail:* enquiries@christianeducation.org.uk
*Web Site:* www.christianeducation.org.uk/cep/
cep_about.htm
*Key Personnel*
Chief Executive Officer: Peter Fishpool
*E-mail:* ceo@christianeducation.org.uk
Senior Editor: Elizabeth Bruce-Whitehorn
*E-mail:* editorial@christianeducation.org.uk
Marketing: Lynette Adjei *E-mail:* marketing@
christianeducation.org.uk
Sales: Jeanne Hayling *E-mail:* sales@
christianeducation.org.uk
Consultant Editor: Colin Johnson *E-mail:* colin@
retoday.org.uk
Design & Production Editor: Liam Purcell
*E-mail:* production@christianeducation.org.uk
Founded: 1809
Subjects: Biblical Studies, Crafts, Games, Hob-
bies, Drama, Theater, Education, Religion -
Protestant
ISBN Prefix(es): 0-7197; 0-85213
Imprints: Hillside
Subsidiaries: International Bible Reading Associa-
tion (IBRA)
*Bookshop(s):* NCEL Bookroom

**Christian Education Movement**, *see* Christian
Education

**Christian Focus**, *imprint of* Christian Focus
Publications Ltd

**Christian Focus Publications Ltd+**
Geanies House, Fearn, Tain, Ross-shire IV20
1TW
*Tel:* (01862) 871 011 *Fax:* (01862) 871 699
*E-mail:* info@christianfocus.com
*Web Site:* www.christianfocus.com
*Key Personnel*
Man Dir: William Mackenzie
*E-mail:* whmmackenzie@christianfocus.com
General Manager: Ian Thompson *Tel:* (01862)
871 022 *E-mail:* ian.thompson@christianfocus.
com

Production Manager: Jonathan Dunbar
*E-mail:* jdunbar@christianfocus.com
Editorial Manager: Willie Mackenzie
*E-mail:* Willie.Mackenzie@christianfocus.com
Children's Editor: Catherine Mackenzie
*E-mail:* cmackenzie@christianfocus.com
Founded: 1979
Evangelical publisher.
Membership(s): Christian Booksellers Association
& Evangelical Christian Publishing Associa-
tion.
Subjects: Fiction, Religion - Protestant, Theology
ISBN Prefix(es): 0-906731; 1-871676; 1-85792
Number of titles published annually: 90 Print
Total Titles: 800 Print; 1 CD-ROM; 1 Audio
*Parent Company:* Balintore Holdings PLC
Imprints: Mentor; Christian Focus; Christian Her-
itage
*U.S. Office(s):* Riverside, 636 South Oak, Iowa
Falls, IA 50126, United States *Fax:* 515-648-
5106 *E-mail:* maureenr@riversidedistributors.
com
Foreign Rep(s): Cook Communications Ministries
(Canada); Family Reading (Australia); Pub-
lishers International Marketing (Asia); Struik
Christian Books (Southern Africa); SU (New
Zealand)

**Christian Heritage**, *imprint of* Christian Focus
Publications Ltd

**Christian Research Association**
Vision Bldg, 4 Footscray Rd, Eltham, London
SE9 2TZ
*Tel:* (020) 8294 1989 *Fax:* (020) 8294 0014
*E-mail:* admin@christian-research.org.uk
*Web Site:* www.christian-research.org.uk
*Key Personnel*
Executive Dir: Dr Peter Brierley
Founded: 1993
Provide resources & undertaking research for
Christian leaders.
Subjects: Management, Religion - Catholic, Reli-
gion - Protestant
ISBN Prefix(es): 1-85321
Number of titles published annually: 5 Print; 1
Online
Total Titles: 19 Print; 1 Online

**The Chrysalis Press+**
7 Lower Ladyes Hills, Kenilworth, Warwicks
CV8 2GN
*Tel:* (01926) 855223
*E-mail:* chrysalis@margaretbuckley.com
*Key Personnel*
Man Dir: Brian Boyd
Founded: 1992
Subjects: Biography, Fiction, Literature, Literary
Criticism, Essays
ISBN Prefix(es): 1-897765
Number of titles published annually: 2 Print; 2
Online; 2 E-Book
Total Titles: 10 Print; 10 Online; 10 E-Book

**Church House Publishing+**
Churchhouse, 31 Great Smith St, London SW1P
3NZ
*Tel:* (020) 7898 1451 *Fax:* (020) 7898 1449
*E-mail:* sales@c-of-e.org.uk
*Web Site:* www.chpublishing.co.uk
*Key Personnel*
Publishing Manager: Alan Mitchell *Tel:* (020)
7898 1450 *E-mail:* alan.mitchell@c-of-e.org.uk
Production Manager: Katharine Allenby
*Tel:* (020) 7898 1452 *E-mail:* katharine.
allenby@c-of-e.org.uk
Sales & Marketing Manager: Matthew Tickle
*Tel:* (020) 7898 1454 *E-mail:* matthew.tickle@
c-of-e.org.uk
Editorial & Copyright Manager: Sarah Roberts
*Tel:* (020) 7898 1578 *E-mail:* sarah.roberts@c-
of-e.org.uk

National Society Publications Off: Hamish Bruce
*Tel:* (020) 7898 1453 *E-mail:* hamish.bruce@c-of-e.org.uk
Contact: Aderyn Watson *E-mail:* aderyn.watson@c-of-e.org.uk
Subjects: Religion - Other
ISBN Prefix(es): 0-7151
Number of titles published annually: 40 Print; 1 CD-ROM
Total Titles: 300 Print; 1 CD-ROM; 1 Audio
*Parent Company:* The Archbishops Council of the Church of England
Imprints: The National Society
Distributed by Novalis (Canada); Charles Paine Pty Ltd (Australia)
*Distribution Center:* Marston Book Services, PO Box 269, Abingdon, Oxon OX14 4YN *Tel:* (01235) 465500 *Fax:* (01235) 465518
*Orders to:* The Canterbury Press, St Mary's Works, St Mary's Plain, Norwich NR3 3BH, Contact: Melanie Cole *Tel:* (01603) 612914 *Fax:* (01603) 624483

**Church Literature Association**, *imprint of* Church Union

**Church Society**
Dean Wace House, 16 Rosslyn Rd, Watford, Herts WD18 0NY
*Tel:* (01923) 235111 *Fax:* (01923) 800362
*E-mail:* enquiries@churchsociety.org
*Web Site:* www.churchsociety.org
*Key Personnel*
Publishing Secretary: David Phillips
Founded: 1835 (present company started in 1950 as an amalgamation of two other similar organizations)
Specialize in books & booklets. Publishers of "Churchmen" quarterly since 1879. A society founded to keep the Church of England faithful to its formularies.
Subjects: Religion - Protestant, Theology
ISBN Prefix(es): 0-85190
Total Titles: 4 Print

**Church Times**, *imprint of* Hymns Ancient & Modern Ltd

**Church Union**
Faith House, 7 Tufton St, London SW1P 3QN
*Tel:* (020) 7222 6952 *Fax:* (020) 7976 7180
*E-mail:* churchunion@care4free.net
*Web Site:* www.churchunion.care4free.net
*Key Personnel*
Contact: Julien Chilcott-Monk
Founded: 1859
Membership(s): Bookseller Association; specialize in religious books; also acts as Bookseller.
Subjects: Religion - Catholic, Religion - Protestant, Religion - Other
ISBN Prefix(es): 0-85191
Imprints: Church Literature Association; Tufton Books
Distributed by SCM - Canterbury Press
*Bookshop(s):* Faith House Bookshop, 7 Tufton St, London SW1P 3QN

**Churchill Livingstone**, *imprint of* Elsevier Ltd

**Cicerone Press**
2 Police Sq, Milnthorpe, Cumbria LA7 7PY
*Tel:* (01539) 562 069 *Fax:* (01539) 563 417
*E-mail:* info@cicerone.co.uk
*Web Site:* www.cicerone.co.uk
*Key Personnel*
Dir, Sales & Marketing: Mrs Lesley Williams *E-mail:* lesley@cicerone.demon.co.uk
Dir, Editorial, Production & Finance: Jonathan E Williams *E-mail:* jonathan@cicerone.demon.co.uk
Founded: 1969

Publish specialized guides to walking, trekking, climbing, mountaineering & biking in the UK, Europe & other world regions.
Subjects: Outdoor Recreation, Travel
ISBN Prefix(es): 0-902363; 1-85284
Number of titles published annually: 20 Print
Total Titles: 280 Print
Distributed by Alpenbooks (USA); Midpoint Trade Books (USA)
*Warehouse:* 2B Summerlands Industrial Estate, North Kendal, Cumbria

**CILIPS**, see Chartered Institute of Library & Information Professionals in Scotland

**CILT, the National Centre for Languages**
Formerly Center for Information on Language Teaching & Research (CILT)
20 Bedfordbury, London WC2N 4LB
*Tel:* (020) 7379 5101; (020) 7379 5110 (resources library & information services) *Fax:* (020) 7379 5082
*E-mail:* publications@cilt.org.uk; library@cilt.org.uk (library information); info@cilt.org.uk
*Web Site:* www.cilt.org.uk
*Key Personnel*
Dir: Isabella Moore *E-mail:* isabella.moore@cilt.org.uk
Publishing Manager: Emma Rees *E-mail:* emma.rees@cilt.org.uk
Founded: 1966
Membership(s): Publishers Association.
Subjects: Education, Language Arts, Linguistics
ISBN Prefix(es): 0-948003; 0-903466; 1-874016; 0-9500528; 1-902031; 1-904243
Number of titles published annually: 15 Print
Total Titles: 100 Print; 2 CD-ROM; 4 Audio
*Showroom(s):* CILT Library *Web Site:* www.cilt.org.uk/publications
*Orders to:* Central Books Ltd, 99 Wallis Rd, London E9 5LN *Tel:* (020) 8458 9910 *Fax:* (020) 8533 5821 *E-mail:* mo@centralbooks.com

**Cinderella**, *imprint of* Novello & Co Ltd

**CIRIA**
Classic House, 174-180 Old St, London EC1V 9BP
*Tel:* (020) 7549 3300 *Fax:* (020) 7253 0523
*E-mail:* enquiries@ciria.org.uk
*Web Site:* www.ciria.org.uk

**CIWEM**, *imprint of* Terence Dalton Ltd

**Clarendon Press**, *imprint of* Oxford University Press

**Clarion**, *imprint of* Elliot Right Way Books

**James Clarke & Co Ltd+**
PO Box 60, Cambridge CB1 2NT
*Tel:* (01223) 350865 *Fax:* (01223) 366951
*E-mail:* publishing@jamesclarke.co.uk
*Web Site:* www.jamesclarke.co.uk
*Key Personnel*
Man Dir: Adrian C Brink
Founded: 1859
Membership(s): IPG, Publishers' Association.
Subjects: Biblical Studies, Biography, History, Library & Information Sciences, Literature, Literary Criticism, Essays, Nonfiction (General), Philosophy, Publishing & Book Trade Reference, Religion - Catholic, Religion - Protestant, Theology
ISBN Prefix(es): 0-227
Number of titles published annually: 4 Print
Total Titles: 300 Print
Imprints: Acorn Editions; Patrick Hardy Books; Lutterworth Press
Distributed by Parkwest Publications Inc

Foreign Rep(s): Keith Ainsworth (Pty) Ltd (Australia); Applied Media (India, Sri Lanka); Catholic Supplies (NK) (New Zealand); CKK (Hong Kong, Indonesia, Malaysia, Philippines, Singapore, Thailand); Iberian Book Services (Portugal, Spain); Parkwest Publications Inc (US); Kelvin van Hasselt Publishing Services (Africa, Caribbean)

**Class Publishing+**
Barb House, Barb Mews, London W6 7PA
*Tel:* (020) 7371 2119 *Fax:* (020) 7371 2878
*E-mail:* post@class.co.uk
*Web Site:* www.class.co.uk
*Key Personnel*
Manager: Richard Warner
Founded: 1989
Membership(s): IPG.
Subjects: Health, Nutrition, Law, Medicine, Nursing, Dentistry
ISBN Prefix(es): 1-872362; 1-859590; 0-9528823
*Book Club(s):* BCA
*Warehouse:* Plymbridge Distributors Ltd, Plymbridge House, Estover Rd, Plymouth, Devon PL6 7PY *Tel:* (01752) 202300 *Fax:* (01752) 202330 *E-mail:* enquiries@plymbridge.com
*Web Site:* www.plymbridge.com

**Classey Books**, *imprint of* E W Classey Ltd

**E W Classey Ltd+**
Oxford House, Marlborough St, Faringdon, Oxon SN7 7JP
Mailing Address: PO Box 93, Faringdon, Oxon SN7 7DR
*Tel:* (01367) 244700 *Fax:* (01367) 244800
*E-mail:* info@classeybooks.com
*Web Site:* www.abebooks.com/home/bugbooks; www.classeybooks.com
*Key Personnel*
Publisher: E W Classey
Contact: Mr P Classey
Founded: 1949
Subjects: Biological Sciences, Earth Sciences, Environmental Studies, Natural History, Science (General), Arachnology, Botany, Entomology, Geology, Natural History, Ornithology, Zoology
ISBN Prefix(es): 0-900848; 0-86096
Imprints: Classey Books; Ferendune; Hedera Press
*Orders to:* Bookmart-Classeybooks, PO Box 93, Faringdon, Oxon SN7 7DR *Tel:* (01367) 244800 *Fax:* (01367) 244700

**Classics**, *imprint of* The Penguin Group UK

**CLB Books**, *imprint of* Colour Library Direct

**CLB Publishing**, *imprint of* Colour Library Direct

**Clever Clogs**, *imprint of* Funfax Ltd

**Cloverleaf**, *imprint of* Evans Brothers Ltd

**CMP Information Ltd**
Riverbank House, Angel Lane, Tonbridge, Kent TN9 1SE
*Tel:* (01732) 377591 *Fax:* (01732) 377440
*Web Site:* www.cmpdata.com
Subjects: Advertising, Architecture & Interior Design, Business, Energy, Film, Video, Health, Nutrition, Publishing & Book Trade Reference
ISBN Prefix(es): 0-86382
Number of titles published annually: 12 Print; 2 CD-ROM; 5 Online
Total Titles: 12 Print; 2 CD-ROM; 5 Online
*Parent Company:* United Business Media

**Coachwise Ltd**
Chelsea Close, Off Amberley Rd, Armley, Leeds
LS12 4HP
*Tel:* (0113) 2311310 *Fax:* (0113) 2319606
*E-mail:* enquiries@coachwise.ltd.uk
*Web Site:* www.coachwise.ltd.uk
*Key Personnel*
Man Dir: Dr Tony Byrne
General Manager: Kath Leonard
Marketing Executive & International Rights
Contact: Melanie Drake *E-mail:* mdrake@
coachwise.ltd.uk
Founded: 1989
Specialize in leisure management & coaching targeting sports professionals.
Membership(s): Direct Marketing Association
(UK) Ltd.
Subjects: Health, Nutrition, Music, Dance, Outdoor Recreation, Sports, Athletics
Total Titles: 40 Print; 1 CD-ROM; 1 Audio
*Parent Company:* National Coaching Foundation

**Cockbird Press+**
PO Box 356, Heathfield TN21 9QF
*Tel:* (01435) 830430 *Fax:* (01435) 830027
*Key Personnel*
Man Dir: Lucy Faridany
General Editor: Diane White
Founded: 1990
Publish prints through catalogues by mail order.
Subjects: Biography, History, Travel
ISBN Prefix(es): 1-873054
Distributed by Seven Hills Book Distributors (US
distributor)

**COIC**, see Careers & Occupational Information
Centre (COIC)

**Adlard Coles Nautical**, *imprint of* A & C Black
Publishers Ltd

**Rosica Colin Ltd+**
One Clareville Grove Mews, London SW7 5AH
*Tel:* (020) 7370 1080 *Fax:* (020) 7244 6441
*Key Personnel*
Dir: Joanna Marston
Founded: 1949
Literary agents.

**Peter Collin Publishing Ltd+**
38 Soho Sq, London W1D 3HB
*Tel:* (020) 7494 2111 *Fax:* (020) 7434 0151
*E-mail:* order@petercollin.com
*Web Site:* www.petercollin.com
*Key Personnel*
Dir: S M H Collin; Peter Collin
Founded: 1985
Specialize in English & bilingual dictionaries.
ISBN Prefix(es): 0-948549; 1-901659
Imprints: Aspect Guides
*U.S. Office(s):* IPG, 814 N Franklin St, Chicago,
IL 60610, United States *Tel:* 312-337-0747
*Fax:* 312-337-5985 *E-mail:* order@petercollin.
com
Distributed by Foucher, Klett
*Shipping Address:* PO Box 1321, Oak Park,
IL 60304, United States *Tel:* 708-366-9553
*Fax:* 708-366-9554 (USA)
*Orders to:* Marston Book Services, PO Box 269,
Abingdon, Oxon OX14 4YN *Tel:* (01235)
465600 *Fax:* (01235) 465655 *E-mail:* sales@
marston.co.uk

**Colonsay Books**, *imprint of* House of Lochar

**ColorCards**, *imprint of* Speechmark Publishing
Ltd

**Colour Library Direct+**
Godalming Business Center, Catteshall Lane,
Woolsack Way, Godalming GU7 1XW
*Tel:* (01483) 426777 *Fax:* (01483) 426947
*E-mail:* prod@quad-pub.co.uk
*Key Personnel*
Man Dir: Brian Phipps
Publishing Dir: Will Steeds
Sales, Rights, Promotions: Des Higgins
Production: Grame Proctor
Production Manager: Karen Staff
Founded: 1959
Subjects: Animals, Pets, Art, Cookery, Environmental Studies, Photography, Travel
ISBN Prefix(es): 0-906558; 0-86283; 0-904681;
1-84100; 1-85833
*Parent Company:* Quadrillion
Imprints: ATAPepperpot Gift; CLB Books; CLB
Publishing; QPI Books
Divisions: Bramley Books; CLB Editions; CLB
Publishing; CLD Direct Marketing; IMC
Video; Pepperpot Gift & Stationary; QPI Publishing; Quadrillion Multimedia Ltd

**Colourpoint Books+**
Colourpoint House, Jubilee Business Park, 21 Jubilee Rd, Newtownards BT23 4YH
*Tel:* (028) 9182 0505 *Fax:* (028) 9182 1900
*E-mail:* info@colourpoint.co.uk; sales@
colourpoint.co.uk
*Web Site:* www.colourpoint.co.uk
*Key Personnel*
Partner: Malcolm Johnston *E-mail:* malcolm@
colourpoint.co.uk; Sheila M Johnston
*E-mail:* sheila@colourpoint.co.uk; Wesley
Johnston
Partner & International Rights: Norman Johnston
*E-mail:* norman@colourpoint.co.uk
Administrator: Michelle Chambers
Sales Manager: Lawrence Greer
Founded: 1993
Specializes in educational textbooks/resources,
transport titles, books of Irish interest.
Membership(s): Publishers Association & Irish
Educational Publishers' Association.
Subjects: Biography, Disability, Special Needs,
Education, Government, Political Science, History, Maritime, Religion - Other, Transportation
ISBN Prefix(es): 1-898392; 1-904242
Number of titles published annually: 30 Print
Total Titles: 120 Print
Distributed by Ian Allan Publishing (England,
Scotland & Wales)
Distributor for Business Enthusiast Publishing; Nostalgia Road; Arthur Southern; Trans-
Pennine Publishing

**Combined Academic Publishers**
15A Lewin's Yard, East St, Chesham, Bucks HP5
1HQ
*Tel:* (01494) 581601 *Fax:* (01494) 581602
*Web Site:* www.combinedacademic.co.uk
*Key Personnel*
Dir: Nicholas Esson *E-mail:* nickesson@
combinedacademic.demon.co.uk
Marketing Manager: Julia Monk
Founded: 1997
Full service sales, marketing & distribution
agency which serves the needs of university &
academic presses seeking promotion/marketing,
field sales representation & distribution in the
UK & Europe.
Imprints: Duke University Press (UK & Europe); Indiana University Press (UK & Europe); McGill-Queens University Press (UK
& Europe); University of Illinois Press (UK &
Europe); University of Nebraska Press (UK &
Europe); University of Texas Press (UK & Europe); University of Washington Press (UK &
Europe)
*Shipping Address:* Marston Book Services
Ltd, 160 Milton Park, PO Box 269, Abing-

don, Oxon OX14 4YN *Tel:* (01235) 465500
*Fax:* (01235) 465555 *E-mail:* trade.orders@
marston.co.uk

**Comedia**, *imprint of* Routledge

**Commission for Racial Equality+**
St Dunstan's House, 201-211 Borough High St,
London SE1 1GZ
*Tel:* (020) 7939 0000 *Fax:* (020) 7939 0001
*E-mail:* info@cre.gov.uk
*Web Site:* www.cre.gov.uk
*Key Personnel*
Chairman: Trevor Phillips
Marketing, Production, Rights & Permissions:
Desrie Thomson
Founded: 1976
Subjects: Human Relations
ISBN Prefix(es): 0-907920; 1-85442; 0-902355
Imprints: CRE
*Branch Office(s)*
Lancaster House, 3rd floor, 67 Newhall St,
Birmingham B3 1NA *Tel:* (0121) 710 3000
*Fax:* (0121) 710 3001
Capital Tower, 3rd floor, Greyfriars Rd, Cardiff
CF10 3AG *Tel:* (02920) 729 200 *Fax:* (02920)
729 220
The Tun, 12 Jackson's Entry off Holyrood Rd,
Edinburgh EH8 8PJ *Tel:* (0131) 524 2000
*Fax:* (0131) 524 2001 *E-mail:* scotland@cre.
gov.uk
Yorkshire Bank Chambers, 1st floor, Infirmary
St, Leeds LS1 2JP *Tel:* (0113) 389 3600
*Fax:* (0113) 389 3601
Maybrook House, 5th floor, 40 Blackfiars St,
M3 2EG Manchester *Tel:* (0161) 835 5500
*Fax:* (0161) 835 5501
*Orders to:* CRE Customer Services, PO Box
29, Norwich NR3 1GN *Tel:* (0870) 240 3697
*Fax:* (0870) 240 3698 *E-mail:* CRE@tso.co.uk

**Commonwealth Secretariat+**
Marlborough House, Pall Mall, London SW1Y
5HX
*Tel:* (020) 7747 6500 *Fax:* (020) 7930 0827
*E-mail:* info@commonwealth.int
*Web Site:* www.thecommonwealth.org
*Key Personnel*
Head of Publications: Mr R Jones-Parry
*E-mail:* r.jones-parry@commonwealth.int
Founded: 1948
Intergovernmental organization with responsibility
for the work & all activities of the Commonwealth.
Membership(s): Publishers' Association.
Subjects: Agriculture, Developing Countries,
Earth Sciences, Economics, Education, Energy,
Environmental Studies, Finance, Government,
Political Science, Law, Management, Public
Administration, Social Sciences, Sociology,
Technology, Women's Studies
ISBN Prefix(es): 0-85092
Number of titles published annually: 40 Print; 2
CD-ROM
Total Titles: 150 Print; 4 CD-ROM; 2 Audio
Foreign Rep(s): Addenda Ltd (New Zealand);
Book Bird (Pakistan); Booker International
(Brunei); Bookwell (India); Buma Kor & Co
Ltd (Cameroon); DCS-Athens (Greece); E
& D Limited (Tanzania); Globe Enterprises
(Malaysia); Grassroots Bookshop (Zimbabwe);
Hargraves Library Services (South Africa);
Iberian Book Services (Spain); Karim International (Bangladesh); Barbie Keene (Zimbabwe);
Prestige Books (Zimbabwe); Publishers Scandinavian Consultancy (Scandinavia); Reimmer
Book Services (Ghana); Renouf Publishing
Company Ltd (Canada); SARDC (Mozambique); Select Books Pte Ltd (Singapore);
Stylus Inc USA (US); Tausco Book Distributors (India); Transglobal Publishers Service Ltd
(Hong Kong); TRIOPS (Germany)

*Warehouse:* York Publishing Services, 64 Hallfield Rd, Layerthorpe, York YO31 72Q, Contact: Duncan Beal *Tel:* (01904) 431 213 *Fax:* (01904) 430 868 *Web Site:* www.yps-publishing.co.uk
*Orders to:* York Publishing Services, 64 Hallfield Rd, Layerthorpe, York YO31 7ZQ *Tel:* (01904) 431 213 *Fax:* (01904) 430 868 *E-mail:* dbeal@yps-publishing.co.uk

### Compass Equestrian Ltd+

Cadborough Farm, Oldberrow, Henley-in-Arden, Warwicks B95 5NX
*Tel:* (0156) 479 5136 *Fax:* (0156) 479 5136
*E-mail:* compbook@globalnet.co.uk
*Web Site:* www.users.globalnet.co.uk/~compbook
*Key Personnel*
Dir: Valerie Wofford Watson
Contact: Clare Harris
Founded: 1996
Specializes in books on equestrian topics.
Subjects: Nonfiction (General)
ISBN Prefix(es): 1-900667
Total Titles: 13 Print
Distributed by Trafalgar Square Publishing

### Compass Maps Ltd

The Coach House, Beech Court, Winford BS40 8DW
*Tel:* (01275) 474737 *Fax:* (01275) 474787
*E-mail:* info@papoutmaps.com
*Web Site:* www.mapgroup.net

### Compendium Publishing+

5 Gerrard St, London W1D 5PF
*Tel:* (020) 72874570 *Fax:* (020) 74940583
*E-mail:* compendium@compuserve.com
*Key Personnel*
Man Dir: Alan Greene
Editorial: Simon Forty
Founded: 1998
Subjects: Aeronautics, Aviation, African American Studies, Anthropology, Antiques, Architecture & Interior Design, Art, Asian Studies, Automotive, Cookery, Crafts, Games, Hobbies, Erotica, History, How-to, Maritime, Military Science, Nonfiction (General), Sports, Athletics, Transportation, Travel
ISBN Prefix(es): 1-902579
Imprints: Wag Books; Windrow & Greene
Divisions: Compendium Publishing Ltd

### Computer Science Press, *imprint of* W H Freeman & Co Ltd

### Computer Step+

Southfield Rd, Southam, Warwicks CV47 0FB
*Tel:* (01926) 817999 *Fax:* (01926) 817005
*E-mail:* publisher@ineasysteps.com
*Web Site:* www.ineasysteps.com
*Key Personnel*
Publisher: Harshad Kotecha
Partner & International Rights: Mrs Sevanti Kotecha *E-mail:* sevanti@computerstep.com
Founded: 1991
Subjects: Business, How-to, Technology, Computers, Educational Software
ISBN Prefix(es): 1-874029; 1-84078
Total Titles: 60 Print; 10 E-Book
Distributed by Computer Bookshops (UK non-booktrade); Federal Publications (Malaysia); IDG Books India (India, Pakistan, Bangladesh); Penguin Books (Australia, New Zealand, South Africa)

### Concrete Information Ltd

Riverside House, 4 Meadows Business Park, Station Approach, Blackwater, Camberley, Surrey GU17 9AB
*Tel:* (01276) 608770 *Fax:* (01276) 37369
*E-mail:* enquiries@concreteinfo.org

*Web Site:* www.concreteinfo.org
*Key Personnel*
Head of Information Service: Edwin Trout *E-mail:* etrout@concreteinfo.org
Founded: 1935
Subjects: Civil Engineering, Engineering (General), Cement, Concrete
ISBN Prefix(es): 0-7210

### Condor Books, *imprint of* Souvenir Press Ltd

### Connections, *imprint of* Eddison Sadd Editions Ltd

### Conran Octopus, *imprint of* Octopus Publishing Group

### Conran Octopus+

Imprint of Octopus Publishing Group
2-4 Heron Quays, London E14 4JP
*Tel:* (020) 7531 8400 *Fax:* (020) 7531 8627
*E-mail:* info@conran-octopus.co.uk
*Web Site:* www.conran-octopus.co.uk
*Telex:* 296249
*Key Personnel*
Sales & Marketing Dir: Catharine Snow *E-mail:* catharine.snow@conran-octopus.co.uk
Publishing Dir: Lorraine Dickey *E-mail:* lorraine.dickey@conran-octopus.co.uk
Creative Dir: Leslie Harrington *E-mail:* leslie.harrington@conran-octopus.co.uk
Publicity & Marketing Assistant: Virginia McIntosh *E-mail:* virginia.mcintosh@conran-octopus.co.uk
UK Sales & Marketing Dir: Martin Hunka *Tel:* (020) 7531 8625 *E-mail:* martin.hunka@conran-octopus.co.uk
Founded: 1984
Subjects: Architecture & Interior Design, Crafts, Games, Hobbies, Gardening, Plants
ISBN Prefix(es): 1-85029; 1-84091
*Distribution Center:* APD Singapore Ptd Limited, 52 Genting Lane #06-05, Hiangkie Complex 1, Singapore 349560, Singapore, Contact: Ian Pringle *Tel:* 749 3551 *Fax:* 749 3552 *E-mail:* apd@pacific.net.sg (Singapore, Malaysia, Indonesia, Vietnam, Burma, Laos & Thailand)
Asia Publishers Services Ltd, 16F Wing Fat Commercial Bldg, 218 Aberdeen Main Rd, Aberdeen, Hong Kong, Contact: Ed Summerson *Tel:* (02553) 2553 9289/9280 *Fax:* (02553) 2554 2912 *E-mail:* apshk@netvigator.com (Hong Kong, China & Taiwan)
Books for Europe, Vosberger Weg 22, 8181 JH, Heerde, Netherlands, Contact: Mr Robert Pleysier *Tel:* (0578) 696 596 *Fax:* (0578) 696 798 *E-mail:* r.j.pleysier.bfe@wxs.nl (Netherlands)
Books for Europe, Via Del Casagrande 22, 6932 Breganzona, Canton Ticino, Switzerland, Contact: Juliusz Komarnicki *Tel:* (091) 967 1539 *Fax:* (091) 966 7865 *E-mail:* juliusz.komarnicki@freesurf.ch (France & Benelux)
CLB Marketing Services, Ktona Jozef utca 41 1/4, Budapest 1137, Hungary, Contact: Csaba Lengyel de Bagota *Tel:* (01) 3405213 *Fax:* (01) 3405213 (Hungary, Czech Republic, Slovakia, Slovenia, Croatia & Poland)
HardieGrant Books, 12 Claremont St, South Yarra, Victoria 3141, Australia *Tel:* (03) 9827 8377 *Fax:* (03) 9827 8766 *E-mail:* jodiemartin@hardiegarnt.com.au (Australia)
Gill Hess Ltd, 15 Church St, Skerries, Co Dublin, Ireland *Tel:* (01) 849 1801 *Fax:* (01) 849 2384 (Ireland)
HRA - Humphrys Roberts Associates, 24 High St, Wanstead, London EII 2AQ, Publishers' Consultant & Representative: Mr Chris Humphrys *Tel:* (020) 8530 5028 *Fax:* (020)

8530 7870 *E-mail:* humph4hra@aol.com (Central America)
HRA - Humphrys Roberts Associates, Caixa Postal 801, AG Jardim da Gloria, 06700/970 Cotia SP, Brazil, Publishers' Consultant & Representative: Mr Terry Roberts *Tel:* (011) 492 4496 *Fax:* (011) 492 6896 *E-mail:* hrabrasil@intercall.com.br (South America)
IKC Korea, 473 19 Deokyo-dong, Mapo-Ku, Seoul 121-210, Republic of Korea *Tel:* (02) 3141 4791 *Fax:* (02) 3141 7733 *E-mail:* ickseoul2@netsgo.com (Korea)
Inter Media Americana, 17 Jeffrey's Place, London NWI 9PP, Contact: Tony Moggach *Tel:* (020) 7267 8054 *Fax:* (020) 7485 8462 *E-mail:* ima@moggach.demon.co.uk (North Africa)
Inter Media Americana, 14 York Rise, London NW5 1ST, Contact: Tony Moggach *Tel:* (020) 7267 8054 *Fax:* (020) 7485 8462 *E-mail:* ima@moggach.demon.co.uk (South America)
Victoria Kalish, 1080 Schooner St, Foster City, CA 94404, United States, Director of Special Markets: Victoria Kalish *Tel:* (650) 573-5732 *Fax:* (650) 618-1535 *E-mail:* VKalishOPG@aol.com (USA)
Marketing Services for Publishers, 57 Sta Teresita, Kapitolyo, Pasig City 1603, Philippines, Contact: Benjie Ocampo *Tel:* (02) 635 3592; 635 3593 *Fax:* (02) 631 4470 *E-mail:* benjie@compass.com.ph (Philippines)
Nilsson & Lamm: Stockholding, Pampuslaan 212, 1382 JS Weesp, Netherlands *Tel:* (0294) 464 949 *Fax:* (0294) 494 455 *E-mail:* nilam@euronet.nl (Netherlands)
Octopus India, PO Box 7208, First Floor, Arun House, 2/25 Ansari Rd, New Delhi 110 002, India, Contact: Ajay Parmer *Tel:* (011) 328 4894 *Fax:* (011) 328 1819 *E-mail:* aparmar@vsnl.com (India & Sri Lanka)
Octopus Publishing Group, 7/30 Hooper St, Randwick, NSW 2031, Australia, Contact: Tina Gitsas *Tel:* (02) 9298 8624 *Fax:* (02) 9298 8624 *E-mail:* tinaoctopus.@bigpond.com (Australia - special sales)
Octopus Publishing Group, 4-7-16-106Kamiuma, Setagaya-ku, Tokyo 150-0011, Japan, Contact: Ms Noriko Skai *Tel:* (0813) 5433 7638 *Fax:* (0813) 5433 7639 *E-mail:* noriko@cool.email.ne.jp (Japan)
Publisher's Agent, 56 Rosebank, Holyport Rd, Fulham, London SW6 6LH, Contact: Penny Padovani *Tel:* (020) 381 3936 *E-mail:* padovanibooks@compuseve.com (Italy, Spain, Portugal & Gibraltar)
Publisher's Services, Ziegenhainer Strasse 169, 60433 Frankfurt, Germany, Contact: Gabrielle Kern *Tel:* (069) 510 694 *Fax:* (069) 510 695 *E-mail:* Gabriele.Kern@publishersservices.de (Germany, Austria & Switzerland)
Quartet Sales & Marketing, Struik House, 7 Wessel Rd, 12 Carmel Avenue, NorthCliff, Gaiteng, Johannesburg, South Africa *Tel:* (011) 782 2034 *Fax:* (011) 782 2053 *E-mail:* shirley.c@mweb.co.za (South Africa)
Reed Publishing (NZ) Ltd, 39 Rawene Rd, Private Bag, Auckland 10, New Zealand *Tel:* (09) 480 4950 *Fax:* (09) 419 1212 *E-mail:* JBrockie@reed.co.nz
Derek Searle Associates Ltd, Progress Business Centre, Unit 13, Whittel Parkway, Burnham, Bucks SL1 6DQ *Tel:* (08) 559 500 *Fax:* (08) 663 876 *E-mail:* Dsapublish@aol.com
Vollmer Communications: Stockholding, Bunsen Strage No 5, 82152, Martinsried Munich, Germany *Tel:* (089) 857 3862 *Fax:* (089) 857 5592 *E-mail:* wv@vollmer-communications.com (Germany)
Peter Ward Book Exports, 4-5 Academy Buildings, Fanshaw Road, London NI 6LQ *Tel:* (020) 7613 5533 *Fax:* (020) 7613 4433

*E-mail:* pwbookex@dircon.co.uk (Middle East, Greece, Israel, Cyprus & Malta)
*Orders to:* Littlehampton Bopok Services Ltd, Faraday Close, Durrington, Worthing, West Sussex BN13 3RB *Tel:* (01933) 828503

**Conservative Policy Forum**
32 Smith Sq Westminster, London SW1P 3HH
*Tel:* (020) 7222 9000
*E-mail:* cpf@conservatives.com
*Web Site:* www.conservatives.com
*Key Personnel*
Dir: Greg Clark
Assistant Dir: Tracy-Jane Malthouse
  *E-mail:* tmalthouse@conservatives.com
Founded: 1945 (as Conservative Political Forum)
Subjects: Economics, Government, Political Science
ISBN Prefix(es): 0-85070

**Constable**, *imprint of* Constable & Robinson Ltd

**Constable & Robinson Ltd+**
3 The Lanchester, 162 Fulham Palace Rd, London W6 9ER
*Tel:* (020) 8741 3663 *Fax:* (020) 8748 7562
*E-mail:* enquiries@constablerobinson.com
*Web Site:* www.constablerobinson.com
*Telex:* 27950 ref 830
*Key Personnel*
Man Dir: Nick Robinson
Editorial: Carol O'Brien *E-mail:* carol@constablerobinson.com
Sales Dir: Andrew Hayward *E-mail:* andrew@constablerobinson.com
Sales Manager: Andrew Sauerwine
  *E-mail:* andrews@constablerobinson.com
Rights Manager: Eryl Humphrey Jones
  *E-mail:* eryl@constablerobinson.com
Founded: 1896
Subjects: Archaeology, Art, Astrology, Occult, Behavioral Sciences, Criminology, Erotica, Gay & Lesbian, Health, Nutrition, History, Humor, Literature, Literary Criticism, Essays, Military Science, Nonfiction (General), Photography, Psychology, Psychiatry, Science Fiction, Fantasy, Travel, Current Affairs
ISBN Prefix(es): 1-85487; 0-09; 1-84119; 1-84529
Number of titles published annually: 130 Print
Imprints: Constable; Robinson; Robinson's Children
*Distribution Center:* TBS Direct, Colchester Rd, Frating Green, Colchester, Essex CO7 7DW
  *Tel:* (01206) 255 678 *Fax:* (01206) 255 930
*Orders to:* TBS Direct, Colchester Rd, Frating Green, Colchester, Essex CO7 7DW
  *Tel:* (01206) 255 777 *Fax:* (01206) 255 914

**Continuum**, *imprint of* The Continuum International Publishing Group Ltd

**The Continuum International Publishing Group Ltd**
The Tower Bldg, 11 York Rd, London SE1 7NX
*Tel:* (020) 7922 0880 *Fax:* (020) 7922 0881
*E-mail:* info@continuum-books.com
*Web Site:* www.continuumbooks.com
*Key Personnel*
Chairman: Philip Sturrock *E-mail:* psturrock@continuumbooks.com
Executive Vice President & General Manager (New York): Ulla Schnell *E-mail:* ulla@continuum-books.com
Vice President Sales & Marketing: Mary Albi
Vice President & Senior Editor: Frank Oveis
  *E-mail:* frank@continuumbooks.com
Publisher-at-Large (New York): Werner Mark Linz
Finance Dir: Frank Roney *E-mail:* froney@continuumbooks.com

Editorial Dir (New York): David Barker
Subjects: Business, Drama, Theater, Education, Government, Political Science, History, Literature, Literary Criticism, Essays, Nonfiction (General), Psychology, Psychiatry, Women's Studies
ISBN Prefix(es): 0-304; 0-7201; 0-8264; 0-7136; 0-225; 0-264; 0-7185; 1-85567; 0-567; 0-485; 1-84127; 1-85805; 0-8044; 0-86175; 0-5670; 0-8601
Number of titles published annually: 300 Print
Imprints: Burns & Oates; Geoffrey Chapman; Continuum; Leicester University Press; Mansell; Morehouse; Mowbray; Pinter; T&T Clark International; Thoemmes; Tycooly
*U.S. Office(s):* The Continuum International Publishing Group Inc, 15 E 26th St, New York, NY 10010, United States *Tel:* 212-953-5858 *Fax:* 212-953-5944
*Orders to:* Orca Book Services, Stanley House, 3 Fleets Lane, Poole, Dorset BH15 3AJ
  *Tel:* (01202) 665432 *Fax:* (01202) 666219

**Conway Maritime Press+**
Division of Chrysalis Group
The Chrysalis Bldg, Bramley Rd, London W10 6SP
*Tel:* (020) 7221 2213; (020) 7314 1469 (sales)
  *Fax:* (020) 7221 6455; (020) 7314 1594 (sales)
*E-mail:* enquiries@chrysalis.com
*Web Site:* www.chrysalisbooks.co.uk
*Key Personnel*
Group Sales & Marketing Dir: Richard Samson
  *Tel:* (020) 7314 1459 *Fax:* (020) 7314 1549
  *E-mail:* rsamson@chrysalisbooks.co.uk
Dir of Marketing: Kate Wood *Tel:* (020) 7314 1496 *E-mail:* kwood@chrysalisbooks.co.uk
Marketing & Publicity Manager: Rachel Armstrong *Tel:* (020) 7314 1605 *Fax:* (020) 7314 1549 *E-mail:* rarmstrong@chrysalisbooks.co.uk
Rights: Candida Buckley *Tel:* (01622) 863117 *Fax:* (01622) 863227 *E-mail:* candidabuckley@aol.com
Permissions: Terry Forshaw *Tel:* (020) 7314 1607 *E-mail:* tforshaw@chrysalisbooks.co.uk
Founded: 1968
Subjects: Maritime
ISBN Prefix(es): 0-85177; 1-84486
*Associate Companies:* Putnam Aeronautical Books

**Leo Cooper**, *imprint of* Pen & Sword Books Ltd

**Leo Cooper+**
Imprint of Pen & Sword Books Ltd
47 Church St, Barnsley, S Yorks S70 2AS
*Tel:* (01226) 734555 *Fax:* (01226) 734438
*E-mail:* enquiries@pen-sword.co.uk
*Web Site:* www.pen-and-sword.co.uk
*Key Personnel*
Man Dir: Charles Hewitt *E-mail:* charles@pen-and-sword.co.uk
Publishing Manager: Henry Wilson *E-mail:* hw@henrywilson.lawlite.net
Book Production Manager: Barbara Bramall
  *E-mail:* production@pen-and-sword.co.uk
Sales Manager: Paula Brennan *E-mail:* sales@pen-and-sword.co.uk
Marketing & Publicity: Jonathan Wright
  *E-mail:* marketing@pen-and-sword.co.uk
Founded: 1990
Subjects: Biography, History, Maritime, Military Science, Nonfiction (General), Travel
ISBN Prefix(es): 0-7232; 0-85052; 1-84415
Number of titles published annually: 100 Print
Total Titles: 350 Print
*Associate Companies:* Wharncliffe Publishing
Distributed by Combined Books (USA); Vanwell Publishing Ltd (Canada)

**Co-operative Union**, *imprint of* Holyoake Books

**Copper Beech Publishing Ltd+**
PO Box 159, East Grinstead, Sussex RH19 4HF
*Tel:* (01342) 314734 *Fax:* (01342) 314794
*E-mail:* sales@copperbeechpublishing.co.uk
*Web Site:* www.btinternet.com/~copperbeechpublishing
*Key Personnel*
Contact: Jan Barnes
Membership(s): IPG.
Subjects: Etiquette, Food & Drink, Victoriana
ISBN Prefix(es): 0-9516295; 1-898617

**Cordee Ltd+**
3a De Montfort St, Leicester, Lincs LE1 7HD
*Tel:* (0116) 2543579 *Fax:* (0116) 2471176
*E-mail:* info@cordee.co.uk
*Web Site:* www.cordee.co.uk
*Key Personnel*
Contact: Ken Vickers *E-mail:* kenvickers@cordee.co.uk
Founded: 1973
Specialist publisher, distributor & wholesaler (worldwide).
Subjects: Outdoor Recreation, Travel
ISBN Prefix(es): 1-871890; 0-904405; 1-904207

**Corgi**, *imprint of* Transworld Publishers Ltd

**Cornwall Books**, *imprint of* Golden Cockerel Press Ltd

**Corwin Press**, *imprint of* SAGE Publications Ltd

**Joanna Cotler Books**, *imprint of* HarperCollins UK

**Cottage Publications**
Laurel Cottage, 15 Ballyhay Rd, Donaghadee, Co Down BT21 0NG
*Tel:* (01247) 888033; (0410) 057990 (mobile)
  *Fax:* (01247) 888063
*E-mail:* info@cottage-publications.com; cottage-publ@online.rednet.co.uk
*Web Site:* www.cottage-publications.com
*Key Personnel*
Contact: Timothy Johnston *E-mail:* tim@cottage-publications.com
Founded: 1990
Specialize in illustrated books on Ireland.
Subjects: Art, History, Regional Interests
ISBN Prefix(es): 0-9516402; 1-900935
Total Titles: 20 Print

**Council for British Archaeology**
Bowes Morrell House, 111 Walmgate, York YO1 9WA
*Tel:* (01904) 671417 *Fax:* (01904) 671384
*E-mail:* archaeology@compuserve.com; cbabooks@dial.pipex.com
*Web Site:* www.britarch.ac.uk
*Key Personnel*
Dir: George Lambrick *E-mail:* georgelambrick@britarch.ac.uk
Publications Officer: Kate Sleight
Founded: 1944
Subjects: Archaeology, Education
ISBN Prefix(es): 0-900312; 0-906780; 1-872414
Number of titles published annually: 12 Print
Total Titles: 65 Print

**Countryside Books**
2 Highfield Ave, Newbury, Berks RG14 5DS
*Tel:* (01635) 43816 *Fax:* (01635) 551004
*E-mail:* info@countrysidebooks.co.uk
*Web Site:* www.countrysidebooks.co.uk
*Key Personnel*
Man Dir, Editorial, Sales & Production: Nicholas Battle
Publicity, Rights & Permissions: Suzanne Battle
Founded: 1976
Publisher of regional interest books within UK

Specialize in walking guides.
Subjects: Genealogy, History, Regional Interests
ISBN Prefix(es): 0-905392; 0-86368; 1-85306
Number of titles published annually: 50 Print
Total Titles: 400 Print
Subsidiaries: Local Heritage Books

**Countyvise Ltd+**
14 Appin Rd, Birkenhead, Merseyside CH41 9HH
*Tel:* (0151) 6473333 *Fax:* (0151) 6478286
*E-mail:* info@countyvise.co.uk
*Web Site:* www.countyvise.co.uk
*Key Personnel*
Man Dir: John Emmerson *E-mail:* je@birkenheadpress.co.uk
Founded: 1981
Subjects: Biography, History, Maritime, Regional Interests, Sports, Athletics, Transportation
ISBN Prefix(es): 0-907768; 1-871201; 0-9516129; 1-873245; 1-901231
Number of titles published annually: 7 Print
Total Titles: 121 Print
Imprints: Liver Press; Merseyside Port Folios; Picton Press (Liverpool)

**Covenant Publishing Co Ltd**
121 Low Etherly, Bishop Auckland, Co Durham DL14 0HA
*Tel:* (01388) 834 395 *Fax:* (01388) 835 957
*E-mail:* admin@britishisrael.co.uk
*Web Site:* www.britishisrael.co.uk
*Key Personnel*
Chairman: M A Clark
Administrator: J B Dowse
Founded: 1922
Subjects: Religion - Other
ISBN Prefix(es): 0-85205

**Richard & Erika Coward Writing & Publishing Partnership+**
16 Sturgess Ave, London NW4 3TS
*Tel:* (020) 8202 9592
*E-mail:* info@writers.net
*Key Personnel*
Author: Richard Coward *E-mail:* richardcoward@onetel.net.uk
Business Manager: Erika Coward
ISBN Prefix(es): 0-9515019

**CRAC,** *imprint of* Hobsons

**CRE,** *imprint of* Commission for Racial Equality

**Creation Books+**
72/80 Leather Lane, 4th floor, London EC1N 7TR
*Tel:* (020) 7430 9878 *Fax:* (020) 7242 5527
*E-mail:* info@creationbooks.com
*Web Site:* www.creationbooks.com
*Key Personnel*
President: James Williamson *E-mail:* james@creationbooks.com
Dir: Laurence Raine *E-mail:* laurence@creationbooks.com
Publishing Executive & Rights: Miranda Filbee *E-mail:* miranda@creationbooks.com
Founded: 1989
Subjects: Biography, Erotica, Fiction, Film, Video, Nonfiction (General), Photography
ISBN Prefix(es): 1-871592; 1-84068; 1-902588
Total Titles: 100 Print
*Associate Companies:* Glitter Books, 85 Clerkenwell Rd, Suite 403, London EC1R 5AR, Contact: James Williamson *Tel:* (020) 7430 9878 *Fax:* (020) 7242 5527 *E-mail:* glitter@creationbooks.com
Imprints: Attack!; Velvet
*U.S. Office(s):* PO Box 1137, New York, NY 10156, United States

c/o Subterranean Co, Box 160, Monroe, OR 97456, United States
Foreign Rep(s): Julian Ashton (Far East, Middle East); Creation Books Tokyo (Japan); Tower Books (Australia, New Zealand)
*Distribution Center:* Consortium Book Sales & Distribution, 1045 Westgate Dr, Saint Paul, MN 55114, United States *Tel:* 651-221-9035 *Fax:* 651-917-6406 *Web Site:* www.cbsd.com
Last Gasp, 777 Florida St, San Francisco, CA 94110, United States *Tel:* 415-824-6636 *Fax:* 415-824-1836 *Web Site:* www.lastgasp.com
Marginal Distribution, 277 George St, Unit 102, North Peterborough, ON K9J 3G9, Canada *Tel:* 705-745-2326 *Fax:* 705-745-2122 *Web Site:* www.marginalbook.com
*Orders to:* Book Clearing House, 46 Purdy St, Harrison, NY 10528, United States *Fax:* 914-835-0398 *E-mail:* bookch@aol.com *Web Site:* www.book-clearing-house.com (US & Canada mail order)
Turnaround, Olympia Trading Estate, Unit 3, Coburg Rd, Wood Green, London N22 6TZ *Tel:* (020) 8829 3000 *Fax:* (020) 8881 5088

**Creative Monochrome,** *imprint of* Creative Monochrome Ltd

**Creative Monochrome Ltd**
20 St Peter's Rd, Croydon CR0 1HD
*Tel:* (020) 8686 3282 *Fax:* (020) 8681 0662
*E-mail:* sales@cremono.com; roger@cremono.demon.co.uk
*Key Personnel*
Man Dir: Roger Maile *E-mail:* roger@cremono.com
Founded: 1992
Membership(s): IPG
Subjects: Photography
ISBN Prefix(es): 1-873319
Total Titles: 24 Print
Imprints: Creative Monochrome; Digital Photoart; Photo Art International
*Distribution Center:* Ingrams & Small Changes Inc (USA & Canada)

**Cressrelles Publishing Company Ltd+**
10 Station Road, Industrial Estate, Colwall, Malvern, Herefordshire WR13 6RN
*Tel:* (01684) 540154 *Fax:* (01684) 540154
*Key Personnel*
Man Dir: Leslie Smith
Business Manager: Simon Smith *E-mail:* simonsmith@cressrelles4drama.fsbusiness.co.uk
Founded: 1973
Subjects: Drama, Theater
ISBN Prefix(es): 0-85956
Number of titles published annually: 3 Print
Total Titles: 48 Print
Imprints: Actinic Press (chiropody); Kenyon-Deane (plays); J Garnet Miller Ltd (plays); New Playwrights Network (plays)
Distributed by Empire Publishing Services
Distributor for Anchorage Press Inc; I E Clark Inc

**Critical Studies in Latin American Culture,** *imprint of* Verso

**Paul H Crompton Ltd+**
Unit 8, The Arena, 1004 Mollison Ave, Enfield EN3 7NL
*Tel:* (020) 88040400 *Fax:* (020) 88040044
*E-mail:* cromptonph@aol.com
*Key Personnel*
Publicity & Rights: Paul Crompton
International Rights: Rose Brookhouse
Founded: 1968
Also produce martial arts videos.

Subjects: Cookery, Crafts, Games, Hobbies, Health, Nutrition
ISBN Prefix(es): 0-901764; 1-874250; 0-9644730
Distributed by Talman Co (North America)
*Orders to:* c/o Airlift Book Co

**Croner CCH Group Ltd**
145 London Rd, Kingston-upon-Thames, Surrey KT2 6SR
*Tel:* (020) 85473333 *Fax:* (020) 85472637
*E-mail:* info@croner.co.uk
*Web Site:* www.croner.co.uk
*Telex:* 267778
*Key Personnel*
Man Dir: H F Staal
Production: George Rankin
Finance Dir: Peter Diggles
Founded: 1941
Subjects: Business, Finance, Health, Nutrition, Labor, Industrial Relations, Law, Transportation
ISBN Prefix(es): 0-900319; 1-85524
*Parent Company:* Wolters Kluwer (UK) PLC
*Ultimate Parent Company:* Wolters Kluwer NV, Netherlands
Subsidiaries: CCH Editions (Bicester)

**Crossbridge Books+**
345 Old Birmingham Rd, Bromsgrove B60 1NX
*Tel:* (0121) 447 7897 *Fax:* (0121) 445 1063
*E-mail:* crossbridgebooks@btinternet.com
*Web Site:* www.crossbridgebooks.com
*Key Personnel*
Publisher & International Rights Contact: Eileen Mohr
Founded: 1995
Publish Christian books.
Membership(s): Christian Booksellers Association; Independent Publishers Guild.
Subjects: Biography, Religion - Protestant, Self-Help
ISBN Prefix(es): 0-9524604
Number of titles published annually: 3 Print
Total Titles: 15 Print
Imprints: Mohr Books

**Crossway,** *imprint of* Inter-Varsity Press

**Crown House Publishing Ltd+**
Crown Buildings, Bancyfelin, Carmarthen SA33 5ND
*Tel:* (01267) 211345 *Fax:* (01267) 211882
*E-mail:* books@crownhouse.co.uk
*Web Site:* www.crownhouse.co.uk
*Key Personnel*
Dir: David Bowman
Marketing Dir: Caroline Lenton
Founded: 1998
Subjects: Business, Education, Psychology, Psychiatry
ISBN Prefix(es): 1-899836; 1-904424; 1-845900
Number of titles published annually: 20 Print
Total Titles: 110 Print
*U.S. Office(s):* 4 Berkeley St, 1st floor, Norwalk, CT 06850, United States
Foreign Rep(s): Everybody's Books (South Africa); Footprint Books (Australia); Mark Tracten (Canada, US)

**The Crowood Press Ltd+**
The Stable Block, Crowood Lane, Ramsbury, Marlborough, Wilts SN8 2HR
*Tel:* (01672) 520320 *Fax:* (01672) 520280
*E-mail:* enquiries@crowood.com
*Web Site:* www.crowood.com
*Key Personnel*
Publisher & Chief Executive: John F Dennis
Man Dir: Ken Hathaway
Sales Office Manager: Julie Sankey *E-mail:* admin@crowood.com
Rights Manager: Madeleine Hacking
Founded: 1982
Subjects: Aeronautics, Aviation, Animals, Pets, Automotive, Crafts, Games, Hobbies, Garden-

ing, Plants, Maritime, Natural History, Outdoor Recreation, Sports, Athletics
ISBN Prefix(es): 0-946284; 1-85223; 1-86126
Imprints: Helmsman Guides
Distributed by Grantham Book Services (United Kingdom); Peter Hyde Associates (South Africa); Motorbooks International (US transport & military titles); Nilsson & Lamm (Netherlands); Peribo Pty Ltd (Australia & New Zealand); Publishers Marketing Services (Singapore); Publishers Marketing Services Pte Ltd (Malaysia); Trafalgar Square Publishing (USA); Vanwell Publishing Ltd (Canada)
Foreign Rep(s): Bookport Associates (Southern Europe); D Richard Bowen (Scandinavia); European Marketing Services (Austria, Belgium, France, Germany, Luxembourg, Switzerland)
Warehouse: Bookpoint Ltd, 39 Milton Park, Abingdon Oxon

## G L Crowther
224 S Meadow Lane, Preston PR1 8JP
Tel: (01772) 257126
Key Personnel
Contact: G L Crowther
Founded: 1984
Specialize in maps showing all navigations, tramways & railways known to have existed in the UK.
Subjects: Geography, Geology, Transportation
ISBN Prefix(es): 1-85615
Number of titles published annually: 20 Print
Total Titles: 125 Print

## Crucible Publishers+
3 Town Barton, Norton St Philip, Bath BA2 7LN
Tel: (01373) 834900 Fax: (01373) 834900
E-mail: sales@cruciblepublishers.com
Web Site: www.cruciblepublishers.com
Key Personnel
Man Dir: Mr Robin Campbell
Founded: 2002
Trade paperbacks, including Crucible Classics.
Subjects: Body, Mind, Environment, Spirit
ISBN Prefix(es): 1-902733
Number of titles published annually: 4 Print
Total Titles: 10 Print

**Crux Press**, *imprint of* Impart Books

## CSA (Cambridge Scientific Abstracts)+
4640 Kingsgate, Cascade Way, Oxford Business Park South, Oxford, Oxon OX4 2ST
Tel: (0865) 336250 Fax: (0865) 336258
E-mail: service@csa.com; marketing@bowker.uk.co
Web Site: www.csa.com
Key Personnel
Man Dir: Jacki Heppard Tel: (01342) 336043 E-mail: jacki.heppard@bowker.co.uk
Marketing Manager: Jo Grange Tel: (01342) 336143 E-mail: jo.grange@bowker.com
Sales Dir: Doug Macmillan Tel: (01342) 336157 E-mail: doug.macmillan@bowker.co.uk
Founded: 1988
Publisher of reference tools & professional development texts for the library & information world & publishing industry.
Subjects: Library & Information Sciences, Publishing & Book Trade Reference
ISBN Prefix(es): 1-85739; 0-8352; 0-85935; 1-88387
Total Titles: 150 Print; 8 CD-ROM; 4 Online; 5 E-Book
Parent Company: Cambridge Information Group
Distributed by D W Thorpe (Australia)
Distributor for R R Bowker LLC (UK, Europe, Middle East, Africa, Southeast Asia)

## CTBI Publications
3rd floor, Bastille Court, 2 Paris Garden, London SE1 8ND

Tel: (020) 7654 7254 Fax: (020) 7654 7222
E-mail: info@ctbi.org.uk
Web Site: www.ctbi.org.uk
Key Personnel
International Rights: Rev D J Rudiger Tel: (020) 7523 2041
Publications Secretary: Rev Collin Davey, PhD Tel: (020) 7523 2154
Founded: 1940 (as BCC Publications)
Subjects: Biblical Studies, Biography, Education, Environmental Studies, History, Microcomputers, Religion - Catholic, Religion - Protestant, Religion - Other, Theology, Women's Studies
ISBN Prefix(es): 0-85169
Parent Company: Churches Together In Britain & Ireland
Distributor for World Council of Churches (UK & Ireland)
Bookshop(s): Church House Bookshop, 31 Great Smith St, London SW1P 3BN Tel: (020) 7898 1306 Fax: (020) 7898 1305 E-mail: bookshop@c-of-e.org.uk

**CTS Publications**, *imprint of* The Catholic Truth Society

## Curiad
The Old Library, County Rd, Pen-y-Groes, Cacrnarfon, Gwynedd LL54 6EY
Tel: (01286) 882166 Fax: (01286) 882692
E-mail: curiad@curiad.co.uk
Web Site: www.curiad.co.uk
Key Personnel
Contact: Dyfed Wyn Edwards
Founded: 1992
Subjects: Music, Dance
ISBN Prefix(es): 1-897664

## Current Science Group+
Middlesex House, 34-42 Cleveland St, London W1T 4LB
Tel: (020) 7323 0323 Fax: (020) 7580 1938
E-mail: info@current-science.com
Web Site: www.current-science-group.com
Key Personnel
Chairman: Vitek Tracz E-mail: vitek@ sciencenow.com
Man Dir: Anne Greenwood E-mail: anne@ sciencenow.com
Operations Dir: Mike Lennie
Marketing Dir: Daryl Rainer
Finance Dir: Brett Hassell E-mail: brett@ sciencenow.com
Human Resources Manager: Cheryl Gambrill E-mail: cheryl@sciencenow.com
Subjects: Biological Sciences, Medicine, Nursing, Dentistry, Science (General)
ISBN Prefix(es): 1-870485; 1-85927
Subsidiaries: Current Drugs Ltd; Science Press
U.S. Office(s): 20 N Third St, Philadelphia, PA 19106-2113, United States Tel: 215-574-2266 Fax: 215-574-2270

## James Currey Ltd+
73 Boxley Rd, Oxford OX2 0BS
Tel: (01865) 244 111 Fax: (01865) 246 454
E-mail: editorial@jamescurrey.co.uk
Web Site: www.jamescurrey.co.uk
Key Personnel
Chairman: James M Currey
Man & Editorial Dir: Dr Douglas H Johnson E-mail: douglas.johnson@jamescurrey.co.uk
Editorial Manager: Lynn Taylor E-mail: lynn.taylor@jamescurrey.co.uk
Founded: 1985
Subjects: Agriculture, Anthropology, Archaeology, Biography, Developing Countries, Drama, Theater, Economics, Education, Environmental Studies, Ethnicity, Foreign Countries, Government, Political Science, History, Law, Philosophy, Social Sciences, Sociology, Africa,

Caribbean, Gender Studies, Literary Criticism, Theatre & Film, Third World Bibliographies
ISBN Prefix(es): 0-85255
Number of titles published annually: 50 Print
Total Titles: 360 Print
Imprints: Hans Zell Bibliographies
Foreign Rep(s): IMA (Africa); Intermedia Americana Ltd (Africa exc South Africa, Middle East exc Israel); David Philip Publishers (Africa)
Orders to: Plymbridge Distributors Ltd, Estover, Plymouth PL6 7PZ Tel: (01752) 202301 Fax: (01752) 202333 E-mail: orders@ plymbridge.com

## CyberClub+
16 St John St, London EC1M 4AY
Tel: (020) 8731 6161 Fax: (020) 8905 5050
Web Site: www.astorlaw.com
Key Personnel
Contact: Richard Astor
Membership(s): Publishers Association (UK).
Subjects: Law
ISBN Prefix(es): 1-873994
Imprints: Bartsky Legal Texts Ltd

**Cyfres y Gair**, *imprint of* Cyhoeddiadau'r Gair

**Cygnus Arts**, *imprint of* Golden Cockerel Press Ltd

## Cyhoeddiadau Barddas
Pen-Rhiw, 71 Ffordd Pentrepoeth, Treforys, Abertawe SA6 6AE
Tel: (01792) 792 829
Key Personnel
Contact: Alan Llwyd
Founded: 1976
Specializes in Welsh language & literature.
Subjects: Literature, Literary Criticism, Essays, Poetry
ISBN Prefix(es): 1-900437

**Cyhoeddiadau FBA**, *imprint of* Francis Balsom Associates

## Cyhoeddiadau'r Gair (Work Publications)+
Cyngor Ysgolion Sul, Ysgol Addsg, Prifysgol Cymru Bangor, Safle'r Normal, Bangor, Gwynedd LL57 2PX
Tel: (01248) 382947 Fax: (01248) 383954
E-mail: eds00e@bangor.ac.uk
Key Personnel
Contact: Aled Davies E-mail: aled.davies@ bangor.ac.uk
Founded: 1992
Specialize in Welsh language Christian books, cards & systems.
Subjects: Biblical Studies, Religion - Protestant
ISBN Prefix(es): 1-85994; 1-874410
Total Titles: 300 Print; 2 CD-ROM
Parent Company: Cyngor Ysgolion Sul
Imprints: Cyfres y Gair
Subsidiaries: Cardiau'r Gair gifts
Distributed by Welsh Books Council
Distributor for Curaid; Gwasg Efeng yl Aidd Cymru
Bookshop(s): Canolfan Addysg Grefyddol, Bangor
Warehouse: Libanus, Bontnewydd

## Cymdeithas Lyfrau Ceredigion+
Ystafell B5, Y Coleg Diwinyddol, Stryd y Brenin, Aberystwyth, Ceredigion SY23 2LT
Tel: (01970) 617776 Fax: (01970) 624049; (01970) 625844
E-mail: clc.gyf@talk21.com
Key Personnel
Contact: Dylan Williams
Founded: 1954
Subjects: Ceredigion Interest

ISBN Prefix(es): 0-901410; 0-948930; 1-902416
*Orders to:* The Distribution Centre, Unit 16, Glan-yr-afon Industrial Estate, Hanbadarn Fawr, Aberystwyth, Ceredigion SY23 3AQ

**Cynulliad Cenedlaethol Cymru,** *imprint of* National Assembly for Wales

**D&B Ltd**
Holmers Farm Way, High Wycombe, Bucks HP12 4UL
*Tel:* (01494) 422000 *Fax:* (01494) 422260
*E-mail:* custserv@dnb.com
*Web Site:* www.dnb.com
*Key Personnel*
Man Dir: Claes Henckel
Sales: Nigel Dickinson
Publicity & Marketing: Barbara James
Founded: 1841
Membership(s): Directory Publishers Association, European Association of Directory Publishers, Booksellers Association & Business Information Network.
ISBN Prefix(es): 0-901491; 0-900714; 1-86071
*Parent Company:* D&B Corporation, 103 JFK Parkway, Short Hills, NJ 07078, United States
*Branch Office(s)*
Bangor
Birmingham
Glasgow
London
Manchester
Newport
Nottingham
Southampton

**Daily Telegraph (map service),** *imprint of* Roger Lascelles

**Dales Large Print Series,** *imprint of* Magna Large Print Books

**Terence Dalton Ltd+**
Water St, Lavenham, Suffolk CO10 9RN
*Tel:* (01787) 249290 *Fax:* (01787) 248267
*E-mail:* tdl@lavenhamgroup.cp.uk
*Web Site:* www.terencedalton.co.uk
*Key Personnel*
Man Dir: Terence Dalton *E-mail:* terence@lavenhamgroup.co.uk
Dir: Mrs Lis Whitehair *E-mail:* lis@lavenhamgroup.co.uk
Marketing Manager: Erica Hammond *E-mail:* erica@lavenhamgroup.co.uk
Business Development Officer: Barney Goodrich *E-mail:* barney@lavenhamgroup.co.uk
Conference & Book Sales: Claire Smith *E-mail:* claire@lavenhamgroup.co.uk
Book Sales: Gail Moss *E-mail:* gail@lavenhamgroup.co.uk
Webmaster: Steve Lodge *E-mail:* steve@lavenhamgroup.co.uk
Founded: 1967
Contract publishers for CIWEM (Chartered Institution of Water & Environmental Management). Some East Anglian, maritime & aviation titles still available.
Subjects: Aeronautics, Aviation, Environmental Studies, Maritime, Regional Interests, Magazines
ISBN Prefix(es): 0-900963; 0-86138; 0-903214; 0-904623
*Parent Company:* The Lavenham Group PLC
*Associate Companies:* The Lavenham Press Ltd, Water St, Lavenham, C010 9RN Sudbury, Suffolk, Contact: Terence Dalton
*Tel:* (01787) 247436 *Fax:* (01787) 248267
*E-mail:* postmaster@lavenhamgroup.co.uk
Imprints: CIWEM; Eastland Press; Mallard Reprints
Distributor for CIWEM

**Dance Books Ltd+**
The Old Bakery, 4 Lenten St, Alton, Hants GU34 1HG
*Tel:* (01420) 86138 *Fax:* (01420) 86142
*E-mail:* dl@dancebooks.co.uk
*Web Site:* www.dancebooks.co.uk
*Key Personnel*
Man Dir, Production, Rights & Permissions: David Leonard
Sales Dir: Richard Holland
Founded: 1960
Publishers & bookkeepers.
Subjects: Music, Dance
ISBN Prefix(es): 0-903102; 1-85273
Number of titles published annually: 10 Print
Total Titles: 130 Print
Distributed by Princeton Book Co; Astam Books
Distributor for Princeton Book Co

**The C W Daniel Co Ltd+**
One Church Path, Saffron Walden, Essex CB10 1JP
*Tel:* (01799) 521909; (01799) 526216 *Fax:* (01799) 513462
*E-mail:* cwdaniel@dial.pipex.com
*Web Site:* www.cwdaniel.com
*Key Personnel*
Man Dir: Ian Miller
Editorial, Rights & Permissions: Jane Miller
Accounts: Jane Goodacre
Marketing, Publicity: Genevieve Miller *Tel:* (01799) 521909
Founded: 1903
Publisher of Mind, Body & Spirit Paperbacks.
Subjects: Animals, Pets, Astrology, Occult, Health, Nutrition, Self-Help
ISBN Prefix(es): 0-85207; 0-85032; 0-85435; 0-85978; 0-85243
Number of titles published annually: 10 Print
Total Titles: 200 Print
Imprints: L N Fowler & Co Ltd; Health Science Press; Neville Spearman Publishers
Distributed by Alternative Books (UK); APA Publications (Singapore); Beekman Publishers Inc (USA); Gemcraft Books (UK); Homeopathic Educational Services; National Book Network (USA); The New Leaf Distributing Co (USA); The Nutri Book Corp (USA); Peaceful Living Publications (UK)
Distributor for Brotherhood of Life, NM; Haug Verlag, Germany
Foreign Rep(s): Angell Eurosales (Northern Europe, Scandinavia); Bookport Associates (Cyprus, Greece, Italy, Portugal, Spain); Kerim Colakoglu (Turkey); Donald MacDonald (Scotland); Tony Moggach (Africa, Eastern Europe, Middle East); National Book Network (Canada, US); Theo Phillips (Hong Kong, Malaysia, Philippines, Singapore, Thailand); David Williams (South America)
Foreign Rights: Angell Euorsales (Northern Europe, Scandinavia); Bookport Associates (Cyprus, Greece, Italy, Portugal, Spain); Kerim Colakoglu (Turkey); Donald MacDonald (Scotland); Genny Kelliher (Northern Ireland); Joe Portelli (Greece, Italy, Portugal, Spain); Tom Moggach (Africa); Tony Moggach (Eastern Europe, Middle East); National Book Network (Canada, US); Theo Philips (Hong Kong, Malaysia, Philippines, Singapore, Thailand); The Segrue Partnership (London); David Williams (South America)
*Warehouse:* Unit 7, Saffron Business Centre, Elizabeth Close, off Elizabeth Way, Saffron Walden, Essex CB10 2BL

**Darf Publishers Ltd**
277 West End Lane, London NW6 1QS
*Tel:* (020) 7431 7009 *Fax:* (020) 7431 7655
*E-mail:* darf@freeuk.com
*Web Site:* home.freeuk.net/darf
*Key Personnel*
Chief Executive: M B Fergiani

Editorial: Usama Al Fergani
Sales, Publicity: Ghassan Fergiani
Production: A Bentaleb
Manager & Rights & Permissions: John Cowen
Founded: 1983
Specialize in reprints of out-of-print & rare books written in the 18th & 19th centuries.
Subjects: Archaeology, History, Religion - Islamic, Travel
ISBN Prefix(es): 1-85077
Number of titles published annually: 10 Print
Total Titles: 200 Print
*Parent Company:* Dar Al Fergian, PO Box 132, Tripoli, Libyan Arab Jamahiriya
Subsidiaries: Dar Al Fergani

**Dartmouth,** *imprint of* Ashgate Publishing Ltd

**Darton, Longman & Todd Ltd+**
One Spencer Court, 140-142 Wandsworth High St, London SW18 4JJ
*Tel:* (020) 8875 0155; (020) 8875 0134 *Fax:* (020) 8875 0133
*E-mail:* tradesales@darton-longman-todd.co.uk
*Web Site:* www.darton-longman-todd.co.uk
*Key Personnel*
Production: Leslie Kay
Sales & Marketing Dir: Alan Mordue
Editorial Dir: Brendan Walsh
Man Editor: Helen Porter
Rights & Permissions: Rachel Davis
Founded: 1959
Subjects: Biblical Studies, Religion - Catholic, Religion - Protestant, Religion - Other, Theology
ISBN Prefix(es): 0-232
*Warehouse:* 9 Amor Way, Dunhams Lane, Letchworth, Herts S96 1U9

**Datapack Books,** *imprint of* E J Morten (Publishers)

**David & Charles Ltd+**
Brunel House, Forde Close, Newton Abbot, Devon TQ12 4PU
*Tel:* (01626) 323200 *Fax:* (01626) 323319
*E-mail:* postermaster@davidandcharles.co.uk
*Web Site:* www.davidandcharles.co.uk
*Telex:* 42904 BOOKS G
*Key Personnel*
Sales & Marketing Dir: Susie Hallam
Non-Executive Dir: Neil McRae
Rights & Book Club Manager: Sue Narramore
Publishing Dir: Piers Spence
Operation Dir & Production Manager: Amanda Newton
Press & Promotions Officer: Susan Hallam
Founded: 1960
Subjects: Animals, Pets, Art, Cookery, Crafts, Games, Hobbies, Gardening, Plants, Health, Nutrition, How-to, Maritime, Outdoor Recreation, Photography, Transportation, Travel
ISBN Prefix(es): 0-7153; 0-907115
*Associate Companies:* Levinson
Imprints: Betterway; How Design; North Light; Popular Woodworking; Writer's Digest
Divisions: The Readers' Union
Distributed by David Batemen Ltd (New Zealand); F & W Publications, Inc (USA & Canada); Kirby Book Distribution (Australia); Trinity Books (South Africa)
Foreign Rep(s): Angell Eurosales (Belgium, Denmark, Netherlands, Finland, France, Iceland, Norway, Sweden); Pat Bence (Botswana, Caribbean, Kenya, Mauritius, The Gambia); Candida Buckley (Denmark, Netherlands, Finland, Norway, Switzerland); Michelle Morrow Curreri (Asia, Latin America, Middle East); Lora Fountain (France); Gabriele Kern (Austria, Germany, Switzerland); Surit Mitra (Bangladesh, Indonesia, Nepal, Sri Lanka); Penny Padovani (France, Gibraltar, Greece,

Italy, Spain); Marta Schooler (Asia, Latin America, Middle East)
*Book Club(s):* Readers Union Ltd
*Orders to:* Exel Logistics, DMS 3, Sheldon Way, Larkfield, Aylesford, Kent ME20 65E

**Christopher Davies Publishers Ltd+**
PO Box 403, Swansea SA1 4YF
*Tel:* (01792) 648825 *Fax:* (01792) 648825
*E-mail:* sales@cdaviesbookswales.com
*Web Site:* www.cdaviesbookswales.com
*Key Personnel*
Man Dir: Christopher Talfan Davies
   *E-mail:* chris@cdaviesbookswales.com
Founded: 1949
Subjects: Cookery, Health, Nutrition, History, Natural History
ISBN Prefix(es): 0-7154; 0-85339

**Dawson Books+**
Subsidiary of Dawson Holdings PLC
Foxhills House, Rushden, Northants NN10 6DB
*Tel:* (01933) 417500 *Fax:* (01933) 417501
*E-mail:* contactus@dawson.co.uk; bksales@ dawsonbooks.co.uk
*Web Site:* www.dawson.co.uk
*Key Personnel*
Man Dir: Diane Kerr
Sales Manager: George Hammond
Customer Service Manager: Tina Atterbury
Senior Team Leader, Customer Service: Sally Barber
Team Leader, Customer Service: Jason Sinclair; Linda Finch
Distribution Manager: Margaret Beresford
Manager Standing Orders: Chris Wilson
IT Manager: Alan Benton
Content Manager: Mark Howard
Marketing Manager: Steven Welch
Founded: 1809
Specialize in international library & information (subscriptions, book, library software); news distribution.
ISBN Prefix(es): 0-946291; 0-9506540
*Associate Companies:* Dawson Books Espana, Pasaje 26 y 28-Nave 4, 28230 Las Rozas (Madrid), Spain *Tel:* (091) 710-42-80 *Fax:* (091) 710-43-57 *E-mail:* libros@ dawson.lci.es; Dawson France, 3, rue Galvani, 91745 Massy Cedex, France *Tel:* (01) 69 19 21 50 *Fax:* (01) 69 19 21 66 *E-mail:* librarie@ dawson.fr; Quality Books Inc, 1003 W Pines Rd, Oregon, IL 61061-9680, United States *Fax:* 815-732-4499

**Debrett's Ltd+**
Brunel House, 55-57 N Wharf Rd, London W2 1LA
*Tel:* (020) 7915 9633 *Fax:* (020) 7753 4212
*E-mail:* people@debretts.co.uk
*Web Site:* www.debretts.co.uk
*Key Personnel*
Editorial, Peerage & Baronetage: Charles Kidd
Editorial: David Williamson
Operations Manager: Andrew Moulder
Business Development: Sharon Tidball
Founded: 1769
Subjects: Biography, Genealogy
ISBN Prefix(es): 1-870520; 0-905649
*Orders to:* Vinehouse Distribution Ltd, Waldenbury, North Common, Chailey, East Sussex BN27 3RP *Tel:* (01825) 723 398 *Fax:* (01825) 724 188

**Decadence from Dedalus**, *imprint of* Dedalus Ltd

**Dedalus European Classics**, *imprint of* Dedalus Ltd

**Dedalus Ltd+**
Langford Lodge, St Judith's Lane, Sawtry, Cambs PE28 5XE
*Tel:* (01487) 832382 *Fax:* (01487) 832382
*E-mail:* info@dedalusbooks.com
*Web Site:* www.dedalusbooks.com
*Key Personnel*
Chief Executive: Eric Lane
Chairman: Juri Gabriel
Editorial Dir: Robert Irwin
Founded: 1983
Subjects: Fiction, Literature, Literary Criticism, Essays
ISBN Prefix(es): 0-946626; 1-873982; 1-903517
Imprints: Dedalus European Classics; Decadence from Dedalus; Dedalus Nobel Prize Winner; Europe 1992-98; Empire of the Senses; Original English Language Fiction
*U.S. Office(s):* Subterranean Co, 265 S Fifth St, Monroe, OR 97651, United States
Distributed by Central Books
Foreign Rep(s): Richard D Bowen (Scandinavia); Michael Geoghegan (Austria, Belgium, Netherlands, France, Germany, Switzerland); Marginal Distribution (Canada); Penny Padovani (Greece, Italy, Portugal, Spain); Peribo Pty Ltd (Australia, New Zealand); SCB Disributors (US)

**Dedalus Nobel Prize Winner**, *imprint of* Dedalus Ltd

**Defiant Publications**
190 Yoxall Rd, Shirley, Solihull, West Midlands B90 3RN
*Tel:* (0121) 745 8421
*E-mail:* info@defiantpublications.co.uk
*Key Personnel*
Proprietor: Peter B Hands
Founded: 1980
Subjects: Humor, Transportation
ISBN Prefix(es): 0-946857

**Delancey Press Ltd+**
4 Delancey Passage, London NW1 7NN
*Tel:* (020) 7387 3544 *Fax:* (020) 8383 5314
*E-mail:* delanceypress@aol.com
*Web Site:* www.delanceypress.com
*Key Personnel*
Man Dir: Tatiana Wilson
Subjects: Fiction, Humor
ISBN Prefix(es): 0-9539119
Number of titles published annually: 2 Print
Total Titles: 4 Print
Distributed by The Book Guild Ltd
*Orders to:* Vine House Distribution

**Delectation**, *imprint of* Delectus Books

**Delectus Books+**
27 Old Gloucester St, London WC1N 3XX
*Tel:* (020) 8963 0979 *Fax:* (020) 8963 0502
*Web Site:* abebooks.com/home/delectus; www. delectusbooks.co.uk
*Key Personnel*
Publisher: Michael R Goss *E-mail:* mgdelectus@ aol.com
Founded: 1988
Subjects: Anthropology, Criminology, Erotica, Gay & Lesbian, Psychology, Psychiatry, Dada, Decadence, Drugs & Alcohol, Ethnology, Fantasy, Folklore, Gothic & Horror, Occult & Witchcraft, Psychoanalysis, Scotland & Ireland, Sexology, Surrealism, Symbolists & the 1890's, True Crime, Vampires & Werewolves
ISBN Prefix(es): 1-897767
Number of titles published annually: 3 Print
Total Titles: 15 Print
Imprints: Delectation
Distributed by Marginal (Canada); Peribo (Australia & New Zealand); Turnaround (UK & Europe)

*Orders to:* Last Gasp of San Francisco, 777 Florida St, San Francisco, CA 94100, United States, Contact: Erick Gilbert *Tel:* 415-824-6636 *E-mail:* gasp@lastgasp.com

**Delta Books (Pty) Ltd+**
Imprint of Jonathan Ball Publishers (Pty) Ltd
Clarendon House, 52 Cornmarket St, Oxford OX1 3HJ
Mailing Address: PO Box 33977, Jeppestown 2043, South Africa
*Tel:* (01865) 304059 *Fax:* (01865) 304035
*E-mail:* mail@premierbookmarketing.com
*Key Personnel*
Publishing & Permissions: Francine Blum
   *E-mail:* fplum@jonathanball.co.za
Marketing: Eugene Ashton
Sales: Alastair Steyn
Founded: 1980
Subjects: Nonfiction (General), General South African
ISBN Prefix(es): 0-908387
*Parent Company:* Nasionale Boekhandel
*Ultimate Parent Company:* Nasionale Pers
*Associate Companies:* Ad Donker (Pty) Ltd
*Warehouse:* Jonathan Ball Publishers, 10-14 Watkins St, Denver Ext 4, Johannesburg 2094, South Africa

**Denor Press+**
PO Box 12913, London N12 0NP
*Tel:* (020) 8343 7368 *Fax:* (020) 8446 4504
*E-mail:* denor@dial.pipex.com
*Web Site:* www.xhf37.dial.pipex.com
*Key Personnel*
Rights Dir: Brendan Beder
Promotion & Marketing Executive: Elizabeth Plumstead
Founded: 1997
Also provides promotion & marketing services.
Membership(s): Publishers' Association.
Subjects: Fiction, Health, Nutrition, Medicine, Nursing, Dentistry, Music, Dance, Nonfiction (General)
ISBN Prefix(es): 0-9526056
Total Titles: 4 Print; 4 Online; 4 E-Book
*Ultimate Parent Company:* Denor Press

**Andre Deutsch Children's Books**, *imprint of* Scholastic Ltd

**Andre Deutsch Ltd+**
20 Mortimer St, London W1N 7RD
*Tel:* (020) 7612 0400 *Fax:* (020) 7612 0401
*Web Site:* www.carlton.com
Founded: 1951
Subjects: Art, Biography, Government, Political Science, History, Humor, Music, Dance, Photography, Sports, Athletics, Travel
ISBN Prefix(es): 0-233; 1-85375 (Prion)
*Parent Company:* Carlton Books Ltd
Imprints: Prion
*Warehouse:* HarperCollins Publishers, PO Box, Glasgow G4 0NB *Tel:* (0141) 306 3100 *Fax:* (0141) 306 3767

**Diagram Visual Information Ltd+**
195 Kentish Town Rd, London NW5 2JU
*Tel:* (020) 7482 3633 *Fax:* (020) 7482 4932
*E-mail:* diagramvis@aol.com
*Key Personnel*
Dir & International Rights: Bruce Robertson
Founded: 1967
Book designer & creator.
Subjects: Art, Crafts, Games, Hobbies
ISBN Prefix(es): 1-900121
Number of titles published annually: 10 Print
Total Titles: 400 Print

**Dial House**, *imprint of* Ian Allan Publishing

**Dickson Price Publishers Ltd**
Unit 9 The Shipyard, Upper Brents, Faversham
ME13 7DZ
*Tel:* (01795) 597800 *Fax:* (01795) 597800
*Key Personnel*
Man Dir, Editorial, Rights & Permissions: Mr K
E Dickson
Production: D S Wanstall
Founded: 1980
Subjects: Computer Science, Electronics, Electrical Engineering
ISBN Prefix(es): 0-85380

**Digital Photoart**, *imprint of* Creative
Monochrome Ltd

**Digital Press**, *imprint of* Elsevier Ltd

**DIME**, *imprint of* Tarquin Publications

**Dinas**, *imprint of* Y Lolfa Cyf

**Discovers**, *imprint of* Moonlight Publishing Ltd

**Discovery Walking Guides Ltd+**
10 Tennyson Close, Dallington, Northampton
NN5 7HJ
*Tel:* (01604) 244869 *Fax:* (01604) 752576
*Web Site:* www.walking.demon.co.uk
*Key Personnel*
Company Secretary: David Brawn
Contact: Ros Brawn
Founded: 1993
Specialize in walking guides, botanical guides,
tour & trail maps.
Membership(s): IPG.
Subjects: Gardening, Plants, Travel
ISBN Prefix(es): 1-899554
Number of titles published annually: 8 Print
Total Titles: 45 Print
Imprints: Tour & Trail Maps; Warm Island Walking Guides
*Distribution Center:* Gardners Books, One Whittle Drive, Eastbourne BN23 6QH *Tel:* (01323)
521555 *Fax:* (01323) 525509

**Disney**, *imprint of* Ladybird Books Ltd

**DIY Publishing**
PO Box 35488, St Johns Wood, London NW8
6WD
*Tel:* (020) 7586 4499 *Fax:* (020) 7722 1068
*E-mail:* info@diypublishing.com
*Web Site:* www.diypublishing.com
Service for authors to publish & sell their publications online.
*Associate Companies:* World Microfilms Publications Ltd

**DMG Business Media Ltd**
Queensway House, 2 Queensway, Redhill, Surrey
RH1 1QS
*Tel:* (01737) 768611 *Fax:* (01737) 855477
*Web Site:* www.dmg.co.uk
*Key Personnel*
Managing Dir: Paul Camp
Subscriptions Mgr: Ben Martin *E-mail:* bmartin@
dmg.co.uk
Subjects: Chemistry, Chemical Engineering, Civil
Engineering, Communications, Engineering
(General), Maritime, Publishing & Book Trade
Reference, Radio, TV, Securities, Transportation
*Parent Company:* DMG World Media
*Associate Companies:* DMG Exhibition Group

**Dobro Publishing**
52 Howcroft Crescent, Finchley, London N3 1PB
*Tel:* (020) 8346 4010

*E-mail:* dobropublishing@aol.com
*Web Site:* www.drsandradelroy.com
*Key Personnel*
Contact: Dr Sandra Delroy
*E-mail:* psychologist@drsandradelroy.com
Subjects: Health, Nutrition, Medicine, Nursing,
Dentistry, Psychology, Psychiatry
ISBN Prefix(es): 0-9527520

**The Dolmen Press Ltd**, see Colin Smythe Ltd

**Dolphin Paperbacks**, *imprint of* Orion Children's
Books

**John Donald Publishers Ltd**, *imprint of* Birlinn
Ltd

**John Donald Publishers Ltd+**
Imprint of Birlinn Ltd
West Newington House, 10 Newington Rd, Edinburgh EH9 1QS
*Tel:* (0131) 668 4371 *Fax:* (0131) 668 4466
*E-mail:* info@birlinn.co.uk
*Web Site:* www.birlinn.co.uk
*Key Personnel*
Man Dir: Hugh Andrew
Founded: 1973
Subjects: History, Regional Interests, Sports, Athletics, Travel
ISBN Prefix(es): 0-85976
Number of titles published annually: 40 Print
Total Titles: 170 Print
*Warehouse:* Book Source, 32 Finlas St, Cowlairs
Estate, Glasgow 922 SDU *Tel:* (0870) 240
2182 *Fax:* (0141) 557 0189
*Orders to:* Book Source, 32 Finlas St, Cowlairs
Estate, Glasgow 922 SDU, Contact: Gerry
McLean *Tel:* (0870) 240 2182 *Fax:* (0141) 557
0189 *E-mail:* orders@booksource.net

**Donhead Publishing Ltd**
Lower Coombe, Donhead St Mary, Shaftesbury,
Dorset SP7 9LY
*Tel:* (01747) 828422 *Fax:* (01747) 828522
*E-mail:* sales@donhead.com
*Web Site:* www.donhead.com
*Key Personnel*
Dir: Jill Pearce
Founded: 1992
Membership(s): IPG.
Subjects: Architecture & Interior Design, Architectural & Building Conservation, Heritage &
Landscapes
ISBN Prefix(es): 1-873394
Number of titles published annually: 7 Print
Total Titles: 50 Print
*Branch Office(s)*
PRG Inc, PO Box 1768, Rockville, MD 20849,
United States (North America only)

**Dorling Kindersley Ltd+**
80 Strand, London WC2R OLR
*Tel:* (020) 7010 3000 *Fax:* (020) 7010 6060
*E-mail:* customer.service@dk.com
*Web Site:* www.dk.com
*Key Personnel*
Chairman: Peter Kindersley
Deputy Chairman: Christopher Davis
International Sales Dir: Ruth Sandys
Group Sales & Marketing Dir: David Holmes
Man Dir, Multi-Media: Alan Buckingham
Production Dir: Martyn Longly
International Sales (Adults): Michael Devenish
Chief Exec: James Middlehurst
Founded: 1974
Subjects: Art, Child Care & Development, Cookery, Crafts, Games, Hobbies, Gardening, Plants,
Health, Nutrition, History, House & Home,
Music, Dance, Nonfiction (General), Photography, Self-Help, Sports, Athletics, Wine &
Spirits

ISBN Prefix(es): 0-7894; 0-86318; 0-7513; 0-
7547; 1-4053
Subsidiaries: DKP Inc; DK Family Library
*Branch Office(s)*
DK Australia & New Zealand
DK Canada
DK France
DK Germany
DK Russia
DK South Africa
*U.S. Office(s):* DK Family Library Inc, 7566
Southland Executive Park, Orlando, FL 32809,
United States
Dorling Kindersley Publishing Inc, 375 Hudson St, New York, NY 10014, United States
*Tel:* 212-213-4800 *Fax:* 212-213-5240
Distributed by Penguin Books
*Bookshop(s):* 10-13 Knox St WC2E 8HN
*Warehouse:* International Book Distributors Ltd,
Magna Park, Coventry Rd, Butterworth, Leics
LE17 4XH

**Doubleday**, *imprint of* Transworld Publishers Ltd

**Alton Douglas Books**, *imprint of* Brewin Books
Ltd

**Drake Educational Associates Ltd+**
Saint Fagans Road, Fairwater, Cardiff CF5 3AE
*Tel:* (029) 2056 0333 *Fax:* (029) 2056 0313
*E-mail:* info@drakeav.com
*Web Site:* www.drakegroup.co.uk
*Key Personnel*
Man Dir: Mr R G Drake
Founded: 1970
Specialize in literacy & languages.
Subjects: Disability, Special Needs, Education
ISBN Prefix(es): 0-86174
*Parent Company:* Drake Group
Distributor for Highsmith Press (USA); Pembroke
Publishers (Canada)

**Dramatic Lines Publishers+**
PO Box 201, Twickenham, Middx TW2 5RQ
*Tel:* (020) 8296 9502 *Fax:* (020) 8296 9503
*E-mail:* mail@dramaticlinespublishers.co.uk
*Web Site:* www.dramaticlines.co.uk
*Key Personnel*
Managing Editor: John Nicholas
Founded: 1994
Drama publisher.
Membership(s): Publishers' Association.
Subjects: Drama, Theater, Education
ISBN Prefix(es): 0-9522224; 0-9537770; 1-
9045571
Number of titles published annually: 6 Print

**Dref Wen**, *imprint of* Gwasg y Dref Wen

**Duck Editions**, *imprint of* Gerald Duckworth &
Co Ltd

**Gerald Duckworth & Co Ltd+**
90-93 Cowcross St, London EC1M 6BF
*Tel:* (020) 7490 7300 *Fax:* (020) 7490 0080
*E-mail:* info@duckworth-publishers.co.uk
*Web Site:* www.ducknet.co.uk
*Key Personnel*
Man Dir: Peter Mayer
Founded: 1898
Specialize in Greek & Latin classics.
Subjects: Fiction, Language Arts, Linguistics, Literature, Literary Criticism, Essays, Maritime,
Nonfiction (General), Philosophy, Psychology,
Psychiatry, Religion - Other, Science (General),
Classics, Linguistics
ISBN Prefix(es): 0-7156; 1-85399; 0-8629
Number of titles published annually: 300 Print
Total Titles: 1,500 Print
Imprints: BCP; Duck Editions

Subsidiaries: Bristol Classical Press
*Warehouse:* Book Sellers International, PO
Box 605, Herndon, VA 20172, United States
*Tel:* 703-434-7064

**Duke University Press**, *imprint of* Combined
Academic Publishers

**Dun & Bradstreet Ltd**, see D&B Ltd

**Dunedin Academic Press+**
Hudson House, 8 Albany St, Edinburgh EH1
3QB
*Tel:* (0131) 473 2397 *Fax:* (01250) 870920
*E-mail:* mail@dunedinacademicpress.co.uk
*Web Site:* www.dunedinacademicpress.co.uk
*Key Personnel*
Dir: Anthony Kinahan *E-mail:* anthony@
dunedinacademicpress.co.uk
Founded: 2000
Membership(s): Scottish Publishers Association.
Subjects: Anthropology, Earth Sciences, Eco-
nomics, Education, Geography, Geology, Gov-
ernment, Political Science, History, Law, Phi-
losophy, Social Sciences, Sociology, Theology
ISBN Prefix(es): 1-903765
Number of titles published annually: 12 Print
Total Titlcs: 30 Print
Foreign Rep(s): Brookside (Ireland); Dar Kreidieh
(Middle East exc Israel); Inbooks (Australia,
Fiji, New Zealand, Papua New Guinea); Inter-
national Specialized Book Services (Canada,
US)

**Gwasg Dwyfor**
Canolfan Sain, Llandwrog, Caernarfon, Gwynedd
LL54 5TG
*Tel:* (01286) 831111 *Fax:* (01286) 831497
*E-mail:* argraff@gwasgdwyfor.demon.co.uk
*Key Personnel*
Partner: J A Ellis; Dafydd Owen; M P Roberts
Founded: 1981
Subjects: Nonfiction (General)
ISBN Prefix(es): 1-870394

**Eagle/Inter Publishing Service (IPS) Ltd+**
6-7 Leapale Rd, Guildford, Surrey GU1 4JX
*Tel:* (01483) 306309 *Fax:* (01483) 579196
*E-mail:* eagle_indeprint@compuserve.com
*Key Personnel*
Man Dir: David Wavre
Editorial Manager: Lynne Barratt
Production Dir: James Ralton
Founded: 1990
Subjects: Religion - Catholic, Religion - Protes-
tant, Religion - Other
ISBN Prefix(es): 0-86347
*Orders to:* STL, Kingstown Broadway, PO Box
300, Carlisle CA3 0QS

**Eaglemoss Publications Ltd+**
5 Cromwell Rd, London SW7 2HR
*Tel:* (020) 7590 8300 *Fax:* (020) 7590 8301
*E-mail:* genenq@eaglemoss.co.uk
*Web Site:* www.eaglemoss.co.uk
*Key Personnel*
Chief Executive: Mark Stanley
Dir: E B Hilton
Commercial Dir: J D Sibley
Financial Dir: S P Rose
Editorial Dir: Maggie Calmels
Marketing Dir: Suzie Deeming
Trade Enquiries: Gary Neale *E-mail:* garyneale@
eaglemoss.co.uk
Founded: 1979
Specialize in publication of Partworks.
Subjects: Art, Computer Science, Cookery, Crafts,
Games, Hobbies, Criminology, Outdoor Recre-
ation, Photography, Sports, Athletics, Trans-
portation

ISBN Prefix(es): 0-947837; 1-85167; 1-85629; 1-
85875
*Branch Office(s)*
Australia
Malaysia
New Zealand
Singapore
South Africa

**EAL**, *imprint of* Training Publications Ltd

**Earthlink**, *imprint of* Simon & Schuster Ltd

**Earthscan**, *imprint of* Earthscan /James & James
(Science Publishers) Ltd

**Earthscan /James & James (Science
Publishers) Ltd+**
8-12 Camden High St, London NW1 0JH
*Tel:* (020) 7387 8558 *Fax:* (020) 7387 8998
*E-mail:* jxj@jxj.com
*Web Site:* www.jxj.com
*Key Personnel*
Publisher: Edward Milford *E-mail:* em@jxj.com
Founded: 1990
Subjects: Agriculture, Archaeology, Architecture
& Interior Design, Civil Engineering, Devel-
oping Countries, Earth Sciences, Economics,
Electronics, Electrical Engineering, Energy, En-
vironmental Studies, Geography, Geology, Gov-
ernment, Political Science, Science (General),
Social Sciences, Sociology
ISBN Prefix(es): 1-85383; 0-907383; 1-873936;
1-902916; 1-84407
Total Titles: 70 Print
Imprints: Earthscan
*U.S. Office(s):* Stylus Publishing LLC, 22883
Quicksilver Drive, Sterling, VA 20166, United
States *Tel:* 703-661-1581 *Fax:* 703-661-1501
*E-mail:* styluspub@aol.com
Distributed by A & I Ltd

**Earthscan Publications Ltd+**
8-12 Camden High St, London NW1 0JH
*Tel:* (020) 7387 8558 *Fax:* (020) 7387 8998
*E-mail:* earthinfo@earthscan.co.uk
*Web Site:* www.earthscan.co.uk
*Key Personnel*
Chief Executive: Jonathan Sinclair-Wilson
Sales Dir for Kogan Page: Julie McNair
Editorial: Frances McDermott
Production: Peter Chadwick
Publicity: Jeannette Hurdle
Marketing Issues/Bulk Orders: Helen Rose
*E-mail:* hrose@earthscan.co.uk
Press/PR Enquiries: Martha Fumagalli
*E-mail:* mfumagalli@kogan-page.co.uk
Press Review Copies: Helen Engstrand
*E-mail:* engstrand@kogan-page.co.uk
Academic Inspection Copy Inquiries: Anna Mur-
phy *E-mail:* amurphy@kogan-copy.co.uk
Founded: 1988
Subjects: Developing Countries, Environmental
Studies
ISBN Prefix(es): 1-85383; 1-84407
*Parent Company:* Kogan Page Ltd, London
*U.S. Office(s):* Kogan Page, 163 Central Ave,
Suite 2, Hopkins Professional Bldg, Dover, NH
03820, United States
Distributed by Island Press (USA)
Distributor for Island Press (outside North Amer-
ica)

**East-West Publications (UK) Ltd+**
2 Regent's Court King's Rd, Burnham-on-Crouch
CM0 8PP
*Tel:* (01621) 782466 *Fax:* (01621) 782466
*Key Personnel*
Chairman: L W Carp
Founded: 1976
Subjects: Music, Dance, Religion - Other

ISBN Prefix(es): 0-85692; 1-872571
*Associate Companies:* Cromwell Book Services
Ltd
Imprints: Britannia Press; Gallery Children's
Books
*Warehouse:* East-West & Britannia, TBS, Frating
Distribution Centre, Frating Green, Colchester
CO7 7DW
Gallery: The Trade Counter, The Airfield, Nor-
wich Rd, Mendlesham IP14 5NA

**Eastland Press**, *imprint of* Terence Dalton Ltd

**Ebury**, *imprint of* Random House UK Ltd

**Ecco**, *imprint of* HarperCollins UK

**Eclipse**, *imprint of* Butterworths Tolley

**The Economist Books**
58A Hatton Garden, London EC1N 8LX
*Tel:* (020) 7404 3001 *Fax:* (020) 7404 3003
*E-mail:* info@profilebooks.co.uk

**The Economist Intelligence Unit+**
15 Regent St, London SW1Y 4LR
*Tel:* (020) 7830 1007 *Fax:* (020) 7830 1023
*E-mail:* london@eiu.com
*Web Site:* www.eiu.com
*Telex:* 266353 *Cable:* EIUG
*Key Personnel*
Man Dir: Nigel Ludlow
Editorial Dir: Daniel Franklin
Founded: 1954
Subjects: Automotive, Business, Developing
Countries, Economics, Finance, Management,
Travel
ISBN Prefix(es): 0-85058; 0-86218; 0-900351
*Parent Company:* The Economist Group
*Branch Office(s)*
60/F Central Plaza, 18 Harbour Rd, Wan-
chai, Hong Kong *Tel:* 2802 7288;
2585 3888 *Fax:* 2802 7638; 2802 7720
*E-mail:* hongkong@eiu.com
Postbus 1254, 1300 BG Almere, Netherlands
*Tel:* (036) 530 0749 *Fax:* (036) 530 1227
*E-mail:* cmf@eiu.com
No 23-01 PWC Bldg, No 8 Cross St 048424,
Singapore *Tel:* 534 5177 *Fax:* 534 5077
*E-mail:* soniayao@eiu.com
*U.S. Office(s):* The Economist Bldg, 111 W
57th St, New York, NY 10019, United States
*Tel:* 212-698-9745 *Fax:* 212-586-1181; 212-
586-1182 *E-mail:* newyork@eiu.com
Foreign Rep(s): Agencia Estado Ltda (Brazil);
Albertina icome Praha (Czech Republic, Slo-
vak Republic); Alex Centre for Multimedia
& Libraries (ACML) (Egypt); Bharat Book
Bureau (India); Business Italy srl (Italy); e-
Tech Solutions de Colombia Ltda (Colombia);
e-Tech Solutions de Ecuador SA (Ecuador);
Edutech Middle East (Gulf States, United Arab
Emirates); Viktor Herman (Bulgaria, Croatia,
Macedonia, Romania, Serbia and Montene-
gro, Slovenia, Bosnia and Herzegovina); IMA
(India Pvt) Ltd (India); INFOESTRATEGICA
(Mexico); InterOPTICS AEE (Cyprus, Greece);
Dariusz Kuzminski (Poland, Ukraine); Latin
Knowledge Consulting (Venezuela); Wanju Lee
(South Korea); Quantec Research (Pty) Ltd
(South Africa); Rayden Research Ltd (Japan);
Rose Systems (CIS, Jordan, Iran, Syria); Sita
International Information Services (India); Tai-
wan Asia Strategy Consulting (Taiwan); THAI-
DTR Co Ltd (Thailand)
*Bookshop(s):* The Economist Bookshop, 25 St
James St, London SW1A 1HG
*Warehouse:* PO Box 200, Harold Hill, Romford
RM3 8UX

**Eddison Sadd Editions Ltd+**
St Chads House, 148 King's Cross Rd, London
WC1X 9DH
*Tel:* (020) 7837 1968 *Fax:* (020) 7837 6844
*E-mail:* reception@eddisonsadd.co.uk
*Web Site:* www.eddisonsadd.co.uk
*Key Personnel*
Man Dir: Nick Eddison
Editorial Dir: Ian Jackson
Founded: 1982
Packagers of international co-editions.
Subjects: Nonfiction (General), Illustrated Books,
Kits
*Associate Companies:* Connections Book Publishing
Imprints: Connections


**Edinburgh City Libraries**
7-9, George IV Bridge, Edinburgh EH1 1EG
*Tel:* (0131) 242 8000 *Fax:* (0131) 242 8009
*E-mail:* elis@cityedin.demon.co.uk
*Web Site:* www.edinburgh.gov.uk/libraries
ISBN Prefix(es): 0-900353


**Edinburgh Project on Extensive Reading**, see
EPER


**Edinburgh University Press Ltd+**
22 George Sq, Edinburgh EH8 9LF
*Tel:* (0131) 650 4223
*E-mail:* marketing@eup.ed.ac.uk; journals@eup.
ed.ac.uk (Orders)
*Web Site:* www.eup.ed.ac.uk
*Key Personnel*
Non-Executive Chair: Tim Rix *E-mail:* tim.rix@
eup.ed.ac.uk
Man Dir, Sales & Marketing Dir: Timothy Wright
*E-mail:* timothy.wright@eup.ed.ac.uk
Deputy Man Dir & Editorial Dir: Jackie Jones
*Tel:* (0131) 6504217 *E-mail:* jackie.jones@eup.
ed.ac.uk
Rights Manager: Alison Bowden *E-mail:* alison.
bowden@eup.ed.ac.uk
Production Manager: Ian Davidson *E-mail:* ian.
davidson@eup.ed.ac.uk
Finance Manager: Jan Thomson *E-mail:* jan.
thomson@eup.ed.ac.uk
Senior Commissioning Editor: Nicola Carr
*E-mail:* nicola.carr@eup.ed.ac.uk
Commissioning Editor: Sarah Edwards
*E-mail:* sarah.edwards@eup.ed.ac.uk
Consultant Editor: John Davey
*E-mail:* jcadavey@btinternet.com
Associate Editor: Roda Morrison *E-mail:* roda.
morrison@eup.ed.ac.uk
Managing Desk Editor: Eddie Clark
*E-mail:* edward.clark@eup.ed.ac.uk; James
Dale *E-mail:* james.dale@eup.ed.ac.uk
Marketing Manager: Charlotte Maxwell
*E-mail:* charlotte.maxwell@eup.ed.ac.uk;
Douglas McNaughton *E-mail:* douglas.
mcnaughton@eup.ed.ac.uk
Sales Administrator: Anna Skinner *E-mail:* anna.
skinner@eup.ed.ac.uk
Founded: 1948
Subjects: Anthropology, Archaeology, Architecture & Interior Design, Art, Computer Science,
Economics, Education, Environmental Studies,
Film, Video, Government, Political Science,
History, Literature, Literary Criticism, Essays,
Music, Dance, Natural History, Philosophy,
Public Administration, Religion - Islamic, Science (General), Social Sciences, Sociology,
Theology, Women's Studies
ISBN Prefix(es): 0-85224; 0-7486
*Parent Company:* The University of Edinburgh
Distributed by Columbia University Press (USA
& Canada)

*Warehouse:* Marston Book Services, PO Box
269, Abingdon, Oxon OX14 4YN *Tel:* (01235)
465500
*Orders to:* Marston Book Services, PO Box 269,
Abingdon, Oxon OX14 4YN *Tel:* (01235)
465500 *Fax:* (01235) 465556


**Edition XII**
23 Arundel Gardens, London W11 2LW
Mailing Address: 10 Regents Wharf, 4th floor,
All Saints St, London N1 9RL
*Tel:* (020) 7229 6471; (020) 7833 0120
*Fax:* (020) 7229 5239; (020) 7923 5500; (020)
7923 5505
*E-mail:* info@editionxii.co.uk
*Web Site:* www.editionxii.co.uk
*Key Personnel*
Man Dir: Edward More O'Ferrall
Marketing Manager: Simon Klemba
Specialize in academic publications.
Subjects: Business, Computer Science, Economics, Education, Engineering (General),
Law, Social Sciences, Sociology
ISBN Prefix(es): 1-86149; 0-9520105; 1-899522
*Parent Company:* Lime House Media Group Ltd,
The Lime House, Unit 2, Chase Side Works,
Chelmsford Rd, Southgate, London N16 4JN
*Orders to:* Mike Sirott, 3691 S 3200 W, West
Valley, UT 84119, United States
Baker & Taylor Books, 44 Kirby Ave,
Somerville, NJ 08876, United States


**Educational Explorers (Publishers) Ltd**
11 Crown St, Reading, Berks RG1 2TQ
Mailing Address: PO Box 3391, Winnersh, Wokingham RG41 5ZD
*Tel:* (0118) 987 3101 *Fax:* (0118) 987 3103
*E-mail:* explorers@cuisenaire.co.uk
*Web Site:* www.cuisenaire.co.uk
*Key Personnel*
Chairman: D M Gattegno
Man Dir: M J Hollyfield *E-mail:* hollyfield@
cuisenaire.co.uk
Founded: 1960
Subjects: Language Arts, Linguistics, Mathematics, Psychology, Psychiatry
ISBN Prefix(es): 0-85225
*Parent Company:* Educational Solutions (UK) Ltd
of Reading
*Associate Companies:* Cuisenaire Co, 11 Crown
St, Reading, Berks RG1 2TQ; Educational Explorers Film Co, 11 Crown St, Reading, Berks
RG1 2TQ; Educational Solutions Inc, 99 University Pl, New York, NY 10003-4555, United
States


**EITB**, *imprint of* Training Publications Ltd


**Eland Publishing Ltd**
61 Exmouth Market, 3rd floor, London EC1R
4QL
*Tel:* (020) 7833 0762 *Fax:* (020) 7833 4434
*E-mail:* info@travelbooks.co.uk
*Web Site:* www.travelbooks.co.uk
*Key Personnel*
Dir: Rose Baring
Subjects: Biography, Fiction, Travel
ISBN Prefix(es): 0-907871
Imprints: Sickle Moon Books
*Warehouse:* Grantham Book Services, Isaac
Newton Way, Alma Park Industrial Estate,
Grantham, Lincs NG31 9SD
*Orders to:* Grantham Book Services, Isaac
Newton Way, Alma Park Industrial Estate,
Grantham, Lincs NG31 9SD


**ELC International**
5 Five Mile Drive, Oxford OX2 8HT
*Tel:* (01865) 513186; (01865) 26520284
*Fax:* (01865) 513186; (01865) 26530180
*E-mail:* snyderpub@aol.com

**Electronic Publishing Services Ltd (EPS)**
26 Rosebery Ave, London EC1R 4SX
*Tel:* (020) 7837 3345 *Fax:* (020) 7837 8901
*E-mail:* eps@epsltd.com
*Web Site:* www.epsltd.com
*Key Personnel*
Chairman: David R Worlock
Dir: David J Powell
Founded: 1985
Research & consultancy company which specializes in electronic publishing strategy development & high-level market research.
Membership(s): The UK Publishers Association.
Subjects: Library & Information Sciences, Publishing & Book Trade Reference
ISBN Prefix(es): 0-9517344
Total Titles: 10 Print


**Element Books Ltd+**
Old School House, The Courtyard, Bell St,
Shaftesbury, Dorset SP7 8BP
*Tel:* (01747) 851448 *Fax:* (01747) 855721
*Key Personnel*
Chairman: Michael Mann
Chief Executive: David Alexander
Man Dir: Julia McCutchen
Sales: Penny Stopa
Publicity: Jenny Carradice
Production Dir: Roger Lane *E-mail:* roger_lane@
iconex.mactel.org
Founded: 1978
Subjects: Art, Astrology, Occult, Biography, Environmental Studies, Health, Nutrition, Literature,
Literary Criticism, Essays, Management, Music, Dance, Philosophy, Psychology, Psychiatry,
Religion - Other, Science (General), Self-Help,
Travel, Women's Studies, Feminist Studies, Zen
ISBN Prefix(es): 1-85230; 1-86204; 0-906540
*U.S. Office(s):* Element Books Inc, 21 Broadway,
Rockport, MA 01966, United States *Tel:* 508-
546-1040
Distributed by India Book Distributors (Bombay)
Ltd; India Book House Pvt Ltd; TBI Publishers' Distributors
*Orders to:* Penguin Books Ltd, Bath Rd, Harmondsworth, West Drayton, Middlesex UB7
0DA *Tel:* (0181) 8994000 *Fax:* (0181) 8994099


**11:9**, *imprint of* Neil Wilson Publishing Ltd


**Elfande Ltd+**
Surrey House, 31 Church St, Leatherhead, Surrey
KT22 7HX
*Tel:* (01372) 220330 *Fax:* (01372) 220340
*E-mail:* sales@contact-uk.com
*Web Site:* www.contact-uk.com
*Key Personnel*
Man Dir: Nick Gould
Administration: Sarah Williams
Founded: 1985
Publish annual image source books in Europe.
Subjects: Architecture & Interior Design, Art,
Photography
ISBN Prefix(es): 1-870458
Number of titles published annually: 6 Print; 3
CD-ROM
Total Titles: 6 Print; 3 CD-ROM; 3 E-Book
*U.S. Office(s):* Tonal Values, 133 N Montclair
Ave, Dallas, TX, United States, Contact: Jill
Peterson *Tel:* 214-943-2569 *Fax:* 214-942-6771
*E-mail:* info@tonalvalues.com


**Edward Elgar Publishing Ltd**
Glensanda House, Montpellier Parade, Cheltenham, Glos GL50 1UA
*Tel:* (01242) 226934 *Fax:* (01242) 262111
*E-mail:* info@e-elgar.co.uk
*Web Site:* www.e-elgar.co.uk
*Key Personnel*
Man Dir: Edward Elgar *E-mail:* edward@e-elgar.
co.uk
Sales & Marketing Manager: Hilary Quinn

Contact: Sandy Elgar *E-mail:* sandy@e-elgar.co.uk
Founded: 1986
A privately owned scholarly publisher with a focus on economics.
Subjects: Business, Developing Countries, Economics, Economics, Environmental Studies, Finance, Government, Political Science, Labor, Industrial Relations
ISBN Prefix(es): 1-85898; 1-85278; 1-84064; 1-84376
Number of titles published annually: 250 Print
Total Titles: 1,360 Print
*U.S. Office(s):* Edward Elgar Publishing Inc, Northhampton, MA 01060, United States, Contact: Rick Henning *Tel:* 413-584-5551 *Fax:* 413-584-9933 *E-mail:* rhenning@e-elgar.com
*Orders to:* DA Book Information Services, 648 Whitehorse Rd, Mitcham, Victoria 3132, Australia *Tel:* (03) 9210 7777 *Fax:* (03) 9210 7788 *E-mail:* Service@dadirect.com.au
Edward Elgar Publishing Inc, 2 Winter Sport Lane, PO Box 574, Williston, VT 05495-0575, United States *Fax:* 802-864-7626 *E-mail:* rhenning@e-elgar.com
Marston Book Services, PO Box 269, Abingdon, Oxon OX14 4YN *Tel:* (01235) 465500 *Fax:* (01235) 465555 *E-mail:* trade@marston.co.uk
Taylor & Francis Asia Pacific, Pines Industrial Bldg, 240 Macpherson Rd 348574, Singapore, Man Dir: Barry Clarke *Tel:* 741 5166 *Fax:* 742 9356 *E-mail:* info@tandf.com.sg
United Publishers Services Ltd, Kenkyu-Sha Bldg, 9 Kanda Surugadai 2-Chome, Chiyoda-Ku, Tokyo, Japan *Tel:* (03) 3291 4541 *Fax:* (03) 3292 8610

**Elkin**, *imprint of* Novello & Co Ltd

**Elliot Right Way Books+**
Kingswood Bldgs, Brighton Rd, Lower Kingswood, Tadworth, Surrey KT20 6TD
*Tel:* (01737) 832202 *Fax:* (01737) 830311
*E-mail:* info@right-way.co.uk
*Web Site:* www.right-way.co.uk
*Key Personnel*
Dir: A Clive Elliot; Malcolm G Elliot
Editor: Judith Mitchell
Founded: 1945 (by Andrew George Elliot, father of the present owners)
Independent Book Publisher.
Subjects: Animals, Pets, Business, Career Development, Cookery, Crafts, Games, Hobbies, Finance, Genealogy, Health, Nutrition, House & Home, How-to, Humor, Self-Help, Sports, Athletics, Transportation, Drawing, Driving, Family Reference, Fishing, Hobbies, Horses, Pets, Public & Social Speaking, Quizzes
ISBN Prefix(es): 0-7160; 1-899606
Number of titles published annually: 20 Print
Total Titles: 120 Print
*Ultimate Parent Company:* Andrew Elliot & Sons Ltd
Imprints: Clarion (Bargain Books); Right Way Books
Foreign Rep(s): Hushion House Publishing Ltd (Canada); Peribo (Australia); Theo Phillips (CKK Ltd) (Asia); Kelvin Van Hasselt (Africa, Caribbean); Peter Ward (Middle East)

**Elliott & Thompson+**
27 John St, London WC1N 2BX
*Tel:* (020) 7831 5013 *Fax:* (020) 7831 5011
*E-mail:* gmo73@dial.pipex.com
*Web Site:* elliottthompson.com
*Key Personnel*
Dir: David Elliott; Brad Thompson
Founded: 2001
Literary works & belles lettres.

Subjects: Art, Biography, History, Humor, Religion - Islamic, Religion - Jewish, Western Fiction
ISBN Prefix(es): 1-904027
Number of titles published annually: 18 Print
Total Titles: 35 Print
Imprints: Elliott & Thompson Gold Editions; Spitfire; Spitfire Originals; Young Spitfire
Foreign Rep(s): BookWorld (US)

**Elliott & Thompson Gold Editions**, *imprint of* Elliott & Thompson

**Aidan Ellis Publishing+**
Whinfield, Herbert Rd, Salcombe, South Devon TQ8 8HN
*Tel:* (01548) 842755
*E-mail:* mail@aidanellispublishing.co.uk
*Web Site:* www.demon.co.uk/aepub
*Key Personnel*
Partner: Aidan Ellis; Lucinda Ellis
Founded: 1971
Subjects: Art, Biography, Gardening, Plants, Literature, Literary Criticism, Essays, Maritime, Natural History, Nonfiction (General)
ISBN Prefix(es): 0-85628
Total Titles: 50 Print
Foreign Rep(s): Keith Ainsworth Pty Ltd (Australia, New Zealand)
*Orders to:* Orca Book Services, 3 Fleets Lane, Poole, Dorset BH15 3AJ *Tel:* (01202) 665 432 *Fax:* (01202) 666 219 *E-mail:* orders@orcabookservices.co.uk

**Elm Publications+**
Seaton House, Kings Ripton, Huntingdon, Cambs PE28 2NJ
*Tel:* (01487) 773254; (01487) 773238
*E-mail:* elm@elm-training.co.uk
*Web Site:* www.elm-training.co.uk
*Key Personnel*
Man Dir & Rights & Permissions: Sheila Ritchie *E-mail:* sritchie@elm-training.co.uk
Production: Lesley Taylor
Founded: 1977
Subjects: Business, History, Law, Library & Information Sciences, Management, Travel, Tourism
ISBN Prefix(es): 0-946139; 1-85450; 0-9505828
Number of titles published annually: 20 Print; 10 Online
Total Titles: 100 Print; 20 Online; 4 E-Book
*Parent Company:* Elm Consulting Ltd
*Associate Companies:* Elm Training

**Elm Tree Books Ltd**, see Hamish Hamilton Ltd

**Elsevier**, *imprint of* Elsevier Ltd

**Elsevier Advanced Technology**, *imprint of* Elsevier Ltd

**Elsevier Advanced Technology+**
Oxford Spires, The Boulevard, Kidlington, Oxon OX5 1GB
*Tel:* (01865) 843000 *Fax:* (01865) 843010
*E-mail:* eatsales@elsevier.co.uk (sales)
*Web Site:* www.elsevier.com
*Key Personnel*
International Sales: Sophie Hayward
Contact: Philippa Sumner *Tel:* (01865) 843828 *Fax:* (01865) 843971 *E-mail:* p.sumner@elsevier.co.uk
Subjects: Business
ISBN Prefix(es): 0-904705; 0-946395; 0-948577; 1-85617
*Parent Company:* Elsevier Science Ltd
*Ultimate Parent Company:* Reed Elsevier plc
Imprints: Trade and Technical Press

*U.S. Office(s):* Elsevier Science Inc, 655 Avenue of the Americas, New York, NY 10010-5107, United States *Tel:* 212-989-5800 *Fax:* 212-633-3990

**Elsevier/Geo Abstracts**, *imprint of* Elsevier Ltd

**Elsevier Ltd+**
The Boulevard, Langford Lane, Kidlington, Oxford OX5 1GB
*Tel:* (01865) 843000 *Fax:* (01865) 843010
*E-mail:* initial.surname@elsevier.com
*Web Site:* www.elsevier.com
*Key Personnel*
Chief Operating Officer: Gavin Howe
Publishing Support & Properties Dir: Anna Moon
Chief Executive Officer, Science & Technology (Books & Journals): Arie Jongejan
Chief Executive Officer, Health Sciences (Books & Journals): Brian Nairn
Man Dir: Philip Shaw
Man Dir (Health Sciences UK/Netherlands): Dominic Vaughan
Founded: 1971
Subjects: Agriculture, Architecture & Interior Design, Behavioral Sciences, Biological Sciences, Business, Chemistry, Chemical Engineering, Communications, Computer Science, Earth Sciences, Economics, Education, Electronics, Electrical Engineering, Energy, Environmental Studies, Health, Nutrition, Library & Information Sciences, Mechanical Engineering, Medicine, Nursing, Dentistry, Technology
ISBN Prefix(es): 0-08; 0-7216; 0-7020; 0-85334; 1-85166; 0-7234; 0-4430; 0-323
*Parent Company:* Reed Elsevier, Netherlands
Imprints: Academic Press; Architectural Press; Bailliere Tindall Ltd; Butterworth Heinemann Ltd; Churchill Livingstone; Digital Press; Elsevier; Elsevier Advanced Technology; Focal Press; Elsevier/Geo Abstracts; Gulf Professional Press; Harcourt Publishers Ltd; JAI; Made Simple Books; Morgan Kauffman; Mosby; Newnes; North Holland; T & AD Poyser Ltd; Saunders
*Branch Office(s)*
Elsevier Ltd (Health Sciences), 32 Jamestown Rd, 111 Queen's Rd, London NW1 7BY
Elsevier Ltd (Health Sciences), Robert Stevenson House, 1-3 Baxters Place, Keith Walk, Edinburgh EH1 3AF
Elsevier Ltd (Science & Technology), 84 Theobald's Road, London WC1X 8RR
Elsevier Ltd (Science & Technology), Linacre House, Jordan Hill, Oxford OX2 8DP
Elsevier/Geo Abstracts, The Old Bakery, 111 Queen's Rd, Norwich NR1 3PL

**Emerald**
60/62 Toller Lane, Bradford, W Yorks BD8 9BY
*Tel:* (01274) 777700 *Fax:* (01274) 785201
*E-mail:* info@emeraldinsight.com; information@emeraldinsight.com (academic sales & enquiries); editorial@emeraldinsight.com (editorial)
*Web Site:* www.emeraldinsight.com
*Key Personnel*
Chairman: Dr Barrie Pettman
Man Dir: Dr Keith Howard
Head of Corporate Communications: Gillian Crawford *E-mail:* gcrawford@emeraldinsight.com
Productions, Rights & Permissions: Tracy Cogan
Publicity: Michelle Kelly
Customer Operations Manager: Suzanne Halliday *E-mail:* shalliday@emeraldinsight.com
Founded: 1969
Subjects: Business, Human Relations, Library & Information Sciences, Management, Marketing
ISBN Prefix(es): 0-86176; 0-905440; 0-903763

**Empire of the Senses**, *imprint of* Dedalus Ltd

**Empiricus Books**, *imprint of* Janus Publishing Co Ltd

**Encyclopaedia Britannica (UK) International Ltd**
Unity Wharf, 2nd floor, London SE1 2BH
*Tel:* (020) 7500 7800; (0845) 075 700 (orders CD or DVD inside UK); (0177) 901 3948 (orders CD or DVD outside UK); (0845) 075 8000 (order books inside UK); (0845) 901 3948 (order books outside UK) *Fax:* (020) 7500 7878
*E-mail:* enquiries@britannica.co.uk
*Web Site:* www.britannica.co.uk
*Telex:* 422084
*Key Personnel*
Man Dir: James Strachan
Marketing Manager: Marcus Missen
ISBN Prefix(es): 0-85229
*Parent Company:* Encyclopaedia Britannica Inc, Britannica Centre, 310 S Michigan Ave, Chicago, IL 60604, United States
*Associate Companies:* Encyclopaedia Britannica (Australia) Inc, Level 1, 90 Mount St, North Sydney NSW 2060, Australia *Tel:* (02) 9923 5600 *Fax:* (02) 9929 3758 *E-mail:* feedbackaccount@brittanica.com.au; Encyclopaedia Britannica (France) Ltd; Encyclopaedia Britannica (India) Pvt. Ltd., Britannica Centre, 55-56 Ydyog Vihar Phase 4, Gurgaon 122016, India *Tel:* (0124) 639 9933 *Fax:* (0124) 639 9942 *E-mail:* corporate@brittanicain.com *Web Site:* www.britannicaindia.com; Encyclopaedia Britannica (Italy) Ltd; Encyclopaedia Britannica (Japan) Inc; Korea Britannica Corp; Encyclopaedia Britannica (Philippines) Inc; Encyclopaedia Britannica SA; Encyclopaedia Britannica de Espana, SA

**The Energy Information Centre+**
Rosemary House, Lanwades Business Park, Newmarket CB8 7PW
*Tel:* (01638) 751 400 *Fax:* (01638) 751 801
*E-mail:* info@eic.co.uk
*Web Site:* www.eic.co.uk
*Key Personnel*
Editorial Dir: Robert Buckley
Commercial Dir: Michael Southin
Founded: 1975
Subjects: Energy
ISBN Prefix(es): 0-905332
*Parent Company:* Cambridge Information & Research Services

**English Teaching Professional**
32-34 Great Peter St, London SW1P 2DB
*Tel:* (020) 7222 1155 *Fax:* (020) 7222 1551
*E-mail:* info@etprofessional.com
*Web Site:* www.etprofessional.com
*Key Personnel*
Editorial Dir: Peter Collin *E-mail:* peter@etprofessional.com
Editor: Helena Gomm *E-mail:* helenagomm@etprofessional.com
Subjects: English as a Second Language
*Parent Company:* First Person Publishing Limited
*Distribution Center:* Marston Lindsay Ross Distribution, Omega Centre Collett Didcot, Oxon OX11 7AW *Tel:* (01235) 515700 *Fax:* (01235) 515777

**Enigma Books**, *imprint of* Severn House Publishers Inc

**Entra**, *imprint of* Training Publications Ltd

**Eos**, *imprint of* HarperCollins UK

**EPER**
21 Hill Pl, Edinburgh EH8 9DP
*Tel:* (0131) 650 6200 *Fax:* (0131) 667 5927
*E-mail:* ials.enquiries@ed.ac.uk

*Web Site:* www.ials.ed.ac.uk
*Key Personnel*
Project Dir: David R Hill
Founded: 1984
Subjects: English as a Second Language, Language Arts, Linguistics
ISBN Prefix(es): 1-871914; 1-871019; 1-871035; 1-871027

**Epworth Press+**
Division of Methodist Publishing House
Methodist Publishing House, 4 John Wesley Rd, Werrington, Peterborough PE4 6ZP
*Tel:* (01733) 325002 *Fax:* (01733) 384180
*Web Site:* www.mph.org.uk
*Key Personnel*
Chair of MPH Board: Eric Jarvis *E-mail:* chair@mph.org.uk
Chief Executive: Martin Stone *E-mail:* chief.exec@mph.org.uk
Commissioning Editor: Dr Natalie K Watson *E-mail:* comm.editor@mph.org.uk
Founded: 1750
Subjects: Biblical Studies, Religion - Protestant, Religion - Other, Theology, Worship
ISBN Prefix(es): 0-7162
Number of titles published annually: 12 Print
Total Titles: 200 Print
*Associate Companies:* SCM-Canterbury Press
*Sales Office(s):* SCM Press Ltd
Distributed by Westminster John Knox
Foreign Rights: SCM Press
*Bookshop(s):* Methodist Bookshop, 25 Marylebone Rd, London
*Distribution Center:* Hymns Ancient & Modern, Norwich
Methodist Publishing House, Peterborough

**ERA Technology Ltd+**
Cleeve Rd, Leatherhead, Surrey KT22 7SA
*Tel:* (01372) 367000 *Fax:* (01372) 367099
*E-mail:* info@era.co.uk
*Web Site:* www.era.co.uk
*Key Personnel*
Divisional Manager: R W H Stafford
Founded: 1920
Specialize in Contract R & D.
Subjects: Aeronautics, Aviation, Automotive, Communications, Computer Science, Electronics, Electrical Engineering, Environmental Studies, Technology, Air Pollution Control, Energy Efficiency, Power Generation
ISBN Prefix(es): 0-7008
Subsidiaries: ERA Technology (Asia) Pte Ltd; ERA Technology Inc

**Ernest Press**
17 Carleton Drive, Glasgow G46 6AQ
*Tel:* (0141) 637 5492 *Fax:* (0141) 637 5492
*E-mail:* sales@ernest-press.co.uk
*Web Site:* www.ernest-press.co.uk
*Key Personnel*
Proprietor: Peter Hodghiss
Subjects: Mountaineering, Mounting Biking Guides
ISBN Prefix(es): 0-948153
*Warehouse:* Cordee, 3A De Montfort St, Leicester LE1 7HD

**Ernst & Young+**
Becket House, One Lambeth Palace Rd, London SE1 7EU
*Tel:* (020) 7951 2000 *Fax:* (020) 7951 1345
*Web Site:* www.ey.com
Also chartered accountants & business advisers.
Subjects: Accounting, Foreign Countries, Management
ISBN Prefix(es): 0-9505745; 1-873278

**The Erskine Press+**
The Old Bakery, Banham, Norwich, Norfolk NR16 2HW

*Tel:* (01953) 88 72 77 *Fax:* (01953) 88 83 61
*E-mail:* erskpres@aol.com
*Web Site:* www.erskine-press.com
*Key Personnel*
Man Dir: Crispin de Boos
Consultant: Stephen Easton
Founded: 1986
Specialize in literature on Antarctic Exploration.
Membership(s): Independent Publishers Guild.
Subjects: Architecture & Interior Design, Art, Astronomy, Cookery, History, Travel
ISBN Prefix(es): 1-85297; 0-948285
Total Titles: 58 Print
*Parent Company:* Archival Facsimiles Ltd

**estamp+**
204 St Albans Ave, London W4 5JU
*Tel:* (020) 8994 2379 *Fax:* (020) 8994 2379
*E-mail:* st@estamp.demon.co.uk
*Key Personnel*
Director: Sylvie Turner
Founded: 1990
Specialize in art publishing, mail order, contemporary print making & paper.
Membership(s): IPG.
ISBN Prefix(es): 1-871831
Total Titles: 17 Print
*Shipping Address:* Central Book, 199 Wallis Rd, London E9 SLN, Contact: Kirsty *Tel:* (020) 8986 7859 *Fax:* (020) 8533 5821

**Estates Gazette**
147-151 Wardour St, London W1V 4BN
*Tel:* (020) 8652 3500; (020) 7411 2540 (edit); (020) 7411 2626 (advertising); (01444) 445335 (subscriptions) *Fax:* (020) 7437 2432; (020) 7437 0294 (edit); (020) 7437 2432 (advertising); (01444) 445567 (subscriptions)
*Key Personnel*
Publisher & Man Dir: James Blazeby
Editorial Dir: Peter Bill *E-mail:* peter.bill@rbi.co.uk
Commissioning Editor: Alison Richards
Founded: 1858
Leading providers of property information.
ISBN Prefix(es): 0-7282; 0-900361
*Parent Company:* Reed Business Information Ltd
*Orders to:* Oakfield House, Perrymount Rd, Haywards Heath, West Sussex RH16 3DM

**Ethics International Press Ltd+**
St Andrews Castle, St Andrews St S, Bury St Edmunds, Suffolk IP33 3PH
*Tel:* (01223) 357458 *Fax:* (01223) 303598
*E-mail:* info@ethicspress.com
*Web Site:* www.ethicspress.com
Founded: 1993
Academic, business & government.
Subjects: Business, Environmental Studies, Film, Video, Government, Political Science, Law, Management, Philosophy, Public Administration, Social Sciences, Sociology
ISBN Prefix(es): 1-871891
Number of titles published annually: 3 Print; 6 CD-ROM; 6 E-Book
Total Titles: 10 Print; 6 CD-ROM; 6 E-Book

**Eurobook Ltd+**
PO Box 52, Wallingford, Oxon OX10 0XU
*Tel:* (01865) 858333 *Fax:* (01865) 858263; (01865) 340087
*E-mail:* eurobook@compuserve.com
*Key Personnel*
Man Dir, Rights & Permissions: Peter S Lowe
Editor: Ruth Spriggs
Sales, Publicity & Advertising: R McFarlane
International Rights: P S Lowe
Founded: 1968
Subjects: Animals, Pets, Gardening, Plants, Natural History, Nonfiction (General), Science (General)

ISBN Prefix(es): 0-85654
Imprints: Peter Lowe

**Euromonitor PLC+**
60-61 Britton St, London EC1M 5UX
*Tel:* (020) 7251 8024 *Fax:* (020) 7608 3149
*E-mail:* info@euromonitor.com
*Web Site:* www.euromonitor.com
*Telex:* 262433 Monref G
*Key Personnel*
Man Dir: Trevor Fenwick
Marketing Dir: David Gudgin
Chairman: Robert Senior
Founded: 1972
Membership(s): UK & European Directory Publishers Associations.
Subjects: Business, Economics, Marketing, Publishing & Book Trade Reference, Demographics, Macro-Economic Data, Market Research Reports
ISBN Prefix(es): 0-903706; 0-86338; 1-84264
Number of titles published annually: 25 Print; 6 CD-ROM
Total Titles: 6 CD-ROM
*Branch Office(s)*
Euromonitor International (Asia) Pte Ltd, Singapore Technologies Bldg, 3 Lim Teck Kim Rd, No 08-02, Singapore 088934, Singapore *Tel:* 6429 0590 *Fax:* 6324 1855 *E-mail:* info@euromonitor.com.sg
Euromonitor International Brazil, Brazil *Tel:* (011) 3771 3490 *Fax:* (011) 5081 5290 *E-mail:* robert.listik@euromonitorintl.com *Web Site:* www.euromonitor.com
*U.S. Office(s):* Euromonitor International Inc, 122 S Michigan Ave, Suite 810, Chicago, IL 60603, United States *Tel:* 312-922-1115 *Fax:* 312-922-1157 *E-mail:* insight@euromonitorintl.com *Web Site:* www.euromonitor.com
Distributed by Gale Research

**Europa**, *imprint of* Taylor & Francis

**Europa Publications**
Member of Taylor & Francis Group
11 New Fetter Lane, London EC4P 4EE
*Tel:* (020) 7842 2110; (020) 7842 2133 (marketing & sales) *Fax:* (020) 7842 2249 (marketing & sales)
*E-mail:* info.europa@tandf.co.uk
*Web Site:* www.europapublications.com
*Key Personnel*
Editorial Dir: Paul Kelly *Fax:* (020) 7842 2391 *E-mail:* edit.europa@tandf.co.uk
Marketing Manager: Mary Sweny
Accounts Manager: Frances Bunting
Founded: 1926
Membership(s): Directory Publishers Association.
Subjects: Developing Countries, Economics, Education, Foreign Countries, Government, Political Science, Publishing & Book Trade Reference, International affairs
ISBN Prefix(es): 0-946653; 1-85743; 0-900362; 0-905118
Number of titles published annually: 30 Print

**Europe 1992-98**, *imprint of* Dedalus Ltd

**European Schoolbooks Ltd**
The Runnings, Cheltenham GL51 9PQ
*Tel:* (01242) 245252 *Fax:* (01242) 224137
*E-mail:* direct@esb.co.uk
*Web Site:* www.eurobooks.co.uk
*Key Personnel*
Man Dir: Frank A Preiss *E-mail:* fap@esb.co.uk
Founded: 1964
Also act as distributor for European publishers.
Subjects: Economics, Environmental Studies, Foreign Countries, Geography, Geology, Language Arts, Linguistics, Social Sciences, Sociology
ISBN Prefix(es): 0-85048; 0-85233

Subsidiaries: European Schoolbooks Publishing
*Bookshop(s):* The European Bookshop, 5 Warwick St, London W1R 5RA *Tel:* (020) 7734 5259 *Fax:* (020) 7287 1720; The Italian Bookshop, 7 Cecil Court, London WC2N 4EZ *Tel:* (020) 7240 1634 *Fax:* (020) 7240 1635 *E-mail:* italbookshop@freenet.co.uk

**The Eurospan Group**
3 Henrietta St, Covent Garden, London WC2E 8LU
*Tel:* (020) 7240 0856 *Fax:* (020) 7379 0609
*E-mail:* info@eurospan.co.uk
*Web Site:* www.eurospan.co.uk
*Key Personnel*
Group Man Dir: Michael Geelan
Chairman: Danny Maher
Operations Manager: Kate Symonds
Business Manager: Patrick Tay
Marketing: Imogen Adams; Sally Greene; Tina Moran; Clare Sutton
Founded: 1963
Subjects: Agriculture, Anthropology, Archaeology, Art, Asian Studies, Behavioral Sciences, Biblical Studies, Biography, Biological Sciences, Business, Chemistry, Chemical Engineering, Child Care & Development, Communications, Computer Science, Developing Countries, Disability, Special Needs, Drama, Theater, Earth Sciences, Economics, Education, Energy, Engineering (General), Environmental Studies, Ethnicity, Film, Video, Finance, Foreign Countries, Gay & Lesbian, Genealogy, Geography, Geology, Government, Political Science, Health, Nutrition, History, Human Relations, Journalism, Labor, Industrial Relations, Language Arts, Linguistics, Law, Library & Information Sciences, Literature, Literary Criticism, Essays, Management, Maritime, Marketing, Mathematics, Medicine, Nursing, Dentistry, Microcomputers, Military Science, Music, Dance, Natural History, Nonfiction (General), Philosophy, Physics, Poetry, Psychology, Psychiatry, Public Administration, Radio, TV, Regional Interests, Religion - Buddhist, Religion - Catholic, Religion - Hindu, Religion - Islamic, Religion - Jewish, Religion - Protestant, Religion - Other, Science (General), Science Fiction, Fantasy, Social Sciences, Sociology, Technology, Theology, Veterinary Science, Women's Studies
Distributor for AMS Press; Aldwych Press; American Academy of Orthopaedic Surgeons; American Enterprise Institute; American Institute for Aeronautics & Astronautics; American Library Association; American Psychiatric Press; American Psychological Association; Amsterdam University Press (The Netherlands); Auburn House; Austin & Winfield; Bergin & Garvey; Boyton/Cook; CSIRO Publishing (Australia); Catholic University of America Press; Da Capo Press; Lawrence Erlbaum Associates Inc; Fordham University Press; Greenwood Press; Hampton Press; Heinemann USA; Human Sciences Press; Idea Group Publishing; International Scholars Publications; Iowa State University Press; Jason Aronson Publishers; Kent State University Press; Krieger Publishing Co; Libraries Unlimited; Louisiana State University Press; Lynne Rienner Publishers; ME Sharpe Publishing; Narosa Publishing House (India); Neal-Schuman Publishers; Rutgers University Press; The New York Academy of Sciences; The University of North Carolina Press; Ohio State University Press; Open Court Publishing Co; PMA Publishing; Penn State Press; Popular Culture Ink; Praeger Publishers; Quorum Books; Scholarly Resources; The Oryx Press; SIR Publishing (New Zealand); Slack Inc; Southern Illinois University Press; Syracuse University Press; Teacher Ideas Press; Teachers College Press; Temple University Press; Thomas International Publishing Co;

University of Alabama Press; University of Georgia Press; University of Massachusetts Press; University of Missouri Press; University of Nevada Press; University of Notre Dame Press; University of Pittsburgh Press; University Press of Florida; University Press of Kansas; University Press of Virginia; University of South Carolina Press; University of Wisconsin Press; Wayne State University Press; Who's Who in Italy (Italy); Facts on File (UK, Ireland & Europe)
*Orders to:* EDS, 3 Henrietta St, London WC2E 8LU

**Evangelical Library of Wales**, *imprint of* Bryntirion Press

**Evangelical Press & Services Ltd**
Grange Close, Faverdale North, Darlington DL3 0PH
*Tel:* (01325) 380232 *Toll Free Tel:* 866-588-6778 (US only) *Fax:* (01325) 466153
*Toll Free Fax:* 866-588-6778 (US only)
*E-mail:* sales@evangelicalpress.org
*Web Site:* www.evangelicalpress.org
*Key Personnel*
General Manager & International Rights: Anthony L Gosling *E-mail:* anthony.gosling@evangelicalpress.org
Founded: 1967
International publisher of Christian, Evangelical & Reformed literature.
Membership(s): Affinity (UK); CBA; ECPA.
Subjects: Biblical Studies, Religion - Protestant, Theology
ISBN Prefix(es): 0-85234; 0-946462; 0-85479
Number of titles published annually: 25 Print
Total Titles: 350 Print
Subsidiaries: Europresse SARL (French publisher)
*U.S. Office(s):* PO Box 825, Webster, NY 14580, United States *E-mail:* usa.sales@evangelicalpress.org
Distributor for Bryntirion Press; Carey Publications; Grace Publications Trust

**Evans Brothers Ltd+**
2A Portman Mansions, Chiltern St, London W1U 6NR
*Tel:* (020) 7487 0920 *Fax:* (020) 7487 0921
*E-mail:* sales@evansbrothers.co.uk
*Web Site:* www.evansbooks.co.uk
*Telex:* 8811713 Evbook G
*Key Personnel*
Dir: B D Jones; A Ojora
Man Dir: Stephen T Pawley *E-mail:* stephenp@evansbrothers.co.uk
Rights Manager: Britta Martins
Production Manager: Jenny Mulvanny
UK Publisher: Su Swallow
Founded: 1908
Subjects: Art, English as a Second Language, Geography, Geology, History, Library & Information Sciences, Mathematics, Music, Dance, Religion - Other, Science (General), Citizenship, Design & Technical, ICT, PSHE, R/E Multifaith, Social Issues
ISBN Prefix(es): 0-237; 1-84089; 1-84234
Number of titles published annually: 120 Print
Total Titles: 730 Print
*Ultimate Parent Company:* Imperial Securities
*Associate Companies:* Evans Brothers (Nigeria Publishers) Ltd, Nigeria
Imprints: Cherrytree; Cloverleaf
Subsidiaries: Evans Brothers (Kenya) Ltd; Zero to Ten Limited
Foreign Rep(s): The British Bookshop (Austria); The Educational Book Service (Botswana, Zambia); Evans Brothers Ltd (Brazil); Pansing Distribution Sdn Bhd (Brunei, Indonesia, Malaysia, Singapore); Reed Educational & Professional Publishing (Australia); Saunders Books Company (Canada); South Pacific Books (Imports) Ltd (New Zealand); TPL Corpora-

tion (HK) Ltd (Hong Kong); Trafalgar Square Publishing (US)
*Orders to:* Thomson Publishing Services, Cheriton House, North Way, Andover, Hants SP10 5BE *Tel:* (01264) 343072 *Fax:* (01264) 342788 *E-mail:* carol.appleton@ thomsonpublishingservices.co.uk *Web Site:* www.thomsonpublishingservices.co.uk

**Ex Libris**, *imprint of* Ex Libris Press

**Ex Libris Press+**
One The Shambles, Bradford on Avon, Wilts BA15 1JS
*Tel:* (01225) 863595 *Fax:* (01225) 863595
*Web Site:* www.ex-librisbooks.co.uk
*Key Personnel*
Proprietor: Roger Jones *E-mail:* roger.jones@ex-librisbooks.co.uk
Founded: 1981
Local & regional press covering west country & Channel Islands, also list of book on country life & lore.
Membership(s): IPG.
Subjects: Biography, Geography, Geology, History, Literature, Literary Criticism, Essays, Walking guides & countryside paperback & occasional hardback
ISBN Prefix(es): 0-9506563; 0-948578; 1-903341
Number of titles published annually: 8 Print
Total Titles: 70 Print
Imprints: Ex Libris; Seaflower Books
Distributed by Halsgrove (UK)

**Helen Exley Giftbooks+**
16 Chalk Hill, Watford, Herts WD19 4BG
*Tel:* (01923) 250505 *Fax:* (01923) 818733
*Toll Free Fax:* 800-440
*E-mail:* enquiry@exleypublications.co.uk
*Key Personnel*
Chairman: Richard Exley
Man Dir & Editorial Dir: Helen Exley
Rights Dir: Sonya Dougan Furnell *E-mail:* sonya@exleypublications.co.uk
Export Sales Manager: Michael Illingworth
Contact: Alyse Bunker *E-mail:* alyse.bunker@ exleypublications.co.uk
Founded: 1976
Specializes in giftbooks, family & relationships, inspirational & biographies.
Subjects: Biography, Human Relations, Humor, Nonfiction (General)
ISBN Prefix(es): 1-85015; 1-86187; 0-905521
Total Titles: 400 Print
*Associate Companies:* Exley Handels GmbH, Schloss Merode, D52379 Langerwehe, Merode, Germany; Exley SA, 13 rue de Genval, B-1301 Bierges, Belgium
Subsidiaries: Exley Giftbooks
Distributed by Exley Handel GmbH (Germany); Exley SA (Belgium)

**Exley Publications Ltd**, see Helen Exley Giftbooks

**Expert Books**, *imprint of* Transworld Publishers Ltd

**Express Newspapers+**
Ludgate House, 245 Blackfriars Rd, London SE1 9UX
*Tel:* (020) 7928 8000 *Fax:* (020) 7922 7966
*Key Personnel*
Licensing Manager: Sue McGeever *Tel:* (020) 7922 7887 *E-mail:* sue.mcgeever@express.co.uk
Subjects: Business, Cookery, Humor, Management, Sports, Athletics
ISBN Prefix(es): 0-85079
*Parent Company:* Northern & Shell

**Eye Books**
51 Boscombe Rd, London W12 9HT
*Tel:* (020) 8743 3276 *Fax:* (020) 8743 3276
*E-mail:* info@eye-books.com
*Web Site:* www.eye-books.com
Membership(s): IPG.
Distributed by Bookwise (Australia & New Zealand); Grantham Book Services (UK)
Foreign Rep(s): Bookwise (Australia)

**Fabbri (GE) Ltd+**
Elme House, 133 Long Acre, London WC2E 9AW
*Tel:* (020) 7836 0519; (020) 7468 5600 *Fax:* (020) 7836 0280
*E-mail:* mailbox@gefabbri.co.uk
*Web Site:* www.gefabbri.co.uk
*Key Personnel*
Man Dir: Peter Edwards
Dir: Liz Glaze
International Dir: Philip Costick
Editorial Dir: Hilary Newstead
Editor-in-Chief: Katie Preston
Marketing Dir: David Lucas
Chief Accountant: Duncan Lewis
Founded: 1987
ISBN Prefix(es): 1-85664; 1-872628
Imprints: GE Fabbri; GE Magazines
Subsidiaries: GE Fabbri; GE Magazines

**Faber & Faber Ltd+**
3 Queen Sq, London WC1N 3AU
*Tel:* (020) 7465 0045 *Fax:* (020) 7465 0034
*Web Site:* www.faber.co.uk *Cable:* FABBAF LONDON WC1
*Key Personnel*
Man Dir: Toby Faber
Publishing Dir: Joanna Mackle
Contract Manager: Alan Winwright
Publisher: Walter Donohue
Head of Sales: Chris McLaren
Founded: 1929
Also distributor.
Subjects: Art, Biography, Drama, Theater, Fiction, Film, Video, History, How-to, Literature, Literary Criticism, Essays, Music, Dance, Philosophy, Poetry, Psychology, Psychiatry, Radio, TV, Religion - Other, Social Sciences, Sociology, Wine & Spirits
ISBN Prefix(es): 0-571
*Parent Company:* Geoffrey Faber Holdings
Subsidiaries: Faber Inc USA
*U.S. Office(s):* Faber & Faber Inc, 50 Cross St, Winchester, MA 01890, United States
*Orders to:* Macmillan Distribution Ltd, Brinel Rd Houndmills Ind Est, Baringstone Harts RG21 6XS *Tel:* (01256) 302692

**Fabian Society**
11 Dartmouth St, London SW1H 9BN
*Tel:* (020) 7227 4900 *Fax:* (020) 7976 7153
*E-mail:* info@fabian-society.org.uk
*Web Site:* www.fabian-society.org.uk
*Key Personnel*
Deputy General Secretary: Adrian Harvey *Tel:* (020) 7227 4908
Finance Officer: Margaret McGillen *Tel:* (020) 7227 4903
General Secretary: Sunder Katwala *Tel:* (020) 7227 4905
Administrator: Claire Willgress
Editorial Manager: Ellie Levenson
Local Societies Officer: Deborah Stoate
Membership Officer: Giles Wright
Events Manager: Emma Burnell
Founded: 1884
Subjects: Economics, Government, Political Science
ISBN Prefix(es): 0-7163
Subsidiaries: NCLC Publishing Society Ltd

**Facet Publishing+**
Imprint of Chartered Institute of Library & Information Professionals (CILIP)
7 Ridgmount St, London WC1E 7AE
*Tel:* (020) 7255 0590 *Fax:* (020) 7255 0591
*E-mail:* info@facetpublishing.co.uk
*Web Site:* www.facetpublishing.co.uk; www.cilip.org.uk
*Key Personnel*
Man Dir & International Rights: Janet Liebster
Publishing Dir: Helen Carley *Tel:* (020) 7255 0592 *E-mail:* helen.carley@facetpublishing.co.uk
Commissioning Editor: Rebecca Casey
Production Manager: Kathryn Beecroft
Sales Manager: Rohini Ramachandran
Founded: 1980
Specialize in library & information science.
Subjects: Computer Science, Library & Information Sciences, Management, Technology
ISBN Prefix(es): 0-85365; 0-85157; 1-85604
*Warehouse:* Bookpoint Ltd, 130 Milton Park, Abingdon OX14 4SB
Neal-Schuman, 100 William St, Suite 2003, New York, NY 10038-4512, United States (North American orders)
*Orders to:* Bookpoint Ltd, 130 Milton Park, Abingdon, Oxon OX14 4SB
Neal-Schuman Publishers Inc, 100 William St, Suite 2003, New York, NY 10038-4512, United States

**The Factory Shop Guide**
34 Park Hill, London SW4 9PB
*Tel:* (020) 7622 3722 *Fax:* (020) 7720 3536
*E-mail:* factshop@macline.co.uk
*Key Personnel*
Partners: Gillian Cutress; Rolf Stricker
Founded: 1985
Subjects: Gardening, Plants, Travel
ISBN Prefix(es): 0-948965

**Fairacres Publication**, *imprint of* SLG Press

**Fairfield**, *imprint of* Novello & Co Ltd

**Falco**, *imprint of* Hawk Books

**Famedram Publishers Ltd+**
PO Box 3, Ellon, Aberdeenshire AB41 9EA
*Tel:* (01651) 842429 *Fax:* (01651) 842180
*E-mail:* adetola@ristol.co.uk
*Web Site:* www.artwork.co.uk
*Key Personnel*
Man Dir: Bill Williams
Production: Eleanor Stewart
Editor (Artwork): Richard Carr
Advertising Sales: Sandra Moore *Tel:* (01436) 675743 *Fax:* (01436) 673327
Founded: 1971
Publisher of Artwork - bimonthly arts newspaper for Scotland & Northern England.
Subjects: Poetry, Travel, Wine & Spirits
ISBN Prefix(es): 0-905489; 0-9501944
Total Titles: 40 Print
Imprints: Northern Books

**Family Law**, *imprint of* Jordan Publishing Ltd

**Family Walks**, *imprint of* Scarthin Books

**Fanny**, *imprint of* Knockabout Comics

**Farsight Press+**
5 Lynette Ave, London SW4 9HE
*Tel:* (020) 8675 1693
*Key Personnel*
Dir & Sole Proprietor: Mr F Knox
Founded: 1996
Research & publication on criminology.
Subjects: Criminology

ISBN Prefix(es): 0-948669
Number of titles published annually: 4 Print
Total Titles: 4 Print

**FBA Publications**, *imprint of* Francis Balsom
Associates

**Feather Books**
PO Box 438, Shrewsbury SY3 0WN
*Tel:* (01743) 872177 *Fax:* (01743) 872177
*E-mail:* john@waddysweb.freeuk.com
*Web Site:* www.waddysweb.com
Founded: 1984
Christian publisher.
Membership(s): Independent Publishers Guild.
Subjects: Drama, Theater, Fiction, Music, Dance,
Poetry, Science Fiction, Fantasy, Hymns
ISBN Prefix(es): 0-947718; 1-84175
Number of titles published annually: 60 Print
Total Titles: 250 Print
*Book Club(s):* The Quill Hedgehog Club

**Ferendune**, *imprint of* E W Classey Ltd

**Fernhurst Books+**
Duke's Path, High St, Arundel, West Sussex
BN18 9AJ
*Tel:* (01903) 882277 *Fax:* (01903) 882715
*E-mail:* sales@fernhurstbooks.co.uk
*Web Site:* www.fernhurstbooks.co.uk
*Key Personnel*
Man Dir: Tim Davison
Founded: 1979
Paperbacks on all aspects of water sports.
Subjects: Maritime
ISBN Prefix(es): 0-906754; 1-898660
Number of titles published annually: 14 Print
Total Titles: 106 Print; 1 CD-ROM
*U.S. Office(s):* Robert Hale, 1803 132 Ave NE,
Suite 4, Bellevue, WA 98005, United States
*Tel:* 425-881-5212 *Fax:* 425-881-0731
*Warehouse:* Clipper Distribution, Windmill Grove,
Porchester, Hants PO16 9HT *Tel:* (02392)
200080 *Fax:* (02392) 200090

**FHG Publications Ltd**
Abbey Mill Business Centre, Seedhill, Paisley
PA1 1TJ
*Tel:* (0141) 8870428 *Fax:* (0141) 8897204
*E-mail:* fhg@ipcmedia.com
*Web Site:* www.holidayguides.com
*Key Personnel*
General Manager: George Pratt
Founded: 1947
Subjects: Travel
ISBN Prefix(es): 1-85055; 0-900365
*Parent Company:* IPC Media Ltd, King's Reach
Tower, Stampford St, London SE19LS
*U.S. Office(s):* Hunter Publishing, 239 S Beach
Rd, Hobe Sound, FL, United States

**Sadie Fields Productions Ltd+**
4C/D West Point, 36/37 Warple Way, London W3
0RG
*Tel:* (020) 8996 9970 *Fax:* (020) 8996 9977
*E-mail:* edith@tangobooks.co.uk
*Key Personnel*
Dir: David Fielder; Sheri Safran
Founded: 1981
Also book packager, childrens novelty (popups,
holograms, touch & feel etc).
*Associate Companies:* Sadie Fields Management
Inc
Divisions: Tango Books

**Financial Times Prentice Hall**, *imprint of*
Pearson Education Europe, Mideast & Africa

**Financial Training Co (FTC)**
New London House, 1st floor, 6 London St, Lon-
don EC3R 7LP
*Tel:* (020) 7481 6050 *Fax:* (020) 7265 0337
*E-mail:* finmkts@financial-training.com
*Web Site:* www.financial-training.com
*Key Personnel*
Man Dir: William Macpherson
Founded: 1978
Subjects: Accounting
ISBN Prefix(es): 1-85179; 1-84390
*Branch Office(s)*
Swift House, Market Place, Berks RG40 1AP
*Tel:* (0118) 977 4922 *Fax:* (0118) 989 4029
Centre City Tower, 1st floor, 7 Hill St, Birming-
ham B5 4UA *Tel:* (0121) 644 4700 *Fax:* (0121)
644 4701 *E-mail:* birmingham@financial-
training.com
26 Berkeley Sq, Clifton, Bristol BS8 1HP
*Tel:* (0117) 925 5266 *Fax:* (0117) 925 5753
*E-mail:* bristol@financial-training.com
Saint David's House, 3rd floor, Wood St, Cardiff
*Tel:* (029) 2038 8067 *Fax:* (029) 2023 7408
*E-mail:* cardiff@financial-training.com
Tempus, 249 Midsummer Blvd, Central Mil-
ton Keynes, Bucks MK 9 1EU *Tel:* (01223)
414514 *Fax:* (01223) 414512
Conference House, 152 Morrison St, The Ex-
change, Edinburgh EH3 8EB *Tel:* (0131) 200
6177 *Fax:* (0131) 200 6200 *E-mail:* scotland@
financial-training.com
112 W George St, 2nd floor, Glasgow G2 1PS
*Tel:* (0141) 333 1101 *Fax:* (0141) 332 4881
*E-mail:* glasgow@financial-training.com
The Shirethorn Centre, Suite R, Prospect St, Hull
HU2 8PX *E-mail:* hull@financial-training.com
49 Saint Pauls St, Leeds LS1 2TE *Tel:* (0113)
245 7455 *Fax:* (0113) 242 8889
*E-mail:* leeds@financial-training.com
Beckville House, 3rd floor, 66 London Rd, lincs
LE2 0QD *Tel:* (0116) 204 5980 *Fax:* (0116)
285 6787 *E-mail:* leicester@financial-training.
com
Cotton House, 4th floor, Old Hall St, Liverpool
L3 9TX *Tel:* (0151) 708 8852 *Fax:* (0151) 709
4264 *E-mail:* liverpool@financial-training.com
18-20 Crucifix Lane, London SE1 3JW
*Tel:* (020) 7407 5000 *Fax:* (020) 7407 0101
*E-mail:* london@financial-training.com
One King St, London W6 9HR *Tel:* (020) 7407
5000 *Fax:* (020) 7407 0101 *E-mail:* london@
financial-training.com
179-191 Borough High St, London SE1 1HR
*Tel:* (020) 7407 5000 *Fax:* (020) 7407 0101
*E-mail:* london@financial-training.com
10-14 White Lion St, London N1 9PD
*Tel:* (020) 7833 0700 *Fax:* (020) 7837 7077
*E-mail:* london@financial-training.com
Saint James Bldg, 6th floor, 79 Oxford St,
Manchester M1 6FQ *Tel:* (0161) 237 3322
*Fax:* (0161) 236 9047 *E-mail:* manchester@
financial-training.com
Provincial House, Northumberland St, Newcastle
Upon Tyne NE1 7DQ *Tel:* (0191) 232 9365
*Fax:* (0191) 232 2115 *E-mail:* newcastle@
financial-training.com
Caer Rhun Hall, Conwy, Gwynedd, North Wales
LL32 8HX *Tel:* (01492) 650797 *Fax:* (01492)
650593 *E-mail:* caerrhunhall@financial-
training.com
74 St Faiths Lane, Norwich NR1 1NE
*Tel:* (01603) 617638 *Fax:* (01603) 761369
*E-mail:* norwich@financial-training.com
Alan House, 3rd floor, 5 Clumber St, Notts NG1
3ED *Tel:* (0115) 853 3600 *Fax:* (0115) 941
5779 *E-mail:* nottingham@financial-training.
com
Crescent House, 2nd floor, 46 Priestgate, Peterborough PE1 1LF *Tel:* (01733) 568666
*Fax:* (01733) 568667 *E-mail:* peterborough@
financial-training.com
Thames Tower, 6th floor, Station Hill, Reading
RG1 1LX *Tel:* (0118) 951 3100 *Fax:* (0118)

989 4029 *E-mail:* reading@financial-training.
com
32a Castle Way, Southampton SO14 2AW
*Tel:* (023) 8022 0852 *Fax:* (023) 8063 4379
*E-mail:* southampton@financial-training.com
Swift House, Market Pl, Wokingham RG40 1AP
*Tel:* (0118) 977 4922 *Fax:* (0118) 989 4029
*E-mail:* wokingham@financial-training.com

**Findhorn Press Inc+**
305a The Park, Findhorn, Forres IV36 3TE
*Tel:* (01309) 690582 *Fax:* (01309) 690036
*E-mail:* info@findhornpress.com
*Web Site:* www.findhornpress.com
*Key Personnel*
Publisher: Thierry Bogliolo *Tel:* (0467) 283488
(France) *Fax:* (0467) 490419 (France)
*E-mail:* thierry@findhornpress.com
Founded: 1971
Publishes books that bring hope, healing & inspi-
ration to the world.
Subjects: Self-Help, Alternative Health, Spiritual-
ity
ISBN Prefix(es): 0-905242; 1-899171; 1-84409
Number of titles published annually: 20 Print
Total Titles: 90 Print; 2 Audio
Distributed by Anthroposophic Press (North
America); Brumby Books (Australia); Deep
Books (UK & Europe); New Horizons (South
Africa); Peaceful Living Publications (New
Zealand)
Foreign Rep(s): Findhorn Publishing Services
(Worldwide)

**Firebird Books Ltd+**
PO Box 327, Poole, Dorset BH15 2RG
*Tel:* (01202) 715349 (sales); (01258) 454675 (edi-
torial) *Fax:* (01202) 736191
*E-mail:* skboorh@bournemouth-net.co.uk
*Key Personnel*
Publisher: Stuart Booth
Production Dir: Kathryn Booth
Sales Dir: Chris Lloyd *E-mail:* chrlloyd@
globalnet.co.uk
Founded: 1987
Subjects: History, Military Science
ISBN Prefix(es): 1-85314
*Associate Companies:* Wise Owl Quiz Promotions
*Sales Office(s):* Chris Lloyd Sales & Marketing,
Poole *Tel:* (01202) 715349

**First & Best in Education Ltd+**
Earlstrees Court, Earlstrees Rd, Corby, Northants
NN17 4HH
*Tel:* (01536) 399004 (editorial); (01536) 399005
(accounts) *Fax:* (01536) 399012
*E-mail:* anne@firstandbest.co.uk
*Web Site:* www.firstandbest.co.uk
*Key Personnel*
Man Dir & Marketing: Tony Attwood
*Tel:* (01536) 399013 *E-mail:* tonyattwood@
hamilton-house.com
Editor: Anne Cockburn
Founded: 1979
Specialize in publishing books on marketing &
direct mail & copiable books for schools &
software for schools.
Subjects: Business, Education
ISBN Prefix(es): 0-906888; 1-898091; 1-86083
Number of titles published annually: 30 Print; 25
CD-ROM
Total Titles: 600 Print; 200 CD-ROM
*Ultimate Parent Company:* Hamilton House Mail-
ings plc
Imprints: School Improvement Reports

**First Discovery**, *imprint of* Moonlight Publishing
Ltd

**First Discovery-Art**, *imprint of* Moonlight
Publishing Ltd

**Fishing News Books Ltd+**
Osney Mead, Oxford OX2 0EL
*Tel:* (01865) 206206 *Fax:* (01865) 721205
*E-mail:* fishing.newsbooks@oxon.
blackwellpublishing.com
*Web Site:* www.fishknowledge.com
*Telex:* 83355 MEDBOK G
*Key Personnel*
Publisher: Nigel Balmforth *E-mail:* nigel.
balmforth@oxon.blackwellpublishing.com
Marketing: Katie Moll *E-mail:* katie.moll@oxon.
blackwellpublishing.com
Founded: 1953
Subjects: Maritime
ISBN Prefix(es): 0-85238
*Parent Company:* Blackwell Scientific Publishing
Ltd, Osney Mead, Oxford OX2 0EL
*Bookshop(s):* Blackwell Book Shops
*Orders to:* Blackwell Publishing Direct Orders,
PO Box 269, Abingdon, Oxfordshire OX14
4YN *Tel:* (01235) 465500 *Fax:* (01235) 455556

**The Fitzjames Press**, *imprint of* Motor Racing
Publications Ltd

**Five Star**, *imprint of* Thomson Gale

**Flambard Press+**
Stable Cottage, East Fourstones, Hexham,
Northumb NE47 5DX
*Tel:* (01434) 674360 *Fax:* (01434) 674178
*Web Site:* www.flambardpress.co.uk
*Key Personnel*
Managing Editor: Peter Lewis
Founded: 1990
Non-commercial publisher mainly for writers
north of England.
Subjects: Fiction, Poetry
ISBN Prefix(es): 1-873226
Number of titles published annually: 7 Print
Total Titles: 68 Print
*Warehouse:* Central Books, London
*Distribution Center:* Central Books, London
*Orders to:* Central Books, London
*Returns:* Central Books, London

**Flame Tree Publishing+**
Crabtree Hall, Crabtree Lane, Fulham, London
SW6 6TY
*Tel:* (020) 7386 4700 *Fax:* (020) 7386 4700
*E-mail:* info@flametreepublishing.com
*Web Site:* www.flametreepublishing.com
*Key Personnel*
Publisher: Nick Wells
Man Dir: Frances Bodiam
Sales Operations Manager: Helen Wall
Founded: 1992
Publishers of books & stationery.
Membership(s): Independent Publishers Guild.
Subjects: Art, Education, History, Music, Dance,
Religion - Other
ISBN Prefix(es): 1-90404; 1-84451; 1-90381
Number of titles published annually: 25 Print
Total Titles: 200 Print
*Parent Company:* The Foundry Creative Media
Co Ltd
*Distribution Center:* Marston Book Services

**Flicks Books+**
29 Bradford St, Trowbridge, Wilts BA14 9AN
*Tel:* (01225) 767 728 *Fax:* (01225) 760 418
*E-mail:* flicks.books@pipex.com
*Key Personnel*
Publisher: Matthew Stevens
Founded: 1986
Subjects: Film, Video, Cinema, TV
ISBN Prefix(es): 0-948911; 1-86236
Total Titles: 70 Print

**Floris Books+**
15 Harrison Gardens, Edinburgh EH11 1SH
*Tel:* (0131) 337 2372 *Fax:* (0131) 347 9919
*E-mail:* floris@floris.books.co.uk
*Web Site:* www.florisbooks.co.uk
*Key Personnel*
Editorial: Christopher Moore
Production, Rights & Permissions: Christian
Maclean
Schools/Libraries: Angelique Fowlie
Contact: Joanne Moore
Founded: 1976
Membership(s): Scottish Publishers Association.
Subjects: Crafts, Games, Hobbies, Religion -
Other, Science (General)
ISBN Prefix(es): 0-903540; 0-86315
*Warehouse:* Scottish Book Source, 32 Finlas
St, Glasgow G22 5DU *Tel:* (0870) 240 2182
*E-mail:* orders@booksource.net

**Focal Press**, *imprint of* Elsevier Ltd

**Fodors**, *imprint of* Random House UK Ltd

**Folens Ltd+**
Boscombe Rd, Dunstable, Beds LU5 4RL
*Tel:* (0870) 609 1237 *Fax:* (0870) 609 1236
*E-mail:* folens@folens.com
*Web Site:* www.folens.com
*Key Personnel*
Man Dir: Malcolm Watson
Dir, Sales & Marketing: Adrian Cockell
Founded: 1986
Publishers of educational books for both teachers
& children up to the age of 18 years.
Subjects: Education
ISBN Prefix(es): 1-85276; 1-84163; 1-84303; 0-
94788; 1-84191; 1-86202
Number of titles published annually: 150 Print;
20 CD-ROM
Total Titles: 1,500 Print; 120 CD-ROM
*Associate Companies:* Educational Publishers
Distributed by Agius + Agius Limited (Malta); Al
Kashkool Bookshop (Jordan); All Prints Dis-
tributors & Publishers (United Arab Emirates);
Al Manahil Educational Consultancy (Oman);
Bacon & Hughes Limited (Canada); Educa-
tional Supplies Pty Ltd (Australia); Incentive
Publications Inc (USA); International Language
Bookshop (Egypt); LKD Educational Resources
(Jordan); Mars Publishing House (Saudi Ara-
bia); Modern Teaching Aids (Australia); Proof
Line (M) Sdn Bhd (Malaysia); Saeed & Samir
Bookstore Co Ltd (Kuwait); September 21 En-
terprise Pte Ltd (Singapore); Social Studies
School Service (USA); South Pacific Books
(Imports) Ltd (New Zealand); Southern Cross
(Australia); Stanford House (ELT Resource
Centre) (Hong Kong); TEK Books (Bookworld
Espana) (Spain); University Book Store (M)
Sdn Bhd (Malaysia)
Foreign Rep(s): IPR Beirut (Lebanon); IPR
Cyprus (Cyprus)
*Distribution Center:* CES Holdings
*E-mail:* info@cesholdings.co.uk
Garnders Books *Tel:* (01323) 521 777
*Fax:* (01323) 521 666 *E-mail:* export@
gardners.com

**Food Trade Press**, *imprint of* Food Trade Press
Ltd

**Food Trade Press Ltd+**
Station House, Hortons Way, Westerham, Kent
TN16 1BZ
*Tel:* (01959) 563944 *Fax:* (01959) 561285
*E-mail:* ftpbooks@aol.com
*Web Site:* foodtradepress.net
*Key Personnel*
Dir: Adrian M Binsted
Founded: 1944
Publisher, distributor & bookseller for the food
trade.
Specialize in food production & technology.
ISBN Prefix(es): 0-900379; 0-903962
Number of titles published annually: 12 Print; 1
CD-ROM
Total Titles: 52 Print; 3 CD-ROM
*Associate Companies:* Attwood & Binsted Ltd
Imprints: Food Trade Press; Food Trade Review
Distributor for Campden & Chorleywood Food
RA (UK); Chemical Publishing (USA); Chiri-
otti Editori (Italy); CTI Publications (USA);
Food & Nutrition Press (USA); Leatherhead
Food RA (UK)

**Food Trade Review**, *imprint of* Food Trade Press
Ltd

**Forbes Publications Ltd+**
26 King St, 2nd floor, Covent Garden, London
WC2E 8JE
*Tel:* (020) 7836 5888 *Fax:* (020) 7836 7349
*E-mail:* editorial@rapportgroup.com
*Key Personnel*
Dir: Judith Bloor; Mary Anne FitzGerald
Founded: 1947
Subjects: Business, Economics, Education,
Health, Nutrition, Human Relations, Science
(General), Technology
ISBN Prefix(es): 0-901762; 1-899527
*Parent Company:* The Rapport Group Ltd
*Orders to:* Plymbridge Distributors, Estover
Rd, Plymouth, Devon PL6 7PZ *Tel:* (01752)
202300 *Fax:* (01752) 202330

**Forensic Science Society**
Clarke House, 18A Mount Parade, Harrogate
HG1 1BX
*Tel:* (01423) 506068 *Fax:* (01423) 566391
*E-mail:* tracey@forensic-science-society.org.uk
*Web Site:* www.forensic-science-society.org.uk
Founded: 1959
Subjects: Forensic science

**Forth Naturalist & Historian**
University of Stirling, Biological Sciences, Stir-
ling FK9 4LA
Mailing Address: 30 Dunmar Drive, Alloa, Clack-
mannan, Scotland FK10 2EH
*Tel:* (01786) 467755 *Fax:* (01786) 464994
*Web Site:* www.stir.ac.uk/departments/
naturalsciences/forth_naturalist
*Telex:* 777557 Stuniv G
*Key Personnel*
Honorary Editor & Secretary: Lindsay Corbett
*Tel:* (01259) 215091 *E-mail:* lindsay.corbett@
stir.ac.uk
Chairman: Prof John Proctor
Founded: 1975
An informal charitable body of the University of
Stirling to promote the environment, heritage &
wildlife of Central Scotland. Specialize in maps
& journals.
Membership(s): Scottish Publishers Association.
Subjects: Environmental Studies, History, Natural
History
ISBN Prefix(es): 0-9506962; 0-9514147; 1-
898008; 0-903650
Number of titles published annually: 1 Print
Total Titles: 30 Print
*Ultimate Parent Company:* University of Stirling
Distributed by Scottish Book Source; Scottish
Publishers Association
Distributor for Clarkmannanshire Libraries; CFSS
(Clarkmannanshire Field Studies Society);
Creag Darach; Falkirk Local History Society;
RIAS/Rutland Press; Stirling District Libraries

**Fostering Network+**
Formerly National Foster Care Association
87 Blackfriars Rd, London SE21 8HA
*Tel:* (020) 7620 6400 *Fax:* (020) 7620 6401
*E-mail:* nfca@fostercare.org.uk
*Key Personnel*
Executive Dir: Gerri McAndrew

Communications Manager: Katrina Phillips
Founded: 1976
Subjects: Child Care & Development
ISBN Prefix(es): 1-897869; 0-946015

**G T Foulis & Co**, *imprint of* Haynes Publishing

**Foulsham Publishers+**
Brunel Rd, Houndmills, Basingstoke RG21 6XS
*Tel:* (01256) 329242 *Fax:* (01256) 812558;
   (01256) 812521
*E-mail:* mdl@macmillan.co.uk
*Telex:* 41671 TCS G
*Key Personnel*
Man Dir & Commissioning Editor: B A R Be-
   lasco *E-mail:* belasco@foulsham.com
Dir, Finance & Export Sales: Graham M Kitchen
   *E-mail:* kitchen@foulsham.com
Production Dir: Roy Mantel *E-mail:* mantel@
   foulsham.com
International Rights & Foreign Rights Manager
   (London): Cathy Miller
Editorial Dir: W Hobson *E-mail:* hobson@
   foulsham.com
Founded: 1819
Subjects: Alternative, Antiques, Astrology, Oc-
   cult, Cookery, Crafts, Games, Hobbies, Educa-
   tion, Film, Video, Finance, Gardening, Plants,
   Health, Nutrition, House & Home, How-to,
   Humor, Self-Help, Technology, Travel, Wine &
   Spirits, Family Reference, Know How, Mind,
   Body, Spirit, Self Improvement
ISBN Prefix(es): 0-572
Number of titles published annually: 100 Print; 2
   E-Book
Total Titles: 300 Print
Imprints: Quantum
*Orders to:* Associated Publishers Group, 1501
   County Hospital Rd, Nashville, TN 37218,
   United States *Tel:* 615-254-2420 *Fax:* 615-254-
   2405

**The Foundational Book Company**
SSI House, Fordbrook Business Centre, Pewsey
   SW9 5NU
*Tel:* (016) 7256 4343
Founded: 1946
Subjects: Biblical Studies, Religion - Other
ISBN Prefix(es): 0-85241
Total Titles: 40 Print
*Distribution Center:* Rare Book Company, PO
   Box 6957, Freehold, NJ 07728, United States,
   Ann Beals *Tel:* 732-364-8043 *Fax:* 732-364-
   8043 *E-mail:* rarebooks@aol.com
The Bookmark, PO Box 801143, Santa Clarita,
   CA 91380-1143, United States *Tel:* 805-298
   7767 *Fax:* 805-250 9227 *E-mail:* order@
   thebookmark.com

**Foundery Press & Chester House Publications**,
   *imprint of* Methodist Publishing House

**Fountain Press**, *imprint of* Newpro UK Ltd

**Four Seasons Publishing Ltd+**
16 Orchard Rise, Kingston Upon Thames, Surrey
   KT2 7EY
*Tel:* (020) 8942 4445 *Fax:* (020) 8942 4446
*E-mail:* info@fourseasons.net
*Key Personnel*
Man Dir: Christopher Shepheard-Walwyn
   *E-mail:* csw@fourseasons.net
Founded: 1988
Expanding range of nonfiction gift books & so-
   cial stationery for the international co-edition
   market.
Membership(s): Independent Publishers Guild.
ISBN Prefix(es): 1-85645

**Fourth Estate+**
Division of HarperCollins UK

Distribution Centre, Colchester Rd Frating Green,
   Colchester C07 7DW
*Tel:* (01206) 256000; (01206) 255678
   *Fax:* (01206) 255715; (01206) 255930
*E-mail:* general@4thestate.co.uk
*Web Site:* www.4thestate.co.uk
*Key Personnel*
Chief Executive Officer & Publisher: Victoria
   Barnsley
Publishing Dir: Christopher Potter
Dep Man Dir: Stephen Page
Rights Dir: Susie Dunlop
Production: Graham Cook
Publicity Dir: Nicky Eaton
Founded: 1984
Subjects: Architecture & Interior Design, Biogra-
   phy, Cookery, Fiction, Gay & Lesbian, History,
   Humor, Literature, Literary Criticism, Essays,
   Radio, TV
ISBN Prefix(es): 0-947795; 1-872180; 1-84115;
   1-85702; 0-00
Imprints: Guardian Books
Distributor for John Brown Publishing; Duncan
   Baird Publisher (UK); Harvill Press (UK); Pro-
   file Books (UK)
*Orders to:* TBS, Frating Green, Colchester C07
   7DW

**L N Fowler & Co Ltd**, *imprint of* The C W
Daniel Co Ltd

**FOYLES**
113-119 Charing Cross Rd, London WC2H 0EB
*Tel:* (020) 7437 5660 *Fax:* (020) 7434 1574
*E-mail:* orders@foyles.co.uk
*Web Site:* www.foyles.co.uk *Cable:* FOYLIBRA
   LONDON WC2
*Key Personnel*
Chairman & Man Dir: WR Christopher Foyle
Marketing Dir: Bill Foyle Samuel *Tel:* (020) 7440
   3226 *E-mail:* bill@foyles.co.uk
General Manager: Sharon Murray
Founded: 1903
Divisions: Archaeology; Art; Astronomy; Auto-
   biographies & Biographies; Children's Books
   - Fiction & Non-Fiction; Cinema; Comput-
   ing; Cookery; Drama; Education; Engineering;
   English Language, EFL, Dictionaries & Ref-
   erence; English Literature; Fiction - Hardback
   & Paperback; Foreign Languages; History; Hu-
   mour; Maths & Physics; Medical, Nursing &
   Veterinary; Music; Natural History & Biology;
   Photography; Rare Books; Sociology; Sport;
   Technical; Theology; Transport; Travel

**Francis Balsom Associates+**
Unit 4, The Science Park, Aberystwyth SY23
   3AH
*Tel:* (01970) 636400 *Fax:* (01970) 636414
*E-mail:* info@fbagroup.co.uk
*Web Site:* www.fbagroup.co.uk
*Key Personnel*
Man Dir: Sue Balsom
Chairman & Company Secretary: Denis Balsom
Business Manager: Priscilla Gibby
Founded: 1989
Subjects: Art, Government, Political Science,
   Health, Nutrition, Sports, Athletics
ISBN Prefix(es): 1-901862
Imprints: Cyhoeddiadau FBA; FBA Publications

**The Fraser Press**
182 Bath St, Glasgow G2 4HG
*Tel:* (0141) 3331992 *Fax:* (0141) 3331992
*Key Personnel*
Proprietor: M Hay
Founded: 1991
Subjects: Architecture & Interior Design, Art
ISBN Prefix(es): 1-873805

**Free Association Books Ltd+**
57 Warren St, London W1T 5NZ

*Tel:* (020) 7388 3182 *Fax:* (020) 7388 3187
*E-mail:* info@fabooks.com
*Web Site:* www.fabooks.com
*Key Personnel*
Chief Executive, Editorial & Man Dir: Tower
   Brown
Publisher: Trevor E Brown
Rights & Permissions: Cathy Miller
Sales & Marketing Manager: Elisabetta Minervini
Founded: 1983
Subjects: Behavioral Sciences, Child Care & De-
   velopment, Ethnicity, Human Relations, Philos-
   ophy, Psychology, Psychiatry, Social Sciences,
   Sociology
ISBN Prefix(es): 0-946960; 1-85343
*U.S. Office(s):* NYUP, Elmer Holmes Bobst Li-
   brary, 70 Washington Sq S, New York, NY
   10012-1091, United States
Foreign Rep(s): Astam Books Pty ltd (Australia,
   New Zealand, Papua New Guinea); Bookworm
   (Israel); Richard Bowen (Scandinavia); Roy de
   Boo (Germany); ISBS (North America); Jordan
   Book Centre (Middle East); Kay Kato (Japan);
   Dineke Kemper (Benelux, Netherlands, France,
   Switzerland); Flavio Marcello (Italy, Portu-
   gal, Spain); STM Publishers Services Pte (Far
   East); Viva Books (India)
Foreign Rights: Cathy Miller Agency
*Warehouse:* The Trade Counter, Unit D, Trading
   Estate Rd, London NW10 7LU
*Distribution Center:* Astam Books Pty Ltd,
   57-61 John St, Leichhardt NSW 2040, Aus-
   tralia, Contact: Chris Player *Tel:* (02) 9566
   4400 *Fax:* (02) 9566 4411 *E-mail:* astam@
   interconnect.com.au
Roy de Boo, Diederik van Altenstraat 12, 5095
   AP Hooge Mierde, Netherlands *Tel:* (13)
   5096033 *Fax:* (13) 5096034 *E-mail:* roy.de.
   boo@inter.nl.net (Germany)
Bookworm, 30 Basel St, Tel Aviv 62744, Israel
   *Tel:* (972) 3546 2714 *Fax:* (972) 3546 2714
   *E-mail:* bookworm@classnet.co.il
Richard Bowen, PO Box 30037, S 200 61 Malmo
   30, Sweden (Scandinavia)
BR&D, Hadleigh Hall, London Rd, Hadleigh SS7
   2DE *Tel:* (01702) 552912 *Fax:* (01702) 556095
Eleanor Cripps, 4 Lytes Cary Rd, Keynsham,
   Bristol BS18 1XD *Tel:* (0117) 983 7326 (Mid-
   lands, Southeast England, Mid & South Wales)
Peter Hampson, 19 Guest Rd, Prestwich, Manch-
   ester M25 3DG *Tel:* (0161) 773 9753 (North
   Wales, North England, Scotland)
ISBS, 5804 NE Hassalo St, Portland, OR 97213-
   3644, United States *Fax:* 503-280-8832
   *E-mail:* fab@isbs.com (North America)
Jordan Book Centre, PO Box 301, Al-Jubeiha,
   Amman 11941, Jordan *Tel:* (6) 5151882
   *Fax:* (6) 5152016 *E-mail:* jbc@go.com.jo
Kay Kato, 5-14 Gokurakuji, 1-Chome, Kamakura
   Kanagawa 248, Japan
Dineke Kemper, Kemper Couseil, Dr Beguin-
   laan 72, NL 2272 AL Voorburg, Nether-
   lands *Tel:* (70) 3868031 *Fax:* (70) 3861498
   *E-mail:* kemper_conseil@dataweb.nl (France,
   Holland, Switzerland, Benelux)
Flavio Marcello, Via Vicenza 36, 35138 Padova,
   Italy (Italy, Spain & Portugal)
Gareth Pottle, 27 Highbury Pl, London N5 1QP
   *Tel:* (020) 7359 0679 (South London, Home
   Counties (South, East Anglia, Northern Ireland,
   Eire))
STM Publishers Services Pte Ltd, 352 Lorong
   Chuan, #01-05 Laurel Park 556783, Sin-
   gapore, Contact: Tony Poh Leong Wah
   *E-mail:* tonypoh@pacific.net.sg
Celia Stocks, 63 Bride St, London N7 8RN
   *Tel:* (020) 7607 4519 (North London, Home
   Counties (North))
Viva Books, 4325/3 Ansari Rd, Darya Ganj, New
   Delhi 110002, India, Contact: Vinod Vashishtha
*Orders to:* ISBS, 5804 NE Hassalo St, Portland,
   OR 97213-3644, United States *Fax:* 503-280-
   8832 *E-mail:* fab@isbs.com

Plymbridge Distributors Ltd, Estover, Plymouth PL6 7PZ *Tel:* (01752) 202301 *Fax:* (01752) 202333 *E-mail:* cservs@plymbridge.com (UK & Europe)

**Free Press**, *imprint of* Simon & Schuster Ltd

**Freedom Ministries**, *imprint of* Moorley's Print & Publishing Ltd

**Freedom Press**
Angel Alley, 84b Whitechapel High St, London E1 7QX
*Tel:* (020) 7247 9249 *Fax:* (020) 7377 9526
*Key Personnel*
Manager: Charles Crute; Vernon Richards
Founded: 1886 (Independent non-profit making publisher)
Subjects: Economics, Government, Political Science, History, Philosophy, Social Sciences, Sociology
ISBN Prefix(es): 0-900384; 1-904491
Number of titles published annually: 7 Print
Total Titles: 80 Print
Distributed by Active Distribution; AK Distribution; Left Bank Distribution
Distributor for AK Press; Calabria Press; Michael E Coughlin; Five Leaves Publications; Left Bank Distribution; Libertarian Education; Phoenix Press; Red Lion Press; See Sharp Press

**W H Freeman**, *imprint of* Palgrave Publishers Ltd

**W H Freeman & Co Ltd**
Brunel Rd, Houndmills, Basingstoke, Hants RG21 6XS
*Tel:* (01256) 302866 *Fax:* (01256) 330688
*E-mail:* orders@palgrave.com
*Web Site:* www.whfreeman.co.uk
*Key Personnel*
Man Dir: Dominic Knight *Tel:* (01256) 302750
Founded: 1959
Subjects: Behavioral Sciences, Biological Sciences, Chemistry, Chemical Engineering, Child Care & Development, Computer Science, Earth Sciences, Economics, Electronics, Electrical Engineering, Environmental Studies, Geography, Geology, Mathematics, Medicine, Nursing, Dentistry, Physical Sciences, Psychology, Psychiatry, Science (General)
ISBN Prefix(es): 0-7167
*Parent Company:* W H Freeman & Co, 41 Madison Ave, 37th floor, New York, NY 10010, United States
*Ultimate Parent Company:* Verlagsgruppe Georg von Holtzbrinck GmbH, Germany
*Holding Company:* Scientific American, 41 Madison Ave, New York, NY 10014, United States
Imprints: Scientific American; Computer Science Press
Distributed by Palgrave (UK, Europe, Africa, Middle East, India & Pakistan)
Distributor for Sirauer Associates; Spectrum; University Science Books; Worth
*Orders to:* Marston Book Services, PO Box 87, Oxford 0X4 1LB
W H Freeman & Co, 41 Madison Ave, New York, NY 10010, United States *Tel:* 212-576-9400 *Fax:* 212-481-1891 *Web Site:* www.whfreeman.com (North America & Far East)
Macmillan Education Publishers Australia Pty Ltd, Levels 4 & 5, 627 Chapel St, South Yarra, Victoria 3141, Australia *Tel:* (03) 9825 1025 *Fax:* (03) 9825 1010 *E-mail:* mea@macmillan.com.au *Web Site:* www.macmillan.com.au (Australia)

**Samuel French Ltd**
52 Fitzroy St, London W1T 5JR

*Tel:* (020) 7387 9373 *Fax:* (020) 7387 2161
*E-mail:* theatre@samuelfrench-london.co.uk
*Web Site:* www.samuelfrench-london.co.uk
*Key Personnel*
Chairman: Charles Van Nostrand
Man Dir: J W Bedding
Dir: Amanda Smith; Paul Taylor
Secretary to Man Dir: Vivien Goodwin
Founded: 1830
Subjects: Drama, Theater
ISBN Prefix(es): 0-573
*Associate Companies:* Samuel French (Canada) Ltd, 100 Lombard St, Lower Level, Toronto, ON, Canada; Samuel French Inc, 45 W 25 St, New York, NY 10010, United States; 7623 Sunset Blvd, Hollywood, CA 90046, United States
*Bookshop(s):* French's Theatre Bookshop, 52 Fitzroy St, London W1P 6JR

**Sigmund Freud Copyrights**
10 Brook St, Wivenhoe, Colchester CO7 9DS
*Tel:* (01206) 225433 *Fax:* (01206) 822990
*E-mail:* info@markpaterson.co.uk
*Web Site:* www.markpaterson.co.uk/sigmund.htm
*Key Personnel*
Dir: Mark Paterson *E-mail:* mark@markpaterson.co.uk
Archivist: Tom Roberts *E-mail:* tom@markpaterson.co.uk
Administrator: S Pearce
ISBN Prefix(es): 0-9507153
*Associate Companies:* Mark Paterson & Associates; Quentin Books Ltd

**The Friendly Press**
26 Cleeve Hill, Bristol BS16 6UL
*Tel:* (0117) 908-2281 *Fax:* (0117) 908-2282
*E-mail:* phgassoc@aol.com
*Key Personnel*
Dir: Anne Hodkinson
Contact: E Anne Lang
Membership(s): Quakers Uniting in Publications Worldwide (QUIP).
Subjects: ELT Books & Materials, Religious Quaker
ISBN Prefix(es): 0-948728
*Parent Company:* PH Group

**From The Portuguese**, *imprint of* Carcanet Press Ltd

**Frontier Publishing Ltd+**
Windetts, Seething Rd, Kirkstead, Norwich NR15 1EG
*Tel:* (01508) 558174
*E-mail:* frontier.pub@macunlimited.net
*Web Site:* www.frontierpublishing.co.uk
*Key Personnel*
Principal: Mr R Barnes
Founded: 1986
Membership(s): IPG.
Subjects: Art, History, Nonfiction (General), Photography, Poetry, Travel
ISBN Prefix(es): 0-85036; 1-872914; 0-9508701
Total Titles: 20 Print
Imprints: Frontier 2000 Series

**Frontier 2000 Series**, *imprint of* Frontier Publishing Ltd

**The FruitMarket Gallery**
45 Market St, Edinburgh EH1 1DF
*Tel:* (0131) 225 2383 *Fax:* (0131) 220 3130
*E-mail:* fruitmarket@fruitmarket.co.uk
*Web Site:* www.fruitmarket.co.uk
*Key Personnel*
Dir: Dr Fiona Bradley
Design & Publishing Manager: Elizabeth McLean
Development Manager: Armida Taylor
Education Manager: Tracy Morgan

Finance Manager: Graham Mannerings
Media & Marketing Manager: Annie Woodman
Founded: 1984
Mission: to bring the work of leading artists worldwide to Scotland & to exhibit the work of Scottish artists in an international context, engaging with contemporary issues.
Subjects: Art
ISBN Prefix(es): 0-947912

**David Fulton Publishers Ltd+**
The Chiswick Centre, 414 Chiswick High Rd, London W4 5TF
*Tel:* (020) 8996 3610 *Fax:* (020) 8996 3622
*E-mail:* mail@fultonpublishers.co.uk
*Web Site:* www.fultonpublishers.co.uk
*Key Personnel*
Chairman: David Fulton *E-mail:* david.fulton@fultonpublishers.co.uk
Man Dir: David Hill *E-mail:* david.hill@fultonpublishers.co.uk
Sales Manager: Rachael Robertson *E-mail:* rachael.robertson@fultonpublishers.co.uk
Publisher: Helen Fairlie *E-mail:* helen.fairlie@fultonpublishers.co.uk
Senior Commissioning Editor: Nina Stibbe *E-mail:* nina.stibbe@fultonpublishers.co.uk
Commissioning Editor (Special Education Needs): Jude Bowen *E-mail:* jude.bowen@fultonpublishers.co.uk
Commissioning Editor: Margaret Haigh *E-mail:* margaret.haigh@fultonpublishers.co.uk
Marketing Executive: Fred O'Connor *E-mail:* fred.oconnor@fultonpublishers.co.uk; Georgina Allan *E-mail:* georgina.allan@fultonpublishers.co.uk
Production Manager: Alan Worth *E-mail:* alan.worth@fultonpublishers.co.uk
Founded: 1987
Specialize in SEN books for teachers.
Subjects: Disability, Special Needs, Education
ISBN Prefix(es): 1-85346
*U.S. Office(s):* Taylor & Francis Inc, 1900 Frost Rd, Suite 101, Bristol, PA 19007-1598, United States *Tel:* 215-785-5800 *Fax:* 215-785-5515
*Foreign Rep(s):* Andrew Durnell (Ireland, Europe, Scandinavia); Karim International (Bangladesh); Viva Group (India); Yale Representation Ltd (England)
*Foreign Rights:* Book Promotions (Pty) Ltd (South Africa); Hemisphere Publication Services (Asia, The Pacific); Macmillan Academic & Reference (Australia); Macmillan Publishers New Zealand Ltd (New Zealand); Taylor & Francis Inc (North America)
*Warehouse:* Marston Book Services Ltd, PO Box 269, Abingdon, Oxon OX14 4YN
*Orders to:* Marston Book Services Ltd, PO Box 269, Abington, Oxon OX14 4YN

**Fun Files**, *imprint of* Funfax Ltd

**Funfax Ltd+**
9 Henrietta St, London WC2E 8PS
*Tel:* (020) 7836 5411 *Fax:* (020) 7836 7570
*E-mail:* clairrey@dk-uk.com
*Key Personnel*
Man Dir & Foreign Rights: Roger Priddy
Commercial Dir: Jonathan Mitchell
Sales Dir: Steve Evans
Chief Editor: Lisa Telford
Production Manager: Mike Kudar
Art Dir: Roger Tainsh
Founded: 1990
ISBN Prefix(es): 1-85597; 0-7547; 1-86208
*Parent Company:* Dorling Kindersley Ltd, 80 Strand, London WC2R ORL
Imprints: Clever Clogs; Fun Files; FX Pax; Junior Funfax; Know Alls; Lettermen; Mad Jack; Magic Joneuery; Microfax

*U.S. Office(s):* Dorling Kindersley Inc, 95 Madison Ave, New York, NY 10016, United States
*Web Site:* www.dk.com
*Warehouse:* International Book Distributors, Magna Park, Coventry Rd, Lutterworth, Lincs LE17

**Furco Ltd**
10 Jewry St, Winchester, Hants SO23 8RZ
*Mailing Address:* PO Box 6109, Harare, Zimbabwe
*Tel:* (04) 726795 *Fax:* (04) 726796
*E-mail:* info@africafilmtv.com
*Web Site:* www.africafilmtv.com
*Key Personnel*
Publisher & Editor: Russell Honeyman
*E-mail:* russell@africafilmtv.com
Sales Dir: Newton Musara *E-mail:* newton@africafilmtv.com
Administration Manager: Martha Musekiwa
*E-mail:* martha@africafilmtv.com
Founded: 1986
Publisher of *Africa Film & TV*, quarterly magazine & annual directory.
Subjects: Film, Video, Radio, TV

**FX Pax**, *imprint of* Funfax Ltd

**Fyfield Books**, *imprint of* Carcanet Press Ltd

**Gaia Books**, *imprint of* Octopus Publishing Group

**Gaia Books Ltd+**
66 Charlotte St, London W1T 4QE
*Tel:* (020) 7323 4010 *Fax:* (020) 7323 0435
*E-mail:* info@gaiabooks.com
*Web Site:* www.gaiabooks.co.uk
*Key Personnel*
Man Dir: Joss Pearson *E-mail:* jpearson@gaiabooks.com
Rights Dir: Rebecca Poulton
UK Publisher: Cathy Grieve
Founded: 1982
Specialize in books that celebrate the vision of Gaia, the self-sustaining living Earth & seek to help their readers live in greater personal & planetary harmony; mainly four-color illustrated titles.
Subjects: Architecture & Interior Design, Environmental Studies, Gardening, Plants, Health, Nutrition, Mind, Body & Spirit, Natural Health & Living
ISBN Prefix(es): 1-85675
Number of titles published annually: 12 Print
Total Titles: 110 Print; 5 Audio
*Branch Office(s)*
20 High St, Stroud, Glos GL5 1AZ, UK Publisher: Lyn Hemming *Tel:* (01453) 752985 *Fax:* (01453) 752987 *E-mail:* addressee@gaiabooks.co.uk
Distributed by Simon & Schuster (USA, Canada, open market excluding Britain & Commonwealth)
*Orders to:* Grantham Book Services, Alma Park Industrial Estate, Isaac Newton Way, Lincolnshire NG31 9SD, Contact: Marilyn Baines *Tel:* (01476) 541080 *Fax:* (01476) 541061

**Gairm Publications**
29 Waterloo St, Glasgow G2 6BZ
*Tel:* (0141) 221 1971 *Fax:* (0141) 221 1971
*Key Personnel*
Editor: Derick S Thomson
Founded: 1952
Specialize in Scottish Gaelic publications.
Subjects: Biography, Fiction, Music, Dance, Poetry, Regional Interests
ISBN Prefix(es): 1-871901; 0-901771
Total Titles: 120 Print

**Galaxy Large Print**, *imprint of* BBC Audiobooks

**Gale**, *imprint of* Thomson Gale

**Gallery Children's Books**, *imprint of* East-West Publications (UK) Ltd

**Galliard**, *imprint of* Stainer & Bell Ltd

**Garden Art Press Ltd**, *imprint of* Antique Collectors' Club Ltd

**Garden Art Press Ltd+**
Imprint of Antique Collectors' Club Ltd
5A Church St, Woodbridge IP12 1DS
*Tel:* (01394) 385501 *Fax:* (01394) 384434
*Key Personnel*
Man Dir: Diana Steel
Subjects: Gardening, Plants
ISBN Prefix(es): 1-870673

**Walter H Gardner & Co**
16 Chalton Dr, London N2 0QW
*Tel:* (20) 8458 3202 *Fax:* (20) 8458 8499
*E-mail:* walterhgardnerco@aol.com
*Key Personnel*
Man Partner: Walter H Gardner
Sales & Marketing: Mrs D Gardner
Founded: 2001
Also acts as remainder & periodical back issue dealer.

**Garland Science**, *imprint of* Taylor & Francis

**Garnet Publishing Ltd+**
8 Southern Court, South St, Reading, Berks RG1 4QS
*Tel:* (0118) 959 7847 *Fax:* (0118) 959 7356
*E-mail:* enquiries@garnet-ithaca.demon.co.uk (general enquiries); orders@garnet-ithaca.demon.co.uk (ordering)
*Web Site:* www.garnet-ithaca.co.uk
*Key Personnel*
Editorial Manager: Emma Hawker
*E-mail:* emmahawker@garnet-ithaca.demon.co.uk
Editor: Anna Hines *E-mail:* annahines@garnet-ithaca.demon.co.uk
Founded: 1991
Subjects: Anthropology, Archaeology, Architecture & Interior Design, Art, Biography, Cookery, English as a Second Language, Foreign Countries, History, Literature, Literary Criticism, Essays, Photography, Religion - Islamic, Travel
ISBN Prefix(es): 1-85964; 1-873938; 1-86372
Total Titles: 300 Print
Imprints: Ithaca Press; South Street Press
Distributed by ISBS (US & Canada)

**Gateway Books+**
Imprint of Gill & Macmillan
The Hollies, Wellow, Bath BA2 8QJ
*Tel:* (01225) 835 127 *Fax:* (01225) 840 012
*E-mail:* sales@gatewaybooks.com
Founded: 1982
Subjects: Anthropology, Earth Sciences, Environmental Studies, Health, Nutrition, Mysteries, Philosophy, Psychology, Psychiatry, Religion - Other, Self-Help
ISBN Prefix(es): 0-946551; 1-85860
*U.S. Office(s):* Gateway Books at WPR, 2819 Tenth St, Berkeley, CA 94710, United States
*Tel:* 510-841-9347
Distributor for Amethyst Books (Banbury, UK)
*Orders to:* Airlift Book Co, 8 The Arena, Mollison Ave, Enfield, Middlesex EN3 7NJ
*Tel:* (0181) 8040 400 *Fax:* (0181) 8040 044

**The Gay Men's Press**, *imprint of* GMP Publishers Ltd

**GE Fabbri**, *imprint of* Fabbri (GE) Ltd

**GE Magazines**, *imprint of* Fabbri (GE) Ltd

**Geddes & Grosset+**
Subsidiary of D C Thomson & Co Ltd
David Dale House, Rosedale St, New Lanark, Lanark ML11 9DJ
*Tel:* (01555) 665000 *Fax:* (01555) 665694
*E-mail:* info@gandg.sol.co.uk
*Key Personnel*
Publisher: Ron B Grosset *E-mail:* ron@gandg.sol.co.uk; Mike Miller *E-mail:* mike@gandg.sol.co.uk
Founded: 1987
Specializes in popular reference & children's books for the mass market.
Membership(s): Scottish Publishers Association.
ISBN Prefix(es): 1-85534
Number of titles published annually: 80 Print
Imprints: Beano Books; Tarantula Books; Waverley Books
Distributed by Book Source; Peter Haddock Ltd

**Geiser Productions+**
7 The Corner, Grange Rd, London W5 3PQ
*Tel:* (020) 8579 4653 *Fax:* (020) 8567 6593
*E-mail:* geiser@gxn.co.uk
*Web Site:* www.geiserproductions.com; www.sidsjournal.com
*Key Personnel*
Dir & International Rights: N H Geiser
Dir: Sidney DuBroff
Founded: 1967
In-house producers of sponsored & commissioned works, who accept assignments in all areas - whether large or small. Areas of endeavour include serious fiction, politics & country sports.
Membership(s): IPG.
Subjects: Fiction, Government, Political Science, Journalism, Outdoor Recreation, Sports, Athletics
ISBN Prefix(es): 0-9503262

**Gembooks**
16 Green Park, 91 Manor Rd, East Cliff, Bournemouth BH1 3HR
*Tel:* (01202) 399729 *Fax:* (01202) 399729
*E-mail:* readbooks@onmail.co.uk
*Key Personnel*
Editor & Author: Peter G Read
Founded: 1995
Specialize in diamond fiction.
Subjects: Criminology, Fiction, Mysteries, Diamond Industry
ISBN Prefix(es): 0-9525315
Total Titles: 3 Print

**Genesis Publications Ltd+**
2 Jenner Rd, Guildford, Surrey GU1 3PL
*Tel:* (01483) 540970 *Fax:* (01483) 304709
*E-mail:* info@genesis-publications.com
*Web Site:* www.genesis-publications.com
*Key Personnel*
Publisher: Brian Roylance
Founded: 1972
Subjects: Art, History, Literature, Literary Criticism, Essays, Natural History, Poetry, Science (General)
ISBN Prefix(es): 0-904351

**Geographers' A-Z Map Company Ltd**
Fairfield Rd, Borough Green, Sevenoaks, Kent TN15 8PP
*Tel:* (01732) 781000 *Fax:* (01732) 780677
*E-mail:* tradesales@a-zmaps.co.uk
*Web Site:* www.azmaps.co.uk

*Key Personnel*
Man Dir: D W Churchill; K Palmer
Founded: 1936
ISBN Prefix(es): 0-85039
*Showroom(s):* 44 Gray's Inn Rd, London WC1X
8HX *Tel:* (020) 7440 9500 *Fax:* (020) 7440
9501 *E-mail:* shop@a-zmaps.co.uk


## The Geographical Association+

160 Solly St, Sheffield S1 4BF
*Tel:* (0114) 296 0088 *Fax:* (0114) 296 7176
*E-mail:* ga@geography.org.uk
*Web Site:* www.geography.org.uk
*Key Personnel*
Marketing Manager: Richard Jones
Senior Administrator: Frances Soar
Founded: 1893
National association for geography teachers with
a membership of over 10,000.
Also book packager.
Subjects: Geography, Geology
ISBN Prefix(es): 0-900395; 0-948512; 1-899085;
1-905448
Number of titles published annually: 25 Print
Total Titles: 120 Print
*Branch Office(s)*
Bedfordshire Branch, Contact: Mr David Cooper
*Tel:* (01536) 710226
Berkhamstead Branch
Birmingham Branch, Contact: Julia Legg
*Tel:* (0114) 2960088
Blackpool & District Branch, Blackpool Sixth
Form College, Blackpool Old Road, High-
furlong, Blackpool, Contact: Joan M Clarke
*Tel:* (01253) 761330
Bradford Branch, Contact: Mr D E Cotton
Brighton & District Branch, Contact: Julia Legg
*Tel:* (0114) 2960088
Cambridge & District Branch, Contact: Richard
Dilley *Tel:* (01480) 461857
Cardiff Branch, Contact: Julia Legg *Tel:* (0114)
2960088
Chester, Halton & Warrington Branch, Contact:
Elaine Jackson *Tel:* (01928) 425489
Durham Branch, Contact: Adam Nichols
*Tel:* (0191) 374 7821
Geographical Association Branch Network,
President: Alison Bailey *Web Site:* www.
digitalbristol.org/members/ga/
Guildford Branch, Contact: Mr R E J Seymour
Hampshire Branch, Contact: Kim Adams
*Tel:* (01962) 852764 *Web Site:* www.
mcnaughtweb.freeserve.co.uk/hantsga/index.htm
Hereford Branch, Contact: Julia Legg *Tel:* (0114)
2960088 *E-mail:* jlegg@geography.org.uk
Hertfordshire GTA Branch
High Weald Branch, Chairman: Peter Goddard
*Tel:* (01580) 764917 *Fax:* (01580) 764917
*E-mail:* c.g.@tobermory.demon.co.uk
Huddersfield & Halifax Branch, Contact: Janet
Clarkson *Tel:* (01484) 608599
Hull & District Branch, Contact: Richard Hurrell
*Tel:* (01482) 711688 *Fax:* (01482) 798991
Isle of Thanet Branch, Chairman: Jan Ingram
*Tel:* (01843) 862845
Kingston-upon-Thames Branch, Contact: Dr An-
nie Hughes
Leicester Branch, Contact: Malcolm Pollard
Lincoln Branch *E-mail:* steephill@btinternet.com
Liverpool & District Branch, Contact: David
Chambers *Tel:* (0151) 420 4941 *Fax:* (0151)
330 3366
Manchester Branch, Contact: Mrs M Blackburn
Norfolk Branch, Contact: Kirsten Remer *Web
Site:* www.norfolkga.org.uk/
North Staffordshire Branch, Alleyne, Stone,
Staffordshire ST15 8DT, Honorary Secre-
tary: Robert G Jones *Tel:* (01785) 354200
*Fax:* (01785) 354222 *E-mail:* robertgjones@
yahoo.com
Oxford Branch, St Edwards School, Woodstock
Road, Oxford OX2 7NN, Contact: Dr G Nagle
*Tel:* (01865) 319231

Plymouth & District Branch, Contact: Miss N S
M Paterson *Tel:* (01752) 668482
Ribblesdale Branch, Contact: Mike Pearson
Tyneside Branch, Inspection & Advisory Service,
Education Department, County Hall, Durham
DH1 5UJ, Contact: Trevor Hemsley *Tel:* (0191)
383 4558
Worcester Branch, Contact: Richard Yarwood
*Web Site:* www.worc.ac.uk/departs/envman/
worcGA/
York & District Branch, 14 St James' Mount,
York YO23 1EL, Secretary: Hilary Arnold
*Tel:* (01904) 655114
Foreign Rep(s): Drake International (Europe, US)


## Geological Society Publishing House

Unit 7, Brassmill Enterprise Centre, Brassmill
Lane, Bath BA1 3JN
*Tel:* (01225) 445046 *Fax:* (01225) 442836
*E-mail:* rebecca.toop@geolsoc.org.uk
*Web Site:* www.geolsoc.org.uk
*Key Personnel*
Dir, Publishing: Neal Marriott *E-mail:* neal.
marriott@geolsoc.org
Editor: Angharad Hills *E-mail:* angharad.hills@
geolsoc.org.uk
Sales: Dawn Angel *E-mail:* dawn.angel@geolsoc.
org.uk
Founded: 1807
Membership(s): European Federation of Geolo-
gists & Association of European Geological
Societies.
Subjects: Civil Engineering, Earth Sciences, Ge-
ography, Geology, Science (General)
ISBN Prefix(es): 0-903317; 1-897799; 1-86239
Number of titles published annually: 30 Print
Total Titles: 250 Print; 2 CD-ROM
*Parent Company:* The Geological Society,
Burlington House, Piccadilly, London W1J
0BG
Distributed by AAPG (North America)
Distributor for American Association of
Petroleum Geologists (European distributor);
Geological Society of America (European dis-
tributor); Society for Sedimentary Geology
(European distributor)
*Orders to:* AAPG Bookstore, PO Box 979, Tulsa,
OK 74101-0979, United States
Affiliated East-West Press PVT Ltd, G-1/16
Ansari Rd, New Delhi 110 002, India, Contact:
Sunny Malik *Tel:* (011) 3279113 *Fax:* (011)
3260538
Kanda Book Trading Co, Cityhouse Tama 204,
Tsurumaki 1-3-10, Tama-Shi, Tokyo 206-0034,
Japan *Tel:* (04) 23577650 *Fax:* (04) 23577651


## George Mann Publications+

8 Birnam Sq, Maidstone ME16 8UN
*Tel:* (01622) 759591 *Fax:* (01622) 209193
*Web Site:* www.gmp.co.uk
*Key Personnel*
Chairman: George Mann
Man Dir: John Arne
Founded: 1972
Subjects: Astrology, Occult, Biography, Fiction,
Human Relations, Nonfiction (General), Philos-
ophy
ISBN Prefix(es): 0-7041
*Parent Company:* Arnefold Editions
Imprints: Arnefold; George Mann; Recollections


**Laura Geringer Books**, *imprint of* HarperCollins
UK


## E J W Gibb Memorial Trust

2 Penarth Pl, Cambridge CB3 9LU
*Tel:* (01985) 213409 *Fax:* (01985) 212910
*Web Site:* www.arisandphillips.com
*Key Personnel*
Secretary to the Trustees: Robin Bligh
Founded: 1902

A charity which supports & publishes books on
the literature, religions, philosophy & history of
the Persian, Turks & Arab peoples.
Subjects: History, Literature, Literary Criticism,
Essays, Philosophy, Religion - Other
ISBN Prefix(es): 0-906094
*Orders to:* c/o Oxbow Books, Park End Place,
Oxford OX1 1HN


## Stanley Gibbons Publications

5 Parkside, Christchurch Rd, Ringwood, Hants
BH24 3SH
*Tel:* (01425) 472363 *Fax:* (01425) 470247
*E-mail:* sales@stangib.demon.co.uk
*Web Site:* www.stanleygibbons.com
*Key Personnel*
Dir: Richard Purkis *E-mail:* rpurkis@
stanleygibbons.co.uk
Editor: Hugh Jeffries *E-mail:* hjeffries@
stanleygibbons.co.uk
General Sales Manager: Brian Case
*E-mail:* bcase@stanleygibbons.co.uk
Founded: 1856
Subjects: Crafts, Games, Hobbies, Philately
ISBN Prefix(es): 0-85259
*Parent Company:* Stanley Gibbons International
Ltd, 399 Strand, London WC2R 0LX


## Ginn & Co+

Division of Harcourt Education International
Halley Court, Jordan Hill, Oxford OX2 8EJ
Mailing Address: PO Box 1127, Freepost (SCE
7554), Oxford OX2 8YY
*Tel:* (01865) 888000 *Fax:* (01865) 314222
*E-mail:* enquiries@ginn.co.uk
*Web Site:* www.myprimary.co.uk
*Key Personnel*
Publishing Dir: Kath Donovan; Rod Theodorou;
Stephen Fahey
Man Dir: Paul Shuter *Tel:* (01865) 311366
*E-mail:* pshuter@ginn.co.uk
UK Sales Manager: Rachel Colyer *Tel:* (01865)
314096
Founded: 1862 (USA, 1920 in London)
Subjects: Education
ISBN Prefix(es): 0-602
Foreign Rep(s): Agius & Agius Ltd (Eu-
rope); Carlos Barbison (Brazil); Basil Bona-
parte (Grenada); Book Link Co Ltd (Thai-
land); Books & Bits (Chile); Bookshop SA
(Uruguay); Brown Onduso (Kenya); Bushbooks
(Australia); Cairo Trade Center - Alexandria
(Egypt); Cairo Trade Center - Cairo (Egypt);
Chris Chirwa (Southern Africa); Susan Chua
(Brunei, Singapore, Sri Lanka, Southeast Asia);
Crownbooks (Africa); George Davis (Jamaica);
Drum Publishers (Tanzania); Editions de L'
Ocean Indien Ltd (Africa); English Book Cen-
ter (Colombia); Carole Ford (Europe, United
Arab Emirates); R Yvonne Gaynes (Caribbean,
Saint Vincent & the Grenadines); Harcourt
Canada (Canada); Heinemann Inc (US); Heine-
mann Botswana (Southern Africa); Carroll
Heinemann (Ireland); Heinemann Educational
Books (Nigeria) Ltd (Nigeria); Heinemann
Educational Botswana (Botswana, Lesotho,
Swaziland); Heinemann Lesotho (Southern
Africa); Heinemann South Africa (South
Africa); Heinemann Southern Africa (South-
ern Africa); Heinemann Swaziland (Southern
Africa); Heinemann UK (UK); Irwin Pub-
lishing (Canada); Louise Jacobs (Africa, Far
East, Middle East); Jango Heinemann (South-
ern Africa); Kel Ediciones SA (Argentina);
Ishmael M Khan & Sons Ltd (Trinidad & To-
bago); Rufus Khodra (Caribbean); Benjamin
Kithyaka (Kenya); Mark Kuo (Cambodia,
Indonesia, Korea, Latin America, Malaysia,
Myanmar, Vietnam); Gerry McCullough
(Southern Africa); Nzomo Educational Supplies
Ltd (Kenya); Onganda Y' Omambo Bookshop
(Southern Africa); Oxford University Press
(India, Pakistan); Publishers Marketing Asso-

ciates (Pakistan); Adam Quilter (Worldwide); R E D I (Africa); Rearden Book Suppliers (Lebanon); Reed Publishing Group (NZ) Ltd (New Zealand); F Reimmer Book Services (Ghana); Rigby Heinemann (Australia); Rorash Educational Publishers (Uganda); Schools Promotion Services (Jamaica); S Seshadra (India); Clare Symonette (Caribbean); Textbook Sales (Pvt) Ltd (Zimbabwe); Transglobal Publishers Service Ltd (Hong Kong); Julie White (Barbados)
*Warehouse:* Unit 1, Block H, Industrial Estate, Long Eaton, Nottingham NG10 1GG

**IL Giornale dell'Arte**, see Umberto Allemandi & Co Publishing

**Glasgow City Libraries Publications+**
The Mitchell Library, North St, Glasgow G3 7DN
*Tel:* (0141) 287 2846 *Fax:* (0141) 287 2815
*Web Site:* www.glasgowlibraries.org
*Key Personnel*
Commercial Manager: Verina Litster
    *E-mail:* verina.litster@cls.glasgow.gov.uk
Founded: 1980
Specialize in local history fact books.
Membership(s): Scottish Publishers' Association.
Subjects: History, Regional Interests
ISBN Prefix(es): 0-906169
*Distribution Center:* The Mitchell Library

**Mary Glasgow Publications**, *imprint of* Nelson Thornes Ltd

**Global Oriental Ltd+**
PO Box 219, Folkestone, Kent CT18 2WP
*Tel:* (01303) 226799 *Fax:* (01303) 243087
*E-mail:* info@globaloriental.co.uk
*Web Site:* www.globaloriental.co.uk
*Key Personnel*
Publisher & Man Dir: Paul Norbury
Sales Manager, International Sales-Marketing: Iris Warr
Founded: 1994
Subjects: Art, Biography, Education, Geography, Geology, Health, Nutrition, History, Language Arts, Linguistics, Literature, Literary Criticism, Essays, Religion - Other, Transportation, Travel, Comparative & Cultural Studies, Media & Cultural Studies, Korea-General Reference, Lafcadio Hearn Studies, Martial Arts, Memoirs
ISBN Prefix(es): 1-86034; 1-901903; 1-898823
Number of titles published annually: 12 Print
Total Titles: 52 Print
Imprints: Renaissance Books
Distributed by University of Hawaii Press (USA & Canada)
Foreign Rep(s): APD Singapore (Southeast Asia); Unifacmanu Trading Co (Taiwan); United Publishers Services Ltd (Japan)
*Distribution Center:* Orca Book Services, Stanley House, 3 Fleets Lane, Poole, Dorset BH15 3AJ *Tel:* (01202) 665432 *Fax:* (01202) 666219 *E-mail:* orders@orcabookservices.co.uk
*Orders to:* Midpoint Trade Books, 1263 Southwest Blvd, Kansas City, KS 66103, United States *Tel:* 913-831-2233 *Fax:* 913-362-7401

**Glowworm Books Ltd+**
Unit 7, Greendykes Industrial Estate, Broxburn EH52 5LH
*Tel:* (01506) 857570 *Fax:* (01506) 858100
*E-mail:* admin@GlowwormBooks.co.uk; sales@amaising.co.uk (packaging); sales@glowwormbooks.co.uk (publishing & schools division)
*Web Site:* www.GlowwormBooks.co.uk
*Key Personnel*
Man Dir: Mrs K Allan
Operations Dir: Mr G Allan
Sales Manager: Mrs Marion Farish

Buyer: Annie Crighton
Founded: 1984
Specialize in publishing children's picture books, also a school supplier for text books & libraries (in Scotland only).
Membership(s): Booksellers Association; Scottish Publishers Association.
ISBN Prefix(es): 1-871512
Number of titles published annually: 3 Print
Total Titles: 43 Print

**GMC Publications Ltd+**
166 High St, Lewes, East Sussex BN7 1XU
*Tel:* (01273) 477374; (01273) 488005
    *Fax:* (01273) 478606
*E-mail:* pubs@thegmcgroup.com; theguild@thegmcgroup.com
*Web Site:* www.thegmcgroup.com/pubsweb/
*Key Personnel*
Senior Man Editor, Books: April McCroskie
    *Fax:* (01273) 487692 *E-mail:* aprilm@thegmcgroup.com
Publish magazines books & videos for general trade.
Subjects: Crafts, Games, Hobbies, Gardening, Plants, How-to, Photography
ISBN Prefix(es): 1-86108
Total Titles: 120 Print
Imprints: Guild of Master Publications Inc
Distributor for Sterling Publishing Co Inc; Taunton Press Publishers
*Warehouse:* Mail International Ltd, Braybon Business Park, Consort Way, Burgess Hill W Sussex

**GMP Publishers Ltd+**
c/o Central Books, 99A Wallis Rd, London E9 5LN
*Tel:* (020) 8986 4854 *Fax:* (020) 8533 5821
*E-mail:* david@gmpub.demon.co.uk
*Web Site:* www.gmppubs.co.uk
*Key Personnel*
Dir, Editorial, Art & Photography: Aubrey Walter
Dir, Editorial, Fiction: David Fernbach
Founded: 1979
Gay fiction & nonfiction.
Subjects: Art, Fiction, Gay & Lesbian, History, Nonfiction (General)
ISBN Prefix(es): 0-85449; 0-907040; 0-946097
*Associate Companies:* Heretic Books Ltd
Imprints: The Gay Men's Press; Editions Aubrey Walter
Distributed by LPC/Inbook (North America)
*Orders to:* Central Books Ltd, 99 Wallis Rd, London E9 5LN *Tel:* (020) 8986 4854 *Fax:* (020) 8533 5821

**Godsfield Press**, *imprint of* Octopus Publishing Group

**Godsfield Press Ltd+**
Division of David & Charles Ltd
Laurel House, Station Approach, Alresford SO24 9JH
*Tel:* (01962) 735633; (01626) 323200 (general enquiries) *Fax:* (01962) 735320; (01626) 323319 (general enquiries)
*E-mail:* mail@davidandcharles.co.uk
*Web Site:* www.davidandcharles.co.uk
*Key Personnel*
Proprietor: Debbie Thorpe *E-mail:* debbie@godsfield.com
Founded: 1995
Subjects: Health, Nutrition, Esoterics/New Age, Divination, Personal Growth, Sacred Living, Spiritual Wisdom
ISBN Prefix(es): 1-899434; 1-84181
Distributed by David & Charles (United Kingdom & Eire)
*Orders to:* HarperCollins Distribution Service, Glasgow GA ONB

**Golden Cockerel Press Ltd+**
The Chandlery, Unit 304, 50 Westminster Bridge Rd, London SE1 7QY
*Tel:* (020) 79538770 *Fax:* (020) 79538738
*E-mail:* aup.uk@btinternet.com
*Telex:* 23565
*Key Personnel*
Man Dir, UK: Andrew Lindesay; Tamar Lindesay
    *E-mail:* lindesay@btinternet.com
Founded: 1979
Subjects: Architecture & Interior Design, Art, Drama, Theater, Film, Video, Government, Political Science, History, Literature, Literary Criticism, Essays, Music, Dance, Philosophy, Social Sciences, Sociology, Theology
ISBN Prefix(es): 0-498
*Associate Companies:* Associated University Presses Inc, 440 Forsgate Dr, Cranbury, NJ 08512, United States
Imprints: Associated University Presses (UK, Europe, India, Australia & New Zealand); Cornwall Books; Cygnus Arts
Distributor for Associated University Presses (UK, Europe, India, Australia & New Zealand)
*Orders to:* Gazelle Book Services, Falcon House, Queen Square, Lancaster LA1 1RN *Tel:* (01524) 68765 *Fax:* (01524) 63232 *E-mail:* gazelle4go@aol.com

**Golden Dawn**, *imprint of* Mandrake of Oxford

**Golden Handshake**, *imprint of* Jay Landesman

**Goldleaf Publishing (Local History)**, *imprint of* Alun Books

**Victor Gollancz**, *imprint of* Cassell & Co

**Victor Gollancz Ltd**, see Gollancz/Witherby

**Gollancz/Witherby+**
Orion House, 5 Upper St Martin's Lane, London WC2H 9EA
*Tel:* (020) 7240 3444 *Fax:* (020) 7240 4822
*E-mail:* info@orionbooks.co.uk
*Web Site:* www.orionbooks.co.uk
*Telex:* 9413701 CASPUB
*Key Personnel*
Sales Dir: Andrew Macmillan
Rights & Permissions: Jane Blackstock
Publisher: Liz Knights
Production: Elizabeth Dobson
Science Fiction: Richard Evans
Children's: Chris Kloet
Subjects: Architecture & Interior Design, Biography, Fiction, History, Music, Dance, Mysteries, Natural History, Nonfiction (General), Outdoor Recreation, Science (General), Science Fiction, Fantasy, Sports, Athletics, Travel
ISBN Prefix(es): 0-575; 0-85493
*Parent Company:* Orion Publishing Group

**Gomer Press (J D Lewis & Sons Ltd)+**
Gwasg Gomer, Llandysul, Ceredigion SA44 4JL
*Tel:* (01559) 362371 *Fax:* (01559) 363758
*E-mail:* gwasg@gomer.co.uk
*Web Site:* www.gomer.co.uk *Cable:* GOMER LLANDYSUL
*Key Personnel*
Man Dir & Rights & Permissions: Jonathan Lewis
Editorial: Mairwen Prys Jones
Sales & Publicity: Meinir Garnon James
Founded: 1892
Specialize in books from Wales, about Wales, in Welsh & English.
Subjects: Education, Fiction, Language Arts, Linguistics, Nonfiction (General), Poetry, Regional Interests
ISBN Prefix(es): 0-86383; 0-85088; 1-85902; 1-84323

Number of titles published annually: 100 Print
Total Titles: 700 Print
*Parent Company:* J D Lewis & Sons Ltd
Imprints: Pont Books
*Bookshop(s):* Gomerian Press, Llandysul, Dyfed

**Goodnight Sleeptight**, *imprint of* Grandreams
Ltd

**A H Gordon**
Priory Cottage, Chetwade, Buckingham MK18
4LB
*Tel:* (01280) 848 650
*Key Personnel*
President: Adam Gordon *E-mail:* adam@
adamgordon.freeewire.co.uk
Founded: 1990
Specialize in Tramways, trolley buses & railways.
Publisher of new books & dealer in second
hand books & ephemera.
Subjects: Transportation, Buses, Railways, Christian
ISBN Prefix(es): 1-874422
Number of titles published annually: 6 Print
Total Titles: 41 Print

**The Robert Gordon University**
Garthdee, Aberdeen AB10 7QE
*Tel:* (01224) 262000 *Fax:* (01224) 263553
*E-mail:* sim@rgu.ac.uk
*Web Site:* www.rgu.ac.uk
*Key Personnel*
Assistant Dean, Aberdeen Business School: Ian
M Johnson
Course Leader (Electronic Publishing): Sarah
Pedersen
Course Leader (Publishing Studies): Josephine M
Royle
Founded: 1967
Subjects: Publishing & Book Trade Education &
Training

**Gower Publishing Ltd**, *imprint of* Ashgate
Publishing Ltd

**Gower Publishing Ltd+**
Imprint of Ashgate Publishing Ltd
Gower House, Croft Rd, Aldershot, Hants GU11
3HR
*Tel:* (01252) 331551 *Fax:* (01252) 344405
*E-mail:* info@gowerpub.com
*Web Site:* www.gowerpub.com
*Key Personnel*
Man Dir: Christopher Simpson
Sales & Marketing Dir: Rachel Maund
Founded: 1967
Subjects: Business, Management
ISBN Prefix(es): 0-566; 0-7045
*Associate Companies:* Dartmouth Publishing Ltd
*Orders to:* Ashgate-Gower Asia Pacific, 3/303
Barrenjoey Rd, Newport, NSW 2107, Australia *Tel:* (02) 9999 2777 *Fax:* (02) 9999 3688
*E-mail:* info@ashgate.com.au (Australia, SE &
NE Asia)
Ashgate Publishing Ltd, 2252 Ridge Rd, Brookfield, VT 05036-9704, United States *Tel:* 802-
276-3162 *Fax:* 802-276-3837 *E-mail:* info@
ashgate.com (North America & South America)
Bookpoint Ltd, Gower Publishing Customer Service, 130 Milton Park, Abingdon, Oxon OX14
4SB *Tel:* (01235) 827730 *Fax:* (01235) 400454
*E-mail:* orders@bookpoint.co.uk/enquiries@
bookpoint.co.uk *Web Site:* pubeasy.books.
bookpoint.co.uk (UK & Europe)

**Gracewing Publishing**
2 Southern Ave, Leominster HR6 0QF
*Tel:* (01568) 616835 *Fax on Demand:* (01568)
613289
*E-mail:* gracewingx@aol.com
*Web Site:* www.gracewing.co.uk

Subjects: Religion - Other, Theology, Church Biography, Ecclesiastical History
ISBN Prefix(es): 0-85244
Distributed by Morehouse (US)
Distributor for Mercer University Press (in UK);
Our Sunday Visitor; Smyth & Helwys; Source;
Templegate

**Graham & Whiteside**, *imprint of* Thomson Gale

**Graham-Cameron Publishing & Illustration+**
The Studio, 23 Holt Rd, Sheringham, Norfolk
NR26 8NB
*Tel:* (01263) 821 333 *Fax:* (01263) 821 334
*E-mail:* enquiry@graham-cameron-illustration.
com
*Web Site:* www.graham-cameron-illustration.com
*Key Personnel*
Partner: Helen Graham-Cameron; Mike Graham-Cameron
Marketing Manager: Duncan Graham-Cameron
Founded: 1985 (Founded as a book publisher, became a packager & illustration agency)
Editorial & production assistance. Approximately
37 freelance professional illustrators under contract.
Membership(s): Independent Publishers Guild
(IPG), Cambridge Book Association (CBA) &
Publishers in Cambridge Association (PICA).
Subjects: Education, English as a Second Language, Language Arts, Linguistics
ISBN Prefix(es): 0-947672

**W F Graham (Northampton) Ltd**
2 Pondwood Close, Moulton Park Industrial Estate, Northampton, Northants NN3 6RT
*Tel:* (01604) 645537 *Fax:* (01604) 648414
*Key Personnel*
Man Dir: R F Graham
Sales Dir: T A Graham
Founded: 1952
ISBN Prefix(es): 1-85128

**Gramophone**, *imprint of* Wilmington Business
Information Ltd

**Granada Media**, *imprint of* Carlton Publishing
Group

**Grandreams Ltd+**
435-437 Edgware Rd, Little Venice, London W2
1TH
*Tel:* (020) 7724 5333 *Fax:* (020) 7724 5777
*E-mail:* wrrake@robert-frederick.co.uk
*Key Personnel*
Rights Manager: Catherine Lyn-Jones
Production Manager: Josie Strong
Founded: 1977
Specialize in international coeditions & mass
market children's books; dictionaries, reference books, foreign language books, novelty books, pop-ups, board books, storybooks,
sticker books, coloring books.
Subjects: Fiction, Nonfiction (General)
ISBN Prefix(es): 0-86227; 1-85830
*Parent Company:* Grandreams Ltd, 435-437 Edgware Rd, Little Venice, London W2 1TH
Imprints: Grandreams USA; Goodnight Sleeptight
*Branch Office(s)*
435-437 Edgware Rd, London W2 1TH
*U.S. Office(s):* 8 Arbor Dr, Wayne, NJ 07470-
6117, United States

**Grandreams USA**, *imprint of* Grandreams Ltd

**Grange Books PLC+**
The Grange, Units 1-6, Kingsnorth Industrial Estate, Hoo, Nr Rochester, Kent ME3 9ND
*Tel:* (01634) 256 000 *Fax:* (01634) 255 500
*E-mail:* grangebooks@aol.com

*Web Site:* www.grangebooks.co.uk
*Key Personnel*
Marketing Manager: Bob Siwecki
General Sales Support & Coordination: Deborah
Duthie *E-mail:* deborah.duthie@grangebooks.
co.uk
Sales (North America): Stephen Ash
*E-mail:* stephen.ash@grangebooks.co.uk
Sales (UK - Southwest & Ireland): Geoff Bailey
Sales (Australia, New Zealand, Far East, India
& South Africa): John Norman *E-mail:* john.
norman@grangebooks.co.uk
Sales (UK - Southeast, East Anglia & London):
Don Peachey
Sales (Middle East, Central & Eastern Europe,
Norway & Baltic States, Spain, Portugal,
Central & South America): Bob Siwecki
*E-mail:* bob.siwecki@grangebooks.co.uk
Sales (UK - Northern England, Scotland, Sweden, Finland, Denmark, Iceland, Holland &
Belgium): Glenn Trueman
Founded: 1972
Discount & promotional book publisher & distributor.
Subjects: Aeronautics, Aviation, Animals, Pets,
Architecture & Interior Design, Art, Astronomy, Automotive, Cookery, Crafts, Games,
Hobbies, Gardening, Plants, Natural History,
Nonfiction (General), Transportation, Travel,
Wine & Spirits
ISBN Prefix(es): 1-85627; 1-84013; 0-9509620
Imprints: Binky (Childrens); Park Lane (Art)
*U.S. Office(s):* Book Club of America, 230 Fifth
Ave, Suite 1405, New York, NY 10001, United
States
*Showroom(s):* Bermondsey, Nr London Bridge
Station *Tel:* (01634) 256 000

**Grant & Cutler Ltd**
55-57 Great Marlborough St, London W1F 7AY
*Tel:* (020) 7734 2012 *Fax:* (020) 7734 9272
*E-mail:* contactus@grantandcutler.com
*Web Site:* www.grantandcutler.com
*Key Personnel*
Dir: R C O Howard *Tel:* (020) 7494 3130
Founded: 1935
Specialize in bookselling & library supplies in
Western European languages. Also specialize
in Critical Guides to French, German, Tamesis
texts, research bibliographies & checklists.
Membership(s): Booksellers Association.
Subjects: Foreign Countries, Literature, Literary
Criticism, Essays
ISBN Prefix(es): 0-7293; 0-900411
Number of titles published annually: 10 Print
Total Titles: 270 Print

**Granta Books+**
2/3 Hanover Yard, Noel Rd, London N1 8BE
*Tel:* (020) 7704 9776 *Fax:* (020) 7704 0474
*E-mail:* info@granta.com
*Web Site:* www.granta.com
*Key Personnel*
Editor: Ian Jack *E-mail:* ijack@granta.com
Deputy Editor: Matt Weiland *E-mail:* mweiland@
granta.com
Associate Editor: Liz Jobey *E-mail:* ljobey@
granta.com
Managing Editor: Fatema Ahmed
*E-mail:* fahmed@granta.com
Sales Dir: Frances Hollingdale
*E-mail:* fhollingdale@granta.com
Publicity: Louise Campbell *E-mail:* lcampbell@
granta.com
Subjects: Biography, Fiction, History, Literature,
Literary Criticism, Essays, Nonfiction (General), Travel
ISBN Prefix(es): 0-14; 1-86207
*Parent Company:* Granta Publications
Imprints: Granta Magazine
*U.S. Office(s):* Granta US, 1755 Broadway, 5th
floor, New York, NY 10019, United States

Distributed by Allen & Unwin (Australia & New Zealand); Penguin Books (India); Raincoast (Canada)
*Foreign Rep(s):* Allen & Unwin Pty Ltd (Australia); Jonathan Ball/Harper Collins (South Africa); Michael Geoghegan (Austria, Belgium, France, Germany, Switzerland); I M A (Africa, Caribbean, Central America, Cyprus, Eastern Europe, Middle East, South America, Turkey); Adam Murray (England, Scotland); Nilsson & Lamm (Netherlands); Penny Padovani (Gibraltar, Greece, Italy, Portugal, Slovenia, Spain); Penguin Books India (Bangladesh, India, Nepal, Pakistan, Sri Lanka); Raincoast Books (Canada); Repforce Ireland (Ireland); Hanne Rotovnik (Scandinavia); Roger Ward (Far East)
*Warehouse:* Macmillan Distribution Ltd, Houndmills Basingstroke, Hants RG21 6XS
*Distribution Center:* Macmillan Distribution Ltd, Houndmills Basingstroke, Hants RG21 6XS
*Tel:* (01256) 302692 *Fax:* (01256) 812521
*E-mail:* mdl@macmillan.co.uk

**Granta Magazine**, *imprint of* Granta Books

**The Greek Bookshop+**
57a Nether St, North Finchley, London N12 7NP
Mailing Address: PO Box 29283, London NI3 5BJ
*Tel:* (020) 8446 1986 *Fax:* (020) 8446 1985
*E-mail:* info@thegreekbookshop.com
*Web Site:* www.thegreekbookshop.com
*Key Personnel*
Partner: Loui D Loizou
   *E-mail:* zenobooksellers@aol.com; Maria Loizou
Founded: 1944
Publish books in Greek & English about Greece & Cyprus. Specialize in books about Byzantium, Modern History of Greece & Cyprus.
Subjects: Archaeology, Art, Cookery, History, Literature, Literary Criticism, Essays, Philosophy, Poetry, Romance, Travel
ISBN Prefix(es): 0-900834; 0-7228; 0-9521246
Total Titles: 25 Print
Subsidiaries: Loizou Publications

**Green Books Ltd+**
Foxhole, Dartington, Totnes, Devon TQ9 6EB
*Tel:* (01803) 863260 *Fax:* (01803) 863843
*E-mail:* greenbooks@gn.apc.org
*Web Site:* www.greenbooks.co.uk
*Key Personnel*
Chairman: Satish Kumar
Publisher (Editorial, Production, Rights): John Elford
Sales & Marketing Manager: Paul Rossiter
Founded: 1987
Subjects: Agriculture, Economics, Environmental Studies, How-to, Philosophy, Self-Help, Ecological, Spiritual & Cultural Issues
ISBN Prefix(es): 1-870098; 1-900322; 0-9527302; 1-903998
*Associate Companies:* Resurgence Magazine
Imprints: Green Earth Books; Resurgence Books; Themis Books
Distributed by Banyan Tree Book Distributors (Australia); Ceres Books
Distributor for Chelsea Green Publishing Co (UK)
*Distribution Center:* Alton Logistics Ltd, Unit 4, Battle Rd, Heathfield, Newton Abbot, Devon TQ12 6RY *Tel:* (01626) 832225 *Fax:* (01626) 832398 (UK & Ireland)
Chelsea Green Publishing, Main St, White River Junction, VT 05001, United States *Tel:* 802-295-6300 *Fax:* 802-295-6444 (USA)

**Green Earth Books**, *imprint of* Green Books Ltd

**Green Print**, *imprint of* The Merlin Press Ltd

**W Green**, *imprint of* Sweet & Maxwell Ltd

**W Green The Scottish Law Publisher+**
21 Alva St, Edinburgh EH2 4PS
*Tel:* (0131) 225 4879 (orders); (0131) 225 4879 (marketing); (020) 7449 1104 (trade customers); (0264) 342 828 (international book orders & information); (0264) 342 766 (international subscription orders & information)
*Fax:* (0131) 225 2104 (orders); (0131) 225 2104 (marketing); (020) 7449 1144 (trade customers); (0264) 342 761 (international book orders & information); (0264) 342 761 (international subscription orders & information)
*E-mail:* enquiries@thomson.com; trade.sales@sweetandmaxwell.co.uk (trade customers)
*Web Site:* www.wgreen.co.uk
*Key Personnel*
Marketing Manager: Mdme Jane Scott
Publisher: Miss Jill Barrington
Dir: Gilly Michie
Man Editor: Stephen Chubb
Marketing Executive: Lyn Minay *E-mail:* lyn.minay@wgreen.co.uk
Subjects: Law
ISBN Prefix(es): 0-414
Total Titles: 140 Print; 1 CD-ROM
*Ultimate Parent Company:* The Thomson Corporation, Suite 2706, Toronto Dominion Bank Tower, PO Box 24, Toronto Dominion Centre, Toronto, ON M5K 1A1, Canada
*Sales Office(s):* Contact: Vicki McGee
   *Tel:* (01578) 730780 *Fax:* (01578) 730780
   *E-mail:* vicki.mcgee@sweetandmaxwell.co.uk (customers in the Lothian, Tayside, Borders, Grampian & Fife areas; that is, postcoded areas: AB/DD/EH/KY/TD)
Contact: Stephen Wilson *Tel:* (01698) 320286
   *Fax:* (01698) 320286 *E-mail:* stephen.wilson@sweetandmaxwell.co.uk (customers in the Central, Strathclyde, Dumfries & Galloway, Northern & Western Isles & Highlands & Islands areas; that is, postcoded areas: DG/G/HS/IV/KW/FK/KA/ML/PA/PH/ZE)
Foreign Rep(s): Barbara Gerken (Scotland)
*Warehouse:* W. Green - ITPS, Cheriton House, North Way, Andover Hants SP10 5BE
*Orders to:* W Green, 100 Ave Rd, Swiss Cottage, London NW3 3PF *Tel:* (020) 7449 1111
   *Fax:* (020) 7449 1155 (customer service)

**Greenhaven Press**, *imprint of* Thomson Gale

**Greenhill Books/Lionel Leventhal Ltd+**
Park House, One Russell Gardens, London NW11 9NN
*Tel:* (020) 8458 6314 *Fax:* (020) 8905 5245
*E-mail:* info@greenhillbooks.com; sales@greenhillbooks.com
*Web Site:* www.greenhillbooks.com
*Key Personnel*
Chief Executive, Man Dir: Lionel Leventhal
Sales Dir: Mark Wray *E-mail:* mark.wray@greenhillbooks.com
Founded: 1984
Also acts as international distribution agent for Presidio Press, Novato, CA; Stackpole Books, Mechanicsburg, PA; Proctor Jones Publishing, San Francisco, CA; Emperor's Press, Chicago, IL; Concord, Hong Kong; Casemate Publishing, Havertown, PA; RZM Imports, Southbury, CT; Medals of America, Fountain Inn, SC; Countrysport Press, Camden, ME.
Subjects: Aeronautics, Aviation, Automotive, History, Maritime, Military Science, Transportation, Military history
ISBN Prefix(es): 1-885119; 0-947898; 1-85367
Number of titles published annually: 30 Print
Total Titles: 200 Print
*Parent Company:* Lionel Leventhal Ltd
Distributed by Peribo Pty Ltd (Australia); Publishers Marketing Services Pte Ltd (Malaysia

& Singapore); South Pacific Books (New Zealand); Stackpole Books (US); Vanwell Publishing Ltd (Canada)

**Greenwich Editions**, *imprint of* Ramboro Books Plc

**Greenwillow Books**, *imprint of* HarperCollins UK

**Gregg International**, *imprint of* Gregg Publishing Co

**Gregg Revivals**, *imprint of* Gregg Publishing Co

**Gregg Publishing Co**
The Old Hospital Ardingly Rd, Chapelfields, Cuckfield, Haywards Heath RH17 5JR
*Tel:* (01444) 445070 *Fax:* (01444) 445050
*E-mail:* Rdowling@gowerpub.com
*Key Personnel*
Contact: Tracy Daborn
Founded: 1960
Subjects: Social Sciences, Sociology
ISBN Prefix(es): 0-576; 0-86127
*Associate Companies:* Ashgate Publishing Group
Imprints: Gregg International; Gregg Revivals
*Orders to:* Ashgate Distribution Services, Unit 3, Lower Farnham Rd, Aldershot, Hants GU12 4DL

**Gresham Books**, *imprint of* Woodhead Publishing Ltd

**Gresham Books Ltd+**
46 Victoria Rd, Summertown, Oxford OX2 7QD
*Tel:* (01865) 513582 *Fax:* (01865) 512718
*E-mail:* info@gresham-books.co.uk
*Web Site:* www.gresham-books.co.uk
*Key Personnel*
Dir: Mr P A Lewis *Fax:* (01865) 452821
   *E-mail:* paul@gresham-books.co.uk; Mrs M L Lewis *Fax:* (01865) 452821 *E-mail:* mary@gresham-books.co.uk
Founded: 1979
Specialize in hymnals, prayer books & school histories.
Subjects: History, Music, Dance, Religion - Catholic, Religion - Protestant, Local History
ISBN Prefix(es): 0-905418; 0-946095; 0-9502121
Number of titles published annually: 30 Print
Total Titles: 350 Print

**Griffith Institute**, *imprint of* Ashmolean Museum Publications

**Grub Street+**
4 Rainham Close, London SW11 6SS
*Tel:* (020) 7924 3966; (020) 7738 1008
   *Fax:* (020) 7738 1009
*E-mail:* post@grubstreet.co.uk
*Web Site:* www.grubstreet.co.uk
*Key Personnel*
Chief Executive & Rights & Permissions: John Davies *E-mail:* john@grubstreet.com.uk
Chief Executive: Anne Dolamore
Founded: 1986
Subjects: Cookery, Health, Nutrition, Nonfiction (General), Wine & Spirits, Military History/Aviation
ISBN Prefix(es): 0-948817; 1-898697; 1-902304; 1-904010
Number of titles published annually: 30 Print
Total Titles: 140 Print
Foreign Rep(s): Capricorn Link Pty Ltd (Australia); Forrester Books (New Zealand); Peter Hyde Associates (South Africa); Seven Hills

Book Distributors (US); Vanwell Publishing (Canada)
*Warehouse:* Littlehampton Book Service (LBS), Faraday Close, Durrington, Worlting, West Sussex BN13 3RB

**Guardian Books**, *imprint of* Fourth Estate

**Guild of Master Publications Inc**, *imprint of* GMC Publications Ltd

**Guinness World Records Ltd**
Division of Guinness Media Inc
338 Euston Rd, London NW1 3BD
*Tel:* (020) 7891 4567 *Fax:* (020) 7891 4501
    *Cable:* MOSTEST ENFIELD
*Key Personnel*
Man Dir: Christopher Irwin
Sales Dir: Fred Buxton
Sales & Marketing Dir: Malcolm Roughead
National Sales Manager: Shaun Elder
Founded: 1954
Subjects: Military Science, Music, Dance, Sports, Athletics
ISBN Prefix(es): 0-900424; 0-85112; 1-892051
*Parent Company:* Diageo plc, 8 Henrietta Pl, London W1G 0NB
*Warehouse:* Macmillan Distribution, Unit 8, Lye Industrial Estate, Pontardulais, Swansea SA4 1QD

**Gulf Professional Press**, *imprint of* Elsevier Ltd

**Gunsmoke Western**, *imprint of* BBC Audiobooks

**Gwasg Carreg Gwalch+**
12 Iard Yr Orsaf, Llanrwst, Conwy LL26 0EH
*Tel:* (01492) 642 031 *Fax:* (01492) 641 502
*E-mail:* llyfrau@carreg-gwalch.co.uk
*Web Site:* www.carreg-gwalch.co.uk
*Key Personnel*
Dir: Myrddin ap Dafydd *E-mail:* myrddin@carreg-gwalch.co.uk
Founded: 1980
Privately owned publisher & printing company.
Subjects: Welsh & Celtic Interest, Welsh Language
ISBN Prefix(es): 0-86381
Number of titles published annually: 70 Print
Total Titles: 1,000 Print
*Branch Office(s)*
Ysgubor Plas, Llwyndyrys, Pwllheli, Gwynedd LL53 6NG *Tel:* (01758) 750440

**Gwasg Gwenffrwd+**
Hendre Bach, Cerrigydrudion, Corwen, Clwyd LL21 9TB
*Tel:* (01490) 420 560; (0845) 330 6754
*Key Personnel*
Man Dir: Dr Goronwy Alun Hughes
Founded: 1947
Specialize in Pacific Islands, Oceanic Languages & Wales.
Membership(s): BLDSC (ASTIC Research Associates).
Subjects: Anthropology, Biography, Foreign Countries, Genealogy, History, Language Arts, Linguistics, Poetry, Regional Interests, Oceanic Languages, Pacific Islands, Wales
ISBN Prefix(es): 0-9501861; 1-85651
Number of titles published annually: 6 Print
Total Titles: 50 Print
Imprints: Astic; Bronant Books; A & Z Hughes; Translations Wales

**Gwasg y Dref Wen+**
28 Church Rd, Yr Eglwys Newydd, Cardiff CF4 2EA
*Tel:* (01222) 617860 *Fax:* (01222) 610507
*E-mail:* gwil-drefwen@btinternet.com

*Key Personnel*
Man Dir, Editorial: Roger Boore
Publicity, Sales: Gwilym Boore
Founded: 1970
Welsh-language publishers.
Membership(s): Union of Welsh Publishers & Booksellers.
ISBN Prefix(es): 0-946962; 0-904910; 1-85596
Number of titles published annually: 50 Print; 4 Audio
Total Titles: 450 Print; 15 Audio
Imprints: Dref Wen

**Peter Haddock Ltd+**
Industrial Estate, Pinfold Lane, Bridlington, East Yorks YO16 6BT
*Tel:* (01262) 678121 *Fax:* (01262) 400043
*E-mail:* enquiries@peterhaddock.com
*Web Site:* www.phpublishing.co.uk
*Key Personnel*
Man Dir: Peter Haddock
Sales Manager: David Haddock
Founded: 1952
ISBN Prefix(es): 0-7105
Imprints: Big Time

**Hakluyt Society**
c/o Map Library, British Library, 96 Euston Rd, London NW1 2DB
*Tel:* (01428) 641850 *Fax:* (01428) 641933
*E-mail:* office@hakluyt.com
*Web Site:* www.hakluyt.com
*Key Personnel*
Administrator: Richard Bateman
Founded: 1846
A registered charity inspired by & named after Richard Hakluyt (1552-1616), the famous collector & editor of narratives of voyages & travels & other documents relating to English interests overseas.
Subjects: Geography, Geology, History, Travel
ISBN Prefix(es): 0-904180
Number of titles published annually: 2 Print
Total Titles: 55 Print
Distributed by Ashgate Publishing Direct Sales

**Peter Halban Publishers Ltd+**
22 Golden Sq, London W1F 9JW
*Tel:* (020) 7437 9300 *Fax:* (020) 7431 9512
*E-mail:* books@halbanpublishers.com
*Web Site:* www.halbanpublishers.com
*Key Personnel*
Man Dir: Martine Halban; Peter Halban
Founded: 1986
Membership(s): Independent Publishers Guild.
Subjects: Biography, Fiction, History, Philosophy, Religion - Other
ISBN Prefix(es): 1-870015
Number of titles published annually: 10 Print
Total Titles: 60 Print
Foreign Rep(s): Orion (Export Sales Dept)
*Shipping Address:* Littlehampton Book Services, Faraday Close, Durrington, Worthing, West Sussex BN13 3RB, Contact: Tim Kinghorn *Tel:* (01903) 828800 *Fax:* (01903) 828801 *E-mail:* info@lbsltd.co.uk *Web Site:* www.lbsltd.co.uk
*Warehouse:* Littlehampton Book Services, Faraday Close, Durrington, Worthing, West Sussex BN13 3RB, Contact: Tim Kinghorn *Tel:* (01903) 828800 *Fax:* (01903) 828801 *E-mail:* info@lbsltd.co.uk *Web Site:* www.lbsltd.co.uk
*Distribution Center:* Littlehampton Book Services
*Orders to:* Littlehampton Book Services, Faraday Close, Durrington, Worthing, West Sussex BN13 3RB, Contact: Rose Mellish *Tel:* (01903) 828800 *Fax:* (01903) 828801 *E-mail:* info@lbsltd.co.uk *Web Site:* www.lbsltd.co.uk

**Haldane Mason Ltd+**
PO Box 34196, London NW10 3YB

*Tel:* (020) 8459 2131 *Fax:* (020) 8728 1216
*E-mail:* haldane.mason@dial.pipex.com
Subjects: Cookery, Health, Nutrition, Sports, Athletics, Lifestyle, New Age
ISBN Prefix(es): 1-902463

**Robert Hale Ltd+**
Clerkenwell House, 45-47 Clerkenwell Green, London EC1R 0HT
*Tel:* (020) 7251 2661 *Fax:* (020) 7490 4958
*E-mail:* enquire@halebooks.com
*Web Site:* www.halebooks.com
*Key Personnel*
Man Dir & Senior Editor: John Hale
Marketing Dir: Martin Kendall
Rights & Permissions Manager: Florence Pinard
Production Dir: Robert Hale
Founded: 1936
Subjects: Art, Biography, Cookery, Fiction, Geography, Geology, History, How-to, Music, Dance, Philosophy, Poetry, Sports, Athletics, Women's Studies
ISBN Prefix(es): 0-85131; 0-7198; 0-7090; 0-7091
Imprints: J A Allen; Horse Books; NAG Press
Distributor for Aperture; International Jewelry; Phoenix
*Warehouse:* Combined Book Services, Units 1/K, Paddock Wood Distribution Centre, Paddock Wood, Tonbridge, Kent TN12 6UU

**GK Hall & Co**, *imprint of* Thomson Gale

**Halldale Publishing & Media Ltd**
84 Alexandra Rd, Farnborough, Hants GU14 6DD
*Tel:* (01252) 532000 *Fax:* (01252) 512714
*Web Site:* www.halldale.com
*Key Personnel*
Publisher: Andrew Smith *E-mail:* andy@halldale.com
General Manager: Janet Llewellyn
Business Manager: Stephen Marston *E-mail:* steve@halldale.com
Founded: 1993
Subjects: Aeronautics, Aviation, Maritime
*U.S. Office(s):* 301 E Pine St, Suite 150, Orlando, FL 32801, United States *Tel:* 407-835-3628

**Halsted Press**, *imprint of* Wiley Europe Ltd

**Hambledon & London Ltd+**
102 Gloucester Ave, London NW1 8HX
*Tel:* (020) 7586 0817 *Fax:* (020) 7586 9970
*E-mail:* office@hambledon.co.uk
*Web Site:* www.hambledon.co.uk
*Key Personnel*
Man Dir: Martin Sheppard *E-mail:* ms@hambledon.co.uk
Commissioning Editor: Tony Morris *Tel:* (020) 7482 2333 *E-mail:* ajm@hambledon.co.uk
Founded: 1981
Subjects: History
ISBN Prefix(es): 0-907628; 1-85285; 0-9506882
Number of titles published annually: 24 Print
Total Titles: 200 Print
*Sales Office(s):* Yale University Press, 23 Pond St, London NW3 2PN *Tel:* (020) 7431 4422 *Fax:* (020) 7431 3755 (UK)
Foreign Rep(s): Michael Geoghegay (Austria, Netherlands, Germany, Switzerland); Andrew Russell (Ireland)
*Distribution Center:* Hoddle, Doyle & Meadows, Station Rd, Linton, Cambs CB1 6UX *Tel:* (1223) 893855 *Fax:* (1223) 893852
Palgrave Macmillan, 175 Fifth Ave, New York, NY 10010, United States *Web Site:* www.palgrave-usa.com

**Hamish Hamilton**, *imprint of* Penguin Books Ltd

**Hamish Hamilton**, *imprint of* The Penguin
Group UK

**Hamish Hamilton Ltd+**
80 Strand, London WCR 0RL
*Tel:* (020) 7010 3000 *Fax:* (020) 7010 6060
*E-mail:* customer.service@penguin.co.uk
*Web Site:* www.penguin.co.uk
*Telex:* 917181; 2
*Key Personnel*
Publisher: Simon Prosser
Export Sales: Max Adam *E-mail:* max.adam@
penquin.co.uk
Founded: 1931
Subjects: Art, Biography, Fiction, History, Music,
Dance
ISBN Prefix(es): 0-14
*Parent Company:* Penguin Books Ltd
Subsidiaries: Elm Tree Books Ltd; Hamish
Hamilton Children's Books Ltd
*Shipping Address:* Bath Road, Harmondsworth,
West Dayton, Middlesex UB7 0DA
*Warehouse:* Bath Road, Harmondsworth, West
Dayton, Middlesex UB7 0DA

**Hamlyn**, *imprint of* Octopus Publishing Group

**Hamlyn+**
Imprint of Octopus Publishing Group
2-4 Heron Quays, London E14 4JP
*Tel:* (020) 7531 8400 *Fax:* (020) 7531 8650
*Web Site:* www.hamlyn.co.uk
*Key Personnel*
Publisher & Man Dir: Alison Goff *Tel:* (020)
7531 8410 *Fax:* (020) 7531 8562
*E-mail:* alison.goff@hamlyn.co.uk
Sales & Marketing Dir: David Inman
*Tel:* (020) 7531 8573 *Fax:* (020) 7537 0514
*E-mail:* david.inman@hamlyn.co.uk
Publicity & Marketing Manager: Sue Bobbermein
*Tel:* (020) 7531 8584 *Fax:* (020) 7537 0514
*E-mail:* sue.bobbermein@hamlyn.co.uk
Export Sales Manager: Caroline Babler
*Tel:* (020) 7531 8574 *Fax:* (020) 7537 0514
*E-mail:* caroline.babler@hamlyn.co.uk
Foreign Rights Manager - France, Spain, Portu-
gal & Italy: John Saunders-Griffiths *Tel:* (020)
7531 8586 *E-mail:* john.saunders-griffiths@
hamlyn.co.uk
Area Rights Manager - Scandanavia: Sarah
French *Tel:* (020) 7531 8587 *E-mail:* sarah.
french@hamlyn.co.uk
Area Rights Manager - Germany, Holland,
Greece, South Africa: Roly Allen *Tel:* (020)
7531 8576 *E-mail:* roly.allen@hamlyn.co.uk
Foreign Rights Executive - Central & Eastern
Europe & Finland: Daniel Bouquet *Tel:* (020)
7531 8575 *E-mail:* daniel.bouquet@hamlyn.co.
uk
North American Rights Manager: Nicole Stephens
*Tel:* (020) 7531 8577 *Fax:* (020) 7537 0514
*E-mail:* nicole.stephens@hamlyn.co.uk
UK Sales Dir: Kevin Hawkins *Tel:* (020) 7531
8582; (0780) 129 2031 *Fax:* (020) 7537 0514
*E-mail:* kevin.hawkins@hamlyn.co.uk
Special Sales Manager: Rebecca Collold
*Tel:* (020) 7531 8585 *E-mail:* rebecca.collold@
hamlyn.co.uk
Premium Sales Executive: Stuart Airley *Tel:* (020)
7531 8580 *E-mail:* stuart.airley@hamlyn.co.uk
Founded: 1947
International publisher of high quality illustrated,
nonfiction for the general market.
Subjects: Architecture & Interior Design, Cook-
ery, Crafts, Games, Hobbies, Fashion, Film,
Video, Gardening, Plants, Health, Nutrition,
History, Music, Dance, Natural History, Nonfic-
tion (General), Sports, Athletics
ISBN Prefix(es): 0-600; 0-601
*Distribution Center:* Little Hampton Book Ser-
vices Ltd, Faraday Close, Durrington, Worthin,
West Sussex BN13 3RB *Tel:* (01903) 825 500
*Fax:* (01903) 828 625

**Handbag Books**, *imprint of* Kenneth Mason
Publications Ltd

**The Handsel Press+**
62 Toll Rd, Kincardine, by Alloa FK10 4QZ
*Tel:* (01202) 665432 *Fax:* (01202) 666219
*E-mail:* orders@orcabookservices.co.uk
*Web Site:* www.handselpress.co.uk
*Key Personnel*
Chairman: David F Wright
Editor: Rev Jock Stein *Tel:* (01236) 723204
Founded: 1976
Subjects: Theology
ISBN Prefix(es): 0-905312; 1-871828
Distributed by Orca Book Services
*Orders to:* Scottish Book Source, 137 Dundee St,
Edinburgh EH11 2QU *Tel:* (0131) 229 6800
*Fax:* (0131) 229 9070

**Hans Zell Bibliographies**, *imprint of* James
Currey Ltd

**Happy Cat Books+**
Imprint of Catnip Publishing Ltd
Islington Business Centre, 3-5 Islington High St,
London N1 9LQ
*Tel:* (020) 7745 2370 *Fax:* (020) 7745 2372
*E-mail:* sales@bouncemarketing.co.uk
*Key Personnel*
Man Dir: Robert Snuggs, Esq *E-mail:* rsnuggs@
bouncemarketing.co.uk
Editorial Dir: Martin C West *Tel:* (01255) 870902
*Fax:* (01255) 870902 *E-mail:* mcwest@
happycat.co.uk
Founded: 2005
Publish picture books for ages under 6, fiction for
5-8 years & 8-11 years.
ISBN Prefix(es): 1-899248; 1-903285
Number of titles published annually: 30 Print
Total Titles: 55 Print
*Orders to:* Macmillan Distribution Ltd, Hound-
mills, Basingstoke, Hants RG21 6X6
*Tel:* (01256) 302692 *Fax:* (01256) 812558

**Harcourt Assessment Inc**
Formerly Psychological Corporation Ltd
Division of Harcourt Education Ltd
Halley Court, Jordan Hill, Oxford, Oxon OX2
8EJ
*Tel:* (01865) 888188 *Fax:* (01865) 314348
*E-mail:* info@harcourt-uk.com
*Web Site:* www.harcourt-uk.com
*Key Personnel*
Contact: Jessica Spencer
Founded: 1921
Subjects: Disability, Special Needs, Language
Arts, Linguistics, Psychology, Psychiatry
ISBN Prefix(es): 0-7491
*Orders to:* Chinese Behavioural Science Corp,
9F-1, 206, Nan-Chuan Rd, Sec 2, Taipei 100
*Tel:* (08862) 2365 6349 *Fax:* (08862) 2365
0525 *E-mail:* cbsc@cm1.hinet.net
Dansk Psykologisk Forlag, Stockholmsgade
29, Copenhagen, Denmark *Tel:* 3538 1655
*Fax:* 3538 1665 *E-mail:* dk-psych@dpf.dk *Web
Site:* www.dpf.dk

**Harcourt Education International+**
Formerly Reed Educational & Professional Pub-
lishing
Member of Reed Elsevier Group
Halley Court, Jordan Hill, Oxford OX2 8EJ
*Tel:* (01865) 311366 *Fax:* (01865) 314641
*E-mail:* uk.schools@harcourteducation.co.uk
*Web Site:* www.harcourteducation.co.uk
*Key Personnel*
Chief Executive Officer: Chris Jones
Chief Operating Officer: Graham Shaw
Chief Financial Officer: Mark Chalmers
Group Human Resources Dir: Andrew Pace

Man Dir, UK & International Schools, Harcourt
Education International: Paul Shuter
Man Dir, Harcourt Asessment: Philip Ellaway
Founded: 2001
Subjects: Education, English as a Second Lan-
guage
ISBN Prefix(es): 1-86391
Divisions: Ginn; Harcourt Education Australia;
Heinemann FE & Vocational UK; Heine-
mann Primary UK; Heinemann Secondary UK;
Heinemann Southern Africa; Reed Publishing
(NZ) Ltd; Rigby UK

**Harcourt Publishers Ltd**, *imprint of* Elsevier Ltd

**Harden's Ltd**
14 Buckingham St, London WC2N 6DF
*Tel:* (020) 7839 4763 *Fax:* (020) 7839 7561
*E-mail:* mail@hardens.com
*Web Site:* www.hardens.com
*Key Personnel*
Dir: Peter Harden; Richard Harden
Founded: 1991
Publish consumer guides, restaurant guides in
particular. Specialize in corporate gift editions.
Membership(s); IPG.
Subjects: Foreign Countries, Travel
ISBN Prefix(es): 1-873721
Number of titles published annually: 5 Print; 2 E-
Book
Total Titles: 10 Print; 2 E-Book

**Patrick Hardy Books**, *imprint of* James Clarke
& Co Ltd

**Patrick Hardy Books**, *imprint of* The
Lutterworth Press

**Patrick Hardy Books+**
Imprint of James Clarke & Co Ltd
PO Box 60, Cambridge CB1 2NT
*Tel:* (01223) 350865 *Fax:* (01223) 366951
*E-mail:* sales@lutterworth.com; publishing@
lutterworth.com
*Web Site:* www.lutterworth.com
*Key Personnel*
Man Dir: Adrian Brink
Subjects: Fiction, Nonfiction (General), Religion -
Other
ISBN Prefix(es): 0-7444
Distributed by Parkwest Publications Inc

**Harley Books+**
Martins, Great Horkesley, Colchester, Essex C06
4AH
*Tel:* (01206) 271216 *Fax:* (01206) 271182
*E-mail:* harley@keme.co.uk
*Web Site:* www.harleybooks.com
*Key Personnel*
Dir: Annette Harley
Founded: 1983
Specialize in natural history, especially entomol-
ogy & botany.
Membership(s): IPG.
Subjects: Biological Sciences, Environmental
Studies, Natural History
ISBN Prefix(es): 0-946589
Number of titles published annually: 3 Print
Total Titles: 7 Print
*Parent Company:* BH & A Harley Ltd

**HarperAudio**, *imprint of* HarperCollins UK

**HarperBusiness**, *imprint of* HarperCollins UK

**HarperCollins**, *imprint of* HarperCollins UK

**HarperCollins Children's Books**, *imprint of*
HarperCollins UK

**HarperCollins UK+**
Subsidiary of News Corporation
77-85 Fulham Palace Rd, Hammersmith, London W6 8JB
*Tel:* (020) 8741 7070 *Toll Free Tel:* (0870) 900 2050 (customer service) *Fax:* (020) 8307 4813 *Toll Free Fax:* (0141) 306 3767 (customer service)
*E-mail:* contact@harpercollins.co.uk
*Web Site:* www.harpercollins.co.uk
*Key Personnel*
Chief Executive Officer & Publisher: Victoria Barnsley
Chief Operating Officer: John Baillie
Man Dir, General Books: Amanda Ridout
Man Dir, Collins: Thomas Webster
Founded: 1819
Membership(s): Publishers Association.
Subjects: Animals, Pets, Anthropology, Art, Astrology, Occult, Behavioral Sciences, Biblical Studies, Biography, Business, Child Care & Development, Cookery, Crafts, Games, Hobbies, English as a Second Language, Fiction, Film, Video, Finance, Foreign Countries, Gardening, Plants, Gay & Lesbian, Government, Political Science, Health, Nutrition, History, House & Home, How-to, Human Relations, Literature, Literary Criticism, Essays, Management, Mysteries, Natural History, Nonfiction (General), Outdoor Recreation, Philosophy, Psychology, Psychiatry, Romance, Science Fiction, Fantasy, Self-Help, Sports, Athletics, Theology, Travel, Wine & Spirits, Women's Studies
ISBN Prefix(es): 0-00; 0-01; 0-246; 0-261; 0-586
*Parent Company:* HarperCollins
Imprints: Access Press; Amistad; Avon; Joanna Cotler Books; Ecco; Eos; Laura Geringer Books; Greenwillow Books; HarperAudio; HarperBusiness; HarperCollins; HarperCollins Children' s Books; HarperEntertainment; HarperFestival; HarperLargePrint; HarperResource; HarperSanFrancisco; HarperTorch; HarperTrophy; William Morrow; Perennial; PerfectBound; Quill; Rayo; ReganBooks; Tempest
*U.S. Office(s):* 10 E 53 St, New York, NY 10022, United States *Tel:* 212-207-7000
*Warehouse:* Westerhill Rd, Bishopbriggs, Glasgow G64 2QT *Tel:* (041) 7723200
*Orders to:* PO Box, Glasgow G4 0NB *Tel:* (0141) 7723200

**HarperEntertainment**, *imprint of* HarperCollins UK

**HarperFestival**, *imprint of* HarperCollins UK

**HarperLargePrint**, *imprint of* HarperCollins UK

**HarperResource**, *imprint of* HarperCollins UK

**HarperSanFrancisco**, *imprint of* HarperCollins UK

**HarperTorch**, *imprint of* HarperCollins UK

**HarperTrophy**, *imprint of* HarperCollins UK

**Hart Advertising Charity Agency**, *imprint of* Hymns Ancient & Modern Ltd

**Hart Publishing**
Salter's Boatyard, Folly Bridge, Abingdon Rd, Oxford OX1 4LB
*Tel:* (01865) 245533 *Fax:* (01865) 794882
*E-mail:* mail@hartpub.co.uk
*Web Site:* www.hartpub.co.uk; www. hartpublishingusa.com

*Key Personnel*
Man Dir: Richard Hart *E-mail:* richard@hartpub. co.uk
Sales & Marketing Dir: Jane Parker *E-mail:* jane@hartpub.co.uk
Customer Services Manager: Joanne Ledger *E-mail:* jo@hartpub.co.uk
Editorial & Production Manager: April Boffin *E-mail:* april@hartpub.co.uk
Finance Manager: Liam Barrett *E-mail:* liam@ hartpub.co.uk
Journals Manager: Barbara Darling *E-mail:* barbara@hartpub.co.uk
Founded: 1996
Subjects: Law
Number of titles published annually: 60 Print
Distributed by Academic Marketing Services (Pty) Ltd (South Africa); Aditya Books Private Ltd (India); Roger Bayliss (Trade Representation (UK) - London, South East, South West, Scotland); Codasat Canada - University of Toronto Press Distribution (Canada); Charles Gibbes (Italy & France); International Specialized Book Services (North America); Intersentia Uitgevers NV (Benelux); IP Communications Pty Ltd (Australia & New Zealand); J & L Watt Publishing Consultants (Arab Middle East, Eastern Mediterranean & North Africa); Kay (Kaoru) Kato (Japan); STM Publisher Services Pte Ltd (China, Hong Kong, Korea, Philippines, Singapore, Taiwan, Thailand, Vietnam); UBS Books (New Zealand)
Foreign Rep(s): Colin Flint (Scandinavia); Iberian Book Services (Portugal, Spain)

**Harvard University Press+**
Fitzroy House, 11 Chenies St, London WC1E 7EY
*Tel:* (020) 7306 0603 *Fax:* (020) 7306 0604
*E-mail:* info@hup-mitpress.co.uk
*Web Site:* www.hup.harvard.edu
*Key Personnel*
General Manager: Ann Sexsmith
Publicity Manager: Lisa Jolliffe
Founded: 1913
Subjects: Anthropology, Asian Studies, Behavioral Sciences, Biological Sciences, Business, Earth Sciences, Economics, Education, Film, Video, Government, Political Science, History, Law, Literature, Literary Criticism, Essays, Medicine, Nursing, Dentistry, Natural History, Nonfiction (General), Philosophy, Psychology, Psychiatry, Religion - Jewish, Science (General), Social Sciences, Sociology, Women's Studies
ISBN Prefix(es): 0-674
Imprints: Belknap
Subsidiaries: The Loeb Classical Library
*U.S. Office(s):* 79 Garden St, Cambridge, MA 02138, United States *Tel:* 617-495-2480 *E-mail:* contact_hup@harvard.edu
*Orders to:* John Wiley & Sons Ltd, Southern Cross Trading Estate, 1 Oldlands Way, Bognor Regis, West Sussex PO22 9SA *Tel:* (01243) 779777 *Fax:* (01243) 820250

**Harvey Map Services Ltd+**
12-22 Main St, Doune, Perthshire FK16 6BJ
*Tel:* (01786) 841202 *Fax:* (01786) 841098
*E-mail:* winni@harveymaps.co.uk; sales@ harveymaps.co.uk
*Web Site:* www.harveymaps.co.uk
*Key Personnel*
Sales Dir: Susan Harvey
Marketing: Catherine Nelson
Founded: 1977
Also acts as mapmakers.
Subjects: Education, Sports, Athletics
ISBN Prefix(es): 1-85137

**Harvill**, *imprint of* Random House UK Ltd

**The Harvill Press+**
Imprint of Random House UK Ltd
Random House, 20 Vauxhall Bridge Rd, London SW1V 2SA
*Tel:* (020) 7840 8893 *Fax:* (020) 7840 6117
*E-mail:* enquiries@randomhouse.co.uk
*Web Site:* www.randomhouse.co.uk/harvill/; www. harvill.com
*Key Personnel*
Publisher: Christopher MacLehose
Sales Dir: Katharina Bielenberg *E-mail:* k. bielenberg@harvill-press.com
Editorial Dir: Margaret Stead; Guido Waldman
Marketing Dir: Paul Baggaley
Founded: 1946
Subjects: Anthropology, Biography, Fiction, Gardening, Plants, History, Literature, Literary Criticism, Essays, Mathematics, Natural History, Nonfiction (General), Philosophy, Photography, Poetry, Self-Help, Travel, African Studies, Anthology, Art History, Crime Fiction, Current Affairs, Letters, Memoirs, Mythology, Politics, Russian Studies
ISBN Prefix(es): 1-86046
Total Titles: 800 Print

**Hassle Free Press**, *imprint of* Knockabout Comics

**Hawk Books+**
Kernick House, Kernick Rd, Penryn, Cornwall TR10 9DT
Mailing Address: PO Box 30, Penryn TR10 9YP
*Tel:* (01326) 376633 *Fax:* (01326) 376669
*Key Personnel*
Dir: P Hawkey
Founded: 1987
Specialize in character merchandise.
Subjects: Art, Humor
ISBN Prefix(es): 0-948248; 1-899441
Imprints: Falco; Sparrowhawk
*Orders to:* Bookpoint Ltd, 39 Milton Park, Abingdon, Oxon OX14 4TD

**Hawker Publications Ltd+**
Culvert House, Culvert Rd, Battersea SW11 5DH
*Tel:* (020) 7720 2108 *Fax:* (020) 7498 3023
*E-mail:* hawker@hawkerpubs.demon.co.uk
*Web Site:* www.careinfo.org
*Key Personnel*
Editor-in-Chief: Dr Richard Hawkins *E-mail:* richard@hawkerpubs.demon.co.uk
Founded: 1985
Specialize in providing a wide range of information to professionals working with elderly people & in the children's nursery sector.
Subjects: Child Care & Development, Medicine, Nursing, Dentistry
ISBN Prefix(es): 1-874790
Number of titles published annually: 12 Print
Total Titles: 18 Print
*Warehouse:* Plymbridge, Estover Rd, Plymouth PL6 7P2 *Fax:* (01752) 202330

**Hawthorn Press+**
Hawthorn House, One Lansdown Lane, Stroud, Glos GL5 1BJ
*Tel:* (01453) 757040 *Fax:* (01453) 751138
*E-mail:* info@hawthornpress.com
*Web Site:* www.hawthornpress.com
*Key Personnel*
Dir: Judith Large; Martin Large
Sales & Accounts: Alan Lord
Project Management & Sales: Rachel Jenkins
Editor: Matthew Barton
Administration & Sales: Lynda McGill
Founded: 1980
Membership(s): Independent Publishers Guild.
Subjects: Behavioral Sciences, Child Care & Development, Crafts, Games, Hobbies, Education, Psychology, Psychiatry, Self-Help, Women's Studies

ISBN Prefix(es): 1-869890; 1-903458; 0-9507062; 1-902069
Number of titles published annually: 12 Print
Total Titles: 100 Print
Distributed by Anthroposophic Press (USA & North America); Astam Books Pty Ltd (Australia); Ceres Books (New Zealand); De Nieuwe Boekerij Import (Holland); Peter Hyde Associates (South Africa); New Leaf Distributing Co (USA & North America); Rudolf Steiner Publications (South Africa); Tri-fold Books (Canada)
*Orders to:* BookSource, 32 Finlas St, Glasgow G22 5DU *Tel:* (0141) 558 1366 *Fax:* (0141) 557 0189 *E-mail:* info@booksource.net

**Hayden Books**, *imprint of* Pearson Education Europe, Mideast & Africa

**Haymarket**, *imprint of* Verso

**Haynes**, *imprint of* Haynes Publishing

**Haynes Publishing+**
Sparkford, Yeovil, Somerset BA22 7JJ
*Tel:* (01963) 442030; (01963) 442080 (trade) *Fax:* (01963) 440001 (trade)
*E-mail:* sales@haynes.co.uk
*Web Site:* www.haynes.co.uk
*Key Personnel*
Chairman: John H Haynes
Group Chief Executive: Eric Oakley
Editorial Dir: Mark Hughes
Sales Dir, UK: Jeremy Yates-Round
Overseas Sales & Rights Dir: Graham Cook
Marketing Dir (Motortrade): David Hermelin
Production: Nigel Clements
Operations Dir: Jon Allen
Finance Dir: James Bunkum
Book Trade Sales Manager: Tony Kemp
Head, UK Sales: Mike Webb
Customer Marketing Mgr: Rebecca Nicholls
Founded: 1960
Subjects: Aeronautics, Aviation, Automotive, Computer Science, History, House & Home, How-to, Maritime, Outdoor Recreation, Technology, Transportation, Motoring, Motorsports, Car & Motorcyle Service & Repair, Restoration
ISBN Prefix(es): 1-85010; 0-85696; 1-56392
Number of titles published annually: 100 Print
Total Titles: 2,280 Print
*Parent Company:* Haynes Publishing Group PLC
Imprints: G T Foulis & Co; Haynes; Patrick Stephens Ltd
Subsidiaries: Editions Haynes SARL; Haynes Manuals Inc; Haynes Publishing Nordiska AB; Sutton Publishing Ltd
Distributor for David Bull Publishing; Duke 'Powersport' Videos; Hazleton Publishing; The Stationery Office
Foreign Rep(s): Graham Cook (Worldwide exc US & Canada)

**Hayward Gallery Publishing**
Royal Festival Hall, Belvedere Rd, London SE1 8XX
*Tel:* (020) 7921 0826 *Fax:* (020) 7401 2664
*E-mail:* dpower@hayward.org.uk
*Web Site:* www.hayward.org.uk
Subjects: Architecture & Interior Design, Photography, Visual Arts
ISBN Prefix(es): 1-85332
Number of titles published annually: 8 Print
*Distribution Center:* Cornerhouse Publications, 70 Oxford St, Manchester M1 5NH

**R Hazell & Co**, *imprint of* Shaw & Sons Ltd

**Hazleton Publishing Ltd+**
Mermaid House, 5th floor, London EC4V 3DS
*Tel:* (020) 7332 2000 *Fax:* (020) 7332 2003

*E-mail:* info@hazletonpublishing.com
*Web Site:* www.hazletonpublishing.com
*Key Personnel*
Chairman: Richard Poulter
Dir: Steven Palmer
Publisher: Nick Poulter
Managing Editor: Robert Yarham
Founded: 1975
Specialize in yearbooks & calendars.
Subjects: Sports, Athletics, Golf, Motor Sports, Tennis
ISBN Prefix(es): 0-905138; 1-874557; 1-903135
Total Titles: 10 Print
*Parent Company:* Profile Media Group PLC

**HB Publications**
PO Box 21660, London SW16 1WJ
*Tel:* (020) 8769 1585 *Fax:* (020) 8769 2320
*E-mail:* sales@hbpublications.com
*Web Site:* www.hbpublications.com
*Key Personnel*
Contact: Lascelles Hussey
Specializes in the production of books for public sector managers.
Subjects: Accounting, Business, Finance, Management, Marketing
ISBN Prefix(es): 1-899448
*Parent Company:* HB Consulting

**Headline**, *imprint of* Headline Book Publishing Ltd

**Headline Book Publishing Ltd+**
338 Euston Rd, London NW1 3BH
*Tel:* (020) 7873 6000 *Fax:* (020) 7873 6124
*E-mail:* headline.books@headline.co.uk
*Web Site:* www.madaboutbooks.com
*Key Personnel*
Chief Executive: Tim Hely Hutchinson
Man Dir: Martin Neild
Deputy Man Dir: Kerr Macrae
Dir, Nonfiction Publishing: Val Hudson
Dir, Production: Bryone Picton
Sales Dir: James Horobin
Dir, Marketing: Julie Manton
Dir, Publicity: Georgina Moore
Dir, Fiction Publishing: Jane Morpeth
Dir, Rights: Sarah Thomson
Dir, Export Sales: Peter Newson
Founded: 1986
Subjects: Biography, Cookery, Fiction, Gardening, Plants, History, Nonfiction (General), Sports, Athletics, Wine & Spirits
ISBN Prefix(es): 0-7472; 0-7553
Number of titles published annually: 410 Print
*Parent Company:* Hodder Headline Ltd
*Ultimate Parent Company:* WH Smith PLC, Greenbridge Rd, Swindon SN3 3LD
Imprints: Headline; Review
*Orders to:* Bookpoint Ltd, 130 Milton Trading Estate, Abingdon, Oxon OX14 4SB *Tel:* (01235) 400400 *Fax:* (01235) 400500

**Headline Specials**, *imprint of* Moorley's Print & Publishing Ltd

**Headlions**, *imprint of* Packard Publishing Ltd

**Health Development Agency+**
Holborn Gate, 330 High Holborn, London WC1V 7BA
*Tel:* (020) 7430 0850 *Fax:* (020) 7061 3390
*E-mail:* communications@hda-online.org.uk
*Web Site:* www.hda-online.org.uk
*Key Personnel*
General Manager & Publisher: Boyd Simon *Tel:* (020) 7413 1846 *Fax:* (020) 7413 2028 *E-mail:* simon.boyd@hea.org.uk
Publishing Manager: Chris Owen *Tel:* (020) 7413 1909 *Fax:* (020) 7413 2028 *E-mail:* chris.owen@hea.org.uk

Man Editor: Delphine Verroest *Tel:* (020) 7413 2613 *Fax:* (020) 7413 2028 *E-mail:* delphine.verroest@hea.org
Sales & Customer Care Manager: Dolores Ashton *Tel:* (020) 7413 1986 *Fax:* (020) 7413 2028 *E-mail:* dolores.ashton@hea.org.uk
Distribution Manager: John Billingham *Tel:* (020) 7413 1892 *Fax:* (020) 7413 2028 *E-mail:* john.billingham@hea.org.uk
New Media Editor & International Rights Contact: Andrea Horth *Tel:* (020) 7413 8986 *Fax:* (020) 7413 2028 *E-mail:* andrea.horth@hea.org.uk
Founded: 1987
Membership(s): Publisher's Association & Educational Publisher's Council.
Subjects: Child Care & Development, Health, Nutrition, Medicine, Nursing, Dentistry, Sports, Athletics, Women's Studies
ISBN Prefix(es): 0-7521; 0-903652; 1-85448
Total Titles: 500 Print
*Warehouse:* Marston Book Services, PO Box 269, Abingdon, Oxon OX14 4YN

**Health Science Press**, *imprint of* The C W Daniel Co Ltd

**Heartland Publishing**, *imprint of* Heartland Publishing Ltd

**Heartland Publishing Ltd**
PO Box 902, Sutton Valence, Kent ME17 3HY
*Tel:* (01622) 843040 *Fax:* (01622) 843040
*E-mail:* publish@heartland.co.uk
*Web Site:* www.heartland.co.uk
*Key Personnel*
Dir: Jeff Horne; Nick Evans
Founded: 1995
A small independent book publisher & visual media consultancy.
Membership(s): Independent Publishers Guild (IPG).
Subjects: Music, Dance, Poetry, Travel
ISBN Prefix(es): 0-9525187
Imprints: Amber Waves; Heartland Publishing

**Hedera Press**, *imprint of* E W Classey Ltd

**William Heinemann**, *imprint of* Random House UK Ltd

**William Heinemann Ltd+**
Imprint of Random House UK Ltd
Random House, 20 Vauxhall Bridge Rd, London SW1V 2SA
*Tel:* (020) 7840 8400 *Fax:* (020) 7828 6681
Founded: 1890
Subjects: Biography, Fiction, Government, Political Science, History, Nonfiction (General), Travel
ISBN Prefix(es): 0-434; 0-437

**Helicon Publishing Ltd+**
Division of RM plc
RM plc, 183 Milton Park, Abingdon, Oxon OX14 4SE
*Tel:* (08709) 200200 *Fax:* (01235) 826999
*E-mail:* helicon@rm.com
*Web Site:* www.helicon.co.uk
*Key Personnel*
Man Dir: David Attwooll
Rights Dir: Clare Painter
Sales & Marketing Dir: Sheila Lambie *E-mail:* sheila@helicon.co.uk
Sales Administration Manager: Hilary Isaac
Founded: 1992
Publishers of general & subject encyclopedias & dictionaries in book, CD-ROM & online form. Text & illustrations on the database are continuously updated offering flexible licensing, coedition & packaging opportunities.

Subjects: Art, Biography, Computer Science, Government, Political Science, History, Language Arts, Linguistics, Music, Dance, Science (General)
ISBN Prefix(es): 0-09; 1-85986
Total Titles: 70 Print; 5 CD-ROM
Imprints: Hutchinson Reference
Distributed by Penguin
*Warehouse:* Bookpoint, 130 Milton Park, Abingdon, Oxon OX14 45B
*Orders to:* Bookpoint, 130 Milton Park, Abingdon, Oxon OX14 45B

**Helion & Co**
26 Willow Rd, Solihull, West Midlands B91 1UE
*Tel:* (0121) 705 3393 *Fax:* (0121) 711 4075
*E-mail:* info@helion.co.uk
*Web Site:* www.helion.co.uk
*Key Personnel*
Owner & Rts Contact: Duncan Rogers
   *E-mail:* duncan@helion.co.uk
Sales: Wilf Rogers *E-mail:* wilfrid@helion.co.uk
Founded: 1992
Specialize in military history; emphasis on German & Austrian history 1675-1945.
Subjects: Biography, History, Nonfiction (General)
ISBN Prefix(es): 1-874622
Total Titles: 15 Print

**Christopher Helm (Publishers) Ltd**, *imprint of* A & C Black Publishers Ltd

**Christopher Helm (Publishers) Ltd+**
Imprint of A & C Black Publishers Ltd
37 Soho Sq, London W1D 3QZ
*Tel:* (020) 7758 0200 *Fax:* (020) 7758 0222
*E-mail:* customerservice@acblack.com; ornithology@acblack.com
*Key Personnel*
Chairman: Nigel Newton
Man Dir: Jill Coleman
Commissioning Editor: Nigel Redman
   *E-mail:* nredman@acblack.com
Rights & Permissions: Paul Langridge
Sales: David Wightman
Production Dir: Oscar Heini
Founded: 1986
Subjects: Natural History, Birds
ISBN Prefix(es): 0-7136; 0-7470; 1-873403; 1-903206
Number of titles published annually: 20 Print
Total Titles: 200 Print
*Ultimate Parent Company:* Bloomsbury Publishing PLC
Imprints: Pica Press; T & AD Poyser Ltd
*Shipping Address:* Brunel Rd, Houndmills, Basingstoke, Hants RG21 6XS *Tel:* (01256) 302692 *E-mail:* mdl@macmillan.co.uk
*Warehouse:* Macmillan Distribution Ltd, Howard Rd, Eaton Socon, Huntingdon, Cambs PE19 3EZ
*Distribution Center:* Macmillan Distribution Ltd
*Orders to:* Brunel Rd, Houndmills, Basingstoke, Hants RG21 6XS *Tel:* (01256) 302692 *E-mail:* mdl@macmillan.co.uk

**Helm Information Ltd+**
The Banks, Mountfield, Nr Robertsbridge, East Sussex TN32 5JY
*Tel:* (01580) 880 561 *Fax:* (01580) 880 541
*Web Site:* www.helm-information.co.uk
*Key Personnel*
Dir: Amanda Helm *E-mail:* amandahelm@helm-information.co.uk; Christopher Helm *E-mail:* christopher.helm@helm-information.co.uk
Editorial, Ornithology: Roger Riddington
Permissions & Promotions Assistant: Elizabeth Imlay *E-mail:* permissions@helm-information.co.uk
Founded: 1990

Membership(s): IPG (Independent Publisher's Guild).
Subjects: History, Literature, Literary Criticism, Essays, Natural History
ISBN Prefix(es): 1-873403; 1-903206
Total Titles: 20 Print
*Associate Companies:* Helm Wood Publishers Pty Ltd, PO Box 666, Wembley WA 601A, Australia
Imprints: A & C

**Helmsman Guides**, *imprint of* The Crowood Press Ltd

**Help Yourself Books**, *imprint of* Hodder & Stoughton Religious

**Hemming Information Services**
32 Vauxhall Bridge Rd, London SW1V 2SS
*Tel:* (020) 7973 6694 *Fax:* (020) 7233 5052
*E-mail:* customer@hqluk.com
*Web Site:* www.h-info.co.uk
*Key Personnel*
Publishing Dir: Graham Bond
Publisher: Yvonne Phillips *E-mail:* y.phillips@hemmings-group.co.uk
Head of Marketing: Susan Kirby *E-mail:* s.kirby@hemmings-group.co.uk
Man Editor: Dean Wanless *E-mail:* d.wanless@hemmings-group.co.uk
Marketing: Phaedra Rees *E-mail:* p.rees@hemmings-group.co.uk
Advertising: David Morris *E-mail:* d.morris@hemmings-group.co.uk
Data Sales: Alethea Wiles *Tel:* (020) 7973 6624 *E-mail:* contacts@hemmings-group.co.uk
Founded: 1939
Membership(s): DMA, DPA & EADP.
Subjects: Cookery, Government, Political Science, Marketing
ISBN Prefix(es): 0-7079
*Parent Company:* Hemming Group Ltd

**Hendon Publishing Co Ltd**
Hendon Mill, Hallam Rd, Nelson, Lancs BB9 8AD
*Tel:* (01282) 613129; (01282) 697725
   *Fax:* (01282) 870215
*Key Personnel*
Chief Executive, Sales: Henry Nelson
Editorial: Dorothy Nelson
Production: Jean Marsden
Publicity, Rights & Permissions: James Nelson
Founded: 1971
Subjects: Cookery, History
ISBN Prefix(es): 0-86067; 0-902907
*Parent Company:* Hendon Mill Co Ltd
*Showroom(s):* Bookmarket, 24 Parker Lane, Burnley, Lancs
*Bookshop(s):* Colne Book Shop, One Newtown St, Colne, Lancs; Bookmarket, 4-6 Market St, Colne, Lancs

**Ian Henry Publications Ltd+**
20 Park Dr, Romford, Essex RM1 4LH
*Tel:* (01708) 736213 *Fax:* (01621) 850862
*Key Personnel*
Man Dir: Ian Wilkes *E-mail:* iwilkes@ianhenry.fsnet.co.uk
Founded: 1975
Subjects: Drama, Theater, Fiction, Genealogy, History, Regional Interests
ISBN Prefix(es): 0-86025
Number of titles published annually: 10 Print
Total Titles: 120 Print
*Branch Office(s)*
PO Box 1132, Studio City 91614-10132, United States
Distributed by Players' Press (USA)
Distributor for Players' Press

**Heraldry Today+**
Parliament Piece, Ramsbury, Wilts SN8 2QH
*Tel:* (01672) 520617 *Fax:* (01672) 520183
*E-mail:* heraldry@heraldrytoday.co.uk
*Web Site:* www.heraldrytoday.co.uk
*Key Personnel*
Head of Firm: Rosemary Pinches
Founded: 1954
Membership(s): Antiquarian Booksellers' Association.
Subjects: Art, Genealogy, History, Armour, Armed Forces, Heraldry, Orders of Knighthood, Peerages, Royalties
ISBN Prefix(es): 0-900455
Distributor for Society of Antiquaries

**Herbert Press Ltd**, *imprint of* A & C Black Publishers Ltd

**Herbert Press Ltd+**
Imprint of A & C Black Publishers Ltd
37 Soho Sq, London W1D 3QZ
*Tel:* (020) 7758 0200 *Fax:* (020) 7758 0222
*E-mail:* customerservices@acblack.com
*Web Site:* www.acblack.com
*Key Personnel*
Publisher: Linda Lambert *Tel:* (020) 7758 0320
   *E-mail:* llambert@acblack.com
Founded: 1975
Specialize in crafts.
Subjects: Archaeology, Architecture & Interior Design, Art, Crafts, Games, Hobbies
ISBN Prefix(es): 0-7136; 0-906969; 1-871569
Number of titles published annually: 3 Print
Total Titles: 100 Print
*Ultimate Parent Company:* Bloomsbury Publishing PLC
Distributed by Allen & Unwin (Australia); Penguin (Europe & Far East)
*Orders to:* MDL (Macmillan Distribution), Houndmills, Basingstoke, Hants RG21 6XS *Tel:* (01256) 302 692

**Heritage**, *imprint of* Osborne Books Ltd

**Heritage House Group Ltd**
Heritage House, Lodge Lane, Derby DE1 3HE
*Tel:* (01332) 347087 *Fax:* (01332) 290688
*E-mail:* sales@hhgroup.co.uk
*Web Site:* www.hhgroup.co.uk
*Key Personnel*
Man Dir: B C Wood
Publications Manager: Nick McCann
Founded: 1950
Specialize in guidebooks to Stately Homes, Castles, Museums, Cathedrals etc, aimed at the tourist industry.
ISBN Prefix(es): 0-85101
Number of titles published annually: 6 Print
Total Titles: 88 Print

**Heritage Press**
4 Buckingham St, Brighton, Sussex BN1 3LT
*Tel:* (01273) 731296 *Fax:* (01273) 731296
*Key Personnel*
International Rights: Ann Dean
Founded: 1991
Heritage Art Guides; specialize in books & postcard books on Burne-Jones, William Morris-Pre-Raphaelites Aubrey Beardsley listed on Book Data.
Subjects: Architecture & Interior Design, Art, Nonfiction (General), Art Travel, Art History, Decorative Arts, Stained Glass, especially William Morris & Burne-Jones
ISBN Prefix(es): 1-873089
Total Titles: 5 Print
Distributed by Strauss Consultants (Canada & USA)
Foreign Rep(s): Roger Ward; David Williams (Austria, Netherlands, Ireland, Far East, France, Germany, Italy, London, Northern Ireland,

Southern Europe, Scandinavia, Spain); Bookport Associates; Books for Europe; Continent Books; Julian Cooper; Emma Ferguson; Hanne Rotovnik; IMA; Alan Levelle; Anthony Mcggach (Austria, UK, China, Far East, France, Germany, Greece, Italy, London, Northern Europe, Northern Ireland, Southern Europe, Scandinavia, Spain, Switzerland, Turkey, US); Tom Moggagh; Hibernian Book Services; MTM; Terry Rule; Strauss Consultants (Canada, US)
*Orders to:* Art Books International Ltd, One Stewart's Court, 220 Stewart's Rd, London SW8 4UD *Tel:* (020) 7720 1503 *Fax:* (020) 7720 3158 *E-mail:* artbooks@a-b-i.demon.co.uk *Web Site:* www.artbooksinternational.co.uk (all countries except USA & Canada)

**Nick Hern Books Ltd+**
The Glasshouse, 49a Goldhawk Rd, London W12 8QP
*Tel:* (020) 8749 4953 *Fax:* (020) 8735 0250
*E-mail:* info@nickhernbooks.demon.co.uk
*Web Site:* www.nickhernbooks.co.uk
*Key Personnel*
Publisher: Nick Hern *E-mail:* nick@nickhernbooks.demon.co.uk
Founded: 1988
Specialist performing arts publisher.
Subjects: Drama, Theater
ISBN Prefix(es): 1 85459
Number of titles published annually: 40 Print
Total Titles: 300 Print
Distributed by Currency Press (Australia); Playwrights Canada Press (Canada); Theatre Communications Group (USA)
Distributor for Drama Book Publishers (USA, Canada & Australia)
*Shipping Address:* Grantham Book Services, Isaac Newton Way, Alma Park Industria, Grantham Lincs NG31 9SD *Tel:* (01476) 54100 *Fax:* (01476) 541060
*Warehouse:* Grantham Book Services, Isaac Newton Way, Alma Park Industria, Grantham Lincs NG31 9SD *Tel:* (01476) 54100 *Fax:* (01476) 541060
*Orders to:* Grantham Book Services, Isaac Newton Way, Alma Park Industria, Grantham Lincs NG31 9SD *Tel:* (01476) 54100 *Fax:* (01476) 541060

**Hertfordshire Publications**, *imprint of* University of Hertfordshire Press

**High Risk**, *imprint of* Serpent's Tail Ltd

**Highland Books Ltd+**
2 High Pines Knoll Rd, Godalming GU7 2EP
*Tel:* (01483) 424560 *Fax:* (01483) 424388
*E-mail:* info@highlandbks.com
*Web Site:* www.highlandbks.com
*Key Personnel*
Dir: Philip Ralli
Founded: 1983
Publish books for Christian market, including "pick-me-ups" (books that encourage & restore).
Subjects: Biography, Religion - Protestant, Self-Help
ISBN Prefix(es): 0-946616; 1-897913
Number of titles published annually: 8 Print
Total Titles: 60 Print
Foreign Rep(s): Methodist Wholesale (South Africa); Scripture Union (New Zealand)
*Shipping Address:* STL Ltd, PO Box 300, Kingstown Broadway Carlisle *Tel:* (01228) 574949
*Warehouse:* STL Ltd, PO Box 300, Kingstown Broadway Carlisle *Tel:* (01228) 574949
*Orders to:* STL Ltd, PO Box 300, Kingstown Broadway Carlisle *Tel:* (01228) 574949

**Hillside**, *imprint of* Christian Education

**Hilmarton Manor Press+**
Calne, Wilts SN11 8SB
*Tel:* (01249) 760208 *Fax:* (01249) 760379
*E-mail:* mailorder@hilmartonpress.co.uk
*Web Site:* www.hilmartonpress.co.uk
*Key Personnel*
Man Dir: C Baile de Laperriere
Founded: 1969
Subjects: Antiques, Architecture & Interior Design, Art, Photography, Wine & Spirits
ISBN Prefix(es): 0-904722; 0-9500508
Distributor for ADEC (France); Arte & Antiques Editions (Germany); Bibliotheque Des Arts (France & Switzerland); Edition Grund (France); Edition Mayer (France); Genlux Holdings; Guide Emer (France); Servedit-Acatos (France); Tardy (France)

**Hippo**, *imprint of* Scholastic Ltd

**Hippopotamus Press+**
22 Whitewell Rd, Frome, Somerset BA11 4EL
*Tel:* (01373) 466653 *Fax:* (01373) 466653
*Key Personnel*
Editor: R John *E-mail:* rjhippopress@aol.com; M Pargitter
Foreign Editor: A Martin
Founded: 1974
Subjects: Literature, Literary Criticism, Essays, Poetry
ISBN Prefix(es): 0-904179
Number of titles published annually: 6 Print
Total Titles: 105 Print

**History-into-Print**, *imprint of* Brewin Books Ltd

**HLT Publications**
Woolwich Rd, Charlton, London SE7 8LN
*Tel:* (020) 8317 6161 *Fax:* (020) 8317 6001
*E-mail:* obp@hltpublications.co.uk
*Web Site:* www.holborncollege.ac.uk/OldbaileyPress.cfm
*Key Personnel*
Chairman: John Grenier
Chief Executive: Prof Cedric Bell
Founded: 1971
Membership(s): Publishers Association of Great Britain.
Subjects: Business, Law
ISBN Prefix(es): 1-85352; 0-7510; 1-85248
*Parent Company:* HLT Group Ltd
Imprints: Old Bailey Press; Wise Owl Books
Subsidiaries: Old Bailey Press Ltd
*Sales Office(s):* Amalgamated Book Services Ltd, Royal Star Arcade, Suite 1, High Street, Maidstone, Kent ME14 1JL *Tel:* (01622) 764 555 *Fax:* (01622) 763 197
*Warehouse:* Antony Rowe Ltd, Vincent Rd, Unit 6, Bumpers Farm Industrial Estate, Chippenham, Wilts SN14 6QA *Tel:* (0118) 950 3911 *Fax:* (0118) 950 5776

**Hobsons+**
159 173 Saint John St, London EC1V 4DR
*Tel:* (020) 7336 6633 *Fax:* (020) 7608 1034
*E-mail:* enquiries@hobsons.co.uk
*Web Site:* www.hobsons.com
*Key Personnel*
Chairman: Martin Morgan
Man Dir: Chris Letcher
Founded: 1974
Publishers under license for the Careers Research & Advisory Centre Ltd.
Subjects: Business, Career Development, Education, Science (General), Technology
ISBN Prefix(es): 1-86017; 0-86021; 1-85324; 0-903161
*Parent Company:* Daily Mail Trust
Imprints: CRAC

*Warehouse:* Biblios 2, Old London Rd, Washington NR Horsham, West Sussex RH20 3EN
*Orders to:* Biblios Publishers' Distribution Service Ltd, Star Rd, Partridge Green, West Sussex RH13 8LD

**Hodder & Stoughton**, *imprint of* Hodder & Stoughton Religious

**Hodder & Stoughton General**
338 Euston Rd, London NW1 3BH
*Tel:* (020) 7873 6000 *Fax:* (020) 7873 6024
*Key Personnel*
Man Dir: Jamie Hodder-Williams *Tel:* (020) 7873 6125 *Fax:* (020) 7873 6198
Dir, Publicity: Karen Geary *Tel:* (020) 7873 6141 *Fax:* (020) 7873 6195
Dir, Sales: Lucy Hale *Tel:* (020) 7873 6159 *Fax:* (020) 7873 6194
Publisher: Nick Sayers *Tel:* (020) 7873 6081 *Fax:* (020) 7873 6198
Publishing Dir: Carolyn Mays *Tel:* (020) 7873 6132 *Fax:* (020) 7873 6198
Publisher, Audio: Rupert Lancaster *Tel:* (020) 7873 6029
Publisher, Sceptre: Carole Welch *Tel:* (020) 7873 6129 *Fax:* (020) 7873 6196
Head of Rights: Briar Silich
Founded: 1868
Subjects: Biography, Child Care & Development, Cookery, Fiction, History, Humor, Military Science, Mysteries, Self-Help, Sports, Athletics, Travel
ISBN Prefix(es): 0-340; 0-450
Total Titles: 5,000 Print; 300 Audio
*Parent Company:* Hodder Headline LTD
*Ultimate Parent Company:* W H Smith PLC
Imprints: Mobius; Sceptre
*Orders to:* Bookpoint Ltd, 130 Milton Park, Abingdon, Oxon OX14 4SB

**Hodder & Stoughton Religious+**
338 Euston Rd, London NW1 3BH
*Tel:* (020) 7873 6000 *Fax:* (020) 7873 6059
*E-mail:* firstname.surname@hodder.co.uk
*Web Site:* www.headline.co.uk
*Key Personnel*
Man Dir: Charles Nettleton
Publishing Dir: Judith Longman
Manager, Publicity: Sarah Dennis
Founded: 1868
Subjects: Biography, Child Care & Development, Human Relations, Humor, Religion - Catholic, Religion - Protestant, Religion - Other, Self-Help, Theology
ISBN Prefix(es): 0-340
*Parent Company:* Hodder Headline Ltd
*Ultimate Parent Company:* WH Smith PLC
Imprints: Help Yourself Books; Hodder Christian Books; Hodder & Stoughton; NIV Bibles
*Distribution Center:* Bookpoint Ltd, 39 Milton Park, Abingdon, Oxon OX14 4BR *Tel:* (01235) 400 400 *Fax:* (01235) 400 500
*Orders to:* Bookpoint Ltd, 39 Milton Park, Abingdon, Oxon OX14 4BR *Tel:* (01235) 400 400 *Fax:* (01235) 400 500 *E-mail:* orders@bookpoint.co.uk

**Hodder Children's Books+**
338 Euston Rd, London NW1 3BH
*Tel:* (020) 7873 6000 *Fax:* (020) 7873 6225
*Web Site:* www.hodderheadline.co.uk
*Key Personnel*
Man Dir: Charles Nettleton
Dir, Publishing: Margaret Conroy
Dir, Marketing: Elisa Offord
Dir, Rights: Andrew Sharp
Dir Sales: Les Phipps
Dir, Fiction, Picture & Gift Publishing: Anne McNeil
Dir, Hodder Wayland: Anne Clarke
Founded: 1868

Subjects: Fiction, Nonfiction (General), Science Fiction, Fantasy
ISBN Prefix(es): 0-340
*Parent Company:* RM plc, Abingdon, Oxon
Imprints: Hodder Wayland
*Orders to:* Bookpoint Ltd, 39 Milton Park, Abingdon, Oxon OX14 4TD

**Hodder Christian Books**, *imprint of* Hodder & Stoughton Religious

**Hodder Education**
338 Euston Rd, London NW1 3BH
*Tel:* (020) 7873 6272 *Fax:* (020) 7873 6299
*E-mail:* joanne.craik@hodder.co.uk
*Web Site:* www.hodderheadline.co.uk
*Key Personnel*
Man Dir: Philip Walters
Dir, Consumer Education: Katie Roden
Dir, Schools Publishing: Lis Tribe
Production & Design Dir: Alyssum Ross
Sales & Marketing Dir: Catherine Newman
Dir, FE/HE, Journals & Reference Books, Health Sciences: Mary Attree
Founded: 1868
Subjects: Biblical Studies, Biological Sciences, Business, Career Development, Chemistry, Chemical Engineering, Computer Science, Crafts, Games, Hobbies, Engineering (General), Geography, Geology, Language Arts, Linguistics, Literature, Literary Criticism, Essays, Mathematics, Natural History, Photography, Physics, Science (General), Sports, Athletics, Theology
ISBN Prefix(es): 0-340; 0-7131; 0-450; 0-7122
*Parent Company:* Hodder Headline PLC
Imprints: Teach Yourself
*Orders to:* Bookpoint Ltd, 130 Milton Park, Abingdon, Oxon OX14 4TD

**Hodder Headline Ltd**
338 Euston Rd, London NW1 3BH
*Tel:* (020) 7873 6000 *Fax:* (020) 7873 6024
*Web Site:* www.hodderheadline.co.uk
*Key Personnel*
Group Chief Executive: Tim Hely Hutchinson
Man Dir, Headline Book Publishing: Martin Neild
Man Dir, Hodder & Stoughton General: Jamie Hodder-Williams
Man Dir, Hodder Children's Books: Mary Tapissier
Man Dir, Hodder & Stoughton Religious: Charles Nettleton
Man Dir, Bookpoint Ltd: Tony Bryars
Man Dir: Hodder Arnold; Philip Walters
Acting Man Dir, John Murray: Martin Neild
Group Financial Dir: Colin Fairbairn
Founded: 1986
ISBN Prefix(es): 0-340; 0-7131; 0-450; 0-7122
*Associate Companies:* Hodder Dargaud Ltd
*Subsidiaries:* Hodder Headline Australia Pty Ltd; Hodder Moa Becket Publishers Limited; Edward Arnold (Publishers) Limited; Bookpoint Limited; Headline Book Publishing Limited; Hodder & Stoughton Limited
*Divisions:* Arnold; Headline Book Publishing; Hodder Children's Books; Hodder & Stoughton Educational; Hodder & Stoughton General; Hodder & Stoughton Religious Books; Hodder Headline Audio
*Orders to:* Bookpoint Ltd, 130 Milton Park, Abingdon, Oxon OX14 4TD *Tel:* (01235) 835001 *Fax:* (01235) 832068

**Hodder Wayland**, *imprint of* Hodder Children's Books

**Holland Enterprises Ltd**
18 Bourne Court, Southend Rd, Woodford Green, Essex IG8 8HD
*Tel:* (020) 8551 7711 *Fax:* (020) 8551 1266

*E-mail:* sales@holland-enterprises.co.uk
*Web Site:* www.holland-enterprises.co.uk
*Key Personnel*
Chairman: William C Holland
Man Dir: Jonathan Holland
ISBN Prefix(es): 1-85038

**Hollis Publishing Ltd**
Harlequin House, 7 High St, Teddington, Middx TW11 8EL
*Tel:* (020) 8977 7711 *Fax:* (020) 8977 1133
*E-mail:* hollis@hollis-pr.co.uk; orders@hollis-pr.co.uk
*Web Site:* www.hollis-pr.co.uk
*Key Personnel*
Man Dir: Gary Zabel
Publishing Dir: Rosie Sarginson
Sales Dir: Jane Ireland
Membership(s): Directory Publishers Association.
Subjects: Advertising, Marketing, Publishing & Book Trade Reference

**Holyoake Books**
Stanford Hall, Loughborough LE12 5QR
*Tel:* (01509) 852333 *Fax:* (01509) 856500
*E-mail:* info@co-opu.demon.co.uk
*Key Personnel*
Publisher & Chief Information Officer: I V Williamson
Founded: 1869 (co-operative union)
Subjects: Human Relations, Social Sciences, Sociology
ISBN Prefix(es): 0-85195
*Parent Company:* Co-operative Union Ltd
Imprints: Co-operative Union

**Home Health Education Service**
Alma Park, Grantham, Lincs NG31 9SL
*Tel:* (01476) 591700; (01476) 539900 (orders) *Fax:* (01476) 577144
*E-mail:* stanborg@aol.com
*Key Personnel*
Secretary: Paul Hammond
Founded: 1892
Subjects: Religion - Other
ISBN Prefix(es): 0-904748; 0-900703; 1-899505
*Parent Company:* Stanborough Press
*U.S. Office(s):* Review & Herald Publishing Association, Hagerstown, MD 21740, United States

**Honeyglen Publishing Ltd+**
56 Durrels House, Warwick Gardens, London W14 8QB
*Tel:* (020) 7602 2876 *Fax:* (020) 7602 2876
*Key Personnel*
Publisher: Nadja Poderegin
Founded: 1982
Membership(s): IPG.
Subjects: Biography, Fiction, History, Philosophy of History
ISBN Prefix(es): 0-907855
Total Titles: 13 Print
*Orders to:* Vine House Distribution Ltd, Waldenbury, North Common, Chailey, East Sussex BN8 4DR, Contact: Richard Squibb
*Tel:* (01825) 723398 *Fax:* (01825) 724188
*E-mail:* sales@vinehouseuk.co.uk

**Honno Welsh Women's Press+**
c/o Canolfan Merched y Wawr, Stryd yr Efail, Aberystwyth SY23 1JH
*Tel:* (01970) 623 150 *Fax:* (01970) 623 150
*E-mail:* post@honno.co.uk
*Web Site:* www.honno.co.uk
*Key Personnel*
Editor: Gwenlian Dafydd; Janet Thomas
Information Officer: Alyson Tyler
Marketing Officer: Heidi Kivekas
Founded: 1986
Specialize in writings by women living in Wales or having a Welsh connection.

Subjects: Biography, Fiction, Nonfiction (General), Poetry
ISBN Prefix(es): 1-870206
Number of titles published annually: 6 Print
Total Titles: 50 Print
*Orders to:* Turnaround Distribution, Unit 3, Olympia Trading Estate, Coburg Rd, London N22 6TZ *Tel:* (020) 8829 3000 *Fax:* (020) 8881 5088 *E-mail:* claire@turnaround-uk.com (England, Scotland, Ireland & overseas)
Welsh Books Council Distribution Centre, Glanyrafon Industrial Estate, Aberystwyth, Ceredigion SSY23 3AQ *Tel:* (01970) 624 455 *Fax:* (01970) 625 506 *E-mail:* canolfan.ddosbarthu@2cllc.org.uk (Wales)

**Hoover's Business Press**
5 Five Mile Dr, Oxford OX2 8HT
*Tel:* (01865) 513186 *Fax:* (01865) 513186
*Web Site:* www.hoovers-europe.com
*Key Personnel*
Man Dir: William Snyder *E-mail:* snyderpub@aol.com
ISBN Prefix(es): 1-57311

**Horizon Scientific Press+**
Rowan House, 28 Queens Rd, Hethersett, Norwich NR9 3DB
Mailing Address: PO Box 1, Wymondham, Norfolk NR18 0EH
*Tel:* (01953) 601106 *Fax:* (01953) 603068
*E-mail:* mail@horizonpress.com
*Web Site:* www.horizonpress.com
*Key Personnel*
Contact: Hugh Griffin
Founded: 1993
Specialize in academic journals & books.
Subjects: Biological Sciences, Medicine, Nursing, Dentistry, Science (General)
ISBN Prefix(es): 1-898486
Number of titles published annually: 8 Print
Total Titles: 30 Print; 2 Online

**Horse Books**, *imprint of* Robert Hale Ltd

**Horus Editions**, *imprint of* Award Publications Ltd

**Hospitality Training Foundation+**
International House, High St, 3rd floor, Ealing, London W5 5DB
*Tel:* (020) 8579 2400 *Fax:* (020) 8840 6217
*E-mail:* info@htf.org.uk
*Web Site:* www.htf.org.uk
*Key Personnel*
Marketing Dir: Paul Hickey
Subjects: Career Development, Hotel & Catering
ISBN Prefix(es): 0-7033
*Branch Office(s)*
PO Box 67, Carmarthern SA31 1YU
    *E-mail:* htfwales@htf.org.uk
28 Castle St, Edinburgh EH2 2HT
    *E-mail:* htfscotland@htf.org.uk

**House of Lochar**
Isle of Colonsay, Argyll PA61 7YR
*Tel:* (01951) 200232 *Fax:* (01951) 200232
*E-mail:* lochar@colonsay.org.uk
*Web Site:* www.houseoflochar.com
*Key Personnel*
Partner: Christa Byrne; Kevin Byrne
    *E-mail:* byrne@colonsay.org.uk; Sophie Byrne
ISBN Prefix(es): 1-899863
Imprints: Colonsay Books; West Highland Series
Distributed by Natural Heritage (Canada); Scottish Book Source

**Hove Foto Books**, *imprint of* Newpro UK Ltd

**How Design**, *imprint of* David & Charles Ltd

**How To Books Ltd+**
3 Newtec Pl, Magdalen Rd, Oxford OX4 1RE
*Tel:* (01865) 793806 *Fax:* (01865) 248780
*E-mail:* info@howtobooks.co.uk
*Web Site:* www.howtobooks.co.uk
*Key Personnel*
Man Dir: Giles Lewis
International Rights: Ros Loten
Founded: 1991
Reference publisher.
Subjects: Business, Career Development, How-to, Management, Self-Help, Living & Working Abroad, Small Business, Successful Writing
ISBN Prefix(es): 1-85703; 1-85876; 1-84528
Number of titles published annually: 50 Print
Total Titles: 300 Print
*Parent Company:* How To Ltd
*Shipping Address:* Grantham Book Distributors
*Warehouse:* Grantham Book Services
*Orders to:* Grantham Book Services, Grantham NG31 9SD

**A & Z Hughes**, *imprint of* Gwasg Gwenffrwd

**Hugo's Language Books Ltd+**
80 Strand, London WC2R 0RL
*Tel:* (020) 7010 3000 *Fax:* (020) 7010 6060
*E-mail:* customerservice@dk.com
*Web Site:* uk.dk.com
*Key Personnel*
Dir Sales: Peter G Lock
Founded: 1875
Subjects: English as a Second Language, How-to, Language Arts, Linguistics
ISBN Prefix(es): 0-85285
*Parent Company:* Dorling Kindersley plc
*Ultimate Parent Company:* Penguin Group UK
*Orders to:* Penguin Direct, Pearson Customer Operations, Edinburgh Gate, Harlow, Essex CM20 2JE *Fax:* (020) 8757 4030 *Web Site:* pubeasy. books.penguin.co.uk
*Returns:* Penguin Books Ltd, Online Returns Department, Pearson Customer Operations, Edinburgh Gate, Harlow, Essex CM20 2JE

**"Huh!" 1991**, *imprint of* Pentathol Publishing

**Human Horizons Series**, *imprint of* Souvenir Press Ltd

**Hunt and Thorpe**, *imprint of* John Hunt Publishing Ltd

**John Hunt Publishing Ltd+**
46a West St, New Alresford, Hants SO24 9AU
*Tel:* (01962) 736880; (01962) 736888 (orders) *Fax:* (01962) 736881
*E-mail:* office@johnhunt-publishing.com
*Web Site:* www.johnhunt-publishing.com
*Key Personnel*
Publisher: John Hunt *Tel:* (01962) 736885 *E-mail:* john@johnhuntpub.demon.co.uk
Sales Manager: Colin Nutt
Financial Controller: Sandra Geary
Edit Manager: Anne O'Rorke
Marketing Administrator: Maria Watson
Founded: 1989
Membership(s): Independent Publishers Guild.
Subjects: Religion - Other, Inspirational, Educational, Children's Books including Novelty & Pop ups
ISBN Prefix(es): 0-85305; 1-85608; 1-903019
Number of titles published annually: 50 Print
Total Titles: 400 Print
Imprints: Hunt and Thorpe; Arthur James Ltd; "O" Books
*Orders to:* STL, Customer Service, PO Box 300, Carlisle, Cumbria CA3 0QS *Tel:* (0800) 282728 *Fax:* (0800) 282530 (UK) *E-mail:* salesline@stl.org

**C Hurst & Co (Publishers) Ltd+**
2nd floor, Africa Centre, Covent Garden, 38 King St, London WC2E 8JZ
*Tel:* (020) 7240 2666 *Fax:* (020) 7240 2667
*E-mail:* hurst@atlas.co.uk
*Web Site:* www.hurstpub.co.uk
*Key Personnel*
Man Dir: Christopher Hurst
Sales & Rights: Michael Dwyer
Founded: 1968
Subjects: Economics, Government, Political Science, History, Regional Interests, Religion - Other
ISBN Prefix(es): 0-905838; 0-903983; 0-900966; 1-85065
Distributed by Alkem Co (S) Pte Ltd (Southeast Asia); Phambili Agencies (South Africa); Unifacmanu Trading Co Ltd (Taiwan); United Publishers Services Ltd (Japan); University & Reference Publishers' Services (UNIREPS) (Australia & New Zealand); Vanguard Books Pvt (Pakistan)
Foreign Rep(s): Cristina de Lara Ruiz (Spain); Peter & Bella Dietschi (Greece); Colin Flint (Denmark, Finland, Iceland, Norway, Sweden); Charles Gibbes (Portugal, Southern France); Ewa Ledochowicz (Eastern Europe, Central Europe); Missing Link (Germany); David Pickering (Italy); James Tovey (Paris, Northern France); Alma van Zaane (Netherlands)
*Shipping Address:* Marston Book Services, PO Box 269, Abingdon, Oxon OX14 4YN *Tel:* (01235) 465500 *Fax:* (01235) 465555 *E-mail:* trade.order@marston.co.uk *Web Site:* www.marston.co.uk

**Hutchinson**, *imprint of* Random House UK Ltd

**Hutchinson Reference**, *imprint of* Helicon Publishing Ltd

**Hutchinson Childrens**, *imprint of* Random House UK Ltd

**Alan Hutchison Ltd**
9 Pembridge Studios, 27A Pembridge Villas, London W11 3EP
*Tel:* (020) 7221 0129
*Telex:* 9419283AHPLTD
*Key Personnel*
Man Dir: Jemima Haddock
Founded: 1979
Subjects: Art
ISBN Prefix(es): 0-905885; 1-85272
*Parent Company:* Crown Products Group PLC
*U.S. Office(s):* Putnam Pub, 200 Madison Ave, New York, NY, United States

**Hutton Press Ltd**
130 Canada Dr, Cherry Burton, Beverly, East Yorks HU17 7SB
*Tel:* (01964) 550573 *Fax:* (01964) 550573
*Key Personnel*
Man Dir: Charles F Brook
Founded: 1979
Subjects: History, Maritime, Regional Interests
ISBN Prefix(es): 0-907033; 1-872167; 1-902709

**Hyden House Ltd+**
The Sustainability Centre, East Meon, Hants GU32 1HR
*Tel:* (01730) 823311 *Fax:* (01730) 823322
*E-mail:* info@permaculture.co.uk
*Web Site:* www.permaculture.co.uk
*Key Personnel*
Man Dir: Madeleine Harland
Creative Dir: Tim Harland
Founded: 1990
Specialize in permaculture & sustainable agriculture.

Subjects: Agriculture, Earth Sciences, Environmental Studies, Gardening, Plants, Permaculture
ISBN Prefix(es): 1-85623
Number of titles published annually: 7 Print
Total Titles: 27 Print
Imprints: Permanent Publications
Distributed by Chelsea Green
Distributor for Candlelight Trust (Australia); Solar Survival Press (USA); Tagari Publications (Australia)

**Hymns Ancient & Modern Ltd+**
St Mary's Works, St Mary's Plain, Norwich NR3 3BH
*Tel:* (01603) 612914 *Fax:* (01603) 624483
*E-mail:* admin@scm-canterburypress.co.uk
*Web Site:* www.scm-canterburypress.co.uk
*Key Personnel*
Chief Executive Officer: Gordon Knights *E-mail:* gordon@scm-canterburypress.co.uk
Founded: 1861 (public company 1975)
Membership(s): IPG.
Subjects: Religion - Other
ISBN Prefix(es): 0-907547; 1-85311
Imprints: Canterbury Press Norwich; Church Times; Hart Advertising Charity Agency; Religious & Moral Education Press; SCM Press
Subsidiaries: G J Palmer & Sons Ltd; SCM-Canterbury Press Ltd
Distributed by Morehouse Publishing (US)
Foreign Rep(s): Churches Stores (New Zealand); Hugh Dunphy (Jamaica, West Indies); International Publishers Marketing (US); Morehouse Publishing (US); Novalis (Canada); Openbook Publishers (Australia); Charles Paine Pty Ltd (Australia); Publishers International Marketing (London)

**Iaith Cyf**
Parc Busnes Aberarad, Uned 3, Castell Newydd Emlyn, Carmarthenshire SA38 9DB
*Tel:* (01239) 711668 *Fax:* (01239) 711698
*E-mail:* ymhol@cwmni-iaith.com
*Web Site:* www.cwmni-iaith.com
*Key Personnel*
Executive Dir: Gareth Ioan
Founded: 1993
Subjects: Education, Welsh Language
ISBN Prefix(es): 0-9522905; 1-900563

**IC Publications Ltd**, see International Communications

**ICC United Kingdom**
12 Grosvenor Pl, London SW1X 7HH
*Tel:* (020) 7838 9363 *Fax:* (020) 7235 5447
*E-mail:* katharinehedger@iccorg.co.uk
*Web Site:* www.iccwbo.org; www.iccuk.net
*Key Personnel*
Chair: Phil Watts
Dir: Andrew Hope
Policy Executive: Tania Baumann
Founded: 1919
Subjects: Advertising, Business, Communications, Economics, Environmental Studies, Finance, Government, Political Science, Law, Marketing
*U.S. Office(s):* US Council of the ICC, 1212 Avenue of the Americas, New York, NY 10036, United States

**Icon Press+**
One Huggetts Lane, Lower Willingdon, Eastbourne, East Sussex BN22 0LZ
*Tel:* (01323) 507270 *Fax:* (01323) 507270
*E-mail:* iconpress@philipbrown.screaming.net
*Web Site:* www.iconpress.co.uk
*Key Personnel*
Dir: Philip Brown
Founded: 1986
Publishers of art manuals, local history & poetry books.

Subjects: Art, Foreign Countries, History, Humor, Poetry, Regional Interests, Travel
ISBN Prefix(es): 1-873812
Number of titles published annually: 2 Print
Total Titles: 20 Print

**ICP**, *imprint of* Wilmington Business Information Ltd

**ICSA Publishing Ltd**
16 Park Crescent, London W1B 1AH
*Tel:* (020) 7612 7020 *Fax:* (020) 7323 1132
*E-mail:* icsa.pub@icsa.co.uk
*Web Site:* www.icsapublishing.co.uk
Founded: 1981
Subjects: Business, Law, Management, Public Administration
ISBN Prefix(es): 1-86072
Number of titles published annually: 20 Print
Total Titles: 70 Print
*Shipping Address:* Extenza-Turpin, Stratton Business Park, Pegasus Drive, Biggleswade, Beds SG18 8QB *Tel:* (01767) 604596
*Warehouse:* Extenza-Turpin, Stratton Business Park, Pegasus Drive, Biggleswade, Beds SG18 8QB *Tel:* (01767) 604596
*Distribution Center:* Extenza-Turpin, Stratton Business Park, Pegasus Drive, Biggleswade, Beds SG18 8QB *Tel:* (01767) 604596
*Orders to:* Extenza-Turpin, Stratton Business Park, Pegasus Drive, Biggleswade, Beds SG18 8QB *Tel:* (01767) 604596
*Returns:* Extenza-Turpin, Stratton Business Park, Pegasus Drive, Biggleswade, Beds SG18 8QB *Tel:* (01767) 604596

**Idol**, *imprint of* Virgin Publishing Ltd

**IEE**, *imprint of* Institution of Electrical Engineers

**Illustrated History Paperbacks**, *imprint of* Sutton Publishing Ltd

**Imago Publishing Ltd**
Member of Imago Group
Albury Court, Albury, Thame, Oxon OX9 2LP
*Tel:* (01844) 337000 *Fax:* (01844) 339935
*E-mail:* sales@imago.co.uk
*Web Site:* www.imago.co.uk
*Key Personnel*
Dir: Richard Hayes *E-mail:* richardh@imago.co.uk
Founded: 1980
Specialize in providing production services to publishers on a world-wide basis.
*Parent Company:* Imago Holdings Ltd
*Ultimate Parent Company:* Imago Investments Ltd
*Branch Office(s)*
Imago Australia, 14 Brown St, Suite 241, Chatswood, Sydney 2067, Australia, Contact: Emma Bell *Tel:* (02) 9415 2713 *Fax:* (02) 9415 2714 *E-mail:* ebell@imagoaus.com
Imago France, 16, rue Charlemagne, 75004 Paris, France, Contact: M Matt Critchlow *Tel:* (01) 42 81 41 24 *Fax:* (01) 42 81 41 24 *E-mail:* mcritchlow@imagogroup.com *Web Site:* www.imago.co.uk
Imago Productions (FE) Pte Ltd, 5 Lorong Bakar Batu, No 05-01, Macpherson Industrial Complex, Singapore 348742, Singapore, Contact: Mr K C Ng *Tel:* 6748 4433 *Fax:* 6748 6082 *E-mail:* kng@imago.com.sg *Web Site:* www.imago.co.uk
Imago Services (HK) Ltd, Tung Chung Factory Bldg, 6th floor, Flat B, 653-659 King's Rd, North Point, Hong Kong, China, Contact: Kendrick Cheung *Tel:* 2811 3316 *Fax:* 2597 5256 *E-mail:* kcheung@imago.com.hk *Web Site:* www.imago.co.uk
*U.S. Office(s):* Imago Sales (USA) Inc, 1431 Broadway-Penthouse, New York, NY 10018,

United States, Contact: Joe Braff *Tel:* 212-921-4411 *Fax:* 212-921-8226 *E-mail:* jbraff@imagousa.com *Web Site:* www.imagosales.com
Imago Sales (USA Mid West) Inc, 17 N Loomis St, No 4A, Chicago, IL 60607, United States, Contact: Ms Ma Yan *Tel:* 312-829-4051 *Fax:* 312-829-4059 *E-mail:* myan@imagousa.com *Web Site:* www.imagosales.com
Imago Sales (USA West Coast) Inc, 31952 Camino Capistrano, Suite C22, San Juan Capistrano, CA 92675, United States, Contact: Greg Lee *Tel:* 949-661-5998 *Fax:* 949-661-8013 *E-mail:* glee@imagousa.com *Web Site:* www.imagosales.com

**Immediate Publishing**
27 Church Rd, Hove BN3 2FA
*Tel:* (01273) 207259; (01273) 207411 *Fax:* (01273) 205612
*Key Personnel*
Contact: Luci Allmark *E-mail:* luci@erlbaum.co.uk
Founded: 1993
Subjects: Computer Science
ISBN Prefix(es): 1-898931
*Warehouse:* Taylor & Francis, Rankin Rd, Basingstoke, Hamps RG24 8PR
*Orders to:* Direct Distribution, 27 Palmeira Mansions, Church Rd, Hove, East Sussex

**Impart Books+**
Gwelfryn, Llanidloes Rd, Newtown, Powys SY16 4HX
*Tel:* (01686) 623484
*E-mail:* impart@books.mid-wales.net
*Web Site:* www.books.mid-wales.net
*Key Personnel*
Proprietor: Alick Hartley
Founded: 1988
Subjects: Accounting, English as a Second Language, Mathematics
ISBN Prefix(es): 1-874155
Number of titles published annually: 3 Print
Total Titles: 50 Print
Imprints: Crux Press

**Imperial College Press+**
57 Shelton St, London WC2H 9HE
*Tel:* (020) 7836 3954 *Fax:* (020) 7836 2002
*E-mail:* edit@icpress.co.uk
*Web Site:* www.icpress.co.uk
*Key Personnel*
Contact: Dr John Navas *E-mail:* john@icpress.demon.co.uk
Founded: 1995
STM publisher of books & journals. Specialize in medicine.
Subjects: Biological Sciences, Chemistry, Chemical Engineering, Electronics, Electrical Engineering, Engineering (General), Mathematics, Medicine, Nursing, Dentistry, Physical Sciences, Science (General)
ISBN Prefix(es): 1-86094
Number of titles published annually: 85 Print; 2 CD-ROM
Total Titles: 175 Print; 2 CD-ROM
Distributed by World Scientific Publishing (Territory: United Kingdom); World Scientific Publishing Co Inc (Territory: United States); World Scientific Publishing Co Pte Ltd (Territories: India, Singapore, Taiwan); World Scientific Publishing (HK) Co Ltd (Territory: Hong Kong)
*Orders to:* World Scientific Publishing, 57 Shelton St, Covent Garden, London WC2H 9HE

**In Old Photographs**, *imprint of* Sutton Publishing Ltd

**The In Pinn**, *imprint of* Neil Wilson Publishing Ltd

**Incorporated Catholic Truth Society**, see The Catholic Truth Society

**Independence Educational Publishers Ltd**
PO Box 295, Cambridge CB1 3XP
*Tel:* (01223) 566 130 *Fax:* (01223) 566 131
*E-mail:* issues@independence.co.uk
*Web Site:* www.independence.co.uk
*Key Personnel*
Publisher: Craig Donnellan
Founded: 1989
Subjects: Social Issues
ISBN Prefix(es): 1-86168; 1-872995

**Independent Voices**, *imprint of* Souvenir Press Ltd

**Independent Writers Publications Ltd+**
97 Geary Rd, Dollis Hill, London NW10 1HS
*Tel:* (020) 8438 0179 *Fax:* (020) 8438 0179
*Key Personnel*
Contact: Alfred Shmueli
Founded: 1993
Subjects: Fiction
ISBN Prefix(es): 1-897894

**Indiana University Press**, *imprint of* Combined Academic Publishers

**Informa Publishing Group Ltd**
Mortimer House, 37-41 Mortimer St, London W1T 3JH
*Tel:* (020) 7017 5000
*E-mail:* publishing.customers@informa.com
*Web Site:* www.informa.com
*Key Personnel*
Executive Chairman: Peter Rigby
Chief Executive: David Gilbertson
Corporate Development Director: Peter Miller
ISBN Prefix(es): 1-85044; 0-904093; 0-907432; 1-84311; 1-85978

**INSPEC**, *imprint of* Institution of Electrical Engineers

**Institute for Fiscal Studies**
7 Ridgmount St, 3rd floor, London WC1E 7AE
*Tel:* (020) 7291 4800 *Fax:* (020) 7323 4780
*E-mail:* mailbox@ifs.org.uk
*Web Site:* www.ifs.org.uk
*Key Personnel*
Dir: Robert Chote
Deputy Dir: Ian Crawford; Rachel Griffith
Research Dir: Richard Blundell
Deputy Research Dir: James Banks
External Relations Manager: Emma Hyman *Tel:* (020) 7291 4850 *E-mail:* emma_h@ifs.org.uk
Executive Administrator: Robert Markless
Founded: 1969
Independent research institute
Publish research findings on all aspects of taxation & economic public policy.
Subjects: Economics, Finance, Public Administration, Working Papers (online only)
ISBN Prefix(es): 1-873357
Number of titles published annually: 15 Print; 10 Online
Total Titles: 200 Print; 100 Online

**Institute of Development Studies**
University of Sussex, Falmer, Brighton, Sussex BN1 9RE
*Tel:* (01273) 606261 *Fax:* (01273) 621202; (01273) 691647
*E-mail:* ids@ids.ac.uk
*Web Site:* www.ids.ac.uk
*Key Personnel*
Head of Information Resource Unit: Geoffrey Barnard *E-mail:* g.barnard@ids.ac.uk

Communications Manager: Rosalind Goodrich
Rights & Permissions: Gary Edwards
    *Tel:* (01273) 678269 *Fax:* (01273) 621202
    *E-mail:* g.edwards@ids.ac.uk
Founded: 1966
Subjects: Agriculture, Developing Countries, Economics, Education, Environmental Studies, Government, Political Science, Public Administration, Women's Studies
ISBN Prefix(es): 0-903354; 0-903715; 1-85864
Number of titles published annually: 50 Print
Total Titles: 500 Print

### Institute of Economic Affairs+
2 Lord North St, London SW1P 3LB
*Tel:* (020) 7799 8900 *Fax:* (020) 7799 2137
*E-mail:* enquiries@iea.org.uk; iea@iea.org.uk
*Web Site:* www.iea.org.uk
*Key Personnel*
Dir General: John Blundell *Tel:* (020) 7799 8911
    *E-mail:* jblundell@iea.org.uk
Editorial Dir: Prof Philip Booth *Tel:* (020) 7799
    8912 *E-mail:* pbooth@iea.org.uk
Development Dir: Jacqueline Baer O'Mahony
    *Tel:* (020) 7799 8904 *E-mail:* jbaer@iea.org.uk
Dir, Marketing & Subscriptions: Adam Myers
    *Tel:* (020) 7799 8920 *E-mail:* amyers@iea.org.uk
Sales Manager: Bob Layson *Tel:* (020) 7799 8909
    *E mail:* books@iea.org.uk
Founded: 1955
Subjects: Economics, Education
ISBN Prefix(es): 0-255

### Institute of Education, University of London+
20 Bedford Way, London WC1H 0AL
*Tel:* (020) 7612 6260 *Fax:* (020) 7612 6560
*E-mail:* info@ioe.ac.uk
*Web Site:* www.ioe.ac.uk/publications
*Key Personnel*
Dir: Prof Geoff Whitty
Publications Officer: Deborah Spring *E-mail:* d.spring@ioe.ac.uk
Founded: 1902
Subjects: Education
ISBN Prefix(es): 0-85473
Number of titles published annually: 15 Print
Total Titles: 80 Print
*Orders to:* Central Books, 99 Wallis Rd, London E9 5LN *Tel:* (020) 8986 4854 *Fax:* (020) 8533 5821

### Institute of Employment Rights
177 Abbeville Rd, London SW4 9RL
*Tel:* (020) 7498 6919 *Fax:* (020) 7498 9080
*E-mail:* office@ier.org.uk
*Web Site:* www.ier.org.uk
*Key Personnel*
Dir: Carolyn Jones
Founded: 1989
Subjects: Disability, Special Needs, Economics, Ethnicity, Government, Political Science, Law, Women's Studies
ISBN Prefix(es): 0-9543781
Number of titles published annually: 8 Print

### Institute of Financial Services+
IFS House, 4-9 Burgate Lane, Canterbury, Kent CT1 2XJ
*Tel:* (01227) 818 687 *Fax:* (01227) 763 788
*E-mail:* institute@ifslearning.com
*Web Site:* www.ifslearning.com
*Key Personnel*
Publishing Manager: Philip Blake
    *E-mail:* pblake@ifslearning.co.uk
Mail Order Manager: Morton Griffiths
    *E-mail:* mgriffiths@ifslearning.co.uk
Founded: 1987 (as Bankers Books Ltd)
Publisher of student & practitioner audiences across the financial services.
Subjects: Business, Finance, Law, Management
ISBN Prefix(es): 0-85297

Number of titles published annually: 90 Print
Total Titles: 190 Print
*Parent Company:* Chartered Institute of Bankers
Imprints: Chartered Institute of Bankers (CIB) Publications
*Bookshop(s):* 90 Bishopsgate, London EC2N 4DQ
*Orders to:* IFS Mail Order, c/o The Chartered Institute of Bankers, Emmanual House, Burgate Lane, Canterbury, Kent CT1 2XJ

### Institute of Food Science & Technology
5 Cambridge Court, 210 Shepherds Bush Rd, London W6 7NJ
*Tel:* (020) 7603 6316 *Fax:* (020) 7602 9936
*E-mail:* info@ifst.org
*Web Site:* www.ifst.org
Founded: 1964
Professional qualifying body & educational charity.
Subjects: Science (General), Technology
ISBN Prefix(es): 0-905367
Number of titles published annually: 2 Print; 1 Online
Total Titles: 10 Print; 1 Online

### Institute of Governance
Chisholm House, High School Yards, Edinburgh EH1 1LZ
*Tel:* (0131) 650 2456 *Fax:* (0131) 650 6345
*Web Site:* www.institute-of-governance.org
*Key Personnel*
Business Manager: Lindsay Adams
    *E-mail:* ladams@ed.ac.uk
Founded: 1976
Subjects: Government, Political Science
ISBN Prefix(es): 0-9518053; 0-9509626

### Institute of Irish Studies, The Queens University of Belfast+
8 Fitzwilliam St, Belfast BT9 6AW
*Tel:* (028) 9027 3386 *Fax:* (028) 9043 9238
*E-mail:* irish.studies@qub.ac.uk
*Web Site:* www.qub.ac.uk/iis
*Key Personnel*
Editor: Margaret McNulty *E-mail:* m.mcnulty@qub.ac.uk
Founded: 1987
A small press & publishing company which publishes academic & semi-academic books relative to all aspects of Irish studies.
Subjects: Anthropology, Archaeology, Art, Biography, Ethnicity, Film, Video, Geography, Geology, Government, Political Science, History, Language Arts, Linguistics, Regional Interests, Religion - Catholic, Religion - Protestant
ISBN Prefix(es): 0-85389
Number of titles published annually: 10 Print
Total Titles: 150 Print
Distributed by Dufour Editions (USA); P D Meaney (1 title only)
Distributor for Van Gorcum (North Ireland & Irish Republic for 1 book only)
Foreign Rep(s): Robert Towers (Ireland); Russell Book Representation (UK)
*Distribution Center:* Central Books Ltd, 99 Wallis Rd, London E9 5LN *Tel:* (020) 8986 4854 *Fax:* (020) 8533 5821 *E-mail:* orders@centralbooks.com (Great Britain & Europe)
Irish Books & Media, Inc, 1433 Franklin Ave E, Minneapolis, MN 55404-2135, United States *Tel:* 612-871-3505 *Fax:* 612-871-3358 *E-mail:* irishbooks@aol.com

### Institute of Physics Publishing+
Dirac House, Temple Back, Bristol BS1 6BE
*Tel:* (0117) 929 7481 *Fax:* (0117) 929 4318
*E-mail:* book.enquiries@iop.org
*Web Site:* www.iop.org; www.iop.org/IOPP/ioppabout.html

*Key Personnel*
Man Dir: Jerry Cowhig *E-mail:* jerry.cowhig@iop.org
Business Dir: Ken Lillywhite *E-mail:* ken.lillywhite@iop.org
Operations Dir: Dr Kurt Paulus *Tel:* (117) 930 1057 *E-mail:* kurt.paulus@iop.org
Finance Dir: Michael Bray *E-mail:* mike.bray@iop.org
Publishing Dir: Richard Roe *E-mail:* richard.roe@iop.org
Head of Book Publishing: Nicki Dennis
    *E-mail:* nicki.dennis@iop.org
Rights: Brenda Trigg *E-mail:* brenda.trigg@iop.org
Sales: Nicola Newey *E-mail:* nicola.newey@iop.org
Founded: 1874
Membership(s): ALPSP, PA & STM.
Subjects: Astronomy, Biography, Computer Science, Electronics, Electrical Engineering, Mathematics, Physical Sciences, Physics, Science (General), Technology
ISBN Prefix(es): 0-7503; 0-85274; 0-85498
Number of titles published annually: 45 Print
Total Titles: 700 Print
*Parent Company:* Institute of Physics
Imprints: Research Studies Press Ltd (RSP)
Subsidiaries: IOP Publishing Inc
*U.S. Office(s):* Institute of Physics Publishing, Inc, Public Ledger Bldg, Suite 1035, 150 S Independence Mall W, Philadelphia, PA 19106, United States *Tel:* 215-627-0880 *Fax:* 215-627-0879 *E-mail:* info@ioppubusa.com
*Warehouse:* Marston Book Services Ltd, PO Box 269, Abingdon OX14 4YN *Tel:* (01235) 465 500 *Fax:* (01235) 465 555
*Orders to:* c/o AIDC, 2 Winter Sport Lane, PO Box 20, Williston, VT 05495-0020, United States

### Institution of Chemical Engineers
Davis Bldg, 165-189 Railway Terrace, Rugby CV21 3HQ
*Tel:* (01788) 578214 *Fax:* (01788) 560833
*E-mail:* jcressey@icheme.org.uk
*Web Site:* www.icheme.org
*Telex:* 311780
*Key Personnel*
Chief Executive & Secretary: Dr T J Evans
Senior Marketing Officer: Jacqueline Cressey
Founded: 1922
Subjects: Chemistry, Chemical Engineering
ISBN Prefix(es): 0-8169; 0-85295
*U.S. Office(s):* American Institute of Chemical Engineers, 345 E 47 St, New York, NY 10017-2300, United States
Distributed by American Institute of Chemical Engineers (Canada & USA only)

### Institution of Electrical Engineers+
Publishing Dept, Michael Faraday House, Six Hills Way, Stevenage, Herts SG1 2AY
*Tel:* (01438) 313311 *Fax:* (01438) 742792
*E-mail:* postmaster@iee.org.uk
*Web Site:* www.iee.org.uk/publish
*Key Personnel*
Man Dir: Steven Mair
Publishing Dir: Robin Mellors-Bourne
Marketing Enquiries: Janet Porter
Commissioning Editor: Roland Harwood
President: David Brown
Founded: 1871
Subjects: Aeronautics, Aviation, Business, Communications, Computer Science, Electronics, Electrical Engineering, Energy, History, Management, Physical Sciences, Technology
ISBN Prefix(es): 0-85296; 0-906048; 0-86341
Number of titles published annually: 30 Print
Total Titles: 240 Print
*Parent Company:* Savoy Pl, London WC2R 0BL
Imprints: IEE; INSPEC; Peter Peregrinus Ltd
*Bookshop(s):* IEE, Savoy Pl, London WC2R 0BL

*Warehouse:* Unit 7, Fulton Close, Argyle Way, Stevenage SG1 2AF *Tel:* (01438) 355029 *Fax:* (01438) 355034
*Orders to:* PO Box 96, Stevenage, Herts SG1 2SD *Tel:* (01438) 767328 *Fax:* (01438) 742792 *E-mail:* sales@ieee.org *Web Site:* www.iee. org/shop/ (Publications Sales Dept)

**The Intef Institute**, *imprint of* Karnak House

**Intellect Ltd+**
PO Box 862, Bristol BS99 1DE
*Tel:* (0117) 9589910 *Fax:* (0117) 9589911
*E-mail:* mail@intellectbooks.com
*Web Site:* www.intellectbooks.com
*Key Personnel*
Chairman: Masoud Yazdani
Dir, Journal Publishing: Robin Beecroft
Founded: 1984
A multidisciplinary publisher for individual & institutional readers.
Membership(s): IPG.
Subjects: Computer Science, Drama, Theater, Film, Video, Language Arts, Linguistics, Regional Interests, Women's Studies
ISBN Prefix(es): 1-871516; 1-84150
Number of titles published annually: 25 Print; 25 E-Book
Total Titles: 450 Print; 100 E-Book
*Branch Office(s)*
Bristol, The Mill, Parnall Rd, Fishponds, Bristol BS16 3JG, Contact: Robin Beecroft *Tel:* (0117) 9589910 *Fax:* (0117) 9589911 *E-mail:* robin@intellectbooks.com *Web Site:* www.intellectbooks.com
Distributed by Astam Books (Australasia); Gardners Books (UK); International Specialised Book Services, Inc (North America)
Foreign Rep(s): Astam Books (Australia); ISBS (US); Kemper Conseil (Netherlands)

**Inter-Varsity Press+**
Norton St, Nottingham NG7 3HR
*Tel:* (0115) 978 1054 *Fax:* (0115) 942 2694
*E-mail:* sales@ivpbooks.com
*Web Site:* www.ivpbooks.com
*Key Personnel*
Chief Executive: B Wilson
Editorial: S Carter
Production: J Mansfield *Tel:* (0115) 978 1054 *Fax:* (0115) 942 2694 *E-mail:* jam@ivpbooks. com
Sales: T Banting *Tel:* (0115) 978 1054 *Fax:* (0115) 942 2694 *E-mail:* trb@ivpbooks. com
Personal Assistant to Chief Executive: Christine Ward *E-mail:* cw@uccf.org.uk
Marketing: V Smith-Dziuba *Tel:* (0115) 978 1054 *Fax:* (0115) 942 2694
Founded: 1928
Publisher of evangelical Christian books.
Subjects: Education, Religion - Other
ISBN Prefix(es): 0-85110; 0-85111
Number of titles published annually: 50 Print
Total Titles: 650 Print
*Parent Company:* UCCF
Imprints: Apollos (Academic books); Crossway (Popular books); IVP (General books)
Distributor for I V Press; DK Religious; Piquant; Third Way
*Distribution Center:* IVP Book Centre, Norton St, Nottingham NG7 3HR *Tel:* (0115) 9781054 *Fax:* (0115) 9422694 *Web Site:* www.ivpbooks. com
*Orders to:* IVP Book Centre, Norton St, Nottingham NG7 3HR *Tel:* (0115) 9781054 *Fax:* (0115) 9422694 *Web Site:* www.ivpbooks. com

**Intercept Ltd**
PO Box 716, Andover, Hants SP10 1YG
*Tel:* (01264) 334748 *Fax:* (01264) 334058

*E-mail:* intercept@andover.co.uk
*Web Site:* www.intercept.co.uk
*Key Personnel*
Manager: Andrew Cook
Founded: 1983
Subjects: Agriculture, Biological Sciences, Environmental Studies, Gardening, Plants, Geography, Geology, Medicine, Nursing, Dentistry, Natural History, Science (General), Technology
ISBN Prefix(es): 0-946707; 1-898298
*Parent Company:* Lavoisier, 14 rue de Provigny, 94236 Cachan, France
Distributor for Exegetics; Natural History Museum (London); Erich Nelson Foundation; NRC Research Press; Polytechnic International Press; Ray Society
*Warehouse:* Unit 2B, Duke Close, West Way, Walworth Industrial Estate, Andover, Hants SP10 5AR

**Interfisc Publishing**
9 Lifford St, London SW15 1NY
*Tel:* (020) 8789 4957 *Fax:* (0845) 330 7249
*E-mail:* aogley@interfisc.com
*Web Site:* www.interfisc.com
*Key Personnel*
Contact: Adrian Ogley *E-mail:* aogley@interfisc. com
Founded: 1993
Professional & academic books on international tax.
Membership(s): Association of Learned & Professional Society of Publishers.
Subjects: Business
ISBN Prefix(es): 0-9520442
Total Titles: 2 Print
*Parent Company:* Interfisc, 27 Old Gloucester St, London WC1N 3XX
Foreign Rep(s): American Distributor (Canada, US)
*Orders to:* International Information Services Inc, PO Box 3490, Silver Spring, MD 20918, United States *Tel:* (301) 565-2975 *Fax:* (301) 565-2973 *E-mail:* orders@interfisc.com (USA & Canada)

**International Affairs**, *imprint of* Royal Institute of International Affairs

**International Bee Research Association**
18 North Rd, Cardiff CF10 3DT
*Tel:* (02920) 372409 *Fax:* (02920) 665522
*E-mail:* mail@cardiff.org.uk
*Web Site:* www.cf.ac.uk/ibra
*Key Personnel*
Dir: Richard Jones
Deputy Dir & Editor: Pamela A Munn, PhD
Founded: 1949
World information specialists on bees.
Membership(s): IUBS.
Subjects: Agriculture, Biological Sciences, Education, Natural History, Bees, Bee Science, Pollination, Conservation
ISBN Prefix(es): 0-86098; 0-900149

**International Biographical Centre**, *imprint of* Melrose Press Ltd

**International Communications**
7 Coldbath Sq, London EC1R 4LQ
*Tel:* (020) 7713 7711 *Fax:* (020) 7713 7898; (020) 7713 7970
*E-mail:* icpubs@africasia.com
*Web Site:* www.africasia.com
*Key Personnel*
Dir: Emena Ben Yedder
Group Publisher: Ahmed Afif Ben Yedder
Sales: Shaunagh Cowell
Founded: 1974
Subjects: Art, Business, Sports, Athletics, Specializes in Current Affairs, Middle East & Africa

ISBN Prefix(es): 0-905268
Number of titles published annually: 4 Print
Subsidiaries: IC Publications

**International Institute for Strategic Studies+**
Arundel House, 13-15 Arundel St, Temple Pl, London WC2R 3DX
*Tel:* (020) 7379 7676 *Fax:* (020) 7836 3108
*E-mail:* iiss@iiss.org
*Web Site:* www.iiss.org
*Telex:* 94081492 G *Cable:* MLINK
*Key Personnel*
Dir: Dr John Chipman *E-mail:* chipman@iiss.org
Assistant Dir: Steven Simon *E-mail:* simon@iiss. org; Terence Taylor *E-mail:* taylor@iiss.org
Manager, Editorial Service: James Green *Tel:* (020) 7379 7676 *E-mail:* green@iiss.org
Founded: 1958
Subjects: Government, Political Science, Military Science
ISBN Prefix(es): 0-86079; 0-900492
Number of titles published annually: 12 Print
*Associate Companies:* Oxford University Press, Great Clarendon St, Oxford OX2 6DP *Tel:* (01865) 267907 *Fax:* (01865) 267485
Imprints: The Military Balance; Strategic Survey; Survival; Adelphi Papers; Strategic Comments
Distributed by Oxford University Press
*Orders to:* Oxford University Press, Journals Marketing, 2001 Evans Rd, Cary, NC 27513, United States
Oxford University Press, Great Clarendon St, Oxford OX2 6DP *Tel:* (01865) 267907 *Fax:* (01865) 267485

**International Labour Office**
Millbank Tower, 21-24 Millbank, London SW1P 4QP
*Tel:* (020) 7828 6401 *Fax:* (020) 7233 5925
*E-mail:* ipu@ilo-london.org.uk; london@ilo-london.org.uk
*Web Site:* www.ilo.org/london
*Key Personnel*
Dir: Juan Somavia
Publications Manager: Nick Evans *E-mail:* evansn@ilo-london.org.uk
Information Officer: Carl David
Founded: 1919
ISBN Prefix(es): 92-2
*Parent Company:* International Labour Organization, 4 Route des Morillons, 1211 Geneva 22, Switzerland

**International Map Trade Association**
5 Spinacre, Becton Lane, Barton on Sea, Hants BH25 7DF
*Tel:* 01425) 620532 *Fax:* (01425) 620532
*Web Site:* www.maptrade.org
*Key Personnel*
Executive Dir: Mike Cranidge *E-mail:* mike. cranidge@btinternet.com

**International Water Association Publishing**, see IWA Publishing

**Interpet Publishing+**
Vincent Lane, Dorking, Surrey RH4 3YX
*Tel:* (01306) 881033 *Fax:* (01306) 885009
*E-mail:* publishing@interpet.co.uk
*Key Personnel*
Publisher: Kevin Kingham
Subjects: Animals, Pets, Gardening, Plants, Veterinary Science
ISBN Prefix(es): 0-948955; 1-86054; 1-84286; 1-902389; 1-903098

**Investment Intelligence**, *imprint of* Wilmington Business Information Ltd

**IOM Communications Ltd**
Subsidiary of The Institute of Materials, Minerals & Mining

One Carlton House Terrace, London SW1Y 5DB
*Tel:* (020) 7451 7300 *Fax:* (020) 7839 1702
*E-mail:* admin@materials.org.uk
*Web Site:* www.iom3.org.uk *Cable:* 451-7300
*Key Personnel*
Chief Executive: Dr Bernie Rickinson
Head of Publishing: Bill Jackson *Tel:* (020) 7451
7305 *E-mail:* bill_jackson@materials.org.uk
Managing Editor: Peter Danckwerts *Tel:* (020)
7451 7310 *E-mail:* peter_danckwerts@
materials.org.uk
Marketing Manager: Peter Richardson *Tel:* (020)
7451 7372 *E-mail:* peter_richardson@materials.
org.uk
Editor, Materials World: Sally Wilkes
Subjects: Chemistry, Chemical Engineering, Engi-
neering (General)
ISBN Prefix(es): 0-904357; 0-900497; 0-901462;
0-901716; 0-903104; 0-903107; 1-86125
*Branch Office(s)*
Shelton House, 12 Stoke Rd, Stoke on Trent ST4
2DR *Tel:* (01782) 221700 *Fax:* (01782) 221722
Danum House, South Parade, Doncaster DN1
2DY *Tel:* (01302) 320486 *Fax:* (01302) 380900
*Distribution Center:* Maney Publishing, Hud-
son Rd, Leeds LS9 7DL *Tel:* (0113) 249 7481
*Fax:* (0113) 248 6983 *E-mail:* maney@maney.
co.uk
*Orders to:* Maney Publishing, Hudson Rd, Leeds
LS9 7DL *Tel:* (0113) 249 7481 *Fax:* (0113)
248 6983 *E-mail:* maney@maney.co.uk

**Iona Community**, see Wild Goose Publications

**IPS**, see Eagle/Inter Publishing Service (IPS) Ltd

**IRL Press**, *imprint of* Oxford University Press

**Isis Publishing Ltd+**
7 Centremead, Osney Mead, Oxford OX2 0ES
*Tel:* (01865) 250 333 *Fax:* (01865) 790 358
*E-mail:* sales@isis-publishing.co.uk
*Web Site:* www.isis-publishing.co.uk
*Key Personnel*
International Rights: Emma Cumberland
*E-mail:* emma.cumberland@isis-publishing.
co.uk
Subjects: Biography, Fiction, Health, Nutrition,
Mysteries, Nonfiction (General), Self-Help,
Western Fiction
ISBN Prefix(es): 1-85089; 1-85695; 0-7531
Number of titles published annually: 192 Print;
192 Audio
*U.S. Office(s):* Ulverscroft Large Print (USA) Inc,
1881 Ridge Rd, PO Box 1230, West Seneca,
NY 14224-1230, United States *Tel:* 716-674-
4270 *Fax:* 716-674-4195

**Islam International Publications Ltd+**
Islamabad, Sheephatch Lane, Tilford, Farnham
GU10 2AQ
*Tel:* (01252) 783155; (01252) 783823
*Fax:* (01252) 783148
*Web Site:* www.alislam.org
*Key Personnel*
Dir: Mr N A Qamar
Founded: 1889
Specialize in books on Islam, various transla-
tions & exegesis of Holy Quran in different
languages.
Subjects: Religion - Islamic, Theology
ISBN Prefix(es): 1-85372
Imprints: Al-Shirkatul Islamiyyah
Subsidiaries: London Mosque Publications
*U.S. Office(s):* The Ahmadiyya Movement in Is-
lam Inc, Masjid Bait-Ur-Rehman, 15000 Good
Hope Rd, Silver Spring, MD 20905, United
States *Tel:* (301) 879-0110 *Fax:* (301) 879-
0115

**Islamic Foundation Publications**
Markfield Conference Centre, Ratby Lane, Mark-
field, Leics LE67 9SY
*Tel:* (01530) 244 944; (01530) 249 230
*Fax:* (01530) 244 946; (01530) 249 656
*E-mail:* info@islamic-foundation.org.uk;
publications@islamic-foundation.com
*Web Site:* www.islamic-foundation.org.uk *Cable:*
ISLAMFOUND LEICESTER UK
*Key Personnel*
Dir General, Editorial: Dr M M Ahsan
Dir Publications: Farooq Murad
Contact: Chowdhury Mueen-Uddin *E-mail:* c.
mueen@islamic-foundation.org.uk
Founded: 1973
Research, publication, post-graduation education,
training.
Subjects: Economics, Education, Government,
Political Science, History, Religion - Islamic
ISBN Prefix(es): 0-86037; 0-9503954
Number of titles published annually: 10 Print
Imprints: Revival Publications
Distributed by International Institute of Islamic
Thought (USA); IPS (Pakistan); Islamic Circle
of North America (USA); Islamic Society of
North America (USA); Sound Vision (USA)
*Orders to:* The Islamic Foundation Publications
Unit, Markfield Dawah Center, Ratby Lane,
Markfield, Leics LE67 9SY

**The Islamic Texts Society**
22A Brooklands Ave, Cambridge CB2 2DQ
*Tel:* (01223) 314387 *Fax:* (01223) 324342
*E-mail:* info@its.org.uk
*Web Site:* www.its.org.uk
*Key Personnel*
Man Dir: Fatima Azzam *E-mail:* fazzam@its.org.
uk
Founded: 1981
Specialize in Islamic literature.
Membership(s): Publishers' Association.
Subjects: Art, Biography, History, Law, Natural
History, Nonfiction (General), Philosophy, Po-
etry, Religion - Islamic
ISBN Prefix(es): 0-946621
Number of titles published annually: 6 Print
Total Titles: 50 Print
Foreign Rep(s): The American University in
Cairo Press (Egypt); Eleanor Brasch Enter-
prises (Australia); Richard Carman (Sub-
Saharan Africa); Iberian Book Services (Portu-
gal, Spain); Independent Publishers Group/Paul
& Co (Canada, US); Publishers International
Marketing (Middle East, Southeast Asia);
Quantum Publishing Solutions Ltd (UK); An-
drew Russell (Ireland, Northern Ireland); Mur-
ray Sutton (Denmark, Iceland, Scandinavia);
Viva Marketing (India)
*Warehouse:* Orca Book Services, Fleets Industrial
Estate, One Willis Way, Poole, Dorset BH15
3SS *Tel:* (01202) 785729 *Fax:* (01202) 666219
*Orders to:* Orca Book Services Ltd, Stanley
House, 3 Fleets Lane, Poole, Dorset BH15
3AJ *Tel:* (01202) 665432 *Fax:* (01202) 666219
*E-mail:* orders@orcabookservices.co.uk

**IT Publications**, *imprint of* ITDG Publishing

**ITDG Publishing+**
Bourton Hall, Bourton-on-Dunsmore, Rugby
CV23 9QZ
*Tel:* (01926) 634501 *Fax:* (01926) 634502
*E-mail:* marketing@itpubs.org.uk; itpubs@itpubs.
org.uk
*Web Site:* www.itdgpublishing.org.uk; www.
developmentbookshop.com
*Key Personnel*
Editorial, Rights & Permissions: Helen Marsden
Sales & Publicity: Toby Harris *E-mail:* tobyh@
itpubs.org.uk
Founded: 1973

Subjects: Agriculture, Business, Developing
Countries, Finance, Social Sciences, Sociology,
Technology
ISBN Prefix(es): 0-903031; 0-946688; 1-85339
Number of titles published annually: 25 Print
Total Titles: 400 Print
*Parent Company:* Intermediate Technology Devel-
opment Group
Imprints: IT Publications
Distributed by Amin al-Abini (Middle East &
North Africa); Astam Books Pty Ltd (Aus-
tralia); Richard Bowen (Finland, Norway, Swe-
den, Iceland, Denmark); Grassroots Books
Pvt Ltd (Zimbabwe); Horizon Books Ltd; In-
terMedia Americana (Central Africa); Lake
House Bookshop (Sri Lanka); Maya Publish-
ers Plc (India); Publishers Marketing Services
Plc (Malaysia, Singapore, Indonesia. Thailand,
Brunei); STM Publishers Services (Taiwan,
Korea, Vietnam, Philippines, Hong Kong, Thai-
land, China); Stylus Publishing Inc (USA)
Distributor for IDRC (Canada); KIT Press (Ams-
terdam, The Netherlands); SKAT (Switzerland)
Foreign Rep(s): Stylus (US)
*Orders to:* Plymbridge Distributors Ltd, Estover
Rd, Plymouth PL6 7PY

**Ithaca Press**, *imprint of* Garnet Publishing Ltd

**IUCN-The World Conservation Union**
Publications Services Unit, 219c Huntingdon Rd,
Cambridge CB3 0DL
*Tel:* (01223) 277894 *Fax:* (01223) 277175
*E-mail:* info@books.iucn.org
*Web Site:* www.iucn.org
*Key Personnel*
Publications Officer: Deborah Murith *Tel:* (022)
999 0119 *Fax:* (022) 999 0010 *E-mail:* dem@
iucn.org
Founded: 1948
ISBN Prefix(es): 2-8317
Divisions:
Distributed by Island Press
Distributor for Cites; Ramsar; World Conservation
Monitoring Centre

**IVP**, *imprint of* Inter-Varsity Press

**IWA Publishing**
Subsidiary of International Water Association
Alliance House, 12 Caxton St, London SW1H
0QS
*Tel:* (020) 7654 5500 *Fax:* (020) 7654 5555
*E-mail:* publications@iwap.co.uk
*Web Site:* www.iwapublishing.com
Subjects: Civil Engineering, Earth Sciences, En-
vironmental Studies, Hydrology, Wastewater,
Water
ISBN Prefix(es): 1-84339
Number of titles published annually: 50 Print; 1
CD-ROM
Total Titles: 250 Print; 5 CD-ROM
Distributed by Portland Press
Foreign Rights: Tony Poh (China, Korea,
Malaysia, Philippines, Singapore, Thailand,
Vietnam)
*Distribution Center:* Portland Customer Ser-
vices, Commerce Way, Colchester CO2 8HP
*Tel:* (01206) 796351 *E-mail:* sales@portland-
services.com
*Returns:* Portland Customer Services, Commerce
Way, Colchester CO2 8HP *Tel:* (01206) 796351

**JAI**, *imprint of* Elsevier Ltd

**JAI Press Ltd+**
38 Tavistock St, Covent Garden, London WC2E
7PB
*Tel:* (01235) 465500 *Fax:* (01235) 465555
*Web Site:* www.jaipress.com
*Telex:* 837515

*Key Personnel*
Marketing in Sales: Della Sar
Founded: 1985
Specialize in research-level serials, monograph series, treatises & journals.
Subjects: Accounting, Behavioral Sciences, Biological Sciences, Business, Chemistry, Chemical Engineering, Child Care & Development, Economics, Education, Government, Political Science, Library & Information Sciences, Management, Psychology, Psychiatry, Social Sciences, Sociology
ISBN Prefix(es): 0-89232; 1-55938; 0-7623
*Parent Company:* Elsevier Science
*Warehouse:* Marston Book Services Ltd, PO Box 269, Abingdon OX14 4YN

**James & James (Publishers) Ltd+**
Gordon House Business Centre, 6 Lissenden Gardens, London NW5 1LX
*Tel:* (020) 7482 8888 *Fax:* (020) 7482 8889
*E-mail:* jxj@jamesxjames.co.uk
*Web Site:* www.jamesxjames.co.uk
*Key Personnel*
Man Dir: Hamish MacGibbon
Project Editor: Susie May
Marketing Manager: Ruth Weinberg
Founded: 1985
Publishers of illustrated books on history & the environment, specifically illustrated histories of companies, schools & other institutions.
Membership(s): IPG.
Subjects: Business, Environmental Studies, History
ISBN Prefix(es): 0-907383
Total Titles: 10 Print
*Associate Companies:* James & James Science Publishers Ltd, Contact: Edward Milford
*Tel:* (020) 7387 8558

**Arthur James Ltd**, *imprint of* John Hunt Publishing Ltd

**Jane's Information Group**
Sentinel House, 163 Brighton Rd, Coulsdon, Surrey CR5 2YH
*Tel:* (020) 8700 3700 *Fax:* (020) 8763 1006
*E-mail:* info.uk@janes.com
*Web Site:* www.janes.com
*Key Personnel*
Man Dir: Alfred Rolington *Tel:* (020) 8700 3701 *Fax:* (020) 8700 3704 *E-mail:* alfred. rolington@janes.com
Publishing Dir, Reference: Ian Kay *Tel:* (020) 8700 3796 *Fax:* (020) 8700 3788 *E-mail:* ian. kay@janes.com
Group Communications Manager: Claire Brunavs *Tel:* (020) 8700 3703 *E-mail:* claire.brunavs@ janes.com
Founded: 1897
Specialize in police, security, geopolitics, risk assessment, technical & infrastructure information. Full online subscription access & CD-ROMS.
Subjects: Aeronautics, Aviation, Foreign Countries, Maritime, Military Science, Transportation
ISBN Prefix(es): 0-7106; 0-309; 0-532; 0-265
Total Titles: 200 Print; 12 CD-ROM; 200 Online; 9 E-Book
*Parent Company:* The Woodbridge Co Ltd
*Branch Office(s)*
78 Shenton Way, No 10-02, Singapore 079120, Singapore, Contact: David Fisher *Tel:* 6325 0866 *Fax:* 6226 1185 *E-mail:* asiapacific@ janes.com
PO Box 3502, Rozelle NSW 2039, Australia, Contact: Pauline Roberts *Tel:* (02) 8587 7900 *Fax:* (02) 8587 7901 *E-mail:* oceania@janes. com
*U.S. Office(s):* Jane's Information Group (US), 110 N Royal St, Suite 200, Alexandria, VA

22314, United States, Contact: Rahul Belani *Tel:* 703-683-3700 *Fax:* 703-836-0029
*E-mail:* rahul.belani@janes.com

**Janus Books**, *imprint of* Janus Publishing Co Ltd

**Janus Publishing Co Ltd+**
105-107 Gloucester Pl, London W1U 6BY
*Tel:* (020) 7580 7664 *Fax:* (020) 7636 5756
*E-mail:* sales@januspublishing.co.uk
*Web Site:* www.januspublishing.co.uk
*Key Personnel*
Man Dir: Sandy Leung
Production: S Legg
Publicity: N Cording
Marketing: S Hughes
Founded: 1991
Publisher of radical ideas founded for authors overlooked by big publishing houses.
*Janus*-subsidized publishing; *Empiricus*-non-subsidized.
Membership(s): IPG.
Subjects: Alternative, Astrology, Occult, Biography, Education, Fiction, Film, Video, Health, Nutrition, Nonfiction (General), Philosophy, Poetry, Religion - Buddhist, Religion - Jewish, Science Fiction, Fantasy, Theology, Social, Academic & Spiritual
ISBN Prefix(es): 1-85756
*Ultimate Parent Company:* Junction Books Ltd
Imprints: Janus Books; Empiricus Books
*U.S. Office(s):* IPG, 140 Union St, Marshfield, MA 02050-6273, United States, Contact: David Gebhart *Tel:* (781) 834-9830
Foreign Rep(s): Richard Bowden (Scandinavia, Sweden); IPG (US)

**Japan Library**, *imprint of* RoutledgeCurzon

**Jarrold Publishing+**
Division of Jarrold & Sons Ltd
Whitefriars, Norwich NR3 1TR
*Tel:* (01603) 763300 *Fax:* (01603) 662748
*E-mail:* info@jarrold.com
*Web Site:* www.jarrold-publishing.co.uk
*Key Personnel*
Man Dir, Rights & Permissions: Caroline Jarrold
Founded: 1770
Specialize in the publishing of books, calendars & stationery.
Subjects: Biography, History, Regional Interests, Travel
ISBN Prefix(es): 0-85306; 0-7117
Number of titles published annually: 30 Print
Total Titles: 250 Print
Imprints: Pathfinder
Distributor for MacMillan Way Association; Northern Ireland Tourist Board; Wales Tourist Board
*Bookshop(s):* Jarrolds, 5 London St, Norwich, Norfolk NR2 1JF *Web Site:* www.britguides.co. uk

**John Wiley & Sons**, *imprint of* Wiley Europe Ltd

**Johnson Publications Ltd+**
21 Picadilly, London W1J 0DQ
*Tel:* (020) 7486 6757 *Fax:* (020) 7487 5436
*Key Personnel*
Dir: M A Murray-Pearce; Z M Pauncefort
Subjects: Advertising, Biography, Marketing
ISBN Prefix(es): 0-85307
*Orders to:* Spring Court, Abbots Rd, Abbots Langley, Herts WD5 0BJ

**Jones & Bartlett International+**
Barb House, Barb Mews, London W6 7PA
*Tel:* (01892) 539356 *Fax:* (01892) 614944
*E-mail:* j&b@class.co.uk
*Web Site:* www.jbpub.com

*Key Personnel*
International Rights: Richard Warner
Founded: 1983
Subjects: Biological Sciences, Computer Science, Earth Sciences, Geography, Geology, Health, Nutrition, Mathematics, Medicine, Nursing, Dentistry
ISBN Prefix(es): 0-86720; 0-7637
*Parent Company:* Jones & Bartlett Publishers, Inc, 40 Tall Pine Dr, Sudbury, MA 01776, United States
Foreign Rep(s): Academic Marketing Services Ltd (South Africa); Alfaomega Grupo Editor (Mexico); Alkem Company (S) Pte Ltd (Indonesia); Blackwell Publishing Asia (Australia, New Zealand); Cranbury International LLC (Caribbean including Puerto Rico, South America); Delaney Global Publishers Services, Inc (Guam, Philippines); Benjamin Ho (China, Hong Kong, Korea, Singapore, Taiwan, Thailand); Interknowledge Books Inc (Japan); International Publishers Representatives (IPR) (Middle East, Iran); Jones & Bartlett Publishers (UK, Canada, Continental Europe); LIDEL - Edicoes Tecnicas Lda (Portugal); Premium Educational Group (Puerto Rico); Publicaciones Educativas (Central America, Mexico); United Publishers Services Ltd (Japan); University Bookstore (Malaysia)
*Orders to:* Plymbridge Distributors, Plymbridge House, Estover Rd, Plymouth, Devon PL6 7PZ
*Tel:* (0752) 695745 *Fax:* (0752) 695699

**John Jones Publishing Ltd+**
Unit 12, Clwydfro Business Centre, Ruthin LL15 1NJ
*Tel:* (01824) 707255 *Fax:* (01824) 705272
*E-mail:* johnjonespublishing.ltd@virgin.net
*Web Site:* www.johnjonespublishing.ltd.uk
*Key Personnel*
Man Dir: John Idris Jones
Founded: 1979
Specialize in paperbacks for the tourist market & books in English with a Welsh background.
Membership(s): IPG.
Subjects: Biography, History, Travel
ISBN Prefix(es): 1-871083
Total Titles: 49 Print
Distributed by John Reed (Australia)
Foreign Rep(s): John Reed Book Distribution

**Jordan Publishing Ltd**
21 St Thomas St, Bristol BS1 6JS
*Tel:* (0117) 918 1491 *Fax:* (0117) 623 0063
*E-mail:* electronic@jordanpublishing.co.uk
*Web Site:* www.jordanpublishing.co.uk
*Telex:* 449119
*Key Personnel*
Man Dir: Richard Hudson
Publishing Dir: Martin West
Managing Editor: Mollie Dickenson
Marketing Manager: David Chaplin
*E-mail:* dchaplin@jordanpublishing.co.uk
Founded: 1863
Subjects: Accounting, Business, Law
ISBN Prefix(es): 0-85308
*Parent Company:* Jordan & Sons Ltd, Bristol
Imprints: Jordans; Family Law
*Branch Office(s)*
20-22 Bedford Row, London WC1R 4JS
*Tel:* (020) 7400 3333 *Fax:* (020) 7400 3366

**Jordans**, *imprint of* Jordan Publishing Ltd

**Michael Joseph**, *imprint of* Penguin Books Ltd

**Michael Joseph Ltd+**
80 Strand, London WC2 0RN
*Tel:* (020) 7416 3000 *Fax:* (020) 7416 3099
*Telex:* 917181
*Key Personnel*
Publishing Dir: Tom Weldon

Marketing Dir: John Bond
Export Sales Dir: Max Adam *E-mail:* max. adam@penguin.co.uk
Rights Dir: Sophie Brewer
Founded: 1936
Subjects: Biography, Fiction, History
ISBN Prefix(es): 0-7181
*Parent Company:* Penguin Books Ltd
Imprints: Mermaid
*Warehouse:* Penguin Group Distribution Ltd, 27 Wrights Lane, London W8 5TZ
*Orders to:* Penguin Group Distribution Ltd, Bath Rd, Harmondsworth, Middlesex UB7 0DA

**Richard Joseph Publishers Ltd**
PO Box 15, Torrington, Devon EX38 8ZJ
*Tel:* (01805) 625750 *Fax:* (01805) 625376
*E-mail:* info@sheppardsworld.com
*Web Site:* www.sheppardsworld.com
*Key Personnel*
Man Dir: Richard Joseph *E-mail:* rjoe01@aol. com
Advertising: Claire Brumham
Founded: 1990
Reference books for the secondhand & antiquarian trades.
Membership(s): IPG.
ISBN Prefix(es): 1-872699
Total Titles: 26 Print; 1 CD-ROM
Imprints: Sheppard
*U.S. Office(s):* Richard Joseph Publishers, PO Box 1350, State College, PA 16804-1350, United States

**Jossey-Bass**, *imprint of* Wiley Europe Ltd

**Junior Funfax**, *imprint of* Funfax Ltd

**Kahn & Averill**
9 Harrington Rd, London SW7 3ES
*Tel:* (020) 8743 3278 *Fax:* (020) 8743 3278
*Key Personnel*
Man Dir: M Kahn
Founded: 1947
Subjects: Music, Dance
ISBN Prefix(es): 0-900707; 1-871082
*Shipping Address:* Bailey Distribution Ltd, Mountfield Industrial Estate, New Romney, Kent TN28 8XU
*Warehouse:* Bailey Distribution Ltd, Mountfield Industrial Estate, New Rowney, Kent TN28 8XU
*Orders to:* Bailey Distribution Ltd, Mountfield Industrial Estate, New Romney, Kent TN28 8XU

**Karnac Books Ltd+**
118 Finchley Rd, London NW3 5HT
*Tel:* (020) 8969 4454 *Fax:* (020) 8969 5585
*E-mail:* books@karnac.demon.co.uk
*Web Site:* www.karnacbooks.com
*Key Personnel*
Man Dir: Cesare D S Sacerdoti
Founded: 1950
Subjects: Psychology, Psychiatry, Social Sciences, Sociology
ISBN Prefix(es): 0-946439; 1-85575; 0-9501647; 0-9507146
Imprints: Maresfield Lib
Distributed by Taylor & Francis (USA)
Distributor for Analytic Press; Clunie Press; Institute of Marital Studies
*Bookshop(s):* 118 Finchley Rd, London NW3 5HJ
*Tel:* (020) 8969 4454 *Fax:* (020) 8969 5585
*E-mail:* shop@karnacbooks.com

**Karnak House+**
300 Westbourne Park Rd, London W11 1EH
*Tel:* (020) 7243 3620 *Fax:* (020) 7243 3620
*E-mail:* connection@karnakhouse.co.uk
*Web Site:* www.karnakhouse.co.uk

*Key Personnel*
Dir: A S Saakana; Seheri Stroude
Founded: 1979
Specialize in African & Caribbean studies worldwide.
Subjects: Anthropology, Education, History, Language Arts, Linguistics, Nonfiction (General), Philosophy, Religion - Other, Science (General), Egyptology
ISBN Prefix(es): 0-907015; 1-872596
Number of titles published annually: 10 Print
Total Titles: 100 Print
Imprints: The Intef Institute
Distributed by Turnaround
*Orders to:* 631 E 75 St, Chicago, IL 60619, United States, Contact: Ras Seko Tafari
*Tel:* 773-651-9888 *Fax:* 773-651-9850

**Kegan Paul International Ltd+**
121 Bedford Court Mansions, Bedford Ave, London WC1B 3SW
Mailing Address: PO Box 256, London WC1B 3SW
*Tel:* (020) 7580 5511 *Fax:* (020) 7436 0899
*E-mail:* books@keganpaul.com
*Web Site:* www.keganpaul.com
*Key Personnel*
Chairman: Peter Hopkins
Editorial Dir: Kaori O'Connor
Founded: 1871
Subjects: Archaeology, Architecture & Interior Design, Art, Photography, Travel, Africa, Arabic Linguistics, Asian Studies, China, Egyptology, Environmental Studies & Natural Science, International Studies & Law, Islam, Japan, Korea, Literature & Poetry, Middle East, Oriental Philosophy & Religion, Pacific
ISBN Prefix(es): 0-7103
Number of titles published annually: 40 Print
Total Titles: 520 Print
*U.S. Office(s):* Columbia University Press, 562 W 113 St, New York, NY 10025, United States
*Tel:* 212-666-1000 *Fax:* 212-316-3100
Distributed by Turpin Distribution
*Shipping Address:* John Wiley & Sons Ltd, Southern Cross Trading Estate, One Oldlands Way, Bognor Regis, West Sussex PO22 9SA, Contact: Diana Butterly *Tel:* (01243) 779777 *Fax:* (01243) 843303
*Warehouse:* John Wiley & Sons Ltd, Southern Cross Trading Estate, Oldlands Way Bagnor Regis, West Sussex PO22 9SA, Contact: Lori Powell *Tel:* (01243) 843223 *Fax:* (01243) 820250
*Orders to:* John Wiley & Sons Ltd, Southern Cross Trading Estate, One Oldlands Way, Bognor Regis, West Sussex PO22 9SA, Contact: Diane Butterly *Tel:* (01243) 843273 *Fax:* (01243) 843303
Columbia University Press, 61 W 62 St, New York, NY 10023, United States *Tel:* 914-591-9111; 800-944-8648 *Fax:* 800-944-1844 *E-mail:* ms1004@columbia.edu *Web Site:* www.columbia.edu/cu/cup (North America)

**Kelly's**
Windsor Court, East Grinstead House, East Grinstead, West Sussex RH19 1XB
*Tel:* (01342) 326972 *Fax:* (01342) 335825
*E-mail:* kellys.mktg@reedinfo.co.uk
*Web Site:* www.kellysearch.com
*Telex:* 95127
*Key Personnel*
Publishing Dr: Brian Gallagher
Founded: 1799
Membership(s): Directory Publishers Association & European Directory Publishers Association.
Subjects: Business
ISBN Prefix(es): 0-610
*Warehouse:* Vale Packaging, 420 Vale Rd, Tonbridge, Kent TN9 1TO

**Kemps Publishing Ltd+**
11 The Swan Courtyard, Charles Edward Rd, Yardley, Birmingham B26 1BU
*Tel:* (0121) 765 4144 *Fax:* (0121) 706 1408
*E-mail:* info@kempsgold.co.uk
*Web Site:* www.kempsgold.co.uk
*Key Personnel*
Contact: Marisha Gorcewicz
Founded: 1912
ISBN Prefix(es): 0-86259; 0-900273; 0-901268; 0-905255

**The Kenilworth Press Ltd+**
Addington, Buckingham, Bucks MK18 2JR
*Tel:* (01296) 715101 *Fax:* (01296) 715148
*E-mail:* customer.services@kenilworthpress.co.uk
*Web Site:* www.kenilworthpress.co.uk
*Key Personnel*
Man Dir: David Blunt *E-mail:* david.blunt@ kenilworthpress.co.uk
Dir: Deirdre Blunt
Founded: 1989
Publisher of instructional equestrian books
Also acts as official publisher to The British Horse Society.
Subjects: Animals, Pets, Natural History, Sports, Athletics, Veterinary Science
ISBN Prefix(es): 1-872082; 0-901366; 1-872119
Number of titles published annually: 10 Print
Total Titles: 100 Print
Imprints: Threshold
Divisions: Threshold Books
Distributed by Half Halt Press Inc (USA)
Distributor for Half Halt Press Inc
*Warehouse:* Hoddle Doyle Meadows, Station Rd, Linton, Cambs CB1 6UX

**Kenyon-Deane**, *imprint of* Cressrelles Publishing Company Ltd

**Kenyon-Deane+**
Imprint of Cressrelles Publishing Company Ltd
Industrial Estate, 10 Station Rd, Colwall, Nr Malvern, Herefordshire WR13 6RN
*Tel:* (01684) 540154 *Fax:* (01684) 540154
*Key Personnel*
Man Dir: Leslie Smith
Founded: 1930
Specialize in plays for women.
Subjects: Drama, Theater
ISBN Prefix(es): 0-7155
Number of titles published annually: 6 Print
Total Titles: 400 Print
*Parent Company:* Cressrelles Publishing Co Ltd
Distributor for Anchorage Press (Europe)

**Kidhaven Press**, *imprint of* Thomson Gale

**Hilda King Educational+**
Ashwells Manor Dr, Penn, Bucks HP10 8EU
*Tel:* (01494) 813947; (01494) 817947
*Fax:* (01494) 813947
*E-mail:* hildaking@clara.co.uk; orders@hilda-king.co.uk
*Web Site:* www.hildaking.clara.net
*Key Personnel*
Dir: Ron King *E-mail:* ron@hilda-king.co.uk
Contact: Hilda King *E-mail:* hilda@hilda-king.co.uk
Founded: 1990
Specializes in photocopiable educational resources.
Membership(s): Publishers Association.
Subjects: Geography, Geology, History, Mathematics, Audio Tapes (phonics); English & French Language; English & French, nursery
ISBN Prefix(es): 1-873533
Total Titles: 100 Print; 8 Audio

**Laurence King Publishing Ltd+**
71 Great Russell St, London WC1B 3BP
*Tel:* (020) 7430 8850 *Fax:* (020) 7430 8880

*E-mail:* enquiries@laurenceking.co.uk
*Web Site:* www.laurenceking.co.uk
*Key Personnel*
Chairman: Robin Hyman
Man Dir: Laurence King
Editorial Dir, Professional Trade Division: Philip
    Cooper
Editorial Dir, College & Fine Art: Lee Ripley
    Greenfield
Rights Manager: Janet Pilch *E-mail:* janet@
    laurenceking.co.uk
Foreign Rights: Sarah Davis *E-mail:* sarah@
    laurenceking.co.uk
Founded: 1976
Also acts as designer & producer of high-quality
    illustrated books
Specialize in international co-editions.
Subjects: Architecture & Interior Design, Art,
    Fashion, Film, Video, House & Home, Religion
    - Other
ISBN Prefix(es): 1-85669
Total Titles: 200 Print
*Warehouse:* Thames & Hudson Ltd, 44 Clock-
    house Rd, Farnborough, Hants GU14 7QZ

**Kingfisher Publications Plc+**
New Penderel House, 283-288 High Holborn,
    London WC1V 7HZ
*Tel:* (020) 7903 9999 *Fax:* (020) 7242 5009
*E-mail:* rights@kingfisherpub.com
*Web Site:* www.kingfisherpub.com
*Key Personnel*
Finance Dir: Geraud de Durand
Production Dir: John Richards
Export Sales Manager: Melissa Johnson
International Sales Dir: Hilary Downie
    *E-mail:* hdownie@kingfisherpub.co.uk
Key Accounts Manager: Sheila O'Sullivan
    *Tel:* (01926) 864 816 *Fax:* (01926) 864 816
UK Trade, Export & Marketing Sales Dir: Robert
    Pearce
UK Rights & Special Sales Dir: Catherine Potter
Export Sales Manager: Melissa Johnson
Sales Office Assistant: Pachi Lopez
Founded: 1974
Subjects: Regional Interests
ISBN Prefix(es): 0-7523; 0-86272; 1-85697; 1-
    85296
Number of titles published annually: 85 Print
*Parent Company:* Houghton Mifflin Co, 222
    Berkeley St, Boston, MA 02116, United States
*Sales Office(s):* Chameleon Group, 5 Milnyard
    Sq, Orton Southgate, Peterborough PE2 6AX
    *Tel:* (01733) 370606 *Fax:* (01733) 370607
Distributed by I K International Pvt Ltd (India);
    Macmillan Distribution Ltd (England); Pans-
    ing Distribution SDN BHD (Brunei, Indone-
    sia, Malaysia, Singapore); Paramount Books
    (PVT) Ltd (Pakistan); Publishers Associates
    Ltd (Hong Kong); Quartet Sales & Marketing
    (South Africa); Scholastic Australia Ltd (Aus-
    tralia); South Pacific Books (Imports) 2001 Ltd
    (New Zealand); Westland Books Pvt Ltd (In-
    dia)
Foreign Rep(s): Ashton International Marketing
    Services (China, Japan, Korea, Taiwan, Thai-
    land); Humphrys Roberts Associates (Central
    America, South America, West Indies); Wal-
    ton Marketing Services (Europe, Israel); Peter
    Ward Book Exports (Middle East)
*Warehouse:* Macmillan Distribution Ltd, Brunel
    Rd, Houndsmill, Basingstoke, Hants R921 2XS
*Orders to:* Macmillan Distribution Ltd, Brunel
    Rd, Houndsmill, Basingstoke, Hants R921 2XS

**King's Fund Publishing+**
11-13 Cavendish Sq, London W1G 0AN
*Tel:* (020) 7307 2400 *Fax:* (020) 7307 2801
*E-mail:* libweb@kingsfund.org.uk
*Web Site:* www.kingsfund.org.uk
*Key Personnel*
Head of Communications & Marketing: Stephen

Lustig *Tel:* (020) 7307 2584 *E-mail:* slustig@
    kingsfund.org.uk
Founded: 1897
Health & social care titles mainly for profession-
    als, managers, academics & libraries
Not for profit charitable foundation.
Subjects: Health, Nutrition, Social Sciences, Soci-
    ology
ISBN Prefix(es): 1-85551; 1-85717; 1-870551; 1-
    870607; 1-873883
Number of titles published annually: 30 Print
Total Titles: 200 Print
*Parent Company:* King's Fund
*U.S. Office(s):* Transaction Publishers, Con-
    tact: Mary Curtis *Tel:* 908-445-2280
    *E-mail:* mcurtis@transactionpub.com

**Jessica Kingsley Publishers**
116 Pentonville Rd, London N1 9JB
*Tel:* (020) 7833 2307 *Fax:* (020) 7837 2917
*E-mail:* post@jkp.com
*Web Site:* www.jkp.com
*Key Personnel*
Man Dir: Jessica Kingsley *E-mail:* jessica@jkp.
    com
Sales Manager: Bill Goodall *E-mail:* bgoodall@
    jkp.com
Founded: 1987
Membership(s): Independent Publishers Guild;
    Publishers Association.
Subjects: Behavioral Sciences, Child Care & De-
    velopment, Criminology, Disability, Special
    Needs, Education, Medicine, Nursing, Den-
    tistry, Psychology, Psychiatry, Self-Help, Social
    Sciences, Sociology, Theology
ISBN Prefix(es): 1-85302; 1-84310
Number of titles published annually: 120 Print; 1
    CD-ROM
Total Titles: 1,000 Print; 3 CD-ROM; 3 Audio
*U.S. Office(s):* Jessica Kingsley Publishers Inc,
    400 Market St, Suite 400, Philadelphia, PA
    19106, United States *Tel:* 215-922-1161
    *Fax:* 215-922-1474 *E-mail:* orders@jkp.com
Foreign Rep(s): Asia Publishers Service Ltd
    (China, Hong Kong, Korea, Philippines, Tai-
    wan); Book Representation & Distribution
    (England, Northern Ireland, Wales); Brookside
    Publishing Services (Ireland); Andrew Durnell
    (Europe); STM Pte Ltd (Thailand)
*Distribution Center:* Book Promotions (Pty) Ltd,
    Unit 1, Section B, Prime Park, Mocke Rd,
    Diep River 7800, South Africa *Tel:* (021) 706
    0949 *Fax:* (021) 706 0940 (South Africa)
Footprint Books Pty Ltd, 4/92A Mona Vale Rd,
    Mona Vale, NSW 2103, Australia *Tel:* (02)
    9997 3973 *Fax:* (02) 9997 3185 *E-mail:* info@
    footprint.com.au *Web Site:* www.footprint.com.
    au (Australia & New Zealand)
Publishers Marketing Services, 28A alan SS
    21/58, Damansara Utama, 47400 Petal-
    ing Jaya, Selangor, Malaysia *Tel:* (03) 717
    6110 *Fax:* (03) 718 7997 (Brunei, Indonesia,
    Malaysia & Singapore)
Publishers Marketing Services, 10-C Jalan Am-
    pas, 07-10 Ho Seng Lee Flatted Warehouse,
    Singapore 329513, Singapore *Tel:* 6256 5166
    *Fax:* 6253 0008 (Brunei, Indonesia, Malaysia
    & Singapore)
UBC Press, Georgetown Terminal Warehouse, 34
    Armstrong Ave, Georgetown, ON L7G 4R9,
    Canada *Tel:* 905-873-9781 *Fax:* 905-873-6170
    *E-mail:* orders@gtwcanada.com (Canada)
United Publishers Services Ltd, 1-32-5 Hugashi-
    shinagawa, Shinagawa-ku, Tokyo 140-0002,
    Japan *Tel:* (03) 5479-7251 *Fax:* (03) 5479-7307
    *E-mail:* info@ups.co.jp (Japan)
Viva Marketing, 4327/3 Ansari Rd, Daryaganj,
    New Delhi 110002, India *Tel:* (011) 327 9280
    *Fax:* (011) 326 7224 (India)

**Kingsway Publications+**
26-28 Lottbridge Drove, Eastbourne, East Sussex
    BN23 6NT

*Tel:* (01323) 437700 *Fax:* (01323) 411970
*E-mail:* office@kingsway.co.uk
*Web Site:* www.kingsway.co.uk
*Key Personnel*
Chief Executive Officer: John Paculabo
Publishing Dir: Richard Herkes
List Administrator: Cathy Williams
Foreign Rights: Chris Jackson
Founded: 1977
Publisher & supplier of Christian books, music,
    crafts & children's ministry resources.
Membership(s): Publishers' Association.
Subjects: Religion - Protestant, Religion - Other,
    Theology
ISBN Prefix(es): 0-86065; 0-85476; 0-902088; 1-
    84291
*Parent Company:* Kingsway Communications Ltd
*Associate Companies:* David C Cook
Distributor for Barbour (USA/Canada); Bethany
    House (USA/Canada); Chariot Victor (USA/
    Canada)
*Orders to:* STL Wholesale, PO Box 300,
    Kingstown Industrial Estates, Kingstown
    Broadway, Carlisle CA3 0JH *Fax:* (01228)
    514949

**Kinship Library**, see Centaur Press (1954)

**Knockabout Comics+**
Unit 24, 10 Acklam Rd, London W10 5QZ
*Tel:* (020) 8969 2945 *Fax:* (020) 8968 7614
*E-mail:* knockcomic@aol.com
*Web Site:* www.knockabout.com
*Key Personnel*
Man Dir: Tony Bennett *E-mail:* tonyknock@aol.
    com
Distribution Manager: Joe Toussaint
International Rights: Lora Fountain *Tel:* (014)
    3562196 *Fax:* (014) 3482272
Founded: 1975
Subjects: Gardening, Plants, Health, Nutrition,
    Humor, Social Sciences, Sociology, Specialize
    in comic books, graphic novels & drug infor-
    mation
ISBN Prefix(es): 0-86166
Number of titles published annually: 6 Print
Total Titles: 110 Print
*Parent Company:* Toskanex Ltd
Imprints: Fanny; Hassle Free Press
Distributor for Last Gasp (North America); Quick
    American Archives (North America); Quick
    Trading Co (North America); Rip Off Press
    (excludes USA & Canada)
Foreign Rights: Lora Fountain (Netherlands,
    France, Germany, Spain)

**Know Alls**, *imprint of* Funfax Ltd

**Kogan Page Ltd+**
120 Pentonville Rd, London N1 9JN
*Tel:* (020) 7278 0433 *Fax:* (020) 7837 6348
*E-mail:* kpinfo@kogan-page.co.uk; kpsales@
    kogan-page.co.uk; orders@kogan-page.co.uk
*Web Site:* www.kogan-page.co.uk
*Key Personnel*
Man Dir: Philip Kogan
Editorial Dir, Business, Trade, Professional &
    Academic: Pauline Goodwin
Export Sales Manager: Lynda Moynihan
    *E-mail:* lmoynihan@kogan-page.co.uk
Finance Dir: Gordon Watts
Rights Manager: Lisa von Fircks *Tel:* (020) 7843
    1967 *E-mail:* lvonfircks@kogan-page.co.uk
Sales & Marketing Dir: Stephen Lustig
    *E-mail:* slustig@kogan-page.co.uk
Founded: 1967
Independent publisher of business & management
    books.
Subjects: Business, Career Development, Educa-
    tion, Finance, Management, Marketing, Self-
    Help, Transportation
ISBN Prefix(es): 0-7494

*Branch Office(s)*
Kogan Page India, c/o Viva Books, 432713 Ansari Rd, New Delhi 10002, India
*U.S. Office(s):* Kogan Page USA Office, 22 Broad St, Suite 34, Milford, CT 06460, United States
*Web Site:* www.earthscan.co.uk
Distributed by Stylus Publishing Inc (USA)
Distributor for American Bankers Association (excluding North & South America)
*Warehouse:* Littlehampton Book Services Ltd, Faraday Close, Durrington, Worthing, West Sussex BN13 3RB *Tel:* (01903) 828 800 *Fax:* (01903) 828 801 *E-mail:* orders@lbsltd.co.uk

**Kuperard+**
Imprint of Bravo Ltd
59 Hutton Grove, London N12 8DS
*Tel:* (020) 8446 2440 *Fax:* (020) 8446 2441
*E-mail:* kuperard@bravo.clara.net
*Web Site:* www.kuperard.co.uk
*Key Personnel*
Publishing: J Kuperard *E-mail:* kuperard@grove.clara.net
Sales & Marketing: Martin Kaye
  *E-mail:* martin@bravo.clara.net
Subjects: Education, Travel
ISBN Prefix(es): 1-85733; 1-870668
Number of titles published annually: 30 Print
Total Titles: 300 Print
*Distribution Center:* Orca Book Services
  *Tel:* (01202) 665432 *Fax:* (01202) 666219
  *E-mail:* orders@orca-book-services.co.uk

**Ladybird**, *imprint of* Penguin Books Ltd

**Ladybird Books Ltd+**
80 Strand, London WC2R 0RL
*Tel:* (020) 7010 2900 *Fax:* (01509) 234672
*Web Site:* www.ladybird.co.uk
*Telex:* 341347
*Key Personnel*
Man Dir: Michael Herridge
Art Dir: Douglas Wilson
Sales Manager, Regional Export & Rights & Coeditions Manager: Yvonne Francis
Sales Manager, Regional Export: Nina Bueno del Carpio
Sales Manager: Ingrid Little
Marketing Dir: Diana Olivant
International Sales Dir: David King
UK Sales Dir: Deborah Wright
Product Manager: Michelle Thurston
Founded: (s)
Children's book publisher.
Subjects: Education, English as a Second Language, Fiction, History, Natural History, Nonfiction (General)
ISBN Prefix(es): 0-7214
*Parent Company:* Penguin Group
Imprints: Disney
Divisions: Ladybird Disney Books
Foreign Rep(s): Penguin Books Deutchland (Austria, Germany); Penguin Books Netherlands (Netherlands); Penguin Books S A (Portugal, Spain); Penguin France (France); Penguin Italia (Italy); Sezai Selek Sokak 10/2 (Bulgaria, Romania, Turkey)

**Jay Landesman+**
8 Duncan Terrace, London N1 8BZ
*Tel:* (020) 7837 7290 *Fax:* (020) 7833 1925
*Key Personnel*
Man Dir: Jay Landesman
Founded: 1977
Subjects: Biography, Humor, Poetry
ISBN Prefix(es): 0-905150
Total Titles: 160 Print
*Associate Companies:* Polytantric Press
Imprints: Golden Handshake; Polytantric Press

**Landy Publishing**
Acorns, 3 Staining Rise, Staining, Blackpool, Lancs FY3 0BU
*Tel:* (01253) 895678 *Fax:* (01253) 895678
*E-mail:* bobdobson@amserve.com
*Key Personnel*
Owner: Bob Dobson
Founded: 1981
Book publisher of regional titles.
Subjects: History, Regional Interests
ISBN Prefix(es): 1-872895
Number of titles published annually: 6 Print
Total Titles: 90 Print

**Allen Lane**, *imprint of* Penguin Books Ltd

**Lang Syne Publishers Ltd+**
120 Carstairs St, Strathclyde Business Centre, Glasgow G40 4JD
*Tel:* (0141) 554 9944 *Fax:* (0141) 554 9955
*E-mail:* enquiries@scottish-memories.co.uk
*Web Site:* www.scottish-memories.co.uk
*Key Personnel*
Dir: Kenneth W Laird
Founded: 1975
Subjects: Business, History, Humor, Music, Dance, Mysteries
ISBN Prefix(es): 0-946264; 1-85217
*Branch Office(s)*
Scott's Highland Enterprises, 1646 Beckworth Ave, London, ON N5V 2K7, Canada *Tel:* 519-453-0892 *Fax:* 519-453-6303
Scottish Flair, Quean Beyan, NSW, Australia *Tel:* (06) 2977-8780

**Language Teaching Publications+**
15 Windmill Grove, Portchester, Fareham PO16 9HT
*Tel:* (023) 9220 0080 *Fax:* (023) 9220 0090
*E-mail:* ltp@ltpwebsite.com
*Web Site:* www.ltpwebsite.com
*Telex:* 250 Elc
*Key Personnel*
Man Dir: Michael Lewis; Jimmie Hill
Founded: 1978
Subjects: English as a Second Language, English as a Foreign Language
ISBN Prefix(es): 0-906717; 1-899396
*Parent Company:* Heinle Publishers, 25 Thomson Pl, Boston, MA 02210, United States
Imprints: LTP
*U.S. Office(s):* Alta Book Center, 14 Adrian Court, Burlingame, CA 94010, United States
Delta Systems Inc, 1400 Miller Parkway, McHenry, IL 60050-7030, United States
*Orders to:* Thomson Learning, Nihonjisyo Brooks Bldg 3-F, 1-4-1, Kudankita, Chiyoda-ku, Tokyo 102-0073, Japan *Tel:* (03) 3511-4390 *Fax:* (03) 3511-4391 (Japan)
Thomson Learning, Seneca 53, Colonia Polanco, 11560 Mexico DF, Mexico *Tel:* (055) 5281-2906 *Fax:* (055) 5281-2656 (Latin America)
Thomson Learning, UIC Bldg, 5 Shenton Way No 01-01, Singapore 068808, Singapore *Tel:* 6410-1200 *Fax:* 6410-1208 (Asia)
Thomson Learning, Distribution Center, 10650 Toebben Dr, Independence, KY 41051, United States (US)

**Languages Information Centre**, *imprint of* Joseph Biddulph Publisher

**Roger Lascelles+**
47 York Rd, Brentford, Middx TW8 0QP
*Tel:* (0181) 8470935 *Fax:* (0181) 5683886
*Key Personnel*
Publisher: Roger Lascelles
Founded: 1970
Membership(s): International Map Trade Association.
Subjects: Travel

ISBN Prefix(es): 0-903909; 1-872815; 1-85879
Imprints: Daily Telegraph (map service)
Distributor for LAC (Italy); Ravenstein (Germany)

**The Latchmere Press**
6 Dundalk Rd, London SE4 2JL
*Tel:* (020) 7639 7282
*Key Personnel*
Dir: Angela Cornforth
Founded: 1996
Subjects: Education
ISBN Prefix(es): 1-901090

**Laurel**, *imprint of* Novello & Co Ltd

**Lawpack Publishing Ltd**
76-89 Alscot Rd, London SE1 3AW
*Tel:* (020) 7394 4040 *Fax:* (020) 7394 4041
*E-mail:* enquiries@lawpack.co.uk
*Web Site:* www.lawpack.co.uk
*Key Personnel*
Man Dir: Thomas Coles *Tel:* (02) 7394 4050
Editor: Jamie Ross
Founded: 1993
Self-help legal publisher.
Subjects: Business, How-to, Law, Management, Self-Help, Taxes
ISBN Prefix(es): 1-898217; 1-902646

**Lawrence & Wishart+**
99a Wallis Rd, London E9 5LN
*Tel:* (020) 8533 2506 *Fax:* (020) 8533 7369
*E-mail:* info@lwbooks.co.uk
*Web Site:* www.l-w-bks.co.uk
*Key Personnel*
Man Editor: Sally J Davison *E-mail:* sally@lwbooks.co.uk
Sales & Publicity: Lindsay Thomas
Financial Dir: Avis Greenaway *E-mail:* avis@lwbooks.co.uk
Permissions: Vanna Derosas *E-mail:* vanna@lwbooks.co.uk
Founded: 1936
Subjects: Economics, Education, Environmental Studies, Ethnicity, Film, Video, Gay & Lesbian, Human Relations, Labor, Industrial Relations, Social Sciences, Sociology
ISBN Prefix(es): 0-85315
Distributed by New York University Press
*Warehouse:* Central Books Ltd *Tel:* (020) 8986 4854 *Fax:* (020) 8533 5821 *E-mail:* orders@centralbooks.com
*Orders to:* Troika Ltd, United House, North Rd, London N7 9DP *Tel:* (020) 7619 0800 *Fax:* (020) 7619 0810

**LCCIEB**, see London Chamber of Commerce & Industry Examinations Board (LCCIEB)

**LDA-Living & Learning (Cambridge) Ltd+**
Abbeygate House, East Rd, Cambridge, Cambs CB1 1DB
*Tel:* (01223) 357788 *Fax:* (01223) 460557
*E-mail:* internationalsales@mcgraw-hill.com
*Key Personnel*
Man Dir: Carole Mills
Marketing Manager: Jayne Harris
  *E-mail:* jayne_harris@mcgraw-hill.com
Founded: 1973
Publisher of educational books, resources & games.
Subjects: Child Care & Development, Education
ISBN Prefix(es): 1-85503; 0-905114
Number of titles published annually: 60 Print
Total Titles: 2,000 Print
*Parent Company:* McGraw-Hill Children's Publishing
Imprints: LDA Multimedia
*Branch Office(s)*
Living & Learning, 5-7 Pembroke Ave, Waterbeach, Cambs, Anita Low *Tel:* (01223) 864886

**LDA Multimedia**, *imprint of* LDA-Living & Learning (Cambridge) Ltd

**Learning Development Aids+**
Abbeygate House, East Rd, Cambridge, Cambs CB1 1DB
*Tel:* (01223) 357788 *Fax:* (01223) 460557
*E-mail:* ldaorders@compuserve.com
*Key Personnel*
Man Dir: Carol Mills
Marketing Dir: Catherine Jeffrey
Founded: 1980
Publish learning materials for numeracy, language, literacy & motivation for primary school children & those with special needs.
Subjects: Health, Nutrition
ISBN Prefix(es): 1-85503; 0-905114
*Parent Company:* Living & Learning (Cambridge) Ltd
*U.S. Office(s):* 4383 Hecktown Rd, Unit GA1, Bethelem, PA 18017, United States
*Bookshop(s):* Chris Lloyd Sales & Marketing Services, 463 Ashley Rd, Poole, Dorset BH14 0AX
*Shipping Address:* Duke St, Wisbech, Cambs PE13 2AE
*Warehouse:* Duke St, Wisbech, Cambs PE13 2AE
*Orders to:* Duke St, Wisbech, Cambs PE13 2AE

**Learning Matters**, *imprint of* Learning Matters Ltd

**Learning Matters Ltd**
33 Southernhay E, Exeter EX1 1NX
*Tel:* (01392) 215560 *Fax:* (01392) 215561
*E-mail:* info@learningmatters.co.uk
*Web Site:* www.learningmatters.co.uk
*Key Personnel*
Man Dir: Jonathan Harris *E-mail:* jonathan@ learningmatters.co.uk
Founded: 1999
Publishers of course books for trainee teachers & social workers.
Membership(s): IPG.
Subjects: Education, Social Sciences, Sociology
ISBN Prefix(es): 1-903300; 1-903337; 1-84445
Number of titles published annually: 30 Print
Total Titles: 120 Print
*Associate Companies:* Law Matters Publishing
Imprints: Learning Matters
*Distribution Center:* BEBC, Albion Close, Parkstone, Poole BH12 3LL *Tel:* (0845) 230 9000 *Fax:* (01202) 715 556

**Learning Together+**
23 Carlston Ave, Cultra, Co Down BT18 0NF
*Tel:* (028) 90402086 *Fax:* (028) 90402086
*E-mail:* info@learningtogether.co.uk
*Web Site:* www.learningtogether.co.uk
*Key Personnel*
Contact: Janet McConkey
Founded: 1989
Specialize in verbal & nonverbal reasoning.
Subjects: Education, Mathematics, Science (General)
ISBN Prefix(es): 1-873385
*Orders to:* Mallard Marketing, Woodside Church Hill, West End Southampton 5030 3AU
*Tel:* (02380) 482528 *Fax:* (02380) 361855 *Web Site:* www.learningtogether.co.uk

**Legal Action Group+**
242 Pentonville Rd, London N1 9UN
*Tel:* (020) 7833 2931 *Fax:* (020) 7837 6094
*E-mail:* lag@lag.org.uk
*Web Site:* www.lag.org.uk
*Key Personnel*
Chief Executive: Andrew Heywood
International Rights: Jonathan Pearce
    *E-mail:* jpearce@lag.org.uk
Founded: 1972

Membership(s): Independent Publishers' Guild.
Subjects: Law
ISBN Prefix(es): 0-905099
Total Titles: 30 Print

**Leicester University Press**, *imprint of* Cassell & Co

**Leicester University Press**, *imprint of* The Continuum International Publishing Group Ltd

**Lemos & Crane+**
20 Pond Sq, London N6 6BA
*Tel:* (020) 8348 8263 *Fax:* (020) 8347 5740
*E-mail:* admin@lemosandcrane.co.uk
*Web Site:* www.lemosandcrane.co.uk
*Key Personnel*
Partner: Paul Crane
Partner & Marketing Manager: Carwyn Gravell
Partner: Gerard Lemos
Founded: 1996
Subjects: Law, Management
ISBN Prefix(es): 1-898001
*Orders to:* Plymbridge Distributors Ltd, Estover Rd, Plymouth PL6 7PZ

**Lennard Publishing**, *imprint of* Queen Anne Press

**Lennard Publishing**
Windmill Cottage, Mackerye End, Harpenden, Herts AL5 5DR
*Tel:* (01582) 715866 *Fax:* (01582) 715121
*E-mail:* lennard@lenqap.demon.co.uk

**Letterbox Library**
71-73 Allen Rd, Stoke Newington, London N16 8RY
*Tel:* (020) 7503 4801 *Fax:* (020) 7503 4800
*E-mail:* info@letterboxlibrary.com
*Web Site:* www.letterboxlibrary.com
*Key Personnel*
Dir: Maikim Stern
Publicity & Marketing: Kerry Mason
Founded: 1983
Specialize in mulitcultural & non-sexist books.
Subjects: Art, Developing Countries, Disability, Special Needs, English as a Second Language, Environmental Studies, Ethnicity, Fiction, Foreign Countries, Gay & Lesbian, Geography, Geology, Health, Nutrition, History, Human Relations, Nonfiction (General), Religion - Hindu, Religion - Islamic, Religion - Jewish, Religion - Protestant, Religion - Other

**Letterland International Ltd**
33 New Rd, Barton, Cambs CB3 7AY
*Tel:* (01223) 262675 *Fax:* (01223) 264126
*E-mail:* info@letterland.com
*Web Site:* www.letterland.com
*Key Personnel*
Man Dir: Mark Wendon
Founded: 1985
Subjects: Education, Language Arts, Linguistics
ISBN Prefix(es): 0-907345; 1-86209
Distributed by Harper Collins Publishers (UK & Eire)

**Lettermen**, *imprint of* Funfax Ltd

**Letts Educational**
Member of Granada Learning Group
The Chiswick Centre, 414 Chiswick High Rd, London W4 5TF
*Tel:* (0845) 602 1937 *Fax:* (020) 8742 8390
*E-mail:* mail@lettsed.co.uk
*Web Site:* www.lettsed.co.uk
*Key Personnel*
Man Dir: Richard Carr
Production Dir: Julia Millette

Administrative Dir: Andrew Riddle
Founded: 1972
Subjects: Accounting, Computer Science, Economics, Finance, Labor, Industrial Relations, Law, Library & Information Sciences, Management, Marketing, Mathematics
ISBN Prefix(es): 1-85805; 1-85758; 1-84315
*Parent Company:* BPP Holdings PLC, Aldine House, Aldine Pl, London W12 8 AW
Subsidiaries: LETTS Educational; BPP Publishing; Blackstone Press
*Warehouse:* c/o The Trade Counter Ltd, The Airfield, Mendlesham 1P14 5NA

**J D Lewis & Sons Ltd**, see Gomer Press (J D Lewis & Sons Ltd)

**John Libbey & Co Ltd+**
PO Box 276, Eastleigh SO50 5YS
*Tel:* (023) 8065 0208 *Fax:* (023) 8065 0259
*E-mail:* johnlibbey@aol.com
*Key Personnel*
Man Dir & Publisher: John Libbey
Marketing Manager: Angie Needs
Founded: 1979
Subjects: Film, Video, Medicine, Nursing, Dentistry, Cinema/Animation, Epilepsy, Neurology, Nuclear Medicine
ISBN Prefix(es): 0-86196; 1-86462
Total Titles: 100 Print
Subsidiaries: John Libbey Eurotext Ltd
*Branch Office(s)*
John Libbey & Co PTY Ltd, Level 10, 15-17 Young St, Sydney, NSW 2000, Australia
*Tel:* (02) 9251 4099 *Fax:* (02) 9251 4428
*E-mail:* jlsydney@mpx.com.au
*U.S. Office(s):* John Libbey at Demos Medical Publishing, 386 Park Ave S, Suite 201, New York, NY 10016, United States *Tel:* 212-683-0072 *Fax:* 212-683-0118
Distributed by Butterworth-Heinemann (Medical titles only); Indiana University Press (North America - film/cinema/animation titles only); Tower Books Wholesalers Pty Ltd (Asia & Southern Hemisphere)
*Orders to:* Plymbridge Distributors Ltd, Plymbridge House, Estover Rd, Plymouth PL6 7PY
*Tel:* (01752) 202301 *Fax:* (01752) 202333
*E-mail:* orders@plymbridge.com (Europe)

**Liberty+**
21 Tabard St, London SE1 4LA
*Tel:* (020) 7403 3888 *Fax:* (020) 7407 5354
*E-mail:* info@liberty-human-rights.org.uk
*Web Site:* www.liberty-human-rights.org.uk
*Key Personnel*
Dir: John Wadham
Founded: 1934
Subjects: Law
ISBN Prefix(es): 0-901108; 0-946088
*Associate Companies:* Civil Liberties Trust

**Libris Ltd+**
26 Lady Margaret Rd, London NW5 2XL
*Tel:* (020) 7482 2390 *Fax:* (020) 7485 2730
*E-mail:* libris@onetel.net.uk
*Web Site:* www.librislondon.co.uk
*Key Personnel*
Dir: Nicholas Jacobs
Founded: 1986
Specialize in German-language literature in translation (pre-1945, from Goethe) & in German author studies (biography, criticism, literary history); German dictionaries.
Subjects: Biography, Fiction, History, Literature, Literary Criticism, Essays, Poetry
ISBN Prefix(es): 1-870352
Number of titles published annually: 3 Print
Total Titles: 42 Print
Distributed by Independent Publishers Group (IPA)
*Shipping Address:* Bookshippers Association Inc, 38 Wilks Ave, Unit 3b, Dartford Trade

Park, Hawley Rd, Dartford, Kent DA1 1JS
*Tel:* (01322) 274414 *Fax:* (01322) 274415
*Orders to:* Central Books Ltd, 99 Wallis Rd,
London E9 5LN, Bill Norris *Tel:* (020) 8986
4854 *Fax:* (020) 8533 5821 *E-mail:* orders@
centralbooks.com

**Frances Lincoln Ltd+**
4 Torriano Mews, Torriano Ave, London NW5
2RZ
*Tel:* (020) 7284 4009 *Fax:* (020) 7485 0490
*E-mail:* reception@frances-lincoln.com
*Web Site:* www.franceslincoln.com
*Telex:* 21376
*Key Personnel*
Man Dir: John Nicoll
Editorial Dir, Adult Nonfiction: Anne Fraser
Editorial Dir, Children's: Janetta Otter-Barry
Production: Siobhan Egan; Kim Oliver
Sales Dir: Martin Oestreicher
Rights (Europe): Janet Martin
Rights (USA): Andrew Dunn
Founded: 1977
Subjects: Architecture & Interior Design, Art,
Child Care & Development, Crafts, Games,
Hobbies, Gardening, Plants, Health, Nutrition,
House & Home, Photography
ISBN Prefix(es): 0-7112; 0-906459
Number of titles published annually: 70 Print
Total Titles: 400 Print
Distributed by ACC (USA); Bookwise (Australia); PGW (USA); Raincoast (Canada);
Walker Books (Australia)
Distributor for Allen & Unwin; Barn Owl;
Tamarind
*Orders to:* Bookpoint Ltd, 130 Milton Park,
Abingdon, Oxon OX14 4SB *Tel:* (01235) 400
400

**Linden Press**, see Centaur Press (1954)

**Linen Hall Library+**
17 Donegall Sq N, Belfast BT1 5GB
*Tel:* (028) 9032 1707 *Fax:* (028) 9043 8586
*E-mail:* info@linenhall.com
*Web Site:* www.linenhall.com
*Key Personnel*
President: Steve Mungavin
Librarian: John Gray
Librarian, Northern Ireland Political Collection:
Yvonne Murphy
Deputy Librarian: John Killen
Irish & Reference Librarian: Mr Gerry Healey
Systems Librarian: Monica McErlane
General Services Manager: Patricia Saunders
Finance Officer: Susan Finlay
Founded: 1788
Subjects: Biography, History, Library & Information Sciences, Literature, Literary Criticism,
Essays
ISBN Prefix(es): 0-9508985; 1-900921
Number of titles published annually: 3 Print
Total Titles: 20 Print; 1 CD-ROM

**Linford Mystery Library Series**, see Ulverscroft
Large Print Books Ltd

**Linford Romance Library Series**, see
Ulverscroft Large Print Books Ltd

**Linford Western Library Series**, see Ulverscroft
Large Print Books Ltd

**Linguaphone Institute Ltd+**
Liongate Enterprise Park, 80 Morden Rd,
Mitcham CR4 4PH
*Tel:* (020) 8687 6010 *Fax:* (020) 8687 6310
*E-mail:* ads@linguaphone.co.uk (advertising);
cst@linguaphone.co.uk (customer support)
*Web Site:* www.linguaphone.co.uk

*Key Personnel*
Chief Executive Officer: Clive Sawkins
Man Dir: Richard Avery *E-mail:* ra@linguaphone.
co.uk
Founded: 1924
Supplier of self-study language courses, products
& services.
Subjects: Language Arts, Linguistics
ISBN Prefix(es): 0-7473
Number of titles published annually: 5 Print; 5
CD-ROM; 1 Audio
Total Titles: 50 Print; 10 CD-ROM; 5 Audio
Imprints: Linguatape
Subsidiaries: Linguapac Distributors Plc; Linguapac Distributors Sdn Bhd; Linguaphone Institute Ltd
*Showroom(s):* Cortina, Inc, 7 Hollyhock Lane,
Wilton, CT 06897, United States *Tel:* 203-762-
2510 *E-mail:* info@cortina_languages.com
*Shipping Address:* Cortina, Inc, 7 Hollyhock Lane, Wilton, CT 06897, United
States *Tel:* 203-762-2510 *E-mail:* info@
cortina_languages.com
*Warehouse:* Cortina, Inc, 7 Hollyhock Lane,
Wilton, CT 06897, United States *Tel:* 203-762-
2510 *E-mail:* info@cortina_languages.com
*Distribution Center:* Cortina, Inc, 7 Hollyhock Lane, Wilton, CT 06897, United
States *Tel:* 203-762-2510 *E-mail:* info@
cortina_languages.com
*Orders to:* Cortina, Inc, 7 Hollyhock Lane,
Wilton, CT 06897, United States *Tel:* 203-762-
2510 *E-mail:* info@cortina_languages.com
*Returns:* Cortina, Inc, 7 Hollyhock Lane, Wilton,
CT 06897, United States *Tel:* 203-762-2510
*E-mail:* info@cortina_languages.com

**Linguatape**, *imprint of* Linguaphone Institute Ltd

**Lion Hudson plc+**
Mayfield House, 256 Banbury Rd, Oxford OX2
7DH
*Tel:* (01865) 302750 *Fax:* (01865) 302757
*E-mail:* enquiries@lionhudson.com
*Web Site:* www.lionhudson.com
*Key Personnel*
Man Dir: Paul Clifford *E-mail:* paulc@
lionhudson.com
Deputy Man Dir: Nick Jones *E-mail:* nickj@
lionhudson.com
International Rights Dir: Tony Wales
*E-mail:* tonyw@lionhudson.com
Sales Dir: John O'Nions *E-mail:* johno@
lionhudson.com
Publishing Dir: Rod Shepherd *E-mail:* rods@
lionhudson.com
Production Dir: Stephen Price *E-mail:* stephenp@
lionhudson.com
Senior International Rights: Paul Whitton
*E-mail:* paulw@lionhudson.com
International Rights: Robert Seath
*E-mail:* roberts@lionhudson.com
Export Sales Manager: Anne Rogers
*E-mail:* anner@lionhudson.com; Robert Wendover *E-mail:* robw@lionhudson.com
Founded: 1971
Specialize in adult religion & spirituality, illustrated reference, biography, health, gift books,
children's books - Bible stories & prayers, information & reference, activity, novelty & picture books.
Subjects: Biblical Studies, Nonfiction (General),
Religion - Catholic, Religion - Protestant, Self-Help, Theology
ISBN Prefix(es): 0-7459; 0-85648; 1-85424; 1-
85985; 0-948902
Number of titles published annually: 200 Print
Total Titles: 800 Print
Imprints: Candle Books; Monarch Books
Distributed by ASAF Import (Netherlands -
Candle/Monarch imprints only); Bookwise
(Australia - Lion Adult/Children imprints
only); Campus Crusade Asia (Singapore -

Candle/Monarch imprints only); Horizon
Books (Singapore - Lion Adult/Children imprints only); Koorong Books (Australia - Candle/Monarch imprints only); Kregel Publications (USA - Candle/Monarch imprints only);
New Holland (New Zealand - Lion Adult/Children imprints only); Novalis (Canada - selected
Lion Adult/Children titles only); Omega Distributors Ltd (New Zealand - Candle/Monarch
imprints only); OMF Literature (Philippines -
All imprints); Pearson (South Africa - Candle
imprint only); Scripture Union New Zealand
(New Zealand - Lion Adult/Children imprints
only); Struik Christian Books (South Africa
- Lion Adult/Children & Monarch imprints
only); Trafalgar Square Publishing (USA - selected Lion Adult/Children titles only)
Foreign Rights: Bridge Communications (Thailand); Richard Carman (Botswana, Middle
East); Infozone Ina Shinwon (Indonesia); Japan
Uni Agency (Japan); Korea Copyright Centre (Korea); Motovun (Japan); Andrew Nurnberg Associates (Mainland China); Eric Yang
Agency (Korea)
*Distribution Center:* Marston Book Services, 160
Milton Park Estate, Abingdon, Oxon OX14
4YN *Tel:* (01235) 465511 *Fax:* (01235) 465518

**Lippincott Williams & Wilkins**
250 Waterloo Rd, London SE1 8RD
*Tel:* (020) 7981 0600 *Fax:* (020) 7981 0601
*Web Site:* www.lww.co.uk
*Key Personnel*
Dir, Journals Publishing: Caroline Black
Sales & Marketing Dir: Ian Banbery
*E-mail:* ibanbery@lww.co.uk
Founded: 1893
Subjects: Medicine, Nursing, Dentistry, Veterinary
Science
ISBN Prefix(es): 0-316; 1-901831
*Parent Company:* Wolters Kluwer
*Branch Office(s)*
Lippincott Williams & Wilkins Pty Ltd, Suite 4,
Level 2, 22-36 Mountain St, Broadway, NSW
2007, Australia *Tel:* (02) 9212-5955 *Fax:* (02)
9212-6966
Lippincott Williams & Wilkins Asia Ltd, Suite
907-910, Wharf T&T Centre, Harbour City, 7
Canton Rd, Tsim Sha Ssui, Kowloon, Hong
Kong *Tel:* 2610-2339 *Fax:* 2421-1123
*U.S. Office(s):* Wolters Kluwer Health, 161 N
Clark St, Suite 4800, Chicago, IL 60601,
United States *Tel:* 312-425-7000
Anatomical Chart Co, 4711 Golf Rd, Suite 650,
Skokie, IL 60076, United States
351 W Camden St, Baltimore, MD 21201, United
States *Tel:* 410-528-4000
16522 Hunters Green Parkway, Hagerstown,
MD 21740, United States *Tel:* 301-223-2300
*Fax:* 301-223-2398 *E-mail:* orders@lww.com
Healthcare Group, 333 Seventh Ave, 19th & 20th
floors, New York, NY 10001, United States
*Tel:* 800-933-6525
Ambler, 323 Norristown Rd, Suite 200, PO Box
808, Ambler, PA 19002-2758, United States
*Tel:* (215) 646-8700 *Fax:* (215) 654-1328
530 Walnut St, Philadelphia, PA 19106-3621,
United States *Tel:* (215) 521-8300 *Fax:* (215)
521-8902 (head office)

**LISU**
Loughborough University, Loughborough, Leics
LE11 3TU
*Tel:* (01509) 635680 *Fax:* (01509) 635699
*E-mail:* lisu@lboro.ac.uk
*Web Site:* www.lboro.ac.uk/departments/dis/lisu/
lisuhp.html
*Key Personnel*
Dir: Dr J Eric Davies *E-mail:* j.e.davies@lboro.
ac.uk
Deputy Dir & Senior Statistician: Claire Creaser
Research Associate & Copyright Adviser: Dr
Sally Maynard

Founded: 1987
Subjects: Library & Information Sciences, Management, Public Administration
ISBN Prefix(es): 0-948848; 0-904924; 1-901786
Number of titles published annually: 7 Print; 4 CD-ROM; 5 Online
Total Titles: 45 Print; 4 CD-ROM; 15 Online
*Parent Company:* Department of Information Science
*Ultimate Parent Company:* Loughborough University

**Little Brown & Co (UK)**, *see* Virago Press

**Little Tiger Press**, *imprint of* Magi Publications

**The Littman Library of Jewish Civilization+**
PO Box 645, Oxford OX2 0UJ
*Tel:* (01865) 514688 *Fax:* (01865) 514688
*E-mail:* info@littman.co.uk
*Web Site:* www.littman.co.uk
*Key Personnel*
Chief Executive Officer: Ludo Craddock
  *Tel:* (01865) 722964 *E-mail:* ludo@littman.co.uk
Dir: Colette Littman; Roby Littman
Editorial: Connie Webber *E-mail:* connie01@globalnet.co.uk
Subjects: Art, Biography, Drama, Theater, Ethnicity, History, Literature, Literary Criticism, Essays, Philosophy, Poetry, Religion - Jewish, Theology
ISBN Prefix(es): 1-874774; 1-904113
*U.S. Office(s):* ISBS, 920 NE 58 Ave, Suite 300, Portland, OR 97213-3786, United States
Distributed by ISBS (Exclusive distributor for the USA & Canada)
*Warehouse:* NBN International, Estover Rd, Plymouth PL6 7PY *Tel:* (01752) 202000 *Fax:* (01752) 202333 *E-mail:* orders@nbninternational.com *Web Site:* www.nbninternational.com

**Liver Press**, *imprint of* Countyvise Ltd

**Liverpool University Press+**
4 Cambridge St, Liverpool L69 7ZU
*Tel:* (0151) 794 2233; (0151) 794 2237 *Fax:* (0151) 794 2235
*E-mail:* j.m.smith@liv.ac.uk
*Web Site:* www.liverpool-unipress.co.uk
*Key Personnel*
Publisher: Robin J C Bloxsidge *Tel:* (0151) 794 2231 *E-mail:* r.j.c.bloxsidge@liv.ac.uk
Sales & Marketing: Simon Bell *Tel:* (0151) 794 2234 *E-mail:* sbell@liv.ac.uk
Production: Andrew Kirk *E-mail:* andrewk@liv.ac.uk
Founded: 1899
Subjects: Archaeology, Architecture & Interior Design, Art, Education, Environmental Studies, Geography, Geology, History, Literature, Literary Criticism, Essays, Medicine, Nursing, Dentistry, Regional Interests, Science (General), Science Fiction, Fantasy, Social Sciences, Sociology, Veterinary Science, Art history, cultural affairs, current events, population studies, urban & regional planning
ISBN Prefix(es): 0-85323
Number of titles published annually: 40 Print
Total Titles: 200 Print
Distributed by International Specialized Book Distributors; University of Pennsylvania Press (USA & Canada)
Distributor for Fremantle Arts Centre Press (Australia)
*Orders to:* Marston Book Services, PO Box 269, Abingdon, Oxon OX14 4YN

**Livewire**, *imprint of* The Women's Press Ltd

**LLP Ltd**
69-77 Paul St, London EC2A 4LQ
*Tel:* (020) 7553 1000 *Fax:* (020) 7553 1109
*E-mail:* info@lloydslist.com
*Web Site:* www.lloydslist.com *Cable:* LLOYDSLIST LONDON EC3
*Key Personnel*
Publishing Dir: Ray Girvan *Tel:* (020) 7553 1751
Chief Executive: David Gilbertson
Executive Editor: Christopher Mayer *Tel:* (020) 7553 1402
Editor: Julian Bray *Tel:* (020) 7553 1374
Production Editor: Linda Roulston *Tel:* (020) 7553 1480
Advertising Dir: Paul Hubbard *Tel:* (020) 7553 1324
Founded: 1973
Business to business international publishers.
Subjects: Finance, Law, Maritime, Insurance
ISBN Prefix(es): 1-85044
*Parent Company:* LLP Ltd, Sheepen Pl, Colchester CO3 3LP
*U.S. Office(s):* LLP Limited, c/o Distributech Fulfillment Services, 41-21 28 St, Unit D, Long Island City, NY 11101, United States *Tel:* 718-786-0076 *Fax:* 718-786-4252

**Local Heritage Books**, *see* Countryside Books

**Ward Lock**, *imprint of* Cassell & Co

**Locomotion Papers**, *imprint of* Oakwood Press

**Lodenek Press**
Trevinette, Chapel Amble, Wadebridge, Cornwall PL27 6ES
*Tel:* (01208) 880850
*Key Personnel*
Man Dir, Sales, Production, Rights & Permissions: D R Rawe
Editorial: H J Ingrey
Founded: 1970
Subjects: Regional Interests
ISBN Prefix(es): 0-902899; 0-946143
Total Titles: 18 Print
Imprints: Chough Series (Educational Packs)
Distributed by Tabb House (in Cornwall only)
Distributor for Tabb House

**Y Lolfa Cyf+**
Talybont, Ceredigion SY24 5AP
*Tel:* (01970) 832 304 *Fax:* (01970) 832 782
*E-mail:* ylolfa@ylolfa.com
*Web Site:* www.ylolfa.com
*Key Personnel*
Man Dir, Production: Garmon Gruffudd *E-mail:* garmon@ylolfa.com
Editorial: Lefi Gruffudd
Administration, Rights & Permissions: Nia Williams
Marketing & Publicity: Dilwyn Phillips
Founded: 1965
Publishers of Welsh books & English books of Welsh & Celtic interest.
Subjects: Cookery, Crafts, Games, Hobbies, Fiction, Language Arts, Linguistics, Music, Dance, Poetry, Regional Interests, Science Fiction, Fantasy
ISBN Prefix(es): 0-86243; 0-904864; 0-9500178
Number of titles published annually: 50 Print
Total Titles: 500 Print; 4 Audio
Imprints: Dinas

**London Chamber of Commerce & Industry Examinations Board (LCCIEB)**
Athena House, 112 Station Rd, Sidcup, Kent DA15 7BJ
*Tel:* (020) 8309 3000 *Fax:* (020) 8302 4169
*E-mail:* custserv@lccieb.org.uk
*Web Site:* www.lccieb.com
*Key Personnel*
Publishing Manager: Christine Winters *E-mail:* christinew@lccieb.org.uk
Publishing arm of the LCCI Examinations Board, publish support materials for students, candidates of LCCI exams (& their teachers), student financial textbooks & teachers handbooks. Specialize in English language for business & secretarial.
Subjects: Business, Finance
Number of titles published annually: 10 Print
Total Titles: 60 Print

**Stacey London**, *imprint of* Stacey International

**Lonely Planet, UK+**
72-82 Rosebery Ave, Clerkenwell, London EC1R 4RW
*Tel:* (020) 7841 9000 *Fax:* (020) 7841 9001
*E-mail:* go@lonelyplanet.co.uk
*Web Site:* www.lonelyplanet.com
*Key Personnel*
Publisher: Tony Wheeler; Maureen Wheeler
Dir: Jim Hart
Manager, UK: Charlotte Hindle
Founded: 1991
Subjects: Travel
ISBN Prefix(es): 1-55992; 0-908086; 0-86442; 2-84070; 1-86450; 1-74104; 1-74059
*Parent Company:* Lonely Planet Publications Pty Ltd, Melbourne, Australia
*Divisions:* Lonely Planet (Australia); Lonely Planet (France); Lonely Planet (United States)
*Warehouse:* Grantham Book Services, Issac Newton Way, Alma Park Industrial Estate, Grantham NU31 9SD
*Orders to:* World Leisure Marketing, West Meadows Industrial Estate, Derby DE2 6HA

**Barry Long Books+**
7 Nichol Pl, Cotford St Luke, Taunton TA4 1JD
Mailing Address: PO Box 574, Mullumbimby, NSW 2482, Australia
*Tel:* (01823) 430061
*E-mail:* contact@barrylongbooks.com
*Web Site:* www.barrylongbooks.com
*Key Personnel*
International Rights: Clive Tempest *Fax:* (01823) 430062 *E-mail:* clive.tempest@btinternet.com
Founded: 1994
Non-profit educational company.
Specialize in the work of spiritual teacher Barry Long.
Subjects: Philosophy, Religion - Other, Self-Help, Spirituality
ISBN Prefix(es): 0-9508050; 1-899324
Number of titles published annually: 2 Print
Total Titles: 20 Print
*Parent Company:* The Barry Long Foundation International, Box 5277, Gold Coast MC, Qld 4217, Australia
*Branch Office(s)*
BCM Box 876, London WC1N 3XX, Contact: Clive Tempest *Tel:* (01823) 430061 *Fax:* (01823) 430062 *E-mail:* contact@barrylongbooks.com *Web Site:* www.barrylongbooks.com
*U.S. Office(s):* 6230 Wilshire Blvd, Suite 251, Los Angeles, CA 90048, United States, Contact: Simon Warwick Smith *Tel:* 707-939-9212 *Fax:* 707-938-3515
Distributed by Brumby Books (Australia); Deep Books (UK & Ireland); New Leaf Distributing Co (US & Canada); Peaceful Living (New Zealand)
Foreign Rights: Daniel Doglioli (Italy)
*Orders to:* Bookworld Services, 1933 Whitfield Park Loop, Sarasota, FL 34243, United States *E-mail:* sales@bookworld.com *Web Site:* www.bookworld.com

**Longman**, *imprint of* Pearson Education Europe, Mideast & Africa

**Lorenz Books+**
Hermes House, 88-89 Blackfriars Rd, London
SE1 8HA
*Tel:* (020) 7401 2077 *Fax:* (020) 7633 9499
*E-mail:* bsp2b@aol.com
*Key Personnel*
Contact: Paul Anness
International Contact: Denise Lie
Subjects: Animals, Pets, Cookery, Crafts, Games,
Hobbies, Gardening, Plants, Health, Nutrition,
How-to, New Age
ISBN Prefix(es): 1-85967; 0-7548
Imprints: Ultimate
Subsidiaries: Anness Publications Pty; Anness
Publications
*U.S. Office(s):* Anness Publishing, 27 W 20 St,
Suite 504, New York, NY 10011, United States
Distributed by Bateman (New Zealand); Five
Mile Press (Australia); Raincoast (Canada)
*Orders to:* Aurum Press, 25 Bedford Ave, London
WC1B 3AT

**Lorna**, *imprint of* Novello & Co Ltd

**Loughborough University**
Dept of Information Science, Ashby Rd, Lough-
borough, Leics LE11 3TU
*Tel·* (01509) 263171; (01509) 223052
*Fax:* (01509) 223053
*E-mail:* dis@lboro.ac.uk
*Web Site:* www.lboro.ac.uk
*Telex:* 34319
*Key Personnel*
Dept Head: Prof Ron Summers
Prof: Christine L Borgman *Tel:* (01509) 223050
*E-mail:* r.summers@lboro.ac.uk; John Feather
*Tel:* (01509) 223058 *E-mail:* j.p.feather@
lboro.ac.uk; Cliff McKnight *Tel:* (01509)
223061 *E-mail:* c.mcknight@lboro.ac.uk; Jack
Meadows *Tel:* (01509) 223082 *E-mail:* a.j.
meadows@lboro.ac.uk; Charles Oppenheim
*Tel:* (01509) 223065 *E-mail:* c.oppenheim@
lboro.ac.uk
ISBN Prefix(es): 0-902761

**Peter Lowe**, *imprint of* Eurobook Ltd

**LTP**, *imprint of* Language Teaching Publications

**Luath Press Ltd+**
543/2 Castlehill, The Royal Mile, Edinburgh EH1
2ND
*Tel:* (0131) 225 4326 *Fax:* (0131) 225 4324
*E-mail:* sales@luath.co.uk
*Web Site:* www.luath.co.uk
*Key Personnel*
Dir: Gavin MacDougall *E-mail:* gavin.
macdougall@luath.co.uk
Founded: 1981
Publisher of *On the Trail of* series.
Membership(s): Scottish Publishers Association.
Subjects: Biography, Fiction, Genealogy, History,
Literature, Literary Criticism, Essays, Natural
History, Nonfiction (General), Outdoor Recre-
ation, Poetry, Regional Interests, Science Fic-
tion, Fantasy, Sports, Athletics, Travel, Wine &
Spirits
ISBN Prefix(es): 0-946487; 1-84282
Number of titles published annually: 30 Print
Total Titles: 80 Print
Distributed by Addenda (New Zealand); Hushion
House (Canada); Midpoint Trade Books (USA
only); Peribo (Australia); Petersen (Germany,
Austria, Switzerland)
*Shipping Address:* Scottish Book Source, 32 Fin-
las St, Glasgow G22 5DU
*Warehouse:* Scottish Book Source, 32 Finlas St,
Glasgow G22 5DU
*Orders to:* Scottish Book Source, 32 Finlas St,
Glasgow G22 5DU, Contact: Gerry McLean
*Tel:* (0141) 558 1366 *Fax:* (0141) 557 0189

*E-mail:* info@booksource.net *Web Site:* www.
booksource.net
*Returns:* Scottish Book Source, 32 Finlas St,
Glasgow G22 5DU

**Lucent Books**, *imprint of* Thomson Gale

**Lucis Press Ltd**
3 Whitehall Court, Suite 54, London SW1A 2EF
*Tel:* (020) 7839 4512; (020) 7839 4513
*Fax:* (020) 7839 5575
*E-mail:* london@lucistrust.org
*Web Site:* www.lucistrust.org
*Key Personnel*
General Secretary: Chris Morgan
Dir: Helen Durant *E-mail:* lucispress@lucistrust.
org
Founded: 1938
Publisher of 24 books of Esoteric Philosophy by
Alice A Bailey.
Subjects: Astrology, Occult, Education, Philoso-
phy, Religion - Other, Social Sciences, Sociol-
ogy
ISBN Prefix(es): 0-85330
Total Titles: 38 Print; 1 CD-ROM
*Parent Company:* Lucis Publishing Co, 120 Wall
St, 24th floor, New York, NY 10005, United
States, Sarah McKechnie
*Associate Companies:* Lucis Trust, One rue de
Varembe 3e, Case Postale 31, 1211 Geneva 20,
Switzerland *Tel:* (022) 734-1252 *Fax:* (022)
740-0911 *E-mail:* geneva@lucistrust.org (for
European translations)
Distributed by Lucis Press SA (South Africa);
Sydney Goodwill Unit of Service (Australia);
The Triangle Centre (New Zealand)
Distributor for Agni Yoga Society

**Lucky Duck Publishing Ltd**
Solar House, Station Rd, Kingswood, Bristol
BS15 4PH
*Tel:* (0117) 947 5150 *Fax:* (0117) 947 5152
*E-mail:* publishing@luckyduck.co.uk
*Web Site:* www.luckyduck.co.uk
Founded: 1988
Educational publisher.
Subjects: Education
ISBN Prefix(es): 1-904315
Number of titles published annually: 20 Print
Total Titles: 100 Print

**Lund Humphries**, *imprint of* Ashgate Publishing
Ltd

**Lund Humphries+**
Imprint of Ashgate Publishing Ltd
Gower House, Croft Rd, Aldershot, Hants GU11
3HR
*Tel:* (01252) 331551 *Fax:* (01252) 344405
*E-mail:* info@lundhumphries.com
*Web Site:* www.lundhumphries.com
*Key Personnel*
Man Dir: Lucy Myers *Tel:* (020) 7841 9800
*Fax:* (020) 7837 6322 *E-mail:* lmyers@
lundhumphries.com
Founded: 1943
Subjects: Architecture & Interior Design, Art,
Crafts, Games, Hobbies, Photography
ISBN Prefix(es): 0-85331
Number of titles published annually: 20 Print
Total Titles: 70 Print
*U.S. Office(s):* Ashgate Publishing, 101 Cherry St,
Suite 420, Burlington, VT 05401-4405, United
States *Tel:* 802-865-7641 *Fax:* 802-865-7847
*E-mail:* info@ashgate.com
Distributor for Hartley & Marks (Europe only);
Powerhouse Publishing, Powerhouse Museum,
Sydney (Outside Australia & New Zealand)
*Warehouse:* Bookpoint Ltd, 130 Milton Park,
Abingdon, Oxon OX14 4SB

**Lutterworth Press**, *imprint of* James Clarke &
Co Ltd

**The Lutterworth Press+**
Imprint of James Clarke & Co
PO Box 60, Cambridge CB1 2NT
*Tel:* (01223) 350865 *Fax:* (01223) 366951
*E-mail:* publishing@lutterworth.com
*Web Site:* www.lutterworth.com
*Key Personnel*
Man Dir, Rights: Adrian C Brink
Sales Manager: Colin Lester
Founded: 1799
Membership(s): IPG; Publishers' Association.
Subjects: Archaeology, Art, Biblical Studies, Bi-
ography, Crafts, Games, Hobbies, Education,
History, Natural History, Nonfiction (General),
Religion - Protestant, Theology
ISBN Prefix(es): 0-7444; 0-7188
Number of titles published annually: 15 Print
Total Titles: 600 Print
Imprints: Acorn Editions; Patrick Hardy Books
Distributed by Parkwest Publications Inc (USA
exclusive; Canada non-exclusive)

**Luxor Press L**, *see* Charles Skilton Ltd

**Lyle Publications Ltd**
4 Shepherds Mill, Selkirk, Selkirkshire TD7 5EA
*Tel:* (01750) 23355 *Fax:* (01750) 23388
*E-mail:* lyle.publications@talk21.com
*Key Personnel*
Dir: Tony Curtis; Annette Curtis
Subjects: Antiques, Art
ISBN Prefix(es): 0-86248; 0-902921

**Thomas Lyster Ltd**
Units 3/4a, Old Boundary Way Industrial Park,
Ormskirk, Lancs L39 2YW
*Tel:* (01695) 575112 *Fax:* (01695) 570120
*E-mail:* books@tlyster.co.uk
*Web Site:* www.tlyster.co.uk
*Key Personnel*
General Manager: Ian Lyster
Founded: 1988
Specialize in offering distribution services to
other smaller publishers.
Membership(s): IPG.
ISBN Prefix(es): 1-871482
Total Titles: 15 Print
*Parent Company:* Plymbridge Distributors Ltd,
Estover Rd, Plymouth DL6 7DY
Distributor for Aquila Books; Broadview Pub-
lishing; Colour Affects Ltd; Cornish Books;
Enanef Ltd; Fort Publishing; Lancashire
Books; Landscape Press; Pigeon Publications;
Royal & Ancient Golf Club; Sheldrake Press;
South Bank University (Distance Learning
Centre); Taghan Publishing

**Macgregor Science**, *imprint of* Thistle Press

**Macmillan**, *imprint of* Pan Macmillan

**Macmillan Audio Books+**
18-21 Cavaye Pl, London SW10 9PG
*Tel:* (020) 7373 6070 *Fax:* (020) 7244 6379
Subjects: Art, Biography, Cookery, Fiction, His-
tory, Military Science, Mysteries, Natural His-
tory, Poetry
ISBN Prefix(es): 0-333
*Parent Company:* Macmillan Publishers Ltd

**Macmillan Children's Books**, *imprint of* Pan
Macmillan

**Macmillan Children's Books+**
Imprint of Pan Macmillan
20 New Wharf Rd, London N1 9RR
*Tel:* (020) 7014 6000 *Fax:* (020) 7014 6142
*Web Site:* www.panmacmillan.com

*Key Personnel*
Man Dir: Kate Wilson
Sales & Marketing Dir: Emma Hopkin
Associate Publisher: Marion Lloyd
Publishing Dir: Sarah Davies
Editorial Dir: Suzanne Carnell
Editorial Dir, Campbell Books: Camilla Reid
Subjects: Fiction, Nonfiction (General), Poetry
ISBN Prefix(es): 0-330; 0-333; 1-405
Number of titles published annually: 200 Print
Total Titles: 2,500 Print
Imprints: Campbell Books; Young Picador
Divisions: Black & White Colour

## Macmillan Heinemann ELT
Macmillan Oxford, Between Towns Rd, Oxford
   OX4 3PP
*Tel:* (01865) 405700 *Fax:* (01865) 405701
*E-mail:* elt@mhelt.com
*Web Site:* www.mhelt.com
*Key Personnel*
Man Dir (Education): Chris Harrison
   *E-mail:* chris.harrison@mhelt.com
Publishing Dir: Sue Bale *E-mail:* sue.bale@mhelt.
   com
Finance Dir: Paul Emmett *E-mail:* paul.emmett@
   mhelt.com
Publishing Dir Educational: Alison Hurbert
Specialize in the publication of core curriculum
   texts for primary, JSS, SSS.
ISBN Prefix(es): 0-435; 0-333
*Parent Company:* Macmillan Education Ltd

## Macmillan Ltd
The Macmillan Bldg, 4 Crinan St, London N1
   9XW
*Tel:* (020) 7833 4000 *Fax:* (020) 7843 4640
*Web Site:* www.macmillan.com
*Key Personnel*
Chief Executive Officer: Richard Charkin
Finance Dir: Geoff Todd
Executive Dir: Mike Barnard; Chris Paterson; Do-
   minic Knight; David North; Annette Thomas
Founded: 1843
An international company focusing on high qual-
   ity academic, scholarly, education & trade pub-
   lishing as well as publishign services for third
   parties.
Subjects: Fiction, Nonfiction (General)
ISBN Prefix(es): 0-312; 0-330; 0-333; 0-283; 0-
   7522; 1-4039; 1-4050
Number of titles published annually: 5,000 Print;
   20 CD-ROM; 1,000 Online; 100 Audio
*Parent Company:* Verlagsgruppe Georg von
   Holtzbrinck
*U.S. Office(s):* Holtzbinck Publishers USA
*Distribution Center:* von Holtzbrinck Publishing
   Services
Macmillan Distribution Services Pty Ltd (Aus-
   tralia)
Macmillan Distribution Ltd
Peninsula Production & Distribution Ltd

## Macmillan Press Ltd, see Palgrave Publishers
Ltd

## Macmillan Publishers (UK) Ltd+
Division of Grove
Brunel Rd, Houndmills, Basingstoke, Hants
   RG21 6XS
*Tel:* (01256) 329242 *Fax:* (01256) 812558
*E-mail:* mdl@macmillan.com
*Web Site:* www.macmillan.com
*Key Personnel*
Chief Executive: R D P Charkin
Rights Dir, Trade: Chantal Noel *E-mail:* c.noel@
   macmillan.co.uk
Founded: 1843
ISBN Prefix(es): 0-333
*Parent Company:* Verlagsgruppe Georg van
   Holtzbrink

*Associate Companies:* Macmillan India Ltd, In-
   dia; Gill & Macmillan Ltd, Ireland; Macmillan
   Publishers Nigeria Ltd, Nigeria; The Northern
   Nigerian Publishing Co Ltd, Nigeria; The Col-
   lege Press plc, Zimbabwe; Pan Macmillan Ltd
*Subsidiaries:* Grove's Dictionaries of Music Ltd;
   Macmillan Education Ltd; Macmillan Mag-
   azines Ltd; Macmillan Press Ltd; Macmil-
   lan Distribution Ltd; Macmillan General
   Books Ltd; Macmillan Children's Books Ltd;
   Stockton Press Ltd; Stockton Press Nether-
   lands BV; Macmillan Publishers Australia Pty
   Ltd; Macmillan Publishers Hong Kong Ltd;
   Macmillan Publishers China Ltd; Peninsula
   Production & Distribution Ltd; Macmillan Lan-
   guage House Co Ltd; Macmillan Shuppan KK;
   Nature Japan KK; Macmillan Kenya Publishers
   Ltd; Editorial Macmillan de Mexico SA de CV;
   Macmillan Publishers New Zealand Ltd; Pans-
   ing Distribution Sdn Bhd; Macmillan Boleswa
   Publishers Pty Ltd; Macmillan Swaziland Na-
   tional Publishing Co Ltd; Nature America Inc;
   St Martin's Press Inc; College Press Pvt Ltd;
   Stockton Press Netherlands Holdings BV
*Orders to:* Macmillan Distribution Ltd, Brunel
   Rd, Houndmills, Basingstoke, Hants RG21
   2XS *Tel:* (0125) 6329242

## Macmillan Reference Ltd
Brunel Rd, Houndmills, Basingstoke, Hants RG21
   6XS
*Tel:* (01256) 329242 *Fax:* (01256) 812558
*E-mail:* mdl@macmillan.co.uk
*Web Site:* www.macmillan.co.uk
*Key Personnel*
Man Dir: Ian Jacobs *E-mail:* i.jacobs@macmillan.
   co.uk
Science Publisher: Gina Fullerlove *E-mail:* g.
   fullerlove@macmillan.co.uk
Art Publisher: Jane Turner *E-mail:* j.turner@
   macmillan.co.uk
Humanities & Social Sciences Publisher: Sara
   Lloyd *E-mail:* s.lloyd@macmillan.co.uk
Marketing: Alex Lankester *E-mail:* a.lankester@
   macmillan.co.uk
Production: Jeremy Macdonald *E-mail:* j.
   macdonald@macmillan.co.uk
Subjects: Art, Economics, Finance, Government,
   Political Science, History, Human Relations,
   Music, Dance, Science (General), Social Sci-
   ences, Sociology
ISBN Prefix(es): 0-333

## Macmillan Reference USA, *imprint of* Thomson
Gale

## Macmillan Technical Publishing USA, *imprint
of* Pearson Education Europe, Mideast &
Africa

## Julia Macrae, *imprint of* Random House UK Ltd

## Mad Jack, *imprint of* Funfax Ltd

## Made Simple Books, *imprint of* Elsevier Ltd

## Magi Publications+
One The Coda Centre, 189 Munster Rd, London
   SW6 6AW
*Tel:* (020) 7385 6333 *Fax:* (020) 7385 7333
*E-mail:* info@littletiger.com
*Web Site:* www.littletigerpress.com
*Key Personnel*
Rights Manager: M S Bhatia
Founded: 1987
Specialize in co-production of children's picture
   books.
Subjects: English as a Second Language, Fiction
ISBN Prefix(es): 1-870271; 1-85430; 1-952246

Imprints: Little Tiger Press
*Orders to:* A & C Black, Howard Rd, Eaton Socon, Huntingdon, Cambs PE19 3EZ

## Magic Joneuery, *imprint of* Funfax Ltd

## Magna Large Print Books+
Magna House, Long Preston, Skipton, N Yorks
   BD23 4ND
*Tel:* (01729) 840 225; (01729) 840 526; (01729)
   840 251 *Fax:* (01729) 840 683
*E-mail:* enquiries@ulverscroft.co.uk
*Web Site:* www.ulverscroft.co.uk
*Key Personnel*
Man Dir: John Cressey
Rights: Diane Allen
Founded: 1973
ISBN Prefix(es): 0-86009; 1-85057; 1-85389; 0-
   7505; 1-84137
Number of titles published annually: 240 Print;
   72 Audio
Total Titles: 1,000 Print
*Parent Company:* The Ulverscroft Group Ltd
Imprints: Dales Large Print Series; Story Sound
   Audio Tapes
*U.S. Office(s):* Ulverscroft (Large Print USA Inc),
   Seneca Pl, 1881 Ridge Rd, West Seneca, NY
   14214, United States
Distributed by Ulverscroft (USA)
*Showroom(s):* Cawdor Books, 96 Dykehead St,
   Queenslie, Glasgow G33 4AQ *Tel:* (01729)
   840225 *Fax:* (01729) 840683

## Mainstream Publishing Co (Edinburgh) Ltd+
7 Albany St, Edinburgh EH1 3UG
*Tel:* (0131) 557 2959 *Fax:* (0131) 556 8720
*E-mail:* enquiries@mainstreampublishing.com
*Web Site:* www.mainstreampublishing.com
*Key Personnel*
Dir: Bill Campbell; Irina MacKenzie; Peter
   MacKenzie
Sales Manager: Raymond Cowie
Sales Administration: Elaine Scott
Founded: 1978
Subjects: Art, Biography, Government, Political
   Science, History, Literature, Literary Criticism,
   Essays, Photography, Sports, Athletics, Travel
ISBN Prefix(es): 1-85158; 1-84018
Distributed by Bill Bailey Publishers' Represen-
   tatives (Europe); Capricorn Link (Australia)
   Pty Ltd (Australia); CKK Ltd (Southeast Asia);
   Hushion House Ltd (Canada); Phambili (South
   Africa); Trafalgar Square (USA); Peter Ward
   Book Exports (Middle East)
*Orders to:* Tiptree, St Luke's Chase, Tiptree,
   Colchester, Essex C05 0SR

## Making Sense of Science, *imprint of* Portland
Press Ltd

## Mallard Reprints, *imprint of* Terence Dalton Ltd

## Management Books 2000 Ltd+
Forge House, Limes Rd, Kemble, Cirencester,
   Glos GL7 6AD
*Tel:* (01285) 771441 *Fax:* (01285) 771055
*E-mail:* mb.2000@virgin.net
*Web Site:* www.mb2000.com
*Key Personnel*
Publisher: James Alexander
Founded: 1986
Publisher & distributor of management guides,
   textbooks & references.
Subjects: Business, Career Development, Manage-
   ment, Marketing, Real Estate
ISBN Prefix(es): 1-85251; 1-85252
Number of titles published annually: 24 Print
Total Titles: 200 Print
Imprints: Mercury Books
*Orders to:* Combined Book Services, Paddock
   Wood Distribution Centre, Paddock Wood Kent
   TN12 6UU *Tel:* (01892) 837171

**Management Pocketbooks Ltd+**
Laurel House, Station Approach, Alresford, Hants SO24 9JH
*Tel:* (01962) 735 573 *Fax:* (01962) 733 637
*E-mail:* sales@pocketbook.co.uk
*Web Site:* www.pocketbook.co.uk
*Key Personnel*
International Rights: Rosalind Baynes
  *E-mail:* ros@pocketbook.co.uk
Founded: 1987
Small, highly accessible management guides written by trainers, full of graphics, mnemonics, bullet points for clarity & ease of recall.
Membership(s): IPG (Independent Publishers Guild).
Subjects: Business, Education, Management
ISBN Prefix(es): 1-870471; 1-903776
Number of titles published annually: 10 Print
Total Titles: 85 Print; 2 Audio
*U.S. Office(s):* Stylus Publishing, 22883 Quicksilver Dr, Sterling, VA 20166-2012, United States, Contact: John von Knorring *Tel:* 703-661-1504; 703-661-1515 (editorial); 703-661-1581 (orders) *Fax:* 703-661-1501
  *E-mail:* styluspub@aol.com
*Distribution Center:* Trade Counter, Unit D, Trading Estate Rd, London NW10 7LU, Denise Johnson *Tel:* (20) 8963 0322

**Manchester United Books**, *imprint of* Carlton Publishing Group

**Manchester University Press+**
Oxford Rd, Manchester M13 9NR
*Tel:* (0161) 275 2310 *Fax:* (0161) 274 3346
*E-mail:* mup@man.ac.uk
*Web Site:* www.manchesteruniversitypress.co.uk
*Key Personnel*
Chief Executive & Production Dir: David Rodgers *E-mail:* d.rodgers@man.ac.uk
Editorial Dir: Matthew Frost *E-mail:* m.frost@man.ac.uk
Editor: Tony Mason *E-mail:* t.mason@man.ac.uk; Alison Welsby *E-mail:* a.welsby@man.ac.uk
Sales & Marketing Dir: Clare Blick *E-mail:* c.blick@man.ac.uk
Rights & Publicity: Alison Sparkes *E-mail:* a.sparkes@man.ac.uk
Founded: 1903
Subjects: Art, Economics, Film, Video, Government, Political Science, History, Literature, Literary Criticism, Essays, Radio, TV, Social Sciences, Sociology, Academic publishers
ISBN Prefix(es): 0-7190
*Associate Companies:* Palgrave, 257 Park Ave S, New York, NY 10010, United States
Imprints: Mandolin
Distributed by University of British Columbia Press (Canada)

**Mandolin**, *imprint of* Manchester University Press

**Mandrake of Oxford+**
PO Box 250, Oxford OX1 1AP
Mailing Address: Po Box 1589, Blaine, WA 98231, United States
*Tel:* (01865) 243671 *Fax:* (01865) 432929
*E-mail:* mandrake@mandrake.uk.net
*Web Site:* www.mandrake.uk.net
*Key Personnel*
Contact: M Morgan
Founded: 1986
Also acts as Bookseller & Mail-Order Subscription Agent.
Subjects: Art, Astrology, Occult, Fiction, Health, Nutrition, Parapsychology, Religion - Hindu, Religion - Other, Science (General), Science Fiction, Fantasy
ISBN Prefix(es): 1-869928
Number of titles published annually: 10 Print
Imprints: Golden Dawn; Nuit-Isis

*Orders to:* Gazelle, White Crown Mills, Hightown, Lancaster LA1 4XS *Tel:* (01524) 68765 *Fax:* (01424) 63232 *E-mail:* Gazelle4go@AOL.com
New Leaf, 401 Thornton Rd, Lithia Springs, GA 30057-1557, United States *Tel:* 770-948-7845 *Fax:* 770-944-2313 (Trade only)

**Maney**, *imprint of* Maney Publishing

**Maney Publishing+**
Hudson Rd, Leeds LS9 7DL
*Tel:* (0113) 249 7481 *Fax:* (0113) 248 6983
*E-mail:* maney@maney.co.uk
*Web Site:* www.maney.co.uk
*Key Personnel*
Man Dir: Michael Gallico *E-mail:* m.gallico@maney.co.uk
Marketing Manager: Lynne Medhurst *E-mail:* l.medhurst@maney.co.uk
Founded: 1900
Academic book & journal publisher.
Subjects: Antiques, Archaeology, Architecture & Interior Design, Art, Drama, Theater, Engineering (General), History, Language Arts, Linguistics, Library & Information Sciences, Literature, Literary Criticism, Essays, Natural History
Number of titles published annually: 25 Print
Total Titles: 300 Print
Imprints: Maney; Northern Universities Press; Modern Humanities Research Association; Pasold Research Fund

**Mango Publishing**
49 Carnabys St, London W1F 9PY
*Tel:* (020) 7292 9000 *Fax:* (020) 7434 1077
*E-mail:* info@mangomedia.net
*Web Site:* www.mangopublishing.net
*Key Personnel*
Contact: Richard Coury *Tel:* (020) 7471 1744 *E-mail:* richard@mangopublishing.net
Subjects: Biography, Literature, Literary Criticism, Essays, Poetry, Poetry, literature & biography by Caribbean heritage writers especially women; literary criticism of Caribbean literature
ISBN Prefix(es): 1-902294
Total Titles: 10 Print

**George Mann**, *imprint of* George Mann Publications

**Mansell**, *imprint of* Cassell & Co

**Mansell**, *imprint of* The Continuum International Publishing Group Ltd

**The Mansk Svenska Publishing Co Ltd+**
17 North View, Peel, Isle of Man 1M5 1DQ
*Tel:* (0162) 4842855 *Fax:* (0162) 844241
*E-mail:* hanneke@advsys.co.uk
*Key Personnel*
Man Dir: G V C Young, OBE
Founded: 1980
Subjects: Biography, Fiction, History
ISBN Prefix(es): 0-907715
*Branch Office(s)*
Spellinge Gard, S-590 20 Mantord, Sweden
*Bookshop(s):* 50 Michael St, Peel 1M5 1HD

**Manson Publishing Ltd+**
73 Corringham Rd, London NW11 7DL
*Tel:* (020) 8905 5150 *Fax:* (020) 8201 9233
*E-mail:* manson@mansonpublishing.com
*Web Site:* www.mansonpublishing.com
*Key Personnel*
Man Dir: Michael Manson
Publishing Coordinator: Clair Chaventre
Founded: 1992

Membership(s): IPG; Publishers' Association.
Subjects: Agriculture, Biological Sciences, Chemistry, Chemical Engineering, Earth Sciences, Medicine, Nursing, Dentistry, Veterinary Science, Microbiology, Plant Science
ISBN Prefix(es): 1-874545; 1-84076
Total Titles: 100 Print; 1 CD-ROM
Subsidiaries: Veterinary Press Ltd
Distributed by Nankodo Co Ltd (Japan - medicine & veterinary medicine books); United Publishers Services Ltd (Japan - Science books only)
Distributor for Schluetersche Verlagsgesellschaft mbH & Co (English-language titles only)
*Orders to:* Marston Book Services Ltd, Unit 160, Milton Park Industrial Centre, Abingdon *Tel:* (01235) 465500 *Fax:* (01235) 465555

**Peter Marcan Publications**
PO Box 3158, London SE1 4RA
*Tel:* (020) 7357 0368
*Key Personnel*
Proprietor: Peter Marcan
Founded: 1978
Membership(s): Author-Publisher Enterprise (UK).
Subjects: Art, History, Music, Dance
ISBN Prefix(es): 0-9510289; 1-871811; 0-9504211

**Marcham Manor Press+**
Appleford, Abingdon, Oxon OX14 4PB
*Tel:* (01235) 848319
*Key Personnel*
Chief Executive, Editorial: G E Duffield
Sales, Publicity: G Elwes
Production: E Collie
Founded: 1963
Subjects: Asian Studies, Biblical Studies, Biography, History, Music, Dance, Philosophy, Religion - Catholic, Religion - Protestant, Theology
ISBN Prefix(es): 0-900531
*Parent Company:* Appleford Publishing Group
*Associate Companies:* Appleford Printers, Courtenay Bookroom
Divisions: Sutton Courtenay Press

**Maresfield Lib**, *imprint of* Karnac Books Ltd

**Maritime Books**
Lodge Hill, Liskeard, Cornwell PL14 4EL
*Tel:* (01579) 343663 *Fax:* (01579) 346747
*E-mail:* editor@navybooks.com
*Web Site:* www.navybooks.com
*Key Personnel*
Chief Executive: M Critchley
Manager: P Garnett
Founded: 1980
Subjects: Maritime
ISBN Prefix(es): 0-907771
Total Titles: 26 Print
Subsidiaries: Warship World Magazine

**The Market Research Society**
15 Northburgh St, London EC1V 0JR
*Tel:* (020) 7490 4911 *Fax:* (020) 7490 0608
*E-mail:* info@mrs.org.uk
*Web Site:* www.mrs.org.uk
*Key Personnel*
Dir General: David Barr
Organization for professional researchers & others engaged or interested in market, social & opinion research.

**Mars Business Associates Ltd**
62 Kingsmead, Lechlade, Glos GL7 3BW
*Tel:* (01367) 252 506 *Fax:* (01367) 252 506
*E-mail:* sales@marspub.co.uk
*Web Site:* www.marspub.co.uk
*Key Personnel*
Contact: Dr John Robertson *E-mail:* johnr@cccp.net
Founded: 1988

Subjects: Accounting, Finance
ISBN Prefix(es): 1-873186

**Marshall Editions Ltd+**
The Old Brewery, 6 Blundell St, London N7 9BH
*Tel:* (020) 7700 6764 *Fax:* (020) 7700 4191
*E-mail:* info@marshalleditions.com
*Web Site:* www.quarto.com/group/companies/
marshalleditions.htm
*Key Personnel*
Chairman: Richard Harman *E-mail:* rharman@
smediakey.u-net.com
Publisher: Barbara Marshall
Chief Executive: Nick Croydon
Sales Dir: Belinda Rasmussen
Founded: 1977
Also acts as book packager.
Subjects: Business, Crafts, Games, Hobbies, Gardening, Plants, Geography, Geology, Health, Nutrition, History, Management, Military Science, Natural History, Religion - Other, Science (General), Travel, Wine & Spirits
ISBN Prefix(es): 0-9507901
*Parent Company:* Quarto

**Marston House**, *imprint of* Marston House

**Marston House+**
Marston Magna, Yeovil, Somerset BA22 8DH
*Tel:* (01935) 851331 *Fax:* (01935) 851372
*Key Personnel*
Man Dir, Production: A E Birks-Hay
Editorial Dir: M L Birks-Hay
Founded: 1991
Subjects: Architecture & Interior Design, Art, Gardening, Plants, Nonfiction (General), crafts
ISBN Prefix(es): 0-9517700; 1-899296
Number of titles published annually: 3 Print
Total Titles: 20 Print
*Parent Company:* Alphabet & Image Ltd
Imprints: Marston House
Foreign Rep(s): Helmut Ecker (Australia, Germany, Switzerland)
*Orders to:* Chris Lloyd Sales & Marketing Services, Stanley House, 1st floor, 3 Fleets Lane, Poole, Dorset BH15 3AJ, Contact: Chris Lloyd
*Tel:* (01202) 649930 *Fax:* (01202) 649950
*E-mail:* chrlloyd@globalnet.co.uk

**Martin Books**, *imprint of* Simon & Schuster Ltd

**Martin Dunitz**, *imprint of* Taylor & Francis

**Kenneth Mason Publications Ltd+**
Dudley House, 12 North St, Emsworth PO10 7DQ
*Tel:* (01243) 377977; (01243) 377978
*Fax:* (01243) 379136
*E-mail:* boatswain@dial.pipex.com
*Key Personnel*
Chairman: Kenneth Mason
Man Dir: Piers Mason
Founded: 1958
Subjects: Astrology, Occult, Child Care & Development, Cookery, Health, Nutrition, House & Home, Law, Maritime, Self-Help
ISBN Prefix(es): 0-85937; 1-873432; 0-900534
Imprints: Handbag Books; Boatswain Press
*Warehouse:* Book Barn

**Mayhew-McCrimmon Ltd**, see McCrimmon Publishing Co Ltd

**MCB University Press Ltd**, see Emerald

**McCrimmon Publishing Co Ltd+**
10-12 High St, Great Wakering, Southend-on-Sea (Essex) SS3 0EQ
*Tel:* (01702) 218956 *Fax:* (01702) 216082

*E-mail:* sales@mccrimmons.com (sales); orders@
mccrimmons.com (orders); permissions@
mccrimmons.com (permission-related
inquiries); clipart@mccrimmons.com (clip art);
accounts@mccrimmons.com-accounts
*Web Site:* www.mccrimmons.com
*Key Personnel*
Dir: Donald McCrimmon; Joan McCrimmon
*E-mail:* mccrimmon@dial.pipex.com
Founded: 1968
Membership(s): PRS, MCPS.
Subjects: Biblical Studies, Education, Music, Dance, Religion - Catholic, Religion - Other, Textbooks-Liturgy
ISBN Prefix(es): 0-85597
Number of titles published annually: 20 Print
Total Titles: 100 Print
Distributed by Liturgical Press (USA)
Distributor for Harcourt Brace; LTP Chicago (USA); Printery House (USA); St Michael's Altar Breads
*Bookshop(s):* All Saints Pastoral Centre Bookshop, London Colney, Herts
*Warehouse:* 10 Terminal Close, Shoeburyness

**Deirdre McDonald Ltd**, *imprint of* Bellew Publishing Co Ltd

**McGill-Queens University Press**, *imprint of* Combined Academic Publishers

**McGraw-Hill Education Europe, Middle East & Africa Group+**
Division of The McGraw-Hill Companies
Shoppenhangers Rd, Maidenhead, Berks SL6 2QL
*Tel:* (01628) 502500 *Fax:* (01628) 777342
*Web Site:* www.mcgraw-hill.co.uk
*Key Personnel*
Man Dir, Europe/MEA: Simon Allen
General Manager Higher Education: Shona Mullen *E-mail:* shona_mullen@mcgraw-hill.com
Director Professional Division: Derek Stordahl *E-mail:* derek_stordahl@mcgraw-hill.com
Schools Division Contact Mainland Europe, Middle East & Africa: Thanos Blintzios *E-mail:* thanos_blintzios@mcgraw-hill.com
Offices in the UK (Headquarters), Greece & Dubai with representatives also in Denmark, Germany, Norway, Netherlands, Sweden, Ireland, Poland, Turkey, Egypt, Lebanon, the United Arab Emirates & Iran.
ISBN Prefix(es): 0-07; 0-335

**McGraw-Hill Publishing Company+**
McGraw Hill House, Shoppenhangers Rd, Maidenhead, Berks SL6 2QL
*Tel:* (01) 628 502500 *Fax:* (01) 628 635895
*Web Site:* www.mcgraw-hill.co.uk
*Telex:* 848484 *Cable:* McGrawHill
*Key Personnel*
Group VP, Northern Europe/MEA: I Raimondi
Publishing Dir: A Waller
Founded: 1899
Subjects: Career Development, Computer Science, Engineering (General), Management, Mathematics, Medicine, Nursing, Dentistry, Psychology, Psychiatry, Science (General), Social Sciences, Sociology
ISBN Prefix(es): 0-07
*Parent Company:* The McGraw-Hill Companies, 1221 Avenue of the Americas, New York, NY 10020, United States
*Associate Companies:* McGraw-Hill Book Co Australia Pty Ltd, Australia; McGraw-Hill Ryerson Ltd, Canada; Editorial McGraw-Hill Latinoamericana SA, Colombia; Tata McGraw-Hill Publishing Co Ltd, India; McGraw-Hill Book Co Japan Ltd, Japan; Libros McGraw-Hill de Mexico SA de CV, Mexico; McGraw-Hill Book Co, New Zealand Ltd, New Zealand;

Editora McGraw-Hill de Portugal Lda, Portugal; Editorial McGraw-Hill Latinoamericana SA, Puerto Rico; McGraw-Hill Interamericana de Espana SA, Spain
Distributed by Amacom (UK, Europe); Berrett-Koehler (UK, Europe); Harvard Business School Press (UK, Europe)

**Meadowfield Press**, *imprint of* Merrow Publishing Co Ltd

**Media Research Publishing Ltd+**
Lister House, 117 Milton Rd, Weston Super Mare, North Somerset BS23 2UX
*Tel:* (01934) 644 309 *Fax:* (01934) 644 402
*Key Personnel*
Chairman: Cliff Dane *E-mail:* cliffd@globalnet.co.uk
Founded: 1993
Specialize in financial aspects of the music industry.
Subjects: Accounting, Business, Music, Dance
ISBN Prefix(es): 0-9521414; 0-9534171
Total Titles: 2 Print

**The Medici Society Ltd**
Grafton House, Hyde Estate Rd, London NW9 6JZ
*Tel:* (020) 8205 2500 *Fax:* (020) 8205 2552
*E-mail:* info@medici.co.uk
*Web Site:* www.medici.co.uk
*Key Personnel*
Chief Executive: Bryan Robertson
Contact: David Hardstaff
Founded: 1908
Subjects: Art, Poetry, Fine Art
ISBN Prefix(es): 0-85503
*Bookshop(s):* The Medici Galleries, 7 Grafton St, London W1X 3LA; 26 Thurloe St, London SW7 2LT

**Willem A Meeuws Publisher**
126-B Milton Park, Abingdon-upon-Thames OX14 4SA
*Tel:* (01235) 821994 *Fax:* (01235) 821994
*E-mail:* thorntons@booknews.demon.co.uk
*Web Site:* www.thorntonsbooks.co.uk
*Key Personnel*
Publisher: Willem A Meeuws
Founded: 1968
Subjects: History
ISBN Prefix(es): 0-902672
Total Titles: 70 Print
Subsidiaries: Thorntons of Oxford Ltd
Distributor for Folio Society; Slavica (USA)
*Orders to:* Thorntons of Oxford Ltd, Oxford

**Melrose Press Ltd+**
St Thomas Pl, Ely, Cambs CB7 4GG
*Tel:* (01353) 646600 *Fax:* (01353) 646601
*E-mail:* tradesales@melrosepress.co.uk; info@
melrosepress.co.uk
*Web Site:* www.melrosepress.co.uk
*Key Personnel*
Chairman: Richard Kay
Man Dir: Nicholas Law
Chief Executive: Jean Pearson
Editorial & Head of Research: Jon Gifford
Founded: 1969
Subjects: Biography
ISBN Prefix(es): 0-948875; 1-903986; 0-900332; 0-9501016
Imprints: International Biographical Centre
*Shipping Address:* Bath Rd, Harmondsworth, West Drayton, Middlesex UB7 0DA

**Mentor**, *imprint of* Christian Focus Publications Ltd

**Mercat Press+**
10 Coates Crescent, Edinburgh EH3 7AL
*Tel:* (0131) 225 5324 *Fax:* (0131) 226 6632

*E-mail:* enquiries@mercatpress.com
*Web Site:* www.mercatpress.com
*Key Personnel*
Man Dir: Sean Costello; Tom Johnstone
Founded: 1970
Membership(s): Scottish Publishers' Association.
Subjects: Cookery, Gardening, Plants, Literature, Literary Criticism, Essays, Music, Dance, Natural History, Nonfiction (General), Outdoor Recreation, Regional Interests
ISBN Prefix(es): 0-901824; 0-906664; 1-873644; 0-902347; 1-85752
Number of titles published annually: 30 Print
Total Titles: 250 Print
*Parent Company:* Mercat Press Ltd

**Merchiston Publishing**
PMPC Dept, Napier University, 10 Colinton Rd, Edinburgh EH10 5DT
*Tel:* (0131) 455 2227 *Fax:* (0131) 455 2299
*Key Personnel*
Contact: Mairi Sutherland *E-mail:* m.sutherland@napier.ac.uk
Founded: 1987
Membership(s): Scottish Publishers' Association.
Subjects: Publishing & Book Trade Reference, Regional Interests
ISBN Prefix(es): 0-9511266; 1-872800

**Mercury Books**, *imprint of* Management Books 2000 Ltd

**Meresborough Books Ltd**
17-25 Station Rd, Rainham, Kent ME8 7RS
*Tel:* (01634) 371591 *Fax:* (01634) 262114
*E-mail:* shop@rainhambookshop.co.uk
*Web Site:* www.rainhambookshop.co.uk
*Key Personnel*
Dir: Hamish Mackay-Miller; Barbara Mackay-Miller
Founded: 1977
Subjects: Regional Interests
ISBN Prefix(es): 0-905270; 0-948193
*Associate Companies:* Rainham Bookshop
Imprints: Bygone Kent

**Meridian Books**
Highfield House, 2 Highfield Ave, Newbury RG14 5DS
*Tel:* (016) 3554 3816 *Fax:* (016) 3555 1004
*E-mail:* jennie@countrysidebooks.co.uk
*Key Personnel*
Contact: Peter Groves
Founded: 1983
Subjects: Travel, Walking
ISBN Prefix(es): 1-869922
Distributed by Local Heritage Books

**The Merlin Press Ltd+**
PO Box 30705, London WC2E 8QD
*Tel:* (020) 7836 3020 *Fax:* (020) 7497 0309
*E-mail:* info@merlinpress.co.uk
*Web Site:* www.merlinpress.co.uk
*Key Personnel*
Dir & Rights: Anthony W Zurbrugg *E-mail:* tz@merlinpress.co.uk
Founded: 1956
Subjects: Economics, Government, Political Science, History, Labor, Industrial Relations, Philosophy, Social Sciences, Sociology, Labor Studies
ISBN Prefix(es): 0-85036; 1-85425
Number of titles published annually: 10 Print
Imprints: Green Print
Distributed by Central Books Ltd (United Kingdom); Independent Publishers Group (USA)

**Mermaid**, *imprint of* Michael Joseph Ltd

**Merrell Publishers Ltd+**
42 Southwark St, London SE1 1UN

*Tel:* (020) 7403 2047 *Fax:* (020) 7407 1333
*E-mail:* mail@merrellpublishers.com; sales@merrellpublishers.com
*Web Site:* www.merrellpublishers.com
*Key Personnel*
Publisher: Hugh Merrell *E-mail:* hm@merrellpublishers.com
Editorial Dir: Julian Honer *E-mail:* jh@merrellpublishers.com
Sales & Marketing Dir: Emilie Amos *E-mail:* ea@merrellpublishers.com
Design Manager: Nicola Bailey *E-mail:* nb@merrellpublishers.com
Production Manager: Michelle Draycott *E-mail:* md@merrellpublishers.com
Founded: 1993
Specialize in all aspects of the visual arts.
Also publishes several exhibition catalogues in association with galleries in Europe & North America.
Subjects: Architecture & Interior Design, Art, Crafts, Games, Hobbies, Photography, Design
ISBN Prefix(es): 1-85894
Number of titles published annually: 35 Print
Total Titles: 90 Print
*U.S. Office(s):* Merrell Publishers USA, 49 W 24 St, New York, NY 10010, United States, Contact: Joan Louise Brookbank *Tel:* 212-929-8344 *Fax:* 212-926-8346 *E-mail:* info@merrellpublishersusa.com
Foreign Rep(s): Ashton International Marketing Services (Japan); Asia Publishers Services Ltd (China, Hong Kong, Korea, Taiwan); Books for Europe (Baltic States, Scandinavia); Bookwise International (Australia, New Zealand); Client Distribution Services (US); Critiques Livres Distribution (France); Humphrys Roberts Associates (Caribbean, Central America, South America); Gabriele Kern (Austria, Germany, Switzerland); Csaba & Jackie Lengyel de Bagota (Eastern Europe); Nilsson & Lamm (Belgium, Netherlands, Luxembourg); Penny Padovani (Greece, Italy, Portugal, Spain); Quartet Books (Southern Africa); Peter Ward Book Exports (Cyprus, Israel, Malta, Middle East, Turkey)
Foreign Rights: Maya Publishers (Bangladesh, India, Nepal, Sri Lanka, Bhutan)
*Orders to:* Marston Book Services, PO Box 269, Abingdon, Oxon OX14 4YN *Tel:* (01235) 465500 *Fax:* (01235) 465555 *E-mail:* trade.order@marston.co.uk; trade.enq@marston.co.uk
Client Distribution Services, 193 Edwards Drive, Jackson, TN 38301, United States (US & Canada)
*Returns:* Marston Book Services, PO Box 269, Abingdon, Oxon OX14 4YN *Tel:* (01235) 465500 *Fax:* (01235) 465555; Client Distribution Services, 193 Edwards Drive, Jackson, TN 38301, United States (US & Canada)

**Merrion Press**
100 Hackford Rd, London SW9 0QU
*Tel:* (020) 7735 7791 *Fax:* (020) 77357 059
*Key Personnel*
Dir: Susan Shaw
Subjects: Art, Literature, Literary Criticism, Essays
ISBN Prefix(es): 0-903560

**Merrow Publishing Co Ltd**
22 Abbey Rd, Darlington, Co Durham DL3 8LR
*Tel:* (01325) 351661 *Fax:* (01325) 351661
*Key Personnel*
Man Dir & Rights: J Gordon Cook
Founded: 1951
Subjects: Mechanical Engineering, Science (General), Technology
ISBN Prefix(es): 0-900541; 0-904095
*Associate Companies:* Meadowfield Press Ltd
Imprints: Meadowfield Press

**Merseyside Port Folios**, *imprint of* Countyvise Ltd

**Meteorology**, *imprint of* Artetech Publishing Co

**Methodist Publishing House**
4 John Wesley Rd, Werrington, Peterborough PE4 6ZP
*Tel:* (01733) 325002 *Fax:* (01733) 384180
*E-mail:* sales@mph.org.uk
*Web Site:* www.mph.org.uk
*Key Personnel*
Chief Executive & Rights: Brian Thornton *E-mail:* chief.exec@mph.org.uk
Founded: 1733
Subjects: Biblical Studies, Religion - Protestant, Theology
ISBN Prefix(es): 0-7162; 0-901027; 0-946550; 1-85852
Number of titles published annually: 40 Print; 1 CD-ROM; 2 Audio
Total Titles: 200 Print; 1 CD-ROM; 10 Audio
*Parent Company:* The Methodist Church of Great Britain
Imprints: Foundery Press & Chester House Publications
Distributor for Upper Room

**Methuen**, *imprint of* Random House UK Ltd

**Methuen+**
215 Vauxhall Bridge Rd, London SW1V 1EJ
*Tel:* (020) 7798 1600 *Fax:* (020) 7828 2098; (020) 7233 9827
*Web Site:* www.methuen.co.uk
*Key Personnel*
Man Dir: Peter Tummons *E-mail:* ptummons@methuen.co.uk
Publishing Dir: Max Eilenberg *E-mail:* maxe@methuen.co.uk
Founded: 1889
Subjects: Archaeology, Biography, Drama, Theater, Fiction, History, Humor, Music, Dance, Travel, Discovery, autobiography
ISBN Prefix(es): 0-413; 0-417
Total Titles: 500 Print
Subsidiaries: Methuen Drama Ltd
*Warehouse:* TBS Distribution Centre, Colchester Rd, Frating Green, Colchester, Essex CO7 7DW *Tel:* (01206) 255678 *Fax:* (01206) 255930

**Metro Books+**
3 Bramber Court, 2 Bramber Rd, London W14 9PB
*Tel:* (020) 7381 0666 *Fax:* (020) 7381 6868
*E-mail:* words@blake.co.uk
*Web Site:* www.blake.co.uk
Founded: 1995
Subjects: Biography, Child Care & Development, Cookery, Gardening, Plants, Health, Nutrition, Nonfiction (General), Psychology, Psychiatry, Travel
ISBN Prefix(es): 1-900512
*Parent Company:* John Blake Publishing Ltd

**Metro Publishing**, *imprint of* John Blake Publishing Ltd

**MGM+**
10 Cumberland Court, Great Cumberland Pl, London W1H 7DP
*Tel:* (020) 7262 8386
*Key Personnel*
Contact: Marcus Gregory
Founded: 1996
Subjects: Poetry, Psychology, Psychiatry
ISBN Prefix(es): 0-9528799
Imprints: Our Wonderful Psychoneural Systems
*U.S. Office(s):* 4500 Seminary Rd, Alexandria, VA 22304-1533, United States, M Y Yassa

**Micelle**, *imprint of* Micelle Press

**Micelle Press+**
10-12 Ullswater Crescent, Weymouth, Dorset
    DT3 5HE
*Tel:* (01305) 781574 *Fax:* (01305) 781574
*E-mail:* tony@wdi.co.uk
*Web Site:* www.wdi.co.uk/micelle
*Key Personnel*
Proprietor: Anthony L L Hunting *E-mail:* tony@
    wdi.co.uk
Founded: 1984
A specialist publisher & bookseller of books on
    cosmetics, toiletries, perfumes, surfactants &
    other specialty materials. In addition to our
    own books, we publish on behalf of the Inter-
    national Federation of Societies of Cosmetic
    Chemists (IFSCC), & represent the Cosmetic,
    Toiletry & Fragrance Association (CTFA) in
    the EC, Quensen & Ourdas for Haarmann &
    Reimer books in the UK, & some other pub-
    lishers.
Membership(s): Independent Publishers Guild.
Subjects: Biological Sciences, Chemistry, Chem-
    ical Engineering, Health, Nutrition, Natural
    History, Physical Sciences, Science (General),
    Technology
ISBN Prefix(es): 1-870228; 0-9608752
Total Titles: 20 Print
Imprints: Micelle
Divisions: Janet Barber Translations
*U.S. Office(s):* PO Box 1519, Port Washington,
    NY 11050-0306, United States, Contact: Art
    Candido *Tel:* 516-767-7171 *Fax:* 516-944-9824
    *E-mail:* art@scholium.com
Distributed by Scholium International Inc (US
    & Canada); Springfields Aromatherapy Pty
    Ltd (Australia); Talulah Books (South Africa);
    United Books & Periodicals (India)
Distributor for CTFA Inc (US, restriction UK
    only); Quensen & Ourdas (Germany, restric-
    tion UK only); H Ziolkowsy GmbH (Germany,
    restriction not Germany)

**Michael Joseph**, *imprint of* The Penguin Group
    UK

**Michelin Tyre PLC, Tourism Dept, Maps &
    Guides Division**
Edward Hyde Bldg, 38 Clarendon Rd, Watford,
    Herts WD1 1SX
*Tel:* (01923) 415000 *Fax:* (01923) 415250
*Web Site:* www.michelin.co.uk
*Key Personnel*
Head of Tourism & Sales Manager: John Lewis
Founded: 1910
Subjects: Travel
ISBN Prefix(es): 0-206
*Parent Company:* Michelin et Cie, France
*U.S. Office(s):* Michelin Travel Publications
    - Michelin Tire Corp, One Parkway S,
    Greenville, SC 29615, United States

**Microfax**, *imprint of* Funfax Ltd

**Microform Academic Publishers**
Division of Microform Imaging Ltd
Main St, East Ardsley, Wakefield, W Yorks WF3
    2AT
*Tel:* (01924) 825700 *Fax:* (01924) 871005
*E-mail:* info@microform.co.uk
*Web Site:* www.microform.co.uk
Subjects: Americana, Regional, Government,
    Political Science, History, Literature, Literary
    Criticism, Essays, Social Sciences, Sociology
Number of titles published annually: 6 CD-ROM
Total Titles: 10 CD-ROM

**Middleton Press**
Easebourne Lane, Midhurst, West Sussex GU29
    9AZ

*Tel:* (01730) 813169 *Fax:* (01730) 812601
*Web Site:* www.middletonpress.co.uk
*Key Personnel*
President & Editor: Vic Mitchell
Founded: 1981
Produce books for the railway & tramway enthu-
    siast & modeller.
Subjects: Military Science, Regional Interests,
    Transportation, Railways, Tramways, Trolley-
    buses
ISBN Prefix(es): 0-906520; 1-873793; 1-901706;
    1-904474

**Midland Publishing+**
Imprint of Ian Allan Publishing Ltd
4 Watling Dr, Hinckley LE10 3EY
*Tel:* (01455) 233747 *Fax:* (01455) 233737
*E-mail:* midlandbooks@compuserve.com
*Web Site:* www.ianallan.com/publishing
*Key Personnel*
Publisher: N P Lewis
Founded: 1992
Subjects: Aeronautics, Aviation, Military Science,
    Transportation
ISBN Prefix(es): 1-85780
*Distribution Center:* Midland Counties Pub-
    lications, 4 Watling Dr, Hinckley, Lincs
    LE10 3EY, Sales Manager: Nigel Passmore
    *Tel:* (01455) 233747 *Fax:* (01455) 233737
    *E-mail:* midlandbooks@compuserve.com

**Miles Kelly Publishing Ltd+**
Bardfield Centre, Great Bardfield, Essex CM7
    4SL
*Tel:* (01371) 811309 *Fax:* (01371) 811393
*E-mail:* info@mileskelly.net
*Web Site:* www.mileskelly.net
ISBN Prefix(es): 1-84236; 1-902947

**The Military Balance**, *imprint of* International
    Institute for Strategic Studies

**Harvey Miller Publishers+**
Imprint of Brepols Publishers NV
Box 269, 2300 Abingdon OX14 4YN
*Tel:* (01235) 465500 *Fax:* (01235) 465555
*E-mail:* harvey.miller@brepols.net
*Key Personnel*
Dir: Harvey Miller
Editorial Dir: Elly Miller
Founded: 1969
Subjects: Art, History
ISBN Prefix(es): 0-905203; 1-872501; 0-85602
*Associate Companies:* G+B Arts International
Distributed by International Publishers Distributor
*Distribution Center:* David Brown Book Co, 28
    Main St, PO Box 511, Oakville, CT 06779,
    United States *Tel:* 860-945-9329 *Fax:* 860-945-
    9468 *E-mail:* david.brown.bk.co@snet.net (US
    & Canada)
Marston Book Services, PO Box 269, Abing-
    don, Oxon OX14 4YN *Tel:* (01235) 465500
    *Fax:* (01235) 465555 (UK)

**J Garnet Miller+**
Imprint of Cressrelles Publishing Company Ltd
Industrial Estate, 10 Station Rd, Colwall,
    Malvern, Herefordshire WR13 6RN
*Tel:* (01684) 540154 *Fax:* (01684) 540154
*Key Personnel*
Man Dir: Leslie Smith
Business Manager: Simon Smith
Founded: 1955
Subjects: Drama, Theater
ISBN Prefix(es): 0-85343
Number of titles published annually: 10 Print
Total Titles: 250 Print
*Parent Company:* Cressrelles Publishing Co Ltd
Distributed by Empire Publishing Services (Re-
    strictions, Africa & Asia)

Distributor for I E Clark Inc (UK & Europe)
Foreign Rights: Bakers Plays (US); DALRO
    (Southern Africa); Play Bureau (New Zealand);
    Warners Chappel (Australia)

**J Garnet Miller Ltd**, *imprint of* Cressrelles
    Publishing Company Ltd

**Miller**, *imprint of* Octopus Publishing Group

**Miller's Publications**
c/o Excel Logistics, Warehouse 1, Sanders Lodge
    Ind Estate, Wellingborough Rd, Rushdon NN10
    6BQ
*Tel:* (01933) 273411 *Fax:* (01933) 229330
*Key Personnel*
General Manager: Valerie Lewis
Executive Editor: Alison Starling
Subjects: Antiques, Architecture & Interior De-
    sign
ISBN Prefix(es): 0-85533; 1-85732; 1-84000; 0-
    86134; 0-905879
*Parent Company:* Octopus Publishing Group
Distributed by Antique Collectors Club (USA)

**MIND Publications+**
15-19 Broadway, London E15 4BQ
*Tel:* (020) 8519 2122 *Fax:* (020) 8522 1725;
    (020) 8534 6399 (orders)
*E-mail:* contact@mind.org.uk; publications@
    mind.org.uk (mail order)
*Web Site:* www.mind.org.uk
*Key Personnel*
Chief Executive: Richard Brook
Information Dir: Anny Brackx *Tel:* (020) 8221
    9660 *Fax:* (020) 7221 9681 *E-mail:* a.brackx@
    mind.org.uk
Founded: 1946
Specialize in mental health, psychiatry, psychol-
    ogy.
Subjects: Psychology, Psychiatry, Self-Help,
    Women's Studies
ISBN Prefix(es): 1-874690; 0-900557
Number of titles published annually: 15 Print
Total Titles: 200 Print; 200 Online; 200 E-Book

**MIT Press Ltd**
Fitzroy House, 11 Chenies St, London WC1E
    7EY
*Tel:* (020) 7306 0603 *Fax:* (020) 7306 0604
*E-mail:* info@hup-mitpress.co.uk
*Web Site:* mitpress.mit.edu
*Key Personnel*
General Manager: Ann Sexsmith
    *E-mail:* asexsmith@hup-mitpress.co.uk
Publicity Manager: Ann Twiselton
    *E-mail:* atwiselton@hup-mitpress.co.uk
Exhibits & Text Manager: Judith Bullent
    *E-mail:* jbullent@hup-mitpress.co.uk
Founded: 1932
Subjects: Architecture & Interior Design, Art,
    Behavioral Sciences, Computer Science, Earth
    Sciences, Economics, Environmental Studies,
    Finance, Language Arts, Linguistics, Philoso-
    phy, Psychology, Psychiatry, Science (General),
    Social Sciences, Sociology, Technology
ISBN Prefix(es): 0-262
Number of titles published annually: 250 Print
*Parent Company:* MIT Press
Imprints: Bradford Books; Semiotext(e); Zone
    Books
*Orders to:* Astam Books, 57-61 John St, Leich-
    hardt, NSW 2040, Australia *Tel:* (02) 9566
    4400 *Fax:* (02) 9566 4411
John Wiley & Sons Ltd, Southern Cross Trad-
    ing Estate, One Oldlands Way, Bognor Regis,
    West Sussex PO22 9SA *Tel:* (01243) 779 777
    *Fax:* (01243) 820 250 *E-mail:* cs-books@wiley.
    co.uk
c/o Triliteral, 100 Maple Ridge Drive, Cumber-
    land, RI 02864, United States *Tel:* 401-658-
    4226 *Fax:* 401-531-2801 *E-mail:* mitpress-
    orders@mit.edu

*Returns:* John Wiley & Sons Ltd, Southern Cross Trading Estate, One Oldlands Way, Bognor Regis, West Sussex PO22 9SA *Tel:* (01243) 779 777 *Fax:* (01243) 820 250 *E-mail:* cs-books@wiley.co.uk

**Mitchell Beazley**, *imprint of* Octopus Publishing Group

**Mobius**, *imprint of* Hodder & Stoughton General

**Modern Humanities Research Association**, *imprint of* Maney Publishing

**Mohr Books**, *imprint of* Crossbridge Books

**Monarch Books**, *imprint of* Lion Hudson plc

**Monarch Books+**
Imprint of Lion Hudson plc
Mayfield House, 256 Banbury Rd, Oxford, London OX2 7DH
*Tel:* (01865) 302750 *Fax:* (01865) 302757
*E-mail:* monarch@lionhudson.com
*Web Site:* www.lionhudson.com
*Key Personnel*
Editorial Dir: Tony Collins *E-mail:* tonyc@lionhudson.com
Founded: 1988
Christian publisher producing up-market paperbacks for the international market.
Subjects: Biblical Studies, Biography, Education, Fiction, Gay & Lesbian, Humor, Psychology, Psychiatry, Religion - Protestant, Self-Help, Theology
ISBN Prefix(es): 0-8254; 1-85424
Number of titles published annually: 35 Print
Total Titles: 130 Print
Distributed by Kregel Publications
*Warehouse:* Kregel Publications, PO Box 2607, Grand Rapids, MI 49501-2607, United States *Tel:* 616-451-4775 *Fax:* 616-451-9330 *E-mail:* kregelbooks@kregel.com *Web Site:* www.kregelpublications.com
*Orders to:* Marston Book Services Ltd, PO Box 269, Abingdon, Oxon OX14 4YN *Tel:* (01235) 465606 *Fax:* (01235) 465509 *E-mail:* salesuk@lionhudson.com
Kregel Publications, PO Box 2607, Grand Rapids, MI 49501-2607, United States *Tel:* 616-451-4774 *Fax:* 616-451-9330 *E-mail:* kregelbooks@kregel.com *Web Site:* www.kregelpublications.com

**Monument**, *imprint of* Witherby & Co Ltd

**Moonlight First Encyclopedia**, *imprint of* Moonlight Publishing Ltd

**Moonlight Publishing Ltd**
36 Stratford Rd, London W8 6QA
*Tel:* (020) 7376 0299 *Fax:* (020) 7937 8921
*Key Personnel*
Dir: Christine Baker; P Stanley Baker; Robin Baker
Founded: 1980
Subjects: Nonfiction (General)
ISBN Prefix(es): 1-85103; 0-907144
Imprints: Discovers; First Discovery; First Discovery-Art; Moonlight First Encyclopedia; Pocket Bears; Pocket Worlds; Tales of Heaven & Earth
*Orders to:* Ragged Bears Ltd, Ragged Appleshaw, Andover, Hants SP11 3HX *Tel:* (01264) 772269

**Moorley's Print & Publishing Ltd+**
23 Park Rd, Ilkeston, Derbys DE7 5DA
*Tel:* (0115) 9320643 *Fax:* (0115) 9320643

*E-mail:* info@moorleys.co.uk
*Web Site:* www.moorleys.co.uk
*Key Personnel*
Chairman & Man Dir: John R Moorley
*E-mail:* john@moorleys.co.uk
Founded: 1966
Subjects: Biblical Studies, Drama, Theater, Music, Dance, Poetry, Religion - Protestant, Theology
ISBN Prefix(es): 0-901495; 0-86071
Number of titles published annually: 12 Print
Total Titles: 320 Print
*Associate Companies:* Truedata Computer Services
Imprints: Freedom Ministries; Headline Specials
Distributor for Cliff College Publishing; Nimbus Press; Pustaka Sufes Sdn Bhd; Social Workers Christian Fellowship; T Young

**Morehouse**, *imprint of* The Continuum International Publishing Group Ltd

**Morgan Kauffman**, *imprint of* Elsevier Ltd

**Morgan Publishing**, *imprint of* Welsh Academic Press

**William Morrow**, *imprint of* HarperCollins UK

**E J Morten (Publishers)+**
6 Warburton St, Didsbury, Manchester M20 6WA
*Tel:* (0161) 445 7629 *Fax:* (0161) 445 7629
*E-mail:* timlovat@aol.com
*Key Personnel*
Man Dir, Rights & Permissions: John Anthony Morten
Founded: 1969
Facsimile reprints undertaken.
Subjects: History, Regional Interests
ISBN Prefix(es): 0-85972; 0-901598
*Parent Company:* E J Morten (Booksellers), Didsbury, Manchester
Imprints: Datapack Books; Pride Publications
Divisions: Morten Hire

**Mosby**, *imprint of* Elsevier Ltd

**Motilal (UK) Books of India**
PO Box 324, Borehamwood, Herts WD6 1NB
*Tel:* (020) 8905 1244 *Fax:* (020) 8905 1108
*E-mail:* info@mlbduk.com
*Web Site:* www.mlbduk.com
*Key Personnel*
Man Dir: Ray McLennan
Founded: 1980
Comprehensive coverage of Indology subjects. Imports from all Indian publishers against special orders. Also acts as UK agent for Motilal Banarsidass, Sundeep Prakashan, Concept Publications, Kant Publications & South Asia Books (India).
Subjects: Archaeology, Architecture & Interior Design, Art, Asian Studies, Education, History, Language Arts, Linguistics, Literature, Literary Criticism, Essays, Philosophy, Religion - Buddhist, Religion - Hindu, Religion - Islamic, Romance, Social Sciences, Sociology, Women's Studies, Specializes in Indology, Hinduism, Buddhism, Jainism, Translations of Sanskrit & Pali texts
ISBN Prefix(es): 81-208; 0-946482
Total Titles: 8,000 Print
*Ultimate Parent Company:* Money Savers (London) Ltd

**Motor Racing Publications Ltd+**
PO Box 1318, Croydon CR9 5YP
*Tel:* (020) 8654 2711 *Fax:* (020) 8407 0339
*E-mail:* mrp.books@virgin.net
*Web Site:* www.motorracingpublications.co.uk

*Key Personnel*
Man Dir, Publicity, Rights & Permissions: John Blunsden
Editorial & Customer Services: John Blunsden
Sales & Production: John Blunsden
Founded: 1948 (restructured & re-established 1968)
Specialize in books on motorsports & passenger cars.
Subjects: Automotive, Technology, Transportation
ISBN Prefix(es): 0-900549; 0-947981; 0-948358; 1-899870
Number of titles published annually: 5 Print
Total Titles: 75 Print
Imprints: The Fitzjames Press
Distributed by MBI Publishing (USA & Canada); Vine House Distribution Ltd (UK & overseas)
Foreign Rep(s): Dr Laszlo Horvath (Croatia, Czech Republic, Greece, Hungary, Slovak Republic, Slovenia); Juliusz Komarnicki (France, Switzerland); Pernille Larsen (Denmark, Finland, Norway, Scandinavia, Sweden); Robbert Pleysier (Austria, Benelux, Germany); Joe Portelli (Gibraltar, Italy, Malta, Portugal, Spain)
*Orders to:* Vine House Distribution Ltd (trade orders)

**Mowbray**, *imprint of* Cassell & Co

**Mowbray**, *imprint of* The Continuum International Publishing Group Ltd

**MQ Publications Ltd**
12 The Ivories, 6-8 Northampton St, London N1 2HY
*Tel:* (020) 7359 2244 *Fax:* (020) 7359 1616
*E-mail:* mail@mqpublications.com
*Web Site:* gustocreative.dsvr.co.uk/mqp-site/home.html
*Key Personnel*
Man Dir: Susan Jenkins; Gerson Kesner
Specialize in gift books.
Subjects: Cookery, Crafts, Games, Hobbies, Health, Nutrition, History, Cultural Reference, Mind, Body & Spirit, Sex
ISBN Prefix(es): 1-84072; 1-897954
*Warehouse:* Biblios, Star Rd, Patridge Green, West Sussex

**MRP**, see Motor Racing Publications Ltd

**Multilingual Matters Ltd+**
Frankfurt Lodge, Clevedon Hall, Victoria Rd, Clevedon BS21 7HH
*Tel:* (01275) 876519 *Fax:* (01275) 871673
*E-mail:* info@multilingual-matters.com
*Web Site:* www.multilingual-matters.com
*Key Personnel*
Man Dir: Mike Grover *E-mail:* mike@multilingual-matters.com
Editorial Manager: Marjukka Grover
*E-mail:* marjukka@multilingual-matters.com
Production Manager: Ken Hall *E-mail:* ken@multilingual-matters.com
Marketing Manager: Kathryn King
*E-mail:* kathryn@multilingual-matters.com
Dir, Sales & Distribution: Tommi Grover
*E-mail:* tommi@multilingual-matters.com
Founded: 1982
Specialize in bilingualism & bilingual education, second & foreign language learning & translation studies, also tourism research.
Membership(s): IPG
Subjects: Education, Environmental Studies, Geography, Geology, Language Arts, Linguistics, Social Sciences, Sociology, Travel, Tourism Research
ISBN Prefix(es): 0-905028; 1-85359; 1-873150; 1-84541
Number of titles published annually: 35 Print
Total Titles: 440 Print
Imprints: Channel View Publications

*Branch Office(s)*
Channel View Publications, 5201 Dufferin
St, North York, ON M3H 5T8, Canada
*Tel:* 416-667-7791 *Fax:* 416-667-7832
*E-mail:* utpbooks@utpress.utoronto.ca (Ameri-
can Distributors)
UTP, 5201 Dufferin St, North York, ON M3H
5T8, Canada *Tel:* 416-667-7791 *Fax:* 416-667-
7832 *E-mail:* utpbooks@utpress.utoronto.ca
*Orders to:* Marston Book Services, PO Box 269,
Abingdon, Oxon OX14 4YN *Tel:* (01235)
465500 *Fax:* (01235) 465555 *E-mail:* direct.
order@marston.co.uk

**James Munro & Co**
4-10 Darnley St, Glasgow G41 2SD
*Tel:* (0141) 429 1234 *Fax:* (0141) 420 1694
*E-mail:* enquiry@skipper.co.uk; sales@skipper.co.
uk (orders)
*Web Site:* www.skipper.co.uk
*Key Personnel*
Sales Dir: L Ingram-Brown
Founded: 1832
Subjects: Maritime
ISBN Prefix(es): 0-85174
*Parent Company:* Brown, Son & Ferguson, Ltd

**Murchison's Pantheon Ltd+**
Murray House, 45 Beech St, London EC2Y 8AD
*Tel:* (020) 7374 2828 *Fax:* (020) 7628 6270
*E-mail:* 100450.1105@compuserve.com
*Key Personnel*
Contact: Charles Blount *E-mail:* charlesblount@
compuserve.com
Specialize in audio travel guides.
Subjects: History, Travel
ISBN Prefix(es): 1-900652

**Murdoch Books UK Ltd**
Erico House, 93-99 Upper Richmond Rd, 6th
floor, Putney, London SW15 2TG
*Tel:* (020) 8785 5995 *Fax:* (020) 8785 5985

**John Murray (Publishers) Ltd+**
338 Euston Rd, London NW1 3BH
*Tel:* (020) 7873 6000 *Fax:* (020) 7873 6446
*E-mail:* enquiries@johnmurrays.co.uk
*Web Site:* www.madaboutbooks.co.uk
*Key Personnel*
Man Dir: Roland Philipps
Head of Rights: Jane Blackstock
Publishing Dir: Gordon Wise
Publicity Dir: Sam Evans
Sales & Marketing: Matt Richell
Founded: 1768
Subjects: Fiction, Nonfiction (General)
ISBN Prefix(es): 0-7195
*Parent Company:* Hodder Headline Ltd
*Ultimate Parent Company:* WHSmith PLC
*Orders to:* Bookpoint Ltd, 130 Milton Park,
Abingdon, Oxon OX14 4TD *Tel:* (01235)
835001 *Fax:* (01235) 832068

**Music Sales Ltd**, see Omnibus Press

**Muslim Welfare House London Publishers**, see
MWH London Publishers

**Muze UK Ltd+**
10 Baker's Yard, Baker's Row, London EC1R
3DD
*Tel:* (0870) 7277 256 *Fax:* (0870) 7277 257
*E-mail:* colin@muze.co.uk
*Web Site:* www.muze.com
*Key Personnel*
President: Colin Larkin
Research Editor: Nic Oliver
Administration: Susan Pipe
Founded: 1990
Subjects: Biography, Music, Dance

ISBN Prefix(es): 1-872747
*Parent Company:* Muze Inc, 304 Hudson St, 8th
floor, New York, NY 10013, United States

**MWH London Publishers+**
233 Seven Sisters Rd, London N4 2DA
*Tel:* (020) 7263 3071 *Fax:* (020) 7281 12687
*E-mail:* info@mwht.org.uk
*Web Site:* www.mwht.org.uk
*Telex:* 8812176
*Key Personnel*
Man Dir: Mohamed Tamin
Founded: 1970
Subjects: Regional Interests
ISBN Prefix(es): 0-906194
*Associate Companies:* Muslim Information Centre
*Orders to:* MIC, London

**NAG Press**, *imprint of* Robert Hale Ltd

**NAG Press+**
Imprint of Robert Hale Ltd
Clerkenwell House, 45-47 Clerkenwell Green,
London EC1R 0HT
*Tel:* (020) 7251 2661 *Fax:* (020) 7490 4958
*E-mail:* enquire@halebooks.com
*Web Site:* www.halebooks.com/n_a_g_press_files.
html
*Key Personnel*
Dir: Martin Kendall
Founded: 1937
Subjects: Horological & Gemmological
ISBN Prefix(es): 0-7198
Total Titles: 100 Print
*Warehouse:* CBS, Units 1/K, Paddockwood
Distribution Centre, Paddock Wood, Kent
TN12 6UU, Contact: Alan Smith *Tel:* (01892)
837171 *Fax:* (01892) 837212 *E-mail:* orders@
combook.co.uk

**NATE**, see National Association for the Teaching
of English (NATE)

**National Archives of Scotland**
H M General Register House, 2 Princes St, Edin-
burgh EH1 3YY
*Tel:* (0131) 535 1334 *Fax:* (0131) 535 1328
*E-mail:* publications@nas.gov.uk; enquiries@nas.
gov.uk
*Web Site:* www.nas.gov.uk
*Key Personnel*
Head of Publications & Education Branch: Rose-
mary Gibson
Publications Officer: Alison Lindsay *Tel:* (0131)
535 1353
Founded: 1787
General historical & educational publications de-
signed to make the holdings of the NAS more
accessible.
Membership(s): Scottish Publishers Association.
Subjects: History
ISBN Prefix(es): 1-870874
Number of titles published annually: 3 Print
Total Titles: 42 Print
*Branch Office(s)*
West Search Room, West Register House, Char-
lotte Square, Edinburgh EH2 4DJ *Tel:* (0131)
535 1413 *Fax:* (0131) 535 1411 *E-mail:* wsr@
nas.gov.uk

**National Assembly for Wales**, *imprint of*
National Assembly for Wales

**National Assembly for Wales**
Cardiff Bay, Cardiff CF99 1NA
*Tel:* (029) 20 825111 *Fax:* (029) 20 825350
*E-mail:* stats.pubs@wales.gsi.gov.uk
*Web Site:* www.wales.gov.uk
*Key Personnel*
Man Dir & General Editor: E Swires-Hennessy

*Tel:* (029) 2082 5087 *Fax:* (029) 2082 5087
*E-mail:* ed.swires-hennessy@wales.gsi.gov.uk
Founded: 1981
Specialize in statistics on Wales.
Subjects: Business, Economics, Education, Gov-
ernment, Political Science, Health, Nutrition,
Public Administration, Social Sciences, Sociol-
ogy
ISBN Prefix(es): 0-7504; 0-86348; 0-903702; 0-
904251
Total Titles: 35 Print
Imprints: Cynulliad Cenedlaethol Cymru; Na-
tional Assembly for Wales

**National Association for Mental Health**, see
MIND Publications

**National Association for the Teaching of
English (NATE)+**
Broadfield Business Centre, 50 Broadfield Rd,
Sheffield S8 OXJ
*Tel:* (0114) 255 5419 *Fax:* (0114) 255 5296
*E-mail:* info@nate.org.uk
*Web Site:* www.nate.org.uk
*Key Personnel*
Development & Communications Dir: Trevor Mil-
lum
Founded: 1963
Specialize in English teaching.
Membership(s): Publishers' Association.
Subjects: Drama, Theater, Education, English as
a Second Language, Film, Video, Literature,
Literary Criticism, Essays, Poetry, Literacy, In-
formation & communication technology
ISBN Prefix(es): 0-901291
Number of titles published annually: 10 Print
Total Titles: 50 Print
Distributed by Australian Reading Association
Distributor for BELTA; Paul Chapman Publish-
ing; Devon County Council; Drake Publishing;
English & Media Centre; Falmer Press; Frame-
work Press/Fultons; David Fulton; Garth Pub-
lishing; Nelsons; Open University Press; PCET
Wallcharts; Thimble Press; Ward Lock

**National Centre for Language & Literacy+**
University of Reading, Bulmershe Court, Reading
RG6 1HY
*Tel:* (0118) 378 8820 *Fax:* (0118) 378 6801
*E-mail:* ncll@reading.ac.uk
*Web Site:* www.ncll.org.uk
*Key Personnel*
Dir: Prof Viv Edwards *E-mail:* v.k.edwards@
reading.ac.uk
Centre Administrator: Pam Brown
Publications: Judy Tallet
Founded: 1969
Specialize in language & literacy learning.
Subjects: Education, English as a Second Lan-
guage, Language Arts, Linguistics
ISBN Prefix(es): 0-7049

**National Childbirth Trust Publishing**
25-27 High St, Chesterton, Cambridge CB4 1ND
*Tel:* (01223) 352790 *Fax:* (01223) 460718
*E-mail:* bpc@bpccam.co.uk
*Web Site:* www.bpccam.co.uk

**National Computing Centre**, see Blackwell
Publishing Ltd

**National Council for Voluntary Organisations
(NCVO)+**
Regent's Wharf, 8 All Saints St, London N1 9RL
*Tel:* (020) 7713 6161 *Fax:* (020) 7713 6300
*E-mail:* ncvo@ncvo-vol.org.uk
*Web Site:* www.ncvo-vol.org.uk
*Key Personnel*
Chief Executive: Stuart Etherington
Head of Marketing & Publications: Jim Minton
Marketing Officer: Lou Large

Online Development Manager: Simon Cope
*Tel:* (020) 7520 2544 *E-mail:* simon.cope@
ncvo-vol.org.uk
Founded: 1919 (NCVO), 1969 (BSP), 1991
(NCVO Publications)
Also publish in association with other organiza-
tions.
Membership(s): IPG; Publishers' Association.
Subjects: Disability, Special Needs, Finance,
Management, Public Administration
ISBN Prefix(es): 0-7199
*Orders to:* Hamilton House Mailings, 17 Staveley
Way, Northampton NN6 7TX

**National Extension College+**
Michael Young Centre, Purbeck Rd, Cambridge
CB2 2HN
*Tel:* (01223) 400 200 *Fax:* (01223) 400 399
*E-mail:* info@nec.ac.uk
*Web Site:* www.nec.ac.uk
*Key Personnel*
Executive Dir: Ros Morpeth
Assistant Dir: Roger Merritt
Founded: 1963
Membership(s): ICDE, NIACE & BAOL.
Subjects: Accounting, Business, Career Devel-
opment, Education, English as a Second Lan-
guage, Environmental Studies, Self-Help
ISBN Prefix(es): 0-86082; 1-85356; 0-902404; 1-
84308
Imprints: NEC

**National Foster Care Association**, see Fostering
Network

**National Foundation for Educational Research**
The Mere Upton Park, Slough SL1 2DQ
*Tel:* (01753) 574123 *Fax:* (01753) 691632
*E-mail:* enquiries@nfer.ac.uk
*Web Site:* www.nfer.ac.uk
*Key Personnel*
Head of Publication: Dr Enver Carim
Founded: 1946
Subjects: Education
ISBN Prefix(es): 0-7005; 0-7087; 0-85633; 0-
901225
*Branch Office(s)*
Slough Rd, Datchet, Berks SL3 9AU *Tel:* (01753)
574123 *Fax:* (01753) 691632 (Please do not
send post to this address)
Genesis 4, York Science Park, University Rd,
Heslington, York YO10 5DG *Tel:* (01904)
433435 *Fax:* (01904) 433436 *E-mail:* j.
harland@nfer.ac.uk
Chestnut House, Tawe Business Village, Phoenix
Way, Enterprise Park, Swansea SA7 9LA
*Tel:* (01792) 459800 *Fax:* (01792) 797815
*E-mail:* scya@nfer.ac.uk

**National Galleries of Scotland+**
Publishing & Picture Library, The Dean Gallery,
73 Belford Rd, Edinburgh EH4 3DS
*Tel:* (0131) 624 6257; (0131) 624 6261
*Fax:* (0131) 315 2963
*E-mail:* publications@nationalgalleries.org
*Web Site:* www.nationalgalleries.org
*Key Personnel*
Head of Publishing & Picture Library: Janis
Adams *E-mail:* jadams@nationalgalleries.org
Subjects: Art, Photography
ISBN Prefix(es): 0-903598; 1-903278; 0-903148
Total Titles: 90 Print; 1 CD-ROM

**National Institute of Adult Continuing
Education (NIACE)+**
Renaissance House, 20 Princess Rd W, Leicester
LE1 6TP
*Tel:* (0116) 204 4200; (0116) 204 4201
*Fax:* (0116) 285-4514
*E-mail:* enquiries@niace.org.uk; niace@niace.org.
uk

*Web Site:* www.niace.org.uk
*Key Personnel*
Dir: Alan Tuckett *E-mail:* alan.tuckett@niace.org.
uk
Dir, Research, Development & Information: Peter
Lavender *E-mail:* peter.lavender@niace.org.uk
Dir, Programmes & Policy: Sue Cara
Dir, Finance: Margaret Conner *E-mail:* margaret.
conner@niace.org.uk
Founded: 1921
NIACE, the national organization for adult learn-
ing, has a broad remit to promote life long
learning opportunities for adults. NIACE works
to develop increased participation in education
& training. It aims to do this for more who do
not have easy access due to class, gender, age,
race, language & culture, learning difficulties,
disabilities or insufficient financial resources.
Subjects: Education
ISBN Prefix(es): 1-872941; 1-86201; 0-900559
Number of titles published annually: 40 Print
Total Titles: 100 Print
*Branch Office(s)*
NIACE Dysgu Cymru, 35 Cathedral Rd,
Ground Floor, Cardiff, Wales CF11 9HB
*Tel:* (0292) 0370900 *Fax:* (0292) 0370909
*E-mail:* enquiries@niacecy.demon.co.uk *Web
Site:* www.niacedc.org.uk

**National Library of Scotland**
George IV Bridge, Edinburgh EH1 1EW
*Tel:* (0131) 226 4531 *Fax:* (0131) 622 4803
*E-mail:* enquiries@nls.uk
*Web Site:* www.nls.uk
*Key Personnel*
Librarian: Martyn Wade
Dir, Public Services: Dr Alan Marchbank
*E-mail:* a.marchbank@nls.uk
Head of Public Programs: Dr Kenneth Gibson
*E-mail:* k.gibson@nls.uk
Subjects: History, Regional Interests
ISBN Prefix(es): 0-902220; 1-872116

**National Library of Wales**
Aberystwyth, Ceredigion SY23 3BU
*Tel:* (01970) 632 800 *Fax:* (01970) 615 709
*E-mail:* holi@llgc.org.uk
*Web Site:* www.llgc.org.uk
*Key Personnel*
President: R Brinley Jones
Vice President: John Phillips
Treasurer: Conrad L Bryant
Editor: Gwyn Jenkins
Librarian: Andrew M W Green
Founded: 1907
Copyright/Legal Deposit Library.
Subjects: Art, Genealogy, Government, Political
Science, Library & Information Sciences, Liter-
ature, Literary Criticism, Essays, Photography,
Publishing & Book Trade Reference
ISBN Prefix(es): 0-907158

**National Museum & Gallery**
Cathays Park, Cardiff CF10 3NP
*Tel:* (029) 2039 7951 *Fax:* (029) 2057 3321
*E-mail:* post@nmgw.ac.uk
*Web Site:* www.nmgw.ac.uk
*Key Personnel*
Contact: John Williams-Davies

**National Museums of Scotland Publishing**, see
NMS Enterprises Ltd - Publishing

**National Portrait Gallery Publications+**
St Martin's Pl, London WC2H 0HE
*Tel:* (020) 7306 0055 (ext 266); (020) 7312 2482
*Fax:* (020) 7306 0092
*Web Site:* www.npg.org.uk
*Key Personnel*
Head of Trading: Robert Carr-Archer
*E-mail:* rcarrarcher@npg.org.uk

Publishing Manager: Celia Joicey
Production Manager: Ruth Muller-Wirth
*E-mail:* rmullerwirth@npg.org.uk
Senior Editor: Anjali Bulley *E-mail:* abulley@
npg.org.uk
Sales & Marketing Officer: Pallavi Vadhia
*E-mail:* pvadhia@npg.org.uk
Founded: 1976 (book publishing division)
Also acts as picture library.
Subjects: Art, Biography, History, Photography
ISBN Prefix(es): 0-904017; 1-85514
Number of titles published annually: 14 Print
Total Titles: 45 Print
*U.S. Office(s):* Antique Collector's Club, Mar-
ket St, Industrial Park, Wappingers Falls, New
York, NY 12590, United States *Fax:* 845-297-
0068
*Warehouse:* Grantham Book Services, Isaac
Newton Way, Alva Park Industrial Estate,
Grantham, Lincs N931 9SD *Tel:* (01476) 541
080 *Fax:* (01476) 541 061

**The National Society**, *imprint of* Church House
Publishing

**National Trust+**
36 Queen Anne's Gate, London SW1H 9AS
*Tel:* (0870) 609 5380 *Fax:* (020) 7222 5097
*Web Site:* www.nationaltrust.org.uk
*Key Personnel*
Publisher: Margaret Willes
Founded: 1987
Subjects: Art, Cookery, Gardening, Plants, His-
tory, Photography, Social Sciences, Sociology,
Travel
ISBN Prefix(es): 0-7078
Number of titles published annually: 12 Print
Total Titles: 75 Print
*Parent Company:* National Trust Enterprises, The
Stable Block, Heywood House, Westbury, Wilts
BA13 4NA
*Branch Office(s)*
Rowallane House, Saintfield, Ballynahinch, Co
Down, Northern Ireland BT24 7LH *Tel:* (028)
9751 0721 *Fax:* (028) 9751 1242
Wemyss House, 28 Charlotte Sq, Edinburgh EH2
4ET *Tel:* (0131) 243 9300 *Web Site:* www.nts.
org.uk/
Hughenden Manor, High Wycombe, Bucks HP14
4LA *Tel:* (01494) 528051 *Fax:* (01494) 463310
*Web Site:* www.nationaltrust.org.uk/regions/
thameschilterns/ (regional office for Thames &
Solent)
The Hollens, Grasmere, Ambleside, Cumbria
LA22 9QZ *Tel:* (0870) 609 5391 *Fax:* (015394)
35353 (regional office for the North West)
Killerton House, Broadclyst, Exeter EX5 3LE
*Tel:* (01392) 881691 *Fax:* (01392) 881954 (re-
gional office for Devon & Cornwall)
Blickling, Norwich NR11 6NF *Tel:* (0870) 609
5388 *Fax:* (01263) 734924 *Web Site:* www.
nationaltrust.org.uk/regions/eastanglia/ (regional
office for East Anglia)
Clumber Park Stableyard, Worksop, Notts S80
3BE *Tel:* (01909) 486411 *Fax:* (01909) 486377
(regional office for the East Midlands)
Attingham Park, Shrewsbury, Salop SY4 4TP
*Tel:* (01743) 708100 *Fax:* (01743) 708150
*E-mail:* sevinfo@stmp.ntrust.org.uk *Web
Site:* www.nationaltrust.org.uk/regions/
westmidlands/ (regional office for the West
Midlands)
Polesden Lacey, Dorking, Surrey RH5 6BO
*Tel:* (01372) 453401 *Fax:* (01372) 452023 (re-
gional office for the South East)
Eastleigh Court, Bishopstrow, Warminster, Wilts
BA12 9HW *Tel:* (01985) 843600 *Fax:* (01985)
843624 *Web Site:* www.nationaltrust.org.
uk/regions/wessex/ (regional office for Wessex)
Goddards, 27 Tadcaster Rd, Dringhouses, York
Y024 1GG *Tel:* (01904) 702021 *Fax:* (01904)
771970 (regional office for Yorkshire & North
East)

Trinity Sq, Llandudno, Wales LL30 2DE
*Tel:* (01492) 860123 *Fax:* (01492) 860233
*U.S. Office(s):* Trafalgar Square Publishing, Howe
Hill Rd, North Pomfret, VT 05053, United
States
*Warehouse:* MacMillian Distribution Ltd, Hound-
mills, Basingstoke R921 GXS, Mrs Beverly
Morris *Tel:* (01256) 329242 *Fax:* (01256)
812558
*Orders to:* MacMillian Distribution Ltd, Hound-
mills, Basingstoke R921 GXS, Hazel Maynard


**National Youth Agency**
17-23 Albion St, Leicester LE1 6GD
*Tel:* (0116) 285 3700 *Fax:* (0116) 285 3777
*E-mail:* nya@nya.org.uk
*Web Site:* www.nya.co.uk
ISBN Prefix(es): 0-86155
Number of titles published annually: 12 Print
Total Titles: 75 Print


**NCVO**, see National Council for Voluntary
Organisations (NCVO)


**NEC**, *imprint of* National Extension College


**Negotiate Ltd+**
99 Caiyside, Edinburgh EH10 7HR
*Tel:* (0131) 445 7571; (0131) 477 7858
  *Fax:* (0131) 445 7572
*E-mail:* florence@negweb.com
*Web Site:* www.negotiate.co.uk
*Key Personnel*
Man Dir: Gavin Kennedy *E-mail:* gavin@negweb.
  com
Founded: 1986
Subsidiaries: Negotiate P S C


**Neil Wilson Publishing Ltd+**
Pentagon Centre, Suite 303, 36 Washington St,
  Glasgow G3 8AZ
*Tel:* (0141) 221 1117 *Fax:* (0141) 221 5363
*E-mail:* info@nwp.co.uk
*Web Site:* www.nwp.co.uk
*Key Personnel*
Man Dir: Neil Wilson *E-mail:* neil@nwp.sol.co.
  uk
Production Editor: Sallie Moffat *E-mail:* sallie@
  nwp.co.uk
Founded: 1992
Membership(s): Scottish Publishers Association.
Subjects: Biography, Cookery, Fiction, History,
  Humor, Music, Dance, Outdoor Recreation,
  Regional Interests, Sports, Athletics, Wine &
  Spirits
ISBN Prefix(es): 1-897784; 1-903238
Number of titles published annually: 15 Print
Total Titles: 100 Print
Imprints: Angels' Share; 11:9; The In Pinn; The
  Vital Spark
Distributed by Interlink Books (USA)
Foreign Rep(s): Interlink Publishing (US); Murray
  Sutton (Scandinavia)
*Warehouse:* Book Source, 32 Finlas St, Cowlairs
  Estate, Glasgow G22 5DU *Tel:* (0870) 240
  2182 *Fax:* (0141) 557 0189 *E-mail:* orders@
  booksource.net *Web Site:* www.booksource.net
*Orders to:* Book Source, 32 Finlas St, Cowlairs
  Estate, Glasgow G22 5DU *Tel:* (0870) 240
  2182 *Fax:* (0141) 557 0189 *E-mail:* orders@
  booksource.net *Web Site:* www.booksource.net


**Nelson Thornes Ltd+**
Delta Pl, 27 Bath Rd, Cheltenham GL53 7TH
*Tel:* (01242) 267100; (01242) 267311
  *Fax:* (01242) 267311
*E-mail:* export@nelsonthornes.com
*Web Site:* www.nelsonthornes.com
*Key Personnel*
Man Dir & General Management: Fred Grainger
Founded: 1972

Subjects: Business, Child Care & Development,
  Education, Environmental Studies, Geography,
  Geology, History, Language Arts, Linguistics,
  Mathematics, Medicine, Nursing, Dentistry,
  Music, Dance, Physics, Religion - Other, Sci-
  ence (General), Social Sciences, Sociology,
  Technology
ISBN Prefix(es): 0-7487; 0-85950; 1-871402
*Parent Company:* Wolters Kluwer PLC
*Ultimate Parent Company:* Wolters Kluwer NV,
  Netherlands
*Associate Companies:* Moorhouse Black; Croner;
  Maps
Imprints: Mary Glasgow Publications
*Warehouse:* Alexandra Industrial Estate, Alexan-
  dra Way, Ashchurch, Tewkesbuy GL20 8PE


**Net.Works**, *imprint of* Take That Ltd


**Network Books**, *imprint of* BBC Worldwide
Publishers


**Neville Spearman Publishers**, *imprint of* The C
W Daniel Co Ltd


**New Cavendish Books+**
3 Denbigh Rd, London W11 2SJ
*Tel:* (020) 7229 6765 *Fax:* (020) 7792 0027
*E-mail:* sales@cavbooks.demon.co.uk
*Web Site:* www.newcavendishbooks.co.uk
*Key Personnel*
Dir: Narisa Chakra *E-mail:* narisa@new-cav.
  demon.co.uk
Founded: 1973
Subjects: Nonfiction (General), Technology, Toys,
  collecting & popular culture
ISBN Prefix(es): 0-904568; 1-872727; 1-904562
Number of titles published annually: 4 Print
Total Titles: 70 Print
Imprints: White Mouse Editions
Distributed by Antique Collectors Club (UK
  & Europe); Antique Collectors Club (USA)
  (USA); Critiques Livres (France); Peribo Pty
  Ltd (Australia)


**New Era Publications UK Ltd+**
Saint Hill Manor, East Grinstead, Sussex RH19
  4JY
*Tel:* (01342) 314 846 *Fax:* (01342) 314 857
*E-mail:* nepuk@newerapublications.com
*Web Site:* www.newerapublications.com
*Key Personnel*
Man Dir: Margaret Blunden
Sales Dir: Nic Webb *E-mail:* nic@nrgw.demon.
  co.uk
Founded: 1985
Subjects: Business, Education, Fiction, Health,
  Nutrition, Management, Nonfiction (General),
  Philosophy, Religion - Other, Science Fiction,
  Fantasy, Self-Help, Western Fiction
ISBN Prefix(es): 1-870451; 1-900944; 1-903820
Total Titles: 90 Print; 1 CD-ROM; 18 Audio
*Parent Company:* New Era Publications Interna-
  tional ApS, Store Kongensgade 53, 1264 Den-
  mark K, Denmark
*Associate Companies:* Author Services Inc, 7051
  Hollywood Blvd, Suite 400, Los Angeles,
  CA 90028, United States *Tel:* 213-466-3310
  *E-mail:* asi@earthlink.net
*Branch Office(s)*
New Era Publications Australia Pty Ltd, 16
  Doraby St, Dundas, NSW 2177, Australia
  *Tel:* (029) 638 30 88 *Fax:* (029) 898 15 88
  *E-mail:* cploanzo@tpg.com.au
New Era Publications Deutschland GmbH, Hitt-
  felder Kirchweg 5, 21220 Seevetal-Maschen,
  Germany *Tel:* (041) 05 683 30 *Fax:* (049) 41
  05 683 3 22 *E-mail:* neweragermany@t-online.
  de
New Era Central Europe, Lenardo Da Vinci u
  8-12, Budapest 1084, Hungary *Tel:* (01) 210

46 13 *Fax:* (01) 210 46 13 *E-mail:* newera@
  menthanet.hu
N E Publications India Pvt Ltd, 96 Gautam Nagar, New Delhi 110049, India *Tel:* (011) 26 60
  15 48 *E-mail:* tgoeldenitz@gmx.net
New Era Publications Italia, Via Cadorna, 61,
  20090 Vimodrone (MI), Italy *Tel:* (02) 274
  09272 *Fax:* (02) 274 09198 *E-mail:* sales@
  newera.it
New Era Publications Japan Inc, Sakei SS Bldg
  2F, 4-38-15, Higashi Ikebukuro, Toshima-
  Ku, Tokyo 170-0013, Japan *Tel:* (03) 5960
  5660 *Fax:* (03) 5960 5561 *E-mail:* nepjp@
  newerapublications.com
New Era Publications Group, Pr Mira, VVC
  Bldg 265, 129223 Moscow, Russian Federation
  *Tel:* (095) 746 64 97 *E-mail:* info@new-era.ru
Continental Publications Pty Ltd, PO Box 27080,
  Benerose, Johannesburg 2011, South Africa
  *Tel:* (011) 331 66 21 *Fax:* (011) 331 66 21
  *E-mail:* nepaf@newerapublications.com
Source Publications Co., 2nd floor 65, Section 4,
  Min-Shen East Rd, Taipei, Taiwan, Province of
  China *Tel:* (062) 25 46 58 51 *Fax:* (062) 25 45
  70 33 *E-mail:* nep.twn@msa.hinet.net
*U.S. Office(s):* Bridge Publications, A751 Foun-
  tain Ave, Los Angeles, CA, United States
*Warehouse:* Bailey Distribution, Learoyd Rd, New
  Romney, Kent TN28 8XU


**New European Publications Ltd+**
14-16 Carroun Rd, London SW8 1JT
*Tel:* (020) 7582 3996 *Fax:* (020) 7582 7021
*Key Personnel*
Dir: Richard Body; John Coleman
Founded: 1987
Specialize in European affairs & subjects with a
  special interest in 'communitarian' politics.
Subjects: Aeronautics, Aviation, Government, Po-
  litical Science, Travel
ISBN Prefix(es): 1-872410
Number of titles published annually: 5 Print
Total Titles: 23 Print
*Orders to:* Central Books Ltd, 99 Wallis Rd, Lon-
  don E9 5LN


**New Holland**, *imprint of* New Holland Publishers
(UK) Ltd


**New Holland Publishers (UK) Ltd+**
Garfield House, 86-88 Edgware Rd, London W2
  2EA
*Tel:* (020) 7724 7773 *Fax:* (020) 7724 6184
*E-mail:* postmaster@nhpub.co.uk
*Web Site:* www.newhollandpublishers.com
*Key Personnel*
Man Dir: John Beaufoy *E-mail:* john@nhpub.co.
  uk
Editorial: Jo Jennings; Yvonne McFarlane; Rose-
  mary Wilkinson
Sales & Marketing Dir: Terry Shaughnessy
  *E-mail:* terry@nhpub.co.uk
Sales Office Manager: Alex Lattes *E-mail:* alex@
  nhpub.co.uk
Publicity & Promotions Manager: Yvonne
  Thynne *E-mail:* yvonnet@nhpub.co.uk
Rights Executive: Anna Thomas *E-mail:* anna@
  nhpub.co.uk
Founded: 1956
Specialize in illustrated books.
Subjects: Cookery, Crafts, Games, Hobbies,
  House & Home, How-to, Natural History,
  Travel
ISBN Prefix(es): 1-85368; 1-85974
*Parent Company:* The New Holland Struik Pub-
  lishing Group (Pty) Ltd, South Africa
Imprints: New Holland
Subsidiaries: New Holland Australia
Distributor for Complete Dive Guides; Juicy
  Books; La Belle Aurore; Pilot Books; SCP
  Publishing; Southern Book Publishers (Eu-
  rope, UK, North America & Asia); Stonebridge

Press (Europe, UK & South Africa); Struik Publishers (Europe, UK & North America); Turtle Press; Weatherhill (Europe, UK & South Africa)
*Shipping Address:* F J Tytherleigh & Co Ltd, Hubert Rd, Brentwood, Essex CM14 4RF
*Orders to:* Littlehampton Book Services Ltd, Faraday Close, Durrington, West Sussex BN13 3RB *Tel:* (01903) 828500 *Fax:* (01903) 828625 *E-mail:* orders@lbsltd.co.uk

**New Orchard Editions**, *imprint of* Cassell & Co

**New Playwrights Network**, *imprint of* Cressrelles Publishing Company Ltd

**New Playwrights' Network+**
Imprint of Cressrelles Publishing Company Ltd
10 Station Rd Industrial Estate, Colwall, Malvern, Herefordshire WR13 6RN
*Tel:* (01684) 540154 *Fax:* (01684) 540154
*Key Personnel*
Managing Proprietor: L G Smith
Founded: 1972
Subjects: Drama, Theater
ISBN Prefix(es): 0-86319; 0-903653; 0-906660
Number of titles published annually: 5 Print
Total Titles: 400 Print

**New Roders**, *imprint of* Pearson Education Europe, Mideast & Africa

**Newnes**, *imprint of* Elsevier Ltd

**Newpro UK Ltd+**
Old Sawmills Rd, Faringdon, Oxon SN7 7DS
*Tel:* (01367) 242411 *Fax:* (01367) 241124
*E-mail:* sales@newprouk.co.uk
*Key Personnel*
Man Dir: Chris Coleman *E-mail:* chriscoleman@ newprouk.co.uk
Founded: 1984
Also distributes for other photography publishers.
Subjects: Crafts, Games, Hobbies, History, Natural History, Photography
ISBN Prefix(es): 0-86343; 0-85245
Imprints: Fountain Press; Hove Foto Books

**Nexus**, *imprint of* Virgin Publishing Ltd

**Nexus Special Interests+**
Nexus House, Azalea Drive, Swanley, Kent BR8 8HU
*Tel:* (01322) 660070 *Fax:* (01322) 667633
*Key Personnel*
Books Manager & International Rights Contact: Bill Burkinshaw *Fax:* (01296) 738704
Customer Services Manager: Jayne Hewish
Specialize in hobby & craft books, magazines, plans, exhibitions & awards evenings.
Subjects: Crafts, Games, Hobbies, Engineering (General), Gardening, Plants, Wine & Spirits
ISBN Prefix(es): 1-87403; 0-85344; 1-85486; 0-85076; 0-85242; 0-900841
Total Titles: 130 Print
*Parent Company:* Nexus Media Ltd
Distributed by Chris Lloyd
Foreign Rep(s): Chris Lloyd
*Warehouse:* Cassell Warehouse, Fleets Industrial Estate, One, Willis Way, Poole, Dorset BH15 3SS

**The NFER-NELSON Publishing Co Ltd+**
The Chiswick Centre, 414 Chiswick High Rd, London W4 5TF
*Tel:* (020) 8996 8444; (020) 8996 8445 (international enquiries) *Toll Free Tel:* (0845) 602 1937 (customer service) *Fax:* (020) 8996 3660 (international enquiries)

*E-mail:* information@nfer-nelson.co.uk; edu&hsc@nfer-Nelson.co.uk (customer service)
*Web Site:* www.nfer-nelson.co.uk
*Telex:* 937400 ONECOM G ref 24966001
*Key Personnel*
Man Dir: Michael Jackson
Commercial Dir: Penn Fiona
Business Development Dir: Ian Florance
Founded: 1981
A joint venture of the National Foundation for Educational Research in England & Wales & the Thomson Corporation.
Subjects: Business, Child Care & Development, Education, Health, Nutrition, Psychology, Psychiatry
ISBN Prefix(es): 0-7005; 0-7087; 0-85633; 0-901225
*Parent Company:* Thomson Corporation
*Associate Companies:* Thomas Nelson & Sons Ltd, Routledge
Divisions: ASE
*Warehouse:* Units 1 & 2, Wyndham Rd, Hawkswoan Estate, Swindon, Wiltshire SN2 1BR
*Distribution Center:* Dansk Psykologisk Forlag, Copenhagen, Denmark
ETCC, Dublin, Ireland
Editions du Centre de Psychologie Appliquee, Paris, France
Malta Union of Professional Psychologists, Valletta, Malta
Nelson Canada, Scarborough, ON, Canada
Nelson Publishers (SEA) plc, Singapore
Norsk Psykologforening, Oslo, Norway
NZCER, Wellington, New Zealand
Occupational & Medical Suppliers, Johannesburg, South Africa
Organizzazioni Speciali, Florence, Italy
Psico, Lisbon, Portugal
Psykologien Kustannus Oy, Helsinki, Finland
PsykologiForlaget AB, Stockholm, Sweden
Stoelting, Dale Wood, IL, United States
Swets Test Services, Lisse, Netherlands
Testzentrale, Gottingen, Germany
Transgobal Publishers Service Ltd, Hong Kong
Universitets Forlaget, Oslo, Norway
HAD Center Ltd, Nicosia, Cyprus
Western Psychological Services, Los Angeles, CA, United States
PJ Professional Resources Ltd, Victoria, Australia
Par Inc, Odessa, FL, United States
NTI, Oman
Manasavan, Delhi, India
Testzentrale, Bern, Switzerland
Verlag Hans Huber AG, Bern, Switzerland
Unifacmanu Trading Co Ltd, Taipai, Taiwan, Province of China

**NIACE**, see National Institute of Adult Continuing Education (NIACE)

**Nico Editions**, *imprint of* Thoemmes Press

**Nielsen BookData**
3rd floor, Midas House, 62 Goldsworth Rd, Woking GU21 6LQ
*Tel:* (0870) 777 8710 *Fax:* (0870) 777 8711
*E-mail:* customerservices@nielsenbooknet.co.uk; helpdesk@nielsenbooknet.co.uk
*Web Site:* www.nielsenbookdata.co.uk
*Key Personnel*
Man Dir: Francis Bennett
Editorial Dir: Michael Healy *E-mail:* michael. healy@nielsenbookdata.co.uk
Head of Sales (UK): Simon Skinner
Head of Marketing: Mo Siewcharran
Founded: 1841
Subjects: Publishing & Book Trade Reference
ISBN Prefix(es): 0-85021
*Parent Company:* VNU Media Measurement & Information

*Associate Companies:* Bookseller Publications
Subsidiaries: The Standard Book Numbering Agency Ltd; Teleordering Ltd; BookTrack Ltd

**Nightingale Books**, *imprint of* Baha'i Publishing Trust

**Nightingale Press**, *imprint of* Wimbledon Publishing Company Ltd

**Nile & Mackenzie Ltd+**
13 John Prince's St, London W1G 0JR
*Tel:* (020) 7493 0351 *Fax:* (020) 7495 0128
*Key Personnel*
Man Dir: Daljit Sehbai
Rights & Permissions: Donna Stewart
Founded: 1974
Subjects: Education
ISBN Prefix(es): 0-86031

**James Nisbet & Co Ltd+**
78 Tilehouse St, Hitchin, Herts SG5 2DY
*Tel:* (01462) 438331 *Fax:* (01462) 713444
*Key Personnel*
Chairman: E M Mackenzie-Wood
Founded: 1810
Subjects: Education
ISBN Prefix(es): 0-7202

**NIV Bibles**, *imprint of* Hodder & Stoughton Religious

**NMS Enterprises Ltd - Publishing+**
National Museums of Scotland, Chambers St, Edinburgh EH1 1JF
*Tel:* (0131) 247 4026 *Fax:* (0131) 247 4012
*E-mail:* publishing@nms.ac.uk
*Web Site:* www.nms.ac.uk
*Key Personnel*
Publishing Dir: Lesley A Taylor *Tel:* (0131) 247 4186 *E-mail:* ltaylor@nms.ac.uk
Marketing: Kate Blackadder
Administrator: Elizabeth Dewar
Founded: 1985 (as National Museums of Scotland Publishing)
Subjects: Archaeology, Art, Biography, Cookery, Geography, Geology, History, Natural History, Nonfiction (General), Poetry, Science (General), Technology, Scottish history & culture, photographic archive
ISBN Prefix(es): 0-948636; 1-901663
Number of titles published annually: 15 Print
Total Titles: 110 Print; 1 CD-ROM; 1 Audio
Distributed by BookSource (Scotland); Codasat Canada Ltd (Canada); Gazelle Book Services (UK except Scotland) & Europe); Arthur Schwartz & Co Inc (US)

**No Exit Press**, *imprint of* Oldcastle Books Ltd

**No Exit Press**, see Oldcastle Books Ltd

**North Holland**, *imprint of* Elsevier Ltd

**North Light**, *imprint of* David & Charles Ltd

**North York Moors National Park**
The Old Vicarage, Bondgate, Helmsley, York YO62 5BP
*Tel:* (01439) 770657 *Fax:* (01439) 770691
*E-mail:* j.renney@northyorkmoors-npa.gov.uk
*Web Site:* www.moors.uk.net
Subjects: Archaeology, Geography, Geology, Natural History, Regional Interests
ISBN Prefix(es): 1-904622; 0-907480

**Northcote House Publishers Ltd+**
Horndon House, Horndon, Tavistock, Devon PL19 9NQ
*Tel:* (01822) 810066 *Fax:* (01822) 810034
*E-mail:* northcote.house@virgin.net

*Web Site:* www.northcotehouse.com
*Key Personnel*
Publisher: Brian Hulme
Founded: 1985
Membership(s): IPG.
Subjects: Drama, Theater, Education, Literature,
  Literary Criticism, Essays, Music, Dance
ISBN Prefix(es): 0-7463
Number of titles published annually: 30 Print
Total Titles: 175 Print
Imprints: Writers & Their Work
Distributed by University Press of Mississippi
  (USA)
*Orders to:* Combined Book Services, Unit
  1/K, Paddock Wood Distribution Centre,
  Paddock Wood, Tonbridge, Kent PL19
  9WQ *Tel:* (01892) 837171 *Fax:* (01892)
  837272 *E-mail:* orders@combook.co.uk *Web
  Site:* www.combook.co.uk

**Northern Books**, *imprint of* Famedram Publishers
Ltd

**Northern Universities Press**, *imprint of* Maney
Publishing

**Norton & Liveright, Countryman Press**,
  *imprint of* W W Norton & Company Ltd

**W W Norton & Company Ltd+**
Castle House, 75/76 Wells St, London W1T 3QT
*Tel:* (020) 7323 1579 *Toll Free Tel:* 800-
  233-4830 (orders) *Fax:* (020) 7436 4553
  *Toll Free Fax:* 800-458-6515 (orders)
*E-mail:* office@wwnorton.co.uk
*Web Site:* www.wwnorton.co.uk
*Key Personnel*
President: W Drake McFeely
Man Dir: R A Cameron
Sales Manager: Judith Pamplin
Publicity: Ariadne Van de Ven
Marketing Manager: Victoria Keown-Boyd
Founded: 1980
Subjects: Architecture & Interior Design, Art,
  Biography, Economics, Government, Political
  Science, History, Literature, Literary Criticism,
  Essays, Maritime, Music, Dance, Photography,
  Psychology, Psychiatry
ISBN Prefix(es): 0-393
Number of titles published annually: 120 Print;
  20 CD-ROM
Total Titles: 4,000 Print
*Parent Company:* W W Norton & Company Inc,
  500 Fifth Ave, New York, NY 10110, United
  States
Imprints: Norton & Liveright, Countryman Press
Distributor for New Directions
Foreign Rep(s): APAC Publishers Services Pte
  Ltd (Indonesia, Malaysia, Singapore, Thailand);
  B K Norton Ltd (Korea, Taiwan); Delaney
  Global Publishers Service (Guam, Philippines);
  M K International Ltd (Japan); Pearson Educa-
  tion New Zealand (New Zealand); Transglobal
  Publishers Service Ltd (Hong Kong); US Pub-
  Rep Inc (Caribbean, Central America, Mexico,
  South America); John Wiley & Sons Australia
  Ltd (Australia)
*Orders to:* John Wiley & Sons Ltd, One Oldlands
  Way, Bognor Regis, West Sussex PO22 9SA

**Norwood Publishers Ltd**
3 Chapel St, Norwood Green, Halifax, W Yorks
HX3 8QU
*Tel:* (01274) 602454
*Key Personnel*
Dir: Mr M H Wolfenden
Secretary: A M Wolfenden
Founded: 1991 (as Norwood Publishers, 2002 as
  Norwood Publishers Ltd)
Subjects: Education, Health, Nutrition, Social Sci-
  ences, Sociology
ISBN Prefix(es): 1-873784

**Novello & Co Ltd+**
8-9 Frith St, London W1D 3JB
*Tel:* (020) 7434 0066 *Fax:* (020) 7287-6329
*E-mail:* music@musicsales.co.uk; media@
  musicsales.co.uk
*Web Site:* www.musicsales.co.uk; www.
  chesternovello.com
*Key Personnel*
Executive Dir: James Rushton *E-mail:* james.
  rushton@musicsales.co.uk
Managing Editor: Howard Friend *E-mail:* howard.
  friend@musicsales.co.uk
Head of Promotion: Gill Graham *E-mail:* gill.
  graham@musicsales.co.uk
Founded: 1811
Subjects: Music, Dance
ISBN Prefix(es): 0-85360
*Parent Company:* Music Sales Ltd
Imprints: Cinderella; Elkin; Fairfield; Laurel;
  Lorna; Paxton
*U.S. Office(s):* c/o Shawnee Press Inc, 49 Waring
  Drive, Delaware Gap, PA 18327-1099, United
  States
*Orders to:* Music Sales Ltd, Newmarket Rd, Bury
  St-Edmunds, Suffolk IP33 3YB *Tel:* (01284)
  702600 *Fax:* (01284) 768301

**NTC Research+**
Farm Rd, Henley-on-Thames, Oxon RG9 1EJ
*Tel:* (01491) 411000 *Fax:* (01491) 571188
*E-mail:* info@ntc.co.uk
*Web Site:* www.ntc-research.com
*Key Personnel*
Man Dir: David Roberts *E-mail:* david_roberts@
  ntc.co.uk
Production Dir: Andrew Denham
Librarian: Alison Haan *E-mail:* alison_haan@ntc.
  co.uk
Founded: 1984
Membership(s): Periodical Publishers Association
  (PPA).
Subjects: Advertising, Economics, Government,
  Political Science, Marketing, Radio, TV
ISBN Prefix(es): 1-870562
*Parent Company:* Information Sciences Ltd
Divisions: NTC Conferences Ltd; NTC Research
  Ltd
*U.S. Office(s):* 1615 "L" St NW, Suite 1220,
  Washington, DC 20036, United States *Tel:* 202-
  778-0680 *Fax:* 202-778-4546

**Nuit-Isis**, *imprint of* Mandrake of Oxford

**"O" Books**, *imprint of* John Hunt Publishing Ltd

**Oakwood Library of Railway History**, *imprint
of* Oakwood Press

**Oakwood Press**
PO Box 13, Usk, Monmouthshire NP15 1YS
*Tel:* (01291) 650444 *Fax:* (01291) 650484
*E-mail:* oakwood-press@dial.pipex.com
*Web Site:* www.oakwood-press.dial.pipex.com
*Key Personnel*
Proprietor, Man Dir & Rights: Jane Kennedy
Founded: 1934
Specialist transport publisher.
Subjects: History, Transportation
ISBN Prefix(es): 0-85361
Number of titles published annually: 20 Print
Total Titles: 150 Print
Imprints: Locomotion Papers; Oakwood Library
  of Railway History
Divisions: Oakwood Video Library

**Oceano Grupo Editorial**, *imprint of* Thomson
Gale

**Octagon Press Ltd+**
PO Box 227, London N6 4EW
*Tel:* (020) 8341 5971 *Fax:* (020) 8348 9392

*E-mail:* octagon@schredds.demon.co.uk
*Web Site:* www.octagonpress.com
*Key Personnel*
Man Dir: George Schrager
Publicity: Patti Schneider
Founded: 1972
Subjects: Anthropology, Asian Studies, Behav-
  ioral Sciences, Education, Philosophy, Poetry,
  Psychology, Psychiatry, Religion - Islamic, Re-
  ligion - Other, Travel, Sufis
ISBN Prefix(es): 0-900860
Number of titles published annually: 2 Print
Total Titles: 150 Print
Distributed by ISHK Book Service (US, North
  America, South America)
*Warehouse:* Suffolk

**Octopus Publishing Group+**
2-4 Heron Quays, London E14 4JP
*Tel:* (020) 7531 8400 *Fax:* (020) 7531 8650
*Web Site:* www.octopus-publishing.co.uk
Subjects: Aeronautics, Aviation, Antiques, Archi-
  tecture & Interior Design, Automotive, Cook-
  ery, Crafts, Games, Hobbies, Drama, Theater,
  Fiction, Film, Video, Gardening, Plants, Geog-
  raphy, Geology, Health, Nutrition, Literature,
  Literary Criticism, Essays, Music, Dance, Mys-
  teries, Natural History, Nonfiction (General),
  Photography, Poetry, Science Fiction, Fantasy,
  Sports, Athletics, Travel, Wine & Spirits
*Parent Company:* Hachette Livre
Imprints: Bounty Books; Gaia Books; Cassell Il-
  lustrated; Conran Octopus; Hamlyn; Miller;
  Mitchell Beazley; Philip; Godsfield Press
*Orders to:* Littlehamptom Book Services Ltd,
  Durrington Worthing, West Sussex BN13 3RB
  *Tel:* (01903) 828800

**Oilfield Publications Ltd**
PO Box 11, Ledbury, Herts HR8 1BN
*Tel:* (01531) 634563 *Fax:* (01531) 634239;
  (01531) 633744
*E-mail:* opl@oilpubs.com
*Web Site:* www.oilpubs.com
*Key Personnel*
Man Dir: Julia Lourd
Publish book & vessel registers for the interna-
  tional offshore oil & gas industry.
Subjects: Energy, Maritime
ISBN Prefix(es): 1-870945
*U.S. Office(s):* Oilfield Publications Inc, 888 W
  Sam Houston Parkway S, Suite 280, Houston,
  TX 77042, United States *Tel:* 713-334-8970
  *Fax:* 713-334-8968 *E-mail:* oplusa@oilpubs.
  com

**Old Bailey Press**, *imprint of* HLT Publications

**Old Pond Publishing**
Dencora Business Centre, 36 White House Rd,
  Ipswich, Suffolk IP1 5LT
*Tel:* (01473) 238200 *Fax:* (01473) 238201
*E-mail:* info@oldpond.com
*Web Site:* www.oldpond.com
Founded: 1998
Subjects: Agriculture, Transportation, Veterinary
  Science
ISBN Prefix(es): 1-903366
Number of titles published annually: 15 Print
Total Titles: 100 Print

**Old Vicarage Publications**
The Old Vicarage, Reades Lane, Dane in Shaw,
  Congleton, Cheshire CW12 3LL
*Tel:* (01260) 279276 *Fax:* (01260) 298913
*Key Personnel*
Proprietor: William Ball *E-mail:* williamball@
  supanet.com
Founded: 1983

Subjects: Ethnicity, Film, Video, Regional Interests, Travel
ISBN Prefix(es): 0-900269; 0-947818; 0-9508635
Imprints: Centaur Books
*U.S. Office(s):* State Book & Periodical Service, New York, NY, United States

**Oldcastle Books Ltd+**
PO Box 394, Harpenden, Herts AL5 1XJ
*Tel:* (01582) 761264 *Fax:* (01582) 761264
*E-mail:* info@noexit.co.uk
*Web Site:* www.noexit.co.uk
*Key Personnel*
Dir & Foreign Rights: Ion Mills
   *E-mail:* ionmills@noexit.co.uk
Founded: 1985
No unsolicited manuscripts.
Subjects: Crafts, Games, Hobbies, Fiction, Mysteries, Noir Fiction, Gambling, Crime Fiction
ISBN Prefix(es): 0-948353; 1-874061; 1-901982; 1-84243
Imprints: No Exit Press
*Sales Office(s):* 21 Great Ormond St, London WC1N 3JB *Tel:* (020) 7430 1021 *Fax:* (020) 7430 0021 *Web Site:* www.thebigbookshop.co.uk
Foreign Rep(s): Capricorn Link (Australia); Codasat (Canada); Four Walls Eight Windows/No Exit Press (North America); Michael Geoghegan (Belgium, France); Gill & Macmillan (Ireland); Gabriele Kern (Austria, Germany, Switzerland); Pernille Larson (Scandinavia); PIMS (Far East, Middle East); Peter Prout (Gibraltar, Spain); PSD Promotions (Pty) Ltd (South Africa); Southern Publishers Group (New Zealand); Trafalgar Square Publishing (US); Turnaround (UK)
Foreign Rights: Shirley Stewart
*Distribution Center:* Turnaround, 3 Olympia Trading Estate, Coburg Rd, London N22 6TZ *Tel:* (020) 8829 3000 *Fax:* (020) 8881 5088 *E-mail:* julie@turnaround-uk.com

**The Oleander Press+**
16 Orchard St, Cambridge CB1 1JT
*Tel:* (01223) 357768
*E-mail:* editor@oleanderpress.com
*Web Site:* oleanderpress.com
*Key Personnel*
Man Dir: Dr Jerry Toner
Founded: 1960
Specialize in travel.
Subjects: Biography, Drama, Theater, History, Language Arts, Linguistics, Literature, Literary Criticism, Essays, Poetry, Regional Interests, Travel, Arabian Peninsula, Games, Monographs
ISBN Prefix(es): 0-900891; 0-902675; 0-906672
Number of titles published annually: 6 Print
Total Titles: 120 Print

**Michael O'Mara Books Ltd+**
9 Lion Yard, Tremadoc Rd, London SW4 7NQ
*Tel:* (020) 7720 8643 *Fax:* (020) 7627 8953 (Editorial); (020) 7627 4900 (Foreign Sales)
*E-mail:* enquiries@michaelomarabooks.com
*Web Site:* www.michaelomarabooks.com
*Key Personnel*
Chairman: Michael O'Mara
Man Dir: Lesley O'Mara
Editorial Dir: Toby Buchan
Editorial Dir (Commissioning): Lindsay Davies
UK Sales Dir: David Crombie
UK Sales Manager: Alison Parker
Foreign Sales Manager: Philippa Slater
Childrens Managing Editor: Philippa Wingate
Production Consultant: David Bann
Founded: 1985
Subjects: Biography, History, Humor, Nonfiction (General), Juvenile
ISBN Prefix(es): 1-85479; 0-948397; 1-84317; 1-904613
Number of titles published annually: 80 Print

Imprints: Buster Books (juvenile list)
Distributed by Andrews McMeel (USA); Littlehampton Book Services
*Orders to:* Grantham Book Services, Isaac Newton Way, Alma Park Industrial Estate, Grantham, Lincs NG31 9SD *Tel:* (01476) 541080 *Fax:* (01476) 541061/63

**Omnibus Press+**
8-9 Frith St, London W1D 3JB
*Tel:* (020) 7434 0066 *Fax:* (020) 7287 6329
*E-mail:* music@musicsales.co.uk
*Web Site:* www.musicsales.com
*Telex:* 21892
*Key Personnel*
Chairman & Man Dir: Robert Wise
Chief Operating Officer: Chris Butler
Finance Dir: Malcolm Grabham
European Sales Dir, Music Sales Ltd: Hilary Power
President, Music Sales Corporation: Barrie Edwards
Vice President, G Schirmer Inc, Associated Music Publishers: Susan Feder
Man Dir, Edition Wilhelm Hansen: Tine Birger Christensen
General Manager, Union Musical Ediciones: German Bartolome
Man Dir, Premiere Music: Claude Duvivier
Man Dir, Bosworth Music GmbH: Michael Ohst
Man Dir, Chester Music Ltd, Novello & Co Ltd: James Rushton
Business Development Dir, Music Sales Ltd: Ian Morgan
Dir of Distribution and IT, Music Sales Ltd: David Vass
Vice President, Administration and Operations, Music Sales Corporation: Denise Maurin
Head of Copyright, Music Sales Limited: Alex Batterbee
Dir of Sales and Marketing, Music Sales Corporation: Steve Wilson
Man Dir, Music in Print: Iain Davidson
Founded: 1979
Subjects: Biography, Music, Dance
ISBN Prefix(es): 0-7119; 0-86001; 0-9657122
*Parent Company:* Music Sales Ltd, London
Imprints: Amsco Publications; Bobcat Books; Proteus; WISE Publications; Zomba Books
Subsidiaries: Music Sales Corp; Music Sales Pty
*Branch Office(s)*
Music Sales Pty Ltd, c/o Bookwise, 54 Coultenden Rd, Fundon, Austria
*U.S. Office(s):* Music Sales Corp, 257 Park Ave S, New York, NY 10010, United States *Tel:* 212-254-2100 *Fax:* 212-254-2013 *E-mail:* info@musicsales.com *Web Site:* www.musicsales.com
Distributor for BBC Music Guides; Firefly; Gramophone; OZONE; Parker Mead; RED Independent Music Press; Rogan House; Showcase Publications
*Warehouse:* Book Sales Ltd, Newmarket Rd, Bury St, Edmunds, Suffolk IP33 3YB
*Distribution Center:* Newmarket Rd, Bury St, Edmonds, Suffolk IP33 3YB *Tel:* (0284) 702600 *Fax:* (0284) 768301
445 Bellvale Rd, PO Box 572, Chester, NY 10918, United States *Tel:* 845-469-2271 *Fax:* 845-469-6952

**Oneworld Publications**
185 Banbury Rd, Oxford OX2 7AR
*Tel:* (01865) 310597 *Fax:* (01865) 310598
*E-mail:* info@oneworld-publications.com
*Web Site:* www.oneworld-publications.com
*Key Personnel*
Partner: Novin Doostdar *E-mail:* ndoostdar@oneworld-publications.com; Juliet Mabey
   *E-mail:* jmabey@oneworld-publications.com
Man Dir: Helen Coward *E-mail:* hcoward@oneworld-publications.com
Founded: 1986

Subjects: Anthropology, Education, History, Philosophy, Psychology, Psychiatry, Religion - Buddhist, Religion - Catholic, Religion - Hindu, Religion - Islamic, Religion - Jewish, Religion - Protestant, Religion - Other, Self-Help
ISBN Prefix(es): 1-85168
Number of titles published annually: 40 Print
Total Titles: 200 Print
*U.S. Office(s):* PO Box 2510, Novato, CA 94948, United States
*Distribution Center:* APD Kuala Lumpur, 18 Jalan SS3/41 PJ 47300, Darul Ehsan, Selangor, Malaysia *Tel:* (03) 7776063 *Fax:* (03) 7773414 *E-mail:* apdkl@tm.net.my (Southeast Asia)
APD Singapore Pte Ltd, 52 Genting Lane, No 06-05 Hiang Kie Complex 1, Singapore 349560, Singapore *Tel:* 7493551 *Fax:* 7493552 *E-mail:* apd@pacific.net.sg (Southeast Asia)
Richard Carman, 16 Chapel Close, Comberbach, Northwich, Cheshire CW9 6BA *Tel:* (1606) 891107 *Fax:* (1606) 891107 (Africa)
Jim Chalmers, 2 Cheviot Rd, Paisley *Tel:* (0141) 884 5322 *Fax:* (0141) 884 5322 *E-mail:* jim@jchalmersassociates.freeserve.co.uk (Scotland, Northeast UK)
Andy Cocks, 13 King Cole Rd, Lexden, Colchester, Essex CO3 5AG *Tel:* (01206) 548515 *E-mail:* acocks@aspects.net (UK)
Lale Colakoglu, Sezai Selek Sok. 10/2, Nisantas, Istanbul 80200, Turkey *Tel:* (0212) 247 85 51 *Fax:* (0212) 247 89 83 *E-mail:* colakoglu@turk.net (Turkey)
Caroline Day, 21 Holtom St, Stratford-on-Avon, Warwicks CV37 6DQ *Tel:* (01789) 266903 (UK)
Durnell Marketing, 2 Linden Close, Tunbridge Wells, Kent TN4 8HH, Contact: Andrew B Durnell *Tel:* (01892) 544272 *Fax:* (01892) 511152 *E-mail:* mail@durnell.co.uk (Europe & Ireland)
InterMedia Americana Limited, PO Box 8734, London SE21 7ZF, Contact: David Williams *Tel:* (020) 8761 5140 *Fax:* (020) 8761 5139 (South America, Caribbean)
ITPS, Cheriton House, North Way, Andover, Hants SP10 5BE *Tel:* (01264) 342832 *Fax:* (01264) 342788 *E-mail:* oneworld@itps.co.uk (outside USA & Canada)
Anwer Iqbal, GPO Box 518, Main Chambers, 3 Temples Rd, Lahore, Pakistan *Tel:* (042) 636 7325 *Fax:* (042) 636 1370 *E-mail:* bookbird@lhr.comsats.net.pk (Pakistan)
Debbie Jones, The Firs, 6 Whitchurch Rd, Tavistock, Devon *Tel:* (01822) 617223 *Fax:* (01822) 610406 (UK)
Felicity Knight, 10 Buckingham Mews, Shoreham-by-Sea, Sussex BN43 6AJ *Tel:* (01273) 453270 (UK)
National Book Network, 15200 NBN Way, Blue Ridge Summit, PA 17214, United States *Tel:* 717-794-3800 *E-mail:* custserv@nbnbooks.com (US & Canada)
Publishers International Marketing, 7 Melton Close, Storrington, West Sussex RH20 4QA *Tel:* (01903) 741 935 *Fax:* (01903) 741 079 *E-mail:* ray@pim1-uk.freeserve.co.uk (Middle East, Japan, Hong Kong)
Research Press, 1st floor, Arun House, 2/25 Ansari, PO 7208, New Delhi 110002, India *Tel:* (011) 328 4894 *Fax:* (011) 328 1819 *E-mail:* aparmar@vsnl.com (India)
The Segrue Partnership, 67B Brent St, Hendon, London NW4 2EA *Tel:* (020) 8202 9452 *Fax:* (020) 8203 9180 (UK)
Mike Wilson, Plas Berw, Pentre Berw, Anglesey LL60 6LL *Tel:* (01248) 421580; (07775) 501986 (mobile) *Fax:* (01248) 421952 (UK)

**Onlywomen Press Ltd+**
40 St Lawrence Terrace, London W10 5ST
*Tel:* (020) 8354 0796 *Fax:* (020) 8960 2817
*E-mail:* onlywomenpress@aol.com
*Web Site:* www.onlywomenpress.com

*Key Personnel*
Man Dir: Lilian Mohin
Founded: 1974
Subjects: Fiction, Gay & Lesbian, History, Poetry, Women's Studies
ISBN Prefix(es): 0-906500
Number of titles published annually: 3 Print
Total Titles: 40 Print
Distributed by Airlift Book Company (UK & Europe); Alamo Square Press (North America); Bulldog Books Pty Ltd (Australia)

**Open Books Publishing Ltd**
Willow Cottage, Cudworth, Ilminster TA19 0PS
*Tel:* (01460) 52565 *Fax:* (01460) 52565
*Key Personnel*
Man Dir: Patrick Taylor *E-mail:* patrickta@aol. com
Founded: 1974
Subjects: Gardening, Plants, Nonfiction (General)
ISBN Prefix(es): 0-7291

**Open Gate Press+**
51 Achilles Rd, London NW6 1DZ
*Tel:* (020) 7431 4391 *Fax:* (020) 7431 5129
*E-mail:* books@opengatepress.co.uk
*Web Site:* www.opengatepress.co.uk
*Key Personnel*
Contact: Jeannie Cohen
Founded: 1988
Subjects: Anthropology, Archaeology, Economics, Government, Political Science, Philosophy, Psychology, Psychiatry, Social Sciences, Sociology
ISBN Prefix(es): 1-871871
*U.S. Office(s):* Paul & Company Publishers Consoritum Inc, PO Box 442, Concord, MA 10742, United States
Distributor for Cambridge International Publishers
*Orders to:* Book Representation & Distribution Ltd, 244-A London Rd, Hadleigh, Essex SS7 2DE

**Open University Press+**
McGraw-Hill House, Shoppenhangers Rd, Maidenhead, Berks SL6 2QL
*Tel:* (01628) 502500; (01628) 502720 (customer service) *Fax:* (01628) 635895 (customer service)
*E-mail:* enquiries@openup.co.uk; emea_orders@ mcgraw-hill.com (orders); emea_queries@ mcgraw-hill.com (customer service)
*Web Site:* mcgraw-hill.co.uk/openup
*Key Personnel*
Man Dir & Publisher: Simon Allen
Financial Dir: Alan Martin
Publishing Dir: Jon Reed *E-mail:* jon_reed@ mcgraw-hill.com
Sales & Marketing Manager: Mark Barratt *E-mail:* mark_barratt@mcgraw-hill.com
Head of Production: Max Elvey *E-mail:* max_elvey@mcgraw-hill.com
Rights & International Sales Executive: Amy Blower *E-mail:* amy_blower@mcgraw-hill.com
Founded: 1977
Subjects: Behavioral Sciences, Criminology, Developing Countries, Education, Government, Political Science, Health, Nutrition, Management, Psychology, Psychiatry, Public Administration, Social Sciences, Sociology, Women's Studies
ISBN Prefix(es): 0-335
*Parent Company:* McGraw-Hill Education

**Open University Worldwide+**
Walton Hall, Milton Keynes MK7 6AA
*Tel:* (01908) 858785 *Fax:* (01908) 858787
*E-mail:* ouwenq@open.ac.uk
*Web Site:* www.open.ac.uk
*Key Personnel*
Dir: Bob Masterton
Marketing Manager: Katherine Bull

Rights & Permissions, Print: Sue Hitchen
Rights & Permissions, Audio Visual: Diana Rualt
Founded: 1977
Subjects: Architecture & Interior Design, Astronomy, Biological Sciences, Chemistry, Chemical Engineering, Computer Science, Developing Countries, Disability, Special Needs, Earth Sciences, Economics, Education, Electronics, Electrical Engineering
ISBN Prefix(es): 0-7492
*Parent Company:* The Open University
*Branch Office(s)*
40 University Rd, Belfast BT7 1SU, Ireland *Tel:* (028) 9024 5025 *Fax:* (028) 9023 0565 *E-mail:* ireland@open.ac.uk
66 High St Harborne, Birmingham *Tel:* (0121) 426 1661 *Fax:* (0121) 427 9484 *E-mail:* west-midlands@open.ac.uk
Cintra House, 12 Hills Rd, Cambridge CB2 1PF *Tel:* (01223) 364721 *Fax:* (01223) 355207 *E-mail:* east-of-england@open.ac.uk
24 Cathedral Rd, Cardiff, Wales CF11 9SA *Tel:* (029) 2039 7911 *Fax:* (029) 2022 7930 *E-mail:* wales@open.ac.uk
St James's House, 150 London Rd, East Grinstead RH19 1HG *Tel:* (01342) 327821 *Fax:* (01342) 317411 *E-mail:* south-east@open. ac.uk
10 Drumsheugh Gardens, Edinburgh, Scotland *Tel:* (0131) 226 3851 *Fax:* (0131) 220 6730 *E-mail:* scotland@open.ac.uk
2 Trevelyan Sq, Boar Lane, Leeds LS1 6ED *Tel:* (0113) 2444431 *Fax:* (0113) 2341862 *E-mail:* yorkshire@open.ac.uk
1-11 Hawley Crescent, Camden Town, London NW1 8NP *Tel:* (020) 7485 6597 *Fax:* (020) 7556 6196 *E-mail:* london@open.ac.uk
Eldon House, Regent Centre, Gosforth, New Castle Upon Tyne NE3 3PW *Tel:* (0191) 284 1611 *Fax:* (0191) 284 6592 *E-mail:* north@open.ac. uk
Foxcombe Hall, Boars Hill, Oxford OX1 5HR *Tel:* (01865) 327000 *Fax:* (01865) 736288 *E-mail:* south@open.ac.uk
351 Altrincham Rd, Sharston, Manchester M22 4UN *Tel:* (0161) 998 7272 *Fax:* (0161) 945 3356 *E-mail:* north-west@open.ac.uk
Clarendon Park, Clumber Ave, Sherwood Rise, Nottingham NG5 1AH *Tel:* (0115) 962 5451 *Fax:* (0115) 971 5575 *E-mail:* east-midlands@ open.ac.uk
*Distribution Center:* Open University Technical & Distribution Services, Unit 16 Denington Industrial Estate, Wellingborough, Northants NN8 2RF *Tel:* (01933) 224911 *Fax:* (01933) 441780

**Opus Book Publishing Ltd**
20 The Strand, Steeple Ashton, Trowbridge, Wilts BA14 6EP
*Tel:* (01380) 871354 *Fax:* (01380) 871354
*E-mail:* opus@dmac.co.uk
*Key Personnel*
Contact: Diana van der Klugt
Subjects: Maritime
ISBN Prefix(es): 1-898574

**Opus Publishing Ltd**
36 Camden Sq, London NW1 9XA
*Tel:* (020) 7267 1034 *Fax:* (020) 7267 6026
*E-mail:* opuspub@btconnect.com
*Key Personnel*
President: Martin Heller

**Orbit**, *imprint of* Time Warner Book Group UK

**Orchard Books**, see The Watts Publishing Group Ltd

**Ordnance Survey**
Customer Contact Centre, Ordnance Survey, Romsey Rd, Southampton SO16 4GU

*Tel:* (08456) 05 05 05 (customer information); (023) 8079 2912 (outside Britain); (023) 8030 5030 (business enquiries) *Fax:* (023) 8079 2615 (trade customer information); (023) 8079 2615 (outside Britain)
*E-mail:* customerservices@ordnancesurvey.co.uk
*Web Site:* www.ordnancesurvey.co.uk
*Key Personnel*
Dir General: Vanessa Lawrence
Head of Marketing: Eric Bates
Head of Sales: Phil Watts
Press Officer: Philip Round
Sales Office Manager: Nicky Long *Tel:* (023) 8030 5278 *E-mail:* nlong@ordsvy.gov.uk
ISBN Prefix(es): 0-319

**Original English Language Fiction**, *imprint of* Dedalus Ltd

**Orion**, *imprint of* Orion Publishing Group Ltd

**Orion Children's Books+**
c/o The Orion Publishing Group, Orion House, 5 Upper St Martins Lane, London WC2H 9EA
*Tel:* (020) 7240 3444 *Fax:* (020) 7240 4822
*E-mail:* info@orionbooks.co.uk
*Web Site:* www.orionbooks.co.uk
*Key Personnel*
Publisher: Fiona Kennedy
Founded: 1993
ISBN Prefix(es): 1-85881
Number of titles published annually: 50 Print
Imprints: Dolphin Paperbacks

**Orion Publishing Group Ltd+**
Orion House, 5 Upper St Martins Lane, London WC2H 9EA
*Tel:* (020) 7240 3444 *Fax:* (020) 7240 4822
*E-mail:* info@orionbooks.co.uk
*Web Site:* orionbooks.co.uk
*Key Personnel*
Chairman: Arnaud Nourry
Chief Executive: Peter Roche
Group Finance Dir: Pierre de Cacqueray
Founded: 1991
Subjects: Archaeology, Art, Biography, Biological Sciences, Business, Crafts, Games, Hobbies, Fiction, Film, Video, History, Management, Mysteries, Nonfiction (General), Poetry, Religion - Other, Romance, Science (General), Science Fiction, Fantasy, Self-Help, Sports, Athletics, Western Fiction
ISBN Prefix(es): 0-7528
*Parent Company:* Hachette Livre
*Associate Companies:* Dent Children; Everyman; Millenium; Phoenix; Phoenix House
Imprints: Orion
Subsidiaries: JM Dent & Sons; Orion Books; Weidenfeld & Nicolson
*Warehouse:* Littlehampton Book Service, 14 Eldon Way, Lineside Estate, Littlehampton, West Sussex BN17 7HE
*Orders to:* Littlehampton Book Service, 14 Eldon Way, Lineside Estate, Littlehampton, West Sussex BN17 7HE

**The Orkney Press Ltd+**
One Linksfield Court, Elgin IV30 5JB
*Tel:* (01343) 540844
*Key Personnel*
Sales Dir: Mrs Sidsel Firth
Founded: 1981
Subjects: Anthropology, Archaeology, History, Maritime, Natural History, Philosophy, Science (General)
ISBN Prefix(es): 0-907618
Imprints: Aurora Northern Classics; Scottish Falcon

**Orpheus Books Ltd+**
2 Church Green, Witney, Oxon OX28 4AW
*Tel:* (01993) 774949 *Fax:* (01993) 700330

*E-mail:* info@orpheusbooks.com
*Web Site:* www.orpheusbooks.com
*Key Personnel*
Chairman: Nicholas Harris *E-mail:* nicholas@
orpheusbooks.com
Founded: 1992
Principally book packagers.
Subjects: Animals, Pets, Astronomy, Earth Sciences, Geography, Geology, History, Natural History, Science (General), Transportation
ISBN Prefix(es): 1-901323
Number of titles published annually: 12 Print

**Osborne Books Ltd**
Unit 1B, Everoak Estate, Bromyard Rd, St Johns, Worcester, Worcs WR2 5HP
*Tel:* (01905) 748071 *Fax:* (0190) 748952
*E-mail:* books@osborne.u-net.com
*Web Site:* www.osbornebooks.co.uk
*Key Personnel*
Contact: Michael Fardon
Founded: 1987
Subjects: Accounting, Business, History, Literature, Literary Criticism, Essays, Photography
ISBN Prefix(es): 1-872962; 0-9510650
Imprints: Heritage

**Osprey Publishing Ltd+**
Elms Court, Chapel Way, Botley, Oxford OX2 9LP
Mailing Address: PO Box 1, Osceola, WI 54020-0001, United States
*Tel:* (01933) 443863 *Toll Free Tel:* 800-826-6600
*Fax:* (01865) 727017
*E-mail:* info@ospreydirect.co.uk; info@
ospreydirectusa.com (USA & Canada)
*Web Site:* www.ospreypublishing.com
*Key Personnel*
Man Dir: William Shepherd
Financial Dir: Sarah Lough
Sales & Marketing Dir: Joanna Sharland
Illustrated military history from around the world with all-time greatest battles of land & air, from antiquity to the present day.
Subjects: Aeronautics, Aviation, Crafts, Games, Hobbies, History, Military Science
ISBN Prefix(es): 1-85532; 0-85045; 0-540; 1-84176
Total Titles: 600 Print
*U.S. Office(s):* Specialty Book Marketing, 443 Park Ave S, New York, NY 10016, United States, Contact: Bill Corsa *Tel:* 212-685-5560 *Fax:* 212-685-5836 *E-mail:* ospreyusa@aol.com
Distributor for Compendium Publishing
*Orders to:* Grantham Book Services, Isaac Newton Way, Alma Park Industrial Estate, Grantham, Lincs NG31 9SD *Tel:* (01476) 541 080 *Fax:* (01476) 541 061
Motorbooks International, 729 Prospect Ave, Osceola, WI 54020-0001, United States *Tel:* 715-294-3345 *Fax:* 715-294-4448

**Our Wonderful Psychoneural Systems,** *imprint of* MGM

**Overstone Press,** *imprint of* Thoemmes Press

**Peter Owen Ltd+**
73 Kenway Rd, London SW5 0RE
*Tel:* (020) 7373 5628; (020) 7370 6093
*Fax:* (020) 7373 6760
*E-mail:* admin@peterowen.com
*Web Site:* www.peterowen.com
*Key Personnel*
Sales & Publicity: Daniel McCabe
  *E-mail:* daniel@peterowen.com; Tom Perrin
  *E-mail:* tom@peterowen.com
Editorial: Antonia Owen *E-mail:* antonia@
peterowen.com
Editorial & Rights: Simon Smith
  *E-mail:* ssmith@peterowen.com

Rights: Peter Owen
Design & Production: Francesca Bechara; Keith Savage
Founded: 1950
Subjects: Art, Biography, Drama, Theater, Fiction, Gay & Lesbian, Language Arts, Linguistics, Literature, Literary Criticism, Essays, Music, Dance, Publishing & Book Trade Reference, Social Sciences, Sociology, Women's Studies
ISBN Prefix(es): 0-7206
Number of titles published annually: 25 Print; 30 Audio
*Distribution Center:* Central Books, 99 Wallis Rd, London E9 5CN *Tel:* (020) 8986 4854 *Fax:* (20) 8533 5821 *E-mail:* orders@
centralbooks.com (UK)
Dufour Editions Inc, PO Box 7, Chester Springs, PA 19425-0007, United States *Tel:* 610-458-5005 *Fax:* 610-458-7103 *E-mail:* info@dufoureditions.com *Web Site:* www.dufoureditions.com (USA)

**Oxfam+**
Member of Oxfam International
Oxfam Supporter Services Dept, Oxfam House, 274 Banbury Rd, Oxford OX2 7DZ
*Tel:* (01865) 313744 *Fax:* (01865) 313713
*E-mail:* oxfam@oxfam.org.uk; publish@oxfam.org.uk
*Web Site:* www.oxfam.org.uk
*Telex:* 83610 *Cable:* OXFAMG OXFORD
*Key Personnel*
Publishing Executive: Robert Cornford *E-mail:* r.cornford@oxfam.org.uk
Marketing: Deborah Logan
Contact: Caroline Knowles
Founded: 1942
Subjects: Developing Countries, Economics, Government, Political Science, Social Sciences, Sociology, Women's Studies
ISBN Prefix(es): 0-85598
Total Titles: 130 Print
Distributed by David Philip Publishers (Southern Africa); Stylus Publishing LLC (US & Canada)
*Orders to:* BEBC, PO Box 1496, Parkstone, Dorset BH12 3YD

**Oxford International Centre for Publishing Studies**
School of Art, Publishing & Music, Oxford Brookes University, The Richard Hamilton Bldg, Headington Hill Campus, Oxford OX3 0BP
*Tel:* (01865) 484951 *Fax:* (01865) 484952
*E-mail:* publishing@brookes.ac.uk
*Web Site:* ah.brookes.ac.uk/publishing/index.php
*Key Personnel*
Dir: Prof Paul Richardson *E-mail:* ptrichardson@
brookes.ac.uk
Founded: 1994
A centre for publishing education, training, consulting & research.

**Oxford Poets,** *imprint of* Carcanet Press Ltd

**Oxford University Press+**
Great Clarendon St, Oxford OX2 6DP
*Tel:* (01865) 556767 *Fax:* (01865) 556646
*E-mail:* webenquiry.uk@oup.com
*Web Site:* www.oup.com
*Telex:* 837330 Oxpres G
*Key Personnel*
Man Dir, ELT: Peter R Mothersole
Man Dir, UK Academic Division: Ivan S Asquith
Group Finance Dir: R C Boning
Group Personal Dir: M J Havelock
Public Affairs Manager: Caroline Scotter Mainprize
Chief Executive: Henry Reece
Man Dir, UK Educational Division: Fiona Clarke
Man Dir, International Division: Susan Froud
President, OUP USA: Edward Barry

Man Dir, OUP Spain: Jesus Lazcano
Founded: 1478
Subjects: Art, Biography, Economics, Education, Engineering (General), Government, Political Science, History, Language Arts, Linguistics, Law, Literature, Literary Criticism, Essays, Mathematics, Medicine, Nursing, Dentistry, Military Science, Music, Dance, Philosophy, Poetry, Psychology, Psychiatry, Publishing & Book Trade Reference, Religion - Other, Science (General), Social Sciences, Sociology
ISBN Prefix(es): 0-19
*Associate Companies:* Cornelsen und Oxford University Press GmbH, Germany
Imprints: Clarendon Press; IRL Press
Subsidiaries: Oxford University Press Inc
*Branch Office(s)*
70 Wynford Dr, Don Mills, ON M3C 1J9, Canada
Warwick House, 18th Floor, Taikoo Place, 979 King's Rd, Hong Kong, China
Oxford University Press Espana SA, Pargue Empresarial San Fernando de Henares: Edificio Atenas la Plantz, San Fernando de Henares, 28830 Madrid, Spain
PO Box 43, New Delhi 110001, India
Oxford University Press KK (Japan), 2-4-8 Kanamecho, Toshima-ku, Toyko 171, Japan
PO Box 72532, Nairobi, Kenya
Penerbit Fajar Bakti Sdn Bhd, Malaysia
PO Box 13033, Karachi 75350, Pakistan
37 Jal an Pemimpin, No 03-03 Union Industrial Bldg B Block A, Singapore 577177, Singapore
PO Box 5299, Dar es Salaam, Thailand
PO Box 1141, Cape Town 8000, South Africa
GPO Box 2784Y, Melbourne, Victoria (Australia & New Zealand)
*Bookshop(s):* 116-117 High St, Oxford OX1 4BZ *Tel:* (01865) 242913
*Orders to:* OUP Distribution Services, Saxon Way West, Corby, Northamptonshire NN18 9ES *Tel:* (01536) 741519 *Fax:* (01536) 746337

**Oxford University Press Children's Books**
Great Clarendon St, Oxford OX2 6DP
*Tel:* (01865) 556767 *Fax:* (01865) 267732
*E-mail:* enquiry@oup.com
*Web Site:* www.oup.co.uk

**Oyster Books Ltd+**
4 Kirlea Farm, Badgworth, Axbridge, Somerset BS26 2QH
*Tel:* (01934) 732251 *Fax:* (01934) 732514
*E-mail:* pearls@oysterbooks.co.uk
*Key Personnel*
Man Dir: Tim Wood
Production Dir: Ali Brooks
Sales Dir: Donna Webber
Sales & Marketing: Rachel Holmes
  *E-mail:* rachel@oysterbooks.co.uk
Founded: 1985
Also acts as book packagers.
Subjects: Fiction, Nonfiction (General)
ISBN Prefix(es): 0-948240

**P N Review,** see Carcanet Press Ltd

**Packard Publishing Ltd+**
Forum House, Stirling Rd, Chichester, West Sussex PO19 7DN
*Tel:* (01243) 537977 *Fax:* (01243) 537977
*E-mail:* info@packardpublishing.co.uk
*Web Site:* www.packardpublishing.com
*Key Personnel*
Man Dir: Michael Packard
Founded: 1977
Academic book publisher & distributor.
Subjects: Agriculture, Architecture & Interior Design, Biological Sciences, Environmental Studies, Gardening, Plants, Geography, Geology, Language Arts, Linguistics, Natural History, Elementary English & French, Landscape Architecture

ISBN Prefix(es): 0-906527; 0-948690; 1-85341
Number of titles published annually: 6 Print
Total Titles: 20 Print
Imprints: Headlions; PPL
Distributed by Stipes Publishing LLC (USA)
Distributor for Librairie DuLiban (UK); Oxy-
graphics Ltd (UK)

**Palgrave Publishers Ltd+**
Brunel Rd, Houndmills, Basingstoke, Hants RG21
6XS
*Tel:* (01256) 329242 *Fax:* (01256) 479476
*E-mail:* orders@palgrave.com (ordering online);
catalogue@palgrave.com (catalogue requests);
conferences@palgrave.com (conference &
exhibition information); rights@palgrave.com
(copyright & permissions); lectureservices@
palgrave.com (inspection copy service);
reviews@palgrave.com (review copy requests);
booksellers@palgrave.com (bookseller queries)
*Web Site:* www.palgrave.com
*Key Personnel*
Man Dir: Dominic Knight *E-mail:* d.knight@
palgrave.com
Publishing Dir, College Publishing Division
(Business, Computer Science & Engineer-
ing): Christopher Glennie *E-mail:* c.glennie@
palgrave.com
Publishing Dir, College Publishing Division (Hu-
manities & Social Science): Frances Arnold
*E-mail:* f.arnold@palgrave.com
Publishing Dir, College Publishing Division (Pro-
fessional & Business Management): Stephen
Rutt *E-mail:* s.rutt@palgrave.com
Publishing Dir, Academic Division: Josie Dixon
*E-mail:* j.dixon@palgrave.com
Sales & Marketing Dir: Margaret Hewinson
*E-mail:* m.hewinson@palgrave.com
Marketing Dir: Carol Monoyios *E-mail:* c.
monoyios@palgrave.com
International Sales Dir: Alastair Gordon
*E-mail:* a.gordon@palgrave.com
UK Sales Dir: Sam Burridge *E-mail:* s.burridge@
palgrave.com
Publishing Services Dir: Tim Fox *E-mail:* t.fox@
palgrave.com
Subjects: Business, Computer Science, Eco-
nomics, Engineering (General), History, Human
Relations, Management, Science (General), So-
cial Sciences, Sociology, Technology
ISBN Prefix(es): 0-312; 0-333; 1-4039
*Parent Company:* Macmillan Ltd
Imprints: W H Freeman
*U.S. Office(s):* 175 Fifth Ave, New York, NY,
NY 10010, United States *Tel:* 212-982-3900
*Fax:* 212-777-6359

**Pallas Athene+**
42 Spencer Rise, London NW5 1AP
*Tel:* (020) 7229 2798 *Fax:* (020) 7792 1067
*Key Personnel*
President & Publisher: Alexander Fyjis-Walker
Founded: 1991
Subjects: Art, Travel
ISBN Prefix(es): 1-873429; 0-9529986
Total Titles: 20 Print
Imprints: Pallas Guides; WOL Books
Foreign Rights: Vincent Vichet-Vadakan Agency
(Worldwide)
*Orders to:* Trafalgar Square Publishing, PO Box
257, Howe Hill Rd, North Pomfret, VT 05053,
United States
Vine House Distribution Ltd, Waldenbury, North
Common, Chailey, East Sussex BN8 4DR

**Pallas Guides**, *imprint of* Pallas Athene

**Pan**, *imprint of* Pan Macmillan

**Pan Books Ltd**, see Pan Macmillan

**Pan Macmillan+**
25 Eccleston Place, London SW1W 9NF
*Tel:* (020) 7881 8000 *Fax:* (020) 7881 8001
*Web Site:* www.panmacmillan.com
*Key Personnel*
Man Dir & Chief Executive: Adrian Soar
*E-mail:* a.soar@macmillan.co.uk
Marketing: Iain Chapple *E-mail:* i.chapple@
macmillan.co.uk
Production: Daria Neklesa *E-mail:* d.neklesa@
macmillan.co.uk
Publicity: Kate Wright-Morris *E-mail:* k.wright-
morris@macmillan.co.uk
International Sales & Marketing: Davina Kimber
*Tel:* (01256) 302942
Marketing Requests: Kate Eshelby *Tel:* (020)
7014 6093
Rights Requests: Michelle Taylor *Tel:* (020) 7014
6155
Special Sales Requests: Katherine Brewster
*Tel:* (020) 7014 6084 *E-mail:* kbrewster@
macmillan.co.uk
Founded: 1947
No unsolicited manuscripts. Query first for appro-
priate contact details & submission process.
New authors & agents for children's books
should go through an agent.
Subjects: Education, Nonfiction (General), Ro-
mance, Self-Help
ISBN Prefix(es): 0-330
*Parent Company:* Macmillan Ltd
*Holding Company:* Macmillan Ltd
*Associate Companies:* Macmillan General Books
Ltd
Imprints: Boxtree; Campbell Books; Channel
4 Books; Macmillan; Macmillan Children's
Books; Pan; Papermac; Picador; Sidgwick &
Jackson
Subsidiaries: Pan Macmillan (Australia) Pty Ltd;
Pan Books New Zealand Ltd; Pan Books Pty
Ltd
*Warehouse:* Houndmills, Basingstoke, Hants
*Tel:* (01256) 464481 *Fax:* (01256) 460675
*Orders to:* Houndmills, Basingstoke, Hants
*Tel:* (01256) 464481 *Fax:* (01256) 460675

**Panaf Books**
75 Weston St, London SE1 3RS
*Tel:* (0870) 333 1192
*E-mail:* zakakembo@yahoo.co.uk
*Web Site:* www.panafbooks.com
Founded: 1968
Academic & general publications.
ISBN Prefix(es): 0-901787
*Ultimate Parent Company:* Panaf Ltd

**Pandora Press**, *imprint of* Rivers Oram Press

**Panos Institute**
9 White Lion St, London N1 9PD
*Tel:* (020) 7278 1111 *Fax:* (020) 7278 0345
*E-mail:* info@panoslondon.org.uk
*Web Site:* www.panos.org.uk
*Key Personnel*
Head of Information: Heather Budge-Reid
Subjects: Developing Countries, Environmental
Studies
ISBN Prefix(es): 1-870670
Distributed by Fernwood Books Ltd (Canada);
Ideas Centre (Australia); Paula & Co (USA);
Russel Friedman Boks (South Africa)

**Papermac**, *imprint of* Pan Macmillan

**Paperstyle Gift Line**, *imprint of* Ryland Peters &
Small Ltd

**Paragon**, *imprint of* BBC Audiobooks

**Parapress**, *imprint of* Parapress Ltd

**Parapress Ltd+**
9 Frant Rd, Tunbridge Wells, Kent TN2 5SD
*Tel:* (01892) 512118 *Fax:* (01892) 512118
*E-mail:* office@parapress.eclipse.co.uk
*Web Site:* www.parapress.co.uk
*Key Personnel*
Man Dir: Elizabeth Imlay *E-mail:* e.imlay.
parapress@virgin.net
General Assistant: James Ewing
Publicity Assistant: David Walsh
Founded: 1999
Specialize in animals, biography, history & mili-
taria.
Membership(s): IPG.
Subjects: Animals, Pets, Biography, Crafts,
Games, Hobbies, Education, Health, Nutri-
tion, History, How-to, Humor, Literature, Liter-
ary Criticism, Essays, Maritime, Military Sci-
ence, Music, Dance, Nonfiction (General), Out-
door Recreation, Self-Help, Sports, Athletics,
Women's Studies
ISBN Prefix(es): 1-898594
Number of titles published annually: 4 Print
Total Titles: 20 Print
Imprints: Parapress

**PARAS+**
64 Sheperds Hill, Unit 3, London N6 5RN
*Tel:* (020) 8342 9600 *Fax:* (020) 8342 9600
*E-mail:* paraspublishing@telco4u.net
*Key Personnel*
Contact: Deborah O'Brien
Founded: 1990
Subjects: Poetry, Spirituality
ISBN Prefix(es): 1-874292
Total Titles: 4 Print

**Park Lane (Art)**, *imprint of* Grange Books PLC

**Parthian Books+**
The Old Surgery, Napier St, Cardigan SA43 1ED
*Tel:* (01239) 612059 *Fax:* (01239) 612059
*E-mail:* parthianbooks@yahoo.co.uk
*Web Site:* www.parthianbooks.co.uk
*Key Personnel*
Dir & International Rights: Richard Davies
Founded: 1993
Specialize in translations from Welsh to English.
Membership(s): Literary Publishers-Wales.
Subjects: Drama, Theater, Fiction
ISBN Prefix(es): 0-9521558; 1-902638
Number of titles published annually: 6 Print
Total Titles: 26 Print
*Owned by:* St Clair Press, PO Box 287, Rozella,
NSW 2039, Australia
Distributed by Dufour Editions (US)
Foreign Rep(s): Dufour Editions Inc (US)
*Orders to:* Dufour Editions, St Clair Press, PO
Box 287, Rozella NSW 2039, Australia

**Partridge Press**, *imprint of* Transworld
Publishers Ltd

**Pasold Research Fund**, *imprint of* Maney
Publishing

**PasTest**
Egerton Court, Parkgate Estate, Knutsford,
Cheshire WA16 8DX
*Tel:* (01565) 752000 *Fax:* (01565) 650264
*E-mail:* enquiries@pastest.co.uk
*Web Site:* www.pastest.co.uk
*Key Personnel*
Dir, Rights: Freydis Campbell
Founded: 1972
Subjects: Business, Medicine, Nursing, Dentistry
ISBN Prefix(es): 0-906896; 1-901198

**Paternoster Periodicals**, *imprint of* Paternoster
Publishing

**Paternoster Press**, *imprint of* Paternoster Publishing

**Paternoster Publishing+**
Subsidiary of Send the Light Ltd
Kingstown Broadway, Carlisle, Cumbria CA3 0QS
Mailing Address: PO Box 300, Carlisle, Cumbria CA3 0QS
*Tel:* (01228) 512512 *Fax:* (01228) 514949; (01228) 593388
*E-mail:* info@paternoster-publishing.com
*Web Site:* www.paternoster-publishing.com
*Key Personnel*
Publisher: Mark Finnie *Tel:* (01228) 512512 ext 2249 *E-mail:* mark.finnie@paternoster-markpublishing.com
General Manager: Rob Cook *Tel:* (01228) 512512 ext 2253 *E-mail:* rob.cook@paternoster-publishing.com
US Sales Manager: John Lewis *Tel:* 706-554-5827 *E-mail:* john@omlit.om.org
Founded: 1936
Specialize in religious (Christian) books & periodicals.
Subjects: History, Philosophy, Religion - Other
ISBN Prefix(es): 0-85364; 1-84227
Total Titles: 200 Print
Imprints: Authentic Lifestyle; Paternoster Periodicals; Paternoster Press; Regnum; Rutherford House

**Pathfinder**, *imprint of* Jarrold Publishing

**Pathfinder London+**
47 The Cut, London SE1 8LF
*Tel:* (020) 7261 1354 *Fax:* (020) 7261 1354
*E-mail:* pathfinderlondon@compuserve.com
*Web Site:* www.pathfinderpress.com
*Key Personnel*
Man Dir: T Hunt
Subjects: Developing Countries, Economics, Government, Political Science, History, Labor, Industrial Relations, Social Sciences, Sociology, Women's Studies
ISBN Prefix(es): 0-87348
*Book Club(s):* Pathfinder Readers Club
*Warehouse:* Plymbridge, Estover, Plymouth PL6 7PZ
*Distribution Center:* Australia Pathfinder, Level 1, 3/281-287 Beamish St, Campsie, NSW 2194, Australia *Tel:* (02) 9718 9698 *Fax:* (02) 9718 0197 *E-mail:* pathfinder_sydney@bigpond.com (Australia, New Zealand, the Pacific, Southeast Asia)
Iceland Pathfinder, Skolavordustig 6B, PO Box 233, Reykjavik IS 121, Iceland *Tel:* 552 5502 *E-mail:* pathfind@mmedia.is
New Zealand Pathfinder, 7 Mason Ave, PO Box 3025, Otahuhu, Auckland, Australia *Tel:* (09) 276 8885 *Fax:* (09) 276 9995 *E-mail:* pathfinder.auck@actrix.co.nz
Pathfinder Press, PO Box 162767, Atlanta, GA 30321-2767, United States *Tel:* 404-669-0600 *Fax:* 707-667-1141 *E-mail:* pathfinderpress@compuserve.com (USA, Caribbean, Latin America, East Asia)
Pathfinder Press Distribution, 2761 Dundas St W, Toronto, ON M6P 1Y4, Canada *Tel:* 416-531-9119 *Fax:* 416-531-9393 *E-mail:* pathdistribcan@bellnet.ca (Canada)
Sweden Pathfinder, Domardrand 16, S-129 04 Hagersten, Sweden *Tel:* (08) 31 69 33 *Fax:* (08) 31 69 33 *E-mail:* pathfbkh@algonet.se
*Orders to:* Pathfinder, c/o Baker & Taylor International, 102 Longueville Rd, Suite 143, Lane Cove, NSW 2066, Australia *Tel:* (02) 9924 0505 *Fax:* (02) 9924 0515 (Australia, New Zealand,the Pacific, Southeast Asia)
Plymbridge Distributors Ltd, Estover Rd, Plymouth PL6 7PZ *Tel:* (01752) 202301

*Fax:* (01752) 202331 *E-mail:* orders@plymbridge.com (Europe, the Middle East, Africa, South Asia)

**Pavilion Books Ltd+**
Division of Chrysalis Group
The Chrysalis Bldg, Bramley Rd, London W10 6SP
*Tel:* (020) 7221 2213; (020) 7314 1469 (sales) *Fax:* (020) 7221 6455; (020) 7314 1594 (sales)
*E-mail:* info@chrysalisbooks.co.uk; enquiries@chrysalis.com
*Web Site:* www.chrysalisbooks.co.uk/books/publisher/pavilion
*Key Personnel*
Group Sales & Marketing Dir: Richard Samson *Tel:* (020) 7314 1459 *Fax:* (020) 7314 1549 *E-mail:* rsamson@chrysalisbooks.co.uk
Dir of Marketing: Kate Wood *Tel:* (020) 7314 1496 *E-mail:* kwood@chrysalisbooks.co.uk
Permissions: Terry Forshaw *Tel:* (020) 7314 1607 *E-mail:* tforshaw@chrysalisbooks.co.uk
Foreign Rights Manager: Emma O'Grady *Tel:* (020) 7314 1447 *E-mail:* eogrady@chrysalisbooks.co.uk
Founded: 1981
Subjects: Art, Biography, Cookery, Film, Video, Gardening, Plants, House & Home, Photography, Travel
ISBN Prefix(es): 1-85145, 1-85793; 0-907516; 1-86205
Total Titles: 200 Print
Foreign Rights: Frank Chambers (Denmark, Far East, Finland, France, Norway, Sweden); Nina de la Mer (Belgium, Netherlands, Germany); Emma O'Grady (Eastern Europe, Italy, Latin America, Portugal, Russia, Spain); John Saunders-Griffiths (Canada, US)
*Orders to:* Littlehampton Book Services, Faraday Close, Off Columbia Dr, Durrington, West Sussex BN13 3HD *Tel:* (01903) 828800 *Fax:* (01903) 828802 *E-mail:* orders@lbsltd.co.uk

**Pavilion Publishing (Brighton) Ltd**
The Ironworks, Cheapside, Brighton, East Sussex BN1 4GD
*Tel:* (01273) 623222 *Fax:* (01273) 625526
*E-mail:* info@pavpub.com
*Web Site:* www.pavpub.com
Subjects: Social Sciences, Sociology, Disability, Health, Nursing, Special Needs
ISBN Prefix(es): 1-84196; 1-900600; 1-871080
Distributed by Gizmo
Distributor for Gizmo; NEC

**Paxton**, *imprint of* Novello & Co Ltd

**PC Publishing+**
Division of Music Technology Books Ltd
Keepers House, Merton, Thetford, Norfolk IP25 6QH
*Tel:* (01953) 889900 *Fax:* (01953) 889901
*E-mail:* info@pc-publishing.com
*Web Site:* www.pc-publishing.co.uk
*Key Personnel*
Publisher: Philip Chapman, Esq
Founded: 1988
Subjects: Computer Science, Electronics, Electrical Engineering, Music, Dance
ISBN Prefix(es): 1-870775
Number of titles published annually: 10 Print
Total Titles: 40 Print
Distributed by Music Software (Australia & New Zealand); O'Reilly (USA & Canada)
*Orders to:* Littlehampton Book Services, Faraday Close, Durrington, Worthing, W Sussex BN13 3RB *Tel:* (01903) 828800 *Fax:* (01903) 828801 *E-mail:* enquiries@lbsltd.co.uk *Web Site:* www.lbsltd.co.uk (UK)

**PCR**, *imprint of* Wilmington Business Information Ltd

**Pearson Education**
128 Long Acre, London WC2 9AN
*Tel:* (020) 7447 2000 *Fax:* (020) 7240 5771
*E-mail:* firstname.lastname@pearsoned-ema.com
*Telex:* 81259
*Key Personnel*
President Professional Education: Peter Marshall
Administration Manager, Prod Ed: Juliane Heineke
Finance Dir, Higher/Prof Ed: John Knight
Vice President, UK Sales & Marketing: Adrian Meillor
Editor-in-Chief, Business & Ref: Richard Stagg
Editor-in-Chief, Computing: Steve Temblett
Founded: 1724
Subjects: Accounting, Aeronautics, Aviation, Agriculture, Anthropology, Art, Biological Sciences, Business, Career Development, Chemistry, Chemical Engineering, Computer Science, Criminology, Economics, Education, Engineering (General), Environmental Studies, Geography, Geology, Government, Political Science, Health, Nutrition, History, Language Arts, Linguistics, Law, Literature, Literary Criticism, Essays, Management, Mathematics, Music, Dance, Natural History, Philosophy, Physics, Poetry, Psychology, Psychiatry, Religion - Other, Science (General), Social Sciences, Sociology, Veterinary Science, Women's Studies
ISBN Prefix(es): 0-582; 0-05
*Parent Company:* Pearson Plc
*Branch Office(s)*
Fourth Ave, Pinnacles, Harlow, Essex CM19 5AA *Tel:* (01279) 623623 *Fax:* (01279) 431067
*Showroom(s):* 5 Bentinck St, London W1M 5RN *Tel:* (020) 7935 0121 *Fax:* (020) 7486 4204
*Distribution Center:* Magna Park, Coventry Rd, Lutterworth, Leics LE17 4XH *Tel:* (01442) 881900 *Fax:* (01442) 882177

**Pearson Education Europe, Mideast & Africa+**
Edinburgh Gate, Harlow, Essex CM20 2JE
*Tel:* (01279) 62 3623 *Fax:* (01279) 41 4130
*E-mail:* firstname.lastname@pearsoned-ema.com
*Web Site:* www.pearsoned.co.uk
*Key Personnel*
President & Chief Executive Officer, Group Executive: Nigel Portwood
Chief Operating Officer, Group Executive: Brian Landers
Vice President, Finance, Group Executive: Lianne Gammon
President, Pearson Education Ltd: Rod Bristow
Rights & Contracts Dir, Pearson Education Ltd: Lynette Owen
VP, Finance, Pearson Education Ltd: John Knight
Senior Vice President, People & Change: Graham Abbey
President, ELT & Schools: Dugie Cameron
Man Dir, ELT Publishing: Gill Negas
Marketing Dir, ELT Marketing: Martha Ware
Man Dir, UK Schools: Jeff Andrew
Dir, International: Kern Roberts
Publishing Dir, International: Jenny Pares
Publishing Dir, UK Schools: Lorna Cocking
President, Higher Education: Jim Green
Vice President, Production: Colin Lander
Head of Facilities Management, Operations: John Fessey
Divisional Coordinator, FM Operations: Miranda Fishburn
Dir, Customer Service, Corporate Services: Jennie Heals
President, Schools EMA: John Penrose
Man Dir, Direct English, Consumer Language Learning: Clive Sawkins
Founded: 1998 (result of merger of Addison Wesley Longman, Financial Times Management & Prentice Hall Europe)

Subjects: Art, Business, Communications, Drama, Theater, Economics, Education, Government, Political Science, History, Language Arts, Linguistics, Medicine, Nursing, Dentistry, Music, Dance, Philosophy, Psychology, Psychiatry, Religion - Other, Science (General), Social Sciences, Sociology, Technology
ISBN Prefix(es): 1-84479
*Parent Company:* Pearson Education
*Ultimate Parent Company:* Pearson PLC
Imprints: Allyn & Bacon; Prentice Hall; Prentice Hall Europe; Prentice Hall Regents; Longman; Addison-Wesley; Financial Times Prentice Hall; Scott Foresman; Que; Que Lycos Books; Ziff-Davis Press; New Roders; Macmillan Technical Publishing USA; Que Education & Training; BradyGames; Sams Publishing; Sams.net; Borland Press; Hayden Books; Adobe Press; Waite Group Press
*Branch Office(s)*
Pearson Education Software Publishing Division, 124 Cambridge Science Park, Milton Rd, Cambridge CB4 4ZS *Tel:* (01223) 425558 *Fax:* (01223) 425349 *E-mail:* info@logo.com
128 Longacre, London WC2 9AN *Tel:* (020) 7477 2000 *Fax:* (020) 7240 5771
Campus 400, Maylands Ave, Hemel Hempstead, Herts HP2 7EZ *Tel:* (01442) 881900 *Fax:* (01442) 882099
*U.S. Office(s):* Pearson Education, One Lake St, Upper Saddle River, NJ 07458, United States

**Peartree Publications**
61 Peartree Lane, Bexhill-un-Sea, East Sussex TN39 4PE
*Tel:* (01424) 844274
*Key Personnel*
Partner: Roger Stepney
Founded: 1986
Subjects: Music, Dance
ISBN Prefix(es): 1-85254
Total Titles: 6 Print; 2 Audio

**Peepal Tree Press Ltd+**
17 Kings Ave, Leeds LS6 1QS
*Tel:* (0113) 245 1703 *Fax:* (0113) 246 8368
*E-mail:* contact@peepaltreepress.com
*Web Site:* www.peepaltreepress.com
*Key Personnel*
Man Editor: Jeremy Poynting *E-mail:* jeremy@peepal.demon.co.uk
Marketing Manager: Hannah Bannister *E-mail:* hannah@peepal.demon.co.uk
Founded: 1985
Specialize in Caribbean, African, South Asian & Black British fiction, poetry & criticism.
Subjects: Education, Fiction, History, Literature, Literary Criticism, Essays, Poetry, Social Sciences, Sociology
ISBN Prefix(es): 0-948833; 0-900715
Imprints: South Asians Overseas Series
*Orders to:* Central Books, 99 Wallis Rd, London E9 5LN
Paul & Co PCS Data Processing Inc, 360 W 31 St, New York, NY 10001, United States

**Pelican History of Art**, *imprint of* Yale University Press London

**Pen & Sword Books Ltd+**
47 Church St, Barnsley, S Yorks S70 2AS
*Tel:* (01226) 734555 *Fax:* (01226) 734438
*E-mail:* enquiries@pen-and-sword.co.uk
*Web Site:* www.pen-and-sword.co.uk
*Key Personnel*
Chairman: Nicholas Hewitt
Man Dir: Charles Hewitt *E-mail:* charles@pen-and-sword.co.uk
Publishing Manager: Henry Wilson *E-mail:* hw@henrywilson.lawlite.net
Production Manager: Barbara Bramall *E-mail:* production@pen-and-sword.co.uk

Sales Manager: Paula Brennan *E-mail:* sales@pen-and-sword.co.uk
Marketing & Publicity: Jonathan Wright *E-mail:* marketing@pen-and-sword.co.uk
Founded: 1990
Subjects: Aeronautics, Aviation, History, Maritime, Military Science, Local History, Military History
ISBN Prefix(es): 0-85052; 1-871647
Imprints: Leo Cooper; Pen & Sword Paperbacks; Wharncliffe Books

**Pen & Sword Paperbacks**, *imprint of* Pen & Sword Books Ltd

**Pencil Press**, *imprint of* Roundhouse Group

**Penguin**, *imprint of* Penguin Books Ltd

**Penguin Books Ltd+**
80 Strand, London WC2R 0RL
*Tel:* (020) 7416 3000 *Fax:* (020) 7416 3099; (020) 7416 3293
*Web Site:* www.penguin.com
*Telex:* 917181
*Key Personnel*
Chief Executive Officer: Anthony Forbes Watson
President: David Wan
Man Dir, Penguin General Division: Helen Fraser
Man Dir, Penguin Press: Andrew Rosenheim
Man Dir, Puffin: Philippa Milnes Smith
Man Dir, Frederick Warne: Sally Floyer
Rights Division (Warne): Susan Winton
Rights Dir (Adult): Sophie Brewer
Publicity Dir: Joanna Prior
Founded: 1935
General trade publisher; baby & toddler titles through to adult.
ISBN Prefix(es): 0-14; 0-7207; 0-14; 0-670; 0-7181
*Parent Company:* Penguin Publishing Co Ltd
*Ultimate Parent Company:* Pearson
Imprints: Viking; Puffin Books; Arkana; Ladybird; Hamish Hamilton; Michael Joseph; Allen Lane; Frederick Warne; Buildings of England; Penguin; Ventura
Divisions: Rough Guides Ltd
*Branch Office(s)*
Penguin USA, 375 Hudson St, New York, NY 10014, United States
*Orders to:* Penguin Group Distribution Ltd, Bath Rd, Harmondsworth, Middlesex UB7 0DA

**The Penguin Group UK+**
80 Strand, London WC2R 0RN
*Tel:* (020) 7010 3000
*E-mail:* editor@penguin.co.uk
*Web Site:* www.penguin.co.uk
*Key Personnel*
Chief Executive Officer, The Penguin Group: John Makinson
Chief Executive Officer, The Penguin Group (UK): Anthony Forbes Watson
Man Dir, Penguin: Helen Fraser
Man Dir, Ventura/Warne: Sally Floyer
Man Dir, Puffin: Francesca Dow
Group Sales & Operations: Peter Brown
Man Dir, Dorling Kindersley: Andrew Welhan
Founded: 1935
ISBN Prefix(es): 0-14; 0-670; 0-7181
*Parent Company:* Pearson PLC
Imprints: Michael Joseph; Hamish Hamilton; Viking; Allen Lane; Rough Guides; Buildings of England; Classics; Puffin
Subsidiaries: LadyBird Books Ltd
Divisions: Penguin General Books; Penguin Press; Frederick Warne; Dorling Kindersley; Puffin
*U.S. Office(s):* Penguin Group (USA) Inc, 375 Hudson St, New York, NY 10014, United States

Distributor for Rough Guides; Wisden
*Warehouse:* Penguin Books Ltd, Bath Rd, Harmondsworth MDDX UB7 (customer services)
*Orders to:* Penguin Books Ltd, Bath Rd, Harmondsworth, Middlesex UB7 0DA

**The Penguin Press**, *imprint of* Viking

**The Pensions Management Institute**
PMI House, 4/10 Artillery Lane, London E1 7LS
*Tel:* (020) 7247 1452 *Fax:* (020) 7375 0603
*E-mail:* enquiries@pensions-pmi.org.uk
*Web Site:* www.pensions-pmi.org.uk
*Key Personnel*
President: Roger Cobley
ISBN Prefix(es): 0-946242; 1-898785

**Pentathol Publishing+**
40 Gibson St, Wrexham, Wrexham County LL13 7NS
Mailing Address: PO Box 92, Wrexham, Wrexham County LL13 7NS
*Key Personnel*
Contact: A E Cowen
Founded: 1991
Membership(s): Publishers Association.
Subjects: Poetry
ISBN Prefix(es): 1-873021
Number of titles published annually: 1 Print
Total Titles: 1 Print
Imprints: "Huh!" 1991

**Perennial**, *imprint of* HarperCollins UK

**PerfectBound**, *imprint of* HarperCollins UK

**Pergamon Flexible Learning+**
Imprint of Butterworth-Heinemann
Linacre House, Jordan Hill, Oxford OX2 8DP
*Tel:* (01865) 310366; (01865) 388190 *Fax:* (01865) 314290
*E-mail:* bhmarketing@repp.co.uk
*Web Site:* www.bh.com/pergamonfl
*Key Personnel*
Dir: Kathryn Grant *E-mail:* kathryn.grant@repp.co.uk
Marketing Manager: Duncan Enright *E-mail:* duncanenright@repp.co.uk
International Marketing Manager: Jacquie Shanahan *E-mail:* jacquie.shanahan@repp.co.uk
UK Sales Manager: Mark Hunt *E-mail:* m.hunt@elsevier.com
Key Accounts Manager, Wholesaler/Library Supplier/Online: Nigel Berkeley *E-mail:* n.berkeley@elsevier.com
Key Accounts Manager, Retail: Chris Hossack *E-mail:* c.hossack@elsevier.com
Field Academic Manager, Scotland & Ireland: Karen McWhirter *E-mail:* k.mcwhirter@elsevier.com
Trade & Academic Representative, Greater London & Home Counties: Tom Waggitt *E-mail:* t.waggitt@elsevier.com
Trade & Academic Representative, South & West: Nicola Haden *E-mail:* n.haden@elsevier.com
Trade & Academic Representative, Midlands & North: Lynne Saunderson *E-mail:* l.saunderson@elsevier.com
National Account Manager, Pergamon Flexible Learning: David Lockley *E-mail:* d.lockley@elsevier.com
European Sales Manager: Rosanna Ramacciotti *E-mail:* r.ramacciotti@elsevier.com
Regional Sales Manager, Germany, Austria & Switzerland: Catherine Anderson *E-mail:* c.anderson@elsevier.com
Sales Representative, Austria & Switzerland: Kai Wuerfl-Davidek *E-mail:* k.wuerfl@elsevier.com
Area Sales Manager, Southern Europe: Miguel Sanchez Gatell *E-mail:* m.sanchez@elsevier.com

Sales Representative, Italy, France & Greece: Nadia Balavoine E-mail: n.balavoine@elsevier.com

Product Manager: Steve Brewster E-mail: s.brewster@elsevier.com

Internet Marketing Manager: Maddie Davis E-mail: m.davis@elsevier.com

Area Sales Manager, Benelux & Scandinavia: Robert Fairbrother E-mail: r.fairbrother@elsevier.com

Sales Representative, Scandinavia: Krista Leppiko E-mail: k.leppiko@elsevier.com

Sales Representative, South Germany: Christiane Leipersberger E-mail: c.leipersberger@elsevier.com

Area Sales Manager, Eastern Europe: Radek Janousek E-mail: r.janousek@elsevier.com

International Sales Manager, Middle East & Africa: Klaus Beran E-mail: k.beran@elsevier.com

Sales Office Manager: Emma Wyatt E-mail: e.wyatt@elsevier.com

Sales Office Coordinator: Emily Mander E-mail: e.mander@elsevier.com

Foreign Rights Manager: Adele Parker E-mail: a.parker@elsevier.com

Foreign Rights Assistant: Annette Fuhrmeister E-mail: a.fuhrmeister@elsevier.com

Special Sales Manager: Judy Chappell E-mail: j.chappell@elsevier.com

Special Sales Executive, Technical Books: Rosie Moss E-mail: r.moss@elsevier.com

Internet Marketing Manager: Maddie Davis E-mail: m.davis@elsevier.com

Founded: 1987

Subjects: Business, Education, Management, Marketing, Customer Service, Sales, Health & Safety, Training & Development, Open Learning Materials

ISBN Prefix(es): 0-08; 0-7506

Parent Company: Butterworth-Heinemann, Linacre House, Jordan Hill, Oxford OX2 8DP

Ultimate Parent Company: Reed

Associate Companies: Butterworth-Heinemann Inc, 313 Washington St, Newton, MA 02158, United States Tel: 617-928-2500 Fax: 617-928-2620

**Permanent Publications**, imprint of Hyden House Ltd

**Perpetuity Press+**
50 Queens Rd, Leicester LE2 1TU
Tel: (0116) 221 7778 Fax: (0116) 221 7171
E-mail: orders@perpetuitypress.com
Web Site: www.perpetuitypress.com
Key Personnel
Publisher: K A Gill
Founded: 1994
Membership(s): IPG.
Subjects: Business, Criminology, Law, Management, Maritime, Security Management, Risk Management & Policing, crime prevention
ISBN Prefix(es): 1-899287

**Peter Peregrinus Ltd**, imprint of Institution of Electrical Engineers

**Pevsner Architectural Guides**, imprint of Yale University Press London

**Phaidon Press Ltd+**
Regent's Wharf, All Saints St, London N1 9PA
Tel: (020) 7843 1234 Fax: (020) 7843 1111
E-mail: esales@phaidon.com
Web Site: www.phaidon.com
Key Personnel
Man Dir: Andrew Price
Export Sales Dir: Sheila McKenna
Operations Dir: Fran Johnson
Publisher: Richard Schlagman

Vice President Sales & Marketing, Phaidon Press Inc: Mary Albi
Deputy Publisher: Amanda Renshaw
Marketing Manager: Truda Spruyt
UK Sales Manager: Simon Kingsley
Sales & Marketing Dir: John Roberts
International Editions Manager: Helen Garrett
Founded: 1923
Subjects: Architecture & Interior Design, Art, Biography, Drama, Theater, History, Photography
ISBN Prefix(es): 0-7148
Subsidiaries: Phaidon Press Inc
U.S. Office(s): 3 Center Plaza, Boston, MA 02108, United States, Contact: Jeremy Raymondjack E-mail: ussales@phaidon.com
Warehouse: Unit 4, Lodge Causeway Trading Estate Fishponds, Bristol, Avon BS16 3JB

**Pharmaceutical Press+**
Division of The Royal Pharmaceutical Society
One Lamberth High St, London SE1 7JN
Tel: (020) 7735 9141 Fax: (020) 7572 2509
E-mail: pharmpress@rpsgb.org
Web Site: www.pharmpress.com
Key Personnel
Dir, Publications: Charles Fry E-mail: charles.fry@rpsgb.org
Editorial Production Manager: John Wilson E-mail: john.wilson@rpsgb.org
Head of Sales & Marketing: Colin Fenton E-mail: colin.fenton@rpsgb.org
Sales Manager, Electronic Products: Peter Goacher Tel: (020) 7735 9141 E-mail: peter.goacher@rpsgb.org
Contracts & Licensing Manager: Jane Mulholland E-mail: jane.mulholland@rpsgb.org
Founded: 1841
Subjects: Chemistry, Chemical Engineering, Health, Nutrition, Law, Medicine, Nursing, Dentistry, Veterinary Science, Pharmaceutical
ISBN Prefix(es): 0-85369
Number of titles published annually: 30 Print; 5 CD-ROM
Total Titles: 60 Print; 7 CD-ROM; 1 Online
U.S. Office(s): 100 S Atkinson Rd, Suite 206, Grayslake, IL 60030-7820, United States
Warehouse: Customer Services Dept, PO Box 151, Wallingford OX10 8QU
Orders to: Customer Services Dept, PO Box 151, Wallingford OX10 8QU
Returns: Customer Services Dept, PO Box 151, Wallingford OX10 8QU

**Philip & Tacey Ltd**
North Way, Andover, Hants SP10 5BA
Tel: (01264) 332171 Fax: (01264) 384808
E-mail: sales@philipandtacey.co.uk
Web Site: www.philipandtacey.co.uk
Key Personnel
Man Dir: Gerry Vaughan
Founded: 1829
Membership(s): BESA.
Subjects: Education
ISBN Prefix(es): 0-902073
Associate Companies: Philograph Publications Ltd, Pottington Industrial Estate, Riverside Rd, Barnstable EX31 1LR
U.S. Office(s): Didax Inc, 395 Main St, Rowley, MA 01969, United States

**Philip**, imprint of Octopus Publishing Group

**Philip's+**
Division of Hachette Livre (France)
11 Salvsbury Rd, London NW6 6RG
Tel: (020) 7644 6900 Fax: (020) 7644 6987
E-mail: philips@philips-maps.co.uk
Web Site: www.philips-maps.co.uk
Key Personnel
Man Dir & Publisher: John Gaisford Tel: (020) 7644 6901 E-mail: john.gaisford@philips-maps.co.uk

Mapping Director: David Gaylard Tel: (020) 7644 6902 E-mail: david.gaylard@philips-maps.co.uk

Trade Sales Dir: Roger Fox E-mail: roger.fox@philips-maps.co.uk

Trade Sales Administrator: Wendy Graham E-mail: wendy.graham@philips-maps.co.uk; Dimity Castellano E-mail: dimity.castellano@philips-maps.co.uk

Rights, Foreign Rights, Premiums & Data Sales Dir: Victoria Dawbarn E-mail: victoria.dawbarn@philips-maps.co.uk

Digital Data Sales: James Mann E-mail: james.mann@philips-maps.co.uk

Founded: 1834

Specialize in world atlases, road & street atlases, astronomy, encyclopedias & illustrated reference.

Membership(s): Royal Geographical Society; International Map Traders Association.

Subjects: Astronomy, Geography, Geology
ISBN Prefix(es): 0-540
Total Titles: 300 Print
Parent Company: Octopus Publishing Group
Ultimate Parent Company: Lagardere Group
Orders to: Littlehampton Book Services, Durrington, Worthing, West Sussex BN13 3RB Tel: (01903) 828500 Fax: (01903) 828625 E-mail: orders@lbsltd.co.uk Web Site: www.lbsltd.co.uk

**Phillimore & Co Ltd+**
Shopwyke Manor Barn, Chichester, West Sussex PO20 2BG
Tel: (01243) 787636 Fax: (01243) 787639
E-mail: bookshop@phillimore.co.uk
Web Site: www.phillimore.co.uk
Key Personnel
Chairman: Philip Harris
Manager & Editorial: Noel H Osborne
Founded: 1897
Subjects: Archaeology, Architecture & Interior Design, History, Regional Interests
ISBN Prefix(es): 0-85033; 0-900592; 1-86077; 0-900809
Associate Companies: British Association for Local History; Historical Publications Ltd

**Philograph Publications Ltd**
Riverside Rd, Pottington Industrial Estate, Barnstaple EX31 1YZ
Tel: (01271) 45061 Fax: (01271) 23076
Key Personnel
Man Dir: Chris Tacey
Founded: 1829
Specialize in teaching aids & resources for primary schools.
ISBN Prefix(es): 0-85370
Parent Company: Philip & Tacey Ltd, North Way, Andover, Hants
U.S. Office(s): Didax Inc, 395 Main St, Rowley, MA 01969, United States
Orders to: Philip & Tracey Ltd, Riverside Rd, Pottington Industrial Estate, Devon EX31 1LR

**Photo Art International**, imprint of Creative Monochrome Ltd

**Phronesis**, imprint of Verso

**Piatkus Books+**
5 Windmill St, London W1T 2JA
Tel: (020) 7631 0710 Fax: (020) 7436 7137
E-mail: info@piatkus.co.uk
Web Site: www.piatkus.co.uk
Key Personnel
Man Dir: Judy Piatkus
Editorial Dir: Gill Bailey
Sales Dir: Philip Cotterell
Publicity Manager: Jana Sommerlad
Production Manager: Simon Colverson
Rights Manager: Jon Mitchell
Founded: 1979

An independent publishing company. Specialize in general trade nonfiction & popular fiction including mass market.
Subjects: Astrology, Occult, Biography, Business, Career Development, Cookery, Criminology, Fashion, Fiction, Health, Nutrition, Humor, Management, Nonfiction (General), Psychology, Psychiatry, Self-Help
ISBN Prefix(es): 0-7499; 0-86188
Number of titles published annually: 175 Print
Total Titles: 3,000 Print
*Parent Company:* Judy Piatkus (Publishers) Ltd
Distributed by Angell Eurosales (Austria, Benelux, France, Germany, Iceland, Scandinavia, Switzerland); Ashton International Marketing Services (Middle East); David Bateman Ltd (New Zealand); Bookport Associates (Gibraltar, Greece, Italy, Malta, Portugal, Spain); General Publishing (Canada); Kelvin van Hasselt (Mauritius, Seychelles & West Africa); Hodder Headline (Australia) Pty Ltd (Australia); India Book Distribution (Bombay) Ltd (India); MTM; Pansing Distribution Sdn Bhd (Malaysia & Singapore); Penguin South Africa (Pty) Ltd (South Africa & Zimbabwe); Ralph & Sheila Summers (Far East)
*Shipping Address:* Grantham Book Services Ltd, Isaac Newton Way, Alma Park Industrial Estate, Grantham, Lincs NG31 9SD *Tel:* (01476) 541044 *Fax:* (01476) 590223
*Warehouse:* Grantham Book Services Ltd, Isaac Newton Way, Alma Park Industrial Estate, Grantham, Lincs N931 9SD *Tel:* (1476) 541000 *Fax:* (1476) 590223
*Orders to:* Grantham Book Services Ltd, Isaac Newton Way, Alma Park Industrial Estate, Grantham, Lincs NG31 9SD *Tel:* (01476) 541000 *Fax:* (01476) 590223

**Pica Press**, *imprint of* A & C Black Publishers Ltd

**Pica Press**, *imprint of* Christopher Helm (Publishers) Ltd

**Picador**, *imprint of* Pan Macmillan

**Piccadilly Press+**
5 Castle Rd, London NW1 8PR
*Tel:* (020) 7267 4492 *Fax:* (020) 7267 4493
*E-mail:* books@piccadillypress.co.uk
*Web Site:* www.piccadillypress.co.uk
*Key Personnel*
Man Dir & Publisher: Brenda Gardner
Senior Editor: Yasemin Ucar
Production: Geoff Barlow
Rights: Margot Edwards
Book Clubs & Special Sales: Lea Garton
Founded: 1983
Independent children's publisher specializing in picture books, teenage fiction, nonfiction & parental books.
Subjects: Fiction, Humor, Nonfiction (General), Parenting
ISBN Prefix(es): 1-85340
Number of titles published annually: 30 Print
Total Titles: 250 Print
Foreign Rights: Akcali Copyright (Turkey); Luigi Bernabo Associates (Italy); The English Agency (Japan) Ltd (Japan); JLM Literary Agency (Greece); KCC (Korea); Jacqueline Miller Agency (France); Andrew Nurnberg Associates (Czech Republic, Hungary, Poland, Romania, Russia); I Pikarski (Israel)
*Orders to:* Ashton International Marketing Services, PO Box 298, Sevenoaks, Kent TN13 1WU *Tel:* (01732) 746 093 *Fax:* (01732) 746 096 (Cambodia, China, Indonesia, Japan, Korea, Laos & Myanmar)
Fields & Associates Ltd, 1/F Prosperous Commercial Bldg, 54 Jardine Bazaar, Causeway Bay, Hong Kong (Hong Kong), Pauline Lau

Forrester Books NZ Ltd, 10 Tarndale Grove, Albany, Private Bag 102907, North Shore Mail Center, Auckland, New Zealand *Tel:* (09) 415 2080 *Fax:* (09) 415 2083 *E-mail:* cath@forrester.co.nz (New Zealand)
Grantham Book Services, Isaac Newton Way, Alma Park Industrial Estate, Grantham NG31 9SD *Tel:* (01476) 541 080 *Fax:* (01476) 541 061 *E-mail:* orders@gbs.tbs-ltd.co.uk (UK)
The Old Whaling House, The Walls, Berwick-upon-Tweed TD15 1HP *Tel:* (01289) 332 934 *Fax:* (01289) 332 935 (France, Benelux, Scandinavia & Iceland)
Peribo, 58 Beaumont Rd, Mount Kuring-Gai, NSW 2080, Australia *Tel:* (02) 9457 0011 *Fax:* (02) 9457 0022 *E-mail:* peribo@bigpond.com (Australia)
Publishers Marketing Service, Unit 509, Block E, Philco Dmansara 1, Jalan 16/11, Off Jalan Damansara, 46350 Petaling Jaya, Selango Darul Ehsan, Malaysia *Tel:* (03) 755 3588 *Fax:* (03) 755 3017 *E-mail:* pmsmal@po.jaring.my (Malaysia)
Publishers Marketing Services, 10c Jalan Ampas 07-01, Ho Seng Lee Flatted Warehouse, Singapore 329513, Singapore *Tel:* 256 5166 *Fax:* 253 0008 *E-mail:* pmssin@mbox3.singnet.com.sg (Singapore)
Rep Force Ireland, 12 Longford Terrace, Monkstown, Co Dublin, Ireland *Tel:* (01) 280 1552 *Fax:* (01) 280 1054 (Ireland)
TBS Ltd, Frating Green, Colchester Rd, Colchester, Essex C07 7DW *Tel:* (01206) 256 000 *Fax:* (01206) 255 715
Trinity Books, PO Box 242, Randburg 2125, South Africa *Tel:* (011) 787 4010; (011) 787 4011 *Fax:* (011) 787 8920 *E-mail:* trinity@africa.com (South Africa)

**Pickering & Chatto Publishers Ltd+**
21 Bloomsbury Way, London WC1A 2TH
*Tel:* (020) 7405 1005 *Fax:* (020) 7405 6216
*E-mail:* info@pickeringchatto.co.uk
*Web Site:* www.pickeringchatto.com
*Key Personnel*
Chairman: Lord Rees-Mogg
Man Dir: James Powell *E-mail:* james@pickeringchatto.co.uk
Editorial Dir: Mark Pollard *E-mail:* mark@pickeringchatto.co.uk
Senior Editor: Michael Middeke *E-mail:* michael@pickeringchatto.co.uk
Marketing Manager: Paul Boland *E-mail:* paul@pickeringchatto.co.uk
Founded: 1985
Also specialize in rare books & journals in facsimile.
Membership(s): IPG.
Subjects: Business, Economics, History, Literature, Literary Criticism, Essays, Philosophy, Women's Studies, History of Science, Politics
ISBN Prefix(es): 1-85196
Number of titles published annually: 20 Print; 5 Online
Total Titles: 25 Online
Imprints: William Pickering
Distributed by Ashgate Publishing Co (North & South America); DA Information Services (Australia & New Zealand); Publishers International Marketing (Singapore, Hong Kong, Indonesia, Philippines, Malaysia & Thailand); Turpin Distribution; Unifacmanu Trading Co Ltd (Taiwan)
Foreign Rep(s): Applied Media (India); Iberian Book Services (Portugal, Spain); Japan Book Associates Co (Japan); Publishers International Marketing (China, Middle East, South Korea)
*Warehouse:* Extenza-Turpin, Stratton Business Park, Pegasus Drive, Biggleswade, Beds SG18 8QG *Tel:* (01767) 604951 *Fax:* (01767) 601640 *E-mail:* books@extenza-turpin.com

**William Pickering**, *imprint of* Pickering & Chatto Publishers Ltd

**Picton Press (Liverpool)**, *imprint of* Countyvise Ltd

**Picture Corgi**, *imprint of* Transworld Publishers Ltd

**Pimlico**, *imprint of* Random House UK Ltd

**Pine Forge Press**, *imprint of* SAGE Publications Ltd

**Pinter**, *imprint of* The Continuum International Publishing Group Ltd

**Pinter, Studio Vista**, *imprint of* Cassell & Co

**Pinwheel Publishing Ltd+**
Subsidiary of Andromeda Holdings Ltd
Station House, 8-13 Swiss Terrace, London NW6 4RR
*Tel:* (020) 7580 8880 *Fax:* (020) 7323 0828
*E-mail:* sales@pinwheel.co.uk
*Web Site:* www.pinwheel.co.uk
*Key Personnel*
Sales Manager: Kristina Dahlqvist *E-mail:* kristina.dahlqvist@pinwheel.co.uk; Giovanna Franchina *E-mail:* giovanna.franchina@pinwheel.co.uk
European Sales Manager: Rachel Pidcock *E-mail:* rachel.pidcock@pinwheel.co.uk
Sales Administrator: Rosie Guard *E-mail:* rosie.guard@pinwheel.co.uk
Commissioning Editor: Shaheen Bilgrami *E-mail:* shaheen.bilgrami@pinwheel.co.uk
Art Dir: Ali Scrivens *E-mail:* ali.scrivens@pinwheel.co.uk
Production Manager: Martin Croshow *E-mail:* martin.croshow@pinwheel.co.uk
Production Editor: Caterina Boselli *E-mail:* caterina.boselli@pinwheel.co.uk
Designer: Ella Butler *E-mail:* ella.butler@pinwheel.co.uk
Founded: 1995
Children's novelty books for preschool age.
ISBN Prefix(es): 1-902249
Number of titles published annually: 15 Print
Total Titles: 60 Print

**Pion Ltd+**
207 Brondesbury Park, London NW2 5JN
*Tel:* (020) 8459 0066 *Fax:* (020) 8451 6454
*E-mail:* sales@pion.co.uk
*Web Site:* www.pion.co.uk
*Key Personnel*
Dir: Dr Jonathan Briggs
Man Dir: Adam Gelbtuch
Senior Editor: Dr Jan Schubert
Sales & Rights Manager: Diana Harrop *E-mail:* sales@pion.co.uk
Founded: 1960
Journal publisher.
Membership(s): ALPSP; IPG.
Subjects: Geography, Geology, Mathematics, Physical Sciences, Physics, Psychology, Psychiatry
ISBN Prefix(es): 0-85086
Total Titles: 15 Print
*Associate Companies:* Turpion Ltd (Joint venture with Institute of Physics Publishing)
Foreign Rights: Japan Uni Agency (Japan)
*Warehouse:* Extenza-Turpin Ltd, Stratton Business Park, Pegasus Dr, Biggleswade, Beds SG18 8QB *Tel:* (01767) 604951 *Fax:* (01767) 601640 *E-mail:* books@extenza-turpin.com (Book orders & Turpin journal orders; Pion Journal orders contact publisher)
*Orders to:* Extenza-Turpin Ltd, Stratton Business Park, Pegasus Dr, Biggleswade, Beds SG18 8QB *Tel:* (01767) 604951 *Fax:* (01767) 601640

*E-mail:* books@extenza-turpin.com (Book orders & Turpion journal orders; Pion Journal orders contact publisher)

**PIRA Intl**
Randalls Rd, Leatherhead, Surrey KT22 7RU
*Tel:* (01372) 802000 *Fax:* (01372) 802238
*E-mail:* publications@pira.co.uk
*Web Site:* www.piranet.com
*Key Personnel*
Contact: Philip Swinden
A consultancy business with major publishing & conference activities, serving the printing, publishing, packaging & paper industries.
Subjects: Publishing & Book Trade Reference, Technology
ISBN Prefix(es): 1-85802; 0-902799
*U.S. Office(s):* Books International, PO Box 605, Herndon, VA 20172, United States *Tel:* 703-689-4204

**Pitkin Unichrome Ltd+**
Healey House, Dene Rd, Andover, Hants SP10 2AA
*Tel:* (01264) 409200 *Fax:* (01264) 334110
*E-mail:* enquiries@pitkin-unichrome.com
*Web Site:* www.britguides.com
*Key Personnel*
Dir: Heather Hook
Founded: 1947
Subjects: Biography, History, Travel
ISBN Prefix(es): 0-85372; 1-871004; 0-9507291; 1-84165
Number of titles published annually: 10 Print; 1 CD-ROM
Total Titles: 280 Print; 1 CD-ROM; 270 Online; 1 E-Book
*Parent Company:* Jarrold Publishing
*Ultimate Parent Company:* Jarrold & Sons Ltd

**PJB Reference Sevices**
Division of PJB Publications Ltd
Suffield House, 9 Paradise Rd, Richmond, Surrey TW9 1SJ
*Tel:* (020) 8332 8970 *Fax:* (020) 8332 8937
*E-mail:* pjbreference@pjbpubs.com
*Web Site:* www.pjbreference.com
Supplier of contact names for the pharmaceutical, biotechnical, medical device, diagnostics & service industries. Details of pharma, biotech, MD & service company addresses worldwide with named senior personnel.
*Ultimate Parent Company:* Informa Group

**Planet+**
PO Box 44, Aberystwyth, Ceredigion SY23 3ZZ
*Tel:* (01970) 611255 *Fax:* (01970) 611197
*E-mail:* planet.enquiries@planetmagazine.org.uk
*Web Site:* www.planetmagazine.org.uk
*Key Personnel*
Chairman & Dir: John Barnie
Founded: 1985
Publishing House.
Subjects: Art, Literature, Literary Criticism, Essays, Poetry
ISBN Prefix(es): 0-9505188
Total Titles: 7 Print
*Parent Company:* Berw Cyf

**Plantin Publishers**, *imprint of* Cardiff Academic Press

**Plantin Publishers+**
St Fagans Rd, Fairwater, Cardiff CF5 3AE
*Tel:* (029) 2056 0333 *Fax:* (029) 2056 0313
*E-mail:* drakegroup@btinternet.com
*Web Site:* www.drakeed.com/cap
*Key Personnel*
Man Dir: R G Drake
Founded: 1987

Specialize in publishing re-prints of out-of-print titles, usually out-of-copyright.
Subjects: Biography, Literature, Literary Criticism, Essays
ISBN Prefix(es): 1-870495
*Parent Company:* Cardiff Academic Press

**Platform 5 Publishing Ltd**
3 Wyvern House, Sark Rd, Sheffield S2 4HG
*Tel:* (0114) 255 8000 *Fax:* (0114) 255 2471
*E-mail:* platform5@platfive.freeserve.co.uk
*Key Personnel*
Publisher & Editor-in-Chief: Peter Fox
Editor: David Haydock
Founded: 1984
Subjects: Transportation
ISBN Prefix(es): 0-906579; 1-872524; 1-902336
Distributor for Quail Map Co (UK, except South of England); South Coast Transport Publishing

**The Playwrights Publishing Co**
70 Nottingham Rd, Burton Joyce, Notts NG14 5AL
*Tel:* (01159) 313356
*E-mail:* playwrightspublishingco@yahoo.com
*Web Site:* www.geocities.com/playwrightspublishingco
*Key Personnel*
Dir: Liz Breeze; Tony Breeze
Founded: 1990
Publisher of one-act & full length plays.
Subjects: Drama, Theater
ISBN Prefix(es): 1-873130
Number of titles published annually: 12 Print; 12 E-Book
Total Titles: 45 Print; 12 E-Book

**Plexus Publishing Ltd+**
55a Clapham Common Southside, London SW4 9BX
*Tel:* (020) 7622 2440 *Fax:* (020) 7622 2441
*E-mail:* info@plexusuk.demon.co.uk
*Web Site:* www.plexusbooks.com
*Key Personnel*
Sales, Production: Terence Porter
Editorial, Rights & Permissions: Sandra Wake
Coordinator Editor: Rebecca Martin
Founded: 1973
Publish illustrated nonfiction books specializing in international co-editions with an emphasis on biography, popular music, rock 'n' roll, popular culture, art, photography & cinema.
Subjects: Biography, Drama, Theater, Fashion, Film, Video, Music, Dance, Photography, Radio, TV
ISBN Prefix(es): 0-85965
Number of titles published annually: 15 Print
Total Titles: 100 Print
Distributed by Publishers Group West (USA & Canada)
*Warehouse:* Bookpoint Ltd, 39 Milton Park, Abingdon, Oxon OX14 4TD *Tel:* (01235) 400 400 *Fax:* (01235) 832 068
*Orders to:* Bookpoint Ltd, 39 Milton Park, Abingdon, Oxon OX14 4TD *Tel:* (01235) 400 400 *Fax:* (01235) 832 068
Publishers Group West, 1700 Fourth St, Berkeley, CA 94710, United States *Tel:* 510-528-1444 *Fax:* 510-528-3444

**Plough Publishing House of Bruderhof Communities in the UK+**
Darvell Bruderhof, Robertsbridge, East Sussex TN32 5DR
*Tel:* (01580) 883 344 *Fax:* (01580) 883 317
*Toll Free Fax:* 800-018-3347
*E-mail:* contact@bruderhof.com
*Web Site:* www.plough.com
*Key Personnel*
Man Dir, Rights & Permissions: Josef Ben Eliezer
Sales, Publicity & Advertising Dir: Stefan Tietze

Founded: 1937
Subjects: Fiction, Poetry, Religion - Other, Self-Help, Theology

**Pluto Books Ltd+**
345 Archway Rd, London N6 5AA
*Tel:* (020) 8348 2724 *Fax:* (020) 8348 9133
*E-mail:* pluto@plutobooks.com
*Web Site:* www.plutobooks.com
*Key Personnel*
President: Roger van Zwanenberg
*E-mail:* rogervz@plutobooks.com
Editorial Dir: Anne Beech *E-mail:* beech@plutobooks.com
Sales Dir: Simon Liebesny *E-mail:* simon@plutobooks.com
Founded: 1987
Subjects: African American Studies, Anthropology, Developing Countries, Economics, Government, Political Science, History, Social Sciences, Sociology
ISBN Prefix(es): 0-7452
Number of titles published annually: 80 Print; 80 Online; 80 E-Book
Total Titles: 450 Print; 250 Online; 250 E-Book
Imprints: Pluto Press
Distributed by University of Michigan Press
Distributor for Autonomedia; Ocean Press; Paradigm; South End Press
*Shipping Address:* Chicago Distribution Center, 11030 S Langley Ave, Chicago, IL 60628, United States
*Warehouse:* Chicago Distribution Center, 11030 S Langley Ave, Chicago, IL 60628, United States
*Distribution Center:* Chicago Distribution Center, 11030 S Langley Ave, Chicago, IL 60628, United States
*Orders to:* Chicago Distribution Center, 11030 S Langley Ave, Chicago, IL 60628, United States
*Returns:* Chicago Distribution Center, 11030 S Langley Ave, Chicago, IL 60628, United States

**Pluto Press**, *imprint of* Pluto Books Ltd

**Pluto Press+**
Imprint of Pluto Books Ltd
345 Archway Rd, London N6 5AA
*Tel:* (020) 8348 2724 *Fax:* (020) 8348 9133
*E-mail:* pluto@plutobooks.com
*Web Site:* www.plutobooks.com
*Key Personnel*
Man Dir: Roger van Zwanenberg
Editorial Dir: Anne Beech
Managing Editor: Robert Webb
Head, Sales & Marketing: Simon Liebesny
*Tel:* (020) 8374 2188 *E-mail:* simon@plutobooks.com
Founded: 1970
Independent progressive publishing.
Subjects: African American Studies, Anthropology, Biography, Criminology, Developing Countries, Economics, Environmental Studies, Ethnicity, Government, Political Science, History, Journalism, Labor, Industrial Relations, Law, Philosophy, Social Sciences, Sociology, Women's Studies
ISBN Prefix(es): 0-85305; 0-86104; 0-7453; 0-902818; 0-904383
Number of titles published annually: 80 Print
Total Titles: 500 Print
*Associate Companies:* Journeyman Press
Distributed by Book Promotions/Horizon Books (South Africa); Footprint Books (Australia); Taylor & Francis Asia Pacific (Far East (excluding Japan)); UBC Press, University of British Columbia (Canada); United Publishers Services Ltd (Japan); University of Michigan Press (USA)
Distributor for Autonomedia Publishers; Ocean Press; Paradigm Publishers; South End Press
Foreign Rep(s): Durnell Marketing (Europe); IPR Publishers Representatives (Middle East); Maya

Publishers Pvt Ltd (India); Vera Medeiros Book Business International (Latin America)
*Distribution Center:* University of Michigan Press, c/o Chicago Distribution Center, 11030 S Langley Ave, Chicago, IL 60628, United States *E-mail:* custserv@press.uchicago.edu
*Orders to:* ITPS, Cheriton House, North Way, Andover, Hants SP10 5BE *Tel:* (01264) 342832 *Fax:* (01264) 342788 *E-mail:* pluto@thomsonpublishingservices.co.uk

**Pocket Bears**, *imprint of* Moonlight Publishing Ltd

**Pocket Biographies**, *imprint of* Sutton Publishing Ltd

**Pocket Books**, *imprint of* Simon & Schuster Ltd

**Pocket Classics**, *imprint of* Sutton Publishing Ltd

**Pocket ColorCards**, *imprint of* Speechmark Publishing Ltd

**Pocket Histories**, *imprint of* Sutton Publishing Ltd

**Pocket Worlds**, *imprint of* Moonlight Publishing Ltd

**Poetica**, *imprint of* Anvil Press Poetry Ltd

**Point**, *imprint of* Scholastic Ltd

**Police Review Publishing Company Ltd**
5th Foor, Celcon House, 289-293 High Holborn, London WC1V 7HZ
*Tel:* (020) 7440 4700 *Fax:* (020) 7405 7167; (020) 7405 7163
*Key Personnel*
Publisher: Fabiana Angelini *E-mail:* fabiana.angelini@policereview.co.uk
Man Dir: Alfred Rolington
Founded: 1893
Subjects: Criminology, Law
ISBN Prefix(es): 0-7106; 0-309; 0-85164
*Parent Company:* The Thomson Corporation
*Associate Companies:* Jane's Information Group, 1340 Braddock Pl, Suite 300, Alexandria, VA 22314-1651, United States *Tel:* 703-683-3700 *Fax:* 703-836-1593

**The Policy Press+**
University of Bristol, Beacon House, 4th floor, Queen's Rd, Bristol BS8 1QU
*Tel:* (0117) 331 4054 *Fax:* (0117) 331 4093
*E-mail:* tpp-info@bristol.ac.uk
*Web Site:* www.policypress.org.uk
*Key Personnel*
Publishing Dir: Alison Shaw *Tel:* (0117) 331 4085 *E-mail:* ali.shaw@bristol.ac.uk
Marketing & Sales Manager: Julia Mortimer *Tel:* (0117) 331 4098 *E-mail:* julia.mortimer@bristol.ac.uk
Editorial Manager: Dawn Louise Rushen *Tel:* (0117) 331 4094 *E-mail:* dawn.l.rushen@bristol.ac.uk
Founded: 1996
A specialist policy studies publisher, publishing books, journals, reports & guides from leading academics & researchers. Publications provide the latest research in accessible formats, reaching those who formulate or implement policy at executive & grass-roots levels, as well as academics & students.
Subjects: Civil Engineering, Disability, Special Needs, Economics, Education, Ethnicity, Geography, Geology, Government, Political Science, Health, Nutrition, Labor, Industrial Relations,

Management, Public Administration, Social Sciences, Sociology, Women's Studies
ISBN Prefix(es): 0-86922; 1-86134; 1-873575
*Associate Companies:* The Joseph Rowntree Foundation
*Orders to:* DA Information Services, 648 Whitehorse Rd, Mitcham, Victoria 3132, Australia *Tel:* (03) 9210 7777 *Fax:* (03) 9210 7788 *E-mail:* service@dadirect.com.au (Australia, New Zealand & Papua New Guinea)
ISBS (International Specialised Book Services), 5824 NE Hassals St, Portland, OR 97213-3644, United States *Fax:* 503-280-8832 *E-mail:* orders@isbs.com *Web Site:* www.isbs.com
Marston Book Services, PO Box 269, Abingdon, Oxon OX14 4YN *Tel:* (01235) 465500 *Fax:* (01235) 465556 *E-mail:* direct.orders@marston.co.uk
Unifacmanu Trading Co Ltd, 4F, 91, Ho-Ping East Rd Section 1, Taipei, Taiwan, Province of China

**Policy Studies Institute (PSI)**
Subsidiary of University of Westminster
100 Park Village E, London NW1 3SR
*Tel:* (020) 7468 0468 *Fax:* (020) 7388 0914
*E-mail:* website@psi.org.uk
*Web Site:* www.psi.org.uk
*Key Personnel*
Dir: Prof Jim Skea *E-mail:* j.skea@psi.org.uk
Founded: 1978
Subjects: Art, Business, Economics, Education, Environmental Studies, Government, Political Science, Labor, Industrial Relations, Public Administration, Social Sciences, Sociology
ISBN Prefix(es): 0-85374; 0-9503317
*Orders to:* BEBC Ltd, PO Box 1496, Poole, Dorset BH12 3YD

**Polity Press**, see Blackwell Publishing Ltd

**Polo Publishing+**
30 Chichester Close, Hampton, Middx TW12 3QJ
*Tel:* (020) 8783 1903 *Fax:* (020) 8979 9425
*Key Personnel*
Contact: Alan Symons
Subjects: History, Religion - Jewish
ISBN Prefix(es): 0-9523751
Distributed by Seven Hills

**Polybooks Ltd+**
2 Caversham St, London SW3 4AH
*Tel:* (020) 7351 4995 *Fax:* (020) 7351 4995
*Key Personnel*
Managing Editor: James Hughes
Founded: 1964
Book publishers.
Subjects: Art, Biography, Communications, Erotica, Fiction, History, Literature, Literary Criticism, Essays, Nonfiction (General), Wine & Spirits
ISBN Prefix(es): 0-284
Total Titles: 20 Print
*Parent Company:* Charles Skilton Publishers
*Associate Companies:* Christchurch Publishers Ltd; Luxor Press

**Polygon**, *imprint of* Birlinn Ltd

**Polygon+**
Imprint of Birlinn Ltd
West Newington House, 10 Newington Rd, Edinburgh EH9 1QS
*Tel:* (0131) 668 4371 *Fax:* (0131) 668 4466
*E-mail:* info@birlinn.co.uk
*Web Site:* www.birlinn.co.uk
*Key Personnel*
Man Dir & International Rights: Hugh Andrew
Founded: 1969
Publisher.

Subjects: Drama, Theater, Fiction, Film, Video, History, Humor, Literature, Literary Criticism, Essays, Music, Dance, Nonfiction (General), Philosophy, Poetry, Women's Studies
ISBN Prefix(es): 0-85224; 0-7486; 0-904919; 0-948275; 0-9501890
Total Titles: 100 Print
*Warehouse:* Scottish Book Source, 32 Finlas St, Glasgow G22 5DU
*Orders to:* 137 Dundee St, Edinburgh *Tel:* (0131) 229 6800 *Fax:* (0131) 229 9070

**Polytantric Press**, *imprint of* Jay Landesman

**Pomegranate Europe Ltd**
Unit 1, Heathcote Business Centre, Hurlbutt Rd, Warwick, Warwicks CV34 6TD
*Tel:* (01926) 430111 *Fax:* (01926) 430888
*E-mail:* sales@pomeurope.co.uk
*Web Site:* www.pomegranate.com
*Key Personnel*
Sales Dir: Ms Ley Bricknell
Founded: 1985
Also acts as distributor of books, calendars, cards, postcards, posters & social stationery throughout Europe.
Subjects: Architecture & Interior Design, Art, Astrology, Occult, Environmental Studies, Ethnicity, Photography, Women's Studies
ISBN Prefix(es): 1-85257

**Pont Books**, *imprint of* Gomer Press (J D Lewis & Sons Ltd)

**Pookie Productions Ltd+**
PO Box 27018, Edinburgh EH10 5YU
*Tel:* (01899) 221868 *Fax:* (01899) 221868
*Key Personnel*
Author & Dir: Ivy Wallace
Man Dir & International Rights: Heather Bonning; Cherry Hope
Founded: 1994
Licensing agent & copyright holders specializing in the work of Ivy Wallace, author & illustrator of the Pookie series & the Animal Shelf series.
Subjects: Fiction
ISBN Prefix(es): 1-872885
Distributed by Scholastic (Australia, New Zealand, Papua New Guinea); Verbatim Distributors (South Africa)
*Orders to:* Biblios Publishers Distribution Services, Star Rd, Partridge Green, West Sussex RH13 8LD

**Popular Woodworking**, *imprint of* David & Charles Ltd

**David Porteous Editions+**
PO Box 5, Chudleigh, Newton Abbot TQ13 OYZ
*Tel:* (01626) 853310 *Fax:* (01626) 853663
*E-mail:* sales@davidporteous.com
*Web Site:* www.davidporteous.com
*Key Personnel*
Publisher: David Porteous
Founded: 1992
Membership(s): IPG.
Subjects: Art, Crafts, Games, Hobbies, How-to
ISBN Prefix(es): 1-870586
Total Titles: 18 Print
Distributed by Keith Ainsworth Pty Ltd (Australia); Everybody's Books CC (Republic of South Africa); Forrester Books NZ Ltd (New Zealand); Vanwell Publishing Ltd (Canada)
*Warehouse:* Parkwest Publications Inc, 451 Communipaw Ave, Jersey City, NJ 07304, United States *Tel:* 201-432-3257 *Fax:* 201-432-3708 *E-mail:* parkwest@parkwestpubs.com *Web Site:* www.parkwestpubs.com
*Orders to:* Parkwest Publications Inc, 451 Communipaw Ave, Jersey City, NJ 07304, United

States *Tel:* 201-432-3257 *Fax:* 201-432-3708
*E-mail:* parkwest@parkwestpubs.com *Web
Site:* www.parkwestpubs.com

**Porthill Publishers**
36 West Way, Edgware, Middx HA8 9LB
Mailing Address: PO Box 311, Edgware, Middx
HA9 9EA
*Tel:* (020) 89586783 *Fax:* (020) 89054516
*Key Personnel*
Publisher: Mr Radomir Putnikovich
Membership(s): British Publishers Association.
Subjects: Art, History, The History of Serbian
Culture
ISBN Prefix(es): 1-870732
Foreign Rep(s): Aleksandar Gacic (US)

**Portland Press Ltd+**
Eagle House, 3rd floor, 16 Procter St, London
WC1V 6NX
*Tel:* (020) 7280 4110 *Fax:* (020) 7280 4169
*E-mail:* editorial@portlandpress.com
*Web Site:* www.portlandpress.com
*Key Personnel*
Man Dir: Rhonda Oliver
Dir, Marketing & Customer Service: Adam Mar-
shall *E-mail:* adam.marshall@portlandpress.
com
Founded: 1990
Membership(s): ALPSP; IPG; UKSG.
Subjects: Biological Sciences, Chemistry, Chem-
ical Engineering, Health, Nutrition, Medicine,
Nursing, Dentistry, Physical Sciences, Science
(General), Biochemistry & Molecular Biology,
school to research level
ISBN Prefix(es): 1-85578; 0-904498
Number of titles published annually: 5 Print; 2
Online
Total Titles: 112 Print; 16 Online; 3 Audio
*Parent Company:* The Biochemical Society, Eagle
House, 3rd floor, 16 Procter St, London WC1V
6NX
Imprints: Making Sense of Science
*Branch Office(s)*
Portland Customer Services, Commerce Way,
Colchester CO2 8HP, Dir, Marketing & Cus-
tomer Services: Adam Marshall *Tel:* (01206)
796351 *Fax:* (01206) 799331 *E-mail:* sales@
portland-services.com *Web Site:* www.portland-
services.com
Distributed by Affiliated East-West Press Pvt Ltd
(India); DA Information Services (Australia,
New Zealand & Papua New Guinea)
Distributor for Bioscientifica Ltd; Energy Institute; Information Today, Inc (Europe); International Water Association Publishing
*Orders to:* Portland Customer Services, Commerce Way, Colchester CO2 8HP *Tel:* (01206)
796351 *Fax:* (01206) 799331 *E-mail:* sales@
portland-services.com *Web Site:* www.portland-
services.com

**T & AD Poyser Ltd+**
Imprint of A & C Black Publishing Ltd
Harcourt Place, 32 Jamestown Rd, London NW1
7BY
*Tel:* (020) 8308 5700 *Fax:* (020) 8308 5702
*E-mail:* cservice@harcourt.com
*Telex:* 25775 Acpres G
*Key Personnel*
Man Dir: Christopher Gibson
Editor & Foreign Rights: Andrew Richford
Founded: 1972
Subjects: Aeronautics, Aviation, Environmental
Studies, Natural History
ISBN Prefix(es): 0-85661
Number of titles published annually: 6 Print
Total Titles: 50 Print

**T & AD Poyser Ltd**, *imprint of* A & C Black
Publishers Ltd

**T & AD Poyser Ltd**, *imprint of* Elsevier Ltd

**PPL**, *imprint of* Packard Publishing Ltd

**PRC Publishing Ltd+**
Kiln House, 210 New King's Rd, London SW6
4NZ
*Tel:* (020) 7700 7799 *Fax:* (020) 7700 0635
*E-mail:* info@chrysalisbooks.co.uk
*Web Site:* www.chrysalisbooks.co.uk/books/
publisher/prc
*Key Personnel*
Man Dir: Joanne Messham *E-mail:* jmessham@
chrysalisbooks.co.uk
Comissioning Editor: Martin Howard
*E-mail:* mhoward@chrysalisbooks.co.uk
Group Sales & Marketing Dir: Richard Samson
*Tel:* (020) 7314 1459 *Fax:* (020) 7314 1549
*E-mail:* rsamson@chrysalisbooks.co.uk
Dir of Marketing: Kate Wood *Tel:* (020) 7314
1496 *Fax:* (020) 7314 1594 *E-mail:* kwood@
chrysalisbooks.co.uk
Permissions: Terry Forshaw *Tel:* (020) 7314 1607
*E-mail:* tforshaw@chrysalisbooks.co.uk
Founded: 1990
Subjects: Architecture & Interior Design, Art,
Cookery, Crafts, Games, Hobbies, Garden-
ing, Plants, How-to, Military Science, Music,
Dance, Natural History, Nonfiction (General),
Transportation, Wine & Spirits
ISBN Prefix(es): 1-85648
*Parent Company:* Chrysalis Books

**Prentice Hall**, *imprint of* Pearson Education
Europe, Mideast & Africa

**Prentice Hall Europe**, *imprint of* Pearson
Education Europe, Mideast & Africa

**Prentice Hall Regents**, *imprint of* Pearson
Education Europe, Mideast & Africa

**Mathew Price Ltd+**
The Old Glove Factory, Bristol Rd, Sherborne,
Dorset DT9 4HP
*Tel:* (01935) 816010 *Fax:* (01935) 816310
*E-mail:* mathewp@mathewprice.com
*Web Site:* www.mathewprice.com
*Key Personnel*
President: Mathew Price
Production Manager: Alis Pugh
Administration Manager: Sarah Newton
Founded: 1983
Subjects: Fiction, Nonfiction (General)
Number of titles published annually: 25 Print
Total Titles: 300 Print

**Pride Publications**, *imprint of* E J Morten
(Publishers)

**Prim-Ed Publishing UK Ltd**
PO Box 2840, Coventry CV6 5ZY
*Tel:* (0870) 876 0151 *Fax:* (0870) 876 0152
*E-mail:* sales@prim-ed.com
*Web Site:* www.prim-ed.com
*Key Personnel*
Administration Manager: Joanne Turnbull
Contact: Seamus McGuinness
Subjects: Education, History, Language Arts, Lin-
guistics, Mathematics, Religion - Other, Sci-
ence (General), Specialize in Geography
Total Titles: 350 Print

**Primary Source Microfilm**, *imprint of* Thomson
Gale

**Primrose Hill Press Ltd+**
Stratton Audley Park, Bicester OX27 9AB
*Tel:* (01869) 277 000 *Fax:* (01869) 277 820

*Web Site:* www.primrosehillpress.co.uk
*Key Personnel*
Dir: William Butler
Man Dir: Brian Hill *E-mail:* bhill@shpub.win-uk.
net
Founded: 1997
Specialize in books dedicated to the art & artists
of fine wood engraving.
Subjects: Animals, Pets, Art, Gardening, Plants,
Poetry, Fine Wood Engraving
ISBN Prefix(es): 1-901648
Number of titles published annually: 10 Print
Total Titles: 28 Print

**The Printed Head**, *imprint of* Atlas Press

**Prion**, *imprint of* Andre Deutsch Ltd

**Prion**, *imprint of* Carlton Publishing Group

**Prion**, *imprint of* Prion Books Ltd

**Prion Books Ltd+**
Brunel Rd, Houndmills, Basingstoke RG21 6XS
*Tel:* (01256) 329242 *Fax:* (01256) 812558;
(01256) 812521
*E-mail:* mdl@macmillan.co.uk
*Key Personnel*
Man Dir: Barry Winkleman
Founded: 1980
Specialize in humor, food & drink, literary &
historical reprints, cultural travel, health & nu-
trition.
ISBN Prefix(es): 1-85375
Number of titles published annually: 50 Print
Total Titles: 200 Print
Imprints: Prion
Distributed by Peter Hyde-Verbatim (South
Africa); Peribo (Australia); South Pacific (New
Zealand); Trafalgar Square (USA)
*Shipping Address:* Macmillan, Basingstoke, Hants
RG21 6XS
*Warehouse:* Macmillan, Houndmills, Basingstoke,
Hampshire RG21 6XS

**Prion-Multimedia**, see Prion Books Ltd

**Prism Press Book Publishers Ltd+**
Stanley House, 3 Fleets Lane, Poole BH15 3AJ
*Tel:* (01202) 665432 *Fax:* (01202) 666219
*E-mail:* orders@orcabookservices.co.uk
*Key Personnel*
Dir: Diana King; Julian King
Founded: 1974
Subjects: Astrology, Occult, Cookery, Environ-
mental Studies, Government, Political Science,
Philosophy, Self-Help, Technology, Wine &
Spirits
ISBN Prefix(es): 0-904727; 0-907061; 1-85327
*U.S. Office(s):* Associated Publishers Group, 1501
County Hospital Rd, Nashville, TN 37218,
United States
*Orders to:* Bailey Distribution Ltd, Units 1A/1B,
Learoyd Rd, Mountfield Industrial Estate, New
Romney, Kent TN28 8XU

**Professional Book Supplies Ltd**
8 Station Yard, Steventon, Abingdon, Oxford
OX13 6RX
*Tel:* (01235) 861234 *Fax:* (01235) 861601
*E-mail:* probooks@aol.com
*Telex:* 9312102446 PB G
*Key Personnel*
Man Dir & Dir of Sales & Marketing: Christo-
pher Smith
Production Dir: Lyn Simister
Founded: 1965
Also acts as second hand law dealers & book
manufacturer.
Subjects: Accounting, Law
ISBN Prefix(es): 0-86205; 0-903486

**Professional, Managerial & Healthcare Publications**
PO Box 100, Chichester, West Sussex PO18 8HD
*Tel:* (01243) 576444 *Fax:* (01243) 576456
*E-mail:* admin@pmh.uk.com
*Web Site:* www.pmh.uk.com
*Key Personnel*
Editor & Publisher: Peter Harkness
Founded: 1994
ISBN Prefix(es): 0-471; 0-9510119; 1-898789
Number of titles published annually: 4 Print
Total Titles: 2 CD-ROM

**Profile Books Ltd+**
58A Hatton Garden, London EC1N 8LX
*Tel:* (020) 7404 3001 *Fax:* (020) 7404 3003
*E-mail:* info@profilebooks.co.uk
*Web Site:* www.profilebooks.co.uk
*Key Personnel*
Publisher & Man Dir: Andrew Franklin
    *E-mail:* andrew.franklin@profilebooks.co.uk
Editorial Dir: Stephen Brough *E-mail:* stephen.
    brough@profilebooks.co.uk
Editorial & International Rights: Penny Daniel
    *E-mail:* penny.daniel@profilebooks.co.uk
Publicity & Marketing: Kate Griffin *E-mail:* kate.
    griffin@profilebooks.co.uk; Ruth Killick
    *E-mail:* ruth.killick@profilebooks.co.uk
Sales: Claire Beaumont *E-mail:* claire.beamont@
    profilebooks.co.uk
Direct Sales: Corinne Anyika
Founded: 1996
Subjects: Biography, Business, Criminology, De-
    veloping Countries, Economics, Environmental
    Studies, Ethnicity, Finance, History, Manage-
    ment, Marketing, Nonfiction (General), Psy-
    chology, Psychiatry, Social Sciences, Sociology,
    Travel, Current Affairs
ISBN Prefix(es): 1-86197
Divisions: The Economist Books
Distributor for The Economist Books
Foreign Rep(s): Allen & Unwin (Australia); APD
    Singapore Pte Ltd (Malaysia, Singapore, Thai-
    land, Vietnam); Asia Publishers Services Ltd
    (China, Hong Kong, Korea, Philippines, Tai-
    wan, Macao); Jonathan Bell Publishers Pty
    Ltd (South Africa); Andrew B Durnell (Eu-
    rope); Faber & Faber (UK); PIM (Japan, Mid-
    dle East); Renouf Publishing (Canada, US);
    Repforce Ireland (Northern Ireland, Republic
    of Ireland); Viva Books Ltd (Bangladesh, India,
    Nepal, Pakistan, Sri Lanka)
*Orders to:* TBS Ltd, Frating Distribution Centre,
    Colchester Rd, Frating Green, Colchester CO7
    7DW *Tel:* (01206) 256 000; (01206) 255 678
    *Fax:* (01206) 255 930

**ProQuest Information & Learning**
Division of ProQuest Co
The Quorum, Barnwell Rd, Cambridge CB5 8SW
*Tel:* (01223) 215512 *Fax:* (01223) 215513
*E-mail:* marketing@proquest.co.uk
*Web Site:* www.proquest.co.uk
*Key Personnel*
Sales Dir: Sue Orchard
Man Dir: Tim Smartt
Subjects: Business, Economics, Electronics, Elec-
    trical Engineering, Management, Marketing,
    Music, Dance, Physics, Science (General), So-
    cial Sciences, Sociology

**Proteus,** *imprint of* Omnibus Press

**PSI,** see Policy Studies Institute (PSI)

**PSP,** *imprint of* BMJ Publishing Group

**Psychological Corporation Ltd,** see Harcourt
    Assessment Inc

**Psychology Press,** *imprint of* Taylor & Francis

**Publishing Training Centre at BookHouse+**
45 E Hill, Wandsworth, London SW18 2QZ
*Tel:* (020) 8874 2718 *Fax:* (020) 8870 8985;
    (020) 7207 5915 (bookings)
*E-mail:* publishing.training@bookhouse.co.uk
*Web Site:* www.train4publishing.co.uk
*Key Personnel*
Chief Executive: Dag Smith; John Whitley
Courses Development Manager: Graham Smith
Founded: 1980
Act as co-publisher with UNESCO & is a mem-
    ber of ABPTOE.
Subjects: Career Development, Publishing &
    Book Trade Reference
ISBN Prefix(es): 0-907706

**Puffin,** *imprint of* The Penguin Group UK

**Puffin Books,** *imprint of* Penguin Books Ltd

**QPI Books,** *imprint of* Colour Library Direct

**Quadrille Publishing Ltd+**
Alhambra House, 27-31 Charing Cross Rd, 5th
    floor, London WC2H 0LS
*Tel:* (020) 7839 7117 *Fax:* (020) 7839 7118
*Web Site:* www.quadrille.co.uk
*Key Personnel*
Man Dir: Alison Cathie
International Sales Manager: Sabine Leon-Dufour
Founded: 1994
Subjects: Architecture & Interior Design, Astrol-
    ogy, Occult, Cookery, Crafts, Games, Hobbies,
    Gardening, Plants, Health, Nutrition, How-to,
    Wine & Spirits
Number of titles published annually: 35 Print
Total Titles: 150 Print

**Quaker Books**
Quaker Book Shop, Friends House, 173-177 Eu-
    ston Rd, London NW1 2BJ
*Tel:* (020) 7663 1000 *Fax:* (020) 7663 1008;
    (020) 7663 1001 (orders)
*E-mail:* bookshop@quaker.org.uk
*Web Site:* www.quaker.org.uk
*Key Personnel*
Book Publishing: Peter Daniels *Tel:* (020) 7663
    1099 *E-mail:* peterd@quaker.org.uk
Founded: 1882
Subjects: Religion - Other
ISBN Prefix(es): 0-85245
*Parent Company:* Religious Society of Friends

**Qualum Technical Services+**
EBC House, Townsend Lane, London NW9 8LL
*Tel:* (0845) 3001 123 *Fax:* (020) 7681 1316
*E-mail:* technical@qualum.com
*Web Site:* qualum.com
*Key Personnel*
Contact: Jonathan Stoppi
Founded: 1993
Subjects: Education, Technology
ISBN Prefix(es): 1-899168
Number of titles published annually: 1 Print
Total Titles: 5 Print

**Quantum,** *imprint of* Foulsham Publishers

**Quartet Books Ltd+**
Member of Namara Group
27 Goodge St, London W1T 2LD
*Tel:* (020) 7636 3992; (020) 7636 0968
    *Fax:* (020) 7637 1866
*E-mail:* quartetbooks@easynet.co.uk
*Key Personnel*
Chairman: Naim Attallah
Man Dir: Jeremy Beale
Publishing Dir: Stella Kane
Editor: Zelfa Hourani; Chris Parker
Publicity: Arielle Gottlieb

Founded: 1972
Subjects: Biography, Fiction, History, Music,
    Dance, Philosophy
ISBN Prefix(es): 0-7043
*Parent Company:* Namara Ltd
*Associate Companies:* Robin Clark Ltd
Subsidiaries: Namara Publications
Distributed by Southern Publishers Group (New
    Zealand); Tower Books (Australia); Trinity
    Books (South Africa)
*Warehouse:* Plymbridge Distributors Ltd, Estover
    Rd, Plymouth, Devon PL6 7PZ *Tel:* (01752)
    202300
*Orders to:* Plymbridge Distributors Ltd, Estover
    Rd, Plymouth, Devon PL6 7PZ *Tel:* (01752)
    202300 *Fax:* (01752) 202333 *E-mail:* orders@
    plymbridge.com

**Quarto Publishing plc+**
The Old Brewery, 6 Blundell St, London N7 9BH
*Tel:* (020) 7700 6700 *Fax:* (020) 7700 4191
*E-mail:* quarto@quarto.com
*Web Site:* www.quarto.com
*Key Personnel*
Chairman & Chief Executive: Laurence F Orbach
Deputy Chief Executive: Robert J Morley
Publisher: Piers Spence *E-mail:* pierss@quarto.
    com
Founded: 1976
International co-editions publisher.
Subjects: Alternative, Animals, Pets, Antiques,
    Art, Astrology, Occult, Crafts, Games, Hobbies,
    Gardening, Plants, Health, Nutrition, House
    & Home, How-to, Natural History, Nonfiction
    (General), Outdoor Recreation, Self-Help, Gar-
    dening; Illustrated, How-To; Interior Design &
    Reference
Number of titles published annually: 50 Print
Total Titles: 5,000 Print
*Parent Company:* Quarto Group Inc, 276 Fifth
    Ave, Suite 206, New York, NY 10001, United
    States
Subsidiaries: Apple Press Ltd; The Artists &
    Illustrators Magazine Ltd; Quarto Children's
    Books; Quintet Publishing Ltd

**Quartz Editions+**
Premier House, 112 Station Rd, Edgware HA8
    7BJ
*Tel:* (020) 8951 5656 *Fax:* (020) 8904 1200
*E-mail:* quartzeditions@btconnect.com
*Key Personnel*
Dir: Susan Pinkus
Founded: 1992
Packager & publisher of high-quality, illustrated
    titles for the international market.
Subjects: Education, Fiction, Nonfiction (General)
ISBN Prefix(es): 0-9534241

**Que,** *imprint of* Pearson Education Europe,
    Mideast & Africa

**Que Education & Training,** *imprint of* Pearson
    Education Europe, Mideast & Africa

**Que Lycos Books,** *imprint of* Pearson Education
    Europe, Mideast & Africa

**Queen Anne Press+**
Windmill Cottage, Mackerye End, Harpenden,
    Herts AL5 5DR
*Tel:* (01582) 715866 *Fax:* (01582) 715121
*E-mail:* queenanne@lenqap.demon.co.uk
*Key Personnel*
Chairman, Man Dir & Editorial Rights: Adrian
    Stephenson *E-mail:* stephenson@lennardqap.co.
    uk
Editor: Celia Kent
Founded: 1976
Specialize in sports.

Subjects: Sports, Athletics
ISBN Prefix(es): 1-85291
Total Titles: 40 Print
*Parent Company:* Lennard Associates
Imprints: Lennard Publishing
Divisions: Lennard Books
*Warehouse:* TBS Book Distribution, Colchester Rd, Frating Green, Colchester Essex CO7 7DW *Tel:* (01206) 255600 *Fax:* (01206) 255930
*Orders to:* Virgin Books, Thames Wharf Studios, Rainville Rd, London W6 9HT *Tel:* (020) 7386 3300 *Fax:* (020) 7386 3360

**Quentin Books Ltd**
10 Brook St, Wivenhoe, Colchester CO7 9DS
*Tel:* (01206) 825433; (01206) 825434
*Fax:* (01206) 822990
*Key Personnel*
Man Dir & International Rights: Mark Paterson
*E-mail:* markpaterson@compuserve.com
Founded: 1978
Also acts as book packager.
Subjects: Geography, Geology, History, Regional Interests
ISBN Prefix(es): 0-947614
*Associate Companies:* Sigmund Freud Copyrights; Mark Paterson & Associates
*Showroom(s):* Alma St, Wivenhoe CO7 9BE
*Bookshop(s):* Alma St, Wivenhoe CO7 9BE

**Quill**, *imprint of* HarperCollins UK

**Quiller Press**, *imprint of* Quiller Publishing Ltd

**Quiller Publishing Ltd+**
Wykey House, Wykey, Shrewsbury SY4 1JA
*Tel:* (01939) 261616 *Fax:* (01939) 261606
*E-mail:* info@quillerbooks.com
*Key Personnel*
Man Dir, Editor & Rights & Permissions: Andrew Johnston
Founded: 2001
Specialize in sponsored books & adult nonfiction.
Subjects: Biography, Business, Cookery, History, House & Home, Humor, Nonfiction (General), Outdoor Recreation, Travel, Country Sports, Equestrian, Falconry, Fishing, Shooting
ISBN Prefix(es): 0-907621; 1-899163; 1-85310; 1-870948; 0-948253; 1-904057
Total Titles: 200 Print
Imprints: Quiller Press; Sportman's Press; Swan Hill Press
Distributed by Peribo Pty Ltd (Australia); Stackpole Books (USA)
*Warehouse:* Grantham Book Services, Isaac Newton Way, Alma Park Industrial Estate, Grantham, Lincs NG31 9SD *Tel:* (01476) 541080 *Fax:* (01476) 541061
*Orders to:* Grantham Book Services, Isaac Newton Way, Alma Park Industrial Estate, Grantham, Lincs NG31 9SD *Tel:* (01476) 541080 *Fax:* (01476) 541061

**Quintessence Publishing Co Ltd+**
Quintessence House, Grafton Rd, New Malden Surrey KT3 3AB
*Tel:* (020) 89496087 *Fax:* (020) 83361484
*E-mail:* info@quintpub.co.uk
*Web Site:* www.quintpub.co.uk
*Key Personnel*
Dir: Joyce Ronald
Managing Dir: Linda Johnson *E-mail:* ljohnson@quintpub.co.uk
Publishing Dir: Paul Smith *E-mail:* psmith@quintpub.co.uk
Customer Services: Andy Johnson
*E-mail:* ajohnson@quintpub.co.uk; Christine McKittrick *E-mail:* cmckittrick@quintpub.co.uk
Marketing & Promotions: Susan Tralls
*E-mail:* stralls@quintpub.co.uk
Founded: 1948

Subjects: Medicine, Nursing, Dentistry
ISBN Prefix(es): 0-86715; 1-85097; 4-87417
*Parent Company:* Quintessenz Verlag Berlin, Germany
*Associate Companies:* Quintessence Publishing Inc, IL, United States; Quintessence Publishing Co, Ltd, Tokyo, Japan

**Quintet Publishing Ltd+**
Division of Quarto Publishing PLC
The Old Brewery Bldg, 6 Blundell St, London N7 9BH
*Tel:* (020) 7700 8001 *Fax:* (020) 7700 4191
*E-mail:* quintet@quarto.com
*Web Site:* www.quarto.com
*Key Personnel*
Chairman & Chief Executive: Laurence F Orbach
Publishing Dir: Oliver Salzmann
*E-mail:* olivers@quarto.com
Founded: 1984
Publishes co-edition books.
Subjects: Crafts, Games, Hobbies, Fashion, Gardening, Plants, Geography, Geology, Health, Nutrition, History, House & Home, How-to, Maritime, Military Science, Music, Dance, Mysteries, Natural History, Outdoor Recreation, Photography, Sports, Athletics, Technology, Transportation, Travel, Wine & Spirits
Number of titles published annually: 60 Print
Total Titles: 750 Print

**RAC Publishing+**
RAC House, Bartlett St, South Croydon, Surrey CR2 6XW
Mailing Address: PO Box 100, South Croydon, Surrey CR2 6XW
*Tel:* (020) 8686 0088 *Fax:* (020) 8688 2882
*Key Personnel*
Publisher: Lynne Elder *E-mail:* lynne@west-one.com
Founded: 1904
Publishers of guides, handbooks & maps for motorists & travelers.
Subjects: Automotive
ISBN Prefix(es): 0-86211; 0-902628
*Parent Company:* RAC Enterprises
*Orders to:* Bookpoint Ltd, 39 Milton Park, Abingdon, Oxon OX14 4TD

**Radcliffe Medical Press Ltd+**
18 Marcham Rd, Abingdon, Oxon OX14 1AA
*Tel:* (01235) 528820 *Fax:* (01235) 528830
*E-mail:* contact.us@radcliffemed.com
*Web Site:* www.radcliffe-oxford.com
*Key Personnel*
Man Dir: Andrew Bax
Editorial Dir: Gill Nineham
Financial Dir: Margaret McKeown
Editorial Manager: Jamie Etherington
*E-mail:* jetherington@radcliffemed.com
Head of Marketing: Gregory Moxon
Founded: 1987
Subjects: Medicine, Nursing, Dentistry
ISBN Prefix(es): 1-870905; 1-85775
Total Titles: 300 Print; 2 CD-ROM

**Ragged Bears Ltd+**
Nightingale House, Queen Camel, Somerset BA22 7NN
*Tel:* (01935) 851590 *Fax:* (01935) 851803
*E-mail:* books@ragged-bears.co.uk
*Web Site:* www.ragged-bears.co.uk
*Key Personnel*
Man Dir: Pamela Shirley
Dir, Editorial & Rights: Henrietta Stickland
Founded: 1985
ISBN Prefix(es): 1-85714; 1-870817
Imprints: Spindlewood
Distributor for ACC - Children's Classics; Allen & Unwin Children's Books; b small Publishing; David Bennett Books; Children's Corner; Chronicle Books; Clunie Press; Era Publica-

tions; Gallery Children's Books; Key Porter Books; Lemniscaat; Lothian Books; Matthew Price Children's Books; Moonlight Publishing; North-South Books; Owl Man; R&S Books; Siphano Picture Books; Star Bright Books; Templar Publishing; Tundra Books; Upland Books; The Wordhouse
*Warehouse:* c/o The Trade Counter, The Airfield, Norwich Rd, Mendlesham, Suffolk IP14 5NA

**Rainham Bookshop**, see Meresborough Books Ltd

**Ramakrishna Vedanta Centre**
Blind Lane, Bourne End, Bucks SL8 5LG
*Tel:* (01628) 526464
*E-mail:* vedantauk@talk21.com
*Web Site:* www.ramakrishna.org; www.vedantauk.com
*Key Personnel*
Book Sales Manager: Tony Leong
Founded: 1948
Subjects: Philosophy, Religion - Hindu
ISBN Prefix(es): 0-902479; 0-7025

**Ramboro Books Plc**
10 Blenheim Court, Brewery Rd, London N7 9NY
*Tel:* (020) 7700 7444 *Fax:* (020) 7700 4552
*E-mail:* enquiries@ramboro.co.uk
*Key Personnel*
Chairman: John Needleman
International Sales Dir: Tim Finch
*E-mail:* tfinch@chrysalisbooks.co.uk
US Sales Dir: Robin Cortie
Founded: 1964
Also remainder dealer, promotion publisher.
Subjects: Art, Cookery, History, Transportation
ISBN Prefix(es): 0-86288; 0-905694
*Associate Companies:* Greenwich Editions
Imprints: Greenwich Editions

**Ramsay Head Press+**
15 Gloucester Pl, Edinburgh EH3 6EE
*Tel:* (0131) 225 5646
*E-mail:* ramsayhead@btinternet.com
*Key Personnel*
Editorial Dir & International Rights: Conrad K Wilson
Contact: Christine Wilson
Founded: 1968
Membership(s): Scottish Publishers Association.
Subjects: Architecture & Interior Design, Art, Biography, Fiction, History, Literature, Literary Criticism, Essays, Poetry
ISBN Prefix(es): 0-902859; 1-873921
Total Titles: 24 Print

**Random House UK Ltd+**
Member of The Random House Group
Random House, 20 Vauxhall Bridge Rd, London SW1V 2SA
*Tel:* (020) 7840 8400 *Fax:* (020) 7233 8791
*E-mail:* enquiries@randomhouse.co.uk
*Web Site:* www.randomhouse.co.uk
*Key Personnel*
Chief Executive: Gail Rebuck
Group Deputy Chairman, General Books Division: Simon Master
President, International Sales Division: Brian Davies
Man Dir, Ebury Special Books Division: Amelia Thorpe
Financial Dir: Anthony McConnell
Group Operations Dir: David Pemberton
Group Sales Dir: Mike Broderick
Man Dir, Century, Hutchinson & Arrow Books: Simon King
Group Marketing Dir: Caroline Michel
Group Production Dir: Stephen Esson
International Dir: Simon Littlewood
Founded: 1987

Subjects: Art, Astrology, Occult, Biography, Cookery, Fashion, Fiction, Government, Political Science, Health, Nutrition, Humor, Nonfiction (General), Philosophy, Poetry, Travel
ISBN Prefix(es): 1-85686; 0-7126
Imprints: Arrow; Audiobooks; Bodley Head CHildrens; Business Books; Jonathan Cape; Jonathan Cape Childrens; Century; Chatto & Windus; Ebury; Fodors; Harvill; William Heinemann; Hutchinson; Hutchinson Childrens; Julia Macrae; Methuen; Pimlico; Red Fox; Rider; Secker & Warburg; Vermilion; Vintage; Yellow Jersey Press
Orders to: The Book Service Ltd, TBS Distribution Centre, Colchester Rd, Frating Green, Colchester, Essex C07 7DW Tel: (01206) 255678

**Ransom Publishing Ltd+**
Rose Cottage, Howe Hill, Watlington, Oxon OX49 5HB
Tel: (01491) 613 711 Fax: (01491) 613 733
E-mail: ransom@ransom.co.uk
Web Site: www.ransom.co.uk
Key Personnel
Man Dir: Jenny Ertle E-mail: jenny@ransom.co.uk
Founded: 1995
Children's multimedia CD-ROM & book publisher.
Subjects: Geography, Geology, Language Arts, Linguistics, English Language
ISBN Prefix(es): 1-86398; 1-900127
Number of titles published annually: 20 Print; 8 CD-ROM
Total Titles: 70 Print; 40 CD-ROM

**Rapra Technology Ltd+**
Shawbury, Shrewsbury, Salop SY4 4NR
Tel: (01939) 250383 Fax: (01939) 251118
E-mail: publications@rapra.net
Web Site: www.rapra.net; www.polymer-books.com
Key Personnel
Chief Executive: Andrew Ward
Publications Sales & Marketing Business Manager: Dr Sarah Ward
Produces books, reports, databases relating to all aspects of rubber & plastics processes, products & properties.
Subjects: Automotive, Chemistry, Chemical Engineering, Science (General), Technology, Polymer Science & Technology
ISBN Prefix(es): 1-85957
Number of titles published annually: 25 Print; 10 Online
Total Titles: 300 Print

**Rationalist Press Association**
One Gower St, London WC1E 6HD
Tel: (020) 7436 1151 Fax: (020) 7079 3588
E-mail: info@rationalist.org.uk
Web Site: www.rationalist.org.uk
Key Personnel
Editor-in-Chief: Jim Herrick E-mail: jim.herrick@rationalist.org.uk
Editor: Frank Jordans
Business Manager: John Metcalf
Founded: 1899
Publisher of New Humanist bimonthly magazine.
Subjects: Literature, Literary Criticism, Essays, Philosophy, Psychology, Psychiatry, Religion - Other, Science (General), Social Sciences, Sociology, From a Humanist Perspective
ISBN Prefix(es): 0-301

**Ravette Publishing Ltd+**
Unit 3, Tristar Centre, Star Rd, Partridge Green, Horsham RH13 8RA
Tel: (01403) 711443 Fax: (01403) 711554
E-mail: ravettepub@aol.com

Key Personnel
Man Dir: Margaret Lamb
Founded: 1980
Subjects: Animals, Pets, Education, Environmental Studies, Fiction, Foreign Countries, Humor, Nonfiction (General), Self-Help
ISBN Prefix(es): 0-906710; 0-948456; 1-85304; 1-84161
Number of titles published annually: 40 Print
Total Titles: 167 Print
Distribution Center: Orca Book Services, Stanley House, 3 Fleets Lane, Poole, Dorset BH15 3AJ, Contact: Jill Caldicott Tel: (01202) 785738 Fax: (01202) 672076

**Rayo,** imprint of HarperCollins UK

**RCGP,** see Royal College of General Practitioners (RCGP)

**Read-Along,** imprint of BBC Audiobooks

**The Reader's Digest Association Ltd**
11 Westferry Circus, Canary Wharf, London E14 4HE
Tel: (020) 7715 8000 Fax: (020) 7715 8181
Web Site: www.readersdigest.co.uk
Telex: 264631
Key Personnel
Marketing Dir: Martin Pasteiner
General Books Editor: Noel Buchanan
Ad Editor: Cortina Butler
Subjects: Animals, Pets, Antiques, Archaeology, Architecture & Interior Design, Cookery, Crafts, Games, Hobbies, Earth Sciences, Fiction, Film, Video, Gardening, Plants, Health, Nutrition, House & Home, How-to, Mysteries, Nonfiction (General), Science (General), Travel
ISBN Prefix(es): 0-276
Parent Company: The Reader's Digest Association Inc, Pleasantville, NY 10570, United States

**Reader's Digest Children's Books+**
11 Westferry Circus, London E14 4HE
Tel: (01225) 312200 Fax: (01225) 460942
Key Personnel
Contact: Jill Eade E-mail: eade@readersdigest.co.uk
Founded: 1981
Subjects: Education
ISBN Prefix(es): 1-85724; 1-84088; 0-907874
Parent Company: Readers Digest Inc
Imprints: Readers Digest Young Families
U.S. Office(s): Readers Digest Young Families, 355 Riverside Ave, Westport, CT 06880, United States
Shipping Address: Littlehampton Book Services, 10-14 Eldon Way, Lineside Estate, Littlehampton, West Sussex BN17 7HE

**Readers Digest Young Families,** imprint of Reader's Digest Children's Books

**Reaktion Books Ltd+**
79 Farringdon Rd, London ECIM 3JU
Tel: (020) 7404 9930 Fax: (020) 7404 9931
E-mail: info@reaktionbooks.co.uk
Web Site: www.reaktionbooks.co.uk
Key Personnel
Editorial Dir: Michael R Leaman
Publicity & Rights Dir: Maria Kilcoyne
  E-mail: maria@reaktionbooks.co.uk
Production Manager: Ken MacPherson
Sales Manager: David Hoek
Designer: Simon McFadden
Picture Researcher: Harry Gilonis
Founded: 1985
Specialize in nonfiction.
Subjects: Architecture & Interior Design, Art, Asian Studies, Film, Video, Geography, Geol-

ogy, Government, Political Science, History, Language Arts, Linguistics, Literature, Literary Criticism, Essays, Nonfiction (General), Photography, Travel
ISBN Prefix(es): 0-948462; 1-86189
Number of titles published annually: 40 Print
Total Titles: 170 Print
U.S. Office(s): University of Chicago Press, 1427 E 60 St, PO Box 976, Chicago, IL 60637, United States, Promotions Manager: Harriett Green Tel: 773-702-4217 Fax: 773-702-9756 E-mail: hgreen@press.uchicago.edu Web Site: www.press.uchicago.edu
Foreign Rep(s): APD Singapore (Malaysia) Ltd (Malaysia); APD Singapore Pte Ltd (Brunei, Cambodia, Indonesia, Philippines, Singapore, Thailand, Vietnam); Consul Books (Netherlands); Michael Geoghegan (Belgium, France); ICK Korea (Korea); Pernille Larson (Denmark, Finland, Iceland, Norway, Sweden); Ewa Ledochowicz (Croatia, Czech Republic, Estonia, Hungary, Poland, Romania, Slovak Republic, Slovenia); Maruzen Company Ltd (Japan); Penny Padovani (Greece, Italy, Portugal, Spain); Stephan Phillip (Pty) Ltd (South Africa); PS Publishers' Services (Austria, Germany, Switzerland); Southern Publishers Group (New Zealand); Unicfacmanu Trading Co (Taiwan); Unireps (Australia); United Publishers Services (Japan); University of Chicago Press (Canada, US); Viva Books Pvt Ltd (India)
Warehouse: Grantham Book Services Ltd, Isaac Newton Way, Alma Park Industrial Estate, Grantham, Lincs NG31 9SD Tel: (01476) 541 080 Fax: (01476) 541 061 E-mail: orders@gbs.tbs-ltd.co.uk

**Reardon Publishing+**
56 Upper Norwood St, Leckhampton, Cheltenham, Glos GL53 0DU
Tel: (01242) 231800
E-mail: reardon@bigfoot.com
Web Site: www.reardon.co.uk; www.coltswoldbookshop.com (bookshop)
Founded: 1976
Subjects: Asian Studies, Foreign Countries, Chinese Culture in America, Cotswolds England, Cycling, Exploring Antarctica, Walking
ISBN Prefix(es): 0-950867; 1-873877
Number of titles published annually: 10 Print; 1 CD-ROM
Total Titles: 100 Print; 2 CD-ROM

**Recollections,** imprint of George Mann Publications

**RED,** imprint of Wilmington Business Information Ltd

**Red Fox,** imprint of Random House UK Ltd

**RED Publishing,** see Retail Entertainment Data Publishing Ltd

**Redcliffe Press Ltd+**
Halsgrove House, Lower Moor Way, Tiverton Business Park, Tiverton EX16 6SS
Tel: (01884) 243242 Fax: (01884) 243325
Key Personnel
Man Dir: John Sansom
Rights & Permissions & Sales: Angela Sansom
Editorial: Clara Sansom
Founded: 1976
Subjects: Art, Literature, Literary Criticism, Essays, Regional Interests
ISBN Prefix(es): 0-905459; 0-948265; 1-872971; 1-900178; 1-904537
Imprints: White Tree Books

**Redstone Press+**
7a St Lawrence Terrace, London W10 5SU
Tel: (020) 7352 1594 Fax: (020) 7352 8749

*Web Site:* www.redstonepress.co.uk
*Key Personnel*
Proprietor: Julian Rothenstein *E-mail:* jr@redstonepress.co.uk
Founded: 1987
Subjects: Art
ISBN Prefix(es): 1-870003
*Associate Companies:* Shambhala Publications (USA)
Subsidiaries: Shambhala Redstone Editions
Distributed by Central Books Ltd; Distribuciones Loring (Spain); Idea Books (Japan & Europe, excluding Spain); Bo Rudin (Scandinavia); Signature Books (UK)
*Orders to:* Central Books Ltd, 99 Wallis Rd, London E9 5LN *Tel:* (020) 8986 4854 *Fax:* (020) 8533 5821 *E-mail:* orders@centralbooks.com

**Reed Business Information**
Quadrant House, The Quadrant, Sutton, Surrey SM2 5AS
*Tel:* (020) 8652 3500 *Fax:* (01342) 335960
*E-mail:* webmaster@rbi.co.uk
*Web Site:* www.reedbusiness.com
*Key Personnel*
Chief Executive: Keith Jones
Chief Operating Officer: Mark Kelsey
Man Dir: James Blazeby; Neil Stiles; Sandy Whetton
Marketing Dir: Jane Burgess
Finance Dir: Carolyn Pickering
ISBN Prefix(es): 0-610; 0-611; 0-948056
*Parent Company:* Reed Elsevier plc, 25 Victoria St, London SW1H 0EX
*Branch Office(s)*
Quadrant House, The Quadrant, Sutton, Surrey SM2 5AS *Tel:* (020) 8652 3500 *Fax:* (020) 8652 8932
Statham House, Talbot Rd, Stretford, Manchester M32 0FP *Tel:* (0161) 877 6399 *Fax:* (0161) 877 6288
24, rue de Milan, Paris 75009, France *Tel:* (01) 55 95 95 13 *Fax:* (01) 55 95 95 15
*U.S. Office(s):* 3730 Kirby Drive, Suite 1030, Houston, TX 77098, United States *Tel:* 713-525-2600 *Fax:* 713-525-2659

**Reed Educational & Professional Publishing**, see Harcourt Education International

**Reed Elsevier Group plc**
Affiliate of Reed Elsevier NV
25 Victoria St, London SW1H 0EX
*Tel:* (020) 7222 8420 *Fax:* (020) 7227 5799
*Web Site:* www.reed-elsevier.com
*Key Personnel*
Chief Executive Officer: Crispin Davis
Chief Financial Officer: Mark Armour
Corporate headquarters, jointly owned by Reed Elsevier plc, London, UK & Reed Elsevier NV, Amsterdam, Netherlands.

**Thomas Reed**, *imprint of* A & C Black Publishers Ltd

**William Reed Directories+**
Broadfield Park, Crawley, West Sussex RH11 9RT
*Tel:* (01293) 613 400 *Fax:* (01293) 610 322
*E-mail:* directories@william-reed.co.uk
*Web Site:* www.william-reed.co.uk
*Key Personnel*
Man Dir: Mark de Lange *E-mail:* mark.delange@william-reed.co.uk
Editorial Manager: Sulann Staniford *E-mail:* sulann.staniford@william-reed.co.uk
Group Sales Manager: Simon Hughes
Marketing Executive: Tracy Larner *E-mail:* tracy.larner@william-reed.co.uk
Founded: 1991
Membership(s): DPA.

Subjects: Business, Catering, Food & Drink
ISBN Prefix(es): 0-901595
*Parent Company:* William Reed Publishing Ltd
*Associate Companies:* Knowledge Store; William Reed International

**ReganBooks**, *imprint of* HarperCollins UK

**Regency House Publishing Ltd+**
Niall House, Rear of 24-26 Boulton Rd, Stevenage, Herts SG1 4QX
*Tel:* (014383) 14488 *Fax:* (014383) 11303
*E-mail:* regencyhouse@btclick.com
*Key Personnel*
Man Dir: Nicolette Trodd
Publisher: Brian Trodd
Founded: 1992
Publisher & packager of mass-market nonfiction.
Subjects: Animals, Pets, Architecture & Interior Design, Art, Automotive, Cookery, Crafts, Games, Hobbies, Nonfiction (General), Photography, Poetry, Regional Interests, Transportation
ISBN Prefix(es): 1-85361
*Parent Company:* Grange Books PLC

**Regency Press CP Ltd**
Gordon House, Lissenden Gardens, London NW5 1LX
*Tel:* (020) 7482 4596 *Fax:* (020) 7485 8353
*E-mail:* info@regency.org
*Web Site:* www.regency.org
*Key Personnel*
Contact: Cristina Paiva *Tel:* (020) 7468 0220 *E-mail:* cp@regency.org
Founded: 1990
Publications intended for developing controls & emerging markets. Specialize in human rights, world health, poverty reduction & racial equality; books for refugees & helping children.
Subjects: Environmental Studies
ISBN Prefix(es): 0-9532905
Number of titles published annually: 10 Print; 1 CD-ROM; 5 Online; 5 E-Book; 1 Audio
Total Titles: 40 Print; 1 CD-ROM; 30 Online; 6 E-Book; 1 Audio
Subsidiaries: The Regency Corporation Ltd
*Branch Office(s)*
Rua Frei Caneca 91 cj 42, 01307-001 Sao Paulo-SP, Brazil *Tel:* (011) 3259 9233 *Fax:* (011) 3259 9233 *E-mail:* info@telecentros.org.br *Web Site:* www.telecentros.org.br

**Regnum**, *imprint of* Paternoster Publishing

**RELATE**
Herbert Gray College, Little Church St, Rugby, Warwicks CV21 3AP
*Tel:* (01788) 573241 *Fax:* (01788) 535007
*E-mail:* enquires@relate.org.uk
*Web Site:* www.relate.org.uk
*Key Personnel*
Chief Executive: Sarah Bowler
Head of Publications: Suzy Powling
Founded: 1938
Subjects: Human Relations, Psychology, Psychiatry, Social Sciences, Sociology
ISBN Prefix(es): 0-85351

**Religious & Moral Education Press**, *imprint of* Hymns Ancient & Modern Ltd

**Religious & Moral Education Press (RMEP)**, *imprint of* SCM-Canterbury Press Ltd

**Renaissance Books**, *imprint of* Global Oriental Ltd

**Research Studies Press Ltd (RSP)+**
Imprint of Institute of Physics Publishing

16 Coach House Cloisters, 10 Hitchin St, Baldock, Herts SG7 6AE
*Tel:* (01462) 895060 *Fax:* (01462) 892546
*E-mail:* info@research-studies-press.co.uk
*Web Site:* www.research-studies-press.co.uk
*Key Personnel*
Publisher: William G Askew
Publishing Dir: Caroline Holmes
Man Dir: Stephen Holmes *E-mail:* stephen@rspltd.demon.co.uk
Founded: 1983
Membership(s): IPG.
Subjects: Automotive, Biological Sciences, Chemistry, Chemical Engineering, Civil Engineering, Communications, Computer Science, Electronics, Electrical Engineering, Energy, Engineering (General), Mathematics, Mechanical Engineering, Microcomputers, Military Science, Technology, Transportation, Botany, Forestry
ISBN Prefix(es): 0-86380
Number of titles published annually: 15 Print; 15 CD-ROM; 50 Online; 50 E-Book
Total Titles: 100 Print; 50 CD-ROM
Foreign Rep(s): Amin Al-abini (Middle East); Book Marketing Services (India); DA Information Services (Australia, New Zealand, Papua New Guinea); Durnell Marketing (Austria, Belgium, UK, Denmark, Netherlands, Ireland, Europe, Finland, France, Germany, Greece, Iceland, Italy, Norway, Portugal, Spain, Sweden, Switzerland); Eastern Book Service Inc (Japan); Humphrys Roberts Associates (Central America, Mexico, South America); Macmillan (China) Ltd (China); Pak Book Corporation (Pakistan); Princeton Selling Group (US); TransQuest Asia Publishers (Hong Kong, Malaysia, Taiwan, Thailand); TransQuest Publishers Pte Ltd (Brunei, Cambodia, Indonesia, Laos, Myanmar, Philippines, Vietnam)
*Orders to:* AIDC, 50 Winter Sport Lane, PO Box 20, Williston, VT 05495, United States *Tel:* 802-862-0095 *Fax:* 802-864-7626 *E-mail:* orders@aidcvt.com (North America)
Marston Book Services Ltd, PO Box 269, Abingdon, Oxon OX14 4YN *Tel:* (01235) 465 500 *Fax:* (01235) 465 555 *E-mail:* direct.order@marston.co.uk (Worldwide (excluding North America))

**Research Studies Press Ltd (RSP)**, *imprint of* Institute of Physics Publishing

**Resurgence Books**, *imprint of* Green Books Ltd

**Retail Entertainment Data Publishing Ltd**
Subsidiary of Wilmington Business Information Ltd
Paulton House, 8 Shepherdess Walk, London N1 7LB
*Tel:* (020) 7566 8216 *Fax:* (020) 7566 8259 (Inquiry); (020) 7566 8316 (Editorial)
*E-mail:* info@redpublishing.co.uk
*Web Site:* www.redpublishing.co.uk
*Key Personnel*
Publisher & Dir: Rory A Cornwell
Publisher: Doug Marshall *Tel:* (020) 7566 8261 *E-mail:* dmarshall@redpublishing.co.uk
Editor: Matthew Garbutt
Sales Manager: Becca Bailey
Founded: 1971
Subjects: Music, Dance
ISBN Prefix(es): 0-904520; 1-900105
*Bookshop(s):* Music Sales, Newmarket Rd, Bury St Edmunds, Suffolk IP33 3YB

**Review**, *imprint of* Headline Book Publishing Ltd

**Revival Publications**, *imprint of* Islamic Foundation Publications

**RIBA Publications+**
Construction House, 56-64 Leonard St, London
EC2A 4LT
*Tel:* (020) 7251 0791 *Fax:* (020) 7608 2375
*Web Site:* www.ribabookshop.com; www.ribac.co.
uk
*Key Personnel*
Man Dir: Geoffrey Denner
Production Dir: M Stribbling
Editor: Mark Lane
Marketing Executive: Diane Williams
  *E-mail:* diane@ribabooks.com
Founded: 1967
Subjects: Architecture & Interior Design
ISBN Prefix(es): 0-900630; 0-947877; 1-85946
*Parent Company:* RIBA Companies Ltd, 66 Port-
land Place, London W1N 4AD
*Associate Companies:* RIBA Information Services
National Building Specification
*Bookshop(s):* RIBA Bookshop, 66 Portland Place,
London W1N 4AD

**The Richmond Publishing Co Ltd+**
PO Box 963, Slough SL2 3RS
*Tel:* (01753) 643104 *Fax:* (01753) 646553
*E-mail:* rpc@richmond.co.uk
*Key Personnel*
Man Dir: Mrs S J Davie
Founded: 1970
Subjects: Environmental Studies, Natural History
ISBN Prefix(es): 0-85546
Total Titles: 100 Print

**RICS Books+**
Surveyor Court, Westwood Business Park, Coven-
try CV4 8JE
*Tel:* (020) 7222 7000 (ext 698) *Fax:* (020) 7334
3851
*E-mail:* weborders@rics.org.uk
*Web Site:* www.ricsbooks.com
*Key Personnel*
Man Dir: Angela Hartland *E-mail:* ahartland@
rics.org.uk
Customer Service Manager: Rita Sparrow
  *Tel:* (020) 7334 3868 *E-mail:* rsparrow@rics.
org.uk
Managing Editor: Toni Gill *Tel:* (020) 7222 7000
(ext 686) *Fax:* (020) 7334 3840 *E-mail:* tgill@
rics.org
Founded: 1981
Specialize in surveying, property, construction &
environment
The Royal Institution of Chartered Surveyors
(RICS).
Subjects: Architecture & Interior Design, Civil
Engineering, Earth Sciences, Environmental
Studies, Real Estate
ISBN Prefix(es): 0-85406
*Parent Company:* RICS Business Services Ltd, 12
Great George St, Westminster, London SW1P
3AD
*Bookshop(s):* 12 Great George St, Parliament
Sq, London SW1P 3AD *Tel:* (020) 7334 3776
*Fax:* (020) 7222 9430 *E-mail:* bookshop@rics.
org.uk

**Rider**, *imprint of* Random House UK Ltd

**Right Way Books**, *imprint of* Elliot Right Way
Books

**Riverrun Press**, *imprint of* Calder Publications
Ltd

**Rivers Oram Press+**
144 Hemingford Rd, London N1 1DE
*Tel:* (020) 7607 0823 *Fax:* (020) 7609 2776
*E-mail:* ro@riversoram.demon.co.uk
*Key Personnel*
Publisher: Elizabeth Fidlom
Editorial Manager: Helen Armitage

Editor: Nicola Chalton
Administration: Margaret Brittain
Founded: 1990
Subjects: Anthropology, Biography, Child Care &
Development, Fashion, Gay & Lesbian, Gov-
ernment, Political Science, History, Nonfiction
(General), Psychology, Psychiatry, Women's
Studies
ISBN Prefix(es): 0-86359; 1-85489
Number of titles published annually: 15 Print
Total Titles: 250 Print
Imprints: Pandora Press
*Foreign Rep(s):* ADDENDA Ltd (New Zealand);
IPG (Independent Publishers Group) (Africa,
Canada, Japan, South America, US); UNIREPS
(University & Reference Publishers' Services)
(Australia)
*Foreign Rights:* Silvia Brunelli (Italy, Spain);
Monica Heyum (Scandinavia); Asako Kawachi
(Japan, Korea); Literarische Agentur Silke
Weniger (Germany)
*Shipping Address:* Clipper Distribution, Wind-
mill Grove, Portchester, Hants PO16 9HT
  *Tel:* (02392) 200080 *Fax:* (02392) 200090
  *E-mail:* office@clipperdistribution.co.uk
*Warehouse:* Clipper Distribution, Windmill Grove,
Portchester, Hants PO16 9HT *Tel:* (02392)
200080 *Fax:* (02392) 200090 *E-mail:* office@
clipperdistribution.co.uk
*Distribution Center:* Clipper Distribution, Wind-
mill Grove, Portchester, Hants PO16 9HT
  *Tel:* (02392) 200080 *Fax:* (02392) 200090
  *E-mail:* office@clipperdistribution.co.uk
*Orders to:* Clipper Distribution, Windmill Grove,
Portchester, Hants PO16 9HT *Tel:* (02392)
200080 *Fax:* (02392) 200090 *E-mail:* office@
clipperdistribution.co.uk
*Returns:* Clipper Distribution, Windmill Grove,
Portchester, Hants PO16 9HT *Tel:* (02392)
200080 *Fax:* (02392) 200090 *E-mail:* office@
clipperdistribution.co.uk

**Roadmaster Publishing**
PO Box 176, Chatham, Kent ME5 9AQ
*Tel:* (01634) 862843 *Fax:* (01634) 201555
*E-mail:* info@roadmasterpublishing.co.uk; sales@
roadmasterpublishing.co.uk
*Key Personnel*
Contact: Malcolm Wright
Subjects: Automotive, Environmental Studies,
Geography, Geology, History, Natural History,
Regional Interests, Transportation

**Robinson**, *imprint of* Constable & Robinson Ltd

**Robinson's Children**, *imprint of* Constable &
Robinson Ltd

**The Robinswood Press Ltd**
30 South Ave, Stourbridge, West Midlands DY8
3XY
*Tel:* (01384) 397475 *Fax:* (01384) 440443
*E-mail:* info@robinswoodpress.com
*Web Site:* www.robinswoodpress.com
*Key Personnel*
Man Dir: Christopher John Marshall
Founded: 1985
Subjects: Disability, Special Needs, Education,
English as a Second Language, Fiction, Nonfic-
tion (General)
Number of titles published annually: 12 Print
Total Titles: 12 Print

**Robson Books+**
Division of Chrysalis Group
The Chrysalis Bldg, Bramley Rd, London W10
6SP
*Tel:* (020) 7221 2213; (020) 7314 1469 (sales)
  *Fax:* (020) 7221 6455; (020) 7314 1594 (sales)
*E-mail:* robson@chrysalisbooks.co.uk

*Web Site:* www.chrysalisbooks.co.uk/books/
publisher/robson
*Key Personnel*
Group Sales & Marketing Dir: Richard Samson
  *Tel:* (020) 7314 1459 *Fax:* (020) 7314 1549
  *E-mail:* rsamson@chrysalisbooks.co.uk
Dir of Marketing: Kate Wood *Tel:* (020) 7314
1496 *E-mail:* kwood@chrysalisbooks.co.uk
Marketing & Publicity Manager: Sharon
Benjamin *Tel:* (020) 7314 1496
  *E-mail:* sbenjamin@chrysalisbooks.co.uk
Permissions: Terry Forshaw *Tel:* (020) 7314 1607
  *E-mail:* tforshaw@chrysalisbooks.co.uk
Founded: 1973
Subjects: Biography, Cookery, Government, Polit-
ical Science, Humor, Military Science, Sports,
Athletics, Travel
ISBN Prefix(es): 0-903895; 0-86051
Number of titles published annually: 75 Print
Total Titles: 800 Print
*Orders to:* HarperCollins Distribution, Campsie
View, Westerhill Rd, Bishopbriggs, Glasgow
G64 2QT *Fax:* (087) 0787 1995

**George Ronald Publisher Ltd+**
24 Gardiner Close, Abington, Oxon OX14 3YA
*Tel:* (01235) 529137
*E-mail:* sales@grbooks.com
*Web Site:* www.grbooks.com
*Key Personnel*
General Manager: Erica Leith *E-mail:* erica@
grooks.com
Founded: 1947
Subjects: Religion - Other
ISBN Prefix(es): 0-85398
*Branch Office(s)*
8325 17 St North, St Petersburg, FL 33702,
United States

**Rooster Books Ltd**
The Old Police Station, Priory Lane, Royston,
Herts SG8 9DU
*Tel:* (01763) 242717 *Fax:* (01763) 243332
*Web Site:* www.solutions-for-books.co.uk/rooster
*Key Personnel*
Dir: Guy Garfit *E-mail:* garfit@roosterbooks.co.
uk
Founded: 1978
Subjects: Fiction, Travel
ISBN Prefix(es): 1-871510
Number of titles published annually: 12 Print

**Rosendale Press Ltd+**
8 Ponsonby Place, London SW1P 4PT
*Tel:* (020) 7834 1123 *Fax:* (020) 7834 1240
*E-mail:* info@rosendale.demon.co.uk
*Key Personnel*
Chairman: Timothy Green
Editorial Dir: Maureen Green *E-mail:* maureen@
rosendale.demon.co.uk
Founded: 1987
Specialize in International co-editions.
Membership(s): IPG.
Subjects: Cookery, Health, Nutrition, Human Re-
lations, Self-Help
ISBN Prefix(es): 0-9509182; 1-872803
*Warehouse:* Littlehampton Book Services Ltd, 10-
14 Eldon Way, Lineside Estate, Littlehampton,
West Sussex BN17 7HE

**RotoVision SA**
Sheridan House, 112-116A Western Rd, Hove,
East Sussex BN3 1DD
*Tel:* (01273) 727 268 *Fax:* (01273) 727 269
*E-mail:* sales@rotovision.com
*Web Site:* www.rotovision.com
*Key Personnel*
Chief Executive: Ken Fund *E-mail:* kenf@
rotovision.com
Publisher: Aidan Walker *E-mail:* aidanw@
rotovision.com
Founded: 1974

Subjects: Advertising, Architecture & Interior Design, Photography
ISBN Prefix(es): 2-88046

**Rough Guides**, *imprint of* The Penguin Group UK

**Rough Guides Ltd+**
Division of Penguin Books Ltd
80 Strand, London WC2R 0RL
*Tel:* (020) 7010 3703 *Fax:* (020) 7010 6767
*E-mail:* mail@roughguides.com
*Web Site:* www.roughguides.com
*Key Personnel*
Publisher: Mark Ellingham
Editorial Dir: Martin Dunford
Rights Dir: Richard Trillo
Founded: 1982
Specialize in worldwide travel guides for independently minded travelers, music & cultural reference books & maps.
Subjects: Developing Countries, Foreign Countries, Geography, Geology, History, Music, Dance, Outdoor Recreation, Travel
ISBN Prefix(es): 1-85828; 1-84353
*Parent Company:* Penguin Books
*Ultimate Parent Company:* Pearson
*Branch Office(s)*
345 Hudson St, 4th floor, New York, NY 10014, United States
Distributed by Penguin Companies
*Orders to:* Penguin Books Australia Ltd, 487 Maroondah Hwy, Ringwood, Victoria 3134, Australia
Penguin Books Canada Ltd, 10 Alcorn Ave, Siuite 300, Toronto, ON M4V 3B2, Canada
Viking Penguin USA, 375 Hudson St, New York, NY 10014-3657, United States

**Roundhall Sweet & Maxwell**, *imprint of* Sweet & Maxwell Ltd

**Roundhouse**, *imprint of* Roundhouse Group

**Roundhouse Group**
Millstone, Limers Lane, Northam, North Devon EX39 2RG
*Tel:* (01237) 474 474 *Fax:* (01237) 474 774
*E-mail:* roundhouse.group@ukgateway.net
*Web Site:* www.roundhouse.net
*Key Personnel*
President & Chief Executive: Alan T Goodworth
Founded: 1991
Distributor of small & medium publisher lists from the USA, Canada, Australia & Singapore.
Also acts as agent & representative for English-language publishers. Full service representation & warehousing for publishers to UK & Europe.
Subjects: Architecture & Interior Design, Art, Asian Studies, Astrology, Occult, Biography, Business, Cookery, Crafts, Games, Hobbies, Criminology, Drama, Theater, Film, Video, Genealogy, Government, Political Science, Health, Nutrition, History, House & Home, Language Arts, Linguistics, Literature, Literary Criticism, Essays, Management, Marketing
ISBN Prefix(es): 1-85710
*Parent Company:* Roundhouse Publishing Ltd
Imprints: Pencil Press; Roundhouse
Subsidiaries: Pencil Press; Roundhouse Reference Books
Distributor for Allen & Unwin (Australia) (UK & Europe); Amadeus Press (UK & Europe); Applause Cinema & Theatre Books (UK & Europe); Archipelago Press (selected titles); Bookworld (UK & Europe); Challis Guides (UK & Europe); Chelsea House (UK & Europe); C-Licence (UK & Europe); CSA Word Audio Books (Europe (excluding UK)); Editions Didier Millet (selected titles); Fairview Press (UK & Europe); Free Spirit Publishing (UK & Europe); Gambit Chess Books (UK & Europe); Ginkgo Press (UK & Europe); Global Exchange (UK & Europe); Graphic Arts Center (UK & Europe); Gryphon House (UK & Europe); Hale & Iremonger (UK & Europe); Harcourt Trade (selected titles); Hardie Grant Books (UK & Europe); Haworth Press (selected titles); Home Planners (UK & Europe); Interlink Publishing (selected titles); Key Porter Books (UK & Europe); Limelight Editions (UK & Europe); Little Hills Press (UK & Europe); Lothian Books (UK & Europe); Marston House Publishers (UK & Europe); Mason Crest (UK & Europe); Mosaic Press (UK & Europe); Newmarket Press (UK & Europe); O Books (UK & Europe); Paragon House (UK & Europe); Quality Medical Publishing (UK & Europe); RDR Books (UK & Europe); J Ross (UK only); Roxbury Publishing (UK & Europe); Santana Books (UK only); Sarasota Press (UK & Europe); Scala/Riverside (UK & Ireland); Self-Counsel Press (UK & Europe); Seven Locks Press (UK & Europe); Sinclair-Stevenson (UK & Europe); Sourcebooks (UK & Europe); SPI Books (selected titles); Ulysses Travel Guides (UK & Europe); University Press of Mississippi (UK & Europe); Visible Ink (UK & Europe); Warwick Publishing (UK & Europe); Whitecap Books (UK & Europe)
*Foreign Rep(s):* Ted Dougherty, Pernille Larsen; Tony Moggarch; Peter Prout
*Shipping Address:* Orca Book Services, Stanley House, Fleets Lane, Poole Dorset BH15 3AJ
*Warehouse:* Orca Book Services, Stanley House, Fleets Lane, Poole Dorset BH15 3AJ

**Routledge**, *imprint of* Taylor & Francis

**Routledge+**
Member of Taylor & Francis Group
11 New Fetter Lane, London EC4P 4EE
*Tel:* (020) 7583 9855 *Fax:* (020) 7842 2298
*E-mail:* info@routledge.co.uk
*Web Site:* www.routledge.com
*Key Personnel*
Chief Executive: A Selby
Publishing Dir: S Neil
IT: Tony Short
Founded: 1988
Represents the publishing interests & activities previously undertaken under the names of Routledge & Kegan Paul Ltd, Methuen Academic, Tavistock Publications Ltd, Croom Helm Ltd & Unwin Hyman Academic.
Subjects: Archaeology, Biography, Business, Communications, Developing Countries, Economics, Education, Film, Video, Geography, Geology, Government, Political Science, History, Language Arts, Linguistics, Law, Literature, Literary Criticism, Essays, Philosophy, Psychology, Psychiatry, Religion - Other, Social Sciences, Sociology, Women's Studies
ISBN Prefix(es): 0-415; 0-7448; 0-7099; 0-85664; 0-416; 0-85362; 0-422
Number of titles published annually: 1,000 Print
Total Titles: 7,000 Print
Imprints: Blueprint; Comedia
*U.S. Office(s):* 29 W 35 St, New York, NY 10001, United States *Tel:* 212-216-7800 *Fax:* 212-564-7854 *E-mail:* info@routledge-ny.com *Web Site:* www.routledge-ny.com
*Orders to:* Copp Clark, 2775 Matheson Blvd East, Mississauga, ON L4W 4P7, Canada
Taylor & Francis, 7625 Empire Dr, Florence, KY, United States *Tel:* 800-634-7064 *Fax:* 800-248-4724 *E-mail:* cserve@routledge-ny.com (US)
Taylor & Francis Customer Services, ITPS, Cheriton House, North Way, Andover, Hants SP10 5BE *Tel:* (01264) 343071 *Fax:* (01264) 343005 *E-mail:* book.orders@tandf.co.uk (UK, Europe & Asia)

**RoutledgeCurzon**, *imprint of* Taylor & Francis

**RoutledgeCurzon**
Member of Taylor & Francis Group
11 New Fetter Lane, London EC4P 4EE
*Tel:* (020) 7583 9855 *Fax:* (020) 7842 2298
*E-mail:* info@routledge.co.uk
*Web Site:* www.routledge.com
*Key Personnel*
Chairman: Malcolm Campbell
Dir: Martina Campbell
Marketing Executive: Digby Halsby *E-mail:* digby.halsby@tandf.co.uk
Senior Editor: Craig Fowlie *E-mail:* craig.fowlie@tandf.co.uk
Founded: 1970
Specialize in Asian & Middle Eastern studies.
Subjects: Anthropology, Asian Studies, Business, Developing Countries, Economics, Ethnicity, Foreign Countries, History, Language Arts, Linguistics, Philosophy, Regional Interests, Religion - Buddhist, Religion - Hindu, Religion - Islamic, Religion - Jewish, Religion - Other, Social Sciences, Sociology, Travel, Women's Studies
ISBN Prefix(es): 0-7007; 1-415
Number of titles published annually: 200 Print
Total Titles: 800 Print
Imprints: Caucasus World; Japan Library
*U.S. Office(s):* 29 W 35 St, New York, NY 10001, United States *Tel:* 212-216-7800 *Fax:* 212-564-7854 *Web Site:* www.routledge-ny.com
Distributed by Paul & Co (Canada & USA, Middle East titles only); University of Hawaii Press (Canada & USA except for Middle East titles)
Distributor for Nordic Institute of Asian Studies (NIAS); University of Hawaii Press (UK, Europe, Africa, Middle East, South Asia)
*Orders to:* ITPS - International Thompson Publishing Service, Cheriton House, North Way, Andover, Hampshire SP10 5BE *Tel:* (01264) 342 991 *Fax:* (01264) 364 418 *E-mail:* curzon@itps.co.uk

**RoutledgeFalmer**, *imprint of* Taylor & Francis

**Joseph Rowntree Foundation**
The Homestead, 40 Water End, York, N Yorks YO30 6WP
*Tel:* (01904) 629241 *Fax:* (01904) 620072
*E-mail:* julia.lewis@jrf.org.uk
*Web Site:* www.jrf.org.uk

**Royal College of General Practitioners (RCGP)+**
14 Princes Gate, Hyde Park, London SW7 1PU
*Tel:* (020) 7581 3232 *Fax:* (020) 7225 3047; (020) 7584 6716 (editorial)
*E-mail:* info@rcgp.org.uk
*Web Site:* www.rcgp.org.uk
*Key Personnel*
Publications Manager: Helen Farrelly *E-mail:* hfarrelly@rcgp.org.uk
Founded: 1952
Subjects: Education, Health, Nutrition, Medicine, Nursing, Dentistry, Psychology, Psychiatry
ISBN Prefix(es): 0-85084
Distributed by San Medrea (Spain)

**Royal Genealogies**, *imprint of* Stacey International

**Royal Institute of International Affairs+**
Chatham House, 10 St James's Sq, London SW1Y 4LE
*Tel:* (020) 7957 5700 *Fax:* (020) 7957 5710
*E-mail:* contact@riia.org
*Web Site:* www.riia.org
*Key Personnel*
Head, Publications: Margaret May *Tel:* (020) 7957 5704 *E-mail:* mmay@riia.org

Media Enquiries: Keith Burnet *Tel:* (020) 7314 2798 *E-mail:* kburnet@riia.org
Founded: 1920
Subjects: Asian Studies, Business, Developing Countries, Economics, Energy, Environmental Studies, Foreign Countries, Government, Political Science
ISBN Prefix(es): 0-905031; 1-86203
Imprints: Chatham House Papers; International Affairs; The World Today
*U.S. Office(s):* Cassell, PO Box 605, Herndon, VA 20172, United States
Chatham House Foundation, 16 Sutton Place 9/A, New York, NY 10022, United States, Contact: Richard W Murphy
Brookings Institution Press, 1775 Massachussetts Ave, NW, Washington, DC 20036, United States
Distributed by Brookings; Cambridge University Press; Cassell Academic; Oxford University Press; Routledge
*Warehouse:* Plymbridge Distributors Ltd, Plymbridge House, Estover Rd, Plymouth, Devon PL6 7PZ *Fax:* (01752) 202 3333
*Orders to:* Plymbridge Distributors Ltd, Plymbridge House, Estover Rd, Plymouth, Devon PL6 7PZ *Fax:* (01752) 202 3333

**Royal Institution of Chartered Surveyors**, see RICS Books

**The Royal Society**
6-9 Carlton House Terrace, London SW1Y 5AG
*Tel:* (020) 7839 5561 *Fax:* (020) 7930 2170
*E-mail:* info@royalsoc.ac.uk
*Web Site:* www.royalsoc.ac.uk
*Key Personnel*
President: Prof Lord May
Executive Secretary: Stephen Cox
 *E-mail:* stephen.cox@royalsoc.ac.uk
Dir of Communications: Dr David Stewart Boak
 *E-mail:* david.boak@royalsoc.ac.uk
Head of Publishing: John Taylor *E-mail:* john. taylor@royalsoc.ac.uk
Founded: 1660
Subjects: Education, Energy, Engineering (General), Geography, Geology, Mathematics, Mechanical Engineering, Physical Sciences, Physics, Psychology, Psychiatry, Science (General)
ISBN Prefix(es): 0-85403

**The Royal Society of Chemistry+**
Burlington House, Piccadilly, London W1J 0BA
*Tel:* (020) 7437 8656 *Fax:* (020) 7437 8883
*E-mail:* sales@rsc.org
*Web Site:* www.rsc.org
*Key Personnel*
Head of Information Services: Robert Welham
Editorial, Books: Dr Robert Andrews
Editorial, Journals: Robert Parker
Editorial, Secondary Services: Sharon Bellard
Sales & Promotion: Barry Anderson; Jenny McCluskey
Production: John Futter
Founded: 1841
Subjects: Chemistry, Chemical Engineering, Engineering (General), Health, Nutrition, Mechanical Engineering
ISBN Prefix(es): 0-85186; 0-85404; 0-85990; 1-870343
*Branch Office(s)*
Thomas Graham House, Science Park, Milton Rd, Cambridge CB4 0WF *Tel:* (01223) 420066 *Fax:* (01223) 423623
Distributed by Springer-Verlag New York Inc (North America)
*Orders to:* Turpin Distribution Services Ltd, Blackhorse Rd, Letchworth, Herts SG6 1HN *Tel:* (01462) 672555 *Fax:* (01462) 480947

**Royal Society of Medicine Press Ltd+**
One Wimpole St, London W1G 0AE
*Tel:* (020) 7290 2921 *Fax:* (020) 7290 2929
*E-mail:* publishing@rsm.ac.uk
*Web Site:* www.rsmpress.co.uk
*Key Personnel*
Man Dir: Peter Richardson
Subjects: Medicine, Nursing, Dentistry
ISBN Prefix(es): 1-85315
Number of titles published annually: 35 Print; 1 E-Book
Total Titles: 500 Print; 1 E-Book
Distributed by Elsevier Australia (Australia, New Zealand & South Pacific); Panther Publishers (India); World Scientific Publishing Co (Japan, Korea & China)
Foreign Rep(s): Bernd Feldmann (Austria, Germany, Switzerland); Frans Janssen (Belgium, Netherlands, Luxembourg); Zoe Kaviani (Africa, Gulf States, Middle East); Jan Norbye (Denmark, Finland, Iceland, Norway, Sweden); Jim Osgerby (Southeast England exc London, Southern England); Judith Rushby (Scotland, Midlands, Northern England)
*Distribution Center:* Jamco Distribution Inc, 1401 Lakeway Drive, Lewisville, TX 75057, United States
Marston Book Services, PO Box 269, Abington, Oxon OX14 4YN (Europe & Middle East)

**RSP**, see Research Studies Press Ltd (RSP)

**The Rubicon Press+**
57 Cornwall Gardens, London SW7 4BE
Mailing Address: PO Box 147, Lytham St Annes, Lancs FY8 3WZ
*Tel:* (020) 7937 6813 *Fax:* (020) 7937 6813
*Key Personnel*
Partner: Juanita Homan; Robin A Page
 *E-mail:* robin.page@whsmithnet.co.uk
Founded: 1985
Specializing in Egyptology & English history.
Membership(s): IPG.
Subjects: Antiques, Archaeology, Biography, Fiction, History, Literature, Literary Criticism, Essays, Travel, Women's Studies
ISBN Prefix(es): 0-948695
*Book Club(s):* Ancient & Medieval History Book Cl; Book Club Associates, Greater London House, Hampstead Rd, London NW1 7TZ, Contact: Michael Greenwood *Tel:* (020) 7760 6500 *Fax:* (020) 7760 6777; The History Guild

**Michael Russell Publishing Ltd+**
Wilby Hall, Wilby, Norwich NR16 2JP
*Tel:* (01953) 887776 *Fax:* (01953) 887762
*Key Personnel*
Man Dir: Michael Russell
 *E-mail:* michaelrussell@waitrose.com
Founded: 1976
Subjects: Nonfiction (General)
ISBN Prefix(es): 0-85955
Number of titles published annually: 15 Print
Total Titles: 135 Print

**Rutherford House**, *imprint of* Paternoster Publishing

**The Rutland Press+**
15 Rutland Sq, Edinburgh EH1 2BE
*Tel:* (0131) 229 7545 *Fax:* (0131) 228 2188
*E-mail:* info@rias.org.uk
*Web Site:* www.rias.org.uk
*Key Personnel*
Sales & Marketing Manager: Eilidh Donaldson
Publishing Manager: Helen Leng *E-mail:* hleng@ rias.org.uk
Publishing Coordinator: Susan Skinner
Founded: 1982
Subjects: Architecture & Interior Design, Travel

ISBN Prefix(es): 1-873190; 0-9501462
*Parent Company:* Royal Incorporation of Architects in Scotland

**Ryland Peters & Small Ltd+**
Kirkman House, 12-14 Whitfield St, London W1T 2RP
*Tel:* (020) 7436 9090 *Fax:* (020) 7436 9790
*E-mail:* info@rps.co.uk
*Web Site:* www.rylandpeters.com
*Key Personnel*
Man Dir: David Peters
Rights Dir: Joanna Everard *E-mail:* joanna. everard@rps.co.uk
Art Dir: Gabriella Le Grazie
Publishing Dir: Alison Starling
Sales Manager: Jacqueline MacEacharn
Founded: 1995
Publish high quality illustrated books for the international market.
Subjects: Architecture & Interior Design, Cookery, Gardening, Plants, Health, Nutrition, House & Home, Self-Help, Wine & Spirits, Lifestyle
ISBN Prefix(es): 1-84172
Number of titles published annually: 100 Print
Total Titles: 250 Print
Imprints: Paperstyle Gift Line
*U.S. Office(s):* Ryland Peters & Small Inc, 519 Broadway, 5th floor, New York, NY 10012, United States *Tel:* 646-613-8682; 646-613-8684; 646-613-8685 *Fax:* 646-613-8683 *E-mail:* info@rylandpeters.com
*Warehouse:* Macmillan Distribution Ltd, Brunel Rd, Houndmills, Basingstoke, Hants RG21 6XS *Tel:* (01256) 329 242 *Fax:* (01256) 327 961 *E-mail:* mdl@macmillam.co.uk
*Distribution Center:* COSI Toll Free *Tel:* 877-342-1478 *Fax:* 201-840-7242 *E-mail:* bookorders@cosi-us.com (US)
Macmillan Distribution Ltd, Brunel Rd, Houndmills, Basingstoke, Hants RG21 6XS *Tel:* (01256) 329 242 *Fax:* (01256) 327 961 *E-mail:* mdl@macmillan.co.uk

**SAGE Publications Ltd+**
One Oliver's Yard, 55 City Rd, London EC1Y 1SP
*Tel:* (020) 7324 8500 *Fax:* (020) 7374 8600
*E-mail:* info@sagepub.co.uk
*Web Site:* www.sagepub.co.uk
*Key Personnel*
Man Dir: Stephen Barr
Non-Executive Dir: Paul Chapman
Production Dir: Richard Fidczuk
Finance Dir: Katharine Jackson
Editorial Dir: Ziyad Marar
Human Resources Dir: Jane Quick
Founded: 1971
Membership(s): IPG.
Subjects: Anthropology, Behavioral Sciences, Biological Sciences, Business, Communications, Computer Science, Criminology, Economics, Education, Engineering (General), Environmental Studies, Ethnicity, Finance, Government, Political Science, Health, Nutrition, History, Human Relations, Language Arts, Linguistics, Management, Marketing, Medicine, Nursing, Dentistry, Philosophy, Psychology, Psychiatry, Religion - Protestant, Social Sciences, Sociology, Women's Studies
ISBN Prefix(es): 0-7591; 0-7619
Imprints: Altamira Press; Paul Chapman Publishing; Corwin Press; Pine Forge Press; Sage Science Press
Divisions: Scolari
*Branch Office(s)*
SAGE Publications India Pvt Ltd, B-42 Panchsheel Enclave, New Delhi 100 017, India *Tel:* (011) 2649 1290 *Fax:* (011) 2649 2117 *E-mail:* sage@vsnl.com *Web Site:* www. indiasage.com

*U.S. Office(s):* SAGE Publications USA, 2455 Teller Rd, Thousand Oaks, CA 91320, United States *Tel:* (805) 499-0721; (805) 499-9774 *Fax:* (805) 499-0871 *E-mail:* info@sagepub. com *Web Site:* www.sagepub.com

**Sage Science Press**, *imprint of* SAGE Publications Ltd

**Sainsbury Publishing Ltd+**
Auldearn Main St, Bleasby, Notts NG14 7GH
*Tel:* (01636) 830499 *Fax:* (01636) 830175
*Key Personnel*
Dir: George Sainsbury *E-mail:* george@gsbooks. demon.co.uk
Founded: 1987
Subjects: Humor, Natural History
ISBN Prefix(es): 1-870655

**Saint Andrew Press+**
121 George St, Edinburgh EH2 4YN
*Tel:* (0131) 225 5722 *Fax:* (0131) 220 3113
*E-mail:* standrewpress@cofscotland.org.uk
*Web Site:* www.churchofscotland.org.uk
*Key Personnel*
Head of Publishing: Ann Crawford
Sales & Production Manager: Derek Auld
Distribution: Ian Dunnet
Marketing & Publicity Officer: Alison Fleming
Founded: 1954
Membership(s): Scottish Publishers Association.
Subjects: History, Regional Interests, Religion - Protestant, Religion - Other, Theology
ISBN Prefix(es): 0-7152; 0-86153
Number of titles published annually: 12 Print
Total Titles: 100 Print
*Parent Company:* The Board of Communication of the Church of Scotland
*Ultimate Parent Company:* The Church of Scotland
Distributor for Church of Scotland Stationery; Pathway Productions; Wild Goose Publications

**St David's Press**, *imprint of* Welsh Academic Press

**St George's Press**
17 Ingatestone Rd, Woodford, Green Essex IG8 9AN
*Tel:* (020) 8504 1199 *Fax:* (020) 8559 0989
*E-mail:* sgp17@aol.com
*Web Site:* www.eppingforest.co.uk/stgeorgespress
Founded: 1969
Specialize in the works of Julian Fane, novelist, short story writer, memorialist & literary figure of distinction.
Subjects: Fiction, Literature, Literary Criticism, Essays
ISBN Prefix(es): 0-14; 0-902619

**St James Press**, *imprint of* Thomson Gale

**St Jerome Publishing**
2 Maple Rd W, Brooklands, Manchester M23 9HH
*Tel:* (0161) 973 9856 *Fax:* (0161) 905 3498
*E-mail:* stjerome@compuserve.com
*Web Site:* www.stjerome.co.uk
*Key Personnel*
Man Dir & International Rights: Ken Baker
Founded: 1994
Specialize in books on interpreting & related fields; intercultural communication.
Memebrship(s): IPG; Publishers' Association.
Subjects: Language Arts, Linguistics, Cultural Studies, Literary Studies
ISBN Prefix(es): 1-900650
Number of titles published annually: 15 Print
Total Titles: 52 Print
Distributed by Binghamton University Press; European Institute for the Media; Exeter Univer-

sity Press; Kent State University Press; Multilingual Matters; Northern Illinois University Press; Rodopi; Routledge; Rutgers University Press

**St Paul's Bibliographies Ltd+**
17 Greenbanks, Lyminge, Kent CT18 8HG
*Tel:* (0130) 386 2258 *Fax:* (0130) 386 2660
*E-mail:* stpauls@stpaulsbib.com
*Web Site:* www.oakknoll.com/spbib.html
*Key Personnel*
Dir: J von Hoelle; R Fleck; C Reynard
Founded: 1979
ISBN Prefix(es): 0-906795; 0-946053; 1-873040
*Parent Company:* Oak Knoll Press, 414 Delaware St, New Castle, DE 19720, United States
Distributed by Oak Knoll Press
Distributor for Oak Knoll Press (USA)
*Orders to:* Scott Brinded, 106 Dover Rd, Folkestone, Kent CT20 1NN *Tel:* (01303) 220567 *Fax:* (01303) 220600

**St Pauls Publishing+**
187 Battersea Bridge Rd, London SW11 3AS
*Tel:* (020) 7978 4300 *Fax:* (020) 7978 4370
*E-mail:* editions@stpauls.org.uk
*Web Site:* www.stpauls.ie
*Key Personnel*
Man Dir & Rights & Permissions: Fr Andrew Pudussery *Tel:* (020) 79784300 *Fax:* (020) 79784370 *E-mail:* vpudussery@tiscali.org.uk
Founded: 1967
Subjects: Human Relations, Humor, Philosophy, Religion - Catholic, Religion - Other, Social Sciences, Sociology, Theology
ISBN Prefix(es): 0-85439
Number of titles published annually: 35 Print
Total Titles: 265 Print
*Parent Company:* Society of St Paul, Via della Fanella 39, 00148 Rome, Italy
*Bookshop(s):* St Pauls, Morpeth Terrace, Victoria, London SW1P 1EP, Sebastian Karamvelil *Tel:* (020) 7828 5582 *Fax:* (020) 7828 3329 *E-mail:* bookshop@stpauls.org.uk
*Distribution Center:* Moyglare Rd, Maynooth, Co Kildare, Ireland, Contact: Sergs Magbanua *Tel:* (01) 6285933 *Fax:* (01) 6289330 *E-mail:* sales@stpauls.ie *Web Site:* www. stpauls.ie

**Salamander Books Ltd+**
Division of Chrysalis Books
Brunel Rd, Houndmills, Basingstoke RG21 6XS
*Tel:* (01256) 329242 *Fax:* (01256) 812558; (01256) 812521
*E-mail:* mdl@macmillan.co.uk
*Web Site:* www.chrysalisbooks.co.uk/books/publisher/salamander
*Key Personnel*
Group Sales & Marketing Dir: Richard Samson *E-mail:* rsamson@chrysalisbooks.co.uk
Dir of Marketing: Kate Wood *E-mail:* kwood@chrysalisbooks.co.uk
Sales Manager: Sharon Pitcher *E-mail:* spitcher@chrysalisbooks.co.uk
Foreign Rights: Candida Buckley *E-mail:* candidabuckley@aol.com
Permissions: Terry Forshaw *E-mail:* tforshaw@chrysalisbooks.co.uk
Founded: 1974
Subjects: Aeronautics, Aviation, Animals, Pets, Architecture & Interior Design, Cookery, Crafts, Games, Hobbies, Gardening, Plants, Health, Nutrition, History, House & Home, Native American Studies, Natural History, Sports, Athletics, Transportation, American History, US Cars & Motorbikes
ISBN Prefix(es): 0-86101; 1-84065; 1-85600
Imprints: Aspect; Vega
*Orders to:* HarperCollins Distribution, Campsie View, Westerhill Rd, Bishopbriggs, Glasgow *Fax:* (087) 0787 1995 (Trade only)

**The Salariya Book Co Ltd+**
25 Marlborough Pl, Brighton, East Sussex BN1 1UB
*Tel:* (01273) 603 306 *Fax:* (01273) 693 857
*E-mail:* salariya@salariya.com
*Web Site:* www.salariya.com
*Key Personnel*
Dir: David Salariya *E-mail:* david.salariya@salariya.com
Editor: Karen Barker Smith *E-mail:* karen.barkersmith@salariya.com; Michael Ford *E-mail:* michael.ford@salariya.com
Finance, Production & Rights: Jo Furse *E-mail:* jo.furse@salariya.com
Founded: 1989
Illustrated children's books for international co-edition market.
Subjects: Architecture & Interior Design, Fiction, Foreign Countries, Geography, Geology, History, Natural History, Science (General), Technology
ISBN Prefix(es): 1-904194
Total Titles: 150 Print
Imprints: Book House

**The Saltire Society**
9 Fountain Close, 22 High St, Edinburgh EH1 1TF
*Tel:* (0131) 556 1836 *Fax:* (0131) 557 1675
*E-mail:* saltire@saltiresociety.org.uk
*Web Site:* www.saltiresociety.org.uk
*Key Personnel*
Administrator: Kathleen Munro
Founded: 1936
Subjects: History, Literature, Literary Criticism, Essays
ISBN Prefix(es): 0-85411
*Branch Office(s)*
Blvd Brand Whitlock 152, BTE 3, 1200 Brussels, Belgium, Convener: Alasdair Geater *Tel:* (02) 735 82 72 *Web Site:* www.amg1.net/scotland.htm (Brussels)
´Eredene´, Huntly Rd, Aboyne, Convener: Ian Kinniburgh *Tel:* (0133) 988 6484 *E-mail:* iankinniburgh@beeb.net (Aberdeen)
Feddans, Cardross G82 5IG, Chair: Alison Cowey *Tel:* (01436) 841 440 (Helensburgh)
Magdalene House, Lochmaben, Dumfries DG11 1PD, Convener: Mdme May McKerrell of Hillhouse *Tel:* (01387) 810439 (Dumfries & Galloway)
1/35 Bothwell House, Edinburgh EH7 5YL, Chairman: Ian MacDonald *Tel:* (0131) 659 6058 (Edinburgh)
14 Cleveden Drive, Glasgow, Convener: Kenneth Thomson *Tel:* (0141) 334 7773
Birchdale, 69 Culduthel Rd, Inverness IV2 4HH, Chairman: Dr Alastair Scott-Brown *Tel:* (01463) 223 294 *E-mail:* ardynsb@onetel.net.uk (Highland)
Lea Cottage, 16 Whiteside, Kirriemuir DD8 4HZ, Chairman: Betty Allan *Tel:* (01575) 574 134 (Kirriemuir)
Solwayside, Harbour Rd, Wigtown, Convener: Mary Norris *Tel:* (01988) 402253 (Galloway)
*Warehouse:* Scottish Book Source, 32 Finlas St, Glasgow G22 5DU
*Orders to:* Scottish Book Source, 32 Finlas St, Glasgow G22 5DU *Tel:* (0131) 229 6800 *Fax:* (0131) 229 9070

**Salvationist Publishing & Supplies Ltd**
117-121 Judd St, London WC1H 9NN
*Tel:* (020) 7387 1656 *Fax:* (020) 7383 3420
*E-mail:* mail_order@sp-s.co.uk
*Web Site:* www.archive.salvationarmy.org.uk
*Key Personnel*
Man Dir: Lieutenant General Michael Williams
Company Secretary: Gordon Camsey
Subjects: Music, Dance, Religion - Other
ISBN Prefix(es): 0-85412
Subsidiaries: S P & S Mail Order (also ordering)

**Sams Publishing**, *imprint of* Pearson Education Europe, Mideast & Africa

**Sams.net**, *imprint of* Pearson Education Europe, Mideast & Africa

**Sangam Books Ltd+**
57 London Fruit Exchange Brushfield St, London E1 6EP
*Tel:* (020) 7377-6399 *Fax:* (020) 7375-1230
*E-mail:* goatony@aol.com
*Key Personnel*
Chief Executive, Sales, Publicity: A A de Souza
Founded: 1981
Membership(s): Publishers Association UK.
Subjects: Fiction, Medicine, Nursing, Dentistry, Nonfiction (General), Science (General), Social Sciences, Sociology, Technology
ISBN Prefix(es): 0-86131; 0-86311; 0-86125; 0-86132
Number of titles published annually: 30 Print
*Parent Company:* Orient Longman Pvt Ltd, India

**Sapphire**, *imprint of* Virgin Publishing Ltd

**Saqi Books+**
26 Westbourne Grove, London W2 5RH
*Tel:* (020) 7221 9347 *Fax:* (020) 7229 7492
*E-mail:* info@saqibooks.com
*Web Site:* www.saqibooks.com
*Key Personnel*
Publisher: Andre Gaspard
Managing Editor: Penny Warburton
Publicity: Rebecca O'Connor
Commissioning Editor: Mitchell Albert
Founded: 1984
Subjects: Art, Asian Studies, Biography, Cookery, Developing Countries, Ethnicity, Fiction, Foreign Countries, Government, Political Science, History, Humor, Language Arts, Linguistics, Literature, Literary Criticism, Essays, Music, Dance, Nonfiction (General), Photography, Social Sciences, Sociology, Travel, Wine & Spirits, Balkan Studies, Middle Eastern Studies
ISBN Prefix(es): 0-86356
Number of titles published annually: 30 Print
Total Titles: 200 Print
Foreign Rep(s): Durnell Marketing (Europe); Horizon Books (Malaysia, Singapore); Palgrave Macmillan (Australia, US)
Foreign Rights: La Nouvelle Agence (France); Pontas Agency (Spain)

**Saunders**, *imprint of* Elsevier Ltd

**KG Saur**, *imprint of* Thomson Gale

**Steve Savage Publishers Ltd+**
Old Truman Brewery, 91 Brick Lane, London E1 6QL
*Tel:* (020) 7770 6083
*E-mail:* mail@savagepublishers.com
*Web Site:* www.savagepublishers.com
Founded: 2001
Subjects: Fiction, Humor, Literature, Literary Criticism, Essays, Nonfiction (General)
ISBN Prefix(es): 0-904246
*Orders to:* Book Source, 32 Finlas St, Glasgow G22 5DU *Tel:* (0141) 558 1366 *Fax:* (0141) 557 0189 *E-mail:* orders@booksource.net

**Savannah Publications**
90 Dartmouth Rd, Forest Hill, London SE23 3HZ
*Tel:* (020) 8244 4350 *Fax:* (020) 8244 2448
*E-mail:* savpub@dircon.co.uk
*Web Site:* www.savannah-publications.com
Subjects: Publishers of military works of reference & military genealogy
ISBN Prefix(es): 1-902366
Total Titles: 100 Print

**Savitri Books Ltd+**
115J Cleveland St, London W1T 6PU
*Tel:* (020) 7436 9932 *Fax:* (020) 7580 6330
*Key Personnel*
Man Dir: M S Srivastava
Founded: 1983
Also acts as packagers.
Subjects: Crafts, Games, Hobbies, How-to, Natural History
ISBN Prefix(es): 0-9534103

**SAWD Publications+**
Suite 1, 62 Bell Rd, Sittingbourne, Kent ME10 4HE
*Tel:* (01795) 472 262 *Fax:* (01795) 422 633
*E-mail:* wainman@sawd.demon.co.uk
*Key Personnel*
Partners: Allison Wainman; Susannah Wainman
Founded: 1989
Subjects: Cookery, Gardening, Plants, Humor, Nonfiction (General)
ISBN Prefix(es): 1-872489

**SB Publications+**
19 Grove Rd, Seaford, East Sussex BN25 1TP
*Tel:* (01323) 893498 *Fax:* (01323) 893860
*E-mail:* sales@sbpublications.swinternet.co.uk
*Key Personnel*
Owner: Lindsay Woods
Founded: 1987
Membership(s): IPG.
Subjects: History, Maritime, Regional Interests, Transportation, Travel, UK local history & guides
ISBN Prefix(es): 1-85770; 1-870708
Number of titles published annually: 25 Print
Total Titles: 140 Print
Imprints: BEN Gunn

**Scarthin Books+**
The Promenade Scarthin, Cromford, Derbys DE4 3QF
*Tel:* (01629) 823272 *Fax:* (01629) 825094
*E-mail:* clare@scarthinbooks.demon.co.uk
*Web Site:* www.scarthinbooks.com; www.books.co.uk
*Key Personnel*
Proprietor: D J Mitchell
Marketing: G N Cooper
Founded: 1981
Membership(s): Booksellers Association of Great Britain & Ireland (BAGBI).
Subjects: History, Outdoor Recreation
ISBN Prefix(es): 0-907758
Number of titles published annually: 5 Print
Total Titles: 110 Print
Imprints: Family Walks

**Sceptre**, *imprint of* Hodder & Stoughton General

**Schirmer Reference**, *imprint of* Thomson Gale

**Schofield & Sims Ltd+**
Dogley Mill, Fenay Bridge, Huddersfield HD8 0NQ
*Tel:* (01484) 607080 *Fax:* (01484) 606815
*E-mail:* post@schofieldandsims.co.uk
*Web Site:* www.schofieldandsims.co.uk
*Key Personnel*
Chairman: John S Nesbitt
Man Dir: J Stephen Platts
Sales Dir: Jack Brierley
Founded: 1901
Membership(s): IPG.
ISBN Prefix(es): 0-7217

**Scholastic Ltd+**
Westfield Rd, Southam, Leamington Spa, Warwicks CV47 0RA
*Tel:* (01926) 887799; (01926) 813910 (warehouse) *Fax:* (01926) 883331

*E-mail:* scholastic@tens.co.uk
*Web Site:* www.scholastic.co.uk
*Key Personnel*
Man Dir: David Kewley
Educational Publishing Dir: Annie Peel
Sales & Marketing Dir: Gavin Lang
Buying Dir, Direct Marketing: Victoria Birkett
Editorial Dir, Children's Books: David Fickling
Senior Commissioning Editor, Educational Books: Gina Nuttall
Editor, Book Clubs: Helen Ward
Editor, Hippo Books: Anne Finnis
Production: Doug Brown
Advertising: Chris Pratt
Finance & Information Technology: Ian Bloodworth
Senior Trade Vice President: Michael Jacobs
Marketing Vice President: Jennifer Pasanen
Founded: 1964
Subjects: Fiction, Nonfiction (General)
ISBN Prefix(es): 0-590
*Parent Company:* Scholastic Inc, 557 Broadway, New York, NY 10012-3999, United States
Imprints: Adlib; Andre Deutsch Children's Books; Hippo; Point
*Branch Office(s)*
Scholastic Childrens Books, Villiers House, Clarendon Ave, Leamington Spa, Warwicks CV32 5PR *Tel:* (01926) 887799

**School Improvement Reports**, *imprint of* First & Best in Education Ltd

**School Improvement Reports**, *see* First & Best in Education Ltd

**School of Oriental & African Studies+**
Thornhaugh St, Russell Sq, London WC1H 0XG
*Tel:* (020) 7637 2388 *Fax:* (020) 7436 3844
*E-mail:* md2@soas.ac.uk; aol@soas.ac.uk
*Web Site:* www.soas.ac.uk *Cable:* SOASUL LONDON WC1
*Key Personnel*
Publications Manager: M J Daly
Publications: Andrew Osmond
Founded: 1916
Subjects: Art, History, Language Arts, Linguistics, Literature, Literary Criticism, Essays, Religion - Other, Asia & Africa
ISBN Prefix(es): 0-901877; 0-7286

**SchoolPlay Productions Ltd+**
15 Inglis Rd, Colchester, Essex CO3 3HU
*Tel:* (01206) 540111 *Fax:* (01206) 766944
*E-mail:* schoolplay@inglis-house.demon.co.uk
*Web Site:* www.schoolplayproductions.co.uk
*Key Personnel*
Man Dir: Jeremy Lucas *E-mail:* jrl@inglis-house.demon.co.uk
Founded: 1989
Specialize in publishing plays & musicals for performance by youth groups & schools; play scripts & musical scores.
Subjects: Drama, Theater, Music, Dance
ISBN Prefix(es): 1-872475; 1-902472
Number of titles published annually: 12 Print
Total Titles: 140 Print

**Science & Technology Letters**, *imprint of* Science Reviews Ltd

**Science Reviews**, *imprint of* Science Reviews Ltd

**Science Reviews Ltd**
PO Box 314, St Albans, Herts AL1 4ZG
*Tel:* (01727) 847322 *Fax:* (01727) 847323
*E-mail:* scilet@scilet.com
*Web Site:* www.scilet.com
*Key Personnel*
Publisher: Dr Peter J Farago

Founded: 1978
Subjects: Chemistry, Chemical Engineering, Environmental Studies, Medicine, Nursing, Dentistry, Science (General)
*Associate Companies:* Science & Technology Letters; Science Reviews Inc, 1115 S Plymouth Court, Suite 412, Chicago, IL 60605, United States *Tel:* 312-913-1404 (also orders)
Imprints: Science Reviews; Science & Technology Letters; Symposium Press


**Scientific American**, *imprint of* W H Freeman & Co Ltd


**SCM-Canterbury Press Ltd+**
Subsidiary of Hymns Ancient & Modern Ltd
9-17 St Albans Pl, London N1 0NX
*Tel:* (020) 7359 8033 *Fax:* (020) 7359 0049
*E-mail:* admin@scm-canterburypress.co.uk
*Web Site:* www.scm-canterburypress.co.uk
*Key Personnel*
Group Chief Executive Officer: Gordon Knights *Tel:* (01603) 612914 ext 203 *E-mail:* gordon@scm-canterburypress.co.uk
Group Financial Controller: Brenda Medhurst *Tel:* (01603) 612914 ext 208 *E-mail:* brenda@scm-canterburypress.co.uk
Customer Services Manager: Louise Hopcroft *Tel:* (01603) 612914 ext 207
Publishing Dir: Christine Smith *Tel:* (020) 7359 8033 *E-mail:* christine@scm-canterburypress.co.uk
Senior Commissioning Editor: Barbara Laing *Tel:* (020) 7354 6217 *E-mail:* barbara@scm-canterburypress.co.uk
Senior Marketing Manager: Michael Addison *Tel:* (020) 7354 6214 *E-mail:* michael@scm-canterburypress.co.uk
Senior Marketing Controller: Anita Manbodh *Tel:* (020) 7354 6292 *E-mail:* anita@scm-canterburypress.co.uk
Key Accounts & UK Sales Manager: Kevin Allard *Tel:* (01603) 612914 *E-mail:* kevin@scm-canterburypress.co.uk
Rights & Permissions Manager: Jenny Willis *Tel:* (020) 7354 6211 *E-mail:* jenny@scm-canterburypress.co.uk
Production Manager: Stephen Rogers *Tel:* (020) 7354 6218 *E-mail:* stephen@scm-canterburypress.co.uk
Friends Administrator: Margaret Tosh *Tel:* (020) 7359 8034 *E-mail:* margaret@scm-canterburypress.co.uk
Founded: 1929 (as SCM Press Ltd)
Membership(s): Publishers Association.
Subjects: Biblical Studies, Biography, Religion - Catholic, Religion - Jewish, Religion - Protestant, Religion - Other, Theology
ISBN Prefix(es): 0-334; 0-7162; 0-907547; 0-900274; 1-85175; 1-85311
Number of titles published annually: 100 Print; 6 CD-ROM; 6 Audio
Total Titles: 3,000 Print; 12 CD-ROM; 12 Audio
Imprints: Canterbury Press; Religious & Moral Education Press (RMEP); SCM Press
Distributor for Deo Publishing (UK); Epworth Press (UK); Tufton Books (UK)
Foreign Rep(s): Columbia Books (Ireland); Hugh Dunphy (West Indies); Durnell Marketing (Europe); Novalis (Canada); Openbook (Australia, New Zealand); Westminster John Knox (US)
*Shipping Address:* St Mary's Works, St Mary's Plain, Norwich, Norfolk NR3 3BH *Tel:* (01603) 612914 *Fax:* (01603) 624483
*Warehouse:* St Mary's Works, St Mary's Plain, Norwich, Norfolk NR3 3BH *Tel:* (01603) 612914 *Fax:* (01603) 624483
*Orders to:* St Mary's Works, St Mary's Plain, Norwich, Norfolk NR3 3BH *Tel:* (01603) 612914 *Fax:* (01603) 624483
*Returns:* St Mary's Works, St Mary's Plain, Norwich, Norfolk NR3 3BH *Tel:* (01603) 612914 *Fax:* (01603) 624483


**SCM Press**, *imprint of* Hymns Ancient & Modern Ltd


**SCM Press**, *imprint of* SCM-Canterbury Press Ltd


**Scott Foresman**, *imprint of* Pearson Education Europe, Mideast & Africa


**Scottish Braille Press**
Division of Royal Blind Asylum & School
Craigmillar Park, Edinburgh EH16 5NB
*Tel:* (0131) 662 4445 *Fax:* (0131) 662 1968
*E-mail:* enquiries@scottish-braille-press.org
*Web Site:* www.scottish-braille-press.org
*Key Personnel*
Manager: John Donaldson *E-mail:* john.donaldson@scottish-braille-press.org
Sales & Marketing Manager: Stewart Connell *E-mail:* stewart.connell@scottish-braille-press.org
Founded: 1891
Also acts as Printer.


**Scottish Council for Research in Education**
61 Dublin St, Edinburgh EH3 6NL
*Tel:* (0131) 557 2944 *Fax:* (0131) 556 9454
*E-mail:* scre.info@scre.ac.uk
*Web Site:* www.scre.ac.uk
*Key Personnel*
Dir: Valerie Wilson *Tel:* (0131) 623 2964 *E-mail:* valerie.wilson@scre.ac.uk
Administrative Services: Moira Simpson
Information Services: John Lewin
Founded: 1932
Research in the service of education, using research series, research reviews & research reports.
ISBN Prefix(es): 0-901116; 0-947833; 1-86003
Total Titles: 153 Print


**Scottish Cultural Press+**
Imprint of SCP Publishers Ltd
Unit 6, Newbattle Abbey Business Annexe, Newbattle Rd, Dalkeith EH22 3LJ
*Tel:* (0131) 660-6366 (editorial); (0131) 660-4757 (editorial); (0131) 660-4666 (orders)
*E-mail:* info@scottishbooks.com
*Web Site:* www.scottishbooks.com
*Key Personnel*
Dir: Avril Gray
Dir & Company Secretary: Brian Pugh
Founded: 1992
Publisher of Scottish nonfiction & fiction.
Subjects: Archaeology, Biography, Environmental Studies, Fiction, History, Literature, Literary Criticism, Essays, Nonfiction (General), Poetry, Regional Interests, Social Sciences, Sociology
ISBN Prefix(es): 80-7239; 1-840170; 1-898827
Total Titles: 100 Print
*Associate Companies:* Scottish Children, Unit 13d, New Battle Abbey Business Annexe, New Battle Rd, Dalkeith EH22 3LT *Tel:* (0131) 660-4757, 660-6414 (Editorial); (0131) 660-4666 (orders) *Fax:* (0131) 660-6414 (editorial); (0131) 660-4666 (orders) *E-mail:* info@scottishbooks.com *Web Site:* www.scottishbooks.com
*U.S. Office(s):* Wilson & Associates, PO Box 2569, Alvin, TX 77512, United States *Tel:* 281-388-0196 *Fax:* 413-683-8503 *E-mail:* info@thebookdistribution.com *Web Site:* www.thebookdistribution.com (Canada & US)
Distributor for Scottish Children's Press; Scottish Cultural Press


**Scottish Executive Library & Information Services**
Saint Andrew's House, Regent Rd, Edinburgh EH1 3GD
*Tel:* (0131) 556 8400 *Fax:* (0131) 244 8240

*E-mail:* ceu@scotland.gov.uk
*Web Site:* www.scotland.gov.uk
*Key Personnel*
Contact: Colin Jardine *E-mail:* colin.jardine@scotland.gov.uk
Founded: 1984
Subjects: Agriculture, Criminology, Disability, Special Needs, Economics, Education, Energy, Environmental Studies, Finance, Government, Political Science, Health, Nutrition, Social Sciences, Sociology, Transportation
Distributed by HMSO Books


**Scottish Falcon**, *imprint of* The Orkney Press Ltd


**Scottish Text Society+**
27 George Sq, Edinburgh EH8 9LD
Mailing Address: School of English Studies, University of Nottingham, Nottingham NG7 2RD *Tel:* (0115) 951 5922
*Tel:* (0115) 951 5922
*E-mail:* sts@arts.gla.ac.uk
*Web Site:* www.scottishtextsociety.org
*Key Personnel*
President: Dr Sally Mapstone
Editorial Secretary: Dr Nicola Royan *E-mail:* nicola.royan@nottingham.ac.uk
Founded: 1882
Subjects: Genealogy, History, Literature, Literary Criticism, Essays, Poetry, Religion - Protestant, Theology, Medieval Literature
ISBN Prefix(es): 0-9500245; 1-897976
Total Titles: 23 Print


**Scribner**, *imprint of* Simon & Schuster Ltd


**Charles Scribner's Sons**, *imprint of* Thomson Gale


**Scripta Technica**, *imprint of* Wiley Europe Ltd


**Scripture Union+**
207-209 Queensway, Bletchley, Milton Keynes, Bucks MK2 2EB
*Tel:* (01908) 856000 *Fax:* (01908) 856111
*E-mail:* info@scriptureunion.org.uk
*Web Site:* www.scriptureunion.org.uk
*Key Personnel*
Publishing Dir: Malcolm Hall *E-mail:* malcolmh@scriptureunion.org.uk
Copyright Permissions, Overseas Rights Administration: Rosemary North *E-mail:* rosemaryn@scriptureunion.org.uk
Founded: 1867
Specialize in holiday club resources.
Subjects: Biblical Studies, Education, Religion - Protestant, Theology
ISBN Prefix(es): 0-85421; 0-86201
Number of titles published annually: 100 Print
Total Titles: 450 Print; 450 Online
*Branch Office(s)*
157 Albertbridge Rd, Belfast BT5 4PS, Ireland *Tel:* (028) 9045 4806 *Fax:* (028) 9073 9758 *E-mail:* admin@suni.co.uk *Web Site:* www.suni.co.uk (Northern Ireland)
87 Lower George's St, Dun Laoghaire, Co Dublin, Ireland *Tel:* (01) 280 2300 *Fax:* (01) 280 2409 *E-mail:* suirl@aol.ie *Web Site:* www.scriptureunion.ie (Republic of Ireland)
9 Canal St, Glasgow, Scotland G4 0ABD *Tel:* (0141) 332 1162 *Fax:* (0141) 332 1162 *E-mail:* info@scriptureunionscotland.org.uk *Web Site:* www.scriptureunionscotland.org.uk (Scotland)
*Orders to:* Scripture Union Mail Order, PO Box 5148, Milton Keynes, MLO MK2 2YZ *Tel:* (01908) 856006 *Fax:* (01908) 856020

*E-mail:* mailorder@scriptureunion.org.uk (UK
& Wales)
Send the Light (STL) Ltd, PO Box 300,
Kingstown Broadway, Carlisle, Cumbria CA3
0GS *Tel:* (01228) 611758

**Seaflower Books,** *imprint of* Ex Libris Press

**Search Press Ltd+**
Wellwood, North Farm Rd, Tunbridge Wells,
Kent TN2 3DR
*Tel:* (01892) 510850 *Fax:* (01892) 515903
*E-mail:* searchpress@searchpress.com
*Web Site:* www.searchpress.com
*Key Personnel*
Man Dir: Martin de la Bedoyere
   *E-mail:* martind@searchpress.com
Commissioning Editor: Rosalind Dace
Production: Inger Arthur
Founded: 1970
Subjects: Art, Crafts, Games, Hobbies, Garden-
   ing, Plants, How-to
ISBN Prefix(es): 0-85532

**Secker & Warburg,** *imprint of* Random House
UK Ltd

**Martin Secker & Warburg+**
Imprint of Random House
20 Vauxhall Bridge Rd, London SW1V 2SA
*Tel:* (020) 7840 8570 *Fax:* (020) 7233 6117
*E-mail:* enquiries@randomhouse.co.uk
*Web Site:* www.randomhouse.co.uk
*Key Personnel*
Editorial Dir: Geoff Mulligan *Fax:* (020) 7233
   6117
Editor: David Milner
Founded: 1910
Subjects: Fiction, Nonfiction (General)
ISBN Prefix(es): 0-436
*Ultimate Parent Company:* Bertelsmann

**SEDA Publications**
Selly Wick House, 59-61 Selly Wick Rd, Selly
   Park, Birmingham B29 7JE
*Tel:* (0121) 415 6801 *Fax:* (0121) 415 6802
*E-mail:* office@seda.ac.uk
*Web Site:* www.seda.ac.uk/publications.htm
Subjects: Education, Professional Development
Number of titles published annually: 8 Print
Total Titles: 38 Print

**Semiotext(e),** *imprint of* MIT Press Ltd

**Senate,** *imprint of* Tiger Books International PLC

**Seren+**
Imprint of Poetry Wales Press Ltd
38-40 Nolton St, 1st & 2nd floors, Bridgend
   CF31 3BN
*Tel:* (01656) 663018 *Fax:* (01656) 649226
*E-mail:* general@seren-books.com
*Web Site:* www.seren-books.com
*Key Personnel*
Chief Executive, Editorial: Cary Archard
Man Dir & International Rights: Mick Felton
   *E-mail:* mickfelton@seren.force9.co.uk
Editor: Robert Minhinnick
Fiction Editor: Will Atkins
Poetry Editor: Amy Wack
Publicity Officer: Simon Hicks
Founded: 1982
Subjects: Art, Biography, Drama, Theater, Fic-
   tion, Government, Political Science, History,
   Literature, Literary Criticism, Essays, Music,
   Dance, Photography, Poetry, Sports, Athletics,
   Women's Studies, Anthologies
ISBN Prefix(es): 0-907476; 1-85411
Number of titles published annually: 30 Print
Total Titles: 200 Print; 1 CD-ROM; 1 Audio

Distributed by Eleanor Brasch Associates (Aus-
   tralia); IPG
*Distribution Center:* Central Books, 99 Wallis
   Rd, London E9 5LN *Tel:* (020) 8986 4854
   *Fax:* (020) 8533 5821 *E-mail:* orders@centbks.
   demon.co.uk (trade)
Welsh Books Council, Uned 16 Stad Glanyra-
   fon, Llanbadarn, Aberystwyth SY23 3AQ
   *Tel:* (01970) 624455 *Fax:* (01970) 625506 *Web
   Site:* www.gwales.com (trade)

**Serif+**
47 Strahan Rd, London E3 5DA
*Tel:* (020) 8981 3990 *Fax:* (020) 8981 3990
*Key Personnel*
Publisher & International Rights: Stephen Hay-
   ward *E-mail:* stephen@serif.demon.co.uk
Founded: 1993
Subjects: Cookery, Developing Countries, For-
   eign Countries, Government, Political Science,
   History
ISBN Prefix(es): 1-897959
*Orders to:* Central Books, 99 Wallis Rd, London
   E9 5LN
Interlink Publishing Group, 46 Crosby St,
   Northampton, MA 01060-1804, United
   States *Tel:* 413-582-7054 *Fax:* 413-582-
   7057 *E-mail:* sales@interlinkbooks.com *Web
   Site:* www.interlinkbooks.com

**Serpent's Tail Ltd+**
4 Blackstock Mews, London N4 2BT
*Tel:* (020) 7354-1949 *Fax:* (020) 7704-6467
*E-mail:* info@serpentstail.com
*Web Site:* www.serpentstail.com
*Key Personnel*
Editorial Dir: Peter Ayrton *E-mail:* pete@
   serpentstail.com
Production: Ruth Petrie
Publicity: Anna Vallois
Sales & Marketing: Jenny Boyce
Founded: 1986
Subjects: African American Studies, Asian Stud-
   ies, Biography, Criminology, Ethnicity, Fiction,
   Gay & Lesbian, Literature, Literary Criticism,
   Essays, Music, Dance, Mysteries, Nonfiction
   (General), Women's Studies, High Risk/Cult
ISBN Prefix(es): 1-85242
Number of titles published annually: 40 Print
Total Titles: 350 Print
Imprints: High Risk
*U.S. Office(s):* Lisa Garbutt Book Promotion, PO
   Box 976, North Kingstown, RI 02852, United
   States *Tel:* 401-885-3482 *Fax:* 401-885-7996
Distributed by Quartet Sales & Marketing (South
   Africa); Tower Books Pty Ltd (Australia)
*Orders to:* LBS, Faraday Close, Durrington, Wor-
   thing, West Sussex BN13 3RB *Tel:* (01903)
   828800 *Fax:* (01903) 828801

**Severn House Publishers Inc+**
Subsidiary of Severn House Publishers Ltd
9-15 High St, Sutton, Surrey SM1 1DF
*Tel:* (020) 8770 3930 *Fax:* (020) 8770 3850
*E-mail:* sales@severnhouse.com; editorial@
   severnhouse.com
*Web Site:* www.severnhouse.com
*Key Personnel*
Chairman: Edwin Buckhalter *E-mail:* edwin@
   severnhouse.com
Publisher: Amanda Stewart *E-mail:* amanda@
   severnhouse.com
Acquisitions Editor: Sheena Craig
   *E-mail:* sheena@severnhouse.com
Rights Manager: Michelle Duff
Founded: 1974
Membership(s): ALA; CWA; RNA; RWA.
Subjects: Fiction, Mysteries, Romance
ISBN Prefix(es): 0-7278
Number of titles published annually: 120 Print
Total Titles: 400 Print

*Ultimate Parent Company:* Severn House Books
   (Holdings) Ltd
Imprints: Enigma Books
*U.S. Office(s):* 595 Madison Ave, 15th floor,
   New York, NY 10022, United States *Tel:* 212-
   935-0966 *Fax:* 212-935-0966 *E-mail:* sales@
   severnhouse.com *Web Site:* www.severnhouse.
   com (regular & large print)
*Warehouse:* Grantham Book Services Ltd, Isaac
   Newton Way, Alma Park Industrial Estate,
   Grantham, Lincs NG31 9SD *Tel:* (01476)
   541080 *Fax:* (01476) 541061
Mercedes Distribution Center, Bldg No 3, Brook-
   lyn Navy Yard, New York, United States, Con-
   tact: Joal Savino or Rena Persaud *Tel:* 718-534-
   3000; 800-830-3044 *Fax:* 718-935-9647
*Orders to:* Grantham Book Services Ltd, Isaac
   Newton Way, Alma Park Industrial Estate,
   Grantham, Lincs NG31 9SD *Tel:* (01476)
   541080 *Fax:* (01476) 541061

**Shakti Communications Ltd**
28a Popin Business Centre, South Way, Wembley
   HA9 0HF
*Tel:* (020) 8903 5442 *Fax:* (020) 8903 4684
*E-mail:* info@shakticom.com
*Web Site:* www.shakticom.com
*Key Personnel*
Man Dir: Mr Ravi Jain *E-mail:* ravi@shakticom.
   com
ISBN Prefix(es): 0-7128; 0-906666; 0-9505709

**Shaw & Sons Ltd**
Shaway House, 21 Bourne Park, Bourne Rd,
   Crayford, Kent DA1 4BZ
*Tel:* (01322) 621100 *Fax:* (01322) 550553
*E-mail:* sales@shaws.co.uk
*Web Site:* www.shaws.co.uk
*Key Personnel*
Publishing Dir: David Hubber
Publications Dir: Crispin Williams
   *E-mail:* crispin.williams@shaws.co.uk
Marketing Manager: Barbara Ferguson
   *E-mail:* barbara.ferguson@shaws.co.uk
Founded: 1750
Membership(s): Publishers' Association.
Subjects: Government, Political Science, Law,
   Nonfiction (General)
ISBN Prefix(es): 0-7219
Number of titles published annually: 10 Print
Total Titles: 60 Print
Imprints: R Hazell & Co

**Shearwater Press Ltd**
45 SlieauDhoo, Tromode Park, Douglas, Isle of
   Man IM2 5LG
*Tel:* (01624) 627727 *Fax:* (01624) 663627
*Telex:* 629824 Bell
*Key Personnel*
Man Dir, Editorial: Peter Crellin
Founded: 1973
Subjects: Art, Fiction, Geography, Geology, His-
   tory, Regional Interests
ISBN Prefix(es): 0-904980

**Sheed & Ward UK+**
The Tower Bldg, 11 York Rd, London SE1 7NX
*Tel:* (020) 7922 0880 *Fax:* (020) 7922 0881
*E-mail:* info@breathemail.net
*Web Site:* www.continuumbooks.com
*Key Personnel*
Dir, UK Publishing Services: Benn Linfield
   *E-mail:* blinfield@econtinuumbokos.com
Founded: 1926
Subjects: History, Philosophy, Religion - Other
ISBN Prefix(es): 0-7220
*Parent Company:* Continuum International Pub-
   lishing Group

**Sheffield Academic Press Ltd+**
Stanley House, 3 Fleets Lane, Poole BH15 3AJ

751

*Tel:* (01202) 665 432 *Fax:* (01202) 666 219
*E-mail:* orders@orcabookservices.co.uk
*Web Site:* www.sheffieldacademicpress.com
*Key Personnel*
Man Dir: Jean Allen
Dir: David J A Clines; Dr Philip R Davies;
  Michael M Mallett
Marketing Manager: Maureen Allum
  *E-mail:* mallum@sheffac.demon.co.uk
Founded: 1976
Subjects: Archaeology, Biblical Studies, Biologi-
  cal Sciences, Chemistry, Chemical Engineering,
  Drama, Theater, Foreign Countries, Language
  Arts, Linguistics, Literature, Literary Criticism,
  Essays, Medicine, Nursing, Dentistry, Religion
  - Jewish, Science (General), Technology, The-
  ology
ISBN Prefix(es): 0-905774; 1-85075; 1-84127
Number of titles published annually: 110 Print
Total Titles: 850 Print
Imprints: Almond Press
Distributor for Worldwide-Semitic Study Aids
  Series of University of Birmingham
Foreign Rep(s): Trevor Brown Associates (Eu-
  rope); Erickson Marketing; Korean Christian
  Book Service (Korea); Justin Moulder (UK);
  Brian Pugh (Ireland, Northern Ireland, Scot-
  land); Russell Book Representation (UK);
  Sheffield Academic Press (Australia, Canada,
  New Zealand); Derek Walker (Northeast Eng-
  land)
*Distribution Center:* Cornell University Press Ser-
  vices, 750 Cascadilla St, PO Box 6525, Ithaca,
  NY 14851, United States

**Sheldon Press**, *imprint of* The Society for
  Promoting Christian Knowledge (SPCK)

**Sheldon Press**
Imprint of The Society for Promoting Christian
  Knowledge (SPCK)
36 Causton St, London SW1P 4ST
*Tel:* (020) 7592 3900 *Fax:* (020) 7592 3939
*E-mail:* director@sheldonpress.co.uk
*Web Site:* www.sheldonpress.co.uk
*Key Personnel*
Publisher: Joanna Moriarty *E-mail:* jmoriarty@
  spck.org.uk
Sales Manager: Susan Kodicek
  *E-mail:* skodicek@spck.org.uk
Founded: 1973
Subjects: Health, Nutrition, Psychology, Psychia-
  try, Self-Help
ISBN Prefix(es): 0-85969
Number of titles published annually: 25 Print
Total Titles: 250 Print
*Warehouse:* Marston Book Services Ltd
*Orders to:* 160 Milton Park Estate, Oxford OX14
  4YN *Tel:* (01235) 465500 *Fax:* (01235) 465555

**Sheldrake Press+**
Imprint of Sheldrake Publications Ltd
188 Cavendish Rd, London SW12 0DA
*Tel:* (020) 8675 1767; (01752) 202301 (orders);
  (01752) 202300 (warehouse) *Fax:* (020) 8675
  7736
*E-mail:* mail@sheldrakepress.demon.co.uk
*Web Site:* www.sheldrakepress.co.uk
*Key Personnel*
Contact: Mr J S Rigge
Founded: 1979
Subjects: Architecture & Interior Design, Cook-
  ery, History, House & Home, Music, Dance,
  Nonfiction (General), Outdoor Recreation,
  Transportation, Travel
ISBN Prefix(es): 1-873329
Number of titles published annually: 2 Print
Total Titles: 30 Print
*Ultimate Parent Company:* Sheldrake Holdings
  Ltd
Distributed by Interlink
Distributor for Inmerc bv

Foreign Rep(s): Bill Baily Publishers (Croatia,
  Cyprus, Czech Republic, Europe, Gibraltar,
  Iceland, Malta, Russia, Slovenia, Turkey)
*Distribution Center:* NBN Plymbridge

**Shelfmark Books**
90 Wallis Rd, London E9 5LN
*Tel:* (020) 8986 4854 *Fax:* (020) 8533 5821
*E-mail:* orders@centralbooks.com
*Key Personnel*
Contact: John Wardroper
Founded: 1994
Subjects: History, Literature, Literary Criticism,
  Essays
ISBN Prefix(es): 0-9526093

**Sheppard**, *imprint of* Richard Joseph Publishers
  Ltd

**Sherbourne Publications+**
Sherbourne, Trefonen Rd, Morda, Oswestery, Sa-
  lop SY10 9AG
*Tel:* (01691) 657 853 *Fax:* (01691) 657 853
*Key Personnel*
Contact: Dorothy McNeil
Founded: 1989
Membership(s): Society of Authors & ALCS In-
  dependent Publishers Guild.
Subjects: Animals, Pets, Poetry
ISBN Prefix(es): 1-872547
Distributor for B Small Publishing (UK); Tarquin
  Publications (UK)

**Sheridan Book Company**, *imprint of* Tiger
  Books International PLC

**Sherwood Publishing+**
Subsidiary of A D International
Sherwood House, 7 Oxhey Rd, Watford, Herts
  WD19 4QF
*Tel:* (01923) 224737 *Fax:* (01923) 210648
*E-mail:* sherwood@adinternational.com
*Web Site:* www.sherwoodpublishing.com
*Key Personnel*
Chief Executive: Julie Hay
Founded: 1993
Subjects: Behavioral Sciences, Career Develop-
  ment, Education, Human Relations, Manage-
  ment, Psychology, Psychiatry, Self-Help, Per-
  sonal development for trainers
ISBN Prefix(es): 0-9521964
*U.S. Office(s):* Sherwood Publishing, 4036 Kerry
  Court, Minnetonka, MN 55343, United States

**Shire Publications Ltd+**
Cromwell House, Church St, Princes Risborough,
  Bucks HP27 9AA
*Tel:* (01844) 344301 *Fax:* (01844) 347080
*E-mail:* shire@shirebooks.co.uk
*Web Site:* www.shirebooks.com
*Key Personnel*
Publisher: John Rotheroe
Sales & General Manager: Sue Ross
Publicity Manager: Patience Dizon
Founded: 1962
Subjects: Antiques, Archaeology, Architecture
  & Interior Design, Biography, Crafts, Games,
  Hobbies, Electronics, Electrical Engineering,
  Ethnicity, Gardening, Plants, Genealogy, His-
  tory, House & Home, Labor, Industrial Re-
  lations, Maritime, Military Science, Music,
  Dance, Natural History, Photography, Social
  Sciences, Sociology, Sports, Athletics, Trans-
  portation, Canals, Coins & Medals, Costume
  & Fashion Accessories, Egyptology, London,
  Scottish Heritage, Furniture & Furnishings,
  Glass, Ceramics, Guide & Walking, Motoring,
  Railway & Steam, Toys, Collectables, Textile
  History
ISBN Prefix(es): 0-85263; 0-7478

Number of titles published annually: 30 Print
Total Titles: 500 Print

**Sickle Moon Books**, *imprint of* Eland Publishing
  Ltd

**Sidgwick & Jackson**, *imprint of* Pan Macmillan

**Sidgwick & Jackson Ltd+**
Imprint of Pan Macmillan
20 New Wharf Rd, London N1 9RR
*Tel:* (020) 7014 6000 *Fax:* (020) 7014 6001
*Key Personnel*
Man Dir: William Armstrong
Publicity: Phillipa McEwan
Promotions Officer: James Strachan
Founded: 1908
Subjects: Archaeology, Biography, Cookery, Eco-
  nomics, Fiction, Government, Political Sci-
  ence, History, Military Science, Music, Dance,
  Sports, Athletics, Travel
ISBN Prefix(es): 0-283
*Orders to:* Macmillan Distribution Ltd, Brunel
  Rd, Houndmills, Basingstoke, Hants RG21
  6XS

**Sigma Leisure**, *imprint of* Sigma Press

**Sigma Press+**
5 Alton Rd, Wilmslow, Cheshire SK9 5DY
*Tel:* (01625) 531035 *Fax:* (01625) 531035
*E-mail:* info@sigmapress.co.uk
*Web Site:* www.sigmapress.co.uk
*Key Personnel*
Man Dir, Production: Graham Beech
Editorial: Diana Beech
Founded: 1980
Specialize in books on all aspects of leisure activ-
  ities, particulary of the outdoors.
Membership(s): IPG.
Subjects: Crafts, Games, Hobbies, Music, Dance,
  Outdoor Recreation, Regional Interests, Sports,
  Athletics, Transportation
ISBN Prefix(es): 1-85058; 0-905104
Total Titles: 250 Print
Imprints: Sigma Leisure
*Warehouse:* Thomas Lyster & Co, Unit 9,
  Ormskirk Industrial Estate, Old Boundary
  Way, Burscough Rd, Ormskirk L39 2TW
  *Tel:* (01695) 575112 *Fax:* (01695) 570120

**Silver Link Publishing Ltd+**
The Trundle, Ringstead Rd, Great Addington,
  Kettering, Northants NN14 4BW
*Tel:* (01536) 330588 *Fax:* (01536) 330469
*E-mail:* sales@nostalgiacollection.com
*Web Site:* www.nostalgiacollection.com
*Key Personnel*
Man Dir: Peter Townsend
Company Secretary: Frances Townsend
Production Manager: Mick Sanders
Founded: 1985
Also acts as book packager.
Subjects: Animals, Pets, Biography, Business,
  Crafts, Games, Hobbies, Health, Nutrition,
  History, Humor, Maritime, Nonfiction (Gen-
  eral), Transportation, Towns/Cities in the UK &
  Farming
ISBN Prefix(es): 0-947971; 1-85794
*Associate Companies:* Past & Present Publishing
  Ltd

**Simon & Schuster Audio**, *imprint of* Simon &
  Schuster Ltd

**Simon & Schuster Ltd+**
Division of Simon & Schuster Inc
Africa House, 4th floor, 64-78 Kingsway, London
  WC2B 6AH
*Tel:* (020) 7316 1900 *Fax:* (020) 7316 0332
*E-mail:* firstname.surname@simonandschuster.co.
  uk

*Web Site:* www.simonsays.co.uk
*Telex:* 21702
*Key Personnel*
Man Dir & Chief Executive Officer: Ian Chapman
  *Fax:* (020) 7316 0331
Publishing Dir, Trade: Susanne Baboneau
Senior Editor, Scribner: Tim Binding
Publisher, Nonfiction: Helen Gummer
Publishing Dir, Children's Books: Ingrid Selberg
Editorial Dir, Martin Books: Janet Copleston
International Publisher: Jonathan Atkins
Sales & Marketing Dir: James Kellow
Rights: Diane Spivey
Production: Karen Ellison
Publicity: Rachael Healey
Dir, Finance: Bob Ness
Founded: 1987
Subjects: Biography, Business, Fiction, Nonfiction
  (General), Science (General)
ISBN Prefix(es): 0-609; 0-689; 0-684; 0-7434; 0-
  7432
Total Titles: 200 Audio
*Parent Company:* Simon & Schuster, 1230 Av-
  enue of the Americas, New York, NY 10020,
  United States
*Ultimate Parent Company:* Viacom Inc, 1515
  Broadway, New York, NY 10036, United States
*Associate Companies:* Simon & Schuster Aus-
  tralia, 20 Barcoo St, East Roseville NSW 2069,
  Australia
*Imprints:* Earthlink; Free Press; Martin Books;
  Pocket Books; Scribner; Simon & Schuster
  Audio; Simon & Schuster's Children's; Touch-
  stone
*Divisions:* Martin Books
*Distributed by* S&S Australia; Distieau
*Distributor for* Pocket Books (US & Europe)
*Shipping Address:* HarperCollins Publishing Ltd,
  Westerhill Rd, Bishopbriggs, Glasgow G64
  2QT
*Warehouse:* IBD Ltd, Magna Park, Coventry Rd,
  Lutterworth, Leics LE17 4XH *Tel:* (01442)
  887900
*Orders to:* HarperCollins Publishing Ltd, Wester-
  hill Rd, Bishopbriggs, Glasgow G64 2Q1
*Returns:* HarperCollins, Westerhill Rd, Bishop-
  briggs, Glasgow G64 2Q1

**Simon & Schuster's Children's,** *imprint of*
Simon & Schuster Ltd

**Charles Skilton Ltd+**
2 Caversham St, London SW3 4AH
*Tel:* (020) 7351 4995 *Fax:* (020) 7351 4995
*Key Personnel*
Man Editor: James Hughes
Publicity Manager: Leonard Holdsworth
Founded: 1943
Subjects: Antiques, Art, Biography, Cookery,
  Erotica, History, Poetry
ISBN Prefix(es): 0-284
Total Titles: 40 Print
Subsidiaries: Albyn Press Ltd; Fortune Press;
  Luxor Press Ltd; Polybooks Ltd

**Skoob Esoterica,** *imprint of* Skoob Russell
Square

**Skoob Pacifica,** *imprint of* Skoob Russell Square

**Skoob Russell Square+**
10 Brunswick Centre, off Bernard St, London
  WC1N 1AE
*Tel:* (020) 7278 8760
*E-mail:* books@skoob.com
*Web Site:* www.skoob.com
*Key Personnel*
President & Editorial Dir: I K Ong *E-mail:* ike@
  skoob.com
Artistic Manager: Mark Lovell *E-mail:* mark@
  skoob.com

Founded: 1987
Independent & multi-media.
Subjects: Anthropology, Antiques, Art, Asian
  Studies, Astrology, Occult, Computer Science,
  Economics, Fiction, Government, Political Sci-
  ence, History, Literature, Literary Criticism, Es-
  says, Mathematics, Philosophy, Poetry, Publish-
  ing & Book Trade Reference, Science (Gen-
  eral), Technology, Secondhand academic books
ISBN Prefix(es): 1-871438
Total Titles: 48 Print
Imprints: Skoob Esoterica; Skoob Seriph; Skoob
  Pacifica
Distributed by APG (USA); Gazelle Book Ser-
  vices Ltd (UK)

**Skoob Seriph,** *imprint of* Skoob Russell Square

**SLG Press** ((Community of) The Sisters of the
  Love of God)+
Convent of the Incarnation, Fairacres, Oxford
  OX4 1TB
*Tel:* (01865) 721301 *Fax:* (01865) 790860
*E-mail:* editor@slgpress.co.uk; orders@slgpress.
  co.uk
*Web Site:* www.slgpress.co.uk
*Key Personnel*
Editor: Sr Isabel Mary
Founded: 1967
Subjects: Religion - Other, Theology
ISBN Prefix(es): 0-7283
Number of titles published annually: 6 Print
Total Titles: 74 Print
*Parent Company:* SLG Charitable Trust Limited
Imprints: Fairacres Publication
Distributed by SCM-Canterbury Press (Australia,
  UK); Cistercian Publications (USA & Canada)

**SLS Legal Publications (NI)**
School of Law, The Queen's University Belfast,
  28 University Sq, Belfast BT7 1NN
*Tel:* (028) 9097 3452 *Fax:* (028) 9097 3376;
  (028) 9097 5040
*E-mail:* law-enquiries@qub.ac.uk
*Web Site:* www.law.qub.ac.uk
*Key Personnel*
Program Dir: Miriam Dudley *E-mail:* m.dudley@
  qub.ac.uk
Publications Editor: Sara Gamble *E-mail:* s.
  gamble@qub.ac.uk
Legal Editor: Deborah McBride *E-mail:* d.
  mcbride@qub.ac.uk
Founded: 1980
Subjects: Law
ISBN Prefix(es): 0-85389

**Jacqui Small,** *imprint of* Aurum Press Ltd

**Smith-Gordon & Co Ltd+**
13 Shalcomb St, London SW10 0HZ
*Tel:* (020) 7351 7042 *Fax:* (020) 7351 1250
*E-mail:* publisher@smithgordon.com
*Web Site:* www.smithgordon.com
*Key Personnel*
Dir & Publisher: Eldred Smith-Gordon
Founded: 1988
Subjects: Health, Nutrition, Medicine, Nursing,
  Dentistry, Science (General), Technology
ISBN Prefix(es): 1-85463
Total Titles: 80 Print
*U.S. Office(s):* Books International Inc, PO Box
  605, Herndon, VA 22106, United States
*Orders to:* Smith-Gordon, 47 Worthing Rd, East
  Preston, Nr Worthing, West Sussex BN16
  1DE, Rosemary Harris *Tel:* (01903) 856646
  *Fax:* (01903) 856646

**Smith Settle Ltd+**
23 Sheep St, Burford OX18 4LS
*Tel:* (01756) 701381 *Fax:* (01524) 251708
*E-mail:* editorial@dalesman.co.uk

*Key Personnel*
Man Dir: Kenneth Smith
Editorial Dir: Mark Whitley
Founded: 1986
Membership(s): IPG.
Subjects: Art, Biography, History, Humor, Nonfic-
  tion (General), Regional Interests
ISBN Prefix(es): 1-870071; 1-85825
Number of titles published annually: 12 Print
Total Titles: 120 Print
Distributor for Spredden Press (UK); Woodstock
  Books (UK)

**Colin Smythe Ltd+**
38 Mill Lane, Gerrards Cross, Bucks SL9 8BA
Mailing Address: PO Box 6, Gerrards Cross,
  Bucks SL9 8XA
*Tel:* (01753) 886000 *Fax:* (01753) 886469
*E-mail:* sales@colinsmythe.co.uk
*Web Site:* www.colinsmythe.co.uk
*Key Personnel*
Man Dir & International Rights: Colin Smythe
  *E-mail:* cs@colinsmythe.co.uk
Production Dir: Leslie Hayward
Founded: 1966
Book publishers & author's agent.
Membership(s): IPG; Publishers' Association.
Subjects: Biography, Drama, Theater, Literature,
  Literary Criticism, Essays, Religion - Catholic,
  Folklore & Mysticism
ISBN Prefix(es): 0-900675; 0-901072; 0-905715;
  0-86140; 0-85105
Number of titles published annually: 12 Print
Total Titles: 480 Print
Distributed by Dufour Editions (USA & Canada);
  Oxford University Press (USA & Canada)
Distributor for ELT Press (Europe); Tir Eolas
  (Britain & Europe)
*Warehouse:* c/o Clipper Distribution Services Ltd,
  Windmill Grove, Portchester, Hants PO16 9HT
  *Tel:* (02392) 200080 *Fax:* (02392) 200090

**Snowbooks Ltd**
239 Old St, London EC1V 9EY
*Tel:* (020) 7553 4473 *Fax:* (020) 7251 3130
*E-mail:* info@snowbooks.com
*Web Site:* www.snowbooks.com
*Key Personnel*
Man Dir: Emma Cahill *Tel:* (079) 0406 2414
  *E-mail:* emma@snowbooks.com
Founded: 2003
Publishes intelligent yet readable, needful fiction
  & nonfiction. Nonfiction categories include
  popular science, business & society.
Membership(s): IPG.
Subjects: Biography, Business, Earth Sciences,
  Fiction, Government, Political Science, Man-
  agement, Nonfiction (General), Philosophy,
  Physics, Psychology, Psychiatry, Science (Gen-
  eral), Science Fiction, Fantasy
*Shipping Address:* 11 Theresas Walk, Sanderstead
  Surrey CR2 0AU
*Warehouse:* 11 Theresas Walk, Sanderstead Sur-
  rey CR2 0AU
*Distribution Center:* 11 Theresas Walk, Sander-
  stead Surrey CR2 0AU, Contact: Emma Cahill
  *Tel:* (079) 0406 *Toll Free Tel:* 2414 *Toll Free
  Fax:* (20) 7251 3130 *E-mail:* emma@snobooks.
  com
*Returns:* 11 Theresas Walk, Sanderstead Surrey
  CR2 0AU

**William Snyder Publishing Associates**
5 Five Mile Drive, Oxford OX2 8HT
*Tel:* (01865) 513186 *Fax:* (01865) 513186
*E-mail:* snyderpub@aol.com
*Key Personnel*
Man Dir: William Snyder *E-mail:* snyderpub@
  aol.com
ISBN Prefix(es): 0-948058
*Associate Companies:* ELC International

**Society for Endocrinology**, *imprint of* Society for Endocrinology

**Society for Endocrinology**
22 Apex Court, Woodlands, Bradley Stoke, Bristol BS32 4JT
*Tel:* (01454) 642200 *Fax:* (01454) 642222
*E-mail:* info@endocrinology.org; sales@endocrinology.org
*Web Site:* www.endocrinology.org
*Key Personnel*
Executive Dir: Sue Thorn *E-mail:* sue.thorn@endocrinology.org
Publications Dir: Steve Byford *E-mail:* steve.byford@endocrinology.org
Sales & Marketing Officer: Lesley Drake
Founded: 1946
Established to promote the study of the endocrine system, publishes journals, books, conference proceedings & newsletters & offers a publication service to pharmaceutical companies
Learned society.
ISBN Prefix(es): 1-898099
Total Titles: 12 Print
Imprints: Bio Scientifica; Society for Endocrinology
Distributed by Portland Press Ltd

**The Society for Promoting Christian Knowledge (SPCK)+**
36 Causton St, London SW1P 4ST
*Tel:* (020) 7592 3900 *Fax:* (020) 7592 3939
*E-mail:* spck@spck.org.uk
*Web Site:* www.spck.org.uk
*Key Personnel*
Publishing Dir: Simon Kingston
*E-mail:* skingston@spck.org.uk
Sales Manager: Susan Kodicek
*E-mail:* skodicek@spck.org.uk
Founded: 1698
Throughout the UK 28 Outlets.
Subjects: Biblical Studies, Biography, Religion - Catholic, Religion - Protestant, Self-Help, Theology
ISBN Prefix(es): 0-85969; 0-281; 1-902694
Number of titles published annually: 80 Print
Total Titles: 500 Print
Imprints: Azure; Sheldon Press
Distributed by The Pilgrim Press (USA)
*Warehouse:* Marston Christian Warehouse
*Orders to:* Marston Book Services, PO Box 269, Abingdon, Oxford OX14 47N *Tel:* (01235) 465511 *Fax:* (01235) 465518

**Society for Research into Higher Education**, see SRHE

**The Society of Metaphysicians Ltd+**
Archers' Court, Stonestile Lane, The Ridge, Hastings, East Sussex TN35 4PG
*Tel:* (01424) 751577 *Fax:* (01424) 751577
*E-mail:* newmeta@btinternet.com; info@metaphysicians.org.uk
*Web Site:* www.newmeta.btinternet.co.uk; www.metaphysicians.org.uk; www.metaphysicalresearchgroup.org.uk
*Key Personnel*
President: J J Williamson
Dir, Research: I D Cumberland
General Secretary: Eleanor Swift
Correspondence Education: Terrance Kiernan
Business Secretary: Trevor Sully
Founded: 1944
Publisher of *Neometaphysical Digest* (quarterly).
Subjects: Astrology, Occult, Earth Sciences, Electronics, Electrical Engineering, Environmental Studies, Government, Political Science, Human Relations, Parapsychology, Philosophy, Physical Sciences, Physics, Psychology, Psychiatry, Science (General), Social Sciences, Sociology, Neometaphysics, Paraphysics
ISBN Prefix(es): 1-85228; 1-85810; 0-900684

Number of titles published annually: 150 Print
Total Titles: 2,330 Print
*Associate Companies:* Istituto Italiano di Ricerche Metafisiche, Triesto, Italy *Tel:* (040) 630315 *Fax:* (040) 630315 *E-mail:* metaresearch@tin.it; Society of Metaphysicians; Society of Metaphysicians (Nigeria) Ltd
Divisions: Metaphysical Research Group
Distributor for Health Research (USA); Sun Books (USA)

**Sophia Books**, *imprint of* Rudolf Steiner Press

**South Asians Overseas Series**, *imprint of* Peepal Tree Press Ltd

**South Street Press**, *imprint of* Garnet Publishing Ltd

**Southgate Publishers+**
The Square, Sandford, Crediton, Devon EX17 4LW
*Tel:* (01363) 776888 *Fax:* (01363) 776889
*E-mail:* info@southgatepublishers.co.uk
*Web Site:* www.southgatepublishers.co.uk
*Key Personnel*
Dir: Drummond Johnstone *E-mail:* dj@southgatepublishers.co.uk
Founded: 1991
Specialize in resources for teachers, home learning & life-long learning.
Subjects: Education, Environmental Studies, Mathematics, Music, Dance, Science (General)
ISBN Prefix(es): 1-85741
Total Titles: 120 Print
Subsidiaries: Mosaic Educational Publications
Distributed by Bacon & Hughes (Canada)

**Souvenir Press Ltd+**
130 Milton Park, Abingdon OX14 4SB
*Tel:* (01235) 400400 *Fax:* (01235) 400500
*E-mail:* orders@bookpoint.co.uk *Cable:* PUBLISHER LONDON WC1
*Key Personnel*
Man Dir, Rights & Permissions: Ernest Hecht
Production: Ken Ruskin
Publicity Executive: James Doyle
Founded: 1951
Membership(s): Publishers' Association.
Subjects: Art, Biography, Fiction, History, How-to, Medicine, Nursing, Dentistry, Music, Dance, Philosophy, Poetry, Psychology, Psychiatry, Religion - Other, Social Sciences, Sociology, Sports, Athletics
ISBN Prefix(es): 0-285
Number of titles published annually: 55 Print
Total Titles: 700 Print
Imprints: Condor Books; Human Horizons Series; Independent Voices; The Story-Tellers
Subsidiaries: Condor Books; Euro-Features Ltd; Pictorial Presentations Ltd; Pop-Universal Ltd; Souvenir Press (Educational & Academic) Ltd; Souvenir Press (Films) Ltd
*Orders to:* BookPoint Ltd, 39 Milton Trading Estate, Abingdon, Oxon OX14 4TD *E-mail:* orders@bookpoint.co.uk

**Sovereign International Books**, *imprint of* Sovereign World Ltd

**Sovereign World Ltd+**
Unit 5, Goblands Farm, Cemetry Lane, Hadlow, Kent TN11 0DP
Mailing Address: PO Box 777, Tonbridge, Kent TN11 0ZS
*Tel:* (01732) 850598 *Fax:* (01732) 851077
*E-mail:* sovereignworldbooks@compuserve.com
*Web Site:* www.sovereign-world.org
*Key Personnel*
President: Chris Mungeam

Man Dir: Tim Pettingale *E-mail:* tim@sovereign-world.com
Founded: 1986
Subjects: Religion - Protestant
ISBN Prefix(es): 1-85240
Imprints: Sovereign International Books

**SPA Books Ltd+**
PO Box 728, Crawley RH10 7WD
*Tel:* (01293) 552727 *Fax:* (01438) 310104
*E-mail:* strongoakpress@hotmail.com
*Key Personnel*
Man Dir: Stephen Apps
Founded: 1980
Also distributor & retailer.
Subjects: Art, Biography, History, Military Science, Nonfiction (General), Regional Interests, Travel
ISBN Prefix(es): 0-907590
*Associate Companies:* The Strong Oak Press
Imprints: Strong Oak Press

**Sparrowhawk**, *imprint of* Hawk Books

**SPCK**, see The Society for Promoting Christian Knowledge (SPCK)

**Speechmark Editions**, *imprint of* Speechmark Publishing Ltd

**Speechmark Publishing Ltd+**
Telford Rd, Bicester OX26 4LQ
*Tel:* (01869) 244644 *Fax:* (01869) 320040
*E-mail:* info@speechmark.net
*Web Site:* www.speechmark.net
*Key Personnel*
Publisher: Ian Franklin *E-mail:* ianf@speechmark.net
Publishing Dir: Sarah Miles *E-mail:* sarahm@speechmark.net
Customer Services Manager: Jan Jervis
*E-mail:* janj@speechmark.net
Marketing Manager: Su Underhill *E-mail:* suu@speechmark.net
Sales Manager: Sally Dickinson *E-mail:* sallyd@speechmark.net
Founded: 1984
Practical handbooks for teachers, speech & language therapists, psychologists, occupational therapists & nursing staff.
Membership(s): IPG; BESA.
Subjects: Behavioral Sciences, Child Care & Development, Disability, Special Needs, Education, Health, Nutrition, Language Arts, Linguistics, Medicine, Nursing, Dentistry, Psychology, Psychiatry, Social Sciences, Sociology, Autism, Early Development, Gerontology, Mental Health, Special Needs, Speech & Language
ISBN Prefix(es): 0-86388
Number of titles published annually: 30 Print
Total Titles: 300 Print; 4 CD-ROM; 1 Online; 1 E-Book; 7 Audio
Imprints: ColorCards; Pocket ColorCards; Speechmark Editions
Distributed by Speechbin

**Spellmount Ltd Publishers+**
Units 1/K, Paddock Wood Distribution Centre, Paddock Wood, Tonbridge TN12 6UU
*Tel:* (01892) 837171 *Fax:* (01892) 837272
*E-mail:* enquiries@spellmount.com
*Key Personnel*
Publisher: Jamie Wilson
Editorial Dir: Jag Wilson
Founded: 1983
Also acts as book packager.
Subjects: Biography, History, Military Science, Nonfiction (General)
ISBN Prefix(es): 0-946771; 1-873376; 1-86227

*Associate Companies:* Tom Donovan Publishing; Howell Press; National Army Museum PUBLICATIONS; Ken Trotman Ltd
*Warehouse:* CBS Ltd, 406 Vale Rd, Tonbridge, Kent TN9 1XR
*Orders to:* Amalgamated Book Services, Royal Star Arcade, High St, Suite 1, Maidstone, Kent ME14 1JL ME14 1JL, Sales Manager: Frank McNamara *Tel:* (01622) 764 555 *Fax:* (01622) 763 197 (North & East Midlands, Scotland, UK & Ireland)
Ashton International Marketing Services, PO Box 298, Sevenoaks, Kent TN13 1WV *Tel:* (01732) 746 093 *Fax:* (01732) 746 096 (Middle East & Far East)
Barry Brittlebank, 17 Whitehall Crescent, Bradford Rd, Wakefield, West Yorkshire WF1 2AF *Tel:* (01622) 764 555 *Fax:* (01622) 763 197 (Northern UK)
Jonathon Brooks, 57 Greenway, Berkhamsted, Herts (London)
D Richard Brown, Post Box 30037, 5-20061 Malmo 30, Sweden *Tel:* (040) 161 200 *Fax:* (040) 161 208 (Denmark, Finland, Iceland, Norway, Sweden)
European Marketing Services, 55 Overhill Rd, Dulwich, London SE22 0PQ *Tel:* (020) 8516-5433 *Fax:* (020) 8516-5434 (Austria, Belgium, France, Germany & Switzerland)
Owen Hazell, 180 Vale Rd, Tonbridge, Kent TN9 1SP (Southeast, East Anglia)
Robin House, 37 From Park, Bartestree, Hereford HR1 4BF (Southwest, Midland & South Wales)
Iberian Book Services, Sector Islas, Bloque 12, 1, B, 28760 Tres Cantos, Madrid, Spain *Tel:* (09) 1803 49 18 *Fax:* (09) 1803 59 36 (Spain & Portugal)
Carr O'Connell, 342 North Circular Rd, Philsboro, Dublin 7, Ireland (Northern Ireland & Ireland)
Penny Padovani, 56 Rosebank, Holyport Rd, Fulham, London SW6 6LH *Tel:* (020) 7381-3936 (Italy & Greece)
Peribo Pty Ltd, 58 Beaumont Rd, Mount Kuringgai, NSW 2080, Australia, Contact: Andrew Coffey *Tel:* (02) 9457 0011 *Fax:* (02) 9457 0022 (Australia & New Zealand)

**Spindlewood**, *imprint of* Ragged Bears Ltd

**Spitfire**, *imprint of* Elliott & Thompson

**Spitfire Originals**, *imprint of* Elliott & Thompson

**Spokesman+**
Imprint of Bertrand Russell Peace Foundation Ltd
Russell House, Bulwell Lane, Notts NG6 0BT
*Tel:* (0115) 9708318; (0115) 9784504 *Fax:* (0115) 9420433
*E-mail:* elfeuro@compuserve.com
*Web Site:* www.spokesmanbooks.com; www.russfound.org
*Key Personnel*
Editorial: Ken Coates
Publications Manager, Rights & Permissions: Anthony Simpson
Production: Ken Fleet
Founded: 1970
Subjects: Business, Economics, Environmental Studies, Government, Political Science, Labor, Industrial Relations, Social Sciences, Sociology, Peace & Human Rights
ISBN Prefix(es): 0-85124
*Associate Companies:* Russell Press Ltd, Radford Mill, Norton St, Notts NG7 3HN

**Spon Press**, *imprint of* Taylor & Francis

**Spon Press**
Member of Taylor & Francis Group

11 New Fetter Lane, London EC4P 4EE
*Tel:* (020) 7583 9855 *Fax:* (020) 7842 2298
*E-mail:* info@routledge.co.uk
*Web Site:* www.sponpress.com
*Key Personnel*
Man Dir: Marianne Russell
Editorial Dir: Phillip Read
Marketing Dir: Robert Creffield
Production: Gavin Macdonald
Sales Manager: Chris Hall
Area Sales Export: Graham Boaler; Mima Birks
Rights & Permissions: Anna Bisztyga
Founded: 1834
Subjects: Architecture & Interior Design, Civil Engineering, Crafts, Games, Hobbies, Environmental Studies, Real Estate, Sports, Athletics, Transportation
ISBN Prefix(es): 0-413; 0-419

**Sportman's Press**, *imprint of* Quiller Publishing Ltd

**Sports Turf Research Institute (STRI)**
St Ives Estate, Bingley, W Yorks BD16 1AU
*Tel:* (01274) 565131 *Fax:* (01274) 561891
*E-mail:* info@stri.co.uk
*Web Site:* www.stri.co.uk
*Key Personnel*
Chief Executive: Dr Gordon McKillop
  *E-mail:* gordon.mckillop@stri.co.uk
Founded: 1929
Independent consultancy & research organization specializing in natural turf grass & sports surfaces.
Subjects: Turfgrass Science for Sports Surfaces
Number of titles published annually: 4 Print; 1 CD-ROM
Total Titles: 2 CD-ROM

**The Sportsman's Press+**
25 King Charles Walk, London SW19 6JA
*Tel:* (020) 8789 0229 *Fax:* (020) 8789 0229
*Key Personnel*
Publisher & Rights: Kenneth Kemp
Founded: 1984
Subjects: Humor, Sports, Athletics, Equestrian, Country Sports
ISBN Prefix(es): 0-948253
*Orders to:* Vine House, Waldenbury, North Common, Chailey, BN8 4DR East Sussex *Tel:* (01825) 723398 *Fax:* (01825) 724188

**Springer-Verlag London Ltd+**
Sweetapple House, Catteshall Rd, Goldaming, Surrey GU7 3DJ
*Tel:* (0483) 418800; (01483) 418822 (sales) *Fax:* (01483) 415151; (01483) 415144
*E-mail:* orders@springer.de
*Key Personnel*
Man Dir: John Watson
Founded: 1987
Subjects: Astronomy, Computer Science, Engineering (General), Mathematics, Medicine, Nursing, Dentistry
ISBN Prefix(es): 1-85233
*Parent Company:* Springer-Verlag GmbH & Co KG, Heidelberger Platz 3, 14197 Berlin, Germany

**Square One Publications+**
The Tudor House, 16 Church St, Upton Office Services, Upton-upon Severn, Worcester WR8 OH7
*Tel:* (01684) 593704 *Fax:* (01684) 594640
*Key Personnel*
Contact: Mary Wilkinson *E-mail:* marywilk@rinyonline.co.uk
Founded: 1988
Subjects: Militaria, autobiographies
ISBN Prefix(es): 1-899955

*Warehouse:* Upton Office Services, 18 Riverside Close Upton-On Severn, Worcester WR8 0JN, Contact: Deidre Thompson *Tel:* (01684) 592035 *E-mail:* deidre@uptonjazz.farmcom.net

**SRHE**
76 Portland Pl, London W1B 1NT
*Tel:* (020) 7637 2766 *Fax:* (020) 7637 2781
*E-mail:* srheoffice@srhe.ac.uk
*Web Site:* www.srhe.ac.uk
*Key Personnel*
Dir: Prof Heather Eggins *E-mail:* heathereggins@srhe.ac.uk
Founded: 1965
The Society is a registered charity & publishes mainly in cooperation with Open University Press.
Subjects: Education
ISBN Prefix(es): 0-9510798

**Stacey International+**
128 Kensington Church St, W8 4BH London
*Tel:* (020) 7221 7166 *Fax:* (020) 7792 9288
*E-mail:* stacey-inter@btconnect.com
*Web Site:* www.stacey-international.co.uk
*Key Personnel*
Chairman: Tom Stacey
Chief Executive: Max Scott
Marketing Manager: Kitty Carruthers
Customer Service: Meave Beckett
  *E-mail:* meave@stacey-international.co.uk
Founded: 1974
Subjects: Archaeology, Architecture & Interior Design, Art, Business, Cookery, Education, Foreign Countries, Gardening, Plants, Genealogy, Geography, Geology, History, Natural History, Religion - Islamic, Travel
ISBN Prefix(es): 0-905743; 0-9503304; 0-900988
Total Titles: 40 Print
*Parent Company:* Stacey Arts Ltd
Imprints: Royal Genealogies; Stacey London
*Distribution Center:* Central Books, 99 Wallis Rd, London E9 5LN, Contact: Katie Sneyd *Tel:* (0845) 458 9911 *Fax:* (0845) 458 9912 *E-mail:* orders@centralbooks.com
Interlink Publishing Group, 46 Crosby St, Northampton, MA 01060-1804, United States *Tel:* 413-582-7054 *Fax:* 413-582-7057 *E-mail:* info@interlinkbooks.com
Portfolio, Unit 5 Perivale Industrial Park, Horsenden Lane S, Greenford, Middlesex UB6 7RL *Tel:* (020) 8997 9000 *Fax:* (020) 8997 9097 *E-mail:* sales@portfoliobooks.co.uk (travel & children's titles)
*Orders to:* Portfolio, Unit 5 Perivale Industrial Park, Horsenden Lane S, Greenford, Middlesex UB6 7RL *Tel:* (020) 8997 9000 *Fax:* (020) 8997 9097 *E-mail:* sales@portfoliobooks.co.uk

**Staff & Educational Development Association**, see SEDA Publications

**Stainer & Bell Ltd**
Victoria House, 23 Gruneisen Rd, London N3 1DZ
Mailing Address: PO Box 110, London N3 1DZ
*Tel:* (020) 8343 3303 *Fax:* (020) 8343 3024
*E-mail:* post@stainer.co.uk
*Web Site:* www.stainer.co.uk
*Key Personnel*
Joint Man Dir, Production: Carol Wakefield
  *E-mail:* carol@stainer.co.uk
Joint Man Dir, Publicity, Rights & Permissions: Keith Wakefield *E-mail:* keith@stainer.co.uk
Publishing Dir: Nicholas Williams
  *E-mail:* nicholas@stainer.co.uk
Founded: 1907
Subjects: Education, Music, Dance, Religion - Other
ISBN Prefix(es): 0-85249
Imprints: Augener; Belton Books; Galliard; A Weekes; Joseph Williams

**Harold Starke Publishers Ltd**
203 Bunyan Court, Barbican, London EC2Y 8DH
*Tel:* (01379) 388334; (020) 7588 5195
    *Fax:* (01379) 388335
*E-mail:* red@eclat.force9.co.uk
*Key Personnel*
Editorial, Rights & Permissions: Miss N Galinski
Export Sales: Harold Starke
Founded: 1960
Membership(s): the British Publishers Association.
Subjects: Medicine, Nursing, Dentistry
ISBN Prefix(es): 0-287; 1-872457
*Distribution Center:* Pixey Green, Stradbroke, Eye, Suffolk IP21 5NG

**The Stationery Office**, see TSO (The Stationery Office)

**Rudolf Steiner Press+**
Imprint of Anthroposophic Press Inc
35 Park Rd, London NW1 6XT
Mailing Address: Hillside House, The Square, Forest Row, East Sussex RH18 5ES
*Tel:* (01342) 824433 *Fax:* (01342) 826437
*E-mail:* office@rudolfsteinerpress.com; editorial@rudolfsteinerpress.com
*Web Site:* www.rudolfsteinerpress.com
*Key Personnel*
Chief Editor: Sevak Gulbekian
Marketing Assistant/Administrator: K Bernard
Founded: 1920
Subjects: Agriculture, Art, Biography, Education, Health, Nutrition, Music, Dance, Philosophy, Self-Help
ISBN Prefix(es): 0-85440; 1-85584
Number of titles published annually: 15 Print
Total Titles: 400 Print
Imprints: Sophia Books
Distributor for BookSource (USA); Mercury Arts Publications (UK); New Knowledge Books (UK)
*Distribution Center:* Anthroposophic Press, PO Box 960, Herndon, VA 20172-0960, United States *E-mail:* service@anthropress.org (US)
Ceres Books, PO Box 11-336, Ellerslie, Auckland 5, New Zealand *Tel:* (09) 574 3356 *Fax:* (09) 527 4513 *E-mail:* info@ceres.co.nz (New Zealand)
Rudolf Steiner Book Centre, 307 Sussex St, Sydney, NSW 2000, Australia *Tel:* (02) 9264 5169 *Fax:* (02) 9267 1225 (Australia)
Rudolf Steiner Publications, PO Box 71925, 235 Bryanston Drive, Bryanston 2021 *Tel:* (011) 706 8544 *Fax:* (011) 706 4136 *E-mail:* steinerp@netactive.co.za (South Africa)
Tri-fold Books, Box 32, Stn Main, Guelph, ON N1H 6J6, Canada *Tel:* 519-821-9901 *Fax:* 519-821-5333 (Canada)
*Orders to:* BookSource, Cowlairs Industrial Estate, 32 Finlas St, Glasgow G22 5DU *Tel:* (0141) 558 1366 *Fax:* (0141) 557 0189 *E-mail:* orders@booksource.net
*Returns:* BookSource, Cowlairs Industrial Estate, 32 Finlas St, Glasgow G22 5DU

**Stenlake Publishing Ltd+**
54-58 Mill Sq, Catrine, Ayrshire KA5 6RD
*Tel:* (01290) 551122 *Fax:* (01290) 551122
*E-mail:* info@stenlake.co.uk
*Web Site:* www.stenlake.co.uk
Founded: 1984
Subjects: History, Maritime, Regional Interests
ISBN Prefix(es): 1-872074; 1-84033
Number of titles published annually: 50 Print
Total Titles: 350 Print

**Patrick Stephens Ltd**, *imprint of* Haynes Publishing

**Sterling Audio Books**, *imprint of* BBC Audiobooks

**Stobart & Son Ltd**, *imprint of* Stobart Davies Ltd

**Stobart Davies Ltd+**
Stobart House Pontyclerc, Penybanc Rd, Ammanford SA18 3HP
*Tel:* (01269) 593100 *Fax:* (01269) 596116
*Web Site:* www.stobartdavies.com
*Key Personnel*
Publicity: Jane Evans *E-mail:* jane@stobartdavies.com
Rights & Permissions: Nigel Evans
Founded: 1989
Subjects: Crafts, Games, Hobbies, How-to, Natural History, Woodwork, Craft & Forestry
ISBN Prefix(es): 0-85442
Number of titles published annually: 5 Print
Total Titles: 65 Print
Imprints: Stobart & Son Ltd

**Stokesby House Publications+**
Stokesby, Norfolk NR29 3ET
*Tel:* (01493) 750645 *Fax:* (01493) 750146
*E-mail:* stokesbyhouse@btinternet.com
*Web Site:* www.stokesbyhouse.co.uk
*Key Personnel*
Contact: Pamela Minett
Subjects: Biological Sciences, Environmental Studies
ISBN Prefix(es): 0-9514490; 1-873600

**Story Sound Audio Tapes**, *imprint of* Magna Large Print Books

**The Story-Tellers**, *imprint of* Souvenir Press Ltd

**Stott's Correspondence College**
POB 35488, St Johns Wood, London NW8 6WD
*Tel:* (020) 586 4499 *Fax:* (020) 722 1068
*E-mail:* microworld@ndirect.co.uk
*Web Site:* www.microworld.ndirect.co.uk
Specialize in correspondence courses.
Subjects: Health, Nutrition, Calligraphy, Dressmaking, Fitness, Locksmithing

**Strategic Comments**, *imprint of* International Institute for Strategic Studies

**Strategic Survey**, *imprint of* International Institute for Strategic Studies

**STRI**, see Sports Turf Research Institute (STRI)

**Strong Oak Press**, *imprint of* SPA Books Ltd

**Studio Editions Ltd+**
Random House, 20 Vauxhall Bridge Rd, London SWIV 2SA
*Tel:* (020) 7973 9690 *Fax:* (020) 7233 6057
*Telex:* 261212
*Key Personnel*
Chairman: Sonia Land
Dir: J Roderick Webb
Rights Dir: K T Forster
Founded: 1982
Subjects: Antiques, Architecture & Interior Design, Art
ISBN Prefix(es): 0-946495; 1-85170; 1-85891
Subsidiaries: BPL Remainders; Studio Designs
*Warehouse:* Grantham Book Services Ltd, Isaac Newton Way, Alma Park Industrial East, Grantham Lincs NG31 9SD

**Sunflower Books**
12 Kendrick Mews, London SW7 3HG
*Tel:* (020) 7589 1862 *Fax:* (020) 7589 1862
*E-mail:* mail@sunflowerbooks.co.uk
*Web Site:* www.sunflowerbooks.co.uk

*Key Personnel*
Joint Man Dir: John Seccombe *Tel:* (01392) 274686; Patricia Underwood
Founded: 1982
Subjects: Travel, Landscapes; walking & touring guides to (mainly) European destinations
ISBN Prefix(es): 0-948513; 1-85691
Number of titles published annually: 6 Print
Total Titles: 48 Print
*Parent Company:* P A Underwood Ltd
Distributed by Hunter Publishing (USA)
*Orders to:* Macmillan Distribution Ltd, Brunel Rd, Houndmills, Basingstoke RG21 6XS *Tel:* (01256) 302692 *Fax:* (01256) 812558

**Supportive Learning Publications+**
23 West View, Chirk, Wrexham LL14 5HL
*Tel:* (01691) 774778 *Fax:* (01691) 774849
*E-mail:* sales@slpuk.demon.co.uk
*Web Site:* www.slpuk.demon.co.uk
*Key Personnel*
Contact: Phil Roberts
Founded: 1988
Subjects: Disability, Special Needs, Drama, Theater, Education, English as a Second Language, Geography, Geology, History, Humor, Mathematics, Poetry, Science (General)
ISBN Prefix(es): 1-86109; 1-871585
Distributed by Galt Educational; Hope Education; The Yorklshire Purchasing Group

**Survival**, *imprint of* International Institute for Strategic Studies

**Sussex Publications**
POB 35488, St Johns Wood, London NW8 6WD
*Tel:* (020) 586 4499 *Fax:* (020) 722 1068
*E-mail:* microworld@ndirect.co.uk
*Web Site:* www.microworld.ndirect.co.uk
Subjects: History, Music, Dance, English
ISBN Prefix(es): 1-86013; 0-905272
Total Titles: 400 Print; 2 CD-ROM

**Sutton Publishing Ltd+**
Subsidiary of Haynes Publishing
Phoenix Mill, Thrupp, Stroud, Glos GL5 2BU
*Tel:* (01453) 731114 *Fax:* (01453) 731117
*E-mail:* sales@sutton-publishing.co.uk; editorial@sutton-publishing.co.uk; publishing@sutton-publishing.co.uk
*Web Site:* www.suttonpublishing.co.uk
*Key Personnel*
Man Dir: Keith Fullman
Publishing Dir, Permissions: Peter Clifford
Sales & Marketing Dir: Jeremy Yates-Round
Foreign Rights Manager: Viktoria Tischer
Contact: Rachel Graham *Tel:* (01453) 732409 *E-mail:* rachelgraham@sutton-publishing.co.uk
Founded: 1979
Subjects: Agriculture, Archaeology, Architecture & Interior Design, Art, Biography, Business, Engineering (General), Fiction, Genealogy, History, House & Home, Human Relations, Labor, Industrial Relations, Literature, Literary Criticism, Essays, Maritime, Military Science, Nonfiction (General), Photography, Regional Interests, Religion - Protestant, Social Sciences, Sociology, Sports, Athletics, Technology, Transportation, Travel
ISBN Prefix(es): 0-86299; 0-904387; 0-7509
Number of titles published annually: 200 Print
Total Titles: 800 Print
Imprints: Pocket Classics; In Old Photographs; Illustrated History Paperbacks; Pocket Biographies; Pocket Histories
Distributor for Army Records Society; History of Parliament Trust
*Distribution Center:* Haynes Publishing, Sparkford, Near Yeoril, Somerset BA22 7JJ

**Swan Hill Press**, *imprint of* Quiller Publishing Ltd

**Sweet & Maxwell**, *imprint of* Sweet & Maxwell Ltd

**Sweet & Maxwell Ltd+**
Cheriton House, North Way, Andover SP10 5BE
*Tel:* (020) 7393 7000; (020) 7449 1104
 *Fax:* (020) 7449 1144
*E-mail:* info@routledge.co.uk
Founded: 1799
Subjects: Law
ISBN Prefix(es): 0-421; 0-420; 0-414
*Parent Company:* Thomson Corporation Publishing Ltd
*Ultimate Parent Company:* The Thomson Corporation, Toronto Dominion Bank Tower, Suite 2706, PO Box 24, Toronto Dominion Centre, Toronto, ON M5K 1A1, Canada
Imprints: Sweet & Maxwell; W Green; Roundhall Sweet & Maxwell
Subsidiaries: W Green; Roundhall Sweet & Maxwell
Distributor for Carswell (Europe); LBC (Europe); WGL (Europe)
*Orders to:* Cheriton House, North Way, Andover, Hants SP10 5BE

**Sydney Jary Ltd+**
9 Upper Belgrave Rd, Clifton, Bristol BS8 2XH
*Tel:* (0117) 974-1640 *Fax:* (0117) 973-7116
*E-mail:* admin@s-jary.co.uk
*Key Personnel*
Contact: Michael C Ross
Founded: 1960
Subjects: Biography, Business, History, Management, Military Science
*Associate Companies:* Avon World Limited

**Symposium Press**, *imprint of* Science Reviews Ltd

**T & AD Poyser Ltd**, *imprint of* Christopher Helm (Publishers) Ltd

**T&T Clark International**, *imprint of* The Continuum International Publishing Group Ltd

**Ta Ha Publishers Ltd**
One Wynne Rd, London SW9 0BB
*Tel:* (020) 7737 7266 *Fax:* (020) 7737 7267
*E-mail:* sales@taha.co.uk
*Web Site:* www.taha.co.uk
Subjects: Religion - Islamic
ISBN Prefix(es): 0-907461; 1-897940; 1-842000
Number of titles published annually: 30 Print
Total Titles: 270 Print; 120 Online
*Bookshop(s):* Islamic Bookstore.com
*Distribution Center:* Islamic Bookstore.com
*Orders to:* 2040-F Lord Baltimore Drive, Baltimore, MD 21244, United States

**Tabb House+**
7 Church St, Padstow, Cornwall PL28 8BG
*Tel:* (01841) 532316 *Fax:* (01841) 532316
*E-mail:* tabbhouse@connexions.co.uk; books@tabb-house.fsnet.co.uk
*Key Personnel*
Chief Executive, Dir: Caroline White
Founded: 1980
Book Publisher.
Subjects: Biography, Fiction, Literature, Literary Criticism, Essays, Nonfiction (General), Poetry, Children's Fiction
ISBN Prefix(es): 0-907018; 1-873951; 0-9534079
Number of titles published annually: 4 Print
Total Titles: 103 Print
Distributed by Tor Mark Press

*Orders to:* Gardeners Books Ltd, One Whittle Dr, Willington Dr, Eastbourne, Sussex BN23 6QH *Tel:* (01323) 521 555 *Fax:* (01323) 521 666 *E-mail:* sales@gardners.com *Web Site:* gardners.com

**The TAFT Group**, *imprint of* Thomson Gale

**Taigh Na Teud Music Publishers**
13 Upper Breakish, Isle of Skye IV42 8PY
*Tel:* (01471) 822528 *Fax:* (01471) 822811
*E-mail:* sales@scotlandsmusic.com
*Web Site:* www.scotlandsmusic.com
*Key Personnel*
Sales Manager: Alasdair Martin
Founded: 1985
Subjects: Music, Dance
ISBN Prefix(es): 1-871931
Number of titles published annually: 6 Print; 2 CD-ROM
Total Titles: 60 Print; 12 CD-ROM

**Take That Ltd**, *imprint of* Verulam Publishing Ltd

**Take That Ltd+**
Imprint of Verulam Publishing Ltd
PO Box 200, Harrogate HG1 2YR
*Tel:* (01423) 507545 *Fax:* (01423) 526035
*E-mail:* shop@takethat.co.uk
*Web Site:* www.takethat.co.uk
*Key Personnel*
Man Dir: Chris Brown
Founded: 1987
Subjects: Business, Computer Science, Finance, Media/Sport, Gambling
ISBN Prefix(es): 1-873668; 0-9516461; 0-9519489; 1-903994
Number of titles published annually: 15 Print; 6 E-Book
Total Titles: 55 Print; 12 E-Book
Imprints: Net.Works
Distributed by Trafalgar Square
Distributor for Cardoza (Europe); Maximedia (UK)
Foreign Rep(s): Trafalgar Square Publishing (US)
*Orders to:* Verulam, 152a Park Street Lane, Park St, St Albans, Herts AL2 2AU

**Tales of Heaven & Earth**, *imprint of* Moonlight Publishing Ltd

**Tango Books+**
Division of Sadie Fields Productions Ltd
4 C/D West Point, 36-37 Warple Way, London W3 ORG
*Tel:* (020) 8996 9970 *Fax:* (020) 8996 9977
*E-mail:* sales@tangobooks.co.uk
*Key Personnel*
Dir: David Fielder *Tel:* (020) 8735 4935
 *E-mail:* david@tangobooks.co.uk; Sheri Safran *Tel:* (020) 8735 4931 *E-mail:* sheri@tangobooks.co.uk
Founded: 1991
ISBN Prefix(es): 1-85707
Imprints: Tango Cards
Distributor for Innovative Kids; Soundprints; Van der Meer
*Warehouse:* The Trade Center Ltd, Mendlesham Industrial Estate, Norwich Rd, Mendlesham, Suffolk IP14 5NA

**Tango Cards**, *imprint of* Tango Books

**Taprobane Ltd**
PO Box 717, London W5 3EY
*Tel:* (020) 8998 3024 *Fax:* (020) 8810 5415
ISBN Prefix(es): 1-873344

**Tarantula Books**, *imprint of* Geddes & Grosset

**Tarquin**, *imprint of* Tarquin Publications

**Tarquin Publications+**
Stradbroke, Diss, Norfolk IP21 5JP
*Tel:* (01379) 384 218 *Fax:* (01379) 384 289
*E-mail:* enquiries@tarquin-books.demon.co.uk
*Web Site:* www.tarquin-books.demon.co.uk
*Key Personnel*
Chief Executive, Editorial, Rights & Permissions: Gerald Jenkins *E-mail:* gerald@tarquin-books.demon.co.uk
Sales: Margaret Jenkins
Founded: 1970
Membership(s): IPG.
Subjects: Education, Mathematics, Science (General)
ISBN Prefix(es): 0-906212; 1-899618
Number of titles published annually: 7 Print
Total Titles: 99 Print
Imprints: Tarquin; DIME

**Taschen Evergreen**, *imprint of* Taschen UK Ltd

**Taschen UK Ltd+**
Subsidiary of Taschen GmbH
13 Old Burlington St, London W1S 3AJ
*Tel:* (020) 7437 4350 *Fax:* (020) 7437 4360
*E-mail:* contact@taschen.com
*Web Site:* www.taschen.com
*Key Personnel*
Public Relations: Christa Urbain *E-mail:* c.urbain@taschen.com
Founded: 1994
Subjects: Art, Fashion, Photography, Architecture, Design
ISBN Prefix(es): 3-8228
*Associate Companies:* TASHEN Deutschland, Hohenzollernring 53, 50672 Cologne, Germany, Public Relations: Dr Christine Waiblinger *Tel:* (0221) 201 80 170 *Fax:* (0221) 201 80 42 *E-mail:* c.waiblinger@taschen-deutschland.com; TASCHEN Espana, c/ Victor Hugo, 1, 2º Dcha, Madrid, Spain, Customer Services: Mr Fernando Gonzalez *Tel:* (091) 360 50 63 *Fax:* (091) 360 50 64 *E-mail:* f.gonzalez@taschen-espana.com; TASCHEN France, 82, Rue Mazarine, 75006 Paris, France, Customer Services: Ms Regina Masanes *Tel:* (01) 40 51 70 93 *Fax:* (01) 43 26 73 80 *E-mail:* r.masanes@taschen-france.com; TASCHEN Japan, Atelier Ark Bldg, 5-11-23, Minami Aoyama Minato-Ku, Tokyo 107-0062, Japan, Public Relations: Ms Asuka Shibata *Tel:* (03) 57 78 30 00 *Fax:* (03) 57 78 30 30 *E-mail:* order@taschen-japan.com
Imprints: Taschen Evergreen
*U.S. Office(s):* Taschen USA, 230 Fifth Ave, Suite 1411, New York, NY 10001, United States, Contact: Paul Norton
*Warehouse:* Grantham Book Services, Isaac Newton Way, Alma Park Industrial Estate, Grantham, Lincs N931 9SD *Tel:* (01476) 541000 (UK only)
*Distribution Center:* Grantham Book Services, Isaac Newton Way, Alma Park Industrial Estate, Grantham, Lincs N931 9SD (UK only)

**Tate Publishing Ltd+**
Millbank, London SW1P 4RG
*Tel:* (020) 7887 8000; (020) 7887 8008
 *Fax:* (020) 7887 8878
*E-mail:* tp.enquiries@tate.org.uk
*Web Site:* www.tate.org.uk *Cable:* TATEGAL LONDON
*Key Personnel*
Chief Executive: Celia Clear *E-mail:* celia.clear@tate.org.uk
Editor: Judith Severne *Tel:* (020) 7887 8868
 *E-mail:* judith.severne@tate.org.uk
Picture Rights: Chris Webster *Tel:* (020) 7887 8867 *Fax:* (020) 7887 8900 *E-mail:* chris.webster@tate.org.uk

Sales & Rights Dir: James Attlee *E-mail:* james.
  attlee@tate.org.uk
Publishing Dir: Roger Thorp *Tel:* (020) 7887
  8617 *E-mail:* roger.thorp@tate.org.uk
Founded: 1931
Publishers of art books, exhibition catalogues &
  gallery guides of modern art & British art since
  1550.
Subjects: Architecture & Interior Design, Art, Ed-
  ucation, Art History
ISBN Prefix(es): 1-85437
Number of titles published annually: 30 Print
Total Titles: 150 Print
*Parent Company:* Tate Enterprises
*Ultimate Parent Company:* Tate Gallery
Subsidiaries: Tate Gallery Liverpool; Tate Gallery
  Modern; Tate Gallery St Ives
Distributed by Thames & Hudson Pty Ltd (Aus-
  tralia); Harry N Abrams Inc (USA & Canada)

**Tauris Academic Studies**, *imprint of* I B Tauris
  & Co Ltd

**I B Tauris & Co Ltd+**
6 Salem Rd, London W2 4BU
*Tel:* (020) 7243 1225 *Fax:* (020) 7243 1226
*E-mail:* mail@ibtauris.com
*Web Site:* www.ibtauris.com
*Key Personnel*
Chairman & Publisher: Iradj Bagherzade
  *E-mail:* ibagherzade@ibtauris.com
Man Dir: Jonathan McDonnell
  *E-mail:* jmcdonnell@ibtauris.com
Financial Controller: Liz Stuckey
  *E-mail:* lstuckey@ibtauris.com
Rights Manager & US Publishing Manager: Is-
  abella Steer *E-mail:* isteer@ibtauris.com
Marketing Manager: Paul Davighi
  *E-mail:* pdavighi@ibtauris.com
Sales Manager: Martin Ashworth
  *E-mail:* mashworth@ibtauris.com
Export Controller: Matthew Fry *E-mail:* mfry@
  ibtauris.com
Production Mgr: Stuart Weir *E-mail:* sweir@
  ibtauris.com
Publicist: Hannah Ross *E-mail:* hross@ibtauris.
  com
Editor: P Brewster; L Crook; D Stonestreet; A
  Wright
Founded: 1983
Independent publisher of both scholarly & general
  interest books
Specialize in Middle East studies, history, poli-
  tics, international relations, film & visual cul-
  ture.
Subjects: Architecture & Interior Design, Asian
  Studies, Developing Countries, Film, Video,
  Geography, Geology, Government, Political
  Science, History, Nonfiction (General), Reli-
  gion - Islamic, Religion - Other, Ancient His-
  tory, ContemporaryArt, Film Studies, Interna-
  tional Relations, Middle East Studies, Politics,
  Visual Culture
ISBN Prefix(es): 1-85043; 1-86064; 1-84511
Number of titles published annually: 175 Print
Imprints: British Academic Press; Tauris Aca-
  demic Studies; Tauris Parke; Tauris Parke Pa-
  perbacks
*U.S. Office(s):* I B Tauris & Co Ltd, Palgrave
  Macmillan, 175 Fifth Ave, New York, NY
  10010, United States *Tel:* 212-982-3900
  *Fax:* 212-777-6359
Palgrave Macmillan, 175 Fifth Ave, New York,
  NY 10010, United States *Tel:* 212-982-3900
  *Fax:* 212-982-5562
Distributor for Emirates Center for Strategic Stud-
  ies & Research (ECSSR) (Worldwide excluding
  Midddle East); The Khalili Collection (World-
  wide); Saqi Books (USA only); Philip Wilson
  Publishers (Worldwide)
*Orders to:* Thomson Publishing Services, Cheri-
  ton House, North Way, Andover SP10 5BE

**Tauris Parke**, *imprint of* I B Tauris & Co Ltd

**Tauris Parke Paperbacks**, *imprint of* I B Tauris
  & Co Ltd

**Taylor & Francis**, *imprint of* Taylor & Francis

**Taylor & Francis+**
Member of Taylor & Francis Group
4 Park Sq, Milton Park, Abingdon, Oxon OX14
  4RN
*Tel:* (01235) 828600 *Fax:* (01235) 828900
*E-mail:* info@tandf.co.uk
*Web Site:* www.tandf.co.uk
*Key Personnel*
Chief Executive: Peter Rigby
Man Dir Books & Journals: Roger Horton
Journal Marketing Dir: Bev Acreman
Books Sales Dir: C Chesher
Man Dir Psychology Press: Mike Forster
Journal Sales: K R Courtney
Founded: 1798
Subjects: Accounting, Art, Business, Computer
  Science, Economics, Education, Engineering
  (General), Finance, Government, Political Sci-
  ence, History, Human Relations, Language
  Arts, Linguistics, Management, Mathematics,
  Medicine, Nursing, Dentistry, Physics, Psy-
  chology, Psychiatry, Religion - Other, Social
  Sciences, Sociology, Transportation
ISBN Prefix(es): 0-85066; 1-85000; 0-7484
Number of titles published annually: 3,000 Print
*Parent Company:* Taylor & Francis Informa
Imprints: Brunner-Routledge; Carfax Publishing;
  Europa; Garland Science; Martin Dunitz; Psy-
  chology Press; Routledge; RoutledgeCurzon;
  RoutledgeFalmer; Spon Press; Taylor & Fran-
  cis; Taylor & Francis Asia Pacific
Subsidiaries: Routledge Inc
Foreign Rep(s): Routledge Inc (North Amer-
  ica); Routledge India Liaison (India); Taylor
  & Francis Group (East Asia, North America);
  United Publishers Services (Japan)
Foreign Rights: David Barrett-Jolley (Botswana);
  Marco Castellan (Central America, France,
  Italy, Portugal, South America, Spain);
  Christoph Chesher (UK); Sandra Collins (Aus-
  tria, Germany, Switzerland); Graham Cross-
  ley (UK); Peter Havinga (Belgium, Nether-
  lands, Greece, Luxembourg); Sophie Hopkin
  (Israel); M Anwer Iqbal (Pakistan); Se-Yung
  Jun (Korea); Barbie Keene (Zimbabwe); Lillian
  Koe (Malaysia); Jeffrey Lim (China, Taiwan);
  Roy Mansell (Lesotho, Namibia, South Africa);
  Vera Medeiros (Brazil); Michelle Swinge (Aus-
  tralia, Asia); Chinke Ojiji (Nigeria); Nick Pep-
  per (Denmark, Finland, Iceland, Norway, Swe-
  den); Ian Pringle (Brunei, Indonesia, Singapore,
  Thailand); Sophie Rogers (London); I J Sagun
  (Philippines); Hema Shah (Eastern Europe); Ed
  Summerson (Hong Kong); Takahiko Kaneko
  (Japan); Rachel Zillig (Caribbean, Middle East,
  North Africa, West Indies)
*Orders to:* ITPS, Cheriton House Northway, An-
  dover SP10 5BE *Tel:* (01264) 342926

**Taylor & Francis Asia Pacific**, *imprint of* Taylor
  & Francis

**Taylor & Francis Group+**
Formerly Taylor & Francis Medical Books
Member of T&F Informa plc
2 Park Square, Milton Park, Abington OX14 4RN
*Tel:* (020) 7583 9855; (020) 7017 6000
  *Fax:* (020) 8842 2298; (020) 7017 6699
*E-mail:* enquiry@tandf.co.uk
*Web Site:* www.taylorandfrancisgroup.com
*Key Personnel*
Head of Medical Publishing: Nick Dunton
  *E-mail:* nick.dunton@tandf.co.uk

Man Dir: Martin Dunitz *E-mail:* martin.dunitz@
  tandf.co.uk
Editor Commissioning: Robert Peden
  *E-mail:* robert.peden@tandf.co.uk
Commissioning Editor: Alan Burgess
  *E-mail:* alan.burgess@tandf.co.uk
Man Editor: Alison Campbell *E-mail:* alison.
  campbell@tandf.co.uk
Production: Rosemary Allen *E-mail:* rosemary.
  allen@tandf.co.uk
Marketing Manager: Daniel Tomkins
  *E-mail:* daniel.tomkins@tandf.co.uk
Journal Sales & Advertising: Ian Mellor
  *E-mail:* ian.mellor@tandf.co.uk
Rights Manager: Carla Oliveira *E-mail:* carla.
  oliveira@tandf.co.uk
Head of Special Sales: Beth Bacchus
  *E-mail:* beth.bacchus@tandf.co.uk
Journal Editorial Enquiries: Maire Collins
  *E-mail:* maire.collins@2tankd.co.uk
Customer Services: Teresa Davey *E-mail:* teresa.
  davey@tandf.co.uk
General Enquiries: Heather Cameron
  *E-mail:* heather.cameron@tandf.co.uk
Founded: 1978 (by Ruth & Martin Dunitz)
Medical publishers of postgraduate books & jour-
  nals.
Recipient of 1991 Queen's Award for Export
  Achievement.
Subjects: Medicine, Nursing, Dentistry, Psychol-
  ogy, Psychiatry
ISBN Prefix(es): 0-906348; 0-948269; 1-85317;
  1-84184
Number of titles published annually: 130 Print
Total Titles: 420 Print; 1 CD-ROM
*Associate Companies:* Isis Medical Media
Distributor for Remedica
*Warehouse:* ITPS, Cheriton House, North Way,
  Andover Hants SP10 5BE *Tel:* (01264) 342937
  *Fax:* (01264) 343005
*Orders to:* ITPS, Cheriton House, North Way,
  Andover Hants SP10 5BE *Tel:* (01264) 342937
  *Fax:* (01264) 343005

**Taylor & Francis Medical Books**, see Taylor &
  Francis Group

**Taylor Graham Publishing**
48 Regent St, Cambridge CB2 1FD
*Web Site:* www.taylorgraham.com
*Key Personnel*
Dir: Peter J Taylor
Founded: 1984
Subjects: Computer Science, Library & Informa-
  tion Sciences, Management, Technology
ISBN Prefix(es): 0-947568
*U.S. Office(s):* PMB 187, 12021 Wilshire Blvd,
  Los Angeles, CA 90025, United States

**Teach Yourself**, *imprint of* Hodder Education

**Teeney Books Ltd+**
Arlington House, 72 Fore St, Trowbridge BA14
  8HD
*Tel:* (01225) 775657 *Fax:* (01225) 775676
*E-mail:* teeneybo@primex.co.uk
*Key Personnel*
Man Dir: Tiny de Vries
Production Dir: Martyn Lewis
Founded: 1990
ISBN Prefix(es): 1-873338; 1-85952

**Telegraph Books+**
One Canada Sq, Canary Wharf, London E14 5DT
*Tel:* (020) 7538 5000 *Fax:* (020) 7538 6064
*Web Site:* www.telegraph.co.uk
*Telex:* 22874 Telldn G
*Key Personnel*
Publisher: Morven Knowles
Product Manager: Clare Sims *E-mail:* clare.
  sims@telegraph.co.uk
Founded: 1930

Subjects: Cookery, Education, Gardening, Plants, Health, Nutrition, How-to, Humor, Journalism, Law, Military Science, Self-Help, Sports, Athletics
ISBN Prefix(es): 0-86367; 0-901684
Number of titles published annually: 50 Print
*Parent Company:* Telegraph Group Ltd
*Ultimate Parent Company:* Hollinger
*Book Club(s):* Telegraph Books Direct (United Kingdom)
*Warehouse:* Units 5 & 6 Industrial Estate, Brecon, Powys LD3 8LA
*Orders to:* Telegraph Books Direct

**Tempest,** *imprint of* HarperCollins UK

**Temple Lodge Publishing Ltd**
Hillside House, The Square, Forest Row, East Sussex RH18 5ES
*Tel:* (01342) 824000 *Fax:* (01342) 826437
*E-mail:* office@templelodge.com
*Web Site:* www.templelodge.com
ISBN Prefix(es): 0-904693; 1-902636
Distributed by Anthroposophic Press (USA); Steinerbooks (New Zealand); Rudolf Steiner Book Centre (Australia); Rudolf Steiner Publications (South Africa); Tri-fold Books (Canada)
*Orders to:* BookSource, 32 Finlas St, Glasgow G22 5DU *Tel:* (0141) 558 1366 *Fax:* (0141) 557 0189 *E-mail:* orders@booksource.net
*Returns:* Scottish BookSource Distribution, 32 Finlas St, Cowlairs Industrial Estate, Glasgow G22 5DU

**Tern Press**
St Mary's Cottage, Great Hales St, Market Drayton, Salop TF9 1JN
*Tel:* (01630) 652153
*Key Personnel*
Rights: Mary Parry; Nicholas Parry
Founded: 1972
Subjects: Biblical Studies, Literature, Literary Criticism, Essays, Natural History, Poetry
Total Titles: 90 Print
*Branch Office(s)*
Joshua Heller Rare Books Inc, PO Box 39114, Washington, DC 20016-9114, United States (US Affiliate)

**Texere Publishing Ltd**
71-77 Leadenhall St, London EC3A 3DE
*Tel:* (020) 7204 3644 *Fax:* (020) 7208 6701
*Web Site:* www.etexere.com
*Key Personnel*
Man Dir: Martin Liu
Dir, Production & Operations: Pom Somkabcharti
Executive Editor: David Wilson
Sales Manager & Administrative Coordinator: James Coulson
Founded: 2000
Total Titles: 80 Print
*U.S. Office(s):* Texere LLC, 440 E 56 St, New York, NY 10022, United States *Tel:* 212-317-5511 *Fax:* 212-317-5178
Distributed by W W Norton

**Textile & Art Publications Ltd+**
12 Queen St, Mayfair, London W1J 5PG
*Tel:* (020) 7499 7979 *Fax:* (020) 7409 2596
*E-mail:* post@textile-art.com
*Web Site:* www.textile-art.com
*Key Personnel*
Publisher: Michael Franses
Founded: 1993
Subjects: Art, Asian Studies, Religion - Buddhist, Textile art
ISBN Prefix(es): 1-898406
Number of titles published annually: 2 Print
Total Titles: 4 Print

**TFPL**
17-18 Britton St, London EC1M 5TL
*Tel:* (020) 7251 5522 *Fax:* (020) 7251 8318
*E-mail:* central@tfpl.com
*Web Site:* www.tfpl.com
*Key Personnel*
Founder & Chief Executive: Nigel Oxbrow
Dir & Senior Advisor: Angela Abell
Marketing Executive: Carmel Boland
   *E-mail:* carmel.boland@tfpl.com
Marketing Manager: Bindy Pease *E-mail:* bindy. pease@tfpl.com
Founded: 1987
Specialist in recruitment, advisory, research & training services company focusing on knowledge, library, information, records, web & content management.
Membership(s): Directory Publishers Association.
Subjects: Communications, Computer Science, Human Relations, Library & Information Sciences
ISBN Prefix(es): 1-870889
Distributor for TFPL Inc

**Thames & Hudson Ltd+**
181A High Holborn, London WC1V 7QX
*Tel:* (020) 7845 5000 *Fax:* (020) 7845 5050
*E-mail:* sales@thameshudson.co.uk
*Web Site:* www.thamesandhudson.com
*Key Personnel*
Man Dir: Thomas Neurath
Editorial: Jamie Camplin
Sales Dir: Trevor Naylor
Production: Neil Palfreyman
Marketing: Anna Vinegrad
Rights: Christian Frederking *E-mail:* c. frederking@thameshudson.co.uk
Publicity: Kate Burvill
Permissions: Naomi Pritchard
Founded: 1949
Subjects: Archaeology, Architecture & Interior Design, Art, Crafts, Games, Hobbies, Ethnicity, Fashion, History, Music, Dance, Philosophy, Photography, Psychology, Psychiatry, Religion - Other, Science (General), Technology, Travel, Graphics, Popular Culture
ISBN Prefix(es): 0-500
*Associate Companies:* Editions Thames & Hudson, 12 Rue du Seine, Paris 75006, France
*Subsidiaries:* Thames & Hudson Ltd (Eastern Mediterranean, Middle East, Pakistan, Italy, Spain, Portugal, Mexico & Central America); Thames & Hudson (S) Private Ltd (Malaysia, Singapore & South-East Asia); Thames & Hudson (Australia) Pty Ltd (Australia); Thames & Hudson (China) Ltd (China & Hong Kong)
*U.S. Office(s):* Thames & Hudson Inc, 500 Fifth Ave, New York, NY 10110, United States
Distributor for Aperture; British Museum Press; Co & Bear; Flammarion; Laurence King; MOMA; National Gallery of Australia; Royal Academy of Arts; Royal Collection Enterprises; Scalo Publishing; Scriptum Editions; Skira Editore; Steidl Verlag; Violette Editions
*Orders to:* 44 Clockhouse Rd, Farnborough, Hants GU14 7QZ *Tel:* (01252) 541602 *Fax:* (01252) 377380

**Tharpa Publications**
Conishead Priory, Ulverston, Cumbria LA12 9QQ
*Tel:* (01229) 588599 *Fax:* (01229) 483919
*E-mail:* tharpa@tharpa.com
*Web Site:* www.tharpa.com
*Key Personnel*
Dir: Hugh Clift
Founded: 1984
Subjects: Religion - Buddhist
ISBN Prefix(es): 0-948006
*Associate Companies:* Editions Tharpa, BP 278, 75525 Paris Cedex 11, France *Tel:* (01) 43 67 87 87 *Fax:* (01) 43 67 87 87 *E-mail:* info@ tharpa.org *Web Site:* www.tharpa.org; Editorial Tharpa Brasil, Rua Mourato Coelho

910, Cep 10.41 7.001, Sao Paulo, SP, Brazil *Tel:* (011) 814 6326 *Fax:* (011) 814 6326 *E-mail:* jangchub@iconet.com.br; Editorial Tharpa Espana, C/Empecinado n2, atico derecha, 41004 Sevilla, Spain *Tel:* (05) 421 1415 *Fax:* (05) 421 1415 *E-mail:* tharpa@ teleline.es; Editorial Tharpa Mexico, Madero No 687 Colonia Centro, CP44100 Guadalajara, Jalisco, Mexico *Tel:* (03) 825 1301 *Fax:* (03) 827 1026 *E-mail:* tharpa@closeup.com.mx; Tharpa Canada Inc, 2255-B Queen St E, Suite 147, Toronto, ON, Canada *Tel:* (416) 504 0966 *Fax:* (416) 504 0966 *E-mail:* 76467.262@ compuserve.com; Tharpa Verlag, Dennlerstr 38, 8047 Zurich, Switzerland *Tel:* (01) 401 0220 *Fax:* (01) 401 0220 *E-mail:* tharpa@tharpa.org *Web Site:* www.tharpa.org
*U.S. Office(s):* Tharpa Books, PO Box 430, 47 Sweeney Rd, Glen Spey, NY 12737, United States *Tel:* 845-856-5102 *Fax:* 845-856-2110 *E-mail:* tharpabooks@aol.com
*Distribution Center:* Banyan Tree, 13 College Rd, Kent Town 5067, Australia *Tel:* (08) 8363 4244 *Fax:* (08) 8363 4255 *E-mail:* banyan@dove.net. au
Buddhist Merit & Wisdom Service, Shop A, Ground Floor, Jenny's Court, 241-3 Sai Yee St, Mongkok, Kowloon, Hong Kong *Tel:* 2391 8143 *Fax:* 2391 1002
Gondwana Books, PO Box 11684, Vorna Valley, Midrand 1686, South Africa *Tel:* (011) 805 6019 *Fax:* (011) 805 3746 *E-mail:* gondwana@ hixnet.co.za
Ingram Book Co, PO Box 3006, One Igngram Blvd, La Vergne, TN 37086-1986, United States
Midpoint Trade Books, 1263 Southwest Blvd, Kansas City, KS 66103, United States *Tel:* 913-362-7400 ext 109 *Fax:* 913-362-7401 *E-mail:* julie@midpt.com
Peaceful Living Publications, PO Box 300, Tauranga, New Zealand *Tel:* (07) 571 8105 *Fax:* (07) 571 8513
PM Associates Pte Ltd, 130 Killiney Rd 239561, Singapore *Tel:* 732 9522 *Fax:* 7323 6076
Tharpa Canada Inc, 2255-B Queen St E, Suite 147, Toronto, ON M4E 1G3, Canada *Tel:* (416) 504 0966 *Fax:* (416) 504 0966 *E-mail:* tsepp@ sympatico.ca

**The Tarragon Press+**
Moss Park, Ravenstone, Whithorn DG8 8DR
*Tel:* (01988) 850368 *Fax:* (01988) 850304
*Key Personnel*
Dir & Editor: David Sumner *E-mail:* dsummer@ gn.apc.org
Founded: 1987
Membership(s): Scottish Publishers Association.
Subjects: Biological Sciences, Environmental Studies, Health, Nutrition, Medicine, Nursing, Dentistry, Physical Sciences, Science (General)
ISBN Prefix(es): 1-870781
*Orders to:* Lavis Marketing, 73 Lime Walk, Headington, Oxford 0X3 7AD

**Themis Books,** *imprint of* Green Books Ltd

**Thistle Press+**
4 Old Mill Cottages, Culsalmond, Insch, Aberdeenshire AB52 6TS
*Tel:* (01464) 821053 *Fax:* (01464) 821053
*E-mail:* info@oldmilldesign.co.uk
*Key Personnel*
Partner & International Rights Contact: Dr Keith Nicholson
Partner: Angela Nicholson
Founded: 1992
Membership(s): Scottish Publishers Association.
Subjects: Archaeology, Biography, Earth Sciences, Environmental Studies, History, Outdoor Recreation, Regional Interests, Travel, Scottish Travel Guides
Total Titles: 10 Print

*Associate Companies:* Scottish Travel Books, West Bank, Western Rd, Insch AB52 6JR
Imprints: Macgregor Science

**Thoemmes**, *imprint of* The Continuum International Publishing Group Ltd

**Thoemmes Press+**
11 Great George St, Bristol BS1 5RR
*Tel:* (0117) 929 1377 *Fax:* (0117) 922 1918
*E-mail:* info@thoemmes.com
*Web Site:* www.thoemmes.com
*Key Personnel*
Publisher: Rudi Thoemmes *E-mail:* rudi@thoemmes.com
Production: Alan Rutherford *E-mail:* arutherford@thoemmes.com
Financial Dir: Linda Keeble
Marketing Manager: Alison Lewis *E-mail:* alisonlewis@thoemmes.com
Editorial: Philip de Bary *E-mail:* pdebary@thoemmes.com; Merilyn Holme *E-mail:* mholme@thoemmes.com; Kirsten Robertson *E-mail:* kroberton@thoemmes.com
Founded: 1989
Specialize in reprints.
Subjects: Business, Education, Geography, Geology, History, Language Arts, Linguistics, Management, Philosophy, Science (General), Social Sciences, Sociology, Theology
ISBN Prefix(es): 1-85506; 1-84371
Number of titles published annually: 60 Print
Total Titles: 1,000 Print
*Parent Company:* Thoemmes Ltd
Imprints: Nico Editions; Overstone Press
*Orders to:* Alton Logistics Ltd, Battle Rd, Unit 4, Heathfeld, Newton Abbot TQ12 6RY
The University of Chicago Press, 1427 60 St, Chicago, IL 60637-2954, United States

**D C Thomson & Co Ltd**
80 Kingsway East, Dundee DD4 8SL
*Tel:* (01382) 223131 *Fax:* (01382) 462097
*E-mail:* shout@dcthomson.co.uk
*Web Site:* www.dcthomson.co.uk
*Key Personnel*
Chairman: Brian H Thompson
Founded: 1905
ISBN Prefix(es): 0-412
*Branch Office(s)*
Courier Buildings, 2 Albert Sq, Dundee DD1 9QJ *Tel:* (01382) 223131 *Fax:* (01382) 322214
144 Port Dundas Rd, Glasgow G4 OHZ *Tel:* (0141) 332 9933 *Fax:* (0141) 331 1595
185 Fleet St, London EC4A 2HS *Tel:* (020) 7400 1030 *Fax:* (020) 7831 9440
137 Chapel St, Manchester M3 6AA *Tel:* (0161) 834 2831 *Fax:* (0161) 833 2884

**Thomson Gale**
50 Milford Rd, Reading, Berks RG1 8LJ
*Tel:* (01264) 342962 *Fax:* (01264) 342763
*Web Site:* www.gale.com
*Telex:* 47214 ITPG
*Key Personnel*
Marketing Manager: Claire Gilman
Head of Sales: Lynne Guthrie
Customer Services Manager: Steven Kempson *Tel:* (0118) 957 7233 *Fax:* (0118) 959 1325 *E-mail:* steven.kempson@gale.com
Founded: 1989
Subjects: Architecture & Interior Design, Art, Biography, Business, Child Care & Development, Drama, Theater, Fashion, Genealogy, History, Literature, Literary Criticism, Essays, Music, Dance, Women's Studies
ISBN Prefix(es): 1-873477
*Parent Company:* Gale Research
Imprints: Blackbirch Press; Five Star; Gale; Graham & Whiteside; Greenhaven Press; GK Hall & Co; Kidhaven Press; Lucent Books; Macmillan Reference USA; Oceano Grupo Editorial;

Primary Source Microfilm; KG Saur; St James Press; Schirmer Reference; Charles Scribner's Sons; The TAFT Group; Thorndike Press; Twayne Publishers; UXL
*Shipping Address:* PO Box 699, Andover, Hants SP10 5YE
*Warehouse:* PO Box 699, Andover, Hants SP10 5YE
*Orders to:* PO Box 699, Andover, Hants SP10 5YE

**Thomson Learning International**
High Holborn House, 50-51 Redford Row, London WC1R 4LR
*Tel:* (020) 7067 2500 *Fax:* (020) 7067 2600
*Web Site:* www.thomsonlearning.co.uk
*Key Personnel*
Contact: Charles Iossi

**Thorndike Press**, *imprint of* Thomson Gale

**Thoth Publications+**
64 Leopold St, Loughborough, Leics LE11 5DN
*Tel:* (01509) 210626 *Fax:* (01509) 238034
*E-mail:* enquiries@thoth.co.uk
*Web Site:* www.thothpublications.com; www.thoth.co.uk
Subjects: New Age
Number of titles published annually: 9 Print
Total Titles: 60 Print

**Thrass (UK) Ltd**
Units 1-3 Tarvin Sands, Barrow Lane, Tarvin, Chester CH3 8JF
*Tel:* (01829) 741413 *Fax:* (01829) 741419
*E-mail:* enquiries@thrass.demon.co.uk
*Web Site:* www.thrass.co.uk
Publish educational books, charts & software, audio & video cassettes.
Subjects: Education
ISBN Prefix(es): 1-904912; 1-876424

**Threshold**, *imprint of* The Kenilworth Press Ltd

**Tiger Books International PLC+**
26A York St, Twickenham, Middx TW1 3LJ
*Tel:* (0181) 8925577 *Fax:* (0181) 8916550
*E-mail:* gp@dial.pipex.com
*Key Personnel*
Dir: Grahame Parish; Sue Parish
Founded: 1985
Specialize in remainders & promotional reprints.
Subjects: Fiction, Nonfiction (General)
ISBN Prefix(es): 1-85501; 1-870461; 1-84056
*Associate Companies:* Sheridan Book Company Ltd
Imprints: Sheridan Book Company; Senate
*Warehouse:* Bartholomews Storage & Distribution Ltd, Woodside Rd, Boyatt Wood Industrial Estate, Eastleigh, Hants SO5 5XZ

**Tigers**, *imprint of* Andersen Press Ltd

**Timber Press Inc+**
2 Station Rd, Swavesey, Cambridge CB4 5QJ
*Tel:* (01954) 232959 *Fax:* (01954) 206040
*E-mail:* timberpressuk@btinternet.com
*Web Site:* www.timberpress.com
*Key Personnel*
Marketing Manager (UK): Pam Segers
Owner & Chief Executive Officer: Bob Conklin
Publisher: Jane Connor
Founded: 1978
Subjects: Agriculture, Gardening, Plants, Music, Dance
ISBN Prefix(es): 0-917304; 0-88192; 0-931340; 0-931146; 1-57467
Imprints: Amadeus Press

*U.S. Office(s):* Timber Press, 133 SW Second Ave, Suite 450, Portland, OR 97204, United States *Tel:* 503-227-2878 *Fax:* 503-227-3070 *E-mail:* info@timberpress.com

**Time-Life Books (UK)+**
Brettenham House, Lancaster Pl, London WC2E 7EN
*Tel:* (020) 7911 8000 *Fax:* (020) 7911 8100
*E-mail:* email@timelife.demon.co.uk; email.uk@timewarnerbooks.co.uk
*Web Site:* www.twbookmark.com; www.timewarnerbooks.co.uk
*Key Personnel*
Man Dir: Joseph Peckl
Rights & Permissions: Curtis Kopf
Dir, Marketing: Alison Lindsay *Tel:* (020) 7911 8062 *E-mail:* alison.lindsay@timewarnerbooks.co.uk
*European Head Off:* Time-Life Books BV, Netherlands.
ISBN Prefix(es): 0-8094; 0-7835; 0-7054; 0-900658
*Parent Company:* Time Warner Inc, United States
*U.S. Office(s):* Time Life Bldg, Rockefeller Center, New York, NY 10020, United States
Time Life Books, 777 Duke St, Alexandria, VA 22314, United States
*Orders to:* Bookpoint Ltd, 39 Milton Park, Abingdon, Oxon OX14 4TD *Tel:* (0235) 835001 *Fax:* (0235) 832068
*Returns:* Time Warner Book Group Returns, 322 S Enterprise Blvd, Lebanon, IN 46052, United States (whole copy returns); WPS/Warner Returns, 3000 University Center Dr, Tampa, FL 33612, United States (stripped returns only)

**Time Out Group Ltd+**
Universal House, 251 Tottenham Court Rd, London W1T 7AB
*Tel:* (020) 7813 3000 *Fax:* (020) 7323 3438
*E-mail:* net@timeout.co.uk
*Web Site:* www.timeout.com
*Key Personnel*
Publisher: Tony Elliott
Man Dir: Mike Hardwick; David Pepper *E-mail:* davidpepper@timeout.com
Financial Dir: Richard Waterlow
Editorial Dir: Pete Fiennes *E-mail:* pete@timeout.com
Group Commercial Dir: Lesley Gill
Marketing Dir: Christine Cort
Production Dir: Steve Proctor
Group General Manager: Nichola Coulthard *Tel:* (020) 7813 6103 *E-mail:* nicholacoulthard@timeout.com
Editor, Time Out Magazine London: Laura Lee Davies
Editor, Time Out New York: Cyndi Stivers
Founded: 1968
Specialize in magazines & guidebooks.
Subjects: Art, Drama, Theater, Fashion, Film, Video, Gay & Lesbian, Poetry, Radio, TV, Travel
Number of titles published annually: 10 Print
Total Titles: 40 Print
Divisions: Time Out Guides; Time Out Magazine
*U.S. Office(s):* Time Out New York, 627 Broadway, 7th floor, New York, NY 10012, United States

**Time Warner Book Group UK+**
Brettenham House, Lancaster Pl, London WC2E 7EN
*Tel:* (020) 7911 8000 *Fax:* (020) 7911 8100
*E-mail:* email.uk@twbg.co.uk
*Web Site:* www.twbg.co.uk
*Key Personnel*
Chief Executive: David Young
Publisher: Ursula Mackenzie
Editorial Dir: Barbara Daniel; Hilary Hale
Publisher, Virago Press: Lennie Goodings

Publishing Dir: Richard Beswick
Publishing Dir, Orbit: Tim Holman
Design Dir: Peter Cotton
Art Dir, Abacus/Virago: Duncan Spilling
International Sales Dir: Richard Kitson
Export Marketing & Publicity Dir: Nicola Hill
Commercial Dir: Karen Blewett
Finance Dir: Nigel Batt
Chief Information Officer: Thura KT Win
Group Marketing Dir: Terry Jackson
Dir of Marketing: Alison Lindsay
Marketing Dir, LB/Abacus/Virago: Roger Cazalet
Personnel Manager: Ann Woodhall
Production Dir: Nick Ross
Group Publicity Dir: Rosalie Macfarlane
Publicity Dir, General: Tamsin Barrack
Publicity Dir, Literary: Susan de Soissons
Publicity Manager, Ireland: Margaret Daly
Rights & Contracts Dir: Diane Spivey
Group Sales Dir: David Kent
UK Sales Dir: Robert Manser
Office Manager: Melanie Rogers
Bibliographic Controller: Sheena-Margot Lavelle
Contracts Manager: Daisy Malaktos
Founded: 1988
Also acts as book distributor.
Subjects: Biography, Business, Fiction, Mysteries, Nonfiction (General), Romance, Science Fiction, Fantasy, Travel
ISBN Prefix(es): 0-8212; 0-316; 0-7515; 1-85723; 1-86049; 1-904233; 1-184149; 1-84408; 1-4055
Number of titles published annually: 400 Print; 24 E-Book; 30 Audio
*Parent Company:* Time Warner Inc, 1271 Avenue of the Americas, New York, NY 10020, United States
Imprints: Abacus; Atom; Orbit; Virago
*Orders to:* TBS Distribution Centre, Colchester Rd, Frating Green, Colchester, Essex CO7 7LW

**Titan Books Ltd+**
Titan House, 144 Southwark St, London SE1 0UP
*Tel:* (020) 7620 0200 *Fax:* (020) 7620 0032
*E-mail:* readerfeedback@titanemail.com
*Web Site:* www.titanbooks.com
*Key Personnel*
Publisher: Nick Landau
Editorial, Rights & Permissions: Katy Wild
Sales & Publicity: Linda Beavis
Production: Robert Kelly
Founded: 1981
Subjects: Art, Biography, Film, Video, Radio, TV, Science Fiction, Fantasy
ISBN Prefix(es): 1-85286; 0-907610; 1-84023
Number of titles published annually: 150 Print
*Parent Company:* Titan Entertainment Group, London
Divisions: Titan Magazines; Titan Merchandise; Titan Studio
*Bookshop(s):* Birmingham; Cambridge; Coventry; Croydon; Edinburgh; Glasgow; Liverpool; London; Newcastle; Southampton

**Tobin Music**
The Old Malthouse, Knight St, Sawbridgeworth, Herts CM21 9AX
*Tel:* (01279) 726625
*E-mail:* candida@tobinmusic.co.uk
*Web Site:* www.candidatobin.co.uk
*Key Personnel*
Man Dir, Editorial: Candida Tobin
    *E-mail:* candida@tobinmusic.co.uk
Sales, Production, Publicity, Rights & Permissions: Christopher Dell
Founded: 1973
Music education books covering all musical theory & simple composition for home & school use for all ages & abilities.
A unique system of teaching using patterns & colors, tutors on various instruments.
Subjects: Education, Music, Dance, Nonfiction (General), Tutors, workbooks & information

books *Specializes In:*Classroom music teaching recorder, classical guitar & piano
ISBN Prefix(es): 0-905684
Total Titles: 31 Print; 1 CD-ROM
Imprints: Tobin Music Books

**Tobin Music Books**, *imprint of* Tobin Music

**Tolley**, *imprint of* Butterworths Tolley

**The Toucan Press**
White Cottage, Rue de Carteret, Castel Guernsey, Channel Islands GY5 7YG
*Tel:* (01481) 57017
*Key Personnel*
Man Dir: G Stevens Cox
Founded: 1850
Subjects: History, Literature, Literary Criticism, Essays
ISBN Prefix(es): 0-85694; 0-900749
Total Titles: 90 Print

**Touchstone**, *imprint of* Simon & Schuster Ltd

**Tour & Trail Maps**, *imprint of* Discovery Walking Guides Ltd

**Towy Publishing**
PO Box 24, Carmarthen SA31 1YS
*Tel:* (01267) 236569 *Fax:* (01267) 220444
*E-mail:* towyfairs@btopenworld.com
Subjects: Antiques
Total Titles: 3 Print

**TPL**, *imprint of* Training Publications Ltd

**Trade and Technical Press**, *imprint of* Elsevier Advanced Technology

**Training Publications**, *imprint of* Training Publications Ltd

**Training Publications Ltd**
3 Finway Court, Whippendell Rd, Watford; Herts WD18 7EN
*Tel:* (01923) 243730 *Fax:* (01923) 213 144
*Key Personnel*
General Manager: Mr B Peck
Editorial, Rights & Permissions: Mrs Lesley Page
    *E-mail:* lpage@emta.org.uk
Warehouse, Distribution: Mr J A Atkinson
Founded: 1965
Subjects: Engineering (General)
ISBN Prefix(es): 0-85083; 1-84019
*Parent Company:* Engineering & Marine Training Authority
Imprints: EAL; EITB; Entra; TPL; Training Publications
*Warehouse:* PO Box 75, Stockport, Chesire SK4 1PH *Tel:* (0161) 480 5285 *Fax:* (0161) 474 7502
*Orders to:* PO Box 75, Stockport, Chesire SK4 1PH *Tel:* (0161) 480 5285 *Fax:* (0161) 474 7502

**Transedition**, *imprint of* Transedition Ltd

**Transedition Ltd+**
43 Henley Ave, Oxford OX4 4DJ
*Tel:* (01865) 396700 *Fax:* (01865) 712500
*E-mail:* enquiries@transed.co.uk
*Web Site:* www.translateabook.com
*Key Personnel*
Sales & Acquisitions: Ed Glover *E-mail:* ed@transed.co.uk
Production: Richard Johnson *Tel:* (020) 8969 4817 *Fax:* (020) 8969 0487 *E-mail:* graphics@dircon.co.uk

Translations: Kathy Pearmain *Tel:* (01865) 396700 *E-mail:* kathy@translateabook.com
Accounts: Yasmin Qureski *E-mail:* yas@transed.co.uk
Founded: 1992
Packaged books & translations, illustrated books.
Membership(s): Motouun.
Subjects: Cookery, Gardening, Plants, History, Religion - Other, Theology
ISBN Prefix(es): 1-898250
Number of titles published annually: 6 Print
Total Titles: 100 Print
Imprints: Transedition
Divisions: Translate-A-Book
Foreign Rights: Illustrata (Portugal, Spain)

**Translations Wales**, *imprint of* Gwasg Gwenffrwd

**Transport Bookman Publications Ltd+**
8 South St, Isleworth TW7 7DH
*Tel:* (020) 8560 2666 *Fax:* (020) 8569 8273
*Key Personnel*
Man Dir: C F Stroud
Founded: 1971
Membership(s): Book Data & Booksellers Association.
Subjects: Transportation
ISBN Prefix(es): 0-85184
*Parent Company:* Chater & Scott Ltd

**Transworld Publishers Ltd**
Division of Random House Group Ltd
61-63 Uxbridge Rd, London W5 5SA
*Tel:* (020) 8579 2652 *Fax:* (020) 8579 5479
*E-mail:* info@transworld-publishers.co.uk
*Web Site:* www.booksattransworld.co.uk
*Telex:* 267974
*Key Personnel*
Deputy Man Dir, Publishing & Bantam Press Publisher: Mark Barty-King
Deputy Man Dir: Patrick Janson-Smith
Editorial Dir, Bantam Press: Ursula Mackenzie
Editorial Dir, Doubleday: Marianne Velmans
Juvenile Editorial Dir: Philippa Dickinson
UK Sales Dir: Garry Prior
Marketing Dir: Larry Finlay
International Sales Dir: John Blake
Publicity Dir: Judy Turner
Rights Dir: Rebecca Winfield
Art Dir: Liz Laczynska
Founded: 1950
Subjects: Biography, Computer Science, Criminology, Fiction, Film, Video, Government, Political Science, Health, Nutrition, Humor, Nonfiction (General), Science Fiction, Fantasy, Sports, Athletics
ISBN Prefix(es): 0-552
*Ultimate Parent Company:* Bertelsmann AG, Germany
*Associate Companies:* Transworld Publishers (Australia) Pty Ltd; Bantam Books (Canada) Inc/Doubleday Canada Ltd, Toronto, ON, Canada; Transworld Publishers (New Zealand) Pty
Imprints: Anchor; Bantam Paperbacks; Bantam Press; Black Swan; Corgi; Doubleday; Expert Books; Picture Corgi; Partridge Press; Young Corgi
*Warehouse:* PO Box 17, Wellingborough, Northants NN8 4BU

**Treehouse Children's Books Ltd+**
The Old Brewhouse, 2nd floor, Lower Charlton Trading Estate, Shepton Mallet, Somerset BA4 5QE
*Tel:* (01749) 330529 *Fax:* (01749) 330544
*E-mail:* ca.baker@virgin.net
*Key Personnel*
Dir: Andrew Bailey; David Bailey; Deborah Bailey; Dawn Powell; Richard Powell
    *E-mail:* richard.powell4@virgin.net
Founded: 1989

ISBN Prefix(es): 1-85576; 1-872300
*Associate Companies:* Emma Books Ltd
*Warehouse:* Macmillan Distribution Ltd, Brunel Rd, Houndmills, Basingstoke, Hants RG21 GX5

**Trentham Books Ltd+**
Westview House, 734 London Rd, Oakhill, Stoke-on-Trent, Staffs ST4 5NP
*Tel:* (01782) 745567; (01782) 844699 *Fax:* (01782) 745553
*E-mail:* tb@trentham-books.co.uk
*Web Site:* www.trentham-books.co.uk
*Key Personnel*
Editorial Dir: Dr Gillian Klein *E-mail:* gillian@trentham-books.co.uk
Dir & Sales Manager: Barbara Wiggins
Production Manager: John Stipling
Founded: 1981
Membership(s): Publishers Association of UK.
Subjects: Child Care & Development, Drama, Theater, Education, Ethnicity, Humor, Law, Psychology, Psychiatry, Social Sciences, Sociology, Technology, Women's Studies, Inclusive Education
ISBN Prefix(es): 0-948080; 1-85856; 0-7287; 0-9507735; 1-897898; 1-904133
Number of titles published annually: 35 Print
Total Titles: 300 Print
Subsidiaries: Trentham Print Design Ltd
Distributor for Arts Council of England

**Trigon Press+**
117 Kent House Rd, Beckenham, Kent BR3 1JJ
*Tel:* (0181) 7780534 *Fax:* (0181) 7767525
*E-mail:* trigon@easynet.co.uk
*Key Personnel*
Man Dir, Sales & Partner: Roger Sheppard
Editorial, Production: Judith Sheppard
Publicity: Angela Roberts
Rights & Permissions: Pat Palmer
Designer: Jacqui Burton
Founded: 1974
Membership(s): Independent Publishers Guild, Bibliographical Society; also acts as distributors for US museums & galleries.
Subjects: Art, Library & Information Sciences, Literature, Literary Criticism, Essays, Science Fiction, Fantasy
ISBN Prefix(es): 0-904929
Total Titles: 4 Print
Subsidiaries: The London Office
Distributed by Oak Knoll Books

**Triumph House**
Imprint of Forward Press
Remus House, Coltsfoot Dr, Woodston, Peterborough PE2 9JX
*Tel:* (01733) 898102 *Fax:* (01733) 313524
*E-mail:* triumphhouse@forwardpress.co.uk
*Web Site:* www.forwardpress.co.uk
Publisher of religious poetry.
Subjects: Poetry, Religion - Other, Christianity
Number of titles published annually: 15 Print
*Ultimate Parent Company:* Forward Press Ltd

**Trotman Publishing+**
2 The Green, Richmond, Surrey TW9 1PL
*Tel:* (0870) 900 2665 *Fax:* (020) 8486 1161
*E-mail:* sales@trotman.demon.co.uk
*Web Site:* www.careers-portal.co.uk/trotmanpublishing
*Key Personnel*
Chairman: Andrew Fiennes Trotman *Tel:* (020) 8486 1170
Dir: Tom Lee *Tel:* (020) 8486 1157
Editorial Dir: Amanda Williams *Tel:* (020) 8486 1168
Man Editor: Rachel Lockhart *Tel:* (020) 8486 1213
Advertising Manager: Alistair Rogers *Tel:* (020) 8486 1164

Marketing Manager: Deborah Jones *Tel:* (020) 8486 1158
Sales & Distribution Manager: Sean McKone *Tel:* (020) 8486 1166
Sales & Distribution Coordinator: Tracy Deadman *Tel:* (020) 8486 1160
Press Officer: Lorna Damiani *Tel:* (020) 8486 1165
Trade Sales Manager: Mike Baggallay *Tel:* (020) 8486 1165
Production Manager: Francisca Perez *Tel:* (020) 8486 1203
Man Dir: Toby Trotman *Tel:* (020) 8486 1171
New Media Manager: Alexis Castillo-Soto *E-mail:* alexis@trotman.co.uk
Founded: 1971
Subjects: Career Development, Education
ISBN Prefix(es): 0-85660
*Parent Company:* Trotman & Co Ltd
*Associate Companies:* Trotman (Australia) Ltd, Sydney, Australia
Subsidiaries: Careers Consultants Ltd; Syston Publishing Co Ltd

**True Crime**, *imprint of* Virgin Publishing Ltd

**TSO (The Stationery Office)+**
51 Nine Elms Lane, London SW8 5DR
*Tel:* (020) 7873 8787
*E-mail:* customer.services@tso.co.uk
*Web Site:* www.tso.co.uk
*Key Personnel*
Chief Executive Officer: Tim Hailstone
Dir, Business Development: Kevan Lawton
Man Dir: Keith Burbage
Editorial: Philip Brooks *Tel:* (01603) 605532 *E-mail:* phil.brooks@theso.co.uk
Chairman: Rupert Pennant-Rea
Chief Financial Officer: Richard Dell
Man Dir: Jeremy Hook; Dr Shane O'Neill
Human Resources Dir: David Orr
Founded: 1786
UK sales agent for most major international organizations.
Subjects: Agriculture, Archaeology, Architecture & Interior Design, Business, Computer Science, Earth Sciences, Economics, Education, Energy, Environmental Studies, Finance, Government, Political Science, Health, Nutrition, History, Law, Library & Information Sciences, Medicine, Nursing, Dentistry, Social Sciences, Sociology, Technology, Transportation
ISBN Prefix(es): 0-10; 0-11; 0-337
*Associate Companies:* The Parliamentary Press - London, Mandela Way, London SE1 5SS *Tel:* (020) 7394 4200; TSO Wales, G50, Phase Two, Government Bldgs, Ty-Glas, Llanishen, Cardiff CF14 5ST *Tel:* (02920) 765892; TSO Content Solutions, 84-90 East St, Epsom, Surrey KT17 1HF *Tel:* (01372) 845700; TSO Ireland, 16 Arthur St, Belfast BT1 4GD, Ireland *Tel:* (02890) 238451 *Fax:* (02890) 235401 *E-mail:* belfast.bookshop@tso.co.uk; TSO - Norwich, St Crispins, Duke St, Norwich NR3 1PD *Tel:* (01603) 622211; TSO Scotland, 71-73 Lothian Rd, Edinburgh EH3 9AZ *Tel:* (0870) 6065566 *Fax:* (0870) 606 5588 *E-mail:* edinburgh.bookshop@tso.co.uk
*Bookshop(s):* 68-69 Bull St, Birmingham B4 6AD, Manager: James Furnival *Tel:* (0121) 236 9696 *Fax:* (0121) 236 9699 *E-mail:* birmingham.bookshop@tso.co.uk; 18-19 High St, Cardiff CF10 1PT *Tel:* (02920) 39 5548 *Fax:* (02920) 38 4347 *E-mail:* cardiff.bookshop@tso.co.uk; 123 Kingsway, London WC2B 6PQ, Manager: Tiffany Holt *Tel:* (020) 7242 6393; (020) 7242 6410 *Fax:* (020) 7242 6394 *E-mail:* london.bookshop@tso.co.uk; 9-21 Princess St, Albert Sq, Manchester M60 8AS, Manager: Ian Penney *Tel:* (0161) 834 7201 *Fax:* (0161) 833 0634 *E-mail:* manchester.bookshop@tso.co.uk; TSO Scotland, 71-73

Lothian Rd, Edinburgh, Scotland EH3 9AZ
*Tel:* (0870) 6065566 *Fax:* (0870) 606 5588
*E-mail:* edinburgh.bookshop@tso.co.uk

**Tuba Press+**
Tunley Cottage, Tunley, Cirencester, Glos GL7 6LW
*Tel:* (01285) 760424 *Fax:* (01285) 760766
*Key Personnel*
Partner, Books: Peter Ellson
Partner, Magazines: Charles Graham
Founded: 1976
Specialize in poetry, chiefly unpublished authors.
Membership(s): Association of Little Presses & Small Press Group of Britain.
Subjects: Fiction, Poetry
ISBN Prefix(es): 0-907155; 0-9505956
Total Titles: 33 Print

**Tuckwell Press Ltd+**
The Mill House, Phantassie, East Linton, East Lothian EH40 3DG
*Tel:* (01620) 860 164 *Fax:* (01620) 860 164
*E-mail:* customerservices@tuckwellpress.co.uk
*Web Site:* www.tuckwellpress.co.uk
*Key Personnel*
Publishing Dir: John Tuckwell
International Rights: Val Tuckwell
Founded: 1995
Specialize in Scottish history; mainly academic with emphasis on Scotland & the North of England.
Subjects: Archaeology, Architecture & Interior Design, Biography, Environmental Studies, History, Literature, Literary Criticism, Essays, Religion - Protestant
ISBN Prefix(es): 1-898410; 1-86232
Number of titles published annually: 40 Print
Total Titles: 150 Print
Imprints: Canongate Academic
Distributed by Footprint (Australia & New Zealand); Hushion House (USA & Canada)
*Warehouse:* Scottish BookSource, 32 Finlas St, Glasgow G22 5DU
*Orders to:* Scottish BookSource, 137 Dundee St, Edinburgh EH11 1BG

**Tufton Books**, *imprint of* Church Union

**Twayne Publishers**, *imprint of* Thomson Gale

**Twelveheads Press**
PO Box 59, Chacewater, Truro, Cornwall TR4 8ZJ
*E-mail:* sales@twelveheads.com
*Web Site:* www.twelveheads.com
Founded: 1978
Subjects: Archaeology, Genealogy, History, Maritime, Regional Interests, Transportation
ISBN Prefix(es): 0-906294
Number of titles published annually: 4 Print
Total Titles: 34 Print
*Distribution Center:* Tor Mark Press, United Downs Industrial Estate, St Day, Redruth TR16 5HY

**Two-Can Publishing Ltd+**
15 New Bridge St, 2nd fl, London EC4V 6AU
*Tel:* (020) 7224 2440 *Fax:* (020) 7224 7005
*E-mail:* helpline@two-canpublishing.com; sales@creativepub.com
*Web Site:* www.two-canpublishing.com
*Key Personnel*
Chairman: Andrew Jarvis
Marketing Dir: Ian Grant
International Rights: Helen Cross
Founded: 1987
Specialize in children's magazines, books & multimedia.
Subjects: Animals, Pets, Geography, Geology, History, Natural History, Physics, Science (General), Technology

ISBN Prefix(es): 1-85434; 1-84301
*Orders to:* Title Book Services, Church Rd, Tiptree, Colchester, Essex C05 0SR

**Tycooly**, *imprint of* Cassell & Co

**Tycooly**, *imprint of* The Continuum International Publishing Group Ltd

**UCL Press Ltd+**
Imprint of Taylor & Francis Group Ltd
11 New Fetter Lane, London EC4P 4EE
*Tel:* (020) 7583 9855 *Fax:* (020) 7842 2298
*E-mail:* info@tandf.co.uk
*Web Site:* www.tandf.co.uk
*Key Personnel*
Publishing Dir: Stephen B Neal *E-mail:* stephen.neal@tandf.co.uk
Senior Editor, Social & Political Sciences: Mari Shullaw
Founded: 1991
Subjects: Archaeology, Art, Environmental Studies, Geography, Geology, Government, Political Science, History, Human Relations, Philosophy, Social Sciences, Sociology, Technology
ISBN Prefix(es): 1-85728; 1-84142
*Orders to:* Taylor & Francis Ltd, Rankine Rd, Basingstoke, Hants RG24 8PR *Tel:* (01256) 813000 *Fax:* (01256) 479438

**UK Academy of Science**, see The Royal Society

**Ulster Historical Foundation+**
12 College Sq E, Belfast BT1 6DD
*Tel:* (028) 90 332288 *Fax:* (028) 90 239885
*E-mail:* enquiry@uhf.org.uk
*Web Site:* www.ancestryireland.com
*Key Personnel*
Chairman: David Clement
Executive Dir: Fintan Mullan
Research Dir: Dr Brian Trainor
Project Manager: Andrew Vaughan
Founded: 1956
Subjects: Education, Genealogy, History, Regional Interests, Conferences, Genealogy, Historical Publishing
ISBN Prefix(es): 0-901905

**Ultimate**, *imprint of* Lorenz Books

**Ulverscroft Large Print Books Ltd+**
The Green Bradgate Rd, Anstey, Leicester LE7 7FU
*Tel:* (0116) 236 4325 *Fax:* (0116) 234 0205
*E-mail:* sales@ulverscroft.co.uk
*Web Site:* www.ulverscroft.co.uk
*Key Personnel*
Chairman: D F Thorpe
Man Dir: Patricia Henderson
Founded: 1964
Publishers of Ulverscroft Large Print Books, Charnwood Library Series, Linford Mystery Library Series, Linford Romance Library Series, Linford Western Library Series.
Subjects: Biography, Fiction, Literature, Literary Criticism, Essays, Mysteries, Nonfiction (General), Romance, Travel, Western Fiction
ISBN Prefix(es): 0-85456; 0-7089
*U.S. Office(s):* Ulverscroft Large Print (USA) Inc, 1881 Ridge Rd, PO Box 1230, West Seneca, NY 14224-1230, United States
Distributor for Magna Large Print (Australia, Canada, New Zealand, South Africa, USA)
*Showroom(s):* Cawdor Books, 96 Dykehead St, Queenslie, Glasgow G33 4QA *Tel:* (01729) 840225 *Fax:* (01729) 840683

**Unicorn Books**
56 Rowlands Ave, Hatch End, Pinner HA5 4BP
*Tel:* (020) 8420 1091 *Fax:* (020) 8428 0125

*Web Site:* www.unicornbooks.co.uk/
*Key Personnel*
Man Dir: Raymond Green
Founded: 1985
Membership(s): Antiquarian Bookseller's Association & Provincial Bookseller's Fairs Association.
Subjects: Military Science, Music, Dance, Transportation
ISBN Prefix(es): 1-85241
*Parent Company:* Factwell Ltd
Subsidiaries: MSR Books
Distributor for Archway Publishing; John Hallewell Publications

**United Writers Publications Ltd+**
Ailsa, Castle Gate, Penzance, Cornwall TR20 8BG
*Tel:* (01736) 365954 *Fax:* (01736) 365954
*E-mail:* info@unitedwriters.co.uk
*Key Personnel*
Man Dir, Editorial, Sales: Malcolm Sheppard *E-mail:* malcolm@unitedwriters.co.uk
Production: Tina Sully
Publicity: Peter Keane
Rights & Permissions: Julian Tremayne
Founded: 1962
Subjects: Biography, Fiction, Sports, Athletics, Travel
ISBN Prefix(es): 0-901976; 1-85200
Number of titles published annually: 6 Print
Total Titles: 150 Print

**Universitas**, *imprint of* Voltaire Foundation Ltd

**The University of Birmingham**
Information Services, Edgbaston, Birmingham B15 2TT
*Tel:* (0121) 414 3344 *Fax:* (0121) 414 3971
*Web Site:* www.general.bham.ac.uk
*Key Personnel*
Dir: Michele Shoebridge *E-mail:* m.i.shoebridge@bham.ac.uk
ISBN Prefix(es): 0-7044; 0-85057; 0-903054

**University of Exeter Press+**
Reed Hall, Streatham Dr, Exeter EX4 4QR
*Tel:* (01392) 263066 *Fax:* (01392) 263064
*E-mail:* uep@ex.ac.uk
*Web Site:* www.ex.ac.uk/uep
*Key Personnel*
Publisher: Simon C Baker *E-mail:* s.c.baker@ex.ae.uk
Marketing & Sales Manager: Genevieve Davey *Tel:* (01392) 264364 *E-mail:* uepsales@exeter.ac.uk
Founded: 1956
Subjects: Archaeology, Drama, Theater, Education, Film, Video, History, Language Arts, Linguistics, Literature, Literary Criticism, Essays, Maritime, Philosophy, Poetry, Regional Interests
ISBN Prefix(es): 0-85989; 0-900771; 0-902414; 0-9501308
Total Titles: 250 Print
Distributed by David Brown Book Co (North America)
Foreign Rep(s): Warren Bertram (Benelux); D Richard Bowen (Scandinavia); Eleanor Brasch Enterprises (Australia, New Zealand); Bernd Feldmann (Austria, Germany, Switzerland); Peter Prout (Gibraltar, Portugal, Spain); Roger Ward (China, Hong Kong, Indonesia, Japan, Korea, Malaysia, Philippines, Singapore, Taiwan, Thailand)
*Orders to:* Plymbridge Distributors Ltd, Estover Rd, Plymouth PL6 7PY *Tel:* (01752) 202301 *Fax:* (01752) 202333 *E-mail:* orders@plymbridge.com

**University of Hertfordshire Press**
University of Hertfordshire, Learning & Information Services, College Lane, Hatfield AL10 9AB
*Tel:* (01707) 284682 *Fax:* (01707) 284666
*E-mail:* uhpress@herts.ac.uk
*Web Site:* www.herts.ac.uk/uhpress
*Key Personnel*
Publisher: Jane Housham
Founded: 1992
Subjects: Biography, Drama, Theater, Education, History, Literature, Literary Criticism, Essays, Mathematics, Medicine, Nursing, Dentistry, Parapsychology
ISBN Prefix(es): 1-902806
Number of titles published annually: 15 Print
Total Titles: 50 Print
Imprints: Hertfordshire Publications
Foreign Rep(s): IPG Chicago (Canada, US)

**University of Illinois Press**, *imprint of* Combined Academic Publishers

**University of London Careers Service**
49-51 Gordon Sq, London WC1H 0PN
*Tel:* (020) 7554 4500 *Fax:* (020) 7383 5876
*E-mail:* careers@lon.ac.uk
*Web Site:* www.careers.lon.ac.uk
*Key Personnel*
Dir: Anne-Marie Martin *E-mail:* directors.office@careers.lon.ac.uk
Communications Services Manager: Ingrid Ross *Tel:* (020) 7554 4521 *E-mail:* i.ross@careers.lon.ac.uk
Head of Systems & Resources: Yanina Hinrichsen
Subjects: Career Development, How to Change Your Career, How to Analyse & Promote Your Skills for Work, How to Complete an Application Form, How to Write a Curriculum Vitae, How to Succeed at Interviews & Other Selection Methods
ISBN Prefix(es): 0-7187
Number of titles published annually: 1 Print
Total Titles: 5 Print

**University of Nebraska Press**, *imprint of* Combined Academic Publishers

**University of Newcastle Upon Tyne**
Registrar's Office, 6 Kensington Terrace, Newcastle Upon Tyne NE1 7RU
*Tel:* (0191) 222 6000 *Fax:* (0191) 222 6229
*Web Site:* www.ncl.ac.uk
*Key Personnel*
Publications Officer: Dinah A Michie *E-mail:* dinah.michie@ncl.ac.uk
Founded: 1963
ISBN Prefix(es): 0-7017; 0-900565

**University of Texas Press**, *imprint of* Combined Academic Publishers

**University of Wales Press** (Gwasg Prifysgol Cymru)+
Member of Literary Publishers (Wales) Ltd
10 Columbus Walk, Brigantine Pl, Cardiff CF10 4UP
*Tel:* (029) 2049-6899 *Fax:* (029) 2049-6108
*E-mail:* press@press.wales.ac.uk
*Web Site:* www.wales.ac.uk/press
*Key Personnel*
Dir: Ashley Drake *E-mail:* a.drake@press.wales.ac.uk
Deputy Dir: Richard Houdmont *E-mail:* r.houdmont@press.wales.ac.uk
Production/Design Manager: Nicola Roper *E-mail:* n.roper@press.wales.ac.uk
Commissioning Editor: Sarah Lewis *E-mail:* s.lewis@press.wales.ac.uk
Sales Support Executive: Bethan James *E-mail:* b.james@press.wales.ac.uk

Founded: 1922
Membership(s): Independent Publishers Guild.
Subjects: Archaeology, Architecture & Interior
  Design, Art, Economics, Education, Geography,
  Geology, History, Language Arts, Linguistics,
  Literature, Literary Criticism, Essays, Philos-
  ophy, Social Sciences, Sociology, Theology,
  Women's Studies
ISBN Prefix(es): 0-7083; 0-900768
Number of titles published annually: 60 Print; 1
  CD-ROM; 20 E-Book
Total Titles: 500 Print; 6 CD-ROM; 200 E-Book
Distributed by Independent Publishers Group
  (IPG) (USA & Canada); UNIREPS (Australia);
  United Publishers Services (UPS) (Japan)
*Distribution Center:* NBN International, Es-
  tover Rd, Plymouth PL6 7PY *Tel:* (01752)
  202301 *Fax:* (01752) 202333 *E-mail:* orders@
  nbninternational.com *Web Site:* www.
  nbninternational.com

**University of Washington Press**, *imprint of*
Combined Academic Publishers

**University Presses of California, Columbia &
  Princeton Ltd**
c/o John Wiley & Sons Ltd, Distribution Centre,
  One Oldlands Way, Bognor Regis, West Sussex
  PO22 9SA
*Tel:* (01243) 843291 *Fax:* (01243) 820250
*E-mail:* lois@upccp.demon.co.uk
*Web Site:* www.ucpress.edu
*Key Personnel*
Office Manager: Lois Edwards *E-mail:* lois@
  upccp.demon.co.uk
Founded: 1976
Subjects: Social Sciences, Sociology
ISBN Prefix(es): 0-520
*Parent Company:* Columbia University Press,
  New York, NY, United States

**Uplands Books+**
One The Uplands, Maze Hill, Saint Leonards
  TN38 0HL
*Tel:* (01424) 422306 *Fax:* (01424) 719879
*E-mail:* sales@upublish.cablenet.co.uk
*Key Personnel*
International Rights: Christopher Maxwell-Stewart
Founded: 1990
Specialize in children's books.
Membership(s): IPG.
ISBN Prefix(es): 1-897951; 0-9512246
*Warehouse:* Trade Counters, Mendelsham Indus-
  trial Estate, Norwich Rd, Mendelsham Suffolk
  1P14 5NA
*Distribution Center:* Ragged Bears Ltd, Ragged
  Appleshaw, Andover, Hants SP11 9HX
*Orders to:* Ragged Bears
*Returns:* Ragged Bears

**Usborne Publishing Ltd+**
Usborne House, 83-85 Saffron Hill, London
  EC1N 8RT
*Tel:* (020) 7430 2800 *Fax:* (020) 7430 1562;
  (020) 7242 0974
*E-mail:* mail@usborne.co.uk
*Web Site:* www.usborne.com
*Key Personnel*
Man Dir: Peter Usborne
General Manager: Robert Jones
Production Manager: Garry Lewis
Publishing Dir: Jenny Tyler
International Rights: Elizabeth Wright
Founded: 1973
ISBN Prefix(es): 0-7460; 0-86020

**UXL**, *imprint of* Thomson Gale

**Vacation Work Publications+**
9 Park End St, Oxford OX1 1HJ
*Tel:* (01865) 241978 *Fax:* (01865) 790885

*E-mail:* info@vacationwork.co.uk
*Web Site:* www.vacationwork.co.uk
*Key Personnel*
Dir & Rights: Charles James
Publicity Dir: David Woodworth
Contact: Andrew James *E-mail:* andrew@
  vacationwork.co.uk
Founded: 1967
Publisher of books for students abroad, the work-
  ing traveler.
Subjects: Advertising, Career Development,
  Crafts, Games, Hobbies, Developing Countries,
  Foreign Countries, Outdoor Recreation, Travel
ISBN Prefix(es): 0-907638; 1-85458; 0-901205
Total Titles: 55 Print
Distributed by Globe Pequot (USA)

**Vacher Dod Publishing Ltd**
One Douglas St, London SW1P 4PA
*Tel:* (020) 7828 7256 *Fax:* (020) 7828 7269
*E-mail:* politics@vacherdod.co.uk
*Web Site:* www.vacherdod.co.uk
*Key Personnel*
Publisher: Andrew Cox *E-mail:* andrewcox@
  vacherdod.co.uk; Edward Peck
Founded: 1832
Publisher of UK Parliamentary Reference.
Subjects: Foreign Countries, Government, Politi-
  cal Science
ISBN Prefix(es): 0-905702

**Vallentine, Mitchell & Co Ltd+**
Subsidiary of Frank Cass Publishers
Suite 314, Premier House, 112-114 Station Rd,
  Edgware, Middx HA8 7AQ
*Tel:* (020) 8952 9526 *Fax:* (020) 8952 9242
*E-mail:* info@vmbooks.com
*Web Site:* www.vmbooks.com
*Key Personnel*
Man Dir: Frank Cass
Editorial: Hilary Hewitts
Trade: Joanna Legg
Production: Ray Green
Publicity: Hayley Osen
Founded: 1950
Subjects: Cookery, History, Literature, Literary
  Criticism, Essays, Religion - Jewish, Theology,
  Military History, Political Science
ISBN Prefix(es): 0-85303
*Associate Companies:* Irish Academic Press; The
  Woburn Press
*Warehouse:* Biblios Distribution, Partridge Green,
  West Sussex RH13 8LD *Tel:* (0403) 710971
  *Fax:* (0403) 711143
*Orders to:* ISBS, 5824 NE Hassalo St, Portland,
  OR 97213-3644, United States *Tel:* 503-287-
  3093 *Fax:* 503-280-8832 *E-mail:* orders@isbs.
  com
Plymbridge Distributors Ltd, Estover Rd,
  Plymouth PL6 7PZ *Tel:* (07152) 202301
  *Fax:* (07152) 202331 *E-mail:* orders@
  plymbridge.com

**ValuSource**, *imprint of* Wiley Europe Ltd

**Van Duren Publishers Ltd**, see Colin Smythe
Ltd

**Van Molle Publishing+**
PO Box 29, Aberteifi, Cardigan, Ceredigion SA43
  1YN
*Tel:* (01239) 851482 *Fax:* (01239) 851482
*Key Personnel*
Contact: Cheryl Foster
Founded: 1995
Subjects: Fiction, Children's Picture Books, Adult
  Fiction (General)
ISBN Prefix(es): 0-9526925
Total Titles: 4 Print

**Variorum**, *imprint of* Ashgate Publishing Ltd

**Vega**, *imprint of* Salamander Books Ltd

**The Vegetarian Society**
Parkdale, Dunham Rd, Altrincham, Cheshire
  WA14 4QG
*Tel:* (0161) 925 2000 *Fax:* (0161) 926 9182
*E-mail:* info@vegsoc.org
*Web Site:* www.vegsoc.org
*Key Personnel*
Chief Executive Officer: Tina Fox *Tel:* (016) 925
  2002 *E-mail:* tina@vegsoc.org
Head of Public Affairs: Samantha Calvert
  *E-mail:* sam@vegsoc.org
Editor: Dave Bowler *E-mail:* editor@vegsoc.org
Founded: 1847
Registered educational charity.
Also publishes in association with HarperCollins,
  Sigma Press & others.
Subjects: Cookery, Education
ISBN Prefix(es): 0-900774

**Veloce Publishing Ltd+**
33 Trinity St, Dorchester, Dorset DT1 1TT
*Tel:* (01305) 260068 *Fax:* (01305) 268864
*E-mail:* info@veloce.co.uk
*Web Site:* www.veloce.co.uk; www.velocebooks.
  com
*Key Personnel*
Publisher: Rod Grainger
Dir: Judith Brooks
Founded: 1991
Also specialize in motorsports & workshop manu-
  als.
Subjects: Automotive, Biography, Mechanical En-
  gineering, Outdoor Recreation, Transportation
ISBN Prefix(es): 1-874105; 1-901295; 1-903706;
  1-904788
Number of titles published annually: 25 Print
Total Titles: 200 Print
Distributed by Motorbooks International Inc
  (USA)
Distributor for Porter Publishing (UK)

**Velvet**, *imprint of* Creation Books

**Ventura**, *imprint of* Penguin Books Ltd

**Venture Press Ltd**
16 Kent St, Birmingham B5 6RD
*Tel:* (0121) 622 3911 *Fax:* (0121) 622 4860
*E-mail:* info@basw.co.uk
*Key Personnel*
Assistant Dir: Sally Arkley
ISBN Prefix(es): 0-900102; 0-9501603; 1-86178;
  1-873878

**Verbatim+**
PO Box 156, Chearsley, Aylesbury, Bucks HP18
  0DQ
*Tel:* (01844) 208474
*Web Site:* www.verbatimbooks.com
*Key Personnel*
Man Dir, Editorial: Laurence Urdang
Sales, Rights & Permissions: Hazel Hall
Founded: 1974
Subjects: Language Arts, Linguistics
ISBN Prefix(es): 0-930454
Total Titles: 17 Print
*Parent Company:* Laurence Urdang Inc
*U.S. Office(s):* Verbatim Books, 4 Laurel Heights,
  Old Lyme, CT 06371-1462, United States,
  Contact: Laurence Urdang *Tel:* 860-434-2104
  *E-mail:* luverbatim@aol.com

**Veritas Foundation Publication Centre+**
63 Jeddo Rd, London W12 9EE
*Tel:* (020) 8749 4957; (020) 8749 4965
  *Fax:* (020) 8749 4965
*E-mail:* veritas@polish.co.uk

*Key Personnel*
Man Dir & Rights: Thomas Wachowiak
  *E-mail:* thomas@veritas.knsc.co.uk
Sales: A Zabihe
Founded: 1947
Also publishes weekly newspaper.
Subjects: Education, Religion - Other
ISBN Prefix(es): 0-948202; 0-901215


**Vermilion**, *imprint of* Random House UK Ltd


**Verso+**
6 Meard St, London W1F 0EG
*Tel:* (020) 7437 3546; (020) 7434 1704; (020)
  7439 8194 *Fax:* (020) 7734 0059
*E-mail:* enquiries@verso.co.uk
*Web Site:* www.versobooks.com
*Key Personnel*
Executive Chairman: George Galfavi
International Rights: Gil McNeil
Founded: 1971
Subjects: Economics, Ethnicity, Film, Video,
  Government, Political Science, History, Lit-
  erature, Literary Criticism, Essays, Nonfiction
  (General), Philosophy, Psychology, Psychiatry,
  Social Sciences, Sociology, Women's Studies
ISBN Prefix(es): 0-86091; 0-85984; 0-902308
Number of titles published annually: 70 Print
*Parent Company:* New Left Review
Imprints: Critical Studies in Latin American Cul-
  ture; Haymarket; Phronesis
*U.S. Office(s):* 180 Varick St, 10th floor,
  New York, NY 10014-4606, United States
  *Tel:* 212-807-9680 *Fax:* 212-807-9152
  *E-mail:* versoinc@aol.com
Distributed by Penguin Books (Canada); W
  W Norton/National Book Company (United
  States)
Foreign Rep(s): APD Singapore Ptd Ltd (Brunei,
  Malaysia, Singapore, Thailand); IMA (South
  America); Macmillan Publishers Australia
  (Australia, New Zealand); Maya Publishers
  Pvt Ltd (India); Missing Link (Germany); B
  K Norton Ltd (China, Hong Kong, Korea, Tai-
  wan); Stephans Philip Publishers Ltd (South
  Africa, Zimbabwe); Publishers European Sales
  Agency (Europe); Segment Book Distributors
  (India); United Publishers Services (Japan);
  James & Lorin Watt (Cyprus, Malta, Middle
  East, Turkey); John Wilde Partnership (Austria,
  Germany, Switzerland)
*Orders to:* Marston Book Services, Unit 160
  Milton Park, Abingdon, Oxford OX14 4SD
  *Tel:* 01235 465500


**Verulam Publishing Ltd**
152A Park Street Lane, Park St, Saint Albans,
  Herts AL2 2AU
*Tel:* (01727) 872770 *Fax:* (01727) 873866
*E-mail:* verulampub@yahoo.co.uk; sales@
  verulampub.demon.co.uk
*Key Personnel*
Man Dir: David Collins *E-mail:* david.collins@
  verulampub.demon.co.uk
Dir: Penny Collins *E-mail:* penny.collins@
  verulampub.demon.co.uk
Founded: 1991
Subjects: Advertising, Animals, Pets, Business,
  Cookery, Humor, Marketing, Photography,
  Sports, Athletics
ISBN Prefix(es): 1-873668; 1-85882; 1-903994;
  1-86019; 1-84067; 1-84186
Imprints: Caxton Publishing Group Ltd; Take
  That Ltd (US)
Distributor for Caxton Publishing Group World
  (US); Cumberland Houe Publishers Europe
  (US); Eric Dobby Publishing Ltd (USA); Rut-
  ledge Hill Press (Europe); Take That Ltd (US);
  Top Floor Publishing Europe (US)
*Distribution Center:* Gazelle Book Services
  Ltd, White Cross Mills, Hightown, South

Rd, Lancaster LA1 4XS *Tel:* (01524)
68765 *Fax:* (01524) 63232 *E-mail:* sales@
gazellebooks.co.uk


**Vif**, *imprint of* Voltaire Foundation Ltd


**Viking**, *imprint of* Penguin Books Ltd


**Viking**, *imprint of* The Penguin Group UK


**Viking+**
27 Wrights Lane, London W8 5TZ
*Tel:* (020) 7416 3000 *Fax:* (020) 7416 3274
*Telex:* 917181
*Key Personnel*
Chief Executive: Peter Mayer
Editorial Dir: Claire Alexander
Production: Joy Harrison
Marketing Dir: Clare Harrington
Rights & Permissions: Ruth Salazar
Founded: 1969
Formerly Allen Lane.
Subjects: Art, Biography, Cookery, Fiction, His-
  tory, Nonfiction (General), Social Sciences,
  Sociology, Travel
ISBN Prefix(es): 0-670
*Parent Company:* Penguin Books Ltd
Imprints: Allen Lane; The Penguin Press
*U.S. Office(s):* 375 Hudson St, New York, NY
  10014, United States *Tel:* 212-366-2000
*Orders to:* Penguin Books, Bath Rd, Har-
  mondsworth, Middlesex UB7 0DA *Tel:* (01)
  7591984


**Viking Children's Books+**
27 Wright's Lane, London W8 5TZ
*Tel:* (020) 7416 3000 *Fax:* (020) 7416 3086
*Telex:* 917181
*Key Personnel*
Chief Executive: Peter Mayer
Editorial Dir: Phillipa Milnes-Smith
Publishing Dir: Elizabeth Attenborough
Rights & Permissions: Nikki Griffiths
Founded: 1969
ISBN Prefix(es): 0-670
*Parent Company:* Penguin Books Ltd
*U.S. Office(s):* Viking Children's Books, 375
  Hudson St, New York, NY 10014, United
  States *Tel:* 212-366-2000
*Orders to:* Penguin Books, Bath Rd, Har-
  mondsworth, Middlesex UB7 0DA *Tel:* (01)
  7591984


**Vintage**, *imprint of* Random House UK Ltd


**Virago**, *imprint of* Time Warner Book Group UK


**Virago Press+**
Brettenham House, Lancaster Pl, London WC2E
  7EN
*Tel:* (020) 7911 8000 *Fax:* (020) 7911 8100
*E-mail:* virago.press@timewarnerbooks.co.uk
*Web Site:* www.virago.co.uk
*Telex:* 885233
*Key Personnel*
Publisher: Ms Lennie Goodings
Senior Editor: Jill Foulston
Founded: 1973
Subjects: Biography, Education, Fiction, Govern-
  ment, Political Science, Health, Nutrition, His-
  tory, Philosophy, Public Administration, Social
  Sciences, Sociology, Travel, Women's Studies
ISBN Prefix(es): 0-86068; 1-86049; 1-85381
*Parent Company:* Little Brown & Co


**Virgin Publishing Ltd+**
Thames Wharf Studios, Rainville Rd, London W6
  9HA
*Tel:* (020) 7386 3300 *Fax:* (020) 7386 3360

*E-mail:* info@virgin-books.co.uk; info@virgin-
  pub.co.uk
*Web Site:* www.virginbooks.com
*Key Personnel*
Chairman: Robert Devereux
Man Dir: Rob Shreeve
Publicity Manager: Susan Atkinson
Marketing Manager: Amy Nelson-Bennett
Sales Dir: Ray Mudie
Export Sales: Natalie Rogers
International Sales & Rights Dir: K T Forster
Editorial Dir: Humphrey Price
Publishing Dir, Travel: Louise Cavanagh
Rights Manager: Helen Monroe
  *E-mail:* hmonroe@virgin-pub.co.uk
Founded: 1990
Specialize in music.
Subjects: Astrology, Occult, Biography, Child
  Care & Development, Criminology, Erotica,
  Film, Video, History, Humor, Music, Dance,
  Nonfiction (General), Radio, TV, Science Fic-
  tion, Fantasy, Sports, Athletics, Travel
ISBN Prefix(es): 0-352; 0-426; 1-85227; 0-7535;
  0-85031; 0-86369
*Parent Company:* Virgin Media Group, 20 Soho
  Square, London W1A 1BS
Imprints: Black Lace; Idol; Nexus; Sapphire; True
  Crime
Distributor for Berlitz Publishing (UK & export)
Foreign Rep(s): Ashton International Marketing
  Services (Far East, India, Middle East); IMA
  (Africa, Eastern Europe); MRA (Brazil, Central
  America, South America, West Indies); Onslow
  Books (Europe)
Foreign Rights: ACER (Spain); Agence Literaire
  Lora Fountain (France); Akcali Copyright
  (Turkey); Bengt Nordin Agency (Scandinavia);
  Big Apple Tuttle Mori Agency (China, Taiwan,
  Thailand); BPA of Israel (Israel); Dilia Literary
  Agency (Czech Republic); Helfa A W Literary
  Agency (Poland); Interrights Literary & Trans-
  lation (Bulgaria); KCC (Korea); Lex Copyright
  (Hungary); Lijnkamp Literary Agency (Nether-
  lands); Living Agency (Italy); Motovun Co
  Ltd (Japan); Read 'n' Right Agency (Greece);
  Thomas Schluck GmbH (Germany); Synopsis
  Literary Agency (Russia); Eric Yang Agency
  (Korea)


**The Vital Spark**, *imprint of* Neil Wilson
Publishing Ltd


**VNU Business Publications**
VNU House, 32-34 Broadwick St, London W1A
  2HG
*Tel:* (020) 7316 9000 *Fax:* (020) 7316 9440
*Web Site:* www.vnu.co.uk
*Key Personnel*
Publishing Dir: Guy Phillips
Associate Publisher: Emma Devine
Man Dir: Brin Bucknor
Production Editor: Francis Abberley
Founded: 1980
Subjects: Accounting, Business, Communications,
  Computer Science, Economics, Finance, Man-
  agement, Technology
ISBN Prefix(es): 0-86271
*Parent Company:* VNU Business Publications,
  Netherlands
Subsidiaries: Learned Information (Europe)
*Orders to:* Booksales Dept, VNU House, 32-34
  Broadwick St, London W1A 2HG


**Voltaire Foundation**, *imprint of* Voltaire
Foundation Ltd


**Voltaire Foundation Ltd+**
University of Oxford, 99 Banbury Rd, Oxford
  OX2 6JX
*Tel:* (01865) 284600 *Fax:* (01865) 284610
*E-mail:* email@voltaire.ox.ac.uk
*Web Site:* www.voltaire.ox.ac.uk

*Key Personnel*
Dir: Dr Nicholas Cronk *Tel:* (01865) 284602
  *E-mail:* nicholas.cronk@voltaire.ox.ac.uk
Publisher: Clare Fletcher *Tel:* (01865) 284601
  *E-mail:* clare.fletcher@voltaire.ox.ac.uk
Deputy Publisher: Janet Godden *Tel:* (01865)
  284606 *E-mail:* janet.godden@voltaire-
  foundation.oxford.ac.uk
Electronic Publishing Manager: Dr Robert Mc-
  Namee *Tel:* (01865) 284603 *E-mail:* robert.
  mcnamee@voltaire.ox.ac.uk
Founded: 1971
Publishing & seminars on the European En-
  lightenment. Specialize in works by & about
  Voltaire & other enlightenment writers.
Subjects: History, Language Arts, Linguistics, Lit-
  erature, Literary Criticism, Essays, Philosophy
ISBN Prefix(es): 0-7294; 0-903588; 0-9502162
Number of titles published annually: 20 Print
Total Titles: 400 Print; 1 CD-ROM; 100 Online
*Parent Company:* University of Oxford
Imprints: Universitas; Vif; Voltaire Foundation
Foreign Rep(s): Aux Amateurs de Livres Interna-
  tional (France)
*Warehouse:* Marston Book Services, 160 Mil-
  ton Park, PO Box 269, Abingdon, Oxon OX14
  4YN *Tel:* (01235) 465500 *Fax:* (01235) 465556
  *E-mail:* direct.orders@marston.co.uk *Web
  Site:* www.marston.co.uk
*Orders to:* Marston Book Services, 160 Milton
  Park, PO Box 269, Abingdon, Oxon OX14
  4YN *Tel:* (01235) 465500 *Fax:* (01235) 465556
  *E-mail:* direct.orders@marston.co.uk
*Returns:* Marston Book Services, 160 Milton
  Park, PO Box 269, Abingdon, Oxon OX14
  4YN

**Wag Books**, *imprint of* Compendium Publishing

**Waite Group Press**, *imprint of* Pearson
  Education Europe, Mideast & Africa

**John Waite Ltd+**
Tower House, Ivychurch, Romney Marsh TN29
  0AX
*Tel:* (1797) 344 283 *Fax:* (01892) 784156
*Key Personnel*
Man Dir: John A Waite
Founded: 1983
Publisher of spoken work CDs & nonfiction.
Subjects: Nonfiction (General)
ISBN Prefix(es): 0-946714
Number of titles published annually: 2 Print

**Walker Books Ltd+**
Brunel Rd, Houndmills, Basingstoke RG21 6XS
*Tel:* (01256) 329242 *Fax:* (01256) 812558;
  (01256) 812521
*E-mail:* enquiry@walker.co.uk
*Web Site:* www.walkerbooks.co.uk
*Key Personnel*
Chairman & Editorial: David Lloyd
Man Dir: David Heatherwick
Merchandising: Judy Burdsall
Publicity Manager: Charlie Price
Foreign Rights: Caroline Muir
Art Dir: Amelia Edwards
Sales, UK: Ian Spanton
Sales & Marketing Dir: Henryk Wesolowski
Founded: 1978
Subjects: Fiction, Nonfiction (General)
ISBN Prefix(es): 1-56402; 0-7636; 0-7445
*U.S. Office(s):* Candlewick Press, 2067 Mas-
  sachusetts Ave, Cambridge, MA 02140, United
  States *Tel:* 617- 661-3330 *Fax:* 617-661-
  0565 *E-mail:* licensing@candlewick.com *Web
  Site:* www.candlewick.com
*Orders to:* Faber Book Services, Burnt Mill, Eliz-
  abeth Way, Harlow, Essex CM20 2HX

**Editions Aubrey Walter**, *imprint of* GMP
  Publishers Ltd

**The Warburg Institute+**
University of London, Woburn Sq, London
  WC1H 0AB
*Tel:* (020) 7862 8949 *Fax:* (020) 7862 8955
*E-mail:* warburg@sas.ac.uk
*Web Site:* www.sas.ac.uk/warburg/
*Key Personnel*
Secretary: Anita Pollard
Founded: 1921
The Institute is a non-commercial organization.
Subjects: Art, History, Philosophy, Science (Gen-
  eral)
ISBN Prefix(es): 0-85481
Number of titles published annually: 2 Print
Total Titles: 37 Print
*Parent Company:* University of London
Distributed by Nino Aragno Editore

**Ward Lock Educational Co Ltd+**
Bic Ling Kee House, One Christopher Rd, East
  Grinstead, West Sussex RH19 3BT
*Tel:* (01342) 318980 *Fax:* (01342) 410980
*E-mail:* wle@lingkee.com
*Web Site:* www.wardlockeducational.com
*Key Personnel*
Chairman: Bak Ling Au
General Manager: Penny Kitchenham
  *E-mail:* psk@lingkee.com
Founded: 1952
Subjects: Computer Science, Geography, Geology,
  History, Mathematics, Music, Dance, Poetry,
  Religion - Other, Science (General)
ISBN Prefix(es): 0-7062
*Parent Company:* Ling Kee Ltd
*Associate Companies:* B L A Publishing Ltd

**Ward Lock Ltd+**
Wellington House, 125 Strand, London WC2R
  OBB
*Tel:* (020) 7420 5555 *Fax:* (020) 7240 7261
*Telex:* 9413701
*Key Personnel*
Chairman & Chief Executive: Philip Sturrock
Publishing Dir: Alison Goff
Founded: 1854
*Overseas Representation:* Australia: New Hol-
  land Publishers Pty Ltd, NSW Australia 2086;
  Canada: Cavendish Books Inc, North Vancou-
  ver, Canada; Caribbean: HRA, London, UK;
  Central Europe: European Marketing Ser-
  vices, London, UK; Southern Europe: Penny
  Padovani, London, UK; Hong Kong, China,
  Korea, Taiwan: APS Ltd, Hong Kong; Hun-
  gary, Czech Republic, Slovakia, Croatia: CLB
  Marketing Services, Kecskemet, Hungary; In-
  dia: Maya Publishers PVT Ltd, New Dehli,
  India; Japan: Ashton International Marketing
  Services, UK; Malaysia: APD Kuala Lumpur,
  Selangor Darul Ehsan, Malaysia; Middle East:
  Ashton International Marketing Services, UK;
  Netherlands: Netherlands: Nilsson & Lamm,
  Netherlands; New Zealand: David Bateman,
  Auckland, New Zealand; Pakistan: Mackwin
  & Co, Karachi, Pakistan; Poland, Russia, Ro-
  mania, Baltic States, Former USSR, Bulgaria:
  Bianca Katris, IMA, Greece; Singapore, In-
  donesia, Thailand: APD Singapore Ltd, Singa-
  pore; Scandinavia: PKB, Glostrup, Denmark;
  South America: HRA, London, UK; South
  Africa: Struik Book Distributors, Cape Town,
  South Africa; USA: Sterling Publishing Co Inc,
  New York, USA.
Subjects: Cookery, Gardening, Plants, Health,
  Nutrition, House & Home, How-to, Nonfic-
  tion (General), Outdoor Recreation, Self-Help,
  Sports, Athletics
ISBN Prefix(es): 0-7063
*Parent Company:* Continuum International Pub-
  lishing Group Ltd

**Warm Island Walking Guides**, *imprint of*
  Discovery Walking Guides Ltd

**Frederick Warne**, *imprint of* Penguin Books Ltd

**Frederick Warne Publishers Ltd+**
80 Strand, London WC2R 0RL
*Tel:* (020) 7010 3000 *Fax:* (020) 7010 6706
*Key Personnel*
Chief Executive: Anthony Forbes-Watson
Marketing: Gill Thomas
Production: Alan Lee
Man Dir: Sally Floyer
Founded: 1865
Specializes in classic characters & licensed mer-
  chandise programs.
ISBN Prefix(es): 0-7232
*Parent Company:* Penguin Books Ltd
*U.S. Office(s):* Penguin USA, 375 Hudson St,
  New York, NY 10014, United States *Tel:* 212-
  366-2000
*Orders to:* Penguin Books Ltd, Bath Rd, Har-
  mondsworth, West Drayton, Middlesex UB7
  0DA *Tel:* (02) 208 757 4000

**Waterlow**, *imprint of* Wilmington Business
  Information Ltd

**A P Watt Ltd**
20 John St, London WC1N 2DR
*Tel:* (020) 7405 6774 *Fax:* (020) 7831 2154
*E-mail:* apw@apwatt.co.uk
*Web Site:* www.apwatt.co.uk
*Key Personnel*
Man Dir: Derek Johns; Caradoc King
Dir: Sheila Crowley; Natasha Fairweather; Geor-
  gia Garrett
Foreign Rights Dir: Linda Shaughnessy
Media: Nick Harris
Founded: 1875

**Franklin Watts**, see The Watts Publishing Group
  Ltd

**The Watts Publishing Group Ltd+**
96 Leonard St, London EC2A 4XD
*Tel:* (020) 7739 2929 *Fax:* (020) 7739 2181
*E-mail:* gm@wattspub.co.uk
*Web Site:* www.wattspub.co.uk
*Key Personnel*
Group Man Dir: Marlene Johnson
Deputy Publishing Dir, Orchard Books: Rosemary
  Davies
Publishing Dir, Franklin Watts: Philippa Stewart
Publishing Dir, Orchard Books: Francesca Dow
Trade Sales Dir, Watts Publishing Group: George
  Spicer
Promotions & Marketing Associate Dir: Linda
  Banner
Royalties & Contracts Manager: Marian Head
Rights Dir: Claire Hurst
Founded: 1969
The Watts Group is comprised of Franklin Watts
  & Orchard Books.
Subjects: Fiction, Nonfiction (General)
ISBN Prefix(es): 0-7496; 1-85213; 1-86039; 0-
  85166; 1-84121; 0-86313
*Parent Company:* Hachette Livre
Subsidiaries: Grolier Australia Pty
*U.S. Office(s):* 387 Park Ave S, New York, NY
  10016, United States
*Orders to:* Littlehampton Book Services, Wor-
  thing, West Sussex, Colchester, Essex C05 0SR

**Waverley Books**, *imprint of* Geddes & Grosset

**Weatherbys Allen Ltd+**
Sanders Rd, Wellingborough, Northants NN8
  4BX
*Tel:* (01933) 440077 (ext 351) *Fax:* (01933)
  270300

*E-mail:* turfnews@weatherbys-group.com
*Web Site:* www.weatherbys-allen.com
*Key Personnel*
Chief Executive: Caroline Burt
Founded: 1926
Subjects: Animals, Pets, Sports, Athletics
ISBN Prefix(es): 0-85131
*Associate Companies:* Mannin Industries Ltd, Isle
of Man
Subsidiaries: The Caduceus Press
Distributor for The Pony Club (UK)
*Bookshop(s):* 4 Lower Grosvenor Place, London
*Warehouse:* The Trade Counter Ltd, 16 Airfield
Norwick Rd, Mendlesham, Suffolk PI4 5NA

**Webb & Bower (Publishers) Ltd+**
9 Duke St, Dartmouth TQ6 9PY
*Tel:* (01803) 835525 *Fax:* (01803) 835552
*Key Personnel*
Man Dir: Richard Webb
Founded: 1975
Subjects: Nonfiction (General)
ISBN Prefix(es): 0-86350; 0-906671
*Parent Company:* R W Ltd
*Associate Companies:* Country Diary of an Ed-
wardian Lady Ltd

**Adrian Webster Ltd**, see Websters International
Publishers Ltd

**Websters International Publishers Ltd+**
Axe & Bottle Court, 70 Newcomen St, London
SE1 1YT
*Tel:* (020) 7940 4700 *Fax:* (020) 7940 4701
*E-mail:* info@websters.co.uk
*Web Site:* www.websters.co.uk; www.ozclarke.
com
*Key Personnel*
Chairman & Publisher: Adrian Webster
*E-mail:* adrianqwe@msmail.websters.eurkom.ie
Man Dir: Jean-Luc Barbanneau
Financial Dir: Alan Fennell
Production Manager: Sara Granger
*E-mail:* saragr@websters.co.uk
Editor-in-Chief: Susannah Webster
Founded: 1983
Specialize in wine information in all formats.
Subjects: Cookery, Health, Nutrition, Travel,
Wine & Spirits
ISBN Prefix(es): 1-870604; 1-85320
Number of titles published annually: 6 Print; 1
CD-ROM
Total Titles: 20 Print
*Associate Companies:* Adrian Webster Ltd; Web-
sters Multimedia Ltd
Distributed by Little Brown & Co (UK) Ltd
Foreign Rights: Elizabeth Brayne Foreign Rights
Agency (Worldwide)

**Websters Multimedia Ltd**, see Websters
International Publishers Ltd

**A Weekes**, *imprint of* Stainer & Bell Ltd

**Welsh Academic Press+**
PO Box 733, Cardiff, Wales CF14 2YX
*Tel:* (029) 2056 0343 *Fax:* (029) 2056 1631
*E-mail:* post@ashleydrake.com
*Web Site:* www.welsh-academic-press.co.uk
*Key Personnel*
Man Dir: Ashley Drake
Dir: Norman Drake; Siwan Drake
Founded: 1994
Specialize in the publishing of scholarly & aca-
demic books that are also accessible to the gen-
eral reader, "International in Outlook...Welsh in
Identity".
Membership(s): Publishers' Association.
Subjects: Biography, Government, Political Sci-
ence, History, Literature, Literary Criticism,
Essays, Celtic Studies

ISBN Prefix(es): 1-86057
Number of titles published annually: 15 Print
Total Titles: 40 Print
*Parent Company:* Ashley Drake Publishing Ltd
Imprints: Morgan Publishing; St David's Press
Foreign Rep(s): Marika Janouskova (Eastern Eu-
rope); Cranbury International (Caribbean, Cen-
tral America, South America); Cristina de Lara
Ruiz (Spain); Ted Dougherty (Austria, Benelux,
Germany, Switzerland); Fathima News Enter-
prise (Singapore); Charles Gibbes (Greece);
Globe Enterprises (Malaysia); Golden Book
Services (Philippines); International Specialized Book Services (US); Maya Publishers Pvt
Ltd (India); Tony Moggach Associates (Sub-
Saharan Africa); Mullet & Fitzpatrick (Ireland);
Onslow Books (Scandinavia); Victor Osorio
(Portugal); David Pickering (Italy); Anthony
Rudkin Associates (Middle East); St. Clair
Press (Australia); James Tovey (France); Uni-
versity of Toronto Press (Canada)
*Warehouse:* International Specialized Book Ser-
vices, Hassalo St, Portland, OR, United States
*Orders to:* International Specialized Book Ser-
vices, Hassalo St, Portland, OR, United States
Orca Book Services Ltd, 3 Fleets Lane, Poole,
Dorset BH15 3AJ *Tel:* (01202) 665432
*Fax:* (01202) 666219 *E-mail:* orders@
orcabookservices.co.uk (Order processing dept)

**Welsh Womens Press**, see Honno Welsh
Women's Press

**West Highland Series**, *imprint of* House of
Lochar

**Westview Press**
PO Box 317, Oxford OX2 9RU
*Tel:* (01865) 865466 *Fax:* (01865) 862763
*E-mail:* perseus@oppuk.co.uk
*Web Site:* www.westviewpress.com
*Telex:* 2 39479 WVP UR
*Key Personnel*
Vice President, Sales & Marketing - Perseus
Books Group: Matthew Goldberg *Tel:* 212-207-
7604 *E-mail:* matty.goldberg@perseusbooks.
com
Manager: Gary Hall; Sue Miller
Founded: 1990
Subjects: Agriculture, Art, Economics, Environ-
mental Studies, Government, Political Science,
History, Social Sciences, Sociology
ISBN Prefix(es): 0-89158; 0-86531; 0-8133
*Parent Company:* Westview Press, 5500 Central
Ave, Boulder, CO 80301, United States, Con-
tact: Cathleen Tetro
Distributed by HarperCollins Publishers Order
Department (New York)
*Orders to:* Perseus Books Group, PO Box
317, Oxford OX2 9RU *Tel:* (01865) 865466
*Fax:* (01865) 862763 *E-mail:* perseus@oppuk.
co.uk
Perseus Books Group Customer Service, 5500
Central Ave, Boulder, CO 80301, United States
*Fax:* 303-449-3356 *E-mail:* westview.orders@
perseusbooks.com

**Wharncliffe Books**, *imprint of* Pen & Sword
Books Ltd

**Wharncliffe Publishing Ltd+**
Imprint of Pen & Sword Books Ltd
47 Church St, Barnsley, S Yorks S70 2AS
*Tel:* (01226) 734222 *Fax:* (01226) 734438
*E-mail:* sales@pen-and-sword.co.uk
*Key Personnel*
Man Dir: Mr C Hewitt *Tel:* (01226) 734555
Founded: 1988
Membership(s): IPG.
Subjects: History, Outdoor Recreation, Regional
Interests, Local History, Countryside Books,
Military History

*Parent Company:* Barnsley Chronicle Holdings
Ltd
Distributed by Casemate
Distributor for National Archives (UK)

**Which? Books**, *imprint of* Which? Ltd

**Which? Ltd+**
2 Marylebone Rd, London NW1 4DF
*Tel:* (020) 7770 7000 *Fax:* (020) 7770 7485;
(020) 7770 7600
*E-mail:* which@which.net
*Web Site:* www.which.net
*Key Personnel*
Head of Publishing: Gill Rowley *Tel:* (020) 7830
7585 *E-mail:* rowleyg@which.co.uk
Founded: 1957
Membership(s): Publishers' Association.
Subjects: Business, Computer Science, Finance,
Gardening, Plants, Health, Nutrition, Law,
Self-Help, Travel, Consumer Advice (Law, Fi-
nance, Practical), Accommodation & Restau-
rant Guides, Do-It-Yourself
ISBN Prefix(es): 0-85202
Total Titles: 80 Print
*Parent Company:* Consumers' Association
Imprints: Which? Books
*Showroom(s):* Castlemead, Gascoyne Way, Hert-
ford, Herts SG14 1LH
*Warehouse:* Castlemead, Gascoyne Way, Hertford,
Herts SG14 1LH
*Distribution Center:* Penguin Books Ltd, 27
Wrights Lane, London W8 5TZ
*Orders to:* Castlemead, Gascoyne Way, Hertford,
Herts SG14 1LH
Penguin Books Ltd, 27 Wrights Lane, London
W8 5TZ

**White Cockade Publishing**
71 Lonsdale Rd, Oxford OX2 7ES
*Tel:* (01865) 510411
*E-mail:* mail@whitecockade.co.uk
*Web Site:* www.whitecockade.co.uk
*Key Personnel*
Dir: Ms Perilla Kinchin
Founded: 1988
Subjects: Antiques, Architecture & Interior De-
sign, Crafts, Games, Hobbies, History, Re-
gional Interests, Social Sciences, Sociology,
Women's Studies, Design History
ISBN Prefix(es): 0-9513124; 1-873487
Number of titles published annually: 1 Print
Total Titles: 12 Print

**White Eagle Publishing Trust+**
New Lands, Brewells Lane, Liss, Hants GU33
7HY
*Tel:* (01730) 893300 *Fax:* (01730) 892235
*E-mail:* enquiries@whiteagle.org
*Web Site:* www.whiteaglelodge.org
*Key Personnel*
Man Dir: Ylana Hayward
Foreign Rights: Geoffrey Dent *E-mail:* geoffrey@
whiteagle.org
Founded: 1953
Subjects: Astrology, Occult, Religion - Other
ISBN Prefix(es): 0-85487
Total Titles: 46 Print; 10 Audio
*Parent Company:* White Eagle Lodge
Distributed by De Vorss & Co Inc (North Amer-
ica)

**White Mouse Editions**, *imprint of* New
Cavendish Books

**White Tree Books**, *imprint of* Redcliffe Press Ltd

**Whiting & Birch Ltd+**
Forest Hill, 90 Dartmouth Rd, London SE23 3HZ
*Tel:* (020) 8244 2421 *Fax:* (020) 8244 2448
*E-mail:* savpub@dircon.co.uk

*Web Site:* www.whitingbirch.com
*Key Personnel*
Man Dir: David Whiting
Founded: 1987
Subjects: Child Care & Development, Criminology, Education, Ethnicity, Language Arts, Linguistics, Literature, Literary Criticism, Essays, Social Sciences, Sociology
ISBN Prefix(es): 1-871177; 1-86177
Number of titles published annually: 8 Print
Total Titles: 50 Print
Foreign Rep(s): Independent Publishers Group (IPG) (Worldwide exc Europe)
Foreign Rights: Independent Publishers Group (IPG) (Worldwide exc Europe)
*Distribution Center:* Independent Publishers Group (IPG), 814 N Franklin St, Chicago, IL 60610, United States *Tel:* 312-337-0747 *Fax:* 312-337-5785 *E-mail:* frontdesk@ipgbook.com *Web Site:* www.ipgbook.com (North America)

**Whittet Books Ltd+**
Hill Farm, Stonham Rd, Cotton, Stowmarket, Suffolk 1P14 4RQ
*Tel:* (01449) 781877 *Fax:* (01449) 781898
*Web Site:* www.whittetbooks.com
*Key Personnel*
Chairman: A Whittet
Man Dir: Annabel Whittet *E-mail:* annabel@whittet.dircon.co.uk
Founded: 1976
Subjects: Animals, Pets, Natural History, Horses
ISBN Prefix(es): 0-905483; 1-873580
*Parent Company:* A Whittet & Co Ltd
Distributed by Diamond Farm Book Publishers (Canada & USA)
*Warehouse:* Biblios, Star Rd, Partridge Green, Horsham, Horsham, West Sussex RH13 8LD

**Whittles Publishing+**
Roseleigh House, Harbour Rd, Latheronwheel, Caithness KW5 6DW
*Tel:* (01593) 741240 *Fax:* (01593) 741360
*E-mail:* info@whittlespublishing.com
*Web Site:* www.whittlespublishing.com
*Key Personnel*
Publisher & Dir: Dr Keith Whittles
Promotions Coordinator: Sue Steven
Founded: 1986
Specialize in engineering, geomatics, surveying, applied science, nature writing & maritime. Also selected fiction noted in the land.
Membership(s): Scottish Publishers Association.
Subjects: Civil Engineering, Maritime, Natural History, Regional Interests, Geomatics
ISBN Prefix(es): 1-870325; 1-904445
Number of titles published annually: 20 Print
Total Titles: 60 Print
Foreign Rep(s): Academic Books (Austria, Germany, Switzerland); Avicenna Partnership (Greece, Middle East, Turkey, Iran); Roy de Boo (Belgium, Netherlands, Luxembourg); DA Information Services Pty Ltd (Australia, New Zealand, Papua New Guinea); Insat Books & Periodicals (India); Marcello sas (France, Italy, Portugal, Spain); STM Publishers Services Pte Ltd (Southeast Asia, Northeast Asia); David Towle International (Baltic States, Scandinavia); John W Wilson (North America)
*Orders to:* BookSource, 32 Finlas St, Cowlairs Industrial Estate, Glasgow G22 5DU
*Tel:* (0141) 558 1355 *Fax:* (0141) 557 0189
*E-mail:* customerservices@booksource.net

**Whurr Publishers Ltd+**
19b Compton Terrace, London N1 2UN
*Tel:* (020) 7359 5979 *Fax:* (020) 7226 5290
*E-mail:* info@whurr.co.uk
*Web Site:* www.whurr.co.uk
*Key Personnel*
Man Dir & Publisher: Colin Whurr

Company Secretary: Lynn Brett
Founded: 1987
Subjects: Business, Education, Medicine, Nursing, Dentistry, Psychology, Psychiatry
Total Titles: 400 Print
Subsidiaries: Cole & Whurr Ltd
Distributed by Elsevier Australia (Australia & New Zealand); Taylor & Francis (exclusive for North America)
*Orders to:* Extenza-Turpin Distribution Services Ltd, Stratton Business Park, Pegasus Drive, Biggleswade, Beds SG18 8QB *Tel:* (01767) 604965 *Fax:* (01767) 601640 *E-mail:* books@extenza-turpin.com *Web Site:* www.extenza-turpin.com

**WI Enterprises Ltd**
104 New Kings Rd, London SW6 4LY
*Tel:* (020) 7371 9300 *Fax:* (020) 7471 9300
*E-mail:* d.page@nfwi.org.uk
*Web Site:* www.womens-institute.co.uk/shop/policies/about.shtml
*Key Personnel*
Chairman: Barbara Gill
Group Manager: Mark Linacre
Sales & Marketing Manager: Dahla Page *E-mail:* d.page@nfwi.org.ok
Company Secretary: David Wood
Founded: 1977
Subjects: Cookery, Crafts, Games, Hobbies, Economics, Gardening, Plants, Women's Studies
ISBN Prefix(es): 0-947990; 0-900556
*Parent Company:* National Federation of Women's Institutes
*Warehouse:* WI Enterprises Ltd, Penzance TR93 0WW *Tel:* (01736) 333 333

**Wild Goose Publications+**
Savoy House, 4th floor, 140 Sauchiehall St, Glasgow G2 3DH
*Tel:* (0141) 332 6292 *Fax:* (0141) 332 1090
*E-mail:* admin@ionabooks.com
*Web Site:* www.ionabooks.com
*Key Personnel*
Publishing Manager: Sandra Kramer *E-mail:* sandra@ionabooks.com
Production Manager: Jane Riley *E-mail:* jane@ionabooks.com
Assistant Publishing Manager: Alex O'Neill *E-mail:* alex@ionabooks.com
Editorial Assistant: Neil Paynter
Administrator: Tri Boi Ta
Founded: 1985
Produces books on social justice, political & peace issues, holistic spirituality, healing & innovative approaches to worship. Part of the IONA community established in the Celtic Christian tradition of Saint Columba.
Membership(s): IPG.
Subjects: Biblical Studies, Music, Dance, Religion - Catholic, Religion - Protestant, Theology
ISBN Prefix(es): 0-947988; 1-901557
Number of titles published annually: 10 Print; 2 Audio
Total Titles: 125 Print; 25 Audio
*Parent Company:* The Iona Community
Distributed by GIA Publications (North America); Novalis Publishing (Canada); Pleroma Christian Supplies (New Zealand); Willow Connection Pty Ltd (Australia)

**Wiley Europe Ltd+**
The Atrium, Southern Gate, Chichester, West Sussex PO19 85Q
*Tel:* (01243) 779777 *Fax:* (01243) 775878
*E-mail:* customer@wiley.co.uk
*Web Site:* www.wiley.co.uk
*Key Personnel*
Man Dir: Dr John Jarvis
Publishing Dir: Dr Steven Mair
STM Book Publishing Dir & Dir of Planning: Dr Ernest Kirkwood

Publisher, Technology: Dr Ann-Marie Halligan
Dir, New Media Development: Dr Rosemary Altoft
STM Journal Publishing Dir: Dr Michael Davis
Publisher, Medicine: Dr Deborah Reece
Publisher, College Division: Dr Simon Plumtree
Publisher, Chemistry: Dr Helen McPherson
Publisher, Medicine: Dr Richard Edelstein
Publisher, Life/Science: Dr Charlotte Brabants
Commercial Dir: Dr Sarah Stevens
Publisher, Psychology: Dr Michael Coombs
Dir Sales, Marketing & Publicity: Dr Robert Long
Publicity & Exhibition Man: Dr Julia Lampam
Production Dir: Helen Balley
Finance Dir: Jim Dicks
IT & Customer Service Dir: Peter Ferris
Marketing Development Dir: Paul Holmes
Sales Dir: Philip Kisray
Publishing Technologies Dir: Cliff Morgan
Human Resource Dir: Angela Poulter
Customer Service Dir: Margaret Radbourne
Distribution Dir: Mike Ridge
Publisher, Earth/Environmental Science: Sally Wilkinson
Senior Publishing Editor, Architecture: Maggie Toy
Founded: 1960
Other Main Office: WILEY-VCH, Pappelallee 3, 69469 Weinheim, Germany. Tel: (06201) 6060; Fax: (06201) 606328
2000 titles in print.
Subjects: Accounting, Architecture & Interior Design, Biological Sciences, Business, Chemistry, Chemical Engineering, Computer Science, Cookery, Earth Sciences, Economics, Finance, Management, Marketing, Mathematics, Mechanical Engineering, Medicine, Nursing, Dentistry, Physics, Psychology, Psychiatry, Religion - Other, Technology
Total Titles: 11,000 Print; 300 E-Book
*Parent Company:* John Wiley & Sons Inc, 111 River St, Hoboken, NJ 07030, United States
*Associate Companies:* John Wiley & Sons Australia Ltd, Australia *Tel:* (07) 3859 9755 *Fax:* (07) 3859 9715; John Wiley & Sons Canada Ltd, ON, Canada *Tel:* (416) 236-4433 *Fax:* (416) 236-4447; WILEY-VCH, Germany *Tel:* (06201) 606 0 *Fax:* (06201) 606 328 *E-mail:* info@wiley-vch.de; John Wiley & Sons (Asia) Pte Ltd, Singapore *Tel:* 463-2400 *Fax:* 463-4603; Tokyo Liaison Office, Kudonshita Tokyu Shin-Sakura, Bldg 6F, 1-3-3 Kudan-Kita, Chiyoda-ku Tokyo 102-0073, Japan *Tel:* (03) 3556 9762 *Fax:* (03) 3556 9763 *E-mail:* fwga5479@mb.infoweb.or.jp
Imprints: Wiley-Interscience; Wiley Liss; John Wiley & Sons; Halsted Press; Scripta Technica; Wiley-Heyden; ValuSource; Jossey-Bass
Distributor for California, Columbia & Princeton University Press (Europe, Middle East, Africa); Indiana University Press (Continental Europe); Kegan Paul International Ltd (Europe); W W Norton & Co Ltd (Europe, Middle East, Africa, Asia, West Indies); O'Reilly UK Ltd (Europe, Middle East, Africa, Asia, West Indies); Research Studies Press Ltd (Europe, Middle East, Africa); Sybex International Corp (Continental Europe); The University of Chicago Press (Europe); Yale University Press (Europe, Middle East, Africa); Harvard University Press/MIT Press Ltd & LOEB Classical Library (Europe, Middle East, Africa)
*Orders to:* John Wiley & Sons Ltd Distribution Center, Southern Cross Trading Estate, One Oldlands Way, Bognor Regis, West Sussex PO22 9SA *Tel:* (01243) 779777 *Fax:* (01243) 820250

**Wiley-Heyden,** *imprint of* Wiley Europe Ltd

**Wiley-Interscience,** *imprint of* Wiley Europe Ltd

**Wiley Liss**, *imprint of* Wiley Europe Ltd

**Joseph Williams**, *imprint of* Stainer & Bell Ltd

**Wilmington Business Information Ltd+**
Paulton House, 8 Shepherdess Walk, London N1
7LB
*Tel:* (020) 7549 8704 *Fax:* (020) 7490 2979
*Web Site:* www.waterlow.com/signature/
*Key Personnel*
Dir: Rory A Conwell; Brian Gilbert; Michael
Harrington; Paul Holden; Peter Lunn; Ahmed
Zahedieh
Business Services Manager: E M Dutta *Tel:* (020)
7566 8277 *E-mail:* sdutta@waterlow.com
Founded: 1843
Membership(s): Directory & Database Publishers
Association.
Subjects: Business, Disability, Special Needs,
Drama, Theater, Fiction, Finance, Law, Music,
Dance
*Parent Company:* Wilmington Group PLC
*Associate Companies:* Wilmington Publishing Ltd
Imprints: Gramophone; ICP; Investment Intelli-
gence; PCR; RED; Waterlow
Subsidiaries: Retail Entertainment Data Publish-
ing Ltd; Waterlow Specialist Information Pub-
lishing Ltd
Divisions: International Company Profile; Invest-
ment Intelligence; RED; Waterlow Co Services;
Waterlow Professional Publishing; Waterlow
Signature: Waterlow Direct Mail

**Philip Wilson Publishers+**
109 The Timber Yard, Drysdale St, London N1
6ND
*Tel:* (020) 7033 9900 *Fax:* (020) 7033 9922
*E-mail:* sales@philip-wilson.co.uk
*Web Site:* www.philip-wilson.co.uk
*Key Personnel*
Man Dir: Philip Wilson *E-mail:* pwilson@
monoclick.co.uk
Sales & Publicity Manager: Juliana Powney
*E-mail:* jpowney@monoclick.co.uk
Commissioning Editor: Anne Jackson
*E-mail:* ajackson@monoclick.co.uk
Production Manager: Norman Turpin
*E-mail:* nturpin@monoclick.co.uk
Founded: 1975
Subjects: Antiques, Archaeology, Architecture &
Interior Design, Art, Fashion
ISBN Prefix(es): 0-85667
Number of titles published annually: 16 Print
Total Titles: 150 Print
Distributed by Antique Collectors Club
Foreign Rep(s): APD Singapore Pte Ltd (Brunei,
Indonesia, Malaysia, Singapore, Thailand); The
Art Book Studio (India); Asia Publishers Ser-
vices Ltd (China, Hong Kong, Japan, Korea,
Taiwan, Macao); Consul Books (Netherlands);
Csaba Lengyel de bagota (Croatia, Czech Re-
public, Hungary, Romania, Serbia and Mon-
tenegro, Slovak Republic, Slovenia, Bosnia and
Herzegovina); Exhibitions International (Bel-
gium); Interart SRL (France); Livraria Gaudi
Ltda (Brazil); Peter Hyde Associates (South
Africa); Thames & Hudson (Australia)
Foreign Rights: Michael Geoghegan (Austria,
Germany, Switzerland); Michael Morris Asso-
ciates (Middle East); Penny Padovani (Greece,
Italy, Portugal, Spain); Hanne Rotovnik (Fin-
land, Iceland, Scandinavia); David Wine (Israel)

**Wimbledon Publishing Company Ltd+**
75-76 Blackfriars Rd, London SE1 8HA
*Tel:* (020) 7401 4200 *Fax:* (020) 7928 4201
*E-mail:* enquiries@wpcpress.com
*Web Site:* www.wpcpress.com
*Key Personnel*
Man Dir: Mr K Sood
Sales & Marketing: Mr N McPherson

Editor, Nightingale Press: Mr L Chaput
Founded: 1993
Specialize in political science & humanities plus
gift & humor books for the discerning wit.
Subjects: Biography, Biological Sciences, Busi-
ness, Economics, Government, Political Sci-
ence, Health, Nutrition, History, Humor, Lan-
guage Arts, Linguistics, Literature, Literary
Criticism, Essays, Self-Help, Women's Studies
ISBN Prefix(es): 1-898855; 1-903222
Number of titles published annually: 50 Print
Total Titles: 150 Print
Imprints: Anthem Press (Academic humanities);
Nightingale Press (Gift books & humor); WPC
Classics (School & college classics); WPC
School Books (Secondary education textbooks)
*U.S. Office(s):* 4117 Hillsboro Pike, Suite 103-
106, Nashville, TN 37215, United States
*Tel:* 801-749-2983 *Fax:* 801-749-2983
*E-mail:* enquiries@wpcpress.com
*Orders to:* Pathway Book Service, 4 White
Brook Lane, Gilsum, NH 03348, United
States *Tel:* 603-357-0236 *Fax:* 603-357-2073
*E-mail:* pbs@pathwaybooks.com

**Windhorse Publications+**
11 Park Rd, Moseley, Birmingham B13 8AB
*Tel:* (0121) 449 9191 *Fax:* (0121) 449 9191
*E-mail:* info@windhorsepublications.com
*Web Site:* www.windhorsepublications.com
*Key Personnel*
Sales & Marketing Manager: Carol Bois
Founded: 1976
Subjects: Religion - Buddhist
ISBN Prefix(es): 0-904766; 1-899579
Number of titles published annually: 9 Print
Total Titles: 100 Print
*Associate Companies:* Windhorse Books, PO Box
574, Newtown, NSW 2042, Australia, Contact:
Ratnajyoti *Tel:* (02) 9519 8826 *Fax:* (02) 9519
8826 *E-mail:* books@windhorse.com.au *Web
Site:* www.windhorse.com.au (Australia)
Distributed by Booksource; Weatherhill Inc
(North America)
*Orders to:* Weatherhill Inc, 41 Monroe Turn-
pike, Trumbull, CT 06611, United States
*Tel:* 800-437-7840 *Fax:* 800-557-5601
*E-mail:* weatherhill@weatherhill.com *Web
Site:* www.weatherhill.com (USA)

**Windrow & Greene**, *imprint of* Compendium
Publishing

**Windsor Books International**
The Boundary, Wheatley Rd, Garsington, Oxford,
Oxon OX44 9EJ
*Tel:* (01865) 361122 *Fax:* (01865) 361133
*E-mail:* sales@windsorbooks.co.uk
*Web Site:* www.windsorbooks.co.uk
*Key Personnel*
Man Dir: A Geoff Cowen *E-mail:* geoffcowen@
windsorbooks.co.uk
Founded: 1991
Also acts as distributor in the UK & Europe for
publishers in the US & other countries.
Subjects: Architecture & Interior Design, Art,
Music, Dance, Radio, TV, Travel
ISBN Prefix(es): 1-874111
Subsidiaries: Springfield Books
Distributor for Allworth Press, New York (UK &
Europe); Billboard Music Books, New York
(UK & Europe); Creative Publishing Inter-
national, Minnesota (UK & Europe); C & T
Publishing, California (UK & Europe); Getty
Publications, California (UK & Europe); The
Globe Pequot Press, Connecticut (UK); Hud-
son Hills Press, New York (UK & Europe);
Hunter Publishing, Florida (UK & Europe);
The Lyons Press, Connecticut (UK); Meyer &
Meyer, Aachen (UK); Sally Milner Publishing,

Australia (UK & Europe); Open Road Publishing, New York (UK & Europe); Watson-Guptill
Publications, New York (UK & Europe)

**Windsor Large Print Bestsellers**, *imprint of*
BBC Audiobooks

**Wise Owl Books**, *imprint of* HLT Publications

**WISE Publications**, *imprint of* Omnibus Press

**Wisley Handbooks**, *imprint of* Cassell & Co

**WIT Press+**
Ashurst Lodge, Ashurst, Southampton S040 7AA
*Tel:* (023) 8029 3223 *Fax:* (023) 8029 2853
*E-mail:* witpress@witpress.com
*Web Site:* www.witpress.com
*Key Personnel*
Chief Executive, Man Dir & Publicity: Prof C
Brebbia
Marketing Manager: Helen Arnold
*E-mail:* marketing@witpress.com
Sales Manager: Graham Presland
*E-mail:* gpresland@witpress.com
Customer Services: Loraine Carter
*E-mail:* lcarter@witpress.com
Founded: 1976
Publisher in advanced engineering subjects, in-
cluding environmental engineering, engineer-
ing analysis & computational methods. Also
publishes the proceedings of conferences orga-
nized by the Wessex Institute of Technology,
edited/authored volumes & journals.
Subjects: Architecture & Interior Design, Auto-
motive, Biological Sciences, Civil Engineering,
Computer Science, Earth Sciences, Electronics,
Electrical Engineering, Engineering (General),
Environmental Studies, Maritime, Mathematics,
Mechanical Engineering, Technology, Trans-
portation, Acoustics, Biomedicine, Earthquake
Engineering, Environmental & Ecological Engi-
neering, Fluid Mechanics, Fracture Mechanics,
Heat Transfer, Marine Engineering, Transport
Engineering
ISBN Prefix(es): 0-931215; 0-945824; 1-56252;
1-85312; 0-905451
Number of titles published annually: 50 Print
Total Titles: 500 Print; 6 CD-ROM
*Parent Company:* Computational Mechanics Inter-
national
*U.S. Office(s):* Computational Mechanics, 25
Bridge St, Billerica, MA 01821, United
States *Tel:* 978-667-5841 *Fax:* 978-667-7582
*E-mail:* infousa@witpress.com

**Witherby**, *imprint of* Cassell & Co

**Witherby & Co Ltd+**
Book Dept, 2nd floor, 32-36 Aylesbury St, Lon-
don EC1R 0ET
*Tel:* (020) 7251 5341 *Fax:* (020) 7251 1296
*E-mail:* books@witherbys.co.uk
*Web Site:* www.witherbys.com
*Key Personnel*
Man Dir: Alan Witherby
Founded: 1740
Membership(s): Bookseller Association; Institute
of Experts.
Subjects: Business, Economics, Management,
Maritime, Technology, Transportation
ISBN Prefix(es): 0-900886; 1-85609
Number of titles published annually: 20 Print; 2
Audio
Total Titles: 250 Print; 1 CD-ROM; 2 Audio
Imprints: Monument
*Bookshop(s):* 20 Aldermanbury, London EC2V
7HY, Contact: Christine Burge *Tel:* (020) 7417
4431 *Fax:* (020) 7417 4431 *E-mail:* books@
witherbys.co.uk

**H F & G Witherby Ltd**, see Gollancz/Witherby

**The Woburn Press+**
Member of Taylor & Francis Group
Subsidiary of Frank Cass Publishers
Crown House, 47 Chase Side, London N14 5BP
*Tel:* (020) 8920 2100 *Fax:* (020) 8447 8548
*E-mail:* info@woburnpress.com
*Web Site:* www.frankcass.com/wp
*Key Personnel*
Man Dir: Stewart Cass
Editorial: Andrew Humphreys
Trade: Joanna Legg
Production: Daphna Weiss
Publicity: Hayley Osen
Founded: 1969
Subjects: Education
ISBN Prefix(es): 0-7130
*Associate Companies:* Vallentine, Mitchell & Co
Ltd; Irish Academic Press
*U.S. Office(s):* 5824 NE Hassalo St, Portland, OR
97213-3644, United States *Tel:* 503-287-3093
*Fax:* 503-280-8832 *E-mail:* wp@isbs.com
*Warehouse:* Biblios Distributions, Star Rd,
Partridge Green, West Sussex RH13 8LD
*Tel:* (403) 710971 *Fax:* (403) 711143

**WOL Books**, *imprint of* Pallas Athene

**Oswald Wolff Books**, *imprint of* Berg Publishers

**The Women's Press Ltd+**
Member of Namara Group
27 Goodge St, London W1T 2LD
*Tel:* (020) 7636 3992 *Fax:* (020) 7637 1866
*E-mail:* sales@the-womens-press.com
*Web Site:* www.the-womens-press.com
*Key Personnel*
Man Dir: Emma Drew *E-mail:* emma@the-
womens-press.com
Founded: 1977
Subjects: Alternative, Art, Biography, Disability,
Special Needs, Environmental Studies, Eth-
nicity, Fiction, Gay & Lesbian, Government,
Political Science, Health, Nutrition, Literature,
Literary Criticism, Essays, Music, Dance, Non-
fiction (General), Psychology, Psychiatry, Self-
Help, Women's Studies
ISBN Prefix(es): 0-7043
Number of titles published annually: 36 Print
Imprints: Livewire (books for teenagers & young
women)
Distributed by Codasat (Canada); Ted Dougherty
(Europe-excluding Spain & Portugal); Iberian
Book Services (Spain & Portugal); IMA
(Africa, Eastern Europe, Caribbean & Latin
America); Quartet (South Africa); Hanne Ro-
tovnik (Scandinavia); Southern Publishers
Group (New Zealand); Tower Books (Aus-
tralia); Trafalgar Square (US)
Foreign Rights: Writer's House (US)
*Orders to:* Plymbridge Distributors Ltd, Estover
Rd, Estover, Plymouth PL6 7PZ *Tel:* (01752)
202301 *Fax:* (01752) 202331 *E-mail:* control@
plymbridge.com

**Woodhead Publishing Ltd+**
Abington Hall, Abington, Cambs CB1 6AH
*Tel:* (01223) 891358 *Fax:* (01223) 893694
*E-mail:* wp@woodhead-publishing.com; info@
woodhead-publishing.com
*Web Site:* www.woodhead-publishing.com
*Key Personnel*
Man Dir: Martin J Woodhead *Tel:* (01223)
891358 (ext 16) *E-mail:* martinw@woodhead-
publishing.com
Editorial Dir: Francis Dodds *Tel:* (01223)
891358 (ext 15) *E-mail:* francisd@woodhead-
publishing.com
Editorial & Production: Mary Campbell; Kristine
Swift
Marketing Manager: Neil MacLeod *Tel:* (01223)
891358 (ext 33) *E-mail:* neilm@woodhead-
publishing.com

Finance Dir: Rob Burleigh *Tel:* (01223) 891358
(ext 11) *E-mail:* robb@woodhead-publishing.
com
Sales Administrator: Jenny Wheeler *Tel:* (01223)
891358 (ext 28)
Founded: 1989
Specialize in engineering materials, welding, food
science, food technology, textiles, environment,
finance & investment.
Membership(s): IPG.
Subjects: Energy, Engineering (General), Finance,
Health, Nutrition, Technology, Food Science
ISBN Prefix(es): 1-85573
Number of titles published annually: 45 Print; 2
CD-ROM; 30 Online; 30 E-Book
Total Titles: 400 Print; 4 CD-ROM; 100 Online;
100 E-Book
Imprints: Abington Publishing; Gresham Books
Distributed by CRC Press LLC
Distributor for American Welding Society
*Warehouse:* Combined Book Services Ltd, Units
I/K, Paddock Wood Distribution Centre, Pad-
dock Wood, Tonbridge TN12 6UU *Tel:* (01892)
837171 *Fax:* (01892) 837272

**Word for Word Audio Books**, *imprint of* BBC
Audiobooks

**Wordsworth Editions**, *imprint of* Wordsworth
Editions Ltd

**Wordsworth Editions Ltd+**
Cumberland House, Crib Street, Ware, Herts
SG12 9ET
*Tel:* (01920) 465167 *Fax:* (01920) 462267
*E-mail:* enquiries@wordsworth-editions.com
*Web Site:* www.wordsworth-editions.co.uk/
distributors.htm
Founded: 1987
Specialize in Wordsworth Editions & Classics
with CD-ROM, folklore, myths & legends.
Subjects: History, Literature, Literary Criticism,
Essays, Poetry
ISBN Prefix(es): 1-85326; 1-84022
Number of titles published annually: 50 Print; 20
CD-ROM
Total Titles: 700 Print; 10 CD-ROM
Imprints: Wordsworth Editions; Wordsworth Edu-
cation
Distributed by Agius & Agius Ltd (Malta &
Gozo); Allphy Book Distributors Ltd (New
Zealand & Fiji); Bohemian Ventures sro (Czech
Republic); Copernicus Diffusion (France); Inter
Orbis Media Dist srl Ed (Italy); NTC/Contem-
porary (USA); OM Books International (In-
dia); Peribo Pty Ltd (Australia & Papua New
Guinea); Readwide Bookshop Ltd (Ghana, The
Gambia, Liberia, Cameroon & Sierra Leone);
Ribera Libros SL (Spain); Slovak Ventures sro
(Slovak Republic); Taschenbuch-Vertrieb Inge-
borg Blank GmbH Lager und Buro (Germany
& Austria)
Foreign Rep(s): Don O'Mahoney (Ireland);
Advanced Global Distribution (US); IMA
(Caribbean, South America); Publishers In-
ternational Marketing (Far East, Middle East)
*Showroom(s):* Cumberland House, Crib Street,
Ware, Herts SG12 9ET
*Warehouse:* Wordsworth Editions, The Airfield,
Mendlesham, Suffolk IP14 5NA

**Wordsworth Education**, *imprint of* Wordsworth
Editions Ltd

**Wordwright Books**, *imprint of* Wordwright
Publishing

**Wordwright Publishing+**
25 Oakford Rd, London NW5 1AJ
*Tel:* (020) 7284 0056 *Fax:* (020) 7284 0041
*E-mail:* wordwright@clara.co.uk

*Key Personnel*
Dir, International Rights: Charles Perkins
*E-mail:* cfp@wordwright.clara.co.uk
Dir: Veronica Davis
Founded: 1987
Also book packager.
Membership(s): Book Packagers Association.
Subjects: Art, Cookery, Gardening, Plants, Geog-
raphy, Geology, History, Humor, Natural His-
tory, Nonfiction (General), Social Sciences,
Sociology, Sports, Athletics, Women's Studies
ISBN Prefix(es): 0-9527128
Total Titles: 40 Print
Imprints: Wordwright Books

**World Microfilms Publications Ltd+**
PO Box 35488, St Johns Wood, London NW8
6WD
*Tel:* (020) 7586 4499; (0845) 606 0612
*Fax:* (020) 7722 1068
*E-mail:* microworld@ndirect.co.uk
*Web Site:* www.microworld.ndirect.co.uk
*Key Personnel*
Man Dir: Stephen C Albert
Founded: 1969
Subjects: Architecture & Interior Design, Art,
Drama, Theater, Economics, Film, Video, His-
tory, Music, Dance, Religion - Other, Science
(General), Self-Help, Microfilm Collections
ISBN Prefix(es): 1-85035; 1-86013; 0-905272
Number of titles published annually: 10 Print
Total Titles: 700 Print; 3 CD-ROM; 400 Audio
*Associate Companies:* Audio-Forum; Pidgeon Au-
dio Visual; Sussex Tapes; Sussex Video; Stotts
Correspondence College
Foreign Rep(s): Norman Ross Publishing Inc
(Canada, US)

**World of Information+**
2 Market St, Saffron Walden, Essex CB10 1HZ
*Tel:* (01799) 521150 *Fax:* (01799) 524805
*E-mail:* queries@worldinformation.com
*Web Site:* www.worldinformation.com
*Key Personnel*
Man Dir & Rights: Anthony Axon
Founded: 1972
Subjects: Business, Economics, Government, Po-
litical Science
ISBN Prefix(es): 1-86217
Number of titles published annually: 140 Print; 1
CD-ROM
Total Titles: 160 Print; 3 CD-ROM
Subsidiaries: Central European Business Ltd
*Distribution Center:* Storgatan 7 B, S-753 31,
Uppsala, Sweden *Tel:* (0) 18 13 36 33 *Fax:* (0)
18 12 36 63

**World of Islam Altajir Trust+**
33 Thurloe Place, London SW7 2HQ
*Tel:* (020) 7581 3522 *Fax:* (020) 7584 1977
*Key Personnel*
Dir: Alistair Duncan
Founded: 1974
Subjects: Archaeology, Art, Religion - Islamic,
Theology
ISBN Prefix(es): 0-905035; 1-901435
*Orders to:* Fox Communications & Publica-
tions, 39 Chelmsford Rd, London E18 2PW
*Tel:* (020) 8498 9768 *Fax:* (020) 8504 2558

**The World Today**, *imprint of* Royal Institute of
International Affairs

**Worldlife Library**, *imprint of* Colin Baxter
Photography Ltd

**WPC Classics**, *imprint of* Wimbledon Publishing
Company Ltd

**WPC School Books**, *imprint of* Wimbledon
Publishing Company Ltd

**Writers & Their Work**, *imprint of* Northcote House Publishers Ltd

**Writer's Digest**, *imprint of* David & Charles Ltd

**Wychwood Press**, *imprint of* Jon Carpenter Publishing

**Y Cyfarwyddwr Urdd Gobaith Cymru**
Swyddfa'r Urdd, Ffordd Llanbadarn, Aberystwyth, Ceredigion SY23 1EY
*Tel:* (01970) 613100 *Fax:* (01970) 626120
*E-mail:* urdd@urdd.org
*Web Site:* www.urdd.org
*Key Personnel*
Chief Executive: Jim O'Rourke *E-mail:* jim@urdd.org
Founded: 1923

**Yale English Monarchs**, *imprint of* Yale University Press London

**Yale University Press London+**
47 Bedford Sq, London WC1B 3DP
*Tel:* (020) 7079 4900 *Fax:* (020) 7079 4901
*E-mail:* sales@yaleup.co.uk
*Web Site:* www.yalebooks.co.uk
*Key Personnel*
Man Dir: Robert Baldock *E-mail:* robert. baldock@yaleup.co.uk
Editorial Dir: Gillian Malpass *E-mail:* gillian. malpass@yaleup.co.uk
Sales & Marketing Dir: Kate Pocock *E-mail:* kate.pocock@yaleup.co.uk
Publicity: Hazel Hutchison
Sales: Andrew Jarmain
Rights: Anne Bihan
Editor: Sally Salvesen
Founded: 1961
Subjects: Anthropology, Architecture & Interior Design, Art, Asian Studies, Biography, Environmental Studies, Government, Political Science, History, Language Arts, Linguistics, Law, Literature, Literary Criticism, Essays, Music, Dance, Natural History, Nonfiction (General), Philosophy, Photography, Physical Sciences, Psychology, Psychiatry, Religion - Jewish, Social Sciences, Sociology, Theology, Women's Studies
ISBN Prefix(es): 0-300
*Parent Company:* Yale University Press, 302 Temple St, PO Box 209040, New Haven, CT 06520-9040, United States
Imprints: Pelican History of Art; Pevsner Architectural Guides; Yale English Monarchs
Subsidiaries: Yale Representation Ltd
Distributor for Metropolitan Museum of Art; National Gallery Publications
*Orders to:* John Wiley & Sons Ltd Distribution Centre, Southern Cross Trading Estate, Bognor Regis, West Sussex PO22 9SA

**Yellow Jersey Press**, *imprint of* Random House UK Ltd

**Anglia Young Books+**
Imprint of Motivation in Learning Ltd (Bangor)
Durham's Farmhouse, Ickleton, Saffron Walden, Essex CB10 1SR
*Tel:* (01799) 531192 *Fax:* (01799) 531192
*Web Site:* www.btinternet.com/~r.hayes
*Key Personnel*
Contact: Rosemary Hayes *E-mail:* r.hayes@btinternet.com
Founded: 1989
Subjects: Disability, Special Needs, Fiction, History, Religion - Other
ISBN Prefix(es): 1-871173
Distributor for Kallisto Ltd
*Orders to:* Broadgali House, 72 Church St, Deeping St James, Peterborough PE6 8HD

**Young Corgi**, *imprint of* Transworld Publishers Ltd

**Young Picador**, *imprint of* Macmillan Children's Books

**Young Spitfire**, *imprint of* Elliott & Thompson

**Zed Books Ltd+**
7 Cynthia St, London N1 9JF
*Tel:* (020) 7837 4014; (020) 7837 0384
*Fax:* (020) 7833 3960
*E-mail:* zedbooks@zedbooks.demon.co.uk
*Web Site:* zedweb.hypermart.net/zed/contact.htm
*Key Personnel*
Sales: Farouk Sohawon
Editor: Robert Molteno; Michael Pallis
Editor, Rights & Permissions: Mohammed Umar *E-mail:* mohammed@zedbooks.demon.co.uk
Marketing: Julian Hosie
Production: Anne Rodford
Founded: 1976
Subjects: Environmental Studies, Social Sciences, Sociology, Women's Studies, Development Studies
ISBN Prefix(es): 0-905762; 0-86232; 1-85649; 1-84277
Total Titles: 350 Print
Distributed by St Martin's Press/Palgrave (USA)
*Shipping Address:* Plymbridge, Estover, Plymouth PL6 7PZ
*Warehouse:* Plymbridge, Estover, Plymouth PL6 7PZ

**Zeno Booksellers**, see The Greek Bookshop

**Ziff-Davis Press**, *imprint of* Pearson Education Europe, Mideast & Africa

**Zomba Books**, *imprint of* Omnibus Press

**Zone Books**, *imprint of* MIT Press Ltd

# Uruguay

## General Information

*Capital:* Montevideo
*Language:* Spanish
*Religion:* Predominantly Roman Catholic
*Population:* 3.1 million
*Bank Hours:* 1300-1700 Monday-Friday
*Shop Hours:* 0900-1200, 1400-1900 Monday-Friday; 0900-1230 Saturday
*Currency:* 100 centesimos = 1 new Uruguayan peso
*Export/Import Information:* Member Southern Cone Common Market (MERCOSUR) No tariffs on books or single copies catalogues but surcharge on advertising matter. Additional surcharge on all imports, plus VAT Cif, plus Stamp Tax of percentage of total invoice value. No import licenses. No exchange controls.
*Copyright:* UCC, Berne, Buenos Aires (see Copyright Conventions, pg xi)

**Albe Libros Technicos**
Cerrito 564/566, Casilla Correos, 1601, Montevideo 11100
*Tel:* (02) 915 75 28; (02) 915 74 85 *Fax:* (02) 915 75 28
*Web Site:* www.bosch.es/puntos_internacional.asp

*Key Personnel*
Contact: Daniel Aljanati
*Branch Office(s)*
Albe Libros Technicos-Salto, Joaquin Suarez 28, Salto

**Editorial Arca SRL+**
Bartolome Mitre 1413, Montevideo 11100
*Tel:* (02) 9166966 int 110 *Fax:* (02) 901887; (02) 930188
*E-mail:* saroya@st.com.uy
*Key Personnel*
Man Dir: Claudio Rama
Founded: 1964
Subjects: Anthropology, Drama, Theater, Economics, Geography, Geology, Health, Nutrition, History, Humor, Music, Dance, Poetry, Regional Interests, Religion - Other, Technology
ISBN Prefix(es): 9974-40

**Arpoador+**
Roque Graseras 693, Montevideo 11300
*Tel:* (02) 707826 *Fax:* (02) 717278
*Key Personnel*
Contact: Martha Paulick
Founded: 1995
Subjects: Economics, History, Literature, Literary Criticism, Essays
ISBN Prefix(es): 9974-7533

**Barreiro y Ramos SA**
Juan Carlos Gomez 1430, Montevideo 11100
*Tel:* (02) 98 66 21 *Fax:* (02) 96 23 58 *Cable:* BAREIRAMOS
*Key Personnel*
Man Dir: Dr Gaston Barreiro Zorrilla
Sales Dir: Raul Catelli
Founded: 1871
Subjects: Literature, Literary Criticism, Essays, Religion - Other
ISBN Prefix(es): 84-8292; 9974-33

**Cotidiano Mujer**
San Jose 1436, 11200 Montevideo
*Tel:* (02) 9018782; (02) 9020393 *Fax:* (02) 4095651
*E-mail:* cotidian@cotidianomujer.org.uy
*Web Site:* chasque.apc.org/cotidian/
*Key Personnel*
Contact: Elena Fonseca
Founded: 1985
Subjects also include ecology, feminism & human rights.
Subjects: Journalism, Women's Studies

**Ediciones de Juan Darien+**
Hocquart 1771, 11800 Montevideo
*Tel:* (02) 2090223
*E-mail:* dayraq@chasque.apc.org
*Key Personnel*
Contact: Dayman Cabrera
Founded: 1990
Subjects: Art, Cookery, Economics, Education, History, Literature, Literary Criticism, Essays, Nonfiction (General), Poetry, Social Sciences, Sociology
ISBN Prefix(es): 9974-580

**Instituto del Tercer Mundo+**
Juan D Jackson 1136, Montevideo 11200
Mailing Address: PO Box 1539, Montevideo 11000
*Tel:* (02) 419 6192 *Fax:* (02) 411 9222
*E-mail:* item@chasque.apc.org; item@item.org.uy
*Web Site:* www.chasque.apc.org/item/
*Key Personnel*
Dir: Roberto Bissio
Editor: Victor Bacchetta *E-mail:* victorb@chasque.apc.org
Founded: 1986
New Zealand/Aotearoa.

Membership(s): Association for Progressive Communications (APC).
Subjects: Human Relations, Civil Society
ISBN Prefix(es): 9974-574
*U.S. Office(s):* Humanities Press International Inc, 165 First Ave, Atlantic Highlands, NJ 07716, United States *Tel:* 908-872-1441 *Fax:* 908-872-0717
DHL, 8424 NW 56 St, Suite MVD 023040, Miami, FL 33166, United States
Distributed by Andenbuch-Romanische Buchhandlung (Alemania); Arning Publications (Norway); CEDIB (Bolivia); Fondo de Cultura Economica (Peru); Hillco Media Group (Sweden); Humanities Press International Inc (US); Ibercultura GmbH (Switzerland); IEPALA (Spain); Instituto del Tercer Mundo (Uruguay); Lamuv Verlag (Germany); Leer Ltda (Colombia); Libreria De La Paz (Argentina); Libreria Lectura SA (Venezuela); Libreria Milnovecientos (Chile); Libri Mundi (Ecuador); MARCIAL PONS Libreros (Spain); Mellemfolkeligt Samvirke (Denmark); NCOS (Belgium); New Internationalist Aotearoa; New Internationalist Australia (Australia); New Internationalist Canada (Canada); New Internationalist Publications (UK); Novib Publications (Netherlands); Oxfam Publications (UK); Sipro (Servicios Informativos Procesados AC) (Mexico); Tyron SA (Argentina)
Distributor for Revista delsur; Social Watch
*Orders to:* Hersilia Fonseca/Marketing

**Departemento de Publicaciones de la Universidad de la Republica**
Jose Enrique Rodo 1827, 11200 Montevideo
*Tel:* (02) 408 2906; (02) 408 5714 *Fax:* (02) 408 0303
*E-mail:* infoed@edic.edu.uy
*Web Site:* www.rau.edu.uy
*Key Personnel*
Dir: Daniel Cabalero
ISBN Prefix(es): 9974-0

**Editorial Dismar+**
18 de Julio 2172/308, 11200 Montevideo
*Tel:* (02) 407946
*Key Personnel*
Editor: Martha Campos
Founded: 1989
Membership(s): Camara Uruguaya del Libro.
Subjects: Journalism, Medicine, Nursing, Dentistry, Psychology, Psychiatry
ISBN Prefix(es): 9974-560

**Editorial Libreria Amalio M Fernandez**
25 de Mayo 589, 11000 Montevideo
*Tel:* (02) 9151782; (02) 295 26 84 *Fax:* (02) 295 17 82
*Key Personnel*
Man Dir & Editorial: Carlos W Deamestoy Perez
Sales: Jorge M Garcia
Founded: 1951
Subjects: Law, Social Sciences, Sociology
ISBN Prefix(es): 84-8293

**La Flor del Itapebi+**
Luis Piera 1917/401, 11300 Montevideo
*Tel:* (02) 710 92 67 *Fax:* (02) 710 92 67
*E-mail:* itapebi@itapebi.com.uy
*Web Site:* www.itapebi.com
*Key Personnel*
Contact: Sra Isabel Grompone
Founded: 1992
Subjects: Computer Science, Fiction, Mathematics
ISBN Prefix(es): 9974-592
*Parent Company:* Olmer SA

**Fundacion de Cultura Universitaria+**
25 de Mayo 568, Casilla de Correo 1155, 11000 Montevideo

*Tel:* (02) 9152532; (02) 959038; (02) 9168360 *Fax:* (02) 9152549
*E-mail:* administrador@fcu.com.uy
*Web Site:* www.fcu.com.uy
*Key Personnel*
Man Dir: Carlos (Fallecido) Fuques
Administrator: Jorge Mahy
Founded: 1968
Subjects: Accounting, Criminology, Economics, Finance, Government, Political Science, History, Law, Regional Interests, Romance, Social Sciences, Sociology
*Branch Office(s)*
Artigas N 1251, regional Norte-Salto

**Hemisferio Sur Edicion Agropecuaria**
Buenos Aires 335, 11000 Montevideo
*Tel:* (02) 916 45 15; (02) 916 45 20 *Fax:* (02) 916 45 20
*E-mail:* librperi@adinet.com.uy
*Key Personnel*
Contact: Sra Margarita Peri
Subjects: Biological Sciences, Natural History
ISBN Prefix(es): 9974-556

**Linardi y Risso Libreria**
Juan Carlos Gomez 1435, Montevideo 11000
*Tel:* (02) 915 71 29; (02) 915 73 28 *Fax.* (02) 915 74 31
*E-mail:* lyrbooks@linardiyrisso.com
*Web Site:* www.linardiyrisso.com/
Founded: 1944
Specialize in Latin American books.
Subjects: Government, Political Science, History, Literature, Literary Criticism, Essays
ISBN Prefix(es): 9974-559
*Orders to:* Linardi Y Risso, 4405 NW 73 Ave, Suite 12-333 4567, Miami, FL 33166-6400, United States

**A Monteverde y Cia SA+**
Treinta y Tres 1475, 11000 Montevideo
*Tel:* (02) 915 2012; (02) 915 2939; (02) 915 8748 *Fax:* (02) 915 2012
*E-mail:* monteverde@monteverde.com.uy
*Web Site:* www.monteverde.com.uy/
*Key Personnel*
Man Dir: Daniel Mussini
Sales Dir: Liliana Mussini
Founded: 1879
Subjects: Astronomy, Biological Sciences, Chemistry, Chemical Engineering, Earth Sciences, Geography, Geology, History, Literature, Literary Criticism, Essays, Mathematics, Music, Dance, Natural History, Philosophy, Physical Sciences, Physics
ISBN Prefix(es): 9974-34
Subsidiaries: Cion; Encuaderna; Impresos; Talleres Graficos
*Bookshop(s):* Palacio del Libro
*Orders to:* Trienta y Tres 1475, 11000 Montevideo *Tel:* (02) 952939

**Mosca Hermanos**
18 de Julio 1578, Montevideo 11100
SAN: 004-2757
*Tel:* (02) 4093141; (02) 4011111 *Fax:* (02) 200 0588
*E-mail:* empresas@mosca.com.uy
*Web Site:* www.mosca.com.uy/ *Cable:* Moscaher
*Key Personnel*
Man Dir: Gustavo Mosca
Sales Dir: Gonzalo Mosca
Founded: 1888
Subjects: Literature, Literary Criticism, Essays, Religion - Other
ISBN Prefix(es): 9974-555; 84-89275

**Nordan-Comunidad+**
Millan 4113, 12900 Montevideo
*Tel:* (02) 305 5609 *Fax:* (02) 308 1640

*E-mail:* nordan@nordan.com.uy; pedidos@nordan.com.uy; info@nordan.com.uy
*Web Site:* www.chasque.net/nordan/; www.nordan.com.uy
*Key Personnel*
Editor: Prieto Ruben
Coordinator: Zaya Arremyr *E-mail:* admin@nordan.com.uy
Subjects: Agriculture, Alternative, Anthropology, Architecture & Interior Design, Communications, Developing Countries, Economics, Education, Environmental Studies, Foreign Countries, Government, Political Science, Health, Nutrition, Language Arts, Linguistics, Literature, Literary Criticism, Essays, Philosophy, Poetry, Psychology, Psychiatry, Radio, TV, Social Sciences, Sociology, Women's Studies
ISBN Prefix(es): 9974-42

**Prensa Medica Latinoamericana+**
Guayabo 1790, Apdo 504, 11200 Montevideo
Mailing Address: Casilla de Correo 6135, Montevideo
*Tel:* (02) 4000 916 *Fax:* (02) 4000 916
*E-mail:* prensmed@adinet.com.uy
Founded: 1988
Subjects: Child Care & Development, Health, Nutrition, Medicine, Nursing, Dentistry, Psychology, Psychiatry
ISBN Prefix(es): 9974-568

**Punto de Encuentro Ediciones**
Andresito Guacarary 1836, 11200 Montevideo
*Tel:* (02) 405167
*Key Personnel*
Editorial: Marylin Dias Capo
Founded: 1989
Subjects: Art, Literature, Literary Criticism, Essays
ISBN Prefix(es): 9974-603

**Luis A Retta Libros**
Paysandu 1827, 11200 Montevideo
Mailing Address: PO Box 591042, Miami, FL 33159-1042, United States
*Tel:* (02) 400-0766 *Fax:* (02) 409-0174
*E-mail:* rettalib@chasque.apc.org
Founded: 1975
Subjects: Anthropology, History, Literature, Literary Criticism, Essays, Poetry, Women's Studies
ISBN Prefix(es): 9974-557

**Rosebud Ediciones+**
Liber Arce 3089, 11300 Montevideo
*Tel:* (02) 771773 *Fax:* (02) 6287111
*E-mail:* zapican@adinet.com.uy
*Key Personnel*
Contact: Jacqueline Listur
Founded: 1993
Subjects: Biography, Ethnicity, Fiction, History, Humor, Nonfiction (General), Poetry, Self-Help
ISBN Prefix(es): 9974-638

**Ediciones Trilce+**
Casilla de correos 12203, 11300 Montevideo
SAN: 002-0230
Mailing Address: Durazno 1888, 11200 Montevideo
*Tel:* (02) 412 77 22; (02) 412 76 62 *Fax:* (02) 412 76 62; (02) 412 77 22
*E-mail:* trilce@adinet.com.uy; infoventas@trilce.com.uy
*Web Site:* www.trilce.com.uy
*Key Personnel*
Dir: Pablo Harari
Founded: 1985
Subjects: Anthropology, Architecture & Interior Design, Biography, Communications, Developing Countries, Economics, Education, Fiction, Government, Political Science, History, Humor, Literature, Literary Criticism, Essays, Music, Dance, Poetry, Psychology, Psychiatry, Regional Interests, Religion - Other, Science

(General), Social Sciences, Sociology, Technology, Women's Studies
ISBN Prefix(es): 9974-32; 84-89269

**La Urpila Editores**
Casilla 5088, Suc 1, Montevideo
*Tel:* (02) 9085347
*Key Personnel*
Dir: Prof Norma Suiffet
Founded: 1979
Subjects: Literature, Literary Criticism, Essays, Poetry
ISBN Prefix(es): 9974-566
*Parent Company:* Casa del Poeta Latinoamericano

**Editia Uruguay+**
Bartolome Mitre 1377, 11000 Montevideo
*Tel:* (02) 915-9633; (02) 915-9759 *Fax:* (02) 916-4419
*E-mail:* edita@adinet.com.uy
*Web Site:* www.editia.com
*Key Personnel*
Contact: Ernesto Sanjines
Founded: 1970
Specialize in computer science & technical books. Also a distributor & wholesaler.
Subjects: Computer Science
ISBN Prefix(es): 9974-621
Distributed by Diana (Mexico, USA, Central America & Colombia)
Distributor for Diana; Editores Mexicanos Unidos (Uruguay, Paraguay & Bolivia); GYR (Uruguay); Marcombo; Prentice Hall

**Vinten Editor+**
Hocquart 1771, 11800 Montevideo
*Tel:* (02) 2090223 *Fax:* (02) 290223
*E-mail:* dayraq@chasque.apc.org
*Web Site:* www.chasque.apc.org/dayraq/vinten
*Key Personnel*
Contact: Dayman Cabrera
Founded: 1976
Subjects: Art, Economics, Education, Literature, Literary Criticism, Essays, Nonfiction (General), Poetry, Social Sciences, Sociology
ISBN Prefix(es): 9974-570

# Uzbekistan

## General Information

*Capital:* Tashkent
*Language:* Uzbek
*Religion:* Predominantly Islamic (mostly Sunni Muslim)
*Population:* 21.6 million
*Bank Hours:* Generally open for short hours between 0930-1230 Monday-Friday
*Shop Hours:* Generally 0900-1800 Monday-Friday; often open weekends
*Currency:* 100 kopeks = 1 rubl

**Izdatelstvo Literatury i isskustva**
ul Navoi 30, 700129 Taskent
*Tel:* (0371) 445172
*Key Personnel*
Dir: Sh Z Usmanhodjayev
Editor-in-Chief: H T Turabekov
Founded: 1926
Subjects: Literature, Literary Criticism, Essays
ISBN Prefix(es): 5-638

**Izdatelstvo Uzbekistan+**
ul Navoi 30, 700129 Taskent
*Tel:* (0371) 443810
*Key Personnel*
Dir: Shomukhitdin Sh Mansurov
Chief Editor: Zufar A Juraev

Founded: 1924
Uzbek Publishing House.
Subjects: Art, Economics, Government, Political Science, History, Law
ISBN Prefix(es): 5-640
*Associate Companies:* Matbaa Uzbek-Turkey JV Rastr Uzbek-Britain JV

# Venezuela

## General Information

*Capital:* Caracas
*Language:* Spanish
*Religion:* Predominantly Roman Catholic
*Population:* 20.7 million
*Bank Hours:* 0830-1130, 1400-1630 Monday-Friday
*Shop Hours:* 0900-1300, 1500-1900 Monday-Saturday
*Currency:* 100 centimos = 1 bolivar
*Export/Import Information:* Member of the Latin American Free Trade Association.
*Copyright:* UCC, Berne (see Copyright Conventions, pg xi)

**Academia Nacional de la Historia**
Palacio de las Academias, Av Universidad, Caracas 1010-A
*Tel:* (0212) 481-34-13; (0212) 483-94-35; (0212) 482-67-20; (0212) 486720 *Fax:* (0212) 481-75-47
*E-mail:* informacion@anhvenezuela.org
*Web Site:* www.anhvenezuela.org
*Telex:* 27252
*Key Personnel*
Dir: Rafael Fernandez Heres
Founded: 1888
ISBN Prefix(es): 980-222

**Alfadil Ediciones+**
Calle Las Flores con calle Paraiso, Edificio Paraiso, PB, Sabana Grande, Caracas 1050
Mailing Address: Apdo 50304, Caracas 1050
*Tel:* (0212) 762-3036; (0212) 761-3576; (0212) 763-5676 *Fax:* (0212) 762-0210
*E-mail:* contacto@alfagrupo.com
*Web Site:* www.alfagrupo.com
*Key Personnel*
Executive President: Leonardo Milla Alcacer
   *E-mail:* leonardomilla@alfagrupo.com
General Administrative: Yolanda de Anuel
   *E-mail:* administracion@alfagrupo.com
Founded: 1978
Subjects: Astrology, Occult, Economics, Fiction, Geography, Geology, History, Journalism, Literature, Literary Criticism, Essays, Music, Dance, Nonfiction (General), Philosophy, Poetry, Self-Help, Social Sciences, Sociology
ISBN Prefix(es): 980-6005; 980-354
*Parent Company:* Alfa, Grupo Editorial
*Associate Companies:* Distribuidora de Ediciones Noray, CA
Subsidiaries: Libreria Ludens
*Bookshop(s):* Ludens, SRL, Torre Polar, Local F, Plaza Venezuela, Caracas

**Armitano Editores CA+**
Cuarta Transversal de la Av principal de Boleita, paralela a la Av Romulo Gallegos, Edificio Centro Industrial Piso 1, Apdo 50853, Caracas 1070
*Tel:* (0212) 2342565; (0212) 2340870; (0212) 2340865 *Fax:* (0212) 2341647
*E-mail:* armiedit@telcel.net.ve
*Web Site:* www.armitano.com *Cable:* ARMITPRESS CARACAS VENEZUELA

*Key Personnel*
Man Dir: E Armitano
Sales Dir: P Salazar
Founded: 1957
Membership(s): Graphic Arts Association of Venezuela.
Subjects: Anthropology, Architecture & Interior Design, Art, Environmental Studies, History
ISBN Prefix(es): 980-216
Number of titles published annually: 12 Print
Total Titles: 350 Print

**Editorial Ateneo de Caracas**
Edificio Ateneo de Caracas, Piso 5, Caracas 1010-A
SAN: 000-4197
Mailing Address: Apdo 662, Caracas 101-A
*Tel:* (0212) 5734622; (0212) 5734400; (0212) 5734600 *Fax:* (0212) 5754475
*E-mail:* webmaster@ateneo.org.ve
*Key Personnel*
President: Maria Teresa Castillo
Editorial Dir, Sales, Production: Antonio Polo
Founded: 1978
Subjects: Art, Government, Political Science, History, Literature, Literary Criticism, Essays, Poetry, Psychology, Psychiatry, Science (General)
ISBN Prefix(es): 980-255; 84-8350
*Bookshop(s):* Libreria Ateneo de Caracas, Edificio Ateneo de Caracas 5 piso, Plaza Morelos Apdo 662, Caracas 1010

**Monte Avila Editores Latinoamericana CA+**
Av Eugenio Mendoza Con Lera Transversal, Qta Cristina, La Castellana, Caracas 1070
Mailing Address: Apdo 70712, Caracas 1070
*Tel:* (0212) 265-6020; (0212) 265-9871
*E-mail:* maelca@telcel.net.ve
*Telex:* 24220 Conac
*Key Personnel*
Man Dir & President: Alexis Marquez Rodrigez
Editorial, Rights & Permissions: Wilfredo Machado
Sales: Glenda Sanchez
Production: Mirna Ferrer
Founded: 1968
Tenemos Una Distribuidora En New York Lectorum Publications Inc, 111 Eighth Ave, Suite 804, New York, NY: Gerente Teresa Mlawer; Libros Sin Fronteras, PO Box 2085, Olympia, WA 98507-2085: Contact Michael Shapiro.
Subjects: Anthropology, Art, Economics, Education, Fiction, Geography, Geology, Government, Political Science, History, Literature, Literary Criticism, Essays, Music, Dance, Philosophy, Poetry, Psychology, Psychiatry, Regional Interests, Science (General), Social Sciences, Sociology
ISBN Prefix(es): 980-01
Distributed by Anahuac (Madrid)
Distributor for Editorial Anthropos Y Visor Libros De Espana; Editorial Montesinos; En Venezuela; Monte Avila Distribuye

**Biblioteca Ayacucho**
Av Urdaneta, Animas a PI Espana, Centro Financiero Latino Piso 12, Ofc 1, 2, 3, Caracas 1010-A
Mailing Address: Apdo 14413/2122, Caracas 1010-A
*Tel:* (0212) 5644402; (0212) 5643583 *Fax:* (0212) 5634223
*Telex:* 26217 B1A4A *Cable:* BIAYACUCHO
*Key Personnel*
President of Editorial Commission, Editorial, Rights & Permissions: Dr Jose Ramon Medina
Editorial Dir: Oswaldo Teejo
Sales, Publicity: Miriam Valdez
Founded: 1975
Subjects: Anthropology, Architecture & Interior Design, Art, Developing Countries, Drama, Theater, Fiction, History, Literature, Literary

Criticism, Essays, Philosophy, Photography,
Poetry
ISBN Prefix(es): 980-276

## Editorial Biosfera CA+
Ave Chama, Qta Coral, PB de Colinas de Bello
Monte, Caracas 1050-A
Mailing Address: Apdo 50634, Caracas 1050-A
*Tel:* (0212) 751 9119; (0212) 753 8892
*Fax:* (0212) 751 9320
*Key Personnel*
Man Dir, Editorial: Dr Serafin Mazparrote
Founded: 1979
Subjects: Art, Biological Sciences, Language
Arts, Linguistics, Mathematics, Nonfiction
(General), Science (General)
ISBN Prefix(es): 980-210
Subsidiaries: Litho-Mundo SA
*Bookshop(s):* Ediciones Amanecer (Libreria) Cen-
tro Polo, Av Principal, Colinas de Bello Monte

## Sociedad Fondo Editorial Cenamec
Esquina de Salas-Edificio Sede del Ministerio de
Educacion, Piso 5, Cultura y Deportes, Caracas
1080-A
Mailing Address: Apdo 75055, Caracas 1080-A
*Tel:* (0212) 563-2591; (0212) 563-3542; (0212)
563-5597; (0212) 563-8155; (0212) 563-9997;
(0212) 563-8244
*E-mail:* cenamec@reacciun.ve
*Web Site:* www.cenamec.org.ve/
*Key Personnel*
President: Dr Enrique Planchart
Vice President: Prof Tania Calderin
Founded: 1974
Subjects: Biological Sciences, Chemistry, Chemi-
cal Engineering, Mathematics, Physics
ISBN Prefix(es): 980-218

## Colegial Bolivariana CA
Av Diego Cisneros (Principal) Los Ruices, Edif
CO-BO, Piso 1, Caracas 1071-A
Mailing Address: PO Box 70324, Caracas 1071-A
*Tel:* (0212) 2391055; (0212) 2391244; (0212)
2391377; (0212) 2391166; (0212) 2391944;
(0212) 2391433; (0212) 2391777; (0212)
2391555 *Fax:* (0212) 2396502; (0212) 2379942
*Web Site:* co-bo.com *Cable:* COLEGIAL
*Key Personnel*
Man Dir: Hans L Schnell
Founded: 1961
ISBN Prefix(es): 980-262
*Branch Office(s)*
Puente Yanes A Tracabordo, Edificio BEL-VEL,
Planta Baja, Caracas 1011
Ave Constitucion, Local No 28, Pto La Cruz
6023 Edo Anzoategui
Calle 97 (Bolivar) No 6-48, Apdo de Correos
834, Maracaibo 4001-A Edo Zulia

## Ediciones Ekare+
Final Ave Luis Roche, Edif Banco del Libro, Al-
tamira Sur 1062
SAN: 001-6780
Mailing Address: Apdo 68284, Caracas 1062
*Tel:* (02) 263 00 80; (02) 263 61 70 *Fax:* (02)
263 00 91 *Fax on Demand:* (02) 263 32 91
*Key Personnel*
President: Carmen Diana Dearden
Edit Dir & Foreign Rights: Maria Francisca Ma-
jobre
Marketing & Sales Manager: Maria Cristina Ser-
rano
Founded: 1978
Specialize in children's picture books. Publish in
Spanish only.
Subjects: Fiction
ISBN Prefix(es): 980-257; 84-8351
Subsidiaries: Ekare Sur; Ekare Espana

## Fundacion Centro Gumilla
Edif Centro Valores PB Local 2, Esquina de La
Luneta-Altagracia, Caracas 1010-A
Mailing Address: Apdo 4838, Caracas 1010-A
*Tel:* (0212) 564 98 03; (0212) 564 58 71; (0212)
562 75 31 *Fax:* (0212) 564 75 57
*E-mail:* comunicacion@gumilla.org.ve; centro@
gumilla.org.ve
*Web Site:* www.gumilla.org.ve
*Key Personnel*
Contact: Klaus Vathroder SJ *E-mail:* vathroder@
gumilla.org.ve
Subjects: Economics, Education, Government,
Political Science, Labor, Industrial Relations,
Religion - Catholic, Social Sciences, Sociology,
Theology
ISBN Prefix(es): 980-250

## Fundacion Servicio para el Agricultor
Av Francisco de Miranda, Edificio Cavendes, Piso
8 Ofc 806, Los Palos Grandes, Caracas 1062
Mailing Address: Apdo 2224, Caracas 1062
*Tel:* (0212) 2843089; (0212) 2841134; (0212)
2852016 *Fax:* (0212) 2853946
*E-mail:* izamora@etheron.net
*Key Personnel*
Contact: Dario Boscan; Jorge M Gonzalez
Founded: 1952
Subjects: Agriculture
ISBN Prefix(es): 980-260

## Grijalbo SA
2 da Av de Campo Claro, Qta Harminia, Caracas
Mailing Address: Ap Correos, 106-62260, Chacao
*Tel:* (0212) 238 15 42; (0212) 238 17 32
*Fax:* (0212) 239 03 08
*E-mail:* griven@etheron.net
*Key Personnel*
Man Dir: Manuel Morales
Founded: 1964
ISBN Prefix(es): 980-293
*Parent Company:* Ediciones Grijalbo SA, Spain

## Editorial Kapelusz Venezolana SA
Ave Cajigal No 29, QTa K, San Bernadino, Apdo
14234, Caracas 1011-A
*Tel:* (0212) 517601; (0212) 526281
*Telex:* 24039 Ekave VC *Cable:* KAPELUSZ
*Key Personnel*
Man Dir: Horacio Perotti Beraldo
Founded: 1963
ISBN Prefix(es): 980-285
*Parent Company:* Editorial Kapelusz SA, Ar-
gentina

## Editorial Labor de Venezuela SA
Ave Andres Bello, Edificio Garten, Caracas
*Tel:* (0212) 7811398; (0212) 7815819
*Key Personnel*
Man Dir: Jaime Salgado Palacio

## McGraw-Hill de Venezuela
2 da Calle de Bello Monte, entre Av Casanova y
Blvd de Sabana Grande, Local G-2, Caracas
1050
Mailing Address: Apdo 50785, Caracas 1050
*Tel:* (0212) 238 3494; (0212) 761 8181; (0212)
761 6992 *Fax:* (0212) 238 2374; (0212) 761
6993
*E-mail:* dpmail@attmail.com
*Telex:* 29976
*Key Personnel*
Man Dir, Bogata: Carlos Marquez
General Manager: Mauricio Mikan
*E-mail:* mikan@attmail.com
Controller-Business Manager: Rafael Ramos
College Division Manager: Javier Lindarte
Market Served: Venezuela.
ISBN Prefix(es): 980-6168

*Parent Company:* The McGraw-Hill Companies,
1221 Avenue of the Americas, New York, NY
10020, United States
*Associate Companies:* Libros McGraw-Hill de
Mexico SA de CV, Bogota, Colombia

## Ministerio de Educacion Biblioteca Central
Esq de Salas, Edif Ministerio, Torre de Servicio,
Edif sede, Carmelitas, Caracas 1010
*Tel:* (0212) 5628970 (ext 8149); (0212) 5621767;
(0212) 5640025 *Fax:* (0212) 5641224
*Telex:* 21943
*Key Personnel*
Dir: Lozada Bernarda
ISBN Prefix(es): 980-02

## Editorial Nueva Sociedad+
Edificio IASA, piso 6 oficina 606, Plaza La
Castellana, Caracas
Mailing Address: Apartado 61712, Caracas 1060-
A
*Tel:* (0212) 2659975; (0212) 2650593 *Fax:* (0212)
2673397
*E-mail:* nuso@nuevasoc.org.ve; nusoven@
nuevasoc.org.ve
*Web Site:* www.nuevasoc.org.ve
*Telex:* 24163
*Key Personnel*
Dir: Dietmar Dirmoser *E-mail:* dirmoser@
nuevasor.org.ve
Man Editor: Sergio Chejfec *E-mail:* chejfec@
nuevasoc.org.ve
Books Coordinator: Helena Gonzalez
*E-mail:* helena@nuevasoc.org.ve
Sales, Promotion: Ester de Rodriguez
*E-mail:* ester@nuevasoc.org.ve
Founded: 1972
Subjects: Developing Countries, Economics, En-
vironmental Studies, Ethnicity, Government,
Political Science, Social Sciences, Sociology,
Technology, Women's Studies
ISBN Prefix(es): 980-6110; 980-317

## OCEI (Oficina Central de Estadistica e Informatica)
Edif Foundacion La Salle, PB, Av Boyaca,
Mariperez, Caracas
Mailing Address: Apdo 4593, San Martin, Cara-
cas 101
*Tel:* (0212) 782 11 33; (0212) 782 12 12; (0212)
782 19 45; (0212) 782 10 31; (0212) 793 71
91; (0212) 782 11 67 *Fax:* (0212) 782 97 55
*Telex:* 21241
*Key Personnel*
Chief, Main Directory: Gustavo Jose Mendez
Boiler *E-mail:* gmendez@platino.gov.ve
General Dir: Miguel Bolivar Chollett
Dir, Social Communication: Ana Maria Rodriguez
Founded: 1978
Specialize in the production of national statistics
& policy information.
ISBN Prefix(es): 980-280
*Warehouse:* O C E I, Sotano 2

## Oficina Central de Estadistics e Informatica,
see OCEI (Oficina Central de Estadistica e
Informatica)

## Editorial Planeta Venezolana
Member of Grupo Planeta
Calle Madrid Entre New York Y Trinidad,
Qta,Toscanella, Las Mercedes, 1050 Caracas
Mailing Address: Apdo 51285, Caracas 1050
*Tel:* (0212) 913982; (0212) 924872 *Fax:* (0212)
913792
*E-mail:* planeta@viptel.com
*Web Site:* www.editorialplaneta.com.ve
*Telex:* 29944
ISBN Prefix(es): 980-271

**Editorial Pomaire Venezuela SA**
Ave Luis Roche, Edif Santa Clara, PB Altamira
    Sur, Apdo 51.960, Caracas 1062
*Tel:* (0212) 2622122; (0212) 2621253 *Fax:* (0212)
    2616962
*Key Personnel*
Man Dir: Jose Luis Garcia Froiz
ISBN Prefix(es): 980-290
*Parent Company:* Editorial Pomaire SA, Spain

**Editorial Reverte Venezolana SA**
Peligro a Pele el Ojo, Edificio Torre Carabobo,
    Local 2, La Candelaria, Caracas 1010
Mailing Address: Apdo 14520, Caracas 1010
*Tel:* (0212) 572 44 68; (0212) 572 66 70
    *Fax:* (0212) 572 25 98
ISBN Prefix(es): 980-294
*Associate Companies:* Editorial Reverte SA,
    Spain

**Teduca, Tecnicas Educativas, CA**
Av Romulo Gallegos, Edificio Zulia, Sector Mon-
    tecristo, piso 1, Caracas 1062
Mailing Address: Apdo 1071, Caracas 1062
*Tel:* (0212) 235 58 78; (0212) 235 43 95; (0212)
    235 62 65 *Fax:* (0212) 239 79 52
*Telex:* 27876 Cpbth Vc
*Key Personnel*
Chairman: Eduardo Robles Piquer
General Manager: Enrique de Polanco Soutullo
Founded: 1977
Subjects: Education
ISBN Prefix(es): 980-275
*Associate Companies:* Santillana SA de Edi-
    ciones, Spain
*Orders to:* Urbanizacion Industrial Cloris, Ave 2,
    Local 84-03 Ave Norte, Guarenas, Edo, Mi-
    randa

**Universidad de los Andes, Consejo de
    Publicaciones**
Edificio Administrativo, Piso 4, Merida
*Tel:* (074) 401111 ext 1998 *Fax:* (074) 274240
    ext 1998
*E-mail:* dsia@ula.ve
*Web Site:* www.ula.ve
*Key Personnel*
Man Dir: Dr Eduardo Zuleto
Sales, Production: Macario Molina
Publicity: Ana Allegue de Pietri
Rights & Permissions: Asunta Briceno
Coordinator: Roberto Donoso Torres
Founded: 1977
Subjects: Medicine, Nursing, Dentistry, Regional
    Interests, Science (General), Social Sciences,
    Sociology, Technology
ISBN Prefix(es): 980-221

**Vadell Hermanos Editores CA+**
Esquina Peligro a Pele el Ojo, Edificio Golden,
    Sotano La Candelaria, Caracas
*Tel:* (0212) 5723108; (0212) 5778110 *Fax:* (0212)
    5725243
*Web Site:* www.vadellhermanos.com/
*Key Personnel*
General Manager: Dr Manuel M Vadell Graterol
Founded: 1973
Membership(s): Association Venezuelan Editors.
Subjects: Computer Science, Economics, Educa-
    tion, Geography, Geology, Psychology, Psy-
    chiatry, Science (General), Social Sciences,
    Sociology, Technology
ISBN Prefix(es): 980-212

**Ediciones Vega SRL**
Av Universitaria Edif Odeon, PB Los Ch-
    aguaramos, Apdo 51662, Caracas 1010-A
*Tel:* (0212) 6622092; (0212) 6621397 *Cable:*
    EDIVEGA
*Key Personnel*
Man Dir: Fernando Vega Alonso

Founded: 1965
ISBN Prefix(es): 980-6044
*Bookshop(s):* Libreria Tecnica Vega

# Viet Nam

## General Information

*Capital:* Hanoi
*Language:* Vietnamese
*Religion:* Predominantly Buddhist
*Population:* 69 million
*Currency:* 100 xu = 1 new dong
*Export/Import Information:* None available at
    present.
*Copyright:* Florence (see Copyright Conventions,
    pg xi)

**Giao Duc Publishing House**
81 Tran Huan Dao, Hanoi
*Tel:* (04) 262011 *Fax:* (04) 262010
*Key Personnel*
Dir: Nguyen Si Ty
Founded: 1957
Subjects: Education

**Lao Dong (Labor) Publishing House**
31, Hai Ba Trung St, Hanoi
*Tel:* (04) 253972

**Pho Thong (Popularization) Publishing House**
Hanoi

**Popular Army Publishing House**
Hanoi
Subjects: Military Science

**Science & Technics Publishing House** (Nha
    Xuat Ban Khoa Hoc Va Ky Thuat)+
70 Tran Hung Dao St, Hanoi 84-4
*Tel:* (04) 9 424 786; (04) 9 423 172; (04)
    8220682; (04) 9423132; (04) 9423128; (04)
    9423543; (04) 9423171 *Fax:* (04) 8 220 658
*E-mail:* nxbkhkt@hn.vnn.vn
*Web Site:* www.nxbkhkt.com.vn
*Key Personnel*
Dir: Prof To Dang Hai, PhD *E-mail:* todanghai@
    hn.vnn.vn
Founded: 1960
Membership(s): Vietnam Publishers Association.
Subjects: Accounting, Advertising, Aeronautics,
    Aviation, Agriculture, Animals, Pets, Archae-
    ology, Architecture & Interior Design, Astron-
    omy, Automotive, Behavioral Sciences, Biolog-
    ical Sciences, Business, Career Development,
    Chemistry, Chemical Engineering, Civil Engi-
    neering, Communications, Computer Science,
    Crafts, Games, Hobbies, Earth Sciences, Eco-
    nomics, Education, Electronics, Electrical Engi-
    neering, Energy, Engineering (General), English
    as a Second Language, Environmental Studies,
    Finance, Gardening, Plants, Geography, Geol-
    ogy, Health, Nutrition, How-to, Management,
    Maritime, Marketing, Mathematics, Mechani-
    cal Engineering, Medicine, Nursing, Dentistry,
    Microcomputers, Natural History, Physical Sci-
    ences, Physics, Radio, TV, Science (General),
    Securities, Technology, Transportation, Veteri-
    nary Science
Number of titles published annually: 280 Print
Total Titles: 10,000 Print
*Branch Office(s)*
28 Dong Khoi St, Q 1 Ho Chi Minh City
    84-8 *Tel:* (08) 8 225 062; (08) 8 296 628
    *E-mail:* chinhanhkhkt@hcm.fpt.vn

*Bookshop(s):* 31-33 Yen Bai St, Danang City
    *Tel:* (04) 8 220 686; 40 Ngo Quyen St, Hanoi
    *Tel:* (04) 9 349 147; 28 Dong Khoi St, Q1, Ho
    Chi Minh City *Tel:* (08) 8 225 062

**Su Hoc (Historical) Publishing House**
Hanoi
Subjects: Government, Political Science, Philoso-
    phy

**Su That (Truth) Publishing House**
24 Quang Trung St, Hanoi
*Tel:* (04) 252008
Founded: 1945
(Under the Central Committee of the Communist
    Party of Viet Nam).
Subjects: Government, Political Science, Philoso-
    phy, Social Sciences, Sociology

**Trung-Tam San Xuat Hoc-Lieu**
Tran-binh-Trong 240, Ho Chi Minh City 5

**Y Hoc Publishing House**
4 Le Thanh Ton, Hanoi
*Tel:* (04) 253274
Subjects: Medicine, Nursing, Dentistry

# Zambia

## General Information

*Capital:* Lusaka
*Language:* English is official language
*Religion:* Most follow traditional animist beliefs
    (70%), about 20% Christian (Protestant and
    Roman Catholic)
*Population:* 8.7 million
*Bank Hours:* 0815-1245 Monday, Tuesday,
    Wednesday, Friday; 0815-1200 Thursday;
    0815-1100 Saturday
*Shop Hours:* Generally 0800-1700 Monday-
    Friday; 0800-1300 Saturday
*Currency:* 100 ngwee = 1 Zambian kwacha
*Export/Import Information:* No tariffs on books
    but all imports subject to sales tax. Single
    copies of advertising free. Import license re-
    quired. Exchange controls.
*Copyright:* UCC, Berne (see Copyright Conven-
    tions, pg xi)

**Aafzam Ltd+**
PO Box 31012, Lusaka
*Tel:* (01) 223261
*Key Personnel*
Chairman: H Earl Johnson
Founded: 1971
Subjects: Biography, Business, Developing Coun-
    tries, Government, Political Science, Music,
    Dance, Wine & Spirits
ISBN Prefix(es): 9982-9903
*Associate Companies:* A Afzamwines Ltd; Satis
    Suppliers Ltd

**Apple Books+**
PO Box 35687, Lusaka 10101
*Tel:* (01) 211216 *Fax:* (01) 224855
*Key Personnel*
Man Dir: G B Mwangilwa
General Manager: Rodrick Chris Chibesa
Founded: 1987
Membership(s): Booksellers & Publishers Asso-
    ciation of Zambia; specialize in book exports;
    also acts as Literary Agent.
Subjects: Biography, Fiction, History, Humor
ISBN Prefix(es): 9982-06
*Parent Company:* Virgo Ltd

**Bookworld Ltd+**
Box 31838, Lusaka 10101
*Tel:* (01) 225 282 *Fax:* (01) 225 195
*E-mail:* bookwld@zamtel.zm
Founded: 1991
Membership(s): Booksellers & Publishers Association of Zambia.
Subjects: Education
ISBN Prefix(es): 9982-16

**Government Printer**
PO Box 30136, 10100 Lusaka
*Tel:* (01) 215401; (01) 215805; (01) 215685; (01) 216972
ISBN Prefix(es): 9982-10

**Historical Association of Zambia**
PO Box 30680, Lusaka
*Key Personnel*
Chairman: Dr Y A Chondoka
Founded: 1969
Subjects: Agriculture, Anthropology, History
ISBN Prefix(es): 9982-802

**Lundula Publishing House+**
Private Bag E 708, Lusaka
*Tel:* (01) 96758496
*Key Personnel*
Man Dir: Ngand 'Osamba Lundula
   *E-mail:* nlundula@yahoo.com
Founded: 1991
French & English language publications.
Membership(s): US & British Library; Zambian Book Sellers & Printers Association.
Subjects: Education, English as a Second Language, Language Arts, Linguistics, Social Sciences, Sociology
ISBN Prefix(es): 9982-9904
Number of titles published annually: 1 Print; 1 CD-ROM
Total Titles: 1 Print; 1 CD-ROM
*Parent Company:* Editions Passou
Distributed by Book World in Zambia; BPAZ (Book & Publishers' Association of Zambia); Enobel Enterprises; Norman Suppliers; Top Shop; University of Zambia Bookshop; Zambia Educational Publishing House
Distributor for Editions Passou (Democratic Republic of the Congo)
*Book Club(s):* US & British Libraries in Zambia; Writer's Association of Zambia

**M & M Management & Labour Consultants Ltd+**
PO Box 35128, Lusaka
*Tel:* (01) 217218 *Fax:* (01) 224495
*Telex:* ZA 40618
*Key Personnel*
Managing Consultant: Tresford K Mwaba
Founded: 1987
Also management consultants.
Subjects: Human Relations, Labor, Industrial Relations, Management
ISBN Prefix(es): 9982-805

**Macmillan Publishers (Zambia) Ltd**
Plot 8357, Sentor Investments Complex, Great North Rd, Luska
Mailing Address: PO Box 320199, Lusaka
*Tel:* (01) 223 669 *Fax:* (01) 223 657; (01) 641 018
*E-mail:* macpub@zamnet.zm
*Web Site:* www.macmillan-africa.com
*Key Personnel*
Man Dir: Miles Banda *E-mail:* mkbanda@zamnet.zm
Sales Manager: Elijah Chimbongwe
Educational publishers.
*Parent Company:* Macmillan Publishers Ltd, United Kingdom
*Branch Office(s)*
Plot No 22, Nawaitwika Rd, Northrise, Ndola

**MFK Management Consultants Services+**
Luangwa House, Cairo Rd, PO Box 31411, Lusaka
*Tel:* (01) 223530; (01) 252934
*Key Personnel*
Author: Frederick K Mwanza
Subjects: Business, Developing Countries, Economics, Finance, Government, Political Science, Management, Philosophy, Social Sciences, Sociology
ISBN Prefix(es): 9982-823

**Movement for Multi-Party Democracy+**
c/o Goodwin Bwalya Mwangilwa, MMD Secretariat, Private Bag E365, Lusaka
*Tel:* (01) 224850; (01) 224851; (01) 224852; (01) 224853 *Fax:* (01) 224855
Founded: 1991
Subjects: Government, Political Science, Public Administration
ISBN Prefix(es): 9982-17

**Multimedia Zambia+**
PO Box 320199, Lusaka
*Tel:* (01) 253666 *Fax:* (01) 363050
*Telex:* 40630 ZA
*Key Personnel*
Executive Dir: Mr Jumbe Ngoma
Founded: 1971
Subjects: Biography, Communications, Cookery, Fiction, Religion - Other, Social Sciences, Sociology
ISBN Prefix(es): 9982-30
*Parent Company:* Christian Council of Zambia/Zambia Episcopal Conference
*Shipping Address:* African Books Collective Ltd, The Jam Factory, 27 Park End St, Oxford OX1 1KU, United Kingdom
*Warehouse:* African Books Collective Ltd, The Jam Factory, 27 Park End St, Oxford OX1 1KU, United Kingdom
*Orders to:* African Books Collective Ltd, The Jam Factory, 27 Park End St, Oxford OX1 1KU, United Kingdom

**Printpak (Z) Ltd**
PO Box 70069, Ndola
*Tel:* (01) 611001; (01) 611002; (01) 600113; (01) 612027 *Fax:* (01) 617096
*Telex:* 41860
*Key Personnel*
Contact: J Muyuni
ISBN Prefix(es): 9982-13

**University of Zambia Press (UNZA Press)**
PO Box 32379, 10101 Lusaka
*Tel:* (01) 213221; (01) 293058; (01) 292884; (01) 293580; (01) 219624; (01) 252514 *Fax:* (01) 253952
*Telex:* ZA 44370 *Cable:* UNZAS
*Key Personnel*
Publisher: Miss M A Sifuniso
Editorial: Christopher Bwalya; Samuel Kasankha
Production: John C Mukuka
Founded: 1938
Subjects: Education, Social Sciences, Sociology
ISBN Prefix(es): 9982-03
*Parent Company:* University of Zambia Company
*Bookshop(s):* University Bookshop

**Yorvik Publishing Ltd+**
Plot 531, David Kaunda Rd, Chingola
Mailing Address: PO Box 10583, Chingola
*Tel:* (02) 311628; (02) 312852; (02) 313707 *Fax:* (02) 311628
*Key Personnel*
Man Dir: A M Morton
Founded: 1993
Subjects: Special Education, Secondary School Sciences
ISBN Prefix(es): 9982-20

*Associate Companies:* Anthony Morton Ltd
*Bookshop(s):* AML Graphics, Armshal Rd, Noola

**Zambia Association for Research & Development (ZARD)**
Zard House Plot No 16, Manchinchi Rd, Northmead, Lusaka
*Tel:* (01) 224536; (01) 222883 *Fax:* (01) 222883
*E-mail:* zard@zamnet.zm; zard@zamtel.zm
*Web Site:* www.zard.org.zm
*Key Personnel*
Contact: Mercy Khozi
Founded: 1984
ZARD's aim is to promote & advance gender development & empowerment of women through research, training & advocacy.
Subjects: Government, Political Science, Health, Nutrition, Social Sciences, Sociology, Women's Studies
ISBN Prefix(es): 9982-818
*Book Club(s):* Booksellers & Publishers Association of Zambia

**Zambia Educational Publishing House+**
Chishango Rd, Lusaka 10101
Mailing Address: PO Box 32708, Lusaka 10101
*Tel:* (01) 229490; (01) 229211 *Fax:* (01) 225073
*E-mail:* zpa@zamnet.zm
*Telex:* ZA 40056 *Cable:* HOUSE LUSAKA
*Key Personnel*
Acting Man Dir: Beninco Mulota
Publishing Manager: R Munamwimbu
Marketing Manager: Alfred Sikabanga
Founded: 1967
Membership(s): Booksellers & Publishers Association of Zambia.
Subjects: Agriculture, Biography, Drama, Theater, Education, Ethnicity, Fiction, Government, Political Science, History, Language Arts, Linguistics, Literature, Literary Criticism, Essays, Poetry, Social Sciences, Sociology
ISBN Prefix(es): 9982-00; 9982-01
Distributed by Dzuka Publishing Co (Malawi); Gamsberg Publishers (Namibia)
Distributor for Longman Zambia; Macmillan Zambia; Multimedia Zambia; Printpak Ltd
*Book Club(s):* Read-a-Book Club

**Zambia Printing Company Ltd (ZPC)+**
Publicity House, Plot No 2349/50, Kabelenga Rd, Fairview, Lusaka
Mailing Address: PO Box 34798, Lusaka
*Tel:* (01) 227673; (01) 227674; (01) 227675 *Fax:* (01) 225026
*Telex:* ZA 40068
*Key Personnel*
Marketing Officer: Langson Siwale
Founded: 1988
Commercial printing also.
Subjects: Agriculture, Child Care & Development, Drama, Theater, Education, Environmental Studies, Gardening, Plants, History, Women's Studies
ISBN Prefix(es): 9982-02
*Parent Company:* Zambia Printing Co Ltd

**Zambian Ornithological Society (ZOS)**
PO Box 33944, 10101 Lusaka
*E-mail:* zos@zamnet.zm
*Web Site:* www.fisheagle.org
Subjects: Natural History
ISBN Prefix(es): 9982-811

ZPC, see Zambia Printing Company Ltd (ZPC)

# Zimbabwe

## General Information

*Capital:* Harare
*Language:* English is the official language. Chishona and Sindebele are major African languages.
*Religion:* Majority (55%) Christian, most of the rest follow traditional beliefs
*Population:* 10 million
*Bank Hours:* 0830-1400 Monday, Tuesday, Thursday, Friday; 0830-1200 Wednesday; 0830-1100 Saturday
*Shop Hours:* 0800 or 0830-1700 Monday-Friday; 0800-1300 Saturday
*Currency:* 100 cents = 1 Zimbabwe dollar
*Export/Import Information:* Surcharge duty of 20% CIF to order, and 12 1/2% tax on retail sales on books. Advertising matter in bulk has duty and VAT charged. Import license is normally required for books and printed matter. Exchange controls.
*Copyright:* Berne (see Copyright Conventions, pg xi)

### Academic Books (Pvt) Ltd+
28 South Ave, Harare
Mailing Address: PO Box 567, Harare
*Tel:* (04) 755034; (04) 754224 *Fax:* (04) 781913
*Key Personnel*
Editorial Dir: Irene Staunton
Membership(s): Zimbabwe Publisher's Association.
Subjects: Art, Education, Fiction, Geography, Geology, History, Literature, Literary Criticism, Essays, Nonfiction (General), Science (General)
ISBN Prefix(es): 0-949229; 0-908311
*Parent Company:* F E I C Ltd
Divisions: Baobab Books
Distributed by ABC (England); David Philip (South Africa)
*Warehouse:* 4 Conald Rd, Graniteside, Harare

### Action Magazine+
PO Box Gt 1274, Graniteside, Harare
*Tel:* (04) 747217 *Fax:* (04) 747409
*E-mail:* action@action.co.zw
*Web Site:* www.action.co.zw
*Key Personnel*
Coordinator: Steve Murray
Founded: 1987
Developing & producing environment & health education materials, training in environmental education.
Subjects: Environmental Studies, Health, Nutrition
*Parent Company:* NGO, Zimbabwe Trust, 4 Lanark Rd, Harare

### Books for Africa Publishing House+
21 Inez Terrace, Harare
Mailing Address: PO Box 3471, Harare
*Tel:* (04) 794329 *Fax:* (04) 61881
*Telex:* 22386
*Key Personnel*
Publishing Manager: Chris Nyabezi
Founded: 1979
Membership(s): the Book Publishers Association.
ISBN Prefix(es): 0-949933

### Anvil Press+
78 Kaguvi St, Harare
Mailing Address: PO Box 4209, Harare
*Tel:* (04) 73-9681; (04) 78-1770; (04) 78-1771; (04) 792551 *Fax:* (04) 75-1202

*Key Personnel*
Man Dir: Paul Brickhill
Manager: Felix Nyabadza
Founded: 1987
Subjects: Drama, Theater, Environmental Studies, Literature, Literary Criticism, Essays, Social Sciences, Sociology
ISBN Prefix(es): 0-7974
*Associate Companies:* Grassroots Books
*Bookshop(s):* Grassroots Books, Africa House, 100 J Moyo Ave, Box A267, Avondale

### Argosy Press
PO Box 2677, Harare 704715
*Tel:* (04) 704715; (04) 704766 *Fax:* (04) 752162
*Telex:* 26334
ISBN Prefix(es): 0-7974; 0-908309
*Associate Companies:* Modus Publications Pvt Ltd

### Bold ADS
PO Box 1027, Harare
*Tel:* (04) 62-1321; (04) 62-1326 *Fax:* (04) 62-1328
*E-mail:* shunidzarira@boldads.co.zw
*Telex:* 26013
*Key Personnel*
General Manager: L M Manduku
Production Manager: N Magadzine
Sales & Marketing: L Ndlovu
Founded: 1950
Subjects: Foreign Countries
*Parent Company:* Zimbabwe Newspapers (Pvt) Ltd
Subsidiaries: B & T Directories (Pvt) Ltd; Publications (C A) (pvt) Ltd
*Branch Office(s)*
PO Box 1027, Bulawayo

### Christian Audio-Visual Action (CAVA)
Box 649, Harare
*Tel:* (04) 752233 *Fax:* (04) 727030
*E-mail:* cava@mango.zw
*Key Personnel*
Contact: Rev H W Murray
Founded: 1977
Subjects: Biblical Studies, Theology

### College Press Publishers (Pvt) Ltd+
Subsidiary of Macmillan Publishers Ltd
15 Douglas Rd, Workington, Harare
Mailing Address: PO Box 3041
*Tel:* (04) 754145; (04) 773231; (04) 773236; (04) 757153; (04) 754255 *Fax:* (04) 754256
*E-mail:* nellym@collegepress.co.zw
*Telex:* 22558 colprs zw *Cable:* LIBRIS
*Key Personnel*
Man Dir: Benias Benison Mugabe
Sales Dir: Cletus Jack Ngwaru
Publishing Manager: Cynthia Sithole *Tel:* (04) 754255 *Fax:* (04) 757150
Production Dir & International Division: Engelbert Lemon Luphahla
Financial Dir: Edwin Busangabanye
Founded: 1968
Primarily an educational publisher.
Membership(s): Zimbabwe Book Publishers Association & APNET.
Subjects: Accounting, Agriculture, Biblical Studies, Biography, Biological Sciences, Business, Chemistry, Chemical Engineering, Child Care & Development, Cookery, Drama, Theater, Economics, English as a Second Language, Environmental Studies, Fiction, Geography, Geology, History, Mathematics, Physics, Poetry, Science (General), Teachers Education
ISBN Prefix(es): 0-86925; 1-77900
Number of titles published annually: 30 Print
Total Titles: 700 Print
Imprints: Scholastic Books; Ventures

*Branch Office(s)*
PO Box 298, Bulawayo, Contact: G Ndlovu
*Tel:* (09) 74174
PO Box 1239, Gweru, Contact: G K Madzime
*Tel:* (054) 23457
PO Box 355, Masvingo, Contact: G Muzenda
*Tel:* (039) 62264
PO Box 963, Mutare, Contact: S J Chikuse
*Tel:* (020) 64211
Distributed by Macmillan Publishers (Worldwide)
Distributor for Macmillan Publishers
Foreign Rep(s): Macmillan Publishers (Worldwide)
*Orders to:* College Press Publishers, Contact: Cletus Ngwaru

### Dorothy Duncan Braille Library & Transcription Library
119 Fife Ave, Harare
Mailing Address: Box CY 1551 Causeway, Harare
*Tel:* (04) 251116; (04) 251117 *Fax:* (04) 251117
*E-mail:* chiedza@samara.co.zw
*Key Personnel*
Coordinator: Sister Catherine Jackson
Founded: 1963
*Parent Company:* Dorothy Duncan Centre for the Blind & Physically Handicapped

### Farm-level Applied Methods for East & Southern Africa (FARMESA)
Robinson House, 9th floor, Union Ave, Harare
Mailing Address: PO Box 3730, Harare
*Tel:* (04) 758051-4 *Fax:* (04) 758055
*E-mail:* fspzim@internet.co.zw; fspzim@harare.iafrica.com
*Web Site:* www.farmesa.co.zw
*Key Personnel*
Project Coordinator: Dr John Dixon *E-mail:* john.dixon@farmesa.co.zw
Information Officer: Margaret Zunguze *E-mail:* margaret.zunguze@farmesa.co.zw
Subjects: Agriculture

FARMESA, see Farm-level Applied Methods for East & Southern Africa (FARMESA)

Flame Lily, *imprint of* The Literature Bureau

### Geological Survey Department
PO Box CY210, Causeway, Harare
*Tel:* (04) 790701; (04) 726342; (04) 726343; (04) 252016; (04) 252017 *Fax:* (04) 739601
*E-mail:* zimeosv@africaonline.co.zw; zgs@samara.co.zw
*Web Site:* www.geosurvey.co.zw
*Telex:* 22416 MINESZW *Cable:* MINES
*Key Personnel*
Dir: Dr J L Orpen
Founded: 1910
Subjects: Geography, Geology
*Parent Company:* Ministry of Mines, Zimbabwe, P Bag 7709, Causeway, Harrare

### The Graham Publishing Company (Pvt) Ltd
PO Box 2931, Harare
*Tel:* (04) 706207 *Fax:* (04) 752439
*Key Personnel*
Man Dir: Gordon M Graham
Founded: 1968
Subjects: Fiction, History, Nonfiction (General), Travel
ISBN Prefix(es): 0-86921

### Legal Resources Foundation Publications Unit
Blue Bridge, 5th floor, Second St, Eastgate, Harare
Mailing Address: PO Box 918, Harare
*Tel:* (04) 251170; (04) 251174 *Fax:* (04) 728213
*E-mail:* lrfhre@mweb.co.zw
*Web Site:* site.mweb.co.zw/lrf

*Key Personnel*
National Dir: Eileen Sawyer
National Administrator: Deborah Barron
   *E-mail:* lrfbyo@mweb.co.zw
Founded: 1984
Subjects: Law
ISBN Prefix(es): 0-908312

**The Literature Bureau**
Ministry of Education, Sport & Culture, Causeway, Harare
Mailing Address: PO Box CY121, Causeway, Harare
*Tel:* (04) 726929; (04) 729120 *Cable:* LITBURO
*Key Personnel*
Chief Publications Officer: B C Chitsike
Principal Editorial Officers: E Tafa; E Bhala
Founded: 1954
Subjects: Animals, Pets, Drama, Theater, Literature, Literary Criticism, Essays, Poetry
ISBN Prefix(es): 0-86926
Imprints: Flame Lily
*Branch Office(s)*
PO Box 828, Bulawayo
*Book Club(s):* Shona Readers' Book Club

**Longman Zimbabwe (Pvt) Ltd+**
Tourle Rd, Southerton, Harare
Mailing Address: PO Box ST 125, Harare Southerton
*Tel:* (04) 621 661; (04) 621 667 *Fax:* (04) 621670
*E-mail:* customeralicek@longman.co.zw
*Web Site:* www.pearsoned.co.uk/contactus/worldwideoffices/africa
*Telex:* 225666 LONZIM *Cable:* Longman Harare Zimbabwe
*Key Personnel*
General Manager: Emily Chandauka
   *E-mail:* emilyc@longman.co.zw
Founded: 1964
Subjects: Accounting, Agriculture, Business, Cookery, Economics, Education, English as a Second Language, Environmental Studies, History, Mathematics, Natural History, Poetry, Religion - Other, Science (General)
ISBN Prefix(es): 0-582; 0-908308; 0-908310; 1-77903
Total Titles: 700 Print
*Parent Company:* Pearson Education, United Kingdom
*Ultimate Parent Company:* Pearson Plc

**Mambo Press+**
Senga Rd, Gweru
Mailing Address: PO Box 779, Gweru
*Tel:* (054) 24016; (054) 25807; (054) 24017; (054) 28351 *Fax:* (054) 21991
*E-mail:* mambo@icon.co.zw
*Web Site:* www.rutenga.com/mambo.htm
*Key Personnel*
General Manager: Fr R Gentile
Editor: Emmanuel Makadho
Marketing Manager: Charles Zhou
Founded: 1958
Subjects: Fiction, History, Natural History, Nonfiction (General), Poetry, Religion - Other
ISBN Prefix(es): 0-86922
Number of titles published annually: 12 Print
Total Titles: 320 Print
Foreign Rep(s): Africa B/Centre (UK); Botswana B/Cecntre (Botswana); Botswana B/Centre (US); Pauline Multimedia (Zambia)
*Bookshop(s):* Mambo Bookshop, Speke Ave/First St, PO Box UA 320, Harare, Contact: Mrs R Mabuza *Tel:* (04) 705899; Mambo Bookshop, PO Box 1010, Masvingo, Contact: Mr H Muromo *Tel:* (039) 64566; Mambo Bookshop, Bulawayo, PO Box FM 87, Bulawayo, Contact: Mrs S Kamutingondo *Tel:* (09) 61162

**Manhattan Publications**
30 Montgomery Rd, Highlands, Harare

Mailing Address: PO Box 5, Harare
*Tel:* (04) 442827; (04) 498206 *Fax:* (04) 496292
*E-mail:* nchudy@zol.co.zw
*Key Personnel*
Proprietor: Alexander Katz
Founded: 1983
Zimbabwe economics.
Subjects: Business, Economics
Number of titles published annually: 2 Print
Total Titles: 15 Print
*Parent Company:* Manhattan Realty (Pvt) Ltd

**Mercury Press Pvt Ltd+**
PO Box 2373, Harare
*Tel:* (04) 75-1515; (04) 75-1084 *Fax:* (04) 73-7670 *Cable:* TUTORIAL
*Key Personnel*
Man Dir & International Rights: D F Sutherland
Founded: 1972
Subjects: Education, English as a Second Language, Language Arts, Linguistics, Poetry
ISBN Prefix(es): 0-7974
*Parent Company:* Central African Correspondence College P/L, Gickon House 22, Kaguvi St, Harare
*Associate Companies:* Phoenix Printers P/L, Gickon House 22, Kaguvi St, Harare

**National Archives of Zimbabwe+**
Borrowdale Rd, Harare
Mailing Address: Private Bag 7729, Causeway, Harare
*Tel:* (04) 792 741 *Fax:* (04) 792 398
*E-mail:* nat.archives@gta.gov.zw
*Web Site:* www.gta.gov.zw
Founded: 1935
Subjects: Ethnicity, Genealogy, History, Nonfiction (General), Social Sciences, Sociology
ISBN Prefix(es): 0-908302

**NAZ**, see National Archives of Zimbabwe

**Nehanda Publishers+**
Union Ave, Harare
Mailing Address: PO Box UA517, Harare
*Tel:* (04) 734415; (04) 727077 *Fax:* (04) 734415
*E-mail:* lenneiye@mweb.co.zw
*Key Personnel*
President: Dr L M Lenneiye
Vice President: Dr Kimani Gecau
Founded: 1984
Subjects: Economics, Environmental Studies, Foreign Countries, Government, Political Science, Literature, Literary Criticism, Essays, Regional Interests
ISBN Prefix(es): 0-908305

**Phantom Publishers+**
PO Box BW59, Borrowdale, Harare
*Tel:* (04) 737241
*Key Personnel*
Author & Publisher: Jeremy Ford
Founded: 1988
Subjects: Poetry
ISBN Prefix(es): 0-7974
*Orders to:* Nationwide, PO Box 1819, Harare

**Sapes Trust Ltd+**
4 Deary Ave, Belgravia, Harare
Mailing Address: PO Box MP111, Mount Pleasant, Harare
*Tel:* (04) 252962; (04) 252963; (04) 252965 *Fax:* (04) 252963
*E-mail:* administrator@sapes.org.zw
*Web Site:* www.sapes.co.zw
*Telex:* 26464 AAPS 2W
*Key Personnel*
Chairperson: Dr Ibbo Mandaza
Head of Publications Division: Mrs J L Kazembe
Founded: 1989
Research, training & publications.

Subjects: Developing Countries, Economics, Environmental Studies, Government, Political Science, Public Administration, Social Sciences, Sociology
ISBN Prefix(es): 1-77905
Number of titles published annually: 5 Print; 1 CD-ROM
Subsidiaries: Southern Africa Publishing & Printing Houses (SAPPHO)
Distributed by African Books Collective
Distributor for CODESRIA

**SAZ**, see Standards Association of Zimbabwe (SAZ)

**Scholastic Books**, *imprint of* College Press Publishers (Pvt) Ltd

**Standards Association of Zimbabwe (SAZ)**
Northridge Park, Northend Close, Borrowdale, Harare
Mailing Address: PO Box 2259, Harare
*Tel:* (04) 885511; (04) 885512; (04) 882021; (04) 882022 *Fax:* (04) 882020
*E-mail:* sazlabs@mall.pcl.co.zw
*Key Personnel*
Dir General: M P Mutasa *Tel:* (04) 885517 *Fax:* (04) 882581 *E-mail:* standards@mail.pci.co.zw
Dir, Operations: Dr O Chinyanakobver *Tel:* (04) 753800; (04) 753802 *Fax:* (04) 749181 *E-mail:* sazlabs@mweb.co.zw
Founded: 1957
Subjects: Agriculture, Automotive, Chemistry, Chemical Engineering, Civil Engineering, Electronics, Electrical Engineering, Energy, Engineering (General), Mechanical Engineering
ISBN Prefix(es): 0-86928
Number of titles published annually: 96 Print
Total Titles: 1,173 Print
*Branch Office(s)*
PO Box 591, Mutare, Contact: Mr P Chiadzwa *Tel:* (020) 60516, (020) 656130 *Fax:* (020) 66252 *E-mail:* sazmutare@technopark.co.zw
PO Box RY 129, Raylton, Bulawayo, Contact: Mr A G Ncube *Tel:* (09) 70447, (09) 71876 *Fax:* (09) 70447 *E-mail:* sazbyo@acacia.mweb.co.zw

**Thomson Publications Zimbabwe (Pvt) Ltd**
130 Harare St, Harare 217373WE
Mailing Address: PO Box 1683, Harare
*Tel:* (04) 736835 *Fax:* (04) 749803
*E-mail:* tpubl@mweb.co.zw
*Telex:* 4705 ZW
*Key Personnel*
General Manager: Brian Gamble *Tel:* (04) 749741
Founded: 1954
Subjects: Accounting, Agriculture, Automotive, Business, Communications, Economics
ISBN Prefix(es): 0-7974
Total Titles: 7 Print
Subsidiaries: Amalgamated Publications

**University of Zimbabwe Library**
PO Box MP 45, Mount Pleasant, Harare
*Tel:* (04) 303211 *Fax:* (04) 335383
*E-mail:* mainlib@uzlib.uz.zw; infocentre@uzlib.uz.ac.zw
*Web Site:* www.uz.ac.zw/library
*Key Personnel*
Librarian: Dr B Mbambo
Founded: 1957
Number of titles published annually: 14,300 Print
Total Titles: 597,356 Print
*Parent Company:* National University of Science & Technology
*Associate Companies:* Africa University; Solusi University College
Divisions: National University of Science & Technology Library

**University of Zimbabwe Publications+**
Main Admin Bldg, 1st floor, West Wing, Mount
Pleasant, Harare
Mailing Address: PO Box MP 167, Mount Pleas-
ant, Harare
*Tel:* (04) 303211 (ext 1236 or 1662) *Fax:* (04)
333407
*E-mail:* uzpub@admin.uz.ac.zn
*Web Site:* www.uz.ac.zw/publications/
*Telex:* 26580 UNIVZ ZW *Cable:* UNIVERSITY
*Key Personnel*
Dir, Publications: M S Mtetwa
Founded: 1969
Subjects: History, Language Arts, Linguistics, Lit-
erature, Literary Criticism, Essays, Medicine,
Nursing, Dentistry, Philosophy, Religion -
Other, Science (General), Social Sciences, So-
ciology, Technology
ISBN Prefix(es): 0-908307; 1-77920; 0-86924
Distributed by African Books Collective (UK)

**Ventures**, *imprint of* College Press Publishers
(Pvt) Ltd

**Vision Publications+**
753 Senga 2, Gweru
Founded: 1996
Subjects: Education, Fiction, Language Arts, Lin-
guistics, Literature, Literary Criticism, Essays,
Nonfiction (General), Poetry, Religion - Protes-
tant, Theology
*Parent Company:* Vision Enterprises

**ZEB**, *imprint of* Zimbabwe Publishing House
(Pvt) Ltd

**Zimbabwe Foundation for Education with
Production (ZIMFEP)+**
Central Ave, Harare
Mailing Address: PO Box 54, Harare
*Tel:* (04) 755991; (04) 771833; (04) 771844;
(04) 771834; (04) 771845; (04) 795679
*Fax:* (04) 749147
*E-mail:* zimfep@africaonline.co.zw

*Key Personnel*
Dir: Patrick Ndlovu
Founded: 1981
Membership(s): Zimbabwe Book Publishers Asso-
ciation.
Subjects: Drama, Theater, Education
ISBN Prefix(es): 0-908303

**Zimbabwe International Book Fair+**
Harare Gardens, J Nyerere Way, Harare
Mailing Address: PO Box CY 1179, Causeway,
Harare
*Tel:* (04) 702104; (04) 702108 *Fax:* (04) 702129
*E-mail:* execdir@zibf.org.zw
*Web Site:* www.zibf.org.zw
*Key Personnel*
Executive Dir: Samuel Matsangaise *Tel:* (04)
704112
Subjects: Developing Countries
Foreign Rep(s): Becky Clarke (Caribbean, Eu-
rope, North America); Vikas Ghai (Asia); Mar-
ilyn Mevana (Lesotho, South Africa, Swazi-
land); Serah Mwanyiky (East Africa); Akoss
Ofori-Mensah (West Africa)

**Zimbabwe Publishing House (Pvt) Ltd+**
183 Arcturus Rd, Kamfinsa Centre, Greendale
Mailing Address: PO Box GD 510, Harre
*Tel:* (04) 495335; (04) 497555 *Fax:* (04) 497554
*E-mail:* trade@zph.co.zw
*Telex:* 6035 Zph Zw
*Key Personnel*
Chairman: Mr D Martin
General Manager: Mwazvita Madondo
Editorial Manager & Rights & Permissions:
Promise Mayo
Founded: 1981
Subjects: Cookery, Education, Geography, Ge-
ology, History, Literature, Literary Criticism,
Essays, Mathematics, Natural History, Science
(General)
ISBN Prefix(es): 0-949225; 0-949932; 0-908300;
1-77901
Total Titles: 187 Print
*Associate Companies:* African Publishing Group,
PO Box 90150, Contact: Helena Perry *Tel:* (04)

497 55518 *Fax:* (04) 497 5554 *E-mail:* apg@
ld.co.zw
Imprints: ZEB; ZPH
Subsidiaries: Zimbabwe Educational Books
*Branch Office(s)*
PO Box 1442, Bulawayo, Contact: Zwelithini
Mpofu *Tel:* (04) 74666
PO Box 384, Masvingo, Contact: Stephan Rubaba
*Tel:* (034) 68137
PO Box 1029, Mutare, Contact: Absalom Kun-
zwu *Tel:* (020) 08716
PO Box 1191, Gweru *Tel:* (054) 24978
*Bookshop(s):* Frontline Bookshop, PO Box 350,
Harare
*Warehouse:* 97 Coventry Rd, Workington Harare
*Tel:* (04) 667170

**Zimbabwe Women Writers+**
78 Kaguvi St, Harare
Mailing Address: PO Box 4209, Harare
*Tel:* (04) 774261 *Fax:* (04) 750282
*E-mail:* zww@telco.co.zw
*Key Personnel*
Contact: Keresia Chateuka
Founded: 1990
Subjects: Nonfiction (General), Poetry
*Orders to:* PO Box 4209, Harare

**Zimbabwe Women's Bureau+**
43 Hillside Rd, Cranborne, Harare
Mailing Address: PO Box CR 120, Cranborne,
Harare
*Tel:* (04) 747905; (04) 747809; (04) 747433;
(263) 720575 *Fax:* (04) 747905
*E-mail:* zwbtc@africaonline.co.zw
*Key Personnel*
Dir: Fiona Mwashita
Founded: 1978
Subjects: Agriculture, Education, Finance, Health,
Nutrition, Human Relations

**ZIMFEP**, see Zimbabwe Foundation for
Education with Production (ZIMFEP)

**ZPH**, *imprint of* Zimbabwe Publishing House
(Pvt) Ltd

# Type of Publication Index

# BELLES LETTRES

# DICTIONARIES, ENCYCLOPEDIAS

# DIRECTORIES, REFERENCE BOOKS

## FINE EDITIONS, ILLUSTRATED BOOKS

# GENERAL TRADE BOOKS - HARDCOVER

## JUVENILE & YOUNG ADULT BOOKS

# LARGE PRINT BOOKS

## PAPERBACK BOOKS - TRADE

## PROFESSIONAL BOOKS

## SCHOLARLY BOOKS

# TEXTBOOKS - ELEMENTARY

## TEXTBOOKS - SECONDARY

## TRANSLATIONS

# UNIVERSITY PRESSES

# VIDEO CASSETTES

# Subject Index

## ADVERTISING

## AERONAUTICS, AVIATION

## AFRICAN AMERICAN STUDIES

## AGRICULTURE

# ANTHROPOLOGY

# ANTIQUES

# ARCHAEOLOGY

# ARCHITECTURE & INTERIOR DESIGN

# ART

## ASTROLOGY, OCCULT

## ASTRONOMY

## BIBLICAL STUDIES

# BIOLOGICAL SCIENCES

## CAREER DEVELOPMENT

## CHEMISTRY, CHEMICAL ENGINEERING

## CHILD CARE & DEVELOPMENT

# CIVIL ENGINEERING

## COMMUNICATIONS

## COMPUTER SCIENCE

# CRAFTS, GAMES, HOBBIES

# CRIMINOLOGY

# DEVELOPING COUNTRIES

## DISABILITY, SPECIAL NEEDS

# EARTH SCIENCES

# ECONOMICS

# EDUCATION

# ELECTRONICS, ELECTRICAL ENGINEERING

# ENERGY

# ENGLISH AS A SECOND LANGUAGE

# ENVIRONMENTAL STUDIES

## FASHION

# FICTION

# FILM, VIDEO

## FOREIGN COUNTRIES

# GARDENING, PLANTS

# GEOGRAPHY, GEOLOGY

# GOVERNMENT, POLITICAL SCIENCE

# HEALTH, NUTRITION

# HISTORY

## HOUSE & HOME

## HUMAN RELATIONS

# HUMOR

# JOURNALISM

# LABOR, INDUSTRIAL RELATIONS

# LANGUAGE ARTS, LINGUISTICS

# LAW

# LIBRARY & INFORMATION SCIENCES

## LITERATURE, LITERARY CRITICISM, ESSAYS

# MARITIME

# MARKETING

## MICROCOMPUTERS

# NATIVE AMERICAN STUDIES

# NATURAL HISTORY

# OUTDOOR RECREATION

# PARAPSYCHOLOGY

# PHILOSOPHY

# PHYSICAL SCIENCES

# PHYSICS

# POETRY

# PSYCHOLOGY, PSYCHIATRY

# PUBLIC ADMINISTRATION

# PUBLISHING & BOOK TRADE REFERENCE

# RELIGION - BUDDHIST

## RELIGION - HINDU

## ROMANCE

## SCIENCE FICTION, FANTASY

# SOCIAL SCIENCES, SOCIOLOGY

## SPORTS, ATHLETICS

## TECHNOLOGY

# VETERINARY SCIENCE

## WESTERN FICTION

## WINE & SPIRITS

## WOMEN'S STUDIES

# Literary Agents

## Argentina

**International Editors' Co**
Ave Cabildo 1156 - 1 A, 1426 Buenos Aires
*Tel:* (011) 4786-0888 *Fax:* (011) 4786-0888
*E-mail:* escritores@lvd.com.ar
Founded: 1939
Agencia Literaria; Subsidiaries in Spain & Brazil.

## Australia

**Australian Licensing Corp**
Affiliate of Little Hare Books Pty Ltd
Unit 4/21 Mary St, Surry Hills, NSW 2010
*Tel:* (02) 9280 2220 *Fax:* (02) 9280 2223
*E-mail:* rodhare@alc-online.com
*Web Site:* www.alc-online.com
Founded: 1999
Membership(s): Australian Publishers Association.
Specializes in children's books.

**Curtis Brown (Australia) Pty Ltd**
27 Union St, Paddington, Sydney, NSW 2021
Mailing Address: PO Box 19, Paddington, NSW 2021
*Tel:* (02) 9331 5301 *Fax:* (02) 9360 3935
*E-mail:* info@curtisbrown.com.au
*Key Personnel*
Man Dir: Fiona Inglis
Dir: Tim Curnow *E-mail:* tim@curtisbrown.com.au
Contact: Garth Nix
Founded: 1967

**Bryson Agency Australia Pty Ltd**
313-315 Flinders Lane, 1st floor, Melbourne 3000
Mailing Address: PO Box 226, Flinders Lane PO, Melbourne 8009
*Tel:* (03) 9620 9100 *Fax:* (03) 9621 2788
*E-mail:* agency@bryson.com.au
*Web Site:* www.bryson.com.au
*Key Personnel*
Contact: Fran Bryson
Book manuscripts only, in hard copy. Must send a sample of first chapters (5000 words maximum), a synopsis (1-2 pages), CV & return postage.

**The Mary Cunnane Agency Pty Ltd**
28 Milina Rd, Matcham, NSW 2250
Mailing Address: PO Box 781, Terrigal, NSW 2260
*Tel:* (02) 438599922 *Fax:* (02) 43651093
*E-mail:* info@cunnaneagency.com
*Web Site:* www.cunnaneagency.com
*Key Personnel*
Dir: Mary Cunnane
Founded: 1999
Entire manuscript & sample chapters in hard copy only after query which may be by mail, phone or email. Adult fiction & nonfiction.

**Diversity Management**
PO Box 1449, Darlinghurst, NSW 1300
*Tel:* (02) 9130 4305 *Fax:* (02) 9365 1426
*Key Personnel*
Agent: Bill Tikos *E-mail:* bill@diversitym.com.au
Specialize in adult nonfiction. Contact via e-mail.

**The Drummond Agency**
PO Box 572, Woodend, Victoria 3442
*Tel:* (03) 5427 3644 *Fax:* (03) 5427 3655
*Key Personnel*
Dir: Sheila Drummond *E-mail:* sheilad@ozemail.com.au
Founded: 1995
Also offers international rights consultancy to publishers.

## Austria

**Literaturagentur Andreas Brunner**
Schaeffergasse 22/4, 1040 Vienna
*Tel:* (01) 5333191 *Fax:* (01) 5333191-15
*E-mail:* brunner@literaturagentur.at
*Web Site:* www.literaturagentur.at
*Key Personnel*
Dir & Owner: Andreas Brunner
Founded: 1996 (as Literary Agency Diana Voigt)
Covering the German language market for US, UK & Canadian publishers & international authors.
Specializes in high quality fiction, psychology, self help, history, politics, theatre, film.

## Barbados

**The Barbados National Trust**
Wildey Great House, Wildey St, St Michael
*Tel:* 246-426-2421 *Fax:* 246-429-9055
*E-mail:* natrust@sunbeach.net
*Web Site:* trust.funbarbados.com
*Key Personnel*
President: John Cole
Executive Dir: Penelope Hynam Roach
Founded: 1961
Specializes in heritage & environmental conservation.

## Belgium

**Toneelfonds J Janssens BVBA**
Te Boelaerlei 107, 2140 Borgerhout, Antwerp
*Tel:* (03) 366 44 00 *Fax:* (03) 366 45 01
*E-mail:* info@toneelfonds.be
*Web Site:* www.toneelfonds.be
*Key Personnel*
Dir: Jessica Janssens *E-mail:* jessica.janssens@toneelfonds.be
Founded: 1880
Publisher of plays & literary agent for playwrights.
Specializes in plays.

## Brazil

**Balcells Mello e Souza Riff Agencia Literaria SC Ltda**, see Agencia Literaria BMSR Ltda

**Agencia Literaria BMSR Ltda** (BMSR Literary Agency)
Rua Visconde de Piraja, 414/1108, 22410-002 Rio de Janeiro-RJ
*Tel:* (021) 2287-6299 *Fax:* (021) 2287-6393
*E-mail:* bmsr@bmsr.com.br
*Web Site:* www.bmsr.com.br
*Key Personnel*
Literary Agent & Executive: Lucia Riff
*E-mail:* lucia@bmsr.com.br
Founded: 1991
Co-agent of foreign publishers & literary agencies.
Specializes in foreign authors for the Brazilian/Portuguese language market & Brazilian authors for Brazil & abroad.

**Pagina da Cultura Agencia Literaria Ideias sobre Linhas Ltda**
Affiliate of Camara Brasileira do Livro
R Coronel Jose Euseblo, 95, Vila Dona Paula Casa 2, 01239-030 Sao Paulo-SP
*Tel:* (011) 31293900
*E-mail:* paginadacultura@pobox.com
*Web Site:* www.paginadacultura.com.br
*Key Personnel*
Contact: Marisa Moura *E-mail:* marisa.moura@paginadacultura.com.br
Founded: 1994
Specializes in business, essays, fiction, history, religions, self-help, children & juvenile books.

**Karin Schindler**
CP 19051, 04505-970 Sao Paulo
*Tel:* (011) 5041-9177 *Fax:* (011) 5041-9077
*E-mail:* kschind@terra.com.br
*Key Personnel*
Contact: Karin Schindler

## Czech Republic

**A R T Dialog**
Michelska 81, 141 00 Prague 4
*Tel:* (0420) 24148 2808 *Fax:* (0420) 24148 1442
*E-mail:* artdialog@mybox.cz
*Web Site:* www.artdialog-literary.wz.cz
*Key Personnel*
Contact: Rene J Tesar *E-mail:* rene.tesar@worldonline.cz; Daniela Vranovska
Founded: 1990
Specializes in import of English & German language literature translation rights to Czech book market.

**Agency Rene Tesar Dialog**, see A R T Dialog

**DILIA**
Kratkeho 1, 19003 Prague 9
*Tel:* (02) 83891587 *Fax:* (02) 826348; (02) 83893599; (02) 83890598; (02) 83890597
*E-mail:* chabr@dilia.cz
*Web Site:* www.dilia.cz *Cable:* DILIA PRAG

*Key Personnel*
Man Dir: Ladislav Simon
Contact: Dr Vera Stranska
Theatrical & literary agency.
Membership(s): Society for Protection of Authors' Rights.

# Denmark

**Bookman Literary Agency**
Bastager 3, 2950 Vedbaek, Copenhagen
*Tel:* 45892520 *Fax:* 45892501
*Web Site:* www.bookman.dk *Cable:* BOOKMAN; COPENHAGEN
*Key Personnel*
Agent: Bebbe Kirsten Lauritzen *E-mail:* bebbel@bookman.dk; Ib H Lauritzen *E-mail:* ihl@bookman.dk
Founded: 1912
Also acts as a literary agent in Denmark, Sweden, Norway, Finland & Iceland for foreign authors.
Specializes in general fiction & non-fiction (business books, golf & tennis), serial sales.

**ICBS**, see ICBS/IBIS ApS

**ICBS/IBIS ApS**
Kvaesthusgade 3F, 1251 Copenhagen
*Tel:* 33114255 *Fax:* 33911167
*E-mail:* icbs@get2net.dk
*Web Site:* www.icbs-ibis.dk
*Key Personnel*
Contact: Virginia Allen Jensen; Johan Broensted
Founded: 1962
Specializes in children's books, co-productions, adult fiction & nonfiction.

**Leonhardt & Hoier Literary Agency ApS**
Studiestr 35, 1455 Copenhagen
*Tel:* 33132523 *Fax:* 33134992
*Web Site:* www.leonhardt-hoier.dk
*Key Personnel*
Dir: Anneli Hoier *E-mail:* anneli@leonhardt-hoier.dk
Contact: Monica Gram *E-mail:* monica@leonhardt-hoier.dk
Representing international publishers & agents in Scandinavia & Scandinavian authors worldwide.
Specializes in modern fiction.

**Licht & Burr Literary Agency**
Klosterstr 21A, 1157 Copenhagen K
*Tel:* 3333 0021 *Fax:* 3333 0521
*E-mail:* mail@licht-burr.de
*Web Site:* www.licht-burr.de
*Key Personnel*
Chief Executive: Anne Burr; Trine Licht
Representing American, Australian, British & Canadian agents & publishers in Denmark, Finland, Iceland, Norway & Sweden & representing Scandanavian authors worldwide.

**Ulla Lohren Literary Agency**
Vaerebrovej 89, 2880 Bagsvaerd
*Tel:* 44494515 *Fax:* 44493515
*E-mail:* ulla.litag@get2net.dk

**Scanvik Books Import ApS**
Esplanaden 8 B, 1263 Copenhagen
*Tel:* 3312 7766 *Fax:* 33 91 28 82
*E-mail:* mail@scanvik.dk; scanvik@bog.dk
*Web Site:* www.scanvik.dk
*Key Personnel*
Dir: John Roberts; Uwe Schultheiss
Founded: 1980

Wholesaler, distributor & agent.
Specializes in maps & travel guides.

# Egypt (Arab Republic of Egypt)

**The Egyptian Society for the Dissemination of Universal Culture & Knowledge (ESDUCK)**
1081 Corniche El Nil, Garden City, Cairo
Mailing Address: PO Box 21, Cairo
*Tel:* (02) 7940295; (02) 7945079 *Fax:* (02) 7940295 *Cable:* ESDUCK
*Key Personnel*
Executive Manager: Dr Amin El-Gamal

**ESDUCK**, see The Egyptian Society for the Dissemination of Universal Culture & Knowledge (ESDUCK)

# Finland

**Werner Soederstrom Osakeyhtio (WSOY)**
Bulevardi 12, 00120 Helsinki
Mailing Address: PO Box 222, 00121 Helsinki
*Tel:* (09) 616 81 *Fax:* (09) 6168 3560
*Web Site:* www.wsoy.fi
*Telex:* 122644 Wsoy *Cable:* WSOY HELSINKI
*Key Personnel*
Foreign Rights Manager: Sirkku Klemola
*Tel:* (09) 6168 3633 *Fax:* (09) 6168 3344
*E-mail:* sirkku@klemola@wsoy.fi
Founded: 1878
Also Publisher.
*Parent Company:* Sanoma WSOY

**WSOY**, see Werner Soederstrom Osakeyhtio (WSOY)

# France

**Agence de l'Est**
11, rue Git-le-Coeur, 75006 Paris
*Tel:* (01) 46334816; (06) 6546 7928 *Fax:* (01) 46334816
*E-mail:* agencedelest1@wanadoo.fr
Founded: 1999
Represents French authors in central & eastern Europe.
Specializes in negotiating between France & Eastern Europe (from Estonia to Albania & from the Czech Republic to Russia) for non-illustrated & illustrated books.

**Eliane Benisti Literary Agency**
80 rue des Sts-Peres, 75007 Paris
*Tel:* (01) 42228533 *Fax:* (01) 45441817
*E-mail:* benisti@elianebenisti.com
*Key Personnel*
Dir: Eliane Benisti

**EAIS Literary Agents**
8/12 rue de l'Abreuvoir, 92400 Courbevoie
*Tel:* (01) 47 88 08 40 *Fax:* (01) 47 88 08 40

*Key Personnel*
Vice President: Vera le Marie *E-mail:* vera.le.marie@wanadoo.fr
Founded: 1983
Representation of American publishers & writers in France, & French publishers & writers in the USA & Russia. Specialize in foreign languages: English, German, French, Dutch, & Polish.
*Parent Company:* EAIS - France
*U.S. Office(s):* European American Information Services Inc, Sarasota, FL 34236, United States, Contact: Dr Allan M Chyrtowski *Tel:* 941-955-3472 *Fax:* 941-955-5365

**European American Information Services Inc**, see EAIS Literary Agents

**Lora Fountain & Associates Literary Agency**
(Agence Litteraire Lora Fountain & Associates)
7 rue de Belfort, 75011 Paris
*Tel:* (01) 43 56 21 96 *Fax:* (01) 43 48 22 72
*E-mail:* agence@fountlit.com
*Web Site:* www.lora-fountain.com
*Key Personnel*
Man Dir: Lora Fountain *E-mail:* lora@fountlit.com
Associate Agent: Alexandre Civico *Tel:* (01) 43 56 10 22 *E-mail:* alexandre@fountlit.com; Sandrine Paccher *Tel:* (01) 43 56 10 22 *E-mail:* sandrine@fountlit.com; Svetlana Ramon *E-mail:* svetlana@fountlit.com
Founded: 1985
No unsolicited manuscripts.
Specializes in French rights sales for English-language publishers (UK, Ireland, USA, Canada, Australia & New Zealand). Also sale of rights to Italy, Netherlands, Spain & Russia. Quality adult fiction & nonfiction, children's literature.

**Agence Hoffman**
77 Blvd St-Michel, 75005 Paris
*Tel:* (01) 43265694 *Fax:* (01) 43263407
*E-mail:* info@agence-hoffman.com
*Telex:* 203605 F *Cable:* AGHOFF PARIS
*Key Personnel*
Contact: Boris Hoffman; Ursula Veit; Georges Hoffman
*Branch Office(s)*
Munich, Germany

**Michelle Lapautre**
6 rue Jean Carries, 75007 Paris
*Tel:* (01) 47348241 *Fax:* (01) 47340090
*E-mail:* lapautre@club-internet.fr
*Parent Company:* Agence Michelle Lapautre

**Montreal-Contacts/The Rights Agency**
70 bd de Picpus, 75012 Paris
*Tel:* (01) 43 40 06 10 *Fax:* (01) 43 40 02 12
*Key Personnel*
Owner: Luc Jutras *Tel:* 450-461-1575 (Canada) *E-mail:* ljutras@montreal-contacts.com
Dir: Anne Confuron *E-mail:* aconfuron@montreal-contacts.com
Represents American, Canadian & other foreign publishers &/or literary exclusively. No author representation.

**La Nouvelle Agence**
7 rue Corneille, 75006 Paris
*Tel:* (01) 43258560 *Fax:* (01) 43254798
*E-mail:* lnaparis@aol.com
*Telex:* 250303 F (Paris Bourse)
*Key Personnel*
Contact: Mary Kling

**Frederique Porretta**
70 rue d'Assas, 75006 Paris
*Tel:* (01) 45448868 *Fax:* (01) 45446936
*E-mail:* f.poretta@wanadoo.fr

*Key Personnel*
Rights Dir: Frederique Poretta
Founded: 1992

**Shelley Power Literary Agency Ltd**
13 rue du Pre Saint Gervais, 75019 Paris
*Tel:* (01) 42383649 *Fax:* (01) 40407008
*Key Personnel*
Dir: Shelley Power *E-mail:* shelley.power@
wanadoo.fr
Founded: 1976
Handles general commercial fiction, quality fiction, business, self-help, health, true crime, investigative exposes, film & entertainment. No scripts, short stories, children's or poetry. Preliminary letter with brief outline of project plus return postage. No reading fee.

**Promotion Litteraire**
12 rue Pergolese, F-75116 Paris
*Tel:* (01) 45004210 *Fax:* (01) 45001018
*E-mail:* promolit@club-internet.fr
*Key Personnel*
Dir: Mariella Giannetti
Specializes in literary translations, book & article translations.

# Germany

**Agence Hoffman**
Bechsteinstr 2, 80804 Munich
*Tel:* (089) 3084807; (089) 3087469 *Fax:* (089) 3082108
*E-mail:* info@agencehoffman.de
*Web Site:* www.agencehoffman.de *Cable:* AGHOFF MUNICH
*Key Personnel*
Contact: Ursula Bender *E-mail:* u.bender@ agencehoffman.de
Literary agents & publishers from UK & USA.
*Branch Office(s)*
Blvd St Michel, 77, 75005 Paris, France

**Asien und Lateinamerika eV**, see Society for the Promotion of African, Asian & Latin American Literature

**Autoren- und Verlags-Agentur GmbH (AVA)**
Seeblickstr 46, 82211 Herrsching-Breitbrunn, Bavaria
*Tel:* (08152) 925883 *Fax:* (08152) 3076
*E-mail:* avagmbh@aol.com
*Key Personnel*
Contact: Claudia von Hornstein
Founded: 1989
Specializes in fiction & nonfiction.

**AVA**, see Autoren- und Verlags-Agentur GmbH (AVA)

**Dr Ivanka Beil, Internationale Handelsvermittlung im Medien- und Verlagswesen**
Schollstr 1, 69469 Weinheim
*Tel:* (06201) 14611 *Fax:* (06201) 17280
Founded: 1984
Specializes in copyright intervention, co-productions, representation of publishing houses, authors, illustrators, children's & young readers' books (also on film & television productions), marketing.
*Branch Office(s)*
Theodor Heuss Str 14, 69469 Weinheim

**The Berlin Agency (Jung-Lindemann & Olechnowitz)**
Niebuhrstr 74, 10629 Berlin
*Tel:* (030) 88702888 *Fax:* (030) 88702889
*E-mail:* junglindemann@berlinagency.de
*Web Site:* www.berlinagency.de
*Key Personnel*
Contact: Ms Frauke Jung-Lindemann
Founded: 1999
Specializes in fiction & nonfiction.

**Cartoon-Caricature-Contor (CCC)**
Rosmarinstr 4, 80939 Munich
*Tel:* (089) 3233669 *Fax:* (089) 3226859
*E-mail:* ccc@c5.net
*Web Site:* www.c5.net
*Key Personnel*
Dir: Arno Koch
Founded: 1977
Acts as agents for cartoons, caricatures & illustrations.
Specializes in cartoons, with stock of about 100,000.

**CCC**, see Cartoon-Caricature-Contor (CCC)

**Copyright International Agency Corina GmbH**
Beerenstr 22A, 14163 Berlin
*Tel:* (030) 80902386 *Fax:* (030) 80902388
*E-mail:* info@corina.com
*Web Site:* www.corina.com
*Key Personnel*
President: Werner B Thiele
Founded: 1998
Internet literary agency. Offers translation rights.
Specializes in literature from & for Middle & Eastern European countries.

**Gesellschaft zur Foerderung der Literatur aus Afrika**, see Society for the Promotion of African, Asian & Latin American Literature

**Gina Schlenz Literatur-Agentur Koln**
Gruenenborn 49, 53797 Lohmar
*Tel:* (02206) 81125 *Fax:* (02206) 81125
*E-mail:* litschlenz@aol.com
*Key Personnel*
Contact: Gina Schlenz
Founded: 1989
Specializes in children & young adults.

**Agentur Literatur Gudrun Hebel**
Behaimstr 20, 10585 Berlin
*Tel:* (030) 34 70 77 67 *Fax:* (030) 34 70 77 68
*E-mail:* info@agentur-literatur.de; gudrun.hebel@ agentur-literatur.de
*Web Site:* www.agentur-literatur.de
*Key Personnel*
Contact: Gudrun Hebel
Representing foreign publishers, agencies & authors in German-language-countries as well as German authors & publishers worldwide.
Specializes in Scandinavian literature.

**IBA International Media & Book Agency**
Heinrich Roller-Str 16 - 17 2 Hof, 10405 Berlin
Mailing Address: Postfach 550 142, 10371 Berlin
*Tel:* (030) 4437 9155 *Fax:* (030) 4437 9199
*E-mail:* office@iba-berlin.de
*Web Site:* www.iba-berlin.de
*Key Personnel*
President & Executive Dir: Ingo-Eric M Schmidt-Braul
Founded: 1991
Also acts as representative of authors & publishing houses.
Specializes in fiction, nonfiction, economics.

**Keil & Keil Literary Agency**
Schulterblatt 58, 20357 Hamburg

*Tel:* (040) 27166892 *Fax:* (040) 27166896
*E-mail:* anfragen@keil-keil.com
*Web Site:* www.keil-keil.com
*Key Personnel*
Agent: Anja Keil *Tel:* (040) 27166894
*E-mail:* ak@keil-keil.com; Bettina Keil
*Tel:* (040) 27166893 *E-mail:* bk@keil-keil.com
Founded: 1995
Email queries preferred (no attachments). Have representatives in all major international markets. No unsolicited manuscripts, query first; provide outline with self-addressed stamped envelope.
Specializes in general trade fiction & nonfiction. No fantasy, sci-fi & children's & young adult..

**Ingrid Anna Kleihues Verlags und Autorenagentur**
Weinbergweg 62A, 70569 Stuttgart
*Tel:* (0711) 6788800 *Fax:* (0711) 6788801
*E-mail:* info@agentur-kleihues.de
Founded: 1990
Specializes in non-fiction.

**LITkom Elisabeth Falk Agentur fur Literatur und Kommunikation** (LITkom Elisabeth Falk Agency for Literature & Communication)
Auf Erden 2, 54610 Buedesheim, Rheinland-Pfalz
*E-mail:* falk@litkom.de
*Web Site:* www.litkom.de *Cable:* LITKOM E.FALK
*Key Personnel*
Agent: Elisabeth Falk
Founded: 1993
Represents authors & handles their manuscripts; exhibits international book art objects; organizes literary events.
Specializes in art books, exhibitions & literary functions.

**MBMS-Bibliography & Management Service**
Postfach 1206, 57271 Hilchenbach
*Tel:* (02733) 7657 *Fax:* (02733) 8492
*Key Personnel*
Contact: Christiane Urlea-Schoen *E-mail:* urlea@ cheerful.com
Founded: 1989
Specializes in literature, medicine, management, business.

**Medienbuero Muenchen** (Media Agency Munich)
Division of Philosophia Verlag GmbH
Gundelindenstr 4, 80805 Munich
Mailing Address: Postfach 221362, 80503 Munich
*Tel:* (089) 299975 *Fax:* (089) 299975
*E-mail:* info@medienbuero-muenchen.com
*Web Site:* www.medienbuero-muenchen.com
*Key Personnel*
Publisher: Ulrich Staudinger *E-mail:* ulrich. staudinger@philosophiaverlag.com
Founded: 2000
Agency for authors & publishers in print, TV, film & new media.
Specializes in nonfiction, science, fiction.

**Merchandising Muenchen KG**
Reichenbachstr 2, 85737 Ismaning
Mailing Address: Postfach 1339, 85767 Unterfohring
*Tel:* (089) 95078600 *Fax:* (089) 95078700
*E-mail:* info.line@merchandising-muenchen.de
*Web Site:* www.merchandisingmedia.com
*Key Personnel*
Contact: Bettina Koeckler *E-mail:* bettina. koeckler@merchandisingmedia.com
Specializes in sales, marketing, business licenses.
*Branch Office(s)*
Hausvogteiplatz 1, 10117 Berlin *Tel:* (030) 20902658 *Fax:* (030) 20902643

**Dr Ray-Gude Mertin Literarische Agentur**
Friedrichstr 1, 61348 Bad Homburg
*Tel:* (06172) 29842 *Fax:* (06172) 29771
*E-mail:* info@mertin-litag.de
*Key Personnel*
Contact: Mrs Ray-Guede Mertin *E-mail:* rg.
mertin@mertin-litag.de
Worldwide representation of authors from Brazil,
Portugal, Africa, Latin America & Spain.
Specializes in fiction & nonfiction.

**Literaturbetreuung Klaus Middendorf (LKM)**
Auerbergweg 8, 86836 Graben
*Tel:* (08232) 78463 *Fax:* (08232) 78468
*E-mail:* lkmcorp@t-online.de
*Web Site:* www.lkmcorp.com
*Key Personnel*
Contact: Klaus Middendorf
Founded: 1986
Author & publisher representation.

**Martina M Oepping Literary Agency**
Wolfsgangstr 34, 60322 Frankfurt am Main
*Tel:* (069) 59790011 *Fax:* (069) 59790012
*E-mail:* litag@oepping.de
*Web Site:* www.oepping.de
*Key Personnel*
Literary Agent: Martina M Oepping
Founded: 1996
Specializes in children's & juvenile books, au-
thors & illustrators.

**Literatur-Agentur Axel Poldner**
Ostpreussentr 27, 81927 Munich
Mailing Address: Raduhner Str 11, 12355 Berlin
*Tel:* (089) 909 558 92 *Fax:* (089) 909 558 91
*E-mail:* info@poldner.de
*Web Site:* www.poldner.de
*Key Personnel*
Contact: Axel Poldner *E-mail:* axel.poldner@
poldner.de
Founded: 1970
Specializes in multimedia projects.

**Quelle Press**
Schoenbergerstr 49, 79227 Schallstadt
Mailing Address: Postfach 1314, 79013 Freiburg/
Br
*Tel:* (07664) 7016 *Fax:* (07664) 60979
*E-mail:* quellepress.germany@gmx.net *Cable:*
QUELLEPRESS -SHALLSTADT
*Key Personnel*
President: Friedrich-Wilhelm Koenig
Founded: 1948
Services include editing advice, reading, transla-
tion & international activities; global licensing
for 50 years; 18,900 copyrights sold.
Specializes in mass market, business books, eso-
teric, holistic, new age, romances, anthologies,
newspaper (serials), books for young readers,
trade books, alternative medicine, basic busi-
ness books, self counsel books, self improve-
ment books, life style books, psychology, reli-
gion, human science, sports, self help books for
young readers.
*Branch Office(s)*
Australia
Bulgaria
China
Croatia
Czech Republic
France
Hungary
India
Indonesia
Italy
Japan
Republic of Korea
Poland
Portugal
Russian Federation (East European Market)
Slovakia

Spain
Taiwan, Province of China

**Thomas Schlueck GmbH**
Hinter der Worth 12, 30827 Garbsen
*Tel:* (05131) 4975-60 *Fax:* (05131) 4975-89
*E-mail:* mail@schlueckagent.com
*Web Site:* www.schlueckagent.com
*Key Personnel*
Agent: Joachim Jessen *E-mail:* j.jessen@
schlueckagent.com; Bastian Schlueck
*E-mail:* b.schlueck@schlueckagent.com;
Thomas Schlueck *E-mail:* t.schlueck@
schlueckagent.com
Agent Children/Juvenile: Tanja Heitmann
*E-mail:* t.heitmann@schlueckagent.com
Founded: 1970
Full representation of Anglo-American, Spanish
& Scandinavian authors, agents & publishers in
German language areas, as well as representa-
tion of German authors. Also handling second
rights of cover illustrations, Europe wide.

**Skandinavia Verlag**
Ithweg 31, 14163 Berlin
*Tel:* (030) 8137006 *Fax:* (030) 8141029
*Key Personnel*
Contact: Marianne Weno
Founded: 1969
Specializes in Scandinavian stage, radio & TV
plays.

**Society for the Promotion of African, Asian &
Latin American Literature**
Reineckstr 3, 60313 Frankfurt am Main
Mailing Address: Postfach 10 01 16, 60001
Frankfurt am Main
*Tel:* (069) 2102247 *Fax:* (069) 2102227
*E-mail:* litprom@book-fair.com
*Web Site:* www.litprom.de
*Key Personnel*
President: Peter Weidhaas *E-mail:* weidhaas@
book-fair.com
Dir: Peter Ripken *Tel:* (0160) 780 38 09
*E-mail:* litprom@book-fair.com
Founded: 1980
The Society seeks to promote German translations
of creative writing from Africa, Asia & Latin
America. It works as a non-profit agency & as
a consultant for German language publishers
& for "Third World" publishers & authors who
have German translation rights to offer. Pub-
lishes *Literaturnachrichten* (Literary News).

**Tipress Deutschland GmbH,** see Tipress
Dienstleistungen fur das Verlagswesen GmbH

**Tipress Dienstleistungen fur das Verlagswesen
GmbH**
Johannes-Fecht-Str 2, 79295 Sulzburg
*Tel:* (07634) 591193 *Fax:* (07634) 591192
*E-mail:* tipress@tipress.com
*Web Site:* www.tipress.com *Cable:* TIPRESS
*Key Personnel*
Chief Executive: Roberto Toso
Assistant: Claudia Robert
Founded: 1980
Specializes in co-editions, illustrated books, hand-
books, encyclopedias, children's books.
*Branch Office(s)*
Tipress Deutschland GmbH, via Cernaia 34,
10122 Turino, Italy, Contact: Ms Claudia
Robert *Tel:* (011) 533487 *Fax:* (011) 535283

# Hungary

**Artisjus**
Meszaros utca 15-17, 1016 Budapest
*Tel:* (01) 488 2600 *Fax:* (01) 212 1544
*E-mail:* info@artisjus.com
*Web Site:* www.artisjus.hu *Cable:* ARTISJUS
*Key Personnel*
Contact: Anita Kenedi
Agency for Theater & Literature of the Hungarian
Bureau for Copyright Protection.

**Katai & Bolza Irodalmi Ugynokseg** (Katai &
Bolza Literary Agents)
Vamhaz Krt 15, 1st floor, No 8, 1093 Budapest
Mailing Address: PO Box 1666, 1465 Budapest
*Tel:* (01) 456-0313 *Fax:* (01) 215-4420
*Web Site:* www.kataibolza.hu
*Key Personnel*
Agent: Peter Bolza *E-mail:* peter@kataibolza.hu;
Katalin Katai *E-mail:* katalin@kataibolza.hu
Founded: 1995
Represents mainly US, British & Italian publish-
ers & agents in the Hungarian market.

# India

**Ajanta Books International**
One U B Jawahar Nagar, Bangalow Rd, Delhi
110007
*Tel:* (011) 23856182 *Fax:* (011) 23856182
*E-mail:* ajantabi@vsnl.com
*Web Site:* ajantabooksinternational.com
*Key Personnel*
Proprietor: Mr S Balwant
Founded: 1975
Specializes in social sciences & humanities, chil-
dren, paperbook.

**Dipak Kumar Guha**
C 1 A / 115 B, Janakpuri, New Delhi 110058
*Tel:* 9810094052 *Fax:* (011) 2-550-0998
*E-mail:* dkguha@eth.net; dkginfo@hgcbroadband.
com (Hong Kong office)
Founded: 1986
Activities also include market evaluation, promo-
tion & public relations, special sales, excess
inventory sales. Now also covering China from
Hong Kong office.
Specializes in east/west rights, co-editions, En-
glish & regional languages, wire services syn-
dication/hook-ups, magazine syndication &
reprint consulting, seek multi-media rights on
CDs, multimedia OEM & distribution market-
ing consulting service.
*Parent Company:* DKG Info Systems, Flat B, 10
Floor, Cheong Fook Mansion, 180 Lai Chi Kok
Road, Mongkok, Kowloon, Hong Kong

# Ireland

**The Office of Public Works, Publications
Branch (OPW)**
51 St Stephen's Green, Dublin 2
*Tel:* (01) 6476000 *Fax:* (01) 6610747
*E-mail:* info@opw.ie
*Web Site:* www.opw.ie
*Key Personnel*
Minister of State, Department of Finance: Tom
Pardon
Irish Government Publications.
Specializes in government publications.

OPW, see The Office of Public Works,
Publications Branch (OPW)


**Jonathan Williams Literary Agency**
Ferrybank House, 6 Park Rd, Dun Laoghaire,
County Dublin
*Tel:* (01) 2803482 *Fax:* (01) 2803482
*Key Personnel*
Dir: Jonathan Williams
Founded: 1981
International coupons, return postage appreciated.
Specializes in works by Irish writers or of Irish
interest.
*Branch Office(s)*
Loecher & Lawrence, Munich, Germany
Lora Fountain, Paris, France
Jan Michael, Amsterdam, Netherlands
Piergiorgio Nicolazzini Literary Agency, Milan,
Italy


# Israel

**The Book Publishers' Association of Israel,
International Promotion & Literary Rights
Department**
29 Carlebach St, 67132 Tel Aviv
Mailing Address: PO Box 20123, 61201 Tel Aviv
*Tel:* (03) 5614121 *Fax:* (03) 5611996
*E-mail:* hamol@tbpai.co.il
*Web Site:* www.tbpai.co.il
*Key Personnel*
Chairman: Shay Hausman
Man Dir: Amnon Ben-Shmuel
Founded: 1939


**Harris-Elon Agency**
43 Emek Refaim St, Jerusalem
Mailing Address: PO Box 8528, 91083 Jerusalem
*Tel:* (02) 563-3237 *Fax:* (02) 561-8711
*E-mail:* litagent@netvision.net.il
*Key Personnel*
Dir: Beth Elon *E-mail:* b_elon@netvision.net.il;
Deborah Harris *E-mail:* d_harris@netvision.net.
il
Managing Editor: Ines Austern *E-mail:* iaustern@
netvision.net.il
Foreign Rights Dir: Efrat Lev *E-mail:* litagent@
netvision.net.il
Founded: 1991


**The Institute for the Translation of Hebrew
Literature**
23 Baruch Hirsch St, Bnei Brak
Mailing Address: PO Box 1005 1, 52001 Ramat
Gan
*Tel:* (03) 579 6830 *Fax:* (03) 579 6832
*E-mail:* hamachon@inter.net.il; litscene@ithl.org.
il
*Web Site:* www.ithl.org.il
*Key Personnel*
Dir: Mrs Nilli Cohen
Founded: 1962
Main activities include promotion of modern He-
brew literature & children's literature in trans-
lation; general literary agency services; sub-
sidies to authors & publishers for translation
of Hebrew literary works & their publication
abroad; assistance in the preparation of an-
thologies of Hebrew literature.
Specializes in Hebrew literature in translation.


# Italy

**Agenzia Letteraria Internazionale**
Via Valpetrosa 1, 20123 Milan
*Tel:* (02) 865445; (02) 861572 *Fax:* (02) 876222
*E-mail:* alidmb@tin.it
*Key Personnel*
President: Dr Donatella Barbieri
Founded: 1898
Right's Representative.


**Luigi Bernabo Associates SRL**
Via Cernaia, 4, 20121 Milan
*Tel:* (02) 45473700 *Fax:* (02) 45473577
*E-mail:* bernabo.luigi@tin.it
*Key Personnel*
Contact: Luigi Bernabo; Daniela Bernabo


**Daniel Doglioli**
Via Lomonaco 15/B, 27100 Pavia
*Tel:* (0382) 529317 *Fax:* (0382) 529317
*Web Site:* www.filastrocche.it/contempo/daniele/
daniele.asp
*Key Personnel*
Contact: Daniel Doglioli *E-mail:* daniel.doglioli@
iol.it
Founded: 1994


**Eulama Literary Agencies**
Via Guido de Ruggiero 28, 00142 Rome
*Tel:* (06) 5407309 *Fax:* (06) 5408772
*E-mail:* eulama@tiscalinet.it *Cable:* EULAROM
*Key Personnel*
President: Harald Kahnemann
Founded: 1967
Also translation agency.
Specializes in architecture, books for young read-
ers, computer science, education, linguistics
& literature, mass-media, philosophy, politics,
psychology, quality fiction, religion, social sci-
ences, Spanish & Latin-American literature,
technology, urban studies.
*Branch Office(s)*
Eulama SA, Germany


**Grandi & Associati SRL**
Via Caradosso 12, 20123 Milan
*Tel:* (02) 4695541; (02) 4818962 *Fax:* (02)
48195108
*E-mail:* agenzia@grandieassociati.it
*Key Personnel*
Contact: Laura Grandi; Stefano Tettamanti; Vi-
viana Vuscovich *E-mail:* viviana.vuscovich@
grandieassociati.it
Represents writers & acts as a subagent for se-
lected publishing houses & agencies outside
Italy. Sells foreign rights & acts as a consultant
for various Italian publishing houses.


**ILA (International Literary Agency) USA**
18010 Terzorio (IM)
*Tel:* (0184) 484048; (0347) 9334966 *Fax:* (0184)
487292
*E-mail:* books@librigg.com
*Key Personnel*
Contact: Tomas D W Friedmann
Founded: 1970
An American agency headquartered in Europe.
Specialize in handling of foreign language
translation rights to multi-volume book & mag-
azine projects, children's books, encyclopedias,
bestsellers, illustrated books on antiques & col-
lectibles (in all European languages).
Specializes in mass market, antiques & col-
lectibles, nonfiction, fiction.


**International Literary Agency**, see ILA
(International Literary Agency) USA


**Living Literary Agency**
Via Poliziano 8, 20154 Milan
*Tel:* (02) 33100584 *Fax:* (02) 33100618
*E-mail:* living@galactica.it
*Key Personnel*
Contact: Elfriede Pexa
Founded: 1976
Specializes in Italian translation rights in books in
English & German.


**Pietro Missorini & Co - Libreria
Commissionaria**
Via Abbeveratoia 63, 43100 Parma PR
Mailing Address: PO Box 326, 43100 Parma PR
*Tel:* (0521) 993919 *Fax:* (0521) 993929
*E-mail:* info@missorini.it
*Web Site:* www.rsadvnet.it/missorini/
*Key Personnel*
Administration: Pietro Missorini
*E-mail:* missorini@rsadvnet.it
Contact: Lucia Missorini
Founded: 1972
Vat nr IT01514140340.
Specializes in food service & technology.


**Natoli Stefan & Oliva Literary Agency**
Corso Plebiscito 12, 20129 Milan
*Tel:* (02) 70 00 16 45 *Fax:* (02) 741277
*E-mail:* natoli.oliva@tiscalinet.it
*Key Personnel*
Partner: Roberta Oliva *E-mail:* roberta.oliva@
tiscali.it
Founded: 1962
Handles foreign publishers, agents authors in Italy
& Italian authors in Italy & worldwide.


**Piergiorgio Nicolazzini Literary Agency**
Via G B Moroni 22, 20146 Milan
*Tel:* (02) 48713365 *Fax:* (02) 48713365
*E-mail:* info@pnla.it
*Web Site:* www.pnla.it
*Key Personnel*
Owner: Piergiorgio Nicolazzini
*E-mail:* piergiorgio.nicolazzini@pnla.it
Founded: 1998
Represents publishers, agents & authors in Italy
& abroad.
Specializes in fiction & nonfiction.


**RCS Rizzoli Libri SpA**
Via Mecenate 91, 20138 Milan
*Tel:* (02) 50951 *Fax:* (02) 5065361
*Web Site:* www.rcs.it
*Telex:* 333543
*Key Personnel*
President: Giorgio Fattori
Dir General: Giovanni Ungarelli
Editorial Dirs: Rosaria Carpinelli; Evaldo Violo
Also publisher & major bookseller.
Specializes in literature, fiction, essays, art, his-
tory.


**Vicki Satlow Literary Agency**
Via Alberto da Giussano 16, 20145 Milan
*Tel:* (02) 48015553
*E-mail:* vickisatlow@tin.it
*Key Personnel*
President: Vicki Satlow
Founded: 1999
Sell translation rights & represents authors from
countries outside of the USA/UK.
Specializes in fiction & narrative non-fiction.


**Susanna Zevi Agenzia Letteraria**
Via Appiani, 19, 20121 Milan
*Tel:* (02) 6570863; (02) 6570867 *Fax:* (02)
6570915
*E-mail:* susiz@tin.it

# Japan

**The Asano Agency, Inc**
Tokuda Bldg 302, 4-44-8 Sengoku, Bunkyo-ku,
Tokyo 112-0011
*Tel:* (03) 39434171 *Fax:* (03) 39437637
*Telex:* 272-2436 ASANO K
*Key Personnel*
President: Kiyoshi Asano *E-mail:* kiyoshi@asano-agency.com
Founded: 1988

**The English Agency (Japan) Ltd**
Sakuragi Bldg 4F, 6-7-3 Minami Aoyama, Minto-ku, Tokyo 107-0062
*Tel:* (03) 3406 5385 *Fax:* (03) 3406 5387
*E-mail:* info@eaj.co.jp
*Key Personnel*
Executive Dir: Junzo Sawa
Man Dir: Hamish Macaskill
Dir: William Miller *E-mail:* villmill@eaj.co.jp;
Peter Thompson
Agent, Adult Books: Yoshinori Kaba; Kaori
Shibayama
Agent, Academic Books: Tsutomu Yawata
Agent, Children's Books: Noriko Hasegawa
Agent, Business Books: Yukako Higuchi
London Representative: Louise Allen-Jones
*Tel:* (020) 7720-2453
Founded: 1979
Sales of book & ancillary rights for translation
mainly into Japanese; author's agent for books
with international appeal by writers living in or
frequently visiting Japan.

**Japan Foreign-Rights Centre (JFC)**
27-18-804 Naka-Ochiai 2-chome, Shinjuku-ku,
Tokyo 161-0032
*Tel:* (03) 59960321 *Fax:* (03) 59960323
*Key Personnel*
Man Dir: Akiko Kurita
Manager, General Books: Harumi Sakai
Manager, Children's Books: Yurika Yokota
Yoshida
Founded: 1981 (as Kurita-Bando Literary
Agency)
Specializes in foreign rights to Japanese books,
co-production, packaging.

**Japan UNI Agency Inc**
Tokyodo-Jinbocho Dai, No 2 Bldg, 1-27 Kanda
Jinbocho, Chiyoda-ku, Tokyo 101-0051
*Tel:* (03) 32950301 *Fax:* (03) 32945173
*E-mail:* info@japanuni.co.jp
*Telex:* J27260 Unilit *Cable:* UNILITERARY
*Key Personnel*
Chairman: Noboru Miyata
President: Yoshio Taketomi
Dir: Ms Tachi Nagasawa *E-mail:* tachi.
nagasawa@japanuni.co.jp; Okimitsu Ohishi
Founded: 1967

**JFC,** see Japan Foreign-Rights Centre (JFC)

**Motovun Co Ltd, Tokyo**
Coop Nomura Ichibancho, No 103, 15-6 Ichiban-cho, Chiyoda-ku, Tokyo 102-0082
*Tel:* (03) 32614002 *Fax:* (03) 32641443
*Key Personnel*
President: Mari Koga *E-mail:* koga_motovun@
mbd.ocn.ne.jp
Dir: Norio Irie *E-mail:* irie_motovun@mbd.ocn.
ne.jp
Founded: 1983
Firm sells rights & co-production between foreign
publishers & Japanese publishers.

**The Sakai Agency Inc**
Papyrus Bldg 4F, 1-58 Kanda-Jinbocho, Chiyoda-ku, Tokyo 101-0051
*Tel:* (03) 32951405 *Fax:* (03) 32954366
*E-mail:* sakai@sakaiagency.com
*Key Personnel*
Contact: Tatemi Sakai
Founded: 1952
Specializes in book rights, serial rights, co-editions, theatrical performing rights, motion
picture rights, TV & radio broadcasting rights,
video rights, merchandising rights; both rights
for export/import market, representing Japanese
authors.

**Tuttle-Mori Agency Inc**
Dai ichi Fuji Bldg, 2-15 Kanda-Jinbocho,
Chiyoda-ku, Tokyo 101-0051
*Tel:* (03) 3230-4081 *Fax:* (03) 3234-5249
*Web Site:* www.tuttlemori.com
*Key Personnel*
President: Ken Mori
Man Dir: Yuji Takeda *E-mail:* yuji@tuttlemori.
com
Executive Dir: Yoshikazu Iwasaki
Financial Dir: Sakae Mino
Specializes in book rights, serial rights, co-productions, motion picture, TV, radio & stage
rights, merchandising rights.
*Branch Office(s)*
5F, No 8, Wu-Chuan Third Rd, Shin-Juang,
Taipei County 242, Taiwan, Province of China
*Tel:* (02) 3234-4255 *Fax:* (02) 3234-4244
Siam Inter Comics Bldg, 6th floor 459 Soi Pi-boonopathum Ladprao 48, Samsen Nok, Huay
Kwang, Bangkok 10310, Thailand *Tel:* (02)
694-3026 *Fax:* (02) 694-3027 *E-mail:* info@
tuttlemori.co.th (Affiliate)
55 Earl's Court Sq, Flat 17, London SW5 9DG,
United Kingdom, Contact: Anne Martyn
*Tel:* (020) 7373-2018 *Fax:* (020) 7286-8629
*U.S. Office(s):* Sanford J Greenburger Asso-ciates Inc, 55 Fifth Ave, New York, NY
10003, United States, Contact: Carol Freder-ick *Tel:* 212-206-5610 *Fax:* 212-627-9281 *Web
Site:* www.greenburger.com
Foreign Rep(s): Anne Martyn & Nina Martyn;
Carol Frederick

# Republic of Korea

**Imprima Korea Agency**
Mijin Bldg, 3rd floor, 464-41 Seokyo-Dong,
Mapo-ku, Seoul 121-210
*Tel:* (02) 325-9155 *Fax:* (02) 334-9160
*E-mail:* imprima@chollian.net
*Web Site:* www.imprima.co.kr
*Key Personnel*
President: Hong Sung-Il
Dir: Duram Kim *E-mail:* duramkim@hnc.net
Founded: 1993
Specializes in publishing newspaper.

**International Publications Service**, see IPS
Copyright Agency (International Publications
Service)

**IPS Copyright Agency (International
Publications Service)**
YBM/Si-sa Bldg 9F, 48-1, Chongro 2-ga,
Chongro-gu, Seoul 110-772
*Tel:* (02) 21158800 *Fax:* (02) 22646936
*E-mail:* copyright@ips-korea.com
*Web Site:* www.ipsbook.com
Founded: 1986
Promoting foreign rights to Korean publishers.

**Mediabank**
Kwanghwamoon, Seoul 110-605
Mailing Address: PO Box 530, Seoul 110-605
*Tel:* (02) 7420425 *Fax:* (02) 7452174
*E-mail:* sales@mediabank.biz
*Web Site:* www.mediabank.pe.kr
*Key Personnel*
President: Jay Sung Rhee *E-mail:* jaysrhee@
nownuri.net
Founded: 1985
Also deals in video rights for home & educational
markets.
Specializes in children's books, el-hi reference
books & instructional multi-media.

**Shin Won Agency Co**
513-12 Paju Book City, Munbal-ri, Gyoha-eup,
Gyeonggi-do, Korea 413-832
*Tel:* (031) 955-2255 *Fax:* (031) 955-2266
*E-mail:* main@shinwonagency.co.kr
*Web Site:* www.shinwonagency.co.kr;
shinwonagency.com
*Key Personnel*
President: Soon Eung Kim
Chairman: Sang Hyung Kim
Dir: Cheol Eung Kim
Founded: 1986
Literary Agency & Editorial Production.

**Time-Space Inc**
Hanyoung Bldg, 57-8 Chungmuro 3 Ga, Jung-gu,
Seoul 100-013
*Tel:* (02) 2272 2381 *Fax:* (02) 2273 8900
*E-mail:* tspace@timespace.co.kr
*Web Site:* www.fotato.com
*Key Personnel*
Contact: Hyang-Ja Yim
Founded: 1984
Specialize in stock photography & royalty free
CD-ROM.
Specializes in photography, arts.

**Universal Publications Agency Press**
UPA Bldg, No 2, Suite 1001, 20 Hyoje-dong,
Chongno-ku, Seoul 110-850
*Tel:* (02) 3672 0044 *Fax:* (02) 3672 1222
*E-mail:* upa@upa.co.kr
*Web Site:* www.upa.co.kr
*Telex:* K 22702 *Cable:* CHANGHOSHIN SEOUL
*Key Personnel*
Chairman: Chang-Ho Shin
President: Kwang-Hoon Cow
Founded: 1958
Also publisher & distributor.
Specializes in advertising, media representation.
*Branch Office(s)*
Will Academia, No 1, Jangkyo-dong, Suite 2613,
Chung-ku, Seoul 100-760

**Eric Yang Agency**
3rd floor, E Bldg, 54-7 Banpo-dong, Seocho-ku,
Seoul 137-803
*Tel:* (02) 5923356 *Fax:* (02) 5923359
*E-mail:* info@ericyangagency.co.kr
*Web Site:* www.ericyangagency.co.kr
*Key Personnel*
President: Eric Yang *E-mail:* ericyang@
ericyangagency.co.kr
Founded: 1994

# Liechtenstein

**Liechtenstein Verlag AG**
PO Box 339, 9490 Vaduz
*Tel:* (0423) 2322414 *Fax:* (0423) 2324340
*E-mail:* flbooks@verlag-ag.lol.li
*Key Personnel*
Man Dir: Albart Piet Schiks

Founded: 1945
Also a publisher.

# Lithuania

**Penki Kontinentai**
Stulginskio-5, 2001 Vilnius
*Fax:* (05) 2664501
*E-mail:* info@5ci.lt
*Web Site:* www.5ci.lt
*Key Personnel*
Contact: Irena Juskauskaite
Founded: 1992
Represents Nordic Council of Ministers, Oxford University Press & Cambridge University Press.

# Netherlands

**Auteursbureau Greta Baars-Jelgersma**
Maasstaete 40, 6585 CB Mook
*Tel:* (024) 6963336 *Fax:* (024) 6963293
*E-mail:* 6963336@hetnet.nl
*Web Site:* home.hetnet.nl/~jelgersma696
Founded: 1951
Literary agent & sworn translator-interpreter.
Specializes in international co-printing of illustrated books, mediation of copyrights, translations from Scandinavian & German languages into Dutch, sworn interpreter/translator Danish, Norwegian, Swedish.

**Foundation for the Production & Translation of Dutch Literature**
Singel 464, 1017 AW Amsterdam
*Tel:* (020) 6206261 *Fax:* (020) 6207179
*E-mail:* office@nlpvf.nl
*Web Site:* www.nlpvf.nl
*Key Personnel*
Man Dir: Henk Propper
Founded: 1991

**Caroline van Gelderen Literary Agency**
Kerkstr 301, 1017 GZ Amsterdam
*Tel:* (020) 6126475 *Fax:* (020) 6180843
*Key Personnel*
Dir: Caroline van Gelderen
   *E-mail:* cvangelderen@carvang.nl
Founded: 1979
Representative of American & English publishers & agents for the Dutch territories.
Specializes in translation rights.

**International Literatuur Bureau BV**
Koninginneweg 2A, 1217 KW Hilversum
Mailing Address: Postbus 10014, 1201 DA Hilversum
*Tel:* (035) 6213500 *Fax:* (035) 6215771
*E-mail:* info@ilb.nu
*Web Site:* www.ilb.nu *Cable:* ILB
*Key Personnel*
Chief Executive: Linda Kohn *E-mail:* lkohn@planet.nl

**Lijnkamp Literary Agents**
Johannes Verhulststr 153-B, 1075 GW Amsterdam
*Tel:* (020) 6207742 *Fax:* (020) 6385298
*E-mail:* info@lijnkamp.nl
*Web Site:* www.lijnkamp.nl
*Key Personnel*
Dir: Marijke Lijnkamp
Assistant Literary Agent: Liz Waters

Founded: 1989
Represents foreign literary agencies & publishing houses in Netherlands. Represents Dutch authors worldwide.
Specializes in The Netherlands & Flemish Belgium as representative areas.

**De Lindenboom/INOR Publikaties**
M A de Ruyterstr 20A, 7482 BZ Haaksbergen
Mailing Address: Postbus 202, 7480 AE Haaksbergen
*Tel:* (053) 5740004 *Fax:* (053) 5729296
*E-mail:* lindeboo@worldonline.nl
*Telex:* 49642 UDOL
Represents Nordic Council of Ministers Publications. Also book distributor.

**Servire BV Uitgevers**
Maliebaan 74, 3581 CV Utrecht
Mailing Address: Postbus 13288, 3507 LG Utrecht
*Tel:* (030) 2349211 *Fax:* (030) 2349247
*E-mail:* info@kosmoszk.nl
*Web Site:* www.servire.nl; www.boekenwereld.com
*Key Personnel*
Chief Executive: Felix Erkelens
Founded: 1921
Also publisher.
Specializes in psychology, health, spirituality.

**Team Double Click Inc Literary**
Subsidiary of Team Double Click Inc
Haringbuis 45, 1483 CP De Rijp
*Toll Free Tel:* 888-827-9129 *Fax:* 262-364-3022
*Web Site:* www.teamdoubleclick.com/literary_agency.html
*Key Personnel*
Proprietor: Gayle Buske
Literary Dir & Agent: A E H Veenman
   *Tel:* (0299) 67-2251 *Fax:* (0299) 67-2257
   *E-mail:* anethea@teamdoubleclick.com
Founded: 2004
Representation of published & unpublished writers in efforts of marketing manuscripts to publishers. Negotiation of auxiliary rights to foreign agents, publishers & producers are included. Submit query letter & synopsis in body of email with first 20 pages in MS Word attached to anethea@teamdoubleclick.com.
Specializes in novel-length manuscripts in general & literary fictions, fantasy, historical fiction, crime/legal thrillers, women's fiction, supernatural, young adult fiction & mystery.
*U.S. Office(s):* W10530 Airport Rd, Lodi, WI 53555, United States, Contact: Gayle Buske *Fax:* 262-364-3022 *E-mail:* literary@teamdoubleclick.com

**Alice Toledo**, see Toledo Creative Management

**Toledo Creative Management**
Binnenkant 20, 1011 BH Amsterdam
*Tel:* (020) 6226873 *Fax:* (020) 6276720
*E-mail:* agency@toledo-cm.nl
Founded: 1991
Literary, TV & film agency. Represents Dutch authors & directors.

# New Zealand

**John Bentley Book Agencies**
14 Montclair Rise, Browns Bay, North Shore 1311
Mailing Address: PO Box 31-328, Auckland 1330
*Tel:* (09) 4736920 *Fax:* (09) 4736920
*E-mail:* sjsb@zip.co.nz

*Key Personnel*
Contact: John Bentley
Founded: 1982
Commission agent acting for publishers on a representation only basis.

**Michael Gifkins & Associates**
PO Box 6496, Auckland 1
*Tel:* (09) 5235032 *Fax:* (09) 5235033
*E-mail:* michael.gifkins@xtra.co.nz
*Key Personnel*
Principal: Michael Gifkins
Founded: 1983
Specializes in general, adult fiction, juvenile, film, television, co-publications.

**Playmarket**
Level 2, 16 Cambridge Terrace, Te Aro, Wellington
Mailing Address: PO Box 9767, Te Aro, Wellington
*Tel:* (04) 382 8462 *Fax:* (04) 382 8461
*E-mail:* info@playmarket.org.nz
*Web Site:* www.playmarket.org.nz
*Key Personnel*
Dir: Mark Amery *Tel:* (04) 382 8464
   *E-mail:* director@playmarket.org.nz
Administrator: Katrina Chandra
Founded: 1973
New Zealand's Playwrights' Agency & Script Advisory Service.

**Richards Literary Agency**
11 Channel View Rd, Campbells Bay, Auckland 1311
Mailing Address: PO Box 31240, Milford, Auckland 9
*Tel:* (09) 479 5681 *Fax:* (09) 479 5681
*E-mail:* rla.richards@clear.net.nz
*Key Personnel*
Partner: Ray Richards; Nicki Richards Wallace
Founded: 1977
Specializes in fiction, nonfiction, educational, academic, juvenile, young adult, films, television, stage, radio.

# Norway

**June Heggenhougen**
Brannpostveien 5, 3014 Drammen
*Tel:* 32832125 *Fax:* 32832125
*Key Personnel*
International Consultant: Gudbrand Heggenhougen *E-mail:* gudbrand@online.no
Publishing Consultant: June Heggenhougen

# Pakistan

**Mirza Book Agency**
65 Shahrah-e-Quaid-e-Azam, Lahore 54000
Mailing Address: PO Box 729, Lahore 54000
*Tel:* (042) 7353601 *Fax:* (042) 5763714
*E-mail:* merchant@brain.net.pk *Cable:* KNOWLEDGE
*Key Personnel*
Proprietor: Mirza Mahmud
Founded: 1949
Deals with foreign publication & government publication; Subscription Agent.
Specializes in educational & professional books, developing countries, dictionaries, reference, social science, scientific, medical.

*Branch Office(s)*
Mirza Book Corporation, 247/A-3, Gulberg-3, Lahore 54660 *Tel:* (042) 5714653 *Fax:* (042) 5763714 *E-mail:* merchant@brain.net.pk

# Romania

**Simona Kessler International Copyright Agency Ltd**
Str Banul Antonache 37, 011663 Bucharest 1
*Tel:* (021) 316 48 06 *Fax:* (021) 316 47 94
*Key Personnel*
President: Simona Kessler *E-mail:* simona@kessler-agency.ro
Founded: 1995
Specializes in subsidiary rights.

# Russian Federation

**RAO**, see Rossijskoye avtorskoye obshestvo

**Rossijskoye avtorskoye obshestvo** (Russian Author's Society)
6-A Bolshaya Bronnaya, K-104, 103670 Moscow
*Tel:* (095) 2033777; (095) 2033260
*E-mail:* rao@rao.ru
*Web Site:* www.rao.ru
*Telex:* 411327 Avtor SU *Cable:* Moscow Avtor
*Key Personnel*
Chairman: V Tverdovsky
Vice Chairman & Dir,Legal Dept: Arkady Tourkine
Dir, Rights & Permissions Dept: G Zareev
*Tel:* (095) 203-06-95
Literary & big rights, internet, mechanical & musical rights; licensing of TV & radio stations.

# Slovakia

**LITA Ochranna Autorska Spolocnost' Agentura**
Mozartova 9, 81530 Bratislava
*Tel:* (07) 62 80 22 48 *Fax:* (07) 62 80 22 46
*E-mail:* lita@lita.sk
*Key Personnel*
Contact: Yvona Vlasata
Slovak Literary Agency: the copyright organization representing Slovak authors in foreign transactions & foreign authors in the territory of Slovakia.
Membership(s): CISAC.

# South Africa

**Frances Bond Literary Services**
14 Grays Inn Crescent, Westville, Kwazulu Natal 3630
Mailing Address: PO Box 223, Westville, Kwazulu Natal 3630
*Tel:* (031) 2662007 *Fax:* (031) 2662007
*E-mail:* fbond@mweb.com.za
*Key Personnel*
Chief Executive: Frances Bond
Chief Editor: Eileen Molver

Founded: 1983
Specializes in adult fiction & nonfiction, children's books.

**Cherokee Literary Agency**
3 Blythwood Rd, Rondebosch, Cape Province 7700
*Tel:* (021) 671-4508 *Fax:* (021) 761-4329
*Key Personnel*
Dir: DonnaKay Lee *E-mail:* dklee@mweb.co.za
Founded: 1988
Specializes in children's picture books.

**The International Press Agency (Pty) Ltd**
Sunrise House, 56 Morningside, Ndabeni, Cape Town 7405
*Tel:* (021) 5311926; (021) 5318197 *Fax:* (021) 5318789
*E-mail:* inpra@iafrica.com
*Web Site:* www.inpra.co.za
*Key Personnel*
Manager & Dir: Terry Temple
Founded: 1934
Specializes in literary agents & press.
*Branch Office(s)*
London, United Kingdom, Contact: Ursula A Bennett *Tel:* (020) 8767-4828

# Spain

**ACER Agencia Literaria**
Amor de Dios, 1, 28014 Madrid
*Tel:* (091) 3692061 *Fax:* (091) 3692052
*Key Personnel*
Contact: Elizbeth Atkins *E-mail:* eatkins@acerliteraria.com; Laure Merle d'Aubigne *E-mail:* lma@acerliteraria.com
Founded: 1959

**Carmen Balcells Agencia Literaria SA** (The Balcells Agency)
Diagonal 580, 08021 Barcelona
*Tel:* (093) 2008565; (093) 2008933 *Fax:* (093) 2007041
*E-mail:* ag-balcells@ag-balcells.com *Cable:* COPYRIGHT BARCELONA
*Key Personnel*
President: Carmen Balcells
Contact: Gloria Gutierrez

**Bookbank SA**
San Martin de Porres, 14, 28035 Madrid
*Tel:* (091) 3733539 *Fax:* (091) 3165591
*E-mail:* bookbank@nexo.es
*Key Personnel*
Contact: Alicia Gonzalez Sterling
Correspondence in Spanish & English.

**International Editors' Co SL**
Rambla de Cataluna 63 - 3 1a, 08007 Barcelona
*Tel:* (093) 2158812 *Fax:* (093) 4873583
*E-mail:* ieco@internationaleditors.com
*Key Personnel*
Manager: Isabel Monteagudo
*Branch Office(s)*
Buenos Aires, Argentina

**Ute Koerner Literary Agent**
Ronda Guinardo 40-3, 08025 Barcelona
*Tel:* (093) 4550414; (093) 4502588 *Fax:* (093) 4365548
*E-mail:* office@uklitag.com
*Web Site:* www.uklitag.com
*Key Personnel*
Founder & Agent: Ute Koerner

Agent: Guenter G Rodewald
Founded: 1984
Representing foreign publishers, authors & agents in Spanish & Portuguese-speaking countries.

**Marcombo SA**
Gran Via de les Corts Catalanes 594, Barcelona 08007
*Tel:* (093) 3180079 (Editor) *Fax:* (093) 3189339
*E-mail:* marcombo.boixareu@marcombo.es
*Web Site:* www.marcombo.es
*Key Personnel*
Man Dir: Josep M Boixareu Vilaplana
Founded: 1945
Specializes in technical books.

**Les Muriers Editions**
Division of Les Muriers Estates SL
Ave Constitucion 8, Apdo 925, Ciutadella de Menorca, Islas Baleares 07760
*Tel:* (0971) 484 423 *Fax:* (0971) 484 423
*Web Site:* www.lmeditions.com
*Key Personnel*
Dir: Janet Greco *E-mail:* janet@lesmuriers.com
Founded: 2003
Work with a small & select group of promising new writers & accomplished authors, writing in English only. Also represent feature-length screenplays.
No unsolicited manuscripts - query first (in English) by e-mail with sample chapters.
Specializes in children's/young readers, commercial fiction (mysteries, political thrillers, thrillers), literary fiction, nonfiction (biography, comedy, cooking, history, how-to, humor, ghosts & graveyards, New Jerseyana, offbeat cooking, popular culture, self development & improvement, writing).
*U.S. Office(s):* 281 Terhune Drive, Wayne, NJ 07470, United States *Tel:* (609) 361-8696

**Pontas Agency**
Formerly Anna Soler-Pont Literary Agency
Seneca, 18, 08006 Barcelona
*E-mail:* info@pontas-agency.com
*Web Site:* www.pontas-agency.com
*Key Personnel*
Agent: Anna Soler-Pont *E-mail:* anna@pontas-agency.com

**RDC Agencia Literaria**
Plaza de Las Salesas 9, 1 izq, 28004 Madrid
*Tel:* (091) 3085585 *Fax:* (091) 3085600
*E-mail:* rdc@idecnet.com
*Key Personnel*
Contact: Raquel de la Concha
Representing Spanish writers & foreign publishers, fiction & nonfiction.

**Mercedes Ros Literary Agency**
Castell 38, 08329 Teia, Barcelona
*Tel:* (093) 5401353 *Fax:* (093) 5401346
*E-mail:* info@mercedesros.com
*Web Site:* www.mercedesros.com
*Key Personnel*
Dir: Mercedes Ros *E-mail:* mercedes@mercedesros.com
Founded: 1996
Represents publishers, packagers & authors all over the world.
Specializes in children: fiction & nonfiction, albums, board books, games & crafts; adults: crafts, hobbies, parenting, self-help & sports.

**Lennart Sane Agency AB**
Paseo de Mejico 65, Las Cumbres-Elvira, 29600 Marbella, Malaga
*Tel:* (0952) 834180 *Fax:* (0952) 833196
*Web Site:* www.lennartsaneagency.com
*Key Personnel*
Pres: Lennart Sane *E-mail:* lennart.sane@lennartsaneagency.com

Agent: Philip Sane *E-mail:* philip.sane@
  lennartsaneagency.com
Associate: Elisabeth Sane
Founded: 1969
The agency was founded in Malmo, Sweden by
  Lennart Sane. The Spanish office was opened
  in 1986.
Lennart Sane Agency AB is a European literary
  agency representing authors in all markets for
  rights in fiction, nonfiction, children's books,
  films & associated rights.
No unsolicited manuscripts.
*Branch Office(s)*
Hollandareplan 9, 374 34 Karlshamn, Sweden
  *Tel:* (0454) 123 56 *Fax:* (0454) 149 20

### Sant Jordi Asociados Agencia
Arquitecte Sert n° 31 5° - 1a, 08005 Barcelona
*Tel:* (093) 2240107 *Fax:* (093) 2254539
*E-mail:* info@santjordi-asociados.com
*Web Site:* www.santjordi-asociados.com
*Key Personnel*
Contact: Monica Antunes
Founded: 1994
Specializes in Latin America authors & Spanish.

### Guillermo Schavelzon & Asociados, Literary Agency
Muntaner, 339 - 5°, 08021 Barcelona
*Tel:* 932 011 310 *Fax:* 932 006 886
*E-mail:* info@schavelzon.com
*Key Personnel*
Principal: Guillermo Schavelzon
  *E-mail:* guillermo@schavelzon.com
Foreign Rights: Barbara Graham
  *E-mail:* barbaragraham@schavelzon.com
Founded: 1998
Specializes in Latin American & Spanish speaking writers (fiction & nonfiction).

### Anna Soler-Pont Literary Agency, see Pontas Agency

### Cristina Vizcaino Literary Agency
Juan de Austria 31 1B, 28010 Madrid
*Tel:* (091) 5944992
*E-mail:* vizcaino@infornet.es
*Key Personnel*
Manager: Cristina Vizcaino
Associate: Paula Serraller
Founded: 1997
Specializes in children & juvenile titles, education, gay & lesbian, literature & reference.

### Julio F Yanez, Agencia Literaria S L
Via Augusta 139 2°, 08021 Barcelona
*Tel:* (093) 2007107; (093) 2005443 *Fax:* (093)
  2094865
*E-mail:* yanezag@retemail.es *Cable:*
  AGENLITER
*Key Personnel*
Dir: Julio F Yanez; Montse F Yanez
Founded: 1960
Covering all Spanish & Portuguese-speaking
  countries.
Specializes in modern literature, documents &
  memoirs; educational: history, art, sociology;
  topical books on modern facts; co-productions.

# Sweden

### Ann-Christine Danielsson Agency
Haeggstigen 17, 24013 Genarpe
*Tel:* (040) 482380 *Fax:* (040) 482190
*E-mail:* acd.agency@swipnet.se

### Monica Heyum Agency
PO Box 3300, Vendelsoe, 136 03 Haninge
*Tel:* (08) 7451934 *Fax:* (08) 7771470
*Key Personnel*
Dir & Literary Agent: Monica Heyum
  *E-mail:* monica@heum-agency.a.se
Founded: 1985

### Kerstin Kvint Literary & Co-Production Agency
PO Box 45164, 104 30 Stockholm
*Tel:* (08) 107014 *Fax:* (08) 107606
Handles foreign rights' sales for individual writers & Scandinavian publishers. Co-productions
  arranged for children's picture books.

### Bengt Nordin Agency
Triewaldsgrand 2, 111 29 Stockholm
Mailing Address: PO Box 2101, 103 13 Stockholm
*Tel:* (08) 57168525 *Fax:* (08) 57168524
*E-mail:* info@nordinagency.se
*Web Site:* www.nordinagency.se
*Key Personnel*
President: Bengt Nordin *E-mail:* bengt.nordin@
  nordinagency.se
Founded: 1990
Specializes in film, TV & literary agency.

### Pan Agency
Division of P A Norstedt & Soner AB
Birger Jarls Torg 5, 111 28 Stockholm
Mailing Address: PO Box 2052, 103 12 Stockholm
*Tel:* (08) 769 87 00 *Fax:* (08) 769 88 04
*Web Site:* www.panagency.se
*Key Personnel*
Rights Dir: Linda Altrov-Berg *E-mail:* linda.
  altrovberg@panagency.com; Lillevi Cederin
  *E-mail:* lillevi.cederin@panagency.se
Rights Director: Magdalena Hedlund
  *E-mail:* magdalena.hedlund@panagency.se
Rights Dir: Agneta Markas *E-mail:* agneta.
  markas@panagency.se; Kerstin Oberg
  *E-mail:* kerstin.oberg@panagency.se
Foreign rights division of P A Norstedt & Sonder, representing Norstedts; Prisma Raben &
  Sjogren; Tiden.

### Lennart Sane Agency AB
Hollandareplan 9, 374 34 Karlshamn
*Tel:* (0454) 123 56 *Fax:* (0454) 149 20
*Web Site:* www.lennartsaneagency.com
*Key Personnel*
Pres: Lennart Sane *E-mail:* lennart.sane@
  lennartsaneagency.com
Agent: Philip Sane *Tel:* (070) 8835245
  *E-mail:* philip.sane@lennartsaneagency.com;
  Lina Hammarling *E-mail:* lina.hammarling@
  lennartsaneagency.com
Associate: Elisabeth Sane
Founded: 1969
The agency was founded in Malmo, Sweden by
  Lennart Sane. The Spanish office was opened
  in 1986 & is located in Marabella.
Lennart Sane Agency AB is a European literary
  agency representing authors in all markets for
  rights in fiction, nonfiction, children's books,
  films & associated rights.
No unsolicited manuscripts.
*Branch Office(s)*
Paseo de Mejico 65, Las Cumbres-Elviria, 29600
  Marbella, Malaga, Spain *Tel:* (0952) 83 41 80
  *Fax:* (0952) 83 31 96

### Sane Toregard Agency
Hollaendareplan 9, 374 34 Karlshamn
*Tel:* (0454) 123 56 *Fax:* (0454) 149 20
*Key Personnel*
Dir: Ulf Toregard *E-mail:* ulf.toregard@
  sanetoregard.se

Founded: 1995
Representing publishers & agents in Scandinavia
  & Holland for rights in fiction & nonfiction.

# Switzerland

### Paul und Peter Fritz AG Literary Agency
Jupiterstr 1, 8032 Zurich
Mailing Address: Postfach 1773, 8032 Zurich
*Tel:* (01) 44 388 41 40 *Fax:* (01) 44 388 41 30
*E-mail:* info@fritzagency.com
*Web Site:* www.fritzagency.com
*Key Personnel*
Man Dir: Peter S Fritz *E-mail:* pfritz@
  fritzagency.com
Founded: 1962
Representation of American & English authors,
  agents & publishers in German-language areas,
  German-language authors worldwide.

### Gaia Media AG/Literary & Media Agency
Spalenvorstadt 13, 4003 Basel
Mailing Address: Postfach 350, 4003 Basel
*Tel:* (061) 2619119 *Fax:* (061) 2619117
*E-mail:* gaiamediaag@access.ch
*Web Site:* www.gaiamedia.org
*Key Personnel*
President: Dieter A Hagenbach *E-mail:* dieter@
  gaiamedia.org
Founded: 1990

### Liepman Agency AG
Maienburgweg 23, 8044 Zurich
*Tel:* (044) 2617660 *Fax:* (044) 2610124
*E-mail:* info@liepmanagency.com
*Key Personnel*
Dir: Eva Koralnik; Ruth Weibel *E-mail:* ruth.
  weibel@liepmanagency.com
Contact: A G Liepman
Founded: 1949
Represent authors, publishers & agents for the
  German language publication rights, & authors
  from manuscript on throughout the world.

### MOHRBOOKS AG, Literary Agency
Klosbachstr 110, 8032 Zurich
*Tel:* (043) 2448626 *Fax:* (043) 2448627
*E-mail:* info@mohrbooks.com
*Web Site:* www.mohrbooks.de
*Key Personnel*
Agent: Sabine Ibach *E-mail:* sabine.ibach@
  mohrbooks.com; Sebastian Ritscher
  *E-mail:* sebastian.ritscher@mohrbooks.com
Agent, Children's Books: Sabina Sciarrone
  *E-mail:* sabina.sciarrone@mohrbooks.com
Contracts & Permissions: Barbara Brachwitz
  *E-mail:* barbara.brachwitz@mohrbooks.com;
  Bettina Kaufmann *E-mail:* bettina.kaufmann@
  mohrbooks.com
*Branch Office(s)*
Am Zirkus 5, 10117 Berlin, Germany
  *Tel:* (030) 28879474 *Fax:* (030) 28879475
  *E-mail:* mohrberlin@mohrbooks.com

### Neue Presse Agentur, see NPA (Neue Presse Agentur)

### Niedieck Linder AG
Zollikerstr 87, 8034 Zurich
*Tel:* (01) 3816592 *Fax:* (01) 3816513
*E-mail:* info@nlagency.ch
*Web Site:* www.nlagency.ch
*Key Personnel*
Contact: Antoinette Matejka
Agent: Leonardo LaRosa *E-mail:* larosa@
  nlagency.ch
Founded: 1975

Representation of German-language authors (including major authors' estates) as well as Italian publishers & agencies on the German language market. Commission: 10-15% of author's gross income.
Specializes in Giulio Einaudi, Bollati Boringhieri, Rusconi Libri, Edizioni EL, Sellerio Editore, Avagliano Editore, Agenzia Letteraria Internazionale, Agenzia Letteraria Agnese Incisa for German speaking countries.

### NPA (Neue Presse Agentur)
Haldenstr 5, Haus am Herterberg, 8500 Frauenfeld-Herten
*Tel:* (052) 7214374 *Cable:* NPA, CH-8500 FRAUENFELD
*Key Personnel*
Contact: Rene Marti
Founded: 1950
Specializes in serialization in newspapers & magazines, especially women's & educational interest, fiction, exclusives.

# Syrian Arab Republic

### Nour E-Sham Book Centre
Omar Al-Mukhtar St, Opp to the Ministry of Education, Damascus
Mailing Address: PO Box 249, Damascus
*Tel:* (011) 4440575 *Fax:* (011) 3324913
*E-mail:* nouresham@mail.sy
*Key Personnel*
Manager: Mr Maher Abul-Zahab
Founded: 1983
Represents the following publishers in Syria: Oxford University Press UK, Cambridge University Press UK, BBC UK, Macmillan UK, Wiley USA, McGraw-Hill USA, McGraw-Hill UK, Penguin UK, Didaco Spain.
Specializes in English language teaching (ELT).
*Branch Office(s)*
Aleppo

# Taiwan, Province of China

### Bardon-Chinese Media Agency
4F, No 230, Hsin-Yi Rd, Sec 2, Taipei
*Tel:* (02) 33932585 *Fax:* (02) 23929577
*Web Site:* www.bardonchinese.com
*Key Personnel*
President: Phillip C Chen *E-mail:* phillip@bardon.com.tw
Contact: Yiwen Chen; Mingming Lu; Jianmei Wang
Founded: 1988
Literary & Rights agency covering Taiwan, Hong Kong, Singapore & China.
Specializes in Chinese language, simplified & complex.

### Big Apple Tuttle-Mori Agency Inc
7F, No 38, Wugong 5th Rd, Wu-Ku Industrial Area, Wugu Township, Taipei County 248
Mailing Address: c/o Anne Martyn, 55 Earl's Court Sq, Flat 17, London SW5 9DG, United Kingdom
*Tel:* (02) 8990-1238 *Fax:* (02) 8990-1129

*E-mail:* bigapple1@worldnet.att.net
*Web Site:* www.bigapple1.info
*Key Personnel*
President: Lily Chen
Executive Vice President: Dr Luc Kwanten
US Representative: Chandler Crawford *Tel:* 212-206-5600
European Representative: Anne Martyn *Tel:* (071) 2868701
Affiliates in all major countries. Rights & authors agent.
*Branch Office(s)*
Chinan, China
Nanking, China
Shanghai, China *Tel:* (021) 6273 4184
Big Apple Tuttle-Mori, 10F No 801, Jeng-Cheng Rd, Jeng-He City, Taipei 235 *Tel:* (02) 506 7828 *Fax:* (02) 506 5827
Big Apple Tuttle-Mori Beijing, Beijing, China *Tel:* (010) 6591 8528
Tuttle-Mori Agency, Fuji Bldg 8F, 2-15 Kanda Jimbocho, Chiyoda-ku, Tokyo, Japan *Tel:* (03) 3230 40181 *Fax:* (03) 3234 5249
Tuttle-Mori Big Apple, Siam Inter Comics Bldg, 6th floor, 459 Soi Piboonupathum Ladprao 48, Samsen Nok, Huay Kwang, Bangkok 10310, Thailand *Tel:* (02) 694 3026 *Fax:* (02) 694 3027

# Thailand

### Silkroad Publishers Agency, Ltd
32/3 Sukhumvit 31 Rd, Bangkok 10110
*Tel:* (02) 2584798; (02) 2588266 *Fax:* (02) 6620553
*E-mail:* silkroad@ji-net.com
*Key Personnel*
Man Dir: Jane Ngarmpun Vejjajiva
Founded: 1994
Specializes in general trade fiction & nonfiction, juvenile.

# Turkey

### Akcali Copyright Agency
Bahariye Caddesi No 8/6, 34714 Kadikoy, Istanbul
*Tel:* (0216) 3388771; (0216) 3485160 *Fax:* (0216) 3490778; (0216) 4142265
*E-mail:* akcali@attglobal.net
*Key Personnel*
President & Dir: Ms Kezban Akcali *E-mail:* kezban@akcalicopyright.com
Handles fiction & nonfiction adult, young adult & children's books.

### Gamma Medya Agency
Eceler Sok, No 6/1, Florya, 34810 Istanbul
*Tel:* (0212) 663 96 80 *Fax:* (0212) 663 96 81
*E-mail:* web@gammamedya.net
*Web Site:* www.gammamedya.net
*Key Personnel*
Man Dir: Zeynep Ataman *E-mail:* zeynep@gammamedya.net
Founded: 1991
Publishing, press & licensing agency.

### Nurcihan Kesim Literary Agency, Inc
Gazeteciler Cemiyeti Basin, Sarayi, No 1 Kat 2, Turkocagi cd, Istanbul
Mailing Address: PO Box 868, 34410 Istanbul
*Tel:* (0212) 5285797; (0212) 5111317; (0212) 5111078 *Fax:* (0212) 5285791

*E-mail:* kesim@superonline.com; contact@nurcihankesim.com
*Web Site:* www.nurcihankesim.com
*Key Personnel*
Man Dir & Executive President: Nurcihan Kesim
Rights & Permissions: Karasuil Asli
Founded: 1971
Specializes in fiction, nonfiction, art works, serials, encyclopedias, licensing, merchandising, music rights, children's books.

### ONK Agency Ltd
Inonu Caddesi, 31/7 Taksim, 34437 Istanbul
Mailing Address: PO Box 983, Sirkeci, 34115 Istanbul
*Tel:* (0212) 2498602; (0212) 2498603 *Fax:* (0212) 2525153
*E-mail:* karaca@onkagency.com
*Web Site:* www.onkagency.com *Cable:* COPYRIGHT ISTANBUL
*Key Personnel*
President: Osman N Karaca *E-mail:* karaca@onkagency.com
Vice President: Mehmet N Karaca
Man Dir: Orsan K Oymen
Rights: Ms Hatice Gok *E-mail:* hatice@onkagency.com
Founded: 1959
Representing Turkish writers, illustrators, playwriters, SACD, many major foreign publishers & agents. Syndicated materials, Sipa press. Literary, dramatic & TV rights.
Specializes in books, (adult/young adult & children books), serials, encyclopedias, comics & cartoons, plays, Dia Positive.

# United Kingdom

### A & B Personal Management Ltd
4th floor, Plasa Suite, 114 Jermyn St, London SW1Y 6HJ
*Tel:* (020) 7839 4433 *Fax:* (020) 7930 5738
*Key Personnel*
Dir: R W Ellis
Founded: 1982
Full-length manuscripts for TV, theatre, cinema; also fiction, nonfiction & performance rights. No unsolicited manuscripts. Send letter first with return postage. No reading fee for synopsis, plays or screenplays, but fee charged for full-length manuscripts.

### The Agency (London) Ltd
24 Pottery Lane, Holland Park, London W11 4LZ
*Tel:* (020) 7727 1346 *Fax:* (020) 7727 9037
*E-mail:* info@theagency.co.uk
*Web Site:* www.writersservices.com/wrhandbook/agency_london.htm
*Key Personnel*
Dir: Stephen Durbridge
Contact: Sebastian Born; Julia Kreitman; Leah Schmidt
Founded: 1995
Works in conjunction with agents in USA & all foreign countries. No adult fiction or nonfiction. Send letter with self-addressed envelope; no reading fee. Commission: Home 10%; USA varies.
Specializes in theater, film, TV, radio, novels, children's fiction.

### Gillon Aitken Associates Ltd
18-21 Cavaye Pl, London SW10 9PT
*Tel:* (020) 7373 8672 *Fax:* (020) 7373 6002
*E-mail:* reception@gillonaitken.co.uk

*Key Personnel*
Dir & Chairman: Gillon Aitken
Contact: Clare Alexander
Founded: 1977
Handles fiction & nonfiction. No plays or scripts.
Send preliminary letter with half page synopsis,
first 30 pages & return postage. No reading fee.
Commission: Home 10%; US 15%; Translation
20%.

**Darley Anderson Literary TV & Film Agency**
Estelle House, 11 Eustace Rd, London SW6 1JB
*Tel:* (020) 7385 6652 *Fax:* (020) 7386 5571;
(020) 7386 9689
*E-mail:* enquiries@darleyanderson.com
*Web Site:* www.darleyanderson.com
*Key Personnel*
President & Contact, Thrillers: Darley Anderson
Foreign Rights Associate & Contact: Lucie
Whitehouse
Contact, TV Film & Children's: Julia Churchill
Contact, Women's & Fiction: Elizabeth Wright
Founded: 1988
Handles commercial fiction & nonfiction, chil-
dren's fiction & selected scripts for film &
TV. Send letter & outline of first three chap-
ters, self-addressed envelope & return postage.
Commission: Home 15%; USA 20%; Transla-
tion 20-25%; TV/Film/Radio 20%.
Specializes in fiction: American & Irish novels,
crime/mystery, humor, thrillers, women's &
male fiction; nonfiction: animals, beauty, biographies, celebrity autobiographies, cookery,
diet, fashions, gardening, health, history, hu-
mor/cartoons, inspirational, popular psychology,
religion, science, self-improvement.
*Branch Office(s)*
Darley Anderson Books

**Book Production Consultants PLC**
25-27 High St, Chesterton, Cambridge CB4 1ND
*Tel:* (01223) 352790 *Fax:* (01223) 460718
*E-mail:* enquiries@bpccam.co.uk
*Web Site:* www.bpccam.co.uk
*Key Personnel*
Director: Tony Littlechild
Founded: 1973
Organization includes project managing, publish-
ing & involvement in all media.
Specializes in book & magazine publishing ser-
vices.
*Branch Office(s)*
The Baltic Exchange, St Mary Axe, London
EC3A 8EX

**Booklink**
Affiliate of Musketeer Books Ltd
43 Maycock Grove, Northwood, Middx HA6 3PU
*Tel:* (01923) 828612 *Fax:* (01923) 828455
*E-mail:* info@booklink.co.uk
*Web Site:* www.booklink.co.uk
*Key Personnel*
President: Evelyne Duval
Founded: 1978
International Rights Agency.
Specializes in foreign rights, co-editions.

**Felicity Bryan**
2A N Parade, Banbury Rd, Oxford OX2 6LX
*Tel:* (01865) 513816 *Fax:* (01865) 310055
*E-mail:* agency@felicitybryan.com
*Key Personnel*
Dir: Felicity Bryan
Associate, Europe: Andrew Nurnberg
Founded: 1988
Handles fiction & nonfiction with emphasis on
history, biography, science & current affairs.
No scripts for TV, radio or theatre; no crafts,
how-to, science fiction or light romance. No
unsolicited manuscripts. No reading fee. Com-
mission: Home 10%; USA & Translation 20%.

**The Buckman Agency**
Ryman's Cottage, Little Tew, Oxford OX7 4JJ
*Tel:* (01608) 683677 *Fax:* (01608) 683449
*Key Personnel*
Contact: Rosemarie Buckman *E-mail:* r.
buckman@talk21.com; Jessica Buckman
*Tel:* (020) 7385 3135 *Fax:* (020) 7385 3137
*E-mail:* j.buckman@talk21.com
Representing American & UK publishers &
agents for the handling of all translation rights.
Specializes in translation rights.

**Bycornute Books**
76a Ashford Rd, Eastbourne BN21 3TE
*Tel:* (01323) 649053
*Key Personnel*
Contact: Asia Haleem *E-mail:* asia@layish.co.uk
Founded: 1986
Specializes in illustrated books on art history, re-
ligion, cosmology, ancient history, mythology,
archaeology, card novelties.

**Campbell Thomson & McLaughlin Ltd**
One King's Mews, London WC1N 2JA
*Tel:* (020) 7242 0958 *Fax:* (020) 7242 2408
*Key Personnel*
Man Dir: John McLaughlin
Contact: Charlotte Bruton
Founded: 1931
No plays, film/TV scripts, articles, short stories or
poetry. No unsolicited manuscripts or synopses.
Preliminary letter with self-addressed envelope
essential. No reading fee.
Specializes in fiction & general nonfiction, ex-
cluding children's.
Foreign Rep(s): Fox Chase Agency; Raines &
Raines

**Carnell Literary Agency**
Danescroft, Goose Lane, Little Hallingbury, Herts
CM22 7RG
*Tel:* (01279) 723626 *Fax:* (01279) 600308
*Key Personnel*
Contact: Pamela Buckmaster
Send letter with outline, two chapters & return
postage.
Specializes in science fiction, fantasy, horror, fic-
tion, nonfiction.

**Casarotto Ramsay & Associates Ltd**
National House, 60-66 Wardour St, London W1V
4ND
*Tel:* (020) 7287 4450 *Fax:* (020) 7287 9128
*E-mail:* agents@casarotto.uk.com
*Web Site:* www.casarotto.uk.com
*Key Personnel*
Man Dir: Giorgio Casarotto
Dir (Film & TV): Jenne Casarotto
Dir (Theatre): Tom Erhardt; Mel Kenyon
Also represent writers, producers, directors & key
technical staff in film, TV & theater.

**Jonathan Clowes Ltd**
10 Iron Bridge House, Bridge Approach, London
NW1 8BD
*Tel:* (020) 7722 7674 *Fax:* (020) 7722 7677
*Key Personnel*
Dir: Ann Evans
Contact: Isobel Creed; Lisa Whadcock
Founded: 1960
Handles fiction, nonfiction & scripts. No
textbooks or children's. No unsolicited
manuscripts, authors come by recommenda-
tion or by successful follow-ups to prelimi-
nary letters. Commission: Home & USA 15%;
Translation 19%.
Specializes in film & TV rights, situation comedy.

**Elspeth Cochrane Agency**
Southbank Commercial Centre, 14/2 2nd floor,
140 Battersea Park Rd, London SW11 4NB

*Tel:* (020) 7622 0314 *Fax:* (020) 7622 5815
*E-mail:* info@elspethcochrane.co.uk
*Key Personnel*
Manager: Elspeth Cochrane
Founded: 1960
Handles fiction, nonfiction, biographies & screen-
plays. Commission: 12 1/2% (negotiable).

**Rosica Colin Ltd**
One Clareville Grove Mews, London SW7 5AH
*Tel:* (020) 7370 1080 *Fax:* (020) 7244 6441
*Key Personnel*
Contact: Johanna Marston
Handles full-length manuscripts, plus theatre,
film, TV & radio. Preliminary letter with return
postage essential. No reading fee. Commission:
Home 10%; USA 15%; Translation 20%.

**Jane Conway-Gordon**
One Old Compton St, London W1D 5JA
*Tel:* (020) 7494 0148 *Fax:* (020) 7287 9264
*Key Personnel*
Contact: Jane Conway-Gordon
Founded: 1982
Works in association with Andrew Mann Ltd.
No poetry or science fiction. Unsolicited
manuscripts welcome; preliminary letter & re-
turn postage essential. No reading fee. Com-
mission: Home 15%; USA & Translation 20%.
Specializes in fiction, general nonfiction.
Foreign Rep(s): McIntosh & Otis, Inc

**Copytrain**
Pitts, Lower End, Great Milton, Oxford, Oxon
OX44 7NF
*Tel:* (01844) 279345 *Fax:* (01844) 279345
*Key Personnel*
Proprietor: Richard Balkwill *E-mail:* rbalkwill@
aol.com
Founded: 1992
Copyrighting & training consultancy.
Specializes in co-publishing, contract review, sup-
plier agreements.

**Rupert Crew Ltd**
One A King's Mews, London WC1N 2JA
*Tel:* (020) 7242 8586 *Fax:* (020) 7831 7914
*E-mail:* rupertcrew@compuserve.com
*Key Personnel*
Chairman & Joint Man Dir: Doreen Montgomery
Joint Man Dir: Caroline Montgomery
Founded: 1927
International representation, handling volume &
subsidiary rights in fiction & nonfiction. No
plays, poetry, journalism or short stories. Pre-
liminary letter & return postage required. Com-
mission: Home 15%; Elsewhere 20%.
Specializes in fiction, nonfiction, major book
projects with international appeal.

**Curtis Brown Group Ltd**
Haymarket House, 28-29 Haymarket, London
SW1Y 4SP
*Tel:* (020) 7393 4400 *Fax:* (020) 7393 4401
*E-mail:* cb@curtisbrown.co.uk
*Key Personnel*
Group Man Dir: Jonathan Lloyd *E-mail:* jlloyd@
curtisbrown.co.uk
Dir: Mark Collingbourne; Jacquie Drewe; Jonny
Geller; Ben Hall; Nick Marston; Peter Robin-
son
Dir (CB Australia): Fiona Inglis
Founded: 1899
Representation of directors, writers, designers,
presenters & actors in theater, film & televi-
sion & a wide range of authors of fiction &
nonfiction. Commission: Home 15%; US &
Translation 20%.

**David Godwin Associates**
55 Monmouth St, London WC2H 9DG

*Tel:* (020) 7240 9992 *Fax:* (020) 7395 6110
*E-mail:* assistant@davidgodwinassociates.co.uk
Founded: 1995
Specializes in fiction & general nonfiction.

**Diagram Visual Information Ltd**
195 Kentish Town Rd, London NW5 2JU
*Tel:* (020) 7482 3633 *Fax:* (020) 7482 4932
*E-mail:* diagramvis@aol.com
*Key Personnel*
Dir: Bruce Robertson
Secretary: Carole A Dease
Founded: 1967

**Drake Educational Associates Ltd**
Saint Fagans Rd, Fairwater, Cardiff CF5 3AE
*Tel:* (029) 2056 0333 *Fax:* (029) 2055 4909
*E-mail:* info@drakeav.com
*Web Site:* www.drakegroup.co.uk; www.drakeed.
com
*Key Personnel*
Man Dir: Mr R G Drake
Specializes in education, children's.

**Toby Eady Associates Ltd**
9 Orme Court, 3rd floor, London W2 4RL
*Tel:* (020) 7792 0092 *Fax:* (020) 7792 0879
*E-mail:* toby@tobyeady.demon.co.uk
*Web Site:* www.tobyeadyassociates.co.uk
*Key Personnel*
Dir: Toby Eady *E-mail:* toby@tobyeady.demon.
co.uk; Jessica Woollard *E-mail:* jessica@
tobyeady.demon.co.uk
Founded: 1968
Commission: UK: 15%; elsewhere 20%.
Specializes in China, Middle East, Africa, India.
handle fiction, nonfiction.
Foreign Rep(s): Ed Breslin; Buckman Agency;
JLM Literary Agency; Katai & Bolza; La Nou-
velle Agence; Jan Michael; Mohrbooks; Kristen
Olson; Prava i Prevodi; Joanne Wang

**Faith Evans Associates**
27 Park Ave North, London N8 7RU
*Tel:* (020) 8340 9920 *Fax:* (020) 8340 9910
*Key Personnel*
Contact: Faith Evans
Founded: 1987
Only accept calls or submissions by recommenda-
tions. Commission: Home 15%; US & Transla-
tion 20%.

**Anne Louise Fisher & Suzy Lucas**
29 D'Arblay St, London W1F 8EP
*Tel:* (020) 7494 4609 *Fax:* (020) 7494 4611
*Key Personnel*
Publisher's Scout: Anne-Louise Fisher
*E-mail:* annelouise@alfisher.co.uk; Suzy Lucas
*E-mail:* suzy@alfisher.co.uk
Literary scout representing Doubleday, Nan
Talese & Broadway Books in US; Librarie
Plon & Poruet in France; Karl Blessing Ver-
lag, Berlin Verlag & Siedler Verlag in Ger-
many; Arnoldo Mondadori Editore in Italy;
Albert Bonniers Bokforlag in Sweden; Octava
in Finland; Gyldendal Norsk Forlag in Norway;
De Boekerij & M Publishers in the Nether-
lands; Plaza y Janes, Editorial Debate, Lumen
& Mondatori Iberica in Spain; Patakis Publica-
tions in Greece.

**French's**
78 Loudoun Rd, London NW8 0NA
*Tel:* (020) 7483 4269 *Fax:* (020) 7722 0574
*Key Personnel*
Contact: Mark Taylor
Founded: 1973
Handles fiction, nonfiction & scripts for all me-
dia, especially novels & screenplays. No re-
ligious or medical books. No unsolicited
manuscripts. For unpublished authors we of-

fer a reading service for a fee per manuscript,
exclusive of postage. Interested authors should
write in the first instance. Commission: Home
10%.

**Blake Friedmann Literary Agency Ltd**
122 Arlington Rd, London NW1 7HP
*Tel:* (020) 7284 0408 *Fax:* (020) 7284 0442
*Web Site:* www.blakefriedmann.co.uk
*Key Personnel*
Joint Man Dir: Carole Blake *E-mail:* carole@
blakefriedmann.co.uk; Julian Friedmann
Finance Dir: Barbara Jones
Dir: Isobel Dixon; Conrad William
Founded: 1977
Handles fiction & nonfiction, scripts for TV, radio
& film. No poetry, juvenile, science fiction or
short stories. Send initial letter with synopsis
& first two chapters. No reading fee. Com-
mission: Home 15%; US & Translation 20%;
Radio/TV/Film 15%.
Specializes in commercial women's fiction, liter-
ary fiction, up-market nonfiction.

**Futerman, Rose & Associates**
Heston Court Business Park, Wimbledon, London
SW19 4UW
*Tel:* (020) 8947 0188 *Fax:* (020) 8605 2162
*Web Site:* www.futermanrose.co.uk
*Key Personnel*
Senior Partner: Guy Rose *E-mail:* guy@
futermanrose.co.uk
Man Dir: Vernon Futerman
Dir: Alexandra Groom
Founded: 1984
Specializes in fiction & academic nonfiction, TV
film & theatre scripts.

**Eric Glass Ltd**
25 Ladbroke Crescent, Notting Hill, London W11
1PS
*Tel:* (020) 7229 9500 *Fax:* (020) 7229 6220
*Key Personnel*
Dir: Janet Glass; Sissi Liechtenstein
Founded: 1934
Handles fiction, nonfiction & scripts for publi-
cation or production in all media. No poetry,
short stories, or children's works. No unso-
licited manuscripts. No reading fee. Commis-
sion: Home 10%; USA & Translation 20%.
Represents Societe des Auteurs et Compositeurs
Dramatiques (SACD), Paris & Societe Civil
des Auteurs Multimedia (SCAM) (formerly
Societe des Gens de Lettres).

**Christine Green Authors' Agent**
6 Whitehorse Mews, Westminster Bridge Rd,
London SE1 7QD
*Tel:* (020) 7401 8844 *Fax:* (020) 7401 8860
*E-mail:* info@christinegreen.co.uk
*Web Site:* www.christinegreen.co.uk
*Key Personnel*
Contact: Christine Green
Founded: 1984
No scripts, poetry or children's. No unsolicited
manuscripts; initial letter & synopsis preferred.
No reading fee but return postage essential.
Commission: Home 10%; USA & Translation
20%.
Specializes in general fiction, general nonfiction
& literary fiction.

**Greene & Heaton Ltd**
37 Goldhawk Rd, London W12 8QQ
*Tel:* (020) 8749 0315 *Fax:* (020) 8749 0318
*Web Site:* www.greeneheaton.co.uk
*Key Personnel*
Contact: Carol Heaton; Judith Murray; Antony
Topping

Contact, Children's: Linda Davis
Handles all types of fiction & nonfiction. No
original scripts for theatre, film or TV. Commission: Home 15%; US & Translation 20%.

**Gregory & Company Authors' Agents**
3 Barb Mews, London W6 7PA
*Tel:* (020) 7610 4676 *Fax:* (020) 7610 4686
*E-mail:* info@gregoryandcompany.co.uk
*Web Site:* www.gregoryandcompany.co.uk
*Key Personnel*
Partner: Jane Gregory *E-mail:* jane@
gregoryandcompany.co.uk
Rights: Jane Barlow *E-mail:* janeb@
gregoryandcompany.co.uk; Claire Morris
Founded: 1987
No original plays, film or TV scripts, no science
fiction, fantasy, poetry, academic or children's
books. No reading fee. Editorial advice given
to own authors. No unsolicited manuscripts;
send a preliminary letter with cover, synopsis, first three chapters & future writing plans
(plus return postage). Short submission by fax
or e-mail. Commission: Home 15%; USA,
Translation, Radio/TV/Film 20%. Represented
throughout Europe, Asia & USA.
Specializes in fiction, general non-fiction, special interest fiction-literary, commercial, crime,
suspense & thrillers.

**David Grossman Literary Agency Ltd**
118B Holland Park Ave, London W11 4UA
*Tel:* (020) 7221 2770 *Fax:* (020) 7221 1445
Founded: 1976
Handles full-length fiction & general nonfiction.
No verse or technical books for students. No
original screenplays or teleplays. Approach by
preliminary letter giving full description of the
work &, in the case of fiction, with the first 50
pages. All material must by accompanied by
return postage. No approaches or submissions
by fax or e-mail. No unsolicited manuscripts.
No reading fee. Material should be addressed
to the Submissions Dept. Commission rates
vary for different markets. Overseas associates
throughout Europe, Asia, Brazil & the USA.
Membership(s): Association of Authors' Agents.

**Gunnar Lie & Associates Ltd**
Roebuck House, 3rd floor, 288 Upper Richmond
Rd W, London SW14 7JG
*Tel:* (020) 8487 9020 *Fax:* (020) 8878 2832
*E-mail:* gunnarlie@compuserve.com
*Key Personnel*
Man Dir: Gunnar Lie
Export Manager: John Edgeler *Tel:* (020) 8487
9021 *E-mail:* johnedgeler@compuserve.com
Founded: 1995
Specializes in international sales & marketing.

**A M Heath & Co Ltd**
79 St Martin's Lane, London WC2N 4RE
*Tel:* (020) 7836 4271 *Fax:* (020) 7497 2561
*E-mail:* amheath@demon.co.uk
*Web Site:* www.amheath.com *Cable:* SCRIPT
LONDON WC2
*Key Personnel*
Chairman: Michael Thomas
Dir: Sara Fisher; William Hamilton; Victoria
Hobbs; Benjamin Mason; Sarah Molloy
Founded: 1919
No dramatic scripts, poetry or short stories. Pre-
liminary letter & synopsis essential. No reading
fee. Commission: Home 10-15%; US & Trans-
lation 20%; Film & TV 15%. Overseas asso-
ciates in the US, Europe, South America, Japan
& the Far East.
Specializes in fiction, general nonfiction & chil-
dren's.

**David Higham Associates Ltd**
5-8 Lower John St, Golden Sq, London W1F
9HA
*Tel:* (020) 7434 5900 *Fax:* (020) 7437 1072
*E-mail:* dha@davidhigham.co.uk
*Web Site:* www.davidhigham.co.uk
*Key Personnel*
Contact, Books: Veronique Baxter; Anthony Goff;
Bruce Hunter; Jacqueline Korn; Lizzy Kremer;
Caroline Walsh
Contact, Scripts: Gemma Hirst; Nicky Lund;
Georgina Ruffhead
Founded: 1935
Handles fiction, nonfiction (biography, history,
current affairs), children's books & scripts.
Preliminary letter with synopsis required. No
reading fee. Commission: Home 15%; US &
Translation 20%.

**Vanessa Holt Ltd**
59 Crescent Rd, Leigh-on-Sea, Essex SS9 2PF
*Tel:* (01702) 473787 *Fax:* (01702) 471890
*E-mail:* vanessa@holtlimited.freeserve.co.uk
*Key Personnel*
Contact: Vanessa Holt
Founded: 1989
No unsolicited material. Handles general fiction,
nonfiction & non-illustrated children's books.
Commission: Home 15%; US & Translation
20%; Radio/TV/Film 15%.
Specializes in commercial & literary fiction,
crime fiction & books with potential for in-
ternational sales.

**Kate Hordern**
18 Mortimer Rd, Clifton, Bristol BS8 4EY
*Tel:* (0117) 923 9368 *Fax:* (0117) 973 1941
*E-mail:* katehordern@blueyonder.co.uk
Handles quality literary & commercial fiction, in-
cluding women's, suspense & genre fictions.
Also general nonfiction. No children's books.
Commission: Home 15%; US & Translation
20%.

**Tanja Howarth Literary Agency**
19 New Row, London WC2N 4LA
*Tel:* (020) 7240 5553 *Fax:* (020) 7379 0969
*E-mail:* tanja.howarth@btinternet.com
Founded: 1970
No children's books, plays or poetry. No unsolicited manuscripts. Preliminary letter preferred.
No reading fee. Established agent for foreign
literature, particularly from the German language. Commission: Home 15%; Translation
20%.
Specializes in fiction & nonfiction from British
authors.

**Hutton-Williams Agency**
58 Melbury Gardens, London SW20 0DJ
*Tel:* (020) 8879 0237 *Fax:* (020) 8879 3831
*Key Personnel*
Contact: Mr C Hutton Williams
*E-mail:* hwagency@email.com
Founded: 1988
Syndication & foreign rights of newspapers, mag-
azines & books throughout the world.
Specializes in annuals, special issues, supplements
& partworks.

**Imrie & Dervis Literary Agency**
7 Carlton Mansions, Holmleigh Rd, London N16
5PX
*Tel:* (020) 8809 3282 *Fax:* (020) 8880 2086
*E-mail:* info@imriedervis.com
*Key Personnel*
Agent: Martina Dervis *E-mail:* martina@
imriedervis.com; Malcolm Imrie
*E-mail:* malcolm@imriedervis.com

**Information Agents Ltd**
26 Rosebery Ave, London EC1R 4SX
*Tel:* (020) 7837 3345 *Fax:* (020) 7837 8901
*E-mail:* eps@epsltd.com
*Web Site:* www.epsltd.com
*Key Personnel*
Chairman: David Worlock
Dir: D J Powell
Founded: 1985
Specializes in negotiating electronic rights.

**Intercontinental Literary Agency**, see PFD

**Intercontinental Literary Agency**
33 Bedford St, London WC2E 9ED
*Tel:* (020) 7379 6611 *Fax:* (020) 7379 6790
*E-mail:* ila@ila-agency.co.uk
*Key Personnel*
Dir: Nicki Kennedy *E-mail:* nicki-kennedy@ila-
agency.co.uk
Founded: 1965
Translation rights only.

**International Scripts Ltd**
1A Kidbrooke Park Rd, Blackheath, London SE3
0LR
*Tel:* (020) 8319 8666 *Fax:* (020) 8319 0801
*Key Personnel*
Man Dir: Bob Tanner
Dir: Jill Lawson
Founded: 1979
Involved in selling UK & Commonwealth, translation & US rights & subsidiary rights. Also
involved in film & TV scripts. Preliminary letter & self-addressed envelope required. Commission: Home 15%; US & Translation 20%.
Specializes in fiction: commerical, women's (contemporary, sagas, romance), mystery & detective, Irish (women's contemporary & sagas),
horror; nonfiction: mind, body & spirit, health
& fitness, biographies, popular business.

**Jane Judd Literary Agency**
18 Belitha Villas, London N1 1PD
*Tel:* (020) 7607 0273 *Fax:* (020) 7607 0623
*Key Personnel*
Contact: Jane Judd
Founded: 1986
Handles general fiction & nonfiction. Also repre-
sents USA companies Avon Books & Mercury
House & USA agents Marian Young & Pen-
guin Canada. No scripts, academic, gardening
or do-it-yourself. Approach with letter, includ-
ing synopsis, first chapter & return postage.
Initial telephone call helpful in the case of
nonfiction. Commission: Home 10%, USA &
Translation 20%.
Specializes in biography, crime, health, humor, in-
vestigative journalism, literary, thrillers, travel,
women's interests.

**The Frances Kelly Agency**
111 Clifton Rd, Kingston-upon-Thames, Surrey
KT2 6PL
*Tel:* (020) 8549 7830 *Fax:* (020) 8547 0051
Founded: 1978
No unsolicited manuscripts. Send letter with brief
synopsis, cover & return postage. Commission:
Home 10%; USA & Translation 20%.
Specializes in nonfiction, including illustrated bi-
ography, history, art, self-help, food & wine,
complementary medicine & therapies, finance
& business; trade, reference, academic.

**Knight Features**
20 Crescent Grove, London SW4 7AH
*Tel:* (020) 7622 1467 *Fax:* (020) 7622 1522
*E-mail:* info@knightfeatures.co.uk
*Web Site:* www.knightfeatures.com

*Key Personnel*
Dir, Proprietor: Peter Knight *E-mail:* peter@
knightfeatures.co.uk
Associate: Gaby Martin *E-mail:* gaby@
knightfeatures.co.uk
Founded: 1985
No poetry, science fiction or cookery. No unsolicited manuscripts. Send cover letter, self-
addressed envelope & synopsis of proposed
work. Commission dependent upon authors &
territories.
Specializes in strip cartoons, major features, serializations, autobiography/memoirs/letters,
biography, astrology, business & economics,
history, humour, formula one racing, puzzles.
*Branch Office(s)*
Peter Knight Literary Agency
Foreign Rep(s): United Media

**LAW Ltd (Lucas Alexander Whitley)**
14 Vernon St, London W14 0RJ
*Tel:* (020) 7471 7900 *Fax:* (020) 7471 7910
*E-mail:* law@lawagency.co.uk
*Key Personnel*
Contact: Julian Alexander *E-mail:* julian@
lawagency.co.uk; Lucinda Cook
*E-mail:* lucinda@lawagency.co.uk; Celia Hay-
ley *E-mail:* celia@lawagency.co.uk; Mark Lu-
cas *E-mail:* mark@lawagency.co.uk; Helen
Mulligan *E-mail:* helen@lawagency.co.uk; Peta
Nightingale *E-mail:* peta@lawagency.co.uk;
Alice Saunders *E-mail:* alice@lawagency.
co.uk; Araminta Whitley *E-mail:* araminta@
lawagency.co.uk
Contact, Children's: Philippa Milnes-Smith
*E-mail:* philippa@lawagency.co.uk
Founded: 1996
Handles full-length commercial & literary fiction,
nonfiction & children's books. No plays, poetry, textbooks or fantasy. Film & TV scripts
handled for established clients only. Unsolicited
manuscripts considered; send brief covering
letter, short synopsis & two sample chapters.
Self-addressed envelope required. No e-mailed
submissions. Commission: Home 15%; USA
& Translation 20%. Overseas associates worldwide.

**Gundhild Lenz-Mulligan**
15 Sandbourne Ave, Merton Park, London SW19
3EW
*Tel:* (020) 8543 7846 *Fax:* (020) 8543 8909
*E-mail:* lenzmulligan@btconnect.com
*Key Personnel*
Contact: Gundhild Lenz-Mulligan
Founded: 1998
Specializes in children's books.

**Barbara Levy Literary Agency**
64 Greenhill, Hampstead High St, London NW3
5TZ
*Tel:* (020) 7435 9046 *Fax:* (020) 7431 2063
*Key Personnel*
Dir: Barbara Levy
Associate: John F Selby
Founded: 1986
Handles fiction, nonfiction & TV presenters. No
unsolicited manuscripts. Send detailed prelim-
inary letter. Commission: Home 10%; USA
20%.

**Litopia Corp Ltd**
186 Bickenhall Mansions, Bickenhall St, London
W1H 3DE
*Tel:* (020) 7224 1748 *Fax:* (020) 7224 1802
*E-mail:* enquiries@litopia.com
*Web Site:* www.litopia.com
*Key Personnel*
Chief Executive Officer: Peter Cox
*E-mail:* peter@litopia.com

Contact: Peggy Brusseau *E-mail:* peggy@litopia. com; Jane Mountbatten *E-mail:* jane@litopia. com
Founded: 1993
Require all submissions to follow the guidelines on website. Commission by negotiation.
Specializes in general, no children's or poetry.

**Christopher Little Literary Agency**
Eel Brook Studios, 125 Moore Park Rd, London SW6 4PS
*Tel:* (020) 7736 4455 *Fax:* (020) 7736 4490
*E-mail:* info@christopherlittle.net
*Web Site:* www.christopherlittle.net
*Key Personnel*
Proprietor: Christopher J Little
   *E-mail:* christopher@christopherlittle.net
Contact: Kellee Nunley *E-mail:* kellee@ christopherlittle.net
Founded: 1979
Handles commercial & literary full-length fiction & nonfiction. Send detailed letter, synopsis &/or first two chapters & self-addressed envelope. Commission: Home 15%; US, Canada, Translation, Audio & Motion Picture 20%.
Specializes in crime, thriller, popular science & narrative & investigative nonfiction.

**London Independent Books**
26 Chalcot Crescent, London NW1 8YD
*Tel:* (020) 7706 0486 *Fax:* (020) 7724 3122
*Key Personnel*
Literary Agent: Carolyn Whitaker
Founded: 1971
All subjects considered except young children's & computer books. Commission: Home 15%; US & Translation 20%.
Specializes in crime fiction, fantasy fiction, travel, young adult fiction.

**Andrew Lownie Literary Agency Ltd**
17 Sutherland St, London SW1V 4JU
*Tel:* (020) 7828 1274 *Fax:* (020) 7828 7608
*E-mail:* lownie@globalnet.co.uk
*Web Site:* www.andrewlownie.co.uk
*Key Personnel*
Chief Executive: Andrew Lownie
Founded: 1988
Specializes in nonfiction, history, biography & current affairs.

**Lucas Alexander Whitley**, see LAW Ltd (Lucas Alexander Whitley)

**Lutyens & Rubinstein**
231 Westbourne Park Rd, London W11 1EB
*Tel:* (020) 7792 4855 *Fax:* (020) 7792 4833
*Key Personnel*
Partner: Sarah Lutyens *E-mail:* sarah@ lutyensrubinstein.co.uk; Felicity Rubinstein *E-mail:* felicity@lutyensrubinstein.co.uk
Submissions: Susannah Godman
   *E-mail:* susannah@lutyensrubinstein.co.uk
Founded: 1993
Membership(s): Association of Authors' Agents.
No TV, film radio or theatre scripts. Unsolicited manuscripts accepted; send introductory letter, cover, two chapters & return postage for all material submitted. No reading fee. Commission: Home 15%; USA & Translation 20%.
Specializes in adult fiction & nonfiction.

**MacLean Dubois Ltd (Writers & Agents)**
Hillend House, Hillend, Edinburgh EH10 7DX
*Tel:* (0131) 445 5885 *Fax:* (0131) 445 5898
*E-mail:* info@whiskymax.co.uk
*Key Personnel*
Dir: Charles MacLean
Founded: 1976

Copywriter, brochures, annual reports & promotional material.
Specializes in Scottish fiction & nonfiction, journalism, writing & related services.

**Adrian Mars**
53 Nassington Rd, London NW3 2TY
*Tel:* (020) 7433 1345 *Fax:* (0870) 164 0870
*E-mail:* a_mars@cix.co.uk
*Key Personnel*
Owner: Mr Adrian Mars
Founded: 2004
Serving US & UK markets.
Proposals should include at least one sample chapter. Complete manuscripts are also accepted.
Specializes in science, technology, health & fiction.

**The Marsh Agency**
11 Dover St, London W1S 4LJ
*Tel:* (020) 7399 2800 *Fax:* (020) 7399 2801
*E-mail:* enquiries@marsh-agency.co.uk
*Web Site:* www.marsh-agency.co.uk
*Key Personnel*
Partner: Paul Marsh; Susanna Nicklin
Rights Manager: Camilla Ferrier
Founded: 1994
Specializes in international rights.

**Blanche Marvin Agency**
21A St Johns Wood High St, London NW8 7NG
*Tel:* (020) 7722 2313 *Fax:* (020) 7722 2313
*Key Personnel*
Editor & Publisher: Blanche Marvin
   *E-mail:* blanchemarvin@madasafish.com
Founded: 1968
Established work only.
Specializes in theater & drama.

**MBA Literary Agents Ltd**
62 Grafton Way, London W1T 5DW
*Tel:* (020) 7387 2076 *Fax:* (020) 7387 2042
*E-mail:* agent@mbalit.co.uk
*Web Site:* www.mbalit.co.uk
*Key Personnel*
Man Dir: Diana Tyler *E-mail:* diana@mbalit.co. uk
Dir: Meg Davis *E-mail:* meg@mbalit.co.uk; Laura Longrigg *E-mail:* laura@mbalit.co.uk; John Richard Parker *E-mail:* john@mbalit.co. uk
Contact: David Riding *E-mail:* david@mbalit.co. uk
Founded: 1971
Handles fiction & nonfiction, TV, film radio & theatre scripts. No poetry. Works in conjunction with agents in most countries. No unsolicted manuscripts. Commission: Home 15%, Overseas 20%; Theatre/TV Radio 10%; Film 10-20%.
Foreign Rep(s): JABberwocky Agency; Donald Maass Agency; Writers House, Inc

**Cathy Miller Foreign Rights Agency**
18 The Quadrangle, 49 Atalanta St, London SW6 6TU
*Tel:* (020) 7386 5473 *Fax:* (020) 7385 1774
*Key Personnel*
Managing Dir: Cathy Miller *E-mail:* cathy@ millerrightsagency.com
Founded: 1981
Consultants to publishers worldwide in the field of translation rights, worldwide market research for publishers interested in European potential, help with negotiating rights contracts & representation.
Specializes in foreign rights.

**William Morris Agency (UK) Ltd**
52/53 Poland St, London W1F 7LX

*Tel:* (020) 7534 6800 *Fax:* (020) 7534 6900
*Web Site:* www.wma.com
*Key Personnel*
Man Dir: Stephanie Cabot
Literary Agent, Books: Eugenie Furniss
Literary Agent, TV: Holly Pie; Hans Schiff
Founded: 1965
Worldwide theatrical & literary agency with offices in New York, Beverly Hills & Nashville & associates in Sydney. Handles TV scripts, fiction & general nonfiction. No unsolicited film, TV or stage material at all. Manuscripts for books with preliminary letter. No reading fee. Commission: TV 10%; UK Books 15%; USA Books & Translation 20%.

**Michael Motley Ltd**
The Old Vicarage Tredington, Tewkesbury, Glos GL20 7BP
*Tel:* (01684) 276390 *Fax:* (01684) 297355
*E-mail:* michael.motley@amserve.com
*Key Personnel*
Contact: Michael Motley
Founded: 1973
Handles full-length fiction & nonfiction only. No unsolicited work considered. New clients by referral only. Commission: Home 10%; US 15%; Translation 20%.

**Negotiate Ltd**
99 Caiyside, Edinburgh EH10 7HR
*Tel:* (0131) 445 7571; (0131) 477 7858
   *Fax:* (0131) 445 7572
*E-mail:* gavin@negotiate.demon.co.uk
*Web Site:* www.negotiate.co.uk
*Key Personnel*
Man Dir: Gavin Kennedy *E-mail:* gavin@negweb. com
Founded: 1986
Negotiation of authors, publishers, agents & contracts.
Specializes in contract negotiation.

**The Maggie Noach Literary Agency**
22 Dorville Crescent, London W6 0HJ
*Tel:* (020) 8748 2926 *Fax:* (020) 8748 8057
*E-mail:* m-noach@dircon.co.uk
*Key Personnel*
Contact: Maggie Noach
Founded: 1982
New clients must live in the UK. No scientific, academic or specialist nonfiction. No poetry, plays, short stories or books for the very young. No unsolicited mmanuscripts. Approach by letter (not by telephone or e-mail), giving a brief description of the book & enclosing a few sample pages. Return postage essential. No reading fee. Commission: Home 15%; USA & Translation 20%.
Specializes in general nonfiction, biography, commercial fiction & non-illustrated children's books for ages 7-12.

**Andrew Nurnberg Associates Ltd**
Clerkenwell House, 45-47 Clerkenwell Green, London EC1R 0QX
*Tel:* (020) 7417 8800 *Fax:* (020) 7417 8812
*E-mail:* all@nurnberg.co.uk
*Telex:* 23353 *Cable:* NURNBOOKS LONDON
*Key Personnel*
Man Dir: Andrew Nurnberg
Dir: Sarah Nundy
Contact: Vicky Mark; D Roger Seaton
Commission: Home 15%; US & Translation 20%.
Specializes in foreign rights.
*Branch Office(s)*
Andrew Nurnberg Associates Baltic, PO Box 77, Riga LV-1011, Latvia, Contact: Tatjana Zoldnere *Tel:* 7289759; 7506495 *Fax:* 7821241; 7506494 *E-mail:* zoldnere@anab.apollo.lv
Andrew Nurnberg Associates Beijing, Room 3404 FLTP, Bldg 19, Xi San Huan Builu, Bei-

jing 100089, China, Contact: Jackie Huang *Tel:* (010) 684-20958 *Fax:* (010) 689-17896 *E-mail:* jhuang@nurnberg.com.cn

Andrew Nurnberg Associates Bucharest, Casa Presei Libere Nr 1, Intrarea A, Etaj 4, Camera 457, Sector 1, Bucharest, Romania *Tel:* (01) 224-0479 *Fax:* (01) 224-0479 *E-mail:* andrew@fx.ro

Andrew Nurnberg Associates Budapest, Hold u 29, 1054 Budapest, Hungary, Contact: Judit Hermann *Tel:* (01) 3026451 *Fax:* (01) 1113948 *E-mail:* jhermann@matavnet.hu

Andrew Nurnberg Associates Prague, Seifertova 81, Prague 3, Czech Republic, Contact: Petra Tobiskova *Tel:* (02) 227 82041 *Fax:* (02) 227 82308 *E-mail:* nurnprg@mbox.vol.cz

Andrew Nurnberg Associates Sofia, 11 Slaveikov Sq, PO Box 453, 1000 Sofia, Bulgaria, Contact: Anna Droumeva *Tel:* (02) 9862819 *Fax:* (02) 9862819 *E-mail:* anas@tea.bg

Andrew Nurnberg Associates Warsaw, UL Milobedzka 10/2, 02-634 Warsaw, Poland, Contact: Aleksandra Matuszak *Tel:* (022) 6465860 *Fax:* (022) 6465860 *E-mail:* aleksandra@literatura.com.pl

Andrew Nurnberg Literary Agency (Moscow), Voprosy Literatury, Bolshoi Gnezdnikovsky 10, Moscow 103009, Russian Federation, Contact: Ludmilla Sushkova *Tel:* (095) 229-5281 *Fax:* (095) 883-6403 *E-mail:* sushkova@adonis.iasnet.ru

## David O'Leary Literary Agents
10 Lansdowne Court, Lansdowne Rise, London W11 2NR
*Tel:* (020) 7229 1623 *Fax:* (020) 7727 9624
*E-mail:* d.o'leary@virgin.net
*Key Personnel*
Contact: David O'Leary
Founded: 1988
Include brief synopsis of subject of novel with initial correspondence. Include self-addressed envelope if return requested. Commission: Home 10%; US 10%.
Specializes in fiction & nonfiction (both literary & commercial), history, popular science & Irish subjects.

## Deborah Owen Ltd
78 Narrow St, Limehouse, London E14 8BP
*Tel:* (020) 7987 5119; (020) 7987 5441
  *Fax:* (020) 7538 4004
*E-mail:* do@deborahowen.co.uk
Founded: 1971
Represents only two authors. No new authors. Commission: Home 10%; US & Translation 15%.

## Paterson Marsh Ltd
Affiliate of Marsh Agency
11 Dover St, London W1S 4LJ
*Tel:* (020) 7399 2800 *Fax:* (020) 7399 2801
*E-mail:* info@markpaterson.co.uk
*Web Site:* www.patersonmarsh.co.uk
*Key Personnel*
Dir: Paul Marsh *E-mail:* paul@patersonmarsh.co.uk; Mark Paterson *E-mail:* mark@patersonmarsh.co.uk
Foreign Rights Manager: Stephanie Ebdon *E-mail:* steph@patersonmarsh.co.uk
Founded: 1961
World rights representatives of authors & publishers.
Specializes in psychology, psychotherapy, psychoanalysis, history.

## John Pawsey
60 High St, Tarring, Worthing, West Sussex BN14 7NR
*Tel:* (01903) 205167 *Fax:* (01903) 205167
*Key Personnel*
Proprietor: John Pawsey

Founded: 1981
Represents American publishers & literary agencies in the UK. Handles nonfiction: biography, politics, current affairs, popular culture, travel, sport, business & music. Also fiction: crime, thrillers & suspense. No children's, science fiction, horror, drama scripts, poetry, academic, short stories or journalism. Send preliminary letter with self-addressed envelope. No reading fee. Commission: Home 10-15%; US & Translation 19-25%.

## Peake Associates
14 Grafton Crescent, London NW1 8SL
*Tel:* (020) 7267 8033 *Fax:* (020) 7267 8033
*E-mail:* tony@tonypeake.com
*Web Site:* www.tonypeake.com/agency/index.htm
*Key Personnel*
Contact: Tony Peake
Currently not accepting new clients.
Specializes in fiction & nonfiction.

## Maggie Pearlstine Associates Ltd
31 Ashley Gardens, Ambrosden Ave, London SW1P 1QE
*Tel:* (020) 7828 4212 *Fax:* (020) 7834 5546
*E-mail:* post@pearlstine.co.uk
*Key Personnel*
Dir: Maggie Pearlstine
Associate: John Oates *E-mail:* john@pearlstine.co.uk
Founded: 1989
Small, selective agency. UK based authors only. Handles general nonfiction & fiction. No children's poetry, horror, science fiction short stories or scripts. Commission: Home 12 1/2% (fiction), 10% (nonfiction); US & Translation 20%; TV, Film & Journalism 20%.
Specializes in biography, current affairs, health & history.

## A D Peters & Co, see PFD

## PFD
Drury House, 34-43 Russell St, London WC2B 5HA
*Tel:* (020) 7344 1000 *Fax:* (020) 7836 9539
*E-mail:* postmaster@pfd.co.uk
*Web Site:* www.pfd.co.uk
*Key Personnel*
Joint Chair: Tim Corrie; Anthony Jones
Man Dir: Anthony Baring
Agent: Annabel Hardman *Tel:* (020) 7344 1054
  *E-mail:* ahardman@pfd.co.uk
Founded: 1988
Handles fiction & children's, plus scripts for film, theatre, radio & TV material. Send letter with a detailed outline & sample chapters. Screenplays & TV scripts should be addressed to the Film & Script Dept, enclose self-addressed envelope. No reading fee. Commission: Home 10%; US & Translation 20%.
Specializes in literary, film & actors agency.
*Parent Company:* CSS Stellar

## Pollinger Ltd
9 Staple Inn, Holborn, London WC1V 7QH
*Tel:* (020) 7404 0342 *Fax:* (020) 7242 5737
*E-mail:* info@pollingerltd.com
*Web Site:* www.pollingerltd.com
*Key Personnel*
Dir: Leigh Pollinger
Man Dir: Lesley Hadcroft Pollinger
  *E-mail:* lesleypollinger@pollingerltd.com
Secretary: John Furzer *E-mail:* johnfurzer@pollingerltd.com
Authors' Agent: Joanna Devereux
  *E-mail:* jdevereux@pollingerltd.com
Founded: 2002
Authors' agents.
Specializes in adult fiction & nonfiction, children's, literary estates.

## Rogers, Coleridge & White Ltd
20 Powis Mews, London W11 1JN
*Tel:* (020) 7221 3717 *Fax:* (020) 7229 9084
*E-mail:* rcwlitagency@rcwlitagency.co.uk *Cable:* DEBROGERS LONDON W11
*Key Personnel*
Dir: Gill Coleridge; David Miller; Deborah Rogers; Peter Straus
Dir, USA: Patricia White
Consultant: Ann Warnford-Davis
Foreign Rights: Stephen Edwards; Laurence Laluyaux
Founded: 1967
No poetry, plays or technical books. No unsolicited manuscripts, no submissions by fax or e-mail. Commission: Home 10%; USA 15%; Translation 20%.
Specializes in fiction, non-fiction & children's.
Foreign Rep(s): ICM

## Elizabeth Roy Literary Agency
White Cottage, Greatford, Near Stamford, Lincs PE9 4PR
*Tel:* (01778) 560672 *Fax:* (01778) 560672
*Key Personnel*
Contact: Elizabeth Roy
Founded: 1990
Send preliminary letter, synopsis, sample chapters, names of previous publishers & agents & return postage. No reading fee. Commission: Home 10-15%; Overseas 20%.
Specializes in children's books (fiction & nonfiction), children's books illustrators.

## The Sayle Literary Agency
8b King's Parade, Cambridge CB2 1SJ
*Tel:* (01223) 303035 *Fax:* (01223) 301638
*Key Personnel*
Contact: Rachel Calder
Preliminary letter & return postage required. No reading fee.
Specializes in full-length literary fiction, crime, suspense & general nonfiction.

## Sheil Land Associates Ltd
43 Doughty St, London WC1N 2LH
*Tel:* (020) 7405 9351 *Fax:* (020) 7831 2127
*E-mail:* info@sheilland.co.uk
*Key Personnel*
Chairman: Anthony Sheil
Chief Executive: Sonia Land
Rights Dir: Laura Susijn
Contact: Luigi Bonomi; Sam Boyce; Vivien Green; Amanda Preston
Founded: 1962
Literary, Theatre & Film Agents. Preliminary letter with self-addressed envelope essential, no reading fee. Commission: Home 15%; US & Translation 20%.
Specializes in commercial & literary fiction & nonfiction, including politics, business, history, military history, gardening, thrillers, crime, romance, fantasy, drama, biography, travel, cookery & humor.
*U.S. Office(s):* Sheil Land Associates in association with George Borchart Inc, 136 E 57 St, New York, NY 10022, United States *Tel:* 212-753-5785
Foreign Rep(s): APA; Georges Borchardt, Inc; CAA; Farrar, Straus & Giroux, Inc

## Caroline Sheldon Literary Agency
Thorley Manor Farm, Thorley, Yarmouth PO41 0S1
*Tel:* (01983) 760205
*Key Personnel*
Literary Agent & Proprietor: Caroline Sheldon
Literary Agent: Penny Holroyde *Tel:* (020) 7336 6550
Founded: 1985

Handles adult fiction, in particular women's (both commercial & literary) & human interest non-fiction. Also full-length children's fiction, younger children's fiction, picture books & picture book artists. No TV/Film scripts unless by book-writing clients. Commission: Home 10-15%; USA & translation 20%. Submissions should be sent to the Isle of Wight address & include a letter describing your ambitions, a well-written synopsis, the first three chapters of your proposal & a self-addressed stamped evelope with sufficient postage for return.
*Branch Office(s)*
70-75 Cowcross St, London EC1M 6EJ, Literary Agent: Penny Holroyde

**Dorie Simmonds Agency**
67 Upper Berkeley St, London W1H 7QX
*Tel:* (020) 7569 8686 *Fax:* (020) 7569 8696
*Key Personnel*
Proprietor: Dorie Simmonds
    *E-mail:* dhsimmonds@aol.com
Rights: Frances Lubbe
Handles a wide range of subjects including general nonfiction & commercial fiction, children's books & associated rights.
Outline required for nonfiction, short synopsis for fiction with 2-3 sample chapters, writing experience & publishing history explained. Include self-addressed stamped envelope if return requested.
Specializes in contemporary personalities, historical biographies, self-help & women's fiction.

**Jeffrey Simmons**
15 Penn House, Mallory St, London NW8 8SX
*Tel:* (020) 7224 8917 *Fax:* (020) 7224 8918
*E-mail:* jas@london-inc.com
*Key Personnel*
Contact: Jeffrey Simmons
Founded: 1978
No science fiction/fantasy, children's books, cookery, crafts, hobbies or gardening. Film scripts handled only if by book-writing clients. Commission: Home 10-15%; US & Foreign 15%.
Specializes in biography & autobiography, cinema & theatre, fiction (both quality & commercial), history, law & crime, politics & world affairs, parapsychology & sport.

**The Stationery Office**, see TSO (The Stationery Office)

**Abner Stein**
10 Roland Gardens, London SW7 3PH
*Tel:* (020) 7373 0456 *Fax:* (020) 7370 6316
*E-mail:* abnerstein@compuserve.com
*Key Personnel*
Contact: Abner Stein
Founded: 1971
No scientific, technical. Commission: Home 10%; US & Translation 20%.
Specializes in children's books, fiction, nonfiction.

**Micheline Steinberg Associates**
104 Great Portland St, London W1W 6PE
*Tel:* (020) 7631 1310 *Fax:* (020) 7631 1146
*E-mail:* info@steinplays.com
*Key Personnel*
Contact: Ginny Sennett; Micheline Steinberg
Founded: 1988
Preliminary letter with self-addressed envelope. Dramatic associate for Laurence Pollinger Limited. Commission: Home 10%; Elsewhere 15%.
Specializes in plays for stage, TV, radio & film.

**J M Thurley Management**
30 Cambridge Rd, Teddington, Middx TW11 8DR
*Tel:* (020) 8977 3176 *Fax:* (020) 8943 2678

*Key Personnel*
Proprietor: J M Thurley *E-mail:* jmthurley@aol.com
Founded: 1976
Specialize in literary & commercial fiction & nonfiction.

**Lavinia Trevor Literary Agency**
The Glasshouse, 49A Goldhawk Rd, London W12 8QP
*Tel:* (020) 8749 8481 *Fax:* (020) 8749 7377
*Key Personnel*
Contact: Lavinia Trevor
Founded: 1993
No poetry, academic, technical or children's books. No TV, film, radio, theatre scripts. Submissions: preliminary letter including brief autobiography, first 50 typewritten pages (double spaced) & plot/structural outline. Send stamped, self-addressed envelope. No reading fee. Commission rate by agreement with author.
Specializes in general fiction & nonfiction, including popular science.

**TSO (The Stationery Office)**
51 Nine Elms Lane, London SW8 5DR
*Tel:* (020) 7873 8787 *Fax:* (0870) 600 5533 (orders)
*E-mail:* customer.services@tso.co.uk
*Web Site:* www.tso.co.uk
*Key Personnel*
Chief Executive Officer: Tim Hailstone
Man Dir: Keith Burbage
Founded: 1996
Provider of information management services.
*Branch Office(s)*
The Parliamentary Press - London, Mandela Way, London SE1 5SS *Tel:* (020) 7394 4200
TSO Wales, G50, Phase Two, Government Bldgs, Ty-Glas, Llanishen, Cardiff CF14 5ST *Tel:* (02920) 765892
TSO Brussels, Martens International Consulting, 70, rue Philippe le Bon, 1000 Brussels, Belgium, Contact: Roger Lecocq *Tel:* (02) 235 0857; (02) 235 0850 *Fax:* (02) 235 0855
TSO Content Solutions, 84-90 East St, Epsom, Surrey KT17 1HF *Tel:* (01372) 845700
TSO Ireland, 16 Arthur St, Belfast BT1 4GD, Ireland *Tel:* (02890) 238451
TSO - Norwich, St Crispins, Duke St, Norwich NR3 1PD *Tel:* (01603) 622211
TSO Scotland, 71-73 Lothian Rd, Edinburgh EH3 9AZ *Tel:* (0870) 6065566
*Bookshop(s):* 16 Arthur St, Belfast BT1 4GD, Ireland *Tel:* (02890) 238451

**Turnaround Publisher Services Ltd**
Unit 3, Olympia Trading Estate, Coburg Rd, Wood Green, London N22 6TZ
*Tel:* (020) 8829 3000 *Fax:* (020) 8881 5088
*E-mail:* enquires@turnaround-uk.com; orders@turnaround-uk.com
*Web Site:* www.turnaround-psl.com
*Key Personnel*
President & Man Dir: Bill Godber *Tel:* (020) 8829 3008 *E-mail:* bill@turnaround-uk.com
Marketing Dir: Claire Thompson *Tel:* (020) 8829 3009 *E-mail:* claire@turnaround-uk.com
Promotions Manager: Matthew Lang *Tel:* (020) 8829 3007 *E-mail:* matthew@turnaround-uk.com
Order Processing Manager: Julie Thelot *Tel:* (020) 8829 3002 *E-mail:* julie@turnaround-uk.com
Finance Dir: Sue Gregg *Tel:* (020) 8829 3006 *E-mail:* sue@turnaround-uk.com
Sales Manager: Andy Webb *Tel:* (020) 8829 3012 *E-mail:* andy@turnaround-uk.com
Founded: 1984

Sales agent & distributor to the UK & continental European booktrade for a wide variety of quality US & UK publishers.
Specializes in black interest, gay interest, American imports, fiction, music, social & political issues, arts.

**Jane Turnbull**
13 Wendell Rd, London W12 9RS
*Tel:* (020) 8743 9580 *Fax:* (020) 8749 6079
*E-mail:* agents@cwcom.net
*Key Personnel*
Contact: Jane Turnbull *E-mail:* jane.turnbull@btintenet.com
Founded: 1986
No science fiction, sagas or romantic fiction. No unsolicited manuscripts or reading fee. Approach with letter in the first instance. Translation rights handled by Gillon Aitken Associates Ltd. Commission: Home 10%; USA & Foreign 20%.
Specializes in biography, history, current affairs, health & diet, fiction & nonfiction.

**Kelvin van Hasselt Publishing Services**
Willow House, The Street, Briningham, Norfolk NR24 2PY
*Tel:* (01263) 862724 *Fax:* (01263) 862803
*E-mail:* kvhbooks@aol.com
*Key Personnel*
Man Dir: Kevin van Hasselt
Order Processing: Gill Hinds
Representing book publishers in Africa, Asia & the Caribbean.
Specializes in academic & professional.

**Van Lear Ltd**
50 Kilmaine Rd, Fulham, London SW6 7JX
Mailing Address: PO Box 21816, Fulham, London SW6 5ZU
*Tel:* (020) 7385 1199 *Fax:* (020) 7385 6262
*E-mail:* evl@vanlear.co.uk
*Key Personnel*
Contact: Anne-Marie Doulton; Elizabeth Van Lear
International publishers representative literary scout.

**Ed Victor Ltd**
6 Bayley St, Bedford Square, London WC1B 3HB
*Tel:* (020) 7304 4100 *Fax:* (020) 7304 4111
*Key Personnel*
Man Dir: Ed Victor
Dir: Graham Greene; Sophie Hicks *E-mail:* sophie@edvictor.com; Leon Morgan; Maggie Phillips; Carol Ryan
Contact: Lizzy Kremer
Founded: 1976
No scripts, academic, poetry. Commission: Home 15%; US 15%; Translation 20%.
Specializes in commercial fiction & nonfiction.

**S Walker Literary Agency**
96 Church Lane, Goldington, Bedford MK41 0AS
*Tel:* (01234) 216229
*Key Personnel*
Partner: Alan Oldfield; Cora-Louise Oldfield
Founded: 1939
No reading fee.
Specializes in full-length fiction.

**Peter Ward Book Exports**
Taylors Yard, Unit 3, 67 Alderbrook Rd, London SW12 8AD
*Tel:* (020) 8772 3300 *Fax:* (020) 8772 3309
*E-mail:* peter@pwbookex.dircon.co.uk
*Key Personnel*
Partner: Peter Ward; Richard Ward *E-mail:* richard@pwbookex.dircon.co.uk
Founded: 1974

Freelance representatives of UK & US publishers. Specializes in Middle East, Cyprus, Turkey, Iran, Greece & Malta.

**Watson, Little Ltd**
Capo Di Monte, Windmill Hill, London NW3 6RJ
*Tel:* (020) 7431 0770 *Fax:* (020) 7431 7225
*E-mail:* enquiries@watsonlittle.com
*Web Site:* www.watsonlittle.net
*Key Personnel*
Dir: Mandy Little *E-mail:* al@watsonlittle.com;
  Sheila Watson *E-mail:* sw@watsonlittle.com;
  Sugra Zaman *E-mail:* sz@watsonlittle.com
Handles fiction & nonfiction. No scripts. Send preliminary letter with synopsis. Commission: Home 15%; US 24%; Translation 19%.
Specializes in business, history, popular science, psychology & self-help.

**A P Watt Ltd**
20 John St, London WC1N 2DR
*Tel:* (020) 7405 6774 *Fax:* (020) 7831 2154
*E-mail:* apw@apwatt.co.uk
*Web Site:* www.apwatt.co.uk
*Key Personnel*
Man Dir: Caradoc King

Foreign Rights Dir: Linda Shaughnessy
Joint Manager: Derek Johns
Founded: 1875
Literary, film & television agents. No unsolicited manuscripts. Commission: home 10%; USA & translation 20%.

**Josef Weinberger Plays**
12-14 Mortimer St, London W1T 3JJ
*Tel:* (020) 7580 2827 *Fax:* (020) 7436 9616
*E-mail:* general.info@jwmail.co.uk
*Web Site:* www.josef-weinberger.com
*Key Personnel*
Manager: Michael Callahan
Founded: 1885
No unsolicited manuscripts; introductory letter essential. No reading fee.
Agent & publisher of scripts for the theatre.

**Dinah Wiener Ltd**
12 Cornwall Grove, Chiswick, London W4 2LB
*Tel:* (020) 8994 6011 *Fax:* (020) 8994 6044
*E-mail:* dinahwiener@enterprise.net
*Key Personnel*
Contact: Dinah Wiener
Founded: 1985

Handles fiction & general nonfiction. No scripts, children's or poetry. Manuscripts submitted must include self-addressed envelope & be typed in double-spacing. Commission: Home 15%; USA & Translation 20%.
Specializes in autobiography, cookery, popular science.

**Zebra Agency**
Broadlands House, One Broadlands, Shevington, Lancs WN6 8DH
*Tel:* (077193) 75575
*E-mail:* admin@zebraagency.co.uk
*Web Site:* www.zebraagency.co.uk
*Key Personnel*
Contact: Dee Jones; Cara Wooi
Nonfiction & general fiction including crime, suspense & drama, murder, mysteries, adventure, thrillers, horror & science fiction, plus scripts for TV/radio/film/theatre. No reading fee. Editorial advice given to authors. No unsolicited manuscripts; send preliminary letter giving publishing history & brief cover, with synopsis (plus self-addressed stamped envelope). No phone calls or submissions by fax or e-mail. Commission: home 10%, USA & translation 15%.

# Translation Agencies & Associations

## Austria

**Oesterreichischer Uebersetzer- und Dolmetscherverband Universitas**
Gymnasiumstr 50, 1190 Vienna
*Tel:* (01) 368 60 60 *Fax:* (01) 368 60 08
*E-mail:* info@universitas.org
*Web Site:* www.universitas.org
*Key Personnel*
President: Florika Griessner
Austrian Association of Interpreters & Translators.

**Uebersetzergemeinschaft Interessengemeinschaft von Uebersetzerinnen und Uebersetzern literarischer und wissenschaftlicher Werke**
(Austrian Association of Literary & Scientific Translators)
Seidengasse 13, 1070 Vienna
*Tel:* (01) 526 204 418 *Fax:* (01) 524 64 35
*E-mail:* ueg@literaturhaus.at
*Key Personnel*
Chairman: Werner Richter
Secretary General: Brigitte Rapp *E-mail:* br@literaturhaus.at
Publication(s): *Literature Infonet* (handbook); *The Translators' Companion*; *Uebersetzerverzeichnis* (directory)

## Bulgaria

**Union of Translators of Bulgaria, Magazin Panorama**
ul Graf Ignatiev 16, Sofia
*Tel:* (02) 65 51 90; (02) 65 61 87
*Key Personnel*
Editor: Gancho Savov
Publication(s): *Panorama* (magazine)
*Branch Office(s)*
Magazine & Publishing House

## China

**Polyglot Translation**
New World Times Center, 904 S Tower, 2191 Guangyuan Rd E, Guangzhou 510500
*Tel:* (020) 8764-1878 *Fax:* (020) 8764-2003
*E-mail:* info@polyglot.com.cn
*Web Site:* www.polyglot.com.cn
A professional translation organization that provides translation, interpretation & simultaneous meeting interpretation in all fields. In addition, we provide localization of websites into Chinese, writing articles in multi-languages, foreign languages recording, proofreading, interpreters/translators recommending, website designing & making & so on. We can provide a large variety of languages translating services such as English, Japanese, French, German, Russian, Korean, Italian, Spanish, Dutch, Swedish, Finnish, Portuguese, Czech, Slovak, Romanian, Polish, Hungarian, Bulgarian, Arabic, Turkish, Cambodian, Malay, Indonesian, Thai, Vietnamese, Nepali, Laotian, Burmese, Mongolian, Indic, Bengalese, Tamil etc. Altogether, we can provide more than 30-languages translation service fast & accurately.

**TAC**, see Translator's Association of China (TAC)

**Translator's Association of China (TAC)**
24 Baiwanzhuang St, Beijing 100037
*Tel:* (010) 68326681
*E-mail:* taccn@163bj.com
*Web Site:* www.tac-online.org.cn
*Key Personnel*
Dir: Sun Chengtang
Publication(s): *Chinese Translators Journal*

## Cuba

**Centro de Traducciones y Terminologia Especializada (CTTE)** (Translation & Specialized Terminology Center)
Dept Comercial y de Marketing, Capitola de la Habana, Prado entre Dragones y San Jose, 10200 La Habana
*Tel:* (07) 862-6531; (07) 860-3411 *Fax:* (07) 862-6531
*E-mail:* comercial@idict.cu
*Web Site:* www.cubaciencia.cu/
*Key Personnel*
Dir: Luis Alberto Gonzalez Moreno
Publication(s): *Catalogo de Cubalingua*

## Czech Republic

**Jednota Tlumocniku a Prekladatelu** (JTP - Union of Interpreters and Translators)
Senovazne Namesti 23, 110 00 Prague 1
*Tel:* (02) 24 142 517 *Fax:* (02) 24 142 312
*E-mail:* info@jtpunion.org
*Web Site:* www.jtpunion.org
*Key Personnel*
President: Dr Andrej Ra'dy
Dir: Peter Kautsky
Press Officer: Jiri Eichler
Glossaries, dictionaries, terminology, proceedings of specialised conferences.
Publication(s): *ToP* (quarterly, bulletin)

**Translators Guild** (Obec Prekladatelu)
Pod nuselskymi schody 3, 120 00 Prague 2
*Tel:* 222 564 082
*E-mail:* info@obecprekladatelu.cz
*Web Site:* www.obecprekladatelu.cz
*Key Personnel*
President: Hana Linhartova

## Egypt (Arab Republic of Egypt)

**Al Ahram Establishment**
6 Al-Galaa' St, Cairo
*Tel:* (02) 5786500; (02) 5786200; (02) 5786300; (02) 5786400 *Fax:* (02) 3941866; (02) 5786126; (02) 5786833
*E-mail:* ahram@ahram.org.eg
*Web Site:* www.ahram.org.eg
*Telex:* 20185-92544
Founded: 1875

**The Egyptian Society for the Dissemination of Universal Culture & Knowledge (ESDUCK)**
1081 Corniche el Nil St, Garden City, Cairo
Mailing Address: PO Box 21, Garden City, Cairo
*Tel:* (02) 3542 0295; (02) 35425079
*Web Site:* www.worldwatch.org
*Telex:* 92548

**ESDUCK**, see The Egyptian Society for the Dissemination of Universal Culture & Knowledge (ESDUCK)

## France

**Societe Francaise des Traducteurs**
Affiliate of Federation Internationale der Traducteurs (FIT)
22 rue des Martyrs, 75009 Paris
*Tel:* (01) 48 78 43 32 *Fax:* (01) 44 53 01 14
*E-mail:* sft@tiscali.fr
*Web Site:* www.sft.fr
*Key Personnel*
President: Maria Lebret-Sanchez
Vice President: Marie-Christine Garcin
Secretary General: Rupert Swyer
Editor-in-Chief: Muriel Valenta *Tel:* (05) 45 36 02 81 *E-mail:* muriel.valenta@wanadoo.fr
Founded: 1947
French Union of Translators.
Publication(s): *Traduire* (quarterly)

## Germany

**BDU**, see Bundesverband der Dolmetscher und Ubersetzer eV (BDU)

**Bundesverband der Dolmetscher und Ubersetzer eV (BDU)** (German Association of Interpreters & Translators)
Kurfuerstendamm 170, 10707 Berlin
*Tel:* (030) 88712830 *Fax:* (030) 88712840
*E-mail:* bgs@bdue.de
*Web Site:* www.bdue.de

*Key Personnel*
President: Barbara Boeer Alves
Publication(s): *Mitteilungsblatt fuer Dolmetscher und Uebersetzer - MDU*

**VDU**, see Verband deutschsprachiger Uebersetzer literarischer und wissenschaftlicher Werke eV (VDUe)

**Verband deutschsprachiger Uebersetzer literarischer und wissenschaftlicher Werke eV (VDUe)** (Association of German-speaking Translators of Literary & Scientific Works)
c/o Sabine Herholz, Verband Deutscher Schriftseller, FB8, Potsdamer Platz 10, 10785 Berlin
*Tel:* (030) 6956-2331 *Fax:* (030) 6956-3655
*Web Site:* www.literaturuebersetzer.de
*Key Personnel*
Secretary: Friedrich Griese

# Ghana

**Bureau of Ghana Languages**
PO Box 1851, Accra
*Tel:* (021) 665461
Also Publisher.
*Branch Office(s)*
PO Box 177, Tamale, Northern Region

# Greece

**EEML**, see Elliniki Etaireia Metafraston Logotechnias

**Elliniki Etaireia Metafraston Logotechnias**
    (Hellenic Society of Translators of Literature)
7 E Tsakona St, Paleo Psychiko, 154 52 Athens
*Tel:* 2106717466 *Fax:* 2106717466
*Key Personnel*
President: Dr Vassilis Vitsaxis
General Secretary: Costas Assimekopoulos
Founded: 1983
Also publish Greek Letters Yearbook containing translations in English, French, German, Italian & Spanish of contemporary Greek literature.
Membership(s): Federation of International Translators (FIT); EWG.
Publication(s): *Greek Letters Yearly* (in English, French, Spanish, Italian & German)

# Hong Kong

**KAMS Information & Publishing Ltd**
PO Box 72050, Kowloon Central Post Office, Kowloon
*Tel:* 23889172 *Fax:* 27716403
*E-mail:* kamsinfo@hkstar.com
*Web Site:* kamsinfo.com
*Key Personnel*
Project Dir: Kam-sun Yiu
Founded: 1989
Specialize in editing, translation & publishing services in more than 20 languages.

**KCL Language Consultancy Ltd**
Shop 1, G/F, 46 Lyndhurst Terrace, Central Hong Kong
*Tel:* (02) 8811368 *Fax:* (02) 8080389
*E-mail:* kcl@iohk.com

*Web Site:* www.iohk.com/userpages/kcl
*Key Personnel*
Dir: Karen Chan

# Hungary

**Magyar Iroszovetseg Konyvtara**
Bajza u 18, 1062 Budapest
*Tel:* (01) 322-8840; (01) 322-0631 *Fax:* (01) 321-3419
*Key Personnel*
President: Marton Kalasz
Library of Hungarian Writers' Union.

# India

**National Institute of Science Communication & Information Resources (NISCAIR)**
14 Satsang Vihar Marg, New Delhi 110 067
*Tel:* (011) 2650141 *Fax:* (011) 26862228
*E-mail:* webmaster@niscair.res.in
*Web Site:* www.niscom.res.in
*Telex:* 031-73099
*Key Personnel*
Dir: Mr V K Gupta *E-mail:* vkgupta@niscair.res.in
Membership(s): FID.
Specializes in translating European & Asian languages into English, library automation, computer networking & database design.
Publication(s): *Annals of Library Science & Documentation*; *Database on Indian Patents (IN-PAT)*; *Databases - Current Contents of Indian Journals*; *Directory of Indian Scientific Periodicals*; *Directory of Scientific Research Institutions in India*; *Indian Science Abstracts*; *Medical & Aromatic Plants Abstracts (MAPA)*; *Metallurgy Index*; *National Union Catalogue of Scientific Serials in India (NUCSSI)*; *Polymer Science Database*
*Branch Office(s)*
Bangalore
Chennai
Kolkata

# Ireland

**Cumann Aistritheoiri nahEireann**, see Irish Translators' & Interpreters' Association

**Ireland Literature Exchange** (Idirmhalartan Litriocht Eireann)
25 Denzille Lane, Dublin 2
*Tel:* (01) 678 8961; (01) 662 5687 *Fax:* (01) 662 5687
*E-mail:* info@irelandliterature.com
*Web Site:* www.irelandliterature.com
*Key Personnel*
Dir: Sinead MacAodha *E-mail:* sinead@irelandliterature.com
Administrator: Maire N Dhonnchadha *E-mail:* maire@irelandliterature.com
Founded: 1994
Not-for-profit organization founded to fund translations of literature from Ireland into foreign languages & foreign literature into English & Irish.

**Irish Translators' & Interpreters' Association**
The Irish Writers' Centre, 19 Parnell Sq, Dublin 1
*Tel:* (01) 8721302 *Fax:* (01) 8726282
*E-mail:* translation@eircom.net
*Web Site:* www.translatorsassociation.ie
*Key Personnel*
FIT Literary Translation Committee Representative: Miriam Lee *Tel:* (01) 2859137
Membership(s): International Federation of Translators (FIT); European Board of Literary Translators Associations (CEATL).
Publication(s): *Transverse*; *Transverse II*

# Israel

**Freund Publishing House Ltd**
PO Box 35010, 61350 Tel Aviv
*Tel:* (03) 562-8540 *Fax:* (03) 562-8538
*E-mail:* h_freund@netvision.net.il
*Web Site:* www.freundpublishing.com
*Key Personnel*
Man Dir & Publisher: Edmund Freund
Founded: 1968

**The Institute for the Translation of Hebrew Literature**
23 Baruch Hirsch St, Bnei Brak
Mailing Address: PO Box 1005 1, 52001 Ramat Gan
*Tel:* (03) 579 6830 *Fax:* (03) 579 6832
*E-mail:* hamachon@inter.net.il
*Web Site:* www.ithl.org.il
*Key Personnel*
Chairman: Prof Ory Bernstein
Man Dir: Nilli Cohen
Office Manager: Debbie Dagan
Founded: 1962
Main activities include promotion of modern Hebrew literature & children's literature in translation & serves as literary agent for a large number of Israeli writers & assists in the preparation of anthologies of Hebrew literature.
Specializes in Hebrew literature in translation.

**Israel Translators' Association**
PO Box 13184, 61131 Tel Aviv
*Tel:* (09) 741 5279 *Fax:* (09) 760 2369
*Web Site:* www.ita.org.il
*Key Personnel*
Chairperson: Ms Sarah Yarkoni *E-mail:* sarahy@netvision.net.il
Association of some 500 translators, mostly freelance. Detailed database of members, with languages & specialties.
Publication(s): *Targima*

# Italy

**AITI (Associazione Italiana Traduttori e Interpreti)** (Association of Italian Translators & Interpreters)
Via dei Prati Fiscali 158, 00141 Rome
*Tel:* (081) 7645362 *Fax:* (081) 7645362
*E-mail:* segreteria@aiti.org
*Web Site:* www.aiti.org
*Key Personnel*
President: Vittoria Lo Faro
Secretary: Grazia Di Bartolomeo
Founded: 1950
Membership(s): Federation Internationale des Traducteurs (FIT).
Publication(s): *Il traduttore nuovo* (biannually, periodical)

**Associazione Italiana Traduttori e Interpreti**, see AITI (Associazione Italiana Traduttori e Interpreti)

# Lebanon

**Ecole de Traducteurs et d'Interpretes de Beyrouth-Universite Saint-Joseph (ETIB)**
Campus des Sciences Humaines, Rue de Damas, BP 17-5208 - Mar Mikhael, Beirut 1104 2020
*Tel:* (01) 611 456 (ext 5512) *Fax:* (01) 611 360
*E-mail:* etib@usj.edu.lb
*Web Site:* www.usj.edu.lb
*Key Personnel*
Dir: Henri Awaiss

# Norway

**The Norwegian Association of Literary Translators**
Postboks 579 Sentrum, 0150 Oslo
*Tel:* 22478090 *Fax:* 22420356
*E-mail:* post@translators.no
*Web Site:* skrift.no/no/english/index.asp; skrift.no/no/index.asp
*Key Personnel*
Contact: Hilde Sveinsson *E-mail:* hilde@translators.no
Founded: 1948

# Poland

**Stowarzyszenie Tlumaczy Polskich** (Association of Polish Translators & Interpreters)
ul Jaworzynska 3 m 22, 00-634 Warsaw
*Tel:* (022) 621 56 78; (022) 825 09 04 *Fax:* (022) 621 56 78
*E-mail:* stp-waw@interkom.pl
*Web Site:* www.stp.org.pl
*Key Personnel*
President: Ryszard Dulinicz
Vice President: Danuta Kierzkowska; Wojciech Dawiec
*Branch Office(s)*
Oddzial Gdanski, ul Gdynskich Kosynierow 11, 80-866 Gdansk *Tel:* (058) 305-30-65 *Fax:* (058) 305-30-65 *E-mail:* stpgdansk@gd.home.pl
Oddzial Katowicki, ul Mlynska 21/23, 40-098 Katowice *Tel:* (032) 253-80-87 *Fax:* (032) 253-80-87 *Toll Free Fax:* stp_ok@poczta.onet.pl
Oddzial Krakowski, ul Dunin-Wasowicza 26/16, 31-112 Krakow *Tel:* (012) 429-26-56 *Fax:* (012) 429-26-56
Oddzial Lodzki, ul Piotrkowska 67, 90-422 Lodz *Tel:* (042) 633-65-80 *Fax:* (042) 633-65-80 *E-mail:* granicki@dawid.com.pl
Oddzial Poznanski, ul Przybyszewskiego 62/1, 60-357 Poznan *Tel:* (061) 867-96-00 *Fax:* (061) 867-96-00 *E-mail:* tomzeb@amu.edu.pl
Oddzial Szczecinski, ul Jagiellonska 8/4, 70-436 Szczecin *Tel:* (091) 43-43-556 *Fax:* (091) 43-43-556 *E-mail:* zespol@biurotlumaczen.pl
Oddzial Warszawski *Tel:* (022) 621-73-76; (022) 629-50-47 *Fax:* (022) 621-73-76 *E-mail:* stpata@medianet.com.pl

**STP**, see Stowarzyszenie Tlumaczy Polskich

# Spain

**Tek Translation International SA**
OneWorld Localization Center, Centro Empresarial El Plantio Ochandiano, 10, 28023 Madrid
*Tel:* (091) 4141111 *Fax:* (091) 4144444
*E-mail:* sales@tektrans.com
*Web Site:* www.tektrans.com
*Key Personnel*
Group Head: Alba Guix
Account Manager: Veit Gunther
Founded: 1961
Technical specialists in over 100 languages, including Chinese, Arabic, Japanese, Russian.

# Sweden

**Exportradet Spraktjanst AB**
Storgatan 19, 114 85 Stockholm
Mailing Address: Box 5513, 114 85 Stockholm
*Tel:* (08) 783 85 00 *Fax:* (08) 662 90 93
*E-mail:* infocenter@swedishtrade.se
*Web Site:* www.swedishtrade.se
*Telex:* 15679
*Key Personnel*
President: Gunnar Lindberg
Translating & interpreting service of the Swedish Trade Council.

**Foereningen Auktoriserade Translatorer** (The Federation of Authorized Translator in Sweden)
Norra Parkvagen 15, 756 45 Uppsala
*E-mail:* info@eurofat.se
*Web Site:* www.eurofat.se
*Key Personnel*
Chairman: Kerstin E Wallin *Tel:* (018) 301658
Secretary: Nadezjda Chekhov *Tel:* (08) 6426124
Founded: 1932
Publication(s): *FATaburen* (in Swedish, 4 issues annually)

# Switzerland

**Association Suisse des Traducteurs Terminologues et Interpretes (ASTTI)** (Swiss Association of Translators & Interpreters)
Postgasse 17, 3011 Berne
*Tel:* (031) 313 88 10 *Fax:* (031) 313 88 99
*E-mail:* astti@astti.ch
*Web Site:* www.astti.ch
*Key Personnel*
President: Doris Schmidt
Vice President: Henry Braun; David Fuhruann
Contact: Marianne Hofmann *E-mail:* m.i.hofmann@bluewin.ch
*Branch Office(s)*
Susenbergstr 111, 8044 Zurich, Ekaterina Ovsiannikova-Keymer *E-mail:* o-key@swissonline.ch

# Taiwan, Province of China

**National Institute for Compilation & Translation**
179 He-ping E Rd, Sec 1, Da-an District, Taipei
*Tel:* (02) 33225558 *Fax:* (02) 33225559
*Web Site:* www.nict.gov.tw
*Key Personnel*
Dir: Shun-Te Lan
Publication(s): *Counter Attack*

# United Republic of Tanzania

**Baraza la Kiswahili la Taifa**
PO Box 4766, Dar Es Salaam
*Tel:* (051) 23452; (051) 24139
*Key Personnel*
Chief Editor: Mastidia Kailembo Mbeo
Translations in English, Kiswahili, Arabic, French, Portuguese & Spanish.

# United Kingdom

**Deborah Adlam**
Member of Edinburgh University & Oxford University
41 W Savile Terrace, Edinburgh EH9 3DP
*Tel:* (0131) 6676048
*Key Personnel*
Contact: Deborah Adlam *E-mail:* deborahadlam@hotmail.com
Founded: 1982
Translation into English carried out from Latin, Russian, French & Classical Greek. Academic, literary, medical, legal & theological texts. Research work also carried out.
Specializes in 12th-19th century Latin legal documents, Classical Greek & Latin texts.

**AE Technical Translation Services**
Ty Coch, Betws Garmon, Caernarfon, Gwynedd LL54 7AQ
*Tel:* (01286) 650667; (01286) 650555 *Fax:* (01286) 650500
*Key Personnel*
Contact: Debra Lockett
Services include interpreting, laser printing, typesetting, color printing, & translations in over 100 language combinations, specializing in rare languages.

**ARADCO VSI Ltd**
132 Cleveland St, London W1T 6AB
*Tel:* (020) 7692 7700 *Fax:* (020) 7692 7711
*Web Site:* www.aradco.com
*Key Personnel*
Contact: R Dawood

## Asgard Publishing Services
One Gledhow Park Grove, Leeds LS7 4JW
*Tel:* (0113) 262 8373 *Fax:* (0113) 262 8373
*Web Site:* www.asgardpublishing.co.uk
*Key Personnel*
Partner: Philip Gardner *E-mail:* philip.gardner@
asgardpublishing.co.uk; Michael Scott Rohan
*Tel:* (01223) 842185 *Fax:* (01223) 842185
*E-mail:* mike.scott.rohan@asgardpublishing.
co.uk; Allan Scott *Tel:* (01449) 741747
*Fax:* (01449) 740118 *E-mail:* allan.scott@
asgardpublishing.co.uk; Andrew Shackleton
*Tel:* (0113) 2741037 *Fax:* (0113) 2741037
*E-mail:* andrew.shackleton@asgardpublishing.
co.uk
Services include editorial, translation, audio-visual
& multimedia.

## Associated Translation & Typesetting
Alexander House, 64 Robin Hood Lane, Hall
Green, Birmingham B28 0JT
*Tel:* (0121) 603 6344 *Fax:* (0121) 603 6399
*E-mail:* info@att-group.com
*Web Site:* www.att-group.com
*Key Personnel*
Dir: Mr S Ahmed
Specializes in translation & typesetting into most
European languages (& vice versa), plus Ara-
bic, Bengali, Chinese (Cantonese, Hakka &
Mandarin) Farsi (Persian), Greek, Hindi, Pun-
jabi, Polish, Russian, Somali, Turkish, Urdu,
Vietnamese & Welsh. Also typesetting of Eu-
ropean, Russian, Vietnamese, Chinese & other
Indian languages. Provide translation services
of multilingual technical translation, documen-
tation, computer manuals, reports, promotional
literature, brochures, packaging & books.

## The Big Word
59 Charlotte St, London W1T 4PE
*Tel:* (0870) 748 8000 *Fax:* (0870) 748 8001
*E-mail:* production@thebigword.com
*Web Site:* www.thebigword.com
*Key Personnel*
Chief Executive Officer: Laurence J Gould
*E-mail:* larry.gould@thebigword.com
Chief Financial Officer: Chris Ball *E-mail:* chris.
ball@thebigword.com
Chief Operations Officer: Diane Miller
*E-mail:* diane.miller@thebigword.com
Chief Technical Officer: Ian Harris *E-mail:* ian.
harris@thebigword.com
Non-Executive Dir: John Westwood *E-mail:* john.
westwood@thebigword.com
Scandinavian Manager: Per Severinsen
*E-mail:* per.severinsen@thebigword.com
Belgium Manager: Rachel Wild *E-mail:* rachel.
wild@thebigword.com
Specialists in Far Eastern Languages.
*Branch Office(s)*
The Big Word Scandinavia, Larsbjrnsstrde 3,
1454 Copenhagen K, Denmark *Tel:* 33 37 71
71 *Fax:* 33 32 43 70
Global Service Center, Belmont House, 20 Wood
Lane, Headingley, Leeds LS6 2AE *Tel:* (0870)
748 8000 *Fax:* (0870) 748 8001; (0870) 748
8002
Mitaka-The Big Word, 30F Shinjuku Park Tower,
3-7-1 Nishi Shinjuku, Shinjuku Ku, Tokyo 163-
1030, Japan *Tel:* (03) 5326 3144 *Fax:* (03)
5326-3001
Park Atrium, 11, Rue des Colonies, 1000 Brussels, Belgium *Tel:* (02) 517 7113 *Fax:* (02) 517
6500
*U.S. Office(s):* The Big Word US, 48 Wall St,
Suite 1100, New York, NY 10005-2902, United
States *Tel:* 212-918-4557 *Fax:* 212-918-4561

## Castle Translations
11 Castle Hill, Lancaster LA1 1YS
*Tel:* (01524) 841169 *Fax:* (01524) 381721
*E-mail:* info@castletranslations.co.uk

*Web Site:* ukpetsearch.freeuk.com/castletrans
*Key Personnel*
Owner: Lynda Burke *E-mail:* lyndaburke@
castletrans.free-online.co.uk
Founded: 1986
Translating & interpreting of all languages; lan-
guage training.

## CBA Translations
Straightway Head, Whimple Nr, Exeter EX5 2QT
*Tel:* (01404) 822284 *Fax:* (01404) 823136
*E-mail:* info@cbatranslations.co.uk
*Web Site:* www.cbatranslations.co.uk
*Key Personnel*
Proprietor: Gerd Ziemer

## Chinese Marketing & Communications
Wuhan House, 5th floor, 16 Nicholas St, Manch-
ester M1 4EJ
*Tel:* (0161) 237 3821 *Fax:* (0161) 236 7558
*E-mail:* support@chinese-marketing.com
*Web Site:* www.chinese-marketing.com
*Key Personnel*
Editor: Jamie Kenny; Shen Yan
Project Manager: David Starway
Marketing materials in Chinese language, market
research & advertising agency.
*Publication(s): Chinese Business Impact* (En-
glish, monthly); *Siyu Chinese Times* (Chinese,
monthly)
*Branch Office(s)*
First Floor West, 90-98 Shaftesbury Ave, London
W1V 7DM

## Conference Interpreters Group
10 Barley Mow Passage, Chiswick, London W4
4PH
*Tel:* (020) 8995 0801 *Fax:* (020) 8742 1066
*E-mail:* ciglondon@aol.com
*Key Personnel*
Executive Secretary: Andrew Brock
*E-mail:* abrock3650@aol.com

## Dutch Connection
196 Prestbury Rd, Macclesfield SK10 3BS
*Tel:* (01625) 610613 *Fax:* (01625) 610613
*E-mail:* dutchconnection@aol.com
*Key Personnel*
Contact: M Kuik
Founded: 1982

## Eastword
16 Pines Close, Northwood, Middx HA6 3SJ
*Tel:* (020) 7582 9349 *Fax:* (020) 7793 0474
*E-mail:* info@eastword.uk.com
*Key Personnel*
Dir: Gladys Ko
Oriental language translation including Chinese,
Japanese, Korean, Thai & Vietnamese.

## Esperanto Translating Service
Kebbell House, Delta Gain, Watford WD19 5BE
Mailing Address: 137 Penrose Ave, Watford WD1
5AA
*Tel:* (020) 84282829 *Fax:* (020) 84282829
*E-mail:* espero@moose.co.uk
*Key Personnel*
Owner & Manager: Peter W Miles
Also provides guide lecturers in approximately 35
languages.

## Euro Translations
6 Field End, Coulsdon, Surrey CR5 2AY
*Tel:* (020) 8668 6133 *Fax:* (020) 8668 6133
*E-mail:* info@euro-translations.net
*Web Site:* www.euro-translations.net
*Key Personnel*
Owner: Mrs P Kain
Founded: 1983

## First Edition Translations Ltd
6 Wellington Ct, Wellington St, Cambridge CB1
1HZ
*Tel:* (01223) 356733 *Fax:* (01223) 321488
*E-mail:* info@firstedit.co.uk
*Web Site:* www.firstedit.co.uk
*Key Personnel*
Dir: Sheila Waller *E-mail:* sheila@firstedit.co.uk
Founded: 1981
Services include copy-editing, proof-reading, in-
dexing, interpreting, voice-overs, typesetting.
Specializes in translations of all material for pub-
lication.

## Michael Fulton Partners
The Chase, Behoes Lane, Woodcote, Reading,
Berks RG8 0PP
*Tel:* (01491) 680042 *Fax:* (01491) 680085
*Web Site:* www.foreignword.biz/cv/410.htm
*Key Personnel*
Senior Partner: Dr Michael Fulton
*E-mail:* mike@fultonm.fsnet.co.uk
Founded: 1968
Translations from Spanish & Portuguese (tech-
nical, scientific, commercial & patents subject
matter); Spanish interpreting.

## GLS Language Services
250 Crow Rd, Glasgow G11 7LA
*Tel:* (0141) 357 6611 *Fax:* (0141) 357 6605
*E-mail:* info@glslanguages.demon.co.uk
*Web Site:* www.glslanguageservices.co.uk
*Key Personnel*
Partner: Dagmar Fortsch
Founded: 1983

## Greek Institute
34 Bush Hill Rd, London N21 2DS
*Tel:* (020) 8360 7968 *Fax:* (020) 8360 7968
*Key Personnel*
Dir: Dr Kypros Tofallis
Publication(s): *Greek Institute Review* (quarterly,
journal)

## Hook & Hatton Ltd
34 Central Ave, Northampton NN2 8DZ
*Tel:* (01604) 847278 *Fax:* (01604) 821486
*E-mail:* hook_hatton@compuserve.com
*Key Personnel*
Chief Executive: Terence Lewis
Specializes in translation of scientific & technical
texts.

## Indo Lingua Services Ltd
125 Poplar High St, London E14 0AE
*Tel:* (020) 7515 3987
*E-mail:* indolingua@compuserve.com
*Key Personnel*
Man Dir: Prithvi Raj
Consultant: Pyare Shivpuri
*Branch Office(s)*
17B Ramesh Nagar, New Delhi 110 015
*Tel:* (011) 5461055 *Fax:* (011) 5461055

## Institute of Linguists
Saxon House, 48 Southwark St, London SE1
1UN
*Tel:* (020) 7940 3100 *Fax:* (020) 7940 3101
*E-mail:* info@iol.org.uk
*Web Site:* www.iol.org.uk
*Key Personnel*
President: Dr John Mitchell
Chairman: John Hammond
Vice Chairman: Ann Corsellis; Keith Moffitt
Chief Executive & Dir: Henry Pavlovich
Membership organization for professional trans-
lators, interpreters, language educationalists &
those using languages in industry & commerce.
Publication(s): *Basic Handbook for the Train-
ing of Public Service Interpreters; Bilingual in
Britain; Careers Using Languages; Glossary of
Educational Terms; Glossary of Social Services*

*Terms*; *Languages & Your Career*; *The Linguist* (bimonthly, journal); *Non-English Speakers & the English Legal System*; *Talk It Through*

**Institute of Translation & Interpreting**
Fortuna House, S Fifth St, Milton Keynes MK9 2EU
*Tel:* (01908) 325250 *Fax:* (01908) 325259
*E-mail:* info@iti.org.uk
*Web Site:* www.iti.org.uk
*Key Personnel*
General Secretary: Alan Wheatley *Tel:* (01908) 325256 *E-mail:* alan@iti.org.uk

**Intercultural Networking Ltd (ICN)**
133 John Trundle Court, London EC2Y 8DJ
*Tel:* (020) 7628 5876 *Fax:* (020) 7628 9147
*E-mail:* icn@dircon.co.uk
*Web Site:* www.users.dircon.co.uk/~icn/
*Key Personnel*
Man Dir: Atsuko Takenaka
Dir: Chieko Takanaka
Specializes in Japanese-English nonfiction book translation through to camera-ready copy.

**International Language & Translation School**
216 Great Portland St, London W1N 5HG
*Tel:* (020) 8882 3362 *Fax:* (020) 8882 3362
*Key Personnel*
Principal: Mr Li Ke-Mo
Tuition in 80 languages by correspondence, oral, telephone, fax & cassette courses. Translation, interpreting in 80 Oriental, European & African languages.

**International Translations Ltd**
Lloyds House, 1st floor, 18-22 Lloyd St, Manchester M2 5WA
*Tel:* (0161) 834 7431 *Fax:* (0161) 832 4717
*E-mail:* admin@ititranslations.co.uk; inttrans@compuserve.com
*Key Personnel*
Dir: Christine Wood
Founded: 1919
Translations in over 30 languages; literary, commercial, technical & legal topics.
Specializes in translation, interpreting, proofreading, typesetting & voice overs.

**Key Language Services**
32 Linford Forum, Rockingham Dr, Linford Wood, Milton Keynes MK14 6LY
*Tel:* (01908) 232101 *Fax:* (01908) 232815
*E-mail:* sales@keylanguageservices.co.uk
*Web Site:* www.keylanguageservices.co.uk
*Key Personnel*
Partner: Sarah Clutton; Gail Farrell
Founded: 1988
*Branch Office(s)*
Business Development Centre, Suite C, Stafford Park 4, Telford TF3 3BA *Tel:* (01952) 293 450 *Fax:* (01952) 290 552

**Language Consultancy Services**
138 Melrose Ave, London NW2 4JX
*Tel:* (020) 8450 5344 *Fax:* (020) 8452 9005
*E-mail:* lucifer@ladet.demon.co.uk
*Key Personnel*
Contact: Lucia Alvarez de Toledo

**Legal & Technical Translation Services**
13 Earl St, Maidstone, Kent ME14 1PL
*Tel:* (01622) 751537; (01622) 751189
   *Fax:* (01622) 754431
*E-mail:* translation@ltts.co.uk
*Web Site:* www.ltts.co.uk
*Key Personnel*
Dir: J M Sallares

**Lexus Ltd**
60 Brook St, Glasgow G402AB
*Tel:* (0141) 2215266 *Fax:* (0141) 2263139
*Web Site:* www.lexusforlanguages.co.uk
*Telex:* 9312134404
*Key Personnel*
Man Dir: Peter Terrell *E-mail:* peterterrell@lexusforlanguages.co.uk
Founded: 1980
Also publisher & packager.
Specializes in bilingual dictionaries.

**Peak Translations**
Shepherd's Bank, Kettleshulme SK23 7QU
*Tel:* (01663) 732074 *Fax:* (01663) 735499
*E-mail:* info@peak-translations.co.uk
*Web Site:* www.peak-translations.co.uk
*Key Personnel*
Contact: Ian Gordon *E-mail:* ian@peak-translations.co.uk
Founded: 1978
Also supply software translation tools for professional translators.

**Marilyn Potts International Language Consultants**
Saint Thomas St, Newcastle-upon-Tyne NE1 4LE
*Tel:* (0191) 222 1775 *Fax:* (0191) 261 6426
*E-mail:* info@marilyn-potts.co.uk
*Web Site:* www.marilyn-potts.co.uk
*Key Personnel*
Contact: Marilyn Potts
Founded: 1987
Services include translations & interpreting.
Membership(s): Institute of Translation & Interpreting.

**Rosie O'Hara German Translations**
PO Box 6064, Nairn IV12 4YH
*Tel:* (01667) 456 222 *Fax:* (01667) 456 222
*Web Site:* www.rosieohara.co.uk/index1.htm
*Key Personnel*
Contact: Rosie O'Hara
Provide translation, interpreting & tuition into & out of German only.

**RWS Translations Ltd**
Marsham Way, Gerrards Cross, Bucks SL9 8BQ
*Tel:* (01753) 480200 *Fax:* (01753) 480280
*E-mail:* rwstrans@rws.com
*Web Site:* www.rws.com
*Key Personnel*
Man Dir: Mr Wojtek Brodnicki
Chief Editor: Ian Watson
Head Foreign Language Operations: George M Dudzinski
Production Manager: Patrick Sutton
Business Development Executive: Nicola Richards
Office Manager: Diane Dye
Service includes medical & pharmaceutical translations in English, German, French, Spanish & Italian.
*Branch Office(s)*
RWS Information Ltd, Tavistock House, Tavistock Sq, London WC1H 9LG *Tel:* (020) 7554 5400 *Fax:* (020) 7554 5454 *E-mail:* rwsinfo@rws.com

**Satrap Publishing & Translation**
271 King St, London W6 9LZ
*Tel:* (020) 8748 9397 *Fax:* (020) 8748 9394
*E-mail:* satrap@btconnect.com
*Web Site:* www.satrap.co.uk
*Key Personnel*
Man Dir: Alex Vahdat
Founded: 1989
A single source for translation, typesetting, publishing, marketing & advertising literature in major languages of the world.
Specializes in Middle & Far Eastern, East & West European languages.

**SDL Agency**
Aspect Court, Pond Hill, Sheffield, S Yorks S1 2BG
*Tel:* (0114) 253 5353 *Toll Free Tel:* 800 917 0044 *Fax:* (0114) 253 5200
*Web Site:* www.sdl.com
*Key Personnel*
Dir: Ray King
Services include foreign language publishing, translating & interpreting.
*U.S. Office(s):* 5700 Granite Parkway, Suite 410, Plano, TX 75024, United States *Tel:* 214-387-9124

**SEL**, see Services for Export & Language (SEL)

**SELTA**, see Swedish-English Literary Translators' Association (SELTA)

**Services for Export & Language (SEL)**
Maxwell Bldg, University of Salford, Manchester M5 4WT
*Tel:* (0161) 7457480 *Fax:* (0161) 2955110
*E-mail:* sales@sel-uk.com
*Web Site:* www.sel-uk.com
*Key Personnel*
Translations Manager: Patrick Murphy *E-mail:* p.m.murphy@salford.ac.uk
Founded: 1986
Service includes translation, foreign language training & interpreting.

**Swedish-English Literary Translators' Association (SELTA)**
14 Grennell Close, Sutton, Surrey SM1 3LU
*Tel:* (020) 8641 8176 *Fax:* (020) 8641 8176
*Web Site:* www.swedishbookreview.com
*Key Personnel*
Honorary Secretary: Tom Geddes
Founded: 1982
SELTA aims to promote the publication of Swedish literature in English & to represent the interests of those involved in its translation.
Publication(s): *Swedish Book Review* (twice a year)

**TransAction Translators Ltd**
Redlands, 3/5 Tapton House Rd, Sheffield S10 5BY
*Tel:* (0114) 2661103 *Fax:* (0114) 2631959
*E-mail:* transaction@transaction.co.uk
*Web Site:* www.transaction.co.uk
*Key Personnel*
Contact: Maryline Tergella
Founded: 1983

**Translators Association**
84 Drayton Gardens, London SW10 9SB
*Tel:* (020) 7373 6642 *Fax:* (020) 7373 5768
*E-mail:* info@societyofauthors.org
*Web Site:* www.societyofauthors.org/translators
*Key Personnel*
Awards Secretary: Dorothy Sym *E-mail:* dsym@societyofauthors.org
The Translators Association is a specialist group within The Society of Authors.
Publication(s): *In Other Words*

**UPS Translations**
111 Baker St, London W1U 6RR
*Tel:* (020) 7837 8300 *Fax:* (020) 7486 3272
*E-mail:* production@upstranslations.com
*Web Site:* www.upstranslations.com
*Key Personnel*
Chairman & Man Dir: Bernard Silver
   *E-mail:* bernard@upstranslations.com
Head of Translation: Sarah Parkhurst
Founded: 1947
Translation company
Membership(s): ATC; ITI; ISO: 9001.

Specializes in translation for publishing, film, video & the media.
*Parent Company:* United Publicity Services PLC

**Sally Walker Language Services**
43 St Nicholas St, Bristol BS1 1TP
*Tel:* (0117) 929 1594 *Fax:* (0117) 929 6033
*E-mail:* translations@sallywalker.co.uk;
    languages@sallywalker.co.uk
*Web Site:* www.sallywalker.co.uk
*Key Personnel*
Man Dir: Sally Walker
Dir: Joseph Walker Cousins
Sales & Marketing Dir: David J Poole
Translations Manager: Loys Heyworth; Gwen
    Parrott

Translations & Marketing Manager: Elizabeth
    Niklewska
Founded: 1969
Translation & interpreting service.
Specializes in 70 languages, all subjects.
Publication(s): *Sallylang* (journal)
*Branch Office(s)*
Perch Bldgs, 9 Mount Stuart Sq, Cardiff CF10
    5EE *Tel:* (029) 204 807 47 *Fax:* (029) 204 887
    36

**Wessex Translations**
Unit A1, The Premier Centre, Abbey Park Indus-
    trial Estate, Romsey, Hants SO51 9AQ
*Tel:* (0870) 1669 300 *Toll Free Tel:* 800 975 5900
    *Fax:* (0870) 1669 299

*E-mail:* sales@wt-lm.com; info@wt-lm.com
*Web Site:* www.wt-languagemanagement.com
*Key Personnel*
Dir: Jonathan Nater *E-mail:* jonathan@wt-lm.com
Contact: Robin Weber
Membership(s): Association of Translation Com-
    panies; Institute of Translations & Interpreters.
Specializes in translations & interpreting software
    localisation, language training, transcription,
    typesetting, telemarketing, editing & proof-
    reading, voice-overs, copywriting, web page
    translation.

**WT Language Management**, see Wessex
    Translations

# Manufacturing

## Complete Book Manufacturing

This section includes companies throughout the world that offer complete book manufacturing services. Those U.S. and Canadian companies with 10% or more of their business done outside North America are also included.

# Australia

**ACI International Ltd**
Queen St, Level 32, Melbourne, Victoria 3000
*Tel:* (03) 6058555
*Key Personnel*
Chairman: Brian W Scott
Man Dir, Security Printing & Computer Services
  Group: I D Reid

# Austria

**ADEVA (Akademische Druck-u Verlagsanstalt)**
Auersperggasse 12, 8010 Graz
*Tel:* (0316) 3644 *Fax:* (0316) 364424
*E-mail:* info@adeva.com
*Web Site:* www.adeva.com *Cable:* ADEVA-GRAZ
*Key Personnel*
Dir: Dr Ursula Struzl
Founded: 1949
Print Runs: 300 min - 10,000 max
Business from Other Countries: 80%
*Branch Office(s)*
Purgleitnergasse 10, Ecke Marburgerstr, 8042
  Graz

**Akademische Druck- u Verlagsanstalt**, see
  ADEVA (Akademische Druck-u Verlagsanstalt)

**Dr Paul Struzl GmbH**, see ADEVA
  (Akademische Druck-u Verlagsanstalt)

# Belgium

**Drukkerij Lannoo NV** (Lannoo Printers)
Kasteelstr 97, 8700 Tielt
*Tel:* (051) 42 42 11 *Fax:* (051) 40 70 70
*E-mail:* lannoo@lannooprint.be
*Web Site:* www.lannooprint.be
*Key Personnel*
General Manager & Marketing Dir: Stefaan Lannoo *E-mail:* stefaan.lannoo@lannooprint.be
Founded: 1909
Turnaround: 10 Workdays
Print Runs: 100 min - 1,000,000 max
Business from Other Countries: 30%

# Canada

**Aardvark Enterprises**
Division of Speers Investments Ltd
204 Millbank Dr SW, Calgary, AB T2Y 2H9
*Tel:* 403-256-4639
*Key Personnel*
Pres: J Alvin Speers
Founded: 1970 (Small Press Pioneers)
Turnaround: 30 Workdays
Print Runs: 10 min - 1,000 max
Business from Other Countries: 25%

**Friesens Corp**
One Printers Way, Altona, MB R0G 0B0
*Tel:* 204-324-6401 *Fax:* 204-324-1333
*E-mail:* friesens@friesens.com
*Key Personnel*
Pres & CEO: David Friesen *E-mail:* davidf@
  friesens.com
Sales Mgr: Frank Friesen *E-mail:* frankf@
  friesens.com
Founded: 1907
Turnaround: 20-25 Workdays
Business from Other Countries: 30%
*Branch Office(s)*
Spectrum Books, 2455 Bennett Valley Rd, Suite
  C-116, Santa Rosa, CA 95405-8568, United
  States, Duncan McCallum *Tel:* 707-542-6044
  *Fax:* 707-542-6045 *E-mail:* specbooks@aol.
  com
528 S Ardmore Ave, Chicago, IL 60181, United
  States *Tel:* 630-834-9954 *Fax:* 815-653-9486
  *E-mail:* dawnw@friesens.com
Four Colour Imports, 2410 Frankfort Ave,
  Louisville, KY 40206, United States, George
  Dick *Tel:* 502-896-9644 *Fax:* 502-896-9594
  *E-mail:* gdick@fourcolour.com
10011 167 Court W, Lakeville, MN 55044,
  United States, Renee Craft *Tel:* 612-435-1997
  *Fax:* 612-898-0227 *E-mail:* reneec@friesens.
  com
Membership(s): BMI

**Mad Dog Design Connection Inc**
22 Saint Leonards Ave, Toronto, ON M4N 1J9
*Tel:* 416-467-0090 *Fax:* 416-484-1140
*E-mail:* maddogs9@rogers.com
*Key Personnel*
Owner & Designer: Linda Pellowe
Designer & Digital Artist: David Szolcsanyi
Founded: 1998
Turnaround: As needed/to deadline
Business from Other Countries: 10%

**Maracle Press Ltd**
1156 King St E, Oshawa, ON L1H 7N4
*Tel:* 905-723-3438 *Toll Free Tel:* 800-558-8604
  *Fax:* 905-428-6024

*E-mail:* info@maraclepress.com
*Web Site:* www.maraclepress.com
*Key Personnel*
Pres & Gen Mgr: Bruce A Fenton
  *E-mail:* bfenton@maraclepress.com
VP, Busn Devt: Ronald G Taylor
  *E-mail:* rtaylor@maraclepress.com
Founded: 1920
Turnaround: 10 Workdays
Print Runs: 500 min - 500,000 max
Business from Other Countries: 25%
Membership(s): BMI; Canadian Printing Industries Association; Ontario Printing & Imaging Association; PIA/GATF

**McLaren Morris & Todd Co**
Subsidiary of Mail-Well
3270 American Dr, Mississauga, ON L4V 1B5
*Tel:* 905-677-3592 *Fax:* 905-677-3675
*Web Site:* www.mmt.ca
*Key Personnel*
Pres & CEO: Tony Sgro
VP, Fin: Tom Englehart
Contact: Anthony Sgro
Founded: 1956
Turnaround: 15 Workdays
Print Runs: 5,000 min - 1,000,000 max
Business from Other Countries: 10%

**PrintWest**
1150 Eighth Ave, Regina, SK S4R 1C9
*Tel:* 306-525-2304 *Toll Free Tel:* 800-236-6438
  *Fax:* 306-757-2439
*E-mail:* general@printwest.com
*Web Site:* www.printwest.com
*Key Personnel*
CEO: Wayne UnRuh
VP, Sales: Ken Benson
Founded: 1992
Turnaround: 15 Workdays
Print Runs: 1,000 min - 100,000 max
Business from Other Countries: 15%
*Branch Office(s)*
Box 2500, 2310 Millar Ave, Saskatoon, SK S7K
  2C4 *Tel:* 306-665-3560 *Fax:* 306-653-1255

**Transcontinental Printing Book Group**
Division of Transcontinental Group
395 Lebeau Blvd, St-Laurent, QC H4N 1S2
*Tel:* 514-337-8560 *Toll Free Tel:* 800-361-3599
  *Fax:* 514-339-5230
*Web Site:* www.transcontinental.com; www.
  transcontinental-printing.com
*Key Personnel*
Sr VP, Book Group: Jacques Gregoire
Dir, Strategic Busn Devt: Denis
  Beaudin *Tel:* 514-339-2220 ext 4101
  *E-mail:* beaudind@transcontinental.ca
Founded: 1976

Turnaround: 10 working days casebound; 7-10
working days softcover
Print Runs: 500 min
Business from Other Countries: 30%
*Branch Office(s)*
614 Yates Ave, Calumet City, IL 60409, United
States, Contact: Kristopher D Levy *Tel:* 708-
832-1528 *Fax:* 708-832-9510 *E-mail:* kris.
levy@transcontinental.ca (Midwest)
3653 W Leland Ave, Suite One W, Chicago,
IL 60625, United States, Contact: Tim Taylor *Tel:* 773-583-8155 *Fax:* 773-583-8162
*E-mail:* tim.taylor@transcontinental.com (Midwest)
393 Highland Ave, Quincy, MA 02170-
4013, United States, Contact: Mike Gazzola *Tel:* 617-696-1435 *Fax:* 617-696-1025
*E-mail:* mikebook@attbi.com (East Coast)
37 Herman Blvd, Franklin Square, NY
11010, United States, Contact: Tom Malloy *Tel:* 516-775-2980 *Fax:* 516-488-0253
*E-mail:* tmmalloy@aol.com (NY)
10 Rountree Dr, PO Box 2551, Duxbury, MA
02331, United States, Contact: Ed Catania *Tel:* 508-881-1119 *Fax:* 508-881-7739
*E-mail:* ecatania@attbi.com (East Coast)
3175 Summit Square Dr, Suite C9, Oakton,
VA 22124, United States, Contact: David
Avesian *Tel:* 703-255-1332 *Fax:* 703-255-1343
*E-mail:* davesian@cox.rr.com (Southeast)
559 Lowrys Rd, Parksville, BC V9P 2R8, Contact: Mike Davies *Tel:* 250-248-9700 *Fax:* 250-
248-2353 *E-mail:* bookguys@shaw.ca (West
Coast)
15373 Victoria Ave, White Rock, BC V4B 1H1,
Contact: Wade Davies *Tel:* 604-535-8800
*Fax:* 604-535-8802 *E-mail:* daviesw@shaw.ca
(West Coast)
490 Wilfred Dr, Peterborough, ON K9K
2H1, Contact: Tom Lang *Tel:* 705-760-
9594 *Fax:* 705-760-9485 *E-mail:* langt@
transcontinental.ca (NY)
395 Lebeau Blvd, St-Laurent, QC H4N 1S2,
Contact: Stephane Lavoie *Tel:* 514-337-
8560 *Fax:* 514-339-2252 *E-mail:* lavoies@
transcontinental.ca
Membership(s): BMI; National Association for
Printing Leadership; PIA/GATF

**Tri-Graphic Printing (Ottawa) Ltd**
485 Industrial Ave, Ottawa, ON K1G 0Z1
*Tel:* 613-731-7441 *Toll Free Tel:* 800-267-9750
*Fax:* 613-731-3741
*Web Site:* www.tri-graphic.com
*Key Personnel*
VP & Gen Mgr: Doug K Doane
*E-mail:* ddoane@tri-graphic.com
VP, Prodn & Servs: Fred Malleau *Tel:* 905-665-
8500 *E-mail:* fmalleau@tri-graphic.com
Founded: 1968
Turnaround: 10-15 Workdays
Print Runs: 1,000 min - 100,000 max
Business from Other Countries: 10%
*Branch Office(s)*
213 Byron St S, Suite 201, Whitby, ON L1N 4P7
*Tel:* 905-665-8500 *Fax:* 905-665-8501

**University of Toronto Press Inc**
Printing Division, 5201 Dufferin St, North York,
ON M3H 5T8
*Tel:* 416-667-7767 *Fax:* 416-667-7803
*E-mail:* printing@utpress.utoronto.ca
*Web Site:* www.utpress.utoronto.ca
*Key Personnel*
Pres & Publr: John Yates
Founded: 1901
Turnaround: 10-15 Workdays
Print Runs: 10 min - 200,000 max
Business from Other Countries: 15%
Membership(s): BMI

**Webcom Limited**
3480 Pharmacy Ave, Toronto, ON M1W 2S7

*Tel:* 416-496-1000 *Toll Free Tel:* 800-665-9322
*Fax:* 416-496-1537
*E-mail:* webcom@webcomlink.com
*Web Site:* www.webcomlink.com
*Key Personnel*
VP, Sales & Mktg: Mike Collinge
Mktg Mgr: Beth Craig
Founded: 1976
Turnaround: 15 Workdays
Print Runs: 50 min - 100,000 max
Business from Other Countries: 40%

# China

**Midas Printing Ltd**
Boluo Yuanzhou Town, Xianan Administration
District, Huizhau, Guangdong
*Tel:* (0752) 6682111 *Fax:* (0752) 6682333
*E-mail:* info@midasprinting.com
*Web Site:* www.midasprinting.com
*Key Personnel*
Chairman: Sheung Chiu Chan
Executive Dir: Michael Wong Chi Sing
Man Dir: Tin Lap Kwong; Ann Li Mee Sum
Deputy Man Dir: Chi Fai Kwok
Sales & Marketing: Paul Tang Chow Ming
*E-mail:* paul@midasprinting.com
Founded: 1990
Turnaround: 14-21 Workdays
Print Runs: 5,000 min - 100,000 max
Business from Other Countries: 25%

# Croatia

**Radin-Repro I Roto**
Zagrebacka 194, 10000 Zagreb
*Tel:* (01) 3869 200 *Fax:* (01) 3862 673
*E-mail:* radin-repro-i-roto@zg.tel.hr
*Web Site:* www.odisej.hr
*Key Personnel*
Dir: Marijan Arambasin
Contact: Sanja Pusec

**Vjesnik dd** (Croatian Printing Plant)
Slavonska Avenija 4, 10 000 Zagreb
*Tel:* (01) 61 66 666; (01) 36 41 111 *Fax:* (01) 61
61 602; (01) 61 61 650
*E-mail:* vjesnik@vjesnik.hr; vjesnik@vjesnik.com
*Web Site:* www.vjesnik.hr; www.vjesnik.com
*Key Personnel*
General Manager: Ivan Bozicevic
Sales Manager: Irena Gnjidic
Technical Manager: Zeljko Bajs; Mijo Paradzik;
Ivan Srsen
Purchasing Manager: Renata Bozickovic
Finance Manager: Koraljka Kokotovic
Founded: 1999 (In 1999 Vjesnik Publishing
Company & Hrvatska tishava dd joined to-
gether to create Vjesnik dd)
Print Runs: 25,000 min - 55,000 max
Business from Other Countries: 1%

# Denmark

**Ingenioeren/Boger** (Engineering Books Danish
Technical Press)
Ingerslevsgade 44, 1705 Copenhagen V
*Tel:* 63 15 17 00 *Fax:* 63 15 17 33
*E-mail:* info@nyttf.dk

*Web Site:* www.bog.ing.dk; www.nyttf.dk
*Key Personnel*
Marketing: Soren Bertelsen

**Nyt Teknisk Forlag**, see Ingenioeren/Boger

# Finland

**Stora Enso Oyj**
Kanavaranta 1, 00101 Helsinki
Mailing Address: PO Box 309, 00101 Helsinki
*Tel:* (09) 2046 131 *Fax:* (09) 2046 214 71
*Web Site:* www.storaenso.com
*Key Personnel*
Sales Manager: Ove Backlund; Aarno Yrjo-
Koskinen

**UPM-Kymmene Ltd**
Subsidiary of UPM-Kymmene Group
Etelaesplanadi 2, 00101 Helsinki
Mailing Address: PO Box 380, 00101 Helsinki
*Tel:* 204 15 111 *Fax:* 204 15 110
*E-mail:* info@upm-kymmene.com
*Web Site:* www.upm-kymmene.com
*Key Personnel*
Communications Officer, Media Relations: Sari
Horkko *Tel:* 204 15 0797

**WS Bookwell Ltd**
Teollisuustie 4, 06100 Porvoo
*Tel:* (019) 21 941 *Fax:* (019) 2194 802
*Web Site:* www.bookwell.fi
*Key Personnel*
Sales Manager: Rainer Poysa *Tel:* (019) 219 4664
*E-mail:* rainer.poysa@bookwell.fi
Founded: 1878
*Parent Company:* Werner Soderstrom Corp
*Ultimate Parent Company:* SanomaWSOY
*Branch Office(s)*
Messdorferstr 127, 53123 Bonn, Germany, Con-
tact: Markku Rapeli *Tel:* (0228) 986 4006
*Fax:* (0228) 986 4008
WS Bookwell AB, Borgveien 2, Ytre Enebakk
1914, Norway, Contact: Kristen Sande
*Tel:* (064) 925 840 *Fax:* (064) 925 841
*E-mail:* k.sande.wsoy@oslo.online.no
PO Box 3, Lowestoft, Suffolk NR33 8EY, United
Kingdom, Contact: David Sowter *Tel:* (1502)
742 038 *Fax:* (1502) 742 039 *E-mail:* ds@
bookwell.co.uk

# France

**Imprimerie Bene**
12 rue Pradier, 30000 Nimes
*Tel:* (04) 66294897 *Fax:* (04) 66382146
*Key Personnel*
President: Jacques Enfer
Print Runs: 100 min - 10,000 max
Business from Other Countries: 20%

**Imprimerie Carlo Descamps SA**
36 place Pierre Delcourt, 59163 Conde sur
l'Escaut
*Tel:* (03) 27400208 *Fax:* (03) 27405683
*Key Personnel*
Contact: Carlo Bertin
Founded: 1830
Turnaround: 2-5 Workdays
Print Runs: 800 min - 20,000 max
Business from Other Countries: 12%

**Plein Chant**
16120 Bassac
*Tel:* (05) 45 81 93 26 *Fax:* (05) 45 81 92 83

*Web Site:* www.nanga.fr
*Key Personnel*
Contact: Edmond Thomas
Founded: 1971
Print Runs: 600 min - 1,000 max
Business from Other Countries: 5%

# Germany

**Adobe Systems GmbH**
Ohmstr 1, 85716 Unterschleissheim
*Tel:* (0180) 2304316 *Fax:* (089) 31705-777
*E-mail:* cic@adobe.de
*Web Site:* www.adobe.de

**Ludwig Auer GmbH**
Heilig-Kreuz-Str 16, 86609 Donauwoerth
Mailing Address: Postfach 1152, 86601 Donau-
  woerth
*Tel:* (0906) 73-0 *Fax:* (0906) 73-130 (manage-
  ment); (0906) 73-184 (sales)
*E-mail:* org@auer-medien.de
*Web Site:* www.auer-medien.de
*Key Personnel*
Manager: Wolfgang Meier *Tel:* (0906) 73-230
Sales Manager: Eduard Steinle *Tel:* (0906) 73-250

**Baader Buch- u Offsetdruckerei GmbH & Co
  KG CL**
Buchrainstr 36, 72525 Muensingen
*Tel:* (07381) 791 *Fax:* (07381) 411412 *Cable:*
  BAADER-MUNSINGEN
Founded: 1835
Turnaround: 1 Workday
Print Runs: 1,000 min - 15,000 max

**Bertelsmann AG**
Carl-Bertelsmannstr 270, 33311 Guetersloh
Mailing Address: Postfach 111, 33311 Guetersloh
*Tel:* (05241) 80-0 *Fax:* (05421) 80-9662; (05421)
  80-9663; (05421) 80-9664
*E-mail:* info@bertelsmann.de
*Web Site:* www.bertelsmann.de
*Key Personnel*
Executive Vice President: Bernd Bauer
Founded: 1835

**Druck & Verlagshaus Fromm GmbH & Co
  KG**
Subsidiary of Neue Osnabruecker Zeitung,
  Druckzentrum Osnabrueck; Verlag A Fromm;
  Fromm International Publ Corp; Edition Inter-
  from AG
Breiter Gang 10-16, 49074 Osnabrueck
*Tel:* (0541) 310-0 *Fax:* (0541) 310315
*E-mail:* info@fromm-os.de
*Web Site:* www.fromm-os.de
*Key Personnel*
Publisher: Leo V Fromm
Chief Executive Officer: A Harms-Hunold
Founded: 1868

**Media-Print Informationstechnologie GmbH**
Schwarzenraben 7, 59558 Lippstadt
*Tel:* (02941) 2 72-300 *Fax:* (02941) 2 72-540
*E-mail:* kg@mediaprint.de
*Web Site:* www.mediaprint.de
*Key Personnel*
Man Dir: Dr Otto W Drosihn *E-mail:* drdrosihn@
  kg.mediaprint.de
Founded: 1993
Turnaround: 5-10 Workdays
Print Runs: 100 min - 30,000 max
Business from Other Countries: 10%

**MOHN Media**
Subsidiary of Bertelsmann AG
Carl-Bertelsmann-Str 161M, 33311 Guetersloh
*Tel:* (05241) 80-4 04 10 *Fax:* (05241) 2 42 82
*E-mail:* mohnmedia@bertelsmann.de
*Web Site:* www.mohnmedia.de
*Key Personnel*
Man Dir: Markus Dohle
Founded: 1824
Business from Other Countries: 25%

**Priese GmbH & Co**
Schwedlerstr 5, 14193 Berlin
*Tel:* (030) 8263024
*Key Personnel*
Contact: Elma Priese; Hans Joachim Priese

**Sankt-Johannis-Druckerei**
Heiligenstr 24, 77933 Lahr
*Tel:* (07821) 581-0 *Fax:* (07821) 581-26
*E-mail:* fels@johannis-druckerei.de
*Web Site:* www.medienverbaende.de
*Telex:* 782122

**Papierfabrik Scheufelen GmbH & Co KG**
Adolf-Scheufelen-Str 26, 73250 Lenningen
*Tel:* (07026) 66-1 *Fax:* (07026) 66-701
*E-mail:* service@scheufelen.de
*Web Site:* www.scheufelen.com

**Strobel Druck & Verlag - A Strobel GmbH &
  Co KG**
Zur Feldmuehle 9-11, 59821 Arnsberg
Mailing Address: PO Box 5654, 59806 Arnsberg
*Tel:* (02931) 89 00 0 *Fax:* (02931) 89 00 38
*E-mail:* leserservice@strobel-verlag.de
*Web Site:* www.ikz.de
*Key Personnel*
Project Manager: Guenther Klauke *E-mail:* g.
  klauke@myshk.com
Print Runs: 2,500 min - 90,000 max

**Topic Verlag GmbH**
Birkenstr 10, 85757 Karlsfeld B Munich
*Tel:* (08131) 97038 *Fax:* (08131) 98404
Founded: 1982
Business from Other Countries: 50%

**Wissenschaftliche Verlagsgesellschaft mbH**
Birkenwaldstr 44, 70191 Stuttgart
*Tel:* (0711) 2582-325 *Fax:* (0711) 2582-290
*E-mail:* service@wissenschaftliche-
  verlagsgesellschaft.de; akimmerle@
  wissenschaftliche-verlagsgesellschaft.de
*Web Site:* www.dav-buchhandlung.de
*Key Personnel*
Man Dir: Dr Christian Rotta

# Hong Kong

**The American Chamber of Commerce in Hong
  Kong**
1904 Bank of America Tower, 12 Harcourt Rd,
  Central Hong Kong
*Tel:* 2526-0165 *Fax:* 2810-1289
*E-mail:* amcham@amcham.org.hk
*Web Site:* www.amcham.org.hk
*Key Personnel*
Publications Manager: Fred Armentrout
  *E-mail:* farmen@amcham.org.hk

**Bright Future Printing Co Ltd**
Sunview Industrial Building, Block D, 5/F, 3 On
  Yip St, Chai Wan
*Tel:* 2515 1776 *Fax:* 2897 2799; 2558 1717

*Key Personnel*
Chairman: Richard Ng
Turnaround: 60 Workdays (including shipping)
Print Runs: 3,000 min - 30,000 max
Business from Other Countries: 30%

**C A Design**, see Communication Art Design &
  Printing Ltd

**C & C Offset Printing Co Ltd**
Subsidiary of C & C Joint Printing Co (HK) Ltd
  under Sino United (Holdings) Hong Kong Ltd
C&C Bldg, 14th floor, 36 Ting Lai Rd, Tai Po,
  New Territories
*Tel:* 2666-4988 *Fax:* 2666-4938
*E-mail:* offsetprinting@candcprinting.com
*Web Site:* www.ccoffset.com
*Key Personnel*
Dir & General Manager: Jackson Leung
Deputy Man Dir: Kee Lee
Deputy General Manager: Ivy Lam
Assistant General Manager: Kit Wong
Senior Sales Manager (Special Project): Francis
  Ho
Founded: 1980
Turnaround: 30-42 Workdays for printing, binding
  & book finishing
Print Runs: 2,000 min - 1,000,000 max
Business from Other Countries: 60%
*Branch Office(s)*
C & C Joint Printing Co (Guangdong) Ltd, 7/F,
  Flat H, Green View Apartment, No 38, Hou
  Guang Ping Hu Tong, Xi Cheng Qu, Beijing
  100035, China *Tel:* (010) 6650-3176 *Fax:* (010)
  6650-3175 *E-mail:* beijing@candcprinting.com
C & C Joint Printing Co (Guangdong) Ltd, Room
  1511, Hua Xin Bldg, East Block, 2 Shuiyin
  Rd, Huanshi East, Guangzhou 510075, China
  *Tel:* (020) 3760-0979 *Fax:* (020) 3760-0977
  *E-mail:* guangzhou@candcprinting.com
C & C Joint Printing Co (Guangdong) Ltd,
  Room 304, Fang Fa Bldg, No 29, 165 Ave,
  Dongzhuanbang Rd, Shanghai 200050, China
  *Tel:* (021) 6240-1305 *Fax:* (021) 6240-2090
  *E-mail:* shanghaioffice@candcprinting.com
C & C Joint Printing Co (Guangdong)
  Ltd, Chunhu Industrial Estate, Pinghu,
  Long Gang, Shenzhen 518111, China
  *Tel:* (0755) 2845-8333 *Fax:* (0755) 2845-9911
  *E-mail:* guangdong@candcprinting.com *Web
  Site:* www.candcprinting.com (Plant)
C & C Offset Printing Co (UK) Ltd, 2 New
  Burlington St, 4th floor, London W1S 2JE,
  United Kingdom, Director: Tracy Broderick
  *Tel:* (020) 7287 7787 *Fax:* (020) 7287 7187
  *E-mail:* tracy@candcoffset.co.uk
C & C Printing Japan Co Ltd, 2-6-12 Hitotsub-
  ashi, Tozaido Bldg 3F, Chiyoda-ku, Tokyo
  101-0003, Japan *Tel:* (03) 5216-4580 *Fax:* (03)
  5216-4610 *E-mail:* mail@candcprinting.co.jp
  *Web Site:* www.candcprinting.com
*U.S. Office(s):* C & C Offset Printing Co (NY)
  Inc, 401 Broadway, Suite 2015, New York, NY
  10013-3004, United States, Dir: Simon M K
  Chan *Tel:* 212-431-4210 *Fax:* 212-431-3960
  *E-mail:* nyinfo@ccoffset.com
C & C Offset Printing Co (USA) Inc, 2632 SE
  25th Ave, Suite E, PO Box 82037, Portland,
  OR 97282-0037, United States, Dir: Charlie
  Clark *Tel:* 503-233-1834 *Fax:* 503-233-7815
  *E-mail:* portlandinfo@ccoffset.com

**Caritas Printing Training Centre**
Caritas House, 3rd floor, Block D, 2 Caine Rd,
  Hong Kong
*Tel:* 2526 1148 *Fax:* 2537 1231
*E-mail:* info@caritas.org.hk
*Web Site:* www.caritas.hk
*Key Personnel*
General Manager: Isaac Mak
Founded: 1953
Print Runs: 1,000 min - 100,000 max
Business from Other Countries: 50%

## Colorprint Offset
Unit 1808-9, 18/F, 8 Commercial Tower, 8 Sun Yip St, Chai Wan
*Tel:* 2896-7777 *Fax:* 2889-6606
*E-mail:* info@cpo.com.hk
*Web Site:* www.cpo.com.hk
*Key Personnel*
Sales Manager: Jennifer Weston *Tel:* 2903-5062
Contact: Eva Lav; Ian Lee
Turnaround: Standard turnaround of 2 weeks
Print Runs: 3,000 min - 100,000 max
Business from Other Countries: 80%
*Branch Office(s)*
Gainsborough House, 81 Oxford St, London W1R 1RB, United Kingdom *Tel:* (020) 7903-5060 *Fax:* (020) 7903-5063 *E-mail:* uk@cpo.com.hk
*U.S. Office(s):* 80 Park Ave, Suite 10N, New York, NY 10016, United States, Lee Moncho *Tel:* 212-681-9400 *Fax:* 212-681-9362 *E-mail:* ny@cpo.com.hk

## Communication Art Design & Printing Ltd
19th floor, China Hong Kong Tower, 8-12 Hennessy Rd, Wan Chai
*Tel:* 2865 6787 *Fax:* 2866 3429
*E-mail:* cadesign@pacific.net.hk
*Key Personnel*
Man Dir: Rosanne Chan
Founded: 1984
Print Runs: 500 min
Business from Other Countries: 50%

## Creative Printing Ltd
Formerly Morris Press Ltd
Wah Ha Industrial Bldg, 15/F, Block C, 8 Shipyard Lane, Quarry Bay
*Tel:* 2563 2187; 2563 2188 *Fax:* 2565 9069
*E-mail:* crprint@netvigator.com
*Web Site:* www.cgan.net/enterprise/crprint
*Key Personnel*
Dir: Raynond Shing
Sales Dir: William Shue *E-mail:* william@creativeprinting.com.hk
Turnaround: 15 Workdays
Print Runs: 5,000 min - 100,000 max
Business from Other Countries: 50%

## Dai Nippon Printing Co (Hong Kong) Ltd
Division of Dai Nippon Printing Co Ltd
Tsuen Wan Industrial Centre, 2-5/F, 220-248 Texaco Rd, Tsuen Wan, New Territories
*Tel:* 2408-0188 *Fax:* 2408-8479
*E-mail:* info@mail.dnp.co.jp
*Web Site:* www.dnp.co.jp *Cable:* DNPICO
*Key Personnel*
Administration & Finance Dir: Mr K Miya
Print Runs: 5,000 min - 200,000 max
Business from Other Countries: 85%
*Branch Office(s)*
Dai Nippon Printing Co (Australia) Pty Ltd, St Martins Tower, Level 10, Suite 1002, 31 Market St, Sydney, NSW 2000, Australia *Tel:* (02) 9267-8166 *Fax:* (02) 9267-9533
DNP America LLC, Los Angeles Office, 3858 Carson St, Suite 300, Torrance, CA 90503, United States *Tel:* 310-540-5123 *Fax:* 310-543-3260
DNP America LLC, New York Office, 335 Madison Ave, 3rd floor, New York, NY 10017, United States *Tel:* 212-503-1060 *Fax:* 212-286-1501
DNP America LLC, Silicon Valley Office, 3235 Kifer Rd, Suite 100, Santa Clara, CA 95051, United States *Tel:* 408-735-8880 *Fax:* 408-735-0453
DNP Corporation USA, New York Office, 335 Madison Ave, 3rd floor, New York, NY 10017, United States *Tel:* 212-503-1850 *Fax:* 212-286-1490
DNP Corporation USA, San Francisco Office, 577 Airport Blvd, Suite 620, Burlingame,

CA 94010, United States *Tel:* 650-558-4050 *Fax:* 650-340-6095
DNP Denmark A/S, Skruegangen 2, 2690 Karlslunde, Denmark *Tel:* 4616-5100 *Fax:* 4616-5200
DNP Electronics America LLC, 2391 Fenton St, Chula Vista 91914, United States *Tel:* 619-397-6700 *Fax:* 619-397-6729
DNP Europa GmbH, Berliner Allee 26, 40212 Dusseldorf, Germany *Tel:* (0211) 8620-180 *Fax:* (0211) 8620-1895
DNP IMS America Corporation, 4524 Enterprise Dr NW, Concord, NC 28027, United States *Tel:* 704-784-8100 *Fax:* 704-784-2777
DNP IMS France SAS, 14, rue da la Violette, 22100 Dinan, France
DNP Korea Co Ltd, Hae sung 2 Bldg 8F, Doechi Dong, Kangnam-ku, Seoul 942-10, Republic of Korea *Tel:* (02) 408-0188 *Fax:* (02) 408-8479
DNP Photomask Europe SpA, Via Olivatti 2/A, 20041 Agrate Brianza, Italy *Tel:* (039) 65493-3000 *Fax:* (039) 65493-215
DNP Singapore Pte Ltd, 896 Dunearn Rd, No 04-09, Sime Darby Centre, Singapore 589472, Singapore *Tel:* 469-7611 *Fax:* 466-8486
DNP Taiwan Co Ltd, Rm D, 6 fl, 44 Chung-Shan N Rd Sec 2, Taipei 104, Taiwan, Province of China *Tel:* (02) 2327-8311 *Fax:* (02) 2327-8283
DNP UK Co Ltd, 27 Throgmorton St, 4th floor, London EC2N 2AQ, United Kingdom *Tel:* (020) 7588 2088 *Fax:* (020) 7588 2089
PT DNP Indonesia, Kawasan Industri Pulogadung, Jalan Pulogadung Kaveling II, Blok H, No 2-3, Jakarta Timur, Indonesia *Tel:* (021) 4610313 *Fax:* (021) 4605795
Tien Wah Press (Pte) Ltd, 4 Pandan Crescent, Singapore 128475, Singapore *Tel:* 466-6222 *Fax:* 469-3894
TWP Sdn Bhd, 89, Jalan Tampoi, Kawasan Perindustrian Tampoi, 80350 Johor Bahru, Johor, Malaysia *Tel:* (07) 2369899 *Fax:* (07) 2363148

## Elgin Consultants Ltd
Crawford Tower, 18B, 99 Jervois St, Sheung Wan
*Tel:* 2815 1680 *Fax:* 2815 1706
Founded: 1983
Turnaround: 21 Workdays
Business from Other Countries: 10%

## Elite Printing Co Ltd
Hong Man Industrial Center, Room 1401-08, 1413 & 1414, 2 Hong Man St, Chai Wan
*Tel:* 2558 0119 *Fax:* 2897 2675
*E-mail:* sales@elite.com.hk
*Web Site:* www.elite.com.hk
*Key Personnel*
Man Dir: Mak Tong Kee
Sales & Marketing Manager: Fred Chu
Founded: 1979
Turnaround: 7-15 Workdays
Print Runs: 2,000 min - 50,000 max
Business from Other Countries: 30%

## Empire Printing Ltd
3 Dai Shun St, Tai Po Ind Estate, Tai Po, New Territories
*Tel:* 2665 5193 *Fax:* 2661 7722
*Key Personnel*
Sales Manager: Lok-Tsang Li
Founded: 1978
Turnaround: 2 Workdays
Print Runs: 2,500 min - 500,000 max
Business from Other Countries: 15%

## Everbest Printing Co Ltd
Ko Fai Industrial Bldg, Block C, Unit 5, 10th floor, Kowloon
*Tel:* 2727 4433 *Fax:* 2772 7687
*E-mail:* sales@everbest.com.hk
*Web Site:* www.everbest.com

*Key Personnel*
Man Dir: Kenneth Chung
Customer Account Executive: Frankie Lee; Ronny Ng
Founded: 1954
Turnaround: 28 Workdays
Print Runs: 1,000 min - 1,000,000 max
Business from Other Countries: 90%
*Branch Office(s)*
100 Macaulay Rd, Stanmore, NSW 2048, Australia, Contact: Lionel Marz *Tel:* 612-9568-5879 *Fax:* 612-9568-5902 *E-mail:* lmarz@onaustralia.com.au (Australian & New Zealand Office)
Everbest Canada, 50 Emblem Court, Scarborough, ON M1S 1B1, Canada, Contact: Connie Chung *Tel:* 416-286-2525 *Fax:* 416-286-2526 *E-mail:* everbestcan@aprinco.com
*U.S. Office(s):* Spectrum Books Inc, 2300 Bethards Dr, Suite C, Santa Rosa, CA 95405-8658, United States, Duncan McCallum *Tel:* 707-542-6044 *Fax:* 707-542-6045 *E-mail:* specbooks@aol.com
Four Colour Imports, 2843 Brownsboro Rd, Suite 102, Louisville, KY 40206, United States, Contact: George Dick *Tel:* 502-896-9644 *Fax:* 502-896-9594 *E-mail:* sales@fourcolour.com *Web Site:* www.fourcolour.com
Everbest Midwest, 6428 Margaret's Lane, Edina, MN 55439, United States, Contact: Dr Josie Lo *Tel:* 612-944-0854 *Fax:* 912-829-7670 *E-mail:* sklo@aol.com

## Golden Cup Printing Co Ltd
Seapower Industrial Centre, 6/F, 177 Hoi Bun Rd, Kwun Tong, Kowloon
*Tel:* 2343 4254 *Fax:* 23415426
*E-mail:* info@goldencup.com.hk
*Web Site:* www.goldencup.com.hk
*Key Personnel*
Man Dir: Yeung Kam Kai
General Manager: W K Ngan
Sales Manager: Mary Yeung *E-mail:* mary@goldencup.com.hk
Founded: 1971
Turnaround: 25 Workdays
Print Runs: 5,000 min - 200,000 max
Business from Other Countries: 80%
*Branch Office(s)*
Dongguan, China
Guangdong, China
Kunming, China
Yunan, China

## Great Wall Graphics Ltd
2/F, 13 Wyndhan St, Hong Kong
*Tel:* 2524 0014 *Fax:* 2845 3588
*Key Personnel*
Dir: Paul Zimmerman
Founded: 1982
Turnaround: 3-28 Workdays
Print Runs: 2,000 min - 500,000 max
Business from Other Countries: 50%

## H & Y Printing Ltd
Blk C, 2/F Shing Tak Industrial Bldg, 44 Wong Chuk Hang Rd, Aberdeen
*Tel:* 2870 2379 *Fax:* 2555 0028
*E-mail:* hyphk@netvigator.com
*Key Personnel*
Contact: Jason Ma
Founded: 1996
Print Runs: 1,000 min - 100,000 max

## Hill & Knowlton Asia Ltd
Subsidiary of WPP
PCCW Tower, 36th floor, Taikoo Pl, 979 King's Rd, Quarry Bay
*Tel:* 2894 6321 *Fax:* 2576 3551
*E-mail:* dmaguire@hillandknowlton.com
*Web Site:* www.hillandknowlton.com
*Telex:* 25763551

*Key Personnel*
Man Dir: Denise Maguire
Founded: 1927
*Branch Office(s)*
Hill & Knowlton Melbourne, 484 St Kilda Rd,
    Level 15, Melbourne, Victoria 3004, Australia,
    General Manager: Rod Nockles *Tel:* (03) 9868
    9370 *Fax:* (03) 9868 9369
Hill & Knowlton (NZ) Ltd, PriceWaterhouse-
    Coopers Centre, Level 15, 66 Wyndham St,
    Auckland, New Zealand *Tel:* (09) 367 6370
    *Fax:* (09) 367 6371
Hill & Knowlton (SEA) Pte Ltd, 100 Beach Rd,
    25-11 Shaw Tower, Singapore, Singapore
Hill & Knowlton (SEA) Sdn Bhd, UBN Tower,
    Lot 6E, 6th floor, 10 Jalan P Ramlee, 50250
    Kuala Lumpur, Malaysia, Man Dir: Julia Ah-
    mad *Tel:* (03) 2026 0899 *Fax:* (03) 2026 0699
Hill & Knowlton Thailand, Q House, Ploenjit
    Bldg, Unit 14C, 14th floor, 598 Ploenchit Rd,
    Lumpini Pathumwan, Bangkok 10330, Thai-
    land, Man Dir: Kanpirom Ungpakorn *Tel:* (02)
    627 3501-6 *Fax:* (02) 627 3510
Hill & Knowlton Zhonglian, Scitech Tower,
    Suite 1901, Beijing 100004, China, Man
    Dir: Annabelle Warren *Tel:* (010) 6512 8811
    *Fax:* (010) 6512 3712
Hill & Knowlton Zhonglian PR Consulting Ltd,
    Westgate Tower, 26th floor, Suite 2606, 1038
    Nanjing West Rd, Shanghai 200041, China,
    General Manager: Carol Yang *Tel:* (021) 6218
    6150 *Fax:* (021) 6218 6125

**Hoi Kwong Printing Co Ltd**
Wah Ha Industry Bldg, 5/F, Block C-D, 8 Ship-
    yard Lane, Quarry Bay
*Tel:* 2562-1641; 2562-1096 *Fax:* 2564-2142
*E-mail:* sales@hoikwong.com
*Web Site:* www.hoikwong.com
*Key Personnel*
Man Dir: David Chan *E-mail:* dchan@hoikwong.
    com
Founded: 1960

**Hong Kong Christian Service**
33 Granville Rd, Kowloon, Hong Kong SAR
*Tel:* 2731-6316 *Fax:* 2731-6333
*E-mail:* info@hkcs.org
*Web Site:* www.hkcs.org
*Key Personnel*
Chief Executive: Mr Ng Shui Lai
Founded: 1952
Turnaround: 40 Workdays
Business from Other Countries: 1%
*Parent Company:* Hong Kong Christian Council

**Hung Hing Off-set Printing Co Ltd**
Subsidiary of Hung Hing Printing Group Ltd
Tai Po Industrial Estate, 17-19 Dai Hei St, New
    Territories
*Tel:* 2664 8682 *Fax:* 2664 2070
*E-mail:* info@hhop.com.hk
*Web Site:* www.hhop.com.hk
*Key Personnel*
Executive Dir: Alvin Chan Siu Man
Founded: 1950
Turnaround: 20-30 Workdays
Print Runs: 5,000 min - 1,000,000 max
Business from Other Countries: 15%

**Icicle/Papercom**
Formerly Paper Communication Printing Express
    Ltd
3rd floor, South West, Warwick House West
    Wing, Taikoo Place, 979 King's Rd, Quarry
    Bay
*Tel:* 2235 2880
*Web Site:* www.papercom.com.hk
*Key Personnel*
Business Development: Bonnie Chan *Tel:* 2235
    2888 *Fax:* 2135 6809 *E-mail:* bonnie.chan@
    icicle.com.hk

Founded: 1981
Turnaround: 28 to 56 Workdays
Print Runs: 1,000 min - 200,000 max
Business from Other Countries: 100%

**Image Printing Company Ltd**
Unit 4, 4/F Cornell Centre, 50 Wing Tai Rd, Chai
    Wan
*Tel:* 2897 8046 *Fax:* 2558 3044
*E-mail:* imageprt@pop3.hknet.com
*Key Personnel*
Man Dir: Philip Chow Sung Ming
Founded: 1992
Print Runs: 1,000 min - 50,000 max
Business from Other Countries: 50%

**Imago Services (HK) Ltd**
Tung Chong Factory Bldg, 6th floor, Flat B, 653-
    659 Kings Rd, North Point
*Tel:* 2811 3316 *Fax:* 2597 5256
*E-mail:* enquiries@imago.com.hk
*Web Site:* www.imago.com.hk
*Key Personnel*
Man Dir: Kendrick Cheung
*Branch Office(s)*
Macpherson Industrial Complex, No 5 Lorong
    Bakar Batu, Hex 05-01, Singapore 348742,
    Singapore *Tel:* 748 4433 *Fax:* 748 6082
Albury Court, Albury, Thame, Oxon 0X9
    2LP, United Kingdom *Tel:* (01844) 337000
    *Fax:* (01844) 339935
*U.S. Office(s):* 31952 Camino Capistrano, Suite
    C22, San Juan Capistrano, CA 92675, United
    States *Tel:* 949-661-5998 *Fax:* 949-661-8013
17 N Loomis St, No 4A, Chicago, IL 60607,
    United States *Tel:* 312-829-4051 *Fax:* 312-829-
    4059
1431 Broadway-Penthouse, New York, NY
    10018, United States *Tel:* 212-921-4411
    *Fax:* 212-921-8226

**Leo Paper Products Ltd**
7/F, Kader Bldg, 22 Kai Cheung Rd, Kowloon
    Bay, Kowloon
*Tel:* 28841374 *Fax:* 25130698
*E-mail:* lpp@leo.com.hk
*Web Site:* www.leo.com.hk
*Key Personnel*
Man Dir: Johnny Fung *E-mail:* johnny@leo.com.
    hk; Michael Leung *E-mail:* michael@leo.com.
    hk
Marketing Dir: Kelly Fok *E-mail:* kelly@leo.com.
    uk
Founded: 1991
Turnaround: 15-30 Workdays
Print Runs: 5,000 min
*Parent Company:* Leo Paper Bags Manufacturing
    Ltd
*Sales Office(s):* Leo Paper Products (Europe)
    BVBA, Keizerstr 5, 2000 Antwerp, Belgium,
    Contact: Jan Van Gijsel *Tel:* (03) 203-0912
    *Fax:* (03) 255-1303 *E-mail:* leo@leo-europe.
    com
Leo Paper USA, 27 W 24 St, Suite 701, New
    York, NY 10010-3204, United States *Tel:* 917-
    305-0708 *Fax:* 917-305-0709 *E-mail:* leo@
    leousanewyork.com
Leo Paper USA, 1180 NW Maple St, Suite 102,
    Issaquah, WA 98027, United States, Contact:
    Bijan Pakzad *Tel:* 425-646-8801 *Fax:* 425-646-
    8805 *E-mail:* leousa@leousa.com
Leo Paper Products (UK) Ltd, St Michaels
    House, 94 High St, Wallingford, Oxon OX10
    0BW, United Kingdom *Tel:* (01844) 274-
    244 *Fax:* (01844) 275-105 *E-mail:* tim.leo@
    btinternet.com

**Literature Ministry Department**
5/F, 128 Castle Peak Rd, Shamshuipo, Kowloon
*Tel:* 2725 8558 *Fax:* 2386 2304
*E-mail:* hkccllmd@hkstar.com
Founded: 1971

Print Runs: 2,000 min - 200,000 max
Business from Other Countries: 50%

**Mei Ka Printing & Publishing Enterprise Ltd**
Cheung Ka Industrial Bldg, Block B, 9th floor,
    179-180 Connaught Rd W, Hong Kong
*Tel:* 2540 1131 *Fax:* 2559 8718; 2559 7137
*E-mail:* mkpp@netvigator.com
*Web Site:* www.meika-printing.com
*Key Personnel*
Dir: Hong Chin Huo
Founded: 1995

**Morris Press Ltd**, see Creative Printing Ltd

**New Island Printing Co Ltd**
New Island Printing Centre, Yuen Long Indus-
    trial Estate, 38 Wang Lee St, Yuen Long, New
    Territories
*Tel:* 2442 8282 *Fax:* 2443 9882; 2443 9883
*E-mail:* info@newisland.com
*Web Site:* www.newisland.com
*Key Personnel*
Local Sales: Pat Lee
China/Overseas Sales: Michelle Hong

**Palace Press International**
Wah Ha Factory Bldg, 10th floor, Block 10, 8
    Shipyard Lane, Quarry Bay
*Tel:* 2357 9019 *Fax:* 415-532-3007
*E-mail:* palacehk@palacepress.ocm; ppihk@
    palacepress.com; info@palacepress.com
*Web Site:* www.palacepress.com
*Key Personnel*
Dir: Lesley Sun *E-mail:* lesley@palacepress.com
Project Manager: Maria Ramos *Tel:* 415-626-
    1080 (ext 208) *E-mail:* maria@palacepress.com
Founded: 1980
*Branch Office(s)*
239C Joo Chiat Rd, Singapore 427496, Sin-
    gapore, Contact: Lesley Sun *Tel:* (0342)
    3117 *Fax:* (0342) 3115 *E-mail:* ppispore@
    palacepress.com *Web Site:* www.palacepress.
    com
*U.S. Office(s):* 1585-A Folsom St, San Fran-
    cisco, CA 94103, United States *Tel:* 415-626-
    1080 *Fax:* 415-626-1510 *E-mail:* ppisfo@
    palacepress.com *Web Site:* www.palacepress.
    com
Palace Press Marin, 17 Paul Dr, San Rafael,
    CA 94903, United States *Tel:* 415-526-
    1370 *Fax:* 415-532-3259 *E-mail:* ppimarin@
    palacepress.com *Web Site:* www.palacepress.
    com
180 Varick St, 10th floor, New York, NY 10014,
    United States *Tel:* 212-462-2622 *Fax:* 212-463-
    9130 *E-mail:* nyoffice@palacepress.com *Web
    Site:* www.palacepress.com

**Paper Art Product Ltd**
Sung Fung Centre, Unit 816, 88 Kwok Shui Rd,
    Kwai Chung
*Tel:* 2481 2929 *Fax:* 2489 2255
*E-mail:* paperart@netvigator.com
*Key Personnel*
Dir: Ho Hok Cheung
Turnaround: 2-4 weeks
Print Runs: 2,000 min - 100,000 max
Business from Other Countries: 80%

**Paper Communication Printing Express Ltd**,
    see Icicle/Papercom

**Paramount Printing Co Ltd**
Member of Paramount Publishing Group Ltd
3 Chun Kwong St, Tseung Kwan O Industrial
    Estate, Kowloon
*Tel:* 2896-8688 *Fax:* 2897-8942
*E-mail:* paraprin@netvigator.com
*Web Site:* www.paramount.com.hk

*Key Personnel*
President: Victor Oh
Account Dir: Kelvin Lai
Founded: 1968
Turnaround: 30-45 Workdays
Print Runs: 1,000 min - 1,000,000 max
Business from Other Countries: 60%
*U.S. Office(s):* Paramount Printing USA Inc, 111
    Chestnut St, Suite 508, San Francisco, CA
    94111, United States, Vice President, Sales:
    Bobby Tan *Tel:* 415-391-9111 *Fax:* 415-398-
    9333 *E-mail:* bobbytan@aol.com
Paramount Printing USA Inc, 386 Park Ave S,
    Room 315, New York, NY 10016, United
    States, President: Jason Cheng *Tel:* 212-696-
    5821 *Fax:* 212-696-5428 *E-mail:* jason3@ix.
    netcom.com

**Professional Publishing Co**
2/F, 65, Wyndham St, Central Hong Kong
*Tel:* 25254623 *Fax:* 28453681
*Key Personnel*
Business Dir: Michael Pak
Founded: 1970
Turnaround: 20-40 Workdays
Print Runs: 5,000 min - 50,000 max
Business from Other Countries: 20%

**Prontaprint Asia Ltd**
Far East Finance Center, Hong Kong
*Tel:* 28657525 *Fax:* 28661064
*E-mail:* postmaster@pronta.com.hk
*Key Personnel*
Man Dir: Clive Howard
Founded: 1986
Business from Other Countries: 40%

**Review Publishing Co Ltd**
Subsidiary of Dow Jones & Co Inc
GPO Box 160, Hong Kong
*Tel:* 2573 7121 *Fax:* 2503 1530
*E-mail:* service@feer.com
*Web Site:* www.feer.com
*Telex:* 75297 *Cable:* REVIEW
*Key Personnel*
Editor: Hugo Restall *E-mail:* hugo.restall@feer.
    com
Founded: 1946

**Sing Cheong Printing Co Ltd**
Tung Chang Fty Bldg, G/F, 655 Kings Rd, North
    Point
*Tel:* 25618801; 25626317 *Fax:* 25659467
*E-mail:* info@singcheong.com.hk
*Key Personnel*
Dir & Manager: Karen Shen Fishel
Founded: 1965
Business from Other Countries: 96%

**Sino Publishing House Ltd**
Valley Centre Room 301-302, 80-82 Morrison
    Hill Rd, Wanchai
*Tel:* 2884 9963 *Fax:* 2884 9321
*E-mail:* benyan@sinophl.com
*Web Site:* www.sinophl.com
*Key Personnel*
Contact: Ben Yan *E-mail:* benyan@sinophl.com
Founded: 1993
Print Runs: 500 min - 500,000 max
Business from Other Countries: 75%

**SNP Leefung Holdings Ltd**
10/F Wing On House, 71 Des Voeux Rd Central,
    Hong Kong
*Tel:* 2810 6801 *Fax:* 2810 5612
*Web Site:* www.leefung-asco.com
*Key Personnel*
Chairman: Peter Yang
General Manager (China Division): Yuan FuYin
Founded: 1960

**South China Printing Co (1988) Ltd**
Subsidiary of Sing Tao Group
Millenium City, 370 Kwun Tong Rd, Suite 3, 9th
    floor, Kowloon 180
*Tel:* 26373611 *Fax:* 26374221
*E-mail:* info@singtao.com
*Web Site:* www.nysingtao.com
*Key Personnel*
General Manager: Dominick Yim
Senior Division Manager: Ivan Cheung
Assistant to General Manager: Athena Yuen
    *E-mail:* ayuen@scpc.com.hk
Founded: 1988
Turnaround: 20 Workdays
Print Runs: 2,000 min - 150,000 max
Business from Other Countries: 98%
*Branch Office(s)*
Sydney, Australia, Contact: Mr Anders Hagberg
    *E-mail:* anders@bigpond.com
Bedfordshire, United Kingdom, Contact: Mr Alan
    Lynch *Tel:* (0152) 523-7455 *Fax:* (0152) 523-
    7756 *E-mail:* alan.lynch@LineOne.net
*U.S. Office(s):* Los Angeles, CA, United States,
    Contact: Mr Moon Chuen Lo *Tel:* (626) 291-
    7398 *Fax:* (626) 285-2870 *E-mail:* moonclo@
    earthlink.com
New York, NY, United States, Contact: Mr Peter
    Lawrence *Tel:* (212) 570-9010 *Fax:* (212) 628-
    0137 *E-mail:* scpco@aol.com

**South Sea International Press Ltd**
3/F, Yip Cheung Centre, 10 Fung Yip St, Chai
    Wan
*Tel:* 2897 1083 *Fax:* 2558 1473
*E-mail:* books@ssip.com.hk
*Web Site:* www.ssip.com.hk
*Key Personnel*
Man Dir: Franky Ho
Contact: George Lo
Founded: 1984
Print Runs: 3,000 min - 500,000 max
Business from Other Countries: 80%

**Speedflex Asia Ltd**
3/F Tianjin Bldg, 167 Connaught Rd W, Hong
    Kong
*Tel:* 2542 2780 *Fax:* 2542 3733
*E-mail:* info@speedflex.com.hk
*Web Site:* www.speedflex.com.hk
Founded: 1981
Turnaround: 1 Workday
Print Runs: 1 min
Business from Other Countries: 20%

**Sunshine Press Ltd**
21/F Fullager Ind Bldg, 234 Aberdeen Main Rd,
    Hong Kong
*Tel:* 25532386 *Fax:* 28732930
*E-mail:* spl@sunshinepress.com.hk
*Key Personnel*
Administrative Assistant: Trevin Tong
Contact: Joney Chan
Founded: 1976
Turnaround: 21-28 Workdays
Print Runs: 3,000 min - 500,000 max
Business from Other Countries: 25%

**Wing King Tong Group**
Leader Industrial Centre, Block I, 3/F, 188-202
    Texaco Rd, Tsuen Wan, New Territories
*Tel:* 2407 3287; 2407 3309; 2407 4547 *Fax:* 2408
    7939; 2407 4130
*E-mail:* printing@wkt.cc; books@wkt.cc
*Web Site:* www.wkt.cc
*Key Personnel*
Man Dir: Alex Yan Tak Chung *E-mail:* ayan@hk.
    super.net
Marketing Dir: Jeremy Kuo
Founded: 1944
Turnaround: 15 Workdays
Print Runs: 1,000 min - 100,000 max
Business from Other Countries: 95%

# Hungary

**Interpress Aussenhandels GmbH**
Bajcsy-Zsilinszky ut 21, 1065 Budapest
*Tel:* (01) 302-7525; (01) 2508267 *Fax:* (01) 302-
    7530
*Key Personnel*
Manager: Miklos Pollak; Sandor Kovacs; Julia
    Kovacs
Founded: 1991

# India

**Hiralal Printing Works Ltd**
Subsidiary of Conway Printers Pvt Ltd
D-41/1 TTC Industrial Area MIDC, opp Turbhe
    tel exchange, Navi Mumbai, Mumbai 400613
*Tel:* (022) 7672726; (022) 7683012 *Fax:* (022)
    7631191
*Key Personnel*
Chairman: G P Agrawal
Man Dir: Mr Rakesh Kumar Agrawal
Founded: 1981
Turnaround: 40-45 Workdays
Print Runs: 5,000 min - 100,000 max
Business from Other Countries: 75%

# Indonesia

**Victory Offset Prima PT**
Jalan Raya Pegangsaan, Dua No 17, Jakarta
    14250
*Tel:* (021) 460-2742; (021) 460-8968; (021) 4682-
    0555 *Fax:* (021) 460-2740; (021) 4682-0551
*E-mail:* info@victoryoffset.com
*Web Site:* www.victoryoffset.com
*Key Personnel*
President: Zainal F Stanley *E-mail:* zainal@
    victoryoffset.com
General Manager: S Wilson Pinady
    *E-mail:* wilson@victoryoffset.com
Founded: 1971
Turnaround: 14 days
Print Runs: 5,000 min
Business from Other Countries: 10%

# Ireland

**Tower Books**
13 Hawthorn Ave, Inniscarra View Estate,
    Ballincollig, County Cork
*Tel:* (021) 4872294 *Fax:* (021) 4872294
*Key Personnel*
Contact: Patricia Daly
Founded: 1970
Turnaround: 7-30 Workdays
Print Runs: 300 min - 2,000 max

# Israel

**Chronicles Publishers Ltd**
24 Haarbaah St, Tel Aviv 61200

Mailing Address: PO Box 20774, Tel Aviv 61200
*Tel:* (03) 5615052 *Fax:* (03) 5624104
*E-mail:* chronicl@inter.net.il
*Key Personnel*
Man Dir: Dr Yehuda Atac
Manager: Farida Yashkuner *Tel:* (03) 5613614
Founded: 1993

**The Government Printer**
One Miriam Ha'hashmonait St, Jerusalem 91007
Mailing Address: PO Box 765, Jerusalem 91007
*Tel:* (02) 5685111; (02) 5685200 *Fax:* (02)
5685226
*Key Personnel*
Comptroller: Shimon Hochster
Founded: 1948

**Har-El Printers & Publishers**
Jaffa Port, Jaffa 61081
Mailing Address: Jaffa Port, PO Box 8053, Jaffa
61081
*Tel:* (03) 681 6834 *Fax:* (03) 681 3563
*Web Site:* www.harelart.com
*Key Personnel*
Manager: Jaacov Har-El
Export Dir: Monique L Har-El *E-mail:* mharel@
harelart.co.il
Founded: 1974
Turnaround: 60-90 Workdays
Print Runs: 30 min - 5,000 max
Business from Other Countries: 70%

**Keterpress Enterprises Jerusalem**
PO Box 7145, 91071 Jerusalem
*Tel:* (02) 6557822 *Fax:* (02) 6528962
*E-mail:* info@keter-books.co.il
*Web Site:* www.keter-books.co.il
*Key Personnel*
Plant Manager: Peter Tomkins *E-mail:* peter@
keter-books.co.il
Sales Manager: Zvi Weller
Print Runs: 500 min - 500,000 max
Business from Other Countries: 10%
*Parent Company:* Keter Publishing House Ltd

**Technosdar Ltd**
5 Levontine St, 65111 Tel Aviv
*Tel:* (03) 560-7418; (03) 560-5951 *Fax:* (03) 560-
4932
*E-mail:* technos@internet-zahav.net
*Key Personnel*
General Manager: Avraham Weiss
Founded: 1972
Turnaround: 7-16 Workdays
Business from Other Countries: 10%

**Youval Tal Ltd**
PO Box 61009, Jerusalem 91610
*Tel:* (02) 6248897 *Fax:* (02) 6245434
*Key Personnel*
Dir: Youval Tal

# Italy

**Calderini SRL**
Subsidiary of Edagricole-Edizioni Agricole
Via Emilia Levante 31/2, 40139 Bologna
*Tel:* (051) 6226822 *Fax:* (051) 549329
*E-mail:* comm@calderini.agriline.it
*Web Site:* www.calderini.it
*Key Personnel*
Editorial Dir: Alberto Perdisa
Founded: 1960

**Canale G e C SpA**
Via Liguria 24, 10071 Borgaro Turin

*Tel:* (011) 40 78 511 *Fax:* (011) 40 78 527
*E-mail:* info@canale.it
*Web Site:* www.canale.it
*Key Personnel*
Dir General: Canale Giacomo *E-mail:* canale@
canale.it
Founded: 1915
Turnaround: 30 Workdays
Print Runs: 3,000 min
Business from Other Countries: 65%

**Dedalo Litostampa SRL**
Viale Luigi Jacobini 5, 70123 Bari
Mailing Address: Casella Postale BA/19, 70123
Bari
*Tel:* (080) 531 14 13; (080) 531 14 00; (080) 531
14 01 *Fax:* (080) 531 14 14
*E-mail:* info@edizionidedalo.it
*Web Site:* www.edizionidedalo.it
*Key Personnel*
Man Dir: Raimondo Coga
General Manager: Sergio Coga *E-mail:* s.coga@
edizionidedalo.it
Founded: 1965
Print Runs: 2,000 min - 10,000 max

**Minerva Medica**
Corso Bramante 83/85, 10126 Turin
*Tel:* (011) 67-82-82 *Fax:* (011) 67-45-02
*E-mail:* minervamedica@minervamedica.it
*Web Site:* www.minervamedica.it
*Key Personnel*
President: Dr Alberto Oliaro
Founded: 1937
Print Runs: 1,000 min - 10,000 max
Business from Other Countries: 8%
*Branch Office(s)*
Via Lamarmora 3, 20122 Milan *Tel:* (02)
551-843-79, 599-000-41 *Fax:* (02) 551-
809-54 *E-mail:* guerrini.minmed.milan@
minervamedica.it
Via Spallanzani 9, 00161 Rome *Tel:* (06) 442-
512-10 *Fax:* (06) 442-915-00 *E-mail:* lucentini.
minmed.rome@minervamedica.it

**Istituto Poligrafico e Zecca Dello Stato**
Piazza Verdi 10, 00198 Rome
*Tel:* (06) 85081 *Toll Free Tel:* 800 864035
*Fax:* (06) 8508-2517
*E-mail:* infoipzs@ipzs.it
*Web Site:* www.ipzs.it
*Telex:* 611008 IPZSRO
*Key Personnel*
Legal Representative: Giovanni Ruggeri
Founded: 1928

**Valdonega SRL**
Via Genova 17, 37024 Arbizzano VR
*Tel:* (045) 6020444 *Fax:* (045) 6020334
*E-mail:* valdonega@valdonega.it
*Web Site:* www.valdonega.it
*Key Personnel*
General Manager: Martino Mardersteig
Founded: 1948
Print Runs: 1,000 min
Business from Other Countries: 70%

# Republic of Korea

**Daehan Printing & Publishing Co Ltd**
41-10, Jamwon-dong, Seacho-gu, Seoul
*Tel:* (031) 730-3850 *Fax:* (031) 735-8104
*E-mail:* mschung@daehane.com
*Web Site:* www.daehane.com
*Key Personnel*
Chief Executive Officer: Hwarg Tae-Rang

Dir: Minsoo Chung *E-mail:* mschung@daehane.
com
Manager: Jin Park *E-mail:* jin@daehane.com
Founded: 1948

# Lithuania

**Spindulys Printing House**
Gedimino 10, 44318 Kaunas
*Tel:* (037) 226243 *Fax:* (037) 208 420
*E-mail:* repro@spindulys.lt
*Web Site:* www.spindulys.lt
*Key Personnel*
Contact: Elena Kapustinskiene
Founded: 1928
Print Runs: 500 min - 100,000 max
Business from Other Countries: 6%

# Madagascar

**Imprimerie Catholique**
127 Rue Lenine-Antanimena, 101 Tananrive
*Tel:* (02) 22304

**Societe Malgache d'Edition**
Route des Hydrocarbures, Ankorondrano, 101
Tananrive
Mailing Address: BP 659, 101 Tananrive
*Tel:* (020) 2222635 *Fax:* (020) 2222254
*E-mail:* tribune@wanadoo.mg
*Web Site:* www.madagascar-tribune.com
*Telex:* (020) 223-40
*Key Personnel*
Dir of Publication: Rahaga Ramaholimihaso
Founded: 1943
Print Runs: 7,000 min - 15,000 max

# Malawi

**Likuni Press**
Division of Odini Bookshop
PO Box 133, Lilongwe
*Tel:* 766022; 721388 *Fax:* 766122
*Key Personnel*
Chief Executive: S P Kalilombe
Managing Editor: P I Akomenji
Bookshop Manager: D H Bvalamwendo
Founded: 1949
Print Runs: 12,000 min - 15,000 max
Business from Other Countries: 5%

# Malta

**Interprint Ltd - Malta**
Subsidiary of Malta Government Investment Ltd
Industrial Estate, Marsa LQA 06
*Tel:* (021) 240169; (021) 222720 *Fax:* (021)
243780; (021) 238115
*Web Site:* www.interprintmalta.com
*Key Personnel*
General Manager: Alfred Azzopardi
*E-mail:* aazzopardi@interprintmalta.com
Commercial Manager: Joseph Bonnici
*E-mail:* jbonnici@interprintmalta.com
Founded: 1963
Turnaround: 15 Workdays

Print Runs: 500 min - 200,000 max
Business from Other Countries: 80%

# Netherlands

**Bosch en Keuning grafische bedrijven**
Ericastr 1, 3742 SG Baarn
Mailing Address: Postbus 1, 3740 AA Baarn
*Tel:* (035) 5412050 *Fax:* (035) 2202446
*Key Personnel*
Contact: P P E Rings

**Collectieve Propaganda van het Nederlandse Boek (CPNB)** (Foundation for the Collective Promotion of the Dutch Book)
Keizersgracht 391, 1016 EJ Amsterdam
*Tel:* (020) 626 49 71 *Fax:* (020) 623 16 96
*E-mail:* info@cpnb.nl
*Web Site:* www.cpnb.nl
*Key Personnel*
Man Dir: Henk Kraima
Founded: 1983

**CPNB**, see Collectieve Propaganda van het Nederlandse Boek (CPNB)

**Foundation of Marginal Printers**, see Stichting Drukwerk in de Marge

**Stichting Drukwerk in de Marge** (Foundation of Marginal Printers)
Bronforel 2, 2318 MD Leiden
Mailing Address: Postbus 16477, 1001 RN Amsterdam
*Tel:* (020) 6227748 *Fax:* (020) 6227748
*E-mail:* didm@jmdendijk.com
*Web Site:* www.drukwerkindemarge.nl
*Key Personnel*
Contact: Jan Molendijk
Founded: 1975

# New Zealand

**Bookprint Consultants Ltd**
Division of Grantham House Publishing
9 Wilkinson St, Apt 6, Oriental Bay, Wellington 6001
*Tel:* (04) 381 3071 *Fax:* (04) 381 3067
*E-mail:* gstewart@iconz.co.nz
*Key Personnel*
Chief Executive: Graham C Stewart
Founded: 1982
Print Runs: 2,000 min - 7,500 max
Business from Other Countries: 10%

**The Caxton Press**
113 Victoria St, Christchurch
*Toll Free Tel:* 800 229 866 *Fax:* (03) 365 7840
*E-mail:* print.design@caxton.co.nz
*Web Site:* www.caxton.co.nz
*Key Personnel*
Man Dir: Bruce Bascand *Tel:* (03) 353 0731
General Manager: Peter Watson *Tel:* (03) 353 0734
Customer Services: Robert Stapleton
Founded: 1935

**PPP Printers Ltd**
339 St Asaph St, Christchurch
*Tel:* (03) 3662727 *Fax:* (03) 3654606
*Key Personnel*
Man Dir: D C Richardson

Founded: 1958
Turnaround: 10 Workdays
Print Runs: 100 min - 100,000 max
Business from Other Countries: 10%

**Rogan McIndoe Print Ltd**
51 Crawford St, Dunedin
Mailing Address: PO Box 1361, Dunedin
*Tel:* (03) 474 0111 *Toll Free Tel:* 800-477-0355
*Fax:* (03) 477 0116
*E-mail:* quality@rogan.co.nz
*Web Site:* www.rogan.co.nz
*Key Personnel*
Man Dir: Brendan A Murphy
Advertising: Amanda Cushen *E-mail:* amanda@mcindoes.co.nz
Founded: 1893
Print Runs: 21 min - 30 max
Business from Other Countries: 1%

# Norway

**ISSN Norway**
Victoria terrasse 11, 0203 Oslo
Mailing Address: National Library of Norway, Oslo Division, PO Box 2674, 0255 Oslo
*Tel:* (023) 27 60 00; (023) 27 60 10 *Fax:* (023) 27 60 50
*E-mail:* nbo@nb.no; nb@nb.no
*Web Site:* www.nb.no
*Key Personnel*
Dir: Vigdis Moe Skarstein

# Philippines

**Cacho Publishing inc**
Pines Cor, Union St, Mandaluyong, Metro Manila
*Tel:* (02) 6318362; (02) 6318363; (02) 6318364; (02) 6318365 *Fax:* (02) 6315244
*E-mail:* cacho@mozcom.com
*Key Personnel*
President: Herbert T Veloso
Founded: 1880
Turnaround: 7-120 Workdays
Print Runs: 500 min - 50,000 max
*Parent Company:* National Book Store

**Reyes Publishing Inc**
4/F Mariwasa Bldg, 717 Aurora Blvd, 1112 Quezon City
*Tel:* (02) 721-8792 *Fax:* (02) 721-8782
*E-mail:* reyesbub@skyinet.net
*Key Personnel*
Operations Manager: Roman Paolo Reyes, V
Founded: 1964
Business from Other Countries: 90%

# Portugal

**Edicoes Silabo**
Rua Cidade de Manchester, 2, 1170 100 Lisbon
*Tel:* (021) 8130345 *Fax:* (021) 8166719
*E-mail:* silabo@silabo.pt
*Web Site:* www.silabo.pt
*Key Personnel*
Marketing Dir: Manuel Robalo
*E-mail:* manuelrobalo@silabo.pt

Founded: 1983
Turnaround: 5 Workdays

# Romania

**Editura si Atelierele Tipografice Metropol SRL**
Str Stefan cel Mare, nr 2, Bucharest
*Tel:* (01) 2104593; (01) 2108433 *Fax:* (01) 2106987
*Key Personnel*
President: Dr Bansoiu Ion
Founded: 1990
Turnaround: 3-20 Workdays
Print Runs: 500 min - 50,000 max
Business from Other Countries: 10%

**Editura Paideia**
2, Sos.Stefan cel Mare, 71216 Bucharest, Sector 1
*Tel:* (01) 2104593 *Fax:* (01) 2106987
*E-mail:* paideia@fx.ro
*Web Site:* www.paideia.ro
*Key Personnel*
President: Ion Bansoiu
Founded: 1990
Turnaround: 3-20 Workdays
Business from Other Countries: 10%

# Singapore

**Alkem Company (S) Pte Ltd**
Division of Toppan Printing Co Ltd
1, Penjuru Close, Jurong Town, Singapore 608617
*Tel:* 6265 6666 *Fax:* 6261 7875
*E-mail:* enquiry@alkem.com.sg
*Web Site:* www.alkem.com.sg
*Key Personnel*
Contact: Mr Takayuki Seki
Man Dir: Chu Bong *E-mail:* chubong@alkem.com.sg
General Manager: M Sonoda
Founded: 1968
Turnaround: 3 - 4 Weeks
Print Runs: 3,000 min - 500,000 max
Business from Other Countries: 70%

**Chong Moh Offset Printing Ltd**
Subsidiary of Chassis Graphic Art Pte Ltd
19 Joo Koon Rd, Jurong Town 628978
*Tel:* 8622701 *Fax:* 8624335
*E-mail:* chongmoh@singnet.com.sg
*Key Personnel*
Chairman: James Ng
Founded: 1946
Turnaround: 10-14 Workdays
Print Runs: 1,000 min
Business from Other Countries: 35%

**CS Graphics Pte Ltd**
10 Tuas Ave 20, Singapore 2263
*Tel:* 861-0100 *Fax:* 861-0190
*Key Personnel*
Man Dir: Mr Lee Sian Tee *E-mail:* stlee@csgraphics-world.com
Founded: 1987
Turnaround: 80 Workdays (with pre-press); 20-60 Workdays (without pre-press)
Print Runs: 1,000 min - 200,000 max
Business from Other Countries: 100%
*Sales Office(s):* 8969 Lake Court, Granite Bay, CA 95746, United States, Contact: Rick Marment *Tel:* 916-791-9066 *Fax:* 916-791-9112
*E-mail:* csgraphics@csi.com

**Eurasia Press (Offset) Pte Ltd**
10 Kampong Ampat, Singapore 368320
*Tel:* 2805522 *Fax:* 2800593; 3825458
*E-mail:* eurasia@mbox3.singnet.com.sg
*Key Personnel*
Marketing Dir: Allan Fong
Founded: 1937
Turnaround: 14 Workdays
Print Runs: 500 min - 100,000 max
Business from Other Countries: 65%

**HB Media Holdings Pte Ltd**
Division of International Printing Division
Subsidiary of HBM Print Ltd
745 Lor 5 TOA Payoh, HBM Bldg, Singapore
  319455
*Tel:* 62591919 *Fax:* 67443895
*Key Personnel*
Chief Operating Officer: Mr Wong Wai Mong
Founded: 1980
Turnaround: 5 Workdays
Business from Other Countries: 97%
*Branch Office(s)*
50 Kallang Bahru No 02-14/23, Kallang Basin
  Industrial Estate, Singapore 339334

**Ho Printing Singapore Pte Ltd**
31 Changi South St One, Changi South Industrial
  Estate, Singapore 486769
*Tel:* 6542 9322 *Fax:* 6542 8322
*E-mail:* marketing@hoprinting.com.sg; sales@
  hoprinting.com.sg
*Web Site:* www.hoprinting.com
*Telex:* RS 39685 HOFSET
*Key Personnel*
Sales Executive: Ho Wah Yuen
Founded: 1951
Turnaround: 35-50 Workdays
Print Runs: 5,000 min - 50,000 max
Business from Other Countries: 30%

**International Press Softcom Ltd**
26 Kallang Ave, Singapore 339417
*Tel:* 2983800; 2952437 *Fax:* 2971668
*Key Personnel*
Marketing Manager: Kok Leong Koo
Founded: 1972
Print Runs: 3,000 min - 50,000 max
Business from Other Countries: 60%

**Khai Wah-Ferco Pte Ltd**
Five Star Bldg, No 61 Yishun Industrial Park A,
  No 02-00, Singapore 768767
*Tel:* 67583313 *Fax:* 67582038
*E-mail:* kwfppi@pacific.net.sg
*Key Personnel*
General Manager: Sim Huat Hoe

**Kim Hup Lee Printing Co Pte Ltd**
22 Lim Teck Boo Rd, Singapore 1953
*Tel:* 2833306 *Fax:* 2889222
*Key Personnel*
Dir: Mr Lim Geok Khoon

**Magenta Lithographic Consultants Pte Ltd**
1093 Lower Delta Rd, No 04-01, Singapore
  169240
*Tel:* 62746288 *Fax:* 62746795
*E-mail:* magenta@singaporebusinessguide.com
*Telex:* RS39478Mlcols
*Key Personnel*
Managing Proprietor: Mr Lim Choon Kiat
Founded: 1975
Turnaround: 2-3 Workdays
Business from Other Countries: 30%

**Markono Print Media Pte Ltd**
Subsidiary of Markono Holdings Pte Ltd
21 Neythal Rd, Singapore 628586
*Tel:* 6281-1118 *Fax:* 6286-6663
*E-mail:* saleslead@markono.com.sg

*Web Site:* www.markono.com.sg
*Key Personnel*
Executive Dir: Mr Ho Tian Lam *Tel:* 393 2338
Associate Dir: Mr Shaun Poh *Tel:* 393 2384
Corporate Affairs: Cindy Gui *Tel:* 393 2359; 393
  2392
Turnaround: 14 Workdays
Print Runs: 1,000 min - 100,000 max
Business from Other Countries: 20%
*Branch Office(s)*
Kin Keong Colour Printing (M) Sdn Bhd, Port
  Klang 539538

**Saik Wah Press (Pte) Ltd**
52 Kallang Bahru, No 07-19/20, Singapore
  339335
*Tel:* 6292 8759 *Fax:* 6296 0638
*E-mail:* sales@saikwah.com.sg
*Web Site:* www.saikwah.com.sg
*Telex:* RS38564
*Key Personnel*
Man Dir: Mr Chin San Hwa
Founded: 1973
Turnaround: 20 Workdays
Print Runs: 1,000 min - 100,000 max
Business from Other Countries: 70%

**SNP SPrint Pte Ltd**
97 Ubi Ave 4, Singapore 408754
*Tel:* 6741-2500 *Fax:* 6744-7098; 6743-9661
*E-mail:* enquiries@snpcorp.com
*Web Site:* www.snpcorp.com
*Telex:* SNPRS14462
*Key Personnel*
Man Dir: Foong Kee Loon
Sales & Operations Dir: Tung Chee Seng
Turnaround: 30 Workdays
Print Runs: 2,000 min - 200,000 max
Business from Other Countries: 40%
*Parent Company:* SNP Corporation Ltd

**Stamford Press Pte Ltd**
209, Kallang Bahru, Singapore 339344
*Tel:* 6294 7227 *Fax:* 6294 4396; 6294 3319
*E-mail:* lynn@stamford.com.sg
*Web Site:* www.stamford.com.sg
*Telex:* RS56414 STAMFO
*Key Personnel*
Dir Sales & Marketing: Mr V Balu *Tel:* 6294
  7227 (ext 228) *E-mail:* balu@stamford.com.sg
Man Dir: Mr R Theyvendran
Founded: 1963
Turnaround: 3-4 Workdays for small jobs; 3-4
  weeks for big jobs
Print Runs: 1,500 min - 50,000 max
Business from Other Countries: 20%

**Times Printers Pte Ltd**
Subsidiary of Times Publishing Group
16 Tuas Ave 5, Singapore 639340
*Tel:* 6311-2888 *Fax:* 682-1313
*E-mail:* enquiry@timesprinters.com
*Web Site:* www.timesprinters.com *Cable:*
  TIMESPRINT
*Key Personnel*
Assistant General Manager: Patsy Tan
Sales Manager: Alexandra Mager
Founded: 1968
Turnaround: 5-25 Workdays
Print Runs: 3,000 min - 300,000 max
Business from Other Countries: 75%

**Viva Lithographers Pte Ltd**
Blk 3 Pasir Panjang Rd, No 06-22/23 Alexandra
  Distripark, Singapore 118483
*Tel:* 2721880 *Fax:* 2735425
*E-mail:* vivasing@singnet.com.sg
*Web Site:* ifc.tp.edu.sg/Project_2000July/Viva
*Key Personnel*
Man Dir: Michael Oh

# Slovenia

**Gorenjski Tisk Printing House**
Mirka Vadnova 6, 4000 Kranj
*Tel:* (04) 2016300 *Fax:* (04) 2016301
*E-mail:* info@go-tisk.si
*Web Site:* www.go-tisk.si
*Telex:* 34560 YU GOTISK
*Key Personnel*
Dir: Kristina Kobal
Commercial Manager: Boris Krist
Founded: 1888
Turnaround: 30 Workdays
Print Runs: 3,000 min - 15,000 max
Business from Other Countries: 50%

# Spain

**Offo SL**
Los Mesejos 23, 28007 Madrid
*Tel:* (01) 5514214 *Fax:* (01) 5010699
*Key Personnel*
Export Manager: Jose A Martinez Minuesa

**Graficas Santamaria SA**
Division of Fotomecanica
Bekolarra, 4 Pol Ali Gobeo, 01010 Vitoria
  Gasteiz
*Tel:* (0945) 229100 *Fax:* (0945) 246393
*E-mail:* grsantamaria@graficassantamaria.com
*Web Site:* www.graficassantamaria.com
*Key Personnel*
Contact: Jesus Alzola Aguinaco
Founded: 1963
Turnaround: 1 Workday
Print Runs: 500 min - 150,000 max
Business from Other Countries: 15%

**Luis Vives (Edelvives)**
Xaudaro, 25, 28034 Madrid
*Tel:* (091) 334 48 83; (091) 334 48 82 *Fax:* (091)
  334 48 92
*E-mail:* dediciones@edelvives.es
*Web Site:* www.grupoeditorialluisvives.com
*Key Personnel*
Production Dir: Jesus Agudo Perez
Founded: 1890
Turnaround: 1 Workday
Business from Other Countries: 25%

# Sri Lanka

**Sarvodaya Vishva Lekha**
41 Lumbini Ave, Ratmalana
*Tel:* (01) 714820; (01) 714829; (01) 731601
  *Fax:* (01) 738932
*E-mail:* sarvs101@sri.lanka.net
*Key Personnel*
Man Dir: Mr Sausiri de Silva
Founded: 1984
Print Runs: 500 min
Business from Other Countries: 5%

**Sumathi Book Printing (Pvt) Ltd**
Division of Sumathi Group
445, Sirimovo Bandaranaike Mawatha, Colombo
  14
*Tel:* (0941) 330-673-5 *Fax:* (0941) 449-593
*E-mail:* lakbima@isplanka.lk
*Web Site:* www.sumathi.lk

*Telex:* 22104 SUMATHI CE SUMATISONS
*Key Personnel*
General Manager: Nawas A Rahim
Business from Other Countries: 75%

# Switzerland

**Autorinnen und Autoren der Schweiz AdS**
  (Association of Swiss Authors)
Nordstr 9, 8035 Zurich
*Tel:* (01) 350 04 60 *Fax:* (01) 350 04 61
*E-mail:* sekretariat@a-d-s.ch
*Web Site:* www.a-d-s.ch
*Key Personnel*
Secretary: Peter A Schmid
Founded: 2002

**Hallwag Kummerly & Frey AG**
Grubenstr 109, 3322 Schoenbuehl, Bern
*Tel:* (031) 332 31 31 *Fax:* (031) 850 31 00
*E-mail:* info@swisstravelcenter.ch
*Web Site:* www.swisstravelcenter.ch
*Telex:* 912-661 HAWA CH
*Key Personnel*
President: Dr Juergen Schad

**IBBY**, see International Board on Books for
  Young People (IBBY)

**International Board on Books for Young
  People (IBBY)**
Nonnenweg 12, 4003 Basel
*Tel:* (061) 272 29 17 *Fax:* (061) 272 27 57
*E-mail:* ibby@ibby.org
*Web Site:* www.ibby.org
*Key Personnel*
President: Peter Schneck
Administrative Dir: Elizabeth Page
Founded: 1953

**Ott Verlag Thun** (Ott Publishers Inc)
Brunngasse 36, 3000 Bern 7
*Tel:* (031) 318 31 33 *Fax:* (031) 318 31 35
*E-mail:* info@hep-verlag.ch
*Web Site:* www.ott-verlag.ch
*Key Personnel*
Man Dir: Hans M Ott

# United Republic of Tanzania

**Peramiho Publications**
PO Box 41, Peramiho
*Tel:* (054) 2730 *Fax:* (054) 2917
*Key Personnel*
Chief Executive: Fr Gerold Rupper
Founded: 1937
Print Runs: 4,000 min - 6,000 max

# Thailand

**J Film Process Co Ltd**
440/7 Soi Ratchawithi 3, Rajthevee, Bangkok
  10400
*Tel:* (02) 248-6888 *Fax:* (02) 247-4719

*Key Personnel*
President: Peer Prayukvong
Vice President: Siriporn Prayukvong
Man Dir: Pira Prayookwongse
Founded: 1970
Turnaround: 6 Workdays
Print Runs: 25,000 min - 65,000 max
Business from Other Countries: 45%

**Phongwarin Printing Company Ltd**
299 Mu 10, Sukhumvit 107, Sumrongnue, Ampur
  Muang, Samutprakarn 10260
*Tel:* (02) 7498934-45; (02) 3994525-31; (02)
  7498275-9 *Fax:* (02) 3994524; (02) 3994255
*E-mail:* somphong@phongwarin.com
*Web Site:* www.phongwarin.com
*Key Personnel*
Man Dir: Mr Somphong Charnsirisaksakul
Founded: 1983
Turnaround: 7 Workdays
Print Runs: 1,000 min - 500,000 max
Business from Other Countries: 5%

**Thai Watana Panich Press Co Ltd**
891 Rama 1 Rd, Bangkok 10330
*Tel:* (02) 2150060-3 *Fax:* (02) 2152360
*E-mail:* twpp@loxinfo.co.th
*Web Site:* www.twppress.com
*Telex:* 72303 Thaiwat th
*Key Personnel*
Man Dir: Thira T Suwan
Founded: 1935
Print Runs: 5,000 min

# United Kingdom

**J W Arrowsmith Ltd**
Winterstoke Rd, Bristol BS3 2NT
*Tel:* (0117) 966 7545 *Fax:* (0117) 963 7829
*E-mail:* jw@arrowsmith.co.uk
*Web Site:* www.arrowsmith.co.uk
*Key Personnel*
Sales Dir: David J Hooper *E-mail:* dhooper@
  arrowsmith.co.uk
Founded: 1854
Turnaround: 15 Workdays
Print Runs: 500 min - 15,000 max
Business from Other Countries: 25%

**BAS Printers Ltd**
115 Tollgate Rd, Salisbury, Wilts SP1 2JG
*Tel:* (01722) 411711 *Fax:* (01722) 411727
*E-mail:* sales@basprint.co.uk
*Web Site:* www.basprint.co.uk
*Key Personnel*
Man Dir: David Gumn
Sales Dir: Paul G Gumn *E-mail:* paul@basprint.
  co.uk
Founded: 1948
Print Runs: 350 min - 40,000 max
Business from Other Countries: 10%

**The Bath Press**
Subsidiary of Bath Press Group PLC
Lower Bristol Rd, Bath BA2 3BL
*Tel:* (01225) 428101 *Fax:* (01225) 312418
*E-mail:* bath@cpi-group.co.uk
*Web Site:* www.cpi-group.net/eng/fichebath.htm
*Key Personnel*
Sales & Marketing Dir: Harry Elson
  *Tel:* (020) 7637 9700 *Fax:* (020) 7637 0183
  *E-mail:* helson@cpi-group.co.uk
Sales Manager: Gordon Reade *Tel:* (020) 7637
  9700 *Fax:* (020) 7637 0183 *E-mail:* greade@
  cpi-group.co.uk

Contact, Commercial: Jonathan Pickering
  *E-mail:* jpickering@cpi-group.co.uk
Founded: 1846
Turnaround: 10-15 Workdays
Print Runs: 3,000 min - 300,000 max
Business from Other Countries: 5%

**BCS Publishing Ltd**
1 Bignell Park Barns, Kirtlington Rd, Bicester,
  Oxford OX6 8TD
*Tel:* (01869) 324423 *Fax:* (01869) 324385
*Key Personnel*
Man Dir: Steve McCurdy
Founded: 1993
Business from Other Countries: 40%

**Bell & Bain Ltd**
303 Burnfield Rd, Thornliebank, Glasgow G46
  7UQ
*Tel:* (0141) 649 5697 *Fax:* (0141) 632 8733
*E-mail:* info@bell-bain.demon.co.uk
*Web Site:* www.bell-bain.co.uk
*Key Personnel*
Man Dir: I Walker
Sales Dir: D Stewart
Founded: 1831
Turnaround: 7-10 Workdays
Print Runs: 100 min - 100,000 max
Business from Other Countries: 25%

**Biddles Ltd**
Division of W & G Baird Ltd
Hardwick Industrial Estate, 24 Rollesby Rd,
  King's Lynn, Norfolk PE30 4LS
*Tel:* (01553) 764 728 *Fax:* (01553) 764 633
*E-mail:* enquiries@biddles.co.uk
*Web Site:* www.biddles.co.uk
*Key Personnel*
Man Dir: Rod Willett *E-mail:* rwillett@biddles.
  co.uk
Founded: 1885
Turnaround: 20 Workdays
Print Runs: 250 min - 50,000 max
Business from Other Countries: 8%

**Roy Bloom Ltd**
Fanshaw House, 3/9 Fanshaw St, London N1
  6HX
*Tel:* (020) 7729 5373 *Fax:* (020) 7729 2375
*E-mail:* info@roybloom.com
*Web Site:* www.roybloom.com
*Key Personnel*
Chairman: Roy Bloom *E-mail:* roybloom@
  roybloom.com
Man Dir: Adam Bloom
Sales Dir: Paul White *E-mail:* paul.white@
  roybloom.com
Founded: 1969
Business from Other Countries: 40%

**Book Creation Services Ltd**
21 Carnaby St, London W1F 7DA
*Tel:* (020) 7287 0214 *Fax:* (020) 7583 9439
*Web Site:* www.bookcreation.com
*Key Personnel*
Chairman: Hal Robinson *E-mail:* hal@librios.com
Founded: 1991
Business from Other Countries: 30%

**Book Production Consultants PLC**
25-27 High St, Chesterton, Cambridge CB4 1ND
*Tel:* (01223) 352790 *Fax:* (01223) 460718
*Web Site:* www.bpccam.co.uk
*Key Personnel*
Dir: Tony Littlechild *E-mail:* tl@bpccam.co.uk;
  Colin Walsh *E-mail:* cw@bpccam.co.uk
Founded: 1973
Turnaround: 50 Workdays
Print Runs: 500 min
Business from Other Countries: 25%

**British Sisalkraft Ltd**
Subsidiary of David S Smith (Holdings)
Commissioners Rd, Rochester, Strood, Kent ME2
    4ED
*Tel:* (01634) 292700 *Fax:* (01634) 291029
*E-mail:* sales@bsk-laminating.com
*Web Site:* www.bsk-laminating.com
*Key Personnel*
Sales & Marketing Dir: Keith Travis
Brand Products Manager: Lawrence Kuhn
Founded: 1937
Business from Other Countries: 27%

**D Brown & Sons Ltd**
14 High St, 2nd floor, Cambridge CF71 7AG
*Tel:* (01446) 771475 *Fax:* (01446) 771476
*Key Personnel*
Dir: J M Whitaker *Tel:* (01446) 774213
Finance Dir: Jane C Brown
Founded: 1895
Business from Other Countries: 5%

**Center Print Ltd**
Colwick Business Park, Private Rd No 2, Col-
    wick, Nottingham NG4 2JR
*Tel:* (0115) 961 2277 *Fax:* (0115) 938 1424
*Key Personnel*
General Manager: Nicola Lesley
Print Runs: 1,000 min - 250,000 max

**Chase Publishing Services**
Mead, Fortescue Rd, Sidmouth, Devon EX10
    9QG
*Tel:* (01395) 514709 *Fax:* (01395) 514709
*E-mail:* r.addicott@btinternet.com
*Key Personnel*
President: Ray Addicott *E-mail:* r.addicott@
    btinternet.com
Founded: 1989

**Clays Ltd**
Subsidiary of St Ives Plc
Popson St, Bungay, Suffolk NR35 1ED
*Tel:* (01986) 893211 *Fax:* (01986) 895293
*E-mail:* sales@clays.co.uk
*Web Site:* www.clays.co.uk
*Key Personnel*
Contact: Sarah Orell
Founded: 1817
Turnaround: 15 Workdays
Print Runs: 1,000 min - 1,000,000 max
Business from Other Countries: 15%

**William Clowes Ltd**
Copland Way, Ellough, Beccles, Suffolk NR34
    7TL
*Tel:* (01502) 712884 *Fax:* (01502) 717003
*E-mail:* william@clowes.co.uk
*Web Site:* www.clowes.co.uk
*Key Personnel*
Man Dir: Alex Evans
Sales Dir: David C Browne *Tel:* (07768) 658820
    *E-mail:* dbrowne@clowes.co.uk
Founded: 1803
Turnaround: 10 Workdays
Print Runs: 2,000 min
Business from Other Countries: 1%
*Sales Office(s):* 2 Fore St, London EC2Y 5DA
    *Tel:* (020) 7588 0754 *Fax:* (020) 7588 0550
    *E-mail:* londonoffice@clowes.co.uk

**Cox & Wyman Ltd**
Cardiff Rd, Reading, Berks RG1 8EX
*Tel:* (0118) 953 0500 *Fax:* (0118) 950 7222
*E-mail:* coxandwyman@cpi-group.net
*Web Site:* www.cpi-group.net
*Key Personnel*
Commercial Contact: Paul Hicks
    *E-mail:* phicks@cpi-group.co.uk; Dave Watkins
    *E-mail:* dwatkins@cpi-group.co.uk
Founded: 1777

Turnaround: 10 workdays
Print Runs: 2,000 min - 2,000,000 max
Business from Other Countries: 12%

**Dorriston Publishers Ltd**
59 Stroud Green Rd, London N4 3EG
*Tel:* (020) 7272 2722 *Fax:* (020) 7272 7274
*Key Personnel*
Man Dir: A G Dicomites

**Edition**
Subsidiary of Cameron Books
PO Box 1, Moffat DG10 9SU
*Tel:* (01683) 220808 *Fax:* (01683) 220012
*E-mail:* sales@cameronbooks.co.uk
*Web Site:* www.cameronbooks.co.uk
*Key Personnel*
Dir: Ian Cameron; Jill Hollis
Founded: 1976

**Export Booksellers Group**
Division of Booksellers Association of the United
    Kingdom & Ireland Ltd
272 Vauxhall Bridge Rd, London SW1V 1BA
*Tel:* (020) 7802 0802 *Fax:* (020) 7802 0803
*E-mail:* mail@booksellers.org.uk
*Web Site:* www.booksellers.org.uk
*Key Personnel*
Meetings Executive: John Parke *E-mail:* john.
    parke@booksellers.org.uk

**Gardenhouse Editions Ltd**
15 Grafton Sq, London SW4 0DQ
*Tel:* (020) 7622 1720 *Fax:* (020) 7720 9114
*Key Personnel*
Man Dir: L Johnson

**Gee & Son (Denbigh) Ltd-Gwasg Gee-Gee's
Press**
Chapel St, Denbigh, Denbigshire LL16 35W
*Tel:* (01745) 812020 *Fax:* (01745) 812825
*Key Personnel*
Man Dir: Emlyn Evans
Founded: 1808

**The Guernsey Press Co Ltd**
Braye Rd, Vale, Guernsey GY1 3EG
Mailing Address: PO Box 57, Vale, Guernsey
    GY1 3BW
*Tel:* (01481) 240240; (01481) 243657 (ISDN)
    *Fax:* (01481) 240282
*E-mail:* books@guernsey-press.com
*Web Site:* www.guernsey-press.com
*Key Personnel*
Manager: Julie Todd
Founded: 1897
Turnaround: 10 Workdays
Print Runs: 2,000 min - 50,000 max
Business from Other Countries: 80%

**Robert Hale Ltd**
45-47 Clerkenwell Green, London EC1R 0HT
*Tel:* (020) 7251 2661 *Fax:* (020) 7490 4958
*E-mail:* webmistress@halebooks.com
*Web Site:* www.halebooks.com
*Key Personnel*
Chairman: John Hare
Marketing Dir: Martin Kendall
Founded: 1936

**Ikon Document Management Services**
Subsidiary of Microgen Holdings Plc
19 The Business Centre, Molly Millars Lane,
    Wokingham, Berks RG41 2QY
*Tel:* (0118) 9770510 *Fax:* (0118) 9770513
*Key Personnel*
Man Dir: Dave Weller
Business Development Dir: Aaron Biggs
Founded: 1972
Turnaround: 2-5 Workdays

Print Runs: 1 min - 5,000 max
Business from Other Countries: 40%
*Branch Office(s)*
Microgen City Park Watchmead, Welwyn Garden
    City, Herts AL7 1LT

**Intype Libra Ltd**
Units 3 & 4, Elm Grove Industrial Estate, Elm
    Grove, Wimbledon SW19 4HE
*Tel:* (020) 8947 7863 *Fax:* (020) 8947 3652
*E-mail:* intype@btconnect.com
*Web Site:* www.intype.co.uk
*Key Personnel*
Man Dir: Tony Chapman *E-mail:* tony.chapman@
    intypelibra.co.uk
Production: Jane Rogers
Founded: 1976
Turnaround: 10-15 Workdays for proofs; 5-10
    Workdays for books
Print Runs: 5 min - 2,500 max
Business from Other Countries: 5%

**ITD**
Rabans Lane Industrial Estate, Faraday Rd, Ayles-
    bury, Bucks HP19 3RY
*Tel:* (01296) 27211 *Fax:* (01296) 392019
*Key Personnel*
Man Dir: Roy Jackson-Moore
Founded: 1976
Turnaround: 7-10 Workdays
Business from Other Countries: 10%

**Gerald Judd Sales Ltd**
Paper House, 47-51 Gillingham St, London
    SW1V 1HS
*Tel:* (020) 7828 8821 *Fax:* (020) 7828 0840
*Key Personnel*
Man Dir: Simon Perks
Sales Dir: Jonathan Addy
Founded: 1936

**The Lavenham Press Ltd**
47 Water St, Lavenham, Suffolk CO10 9RN
*Tel:* (01787) 247436; (01787) 248046 (ISDN)
    *Fax:* (01787) 248267
*Web Site:* www.lavenhampress.co.uk
*Key Personnel*
Man Dir: Terence Dalton *E-mail:* terence@
    lavenhamgroup.co.uk
Sales Dir: Nic Waller *E-mail:* nic@
    lavenhamgroup.co.uk
Publishing Dir: Lis Whitehair *E-mail:* lis@
    lavenhamgroup.co.uk
Founded: 1953
Business from Other Countries: 1%

**Charles Letts & Co Ltd**
Thorneybank Industrial Estate, Dalkeith, Midloth-
    ian EH22 2NE
*Tel:* (0131) 663 1971 *Fax:* (0131) 660 3225
*E-mail:* sales@letts.co.uk; diaries@letts.co.uk
*Web Site:* www.letts.co.uk
*Key Personnel*
Man Dir: Gordon Presly
Founded: 1796

**Masons Design & Print**
Viscount House, River Lane, Saltney, Chester
    CH4 8RH
*Tel:* (01244) 674433 *Fax:* (01244) 674274
*Key Personnel*
Man Dir: Timothy Leaman
Founded: 1908
Turnaround: 5-10 Workdays
Print Runs: 500 min - 500,000 max

**MPG Books Ltd**
Division of MPG Ltd
Victoria Sq, Bodmin, Cornwall PL31 1EB
*Tel:* (01208) 73266; (01208) 72008 (ISDN)
    *Fax:* (01208) 73603
*E-mail:* print@mpg-books.co.uk

*Web Site:* www.mpg-books.com
*Key Personnel*
Man Dir: Tony Chard *E-mail:* tchard@mpg-books.co.uk
Deputy Managing Dir: Jeff Swift *Tel:* (01869) 324 992 *Fax:* (01869) 324 992 *E-mail:* jswift@mpg-books.co.uk
Sales Executive: Roy Skinner *Tel:* (01843) 231 029 *E-mail:* rskinner@mpg-books.co.uk
Sales & Marketing Development Manager: Colin Porter *Tel:* (0117) 968 8838 *Fax:* (0117) 968 8838 *E-mail:* cporter@mpg-books.co.uk
Founded: 1967
Turnaround: 10-15 days
Print Runs: 400 min - 10,000 max
Business from Other Countries: 5%
*Ultimate Parent Company:* Martins Printing Group

**NES Arnold Ltd**
Subsidiary of Group Holdings PLC
Findel House, Excelsior Rd, Ashby Park, Ashby de la Zouch, Leics LE65 1NG
*Tel:* (0845) 120 4525 *Fax:* (0800) 328 0001
*E-mail:* enquiries@nesarnold.co.uk
*Web Site:* www.nesarnold.co.uk
*Telex:* (0602) 377082
*Key Personnel*
Marketing Manager: Anita Ladva
    *E-mail:* aladva@novara.co.uk
Sales: Jane Smithson

**Page Bros Ltd (Norwich)**
Subsidiary of Milex Ltd
Mile Cross Lane, Norwich, Norfolk NR6 6SA
*Tel:* (01603) 429141 *Fax:* (01603) 485126
*Key Personnel*
Sales Dir: Steve Commons
Founded: 1750
Turnaround: 10 Workdays
Print Runs: 100 min - 30,000 max
Business from Other Countries: 20%
*Branch Office(s)*
105-A Euston St, London NW1 2ET *Tel:* (020) 7383 2212 *Fax:* (020) 7383 4145

**Paternoster Publishing**
Subsidiary of STL Ltd
9 Holdom Ave, Bletchley, Milton Keynes MK1 1QR
*Tel:* (01905) 357780
*E-mail:* info@paternoster-publishing.com
*Web Site:* www.paternoster-publishing.com
*Key Personnel*
Commissioning Editor: Robin Parry
Founded: 1935
Print Runs: 3,000 min - 10,000 max

**Pensord Press Ltd**
Tram Rd, Pontllanfraith, Blackwood NP12 2YA
*Tel:* (01495) 223721; (01495) 222020 (customer service) *Fax:* (01495) 220672
*E-mail:* sales@pensord.co.uk
*Web Site:* www.pensord.co.uk
*Key Personnel*
International Sales, Coordinator: Louise Williams
    *E-mail:* louise.williams@pensord.co.uk

**Polestar Purnell Ltd**
Subsidiary of BPC Ltd
Paulton, Bristol BS39 7LQ
*Tel:* (01761) 404142 *Fax:* (01761) 404191
*Web Site:* www.polestar-group.com/purnell
*Key Personnel*
Chairman: Thomas Middelhoff
Man Dir: Tony Hall
Production Manager: Andy Casling
Manufacturing Dir: Tony Kington
Finance Dir: Gerald Richardson
Founded: 1839

**Precision Publishing Papers Ltd**
Subsidiary of Ekman Cleave Group Ltd
Court Ash House, Court Ash, Yeovil, Somerset BA20 1HG
*Tel:* (01935) 431800; (732) 563-9292 (USA & other) *Fax:* (01935) 431805
*E-mail:* precisionpub@pppl.co.uk
*Web Site:* www.hspg.com/precision
*Key Personnel*
Man Dir: David Darwood

**The Q Group Plc**
Calverley House, 45 Dane St, Bishop's Stortford, Herts CM23 3BT
*Tel:* (01279) 719070 *Fax:* (01279) 757409
*E-mail:* marketing@qgroupplc.com; support@qgroupplc.com
*Web Site:* www.qgroupplc.com
*Key Personnel*
Man Dir: P F Poulter *E-mail:* ppoulter@qgroupplc.com
Founded: 1993

**F J Ratchford Ltd**
Subsidiary of Bookcraft Supplies Ltd
Kennedy Way, Green Lane, Stockport, Cheshire SK4 2JX
*Tel:* (0161) 4808484 *Fax:* (0161) 4803679
*E-mail:* info@fjratchford.co.uk
*Web Site:* www.fjratchford.co.uk
*Key Personnel*
Dir: J P Ratchford
Founded: 1889

**Antony Rowe Ltd**
Bumper's Farm Industrial Estate, Chippenham, Wilts SN14 6LH
*Tel:* (01249) 659 705 *Fax:* (01249) 448 900
*E-mail:* sales@antonyrowe.co.uk
*Web Site:* www.antonyrowe.co.uk
*Key Personnel*
Chief Executive: Ralph Bell
Production Dir: Mike Bando
Technical Dir: Andy Burns
Founded: 1983
Turnaround: 20 Workdays
Print Runs: 50 min - 2,000 max
Business from Other Countries: 2%

**Scottish Braille Press**
Craigmillar Park, Edinburgh EH16 5NB
*Tel:* (0131) 662 4445 *Fax:* (0131) 662 1968
*E-mail:* enquiries@scottish-braille.press.org
*Web Site:* www.scottish-braille-press.org
*Key Personnel*
Manager: John Donaldson *E-mail:* john.donaldson@scottish-braille-press.org
Sales & Marketing Manager: Stewart Connell
    *E-mail:* stewart.connell@dial.pipex.com
Founded: 1891
Turnaround: 15-20 Workdays
*Parent Company:* Royal Blind Asylum & School

**Society of Authors**
84 Drayton Gardens, London SW10 9SB
*Tel:* (020) 7373 6642 *Fax:* (020) 7373 5768
*E-mail:* info@societyofauthors.org
*Web Site:* www.societyofauthors.net
*Key Personnel*
Chairman: Antony Beevor
General Secretary: Mark Le Fanu
Founded: 1884

**M & A Thomson Litho Ltd**
Kelvin Industrial Estate, 2-16 Colvilles Pl, East Kilbride, Glasgow G75 0SN
*Tel:* (01355) 233081 *Fax:* (01355) 245 039
*E-mail:* enquiries@thomsonlitho.com
*Web Site:* www.thomsonlitho.com

*Key Personnel*
Contact: Ken Thomson
Deputy Chairman: Gary Thomson

**TJ International Ltd**
Subsidiary of Ulverscroft Large Print Books
Trecerus Industrial Estate, Padstow, Cornwall PL28 8RW
*Tel:* (01841) 532691 *Fax:* (01841) 532862
*E-mail:* sales@tjinternational.ltd.uk
*Web Site:* www.tjinternational.ltd.uk
*Key Personnel*
Chief Executive Officer: Angus Clark
    *E-mail:* angus@tjinternational.ltd.uk
Founded: 1970
Turnaround: 15 Workdays
Business from Other Countries: 5%

**Toppan Printing Co (UK) Ltd**
Subsidiary of Toppan Printing Co Ltd
Gillingham House, 38-44 Gillingham St, London SW1V 1HU
*Tel:* (020) 7828 7292; (020) 7828 7296
*Fax:* (020) 7828 5310
*E-mail:* kawamura@toppan.co.uk; info.e@toppan.co.jp
*Web Site:* www.toppan.co.jp
*Key Personnel*
President: Mr K Jo
Manager: Mr P Harty
Founded: 1983

**UK Serials Group-UKSG**
The Old Brewery, Priory Lane, Burford, Oxon OX18 4SG
*Tel:* (01635) 254292 *Fax:* (01635) 253826
*E-mail:* alison@uksg.org
*Web Site:* www.uksg.org
*Key Personnel*
Business Manager: Alison Whitehorn
Founded: 1978

**UKSG,** see UK Serials Group-UKSG

**United Kingdom Serials Group,** see UK Serials Group-UKSG

**Vista Computer Services Ltd**
Link House, 19 Colonial Way, Watford, Herts WD24 4JL
*Tel:* (01923) 830200 *Fax:* (01923) 238789
*E-mail:* solutions@vistacomp.com
*Web Site:* www.vistacomp.com
*Key Personnel*
Chairman: Denis Bennett
Man Dir: Colin Bottle
Marketing Manager: Marlyn Daniels
Founded: 1977
Business from Other Countries: 50%
*Associate Companies:* Vista Computer Services Inc, 80 Cottontail Lane, 4th floor, Somerset, NJ 08873, United States *Tel:* 732-563-9292 *Fax:* 732-563-9044; Vista Computer Services Pty, 5 Alexander St, Crows Nest, Sydney, NSW 2065, Australia *Tel:* (02) 9906 1222 *Fax:* (02) 9906 1441

**Watkiss Automation Ltd**
Subsidiary of The Watkiss Group
Watkiss House, Blaydon Rd, Middlefield Industrial Estate, Sandy, Beds SG19 1RZ
*Tel:* (01767) 682177 *Fax:* (01767) 691769
*E-mail:* info@watkiss.com
*Web Site:* www.watkiss.com
*Key Personnel*
Technical Dir: M Watkiss
Contact: Jo Watkiss
Founded: 1959
Print Runs: 200 min - 10,000 max
Business from Other Countries: 5%

## The Word Factory

Syntax House, PO Box 186, Nottingham NG11 6DU
*Tel:* (0115) 914 5654 *Fax:* (0115) 914 5675
*E-mail:* info@thewordfactory.co.uk
*Web Site:* www.thewordfactory.co.uk
*Key Personnel*
Contact: Rory Baxter *E-mail:* roryb@ thewordfactory.co.uk

## Zoe Books Ltd

15 Worthy Lane, Winchester, Hants SO23 7AB
*Tel:* (01962) 851318 *Fax:* (01962) 843015
*E-mail:* enquiries@zoebooks.co.uk
*Web Site:* www.zoebooks.co.uk
*Key Personnel*
Man Dir: Imogen Dawson *E-mail:* imogen@ easynet.co.uk
Founded: 1990
Business from Other Countries: 75%

# United States

## A-R Editions Inc

8551 Research Way, Suite 180, Middleton, WI 53562
*Tel:* 608-836-9000 *Toll Free Tel:* 800-736-0070 (US book orders only) *Fax:* 608-831-8200
*E-mail:* info@areditions.com
*Web Site:* www.areditions.com
*Key Personnel*
Pres & CEO: Patrick Wall
Dir, Sales & Mktg: James L Zychowicz
    *E-mail:* james.zychowicz@areditions.com
Founded: 1962
Business from Other Countries: 10%

## ADR/BookPrint Inc

2012 Northern Ave E, Wichita, KS 67216
*Tel:* 316-522-5599 *Toll Free Tel:* 800-767-6066 *Fax:* 316-522-5445
*E-mail:* info@adrbookprint.com
*Web Site:* www.adrbookprint.com
*Key Personnel*
Pres: Grace M Rishel *E-mail:* grace@ adrbookprint.com
VP: James E Rishel
Prodn Mgr: Marc Seiwert
Founded: 1978
Print Runs: 50 min - 25,000 max
Business from Other Countries: 10%

## American Pizzi Offset Corp

Subsidiary of Arti Grafiche Amilcare Pizzi (Milan)
370 Lexington Ave, Suite 1505, New York, NY 10017
*Tel:* 212-986-1658 *Fax:* 212-286-1887
*E-mail:* info@americanpizzi.com
*Key Personnel*
Pres: Massimo Pizzi
Sales Mgr, New York: Barbara Sadick
Sales Mgr, Italy: Elena Gaiardelli
Founded: 1914
Business from Other Countries: 50%

## Asia Pacific Offset Inc

1332 Corcoran St NW, Suite 6, Washington, DC 20009
*Tel:* 202-462-5436 *Toll Free Tel:* 800-756-4344 *Fax:* 202-986-4030
*Web Site:* www.asiapacificoffset.com
*Key Personnel*
Pres: Andrew Clarke *E-mail:* andrew@ asiapacificoffset.com
Dir, Sales (NY Office): Timothy Linn
    *Tel:* 212-941-8300 *Fax:* 212-941-9810
    *E-mail:* timothy@asiapacificoffset.com

Founded: 1997
Turnaround: 104 Workdays including color separation & shipping
Print Runs: 2,000 min
Business from Other Countries: 100%
*Branch Office(s)*
Phoenix Offset, Unit F1-2 2nd fl, Yeung Yiu Chung No 8 Industrial Bldg, 20 Wang Hoi Rd, Kowloon Bay, Hong Kong, Contact: Edmond Chan *Tel:* 2751-9962 *Fax:* 2755-8408 *E-mail:* edmond.chan@phoenixoffset.com
*Sales Office(s):* 270 Lafayette St, Suite 502, New York, NY 10012, Timothy Linn *Tel:* 212-941-8300 *Fax:* 212-941-9810 *E-mail:* timothy@ asiapacificoffset.com *Web Site:* www. asiapacificoffset.com
870 Market St, Suite 801, San Francisco, CA 94102, Dir, Sales: Amy Armstrong *Tel:* 415-433-3488 *Fax:* 415-433-3489 *E-mail:* amy@ asiapacificoffset.com *Web Site:* www. asiapacificoffset.com

## BookBuilders New York Inc

16 Sabal Bend, Palm Coast, FL 32137
*Tel:* 386-447-8692 *Fax:* 386-447-8746
*Web Site:* www.mcabooks.com
*Key Personnel*
Pres: Martin Cook *E-mail:* martin@mcabooks. com
Founded: 1977
Turnaround: 30-45 Workdays
Print Runs: 2,000 min - 500,000 max
Business from Other Countries: 60%

## C & C Offset Printing Co Ltd

Subsidiary of C & C Joint Printing Co (HK) Ltd under Sino United Publishing (Holdings) Ltd
2632 SE 25 Ave, Suite E, Portland, OR 97202
Mailing Address: PO Box 82037, Portland, OR 97282-0037
*Tel:* 503-233-1834 *Fax:* 503-233-7815
*E-mail:* portlandinfo@ccoffset.com
*Web Site:* www.ccoffset.com
*Key Personnel*
Dir, C & C Offset Printing Co (USA) Inc, Portland, OR, USA: Charles H Clark, IV
    *E-mail:* cclark@ccoffset.com
Devt Mgr, C & C Offset Printing Co (USA) Inc, Portland, OR, USA: Jenny Whittier
    *E-mail:* jwhittier@ccoffset.com
Dir & Exec VP, C & C Offset Printing Co (NYC) Inc, New York, NY, USA: Simon Chan
    *E-mail:* schan@ccoffset.com
Cust Serv Mgr, C & C Offset Printing Co (USA) Inc, Portland, OR, USA: Ernest Li
    *E-mail:* ernestli@ccoffset.com
Cust Serv Mgr, C & C Offset Printing Co (NYC) Inc, New York, NY, USA: Frances Harkness
    *E-mail:* fharkness@ccoffset.com
Dir & Gen Mgr, Hong Kong Head Office: Zhang Yue Ming
Deputy Man Dir, Hong Kong Head Office: Ken Lee
Deputy Gen Mgr, Hong Kong Head Office: Ivy Lam
Asst Gen Mgr, Hong Kong Head Office: Kit Wong
Sr Sales Mgr (Special Projects), Hong Kong Head Office: Francis Ho
Dir & Gen Mgr, C & C Joint Printing Co (Guangdong) Ltd, Shenzhen, China: Jackson Leung
Dir, C & C Offset Printing Co (France) Ltd: Michele Olson Niel
Pres, C & C Printing Japan Co Ltd, Tokyo, Japan: Yamamoto Masaaki
Man Dir, C & C Joint Printing Co (Beijing) Ltd, Beijing, China: Zhang Lin Gui
Dir, C & C Offset Printing Co (UK) Ltd: Tracy Broderick
Acct Mgr, C & C Offset Printing Co (UK) Ltd: Fia Fornari
Australian Sales Rep Off: Lena Frew

Founded: 1980
Turnaround: varies
Print Runs: 2,000 min - 1,000,000 max
Business from Other Countries: 70%
*Branch Office(s)*
C & C Printing Co (NY) Inc, 401 Broadway, Suite 2015, New York, NY 10013-3016 *Tel:* 212-431-4210 *Fax:* 212-431-3960 *E-mail:* newyorkinfo@ccoffset.com (New York City office)

## Codra Enterprises Inc

5912 Bolsa Ave, Suite 200, Huntington Beach, CA 92649
*Tel:* 714-891-5652 (ext 30) *Fax:* 714-891-5642
*E-mail:* codra@codra.com; sales@codra.com
*Web Site:* www.codra.com
*Key Personnel*
Gen Mgr: Jay Kim *E-mail:* jaykim@codra.com
Sales: Chris Sanatar *E-mail:* chriss@codra.com
Founded: 1985
Turnaround: 4-6 Weeks
Print Runs: 5,000 min
Business from Other Countries: 10%
Membership(s): Independent Publishers Association; Pacific Northwest Booksellers Association; Publishers Association of the West

## Colorprint Offset Inc

Division of Colorprint Offset (Hong Kong)
80 Park Ave, Suite 10-N, New York, NY 10016
*Tel:* 212-681-9400 *Fax:* 212-681-9362
*E-mail:* ny@cpo.com.hk
*Web Site:* www.hq.cpo.bz
*Key Personnel*
Pres: Lee Moncho *E-mail:* lee@colorprintoffset. com
Prod Dir & Cust Serv Mgr: Kate Brady
    *E-mail:* kate@colorprintoffset.com
Founded: 1986
Turnaround: 15 Workdays
Print Runs: 100 min - 50,000 max
Business from Other Countries: 65%

## Consolidated Printers Inc

2630 Eighth St, Berkeley, CA 94710
*Tel:* 510-843-8524; 510-843-8565 *Fax:* 510-486-0580
*E-mail:* cpi@consoprinters.com
*Web Site:* www.consoprinters.com
*Key Personnel*
CEO: Lawrence A Hawkins
Founded: 1952
Turnaround: 2-20 Workdays
Print Runs: 2,000 min - 500,000 max
Business from Other Countries: 15%

## Martin Cook Associates Inc

16 Sabal Bend, Palm Coast, FL 32137
*Tel:* 386-447-8692 *Fax:* 386-447-8746
*E-mail:* mcanewcity@aol.com
*Web Site:* www.mcabooks.com
*Key Personnel*
Pres: Martin Cook *E-mail:* mcanewcity@aol.com
Founded: 1977
Turnaround: 30-45 Workdays
Print Runs: 2,000 min - 500,000 max
Business from Other Countries: 15%

## CS Graphics USA Inc

Subsidiary of CS Graphics Pte Ltd Singapore
9748 Weddington Circle, Granite Bay, CA 95746
*Tel:* 916-791-9066 *Fax:* 916-791-9112
*Key Personnel*
Mgr, Sales & Mktg: Rick Marment
    *E-mail:* rick@csgraphics.us
Founded: 1980
Turnaround: 80 Workdays
Print Runs: 1,000 min - 75,000 max
Business from Other Countries: 30%

**DNP America LLC**
Subsidiary of Dai Nippon Printing Co Ltd
335 Madison Ave, 3rd fl, New York, NY 10017
*Tel:* 212-503-1060 *Fax:* 212-286-1505
*Web Site:* www.dnp.co.jp/ *Cable:* DAIPRINTS
  NY
*Key Personnel*
Pres: Yoji Yamakawa
VP & Gen Mgr, Graphic Printing: Kazuteru Arai
  *E-mail:* arai-k@mail.dnp.co.jp
Founded: 1974
Print Runs: 1,000 min
Business from Other Countries: 54%

**Elegance Printing & Book Binding (USA)**
Member of The Elegance Printing Group
708 Glen Cove Ave, Glen Head, NY 11545
*Tel:* 516-676-5941 *Fax:* 516-676-5973
*Web Site:* www.elegancebooks.com
*Key Personnel*
Man Dir: Frank DeLuca *E-mail:* frank@
  elegancebooks.com
Founded: 1977
Turnaround: Reprints ship within 14 days. New
  bks artwork to press within 2 wks-ship within
  30 days
Print Runs: 1,000 min - 1,000,000 max
Business from Other Countries: 40%

**Express Media Corp**
1419 Donelson Pike, Nashville, TN 37217
*Tel:* 615-360-6400 *Toll Free Tel:* 800-336-2631
  *Fax:* 615-360-3140
*E-mail:* info@expressmedia.com
*Web Site:* www.expressmedia.com
*Key Personnel*
Pres: Andrew Cameron
Exec VP: Andrew S Cameron
  *E-mail:* ascameron@expressmedia.com
Founded: 1996
Turnaround: 3 Workdays
Print Runs: 1 min - 10,000 max
Business from Other Countries: 10%

**The Floating Gallery & Advanced Self
  Publishing**
244 Madison Ave, Suite 254, New York, NY
  10016
*Toll Free Tel:* 877-822-2500
*E-mail:* floatingal@aol.com
*Web Site:* www.thefloatinggallery.com
*Key Personnel*
Owner: Joel Hochman; Laurence Leichman
  *E-mail:* larrydtp@aol.com
Mktg Dir: Olga Vladimizov
Founded: 1992
Turnaround: 21 Workdays; 1-7 for art
Print Runs: 1 min - 1,000,000 max
Business from Other Countries: 15%

**Hamilton Printing Co**
22 Hamilton Way, Castleton-on-Hudson, NY
  12033
*Tel:* 518-732-4491 *Toll Free Tel:* 800-242-4222
  *Fax:* 518-732-7714
*Key Personnel*
Pres: Brian F Payne
VP, Fin: Michael H Hart
VP, Mfg: Rick Dunn
Prod Mgr: Judy Rappold
Sales Rep: Stephen H Feuer; Tom Plain; Larry
  Ritchie; Michael C Rosenhack *E-mail:* miker@
  hpcbook.com
Founded: 1912
Turnaround: Flexible, time-sensitive scheduling
Business from Other Countries: 10%
Membership(s): BMI

**IBT Global Ltd**, see Integrated Book Technology
Inc

**Imago**
1431 Broadway, Penthouse, New York, NY 10018
*Tel:* 212-921-4411 *Fax:* 212-921-8226
*E-mail:* sales@imagousa.com
*Web Site:* www.imagousa.com
*Key Personnel*
Pres: Joseph E Braff *E-mail:* jbraff@imagousa.
  com
Northeast Sales: Linda Readerman
  *E-mail:* lreaderman@imagousa.com
USA Prodn Dir: Howard R Musk
  *E-mail:* hmusk@imagousa.com
Founded: 1985
Turnaround: 14 Workdays for color separations; 6
  Weeks for printing & binding
Print Runs: 5,000 min
Business from Other Countries: 100%
*Branch Office(s)*
Imago West Coast, 31952 Camino Capistrano,
  Suite C22, San Juan Capistrano, CA 92675,
  West Coast Sales: Greg Lee *Tel:* 949-661-5998
  *Fax:* 949-661-8013 *E-mail:* glee@imagousa.
  com
Imago Midwest, 17 N Loomis St, Unit 4A,
  Chicago, IL 60607, Midwest Sales: Ma
  Yan *Tel:* 312-829-4051 *Fax:* 312-829-4059
  *E-mail:* myan@imagousa.com
Imago Australia, 14 Brown St, Suite 241,
  Chatswood, Sydney 2067, Australia, Contact:
  Emma Bell *Tel:* (02) 9415 2713 *Fax:* (02) 9415
  2714 *E-mail:* sales@imagoaus.com
Imago France, 6 eme Etage, 42, rue le Peletier,
  75009 Paris, France, Contact: Matt Critchlow
  *Tel:* (1) 42 81 41 24 *Fax:* (1) 42 81 41 24
  *E-mail:* sales@imagogroup.com
Imago Services (HKG) Ltd, 653-659 Kings
  Rd, 6th fl, Flat B, North Point, Hong Kong,
  Contact: Kendrick Cheung *Tel:* 2811 3316
  *Fax:* 2597 5256 *E-mail:* enquiries@imago.com.
  hk
Imago Productions (FE) Pte Ltd, MacPherson
  Industrial Complex, Suite 05-01, 5 Lorong
  Bakar Batu, Singapore 348742, Singapore,
  Contact: K C Ng *Tel:* 6748 4433 *Fax:* 6748
  6082 *E-mail:* enquiries@imago.com.sg
Imago (UK/Europe) Publishing Ltd, Albury Ct,
  Albury Thame, Oxfordshire OX9 2LP, United
  Kingdom, Contact: Colin Risk *Tel:* (01844)
  337000 *Fax:* (01844) 339935 *E-mail:* sales@
  imago.co.uk *Web Site:* www.imago.co.uk

**Integrated Book Technology Inc**
Subsidiary of The IBT Group
18 Industrial Park Rd, Troy, NY 12180
*Tel:* 518-271-5117 *Fax:* 518-266-9422
*E-mail:* mail@integratedbook.com
*Web Site:* www.integratedbook.com
*Key Personnel*
CEO & Pres: John R Paeglow *E-mail:* johnp@
  integratedbook.com
VP & Chief Technol Officer: William Clockel
  *E-mail:* billc@integratedbook.com
VP, Sales & Mktg: Robert Lindberg
  *E-mail:* bobl@integratedbook.com
Dir, Info Technol: Michael Whalen
  *E-mail:* mikew@integratedbook.com
Regl Sales: Ledner Cunningham
  *E-mail:* lednerc@integratedbook.com
Founded: 1991
Turnaround: 1-15 Workdays
Print Runs: 10 min - 2,500 max
Business from Other Countries: 20%
*Branch Office(s)*
The IBT Global Ltd, Rollesby Rd, London N4-
  2JZ, United Kingdom, Intl Strategist: Pe-
  ter Kenyon *Tel:* (020) 7354 3332 *Fax:* (020)
  73543332
Membership(s): BMI

**Jinno International Group**
3 Christine Dr, Chestnut Ridge, NY 10977-6802
*Tel:* 845-735-4666 *Fax:* 617-344-5905
*E-mail:* jinno@hotmail.com

*Key Personnel*
Pres: Yoh Jinno
VP: Sharon Jinno
Founded: 1989
Turnaround: 21-30 Workdays US; 45-75 Work-
  days overseas
Print Runs: 500 min - 3,000,000 max
Business from Other Countries: 98%
*Branch Office(s)*
Hindy's Enterprise, Melbourne Industrial Bldg, 16
  Westlands Rd, Block A, 20th fl, Quarry Bay,
  Hong Kong *Tel:* 516-6318 *Fax:* 516-5161
Wing Yiu Printing Co, Melbourne Industrial
  Bldg, 6th fl, Block A, 16 Westlands Rd, Quarry
  Bay, Hong Kong, Contact: Law Ming Wah
  *Tel:* 561 0283 *Fax:* 565 8233
c/o Eurasia Press Pte Ltd, 10/14 Kampong Am-
  pat, Singapore 1336, Singapore, Contact: Allan
  Fong *Tel:* 280 5522 *Fax:* 280 0593
Jinno International Singapore, 710 Ang Mo Kio,
  Ave 8, Suite 07-2615, Singapore 2056, Singa-
  pore *Tel:* 458 0778

**Leo Paper USA**
1180 NW Maple St, Suite 102, Issaquah, WA
  98027
*Tel:* 425-646-8801 *Fax:* 425-646-8805
*E-mail:* leo@leousa.com; sales@leousa.com
*Web Site:* www.leousa.com
*Key Personnel*
VP: Peter R Gillies *Tel:* 425-646-8801 ext 21
  *E-mail:* peter@leousa.com
Sales: Tom Leach *E-mail:* tom@leousa.com; Greg
  Witt *E-mail:* greg@leousa.com
Founded: 1982
Turnaround: 90 Workdays
Print Runs: 3,500 min - 2,000,000 max
Business from Other Countries: 20%
*Branch Office(s)*
27 W 24 St, Suite 701, New York, NY 10010,
  Contact: Jeanine Laborne *Tel:* 917-305-
  0708 *Fax:* 917-305-0709 *E-mail:* sales@
  leoausanewyork.com

**LK Litho**
Division of The Linick Group Inc
Linick Bldg, 7 Putter Lane, Middle Island, NY
  11953
Mailing Address: PO Box 102, Middle Island,
  NY 11953-0102
*Tel:* 631-924-3888
*E-mail:* linickgrp@att.net
*Web Site:* www.lgroup.addr.com/lklitho.htm
*Key Personnel*
VP: Roger Dextor
Founded: 1968
Turnaround: 10 Workdays
Print Runs: 2,500 min - 2,000,000 max
Business from Other Countries: 20%

**Marrakech Express Inc**
720 Wesley Ave, No 10, Tarpon Springs, FL
  34689
*Tel:* 727-942-2218 *Toll Free Tel:* 800-940-6566
  *Fax:* 727-937-4758
*E-mail:* print@marrak.com
*Web Site:* www.marrak.com
*Key Personnel*
CEO: Peter Henzell
Prodn Mgr: Steen Sigmund
Sales/Estimator: Shirley Copperman
Founded: 1976
Turnaround: 10 days
Print Runs: 500 min - 25,000 max
Business from Other Countries: 12%

**Mazer Publishing Services**
Division of The Mazer Corporation
6680 Poe Ave, Dayton, OH 45414
*Tel:* 937-264-2600 *Fax:* 937-264-2624
*E-mail:* info@mazer.com
*Web Site:* www.mazer.com

*Key Personnel*
Pres: William Franklin *E-mail:* bill_franklin@ mazer.com
Exec VP: Ken Fultz *E-mail:* ken_fultz@mazer. com
VP & Gen Mgr, Creative Servs: Bill Scroggie
Exec Dir, Sales: Bill Faber *Fax:* 937-264-2622 *E-mail:* bill_faber@mazer.com
Founded: 1964
Print Runs: 50 min - 25,000 max
Business from Other Countries: 10%
*Branch Office(s)*
2460 Sand Lake Rd, Orlando, FL 32809, Contact: Brian Blakley *Tel:* 407-859-5552 *Fax:* 407-859-0643 *E-mail:* brian_blakley@mazer.com
224 Lexington Ave, Fox River Grove, IL 60021, Contact: Dennis Bowman *Tel:* 847-639-1555 *Fax:* 847-639-1562 *E-mail:* dennis_bowman@ mazer.com
22 Lehigh Rd, Wellesley, MA 02181, Contact: Ken Leahy *Tel:* 781-237-4112 *Fax:* 781-431-6184 *E-mail:* ken_leahy@mazer.com
22 Laurel Place, Upper Montclair, NJ 07043, Contact: John Martel *Tel:* 973-744-4320 *Fax:* 973-746-5608 *E-mail:* john_martel@ mazer.com
3081 Glenmere Ct, Kettering, OH 45440, Contact: Mark Brewer *Tel:* 937-299-5746 *Fax:* 937-299-5761 *E-mail:* mark_brewer@mazer.com
Membership(s): BMI

**Midas Printing International Ltd**
Subsidiary of Midas Printing Group Ltd
35 Belleview Ave, Ossining, NY 10562
*Tel:* 914-941-2041
*E-mail:* info@midasprinting.com
*Web Site:* www.midasprinting.com
*Key Personnel*
US Contact: Gerald B Levine
    *E-mail:* gerald_levine@midasprinting.com
Dir, Sales & Mktg, Hong Kong: Paul Tang
    *Tel:* 24084040 *Fax:* 24065890 *E-mail:* paul@ midasprinting.com
Busn Devt Mgr, China: Ian Lee *Tel:* 24084048
    *Fax:* 24065874 *E-mail:* ian@midasprinting.com
Founded: 1990
Turnaround: 2 weeks for paperbound; 3 weeks for hardbound
Print Runs: 3,000 min
Business from Other Countries: 85%
*Branch Office(s)*
1/F, 100 Texaco Rd, Tsuen Wan, New Territories, Hong Kong *Tel:* 24076888 *Fax:* 24080611 (headquarters, send all inquires to this address)
Membership(s): Graphic Arts Association of Hong Kong

**Milanostampa/New Interlitho USA Inc**
Subsidiary of Milanostampa New Interlitho Italia SpA
299 Broadway, Suite 901, New York, NY 10007
*Tel:* 212-964-2430 *Fax:* 212-964-2497
*Web Site:* www.milanostampa.com
*Key Personnel*
Chmn & Sales Rep: Rino Varrasso *Tel:* 917-225-9460 *E-mail:* rvarrasso@milanostampa-usa.com
Founded: 1998
Turnaround: 30 Workdays
Print Runs: 1,000 min - 3,000,000 max
Business from Other Countries: 75%

**Overseas Printing Corporation**
99 The Embarcadero, San Francisco, CA 94105
*Tel:* 415-835-9999 *Fax:* 415-835-9899
*Web Site:* www.overseasprinting.com
*Key Personnel*
Pres: Hal Belmont *E-mail:* hal@ overseasprinting.com
VP: Vito Badalamenti *E-mail:* vito@ overseasprinting.com
Founded: 1972
Complete hardcover & softcover book, calendar & catalog manufacturing. Full color separation with press proofs. We specialize in high quality museum, art & photography books, catalogs & calendars. As part of our comprehensive service, we perform traditional & side sewing, notch & perfect binding, spiral & twin wire-O, saddle stitching & 4-, 5- & 6- color printing. We represent sheetfed & web printing plants in Korea, Hong Kong/China, Singapore, Italy, Canada & the US. We specialize in the traditional & excel in the unusual & difficult jobs.
Print Runs: 500-150,000 sheetfed; 50,000-3,000,000 web printing.
Turnaround: 8 - 12 Weeks, or shorter depending on job requirements
Business from Other Countries: 10%

**Palace Press International - Corporate Headquarters**
17 Paul Dr, San Rafael, CA 94903
*Tel:* 415-526-1370 *Fax:* 415-526-1394
*E-mail:* info@palacepress.com
*Web Site:* www.palacepress.com
*Key Personnel*
CEO: Raoul Goff *E-mail:* raoul@palacepress.com
Gen Mgr: Michael Madden *E-mail:* michael@ palacepress.com
Founded: 1984
Turnaround: 90 Workdays
Print Runs: 3,000 min - 1,000,000 max
Business from Other Countries: 20%
*Branch Office(s)*
Palace Press International Los Angeles, 1499 Huntington Dr, Suite 408, South Pasadena, CA 91030, Contact: Roger Ma *Tel:* 626-282-8877 *Fax:* 626-282-6880 *E-mail:* roger@palacepress. com
Palace Press International New York, 180 Varick St, 10th fl, New York, NY 10014, Contact: Jessica Jones *Tel:* 212-462-2622 *Fax:* 212-463-9130 *E-mail:* jessica@palacepress.com

**Printing Corp of the Americas Inc**
620 SW 12 Ave, Fort Lauderdale, FL 33312
*Tel:* 954-781-8100 *Fax:* 954-781-8421
*Key Personnel*
Pres: Jan Tuchman
Founded: 1979
Turnaround: 5-10 Workdays
Print Runs: 500 min - 100,000 max
Business from Other Countries: 10%

**Taylor Publishing Company**
1550 W Mockingbird Lane, Dallas, TX 75235
*Tel:* 214-819-8226 *Toll Free Tel:* 800-677-2800
    *Fax:* 214-630-1852

*E-mail:* info@taylorpub.com
*Web Site:* www.taylorpub.com
*Key Personnel*
CEO: Dave Fiore
Dir, Fine Books & Div Sales Mgr: Jay Love
Founded: 1939
Turnaround: 45 Workdays
Print Runs: 300 min - 25,000 max
Business from Other Countries: 10%

**Times International Publishing**
Division of Times Publishing Ltd/Singapore
99 White Plains Rd, Tarrytown, NY 10591
*Tel:* 914-366-9888 *Fax:* 914-366-9898
*Web Site:* www.tpl.com.sg
*Key Personnel*
Cust Serv Exec: Bonnie Stone *E-mail:* bstone@ marshallcavendish.com
Sales Mgr: Suresh Kumar *E-mail:* skumar@ marshallcavendish.com
Founded: 1965
Print Runs: 2,000 min - 1,000,000 max
Business from Other Countries: 90%

**Toppan Printing Co America Inc**
Subsidiary of Toppan Printing Co Ltd
1110 Randolph Rd, Somerset, NJ 08873
*Tel:* 732-469-8400 *Fax:* 732-469-1868
*E-mail:* njsales@ta.toppan.com
*Web Site:* www.ta.toppan.com
*Key Personnel*
Pres & CEO: Seishi Tanoue
Sr VP, Sales: Al Starzyk
Sales Mgr: Rob Sternau
Founded: 1970
Turnaround: 3-5 Months
Business from Other Countries: 10%
*Branch Office(s)*
4551 Glencoe AveSuite 110, Marina del Rey, CA 90292, Sales Mgr: Yoshihei Okamoto *Tel:* 310-823-0050 *Fax:* 310-823-0777
650 Fifth Ave, 12th fl, New York, NY 10019

**Vicks Lithograph & Printing Corp**
5166 Commercial Dr, Yorkville, NY 13495
Mailing Address: PO Box 270, Yorkville, NY 13495-0270
*Tel:* 315-736-9344 *Fax:* 315-736-1901
*Web Site:* www.vickslitho.com
*Key Personnel*
Chmn: Dwight E "Duke" Vicks, Jr
Pres: Dwight E Vicks, III
Sales: Rick A Anderson *Tel:* 315-272-2489
    *E-mail:* randerson@vickslitho.com
Founded: 1918
Turnaround: 10-20 Workdays
Print Runs: 1,000 min - 100,000 max
Business from Other Countries: 10%
Membership(s): BMI; PIA/GATF

# Uruguay

**Barreiro y Ramos SA**
25 de Mayo, Esq J C Gomez, Casilla Correos, 15, 1430 Montevideo
*Tel:* (02) 96 23 58 *Fax:* (02) 96 23 58
*Telex:* 23901PB.CVJA.UY *Cable:* BAREIRAMOS
*Key Personnel*
President: Gaston Barreiro
Vice President: Guzman Barreiro
Founded: 1837
Print Runs: 1,000 min - 50,000 max
Business from Other Countries: 10%

# Prepress Services Index

# Prepress Services

This section includes companies throughout the world that offer a variety of prepress services. Those U.S. and Canadian companies with 10% or more of their business done outside North America are also included. Immediately preceding this section is an index classifying companies by services offered.

# Austria

**ADEVA (Akademische Druck-u Verlagsanstalt)**
Auersperggasse 12, 8010 Graz
Mailing Address: Postfach 598, 8011 Graz
*Tel:* (0316) 3644 *Fax:* (0316) 364424
*E-mail:* info@adeva.com
*Web Site:* www.adeva.com *Cable:* ADEVA-GRAZ
*Key Personnel*
Editor: Dr Michael Struzl *E-mail:* struzl@adeva.com
General Manager: Dr Ursula Struzl
 *E-mail:* struzl@adeva.com
Founded: 1949
Print Runs: 300 min - 10,000 max
Business from Other Countries: 80%
*Branch Office(s)*
Purgleitnergasse 10, Ecke Marburgerstr, 8042 Graz

**Akademische Druck- u Verlagsanstalt**, see ADEVA (Akademische Druck-u Verlagsanstalt)

**Dr Paul Struzl GmbH**, see ADEVA (Akademische Druck-u Verlagsanstalt)

# Belgium

**IMPF bvba**
Sint-Amandstr 18, 9000 Ghent
*Tel:* (09) 225 44 29 *Fax:* 058 315 77
*E-mail:* maarten@fotobeurs.com
*Web Site:* www.fotobeurs.com
*Key Personnel*
Manager: Xavier Dewulf
Founded: 1958
Business from Other Countries: 10%

**Drukkerij Lannoo NV** (Lannoo Printers)
Kasteelstr 97, 8700 Tielt
*Tel:* (051) 42 42 11 *Fax:* (051) 40 70 70
*E-mail:* lannoo@lannooprint.be
*Web Site:* www.lannooprint.be
*Key Personnel*
General Manager & Marketing Dir: Stefaan Lannoo *E-mail:* stefaan.lannoo@lannooprint.be
Founded: 1909
Turnaround: 10 Workdays
Print Runs: 100 min - 1,000,000 max
Business from Other Countries: 30%

# Canada

**Aardvark Enterprises**
Division of Speers Investments Ltd
204 Millbank Dr SW, Calgary, AB T2Y 2H9
*Tel:* 403-256-4639
*Key Personnel*
Pres: J Alvin Speers
Founded: 1970 (Small Press Pioneers)

Turnaround: 30 Workdays
Print Runs: 10 min - 1,000 max
Business from Other Countries: 25%

**Barcode Graphics Inc**
25 Brodie Dr, Unit 5, Richmond Hill, ON L4B 3K7
*Tel:* 905-770-1154 *Toll Free Tel:* 800-263-3669
 *Fax:* 905-787-1575
*E-mail:* info@barcodegraphics.com
*Web Site:* www.barcodegraphics.com
*Key Personnel*
Pres: John Herzig *E-mail:* jherzig@barcodegraphics.com
Founded: 1981
Turnaround: 1-2 Workdays
Print Runs: 2,000,000 max
Business from Other Countries: 10%

**David Berman Developments Inc**
283 Ferndale, Ottawa, ON K1Z 6P9
*Tel:* 613-728-6777 *Fax:* 613-728-2867
*E-mail:* info@timewise.net
*Web Site:* www.timewise.net
*Key Personnel*
Pres: David Berman
Founded: 1987
Business from Other Countries: 50%

**Coach House Printing**
401 Huron St, Rear, Toronto, ON M5S 2G5
*Tel:* 416-979-2217 *Fax:* 416-977-1158
*E-mail:* mail@chbooks.com
*Web Site:* www.chbooks.com
*Key Personnel*
Publr: Stan Bevington
Edit Consultant: Darren Wershler-Henry
Founded: 1965
Turnaround: 14 Workdays
Print Runs: 200 min - 2,000 max
Business from Other Countries: 10%

**Leanne Franson**
4323 Parthenais, Montreal, QC H2H 2G2
*Tel:* 514-526-4236 *Fax:* 514-526-0972
*E-mail:* inksports@videotron.ca
*Web Site:* www.theispot.com/artist/LFranson
Founded: 1991
Turnaround: 3-7 plus Workdays
Business from Other Countries: 50%
Membership(s): Association des Illustrateurs et d'Illustratries du Quebec

**Girol Books Inc**
120 Somerset St W, Ottawa, ON K2P 0H8
Mailing Address: Box 5473, Sta F, Ottawa, ON K2C 3M1
*Tel:* 613-233-9044 *Fax:* 613-233-9044
*E-mail:* info@girol.com
*Web Site:* www.girol.com
*Key Personnel*
Owner: Miguel Angel Giella; Peter Roster
Mgr: Leslie Roster *E-mail:* lroster@girol.com
Founded: 1975
Business from Other Countries: 30%

**Celia Godkin**
Mod 6, Comp 12, 10 James St, Frankville, ON K0E 1H0
*Tel:* 613-275-7204 *Fax:* 613-275-7204

*E-mail:* celiagodkin@ripnet.com
*Web Site:* www.canscaip.org/bios/godkin.html
Founded: 1983
Business from Other Countries: 10%
Membership(s): CANSCAIP; The Writers' Union of Canada

**Maracle Press Ltd**
1156 King St E, Oshawa, ON L1H 7N4
Mailing Address: Box 606, Oshawa, ON L1H 7N4
*Tel:* 905-723-3438 *Toll Free Tel:* 800-558-8604
 *Fax:* 905-428-6024
*E-mail:* info@maraclepress.com
*Web Site:* www.maraclepress.com
*Key Personnel*
Pres & Gen Mgr: Bruce A Fenton
 *E-mail:* bfenton@maraclepress.com
VP, Busn Devt: Ronald G Taylor
 *E-mail:* rtaylor@maraclepress.com
Founded: 1920
Turnaround: 10 Workdays
Print Runs: 500 min - 500,000 max
Business from Other Countries: 25%
Membership(s): BMI

**Preney Print & Litho Inc**
1457 Lauzon Rd, Windsor, ON N8S 3N2
*Tel:* 519-966-3412 *Toll Free Tel:* 877-870-4164
 *Fax:* 519-966-4996
*E-mail:* contactus@preneyprint.com
*Web Site:* www.preneyprint.com
Founded: 1972
Turnaround: 15 Workdays
Print Runs: 2,000 min
Business from Other Countries: 20%

**Printcrafters Inc**
78 Hutchings St, Winnipeg, MB R2X 3B1
*Tel:* 204-633-7117 *Fax:* 204-694-1519
*E-mail:* info@printcraftersinc.com
*Web Site:* www.printcraftersinc.com
*Key Personnel*
Pres: Bob Payne *Tel:* 204-633-7117 ext 223
 *Fax:* 204-694-1594 *E-mail:* bpayne@printcraftersinc.com
Founded: 1996 (Employee owned)
Turnaround: 5-20 Workdays
Print Runs: 200,000 min - 500,000 max
Business from Other Countries: 30%
Membership(s): Canadian Printing Industries Association

**PrintWest**
1150 Eighth Ave, Regina, SK S4R 1C9
*Tel:* 306-525-2304 *Toll Free Tel:* 800-236-6438
 *Fax:* 306-757-2439
*E-mail:* general@printwest.com
*Web Site:* www.printwest.com
*Key Personnel*
CEO: Wayne UnRuh
VP, Sales: Ken Benson
Founded: 1992
Turnaround: 15 Workdays
Print Runs: 1,000 min - 100,000 max
Business from Other Countries: 15%
*Branch Office(s)*
Box 2500, 2310 Millar Ave, Saskatoon, SK S7K 2C4 *Tel:* 306-665-3560 *Fax:* 306-653-1255

**Schawk**
543 Richmond St W, Suite 125, Toronto, ON
M5V 1Y6
*Tel:* 416-703-1445 *Fax:* 416-703-1494
*Web Site:* www.schawk.com
*Key Personnel*
Pres: Bob Cockerill
Founded: 1965
Business from Other Countries: 10%

**David Shaw & Associates Ltd**
108 Ranleigh Ave, Toronto, ON M4N 1W9
*Tel:* 416-487-2019 *Fax:* 416-486-1744
*E-mail:* djshaw@simpatico.ca
*Key Personnel*
Pres: David Shaw
Founded: 1977
Business from Other Countries: 25%

**Barbara Spurll Illustration**
1180 Danforth Ave, Toronto, ON M4J 1M3
*Tel:* 416-594-6594
*E-mail:* bspurll@yahoo.ca
*Web Site:* www.barbaraspurll.com
*Key Personnel*
Contact: Barbara Spurll
Founded: 1975
Business from Other Countries: 70%

**Transcontinental Printing Book Group**
Division of Transcontinental Group
395 Lebeau Blvd, St-Laurent, QC H4N 1S2
*Tel:* 514-337-8560 *Toll Free Tel:* 800-361-3599
*Fax:* 514-339-5230
*Web Site:* www.transcontinental.com; www.
transcontinental-printing.com
*Key Personnel*
VP, Book Group: Jacques Gregoire
Dir, Strategic Busn Devt: Denis
Beaudin *Tel:* 514-339-2220 ext 4101
*E-mail:* beaudind@transcontinental.ca
Founded: 1976
Turnaround: 4 weeks casebound; 3 weeks soft-
cover
Print Runs: 1,000 min
Business from Other Countries: 15%
*Branch Office(s)*
614 Yates Ave, Calumet City, IL 60409, United
States, Contact: Kristopher D Levy *Tel:* 708-
832-1528 *Fax:* 708-832-9510 *E-mail:* kris.
levy@transcontinental.ca (Midwest)
3653 W Leland Ave, Suite One W, Chicago,
IL 60625, United States, Contact: Tim Taylor *Tel:* 773-583-8155 *Fax:* 773-583-8162
*E-mail:* tim.taylor@transcontinental.ca (Midwest)
10 Rountree Dr, PO Box 2551, Duxbury, MA
02331, United States, Contact: Ed Catania
*Tel:* 508-881-1119 *E-mail:* ecatania@attbi.com
(East Coast)
393 Highland Ave, Quincy, MA 02170-
4013, United States, Contact: Mike Gazzola *Tel:* 617-696-1435 *Fax:* 617-696-1025
*E-mail:* mikebook@attbi.com (East Coast)
37 Herman Blvd, Franklin Square, NY
11010, United States, Contact: Tom Malloy *Tel:* 516-775-2980 *Fax:* 516-488-0253
*E-mail:* tmmalloy@aol.com (NY)
3175 Summit Square Dr, Suite C9, Oakton,
VA 22124, United States, Contact: David
Avesian *Tel:* 703-255-1332 *Fax:* 703-255-1343
*E-mail:* davesian@cox.rr.com (Southeast)
559 Lowrys Rd, Parksville, BC V9P 2R8, Contact: Mike Davies *Tel:* 250-248-9700 *Fax:* 250-
248-2353 *E-mail:* bookguys@shaw.ca (West
Coast)
15373 Victoria Ave, White Rock, BC V4B 1H1,
Contact: Wade Davies *Tel:* 604-535-8800
*Fax:* 604-535-8802 *E-mail:* daviesw@shaw.ca
(West Coast)

490 Wilfred Dr, Peterborough, ON K9K
2H1, Contact: Tom Lang *Tel:* 705-760-
9594 *Fax:* 705-760-9485 *E-mail:* langt@
transcontinental.ca (NY)

**Tri-Graphic Printing (Ottawa) Ltd**
485 Industrial Ave, Ottawa, ON K1G 0Z1
*Tel:* 613-731-7441 *Toll Free Tel:* 800-267-9750
*Fax:* 613-731-3741
*Web Site:* www.tri-graphic.com
*Key Personnel*
VP & Gen Mgr: Doug K Doane
*E-mail:* ddoane@tri-graphic.com
VP, Prodn & Servs: Fred Malleau *Tel:* 905-665-
8500 *E-mail:* fmalleau@tri-graphic.com
Founded: 1968
Turnaround: 10-15 Workdays
Print Runs: 1,000 min - 100,000 max
Business from Other Countries: 10%
*Sales Office(s):* 213 Byron St S, Suite 201,
Whitby, ON L1N 4P7, VP Prod Devt: Fred
Malleau *Tel:* 905-665-8500 *Fax:* 905-665-8501
*E-mail:* fmalleau@tri-graphic.com
Membership(s): BMI

**University of Toronto Press Inc**
Printing Division, 5201 Dufferin St, North York,
ON M3H 5T8
*Tel:* 416-667-7767 *Fax:* 416-667-7803
*E-mail:* printing@utpress.utoronto.ca
*Web Site:* www.utpress.utoronto.ca
*Key Personnel*
Pres & Publr: John Yates
Founded: 1901
Turnaround: 10-15 Workdays
Print Runs: 10 min - 200,000 max
Business from Other Countries: 15%
Membership(s): BMI

# Denmark

**Bianco Lunos Bogtrykkeri AS**
Subsidiary of Carl Allers Etablissement AS
Otto Monsteds Gade 3, 1571 Copenhagen V
*Tel:* (03) 615 3300 *Fax:* (03) 615 3301
*E-mail:* direktionen@aller.dk
*Web Site:* www.aller.dk
*Key Personnel*
General Manager: J Heede Sorensen
Founded: 1871

# Finland

**Gummerus Printing**
Division of Gummerus Kirjapaino Oy
Subsidiary of Gummerus Oy
Alasinkatu 1-3, 40351 Jyvaskyla
Mailing Address: PO Box 444, 40351 Jyvaskyla
*Tel:* (014) 683 525 *Fax:* (014) 685 166
*E-mail:* printing@gummerus.fi
*Web Site:* www.gummerus.fi
*Key Personnel*
Marketing Dir: Mr Martti Aaltonen
*E-mail:* martti.aaltonen@gummerus.fi
Man Dir: Mr Jarmo Porkka
Founded: 1872
Turnaround: 20-60 Workdays
Print Runs: 1,000 min - 100,000 max
Business from Other Countries: 15%

# France

**Signes du Monde**
1424 ch du Dupere Hubert Saint-Genez, 40380
Povartin
*Tel:* (06) 12 99 73 37 *Fax:* (0561) 575717
*Key Personnel*
Production: Hubert Saint-Genez

# Germany

**Baader Buch- u Offsetdruckerei GmbH & Co
KG CL**
Gutenbergstr 1, 72522 Muensingen Wurh
*Tel:* (07381) 791 *Fax:* (07371) 4114 *Cable:*
BAADER-MUNSINGEN
Founded: 1835
Turnaround: 1 Workday
Print Runs: 1,000 min - 15,000 max

**Fachhochschule Stuttgart - Hochschule der
Medien (HdM)**
Nobelstr 10, 70569 Stuttgart
*Tel:* (0711) 685 2807 *Fax:* (0711) 685 6650
*E-mail:* info@hdm-stuttgart.de
*Web Site:* www.hdm-stuttgart.de
*Telex:* 725 185 fhd d
*Key Personnel*
Contact: Prof Eduard H Schoenstedt

**Hochschule der Medien (HdM)**, see
Fachhochschule Stuttgart - Hochschule der
Medien (HdM)

**C Maurer Druck und Verlag**
Schubartstr 21, 73312 Geislingen/Steige
*Tel:* (07331) 930-0 *Fax:* (07331) 93 0-190
*Web Site:* www.maurer-online.de
*Key Personnel*
Management: Carl-Otto Maurer *Tel:* 930-112
*E-mail:* c.maurer@maurer-online.de
Sales: Christoph Traub *Tel:* 930-120
*E-mail:* traub@maurer-online.de
Founded: 1856

**Media-Print Informationstechnologie GmbH**
Eggertstr 28, 33100 Paderborn
*Tel:* (05251) 522 300 *Fax:* (05251) 522 480
*E-mail:* rings@mediaprint-pb.de
*Web Site:* www.mediaprint-pb.de
*Key Personnel*
Man Dir: Rainer Rings *Tel:* (05251) 522-460
*E-mail:* rings@mediaprint.de
Contact: Udo Sengstock *E-mail:* sengst@
mediaprint.de
Founded: 1993
Turnaround: 5-10 Workdays
Print Runs: 100 min - 30,000 max
Business from Other Countries: 10%

**MOHN Media**
Subsidiary of Bertelsmann AG
Carl-Bertelsmann-Str 161M, 33311 Guetersloh
*Tel:* (05241) 80 56 29 *Fax:* (05241) 1 66 92
*E-mail:* mohnmedia@bertelsmann.de
*Web Site:* www.mohnmedia.de
*Key Personnel*
Contact: Alfred Hahn
Founded: 1824
Business from Other Countries: 25%

**Oertel & Sporer GmbH & Co**
Burgstr 1-7, 72764 Reutlingen
*Tel:* (07121) 302555 *Fax:* (07121) 302558

*Key Personnel*
Publisher: Valdo Lehari
Manager & Printer: Ermo Lehari
Print Runs: 500 min - 50,000 max

**Priese GmbH & Co**
Auerbacher Str 9, 14193 Berlin
*Tel:* (030) 8263024 *Fax:* (030) 3249630
*Key Personnel*
Contact: Elma Priese; Hans Joachim Priese

**Topic Verlag GmbH**
Birkenstr 10, 85757 Karlsfeld B Munich
*Tel:* (08131) 97038 *Fax:* (08131) 98404
Founded: 1982
Business from Other Countries: 50%

**Vier-Tuerme GmbH Benedikt Press**
Schweinfurter Str 40, 97359 Muensterschwarzach
  Abtei
*Tel:* (09324) 20292 *Fax:* (09324) 20495
*E-mail:* info@vier-tuerme.de
*Web Site:* www.vier-tuerme.de
*Key Personnel*
Contact: Josef Stoecklein
Founded: 1951
Turnaround: 8-16 Workdays
Print Runs: 300 min - 20,000 max
Business from Other Countries: 5%

# Hong Kong

**Bookbuilders Ltd**
Unit J 13/F Yeung Yiu Chung No 8 Industrial Bldg, 20 Wang Hoi Rd, Kowloon Bay, Kowloon
*Tel:* 27968123 *Fax:* 27968267; 27968690
*E-mail:* lph@netvigator.com
*Key Personnel*
Man Dir: Leslie Henman
General Manager: Edward Chan

**Bright Arts Hong Kong Ltd**
Tung Chong Factory Bldg, 11/F, Block D, 659 Kings Rd, North Point
*Tel:* 25620119 *Fax:* 25657031
*E-mail:* william@brightartshk.com
*Web Site:* www.brightartshk.com
*Key Personnel*
Man Dir: Sunny Shum
Dir, China Operations: Jimmy Wong
Customer Service Manager, China: Tino Kwok
Customer Service Manager, Hong Kong: William Yue

**Bright Future Printing Co Ltd**
Sunview Industrial Building, Block D, 5/F, 3 On Yip St, Chai Wan
*Tel:* 2515 1776 *Fax:* 2897 2799; 2558 1717
*Key Personnel*
Chairman: Richard Ng
Turnaround: 60 Workdays (including shipping)
Print Runs: 3,000 min - 30,000 max
Business from Other Countries: 30%

**C & C Offset Printing Co Ltd**
Subsidiary of C & C Joint Printing Co (HK) Ltd under Sino United (Holdings) Hong Kong Ltd
C&C Bldg, floors 1-9, 36 Ting Lai Rd, Tai Po, New Territories
*Tel:* 2666-4988 *Fax:* 2666-4938
*E-mail:* offsetprinting@candcprinting.com
*Web Site:* www.ccoffset.com
*Key Personnel*
Dir & General Manager: Jackson Leung
Deputy Man Dir: Kee Lee

Deputy General Manager: Ivy Lam
Assistant General Manager: Kit Wong
Senior Sales Manager (Special Project): Francis Ho
Dir & Executive Vice President, C & C Offset Printing Co (USA) Inc, Portland OR, USA: Charles H Clark, IV *E-mail:* cclark@ccoffset.com
Development Manager, C & C Offset Printing Co (USA) Inc, Portland, OR, USA: Jenny Whittier *E-mail:* jwhittier@ccoffset.com
Customer Service Manager, C & C Offset Printing Co (USA) Inc, Portland, OR, USA: Ernest Li *E-mail:* ernestli@ccoffset.com
Dir & Executive Vice President, C & C Offset Printing Co (NY) Inc, New York, NY, USA: Simon Chan *E-mail:* schan@ccoffset.com
Assistant General Manager-China Sales, C & C Joint Printing Co (Ghuangdong) Ltd, Shenzhen, China: Simon Zhang
President, C & C Printing Japan Co Ltd, Tokyo, Japan: Yamamoto Masaaki
Customer Service Manager, C & C Offset Printing Co (NYC), Inc, New York, NY: Frances Harkness *E-mail:* fharkness@ccoffset.com
Man Dir, C & C Joint Printing Co (Beijing), Ltd, Beijing, China: Zhang Lin Gui
Dir, C & C Offset Printing Co (UK), Ltd: Tracy Broderick
Account Manager, C & C Offset Printing Co (UK) Ltd: Fia Fornari
Founded: 1980
Turnaround: 30-42 Workdays for printing, binding & book finishing
Print Runs: 2,000 min - 1,000,000 max
Business from Other Countries: 60%
*Branch Office(s)*
C & C Joint Printing Co (Guangdong) Ltd, Chunhu Industrial Estate, Pinghu, Long Gang, Shenzhen 518111, China *Tel:* (0755) 2845-8333 *Fax:* (0755) 2845-9911 *E-mail:* guangdong@candcprinting.com *Web Site:* www.candcprinting.com (Plant)
C & C Printing Japan Co Ltd, 2-6-12 Hitotsubashi, Tozaido Bldg 3F, Chiyoda-ku, Tokyo 101-0003, Japan *Tel:* (03) 5216-4580 *Fax:* (03) 5216-4610 *E-mail:* mail@candcprinting.co.jp *Web Site:* www.candcprinting.co.jp
C & C Joint Printing Co (Guangdong) Ltd, 7/F, Flat H, Green View Apartment, No 38, Hou Guang Ping Hu Tong, Xi Cheng Qu, Beijing 100035, China *Tel:* (010) 6650-3176 *Fax:* (010) 6650-3175 *E-mail:* beijingoffice@candcprinting.com
C & C Joint Printing Co (Guangdong) Ltd, Room 304, Fang Fa Bldg, No 29, 165 Ave, Dongzhuanbang Rd, Shanghai 200050, China *Tel:* (021) 6240-1305 *Fax:* (021) 6240-1305 *E-mail:* shanghaioffice@candcprinting.com
C & C Offset Printing Co (UK) Ltd, 2 New Burlington St, 4th floor, London W1S 2JE, United Kingdom, Dir: Tracy Broderick *Tel:* (020) 7287 7787 *Fax:* (020) 7287 7187 *E-mail:* tracy@candcoffset.co.uk
*U.S. Office(s):* C & C Offset Printing Co (USA) Inc, 2632 SE 25th Ave, Suite D, Portland, OR 97202, United States *Tel:* 503-233-1834 *Fax:* 503-233-7815 *E-mail:* portlandinfo@ccoffset.com (shipping)
C & C Offset Printing Co (NY) Inc, 401 Broadway, Suite 2015, New York, NY 10013-3004, United States *Tel:* 212-431-4210 *Fax:* 212-431-3960 *E-mail:* newyorkinfo@ccoffset.com

**Caritas Printing Training Centre**
Caritas House, 3rd floor, Block D, 2 Caine Rd, Hong Kong
*Tel:* 25261148 *Fax:* 25371231
*E-mail:* info@caritas.org.hk
*Web Site:* www.caritas.hk
*Key Personnel*
General Manager: Isaac Mak

Print Runs: 1,000 min - 100,000 max
Business from Other Countries: 50%

**Colorprint Offset**
Unit 1808-9, 18/F, 8 Commercial Tower, 8 Sun Yip St, Chai Wan
*Tel:* 2896-7777 *Fax:* 2889-6606
*E-mail:* info@cpo.com.hk
*Web Site:* www.cpo.com.hk
*Key Personnel*
Sales Manager: Jennifer Weston *Tel:* 2903-5062
Contact: Eva Lav; Ian Lee
Turnaround: 30-40 Workdays
Print Runs: 3,000 min - 100,000 max
Business from Other Countries: 80%
*Sales Office(s):* Gainsborough House, 81 Oxford St, London W1R 1RB, United Kingdom *Tel:* (02) 7903-5060 *Fax:* (02) 7903-5063 *E-mail:* uk@cpo.com.hk
80 Park Ave, Suite 10N, New York, NY 10016, United States *Tel:* 212-681-9400 *Fax:* 212-681-9362 *E-mail:* ny@cpo.com.hk

**Cristy's Atelier**
37-39 Jervois St, Sheung Wan
*Tel:* 25418609 *Fax:* 28540995
*E-mail:* cristys@intercon.net
Founded: 1982

**Dai Nippon Printing Co (Hong Kong) Ltd**
Division of Dai Nippon Printing Co Ltd
Tsuen Wan Industrial Centre, 2-5/F, 220-248 Texaco Rd, Tsuen Wan, New Territories
*Tel:* 2408-0188 *Fax:* 2408-8479
*E-mail:* info@mail.dnp.co.jp
*Web Site:* www.dnp.co.jp *Cable:* DNPICO
*Key Personnel*
Administration & Finance Dir: Mr K Miya
Print Runs: 5,000 min - 200,000 max
Business from Other Countries: 85%
*Branch Office(s)*
DNP IMS America Corp, 4524 Enterprise Dr NW, Concord, NC 28027, United States *Tel:* 704-784-8100 *Fax:* 704-784-2777
Dai Nippon Printing Co Ltd, 1-1-1, Ichigaya-Kagacho, Shinjuku-ku, Tokyo, Japan
Dai Nippon Printing Co (Australia) Pty Ltd, St Martins Tower, Level 10, Suite 1002, 31 Market St, Sydney, NSW 2000, Australia *Tel:* (02) 9267-8166 *Fax:* (02) 9267-9533
Dai Nippon Printing Co (Singapore) Pte Ltd, 896 Dunearn Rd, No 04-09, Sime Darby Centre, Singapore 589472, Singapore *Tel:* 469-7611 *Fax:* 469-8486
Dai Nippon Printing Co (UK) Ltd, 27 Throgmorton St, 4th floor, London EC2N 2AQ, United Kingdom *Tel:* (020) 7588-2088 *Fax:* (020) 7588-2089
DAI Nippon Printing (Europe) GmbH, Berliner Allee 26, 40212 Dusseldorf, Germany *Tel:* (0211) 8620-180 *Fax:* (0211) 8620-1895
DAI Nippon Printing (Taiwan) Co, LTD, 44 Chung-Shan N Rd, RMD 6th floor, Sec 2 Taipei 104, Taiwan, China *Tel:* (02) 2327-8311 *Fax:* (02) 2327-8283
DNP Denmark A/S, Skruegangen 2, DK-2690 Karlslunde, Denmark *Tel:* 4616-5100 *Fax:* 4616-5200
P T Dai Nippon Printing Indonesia, Kawasan Industri Pulogadung, Jalan Pulogadung Kaveling II, Blok H No 2-3, Jakarta Timur, Indonesia *Tel:* (021) 4610313 *Fax:* (021) 4605795
PT Tien Wah Press Indonesia, Janlan Tenaru, Desa Cangkir, Kec Driyorejo, Gresik 61177, Indonesia *Tel:* (031) 7507403
TWP Sdn Bhd, 89, Jalan Tampoi, Kawasan Perindustrian Tampoi, 80350 Johor Bahru, Johor, Malaysia *Tel:* (07) 2369899 *Fax:* (07) 2363148
Tien Wah Press Pte Ltd, 4 Pandan Crescent, Singapore 128475, Singapore *Tel:* 466-6222 *Fax:* 469-3894

*Sales Office(s):* DNP America LLC, Los Angeles Office, 3858 Carson St, Suite 300, Torrance, CA 90503, United States *Tel:* 310-540-5123 *Fax:* 310-543-3260

DNP America LLC, Silicon Valley Office, 3235 Kifer Rd, Suite 100, Santa Clara, CA 95051, United States *Tel:* 408-735-8880 *Fax:* 408-735-0453

*U.S. Office(s):* DNP Corporation USA, San Francisco Office, 577 Airport Blvd, Suite 620, Burlingame, CA 94010, United States *Tel:* 650-558-4050 *Fax:* 650-340-6095

DNP Corporation USA, New York Office, 335 Madison Ave, 3rd floor, New York, NY 10017, United States *Tel:* 212-503-1850 *Fax:* 212-286-1490

### Elegance Finance Printing Services Ltd
Subsidiary of Elegance Printing Company Limited
2401 Alexandra House, 16-20 Chater Rd, Central Hong Kong
*Tel:* 2283 2222 *Fax:* 2521 3616
*E-mail:* saledept@elegancefinptg.com
Print Runs: 500 min - 7,200 max
Business from Other Countries: 2%

### Everbest Printing Co Ltd
Ko Fai Industrial Bldg, Block C5, 10th floor, 7 Ko Fai Rd, Yau Tong, Kowloon
*Tel:* 2727 4433 *Fax:* 2772 7687
*E-mail:* sales@everbest.com.hk
*Web Site:* www.everbest.com
*Key Personnel*
Man Dir: Kenneth Chung
Customer Account Executive: Frankie Lee; Ronny Ng
Founded: 1954
Turnaround: 28 Workdays
Print Runs: 1,000 min - 1,000,000 max
Business from Other Countries: 90%
*Branch Office(s)*
Everbest Printing, 100 Macauley Rd, Stanmore, NSW 2048, Australia, Contact: Lionel Marz *Tel:* (02) 9568-5879 *Fax:* (02) 9568-8694 *E-mail:* lmarz@onaustralia.com.au (Australia & New Zealand office)
Everbest Canada, 50 Emblem Court, Scarborough, ON M1S 1B1, Canada, Connie Chung *Tel:* 416-286-2525 *Fax:* 416-286-2526 *E-mail:* everbestcan@aprinco.com
*U.S. Office(s):* Spectrum Books Inc, 2300 Bethards Dr, Suite C, Santa Rosa, CA 95405-8658, United States, Contact: Duncan McCallum *Tel:* 707-542-6044 *Fax:* 707-542-6045 *E-mail:* specbooks@aol.com
Four Colour Imports, 2843 Brownsboro Rd, Suite 102, Louisville, KY 40206, United States, George Dick *Tel:* 502-896-9644 *Fax:* 502-896-9594 *E-mail:* sales@fourcolor.com *Web Site:* www.fourcolor.com
Everbest Midwest, 6428 Margaret's Lane, Edina, MN 55439, United States, Dr Josie Lo *Tel:* 612-944-0854 *Fax:* 912-829-7670 *E-mail:* sklo@aol.com

### Golden Cup Printing Co Ltd
Seapower Industrial Centre, 6/F, 177 Hoi Bun Rd, Kwun Tong, Kowloon
*Tel:* 2343 4254; 23434255 *Fax:* 23415426
*E-mail:* sales@goldencup.com.hk
*Web Site:* www.goldencup.com.hk
*Key Personnel*
Man Dir: Yeung Kam Kai
General Manager: W K Ngan
Sales Manager: Mary Yeung *E-mail:* mary@goldencup.com.hk
Founded: 1971
Turnaround: 25 Workdays
Print Runs: 5,000 min - 200,000 max
Business from Other Countries: 80%

*Branch Office(s)*
Dongguan, China
Guangdong, China
Kunming, China
Yunan, China

### The Green Pagoda Press Ltd
13/F Block A, Tung Chong Factory Bldg, 633-655 King's Rd, North Point
*Tel:* 2561 1924 *Fax:* 2811 0946
*E-mail:* gpinfo@gpp.com.hk
*Web Site:* www.greenpagoda.com
*Key Personnel*
Man Dir: Derek Yip
Founded: 1957
Turnaround: 1-14 days
Print Runs: 10 min - 500,000 max
Business from Other Countries: 30%

### H K Scanner Arts International Ltd
Block B1, 6/F Fortune Factory Bldg, 40 Lee Chung St, Chai Wan
*Tel:* 29760289 *Fax:* 29760292
*E-mail:* hksagp@netvigator.com
*Key Personnel*
Dir, Sales & Marketing: Wayne C Ling
Man Dir: Y C Luk

### Hindy's Enterprise Co Ltd
Flat A 20/F, Melbourne Industrial Bldg, 16 Wetlands Rd, Quarry Bay
*Tel:* 25166318 *Fax:* 25165161
*Key Personnel*
General Manager: Cecilia Chung

### Hung Hing Off-set Printing Co Ltd
Subsidiary of Hung Hing Printing Group Ltd
Tai Po Industrial Estate, 17-19 Dai Hei St, New Territories
*Tel:* 2664 8682 *Fax:* 2664 2070
*E-mail:* info@hhop.com.hk
*Web Site:* www.hhop.com.hk
*Key Personnel*
Man Dir: Matthew Yum *E-mail:* matthew@hhop.com.hk
Contact: Yam Cheong Hung
Founded: 1950
Turnaround: 20-30 Workdays
Print Runs: 5,000 min - 1,000,000 max
Business from Other Countries: 15%

### Icicle/Papercom
Formerly Paper Communication Printing Express Ltd
3rd floor, South West, Warwick House West Wing, Taikoo Place, 979 King's Rd, Quarry Bay
*Tel:* 2235 2880
*Web Site:* www.papercom.com.hk
*Key Personnel*
Business Development: Bonnie Chan *Tel:* 2235 2888 *Fax:* 2135 6809 *E-mail:* bonnie.chan@icicle.com.hk
Founded: 1981
BISAC compatible software
Turnaround: 28 to 56 Workdays
Print Runs: 1,000 min - 3,000,000 max
Business from Other Countries: 90%

### Image Printing Company Ltd
Unit 4, 4/F Cornell Centre, 50 Wing Tai Rd, Chai Wan
*Tel:* 2873 2633 *Fax:* 2558 3044
*E-mail:* imageprt@pop3.hknet.com
*Key Personnel*
Man Dir: Philip Chow Sung Ming
Founded: 1992
Print Runs: 1,000 min - 50,000 max
Business from Other Countries: 50%

### Leo Paper Products Ltd
7/F, Kader Bldg, 22 Kai Cheung Rd, Kowloon Bay, Kowloon
*Tel:* 28841374 *Fax:* 25130698
*E-mail:* lpp@leo.com.hk
*Web Site:* www.leo.com.hk
*Key Personnel*
Deputy Man Dir: Burman Tam *E-mail:* burman@leo.com.hk
Founded: 1991
Turnaround: 15-30 Workdays
Print Runs: 5,000 min
*Parent Company:* Leo Paper Bags Manufacturing Ltd
*Branch Office(s)*
Leo Paper USA, 1180 NW Maple St, Suite 102, Issaquah, WA 98027, United States, Contact: Bijan Pakzad *Tel:* 425-646-8801 *Fax:* 425-646-8805 *E-mail:* sales@leousa.com
Leo Paper USA - New York, 27 W 24 St, Suite 701, New York, NY 10010-3204, United States *Tel:* 917-305-0708 *Fax:* 917-305-0709 *E-mail:* sales@leousanewyork.com
*Sales Office(s):* Leo Paper Products (Europe) BVBA, Keizerstr 5, 2000 Antwerp, Belgium, Sales Dir: Jan Van Gijsel *Tel:* (03) 203-0912 *Fax:* (03) 255-1303 *E-mail:* leo@leo-europe.com
Leo Paper Products (UK) Ltd, St Michaels House, 94 High St, Wallingford, Oxon OX10 0BW *Tel:* (01491) 827827 *Fax:* (01491) 837127 *E-mail:* info@leouk.com

### Leo Reprographic Ltd
7/F Kader Bldg, 22 Kai Cheung Rd, Kowloon Bay, Kowloon
*Tel:* (02) 25696293 *Fax:* (02) 25138400
*E-mail:* lrg@leo.com.hk
*Web Site:* www.leo.com.hk
*Key Personnel*
Managing Deputy Dir: Burman Tam *E-mail:* burman@leo.com.hk
Founded: 1991
Turnaround: 7 Workdays for 128pp A4 size
*Parent Company:* Leo Paper Bags Manufacturing Ltd
*Sales Office(s):* Leo Marketing Ltd, The Malthouse, Malthouse Sq, Princes Risborough, Bucks HP27 9AB, United Kingdom, Director: Sally Wood *Tel:* (018) 274-244 *Fax:* (018) 275-105 *E-mail:* sallywood.leo@btinternet.com
Leo Paper Products (Europe) BVBA, De Wilde Zee, Wiegstraat 19, 2000 Antwerp, Belgium, Sales Director: Jan Van Gijsel *Tel:* (03) 203-0912 *Fax:* (03) 255-1303 *E-mail:* leo@leo-europe.com
*U.S. Office(s):* Leo Paper USA, 1180 NW Maple St, Suite 102, Issaquah, WA 98027, United States, Contact: Bijan Pakzad *Tel:* 425-646-8801 *Fax:* 425-646-8805 *E-mail:* sales@leousa.com

### Mei Ka Printing & Publishing Enterprise Ltd
Cheung Ka Industrial Bldg, 9/F Block B, 180 Connaught Rd W, West Hong Kong
*Tel:* 2540 1131 *Fax:* 2559 8718; 2559 7137
*E-mail:* mkpp@netvigator.com
*Web Site:* www.meika-printing.com
*Key Personnel*
Dir: Hong Chin Huo

### Midas Printing Ltd
1/F, 100 Texaco Rd, Tsuen Wan, New Territories
*Tel:* 2407 6888 *Fax:* 2408 0611
*E-mail:* info@midasprinting.com
*Web Site:* www.midasprinting.com
*Key Personnel*
Project Manager: Raymond Chan
Executive Dir: Gloria Y P Kan
Contact: Annie Wong *E-mail:* annie@midasprinting.com
Founded: 1990

Turnaround: 14-21 Workdays
Print Runs: 5,000 min - 100,000 max
Business from Other Countries: 25%

**New Arts Graphic Reproduction Co Ltd**
Loks Industrial Bldg, 4/F, 204 Tsat Tse Mui Rd,
    North Point
*Tel:* 25641323; 25618161 *Fax:* 25658262
*E-mail:* newarts@writeme.com
*Key Personnel*
Man Dir: Paul Sik-Kwong Choy
Manager: Andrew Choy *E-mail:* andchoy@
    netvigator.com
Founded: 1970
Business from Other Countries: 50%

**Paper Communication Printing Express Ltd**,
    see Icicle/Papercom

**Rainbow Graphic & Printing Co Ltd**
Tseung Kwan O Industrial Estate, 8 Chun Ying
    St, 4/F, Kowloon
*Tel:* 27523423 *Fax:* 28974890
*E-mail:* rgarts@netvigator.com
*Telex:* 61310 RBART HX
*Key Personnel*
General Manager: Willie Lim *E-mail:* willylim@
    netvigator.com
Business from Other Countries: 90%

**SNP Best-Set Typesetter Ltd**
Wing On House, 10th floor, 71 Des Voeux Rd C,
    Central
*Tel:* 2897 6033 *Fax:* 2897 5170
*E-mail:* bestset@snpcorp.com
*Web Site:* www.bestset-typesetter.com
*Key Personnel*
Dir (Hong Kong): Johnson Yeung *Tel:* 852-289-
    6033 *E-mail:* johnson@bestset-typesetter.com
Manager: Cynthia Hui *E-mail:* cynthiahui@
    snpcorp.com
Sales Rep: Wai Man Yeung
    *E-mail:* waimanyeung@snpcorp.com
Founded: 1986
Turnaround: 5 workdays
Print Runs: 100 min - 200,000 max
Business from Other Countries: 98%
*Branch Office(s)*
3 Da Song Jiang nan Main Ave C, 3rd floor,
    Guangzhou, China, Contact: Patrick Au
    *Tel:* (020) 8441 5873 *Fax:* (020) 8441 5874
    *E-mail:* gzbestset@snpcorp.com
*Sales Office(s):* 50 S Buckhout St, Suite 208, Ir-
    vington, NY 10533, United States, Contact: Wai
    Man Yeung *Tel:* 914-961-6223 *Fax:* 914-961-
    8212 *E-mail:* waimanyeung@snpcorp.com
33 Alpin Way, TW7 4RJ Isleworth, Middlesex,
    United Kingdom, Contact: Keith Harrocks
    *Tel:* (0208) 847-4947 *Fax:* (0208) 847-4947
    *E-mail:* keithharrocks@snpcorp.com

**Sota Graphic Arts Co Ltd**
Seapower Industrial Centre, 6/F, 177 Hoi Bun Rd,
    Kwun Tong
*Tel:* 23421083 *Fax:* 23415426
*E-mail:* sales@goldencup.com.hk
*Web Site:* www.goldencup.com.hk
*Key Personnel*
Man Dir: K K Yeung
General Manager: Wai Kwong Ngan
Assistant Manager: Mary Yeung *E-mail:* mary@
    goldencup.com.hk
Founded: 1985
Turnaround: 10 Workdays
Print Runs: 2,000 min
Business from Other Countries: 90%

**South Sea International Press Ltd**
3/F, Yip Cheung Centre, 10 Fung Yip St, Chai
    Wan
*Tel:* 2897 1083 *Fax:* 2558 1473

*E-mail:* books@ssip.com.hk
*Web Site:* www.ssip.com.hk
*Key Personnel*
Man Dir: P Y Lee; Franky Ho
Founded: 1984
Print Runs: 3,000 min - 500,000 max
Business from Other Countries: 80%
*Branch Office(s)*
Haverdreef 39, 7006 LH, Doetinchen, Nether-
    lands, Contact: Buro Doral *Tel:* (0314) 35 40
    40 *Fax:* (0314) 35 46 00 *E-mail:* info@ssip-
    holland.nl *Web Site:* www.ssip-holland.nl
The High Barn, Snailing Lane, Hawkley GU33
    6NJ, United Kingdom, Contact: Myles Wells
    *Tel:* (01) 730 827 326 *Fax:* (01) 730 827 537
    *E-mail:* mwells@eastwest.fsworld.co.uk

**Sunshine Press Ltd**
21/F Fullager Ind Bldg, 234 Aberdeen Main Rd,
    Hong Kong
*Tel:* 25532386 *Fax:* 28732930
*E-mail:* spl@sunshinepress.com.hk
*Key Personnel*
Administrative Assistant: Trevin Tong
Contact: Joney Chan
Founded: 1976
Turnaround: 21-28 Workdays
Print Runs: 3,000 min - 500,000 max
Business from Other Countries: 25%

**Toppan Printing Co (HK) Ltd**
Division of Toppan Printing Co Ltd
Yuen Long Industrial Estate, One Fuk Wang St,
    Yuen Long, New Territories
*Tel:* 2475-5666; 2561-0101 *Fax:* 2475-4321
*E-mail:* info@toppan.co.jp
*Web Site:* www.toppan.co.jp
*Key Personnel*
Man Dir: James Lee Lee
Sales Manager: Yukata Ito
Founded: 1963
Turnaround: 30 Workdays
Business from Other Countries: 25%

**Wing King Tong Group**
Leader Industrial Centre, Block I, 3/F, 188-202
    Texaco Rd, Tsuen Wan, New Territories
*Tel:* 2407 3287; 2407 3309; 24074547
    *Fax:* 24074130; 2408 7939
*E-mail:* printing@wkt.cc; books@wkt.cc
*Web Site:* www.wkt.cc
*Key Personnel*
Man Dir: Alex Yan Tak Chung *E-mail:* ayan@hk.
    super.net
Marketing Dir: Jeremy Kuo
Founded: 1944
Turnaround: 15 Workdays
Print Runs: 1,000 min - 100,000 max
Business from Other Countries: 95%

**Ying Tat Co**
Division of Quality Printing & Paper Products
Flat K, 17/f, Block 1, Vigor Industrial Bldg, 49-
    53 Ta Chuen Ping St, Kwai Chung, Hong Kong
*Tel:* 24227872 *Fax:* 248500287
*Key Personnel*
Chief Executive Officer: William Wong
Founded: 1968
Turnaround: 7-10 Workdays
Print Runs: 1,000 min - 1,000,000 max
Business from Other Countries: 30%

# India

**Hiralal Printing Works Ltd**
Subsidiary of Conway Printers Pvt Ltd
D-41/1 TTC Industrial Area MIDC, opp Turbhe
    tel exchange, Navi Mumbai, Mumbai 400613

*Tel:* (022) 7672726
*Key Personnel*
Chairman: G P Agrawal
Man Dir: Mr Rakesh Kumar Agrawal
Founded: 1981
Turnaround: 40-45 Workdays
Print Runs: 5,000 min - 100,000 max
Business from Other Countries: 75%

**IBH Publishing Services**
Unit of India Book House Pvt Ltd
Fleet Bldg, Marol Naka, M V Rd, Mumbai 400
    059
*Tel:* (022) 2852-7619 *Fax:* (022) 2852-9473
*Web Site:* www.ibhsolves.com
*Key Personnel*
Chief Executive: Dilip Mirchandani *Tel:* 917-
    779-8255 *Fax:* 973-783-7164 *E-mail:* dkm@
    ibhsolves.com
Production Manager: Nizam Ahmed *Tel:* (022)
    2850-7189 *E-mail:* nizam.a@ibhsolves.com
Sales Manager: Madhukar Gandhi *Tel:* (022)
    2852-1921 *E-mail:* madhukar.g@ibhsolves.com
Technology Manager: Samuel Vinodkumar
    *Tel:* (022) 2850-8644 *E-mail:* sam.v@
    ibhsolves.com
Founded: 2004
Business from Other Countries: 100%

**Paragon Prepress Inc**
N-31, Kalkaji, New Delhi 110019
*Tel:* (011) 2622 44 51; (011) 5160 1485
    *Fax:* (011) 2622 44 51
*E-mail:* information@paragonpress.com
*Web Site:* www.paragonpress.com
*Key Personnel*
Chief Executive Officer: Shailander Malhotra
    *E-mail:* shailander@paragonpress.com
Production Manager: T Malhotra *E-mail:* tarun@
    paragonpress.com
Founded: 1991

# Indonesia

**Ichtiar Baru van Hoeve**
Jalan Raya Pasar Jumat 38 D-E, Pondok Pinang,
    Jakarta 12013
*Tel:* (021) 7511856; (021) 7511901 *Fax:* (021)
    7511855
*E-mail:* redaksi@ibvh.com
*Web Site:* www.ibvh.com
Founded: 1972
Turnaround: 6 Workdays
Print Runs: 500 min - 18,000 max

**Victory Offset Prima PT**
Jalan Raya Pegangsaan, Dua No 17, Jakarta
    14250
*Tel:* (021) 460-2742; (021) 460-8968; (021) 4682-
    0555 *Fax:* (021) 460-2740; (021) 4682-0551
*E-mail:* info@victoryoffset.com
*Web Site:* www.victoryoffset.com
*Key Personnel*
President: Zainal F Stanley *E-mail:* zainal@
    victoryoffset.com
General Manager: S Wilson Pinady
    *E-mail:* wilson@victoryoffset.com
Founded: 1971
Turnaround: 14 days
Print Runs: 5,000 min
Business from Other Countries: 10%

# Ireland

**Doyle Graphics**
Esker House, Patrick St, Tullamore, Co Offaly
*Tel:* (0506) 21970 *Fax:* (0506) 51323
*Key Personnel*
Contact: Desmond Doyle
Production Manager: Tom Clarke

**Graphic Reproductions Ltd**
Westlink House, Old Lucan Rd, Palmerstown,
  Dublin 20
*Tel:* (01) 6230101 *Fax:* (01) 6166598; (01)
  6166599
*Key Personnel*
Contact: David Malone; Tim Hurley
*Branch Office(s)*
Graphic Reproductions, 475 Park Ave S, New
  York, NY 10016, United States *Tel:* 212-679-
  4351 *Fax:* 212-679-4352

**ICPC Ltd**
Subsidiary of The Irish Times
Greencastle Parade, Coolock, Dublin 17
*Tel:* (01) 8474711 *Fax:* (01) 8474546
*Web Site:* www.icpc.ie
*Key Personnel*
Man Dir: Seamus McCague *E-mail:* seamus@
  icpc.ie
Production Manager: Wayne Nial
  *E-mail:* wayne@icpc.ie
Founded: 1976
Turnaround: 10 Workdays
Business from Other Countries: 95%

**Kilkenny People/Wellbrook Press**
34 High St, Kilkenny
*Tel:* (056) 63366 *Fax:* (056) 63388
*Web Site:* www.srhplc.com; www.kilkennypeople.
  ie
*Key Personnel*
Man Dir: Joe Hayes *E-mail:* jhayes@
  kilkennypeople.ie
Sales Manager: Martin Brett
Founded: 1892
Business from Other Countries: 10%
*Ultimate Parent Company:* Scottish Radio Hold-
  ings

**SciPrint Ltd**
Bay 93, Shannon Industrial Estate, Shannon, Co
  Clare
*Tel:* (061) 472114; (061) 472520 *Fax:* (061)
  472021
*Key Personnel*
Man Dir, Sales: M K Parsons
Chairman: B Lane
Founded: 1974
Turnaround: 15-20 Workdays
Print Runs: 300 min - 10,000 max
Business from Other Countries: 95%

**Smurfit Print**
Beech Hill, Clonskeagh, Dublin 4
*Tel:* (01) 202-7000 *Fax:* (01) 269-4481
*Web Site:* www.smurfit.ie
*Key Personnel*
Sales Manager: Donal Greene *E-mail:* dgreene@
  smurfitprint.ie
Print Runs: 200 min - 5,000,000 max
Business from Other Countries: 20%
*Parent Company:* Jefferson Smurfit Group plc

**Ultragraphics**
Unit 78A, Cookstown Industrial Estate, Tallaght,
  Dublin 24
*Tel:* (01) 4599133 *Fax:* (01) 4512368
*Key Personnel*
President: Tony Lovett

Turnaround: 4-5 Workdays
Business from Other Countries: 80%

# Israel

**Har-El Printers & Publishers**
Jaffa Port, Jaffa 61081
Mailing Address: Jaffa Port, PO Box 8053, Jaffa
  61081
*Tel:* (03) 681 6834 *Fax:* (03) 681 3563
*E-mail:* mharel@harelart.co.il
*Web Site:* www.harelart.com
*Key Personnel*
Manager: Jaacov Har-El
Founded: 1974
Turnaround: 60-90 Workdays
Print Runs: 30 min - 5,000 max
Business from Other Countries: 70%

**Keterpress Enterprises Jerusalem**
PO Box 7145, 91071 Jerusalem
*Tel:* (02) 6521201 *Fax:* (02) 6527956
*E-mail:* info@keter-books.co.il
*Web Site:* www.keter-books.co.il
*Key Personnel*
Plant Manager: Peter Tomkins *E-mail:* peter@
  keter-books.co.il
Sales Manager: Zvi Weller
Print Runs: 500 min - 500,000 max
Business from Other Countries: 10%
*Parent Company:* Keter Publishing House Ltd

**Monoline Ltd**
3 Avnei Nezer, Kiryat Sefer
*Tel:* (08) 9741456 *Fax:* (08) 9741454
*Key Personnel*
Dir: S J Colthof
Founded: 1959
Business from Other Countries: 30%

**Technosdar Ltd**
5 Levontine St, 65111 Tel Aviv
Mailing Address: PO Box 31684, Tel Aviv 61316
*Tel:* (03) 560-7418; (03) 5605951 *Fax:* (03)
  5605951
*Key Personnel*
General Manager: Avraham Weiss
Founded: 1972
Turnaround: 7-16 Workdays
Business from Other Countries: 10%

# Italy

**Canale G e C SpA**
Subsidiary of Istituto Grafico Bertello SpA
Via Liguria 24, 10071 Borgaro Turin
*Tel:* (011) 40 78 511 *Fax:* (011) 40 78 527
*E-mail:* info@canale.it
*Web Site:* www.canale.it
*Key Personnel*
Dir General: Canale Giacomo *E-mail:* canale@
  canale.it
Founded: 1915
Turnaround: 30 Workdays
Print Runs: 3,000 min
Business from Other Countries: 65%
*Parent Company:* Ledi Srl; PPG Srl

**Dedalo Litostampa SRL**
Viale Luigi Jacobini 5, 70123 Bari
Mailing Address: Casella Postale BA/19, 70123
  Bari

*Tel:* (080) 531 14 13; (080) 531 1400 *Fax:* (080)
  531 14 14
*E-mail:* info@edizionidedalo.it
*Web Site:* www.edizionidedalo.it
*Key Personnel*
Man Dir: Raimondo Coga
General Manager: Sergio Coga *E-mail:* s.coga@
  edizionidedalo.it
Founded: 1965
Print Runs: 2,000 min - 15,000 max

**Milanostampa SpA**
Corso Ferrero, 5, 12060 Farigliano
*Tel:* (0173) 746111 *Fax:* (0173) 746248; (0173)
  746249
*E-mail:* info@milanostampa.com; sales@
  milanostampa.com
*Web Site:* www.milanostampa.com
*Telex:* 212428
*Key Personnel*
Commercial Dir: Riccardo Sardo
Man Dir: Fuad Lahham
Founded: 1965
Turnaround: 15 Workdays
Print Runs: 3,000 min - 80,000 max
Business from Other Countries: 65%
*Branch Office(s)*
Via Statuto, 4, 20121 Milan *Tel:* (02) 6200 1311
  *Fax:* (02) 6200 1313

**Nuovo Instituto Italiano d'Arti Grafiche**
Via Zanica 92, 24126 Bergamo
*Tel:* (035) 329111 *Fax:* (035) 329346
*E-mail:* artigraf@bertelsmann.de
*Telex:* (035) 300114
Founded: 1871
Turnaround: 10 Workdays
Business from Other Countries: 30%

**Amilcare Pizzi SpA**
Via A Pizzi, 14, 20092 Cinisello Balsamo
*Tel:* (02) 61836 1 *Fax:* (02) 61836 283
*E-mail:* info@amilcarepizzi.it
*Web Site:* www.amilcarepizzi.it
*Key Personnel*
Chief Executive Officer: Massimo Pizzi
Founded: 1914
Business from Other Countries: 45%
*Branch Office(s)*
American Pizzi Offset Corp, 370 Lexington Ave,
  Suite 505, New York, NY 10017, United States
  *Tel:* 212-986-1658 *Fax:* 212-286-1887

# Republic of Korea

**Daehan Printing & Publishing Co Ltd**
41-10, Jamwon-dong, Seacho-gu, Seoul
*Tel:* (0822) 34 75 3800 *Fax:* (0822) 541 8158
*E-mail:* mschung@daehane.com
*Web Site:* www.daehane.com
*Key Personnel*
Manager: Jongjun Yu
President & Chief Executive Officer: Tae-Rang
  Hwang
Founded: 1948
*U.S. Office(s):* 3271 Sawtelle Blvd No 104, Los
  Angeles, CA 90066, United States *Tel:* 310-
  737-0058 *Fax:* 310-737-9213 (sales)

**Pyunghwa Dang Printing Co Ltd**
60 Kyunji-Dong, Chongro-ku, Seoul 110-170
*Tel:* (02) 735-4011 *Fax:* (02) 734-5201
*E-mail:* comuser@hitel.kol.co.kr *Cable:*
  PHDPRINTCO SEOUL
*Key Personnel*
President: Mr Il Soo Lee

Vice President: Mr Hae Kun Oh
Executive Dir: Mr Sang Woo Lee
Founded: 1923
Turnaround: 10 Workdays
Print Runs: 2,000 min - 500,000 max
Business from Other Countries: 7%

# Lithuania

**Spindulys Printing House**
Gedimino g 10, 44318 Kaunas
*Tel:* (037) 226243; (037) 386737 *Fax:* (037) 204970
*E-mail:* spindul@kaunas.aiva.lt
*Key Personnel*
Contact: Elena Kapustinskiene
Founded: 1928
Print Runs: 500 min - 100,000 max
Business from Other Countries: 6%

# Madagascar

**Societe Malgache d'Edition**
Route des Hydrocarbures, Ankorondrano, 101 Tananrive
Mailing Address: BP 659, 101 Tananrive
*Tel:* (020) 2222635 *Fax:* (020) 2222254
*E-mail:* tribune@bow.dts.mg
*Web Site:* www.madagascar-tribune.com
*Telex:* (020) 223-40
*Key Personnel*
Dir of Publication: Rahaga Ramaholimihaso
Founded: 1943
Print Runs: 7,000 min - 15,000 max

# Netherlands

**Bosch en Keuning grafische bedrijven**
Ericastr 1, 3742 SG Baarn
*Tel:* (035) 5417979
*Key Personnel*
Dir: Jaap Atema

# New Zealand

**Egan-Reid Ltd**
Level 2, 38 Ireland St, Freemans Bay, Auckland 1001
*Tel:* (09) 3784100 *Fax:* (09) 3784300
*E-mail:* publishing@eganreid.com
*Web Site:* www.egan-reid.com
*Key Personnel*
Man Dir: Gerard Reid *E-mail:* gerard@eganreid.co.nz
Contact: Mary Egan *E-mail:* mary@eganreid.co.nz
Founded: 1988
Turnaround: 2 Workdays
Business from Other Countries: 75%

**PPP Printers Ltd**
PO Box 22785, Christchurch
*Tel:* (03) 3662727 *Fax:* (03) 3654606
*Key Personnel*
Man Dir: D C Richardson
Founded: 1958

Turnaround: 10 Workdays
Print Runs: 100 min - 100,000 max
Business from Other Countries: 10%

**Rogan McIndoe Print Ltd**
51 Crawford St, Dunedin 9001
Mailing Address: PO Box 1361, Dunedin
*Tel:* (03) 474 0111 *Toll Free Tel:* 800-477-0355 *Fax:* (03) 474 0116
*E-mail:* quality@rogan.co.nz
*Web Site:* www.rogan.co.nz
*Key Personnel*
Man Dir: Brendan A Murphy
Founded: 1893
Print Runs: 21 min - 30 max
Business from Other Countries: 1%
*Branch Office(s)*
73 Durham St, Sydenham, Christchurch *Tel:* (03) 377 4637 *Fax:* (03) 377 4639

# Philippines

**Naldoza Printers**
362 Tupaz St, 6000 Cebu City
*Tel:* (032) 261-7326 *Fax:* (032) 261-7326
*E-mail:* naldoza@ebu.skyinet.net
*Key Personnel*
Chief Executive Officer: John R Naldoza
Founded: 1989
*Parent Company:* Business Developers Inc

**Reyes Publishing Inc**
4/F Mariwasa Bldg, 717 Aurora Blvd, 1112 Quezon City
*Tel:* (02) 721-8782 *Fax:* (02) 721-8782
*E-mail:* reyesbub@skyinet.net
*Key Personnel*
Operations Manager: Roman Paolo Reyes, V
Founded: 1964
Business from Other Countries: 90%

# Portugal

**Edicoes Silabo**
Rua Cidade de Manchester, 2, 1170 100 Lisbon
*Tel:* (021) 316 12 81 *Fax:* (021) 314 58 80
*E-mail:* silabo@silabo.pt
*Web Site:* www.silabo.pt
*Key Personnel*
Marketing Dir: Manuel Robalo
 *E-mail:* manuelrobalo@silabo.pt
Founded: 1983
Turnaround: 5 Workdays

# Puerto Rico

**Publishing Resources Inc**
373 San Jorge St, 2nd floor, Santurce 00912
Mailing Address: PO Box 41307, Santurce 00940
*Tel:* 787-268-8080 *Fax:* 787-774-5781
*E-mail:* pri@tld.net
*Key Personnel*
Owner & President: Ronald J Chevako
Editorial Dir: Anne W Chevako
Founded: 1976
Print Runs: 500 min - 10,000 max
Business from Other Countries: 5%

# Singapore

**Alkem Company (S) Pte Ltd**
1, Penjuru Close, Jurong Town, Singapore 608617
*Tel:* 6265 6666 *Fax:* 6261 7875
*E-mail:* enquiry@alkem.com.sg
*Web Site:* www.alkem.com.sg
*Key Personnel*
Man Dir: Chu Bong *E-mail:* chubong@alkem.com.sg
Founded: 1998
Turnaround: 15 Workdays
Print Runs: 1,000 min - 1,000,000 max
Business from Other Countries: 90%

**Chong Moh Offset Printing Ltd**
Subsidiary of Chassis Graphic Art Pte Ltd
19 Joo Koon Rd, Jurong Town 628978
*Tel:* 8622701 *Fax:* 8624335
*E-mail:* chongmoh@singnet.com.sg
*Key Personnel*
Chairman: James Ng
Founded: 1946
Turnaround: 10-14 Workdays
Print Runs: 1,000 min
Business from Other Countries: 35%

**Chroma Graphics (Overseas) Pte Ltd**
Blk 12, Lorong Bakar Batu, No 05-08/10, Singapore 348745
*Tel:* 67423706 *Fax:* 67484097
*Telex:* 55962 CG SEP
*Key Personnel*
Man Dir: Thomas K P Chan
 *E-mail:* thomaschan@chromographics.com.sg
Founded: 1978
Turnaround: 7-10 Workdays
Business from Other Countries: 85%

**Craft Print Pte Ltd**
9 Joo Koon Circle, Jurong, Singapore 629041
*Tel:* 861 4040 *Fax:* 861 0530
*E-mail:* craftprt@singet.com.sg
*Key Personnel*
Man Dir: Charlie Chan

**CS Graphics Pte Ltd**
10 Tuas Ave 20, Singapore 2263
*Tel:* 6865 2010 *Fax:* 6861 0190
*Web Site:* ourworld.compuserve.com/homepages/csgraphics
*Key Personnel*
Man Dir: Mr Lee Sian Tee *E-mail:* stlee@csgraphics-world.com
Founded: 1980
Turnaround: 80 Workdays
Print Runs: 1,000 min - 100,000 max
Business from Other Countries: 100%

**Eurasia Press (Offset) Pte Ltd**
10 Kampong Ampat, Singapore 368320
*Tel:* 2805522 *Fax:* 2800593; 3825458
*E-mail:* eurasia@mbox3.singnet.com.sg
*Key Personnel*
Marketing Dir: Allan Fong
Founded: 1937
Turnaround: 14 Workdays
Print Runs: 500 min - 100,000 max
Business from Other Countries: 65%

**Ho Printing Singapore Pte Ltd**
31 Changi South St One, Changi South Industrial Estate, Singapore 486769
*Tel:* 6542 9322 *Fax:* 6542 8322
*E-mail:* marketing@hoprinting.com.sg; sales@hoprinting.com.sg
*Web Site:* www.hoprinting.com
*Telex:* RS 39685 HOFSET

*Key Personnel*
Man Dir: Ho Wai Hoi
Founded: 1951
Turnaround: 35-50 Workdays
Print Runs: 5,000 min - 50,000 max
Business from Other Countries: 30%

**Markono Print Media Pte Ltd**
Subsidiary of Markono Holdings Pte Ltd
21 Neythal Rd, Singapore 628586
*Tel:* 6281-1118 *Fax:* 6286-6663
*E-mail:* saleslead@markono.com.sg
*Web Site:* www.markono.com.sg
*Key Personnel*
Dir: Bob Lee Song Tioh *E-mail:* blee@markono.
   com.sg
Turnaround: 14 Workdays
Print Runs: 1,000 min - 100,000 max
Business from Other Countries: 20%
*Branch Office(s)*
Kin Keong Colour Printing (M) Sdn Bhd, Port
   Klang 539538

**Pica Digital Pte Ltd**
Block 55, 2nd floor, 11-22 Ayer Rajah Crescent,
   Singapore 139949
*Tel:* 67761311 *Fax:* 67793055
*E-mail:* picaosea@singnet.com.sg
*Key Personnel*
Dir: Thomas Ling
Founded: 1977
Turnaround: 4 Workdays
Business from Other Countries: 60%

**Sang Choy International Pte Ltd**
Harrison Ind Bldg, 05-01, 9 Harrison Rd, Singa-
   pore 369651
*Tel:* (065) 6289 0829 *Fax:* (065) 6282 7673
*E-mail:* marketing@sc-international.com.sg
*Web Site:* www.sc-international.com.sg
*Key Personnel*
Dir of Operations: Almond Ko
Founded: 1992
Business from Other Countries: 90%

**SNP SPrint Pte Ltd**
97 Ubi Ave 4, Singapore 408754
*Tel:* 6826-9600 *Fax:* 6820-3341
*E-mail:* enquiries@snpcorp.com
*Web Site:* www.snp-corp.com
*Telex:* SNPRS14462
*Key Personnel*
Chief Executive Officer & President: Yeo Chee
   Tong
Executive Vice President Security Printing: Paul
   Wong Pao Lu *E-mail:* paulwong@snp.com.sg
US Sales Manager: Patrick Chung
Turnaround: 30 Workdays
Print Runs: 2,000 min - 200,000 max
Business from Other Countries: 40%
*Parent Company:* SNP Corporation Ltd

**Stamford Press Pte Ltd**
209, Kallang Bahru, Singapore 339344
*Tel:* 6294 7227 *Fax:* 6294 4396; 6294 3319
*E-mail:* stamfad@singnet.com.sg
*Web Site:* www.stamford.com.sg
*Telex:* RS56414 STAMFO
*Key Personnel*
Dir: Mr L Rajesh *Tel:* 6294 7227 (ext 233)
   *E-mail:* rajesh@stamford.com.sg
Founded: 1963
Turnaround: 3-4 Workdays for small jobs; 3-4
   weeks for big jobs
Print Runs: 1,500 min - 50,000 max
Business from Other Countries: 20%

**Times Graphics**
Division of Times Printers Pte Ltd
Subsidiary of Times Publishing Ltd

Times Centre, One New Industrial Rd, Singapore
   536196
*Tel:* 6213-9288 *Fax:* 6284 4733; 6288 1186
*E-mail:* tpl@tpl.com.sg
*Web Site:* www.tpl.com.sg
*Telex:* RS 25713
*Key Personnel*
Manager: Andrew Wong Weng Fook
Founded: 1986
Turnaround: 15 Workdays
Business from Other Countries: 40%

**Times Printers Pte Ltd**
Subsidiary of Times Publishing Group
16 Tuas Ave 5, Singapore 639340
*Tel:* 6311-2888 *Fax:* 6862-1313
*E-mail:* tp@timesprinters.com; enquiry@
   timesprinters.com
*Web Site:* www.timesprinters.com; www.tpl.com.
   sg *Cable:* TIMESPRINT
*Key Personnel*
Corporate General Manager: Ronald Pereira
   *E-mail:* ronaldpereira@tpl.com.sg
Head of Sales: Patsy Tan *Tel:* 63112 763
   *E-mail:* patsytan@timesprinters.com
Sales Manager: Koo Kok Leong
Founded: 1968
Turnaround: 5-25 Workdays
Print Runs: 3,000 min - 300,000 max
Business from Other Countries: 75%

# Slovenia

**Gorenjski Tisk Printing House**
Mirka Vadnova 6, 4000 Kranj
*Tel:* (04) 2016300 *Fax:* (04) 2016301
*E-mail:* info@go-tisk.si
*Web Site:* www.go-tisk.si
*Telex:* 34560 YU GOTISK
*Key Personnel*
Dir: Kristina Kobal
Commercial Manager: Boris Krist
Founded: 1888
Turnaround: 30 Workdays
Print Runs: 3,000 min - 15,000 max
Business from Other Countries: 50%

# South Africa

**CTP Book Printers (Pty) Ltd**
Caxton St, Parow, Cape Town 7500
*Tel:* (011) 8890600 *Fax:* (011) 8890922
*E-mail:* ctpjhb@iafrica.com

# Spain

**Graficas Santamaria SA**
Division of Fotomecanica
Bekolarra, 4 Pol Ali Gobeo, 01010 Vitoria
   Gasteiz
*Tel:* (0945) 229100 *Fax:* (0945) 246393
*E-mail:* grsantamaria@sea.es; grsantamaria@
   graficassantamaria
*Web Site:* www.graficassantamaria.com
*Key Personnel*
Contact: Jesus Alzola Aguinaco
Founded: 1963
Turnaround: 1 Workday
Print Runs: 500 min - 150,000 max
Business from Other Countries: 15%

# Sri Lanka

**Sumathi Book Printing (Pvt) Ltd**
Division of Sumathi Group
445, Sirimovo Bandaranaike Mawatha, Colombo
   14
*Tel:* (0941) 330-673-5 *Fax:* (0941) 449-593
*E-mail:* lakbima@isplanka.lk
*Web Site:* www.sumathi.lk
*Telex:* 22104 SUMATHI CE SUMATISONS
*Key Personnel*
General Manager: Nawas A Rahim
Founded: 1980
Business from Other Countries: 75%

# Switzerland

**Hallwag Kummerly & Frey AG**
Grubenstr 109, 3322 Schoenbuehl, Bern
*Tel:* (031) 850 31 31 *Fax:* (031) 850 31 00
*E-mail:* info@swisstravelcenter.ch
*Web Site:* www.swisstravelcenter.ch; www.
   hallwag.com
*Telex:* 912-661 HAWA CH
*Key Personnel*
Chief Executive Officer: Peter Niederhauser
Marketing, Public Relations: Danielle Zingg
Sales: Juerg Burri; Benro Paul Meyerhans

**Photolitho AG**
Industriestr 12, 8625 Gossau ZH
*Tel:* (043) 833 70 20 *Fax:* (043) 833 70 30
*E-mail:* info@photolitho.ch
*Web Site:* www.photolitho.ch
*Key Personnel*
President: Michael von Eicke *Tel:* (043) 833 70
   22 *E-mail:* voneicke@photolitho.ch
Administrator: Werner Holliger *Tel:* (043) 833 70
   23 *E-mail:* w.holliger@photolitho.ch
Founded: 1965
Business from Other Countries: 50%

# United Republic of Tanzania

**Peramiho Publications**
PO Box 41, Peramiho
*Tel:* (054) 2730 *Fax:* (054) 2917
*Key Personnel*
Chief Executive: Fr Gerold Rupper
Founded: 1937
Print Runs: 4,000 min - 6,000 max

# Thailand

**Phongwarin Printing Company Ltd**
299 Mu 10, Sukhumvit 107, Sumrongnue, Ampur
   Muang, Samutprakarn 10260
*Tel:* (02) 7498934-45; (02) 3994525-31; (02)
   7498275-9 *Fax:* (02) 3994524; (02) 3994255
*E-mail:* somphong@phongwarin.com
*Web Site:* www.phongwarin.com

*Key Personnel*
Man Dir: Mr Somphong Charnsirisaksakul
Founded: 1983
Turnaround: 7 Workdays
Print Runs: 1,000 min - 500,000 max
Business from Other Countries: 5%

# United Kingdom

**Adroit Birmingham Ltd**
Cecil St, Birmingham B19 3ST
*Tel:* (0121) 3596831 *Fax:* (0121) 3593974
*Key Personnel*
Sales Manager: Jackie Robotham

**The Alden Group Ltd**
Osney Mead, Oxford OX2 0EF
*Tel:* (01865) 253 200 *Fax:* (01865) 249 070
*E-mail:* information@alden.co.uk
*Web Site:* www.alden.co.uk
*Key Personnel*
Group Technical/Development Dir: Robert Hay
Sales Dir: Michael Angless
Marketing Administrator: Gemma Webb
   *E-mail:* gwebb@alden.co.uk

**AlpnetCompuType Ltd**
Horton Parade Horton Rd, West Drayton UB7 8EP
*Tel:* (01895) 440791 *Fax:* (01895) 441500
*E-mail:* computype@computype.co.uk
*Key Personnel*
Business Manager: Brian Trowse
Founded: 1976

**ARADCO VSI Ltd**
Aradco House, 132 Cleveland St, London W1T 6AB
*Tel:* (020) 7692 7700 *Fax:* (020) 7692 7711
*E-mail:* aradco@compuserve.com
*Web Site:* www.aradco.com
*Key Personnel*
Contact: R Dawood
Founded: 1958
Business from Other Countries: 20%

**J W Arrowsmith Ltd**
Winterstoke Rd, Bristol BS3 2NT
*Tel:* (0117) 966 7545 *Fax:* (0117) 963 7829
*E-mail:* jw@arrowsmith.co.uk
*Web Site:* www.arrowsmith.co.uk
*Key Personnel*
Sales Dir: David J Hooper *E-mail:* dhooper@ arrowsmith.co.uk
Founded: 1854
Turnaround: 15 Workdays
Print Runs: 500 min - 15,000 max
Business from Other Countries: 40%

**Associated Translation & Typesetting**
Alexander House, 64 Robin Hood Lane, Hall Green, Birmingham B28 0JT
*Tel:* (0121) 603 6344 *Fax:* (0121) 603 6399
*E-mail:* ATTEuro@aol.com (European translation); ATTAsia@aol.com (Eastern/Asian translation); info@att-group.com
*Web Site:* www.att-group.com
*Key Personnel*
Dir: Mr S Ahmed
Founded: 1971
Business from Other Countries: 50%

**Axicon Auto ID Ltd**
Weston on the Green, Bicester, Church Rd, Oxford OX25 3QP
*Tel:* (01869) 351155 *Fax:* (01869) 351205
*E-mail:* sales@axicon.com
*Web Site:* www.axicon.com
*Key Personnel*
Dir: Jenny Hicks *E-mail:* jmh@axicon.com
Founded: 1981
Turnaround: 1-2 Workdays
Business from Other Countries: 30%

**W & G Baird Ltd**
Subsidiary of The Baird Group
Greystone Press, Caulside Dr, Antrim BT41 2RS
*Tel:* (028) 9446 3911 *Fax:* (028) 9446 6250
*E-mail:* wgbaird@wgbaird.com
*Web Site:* www.wgbaird.org
*Key Personnel*
Man Dir: Dairmuid McGarry *E-mail:* dairmuid. mcgarry@wgbaird.com
Founded: 1863
Print Runs: 500 min - 100,000 max
Business from Other Countries: 45%
*Branch Office(s)*
Textflow, Belfast, Ireland
MSO, Belfast, Ireland
Biddles Ltd, Woodbridge Park, Woodbridge Rd, Guildford, Surrey GU1 1DA

**BAS Printers Ltd**
115 Tollgate Rd, Salisbury, Wilts SP1 2JG
*Tel:* (01722) 411711 *Fax:* (01722) 411727
*E-mail:* sales@basprint.co.uk
*Web Site:* www.basprint.co.uk
*Key Personnel*
Man Dir: David Gumn
Sales Dir: Paul G Gumn *E-mail:* paul@basprint. co.uk
Founded: 1948
Print Runs: 350 min - 40,000 max
Business from Other Countries: 10%

**Baseline Creative Ltd**
60A Northumbria Dr, Henleaze, Bristol BS9 4HW
*Tel:* (0117) 962 0006 *Fax:* (0117) 962 5006
*E-mail:* contact@base.co.uk
*Web Site:* www.base.co.uk
*Key Personnel*
Man Dir & Creative Dir: John Buchmueller
   *E-mail:* john@base.co.uk
Account Manager: Nicholas J Wood
   *E-mail:* nick@base.co.uk
Senior Designer: David Sheppard *E-mail:* david@ base.co.uk; Rob Wilkins *E-mail:* rob@base.co. uk
Founded: 1985
Turnaround: 30 Workdays

**The Bath Press**
Subsidiary of Bath Press Group PLC
Lower Bristol Rd, Bath BA2 3BL
*Tel:* (01225) 428101 *Fax:* (01225) 312418
*E-mail:* bath@cpi-group.co.uk
*Web Site:* www.cpi-group.net
*Key Personnel*
Man Dir: Peter Palframan
Marketing Dir: Keith Johnson; Jack McCabe
   *E-mail:* jmccabe@bathpress.co.uk
Founded: 1846
Turnaround: 10-15 Workdays
Print Runs: 3,000 min - 300,000 max
Business from Other Countries: 5%

**BCS Publishing Ltd**
One Bignell Park Barns, Kirtlington Rd, Bicester, Oxon OX6 8TD
*Tel:* (01869) 324423 *Fax:* (01869) 324385
*Key Personnel*
Man Dir: Steve McCurdy

Founded: 1993
Business from Other Countries: 40%

**Bell & Bain Ltd**
303 Burnfield Rd, Thornliebank, Glasgow G46 7UQ
*Tel:* (0141) 649 5697 *Fax:* (0141) 632 8733
*E-mail:* info@bell-bain.demon.co.uk
*Web Site:* www.bell-bain.co.uk
*Key Personnel*
Man Dir: I Walker
Sales Dir: D Stewart
Turnaround: 7-10 Workdays
Print Runs: 100 min - 100,000 max
Business from Other Countries: 25%

**Black Bear Press Ltd**
King's Hedges Rd, Cambridge CB4 2PQ
*Tel:* (01223) 424571 *Fax:* (01223) 426877
*E-mail:* enquiries@black-bear-press.com
*Web Site:* www.black-bear-press.com
*Key Personnel*
Man Dir: K Fentiman
Sales Manager: Mike Hallam
Contact: Mary Simpson

**Blackmore Ltd**
Longmead Industrial Estate, Shaftesbury, Dorset SP7 8PX
*Tel:* (01747) 853034 *Fax:* (01747) 854500
*E-mail:* sales@blackmore.co.uk
*Web Site:* www.blackmore.co.uk
*Key Personnel*
Group Chief Executive: Chris Brickell
Man Dir: Peter Smith
Sales Dir: Aubrey Aviss

**Book Creation Services Ltd**
Mitre House, 44-46 Fleet St, London EC4Y 1BN
*Tel:* (020) 7583 0553 *Fax:* (020) 7583 9439
*E-mail:* info@librios.com
*Web Site:* www.librios.com
*Key Personnel*
Chairman: Hal Robinson *E-mail:* hal@librios.com
Founded: 1991
Business from Other Countries: 30%

**Book Production Consultants PLC**
25-27 High St, Chesterton, Cambridge CB4 1ND
*Tel:* (01223) 352790 *Fax:* (01223) 460718
*E-mail:* bpc@bpccam.co.uk
*Web Site:* www.bpccam.co.uk
*Key Personnel*
Dir: Tony Littlechild *E-mail:* tl@bpccam.co.uk; Colin Walsh
Founded: 1973
Print Runs: 500 min
Business from Other Countries: 25%

**D Brown & Sons Ltd**
North Rd, Bridgend Industrial Estate, Bridgend CF31 3TP
*Tel:* (01656) 652447 *Fax:* (01656) 676509
*Key Personnel*
Dir: J M Whitaker *Tel:* (01446) 774213
Finance Dir: Jane C Brown
Founded: 1895
Print Runs: 1 min - 1,000,000 max
Business from Other Countries: 20%
*Branch Office(s)*
Eastgate Press, 62 Eastgate, Cowbridge, S Glam CF7 7AB

**Butler & Tanner Ltd**
Selwood Printing Works, Caxton Rd, Frome, Somerset BA11 1NF
*Tel:* (01373) 451500 *Fax:* (01373) 451333
*E-mail:* info@butlerandtanner.com
*Web Site:* www.butlerandtanner.com
*Key Personnel*
President: John Clare *Tel:* (01373) 463366

Joint Man Dir: A Huett
Sales Dir: N White

**Caledonian International Book Manufacturing**
Westerhill Rd, Bishopbriggs, Glasgow G64 2QR
*Tel:* (0141) 7623000 *Fax:* (0141) 7620922
*E-mail:* 101622.235@compuserve.com
*Key Personnel*
Man Dir: Kevin McKenna
Commercial Dir: G Morrison
Group Sales Manager: Martin Platt
    *E-mail:* martin@platt44.freeserve.co.uk
Founded: 1819

**Cambridge University Press - Printing Division**
Division of Cambridge University Press
University Printing House, Edinburgh Bldg,
    Shaftesbury Rd, Cambridge CB2 2RU
*Tel:* (01223) 312393 *Fax:* (01223) 315052
*E-mail:* printing@cambridge.org
*Web Site:* www..cambridgeprinting.org
*Key Personnel*
Executive Dir: Sandra Ward *Tel:* (01223) 325608
    *E-mail:* sward@cambridge.org
Founded: 1534
Print Runs: 1 min

**Center Print Ltd**
Subsidiary of Beshara Press
Private Rd 2, Colwich Business Park, Colwich,
    Nottingham NG4 2JR
*Tel:* (0115) 961 2277 *Fax:* (0115) 938 1424
*E-mail:* cprint@besharapress.co.uk
*Web Site:* www.besharapress.com
*Key Personnel*
General Manager: Nicola Lesley
Print Runs: 1,000 min - 250,000 max

**The Charlesworth Group**
Flanshaw Lane, Wakefield WF2 9LP
*Tel:* (01924) 204830 *Fax:* (01924) 332637
*E-mail:* sales@charlesworth.com
*Web Site:* www.charlesworth.com
*Key Personnel*
Marketing Manager: Sarah Philp
    *E-mail:* s_philp@charlesworth.com
Founded: 1928
Turnaround: 1 to 10 Workdays
Print Runs: 1 min - 10,000 max
Business from Other Countries: 30%

**Chase Publishing Services**
Mead, Fortescue Rd, Sidmouth, Devon EX10
    9QG
*Tel:* (01395) 514709 *Fax:* (01395) 514709
*Key Personnel*
President: Ray Addicott *E-mail:* r.addicott@
    btinternet.com
Founded: 1989

**William Clowes Ltd**
Beccles, Suffolk NR34 9QE
*Tel:* (01502) 712884 *Fax:* (01502) 717003
*E-mail:* william@clowes.co.uk
*Web Site:* www.clowes.co.uk
*Key Personnel*
Chief Executive Dir: Alex Evans
Sales Dir: David C Browne *Tel:* (07768) 658820
    *E-mail:* dbrowne@clowes.co.uk
Contact: Tracy Humphrey
Founded: 1803
Turnaround: 10 Workdays
Print Runs: 2,000 min
Business from Other Countries: 1%

**Cooper Dale**
1a Dalling Rd, London W6 0RA
*Tel:* (020) 8995 3157 *Fax:* (020) 8748 5689
*Web Site:* www.cooperdale.com

*Key Personnel*
Design Dir: Roger Pring *E-mail:* roger@
    cooperdale.com
Founded: 1985
Print Runs: 1 min - 1,000,000 max
Business from Other Countries: 10%

**Cox & Wyman Ltd**
Cardiff Rd, Reading, Berks RG1 8EX
*Tel:* (0118) 953 0500 *Fax:* (0118) 950 7222
*E-mail:* coxandwyman@cpi-group.net
*Web Site:* www.cpi-group.net
*Key Personnel*
General Manager: Tom Roberts
Sales Manager: Paul Hicks
Sales Executive: Ruth Goodman
Founded: 1777
Turnaround: 10 Workdays reprints/15 workdays
    new books
Print Runs: 2,000 min - 2,000,000 max
Business from Other Countries: 5%
*Parent Company:* Chevrillon Philippe Industrie

**Cradley Print Ltd**
Chester Rd, Cradley Heath, Warley, West Mid-
    lands B64 6AB
*Tel:* (01384) 414100; (01384) 414102 (sales)
    *Fax:* (01384) 414102
*E-mail:* sales@cradleygp.co.uk
*Web Site:* www.cradleygp.co.uk
*Key Personnel*
Man Dir: Chris Jordan
Turnaround: 5 Workdays
Print Runs: 1,000 min - 500,000 max
Business from Other Countries: 7%
*Branch Office(s)*
Quadcolor Repro

**The Diagram Group**
195 Kentish Town Rd, London NW5 2JU
*Tel:* (020) 7482 3633 *Fax:* (020) 7482 4932
*E-mail:* diagramuis@aol.com
*Key Personnel*
Contact: Bruce Robertson
Secretary: C A Dease
Founded: 1967
Business from Other Countries: 80%

**Edition**
Subsidiary of Cameron Books
PO Box 1, Moffat DG10 9SU
*Tel:* (01683) 220808 *Fax:* (01683) 220012
*E-mail:* editorial@cameronbooks.co.uk; sales@
    cameronbooks.co.uk
*Web Site:* www.cameronbooks.co.uk
*Key Personnel*
Dir: Ian Cameron; Jill Hollis
Founded: 1976

**Fern House**
19 High St, Haddenham, Ely, Cambs CB6 3XA
*Tel:* (01353) 740222 *Fax:* (01353) 741987
*E-mail:* info@fernhouse.com
*Web Site:* www.fernhouse.com
*Key Personnel*
Contact: Rodney Dale
Founded: 1976

**The Guernsey Press Co Ltd**
Braye Rd, Vale, Guernsey GY1 3EG
Mailing Address: PO Box 57, Vale, Guernsey
    GY1 3BW
*Tel:* (01481) 240240; (01481) 243657 (ISDN)
    *Fax:* (01481) 240290; (01481) 240275
*E-mail:* books@guernsey-press.com
*Web Site:* www.guernsey-press.com
*Key Personnel*
Editor: Richard Digard
Contact: Mr T A R Duquemin
Founded: 1897
Turnaround: 10 Workdays

Print Runs: 2,000 min - 50,000 max
Business from Other Countries: 80%

**Hammond Packaging Ltd**
Division of Hammond Bindery Ltd
Flanshaw Way, Flanshaw Lane, Wakefield WF2
    9LP
*Tel:* (01924) 204830 *Fax:* (01924) 332637;
    (01924) 339107
*E-mail:* sales@hammond-bindery.co.uk
*Web Site:* www.hammond-bindery.co.uk
*Key Personnel*
Man Dir: Steve Allan *E-mail:* s_allan@hammond-
    bindery.co.uk
Sales Manager: Susan Sheldon
    *E-mail:* s_sheldon@hammond-bindery.co.uk
Founded: 1991
Turnaround: 5-15 Workdays
Print Runs: 100 min - 500,000 max

**Headley Brothers Ltd**
The Invicta Press, Queens Rd, Ashford, Kent
    TN24 8HH
*Tel:* (01233) 623131 *Fax:* (01233) 612345
*E-mail:* printing@headley.co.uk
*Web Site:* www.headley.co.uk
*Key Personnel*
Sales Manager: Bruce Finn *E-mail:* bruce.finn@
    headley.co.uk
Commercial Dir: Jon Pitt *E-mail:* jon.pitt@
    headley.co.uk
European Sales: Ingrid Eissfeldt
Man Dir: Roger Pitt *E-mail:* roger.pitt@headley.
    co.uk
Founded: 1881
Print Runs: 1,000 min - 200,000 max
Business from Other Countries: 5%

**Heyden & Son**, see Securit World Ltd

**Hobbs The Printers Ltd**
Brunel Rd, Totton, Hants SO40 3WX
*Tel:* (023) 8066 4800 *Fax:* (023) 8066 4801
*E-mail:* info@hobbs.co.uk
*Web Site:* www.hobbstheprinters.co.uk; www.
    hobbs.uk.com
*Key Personnel*
Man Dir: David Hobbs *E-mail:* d.a.hobbs@hobbs.
    uk.com
Commercial Dir: Terry Ozanne *E-mail:* t.
    ozanne@hobbs.uk.com
Sales Manager: Sajid Ali *E-mail:* s.ali@hobbs.uk.
    com
Founded: 1884
Turnaround: 5-10 days litho; up to 5 days digital
Print Runs: 10 min - 50,000 max
Business from Other Countries: 4%

**Holbrook Design**
Holbrook House, 105 Rose Hill, Oxford OX4
    4HT
*Tel:* (01865) 459000 *Fax:* (01865) 459006
*E-mail:* info@holbrook-design.co.uk
*Web Site:* www.holbrook-design.co.uk
*Key Personnel*
Design Dir: Peter Tucker *E-mail:* pgt@holbrook-
    design.co.uk
Founded: 1974
Business from Other Countries: 20%

**Ikon Document Management Services**
Subsidiary of Microgen Holdings Plc
19 The Business Centre, Molly Millars Lane,
    Wokingham, Berks RG41 2QY
*Tel:* (0118) 9770510 *Fax:* (0118) 9770513
*E-mail:* pamh@ikonds.co.uk
*Web Site:* www.ikon.com
*Key Personnel*
Man Dir: Dave Weller
Business Development Dir: Aaron Biggs
Founded: 1972

Turnaround: 2-5 Workdays
Print Runs: 1 min - 5,000 max
Business from Other Countries: 40%
*Branch Office(s)*
Microgen City Park Watchmead, Welwyn Garden
City, Herts AL7 1LT

## Image & Print Group Ltd
Unit 9, Oakbank Industrial Estate, Garscube Rd,
Glasgow G20 7LU
*Tel:* (0141) 353 1900 *Fax:* (0141) 353 8611
*E-mail:* info@imageandprint.co.uk
*Web Site:* www.imageandprint.co.uk
*Key Personnel*
Man Dir: Ken Roberts; Stephen McPhee
*Tel:* (0141) 353-8609 *E-mail:* stephen@
imageandprint.co.uk
Founded: 1975
Turnaround: 5 Workdays
Print Runs: 1,000 min - 250,000 max

## Intype Libra Ltd
Units 3 & 4, Elm Grove Industrial Estate, Elm
Grove, Wimbledon SW19 4HE
*Tel:* (020) 8947 7863 *Fax:* (020) 8947 3652
*E-mail:* intype@btconnect.com
*Key Personnel*
Man Dir: Tony Chapman *E-mail:* tony.chapman@
intypelibra.co.uk
Production: Richard Mayne
Dir: Alan Johnson
Founded: 1976
Turnaround: 10-15 Workdays for proofs; 5-10
Workdays for books
Print Runs: 25 min - 1,000 max
Business from Other Countries: 5%

## Keytec Typesetting Ltd
Unit 2-5, Hounsell Bldgs, North Mills Trading
Estate, Bridport, Dorset DT6 3BE
*Tel:* (01308) 427580 *Fax:* (01308) 421961
*E-mail:* all@keytectype.co.uk
*Web Site:* www.keytectype.co.uk
*Key Personnel*
Man Dir: Mark Riddington
Founded: 1983

## Linden Artists Ltd
41 Battersea Business Centre, 103 Lavender Hill,
London SW11 5QL
*Tel:* (020) 7738 2505 *Fax:* (020) 7738 2513
*E-mail:* lindenartists@aol.com
*Web Site:* www.lindenartists.co.uk
*Key Personnel*
Dir: Dennis J Bosdet; Martin J Gibbs; Sheila
Wall
Founded: 1962
Business from Other Countries: 30%

## Lowfield Printing Co Ltd
9 Kennet Rd, Dartford, Kent DA1 4QT
*Tel:* (01322) 522216 *Fax:* (01322) 555362
*E-mail:* lowfield@compuserve.com
*Key Personnel*
Dir: Ian J Starkey
Founded: 1964
Print Runs: 500 min - 20,000 max

## Maney Publishing
Subsidiary of The Charlesworth Group of Compa-
nies
Hudson Rd, Leeds LS9 7DL
*Tel:* (0113) 249 7481 *Fax:* (0113) 248 6983
*E-mail:* maney@maney.co.uk
*Web Site:* www.maney.co.uk
*Key Personnel*
Man Dir: Michael Gallico *E-mail:* m.gallico@
maney.co.uk
Founded: 1900
Print Runs: 350 min - 100,000 max
Business from Other Countries: 2%

## MPG Ltd
Division of Martins Printing Group
The Gresham Press, Old Woking, Surrey GU22
9LH
*Tel:* (01483) 757501 *Fax:* (01483) 724629
*E-mail:* print@mpgltd.co.uk
*Web Site:* www.mpgltd.co.uk
*Key Personnel*
Chairman: Sir Clive Martin
Founded: 1945
Turnaround: 5 Workdays
Print Runs: 3,000 min - 75,000 max
Divisions: MPG Books Ltd; Unwin Brothers Ltd
*Branch Office(s)*
Bodmin
Peterborough
Rochester
St Albans
Wimbledon
Woking

## Multiplex Medway Ltd
Lordswood Industrial Estate, Gleaming Wood Dr,
Walderslade, Kent ME5 8XT
*Tel:* (01634) 684371 *Fax:* (01634) 683840
*E-mail:* enquiries@multiplex-medway.co.uk
*Web Site:* www.multiplex-medway.co.uk
*Key Personnel*
Dir: Jon Chandler
Sales Manager: Paul Abson

## Page Bros Ltd (Norwich)
Subsidiary of Milex Ltd
Mile Cross Lane, Norwich NR6 6SA
*Tel:* (01603) 778800 *Fax:* (01603) 778801
*E-mail:* info@pagebros.co.uk
*Web Site:* www.pagebros.co.uk
*Key Personnel*
Sales Dir: Steve Commons
Founded: 1750
Turnaround: 10 Workdays
Print Runs: 100 min - 30,000 max
Business from Other Countries: 20%
*Branch Office(s)*
105-A Euston St, London NW1 2ET *Tel:* (020)
7383 2212 *Fax:* (020) 7383 4145

## Redwood Books Ltd
Division of CPI (UK) Ltd
Kennet Way, Trowbridge, Wilts BA14 8RN
*Tel:* (01225) 769979 *Fax:* (01225) 769050
*E-mail:* enquiries@redwood-books.co.uk
*Web Site:* www.cpi-group.net
*Key Personnel*
General Manager: Trevor Gee
Commercial Manager: Tony Warner
*E-mail:* tony@redwood-books.co.uk
Production Manager: Peter Grant
Founded: 1993
Turnaround: 10 Workdays
Print Runs: 10 min - 20,000 max
Business from Other Countries: 8%
*Parent Company:* CPI France
*Branch Office(s)*
London Sales Office, 22 Bloomsbury Sq, London
WC1A 2NS *Tel:* (020) 7580 9328 *Fax:* (020)
7580 9337

## J R Reid Print & Media Group, see J R Reid
Printing Group Ltd

## J R Reid Printing Group Ltd
79-99 Glasgow Rd, Blantyre, Glasgow G72 0YL
*Tel:* (01698) 826000 *Fax:* (01698) 824944
*E-mail:* office@reid-print-group.co.uk
*Web Site:* www.reid-print-group.co.uk
*Key Personnel*
Joint Man Dir: John R Reid *E-mail:* johnreid@
reid-print-group.co.uk

## Antony Rowe Ltd
Division of Rexam Plc
Bumper's Farm Industrial Estate, Chippenham,
Wilts SN14 6LH
*Tel:* (01249) 659 705 *Fax:* (01249) 448 900
*E-mail:* sales@antonyrowe.co.uk
*Web Site:* www.antonyrowe.co.uk
*Key Personnel*
Chief Executive: Ralph Bell
Sales Manager: Andrew Copley
Founded: 1897
Turnaround: 10 Workdays
Print Runs: 50 min - 100,000 max
Business from Other Countries: 10%

## Santype International Ltd
Netherhampton Rd, Salisbury, Wilts SP2 8PS
*Tel:* (01722) 334261 *Fax:* (01722) 333171
*E-mail:* info@santype.com
*Web Site:* www.santype.com
*Key Personnel*
Sales Dir: John Roost *Fax:* (0870) 1372738
*E-mail:* jroost@santype.co.uk
Business from Other Countries: 35%

## Securit World Ltd
Formerly Heyden & Son
Spectrum House, Hillview Gardens, London NW4
2JQ
*Tel:* (020) 8266 3300 *Fax:* (020) 8203 1027
*E-mail:* sales@securitworld.com
*Web Site:* www.securitworld.com
*Key Personnel*
Dir: Edward Heyden

## Severnside Printers Ltd
Olympus Business Park, Quedgeley, Glos GL2
4NF
*Tel:* (01452) 720250 *Fax:* (01452) 723012
*E-mail:* info@ssl-uk.net
*Web Site:* www.ssl-uk.net
*Key Personnel*
President & Chief Executive: Norman H Beechey
Turnaround: 14-20 Workdays
Print Runs: 500 min - 5,000 max
Business from Other Countries: 10%

## Thomas Technology Solutions (UK) Ltd
Lee House, 1st floor, 109 Hammersmith Rd, Lon-
don W14 0QH
*Tel:* (020) 7070 7550 *Fax:* (020) 7070 7551
*E-mail:* marketing@thomastechsolutions.com
*Web Site:* www.thomastechsolutions.com
*Key Personnel*
Man Dir: Peter Camilleri
Founded: 1964
*Parent Company:* Thomas Publishing Co, LLC,
5 Penn Plaza, New York, NY 10001, United
States
*U.S. Office(s):* Thomas Technology Solutions Inc,
One Progress Drive, Horsham, PA 19044-8014,
United States *Tel:* 215-682-5000; 800-872-2828

## M & A Thomson Litho Ltd
Kelvin Industrial Estate, 2-16 Colvilles Pl, East
Kilbride, Glasgow G75 0SN
*Tel:* (01355) 233 081 *Fax:* (01355) 245 039
*Web Site:* www.thomsonlitho.com
*Key Personnel*
Contact: Ken Thomson
Environment Quality Dir: Angela Hart
*E-mail:* ahart@tlitho.co.uk

## Tradespools Ltd
Vallis House, Robins Lane, Frome, Somerset
BA11 3EG
*Tel:* (01373) 461475 *Fax:* (01373) 474112
*E-mail:* admin@tradespools.co.uk
*Web Site:* www.tradespools.co.uk
*Key Personnel*
Sales Dir: Roger Carraher
Founded: 1967

Print Runs: 1 min - 10,000 max
Business from Other Countries: 30%
*Ultimate Parent Company:* Antony Rowe Group

**Watkiss Automation Ltd**
Subsidiary of The Watkiss Group
Watkiss House, Blaydon Rd, Middlefield Industrial Estate, Sandy, Beds SG19 1RZ
*Tel:* (01767) 682177 *Fax:* (01767) 691769
*E-mail:* info@watkiss.com
*Web Site:* www.watkiss.com
*Key Personnel*
Technical Dir: M Watkiss
Founded: 1959
Print Runs: 200 min - 10,000 max
Business from Other Countries: 5%

# United States

**A-R Editions Inc**
8551 Research Way, Suite 180, Middleton, WI 53562
*Tel:* 608-836-9000 *Toll Free Tel:* 800-736-0070 (US book orders only) *Fax:* 608-831-8200
*E-mail:* info@areditions.com
*Web Site:* www.areditions.com
*Key Personnel*
Pres & CEO: Patrick Wall
Dir, Sales & Mktg: James L Zychowicz
    *E-mail:* james.zychowicz@areditions.com
Founded: 1962
Business from Other Countries: 10%

**ADR/BookPrint Inc**
2012 Northern Ave E, Wichita, KS 67216
*Tel:* 316-522-5599 *Toll Free Tel:* 800-767-6066
    *Fax:* 316-522-5445
*E-mail:* info@adrbookprint.com
*Web Site:* www.adrbookprint.com
*Key Personnel*
Pres: Grace M Rishel *E-mail:* grace@
    adrbookprint.com
VP: James E Rishel
Prodn Mgr: Marc Seiwert
Founded: 1978
Print Runs: 50 min - 20,000 max
Business from Other Countries: 10%
Membership(s): DMIA; PIA/GATF

**Alpina Color Graphics Inc**
Subsidiary of Alpina International Inc
27 Cliff St, 2nd fl, New York, NY 10038
*Tel:* 212-285-2700 *Fax:* 212-285-2704
*E-mail:* info@alpina.net
*Web Site:* www.alpina.net
*Key Personnel*
Contact: Raj Sawhney *E-mail:* raj@alpinanyc.com
Founded: 1980
Turnaround: 2-3 Workdays
Print Runs: 1,000 min - 200,000 max
Business from Other Countries: 20%

**American Pizzi Offset Corp**
Subsidiary of Arti Grafiche Amilcare Pizzi (Milan)
370 Lexington Ave, Suite 1505, New York, NY 10017
*Tel:* 212-986-1658 *Fax:* 212-286-1887
*E-mail:* info@americanpizzi.com
*Key Personnel*
Pres: Massimo Pizzi
Sales Mgr, New York: Barbara Sadick
Founded: 1914
Business from Other Countries: 50%

**Any Photo Type**
242 W 30 St, New York, NY 10001

*Tel:* 212-244-1130 *Fax:* 212-594-4697
*Key Personnel*
Pres: Harold Katzman
Founded: 1977
Turnaround: 1-2 Workdays
Business from Other Countries: 15%

**Asia Pacific Offset Inc**
1332 Corcoran St NW, Suite 6, Washington, DC 20009
*Tel:* 202-462-5436 *Toll Free Tel:* 800-756-4344
    *Fax:* 202-986-4030
*Web Site:* www.asiapacificoffset.com
*Key Personnel*
Pres: Andrew Clarke *E-mail:* andrew@
    asiapacificoffset.com
Dir, Sales (NY Office): Timothy Linn
    *Tel:* 212-941-8300 *Fax:* 212-941-9810
    *E-mail:* timothy@asiapacificoffset.com
Founded: 1997
Turnaround: 105 Workdays including color separation & shipping
Print Runs: 2,000 min
Business from Other Countries: 100%
*Branch Office(s)*
Phoenix Offset, Unit F1-2 2nd fl, Yeung Yiu Chung No 8 Industrial Bldg, 20 Wang Hoi Rd, Kowloon Bay, Hong Kong, Contact: Edmond Chan *Tel:* 852-2751-9962 *Fax:* 852-2755-8408
    *E-mail:* Phoffset@netvigator.com
*Sales Office(s):* 870 Market St, Suite 801, San Francisco, CA 94102, Dir of Sales: Rick Conant *Tel:* 415-433-3488 *Fax:* 415-433-3489
    *E-mail:* Rick@asiapacificoffset.com
270 Lafayette St, Suite 502, New York, NY 10012 *Tel:* 212-941-8300 *Fax:* 212-941-9810
    *E-mail:* Timothy@asiapacificoffset.com

**Bang Printing Co Inc**
3323 Oak St, Brainerd, MN 56401
Mailing Address: PO Box 587, Brainerd, MN 56401-0587
*Tel:* 218-829-2877 *Toll Free Tel:* 800-328-0450
    *Fax:* 218-829-7145
*Web Site:* www.bangprinting.com
*Key Personnel*
VP, Sales: Todd Vanek *Tel:* 218-822-2124
    *E-mail:* toddv@bangprinting.com
Founded: 1899
Turnaround: 10-25 Workdays
Print Runs: 500 min - 100,000 max
Business from Other Countries: 50%

**BookBuilders New York Inc**
16 Sabal Bend, Palm Coast, FL 32137
*Tel:* 845-639-5316 *Fax:* 845-639-5318
*Web Site:* www.mcabooks.com
*Key Personnel*
Pres: Martin Cook *E-mail:* martin@mcabooks.com
Founded: 1977
Turnaround: 30-45 Workdays
Print Runs: 2,000 min - 500,000 max
Business from Other Countries: 60%

**C & C Offset Printing Co Ltd**
Subsidiary of C & C Joint Printing Co (HK) Ltd under Sino United Publishing (Holdings) Ltd
2632 SE 25 Ave, Suite E, Portland, OR 97202
Mailing Address: PO Box 82037, Portland, OR 97282-0037
*Tel:* 503-233-1834 *Fax:* 503-233-7815
*E-mail:* portlandinfo@ccoffset.com
*Web Site:* www.ccoffset.com
*Key Personnel*
Dir, C & C Offset Printing Co (USA) Inc, Portland, OR, USA: Charles H Clark, IV
    *E-mail:* cclark@ccoffset.com
Devt Mgr, C & C Offset Printing Co (USA) Inc, Portland, OR, USA: Jenny Whittier
    *E-mail:* jwhittier@ccoffset.com

Dir & Exec VP, C & C Offset Printing Co (NYC) Inc, New York, NY, USA: Simon Chan
    *E-mail:* schan@ccoffset.com
Cust Serv Mgr, C & C Offset Printing Co (USA) Inc, Portland, OR, USA: Ernest Li
    *E-mail:* ernestli@ccoffset.com
Cust Serv Mgr, C & C Offset Printing Co (NYC) Inc, New York, NY, USA: Frances Harkness
    *E-mail:* fharkness@ccoffset.com
Dir & Gen Mgr, Hong Kong Head Office: Zhang Yue Ming
Deputy Man Dir, Hong Kong Head Office: Ken Lee
Deputy Gen Mgr, Hong Kong Head Office: Ivy Lam
Asst Gen Mgr, Hong Kong Head Office: Kit Wong
Sr Sales Mgr (Special Projects), Hong Kong Head Office: Francis Ho
Dir & Gen Mgr, C & C Joint Printing Co (Guangdong) Ltd, Shenzhen, China: Jackson Leung
Asst Gen Mgr, C & C Joint Printing Co (Guangdong) Ltd, Shenzhen, China: Simon Zhang
Pres, C & C Printing Japan Co Ltd, Tokyo, Japan: Yamamoto Masaaki
Man Dir, C & C Joint Printing Co (Beijing) Ltd, Beijing, China: Zhang Lin Gui
Dir, C & C Offset Printing Co (UK) Ltd: Tracy Broderick
Acct Mgr, C & C Offset Printing Co (UK) Ltd: Fia Fornari
Founded: 1980
Turnaround: varies
Print Runs: 2,000 min - 1,000,000 max
Business from Other Countries: 70%
*Branch Office(s)*
C & C Printing Co (NY) Inc, 401 Broadway, Suite 2015, New York, NY 10013-3016 *Tel:* 212-431-4210 *Fax:* 212-431-3960
    *E-mail:* newyorkinfo@ccoffset.com (New York City office)
C & C Joint Printing Co (Guangdong) Ltd, 7/Fl, Flat H, Greenview Apt No 38, Hou Guang Ping Hu Tong, Xi Cheng Ou, Beijing 100035, China, Contact: Mr Xiao Mungshen *Tel:* (010) 6650 3176 *Fax:* (010) 6650 3175
    *E-mail:* beijing@cancprinting.com (regional office)
C & C Joint Printing Co (Beijing) Ltd, Beijing Economic & Technological Development Area (BDA), No 3, Donghuan North Rd, Beijing 100176, China, Dir & Gen Mgr: Mr Zhang Lin Gui *Tel:* (010) 6787 6655 *Fax:* (010) 6787 8255 *E-mail:* beijing@cancprinting.com
C & C Offset Printing Co Ltd, C & C Bldg, 36 Ting Lai Rd, Tai Po, New Territories, Hong Kong *Tel:* 2666-4988 *Fax:* 2666-4938
    *E-mail:* offsetprinting@candcprinting.com (corporate headquarters)
C & C Joint Printing Co (Guangdong) Ltd (Changsha Office), The Building of Changsha City, Commercial Bank, No 1, Foreing Middle Rd, Rm 1218, Changsha, Hunan 41005, China, Contact: Ms Chen Jian *Tel:* (0731) 225 0288 *Fax:* (0731) 225 0178 *E-mail:* changsha@candcprinting.com (regional office)
Shanghai C & C Joint Printing Co Ltd, Fang Fa Bldg, No 29, Rm 304, 165 Dongzhu Anbin Rd, Shanghai 200050, China, Contact: Ms Wu Hiaohung *Tel:* (021) 6240-1305 *Fax:* (021) 6240-2090 *E-mail:* shanghai@candcprinting.com (regional office)
C & C Joint Printing Co (Guangdong) Ltd, Chunhu Industrial Estate, Pinghu, Long Gang, Shenzhen 518111, China *Tel:* (0755) 2845-8333 *Fax:* (0755) 2885-9911
    *E-mail:* guangdong@candcprinting.com (plant)
C & C Printing Japan Co Ltd, Tozaido Bldg, 3F, 2-6-12 Hitotsubashi, Chiyoda-ku, Tokyo 101-0003, Japan, Contact: Mr Yamamoto Masaaki *Tel:* (03) 5216-4580 *Fax:* (03) 5216-4610 *E-mail:* mail@candcprinting.co.jp *Web Site:* www.candcprinting.co.jp (regional office)

C & C Joint Printing Co (Guangdong) Ltd (Xian Office), 10 Xuanfengquiao, Jianguo Rd, Xian 710001, China *Tel:* (029) 741 8407 *Fax:* (029) 743 5730 *E-mail:* xian@candcprinting.co (regional office)

C & C Joint Printing Co (Guangdong) Ltd, Hua Xin Bldg E Block, Rm 1511, 2 Shuiyin Rd, Huanshi East, Guangzhou 510075, China, Contact: Mr Peng Ji Shan *Tel:* (020) 3760 0979; (020) 3760 0980 *Fax:* (020) 3760 0977 *E-mail:* guangzhou@candcprinting.com (regional office)

C & C Offset Printing Co (UK) Ltd, 2 New Burlington St, 4th fl, London W1S 2JE, United Kingdom, Dir: Tracy Broderick *Tel:* (020) 7287 7787 *Fax:* (020) 7287 7187 *E-mail:* tracy@candcoffset.co.uk

C & C Offset Printing Co Ltd, 150-154 Thistlethwaite St, South Melbourne, Victoria 3205, Australia, Contact: Lena Frew *Tel:* (03) 9699 7955 *Fax:* (03) 9699 1574 *E-mail:* lena.frew@candcprinting.com

**Colorprint Offset Inc**
80 Park Ave, Suite 10-N, New York, NY 10016
*Tel:* 212-681-9400 *Fax:* 212-681-9362
*E-mail:* ny@cpo.com.hk
*Web Site:* www.hq.cpo.bz
*Key Personnel*
Pres: Lee Moncho *E-mail:* lee@colorprintoffset.com
Prod Dir & Cust Serv Mgr: Kate Brady
   *E-mail:* kate@colorprintoffset.com
Founded: 1986
Turnaround: 15 Workdays
Print Runs: 100 min - 50,000 max
Business from Other Countries: 65%

**Martin Cook Associates Inc**
16 Sabal Bend, Palm Coast, FL 32137
*Tel:* 386-447-8692 *Fax:* 386-447-8746
*E-mail:* mcanewcity@aol.com
*Web Site:* www.mcabooks.com
*Key Personnel*
Pres: Martin Cook
Founded: 1977
Turnaround: 30-45 Workdays
Print Runs: 2,000 min - 300,000 max
Business from Other Countries: 15%
Membership(s): Bookbinders Guild of New York

**CS Graphics USA Inc**
Subsidiary of CS Graphics Pte Ltd Singapore
9748 Weddington Circle, Granite Bay, CA 95746
*Tel:* 916-791-9066 *Fax:* 916-791-9112
*Key Personnel*
Mgr, Sales & Mktg: Rick Marment
   *E-mail:* rick@csgraphics.us
Founded: 1980
Turnaround: 80 Workdays
Print Runs: 1,000 min - 75,000 max
Business from Other Countries: 30%

**Custom Services**
Subsidiary of Nationwide Custom Services Inc
77 Main St, Tappan, NY 10983
Mailing Address: PO Box 76, Tappan, NY 10983
*Tel:* 845-365-0414 *Fax:* 845-365-0864
*Key Personnel*
Owner & Pres: Norman Shaifer
VP & Mgr: Helen Newman
VP: Harry Title
Founded: 1960
Print Runs: 500 min - 10,000 max
Business from Other Countries: 30%

**Datapage Technologies International Inc**
222 Turner Blvd, St Peters, MO 63376-1079
*Tel:* 636-278-8888 *Toll Free Tel:* 800-876-3844
   *Fax:* 636-278-2180
*Web Site:* www.datapage.com

*Key Personnel*
Pres: Jack M Delo
VP, Sales: John E Ingerslew
VP, Publg: Linda S Blevins *E-mail:* lindab@datapage.com
VP, Info Systems: Ron McCafferty
Founded: 1969
Turnaround: 1-15 Workdays
Business from Other Countries: 10%

**Desktop Miracles Inc**
112 S Main, PMB 294, Stowe, VT 05672
*Tel:* 802-253-7900 *Fax:* 802-253-1900
*Web Site:* www.desktopmiracles.com
*Key Personnel*
Pres & CEO: Barry T Kerrigan *E-mail:* barry@desktopmiracles.com
Founded: 1994
Turnaround: 10-15 Workdays
Print Runs: 2,500 min
Business from Other Countries: 10%

**DNP America LLC**
Subsidiary of Dai Nippon Printing Co Ltd
335 Madison Ave, 3rd fl, New York, NY 10017
*Tel:* 212-503-1060 *Fax:* 212-286-1505
*Web Site:* www.dnp.co.jp/ *Cable:* DAIPRINTS NY
*Key Personnel*
Pres: Yoji Yamakawa
VP & Gen Mgr, Graphic Printing: Kazuteru Arai
   *E-mail:* arai-k@mail.dnp.co.jp
Founded: 1974
Turnaround: 30-60 Workdays
Print Runs: 1,000 min - 1,000,000 max
Business from Other Countries: 54%
*Branch Office(s)*
577 Airport Blvd, Suite 620, Burlingame, CA 94010, Gen Mgr: Kosuke Tago *Tel:* 650-340-6061 *Fax:* 650-340-6090

**Elegance Printing & Book Binding (USA)**
Member of The Elegance Printing Group
708 Glen Cove Ave, Glen Head, NY 11545
*Tel:* 516-676-5941 *Fax:* 516-676-5973
*Web Site:* www.elegancebooks.com
*Key Personnel*
Man Dir: Frank DeLuca *E-mail:* frank@elegancebooks.com
Founded: 1977
Turnaround: CTP projects, disk to proof 5 days. Reprints ship within 14 days. Proof to board books, ready to ship 3 weeks
Print Runs: 1,000 min - 1,000,000 max
Business from Other Countries: 40%

**Express Media Corp**
1419 Donelson Pike, Nashville, TN 37217
*Tel:* 615-360-6400 *Toll Free Tel:* 800-336-2631
   *Fax:* 615-360-3140
*E-mail:* info@expressmedia.com
*Web Site:* www.expressmedia.com
*Key Personnel*
Pres: Andrew Cameron
Founded: 1996
Turnaround: 3 Workdays
Print Runs: 1 min - 10,000 max
Business from Other Countries: 10%

**Fairfield Marketing Group Inc**
Subsidiary of FMG Inc
830 Sport Hill Rd, Easton, CT 06612-1250
*Tel:* 203-261-5585; 203-261-5568 *Fax:* 203-261-0884
*E-mail:* ffldmktgrp@aol.com
*Web Site:* www.fairfieldmarketing.com
*Key Personnel*
CEO & Pres: Edward P Washchilla *E-mail:* fmg.inc@aol.com
VP, Fin: Pamela L Johnson

VP, Fulfillment: Jason Paul Miller *Tel:* 203-261-5585 ext 203
Cust Servs Rep: Mike Lozada *Tel:* 203-261-5585 ext 204
Founded: 1987
Turnaround: 5-10 Workdays
Print Runs: 2,500 min - 1,000,000 max
Business from Other Countries: 10%
Membership(s): ABA; Association of Educational Publishers; The Direct Marketing Association; Direct Marketing Club of New York; Hudson Valley Direct Marketing Association; International Reading Association; National School Supply & Equipment Association; United States Chamber of Commerce

**The Floating Gallery & Advanced Self Publishing**
244 Madison Ave, Suite 254, New York, NY 10016
*Toll Free Tel:* 877-822-2500
*E-mail:* floatingal@aol.com
*Web Site:* www.thefloatinggallery.com
*Key Personnel*
Owner: Joel Hochman; Laurence Leichman
   *E-mail:* larrydtp@aol.com
Mktg Dir: Olga Vladimizov
Founded: 1992
BISAC compatible software
Turnaround: 21 Workdays; 1-7 for art
Print Runs: 1 min - 1,000,000 max
Business from Other Countries: 15%

**The Font Bureau Inc**
326 "A" St, Boston, MA 02210
*Tel:* 617-423-8770 *Fax:* 617-423-8771
*E-mail:* info@fontbureau.com
*Web Site:* www.fontbureau.com
*Key Personnel*
Retail Sales Mgr: Harry Parker
Founded: 1989
Turnaround: 1 Workday
Business from Other Countries: 20%

**Huron Valley Graphics Inc**
4597 Platt Rd, Ann Arbor, MI 48108
*Tel:* 734-477-0448 *Toll Free Tel:* 800-362-9655
   *Fax:* 734-477-0393
*E-mail:* custserv@hvg.com
*Web Site:* www.hvg.com
*Key Personnel*
Pres: Claudia Lybrink
Prodn Mgr: Kathryn C Steiner
Founded: 1971
Turnaround: 15 Workdays
Business from Other Countries: 10%

**IBT Global Ltd**, see Integrated Book Technology Inc

**Ikon Document Services**, see TEC Doc Publishing Inc

**Innodata Isogen Inc**
Three University Plaza, Hackensack, NJ 07601
*Tel:* 201-488-1200 *Toll Free Tel:* 800-567-4784
   *Fax:* 201-488-9099
*E-mail:* solutions@innodata-isogen.com
*Web Site:* www.innodata-isogen.com
*Key Personnel*
CEO: Jack Abuhoff
Exec VP: George Kondrach
VP, Sales: Martin Korsin
VP: Jan Palmen
VP, Mktg & Communs: Al Girardi
VP, Fin: Steven Agress
Founded: 1989
Turnaround: As little as 12 hours
Business from Other Countries: 25%
Membership(s): AAP; ALA; Center for Information Development & Content Management

Strategies; International Digital Enterprise Alliance; Localization Industry Standards Association; National Initiative for a Networked Cultural Heritage; Organization of Advancement of Structured Information Standards; Society for Scholarly Publishing; Software & Information Industry Association; World Wide Web Consortium

**Integrated Book Technology Inc**
Division of The IBT Group
18 Industrial Park Rd, Troy, NY 12180
*Tel:* 518-271-5117 *Fax:* 518-266-9422
*E-mail:* mail@integratedbook.com
*Web Site:* www.integratedbook.com
*Key Personnel*
CEO & Pres: John R Paeglow *E-mail:* johnp@integratedbook.com
VP & Chief Technol Officer: William Clockel *E-mail:* billc@integratedbook.com
VP, Sales & Mktg: Robert Lindberg *E-mail:* bobl@integratedbook.com
Dir, Info Technol: Michael Whalen *E-mail:* mikew@integratedbook.com
Regl Sales: Ledner Cunningham *E-mail:* lednerc@integratedbook.com
Founded: 1991
Turnaround: 1-15 Workdays
Print Runs: 10 min - 3,000 max
Business from Other Countries: 20%
*Branch Office(s)*
Rollesby Rd, King's Lynn, Norfolk PE3 3NR, United Kingdom *Tel:* (015) 5376 9072
Membership(s): BMI

**ITC**
Division of Software Services
2921 W Cypress Creek Rd, Fort Lauderdale, FL 33309
*Tel:* 954-623-3101 *Fax:* 954-623-3122
*E-mail:* team@inttype.com
*Web Site:* www.inttype.com
*Key Personnel*
Pres: Mukesh Narang
Dir, Sales & Mktg: Jane Stark *E-mail:* janes@inttype.com
Founded: 1995
BISAC compatible software
Turnaround: 10-20 workdays - rush service available (48 hr turnaround)
Business from Other Countries: 10%

**Leo Paper USA**
Unit of Leo Paper Group
1180 NW Maple St, Suite 102, Issaquah, WA 98027
*Tel:* 425-646-8801 *Fax:* 425-646-8805
*E-mail:* leo@leousa.com
*Web Site:* www.leopaper.com
*Key Personnel*
Sales: Tom Leach *E-mail:* tom@leousa.com
Founded: 1983
Turnaround: 90 Workdays
Print Runs: 3,500 min - 2,000,000 max
Business from Other Countries: 20%
*Branch Office(s)*
27 W 24 St, Suite 701, New York, NY 10010-3204, Contact: John Di Masi *Tel:* 917-783-3065 *Fax:* 917-305-0709

**Linick International Inc**
Division of The Linick Group Inc
Linick Bldg, 7 Putter Lane, Middle Island, NY 11953
Mailing Address: PO Box 102, Middle Island, NY 11953-0102
*Tel:* 631-924-3888 *Fax:* 631-924-3890
*E-mail:* linickgrp@att.net
*Web Site:* www.lgroup.addr.com
*Key Personnel*
Chmn & CEO: Andrew S Linick, PhD
Treas: Marvin Glickman

Exec VP: Roger Dextor
Founded: 1972
Turnaround: 21-30 Workdays
Print Runs: 2,500 min - 100,000 max
Business from Other Countries: 30%

**LK Litho**
Division of The Linick Group Inc
Linick Bldg, 7 Putter Lane, Middle Island, NY 11953
Mailing Address: PO Box 102, Middle Island, NY 11953-0102
*Tel:* 631-924-3888
*E-mail:* linickgrp@att.net
*Web Site:* www.lgroup.addr.com/lklitho.htm
*Key Personnel*
VP: Roger Dextor
Founded: 1968
BISAC compatible software
Turnaround: 7-10 Workdays depending on job
Print Runs: 5,000 min - 2,000,000 max
Business from Other Countries: 20%
Membership(s): Copywriters Council of America; The Direct Marketing Association; LIAC

**Mazer Publishing Services**
Division of The Mazer Corporation
6680 Poe Ave, Dayton, OH 45414
*Tel:* 937-264-2600 *Fax:* 937-264-2624
*E-mail:* info@mazer.com
*Web Site:* www.mazer.com
*Key Personnel*
Pres: William Franklin *E-mail:* bill_franklin@mazer.com
Exec VP: Ken Fultz *E-mail:* ken_fultz@mazer.com
Exec Dir, Sales: Bill Faber *Fax:* 937-264-2622 *E-mail:* bill_faber@mazer.com
Founded: 1964
Print Runs: 50 min - 25,000 max
Business from Other Countries: 10%
*Branch Office(s)*
2460 Sand Lake Rd, Orlando, FL 32809, Contact: Bryan Blakley *Tel:* 407-859-5552 *Fax:* 407-859-0643 *E-mail:* bryan_blakley@mazer.com
224 Lexington Ave, Fox River Grove, IL 60021, Contact: Dennis Bowman *Tel:* 847-639-1555 *Fax:* 847-639-1562 *E-mail:* dennis_bowman@mazer.com
22 Lehigh Rd, Wellesley, MA 02181, Contact: Ken Leahy *Tel:* 781-237-4112 *Fax:* 781-431-6184 *E-mail:* ken_leahy@mazer.com
22 Laurel Place, Upper Montclair, NJ 07043, Contact: John Martel *Tel:* 973-744-4320 *Fax:* 973-746-5608 *E-mail:* john_martel@mazer.com
3081 Glenmere Ct, Kettering, OH 45440, Contact: Mark Brewer *Tel:* 937-299-5746 *Fax:* 937-299-5761 *E-mail:* mark_brewer@mazer.com
Membership(s): BMI

**Midas Printing International Ltd**
Subsidiary of Midas Printing Group Ltd
35 Belleview Ave, Ossining, NY 10562
*Tel:* 914-941-2041
*E-mail:* info@midasprinting.com
*Web Site:* www.midasprinting.com
*Key Personnel*
US Contact: Gerald B Levine *E-mail:* gerald_levine@midasprinting.com
Dir, Sales & Mktg, Hong Kong: Paul Tang *Tel:* 24084040 *Fax:* 24065890 *E-mail:* paul@midasprinting.com
Busn Devt Mgr, China: Ian Lee *Tel:* 24084048 *Fax:* 24065874 *E-mail:* ian@midasprinting.com
Founded: 1990
Turnaround: 1 Week
Print Runs: 3,000 min
Business from Other Countries: 85%
*Branch Office(s)*
1/F, 100 Texaco Rd, Tsuen Wan, New Territo-

ries, Hong Kong *Tel:* 24076888 *Fax:* 24080611 (headquarters, send all inquires to this address)
Membership(s): Graphic Arts Association of Hong Kong

**Milanostampa/New Interlitho USA Inc**
Unit of Milanostampa New Interlitho AGG Printing Stars SRL
299 Broadway, Suite 901, New York, NY 10007
*Tel:* 212-964-2430 *Fax:* 212-964-2497
*Web Site:* www.milanostampa.com
*Key Personnel*
Chmn: Maria Rosa Filippino
Chmn & Sales Rep: Rino Varrasso *Tel:* 917-225-9460 *E-mail:* rvarrasso@milanostampa-usa.com
Founded: 1974
Turnaround: 30 Workdays
Print Runs: 1,000 min - 3,000,000 max
Business from Other Countries: 75%

**Pageworks**
4 Gibbons Circle, Old Saybrook, CT 06475
*Tel:* 860-395-5022; 860-434-3605 *Fax:* 860-388-4353
*Key Personnel*
Owner: Maggie Dana *E-mail:* maggiedana@aol.com; Jamie Temple *E-mail:* j23hc@sbcglobal.net
Founded: 1987
Business from Other Countries: 10%

**Palace Press International - Corporate Headquarters**
17 Paul Dr, San Rafael, CA 94903
*Tel:* 415-526-1370 *Fax:* 415-526-1394
*E-mail:* info@palacepress.com
*Web Site:* www.palacepress.com
*Key Personnel*
CEO: Raoul Goff *E-mail:* raoul@palacepress.com
Gen Mgr: Michael Madden *E-mail:* michael@palacepress.com
Founded: 1984
Turnaround: 90 Workdays
Print Runs: 3,000 min - 1,000,000 max
Business from Other Countries: 20%
*Branch Office(s)*
Palace Press International Los Angeles, 1499 Huntington Dr, Suite 408, South Pasadena, CA 91030, Contact: Roger Ma *Tel:* 626-282-8877 *Fax:* 626-282-6880 *E-mail:* roger@palacepress.com
Palace Press International New York, 180 Varick St, 10th fl, New York, NY 10014, Contact: Jessica Jones *Tel:* 212-462-2622 *Fax:* 212-463-9130 *E-mail:* jessica@palacepress.com

**Photoengraving Inc**
502 N Willow Ave, Tampa, FL 33606
*Tel:* 813-253-3427 *Fax:* 813-253-5491
*Web Site:* www.photoengravinginc.com
*Key Personnel*
Owner: Ed Dalton, Jr *E-mail:* eddalton@photoengravinginc.com
Founded: 1953
Turnaround: 3 Workdays
Business from Other Countries: 25%

**PrePress Imaging Inc**
1864 Scherer Pkwy, St Charles, MO 63303
*Tel:* 636-940-9146 *Toll Free Tel:* 800-886-6122 *Fax:* 636-896-8107
*E-mail:* mail@ppi-stl.com
*Web Site:* www.ppi-stl.com
*Key Personnel*
Pres & Owner: Wayne Kissel *E-mail:* wkissel@ppi-stl.com
Account Mgr: Christine Merrick *E-mail:* cmerrick@ppi-stl.com
Founded: 1989
Business from Other Countries: 20%

**Printing Corp of the Americas Inc**
620 SW 12 Ave, Fort Lauderdale, FL 33312
*Tel:* 954-781-8100 *Fax:* 954-781-8421
*Key Personnel*
Pres: Jan Tuchman
Founded: 1979
Turnaround: 5-10 Workdays
Print Runs: 500 min - 100,000 max
Business from Other Countries: 15%

**Quantum Colorgraphics**
166 Midland Ave, Montclair, NJ 07042
*Tel:* 973-783-0462 *Fax:* 973-783-0637
*Key Personnel*
Sr Acct Exec: Jeffrey Sestilio *E-mail:* jeff.cgi@
verizon.net
Print Runs: 1,000 min - 300,000 max
Business from Other Countries: 30%

**Sencor**
One W 34 St, Suite 1104, New York, NY 10001
*Tel:* 212-947-5601 *Fax:* 212-947-5604
*E-mail:* sales@sencor.net
*Web Site:* www.sencor.net
*Key Personnel*
Pres & CEO: George Martel *E-mail:* gmartel@
sencor.net
VP: Michael Martel *E-mail:* mvmartel@sencor.
net
Founded: 1984
BISAC compatible software
Turnaround: 5 Workdays
Business from Other Countries: 10%
*Branch Office(s)*
1991 Taft Ave, Pasay City, Manila 1306, Philip-
pines

**SNP Best-Set Typesetter Ltd**
Subsidiary of SNP Corp Ltd
50 S Buckhout St, Suite 208, Irvington, NY
10533
*Tel:* 914-693-1565 *Toll Free Tel:* 866-888-8767
*Fax:* 914-674-5923
*Web Site:* www.bestset-typesetter.com
*Key Personnel*
Dir (Hong Kong): Johnson Yeung *Tel:* 852-289-
6033 *E-mail:* johnson@bestset-typesetter.com
Sales Rep: Wai Man Yeung
*E-mail:* waimanyeung@snpcorp.com
Founded: 1986

Turnaround: 5 Workdays
Print Runs: 100 min - 200,000 max
Business from Other Countries: 98%
*Branch Office(s)*
3 Jiang nan Main Ave C, 3rd fl, Guangzhou,
China
10/F Wing On House, 71 Des Voeux Road C,
Central, Hong Kong
33 Alpin Way, TW7 4RJ Isleworth, Middlesex,
United Kingdom

**SpectraComp**
1609 Main St, Mechanicsburg, PA 17055
*Tel:* 717-697-8600 *Toll Free Tel:* 800-666-2662
*Fax:* 717-691-0433
*E-mail:* info@spectracomp.com
*Web Site:* www.spectracomp.com
*Key Personnel*
Pres: Terry Fackler *E-mail:* tfackler@
spectracomp.com
VP, Opers: Jeffrey Fackler
Founded: 1966
Turnaround: 1-10 Workdays
Business from Other Countries: 10%

**Square Two Design Inc**
2325 Third St, Suite 401, San Francisco, CA
94107
*Tel:* 415-437-3888 *Fax:* 415-437-3880
*E-mail:* sq2d@square2.com
*Web Site:* www.square2.com
*Key Personnel*
Pres: Eddie Lee
Founded: 1992
Business from Other Countries: 10%

**Studio 31**
2740 SW Martha Downs Blvd, No 358, Palm
City, FL 34990
*Tel:* 772-781-7195 *Fax:* 772-781-6044
*E-mail:* studio31@mindspring.com
*Web Site:* www.studio31.com
*Key Personnel*
Pres: Jim Wasserman
Founded: 1977
Business from Other Countries: 15%

**Taylor Publishing Company**
1550 W Mockingbird Lane, Dallas, TX 75235

*Tel:* 214-819-8226 *Toll Free Tel:* 800-677-2800
*Fax:* 214-630-1852
*E-mail:* info@taylorpub.com
*Web Site:* www.taylorpub.com
*Key Personnel*
CEO: Dave Fiore
Dir, Fine Books & Div Sales Mgr: Jay Love
Founded: 1939
Turnaround: 45 Workdays
Print Runs: 300 min - 25,000 max
Business from Other Countries: 10%

**TEC Doc Publishing Inc**
Formerly Ikon Document Services
399 River Rd, Hudson, MA 01749-2627
*Tel:* 978-567-6000 *Fax:* 978-562-4304
*Web Site:* www.tecdocpub.com
Founded: 1973
Turnaround: 3 Workdays
Print Runs: 10 min - 5,000 max
Business from Other Countries: 10%

**Times International Publishing**
Division of Times Publishing Ltd/Singapore
99 White Plains Rd, Tarrytown, NY 10591
*Tel:* 914-366-9888 *Fax:* 914-366-9898
*Web Site:* www.tpl.com.sg
*Key Personnel*
Cust Serv Exec: Bonnie Stone *E-mail:* bstone@
marshallcavendish.com
Sales Mgr: Suresh Kumar *E-mail:* skumar@
marshallcavendish.com
Founded: 1965
Print Runs: 2,000 min - 500,000 max
Business from Other Countries: 90%

**Fred Weidner & Daughter Printers**
15 Maiden Lane, Suite 1505, New York, NY
10038
*Tel:* 212-964-8676 *Fax:* 212-964-8677
*E-mail:* info@fwdprinters.com
*Web Site:* www.fwdprinters.com
*Key Personnel*
Pres: Fred Weidner, III
Exec VP: Cynthia Weidner *E-mail:* cynthia@
fwdprinters.com
Creative Dir: Carol Mittelsdorf
Founded: 1860
Turnaround: 5-10 Workdays
Print Runs: 1,000 min - 500,000 max
Business from Other Countries: 25%

# Printing, Binding & Book Finishing Index

# BOOK PRINTING - HARDBOUND

# BOOK PRINTING - SOFTBOUND

## HOLOGRAMS

## JOURNAL PRINTING

## LETTERPRESS

# Printing, Binding & Book Finishing

This section includes companies throughout the world that offer printing, binding and/or book finishing services. Those U.S. and Canadian companies with 10% or more of their business done outside North America are also included here. Immediately preceding this section is an index classifying companies by services offered.

## Australia

**Southwood Press Pty Ltd**
76-82 Chapel St, Marrickville, NSW 2204
*Tel:* (02) 9560 5100 *Fax:* (02) 9550 0097
*E-mail:* info@southwoodpress.com.au
*Web Site:* www.southwoodpress.com.au
*Key Personnel*
Production Manager: Patrick Jayatilake
Sales Manager: Elizabeth Finniecome
Founded: 1966
Turnaround: 15-20 workdays
Print Runs: 500 min - 20,000 max
Business from Other Countries: 1%

## Austria

**ADEVA (Akademische Druck-u Verlagsanstalt)**
Auersperggasse 12, 8010 Graz
Mailing Address: Postfach 598, 8011 Graz
*Tel:* (0316) 3644 *Fax:* (0316) 364424
*E-mail:* info@adeva.com
*Web Site:* www.adeva.com *Cable:* ADEVA-GRAZ
*Key Personnel*
Dir: Dr Ursula Struzl
Founded: 1949
Print Runs: 300 min - 10,000 max
Business from Other Countries: 80%
*Branch Office(s)*
Purgleitnergasse 10, Ecke Marburgerstr, 8042
  Graz

**Akademische Druck- u Verlagsanstalt**, see
  ADEVA (Akademische Druck-u Verlagsanstalt)

**Dr Paul Struzl GmbH**, see ADEVA
  (Akademische Druck-u Verlagsanstalt)

## Belgium

**Delabie Europrint SA**
Blvd de l'Eurozone 8, 7700 Mouscron
*Tel:* (056) 84 10 00
*Key Personnel*
PDG: D M Delabie
Sales Manager: Willem Mandeville
Finance: Luc Haspeslagh
Production: Debie Bertrand
Founded: 1964
Turnaround: 8 Workdays
Print Runs: 100,000 min - 1,000,000 max
Business from Other Countries: 60%

**IMPF bvba**
Sint-Amandstr 18, 9000 Ghent
*Tel:* (09) 225 44 29
*Key Personnel*
Manager: Xavier Dewulf
Founded: 1958
Business from Other Countries: 10%

**Drukkerij Lannoo NV** (Lannoo Printers)
Kasteelstr 97, 8700 Tielt
*Tel:* (051) 42 42 11 *Fax:* (051) 40 70 70
*E-mail:* lannoo@lannooprint.be
*Web Site:* www.lannooprint.be
*Key Personnel*
General Manager & Marketing Dir: Stefaan Lannoo *E-mail:* stefaan.lannoo@lannooprint.be
Founded: 1909
Turnaround: 10 Workdays
Print Runs: 100 min - 1,000,000 max
Business from Other Countries: 30%

## Canada

**Aardvark Enterprises**
Division of Speers Investments Ltd
204 Millbank Dr SW, Calgary, AB T2Y 2H9
*Tel:* 403-256-4639
*Key Personnel*
Pres: J Alvin Speers
Founded: 1970 (Small Press Pioneers)
Turnaround: 30 Workdays
Print Runs: 10 min - 1,000 max
Business from Other Countries: 25%

**Appleby's Bindery Ltd**
1303 Rte 102, Upper Gagetown, NB E5M 1R5
*Tel:* 506-488-2086 *Toll Free Tel:* 800-561-2005
  (Canada only) *Fax:* 506-488-2086
*E-mail:* applbind@nbnet.nb.ca
*Key Personnel*
Pres & Owner: David E Appleby
Mgr: Edward Appleby
Founded: 1976
Turnaround: 30 Workdays
Business from Other Countries: 10%

**Blitzprint Inc**
1235 64 Ave SE, Calgary, AB T2H 2J7
*Tel:* 403-253-5151 *Toll Free Tel:* 866-479-3248
  *Fax:* 403-253-5642
*E-mail:* blitzprint@blitzprint.com
*Web Site:* www.blitzprint.com
*Key Personnel*
Pres: Kevin Lanuke *E-mail:* klanuke@blitzprint.
  com
COO & VP: Peter Friebel *E-mail:* pfriebel@
  blitzprint.com
Turnaround: 10
Print Runs: 1 min - 10,000 max
Business from Other Countries: 50%
Membership(s): Association of Book Publishers
  of British Columbia; Canadian Booksellers Association

**Coach House Printing**
401 Huron St, Rear, Toronto, ON M5S 2G5
*Tel:* 416-979-2217 *Fax:* 416-977-1158
*E-mail:* mail@chbooks.com
*Web Site:* www.chbooks.com
*Key Personnel*
Publr: Stan Bevington
Founded: 1965
Turnaround: 14 Workdays
Print Runs: 200 min - 2,000 max
Business from Other Countries: 10%

**Maracle Press Ltd**
1156 King St E, Oshawa, ON L1H 7N4
*Tel:* 905-723-3438 *Toll Free Tel:* 800-558-8604
  *Fax:* 905-428-6024
*E-mail:* info@maraclepress.com
*Web Site:* www.maraclepress.com
*Key Personnel*
Pres & Gen Mgr: Bruce A Fenton
  *E-mail:* bfenton@maraclepress.com
VP, Busn Devt: Ronald G Taylor
  *E-mail:* rtaylor@maraclepress.com
Founded: 1920
Turnaround: 10 Workdays
Print Runs: 500 min - 500,000 max
Business from Other Countries: 25%
Membership(s): BMI; Canadian Book Manufacturer Association; Canadian Printing Industries
  Association; Ontario Printing & Imaging Association; PIA/GATF

**McLaren Morris & Todd Co**
3270 American Dr, Mississauga, ON L4V 1B5
*Tel:* 905-677-3592 *Fax:* 905-677-3675
*Web Site:* www.mmt.ca
*Key Personnel*
Pres & CEO: Tony Sgro
Cont: Nancy Marquis *Tel:* 905-677-3592 ext 247
Founded: 1956
Turnaround: 15 Workdays
Print Runs: 5,000 min - 1,000,000 max
Business from Other Countries: 10%

**Preney Print & Litho Inc**
1457 Lauzon Rd, Windsor, ON N8S 3N2
*Tel:* 519-966-3412 *Toll Free Tel:* 877-870-4164
  *Fax:* 519-966-4996
*E-mail:* contactus@preneyprint.com
*Web Site:* www.preneyprint.com
*Key Personnel*
Pres: John Preney
Founded: 1972
Turnaround: 15 Workdays
Print Runs: 2,000 min
Business from Other Countries: 20%

**Printcrafters Inc**
78 Hutchings St, Winnipeg, MB R2X 3B1
*Tel:* 204-633-7117 *Fax:* 204-694-1519
*E-mail:* info@printcraftersinc.com
*Web Site:* www.printcraftersinc.com
*Key Personnel*
Pres: Bob Payne *Tel:* 204-633-7117 ext 223
  *Fax:* 204-694-1594 *E-mail:* bpayne@
  printcraftersinc.com
Founded: 1996 (Employee owned)
Turnaround: 5-20 Workdays
Print Runs: 500,000 min
Business from Other Countries: 30%
Membership(s): Canadian Printing Industries Association

**Schawk**
543 Richmond St W, Suite 125, Toronto, ON
  M5V 1Y6
*Tel:* 416-703-1445 *Fax:* 416-703-1494
*Web Site:* www.schawk.com
*Key Personnel*
Pres: Bob Cockerill
Founded: 1965
Business from Other Countries: 10%

**Transcontinental Printing Book Group**
Division of Transcontinental Group
395 Lebeau Blvd, St-Laurent, QC H4N 1S2
*Tel:* 514-337-8560 *Toll Free Tel:* 800-361-3599
*Fax:* 514-339-2252
*Web Site:* www.transcontinental.com; www.
transcontinental-printing.com
*Key Personnel*
Sr VP, Book Group: Jacques Gregoire
Dir, Strategic Busn Devt: Denis
Beaudin *Tel:* 514-339-2220 ext 4101
*E-mail:* beaudind@transcontinental.ca
Founded: 1976
Turnaround: 15-20 workdays casebound; 10-15
workdays softcover
Print Runs: 1,000 min
Business from Other Countries: 30%
*Branch Office(s)*
3653 W Leland Ave, Suite One, West Chicago,
IL 60625, United States, Contact: Tim Tay-
lor *Tel:* 773-583-8155 *Fax:* 773-583-8162
*E-mail:* tim.taylor@transcontinental.ca (Mid-
west)
10 Rountree Dr, PO Box 2551, Duxbury, MA
02331, United States, Contact: Joe Pisco
*Tel:* 781-585-6781 *E-mail:* joseph.pisco@
transcontinental.ca (East Coast)
393 Highland Ave, Quincy, MA 02170-4013,
United States, Contact: Mike Gazzola
*Tel:* 617-770-1435 *E-mail:* mike.gazzola@
transcontinental.ca (East Coast)
37 Herman Blvd, Franklin Square, NY 11010,
United States, Contact: Tom Malloy *Tel:* 516-
775-2980 *Fax:* 516-488-0253 *E-mail:* mallyt@
transcontinental.ca (NY)
175 W 79 St, No 8-E, New York, NY 10024,
United States, Contact: Ellen Lerner
*E-mail:* ellen.lerner@transcontinental.ca
109 Gallagher Dr, Franklin, TN 37064, United
States (Southeast), Contact: Steve Absher
1485 Stevens St, White Rock, BC V4B 4Y3,
Contact: Wade Davies *Tel:* 604-535-8800
*Fax:* 604-535-8802 *E-mail:* daviesw@
transcontinental.ca (West Coast)
Membership(s): BMI; National Association for
Printing Leadership; PIA/GATF

**Tri-Graphic Printing (Ottawa) Ltd**
485 Industrial Ave, Ottawa, ON K1G 0Z1
*Tel:* 613-731-7441 *Toll Free Tel:* 800-267-9750
*Fax:* 613-731-3741
*Web Site:* www.tri-graphic.com
*Key Personnel*
VP & Gen Mgr: Doug K Doane
*E-mail:* ddoane@tri-graphic.com
VP, Prodn & Servs: Fred Malleau *Tel:* 905-665-
8500 *E-mail:* fmalleau@tri-graphic.com
Founded: 1968
Turnaround: 10-15 Workdays
Print Runs: 1,000 min - 100,000 max
Business from Other Countries: 10%
*Branch Office(s)*
213 Byron St S, Suite 201, Whitby, ON L1N 4P7
*Tel:* 905-665-8500 *Fax:* 905-665-8501

**University of Toronto Press Inc**
Printing Division, 5201 Dufferin St, North York,
ON M3H 5T8
*Tel:* 416-667-7767 *Fax:* 416-667-7803
*E-mail:* printing@utpress.utoronto.ca
*Web Site:* www.utpress.utoronto.ca
*Key Personnel*
Pres & Publr: John Yates
Founded: 1901
Turnaround: 10-15 Workdays
Print Runs: 10 min - 200,000 max
Business from Other Countries: 15%
Membership(s): BMI

**Webcom Limited**
3480 Pharmacy Ave, Toronto, ON M1W 2S7
*Tel:* 416-496-1000 *Toll Free Tel:* 800-665-9322
*Fax:* 416-496-1537
*E-mail:* webcom@webcomlink.com
*Web Site:* www.webcomlink.com
*Key Personnel*
VP, Sales & Mktg: Mike Collinge
Mktg Mgr: Beth Craig
Founded: 1976
Turnaround: 15 Workdays
Print Runs: 50 min - 100,000 max
Business from Other Countries: 40%

# Czech Republic

**GRASPO CZ AS - Druckerei und
Buchbinderei**
Pod Sternberkem 324, 76302 Zlin
*Tel:* (0577) 606111 *Fax:* (0577) 104052
*E-mail:* graspo@graspo.com
*Web Site:* www.graspo.com
*Key Personnel*
Contact: Marie Polaskova
Founded: 1995
Print Runs: 1,000 min
Business from Other Countries: 50%
*Branch Office(s)*
Racianska 109/c, 83102 Bratislava
Sinkulova 48, 14000 Prague 4

# Denmark

**Bianco Lunos Bogtrykkeri AS**
Subsidiary of Carl Allers Etablissement AS
Otto Monsteds Gade 3, 1571 Copenhagen V
*Tel:* 33140781 *Fax:* 33913808
*Key Personnel*
General Manager: J Heede Sorensen
Founded: 1871

# Finland

**Gummerus Printing**
Subsidiary of Gummerus Oy
Alasinkatu 1-3, 40320 Jyvaskyla
Mailing Address: PO Box 444, 40351 Jyvaskyla
*Tel:* (014) 683 525 *Fax:* (014) 685 166
*E-mail:* printing@gummerus.fi
*Web Site:* www.gummerus.fi
*Key Personnel*
Marketing Dir: Mr Martti Aaltonen
*E-mail:* martti.aaltonen@gummerus.fi
Founded: 1872
Turnaround: 20-60 Workdays
Print Runs: 1,000 min - 100,000 max
Business from Other Countries: 15%

**WS Bookwell Ltd**
Teollisuustie 4, 06100 Porvoo
*Tel:* (019) 21 941 *Fax:* (019) 219 4800
*E-mail:* pekka.tykkylainen@bookwell.fi
*Web Site:* www.bookwell.fi
*Key Personnel*
Man Dir: Magnus Breitenstein *Tel:* (019) 2194
608 *E-mail:* magnus.breitenstein@bookwell.fi
Marketing Manager: Pekka Tykkyloinen
*Tel:* (019) 219 4663 *E-mail:* pekka.
tykkylainen@bookwell.fi
Founded: 1878
Business from Other Countries: 50%
*Parent Company:* WSOY

*Ultimate Parent Company:* Sanoma WSOY
*Branch Office(s)*
Messdorferstr 127, 53123 Bonn, Germany, Con-
tact: Markku Rapeli *Tel:* (0228) 986 4006
*Fax:* (0228) 986 4008
PO Box 3, Lowestoft, Suffolk NR33 8EY, United
Kingdom *Tel:* (502) 742 038 *Fax:* (502) 742
039

# France

**Imprimerie Bene**
12 rue Pradier, 30000 Nimes
*Tel:* (04) 66294897 *Fax:* (04) 66382146
*Key Personnel*
President: Jacques Enfer
Print Runs: 100 min - 10,000 max
Business from Other Countries: 20%

**Imprimerie Gaignault**
Route De Levroux, 36100 Issoudun

**Plein Chant**
16120 Bassac
*Tel:* (05) 45 81 93 26 *Fax:* (05) 45 81 92 83
*Web Site:* www.lelibraire.com
*Key Personnel*
Contact: Edmond Thomas
Founded: 1971
Print Runs: 600 min - 1,000 max
Business from Other Countries: 5%

**Signes du Monde**
69 rue St Gizons, 40700 Hagetmau
*Tel:* (05) 58 79 54 90
*Key Personnel*
Production: Hubert Saint-Genez

# Germany

**Baader Buch- u Offsetdruckerei GmbH & Co
KG CL**
Gutenbergstr 1, 72522 Muensingen Wurh
*Tel:* (07381) 791 *Cable:* BAADER-MUNSINGEN
Founded: 1835
Turnaround: 1 Workday
Print Runs: 1,000 min - 15,000 max

**Fachhochschule Stuttgart - Hochschule der
Medien (HdM)**
Nobelstr 10, 70569 Stuttgart
*Tel:* (0711) 685 2807 *Fax:* (0711) 685 6650
*E-mail:* info@hdm-stuttgart.de
*Web Site:* www.hdm-stuttgart.de
*Telex:* 725 185 fhd d
*Key Personnel*
Contact: Prof Eduard H Schoenstedt

**G Braun (vormals G Braun'sche
Hofbuchdruckerei und Verlag)**
Karl-Friedrichstr 14-18, 76 133 Karlsruhe
*Tel:* (0721) 1607320 *Fax:* (0721) 1607321
*E-mail:* info@gbraun-immo.de
*Web Site:* www.gbraun.de; www.gbraun-immo.de
*Telex:* 7 826 904
*Key Personnel*
Contact: Michael Schimmele

**Hochschule der Medien (HdM)**, see
Fachhochschule Stuttgart - Hochschule der
Medien (HdM)

**C Maurer Druck und Verlag**
Schubartstr 21, 73312 Geislingen/Steige
*Tel:* (07331) 9300
*Web Site:* www.maurer-online.de
*Key Personnel*
Contact: Carl Otto Maurer *Tel:* (07331) 930-112
Founded: 1856

**Media-Print Informationstechnologie GmbH**
Unit of Media-Print GmbH & Co KG
Schwarzenraben 7, 59558 Lippstadt
*Tel:* (02941) 2 72-300 *Fax:* (02941) 2 72-540
*E-mail:* kg@mediaprint.de
*Web Site:* www.mediaprint.de
*Key Personnel*
Man Dir: Dr Otto W Drosihn *E-mail:* drdrosihn@ kg.mediaprint.de
Founded: 1993
Turnaround: 5-10 Workdays
Print Runs: 100 min - 300,000 max
Business from Other Countries: 10%

**MOHN Media**
Subsidiary of Bertelsmann AG
Carl-Bertelsmann-Str 161M, 33311 Guetersloh
*Tel:* (05241) 80-4 04 10 *Fax:* (05241) 2 42 82
*E-mail:* mohnmedia@bertelsmann.de
*Web Site:* www.mohnmedia.de
*Key Personnel*
Man Dir: Markus Dohle
Founded: 1824
Business from Other Countries: 25%

**Oertel & Sporer GmbH & Co**
Burgstr 1-7, 72764 Reutlingen
Mailing Address: Postfach 1642, D-72706 Reutlingen
*Tel:* (07121) 302555 *Fax:* (07121) 302558
*Key Personnel*
Publisher: Valdo Lehari
Manager & Printer: Ermo Lehari
Print Runs: 500 min - 50,000 max

**Priese GmbH & Co**
Schwedlerstr 5, 14193 Berlin
*Tel:* (030) 8263024 *Fax:* (030) 8266024
*Key Personnel*
Contact: Elma Priese; Hans Joachim Priese

**Vier-Tuerme GmbH Benedikt Press**
Schweinfurter Str 40, 97359 Muensterschwarzach Abtei
*Tel:* (09324) 20214 *Fax:* (09324) 20444
*E-mail:* br.sturmius@vier-tuerme.de.oder; w. stafflinger@vier-tuerme.de
*Web Site:* www.vier-tuerme.de/benedictpress
*Key Personnel*
Contact: Josef Stoecklein
Founded: 1951
Turnaround: 8-16 Workdays
Print Runs: 300 min - 20,000 max
Business from Other Countries: 5%

# Hong Kong

**Bookbuilders Ltd**
Unit J 13/F Yeung Yiu Chung No 8 Industrial Bldg, 20 Wang Hoi Rd, Kowloon Bay, Kowloon
*Tel:* 27968123 *Fax:* 27968267; 27968690
*E-mail:* lph@netvigator.com
*Key Personnel*
Man Dir: Leslie Henman
General Manager: Edward Chan

**C & C Offset Printing Co Ltd**
Subsidiary of C & C Joint Printing Co (HK) Ltd under Sino United (Holdings) Hong Kong Ltd
C&C Bldg, floor 14, 36 Ting Lai Rd, Tai Po, New Territories
*Tel:* 2666-4988 *Fax:* 2666-4938
*E-mail:* offsetprinting@candcprinting.com
*Web Site:* www.ccoffset.com
*Key Personnel*
Dir & General Manager: Jackson Leung
Deputy Man Dir: Kee Lee
Deputy General Manager: Ivy Lam
Assistant General Manager: Kit Wong
Senior Sales Manager (Special Project): Francis Ho
Dir & Executive Vice President, C & C Offset Printing Co (USA) Inc, Portland OR, USA: Charles H Clark, IV *E-mail:* cclark@ccoffset. com
Development Manager, C & C Offset Printing Co (USA) Inc, Portland, OR, USA: Jenny Whittier *E-mail:* jwhittier@ccoffset.com
Customer Service Manager, C & C Offset Printing Co (USA) Inc, Portland, OR, USA: Ernest Li *E-mail:* ernestli@ccoffset.com
Dir & Executive Vice President, C & C Offset Printing Co (NY) Inc, New York, NY, USA: Simon Chan *E-mail:* schan@ccoffset.com
Assistant General Manager-China Sales, C & C Joint Printing Co (Ghuangdong) Ltd, Shenzhen, China: Simon Zhang
President, C & C Printing Japan Co Ltd, Tokyo, Japan: Yamamoto Masaaki
Customer Service Manager, C & C Offset Printing Co (NYC), Inc, New York, NY: Frances Harkness *E-mail:* fharkness@ccoffset.com
Man Dir, C & C Joint Printing Co (Beijing), Ltd, Beijing, China: Zhang Lin Gui
Dir, C & C Offset Printing Co (UK), Ltd: Tracy Broderick
Account Manager, C & C Offset Printing Co (UK) Ltd: Fia Fornari
Founded: 1980
Turnaround: 30-42 Workdays
Print Runs: 2,000 min - 1,000,000 max
Business from Other Countries: 60%
*Branch Office(s)*
C & C Offset Printing Co (USA) Inc, 2632 SE 25th Ave, Suite D, Portland, OR 97202, United States *Tel:* 503-233-1834 *Fax:* 503-233-7815 *E-mail:* portlandinfo@ccoffset.com (shipping)
C & C Offset Printing Co (NY) Inc, 401 Broadway, Suite 2015, New York, NY 10013-3004, United States *Tel:* 212-431-4210 *Fax:* 212-431-3960 *E-mail:* newyorkinfo@ccoffset.com
C & C Joint Printing Co (Guangdong) Ltd, Chunhu Industrial Estate, Pinghu, Long Gang, Shenzhen 518111, China *Tel:* (0755) 2845-8333 *Fax:* (0755) 2845-9911 *E-mail:* guangdong@candcprinting.com *Web Site:* www.candcprinting.com (Plant)
C & C Printing Japan Co Ltd, 2-6-12 Hitotsubashi, Tozaido Bldg 3F, Chiyoda-ku, Tokyo 101-0003, Japan *Tel:* (03) 5216-4580 *Fax:* (03) 5216-4610 *E-mail:* mail@candcprinting.co.jp *Web Site:* www.candcprinting.com
C & C Joint Printing Co (Guangdong) Ltd, 7/F, Flat H, Green View Apartment, No 38, Hou Guang Ping Hu Tong, Xi Cheng Qu, Beijing 100035, China *Tel:* (010) 6650-3176 *Fax:* (010) 6650-3175 *E-mail:* beijing@candcprinting.com
C & C Joint Printing Co (Guangdong) Ltd, Room 304, Fang Fa Bldg, No 29, 165 Ave, Dongzhuanbang Rd, Shanghai 200050, China *Tel:* (021) 6240-1305 *Fax:* (021) 6240-2090 *E-mail:* shanghaioffice@candcprinting.com
C & C Joint Printing Co (Guangdong) Ltd, Room 1511, Hua Xin Bldg, East Block, 2 Shuiyin Rd, Huanshi East, Guangzhou 510075, China *Tel:* (020) 3760-0979 *Fax:* (020) 3760-0977 *E-mail:* quangzhou@candcprinting.com
C & C Offset Printing Co (UK) Ltd, 2 New Burlington St, 4th floor, London W1S 2JE,

United Kingdom, Dir: Tracy Broderick
*Tel:* (020) 7287 7787 *Fax:* (020) 7287 7187
*E-mail:* tracy@candcoffset.co.uk

**Caritas Printing Training Centre**
Caritas House, 3rd floor, Block D, 2 Caine Rd, Hong Kong
*Tel:* 2526 1148 *Fax:* 2537 1231
*Key Personnel*
General Manager: Isaac Mak
Print Runs: 1,000 min - 100,000 max
Business from Other Countries: 50%

**Colorprint Offset**
Unit 1808-9, 18/F, 8 Commercial Tower, 8 Sun Yip St, Chai Wan
*Tel:* 2896-7777 *Fax:* 2889-6606
*E-mail:* info@cpo.com.hk
*Web Site:* www.cpo.com.hk
*Key Personnel*
Sales Manager: Jennifer Weston *Tel:* 2903-5062
Contact: Eva Lav; Ian Lee
Turnaround: Standard 2 week turnaround
Print Runs: 3,000 min - 100,000 max
Business from Other Countries: 80%
*Sales Office(s):* Gainsborough House, 81 Oxford St, London W1R 1RB, United Kingdom
80 Park Ave, Suite 10N, New York, NY 10016, United States

**Commercial Colorlab Ltd**
Block A 7/F, Aik San Factory Bldg, 14 Westland Rd, Quarry Bay
*Tel:* 2880 5128
*Key Personnel*
Dir: Simon Wong; Fong Lee Yong
Turnaround: 10 Workdays
Business from Other Countries: 30%
*Branch Office(s)*
5/F, Block E, Finance Bldg, 254-256 Des Voeux Rd, Central

**Creative Printing Ltd**
Formerly Morris Press Ltd
Wah Ha Industrial Bldg, 12/F, Block B, 8 Shipyard Lane, Quarry Bay
*Tel:* 25632187; 2563 2188 *Fax:* 25659069
*Key Personnel*
President & Contact: Suzy P Morris
*Tel:* 732-572-5185 *Fax:* 732-572-5150
*E-mail:* spmorris@ix.netcom.com
Dir: Raymond Shing; Raynond Shing
Contact: William M F Shui
Turnaround: 20 Workdays
Print Runs: 5,000 min - 100,000 max
Business from Other Countries: 50%

**Dai Nippon Printing Co (Hong Kong) Ltd**
Division of Dai Nippon Printing Co Ltd
Tsuen Wan Industrial Centre, 2-5/F, 220-248 Texaco Rd, Tsuen Wan, New Territories
*Tel:* 2408-0188 *Fax:* 2614-7585; 2407-6201
*E-mail:* info@mail.dnp.co.jp
*Web Site:* www.dnp.co.jp *Cable:* DNPICO
*Key Personnel*
Administration & Finance Dir: Mr K Miya
Print Runs: 5,000 min - 200,000 max
Business from Other Countries: 85%
*Branch Office(s)*
Dai Nippon Printing Co (Australia) Pty Ltd, St Martins Tower, Suite 1002, Level 10, 31 Market St, Sydney, NSW 2000, Australia *Tel:* (02) 9267-8166 *Fax:* (02) 9267-9533
DNP America LLC, Los Angeles Office, 3858 Carson St, Suite 300, Torrance, CA 90503, United States *Tel:* 310-540-5123 *Fax:* 310-543-3260
DNP America LLC, New York Office, 335 Madison Ave, 3rd floor, New York, NY 10017, United States *Tel:* 212-503-1060 *Fax:* 212-286-1501
DNP America LLC, Silicon Valley Office, 3235 Kifer Rd, Suite 100, Santa Clara, CA 95051,

United States *Tel:* 408-735-8880 *Fax:* 408-735-0453

DNP Corporation USA, New York Office, 335 Madison Ave, 3rd floor, New York, NY 10017, United States *Tel:* 212-503-1850 *Fax:* 212-286-1490

DNP Corporation USA, San Francisco Office, 577 Airport Blvd, Suite 620, Burlingame, CA 94010, United States *Tel:* 650-558-4050 *Fax:* 650-340-6095

DNP Denmark A/S, Skruegangen 2, 2690 Karlslunde, Denmark *Tel:* 4616-5100 *Fax:* 4616-5200

DNP Electronics America LLC, 2391 Fenton St, Chula Vista 91914, United States *Tel:* 619-397-6700 *Fax:* 619-397-6729

DNP Europa GmbH, Berliner Allee 26, 40212 Dusseldorf, Germany *Tel:* (0211) 8620-180 *Fax:* (0211) 8620-1895

DNP IMS America Corporation, 4524 Enterprise Dr NW, Concord, NC 28027, United States *Tel:* 704-784-8100 *Fax:* 704-784-2777

DNP IMS France SAS, 14, rue da la Violette, 22100 Dinan, France

DNP Photomask Europe SpA, Via Olivatti 2/A, 20041 Agrate Brianza, Italy *Tel:* (039) 65493-3000 *Fax:* (039) 65493-215

DNP Singapore Pte Ltd, 896 Dunearn Rd, No 04-09, Sime Darby Centre, Singapore 589472, Singapore *Tel:* 469-7611 *Fax:* 466-8486

DNP Taiwan Co Ltd, Rm D, 6 fl, 44 Chung-Shan N Rd Sec 2, Taipei 104, Taiwan, Province of China *Tel:* (02) 2327-8311 *Fax:* (02) 2327-8283

DNP UK Co Ltd, 27 Throgmorton St, 4th floor, London EC2N 2AQ, United Kingdom *Tel:* (020) 7588 2088 *Fax:* (020) 7588 2089

PT DNP Indonesia, Kawasan Industri Pulogadung, Jalan Pulogadung Kaveling II, Blok H, No 2-3, Jakarta Timur, Indonesia *Tel:* (021) 4610313 *Fax:* (021) 4605795

Tien Wah Press (Pte) Ltd, 4 Pandan Crescent, Singapore 128475, Singapore *Tel:* 466-6222 *Fax:* 469-3894

TWP Sdn Bhd, 89, Jalan Tampoi, Kawasan Perindustrian Tampoi, 80350 Johor Bahru, Johor, Malaysia *Tel:* (07) 2369899 *Fax:* (07) 2363148

**Everbest Printing Co Ltd**
Ko Fai Industrial Bldg, Block C5, 10th floor, 7 Ko Fai Rd, Yau Tong, Kowloon
*Tel:* 2727 4433 *Fax:* 2772 7687
*E-mail:* sales@everbest.com.hk
*Web Site:* www.everbest.com
*Key Personnel*
Man Dir: Kenneth Chung
Customer Account Executive: Frankie Lee; Ronny Ng
Founded: 1954
Turnaround: 28 Workdays
Print Runs: 1,000 min - 1,000,000 max
Business from Other Countries: 90%
*Branch Office(s)*
Everbest Printing (Australian & New Zealand Office), 100 Macaulay Rd, Stanmore, NSW 2048, Australia, Lionel Marz *Tel:* 612-9568-5879 *Fax:* 612-9568-5902 *E-mail:* lmarz@onaustralia.com.au
Everbest Canada, 50 Emblem Court, Scarborough, ON M1S 1B1, Canada, Connie Chung *Tel:* 416-286-2525 *Fax:* 416-286-2526 *E-mail:* everbest@aprinco.com
*U.S. Office(s):* Spectrum Books Inc, 2300 Bethards Dr, Suite C, Santa Rosa, CA 95405-8658, United States, Duncan McCallum *Tel:* 707-542-6044 *Fax:* 707-542-6045 *E-mail:* specbooks@aol.com
Four Colour Imports, 2843 Brownsboro Rd, Suite 102, Louisville, KY 40206, United States, George Dick *Tel:* 502-896-9644 *Fax:* 502-896-9594 *E-mail:* sales@fourcolour.com *Web Site:* www.fourcolour.com

Everbest Midwest, 6428 Margaret's Lane, Edina, MN 55439, United States, Dr Josie Lo *Tel:* 612-944-0854 *Fax:* 912-829-7670 *E-mail:* sklo@aol.com

**Golden Cup Printing Co Ltd**
Seapower Industrial Centre, 6/F, 177 Hoi Bun Rd, Kwun Tong, Kowloon
*Tel:* 2343 4254; 23434255 *Fax:* 23415426
*E-mail:* sales@goldencup.com.hk
*Web Site:* www.goldencup.com.hk
*Key Personnel*
Man Dir: Yeung Kam Kai
General Manager: W K Ngan
Sales Manager: Mary Yeung *E-mail:* mary@goldencup.com.hk
Founded: 1971
Turnaround: 25 Workdays
Print Runs: 5,000 min - 200,000 max
Business from Other Countries: 80%
*Branch Office(s)*
Dongguan, China
Guangdong, China
Kunming, China
Yunan, China

**The Green Pagoda Press Ltd**
9/F, Block B, Tung Chong Factory Bldg, 653-655 King's Rd, North Point
*Tel:* 2561 1924 *Fax:* 2811 0946
*E-mail:* gpinfo@gpp.com.hk
*Web Site:* www.gpp.com.hk
*Key Personnel*
Man Dir: Derek Yip
Founded: 1957
Turnaround: 1-14 days
Print Runs: 10 min - 500,000 max
Business from Other Countries: 30%

**Hindy's Enterprise Co Ltd**
Flat A 20/F, Melbourne Industrial Bldg, 16 Wetlands Rd, Quarry Bay
*Tel:* 25166318 *Fax:* 25165161
*Key Personnel*
General Manager: Cecilia Chung

**Hing Yip Printing Co Ltd**
Shing Tak Ind Bldg, 6/F, Block C & D, 44 Wong Chuk Hang Rd, Aberdeen
*Tel:* 25532432; 25532828 *Fax:* 28147887
*Key Personnel*
General Manager: Louis Ma
Contact: Ma Kai Chiu
Founded: 1963
Print Runs: 1,000 min - 100,000 max
Business from Other Countries: 95%

**Hoi Kwong Printing Co Ltd**
Wah Ha Industry Bldg, 5/F, Block C-D, 8 Shipyard Lane, Quarry Bay
*Tel:* 2562-1641; 2562-1096 *Fax:* 2564-2142
*E-mail:* sales@hoikwong.com
*Web Site:* www.hoikwong.com
*Key Personnel*
Man Dir: David Chan *E-mail:* dchan@hoikwong.com

**Hua Yang Printing Holding Co Ltd**
Tai Ping Industrial Centre, Unit B, 25/F, Block 1, 57 Ting Kok Rd, Tai Po, New Territories
*Tel:* 24167591 *Fax:* 24110235
*Key Personnel*
Man Dir: Mr Chan Kok Wai
Sales & Marketing: Carl Chan
Contact: Ng Kwok Cheong

**Hung Hing Off-set Printing Co Ltd**
Subsidiary of Hung Hing Printing Group Ltd
Tai Po Industrial Estate, 17-19 Dai Hei St, New Territories
*Tel:* 2664 8682 *Fax:* 2664 2070

*E-mail:* info@hhop.com.hk
*Web Site:* www.hhop.com.hk
*Key Personnel*
Man Dir: Matthew Yum *E-mail:* matthew@hhop.com.hk
Founded: 1950
Turnaround: 20-30 Workdays
Print Runs: 5,000 min - 1,000,000 max
Business from Other Countries: 15%

**Icicle/Papercom**
Formerly Paper Communication Printing Express Ltd
3rd floor, South West, Warwick House West Wing, Taikoo Place, 979 King's Rd, Quarry Bay
*Tel:* 2235 2880
*Web Site:* www.papercom.com.hk
*Key Personnel*
Business Development: Bonnie Chan *Tel:* 2235 2888 *Fax:* 2135 6809 *E-mail:* bonnie.chan@icicle.com.hk
Founded: 1981
Turnaround: 28 to 56 Workdays
Print Runs: 1,000 min - 100,000 max
Business from Other Countries: 10%

**Image Printing Company Ltd**
Unit 4, 4/F Cornell Centre, 50 Wing Tai Rd, Chai Wan
*Tel:* 2873 2633 *Fax:* 2558 3044
*E-mail:* imageprt@pop3.hknet.com
*Key Personnel*
Man Dir: Philip Chow Sung Ming
Founded: 1992
Print Runs: 1,000 min - 50,000 max
Business from Other Countries: 50%

**Lammar Offset Printing Co**
Flat C, 16/F Aik Sun Factory Bldg, 14 Westlands Rd, Quarry Bay
*Tel:* 25631068 *Fax:* 28113375
*Key Personnel*
Man Dir: Mr Wu Yuk Ting

**Leo Paper Products Ltd**
7/F, Kader Bldg, 22 Kai Cheung Rd, Kowloon Bay, Kowloon
*Tel:* 28841374 *Fax:* 25130698
*E-mail:* lpp@leo.com.hk
*Web Site:* www.leo.com.hk
*Key Personnel*
Man Dir: Johnny Fung *E-mail:* johnny@leo.com.hk; Michael Leung *E-mail:* michael@leo.com.hk
Marketing Dir: Kelly Fok *E-mail:* kelly@leo.com.uk
Founded: 1991
Turnaround: 15-30 Workdays
Print Runs: 5,000 min
*Parent Company:* Leo Paper Bags Manufacturing Ltd
*Branch Office(s)*
Leo Paper USA, 1180 NW Maple St, Suite 102, Issaquah, WA 98027, United States, Contact: Bijan Pakzad *Tel:* 425-646-8801 *Fax:* 425-646-8805 *E-mail:* bijan@pacificpier.com
*Sales Office(s):* Leo Paper Products (Europe) BVBA, Keizerstr 5, 2000 Antwerp, Belgium, Contact: Jan Van Gijsel *Tel:* (03) 203-0912 *Fax:* (03) 255-1303 *E-mail:* leo@leo-europe.com
Leo Paper Products (UK) Ltd, St Michaels House, 94 High St, Wallingford, Oxon OX10 0BW, United Kingdom *Tel:* (01491) 827827 *Fax:* (01491) 837127 *E-mail:* infoleouk@btconnect.com

**Liang Yu Printing Factory Ltd** (Good Friend's Printing Factory Ltd)
1/F, 9-11 Sai Wan Ho St, Shaukiwan
*Tel:* 25604453; 25677563 *Fax:* 28858099

*E-mail:* liangyup@netvigator.com
*Key Personnel*
Man Dir: Eric Yat-Sum Hui
Print Runs: 5,000 min - 100,000 max
Business from Other Countries: 40%
*U.S. Office(s):* 3616 167th Pl SW, Lynnwood, WI
98037, United States, Contact: Alvin Hui

**Midas Printing Ltd**
1/F, 100 Texaco Rd, Tsuen Wan, New Territories
*Tel:* 24084024 *Fax:* 24065897
*Web Site:* www.midasprinting.com
*Key Personnel*
Project Manager: Raymond Chan
Executive Dir: Gloria Y P Kan
Contact: Annie Wong *E-mail:* annie@
midasprinting.com
Founded: 1990
Turnaround: 14-21 Workdays
Print Runs: 5,000 min - 100,000 max
Business from Other Countries: 25%

**Morris Press Ltd**, see Creative Printing Ltd

**Nordica Printing Co Ltd**
Melbourne Industrial Bldg, 1-2/F, Block C, 16
Westlands Rd, Quarry Bay
*Tel:* 25648444; 25648446 *Fax:* 25656445
*Key Personnel*
Executive Officer, Nordica Group: Benny Kwan
Dir: Alan Wong
Manager: K P Chow
Contact: Ng Tsai On

**Paper Art Product Ltd**
Sung Fung Centre, Unit 816, 88 Kwok Shui Rd,
Kwai Chung
*Tel:* 2481 2929 *Fax:* 2489 2255
*E-mail:* paperart@netvigator.com
Turnaround: 4-8 weeks
Print Runs: 3,000 min - 1,000,000 max
Business from Other Countries: 80%

**Paper Communication Printing Express Ltd**,
see Icicle/Papercom

**Paramount Printing Co Ltd**
3 Chun Kwong St, Tseung Kwan O Industrial
Estate, Kowloon
*Tel:* 2896-8688 *Fax:* 2897-8942
*E-mail:* paraprin@netvigator.com
*Web Site:* www.paramount.com.hk
*Key Personnel*
President: Victor Oh
Account Dir: Kelvin Lai
Founded: 1968
Turnaround: 30-45 Workdays
Print Runs: 1,000 min - 1,000,000 max
Business from Other Countries: 60%
*Branch Office(s)*
Paramount Printing USA Inc, 386 Park Ave S,
Room 315, New York, NY 10016, United
States, President: Jason Cheng *Tel:* 212-696-
5821 *Fax:* 212-696-5428 *E-mail:* jason3@ix.
netcom.com

**Prontaprint Asia Ltd**
Far East Finance Center, Hong Kong
*Tel:* 28657525 *Fax:* 28661064
*E-mail:* postmaster@pronta.com.hk
*Key Personnel*
Man Dir: Clive Howard
Founded: 1986
Business from Other Countries: 40%

**Sheck Wah Tong Printing Press Ltd**
653-659 Kings Rd, 1/F, North Point
*Tel:* 25628293 *Fax:* 25655431
*Web Site:* www.sheckwahtong.com

*Key Personnel*
Deputy Man Dir: K C Chiu *E-mail:* kcchiu@swt.
com.hk
Founded: 1911
Turnaround: 20 Workdays
Print Runs: 3,000 min - 200,000 max

**Sing Cheong Printing Co Ltd**
Tung Chang Fty Bldg, G/F, 655 Kings Rd, North
Point
*Tel:* 25618801; 25626317 *Fax:* 25659467
*E-mail:* info@singcheong.com.hk
*Key Personnel*
Dir & Manager: Karen Shen Fishel
Founded: 1965
Business from Other Countries: 96%

**Sino Publishing House Ltd**
Valley Center, Room 301 & 302, 80-82 Morrison
Hill Rd, Wanchai
*Tel:* 2884 9963 *Fax:* 2884 9321
*Web Site:* www.sinophl.com
*Key Personnel*
Contact: Ben Yan *E-mail:* benyan@sinophl.com
Founded: 1993
Print Runs: 500 min - 500,000 max
Business from Other Countries: 75%

**SNP Best-Set Typesetter Ltd**
Wing on House, 10th floor, 71 Des Voeux Rd C,
Central
*Tel:* 2897 6033 *Fax:* 2897 5170
*E-mail:* bestset@snpcorp.com
*Web Site:* www.bestset-typesetter.com
*Key Personnel*
Manager: Cynthia Hui *E-mail:* cynthiahui@
snpcorp.com
Dir: Johnson Yeung *Tel:* 2975 1012
Sales Representative: Wai Man Yeung *Tel:* 914
961 6223 *Fax:* 914 961 8212
Founded: 1986
Turnaround: 14 workdays
Print Runs: 500 min - 5,000,000 max
Business from Other Countries: 99%
*Branch Office(s)*
3rd floor, No 3 Da Song Jiang Nan Main Ave
C, Guangzhou, China, Contact: Patrick Au
*Tel:* (020) 8441 5873 *Fax:* (020) 8441 5874
*E-mail:* gzbestset@snpcorp.com
*Sales Office(s):* 157 Fisher Ave, Suite 6,
Eastchester, NY 10709, United States, Con-
tact: Wai Man Yeung *Fax:* 914-961-8212
*E-mail:* waimanyeung@snpcorp.com

**Sota Graphic Arts Co Ltd**
Seapower Industrial Centre, 6/F, 177 Hoi Bun Rd,
Kwun Tong
*Tel:* 23434254 *Fax:* 23415426
*E-mail:* sales@goldencup.com.hk
*Web Site:* www.goldencup.com.hk
*Key Personnel*
Man Dir: K K Yeung
General Manager: Wai Kwong Ngan
Assistant Manager: Mary Yeung *E-mail:* mary@
goldencup.com.hk
Founded: 1985
Turnaround: 10 Workdays
Print Runs: 2,000 min
Business from Other Countries: 90%

**South Sea International Press Ltd**
3/F, Yip Cheung Centre, 10 Fung Yip St, Chai
Wan
*Tel:* 2897 1083 *Fax:* 2558 1473
*E-mail:* ssiphk@hk.super.net
*Key Personnel*
Man Dir: P Y Lee; Franky Ho
Founded: 1984
Print Runs: 3,000 min - 500,000 max
Business from Other Countries: 80%

**Speedflex Asia Ltd**
3/F Tianjin Bldg, 167 Connaught Rd W, Hong
Kong
*Tel:* 2542 2780 *Fax:* 2542 3733
*E-mail:* info@speedflex.com.hk
*Web Site:* www.speedflex.com.hk
Founded: 1981
Turnaround: 1 Workday
Print Runs: 1 min
Business from Other Countries: 20%

**Sun Fung Offset Binding Co Ltd**
Westlands Centre, Suites 801-803, 8/F, 20 West-
lands Rd, Quarry Bay
*Tel:* 25618109; 25623381; 25621925
*Fax:* 28110638
*E-mail:* sunfung@sunfung.com.hk
*Web Site:* www.sunfung.com.hk
*Key Personnel*
Marketing Manager: Raymond Chau
Marketing Executive: Maria Tsang

**Sunny Printing (Hong Kong) Co Ltd**
Ming Pao Industrial Centre, Room 12, 2/F, Block
A, 18 Ka Yip St, Chai Wan
*Tel:* 25578663 *Fax:* 28898070
*E-mail:* enquiry@sunnyprinting.com.hk
*Web Site:* www.sunnyprinting.com.hk
*Key Personnel*
Man Dir: Albert T W Chan
Founded: 1991

**Sunshine Press Ltd**
21/F Fullager Ind Bldg, 234 Aberdeen Main Rd,
Hong Kong
*Tel:* 25530228; 25532303 *Fax:* 28732930
*E-mail:* spl@sunshinepress.com.hk
*Key Personnel*
Administrative Assistant: Trevin Tong
Contact: Joney Chan
Founded: 1976
Turnaround: 21-28 Workdays
Print Runs: 3,000 min - 500,000 max
Business from Other Countries: 25%

**Toppan Printing Co (HK) Ltd**
Division of Toppan Printing Co Ltd
Yuen Long Industrial Estate, One Fuk Wang St,
Yuen Long, New Territories
*Tel:* 2561-0101 *Fax:* 24754321
*E-mail:* info@toppan.co.jp
*Web Site:* www.toppan.co.jp
*Key Personnel*
Man Dir: James Lee Lee
Sales Manager: Yukata Ito
Founded: 1963
Turnaround: 30 Workdays
Business from Other Countries: 25%

**Wing King Tong Group**
Leader Industrial Centre, Block I, 3/F, 188-202
Texaco Rd, Tsuen Wan, New Territories
*Tel:* 2407 3287 *Fax:* 24074130; 2408 7939
*E-mail:* printing@wkt.cc; books@wkt.cc
*Web Site:* www.wkt.cc
*Key Personnel*
Man Dir: Alex Yan Tak Chung *E-mail:* ayan@hk.
super.net
Marketing Dir: Jeremy Kuo
Founded: 1944
Turnaround: 15 Workdays
Print Runs: 1,000 min - 100,000 max
Business from Other Countries: 95%

# Hungary

**Interpress Aussenhandels GmbH**
Subsidiary of ADWEST
Bajcsy-Zsilinszky ut 21, 1065 Budapest
Mailing Address: PF 290, 1364 Budapest
*Tel:* (01) 302-7525 *Fax:* (01) 302-7530
*E-mail:* office@interpress.hu
*Web Site:* www.interpress.hu
*Key Personnel*
Manager: Julia Kovacs; Sandor Kovacs; Miklos
   Pollak
Founded: 1991

**Kultura**
PO Box 149, 1389 Budapest
*Tel:* (01) 2501194 *Fax:* (01) 2500233
*Key Personnel*
Manager: Katalin Multas

# India

**Hiralal Printing Works Ltd**
Subsidiary of Conway Printers Pvt Ltd
D-41/1 TTC Industrial Area MIDC, opp Turbhe
   tel exchange, Navi Mumbai, Mumbai 400613
*Tel:* (022) 7672726; (022) 7683012
*Key Personnel*
Chairman: G P Agrawal
Man Dir: Mr Rakesh Kumar Agrawal
Founded: 1981
Turnaround: 40-45 Workdays
Print Runs: 5,000 min - 100,000 max
Business from Other Countries: 75%

# Indonesia

**Ichtiar Baru van Hoeve**
Jalan Raya Pasar Jumat 38 D-E, Pondok Pinang,
   Jakarta 12013
*Tel:* (021) 7511856; (021) 7511901 *Fax:* (021)
   7511855
Founded: 1972
Turnaround: 6 Workdays
Print Runs: 500 min - 18,000 max

**Victory Offset Prima PT**
Jalan Raya Pegangsaan, Dua No 17, Jakarta
   14250
*Tel:* (021) 460-8968; (021) 460-2742; (021) 4682-
   0555 *Fax:* (021) 460-2740; (021) 4682-0551
*E-mail:* info@victoryoffset.com
*Web Site:* www.victoryoffset.com
*Key Personnel*
President: Zainal F Stanley *E-mail:* zainal@
   victoryoffset.com
General Manager: S Wilson Pinady
   *E-mail:* wilson@victoryoffset.com
Founded: 1971
Turnaround: 14 days
Print Runs: 5,000 min
Business from Other Countries: 20%

# Ireland

**Kilkenny People/Wellbrook Press**
34 High St, Kilkenny
*Tel:* (056) 77 21015 *Fax:* (056) 77 21414

*E-mail:* info@kilkenny-people.ie
*Web Site:* www.medialive.ie/press/provincial/
   kilkenny.html
*Key Personnel*
Advertising Manager: Peter Seaver
Founded: 1892
Business from Other Countries: 10%

**Smurfit Print**
Beech Hill, Clonskeagh, Dublin 4
*Tel:* (01) 202 7000 *Fax:* (01) 269 4481
*Web Site:* www.smurfit.ie
*Key Personnel*
Chief Executive: G W McGann
Print Runs: 200 min - 5,000,000 max
Business from Other Countries: 20%
*Parent Company:* Jefferson Smurfit Group plc

**Ultragraphics**
Unit 78A, Cookstown Industrial Estate, Tallaght,
   Dublin 24
*Tel:* (01) 4599133 *Fax:* (01) 4512368
*Key Personnel*
President: Tony Lovett
Turnaround: 4-5 Workdays
Business from Other Countries: 80%

# Israel

**Har-El Printers & Publishers**
Jaffa Port, PO Box 8053, Jaffa 61081
*Tel:* (03) 681 6834 *Fax:* (03) 681 3563
*E-mail:* mharel@harelart.co.il
*Web Site:* www.harelart.com
*Key Personnel*
Export Dir: Monique L Har-El *E-mail:* mharel@
   harelart.co.il
Founded: 1974
Turnaround: 60-90 Workdays
Print Runs: 30 min - 5,000 max
Business from Other Countries: 70%

**Keterpress Enterprises Jerusalem**
PO Box 7145, 91071 Jerusalem
*Tel:* (02) 6521201 *Fax:* (02) 6536811
*E-mail:* info@keter-books.co.il
*Web Site:* www.keter-books.co.il
*Key Personnel*
Plant Manager: Peter Tomkins *E-mail:* peter@
   keter-books.co.il
Sales Manager: Zvi Weller
Print Runs: 500 min - 500,000 max
Business from Other Countries: 10%
*Parent Company:* Keter Publishing House Ltd

**Monoline Ltd**
3 Avnei Nezer, Kiryat Sefer
*Tel:* (08) 9741456 *Fax:* (08) 9741454
*Key Personnel*
Dir: S J Colthof
Founded: 1959
Business from Other Countries: 30%

**Technosdar Ltd**
PO Box 31684, Tel Aviv 61316
*Tel:* (03) 560-7418 *Fax:* (03) 560-4932
*E-mail:* technos@zahav.net.il
*Key Personnel*
General Manager: Avraham Weiss
Founded: 1972
Turnaround: 7-16 Workdays
Business from Other Countries: 10%

# Italy

**Canale G e C SpA**
Subsidiary of Istituto Grafico Bertello SpA
Via Liguria 24, 10071 Borgaro Turin
*Tel:* (011) 40 78 511 *Fax:* (011) 40 78 527
*E-mail:* info@canale.it
*Web Site:* www.canale.it
*Key Personnel*
Dir General: Canale Giacomo *E-mail:* canale@
   canale.it
Founded: 1915
Turnaround: 30 Workdays
Print Runs: 3,000 min
Business from Other Countries: 65%

**Dedalo Litostampa SRL**
Viale Luigi Jacobini 5, 70123 Bari
Mailing Address: Casella Postale BA/19, 70123
   Bari
*Tel:* (080) 531 14 13; (080) 531 14 00; (080) 531
   14 01 *Fax:* (080) 531 14 14
*E-mail:* info@edizionidedalo.it
*Web Site:* www.edizionidedalo.it
*Key Personnel*
Man Dir: Raimondo Coga
General Manager: Sergio Coga *E-mail:* s.coga@
   edizionidedalo.it
Founded: 1965
Print Runs: 2,000 min - 15,000 max

**Mariani Ritti Grafiche SRL**
Via Rontgen 16, 20136 Milan
*Tel:* (02) 58310004 *Fax:* (02) 58310408
*E-mail:* ritti@tiw.it
*Key Personnel*
Manager: Giorgio Ritti
Founded: 1959
Business from Other Countries: 25%

**Milanostampa SpA**
Corso Ferrero 5, 12060 Farigliano (Cuneo)
*Tel:* (0173) 746111 *Fax:* (0173) 746248; (0173)
   746249
*E-mail:* info@milanostampa.com
*Web Site:* www.milanostampa.it
*Telex:* 212428
*Key Personnel*
Commercial Dir: Riccardo Sardo
Man Dir: Fuad Lahham
Founded: 1965
Turnaround: 15 Workdays
Print Runs: 3,000 min - 80,000 max
Business from Other Countries: 65%

**Minerva Medica**
Corso Bramante 83/85, 10126 Turin
*Tel:* (011) 67-82-82 *Fax:* (011) 67-45-02
*E-mail:* minervamedica@minervamedica.it
*Web Site:* www.minervamedica.it
*Key Personnel*
President: Dr Alberto Oliaro
Founded: 1937
Print Runs: 1,000 min - 10,000 max
Business from Other Countries: 8%
*Branch Office(s)*
Via Spallanzani 9, 00161 Rome *Tel:* (06)
   44251210 *Fax:* (06) 44291500
   *E-mail:* lucentini.minmed.rome@
   minervamedica.it

**Nuovo Instituto Italiano d'Arti Grafiche**
Via Zanica 92, 24126 Bergamo
*Tel:* (035) 329111 *Fax:* (035) 329322
*E-mail:* info.niiag@arvato.it
*Web Site:* artigrafiche.bergamo.it; www.arvato.it
*Telex:* (035) 300114
Founded: 1873
Turnaround: 10 Workdays
Business from Other Countries: 30%

**Amilcare Pizzi SpA**
Via A Pizzi, 14, 20092 Cinisello Balsamo
*Tel:* (02) 61836 1 *Fax:* (02) 61836 283
*E-mail:* info@amilcarepizzi.it
*Key Personnel*
Chief Executive Officer: Massimo Pizzi
Founded: 1914
Business from Other Countries: 45%
*U.S. Office(s):* American Pizzi Offset Corp,
 370 Lexington Ave, Suite 505, New York,
 NY 10017, United States *Tel:* 212-986-1658
 *Fax:* 212-286-1887

# Japan

**Dai Nippon Printing Co Ltd**
1-1, Ichigaya Kagacho 1-chome, Shinjuku-ku,
 Tokyo 162-8001
*Tel:* (03) 3266 2111
*E-mail:* info@mail.dnp.co.jp
*Web Site:* www.dnp.co.jp *Cable:* DNPRINT
 TOKYO
*Key Personnel*
President: Kitajima Yoshitoshi
Dir, International Operations: Satoshi Saruwatari
Founded: 1876
Print Runs: 5,000 min - 200,000 max
Business from Other Countries: 85%
*Branch Office(s)*
DNP America LLC, 3858 Carson St, Suite 300,
 Torrance, CA 90503, United States *Tel:* 310-
 540-5123 *Fax:* 310-543-3260
DNP Europa GmbH, Berliner Allee 26, 40212
 Duesseldorf, Germany *Tel:* (0211) 8620-180
 *Fax:* (0211) 8620-1892
DNP UK Co Ltd, 27 Throgmorton St, 4th
 floor, London EC2N 2AN, United Kingdom
 *Tel:* (020) 7588 2088 *Fax:* (020) 7588 2089
*Sales Office(s):* Sydney, Australia
San Francisco, CA, United States
Santa Clara, CA, United States
New York, NY, United States

**Nissha Printing Co Ltd**
3 Mibu Hanai-cho, Nakagyo-ku, Kyoto 604-8551
*Tel:* (075) 811-8111 *Fax:* (075) 801-8250
*E-mail:* print-info@nissha.co.jp
*Web Site:* www.nissha.co.jp
*Key Personnel*
Chairman: Mr Shozo Suzuki
President: Mr Hiroshi Furukawa
International Division: Ms Yuri Miura
Founded: 1929

# Republic of Korea

**Daehan Printing & Publishing Co Ltd**
41-10, Jamwon-dong, Seacho-gu, Seoul
*Tel:* (031) 730-3850; (031) 730-3813 *Fax:* (031)
 735-8104
*Web Site:* www.dhpop.com; www.daehane.com
*Key Personnel*
Dir: Minsoo Chung *E-mail:* mschung@daehane.
 com
Founded: 1948

**Pyunghwa Dang Printing Co Ltd**
60 Kyunji-Dong, Chongro-Ku, Seoul 110-170
*Tel:* (02) 735 4011 *Fax:* (02) 734 5201
*E-mail:* comuser@hitel.kol.co.kr
*Key Personnel*
President: Mr Il Soo Lee

Vice President: Mr Hae Kun Oh
Executive Dir: Mr Sang Woo Lee
Founded: 1923
Turnaround: 10 Workdays
Print Runs: 2,000 min - 500,000 max
Business from Other Countries: 7%

# Lithuania

**Spindulys Printing House**
Gedimino g 10, 44318 Kaunas
*Tel:* (037) 226243 *Fax:* (037) 204970
*E-mail:* spaustuve@spindulys.lt
*Web Site:* www.spindulys.lt
*Key Personnel*
Contact: Elena Kapustinskiene
Founded: 1928
Print Runs: 500 min - 100,000 max
Business from Other Countries: 6%

# Madagascar

**Societe Malgache d'Edition**
Route des Hydrocarbures, Ankorondrano, 101
 Tananrive
Mailing Address: BP 659, 101 Tananrive
*Tel:* (020) 2222635 *Fax:* (020) 2222254
*E-mail:* tribune@wanadoo.com
*Web Site:* www.madagascar-tribune.com
*Telex:* (020) 223-40
*Key Personnel*
Dir of Publication: Rahaga Ramaholimihaso
Founded: 1943
Print Runs: 7,000 min - 15,000 max

# Malaysia

**Web Printers Sdn Bhd**
42 Jln 13/4 Sekn 13, 46200 Petaling Jaya
*Tel:* (03) 7956 3577 *Fax:* (03) 7726 3563
*Key Personnel*
General Manager: Hashim Natt
Marketing Manager: Ashraf Ali

# Malta

**Interprint Ltd - Malta**
Subsidiary of Malta Government Investment Ltd
Industrial Estate, Marsa LQA 06
*Tel:* (021) 240169; (021) 222720 *Fax:* (021)
 243780; (021) 238115
*Web Site:* www.interprintmalta.com
*Key Personnel*
General Manager: Alfred Azzopardi
 *E-mail:* aazzopardi@interprintmalta.com
Commercial Manager: Joseph Bonnici
 *E-mail:* jbonnici@interprintmalta.com
Founded: 1963
Turnaround: 15 Workdays
Print Runs: 500 min - 20,000 max
Business from Other Countries: 80%

# Netherlands

**Bosch en Keuning grafische bedrijven**
Ericstr 1, 3742 SG Baarn
Mailing Address: Postbus 1, 3740 AA Baarn
*Tel:* (035) 5412050 *Fax:* (035) 2202446
*Key Personnel*
Contact: P P E Rings

**Koninklijke Wohrmann Bv**
Estlandsestr 1, 7202 CP Zutphen
*Tel:* (0575) 582121 *Fax:* (0575) 582128
*E-mail:* secretariaat@wohrmann.nl
*Web Site:* www.wohrmann.nl

# New Zealand

**Bookprint Consultants Ltd**
Division of Grantham House Publishing
9 Wilkinson St, Apt 6, Oriental Bay, Wellington
 6001
*Tel:* (04) 381 3071 *Fax:* (04) 381 3067
*E-mail:* gstewart@iconz.co.nz
*Key Personnel*
Chief Executive: Graham C Stewart
Founded: 1982
Print Runs: 2,000 min - 7,500 max
Business from Other Countries: 10%

**PPP Printers Ltd**
PO Box 22785, Christchurch
*Tel:* (03) 3662727 *Fax:* (03) 3654606
*Key Personnel*
Man Dir: D C Richardson
Founded: 1958
Turnaround: 10 Workdays
Print Runs: 100 min - 100,000 max
Business from Other Countries: 10%

**Rogan McIndoe Print Ltd**
51 Crawford St, Dunedin 9001
*Tel:* (03) 474 0111 *Fax:* (03) 474 0116
*E-mail:* quality@rogan.co.nz
*Web Site:* www.rogan.co.nz
*Key Personnel*
Man Dir: Brendan A Murphy
Founded: 1893
Print Runs: 21 min - 30 max
Business from Other Countries: 1%

# Peru

**Industrias del Envase SA**
Subsidiary of Cerveceria Backus & Johnson SA
Av Elmer Faucett 4766, Callao
*Tel:* (01) 574-1150 *Fax:* (01) 574-1287
*E-mail:* webmast@envase.com.pe
*Web Site:* www.envase.com.pe
*Key Personnel*
General Manager: Jose Santa Maria Zuniga
 *E-mail:* jsanta@envase.com.pe
Administrative & Finance Manager: Gustavo
 Domecq *E-mail:* gdomecq@envase.com.pe
Marketing & Sales Manager: Adolfo Vasquez
 Quijada *E-mail:* avasquez@envase.com.pe
Manufacturing & Project Manager: Gustavo Man-
 cilla Mundaca *E-mail:* gman@envase.com.pe
Founded: 1971
Turnaround: 2 Workdays
Print Runs: 15,000 min - 1,200,000 max
Business from Other Countries: 5%

# Philippines

**Cacho Publishing inc**
Pines Cor, Union St, Mandaluyong, Metro Manila
*Tel:* (02) 783011-13 *Fax:* (02) 6315244
*E-mail:* cacho@mozcom.com
*Key Personnel*
President: Herbert T Veloso
Founded: 1880
Turnaround: 7-120 Workdays
Print Runs: 500 min - 50,000 max
*Ultimate Parent Company:* National Book Store

**JF Printhaus**
Km 83.38 Maharlika Hi-way, Brgy San Francisco,
    4000 San Pablo City
*Tel:* (049) 800-3961 *Fax:* (049) 562-0916
*Key Personnel*
President: Victorino F Javier, Jr
Founded: 1982
*Parent Company:* JF Corporation

**Naldoza Printers**
362 Tupaz St, 6000 Cebu City
*Tel:* (032) 261-7326 *Fax:* (032) 261-7326
*E-mail:* naldoza@ebu.skyinet.net
*Key Personnel*
Chief Executive Officer: John R Naldoza
Founded: 1989
*Parent Company:* Business Developers Inc

**Philippine Graphic Arts Inc**
163 Tandang Sora St, 1400 Caloocan City
*Tel:* (02) 364-4591 *Fax:* (02) 631-9733
*E-mail:* philippinegraphicarts@yahoo.com
*Key Personnel*
Pres & Gen Mgr: Igmedio R Silverio

# Portugal

**Printer Portuguesa Industria Grafica Lda**
Sao Carlos, 2725 Mem Martins
*Tel:* (01) 9216025 *Fax:* (01) 9218363
*E-mail:* lissabon.printerportuguesa@bertelsmann.
    de
*Key Personnel*
Contact: Albert Lutz

**Edicoes Silabo**
Rua Cidade de Manchester, 2, 1170 100 Lisbon
*Tel:* (021) 8130345 *Fax:* (021) 8166719
*E-mail:* silabo@silabo.pt
*Web Site:* www.silabo.pt
*Key Personnel*
Marketing Dir: Manuel Robalo
    *E-mail:* manuelrobalo@silabo.pt
Founded: 1983
Turnaround: 5 Workdays

# Puerto Rico

**Publishing Resources Inc**
373 San Jorge St, 2nd floor, Santurce 00912
Mailing Address: PO Box 41307, Santurce 00940
*Tel:* 787-268-8080 *Fax:* 787-774-5781
*E-mail:* publishingresources@worldnet.att.net
*Key Personnel*
Owner & President: Ronald J Chevako
Editorial Dir: Anne W Chevako
Founded: 1976

Print Runs: 500 min - 10,000 max
Business from Other Countries: 5%

# Singapore

**Chong Moh Offset Printing Ltd**
Subsidiary of Chassis Graphic Art Pte Ltd
19 Joo Koon Rd, Jurong Town 628978
*Tel:* 8622701 *Fax:* 8624335
*E-mail:* chongmoh@singnet.com.sg
*Key Personnel*
Chairman: James Ng
Founded: 1946
Turnaround: 10-14 Workdays
Print Runs: 1,000 min
Business from Other Countries: 35%

**Columbia Overseas Marketing Pte Ltd**
Subsidiary of Columbia Offset Platemaking Co
77 Lorong 19 Geylang, No 02-00/05 Wing Yip
    Bldg, Singapore 388513
*Tel:* 7478607 *Fax:* 7458668
*Key Personnel*
Man Dir: Mr Eujin Chua
Founded: 1969
Print Runs: 1,000 min - 20,000 max
Business from Other Countries: 40%
*Branch Office(s)*
Columbia Binding Pte Ltd (Binding)
Columbia Laserart Pte Ltd (Printing)
Columbia Lasermould Pte Ltd (Die-cutting)

**Craft Print Pte Ltd**
9 Joo Koon Circle, Jurong, Singapore 629041
*Tel:* 861 4040 *Fax:* 861 0530
*E-mail:* info@craftprint.com
*Web Site:* www.craftprint.com
*Key Personnel*
Man Dir: Charlie Chan
Marketing Manager: Desmond Chan

**CS Graphics Pte Ltd**
10 Tuas Ave 20, Singapore 2263
*Tel:* 861-0100 *Fax:* 861-0190
*Web Site:* www.csgraphics.us
*Key Personnel*
Man Dir: Mr Lee Sian Tee *E-mail:* stlee@
    csgraphics-world.com
Founded: 1987
Turnaround: 20-30 Workdays
Print Runs: 1,000 min - 200,000 max
Business from Other Countries: 100%

**Eurasia Press (Offset) Pte Ltd**
10/14 Kg Ampat, Singapore 368318
*Tel:* 2805522 *Fax:* 2800593
*Key Personnel*
Man Dir: Peter Ho *Tel:* hopeter@singapore.com
Founded: 1937
Turnaround: 14 Workdays
Print Runs: 500 min - 100,000 max
Business from Other Countries: 65%

**Fong & Sons Printers Pte Ltd**
40 Pandan Rd, Singapore 609282
*Tel:* 2663688 *Fax:* 2664988
*Key Personnel*
Man Dir: Tony Fong

**Ho Printing Singapore Pte Ltd**
31 Changi South St One, Changi South Industrial
    Estate, Singapore 486769
*Tel:* 6542 9322 *Fax:* 6542 8322
*E-mail:* marketing@hoprinting.com.sg; sales@
    hoprinting.com.sg
*Web Site:* www.hoprinting.com

*Telex:* RS 39685 HOFSET
*Key Personnel*
Man Dir: Mr Ho Wai Hoi
Founded: 1951
Turnaround: 35-50 Workdays
Print Runs: 5,000 min - 50,000 max
Business from Other Countries: 30%

**Huntsmen Offset Printing Pte Ltd**
2 Fan Yoong Rd, Jurong Town, Singapore 629780
*Tel:* 2650600 *Fax:* 2658575
*Key Personnel*
General Manager: Heung Yam Yuen
Founded: 1970
Turnaround: 30 Workdays
Business from Other Countries: 60%

**International Press Softcom Ltd**
26 Kallang Ave, Singapore 339417
*Tel:* 2983800; 2952437 *Fax:* 2971668
*Key Personnel*
Marketing Manager: Kok Leong Koo
Founded: 1972
Print Runs: 3,000 min - 50,000 max
Business from Other Countries: 60%

**Kyodo Printing Co (S'pore) Pte Ltd**
112 Neythal Rd, Jurong Town, Singapore 628599
*Tel:* 6265 2955 *Fax:* 6264 4939
*E-mail:* cschong@kyodoprinting.com.sg
*Web Site:* kyodosing.com
*Telex:* KSPRINT RS22144 *Cable:* SHINGPRESS
*Key Personnel*
Executive Secretary: Mr Ng Soo Siah

**Markono Print Media Pte Ltd**
Subsidiary of Markono Holdings Pte Ltd
21 Neythal Rd, Singapore 628586
*Tel:* 6281-1118 *Fax:* 6286-6663
*E-mail:* saleslead@markono.com.sg
*Web Site:* www.markono.com.sg
*Key Personnel*
Founder & Chairman: Ng Siow How
Dir: Bob Lee Song Tioh *E-mail:* blee@markono.
    com.sg
Turnaround: 7 Workdays
Print Runs: 500 min - 150,000 max
Business from Other Countries: 20%
*Branch Office(s)*
Kin Keong Colour Printing (M) Sdn Bhd, Port
    Klang 539538

**PacPress Media Pte Ltd**
Blk 1200 Depot Close, No 01-21/27 (off Depot
    Rd), Telok Blangah Industrial Estate, Singapore
    0410 109675
*Tel:* 2768090; 2730756 *Fax:* 2730060
*Key Personnel*
Man Dir: Mr T H Oh

**SNP SPrint Pte Ltd**
97 Ubi Ave 4, Singapore 408754
*Tel:* 6741 2500 *Fax:* 6744 3770
*E-mail:* enquiries@snpcorp.com
*Web Site:* www.snpcorp.com
*Telex:* rs56289epb
*Key Personnel*
Chief Executive Officer & President: Yeo Chee
    Tong
Chief Operating Officer: Tan Jin Yan
US Sales Manager: Patrick Chung
Turnaround: 30 Workdays
Print Runs: 2,000 min - 200,000 max
Business from Other Countries: 40%
*Parent Company:* SNP Corporation Ltd

**Stamford Press Pte Ltd**
209, Kallang Bahru, Singapore 339344
*Tel:* 6294 7227 *Fax:* 6294 4396; 6294 3319
*E-mail:* lynn@stamford.com.sg
*Web Site:* www.stamford.com.sg
*Telex:* RS56414 STAMFO

*Key Personnel*
Dir: Mr L Rajesh *Tel:* 6294 7227 (ext 233)
    *E-mail:* rajesh@stamford.com.sg
Founded: 1963
Turnaround: 3-4 Workdays for small jobs; 3-4
    weeks for big jobs
Print Runs: 1,500 min - 50,000 max
Business from Other Countries: 20%

**Tien Wah Press Pte Ltd**
4 Pandan Crescent, Singapore 128475
*Tel:* 466-6222 *Fax:* 469-3894
*Web Site:* www.dnp.co.jp
*Key Personnel*
Man Dir: Makoto Takakura
Marketing Dir: Mrs Campos-Chia Chiu Leng
Founded: 1935
Business from Other Countries: 80%
*Ultimate Parent Company:* Dai Nippon Printing
    Co Ltd
*Branch Office(s)*
Tien Wah Press Aust Pty Ltd, Unit 10, 130 Pa-
    cific Highway, St Leonards, 2085 Sydney,
    NSW, Australia *Tel:* (02) 9436-0255 *Fax:* (02)
    9438-5381
Tien Wah Press France, 62 Rue Ducourdic, 75014
    Paris, France *Tel:* (01) 4279-0700 *Fax:* (01)
    4279-8090
Tien Wah Press, 84 Wooster St, Suite 505, New
    York, NY 10012, United States *Tel:* 212-274-
    8090 *Fax:* 212-274-0771
TWP America Inc, 2550 Ninth St, Suite 111,
    Berkeley, CA 94710, United States *Tel:* 510-
    845-9532 *Fax:* 510-845-8580
Tien Wah Press (UK) Ltd, Unit 23, The Ivories,
    6-8 Northampton St, London N1 2HY, United
    Kingdom *Tel:* (020) 7354-3323 *Fax:* (020)
    7359-8777

**Times Printers Pte Ltd**
Subsidiary of Times Publishing Group
16 Tuas Ave 5, Singapore 639340
*Tel:* 6862 3333 *Fax:* 6862 1313
*E-mail:* tp@timesprinters.com
*Web Site:* www.tpl.com.sg *Cable:* TIMESPRINT
*Key Personnel*
Senior Vice President & Head of Printing Divi-
    sion: Mr Leong Kwok Sun
Head of Sales: Patsy Tan *Tel:* 63112 763
    *E-mail:* patsytan@timesprinters.com
Founded: 1968
Turnaround: 5-25 Workdays
Print Runs: 3,000 min - 300,000 max
Business from Other Countries: 75%

**World Publications Printers Pte Ltd**
Subsidiary of World Publications Distributors, Pte
    Ltd
39 Ubi Rd 1, World Publications Bldg, Singapore
    408695
*Tel:* 7442778 *Fax:* 8468256
*E-mail:* enquiries@knscom.com
*Telex:* RS 39283 WPD
*Key Personnel*
Chief Executive Officer & President: Mr S K Ng
Finance Dir: Mrs S K Ng
Vice President, Sales & Marketing: Ms Chan Sew
    Chu
Vice President, Corporate Affairs, Human Re-
    sources & Administration: Ms Dot Loh
Founded: 1982
Turnaround: 7-14 Workdays
Print Runs: 1 min - 70,000 max
Business from Other Countries: 80%

# Slovenia

**Gorenjski Tisk Printing House**
Mirka Vadnova 6, 4000 Kranj

*Tel:* (04) 2016300 *Fax:* (04) 2016301
*E-mail:* info@go-tisk.si
*Web Site:* www.go-tisk.si
*Telex:* 34560 YU GOTISK
*Key Personnel*
Chief Executive Officer: Kristina Kobal
Founded: 1888
Turnaround: 30 Workdays
Print Runs: 3,000 min - 15,000 max
Business from Other Countries: 50%

# South Africa

**CTP Book Printers (Pty) Ltd**
Caxton St, Parow, Cape Town 7500
*Tel:* (021) 930 8820 *Fax:* (021) 939 1559
*E-mail:* ctp@ctpbooks.co.za
*Key Personnel*
Managing Director: Caroline Sturgeon
    *E-mail:* carolines@ctpbooks.co.za
Operations Director: Colin Sturgeon
    *E-mail:* colins@ctpbooks.co.za
Founded: 1947

# Spain

**Eurohueco SA**
Subsidiary of Arvato AG (Bertelsmann)
Apdo 30099, 08080 Barcelona
*Tel:* (093) 7730700 *Fax:* (093) 7730708
*Web Site:* www.eurohueco.es
*Key Personnel*
Vice President, Sales: Clemens Brauer *Tel:* (093)
    7730703 *E-mail:* c.brauer@eurohueco.es
Founded: 1985
Print Runs: 200,000 min - 15,000,000 max
Business from Other Countries: 17%

**Grafos SA Arte Sobre Papel**
Zona Franca, Sector C, calle D 36, 08040
    Barcelona
*Tel:* (093) 261 87 50 *Fax:* (093) 263 10 04
*E-mail:* info@grafos-barcelona.com
*Web Site:* www.grafos-barcelona.com
*Key Personnel*
Man Dir: Bernardo G Masana
    *E-mail:* bgmasana@compuserve.com
Domestic Sales Dir: Alberto Monclus
Packaging Sales Dir: Alejandro Hijar
Founded: 1934
Turnaround: 30 Workdays
Print Runs: 3,000 min - 60,000 max
Business from Other Countries: 45%

**Printer Industria Grafica SA**
Ctra N-II, Km 600, 08620 Sant Vicenc dels
    Horts, Barcelona
*Tel:* (093) 631 01 23 *Fax:* (093) 631 02 05; (093)
    631 02 06
*E-mail:* info.printer@arvato-print.es
*Web Site:* www.printer-spain.com
*Key Personnel*
President: Joaquin Roca Ferrer
Business from Other Countries: 30%
*Branch Office(s)*
Cobrhi SA, Madrid
Rotedic SA, Madrid

**Mercedes Ros Literary Agency**
Castell 38, 08329 Teia, Barcelona
*Tel:* (093) 540 13 53 *Fax:* (093) 540 13 46
*E-mail:* info@mercedesros.com

*Web Site:* www.mercedesros.com
*Key Personnel*
Owner: Mercedes Ros *E-mail:* mercedes@
    mercedesros.com

**Rotedic SA**
Subsidiary of Novo Sistema
Ronda de Valdecarrizo, 13, 28760 Tres Cantos,
    Madrid
*Tel:* (091) 8031676 *Fax:* (091) 8038316
*Web Site:* www.rotedic.com
*Key Personnel*
Chief Executive Officer: Antonio de Haro
    *E-mail:* antonio@rotedic.com
President: Gregorio Juarez de Haro
Sales Manager & Commercial Dir: Francisco J de
    Haro
Founded: 1974
Print Runs: 50,000 min
Business from Other Countries: 7%

**Graficas Santamaria SA**
Division of Fotomecanica
Bekolarra, 4 Pol Ali Gobeo, 01010 Vitoria
    Gasteiz
*Tel:* (0945) 229100 *Fax:* (0945) 246393
*E-mail:* grsantamaria@graficassantamaria.com
*Web Site:* www.graficassantamaria.com
*Key Personnel*
Contact: Jesus Alzola Aguinaco
Founded: 1963
Turnaround: 1 Workday
Print Runs: 500 min - 150,000 max
Business from Other Countries: 15%

**Luis Vives (Edelvives)**
Xaudaro, 25, 28034 Madrid
*Tel:* (091) 334 48 83 *Fax:* (091) 334 48 92
*E-mail:* dediciones@edelvives.es
*Web Site:* www.grupoeditorialluisvives.com
*Key Personnel*
Production Dir: Jesus Agudo Perez
Founded: 1890
Turnaround: 1 Workday
Business from Other Countries: 25%

# Sri Lanka

**Sumathi Book Printing (Pvt) Ltd**
Division of Sumathi Group
445, Sirimovo Bandaranaike Mawatha, Colombo
    14
*Tel:* (0941) 330-673-5 *Fax:* (0941) 449-593
*E-mail:* lakbima@isplanka.lk
*Web Site:* www.sumathi.lk
*Telex:* 22104 SUMATHI CE SUMATISONS
*Key Personnel*
General Manager: Nawas A Rahim
Business from Other Countries: 75%

# Switzerland

**Hallwag Kummerly & Frey AG**
Grubenstr 109, 3322 Schoenbuehl, Bern
*Tel:* (031) 850 31 31 *Fax:* (031) 850 31 00
*E-mail:* info@swisstravelcenter.ch
*Web Site:* www.swisstravelcenter.ch
*Telex:* 912-661 HAWA CH
*Key Personnel*
Chief Executive Officer: Peter Niederhauser

**Photolitho AG**
Industriestr 12, 8625 Gossau ZH
*Tel:* (043) 833 70 20 *Fax:* (043) 833 70 30
*E-mail:* info@photolitho.ch

*Web Site:* www.photolitho.ch
*Key Personnel*
President: Michael von Eicke *Tel:* (043) 833 70
22 *E-mail:* voneicke@photolitho.ch
Administrator: Werner Holliger *Tel:* (043) 833 70
23 *E-mail:* w.holliger@photolitho.ch
Founded: 1965
Business from Other Countries: 50%

# Taiwan, Province of China

**Taipei Yung Chang Printing**
No 9, Lane 252, Sec 3, Chung Ching N Rd,
Taipei 10318
*Tel:* (02) 5932392 *Fax:* (02) 5932763

# United Republic of Tanzania

**Peramiho Publications**
PO Box 41, Peramiho
*Tel:* (054) 2730 *Fax:* (054) 2917
*Key Personnel*
Chief Executive: Fr Gerold Rupper
Founded: 1937
Print Runs: 4,000 min - 6,000 max

# Thailand

**J Film Process Co Ltd**
440/7 Soi Ratchawithi 3, Rajthevee, Bangkok
10400
*Tel:* (02) 248-6888 *Fax:* (02) 247-4719
*Key Personnel*
President: Peer Prayukvong
Vice President: Siriporn Prayukvong
Man Dir: Pira Prayookwongse
Founded: 1980
Turnaround: 6 Workdays
Print Runs: 25,000 min - 65,000 max
Business from Other Countries: 45%

**Mavisu International Co Ltd**
11 Soi Prachanimit, Pradpatrd Phayathai,
Bangkok 10400
*Tel:* (02) 2711148 *Fax:* (02) 2711168
*Key Personnel*
Man Dir: Vipavee Charoensidhi
Chairman: Marshall French
Founded: 1986
Print Runs: 15 min - 40 max
Business from Other Countries: 100%

**Phongwarin Printing Company Ltd**
299 Mu 10, Sukhumvit 107, Sumrongnue, Ampur
Muang, Samutprakarn 10260
*Tel:* (02) 7498934-45; (02) 3994525-31; (02)
7498275-9 *Fax:* (02) 3994524; (02) 3994255
*E-mail:* somphong@phongwarin.com
*Web Site:* www.phongwarin.com

*Key Personnel*
Man Dir: Mr Somphong Charnsirisaksakul
Founded: 1983
Turnaround: 7 Workdays
Print Runs: 1,000 min - 500,000 max
Business from Other Countries: 5%

# United Arab Emirates

**Emirates Printing Press (LLC)**
Member of Al Shirawi Group
PO Box 5106, Al Quoz, Dubai
*Tel:* (04) 347 5550; (04) 347 5544 *Fax:* (04) 347
5959
*E-mail:* eppdubai@emirates.net.ae
*Web Site:* www.eppdubai.com
Founded: 1974
*Sales Office(s):* Emirates Printing Press (UK)
Ltd, Baylis House, Stoke Poges Lane,
Slough, Berkshire SL1 3PB, United King-
dom, Sales Manager, UK & USA: Ron Nunn
*Tel:* (01753) 505612 *Fax:* (01753) 505613
*E-mail:* eppeurope@aol.com (Europe & USA)

# United Kingdom

**The Alden Group Ltd**
Osney Mead, Oxford OX2 0EF
*Tel:* (01865) 253 200 *Fax:* (01865) 249 070
*E-mail:* information@alden.co.uk
*Web Site:* www.alden.co.uk
*Key Personnel*
Man Dir: William Alden
Founded: 1832

**J W Arrowsmith Ltd**
Winterstoke Rd, Bristol BS3 2NT
*Tel:* (0117) 966 7545 *Fax:* (0117) 963 7829
*E-mail:* jw@arrowsmith.co.uk
*Web Site:* www.arrowsmith.co.uk
*Key Personnel*
Sales Dir: David J Hooper *E-mail:* dhooper@
arrowsmith.co.uk
Founded: 1854
Turnaround: 15 Workdays
Print Runs: 500 min - 15,000 max
Business from Other Countries: 40%

**W & G Baird Ltd**
Subsidiary of The Baird Group
The Greystone Press, Caulside Dr, Antrim BT41
2RS
*Tel:* (028) 9446 3911 *Fax:* (028) 9446 6250
*E-mail:* wgbaird@wgbaird.com
*Web Site:* www.wgbaird.org
*Key Personnel*
Man Dir: Dairmuid McGarry *E-mail:* dairmuid.
mcgarry@wgbaird.com
Founded: 1863
Print Runs: 500 min - 100,000 max
Business from Other Countries: 45%
Divisions: Biddles Ltd
*Branch Office(s)*
MSO, Belfast, Ireland

**BAS Printers Ltd**
115 Tollgate Rd, Salisbury, Wilts SP1 2JG
*Tel:* (01722) 411711 *Fax:* (01722) 411727
*E-mail:* sales@basprint.co.uk

*Web Site:* www.basprint.co.uk
*Key Personnel*
Man Dir: David Gumn
Sales Dir: Paul G Gumn *E-mail:* paul@basprint.
co.uk
Founded: 1948
Print Runs: 350 min - 40,000 max
Business from Other Countries: 10%

**Ebenezer Baylis & Son Ltd**
The Trinity Press, London Rd, Worcester, Worcs
WR5 2JH
*Tel:* (01905) 357979 *Fax:* (01905) 354919
*E-mail:* theworks@ebaylis.demon.co.uk
*Key Personnel*
Man Dir: Ian Cranston

**Bell & Bain Ltd**
303 Burnfield Rd, Thornliebank, Glasgow G46
7UQ
*Tel:* (0141) 649 5697 *Fax:* (0141) 632 8733
*E-mail:* info@bell-bain.co.uk
*Web Site:* www.bell-bain.co.uk
*Key Personnel*
Man Dir: I Walker
Sales Dir: D Stewart
Founded: 1831
Turnaround: 5-10 Workdays
Print Runs: 100 min - 100,000 max
Business from Other Countries: 25%

**Bemrose Booth**
Wayzgoose Dr, Derby DE21 6XG
Mailing Address: PO Box 18, Derby DE21 6XG
*Tel:* (01332) 294242; (01332) 267245
*Fax:* (01332) 295848; (01332) 290367
*Web Site:* www.bemrose.co.uk
*Key Personnel*
Business Development Dir: Joe Pleshek
*E-mail:* pleshek@bemrosebooth.com

**Biddles Ltd**
Division of W & G Baird Ltd
Hardwick Industrial Estate, 24 Rollesby Rd,
King's Lynn, Norfolk PE30 4LS
*Tel:* (01553) 764 728 *Fax:* (01553) 764 633
*E-mail:* enquiries@biddles.co.uk
*Web Site:* www.biddlesbooks.co.uk
*Key Personnel*
Customer Service Manager: Nick Faux
Founded: 1885
Turnaround: 20 Workdays
Print Runs: 250 min - 50,000 max
Business from Other Countries: 8%

**Black Bear Press Ltd**
King's Hedges Rd, Cambridge CB4 2PQ
*Tel:* (01223) 424571 *Fax:* (01223) 426877
*E-mail:* enquiries@black-bear-press.com
*Web Site:* www.black-bear-press.com
*Key Personnel*
Man Dir: K Fentiman
Sales Manager: Mike Hallam

**Blackmore Ltd**
Longmead Industrial Estate, Shaftesbury, Dorset
SP7 8PX
*Tel:* (01747) 853034 *Fax:* (01747) 854500
*E-mail:* sales@blackmore.co.uk
*Web Site:* www.blackmore.co.uk
*Key Personnel*
Group Chief Executive: Chris Brickell
Man Dir: Peter Smith
Sales Dir: Aubrey Aviss

**Blockfoil Ltd**
Foxtail Rd, Ransomes Park, Ipswich IP3 9RT
*Tel:* (01473) 721701 *Fax:* (01473) 270705
*E-mail:* info@blockfoil.com

*Web Site:* www.blockfoil.com
*Key Personnel*
Man Dir: Barry Corbett *E-mail:* barrycorbett@
   blockfoil.com


**Book Creation Services Ltd**
Mitre House, 44-46 Fleet St, London EC4Y 1BN
*Tel:* (01223) 424571 *Fax:* (01223) 426877
*Key Personnel*
Chairman: Hal Robinson *E-mail:* hal@librios.com
Founded: 1991
Business from Other Countries: 30%


**J W Braithwaite & Son Ltd**
Pountney St, Wolverhampton WV2 4HY
*Tel:* (01902) 452209 *Fax:* (01902) 352918
*Key Personnel*
Man Dir: Bruce Kidson *E-mail:* brucekidson@
   jwbraithwaite.co.uk
Founded: 1901


**D Brown & Sons Ltd**
North Rd, Bridgend Industrial Estate, Bridgend
   CF31 3TP
*Tel:* (01656) 652447 *Fax:* (01656) 676509
*Key Personnel*
Dir: J M Whitaker *Tel:* (01446) 774213
Finance Dir: Jane C Brown
Founded: 1895
Print Runs: 1 min - 1,000,000 max
Business from Other Countries: 20%
*Branch Office(s)*
Eastgate Press, 62 Eastgate, Cowbridge, S Glam
   CF7 7AB


**Butler & Tanner Ltd**
Caxton Rd, Frome, Somerset BA11 1NF
*Tel:* (01373) 451500 *Fax:* (01373) 451333
*E-mail:* manufacturing@butlerandtanner.com
*Web Site:* www.butlerandtanner.com
*Key Personnel*
Joint Man Dir: A Huett
Sales Dir: N White
Founded: 1850


**Caledonian International Book Manufacturing**
Westerhill Rd, Bishopbriggs, Glasgow G64 2QR
*Tel:* (0141) 7623000 *Fax:* (0141) 7620922
*E-mail:* 101622.235@compuserve.com
*Key Personnel*
Man Dir: Kevin McKenna
Commercial Dir: G Morrison
Group Sales Manager: Martin Platt
   *E-mail:* martin@platt44.freeserve.co.uk
Founded: 1819


**Cambridge University Press - Printing Division**
Division of Cambridge University Press
University Printing House, Edinburgh Bldg,
   Shaftesbury Rd, Cambridge CB2 2RU
*Tel:* (01223) 312393 *Fax:* (01223) 315052
*Web Site:* uk.cambridge.org
*Key Personnel*
Executive Dir: Sandra Ward *Tel:* (01223) 325608
   *E-mail:* sward@cambridge.org
Corporate Relations: Helen Bradbury
Founded: 1534
Print Runs: 1 min


**CB Print Finishers Ltd**
North Tyne Industrial Estate, Whitley Rd, Long-
   benton, Newcastle upon Tyne NE12 9TG
*Tel:* (0191) 2150101 *Fax:* (0191) 2701651
*E-mail:* sales@cbprint.co.uk
*Web Site:* www.cbprint.co.uk
*Key Personnel*
Man Dir: Paul Laidler *E-mail:* paul@cbprint.co.
   uk
Founded: 1921


**Center Print Ltd**
Subsidiary of The Boots Co PLC
Private Rd 2, Colwich Business Park, Colwich,
   Nottingham NG4 2JR
*Tel:* (0115) 961 2277 *Fax:* (0115) 938 1424
*E-mail:* cprint@besharapress.co.uk
*Key Personnel*
General Manager: Nicola Lesley
Print Runs: 1,000 min - 250,000 max


**The Charlesworth Group**
Flanshaw Lane, Wakefield WF2 9LP
*Tel:* (01924) 204830 *Fax:* (01924) 332637;
   (01924) 339107
*E-mail:* sales@charlesworth.com
*Web Site:* www.charlesworth.com
*Key Personnel*
Chief Executive Officer: Graham Lawley
Marketing Manager: Sarah Philp
   *E-mail:* s_philp@charlesworth.com
Founded: 1928
Turnaround: 1-10 Workdays
Print Runs: 1 min - 10,000 max
Business from Other Countries: 30%


**Cedric Chivers Ltd**
Subsidiary of Information Preservation Ltd
One Beaufort Trade Park, Pucklechurch, Bristol
   BS16 9QH
*Tel:* (0117) 9371910 *Fax:* (0117) 9371920
*E-mail:* info@cedricchivers.co.uk
*Web Site:* www.cedricchivers.co.uk
*Key Personnel*
Sales & Marketing Dir: Russell Pocock
Founded: 1878
Turnaround: 15 Workdays
Print Runs: 1 min - 100 max


**Clays Ltd**
Subsidiary of St Ives Plc
Popson St, Bungay, Suffolk NR35 1ED
*Tel:* (01986) 893211 *Fax:* (01986) 895293
*E-mail:* sales@clays.co.uk
*Web Site:* www.clays.co.uk
*Key Personnel*
Sales Dir: Andrew Clay
Vice President, Sales-Clays USA: Andrew Copley
Founded: 1817
Turnaround: 15 Workdays
Print Runs: 1,000 min - 1,000,000 max
Business from Other Countries: 15%
*U.S. Office(s):* Clays, St Ives Burrups, 75 Ninth
   Ave, New York, NY 10011, United States
   *Tel:* 212-414-7520


**William Clowes Ltd**
Copland Way, Ellough, Beccles NR34 7TL
*Tel:* (01502) 712884 *Fax:* (01502) 717003
*E-mail:* william@clowes.co.uk
*Web Site:* www.clowes.co.uk
*Key Personnel*
Man Dir: Ian Foyster *E-mail:* ifoyster@clowes.co.
   uk
Sales Dir: David C Browne *Tel:* (07768) 658820
   *E-mail:* dbrowne@clowes.co.uk
Founded: 1803
Turnaround: 10 Workdays
Print Runs: 2,000 min
Business from Other Countries: 1%


**Cox & Wyman Ltd**
Subsidiary of Rexam Plc
Cardiff Rd, Reading, Berks RG1 8EX
*Tel:* (0118) 953 0500 *Fax:* (0118) 950 7222
*E-mail:* coxandwyman@cpi-group.net
*Web Site:* www.cpi-group.net
*Key Personnel*
Commercial Contact: Dave Watkins
   *E-mail:* dwatkins@cpi-group.co.uk
Founded: 1777
Turnaround: 10 Workdays

Print Runs: 2,000 min - 2,000,000 max
Business from Other Countries: 12%


**Cradley Print Ltd**
Chester Rd, Cradley Heath, West Midlands B64
   6AB
*Tel:* (01384) 414100 *Fax:* (01384) 414102
*E-mail:* sales@cradleygp.co.uk
*Web Site:* www.cradleygp.co.uk
*Key Personnel*
Man Dir: Chris Jordan
Turnaround: 5 Workdays
Print Runs: 1,000 min - 500,000 max
Business from Other Countries: 7%
*Branch Office(s)*
Quadcolor Repro


**R R Donnelley**
Global Media Solutions, High Barn, Midgeley
   Lane, Goldsborough, Knaresborough HG5 8NN
*Tel:* (01423) 796100; (01423) 866132 (ISDN)
   *Fax:* (01423) 796101
*E-mail:* gms.sales@rrd.com
*Web Site:* www.rrdonnelley.co.uk
*Key Personnel*
Man Dir: Roy Houston


**Eagle Press**
Riverside Way, Nottingham NG2 1DP
*Tel:* (0115) 9552335 *Fax:* (0115) 9552336
*Key Personnel*
Man Dir: S Keilpinski


**Furnival Press**
61 Lilford Rd, London SE5 9HY
*Tel:* (020) 7274 2067 *Fax:* (020) 7274 6984
*E-mail:* furnprint@aol.com
*Key Personnel*
Dir: Johnny Gumb


**Green Street Bindery**
9 Green St, Oxford, Oxon OX4 1YB
*Tel:* (01865) 243297 *Fax:* (01865) 791329
*Key Personnel*
Contact: Garry Phipps
Turnaround: 10-15 Workdays
Print Runs: 1 min - 10,000 max
Business from Other Countries: 5%


**The Guernsey Press Co Ltd**
Braye Rd, Vale, Guernsey GY1 3EG
Mailing Address: PO Box 91, Vale, Guernsey
   GY1 3EG
*Tel:* (01481) 240240; (01481) 243657 (ISDN)
   *Fax:* (01481) 240282
*E-mail:* books@guernsey-press.com
*Web Site:* www.guernsey-press.com
*Key Personnel*
Manager: Julie Todd
Founded: 1897
Turnaround: 10 Workdays
Print Runs: 2,000 min - 50,000 max
Business from Other Countries: 80%


**Hammond Bindery Ltd**
Subsidiary of The Charlesworth Group
Flanshaw Way, Flanshaw Lane, Wakefield WF2
   9LP
*Tel:* (01924) 204830 *Fax:* (01924) 339107;
   (01924) 332637
*E-mail:* sales@hammond-bindery.co.uk
*Web Site:* www.hammond-bindery.co.uk
*Key Personnel*
Man Dir: Steve Allan *E-mail:* s_allan@hammond-
   bindery.co.uk
Technical Sales Dir: Brian Quarmby
   *E-mail:* b_quarmby@hammond-bindery.co.uk
Founded: 1974
Turnaround: 3-10 Workdays
Print Runs: 100 min - 250,000 max
Divisions: Hammond Packaging Ltd

**Hammond Packaging Ltd**
Division of Hammond Bindery Ltd
Flanshaw Way, Flanshaw Lane, Wakefield WF2
9LP
*Tel:* (01924) 204830 *Fax:* (01924) 339107;
(01924) 332637
*E-mail:* sales@hammond-bindery.co.uk
*Web Site:* www.hammond-bindery.co.uk
*Key Personnel*
Man Dir: Steve Allan *E-mail:* s_allan@hammond-
bindery.co.uk
Sales Manager: Kirk Allan *E-mail:* k_allan@
hammond-bindery.co.uk
Founded: 1991
Turnaround: 5-15 Workdays
Print Runs: 100 min - 500,000 max

**Norman Hardy Printing Group**
Granville House, 112 Bermondsey St, London
SE1 3TX
*Tel:* (020) 7378 1579 *Fax:* (020) 7378 6422
*E-mail:* info@thehardygroup.co.uk
*Key Personnel*
Man Dir: Stuart Hardy
Contact: Ken Stanger *E-mail:* ken@hardyprinting.
co.uk
Founded: 1946

**Harveys Ltd**
Edgefield Road, Loanhead Midlothian EH20 9SX
*Tel:* (0131) 440 0074 *Fax:* (0131) 440 3478
*E-mail:* websales@harveys.ltd.uk
*Web Site:* www.harveys.ltd.uk
*Telex:* 727985
*Key Personnel*
Chairman: Tom Domke *E-mail:* tom@harveys.ltd.
uk
Joint Man Dir: Tom Dalgleish *E-mail:* tom.
dalgleish@harveys.ltd.uk; Peter McCraw
*E-mail:* peter@harveys.ltd.uk
Sales Dir: Ross Porter *E-mail:* ross@harveys.ltd.
uk
Dir Customer Service: Craig Linton
*E-mail:* craig@harveys.ltd.uk
Founded: 1856
Print Runs: 100 min - 250,000 max
Business from Other Countries: 10%

**Headley Brothers Ltd**
The Invicta Press, Queens Rd, Ashford, Kent
TN24 8HH
*Tel:* (01233) 623131 *Fax:* (01233) 612345
*E-mail:* printing@headley.co.uk
*Web Site:* www.headley.co.uk
*Key Personnel*
Sales Manager: Bruce Finn *E-mail:* bruce.finn@
headley.co.uk
Commercial Dir: Jon Pitt *E-mail:* jon.pitt@
headley.co.uk
Man Dir: Roger Pitt *E-mail:* roger.pitt@headley.
co.uk
Editor: Richard Rice
Founded: 1881
Print Runs: 1,000 min - 200,000 max
Business from Other Countries: 5%

**Hobbs The Printers Ltd**
Brunel Rd, Totton, Hants SO40 3WX
*Tel:* (023) 8066 4800 *Fax:* (023) 8066 4801
*E-mail:* info@hobbs.uk.com
*Web Site:* www.hobbs.uk.com
*Key Personnel*
Man Dir: David Hobbs *E-mail:* d.a.hobbs@hobbs.
uk.com
Commercial Dir: Terry Ozanne *E-mail:* t.
ozanne@hobbs.uk.com
Founded: 1884
Turnaround: 5-10 days litho; up to 5 days digital
Print Runs: 10 min - 50,000 max
Business from Other Countries: 4%

**Hunter & Foulis Ltd**
Unit 3, Gateside Commerce Park, Haddington,
East Lothian EH41 3ST
*Tel:* (01620) 826379 *Fax:* (01620) 829485
*E-mail:* mail@hunterfoulis.co.uk
*Web Site:* www.hunterfoulis.co.uk
*Key Personnel*
Man Dir: Richard Beese
Founded: 1857

**Ikon Document Management Services**
Subsidiary of Microgen Holdings Plc
19 The Business Centre, Molly Millars Lane,
Wokingham, Berks RG41 2QY
*Tel:* (0118) 9770510 *Fax:* (0118) 9770513
*Web Site:* www.ikon.com
*Key Personnel*
Chief Executive Officer: Matthew J Espe
Vice President: Kathleen Burns
Founded: 1972
Turnaround: 2-5 Workdays
Print Runs: 1 min - 5,000 max
Business from Other Countries: 40%
*Branch Office(s)*
Microgen City Park Watchmead, Welwyn Garden
City, Herts AL7 1LT

**Image & Print Group Ltd**
Unit 9, Oakbank Industrial Estate, Garscube Rd,
Glasgow G20 7LU
*Tel:* (0141) 353 1900; (0141) 353 8620 (ISDN)
*Fax:* (0141) 353 8611
*E-mail:* info@imageandprint.co.uk
*Web Site:* www.imageandprint.co.uk
*Key Personnel*
Man Dir: Stephen McPhee *Tel:* (0141) 353-8609
*E-mail:* stephen@imageandprint.co.uk
Production Dir: Frank Boyle *Tel:* (0141) 353-
8606 *E-mail:* frank@imageandprint.co.uk
Founded: 1975
Turnaround: 5 Workdays
Print Runs: 1,000 min - 250,000 max

**Intype Libra Ltd**
Units 3 & 4, Elm Grove Industrial Estate, Elm
Grove, Wimbledon SW19 4HE
*Tel:* (020) 8947 7863 *Fax:* (020) 8947 3652
*E-mail:* intype@btconnect.com
*Key Personnel*
Man Dir: Tony Chapman *E-mail:* tony.chapman@
intypelibra.co.uk
Production: Richard Mayne
Dir: Alan Johnson
Founded: 1976
Turnaround: 10-15 Workdays for proofs; 5-10
Workdays for books
Print Runs: 25 min - 1,000 max
Business from Other Countries: 5%

**The Lavenham Press Ltd**
Affiliate of Terence Dalton Ltd
47 Water St, Lavenham, Suffolk CO10 9RN
*Tel:* (01787) 247436; (01787) 248046 (ISDN)
*Fax:* (01787) 248267
*E-mail:* lpl@lavenhamgroup.co.uk
*Web Site:* www.lavenhampress.co.uk
*Key Personnel*
Man Dir: Terence Dalton *E-mail:* terence@
lavenhamgroup.co.uk
Founded: 1953
Business from Other Countries: 1%
*Parent Company:* The Lavenham Group PLC

**Charles Letts & Co Ltd**
Thorneybank Industrial Estate, Dalkeith, Midloth-
ian EH22 2NE
*Tel:* (0131) 663 1971 *Fax:* (0131) 660 3225
*E-mail:* diaries@letts.co.uk
*Web Site:* www.letts.co.uk
*Key Personnel*
Man Dir: Gordon Presly
Founded: 1796

**Lowfield Printing Co Ltd**
9 Kennet Rd, Thames Rd, Dartford, Kent DA1
4QT
*Tel:* (01322) 522216
*E-mail:* lowfield@compuserve.com
*Web Site:* www.applegate.com
*Key Personnel*
Sales Manager: James Dow
Founded: 1964
Print Runs: 500 min - 20,000 max

**MacKays of Chatham PLC**
Badger Rd, Lordswood, Chatham, Kent ME5
8TD
*Tel:* (01634) 864 381 *Fax:* (01634) 867 742
*E-mail:* mackays@cpi-group.co.uk
*Web Site:* www.cpi-group.net
*Key Personnel*
Sales Dir: Paul Hicks

**The Malvern Press Ltd**
71 Dalston Lane, London E8 2NG
*Tel:* (020) 7249 2991 *Fax:* (020) 7254 1720
*E-mail:* admin@malvernpress.com
*Web Site:* www.malvernpress.com
*Key Personnel*
Man Dir: Leslie Wynn *E-mail:* les@malvernpress.
com
Marketing Dir: Peter Wynn *E-mail:* peter@
malvernpress.com
Founded: 1953
Turnaround: 10-15 Workdays
Print Runs: 100 min
Business from Other Countries: 15%

**MPG Books Ltd**
Division of MPG Ltd
Victoria Sq, Bodmin, Cornwall PL31 1EB
*Tel:* (01208) 73266 *Fax:* (01208) 76515
*E-mail:* print@mpg-books.co.uk
*Web Site:* www.mpg-books.com
*Key Personnel*
Man Dir: Tony Chard *E-mail:* tchard@mpg-
books.co.uk
Deputy Managing Dir: Jeff Swift *Tel:* (01869)
324 992 *Fax:* (01869) 324 992 *E-mail:* jswift@
mpg-books.co.uk
Sales Executive: Roy Skinner *Tel:* (01843) 231
029 *E-mail:* rskinner@mpg-books.co.uk
Sales & Marketing Development Manager: Colin
Porter *Tel:* (0117) 968 8838 *Fax:* (0117) 968
8838 *E-mail:* cporter@mpg-books.co.uk
Founded: 1967
Turnaround: 10-15 days
Print Runs: 400 min - 10,000 max
Business from Other Countries: 5%
*Ultimate Parent Company:* Martins Printing
Group

**MPG Ltd**
Division of Martins Printing Group
The Gresham Press, Old Woking, Surrey GU22
9LH
*Tel:* (01483) 757501 *Fax:* (01483) 724629
*E-mail:* print@mpgltd.co.uk
*Web Site:* www.mpgltd.co.uk
*Key Personnel*
Chairman: Sir Clive Martin
Chief Executive: Mike Milton
Founded: 1945
Turnaround: 5 Workdays
Print Runs: 3,000 min - 75,000 max
Divisions: MPG Books Ltd; Unwin Brothers Ltd
*Branch Office(s)*
Woking
Rochester
St Albans
Wimbledon
Bodmin
Peterborough

**Multiplex Medway Ltd**
Lordswood Industrial Estate, Gleaming Wood Dr,
    Walderslade, Kent ME5 8XT
*Tel:* (01634) 684371; (01634) 671687 (ISDN)
    *Fax:* (01634) 683840
*E-mail:* enquiries@multiplex-medway.co.uk
*Web Site:* www.multiplex-medway.co.uk
*Key Personnel*
Dir: Jon Chandler
Sales Manager: Paul Abson

**George Over Ltd**
20 Somers Rd, Rugby, Warwicks CV22 7DH
*Tel:* (01788) 573621 *Fax:* (01788) 578738
*E-mail:* xuz23@dial.pinex.com
*Key Personnel*
Man Dir: A E H Gilbert
Sales Dir: Richard Gilbert

**Page Bros Ltd (Norwich)**
Subsidiary of Milex Ltd
Mile Cross Lane, Norwich NR6 6SA
*Tel:* (01603) 778800 *Fax:* (01603) 778801
*E-mail:* info@pagebros.co.uk
*Web Site:* www.pagebros.co.uk
*Key Personnel*
Sales Dir: Steve Commons
Founded: 1750
Turnaround: 10 Workdays
Print Runs: 100 min - 30,000 max
Business from Other Countries: 20%
*Branch Office(s)*
105-A Euston St, London NW1 2ET *Tel:* (020)
    7383 2212 *Fax:* (020) 7383 4145

**Peak Technologies UK Ltd**
Silwood Park, Buckhurst Rd, Ascot, Berks SL5
    7PW
*Tel:* (01344) 290000 *Fax:* (01344) 290001
*E-mail:* info@peakeurope.com
*Web Site:* www.peakeurope.com/uk
*Key Personnel*
Man Dir: Paul O'Donnell
*Parent Company:* Moore Corp Ltd

**Printafoil Ltd**
85 Mitcham Industrial Estate, Streatham Rd,
    Mitcham, Surrey CR4 2AP
*Tel:* (020) 8640 3075 *Fax:* (020) 8640 2136
*Key Personnel*
Dir: Simon Flower

**Redwood Books Ltd**
Division of CPI (UK) Ltd
Kennet Way, Trowbridge, Wilts BA14 8RN
*Tel:* (01225) 769979 *Fax:* (01225) 769050
*E-mail:* enquiries@redwood-books.co.uk
*Key Personnel*
General Manager: Trevor Gee
Commercial Manager: Tony Warner
    *E-mail:* tony@redwood-books.co.uk
Production Manager: Peter Grant
Founded: 1993
Turnaround: 10 Workdays
Print Runs: 10 min - 20,000 max
Business from Other Countries: 8%
*Branch Office(s)*
London Sales Office, 22 Bloomsbury Sq, London
    WC1A 2NS *Tel:* (020) 7580-9328 *Fax:* (020)
    7580-9337

**J R Reid Print & Media Group**, see J R Reid
    Printing Group Ltd

**J R Reid Printing Group Ltd**
79-99 Glasgow Rd, Blantyre, Glasgow G72 0YL
*Tel:* (01698) 826000 *Fax:* (01698) 824944
*E-mail:* printsales@reid-print-group.co.uk
*Web Site:* www.reid-print-group.co.uk

*Key Personnel*
Joint Man Dir: Ian Johnstone; John R Reid
    *E-mail:* johnreid@reid-print-group.co.uk
Founded: 1972
Business from Other Countries: 1%

**Antony Rowe Ltd**
Bumper's Farm Industrial Estate, Chippenham,
    Wilts SN14 6LH
*Tel:* (01249) 659 705 *Fax:* (01249) 448 900
*E-mail:* sales@antonyrowe.co.uk
*Web Site:* www.antonyrowe.co.uk
*Key Personnel*
Chief Executive: Ralph Bell
Production Dir: Mike Bando
Technical Dir: Andy Burns
Founded: 1983
Turnaround: 20 Workdays
Print Runs: 50 min - 2,000 max
Business from Other Countries: 2%

**Selwood Printing**
Subsidiary of Lloyd's Register of Shipping
Edward Way, Burgess Hill, West Sussex RH15
    9UA
*Tel:* (01444) 236060 *Fax:* (01444) 245043
*E-mail:* sales@selwood.com
*Key Personnel*
Man Dir: Andrew Lowden

**Severnside Printers Ltd**
Olympus Business Park, Quedgeley, Glos GL2
    4NF
*Tel:* (01452) 720250 *Fax:* (01452) 723012
*E-mail:* info@ssl-uk.net
*Web Site:* www.ssl-uk.net
*Key Personnel*
President & Chief Executive: Norman H Beechey
Turnaround: 14-20 Workdays
Print Runs: 500 min - 5,000 max
Business from Other Countries: 10%

**Stott Brothers Ltd**
Lister Lane, Halifax, W Yorks HX1 5AJ
*Tel:* (01422) 362184 *Fax:* (01422) 353707
*E-mail:* stottbros@aol.com
*Key Personnel*
Man Dir: Ian Bullough

**M & A Thomson Litho Ltd**
Kelvin Industrial Estate, 2-16 Colvilles Pl, East
    Kilbride, Glasgow G75 0SN
*Tel:* (01355) 233081 *Fax:* (01355) 245 039
*Web Site:* www.thomsonlitho.com
*Key Personnel*
Deputy Chairman: Gary Thomson
Contact: Ken Thomson
Environment Quality Dir: Angela Hart
    *E-mail:* ahart@tlitho.co.uk

**TJ International Ltd**
Subsidiary of Ulverscroft Large Print Books
Trecerus Industrial Estate, Padstow, Cornwall
    PL28 8RW
*Tel:* (01841) 532691 *Fax:* (01841) 532862
*E-mail:* sales@tjinternational.ltd.uk
*Web Site:* www.tjinternational.ltd.uk
*Key Personnel*
Chief Executive Officer: Angus Clark
    *E-mail:* angus@tjinternational.ltd.uk
Founded: 1970
Turnaround: 15 Workdays
Business from Other Countries: 5%

**Watkiss Automation Ltd**
Subsidiary of The Watkiss Group
Watkiss House, Blaydon Rd, Middlefield Indus-
    trial Estate, Sandy, Beds SG19 1RZ
*Tel:* (01767) 682177 *Fax:* (01767) 691769
*E-mail:* info@watkiss.com
*Web Site:* www.watkiss.com

*Key Personnel*
Technical Dir: M Watkiss
Founded: 1959
Print Runs: 200 min - 10,000 max
Business from Other Countries: 5%

**WH Trade Binders Ltd**
Units 1-4, South March, Long March Idustrial
    Estate, Daventry, Northants NN11 4PH
*Tel:* (01327) 704911 *Fax:* (01327) 872588
*E-mail:* wh@whtradebinders.demon.co.uk
*Key Personnel*
Man Dir: Roger Westrop
Financial Manager: Adrian Johnson
    *E-mail:* adrian@whtradebinders.demon.co.uk
Founded: 1981
Print Runs: 10,000 min
Business from Other Countries: 1%

# United States

**ADR/BookPrint Inc**
2012 Northern Ave E, Wichita, KS 67216
*Tel:* 316-522-5599 *Toll Free Tel:* 800-767-6066
    *Fax:* 316-522-5445
*E-mail:* info@adrbookprint.com
*Web Site:* www.adrbookprint.com
*Key Personnel*
Pres: Grace M Rishel *E-mail:* grace@
    adrbookprint.com
VP: James E Rishel
Prodn Mgr: Marc Seiwert
Founded: 1978
Print Runs: 250 min - 5,000 max
Business from Other Countries: 10%
Membership(s): PIA/GATF

**Asia Pacific Offset Inc**
1332 Corcoran St NW, Suite 6, Washington, DC
    20009
*Tel:* 202-462-5436 *Toll Free Tel:* 800-756-4344
    *Fax:* 202-986-4030
*Web Site:* www.asiapacificoffset.com
*Key Personnel*
Pres: Andrew Clarke *E-mail:* andrew@
    asiapacificoffset.com
Dir, Sales (NY Office): Timothy Linn
    *Tel:* 212-941-8300 *Fax:* 212-941-9810
    *E-mail:* timothy@asiapacificoffset.com
Founded: 1997
Turnaround: 105 Workdays including color sepa-
    ration & shipping
Print Runs: 2,000 min
Business from Other Countries: 100%
*Branch Office(s)*
Phoenix Offset, Unit F1-2 2nd fl, Yeung Yiu
    Chung No 8 Industrial Bldg, 20 Wang Hoi Rd,
    Kowloon Bay, Hong Kong, Contact: Edmond
    Chan *Tel:* 852-2751-9962 *Fax:* 852-2755-8408
    *E-mail:* Phoffset@netvigator.com
*Sales Office(s):* 870 Market St, Suite 801, San
    Francisco, CA 94102, Dir, Sales: Amy Arm-
    strong *Tel:* 415-433-3488 *Fax:* 415-433-3489
    *E-mail:* Amy@asiapacificoffset.com
270 Lafayette St, Suite 502, New York, NY
    10012, Dir, Sales: Timothy Linn *Tel:* 212-941-
    8300 *Fax:* 212-941-9810 *E-mail:* Timothy@
    asiapacificoffset.com

**Bind-It Corp**
150 Commerce Dr, Hauppauge, NY 11788
*Tel:* 631-234-2500 *Toll Free Tel:* 800-645-5110
*Web Site:* www.bindit.com
*Key Personnel*
Contact: Matt Caleca *E-mail:* m.caleca@bindit.
    com
Founded: 1973
Turnaround: 14 Workdays
Business from Other Countries: 20%

*Branch Office(s)*
5601 W Slauson Ave, Suite 101, Los Angeles, CA 90230, Contact: Theresa LaVerne *Tel:* 310-342-6767 *Fax:* 310-342-6760 *E-mail:* t. scheer@bindit.com

760 Market St, Suite 337, San Francisco, CA 94104, Contact: Mike Rose *Tel:* 415-981-9392 *Fax:* 415-981-0321 *E-mail:* m.rose@bindit.com

275 Carpenter Dr, Atlanta, GA 30328, Contact: Jeff Driscoll *Tel:* 404-851-9720 *Fax:* 404-851-9722 *E-mail:* jeffstern@bindit.com

1820 Ridge Rd, Suite 205, Homewood, IL 60430, Br Mgr: Leo Corrigan *Tel:* 708-798-6600 *Fax:* 708-798-3502 *E-mail:* l.corrigan@bindit. com

165 "M" New Boston St, Suite 248, Woburn, MA 01801, Contact: Jeff Stern *Tel:* 781-938-9296 *Fax:* 781-938-9310 *E-mail:* jeffstern@bindit. com

9 Gaylord Lane, Marlton, NJ 08053, Br Mgr: Mark O'Dea *Tel:* 856-983-1010 *Fax:* 856-983-0986 *E-mail:* m.odea@bindit.com

7 Penn Plaza, 4th fl, New York, NY 10001, Contact: Jeff Stern *Tel:* 212-629-6500 *Fax:* 212-629-5043 *E-mail:* jeffstern@bindit.com

## BookBuilders New York Inc
16 Sabal Bend, Palm Coast, FL 32137
*Tel:* 845-639-5316 *Fax:* 845-639-5318
*E-mail:* mcanewcity@aol.com
*Web Site:* www.mcabooks.com
*Key Personnel*
Pres: Martin Cook *E-mail:* martin@mcabooks. com
Founded: 1977
Turnaround: 30-45 Workdays
Print Runs: 2,000 min - 500,000 max
Business from Other Countries: 60%

## Butler & Tanner Inc
1776 Broadway, Suite 1710, New York, NY 10019
*Tel:* 212-262-4753 *Fax:* 212-262-4779
*E-mail:* sales@nyc.butlerandtanner.com
*Web Site:* www.butlerandtanner.com
*Key Personnel*
Dir, US Sales: Laura Callegari
Founded: 1850
Turnaround: 10 Days
Print Runs: 1,000 min - 200,000 max
Business from Other Countries: 10%
*Parent Company:* Butler & Tanner Ltd (UK)

## C & C Offset Printing Co Ltd
Subsidiary of C & C Joint Printing Co (HK) Ltd under Sino United Publishing (Holdings) Ltd
2632 SE 25 Ave, Suite E, Portland, OR 97202
Mailing Address: PO Box 82037, Portland, OR 97282-0037
*Tel:* 503-233-1834 *Fax:* 503-233-7815
*E-mail:* portlandinfo@ccoffset.com
*Web Site:* www.ccoffset.com
*Key Personnel*
Dir, C & C Offset Printing Co (USA) Inc, Portland, OR, USA: Charles H Clark, IV
*E-mail:* cclark@ccoffset.com
Devt Mgr, C & C Offset Printing Co (USA) Inc, Portland, OR, USA: Jenny Whittier
*E-mail:* jwhittier@ccoffset.com
Dir & Exec VP, C & C Offset Printing Co (NYC) Inc, New York, NY, USA: Simon Chan
*E-mail:* schan@ccoffset.com
Cust Serv Mgr, C & C Offset Printing Co (USA) Inc, Portland, OR, USA: Ernest Li
*E-mail:* ernestli@ccoffset.com
Cust Serv Mgr, C & C Offset Printing Co (NYC) Inc, New York, NY, USA: Frances Harkness
*E-mail:* fharkness@ccoffset.com
Dir & Gen Mgr, Hong Kong Head Office: Zhang Yue Ming
Deputy Man Dir, Hong Kong Head Office: Ken Lee

Deputy Gen Mgr, Hong Kong Head Office: Ivy Lam
Asst Gen Mgr, Hong Kong Head Office: Kit Wong
Sr Sales Mgr (Special Projects), Hong Kong Head Office: Francis Ho
Dir & Gen Mgr, C & C Joint Printing Co (Guangdong) Ltd, Shenzhen, China: Jackson Leung
Asst Gen Mgr, C & C Joint Printing Co (Guangdong) Ltd, Shenzhen, China: Simon Zhang
Pres, C & C Printing Japan Co Ltd, Tokyo, Japan: Yamamoto Masaaki
Man Dir, C & C Joint Printing Co (Beijing) Ltd, Beijing, China: Zhang Lin Gui
Dir, C & C Offset Printing Co (UK) Ltd: Tracy Broderick
Acct Mgr, C & C Offset Printing Co (UK) Ltd: Fia Fornari
Founded: 1980
Turnaround: varies
Print Runs: 2,000 min - 1,000,000 max
Business from Other Countries: 70%
*Branch Office(s)*
C & C Printing Co (NY) Inc, 401 Broadway, Suite 2015, New York, NY 10013-3016 *Tel:* 212-431-4210 *Fax:* 212-431-3960 *E-mail:* newyorkinfo@ccoffset.com (New York City office)
C & C Joint Printing Co (Guangdong) Ltd, 7/Fl, Flat H, Greenview Apt No 38, Hou Guang Ping Hu Tong, Xi Cheng Ou, Beijing 100035, China, Contact: Mr Xiao Mungshen *Tel:* (010) 6650 3176 *Fax:* (010) 6650 3175 *E-mail:* beijing@candcprinting.com (regional office)
C & C Joint Printing Co (Beijing) Ltd, Beijing Economic & Technological Development Area (BDA), No 3, Donghuan North Rd, Beijing 100176, China, Dir & Gen Mgr: Mr Zhang Lin Gui *Tel:* (010) 6787 6655 *Fax:* (010) 6787 8255 *E-mail:* beijing@candcprinting.com
C & C Offset Printing Co Ltd, C & C Bldg, 36 Ting Lai Rd, Tai Po, New Territories, Hong Kong *Tel:* 2666-4988 *Fax:* 2666-4938 *E-mail:* offsetprinting@candcprinting.com (corporate headquarters)
C & C Joint Printing Co (Guangdong) Ltd (Changsha Office), The Building of Changsha City, Commercial Bank, No 1, Frong Middle Rd, Rm 1218, Changsha, Hunan 41005, China, Contact: Ms Chen Jian *Tel:* (0731) 225 0288 *Fax:* (0731) 225 0178 *E-mail:* changsha@candcprinting.com *Web Site:* www.candcprinting.com (regional office)
Shanghai C & C Joint Printing Co Ltd, Fang Fa Bldg, No 29, Rm 304, 165 Dongzhu Anbin Rd, Shanghai 200050, China, Contact: Ms Wu Hiaohung *Tel:* (021) 6240 1305 *Fax:* (021) 6240 2090 *E-mail:* shanghai@candcprinting. com (regional office)
C & C Joint Printing Co (Guangdong) Ltd, Chunhu Industrial Estate, Pinghu, Long Gang, Shenzhen 518111, China *Tel:* (0755) 2845 8333 *Fax:* (0755) 2845 9111 *E-mail:* guangdong@candcprinting.com *Web Site:* www.candcprinting.com (plant)
C & C Printing Japan Co Ltd, Tozaido Bldg, 3F, 2-6-12 Hitotsubashi, Chiyoda-ku, Tokyo 101-0003, Japan, Pres: Yamamoto Masaaki *Tel:* (03) 5216 4580 *Fax:* (03) 5216 4610 *E-mail:* mail@candcprinting.co.jp *Web Site:* www.candcprinting.co.jp (regional office)
C & C Joint Printing Co (Guangdong) Ltd (Xian Office), 10 Xuanfengquiao, Jianguo Rd, Xian 710001, China *Tel:* (029) 741 8407 *Fax:* (029) 743 5730 *E-mail:* xian@candcprinting.com (regional office)
C & C Joint Printing Co (Guangdong) Ltd, Hua Xin Bldg E Block, Rm 1511, 2 Shuiyin Rd, Huanshi East, Guangzhou 510075, China, Contact: Mr Peng Ji Shan *Tel:* (020) 3760 0979; (020) 3760 0980 *Fax:* (020) 3760 0977

*E-mail:* guangzhou@candcprinting.com (regional office)
C & C Offset Printing Co (UK) Ltd, 2 New Burlington St, 4th fl, London W1S 2JE, United Kingdom, Dir: Tracy Broderick *Tel:* (020) 7287 7787 *Fax:* (020) 7287 7187 *E-mail:* tracy@candcoffset.co.uk
C & C Offset Printing Co Ltd, 150-154 Thistlethwaite St, South Melbourne, Victoria 3205, Australia, Contact: Lena Frew *Tel:* (03) 9699 7955 *Fax:* (03) 9699 1574 *E-mail:* lena.frew@candcprinting.com

## Carvajal International Inc
Division of Carvajal Inversiones
901 Ponce de Leon Blvd, 6th fl, Suite 601, Coral Gables, FL 33134
*Tel:* 305-448-6875 *Toll Free Tel:* 800-622-6657 *Fax:* 305-448-9942
*E-mail:* info@cargraphics.com
*Web Site:* www.carvajal.com.co
*Key Personnel*
Gen Mgr: David Ashe *Tel:* 305-448-6875 ext 231
Founded: 1904
Print Runs: 3,000 min - 250,000 max
Business from Other Countries: 30%
*Branch Office(s)*
Carvajal S A, Calle 29 N 1, 6A-40 Cali, Colombia, Alvaro Lopez *Tel:* 572-661-8150

## Colorprint Offset Inc
Division of Colorprint Offset (Hong Kong)
80 Park Ave, Suite 10-N, New York, NY 10016
*Tel:* 212-681-9400 *Fax:* 212-681-9362
*E-mail:* ny@cpo.com.hk
*Web Site:* www.hq.cpo.bz
*Key Personnel*
Pres: Lee Moncho *E-mail:* lee@colorprintoffset. com
Prod Dir & Cust Serv Mgr: Kate Brady
*E-mail:* kate@colorprintoffset.com
Founded: 1986
Turnaround: 15 Workdays
Print Runs: 100 min - 50,000 max
Business from Other Countries: 65%

## Consolidated Printers Inc
2630 Eighth St, Berkeley, CA 94710
*Tel:* 510-843-8524; 510-843-8565 *Fax:* 510-486-0580
*E-mail:* cpi@consoprinters.com
*Web Site:* www.consoprinters.com
*Key Personnel*
CEO: Lawrence A Hawkins
Founded: 1952
Turnaround: 2-20 Workdays
Print Runs: 2,000 min - 500,000 max
Business from Other Countries: 15%

## Martin Cook Associates Inc
16 Sabal Bend, Palm Coast, FL 32137
*Tel:* 386-447-8692 *Fax:* 386-447-8746
*E-mail:* mcanewcity@aol.com
*Web Site:* www.mcabooks.com
*Key Personnel*
Pres: Martin Cook
Founded: 1977
Turnaround: 30-45 Workdays
Print Runs: 2,000 min - 500,000 max
Business from Other Countries: 15%
Membership(s): Bookbinders Guild of New York

## CS Graphics USA Inc
Subsidiary of CS Graphics Pte Ltd Singapore
9748 Weddington Circle, Granite Bay, CA 95746
*Tel:* 916-791-9066 *Fax:* 916-791-9112
*Key Personnel*
Mgr, Sales & Mktg: Rick Marment
*E-mail:* rick@csgraphics.us
Founded: 1980
Turnaround: 80 Workdays
Print Runs: 1,000 min - 75,000 max
Business from Other Countries: 30%

**D & K Group**
1795 Commerce Dr, Elk Grove Village, IL 60007
*Tel:* 847-956-0160 *Toll Free Tel:* 800-632-2314
*Fax:* 847-956-8214
*E-mail:* info@dkgroup.net
*Web Site:* www.dkgroup.com
*Key Personnel*
Pres: Karl Singer
VP, Sales & Mktg: Marge Hayes
Mktg Communs Coord: Holli Hagene
*E-mail:* holli.hagene@dkgroup.net
Founded: 1979
Business from Other Countries: 15%

**Dix**
200-B Gateway Park Dr, North Syracuse, NY
13212
*Tel:* 315-478-4700 *Fax:* 315-703-0119
*Web Site:* www.dixtype.com
*Key Personnel*
Pres: Scott Wenger *E-mail:* swenger@dixtype.
com
Acct Exec, Sales & Mktg: Kelly Farley
*E-mail:* kfarley@dixtype.com
Founded: 1923
Turnaround: 2-10 Workdays
Business from Other Countries: 30%

**DNP America LLC**
Subsidiary of Dai Nippon Printing Co Ltd
335 Madison Ave, 3rd fl, New York, NY 10017
*Tel:* 212-503-1074 *Fax:* 212-286-1505
*Web Site:* www.dnp.co.jp/ *Cable:* DAIPRINTS
NY
*Key Personnel*
Pres: Yoji Yamakawa
VP & Gen Mgr, Graphic Printing: Kazuteru Arai
*E-mail:* arai-k@mail.dnp.co.jp
Founded: 1974
Turnaround: 30-60 Workdays
Business from Other Countries: 54%

**Elegance Printing & Book Binding (USA)**
Member of The Elegance Printing Group
708 Glen Cove Ave, Glen Head, NY 11545
*Tel:* 516-676-5941 *Fax:* 516-676-5973
*Web Site:* www.elegancebooks.com
*Key Personnel*
Man Dir: Frank DeLuca *E-mail:* frank@
elegancebooks.com
Founded: 1977
Turnaround: 3-4 weeks for CTP projects. Reprints
ship within 14 days
Print Runs: 1,000 min - 1,000,000 max
Business from Other Countries: 40%

**EP Graphics**
169 S Jefferson St, Berne, IN 46711
*Tel:* 260-589-2145 *Toll Free Tel:* 877-589-2145
*Fax:* 260-589-2810
*Web Site:* www.epgraphics.com
*Key Personnel*
Pres: Thomas Muselman
Founded: 1925
Turnaround: 15 Workdays
Print Runs: 25,000 min - 500,000 max
Business from Other Countries: 80%

**Express Media Corp**
1419 Donelson Pike, Nashville, TN 37217
*Tel:* 615-360-6400 *Toll Free Tel:* 800-336-2631
*Fax:* 615-360-3140
*E-mail:* info@expressmedia.com
*Web Site:* www.expressmedia.com
*Key Personnel*
Pres: Andrew Cameron
Founded: 1996
Turnaround: 3 Workdays
Print Runs: 1 min - 10,000 max
Business from Other Countries: 10%

**Fairfield Marketing Group Inc**
Subsidiary of FMG Inc
830 Sport Hill Rd, Easton, CT 06612-1250
*Tel:* 203-261-5585; 203-261-5568 *Fax:* 203-261-
0884
*E-mail:* ffldmktgrp@aol.com
*Web Site:* www.fairfieldmarketing.com
*Key Personnel*
CEO & Pres: Edward P Washchilla *E-mail:* fmg.
inc@aol.com
VP, Fin: Pamela L Johnson
VP, Fulfillment: Jason Paul Miller *Tel:* 203-261-
5585 ext 203
Cust Servs Rep: Mike Lozada *Tel:* 203-261-5585
ext 204
Founded: 1987
Turnaround: 1-7 Workdays
Print Runs: 2,500 min - 10,000,000 max
Business from Other Countries: 10%
Membership(s): ABA; Association of Educational
Publishers; The Direct Marketing Association;
Direct Marketing Club of New York; Hudson
Valley Direct Marketing Association; Interna-
tional Reading Association; National School
Supply & Equipment Association; United
States Chamber of Commerce

**The Floating Gallery & Advanced Self
Publishing**
244 Madison Ave, Suite 254, New York, NY
10016
*Toll Free Tel:* 877-822-2500
*E-mail:* floatingal@aol.com
*Web Site:* www.thefloatinggallery.com
*Key Personnel*
Owner: Joel Hochman; Laurence Leichman
*E-mail:* larrydtp@aol.com
Mktg Dir: Olga Vladimizov
Founded: 1992
Turnaround: 21 Workdays; 1-7 for art
Print Runs: 1 min - 1,000,000 max
Business from Other Countries: 15%

**Global Interprint**
589 Mendocino Ave, Santa Rosa, CA 95401
*Tel:* 707-545-1220 *Fax:* 707-545-1210
*Web Site:* www.globalinterprint.com
*Key Personnel*
Pres: Ken Coburn *E-mail:* ken@globalinterprint.
com
Founded: 1979
Business from Other Countries: 65%

**Hamilton Printing Co**
22 Hamilton Way, Castleton-on-Hudson, NY
12033
*Tel:* 518-732-4491 *Toll Free Tel:* 800-242-4222
*Fax:* 518-732-7714
*Key Personnel*
Pres: Brian F Payne
VP, Fin: Michael H Hart
VP, Mfg: Rick Dunn
Prod Mgr: Judy Rappold
Sales Rep: Stephen H Feuer; Tom Plain; Larry
Ritchie; Michael C Rosenhack *E-mail:* miker@
hpcbook.com
Founded: 1912
Turnaround: Flexible, time sensitive scheduling
Business from Other Countries: 10%
Membership(s): BMI

**IBT Global Ltd**, see Integrated Book Technology
Inc

**Ikon Document Services**, see TEC Doc
Publishing Inc

**Imago**
1431 Broadway, Penthouse, New York, NY 10018
*Tel:* 212-921-4411 *Fax:* 212-921-8226
*E-mail:* sales@imagousa.com

*Web Site:* www.imagousa.com
*Key Personnel*
Pres: Joseph E Braff *E-mail:* jbraff@imagousa.
com
Northeast Sales: Linda Readerman
*E-mail:* lreaderman@imagousa.com
USA Prodn Dir: Howard R Musk
*E-mail:* hmusk@imagousa.com
Founded: 1985
Turnaround: 14 Workdays for color separations; 6
Weeks for printing & binding
Print Runs: 5,000 min
Business from Other Countries: 100%
*Branch Office(s)*
Imago West Coast, 31952 Camino Capistrano,
Suite C22, San Juan Capistrano, CA 92675,
West Coast Sales: Greg Lee *Tel:* 949-661-5998
*Fax:* 949-661-8013 *E-mail:* glee@imagousa.
com
Imago Midwest, 17 N Loomis St, Unit 4A,
Chicago, IL 60607, Midwest Sales: Ma
Yan *Tel:* 312-829-4051 *Fax:* 312-829-4059
*E-mail:* myan@imagousa.com
Imago Australia, 14 Brown St, Suite 241,
Chatswood, Sydney 2067, Australia, Contact:
Emma Bell *Tel:* (02) 9415 2713 *Fax:* (02) 9415
2714 *E-mail:* sales@imagoaus.com
Imago France, 6 eme Etage, 42, rue le Peletier,
75009 Paris, France, Contact: Matt Critchlow
*Tel:* (1) 42 81 41 24 *Fax:* (1) 42 81 41 24
*E-mail:* sales@imagogroup.com
Imago Services (HKG) Ltd, 653-659 Kings
Rd, 6th fl, Flat B, North Point, Hong Kong,
Contact: Kendrick Cheung *Tel:* 2811 3316
*Fax:* 2597 5256 *E-mail:* enquiries@imago.com.
hk
Imago Productions (FE) Pte Ltd, MacPherson
Industrial Complex, Suite 05-01, 5 Lorong
Bakar Batu, Singapore 348742, Singapore,
Contact: K C Ng *Tel:* 6748 4433 *Fax:* 6748
6082 *E-mail:* enquiries@imago.com.sg
Imago (UK/Europe) Publishing Ltd, Albury Ct,
Albury Thame, Oxfordshire OX9 2LP, United
Kingdom, Contact: Colin Risk *Tel:* (01844)
337000 *Fax:* (01844) 339935 *E-mail:* sales@
imago.co.uk *Web Site:* www.imago.co.uk

**Integrated Book Technology Inc**
Division of The IBT Group
18 Industrial Park Rd, Troy, NY 12180
*Tel:* 518-271-5117 *Fax:* 518-266-9422
*E-mail:* mail@integratedbook.com
*Web Site:* www.integratedbook.com
*Key Personnel*
CEO & Pres: John R Paeglow *E-mail:* johnp@
integratedbook.com
VP & Chief Technol Officer: William Clockel
*E-mail:* billc@integratedbook.com
VP, Sales & Mktg: Robert Lindberg
*E-mail:* bobl@integratedbook.com
Dir, Info Technol: Michael Whalen
*E-mail:* mikew@integratedbook.com
Regl Sales: Ledner Cunningham
*E-mail:* lednerc@integratedbook.com
Founded: 1991
Turnaround: 1-15 Workdays
Print Runs: 10 min - 2,000 max
Business from Other Countries: 20%
*Branch Office(s)*
The IBT Global Ltd, Rollesby Rd, London N4-
2JZ, United Kingdom, Intl Strategist: Peter
Kenyon *Tel:* (020) 7354 3332 *Fax:* (020) 7354
3332 *E-mail:* peterk@integratedbook.com
Membership(s): BMI

**Jinno International Group**
3 Christine Dr, Chestnut Ridge, NY 10977-6802
*Tel:* 845-735-4666 *Fax:* 617-344-5905
*E-mail:* jinno@hotmail.com
*Key Personnel*
Pres: Yoh Jinno
VP: Sharon Jinno
Founded: 1989

Turnaround: 21-30 Workdays US; 45-75 Work-
days overseas
Print Runs: 500 min - 3,000,000 max
Business from Other Countries: 98%
*Branch Office(s)*
Hindy's Enterprise, Melbourne Industrial Bldg, 16
Westlands Rd, Block A, 20th fl, Quarry Bay,
Hong Kong *Tel:* 516-6318 *Fax:* 516-5161
Wing Yiu Printing Co, Melbourne Industrial
Bldg, 6th fl, Block A, 16 Westlands Rd, Quarry
Bay, Hong Kong, Contact: Law Ming Wah
*Tel:* 561 0283 *Fax:* 565 8233
Jinno International Singapore, 710 Ang Mo Kio,
Ave 8, Suite 07-2615, Singapore 2056, Singa-
pore *Tel:* 458 0778

**Leo Paper USA**
Unit of Leo Paper Group
1180 NW Maple St, Suite 102, Issaquah, WA
98027
*Tel:* 425-646-8801 *Fax:* 425-646-8805
*E-mail:* leo@leousa.com
*Web Site:* www.leopaper.com
*Key Personnel*
Sales: Tom Leach *E-mail:* tom@leousa.com
Founded: 1983
Turnaround: 90 Workdays
Print Runs: 3,500 min - 2,000,000 max
Business from Other Countries: 20%
*Branch Office(s)*
27 W 24 St, Suite 701, New York, NY 10010,
Contact: John Di Masi *Tel:* 917-783-3065
*Fax.* 917-305-0709 *E-mail:* john@leousa.com

**Linick International Inc**
Division of The Linick Group Inc
Linick Bldg, 7 Putter Lane, Middle Island, NY
11953
Mailing Address: PO Box 102, Middle Island,
NY 11953-0102
*Tel:* 631-924-3888 *Fax:* 631-924-3890
*E-mail:* linickgrp@att.net
*Web Site:* www.lgroup.addr.com
*Key Personnel*
Chmn & CEO: Andrew S Linick, PhD
Treas: Marvin Glickman
Exec VP: Roger Dextor
Founded: 1972
Turnaround: 21-30 Workdays
Print Runs: 2,500 min - 100,000 max
Business from Other Countries: 30%

**LK Litho**
Division of The Linick Group Inc
Linick Bldg, 7 Putter Lane, Middle Island, NY
11953
Mailing Address: PO Box 102, Middle Island,
NY 11953-0102
*Tel:* 631-924-3888
*E-mail:* linickgrp@att.net
*Web Site:* www.lgroup.addr.com/lklitho.htm
*Key Personnel*
VP: Roger Dextor
Founded: 1968
Turnaround: 10 Workdays or may vary according
to job
Print Runs: 2,500 min - 2,000,000 max
Business from Other Countries: 20%

**Maps.com**
6464 Hollister Ave, Santa Barbara, CA 93117
*Tel:* 805-685-3100 *Toll Free Tel:* 800-929-4MAP
(929-4627 sales) *Fax:* 805-685-3330
*E-mail:* publishing@maps.com
*Web Site:* www.maps.com
*Key Personnel*
CEO & Chmn: Robert Tempkin
*E-mail:* tempkinr@maps.com
Exec VP, Sales & Custom Mapping: Char-
lie Regan *Tel:* 805-685-3100 ext 124
*E-mail:* reganc@maps.com

Dir, Mktg: Diane Rivera *Tel:* 805-685-3100 ext
136
Founded: 1991
Print Runs: 1,000 min
Business from Other Countries: 10%
Membership(s): Association of Directory Pub-
lishers; International Map Trade Association;
Yellow Pages Publishers Association

**Marrakech Express Inc**
720 Wesley Ave, No 10, Tarpon Springs, FL
34689
*Tel:* 727-942-2218 *Toll Free Tel:* 800-940-6566
*Fax:* 727-937-4758
*E-mail:* print@marrak.com
*Web Site:* www.marrak.com
*Key Personnel*
CEO: Peter Henzell
Prodn Mgr: Steen Sigmund
Sales/Estimator: Shirley Copperman
Founded: 1976
Turnaround: 7-10 Workdays
Print Runs: 500 min - 25,000 max
Business from Other Countries: 10%

**Mazer Publishing Services**
Division of The Mazer Corporation
6680 Poe Ave, Dayton, OH 45414
*Tel:* 937-264-2600 *Fax:* 937-264-2624
*E-mail:* info@mazer.com
*Web Site:* www.mazer.com
*Key Personnel*
Pres: William Franklin *E-mail:* bill_franklin@
mazer.com
Exec VP: Ken Fultz *E-mail:* ken_fultz@mazer.
com
Exec Dir, Sales: Bill Faber *Fax:* 937-264-2622
*E-mail:* bill_faber@mazer.com
Founded: 1964
Print Runs: 50 min - 25,000 max
Business from Other Countries: 10%
*Branch Office(s)*
2460 Sand Lake Rd, Orlando, FL 32809, Contact:
Bryan Blakley *Tel:* 407-859-5552 *Fax:* 407-
859-0643 *E-mail:* bryan_blakley@mazer.com
224 Lexington Ave, Fox River Grove, IL 60021,
Contact: Dennis Bowman *Tel:* 847-639-1555
*Fax:* 847-639-1562 *E-mail:* dennis_bowman@
mazer.com
22 Lehigh Rd, Wellesley, MA 02181, Contact:
Ken Leahy *Tel:* 781-237-4112 *Fax:* 781-431-
6184 *E-mail:* ken_leahy@mazer.com
22 Laurel Place, Upper Montclair, NJ 07043,
Contact: John Martel *Tel:* 973-744-4320
*Fax:* 973-746-5608 *E-mail:* john_martel@
mazer.com
3081 Glenmere Ct, Kettering, OH 45440, Contact: Mark Brewer *Tel:* 937-299-5746 *Fax:* 937-
299-5761 *E-mail:* mark_brewer@mazer.com
Membership(s): BMI

**Midas Printing International Ltd**
Subsidiary of Midas Printing Group Ltd
35 Belleview Ave, Ossining, NY 10562
*Tel:* 914-941-2041
*E-mail:* info@midasprinting.com
*Web Site:* www.midasprinting.com
*Key Personnel*
US Contact: Gerald B Levine
*E-mail:* gerald_levine@midasprinting.com
Dir, Sales & Mktg, Hong Kong: Paul Tang
*Tel:* 24084040 *Fax:* 24065890 *E-mail:* paul@
midasprinting.com
Busn Devt Mgr, China: Ian Lee *Tel:* 24084048
*Fax:* 24065874 *E-mail:* ian@midasprinting.com
Founded: 1990
Turnaround: 2 Weeks for paperbound; 3 Weeks
for hardbound
Business from Other Countries: 85%
*Branch Office(s)*
1/F, 100 Texaco Rd, Tsuen Wan, New Territo-

ries, Hong Kong *Tel:* 24076888 *Fax:* 24080611
(headquarters, send all inquires to this address)
Membership(s): Graphic Arts Association of
Hong Kong

**Milanostampa/New Interlitho USA Inc**
Subsidiary of Milanostampa New Interlitho Italia
SpA
299 Broadway, Suite 901, New York, NY 10007
*Tel:* 212-964-2430 *Fax:* 212-964-2497
*Web Site:* www.milanostampa.com
*Key Personnel*
Chmn: Riccardo Sardo
Chmn & Sales Rep: Rino Varrasso *Tel:* 917-225-
9460 *E-mail:* rvarrasso@milanostampa-usa.com
Founded: 1974
Turnaround: 30 Workdays
Print Runs: 1,000 min - 3,000,000 max
Business from Other Countries: 75%

**Naturegraph Publishers Inc**
3543 Indian Creek Rd, Happy Camp, CA 96039
Mailing Address: PO Box 1047, Happy Camp,
CA 96039
*Tel:* 530-493-5353 *Toll Free Tel:* 800-390-5353
*Fax:* 530-493-5240
*E-mail:* nature@sisqtel.net
*Web Site:* www.naturegraph.com
*Key Personnel*
Owner & Mgr: Barbara Brown
Founded: 1946
Turnaround: 20-30 Workdays
Print Runs: 500 min - 10,000 max
Business from Other Countries: 10%

**Outskirts Press**
10940 S Parker Rd, Suite 515, Parker, CO 80134
*Toll Free Tel:* 888-672-6657
*E-mail:* info@outskirtspress.com
*Web Site:* www.outskirtspress.com
*Key Personnel*
Pres: Brent Sampson
Acqs: Jeanine Laiza
Ed: Mindy Pellegrino
Founded: 1999
Turnaround: 21 Workdays
Print Runs: 1 min
Business from Other Countries: 20%

**Palace Press International - Corporate
Headquarters**
17 Paul Dr, San Rafael, CA 94903
*Tel:* 415-526-1370 *Fax:* 415-526-1394
*E-mail:* info@palacepress.com
*Web Site:* www.palacepress.com
*Key Personnel*
CEO: Raoul Goff *E-mail:* raoul@palacepress.com
Gen Mgr: Michael Madden *E-mail:* michael@
palacepress.com
Founded: 1984
Turnaround: 90 Workdays
Print Runs: 3,000 min - 1,000,000 max
Business from Other Countries: 20%
*Branch Office(s)*
Palace Press International Los Angeles, 1499
Huntington Dr, Suite 408, South Pasadena, CA
91030, Contact: Roger Ma *Tel:* 626-282-8877
*Fax:* 626-282-6880 *E-mail:* roger@palacepress.
com
Palace Press International New York, 180 Var-
ick St, 10th fl, New York, NY 10014, Contact:
Jessica Jones *Tel:* 212-462-2622 *Fax:* 212-463-
9130 *E-mail:* jessica@palacepress.com

**Printing Corp of the Americas Inc**
620 SW 12 Ave, Fort Lauderdale, FL 33312
*Tel:* 954-781-8100 *Fax:* 954-781-8421
*Key Personnel*
Pres: Jan Tuchman
Founded: 1979
Turnaround: 5-10 Workdays
Print Runs: 500 min - 100,000 max
Business from Other Countries: 15%

**RSG Industrial Printing**
13577 Coachella Rd, Apple Valley, CA 92308-
6022
*Tel:* 760-961-0803 *Toll Free Tel:* 866-743-4066
*Fax:* 760-961-0813
*E-mail:* sales@rsg123.com
*Web Site:* www.rsgindustrialprinting.com
*Key Personnel*
Owner: Robert S Giovannucci *E-mail:* bob@
rsg123.com
Founded: 1996
Print Runs: 5,000,000 min
Business from Other Countries: 10%
*Sales Office(s):* National Sales & Marketing Cen-
ter, 13577 Coachella Rd, Apple Valley, CA
92308-6022
Membership(s): PIA/GATF; Web Offset Associa-
tion

**Spraymation Inc**
5320 NW 35 Ave, Fort Lauderdale, FL 33309-
6314
*Tel:* 954-484-9700 *Toll Free Tel:* 800-327-4985
*Fax:* 954-484-9778
*E-mail:* sales@spraymation.com
*Web Site:* www.spraymation.com
*Key Personnel*
VP & Gen Mgr: Richard A Griffin
Founded: 1958
Business from Other Countries: 20%

**Taylor Publishing Company**
1550 W Mockingbird Lane, Dallas, TX 75235
*Tel:* 214-819-8226 *Toll Free Tel:* 800-677-2800
*Fax:* 214-630-1852
*E-mail:* info@taylorpub.com
*Web Site:* www.taylorpub.com
*Key Personnel*
CEO: Dave Fiore
Dir, Fine Books & Div Sales Mgr: Jay Love
Founded: 1939
Turnaround: 45 Workdays
Print Runs: 300 min - 25,000 max
Business from Other Countries: 10%

**TEC Doc Publishing Inc**
Formerly Ikon Document Services
Division of Ikon Office Solutions
399 River Rd, Hudson, MA 01749-2627
*Tel:* 978-567-6000 *Fax:* 978-562-4304
*Web Site:* www.tecdocpub.com
*Key Personnel*
Sales Mgr: Jeff Kalb
Founded: 1973
Turnaround: 3 Workdays
Print Runs: 5 min - 5,000 max
Business from Other Countries: 10%

**Times International Publishing**
Division of Times Publishing Ltd/Singapore
99 White Plains Rd, Tarrytown, NY 10591
*Tel:* 914-366-9888 *Fax:* 914-366-9898
*Web Site:* www.tpl.com.sg
*Key Personnel*
Cust Serv Exec: Bonnie Stone *E-mail:* bstone@
marshallcavendish.com
Sales Mgr: Suresh Kumar *E-mail:* skumar@
marshallcavendish.com
Founded: 1965
Print Runs: 2,000 min - 500,000 max
Business from Other Countries: 90%

**Tobias Associates Inc**
50 Industrial Dr, Ivyland, PA 18974-1433
Mailing Address: PO Box 2699, Ivyland, PA
18974-0347
*Tel:* 215-322-1500 *Toll Free Tel:* 800-877-3367
*Fax:* 215-322-1504
*E-mail:* sales@tobiasinc.com
*Web Site:* www.densitometer.com
*Key Personnel*
Pres: Philip Tobias
Founded: 1960
Business from Other Countries: 10%

**Vicks Lithograph & Printing Corp**
5166 Commercial Dr, Yorkville, NY 13495
Mailing Address: PO Box 270, Yorkville, NY
13495-0270
*Tel:* 315-736-9344 *Fax:* 315-736-1901

*Web Site:* www.vickslitho.com
*Key Personnel*
Chmn: Dwight E "Duke" Vicks, Jr
Pres: Dwight E Vicks, III
Sales: Rick A Anderson *Tel:* 315-272-2489
*E-mail:* randerson@vickslitho.com
Founded: 1918
Turnaround: 10-20 Workdays
Print Runs: 25 min - 100,000 max
Business from Other Countries: 10%
Membership(s): BMI; PIA/GATF

**Fred Weidner & Daughter Printers**
15 Maiden Lane, Suite 1505, New York, NY
10038
*Tel:* 212-964-8676 *Fax:* 212-964-8677
*E-mail:* info@fwdprinters.com
*Web Site:* www.fwdprinters.com
*Key Personnel*
Pres: Fred Weidner, III
Exec VP: Cynthia Weidner *E-mail:* cynthia@
fwdprinters.com
Creative Dir: Carol Mittelsdorf
Founded: 1860
Turnaround: 5-10 Workdays
Print Runs: 1,000 min - 500,000 max
Business from Other Countries: 25%

# Uruguay

**Barreiro y Ramos SA**
Juan Carlos Gomez, Montevideo 1430
*Tel:* (02) 986621 *Fax:* (02) 962358
*Telex:* 23901PB.CVJA.UY *Cable:*
BAREIRAMOS
*Key Personnel*
President: Gaston Barreiro
Vice President: Guzman Barreiro
Founded: 1837
Print Runs: 1,000 min - 50,000 max
Business from Other Countries: 10%

# Manufacturing Materials Index

# Manufacturing Materials

This section includes companies throughout the world involved in the production of book manufacturing materials such as paper and book cover material. Those U.S. and Canadian companies with 10% or more of their business done outside North America are also included here. Immediately preceding this section is an index classifying companies by materials manufactured.

# Belgium

**Imprimerie Bietlot Freres SA**
rue du Rond Point 185, 6060 Gilly
*Tel:* (071) 283611 *Fax:* (071) 283620
*E-mail:* info@bietlot.be
*Web Site:* www.bietlot.be
*Key Personnel*
Man Dir: A Franquin
Founded: 1988
Business from Other Countries: 35%

# Canada

**Appleby's Bindery Ltd**
1303 Rte 102, Upper Gagetown, NB E5M 1R5
*Tel:* 506-488-2086 *Toll Free Tel:* 800-561-2005 (Canada only) *Fax:* 506-488-2086
*E-mail:* applbind@nbnet.nb.ca
*Key Personnel*
Pres & Owner: David E Appleby
Mgr: Edward Appleby
Founded: 1976
Business from Other Countries: 10%

**McLaren Morris & Todd Co**
3270 American Dr, Mississauga, ON L4V 1B5
*Tel:* 905-677-3592 *Fax:* 905-677-3675
*Web Site:* www.mmt.ca
*Key Personnel*
Pres & CEO: Tony Sgro
VP, Fin: Tom Englehart
Founded: 1956
Business from Other Countries: 10%

**Printcrafters Inc**
78 Hutchings St, Winnipeg, MB R2X 3B1
*Tel:* 204-633-7117 *Fax:* 204-694-1519
*E-mail:* info@printcraftersinc.com
*Web Site:* www.printcraftersinc.com
*Key Personnel*
Pres: Bob Payne *Tel:* 204-633-7117 ext 223 *Fax:* 204-694-1594 *E-mail:* bpayne@printcraftersinc.com
Founded: 1996 (Employee owned)
Business from Other Countries: 30%
Membership(s): Canadian Printing Industries Association

**PrintWest**
1150 Eighth Ave, Regina, SK S4R 1C9
*Tel:* 306-525-2304 *Toll Free Tel:* 800-236-6438 *Fax:* 306-757-2439
*E-mail:* general@printwest.com
*Web Site:* www.printwest.com
*Key Personnel*
CEO: Wayne UnRuh
VP, Sales: Ken Benson
Founded: 1992
Business from Other Countries: 15%
*Branch Office(s)*
Box 2500, 2310 Millar Ave, Saskatoon, SK S7K 2C4 *Tel:* 306-665-3560 *Fax:* 306-653-1255

**St Armand Paper Mill**
3700 St Patrick, Montreal, QC H4E 1A2
*Tel:* 514-931-8338 *Fax:* 514-931-5953
*Web Site:* www.st-armand.com
*Key Personnel*
Prop: David Carruthers
Founded: 1979
Business from Other Countries: 40%
Cover Line(s) Milled: Canal Press; St Armand Colours
Membership(s): Canadian Marketing Association; NAMTA

**Tembec Paperboard Group**
Division of Tembec
800 Rene Levesque blvd W, Suite 1050, Montreal, QC H3B 1X9
*Tel:* 514-871-0137 *Toll Free Tel:* 800-411-7011 *Fax:* 514-397-0896
*Web Site:* www.tembec.com; www.kallimapaper.com
*Key Personnel*
Pres: Mel Zangwill *Tel:* 514-871-2311 *E-mail:* mel.zangwill@tembec.com
VP, Sales: Phil Glatfelter *Tel:* 717-817-0300 *Fax:* 717-793-8035 *E-mail:* philip.glatfelter@tembec.com
Mktg Dir: Renee Yardley *Tel:* 514-397-3926 *E-mail:* renee.yardley@tembec.com
Founded: 1990
Business from Other Countries: 90%
Cover Line(s) Milled: Kallima® Coated Cover C1S Plus; Kallima® Web Coated Cover C1S Plus
Cover Line(s) Sold: Kallima® Coated Cover C1S Plus; Kallima® Web Coated Cover C1S Plus

**Transcontinental Printing Book Group**
395 Lebeau Blvd, St-Laurent, QC H4N 1S2
*Tel:* 514-337-8560 *Toll Free Tel:* 800-361-3599 *Fax:* 514-339-5230
*Web Site:* www.transcontinental.com; www.transcontinental-printing.com
*Key Personnel*
VP, Book Group: Jacques Gregoire
US Sales Mgr: Denis Beaudin *Tel:* 514-339-2220 ext 4101 *E-mail:* beaudind@transcontinental.ca
Founded: 1976
Business from Other Countries: 15%
*Branch Office(s)*
614 Yates Ave, Calumet City, IL 60409, United States, Contact: Kristopher D Levy *Tel:* 708-832-1528 *Fax:* 708-832-9510 *E-mail:* kris.levy@transcontinental.ca (Midwest)
3653 W Leland Ave, Suite One W, Chicago, IL 60625, United States, Contact: Tim Taylor *Tel:* 773-583-8155 *Fax:* 773-583-8162 *E-mail:* tim.taylor@transcontinental.ca (Midwest)
10 Rountree Dr, PO Box 2551, Duxbury, MA 02331, United States, Contact: Ed Catania *Tel:* 617-696-1119 *Fax:* 508-881-7739 *E-mail:* ecatania@attbi.com (East Coast)
393 Highland Ave, Quincy, MA 02170-4013, United States, Contact: Mike Gazzola *Tel:* 617-696-1435 *Fax:* 617-696-1025 *E-mail:* mikebook@attbi.com (East Coast)
37 Herman Blvd, Franklin Square, NY 11010, United States, Contact: Tim Malloy *Tel:* 516-775-2980 *Fax:* 516-488-0253 *E-mail:* tmmalloy@aol.com (NY)
3175 Summit Square Dr, Suite C9, Oakton, VA 22124, United States, Contact: David Avesian *Tel:* 703-255-1332 *Fax:* 703-255-1343 *E-mail:* davesian@cox.rr.com (Southeast)
559 Lowrys Rd, Parksville, BC V9P 2R8, Contact: Mike Davies *Tel:* 250-248-9700 *Fax:* 250-248-2353 *E-mail:* bookguys@shaw.ca (West Coast)
15373 Victoria Ave, White Rock, BC V4B 1H1, Contact: Wade Davies *Tel:* 604-535-8800 *Fax:* 604-535-8802 *E-mail:* davies@shaw.ca (West Coast)
490 Wilfred Dr, Peterborough, ON K9K 2H1, Contact: Tom Lang *Tel:* 705-760-9594 *Fax:* 705-760-9485 *E-mail:* langt@transcontinental.ca (NY)

**University of Toronto Press Inc**
Printing Division, 5201 Dufferin St, North York, ON M3H 5T8
*Tel:* 416-667-7767 *Fax:* 416-667-7803
*E-mail:* printing@utpress.utoronto.ca
*Web Site:* www.utpress.utoronto.ca
*Key Personnel*
Pres & Publr: John Yates
Founded: 1901
Business from Other Countries: 15%
Membership(s): BMI

# Denmark

**Bianco Lunos Bogtrykkeri AS**
Subsidiary of Carl Allers Etablissement AS
Otto Monsteds Gade 3, 1571 Copenhagen V
*Tel:* 36 15 33 00 *Fax:* 36 15 33 01
*Key Personnel*
General Manager: J Heede Sorensen
Founded: 1871

# Finland

**WS Bookwell Ltd**
Subsidiary of Werner Soderstrom Corp
Teollisuustie 4, 06100 Porvoo
*Tel:* (019) 21 941 *Fax:* (019) 219 4800
*Web Site:* www.bookwell.fi
*Key Personnel*
Sales Manager: Rainer Poysa *Tel:* (019) 219 4664 *E-mail:* rainer.poysa@bookwell.fi
Founded: 1999
Business from Other Countries: 70%
*Branch Office(s)*
Messdorferstr 127, 53123 Bonn, Germany, Contact: Markku Rapeli *Tel:* (0228) 986 4006 *Fax:* (0228) 986 4008
WS Bookwell AB, Borgveien 2, Ytre Enebakk 1914, Norway, Kristen Sande *Tel:* (064) 925840 *Fax:* (064) 925841 *E-mail:* k.sande.wsoy@oslo.online.no

PO Box 3, Lowestoft, Suffolk NR33 8EY, United Kingdom, David Sowter *Tel:* (01502) 742 038 *Fax:* (01502) 742 039 *E-mail:* ds@bookwell. co.uk

# Germany

**Baader Buch- u Offsetdruckerei GmbH & Co KG CL**
Buchrainstr 36, 72525 Muensingen
*Tel:* (07381) 791 *Fax:* (07381) 411412 *Cable:* BAADER-MUNSINGEN
Founded: 1835

**MOHN Media**
Subsidiary of Bertelsmann AG
Carl-Bertelsmann-Str 161M, 33311 Guetersloh
*Tel:* (05241) 80-4 04 10 *Fax:* (05241) 2 42 82
*E-mail:* mohnmedia@bertelsmann.de
*Web Site:* www.mohnmedia.de
*Key Personnel*
Man Dir: Markus Dohle
Founded: 1824
Business from Other Countries: 25%

**Priese GmbH & Co**
Schwedlerstr 5, 14193 Berlin
*Tel:* (030) 8263024 *Fax:* (030) 3249630
*Key Personnel*
Contact: Elma Priese; Hans Joachim Priese

# Hong Kong

**Caritas Printing Training Centre**
Caritas House, 3rd floor, Block D, 2 Caine Rd, Hong Kong
*Tel:* 2524 2701 (ext 647) *Fax:* 2530 3065
*Web Site:* vtes.caritas.org.hk
*Key Personnel*
General Manager: Isaac Mak
Business from Other Countries: 50%

**Dai Nippon Printing Co (Hong Kong) Ltd**
Division of Dai Nippon Printing Co Ltd
Tsuen Wan Industrial Centre, 2-5/F, 220-248 Texaco Rd, Tsuen Wan, New Territories
*Tel:* 2408-0188 *Fax:* 2614-7585; 2407-6201
*Web Site:* www.dnp.co.jp *Cable:* DNPICO
*Key Personnel*
Administration & Finance Dir: Mr K Miya
Business from Other Countries: 85%
*Branch Office(s)*
Dai Nippon Printing Co (Australia) Pty Ltd, St Martins Tower, Suite 1002, Level 10, 31 Market St, Sydney, NSW 2000, Australia *Tel:* (02) 9267-8166 *Fax:* (02) 9267-9533
DNP America LLC, Los Angeles Office, 3858 Carson St, Suite 300, Torrance, CA 90503, United States *Tel:* 310-540-5123 *Fax:* 310-543-3260
DNP America LLC, New York Office, 335 Madison Ave, 3rd floor, New York, NY 10017, United States *Tel:* 212-503-1060 *Fax:* 212-286-1501
DNP America LLC, Silicon Valley Office, 3235 Kifer Rd, Suite 100, Santa Clara, CA 95051, United States *Tel:* 408-735-8880 *Fax:* 408-735-0453
DNP Corporation USA, New York Office, 335 Madison Ave, 3rd floor, New York, NY 10017, United States *Tel:* 212-503-1850 *Fax:* 212-286-1490

DNP Corporation USA, San Francisco Office, 577 Airport Blvd, Suite 620, Burlingame, CA 94010, United States *Tel:* 650-558-4050 *Fax:* 650-340-6095
DNP Denmark A/S, Skruegangen 2, 2690 Karlslunde, Denmark *Tel:* 4616-5100 *Fax:* 4616-5200
DNP Electronics America LLC, 2391 Fenton St, Chula Vista 91914, United States *Tel:* 619-397-6700 *Fax:* 613-397-6729
DNP Europa GmbH, Berliner Allee 26, 40212 Dusseldorf, Germany *Tel:* (0211) 8620-180 *Fax:* (0211) 8620-1895
DNP IMS America Corporation, 4524 Enterprise Dr NW, Concord, NC 28027, United States *Tel:* 704-784-8100 *Fax:* 704-784-2777
DNP IMS France SAS, 14, rue da la Violette, 22100 Dinan, France
DNP Photomask Europe SpA, Via Olivatti 2/A, 20041 Agrate Brianza, Italy *Tel:* (039) 65493-3000 *Fax:* (039) 65493-215
DNP Singapore Pte Ltd, 896 Dunearn Rd, No 04-09, Sime Darby Centre, Singapore 589472, Singapore *Tel:* 469-7611 *Fax:* 466-8486
DNP Taiwan Co Ltd, Rm D, 6 fl, 44 Chung-Shan N Rd Sec 2, Taipei 104, Taiwan, Province of China *Tel:* (02) 2327-8311 *Fax:* (02) 2327-8283
DNP UK Co Ltd, 27 Throgmorton St, 4th floor, London EC2N 2AQ, United Kingdom *Tel:* (020) 7588 2088 *Fax:* (020) 7588 2089
PT DNP Indonesia, Kawasan Industri Pulogadung, Jalan Pulogadung Kaveling II, Blok H, No 2-3, Jakarta Timur, Indonesia *Tel:* (021) 4610313 *Fax:* (021) 4605795
Tien Wah Press (Pte) Ltd, 4 Pandan Crescent, Singapore 128475, Singapore *Tel:* 466-6222 *Fax:* 469-3894
TWP Sdn Bhd, 89, Jalan Tampoi, Kawasan Perindustrian Tampoi, 80350 Johor Bahru, Johor, Malaysia *Tel:* (07) 2369899 *Fax:* (07) 2363148

**Everbest Printing Co Ltd**
Ko Fai Industrial Bldg, Block C5, 10th floor, 7 Ko Fai Rd, Yau Tong, Kowloon
*Tel:* 2727 4433 *Fax:* 2772 7687
*E-mail:* sales@everbest.com.hk
*Web Site:* www.everbest.com
*Key Personnel*
Founder: James Chung
Man Dir: Kenneth Chung
Customer Account Executive: Ronny Ng; Frankie Lee
Founded: 1954
Business from Other Countries: 90%
*Branch Office(s)*
Everbest Canada, 50 Emblem Court, Scarborough, ON M1S 1B1, Canada, Contact: Ms Connie Chung *Tel:* 416-286-2525 *Fax:* 416-286-2526 *E-mail:* everbestcan@aprinco.com
Everbest Printing (Australian & New Zealand Office), 100 Macaulay Rd, Stanmore, NSW 2048, Australia, Contact: Lionel Marz *Tel:* (02) 9568-5879 *Fax:* (02) 9568-5902 *E-mail:* lmarz@onaustralia.com.au
*U.S. Office(s):* Everbest Midwest, 6428 Margaret's Lane, Edina, MN 55439, United States, Contact: Dr Josie Lo *Tel:* 612-944-0854 *Fax:* 612-829-7670 *E-mail:* sklo@aol.com
Four Colour Imports, 2843 Brownsboro Rd, Suite 102, Louisville, KY 40204, United States, Contact: George Dick *Tel:* 502-896-9644 *Fax:* 502-896-9594 *E-mail:* sales@fourcolour.com *Web Site:* www.fourcolour.com
Spectrum Books Inc, 2300 Bethards Drive, Suite C, Santa Rosa, CA 95405-8658, United States, Contact: Duncan McCallum *Tel:* 707-542-6044 *Fax:* 707-542-6045 *E-mail:* specbooks@aol.com

**Golden Cup Printing Co Ltd**
Seapower Industrial Centre, 6/F, 177 Hoi Bun Rd, Kwun Tong, Kowloon
*Tel:* 2343 4254 *Fax:* 2341 5426
*E-mail:* sales@goldencup.com.hk
*Web Site:* www.goldencup.com.hk
*Key Personnel*
Man Dir: Yeung Kam Kai
General Manager: W K Ngan
Sales Manager: Mary Yeung *E-mail:* mary@goldencup.com.hk
Founded: 1969
Business from Other Countries: 80%
*Branch Office(s)*
Dongguan, China
Guangdong, China
Kunming, China
Yunan, China

**The Green Pagoda Press Ltd**
9/F, Block B, Tung Chong Factory Bldg, 653-655 King's Rd, North Point
*Tel:* 2561 1924 *Fax:* 2811 0946
*E-mail:* gpinfo@gpp.com.hk
*Web Site:* www.greenpagoda.com
*Key Personnel*
Man Dir: Derek Yip
Founded: 1957
Business from Other Countries: 30%

**Image Printing Company Ltd**
Unit 4, 4/F Cornell Centre, 50 Wing Tai Rd, Chai Wan
*Tel:* 2897 8046 *Fax:* 2558 3044
*E-mail:* imageprt@pop3.hknet.com
*Key Personnel*
Man Dir: Philip Chow Sung Ming
Founded: 1992
Business from Other Countries: 50%

**Mei Ka Printing & Publishing Enterprise Ltd**
Cheung Ka Industrial Bldg, Block B, 9th floor, 179-180 Connaught Rd W, Hong Kong
*Tel:* 2540 1131 *Fax:* 2559 8718; 2559 7137
*E-mail:* mkpp@netvigator.com
*Web Site:* www.meika-printing.com
*Key Personnel*
Dir: Hong Chin Huo

**Prontaprint Asia Ltd**
Far East Finance Center, Hong Kong
*Tel:* 28657525 *Fax:* 28661064
*Key Personnel*
Man Dir: Clive Howard
Founded: 1986
Business from Other Countries: 40%

**Sino Publishing House Ltd**
Valley Centre, Room 301-302, 80-82 Morrison Hill Rd, Wanchai
*Tel:* 2884 9963 *Fax:* 2884 9321
*Web Site:* www.sinophl.com
*Key Personnel*
Contact: Ben Yan *E-mail:* benyan@sinophl.com
Founded: 1993
Business from Other Countries: 75%

**Speedflex Asia Ltd**
3/F Tianjin Bldg, 167 Connaught Rd W, Hong Kong
*Tel:* 2542 2780 *Fax:* 2542 3733
*E-mail:* info@speedflex.com.hk
*Web Site:* www.speedflex.com.hk
Founded: 1981
Business from Other Countries: 20%

**Wing King Tong Group**
Leader Industrial Centre, Block I, 3/F, 188-202 Texaco Rd, Tsuen Wan, New Territories
*Tel:* 2407 3287 *Fax:* 24074130; 2408 7939
*E-mail:* printing@wkt.cc; books@wkt.cc
*Web Site:* www.wkt.cc

## Key Personnel
Man Dir: Alex Yan Tak Chung *E-mail:* ayan@hk.
super.net
Marketing Dir: Jeremy Kuo
Founded: 1944
Business from Other Countries: 95%

**Ying Tat Co**
Division of Quality Printing & Paper Products
Wing Wah Industrial Bldg, 8th floor, 677 Kings
Rd, North Point
*Tel:* 25645980; 25645963; 25639981
*Fax:* 28111280
*Key Personnel*
Contact: Chan Dun Yin
Founded: 1968
Business from Other Countries: 30%

# Hungary

**Interpress Aussenhandels GmbH**
Subsidiary of ADWEST
Bajcsy-Zsilinszky ut 21, 1065 Budapest
*Tel:* (01) 302-7525 *Fax:* (01) 302-7530
*E-mail:* office@interpress.hu
*Web Site:* www.interpress.hu
*Key Personnel*
Manager: Julia Kovacs; Sandor Kovacs; Miklos
Pollak
Founded: 1991

# Indonesia

**Ichtiar Baru van Hoeve**
Jalan Raya Pasar Jumat 38 D-E, Pondok Pinang,
Jakarta 12013
*Tel:* (021) 7511901
Founded: 1972

**Victory Offset Prima PT**
Jalan Raya Pegangsaan, Dua No 17, Jakarta
14250
*Tel:* (021) 460-2742; (021) 460-8968; (021) 4682-
0555 *Fax:* (021) 460-2740; (021) 4682-0551
*E-mail:* info@victoryoffset.com
*Web Site:* www.victoryoffset.com
*Key Personnel*
President: Zainal F Stanley *E-mail:* zainal@
victoryoffset.com
General Manager: S Wilson Pinady
*E-mail:* wilson@victoryoffset.com
Founded: 1971
Business from Other Countries: 10%

# Ireland

**SciPrint Ltd**
Bay 93, Shannon Industrial Estate, Shannon, Co
Clare
*Tel:* (061) 472114; (061) 472520 *Fax:* (061)
472021
*Key Personnel*
Man Dir, Sales: M K Parsons
Chairman: B Lane
Founded: 1974
Business from Other Countries: 95%

# Israel

**Keterpress Enterprises Jerusalem**
PO Box 7145, 91071 Jerusalem
*Tel:* (02) 655 7822 *Fax:* (02) 6536811
*E-mail:* info@keter-books.co.il
*Web Site:* www.keter-books.co.il
*Key Personnel*
Plant Manager: Peter Tomkins *E-mail:* peter@
keter-books.co.il
Sales Manager: Zvi Weller
Business from Other Countries: 10%
*Parent Company:* Keter Publishing House Ltd

# Italy

**Dedalo Litostampa SRL**
Viale Luigi Jacobini 5, 70123 Bari
Mailing Address: Casella Postale BA/19, 70123
Bari
*Tel:* (080) 531 14 13; (080) 531 14 01; (080) 531
14 00 *Fax:* (080) 531 14 14
*E-mail:* info@edizionidedalo.it
*Web Site:* www.edizionidedalo.it
*Key Personnel*
Man Dir: Raimondo Coga
General Manager: Sergio Coga *E-mail:* s.coga@
edizionidedalo.it
Founded: 1965

**Milanostampa SpA**
Corso Ferrero 5, 12060 Farigliano (Cuneo)
*Tel:* (0173) 746111 *Fax:* (0173) 746248; (0173)
746249
*E-mail:* info@milanostampa.com
*Web Site:* www.milanostampa.com
*Telex:* 212428
*Key Personnel*
Commercial Dir: Riccardo Sardo
Man Dir: Fuad Lahham
Founded: 1965
Business from Other Countries: 65%
*U.S. Office(s):* 299 Broadway, Suite 901, New
York, NY 10007, United States *Tel:* 212-964-
2430 *Fax:* 212-964-2497 *E-mail:* rvarrasso@
milanostampa.com (North American Sales &
Production Office)

# Republic of Korea

**Daehan Printing & Publishing Co Ltd**
344-12, Sangdaewon-dong, Jungwon-gu,
Sungnam-City, Kyunggi-do
*Tel:* (031) 730-3850 *Fax:* (031) 735-8104
*Web Site:* www.daehane.com
*Key Personnel*
Dir: Minsoo Chung *E-mail:* mschung@daehane.
com
Manager: S M Bae *E-mail:* smbae@daehane.com;
Jin Park *E-mail:* jin@daehane.com
Founded: 1948
*U.S. Office(s):* 3271 Sawtelle Blvd, No 104, Los
Angeles, CA 90066, United States *Tel:* 310-
737-0058 *Fax:* 310-737-9213

# Netherlands

**BN International BV**
Rokerijweg 5, 1271 AH Huizen
Mailing Address: PO Box 2, 1270 AA Huizen
*Tel:* (035) 524 84 00 *Fax:* (035) 525 60 04
*Web Site:* www.bninternational.com
*Key Personnel*
Sales & Marketing Manager: Henk Bunschoten
Founded: 1938
Business from Other Countries: 95%
*Branch Office(s)*
BN International UK, Unit 38, The Metro Centre,
Tolpits Lane, Watford, Herts WD1 8SB, United
Kingdom *Tel:* (01923) 219132 *Fax:* (01923)
219134

# New Zealand

**Bookprint Consultants Ltd**
Division of Grantham House Publishing
9 Wilkinson St, Apt 6, Oriental Bay, Wellington
6001
*Tel:* (04) 381 3071 *Fax:* (04) 381 3067
*E-mail:* gstewart@iconz.co.nz
*Key Personnel*
Chief Executive: Graham C Stewart
Founded: 1982
Business from Other Countries: 10%

**Rogan McIndoe Print Ltd**
51 Crawford St, Dunedin 9001
Mailing Address: PO Box 1361, Dunedin 9015
*Tel:* (03) 474 0111 *Toll Free Tel:* 800 477 0355
*Fax:* (03) 474 0116
*E-mail:* quality@rogan.co.nz
*Web Site:* www.rogan.co.nz
*Key Personnel*
Man Dir: Brendan A Murphy
Founded: 1893
Business from Other Countries: 1%

# Singapore

**Alkem Company (S) Pte Ltd**
1, Penjuru Close, Jurong Town, Singapore 608617
*Tel:* 6265 6666 *Fax:* 6261 7875
*E-mail:* enquiry@alkem.com.sg
*Web Site:* www.alkem.com.sg
*Key Personnel*
Man Dir: Chu Bong *E-mail:* chubong@alkem.
com.sg
Dir: Mr Ee Long Tear
Business Manager: Eugene Koh
Founded: 1973
Business from Other Countries: 70%

**CS Graphics Pte Ltd**
10 Tuas Ave 20, Singapore 2263
*Tel:* 6865 2010 *Fax:* 6861 0190
*E-mail:* rick@csgraphics.us
*Web Site:* www.csgraphics.us
*Key Personnel*
Man Dir: Mr Lee Sian Tee *E-mail:* stlee@
csgraphics-world.com
Founded: 1981
Business from Other Countries: 100%

**Eurasia Press (Offset) Pte Ltd**
10 Kampong Ampat, Singapore 368320
*Tel:* 2805522 *Fax:* 2800593
*E-mail:* eurasia@mbox3.singnet.com.sg

*Key Personnel*
Marketing Dir: Allan Fong
Founded: 1937
Business from Other Countries: 65%

**Ho Printing Singapore Pte Ltd**
31 Changi South St One, Changi South Industrial
Estate, Singapore 486769
*Tel:* 5429322 *Fax:* 5428322
*E-mail:* marketing@hoprinting.com.sg; sales@
hoprinting.com.sg
*Web Site:* www.hoprinting.com
*Telex:* RS 39685 HOFSET
*Key Personnel*
Man Dir: Ho Wai Hoi
Sales Executive: Ho Wah Yuen
Founded: 1951
Business from Other Countries: 30%

**International Press Softcom Ltd**
26 Kallang Ave, Singapore 339417
*Tel:* 2983800 *Fax:* 2971668
*Key Personnel*
Marketing Manager: Kok Leong Koo
Founded: 1972
Business from Other Countries: 60%

**Markono Print Media Pte Ltd**
Subsidiary of Markono Holdings Pte Ltd
21 Neythal Rd, Singapore 628586
*Tel:* 6281-1118 *Fax:* 6286-6663
*E-mail:* saleslead@markono.com.sg
*Web Site:* www.markono.com.sg
*Key Personnel*
Founder & Chairman: Ng Siow How
Dir: Bob Lee Song Tioh *E-mail:* blee@markono.
com.sg
Founded: 1967
Business from Other Countries: 20%
*Branch Office(s)*
Kin Keong Colour Printing (M) Sdn Bhd, Port
Klang 539538

**SNP SPrint Pte Ltd**
97 Ubi Ave 4, Singapore 408754
*Tel:* 6741-2500 *Fax:* 6744-7098
*E-mail:* enquiries@snpcorp.com
*Web Site:* www.snpcorp.com
*Telex:* SNPRS14462
*Key Personnel*
Chief Executive Officer & President: Yeo Chee
Tong
US Sales Manager: Patrick Chung
Business from Other Countries: 40%
*Parent Company:* SNP Corporation Ltd

**Times Printers Pte Ltd**
Subsidiary of Times Publishing Group
16 Tuas Ave 5, Singapore 639340
*Tel:* 6311-2888 *Fax:* 6862-1313
*E-mail:* enquiry@timesprinters.com
*Web Site:* www.timesprinters.com *Cable:*
TIMESPRINT
*Key Personnel*
Man Dir: Leong Kwok Sun *Tel:* 6311-2701
*E-mail:* ksleong@timesprinters.com
Assistant General Manager: Patsy Tan
Assistant General Manager, Manufacturing: G G
Krishnan *Tel:* 6311-2720 *E-mail:* ggkrishnan@
timesprinters.com
Founded: 1968
Business from Other Countries: 75%

# Slovenia

**Gorenjski Tisk Printing House**
Mirka Vadnova 6, 4000 Kranj

*Tel:* (064) 263 0 *Fax:* (064) 241 323
*E-mail:* info@go-tisk.si
*Web Site:* www.go-tisk.si
*Telex:* 34560 YU GOTISK
*Key Personnel*
Dir: Kristina Kobal
Commercial Manager: Boris Krist
Founded: 1888
Business from Other Countries: 50%

# Spain

**Grafos SA Arte Sobre Papel**
Zona Franca, Sector C, calle D 36, 08040
Barcelona
*Tel:* (093) 261 87 50 *Fax:* (093) 263 10 04
*E-mail:* info@grafos-barcelona.com
*Web Site:* www.grafos-barcelona.com
*Key Personnel*
Man Dir: Bernardo G Masana
*E-mail:* bgmasana@compuserve.com
Domestic Sales Dir: Alberto Monclus
Packaging Sales Dir: Alejandro Hijar
Founded: 1934
Business from Other Countries: 45%

**Guarro Casas SA**
Subsidiary of ArjoWiggins Appleton
Can Guarro s/n, 08790 Gelida (Barcelona)
*Tel:* (093) 7767676 *Fax:* (093) 7767677
*E-mail:* guarro@guarro.com
*Web Site:* www.guarro.com
*Key Personnel*
Export Executive Dir: Manuel Freijomil
*E-mail:* mfreijomil@guarro.com
Founded: 1698
Business from Other Countries: 60%

# United
# Kingdom

**Bell & Bain Ltd**
303 Burnfield Rd, Thornliebank, Glasgow G46
7UQ
*Tel:* (0141) 649 5697 *Fax:* (0141) 632 8733
*E-mail:* info@bell-bain.demon.co.uk
*Web Site:* www.bell-bain.co.uk
*Key Personnel*
Man Dir: I Walker
Sales Dir: D Stewart
Founded: 1831
Business from Other Countries: 25%

**Biddles Ltd**
Division of W & G Baird Ltd
Hardwick Industrial Estate, 24 Rollesby Rd,
King's Lynn, Norfolk PE30 4LS
*Tel:* (01553) 764 728 *Fax:* (01553) 764 633
*E-mail:* sales@biddles.co.uk; enquiries@biddles.
co.uk
*Web Site:* www.biddles.co.uk
*Key Personnel*
Man Dir: Rod Willett *E-mail:* rwillett@biddles.
co.uk
Founded: 1885
Business from Other Countries: 8%

**Book Creation Services Ltd**
Mitre House, 44-46 Fleet St, London EC4Y 1BN
*Tel:* (020) 7583 0553 *Fax:* (020) 7583 9439
*E-mail:* info@librios.com
*Web Site:* www.librios.com

*Key Personnel*
Chairman: Hal Robinson *E-mail:* hal@librios.com
Founded: 1991
Business from Other Countries: 30%

**Clays Ltd**
Subsidiary of St Ives Plc
Popson St, Bungay, Suffolk NR35 1ED
*Tel:* (01986) 893211 *Fax:* (01986) 89529
*E-mail:* sales@clays.co.uk
*Web Site:* www.st-ives.co.uk; www.clays.co.uk
*Key Personnel*
Contact: Sarah Orell
Founded: 1817
Business from Other Countries: 15%

**William Clowes Ltd**
Copland Way, Ellough Beccles, Suffolk NR34
9QE
*Tel:* (01502) 712884 *Fax:* (01502) 717003
*E-mail:* william@clowes.co.uk
*Web Site:* www.clowes.co.uk
*Key Personnel*
Man Dir: Ian Foyster *E-mail:* ifoyster@clowes.co.
uk
Sales Dir: David C Browne *Tel:* (07768) 658820
*E-mail:* dbrowne@clowes.co.uk
Founded: 1803
Business from Other Countries: 1%

**Cox & Wyman Ltd**
Cardiff Rd, Reading, Berks RG1 8EX
*Tel:* (0118) 953 0500 *Fax:* (0118) 950 7222
*E-mail:* coxandwyman@cpi-group.net
*Web Site:* www.cpi-group.net
*Key Personnel*
Commercial Contact: Paul Hicks
*E-mail:* phicks@cpi-group.co.uk; Dave Watkins
*E-mail:* dwatkins@cpi-group.co.uk
Founded: 1777
Business from Other Countries: 12%
*Parent Company:* Chevrillon Philippe Industrie of
France

**FiberMark Red Bridge International Ltd**
Ainsworth, Bolton BL2 5PD
*Tel:* (01204) 556900 *Fax:* (01204) 384754
*E-mail:* sales@redbridge.co.uk
*Web Site:* www.redbridge.co.uk
*Key Personnel*
Man Dir: Denis Wolstenholme
Sales & Marketing Dir: Derek Ives
*E-mail:* dives@redbridge.co.uk
Business from Other Countries: 35%
*Parent Company:* Rexam
*U.S. Office(s):* FiberMark, 161 Wellington Rd,
PO Box 498, Brattleboro, VT 05302, United
States *Tel:* 802-257-0365 *Fax:* 802-257-5900
*E-mail:* info@fibermark.com

**Furnival Press**
61 Lilford Rd, London SE5 9HY
*Tel:* (020) 7274 2067 *Fax:* (020) 7274 6984
*E-mail:* furnprint@aol.com
*Key Personnel*
Man Dir: Keith Herbert

**The Guernsey Press Co Ltd**
Braye Rd, Vale, Guernsey GY1 3EG
Mailing Address: PO Box 57, Vale, Guernsey
GY1 3BW
*Tel:* (01481) 240240; (01481) 243657 (ISDN)
*Fax:* (01481) 240275
*E-mail:* books@guernsey-press.com
*Web Site:* www.guernsey-press.com
*Key Personnel*
Contact: Mr T A R Duquemin
Founded: 1897
Business from Other Countries: 80%

**Hammond Bindery Ltd**
Subsidiary of The Charlesworth Group
Unit 2, Flanshaw Way, Flanshaw Lane, Wake-
field, W Yorks WF2 9LP
*Tel:* (01924) 204830 *Fax:* (01924) 332637;
(01924) 339107
*E-mail:* sales@hammond-bindery.co.uk
*Web Site:* www.hammond-bindery.co.uk
*Key Personnel*
Man Dir: Steve Allan *E-mail:* s_allan@hammond-
bindery.co.uk
Sales Manager: Kirk Allan *E-mail:* k_allan@
hammond-bindery.co.uk
Technical Sales Dir: Brian Quarmby
*E-mail:* b_quarmby@hammond-bindery.co.uk
Customer Service Manager: Val Freeman
*Tel:* (01924) 204850 *E-mail:* val@hammond-
bindery.co.uk
Founded: 1972


**Harveys Ltd**
Edgefield Road, Loanhead Midlothian EH20 9SX
*Tel:* (0131) 440 0074; (0131) 440 0014
*Fax:* (0131) 440 3478
*E-mail:* websales@harveys.ltd.uk
*Web Site:* www.harveys.ltd.uk
*Key Personnel*
Chairman: Tom Domke *E-mail:* tom@harveys.ltd.
uk
Joint Man Dir: Tom Dalgleish *E-mail:* tom.
dalgleish@harveys.ltd.uk; Peter McCraw
*E-mail:* peter@harveys.ltd.uk
Dir Customer Service: Craig Linton
*E-mail:* craig@harveys.ltd.uk
Sales Dir: Ross Porter *E-mail:* ross@harveys.ltd.
uk
Sales Manager: Gavin Lowe *E-mail:* sales@
harveys.ltd.uk
Sales Executive: Frank Johnstone *E-mail:* sales@
harveys.ltd.uk; Alasdair Ponton *E-mail:* sales@
harveys.ltd.uk; Chris Seaton *E-mail:* chris@
harveys.ltd.uk
Founded: 1856
Business from Other Countries: 10%


**Hobbs The Printers Ltd**
Brunel Rd, Totton, Hants SO40 3WX
*Tel:* (023) 8066 4800 *Fax:* (023) 8066 4801
*E-mail:* info@hobbs.uk.com
*Web Site:* www.hobbs.uk.com; www.
hobbstheprinters.co.uk
*Key Personnel*
Man Dir: David Hobbs *E-mail:* d.a.hobbs@hobbs.
uk.com
Commercial Dir: Terry Ozanne *E-mail:* t.
ozanne@hobbs.uk.com
Founded: 1884
Business from Other Countries: 4%


**Hunter & Foulis Ltd**
Unit 3, Gateside Commerce Park, Haddington,
East Lothian EH41 3ST
*Tel:* (01620) 826 379 *Fax:* (01620) 829 485
*E-mail:* mail@hunterfoulis.co.uk
*Web Site:* www.hunterfoulis.co.uk
*Key Personnel*
Man Dir: Richard Beese
Production Dir: David Bisset
Founded: 1857


**Image & Print Group Ltd**
Unit 9, Oakbank Industrial Estate, Garscube Rd,
Glasgow G20 7LU
*Tel:* (0141) 353 1900; (0141) 353 8620 (ISDN)
*Fax:* (0141) 353 8611
*E-mail:* info@imageandprint.co.uk
*Web Site:* www.imageandprint.co.uk
*Key Personnel*
Man Dir: Stephen McPhee *Tel:* (0141) 353-8609
*E-mail:* stephen@imageandprint.co.uk
Production Dir: Frank Boyle *Tel:* (0141) 353-
8606 *E-mail:* frank@imageandprint.co.uk

Sales Dir: Kevin Traynor *E-mail:* kevin@
imageandprint.co.uk
Founded: 1975


**Intype Libra Ltd**
Units 3 & 4, Elm Grove Industrial Estate, Elm
Grove, Wimbledon SW19 4HE
*Tel:* (020) 8947 7863 *Fax:* (020) 8947 3652
*E-mail:* intype@btconnect.com
*Key Personnel*
Man Dir: Tony Chapman *E-mail:* tony.chapman@
intypelibra.co.uk
Production: Moya Birchell; Richard Mayne
Founded: 1976
Business from Other Countries: 5%


**The Malvern Press Ltd**
71 Dalston Lane, London E8 2NG
*Tel:* (020) 7249 2991 *Fax:* (020) 7254 1720
*E-mail:* admin@malvernpress.com
*Web Site:* www.malvernpress.com
*Key Personnel*
Man Dir: Leslie Wynn *E-mail:* les@malvernpress.
com
Marketing Dir: Peter Wynn *E-mail:* peter@
malvernpress.com
Founded: 1953
Business from Other Countries: 15%


**Page Bros Ltd (Norwich)**
Subsidiary of Milex Ltd
Mile Cross Lane, Norwich, Norfolk NR6 6SA
*Tel:* (01603) 778800 *Fax:* (01603) 778801
*E-mail:* info@pagebros.co.uk
*Web Site:* www.milex.co.uk
*Key Personnel*
Sales Dir: Steve Commons
Founded: 1750
Business from Other Countries: 20%
*Branch Office(s)*
105-A Euston St, London NW1 2ET *Tel:* (020)
7383 2212 *Fax:* (020) 1383 4145


**Printafoil Ltd**
Foxtail Rd, Ransomes Park, Ipswich IP3 9RT
*Tel:* (01473) 721701 *Fax:* (01473) 270705
*E-mail:* printafoil@blockfoil.com
*Web Site:* www.blockfoil.com
*Key Personnel*
Dir: Simon Flower
General Manager: Jonathan Higgs
*E-mail:* jonhiggs@blockfoil.com
Sales Executive: Barry Fairservice
Production: Norman Eyles *E-mail:* normaneyles@
blockfoil.com; Simon Piddock
*E-mail:* simonpiddock@blockfoil.com
Estimator: Carl Thomas


**J R Reid Print & Media Group**, see J R Reid
Printing Group Ltd


**J R Reid Printing Group Ltd**
79-99 Glasgow Rd, Blantyre, Glasgow G72 0YL
*Tel:* (01698) 826000 *Fax:* (01698) 824944
*E-mail:* info@reid-print-group.co.uk
*Web Site:* www.reid-print-group.co.uk
*Key Personnel*
Joint Man Dir: John R Reid *E-mail:* johnreid@
reid-print-group.co.uk
Founded: 1972


**Antony Rowe Ltd**
Bumper's Farm Industrial Estate, Chippenham,
Wilts SN14 6LH
*Tel:* (01249) 659 705; (01249) 445 535 (ISDN)
*Fax:* (01249) 448 900
*E-mail:* sales@antonyrowe.co.uk
*Web Site:* www.antonyrowe.co.uk
*Key Personnel*
Chief Executive: Ralph Bell
Production Dir: Mike Bando

Technical Dir: Andy Burns
Founded: 1983
Business from Other Countries: 2%
*Branch Office(s)*
Highfield Industrial Estate, 2 Whittle Dr, East-
bourne, East Sussex BN23 6QH *Tel:* (01323)
500040 *Fax:* (01323) 521117 *E-mail:* bob.
hunt@antonyrowe.co.uk


**Stott Brothers Ltd**
Lister Lane, Halifax, W Yorks HX1 5AJ
*Tel:* (01422) 362184 *Fax:* (01422) 353707
*E-mail:* stottbros@aol.com
*Key Personnel*
Man Dir: Ian Bullough


**M & A Thomson Litho Ltd**
Kelvin Industrial Estate, 2-16 Colvilles Pl, East
Kilbride, Glasgow G75 0SN
*Tel:* (01355) 233081 *Fax:* (01355) 245 039
*Web Site:* www.thomsonlitho.com
*Key Personnel*
Man Dir: John Williamson
Sales: Vincent Whittet
*Sales Office(s):* Obrechtstr 35A, Clobe 2nd floor,
5344 AT Oss, Netherlands *Tel:* (0412) 465190
*Fax:* (0412) 465 191
Gibbs House, Kennel Ride, Ascot Berks SL5
7NT *Tel:* (01344) 893 885 *Fax:* (01344) 893
887


**Watkiss Automation Ltd**
Subsidiary of The Watkiss Group
Watkiss House, Blaydon Rd, Middlefield Indus-
trial Estate, Sandy, Beds SG19 1RZ
*Tel:* (01767) 682177 *Fax:* (01767) 691769
*E-mail:* info@watkiss.com
*Web Site:* www.watkiss.com
*Key Personnel*
Technical Dir: M Watkiss
Founded: 1959
Business from Other Countries: 5%


**Winter & Co UK Ltd**
Stonehill, Huntingdon, Cambs PE29 6ED
*Tel:* (01480) 377177 *Fax:* (01480) 377166
*E-mail:* sales@winteruk.com
*Web Site:* www.winteruk.com
*Key Personnel*
Man Dir: Richard Higgins *E-mail:* richardh@
winteruk.com
Sales Dir: Steve Burdett *E-mail:* steveb@
winteruk.com
Founded: 1892


# United States

**Bang Printing Co Inc**
3323 Oak St, Brainerd, MN 56401
Mailing Address: PO Box 587, Brainerd, MN
56401-0587
*Tel:* 218-829-2877 *Toll Free Tel:* 800-328-0450
*Fax:* 218-829-7145
*Web Site:* www.bangprinting.com
*Key Personnel*
VP, Sales: Todd Vanek *Tel:* 218-822-2124
*E-mail:* toddv@bangprinting.com
Founded: 1899
Business from Other Countries: 50%


**BookBuilders New York Inc**
16 Sabal Bend, Palm Coast, FL 32137
*Tel:* 845-639-5316 *Fax:* 845-639-5318
*Web Site:* www.mcabooks.com
*Key Personnel*
Pres: Martin Cook *E-mail:* martin@mcabooks.
com

Founded: 1977
Business from Other Countries: 60%

**Conservation Resources International Inc**
5532 Port Royal Rd, Springfield, VA 22151
*Tel:* 703-321-7730 *Toll Free Tel:* 800-634-6932
    *Fax:* 703-321-0629
*E-mail:* crisales@conservationresources.com
*Web Site:* www.conservationresources.com
*Key Personnel*
Pres: William K Hollinger, Jr
VP: Lavonia Hollinger
Dir, Mktg: Abby A Shaw *Tel:* 800-639-8422
    *E-mail:* crisales@aol.com
Business from Other Countries: 30%
Membership(s): AIC

**Martin Cook Associates Inc**
16 Sabal Bend, Palm Coast, FL 32137
*Tel:* 386-447-8692 *Fax:* 386-447-8746
*E-mail:* mcanewcity@aol.com
*Web Site:* www.mcabooks.com
*Key Personnel*
Pres: Martin Cook *E-mail:* mcanewcity@aol.com
Founded: 1977
Business from Other Countries: 15%
Membership(s): Bookbinders Guild of New York

**CS Graphics USA Inc**
Subsidiary of CS Graphics Pte Ltd Singapore
9748 Weddington Circle, Granite Bay, CA 95746
*Tel:* 916-791-9066 *Fax:* 916-791-9112
*Key Personnel*
Mgr, Sales & Mktg: Rick Marment
    *E-mail:* rick@csgraphics.us
Founded: 1980
Business from Other Countries: 30%

**D & K Group**
1795 Commerce Dr, Elk Grove Village, IL 60007
*Tel:* 847-956-0160 *Toll Free Tel:* 800-632-2314
    *Fax:* 847-956-8214
*E-mail:* info@dkgroup.net
*Web Site:* www.dkgroup.com
*Key Personnel*
Pres: Karl Singer
VP, Sales & Mktg: Marge Hayes
Mktg Communs Coord: Holli Hagene
    *E-mail:* holli.hagene@dkgroup.net
Founded: 1979
Business from Other Countries: 15%

**Desktop Miracles Inc**
112 S Main, PMB 294, Stowe, VT 05672
*Tel:* 802-253-7900 *Fax:* 802-253-1900
*Web Site:* www.desktopmiracles.com
*Key Personnel*
Pres & CEO: Barry T Kerrigan *E-mail:* barry@
    desktopmiracles.com
VP: Virginia Kerrigan *E-mail:* virginia@
    desktopmiracles.com
Founded: 1994
Business from Other Countries: 10%

**DNP America LLC**
Subsidiary of Dai Nippon Printing Co Ltd
335 Madison Ave, 3rd fl, New York, NY 10017
*Tel:* 212-503-1060 *Fax:* 212-286-1505
*Web Site:* www.dnp.co.jp/ *Cable:* DAIPRINTS
    NY
*Key Personnel*
Pres: Yoji Yamakawa
VP & Gen Mgr, Graphic Printing: Kazuteru Arai
    *E-mail:* arai-k@mail.dnp.co.jp
Founded: 1974
Business from Other Countries: 54%
*Branch Office(s)*
577 Airport Blvd, Suite 620, Burlingame, CA
    94010, Gen Mgr: Kosuke Tago *Tel:* 650-340-
    6061 *Fax:* 650-340-6090

**Elegance Printing & Book Binding (USA)**
Member of The Elegance Printing Group
708 Glen Cove Ave, Glen Head, NY 11545
*Tel:* 516-676-5941 *Fax:* 516-676-5973
*Web Site:* www.elegancebooks.com
*Key Personnel*
Man Dir: Frank DeLuca *E-mail:* frank@
    elegancebooks.com
Founded: 1977
Business from Other Countries: 40%

**Fibre Leather Manufacturing Corp**
686 Belleville Ave, New Bedford, MA 02745
*Tel:* 508-997-4557 *Toll Free Tel:* 800-358-6012
    *Fax:* 508-997-7268
*E-mail:* fibreleather@earthlink.net
*Key Personnel*
Pres: Thomas Costella
VP, Sales & Mktg: Rick Plaut
Admin Asst: Carol Gutowski
Founded: 1927
Business from Other Countries: 20%

**Graphic Services Corp**
153 S Main St, Newtown, CT 06470
*Tel:* 203-426-0399 *Fax:* 203-270-1578
*Web Site:* www.independentcartongroup.com
*Key Personnel*
Pres: Jay Willie *E-mail:* jwilliegsc@aol.com
Off Mgr: Kathy Renzulli *E-mail:* krenzulli@
    independentcartongroup.com
Founded: 1990
Business from Other Countries: 10%
Membership(s): Independent Carton Group

**IBT Global Ltd**, see Integrated Book Technology
    Inc

**ICG/Holliston**
Subsidiary of Industrial Coatings Group
Hwy 11-W, Holliston Mills Rd, Church Hill, TN
    37642
Mailing Address: PO Box 478, Kingsport, TN
    37662-0478
*Tel:* 423-357-6141 *Toll Free Tel:* 800-251-0451
    *Fax:* 423-357-8840 *Toll Free Fax:* 800-325-
    0351
*E-mail:* custserv@icgholliston.com
*Web Site:* www.icgholliston.com
*Key Personnel*
Pres: Robert Dwyer
VP, Sales & Mktg: Joann Scherf
    *E-mail:* jscherf@holliston.com
Founded: 1897
Business from Other Countries: 10%
Cover Line(s) Milled: Arrestox/Roxite B; Im-
    perium; Kennett; Pearl Linen; Sturdite

**Imago**
1431 Broadway, Penthouse, New York, NY 10018
*Tel:* 212-921-4411 *Fax:* 212-921-8226
*E-mail:* sales@imagousa.com
*Web Site:* www.imagousa.com
*Key Personnel*
Pres: Joseph E Braff *E-mail:* jbraff@imagousa.
    com
Northeast Sales: Linda Readerman
    *E-mail:* lreaderman@imagousa.com
USA Prodn Dir: Howard R Musk
    *E-mail:* hmusk@imagousa.com
Founded: 1985
Business from Other Countries: 100%
*Branch Office(s)*
Imago West Coast, 31952 Camino Capistrano,
    Suite C22, San Juan Capistrano, CA 92675,
    West Coast Sales: Greg Lee *Tel:* 949-661-5998
    *Fax:* 949-661-8013 *E-mail:* glee@imagousa.
    com
Imago Midwest, 17 N Loomis St, Unit 4A,
    Chicago, IL 60607, Midwest Sales: Ma

Yan *Tel:* 312-829-4051 *Fax:* 312-829-4059
    *E-mail:* myan@imagousa.com
Imago Australia, 14 Brown St, Suite 241,
    Chatswood, Sydney 2067, Australia, Contact:
    Emma Bell *Tel:* (02) 9415 2713 *Fax:* (02) 9415
    2714 *E-mail:* sales@imagoaus.com
Imago France, 6 eme Etage, 42, rue le Peletier,
    75009 Paris, France, Contact: Matt Critchlow
    *Tel:* (1) 42 81 41 24 *Fax:* (1) 42 81 41 24
    *E-mail:* sales@imagogroup.com
Imago Services (HKG) Ltd, 653-659 Kings
    Rd, 6th fl, Flat B, North Point, Hong Kong,
    Contact: Kendrick Cheung *Tel:* 2811 3316
    *Fax:* 2597 5256 *E-mail:* enquiries@imago.com.
    hk
Imago Productions (FE) Pte Ltd, MacPherson
    Industrial Complex, Suite 05-01, 5 Lorong
    Bakar Batu, Singapore 348742, Singapore,
    Contact: K C Ng *Tel:* 6748 4433 *Fax:* 6748
    6082 *E-mail:* enquiries@imago.com.sg
Imago (UK/Europe) Publishing Ltd, Albury Ct,
    Albury Thame, Oxfordshire 0X9 2LP, United
    Kingdom, Contact: Colin Risk *Tel:* (01844)
    337000 *Fax:* (01844) 339935 *E-mail:* sales@
    imago.co.uk *Web Site:* www.imago.co.uk

**Integrated Book Technology Inc**
Division of The IBT Group
18 Industrial Park Rd, Troy, NY 12180
*Tel:* 518-271-5117 *Fax:* 518-266-9422
*E-mail:* mail@integratedbook.com
*Web Site:* www.integratedbook.com
*Key Personnel*
CEO & Pres: John R Paeglow *E-mail:* johnp@
    integratedbook.com
VP & Chief Technol Officer: William Clockel
    *E-mail:* billc@integratedbook.com
VP, Sales & Mktg: Robert Lindberg
    *E-mail:* bobl@integratedbook.com
Dir, Info Technol: Michael Whalen
    *E-mail:* mikew@integratedbook.com
Regl Sales: Ledner Cunningham
    *E-mail:* lednerc@integratedbook.com
Founded: 1991
Business from Other Countries: 20%
*Branch Office(s)*
The IBT Global Ltd, Rollesby Rd, London N4-
    2JZ, United Kingdom, Intl Strategist: Peter
    Kenyon *Tel:* (020) 7351 3332 *Fax:* (020) 7351
    3332 *E-mail:* bobl@integratedbook.com
Membership(s): BMI

**Jinno International Group**
3 Christine Dr, Chestnut Ridge, NY 10977-6802
*Tel:* 845-735-4666 *Fax:* 617-344-5905
*E-mail:* jinno@hotmail.com
*Key Personnel*
Pres: Yoh Jinno
VP: Sharon Jinno
Founded: 1989
Business from Other Countries: 98%
*Branch Office(s)*
Hindy's Enterprise, Melbourne Industrial Bldg, 16
    Westlands Rd, Block A, 20th fl, Quarry Bay,
    Hong Kong *Tel:* 516-6318 *Fax:* 516-5161
Wing Yiu Printing Co, Melbourne Industrial
    Bldg, 6th fl, Block A, 16 Westlands Rd, Quarry
    Bay, Hong Kong, Contact: Law Ming Wah
    *Tel:* 561 0283 *Fax:* 565 8233
c/o Eurasia Press Pte Ltd, 10/14 Kampong Am-
    pat, Singapore 1336, Singapore, Contact: Allan
    Fong *Tel:* 280 5522 *Fax:* 280 0593
Jinno International Singapore, 710 Ang Mo Kio,
    Ave 8, Suite 07-2615, Singapore 2056, Singa-
    pore *Tel:* 458 0778

**Linick International Inc**
Division of The Linick Group Inc
Linick Bldg, 7 Putter Lane, Middle Island, NY
    11953
Mailing Address: PO Box 102, Middle Island,
    NY 11953-0102

*Tel:* 631-924-3888 *Fax:* 631-924-3890
*E-mail:* linickgrp@att.net
*Web Site:* www.lgroup.addr.com
*Key Personnel*
Chmn & CEO: Andrew S Linick, PhD
Treas: Marvin Glickman
Exec VP: Roger Dextor
Founded: 1972
Business from Other Countries: 30%
Paper Type(s) Sold: Acid Free; Recycled

### LK Litho
Division of The Linick Group Inc
Linick Bldg, 7 Putter Lane, Middle Island, NY 11953
Mailing Address: PO Box 102, Middle Island, NY 11953-0102
*Tel:* 631-924-3888
*E-mail:* linickgrp@att.net
*Web Site:* www.lgroup.addr.com/lklitho.htm
*Key Personnel*
VP: Roger Dextor
Founded: 1968
Business from Other Countries: 20%

### Mazer Publishing Services
Division of The Mazer Corporation
6680 Poe Ave, Dayton, OH 45414
*Tel:* 937-264-2600 *Fax:* 937-264-2624
*E-mail:* info@mazer.com
*Web Site:* www.mazer.com
*Key Personnel*
Pres: William Franklin *E-mail:* bill_franklin@mazer.com
Exec VP: Ken Fultz *E-mail:* ken_fultz@mazer.com
Exec Dir, Sales: Bill Faber *Fax:* 937-264-2622 *E-mail:* bill_faber@mazer.com
Founded: 1964
Business from Other Countries: 10%
*Branch Office(s)*
2460 Sand Lake Rd, Orlando, FL 32809, Contact: Bryan Blakley *Tel:* 407-859-5552 *Fax:* 407-859-0643 *E-mail:* bryan_blakley@mazer.com
224 Lexington Ave, Fox River Grove, IL 60021, Contact: Dennis Bowman *Tel:* 847-639-1555 *Fax:* 847-639-1562 *E-mail:* dennis_bowman@mazer.com
22 Lehigh Rd, Wellesley, MA 02181, Contact: Ken Leahy *Tel:* 781-237-4112 *Fax:* 781-431-6184 *E-mail:* ken_leahy@mazer.com
22 Laurel Place, Upper Montclair, NJ 07043, Contact: John Martel *Tel:* 973-744-4320 *Fax:* 973-746-5608 *E-mail:* john_martel@mazer.com

3081 Glenmere Ct, Kettering, OH 45440, Contact: Mark Brewer *Tel:* 937-299-5746 *Fax:* 937-299-5761 *E-mail:* mark_brewer@mazer.com
Membership(s): BMI

### Midas Printing International Ltd
Subsidiary of Midas Printing Group Ltd
35 Belleview Ave, Ossining, NY 10562
*Tel:* 914-941-2041
*E-mail:* info@midasprinting.com
*Web Site:* www.midasprinting.com
*Key Personnel*
US Contact: Gerald B Levine *E-mail:* gerald_levine@midasprinting.com
Dir, Sales & Mktg, Hong Kong: Paul Tang *Tel:* 24084040 *Fax:* 24065890 *E-mail:* paul@midasprinting.com
Busn Devt Mgr, China: Ian Lee *Tel:* 24084048 *Fax:* 24065874 *E-mail:* ian@midasprinting.com
Founded: 1990
Business from Other Countries: 85%
*Branch Office(s)*
1/F, 100 Texaco Rd, Tsuen Wan, New Territories, Hong Kong *Tel:* 24076888 *Fax:* 24080611 (headquarters, send all inquires to this address)
Membership(s): Graphic Arts Association of Hong Kong

### Milanostampa/New Interlitho USA Inc
Subsidiary of Milanostampa New Interlitho Italia SpA
299 Broadway, Suite 901, New York, NY 10007
*Tel:* 212-964-2430 *Fax:* 212-964-2497
*Web Site:* www.milanostampa.com
*Key Personnel*
Chmn & Sales Rep: Rino Varrasso *Tel:* 917-225-9460 *E-mail:* rvarrasso@milanostampa-usa.com
Founded: 1974
Business from Other Countries: 75%

### Palace Press International - Corporate Headquarters
17 Paul Dr, San Rafael, CA 94903
*Tel:* 415-526-1370 *Fax:* 415-526-1394
*E-mail:* info@palacepress.com
*Web Site:* www.palacepress.com
*Key Personnel*
CEO: Raoul Goff *E-mail:* raoul@palacepress.com
Gen Mgr: Michael Madden *E-mail:* michael@palacepress.com
Founded: 1984
Business from Other Countries: 20%
*Branch Office(s)*
Palace Press International Los Angeles, 1499 Huntington Dr, Suite 408, South Pasadena, CA 91030, Contact: Roger Ma *Tel:* 626-282-8877

*Fax:* 626-282-6880 *E-mail:* roger@palacepress.com
Palace Press International New York, 180 Varick St, 10th fl, New York, NY 10014, Contact: Jessica Jones *Tel:* 212-462-2622 *Fax:* 212-463-9130 *E-mail:* jessica@palacepress.com

### Printing Corp of the Americas Inc
620 SW 12 Ave, Fort Lauderdale, FL 33312
*Tel:* 954-781-8100 *Fax:* 954-781-8421
*Key Personnel*
Pres: Jan Tuchman
Founded: 1979
Business from Other Countries: 15%

### Taylor Publishing Company
1550 W Mockingbird Lane, Dallas, TX 75235
*Tel:* 214-819-8226 *Toll Free Tel:* 800-677-2800 *Fax:* 214-630-1852
*E-mail:* info@taylorpub.com
*Web Site:* www.taylorpub.com
*Key Personnel*
CEO: Dave Fiore
Dir, Fine Books & Div Sales Mgr: Jay Love
Founded: 1939
Business from Other Countries: 10%

### Times International Publishing
Division of Times Publishing Ltd/Singapore
99 White Plains Rd, Tarrytown, NY 10591
*Tel:* 914-366-9888 *Fax:* 914-366-9898
*Web Site:* www.tpl.com.sg
*Key Personnel*
Cust Serv Exec: Bonnie Stone *E-mail:* bstone@marshallcavendish.com
Sales Mgr: Suresh Kumar *E-mail:* skumar@marshallcavendish.com
Founded: 1965
Business from Other Countries: 90%

# Uruguay

### Barreiro y Ramos SA
25 de Mayo, Esq J C Gomez, Casilla Correos, 15, 1430 Montevideo
*Tel:* (02) 96 23 58 *Fax:* (02) 96 23 58
*Telex:* 23901PB.CVJA.UY *Cable:* BAREIRAMOS
*Key Personnel*
President: Gaston Barreiro
Vice President: Guzman Barreiro
Founded: 1837
Business from Other Countries: 10%

# Manufacturing Services & Equipment Index

# Manufacturing Services & Equipment

This section includes companies throughout the world that offer manufacturing services & equipment. Those U.S. and Canadian companies with 10% or more of their business done outside North America are also included here. Immediately preceding this section is an index classifying companies by services offered.

## Belgium

**IMPF bvba**
Sint-Amandstr 18, 9000 Ghent
*Tel:* (09) 225 44 29; (09) 265 99 00 *Fax:* (09) 233 13 38
*E-mail:* impf@xs4all.be
*Key Personnel*
Manager: Xavier Dewulf
Founded: 1958
Business from Other Countries: 10%

## Canada

**Appleby's Bindery Ltd**
1303 Rte 102, Upper Gagetown, NB E5M 1R5
*Tel:* 506-488-2086 *Toll Free Tel:* 800-561-2005 (Canada only) *Fax:* 506-488-2086
*E-mail:* applbind@nbnet.nb.ca
*Key Personnel*
Pres & Owner: David E Appleby
Mgr: Edward Appleby
Founded: 1976
Business from Other Countries: 10%

**Master Flo Technology Inc**
1233 Tessier St, Hawkesbury, ON K6A 3R1
*Tel:* 613-636-0539 *Fax:* 613-636-0762
*E-mail:* info@mflo.com
*Web Site:* www.mflo.com
*Key Personnel*
VP, Opers: Tim Duffy
Founded: 1984
Business from Other Countries: 75%

**Printcrafters Inc**
78 Hutchings St, Winnipeg, MB R2X 3B1
*Tel:* 204-633-7117 *Fax:* 204-694-1519
*E-mail:* info@printcraftersinc.com
*Web Site:* www.printcraftersinc.com
*Key Personnel*
Pres: Bob Payne *Tel:* 204-633-7117 ext 223
    *Fax:* 204-694-1594 *E-mail:* bpayne@printcraftersinc.com
Founded: 1996 (Employee owned)
Business from Other Countries: 30%

**PrintWest**
1150 Eighth Ave, Regina, SK S4R 1C9
*Tel:* 306-525-2304 *Toll Free Tel:* 800-236-6438
    *Fax:* 306-757-2439
*E-mail:* general@printwest.com
*Web Site:* www.printwest.com
*Key Personnel*
CEO: Wayne UnRuh
VP, Sales: Ken Benson
Founded: 1992
Business from Other Countries: 15%
*Branch Office(s)*
Box 2500, 2310 Millar Ave, Saskatoon, SK S7K 2C4 *Tel:* 306-665-3560 *Fax:* 306-653-1255

**Transcontinental Printing Book Group**
Division of Transcontinental Group

395 Lebeau Blvd, St-Laurent, QC H4N 1S2
*Tel:* 514-337-8560 *Toll Free Tel:* 800-361-3599
    *Fax:* 514-339-5230
*Web Site:* www.transcontinental.com
*Key Personnel*
VP, Book Group: Jacques Gregoire
Dir, Strategic Busn Devt: Denis Beaudin *Tel:* 514-339-2220 ext 4101
    *E-mail:* beaudind@transcontinental.ca
Founded: 1976
Business from Other Countries: 15%
*Branch Office(s)*
614 Yates Ave, Calumet City, IL 60409, United States, Contact: Kristopher D Levy *Tel:* 708-832-1528 *Fax:* 708-832-9510 *E-mail:* kris.levy@transcontinental.ca (Midwest)
3653 W Leland Ave, Suite One W, Chicago, IL 60625, United States, Contact: Tim Taylor *Tel:* 773-583-8155 *Fax:* 773-583-8162 *E-mail:* tim.taylor@transcontinental.ca (Midwest)
10 Rountree Dr, PO Box 2551, Duxbury, MA 02331, United States, Contact: Ed Catania *Tel:* 508-881-1119 *Fax:* 508-881-7739 *E-mail:* ecatania@attnbi.com (East Coast)
393 Highland Ave, Quincy, MA 02170-4013, United States, Contact: Michael Gazzola *Tel:* 617-696-1435 *Fax:* 617-696-1025 *E-mail:* mikebook@attbi.com (East Coast)
37 Herman Blvd, Franklin Square, NY 11010, United States, Contact: Tom Malloy *Tel:* 516-775-2980 *Fax:* 516-488-0253 *E-mail:* tmmalloy@aol.com (NY)
3175 Summit Square Dr, Suite C9, Oakton, VA 22124, United States, Contact: David Avesian *Tel:* 703-255-1332 *Fax:* 703-255-1343 *E-mail:* davesian@cox.rr.com (Southeast)
559 Lowrys Rd, Parksville, BC V9P 2R8, Contact: Mike Davies *Tel:* 250-248-9700 *Fax:* 250-248-2353 *E-mail:* bookguys@shaw.ca (West Coast)
15373 Victoria Ave, White Rock, BC V4B 1H1, Contact: Wade Davies *Tel:* 604-535-8800 *Fax:* 604-535-8802 *E-mail:* daviesw@shaw.ca (West Coast)
490 Wilfred Dr, Peterborough, ON K9K 2H1, Contact: Tom Lang *Tel:* 705-760-9594 *Fax:* 705-760-9485 *E-mail:* langt@transcontinental.ca (New York)

**Webcom Limited**
3480 Pharmacy Ave, Toronto, ON M1W 2S7
*Tel:* 416-496-1000 *Toll Free Tel:* 800-665-9322
    *Fax:* 416-496-1537
*E-mail:* webcom@webcomlink.com
*Web Site:* www.webcomlink.com
*Key Personnel*
VP, Sales & Mktg: Mike Collinge
Mktg Mgr: Beth Craig
Founded: 1976
Business from Other Countries: 40%
Membership(s): BMI; Canadian Book & Periodical Council; Canadian Printing Industries Association; PIA/GATF

## France

**Critiques Livres Distribution SAS**
24 Rue Malmaison, BP 93, 93172 Bagnolet Cedex
*Tel:* (014) 360-3910 *Fax:* (014) 897-3706
*E-mail:* critiques.livres@wanadoo.fr
*Key Personnel*
President: Rosalind Fay-Boehlinger
Founded: 1976
Business from Other Countries: 100%

## Germany

**Baader Buch- u Offsetdruckerei GmbH & Co KG CL**
Buchrainstr 36, 72525 Muensingen
*Tel:* (07381) 791 *Fax:* (07381) 411412 *Cable:* BAADER-MUNSINGEN
Founded: 1835

**Priese GmbH & Co**
Schwedlerstr 5, 14193 Berlin
*Tel:* (030) 8263024 *Fax:* (030) 8266024
*Key Personnel*
Contact: Elma Priese; Hans Joachim Priese

## Hong Kong

**Co-Fine Promotions**
1407 & Mezz floor, Shiu Fat Bldg, 139-141 Wai Yip St Kwun Tong, Kowloon
*Tel:* 2518 0383 *Fax:* 2518 0361
*E-mail:* cofine@netvigator.com
*Key Personnel*
Contact: Kenneth Derek Kan
Founded: 1988
Business from Other Countries: 30%

**Colorcraft Ltd**
Unit 8-9, 16/F Kodak House Phase II, 321 Java Rd, North Point
*Tel:* 25909033 *Fax:* 25909005; 25909271
*E-mail:* info.cc@colorcraft.com.hk
*Web Site:* www.colorcraft.com.hk
*Key Personnel*
Contact: Ms Bundy Walker
Business from Other Countries: 100%

**Elegance Finance Printing Services Ltd**
Subsidiary of Elegance Printing Company Limited
2401 Alexandra House, 16-20 Chater Rd, Central Hong Kong
*Tel:* 2283 2222 *Fax:* 2283 2283; 2521 3616
*Web Site:* www.eleganceholdings.com
*Key Personnel*
Contact: Rita Chan *E-mail:* rita.chan@eleganceholdings.com
Business from Other Countries: 2%

**Golden Cup Printing Co Ltd**
Seapower Industrial Centre, 6/F, 177 Hoi Bun Rd, Kwun Tong, Kowloon
*Tel:* 2343 4254 *Fax:* 223415426
*E-mail:* info@goldencup.com.hk; sales@ goldencup.com.hk
*Web Site:* www.goldencup.com.hk
*Key Personnel*
Man Dir: Yeung Kam Kai
General Manager: W K Ngan
Sales Manager: Mary Yeung *E-mail:* mary@ goldencup.com.hk
Founded: 1969
Business from Other Countries: 80%
*Branch Office(s)*
Dongguan, China
Guangdong, China
Kunming, China
Yunan, China

**Hong Kong Christian Service**
33 Granville Rd, Kowloon, Hong Kong SAR
*Tel:* 2731-6316 *Fax:* 2731-6333
*E-mail:* info@hkcs.org
*Web Site:* www.hkcs.org
*Key Personnel*
Chief Executive: Mr Ng Shui Lai
Founded: 1952
Business from Other Countries: 1%

**Prontaprint Asia Ltd**
Far East Finance Center, Hong Kong
*Tel:* 28657525 *Fax:* 28661064
*Key Personnel*
Man Dir: Clive Howard
Founded: 1986
Business from Other Countries: 40%

**Sino Publishing House Ltd**
Room 301-302 Valley Centre, 80-82 Morrison Hill Rd, Wanchai, Hong Kong
*Tel:* 2884 9963 *Fax:* 2884 9321
*E-mail:* benyan@sinophl.com
*Web Site:* www.sinophl.com
*Key Personnel*
Contact: Ben Yan *E-mail:* benyan@sinophl.com
Founded: 1993
Business from Other Countries: 75%

# Israel

**Monoline Ltd**
3 Avnei Nezer, Kiryat Sefer
*Tel:* (08) 9741456 *Fax:* (08) 9741454
*Key Personnel*
Dir: S J Colthof
Founded: 1959
Business from Other Countries: 30%

# New Zealand

**Bookprint Consultants Ltd**
Division of Grantham House Publishing
9 Wilkinson St, Apt 6, Oriental Bay, Wellington 6001
*Tel:* (04) 381 3071 *Fax:* (04) 381 3067
*E-mail:* gstewart@iconz.co.nz
*Key Personnel*
Chief Executive: Graham C Stewart
Founded: 1982
Business from Other Countries: 10%

**Egan-Reid Ltd**
Level 2, 38 Ireland St, Freemans Bay, Auckland 1001
*Tel:* (09) 3784100 *Fax:* (09) 3784300
*E-mail:* publishing@eganreid.co.nz
*Web Site:* www.egan-reid.com
*Key Personnel*
Man Dir: Gerard Reid *E-mail:* gerard@eganreid. co.nz
Contact: Mary Egan *E-mail:* mary@eganreid.co. nz
Founded: 1988
Business from Other Countries: 75%

**Rogan McIndoe Print Ltd**
51 Crawford St, Dunedin
Mailing Address: PO Box 1361, Dunedin
*Tel:* (03) 474 0111 *Toll Free Tel:* (0800) 477 0355 *Fax:* (03) 474 0116
*E-mail:* production@rogan.co.nz
*Web Site:* www.rogan.co.nz
*Key Personnel*
Man Dir: Brendan A Murphy
Founded: 1893
Business from Other Countries: 1%

# Portugal

**Edicoes Silabo**
Rua Cidade de Manchester, 2, 1170 100 Lisbon
*Tel:* (021) 8130345 *Fax:* (021) 8166719
*E-mail:* silabo@silabo.pt
*Web Site:* www.silabo.pt
*Key Personnel*
Marketing Dir: Manuel Robalo *E-mail:* manuelrobalo@silabo.pt
Founded: 1983

# Puerto Rico

**Publishing Resources Inc**
373 San Jorge St, 2nd floor, Santurce 00912
*Tel:* (787) 727-1800 *Fax:* (0787) 727-1823
*E-mail:* pri@chevako.net
*Key Personnel*
Owner & President: Ronald J Chevako
Editorial Dir: Anne W Chevako
Founded: 1976
Business from Other Countries: 5%

# Singapore

**Craft Print Pte Ltd**
9 Joo Koon Circle, Jurong, Singapore 629041
*Tel:* 861 4040 *Fax:* 861 0530
*E-mail:* info@craftprint.com
*Web Site:* www.craftprint.com
*Key Personnel*
Man Dir: Charlie Chan
Marketing Manager: Desmond Chan

**Eurasia Press (Offset) Pte Ltd**
10/14 Kg Ampat, Singapore 368318
*Tel:* 2805522 *Fax:* 2800593
*Key Personnel*
Marketing Dir: Allan Fong
Founded: 1937
Business from Other Countries: 65%

**Ho Printing Singapore Pte Ltd**
31 Changi South St One, Changi South Industrial Estate, Singapore 486769
*Tel:* 6542 9322 *Fax:* 6542 8322
*E-mail:* sales@hoprinting.com.sg; marketing@ hoprinting.com.sg
*Web Site:* www.hoprinting.com
*Telex:* RS 39685 HOFSET
*Key Personnel*
Man Dir: Ho Wai Hoi
Sales Executive: Ho Wah Yuen
Founded: 1951
Business from Other Countries: 30%

**Imago Productions (Far East) Pte Ltd**
5 Lorong Bakar Batu, Hex 05-01, MacPherson Industrial Complex, Singapore 348742
*Tel:* 67484433 *Fax:* 67486082
*E-mail:* enquires@imago.com.sg
*Web Site:* www.imago.co.uk
*Key Personnel*
Man Dir: K C Ng
*Branch Office(s)*
Imago Sales USA Inc, 310 Madison Ave, Suite 2103, New York, NY 10017, United States
*Tel:* 212-921-4411 *Fax:* 212-370-4542

**Markono Print Media Pte Ltd**
Subsidiary of Markono Holdings Pte Ltd
21 Neythal Rd, Singapore 628586
*Tel:* 6281-1118 *Fax:* 6286-6663
*E-mail:* saleslead@markono.com.sg
*Web Site:* www.markono.com.sg
*Key Personnel*
Founder & Chairman: Ng Siow How
Dir: Bob Lee Song Tioh *E-mail:* blee@markono. com.sg
Founded: 1967
Business from Other Countries: 20%
*Branch Office(s)*
Kin Keong Colour Printing (M) Sdn Bhd, Port Klang 539538

**SNP SPrint Pte Ltd**
97 Ubi Ave 4, Singapore 408754
*Tel:* 6741-2500 *Fax:* 6744-7098
*E-mail:* enquiries@snpcorp.com
*Web Site:* www.snpcorp.com
*Telex:* SNPRS14462
*Key Personnel*
President & Chief Executive Officer: Yeo Chee Tong
Group Chief Financial Officer: Koo Tse Chia
Business from Other Countries: 40%
*Parent Company:* SNP Corporation Ltd

**Times Printers Pte Ltd**
Subsidiary of Times Publishing Group
16 Tuas Ave 5, Singapore 639340
*Tel:* 6311-2888 *Fax:* 6862-1313
*E-mail:* enquiry@timesprinters.com
*Web Site:* www.timesprinters.com *Cable:* TIMESPRINT
*Key Personnel*
Senior Vice President: Leong Kwok Sun
General Manager: Tay Kiah Chiew
Sales Manager: Wendy Woo
Assistant General Manager: Patsy Tan
Founded: 1968
Business from Other Countries: 75%

# Slovenia

**Gorenjski Tisk Printing House**
Mirka Vadnova 6, 4000 Kranj
*Tel:* (0386) 4 20 16 333 *Fax:* (064) 241 323
*E-mail:* info@go-tisk.si
*Web Site:* www.go-tisk.si
*Telex:* 34560 YU GOTISK

*Key Personnel*
Chief Executive Officer: Kristina Kobal
Founded: 1888
Business from Other Countries: 50%

# Spain

**Luis Vives (Edelvives)**
Xaudaro, 25, 28034 Madrid
*Tel:* (091) 334 48 83 *Fax:* (091) 334 48 82
*E-mail:* dediciones@edelvives.es
*Web Site:* www.grupoeditorialluisvives.com
*Key Personnel*
Production Dir: Jesus Agudo Perez
Founded: 1890
Business from Other Countries: 25%

# Switzerland

**Schweizer Buchzentrum** (Swiss Book Centre)
Buchzentrum AG (BZ), Domizil Industriestr Ost
    10, 4614 Haegendorf
*Tel:* (062) 2092525; (062) 2092644 *Fax:* (062)
    2092627; (062) 2092760
*E-mail:* info@sbz.ch
*Web Site:* www.sbz.ch
*Key Personnel*
Dept Manager: Michael Taylor
Founded: 1882

**Centre Suisse du Livre**, see Schweizer
    Buchzentrum

**Centro Svizzero del Libro**, see Schweizer
    Buchzentrum

**Swiss Book Centre**, see Schweizer Buchzentrum

# United Republic of Tanzania

**Peramiho Publications**
PO Box 41, Peramiho
*Tel:* (054) 2730 *Fax:* (054) 2917
*Key Personnel*
Chief Executive: Fr Gerold Rupper
Founded: 1937

# Thailand

**J Film Process Co Ltd**
440/7 Soi Ratchawithi 3, Rajthevee, Bangkok
    10400
*Tel:* (02) 248-6888 *Fax:* (02) 247-4719
*Key Personnel*
President: Peer Prayukvong
Vice President: Siriporn Prayukvong
Man Dir: Pira Prayookwongse
Founded: 1970
Business from Other Countries: 45%

# United Kingdom

**J W Arrowsmith Ltd**
Winterstoke Rd, Bristol BS3 2NT
*Tel:* (0117) 966 7545 *Fax:* (0117) 963 7829
*E-mail:* jw@arrowsmith.co.uk
*Web Site:* www.arrowsmith.co.uk
*Key Personnel*
Sales Dir: David J Hooper *E-mail:* dhooper@
    arrowsmith.co.uk
Founded: 1854
Business from Other Countries: 40%

**The Bath Press**
Subsidiary of Bath Press Group PLC
Lower Bristol Rd, Bath BA2 3BL
*Tel:* (01225) 428101 *Fax:* (01225) 312418
*E-mail:* bath@cpi-group.co.uk
*Web Site:* www.cpi-group.net
*Key Personnel*
Contact, Commercial: Jonathan Pickering
    *E-mail:* jpickering@cpi-group.co.uk
Founded: 1846
Business from Other Countries: 5%

**Book Production Consultants PLC**
25-27 High St, Chesterton, Cambridge CB4 1ND
*Tel:* (01223) 352790; (01223) 323092 (ISDN)
    *Fax:* (01223) 460718
*E-mail:* enquiries@bpccam.co.uk
*Web Site:* www.bpccam.co.uk
*Key Personnel*
Dir: Tony Littlechild *E-mail:* tl@bpccam.co.uk;
    Colin Walsh *E-mail:* cw@bpccam.co.uk
Founded: 1973
Business from Other Countries: 25%

**Butler & Tanner Ltd**
Caxton Rd, Frome, Somerset BA11 1NF
*Tel:* (01373) 451500 *Fax:* (01373) 451333
*E-mail:* info@butlerandtanner.com
*Web Site:* www.butlerandtanner.com
*Key Personnel*
Joint Man Dir: A Huett
Sales Dir: N White

**Cambridge University Press - Printing Division**
Division of Cambridge University Press
University Printing House, Edinburgh Bldg,
    Shaftesbury Rd, Cambridge CB2 2RU
*Tel:* (01223) 312393 *Fax:* (01223) 315052
*E-mail:* printing@cambridge.org
*Web Site:* uk.cambridge.org
*Key Personnel*
Executive Dir: Sandra Ward *Tel:* (01223) 325608
    *E-mail:* sward@cambridge.org
Corporate Relations: Helen Bradbury
Founded: 1534

**Clays Ltd**
Subsidiary of St Ives Plc
Popson St, Bungay, Suffolk NR35 1ED
*Tel:* (01986) 893211 *Fax:* (01986) 895293
*E-mail:* sales@clays.co.uk
*Web Site:* www.clays.co.uk
*Key Personnel*
Contact: Sarah Orell
Founded: 1817
Business from Other Countries: 15%

**William Clowes Ltd**
Customer Service & Manufacturing Centre, Cop-
    land Way, Ellough Beccles, Suffolk NR34 7TL
*Tel:* (01502) 712884 *Fax:* (01502) 717003
*E-mail:* william@clowes.co.uk
*Web Site:* www.clowes.co.uk

*Key Personnel*
Man Dir: Ian Foyster *E-mail:* ifoyster@clowes.co.
    uk
Sales Dir: David C Browne *Tel:* (07768) 658820
    *E-mail:* dbrowne@clowes.co.uk
Founded: 1803
Business from Other Countries: 1%

**Cradley Print Ltd**
Chester Rd, Cradley Heath, Warley, West Mid-
    lands B64 6AB
*Tel:* (01384) 414100 *Fax:* (01384) 414102
*Web Site:* www.cradleygp.co.uk
*Key Personnel*
Man Dir: Chris Jordan
Founded: 1873
Business from Other Countries: 7%
*Branch Office(s)*
Quadcolor Repro

**Hammond Bindery Ltd**
Subsidiary of The Charlesworth Group
Unit 2, Flanshaw Way, Flanshaw Lane, Wake-
    field, W Yorks WF2 9LP
*Tel:* (01924) 204830 *Fax:* (01924) 339107;
    (01924) 332637
*E-mail:* sales@hammond-bindery.co.uk
*Web Site:* www.hammond-bindery.co.uk
*Key Personnel*
Man Dir: Steve Allan *E-mail:* s_allan@hammond-
    bindery.co.uk
Sales Manager: Kirk Allan *E-mail:* k_allan@
    hammond-bindery.co.uk
Technical Sales Dir: Brian Quarmby
    *E-mail:* b_quarmby@hammond-bindery.co.uk
Founded: 1972

**Headley Brothers Ltd**
The Invicta Press, Queens Rd, Ashford, Kent
    TN24 8HH
*Tel:* (01233) 623131 *Fax:* (01233) 612345
*E-mail:* printing@headley.co.uk
*Web Site:* www.headley.co.uk
*Key Personnel*
Man Dir: Roger Pitt *E-mail:* roger.pitt@headley.
    co.uk
Commercial Dir: Jon Pitt *E-mail:* jon.pitt@
    headley.co.uk
Sales Manager: Bruce Finn *E-mail:* bruce.finn@
    headley.co.uk
Founded: 1881
Business from Other Countries: 5%
*Branch Office(s)*
3rd floor West, High Holborn House, 52-54 High
    Holborn, London WC1V 6LR

**Hobbs The Printers Ltd**
Brunel Rd, Totton, Hants SO40 3WX
*Tel:* (023) 8066 4800 *Fax:* (023) 8066 4801
*E-mail:* info@hobbs.uk.com
*Web Site:* www.hobbs.uk.com; www.
    hobbstheprinters.co.uk
*Key Personnel*
Man Dir: David Hobbs *E-mail:* d.a.hobbs@hobbs.
    uk.com
Commercial Dir: Terry Ozanne *E-mail:* t.
    ozanne@hobbs.uk.com
Operations Dir: Graham Bromley *E-mail:* g.
    bromley@hobbs.uk.com
Operations Manager: Russell Hack *E-mail:* r.
    hack@hobbs.uk.com
Production Manager: Dave Smith *E-mail:* d.
    smith@hobbs.uk.com
Sales Representative: Sajid Ali *E-mail:* s.ali@
    hobbs.uk.com
Founded: 1884
Business from Other Countries: 4%

**Ikon Document Management Services**
Subsidiary of Microgen Holdings Plc

Telephone House, 69-77 Paul St, London EC2A
4NW
*Tel:* (020) 7336 6509 *Fax:* (020) 7336 7840
*Web Site:* www.uk.ikon.com
*Key Personnel*
Man Dir: Dave Weller
Business Development Dir: Aaron Biggs
Founded: 1972
Business from Other Countries: 40%
*Branch Office(s)*
Microgen City Park Watchmead, Welwyn Gar-
den City, Herts AL7 1LT *Tel:* (01707) 355 555
*Fax:* (01707) 338 970

**Multiplex Medway Ltd**
Lordswood Industrial Estate, Gleaming Wood Dr,
Walderslade, Kent ME5 8XT
*Tel:* (01634) 684371 *Fax:* (01634) 683840
*E-mail:* enquiries@multiplex-medway.co.uk
*Web Site:* www.multiplex-medway.co.uk
*Key Personnel*
Dir: Jon Chandler
Sales Manager: Paul Abson

**Page Bros Ltd (Norwich)**
Subsidiary of Milex Ltd
Mile Cross Lane, Norwich, Norfolk NR6 6SA
*Tel:* (01603) 778800 *Fax:* (01603) 778801
*E-mail:* info@pagebros.co.uk
*Web Site:* www.milex.co.uk
*Key Personnel*
Sales Dir: Steve Commons
Founded: 1750
Business from Other Countries: 20%
*Branch Office(s)*
105-A Euston St, London NW1 2ET *Tel:* (020)
7383 2212 *Fax:* (020) 7383 4145

**Pillar Publications Ltd**
Division of Pillar Publications Ltd
66 York Rd, Weybridge, Surrey KT13 9DY
*Tel:* (01932) 852776 *Fax:* (01932) 858035
*E-mail:* hu@bjhc.demon.co.uk
*Key Personnel*
Owner: Dr H de Glanville
Founded: 1981
Business from Other Countries: 10%

**Antony Rowe Ltd**
Division of Rexam Plc
Bumper's Farm Industrial Estate, Chippenham,
Wilts SN14 6LH
*Tel:* (01249) 659 705; (01249) 445 535 (ISDN)
*Fax:* (01249) 448 900
*E-mail:* sales@antonyrowe.co.uk
*Web Site:* www.antonyrowe.co.uk
*Key Personnel*
Chief Executive: Ralph Bell
Sales Manager: Andrew Copley
Founded: 1897
Business from Other Countries: 10%

**TMS Development International Ltd**
128 Holgate Rd, York YO24 4FL
*Tel:* (01904) 641640 *Fax:* (01904) 640076
*E-mail:* enquiry@tmsdi.com
*Web Site:* www.tmsdi.com
*Key Personnel*
Man Dir: Catherine Hick
Marketing Manager: Pat Anslow
Founded: 1989
Business from Other Countries: 30%

**Turnaround Publisher Services Ltd**
Unit 3, Olympia Trading Estate, Coburg Rd,
Wood Green, London N22 6TZ
*Tel:* (020) 8829 3000 *Fax:* (020) 8881 5088
*E-mail:* enquires@turnaround-uk.com
*Web Site:* www.turnaround-uk.com

*Key Personnel*
Man Dir: Bill Godber *Tel:* (020) 8829 3008
*E-mail:* bill@turnaround-uk.com
Marketing Dir: Claire Thompson *Tel:* (020) 8829
3009 *E-mail:* claire@turnaround-uk.com
Finance Dir: Sue Gregg *Tel:* (020) 8829 3006
*E-mail:* sue@turnaround-uk.com
Founded: 1984
Business from Other Countries: 50%

**Watkiss Automation Ltd**
Subsidiary of The Watkiss Group
Watkiss House, Blaydon Rd, Middlefield Indus-
trial Estate, Sandy, Beds SG19 1RZ
*Tel:* (01767) 682177 *Fax:* (01767) 691769
*E-mail:* info@watkiss.com
*Web Site:* www.watkiss.com
*Key Personnel*
Technical Dir: M Watkiss
Founded: 1959
Business from Other Countries: 5%

**John Wilson Booksales**
One High St, Princes Risborough, Bucks HP27
0AG
*Tel:* (01844) 275927 *Fax:* (01844) 274402
*E-mail:* jw@jwbs.co.uk
*Key Personnel*
Contact: John S Wilson
Founded: 1982

# United States

**A-R Editions Inc**
8551 Research Way, Suite 180, Middleton, WI
53562
*Tel:* 608-836-9000 *Toll Free Tel:* 800-736-0070
(US book orders only) *Fax:* 608-831-8200
*E-mail:* info@areditions.com
*Web Site:* www.areditions.com
*Key Personnel*
Pres & CEO: Patrick Wall
Dir, Sales & Mktg: James L Zychowicz
*E-mail:* james.zychowicz@areditions.com
Founded: 1962
Business from Other Countries: 10%

**AWT World Trade**
4321 N Knox, Chicago, IL 60641
*Tel:* 773-777-7100 *Fax:* 773-777-0909
*E-mail:* sale@awt-gpi.com
*Web Site:* www.awt-gpi.com
*Key Personnel*
Pres: Michael Green
Business from Other Countries: 25%
*Sales Office(s):* 8984 NW 105 Way, Medley, FL
*Tel:* 305-887-7500 *Fax:* 305-887-2300
AWT World Trade Europe BV, Antennestr 86,
1322 AS Almere, Netherlands *Tel:* (036)
5463070 *Fax:* (036) 5463071 *E-mail:* info@
awt-europe.com

**BookBuilders New York Inc**
16 Sabal Bend, Palm Coast, FL 32137
*Tel:* 845-639-5316 *Fax:* 845-639-5318
*Web Site:* www.mcabooks.com
*Key Personnel*
Pres: Martin Cook *E-mail:* martin@mcabooks.
com
Founded: 1977
Business from Other Countries: 60%

**Challenge Machinery Co**
6125 Norton Center Dr, Norton Shores, MI 49441
*Tel:* 231-799-8484 *Fax:* 231-798-1275
*E-mail:* info@challengemachinery.com
*Web Site:* www.challengemachinery.com

*Key Personnel*
Dir, Sales & Mktg: Britt Cary *E-mail:* bcary@
challengemachinery.com
Founded: 1870
Business from Other Countries: 10%

**The Cleveland Vibrator Co**
2828 Clinton Ave, Cleveland, OH 44113
*Tel:* 216-241-7157 *Toll Free Tel:* 800-221-3298
*Fax:* 216-241-3480
*Web Site:* www.clevelandvibrator.com
*Key Personnel*
Gen Sales Mgr: Jack Steinbuch
Mktg Spec: Sue Kobylski
Founded: 1923
Business from Other Countries: 12%

**Martin Cook Associates Inc**
16 Sabal Bend, Palm Coast, FL 32137
*Tel:* 386-447-8692 *Fax:* 386-447-8746
*E-mail:* mcanewcity@aol.com
*Web Site:* www.mcabooks.com
*Key Personnel*
Pres: Martin Cook *E-mail:* mcanewcity@aol.com
Founded: 1977
Business from Other Countries: 15%
Membership(s): Bookbinders Guild of New York

**Crathern Machinery Group Inc**
215 Canal St, Manchester, NH 03101
Mailing Address: PO Box 1180, Manchester, NH
03105-1180
*Tel:* 603-314-0444 *Fax:* 603-314-0431
*E-mail:* info@crathern.com
*Web Site:* www.crathern.com
*Key Personnel*
Pres: Larry Pitsch
Business from Other Countries: 40%

**D & K Group**
1795 Commerce Dr, Elk Grove Village, IL 60007
*Tel:* 847-956-0160 *Toll Free Tel:* 800-632-2314
*Fax:* 847-956-8214
*E-mail:* info@dkgroup.net
*Web Site:* www.dkgroup.com
*Key Personnel*
Pres: Karl Singer
VP, Sales & Mktg: Marge Hayes
Mktg Communs Coord: Holli Hagene
*E-mail:* holli.hagene@dkgroup.net
Founded: 1979
Business from Other Countries: 15%

**Desktop Miracles Inc**
112 S Main, PMB 294, Stowe, VT 05672
*Tel:* 802-253-7900 *Fax:* 802-253-1900
*Web Site:* www.desktopmiracles.com
*Key Personnel*
Pres & CEO: Barry T Kerrigan *E-mail:* barry@
desktopmiracles.com
Founded: 1994
Business from Other Countries: 10%

**Express Media Corp**
1419 Donelson Pike, Nashville, TN 37217
*Tel:* 615-360-6400 *Toll Free Tel:* 800-336-2631
*Fax:* 615-360-3140
*E-mail:* info@expressmedia.com
*Web Site:* www.expressmedia.com
*Key Personnel*
Pres: Andrew Cameron
Founded: 1996
Business from Other Countries: 10%

**Fairfield Marketing Group Inc**
Subsidiary of FMG Inc
830 Sport Hill Rd, Easton, CT 06612-1250
*Tel:* 203-261-5585; 203-261-5568 *Fax:* 203-261-
0884
*E-mail:* ffijmktgrp@aol.com
*Web Site:* www.fairfieldmarketing.com

*Key Personnel*
CEO & Pres: Edward P Washchilla *E-mail:* fmg.
inc@aol.com
VP, Fin: Pamela L Johnson
VP, Fulfillment: Jason Paul Miller *Tel:* 203-261-
5585 ext 203
Cust Servs Rep: Mike Lozada *Tel:* 203-261-5585
ext 204
Founded: 1987
Business from Other Countries: 10%
Membership(s): ABA; Association of Educational
Publishers; The Direct Marketing Association;
Direct Marketing Club of New York; Hudson
Valley Direct Marketing Association; International Reading Association; National School
Supply & Equipment Association; United
States Chamber of Commerce

**Hamilton Printing Co**
22 Hamilton Way, Castleton-on-Hudson, NY
12033
*Tel:* 518-732-4491 *Toll Free Tel:* 800-242-4222
*Fax:* 518-732-7714
*Key Personnel*
Pres: Brian F Payne
VP, Mfg: Rick Dunn
VP, Fin: Michael H Hart
Prod Mgr: Judy Rappold
Sales Rep: Stephen H Feuer; Tom Plain; Larry
Ritchie; Michael C Rosenhack *E-mail:* miker@
hpcbook.com
Founded: 1912
Business from Other Countries: 10%
Membership(s): BMI

**IBT Global Ltd**, see Integrated Book Technology
Inc

**Integrated Book Technology Inc**
Division of The IBT Group
18 Industrial Park Rd, Troy, NY 12180
*Tel:* 518-271-5117 *Fax:* 518-266-9422
*Web Site:* www.integratedbook.com
*Key Personnel*
CEO & Pres: John R Paeglow *E-mail:* johnp@
integratedbook.com
VP & Chief Technol Officer: William Clockel
*E-mail:* billc@integratedbook.com
VP, Sales & Mktg: Robert Lindberg
*E-mail:* bobl@integratedbook.com
Dir, Info Technol: Michael Whalen
*E-mail:* mikew@integratedbook.com
Regl Sales: Ledner Cunningham
*E-mail:* lednerc@integratedbook.com
Founded: 1991
Business from Other Countries: 20%
*Branch Office(s)*
The IBT Global Ltd, Rollesby Rd, London N4-
2JZ, United Kingdom, Intl Strategist: Peter
Kenyon *Tel:* (020) 7354 3332 *Fax:* (020) 7354
3332 *E-mail:* peterk@integratedbook.com
Membership(s): BMI

**Linick International Inc**
Division of The Linick Group Inc
Linick Bldg, 7 Putter Lane, Middle Island, NY
11953
Mailing Address: PO Box 102, Middle Island,
NY 11953-0102
*Tel:* 631-924-3888
*E-mail:* linickgrp@att.net
*Web Site:* www.lgroup.addr.com
*Key Personnel*
Chmn & CEO: Andrew S Linick, PhD
Treas: Marvin Glickman
Exec VP: Roger Dextor
Founded: 1972
Business from Other Countries: 30%

**LK Litho**
Division of The Linick Group Inc

Linick Bldg, 7 Putter Lane, Middle Island, NY
11953
Mailing Address: PO Box 102, Middle Island,
NY 11953-0102
*Tel:* 631-924-3888
*E-mail:* linickgrp@att.net
*Web Site:* www.lgroup.addr.com/lklitho.htm
*Key Personnel*
VP: Roger Dextor
Founded: 1968
Business from Other Countries: 20%

**Marrakech Express Inc**
720 Wesley Ave, No 10, Tarpon Springs, FL
34689
*Tel:* 727-942-2218 *Toll Free Tel:* 800-940-6566
*Fax:* 727-937-4758
*E-mail:* print@marrak.com
*Web Site:* www.marrak.com
*Key Personnel*
CEO: Peter Henzell
Prodn Mgr: Steen Sigmund
Sales/Estimator: Shirley Copperman
Founded: 1976
Business from Other Countries: 10%

**Maxcess International**
222 W Memorial Rd, Oklahoma City, OK 73114
Mailing Address: 2305 SE Eighth Ave, Camas,
WA 98607
*Tel:* 405-755-1600 *Toll Free Tel:* 800-639-3433
*Fax:* 405-755-8425
*E-mail:* sales@maxcessintl.com
*Web Site:* www.maxcessintl.com
*Key Personnel*
Media Mgr: Kasey Morales *E-mail:* kmorales@
maxcessintl.com
VP Sales & Mktg: Marcel Hage
Natl Sales Mgr: Randy Adams
Dir, Mktg: Stephanie Tuggle
Business from Other Countries: 35%
Membership(s): Paper Industry Machine Association; Technical Association of the Pulp &
Paper Industry

**Mazer Publishing Services**
Division of The Mazer Corporation
6680 Poe Ave, Dayton, OH 45414
*Tel:* 937-264-2600 *Fax:* 937-264-2624
*E-mail:* info@mazer.com
*Web Site:* www.mazer.com
*Key Personnel*
Pres: William Franklin *E-mail:* bill_franklin@
mazer.com
Exec VP: Ken Fultz *E-mail:* ken_fultz@mazer.
com
Founded: 1964
Business from Other Countries: 10%
*Branch Office(s)*
2460 Sand Lake Rd, Orlando, FL 32809, Contact:
Bryan Blakley *Tel:* 407-859-5552 *Fax:* 407-
859-0643 *E-mail:* bryan_blakley@mazer.com
224 Lexington Ave, Fox River Grove, IL 60021,
Contact: Dennis Bowman *Tel:* 847-639-1555
*Fax:* 847-639-1562 *E-mail:* dennis_bowman@
mazer.com
22 Lehigh Rd, Wellesley, MA 02181, Contact:
Ken Leahy *Tel:* 781-237-4112 *Fax:* 781-431-
6184 *E-mail:* ken_leahy@mazer.com
22 Laurel Place, Upper Montclair, NJ 07043,
Contact: John Martel *Tel:* 973-744-4320
*Fax:* 973-745-5608 *E-mail:* john_martel@
mazer.com
3081 Glenmere Ct, Kettering, OH 45440, Contact: Mark Brewer *Tel:* 937-299-5746 *Fax:* 937-
299-5761 *E-mail:* mark_brewer@mazer.com
Membership(s): BMI

**Midas Printing International Ltd**
Subsidiary of Midas Printing Group Ltd
35 Belleview Ave, Ossining, NY 10562
*Tel:* 914-941-2041

*E-mail:* info@midasprinting.com
*Web Site:* www.midasprinting.com
*Key Personnel*
US Contact: Gerald B Levine
*E-mail:* gerald_levine@midasprinting.com
Dir, Sales & Mktg, Hong Kong: Paul Tang
*Tel:* 24084040 *Fax:* 24065890 *E-mail:* paul@
midasprinting.com
Busn Devt Mgr, China: Ian Lee *Tel:* 24084048
*Fax:* 24065874 *E-mail:* ian@midasprinting.com
Founded: 1990
Business from Other Countries: 85%
*Branch Office(s)*
1/F, 100 Texaco Rd, Tsuen Wan, New Territories, Hong Kong *Tel:* 24076888 *Fax:* 24080611
(headquarters, send all inquires to this address)
Membership(s): Graphic Arts Association of
Hong Kong

**Odyssey Press Inc**
22 Nadeau Dr, Gonic, NH 03839-7307
Mailing Address: PO Box 7307, Gonic, NH
03839-7307
*Tel:* 603-749-4433 *Fax:* 603-749-1425
*E-mail:* info@odysseypress.com
*Web Site:* www.odysseypress.com
*Key Personnel*
Pres: Tad Parker *E-mail:* tad@odysseypress.com
VP: Kevin Pirkey *E-mail:* kevin@odysseypress.
com
Founded: 1989
Business from Other Countries: 10%

**Palace Press International - Corporate
Headquarters**
17 Paul Dr, San Rafael, CA 94903
*Tel:* 415-526-1370 *Fax:* 415-526-1394
*E-mail:* info@palacepress.com
*Web Site:* www.palacepress.com
*Key Personnel*
CEO: Raoul Goff *E-mail:* raoul@palacepress.com
Gen Mgr: Michael Madden *E-mail:* michael@
palacepress.com
Founded: 1984
Business from Other Countries: 20%
*Branch Office(s)*
Palace Press International Los Angeles, 1499
Huntington Dr, Suite 408, South Pasadena, CA
91030, Contact: Roger Ma *Tel:* 626-282-8877
*Fax:* 626-282-6880 *E-mail:* roger@palacepress.
com
Palace Press International New York, 180 Varick St, 10th fl, New York, NY 10014, Contact:
Jessica Jones *Tel:* 212-462-2622 *Fax:* 212-463-
9130 *E-mail:* jessica@palacepress.com

**Times International Publishing**
Division of Times Publishing Ltd/Singapore
99 White Plains Rd, Tarrytown, NY 10591
*Tel:* 914-366-9888 *Fax:* 914-366-9898
*Web Site:* www.tpl.com.sg
*Key Personnel*
Cust Serv Exec: Bonnie Stone *E-mail:* bstone@
marshallcavendish.com
Sales Mgr: Suresh Kumar *E-mail:* skumar@
marshallcavendish.com
Founded: 1965
Business from Other Countries: 90%

**Tobias Associates Inc**
50 Industrial Dr, Ivyland, PA 18974-1433
Mailing Address: PO Box 2699, Ivyland, PA
18974-0347
*Tel:* 215-322-1500 *Toll Free Tel:* 800-877-3367
*Fax:* 215-322-1504
*E-mail:* sales@tobiasinc.com
*Web Site:* www.densitometer.com
*Key Personnel*
Pres: Philip Tobias
VP: Eric Tobias
Founded: 1960
Business from Other Countries: 10%

**US Lithograph Inc**
915 Broadway, 4th fl, New York, NY 10010
*Tel:* 212-673-3210 *Fax:* 212-673-5261
*Web Site:* www.uslithograph.com
*Key Personnel*
Pres: Scott Kelly *E-mail:* scottkelly@uslitho.com
Business from Other Countries: 20%

**Fred Weidner & Daughter Printers**
15 Maiden Lane, Suite 1505, New York, NY
  10038
*Tel:* 212-964-8676 *Fax:* 212-964-8677
*E-mail:* info@fwdprinters.com
*Web Site:* www.fwdprinters.com

*Key Personnel*
Pres: Fred Weidner, III
Exec VP: Cynthia Weidner *E-mail:* cynthia@
  fwdprinters.com
Creative Dir: Carol Mittelsdorf
Founded: 1860
Business from Other Countries: 25%

# Uruguay

**Barreiro y Ramos SA**
25 de Mayo, Esq J C Gomez, Casilla Correos, 15,
  Montevideo
*Tel:* (02) 96 23 58 *Fax:* (02) 96 23 58
*Telex:* 23901PB.CVJA.UY *Cable:*
  BAREIRAMOS
*Key Personnel*
President: Gaston Barreiro
Vice President: Guzman Barreiro
Founded: 1837
Business from Other Countries: 10%

# Book Trade Information

## Book Clubs

## Austria

**Deutsche Buch-Gemeinschaft C A Koch's Verlag Nachfolger**
Vivenotgasse 2, 1120 Vienna
*Tel:* (01) 8123730 *Fax:* (01) 811024
*Telex:* 31405
*Branch Office(s)*
Deutsche Buch-Gemeinschaft C A Koch's Verlag
Nachfolge, Germany

**Buchgemeinschaft Donauland Kremayr & Scheriau**
Niederhofstr 37, 1121 Vienna
*Tel:* (01) 811 02 348 *Fax:* (01) 811 02 680
*E-mail:* donauland@donauland.at
*Web Site:* www.donauland.at
*Telex:* 131405

**Buchgemeinschaft Donauland Kremayr & Scheriau**, see Buchgemeinschaft Donauland Kremayr & Scheriau

## Brazil

**Circulo do Livro SA**
Alameda Ministro Rocha de Azeredo 346, 01410
Sao Paulo
*Tel:* (011) 8513644 *Fax:* (011) 2827273
*Telex:* 31747 *Cable:* Cirlivro
*Key Personnel*
Man Dir: Rene Cesar Xavier dos Santos
Editorial Dir: Esnider Pizzo
*Owned by:* Bertelsmann AG, Germany; Abril SA
Cultural e Industrial

**Editora Universidade De Brasilia** (J)
SCS Qd 02, Bloco C N°78, 2° andar-Ed OK,
70302-907 Brasilia-DF
*Tel:* (061) 3035-4200 *Fax:* (061) 323-1017
*E-mail:* editora@unb.br
*Web Site:* www.livrariauniversidade.unb.br *Cable:*
UNIVERBRASILIA EDITORA
*Owned by:* Fundacao Universidade de Brasilia

## Chile

**Clubs de Lectores Andres Bello**
Ave Ricardo Lyon 946, Casilla de Correo, Providencia, Santiago
*Tel:* (02) 2049900; (02) 2049901 *Fax:* (02)
2253600
*Telex:* 240901 Edjur

*Key Personnel*
General Manager: Julio Serrano Lamas
Commercial Manager: Marta Mallea Araya
Established: 1947
There are two clubs: one for children (membership 20,000), the other for adults (membership 25,000).
*Owned by:* Editorial Andres Bello/Editorial Juridica de Chile

## Colombia

**Circulo de Lectores SA**
Calle 57 No 6-35, Apdo Aereo 52111, Bogota
*Tel:* 2173211; 2177720 *Fax:* 2178157
*Web Site:* www.comercial-eltiempo.com
*Telex:* 41255 *Cable:* CIRLEC
*Key Personnel*
Dir: Eduardo Polo, Sr
Marketing: Rafael Vargas
Established: 1970
Number of Members: 650,000
*Owned by:* Casa Editorial El Tiempo

## Czech Republic

**ERB**
Vaclavske nam 17, 11258 Prague 1
*Tel:* 224 810 053 *Fax:* 224 811 566
*Web Site:* www.prace.cz
*Telex:* 121442 *Cable:* 1106
Established: 1968
Number of Members: 67,835
*Owned by:* Prace

**Friends of Antiquity**
Na Florenci 3, 11303 Prague 1
*Tel:* (02) 24811549; (02) 24225143 *Fax:* (02)
24226026
*Key Personnel*
Manager: Stefan Szerynski
Established: 1969
Number of Members: 6,000
*Owned by:* Nakladatelstvi Svoboda

**KM C**
c/o Albatros, Napankraci 30, 14000 Prague 4
*Tel:* 234 633 274
*Web Site:* www.albatros.cz
*Key Personnel*
Man Dir: Dr Martin Slavik
Young Readers' Club.
*Owned by:* Albatros

**Odeon Buch- und Phonoclub**
Narodni tr 36, 11000 Prague 1
*Tel:* (02) 264100 *Fax:* (02) 24225254
*E-mail:* odeon@comp.cz
*Web Site:* www.odeon.cz
*Key Personnel*
Editorial Dir: Dr Jiri Nasinec
Established: 1953
Subjects: Fiction, Art
Number of Members: 250,000
*Owned by:* Odeon; nakladatelstvi krasne literatury
a umeni

## Denmark

**Egmont Lademann A/S** (J)
Vognmagergade 11, 1148 Copenhagen V
*Tel:* 3615 6600 *Fax:* 3644 1162
*Web Site:* www.egmontbogklub.dk
Subjects: Management, Children's Books, Commercial Fiction, True Stories
*Book Club(s):* Bogsamleren; Bolig Og Livsstil;
DisneyKlubben; Disney's Borneleksikon;
Egmont Bogklubben; Girls Only; Hobbyklubben; Livsenergi Klubben; Paperback Bogklubben; Virkelighedens Verden; Bogsamleren;
Bolig Og Livsstil; DisneyKlubben; Disney's
Borneleksikon; Egmont Bogklubben; Girls
Only; Hobbyklubben; Livsenergi Klubben; Paperback Bogklubben; Virkelighedens Verden

**Fiction Factory International Ltd**
Klareboderne 3, 1001 Copenhagen K
*Tel:* (043) 33 75 55 60 *Fax:* (043) 33 75 55 22
*E-mail:* information@gyldendal.dk
*Web Site:* www.gyldendal-uddannelse.dk
*Key Personnel*
Publisher: Jens Bendtsen *E-mail:* jens_bendtsen@
gyldendal.dk
Established: 1987
Subjects: Children's, Adolescent, Adult (in English)
*Publication(s): Fiction Factory* (materials for
teaching of modern languages)
*Owned by:* Kaleidoscope Publishers Ltd

**Gyldendals Babybogklubben** (J)
Postboks 176, 1005 Copenhagen K
*Tel:* 70 11 00 33 *Fax:* 70 11 01 33
*E-mail:* boernebogklub@gyldendal.dk
*Web Site:* www.gyldendal.dk
*Owned by:* Gyldendalske Boghandel - Nordisk
Forlag A/S

**Gyldendals Bogklubben** (J)
Postboks 176, 1005 Copenhagen K
*Tel:* 70 11 00 33 *Fax:* 70 11 01 33
*E-mail:* gyldendals-bogklub@gyldendal.dk
*Web Site:* www.gyldendal.dk

*Telex:* 15887 gyldal dk *Cable:*
  GYLDENDALSKE
Subjects: Fiction, Nonfiction (General)
*Owned by:* Gyldendalske Boghandel - Nordisk
  Forlag A/S

**Gyldendals Borne Bogklubben** (J)
Postboks 176, 1005 Copenhagen K
*Tel:* 70 11 00 33 *Fax:* 70 11 01 33
*E-mail:* boernebogklub@gyldendal.dk
*Web Site:* www.gyldendal.dk
*Telex:* 15887 gyldal dk *Cable:*
  GYLDENDALSKE
*Owned by:* Gyldendalske Boghandel - Nordisk
  Forlag A/S

**Gyldendals Junior Bogklubben** (J)
Postboks 176, 1005 Copenhagen K
*Tel:* 70 11 00 33 *Fax:* 70 11 01 33
*E-mail:* boernebogklub@gyldendal.dk
*Web Site:* www.gyldendal.dk
*Owned by:* Gyldendalske Boghandel - Nordisk
  Forlag A/S

**Samlerens Bogklub** (J)
Postboks 176, 1005 Copenhagen K
*Tel:* 70 11 00 33 *Fax:* 70 11 01 33
*E-mail:* samlerens-bogklub@gyldendal.dk
*Web Site:* www.samlerens-bogklub.dk; www.
  gyldendal.dk
*Telex:* 15887 gyldal dk *Cable:*
  GYLDENDALSKE
Subjects: Fiction, Government, Political Science,
  Nonfiction (General)
*Owned by:* Gyldendalske Boghandel - Nordisk
  Forlag A/S

**Bogklubben 12 Boget A/S**
Pilestraede 52, 1112 Copenhagen K
*Tel:* 33695000 *Fax:* 33695051
*E-mail:* b12b@bogklubben-12-boget.dk
*Web Site:* www.lrforlag.dk
*Key Personnel*
Man Dir: Jette Juliusson
Established: 1988
Subjects: General nonfiction
*Owned by:* Lindhardt & Ringhof I/S, Munksgaard

# Finland

**Aikamedia Oy** (Aikamedia Ltd)
Heikkilantie 177, 42701 Keuruu
Mailing Address: PL 99, 42701 Keuruu
*Tel:* (020) 7619 800 *Fax:* (014) 7514 757
*E-mail:* asiakaspalvelu@aikamedia.fi
*Web Site:* www.aikamedia.fi
*Key Personnel*
President: Jari Vieltojarvi *Tel:* (040) 0533 036
  *E-mail:* jari.vieltojarvi@aikamedia.fi
Publishing Manager: Outi Katto *Tel:* (040) 0618
  601 *E-mail:* outi.katto@aikamedia.fi
Established: 1995
Christian books, music & periodicals.
*Owned by:* Ristin Voitto ry
Imprints: Hengellinen Laulukirja; Raamatun Ti-
  etosarja

**Hengellinen Laulukirja**, *imprint of* Aikamedia
  Oy

**Raamatun Tietosarja**, *imprint of* Aikamedia Oy

**Suuri Suomalainen Kirjakerho Oy** (Great
  Finnish Book Club Ltd)
PL 120, 00241 Helsinki

*Tel:* (09) 2705 0077; (09) 1566 830 *Fax:* (09) 145
  510
*E-mail:* sskk.palaute@sskk.fi
*Web Site:* www.sskk.fi
*Key Personnel*
President: Pauli A Leimio *Tel:* (09) 1566 316
  *E-mail:* pauli.leimio@kuvalehdet.fi
Number of Members: 280,000
*Owned by:* Otava Kustannusosakeyhtioe, Uuden-
  maankatu 10, Helsinki 00120
*Parent Company:* Yhtyneet Kuvalehdet Oy
  (United Magazines Ltd)
*Ultimate Parent Company:* Otava-Kuvalehdet Oy

**Uudet Kirjat**
Bulevardi 12, 00120 Helsinki
Mailing Address: PL 15, 00121 Helsinki
*Tel:* (09) 6168 3370
*E-mail:* uudetkirjat@wsoy.fi
*Web Site:* www.uudetkirjat.fi
*Telex:* 122644 Wsoy
*Key Personnel*
Contact: Raija Hynynen
The New Books.
Number of Members: 110,000
*Owned by:* Werner Soederstroem Osakeyhtio
  (WSOY)

# France

**L'Amitie par le Livre**
BP 1031, 25001 Besancon Cedex
*Tel:* (03) 81820894 *Fax:* (03) 81820894
First book club founded in France in 1930, by
  people in the teaching profession. It is non-
  profitmaking & run by voluntary effort.
*Owned by:* L'Amitie par le Livre

**Club du Livre SA**
28 rue Fortuny, 75017 Paris
*Tel:* (01) 47638055 *Fax:* (01) 44404865
*Key Personnel*
Man Dir: Philippe Lebaud
Subjects: Art, De Luxe Editions

**Jean Grassin Editeur**, *imprint of* Poetes Presents

**Nouveau Cercle Parisien du Livre**
6 rue Bonaparte, 75006 Paris
*Tel:* (01) 43547195 *Fax:* (01) 40518288
*Web Site:* zalber.free.fr
*Key Personnel*
President: Charles Zalber
Club is associated with publisher Galerie Lucie
  Weill.
Subjects: Olivier Debre Illustrations, Edmond
  Jabese Texts
*Owned by:* Au Pont des Arts; Galerie Lucie Weill

**PEMF**, see Publications de l'Ecole Moderne
  Francaise (PEMF)

**Poetes Presents**
Pl de Port-en-Dro, 56342 Carnac Cedex
Mailing Address: BP 75, 56342 Carnac Cedex
*Tel:* (02) 97 52 93 63 *Fax:* (02) 97 52 83 90
*Web Site:* perso.wanadoo.fr/j.grassin
*Key Personnel*
President: Jean Grassin
Established: 1957
Subjects: Poetry
*Book Club(s):* Club de Selection des Meilleurs
  Livre de Poesie; Club de Selection des
  Meilleurs Livre de Poesie
Number of Members: 1,500
*Owned by:* Jean Grassin Editeur
Imprints: Jean Grassin Editeur

**Publications de l'Ecole Moderne Francaise**
  **(PEMF)**
06376 Mouans Sartoux Cedex
*Tel:* (04) 92284284 *Fax:* (016) 92921804
*E-mail:* commercial@pemf.fr
*Web Site:* www.pemf.fr *Cable:* PEMF
This company runs five book clubs supplying series of books for children: aged 8-12 (BTJ),
  aged 10-15 (BT), aged over 15 (BT2); for
  teachers (L'Educateur) & for audiovisual supplies (BT Son).

**Gerard Varin**, see L'Amitie par le Livre

# Germany

**Bertelsmann Club**
PO Box 7777, 33300 Gutersloh
*Tel:* (05) 415 233 *Fax:* (05) 415 744
*E-mail:* service@derclub.de
*Web Site:* www.bertelsmann-club.de
*Telex:* 931149
*Key Personnel*
Contact: Dr Stephan Kruemmer
Number of Members: 5,600,000
*Owned by:* Bertelsmann AG
*Branch Office(s)*
290 Club-Filialen/Bertelsmann Club

**Buechergilde Gutenberg**
Stuttgarter Str 25-29, 60329 Frankfurt am Main
*Tel:* (069) 27 39 08-0 *Fax:* (069) 27 39 08-25;
  (069) 27 39 08-26
*E-mail:* service@buechergilde.de
*Web Site:* www.buechergilde.de
*Owned by:* Buechergilde Gutenberg Verlagsge-
  sellschaft mbH

**Deutscher Buchkreis**
Am Apfelberg 18, 72076 Tuebingen
*Tel:* (07071) 4070-0 *Fax:* (07071) 4070-26
*E-mail:* info@grabertverlag.de
*Web Site:* www.hohenrain.de
*Key Personnel*
Publisher: Wigbert Grabert
*Owned by:* Grabert-Verlag Wigbert Grabert

**EBG Verlags GmbH**
Wolframstr 36, 70191 Stuttgart
*Tel:* (07154) 1340
*Telex:* 17715410 ebege d
Established: 1950
Number of Members: 1,300,000
*Owned by:* Bertelsmann AG

**Europaeische Bildungsgemeinschaft Verlags**
  **GmbH**, see EBG Verlags GmbH

**Herder-Buchgemeinde**
Hermann-Herder-Str 4, 79104 Freiburg
*Tel:* (0761) 2717440 *Fax:* (0761) 2717360
*E-mail:* kundenservice@herder.de
*Web Site:* www.herder.de
Established: 1952
Subjects: Fiction & poetry, picture books
*Owned by:* Verlag Herder GmbH & Co KG

**Wissenschaftliche Buchgesellschaft** (Scientific
  Book Society) (J)
Hindenburgstr 40, 64295 Darmstadt
*Tel:* (06151) 33 08-0 *Fax:* (06151) 31 41 28
*E-mail:* service@wbg-darmstadt.de
*Web Site:* www.wbg-darmstadt.de
Established: 1949
Number of Members: 140,000

# Greece

**Sport & Hobby Book Club**
19 Iperidou, 105 58 Athens
Mailing Address: PO Box 30564, 100 33
    Athens
*Tel:* 2103234217 *Fax:* 2103232082
*E-mail:* hcp@photography.gr
*Key Personnel*
President: Stavros Moressopoulos *E-mail:* mores.
    s@altavista.net
Established: 1986
Subjects: Photography, Sports, Hobbies, How-to,
    Music, Travel, Wine & Spirits, Animals
Number of Members: 780
*Owned by:* Moressopoulos SA Organizing, Pub-
    lishing, Advertising, Education

# Iceland

**The AB Book Club (BAB)**
Suaurlandsbraut 12, 108 Reykjavik
*Tel:* 522 2138 *Fax:* 522 2026
*Web Site:* www.ab.is
*Key Personnel*
President: Fridrik Fridriksson
Editor: Bjarni Thorsteinsson *E-mail:* bjarni.
    thorsteinsson@edda.is
Established: 1974
Number of Members: 8,500
*Owned by:* AB Almenna bokafelagid

**BAB**, see The AB Book Club (BAB)

**Gulur Raudur Grenn og Blar Childrens
    Bookclub**
Sidumula 7-9, 108 Reykjavik
*Tel:* 5102525 *Fax:* 5102525
*E-mail:* malogmenning@edda.is
*Web Site:* www.malogmenning.is
*Key Personnel*
Contact: Thorhildur Gardosdottir
Number of Members: 10,000
*Owned by:* MM Mal og menning

**Heima er Bezt Book Club**
Armuli 23, 108 Reykjavik
Mailing Address: Postholf 8427, 128 Reykjavik
*Tel:* 5531599; 5882400 *Fax:* 5888994
*Key Personnel*
Editor: G Baldvinsson
*Owned by:* Skjaldborg Ltd

**The MAB Cookery Book Club**
Suaurlandsbraut 12, 108 Reykjavik
*Tel:* 522 2138 *Fax:* 522 2026
*Web Site:* www.ab.is
Established: 1984
Number of Members: 11,500
*Owned by:* AB Almenna bokafelagid

**MM Mal og menning**
Sudurlandsbraut 12, 108 Reykjavik
*Tel:* 522 2000 *Fax:* 522 2022; 522 2026
*E-mail:* malogmenning@edda.is
*Web Site:* www.malogmenning.is
*Key Personnel*
Contact: Pall Valsson
Number of Members: 24,000
Publication(s): *Booksellers*

**Uglan Islenski Kiljuklubburinn**
Sudurlandsbraut 12, 108 Reykjavik
*Tel:* 522 2000 *Fax:* 522 2022
*E-mail:* edda@edda.is

*Web Site:* www.edda.is
Paperback Book Club.
Number of Members: 10,000
*Owned by:* Edda Utgafa hf

**Particip Verold**
Njoervasundisa 15a, 104 Reykjavik
*Tel:* 5688433 *Fax:* 5688142
*E-mail:* fjolvi@fjolvi.is
*Web Site:* www.fjolvi.is
*Owned by:* Fjolvi; bokautgafa

# India

**Anand Book Club**
c/o Vision Books Pvt Ltd, Videsh Sanchar Bha-
    van Bangla Saheb Rd, New Delhi 110001
*Tel:* (011) 5550-2222
*E-mail:* customerservice@vsnl.com
*Web Site:* www.vsnl.in
*Key Personnel*
Dir: Sudhir Malhotra
Number of Members: 22,000
*Owned by:* Vision Books Pvt Ltd

**Book Lovers Club**
A-59 Okhla Industrial Area, Phase II, New Delhi
    110020
*Tel:* (011) 26387070; (011) 26386209 *Fax:* (011)
    26383788
*E-mail:* ghai@nde.vsnl.net.in
*Web Site:* www.sterlingpublishers.com *Cable:*
    PAPERBACKS
Established: 1986
Number of Members: 1,076
*Owned by:* Sterling Publishers Pvt Ltd

**DC Book Club**
Good Shepherd St, Kottayam, Kerala 686001
Mailing Address: PO Box 212, Kottayam, Kerala
    686001
*Tel:* (0481) 2563114; (0481) 2563226; (0481)
    2578214 *Fax:* (0481) 2564758
*E-mail:* info@dcbooks.com
*Web Site:* www.dcbooks.com
*Key Personnel*
Chief Executive Officer: Ravi Deecee *Tel:* (0481)
    2301614
Established: 1975
Number of Members: 2,500
*Owned by:* D C Books, Printers, Publishers &
    Booksellers

**Orient Book Club** (J)
c/o Vision Books Pvt Ltd, Videsh Sanchar Bha-
    van Bangla Saheb Rd, New Delhi 110 001
*Tel:* (011) 5550-2220
*E-mail:* customerservice@vsnl.com
*Web Site:* www.vsnl.in
*Key Personnel*
Dir: Sidharth Malhotra
Established: 1979
Subjects: Cookery, How-to, Fiction, Health & Fit-
    ness, Self Help, Children's Books, Investment
    Personal Finance
Number of Members: 40,000
*Parent Company:* Vision Books Pvt Ltd

**Star Publisher's Distributors** (J)
4/5 B Asaf Ali Rd, New Delhi 110002
*Tel:* (011) 23286757; (011) 23268651; (011)
    23261696; (011) 23258993 *Fax:* (011)
    23273335; (011) 26481565
*E-mail:* starpub@satyam.net.in
*Web Site:* www.starpublic.com
*Key Personnel*
Chairman: Mr Amar Nath Varma

Subjects: Books in English, Hindi & other Indian
    Languages, Children's Books, Linguistics, So-
    cial Sciences
Number of Members: 15,000
*Owned by:* Star Publications (P) Ltd
*Branch Office(s)*
55 Warren St, London W1T 5NW, United King-
    dom *Tel:* (020) 7380 0622; (020) 7419 9169
    *Fax:* (020) 7419 9169 *E-mail:* indbooks@aol.
    com

# Indonesia

**Himpunan Masyarakat Pencinta Buku**
Jin Hasanuddin 9, Bandung, Jawa Barat
*Tel:* (022) 470821; (022) 470287
Established: 1979
The Association of Bibliophiles.
Number of Members: 14,300
*Owned by:* Eresco PT

**KPI**
Jln Dr Wahidin 1, Jakarta
Mailing Address: PO Box 29, Jakarta
*Tel:* (021) 361701; (021) 41701
*Telex:* 45905 Prumbp Ia
Established: 1982
Klub Perpustakaan Indonesia.
Number of Members: 4,500

# Israel

**Ma'ariv Book Guild (Sifriat Ma'ariv)**
3a Yoni Netanyahu St, Or-Yehuda 60376
*Tel:* (03) 5383313 *Fax:* (03) 6343205
*Telex:* 033735 *Cable:* MA'ARIV TELAVIV
*Key Personnel*
Man Dir: Eli Shimoni *E-mail:* shimoni@hed-arzi.
    co.il
*Owned by:* Ma'ariv Book Guild

# Italy

**Isper Club** (J)
Corso Dante 122, 10126 Turin
*Tel:* (011) 66 47 803 *Fax:* (011) 66 70 829
*E-mail:* isper@isper.org
*Web Site:* www.isper.org
*Key Personnel*
Contact: Marco Actis Grosso *E-mail:* marco.
    actisgrosso@isper.org
*Owned by:* ISPER

**Edi Thule Club**
Via Gravina 95, I-90139 Palermo
*Tel:* (091) 323699
*Owned by:* Edizioni Thule
Imprints: Thule Spiritualita E Letteratura

**Thule Spiritualita E Letteratura**, *imprint of* Edi
    Thule Club

# Japan

**Fukuinkan Ehon Library**
c/o Fukuinkan Shoten Publishers Inc, 6-3 Hon-
     Komagome 6 chome, Bunkyo-ku, Tokyo 113
*Tel:* (03) 39421226 *Fax:* (03) 39429691
*Web Site:* www.fukuinan.co.jp
*Telex:* J33597 Aab Forchild *Cable:*
     FUKUINKANSHOTEN TOKYO
Subjects: Children's Books
*Owned by:* Fukuinkan Shoten Publishers Inc

**Kodansha Disney Children's Book Club** (J)
2-12-21 Otowa, Bunkyo-ku, Tokyo 112-8001
*Tel:* (03) 3946-6201 *Fax:* (03) 3944-9915
*Web Site:* www.kodansha.co.jp; www.kodanclub.
     com
*Key Personnel*
President: Sawako Noma
*Owned by:* Kodan-Sha International
*Branch Office(s)*
Paris Liaison Office, 4, pl de l'Opera, 75002
     Paris, France *Tel:* (01) 42 66 55 73 *Fax:* (01)
     42 66 55 91
*U.S. Office(s):* 575 Lexington Ave, New York,
     NY 10022, United States *Tel:* 917-322-6223
     *Fax:* 212-935-6529

**Bookclub Psyche**
2-5 Kami-Takaido 1 chome, Suginami-ku, Tokyo
     168
*Tel:* (03) 33290031 *Fax:* (03) 53747186
*Web Site:* www.seiwa-pb.co.jp
Subjects: Psychiatry
*Owned by:* Seiwa Shoten

# Mexico

**Bertelsmann de Mexico SA**
Ave de la Paz No 26, Col San Angel, 01000
     Mexico, DF
*Tel:* (05) 5501620; (05) 5489048
*Telex:* 1761195 Cileme
Number of Members: 200,000
*Owned by:* Bertelsmann AG, Germany

**Club de Lectores Extemporaneos**
Poniente 126-A-400, No 400, Colonia Nueva
     Vallejo, 07750 Mexico, DF
*Tel:* (05) 5875424; (05) 5878785
*Owned by:* Editorial Extemporaneos SA

# Myanmar

**Sarpay Beikman Book Club**
529 Merchant St, Rangoon
*Tel:* (01) 283277
*Owned by:* Sarpay Beikman Board

# Netherlands

**ECI voor Boeken en platen BV**
Laanakkerweg 14-16, 4131 PB Vianen
*Tel:* (0347) 379214 *Fax:* (0347) 379380
*Web Site:* www.nbc-club.nl
*Telex:* 47449

*Book Club(s):* Nederlandse Boekenclub; Neder-
     landse Lezerskring Boek en Plaat BV; Neder-
     landse Boekenclub; Nederlandse Lezerskring
     Boek en Plaat BV

**Nederlandse Boekenclub** (Netherlands Book
     Club) (J)
Postbus 2394, 3500 GJ Utrecht
*Tel:* (03473) 6 11 22 *Fax:* (03473) 79380
*E-mail:* service@nbc-club.nl
*Web Site:* www.nbc-club.nl
*Key Personnel*
Manager: A L P Bongaards
Established: 1967
Subjects: Fiction, Nonfiction (General)
Number of Members: 350,000
*Owned by:* ECI voor Boeken en Platen BV

**Nederlandse Lezerskring Boek en Plaat BV**
Laanakkerweg 14-18, 413 1EB Vianen Zh
Mailing Address: PO Box 400, 4130 EK Vianen
     Zh
*Tel:* (03473) 79214 *Fax:* (03473) 79380
Established: 1966
Number of Members: 500,000
*Owned by:* ECI voor Boeken en Platen BV

**VCL**
POB 5018, 8260 GA Kampen
*Tel:* (038) 3392555
*Web Site:* www.kok.nl
*Key Personnel*
Contact: Mrs M Boltje *Tel:* (038) 3392524
     *E-mail:* mboltje@kok.nl
*Owned by:* Uitgeefmaatschappij J H Kok BV

# New Zealand

**Doubleday New Zealand Ltd, Book Club
     Division**
One Parkway Dr, Mairangi Bay Industrial Estate,
     Auckland 10
Mailing Address: Private Bag 102947, North
     Shore Mail Centre, Auckland 1333
*Tel:* (09) 4782846 *Fax:* (09) 4781609
*Web Site:* www.doubleday.com.au
*Telex:* NZ60589
Operated by Doubleday Australia Pty Ltd, Aus-
     tralia. Ultimate Parent Company: Bertelsmann
     AG, Germany.
*Book Club(s):* Book New Zealand; Book of the
     Month Club; Doubleday Book Club; Double-
     day History Book Club; Doubleday Military
     Book Club; The Literary Guild; Doubleday
     Children's Book Club; Book New Zealand;
     Book of the Month Club; Doubleday Book
     Club; Doubleday History Book Club; Double-
     day Military Book Club; The Literary Guild;
     Doubleday Children's Book Club

# Nigeria

**Amebo Book Club**
PO Box 1970, Ibadan
*Owned by:* Adebara Publishing House

**Onibon-Oje Book Club**
Felele Layout, Molete, Ibadan
Mailing Address: PO Box 3109, Ibadan
*Tel:* (022) 313956
Subjects: Fiction, Drama
*Owned by:* Onibon-Oje Publishers

**Varsity Book Club**
11 Central School Rd, Onitsha
Mailing Address: PO Box 386, Onitsha
*Tel:* (046) 210013
*Key Personnel*
President: F C Ogbalu
Vice President: S U Ogbalu
Established: 1960
Subjects: Igbo, English including Primary, Sec-
     ondary & Tertiary Subjects
*Owned by:* Varsity Industrial Press
*Branch Office(s)*
14 Owerri-Orlu Rd, Owerri, Imo State

# Norway

**Absolutt Kontroll** (J)
Formerly Absolutt Krim
Fridtjof Nansens vei 14, 0055 Oslo
*Tel:* 24051010 *Fax:* 24051099
*E-mail:* post@damm.no
*Web Site:* www.dammbokklubb.no
*Key Personnel*
Man Dir: Cato Praner
Established: 1978
Subjects: Crime Fiction
*Owned by:* N W Damm & Son A/S

**Absolutt Krim**, see Absolutt Kontroll

**Peter Asschenfeldts Bokklubb**
Postboks 1755 Vika, 0122 Oslo
*Tel:* 22429165 *Fax:* 22471098
*Telex:* 77074
*Key Personnel*
Manager: Willy Fordet
Established: 1978
Fiction.
*Owned by:* Hjemmets Bokforlag A/S

**Barnas Hobbyklubb**, see Bokklubben Energica

**Bokklubben Bedre Ledelse** (J)
Fridtjof Nansens vei 14, 0055 Oslo
*Tel:* 24051010 *Fax:* 24051099
*E-mail:* post@damm.no
*Web Site:* www.dammbokklubb.no
*Key Personnel*
Publishing Manager: Gerhard Anthun
Established: 1978
Subjects: Literature, Literary Criticism, Essays,
     Management
*Owned by:* N W Damm & Son A/S

**Bokklubben Energica** (J)
Formerly Barnas Hobbyklubb
Fridtjof Nansens vei 14, 0055 Oslo
*Tel:* 24051010 *Fax:* 24051099
*E-mail:* post@damm.no
*Web Site:* www.dammbokklubb.no
*Owned by:* N W Damm & Son A/S

**De norske Bokklubbene A/S** (J)
Gullhaug Torg 1, 0040 Oslo
*Tel:* 02299 *Fax:* 02212
*Web Site:* www.bokklubbene.no
*Telex:* 74213 Bokkl n
*Key Personnel*
Vice President: Jon Oestboe
Contact: Aud Norlin
Subjects: Fiction, Nonfiction (General)
*Book Club(s):* Bokklubben Krim og Spenning;
     Bokklubben Kunst & Interior; Bokklubben
     Kursiv; Bokklubben Mat- og Vinglede;
     Bokklubben Nye Boker; Bokklubbens Barn;
     Bokklubben Villmarksliv; Dagens Boker;
     Den Norske Bokklubben; Den Norske

Lyrikklubben; Lydbokklubben; Ungdoms-
bokklubben; Bokklubben Krim og Spenning;
Bokklubben Kunst & Interior; Bokklubben
Kursiv; Bokklubben Mat- og Vinglede;
Bokklubben Nye Boker; Bokklubbens Barn;
Bokklubben Villmarksliv; Dagens Boker; Den
Norske Bokklubben; Den Norske Lyrikklubben;
Lydbokklubben; Ungdomsbokklubben
Number of Members: 550,000
*Owned by:* H Aschehoug & Co (W Nygaard)
A/S; Gyldendal Norsk Forlag A/S; Tiden Norsk
Forlag A/S

**Boksamleren**
Fridtjof Nansens vei 14, 0055 Oslo
*Tel:* 24051010 *Fax:* 24051099
*E-mail:* post@damm.no
*Web Site:* www.dammbokklubb.no
*Owned by:* N W Damm & Son A/S

**Donald Duck's Bokklubb** (J)
Fridtjof Nansens vei 14, 0055 Oslo
*Tel:* 24051010 *Fax:* 24051099
*E-mail:* post@damm.no
*Web Site:* www.dammbokklubb.no
*Key Personnel*
Publishing Manager: Gerhard Anthun
Established: 1978
Subjects: Fiction
*Owned by:* N W Damm & Son A/S

**Hobbyglede**
Fridtjof Nansens vei 14, 0055 Oslo
*Tel:* 24051010 *Fax:* 24051099
*E-mail:* post@damm.no
*Web Site:* www.dammbokklubb.no
*Owned by:* N W Damm & Son A/S

**Bokklubben Natur og Kultur**
Gullhaug Torg 1, 0040 Oslo
*Tel:* 02299
*Web Site:* www.bokklubben.no
*Key Personnel*
Editor: Hans Tarjei Skaare
*Owned by:* Grondahl OG Dreyers Forlag AS

**Ole Brumm** (J)
Fridtjof Nansens vei 14, 0055 Oslo
*Tel:* 24051010 *Fax:* 24051099
*E-mail:* post@damm.no
*Web Site:* www.dammbokklubb.no
*Owned by:* N W Damm & Son A/S

# Philippines

**Alemar's Best Sellers Club**
Northmall Bldg, Makati Commercial Center,
Makati, Metro Manila
*Tel:* (02) 592617
Established: 1977
Number of Members: 2,400
*Owned by:* Alemar's (Sibal & Son's Inc)

# Portugal

**Circulo de Leitores**
Rua Prof Jorge da Silva Horta, 1, 1500-499 Lis-
bon
*Tel:* 217 626 100 *Fax:* 217 607 149
*E-mail:* correio@circuloleitores.pt
*Web Site:* www.circuloleitores.pt
*Telex:* 18343 cilecl p

*Key Personnel*
Man Dir: Dr Rui Beja
Editor: Guilhermina Gomes
Subjects: Fiction, Biography, Juvenile, Encyclope-
dias, Scientific, Historical, General Nonfiction,
Special Editions, Magazines
Number of Members: 500,000
*Owned by:* Bertelsmann AG, Germany
*Branch Office(s)*
Lexicultural

# Serbia and Montenegro

**Book Lovers' Club**
Bulevar Vojvode Misica 17, 11000 Belgrade
*Tel:* (011) 651666; (011) 650399
*Owned by:* Beogradski Izdavacko-Graficki Zavod

**Prosveta-Izdavako preduzece**
Cika Ljubina 1, 11000 Belgrade
*Tel:* (011) 629 843; (011) 631 566; (011) 625760
*Fax:* (011) 627465

# Slovakia

**Club of Young Readers**
Sasinkova 5, 815 19 Bratislava 1
*Tel:* (02) 502 272 25 *Fax:* (02) 555 718 94
*E-mail:* spn@spn.sk
*Web Site:* www.mlade-leta.sk
*Telex:* 093 421
*Key Personnel*
Dir: Ing Oldrich Polak
Established: 1963
Subjects: Fairy Tales, Original Slovak Litera-
ture, Prose, Poetry, Anthologies, Translations
of World Literature, Scientific Literature, Cri-
tiques
Number of Members: 55,000
*Owned by:* Mlade leta

# South Africa

**Klub-Dagbreek**
127 Mirn Rd, Newlands, Johannesburg 2092
*Tel:* (011) 6736725 *Fax:* (011) 6736719
Subjects: Fiction
*Owned by:* Perskor-uitgewery

**Eike-Boekklub**
380 Bosman St, Pretoria 0002
Mailing Address: PO Box 123, Pretoria 0001
*Tel:* (012) 401 0700 *Fax:* (012) 3255498
*E-mail:* lapa@atkv.org.za
*Key Personnel*
Publication & Administrative Officer: Esme Smith
*E-mail:* esmes@atkv.org.za
Subjects: Fiction, Novels
*Parent Company:* LAPA Publishers (Pty) Ltd
*Ultimate Parent Company:* ATKV, Dover St,
Randburg 2194

**Keurbiblioteek**
380 Bosman St, Pretoria 0002
Mailing Address: PO Box 123, Pretoria 0001
*Tel:* (012) 401 0700 *Fax:* (012) 3255498
*E-mail:* lapa@atkv.org.za

*Key Personnel*
Publication & Administrative Officer: Esme Smith
*E-mail:* esmes@atkv.org.za
Subjects: Fiction
*Parent Company:* LAPA Publishers (Pty) Ltd
*Ultimate Parent Company:* ATKV, Dover St,
Randburg 2194

**New Day Readers Circle**
33 Waterkant St, Cape Town 8000
Mailing Address: PO Box 1822, Cape Town 8000
*Tel:* (021) 421 5540 *Fax:* (021) 419 1865
*E-mail:* luxverbi.publ@kingsley.co.za
*Web Site:* www.luxverbi.com
*Telex:* 526922
*Owned by:* Lux Verbi

**President Boekklub**
380 Bosman St, Pretoria 0002
Mailing Address: PO Box 123, Pretoria 0001
*Tel:* (012) 401 0700 *Fax:* (012) 3255498
*E-mail:* lapa@atkv.org.za
*Web Site:* www.lapauitgewers.org.za
*Key Personnel*
Publications & Administrative Officer: Esme
Smith *E-mail:* esmes@atkv.org.za
*Parent Company:* LAPA Publishers (Pty) Ltd
*Ultimate Parent Company:* ATKV, Dover St,
Randburg 2194

**Klub Saffier**
127 Mirn Rd, Newlands, Johannesburg 2092
*Tel:* (011) 6736725 *Fax:* (011) 6736719
Subjects: Fiction
*Owned by:* Perskor-uitgewery

**Klub 707**
127 Mirn Rd, Newlands, Johannesburg 2092
*Tel:* (011) 6736725 *Fax:* (011) 6736719
Subjects: Fiction: especially Suspense, Espionage,
Detective, Thrillers (in Afrikaans)
*Owned by:* Perskor-uitgewery

**Treffer-Boekklub**
380 Bosman St, Pretoria 0002
Mailing Address: PO Box 123, Pretoria 0001
*Tel:* (012) 401 0700 *Fax:* (012) 3255498
*E-mail:* lapa@atkv.org.za
*Key Personnel*
Publications & Administrative Officer: Esme
Smith *E-mail:* esmes@atkv.org.za
Subjects: Fiction
*Parent Company:* LAPA Publishers (Pty) Ltd
*Ultimate Parent Company:* ATKV, Dover St,
Randburg 2194

# Spain

**Circulo de Lectores SA**
Travessera de Gracia, 47-49, 08021 Barcelona
*Tel:* (0902) 22 33 55
*E-mail:* atencion-socios@circulo.es
*Web Site:* www.circulo.es
*Key Personnel*
Dir General: Hans Meinke
Literary Dir: Jordi Nadal
Marketing Dir: Bengt Johansson
Financial Dir: Pedro Piella
Number of Members: 1,540,000
*Owned by:* Bertelsmann AG, Germany

# Sri Lanka

**Book Club of the Dept of Cultural Affairs of Sri Lanka**
8th floor, Sethsiripaya, Battaramulla 1
*Tel:* (01) 872035 *Fax:* (01) 872035
*E-mail:* pltm1950@sltnet.lk; gsk@sltnet.lk
*Web Site:* www.mca.gov.lk
*Key Personnel*
Dir. Mr Laxman Perera
*Owned by:* Department of Cultural Affairs

# Sweden

**Allt om Hobbys Publishing Co**
Box 90133, 120 21 Stockholm
*Tel:* (08) 99 93 33 *Fax:* (08) 99 88 66
*E-mail:* order@hobby.se
*Web Site:* www.hobby.se
*Key Personnel*
President: Freddy Stenbom *E-mail:* freddy.
stenbom@hobby.se
*Publication(s): Allt om Hobby*
*Owned by:* Allt om Hobby AB

**Barnens Bokklubb**
Box 3486, 10369 Stockholm
*Tel:* (08) 506 304 00 *Fax:* (08) 506 304 01
*E-mail:* redaktionen@barnensbokklubb.se
*Web Site:* www.barnensbokklubb.se
*Key Personnel*
Contact: Gunilla Halkjaer Olofsson
Subjects: Children's Books
Number of Members: 150,000
*Publication(s): Barn Posten; Laese Posten*
*Owned by:* AB Raben och Sjoegren Bokfoerlag;
Bokfoerlaget Opal AB; Astrid Lindgren; Mari-
anne von Baumgarten-Lindberg

**Battre Ledarskap** (J)
c/o Liber Distribution AB, 16289 Stockholm
*Tel:* (08) 690 93 30 *Fax:* (08) 690 93 01; (08)
690 93 02
*E-mail:* kundtjanst.liberab@liber.se
*Web Site:* www.battreledarskap.net
*Telex:* 12801 S
*Key Personnel*
Contact: Lars Abramson *E-mail:* lars.abramson@
liber.se
Subjects: Business, Economics, Management
Number of Members: 3,500
*Owned by:* Liber AB

**Bokklubb Bra Bockesr**
Soedra Vaegen, 263 80 Hoeganaes
*Tel:* (042) 339000 *Fax:* (042) 330504 *Cable:*
BEBE BOOKS
*Owned by:* Bokfoerlaget Bra Boecker AB

**Bonniers Bokklubb** (J)
PO Box 3159, 103 63 Stockholm
*Tel:* (08) 696 87 80 *Fax:* (08) 442 17 40; (08)
442 17 49
*E-mail:* medlemsservice@bbk.bonnier.se; best@
bbk.bonnier.se; avbest@bbk.bonnier.se
*Web Site:* www.bonniersbokklubb.se
*Telex:* 14546 Bonbook S *Cable:* BONNIERS
*Key Personnel*
Editor-in-Chief: Ingrid Carroll
Book Club Manager: Richard Ekstroem
*Publication(s): Bokspegeln* (The Book Mirror)
*Owned by:* Albert Bonniers Forlag AB

**Delta Science Fiction Bok Klubb**
Box 15123, 161 15 Bromma

*Tel:* (08) 254781
*Owned by:* Delta Foerlags AB

**Manadens Bok** (J)
Sankt Eriksgatan 63, 104 20 Stockholm
Mailing Address: Box 8090, 104 20 Stockholm
*Tel:* (08) 696 85 50 *Fax:* (08) 442 17 45
*E-mail:* info@manadensbok.se
*Web Site:* www.manadensbok.se
*Key Personnel*
Vice-Dir: Gabriella Hedlund

**Reader's Digest AB**
Lasarbidrag, 11597 Stockholm
*Tel:* (08) 58710900 *Fax:* (08) 58710990
*E-mail:* red@readersdigest.se
*Web Site:* www.readersdigest.se

**Richters Forlag**
c/o Richter Egmont, Sallerupsvaegen 9, 205 75
Malmo
*Tel:* (040) 38 06 80 *Fax:* (040) 29 43 50
*E-mail:* kundservice@richters.se
*Web Site:* www.egmontrichter.com
*Telex:* 33180 richt s
*Key Personnel*
Contact: Sara Hemmel
*Book Club(s):* Girls Only; Hem & Livsstil;
Livsenergi; Livsutveckling; Richters Bokklubb;
Bokklubben Skaparglaedje; Girls Only; Hem
& Livsstil; Livsenergi; Livsutveckling; Richters
Bokklubb; Bokklubben Skaparglaedje

**Serie-pocket-klubben**
Landsvaegen 57, 172 22 Sundbyberg
Mailing Address: PO Box 1074, Sundbyberg
*Tel:* (08) 7993110 *Fax:* (08) 7645764
*Telex:* 17370 semic s *Cable:* SEMICPRESS
SUNDBYBERG
*Owned by:* Semic Press AB

**Stora Familjebokklubben** (J)
Sveavaegen 56, 103 63 Stockholm
Mailing Address: Box 3159, 103 63 Stockholm
*Tel:* (08) 696 88 30 *Fax:* (08) 442 17 41
*E-mail:* medlemsservice@sfbk.bonnier.se; info@
sfbk.bonnier.se
*Web Site:* www.storafamiljebokklubben.se
*Telex:* 14546 Bonbook s *Cable:* BONNIERS
*Owned by:* Albert Bonniers Forlag AB

**Stora Romanklubben** (J)
Sveavaegen 56, 103 63 Stockholm
Mailing Address: Box 3159, 103 63 Stockholm
*Tel:* (08) 696 88 40 *Fax:* (08) 442 17 43
*E-mail:* medlemsservice@srk.bonnier.se
*Web Site:* www.storaromanklubben.se
*Owned by:* Albert Bonniers Forlag AB

**Bokklubben Svalan** (J)
Sveavaegen 56, 103 63 Stockholm
Mailing Address: Box 3159, 103 63 Stockholm
*Tel:* (08) 696 88 00 *Fax:* (08) 696 83 76
*E-mail:* medlemsservice@svalan.bonnier.se
*Web Site:* www.bokklubbensvalan.se
*Telex:* 14546 Bonbook S *Cable:* BONNIERS
*Owned by:* Albert Bonniers Forlag AB

# Switzerland

**Buchergilde Gutenberg AG**
4601 Olten
*Owned by:* Edition Gutenberg

**Europaring der Buch- und Schallplattenfreunde**
Worblentalstr 33, 3063 Ittigen, Bern
*Tel:* (031) 584466
*Owned by:* Bertelsmann AG

**NSB Buch- und Phonoclub**
Schweizer Verlagshaus AG, Klausstr 10, 8008
Zurich
*Tel:* (01) 3833622
*Key Personnel*
General Manager: F Rothacher
Affiliated with Schweizer Verlagshaus AG.

**Punktum AG**
Klusstr, 508032 Zurich
*Tel:* (01) 422 45 40
This club deals exclusively with children's books,
intended as gifts.
*Owned by:* Rada Matija AG

# Thailand

**Science Fiction Magazine Club**
105/19-2 Naret Rd, Bangkok 10500
*Tel:* (02) 2330302; (02) 2356931
*Telex:* 20657 Graphic Th
*Owned by:* Graphic Art Publications

# United Kingdom

**BCA**, see Book Club Associates

**Bibliophile Books** (J)
Thomas Rd, Unit 5, London E14 7BN
*Tel:* (020) 7515 9222 *Fax:* (020) 7538 4115
*E-mail:* customercare@bibliophilebooks.co.uk;
orders@bibliophilebooks.co.uk
*Web Site:* www.bibliophilebooks.com
*Key Personnel*
General Manager: Anne Quigley
Established: 1978

**Book Club Associates**
Guild House, Farnsby St, Swindon Wilts SN1
5DD
Mailing Address: Greater London House, Hamp-
stead Rd, London NW1 7TZ
*Tel:* (0870) 165 0292; (020) 7760 6500
*Fax:* (0870) 165 0222; (044) 1793 567711
*E-mail:* e-support@booksdirect.co.uk
*Web Site:* www.bca.co.uk
*Telex:* 24359 B CALON *Cable:* Booklub
*Key Personnel*
Chief Executive: Christian Friege
*Book Club(s):* Ancient & Medieval History Book
Club; Arts Guild; Children's Book of the
Month Club; Classical Selection Club (Au-
dio); EBC (Netherlands); Encounters; English
Book Club (France); English Book Club (Ger-
many); English Book Club (Norway); English
Book Club (Sweden); Executive World; His-
tory Guild; Home Computer - Amiga; Home
Computer - Amstrad; Home Computer - Com-
modore 64; Home Computer - PC; Home Com-
puter - Spectrum Sinclair; Home Computer
Atari St; Irish Book Club; Leisure Circle; Lit-
erary Guild (F); Literary Guild (M); Literary
Guild Gold; Military and Aviation Book Society; Music Direct (Cass); Music Direct (R/CD);
Music Direct Gold; Mystery and Thriller Guild;

On the Road; Paperbacks; Plate Series; Railway Book Club; Video Direct; World Books (F); World Books (M); Ancient & Medieval History Book Club; Arts Guild; Children's Book of the Month Club; Classical Selection Club (Audio); EBC (Netherlands); Encounters; English Book Club (France); English Book Club (Germany); English Book Club (Norway); English Book Club (Sweden); Executive World; History Guild; Home Computer - Amiga; Home Computer - Amstrad; Home Computer - Commodore 64; Home Computer - PC; Home Computer - Spectrum Sinclair; Home Computer Atari St; Irish Book Club; Leisure Circle; Literary Guild (F); Literary Guild (M); Literary Guild Gold; Military and Aviation Book Society; Music Direct (Cass); Music Direct (R/CD); Music Direct Gold; Mystery and Thriller Guild; On the Road; Paperbacks; Plate Series; Railway Book Club; Video Direct; World Books (F); World Books (M)
*Owned by:* Reed International Books Ltd (parent company Reed Elsevier Plc); Doubleday & Company Inc, USA (parent company Bertelsmann AG, Germany)
Imprints: Guild Publishing

### Bookmarks Club
265 Seven Sisters Rd, Finsbury Park, London N4 2DE
*Tel:* (020) 7536 9696 *Fax:* (020) 7538 0018
*E-mail:* bookmarks@internationalsocialist.org
*Web Site:* www.internationalsocialist.org
Subjects: Politics, Socialism
*Owned by:* IS Books Ltd
*Branch Office(s)*
PO Box 16085, Chicago, IL 60616, United States
  *Tel:* (773) 665 9601 *Fax:* (773) 665 9651

### Books Exports
137 Hale Lane, Edgware, Middx HA8 9QP
*Tel:* (020) 8931 2359; (020) 8959 2137
  *Fax:* (0181) 9592137
*E-mail:* roshanbp@aol.com
*Key Personnel*
Partner & Man Dir: Mr B P Lakhani
Established: 1978
Remainders at competitive prices.

### Books for Children
Brettenham House, Lancaster Pl, London SE1 5SF
*Tel:* (020) 7911 8000 *Fax:* (020) 7911 8100
*E-mail:* uk@twbg.co.uk
*Web Site:* www.twbg.co.uk
Established: 1977
*Owned by:* Time-Warner

### The Bookworm Club
Rustat House, 60 Clifton Rd, Cambridge CB2 4GZ
*Tel:* (01223) 568650 *Fax:* (01223) 568591
*E-mail:* clubs@heffers.co.uk
*Web Site:* www.heffers.co.uk
*Key Personnel*
Contact: Fran Whiting
Subjects: Paperbacks for children age 8 up to the age of 13 (children's club in schools)
*Owned by:* W Heffer & Sons Ltd, 20 Trinity St, Cambridge CB2 3NG

**English Book Club**, see Book Club Associates

### The Folio Society
44 Eagle St, London WC1R 4FS
*Tel:* (020) 7400 4200 *Fax:* (020) 7400 4242
*E-mail:* enquiries@foliosoc.co.uk
*Web Site:* www.foliosoc.co.uk
*Key Personnel*
Editorial Dir: Sue Bradbury
Rights & Permissions: Gilly Vincent

Contact: Kerry Davidson
Subjects: Fiction, Poetry, Biography, History

### Godfrey Cave Associates
27 Wrights Lane, London W8 5TZ
*Tel:* (020) 7416 3000 *Fax:* (020) 7416 3289
*Key Personnel*
Man Dir: Kevin Binston

**Guild Publishing**, *imprint of* Book Club Associates

### Letterbox Library
71-73 Allen Rd, Stoke Newington, London N16 8RY
*Tel:* (020) 7503 4801 *Fax:* (020) 7503 4800
*E-mail:* info@letterboxlibrary.com
*Web Site:* www.letterboxlibrary.com
*Key Personnel*
Dir: Maikim Stern
Publicity & Marketing: Kerry Mason
Children's book club producing quarterly catalogue & newsletter. Once-off joining fee L5.
Subjects: Non-Sexist & Multi-Cultural Children's Books

### 9-12 Club
Red House School Book Club, Windough Pk, Witney, Oxon OX8 5YZ
*Tel:* (0845) 6039091 *Fax:* (0845) 6039092
*E-mail:* sbenquiries@scholastic.co.uk
*Web Site:* www.scholastic.co.uk
*Key Personnel*
Man Dir: D M R Kewley
Subjects: Books for school children (9-12 years)
*Owned by:* Scholastic Publications Ltd

### The Poetry Book Society Ltd
2 Tavistock Place, 4th floor, London WC1H 9RA
*Tel:* (020) 7833 9247 *Fax:* (020) 7833 5990
*E-mail:* info@poetrybooks.co.uk
*Web Site:* www.poetrybooks.co.uk
*Key Personnel*
Dir: Chris Holifield *E-mail:* chris@poetrybooks. co.uk
Membership organization which promotes selected poetry at discounted prices.
Subjects: Poetry
Number of Members: 2,200
Publication(s): *The Bulletin* (quarterly)

### Puffin Book Clubs
c/o Penguin Books Ltd, 80 Strand, London WC2R 0RL
*Tel:* (020) 7416 3000 *Toll Free Tel:* (0500) 454 444 *Fax:* (020) 7010 6667
*E-mail:* pbccustomerservice@penguin.co.uk
*Web Site:* www.penguin.co.uk; www. puffinbookclub.co.uk
*Key Personnel*
Contact: Michelle Edmonds *E-mail:* michelle. edmonds@penguin.co.uk
Incorporating Fledgling (for up to 6-year-olds), Kite (for 6 to 9-year-olds) & Post (for 9 to 13-year-olds) book clubs.
*Owned by:* Penguin Books Ltd

### Readers Union
Berkeley Square House, Berkeley Sq, London W1X 6AB
*Tel:* (020) 7629 8144 *Fax:* (020) 7499 9751
*Telex:* 264631 *Cable:* BOOKS NABBOT
*Key Personnel*
Marketing Dir: Lesley Godwin
Established: 1937
*Book Club(s):* Anglers Book Society; Belief the Religious Book Society; Birds and Natural History Book Society; Country Book Society; Country Book Society Incorporating Arena; Craft & Country Style Book Society; Craft Book Society; Craftsman Book Society; Design

Book Club; Equestrian Book Society; Fieldsports Book Society; Gardeners Book Society; Golf Book Club; Maritime Book Society; Music Book Society; Nationwide & Phoenix Book Service; Needlecraft Book Society; Photographic Book Society; Ramblers & Climbers Book Society; World of Nature Book Club; World of Nature Incorporating Travel & Exploration Book Society; Anglers Book Society; Belief the Religious Book Society; Birds and Natural History Book Society; Country Book Society; Country Book Society Incorporating Arena; Craft & Country Style Book Society; Craft Book Society; Craftsman Book Society; Design Book Club; Equestrian Book Society; Fieldsports Book Society; Gardeners Book Society; Golf Book Club; Maritime Book Society; Music Book Society; Nationwide & Phoenix Book Service; Needlecraft Book Society; Photographic Book Society; Ramblers & Climbers Book Society; World of Nature Book Club; World of Nature Incorporating Travel & Exploration Book Society
*Owned by:* Reader's Digest Associates Ltd

### The Red House Books Ltd
PO Box 142, Bangor LL57 4ZP
*Tel:* (0870) 191 99 80 *Fax:* (0870) 6077720
*E-mail:* enquiries@redhouse.co.uk
*Web Site:* www.redhouse.co.uk
*Key Personnel*
Man Dir: David Teale
Subjects: Children's
Number of Members: 350,000
*Owned by:* Red House Books Ltd

### Scholastic Publications Ltd (J)
Windrush Park, Range Rd, Witney, Oxon OX29 0YZ
*Tel:* (0845) 6039091; (01993) 893475 (outside UK) *Fax:* (0845) 6039092; (01993) 893424 (outside UK)
*E-mail:* sbcenquiries@scholastic.co.uk
*Web Site:* www.scholastic.co.uk/schoolbookclub
*Key Personnel*
Man Dir: D M R Kewley
Publishing Dir, Education Division: Ann Peel
Editorial Dir, Scholastic Children's Books: Richard Scrivener
Finance Dir: Ian Bloodworth
Trade Sales & Marketing: Gavin Lang
Operations & Distribution Dir: Philip Owen
Office Manager: Deborah Shrives
  *E-mail:* dshrives@scholastic.co.uk
Subjects: Education
*Book Club(s):* Arrow (children aged 9 to 11); Cover2Cover (children aged 11 to 14 at secondary schools); Firefly (children aged 5 to 7); Lucky (children aged 7 to 9); Seesaw (children aged 3 to 5); Arrow (children aged 9 to 11); Cover2Cover (children aged 11 to 14 at secondary schools); Firefly (children aged 5 to 7); Lucky (children aged 7 to 9); Seesaw (children aged 3 to 5)
*Owned by:* Scholastic Inc, 557 Broadway, New York, NY 10012, United States

### 6-9 Club
Red House School Book Club, Windough Pk, Witney, Oxon OX8 5YZ
*Tel:* (0845) 6039091 *Fax:* (0845) 6039090
*E-mail:* sbenquiries@scholastic.co.uk
*Web Site:* www.scholastic.co.uk
*Key Personnel*
Man Editor: D M R Kewley
Subjects: Books for school children (6-9 years)
*Owned by:* Scholastic Publications Ltd

### Teachers Book Club (J)
Westfield Rd, Southam, Leamington Spa CV33 0JH
*Tel:* (01926) 813910 *Fax:* (01926) 817727

*E-mail:* enquiries@scholastic.co.uk
*Web Site:* www.scholastic.co.uk/teach_index.html
*Key Personnel*
Man Dir: D M R Kewley
Office Manager: Deborah Shrives
   *E-mail:* dshrives@scholastic.co.uk
Books & resource materials for primary teachers.
*Owned by:* Scholastic Ltd


**The Women's Press Book Club**
27 Goodge St, London W1T 2LD
*Tel:* (020) 7636 3992 *Fax:* (020) 7637 1866
*E-mail:* sales@the-womens-press.com
*Web Site:* www.the-womens-press.com

*Key Personnel*
Manager: Kay Stirling *Tel:* (020) 7553 9273
Subjects: Books by & about women, with emphasis on fiction, women's studies, art, politics, health, biography
Number of Members: 7,000
*Owned by:* The Women's Press Ltd

# Zambia

**Read-a-Book Club**
Chishango Rd, Lusaka 10101
Mailing Address: PO Box 32708, 10101 Lusaka
*Tel:* (01) 222324; (01) 236629 *Fax:* (01) 225073
*Telex:* 40056 *Cable:* HOUSE
*Key Personnel*
Man Dir: Beniko Mulota
Publishing Manager: Ray Munamwimbu
   *E-mail:* raymuna2@yahoo.co.uk
Established: 1966
Publishing, printing & distribution.
*Owned by:* Zambia Educational Publishing House

# Book Trade Organizations

The organizations listed below include publisher and bookseller associations and ISBN agencies as well as book trade and allied organizations. Listings appear under the country in which they are physically located. Some of the organizations are specific to a particular country; others are international in nature.

† indicates those organizations that are international in scope.

‡ indicates United Nations agencies with publishing activities.

◇ indicates other international organizations with publishing activities.

Additional book trade associations can be found in the sections **Literary Associations & Societies** and **Library Associations**.

## Albania

◇**Lidhja e Shkrimtareve dhe e Artisteve toe Shqiperise** (Union of Writers & Artists of Albania)
Baboci 37 z, Tirana
*Tel:* (042) 23843 *Fax:* (042) 23843
*E-mail:* bashan@natlib.tirana.al
*Key Personnel*
President: Dritero Agolli
Publication(s): *Albanaises* (quarterly, in French); *Drita* (weekly); *International Literatur* (quarterly); *Kultur Popullore* (annually, in Albanian & French); *Nentori* (monthly)

## Algeria

**Agence ISBN**, see Bibliotheque Nationale d'Algerie

**Bibliotheque Nationale d'Algerie**
BP 127 El Hamma Les Anasser, 16000 Algiers
*Tel:* (021) 671967; (021) 675781; (021) 671867
*Fax:* (021) 672999
*Key Personnel*
Dir: Mahamed Aissamoussa
Founded: 1835

## Andorra

**Andorran Standard Book Numbering Agency**
Placeta Sant Esteve s/n, Andorra la Vella
*Tel:* 826445 *Fax:* 829445
*E-mail:* bncultura.gov@andorra.ad
*Web Site:* bibnac.andorra.ad
*Key Personnel*
Dir: Pilar Burgues

## Angola

**UEA**, see Uniao dos Escritores Angolanos (UEA)

**Uniao dos Escritores Angolanos (UEA)** (Union of Angolan Writers)
Rua Ho Chi Min (Zona Escolar), CP 2767-C, Luanda
*Tel:* (02) 323205; (02) 322421 *Fax:* (02) 323205

*E-mail:* uea@uea-angola.org
*Web Site:* www.uea-angola.org
*Telex:* 3056
*Key Personnel*
Secretary General: Luandino Vieira

## Argentina

**Agencia Argentina ISBN**, see Camara Argentina del Libro

**Argentine Society of Authors**, see Sociedad General de Autores de la Argentina (SGAA)

**Camara Argentina del Libro** (Argentine Book Association)
Ave Belgrano 1580 - Piso 4°, 1093 Buenos Aires
*Tel:* (011) 4381-8383 *Fax:* (011) 4381-9253
*E-mail:* cal@editores.org.ar
*Web Site:* www.editores.org.ar *Cable:* 381-9253
*Key Personnel*
Dir: Noberto J Pou
Founded: 1938
Publication(s): *LEA*

**Fundacion El Libro**
Hipolito Yrigoyen 1628, 5° Piso, 1089 Buenos Aires
*Tel:* (011) 43743288 *Fax:* (011) 43750268
*E-mail:* fundacion@el-libro.com.ar
*Web Site:* www.el-libro.com.ar
*Key Personnel*
President: Carlos Alberto Pazos
Dir: Marta V Diaz

**SGAA**, see Sociedad General de Autores de la Argentina (SGAA)

**Sociedad General de Autores de la Argentina (SGAA)**
Pacheco de Melo 1820, 1126 Buenos Aires
*Tel:* (011) 4811-2582; (011) 4812-9996
*Fax:* (011) 4812-6954
*E-mail:* info@argentores.org.ar
*Web Site:* www.argentores.org.ar
*Key Personnel*
President: Elio Vicente Gallipoli
Secretary: Julia Mercedes Ferradas
Founded: 1910
Text in Spanish.

**Standard Book Numbering Agency**
Camara Argentina del Libro, Ave Belgrano 1580 - 4° Piso, 1093 Buenos Aires
*Tel:* (011) 4381-8383 *Fax:* (011) 4381-9253

*E-mail:* registrolibros@editores.com
*Web Site:* www.editores.com
*Key Personnel*
ISBN Administrator: Norberto Pou, Sr
Publication(s): *ISBN Directory*

## Armenia

**Gosudarstvenny Komitet Armjamskoj SSR po delam izdatel'stv, poligrafii, kniznoj targovli**
Terjan 89, 375009 Erevan 9
*Tel:* (02) 528660
*E-mail:* grapalat@arminco.com
*Telex:* 411871 Kniga
*Key Personnel*
Chairman: M F Nenashev
The USSR State Committee for Publishing, Printing & the Book Trade.

## Australia

**ANZAAB**, see The Australian & New Zealand Association of Antiquarian Booksellers

**Australia Council Literature Board**
372 Elizabeth St, Surry Hills NSW 2010
Mailing Address: PO Box 788, Strawberry Hills NSW 2012
*Tel:* (02) 9215 9000 *Toll Free Tel:* 800 226 912
*Fax:* (02) 9215 9111
*E-mail:* mail@ozco.gov.au
*Web Site:* www.ozco.gov.au
*Key Personnel*
Manager: Gail Cork *Tel:* (02) 9215 9058
*E-mail:* g.cork@ozco.gov.au
The Literature Board supports the writing of all forms of creative literature, including novels, short stories, poetry, publishing & promotion, plays & nonfiction (especially biography, autobiography, essays, histories, literary criticism or other expository or analytical prose). All applicants must use the Literature Board's application forms.
Publication(s): *Australia Council Support for the Arts Handbook* (1997)

**The Australian & New Zealand Association of Antiquarian Booksellers**
Affiliate of International League of Antiquarian Booksellers (ILAB)
604 High St, Prahran, Victoria 3181
*Tel:* (03) 9525 1649 *Fax:* (03) 9529 1298
*E-mail:* admin@anzaab.com; bookshop@hincebooks.com.au

*Web Site:* www.anzaab.com
*Key Personnel*
President: Lovella Kerr
Vice President: Peter Tinslay
Founded: 1977

**Australian Booksellers Association Inc**
828 High St, Unit 9, Kew East, Victoria 3102
*Tel:* (03) 9859 7322 *Fax:* (03) 9859 7344
*E-mail:* mail@aba.org.au
*Web Site:* www.aba.org.au
*Key Personnel*
President: Tim Peach
Executive Dir: Celia Pollock
The ABA is a federal association with branches in every state & represents booksellers' interests to government bodies, publishers & other organizations.
Publication(s): *Economic Survey* (annually)

◇**Australian Copyright Council**
245 Chalmers St, Suite 3, Redfern, NSW 2016
Mailing Address: PO Box 1986, Strawberry Hills, NSW 2012
*Tel:* (02) 9318 1788 (copyright); (02) 9699 3247 (sales) *Fax:* (02) 9698 3536
*E-mail:* info@copyright.org.au
*Web Site:* www.copyright.org.au
*Key Personnel*
Chairman: Peter Banki
Executive Officer: Libby Baulch
Office Manager & Events Coordinator: Vickie James
Publication(s): *Copyright Reporter*; *Practical Guide* (Discussion paper)
ISBN Prefix(es): 0-9595513

**Australian Press Council**
117 York St, Suite 10-02, Sydney, NSW 2000
*Tel:* (02) 9261 1930 *Toll Free Tel:* 800-02-5712 *Fax:* (02) 9267 6826
*E-mail:* info@presscouncil.org.au
*Web Site:* www.presscouncil.org.au
*Key Personnel*
Executive Secretary: Jack R Herman
Office Manager: Deborah Kirkman

**Australian Publishers Association Ltd**
60/89 Jones St, Ultimo, NSW 2007
*Tel:* (02) 9281 9788 *Fax:* (02) 9281 1073
*E-mail:* apa@publishers.asn.au
*Web Site:* www.publishers.asn.au
*Key Personnel*
Chief Executive Officer: Susan Bridge
Information Officer: Michaela Purcell
  *E-mail:* michaela.purcell@publishers.asn.au
Founded: 1948
Trade association representing Australian book publishers.
Publication(s): *Directory of Members*; *Introduction to Book Publishing*

**The Australian Society of Authors Ltd**
PO Box 1566, Strawberry Hills NSW 2012
*Tel:* (02) 93180877 *Fax:* (02) 93180530
*E-mail:* office@asauthors.org
*Web Site:* www.asauthors.org/cgi-bin/asa/information.cgi
*Key Personnel*
Executive Dir: Jeremy Fisher *E-mail:* jeremy@asauthors.org
Founded: 1963
Publication(s): *Australian Author* (trianually, magazine, magazine for writers, readers & people who love books); *Australian Book Contracts* (step-by-step guide to publishing contracts for authors)

**Australian Society of Indexers**
GPO Box 2069, Canberra, ACT 2601
*Tel:* (02) 4268-5335

*Web Site:* www.aussi.org
*Key Personnel*
President: Lynn Farkas *Tel:* (02) 6286 4818
  *Fax:* (02) 6286 6570 *E-mail:* president@aussi.org
Vice President: Clodagh Jones *Tel:* (03) 6225 3848 *E-mail:* vicepres@aussi.org
Secretary: Shirley Campbell *Tel:* (02) 6285 1006
  *E-mail:* secretary@aussi.org
Treasurer: Penelope Whitten *Tel:* (02) 6241 4289
  *E-mail:* treasurer@aussi.org
President, ACT Branch: Geraldine Triffitt
  *Tel:* (02) 6231 4975 *E-mail:* geraldine.triffitt@alianet.alia.org.au
Affiliated with indexing societies in Britain, Canada, China, South Africa & USA.
Publication(s): *Australian Society of Indexers' Newsletter* (10 times/yr); *Indexers Available*
Associate Companies: American Society of Indexers; Association of Southern African Indexers & Bibliographers (ASAIB); China Society of Indexers; Indexing & Abstracting Society of Canada; Society of Indexers, United Kingdom
*Branch Office(s)*
PO Box R598, Royal Exchange, NSW 1225, Branch President: Caroline Colton
  *Tel:* (02) 4285 7199 *Fax:* (02) 4285 7199
  *E-mail:* nswbranch@aussi.org
GPO Box 1251, Melbourne, Victoria 3000, Branch President: Ann Philpott *Tel:* (03) 9830 0494 *Fax:* (03) 9830 0494 *E-mail:* vicbranch@aussi.org

†◇**Bibliographical Society of Australia & New Zealand (BSANZ)**
PO Box 1463, Wagga Wagga, NSW 2650
*Tel:* (02) 6931 8669 *Fax:* (02) 6931 8669
*E-mail:* rsalmond@pobox.com
*Web Site:* www.csu.edu.au/community/BSANZ/
*Key Personnel*
President: Paul Eggert *E-mail:* p.eggert@adfa.edu.au
Founded: 1969
Publication(s): *Broadsheet* (newsletter); *Bulletin* (quarterly, journal)
ISBN Prefix(es): 0-9598271

**BSANZ**, see Bibliographical Society of Australia & New Zealand (BSANZ)

**Christian Bookselling Association of Australia Inc**
Suite 2, 7-9 President Ave, Caringbah NSW 2229
Mailing Address: PO Box 576, Caringbah NSW 2229
*Tel:* (02) 9524 3347 *Fax:* (02) 9540 3001
*E-mail:* info@cbaa.com.au
*Web Site:* www.cbaa.com.au
*Key Personnel*
Executive Secretary: Jan Holt
Founded: (In existence for 28 years)
Membership: Christian Booksellers Association (USA).
Publication(s): *CBAA News*

**Copyright Agency Ltd**
157 Liverpool St, Level 19, Sydney, NSW 2000
*Tel:* (02) 93947600 *Fax:* (02) 93947601
*E-mail:* info@copyright.com.au
*Web Site:* www.copyright.com.au
*Key Personnel*
Chief Executive: Michael Fraser
General Manager, Client Services Division: Jill Connell
Acts as a copyright collecting society.

†◇**International Association of School Librarianship**
IASL Secretariat, PO Box 587, Carlton North 3054
*Fax:* (03) 9428 7612

*E-mail:* iasl@rockland.com
*Web Site:* www.iasl-slo.org
*Key Personnel*
Executive Dir: Dr Penny Moore
President: Peter Genco *Fax:* 814-474-1115
  *E-mail:* iaslpres@hotmail.com
Vice President, Association Operations: Dr Diljit Singh *E-mail:* diljit@um.edu.my
Administrative Manager: Karen Bonanno
Founded: 1971
Publication(s): *Annual Conference Proceedings*; *Newsletter of the International Association of School Librarianship* (quarterly); *School Libraries Worldwide* (biannually, journal)

**International Standard Book Numbering Agency**, see ISBN Agency Australia

**ISBN Agency Australia**
Bldg C3, 85 Turner St, Port Melbourne, Victoria 3207
*Tel:* (03) 8645-0385 *Fax:* (03) 8645-0393
*E-mail:* isbn.agency@thorpe.com.au
*Web Site:* www.thorpe.com.au
*Key Personnel*
ISBN Coordinator: Maria Watt
Publication(s): *Australian Books In Print*
*Parent Company:* D W Thorpe

**Mardev**
Tower 2, 475 Victoria Ave, Chatswood, NSW 2067
*Tel:* (02) 9422 2644 *Fax:* (02) 9422 2633
*E-mail:* mardevlists@reedbusiness.com.au
*Web Site:* www.mardevlists.com
*Key Personnel*
General Manager, UK: Nick Martin
List Manager: Maureen Ryan *E-mail:* maureen.ryan@reedbusiness.com.au
*Parent Company:* Reed Elsevier plc
*Branch Office(s)*
The Signature, 51 Changi Business Park Central 2, No 07-01, Singapore 486066, Singapore *Tel:* 6588 3978 *Fax:* 6588 3866
Quadrant House, Sutton, Surrey SM2 5AS, United Kingdom *Tel:* (020) 8652 3899 *Fax:* (020) 8652 4597 *E-mail:* enquiries@mardev.com
2 Rector St, 26th floor, New York, NY 10006, United States *Tel:* 212-584-9370 *Fax:* 212-584-9371 *E-mail:* sales@mardevlists.com

**Public Lending Right Scheme**
GPO Box 3241, Canberra, ACT 2601
*Tel:* (02) 6271 1650 *Toll Free Tel:* 800 672 842 (Australia only) *Fax:* (02) 6271 1651
*E-mail:* plr.mail@dcita.gov.au
*Web Site:* www.dcita.gov.au
*Key Personnel*
PLR Administrator: Paul Bootes *Tel:* (02) 6271 1635 *E-mail:* paul.bootes@dcita.gov.au
*Parent Company:* Department of Communications, Information Technology & the Arts

◇**Society of Women Writers NSW Inc**
GPO Box 1388, Sydney, NSW 2001
*Tel:* (03) 63310267
*Web Site:* www.womenwritersnsw.org
*Key Personnel*
Federal President: Valerie Pybus
Editor: Marilyn Arnold
Founded: 1925
Publication(s): *The Woman Writer* (bi-monthly, newsletter)
ISBN Prefix(es): 0-9587871; 0-9591144; 0-9598432
Associate Companies: Society of Women Writers & Journalists London

◇**UNILINC**
Level 9, 210 Clarence St, Sydney, NSW 2000
*Tel:* (02) 9283 1488 *Fax:* (02) 9267 9247

*E-mail:* info@unilinc.edu.au
*Web Site:* www.unilinc.edu.au
*Key Personnel*
Executive Dir & Chief Executive Officer: Rona
  Wade *E-mail:* rona@unilinc.edu.au
Founded: 1978

# Austria

†**CIE (International Commission on
  Illumination Central Bureau)**
Kegelgasse 27, 1030 Vienna
*Tel:* (01) 714 31 87 0 *Fax:* (01) 713 08 38 18
*E-mail:* ciecb@ping.at
*Web Site:* www.cie.co.at/cie
*Key Personnel*
President: Wout van Bommel
General Secretary: Christine Hermann
Founded: 1913
Subjects: Lighting

**Fachverband der Buch und Medienwirtschaft**
Wiedner-Hauptstr 63, Postfach 440, 1045 Vienna
*Tel:* (01) 50105 DW 3331; (01) 50105 DW 3333
  *Fax:* (01) 50105 DW 3043
*E-mail:* buchwirtschaft@wko.at
*Web Site:* www.buchwirtschaft.at
*Key Personnel*
President: Bernhard Weis
Vice President: Gustav Glockler

†◇**Federation Internationale des Traducteurs
  (FIT)**
Dr Heinrich Maierstr 9, 1180 Vienna
*Tel:* (01) 4403607; (01) 4709819 *Fax:* (01)
  4403756; (01) 4708194
*E-mail:* info@fit.org
*Web Site:* www.fit-ift.org/
*Key Personnel*
President: Betty Cohen
Vice President: Peter Bush
Secretary General: Miriam Lee *E-mail:* secgen@
  fit-ift.org
International Federation of Translators.
Publication(s): *Babel* (International journal of
  translation); *Translatio* (FIT Newsletter)

**FIT**, see Federation Internationale des
  Traducteurs (FIT)

◇**Hauptverband des Oesterreichischen
  Buchhandels** (Austrian Publishers' &
  Booksellers' Association)
Grunangergasse 4, 1010 Vienna
*Tel:* (01) 512 15 35 *Fax:* (01) 512 84 82
*E-mail:* hvb@buecher.at
*Web Site:* www.buecher.at
*Key Personnel*
President: Dr Alexander Potyka
Publication(s): *Adressbuch des oesterreichis-
  chen Buchhandels* (Directory of Austrian Book
  Trade); *Anzeiger des oesterreichischen Buch-
  handels* (Austrian Book Trade Gazette, bi-
  monthly)
*Associate Companies:* Verband der Antiquare
  Oesterreichs; Verband der oesterreichischen
  Buch- und Presse-Grossisten und der Wer-
  benden Zeitschriftenhaendler; Oesterreichis-
  cher Verlegerverband; Oesterreichischer Buch-
  haendlerverband; Verband von selbstaendigen
  Verlagsvertretern Oesterreichs; Standard Book
  Numbering Agency

**IAEA**, see International Atomic Energy Agency
  (IAEA)

†‡**International Atomic Energy Agency (IAEA)**
Wagramer Str 5, 1400 Vienna
Mailing Address: PO Box 100, 1400 Vienna
*Tel:* (0222) 2600-0 *Fax:* (0222) 2600-7
*E-mail:* official.mail@iaea.org; info@iaea.org
*Web Site:* www.iaea.org
*Key Personnel*
Editorial: M F Boemeke
Dir, Public Information: Mark Gwozdecky
  *Tel:* (01) 2600-21270
Senior Information Officer: Melissa Fleming
  *Tel:* (01) 2600-21275 *Fax:* (01) 2600-29610
  *E-mail:* m.fleming@iaea.org
Sales, Publicity: A Bugno; G Cazier
Founded: 1957
The International Atomic Energy Agency is an
  international organization within the United
  Nations family, having the general purpose of
  seeking to accelerate & enlarge the contribution
  of atomic energy to peace, health & prosperity
  throughout the world. The Agency's publica-
  tions result, almost exclusively, from its own
  activities; published material is of intense inter-
  est only to a relatively small group of scientists
  & technicians
*Membership:* Intergovernmental Organization in
  Family of United Nations.
Subjects: Life Sciences, Nuclear Safety & Environmental Protection, Physics, Chemistry,
  Geology & Raw Materials, Reactors & Nuclear
  Power, Industrial Applications, Miscellaneous
Publication(s): *Meetings in Atomic Energy* (quar-
  terly); *Nuclear Fusion* (monthly)
ISBN Prefix(es): 92-0

**International Commission on Illumination
  Central Bureau**, see CIE (International
  Commission on Illumination Central Bureau)

†◇**International Federation for Information
  Processing (IFIP)**
c/o Plamen Nedkov, Hofstr 3, 2361 Laxenburg
*Tel:* (02236) 73616 *Fax:* (02236) 736169
*E-mail:* ifip@ifip.or.at
*Web Site:* www.ifip.or.at

†‡**International Institute for Children's
  Literature & Reading Research (UNESCO
  category C)**
Mayerhofgasse 6, 1040 Vienna
*Tel:* (01) 505 03 59; (01) 505 28 31 *Fax:* (01)
  505 03 59-17; (01) 505 28 31-17
*E-mail:* office@jugendliteratur.net
*Web Site:* www.jugendliteratur.net
*Key Personnel*
President: Dr Hilde Hawlicek
Vice President: Alois Almer
Dir: Mag Karin Haller *E-mail:* karin.haller@
  jugendliteratur.net
Secretary: Barbara Mladek *E-mail:* barbara.
  mladek@jugendliteratur.net
Founded: 1965
Internationales Institut fur Jugendliteratur und
  Leseforschung.
Subjects: Children & Youth Literature, Research
Publication(s): *1000 und 1 Buch* (4 times/yr)

†**International Union of Geological Sciences
  (IUGS)** (Union internationale des Sciences
  Geologiques)
Rasumofskygasse 23, 1031 Vienna
Mailing Address: PO Box 127, 1031 Vienna
*Tel:* (01) 712 56 74 (ext 180) *Fax:* (01) 712 56
  74 56
*Web Site:* www.iugs.org
*Telex:* 55417 NGU N
*Key Personnel*
President: Prof Zhang Hongren *E-mail:* zhang.
  iugs@gmail.com
Secretary General: Dr Peter T Bobrowsky
  *E-mail:* pbobrows@nrcan.gc.ca
Founded: 1961

Subjects: Earth Sciences
Publication(s): *Episodes* (quarterly)

**IUGS**, see International Union of Geological
  Sciences (IUGS)

**Literar-Mechana, Wahrnehmungsgesellschaft
  fuer Urheberrechte GmbH**
Linke Wienzeile 18, 1060 Vienna
*Tel:* (01) 5872161-0 *Fax:* (01) 5872161-9
*E-mail:* literar.mechana@netway.at
*Key Personnel*
Man Dir: Franz Leo Popp
Organization for Copyright Protection.

**Standard Book Numbering Agency**
Grunangergasse 4, 1010 Vienna
*Tel:* (01) 512 15 35 *Fax:* (01) 512 84 82
*E-mail:* isbn@hvb.at
*Web Site:* www.buecher.at
*Key Personnel*
Contact: Herma Papovschek
ISBN Prefix(es): 3-85103

◇**Verband der Antiquare Oesterreichs**
  (Antiquarian Booksellers Association of
  Austria)
Grunangergasse 4, 1010 Vienna
*Tel:* (01) 512 15 35 *Fax:* (01) 512 84 82
*E-mail:* sekretariat@hvb.at
*Web Site:* www.antiquare.at
*Key Personnel*
President: Norbert Donhofer *E-mail:* donhofer@
  oebv.co.at
Vice President: Michael Sulzmann
  *E-mail:* antiquariat.ms@chello.at
Publication(s): *Anzeiger des Verbandes der An-
  tiquare Oesterreichs* (Austrian Antiquarian
  Booksellers' Association Gazette)

**Verband der Oesterreichischen Buch-und
  Presse- Grossisten und der Werbenden
  Zeitschriftenhaendler**
Grunangergasse 4, 1010 Vienna
*Tel:* (01) 512 15 35 *Fax:* (01) 512 84 82
*E-mail:* hvb@buecher.at
*Web Site:* www.buecher.at
*Key Personnel*
President: Dr Alexander Potyka

**Verband von selbstaendigen Verlagsvertreten
  Oesterreichs** (Association of Independent
  Publishers Representing Austria)
Grunangergasse 4, 1010 Vienna
*Tel:* (01) 512 15 35 *Fax:* (01) 512 84 82
*E-mail:* hvb@buecher.at
*Web Site:* www.buecher.at
*Key Personnel*
President: Hans Jobst

# Bangladesh

**National Library**
32 Justice S M Morshed Sarani, Sher-e-Bangla
  Nagar Agargaon, Dhaka 1207
*Tel:* (02) 9129992; (02) 9112733 *Fax:* (02)
  9118704
*Key Personnel*
Contact: Mr Shahabuddin Khan
Publication(s): *Boi* (text in Bengali)

**Standard Book Numbering Agency**, see
  National Library

# Belarus

**National Book Chamber of Belarus**
11 Masherow Ave, 220600 Minsk
*Tel:* (172) 235839 *Fax:* (172) 235825
*E-mail:* palata@palata.belpak.minsk.by
*Key Personnel*
Contact: Anatoli Voronko
*Parent Company:* Republic of Belarus

**Standard Book Numbering Agency**, see
National Book Chamber of Belarus

# Belgium

**Association des Editeurs Belges** (Belgian
Publishers' Association)
140 Blvd Lambermont, bte 1, 1030 Brussels
*Tel:* (02) 241 65 80 *Fax:* (02) 216 71 31
*E-mail:* adeb@adeb.be
*Web Site:* www.adeb.irisnet.be
*Key Personnel*
President: Jean Vandeveld
Dir: Bernard Gerard
Publication(s): *Annuaire des Editeurs belges de
Langue francaise* (Belgian Publishers in French
Language Annual); *Catalogue des Editeurs
scientifiques*; *Donnees statistiques sur le livre
belge de langue francaise*

**Boek.be**
Hof ter Schrieckaan 17, 2600 Berchem, Antwerp
*Tel:* (03) 230 89 23 *Fax:* (03) 281 22 40
*E-mail:* info@boek.be
*Web Site:* www.boek.be
*Key Personnel*
President: Andre Van Halewyck
Dir: Rene Van Loon *E-mail:* rene.van.loon@boek.
be
Association for the promotion of Dutch language
books/books from Flanders.
Publication(s): *Adresgids voor het Boekenvan* (list
of publishers & booksellers); *De Boekentrom-
mel* (list of new children's books); *Het Boek
in Vlaanderen* (list of new books); *Lijstenboek*
(list of publishers & booksellers); *Tijdingen*
(news)

†‡**Centre for European Policy Studies**
One Place du Congres, 1000 Brussels
*Tel:* (02) 2293911 *Fax:* (02) 2194151; (02)
2293971
*E-mail:* info@ceps.be
*Web Site:* www.ceps.be
*Key Personnel*
President: Peter Ludlow
General Manager: Catherine Chanut
Corporate Relations Manager: Staffan Jerneck
Finances & Administration Dir: Willem Roekens
Editor: Anne Harrington
Founded: 1983
Subjects: Politics, Economics, Business

**EBF**, see European Booksellers Federation (EBF)

†◇**European Association of Directory &
Database Publishers** (Association Europeenne
des Editeurs d'Annuaires/Europaeischer
Adressbuchverleger-Verband)
127 Ave Franklin Roosevelt, 1050 Brussels
*Tel:* (02) 6463060 *Fax:* (02) 6463637
*E-mail:* mailbox@eadp.org
*Web Site:* www.eadp.be
*Key Personnel*
President: Dr Christoph Dumrath

Secretary-General: Anne Lerat
Public Relations: Annie Komaromi
*E-mail:* anniekomaromi@eadp.org
Founded: 1966
Publication(s): *Directories in Europe* (annually,
list of members)

†◇**European Booksellers Federation (EBF)**
Chaussee de Charleroi, 51b Boite 1, 1060 Brus-
sels
*Tel:* (02) 223 49 40 *Fax:* (02) 223 49 38
*E-mail:* eurobooks@skynet.be
*Web Site:* www.ebf-eu.org
*Key Personnel*
President: John McNamee *Tel:* (050) 22-04-66
*Fax:* (09) 63-50-48
Vice President: Juancho Pons *Tel:* (0976) 55-49-
20 *Fax:* (0976) 35-60-72
Dir: Fran Dubrville *E-mail:* frandubruille.
eurobooks@skynet.be

†◇**Federation of European Publishers (FEP)**
Av de Tervueren 204, 1150 Brussels
*Tel:* (02) 7701110 *Fax:* (02) 7712071
*Web Site:* www.fep-fee.be
*Key Personnel*
President: Dr Arne Bach
Dir General: Anne Bergman-Tahon
*E-mail:* abergman@fep-fee.be
Founded: 1967
The Federation consists of the book associations
of the European Communities & European
Econo mic Area (EEA) & aims at represent-
ing jointly the interests of the European pub-
lishers for all matters arising from the Treaty
of Rome, Maastricht & Amsterdam & Nice (or
the Treaties).

**FEP**, see Federation of European Publishers
(FEP)

†◇**FIAF (International Federation of Film
Archives)** (Federation internationale des
archives du film)
One Rue Defacqz, 1000 Brussels
*Tel:* (02) 538 3065 *Fax:* (02) 534 4774
*E-mail:* info@fiafnet.org
*Web Site:* www.fiafnet.org
*Key Personnel*
Executive Secretary: Brigitte van der Elst
Senior Administrator: Christian Dimitriu
Founded: 1938
Dedicated to the rescue, collection, preservation
& screening of moving images.
Publication(s): *Bibliography of National Filmo-
graphies*; *Cataloguing Rules for Film Archives*;
*Glossary of Filmographic Terms, Version II*;
*Handbook for Film Archives*; *Handling, Storage
& Transport of Cellulose Nitrate Film*; *Interna-
tional Directory of Film & TV Documentation
Collections*; *International Film Archive CD-
ROM*; *Journal of Film Preservation*; *Preserva-
tion & Restoration of Moving Images & Sound*;
*Technical Manual of the FIAF Preservation
Commission*; *The International Index to Film &
Television Periodicals*

**IBF**, see International Booksellers Federation
(IBF)

**IFRRO**, see International Federation of
Reproduction Rights Organisations (IFRRO)

†◇**International Booksellers Federation (IBF)**
Chaussee de Charleroi 51b, Boite 1, 1060 Brus-
sels
*Tel:* (02) 223 49 40 *Fax:* (02) 223 49 38
*E-mail:* ibf.booksellers@skynet.be
*Web Site:* www.ibf-booksellers.org

*Key Personnel*
President: Eric Hardin *E-mail:* hardin@club-
internet.fr
Dir: Francoise Dubruille
Founded: 1955
International, non-governmental organization of
booksellers associations & booksellers from
around the world. Its purpose is to enable
booksellers associations & individual booksellers to connect.
Publication(s): *Booksellers International* (different
country reports); *The IBF* (IBF list of members)

†‡**International Catholic Organization for
Cinema & Audiovisual (OCIC)**
8, rue de l'Orme, 1040 Brussels
*Tel:* (02) 7344294 *Fax:* (02) 7343207
*E-mail:* sg@ocic.org
*Web Site:* www.ocic.org *Cable:*
OCIC.BRUXELLES
*Key Personnel*
President: Henk Hoegstra
Secretary General: Robert Molhant
Founded: 1928
Subjects: African Cinema, Cinema & Religion,
Video & Religion, World Cinema
Publication(s): *Cineamedia* (bimonthly, magazine)
ISBN Prefix(es): 92-9080

**International Federation of Film Archives**, see
FIAF (International Federation of Film
Archives)

†◇**International Federation of Reproduction
Rights Organisations (IFRRO)**
Rue de Prince Royal 87, 1050 Brussels
*Tel:* (02) 551 08 99 *Fax:* (02) 551 08 95
*E-mail:* iffro@skynet.be; secretariat@ifrro.be
*Web Site:* www.ifrro.org
*Key Personnel*
President: Peter F Shepherd
Vice President: Michael Fraser
General Secretary: Olav Stokkmo *E-mail:* olav.
stokkmo@ifrro.be
Information Officer: Marie-Agnes Lenoir
*E-mail:* marie.agnes.lenoir@ifrro.be
IFRRO links together all national Reproduction
Rights Organizations (RROs) & national & international associations of rightsholders. RROs
are organizations engaged in the conveyance
of photocopying authorizations & royalties
between rightsholders & users. IFRRO's purposes are to foster the creation of RROs worldwide; to facilitate the development of formal
agreements & informal relationships between,
among & on behalf of its members; & to increase public awareness of copyright & the
need for effective mechanisms for convey-
ing rights & royalties between rightsholders
& users.

**OCIC**, see International Catholic Organization
for Cinema & Audiovisual (OCIC)

†‡**Tantalum-Niobium International Study
Center**
40 Rue Washington, 1050 Brussels
*Tel:* (02) 6495158 *Fax:* (02) 6496447
*E-mail:* info@tanb.org
*Web Site:* www.tanb.org
*Key Personnel*
Secretary General: Judith Wickens
Subjects: Metals
ISBN Prefix(es): 92-9093

**TIC**, see Tantalum-Niobium International Study
Center

**VBB**, see Vlaamse Boekverkopersbond (VBB)

◇**Vlaamse Boekverkopersbond (VBB)** (Flemish Booksellers' Association)
Hof ter Schrieecklaan 17, 2600 Berchem, Antwerp
*Tel:* (03) 230 89 23 *Fax:* (03) 281 22 40
*E-mail:* info@boek.be
*Web Site:* www.boek.be
*Key Personnel*
General Secretary: Luc Tessens *E-mail:* luc. tessens@vbvb.be

**Vlaamse Uitgevers Vereniging (VUV)** (Publishers From Flanders)
Hof ter Schrieecklaan 17, 2600 Antwerp
*Tel:* (03) 2308923 *Fax:* (03) 2812240
*E-mail:* info@boek.be
*Web Site:* www.vbvb.be
*Key Personnel*
Secretary: Jan Vanderheyden *E-mail:* jan. vanderheyden@vbvb.be
Association of Publishers of Dutch Language Books.

**VUV**, see Vlaamse Uitgevers Vereniging (VUV)

# Bolivia

**Camara Boliviana del Libro** (Bolivian Booksellers' Association)
Calle Capitan Ravelo 2116, 682 La Paz
*Tel:* (02) 44 4239; (02) 44 4077 *Fax:* (02) 44 1523
*E-mail:* cabolib@ceibo.entelnet.bo
*Key Personnel*
President & Dir: Rolando Condori Salinas
Vice President: Nancy C de Montoya
Secretary: Teresa G de Alvarez
Distributions: Miguel Martinez
Sales: Jose Carlos Ciappesoni
Editorial: Nestor Castillo
Retail Sales: Walter Mercado

# Botswana

**Standard Book Numbering Agency (Botswana)**
Botswana National Library Service, Pvt Bag 0036, Gaborone
*Tel:* 3952 397; 3952 288 *Fax:* 3957 108; 3901 149
*Telex:* 2414 pula bd *Cable:* BONALIBS
*Key Personnel*
ISBN Administrator: G K Mulindwa

# Brazil

**ABEU**, see Associacao Brasileira dar Editoras Universitarias (ABEU)

**Agencia Brasileira do ISBN**
c/o Biblioteca Nacional, Av Rio Branco, 219-1°, 20040-008 Rio de Janeiro-RJ
*Tel:* (021) 2220-9367 *Fax:* (021) 2220-4173
*E-mail:* isbn@bn.br
*Web Site:* www.bn.br
*Telex:* 2122941bnrjbr
*Key Personnel*
Contact: Sueli Ferreira Aleixo

**Associacao Brasileira dar Editoras Universitarias (ABEU)**
Praca da Se 108 5° andar, 01001-900 Centro, Sao Paulo
*Tel:* (011) 32427171 *Fax:* (011) 32427172
*E-mail:* feu@editora.unesp.br
*Telex:* (0482) 240
*Key Personnel*
President: Alcides Buss
Brazilian Association of Academic Publishers.

**Brazilian National Library**, see Departamento Nacional do Livro

**Camara Brasileira do Livro** (Brazilian Book Association)
Cristiano Viana, 91, 05411-000 Sao Paulo-SP
*Tel:* (011) 3069-1300 *Fax:* (011) 3069-1300
*E-mail:* cbl@cbl.org.br
*Web Site:* www.cbl.org.br
*Telex:* 24788 Vrli
*Key Personnel*
President: Oswaldo Siciliano
Dir: H Carlos Dias
General Manager: Aloysio T Costa

**Departamento Nacional do Livro** (National Books Department)
Affiliate of Ministerio da Cultura Republica Federativa do Brazil
c/o Fundacao Biblioteca Nacional, Avenida Rio Branco, 219-1 andar, 20040-008 Rio de Janeiro-RJ
*Tel:* (021) 2220-1707; (021) 2220-1683 *Fax:* (021) 2220-1702
*E-mail:* dnl@bn.br
*Web Site:* www.bn.br
*Key Personnel*
Dir: Elmer Correa Barbosa *E-mail:* elmer@bn.br

**Livraria Kosmos Editora Ltda**
Rua do Rosario 135-137, Centro, CP 3481, 20041-005 Rio de Janeiro-RJ
*Tel:* (021) 224-8616 *Fax:* (021) 221-4582
Brazilian Association of Antiquarian Booksellers.
ISBN Prefix(es): 85-7096

**Sindicato Nacional dos Editores de Livros (SNEL)** (Brazilian Publishers' Association)
Av Rio Branco 37, Sala 1.504, 20090-003 Rio de Janeiro-RJ
*Tel:* (021) 2233-6481 *Fax:* (021) 2253-8502
*E-mail:* snel@snel.org.br
*Web Site:* www.snel.org.br
*Key Personnel*
President: Paulo Roberto Rocco
Dir Secretary: Francisco Bilac Pinto
Manager: Nilson Lopes da Silva
Publication(s): *Informativo Bibliografico* (annually); *Jornal do SNEL* (bimonthly); *Producao Editorial Brasileira* (Brazilian Publishing Output, annually)

**SNEL**, see Sindicato Nacional dos Editores de Livros (SNEL)

**Standard Book Numbering Agency**, see Agencia Brasileira do ISBN

# Brunei Darussalam

**Standard Book Numbering Agency**
Bandar Seri Begawan 2064, Negara
*Tel:* (02) 382511 *Fax:* (02) 381817

*Telex:* bu 2774
*Key Personnel*
Contact: Ms Nellie Dato Paduka Haji Sunny

# Bulgaria

**Bulgarian National ISSN Centre**
c/o St Cyril & Methodius National Library, Vassil Levski 88, 1037 Sofia
*Tel:* (02) 9461165; (02) 9882811 *Fax:* (02) 435495
*E-mail:* issn@nationallibary.bg
*Web Site:* www.nationallibrary.bg
*Telex:* 22432
*Key Personnel*
Dir: Antoaneta Totomanova *E-mail:* totomanova@ nationallibrary.bg
*Parent Company:* St St Cyril & Methodius

◇**National ISBN Agency**
St Cyril & St Methodius National Library, Boul Vasil Leveski 88, 1037 Sofia
*Tel:* (02) 9882811; (02) 9882362 *Fax:* (02) 435495
*E-mail:* nl@nationallibrary.bg
*Web Site:* www.nationallibrary.bg
*Telex:* 22432 natlib
*Key Personnel*
ISBN Administrator: Tatjana Dermendzieva *E-mail:* isbn@nationallibrary.bg
Publication(s): *Novini ISBN i ISSN* (monthly); *Spravocnik na izdatelstva, redakcii i pecatnici v Baelgarija* (annually, directory)

**Standard Book Numbering Agency**, see National ISBN Agency

# Cameroon

†◇**Centre Regional pour la Promotion du Livre en Afrique (CREPLA)**
POB 1646, Yaounde
*Tel:* 224782; 2936
*Key Personnel*
Secretary: William Moutchia
Founded: 1962
Regional Centre for Book Promotion in Africa (co-sponsored by UNESCO).
Publication(s): *CREPLA Bulletin*

**CREPLA**, see Centre Regional pour la Promotion du Livre en Afrique (CREPLA)

**IFORD**, see Institut de Formation et de Recherche Demographiques (IFORD)

†‡**Institut de Formation et de Recherche Demographiques (IFORD)**
BP 1556, Yaounde
*Tel:* (023) 222471; (023) 231917 *Fax:* (023) 226793
*E-mail:* wyaounde@un.cm; jtsoyenk@un.cm
*Web Site:* www.un.cm/iford
*Telex:* S/C PNUD 8304 KN
*Key Personnel*
Dir: Dr Eliwo Mandjale Akoto
Founded: 1972
Subjects: Demography, Population Studies
ISBN Prefix(es): 2-905327

**PAID**, see Pan African Institute for Development (PAID)

†**Pan African Institute for Development (PAID)**
BP 4056, Douala
Mailing Address: PO Box 133, Buca
*Tel:* 332 28 06 *Fax:* 332 28 06
*E-mail:* info@paid-wa.org
*Web Site:* www.irc.nl/page/6919
*Telex:* 6048
*Key Personnel*
President, Governing Council: Dr Mbuki V T
    MWamufiya
Dir: Rosetta B Thompson
Founded: 1964
Subjects: Rural Development
Publication(s): *An Integrated Approach to Ru-
    ral Development* (IRD); *Community Health &
    Nutrition* (CHN); *Drought & Famine Prepared-
    ness & Response* (DFPR); *Food Self Sufficiency
    & Agricultural Development* (FSS); *Informal
    Sector & Small Scale Enterprises* (ISSE); *Pop-
    ular Participation & the Promotion & Manage-
    ment of NGOs* (NGO); *Promoting Active Train-
    ing Methods* (ATM); *Strengthening African
    Training & Research Institutions*; *Towards a
    Support Methodology* (SM); *Women & Health
    Programme* (W/H); *Women in Development*
    (WiD)

# Canada

†◇**International Fiction Review**
University of New Brunswick, Dept of Culture &
    Language Studies, PO Box 4400, Fredericton,
    NB E3B 5A3
*Tel:* 506-453-4636 *Fax:* 506-447-3166
*E-mail:* ifr@unb.ca
*Web Site:* www.lib.unb.ca/Texts/IFR
*Key Personnel*
Editor: Chris Lorey *E-mail:* lorey@unb.ca
Founded: 1974
Publication(s): *The International Fiction Review*
    (annually)

# Chile

**Camara Chilena del Libro AG**
Av Libertador Bernardo O'Higgins 1370 Oficina
    501, Santiago
*Tel:* (02) 6989519; (02) 6724088 *Fax:* (02)
    6989226
*E-mail:* prolibro@tie.cl
*Web Site:* www.camlibro.cl
*Key Personnel*
President: Eduardo Castillo Garcia
Chilean association of publishers, distributors &
    booksellers. Also acts as Standard Book Num-
    bering Agency.

**CELADE**, see Centro Latinoamericano de
    Demografia (CELADE)

†‡**Centro Latinoamericano de Demografia
    (CELADE)**
Edeficio Naciones Unidas, Avda Dag Ham-
    marskjoeld 3477, Vitacura, Santiago
Mailing Address: Casilla 179-D, Santiago
*Tel:* (02) 4712000; (02) 2102000; (02) 2085051
    *Fax:* (02) 2080252; (02) 2081946
*E-mail:* secepal@eclac.cl
*Web Site:* www.eclac.org
*Telex:* 340295 UNSTGOCK *Cable:* UNATIONS
*Key Personnel*
Dir: Reynaldo F Bajraj

Subjects: Demography, Statistics, Sociology, Pop-
    ulation Information & Data Processing, Period-
    icals
Publication(s): *Boletin Demografico* (biennially);
    *Notas de Poblacion* (biennially); *Revista Doc-
    pal* (annually)

**PROLIBRO**, see Camara Chilena del Libro AG

**Standard Book Numbering Agency**
c/o Camara Chilena del Libro A G, Av Libertador
    Bernardo O'Higgins 1370 Oficina 501, Santi-
    ago
*Tel:* (02) 6989519; (02) 6724088 *Fax:* (02)
    6989226
*E-mail:* camlibro@terra.cl; prolibro@ctcreuna.cl
*Web Site:* www.camlibro.cl
*Key Personnel*
President: Eduardo Castillo Garcia
Publication(s): *Catalogo ISBN Libros Chilenos
    (Ultima Publicacion 1996)*

# China

**China ISBN Agency**
85 Dongsi Nan Dajie, Beijing 100703
*Tel:* (010) 65127806; (010) 65212832 *Fax:* (010)
    65127875
*Telex:* 22024 cpmcp cn
*Key Personnel*
ISBN Contact: Yang Muzhi

**Press & Publication Administration of the
    People's Republic of China**
85 Dongsi Nandajie, Beijing 100703
*Tel:* (010) 5127809 *Fax:* (010) 5127875
*Key Personnel*
President: Song Muwen
Chief Foreign Affairs Dept: Wei Hong

**Standard Book Numbering Agency**, see China
    ISBN Agency

# Colombia

**Agencia Colombiana del ISBN, Camara
    Colombiana del Libro**
Calle 40 No 21-31, Bogota DC
*Tel:* (01) 288-6188 *Fax:* (01) 287-3320
*E-mail:* agenciaisbn@camlibro.com.co
*Web Site:* www.camlibro.com.co
*Key Personnel*
Contact: Sr Jaime Bravo Navarrete
Also acts as Standard Book Numbering Agency.

◇**Camara Colombiana del Libro**
Calle 40 No 21-31, Bogota DC
*Tel:* (01) 288 6188 *Fax:* (01) 287 3320
*E-mail:* camlibro@camlibro.com.co
*Web Site:* www.camlibro.com.co
Colombian Book Association.
Publication(s): *Correo Editorial - Boletin Bibli-
    ografico ISBN*
*Associate Companies:* Agencia Colombiana Del
    ISBN
*Branch Office(s)*
Camara Colombiana Del Libro Seccional Occi-
    dente

†◇**Centro Regional para el Fomento del Libro
    en America Latina y el Caribe** (Regional
    Center for the Promotion of Books in Latin
    America & the Caribbean)

Calle 70 No 9-52, Bogota DC
Mailing Address: Apdo Aereo 57348, Bogota 2
*Tel:* (01) 212-6056; (01) 249-5141 *Fax:* (01) 255-
    4614; (01) 321-7503
*E-mail:* libro@cerlalc.org
*Web Site:* www.cerlalc.org
*Key Personnel*
Dir: Carmen Barvo
Founded: 1971
ISBN Prefix(es): 92-9057; 958-671

**CERLALC**, see Centro Regional para el
    Fomento del Libro en America Latina y el
    Caribe

**Standard Book Numbering Agency**
Camara Colombiana del Libro, Carrera 17A, No
    37-27, Bogota
Mailing Address: Apdo Aereo 8998, Bogota
*Tel:* (01) 2886188 *Fax:* (01) 2873320
*E-mail:* agenciaisbn@camlibro.com.co
*Web Site:* www.camlibro.com.co
*Key Personnel*
Dir: Sandra Del Mar Sacanamboy Franco
Publication(s): *Libros Registrados En Colombia;
    Periodico Tinta Fresca*

# Costa Rica

†◇**AIBDA**
Apdo 55, 2200 Coronado
*Tel:* (0506) 2160222 *Fax:* (0506) 2294741; (0506)
    2160233
*E-mail:* iicahq@iica.ac.cr
*Web Site:* www.iica.int/
*Telex:* 2144 IICACR *Cable:* IICASANJOSE
*Key Personnel*
Executive Secretary: Aura Mata
Founded: 1965
Publication(s): *AIBDA Actualidades* (irregularly);
    *Boletin Informativo* (triannually); *Boletin Tec-
    nico* (irregularly); *Guia para Bibliotecas Agri-
    colas*; *Quienes Quien en AIBDA*

**Asociacion Interamericana de Bibliotecarios y
    Documentalistas Agricolas**, see AIBDA

†‡**Instituto Interamericano de Cooperacion
    para la Agricultura (IICA)**
Apdo 55, 2200 Coronado, San Jose
*Tel:* (0506) 2160222 *Fax:* (0506) 2160233
*E-mail:* iicahq@iica.ac.cr
*Web Site:* www.iica.int
*Telex:* 2144 Iica *Cable:* IICASANJOSE
*Key Personnel*
Editor, General Publishing: Susana Raine
Founded: 1942
In every Latin American & Caribbean country,
    Canada & USA.
ISBN Prefix(es): 92-9039

**Standard Book Numbering Agency**
Biblioteca Nacional, 1000 San Jose
Mailing Address: Apdo Postal 10008, San Jose
    1000
*Tel:* (0506) 2212436; (0506) 2212479 *Fax:* (0506)
    2235510
*E-mail:* proctec@racsa.co.cr
*Key Personnel*
General Manager: Isidro Serrano Rodriguez
Publication(s): *Catalogo Nacional ISBN*

# Cote d'Ivoire

**†African Publishers' Network (APNET)**
7e etage, Immeuble Roume Blvd, Abidjan 01
Mailing Address: BP 3429, Abidjan 01
*Tel:* 20211801; 20211802 *Fax:* 20211803
*E-mail:* apnetes@yahoo.com
*Web Site:* www.freewebs.com/africanpublishers
*Key Personnel*
Chairman: Mamadou Aliou Sow
Executive Secretary: Akin Fasemore *E-mail:* es@
apnet.org
Membership & Trade Promotion Officer: Tainie
Mundondo *E-mail:* apnettrade@yahoo.com
Treasurer: Janet Njoroge
Training Coordinator: Alice Mouko
*E-mail:* apnettraining@yahoo.fr
Founded: 1992
Publication(s): *African Publishing Review* (6
times/yr); *Indaba Papers*; *Thematic Catalogues*;
*Trade Directory 2000* (Repertoire Commer-
cial/O Directorio Comercial, biannually, book,
2000)
*Branch Office(s)*
CP 1248, Luanda, Angola, Contact: Antonio de
Brito *Tel:* (02) 331371 *Fax:* (02) 895162; (02)
332714 *E-mail:* infosec@ebonet.net
BP 1501, Yaounde, Cameroon, Contact: Freddy
Ngandu *Tel:* 223554; 2223554 *Fax:* 2221761
*E-mail:* ngan_fred@yahoo.fr
PO Box 33 Panorama, Cairo, Egypt (Arab Re-
public of Egypt), Contact: Ashraf Hamouda
*Tel:* (02) 4023399 *Fax:* (02) 4037567
*E-mail:* ahamouda@link.net
BP 542, Conakry, Guinea, Contact: Mamadou
Aliou Sow *Tel:* 463507; 402849 *Fax:* 412012;
463507 *E-mail:* ganndal@mirinet.net.gn
PO Box 18033, Nairobi, Kenya, Contact: Janet
Njoroge *Tel:* (02) 533665 *Fax:* (02) 540037
*E-mail:* longhorn@iconnect.co.ke
Private Bag 39, Blantyre, Malawi, Con-
tact: Egidio Mpanga *Tel:* 670880; 670855
*Fax:* 671114 *E-mail:* dzuka@malawi.net
Ighodaro Rd, No 1, Jericho Layout, PMB 5205,
Ibadan, Nigeria, Contact: Ayo Ojeniyi *Tel:* (02)
2412268; (02) 2410943 *Fax:* (02) 2411089;
(02) 2413237 *E-mail:* info@heinemannbooks.
com

**APNET**, see African Publishers' Network
(APNET)

# Croatia

**†Croatian ISBN Agency**
Hrvatske bratske zajednice 4, 10000 Zagreb
*Tel:* (01) 6164087; (01) 6164288 *Fax:* (01)
6164371
*E-mail:* isbn@nsk.hr
*Web Site:* www.nsk.hr
*Key Personnel*
Contact: Ms Jasenka Zajec
Founded: 1992
Registers publishers in Croatia in the ISBN
System; maintains the Croatian Publishers
Database; holds statistics on book publishing
in Croatia.
Membership(s): International ISBN Agency.
Subjects: National ISBN Agency
Publication(s): *Book & Music Publishers in Croa-
tia: Directory*
*Parent Company:* National & University Library
in Zagreb

**Croatian ISMN Agency**, see Croatian ISBN
Agency

# Cuba

**Agencia Cubana del ISBN**
Camara Cubana del Libro, Calle 15 No 602 esq
C, Vedado, Ciudad Havana
*Tel:* (07) 36034 *Fax:* (07) 333441
*E-mail:* cclfilh@ceniai.cu
*Telex:* 511881 feria cu
*Key Personnel*
Contact: Jose A Robert Gasset

**Standard Book Numbering Agency**, see
Agencia Cubana del ISBN

◇**Union de Escritores y Artistas de Cuba**
(Union of Writers & Artists of Cuba)
Calle 17 No 354, Plaza de la Revolucion, Havana
*Tel:* (07) 555081 *Fax:* (07) 333158
*E-mail:* informatica@uneac.co.cu
*Web Site:* www.uneac.com
*Telex:* 051156364
*Key Personnel*
Secretary: Armando Cristobal
Publication(s): *Union, La Gaceta de Cuba, Re-
vista de Literatura Cubana*

# Cyprus

**Standard Book Numbering Agency**
c/o Cyprus Centre for Registration of Books &
Serials, The Cyprus Library, Byron Ave 20,
1437 Nicosia
*Tel:* (022) 303337 *Fax:* (022) 443565
*E-mail:* antonism@ucy.ac.cy
*Key Personnel*
Dir: Dr Antonis Maratheftis
*E-mail:* amaratheftis@hotmail.com
Founded: 1987
National library.
Membership(s) IFLA.
Subjects: Cyprus bibliography
ISBN Prefix(es): 9963-0

# Czech Republic

**ACBP**, see Svaz ceskych knihkupcu a nakladatelu
(SCKN)

**Ceske Narodni Stredisko ISSN** (Czech National
ISSN Center)
Division of Statni Technicka Knihovna
Marianske nam 5, 110 01 Prague 1
Mailing Address: PO Box 206, 110 01 Prague 1
*Tel:* (02) 21 663 440 *Fax:* (02) 2222 1340
*E-mail:* issn@stk.cz
*Web Site:* www.stk.cz/en/issn/index.htm
*Key Personnel*
Dir: Dr Jan Bayer, PhD *Tel:* (02) 21 663 480
*E-mail:* j.bayer@stk.cz

◇**Ministerstvo Kultury C R, Oddeleni Tisku
Oddeleni Knizi Kultury** (Czech Ministry of
Culture, Production Department, Publishing &
Trade Book)
Milady Horakove 139, 160 41 Prague 6
*Tel:* (02) 57 085 111 *Fax:* (02) 24 318 155
*E-mail:* minkult@mkcr.cz
*Web Site:* www.mkcr.cz
Publication(s): *Books in Czech Republic*

**Narodni agentura ISBN v CR**
Klementinum 190, 11001 Prague 1
*Tel:* (02) 21663262 *Fax:* (02) 21663261
*E-mail:* isbn@nkp.cz
*Web Site:* www.nkp.cz
*Key Personnel*
ISBN Administrator: Mr Antonin Jerabek
Publication(s): *Soupis ucastniku systemu mezinar-
odniho standardniho cislovani knih - ISBN - v
Ceske republice* (annually, directory of Czech
publishers)
*Parent Company:* Narodni Knihovna Ceske re-
publiky
*Associate Companies:* Narodna agentura ISBN v
SR

**SCKN**, see Svaz ceskych knihkupcu a
nakladatelu (SCKN)

**Standard Book Numbering Agency**, see
Narodni agentura ISBN v CR

**Svaz Antikvaru CR**
Karlova 2, 110 00 Prague 1
*Tel:* (02) 22220286 *Fax:* (02) 22220286
*E-mail:* info@meissner.cz
*Web Site:* www.meissner.cz
*Key Personnel*
President: Petr Meissner
Contact: Vaclav Prosek
Membership(s): ILAB (International League of
Antiquarian Booksellers).

◇**Svaz ceskych knihkupcu a nakladatelu
(SCKN)** (Association of Czech Booksellers &
Publishers (ACBP))
Jana Masaryka 56, 120 00 Prague 2
*Tel:* (02) 24 219 944 *Fax:* (02) 24 219 942
*E-mail:* sckn@sckn.cz
*Web Site:* www.sckn.cz
*Key Personnel*
Chairman: Jitka Undeova
Chairman of Booksellers Section, 1st Vice Chair-
man: Jiri Seidl
Founded: 1879 (renewed 1990)
Membership(s): IPA.
Publication(s): *Bookseller & Publisher* (Knihku-
pec a nakladatel, monthly); *Czech Books In
Print (Katalog kladovanych Knih)* (annually)
ISBN Prefix(es): 80-902495
*Associate Companies:* Svet knihy S R O (Book
World Ltd)

# Denmark

**Dansk ISBN - Kontor (the Danish ISBN
Agency)**
Dansk Biblioteks Center, Tempovej 7-11, 2750
Ballerup
*Tel:* 44867725 *Fax:* 44867853
*E-mail:* isbn@dbc.dk
*Web Site:* www.isbn-kontoret.dk
*Key Personnel*
ISBN Administrator: Mrs Lone Olsen
*E-mail:* lo@dbc.dk

**Den Danske Boghandlerforening** (The Danish
Booksellers Association)
Siljangade 6 3, DK 2300 Copenhagen S
*Tel:* 32542255 *Fax:* 32540041
*E-mail:* ddb@bogpost.dk
*Web Site:* www.bogguide.dk
*Key Personnel*
President: Jesper Moller
Dir: Olaf Winslow

Memberships: European Booksellers Federation
(EBF); International Booksellers Federation
(IBF).
Publication(s): *Bogmarkedet* (The Booktrade, The
Danish Book Market with Den Danske For-
laeggerforening)

◇**Den Danske Forlaeggerforening** (Danish
Publishers' Association)
18/1 Kompagnistr, 1208 Copenhagen K
*Tel:* 33 15 66 88 *Fax:* 33 15 65 88
*E-mail:* publassn@webpartner.dk; jh@carlsen.dk
*Key Personnel*
President: Mr Jesper Holm *E-mail:* jh@carlsen.dk
Dir: Ib Tune Olsen
Publication(s): *Det Danske Bogmarked* (The Dan-
ish Book Market with Den Danske Boghan-
dlerforening); *Fortegnelse over Samhandels
berettigede Boghandlere MV* (Register of Li-
censed Booksellers, etc)

◇**Forening for Boghaandvaerk, Nordjysk
afdeling** (Association of Book Crafts, North
Jutland Branch)
c/o Riget Consult, Thorshavnsgade 22, kld, 2300
Copenhagen
*Tel:* 32 95 85 15
*Web Site:* www.boghaandvaerk.dk
*Key Personnel*
President: Bent Joergensen *E-mail:* bj@kb.dk
Treasurer & Secretary: Lilli Riget
Founded: 1888
Danish Bookcraft Association.
Publication(s): *Arets bogarbejde* (Selected Books
of the Year, yearbook); *Bogvennen* (The Book
Lover, yearbook)
*Parent Company:* Forening for Boghaandvoerk

†◇**International Association for Mass
Communication Research**
Aalborg Universitet, Fredrik Bajers Vej 5, 9100
Aalborg
Mailing Address: Postboks 159, 9100 Aalborg
*Tel:* (045) 9635 8080 *Fax:* (045) 9815 6864
*E-mail:* prehn@hum.auc.dk
*Web Site:* www.auc.dk/fak-hum
*Key Personnel*
President: Prof Cees Hamelink
Administrative Secretary: Peggy Gray
Secretary General: Ole Prehn *E-mail:* prehn@
hum.auc.dk
Association internationale des etudes et
recherches sur l'information.
Publication(s): *Communication & Democracy*;
*Directions in Research*; *Mass Media & Man's
View of Society*; *Mass Media & National Cul-
tures*; *Mass Media & Socialization*; *New Struc-
tures of International Communication*; *The
Role of Research*; *Social Communication &
Global Problems*

†‡**Nordic Council of Ministers Publications**
Store Strandstr 18, 1255 Copenhagen K
*Tel:* 33960200 *Fax:* 33960202
*E-mail:* nmr@nmr.dk
*Web Site:* www.norden.org
*Telex:* 15544 nordmr dk
*Key Personnel*
Secretary General: Soren Christensen
Head, Publishing Department: Agneta Sverkel-
Osterberg *Tel:* 33960410 *E-mail:* aso@nmr.dk
Founded: 1971
ISBN Prefix(es): 92-893
Number of titles published annually: 200 Print

**Standard Book Numbering Agency**, see Dansk
ISBN - Kontor (the Danish ISBN Agency)

# Ecuador

**Camara Ecuatoriana del Libro**
Nucleo de Pichincha, Avda Eloy Alfaro, N29-61
e Inglaterra piso N 9, Quito
*Tel:* (02) 553311; (02) 553314 *Fax:* (02) 222150
*E-mail:* celnp@hoy.net
*Web Site:* www.celibro.org.ec
*Key Personnel*
Presidenta Ledo: Luis Mora Ortega

**Standard Book Numbering Agency**, see Camara
Ecuatoriana del Libro

# Egypt (Arab Republic of Egypt)

**General Egyptian Book Organization**
Corniche el-Nil - Ramlet Boulac, Cairo 11221
*Tel:* (02) 5775436; (02) 5775228; (02) 5775109;
(02) 5775367; (02) 5775436; (02) 5775545;
(02) 5775000 *Fax:* (02) 5765058
*E-mail:* info@cgyptianbook.org
*Web Site:* www.egyptianbook.org
*Key Personnel*
Chmn: Dr Nasser El Ansary
VChmn: Dr Waheed Abdel Majeed
Also Publisher.
ISBN Prefix(es): 977-01

†**National Information & Documentation
Centre (NIDOC)**
Al Tahrir St, Dokki, Cairo
*Tel:* (02) 3371696
*Telex:* 92111 Alsun
*Key Personnel*
Dir: Dr Mostago Esmat El Sarha

**NIDOC**, see National Information &
Documentation Centre (NIDOC)

**Standard Book Numbering Agency**
National Library & Archives, Corniche El Nil,
Ramlet Boulac, Cairo
*Tel:* (02) 5751078; (02) 5750886; (02) 5752883
*Fax:* (02) 5765634
*E-mail:* libmang@darelkotob.org
*Telex:* 93932

# Estonia

**Estonian Publishers Association**
Roosikrantsi 6, 10119 Tallinn
*Tel:* (02) 6449866 *Fax:* (02) 6411443
*E-mail:* astat@eki.ee
*Key Personnel*
Dir: Ms A Trummal
Affiliate member of International Publishers As-
sociation.

**Standard Book Numbering Agency**
Eesti Rahvusraamatukogu, National Library, Ton-
ismagi 2, 15189 Tallinn
*Tel:* (02) 630 7372 *Fax:* (02) 631 1200
*E-mail:* eraamat@nlib.ee; nlib@nlib.ee

*Web Site:* www.nlib.ee
*Key Personnel*
Contact: Ms Mai Valtna *E-mail:* mai.valtna@nlib.
ee

# Ethiopia

†‡**United Nations Economic Commission for
Africa, ECA**
PO Box 3001, Addis Ababa
*Tel:* (01) 44 31 14 *Fax:* (01) 51 03 65
*E-mail:* ecainfo@uneca.org
*Web Site:* www.uneca.org
*Telex:* 21029 *Cable:* ECA ADDIS ABABA
*Key Personnel*
Librarian: Abdel-Rahman M Tahir

# Faroe Islands

**Foroya Landsbokasavn** (National Library of the
Faroe Islands)
J C Svabosgotu 16, 110 Torshavn
Mailing Address: PO Box 61, 110 Torshavn
*Tel:* (031) 311626 *Fax:* (031) 318895
*E-mail:* utlan@flb.fo
*Web Site:* www.flb.fo
*Key Personnel*
Contact: Mr Arnbjoern O Dalsgard
*E-mail:* arndal@flb.fo

**Standard Book Numbering Agency**, see Foroya
Landsbokasavn

# Fiji

**Regional ISBN Centre The ISBN Officer**
The University of the South Pacific Library, PO
Box 1168, Suva
*Tel:* 3313 900 *Fax:* 3300 830
*E-mail:* mamtora_j@usp.ac.fj; library@usp.ac.fj
*Web Site:* www.usp.ac.fj
*Telex:* fj 2276

# Finland

**The Finnish Book Publishers' Association**, see
Suomen Kustannusyhdistys

◇**Finnish ISBN Agency**
Helsinki University Library, Teollisuuskatu 23,
00014 Helsinki
Mailing Address: PO Box 26, University of
Helsinki, 00014 Helsinki
*Tel:* (09) 19144327 *Fax:* (09) 19144341
*E-mail:* isbn-keskus@helsinki.fi
*Web Site:* www.lib.helsinki.fi
*Key Personnel*
ISBN Administrator: Maarit Huttunen
The Finnish ISSN Center is located at the same
address.

**Kirjakauppaliitto Ry** (The Booksellers'
Association of Finland)
Eerikinkatu 15-17 D 43-44, 00100 Helsinki

*Tel:* (09) 6859 9110; (050) 540 6451 *Fax:* (09) 6859 9119
*E-mail:* toimisto@kirjakauppaliitto.fi
*Web Site:* www.kirjakauppaliitto.fi
*Key Personnel*
President: Stig-Bjorn Nyberg *E-mail:* stig-bjorn@stockmann.fi
Vice President: Arto Lahdenpera *E-mail:* arto.lahdenpera@info.fi; Jarmo Oksaharju *E-mail:* jarmo.oksaharju@suomalainenkk.fi
Dir: Olli Erakivi *E-mail:* olli.erakivi@kirjakauppaliitto.fi
Publication(s): *Kirja-ja Paperialan kalenteri* (Book & Paperbranch register); *Kirjakauppaliitto* (magazine)
*Parent Company:* Kirjakauppalehden Julkaisu Oy
*Associate Companies:* Suomen Kirjakaupan Saatio

**Standard Book Numbering Agency**, see Finnish ISBN Agency

**Suomen Kirjailijaliitto** (Association of Finnish Authors)
Runeberginkatu 32 C 28, 00100 Helsinki
*Tel:* (09) 445392 *Fax:* (09) 492278
*E-mail:* info@suomenkirjailijaliitto.fi
*Web Site:* www.suomenkirjailijaliitto.fi
*Key Personnel*
President: Jarkko Laine
Executive Secretary: Ms Paeivi Liedes
Publication(s): *Suomen Runotar*

**Suomen Kustannusyhdistys**
PO Box 177, 00121 Helsinki
*Tel:* (09) 22877250 *Fax:* (09) 6121226
*Web Site:* www.skyry.net
*Key Personnel*
Dir: Veikko Sonninen *E-mail:* veikko.sonninen@skyry.net
Membership(s): International Publishers Association; Federation of European Publishers.
Publication(s): *Vuoden Kirjat* (List of books published in Finland)

# France

◇**ADAGP (Societe des Auteurs dans les Arts Grarphiques et Plastiques)**
11 rue Berryer, 75008 Paris
*Tel:* (01) 43590979 *Fax:* (01) 45634489
*E-mail:* adagp@adagp.fr
*Web Site:* www.adagp.fr
*Key Personnel*
Dir: Jean-Marc Gutton
Founded: 1953
To administer & protect the rights of visual artists (painters, sculptors, engravers, architechts, graphists, photographers, illustrators) in matters of copyright in France.

**ADELF**, see Association des Ecrivains de Langue Francaise (ADELF)

**ADMICAL (Association pour le Developpement du Mecenat Industriel et Commercial)**
16 Rue Girardon, 75018 Paris
*Tel:* (01) 42552001 *Fax:* (01) 42557132
*E-mail:* contact@admical.org
*Web Site:* www.admical.org
*Key Personnel*
Dir: Marianne Eshet
Association for the development of business sponsorship.
Publication(s): *Cultural Sponsorship in Europe* (1999); *Le Guide Juridique et Fiscal du Mece-*nat; *L'Actualite du Mecenat* (4 times/yr); *Le Repertoire du Mecenat 2001/2002* (biennially)
ISBN Prefix(es): 2-907507

**AFNIL**, see Agence Francophone pour la Numerotation Internationale du Livre (AFNIL)

**Agence Francophone pour la Numerotation Internationale du Livre (AFNIL)**
35 rue Gregoire de Tour, 75279 Paris Cedex 06
*Tel:* (01) 44 41 29 19 *Fax:* (01) 44 41 29 03
*E-mail:* afnil@electre
*Web Site:* www.afnil.org; www.afnil.com
*Key Personnel*
Contact: Joelle Aernoudt

**AIEF**, see Association Internationale des Etudes Francaises (AIEF)

**ASFORED (Association Nationale pour la Formation et le Perfectionnement Professionnels dans les Metiers de l'Edition)**
21 rue Charles-Fourier, 75013 Paris
*Tel:* (01) 45883981 *Fax:* (01) 45815492
*E-mail:* info@asfored.org
*Web Site:* www.asfored.org
*Key Personnel*
President: Francois (de) Waresquiel
Dir: Aida Diab *E-mail:* aida.diab@asfored.org

**Association des Auteurs Autoedites** (Association of Self-Published Authors)
23 rue de la Sourdiere, 75001 Paris
*Tel:* (01) 47 03 36 64 *Fax:* (01) 43 27 20 35
*Web Site:* www.auteurs-autoedites.com
*Key Personnel*
President: Robert Hentsch *Tel:* (01) 47 45 19 73 *E-mail:* rhentsch@club-internet.fr
Founded: 1975
500 authors members. Publications include poetry, art, novels, philosophy, science, teaching health.
Number of titles published annually: 130 Print

†◇**Association Internationale de Bibliophilie** (International Association of Bibliophiles)
c/o Electre-Editions du Cercle de la Librairie, 35 rue Gregoire de Tours, 75006 Paris
*Tel:* (01) 44412800 *Fax:* (01) 43296895
*Key Personnel*
Secretary-General: Jean-Marc Chatelain
Founded: 1834
Publication(s): *Le Bulletin du Bibliophile* (biannually)

**Association internationale des Critiques litteraires (NGO)**, see International Association of Literary Critics

†◇**Association Internationale des Etudes Francaises (AIEF)** (International Association of French Studies)
One rue Victor-Cousin, 75230 Paris Cedex 05
*Fax:* (01) 40462588
*Web Site:* www.aief.eu.org
*Key Personnel*
Contact: Prof Antoine Compagnon *E-mail:* compagnon@aief.eu.org
Founded: 1949
Publication(s): *Cahiers de l'AIEF* (annually)
ISBN Prefix(es): 2-913718
Number of titles published annually: 1 Print
*Bookshop(s):* Les Belles Lettres, 95 Bd Raspail, 75006 Paris

**Cercle de la Librairie**
35 rue Gregoire-de-Tours, 75006 Paris
*Tel:* (01) 44 41 28 00 *Fax:* (01) 44 41 28 65
*E-mail:* commercial@electre.com
*Web Site:* www.electre.com

*Telex:* Lifran 270838 F
*Key Personnel*
President: Charles Henri Flammarion
Publication(s): *La Bibliographie de la France* (Bibliography of France); *Catalogue general des ouvrages parus en langue francaise* (General Catalog of Works Which Have Appeared in the French Language); *Donnees statistiques sur l'edition du Livre en France* (French Book Production Statistics); *Les Livres Disponibles* (French Books in Print); *Repertoire des Livres au Format de Poche* (List of Paperback or Pocket Edition Books); *Le Repertoire International des Editeurs et Diffuseurs de Langue Francaise* (International List of French Language Publishers & Distributors); *Repertoire international des Librairies de Langue francaise* (International List of French Language Bookshops)
*Associate Companies:* Booksellers' Circle Association of Book Trades & Industries

†◇**CISAC (Confederation Internationale des Societes d'Auteurs et de Compesiteurs)** (International Confederation of Societies of Authors & Composers)
20-26 Blvd du Parc, 92200 Neuilly/sur/Seine
*Tel:* (01) 55 62 08 50 *Fax:* (01) 55 62 08 60
*E-mail:* cisac@cisac.org
*Web Site:* www.cisac.org
*Key Personnel*
Secretary General: Eric Baptiste
President: Jean Louis Tournier
Founded: 1926

**CITL**, see College International des Traducteurs Litteraires (CITL)

**College International des Traducteurs Litteraires (CITL)** (International College of Literary Translators)
Espace Van Gogh, 13200 Arles
*Tel:* (04) 90 52 05 50 *Fax:* (04) 90 93 43 21
*E-mail:* citl@provnet.fr
*Key Personnel*
Dir: Claude Bleton
Publication(s): *Actes des Assises de la Traduction Litteraire a Arles* (1 volume annually)
*Parent Company:* Assises de la Traduction Litteraire A Arles

**Confederation Internationale des Societes d'Auteurs et de Compesiteurs**, see CISAC (Confederation Internationale des Societes d'Auteurs et de Compesiteurs)

**COPACEL**, see Groupements Francais des Fabricants de Papiers d'Impression-Ecriture (COPACEL)

†**Council of Europe Publishing**
Palais de l'Europe, 67075 Strasbourg Cedex
*Tel:* (03) 88 41 25 81 *Fax:* (03) 88 41 39 10
*E-mail:* publishing@coe.int
*Web Site:* book.coe.int
*Telex:* 870943F
*Key Personnel*
Head of Division: Mrs E Lejard-Boutsavath
Marketing & Promotion: Sophie Lobey *Tel:* (03) 88 41 22 63 *E-mail:* sophie.lobey@coe.int
Rights & Permissions Manager: Charalambos Papadopoulos *Tel:* (03) 88 412952 *E-mail:* charalambos.papadopoulos@coe.int
Founded: 1949
Official publisher of the Council of Europe & reflects many different aspects of the Council's work, addressing the main challenges facing European society & the world today. Our catalogue of over 1200 title in French & English includes topics ranging from international law, human rights, ethical & moral issues, society, environment, health, education & culture.

Subjects: Human Rights, Law, Criminology, Public Health, Sociology, Nature, Consumer Protection, Education, Sports, Culture, Social Security, Youth, Local Authorities
ISBN Prefix(es): 92-871

**CPE (Conseil Permanent des Ecrivains)**
53 rue de Verneuil, 75007 Paris
*Tel:* (01) 49 54 68 80 *Fax:* (01) 42 84 20 87
*Key Personnel*
President. Maurice Cury *Tel:* (01) 40 35 87 06

◇**Dilicom**
20, rue des Grands-Augustins, 75006 Paris
*Tel:* (01) 43 25 43 35 *Fax:* (01) 43 29 76 88
*E-mail:* contact@dilicom.net
*Web Site:* www.dilicom.net
*Key Personnel*
Dir General: Bernard de Freminville
Specialize in teleordering & teleinformation between booksellers & publishers
Electra Transmittal.

**Conseil Permanent des Ecrivains**, see CPE (Conseil Permanent des Ecrivains)

**Association des Ecrivains de Langue Francaise (ADELF)** (French Language Writers' Association)
14, rue Broussais, 75014 Paris
*Tel:* (01) 43 21 95 99 *Fax:* (01) 43 20 12 22
*Key Personnel*
President: Edmond Jouve
Secretary General: Simone Freyfus
Founded: 1926
French Language Writers' Association.
Publication(s): *Lettres et cultures de langue francaise* (biannually)

**Editions du Conseil de l'Europe**, see Council of Europe Publishing

**Federation de l'Imprimerie et de la Communaute Graphique-FICG** (Federation of French Printers & Trade Writers)
115, blvd Saint-Germain, 75006 Paris
*Tel:* (01) 46 34 21 15 *Fax:* (01) 46 33 73 34
*E-mail:* ficg@ficg.fr
*Web Site:* www.ficg.fr
*Key Personnel*
President: Francois Gutle
Chief Executive: Pascal Bovero

**Federation francaise des syndicats de librairies**, see FFSL (Federation francaise des syndicats de libraires)

**FFSL (Federation francaise des syndicats de libraires)**
43 rue de Chateaudun, 75009 Paris
*Tel:* (01) 42 82 00 03 *Fax:* (01) 42 82 10 51
*Key Personnel*
President: Jean-Luc Dewas

**FNPS (Federation nationale depresse d'information specialisee)**
37 rue de Rome, 75008 Paris
*Tel:* (01) 44 90 43 60 *Fax:* (01) 44 90 43 72
*E-mail:* contact@fnps.fr
*Web Site:* www.fnps.fr
*Key Personnel*
President: Jean-Marc Detailleur
Dir: Jean-Michel Huan
French National Federation of Special Interest Press.

◇**France Edition**
115, bd Saint-Germain, 75006 Paris
*Tel:* (01) 44 41 13 13 *Fax:* (01) 46 34 63 83
*E-mail:* info@franceedition.org
*Web Site:* www.franceedition.org
*Telex:* Lifran 270838 F
*Key Personnel*
President: Liana Levi
Dir General: Jean-Guy Boin
Specializing in promoting French books around the world, the organization of trade fairs, exhibitions, symposia, conferences & training sessions, production of catalogues devoted to specific themes, publication of a newsletter & marketing studies.
Publication(s): *La Lettre de France Edition* (marketing studies)
*Branch Office(s)*
30, rue Dinh Ngang, Hanoi, Viet Nam
*Tel:* (04) 826 4862 *Fax:* (04) 825 3411
*E-mail:* lanfevn@hn.vnn.vn
*U.S. Office(s):* French Publishers Agency/France Edition Inc, 853 Broadway, Suite 1509, New York, NY 10003-4703, United States *Tel:* 212-254-4540 *Fax:* 212-254-4540 *Web Site:* www.frenchpubagency.com

**GFFDIE**, see Groupements Francais des Fabricants de Papiers d'Impression-Ecriture (COPACEL)

**Groupements Francais des Fabricants de Papiers d'Impression-Ecriture (COPACEL)**
154, bd Haussmann, 75008 Paris
*Tel:* (01) 53 89 24 00 *Fax:* (01) 53 89 24 01
*E-mail:* info@copacel.fr
*Web Site:* www.copacel.fr
*Telex:* 651544
*Key Personnel*
President: M Claude Prince
French Manufacturer of Pocket Editions Group.

**IIEP**, see International Institute for Educational Planning (IIEP)

**Intergovernmental Copyright Committee**, see United Nations Educational, Scientific & Cultural Organization (UNESCO)

†◇**International Association of Literary Critics**
Affiliate of UNESCO
Hotel de Massa, 38, rue du Faubourg, St Jacques, 75014 Paris
*Tel:* (01) 40513300 *Fax:* (01) 43549299
*E-mail:* aicl.org@tiscalinet.it
*Web Site:* www.aicl.org
*Telex:* 206963
*Key Personnel*
President: Neria De Giovanni
Vice President: Fernando Martinho; Ryszard Matuszewski
Founded: 1970
Publication(s): *Revue* (biannually)

†‡**International Association of Universities**
One Rue Miollis, 75732 Paris Cedex 15
*Tel:* (01) 45 68 48 00 *Fax:* (01) 47 34 76 05
*E-mail:* iau@unesco.org
*Web Site:* www.unesco.org/iau
*Key Personnel*
Secretary General: Eva Egron-Polak *E-mail:* eegron.iau@unesco.org
Dir, Research: Guy R Neave *E-mail:* neave.iau@unesco.org
Founded: 1950
International non-governmental organization.
Publication(s): *Higher Education Policy* (quarterly, journal); *International Handbook of Universities* (biannually); *Monographs: Issues in Higher Education* (biannually); *World List of Universities*

†‡**International Chamber of Commerce**
38 Cours Albert 1er, 75008 Paris

*Tel:* (01) 49 53 28 28 *Fax:* (01) 49 53 28 59
*E-mail:* icclib@ibnet.com; icc@iccwbo.org
*Web Site:* www.iccwbo.org
*Telex:* 650770 ICCHQ *Cable:* INCOMERC-PARIS
*Key Personnel*
Secretary General: Maria Livanos
General Counsel: Emmanuel Jolivet
ISBN Prefix(es): 92-842

†◇**International Council on Archives** (Conseil International des Archives)
60 rue des Francs-Bourgeois, 75003 Paris
*Tel:* (01) 40 27 63 49; (01) 40 27 63 06; (01) 40 27 61 34 *Fax:* (01) 42 72 20 65
*E-mail:* ica@ica.org
*Web Site:* www.ica.org
*Key Personnel*
Secretary General: Mrs Joan Van Albada *Tel:* (01) 40276349 *E-mail:* vanalbada@ica.org
Publication(s): *Archivum*; *Janus*; *N'Existe Plus*

†‡**International Institute for Educational Planning (IIEP)**
7-9, rue Eugene-Delacroix, 75116 Paris
*Tel:* (01) 45 03 77 00 *Fax:* (01) 40 72 83 66
*E-mail:* information@iiep.unesco.org
*Web Site:* www.unesco.org/iiep
*Telex:* 620074 *Cable:* EDUPLAN PARIS
*Key Personnel*
Assistant Programme Specialist: Estelle Zadra *E-mail:* e.zadra@iiep.unesco.org
Chief, Communication & Publications: Ian Denison
Founded: 1963
Established by UNESCO, IIEP is an international center for advanced training & research in educational planning. The Institute's aim is to contribute to the development of education by expanding both knowledge & the supply of competent professionals in the field of educational planning. In this endeavor the Institute cooperates with interested training & research institutions throughout the world. IIEP is financed by UNESCO & by voluntary contributions from individual member states. The program & budget of the Institute are approved by its own Governing Board. A catalogue of publications is available on request.
Subjects: Educational Planning (Administration & Management, Methologies, Manpower & Employment, School Locations, Non-formal, Adult & Rural Education & Literacy)
ISBN Prefix(es): 92-803

†**ISSN International Centre**
20 rue Bachaumont, 75002 Paris
*Tel:* (01) 44 88 22 20 *Fax:* (01) 44 88 60 96; (01) 40 26 32 43
*E-mail:* issnic@issn.org
*Web Site:* www.issn.org
*Key Personnel*
Dir: Francoise Pelle *E-mail:* pelle@issn.org
International Bibliographic database regarding serial publications.
Publication(s): *ISSN Register* (quarterly on CD-ROM (ISSN compact) or frequently on the web (ISSN online)); *List of Serial Title Word Abbreviations-Cumulated Edition* (1998)

**Ministere des Affaires Etrangeres Division de L'Ecrit et des Mediatheques**
244, bd Saint-Germain, 75007 Paris
*Tel:* (01) 43 17 53 53 *Fax:* (01) 43 17 88 83
*Web Site:* www.france.diplomatie.gouv.fr
*Key Personnel*
Dir: Yves Mabin
Ministry of Foreign Affairs.
*Parent Company:* Association pour la diffusion de la pensee francaise (ADPF), 6 rue Ferrus, 75683 Paris Cedex 14

**OECD**, see Organization for Economic Cooperation & Development (OECD)

**†Office International des Epizooties** (World Organisation for Animal Health)
12 Rue de Prony, 75017 Paris
*Tel:* (01) 44 15 18 88 *Fax:* (01) 42 67 09 87
*E-mail:* oie@oie.int
*Web Site:* www.oie.int
*Telex:* EPIZOTI 642285F
*Key Personnel*
Editorial Dir: Dr Bernard Vallat
Sales & Marketing Agent: Ms Tamara Benicasa
Founded: 1924
Subjects: Veterinary science & world animal health
Publication(s): *Disease Information* (weekly, periodical); *World Animal Health in 2001* (periodical, 2002)
ISBN Prefix(es): 92-9044
Total Titles: 44 Print
Distributed by SMPF Inc

**†Organization for Economic Cooperation & Development (OECD)**
2, rue Andre-Pascal, 75775 Paris Cedex 16
*Tel:* (01) 45 24 82 00 *Fax:* (01) 45 24 85 00
*E-mail:* news.contact@oecd.org
*Web Site:* www.oecd.org
*Telex:* 640048 *Cable:* DEVELOPECONOMIE
*Key Personnel*
Secretary General: Donald Johnston
Founded: 1960
Subjects: Economics, Statistics, Environment, Energy, Education, Transportation, Agriculture, Development, Finance, Urban Affairs, Labor, Science & Technology, Tourism, Consumer policy, Social problems
ISBN Prefix(es): 92-64; 92-821
*Showroom(s):* 33 rue Octave Feuillet, 75016 Paris
*Bookshop(s):* 33 rue Octave Feuillet, 75016 Paris

**SACEM (Societe des Auteurs Copositeurs et Editeurs de Musique)**
225 av Charles de Gaulle, 92528 Neuilly-sur-Seine Cedex
*Tel:* (01) 47 15 47 15 *Fax:* (01) 47 15 47 86
*E-mail:* communication@sacem.fr
*Web Site:* www.sacem.fr
*Telex:* 630 312 musica
*Key Personnel*
President: Jacques Demarny

**SELF Syndicate of French Language Authors**
18 rue Theodore Deck, 75015 Paris
*Tel:* (01) 40600501 *Fax:* (01) 46707395
*Key Personnel*
President: Benjamin Lambert; Victoria Therame; Maguelonne Toussaint-Samat
Secretary General: Gerard Gaillaguet
Publication(s): *Ecrivains*

**SLAM**, see Syndicat National de la Librairie Ancienne et Moderne (SLAM)

**SLUT**, see Syndicat des Libraires Universitaires et Techniques

**Societe des auteurs dans les arts graphiques, plastiques et photographiques**, see ADAGP (Societe des Auteurs dans les Grarphiques et Plastiques)

**Societe des Auteurs Compositeurs et Editeurs de Musique**, see SACEM (Societe des Auteurs Copositeurs et Editeurs de Musique)

**Standard Book Numbering Agency**, see Agence Francophone pour la Numerotation Internationale du Livre (AFNIL)

**Standard Book Numbering Agency**, see Unesco Books & Copyright Division, USBN agency

**Syndicat des ecrivains de langue francaise**, see SELF Syndicate of French Language Authors

**Syndicat des Libraires Universitaires et Techniques**
40, rue Gregoire de Tours, 75006 Paris
*Tel:* (01) 43 29 88 79 *Fax:* (467) 525905
*Key Personnel*
President: Dominique Torreilles
Secretary: Janine de Puniet

**Syndicat National de la Librairie Ancienne et Moderne (SLAM)** (National Association of Antiquarian & Modern Booksellers)
4, rue Git-le-Coeur, 75006 Paris
*Tel:* (01) 43 29 46 38 *Fax:* (01) 43 25 41 63
*E-mail:* slam-livre@wanadoo.fr
*Web Site:* www.slam-livre.fr
*Key Personnel*
President: Alain Marchiset
Publication(s): *Guide du Livre Ancien et des libraires membres du Syndicat national de la Librairie Ancienne et Moderne*

**◇Syndicat National de l'Edition** (National Union of Publishers)
115 Blvd Saint-Germain, 75006 Paris
*Tel:* (01) 4441 4050 *Fax:* (01) 4441 4077
*Web Site:* www.snedition.fr
*Key Personnel*
President: Serge Eyrolles
Deputy General: Jean Sarzana
Publication(s): *Abeviations des principales references en matiere juridique* (1993); *Actes du colloque sur l'edition scientifique francaise*; *L'edition de livres en France* (annually, statistics); *Fiches techniques-pays (etudes du marche du livre a l'etranger)* (RFA, Espagne, Royaume-Uni); *Plaquette de representation de l'edition francaise*
ISBN Prefix(es): 2-909677

**ULF (Union des Libraires de France)**, see Union des Libraires de France (ULF)

**UNESCO**, see United Nations Educational, Scientific & Cultural Organization (UNESCO)

**Unesco Books & Copyright Division, USBN agency**
35 rue Gregoire de Tour, 75279 Paris Cedex 06
*Tel:* (01) 44 41 29 19 *Fax:* (01) 44 41 29 03
*E-mail:* afnil@electre.com
*Web Site:* www.afnil.org; www.afnil.com
*Telex:* 204461; 270602
*Key Personnel*
Contact: Michele Fournier

**Union des Libraires de France (ULF)**
40 rue Gregoire-de-Tours, 75006 Paris
*Tel:* (01) 43 29 88 79 *Fax:* (01) 43 29 88 79
*Key Personnel*
President: Eric Hardin
General Delegate: Marie-Dominique Doumenc
Union of French Booksellers.
Publication(s): *La Voix des Libraires*; *Le Bullentin de l'ULF*

**†◇United Nations Educational, Scientific & Cultural Organization (UNESCO)**
7 Place de Fontenoy, 75352 Paris
*Tel:* (01) 45 68 10 00 *Fax:* (01) 45 67 16 90
*E-mail:* clearing-house@unesco.org
*Web Site:* www.unesco.org
*Telex:* 204461; 270602 *Cable:* UNESCO PARIS
*Key Personnel*
Dir-General: Koichiro Matsuura

Dir, UNESCO Publishing: Milagros Del Corral
Rights: Alastair McLurg; Michiko Tanaka
Promotion: Cristina Laje; Jeanette Coulibaly
Founded: 1946
To date, UNESCO books have been translated into more than seventy languages. UNESCO acts as Standard Book Numbering Agency, administering ISBNs for UN publications. It also maintains responsibility, within its Copyright Division, for the Intergovernmental Copyright Committee. UNESCO publishes seven periodicals, including the illustrated monthly reviews, The Unesco Courier & World Heritage Review.
Subjects: Education, Science, Technology, Social Science, Culture, Communications, Human Rights, Art
ISBN Prefix(es): 92-3
Number of titles published annually: 152 Print
Total Titles: 6,000 Print

# Gambia

**Standard Book Numbering Agency**
Gambia National Library, RG Pye Lane, Banjul
*Tel:* 226491 *Fax:* 223776
*E-mail:* national.library@ganet.gm
*Key Personnel*
Chief Librarian: Abdou Wally Mbye
Founded: 1946
National/public library service.
*Branch Office(s)*
Brikama Branch Library *Tel:* 484111 (Western division)

# Germany

**AG BDB**, see Arbeitsgemeinschaft der Blindenschrift-Druckereien und Bibliotheken (AG BDB)

**Arbeitsgemeinschaft der Blindenschrift-Druckereien und Bibliotheken (AG BDB)** (Association of Braille Publishing Houses & Libraries)
c/o Deutsche Blindenstudienanstalt (BLISTA), Am Schlag 8, 35037 Marburg
*Tel:* (06421) 60 60 *Fax:* (06421) 60 62 29
*E-mail:* info@blista.de
*Web Site:* www.blista.de
*Key Personnel*
President: Rainer F V Witte

**Arbeitsgemeinschaft von Jugendbuchverlagen e v** (The Alliance of Publishers of Children's Books)
c/o Thienemann Verlag, Blumenstr 36, 70182 Stuttgart
*Tel:* (0711) 2843 440 *Fax:* (0711) 2483 622
*E-mail:* info@avj-online.de
*Web Site:* www.avj-online.de
*Key Personnel*
Chairman: Mathias Berg
Manager: Susanne Ziemer
Publication(s): *Kinder und Jugendbuchverlage von A bis Z*

**Arbeitskreis fur Jugendliteratur eV**
Metzstr 14c, 81667 Munich
*Tel:* (089) 45 80 80 6 *Fax:* (089) 45 80 80 88
*E-mail:* info@jugendliteratur.org
*Web Site:* www.jugendliteratur.org

*Key Personnel*
Man Dir: Franz Meyer
Youth Literature Committee (Section of IBBY).
Publication(s): *Auswahlliste zum Deutschen Jugendliteraturpreis* (annually); *Buch der Jugend* (annually); *Das Bilderbuch*; *Das blane Buch*; *Das Kinderbuch*; *Julet* (quarterly)

### ◇Borsenverein des Deutschen Buchhandels eV
Grosser Hirschgraben 17-21, 60313 Frankfurt am Main
*Tel:* (069) 1306-0 *Fax:* (069) 1306-201
*E-mail:* info@boev.de
*Web Site:* www.boev.de
*Key Personnel*
General Manager: Dr Harald Heker
Head Information Department: Eugen Emmerling
  *Tel:* (069) 1306-291 *Fax:* (069) 1306-294
  *E-mail:* emmerling@boev.de
Publication(s): *Adressbuch fuer den deutschsprachigen Buchhandel* (German-Speaking Book Trade Directory); *Archiv fuer Geschichte des Buchwesens* (Book History Archives); *Boersenblatt fuer den Deutschen Buchhandel* (German Book Trade Journal); *Buch und Buchhandel in Zahlen* (Books & the Book Trade in Figures); *BuchJournal* (a general magazine for booksellers' customers); *Deutsche Bibliographie* (German Bibliography); *Neuerscheinungen-Sofortdienst (CIP)* (New Titles Express Service CIP); *VLB Verzeichnis lieferbarer Buecher* (German Books in Print)
*Branch Office(s)*
Berliner Bureau, Schiffbauerdamm 5, 10117 Berlin *Tel:* (030) 2800783-0 *Fax:* (030) 2800783-50
Leipziger Buero, Gerichtsweg 28, 04103 Leipzig *Tel:* (0341) 9954-110 *Fax:* (0341) 9954-113

### Boersenverein des Deutschen Buchhandels, Landesverband Baden-Wuerttemberg eV
(Association of Publishers & Booksellers in Baden-Wuerttemberg eV)
Paulinenstr 53, 70178 Stuttgart
*Tel:* (0711) 61941-0 *Fax:* (0711) 61941-44
*E-mail:* post@buchhandelsverband.de
*Web Site:* www.buchhandelsverband.de
*Key Personnel*
Man Dir: Johannes Scherer
Association of Publishers & Booksellers in Baden-Wuerttemberg.

### Borromausverein eV
Wittelsbacherring 9, 53115 Bonn
*Tel:* (0228) 7258-0 *Fax:* (0228) 7258-189
*E-mail:* info@borro.de
*Web Site:* www.borro.de
*Key Personnel*
President: Norbert Trippen
Publisher: Rolf Pitsch

### Bundesverband Deutscher Kunstverleger eV
(Association of German Art Editors)
Darmstaedter Landstr 3, 60594 Frankfurt Main
Mailing Address: Postfach 700 210, 60552 Frankfurt Main
*Tel:* (069) 629120 *Fax:* (069) 629120
*Web Site:* www.bdkv.de
*Key Personnel*
Chairman: Klaus Gerrit Friese; Ruth Leuchter
Contact: Birgit Maria Sturm *E-mail:* sturm@bdkv.de
Founded: 1989
The Federal Association of German Art Publishers is the ideal Sponsor of Kunstkoeln-International Art Fair for Art Brut, Editions & Art after 1980.
Membership(s): Arbeitskreis Deutscher Kusthandelsverbande.

### †◇Conseil International des Associations de Bibliotheques de Theologie
Postfach 250104, 50517 Cologne
*Tel:* (0221) 3382109 *Fax:* (0221) 3382103
*Key Personnel*
President: Dr Andre J Geuns
Secretary: Dr I Dumke

### Deutscher Komponisten-Interessenverband eV
(German Composers Association)
kadettenweg 80 b, 12205 Berlin
*Tel:* (030) 84 31 05 80 *Fax:* (030) 84 31 05 82
*E-mail:* info@komponistenverband.org
*Web Site:* www.dkiv.allmusic.de
*Key Personnel*
President: Karl Heinz Wahren
Vice President: Prof Harald Banter
Manager: Manuel Neuendorf
Publication(s): *Handbuch "Komponisten der Gegnwart im Deutschen Komponisten-Interessenverband"* (1995)

### †◇Gutenberg-Gesellschaft eV (Gutenberg Society)
Liebfrauenplatz 5, 55116 Mainz
*Tel:* (06131) 22 64 20 *Fax:* (06131) 23 35 30
*E-mail:* gutenberg-gesellschaft@freenet.de
*Web Site:* www.gutenberg-gesellschaft.uni-mainz.de
*Key Personnel*
President: Jens Beutel
Vice President: Hannetraud Schultheiss
Secretary General: Karl Delorme
Founded: 1901
International Association for Past & Present History of the Art of Printing.
Subjects: Past & Present History of the Art of Printing & of the Book
Publication(s): *Gutenberg-Jahrbuch*; *Kleine Drucke*; *Sonder-Veroeffentlichungen*
ISBN Prefix(es): 3-7755

### Hessischer Verleger- und Buchhandler-Verband eV
Hessischer Verleger-und Buchhandler-Verband eV, Villa Clementine, Frankfurterstr 1, 65189 Wiesbaden
*Tel:* (0611) 166 600 *Fax:* (0611) 166 6059
*E-mail:* briefe@hessenbuchhandel.de
*Web Site:* www.hessenbuchhandel.de
*Key Personnel*
Chairman: Michael Lemling
Manager: Peter Brunner
Hessen Publishers' & Booksellers' Federation.

I A S A, see International Association of Sound & Audiovisual Archives

### †International Association of Sound & Audiovisual Archives
c/o Suedwestrundfunk, Documentation & Archives Dept, 76522 Baden-Baden
Mailing Address: Postfach 820, 76522 Baden-Baden
*Tel:* (07221) 9293487 *Fax:* (07221) 9294199
*Web Site:* www.llgc.org.uk/iasa/
*Key Personnel*
Secretary General: Albrecht Haefner
  *E-mail:* albrecht.haefner@swr.de
Founded: 1969
A non-governmental UNESCO-affiliated organization established to function as a medium for international co-operation between archives which preserve recorded sound & audiovisual documents.
Publication(s): *IASA Information Bulletin* (quarterly); *IASA Journal* (biannual)
ISBN Prefix(es): 0-946475

### International Council of Theological Library
**Associations**, see Conseil International des Associations de Bibliotheques de Theologie

### †◇International ISBN Agency, International ISMN Agency
Staatsbibliothek zu Berlin - Preussischer Kulturbesitz, Potsdamerstr 33, 10785 Berlin
*Tel:* (030) 266-2498; (030) 266-2496; (030) 266-2336 *Fax:* (030) 266-2378
*E-mail:* isbn@sbb.spk-berlin.de; ismn@sbb.spk.berlin.de
*Web Site:* isbn-international.org; ismn-international.org
*Key Personnel*
Dir: Dr Hartmut Walravens
ISMN Coordinator: Katrin Spitzer; Dr Ulrich Wegner
Founded: 1972
This is the international ISBN office. For national offices & further details please see the ISBN System section of this book.
Publication(s): *International ISBN Users' Manual*; *International ISMN Users' Manual*; *ISBN Newsletter*; *ISMN Newsletter*; *Music Publishers' International ISMN Directory*; *Publishers' International ISBN Directory*; *The ISBN & its Uses* (video-film & sound-slide-show)

### †International ISMN Agency
Potsdamer Str 33, 10785 Berlin
*Tel:* (030) 266-2496; (030) 266-2498; (030) 266 2338 *Fax:* (030) 266-2378
*E-mail:* ismn@sbb.spk.berlin.de
*Web Site:* ismn-international.org
*Key Personnel*
Dir: Dr Hartmut Walravens
Founded: 1994
Agency for the standard numbering of sheet music.
Publication(s): *ISMN Newsletter*; *ISMN Users' Manual*; *Publishers' International ISMN Directory*

### †◇Internationale Jugendbibliothek
(International Youth Library)
Schloss Blutenburg, 81247 Munich
*Tel:* (089) 891211-0 *Fax:* (089) 8117553
*E-mail:* bib@ijb.de
*Web Site:* www.ijb.de
*Key Personnel*
Chairwoman Foundations Board of Governors: Christa Spangenberg
Dir: Dr Barbara Scharioth
Publicity: Carola Gade *Tel:* (089) 891211-30
  *E-mail:* presse@ijb.de
Founded: 1949
Publication(s): *IJB Report* (biannually); *The White Ravens* (annual selection of international children's & youth literature)

### Internationale Vereinigung fuer Geschichte und Gegenwart der Druckkunst eV, see Gutenberg-Gesellschaft eV

**ISBN**, see International ISBN Agency, International ISMN Agency

**ISMN**, see International ISMN Agency

### Landesverband der Verleger und Buchhaendler Rheinland-Pfalz eV
Frankfurter Str 1, 65189 Wiesbaden
*Tel:* (06131) 234035 *Fax:* (06131) 230364
Rhineland-Palatinate Provincial Federation of Publishers & Booksellers.

**LIBER**, see Ligue des Bibliotheques Europeennes de Recherche (LIBER)

†◇**Ligue des Bibliotheques Europeennes de Recherche (LIBER)** (League of European Research Libraries)
Universitat Bremen, FB 10, GW 1, B 1200, 28334 Bremen
Mailing Address: Postfach 330440, 28334 Bremen
*Tel:* (0421) 2183361
*Web Site:* www.kb.dk/guests/intl/liber
*Key Personnel*
President: Erland Kolding Nielsen *Tel:* (045) 33 47 4301 *Fax:* (045) 33 32 98 46 *E-mail:* ekn@kb.dk
Vice President: Hans Geleijnse *Tel:* (031) 13 466 2240 *E-mail:* hans.geleijnse@uvt.nl
Publication(s): *European Research Libraries Co-operation* (The Liber Quarterly)

**Norddeutscher Verleger- und Buchhaendler-Verband eV**
Schwanenwik 38, 22087 Hamburg
*Tel:* (040) 22 54 79 *Fax:* (040) 2 29 85 14
North German Publishers' and Booksellers' Federation.

◇**O Gracklauer Verlag und Bibliographische Agentur GmbH** (O Gracklauer Publishers & Bibliographic Agency)
Wallotstr 7A, 14193 Berlin
*Tel:* (030) 825 81 39 *Fax:* (030) 826 20 39
*E-mail:* info@gracklauer.de
*Web Site:* www.gracklauer.de
*Key Personnel*
Owner & Man Dir: Rose M Meerwein
Suppliers of bibliographic information, title & copyright research.

†◇**PEN Club-German Speaking Writers Abroad**
PO Box 420, 248, 50896 Cologne
*E-mail:* intpen@dircon.co.uk
*Web Site:* www.exilpen.de
*Key Personnel*
Secretary: Uwe Westphal
Contact: Peter Finkelgruen
Founded: 1934
Writers association.

**Presse-Grosso**, see Presse-Grosso-Bundesverband Deutscher Buch-, Zeitungs-und Zeitschriften-Grossisten eV

**Presse-Grosso-Bundesverband Deutscher Buch-, Zeitungs-und Zeitschriften-Grossisten eV**
Haendelstr 25-29, 50674 Cologne
*Tel:* (0221) 9213370 *Fax:* (0221) 92133744
*E-mail:* bvpg@bvpg.de
*Web Site:* www.pressegrosso.de
*Key Personnel*
Chairman: Weiner Schiessl
Manager: Gerd Kapp
Founded: 1950
Federation of German Wholesalers of Books, Newspapers and Periodicals (also known as Presse-Grosso).

**International Standard Book Numbering Agency**, see International Standard Buchnummer GmbH

**International Standard Buchnummer GmbH**
Grosser Hirschbraben 17-21, 60311 Frankfurt am Main
Mailing Address: Postfach 100442, 60004 Frankfurt am Main
*Tel:* (069) 1306-387 *Fax:* (069) 1306-258
*E-mail:* lehr@bhv.de
*Web Site:* www.german-isbn.org

*Key Personnel*
Dir: Manfred Gravelius
The Booksellers' Association, Documentation & Data Processing Department (Standard Book Numbering Agency).

**Stiftung Lesen**
Fischtorplatz 23, 55116 Mainz
*Tel:* (06131) 2 88 90-0 *Fax:* (06131) 23 03 33
*E-mail:* mail@stiftunglesen.de
*Web Site:* www.stiftunglesen.de
*Key Personnel*
Manager: Prof Hilmar Hoffmann

**UIE**, see UNESCO Institute for Education (UIE)

†◇**UNESCO Institute for Education (UIE)**
Feldbrunnenstr 58, 20148 Hamburg
*Tel:* (040) 4480410 *Fax:* (040) 4107723
*E-mail:* uie@unesco.org
*Web Site:* www.unesco.org/education/uie
*Key Personnel*
Dir: Dr Adama Ouane *E-mail:* a.ouane@unesco.org
Founded: 1951
The UIE was created in 1951 with the financial support of UNESCO & a number of member states. It is funded by Germany, UNESCO & other donors, & housed in premises provided by the City of Hamburg. It is a research, training & dissemination center which has enabled more than 2000 scholars to participate in international cooperative research projects & has developed a particular interest in lifelong education. Major areas of the current research program include the development of nonconventional approaches to primary education for out-of-school children, post-literacy & functional literacy for adults & young people, monitoring & evaluation of nonformal education programs, literacy exchange network, the legislative environment for adult education, the empowerment of women through education. Publications include over 120 titles in English, French, Spanish & Arabic & the bimonthly International Review of Education, for which there are concessionary subscription rates for developing countries. In the field of lifelong education & related aspects, it has published over 60 books under the series of UIE Monographs, Case Studies, Advances in Lifelong Education, UIE-Studies on Post-literacy in Industrialized Countries, other theoretical studies on Post-literacy & Continuing Education, & UIE-Studies on Functional Illiteracy in Industrialized Countries & Handbooks & Reference books, based on both theoretical & operational research.
Subjects: Literacy, Non Formal Basic Education, Continuing Education, Functional Illiteracy in Industrialized Countries, Nonformal Education, Adult Education & lifelong learning
ISBN Prefix(es): 92-820
*Parent Company:* UNESCO, Paris, France

**Verband der Schulbuchverlage eV** (Association of Text Book Publishers)
Zeppelinallee 33, 60325 Frankfurt am Main
*Tel:* (069) 70 30 75 *Fax:* (069) 70 79 01 69
*E-mail:* verband@vds-bildungsmedien.de
*Web Site:* www.vds-bildungsmedien.de
*Key Personnel*
Chairman: Gerd-Dietrich Schmidt
Man Dir: Andreas Baer *E-mail:* baer@vds-bildungsmedien.de

**Verband der Verlage- und Buchhaendlungen Berlin-Brandenburg eV**
Luetzowstr 33, 10785 Berlin
*Tel:* (030) 26 39 18 0 *Fax:* (030) 26 39 18 18
*E-mail:* verband@berliner-buchhandel.de

*Web Site:* www.berliner-buchhandel.de
*Key Personnel*
President: Dietrich Simon
Manager: Detlef Bluhm
Publishers' & Booksellers' Association Berlin-Brandenburg.

**Verband der Verlage und Buchhandlungen in Nordrhein-Westfalen eV** (Association of Publishers & Booksellers at North Rhine Westphalia)
Marienstr 41, 40210 Duesseldorf
*Tel:* (0211) 8 64 45-22 *Fax:* (0211) 32 44 97
*E-mail:* info@buchnrw.de
*Web Site:* www.buchnrw.de
*Key Personnel*
Secretary: Herbert Becker

◇**Verband Deutscher Antiquare eV** (German Antiquarian Booksellers' Association)
Geschaftsstelle, Herr Norbert Munsch, Seeblick 1, 56459 Elbingen
*Tel:* (06435) 909147 *Fax:* (06435) 909148
*E-mail:* buch@antiquare.de
*Web Site:* www.antiquare.de
*Key Personnel*
President: Herrn Jochen Granier
Vice President: Fr Inge Utzt
Founded: 1952
Publication(s): *Katalog zur Stuttgarter Antiquariatsmesse* (annually); *Mitgliederverzeichnis* (biannually); *zur Koelner Antiquariatsmesse empfohlen von der Internationalen Liga der Antiquariatsbuchhaendler ILAB; Katalog zu den Antiquariatstagen in Koeln* (annually)

**Verband Deutscher Auskunfts und Verzichnismedien**
Heerdter Sandberg 30, 40549 Duesseldorf
*Tel:* (0211) 577995-0 *Fax:* (0211) 577995-44
*E-mail:* info@vdav.org
*Web Site:* www.vdav.de
*Key Personnel*
Dir: Stephanie Hollstein *E-mail:* redaktion@vdav.de
Association of German Directory Publishers.

**Verband katholischer Verleger und Buchhaendler eV**
Adenaueralle 176, 53113 Bonn
*Tel:* (0228) 2421560 *Fax:* (0228) 2421561
*E-mail:* vkb2000@aol.com
*Key Personnel*
Manager: Peter J Kerp
Federation of Catholic Publishers & Booksellers.

**Verlegervereinigung Rechtsinformatik eV**
c/o Carl Heymanns Verlag, Luxemburger Str 449, 50939 Cologne
*Tel:* (0221) 94373-0 *Fax:* (0221) 94373-901
*E-mail:* marketing@heymanns.com
*Web Site:* www.heymanns.com
*Key Personnel*
Chairman: Bertram Gallus
Association of Publishers of Legal Documentation.

**Verwertungsgesellschaft Wort** (Collecting Society Word)
Goethestr 49, 80336 Munich
*Tel:* (089) 5 14 12-0 *Fax:* (089) 5141258
*E-mail:* vgw@vgwort.de
*Web Site:* www.vgwort.de
*Key Personnel*
Chairman: Lutz Franke
General Manager: Prof Ferdinand Melichar, PhD *E-mail:* f.melichar@vgwort.de
Founded: 1958
Copyright society representing authors & publishers of literary & scientific works.
*Branch Office(s)*
Verwertungsgesellschaft Wort Berliner

Buero, Koethener Str 44, 10963 Berlin
*Tel:* (030) 261 27 51 *Fax:* (030) 23 00 36 29
*E-mail:* vgbuero@t-online.de

# Ghana

**†Association of African Universities**
(Association des Universites Africaines)
African Universities House, 11 Aviation Rd, Airport Residential Area, Accra
Mailing Address: PO Box 5744, Accra-North
*Tel:* (021) 774495; (021) 761588 *Fax:* (021) 774821
*E-mail:* info@aau.org
*Web Site:* www.aau.org
*Telex:* 2284 Adua *Cable:* AFUNIV ACCRA
*Key Personnel*
President: Prof George Benneh
Secretary-General: Prof Akilagpa Sawyerr
*E-mail:* secgen@aau.org
Founded: 1967
Subjects: Higher Education in Africa

**Standard Book Numbering Agency**
c/o Ghana Library Board, George Padmore Research Library on African Affairs, PO Box 2970, Accra
*Tel:* (021) 223526; (021) 228402 *Fax:* (021) 247768
*E-mail:* GeorgePadmore@Africanmail.com; Padmoreslib@yahoo.co.uk
*Key Personnel*
Contact: Sarah Dorothy Kanda; Omari Mensah Tenkovang
*Parent Company:* Ghana Library Board

**†◇Union of Writers of the African Peoples**
(Union des Ecrivains Negro Africains)
c/o Ghana Association of Writers, PO Box 4414, Accra
*Tel:* (021) 774944 *Fax:* (021) 774250
*Key Personnel*
President: Atukwei Okai
General Secretary: J E Allotey-Pappoe
Objectives include the operation of a writers' publishing co-operative & the encouragement of the use of Swahili as the common language of all black African peoples.
Publication(s): *African World Alternatives*

**†◇University Bookshop**
University of Ghana, PO Box 25, Legon
*Tel:* (021) 500398 *Fax:* (021) 500398
*E-mail:* unibks@ug.gn.apc.org
*Key Personnel*
Manager: Emmanuel K H Tonyigah
Founded: 1948

# Greece

**Hellenic Federation of Publishers & Booksellers**
73 Themistocleous St, 106 83 Athens
*Tel:* 2103300924; 213300926 *Fax:* 213301 617
*E-mail:* poev@otenet.gr
*Key Personnel*
President: Georgios Dardanos
Dir: Ms E Filippopoulos
Membership(s): International Association of Publishers; Federation of European Publishing; Federation of European Booksellers.
Publication(s): *Catalogue of the Greek Children's Books*; *General Catalogue of Greek Publishers*

**Standard Book Numbering Agency**
National Library of Greece, National Centre of ISBN, 32 Panepistimiou Ave, 106 79 Athens
*Tel:* 2103382601; 2103382581 *Fax:* 2103608 495
*E-mail:* ebe@nlg.gr
*Web Site:* www.nlg.gr
*Telex:* 216270 ypth gr
*Key Personnel*
ISBN Administrator: Mrs Stauroula Verveniotou
*E-mail:* verveniotou@nlg.gr

**Syllogos Ekdoton Bibliopolon Athinon**
(Publishers & Booksellers' Association of Athens)
73 Themistokleous St, 106 83 Athens
*Tel:* 2103830029; 2103303268 *Fax:* 210 3823222
*E-mail:* seva@otenet.ge
*Key Personnel*
President: Eleni Kanaki
Membership(s): Hellenic Federation of Publishers & Booksellers.
Subjects: Issues concerning the book industry

# Guatemala

**Comite Gremial de Editores de Guatemala**
10a Calle 7-55 Z, Zona 1, Guatemala City
*Tel:* (02) 82 68 15 *Fax:* (02) 2329053; (02) 2518381
*Key Personnel*
President: Santa Irene Piedra

# Guinea

**SAEC**, see La Societe Africaine d'Edition et de Communication (SAEC)

**La Societe Africaine d'Edition et de Communication (SAEC)**
BP 6826, Conakry
*Tel:* 45 34 44 *Fax:* 45 34 44
*E-mail:* dtniane@eti-bull.net
*Key Personnel*
PDG de la SAEC: Mr Djibril Tamsir Niane
Editorial Secretary: Mr Daouda Tamsir Niane

# Guyana

**CARICOM**, see Regional ISBN Agency (CARICOM)

**Regional ISBN Agency (CARICOM)**
Caribbean Community Secretariat, Avenue of the Republic, Georgetown
Mailing Address: PO Box 10827, Georgetown
*Tel:* (02) 226 9280 *Fax:* (02) 226 7816
*E-mail:* carisec1@caricom.org; carisec2@caricom.org; carisec3@caricom.og
*Web Site:* www.caricom.org *Cable:* CARIBSEC GUYANA
*Key Personnel*
ISBN Administrator: Maureen Newton *Tel:* (02) 223 7127
Publication(s): *Aging in the Commonwealth Caribbean*; *The Caribbean Community in the 1980s: report by a group of Caribbean experts*; *Caribbean development to the Year 2000: chal-*

*lenges, prospects and policies*; *CARICOM Model Legislation on Citzenship; Domestic Violence; Equality for Women in Employment; Equal Pay; Inheritance; Maintenance & Maintenance Order: Sexual Harassment & Sexual Offences*; *CARICOM Perspective*; *CARICOM Secretary-General's report* (annually); *CARICOM'S trade: a quick reference to some summary data: 1980-1996; CCS Current Awareness Service: New Additions: Articles* (occasional); *Charter of Civil Society for the Caribbean Community; Common External Tariff of the Caribbean Common Market: based on the Harmonised Commodity Description & Coding System (HS) 2nd ed; Curriculum Guidelines for Family Life Education in the Caribbean: Education for Living; Directory of Caribbean Publishers, 3rd ed; Employment Problem in CARICOM Countries: the Role of Education & Training in its Existence & its Solution; External Public Debt & Balance of Payment of CARICOM Member States 1980-1996; National Accounts Digest 1980-1994; Regional Census Office, Volume of Basic Tables for Sixteen CARICOM Countries; Regional Cultural Policy of the Caribbean Community; Removing the Barriers: facts on the CARICOM Single Market & Economy; Report on a Comprehensive Review of the Programmes, Institutions & Organisations of the Caribbean Community; Socio-economic Conditions of Children & Youth in CARICOM Countries: a Situational Analysis; Towards Equity in Development: a Report on the Status of Women in Sixteen Commonwealth Caribbean Countries; Treaty Establishing the Caribbean Community, Chaguaramas, 4th July 1973*

**Standard Book Numbering Agency**, see Regional ISBN Agency (CARICOM)

# Hong Kong

**Books Registration Office**
Leisure & Cultural Services Dept, Room 805, 8/F, Lai Chi Kok Government Offices, 19 Lai Wan Rd, Lai Chi Kok, Kowloon
*Tel:* 218 09 145; 218 09 146 *Fax:* 218 09 841
*E-mail:* bro@lcsd.gov.hk
*Web Site:* www.lcsd.gov.hk
*Key Personnel*
ISBN Administrator & Librarian: Miss Chow Kam-sheung

**Government Information Services**
3rd-8th floors, Murray Bldg, Garden Road, Central
*Tel:* 2842 8777 *Fax:* 2845 9078
*Web Site:* www.info.gov.hk/isd
*Key Personnel*
Dir of Information Services: Yvonne Ying Pik Choi *Tel:* 2842 8728
Deputy Dir of Information Services: Juliana Wai Fan Chen Yam; Mr Kwok Wah Mak

**Standard Book Numbering Agency**, see Books Registration Office

# Hungary

**Magyar Iroszoevetseg**
Bajza utca 18, 1062 Budapest

Mailing Address: Pf 546, 1397 Budapest
*Tel:* (01) 322-8840; (01) 322-0631 *Fax:* (01) 321-3419
*Key Personnel*
President: Marton Kalasz
Hungarian Writers' Association.
Publication(s): *Kortars*; *Magyar Naplo* (journal)

◇**Magyar Koenyvkiadok es Koenyvterjesztoek Egyesuelese**
Kertesz u 41, 1073 Budapest
*Tel:* (01) 343 25 40 *Fax:* (01) 343 25 41
*E-mail:* mkke@mkke.hu
*Web Site:* www.mkke.hu
*Key Personnel*
President: Istvan Bart
Secretary General: Peter Zentai
Editor-in-Chief: Tarjan Tamas
Publication(s): *Koenyvvilag*
ISBN Prefix(es): 963-7002; 963-7409

**Orszagos Szechenyi Konyvtar** (National Szechenyi Library)
Budavari Palota F epuelet, 1827 Budapest
*Tel:* (01) 224-3700 *Fax:* (01) 202-0804
*E-mail:* isbn@oszk.hu
*Web Site:* www.oszk.hu
*Key Personnel*
Head of Division: Susanne Berke *E-mail:* berk@oszk.hu
ISBN Prefix(es): 963-201

**Standard Book Numbering Agency**, see
Orszagos Szechenyi Konyvtar

# Iceland

**Felag Islenskra Bokautgefenda** (Icelandic Publishers' Association)
Baronsstig 5, 101 Reykjavik
*Tel:* 511 8020 *Fax:* 511 5020
*E-mail:* baekur@mmedia.is
*Key Personnel*
Chairman: Sigurdur Svavarsson
General Manager: Vilborg Hardardottir
Founded: 1889
Publication(s): *Bokatidindi* (annually)

**Standard Book Numbering Agency of Iceland**
National & University Library of Iceland, Arngrimsgata 3, 107 Reykjavik
*Tel:* 525 5600 *Fax:* 525 5615
*E-mail:* lbs@bok.hi.is; isbn@bok.hi.is
*Web Site:* www.bok.hi.is
*Telex:* 2111 iskult
*Key Personnel*
Departmental Chief: Ms Nanna Bjarnadottir
*E-mail:* nannab@bok.hi.is

# India

**AABC**, see Afro-Asian Book Council (AABC)

†◇**Afro-Asian Book Council (AABC)**
4835/24 Ansari Rd, Daryaganj, New Delhi 110002
*Tel:* (011) 3261487 *Fax:* (011) 3267437
*E-mail:* sdas@ubspd.com
*Key Personnel*
Secretary General: Sukumar Das
Dir: Abul Hasan *E-mail:* kiran@ubspd.com
Founded: 1990

Nonprofit book promotion organization for South-South dialogue for the development of indigenous authorship & national book industries in Asia & Africa; International Book Development.
Membership(s): African Publishers Network (APNET), Asia-Pacific Cooperative Programme for Reading Promotion & Book Development (APPREB), World Intellectual Property Organisation (WIPO)
Publication(s): *AABC Newsletter* (quarterly, newsletter)
Number of titles published annually: 3 Print
Total Titles: 8 Print

**Assam Publishers' Association**
College Hostel Rd, Panbazar, Guwahati 781 001
*Tel:* (0361) 23995
Founded: 1977

**Delhi State Booksellers' & Publishers' Association**
3027/7H Ranjit Nagar, Shiv Chowk, New Delhi 110008
*Tel:* (011) 231867; (011) 2515726 *Fax:* (011) 2936758
*Key Personnel*
President: Devendra Sharma
Honorary Secretary: Bhupinder Chowdhri

**Federation of Indian Publishers**
18/1C, Institutional Area, Aruna Asaf Ali Marg, New Delhi 110067
*Tel:* (011) 26964847; (011) 26852263 *Fax:* (011) 26864054
*E-mail:* fip1@satyam.net.in
*Web Site:* www.fiponweb.com
*Key Personnel*
President: Shri Anand Bhushan
Vice President (E): Amitabha Sen
Vice President (S): Prof H R Dase Gowda
Vice President (N): Shri Narender Kumar
Vice President (W): Shri Anil Gala
Publication(s): *Indian Book Industry Journal*

**Gujarat Book Trade Federation**
Navajivan Trust, PO Navajivan, Ahmedabad 380014
*Tel:* (079) 447 634; (079) 447 635
*Key Personnel*
Honorary Secretary: R N Shah
Representative body of the book trade in Gujarat.

**ICRISAT**, see International Crops Research Institute for the Semi-Arid Tropics (ICRISAT)

†‡**International Crops Research Institute for the Semi-Arid Tropics (ICRISAT)**
Patancheru 502 No 324, Andhra Pradesh
*Tel:* (040) 3296161 *Fax:* (040) 3241239; (040) 3296182
*E-mail:* icrisat@cgnet.com
*Web Site:* www.icrisat.org
*Key Personnel*
Dir General: William D Dar *E-mail:* w.dar@cgiar.org
Manager: C Geetha *E-mail:* c.geetha@cgiar.org
Subjects: Agriculture
ISBN Prefix(es): 92-9066

**Meerut Publishers' Association**
Shivaji Rd, Meerut, 250 002 Uttar Pradesh
*Tel:* (0121) 51 0688; (0121) 51 6080 *Fax:* (0121) 52 1545
*E-mail:* vrastogi@vsnl.com
*Telex:* 0549-209
*Key Personnel*
Partner: Mr Vipin Rastogi
Specializes in the field of bio-sciences, agriculture, environment & genetics for undergraduate

& post graduate courses of studies in colleges & universities.
*Parent Company:* M/S Rastogi Publications
*Associate Companies:* M/S Pioneer Printers, Shiuasi Rd, Meerut

**National Agency for ISBN**
Ministry of Human Resource Development, Government of India, New Delhi 110001
Mailing Address: A2, W4 Curzon Rd Barracks, New Delhi 110001
*Tel:* (011) 2338-4687 *Fax:* (011) 2338 7934
*E-mail:* isbn@sb.nic.in
*Telex:* 031-61336
*Key Personnel*
Contact: Dr Suresh Chand
Publication(s): *National Catalogue of ISBN Titles*

**Standard Book Numbering Agency**, see
National Agency for ISBN

# Indonesia

**IKAPI**, see Ikatan Penerbit Indonesia (IKAPI)

**Ikatan Penerbit Indonesia (IKAPI)**
Jl Kalipasir 32, Jakarta 10330
*Tel:* (021) 3141907; (021) 3146050 *Fax:* (021) 3146050
*E-mail:* sekretariat@ikapi.or.id
*Web Site:* www.ikapi.or.id
*Key Personnel*
President: Arselan Harahap
Secretary General: Robinson Rusdi
Association of Indonesian Book Publishers.

**Indonesian ISBN Agency**
Jl Salemba Raya 28A, Jakarta Pusat 10430
*Tel:* (021) 3154864; (021) 3154870 *Fax:* (021) 3103554
*E-mail:* info@pnri.go.id
*Web Site:* www.pnri.go.id
*Telex:* 07345875
*Key Personnel*
Head, Sub Directorate of Bibliography: Sauliah Saleh *E-mail:* sauliah@pnri.go.id

**Standard Book Numbering Agency**, see
Indonesian ISBN Agency

# Islamic Republic of Iran

**Standard Book Numbering Agency**
1178 Enqulab Ave, Tehran 13156
*Tel:* (021) 6414991 *Fax:* (021) 6415360
*E-mail:* dariushmatlabi@yahoo.com; isbn@ketab.org.ir; dmatlabi@yahoo.com
*Web Site:* www.ketab.org.ir
*Telex:* 224581-IBFS-IR
*Key Personnel*
Contact: Mr Vahraz Nowruzpur Deilami

# Ireland

**CLE: The Irish Book Publishers' Association**
43/44 Temple Bar, Dublin 2
*Tel:* (01) 670-7393 *Fax:* (01) 670-7642
*E-mail:* info@publishingireland.com
*Web Site:* www.publishingireland.com
*Key Personnel*
President: Tony Farmar
Treasurer: Marie Maguire

**Cumann Leabharfhoilsitheoiri Eireann**, see
CLE: The Irish Book Publishers' Association

**Irish Educational Publishers' Association**
c/o Gill & Macmillan Ltd, 10 Hume Ave, Park
West, Dublin 12
*Tel:* (01) 500 9509; (01) 500 9555 (cust serv)
*Fax:* (01) 500 9598; (01) 500 9596 (cust serv)
*Key Personnel*
Secretary: Hubert Mahony *E-mail:* hmahony@
gillmacmillan.ie

# Israel

**Book & Printing Center - Israel Export
Institute**
29 Hamered St, 61500 Tel Aviv
Mailing Address: PO Box 50084, 61500 Tel Aviv
*Tel:* (03) 514 2830 *Fax:* (03) 514 2902; (03) 514
2815
*E-mail:* export-institute@export.gov.il; pama@
export.gov.il
*Web Site:* www.export.gov.il; duns100.dundb.co.il/
1483
*Telex:* 35613 *Cable:* MEMEX
*Key Personnel*
Chairman of the Board: Shraga Brosh
Dir General: Yechiel Assia
Founded: 1958
Division of the Israel Export Institute. Organizes
& promotes activities relating to the export of
Israeli books, publishing & printing services.
Publication(s): *Israel Book Trade Directory* (bien-
nially)

**Book Publishers' Association of Israel**
29 Carlebach St, 67132 Tel Aviv
Mailing Address: PO Box 20123, 61201 Tel Aviv
*Tel:* (03) 5614121 *Fax:* (03) 5611996
*E-mail:* info@tbpai.co.il
*Web Site:* www.tbpai.co.il
*Key Personnel*
Man Dir: Amnon Ben-Shmuel
Chairman: Shai Hausman
Key Representative: Lorna Soifer
The Association administers two subsidiary co-
operative associations & two joint publishing
companies - Ma'alot & Yachdav.

**Hebrew Writers Association of Israel**
PO Box 7098, 61070 Tel Aviv
*Tel:* (03) 6953256 *Fax:* (03) 6919681
*Key Personnel*
President: Nathan Yonathan
Chairman: Dr Zahava Ben-Dov
Publication(s): *Moznayim* (monthly)

**The Institute for the Translation of Hebrew
Literature**
23 Baruch Hirsch St, Bnei Brak
Mailing Address: PO Box 1005 1, 52001 Ramat
Gan
*Tel:* (03) 579 6830 *Fax:* (03) 579 6832
*E-mail:* hamachon@inter.net.il
*Web Site:* www.ithl.org.il

*Key Personnel*
Man Dir: Nilli Cohen
Office Manager: Debbie Dagan
Activities of the Institute include promotion of
modern Hebrew literature in translation & co-
publishing projects, literary agency services,
subsidies to authors & publishers for transla-
tions of Hebrew literary works & their publica-
tion abroad
Also acts as literary agent.
Publication(s): *Bibliography of Modern Hebrew
Literature in Translation* (annually); *Modern
Hebrew Literature* (semiannually)

**Israel ISBN Group Agency**
Israeli Center for Libraries, 5 Havazelet St, 91002
Jerusalem
Mailing Address: PO Box 801, Bnei Brak 51108
*Tel:* (03) 6180151 *Fax:* (03) 5798048
*E-mail:* isbn@ici.org.il; icl@icl.org.il
*Web Site:* www.icl.org.il
*Key Personnel*
Dir, Consulting & Publication: Ariella Z Barrett
*Tel:* (03) 6180151 (ext 106)
Contact: Haviva Shmueli *Tel:* (03) 6180151 (ext
115)
*Parent Company:* Israeli Center for Libraries
*Branch Office(s)*
28 Baruch Hirsh St, 51131 Bnei Brak *Tel:* (03)
6180151 (ext 106) *E-mail:* ariella@icl.org.il
*Web Site:* www.icl.org.il

**Standard Book Numbering Agency**, see Israel
ISBN Group Agency

# Italy

◇**Agenzia ISBN per l'Area di Lingua Italiana**
(ISBN Agency for the Area of Italian
Language)
Vie Bergonzoli 1/5, 20127 Milan
*Tel:* (02) 28315996 *Fax:* (02) 28315906
*E-mail:* bibliografica@bibliografica.it
*Web Site:* www.aie.it/ISBN/intro.asp
*Key Personnel*
ISBN Administrator: Dr Michele Costa
*E-mail:* michele.costa@bibliografica.it
Run by Editrice Bibliografica.
*Parent Company:* Associazione Italiana Editori

**ALAI**, see Associazione Librai Antiquari d'Italia

**Associazione Italiana Editori**
Via delle Erbe 2, 20121 Milan
*Tel:* (02) 86463091 *Fax:* (02) 89010863
*E-mail:* aie@aie.it
*Web Site:* www.aie.it
*Key Personnel*
Dir: Ivan Cecchini *E-mail:* ivan.cecchini@aie.it
Italian Publishers' Association.
Publication(s): *Catalogo dei Libri Italiani in
Commercio*; *Giornale Della Libreria*
*Branch Office(s)*
Via Crescenzio 19, 00193 Rome
*Tel:* (06) 68806298 *Fax:* (06) 6872426
*E-mail:* aieroma@aie.it

**Associazione Librai Antiquari d'Italia**
(Antiquarian Booksellers' Association of Italy)
Via del Parione, 11, 50123 Florence
*Tel:* (055) 282635 *Fax:* (055) 214831
*E-mail:* alai@alai.it
*Web Site:* www.alai.it
*Key Personnel*
President: Umberto Pregliasco *E-mail:* preglias@
fileita.it
Vice President: Marco Cicolini

†‡**Food & Agriculture Organization of the
United Nations (FAO)**
Viale delle Terme di Caracalla, 00100 Rome
*Tel:* (06) 57054350 *Fax:* (06) 57053360
*E-mail:* telex-room@fao.org
*Web Site:* www.fao.org
*Telex:* 610181 FAO I *Cable:* FOODAGRI ROME
*Key Personnel*
Dir General: Dr Jacques Diouf
Dir Information: Christina Engfeldt
Chief, Sales & Marketing Group: R Sutton
Founded: 1945
FAO Publications reflect the Organization's prin-
cipal aims: to increase world agriculture pro-
duction; raise levels of nutrition; & improve the
conditions of rural populations. Titles include
books, monographs, periodicals, technical documents, annuals, yearbooks & reports of FAO
conferences & meetings. Major publications
are produced in the five official UN languages
(Arabic, Chinese, English, French & Spanish)
& all publications & documents are available
on microfiche. Unsolicited manuscripts are
automatically rejected. Articles of a technical
nature of no more than 2500 words on international aspects of the animal industry, food
& nutrition are occasionally accepted. No payment is made.
Subjects: Agriculture, Plant Production & Protection, Animal Production & Health, Forestry,
Fisheries, Land & Water Development, Economic & Social Development, Food & Nutrition, Computerized Information Series, Educational & Training Materials
ISBN Prefix(es): 92-5; 92-851; 92-852; 92-853;
92-854; 92-855

**Institute Propaganda Libraria**, see IPL -
Istituto Propaganda Libraria

†**International Centre Study Preservation &
Restoration of Cultural Property (ICCROM)**
Via di San Michele 13, 00153 Rome
*Tel:* (06) 585531 *Fax:* (06) 58553349
*E-mail:* iccrom@iccrom.org
*Web Site:* www.iccrom.org
*Key Personnel*
Dir General: Nicholas Stanley-Price
Founded: 1959
Subjects: Heritage Preservation & Intergovern-
mental Organization
ISBN Prefix(es): 92-9077

◇**IPL - Istituto Propaganda Libraria** (Institute
of Bookshop Advertising)
Via Mercalli 23, 20122 Milan
*Tel:* (02) 58301960 *Fax:* (02) 58301960
*Key Personnel*
Editorial Dir: Nicola Cerbino
Subjects include literature, literary criticism, fic-
tion, history, essays, religion & philosophy.

**Standard Book Numbering Agency**, see
Agenzia ISBN per l'Area di Lingua Italiana

# Jamaica

**Booksellers' Association of Jamaica**
c/o Noveltry Trading Co Ltd, 53 Hanover St,
Kingston
Mailing Address: PO Box 80, Kingston
*Tel:* (876) 922-5883 *Fax:* (876) 922-4743
*Key Personnel*
President: Keith Shervington

**COMLA**, see The Commonwealth Library Association (COMLA)

**†◇The Commonwealth Library Association (COMLA)**
PO Box 144, Mona, Kingston 7
*Tel:* (876) 927-2123 *Fax:* (876) 927-1926
*E-mail:* nkpodo@uwimona.edu.jm
*Key Personnel*
President: Anthony Evans
Vice President: Elizabeth Watson
Executive Secretary: Norma Y Amenu-Kpodo
Founded: 1972
Publication(s): *COMLA Newsletter* (3 issues/yr, newsletter)

**◇University of the West Indies Publishers' Association**
PO Box 42, Mona, Kingston
*Tel:* (876) 977-2659 *Fax:* (876) 977-2660
*Key Personnel*
Publication Officer: Annie Paul
University of the West Indies, Mona Campus.
Publication(s): *Caribbean Geography*

# Japan

**ACCU**, see Asia/Pacific Cultural Centre for UNESCO (ACCU)

**Antiquarian Booksellers' Association of Japan**
29 San-ei-cho, Shinjuku-ku, Tokyo 160-0008
*Tel:* (03) 3357-1411 *Fax:* (03) 3351-5855
*E-mail:* kikuo@sc4.so-net.ne.jp
*Web Site:* www.abaj.gr.jp
*Key Personnel*
President: Mitsuo Nitta
Founded: 1964

**†‡Asia/Pacific Cultural Centre for UNESCO (ACCU)**
Japan Publishers Bldg, 6 Fukuromachi, Shinjuku-ku, Tokyo 162-8484
*Tel:* (03) 3269-4435 *Fax:* (03) 3269-4510
*E-mail:* general@accu.or.jp
*Web Site:* www.accu.or.jp *Cable:* ASCULCENTRE TOKYO
*Key Personnel*
Dir General: Muneharu Kusaba
Founded: 1971
Asian/Pacific Copublication Programme (ACP) is a joint program of UNESCO member states in Asia & the Pacific to produce good children's books. Regional training course on book production organized annually & Noma Concours for Picture Book Illustrations biennially.
Publication(s): *Asian/Pacific Book Development (ABD)*; *Asian/Pacific Culture (APC)*
ISBN Prefix(es): 4-946438

**†The Asian Productivity Organization**
1-2-10 Hirakawacho, Chiyoda-ku, Tokyo 102-0093
*Tel:* (03) 5226 3920 *Fax:* (03) 5226 3950
*E-mail:* apo@apo-tokyo.org
*Web Site:* www.apo-tokyo.org
*Key Personnel*
Secretary General: Shigeo Takenaka
Dir, Administration & Finance Department: Kenneth Mok
Dir, Information & Public Relations: Nagre Gamage Kularatne *Tel:* (03) 5226 3927
*E-mail:* ipr@apo-tokyo.com
Founded: 1961
Subjects: Productivity Improvement in APO Member Countries

ISBN Prefix(es): 92-833
*Bookshop(s):* Quality Resources, One Water St, White Plains, NY 10601, United States *Tel:* 212-979-8600 *Fax:* 914-791-9467

**JAIP**, see Japan Association of International Publications

**◇Japan Association of International Publications**
Chiyoda Kaikan, 21-4 Nihonbashi 1-chome, Chuo-ku, Tokyo 103-0027
*Tel:* (03) 3271 6901 *Fax:* (03) 3271 6920
*E-mail:* jaip@poppy.ocn.ne.jp
*Web Site:* www.jaip.gr.jp
*Key Personnel*
Chairman Board: Seishiro Murata
Secretary General: Hiroshi Takahashi
Founded: 1941
Association of those who import & sell foreign publications, represent foreign publishers & support import of such publications.
Publication(s): *JAIP Directory*
ISBN Prefix(es): 4-931516

**Japan Book Publishers Association**
6 Fukuro-machi, Shinjuku-ku, Tokyo 162-0828
*Tel:* (03) 3268-1303 *Fax:* (03) 3268-1196
*E-mail:* rd@jbpa.or.jp
*Web Site:* www.jbpa.or.jp *Cable:* SHOSEKIKYO TOKYO
*Key Personnel*
President: Mr Kunizo Asakura
Executive Dir: Tadashi Yamashita
Founded: 1957
Publication(s): *Bulletin of Japan Book Publishers Association*; *The Catalogue of Books in the Near Future*; *Introduction to Publishing in Japan 2002-2003*; *Japanese Books in Print CD-ROM Edition*

**Japan Electronic Publishing Association (JEPA)**
Tomodasanwa Bldg 5F, 1-37 Kanda Jinbo-cho, Chiyoda-ku, Tokyo 101-0051
*Tel:* (03) 3219-2958 *Fax:* (03) 3219-2940
*Web Site:* www.jepa.or.jp
*Key Personnel*
Chairman of Board: Mr Hideki Hasegawa

**Japan ISBN Agency**
c/o Japan Library Publishers Bldg, 6 Fukuro-machi, Shinjuku-ku, Toyko 162-0828
*Tel:* (03) 326 72 301 *Fax:* (03) 326 72 304
*E-mail:* info@isbn-center.jp
*Web Site:* www.isbn-center.jp
*Key Personnel*
Secretary General: Naotoshi Matsudaira

**JEPA**, see Japan Electronic Publishing Association (JEPA)

**Nihon Shoten Shogyo Kumiai Rengokai**
2 Kanda-Surugadai 1 chome, Chiyoda-ku, Tokyo 101
*Tel:* (03) 32940388
Japan Federation of Commercial Co-operative of Bookstores.
Publication(s): *Kodomonohon Long-seller-list* (Children's Books: A List of Best Sellers); *Zenkoku Shoten Meibo* (Address Book of Japan Booksellers); *Zenkoku Shoten Shinbun* (Newspaper for booksellers)

**◇Publishers' Association for Cultural Exchange (PACE) Japan**
1-2-1, Sarugaku-cho, Chiyoda-ku, Tokyo 101-0064
*Tel:* (03) 32915685 *Fax:* (03) 32333645
*E-mail:* office@pace.or.jp

*Web Site:* www.pace.or.jp
*Key Personnel*
President: Tatsuro Matsumae
Man Dir: Yasuko Korenaga
Founded: 1953
*European Representation:* Euro-Japanische Gesellschaft e.V. (Ohnichi Kyokai), Rossmarkt 15, 6000 Frankfurt am Main 1, Germany. Tel: (069) 285644.
Publication(s): *Directory of Japanese Publishers* (biennially); *Practical Guide to Publishing in Japan* (annually)

**Standard Book Numbering Agency**, see Japan ISBN Agency

# Kazakstan

**Book Chamber of Kazakhstan ISBN Agency**
Ulica Puskina 2, Almaty 480016
*Tel:* (03272) 306 421 *Fax:* (03272) 304 265
*E-mail:* rntb@kaznet.kz
*Web Site:* www.isbn-international.org
*Key Personnel*
Contact: Ms K M Mukhataeva

**Standard Book Numbering Agency**, see Book Chamber of Kazakhstan ISBN Agency

# Kenya

**†◇Eastern & Southern Africa Regional Branch of the International Council on Archives (ESARBICA)**
c/o Kenya National Archives & Documentation Service Archives Bldg, Moi Ave, Nairobi
Mailing Address: PO Box 49210, Nairobi 00100
*Tel:* (02) 228959 *Fax:* (02) 240059
*E-mail:* knarchives@form-net.com
*Web Site:* www.kenyarchives.go.ke *Cable:* ARCHIVES NAIROBI

**ESARBICA**, see Eastern & Southern Africa Regional Branch of the International Council on Archives (ESARBICA)

**†International Livestock Research Institute**
Old Naivasha Rd, Nairobi
Mailing Address: PO Box 30709, Nairobi
*Tel:* (020) 630 743 *Fax:* (020) 631 499
*E-mail:* ilri-kenya@cgiar.org
*Web Site:* www.cgiar.org/ilri
*Key Personnel*
Dir General: Carlos Sere
Sales, Production, Information, Rights & Permissions: Michael Smalley
Founded: 1974
Subjects: Livestock Research & Development in Africa
ISBN Prefix(es): 92-9053
*Branch Office(s)*
PO Box 5689, Addis Ababa, Ethiopia *Tel:* (01) 463 215 *Fax:* (01) 461 252 *E-mail:* ilri-ethiopia@cgiar.org

**Kenya Literature Bureau**
PO Box 30022, Nairobi
*Tel:* (020) 333763 *Fax:* (020) 340954
*E-mail:* klb@onlinekenya.co.ke
*Key Personnel*
Man Dir: M A Karauri
Chief Editor: A S Githenji
Founded: 1980
ISBN Prefix(es): 9966-44

**Kenya Publishers Association**
Occidental Plaza, 4th floor, Westlands, Nairobi
Mailing Address: PO Box 42767, Nairobi 00100
*Tel:* (020) 375 2344 *Fax:* (020) 375 4076
*E-mail:* kenyapublishers@wananchi.com
*Web Site:* www.kenyabooks.org
*Key Personnel*
Executive Secretary: Lynnette Kariuki
Founded: 1971
Membership(s): National Book Development
 Council of Kenya.

**Standard Book Numbering Agency**
Kenya National Library Services, Ngong Rd,
 Nairobi
Mailing Address: PO Box 30573, Nairobi
*Tel:* (02) 718012; (02) 718013; (02) 725550
 *Fax:* (02) 721749
*E-mail:* knls@nbnet.co.ke
*Web Site:* www.knls.or.ke
*Telex:* 23278 afrec ke
*Key Personnel*
Dir: S K Nganga
Publication(s): *Kenya National Bibliography*

**UNEP**, see United Nations Environment
 Programme (UNEP)

**†‡United Nations Environment Programme
 (UNEP)**
PO Box 30552, Nairobi
*Tel:* (02) 621234 *Fax:* (02) 624489; (02) 624490
*E-mail:* eisinfo@unep.org
*Web Site:* www.unep.org
*Telex:* 22068 *Cable:* UNITERRA NAIROBI
*Key Personnel*
Editor: Naomi Poulton *E-mail:* naomi.poulton@
 unep.org
Founded: 1972
Subjects: Environmental Literature
ISBN Prefix(es): 92-807
Number of titles published annually: 100 Print
*U.S. Office(s):* United Nations Environment Pro-
 gramme, Regional Office for North America,
 1707 "H" St NW, Suite 300, Washington,
 DC 20006, United States *Tel:* 202-785-0465
 *E-mail:* brennan.vandyke@rona.unep.org

# Republic of Korea

**ISBN Agency - Korea**
The National Library of Korea, 60-1 Banpo-dong,
 Seocho-gu, Seoul 137-702
*Tel:* (02) 590 06 27; (02) 590 06 28 *Fax:* (02)
 590 06 22; (02) 590 06 21
*E-mail:* ISSNKC@mail.nl.go.kr
*Web Site:* www.nl.go.kr
*Key Personnel*
Contact: Mrs Nam-Sook Kim
Founded: 1990

**Korean Publishers Association**
105-2 Sagan-Dong, Chongno-Gu, Seoul 110-190
*Tel:* (02) 735-2701; (02) 735-2704 *Fax:* (02) 738-
 5414
*E-mail:* kpa@kpa21.or.kr
*Web Site:* www.kpa21.or.kr
*Key Personnel*
President: Choon Ho Na
Secretary General: Jong Jin Jung
Founded: 1947
ISBN Prefix(es): 89-85231

**Korean Publishing Research Institute**
3 F Daehan Chulpan Munhwa Hoegwan, 105-2
 Sagan-dong, 110-190 Jongro-gu, Seoul
*Tel:* (02) 7399040 *Fax:* (02) 7376187
*E-mail:* p715@chollian.net
*Key Personnel*
Chief Dir: Yoon Chung-Kwang
Researcher: Park Hyun-Na

**Standard Book Numbering Agency**, see ISBN
 Agency - Korea

# Kuwait

**†‡Arab Centre for Medical Literature**
PO Box 5225, Safat 13053
*Tel:* 5338610; 5338611 *Fax:* 5338618; 5338619
*Key Personnel*
Secretary General: Dr Abdel Rahman Al-Awadi
Subjects: Arabizing Medical Literatures
Publication(s): *Atlas of Eye Diseases in Arab
 Countries* (undergoing publication); *Lecture
 Notes on Gynaecology*; *Teeth & Health*

# Latvia

**†Latvian Publishers Association** (Latvieas
 Gramatizdevefu Asociacifa)
K Barona iela 36-4, LV-1011 Riga
*Tel:* (0371) 7282392 *Fax:* (0371) 7280549
*E-mail:* lga@gramatizdeveji.lv
*Web Site:* www.gramatizdeveji.lv
*Key Personnel*
President: Leva Jansone
Executive Dir: Dace Pugaca
Founded: 1993
Protection of rights & interests of publishers.
Membership(s): International Publishers Associa-
 tion.

**Standard Book Numbering Agency**
Unit of Latvijas bibliografijas Instituts
Latvijas Bibliografijas Instituts, Anglikanu St 5,
 Riga LV-1816
*Tel:* (02) 721 26 68 *Fax:* (02) 722 45 87
*Web Site:* www.lnb.lv
*Key Personnel*
Dir, Latvian ISBN Agency: Ms Laimdota Pruse
 *E-mail:* laimdotap@lbi.lnb.lv
Founded: 1993
ISBN Numbering.
*Parent Company:* National Library of Latvia, K
 Barona 14, Riga LV-1235
*Ultimate Parent Company:* Ministry of Culture of
 the Republic of Latvia

# Lesotho

**◇Standard Book Numbering Agency**
National University of Lesotho Library, Thomas
 Mofolo Library, Roma
Mailing Address: National University of Lesotho,
 PO Roma 180, Roma
*Tel:* (022) 340601; (022) 340468 *Fax:* 340000
*E-mail:* isbn@lib.nul.ls
*Web Site:* www.nul.ls
*Telex:* 4303 lo
*Key Personnel*
Contact: Ms Mamothepane Kotele *E-mail:* mt.
 kotele@nul.ls

Founded: 1964
Education, humanities, law, science & technology,
 social sciences, agriculture & health sciences.

# Lithuania

**Lithuanian ISBN Agency**
Centre of Bibliography & Book Science, Ged-
 imino pr 51, 2600 Vilnius
*Tel:* (05) 2497023 *Fax:* (05) 2496129
*E-mail:* isbnltu@lnb.lt
*Web Site:* www.lnb.lt
*Key Personnel*
Head of Agency: Dalia Smoriginiene
ISBN Prefix(es): 9986-530

**Lithuanian Publishers' Association**
Ave Jaksto 22-13, 01105 Vilnius
*Tel:* (05) 2617740 *Fax:* (05) 2617740
*E-mail:* lla@centras.lt
*Web Site:* www.lla.lt
*Key Personnel*
President: Arvydas Andrijauskas
Secretary: Violeta Misiuniene
Represents the interests of Lithuanian publishers.

# Luxembourg

**Federation Luxembourgeoise des Editeurs de
 Livres, ASBL**
7 Rue Alcide de Gasperi, 2014 Luxemburg
Mailing Address: BP 482, 2014 Luxembourg
*Tel:* 439444 *Fax:* 439450
*E-mail:* promoculture@ibm.net
*Key Personnel*
General Secretary: Jean-Paul Schortgen
Economic Advisor: Romain Jeblick
Luxemburgish Publishers' Association.
*Parent Company:* Confederation Luxembour-
 geoise du Commerce

**ISBN Agency - Luxembourg**
Bibliotheque Nationale, 37 Blvd F D Roosevelt,
 L-2450 Luxembourg
*Tel:* 22 97 55-1 *Fax:* 47 56 72
*E-mail:* bib.nat@bi.etat.lu
*Web Site:* www.bnl.lu
*Key Personnel*
Dir: F F Monique Kieffer
*Parent Company:* Bibliotheque nationale

**†Office des Publications Officielles des
 Communautes Europeennes** (Office for
 Official Publications of the European
 Communities)
2, rue Mercier, 2985 Luxembourg
*Tel:* 2929-1 *Fax:* 292944619
*E-mail:* opoce-info-info@cec.eu.int
*Web Site:* www.eur-op.eu.int
*Key Personnel*
Dir: Lucien Emringer
Chief of Sales: Serge Brack
Chief of Marketing: N Reinert
Founded: 1969
Subjects: Economy, Law, Finance, Enterprises
 & Business, Energy, Foreign Relations, Agri-
 culture, Fishing, Forestry, Tax, Employment,
 Labor, Environment, Scientific Research &
 Techniques, Information, Education, Culture,
 Statistics
*U.S. Office(s):* Unipub, 4611-F Assembly Dr,
 Lanham, MD 20706-4391, United States
 *Tel:* 800-274-4888 *Fax:* 301-459-0056

**Standard Book Numbering Agency**, see ISBN Agency - Luxembourg

# The Former Yugoslav Republic of Macedonia

**Standard Book Numbering Agency**
Narodna i Univerzitetska Biblioteka, Bul Goce Delcev, br 6, 91000 Skopje
*Tel:* (02) 3115 177; (02) 3133 418 *Fax:* (02) 3226 846
*E-mail:* kliment@nubsk.edu.mk
*Web Site:* www.nubsk.edu.mk
*Key Personnel*
Dir: Vera Kaljlieva

# Madagascar

**Fiantsorohana NY Boky Malagasy, Office du Livre Malgache**
Lot 111, H29 Andrefran' Ambohijanahary, 101 Tananrive
Mailing Address: BP 617, 101 Tananrive
*Tel:* (02) 24449
*Key Personnel*
Secretary General: Juliette Ratsimandrava
    *E-mail:* ratsimandrav@initel.refer.org

# Malawi

**ISBN Agency (International Standard Book Number National Agency)**
National Archives of Malawi, PO Box 62, Zomba
*Tel:* (01) 525 240; (01) 524 148; (01) 524 184
    *Fax:* (01) 525 362; (01) 524 148
*E-mail:* archives@sdnp.org.mw
*Web Site:* chambo.sdnp.org.mw
*Key Personnel*
Acting Dir: Mr O W Ambali
Administer the issuing of ISBNs to publishers in Malawi.
Membership(s): ICA (International Council on Archives).
Publication(s): *National Bibliography Archives of Malawi, Zomba* (annually)
*Parent Company:* Ministry of Sports & Culture, Pvt Bag 384, Lilongwe 3

**Standard Book Numbering Agency**, see ISBN Agency (International Standard Book Number National Agency)

# Malaysia

**Malaysian Book Importers & Distributors Association**
45 Jalan Tun Mudh 2, Taman Tun Dr Ismail, 60000 Kuala Lumpur

*Tel:* (03) 7193485 *Fax:* (03) 7181664
*Key Personnel*
President: Mr K Arul
Secretary: Mr Leong Fook Kwong

**Malaysian Book Publishers' Association**
No 39, Jln Nilam 1/2, Subang Square, Subang High-Tech Industrial Park Batutiga, 40000 Shah Alam, Selangor
*Tel:* (03) 56379044 *Fax:* (03) 56379043
*E-mail:* inquiry@cerdik.com.my
*Web Site:* www.mabopa.com.my
*Key Personnel*
President: Ng Tieh Chuan
Vice President: Peter Paul
Honorary Secretary: Zainora Muhamad
Honorary Treasurer: Guan Swee Leong
Founded: 1969
Publish textbooks, revision course books, workbooks, encyclopedias, readers, magazines & multimedia products.
Publication(s): *Malaysian Publishers Directory*

**SARBICA**, see Southeast Asian Regional Branch of the International Council on Archives (SARBICA)

†◇**Southeast Asian Regional Branch of the International Council on Archives (SARBICA)**
c/o National Archives of Malaysia, Jalan Duta, 50568 Kuala Lumpur
*Tel:* (03) 62010688 *Fax:* (03) 62015679
*Web Site:* arkib.gov.my/sarbica/index.html; www. arkib.gov.my
*Key Personnel*
Chairman, Malaysia: Lily Tan
Dir General: Mrs Hajjah Rahani Jamil
    *E-mail:* rahani@arkib.gov.my
Founded: 1968
Publication(s): *Southeast Asian Archives*; *Southeast Asian Microfilms Newsletter*

**Standard Book Numbering Agency**
c/o National Library of Malaysia, 232, Jalan Tun Razak, 50572 Kuala Lumpur
*Tel:* (03) 26871700 *Fax:* (03) 26927082
*E-mail:* pnmweb@www1.pnm.my
*Web Site:* www.pnm.my
*Telex:* MA 30092 *Cable:* NATLIB KUALALUMPUR

# Maldive Islands

**Standard Book Numbering Agency**
Ministry of Education, Ghaazee Bldg, Ameeru Ahmed Magu, Male 20-05
*Tel:* 323261 *Fax:* 321201
*E-mail:* educator@dhivehinet.net.mv
*Web Site:* www.moe.gov.mv

# Malta

**Maltese Publishers Association**, see Periodical & Book Publishers Association

◇**Periodical & Book Publishers Association**
The Terrace, Ta'Xbiex MSD 11
*Fax:* (507) 295 9217
*E-mail:* bookpub@cwebdesign.com
*Web Site:* www.cwebdesign.com/pbpa
*Key Personnel*
Founder & Chairman: Joseph John Meli

Founded: 1989
Member association of "Kopjamalt" - the Copyright Licensing Agency for the Maltese Islands.

**Standard Book Numbering Agency**
Publishers Enterprises Group (PEG) Inc, PEG Bldg, UB 7 Industrial Estate, San Gwann SGN 09
*Tel:* (021) 440083; (021) 448539; (021) 490540
    *Fax:* (021) 488908
*E-mail:* contact@peg.com.mt
*Web Site:* www.peg.com.mt
*Key Personnel*
Man Dir: Emanuel Debattista
Publishers & printers.

# Mauritius

**National ISBN Agency**
Editions de l'Ocean Indien Ltee, Stanley, Rose Hill
*Tel:* (0230) 4646761; (0230) 4643959; (0230) 4643452 *Fax:* (0230) 4643445
*E-mail:* eoibooks@intnet.mu
*Telex:* mesynd 4739
*Key Personnel*
Contact: Mr C Colimalay
Publishers & Distributors of books/private company.
ISBN Prefix(es): 99903-0
*Parent Company:* Editions de L'Ocean Indien Ltee (Publishers & Distributors)
*Associate Companies:* Mauritius Printing Specialists (Pte) Ltd, Stanley, Rose-Hill
*Branch Office(s)*
Curepipe
Flacq
Goodlands
Port Louis
Rose Hill

**Standard Book Numbering Agency**, see National ISBN Agency

# Mexico

**Camara Nacional de la Industria Editorial Mexicana**
Holanda No 13, col San Diego Churubusco, Del Coyoacan, 04120 Mexico
*Tel:* (05) 6 88 24 34; (05) 6 88 22 21; (05) 6 88 2011 *Toll Free Tel:* (800) 714-5352 *Fax:* (055) 5604-4347; (05) 6 04 31 47
*E-mail:* cepromex@caniem.com
*Web Site:* www.caniem.com
*Telex:* 1772969
*Key Personnel*
Dir: R Servin
President: A H Gayosso; J C Cramerez
Mexican Publishers' Association.
Publication(s): *Books of Mexico; How to obtain Mexican books and periodicals*

**Centro Nacional de Informacion, Agencia Nacional ISBN**
Calle Dinamarca 84, 2° Piso Colonia Juarez Delegacion Cuauhtemoc, 06600 Mexico, DF
*Tel:* (0555) 230 7632 *Fax:* (0555) 230 7634
*Web Site:* www.sep.gob.mx
*Telex:* 1773860 psep me
*Key Personnel*
ISBN Administrator: Alejandra Martinez Gamboa; Ketty Garcia Agut
National Center of Information, National Agency ISBN.

## MEXICO (continued)

†◇**Consejo Interamericano de Archiveros (CITA)**
c/o Archivo General de la Nacion, Eduardo Molina y Albaniles s/n Col Penitenciaria Ampliacion, Delegacion Venustiano Carranza, 15350 Mexico, DF
*Tel:* (05) 51 33 99 00 (ext 19327); (05) 57 95 70 80 (ext 19424) *Fax:* (05) 57 89 52 96
*Web Site:* www.agn.gob.mx
*Key Personnel*
Dir General: Patricia Galeana
Publication(s): *Boletin del AGN y Colecciones Graficas*; *Documentos de Archivonomia*; *Estudios Historicos*; *Guias y Catalogos*; *Informacion de Archivos Estatales y Municipales*

**Standard Book Numbering Agency**, see Centro Nacional de Informacion, Agencia Nacional ISBN

# Republic of Moldova

**Camera Nationala a Cartii din Republica Moldova**, see Chambre Nationale du Livre Agence ISBN

**Chambre Nationale du Livre Agence ISBN**
Subsidiary of Ministry of Culture
bd Stefan cel Mare 180, 2004 Chisinau
*Tel:* (02) 24 65 42 *Fax:* (02) 24 65 11
*E-mail:* cncm@moldova.cc
*Web Site:* www.iatp.md/cnc
*Key Personnel*
Dir: Valentina Chitoroaga *E-mail:* chitoroaga_v@moldova.cc
Founded: 1957
ISBN Prefix(es): 9975-9532

**Standard Book Numbering Agency**, see Chambre Nationale du Livre Agence ISBN

# Morocco

**Agence Marocaine de l'ISBN**
Bibliotheque Generale et Archives, Service du depot legal, Av Ibn Battouta, Rabat
Mailing Address: BP 1003, Rabat
*Tel:* (07) 771 890; (07) 772 152 *Fax:* (07) 776 062
*E-mail:* biblio1@onpt.net.ma
*Key Personnel*
ISBN Dir: Ahmed Toufiq
Contact: Meryem Moussaid
ISBN Agency of Morocco.
Publication(s): *Bibliographie Nationale Retrospective du Marco* (1986-1995)
*Parent Company:* Biliotheque Generale et Archives

†◇**Centre Africain de Formation et de Recherche Administratives pour le Developpement, Centre de Documentation** (African Training and Research Centre in Administration for Development, Documentation Centre)
PO Box 310, 90001 Tangier
*Tel:* (061) 30 72 69 *Fax:* (039) 32 57 85
*E-mail:* cafrad@cafrad.org
*Web Site:* www.cafrad.org
*Telex:* 33664 *Cable:* CAFRAD TANGIER

*Key Personnel*
President: Mansouri Messaoud
Publication(s): *Directory of Administrative Information Services in Africa*

**Standard Book Numbering Agency**, see Agence Marocaine de l'ISBN

# Namibia

**ISBN Agency - Namibia**
National Library of Namibia, Pvt Bag 13349, 9000 Windhoek
*Tel:* (061) 293 53 05 *Fax:* (061) 293 53 08
*Web Site:* www.isbn-international.org
*Key Personnel*
Contact: Werner Hillebrecht
  *E-mail:* whillebrecht@mec.gov.na
Publication(s): *Namibia National Bibliography* (1996-)

**Standard Book Numbering Agency**, see ISBN Agency - Namibia

# Nepal

◇**National Federation of Standard Editor's Association in Nepal (NAFSEEN)**
Kamabakshee Tole, Gha 3-333, Kathmandu 44601-3000
Mailing Address: PO Box 3000-NFSEA Katmandu-3-30-15B, Kathmandu 44601-3000
*Tel:* (01) 212289; (01) 223036; (01) 224005 *Fax:* (01) 223036
*Telex:* 3000 1-SB-ASS-NP *Cable:* NAFSEAN
*Key Personnel*
Secretary General: Ganesh Lall Chhipa
Editorial Dir: Ganesh Dass Chhipa
*Branch Office(s)*
09/63-09 Dathwee Chhen Twa Gallee, Chowk Bhitra 2nd Floor Puranco Bazaar, Arniiko-Barhabise VDC-9, Arniko Rajmarg-87 KM, Bagmati Anchal, Barhabise Mail PO Code 45303, Kathmandu Mail Centre

**National Federation of Standard Periodicals Publishers Association of Nepal**
Kamabakohee Tole, GHA 3-333, Kathmandu 44601-3000
Mailing Address: PO Box 3000-NFFSPP Kathmandu-3-30-15B, Kathmandu 44601-3000
*Tel:* (01) 212289; (01) 223036; (01) 224005 *Fax:* (01) 223036
*Telex:* 3000 1-SB-ASS-NP *Cable:* NAPSPEPAN
*Key Personnel*
Secretary General: Ganesh Lall Singh
Dir: Ganesh Dass
*Branch Office(s)*
Arniko-Barhabise VDC-9, Arniko Rajmarg-87 KMArniko Rajmarg-87 KM, Bagmati Anchal Barhamise Mail

◇**National Federation of Standard Translator's Association in Nepal**
Kamabakshee Tole, Gha 3-333, Kathmandu 44601-3000
Mailing Address: PO Box 3000-NFSTA Kathmandu-3-30-15B, Kathmandu 44601-3000
*Tel:* (01) 212289; (01) 223036; (01) 224005 *Fax:* (01) 223036 ISB-ASS
*Telex:* 3000 1-SB-ASS-NP *Cable:* NAFSTAN
*Key Personnel*
Secretary General: Ganesh Lall Chhipa

Dir: Ganesh Dass Chhipa
*Branch Office(s)*
09/63-16 Dathwee Chhen Twa Gallee, Chowk Bhitra 4th Floor Puranco Bazaar, Arniiko-Barhabise VDC-9, Arniko Rajmarg-87 KM, Bagmati Anchal, Barhabise Mail PO Code 45303, Kathmandu Mail Centre

◇**National Standards Wholesaler's Distributor's & Subscriber's Association of Nepal (NASWDISAN)**
Kamabakshcc Tole, Gha 3-333, Kathmandu 44601-3000
Mailing Address: PO Box 3000-NSWDS Kathmandu-3-30-15B, Kathmandu 44601-3000
*Tel:* (01) 212289; (01) 223036; (01) 224005 *Fax:* (01) 223036
*Telex:* 3000 1-SB-ASS-NP
*Key Personnel*
Secretary General: Ganesh Lall Chhipa
Dir: Ganesh Dass Chhipa
*Branch Office(s)*
09/63-08 Dathwee Chhen Twa Gallee, Chowk Bhitra 5th floor Puranco Bazaar, Arniiko-Barhabise VDC-9, Arniko Rajmarg-87 KM, Bagmati anchal, Barhabise Mail PO Code 45303, Kathmandu Mail Centre

# Netherlands

**Centraal Boekhuis BV**
Erasmusweg 10, 4104 AK Culemborg
Mailing Address: Postbus 125, 4100 AC Culemborg
*Tel:* (0345) 47 59 11 *Fax:* (0345) 47 56 90
*E-mail:* info@centraal.boekhuis.nl
*Web Site:* www.centraalboekhuis.nl
*Key Personnel*
Man Dir: C J Hagenbeek
Dir, Sales & Marketing: S Berkina
Contact: Jaco Gulmans *Tel:* (0345) 47 56 50
  *E-mail:* j.gulmans@centraal.boekhuis.nl

**Collectieve Propaganda van het Nederlandse Boek (CPNB)** (Foundation for the Collective Promotion of the Dutch Book)
Keizersgracht 391, 1016 EJ Amsterdam
Mailing Address: Postbus 10576, 1001 EN Amsterdam
*Tel:* (020) 626 49 71 *Fax:* (020) 623 16 96
*E-mail:* info@cpnb.nl
*Web Site:* www.cpnb.nl
*Key Personnel*
Man Dir: Henk Kraima
Publication(s): *Children's Bookweek*; *Kinderboekenmolen, Voorleesgids* (annually); *Premium Bookweek*

†‡**Cour Internationale de Justice**
Palais de la Paix/Peace Palace, 2517 KJ The Hague
*Tel:* (070) 302 23 23 *Fax:* (070) 364 99 28
*E-mail:* mail@icj-cij.org; information@icj-cij.org
*Web Site:* www.icj-cij.org
*Telex:* 32323 *Cable:* INTERCOURT THE HAGUE
*Key Personnel*
Registrar & Contact: M Philippe Couvreur

**CPNB**, see Collectieve Propaganda van het Nederlandse Boek (CPNB)

**ESOMAR**, see European Society for Opinion & Marketing Research

†‡**Universala Esperanto-Asocio** (World Esperanto Association)
176 Nieuwe Binnenweg, 3015 BJ Rotterdam
*Tel:* (010) 4361044 *Fax:* (010) 4361751
*E-mail:* info@uea.org
*Web Site:* www.uea.org *Cable:* ESPERANTO ROTTERDAM
*Key Personnel*
President: Dr Renato Corsetti
Vice President: Prof Lee Chong-Yeong; Prof Humphrey Tonkin
Secretary General: Ivo Osibov
Editor: Stano Marchek
Founded: 1908
Subjects: Language problems & Esperanto as a possible solution
ISBN Prefix(es): 92-9017

†◇**European Association for Health Information & Libraries**
EAHIL Secretariat, c/o NVB Bureau, Nieuwegracht 15, 3512 LC Utrecht
*Tel:* (030) 2619663 *Fax:* (030) 2311830
*E-mail:* EAHIL-secr@nic.surfnet.nl
*Web Site:* www.eahil.org
*Key Personnel*
President: Arne Jakobsson
Secretary: Suzanne Bakker

**European Association of Information Services**, see EUSIDIC (European Association of Information Services)

†**European Society for Opinion & Marketing Research**
Vondelstr 172, 1054 GV Amsterdam
*Tel:* (020) 664 21 41 *Fax:* (020) 664 29 22
*E-mail:* email@esomar.nl
*Web Site:* www.esomar.org
*Key Personnel*
President: Jose Wertortega
Dir General: Ted Vonk *E-mail:* t.vonk@esomar.org
Founded: 1948
Subjects: Marketing & opinion research

†◇**EUSIDIC (European Association of Information Services)**
CAOS, WG Plein 475, 1054 SH Amsterdam
*Tel:* (020) 589 32 32 *Fax:* (020) 589 32 30
*E-mail:* eusidic@caos.nl
*Web Site:* www.eusidic.org
*Key Personnel*
Chair: Johan van Halm *Tel:* (033) 47 00671 *Fax:* (033) 47 01123 *E-mail:* johanvanhalm@cs.com
Vice Chair: Frank Spellerberg *Tel:* (0170) 3821 779 *Fax:* (06198) 57 66 95 *E-mail:* spellerberg.frank@web.de

**IEA**, see International Association for the Evaluation of Educational Achievement (IEA)

**IFLA**, see International Federation of Library Associations & Institutions (IFLA)

**International Association for the Evaluation of Educational Achievement (IEA)**
Herengracht 487, 1017 BT Amsterdam
*Tel:* (020) 6253625 *Fax:* (020) 4207136
*E-mail:* department@iea.nl
*Web Site:* www.iea.nl
*Key Personnel*
Chairman: Dr Seamus Hegarty *E-mail:* s.hegarty@nfer.ac.uk
Executive Dir: Dr Hans Wagemaker *E-mail:* hanswagemaker@compuserve.com
Manager Membership Relations: Dr Barbara Malak-Minkiewicz *E-mail:* b.malak@iea.nl
Founded: 1954
Research on educational outcomes.

Subjects: Education & various school subjects
Publication(s): *International Reports of IEA Studies*

†◇**International Association of Scientific, Technical & Medical Publishers (STM)**
Prins Willem Alexanderhof 5, 2595 BE The Hague
Mailing Address: POB 90407, 2509 LK The Hague
*Tel:* (070) 314 09 30 *Fax:* (070) 314 09 40
*E-mail:* info@stm-assoc.org
*Web Site:* www.stm-assoc.org
*Key Personnel*
Chairman: Eric Swanson
Secretary: Lex Lefebvre
International Trade Organization for STM, professional & scholarly publishers. Focus on copyright & legal issues, technology development & industry standards & library & users relations.

**International Court of Justice**, see Cour Internationale de Justice

†◇**International Federation of Library Associations & Institutions (IFLA)**
(Federation internationale des associations de bibliothecaires et des bibliotheques)
PO Box 95312, 2509 CH The Hague
*Tel:* (070) 3140884 *Fax:* (070) 3834827
*E-mail:* ifla@ifla.org
*Web Site:* www.ifla.org
*Key Personnel*
President: Kay Raseroka
Secretary General: R Ramachandran
Founded: 1927
Publication(s): *IFLA Annual Report*; *IFLA Directory* (biennially); *IFLA Journal*; *IFLA Professional Reports*; *IFLA Publications* (series of monographs, published by K G Saur Verlag KG, Germany); *International Cataloguing & Bibliographic Control* (quarterly)

**Bureau ISBN**
Centraal Boekhuis, Erasmusweg 10, 4104 AK Culemborg
Mailing Address: Postbus 360, 4100 AJ Culemborg
*Tel:* (0345) 475855 *Fax:* (0345) 475895
*E-mail:* isbn@centraal.boekhuis.nl
*Web Site:* www.isbn.nl
*Key Personnel*
ISBN Administrator: Ben Klomp
Contact: Mr M G van den Heuvel *E-mail:* heuvm@centraal.boekhuis.nl
Publication(s): *ISBN Manual* (2004); *ISBN Publishers List* (on diskette & computer printout)
*Parent Company:* Centraal Boekhuis BV

**KVB Koninklijke Vereeniging van het Boekenvak** (Royal Dutch Book Trade Organization)
Fredriksplein 1, 1017 XK Amsterdam
Mailing Address: Postbus 15007, 1001 MA Amsterdam
*Tel:* (020) 624 02 12 *Fax:* (020) 620 88 71
*E-mail:* info@kvb.nl
*Web Site:* www.kvb.nl
*Key Personnel*
Executive Dir: Mrs C Verberne
Founded: 1815
Association for the Promotion of the Interests of Booksellers & Publishers.
Publication(s): *Adresboek* (Address book for the Dutch Book Trade); *Boekblad* (News Magazine for the Book Trade, weekly & monthly & website www.boekblad.nl)

**Nederlands Uitgeversverbond** (Dutch Publishers Association)
Atlas Kantorenpark, gebouw Azie, Hoogoorddreef 5, 1101 BA Amsterdam
Mailing Address: Postbus 12040, 1100 AA Amsterdam
*Tel:* (020) 43 09 150 *Fax:* (020) 43 09 179
*E-mail:* info@nuv.nl
*Web Site:* www.nuv.nl; www.uitgeversverbond.nl
*Key Personnel*
President: Prof Henk J L Vonhoff
Man Dir: J Bommer
Public Relations Secretary: Jaap Roorda *E-mail:* j.roorda@uitgeversverbond.nl
Founded: 1880
Royal Dutch Publishers' Association.

**Nederlandsche Vereeniging van Antiquaren** (Dutch Antiquarian Booksellers' Association)
Postbus 364, 3500 AJ Utrecht
*Tel:* (030) 231 92 86 *Fax:* (030) 234 33 62
*E-mail:* bestbook@wxs.nl
*Web Site:* www.nvva.nl
*Key Personnel*
President: Ton Kok *E-mail:* kok@xs4all.nl
Secretary: Drs PAGWE Pruimers
Founded: 1935

**Nederlandsche Vereeniging voor Druk- en Boekkunst**
van Banningstraas 2c, 2381 AV Zoeterwoude
*Tel:* (071) 5809634
*Key Personnel*
Secretary: Kees Thomassen
Netherlands Society for the Art of Printing and Book Production.
Publication(s): *Mededelingen* (irregularly)

**Nederlandse Boekverkopersbond** (Dutch Booksellers Association)
Prins Hendriklaan 72, 3721 AT Bilthoven
*Tel:* (030) 228 79 56 *Fax:* (030) 228 45 66
*E-mail:* nbb@boekbond.nl
*Web Site:* www.boekbond.nl
*Key Personnel*
President: W Karssen
Executive Secretary: Mr A C Doeser

**Speurwerk Stitching betreffende het Boek**
Frederiksplein 1, 1017 XK Amsterdam
*Tel:* (020) 625 49 27 *Fax:* (020) 620 88 71
*E-mail:* info@speurwerk.kvb.nl
*Web Site:* www.speurwerk.nl
*Key Personnel*
Dir: A A Herpers
Foundation for Bookmarket Research in the Netherlands.
Publication(s): *Boekenvakboek 1980, 1986-88* (Publishing Industry Statistics); *Gids voor de Informatiesector 1990, 1991, 1992, 1993, 1994*; *Speurwerk Boeken Omnibus* (quarterly, The Dutch Book Market); *Structural Analysis of the Book Market in Netherlands*
*Branch Office(s)*
Documentation Department Speurwerk/FE, Herengracht 330, 1016 CE Amsterdam, 1016 CE Amsterdam *Tel:* (020) 6247676 *Fax:* (020) 6238869

**Standard Book Numbering Agency**, see Bureau ISBN

**STM**, see International Association of Scientific, Technical & Medical Publishers (STM)

†**Technical Centre for Agricultural & Rural Co-operation**
Agro Business Park 2, Wageningen
Mailing Address: Postbus 380, 6700 AJ Wageningen
*Tel:* (0317) 467100 *Fax:* (0317) 460067

*E-mail:* cta@cta.nl
*Web Site:* www.cta.nl
*Key Personnel*
Head: A C Jackson *Tel:* (0317) 467127
   *E-mail:* jackson@cta.nl
Founded: 1984
Subjects: Tropical Agriculture, Rural Development & Information & Communication Management
ISBN Prefix(es): 92-9081
*Branch Office(s)*
Rue Montoyer, 39, 1000 Brussels, Belgium
   *Tel:* (02) 5137436 *Fax:* (02) 580868

# Netherlands Antilles

†**Bureau Intellectual Property**
Berg Carmelweg 10-A, Curacao
*Tel:* (09) 465 7800 *Fax:* (09) 465 7692
*E-mail:* bipantil@curinfo.an
*Key Personnel*
Dir: Mr Juny J Sluis
Founded: 1893
Registration of trademarks.
Publication(s): *Merkenblad* (Trademark journal)
Number of titles published annually: 161 Print
Total Titles: 296 Print

# New Zealand

**Booksellers New Zealand**
Level 1, Survey House, 21-29 Broderick Rd, Wellington
Mailing Address: PO Box 13 248, Wellington
*Tel:* (04) 478 5511 *Fax:* (04) 478 5519
*E-mail:* enquiries@booksellers.co.nz
*Web Site:* www.booksellers.co.nz
*Key Personnel*
Chairperson: Tony Moores
Chief Executive: Alice Heather

**Booksellers New Zealand**
Level 1, E Wing Survey House, 21-29 Broderick Rd, Johnsonville 9
Mailing Address: PO Box 13-248, Johnsonville 1
*Tel:* (04) 4478-5511 *Fax:* (04) 4478-5519
Publication(s): *NZ Publishing News* (members only)
*Associate Companies:* Copyright Licensing Ltd

**Christian Booksellers' Association (NZ Chapter)**
71 Rata St, Matamata 2711
*Tel:* (07) 888 6010
*E-mail:* info@cbaonline.org
*Web Site:* www.cbaonline.org
*Key Personnel*
Secretary & Treasurer: Roger McRae
Currently have 54 retail members & 27 wholesale members.
Publication(s): *Newsletters* (bimonthly)

**IAML**, see International Association of Music Libraries, Archives & Documentation Centres (IAML)

†◇**International Association of Music Libraries, Archives & Documentation Centres (IAML)**
National Library of New Zealand, PO Box 1467, Wellington

*Tel:* (04) 474 3039 *Fax:* 613-520-2750
*Web Site:* www.iaml.info
*Key Personnel*
Secretary General: Roger Flury *E-mail:* roger.flury@natlib.govt.nz
Founded: 1951
Association internationale des bibliotheques, archives et centres de documentation musicaux (AIBM)
Internationale Vereinigung der Musikbibliotheken, Musikarchive und Musikdokumentations Zentren (IVMB).
Publication(s): *Fontes artis musicae*

◇**New Zealand Council for Educational Research**
10th floor, West Block, Education House, 178-182 Willis St, Wellington
Mailing Address: PO Box 3237, Wellington
*Tel:* (04) 384 7939 *Fax:* (04) 384 7933
*Web Site:* www.nzcer.org.nz
*Key Personnel*
Dir: Robyn Baker *E-mail:* robyn.baker@nzcer.org.nz
Publications Officer: Peter Ridder
Founded: 1934
Publication(s): *New Zealand Journal of Educational Studies* (set)
ISBN Prefix(es): 0-908567; 0-908916; 1-877140

**New Zealand Press Council**
79 Boulcott St, Wellington
Mailing Address: Box 10879, The Terrace, Wellington
*Tel:* (04) 4735220 *Fax:* (04) 4711785
*E-mail:* presscouncil@asa.co.nz
*Web Site:* www.presscouncil.org.nz
*Key Personnel*
Chairman: Sir John Jeffries
Secretary: Mary Major
Founded: 1972

†◇**South Pacific Association for Commonwealth Literature & Language Studies (SPACLALS)**
University of Waikato, Private Bag 3105, Hamilton
*Tel:* (07) 838-4466 *Fax:* (07) 838 4722
Founded: 1975
Publication(s): *Journal & Spaccals* (biannually); *Span*

**SPACLALS**, see South Pacific Association for Commonwealth Literature & Language Studies (SPACLALS)

**Standard Book Numbering Agency**
National Library of New Zealand, Molesworth & Aitken Sts, Wellington 6001
Mailing Address: PO Box 1467, Wellington 6001
*Tel:* (04) 474 3074 *Fax:* (04) 474 3161
*E-mail:* isbn@natlib.govt.nz
*Web Site:* www.natlib.govt.nz
*Key Personnel*
ISBN Librararian: Joy Grove

# Nigeria

**Children's Literature Association of Nigeria**
c/o Institute of African Studies, University of Ibadan, Ibadan, Oyo State
*Tel:* (022) 400550; (022) 400614 *Fax:* (022) 711254
*Key Personnel*
President: Mabel Segun

**Children's Literature Documentation & Research Centre, Ibadan**
UIPO Box 20744, Ibadan, Oyo State
*Fax:* (022) 711254
*Key Personnel*
Dir: Mabel Segun

**Christian Booksellers Association of Nigeria**
c/o Potters House Bookshop, PO Box 13328, Jos, Plateau State
*Tel:* (073) 452387
*E-mail:* cban@bwave.net
*Web Site:* www.cbaonline.org
*Key Personnel*
President: Thomas A Sule
Administrative Secretary: Justice Okonkwo
*Parent Company:* Christian Booksellers Association USA, United States

**CLIDORC**, see Children's Literature Documentation & Research Centre, Ibadan

**Nigerian Book Development Council**
6, Obanta Rd, Apapa, Lagos
*Tel:* (01) 862269; (01) 862272
*Key Personnel*
Secretary: Alhaja M M Musa

**Nigerian ISBN Agency**
National Library of Nigeria, Ijora Lilipond Office, Otto Rd, Ijora Olopa, Lagos
Mailing Address: PMB 12626, Lagos
*Tel:* (01) 5850657; (01) 5850649
*Web Site:* www.nlbn.org
*Telex:* 21746 *Cable:* Biblios
*Key Personnel*
Agency Head: S E A Sonaike
Publication(s): *Nigerian ISBN Manual & Directory*

**Nigerian Publishers Association**
Book House: Quarter 673, Jericho GRA, Old Bodija, Ibadan
Mailing Address: GPO Box 2541, Ibadan
*Tel:* (02) 2414427 *Fax:* (02) 2413396
*E-mail:* nigpa@skannet.com; nigpa@steineng.net; nigpa@freemail.nig.com
*Telex:* 31113
*Key Personnel*
President: V Nwankwo
Chief: Mrs F O Orikan
Publication(s): *The Publisher* (biannually)

**SCAUL**, see Standing Conference of African University Libraries (SCAUL)

**Standard Book Numbering Agency**, see Nigerian ISBN Agency

†◇**Standing Conference of African University Libraries (SCAUL)**
c/o E Bejide Bankole, Editor African Journal of Academic Librarianship, University of Lagos, Akoka, Yaba, Lagos
Mailing Address: PO Box 46, Akoka, Yaba, Lagos
*Tel:* (01) 524968 *Fax:* (01) 822644

**University Booksellers Association of Nigeria**
c/o Benin University Bookshop, PMB 1154, Ugbowo Campus, Benin City
*Tel:* (052) 200250 (Ugbowo); (052) 200480 (Ekehuan) *Fax:* (052) 241156
*Telex:* 41365

# Norway

**Bok Og Papiransattes Forening**
Ovre Vollgate 15, 0158 Oslo
*Tel:* 22205197 *Fax:* 22400033
Norwegian Book Trade Employees' Association.
Publication(s): *Norsk Bokhandlermatrikkel*; *Norsk Boknokkel*

**Den Norske Bokhandlerforening** (Norwegian Booksellers Association)
Ovre Vollgt 15, 0158 Oslo
*Tel:* 22 00 75 80 *Fax:* 22 33 38 30
*E-mail:* dfn@forleggerforeningen.no
*Web Site:* www.forleggerforeningen.no
*Key Personnel*
Dir: Kristin C Slordahl *E-mail:* kristin.slordahl@
forleggerforeningen.no
Publication(s): *Bok og Samfunn*

**ISBN-Kontoret Norge**
National Library of Norway Oslo Division, Postbox 2674, N-0203 Oslo
*Tel:* 23 27 62 17 *Fax:* 23 27 60 10
*E-mail:* isbn-kontoret@nb.no
*Web Site:* www.nb.no
*Telex:* 76078 ub n
*Key Personnel*
Administrator & Senior Librarian: Ms Ingebjoerg Rype
ISBN Agency.
Publication(s): *ISBN-Internasjonalt standard boknummer*
*Parent Company:* National Library of Norway

**Norsk Musikkforleggerforening** (Norwegian Music Publishers' Association)
c/o Musikk-Husets Forlag AS, PO Box 822, Sentrum, 0104 Oslo
*Tel:* (022) 42 50 90 *Fax:* (022) 42 55 41
*E-mail:* info@mic.no
*Web Site:* www.mic.no

**Den Norske Forfatterforening**
Radhusgata 7, Oslo
Mailing Address: Boks 327 Sentrum, N-0103 Oslo
*Tel:* 23357620; 22 42 40 77; 22 41 11 97 *Fax:* 22 42 11 07
*E-mail:* post@forfatterforeningen.no; forfatterforeningen@online.no
*Web Site:* skrift.no/dnf
*Key Personnel*
Secretary General: Lars Haavik
Office Manager: Tordis Fjeldstad
Founded: 1893
Norwegian Authors' Union.

**Den Norske Forleggerforening**
Ovre Vollgt 15, 0158 Oslo
*Tel:* 22 00 75 80 *Fax:* 22 33 38 30
*E-mail:* dnf@forleggerforeningen.no
*Web Site:* www.forleggerforeningen.no
*Key Personnel*
Permission: Kristin Cecilie Slordahl
*E-mail:* kristin.shordahl@forleggerforeningen.
no
Secretary: Astri Skarde *E-mail:* astri.skarde@
forleggerforeningen.no
Memberships: IPA; FEP.

**Standard Book Numbering Agency**, see ISBN-Kontoret Norge

# Pakistan

**Standard Book Numbering Agency**
National Library of Pakistan, Constitution Ave, Islamabad 44000
Mailing Address: PO Box 1982, Islamabad 44000
*Tel:* (051) 921 4523; (051) 920 2544; (051) 920 2549 *Fax:* (051) 922 1375
*E-mail:* nlpiba@paknet2.ptc.pk
*Web Site:* www.nlp.gov.pk
*Key Personnel*
Dir General: Mr M A Zaheer

**Urdu Science Board**
299 Upper Mail, Lahore
*Tel:* (042) 5758674; (042) 878168 *Fax:* (042) 5758674
*Branch Office(s)*
Gari Khata, Manzoor Chambers, Hyderabad
Khyber Bazar, Peshawar Branch, Peshawar

# Papua New Guinea

**Standard Book Numbering Agency**
National Library Service of Papua New Guinea, 131, National Capital District, Waigani
Mailing Address: PO Box 734, Waigani
*Tel:* 3256200 *Fax:* 3251331
*E-mail:* paraide@datec.com.pg
*Web Site:* www.dg.com.pg/ola
*Telex:* NE 22234
*Key Personnel*
Contact: Mr Chris Kelly Meti
Publication(s): *ISBN Users Manual* (Second Edition, 1991)

# Peru

**Camara Peruana del Libro** (Peruvian Publishers' Association)
Av Abancay 4ta cuadra, Lima
*Tel:* (01) 428 7690; (01) 428 7696 *Fax:* (01) 427 7331
*E-mail:* dn@binape.gob.pe
*Web Site:* www.binape.gob.pe
*Key Personnel*
President: Julio Cesar Flores Rodriguez
Executive Dir: Dra Loyda Moran Bustamente
Administrator: Guerra Raul Guerra

**Standard Book Numbering Agency**, see Camara Peruana del Libro

# Philippines

**†◇Congress of South-East Asian Librarians IV (CONSAL IV)**
National Historic Institute of the Philippines, T M Kalaw St, 100 Ermita, Manila
Mailing Address: PO Box 2926, 100 Ermita, Manila
*Tel:* (02) 590646 *Fax:* (02) 572644
*Key Personnel*
Chairman: Dr Serafin D Quiason

**Philippine Educational Publishers' Association**
84 P Florentino St, Sta Mesa Heights, Quezon City
*Tel:* (02) 7124106 *Fax:* (02) 7313448; (02) 7437687
*Web Site:* nbdb.gov.ph/pubindust.htm
*Key Personnel*
President: Dominador D Buhain
*E-mail:* dbuhain@cnl.net
Founded: 1950
Memberships: International Trade Association; IPA.

**Standard Book Numbering Agency, The National Library of the Philippines**
Division of Bibliographic Services Division
TM Kalaw St, 1000 Ermita, Manila
Mailing Address: PO Box 2926, Manila
*Tel:* (02) 5253196; (02) 5251748 *Fax:* (02) 5242324
*E-mail:* director@nlp.gov.ph
*Web Site:* www.nlp.gov.ph
*Telex:* 40726 nalib pm
*Key Personnel*
ISBN Administrator: Leonila DA Tominez
*E-mail:* leat@nlp.gov.ph
Founded: 1900
National library.
Publication(s): *Directory of Printers & Publishers*; *Philippine National Bibliography* (annually, Bibliography of works written by Filipino authors about the Philippines, cumulated quarterly)
*Parent Company:* The National Library of the Philippines
*Ultimate Parent Company:* National Commission for Culture & the Arts

# Poland

**AGPOL (Przedsiebiorstwo Reklamy i Wydawnictw Handlu Zagranicznego)**
ul St Kierbedzia 4, skr poczt 7, 00-957 Warsaw
*Tel:* (022) 416061 *Fax:* (022) 405607
*Telex:* 813364 *Cable:* Agpol Warszawa
*Key Personnel*
Dir: Mieczyslaw Kroker
Founded: 1956
Offers publicity services abroad for Polish foreign trade & in Poland for foreign companies.

**Krajowe Biuro Miedzynarodowego Numeru Ksiazki ISBN**
Biblioteka Narodowa, Institute Bibliograficzny, International Document Numbers Dept, al Niepodleglosci 213, 02-086 Warsaw
*Tel:* (022) 608 2432 *Fax:* (022) 825 5729
*Web Site:* www.bn.org.pl
*Key Personnel*
Contact: Hanna Zawado *E-mail:* hzawado@bn.org.pl

**National ISBN Agency**, see Krajowe Biuro Miedzynarodowego Numeru Ksiazki ISBN

**Polish Chamber of Books**
Krakowskie Przdmiescie 7, PL-00 068 Warsaw
*Tel:* (022) 826 12 01 *Fax:* (022) 826 78 55
*E-mail:* pik@arspolona.com.pl
*Web Site:* www.pik.org.pl
*Key Personnel*
President: Mr Andrzej Nowakowski
Vice President: Grzegorz Majerowicz; Krzysztof Raniowski
Executive Dir: Regina Malgorzata Greda
Founded: 1990
Chamber of Commerce.

**Polskie Towarzystwo Wydawcow Ksiazek**
Mazowiecka 2/4, 00-048 Warsaw
*Tel:* (022) 826 72 71 (ext 345); (022) 826 07 35
   *Fax:* (022) 826 07 35 *Cable:* PETEWUKA
*Key Personnel*
President: Janusz Fogler
Deputy President: Aniela Topulos
General Secretary: Donat Chruscicki
Dir: Maria Kuisz
Polish Society of Book Editors.

**Przedsiebiorstwo Reklamy i Wydawnictw**
   **Handlu Zagranicznego**, see AGPOL
(Przedsiebiorstwo Reklamy i Wydawnictw
Handlu Zagranicznego)

**Stowarzyszenie Ksiegarzy Polskich** (Association
of Polish Booksellers)
ul Mokotowska 4/6, 00-641 Warsaw
*Tel:* (022) 252-874; (022) 256-061
*Web Site:* www.bookweb.org/orgs/1322.html
*Key Personnel*
President: Tadeusz Hussak
Social organization for State book trade employ-
ees.
Publication(s): *Ksiegarz*
ISBN Prefix(es): 83-85020

**Zwiazek Literatow Polskich** (Union of Polish
   Letters)
Krakowskie Przedmiescie 87/89, 00-079 Warsaw
*Tel:* (022) 8260589; (022) 8260866; (022)
   8262504
*Key Personnel*
President: Piotr Kuncewicz
Founded: 1920
Union of Polish Writers.
Membership(s): EWC (European Writers'
   Congress).

# Portugal

**Associacao Portuguesa de Editores e Livreiros**
   (Portuguese Publishers & Booksellers
   Association)
Av dos Estados Unidas da America, n° 97, 6°
   Esq°, 1700-167 Lisbon
*Tel:* (021) 843 51 80 *Fax:* (021) 848 93 77
*E-mail:* geral@apel.pt
*Web Site:* www.apel.pt
*Telex:* 62735 Apel P *Cable:* APEL
*Key Personnel*
President: Graca Didier
Secretary: Joao Miguel Guedes; Vasco Teixeira
Publication(s): *Livros Disponiveis*; *Livros de Por-
tugal, Boletim Bibliografico* (Portuguese Books
in Print, monthly)

**Standard Book Numbering Agency**
Associacao Portuguesa de Editores e Livreiros,
   Av dos Estados Unidos da America, n° 97, 6°
   Esq°, 1700-167 Lisbon
*Tel:* (021) 843 51 80 *Fax:* (021) 848 93 77
*E-mail:* isbn@apel.pt
*Web Site:* www.apel.pt
*Key Personnel*
ISBN Administrator: Ms Conceicao Tome
Publication(s): *Livros Disponiveis* (Books in
Print); *Portuguese Books* (CD Rom)

# Puerto Rico

†◇**ACURIL**
PO Box 23317, UPR Station, San Juan 00931-
3317
*Tel:* (787) 790-8054; (787) 764-0000 (ext 3319)
   *Fax:* (787) 764-2311
*E-mail:* acuril@rrpac.upr.clu.edu; acuril@coqui.
net
*Web Site:* acuril.rrp.upr.edu
*Key Personnel*
President: Lucero Arboleda De Roa
Executive Secretary: Oneida R Ortiz
Treasurer: Neida Pagan-Jimenez
Association of Caribbean University, Research &
   Institutional Libraries.
Publication(s): *ACURIL Newsletter*; *Proceedings
of Annual Conference*

**Association of Caribbean University, Research
   & Institutional Libraries**, see ACURIL

**Ateneo Puertorriqueno**
PO Box 9021180, San Juan 00902-1180
*Tel:* (787) 722-4839; (787) 721-3877 *Fax:* (809)
   725-3873
*E-mail:* ateneopr@caribe.net
*Web Site:* www.ateneopr.com
*Key Personnel*
President: Eduardo Morales, Esq
Vice President: Eladio Rivera Quinones
Executive Dir: Prof Roberto Ramos Perea
Founded: 1876
Puerto Rican Society of Writers. A depository of
   treasures in works of art, literature, historical
   documents & memorabilia. Offers literary con-
   tests, annual art competitions & short academic
   courses.

# Qatar

**Standard Book Numbering Agency**
Qatar National Library, PO Box 205, Doha
*Tel:* 42 9955 *Fax:* 42 9976
*E-mail:* qanali@qatar.net.qa
*Telex:* 4743 qanali
*Key Personnel*
Contact: Mr Sami Abdel Jawad

# Romania

†‡**Centre Europeen pour l'Enseignement
   Superieur (CEPES)** (European Centre for
   Higher Education)
39, Stirbei Voda St, 70732 Bucharest
*Tel:* (01) 3130839; (01) 3130698; (01) 3159956
   *Fax:* (01) 3123567
*E-mail:* cepes@cepes.ro
*Web Site:* www.cepes.ro
*Key Personnel*
Dir: Jan Sadlak
Founded: 1972
Subjects: Higher Education
ISBN Prefix(es): 0-379
Number of titles published annually: 6 Print
Total Titles: 42 Print

**Centrul National de Numerotare Standardizata
   Biblioteca Nationala** (National Centre for
   Standard Numbering ISBN-ISSN-CIP)
Unit of Biblioteca Nationala A Romaniei
Str Ion Ghica 4, sect 3, 79708 Bucharest

*Tel:* (021) 3112635 *Fax:* (021) 3124990
*E-mail:* isbn@bibnat.ro; issn@bibnat.ro
*Web Site:* www.bibnat.ro
*Key Personnel*
Coordinator & Librarian: Aurelia Persinaru
CIP, Librarian: Laura Margarit
ISBN Librarian: Mihaela Laura Stanciu
Activities for a national ISBN & ISSN agency
   (record all the Romanian publishers, assign
   ISBN & ISSN codes, etc). In charge with the
   management of Romanian Cataloguing in Pub-
   lication Programme & editor of CIP National
   Bibliography.
Membership(s):ISBN International Agency, ISSN
   International Centre.
Publication(s): *Bibliografia Cartilor in Curs de
Aparitie* (monthly, journal)
ISBN Prefix(es): 973

**Societa Ziaristilor din Romania** (Journalists
   Society of Romania)
Piata Presei Libere 1, 71341 Bucharest
Mailing Address: Oficial Postal 33, 71341
   Bucharest
*Tel:* (01) 222 83 51; (01) 222 38 71; (01) 315 24
   82 *Fax:* (01) 222 42 66
*E-mail:* szrpress@moon.ro
*Key Personnel*
President: Cornelius Popa
First Vice President: Radu Sorescu

**Standard Book Numbering Agency**, see Centrul
   National de Numerotare Standardizata
   Biblioteca Nationala

**Uniunea Scriitorilor din Romania** (Romanian
   Writer's Union)
Piata Sf Gheorghe, nr3, 1900 Timisoara
*Tel:* (0256) 294895 *Fax:* (0256) 294895
*Web Site:* www.infotim.ro/usrt/usrt.htm
*Telex:* 11796
*Key Personnel*
President: Laurentiu Ulici
Secretary: Cornel Ungureanu
Publication(s): *Convorbiri Literare* (Literary Con-
   versations); *Igaz Szo*; *Knijevni Jivot*; *Lucea-
farul*; *Neue Literatur*; *Orizont* (Horizon); *Ro-
mania Literara* (Literary Romania); *Secolul XX*
   (Twentieth Century); *Steaua* (The Star); *Utunk*;
   *Vatra*; *Viata Romaneasca* (Romanian Life)

# Russian Federation

†◇**Association of Research Libraries &
   Libraries for Science & Technology in the
   CIS**
c/o Russian National Public Library for Science
   & Technology, 12 Kuznetski most, 103919
   Moscow
*Tel:* (095) 925 9288; (095) 924 9458 *Fax:* (095)
   921 9862; (095) 925 9750
*E-mail:* gpntb@gpntb.ru
*Web Site:* www.gpntb.ru
*Key Personnel*
President: Andrei Zemskov

†◇**International Association of Orientalist
   Librarians**
Oriental Center, Russian State Library, 3/5 Vozd-
   vizhenka St, 119019 Moscow
*Tel:* (095) 2028852 *Fax:* (095) 2029187
*E-mail:* oricen@mail.ru

*Key Personnel*
Librarian: Mrs Benedicte Vaerman
  *E-mail:* benedicte.vaerman@bib.kuleuven.ac.be
Publication(s): *International Association of Orientalist Librarians Bulletin* (biannually)

**International Community of Writers' Unions**
Ul Povarskaja 52, 121825 Moscow
*Tel:* (095) 2916307 *Fax:* (095) 2919760
*Key Personnel*
First Secretary: T Pulator

◇**The Press & Publishing Engineering Society**
c/o Union of Scientific and Engineering Associations, Kursovoi per 17, 119034 Moscow
*Tel:* (095) 291 59 43; (095) 291-42-42 *Fax:* (095) 291-85-06
*E-mail:* sitsev@mail.sitek.ru
*Web Site:* usea.mailru.com
*Key Personnel*
Chairman: A Yu Ishlinskii
Scientific & production activities in book publishing.
*Parent Company:* Union of Scientific & Engineering Societies
*Associate Companies:* Ministry of Printing & Information of the Russian Federation

**Publishers Association**
B Nikitskaya St 44, 121069 Moscow
*Tel:* (095) 2021174 *Fax:* (095) 2023989
*Key Personnel*
Dir: Mr V Shibaev
Contact: Mr I Laptev

**Publishing Council of the Academy of Sciences of the Russian Academy of Sciences**
Leninsky prospekt 14, 117901 Moscow
*Tel:* (095) 952905 *Fax:* (095) 2379107

◇**Rossiiskaya Knizhnaya Palata** (Russian Book Chamber)
ul Ostozhenka, d ya, 119034 Moscow
*Tel:* (095) 291-12-78; (095) 291-96-30 *Fax:* (095) 291-96-30; (095) 202-67-25
*E-mail:* bookch@postman.ru; bci@aha.ru
*Web Site:* www.bookchamber.ru
The Russian Book Chamber
All books & publications are registered & described.
Chamber also administers Russian National ISBN Agency.
Publication(s): *Knizhnava Letopis'* (Book Chronicle, weekly bulletin & 5 indexes, journal, 2002, informs about all types of books & booklets published in Russia)

**Standard Book Numbering Agency**
Russian ISBN Agency, Russian Book Chamber, Kremlevskaja Nab 1/9, 119019 Moscow
*Tel:* (095) 2034653; (095) 2035608 *Fax:* (095) 2982576; (095) 2982590
*E-mail:* chamber@aha.ru
*Key Personnel*
ISBN Administrator: N Smourova
Dir General: Boris Lenski

# Saudi Arabia

**Standard Book Numbering Agency**
King Fahd National Library, Registration & Book Numbering Department, Riyadh 11472
Mailing Address: PO Box 7572, Riyadh 11472
*Tel:* (01) 464 51 97; (01) 462 48 88 (ext 224); (01) 462 48 88 (ext 601); (01) 462 48 88 (ext 238) *Fax:* (01) 464 53 41; (01) 462 27 07

*E-mail:* saudi-isbn@kfnl.gov.sa *Cable:* 407599 KFNLR S.J.
*Key Personnel*
General Dir: Mr Ali S Al-Sowaine

# Senegal

†◇**Commission des Bibliotheques de l'AIDBA**
BP 375, Dakar
*Tel:* 240954
*Key Personnel*
Secretary: Emmanuel K W Dadzie
Association internationale pour le Developpement de la Documentation des Bibliotheques et des Archives en Afrique
International Association for the Development of Libraries and Archives in Africa.

†◇**Standing Conference of African Library Schools (SCALS)**
Universite Cheikh Anta Diop de Darkar, BP 5005, Dakar
*Tel:* (08) 250530 *Fax:* (08) 255219
*Telex:* 51-262

# Serbia and Montenegro

**Association of Serbia & Montenegro Publishers & Booksellers**
Kneza Milosa 25, 11000 Belgrade
Mailing Address: POB 570, 11000 Belgrade
*Tel:* (011) 2642-533; (011) 2642-248 *Fax:* (011) 2686-539; (011) 2646-339
*E-mail:* uikj@eunet.yu
*Web Site:* www.beobookfair.co.yu
*Key Personnel*
General Dir: Mr Zivadin Mitrovic
Book Fairs, Department Manager: Marina Radojicic
Founded: 1954
Voluntary non-governmental organization. Represents members at home, abroad & by international organizations (IPA, Geneva). Organizer of the International Book Fair in Belgrade, Publishing activities
Membership(s): International Publishers Association, Geneva.
Publication(s): *Catalog of Yugoslav Books in Print*; *Catalogue of Book Fairs in Belgrade*; *Directory of Exhibitors at the International Book Fair in Belgrade*; *Directory of Members of the Association of Yugoslav Publishers & Booksellers* (annually)
ISBN Prefix(es): 86-7115

**Jugoslovenski Bibliografsko-informacijski institut, Yubin, Agencija za ISBN** (Yugoslav Institute for Bibliography & Information)
Skerliceva 1, 11000 Belgrade
*Tel:* (011) 2451 242 *Fax:* (011) 459 444
*E-mail:* yubin@jbi.bg.ac.yu
*Web Site:* www.jbi.bg.ac.yu/
*Key Personnel*
Dir: Dr Radomir Glavicki
Head of International Exchange Dept: Tanja Ostojic *E-mail:* tanya@jbi.bg.ac.yu
Founded: 1950
Specializes in the production of National bibliography.
Publication(s): *Bibliography of Yugoslavia* (Bibliografija Jugoslavije)

Number of titles published annually: 8 Print
Total Titles: 8 Print

**Standard Book Numbering Agency**, see Jugoslovenski Bibliografsko-informacijski institut, Yubin, Agencija za ISBN

# Singapore

**SBPA**, see Singapore Book Publishers' Association

**Singapore Book Publishers' Association**
c/o Cannon International, Block 86, Marine Parade Central No 03-213, Singapore 440086
*Tel:* (065) 3447801; (065) 4407409 *Fax:* (065) 4470897
*E-mail:* twcsbpa@singnet.com.sg
*Key Personnel*
President: K P Siram
Dir: Mr Tan Wu Cheng
Founded: 1966
Memberships: International Publishers Association (Geneva); Asia Pacific Publishers Association (Seoul).

**Standard Book Numbering Agency**
National Library Board, No 3 Changi South St 2, Tower B, Level 3, Singapore 486548
*Tel:* 6546 7271 *Fax:* 6546 7262
*E-mail:* legaldep@nlb.gov.sg
*Web Site:* www.nlb.gov.sg
*Telex:* Rs 26620 *Cable:* NATLIB SINGAPORE
*Key Personnel*
ISBN Administrators: Mrs Lim Siew Kim; Ms N Dana Lashmi
Publication(s): *Books About Singapore* (biannually); *Singapore National Bibliography* (quarterly/annually); *Singapore: National Library*; *Singapore Periodicals Index* (annually)

# Slovakia

**ISBN National Agency**
Slovak National Library, Nam J C Hronskeho 1, 036 01 Martin
*Tel:* (043) 430 1803; (043) 430 1802 (secretary) *Fax:* (043) 422 4983; (043) 422 0720
*E-mail:* naisbn@snk.sk; poloncova@snk.sk
*Web Site:* www.snk.sk
*Key Personnel*
Contact: Jarmila Majerova *E-mail:* majerova@snk.sk
Founded: 1989
*Parent Company:* Slovak National Library

◇**Spolok slovenskych spisovatel'ov**
Laurinska 2, 815 08 Bratislava
*Tel:* (07) 533 53 71
*Key Personnel*
Honor Chairman: Ladislav Tazky
Chairman: Jaroslav Reznik
President: Mr Vincent Sikula
Founded: 1949
Association of Slovak Writers.
Publication(s): *Literarny Tyzdhennik* (Literary Weekly)
*Associate Companies:* Asociacia organizacii1 Slovenska, Ste Fanikova 14, 81508 Bratislava

# Slovenia

**Gospodarska Zbornica Slovenije**, see Zdruzenie
Zaloznikov in Knjigotrzcev Slovenije
Gospodarska Zbornica Slovenije

**Standard Book Numbering Agency**
National & University Library, Turjaska 1, p p
259, 1000 Ljubljana
*Tel:* (01) 5861 333; (01) 2001 110; (01) 5861 300
*Fax:* (01) 5861 311
*E-mail:* isbn@nuk.uni-lj.si
*Web Site:* www.nuk.uni-lj.si
*Key Personnel*
Contact: Ms Alenka Kanic *E-mail:* alenka.kanic@
nuk.uni-lj.si

◇**Zdruzenie Zaloznikov in Knjigotrzcev**
**Slovenije Gospodarska Zbornica Slovenije**
(Association of Publishers & Booksellers of
Slovenia)
Dimiceva 13, Ljubljana 1504
*Tel:* (01) 5898 474 *Fax:* (01) 5898 100
*E-mail:* info@gzs.si
*Web Site:* www.gzs.si
*Key Personnel*
President, Association: Milan Matos
Membership(s): International Publishers Associa-
tion.
Publication(s): *Knjiga*

# South Africa

**CDNL**, see Conference of Directors of National
Libraries (CDNL)

†◇**Conference of Directors of National**
**Libraries (CDNL)**
The State Library of South Africa, Andries &
Vermeulen Sts, Pretoria 0001
Mailing Address: PO Box 397, Pretoria 0001
*Tel:* (012) 21 8931 *Fax:* (012) 32 5594
*E-mail:* postmaster@statelib.pwv.gov.za
*Key Personnel*
Chairperson: P J Lor
Vice Chairperson: M A Kadir; W van Drimmelen
Founded: 1980

**International Standard Book Numbering**
**Agency**
National Library of South Africa, PO Box 397,
Pretoria 0001
*Tel:* (012) 401 9718 *Fax:* (012) 324 2441
*E-mail:* isn@nlsa.ac.za
*Web Site:* www.nlsa.ac.za
*Key Personnel*
Contact: Magret Kibido *E-mail:* magret.kibido@
nlsa.ac.za

**PASA**, see Publishers' Association of South
Africa (PASA)

**Publishers' Association of South Africa (PASA)**
Centre for the Book, 62 Queen Victoria St, Cape
Town 8000
Mailing Address: PO Box 15277, Vlaeberg 8018
*Tel:* (021) 426 2728; (021) 426 1726 *Fax:* (021)
426 1733
*E-mail:* pasa@publishsa.co.za
*Web Site:* www.publishsa.co.za
*Key Personnel*
Manager: Samantha Faure *E-mail:* samantha@
publishsa.co.za
Administrator: Desiree Murdoch
*E-mail:* desiree@publishsa.co.za

Founded: 1992
Publication(s): *PASA Directory* (annually, list of
members)

**South African Booksellers' Association**
PO Box 870, Bellville 7530
*Tel:* (021) 918 8616 *Fax:* (021) 951 4903
*E-mail:* fnel@naspers.com
*Web Site:* sabooksellers.com
*Key Personnel*
Chairman & President: Guru Redhi
Secretary: Peter Adams
Founded: 1998

# Spain

**Agencia Espanola del ISBN**
Santiago Rusinol, 8, 28040 Madrid
*Tel:* (091) 536 88 00 *Fax:* (091) 553 99 90
*Web Site:* www.mcu.es/bases/spa/isbn/ISBN.html
*Telex:* 47891 fcli e
*Key Personnel*
Head of Service: Maria Yribarren *E-mail:* maria.
yribarren@cll.mcu.es
Ministerio de Educacion y Cultura.

**Asociacion de Escritores y Artistas Espanoles**
(Spanish Writers' & Artists' Association)
Leganitos 10, 28013 Madrid
*Tel:* (091) 5599067 *Fax:* (091) 5599067
*Key Personnel*
Secretary: Jose Lopez Martinez
ISBN Prefix(es): 84-404; 84-398; 84-87857

**Associacio d'Editors en Llengua Catalana**
(Association of Publishers in Catalan)
Valencia 279, 1r, 08009 Barcelona
*Tel:* (093) 155091 *Fax:* (093) 155273
*E-mail:* info@gremieditorscat.es
*Web Site:* www.gremieditorscat.es

**Federacion de Gremios de Editores de Espana**
(FGEE) (Spanish Publishers Association)
Cea Bermudez, 44-2° Dche, 2003 Madrid
*Tel:* (091) 534 51 95 *Fax:* (091) 535 26 25
*E-mail:* fgee@fge.es
*Web Site:* www.federacioneditores.org
*Key Personnel*
President: D Emiliano Martinez
Executive Dir: Antonio Ma Avila
Founded: 1978
Professional Association of Publishers.
Subjects: To represent & defend the general inter-
ests of the Spanish publishing industry

**Standard Book Numbering Agency**, see
Agencia Espanola del ISBN

**UMA**, see World Blind Union (WBU) - Union
Mondiale des Aveugles (UMA)

**WBU**, see World Blind Union (WBU) - Union
Mondiale des Aveugles (UMA)

†◇**World Blind Union (WBU) - Union**
**Mondiale des Aveugles (UMA)**
Jose Ortega y Gasset 22-24, 4°, 28006 Madrid
*Tel:* (091) 436 5366; (091) 589 4533 *Fax:* (091)
589 4749
*E-mail:* umc@once.es
*Web Site:* umc.once.es
*Key Personnel*
Secretary General: Enrique Perez

Founded: 1984
Publication(s): *The World Blind* (2 times/yr, Les
Aveugles dans le Monde & Los Ciegos en el
Mundo)

# Sri Lanka

†◇**The International Water Management**
**Institute**
127, Sunil Mawatha, Pelawatte, Battaramulla
Mailing Address: PO Box 2075, Colombo
*Tel:* (011) 2787404; (011) 2784080 *Fax:* (011)
2786854
*E-mail:* iwmi@cgiar.org
*Web Site:* www.iwmi.cgiar.org
*Telex:* 22318; 22907 IIMIHQCE
*Key Personnel*
Dir General: Prof Frank Rijsberman
Head of Information: Dr James K Lenahan
Founded: 1956
An autonomous nonprofit International Organiza-
tion.
Membership(s): The Consultative Group on Inter-
national Agricultural Research (CGIAR).
ISBN Prefix(es): 92-9090

**Sri Lanka Association of Publishers**
112 S Mahinda Mawatha, Colombo 10
*Tel:* (01) 695773 *Fax:* (01) 696653
*Key Personnel*
Dir: Dayawansa Jayakody
*E-mail:* dayawansajay@hotmail.com
General Secretary: Gamini Wijesuriya
Publication(s): *Hela Bima* (newspaper); *Publish-
ing Scene* (newsletter)

†◇**Standard Book Numbering Agency (ISBN**
**Agency-Sri Lanka)**
14 Independence Ave, Colombo 7
Mailing Address: PO Box 1764, Colombo
*Tel:* (01) 698847; (01) 685198 *Fax:* (01) 685201
*E-mail:* natlib@slt.lk *Cable:* NATLIB
*Key Personnel*
Dir: Matarage Sarath Upali Amarasiri
Founded: 1990
Subjects: Social Sciences, Humanities, Science
& Technology, Computer Science, Library &
Information Science, Literature, Regional Inter-
ests, Mass Communication (mainly material on
Sri Lanka)
Publication(s): *International Standard Book num-
bering in Sri Lanka* (2nd edition, brochure); *Sri
Lanka (ISBN) Publishers Directory* (1991 &
1999 editions)
ISBN Prefix(es): 955-9011

# Sudan

**Sudanese Publishers' Association**
c/o Institute of African & Asian Studies, Khartoum University, PO Box 321, Khartoum
11115
*Tel:* (0249) 11-7780031 *Fax:* (0249) 11-770358
*Key Personnel*
Dir: Abel Rahim Makkawi *E-mail:* makkawi@
sudanmail.net

# Suriname

**Standard Book Numbering Agency**
Publishers' Association Suriname, Domineestr 32
boven, Paramaribo
Mailing Address: PO Box 1841, Paramaribo
*Tel:* 472545 *Fax:* 410563
*E-mail:* postmaster@interfundgroup.com
*Telex:* 123 inco-sn
*Key Personnel*
ISBN Administrator: Mr E Hogenboom
ISBN Prefix(es): 99914

# Swaziland

**The Librarian, University College of Swaziland**
Private Bag 4, Kwaluseni
*Tel:* 5184011 *Fax:* 5185276
*E-mail:* pmuswazi@uniswa.sz; paiki@uniswacc.
uniswa.sz
*Web Site:* www.uniswa.sz
*Telex:* 2087
*Key Personnel*
Librarian: M R Mavuso *E-mail:* mmavuso@
uniswac1.uniswa.sz

**Standard Book Numbering Agency**, see The
Librarian, University College of Swaziland

# Sweden

**Foreningen Svenska Laromedelsproducenter
(The Swedish Association of Educational
Publishers**
Drottninggatan 97, 2nd floor, 113 60 Stockholm
*Tel:* (08) 736 19 40 *Fax:* (08) 736 19 44
*E-mail:* fsl@fsl.se
*Web Site:* www.fsl.se
*Key Personnel*
Dir: Jerker Fransson *Tel:* (08) 736 19 46
    *E-mail:* jerker.fransson@forlagskansli.se
Founded: 1974
Trade association for educational publishers.
ISBN Prefix(es): 91-85386
*Associate Companies:* The Swedish Publishers
    Association

**Svenska Forlaggareforeningen** (Swedish
    Publishers' Association)
Drottninggatan 97, 113 60 Stockholm
*Tel:* (08) 736 19 40 *Fax:* (08) 736 19 44
*E-mail:* info@forlaggareforeningen.se
*Web Site:* www.forlaggareforeningen.se
*Key Personnel*
Dir: Kristina Ahlinder
Founded: 1843
Publication(s): *Svensk Bokhandel* (jointly with the
    Swedish Booksellers' Association)

**The Swedish Association of Educational
Publishers (Foreningen Svenska
Laromedelsproducenter)**, see Foreningen
Svenska Laromedelsproducenter (The Swedish
Association of Educational Publishers

# Switzerland

**AIESI**, see Association Internationale des Ecoles
des Sciences de l'Information

**ASELF**, see Association Suisse des Editeurs de
Langue Francaise

**†◇Association Internationale des Ecoles des
Sciences de l'Information** (International
Association of Information Science Schools)
Unit of Agence Universitaire de la Francophonie
Haute Ecole de Gestion, Information et documen-
    tation, 7, route de Drize, 1227 Carouge
*Tel:* (022) 705 99 77 *Fax:* (022) 705 99 98
*Web Site:* www.aiesi.refer.org
*Key Personnel*
President: Jacqueline Deschamps *Tel:* (022) 705
    99 69 *E-mail:* jacqueline.deschamps@heg.ge.ch
Founded: 1977

**Association Suisse des Editeurs de Langue
Francaise** (Swiss Publishers' Association
(French Language))
2, ave Agassiz, 1001 Lausanne
*Tel:* (021) 319 71 11 *Fax:* (021) 319 79 10
*Telex:* 455730
*Key Personnel*
Secretary General: Philippe Schibli
    *E-mail:* pschibli@centrezational.cl
ISBN Prefix(es): 2-88303

**Association Suisse des Libraires de Langue
Francaise** (Association of Swiss
French-Language Bookshops)
2 ave Agassiz, 1001 Lausanne
*Tel:* (021) 319 71 11 *Fax:* (021) 319 79 10
*E-mail:* aself@centrezational.cl
*Telex:* 455730
*Key Personnel*
Secretary: Philippe Schibli *E-mail:* pschibli@
    centrezational.cl
ISBN Prefix(es): 2-88303

**Association Suisse Romande des Diffuseurs et
Distributeurs de Livres** (Association of Book
Distributors of French-Speaking Switzerland)
2 ave Agassiz, 1001 Lausanne
*Tel:* (021) 319 71 11 *Fax:* (021) 319 79 10
*E-mail:* aself@centrezational.ch
*Telex:* 455730
*Key Personnel*
President: Antonio Jaccheo
Contact: Philippe Schibli *E-mail:* pschibli@
    centrezational.cl

**Buchverleger-Verband der Deutschsprachigen
Schweiz (VVDS)** (Swiss Publishers
Association)
Alderstr 40, 8034 Zurich
*Tel:* (01) 421 28 00 *Fax:* (01) 421 28 18
*E-mail:* sbvv@swissbooks.ch
*Web Site:* www.swissbooks.ch
*Key Personnel*
ISBN Administrator: Stefanie Nuebling *Tel:* (01)
    421 28 01 *E-mail:* isbn@swissbooks.ch
This is the agency for German-language ISBNs.
*Parent Company:* Swiss Booksellers & Publishers
    Association

**†Conference of European Churches**
150 route de Ferney, 1211 Geneva 2
Mailing Address: PO Box 2100, 1211 Geneva 2
*Tel:* (022) 791 61 11 *Fax:* (022) 791 62 27
*E-mail:* cec@cec-kek.org
*Web Site:* www.cec-kek.org
*Telex:* 415 730 0IK CH *Cable:* OIKOUMENE,
    GENEVA

*Key Personnel*
General Secretary: Rev Keith Winston Clements
Associate General Secretary: Rev Ruediger Noll
Communications Secretary: Mr Robin Gurney
    *Tel:* (022) 791 6485 *E-mail:* reg@cec-kek.org
Founded: 1959
Subjects: Ecumenical Theology, International Re-
    lationships
Publication(s): *God Unites; In Christ a New
    Creation* (1992, English, French & German);
    *Springs Within the Valleys* (1997, English,
    French & German); *Working Together With
    Him* (1997, English, French & German)
ISBN Prefix(es): 2-88070
*Branch Office(s)*
Strasbourg, France
Brussels, Belgium

**†◇Distripress**
Beethovenstr 20, 8002 Zurich
*Tel:* (01) 202 41 21 *Fax:* (01) 202 10 25
*E-mail:* info@distripress.ch
*Web Site:* www.distripress.ch
*Key Personnel*
Man Dir: Dr Peter Emod *E-mail:* peter.emod@
    distripress.ch
Founded: 1955
Association pour la Promotion de la Diffusion
    Internationale de la Presse
Vereinigung zur Foerderung des internationalen
    Pressevertriebes
Membership(s): World Association of Newspa-
    pers; European Newspaper Publishers' Associa-
    tion.
Publication(s): *Distripress Gazette* (3 times/yr);
    *Who's Who in Distripress* (annually)

**IBBY**, see International Board on Books for
    Young People (IBBY)

**ILO**, see International Labour Organization (ILO)

**†Inter-Parliamentary Union**
5, chemin du Pommier, 1218 Le Grand Saconnex/
    Geneva
Mailing Address: PO Box 330, 1218 Le Grand
    Saconnex/Geneva
*Tel:* (022) 919 41 50 *Fax:* (022) 919 41 60
*E-mail:* postbox@mail.ipu.org
*Web Site:* www.ipu.org
*Key Personnel*
Secretary General: Anders B Johnsson
Information Officer: Luisa Ballin *Tel:* (022) 919
    41 16 *E-mail:* lb@mail.ipu.org
Founded: 1889
World organization of national parliaments.
Publication(s): *Codes of Conduct for Elections*
    (1998, CS Goodwin-Gill); *The Conference
    of Presiding Officers of National Parliaments*
    (2001); *Declaration on Criteria for Free &
    Fair Elections* (1994); *Democracy: Its Princi-
    ples & Achievement* (1998); *Free & Fair Elec-
    tions: International Law & Practice* (1994,
    GS Goodwin-Gill); *Handbook for Parliamen-
    tarians: Eliminating the Worst Forms of Child
    Labour* (2002); *Handbook for Parliamentar-
    ians: Refugee Protection, A Guide to Inter-
    national Refugee Law* (2001); *Handbook for
    Parliamentarians: Respect for International
    Humanitarian Law* (1999); *The Parliamentary
    Mandate* (2000); *Presiding Officers of National
    Parliamentary Assemblies* (1997, G Bergoug-
    nous); *Universal Declaration on Democracy*
    (1997)
ISBN Prefix(es): 92-9142

**†◇International Board on Books for Young
People (IBBY)**
Nonnenweg 12, 4003 Basel
*Tel:* (061) 272 29 17 *Fax:* (061) 272 27 57
*E-mail:* ibby@ibby.org

*Web Site:* www.ibby.org
*Key Personnel*
Executive Dir: Kimete Basha
Administrative Dir: Elizabeth Page
Founded: 1953
Publication(s): *Bookbird: A Journal of International Children's Literature* (quarterly); *Congress Proceedings* (biennially); *IBBY Honour List* (biennially)

### †‡International Commission of Jurists
81a Ave de Chatelaine, 1219 Geneva
Mailing Address: PO Box 216, 1219 Geneva
*Tel:* (022) 979 38 00 *Fax:* (022) 979 38 01
*E-mail:* info@icj.org
*Web Site:* www.icj.org
*Telex:* 418 531 ICJ CH *Cable:* INTERJURISTS, GENEVA
*Key Personnel*
Secretary-General: Ernst Lueber
Founded: 1952
Subjects: Human Rights, International Law
Publication(s): *ICJ Newsletter; The Review*
ISBN Prefix(es): 92-9037

### †‡International Institute for Labour Studies
4, route des Morillons, 1211 Geneva 22
*Tel:* (022) 799 6111 *Fax:* (022) 798 8685
*E-mail:* ilo@ilo.org
*Web Site:* www.ilo.org
*Telex:* 415647 ilo ch
*Key Personnel*
Dir: Padmanabha Gopinath
Founded: 1960
Publication(s): *The Bibliography Series; Discussion Papers; Organized Labour in the 21st Century; The Research Series*

### †◇International Labour Organization (ILO)
4, route des Morillons, 1211 Geneva 22
*Tel:* (022) 799 6111 *Fax:* (022) 798 8685
*E-mail:* ilo@ilo.org
*Web Site:* www.ilo.org
*Telex:* 415 647 ilo ch *Cable:* INTERLAB GENEVA
*Key Personnel*
Dir: Ms L Stoddart *Tel:* (022) 799 6092
  *E-mail:* stoddart@ilo.org
Dir-General: Michel Hansenne
Chief, Publications Bureau: David Freedman
Chief, Marketing Operations: Luisito Cabrera
Rights Services: Susan Peters
Business Manager: Neal Thornton
Production Editor: May Ballerio
Editor: Francois Crozon; John Myers; Lillian Nell; Carlos Sebilla
Sales: Denis Brodier; Gloria Manghinang; Nicole Vallee
Founded: 1919
From the creation of the ILO in 1919, publishing has formed an important part of its activities. The ILO publishes books, reports & periodicals of international interest on major social, labor & economic problems & trends falling within their competence. This substantial publishing program has over 1300 titles in English, 827 in French & 650 in Spanish (editions in print) which cover studies, monographs, handbooks, training materials & periodicals.
Subjects: Reports for the *International Labor Conference,* Regional Conferences & Sectoral Meetings, Equality of Rights, International Labor Standards, Conditions of Work & Welfare Facilities, Cooperatives, Developing Countries & Technical Cooperation, Economics, Industrial Relations, Intermediate Technology, Employment & Development, Structural Adjustment, Rural Development & Employment Planning, Human Rights & Apartheid, Labor Law & Labor Administration, International Migration & Population Questions, Multinationals, Productivity & Management Development &

Training, Occupational Safety & Health, Social Security, Trade Unions, Vocational Guidance & Training, Wages & Hours of Work, Vocational Rehabilitation, Workers' Education, Women's Questions, Labor Information, Statistics, Bibliographies & Periodicals, Audiovisual Material, Microfiches & CD-ROM
ISBN Prefix(es): 92-2
*Branch Office(s)*
Guillermo Prieto No 94, Colonia San Rafael, Ave Cordoba 950, 06470 Mexico DF, Mexico
Piso 13 y 14, 1054 Buenos Aires, Argentina
Hohenzollernstr 21, 53173 Bonn, Germany
East Court, 3rd floor, India Habitat Centre, Lodi Rd, New Delhi 110 003, India
8th floor, UNU Headquarters Bldg, 53-70 Jingumae 5-chome, Shibuya-ku, Toyko 150, Japan
Millbank Tower, 21-24 Millbank, London SWIP 4QP, United Kingdom
*U.S. Office(s):* ILO Publications Center, 49 Sheridan Ave, Albany, NY 12210, United States

### †International Organization for Standardization (ISO)
CP 56, One rue de Varembe, 1211 Geneva 20
*Tel:* (022) 749 01 11 *Fax:* (022) 733 34 30
*E-mail:* central@iso.org
*Web Site:* www.iso.org
*Key Personnel*
Secretary General: Alan Bryden
Founded: 1947
Worldwide Federation of national standards bodies with some 140 members (one per country).
Subjects: Development of International Standards in all fields except electrical & electronic engineering
ISBN Prefix(es): 92-67
*U.S. Office(s):* American National Standards Institute (ANSI), 1819 "L" St, NW, Washington, DC 20036, United States *Tel:* 212-642-4900 *Fax:* 212-398-0023 *E-mail:* info@ansi.org *Web Site:* www.ansi.org (Postal Address: 25 W 23 St, 4th floor, New York, NY 10036)

### †◇International Publishers Association
Av de Miremont 3, 1206 Geneva
*Tel:* (022) 346 3018 *Fax:* (022) 347 5717
*E-mail:* secretariat@ipa-uie.org; info@ipa-uie.org
*Web Site:* www.ipa-uie.org
*Key Personnel*
President: Pere Vicens Rahola
Vice President: Dr Ana Maria Cabanellas de las Cuevas; Asoke K Ghosh
Treasurer: Hans-Peter Thur
Secretary General: Jens Bammel
Founded: 1896

### †‡International Road Federation
chemin de Blandonnet 2, 1214 Vernier (Geneva)
*Tel:* (022) 306 0260 *Fax:* (022) 306 0270
*E-mail:* info@irfnet.org
*Web Site:* www.irfnet.org
*Key Personnel*
Dir General & Chief Executive Officer: Wim Westerhuis
President: Alain Dupont
Publications: C de Jong Bozkurt
Founded: 1948
Subjects: Road Transport; Road Infrastructure
ISBN Prefix(es): 92-9106
*U.S. Office(s):* The Watergate Office Bldg, 2600 Virginia Ave NW, Suite 208, Washington, DC 20037, United States *Tel:* 202-338-4641 *Fax:* 202-338-8104

### †‡International Telecommunication Union (ITU)
Place des Nations, 1211 Geneva 20
*Tel:* (022) 730 5111 *Fax:* (022) 733 7256
*E-mail:* itumail@itu.int
*Web Site:* www.itu.int/home/contact/index.html
*Telex:* 421000 Uit

*Key Personnel*
Executive Manager: Claus Ilg *E-mail:* claus.ilg@itu.int
The ITU was founded in 1865 as the International Telegraphic Union. It became the International Telecommunication Union in 1934 & a specialized agency of the UN in 1947. Structure: 4 permanent organizations - General Secretariat, International Telegraph & Telephone Consultative Committee (CCITT), International Radio Consultative Committee (CCIR) & the International Frequency Registration Board (IFRB). It regulates, plans, coordinates & standardizes international telecommunications.
ISBN Prefix(es): 92-61; 92-71; 92-72; 92-73; 92-74

### †‡International Union Against Cancer
Affiliate of Council for International Organizations of Medical Sciences
3 Rue du Conseil General, 1205 Geneva
*Tel:* (022) 809 18 11 *Fax:* (022) 809 18 10
*E-mail:* info@uicc.org
*Web Site:* www.uicc.org
*Key Personnel*
Communications Manager: Steve Donnet
  *Tel:* (022) 809 18 75 *E-mail:* donnet@uicc.org
Founded: 1933
Objectives are to advance scientific & medical knowledge in research, diagnosis, treatment & prevention of cancer & promote all other aspects of the campaign against cancer throughout the world.
Publication(s): *Association of UICC Fellows Membership Directory* (2000); *International Directory of Cancer Institutes & Organizations* (online only)

**ISO,** see International Organization for Standardization (ISO)

**IUCN,** see World Conservation Union (IUCN)

### ◇Schweizerischer Buchhaendler- und Verleger-Verband SBVV (Swiss Booksellers' & Publishers' Association (German Language))
Alderstr 40, 8034 Zurich
*Tel:* (01) 421 28 00 *Fax:* (01) 421 28 18
*E-mail:* sbvv@swissbooks.ch
*Web Site:* www.swissbooks.ch
*Key Personnel*
Executive Dir: Dr Martin Jann
Secretary: Eva Heberlein
Further Education: Susanne Weibel
Accountant: Ernst Kaeppeli
ISBN Agentur: Stefanie Nuebling
  *E-mail:* stefanie.nuebling@swissbooks.ch
Publication(s): *Adressbuch des Schweizer Buchhandels; Das Schweizer Buch; Der Schweizer Buchhandel* (bimonthly, Official organ of this association, also its French equivalent SLESR & its Italian equivalents SESI & ALSI); *Schweizer Buecherverzeichnis; Verzeichnis der Auslieferungsstellen*

**SLESR,** see Societe des Libraires et Editeurs de la Suisse Romande (SLESR)

### Societe des Libraires et Editeurs de la Suisse Romande (SLESR) (Booksellers' & Publishers' Association of French-Speaking Switzerland)
2 Ave Agassiz, 1001 Lausanne
*Tel:* (021) 319 71 11 *Fax:* (021) 319 79 10
*E-mail:* aself@centrezational.cl
*Web Site:* www.culturactif.ch/editions/asef1.htm
*Key Personnel*
Dir: Philippe Schibli
Publication(s): *La Librairie suisse* (official organ of this association, also its German equivalent SBVV & its Italian equivalents SESI & ALSI)
ISBN Prefix(es): 2-88303

**Standard Book Numbering Agency**, see Buchverleger-Verband der Deutschsprachigen Schweiz (VVDS)

**UNCTAD**, see United Nations Conference on Trade and Development (UNCTAD)

**UNECE**, see United Nations Economic Commission for Europe (UNECE)

**Union Interparlementaire**, see Inter-Parliamentary Union

**†‡United Nations Conference on Trade and Development (UNCTAD)**
Palais des Nations, 8-14, Av de la Paix, 1211 Geneva 10
*Tel:* (022) 917 1234; (022) 917 5809 *Fax:* (022) 907 0043
*E-mail:* info@unctad.org
*Web Site:* www.unctad.org
*Telex:* 412962 *Cable:* UNATIONS GENEVA
*Key Personnel*
Secretary-General: Edna Dos Santos-Duisenberg
Chief Reference Service: A Von Wartensleben
    *E-mail:* wartensleben@unctad.org
Founded: 1964
Subjects: Trade & Development

**†‡United Nations Economic Commission for Europe (UNECE)**
Palais des Nations, 1211 Geneva 10
*Tel:* (022) 917 12 34 *Fax:* (022) 917 05 05
*E-mail:* info.ece@unece.org
*Web Site:* www.unece.org
*Telex:* 41 29 62
*Key Personnel*
Executive Secretary: Brigita Schmoegnerova
Information Officer: Jean Michel Jakobowicz
Founded: 1947
Provides technical assistance to countries in transition & regional framework for the elaboration of conventions, norms & standards.
Subjects: Economic Analysis, Environmental, Transport, Energy, Timber, Statistics, Trade
ISBN Prefix(es): 92-1
*U.S. Office(s):* Regional Commissions New York Office, New York, NY 10017, United States, Director: Ms S Al-Bassam *Tel:* 212-963-8090 *Fax:* 212-963-1500 *E-mail:* rcnyo@un.org

**†‡United Nations Research Institute for Social Development (UNRISD)**
Palais des Nations, 1211 Geneva 10
*Tel:* (022) 917 3020 *Fax:* (022) 917 0650
*E-mail:* info@unrisd.org
*Web Site:* www.unrisd.org
*Telex:* 412962 UNOCH *Cable:* UNATIONS GENEVA
*Key Personnel*
Dir: Thandika Mkandawire
Deputy Dir: Peter Utting
Information Officer: Nicolas Bovay *Tel:* (022) 917 1143 *E-mail:* bovay@unrisd.org
Founded: 1963
Engages in multidisciplinary research on the social dimensions of contemporary problems affecting development.
Subjects: Technology & society; social policy & development; civil society & social movements; democracy & human rights; identities, conflict & cohesion
Publication(s): *The Accommodation of Cultural Diversity* (Case studies & public policy); *Agricultural Expansion & Tropical Deforestation: Poverty, International Trade & Land Use*; *Cambodia Reborn? The Transition to Democracy & Development*; *Derechos@Glob.net: Globalizacion y derechos humanos en America latina*; *Discours et realites des politiques participatives de gestion*

*de l'environnement: Le cas du Senegal*; *Discours et Realites des Politiques Participatives de Geston de L'Environment*; *Ethnic Diversity & Public Policy: A Comparative Inquiry*; *Forest Policy & Politics in the Philippines: The Dynamics of Participatory Conservation*; *Gendered Poverty & Well-Being*; *Ghana's Adjustment Experience*; *La mano visible: Asumir la responsabilidad por el desarrollo social*; *Land Reform & Peasant Livelihoods: The Social Dynamics of Rural Poverty & Agrarian Reforms in Developing Countries*; *Le conflit libanais: Communautes religieuses, classes sociales et identite nationale*; *Lima megaciudad: Democracia, desarrollo y descentralizacion en sectores populares*; *Mains visibles: Assumer la responsabilite du developpement social*; *Missionaries & Mandarins: Feminist Engagement with Development Institutions*; *The Native Tourists: Mass Tourism within Developing Countries*; *Post-Conflict Eritrea: Prospects for Reconstruction & Development*; *Rebuilding Social & Economic Progress in Africa: Essays in the Memory of Philip Ndegwa*; *Renewing Social & Economic Transformation in East Central Europe*; *Rights@Glob.Net: Globalization & Human Rights in Latin America*; *Social Development & Public Policy*; *UNRISD News* (biannually, newsletter); *Visible Hands: Taking Responsibility for Social Development*; *Whose Land? Civil Society Perspective on Land Reform & Rural Poverty Reduction, Regional Experiences from Africa, Asia & Latin America*
ISBN Prefix(es): 92-9085
Total Titles: 95 Print

**†‡Universal Postal Union (UPU)**
CP 13, 3000 Berne 15
*Tel:* (031) 350 31 11 *Fax:* (031) 350 31 10
*E-mail:* info@upu.int
*Web Site:* www.upu.int *Cable:* UPU BERNE
*Key Personnel*
Dir-General: Thomas E Leavey
Head External Communications: James H Gunderson *Tel:* (031) 350 32 01 *E-mail:* james.gunderson@upu.int
Founded: 1874
Subjects: Postal matters
Publication(s): *Union Postale* (quarterly)
ISBN Prefix(es): 92-62

**UNRISD**, see United Nations Research Institute for Social Development (UNRISD)

**UPU**, see Universal Postal Union (UPU)

**Vereinigung der Buchantiquare und Kupferstichhaendler in der Schweiz**
(Association of Swiss Antiquarian Book & Print Dealers)
Kirchgasse 22, 8001 Zurich
Mailing Address: PO Box 675, 8001 Zurich
*Tel:* (01) 261 57 50 *Fax:* (01) 793 19 33
*E-mail:* eos@eos.ch
*Web Site:* www.vebuku.ch
*Key Personnel*
President: Marcus Benz
Founded: 1939
Membership(s): International League of Antiquarian Booksellers (ILAB).

**Vereinigung des katholischen Buchandels der Schweiz**
Perolles 42, CH-1705 Fribourg
*Tel:* (026) 4 26 43 11 *Fax:* (026) 4 26 43 00
Association of Swiss Catholic Booksellers & Publishers.

**VVDS**, see Buchverleger-Verband der Deutschsprachigen Schweiz (VVDS)

**WARC**, see World Alliance of Reformed Churches

**Weltverband der Lehrmittelfirmen**, see Worlddidac

**WHO**, see World Health Organization (WHO)

**WIPO**, see World Intellectual Property Organization (WIPO)

**WMO**, see World Meteorological Organization

**†World Alliance of Reformed Churches**
150 Route de Ferney, 1211 Geneva 2
Mailing Address: PO Box 2100, 1211 Geneva 2
*Tel:* (022) 791 6240 *Fax:* (022) 791 6505
*E-mail:* warc@warc.ch
*Web Site:* www.warc.ch *Cable:* WARC GENEVA
*Key Personnel*
Secretary General: Rev Setri Nyomi
Administrative Assistant & Communications Office: Sally J Redondo *Tel:* (022) 791 6235
    *E-mail:* sjr@warc.ch
Founded: 1875
Subjects: Biblical Studies, Regional Interests, Protestant Religion, Theology, Women's Studies, Ecological Issues, Economic & Social Justice
Publication(s): *Reformed World* (quarterly, journal, Annual subscription); *Update* (quarterly, newsletter, Annual subscription)
ISBN Prefix(es): 92-9075

**World Association of Publishers, Manufacturers & Distributors of Educational Materials**, see Worlddidac

**†World Conservation Union (IUCN)**
Rue Mauverney 28, 1196 Gland
*Tel:* (022) 999 0000 *Fax:* (022) 999 0002
*E-mail:* mail@iucn.org
*Web Site:* www.iucn.org *Cable:* IUCNATURE GLAND
*Key Personnel*
President: Yolanda Kakabadse Navarro
    *E-mail:* president@iucn.org
Dir-General: Achim Steiner *Tel:* (022) 999 0297 *Fax:* (022) 999 0029 *E-mail:* achim.steiner@iucn.org
Founded: 1948
Subjects: Analytical reports on Eastern Europe; Biodiversity; Ecosystems; Forests; Mountains; Wetlands, Coastal & Marine Areas; Environmental Education; Environmental Law & Policy; Social Policy; Sustainable use initiatives & threatened species
ISBN Prefix(es): 2-8317; 2-88032

**†‡World Health Organization (WHO)**
(Organisation mondiale de la Sante)
Ave Appia, 20, 1211 Geneva 27
*Tel:* (022) 791 2111 *Fax:* (022) 791 3111
*E-mail:* publications@who.int
*Web Site:* www.who.int
*Telex:* 415 416 *Cable:* UNISANTE-GENEVE
*Key Personnel*
Dir General: Dr G H Brundtland
Chief, Marketing: A C Wieboldt *Tel:* (022) 791 2476 *E-mail:* wieboldta@who.int
Founded: 1948
The WHO is a specialized agency of the United Nations with primary responsibility for international health matters & public health. Through this organization the health professions of member states exchange their knowledge & experience with the aim of making possible the attainment by all citizens of the world of a level of health that will permit them to lead a socially & economically productive lives.

Subjects: Public Health, Reference, Medicine, Environmental Health
ISBN Prefix(es): 92-4
Number of titles published annually: 100 Print
Total Titles: 10,000 Print
*Parent Company:* Publicacoes Europa-America
*U.S. Office(s):* WHO Publications Center, 49 Sheridan Ave, Albany, NY 12210, United States *Tel:* 518-436-9686 *Fax:* 518-436-7433
*E-mail:* qcorp@compuserve.com

**†◇World Intellectual Property Organization (WIPO)**
34, chemin des Colombettes, 1211 Geneva 20
Mailing Address: PO Box 18, 1211 Geneva 20
*Tel:* (022) 338 95 20 *Fax:* (022) 740 14 29
*E-mail:* info@wipo.int
*Web Site:* www.wipo.org
*Key Personnel*
Dir General: Dr Kamil Idris
Founded: 1967
World Intellectual Property Organization (WIPO)
Responsible for the promotion of the protection of intellectual property (industrial property & copyright & neighboring rights) throughout the world. Administers, among other international conventions, the Paris Convention for the Protection of Industrial Property & the Berne Convention for the Protection of Literary & Artistic Works.
Publication(s): *Industrial Property & Copyright* (La Propriete industrielle et le Droit d'auteur, monthly in English & French, bimonthly in Spanish); *Intellectual Property in Asia & the Pacific* (quarterly in English); *International Designs Bulletin* (monthly, bilingual French & English); *PCT Gazette* (weekly in English & French); *PCT Newsletter* (monthly in English); *WIPO Gazette of International Marks-Gazette OMPI des Marques internationales* (monthly in English & French)

**†◇World Meteorological Organization**
CP 2300, 1211 Geneva 2
*Tel:* (022) 730 8111 *Fax:* (022) 730 8181
*E-mail:* pubsales@gateway.wmo.ch; wmo@wmo.int
*Web Site:* www.wmo.int
*Telex:* 44 41 99 OMM CH *Cable:* METEOMOND GENEVE
*Key Personnel*
President: John Zillman
Secretary General: G O P Obasi
The publications of WMO include basic documents, operational publications, official records, WMO guides, technical notes, annual reports & the WMO Bulletin.
ISBN Prefix(es): 92-63
*U.S. Office(s):* AMS, 45 Beacon St, Boston, MA 02108, United States *Tel:* 617-227-2425 *Fax:* 617-742-8718 *E-mail:* wmopubs@9metsoc.org

**World Trade Organization**, see WTO (World Trade Organization)

**†◇Worlddidac**
Bollwerk 21, 3001 Bern
*Tel:* (031) 311 76 82 *Fax:* (031) 312 17 44
*E-mail:* info@worlddidac.org
*Web Site:* www.worlddidac.org
*Key Personnel*
Dir: Beat Jost

**†‡WTO (World Trade Organization)**
Centre William Rappard, 154 rue de Lausanne, 1211 Geneva 21
*Tel:* (022) 739 51 11 *Fax:* (022) 731 42 06
*E-mail:* info@wto.org
*Web Site:* www.wto.org

*Telex:* 412324 OMC; WTOCH *Cable:* OMC/WTO GENEVE
*Key Personnel*
Dir General: Dr Supachai Panitchpakdi
Dir Information: Keith Rockwell
Founded: 1948
Accord general sur les Tarifs douaniers et le Commerce; Examination & negotiations of various aspects of international trade policies & practices.
Publication(s): *Basic Instruments & Selected Documents (BISD) Series* (annually); *GATT Activities* (annually); *The International Markets for Meat* (annually); *International Trade Report* (annually); *International Trade Statistics* (annually); *Trade Policy Review series* (about 14 countries reviewed annually); *The World Market for Dairy Products* (annually)
ISBN Prefix(es): 92-870

# Taiwan, Province of China

**Standard Book Numbering Agency**
National Central Library, 20 Chungshan S Rd, Taipei 100-01
*Tel:* (02) 3822613 *Fax:* (02) 3115330
*E-mail:* isbn@msg.ncl.edu.tw
*Web Site:* www.ncl.edu.tw/isbn
*Key Personnel*
Dir: Dr Chuang Fang-Jung
Contact: Ms Li-chien Lee
Publication(s): *ISBN Publishers' Directory* (annually); *National Central Library Newsletter* (quarterly, newsletter)

# United Republic of Tanzania

**National Bibliographic Agency**
Tanzania Library Service, 51 Uporoto St, Ursino Estates, Dar Es Salaam
Mailing Address: PO Box 31226, Dar Es Salaam
*Tel:* (051) 150048; (051) 110573 *Fax:* (022) 2151100
*E-mail:* tlsb@africaonline.co.tz; library@esrf.or.tz
*Key Personnel*
Dir: E A Mwinyimvua
ISBN Administrator: Mr M S Mkenga

**Standard Book Numbering Agency**, see Tanzania Library Service

**Tanzania Library Service**
PO Box 9283, Dar es Salaam
*Tel:* (022) 215 09 23; (022) 215 00 48 *Fax:* (022) 215 11 00
*E-mail:* tlsb@africaonline.co.tz
*Key Personnel*
Head, Bibliographic & Documentation Service
 Dir: Irene Minja
ISBN Prefix(es): 9976-65

# Thailand

**National Library**
Samsen Rd, Bangkok 10300
*Tel:* (02) 2810263; (02) 2815999; (02) 2815450 *Fax:* (02) 2810263; (02) 2815999; (02) 2815450
*E-mail:* suwaksin@emisc.moe.go.th
*Web Site:* www.natlib.moe.go.th
*Telex:* 84189 depfiar th
*Key Personnel*
Dir: Suwakhon Siriwongworawat
Also acts as Standard Book Numbering Agency.

**Publishers' & Booksellers' Association of Thailand**
947/158-159 Moo 12, Bang Na-Trad Rd, Bang Na, Bangkok 10260
*Tel:* (02) 954-9560-4 *Fax:* (02) 954-9565-6
*E-mail:* info@pubat.or.th
*Web Site:* www.pubat.or.th

**C/O Seames**, see Southeast Asian Ministers of Education Organization Regional Language Centre (SEAMEO RELC)

**†◇Southeast Asian Ministers of Education Organization Regional Language Centre (SEAMEO RELC)**
Mom Luang Pin Malakul Centenery Bldg, 920 Sukhumvit Rd, Bangkok 10110
*Tel:* (02) 3910144; (02) 3910554; (02) 3916413 *Fax:* (02) 3812587
*E-mail:* secretariat@seameo.org
*Web Site:* www.seameo.org
*Key Personnel*
Dir: Dr Arief S Sadiman
Publications Officer: Wilfredo O Pascual, Jr
Founded: 1965
Subjects: Language Teaching & Research, Linguistics, English in multilingual, multicultural situations

**Standard Book Numbering Agency**
The National Library of Thailand, Samsen Rd, Bangkok 10300
*Tel:* (02) 2810263; (02) 6285196 *Fax:* (02) 2810263
*E-mail:* suwksir@emisc.moe.go.th; suwaksir@yahoo.com
*Web Site:* www.isbn.org
*Telex:* 84189 Natlib Th
*Key Personnel*
Dir: Suwakhon Siriwongorawat *Tel:* (062) 2817543

**†‡United Nations Library, Bangkok**
United Nations Bldg, Rajadamnern Ave, Bangkok 10200
*Tel:* (02) 2881360; (02) 2881341 *Fax:* (02) 2883036
*E-mail:* libweb@un.org; library-escap@un.org
*Web Site:* www.unescap.org/unis/lib.htm; www.unescap.org/unis/library/net08.asp
*Telex:* 82392; 82315 Escap *Cable:* ESCAP BANGKOK
*Key Personnel*
Chief Librarian: Domingo Barker *Tel:* (02) 2881799 *E-mail:* domingo-barker@un.org
Founded: 1950
Subjects: Economic & Social Development in Asia & the Pacific Region
Publication(s): *Asia & Pacific Bibliography* (biannually); *ESCAP Publications* (biannually)

# Tunisia

**Agence Tunisienne de l'ISBN**
Bibliotheque Nationale, 20 Souk El Attarine,
1008 Tunis
Mailing Address: BP 42, 1008 Tunis
*Tel:* 71572706 *Fax:* 71572887
*E-mail:* bibliotheque.nationale@email.ati.tn
*Web Site:* www.bibliotheque.nat.tn
*Key Personnel*
Contact: Mdme Ben Sedrine Nabiha
Founded: 1988

**Standard Book Numbering Agency**, see Agence
Tunisienne de l'ISBN

# Turkey

**Standard Book Numbering Agency**
Kultur Bakanligi, Kutuphaneler Genel Mudurlugu,
Necatibey Cad No:55, 06440 Ankara
*Tel:* (0312) 231 78 26; (0312) 231 78 29; (0312)
232 27 60 *Fax:* (0312) 231 35 64
*E-mail:* kultur@kutuphanelergm.gov.tr; isbn@
kultur.gov.tr
*Web Site:* www.kutuphanelergm.gov.tr
*Key Personnel*
General Dir: Ms Gokcin Yalcin

**Tuerk Editoerler Dernegi**
No 12-3 Cagaloglu, Istanbul
*Tel:* (0212) 5125602 *Fax:* (0212) 5117794
Turkish Publishers' Association.

# Uganda

**Standard Book Numbering Agency**, see Uganda
Publishers & Booksellers Association

**Uganda Publishers & Booksellers Association**
PO Box 7732, Kampala
*Tel:* (041) 259 163 *Fax:* (041) 251 160
*E-mail:* mbd@infocom.co.ug
*Telex:* 61272
*Key Personnel*
Contact: Martin Okia
ISBN Prefix(es): 9970-04

# Ukraine

**Book Chamber of Ukraine, National ISBN
Agency**
Knyzkova Palata Ukrainy, 27 Yuri Gagarin Ave,
Kiev 02660
*Tel:* (044) 552-0134; (044) 573-0184 *Fax:* (044)
552-0143
*E-mail:* office@ukrbook.net
*Web Site:* www.ukrbook.net
*Key Personnel*
Head of ISBN Agency: Iryna Pogorelovska
Publication(s): *Economics, Economic Science*;
*Germans in Ukraine*; *Market Economy*; *New
Editions of Ukraine*; *Politics, Political Sciences*;
*Publishing Business*; *Tartars in Ukraine*; *Turks
in Ukraine*; *Ukraine's Ethnic Communities*

**Standard Book Numbering Agency**, see Book
Chamber of Ukraine, National ISBN Agency

# United Kingdom

**†African Books Collective Ltd**
Kings Meadow, Unit 13, Ferry Hinksey Rd, Ox-
ford OX2 ODP
*Tel:* (01865) 726686 *Fax:* (01865) 793298
*E-mail:* abc@africanbookscollective.com
*Web Site:* www.africanbookscollective.com
*Key Personnel*
Head: Mary Jay *E-mail:* mary.jay@
africanbookscollective.com
Marketing: Ejemhen Esangbedo
Customer Services: Krisia Cook *E-mail:* krisia.
cook@africanbookscollective.com; Naomi
Robertson
Founded: 1989
Donor-funded organization owned by member
publishers. Has exclusive distribution rights of
member publishers titles outside Africa.
Subjects: Scholarly & Academic, Literary (including Criticism), Children's Books
ISBN Prefix(es): 91-7106; 0-949229; 0-908311;
9966-831; 1-870784; 978-2601; 978-2266;
0-947479; 0-947009; 978-2264; 978-2299;
978-2321; 978-2494; 9964-970; 978-2711; 1-
870716; 0-949225; 99916-31; 0-908307; 0-
949932; 0-906968; 99911-31; 9964-978; 978-
2492; 978-2323; 978-2276

**ALPSP**, see Association of Learned &
Professional Society Publishers

**Antiquarian Booksellers' Association**
Sackville House, 40 Piccadilly, London W1J 0DR
*Tel:* (020) 7439 3118 *Fax:* (020) 7439 3119
*E-mail:* admin@aba.org.uk
*Web Site:* www.aba.org.uk
*Key Personnel*
President: Jonathan Potter
Administrator: Philippa Gibson; Deborah Strat-
ford

**Association of Authors' Agents**
AP Watt Ltd, 20 John St, London WC1N 2DR
*Tel:* (020) 7405 6774 *Fax:* (020) 7836 9541
*E-mail:* aaa@apwatt.uk
*Web Site:* www.agentsassoc.co.uk
*Key Personnel*
President: Derek Jones
Treasurer: Barbara Levy
Secretary: Anna Power
Trade association representing the interests of UK
based literary agents.

**Association of Learned & Professional Society
Publishers**
South House, The Street, Clapham, Worthing,
West Sussex BN13 3UU
*Tel:* (01903) 871 686 *Fax:* (01903) 871 457
*Web Site:* www.alpsp.org/default.htm
*Key Personnel*
Secretary-General: Sally Morris *E-mail:* sally.
morris@alpsp.org
Business Manager: Jill Tolson
Editor: Robert Welham
Trade association for not-for-profit publishers in-
ternational.
Publication(s): *ALPSP Alert* (monthly); *Learned
Publishing* (quarterly); *Serial Publications* (2nd
Edition, 2003)

**Association of Little Presses**
86 Lylton Rd, Oxford OX4 3N2
*Tel:* (01865) 718266
*E-mail:* alp@melloworld.com
*Web Site:* www.melloworld.com/alp
*Key Personnel*
Chairman: Lawrence Upton
Coordinator & Membership Secretary: Chris
Jones
Treasurer: Peter Finch
Editor: Paul Green; Stan Trevor
Founded: 1971
Organizes book fairs.
Publication(s): *Catalogue of Little Press Books
in Print* (biennially); *Getting Your Poetry
Published*; *Poetry & Little Press Information
(PALPI)* (biannually); *Publishing Yourself-Not
Too Difficult After All*; *Small Presses and Little
Publications of the UK and Ireland - an Ad-
dress list*
*Branch Office(s)*
Consortium of London Presses, 89a Petherton Rd,
London N5 2QT

**Authors' Licensing & Collecting Society**
Marlborough Court, 14-18 Holborn, London
EC1N 2LE
*Tel:* (020) 7395 0600 *Fax:* (020) 7395 0660
*E-mail:* alcs@alcs.co.uk
*Web Site:* www.alcs.co.uk
*Key Personnel*
Chief Executive: Jane Carr *E-mail:* chief.
executive@alcs.co.uk
Head of Communications: Sandy Teli
Founded: 1977

**Book Development Council International
(BDCI)**
29B Montague St, London WC1B 5BH
*Tel:* (020) 7691 9191 *Fax:* (020) 7691 9199
*E-mail:* mail@publishers.org.uk
*Web Site:* www.publishers.org.uk
*Key Personnel*
Chairman: Chris Paterson
Dir: Ian Taylor *Tel:* (020) 7691 1373
*E-mail:* itaylor@publishers.org.uk
Executive Assistant: Kate Bostock *Tel:* (020)
7691 1375 *E-mail:* kbostock@publishers.org.uk
International Division of the Publishers Associa-
tion.
*Parent Company:* International Division of the
Publishers Association UK

**†◇Book Industry Communication**
39-41 North Rd, London N7 9DP
*Tel:* (020) 7607 0021 *Fax:* (020) 7607 0415
*Web Site:* www.bic.org.uk
*Key Personnel*
Chairman: Roger Woodham
Managing Agent: Brian Green *E-mail:* brian@bic.
org.uk

**Book Marketing Ltd**
7 John St, London WC1N 2ES
*Tel:* (020) 7440 8930 *Fax:* (020) 7242 7485
*E-mail:* bml@bookmarketing.co.uk
*Web Site:* www.bookmarketing.co.uk
*Key Personnel*
Man Dir: Jo Henry
Chairman: Tim Rix
Deputy Chairman: Clare Harrison
Founded: 1989
Market research agency specializing in the book
industry.
ISBN Prefix(es): 1-873517

**Book Tokens Ltd**
Minster House, 272-274 Vauxhall Bridge Rd,
London SW1V 1BA
*Tel:* (020) 7802 0802 *Fax:* (020) 7802 0803
*E-mail:* mail@booksellers.org.uk
*Web Site:* www.booksellers.org.uk

*Key Personnel*
Man Dir: Stuart Mathews *E-mail:* stuart.
mathews@booktokens.co.uk
Marketing & Sales Dir: Matthew Graham-Clare
*E-mail:* matthew.graham-clare@booktokens.co.
uk
Serves more than 3000 bookshops.
*Parent Company:* Booksellers Association of
Great Britain & Ireland
*Associate Companies:* Booksellers Clearing
House

## The Book Trade Benevolent Society
Dillon Lodge, The Retreat, Abbots Rd, Kings
Langley, Herts WD4 8LT
*Tel:* (01923) 263128 *Fax:* (01923) 270732
*E-mail:* btbs@booktradecharity.demon.co.uk
*Web Site:* www.booktradecharity.demon.co.uk
*Key Personnel*
President: Sally Whitaker
Chief Executive: David Hicks *Tel:* (01923)
299731
Founded: 1837
Charity-Occupational Benevolent Fund.

## Books for Keeps
6 Brightfield Rd, Lee, London SE12 8QF
*Tel:* (020) 8852 4953 *Fax:* (020) 8318 7580
*E-mail:* enquiries@booksforkeeps.co.uk
*Web Site:* www.booksforkeeps.co.uk
*Key Personnel*
Man Dir: Richard Hill
Founded: 1976
Children's Book Review Magazine.
*Publication(s):* *Books for Keeps* (bimonthly);
*Children's Books About Bullying*; *A Multicul-
tural Guide to Children's Books: 0-16*; *Poetry
0-13*
*Parent Company:* School Bookshop Association

## ◇Booktrust
45 East Hill, London SW18 2QZ
*Tel:* (020) 8516 2977 *Fax:* (020) 8516 2978
*Web Site:* www.booktrust.org.uk
*Key Personnel*
Prizes Administrator: Tarryn McKay *Tel:* (020)
8516 2972 *E-mail:* tarryn@booktrust.org.uk
Prizes Manager: Kate Mervyn-Jones *Tel:* (020)
8516 2973 *E-mail:* kate@booktrust.org.uk
Supported by the Arts Council of England with
activities which include literary prizes such
as The Man Booker Prize, The Orange Prize
for Fiction & the Nestle Smarties Book Prize.
Booktrust also runs the Book Information Ser-
vice.
*Publication(s):* *The Authors & Bank Directory*;
*Children's Books of the Year*; *Grants & Awards
Annotated*; *Guide to Literary Prizes*
Divisions: Children's Literature Team at Booktrust (Reading-based projects & publications
related to children under 16)

**BPIF**, see British Printing Industries Federation
(BPIF)

## British Association of Communicators in Business Ltd (CIB)
Suite A, 1st floor, Auriga Bldg, Davy Ave,
Knowlhill, Milton Keynes MK5 8ND
*Tel:* (0870) 121 7606 *Fax:* (0870) 121 7601
*E-mail:* enquiries@cib.uk.com
*Web Site:* www.cib.uk.com
*Key Personnel*
Chairman: Alison Crossley
President: Alan Peaford
Secretary General: Kathie Jones *E-mail:* kathie@
cib.uk.com
Founded: 1949
*Publication(s):* *CiB News* (monthly); *Communica-
tors in Business Magazine* (quarterly)

## British Copyright Council
29-33 Berners St, London W1T 3AB
*Tel:* (020) 788 122 *Fax:* (020) 788 847
*E-mail:* secretary@britishcopyright.org
*Web Site:* www.britishcopyright.org
*Key Personnel*
Vice President: Geoffrey Adams; Maureen Duffy

## British Guild of Travel Writers
BGTW Secretariat, 51b Askew Crescent, London
W12 9DN
*Tel:* (020) 8749 1128 *Fax:* (020) 8749 1128
*E-mail:* bgtw@garlandintl.co.uk
*Web Site:* www.bgtw.org
*Key Personnel*
Chairman: Mary Johns
Secretary: Melissa Shales
Founded: 1960
*Publication(s):* *Year Book* (annually)

## British Printing Industries Federation (BPIF)
Farringdon Point, 29-35 Farringdon Rd, London
EC1M 3JF
*Tel:* (0870) 240 4085 *Fax:* (020) 7405 7784
*E-mail:* info@bpif.org.uk
*Web Site:* www.britishprint.com
*Key Personnel*
Chief Executive: Michael Johnson
Dir General: Tom Machin
Deputy Dir: David Padbury
Marketing Executive: Ruth Yarnit *E-mail:* ruth.
yarnit@bpif.org.uk
*Publication(s):* *Introduction to Printing Technol-
ogy*; *Print Buyers Directory*; *Printing Industries*
(monthly); *UK Periodical Printers*

## Bryntirion Press
Bryntirion, Bridgend CF31 4DX
*Tel:* (01656) 655886 *Fax:* (01656) 656095
*E-mail:* office@emw.org.uk
*Key Personnel*
Press Manager: Huw Kinsey *Tel:* (01656) 665916
*E-mail:* huw@emw.org.uk
Secretary: Manon Lloyd Owen *Tel:* (01656)
665911 *E-mail:* manon@mudiad-efengylaidd.
org
*Publication(s):* *Christian Handbook*; *From Shore
to Shore*; *Heaven*; *Heirs of Salvation*; *A Light
in the Land*; *On the Wings of the Dove*
ISBN Prefix(es): 0-900898; 1-85049

## BSI British Standards Institution
389 Chiswick High Rd, London W4 4AL
*Tel:* (020) 8996 9000 *Fax:* (020) 8996 7001
*E-mail:* info@bsi-global.com; cservices@bsi-
global.com
*Web Site:* www.bsi-global.com
*Telex:* 266933
*Key Personnel*
Chairman: David John
Man Dir: Stevan Breeze
Secretary: Stanley Williams
Founded: 1901
National Standards Body.
*Publication(s):* *Business Standards Magazine*;
*13,000 British Standards*
*U.S. Office(s):* BSI Inc, 12110 Sunset Hills Rd,
Suite 140, Reston, VA 20190-2131, United
States

**BTBS The Book Trade Charity**, see The Book
Trade Benevolent Society

## †CAB International
Nosworthy Way, Wallingford, Oxon OX10 8DE
*Tel:* (01491) 832111 *Fax:* (01491) 833508
*E-mail:* corporate@cabi.org
*Web Site:* www.cabi.org
*Telex:* 847964 Comagg *Cable:* COMAG
*Key Personnel*
Dir General: Dr Denis Blight

Assistant Dir: Dr Ruth Ibbotson
Distribution Manager: Roger Farnell
Journals Production Manager: Pippa Smart
Contact: Angie Barker *E-mail:* a-barker@cabi.org
Publisher: Tim Hardwick *E-mail:* t.hardwick@
cabi.org
Founded: 1929
Subjects: Agriculture, Agricultural Economics,
Animal Health, Animal Science, Forestry, Ru-
ral Sociology, Nutrition, Environmental Sci-
ence, Human, Horticulture Health
ISBN Prefix(es): 0-85198; 0-85199

## †◇The Lewis Carroll Society
The Secretary, 69 Cromwell Rd, Hertford, Herts
SG13 7DP
*E-mail:* aztec@compuserve.com
*Web Site:* lewiscarrollsociety.org.uk
*Key Personnel*
Honorary Secretary: Alan White
Chairman: Mark Richards
Treasurer: Roger Allen
Founded: 1969
The Ellis Hillman Memorial Award was estab-
lished to honour significant & original con-
tributions to the appreciation & enjoyment of
Lewis Carroll & his works.

## Chartered Institute of Journalists (CIJ)
2 Dock Offices, Surrey Quays Rd, London SE16
2XU
*Tel:* (020) 7252 1187 *Fax:* (020) 7232 2302
*E-mail:* memberservices@ioj.co.uk
*Web Site:* www.ioj.co.uk
*Key Personnel*
President: M Moriarty
General Secretary: C J Underwood
Founded: 1884
Professional body/independent trade union.
Subjects: Journalism & Broadcasting
*Publication(s):* *The Journal*

## Children's Book Circle
80 Strand, London WC2R 0RL
*Tel:* (020) 7416 3130 *Fax:* (020) 7739 2318
*Web Site:* www.booktrusted.com/handbook/
journals/bookskeeps.html
*Key Personnel*
Co-Chairperson: Susan Barry *E-mail:* susan.
barry@wattspub.co.uk; Kirsten Grant

## Children's Writers & Illustrators Group
Society of Authors, 84 Drayton Gardens, London
SW10 9SB
*Tel:* (020) 7373 6642 *Fax:* (020) 7373 5768
*Web Site:* www.booktrusted.com/booklists/
listindex.html; www.societyofauthors.net
*Key Personnel*
Secretary: Jo Hodder *Tel:* (020) 7373 6647
*E-mail:* johodder@societyofauthors.org
*Parent Company:* The Society of Authors

## Christian Booksellers Association
Grampian House, 144 Deansgate, Manchester M3
3ED
Mailing Address: PO Box 30, Manchester M60
3BX
*Tel:* (0161) 434 7000 *Fax:* (0161) 445 2911
*E-mail:* info@cba-ukeurope.org
*Web Site:* www.cba-ukeurop.org
*Key Personnel*
Executive Vice Chairman: John F Macdonald
General Secretary: Barry Holmes
Founded: 1984
International trade association. Not for profit, of-
fering a trade service to the Christian sector &
some at the general sector of publishing, distri-
bution, retailing. In UK & over 70 countries.
*Publication(s):* *Christian Bookstore Journal*
(monthly, trade publications)

**CICI**, see Confederation of Information Communication Industries

**CIJ**, see Chartered Institute of Journalists (CIJ)

**Circle of Wine Writers**
393 Ham Green, Holt, Trowbridge, Wilts BA14 6PX
*Tel:* (01225) 783007 *Fax:* (01225) 783152
*E-mail:* administrator@winewriters.org
*Web Site:* www.winewriters.org
*Key Personnel*
President: Hugh Johnson
Chairman: Andrew Henderson *E-mail:* andyh@mailbox.co.uk; Steven Spurrier
Honorary Secretary: Christopher Fielden *E-mail:* secretary@winewriters.org

**†CODE - Europe**
The Jam Factory, 27 Park End St, Oxford OX1 1HU
*Tel:* (01865) 202438 *Fax:* (01865) 2024390
*E-mail:* code_europe@compuserve.com
*Web Site:* www.oneworld.org/code_europe/code_news10.html
*Key Personnel*
Editor: Kevin Smith
Publication(s): *Tailor-Made Textbooks*

**Comhairle nan Leabhraichean - The Gaelic Books Council**
22 Mansfield St, Glasgow G11 5QP
*Tel:* (0141) 337 6211 *Fax:* (0141) 341 0515
*E-mail:* fios@gaelicbooks.net
*Web Site:* www.gaelicbooks.net
*Key Personnel*
Chairman: Donalda MacKinnon
Dir: Ian MacDonald
Retails all Gaelic & Gaelic related titles in print.
Publication(s): *Catalog of Gaelic Books in print*; *Gaelic Poetry Posters*

**Confederation of Information Communication Industries**
39-41 North Rd, London N7 9DP
*Tel:* (020) 7607 0021 *Fax:* (020) 7607 0415
*Key Personnel*
Manager: Brian Green *E-mail:* brian@bic.org.uk
Chairman: Peter Lalster
Dir: Clive Bradley
Operates CICInet, containing reference databases.

**◇Copyright Licensing Agency**
90 Tottenham Court Rd, London W1T 4LP
*Tel:* (020) 7631 5555 *Fax:* (020) 7631 5500
*E-mail:* cla@cla.co.uk
*Web Site:* www.cla.co.uk
*Key Personnel*
Office Manager: K Gardner
Collective administration of rights. Membership(s): International Federation of Reproduction Rights Organizations (IFRRO).
Publication(s): *CLArion* (biannually)
*Associate Companies:* Authors' Licensing & Collecting Society; Publishers Licensing Society

**◇Council of Academic & Professional Publishers**
Division of The Publishers Association
29 B Montague St, London WC1B SBH
*Tel:* (020) 4691 9191 *Fax:* (020) 7691 9199
*E-mail:* mail@publishers.org.uk
*Web Site:* www.publishers.org.uk
*Key Personnel*
Chairman: Philip Shaw
Vice Chairman: Richard Stileman
Dir: Graham Taylor
Founded: 1977
Academic/Professional Publishing Division of The Publishers Association.
*Associate Companies:* Serial Publishers Executive

**Crime Writers' Association**
PO Box 63, Wakefield WF2 0YW
*E-mail:* info@theCWA.co.uk
*Web Site:* www.thecwa.co.uk
*Key Personnel*
Chairman: Danuta Reah
Secretary: Judith Cutler *Tel:* (07227) 709 782 *E-mail:* judith.cutler@virgin.net
Founded: 1953

**Cyngor Llyfrau Cymru**, see Welsh Books Council

**Cyngor Llyfrau Cymru Canolfan Dosbarthu**, see Welsh Books Council

**DACS**, see Design & Artists Copyright Society (DACS)

**Design & Artists Copyright Society (DACS)**
33 Great Sutton St, London EC1V 0DX
*Tel:* (020) 7336 8811 *Fax:* (020) 7336 8822
*E-mail:* info@dacs.co.uk
*Web Site:* www.dacs.co.uk
*Telex:* 885130 FABRIX G
*Key Personnel*
Chief Executive: Rachel Duffield

**Directory & Database Publishers Association**
Queens House, 28 Kingsway, London WC 2B 6JR
*Tel:* (020) 7405 0836 *Fax:* (020) 7404 4167
*Web Site:* www.directory-publisher.co.uk
*Key Personnel*
Chairman: John Condron
Secretary: Rosemary Pettit *E-mail:* RosemaryPettit@onetel.net.uk
Founded: 1970
Trade association for directory & database publishers
Membership(s): Advertising Association, Periodical Publishers Association, European Association of Directory Publishers, Advertising Standards Board of Finance, Confederation of Information Communication Industries, Digital Content Forum, Publishing National Training Organization.
Publication(s): *DPA News* (quarterly, newsletter); *Membership Book* (annually)
ISBN Prefix(es): 0-906247; 0-900247

**Educational Publishers Council**
29B Montague St, London WC1B 6BH
*Tel:* (020) 7691 9191 *Fax:* (020) 7691 9199
*E-mail:* mail@publishers.org.uk
*Web Site:* www.publishers.org.uk *Cable:* PUBLASOC, LONDON WC1
*Key Personnel*
Chairman: Philip Walters
Dir: Graham Taylor
School Books Division of The Publishers Association.
*Parent Company:* The Publishers Association

**Educational Writers' Group**
84 Drayton Gardens, London SW10 9SB
*Tel:* (020) 7373 6642 *Fax:* (020) 7373 5768
*E-mail:* info@societyofauthors.org
*Web Site:* www.societyofauthors.org
*Key Personnel*
General Secretary: Mark Le Fanu
*Parent Company:* The Society of Authors

**Effective Publishing**
58 Saint Wulszan Way, Southam, Leamington Spa, Warks CV33 OTQ
*Tel:* (01926) 812110
*Key Personnel*
Dir: Mr Chris Pratt

ISBN Prefix(es): 0-9518558; 1-900319
*Associate Companies:* Effective Services

**†European Information Association**
Central Library, Saint Peter's Sq, Manchester M2 5PD
*Tel:* (0161) 228 3691 *Fax:* (0161) 236 6547
*E-mail:* eia@libraries.manchester.gov.uk
*Web Site:* www.eia.org.uk/
*Key Personnel*
Manager: Catherine Webb *E-mail:* cwebb@librairies.manchester.gov.uk
Founded: 1991
Subjects: European Union Information
Publication(s): *Basic Sources of EU Information*; *EIA European Information Guides*; *EIA Quick Guides* (self-help reference cards series)
ISBN Prefix(es): 0-948272

**Federation of Children's Book Groups**
2 Bridge Wood View, Horsforth Leeds, W Yorks LS18 5PE
*Tel:* (0113) 2588910 *Fax:* (0113) 2588920
*E-mail:* info@fcbg.org.uk
*Web Site:* www.fcbg.org.uk
*Key Personnel*
Secretary: Alison Dick

**†◇The Folklore Society**
Warburg Institute, Woburn Sq, London WC1H 0AB
*Tel:* (020) 7862 8564; (020) 7862 8562
*E-mail:* folklore.society@talk21.com
*Web Site:* www.folklore-society.com
*Key Personnel*
President: Dr Marion Bowman
Vice President: Prof W F H Nicolaisen; Dr Jacqueline Simpson
Secretary: Juliette Wood
Treasurer: Robert McDowall
Information Officer, Librarian: Caroline Oates *E-mail:* c.oates@folklore-society.com
Administrator: Susan Vass *E-mail:* s.vass@folklore-society.com
Founded: 1878
Publication(s): *Aspect of British Calendar Customs*; *Folklore (Journal of the Folklore Society)* (FLS News); *Ribbons, Bells & Squeaking Fiddlers*

**The Gaelic Books Council**, see Comhairle nan Leabhraichean - The Gaelic Books Council

**IATUL**, see International Association of Technological University Libraries (IATUL)

**IBD**, see International Book Development (IBD)

**IMO**, see International Maritime Organization (IMO)

**Independent Publishers Guild**
PO Box 93, Royston SG8 5GH
*Tel:* (01763) 247014 *Fax:* (01763) 246293
*E-mail:* info@ipg.uk.com
*Web Site:* www.ipg.uk.com/
*Key Personnel*
Secretary: Y S Messenger

**Institute of Printing**
The Mews, Hill House, Clanricarde Rd, Tunbridge Wells, Kent TN1 1NU
*Tel:* (01892) 538118 *Fax:* (01892) 518028
*E-mail:* admin@instituteofprinting.org
*Web Site:* www.instituteofprinting.org/
*Key Personnel*
Chairman: Tony White
Secretary General & Administrator: David Freeland
Marketing: Sally Winser

Founded: 1980
Publication(s): *Professional Printer*

## Institute of Scientific & Technical Communicators (ISTC)
PO Box 522, Peterborough PE2 5WX
*Tel:* (01733) 390141 *Fax:* (01733) 390126
*E-mail:* istc@istc.org.uk
*Web Site:* www.istc.org.uk
*Key Personnel*
President: Iain Wright *E-mail:* president@istc.org.uk
Editor: Colin Battson
Executive Secretary: Carol Battson
Founded: 1972
Subjects: Technical & Communication
Publication(s): *Communicator Journal* (quarterly)

## †International African Institute
SOAS, Thornhaugh St, Russell Sq, London WC1H 0XG
*Tel:* (020) 7898 4420 (general); (020) 7898 4435 (publications) *Fax:* (020) 7898 4419
*E-mail:* iai@soas.ac.uk (general); ed2@soas.ac.uk (publications)
*Web Site:* www.iaionthe.net
*Key Personnel*
Chairman: Prof V Y Mudimbe
Chairman, Publications Committee: Dr Elizabeth Dunstan *Tel:* (020) 7898 4435
Honorary Dir: Prof Paul Spencer
Honorary Editor, Africa: Prof Richard Fardon
Founded: 1926
1200 institutions & individuals are subscribing & the Council includes representatives from Africa & elsewhere.
Subjects: Academic books on Africa, including History, Ethnography, Environmental Studies, Bibliography
Publication(s): *Africa* (quarterly, journal); *The Africa Bibliography* (annually); *African Issues* (biannually, paperback); *Classics in African Anthropology Series*; *International African Library Series* (biannually, paperback); *International African Seminars*; *Monographs from the IAI*
ISBN Prefix(es): 0-85302

## †◇International Association of Agricultural Information Specialists (Association Internationale des Specialistes de l'Information Agricoles)
14 Queen St, Wallingford, Dorchester-on-Thames OX10 7HR
*Tel:* (01865) 340054
*Web Site:* www.iaald.org
*Key Personnel*
Secretary-Treasurer: Margot Bellamy
*E-mail:* margot.bellamy@fritillary.demon.co.uk
Founded: 1955
Publication(s): *Quarterly IAALD Bulletin* (2/yr (one combined issue), newsletter, 2000); *World Directory of Agricultural Information Resource Centres* (1/5 yrs, 2000, Available in hard copy & on CD Rom)

## †International Association of Technological University Libraries (IATUL)
c/o Heriot-Watt University Library, EH14 4AS Edinburgh
Mailing Address: Radcliffe Science Library, Oxford University, Parks Rd, Oxford OX1 3QP
*Tel:* (0131) 449 5111 *Fax:* (0131) 451 3164
*E-mail:* iatul@qut.edu.au
*Web Site:* www.iatul.org
*Key Personnel*
President: Michael L Breaks *E-mail:* m.l.breaks@hw.ac.uk
Secretary: Judith Palmer *E-mail:* judith.palmer@bodley.ox.ac.uk

Founded: 1955
Publication(s): *IATUL Conference Proceedings*; *IATUL News* (quarterly)

## International Book Development (IBD)
CfBT, 60 Queens Rd, Reading RG1 4BS
*Tel:* (0118) 902 1000 *Fax:* (0118) 902 1434
*E-mail:* enquiries@cfbt.com
*Web Site:* www.cfbt.com
*Key Personnel*
Man Dir: Tony Read
Dir: Amanda Buchan; Carmelle Denning; David Foster; Euan Henderson
Founded: 1990 (Now owned by the Centre for British Teachers (CfBT))
Provides consultancy, advisory, research, management & training services to international agencies, governments & trade organisations.

## †‡International Maritime Organization (IMO)
4 Albert Embankment, London SE1 7SR
*Tel:* (020) 7735 7611 *Fax:* (020) 7587 3210
*E-mail:* publications-sales@imo.org
*Web Site:* www.imo.org
*Telex:* 04423588 *Cable:* INTERMAR
*Key Personnel*
Information Officer: Roger Kohn *E-mail:* rkohn@imo.org
Head of Publications: Harald Grell
Founded: 1959
Subjects: Texts of International Maritime Treaties concluded under its auspices, Maritime Technical Publications, Oil Pollution Prevention, Maritime Safety
ISBN Prefix(es): 92-801

## †‡The International Molinological Society
125 Parkside Dr, Watford, Herts WD17 3BA
Mailing Address: Groothertoginnelaan 174B, 2517 EV The Hague, Netherlands
*Tel:* (070) 3460885
*Web Site:* tims.geo.tudelft.nl
*Key Personnel*
President: Michael Harverson
*E-mail:* HarversonTims@aol.com
Publications Officer: Leo van der Drift
*E-mail:* leo.diederik@consunet.nl
Founded: 1973
Subjects: Mills (Windmills, Watermills, Animal-Powered Mills) Technique, History, Sociology

## †◇International PEN
9-10 Charterhouse Bldgs, Goswell Rd, London EC1M 7AT
*Tel:* (020) 7253 4308 *Fax:* (020) 7253 5711
*E-mail:* info@internationalpen.org.uk
*Web Site:* www.internationalpen.org.uk
*Key Personnel*
International President: Homero Aridjis
General-Secretary: Terry Carlbom
Contact: Sara Whyatt
Founded: 1921
A World Association of Writers.
Publication(s): *PEN International* (in English & French, issued with the assistance of UNESCO)

**IOJ**, see Chartered Institute of Journalists (CIJ)

## ISSN UK Centre
British Library, Boston Spa, Wetherby, W Yorks LS23 7BQ
*Tel:* (0870) 444 1500 *Fax:* (01937) 546562
*E-mail:* issn-uk@bl.uk
*Web Site:* www.bl.uk/services/bibliographic/issn.html
*Telex:* 557381
*Key Personnel*
Director: David Baron
Allocates International Standard Serial Numbers (ISSN) to serials published in UK.

**ISTC**, see Institute of Scientific & Technical Communicators (ISTC)

**LAB**, see Latin America Bureau

## †◇Latin America Bureau
One Amwell St, London EC1R 1UL
*Tel:* (020) 7278 2829 *Fax:* (020) 7833 0715
*E-mail:* contactlab@lab.org.uk
*Web Site:* www.lab.org.uk
*Key Personnel*
Researcher & Editor: Marcela Lopez
Founded: 1977
Subjects: Political, Social & Economic Issues in contemporary Latin America & the Caribbean, Environmental & Women's studies

## †◇Maritime Information Association
c/o Marine Society, 202 Lambeth Rd, London SE1 7JW
*Tel:* (020) 7261 9535 *Fax:* (020) 7401 2537
*E-mail:* enq@marine-society.org
*Web Site:* www.marine-society.org.uk/
*Key Personnel*
Dir: Jeremy Howard
Founded: 1972
Publication(s): *Marine Information* (guide to libraries & sources of information in the UK)

## ◇Music Publishers Association
20 York Bldg, 3rd floor, London WC2N 6JU
*Tel:* (020) 7839 7779 *Fax:* (020) 7839 7776
*E-mail:* info@mpaonline.org.uk
*Web Site:* www.mpaonline.org.uk
*Key Personnel*
Chairman: Andrew Potter
Deputy Chair: Jane Dyball
Chief Executive: Sarah Faulder
Trade organization for music publishers.
Publication(s): *Catalogue of Printed Music on CD-ROM*; *List of Members*; *Printed Music Distributors*

## National Acquisitions Group
12 Holm Oak Dr, Madeley, Nr Crewe CW3 9HR
*Tel:* (01782) 750462 *Fax:* (01782) 750462
*E-mail:* nag@btconnect.com
*Web Site:* www.nag.org.uk
*Key Personnel*
Chair: Jo Grocott
Administration: Marie Hackett; Diane Roberts
Publication(s): *Directory of Acquisitions Librarians in the UK & Republic of Ireland* (biannually); *NAG News* (quarterly); *Taking Stock* (biannually)

## National Federation of Retail Newsagents
Yeoman House, Sekforde St, London EC1R 0HF
*Tel:* (020) 7253 4225 *Fax:* (020) 7250 0927
*E-mail:* info@nfrn.org.uk
*Web Site:* www.nfrn.org.uk
*Key Personnel*
Dir: David Daniels

## National Union of Journalists (Book Branch)
Headland House, 308 Gray's Inn Rd, London WC1X 8DP
*Tel:* (020) 7278 7916 *Fax:* (020) 7873 8143
*E-mail:* book_branch@hotmail.com
*Web Site:* www.nujbook.org
*Key Personnel*
National Organization: Mike Sherrington
*E-mail:* mikes@nuj.org.uk
Branch Secretary: Nick Bardsley
Membership Secretary: Cath Rasbash
Founded: 1973
Trade Union.
Publication(s): *Comrade Moss* (1990, biography)

## †◇PEN Club-Writers in Exile London Branch
10 Melfort Dr, Leighton Buzzard, Beds LU7 7XN
*Tel:* (020) 8340 5279

*Key Personnel*
President: Velta Snikere
Secretary: Robert Fearnley
Total Titles: 8 Print

**Picture Research Association**
One Willow Court, off Willow St, London EC2A 4QB
*Tel:* (01883) 730123 *Fax:* (01883) 730144
*E-mail:* chair@picture-research.org.uk
*Web Site:* www.picture-research.org.uk
*Key Personnel*
Chair: Charlotte Lippmann
Treasurer: Christine Hinze *E-mail:* christine@ hinze.fsbusiness.co.uk
*Publication(s): Montage* (quarterly, magazine)

**PLA**, see Private Libraries Association (PLA)

**†◇Private Libraries Association (PLA)**
49 Hamilton Park W, London N5 1AE
*Web Site:* www.the-old-school.demon.co.uk/pla. htm
*Key Personnel*
Executive Secretary: James Brown
American Membership Secretary: William A Klutts *Tel:* 901-635-2544
Canadian Membership Secretary: Alan J Horne
Editor, Private Press Books: Paul W Nash
Founded: 1956
An international society of book collectors.
*Publication(s): The Private Library* (journal); *Private Press Books* (checklist of privately printed books)

**Public Lending Right**
Richard House, Sorbonne Close, Stockton-on-Tees, Cleveland TS17 6DA
*Tel:* (01642) 604699 *Fax:* (01642) 615641
*E-mail:* registrar@plr.uk.com
*Web Site:* www.plr.uk.com
*Key Personnel*
Registrar: Dr James Parker *E-mail:* jim.parker@ plr.uk.com
Reports & Press Releases.
*Publication(s): Report on the Public Lending Right Scheme, 2000-01* (annually, 2002); *Whose Loan Is It Anyway? Essays in Celebration of PLR's 20th Anniversary* (1998)

**The Publishers Association**
29b Montague St, London WC1B 5BH
*Tel:* (020) 7691 9191 *Fax:* (020) 7691 9199
*E-mail:* mail@publishers.org.uk
*Web Site:* www.publishers.org.uk
*Key Personnel*
President: Anthony Forbes-Watson
Chief Executive: Ronnie Williams
   *E-mail:* rwilliams@publishers.org.uk
Dir: Graham Taylor *E-mail:* gtaylor@publishers. org.uk; Ian Taylor *E-mail:* itaylor@publishers. org.uk
Trade association for UK publishers of books, journals & electronic publications.
*Publication(s): Annual Book Trade Year Book*

**Publishers Licensing Society Ltd**
37-41 Gower St, London WC1E 6HH
*Tel:* (020) 7299 7730 *Fax:* (020) 7299 7780
*E-mail:* pls@pls.org.uk
*Web Site:* www.pls.org.uk
*Key Personnel*
Chairman: Neil McRae
Consultant: Richard Balkwill
Chief Executive: Jens Bammel
Founded: 1981
PLS has non-exclusive licences from 1600 publishers to include their works in photocopying & digitisation licences negotiated by the Copyright Licensing Agency. PLS ensures publishers receive their share of fees collected by CLA.

*Publication(s): PLS Plus* (newsletter)
*Associate Companies:* Copyright Licensing Agency

**SCOLMA**, see Standing Conference on Library Materials on Africa

**Scottish Book Marketing Group**
Scottish Book Centre, 137 Dundee St, Edinburgh EH11 1BG
*Tel:* (0131) 228 6866 *Fax:* (0131) 228 3220
*Publication(s): Directory of Publishing in Scotland* (annually); *New Scottish Books* (bimonthly, leaflet); *Scottish Bestseller List* (fortnightly listing of bestselling books on Scotland); *Scottish Books Direct* (Home-Shopping facility for readers at home & abroad)
*Associate Companies:* Scottish Publishers Association *E-mail:* enquiries@scottishbooks.org *Web Site:* www.scottishbooks.org

**Scottish Book Trust**
Sandeman House, Trunk's Close, 55 High St, Edinburgh EH1 1SR
*Tel:* (0131) 524 0160 *Fax:* (0131) 524 0161
*E-mail:* info@scottishbooktrust.com
*Web Site:* www.scottishbooktrust.com
*Key Personnel*
Chief Executive Officer: Marc Lambert
   *Tel:* (0131) 524 0162
*Publication(s): Off The Shelf: A Guide To Books & Writers for Children From Scotland; Shelf Life: Information, Author Information, Reviews on Books for Children in Scotland*
*Parent Company:* Book Trust

**Scottish Newspaper Publishers Association**
48 Palmerston Pl, Edinburgh EH12 5DE
*Tel:* (0131) 220 4353 *Fax:* (0131) 220 4344
*E-mail:* info@snpa.org.uk
*Web Site:* www.snpa.org.uk
*Key Personnel*
Dir: Mr J B Raeburn *E-mail:* jraeburn@spef.org. uk
Trade association representing publishers of local newspapers throughout Scotland.

**◇Scottish Publishers Association**
Scottish Book Centre, 137 Dundee St, Edinburgh EH11 1BG
*Tel:* (0131) 2286866 *Fax:* (0131) 2283220
*E-mail:* info@scottishbooks.org
*Web Site:* www.scottishbooks.org
*Key Personnel*
Dir: Lorraine Fannin
Chairman: Timothy Wright
Founded: 1973
Trade association with 80 members.
*Publication(s): Directory of Publishing in Scotland* (annually); *New Scottish Books* (6 times/ yr)
*Associate Companies:* Scottish Book Marketing Group

**SIBMAS**, see Societe Internationale des Bibliotheques et des Musees des Arts du Spectacle (SIBMAS)

**†◇Societe Internationale des Bibliotheques et des Musees des Arts du Spectacle (SIBMAS)**
(International Association of Libraries & Museums of the Performing Arts)
Theatre Museum, 1E Tavistock St, London WC2E 7PR
*Tel:* (020) 7943 4720 *Fax:* (020) 7943 4777
*Web Site:* www.theatrelibrary.org/sibmas/sibmas. html
*Key Personnel*
President: Claire Hudson *E-mail:* c.hudson@vam. ac.uk
Secretary General: Maria Teresa Iovinelli

Founded: 1954
International Society of Libraries & Museums for the Performing Arts.
Subjects: Performing Arts Collections, Worldwide
*Publication(s): Proceedings Bi-Annual Congresses; SIBMAS International Directory of Performing Arts Collections/Emmett Publishing Ltd (Haslemere 1996)*

**Society of Authors**
84 Drayton Gardens, London SW10 9SB
*Tel:* (020) 7373 6642 *Fax:* (020) 7373 5768
*E-mail:* info@societyofauthors.org
*Web Site:* www.societyofauthors.net
*Key Personnel*
General Secretary: Mark Le Fanu
Manager: Kate Pool *E-mail:* kpool@ societyofauthors.org
*Publication(s): The Author* (quarterly)

**Society of Indexers**
Blades Enterprise Centre, John St, Sheffield S2 4SU
*Tel:* (0114) 292 2350 *Fax:* (0114) 292 2351
*E-mail:* admin@indexers.org.uk
*Web Site:* www.socind.demon.co.uk
*Key Personnel*
President: Doreen Blake
Secretary: Liza Weinkoe
Administrator: P W Burrow
Founded: 1957
*Publication(s): The Indexer; Training in Indexing*
*Associate Companies:* American Society of Indexers; Australian Society of Indexers; Indexing & Abstracting Society of Canada; Association of Southern African Indexers & Bibliographers

**†◇Standing Conference on Library Materials on Africa**
Commonwealth Secretariat, Marlborough House, Pall Mall, London SW1Y 5HX
*Tel:* (020) 7747 6253 *Fax:* (020) 7747 6168
*E-mail:* scolma@hotmail.com
*Web Site:* www.lse.ac.uk/library/scolma/
*Key Personnel*
Chair: Sheila Allcock *E-mail:* sheila.allcock@qeh. ox.ac.uk
Secretary: Iain Cooke
*Publication(s): African Research & Documentation*

**UK International Standard Book Numbering Agency Ltd**
Woolmead House W Bear Lane, Farnham GU9 7LG
*Tel:* (01252) 742525 *Fax:* (01252) 742526
*E-mail:* isbn@whitaker.co.uk
*Web Site:* www.whitaker.co.uk/isbn.htm
*Key Personnel*
Manager: Stella Griffiths
*Publication(s): International Standard Book Numbering*
*Parent Company:* J Whitaker & Sons Ltd

**Union of Welsh Publishers & Booksellers**
c/o Gomer Press, Llandysul, Ceredigion SA44 4BQ
*Tel:* (01559) 362371 *Fax:* (01559) 363758

**†VSO Books**
Voluntary Service Overseas, 317 Putney Bridge Rd, London SW15 2PN
*Tel:* (020) 8780 7200 *Fax:* (020) 8780 7300
*E-mail:* enquiry@vso.org.uk
*Web Site:* www.vso.org.uk
*Key Personnel*
Editor: Silke Bernau *Tel:* (020) 8780 7342
Founded: 1990
Subjects: Education, Development (Health, Agriculture, Technical, Community Development)
ISBN Prefix(es): 0-9509050; 1-903697

Number of titles published annually: 3 Print
Total Titles: 22 Print

**Welsh Books Council** (Cyngor Llyfrau Cymru)
Castell Brychan, Aberystwyth, Ceredigion SY23
2JB
*Tel:* (01970) 624151 *Fax:* (01970) 625385
*E-mail:* castellbrychan@wbc.org.uk
*Web Site:* www.cllc.org.uk
*Key Personnel*
Dir: Gwerfyl Pierce Jones
Head of Marketing: D Philip Davies *E-mail:* phil.
davies@wbc.org.uk
Founded: 1963
*Branch Office(s)*
Distribution Center, Glanyrafon Enterprise
Park, Aberystwyth, Ceredigion SY23 3AQ
*E-mail:* distribution.centre@cllc.org.uk

**Women in Publishing**
Membership Officer, PO Box 402, West Byfleet
KT14 7ZF
*E-mail:* wipub@hotmail.com; info@wipub.org.uk
*Web Site:* www.cyberiacafe.net/wip
*Key Personnel*
Membership Secretary: Natalie McCormack
*Tel:* (020) 8923 2386 *E-mail:* nmccormack@
waterlow.com
Founded: 1979
Promote the status of women within publishing &
related fields.

**†◇Writers & Scholars International**
6-8 Amwell St, London EC1R 1UQ
*Tel:* (020) 7278 2313 *Fax:* (020) 7278 1878
*E-mail:* natasha@indexoncensorship.org
*Web Site:* www.indexonline.org/
*Key Personnel*
Editor: Ursula Owen
Marketing Dir: Henderson Mullin
Founded: 1972
Information about censorship in the world today,
covering subjects such as free speech, human
rights, literature, freedom of information.
Subjects: Censorship, Current Affairs, Literature,
Politics
Publication(s): *Index on Censorship* (quarterly,
magazine)
Number of titles published annually: 4 Print

**Writers' Guild of Great Britain**
15 Britannia St, London WC1X 9JN
*Tel:* (020) 7833 0777 *Fax:* (020) 7833 4777
*E-mail:* admin@writersguild.org.uk
*Web Site:* www.writersguild.org.uk
*Key Personnel*
President: John Wilsher
Chairman: Bill Morrison
General Secretary: Bernie Corbett
*E-mail:* corbett@writersguild.org.uk

# United States

**†American-Scandinavian Foundation**
58 Park Ave, New York, NY 10016
*Tel:* 212-879-9779 *Fax:* 212-879-2301
*E-mail:* info@amscan.org; asf@amscan.org
*Web Site:* www.amscan.org
*Key Personnel*
Executive Vice President: Lynn Carter
*E-mail:* carter@amscan.org
Publication(s): *Scan* (quarterly, newsletter); *Scan-
dinavian Review* (triannually, cultural/liter-
ary/political magazine)

**†Bernan Associates, Div of Kraus
Organization, Ltd**
4611-F Assembly Dr, Lanham, MD 20706-4391
*Tel:* 301-459-7666 *Toll Free Tel:* 800-274-4888
(USA); 800-233-0504 (Canada) *Fax:* 301-459-
0056
*E-mail:* query@berman.com
*Web Site:* www.eurunion.org/publicat/sales.htm
*Telex:* 7108260418
*Key Personnel*
Sales & Publicity: Christopher Zahn
There are OAS offices/bookstores in 31 countries
outside the USA.
Subjects: Development of American Nations (Re-
gional, Social, Historical), Bibliography, Cul-
tural Affairs, Economics, Education, Human
Rights, Law, Sciences, Statistics
Publication(s): *Inter-American Review of Bibliog-
raphy*
ISBN Prefix(es): 0-8270; 0-8171

**IALL**, see International Association of Law
Libraries (IALL)

**IASP**, see International Association of Scholarly
Publishers (IASP)

**ILAB**, see International League of Antiquarian
Booksellers (ILAB)

**†◇International Association of Law Libraries
(IALL)** (Association Internationale des
Bibliotheques de Droit)
PO Box 5709, Washington, DC 20016-1309
*Tel:* 804-924-3384 *Fax:* 804-982-2232
*E-mail:* lbw@virginia.edu
*Web Site:* www.iall.org
*Key Personnel*
President: Holger Knudsen *Tel:* 856-225-6457
*E-mail:* knudsen@mpipriv-hh.mpg.de
Treasurer: Gloria F Chao
Secretary: Ann Morrison *Tel:* 902-494-2640
*E-mail:* morriso6@is.dal.ca
Founded: 1959
Publication(s): *The IALL Messenger* (irregularly);
*International Journal of Legal Information* (tri-
annually, Membership)

**†◇International Association of Scholarly
Publishers (IASP)**
c/o Michigan State University Press, 1405 S Har-
rison Rd, East Lansing, MI 48823-5202
*Tel:* 517-355-9543 *Fax:* 517-432-2611
*E-mail:* bohm@pilot.msu.edu
*Key Personnel*
Dir: Mr F C Bohm
Founded: 1972

**†◇International Comparative Literature
Association** (Association Internationale de
Litterature Comparee)
Catholic University, Washington, DC 20064
*Tel:* 416-487-6727 *Fax:* 416-487-6786
*E-mail:* icla@byu.edu
*Web Site:* www.byu.edu/~icla
*Key Personnel*
President: Kawamoto Koji *E-mail:* kojik@aurora.
dti.ne.jp
Vice President: Virgil Nemoianu
*E-mail:* nemoianu@cua.edu
Founded: 1954

**†◇International Institute of Iberoamerican
Literature**
University of Pittsburgh, 728 Cathedral of Learn-
ing, Pittsburgh, PA 15260-0001
*Tel:* 412-624-5246; 412-624-6100 *Fax:* 412-624-
0829
*E-mail:* iili+@pitt.edu
*Web Site:* www.pitt.edu

*Key Personnel*
Dir: Jinx P Walton *E-mail:* jpw@pitt.edu
Administrator: Erika Braga
Contact: Mabel Morana *E-mail:* mabel@pitt.edu
Founded: 1938
Publication(s): *Memorias*; *Revista Iberoamericana*
(quarterly, 1938, literary criticism journal)

**†◇International League of Antiquarian
Booksellers (ILAB)**
400 Summit Ave, St Paul, MN 55102
*Tel:* 800-441-0076; 612-290-0700 *Fax:* 612-290-
0646
*E-mail:* info@ilab-lila.com
*Web Site:* www.ilab.org
*Key Personnel*
Secretary General: Steven Temple *Tel:* 416-703-
9908 *E-mail:* books@steventemplebooks.com
Founded: 1947
Publication(s): *Dictionary of the Antiquarian
Book Trade* (in Danish, Dutch, English, French,
German, Italian, Japanese, Spanish, Swedish);
*International Directory of Antiquarian Book-
sellers*

**†International Monetary Fund**
700 19 St NW, Washington, DC
*Tel:* 202-623-7000; 202-623-7430 *Fax:* 202-623-
4661; 202-623-7201
*E-mail:* publicaffairs@imf.org
*Web Site:* www.imf.org
*Key Personnel*
Acting Man Dir: Anne O Krueger
Chief, Publication Services: Lori Michele New-
som
Editor, Rights & Permissions: Ian S McDonald
Founded: 1946
Subjects: Economics, International monetary &
trade issues, Domestic fiscal & monetary top-
ics, Activities & operations of the International
Monetary Fund, Balance of payments & exter-
nal adjustment problems, International finance,
International statistics
Publication(s): *Annual Report on Exchange Ar-
rangements & Exchange Restrictions*; *Direction
of Trade Statistics*; *Finance & Development*
(published jointly with World Bank); *World
Economic Outlook*
ISBN Prefix(es): 0-939934; 1-55775

**†◇International Reading Association**
800 Barksdale Rd, Newark, DE 19714
Mailing Address: PO Box 8139, Newark, DE
19714-8139
*Tel:* 302-731-1600 *Toll Free Tel:* 800-336-7323
*Fax:* 302-731-1057
*E-mail:* pubinfo@reading.org
*Web Site:* www.reading.org
*Telex:* 5106002813
*Key Personnel*
President: Lesley Mandel Morrow
Executive Dir: Alan Farstrup
Public Information Associate: Janet Butler
*Tel:* 302-731-1600 (ext 293) *E-mail:* jbutler@
reading.org
Founded: 1956
Publication(s): *Journal of Adolescent & Adult Lit-
eracy*; *Lectura y vida*; *Newspaper Reading To-
day*; *Reading Research Quarterly*; *The Reading
Teacher*

**†◇Middle East Librarians Association**
University of Washington Libraries, Monographic
Services, Campus Box 352900, Seattle, WA
98195-2900
*Tel:* (206) 543-8407 *Fax:* (206) 685-8049
*Web Site:* www.depts.washington.edu/wsx9/
melahp.html
*Key Personnel*
Editor, Near East Division: Jonathan Rodgers
*Tel:* (734) 764-7555 *Fax:* (734) 763-6743
*E-mail:* jrodgers@umich.edu

Secretary-Treasurer: Janet Heineck
*Tel:* (206) 543-1642 *Fax:* (206) 685-8782
*E-mail:* janeth@u.washington.edu
Publication(s): *MELA Notes* (Journal of Middle
Eastern Librarianship)

**SALALM**, see Seminar on the Acquisition of
Latin American Library Materials (SALALM)

†◇**Seminar on the Acquisition of Latin
American Library Materials (SALALM)**
Secretariat, General Library, University of New
Mexico, Albuquerque, NM 87131-1466
*Tel:* 505-277-5102 *Fax:* 505-277-0646
*Key Personnel*
Executive Secretary: Sharon A Moynahan
Publication(s): *Bibliography & Reference Series*

†◇**United Nations Publications**
Two UN Plaza, Room DC2-853, New York, NY
10017
*Tel:* 212-963-8302 *Toll Free Tel:* 800-253-9646
(orders US only) *Fax:* 212-963-3489
*E-mail:* publications@un.org
*Web Site:* www.un.org/Pubs/sales.htm
*Telex:* 62450 *Cable:* UNATIONS NYK
*Key Personnel*
Chief of Section: Susanna H Johnston
Marketing & Product Development: Christopher
Woodthorpe
Rights & Permissions, US: Claudia Kaiser
*Tel:* 212-963-5455 *Fax:* 212-963-4116
*E-mail:* kaiser@un.org
Rights & Permissions, Geneva: Patricia Piguet
External Publications Officer: Renata Morteo
*Tel:* 212-963-5455 *Fax:* 212-963-3489
Founded: 1945
Since 1946, United Nations has published more
than 10,000 reports, studies, annual surveys,
yearbooks & monthly & quarterly periodi-
cals in addition to the United Nations Official
Records.
Reflecting the varied work of the Organization,
the subjects include international trade, world
& regional economic questions, international
law, social questions, atomic energy, public ad-
ministration & literature concerning the role &
activities of the United Nations.
Subjects: Reference, Economics, International
Trade, International Law, Political Science, So-
cial Science, Environment, Educational
ISBN Prefix(es): 92-1
*Branch Office(s)*
Publications des Nations Unies, Section des
Ventes et Commercialisation, Bureau E-4,
1211 Geneva 10, Switzerland *Tel:* (022) 917
2600; (022) 917 2614 *Fax:* (022) 917 0027
*E-mail:* unpubli@unog.ch
*Bookshop(s):* United Nations Bookshop, United
Nations Concourse Level, First Ave & 46 St -
Visitors Entrance, New York, NY 10017

# Uruguay

**Camara Uruguaya del Libro** (Uruguayan
Publishers' Association)
Juan D Jackson 1118, 11 200 Montevideo
*Tel:* (082) 41 57 32 *Fax:* (082) 41 18 60
*E-mail:* camurlib@adinet.com.uy
*Key Personnel*
President: Ernesto Sanjines

**Standard Book Numbering Agency**
Biblioteca Nacional, Casilla de Correo 452,
11200 Montevideo
*Tel:* (02) 402 08 12; (02) 408 50 30 *Fax:* (02)
409 69 02; (02) 401 67 16
*E-mail:* bibna@adinet.com.uy
*Telex:* 26991 biname uy
*Key Personnel*
Dir General: Luis Alberto Musso

# Venezuela

**Camara Venezolana del Libro** (Venezuelan
Publishers' Association)
Ave Andres Bello, Edificio Centro Andres Bello,
Torre Oeste 11, piso 11, ofic 112-0, Caracas
1050
*Tel:* (0212) 7931347; (0212) 7931368 *Fax:* (0212)
7931368
*E-mail:* cavelibro@cantv.net
*Key Personnel*
Dir: M P Vargas

**Standard Book Numbering Agency**
Parque Central, Torre Este, Piso 3, Caracas 1011
*Tel:* (0212) 576 5650; (0212) 576 5370; (0212)
576 7120; (0212) 577 5106 *Fax:* (0212) 576
3424
*E-mail:* isbn_cenal@platino.gov.ve;
isbnvenezuela@cenal.gov.ve
*Web Site:* www.bnv.bib.ve; www.cenal.gov.ve
*Telex:* 24621 iabn vc
*Key Personnel*
Contact: Angela Negrin
*Parent Company:* Ubicacion del Centro Nacional
del Libro

# Zambia

**Booksellers' & Publishers' Association of
Zambia (BPAZ)**
Haile Selassie Ave, Lusaka
Mailing Address: PO Box 31838, Lusaka
*Tel:* (01) 225282 *Fax:* (01) 225195
*E-mail:* bpaz@zamnet.zm; longman@zamnet.zm
*Key Personnel*
Executive Dir: Basil Mbewe
Contact: Christine Kasonde

**BPAZ**, see Booksellers' & Publishers'
Association of Zambia (BPAZ)

**Standard Book Numbering Agency**
c/o University of Zambia Library, PO Box 32379,
Lusaka
*Tel:* (01) 292 837 (ext 1342); (01) 253 952; (01)
250 845 *Fax:* (01) 295 038
*E-mail:* library@unza.zm
*Web Site:* www.unza.zm/
*Telex:* ZA 40370 *Cable:* UNZA
*Key Personnel*
ISBN Administrator: Dr H Mwacalimba
*Parent Company:* Booksellers & Publishers Asso-
ciation of Zambia

# Zimbabwe

**Standard Book Numbering Agency**
National Archives of Zimbabwe, Causeway, Pri-
vate Bag 7729, Harare
*Tel:* (04) 792 741 *Fax:* (04) 792 398
*E-mail:* nat.archives@gta.gov.zw
Publication(s): *Zimbabwe National Bibliography*

**ZBPA**, see Zimbabwe Book Publishers
Association (ZBPA)

**Zimbabwe Book Publishers Association
(ZBPA)**
Fidelity Life Tower, 4th floor, Corner Raleigh/
Luck Sts, Harare
Mailing Address: PO Box 3041, Harare
*Tel:* (04) 754256 *Fax:* (04) 754256
*E-mail:* engelbert@collegepress.co.zw
Publication(s): *Directory of Zimbabwe Publish-
ers 1995; Making Books; Zimbabwe: Books In
Print 1995*

# Major Book Dealers

This section contains active book dealers in one or more of the following categories: distribution, exporting, importing, major book chains, major independent booksellers, remainder dealers, and wholesalers.

# Argentina

**Librerias ABC SA**
Ave Cordoba 685, 1054 Buenos Aires
Mailing Address: Casilla Correo Central 4452, 1000 Buenos Aires
*Tel:* (011) 4314-8106 *Fax:* (011) 4314-8106
*E-mail:* libabcc@datamarkets.com.ar
*Web Site:* www.libreriasabc.com.ar *Cable:* MOLAGENT
*Key Personnel*
President: Horst Stephan
Founded: 1969

**Cosmos Libros SRL**
Av Callao 737, 1023 Buenos Aires
*Tel:* (011) 48127364; (011) 48155347
*E-mail:* contactenos@cosmoslibros.com.ar
*Web Site:* www.cosmoslibros.com.ar
*Key Personnel*
Dir: Hugo Emilio Palacios
    *E-mail:* palacioshugo@arnet.com.ar
Founded: 1984
Subjects: Specialize in education
Type of Business: Distributor, Exporter, Importer, Major Independent Bookseller

**Cuspide Libros SA**
Suipacha 764 Piso Bajo Oficina 2, 1008 Buenos Aires
*Tel:* (011) 43228868 *Fax:* (011) 43223456
*E-mail:* ventas@cuspide.com
*Web Site:* www.cuspide.com
*Telex:* 25477 Dicus
*Key Personnel*
President: Joaquin M Gil Paricio
Founded: 1960
*Branch Office(s)*
Suipacha 1045, 1008 Buenos Aires *Tel:* (011) 3130486
Portugal 18 Santiago, Chile *Tel:* (02) 2224978
    *Fax:* (02) 2250435

**Libreria Huemul SA**
Ave Santa Fe 2237, 1123 Buenos Aires
*Tel:* (011) 4822-1666; (011) 4825-2290
    *Fax:* (011) 822-1666
*E-mail:* libreriahuemul@arnet.com.ar
*Key Personnel*
President & Manager: Antonio Rego
Also Publisher.

**Libreria Kier**
Don Felipe 9, 1059 Buenos Aires
*Tel:* (091) 5227335
*E-mail:* info@libreriakier.com
*Web Site:* www.libreriakier.com
Founded: 1907
Type of Business: Distributor, Exporter, Importer, Major Independent Bookseller
*Owned by:* Editorial Kier SACIFI

**H F Martinez de Murguia SAC y E**
Av Cordoba 2270, 1120 Buenos Aires
*Tel:* (011) 4952-1088; (011) 4952-6173 (sales)
    *Fax:* (011) 4952-1088
*E-mail:* info@murguia.com.ar

*Web Site:* www.murguia.com.ar
*Key Personnel*
President: Agustin T Aparicio

**Nueva Vision**
Tucaman 3748, 1189 Buenos Aires
*Tel:* (011) 8631461; (011) 8635980
*Key Personnel*
Manager: Hector Yanover

**Libreria General de Tomas Pardo SRL**
Maipu 618, 1006 Buenos Aires
*Tel:* (011) 4322-0496 *Fax:* (011) 4393-6759

**Riverside Agency SAC**
Mexico 3080 PB, C1223ABL Buenos Aires
*Tel:* (011) 4957-2336 *Fax:* (011) 4956-1985
*E-mail:* riverside@laisla.net
*Key Personnel*
President: Juan Carlos Zaragoza
Vice President: Carlos Miguel Zaragoza
Dir: Gabriela Zaragoza
Founded: 1958
Type of Business: Distributor, Importer, Wholesaler

**Libreria Rodriguez SA, Dto Suscripciones**
Sarmiento 835, 1041 Buenos Aires
*Tel:* (011) 4326-3725; (011) 4326-3826
    *Fax:* (011) 4326-1959
*E-mail:* librerod@ssdnet.com.ar
*Telex:* 22087 Elerre
*Key Personnel*
General Manager: Bautista L Tello
Founded: 1903
Also Publisher (see Ediciones L R SA).

**Libreria Santa Fe**
Ave Santa Fe 2582, 1123 Buenos Aires
*Tel:* (011) 4824-5005; (011) 4829-2545 (virtual store) *Fax:* (011) 824-7932
*E-mail:* info@lsf.com.ar
*Web Site:* www.lsf.com.ar; www.libreriasantafe.com
*Key Personnel*
Contact: Juan Pablo Aisenberg; Ruben Aisenberg
Founded: 1957
Type of Business: Importer
*Branch Office(s)*
Ave Santa Fe 2376, Buenos Aires *Tel:* (011) 4827-0100
Alto Palermo Shopping Local 78, Ave Santa Fe 3253, Buenos Aires *Tel:* (011) 5777-8078
Ave Callao 335, Buenos Aires *Tel:* (011) 4371-8391
Ave Cordoba 2064, Buenos Aires *Tel:* (011) 4372-7609

# Australia

**Academic & General Bookshop**
259 Swanston St, Melbourne, Victoria 3000
*Tel:* (03) 9663 3231 *Fax:* (03) 9663 7234
*E-mail:* info@academicbooks.com.au
*Key Personnel*
Owner: Anthony Kyriacou

Founded: 1974
*Branch Office(s)*
Caledonia Lane, Melbourne, Victoria *Tel:* (03) 9663 7229 *Fax:* (03) 9663 7234
*Bookshop(s):* 196 Elgin St, Carlton 3053

**Angus & Robertson Bookshops**
379 Collins St, Level 14, Melbourne, Victoria 3000
Mailing Address: GPO Box 82A, Melbourne, Victoria 3001
*Tel:* (03) 8623 1111 *Fax:* (03) 8623 1150
*E-mail:* info@angusrobertson.com.au
*Web Site:* www.angusrobertson.com.au
*Key Personnel*
General Manager: David Conners
Founded: 1882
170 stores in Australia & online bookstore.
*Owned by:* Brasch Pty Ltd

**Australian Book Collector**, *imprint of* Burnet's Books

**Banyan Tree Book Distributors**
PO Box 566, Sumner Park, Qld 4074
*Tel:* (07) 3279 1877 *Fax:* (07) 3279 2871
*E-mail:* enquiries@banyantreebooks.com.au; orders@banyantreebooks.com.au
*Web Site:* www.banyantreebooks.predelegation.com.au
*Key Personnel*
Dir: Susan Vanderheiden
Founded: 1989
Large, independent national Australian distributor of spiritual books.
Type of Business: Distributor

**James Bennett Pty Ltd**
3 Narabang Way, Belrose, NSW 2085
Mailing Address: Locked Bag 537, Frenchs Forest, NSW 2086
*Tel:* (02) 9986 7000 *Fax:* (02) 9986 7031
*E-mail:* customerservice@bennett.com.au
*Web Site:* www.bennett.com.au
*Key Personnel*
Man Dir: Chris von Hinckeldey *Tel:* (02) 9986 7036 *E-mail:* cvh@bennett.com.au
National Sales & Marketing Manager: Nada Novakov *Tel:* (02) 9986 7064 *E-mail:* nada@bennett.com.au
Operations & Logistics Controller: Frank Peard *Tel:* (02) 9986 7054 *E-mail:* fpeard@bennett.com.au
Founded: 1958
Library supplier.
Type of Business: Distributor, Exporter, Importer, Wholesaler
*Owned by:* B H Blackwell Ltd

**Bibliotech International Pty Ltd**
Division of ANUTECH
17 Keith St, Hampton East, Victoria 3188
*Tel:* (03) 9502 3056 *Fax:* (03) 9502 3057
*E-mail:* bibliotech@bibliotech.com.au
*Web Site:* www.bibliotech.com.au
*Key Personnel*
Manager: Cathy Teager *Tel:* (02) 6249 4005
    *E-mail:* cathy.teager@anutech.com.au
Book Distribution Service.

Type of Business: Distributor
*Bookshop(s):* Anutech Court, CNR Barry Dr & Daley Rd, Canberra ACT 2601 *Web Site:* www.anutech.com.au

**Biramo Book Distributors**
5 King St, Warners Bay, NSW 2282
Mailing Address: PO Box 95, Warners Bay, NSW 2282
*Tel:* (02) 49542626 *Fax:* (02) 49565398
*E-mail:* biramobooks@tpg.com.au
*Key Personnel*
Dir: Mr A F Rich
Founded: 1985
Type of Business: Distributor, Exporter, Importer, Wholesaler
*Branch Office(s)*
PO Box 14 640, Panmure, Auckland, New Zealand *Tel:* (09) 570 9089 *Fax:* (09) 570 4604

**Birchalls**
PO Box 170, Launceston, Tas 7250
*Tel:* (03) 63313011 *Toll Free Tel:* 800 806867
  *Fax:* (03) 63317165
*E-mail:* enquiry@birchalls.com.au
*Web Site:* www.birchalls.com.au
*Key Personnel*
Man Dir: Graeme R Tilley *E-mail:* gtilley@birchalls.com.au
Founded: 1844
Australia's oldest online bookseller.
Type of Business: Importer, Major Book Chain Headquarters, Major Independent Bookseller, Wholesaler
*Branch Office(s)*
Students Bookshop, Burnie Tafe College, Mooreville Rd, Burnie *Tel:* (03) 64333602 *Fax:* (03) 64333716
Students Bookshop, Devonport Tafe College, 20 Valley Rd, Devonport *Tel:* (03) 64215518 *Fax:* (03) 64242581
Students Bookshop, Don College, Watkinson St, Devonport *Tel:* (03) 64244072 *Fax:* (03) 64244072
Birchalls Education Centre, 147 Bathurst St, Hobart, Tasmania 7250 *Tel:* (03) 62342122 *Fax:* (03) 62348719
Hobart Tafe Student Bookshop, 75 Campbell St, Hobart, Tasmania *Tel:* (03) 62337405 *Fax:* (03) 62311067
*Bookshop(s):* Students Bookshop, Alanvale Tafe College, Alanvale, Tasmania *Tel:* (03) 63364284 *Fax:* (03) 63364284

**Books Australasia**, see Gaston Renard Pty Ltd

**Bookwise International**
174 Cormack Rd, Wingfield SA 5013
Mailing Address: PO Box 2164, Regency Park SA 5942
*Tel:* (08) 8268 8222 *Fax:* (08) 8268 8704
*E-mail:* customer.service@bookwise.com.au
*Web Site:* www.bookwise.com.au
*Key Personnel*
Man Dir: Patricia Genat *E-mail:* patricia.genat@bookwise.com.au
Marketing Dir: Andrew Easton *E-mail:* andrew.easton@bookwise.com.au
Founded: 1957
Type of Business: Wholesaler
*Branch Office(s)*
62 Wellington Parade, East Melbourne, Victoria 3002
4124 Hood St, Sherwood 4075
428 George St, Sydney 2000

**Burgewood Books**
4 Diane Court, Warrandyte, Victoria 3113
*Tel:* (03) 98442512 (Australia); (03) 9844 2512 (International) *Fax:* (03) 98440664 (Australia); (03) 9844 0664 (International)

*Key Personnel*
President & Partner: Doreen Burge
  *E-mail:* dburge@iprimus.com.au
Vice President: Nell Charlwood
Author: Don Charlwood
Founded: 1996
Publishing.

**Burnet's Books**
100 Bridge St, Uralla, NSW 2358
*Tel:* (02) 6778 4682 *Fax:* (02) 6778 4516
*E-mail:* burnet@ozbook.com
*Web Site:* www.ozbook.com
*Key Personnel*
Man Dir & Editor: Ross Burnet *E-mail:* burnet@ozbook.com
Founded: 1986
Antiquarian & secondhand bookdealer.
Type of Business: Distributor, Exporter, Importer, Major Independent Bookseller, Wholesaler
Imprints: Australian Book Collector; Idriess Enterprises
*Branch Office(s)*
Gatherum Books, 62 Bridge St, Uralla, NSW 2358 *Tel:* (02) 6778 4376 *E-mail:* gatherum@dodo.com.au

**Collins Booksellers Pty Ltd**
86 Bourke St, 2nd floor, Melbourne, Victoria 3000
*Tel:* (03) 96629472 *Fax:* (03) 96622527
*E-mail:* enquiries@collinsbooks.com.au
*Web Site:* www.collinsbooks.com.au
*Key Personnel*
Chairman & Chief Executive, OBE: Michael G Zifcak
Secretary: T J McCarthy
Founded: 1929
Type of Business: Major Book Chain Headquarters
*Branch Office(s)*
Canberra
New South Wales
Victoria, Queensland
Western Australia (Western Australia)

**Continental Bookshop**
1292 Malvern Rd, Malvern, Victoria 3144
*Tel:* (03) 98247711 *Fax:* (03) 98247855
*Key Personnel*
Owner: Harry Raynor
Owner & Mgr: Christopher Raynor
  *E-mail:* audio@vicnet.com.au
Founded: 1962
Foreign language books & language learning media.
Type of Business: Distributor, Exporter, Importer, Major Independent Bookseller

**DA Information Services Pty Ltd**
648 Whitehorse Rd, Mitcham, Victoria 3132
Mailing Address: PO Box 163, Mitcham, Victoria 3132
*Tel:* (03) 9210-7777 *Fax:* (03) 9210-7788
*E-mail:* service@dadirect.com.au
*Web Site:* www.dadirect.com.au
*Key Personnel*
Chief Executive: Kim Hunt
Founded: 1951
Subscription agents, Library suppliers, Electronic Information Suppliers.
Type of Business: Distributor, Importer

**Daltons Books**
54 Marcus Clarke St, Canberra City, ACT 2601
Mailing Address: GPO Box 549, Canberra City ACT 2601
*Tel:* (02) 62491844 *Fax:* (02) 62475753
*E-mail:* daltons@daltons.com.au
*Web Site:* www.daltons.com.au

*Key Personnel*
Dir: Meredith Wright *E-mail:* meredith@daltons.com.au
Founded: 1968
Computer & Business, Book Specialists, Rare & Limited Edition Books.
Type of Business: Distributor, Exporter, Importer, Major Independent Bookseller
*Owned by:* T J Dalton Pty Ltd, PO Box 189, Claremont, WA 6010
*Branch Office(s)*
Dalton Books Pty Ltd

**Dominie**
8 Cross St, Brookvale, NSW 2100
Mailing Address: PO Box 33, Brookvale, NSW 2100
*Tel:* (02) 9050201 *Fax:* (02) 9055209

**Dymocks Pty Ltd**
428 George St, 6th floor, Sydney, NSW
Mailing Address: GPO Box 1521, Sydney, NSW 2001
*Tel:* (02) 9224 0411 *Toll Free Tel:* 800 805 711
  *Fax:* (02) 9224 9401
*E-mail:* feedback@dymocks.com.au; service@dymocks.com.au
*Web Site:* www.dymocks.com.au
*Key Personnel*
Chairman: J P C Forsyth
Man Dir: K B Terry

**Foreign Language Bookshop**
259 Collins St, Melbourne, Victoria 3000
*Tel:* (03) 96542883 *Fax:* (03) 96507664
*E-mail:* flb@ozonline.com.au
*Web Site:* www.languages.com.au
*Key Personnel*
Man Dir: Annette Monester
Founded: 1938
Bookstore with stock in 90 languages-books, audio learning kits software.
Type of Business: Exporter, Importer, Major Independent Bookseller

**Gaanetgetal Books**
21 National St, Leichhardt, NSW 2040
*Tel:* (02) 4234-0865 *Fax:* (02) 4234-0875
*E-mail:* enquiries@books-on-rugs.com
*Key Personnel*
President: Geoffrey Long
Vice President: Ann Long
Manager: Naomi Jacobs
Type of Business: Distributor, Importer, Major Independent Bookseller, Wholesaler
*Branch Office(s)*
Bolvanna, Lot 2, Foxground Rd, Foxground, NSW 2536
*Bookshop(s):* 22 National St, Leichhardt, NSW 2040

**Gaston Renard Pty Ltd**
PO Box 1030, Ivanhoe, Melbourne, Victoria 3079
*Tel:* (03) 9459 5040 *Fax:* (03) 9459 6787
*E-mail:* books@gastonrenard.com.au
*Web Site:* www.gastonrenard.com.au
*Key Personnel*
Owner: Julien Renard
Founded: 1945
Specialize in antiquarian bookseller & publisher
Membership(s): ANZAAB.
Type of Business: Distributor, Exporter, Importer, Major Independent Bookseller

**Grahames Bookshop**
Division of Horwitz Grahame Pty Ltd
506 Miller St, Cammeray, NSW 2062
*Tel:* (02) 9296144 *Fax:* (02) 9571814
Ten company & franchise stores nationwide.

*Branch Office(s)*
MLC Bldg, 105 Miller S, North Sydney, NSW 2060
Bankstown Shopping Square, Bankstown, NSW 2200
Imperial Centre, Gosford, NSW 2250
City Tatts, 200 Pitt St, Sydney, NSW 2000
Mid-City Centre, 197 Pitt St, Sydney, NSW 2000

**Identic Books**
PO Box 323, Pymble NSW 2073
*Tel:* (02) 8901 3466 *Fax:* (02) 8901 3404
*E-mail:* enquiries@identic.com.au
*Web Site:* www.identic.com.au
*Key Personnel*
Man Dir: W A T Mason
Dir & Secretary: D W Mason
Founded: 1967
Type of Business: Distributor, Exporter, Importer, Major Independent Bookseller

**Idriess Enterprises**, *imprint of* Burnet's Books

**Kirby Book Co Pty Ltd**
19 Bowden St, Alexandria, NSW 2015
Mailing Address: Private Bag No 19, PO Alexandria, Sydney, NSW 2067
*Tel:* (02) 9698 2377 *Toll Free Tel:* 800 225271 *Fax:* (02) 9698 8748
*Key Personnel*
Chairman: John D C Reid
Co Man Dir: John A D Reid; Peter N D Reid *E-mail:* preid@kirby.com.au
Founded: 1951
Specialist wholesale distributor of overseas publications.
Type of Business: Wholesaler

**Koorong Books Pty Ltd**
28 West Parade, West Ryde, NSW 2114
*Tel:* (02) 9857 4477 *Fax:* (02) 9857 4499
*E-mail:* west_ryde@koorong.com.au; koorong@koorong.com.au
*Web Site:* www.koorong.com.au
*Key Personnel*
Managing Dir: Paul Bootes *E-mail:* pb@koorong.com.au
Buying & Marketing Manager: Gavin Shume *E-mail:* ga@koorong.com.au
Store Manager: Rob Morris *E-mail:* ro@koorong.com.au
Founded: 1975
Type of Business: Importer, Major Book Chain Headquarters
*Branch Office(s)*
198 Waymouth St, Adelaide, SA 5000, Store Manager: Christine DeBruyn *Tel:* (08) 8239 6777 *Fax:* (08) 8239 6788 *E-mail:* adelaide@koorong.com.au
120 Rusden St, Armidale, NSW 2350, Store Manager: Pete Hansen *Tel:* (02) 6772 2622 *Fax:* (02) 6772 7608 *E-mail:* armidale@koorong.com.au
4-8 Vicki St, Blackburn South, Victoria 3130, Store Manager: Matthew Hart *Tel:* (03) 9262 7444 *Fax:* (03) 9262 7499 *E-mail:* blackburn@koorong.com.au
Unit 1, 26 Maryborough St, Fyshwick, ACT 2609, Store Manager: Rod Brewe *Tel:* (02) 6280 3477 *Fax:* (02) 6280 3488 *E-mail:* fyshwick@koorong.com.au
31 Criterion St, Hobart, Tas 7000, Store Manager: Peter Atkinson *Tel:* (03) 6231 0992 *Fax:* (03) 6231 0993 *E-mail:* hobart@koorong.com.au
434 Lord St, Mount Lawley, WA 6050, Store Manager: Sheila Fitch *Tel:* (08) 9427 9777 *Fax:* (08) 9427 9788 *E-mail:* sf@koorong.com.au
Unit 3b, Henry Lawson Centre, 61-79 Henry St, Penrith, NSW 2750, Store Manager: Warren Ward *Tel:* (02) 4724 4477 *Fax:* (02) 4724 4488 *E-mail:* ww@koorong.com.au

141 Gordon St, Port Macquarie, NSW 2444, Store Manager: Rod Lampard-Mills *Tel:* (02) 6584 4977 *Fax:* (02) 6583 6235 *E-mail:* port-macquarie@koorong.com.au
837 Ruthven St, Toowoomba, Qld 4350, Store Manager: Cheryl Hansen *Tel:* (07) 4636 2177 *Fax:* (07) 4636 2188 *E-mail:* ch@koorong.com.au
7 Broadway St, Wooloongabba, Qld 4102, Store Manager: Jenny Graf *Tel:* (07) 3896 8777 *Fax:* (07) 3896 8788 *E-mail:* wooloongabba@koorong.com.au

**Landmark Education Supplies Pty Ltd**
Princes Hwy, Drouin, Victoria 3818
*Tel:* (056) 251701
*Key Personnel*
Owner: Russell Porch

**Language Book Centre**
Division of Abbey's Bookshops Pty Ltd
131 York St, Sydney, NSW 2000
*Tel:* (02) 92671397 *Toll Free Tel:* 800 802 432 (outside Sydney & within Australia) *Fax:* (02) 92648993
*E-mail:* language@abbeys.com.au
*Web Site:* www.languagebooks.com.au
*Key Personnel*
Manager: Jacqueline Rychner *E-mail:* jacquir@abbeys.com.au
Man Dir: Jack Winning *Tel:* (02) 9264 3260 *E-mail:* jackw@abbeys.com.au
Founded: 1976
Type of Business: Major Independent Bookseller

**Magpie Books**
PO Box 2038, Brighton 3186
*Tel:* (03) 95929931 *Fax:* (03) 95922045
*E-mail:* admin01@magpiebooks.com.au
*Web Site:* www.magpiebooks.com.au
*Key Personnel*
Proprietor: Brian Howes *E-mail:* brhowes@dove.net.au
Founded: 1986
Publishers of directories & price guides for the antiquarian book trade.
Type of Business: Distributor
*Bookshop(s):* Barossa Vintage Books, 111 Murray St, Angaston 5353 *Tel:* (08) 8564 3633 *E-mail:* brhowes@ozemail.com.au

**Robert Muir Old & Rare Books**
69 Broadway, Nedlands 6009
*Tel:* (08) 9386 5842 *Fax:* (08) 9386 8211
*E-mail:* books@muirbooks.com
*Web Site:* www.muirbooks.com
*Key Personnel*
Owner: Helen Muir; Robert Muir
Founded: 1973
Membership(s): ILAB, ABA, ANZAAB.
Type of Business: Exporter, Importer, Major Independent Bookseller

**The Open Book**
110 Gawler Pl, Adelaide, SA 5000
Mailing Address: GPO Box 1368, Adelaide, SA 5001
*Tel:* (08) 8124 0049 *Fax:* (08) 8223 4552
*E-mail:* openbook@openbook.com.au; service@openbook.com.au
*Web Site:* www.openbook.com.au
*Key Personnel*
National Retail Manager: Kevin Reichelt *Tel:* (08) 82239140 *E-mail:* kreichelt@openbook.com.au
Trade Sales Manager: Mike Grieger *E-mail:* mgrieger@openbook.com.au
Founded: 1913
Christian, religious bookstore - theological books & resources - specialty. Branch offices in Aubury, Brisbane, Hamilton, Melbourne, Sydney, Tanunda, & Toowoomba.

Type of Business: Distributor, Exporter, Importer, Major Book Chain Headquarters, Major Independent Bookseller, Wholesaler
*Owned by:* Openbook Publishers, 205 Halifax St, Adelaide, SA 5000

**Soundbooks**
1292 Malvern Rd, Malvern, Victoria 3144
*Tel:* (03) 98247711 *Fax:* (03) 98247855
*E-mail:* audio@soundbooks.com.au
*Web Site:* www.soundbooks.com.au
*Key Personnel*
Dir: Christopher Raynor
Founded: 1982
Specialize in audiobooks.
Type of Business: Distributor, Exporter, Importer, Major Independent Bookseller

**Michael Treloar Antiquarian Booksellers**
196 North Terrace, Adelaide SA 5000
Mailing Address: GPO Box 2289, Adelaide SA 5001
*Tel:* (08) 82231111 *Fax:* (08) 82236599
*E-mail:* treloars@treloars.com
*Web Site:* www.treloars.com
*Key Personnel*
Owner: Michael Treloar
Founded: 1976
Type of Business: Major Independent Bookseller

**La Trobe University Bookshop**
La Trobe University, Plenty Rd, The Agora, Bundoora, Victoria 3083
*Tel:* (03) 94791234 *Fax:* (03) 94702011
*E-mail:* enquiries@bookshop.latrobe.edu.au
*Web Site:* www.bookshop.latrobe.edu.au
*Key Personnel*
General Manager: I Patterson
*Branch Office(s)*
La Trobe University Bendigo Campus, Edwards Rd, Student Union floor, Bendigo 3550 *Tel:* (03) 5444 7516 *Fax:* (03) 5444 7825 *E-mail:* bendigo@bookshop.latrobe.edu.au
Wodonga TAFE Campus, 15 McKoy St, Wodonga 3690 *Tel:* (02) 6058 3899 *Fax:* (02) 6056 2380 *E-mail:* wodonga@bookshop.latrobe.edu.au

**University Co-operative Bookshop Ltd**
235 Jones St, Level 10, Ultimo NSW 2007
*Tel:* (02) 93259600 *Fax:* (02) 92123372
*E-mail:* webhelp@coop-bookshop.com.au
*Web Site:* www.coop-bookshop.com.au
*Key Personnel*
Chief Executive Officer: Duncan Maclellan
Founded: 1958
Over 40 co-op stores located across Australia.
Type of Business: Major Book Chain Headquarters, Major Independent Bookseller

# Austria

**Aichinger, Bernhard & Co GmbH**
Weihburggasse 16, 1010 Vienna
*Tel:* (01) 5128853 *Fax:* (01) 5128853-13
*Key Personnel*
Manager: Mag Veronika Aichinger

**Buchhandlung Bayer**
Kreuzgasse 6, 6800 Feldkirch
*Tel:* (05522) 74770 *Fax:* (05522) 74770
*E-mail:* bayer.buch@utanet.at
*Key Personnel*
Contact: Irmgard Neugebauer
Founded: 1973
Also library supplier.
Type of Business: Distributor, Exporter, Importer, Major Independent Bookseller
*Parent Company:* W Neugebauer Verlag GesmbH

**Blackwell & Hadwiger GesmbH British Bookshop**
Weihburggasse 24-26, 1010 Vienna
*Tel:* (01) 5121945; (01) 5132933 *Fax:* (01) 5121026
*E-mail:* britbook@netway.at
*Key Personnel*
Contact: Margaret Hofmaier
Founded: 1974
Type of Business: Importer, Major Independent Bookseller

**British Bookshop**, see Blackwell & Hadwiger GesmbH British Bookshop

**Bucher-Stierle GesmbH**
Kaigasse 1 - Mozartplazt, 5010 Salzburg
Mailing Address: Postfach 245, 5010 Salzberg
*Tel:* (0662) 840114 *Fax:* (0662) 8401149
*E-mail:* buecher-stierle@members.debis.at
*Key Personnel*
Owner: Vivienne Stierle
Founded: 1988
Type of Business: Exporter, Importer, Major Independent Bookseller

**Der Buchfreund Universitats-Buchhandlung u Antiquariat Walter R Schaden**
Sonnenfelsgasse 4, 1010 Vienna
*Tel:* (01) 512 48 56; (01) 513 82 89 *Fax:* (01) 512 60 28
*E-mail:* buch.schaden@vienna.at
*Web Site:* www.buch-schaden.at
*Key Personnel*
Owner: Rainer Schaden
Founded: 1955
Membership(s): JLAB.
Type of Business: Importer, Major Independent Bookseller
*Owned by:* Rainer Schaden
*Bookshop(s):* Lugeck 7, 1010 Vienna

**Dietz GmbH**
Bahnstr 1, 2351 Wiener Neudorf
*Tel:* (02236) 22596 *Fax:* (02236) 47127
*Key Personnel*
Manager: Horst Jansa; Walter Dietz
Founded: 1978
Type of Business: Importer, Wholesaler
*Branch Office(s)*
Airport Vienna, Vienna
Graz
Salzburg
*Bookshop(s):* American Discount, Rechte Wienzeile 5, 1040 Vienna

**Fachbuchhandlung fur Wirtschaft und Recht Dr Karl Stropek GmbH**
Waehringerstr 122, Postfach 84, A-1181 Vienna
*Tel:* (01) 4795495 *Fax:* (01) 4796230
*Key Personnel*
Proprietor: Eleonore Stropek
Founded: 1863
Library supplier.
Type of Business: Major Independent Bookseller

**Gerold & Co**
Graben 13, 1010 Vienna
Mailing Address: Postfach 597, 1011 Vienna
*Tel:* (01) 5335014-0
*E-mail:* office@gerold.at
*Web Site:* www.gerold.at
*Telex:* 847136157 Gerol *Cable:* Geroldbuch Vienna
*Key Personnel*
Man Dir: Hans Neusser
Subscription agent & library jobber for European books & periodicals; also publisher.

**Hans Furstelberger**
Kaufmaennisches Vereinhaus, Landstr 49, 4013 Linz
*Tel:* (0732) 773177 *Fax:* (0732) 784485
Type of Business: Major Independent Bookseller

**A Hartleben Inhaber Dr Walter Rob**
Schwarzenbergstr 6, Postfach 309, 1010 Vienna
*Tel:* (01) 512-62-41 *Fax:* (01) 513-94-98
*Key Personnel*
Owner: Dr Walter Rob; Dr Marion Unger-Rob
Founded: 1803
Type of Business: Distributor, Importer, Major Independent Bookseller
*Branch Office(s)*
Huetteldorfer Str 114, 1140 Vienna

**Verlag Johannes Heyn**
Kramergasse 2-4, 9020 Klagenfurt
*Tel:* (0463) 54249 *Fax:* (0463) 5424941
*E-mail:* buch@heyn.at; technik@heyn.at
*Web Site:* www.heyn.at
*Key Personnel*
Owner: Gert Zechner; Volkmar Zechner
Type of Business: Major Independent Bookseller

**Buchhandlung Karl Hofbauer KG**
Hauptplatz 31, 8430 Leibnitz
*Tel:* (03452) 82793; (03452) 82177 *Fax:* (03452) 71218
*E-mail:* hofbauer.buch@magnet.at
*Key Personnel*
Manager: Jutta Hofbauer
Founded: 1963
Type of Business: Importer, Major Independent Bookseller
*Branch Office(s)*
A-8430 Leibnitz, Grazerg 73 *Tel:* (03452) 83166

**Friedrich Hofmeister-Figaro Verlag Grossortiment und Musikalienhandlung GesmbH**
Seikrgasse 12, 1015 Vienna
*Tel:* (01) 50576510 *Fax:* (01) 5059185
*Key Personnel*
Contact: Ferdinand Walcher
Type of Business: Importer, Wholesaler

**Innverlag + Gatt**
Hunoldstr 12, 6020 Innsbruck
*Tel:* (0512) 34 53 31 *Fax:* (0512) 34 12 90
*E-mail:* info@innverlag.at
*Web Site:* www.innverlag.at
*Key Personnel*
Production: Klaus Hagleitner
Founded: 1947
Type of Business: Distributor, Importer, Major Independent Bookseller, Wholesaler

**Alexander Kerbiser KG**
Wiener Str 17, Hammerpark 10, 8680 Muerzzuschlag
*Tel:* (03852) 2204 *Fax:* (03852) 5349
*Key Personnel*
Contact: E M Mueck
Founded: 1936
Type of Business: Major Independent Bookseller

**Walter Klugel**
Gumpendorferstr 33, 1060 Vienna
*Tel:* (0222) 573 03 42
Founded: 1921
Type of Business: Major Independent Bookseller

**Antiquariat Walter Krieg Verlag**
Karntner Str 4/III, 1010 Vienna
*Tel:* (01) 5121093 *Fax:* (01) 5123266
Also library supplier.
Type of Business: Exporter

**Leopold Stocker Verlag**
Hofgasse 5, 8011 Graz
Mailing Address: Postfach 189, 8011 Graz
*Tel:* (0316) 82 16 36 *Fax:* (0316) 83 56 12
*E-mail:* buecherquelle@stocker-verlag.com
*Web Site:* www.buecherquelle.at
*Key Personnel*
Publisher: Wolfgang Dvorak-Stocker
Founded: 1917
Type of Business: Major Independent Bookseller
*Bookshop(s):* Buecherquelle Buchhandlungs GmbH, Graz

**MANZ'sche Verlags- und Universitaetsbuchhandlung GMBH**
Kohlmarkt 16, Postfach 163, 1010 Vienna
*Tel:* (01) 531 61-100 *Fax:* (01) 531 61-181
*E-mail:* bestellen@manz.at
*Web Site:* www.manz.at
*Telex:* 75310631
Also publisher & library supplier.
Type of Business: Exporter

**Mohr-ZA Verlagsauslieferungen Ges mbH**
Singerstr 12, 1010 Vienna
Mailing Address: Postfach 771, 1010 Vienna
*Tel:* (01) 5121676; (01) 5125711; (01) 5126994 *Fax:* (01) 111859
*Key Personnel*
Proprietor: Dr Gottfried Berger
Type of Business: Wholesaler

**Osterreichische Bibelgesellschaft** (Austrian Bible Society)
Breite Gasse 8, 1070 Vienna
*Tel:* (01) 5238240 *Fax:* (01) 5238240-20
*E-mail:* bibelhaus@bibelgesellschaft.at
*Web Site:* www.bibelgesellschaft.at
*Key Personnel*
Contact: Dr Jutta Henner
Founded: 1970
Type of Business: Major Independent Bookseller

**Max Pock, Universitaetsbuchhandlung**
Hauptplatz 1, 8010 Graz
*Tel:* (0316) 825254-0 *Fax:* (0316) 825258; (0316) 825254-8
*Telex:* 031873
*Key Personnel*
Manager: Dr Maximilian Pock
Also library supplier.
Type of Business: Exporter

**Georg Prachner KG**
Kaerntner Str 30, 1015 Vienna
*Tel:* (01) 5128549-0 *Fax:* (01) 5120158
*Key Personnel*
Man Dir: O G Prachner
Also Publisher.
Type of Business: Exporter, Importer, Major Independent Bookseller, Wholesaler

**Styria Medien AG**
Schonaugasse 64, 8010 Graz
*Tel:* (0316) 8063-1012 *Fax:* (0316) 8063-3034
*E-mail:* medien.ag@styria.com
*Web Site:* www.styria.com
*Key Personnel*
Contact: Wolfgang Habenschuss
*Owned by:* Styria Druck und Verlagshaus
*Branch Office(s)*
Hauptpl 15, 8720 Judenburg, Australia
Kaerntnerstr 2, 8720 Knittelfeld
Wollzeile 2, 1010 Vienna

**J G Sydy's Buchhandlung Ludwig Schubert GmbH Nachfolge KG**
Wienerstr 19, 3100 St Poelten
*Tel:* (02742) 35 31 89 *Fax:* (02742) 35 31 89; (02742) 35 31 85

*E-mail:* schubert.sydys@aon.at; info@
buchhandlung-schubert.at
*Web Site:* www.buchhandlung-schubert.at
*Key Personnel*
Contact: Susanne Sandler
Founded: 1837
Membership(s): Hauptverband des Oesterreichis-
chen Buchhandels.
Type of Business: Exporter, Importer, Major Inde-
pendent Bookseller

**Tyrolia Verlagsanstalt GmbH**
Exlgasse 20, 6020 Innsbruck
*Tel:* (0512) 2233-0 *Fax:* (0512) 2233-501
*E-mail:* tyrolia@tyrolia.at
*Web Site:* www.tyrolia.at
*Telex:* 053620
*Key Personnel*
Manager: Thaler Franz
*Owned by:* Verlagsanstalt Tyrolia
*Branch Office(s)*
Ehrwald
Fulpmes
Imst
Kufstein
Landeck
Lienz
Mayrhofen
Reutte
Schwaz
St Johann
Telfs
Vienna
Wattens
Woergl

**Urban und Schwarzenberg GmbH**
Frankgasse 4, 1096 Vienna
*Tel:* (01) 4052731 *Fax:* (01) 405272441
*Key Personnel*
Manager: Gunter Royer
Also Publisher.
*Owned by:* Williams & Wilkins Ltd

**Buchhandlung Veritas**
Hafenstr 1-3, 4010 Linz
Mailing Address: Postfach 50, 4010 Linz
*Tel:* (0732) 776451-280 *Fax:* (0732) 776451-239
*E-mail:* veritas@veritas.at
*Web Site:* www.veritas.at
*Key Personnel*
Manager: Klaus Radler
*Owned by:* Veritas GesmbH & Co KG

**Wagner'sche Universitaetsbuchhandlung**
Museumstr 4, 6020 Innsbruck
*Tel:* (0512) 59505-0 *Fax:* (0512) 59505-38
*E-mail:* buch@wagnersche.at
*Web Site:* www.wagnersche.at
*Telex:* 75311457
*Key Personnel*
Dir: Martin Flatscher
Also library supplier.
Type of Business: Exporter

**Rupertusbuchhandlung Augustin Weis und
Soehne KG**
Dreifaltigkeitsgasse 12, A-5024 Salzburg
*Tel:* (0662) 878733-0 *Fax:* (0662) 871661
*E-mail:* info@rupertusbuch.at
*Key Personnel*
Manager: Bernhard Weis *E-mail:* b.weis@
rupertusbuch.at
Also library supplier.
Type of Business: Exporter

**Kunstverlag Wolfrum**
Augustinerstr 10, 1010 Vienna
*Tel:* (01) 5125398-0 *Fax:* (01) 5125398-57
*E-mail:* your-welcome@wolfrum.at
*Web Site:* www.wolfrum.at

*Telex:* 75311081 Wolb *Cable:* WITWOLF
VIENNA
*Key Personnel*
Man Dir: Monika Engel
Manager: Peter Engel; Erich Pospisil
Founded: 1919
Also Publisher of posters, note-cards, calendars &
library supplier of art books.
Type of Business: Distributor, Exporter, Importer,
Major Independent Bookseller
*Owned by:* Monika Engel & Hubert Wolfrum

# Bangladesh

**Adeyle Brothers & Co**
60 Patuatuly, Dhaka 1100
*Tel:* (02) 233508
*Owned by:* Genclik Kitabevi

**Bangladesh Books International Ltd**
73-74 Patuatuli, Dhaka 1100
*Tel:* (02) 232252 (ext 31); (02) 232229; (02)
256071 (ext 19)
*Key Personnel*
Manager: Abdul Hafiz
Also publisher.

**Dhaka Book Mart**
38-2 Banglabazar, Dhaka 1100
*Tel:* (02) 259173

**Kathakali** (Bud of Spoken World)
18 Momin Rd, Chittagong 4000
*Tel:* (031) 619476; (031) 619006; (031) 612625
*Key Personnel*
Dir, Author & Editor: Mahbubul Haque
*E-mail:* mhaque@abnetbd.com
Founded: 1982
Managing Authority of Chittagong University
Book Center, Publisher of Chittagong Guide.
Membership(s): Bangladesh Book Sellers' & Pub-
lishers' Association.
Type of Business: Distributor, Importer, Major
Independent Bookseller, Wholesaler
*Owned by:* Mashuda Yasmin

**Mullick Bros**
160-161 Dhaka New Market, Dhaka 1205
*Tel:* (02) 8619125; (02) 507434 *Fax:* (02)
8610562
*E-mail:* mullick@bd.com
Also Publisher.

**Puthigar Ltd**
74 Farashganj, Dhaka 1100
*Tel:* (02) 231374; (02) 235333; (02) 259867

# Barbados

**The Book Source**
9100407 Barbados Community College Campus,
Howells Cross Rd, St Michael
Mailing Address: PO Box 964E, Belleville, Saint
Michael
*Tel:* 4310379 *Fax:* 4261855
*E-mail:* bksource@caribsurf.com
*Web Site:* www.booksourceonline.com
*Key Personnel*
Dir: Beverly Smith-Hinkson *E-mail:* beverly.
bksource@caribsurf.com
Founded: 1989

Book ordering service; college bookshop; online
bookstore.
Type of Business: Major Independent Bookseller
*Owned by:* Datalore Inc

**Christian Literature Crusade**
Constitution Rd, Bridgetown
Mailing Address: PO Box 1239, Bridgetown
*Tel:* 429-5630 *Fax:* 426-9254
*Key Personnel*
Manager: Pauline Sealy
Founded: 1941
Type of Business: Distributor, Importer, Major
Book Chain Headquarters

**Cloister Bookstore Ltd**
Hincks & Cowell Sts, Bridgetown
*Tel:* (246) 426-2662 *Fax:* (246) 429-7269
*E-mail:* cloisterbookstore@caribsurf.com
*Key Personnel*
Man Dir: A Musgrave
Founded: 1957
Type of Business: Distributor, Importer, Major
Independent Bookseller, Wholesaler

# Belgium

**Uitgeverij Acco**
Tiensestr 134, 3000 Leuven
*Tel:* (016) 29 11 00 *Fax:* (016) 20 73 89
*E-mail:* papierhandel@acco.be
*Web Site:* www.acco.be
*Key Personnel*
Dir: Herman Peeters *Tel:* (016) 62 80 10
*E-mail:* herman.peeters@acco.be
Founded: 1960
Type of Business: Distributor, Exporter, Major
Independent Bookseller, Wholesaler

**Agence et Menageries de la Prense**
One Rue de Petite Ile, 1070 Brussels
*Tel:* (02) 52 51 641 *Fax:* (02) 52 34 863
*Key Personnel*
Contact: Jean-Pierre Verbeeck; Mr Sheridan
Founded: 1850
Type of Business: Distributor, Exporter, Importer,
Major Book Chain Headquarters, Wholesaler

**Agora bvba**
Ninovesteenweg 24, 9320 Aalst-Erembodegem
*Tel:* (053) 78-87-00 *Fax:* (053) 78-26-91
*E-mail:* info@agorabooks.com
*Web Site:* www.agorabooks.com
*Key Personnel*
Dir: Jacques Van Mello
Founded: 1985
Type of Business: Distributor, Importer, Major
Independent Bookseller

**Altiora Averbode Uitgeverij nv**
PB 54, 3271 Averbode
*Tel:* (013) 780 182 *Fax:* (013) 780 179
*E-mail:* averbode.publ@verbode.be
*Web Site:* www.averbode.be
*Key Personnel*
Contact: Karolien Van Geldre

**Artis-Historia**
One rue Carli, 1140 Brussels
*Tel:* (02) 2409200 *Fax:* (02) 2480818
*E-mail:* info@artis-historia.be
Also acts as publisher.

**Audivox**
Rubenslei 23, 2018 Antwerp
*Tel:* (03) 470 1784
*E-mail:* info@audivox.net

*Key Personnel*
Dir: Robert Gonnissen
Founded: 1953
Specialize in the import & distribution of English
& American books.

**Bredero**
Rozenberg 15, 2400 Mol
*Tel:* (014) 31-84-61 *Fax:* (014) 70-02-05
*Web Site:* www.bredero.be
*Key Personnel*
Contact: E De Ridder
Type of Business: Major Independent Bookseller

**De Plukvogel nv**
Mechelsesteenweg 9, 1800 Vilvoorde
*Tel:* (02) 253-06-58 *Fax:* (02) 253-06-58
*Key Personnel*
Contact: P Steyaert

**Exhibitions International NV/SA**
Kolonel Begaultlaan 17, 3012 Leuven (Wilsele)
*Tel:* (016) 296900 *Fax:* (016) 296129
*E-mail:* orders@exhibitionsinternational.be
*Web Site:* www.exhibitionsinternational.be
*Key Personnel*
Dir: Marleen Geukens *E-mail:* marleen.geukens@
exhibitionsinternational.be
Founded: 1988
Acts as distributor for art books, catalogues & il-
lustrated books on gardens, travel, architecture,
design, etc.
Type of Business: Distributor

**Uitgeverij Het-Volk**
Forelstr 22, 9000 Ghent
*Tel:* (09) 2656424; (09) 2656420 *Fax:* (09)
2258406
*Key Personnel*
Publishing Dept Manager: F Nauwelaerts
General Manager: E Korntheuer
Publishers of newspapers, magazines, books &
comics.
*Owned by:* Drukkerij Het Volk NV
*Bookshop(s):* Brusselsestr 11, 9200 Dender-
monde; Kortedagsteeg 16, 9000 Ghent; Rijsel-
str 20, 8900 Ieper; Marktstr 24, 8870 Izegem;
Voorstr 35, 8500 Kortrijk; Noordstr 6, 8800
Roeselare; Maastrichtstr 65, 3700 Tongeren;
Korte Gasthuisstr 13, 2300 Turnhout

**J Story-Scientia BVBA**
Van Duyseplein 8, 9000 Ghent
*Tel:* (09) 2255757 *Fax:* (09) 2331409
*E-mail:* bookshop@story.be
*Web Site:* www.story.be
*Key Personnel*
Manager: J Story
Founded: 1962
Scientific booksellers & subscription agents &
publishers.
Type of Business: Distributor, Exporter, Importer,
Major Independent Bookseller

**Boekhandel Johannes**
Alfons Smetsplein 10, 3000 Leuven
*Tel:* (016) 229501 *Fax:* (016) 208419
*E-mail:* info@johannes.be
*Web Site:* www.johannes.be
*Key Personnel*
Manager: Jos Maes *E-mail:* jos.maes@johannes.
be
Founded: 1977
Type of Business: Distributor, Importer, Major
Independent Bookseller
*Owned by:* Aquila bvba, de Beriotstr 2, 3000
Leuven
*Branch Office(s)*
Boekhandel de Kleine Johannes, Tiensestr 47,
3000 Leuven *Tel:* (016) 206046 *Fax:* (016)
208419

**Librairie des Presses Universitaires de
Bruxelles**
42 ave Paul Heger, 1000 Brussels
*Tel:* (02) 641 1440 *Fax:* (02) 647 7962
*Web Site:* www.ulb.ac.be
*Key Personnel*
Contact: Paulette Biondi *E-mail:* paulette.biondi@
ulb.ac.be
Scientific books.
*Owned by:* Presses universitaires de Bruxelles
ASBL

**Licap CVBA**
Guimardstraat 1, 1040 Brussels
*Tel:* (02) 5099672 *Fax:* (02) 5099704; (02)
5099780
*E-mail:* info@licap.be
*Key Personnel*
Contact: Herman Deben
Founded: 1973
Type of Business: Major Independent Bookseller

**Maison des Langues Vivantes-Intertaal SA**
Steenstraat, 9, Rue des Pierres, 1000 Brussels
*Tel:* (02) 5117117 *Fax:* (02) 5145820
*E-mail:* mlv.i@skynet.be
*Web Site:* maison-des-langues.com
*Key Personnel*
Man Dir: Pierre De Laet
Founded: 1960
Specialize in modern languages.
Type of Business: Importer, Major Independent
Bookseller

**Oneindige Verhaal, t bvba** (The Neverending
Story)
Nieuwstraat 17, 9100 Sint-Niklaas
*Tel:* (03) 7765225 *Fax:* (03) 7765225
*E-mail:* oneindigeverhaal@boekenbank.be
*Key Personnel*
Dir: Herwig Staes
Assistant Manager: Tim Staes *Tel:* (03) 7651730
*E-mail:* timstaes@planetinternet.be
Founded: 1996
Bookstore.

**Pijl Boekbedrijf nv**
Bleekhofstraat 87, 2140 Antwerp
*Tel:* (03) 236-98-30; (03) 270-02-70 *Fax:* (03)
235-90-02
*E-mail:* booksell@innet.be
*Key Personnel*
Contact: Johan Van Hemeldonck
Type of Business: Major Book Chain Headquar-
ters, Wholesaler

**Simon Stevin NV**
Zennestraat 37, 1000 Brussels
*Tel:* (02) 5121085; (02) 5138295 *Fax:* (02)
5117015
*Key Personnel*
Dirs: L Van Hoorick; J De Hertogh
Founded: 1930

**Libris Toison d'Or SA**
Espace Louise, 40-42 ave de la Toison d'Or, 1050
Brussels
*Tel:* (02) 5116400 *Fax:* (02) 5140961
*Key Personnel*
Manager: Jacqueline Evrard
Founded: 1961
Type of Business: Major Book Chain Headquar-
ters, Wholesaler
*Owned by:* Librairies du Savoir

**VTB-Travel Bookshop**
Division of Tui Germany
Osystraat 35, 2060 Antwerp
*Tel:* (03) 224 10 52 *Fax:* (03) 224 10 56
*E-mail:* info.cultuur@vtb.be
*Web Site:* www.vtb.be

*Key Personnel*
Manager: Bert van Uytsel *Tel:* (03) 220-33-68
*E-mail:* bert.vanuytsel@vtb.be
Founded: 1929
Travel Bookshop; Travel Guides-Maps-Travel Ne-
cessities.
Membership(s): IMTA; VBVB.
Type of Business: Major Book Chain Headquar-
ters, Major Independent Bookseller, Wholesaler

**Wouters Import NV**
Naamsestraat 48, 3000 Leuven
*Tel:* (016) 202944 *Fax:* (016) 237785
*E-mail:* info@fonteynsciences.com
*Web Site:* www.wouters.be
*Key Personnel*
Dir: L Verwimp *E-mail:* ludov@bookshop.
wouters.be
Founded: 1989
Type of Business: Distributor, Exporter, Importer,
Wholesaler
*Owned by:* Wouters BVBA

# Benin

**Libraira-Papeterie ABM**
BP 889, Cotonou
*Tel:* 330690 (voice & fax)
*Key Personnel*
Vice President: Michel Goussanou
Type of Business: Distributor, Exporter, Importer,
Wholesaler
*Owned by:* Maison d'Edition ABM
*Branch Office(s)*
Porto Novo
*Bookshop(s):* BP 889, C138 Guinkomey, Cotonou

# Bolivia

**Libreria los Amigos del Libro**
Casilla de Correo 450, Cochabamba 15
*Tel:* (04) 4504150; (04) 4504151 *Fax:* (04)
4115128
*E-mail:* gutten@amigol.bo.net *Cable:* AMIGOL
*Key Personnel*
Owner: Ingrid Guttentag
Manager: Petra Guttentag; Sonia Laguna
Founded: 1945
Type of Business: Distributor, Exporter, Importer,
Major Book Chain Headquarters, Wholesaler
*Branch Office(s)*
Airport Jorge Wilstermann, Cochabamba
Shopping Center S O F E R, Cochabamba
Av Ayacucho S-0156, Cochabamba
Bookstore San Miguel, La Paz
Bookstore en Avd 16 de Julio Edificio Alameda,
La Paz
Bookstore Calle, Ingavi No 14, Santa Cruz
Calle Mercado 1315, Aerport E1 Alto, La Paz

**Gisbert y Cia SA**
Comercio 1270, La Paz
Mailing Address: Casilla Postal 195, La Paz
*Tel:* (02) 220 26 26 *Fax:* (02) 220 29 11
*E-mail:* libgis@ceibo.entelnet.bo
*Key Personnel*
President: Javier Gisbert
Founded: 1907
Also Publisher.
Type of Business: Distributor, Importer, Major
Independent Bookseller, Wholesaler

**Libreria Juventud**
Plaza Murillo 519, Casilla de Correo 1489, La Paz
*Tel:* (02) 2406248 *Fax:* (02) 2406248
*Key Personnel*
Manager: Gustavo Urquizo Mendoza
Founded: 1948
Type of Business: Importer, Wholesaler
*Owned by:* Libreria y Editorial Juventud

**Libreria la Paz**
Calle Colon 618, Casilla, 539 La Paz
*Tel:* (02) 353323; (02) 357109 *Fax:* (02) 391513
*Key Personnel*
Manager: Carlos Burgos Munoz
Founded: 1900
Type of Business: Distributor, Importer, Major Independent Bookseller, Wholesaler

# Bosnia and Herzegovina

**Veselin Maslesa**
UI Obala V Stepe Br 4, 71000 Sarajevo
Mailing Address: Pro Boks 237, 71000 Sarajevo
*Tel:* (071) 214633
*Telex:* 41154
Also publisher.
Type of Business: Exporter, Importer
*Branch Office(s)*
Maksima Gorkog 2, Pavla Goranina 2, Sarajevo
Terazije 38, Belgrade, Serbia and Montenegro
  (over 30 group bookshops)

**Sarajevo Publishing**, see Veselin Maslesa

**Svjetlost**
Muhamede Kantardzica 3, 71000 Sarajevo
*Tel:* (071) 443 419; (071) 664 535; (071) 664 066; (071) 214 578; (071) 207 352 *Fax:* (071) 443 435
Also Publisher.
Type of Business: Exporter, Importer

# Botswana

**Botswana Book Centre**
The Mall, PO Box 91, Gaborone
*Tel:* 3974315
*E-mail:* pulapress@botsnet.bw
*Telex:* 2327 Books *Cable:* Books
*Key Personnel*
Manager: Sedilame Dhliwayo
Founded: 1826
Membership(s): BOPIA.
Also acts as publisher.
*Owned by:* Botswana Book Centre Trust
*Bookshop(s):* Botswana Book Centre-Westgate *Tel:* 3500290; Francistown Shop; Lobatse Book Shop; Maun Shop
*Warehouse:* Broadhurst Industrial, Gaborone *Tel:* 3912130 *Fax:* 3912029
  *E-mail:* bookcenter@botsnet.bw

# Brazil

**Livraria Alema Buecherstube Brooklin Ltda**
Rua Bernardino de Campos, 215, Brooklin, Sao Paulo-SP CEP 04620-001

*Tel:* (011) 5543 3829 *Fax:* (011) 5041 4315
*E-mail:* buchlbb@uol.com.br
*Web Site:* www.buchlbb.com/
*Key Personnel*
Contact: Ursula Hellner; Erica Richter

**Livraria Brasiliense Editora SA**
Av Marques do Sao Vicente 1771, 01139-003 Sao Paulo-SP
*Tel:* (011) 8250122 *Fax:* (011) 673024
*Telex:* 33271 *Cable:* DBL
*Key Personnel*
Contact: Claiton Celso Guerrato; Caio Graco Prado
Founded: 1943
*Owned by:* Editora Brasiliense SA

**Livraria Cientifica Ernesto Reichmann Ltda**
Rua Dom Jose de Barros 158 andar-Centro, 01.038-000 Sao Paulo SP
Mailing Address: PO Box 3935, 01038 Sao Paulo
*Tel:* (011) 3255-1342; (011) 3214-3167
  *Fax:* (011) 3255-7501
*E-mail:* rrr@erdl.com
*Web Site:* www.ernestoreichmann.com.br
*Key Personnel*
Manager: Antonio Francisco; Hannelore Reichmann; Renato Reichmann
Founded: 1936
Specialize in Medical & Allied Literature.
Type of Business: Distributor, Exporter, Importer, Major Book Chain Headquarters, Wholesaler
*Branch Office(s)*
Rua Pedro de Toledo, 597-Vila Mariana, 04.039-031 Sao Paulo SP *Tel:* (011) 5575-8283
  *Fax:* (011) 5575-9037

**COLIVRO - Comercio e Distribuicao de Livros Ltda**
Rua Miquel Couto, 35 SL 201/7, 20070-030 Rio de Janeiro
*Tel:* (021) 2243177 *Fax:* (021) 2424517
*Key Personnel*
Manager: Fernando Jorge da Silva
Type of Business: Distributor, Wholesaler

**Columbus Cultural Editora Comercial Importacao e Exporta**
Rua Alves Guimaraes, 1297 Jardim America, 05410-002 Sao Paulo-SP
*Tel:* (011) 8648777 *Fax:* (011) 8646531
*Key Personnel*
Editor: Luiz Carlos Cardoso
Editor Assistant: Renata Farhat Borges
Founded: 1987
Type of Business: Exporter, Importer, Major Independent Bookseller
*Owned by:* Grupo Cardapio de Alimentacao

**Cortez Editora e Livraria Ltda**
Rua Bartira, 317 Perdizes, 05009-000 Sao Paulo-SP
*Tel:* (011) 3864 0111 *Fax:* (011) 3864 4290
*E-mail:* livraria@cortezeditora.com.br
*Web Site:* www.cortezeditora.com.br; www.livrariacortez.com.br
*Key Personnel*
Proprietor: Jose Xavier Cortez; Potira Beserra X Cortez
Editor: Danilo A Morales
Founded: 1980
Membership(s): Brazilian Book Association.

**Livraria Cultura Editora Ltda**
Av Paulista, 2073 Conjunto Nacional, 01311-940 Sao Paulo-SP
*Tel:* (011) 3170-4033 *Fax:* (011) 3285-4457
*E-mail:* livros@livrariacultura.com.br
*Telex:* 1138632 *Cable:* BOOKS-S.PAULO
*Key Personnel*
Dir: Pedro Herz

Founded: 1969
Type of Business: Importer

**Disal S/A Distribuidores Associados de Livros**
Av Marques de Sao Vicente 182, 01139-000 Sao Paulo SP
*Tel:* (011) 3226-3111 *Fax:* (011) 0800-7707106
*E-mail:* disal@disal.com.br
*Web Site:* www.disal.com.br
*Key Personnel*
President: Francisco S Canato
Founded: 1968
Type of Business: Distributor, Importer, Wholesaler
*Bookshop(s):* Rua Marcondes Salgado, 1.209, Centro, 14010-150 Ribeirao Preto/SP *Tel:* (016) 610-6536 *Fax:* (016) 3931-3031; Rua Maria Antonia, 380, 01222-010 Sao Paulo/SP *Tel:* (011) 3256-7293; (011) 3256-0264 *Fax:* (011) 3256-4127; Rua Deputado Lacerda Franco, 365, 05418-000 Sao Paulo/SP *Tel:* (011) 3816-6096 *Fax:* (011) 3813-5761; Rua Brasilia Castanho de Oliveira, 141, 07115-010 Sao Paulo *Tel:* (011) 6440-0555 *Fax:* (011) 6409-1753; Rua Emilio Malet, 1.196, 03320-001 Sao Paulo *Tel:* (011) 6193-0233 *Fax:* (011) 6192-4062

**Livraria Duas Cidades Ltda**
Rua Bento Freitas, 158, 01220-000 Sao Paulo
*Tel:* (011) 3331-5134 *Fax:* (011) 3331-4702
Also Publisher.

**Editora Letraviva Importacao Distribuidora Livros Ltd**
Av Reboucas 1986, 05402-300 Sao Paulo-SP
*Tel:* (011) 3088 7992; (011) 3088 7832
  *Fax:* (011) 3088 7780
*E-mail:* letraviva@letraviva.com.br
*Web Site:* www.letraviva.com.br
*Key Personnel*
Contact: Bernardo J I Gurbanov
Founded: 1979
Type of Business: Distributor, Importer

**Livraria Editora Tecnica Ltd**, see LITEC (Livraria Editora Tecnica) Ltda

**Global Editora e Distribuidora Ltda**
Rua Pirapitingui 111, CEP 01508-020 Liberdade, Sao Paulo
*Tel:* (011) 3277-7999
*Key Personnel*
Man Dir, Sales: Luis Alves, Jr
Founded: 1973
Type of Business: Distributor, Exporter, Importer

**Livro Ibero-Americano Ltda**
Rua Hermenegildo de Barros 40, 20241-040 Rio de Janeiro
*Tel:* (021) 252 8814 *Fax:* (021) 232 5248
*E-mail:* livo-ibero@uol.com.br *Cable:* NEBRIJA
*Key Personnel*
Man Dir: Sir Joao Francisco J Gomes
Founded: 1946
Also Publisher.
Type of Business: Distributor, Importer, Wholesaler
*Branch Office(s)*
Rua Conselheiro Crispiniano 29 - 1 pav, Sao Paulo-SP

**ISAEC**, see Editora Sinodal

**Livraria Kosmos Editora Ltda**
Rua do Rosario 155 Centro, 20041-005 Rio de Janeiro
*Tel:* (021) 2224-8616 *Fax:* (021) 2221-4582
*Cable:* EIKOS

Founded: 1935
Type of Business: Distributor, Exporter, Importer, Major Book Chain Headquarters

**LITEC (Livraria Editora Tecnica) Ltda**
Rua Vitoria, 374, Santa Ifigenia, 01210-001 Sao Paulo
*Tel:* (011) 223-7872 *Fax:* (011) 222-6728
*E-mail:* litec@litec.com.br
*Web Site:* www.litec.com.br
*Key Personnel*
Manager: Vainer Cavalheri; Antonio Clara Dos Santos
Founded: 1971
Type of Business: Importer
*Owned by:* Livraria Editora Tecnica Ltda
*Branch Office(s)*
Rua Marechal Floriano, 151 Centro, 20080-005 Rio de Janeiro-RJ *Tel:* (021) 2223-9025 *Fax:* (021) 2253-8005

**Livraria Nobel S/A**
Rua Pedroso Alvarenga, 1046 9 andar, Sao Paulo CEP 04531-004
*Tel:* (011) 3706 1469 *Fax:* (011) 3218-2833
*E-mail:* ary@editoranobel.com.br
*Web Site:* www.livrarianobel.com.br
*Key Personnel*
Dir, Publicity: Ary Kuflik Benclowicz
Founded: 1943
Number of titles published annually: 80 Print
Total Titles: 230 Print
Type of Business: Distributor

**Papirus Editora**
R Dr Gabriel Penteado, 253, Campinas SP CEP 13001 970
Mailing Address: Caixa postal 736, CEP 13001 970 Campinas SP
*Tel:* (0192) 3272 4500; (0192) 3272 4534 *Fax:* (0192) 3272 7578
*E-mail:* editora@papirus.com.br
*Web Site:* www.papirus.com.br/
*Key Personnel*
Contact: Eliane Camargo
Founded: 1976
*Branch Office(s)*
Rua Jose Antonio Coelho, 386 Sao Paulo SP
*Bookshop(s):* Rua Sacramento 202, Campinas SP; Rua Sacramento 114, Campinas SP; Rua Barao de Jaguara 1331, Campinas SP

**PTI**, see PTI - Publicacoes Tecnicas Internacionais Ltda

**PTI - Publicacoes Tecnicas Internacionais Ltda**
Rua Peixoto Gomide, 209, 01409-901 Sao Paolo SP
*Tel:* (011) 3159 2535 *Fax:* (011) 3159 2450
*E-mail:* info@pti.com.br
*Web Site:* www.pti.com.br
*Key Personnel*
Contact: Pierre Grossmann
Founded: 1972
Type of Business: Distributor, Exporter, Importer
*Branch Office(s)*
Rua Herculano De Freitas 390, Sao Paulo, SP

**Ernesto Reichmann Distribuidores de Livros LTDA**
Rua Coronel Marques, 335, Tatuape, 03440-000 Sao Paulo
*Tel:* (011) 61982122 *Fax:* (011) 61982122
*E-mail:* rrr@erdl.com
*Key Personnel*
Dir: Reichmann Renato
Manager: Antonio Francisco; Hannelore Reichmann
Founded: 1936
Specialize in Medical & Allied Literature.

Subjects: Health & Fitness; Medical; Psychology & Psychiatry
Type of Business: Distributor, Exporter, Importer, Wholesaler
*Branch Office(s)*
Livraria Cientifica Ernesto Reichmann LTDA, R Pedro de Toledo, 597, V Mariana, 04039-031 Sao Paulo-SP
*Bookshop(s):* Livraria Cientifica Ernesto Reichmann LTDA, Rua Dom Jose de Barros, 158, Centro, 01038-000 Sao Paulo-SP

**Sagra-D C Luzzatto Livreiros, Editores e Distribuidores Ltda**
Rua Joao Alfredo, 448 Cidade Baixa, 90050-230 Porto Alegre-RS
*Tel:* (051) 3227 5222 *Fax:* (051) 3227 4438
*E-mail:* atendimento@sagra-luzzatto.com.br
*Web Site:* www.sagra-luzzatto.com.br
*Key Personnel*
Dir: Antonio Wenzel Luzzatto; Fernanda Dora Luzzatto
Founded: 1967
Type of Business: Distributor, Exporter, Importer

**Saraiva SA, Livreiros Editores**
Rua Maestro Gabriel Migliori 380, 02712-140 Bairro Limao
*Tel:* (011) 3933-3300 *Fax:* (011) 3662-2062
*E-mail:* atendimento@livrariasaraiva.com.br
*Web Site:* www.livrariasaraiva.com.br; www.saraiva.com.br
*Telex:* 1126789
*Key Personnel*
Man Dir: Wander Soares
Founded: 1914
Subjects: Auxiliary textbooks; administration; economics; legal; primary & secondary school books
Type of Business: Distributor

**Editora Sinodal**
Rua Amadeo Rossi, 93001-970 Sao Leopoldo-RS
Mailing Address: 467 Caixa Postal 11, 93001-970 Sao Leopoldo-RS
*Tel:* (051) 590 2366 *Fax:* (051) 590 2664
*E-mail:* editora@editorasinodal.com.br
*Web Site:* www.editorasinodal.com.br
*Key Personnel*
General Dir: Eloy Teckemeier *E-mail:* diretor@editorasinodal.com.br
Founded: 1948
Type of Business: Exporter, Wholesaler

**Sulina Livraria Editora**
Av Borges de Medeiros 1030-1036, 90000 Porto Alegre RS
*Tel:* (0512) 254765; (0512) 250287 *Fax:* (0512) 280734
*Key Personnel*
President: Vilson Nailor Noer
Founded: 1946
Type of Business: Distributor, Exporter, Importer, Major Book Chain Headquarters
*Owned by:* Organizacao Sulina de Representacoes SA (see Livraria Sulina Editora)
*Branch Office(s)*
Rua Julio de Castilbos 1657, Caxias do Sul (nine other bookshops in Porto Alegre)
AV: Nacoes Unidas, 2001 Lj 1062

**Livraria Triangulo Ltda**
Rua Barao de Itapetininga, Galeria California Loja 24 - Centro, Cep 01042-000 Sao Paulo-SP
*Tel:* (011) 3231-0922; (011) 3231-0362; (011) 3231-0552 *Fax:* (011) 3231-0162
*E-mail:* atendimento@livrariatriangulo.com.br
*Web Site:* www.livrariatriangulo.com.br
*Key Personnel*
Contact: Carlos Roberto Gomes

Founded: 1985
Type of Business: Importer

# Brunei Darussalam

**The Brunel Press**
PO Box 69, Kuala Belait
*Tel:* (03) 2344
*Key Personnel*
Manager: Ian MacGregor
Stockists & dealers for books handled by the Strait Times Press, Singapore.

# Bulgaria

**Hemus Co Inc**
14 Benkovski Str, 1000 Sofia
*Tel:* (02) 981 1769 *Fax:* (02) 981 3341
*E-mail:* hemusb@pbitex.com
*Telex:* 22267 Hemkik
*Key Personnel*
Executive Dir: Anastasia Boneva
Founded: 1967
Art products, souvenirs, photo materials, records, compact discs, numismatic items, musical instruments. State owned.
Type of Business: Distributor, Exporter, Importer, Major Independent Bookseller
*Bookshop(s):* Hemus Books, 1b Raiko Daskalov Sq, Sofia 1000

# Burundi

**Imparudi (Imprimerie et Papeterie du Burundi)**
BP 3010, Bujumbura
*Tel:* (02) 3125; (02) 7381 *Fax:* (02) 2572
*Key Personnel*
Contact: Mutambuka Theoneste
Type of Business: Distributor, Exporter, Importer, Wholesaler

# Cameroon

**Librairie Bilingue/The Bilingual Bookshop**
BP 727, Yaounde
*Tel:* 224899 *Fax:* 232903
*Telex:* 8438 kn
Type of Business: Distributor, Importer, Major Independent Bookseller, Wholesaler
*Owned by:* Buma Kor & Co Ltd (SARL)
*Branch Office(s)*
Bomenda
Limbe

**Presbyterian Book Depot & Printing Press Ltd (PRESBOOK)**
BP 13, Limbe
*Tel:* 332114 *Fax:* 332694
*Telex:* 5952 *Cable:* PRESBOOK
*Key Personnel*
General Manager: W Abange
Founded: 1968
Also publishers & printers.

Type of Business: Distributor, Importer
*Owned by:* Presbyterian Church in Cameroon
*Branch Office(s)*
Presbook Mankon, BP 39, Bamenda
Presbook Buea, BP 19, Buea
Presbook Douala, BP 18, Douala
Presbook Kumba, BP 87, Kumba
Presbook Kumbo, BP 4, Kumbo
Presbook Mamfe, BP 114, Mamfe
Presbook Tiko, BP 28, Tiko
Presbook Yaounde, BP 1467, Yao Unde

# Chile

**Libreria Eduardo Albers Ltda**
Vitacura 5648, 6640785 Santiago
Mailing Address: Casilla 17, Santiago 30
*Tel:* (02) 218 5371 *Fax:* (02) 218 1458
*Web Site:* www.albers.cl
*Key Personnel*
Manager: Eduardo Albers *E-mail:* ealbers@albers.cl
Founded: 1943
Type of Business: Distributor, Exporter, Importer, Major Independent Bookseller, Wholesaler

**Libreria Andres Bello**
Editorial Juridica de Chile, Avda Ricardo Lyon, 946, 4256 Casilla
*Tel:* (02) 2049900 *Fax:* (02) 2253600
*Key Personnel*
Manager: Francisco Hoyl Sotomayor

**Berenguer Editorial**
Correo 9, Casilla 16598-9, Santiago

**Editorial Francesa Espanola SA**
Huelen 10 piso 3 of A, Santiago
*Tel:* (02) 235-0911; (02) 235-9734 *Fax:* (02) 236-0900
*Key Personnel*
General Manager: Maria Isabel Castillo
Dir, Administration & Finance: Manuel Prietu
Type of Business: Distributor, Exporter, Importer, Wholesaler
*Branch Office(s)*
Av Valparaiso 152, Vina del Mar

**Libreria Esoterica**
Huerfanos 786, Local 19, Santiago
*Tel:* (02) 6338430 *Fax:* (02) 6397933
*E-mail:* wzzdarmd@entelchile.net
*Telex:* 240201
*Key Personnel*
Owner: Walter Zuniga Zavala
Founded: 1985
Type of Business: Distributor, Exporter, Importer, Major Independent Bookseller, Wholesaler

**Feria Chilena del Libro Ltda**
Huerfanos 623, Casilla 10225, Santiago
*Tel:* (02) 632 7334; (02) 639 6758 *Fax:* (02) 633 9374
*E-mail:* ventas@feriachilenadellibro.cl
*Web Site:* www.feriachilenadellibro.cl
*Key Personnel*
Chief Executive Officer: Juan Aldea Perez
*Tel:* (0562) 6323465 *E-mail:* juanaldeap@feriachilenadellibro.cl
Head: Manuel Vilches
Sales Manager: Carlos Diaz
Founded: 1952
Type of Business: Distributor, Importer, Major Book Chain Headquarters, Wholesaler
*Branch Office(s)*
Isidora Goyenechea 3162, Las Condes, Santiago, Head: Eric Maxwell *Tel:* (02) 335 3693; (02)

335 3647 *Fax:* (02) 335 3694 *E-mail:* isidora@feriachilenadellibro.cl
Santa Magdalena 50, Providencia, Santiago, Head: Mirta Aldea *Tel:* (02) 232 1422; (02) 232 1426 *Fax:* (02) 232 1422 *E-mail:* magdalena@feriachilenadellibro.cl
Nueva York 3, Santiago, Head: Matilde Garay *Tel:* (02) 687 4270; (02) 697 2751 *Fax:* (02) 697 2751 *E-mail:* nuevayork@feriachilenadellibro.cl
Providencia 2124, Santiago, Head: Juan Carlos Fau *Tel:* (02) 335 3697; (02) 231 7197 *Fax:* (02) 231 7197 *E-mail:* drugstore@feriachilenadellibro.cl
Agustinas 859, Santiago, Sales Manager: Jorge Godoy *Tel:* (02) 664 3371; (02) 639 5354 *Fax:* (02) 639 5354 *E-mail:* agustinas@feriachilenadellibro.cl
Estado 22, Santiago, Sales Manager: Eduardo Jara *Tel:* (02) 639 6396; (02) 639 6536 *Fax:* (02) 639 6536 *E-mail:* estado@feriachilenadellibro.cl
Galeria Pleno Centro, Av Valparaiso 595, Vina del Mar, Sales Manager: Luis Cisternas *Tel:* (032) 694583; (032) 683093 *Fax:* (032) 683093 *E-mail:* vina@feriachilenadellibro.cl
Mall Marina Arauco Local 108, Vina del Mar, Sales Manager: Rafael Gonzalez *Tel:* (032) 382266; (032) 382267 *Fax:* (032) 382267 *E-mail:* marina@feriachilenadellibro.cl

**Fondo de Cultura Economica SA**
Paseo Bulnes 152, Casilla 10249
*Tel:* (02) 695 4843
*E-mail:* fcechile@ctcinternet.cl
Founded: 1953
Type of Business: Distributor, Exporter, Importer

**Libreria Internacional Estudio**
Anibal Pinto 345, Concepcion
*Tel:* (041) 225 533 *Fax:* (041) 244 542
*Key Personnel*
Contact: Jorge Jimenez Arriola
Founded: 1962
Type of Business: Major Independent Bookseller

**Libreria Universitaria**
Maria Luisa Santander 0447, Cassilla de Correo, Providencia, Santiago 10220
*Tel:* (02) 2234555; (02) 2236980 *Fax:* (02) 2099455; (02) 499455
*Telex:* 10220
*Owned by:* Editorial Universitaria SA

**Lila Libreria de Mujeres**
Providencia 1652, Local 3, Santiago
*Tel:* (02) 2361725 *Fax:* (02) 2361725
*Key Personnel*
Manager: Jimena Pizarro
Type of Business: Major Independent Bookseller

**Libreria San Pablo**
Avda L B O'Higgins 1626, Casilla 3746, Correo Central, Santiago
*Tel:* (02) 698 9145 *Fax:* (02) 671 6884
*E-mail:* alameda@san-pablo.cl
*Web Site:* www.san-pablo.cl
*Key Personnel*
Manager: Antonio Taconi
Type of Business: Distributor, Exporter, Importer, Wholesaler
*Owned by:* Ediciones San Pablo
*Branch Office(s)*
Benavente 383, Puerto Montt *Tel:* (065) 310154 *E-mail:* pmontt@san-pablo.cl
Av Vicuna Mackenna 779, Temuco *Tel:* (045) 210371 *E-mail:* temuco@san-pablo.cl
Avda Providencia 2343, Casilla 3746, Santiago *Tel:* (02) 232 4350 *E-mail:* providencia@san-pablo.cl

Gamero 498 Esquina Campos, Rancagua *Tel:* (072) 221063 *Fax:* (072) 221828 *E-mail:* rancagua@san-pablo.cl
Lautaro 517, Los Angeles *Tel:* (043) 315626

# China

**China Foreign Language Publishing & Distribution Administration,** see China International Book Trading Corporation (CIBTC)

**China International Book Trading Corporation (CIBTC)**
35 Chegongzhuang Xilu, Beijing 100044
Mailing Address: PO Box 399, Beijing 100044
*Tel:* (010) 684133078; (010) 68413849 *Fax:* (010) 68412166
*E-mail:* sinda@mail.cnokay.com
*Web Site:* chinabooks.cnokay.com; www.cnokay.com *Cable:* CIBTC BEIJING
*Key Personnel*
President: Zhi Bin Liu
Contact: Ming Liang Yang
Founded: 1949
Type of Business: Distributor, Exporter, Importer, Major Independent Bookseller, Wholesaler
*Branch Office(s)*
Librairie Grande Muraille, 5 Galerie rue de Ruysbroeck, 1000 Brussells, Belgium *Tel:* (02) 512 1456 *Fax:* (02) 513 8337 *E-mail:* grande_muraille@swing.be
China International Book Trading Corporation Shanghai, F9 Shanghai Cultural Plaza, 355 Fuzhou Rd, Shanghai 200001 *Tel:* (021) 63747048 *E-mail:* cibtcsh@shtel.net.cn
China International Book Trading Corporation Guangzhou, 38 Tangzigangbei Rd, F4/No 2, Guangzhou 510410 *Tel:* (020) 36228658 *E-mail:* cibtcgz@21cn.com
China International Book Trading Corporation Shenzhen, Rm 210 West, Xincheng Mansion, Shennan Zhonglu 1027 *Tel:* (0755) 2050762 *E-mail:* cibtcsz@public.szptt.net.cn
China Book Trading GmbH, Max Planckstr 6a, 63322 Rodermark, Germany *Tel:* (06074) 95564 *Fax:* (06074) 95271 *E-mail:* chinabook@aol.com
Peace Book Co Ltd, Wing On House, 71 Des Vouex Rd, Rm 901-3 & 916, Central, Hong Kong, Hong Kong *Tel:* 28046687 *Fax:* 28046409 *E-mail:* pbcimp@netvigator.com
Sebunsuta Manshon Dai, 2 Aobadai, Room 306, 1-29-12 Aobadai Meguro-ku, Tokyo, Japan *Tel:* (03) 57216536 *Fax:* (03) 57216537 *E-mail:* aac14940@pop17.odn.ne.jp
Cyress Book Co Ltd, Port Royal Metro Centre, Britannia Way, Coronation Rd, London NW10 7PA, United Kingdom *E-mail:* sales@cypressbooks.com *Web Site:* www.cypressbooks.co.uk
Cypress Book (US) Company Inc, 3450 Third St, Unit 4B, San Francisco, CA 94124, United States *Tel:* 415-821-3582 *Fax:* 415-821-3523 *E-mail:* mqxu@cypressbook.com
Great Wall Books & Arts Co, 970 N Broadway, No 104, Los Angeles, CA 90012, United States *Tel:* 213-617-2817 *Fax:* 213-617-2827 *E-mail:* info@gwbooks.net

**China National Publications Import & Export (Group) Corp**
Member of China Publishing Group
16 Gongti East Rd, Chaoyang District, Beijing 100020
*Tel:* (010) 65082324; (010) 65086873; (010) 65086874 *Fax:* (010) 65086860
*E-mail:* info-center@cnpeak.com

*Web Site:* www.cnpiec.com.cn
*Telex:* 22313 CPC CN *Cable:* PUBLIMEX
*Key Personnel*
President: Chen Weijiang
Type of Business: Distributor, Exporter, Importer, Wholesaler
*Branch Office(s)*
Dalian Branch, No 15 Mingze St, Zhongshan District, Dalian 116001 *Tel:* (0411) 2807891; (0411) 2645663 *Fax:* (0411) 2650090 *E-mail:* cdtl@mail.dlptt.ln.cn
Guangzhou Branch, 20 W Guangyuan Rd, Guangzhou, Guangdong Province 510300 *Tel:* (020) 86522185 *Fax:* (020) 86505965 *E-mail:* gzcnpiec@public.guangzhou.gd.cn
Shanghi Branch, 555 Wu Ding Rd, Shanghai 200040 *Tel:* (021) 62551599 *Fax:* (021) 62552697
Xi'an Branch, No 17, South St, Xi'an 710001 *Tel:* (029) 7279746 *Fax:* (029) 7279755 *E-mail:* cnpiecx@public.xa.sn.cn
Zhejiang Branch, Rm 8, No 10 Bldg, Baoshiyilu Rest House, Provincial Organs Management Bureau, Hangzhou, Zhejiang 100020 *Tel:* (0571) 5114218 *Fax:* (0571) 5211780 *E-mail:* sales@cnpzjb.com *Web Site:* www.cnpzjb.com

**CNPIEC**, see China National Publications Import & Export (Group) Corp

**Hubei Publications Import & Export Corporation**
11, Zhongnan Rd, Wuchang, Wuhan 430071-027
*Tel:* (027) 87825561 *Fax:* (027) 87815557
*E-mail:* hbwwsdjkb@163.com
*Key Personnel*
Manager, Import & Export Dept: Shao-Zhang He
Founded: 1994
State owned company specializing in book printing materials, audio-video products & other related goods both in wholesale & retail.
Type of Business: Distributor, Exporter, Importer, Major Independent Bookseller, Wholesaler

**Jiang Xi Copyright Agency**
Xin Wei Rd, Suite 17, Nanchang City, Jiang Xi Province 330002
*Tel:* (0791) 8528405 *Fax:* (0791) 8508901
*E-mail:* jxcopyright@hotmail.com
*Web Site:* www.jxbqzx.com
*Key Personnel*
Dir: Nie Wen Xing *Tel:* (0791) 8508901
Manager: Maggie Wan; Jiang Zhi Fei
Founded: 2001
Import foreign copyrights to all Jiang Xi Provincial publishers & export provincial copyrights to foreign publishers. Organize Jiang Xi Province News & Publishing Delegates to visit foreign counterparts, attend book exhibitions & have training.
Type of Business: Exporter, Importer
*Parent Company:* Jiang Xi Province Copyright Bureau

**Xiamen International Book Exchange Center**
No 809, East Section, South Hubin Rd, Xiamen, Fujian 361004
*Tel:* (0592) 5061401 *Fax:* (0592) 5061400
*E-mail:* xibc@xpublic.fz.fj.cn
*Key Personnel*
President: Shu Yan Zhang
Type of Business: Distributor, Exporter, Importer, Major Independent Bookseller, Wholesaler

# Colombia

**Libreria Aguirre**
Obispo Aguirre, 8, 27002 Lugo
*Tel:* (04) 2220336 *Cable:* Laguirre
*Key Personnel*
Manager: Aura Lopez Posada
Type of Business: Importer, Major Independent Bookseller

**Circulo de Lectores SA**
Calle 57 No 6-35, Apdo 52111, Bogota
*Tel:* (01) 2173211; (01) 2177720 *Fax:* (01) 2178157
*Telex:* 41255
*Key Personnel*
General Manager: Eduardo Polo
Dir Marketing: Rafael Vargas
Founded: 1969
Also Book Club. Branch offices in Barranquilla, Bogota, Cali, Cartagena, Manizales, Medellin, Pereira, & Tunja.
Type of Business: Distributor, Exporter, Importer, Major Book Chain Headquarters, Wholesaler
*Owned by:* Diario el Tiempo

**Distribuidoras Unidas SA**
Transversal 93 Nº 52-03, Bogota
*Tel:* 413 8079 *Fax:* 413 8502
*E-mail:* ibernal@disunidas.com.co
*Web Site:* www.disunidas.com.co
*Key Personnel*
Contact: Sr Hernando Trivino

**Eurolibros**
Calle 40 No 20-27, Bogota
*Tel:* (01) 2886400 *Fax:* (01) 2450291; (01) 3401811; (01) 3401830; (01) 2886400
*Key Personnel*
General Dir: Carlos Roberto Jimenez
    *E-mail:* carlosji@latino.net.co
Founded: 1983
Type of Business: Distributor, Wholesaler

**Grupo Editorial Iberoamerica de Colombia SA**
Carrer 2a1 No 54-78, Bogota
Mailing Address: Apdo Aereo 513, Bogota
*Tel:* (01) 3106553 *Fax:* (01) 3106553
*E-mail:* geicol@colomsat.net.co
*Key Personnel*
Dir General: Hernandez Rico Victor Manuel
Founded: 1991
Type of Business: Distributor, Exporter, Importer, Wholesaler

**Grupo Noriega Editores de Colombia Ltda**
Calle 40 No 22-44, Bogota
*Tel:* (01) 3689036 *Fax:* (01) 3377788
*E-mail:* gnoriega@unete.com.co
*Key Personnel*
Legal Representative: Gustavo Rodriguez Garcia
Founded: 1993
Type of Business: Distributor, Importer, Wholesaler
*Owned by:* Editorial Limusa SA DE CV

**Editorial y Libreria Herder Ltda**
Carrera 11, No 73-61, Bogota
*Tel:* (01) 3344853 *Fax:* (01) 2832272
*Key Personnel*
Legal Representative: Alvaro Gomez Robayo
Type of Business: Distributor, Exporter, Importer
*Owned by:* Hermann Herder e Instituto Literario

**Libreria Nacional Ltda**
Unicentro-Local 1-146, Bogota
*Tel:* (01) 825829; (01) 833849; (01) 2139842; (01) 2139882 *Fax:* (01) 822404; (01) 2138404
    *Cable:* LINALCO AA CALI

*Key Personnel*
Manager: Hernando Ordonez
Administrator General: Aura Bustamante
Gerente Bogota: Felipe Ossa
Administrador Libreria Barranquilla: Edgar Ramirez
*Branch Office(s)*
Carrera 53 No 75-129, Barranquilla
Unicentro Local No 1-146, Apdo Aereo 100778, Bogota *Fax:* (01) 2130484

**Libreria y Distribuidora Lerner Ltda**
Av Jimenez No 4-35, Bogota DC
Mailing Address: Apdo 8304, Bogata DC
*Tel:* (01) 243 0567; (01) 334 7826 *Fax:* (01) 281 4319
*Telex:* 43195
*Key Personnel*
Manager: Luis A Burgos H
Founded: 1957
Type of Business: Importer, Major Independent Bookseller
*Branch Office(s)*
Calle 92 No 15-23, Cundinamarca, Bogota
*Tel:* (01) 2360580 *Fax:* (01) 6364362
*E-mail:* lerner-norte@librerialerner.com.co

**Panamericana Libreria y Papeleria SA**
    (Panamericana Bookshop & Stationery Shop)
Calle 12, No 34-20, Apdo Aereo 6210, Cundinamarca
*Tel:* (01) 3649000 (ext 213) *Fax:* (01) 3600885
*E-mail:* servicliente@panamericana.com.co
*Web Site:* www.panamericana.com.co
*Key Personnel*
Contact: Carlos Federico Ruiz *Tel:* (01) 3649000 (ext 257); Fernando Rojas Acosta
    *E-mail:* frojas@panamericana.com.co
Founded: 1997
Type of Business: Exporter, Importer, Major Independent Bookseller
*Bookshop(s):* Panamericana Libreria y Paleria Contamos Con

**Ediciones Paulinas (Libreria San Pablo)**
Carrera 46 No 22A-90, Bogota
*Tel:* (01) 2444516 *Fax:* (01) 2684288
*Key Personnel*
Manager: Esther Guzman
Branch offices in Barranquilla, Bogota, Cali, Cucuta, Manizales, & Medellin.
Type of Business: Distributor, Exporter, Importer, Major Book Chain Headquarters, Wholesaler
*Branch Office(s)*
Barranquilla
Medellin
Bogota
Cali
Cucuta
Manizales
*Bookshop(s):* Carrera 13 No 72-41, Bogota; Carrera 32 No 161A-04, Bogota

**Libreria Temis SA**
Calle 13, No 6-45, Apdo Aereo, 5941 y 12008, 1 Bogota
*Tel:* (01) 341 3225 *Fax:* (01) 269 0793
Founded: 1951
Type of Business: Distributor, Exporter, Importer, Wholesaler
*Owned by:* Editorial Temis SA, Transv 39B 17-98, SantaFe de Bogota; Nomos Impresores, SA
*Branch Office(s)*
Calle 52 No 42-68, Medellin
Calle 12 No 5-33, Avda Pepe Sierra No 24-25

**Libreria Tercer Mundo**
Transv 2a A, No 67-27, Bogota
*Tel:* (01) 255 1539; (01) 255 0737 *Fax:* (01) 212 5976
*E-mail:* tmundoed@polcola.com.co

*Key Personnel*
General Manager: Santiago Pombo Vejarano
Library Dir: Juan Manuel Borda de Francisco
Founded: 1962
*Owned by:* Tercer Mundo Editores SA
*Bookshop(s):* Cra 7, No 16-91, Bogota; Cra 13,
  No 44-70, Bogota

**Libreria Uniandes**
Carrera 1 No 18A82, Bogota
*Tel:* (01) 2824066 (ext 2197); (01) 2824066 (ext
  2198) *Fax:* (01) 2841890 *Cable:* UNIANDES
*Key Personnel*
General Manager: Arcesio Rodriguez P
Marketing & Sales Manager: Cesar Augusto Pena
International Trade: Luz Marina Cortes
Spanish & Latin American trade books; importers
  & subscription agents of academic & scientific
  publications.
Type of Business: Importer

# Congo

**Office national des Librairies Populaires
  (ONLP)**
PB 1489, Brazzaville
*Tel:* 833 485 *Fax:* 831 879
*Telex:* 5379 *Cable:* Lipolaire Brazzaville
*Key Personnel*
Dir General: Ignace Taliane-Tchibamba

**ONLP**, see Office national des Librairies
  Populaires (ONLP)

# The Democratic Republic of the Congo

**Librairie des Presses Universitaires**
Blvd du 30 Juin 4113, Kinshasa
Mailing Address: BP 1682, Kinshasa
*Tel:* (012) 30652
*Owned by:* Presses universitaires du Zaiire et
  l'Office du Livre (PUZ)

**Librairie les Volcans**
22 Ave President Mobutu, Goma
Mailing Address: BP 105, Goma
*Tel:* 366
*Key Personnel*
President: Kakule Tatsopa wa Mughalitsa
Type of Business: Distributor, Major Independent
  Bookseller
*Owned by:* Librairie Les Volcans, Publisher
*Bookshop(s):* Cereva

**Okapi Centre de Diffusion**
BP 11398, Kinshasa
*Tel:* (012) 31457

**Librairie Saint-Paul**
c/o Editions Paulines, Ave du Commerce 76, BP
  335, Kinshasa
Mailing Address: BP 8505, Kinshasa
*Tel:* 77726
Founded: 1958

Type of Business: Distributor, Exporter, Importer,
  Major Independent Bookseller, Wholesaler
*Owned by:* Filles de Saint Paul - Congr. In-
  ternat. au service de la promotion et de
  l'evangelisation par les medias
*Branch Office(s)*
BP 505, Kisangani
BP 2447, Lubumbashi

# Costa Rica

**Libreria Universal Carlos Federspiel**
Apdo 1532, Edificio Central, San Jose

**Libreria Imprenta y Litografia Lehmann SA**
Apdo 10011, San Jose
*Tel:* 2231212
Also Publisher.

**Libreria Trejos SA**
Apdo 10096, 1000 San Jose
*Tel:* 2242411 *Fax:* 2241528
*Telex:* 2858 Ltsa
*Key Personnel*
Manager: A Trejos

# Cote d'Ivoire

**CEDA**, see Centre d'Edition et de Diffusion
  Africaines

**Centre d'Edition et de Diffusion Africaines**
BP 541, Abidjan 04
*Tel:* 22 22 42; 22 20 55 *Fax:* 21 72 62
*Web Site:* www.mbendi.co.za/orgs/cg01.htm
*Key Personnel*
Dir: Mr Venance Kacou
Also publisher.
Type of Business: Distributor, Exporter, Importer,
  Wholesaler

# Croatia

**Tehnicka Knjiga**
Jurisiceva 10, 10000 Zagreb
*Tel:* (041) 4810819; (041) 4810820 *Fax:* (041)
  4810821
*Key Personnel*
General Manager: Zvonimir Vistricka

# Cuba

**Ediciones Cubanas**
Obispo No 527 (altos) esq a Bernaza, Habana
  Vieja, Habana
*Tel:* (07) 63 1981; (07) 33 8942; (07) 63 1989
  *Fax:* (07) 338 943
*E-mail:* edicuba@artsoft.cult.cu
*Telex:* 0512337 *Cable:* LIBROCUBA
*Key Personnel*
Dir: Nancy Matos Lacosta
Books, periodicals & printing material.
Type of Business: Distributor, Exporter, Importer,
  Major Book Chain Headquarters, Wholesaler

*Owned by:* Empresa de Comercio Exterior de
  Publicaciones
*Bookshop(s):* Libreria Internacional, Obispo No
  528 e/ Vernaza y Villegas, Habana; Libreria
  La Bella Habana, Palacio del Segundo Cabo,
  O'Reilly No 4 Esq a Tacon, Habana Vieja

# Cyprus

**K P Kyriakou (Books - Stationery) Ltd**
Panagides Bldg, 3 Crivas Digenis Ave, 3601 Li-
  massol
Mailing Address: PO Box 159, 3601 Limassol
*Tel:* (025) 747555 *Fax:* (025) 747047
*E-mail:* cybooks@logos.cy.net
*Web Site:* www.logos.cy.net
*Key Personnel*
Man Dir: Kyriakos P Kyriakou
  *E-mail:* kyriakospk@webnmedia.com
Founded: 1947
Type of Business: Distributor, Exporter, Importer,
  Major Independent Bookseller, Wholesaler

**MAM (The House of Cyprus & Cyprological
  Publications)**
19 Konstantinou Palaiologou Ave, 1015 Nicosia
Mailing Address: PO Box 21722, 1512 Nicosia
*Tel:* (022) 753536
*E-mail:* mam@mam.com.cy
*Web Site:* www.mam.com.cy
*Key Personnel*
Manager: Fryni Michaelidou
Secretary: Mikis Michaelides
Founded: 1965
Specialize in all kinds of publications on Cyprus
  & in all publications by Cypriots. Authorized
  distributors of Cyprus Government publications
  & other Cypriot publishers.
Also publisher.
Type of Business: Distributor, Exporter, Importer,
  Wholesaler
*Bookshop(s):* MAM Cyprus Publications, Stoa tou
  Vivliou, 5 Pesmazoglou, 105 64 Athens, Greece,
  Contact: Ms Koula Kyziakou

**K Rustem & Bro**
21-26 Kyrenia St, Nicosia
Mailing Address: PO Box 239, Nicosia
*Tel:* (022) 71041; (022) 71418; (022) 52085
  *Cable:* RUSTEM BR 4
*Bookshop(s):* Tofarides Bookshop, PO Box 278,
  Larnaca *Tel:* (041) 54144

# Czech Republic

**Knihkupectvi - Antikvariat Galerie**
Masarykova 15, 415 01 Teplice
*Tel:* (0417) 537 370 *Fax:* (0417) 537 370
*E-mail:* kniha.ln@antikteplice.cz; kniha.ln@
  worldonline.cz
*Web Site:* www.antikteplice.cz/
*Key Personnel*
Manager: Milos Novotny
*Owned by:* Martina Uldrychova
*Branch Office(s)*
Teplice, Kapelnii 4

# Denmark

## Arnold Busck International Boghandel A/S
Kobmagergade 49, 1150 Copenhagen K
*Tel:* 33 73 35 00 *Fax:* 33 73 35 35
*E-mail:* arnold@busck.dk
*Web Site:* www.busck.dk
*Key Personnel*
Manager & Bookseller: Troels Bek *Tel:* 33733525
Founded: 1896
Export Division is at above address.
Type of Business: Exporter, Major Book Chain
  Headquarters, Major Independent Bookseller
*Owned by:* Ole Arnold Busck

## Gads Forlag
Kloster Str 9, 1157 Copenhagen K
*Tel:* 77 66 00 00 *Fax:* 77 66 60 01
*E-mail:* kundeservice@gads-forlag.dk.ell
*Web Site:* www.gads-forlag.dk
*Key Personnel*
Dir: Peter Hartmann
Manager: Erling Sievert *E-mail:* ES@gad.dk
*Owned by:* G E C Gads Foundation (see also G E
  C Gads Forlag)

## Magasin du Nord A/S
Kongens Nytorv 13, 1095 Copenhagen K
*Tel:* 33 11 44 33 *Fax:* 33 15 18 40
*E-mail:* kundeservice@magasinkort.dk
*Web Site:* www.magasin.dk *Cable:*
  MAGDUNORD TELEX 15975
*Key Personnel*
Buyer: Alfred Jensen *Tel:* 033 182121 *Fax:* 033
  182215

## Nyt Nordisk Forlag Arnold Busck A/S,
**Publishers**, see Arnold Busck International
Boghandel A/S

## Polyteknisk Boghandel og Forlag
Anker Engelunds Vej 1, Bygn 101 A, 2800 Lyngby
*Tel:* 77 42 44 44 *Fax:* 77 42 43 54
*E-mail:* polybog@pb.dtu.dk
*Web Site:* www.pf.dtu.dk/
*Key Personnel*
Dir: Lotte Lonver *E-mail:* lotte@poly.dtu.dk
Founded: 1960
Type of Business: Distributor, Importer, Major
  Independent Bookseller, Wholesaler

## C A Reitzel Boghandel & Forlag A/S
Norregade 20, 1165 Copenhagen K
*Tel:* 33 12 24 00 *Fax:* 33 14 02 70
*Web Site:* www.careitzel.dk
*Key Personnel*
Man Dir: Svend Olufsen
Supplies universities, scientific libraries & institu-
  tions worldwide
Also Publisher.
Type of Business: Exporter, Importer

## Scanvik Books Import ApS
Esplanaden 8 B, 1263 Copenhagen K
*Tel:* 33 12 77 66 *Fax:* 33 91 28 82
*E-mail:* mail@scanvik.dk
*Web Site:* www.scanvik.dk
*Key Personnel*
Dir: John Roberts; Uwe Schultheiss
Founded: 1980
Also agent.
Type of Business: Distributor, Exporter, Importer,
  Wholesaler

## SKT's Boghandel
Lautrupvang 15, 2750 Ballerup
*Tel:* 44686662 *Fax:* 44686660
*E-mail:* skt@sktbooks.dk

*Web Site:* www.sktbooks.dk
*Key Personnel*
Contact: Mark Bentley
Founded: 1968
Type of Business: Major Independent Bookseller

## Studenterboghandelen ved Odense Universitet
Campusvej 55, 5230 Odense M
*Tel:* 6550 1700 *Fax:* 6550 1701
*E-mail:* studenter@boghandel.sdu.dk
*Web Site:* www.boghandel.sdu.dk/
*Key Personnel*
Man Dir: Niels Lindberg
Founded: 1981
Type of Business: Importer, Major Independent
  Bookseller

## Svensk-Norsk Bogimport A/S (Swedish
  Norwegian Bookimport)
Esplanaden 8 B, 1263 Copenhagen K
*Tel:* 33142666 *Fax:* 33143588
*E-mail:* snb@bog.dk
*Web Site:* www.snbog.dk
*Key Personnel*
President: Poul Brehmer
Founded: 1968
Type of Business: Distributor, Exporter, Importer,
  Major Independent Bookseller, Wholesaler

## Tysk Bogimport ApS
Storeholm 51, 2670 Greve
*Tel:* 7020 4990 *Fax:* 7020 4991
*E-mail:* tyskforlaget@tyskforlaget.dk
*Web Site:* www.tyskforlaget.dk
*Key Personnel*
Contact: Eberhard Riedel
Founded: 1958
Type of Business: Distributor, Importer, Major
  Independent Bookseller, Wholesaler

## Universitetsbogladen
Blegdamsvej 3, 2200 Copenhagen N
Mailing Address: Postboks 716, 2200 Copen-
  hagen N
*Tel:* 3524 0444; 3532 6570 *Fax:* 3532 6571
*E-mail:* panum@unibog.dk
*Web Site:* www.universitetsbogladen.dk
*Key Personnel*
Manager: Henrik Larsen
Founded: 1968
Type of Business: Exporter, Importer, Major Inde-
  pendent Bookseller
*Branch Office(s)*
Universitetsparken 13, 2100 Copenhagen O
  *Tel:* 3537 1133; 3532 0035 *Fax:* 3539 5459

# Dominican Republic

## Editorial Padilla
Prol Ave 27 de Febrero, Santo Domingo
Mailing Address: Apdo Postal 468, Santo
  Domingo
*Tel:* 809-379-1550 *Fax:* 809-379-2631
*E-mail:* edpadilla@codetel.net.do
*Key Personnel*
Contact: Carretera Manoguayabo, Esq
Also publisher.
*Branch Office(s)*
El Conde 109, Santo Domingo *Tel:* 809-688-0303

# Ecuador

## CD Remain Cia Ltda
Ave Repulbica 740 y Eloy Alfaro, Profesional
  Piso 7, Ofc 702 Casilla, 17-17-1548 Quito
*Tel:* (02) 224973; (02) 239328 *Fax:* (02) 505760
Type of Business: Distributor

## Libreria Cientifica SA
Casilla 2905, Quito
*Tel:* (02) 12556
*Key Personnel*
Manager: Alicia de Pino
*Branch Office(s)*
Luque 223, Guayaquil *Tel:* (04) 324650

## Libreria Cima
Carlos Ibarra 200 y 10 de Agosto, Casilla 17-15-
  87C, Quito
*Tel:* (02) 571218; (02) 571318 *Cable:* CIMALE
*Key Personnel*
Manager: Luis A Carrera
Assistant Manager: Edgar R Freire
Type of Business: Exporter

## De Cervantes Ediciones SA
Orellana 1811 y 10 de Agosto, primer piso, Quito
*Tel:* (02) 522 956 *Fax:* (02) 523 452; (02) 223
  062
*Key Personnel*
Contact: Ismael Cervantes Quintero
Type of Business: Distributor, Exporter, Importer

## Ecuazeta De Publicaciones Cia Ltda
Av 10 de Agosto N38-60y, Quito
*Tel:* (02) 2546 149 *Fax:* (02) 2902 693
*E-mail:* ecuazeta@interactive.net.ec
*Key Personnel*
President: Jorge Zavaleta Salvador
Manager: Rocio Vacas de Alvarez
Founded: 1989
Type of Business: Distributor, Importer, Whole-
  saler

## Edimecien Cia Ltda
Gral Aguirre 178 y Av 10 de Agosto, Quito
*Tel:* (02) 2502 427; (02) 2502 428; (02) 2502 431
  *Fax:* (02) 2502 429
*Key Personnel*
Contact: Sr Alfredo Montoya *E-mail:* amontoya@
  lexusec.com
Type of Business: Distributor, Importer, Whole-
  saler

## Promociones Culturales Gitral SA
Ave Machala 1024 y Velez Casilla, 09-01-7278
  Guayaquil
Mailing Address: PO Box 09-01-7278, Guayaquil
*Tel:* (02) 510510; (02) 532060; (02) 32644
  *Fax:* (02) 510510; (02) 326733
*Key Personnel*
President: Ramon Cedeno Galarza
Type of Business: Distributor, Importer

## Libreria Universitaria
Garcia Moreno 739, Apdo 2982, Quito
*Tel:* (02) 212521
*Key Personnel*
Dir: Ing Carlos E Wong Flores
Founded: 1951
Type of Business: Distributor, Exporter, Importer,
  Wholesaler

## Ediciones Monserrat
Ave 10 de Agosto 1831 y San Gregorio, Quito
*Tel:* (02) 2222 567; (02) 2505 685 *Fax:* (02) 2222
  567
*E-mail:* claudio@uio.satnet.net

*Key Personnel*
Contact: Monica Claudio Cando
Type of Business: Distributor

# Egypt (Arab Republic of Egypt)

**Al Arab Bookshop**
Add 29, El Fagalah St, Cairo
*Tel:* (02) 5915315 *Cable:* ARABUKSHOP
  CAIRO
*Key Personnel*
Manager: Prof Saladin Boustany, PhD
Founded: 1900
Agent of the Library of Congress PL 480.
Type of Business: Distributor, Exporter
*Owned by:* Al Arab Publishing House

**FHB Exporter**
Ramsis Center, PO Box 159-11794, Cairo
*Tel:* (02) 2358329 *Fax:* (02) 2358329
*E-mail:* fhb@link.net
*Key Personnel*
Manager: Fouad H Baskharoun
Founded: 1970
Books, magazines & periodicals published in
  Egypt & the Arab World.
Type of Business: Distributor, Exporter, Whole-
  saler

**Lehnert & Landrock Bookshop**
44 Sherif St, Cairo 11511
*Tel:* (02) 3927606; (02) 3935324 *Fax:* (02)
  3934421
*Key Personnel*
Owner & Manager: Dr E Lambelet
Manager: Mahmud Abdel Aziz
Founded: 1924
Type of Business: Importer, Major Independent
  Bookseller, Wholesaler
*Owned by:* Edouard Lambelet & Co

**Livres de France**
36 rue Kasr el-Nil, Cairo
*Tel:* (02) 3935512

**Misr Bookshop**
3 Kamel Sidkey St, Al-Fagalah, Cairo
*Tel:* (02) 908920
*Key Personnel*
Manager: Amir Saiid El-Sahhar

# El Salvador

**Clasicos Roxsil Editorial SA de CV**
Cuarta Avenida Sur 2-3, La Libertad, Santa Tecla
*Tel:* 228 1832; 229 3621 *Fax:* 228 1212
  *Fax on Demand:* 228 1212
*Key Personnel*
Manager: Rosa Serrano de Lopez
Chief Editorial Dept: Roxana Beatriz Lopez
  *E-mail:* roxanabe@navegante.com.sv
Founded: 1969
Type of Business: Distributor, Exporter, Importer,
  Wholesaler

**Libreria UCA**
Universidad Centroamericana Jose Simeon Canas,
  Autopista Sur, Jardines de Guadalupe, Boule-
  vard Los Proceres, 168 San Salvador
*Tel:* 2210-6600 *Fax:* 2210-6655
*E-mail:* correo@uca.edu.sv
*Web Site:* www.uca.edu.sv

**Libreria Universitaria de l'Universidad de El
  Salvador**
Ciudad Universitaria, Apdo 1703, San Salvador
*Tel:* 259427; 256604 *Fax:* 259427
*Telex:* 20794

# Ethiopia

**ECA Bookshop Co-op Society**
PO Box 3001, Addis Ababa
*Tel:* (01) 517200 *Fax:* (01) 510365; (212) 963-
  4957 (New York)
*E-mail:* ecainfo@uneca.org
*Web Site:* www.uneca.org *Cable:* ECA ADDIS
  ABABA

# Finland

**Akateeminen Kirjakauppa**
Keskuskatu 1, Pohjoisesplanadi 39, PL 128,
  00101 Helsinki
*Tel:* (09) 121 4252 *Fax:* (09) 121 4322
*E-mail:* tilaukset@akateeminen.com
*Web Site:* www.akateeminen.com *Cable:*
  AKATEEMINEN
*Key Personnel*
Chief Executive: Stig-Bjorn Nyberg
Assistant: Anu Hantala
Founded: 1893
Subscriptions, CD-ROM.
Type of Business: Major Book Chain Headquar-
  ters, Major Independent Bookseller
*Owned by:* OY Stockmann AB
*Branch Office(s)*
Itakeskus, Itakatu 1 C, 00930 Helsinki *Tel:* (09)
  121 4761
Tampere, Hameenkatu 6, 33100 Tampere
  *Tel:* (03) 248 0300 *Fax:* (03) 222 8602
Tapiola, Lansituulentie 10, 02100 Espoo *Tel:* (09)
  121 451 *Fax:* (09) 121 4520
Turku, Eerikinkatu 15, 20100 Turku *Tel:* (02) 265
  6811 *Fax:* (02) 265 6820

**Oy Satusiivet - Sagovingar AB (Lasten Parhaat
  Kirjat)**
Urho Kekkosen katu 4-6 E, 00100 Helsinki
*Tel:* (09) 6937 621 *Fax:* (09) 6937 6266
*Web Site:* www.tammi.net
*Key Personnel*
President: Ritva Lemonen
Editoial Manager: Leena Jaervenpaeae
Children's Bookclub.
*Owned by:* Kustannus Oy Tammi

**Suomalainen Kirjakauppa Oy**
Verkkokauppa, Koivuvaarankuja 2, 01640 Vantaa
*Tel:* (09) 852 751 *Fax:* (09) 852 7980
*E-mail:* etunimi.sukunimi@suomalainenkk.fi
*Web Site:* www.suomalainen.com
*Telex:* 121841
*Key Personnel*
Man Dir: Hannu Syrjaenen
Marketing Manager: Lisbeth Kuitunen; Alto Lah-
  denpere

Contact: Toimitusjohtaja Raimo Kurri
  *E-mail:* raimo.kurri@suomalainenkk.fi
Branch offices in Espoo (3), Forssa, Hameen-
  linna, Hamina, Heinola, Helsinki (11), Iisalmi,
  Imatra, Javenpaa, Joensuu, Jyvaskyla, Ka-
  jaani, Kerava, Kotka (3), Kouvola, Kuopio,
  Lahti, Lappeenranta, Mikkeli (2), Pori, Raahe,
  Rovaniemi, Salo, Savonlinni, Seinaajoki, Tam-
  pere, Turku, Vaasa, Vantaa, Varkaus.
Type of Business: Major Book Chain Headquar-
  ters
*Owned by:* Rautakirja Oy

**Tampereen Kirjakauppa Oy**
Haemeenkatu 27, PL 21, 33200 Tampere
*Tel:* (03) 2128380 *Fax:* (03) 2122136
*E-mail:* trekirja@vip.fi
*Web Site:* www.tampereenkirjakauppa.fi
*Key Personnel*
Manager: Martti Helminen
Founded: 1910
Type of Business: Exporter, Importer, Major Inde-
  pendent Bookseller

**Turun Kansallinen Kirjakauppa Oy**
Linnankatu 16, 20101 Turku
Mailing Address: PL 135, 20101 Turku
*Tel:* (02) 2831000 *Fax:* (02) 2831010
*E-mail:* info@kansallinenkirjakauppa.fi
*Web Site:* www.kansallinenkirjakauppa.fi
*Key Personnel*
Manager: Paula Palmroth *E-mail:* paula.
  palmroth@kansallinenkirjakauppa.fi
*Branch Office(s)*
Hameenkatu 7, Turku *Tel:* (02) 2831 050
  *Fax:* (02) 2831 051
Lansikeskus Viilarinkatu 1, Turku *Tel:* (02) 2831
  060

# France

**Critiques Livres Distribution SAS**
24 rue Malmaison, BP 93, 93172 Bagnolet Cedex
*Tel:* (01) 43603910 *Fax:* (01) 48973706
*E-mail:* critiques.livres@wanadoo.fr
*Key Personnel*
President: Rosalind Fay-Boehlinger
Founded: 1976
Books in the visual arts in English, French, Ger-
  man & Italian.
Type of Business: Distributor, Exporter, Importer,
  Wholesaler

**Distique**
5, rue du Mal Leclerc, 28600 Luisant
*Tel:* (02) 3730 5700 *Fax:* (02) 3730 5712
Type of Business: Distributor

**Flammarion**
26, rue Racine, 75278 Paris Cedex 06
*Tel:* (01) 40 51 31 00; (01) 40 51 30 41 *Fax:* (01)
  43 29 21 48
*Web Site:* www.flammarion.com/
*Telex:* Flamlyo 300460 F
*Key Personnel*
Manager: Jean-Noel Flammarion
Also Publisher. Branches in Bordeaux, Dijon,
  Grenoble, Lyon, Marseilles, Montreal (Canada),
  & Paris.

**A Van Ginneken**
BP 532, 21014 Dijon Cedex
*Tel:* (0380) 789595 *Fax:* (0380) 740700
*E-mail:* hexalivre@axnet.fr
*Telex:* 341429
*Key Personnel*
Man Dir: Andries Van Ginneken
Type of Business: Distributor, Exporter, Importer,
  Wholesaler

**Hachette Livre SA - H E D**
43, Quai de Grenelle, 75905 Paris Cedex 15
*Tel:* (01) 43923000 *Fax:* (01) 43923030
*Web Site:* www.hachette.com
*Key Personnel*
Director: Isabelle Magnac

**Editions Lavoisier**
14 rue de Provigny, 94236 Cachan Cedex
*Tel:* (01) 47 40 67 00 *Fax:* (01) 47 40 67 03
*E-mail:* edition@tec-et-doc.com
*Web Site:* www.tec-et-doc.com/fr
*Telex:* 632020 F TDL
*Key Personnel*
Dir: Jacques Besnault
Founded: 1947
Type of Business: Distributor, Exporter, Importer, Major Independent Bookseller

**Librairie FNAC**
95, bd Jean-Jaures, 92110 Clichy Cedex
*Tel:* (01) 42 70 56 90
*E-mail:* service-clientele@fnac.com
*Web Site:* www.fnac.com
*Key Personnel*
Manager: Bertrand Picard
Assistant Dir: Garrigou Martine *E-mail:* marie-martine.garrigou@fnac.tm.fr

**Librairie Generale des PUF**
49 blvd Saint-Michel, 75005 Paris
*Tel:* (01) 44 41 81 20 *Fax:* (01) 43 54 64 81
*E-mail:* puf-lib@puf.worldnet.net
*Web Site:* www.puf.com
*Owned by:* Presses Universitaires de France, 12 rue Jean de Beauvais, 75006 Paris

**Librairie la Hune**
170, Blvd Saint-Germain, 75006 Paris
*Tel:* (01) 45 48 35 85
*Key Personnel*
Man Dir: Georges Dupre
*Owned by:* Flammarion

**Librairie Mollat**
11-15 rue Vital Carles, 33080 Bordeaux Cedex
*Tel:* (0556) 564040 *Fax:* (0556) 564088
*E-mail:* mollat@mollat.com
*Web Site:* www.mollat.com
*Telex:* 541542 F
*Branch Office(s)*
83-91 rue Porte-Dijeaux, 33080 Bordeaux Cedex

**Office International de Documentation et Librairie (OFFILIB)**
48, rue Gay Lussac, 75240 Paris Cedex 05
*Tel:* (01) 55 42 73 00 *Fax:* (01) 43 29 91 67
*E-mail:* info@offilib.com
*Web Site:* www.offilib.com
*Key Personnel*
Dir: Stephanie Boudon
Type of Business: Importer, Major Independent Bookseller

**OFFILIB**, see Office International de Documentation et Librairie (OFFILIB)

**Librairie Sauramps Medical**
11 Bd Henri IV, 34000 Montepellier
*Tel:* (04) 67 63 68 80 *Fax:* (04) 67 52 59 05
*E-mail:* christelle.itasse@livres-medicaux.com
*Web Site:* www.livres-medicaux.com
*Telex:* (04) 480728
*Key Personnel*
Manager: Dominique Torreilles
Founded: 1977
Also acts as publisher.
Subjects: Specialize in medicine
Type of Business: Importer, Major Independent Bookseller

**Librairie de l'Universite**
2 place Dr Leon Martin, 38000 Grenoble Cedex
*Tel:* (0476) 46 61 63 *Fax:* (0476) 46 14 59
Founded: 1964
Type of Business: Major Independent Bookseller
*Owned by:* Flammarion

# Gambia

**The Gambia Methodist Bookshop Ltd**
16 Nelson Mandela St, Banjul
Mailing Address: PO Box 203, Banjul
*Tel:* 28179
*Key Personnel*
Manager: James Heffernan

# Germany

**Artibus et Literis**
Friedrichstr 22-26, 40001 Duesseldorf
*Tel:* (0211) 388-10 *Fax:* (0211) 3881280
*E-mail:* webmaster@artibus.de
*Web Site:* www.artibus.de
*Key Personnel*
Managing Partner: Horst Janssen; Klaus Janssen
Books & journals.
Type of Business: Exporter, Importer

**Buchhandlung G D Baedeker**
Kettwiger Str 35, 45127 Essen
*Tel:* (0201) 20680 *Fax:* (0201) 2068-100
*E-mail:* service.gdb.essen@baedeker.de
*Web Site:* www.baedeker.de

**Bertelsmann Distribution GmbH**
And der Autobahn, 33310 Gutersloh
Mailing Address: PO Box 7777, 33310 Gutersloh
*Tel:* (05241) 805 718 *Fax:* (05241) 46970
*Web Site:* www.bertelsmann-distribution.de
*Telex:* 933827
*Key Personnel*
Man Dir: Dr Hans-Joachim Herzog; Hartmut Ostrowski
Also publishers' delivery service.
Type of Business: Wholesaler
*Owned by:* Bertelsmann AG

**Blazek und Bergmann**
c/o Hunzinger Information AG, Holzhausenstr 21, 60322 Frankfurt
Mailing Address: Postfach 50 05 54, 60394 Frankfurt
*Tel:* (069) 152003-0 *Fax:* (069) 152003-44
*E-mail:* info@blazek-und-bergmann.de
*Web Site:* www.blazek-und-bergmann.de
*Owned by:* Hunziger Information AG

**Bouvier GmbH & Co KG**
Am Hof 28, 53113 Bonn
*Tel:* (0228) 72901-0; (01803) 258940 (orders) *Fax:* (0228) 72901-178
*E-mail:* bouvier@books.de
*Web Site:* www.books.de
*Key Personnel*
Manager: Thomas Grundmann
Man Dir: Richard Feldmann
Type of Business: Major Independent Bookseller
*Branch Office(s)*
Bouvier Buechermarkt, Am Hof 20, 53113 Bonn *Tel:* (0228) 72901-156 *Fax:* (0228) 72901-178
Bouvier Duisdorf, Rochusstr 175, 53123 Bonn *Tel:* (0228) 72901-510 *Fax:* (0228) 72901-511

Bouvier Hamm, Richard-Matthaei-Platz 1, 59065 Hamm *Tel:* (02381) 92021-0 *Fax:* (02381) 92021-530
Bouvier Juridicum, Nassestr 1, 53113 Bonn *Tel:* (0228) 2420772 *Fax:* (0228) 72901-178
Bouvier Koblenz, Loehrstr 30, 56068 Koblenz *Tel:* (0261) 30337-0 *Fax:* (0261) 30337-577
Bouvier Science-Center, Endenicher Allee 19, 53115 Bonn *Tel:* (0228) 72901-158 *Fax:* (0228) 72901-178
Bouvier Siegburg, Markt 16-19, 53721 Siegburg *Tel:* (02241) 9667-0 *Fax:* (02241) 9667-524
Buchhaus Gonski, Neumarkt Passage, Neumarkt 18a, 50667 Cologne *Tel:* (0221) 20909-0 *Fax:* (0221) 20909-359

**Fachverlag Hans Carl GmbH**
Andernacher Str 33a, 90411 Nuernberg
*Tel:* (0911) 95285-0 *Fax:* (0911) 95285-48
*E-mail:* info@hanscarl.com
*Web Site:* www.hanscarl.com *Cable:* CARLVERLAG
*Key Personnel*
Contact: Wolfgang Illguth; Traudel Schmitt
Founded: 1861
Type of Business: Distributor, Major Independent Bookseller

**Dokumente Verlag Import-Exportbuchhandlung**, see Dokumente Verlag Versandbuchhandlung Librairie

**Dokumente Verlag Versandbuchhandlung Librairie**
Hildostr 4, 77603 Offenburg
*Tel:* (0781) 923699-0 *Fax:* (0781) 923699-70
*E-mail:* info@dokumente-verlag.de
*Web Site:* www.dokumente-verlag.de
*Key Personnel*
President: Michael Schlageter *Tel:* (0781) 92369918 *E-mail:* ms@dokumente-verlag.de
Contact: Heribert Jager
Founded: 1945
Library.
*Owned by:* Michael Schlageter & Heribert Jager

**Erich-Weinert Universitatsbuchhandlung**
Ulrichplatz 4-6, 39104 Magdeburg
*Tel:* (0391) 568590 *Fax:* (0391) 5685923
*E-mail:* e.angerer@weinert.de
*Web Site:* www.weinert.de
Founded: 1960
Type of Business: Major Independent Bookseller
*Owned by:* Ernst Angerer

**Werner Flach Internationale Fachbuchhandlung**
Humboldstr 57, 60318 Frankfurt am Main
*Tel:* (069) 9591750 *Fax:* (069) 95917522
*E-mail:* fachbuch@flachbuch.com
*Web Site:* www.flachbuch.com
*Key Personnel*
President: Werner Flach
Founded: 1957
Type of Business: Major Independent Bookseller

**R Friedlaender & Sohn GmbH Buchhaunlung & Antiquariat**
Dessauer St 28-29, 10963 Berlin
*Tel:* (030) 2622328
*Key Personnel*
International Rights: Hans-Werner Kyrieleis

**Graff Buchhandlung**
Sack 15, 38100 Braunschweig
*Tel:* (0531) 480 89-0 *Fax:* (0531) 480 89-89
*E-mail:* infos@graff.de
*Web Site:* www.graff.de
*Key Personnel*
Contact: Joachim Wrensch; Thomas Wrensch

Founded: 1867
Type of Business: Major Independent Bookseller

**Otto Harrassowitz KG Wissenschaftliche Buchhandlung & Zeitschriftenagentur**
Kreuzberger Ring 7 b-d, 65205 Wiesbaden
*Tel:* (0611) 5300 *Fax:* (0611) 530560
*E-mail:* service@harrassowitz.de
*Web Site:* www.harrassowitz.de
*Key Personnel*
Dir & Managing Partner: Dr Knut Dorn
  *Tel:* (0611) 530800 *E-mail:* kdorn@
  harrassowitz.de
EDP: Friedemann Weigel
Administrative Dir: Detlef Dorn
Accounting & Finances: Ruth Becker-Scheicher
Founded: 1872
Service of Books & Scholarly Journals to Academic & Research Libraries.
Subjects: Library Service Agency; Subscription Agency
Type of Business: Exporter, Importer, Major Independent Bookseller
*Owned by:* Ruth Becker-Scheicher, Dr Knut Dorn, Friedemann Weigel

**Anton Hiersemann, Verlag**
Haldenstr 30, 70376 Stuttgart
*Tel:* (0711) 5499710; (0711) 5499711 *Fax:* (0711) 54997121
*E-mail:* hiersemann.hauswedell.verlage@t-online.de
*Web Site:* www.hiersemann.de
*Key Personnel*
Contact: Karl G Hiersemann
Founded: 1884
*Owned by:* Dr Ernst Hauswedell und Co

**Buchhandlung Heinrich Hugendubel GmbH & Co KG**
Nymphenburger Str 25 - 29, 80335 Munich
*Tel:* (01801) 484484 *Fax:* (01801) 484585
*E-mail:* service@hugendubel.de
*Web Site:* www.hugendubel.de *Cable:* HUGENDUBEL MUNICH

**Iberoamericana Editorial Vervuert**
Wielandstr 40, 60318 Frankfurt
*Tel:* (069) 5974617 *Fax:* (069) 5978743
*E-mail:* info@iberoamericanalibros.com
*Web Site:* www.ibero-americana.net
Founded: 1975
Specialize in books & journals, Latin American & Spanish books.
Type of Business: Distributor, Exporter, Importer, Major Independent Bookseller
*Parent Company:* Iberoamericana de Libros y Ediciones, Amor de Dios 1, 28014 Madrid, Spain

**Von Kloeden KG**
Wielandstr 24, 10707 Berlin-Charlottenburg
*Tel:* (030) 887 125 18 *Fax:* (030) 887 125 19
*E-mail:* vkloeden@t-online.de
*Web Site:* www.vonkloeden.de
*Key Personnel*
Man Dir, Rights & Permissions: Friedrich Von Kloeden
Editorial: Uta Grabe Von Kloeden
Founded: 1967
*Bookshop(s):* Berlin

**Koch, Neff und Oetinger & Co**
Schockenriedstr 37, 70565 Stuttgart
*Tel:* (0711) 78600 *Fax:* (0711) 78602800
*Web Site:* www.buchkatalog.de
*Telex:* 07255684 knov d stgt
Subjects: Bibliography
Type of Business: Distributor, Wholesaler

**Kreuz Verlag GmbH & Co KG**
Liebknechtstr 33, 70565 Stuttgart
*Tel:* (0711) 788030 *Fax:* (0711) 7880310
*E-mail:* service@kreuzverlag.de
*Web Site:* www.kreuzverlag.de
*Key Personnel*
Manager: Olaf Carstens; Bernd Friedrich; Sabine Schubert
Sales: Heike Donner
Editor: Thomas Schmitz
Founded: 1945
*Owned by:* Verlagsgruppe Dornier, Dircksenstr 48, 10178 Berlin

**Kubon & Sagner Buchexport-Import GmbH**
Hessstr 39/41, 80798 Munich
*Tel:* (089) 54 218-0 *Fax:* (089) 54 218-218
*E-mail:* postmaster@kubon-sagner.de
*Web Site:* www.kubon-sagner.de
*Key Personnel*
Manager: Otto Sagner; Sabine Sagner-Weigl
Founded: 1947
Specialize in publications from East & Southeast Europe.
Subjects: Albanian, Hungarian, Romanian & Slavic studies
Type of Business: Distributor, Exporter, Importer, Major Independent Bookseller, Wholesaler
Subsidiaries: Verlag Otto Sagner

**Lange & Springer Antiquariat**
Hegelplatz 1, 10117 Berlin
*Tel:* (030) 31504196; (030) 3422011 *Fax:* (030) 3410440; (030) 31504197
*E-mail:* buchladen@lange-springer-antiquariat.de
*Web Site:* www.lange-springer-antiquariat.de
Founded: 1980
Type of Business: Major Independent Bookseller

**Georg Lingenbrink GmbH & Co, Libri**
Friesenweg 1, 22763 Hamburg
*Tel:* 0180-53 69 800 *Fax:* (040) 853 98 300
*E-mail:* service@libri.de
*Web Site:* www.libri.de
*Key Personnel*
Manager: Alfred Becht; Holger Bellmann; Dr Markus Conrad; Dr Gerhard Dust; Marga Winkler
Founded: 1928
Type of Business: Exporter, Importer, Wholesaler
*Branch Office(s)*
August-Schanz-Str 33, 60433 Frankfurt *Tel:* (069) 954 22 0 *Fax:* (069) 954 22 300
Europaeallee, 36244 Bad Hersfeld *Tel:* (06621) 890 *Fax:* (06621) 89 13 12

**J A Mayersche Buchhandlung GmbH & Co KG Abt Verlag**
Matthiashofstr 28-30, 52064 Aachen
*Tel:* (0241) 4777 499 *Fax:* (0241) 4777 467
*E-mail:* info@mayersche.de
*Web Site:* www.mayersche.de
*Key Personnel*
Man Dir, Publicity: Helmut Falter
Founded: 1817
Branch offices in Bochum, Cologne, Dortmund, Duisburg, Essen, Gelsenkirchen & Monchengladbach.
Type of Business: Distributor, Exporter, Importer, Major Independent Bookseller

**Minerva KG Internationale Fachliteratur fur Medizin und Naturwissenschaften Neue Medien**
Bunsenstr 6, 64293 Darmstadt
*Tel:* (06151) 9880 *Fax:* (06151) 98839
*E-mail:* minerva@minerva.de
*Web Site:* www.minerva.de
*Key Personnel*
Contact: Christoph Gude *E-mail:* c.gude@
minerva.de; Stefan Gude *E-mail:* s.gude@
minerva.de
Founded: 1949
Type of Business: Distributor, Major Independent Bookseller
*Owned by:* Helmut Gude

**Heinrich Petersen Hans Buchimport GmbH**
Meessen 10, 22113 Oststeinbek
Mailing Address: Postfach 1119, 22109 Oststeinbek
*Tel:* (040) 71003-0 *Fax:* (040) 71003-141
*E-mail:* vertrieb@petersen-buchimport.com
*Web Site:* www.petersen-buchimport.com
*Key Personnel*
Contact: Johann Christian Peterson

**Pociao's Books**
Prinz Albrechtstr 65, 53113 Bonn
Mailing Address: Postfach 190136, 53037 Bonn
*Tel:* (0228) 229583 *Fax:* (0228) 219507
*E-mail:* pociao@t-online.de
*Web Site:* www.sanssoleil.de
Founded: 1975
Type of Business: Distributor, Exporter, Importer, Major Independent Bookseller
*Owned by:* Expanded Media Editions Sans Soleil

**Sachse & Heinzelmann Kunst- und Buchhandlung GmbH**
Koenigstr 20, 30175 Hannover
*Tel:* (0511) 360240 *Fax:* (0511) 324167
*E-mail:* info@sachse-heinzelmann.de
*Web Site:* www.sachse-heinzelmann.de
Type of Business: Major Independent Bookseller

**Sandila Import-Export Handels-GmbH**
Sagestr 37, 79737 Herrischried
*Tel:* (07764) 93970 *Fax:* (07764) 939739
*E-mail:* info@sandila.de
*Web Site:* www.sandila.de
Founded: 1984
Type of Business: Distributor, Exporter, Importer, Wholesaler

**Kurt Scholl**
Steinhofweg 20, 69123 Heidelberg
*Tel:* (06221) 707661
Founded: 1964
Type of Business: Major Independent Bookseller

**SPS Verlaggsservice GmbH**
Karl-Mand-Str 2, 56070 Koblenz
*Tel:* (0261) 80706-0 *Fax:* (0261) 80706-54
*Key Personnel*
Owner: Hansjochen Keilholz
Founded: 1979
Type of Business: Distributor

**Stern-Verlag Janssen & Co**
Friedrichstr 24-26, 40001 Duesseldorf
*Tel:* (0211) 3881-0 *Fax:* (0211) 3881-200
*E-mail:* service@buchsv.de
*Web Site:* www.buchsv.de
*Key Personnel*
Managing Partner: Horst Janssen; Klaus Janssen
Founded: 1900
New & antiquarian/second-hand books; journals.
Type of Business: Distributor, Exporter, Importer
*Bookshop(s):* Friedrichstr 22-26, 40217 Duesseldorf; Universitatsbuchhandlung, Universitatsstr 1, 40225 Duesseldorf *Tel:* (0211) 346161 *Fax:* (0211) 340360 *E-mail:* unibuch@
buchhaus-sternverlag.de

**G Umbreit GmbH & Co KG**
Mundelsheimer Str 3, 74321 Bietigheim-Bissingen
*Tel:* (07142) 596-0 *Fax:* (07142) 596-200
*E-mail:* info@umbreit-kg.de

*Web Site:* www.umbreit-kg.de
*Key Personnel*
Man Dir & Associate: Thomas Bez
Assistant Mgr, Buying Department: Martina
    Schlaud-Weisensee
Contact: Torben Merklinghaus *Tel:* (07142) 596
    115
Founded: 1912
Type of Business: Distributor, Wholesaler

**Vervuert Verlag**, see Iberoamericana Editorial
    Vervuert

**Berthold Winter**
Wilzenweg 17, 13595 Berlin
*Tel:* (030) 362 35 30 *Fax:* (030) 362 96 93
Founded: 1920
Type of Business: Distributor, Exporter, Importer,
    Wholesaler

**Verlags -und Sortiments-Buchhandlung
    Konrad Wittwer GmbH & Co KG**
Postfach 105343, 70046 Stuttgart
*Tel:* (0711) 25 07 0 *Fax:* (0711) 25 07 145
*E-mail:* info@wittwer.de
*Web Site:* www.wittwer.de
*Key Personnel*
Man Dir: Christian Wittwer; Dr Konrad M Wit-
    twer; Konrad P Wittwer; Michael Wittwer
Founded: 1867
Type of Business: Major Independent Bookseller
*Branch Office(s)*
Koenigstr 30, 70173 Stuttgart *E-mail:* buchhans@
    wittwer.de *Web Site:* www.wittwer.de

# Ghana

**Ghana Publishing Corporation, Distribution
    and Sales Division**
c/o Publishing Div, Private Post Bag, Tema
*Tel:* (022) 812921
Branches throughout Ghana.

**Presbyterian Book Depot Ltd**
Box 195, Thorpe Rd, Accra
*Tel:* (021) 663124 *Fax:* (021) 662415
*E-mail:* pcg@africaonline.com.gh
*Telex:* 2525 *Cable:* BOOKS ACCRA
*Key Personnel*
Man Dir: E Anim-Ansah
Founded: 1870
The organization comprises bookselling, sta-
    tionery supply, printing (Presbyterian Press)
    & publishing activities (see Waterville Publish-
    ing House) Newspapers-Christian Messenger &
    The Presbyterian.
Type of Business: Distributor, Importer, Major
    Book Chain Headquarters, Major Independent
    Bookseller, Wholesaler
*Owned by:* Presbyterian Church of Ghana, PO
    Box 1800, Accra
*Branch Office(s)*
PO Box GP 195, Accra, Contact: Twum Barima J
    *Tel:* (021) 663124
PO Box 70, Akim Oda, Contact: Mr Boakye Yi-
    adom *Tel:* (0882) 2181
PO Box 10, Berekum, Contact: Mr Francis
    Yeboan *Tel:* (0642) 22029
PO Box 219, Koforidua, Contact: Ms Makafui
    Acolatse *Tel:* (081) 22434
PO Box 1999, Kumasi, Contact: Mr G K Aboa
    *Tel:* (051) 28145
PO Box 16, Nkawkaw, Contact: S O Lartey
    *Tel:* (0842) 22010
PO Box 7, Odumase, Contact: Mr F T Lowor
PO Box 27, Tamale, Contact: K Mate *Tel:* (071)
    22382

**Queensway Bookshop & Stores Ltd**
Bank Lane, Accra
Mailing Address: PO Box 4276, Accra
*Tel:* (021) 62707 *Cable:* Success Accra
*Key Personnel*
Manager: Kwaku Mensah
Suppliers of educational, library & HMSO publi-
    cations.
*Branch Office(s)*
Bank St, PO Box 20, Kumasi *Tel:* (051) 4047

**University Bookshop**
Kwame Nkrumah University of Science & Tech-
    nology, University Post Office, Kumasi
*Tel:* (051) 60223 *Fax:* (051) 60137
*E-mail:* library@knust.edu.gh
*Web Site:* www.knust.edu.gh *Cable:*
    KUMASITECH KUMASI
*Key Personnel*
Manager: Robert Reddick Mensah
Type of Business: Major Independent Bookseller

**University Bookshop**
University Sq, University of Ghana, PO Box LG
    1, Legon
*Tel:* (021) 500398 *Fax:* (021) 500774
*E-mail:* bookshop@ug.edu.gh
*Web Site:* www.ghanaweb.com/GhanaHomePage/
    education/legon.html
*Key Personnel*
Manager: Emmanuel Tonyigah
Founded: 1950
Type of Business: Major Independent Bookseller
*Owned by:* University of Ghana, PO Box LG 25,
    Legon

# Gibraltar

**Gibraltar Bookshop**
300 Main St, Gibraltar
*Tel:* 71894 *Fax:* 75554
*Key Personnel*
Manager: A Benady
Founded: 1973
Type of Business: Distributor, Major Independent
    Bookseller

# Greece

**Agyra** (Atkypa)
271 Lamprou Katsoni & G Papandreou St, Ag
    Anargiri, 135 62 Athens
*Tel:* 2102693800 *Fax:* 2102693805
*E-mail:* info@agyra.gr
*Web Site:* www.agyra.gr
*Bookshop(s):* Pesmazoglou 5, Athens 105 64
    *Tel:* 2103213507

**Aithra Scientific Bookstore**
One Messologiou St, 106 81 Athens
*Tel:* 2103301269 *Fax:* 2103302622
*Key Personnel*
President: Prof Vangelis Spourdagos
Founded: 1984
Specialize in books on mathematics, physics,
    chemistry, astronomy, geology & meteorology.
Type of Business: Exporter, Importer, Major Inde-
    pendent Bookseller, Wholesaler

**Akti-Oxy Publications**
278 Mithymnis, 112 57 Athens
*Tel:* 2108658502; 2108676125 *Fax:* 210
    3802030

*E-mail:* info@oxy.gr
*Web Site:* www.oxy.gr
*Key Personnel*
President: Nikos Hatzopoulos
Vice President: Paris Coutsikos
Editor: Arhondi Korka; Tassos Nickogiannis
Founded: 1995
Experimental, cultural & underground publication.
*Bookshop(s):* Oxy, Asklipiou 22, 106 80 Athens

**Alexiadou Vefa**
4 Leonidou, 144 52 Athens
*Tel:* 2102848086 *Fax:* 2102849689
*E-mail:* vefaeditions@ath.forthnet.gr
*Web Site:* www.addgr.com/comp/vefa/index.htm
*Key Personnel*
President, Author & Editor: Vefa Alexiadou
Vice President: Koszas Alexiades
Marketing Dir: Alexia Alexiadou
Founded: 1979
Type of Business: Exporter, Wholesaler
*Branch Office(s)*
Nevrokopiou 16, Thessaloniki

**Alpha-Delta**
6, Sarantaporou St, 111 44 Athens
*Tel:* 2102280027 *Fax:* 2102280027
*Key Personnel*
President: Dr Ath I Delikostopoulos
Founded: 1966
Type of Business: Wholesaler
*Owned by:* Alamoheilas Ltd

**Anastasiadis Publications**
306 Patission St, 111 41 Athens
*Tel:* 2102284013 *Fax:* 2102236442
*Key Personnel*
Contact: Pantelis Anastasiadis
Type of Business: Distributor, Wholesaler

**Angeletos Sokzates**
68-70 Ipirou St, 163 42 Ilioupoli, Athens
*Tel:* 2109928100 *Fax:* 2109940530

**Aquarious**
One Notara, 106 83 Athens
*Tel:* 2103842354; 2103617360 *Fax:* 210
    3303890

**Athina**
2 N Plastira, 171 21 Athens
*Tel:* 21009341166
*Key Personnel*
Contact: Mary G Mavrogianni
Type of Business: Exporter
*Owned by:* George Mavrogianni, 27, Emm Be-
    naki St, 106 81 Athens

**Bacharakis**
31 Tsimiski, 546 23 Thessaloniki
Mailing Address: Imeras 4, 552 36 Panorama,
    Thessaloniki
*Tel:* 2310220160 *Fax:* 2310263776
Founded: 1967
Also publisher.
Type of Business: Distributor, Wholesaler

**Typothito G Dardanos**
37 Didotou, 106 80 Athens
*Tel:* 2103642003 *Fax:* 2103642030
*E-mail:* info@dardanosnet.gr
*Web Site:* www.dardanosnet.gr
Founded: 1993
Also acts as Publisher.
Type of Business: Distributor, Exporter, Importer,
    Major Book Chain Headquarters, Major Inde-
    pendent Bookseller

**Diavlos**
10 Valtetsiou St, 106 80 Athens

*Tel:* 2103631169; 2103625315 *Fax:* 210
  3617473
*E-mail:* info@diavlos-books.gr
*Web Site:* www.diavlos-books.gr
*Key Personnel*
President & Man Dir: Mr E Deligiannakis
Founded: 1988
Publication of scientific, computer, popular sci-
  ence, academic, short guides, humor books.
Type of Business: Distributor, Exporter, Major
  Independent Bookseller
*Bookshop(s):* 5 Pesmazoglov St, 105 64 Athens

**Dion**
39 Filikis Etaireias, 546 21 Thessaloniki
*Tel:* 2310265042 *Fax:* 2310265083
*E-mail:* info@psarasbooks.gr
*Web Site:* www.psarasbooks.gr
*Key Personnel*
Public Relations: Maria Psara
Founded: 1978
Bookshop & publications.
Type of Business: Distributor, Major Independent
  Bookseller, Wholesaler
*Owned by:* Psaras Evangelos
*Parent Company:* Bookshop Psaras, Albania
*Warehouse:* Tzabela 25, Thessaloniki

**Efstathiadis Group SA**
88 Drakontos St, 104 42 Athens
*Tel:* 2105154650 *Fax:* 2105154657
*E-mail:* info@efgroup.gr
*Web Site:* www.efgroup.gr
*Telex:* 216176
*Key Personnel*
President: Panos Efstathiadis
Vice President & Sales Dir: Thanos Efstathiadis
Founded: 1930
Type of Business: Distributor, Exporter, Importer,
  Wholesaler
*Branch Office(s)*
14 Valtetsious St, 106 80 Athens
4 C Cristali St, Antigonidon Sq, 546 30 Thessa-
  loniki
*Bookshop(s):* 84 Academias St, 106 78 Athens;
  14 Ethnikis Aminis St, 546 21 Thessaloniki

**Eleftheri Skepsis**
112 Ippokratous St, 114 72 Athens
*Tel:* 2103614736; 2103630697
*E-mail:* info@eleftheriskepsis.gr
*Web Site:* www.eleftheriskepsis.gr

**G C Eleftheroudakis Co Ltd**
International Bookstore, Constitution Sq, Nikis 4,
  105 63 Athens
*Tel:* 2103222255; 2103229388 *Fax:* 210
  3231401; 2103229388
*Key Personnel*
Man Dir: Virginia Eleftheroudakis-Gregou
Also publisher.

**Enalios**
4 El Venizelou, 143 43 Athens
*Tel:* 2102531614 *Fax:* 2102184854
Founded: 1996
Type of Business: Wholesaler
*Owned by:* Eleni Kekropoulou

**Erevnites**
3-5 Gravias St, 105 52 Athens
*Tel:* 2105234415; 2105234232
  *Fax:* 2105241863
*E-mail:* erevnite@otenet.gr
*Web Site:* www.erevnites.gr
Founded: 1991

**Esoptron**
14 Armodiou St, 105 52 Athens
*Tel:* 2103236852 *Fax:* 2103210472

*Key Personnel*
Publisher: Stamos Stinis; Pavlos Voudouris
Type of Business: Wholesaler
*Bookshop(s):* 49 Panepistimiou Str, 106 78
  Athens (Stoa Orfeos)

**Eurodiastasi**
49 Kallifrona, 106 77 Athens
*Tel:* 2103844695 *Fax:* 2103844888
*E-mail:* eurodiastasi@internet.gr; eurodiastasi@
  galaxynet.gr
*Web Site:* www.eurodiastasi.gr
*Key Personnel*
Sales Manager: Yanni Mitsios
Type of Business: Exporter, Wholesaler
*Owned by:* Loukia Mitsa & Takis Michalopoulos

**Filistor Publishing**
31 Themistokleous St, 106 77 Athens
*Tel:* 2103818457
Founded: 1995
*Owned by:* Charalabos Grammenos

**Grivas Publications**
3 Irodotou St, 193 00 Aspropyrgos, Attiki
Mailing Address: PO Box 72, 193 00 Aspropyr-
  gos, Attiki
*Tel:* 2105573470 *Fax:* 2105573076
*E-mail:* info@grivas.gr
*Web Site:* www.grivas.gr
*Key Personnel*
Man Dir: N Grivas *E-mail:* grivas@otenet.gr
Founded: 1985
Publisher of ELT books.
*Owned by:* Nick & Costas Grivas

**Harry Joe Patsis' European Publications'
Center Ltd**
62 Panepistimiou Str, 106 77 Athens
*Tel:* 2103841040; 2103841050 *Fax:* 210
  6232194; 2103841050
*Key Personnel*
Foreign Affairs Dir: Harry Joe Patsis
Contact: Helen Patsis; Theoharis Patsis
Founded: 1996
Type of Business: Distributor, Exporter, Importer,
  Major Book Chain Headquarters, Major Inde-
  pendent Bookseller, Wholesaler
*Showroom(s):* 62 Panepistiniou Str, Athens 106
  77 (Same location for bookshop)

**Iamvlichos**
41 Valtetsiou, 106 81 Athens
*Tel:* 2103807180 *Fax:* 2103807828; 2103807
  435
*Key Personnel*
General Manager: P Michalitsis
Sales Manager: K Pachidis
Founded: 1981
*Owned by:* P Michalitsis, K Pachidis, K
  Kalogeropoulos & D Doulgaridis
*Bookshop(s):* Sirius, Marni S, 10433 Athens

**Ikaros**
4 Voulis St, 105 62 Athens
*Tel:* 2103225152 *Fax:* 2103235262
Founded: 1943
*Owned by:* K Karydi & Ch Karydi

**J M Pantelides Booksellers Ltd**
11 Amerikis St, 106 72 Athens
*Tel:* 2103639560 *Fax:* 2103636453
*Telex:* 224609 Paza gr
*Key Personnel*
Man Dir: Mrs Maro Pantelides
Founded: 1948
Type of Business: Importer, Major Book Chain
  Headquarters, Major Independent Bookseller,
  Wholesaler

**Kanakis Publications & Bookshop**
24 Z Pigis St, 105 61 Athens
*Tel:* 2103302385 *Fax:* 2103811902

**Kapon Editions**
23-27 Makriyanni St, 117 42 Athens
*Tel:* 2109235098 *Fax:* 2109214089
*Web Site:* www.homemarket.gr
*Key Personnel*
Contact: Rachel Kapon *E-mail:* kapon_ed@
  otenet.gr
Founded: 1970
Also publisher.
Type of Business: Wholesaler

**Kritiki**
1-3 Tsamadou St, 106 83 Athens
*Tel:* 2103803730 *Fax:* 2103803740
*E-mail:* biblia@kritiki.gr
*Web Site:* www.kritiki.gr

**Kyriakidis Brothers sa**
Melenikou 5, 546 35 Thessaloniki
*Tel:* 2310208540 *Fax:* 2310245541
*E-mail:* info@kyriakidis.gr
*Web Site:* www.kyriakidis.gr
Type of Business: Major Independent Bookseller,
  Wholesaler
*Owned by:* Dimitrios Kyriakidis; Tasos Kyriakidis

**Librairie Kaufmann SA**
28, Stadiou St, 105 64 Athens
*Tel:* 2103236817 *Fax:* 2103230320
*E-mail:* ccaldi@otenet.gr
*Telex:* 218187
*Branch Office(s)*
Academias 76, 106 78 Athens *Tel:* 2103627844
Siha 54, 106 72 Athens *Tel:* 2103643433

**Malliaris - Pedia**
10 Aristotelous St, 546 24 Thessaloniki
*Tel:* 2310262485 *Fax:* 2310264856
*E-mail:* info@malliaris.gr
*Web Site:* www.malliaris.gr
*Key Personnel*
President: Antonis Malliaris
Founded: 1985
*Branch Office(s)*
11 Mavromihalis St, Athens *Tel:* 2103605874
Aristotelous Corner & Ermou 53, Thessaloniki
  *Tel:* 2310252888 *Fax:* 2310252890
*Bookshop(s):* 11 Saint Minas St, 546 24 Thessa-
  loniki; 57 So Fouli St, Kalamaria, Thessaloniki
  *Tel:* 2310424277 *Fax:* 2310424294; 22
  Kolokotronis St, Stavroupoli *Tel:* 2310640755
  *Fax:* 22310640757

**Mavrogianni Publications**
27 Emm Benaki & Solonos St, 106 81 Athens
*Tel:* 2103304628 *Fax:* 2103304628

**Melissa Publishing House**
58 Skoufa St, 106 80 Athens
*Tel:* 2103611692 *Fax:* 2103600865
*E-mail:* webmaster@melissabooks.com
*Web Site:* www.melissabooks.com
Founded: 1954

**Olkos Editions**
56 Sina Str, 106 72 Athens
*Tel:* 2103621379 *Fax:* 2103625576
*Web Site:* www.olkos.gr
*Key Personnel*
Contact: Irene Louvzou
Founded: 1973
Type of Business: Distributor, Major Independent
  Bookseller, Wholesaler
*Showroom(s):* 5 Pezmantzoglou St, 105 64
  Athens
*Bookshop(s):* 5 Pezmantzoglou St, 105 64 Athens

**Pournaras Panagiotis**
12 Kastritsiou Str, 546 23 Thessaloniki
*Tel:* 2310270941 *Fax:* 2310228922
*E-mail:* pournarasbooks@the.forthnet.gr
Founded: 1962
International library suppliers & publisher.
Type of Business: Distributor, Exporter, Importer,
   Major Independent Bookseller

**Press Photo Publications**
One Tpounakn, 104 45 Athens
*Tel:* 2108541400 *Fax:* 2108541485
*E-mail:* photomag@photo.gr
*Web Site:* www.photo.gr
Founded: 1989
Type of Business: Major Independent Bookseller

**Road Editions**
39 Ippokratous Str, 106 80 Athens
*Tel:* 2103613242 *Fax:* 2103614681
*E-mail:* roadsales@road.gr
*Web Site:* www.road.gr
*Key Personnel*
President & General Manager: Stephanos Psi-
   menos
Editor: Ioannis Tegopoulos
Founded: 1994
Publish & retailer of maps & travel guides.
Type of Business: Exporter

**Salto Publishers**
33, Angelaki St, 546 21 Thessaloniki
*Tel:* 2310262854 *Fax:* 2310285879
*E-mail:* saltos@spocrk.net.gr
*Key Personnel*
Contact: Marina Mouratidou

**Vlassi**
116 Solwnos & 2-4 Lontoy, 106 81 Athens
*Tel:* 2103812900; 2103833013 *Fax:* 210
   3827557
*Web Site:* www.vlassi.gr
*Key Personnel*
President: Nikos Vlassis
Author: G R Enopoulos; K Palamas; S Melas;
   Oswalt Kolle
Founded: 1964

**Votsis Nikos**
16 Emm Benaki St, 106 78 Athens
*Fax:* 2103820646
*E-mail:* mvotsis@otenet.gr
Founded: 1958
Type of Business: Importer, Wholesaler

**IE Zachariadou OHG (Bucherstube)**
Prox Koromila 20, 546 22 Thessaloniki
*Tel:* 2310276334 *Fax:* 2310229936
*E-mail:* info@lillisbookstore.gr
*Web Site:* www.lillisbookstore.gr
*Key Personnel*
Owner: Evangelia (Lilli) Zachariadou
   *E-mail:* lilli@lillisbookstore.gr
Founded: 1972
German book & information center, Greek gen-
   eral bookstore, Italian bookstore.
Type of Business: Exporter, Importer, Major Inde-
   pendent Bookseller

# Guatemala

**Piedra Santa Editorial**
5 Calle, 7-55, Zona 1, Guatemala City
*Tel:* (02) 29053
*E-mail:* piedrasanta@guate.net

*Key Personnel*
Dir: Irene Piedra Santa
   *E-mail:* irene_piedra_santa@hotmail.com
Founded: 1947
Also acts as publisher.
Type of Business: Distributor, Exporter, Importer,
   Major Book Chain Headquarters
*Showroom(s):* 11 Calle 6-50, Zona 1, Guatemala
   City

**Libreria Tuncho Granados G**
Apdo 13, Guatemala City
*Tel:* (02) 24736; (02) 27269; (02) 21181
*Branch Office(s)*
La Plaza del Sol, Calle Montufar y 2 Ave, Zona 9
   Guatemala City CA

**Libreria Universal**
13 Calle 4-16, Zona 1, Guatemala City
*Tel:* (02) 28 484
*Key Personnel*
Manager: Olga A de Manrique
*Owned by:* Distribuidora General Universal

# Guyana

**Austin's Book Services**
190 Church St, South Cummingsburg, George-
   town
*Tel:* (02) 277 395; (02) 267 350 *Fax:* (02) 277
   369
*E-mail:* austins@guyana.net.gy
*Key Personnel*
Man Dir: Lloyd F Austin
Founded: 1993
Type of Business: Distributor, Importer, Major
   Independent Bookseller

**Christian Book Service**
242 Albert St & South Rd, Border, Georgetown
*Tel:* (02) 52521 *Fax:* (02) 54039
*Key Personnel*
Manager: Wesley Rowe
Type of Business: Major Independent Bookseller
*Owned by:* Full Gospel Fellowship

**National Bookseller**
78 Church St, Georgetown
*Tel:* (02) 71244 *Fax:* (02) 57309

# Honduras

**Libreria Universitaria Jose T Reyes**
Universidad Nacional Autonoma de Honduras,
   Blvd Suyapa, Edificio Administrativo, Planta
   Baja, Tegucigalpa DC
*Tel:* 232-2110 *Fax:* 235-3361
*Web Site:* www.unah.hn
*Telex:* 1289

**University Library,** see Libreria Universitaria
   Jose T Reyes

# Hong Kong

**Enterprise International**
1604 Eastern Commercial Centre, 16th floor, 393-
   407 Hennessy Rd, Wan Chai

*Tel:* 25734161 *Fax:* 28383469 *Cable:* EINPRISE
   HONG KONG
*Key Personnel*
Proprietor: C P Ho
Founded: 1978

**Hong Kong Book Centre Ltd**
On Lok Yuen Bldg, Basement, 25 Des Voeux Rd,
   Central Hong Kong
*Tel:* 2522-7064 *Fax:* 2868-5079
*E-mail:* orders@hkbookcentre.com.hk
*Web Site:* www.swindonbooks.com
*Key Personnel*
Dir: Annabella Lee
Founded: 1962

**Swindon Book Co Ltd**
13-15 Lock Rd, Kowloon
*Tel:* 2366 8001 *Fax:* 2739 4978
*E-mail:* swindon@netvigator.com
*Web Site:* www.swindonbooks.com
*Telex:* 50441 swin hx *Cable:* SWINDON
*Key Personnel*
Dir: Annabella Li
Manager: Daisy K Y Li
Book & stationery retail & distribution; filofax
   agency; OECD publications.
*Branch Office(s)*
University Book Store

# Hungary

**Talentum Konyves es Kereskedo Kft**
Bajcsy-Zsilinszky ut 66, 1054 Budapest
*Tel:* (01) 3118824
Type of Business: Distributor, Importer, Whole-
   saler

# Iceland

**Bokabud Mals og menningar**
Laugavegi 18, 101 Reykjavik
*Tel:* 552 4240 *Fax:* 562 3523
*Key Personnel*
Manager: Arni Einarsson
Founded: 1937
Type of Business: Distributor, Exporter, Importer,
   Wholesaler
*Owned by:* Mal og menning
*Branch Office(s)*
Sidumula 7-9, 108 Reykjavik

**Boksala Studenta (The University Bookstore)**
V/Hringbraut, 101 Reykjavik
*Tel:* (05) 700 777 *Fax:* (05) 700 778
*E-mail:* boksala@boksala.is
*Web Site:* www.boksala.is
*Key Personnel*
Man Dir: Sigurdur Palsson
Buyer: Eysteinn Bjornsson
Founded: 1968
All subjects with a concentration on Academic &
   Professional Literature, Textbooks.
Type of Business: Distributor, Importer, Major
   Independent Bookseller
*Owned by:* Felagsstofnun Studenta

**Vaka-Helgafell**
Sueurlandsbraut 12, 108 Reykjavik
*Tel:* 522 2000 *Fax:* 522 2022
*E-mail:* edda@edda.is
*Web Site:* vaka.is

## Key Personnel
Chairman of the Board: Olafur Ragnarsson
Man Dir: Bernhard Petersen
Dir, Publishing & Rights: Petur Mar Olafsson
Marketing Manager: Kjartan Orn Olafsson
Editor-in-Chief: Bjarni Thorsteinsson
Production Manager: Unnur Agustsdottir
Founded: 1981
Type of Business: Distributor, Importer, Wholesaler

# India

## Affiliated East West Press Pvt Ltd
104 Nirmal Tower, 26 Barakhamba Rd, New Delhi 110 001
*Tel:* (011) 23279113; (011) 23264180 *Fax:* (011) 23260538
*E-mail:* affiliat@vsnl.com
*Key Personnel*
Man Dir: Sunny Malik
Founded: 1962
Expertise in society publications & distribution; publishers of undergraduate & graduate STM Books.
Type of Business: Distributor, Importer, Wholesaler

## Allied Publishers Pvt Ltd
13-14 Asaf Ali Rd, New Delhi 110002
*Tel:* (011) 3239001; (011) 3233002; (011) 3233004; (011) 323006667 *Fax:* (011) 3235967
*E-mail:* aplcmd@ndf.vsnl.net.in
*Web Site:* www.alliedpublishers.com
*Key Personnel*
Man Dir: S M Sachdev
Dir: Ravi Sachdev; Sunil Sachdev
Founded: 1934
Also printers.
Type of Business: Distributor, Exporter, Importer, Wholesaler
*Owned by:* Allied Chambers (India) Ltd
*Branch Office(s)*
Prarthana Flats, Navrangpura, Ahmedabad 380009 *Tel:* (079) 646 5916; (079) 663 0079 *Fax:* (079) 646 5916
5th Main Rd, Gandhinagar, Bangalore 560009
750 Anna Salai, Chennai 600002 *Tel:* (044) 8523938; (044) 8523958 *Fax:* (044) 8520649 *E-mail:* allied.mds@smb.sprintrpg.ems.vsnl.net.in
3-5-1129 Kachiguida Cross Rd, Hyderabad 500027 *Tel:* (040) 4619079; (040) 4619081 *Fax:* (040) 4619079; (040) 4619081
Patiala House, 16-A Ashok Marg, Lucknow 226001 *Tel:* (0522) 214253; (0522) 280358 *Fax:* (0522) 214253
Ballard Estate, 15, JN Heredia Marg, Mumbai 400038 *Tel:* (022) 2617926; (022) 2617927 *Fax:* (022) 2617928 *E-mail:* alliedpl@vsnl.com
18 Hill Rd, Ramnagar, Nagpur 440010 *Tel:* (0712) 521122; (0712) 542625 *Fax:* (0712) 542625

## Atma Ram & Sons
Kashmere Gate, Delhi 110006
*Tel:* (011) 223092 *Cable:* BOOKS
*Key Personnel*
Man Dir, Publicity, Rights & Permissions: Sushil Kumar Puri
Also publisher.
Type of Business: Importer

## Biblia Impex Pvt Ltd
2/18 Ansari Rd, New Delhi 110002
*Tel:* (011) 327-8034; (011) 326-2515 *Fax:* (011) 328-2047
*E-mail:* info@bibliaimpex.com

*Web Site:* www.bibliaimpex.com *Cable:* ELYSIUM
*Key Personnel*
Man Dir: P K Goel
Founded: 1980
International bookseller & subscription agent.
Type of Business: Distributor, Exporter, Major Independent Bookseller

## Books & Periodicals Agency
B-1 Inder Puri, New Delhi 110012
*Tel:* (011) 205624 *Fax:* 801-881-6189 (US Fax)
*E-mail:* bpage@del2.vsnl.net.in
*Web Site:* www.bpagency.com *Cable:* BACKVOLUME
*Key Personnel*
Proprietor: Girish Gupta
Founded: 1973
Exporter of books on South Asia & Southeast Asia. Over 100,000 titles in 356 subjects at www.bpagency.com.
Type of Business: Distributor, Exporter, Major Independent Bookseller

## Books India
135 Coral Merchant St, Chennai 600001
*Tel:* (011) 327 7463 *Fax:* (011) 241 2912
*Key Personnel*
Dir: Mr Baxi Himanshu
Founded: 1969
Type of Business: Exporter, Major Independent Bookseller

## Nem Chand & Bros
Civil Lines, Roorkee 247667
*Tel:* (01332) 272258; (01332) 272752; (01322) 264343 *Fax:* (01332) 273258
*E-mail:* ncb_rke@rediffmail.com *Cable:* ENGINJOUR
Founded: 1951
Type of Business: Distributor, Exporter, Importer, Major Independent Bookseller, Wholesaler

## Current Technical Literature Co (Pvt) Ltd
Malhotra House, Opp GPO, Mumbai, Maharashtra 400 001
Mailing Address: PO Box 1374, Mumbai, Maharashtra 400 001
*Tel:* (022) 2611045 *Fax:* (022) 2679786
*Cable:* Cutelico
*Key Personnel*
Man Dir: R K Murti
Scientific, technical & medical books.
*Branch Office(s)*
Narayanguda, Opp Blood Bank, PO Box No 1030, Hyderabad 500 029 *Tel:* (040) 591516
152 Thambu Chetti St, PO Box No 128, Chennai 600 001 *Tel:* (044) 5342897
22 Chittaranjan Ave, Kolkata 700 072 *Tel:* (033) 273138
4676 Ansari Rd, 21 Daryaganj, PO Box No 7008, New Delhi 110 002 *Tel:* (011) 3278737

## DK Agencies (P) Ltd
A/15-17 DK Ave, Mohan Garden, Najafgarh Rd, New Delhi 110 059
*Tel:* (011) 2535-7104; (011) 2535-7105 *Fax:* (011) 2535-7103
*E-mail:* custserv@dkagencies.com
*Web Site:* www.dkagencies.com
*Key Personnel*
Dir: Jaswant Rai Mittal; Ramesh K Mittal *E-mail:* rkmittal@dkagencies.com
Senior Executive: Surya P Mittal *E-mail:* surya@dkagencies.com
Founded: 1968
Indian books, periodicals & multi-media (audio, video, CDs & microfilms from India). Also publisher & subscription agent.
Type of Business: Distributor, Exporter, Major Independent Bookseller, Wholesaler

*Branch Office(s)*
4788-90/23 Ansari Rd, Daryagarj, New Delhi 110 002 *Tel:* (011) 2326-6890
*Bookshop(s):* 4788-90/23 Ansari Rd, Darya Ganj, New Delhi 110002 *Tel:* (011) 2326-6890

## E D Galgotia & Sons
17-B Connaught Pl, New Delhi 110 001
*Tel:* (011) 3322876 *Fax:* (011) 3755150
*E-mail:* galgotia@ndf.vsnl.net.in
*Telex:* 71161 Star In
*Key Personnel*
Dir: Suneel Galgotia; Neeraj Galgotia
Manager: P Paul
Subjects: Technical, scientific, medical & management
Type of Business: Importer, Major Independent Bookseller, Wholesaler

## English Book Store
17-L Connaught Circus, New Delhi 110001
*Tel:* (011) 332 9126 *Fax:* (011) 332 1731
*Key Personnel*
Proprietor: Bhupinder Chowdhri
Importer - military science, aviation, nursing, foreign languages, travel, religion.

## General Book Depot
1691 Nai Sarak, Delhi 110007
*Tel:* (011) 3263695; (011) 3250635 *Fax:* (011) 2394 0861

## German Book Centre
8 II Main Rd CIT (East), Chennai 600 035
*Tel:* (044) 2434-6244; (044) 2434-6266 *Fax:* (044) 2434-6529
*E-mail:* germanbk@vsnl.com
*Web Site:* germanbookcentre.com
*Key Personnel*
Contact: R Seshadri
Type of Business: Distributor, Importer, Wholesaler

## Giri Trading Agency Pvt Ltd
58/2 TSV Koil St, Mylapore, Chennai 600004
*Tel:* (044) 24943551; (044) 24953817; (044) 24953823 *Fax:* (044) 24953823
*E-mail:* giritrading@vsnl.com
*Web Site:* www.giritrading.com
*Key Personnel*
Dir: T S V Hari *Tel:* (044) 46116110 *E-mail:* tsvhari@eth.net; T S Srinivasan
General Manager: V Subramanian
Founded: 1951
Producers of audio cassettes specializing in all (A-Z) items pertaining to Hindu Religion; also acts as publisher of English & all South Indian language books. Supplier of all items pertaining to Hindu worship.
Membership(s): Booksellers & Publishers of South India.
Type of Business: Distributor, Exporter, Major Independent Bookseller, Wholesaler
*Owned by:* Giri Publications; Gitaa Cassettes, T S Ranganathan; Kamakoti-Tamil Monthly Magazine
*Parent Company:* Giri Trading Agency
*Ultimate Parent Company:* Giri Trading Agency Pvt Ltd
*Branch Office(s)*
Modi Nivas, Bhandarkar Rd, Matunga, Mumbai 400019 *Tel:* (022) 24141344; 24122316 *Fax:* (022) 24143140 *E-mail:* giri@bom8.vsnl.net.in
Ram Nagar, Near Sagar Dairy, Dombivili (E), Mumbai 421201
2 Siddhi Vinayak Apartments, Bangur Nagar, Goregon (W), Mumbai 400062 *Tel:* (022) 28767298
SIES Engineering & Computer College Complex, Anjaneyar Temple, Nehrul, Navi Mumbia
*Bookshop(s):* 10 Kapaleshwarar Sannidhi St, Mylapore, Chennai 600004 *Tel:* (044) 24940376;

(044) 24942530; (044) 24953820; No 8, Tenth St, Near Anjaneyar Temple & Ragavender Temple, Nanganallur, Chennai 600061 *Tel:* (044) 22311735; Shop F6, T M House, 92, Thruvenkatasami Sala W, Near Kamakshi Amman Koil, R S Puram, Coimbatore 641002 *Tel:* (0422) 2541523; No 5, Kamakshi Amman Sannadhi St, Kanchipuram 631502 *Tel:* (04112) 224415; Sri Subramanya Swamy Devalayam, Padmarao Nagar, Skandagiri, Secunderabad 500061 *Tel:* (040) 27503046

**GOYL Saab, Publishers & Distributors**, see General Book Depot

**Health-Harmony**, *imprint of* B Jain Publishers Overseas

**Higginbothams Ltd**
814 Anna Salai, Chennai 600 002
*Tel:* (044) 852 1841 *Fax:* (044) 852 8101 *Cable:* BOOKLOVER
*Key Personnel*
Dir: K A Arjun
Type of Business: Importer

**Hindi Book Centre**
4/5-B Asaf Ali Rd, New Delhi 110 002
*Tel:* (011) 23286757; (011) 23258993; (011) 23261696; (011) 23268651 *Fax:* (011) 23273335; (011) 26481565
*E-mail:* info@hindibook.com
*Web Site:* www.hindibook.com *Cable:* STARPUBLIS
*Key Personnel*
Executive Dir Sales: Mr Anil Varma
General books in Hindi.
*Owned by:* Star Publications (Pvt) Ltd, 55 Warren St, London W1T 5NW, United Kingdom

**Hindustan Book Agency**
P19, Green Park Extension, New Delhi 110 016
*Tel:* (011) 6163294; (011) 6163296 *Fax:* (011) 6193297
*E-mail:* hindbook@nda.vsnl.net.in
*Web Site:* www.hindbook.com
*Key Personnel*
Partner: D K Jain; J K Jain
Founded: 1947
American Mathematical Society, Birkhauser Verlag, Cambridge University Press, IOP, Kluwer Academic Publisher, Oxford University Press, Princeton University Press, Springer Verlag, Elsevier Science.
Type of Business: Distributor

**International Book House Pvt Ltd**
Indian Mercantile Mansions (Extn), 6th floor, Madame Cama Rd, Opp Regal Cinema, Colaba, Mumbai 400 001
*Tel:* (022) 22021634; (022) 22020765 *Fax:* (022) 22851109
*E-mail:* ibh@vsnl.com; 1ibh@vsnl.in
*Web Site:* www.intbh.com *Cable:* Interbook
*Key Personnel*
Dir: Sanjeev Gupta
Manager: T R B Vathsal
Founded: 1941
Trade books, book distributors, retailers, direct mail, direct to home, magazine subscriptions.
Type of Business: Distributor, Importer
*Branch Office(s)*
97 Residency Rd, Bangalore 560 025 *Tel:* (080) 22210193
Shop 5 Palace Court, One Kyd St, Kolkata 700 016 *Tel:* (033) 22294493
*Bookshop(s):* 13, S N Banejeer Rd, 2nd floor, Kolkata 700 013 *Tel:* (033) 216 26 78

**Jaico Publishing House**
127 Mahatma Gandhi Rd, Mumbai 400 023

*Tel:* (022) 267 6702; (022) 267 6802; (022) 267 4501 *Fax:* (022) 265 6412
*E-mail:* jaicowbd@vsnl.com
*Web Site:* www.jaicobooks.com
*Telex:* 118-6398 JAI IN *Cable:* JAICOBOOKS
*Key Personnel*
Man Dir: Ashwin Shah
Assistant General Manager: D M Patel
Editor: R H Sharma
Type of Business: Importer
*Owned by:* Jaico Publishing House
*Branch Office(s)*
Jaico Book Agency, No 57, Dr Giri Rd, T Nagar, Chennai 600 017, Manager: Mr A R Sivaraman *Tel:* (044) 2826 2874; (044) 2822 2653; (044) 2822 4582 *E-mail:* jaicoche@md3.vsnl.net.in
Jaico Book Distributors, 194, Patpar Ganj Indl Area, Delhi *Tel:* (011) 2214 4204; (011) 2214 4205 *Fax:* (011) 2214 4206 *E-mail:* jaicobook@vsnl.net
Jaico Book Distributors, G-2, 16 Ansari Rd, Darya Ganj, New Delhi 110 002, Manager: Mr Sanjay Verma *Tel:* (011) 2326 0651; (011) 2326 0618; (011) 2326 4748 *Fax:* (011) 2327 8469 *E-mail:* sethidel@del6.vsnl.net.in
Jaico Book Enterprises, 302, Acharya Prafulla Chandra Roy Rd, Kolkata 700 009, Manager: Mr M K Bal *Tel:* (033) 2360 0542; (033) 2360 0543 *E-mail:* jaicocal@cal2.vsnl.net.in
Jaico Book House, 14/1 1st Main Rd, 6th Cross, Gandhi Nagar, Bangalore 560 009, Manager: Mr Hemant Sharma *Tel:* (080) 226 7016; (080) 225 7083 *Fax:* (080) 228 5492 *E-mail:* jaicobgr@blr.vsnl.net.in
Jaico Book House, 3-4-494/1/2 Barkatpura, Hyderabad 500 027, Manager: Mr K S Anand *Tel:* (040) 2755 1992 *E-mail:* hyd1_jaicohyd@sancharnet.in
Jaicos' Wholesale Book Distributors, ELGI House, 2 Mill Officers' Colony, Ahmedabad 380 009, Contact: Mr Sujesh Kumar *Tel:* (079) 657 9865; (079) 657 5262 *E-mail:* jaicoahm@vsnl.com

**B Jain Publishers Overseas**
1921/10, Chuna Mandi, Paharganj, New Delhi 110055
*Tel:* 23581100; 23581300 *Fax:* (011) 23580471
*E-mail:* bjain@vsnl.com; info@bjainbooks.com
*Web Site:* www.bjainbooks.com
*Key Personnel*
Owner: Dr P N Jain *Tel:* (011) 22542967
Chief Executive Officer: Sh Kuldeep Jain *E-mail:* kuldeep@bjainbooks.com
Founded: 1967
Books, handcraft items & globules.
Subjects: Medical, health & new age
Imprints: Health-Harmony
*Branch Office(s)*
7, FIE Patparganj, Delhi 110092

**Krishnamurthy K**
23 Thanikachalam Rd, Chennai 600 017
*Tel:* (044) 2434 4519 *Fax:* (044) 2434 2009
*E-mail:* service@kkbooks.com
*Web Site:* www.kkbooks.com
Founded: 1944
Type of Business: Importer
*Branch Office(s)*
Shop No 31, Lal Bahadur Stadiom, Hyderabad 500001 *Tel:* (040) 231447

**The Modern Book Depot**
15A, J L Nehru Rd, Kolkata 700013
*Tel:* (033) 2493102; (033) 2490933 *Fax:* (033) 2497455
*E-mail:* modcal@vsnl.com
*Key Personnel*
Owner: Dewan Chand; Prem Prakash
Founded: 1949
Type of Business: Importer, Major Independent Bookseller, Wholesaler

*Owned by:* Om Prakash
*Branch Office(s)*
Station Sq, Unit III, Bhubaneswar, Orissa 751001 *E-mail:* modbooks@cal2.vsnl.net.in

**Motilal Banarsidass**
41-UA Bungalow Rd, Jawahar Nagar, Delhi 110 007
*Tel:* (011) 23851985; (011) 23858335; (011) 23854876; (011) 23852747 *Fax:* (011) 23850689; (011) 25797221
*E-mail:* mlbd@vsnl.com
*Web Site:* www.mlbd.com *Cable:* GLORYINDIA
*Key Personnel*
Managing Partner: R P Jain
Founded: 1903
Indological books including Indian literature, religion, philosophy, history, culture, etc; also a publisher.
Type of Business: Distributor, Exporter, Importer, Wholesaler
*Branch Office(s)*
236, Ninth Main III Block, Jayanagar, Bangalore 560 0111 *Tel:* (080) 6542591 *E-mail:* mlbdbgl@vsnl.com
120 Royapettah High Rd, Mylapore, Chennai 600004 *Tel:* (044) 4982315 *Fax:* (044) 4940066 FDA 48 *E-mail:* mlbdbook@sancharnet.in
PO Box 75, Chowk, Varanasi 221 001 *Tel:* (0542) 352331 *Fax:* (0542) 321806 *E-mail:* varanasi@mlbd.com
8 Camac St, Kolkata 700 017 *Tel:* (033) 2434874; (033) 2427457 *Fax:* (033) 2425291 *E-mail:* bpp_kol@vsnl.net
8 Mahalakshmi Chambers, 22 Warden Rd, Mumbai 400026 *Tel:* (022) 4923526; (022) 4982583 *Fax:* (022) 4963850 *E-mail:* mlbdmumbai@vsnl.net
Ashok Raipath, opposite Patna College, Patna, Bihar 800 004 *Tel:* (0612) 671442 *Fax:* (0612) 657641 *E-mail:* patna@mlbd.com
Sanas Plaza, Shop 11-12, 1302 Baji Rao Rd, Pune 411 002 *Tel:* (0212) 4486190 *Fax:* (0212) 660557 *E-mail:* mlbdpune@vsnl.net

**Munshiram Manoharlal Publishers Pvt Ltd**
54 Rani Jhansi Rd, New Delhi 110055
Mailing Address: PO Box 5715, New Delhi 110055
*Tel:* (011) 513841
*E-mail:* mml@mantraonline.com *Cable:* LITERATURE NEW DELHI
*Key Personnel*
Man Dir: Devendra Jain
Sales Dir: Ashok Jain; Pankaj D Jain
Founded: 1952
Also acts as publisher.
Type of Business: Major Independent Bookseller
*Bookshop(s):* 4416 Nai Sarak, Delhi 110006

**Narosa Book Distributors Pvt Ltd**
22, Daryaganj, Delhi Medical Association Rd, Delhi 110002
*Tel:* (011) 23243224; (011) 23243415; (011) 23243416 *Fax:* (011) 23243225; (011) 23258934
*E-mail:* narosa@ndc.vsnl.net.in/narosadl@nda.vsnl.net.in
*Web Site:* www.narosa.com *Cable:* NAROSA NEW DELHI
*Key Personnel*
Man Dir: N K Mehra
Marketing Manager: S Mehra
Senior Executive: P.K. Chopra
*Branch Office(s)*
35-36 Greams Rd, Thousand Lights, Chennai 600 006 *Tel:* (044) 28295362 *Fax:* (044) 28290377 *E-mail:* narosamds@vsnl.net

2F-2G Shivam Chambers, 53 Syed Amir Ali Ave, Kolkata 700 019 *Tel:* (033) 22814809 *Fax:* (033) 22814778
306 Shiv Centre, DBC Sector 17, PO KU Bazar, New Bombay 400 705 *Tel:* (022) 27890977 *Fax:* (022) 27891930

## Navakarnataka Publications (P) Ltd
Embassy Centre, 11 Crescent Rd, Kumara Park East, PB 5159, Bangalore, Karnataka 560001
*Tel:* (080) 22203580; (080) 22203581; (080) 22203582 *Fax:* (080) 22203582
*E-mail:* nkp@bgl.vsnl.net.in
*Web Site:* www.navakarnatakabooks.com
*Cable:* BOOKCENTRE
*Key Personnel*
Man Dir: R S Rajaram
Founded: 1960
Subscriptions, publications & distribution.
Type of Business: Distributor, Exporter, Importer, Major Independent Bookseller, Wholesaler
*Branch Office(s)*
5th Main, Gandhinagar, Bangalore, Karnataka 560009 *Tel:* (080) 22251382
Moquaddam Trade Centre, Station Rd, Gulbarga, Karnataka 585102 *Tel:* (08472) 224302
K S R Road, Mangalore, Karnataka 575001 *Tel:* (0824) 2441016
Ramaswamy Circle, Mysore, Karnataka 570024 *Tel:* (0821) 2424094

## Oxford & IBH Publishing Co Pvt Ltd
66 Janpath, New Delhi 110001
*Tel:* (011) 321035
*E-mail:* oxfordpubl@axcess.net.in *Cable:* INDAMER
*Key Personnel*
Man Dir: Gulab Primlani
Founded: 1921
Distributing agents for FAO, ICAO, OECD, IDRC.
Type of Business: Exporter, Importer, Major Independent Bookseller, Wholesaler
*Owned by:* Oxford & IBH Publishing Co Pvt Ltd
*Branch Office(s)*
17 Park St, Kolkata 700016

## Popular Book Depot
217 Raja Rammohan Roy Marg, Mumbai 400 007
*Tel:* (022) 382 9401; (022) 382 6762
*Key Personnel*
Partner: Manmohan S Bhatkal *E-mail:* bhatkal@vsnl.com
Founded: 1924
Distribution of books, journals & educational aids.
Type of Business: Exporter, Importer
*Branch Office(s)*
Subscription Division, Saraswati Mandir, Jaganath Shankarshet Rd, Mumbai *Tel:* (022) 3879402
*Bookshop(s):* Nehru Planetarium, Worli, Mumbai 400018 *E-mail:* bhatkal@vsnl.com

## Prints India
Prints House, 11 Darya Ganj, New Delhi 110 002
*Tel:* (011) 3268645 *Fax:* (011) 3275542
*Telex:* 31-61087 *Cable:* INDOLOGY
*Key Personnel*
Contact: V K Gupta
Founded: 1966
Also subscription agent & publisher.
Type of Business: Distributor, Exporter, Major Book Chain Headquarters, Major Independent Bookseller, Wholesaler
*Owned by:* MD Publications Pvt Ltd Co, MD House, 11 Darya Ganj, New Delhi 110 002

## Rupa & Co
7/16 Ansari Rd, Darya Ganj, New Delhi 110 002

Mailing Address: PO Box 7071, Daryaganj, New Delhi 110 002
*Tel:* (011) 23272161; (011) 23270260 *Fax:* (011) 23277294
*E-mail:* rupa@ndb.vsnl.net.in
*Telex:* 3166641 *Cable:* RUPANCO
*Key Personnel*
Man Dir: D Mehra
Also acts as publisher.
Type of Business: Distributor, Exporter, Importer, Wholesaler
*Branch Office(s)*
94 South Malaka, Allahabad
G1 & 2 Ghaswalla Tower, P G Solanki Path, Off Lamington Rd, Near Minerva Cinema, Mumbai 400 007

## Scientific Book Agency
49/13, Hindusthan Park, Calcutta 70029
Mailing Address: PO Box 239, Kolkata 700001
*Tel:* (033) 2292915; (033) 24642206; (033) 24638273
*Key Personnel*
Editor: J Sinha; Mrs Prakriti Sinha
Founded: 1954
Also acts as publisher.
Type of Business: Distributor, Exporter, Importer, Major Independent Bookseller, Wholesaler
*Parent Company:* J Sinha Publishers

## R R Sheth & Co
PO Box 4060, Ashram Rd, Riverside, Ahmedabad 380009
*Tel:* (079) 5356573
*E-mail:* chintan@rrsheth.com
*Web Site:* www.rrsheth.com
*Key Personnel*
Proprietor: Bhagatbhai Bhuralal Sheth *Tel:* (022) 6183182
Export Manager: P V Katira
Founded: 1926
Gujarati & Hindi books, also publisher.
Type of Business: Wholesaler
*Branch Office(s)*
Opp Phuvara, Gandhi Marg, Ahmedabad 380001 *Tel:* (079) 5356573

## Star Publications (P) Ltd
4/5 B Asaf Ali Rd, New Delhi 110002
*Tel:* (011) 328 6757; (011) 23258993; (011) 326 1696; (011) 326 8651 *Fax:* (011) 23273335; (011) 648 1565
*E-mail:* starpub@satyam.net.in
*Web Site:* www.starpublic.com *Cable:* STARPUBLIS
*Key Personnel*
Man Dir: Mr Amarnath Varma
All types of Indian Books, in all Indian languages & English
Also acts as publisher.
Type of Business: Distributor, Exporter

## Super Book House
Sind Chambers, Shahid Bhagat Singh Rd, Colaba, Mumbai, Maharashtra 400 005
*Tel:* (022) 2830560 *Fax:* (022) 2834452
*Telex:* 011-83850
*Key Personnel*
Contact: Shoaib S Ranalui; M S Lehri
*Branch Office(s)*
5-8-548/A, 1st floor, Arastu Trust Bldg, Abid Rd, Hyderabad 500 001 *Tel:* (040) 203123
27/25 Shakti Nagar, New Delhi 110 007 *Tel:* (040) 203123 *Fax:* (040) 203724
*Bookshop(s):* Ideas, 1st floor, Doli Chambers, Next to Strand Cinema, Mumbai 400005

## TBI Publishers' Distributors
M-33, Connaught Place, New Delhi 110 001
*Tel:* (011) 3325247 *Fax:* (011) 3325247

*Key Personnel*
Contact: Ravi Sabharwal
Founded: 1985
Type of Business: Distributor, Importer, Wholesaler
*Branch Office(s)*
46 Housing Society, South Extension I, New Delhi 110 001 *Tel:* (011) 4632903

## N M Tripathi Pvt Ltd Publishers & Booksellers
164 Shamaldas Gandhi Marg, Mumbai 400002
*Tel:* (022) 22013651; (022) 22050048
*Key Personnel*
Man Dir: Kartik R Tripathi
Founded: 1888
Only Gujrati literature & publications. Gujrati is a local Indian language.

## UBS Publishers' Distributors Pvt Ltd
5 Ansari Rd, New Delhi 110002
Mailing Address: PO Box 7015, New Delhi 110002
*Tel:* (011) 23273601; (011) 23266646 *Fax:* (011) 23276593; (011) 23274261
*E-mail:* ubspd@ubspd.com
*Web Site:* www.gobookshopping.com *Cable:* ALLBOOKS
*Key Personnel*
Chairman: Mr C M Chawla
Man Dir: Mr Sukumar Das *Tel:* (011) 3276585 *E-mail:* sdas@ubspd.com
Dir: M K Kalsi *Tel:* (011) 3245477 *E-mail:* mkkalsi@ubspd.com
General Manager, Export Marketing: Amrit Sharma *Tel:* (011) 3271485 *E-mail:* alsharma@ubspd.com
Founded: 1963
Type of Business: Distributor, Exporter, Importer, Wholesaler
*Branch Office(s)*
10 First Main Rd, PO Box 9713, Gandhi, Nagar, Bangalore 560 009 *Tel:* (080) 2253903; (080) 2263901; (080) 2263902 *Fax:* (080) 2263904 *E-mail:* ubspdbng@bgl.vsnl.net.in
143, M P Nagar, Zone 1, Bhopal 462011 *Tel:* (0755) 5203183; (0755) 5203193; (0755) 2555228 *Fax:* (0755) 2555285 *E-mail:* ubspdbhp@sancharnet.in
No 60, Nelson Manickam Rd, Aminji Karai, Chennai 600029 *Tel:* (044) 3746222; (044) 3746351 *Fax:* (044) 3746287 *E-mail:* ubspd@che.ubspd.com
No 40/7940, Convent Rd, Ernakulam 682035 *Tel:* (0484) 2353901; (0484) 2363905 *Fax:* (0484) 2365511
8/1-B, Chowringhee Lane, Kolkata 700 016 *Tel:* (033) 22521821; (033) 22522910; (033) 22529473 *Fax:* (033) 22523027 *E-mail:* ubspdcal@cal.vsnl.net.in
Halwasiya Court Annexe, 1st floor, 11 M G Marg, Hazratganj, Lucknow 226001 *Tel:* (0522) 2294133; (0522) 2294134 *Fax:* (0522) 2294133 *E-mail:* ubspdlko@lko.ubspd.com
Apeejay Chambers, 2nd floor, 5 Wallace St, Fort, Mumbai 400001 *Tel:* (022) 56376922; (022) 56376923 *Fax:* (022) 56376921 *E-mail:* ubspdmum@mum.ubspd.com
5A, Rajendra Nagar, Patna 800016 *Tel:* (0612) 2672856; (0612) 2673973; (0612) 2686170 *Fax:* (0612) 2686169 *E-mail:* ubspdpat1@sancharnet.in

## Universal Book Shop
c/o Chugh Publications, PB No 101, 2 Starchey Rd, Civil Lines, Allahabad 21101
*Tel:* (0532) 603012
*Key Personnel*
Partner: Ramesh Chugh
*Owned by:* Chugh Publications

## Universal Book Traders

80 Gokhale Market, Opp Tishazari Courts, Delhi
110 054
*Tel:* (011) 2396 1288; (011) 2391 1966; (011)
2399 0487 *Fax:* (011) 2392 4152; (011) 2745
9023
*E-mail:* unilaw@vsnl.com
*Web Site:* www.unilawbooks.com
*Key Personnel*
Partner: Manish Arora; M G Arora; Pradeep
Arora; Sanjeev Arora
Founded: 1956
Type of Business: Distributor, Exporter, Importer,
Major Independent Bookseller, Wholesaler
*Branch Office(s)*
C-27, Connaught Pl, (between Odeon & Plaza)
Middle Circle, New Delhi 110 001 *Tel:* (011)
2341 6277; (011) 2341 8671 *Fax:* (011) 2341
8014

## Visalaandhra Publishing House

4-1-435, Vignana Bhavan, Bank St, Hyderabad
500 001
*Tel:* (040) 4744580 *Fax:* (040) 4735905
*E-mail:* visalaandhraph@yahoo.com
*Key Personnel*
Manager: Mr Rajeswara Rao
Founded: 1953
Publishing & marketing of general books in Tel-
ugu language.
Type of Business: Distributor, Importer, Whole-
saler
*Branch Office(s)*
Sultan Bazar, Hyderabad 500 095 *Tel:* (040)
24751462
Visalaandhra Book House, College Rd, Anantapur
515001 *Tel:* (08554) 220614
Visalaandhra Book House, Arundelpet, Guntur
522 002 *Tel:* (0863) 2233297
Visalaandhra Book House, Main Rd, Han-
makonda 506 001 *Tel:* (08712) 2577156
Visalaandhra Book House, Bank St, Hyderabad
500001 *Tel:* (040) 24602946
Visalaandhra Book House, Kakinada 533 001
*Tel:* (0884) 2378992
Visalaandhra Book House, Gandhi Rd, Tirupati
517 501 *Tel:* (08574) 2222475
Visalaandhra Book House, Karl Marx Rd, Vi-
jayawada 520002 *Tel:* (0866) 2572949
Visalaandhra Book House, Main Rd, Visakhapat-
nam 530002 *Tel:* (0891) 2502534

# Indonesia

## C V Toko Buku Tropen

Jl Pasar Baru 113, Jakarta 10710
Mailing Address: Tromol Pos 3604, Jakarta
10036
*Tel:* (021) 381 1669; (021) 381 3543; (021) 380
5938 *Fax:* (021) 380 0566
*E-mail:* tropen@cbn.net.id
*Telex:* 44122 Tropen IA *Cable:* TROPEN
*Key Personnel*
General Manager: Mr Yohan Slamet
Man Dir: Jani Dipokusumo
Founded: 1939
Type of Business: Distributor, Exporter, Importer,
Major Independent Bookseller, Wholesaler

## Effendi Harahap Bookstore

Jl Abimanyu Raya 17-19, Semarang
*Tel:* (024) 3544694

## Gramedia Bookshop

109 Jln Palmerah, Selatan 22, Lantai IV, Jakarta
10270
*Tel:* (021) 5300545 *Fax:* (021) 5486085

*Key Personnel*
General Manager: Indra Gunawan
*Owned by:* PT Gramedia
*Branch Office(s)*
Jl Merdeka 43, Bandung
Jl Melawai IV/13, Jakarta
Jl Pintu Air 72, Jakarta
Jl Jendral Sudirman 56, Jogjakarta
Jl Basuki Rachmat 95, Surabaya

## PT BPK Gunung Mulia (Gunung Mulia
Christian Publishing House Limited Company)

Jl Kwitang 22-23, Jakarta Pusat 10420
*Tel:* (021) 3901208 *Fax:* (021) 3901633
*Fax on Demand:* (021) 3901633
*E-mail:* corp.off@bpkgm.com
*Web Site:* www.bpkgm.com
*Key Personnel*
President & Dir: Ichsan Gunawan
*E-mail:* ichsan@bpkgm.com
Finance & Administration Dir: Viveka Nanda
Leimena
Founded: 1951
Also publisher & printer.
Membership(s): CBA.
Type of Business: Distributor, Importer, Major
Book Chain Headquarters, Major Independent
Bookseller
*Owned by:* PT BPK Gunung Mulia
*Branch Office(s)*
Istana Trade Center, Kosambi Kav G21, Jl
Baranangsiang, Bandung 40122 *Tel:* (022)
4222182; (022) 4262134 *Fax:* (022) 4262134
*E-mail:* bandung@bpkgm.com
Jl Cendrawasih 267 B-C-D, Makassar, South Su-
lawesi 90134 *Tel:* (0411) 853586 *Fax:* (0411)
855717 *E-mail:* makassar@bpkgm.com
Jl Nibung II/78, Komp Medan Plaza, Medan
20112 *Tel:* (061) 4567973 *Fax:* (061) 4567973
*E-mail:* medan@bpkgm.com
Jl Sektor I, Blok C1 No 3-4, Bumi Serpong
Damai, Serpong 15310 *Tel:* (021) 5377179
*Fax:* (021) 5377179 *E-mail:* serpong@bpkgm.
com
Jl Genteng Besar No 28, Surabaya, East Java
60275 *Tel:* (031) 5342534 *Fax:* (031) 546884
*E-mail:* surabaya@bpkgm.com

## PT Indira

Jln Borobudur 20, Jakarta
*Tel:* (021) 3148868; (021) 3904290 *Fax:* (021)
3929373
*E-mail:* indirawb@mweb.co.id
Importers of General/Trade books & Educa-
tional/Scientific/Technical books & textbooks.
Library suppliers to foreign libraries of Indone-
sian printed books; also publisher.
Type of Business: Distributor
*Branch Office(s)*
Jogjakarta
*Bookshop(s):* JLn Borobudur 20, Jakarta

## Java Books

PT Wira Mandala Pustaka, Kepala Cading Kiram
Blok A-14 No 17, Jakarta 14240
*Tel:* (021) 4515351 (Hunting) *Fax:* (021) 4534987
*E-mail:* mndl@indo.net.id
*Key Personnel*
Contact: Eric Oey; Johannes Minarwan; Judo
Suwidji
Founded: 1985
Type of Business: Distributor, Importer
*Branch Office(s)*
Bali
Bandung
Jakarta
Lombok
Medan
Surabaya
Ujung Pandang
Yogyakarta

## Pembimbing Masa PT

Pusat Perdagangan Senen, Blok 1, Lantai IV No
2, Jakarta Pusat
Mailing Address: PO Box 3281, Jakarta Pusat
*Tel:* (021) 367645
Bookshop, subscription agency.
Type of Business: Importer
*Owned by:* Pembimbing Masa PT
*Branch Office(s)*
Jl Raya Pajajaran 7, Bogor

## PT Pradnya Paramita

Jln Bunga No 8 A Matraman, Jakarta 13140
*Tel:* (021) 8583369 *Fax:* (021) 8583369
*Cable:* PRADNYA JKT
*Key Personnel*
General Manager: Soehardjo
Administration Manager: W Moedjiono
Marketing Manager: M N Supomo
Production Manager: R E S Bujung
Also publisher.
*Branch Office(s)*
Jl Kyai Maja 2A, Kebayoran Baru, Jakarta 12120,
India

# Islamic Republic of Iran

## Nayiri Bookshop

1022 Enghelab Ave, Tehran 11339
Mailing Address: PO Box 11365-4631, Tehran
11339
*Tel:* (021) 677578; (021) 7536802; (021) 7537029
*Fax:* (021) 677578
*Key Personnel*
President: Sebouh Amirkhanian
Vice President: Mrs Seda Hartounian
Founded: 1931
Printing & Publishing of Magazines, Newspapers,
in many languages, Greeting Cards, Gregorian-
Armenian Art Calendars.
Type of Business: Distributor, Exporter, Importer,
Major Independent Bookseller, Wholesaler

# Ireland

**AIS**, see Bord na Gaeilge

## Book Stop

Dun Laoghaire Shopping Centre, Dun Laoghaire,
Dublin
*Tel:* (01) 2809917 *Fax:* (01) 2844863
*E-mail:* bookstop@indigo.ie
*Key Personnel*
Manager: John Davey
*Branch Office(s)*
Blackrock Shopping Centre, Blackrock, Co
Dublin *Tel:* (01) 2832193 *Fax:* (01) 2782796
*E-mail:* bookstopbr@indigo.ie
Craysfort Park, Blackrock Teachers Center

## Bord na Gaeilge

Formerly AIS
7 Merrion Sq, Dublin 2
*Tel:* (01) 6616522 *Fax:* (01) 6612378
Type of Business: Distributor

## The Columba Bookservice Ltd

55A Spruce Ave, Stillorgan Industrial Park,
Blackrock, Dublin

Tel: (01) 2942556 Fax: (01) 2942564
E-mail: info@columba.ie
Web Site: www.columba.ie
Key Personnel
Sales Dir: Cecilia West E-mail: west@columba.ie
Founded: 1986
Type of Business: Distributor

**Eason & Son Ltd**
80 Middle Abbey St, Dublin 1
Tel: (01) 858-3800 Fax: (01) 858-3806
E-mail: info@eason.ie
Web Site: www.eason.ie
Telex: 32566
Key Personnel
Chairman: Michael Ryder
Man Dir: Gordon Bolton
Founded: 1856
45 outlets in both the Republic of Ireland &
   Northern Ireland.
Type of Business: Distributor, Importer, Major
   Book Chain Headquarters, Major Independent
   Bookseller, Wholesaler

**Gill & Macmillan Distribution**
10 Hume Ave, Park West, Dublin 12
Tel: (01) 500 9500 Fax: (01) 500 9596
E-mail: sales@gillmacmillan.ie
Web Site: www.gillmacmillan.ie
Key Personnel
Sales Manager: Paul Neilan E-mail: pneilan@
   gillmacmillan.ie
Type of Business: Distributor
Owned by: Gill & Macmillan Ltd

**Greene's Bookshop Ltd**
16 Clare St, Dublin 2
Tel: (01) 6762554 Fax: (01) 6789091
E-mail: info@greenesbookshop.com
Web Site: www.greenesbookshop.com
Key Personnel
Man Dir: David H Pembrey Tel: (01) 6760476
   E-mail: dave@greenesbookshop.com
Dir & Financial Controller: Diarmuid Byrne
   E-mail: diarmuuid@greenesbookshop.com
Secondhand & Antiquarian Books: Fred Collins
   E-mail: fred@greenesbookshop.com
Library & Special Order Dept: Catherine Boyd
   E-mail: catherine@greenesbookshop.com
Founded: 1843
New & secondhand booksellers.
Type of Business: Major Independent Bookseller

**Hodges Figgis & Co**
56-58 Dawson St, Dublin 2
Tel: (01) 6774754 Fax: (01) 6792810; (01)
   6793402
E-mail: books@hfiggis.ir
Key Personnel
Manager: Walter Pohli
Deputy Manager: Joseph Collins
Bookstall, National Institute of Higher Education,
   Dublin 9.
Owned by: EMI Group
Bookshop(s): Dublin City University, Dublin 9

**The Library Shop**
Trinity College, College St, Dublin 2
Tel: (01) 608 1000 Fax: (01) 6081016
E-mail: library.shop@tcd.ie
Web Site: www.tcd.ie/library/shop/
Telex: 93782
Key Personnel
Manager: J G Duffy Tel: (01) 608 1650
   E-mail: jduffy@tcd.ie
Contact: Paul Corrigan E-mail: paul.corrigan@
   tcd.ie
Type of Business: Major Independent Bookseller

**O'Mahony & Co Ltd**
120 O'Connell St, Limerick

Tel: (061) 418155 Fax: (061) 414558
E-mail: info@omahonys.ie
Web Site: www.omahonys.ie
Key Personnel
Chairman: David O'Mahony
Man Dir: Frank O'Mahony E-mail: frank.
   omahony@omahonys.ie
Founded: 1902
School & library suppliers.
Type of Business: Major Independent Bookseller
Branch Office(s)
Merchant Square, Ennis, Co Clare Tel: (065)
   6828355 Fax: (065) 6820074 E-mail: ennis.
   branch@omahonys.ie
University of Limerick Bookshop, Plassey Tech-
   nological Park, Limerick Tel: (061) 202048
   Fax: (061) 335147 E-mail: university.branch@
   omahonys.ie
Castle St, Tralee, Co Kerry Tel: (066) 7122266
   Fax: (066) 7129442 E-mail: tralee.branch@
   omahonys.ie

**Veritas Co Ltd**
Veritas House, 7-8 Lower Abbey St, Dublin 1
Tel: (01) 878 8177 Fax: (01) 874 4913
E-mail: sales@veritas.ie
Web Site: www.veritas.ie
Key Personnel
Dir: Maura Hyland
Sales & Operations Manager: Maureen Sanders
Owned by: The Catholic Communications Insti-
   tute of Ireland
Branch Office(s)
Carey's Lane, Cork Tel: (021) 425 1255
   Fax: (021) 427 9165
Butcher St, Derry BT48 6HL Tel: (028) 71 266
   888 Fax: (028) 71 365 120
Unit 309, Blanchardstown Centre, Dublin 15
   Tel: (01) 8864030 Fax: (01) 8864031
83 O'Connell St, Ennis, Co Clare Tel: (065) 682
   8696 Fax: (065) 682 0176
13 Lower Main St, Letterkenny, Co Donegal
   Tel: (074) 91 24814 Fax: (074) 91 22716
16-18 Park St, Monaghan, Co Monaghan
   Tel: (047) 84077 Fax: (047) 84019
Adelaide St, Sligo Tel: (071) 91 61800 Fax: (071)
   91 60121

# Israel

**Academon Publishing House**
PO Box 24130, Jerusalem
Tel: (02) 5811326 Fax: (02) 5811329
Web Site: www.academon.co.il
Key Personnel
Import Manager: Richard Sherman
   E-mail: richard@academon.co.il
Founded: 1952
Academic & general bookstore chain serving He-
   brew University.
Type of Business: Importer, Major Book Chain
   Headquarters

**Librairie Francaise Alcheh**
55 Nahalat Benjamin St, 65163 Tel Aviv
Mailing Address: PO Box 1550, Tel Aviv
Tel: (03) 5604173 Fax: (03) 6 994526
E-mail: alcheh@zahav.net.il
Key Personnel
Man Dir: Yohanan Djerassi
Founded: 1939
French & English Books.
Type of Business: Major Book Chain Headquar-
   ters
Branch Office(s)
30, Jaffa Rd, Jerusalem
55 Nachlat Banyamin St, 68020 Tel Aviv-Jaffa
   Tel: (03) 5609817 Fax: (03) 5606218

**Books International**
1204/1 Grofit St (Commercial Center), Eilat
Mailing Address: PO Box 1950, Eilat 88000
Tel: (08) 633 0205 Fax: (08) 633 0204
E-mail: info@booksinternational.com
Web Site: www.booksinternational.com
Key Personnel
Man Dir: Shulamit Koretz
Exporter of Israeli books.
Type of Business: Distributor, Exporter

**Eric Cohen Books Ltd**
27 Hata'asia St, Ra'anana 43650
Mailing Address: PO Box 2325, Ra'anana 43650
Tel: (09) 747 8000 Fax: (09) 747 8001
E-mail: info@ecb.co.il
Web Site: www.ecb.co.il
Key Personnel
Man Dir: Eric Cohen

**Dyonon/Papyrus Publishing House of the
   Tel-Aviv**
Tel Aviv University, Entin Plaza, Gate 7, Tel Aviv
   61392
Mailing Address: University Student's Union, PO
   Box 39287, Tel Aviv 61392
Tel: (03) 6410351; (03) 6410352; (03) 6427545
   (head office); (03) 6422667 (import office)
   Fax: (03) 6423149
Telex: 342171 Versy Il attn Dyonon
Key Personnel
General Manager: Eitan Zinger
Import Manager: Rachel Hamo
Founded: 1972
Also publisher.
Type of Business: Distributor, Exporter, Importer,
   Major Book Chain Headquarters, Major Inde-
   pendent Bookseller, Wholesaler
Branch Office(s)
Bar-Ilan University Campus

**F Fischer Book Service**
PO Box 7346, Haifa 31071
Tel: (04) 255830 Fax: (04) 244970
Key Personnel
Manager: F Fischer
Founded: 1941
Type of Business: Importer, Major Independent
   Bookseller

**Yozmot Heiliger Ltd**
PO Box 56055, Tel Aviv 61560
Tel: (03) 5284851 Fax: (03) 5285397
E-mail: books@yozmot.com
Web Site: www.yozmot.com
Key Personnel
Dir: Avi Chamo; Jacob Merynger
Founded: 1989
Subscription center. Specialize in scientific &
   medical books.
Type of Business: Distributor, Exporter, Importer,
   Major Book Chain Headquarters, Major Inde-
   pendent Bookseller, Wholesaler

**Israbook**
Gefen Publishing House, PO Box 36004,
   Jerusalem 91360
Tel: (02) 5380247 Fax: (02) 5388423
E-mail: isragefen@netmedia.net.il
Web Site: www.israelbooks.com
Key Personnel
Publisher: Dror Greenfield; Ilan Greenfield
Founded: 1981
Type of Business: Distributor, Importer, Major
   Book Chain Headquarters, Major Independent
   Bookseller, Wholesaler
Owned by: Greenfield

**Jerusalem Books Ltd**
PO Box 26190, Jerusalem 91261
Tel: (02) 643-3580 Fax: (02) 643 3580

*E-mail:* jerbooks@netmedia.co.il
*Web Site:* www.jerusalembooks.co.il
*Key Personnel*
Contact: Jeffrey Spitzer
Type of Business: Distributor, Exporter

**Lonnie Kahn Ltd**
20 Eliyahu Eitan St, Rishon Lezion 75703
*Tel:* (03) 9518418 *Fax:* (03) 9518415; (03)
  9518416
*E-mail:* lonikahn@netvision.net.il
*Key Personnel*
General Manager: Mr Itamar Karlinski
Founded: 1943
Type of Business: Distributor, Importer, Major
  Independent Bookseller, Wholesaler

**Landsberger**
9 Ben-Yehuda St, Tel Aviv
*Tel:* (03) 5176330 *Fax:* (03) 5222646
*Key Personnel*
Man Dir: Esther Parnes

**Ludwig Mayer Jerusalem Ltd**
4 Shlomzion Hamalka St, 91010 Jerusalem
Mailing Address: PO Box 1174, 91010 Jerusalem
*Tel:* (02) 625-2628 *Fax:* (02) 623-2640
*E-mail:* mayerbks@netvision.net.il
*Key Personnel*
Contact: Marcel Marcus
Founded: 1908
Academic bookstore.
Type of Business: Exporter, Importer

**Michlol Ltd**
Technion, Haifa 32000
*Tel:* (04) 8322970 *Fax:* (04) 8223854
*E-mail:* ws2@isdn.net.il
*Key Personnel*
General Dir: Samuel Weissbach
Import Manager: Daniel Ran *Tel:* (04) 8322970

**Mosad Harav Kook**, see Rav Kook Institute

**Palphot Ltd**
PO Box 2, Herzlia 46100
*Tel:* (09) 9525252 *Fax:* (09) 9525277
*E-mail:* palphot@palphot.com
*Web Site:* www.palphot.com
Founded: 1934
Type of Business: Distributor, Exporter, Importer,
  Wholesaler

**Rav Kook Institute**
Maimon St, Jerusalem 910066
Mailing Address: PO Box 642, Jerusalem 910066
*Tel:* (02) 6526231 *Fax:* (02) 6526968
*E-mail:* mosad-haravkook@neto.bezeqint.net
*Key Personnel*
Chairman: Yehuda Raphael
Executive Dir: Yosef Movshovitz
Founded: 1935
Type of Business: Exporter, Wholesaler

**J Robinson & Co**
31 Nachlat Benyamin St, Tel Aviv 65162
Mailing Address: PO Box 4308, Tel Aviv 61042
*Tel:* (03) 5605461; (03) 5601626 *Fax:* (03)
  5660439
*E-mail:* rob_book@netvision.net.il
*Web Site:* www.robinson.co.il
*Key Personnel*
Owner: Judah Robinson
Man Dir: Yehuda Robinson
Founded: 1889
Also antiquarian bookseller.
Total Titles: 100,000 Print
Type of Business: Exporter

*Bookshop(s):* Safra Tava Baita, 140 Ibn Gvirol St,
  Tel Aviv *Tel:* (03) 6021391; Sfat Em, 54 Ibn
  Gvirol St, Tel Aviv *Tel:* (03) 6961074; Vayikra,
  90 Frishman St, Tel Aviv *Tel:* (03) 5238501

**Rubin Mass Ltd**
PO Box 990, Jerusalem 91009
*Tel:* (02) 627-7863 *Fax:* (02) 627-7864
*E-mail:* rmass@barak.net.il
*Web Site:* www.rubin-mass.com
*Key Personnel*
Man Dir: Mr Oren Mass *E-mail:* rmass@barak.
  net.il
Contact: Ilana Zin
Founded: 1927
Exporter of all Israeli books & periodicals.
Type of Business: Distributor, Exporter, Major
  Independent Bookseller, Wholesaler

**Steimatzky Group Ltd**
11 Hakishon St, 51114 Bnei Brak
Mailing Address: PO Box 1444, 51114 Bnei Brak
*Tel:* (03) 5775777 *Fax:* (03) 5794567
*E-mail:* info@steimatzky.co.il
*Web Site:* www.steimatzky.com
*Key Personnel*
Chairman: Eri M Steimatzky
Founded: 1925
Also publisher & publishers' representative.
Type of Business: Distributor, Exporter, Importer,
  Major Book Chain Headquarters, Wholesaler

**Yavneh Publishing House Ltd**
4 Mazeh St, 65213 Tel Aviv
*Tel:* (03) 6297856 *Fax:* (03) 6293638
*E-mail:* yahneh@attglobal.net
*Key Personnel*
Man Dir: Eliav Cohen
Founded: 1932
Type of Business: Distributor, Exporter, Importer,
  Major Book Chain Headquarters, Major Inde-
  pendent Bookseller, Wholesaler
*Owned by:* Aushalom Orenstein, Nira Prieskel

# Italy

**Libreria All'Accademia di Randi Lorenzo &
  Elena snc**
Via S Lucia 1, 35139 Padova
*Tel:* (049) 8760306 *Fax:* (049) 8751825
*E-mail:* libreria@libreriadraghi.it *Cable:*
  DRAGHI PADOVA
*Key Personnel*
Manager: Lorenzo Randi; Elena Randi
Type of Business: Exporter, Importer, Major
  Book Chain Headquarters, Major Independent
  Bookseller
*Bookshop(s):* Libreria Draghi-Randi, Via Cavour
  17-19, 1, 35122 Padova (established 1850; gen-
  eral bookshop, foreign dept, art books, law,
  finance); Libreria Universitaria, Via 8 Feb-
  braio 10, 35122 Padova *Tel:* (049) 8757244
  (law, literature, university textbooks); Libreria DRAGHI-GALLERIA, Galleria S Lucia 6,
  35122 Padova (children books, guide books,
  dictionary, VHS films, gadgets, law, finance)

**Athesia Buchhandlung**
Via Portici, 41, 39100 Bozen
*Tel:* (0471) 927111 *Fax:* (0471) 927215
*E-mail:* buch@athesia.it
*Web Site:* www.athesiabuch.it
*Telex:* 400161
*Key Personnel*
Head of Library: Peter Matzneller
Founded: 1907

Type of Business: Distributor, Importer, Major
  Book Chain Headquarters, Major Independent
  Bookseller, Wholesaler
*Owned by:* Athesiabuch GmbH
*Branch Office(s)*
Via Torre bianca, 39042 Bressanone *Tel:* (0472)
  837 110 *Fax:* (0472) 838 244 *E-mail:* brixen.
  buch@athesia.it
Via Centrale 4, 39031 Brunico *Tel:* (0474) 413
  200 *Fax:* (0474) 413 225 *E-mail:* bruneck.
  buch@athesia.it
Via Argentiere 21/e, 39100 Bolzano
  *Tel:* (0471) 927 242 *Fax:* (0471) 927 244
  *E-mail:* ferrariauer.buch@athesia.it
Via Portici 186, 39012 Meran *Tel:* (0473) 231
  444 *Fax:* (0473) 231 313 *E-mail:* meran.buch@
  athesia.it
Via Principale 51, 39028 Silandro *Tel:* (0473) 730
  216 *Fax:* (0473) 621 616 *E-mail:* schlanders.
  buch@athesia.it
Citta vecchia 9, 39049 Vipiteno *Tel:* (0472) 765
  300 *Fax:* (0472) 767 240 *E-mail:* sterzing.
  buch@athesia.it

**Casalini Libri**
Via Benedetto da Maiano, Suite 3, 50014 Flo-
  rence
*Tel:* (055) 5018 1 *Fax:* (055) 5018 201
*E-mail:* info@casalini.it
*Web Site:* www.casalini.it
*Key Personnel*
Man Dir: Barbara Casalini *E-mail:* barbara@
  casalini.it; Michele Casalini *E-mail:* michele@
  casalini.it
Dir of Sales & Customer Services: Joachim Bartz
  *E-mail:* jbartz@casalini.it
Also publisher.
Type of Business: Exporter

**Libreria Dante di A M Longo**
Via P Costa, 39, 48100 Ravenna
*Tel:* (0544) 217026 *Fax:* (0544) 217554
*E-mail:* longo-ra@linknet.it
*Web Site:* www.longo-editore.it
*Key Personnel*
Manager: Alfio Longo
Founded: 1950
Type of Business: Exporter, Importer, Major Inde-
  pendent Bookseller
*Owned by:* Angelo Longo Editore

**DEA**, see DEA Diffusione Edizioni
  Anglo-Americane

**DEA Diffusione Edizioni Anglo-Americane**
Sede Legale e Amministrativa, Via Lima, 28,
  00198 Rome
*Tel:* (06) 852121 *Fax:* (06) 8543228
*E-mail:* deanet@deanet.it; info@deanet.it
*Web Site:* www.deanet.it
*Key Personnel*
Contact: Enrico Ligi
Subjects: agriculture, architecture, archaeology,
  arts, astronomy, biology, botany, business,
  chemistry, computer science, earth sciences,
  economics, engineering, environment, fiction,
  finance, geography, history, languages, law,
  library science, literature, management, mathematics, medicine, philosophy, physics, political
  science, psychology, reference, religion, social
  science, sports & travel, veterinary, zoology

**Librerie Feltrinelli SpA**
via Tucidide, 56, 20134 Milan
*Tel:* (02) 7529151; (02) 748151 *Fax:* (02)
  74815339
*E-mail:* info@lafeltrinelli.it
*Web Site:* www.lafeltrinelli.it
*Branch Office(s)*
Piazza Porta Ravegnana 1, Bologna
Via Cavour 12-20, 50129 Florence *Tel:* (055)
  292196
Via Carlo Alberto 2, Turin

**Libreria S F Flaccovio**
di via Ruggiero Settimo, 37, a Palermo
*Tel:* (091) 589442 *Fax:* (091) 331992
*E-mail:* info@flaccovio.com
*Web Site:* www.flaccovio.com
*Key Personnel*
Administrator: Sergio Flaccovio
Manager: Francesco Flaccovio
Founded: 1938
*Owned by:* S F Flaccovio Editore
*Branch Office(s)*
Libreria Dante, Quattro Canti di Citta, a Palermo
*Tel:* (091) 585927 *Fax:* (091) 323103
P zza Vittorio Emanuele Orlando, 15/19, a
Palermo *Tel:* (091) 334323 *Fax:* (091) 6112750
di via Ernesto Basile, 136, a Palermo *Tel:* (091)
420363 *Fax:* (091) 420363
Aeroporto Falcone Borsellino, Punta Raisi
*Tel:* (091) 6525052

**Libreria FMR**
Via Benedetto Croce 38, 80134 Naples
*Tel:* (081) 5802279 *Fax:* (081) 5802279
*E-mail:* commerciale@fmrnapoli.it
*Web Site:* www.fmrnapoli.it
*Key Personnel*
President: Franco Maria Ricci *E-mail:* ricci@
fmrmagazine.it
Contact: Raffaella Russo
*Bookshop(s):* Via Farini 27, Bologna 40124
*Tel:* (051) 231811; Via Delle Donne 412, Flo-
rence 50123 *Tel:* (055) 283312; Via Durini 19,
Milan 20122 *Tel:* (02) 798444; Via Affio 1,
Parma 43100 *Tel:* (0521) 287023; Via Bor-
gognona 48, Rome 00187 *Tel:* (06) 6793466;
Via Del Babbuino 48, Rome *Tel:* (06) 3270126;
Viale Parioli 24, Rome *Tel:* (06) 36001899;
(06) 36001842; Via Carlo Alberto 12, Turin
10123 *Tel:* (011) 5629171

**Gregoriana Libreria Editrice**
Via Roma, 82, 35122 Padova
*Tel:* (049) 657493 *Fax:* (049) 8786435
*E-mail:* seicom@mclink.it
Founded: 1922
Type of Business: Major Independent Bookseller
*Owned by:* Euganea Editoriale Comunicazioni
SRL, Via Roma, 82, 35122 Padova
*Branch Office(s)*
Via Vescovado 33, 35100 Padua
Piazza Duomo 5, 35100 Padua

**Herder Editrice e Libreria**
Piazza Montecitorio 120, 00186 Rome
*Tel:* (06) 679 53 04; (06) 679 46 28 *Fax:* (06)
678 47 51
*E-mail:* distr@herder.it; distr@herder.it
*Web Site:* www.herder.it
*Key Personnel*
Manager: Bettina Bolli
Administration: Paul Hermann Koellner
Founded: 1925
Book commerce, publishing house & distributor.
Type of Business: Distributor, Exporter, Importer,
Major Independent Bookseller

**Ilisso Edizioni di Vanna Fois & CSNC**
Via Guerrazzi 6, 08100 Nuoro
*Tel:* (0784) 33033 *Fax:* (0784) 35413
*E-mail:* ilisso@ilisso.it
*Web Site:* www.ilisso.it
*Key Personnel*
Contact: Tiziana Serra
Founded: 1985
Specialize in art books.
Subjects: Art
*Owned by:* Sebastiano Congiu & Vanna Fois

**Libreria Editrice Minerva**
Vicolodeli Archi 1, 1-06081 Assisi
*Tel:* (075) 812381 *Fax:* (075) 816564

**Opus Libri SRL**
Via della Torretta 16, 50137 Florence
*Tel:* (055) 660833 *Fax:* (055) 670604
*E-mail:* opuslib@dada.it
*Key Personnel*
Contact: Piero Riccetti
Founded: 1980
Type of Business: Distributor, Exporter, Importer,
Major Independent Bookseller, Wholesaler

**Libreria Commissionaria Internazionale di
Raffaele Pancaldi**
Via San Petronio Vecchio n 3, 40125 Bologna
*Tel:* (051) 229466 *Fax:* (051) 229466
*Key Personnel*
Manager: Raffaele Pancaldi
Founded: 1975
Type of Business: Importer, Major Independent
Bookseller, Wholesaler

**Libreria Internazionale Patron**
Via Zamboni, 24, Bologna
*Tel:* (051) 223208 *Fax:* (051) 223208
*Owned by:* Patron Editore SRL

**Libreria Rizzoli della Rizzoli Editore SpA**
Via Mecenate, 91, 20138 Milan
*Tel:* (02) 50951 *Fax:* (02) 5065361
*Key Personnel*
Manager: Aldo Allegri
*Owned by:* R C S Rizzoli Libri SpA
*Branch Office(s)*
Libreria Internazionale Rizzoli SRL, Galleria
Colonna, Largo Chigi 15, Rome *Tel:* (06)
6796641

**Rosenberg e Sellier SpA**
Via Andrea Doria 14, 10123 Turin
*Tel:* (011) 812 76 56 *Fax:* (011) 812 77 44
*Key Personnel*
Proprietor: Ugo Gianni Rosenberg; Elvi Rosen-
berg
International bookseller & subscription agent.
Type of Business: Exporter, Importer

**Rux Guru srl**
Via A Manna, 25/27, 06132 Perugia
*Tel:* (075) 5270257; (075) 5270258 *Fax:* (075)
5288244
*E-mail:* ruxinfo@rux-distribuzione.com
*Web Site:* www.rux-distribuzione.com
*Key Personnel*
President: Gastone Chellini
Administrator: Sara Maria Chellini
Founded: 1989
Distributor of books & didactical material for
learning Italian as a foreign language. Media
formats include audio, books, CD-ROM, online
& video.
Subjects: linguistics
Type of Business: Distributor, Wholesaler

**Libreria Internazionale Sperling e Kupfer**
Via Durazzo, 4, 20134 Milan
*Tel:* (02) 21721-1 *Fax:* (02) 21721-277
*Web Site:* www.sperling.it
*Key Personnel*
Manager: Francesco Bogliari

**Ulrico Hoepli - Libreria Internazionale**
Via Hoepli 5, 20121 Milan
*Tel:* (02) 864871 *Fax:* (02) 8052886; (02) 864322
(library)
*E-mail:* libreria@hoepli.it
*Web Site:* www.hoepli.it *Cable:* HOEPLI MILAN
*Key Personnel*
Manager: Dr Ulrico Carlo Hoepli; Susanna
Schwarz; Roberto Taneggi
Contact: Daniela Grazi

Founded: 1870
*Owned by:* Casa Editrice Libraria Ulrico Hoepli
SpA

# Jamaica

**Bolivar Bookshop**
1D Grove Rd, Kingston 10
*Tel:* (876) 926-8799 *Fax:* (876) 968-1874
*E-mail:* bolivar-jamaica@colis.com
*Key Personnel*
Owner & Manager: Hugh Dunphy
Founded: 1965
Bookshop, Art Gallery & Antique Shop.
*Parent Company:* Jacaranda Holdings Ltd

**Kingston Bookshop Ltd**
74 King St, Kingston
*Tel:* 876-938-0005
*E-mail:* info@kingstonbookshop.com
*Web Site:* www.kingstonbookshop.com *Cable:*
FUTURITY JAMAICA
*Key Personnel*
Chief Executive Officer & Man Dir: Steadman
Fuller
Dir & Administrator: Sonia Fuller
*Branch Office(s)*
The Pavillon Shopping Center, Halfway Tree
Kingston *Tel:* 876-960-5376; 876-968-4591
*Fax:* 876-968-2325
*Bookshop(s):* Postal Corporation Commercial
Centre, Liguanea, Kingston 6 *Tel:* 876-978-
7261 *Fax:* 876-946-0914; The Springs, 17 Con-
stant Spring Rd, Kingston 10 *Tel:* 876-920-
1529; 876-960-7104 *Fax:* 876-968-6277

**Sangster's Book Stores Ltd**
101-103 Water Lane, Kingston
*Tel:* 876-922-3648; 876-922-3640
*Toll Free Tel:* 888-269-2665 *Fax:* 876-922-3813
*E-mail:* info@sangstersbooks.com
*Web Site:* www.sangstersbooks.com
*Key Personnel*
Man Dir: S Kumaraswamy
Publishing & Publisher Representation.
*Owned by:* Gleaner Co Ltd, 7 North St, PO Box
40, Kingston
*Branch Office(s)*
33 King St, Kingston *Tel:* 876-967-1930; 876-
967-1931 *Fax:* 876-967-9776
Mall Plaza, 20 Constant Spring, Kingston 10
*Tel:* 876-926-2271 *Fax:* 876-968-7155
Soverign Centre, 106 Hope Rd, Kingston 6
*Tel:* 876-978-7825
97 Harbour St, Kingston *Tel:* 876-922-3810
*Fax:* 876-922-3813
2 St James St, Montego Bay, St James *Tel:* 876-
952-0319 *Fax:* 876-940-0182
Lot 8 Portmore Plaza, St Catherine *Tel:* 876-704-
5450; 876-704-5371 *Fax:* 876-704-5459
*Bookshop(s):* Springs Plaza, Shop 6, 17 Constant Spring Rd, Kingston 10 *Tel:* 876-926-
1800 *Fax:* 876-968-5516; 28 Barbados Ave,
Kingston 5 *Tel:* 876-950-2489 *Fax:* 876-960-
2490; Spanish Town, Shop 28, 17 Burke Rd, St
Catherine *Tel:* 876-984-5003

# Japan

**Academia Scientific Book Inc**
Shichi Bldg, 2-10-15 Kasuga, Bunkyo-Ku, Tokyo
*Tel:* (03) 3819805 *Fax:* (03) 38128509

*Key Personnel*
Owner: Satoshi Nakai
*Branch Office(s)*
Ohhomachi Hanahata 3-9-21, Tsukuba-City

## Asahiya Shoten Ltd (Booksellers)

Asahi Bldg, 3-17-19 Toyosaki, Kita-ku, Osaka
531-0072
*Tel:* (06) 3131191; (06) 3727251; (06) 3727253
*Fax:* (06) 3755650
*Key Personnel*
President: Takeshi Hayashima

## Bookman's & Co Ltd

Yodogawa Bldg, 3-1-18 toyosaki, Chome 1-18,
Kita-ku, Osaka 531-0072
*Tel:* (06) 6371-4164 *Fax:* (06) 6371-4174
*E-mail:* info@bookmans.co.jp
*Web Site:* www.bookmans.co.jp
*Key Personnel*
President: Mr Mitsunobu Nakamura
Founded: 1967
Art & architecture & graphical, industrial design
photography. Textile, fashion, interior design &
human science.
Subjects: Human Science: Art & Architecture,
Graphic design Industrial Design, Social Sci-
ence
Type of Business: Importer, Wholesaler
*Owned by:* Mr M Nakamura

## Christian Literature Society of Japan, see
Kyobunkan Inc (Christian Literature Society of
Japan)

## France Tosho

1-12-9, Nishi-Shinjuku, Shinjuku-ku, Tokyo 160-
0023
Mailing Address: PO Box 103, Shinjuuku, Tokyo
*Tel:* (03) 3346-0396 *Fax:* (03) 3346-9154
*E-mail:* frtosho@blue.ocn.ne.jp
*Web Site:* www.francetosho.com
*Key Personnel*
Chief of the Purchase Section: Fumisate Konodo
Founded: 1967
Type of Business: Importer, Major Independent
Bookseller, Wholesaler

## Ikubundo Publishing Co Ltd

Hongo 5-30-21, Bunkyo-ku, Tokyo 113-0033
*Tel:* (03) 3814-5571 *Fax:* (03) 3814-5576
*E-mail:* webmaster@ikubundo.com
*Web Site:* www.ikubundo.com

## Japan Publications Trading Co Ltd (Import &
Export)

1-2-1 Sarugaku-cho, Chiyoda-ku, Tokyo 101-0064
*Tel:* (03) 3292-3751 *Fax:* (03) 3292-0410
*E-mail:* jpt@jptco.co.jp
*Web Site:* www.jptco.co.jp
*Key Personnel*
President: Toyohiko Ayamori
Export Dir: Masatoshi Sato
Import Dir: Akira Sugiyama
Founded: 1942
Importer & exporter of general & academic books
& periodicals, language learning textbooks &
materials, audio/visual discs & other general
merchandise. Also deals in rental & manage-
ment of real estate.
Type of Business: Distributor, Exporter, Importer,
Wholesaler
*Sales Office(s):* Maeda Bldg, 5-40-11 Maidashi,
Higashi-ku, Fukuoka 812-0054 *Tel:* (092) 651-
3785 *Fax:* (092) 651-1191 *E-mail:* kyushu@
jptco.co.jp
701 Arai Bldg No 10, 3-5-2 Nishi-Nakajima,
Yodogawa-ku, Osaka 532-0011 *Tel:* (06) 6886-
7177 *Fax:* (06) 6886-7131 *E-mail:* osaka@
jptco.co.jp

## Kaigai Publications Ltd (Kaigai Shuppan
Boeki Kabushiki Kaisha)

2-21 Kanda-Tsukasa-cho, Chiyoda-ku, Tokyo
101-0048
*Tel:* (03) 32924271 *Fax:* (03) 32924278
*E-mail:* admin@kaigai-pub.co.jp *Cable:*
OVERSISPUB TOKYO
Founded: 1949
Type of Business: Importer, Major Independent
Bookseller
*Branch Office(s)*
Sendai
Tsukuba

## Kaigai Shuppan Boeki Kabushiki Kaisha, see
Kaigai Publications Ltd (Kaigai Shuppan Boeki
Kabushiki Kaisha)

## Kinokuniya Co Ltd

3-17-7 Shinjuku, Shinjuku-ku, Tokyo 163-8636
*Tel:* (03) 3354-0131 *Fax:* (03) 3354-0275
*E-mail:* info@kinokuniya.co.jp
*Web Site:* www.kinokuniya.co.jp
*Key Personnel*
President: Osamu Matsubara
Founded: 1927
Also publisher.
Type of Business: Distributor, Exporter, Importer,
Major Book Chain Headquarters, Wholesaler

## KPT InfoTrader Inc

501 Naniwasuji Bldg, 1-20-13, Utsubohonmachi,
Nishi-Ku, Osaka 550-0004
Mailing Address: CPO Box 936, Osaka 530-8694
*Tel:* (06) 6479 7160 *Fax:* (06) 6479 7163
*E-mail:* osaka@infotrader.jp
*Web Site:* www.infotrader.jp
*Key Personnel*
Chief Executive Officer: Yoshitaka Kitao
Chief Operating Officer: Yukichi Ohtsuka
Founded: 1956
Importing books & periodicals from all over the
world, for world-famous enterprises, universi-
ties, government organizations, on firm-order
basis.
Type of Business: Importer
*Branch Office(s)*
Tokyo *Tel:* (03) 5842 3150 *Fax:* (03) 5842 3153
*E-mail:* tokyo@infotrader.jp
Tsukuba *Tel:* (0298) 51 8145 *Fax:* (0298) 52
9873 *E-mail:* tsukuba@infotrader.jp

## Kyobunkan Inc (Christian Literature Society
of Japan)

4-5-1, Chuo-ku, Ginza, Tokyo 104-0061
*Tel:* (03) 3561-8449 *Fax:* (03) 5250-5109
*E-mail:* fbooks@kyobunkwan.co.jp
*Web Site:* www.kyobunkwan.co.jp
*Key Personnel*
Vice President: Hideo Usui
Founded: 1885
Branch offices in Fukuoka, Hiroshima, Kanazawa,
Kobe, Kyoto, London (UK), Nagoya, New
York (USA), Okayama, Osaka, Sapporo,
Sendai, Singapore, Tsukuba, & Yokohama.
Type of Business: Distributor, Importer, Major
Independent Bookseller, Wholesaler

## Maruzen Co Ltd

9-2, Nihombashi 3-chome, Chuo-ku, Tokyo 103-
8244
Mailing Address: PO Box 5050, Tokyo Interna-
tional 100-3191
*Tel:* (03) 3273-6191 *Fax:* (03) 3273-6192
*E-mail:* sd-data@maruzen.co.jp
*Web Site:* www.maruzen.co.jp *Cable:* MARUYA
TOKYO
*Key Personnel*
President: Seishiro Murata
Executive Dir: Atsushi Suzuki
Senior General Manager: Yusaku Takahashi

General Manager, Information Resources
Navigation Division: Tetsuro Konno
*E-mail:* t_konno@maruzen.co.jp
Dir, Information Resources Navigatioin Division:
Nobuji Ebisui
Founded: 1869
Sales of foreign & Japanese books & journals;
scientific information retrieval services; publishing.
Type of Business: Exporter, Importer
*Bookshop(s):* 6F Lumine 42-2 Senju Asahi-
cho, Adachi ku, Tokyo 120-0026 *Tel:* (03)
3879-1861 *Fax:* (03) 3879-1237 *E-mail:* sd-
kitasenjyu@maruzen.co.jp; 1F AER 3-1 Chuou
1, Aoba-ku, Sendai Miyagi 980-6104 *Tel:* (022)
264-0151 *Fax:* (022) 264-0112 *E-mail:* sd-
aer@maruzen.co.jp; 4F Fashion Dome 141,
11-1 Ichibancho 4, Aoba-ku, Sendai Miyagi
980-0811 *Tel:* (022) 268-8231 *Fax:* (022) 268-
8232 *E-mail:* sd-141@maruzen.co.jp; 5F Fu-
jisaki Dept Store, 2-17 Ichibancho 3, Aoba-
ku, Sendai Miyagi 980-8652 *Tel:* (022) 221-
5001 *Fax:* (022) 221-5039; 4F DUO-1 6-2
Atsubetsu Chuo 2 Ave 5, Atsubetsu-ku, Sapporo 004-8515 *Tel:* (011) 890-2586 *Fax:* (011)
895-7251 *E-mail:* sd-duo@maruzen.co.jp;
2 & 4F Marunouchi Bldg 4-1 Marunouchi
2, Chiyoda-ku, Tokyo 100-6304 *Tel:* (03)
5220-7551 *Fax:* (03) 5220-7556 *E-mail:* sd-
maru@maruzen.co.jp; 1F Segawa Bldg, 2-8
Kanda Surugadai, Chiyoda-ku, Tokyo 101-
0062 *Tel:* (03) 3295-5581 *Fax:* (03) 3295-
6036 *E-mail:* sd-ochanomizu@maruzen.co.jp;
2 & 3F Fukuoka Bldg, 11-17 Tenjin 1, Chuo-
ku, Fukuoka 810-0001 *Tel:* (092) 731-9000
*Fax:* (092) 731-8996 *E-mail:* sd-fukuoka@
maruzen.co.jp; 3-2 Bakurocho 3, Chuo-ku, Osaka 541-0059 *Tel:* (06) 6251-2700 *Fax:* (06)
6245-3742 *E-mail:* sd-osaka@maruzen.co.jp;
3-8 Minami-Ichijo Nishi, Chuo-ku, Sapporo
060-0061 *Tel:* (011) 241-7251 *Fax:* (011)
241-6015 *E-mail:* sd-sapporo@maruzen.co.
jp; 7F Isetan Dept Store 41-2, Miyamachi
1, Fuchu, Tokyo 183-0023 *Tel:* (042) 351-
9066 *Fax:* (042) 351-9067 *E-mail:* sd-fuchu@
maruzen.co.jp; 6F May-One 6-1 Sunayamacho,
Hamamatsu Shizuoka 430-0926 *Tel:* (0534)
57-4811 *Fax:* (0534) 57-4852 *E-mail:* sd-
mayone@maruzen.co.jp; 2F Aero Plaza
Takashimaya Senshu Airport-North No 1, Izu-
misano, Osaka 549-0001 *Tel:* (0724) 56-8155
*Fax:* (0724) 56-8157; 6F Takashimaya Station
Mall, 1-1 Suehirocho, Kashiwa, Chiba 277-
8550 *Tel:* (04) 7147-9836 *Fax:* (04) 7148-
2295 *E-mail:* sd-kashiwa@maruzen.co.jp;
9F Usui Dept Store 13-1, Nakamachi, Ko-
riyama, Fukushima 963-8004 *Tel:* (024) 935-
8034 *Fax:* (024) 935-8034; 6F Kawatoku
Dept Store 1-10-1, Saien, Morioka, Iwate
020-8655 *Tel:* (019) 621-8844 *Fax:* (019)
621-8845 *E-mail:* sd-morioka@maruzen.
co.jp; 3F Ark Mori Bldg 12-32 Akasaka 1,
Minato-ku, Tokyo 107-6003 *Tel:* (03) 3589-
1772 *Fax:* (03) 3589-2247 *E-mail:* sd-ark@
maruzen.co.jp; Takoyakushi-Agaru, Kawara-
machi Ave, Nakagyo-ku, Kyoto 604-8033
*Tel:* (075) 241-2161 *Fax:* (075) 241-0653
*E-mail:* sd-kyoto@maruzen.co.jp; 2-7 Sakae 3,
Naka-ku, Nagoya Aichi 460-0008 *Tel:* (052)
261-2251 *Fax:* (052) 264-4400 *E-mail:* sd-
nagoya@maruzen.co.jp; 5F Matsuzakaya-South,
16-1 Sakae 3, Naka-ku, Nagoya Aichi 460-
8430 *Tel:* (052) 264-2730 *Fax:* (052) 264-2735
*E-mail:* sd-nmatsu@maruzen.co.jp; 5F Ocat
Mall, Osaka City Air Terminal Bldg, 4-1 Mi-
nato 1, Naniwa-ku, Osaka 556-0017 *Tel:* (06)
6635-3225 *Fax:* (06) 6635-3224 *E-mail:* sd-
ocat@maruzen.co.jp; 2 & 3F Block-B 7-1
Yatsu 7, Narashino, Chiba 275-0026 *Tel:* (047)
470-8311 *Fax:* (047) 470-8316 *E-mail:* sd-
tsudanuma@maruzen.co.jp; B1F Symphony
Bldg 5-1, Omotecho 1, Okayama 700-0822
*Tel:* (086) 233-4650 *Fax:* (086) 233-4610
*E-mail:* sd-symphony@maruzen.co.jp; 3F

Passenger Terminal Senshu Airport-Central No 1 Tajiricho, Sen-nan-gun, Osaka 549-0011 *Tel:* (0724) 56-8155 *Fax:* (0724) 56-8157 *E-mail:* sd-kanku@maruzen.co.jp; 2 & 7F Tokyu Dept Store, 24-1 Dogenzaka 2, Shibuya-ku, Tokyo 150-8019 *Tel:* (03) 3477-3524 *Fax:* (03) 5428-3802; 8F Keio Dept Store, 1-4 Nishi-Shinjuku 1, Shinjuku-ku, Tokyo 160-0023 *Tel:* (03) 5321-4685 *Fax:* (03) 5321-4686 *E-mail:* sd-shinjyuku@maruzen.co.jp; 4F Shin-Shizuoka Center 1-1 Takajo 1, Shizuoka 420-0839 *Tel:* (054) 255-1851 *Fax:* (054) 255-2028 *E-mail:* sd-shizuoka@maruzen.co.jp; 6F Isetan Dept Store, 2-5-1 Akebono-Cho, Tachikawa, Tokyo 190-0012 *Tel:* (042) 540-7355 *Fax:* (042) 540-7356 *E-mail:* sd-tachikawa@maruzen.co.jp; B1F Tameike-Sanno Station, Tokyo *Tel:* (03) 5114-0604 *Fax:* (03) 5114-0605; 1F Ikspiari 1-4, Maihama, Urayasu, Chiba 279-8529 *Tel:* (047) 305-5808 *Fax:* (047) 305-5765 *E-mail:* sd-ikspiari@maruzen.co.jp

**Nankodo Co Ltd**
42-6, Hongo 3-Chome, Bunkyo-ku, Tokyo 113-8410
*Tel:* (03) 3811-7140 *Fax:* (03) 3811-7265
*E-mail:* yoshohp@nankodo.co.jp
*Web Site:* www.nankodo.co.jp
*Key Personnel*
President: Nobuhiko Hongo
Executive Dir, Foreign Division: Masao Takahashi
Founded: 1879
Also medical publishers.
Type of Business: Distributor, Importer, Wholesaler

**Nauka Ltd**
1-36-7 E Ikebukuro, Toshima-ku, Tokyo 170-0013
*Tel:* (03) 3981-5261 *Fax:* (03) 3981-5361
*E-mail:* tokyo@nauka.co.jp
*Web Site:* www.nauka.co.jp
*Telex:* 524432 *Cable:* NAUKAINCO TOKYO
*Key Personnel*
President: Shuichi Sugawara
Founded: 1952
Type of Business: Distributor, Exporter, Importer, Major Book Chain Headquarters, Wholesaler
*Bookshop(s):* 1-34 Kanda-Jinbocho, Chiyoda-ku, Tokyo 101-0051 *Tel:* (03) 5259-2711 *Fax:* (03) 5259-2714 *E-mail:* shop@nauka.co.jp

**Nihon-Shoseki Ltd**
4-14-24 Koishikawa-ku, Tokyo 112-0002
*Tel:* (03) 3813-8111 *Fax:* (03) 3818-5665
*Web Site:* www.nihon-shoseki.co.jp
*Key Personnel*
President: Humiya Yamada
Purchasing Manager: I Tamaki
Founded: 1959
Scientific backfiles, rare & modern books, microforms & electromedias.
Membership(s): Japan Association of International Publications.
Type of Business: Distributor, Exporter, Wholesaler
*Branch Office(s)*
Toyko

**Nippon Shuppan Hanbai Inc**
4-3 Kandasurugadai, Chiyoda-ku, Tokyo 101-0062
*Tel:* (03) 3233-1111 *Fax:* (03) 3292-8521
*E-mail:* info@nippon.co.jp
*Web Site:* www.nippon.co.jp
*Key Personnel*
Chairman: Tetsuo Suga
President & Chief Executive Officer: Naomasa Turuta
Executive Vice President, Finance & Human Resources: Katsumi Shibata

Founded: 1949
Type of Business: Distributor, Exporter, Importer

**Osaka Oviss Inc**
Central PO Box 292, Osaka 530-8692
*Tel:* (06) 352 7090 *Fax:* (06) 352 8898
*E-mail:* ovissbk@osk.3web.ne.jp
Type of Business: Importer, Major Independent Bookseller

**Sanseido Bookstore Ltd**
1-1 Kanda Jimbocho, Chiyoda-ku, Tokyo 101
*Tel:* (03) 3233 3312 *Fax:* (03) 3291 3033
*E-mail:* fbook_stock@mail.books-sanseido.co.jp
*Web Site:* www.books-sanseido.co.jp
*Key Personnel*
President: Tadao Kamei
Dir, Sales Dept: Ryosuke Suzuki
Manager: Osamu Suzuki
Founded: 1881
Membership(s): Japan Association of International Publications.
Type of Business: Importer, Major Book Chain Headquarters, Major Independent Bookseller

**Sanyo Shuppan Boeki Co Inc**
Taiko Bldg 3F 11-16, 3 Nishishinjuku, Shinjuku-ku, Tokyo 160-0023
*Tel:* (03) 5351 3021 *Fax:* (03) 5351 3028
*E-mail:* ssb01@mx1.alpha-web.ne.jp
*Key Personnel*
President: Takeshi Katsukawa
Senior Man Dir: Koichi Ohnishi
Founded: 1956
Also publisher.
Type of Business: Distributor, Importer, Major Independent Bookseller, Wholesaler
*Branch Office(s)*
Niihama
Osaka

**Shinko Tsusho Co Ltd**
1-7-1 Wakaba, Shinjuku-ku, Tokyo 160
*Tel:* (03) 33531751 *Fax:* (03) 33532205
*E-mail:* shinko@tokyo.e-mail.ne.jp
*Key Personnel*
President: Ms Keiko Nagato
Founded: 1960
Type of Business: Distributor, Importer, Wholesaler

**Shiseido Booksellers Ltd**
55 Koyama-Minamikazusa, Kita-ku, Kyoto 603-8149
*Tel:* (075) 431 2345 *Fax:* (075) 432 6588
*E-mail:* shiseido@jd5.so-net.ne.jp
*Web Site:* www.shiseido-book.co.jp
*Key Personnel*
President: Tatsuro Sugaura
Import Dir: Hiromitsu Hori
Founded: 1947
Booksellers for scholars on the field of humanities
Membership(s): Japan Association of International Publications.
Type of Business: Importer, Major Independent Bookseller

**Tohan Corporation**
6-24 Higashigoken-cho, Shinjuku-ku, Tokyo 162-0813
*Tel:* (03) 3269-6111 *Fax:* (03) 3235-1337
*Key Personnel*
President: Hirotaka Kotaki
Manager, Overseas Business Dept: Kainan Tanaka
Overseas Business Development: Takako Yuasa *Tel:* (03) 3266-9593 *Fax:* (03) 3266-8943
Overseas Sales Div: *Tel:* (03) 3266-9573 *Fax:* (03) 3266-8943

Also acts as literary agent.
Type of Business: Distributor, Exporter, Wholesaler

**Tokyo Publications Service Ltd**
Daiichi-Takiguchi Bldg, 20-7, Ginza 1-chome, Chuo-ku, Tokyo 104-0061
*Tel:* (03) 3561-9741 *Fax:* (03) 3561-9743
*E-mail:* info@tokyoyosho.com
*Web Site:* www.tokyoyosho.com
*Key Personnel*
President: Kensaku Kihara
Chairman: Kunio Kihara
Dir, Sales: Juniihiro Hirakata
Founded: 1968
Retail & wholesale.
Type of Business: Distributor, Exporter, Importer, Major Independent Bookseller, Wholesaler

**Tuttle Bookshop**
1-3 Kanda Jimbocho, Chiyoda-ku, Tokyo 101-0051
*Tel:* (03) 3291-7071 *Fax:* (03) 3293-8005
*E-mail:* kanda@bookshop.co.jp
*Web Site:* www.bookshop.co.jp/kandamap.html
Retail outlet of publisher Charles E Tuttle Company.
*Owned by:* Charles E Tuttle Co Inc
*Branch Office(s)*
American Club Shop, 1-2 Azabu-dai 2-chome, Minato-ku, Tokyo 106 *Tel:* (03) 5848938
Okinawa Plaza Book Shop, 242 Yamazato, Okinawa-shi, Okinawa 904 *Tel:* (0988) 333520

**Charles E Tuttle Publishing Co Inc**
Member of Periplus Publishing Group
5-4-12 Osaki, Shinagawa-ku, Tokyo 153
*Tel:* (03) 5437-0171 *Fax:* (03) 5437-0755
*E-mail:* info@tuttlepublishing.com
*Web Site:* www.tuttlepublishing.com
*Key Personnel*
President, Singapore: Eric Oey
Man Dir: Kazuo Maekawa
Founded: 1948
English-language books in Japan.
Type of Business: Distributor, Exporter, Importer, Major Independent Bookseller, Wholesaler
*Branch Office(s)*
Jakarta, Indonesia
Osaka
Berkeley Books Pte Ltd, No 06-01/03 Olivine Bldg, 130 Joo Seng Rd, Singapore 368357, Singapore *Tel:* (06) 280-3320 *Fax:* (06) 280-6290
*Sales Office(s):* Airport Industrial Park, 364 Innovation Dr, North Clarendon, VT 05759-9436, United States
*U.S. Office(s):* 153 Milk St, Boston, MA 02109, United States *Fax:* 617-951-4045
*Bookshop(s):* Kanda Shop, 1-3 Kanda-Jimbocho, Chiyoda-ku, Tokyo 100

**United Publishers Services Ltd**
Member of Times Publishing Group, Republic of Singapore
1-32-5 Higashi-shinagawa, Shinagawa-ku, Tokyo 140-0002
*Tel:* (03) 5479-7251 *Fax:* (03) 5479-7307
*E-mail:* general@ups.co.jp
*Web Site:* www.ups.co.jp
*Key Personnel*
President: Mark Gresham
Vice President: Junichi Takayori
Type of Business: Distributor, Importer, Wholesaler
*Owned by:* Times Publishing Ltd, Singapore

**Yohan Inc**
Akasaka Community Bldg, 1-1-8 Moto-Akasaka, Minato-ku, Tokyo 107-0051
*Tel:* (03) 5786-7426 *Fax:* (03) 5770-2440

*Web Site:* www.yohan.co.jp
*Key Personnel*
President & Chief Executive Officer: Hiroshi Kagawa
Vice President & Chief Financial Officer: J P Kiyota
Founded: 1953
Import, sell & market foreign books & magazines.
Affiliates: ICG-Muse Inc; Intercultural Group; School Book Services; IBC Publishing Inc; Heian International Inc (US); Stone Bridge Press (US).
Type of Business: Distributor, Importer, Wholesaler
*Branch Office(s)*
Fukuoka
Nagoya
Okinawa
Osaka
Sapporo
Yokohama
London, United Kingdom
*U.S. Office(s):* NY, United States

**Yushodo Co Ltd**
29, San-ei-Cho, Shinjuku-ku, Tokyo 160-0008
*Tel:* (03) 3357-1411 *Fax:* (03) 3351-5855
*E-mail:* ysdhp@yushodo.co.jp; antiq@yushodo.co.jp; intl@yushodo.co.jp
*Web Site:* www.yushodo.co.jp
*Telex:* 02324136
*Key Personnel*
President: Mitsuo Nitta
Founded: 1932
Branch offices in Kansai, Ohtsuka, & Toyko. Importer & Exporter of Western Antiquarian & Rare Books.
Type of Business: Distributor, Exporter, Importer, Wholesaler

# Jordan

**Jordan Book Centre Co Ltd**
University St, Amman 11941
Mailing Address: PO Box 301 (Al-Jubeiha), Amman 11941
*Tel:* (06) 5151882; (06) 5155882 *Fax:* (06) 5152016
*E-mail:* jbc@go.com.jo
*Telex:* 21153 *Cable:* JORDAN BOOK CENTRE/AMMAN
*Key Personnel*
Chief Executive: I Sharbain
Founded: 1958
Also publisher.
Subjects: education, historical fiction, history, religion, theology, science, biology, chemistry, technology, engineering
Type of Business: Distributor, Wholesaler

**Jordan Distribution Agency Co Ltd**
PO Box 375, Amman 11118
*Tel:* (06) 4630191; (06) 4630192 *Fax:* (06) 4635152
*E-mail:* jda@go.com.jo
*Telex:* 22083 Distag Jo *Cable:* JODISTAG AMMAN
*Key Personnel*
Chairman: Raja Elissa
General Manager: Wadie Sayegh
Founded: 1951
Type of Business: Distributor, Exporter, Importer, Major Book Chain Headquarters, Major Independent Bookseller, Wholesaler
*Owned by:* Raja Elissa
*Bookshop(s):* Hotel Jordan Intercontinental, Amman

**Sharbain's Bookshop**
Jebel Amman, 1st Circle, Rainbow St, Amman
Mailing Address: PO Box 2427, Amman
*Tel:* (06) 638709 *Fax:* (06) 699119
*Telex:* 21153 sharbn jo-Bgrh-Inh *Cable:* SHARBAIN, AMMAN
*Key Personnel*
Owner: J I Sharbain
Founded: 1963
Type of Business: Distributor, Exporter, Importer, Major Independent Bookseller, Wholesaler

**University of Jordan Bookshop**
University of Jordan, Amman 11943
Mailing Address: PO Box 13307, Amman
*Tel:* (06) 843555 (ext 3339) *Fax:* (06) 836446
*E-mail:* admin@ju.edu.jo
*Telex:* 21153 *Cable:* UNIVERSITY OF JORDAN BOOKSHOP/AMMAN
*Key Personnel*
President: J J Sharbain
Founded: 1978
*Owned by:* JBC Co Ltd
*Bookshop(s):* PO Box 19903, Amman

# Kenya

**Book Sales (K) Ltd**
Rivron House, Ground floor, Ronald Nigala St, Nairobi
*Tel:* (02) 221031; (02) 226543
*Key Personnel*
Chief Executive: Adrian Louis
Founded: 1976
Also Publishes.

**Bookpoint Ltd**
Loans House, Moi Ave, GPO 00100 Nairobi
Mailing Address: PO Box 46449, GPO 00100 Nairobi
*Tel:* (02) 211156; (02) 220221; (02) 226680 *Fax:* (02) 211029
*E-mail:* books@africaonline.co.ke
*Key Personnel*
Chairman: Mohinderlal Shah
Chief Executive: Sudhir Shah
Dir: Dipak Shah
Retail booksellers & stationers.
Type of Business: Exporter, Importer, Major Independent Bookseller, Wholesaler

**City Bookshop Ltd**
Nkrumah Rd, Mombasa, City Centre
Mailing Address: PO Box 90512, Mombasa, City Centre
*Tel:* (011) 313 149; (011) 225548 *Fax:* (011) 314815 *Cable:* CITYBOOK
*Key Personnel*
Man Dir: Moez T Dungerwalla
Founded: 1953
Subjects: fiction, non fiction, magazines, greeting cards
Type of Business: Distributor, Importer, Major Independent Bookseller, Wholesaler

**Keswick Books & Gifts Ltd**
Bruce House, Kaunda St, Nairobi
Mailing Address: PO Box 10242, Nairobi
*Tel:* (02) 226-047; (02) 331-692 *Fax:* (02) 728-557
*E-mail:* keswick@swiftkenya.com
*Key Personnel*
Chief Executive: Margareta Hakanson
Founded: 1959

Type of Business: Distributor, Importer, Major Independent Bookseller
*Branch Office(s)*
Gospel Centre, Box 90310, Mombasa

**Prestige Booksellers & Stationers**
Mama Ngina St Prudential Bldg, Nairobi
Mailing Address: PO Box 45425, Nairobi
*Tel:* (02) 223515 *Fax:* (02) 2246796
*E-mail:* prest@iconnect.co.ke
*Key Personnel*
Chief Executive: R M Upadhyay
Contact: Dipak Upadhyay
Founded: 1972
Type of Business: Exporter, Importer, Major Independent Bookseller

**Text Book Centre Ltd**
Kijabe St, Nairobi
Mailing Address: PO Box 47540, Nairobi
*Tel:* (02) 330340 *Fax:* (02) 225779
*E-mail:* admin@tbc.co.ke
*Web Site:* www.saritcentre.com/text_book_centre.htm *Cable:* TEXTBOOKS
*Key Personnel*
General Manager: C D Shah
Founded: 1964
Also publisher.
Type of Business: Distributor, Exporter, Importer, Major Independent Bookseller, Wholesaler
*Branch Office(s)*
Sarit Centre, Westlands, Nairobi

**University of Nairobi Bookshop**
PO Box 30197, Nairobi
*Tel:* (02) 334244 *Fax:* (02) 336885
*E-mail:* webmaster@uonbi.ac.ke
*Web Site:* www.uonbi.ac.ke
*Telex:* 22095 VARSITY KE
*Key Personnel*
Contact: Mrs M N Muriuki
Founded: 1974
Bookseller.
*Owned by:* University of Nairobi

# Democratic People's Republic of Korea

**Korea Publications Export & Import Corporation**
Yonggwang St, Central District, Yokjon-dong, Pyongyang
*Tel:* (02) 3818536 *Fax:* (02) 3814404; (02) 3814410
*Telex:* 36062 CH KP *Cable:* CHULPHANMUL, PYONGYANG
*Key Personnel*
Dir: Ri Yong
Head of Export Dept: Sin Hak Chol
Head of Import Dept: Jong Yong
Exporter: Mrs Kim Hye Son
Type of Business: Distributor, Exporter, Importer, Major Book Chain Headquarters, Major Independent Bookseller, Wholesaler
*Bookshop(s):* Changgwang Bookshop, Chollima St, Central District, Dongsong-dong

# Republic of Korea

**Daejon Trading Co Ltd**
783-20 Pangbae-bondong, Socho-ku, Seoul
*Tel:* (02) 536-9555 *Fax:* (02) 536-0025
*Key Personnel*
Contact: Yoo Jung-Sun
Founded: 1981
Type of Business: Distributor, Importer

**International Publications Service Inc (IPS)**
Gongpyong Bldg, 11th floor, 5-1 Gongpyong-
dong, Jongro-gu, Seoul 110-160
Mailing Address: KPO Box 496, Seoul 110-604
*Tel:* (02) 2115-8800 *Fax:* (02) 2273-8048
*Web Site:* www.ipsbook.com
*Key Personnel*
President: Yong-Kook Kim
General Manager: Dong-Hyun Lee
Founded: 1983
Distributions & subscription promotions for for-
eign publications.
Exclusive distributor for Newsweek, Reader's Di-
gest, National Geographic & 63 other foreign
periodicals.
Type of Business: Distributor, Importer, Whole-
saler
*Branch Office(s)*
Kwangju
Kyungin
Pusan
Taejon
Taeku

**IPS Inc**, see International Publications Service
Inc (IPS)

**Kyobo Book Centre Co Ltd**
1, 1-Ka Chongno, Chongno-ku, Seoul 110-714
*Tel:* (02) 397-3481; (02) 397-3482; (02) 397-
3483; (02) 397-3484; (02) 397-3485 *Fax:* (02)
735-0030
*E-mail:* kyobofbd@kyobobook.co.kr
*Key Personnel*
President: Kun-Lyu
Dir: Byung Ha-Yu; Seong Ryoung-Kim
Supervisor: Sang Sik-Ahn
Vice President: Mun Jae-Shin
Manager Information Business Team: Mr T K
Kim
Type of Business: Distributor, Exporter, Importer,
Major Book Chain Headquarters, Wholesaler
*Owned by:* Kyobo Life Insurance Co Ltd

**Panmun Book Co Ltd**
40, Chongro 1-ka, Chongro-ku, Seoul
Mailing Address: CPO Box 1016, 136-074
Sungbuk-ku, Seoul
*Tel:* (02) 953-2451-5 *Fax:* (02) 953-2456-7
*E-mail:* panmunex@unitel.co.kr
*Telex:* K27546 *Cable:* PANMUSE
*Branch Office(s)*
16 Kwangbok-dong, 1-ka Pusan

**Science Publications Centre**
201 Taegyeong Bldg 364-28, Habjeong-dong,
Mapo-gu, Seoul 121-220
*Tel:* (02) 3254015; (02) 7336719; (02) 3254017
*Fax:* (02) 3335799

**Sophia Book Service**
Golden Tower 1319, 191, 2-ka Chung Jung Rd,
Sodaemun Ku, Seoul 120-722
*Tel:* (02) 362-2036 *Fax:* (02) 362-2036
*Key Personnel*
Owner: Eui-Soon Chang

General Manager: Hwan Kyu Paik
Founded: 1957
Type of Business: Distributor, Exporter, Importer,
Wholesaler

**Universal Publications Agency Press**
54, Gyeonji-dong, Jongro-gu, Seoul 110-170
*Tel:* (02) 32-8175 *Fax:* (02) 32-8176
*E-mail:* upa@upa.co.kr
*Web Site:* www.upa.co.kr
*Telex:* K28504 Unipub *Cable:* CHANGHOSHIN
SEOUL
*Key Personnel*
Chairman: Chang-Ho Shin
Also acts as publisher.
Type of Business: Distributor

# Kuwait

**The Kuwait Book Shop Company Ltd**
Sour-Al-Ghanem Bldg, Al-Sour St, Ahmadi-Souk
Al-Ahmadi
Mailing Address: PO Box 2942, 13030 Safat
*Tel:* 2424687; 2424266 *Fax:* 2420558
*E-mail:* kbs@ncc.moc.kw
*Telex:* 30860 *Cable:* FARATOURS
*Key Personnel*
Owner: Bashir N Khatib

# Lebanon

**Librairies Antoine SAL/Librairie Antoine, A.
Naufal & Freres**
BP 11-656, Beirut
*Tel:* (01) 48 10 72; (01) 48 35 13 *Fax:* (01) 49 26
25

**Librairie du Liban Publishers (Sal)**
Sayegh Bldg Zouk Mosbeh, Kesrouwan
Mailing Address: PO Box 11-9232, Beirut
*Tel:* (09) 217 735; (09) 217 944; (09) 217 945;
(09) 217 946 *Fax:* (09) 217 734
*E-mail:* info@ldlp.com
*Web Site:* www.ldlp.com
*Telex:* 45297 Libsay
*Key Personnel*
Man Dir: Pierre Sayegh *E-mail:* psayegh@ldlp.
com
Founded: 1944
Bookseller
Also acts as Publisher.
Type of Business: Distributor, Exporter, Importer,
Major Independent Bookseller, Wholesaler
*Branch Office(s)*
Arab Gulf Education, Al Twar Center, Al Nahda
St, Al Qussais 2, PO Box 86865, Dubai,
United Arab Emirates *Tel:* (04) 2617373
*Fax:* (04) 2617557 *E-mail:* agedu@emirates.
net.ae
Petra International Publishers, H & M Bldg, No
157, Al-Jame'ah St, PO Box 6587, Amman
11118, Jordan *Tel:* (06) 5685827 *Fax:* (06)
5685819 *E-mail:* pip@go.com.jo
Sphinx Publishing Co, 127 Horriya St, Al
Shallalat, Alexandria, Egypt (Arab Re-
public of Egypt) *Tel:* (03) 4940539; (03)
4930356 *Fax:* (03) 4924839 *E-mail:* sphinx@
internetalex.com
Sphinx Publishing Co, 3, Shawarby Str, Apt
305, Cairo, Egypt (Arab Republic of Egypt)
*Tel:* (02) 3924616 *Fax:* (02) 3918002
*E-mail:* sphinx@intouch.com
Sphinx Publishing Co, Higher Education Division, Cairo, Egypt (Arab Republic of

Egypt) *Tel:* (02) 3909169 *Fax:* (02) 3909169
*E-mail:* hesphinx@link.net
Sphinx Publishing Co, Zahra'a St, Al Dokki,
Cairo, Egypt (Arab Republic of Egypt)
*Tel:* (02) 7494998 *Fax:* (02) 3389595
*E-mail:* zahraasp@intouch.com
Sayegh Bldg, Baabdat-Al Metn *Tel:* (04)
820 804; (04) 820 728 *Fax:* (04) 977 435
*E-mail:* ksayegh@ldlp.com
Rubeiz Bldg, Hamra St, Beirut *Tel:* (01) 344 070
Riad El Solh Sq, Beirut
Diab Bldg, Al-Taif Str, Al-Salihiya, PO Box
704, Damascus, Syrian Arab Republic
*Tel:* (011) 4422973 *Fax:* (011) 4423236
*E-mail:* sayeghbook@net.sy
*Bookshop(s):* 42 Bliss St, Ras Beirut *Tel:* (01)
344 968

# Lesotho

**Mazenod Book Centre**
PO Box 39, Mazenod 160
*Tel:* 35 0224; 35 0465 *Fax:* 35 0010 *Cable:*
Mazbooks
*Key Personnel*
Manager: Rev Fr M Gareau

**Morija Sesuto Book Depot**
Church St, PO Box 4, Morija 190
*Tel:* 360204 *Fax:* 360001
Book & stationery retailer. Also publisher.
*Parent Company:* Lesotho Evangelical Church
(KEL), PO Box 260, Masery

# Liberia

**University Bookstore**
University of Liberia, Monrovia
Mailing Address: PO Box 9020
*Tel:* 224671

# Lithuania

**Giliukas Ltd**
S Lozoraicio 13, 3009 Kaunas
*Tel:* (07) 709560 *Fax:* (07) 709560
*E-mail:* giliukas@isi.kvn.lt
*Key Personnel*
Dir: Vyturys Jarutis
Founded: 1991
Type of Business: Distributor, Exporter, Importer,
Wholesaler

**Humanitas Ltd**
Donelaicio 52, 3000 Kaunas
*Tel:* (07) 220333 *Fax:* (07) 423653
*E-mail:* info@humanitas.lt
*Web Site:* www.humanitas.lt
*Key Personnel*
Dir: Saulius Stogevicius
Founded: 1994
Type of Business: Distributor, Importer, Major
Book Chain Headquarters, Wholesaler
*Bookshop(s):* Tunstantis ir Viena Naktis Book-
shop, Vilnius g 11, 3000 Kaunas; Vilnius Art
Bookshop, Vokieciy 2, Vilnius

# Luxembourg

**Librairie Bourbon**
11, rue Bourbon, 1249 Luxembourg
*Tel:* 40 30 30-21 *Fax:* 40 30 30-45
*E-mail:* librairies@isp.lu
*Web Site:* www.librairie.lu
*Key Personnel*
Manager: Charles Jourdain
Founded: 1982
*Owned by:* Imprimerie Saint-Paul SA, 2988

**Ernster Sarl**
27 rue du Fosse, 1536 Luxembourg
*Tel:* 22 50 77-1 *Fax:* 22 50 73
*E-mail:* librairie@ernster.com
*Web Site:* www.ernster.com
*Key Personnel*
Manager: Fernand Ernster
Founded: 1889
Stationary: supplies for schools, bookshop.
*Bookshop(s):* Librairie Ernster City Concorde, 80,
route de Longwy, 8060 Bertrange *Tel:* 26 44 04
24 *Fax:* 26 44 04 33 *E-mail:* city.concorde@
ernster.com; Librairie Ernster La Belle Etoile,
8050 Bertrange *Tel:* 31 13 77-1 *Fax:* 31 16 73
*E-mail:* belle.etoile@ernster.com

**Librairie Promoculture**
14 rue Duchscher, 1424 Luxembourg
Mailing Address: BP 1142, L-1011 Luxembourg
*Tel:* 480691 *Fax:* 400950
*E-mail:* info@promoculture.lu
*Web Site:* www.promoculture.lu
*Key Personnel*
Dir: Albert P Daming *E-mail:* daming@pt.lu
Founded: 1972
Subscription agency & technical bookshop. Also
book publisher.
Subjects: Law
Type of Business: Major Independent Bookseller
*Owned by:* Albert Daming, 4, Avalaon St, Lux-
embourg L-1159

# The Former Yugoslav Republic of Macedonia

**Kultura**
Bul Sv Kliment Ohridski 68A, 91000 Skopje
*Tel:* (02) 111-332 *Fax:* (02) 228-608
*E-mail:* ipkultura@unet.com.mk
*Web Site:* www.kultura.com.mk/en
*Key Personnel*
Dir: Dimitar Basevski
Commercial Dir: Arso Kokaleski
Editor-in-Chief: Gligor Stojkovski
Editor: Lence Milosevska
Founded: 1945
Also publisher & stationery goods supplier.
Type of Business: Distributor, Exporter, Importer,
Major Independent Bookseller, Wholesaler

**Makedonska kniga**
11-ti Oktomvri, 1000 Skopje
*Tel:* (02) 1164 73 *Fax:* (02) 1212 77
*Telex:* 51637
*Key Personnel*
Man Dir: Branislav Mihajlovic

Thirty-one bookshops in Skopje & in all major
towns in Macedonia.
Type of Business: Exporter, Importer, Wholesaler
*Owned by:* Makedonska kniga (Knigoizdatelstvo)

# Madagascar

**La Librairie de Madagascar**
38 Ave de l'Independance, 101 Tananrive
Mailing Address: BP 402, 101 Tananrive
*Tel:* (020) 222454 *Fax:* (020) 2264395; (020)
224395
*Key Personnel*
Manager: Yves Balanche
Founded: 1936

**Librairie Mixte Sarl**
37 bis, av 26 Jona Analakely, 101 Antananarivo
*Tel:* (020) 22 251 30 *Fax:* (020) 22 376 16
*E-mail:* librairiemixte@dts.mg
*Key Personnel*
Manager: Jean Razakasoa

**Librairie Universitaire**
BP 566, 101 Tananrive
*Tel:* (020) 24114

**Societe Malgache d'Edition**
Route des Hydrocarbures, Ankorondrano, 101
Tananrive
Mailing Address: BP 659, 101 Tananrive
*Tel:* (020) 2222635 *Fax:* (020) 2222254
*E-mail:* tribune@wanadoo.mg
*Web Site:* www.madagascar-tribune.com
*Telex:* 22340 RAMEX MG TANANARIVE
*Key Personnel*
Dir of Publication: Rahaga Ramaholimihaso
Founded: 1943
Also Publisher.
Type of Business: Exporter

**Trano Printy Fiangonana Loterana Malagasy
(TPFLM)-(Imprimerie Lutherienne)**
9 ave Grandidier, 101 Tananrive
Mailing Address: BP 533, 101 Tananrive
*Tel:* (020) 223340; (020) 24569
Also Publisher.

# Malawi

**Central Bookshop Ltd**
PO Box 264, Blantyre
*Tel:* 621 447 *Fax:* 633 863
*Key Personnel*
Man Dir: A Hamid Sacranie *E-mail:* hamidcbs@
malawi.net
Founded: 1960
School supplies, books, stationary & cards,
Africana.
Type of Business: Distributor, Importer, Major
Independent Bookseller
*Branch Office(s)*
City Centre, Lilongwe *Tel:* 784 343
*Bookshop(s):* Livingston Ave, Blantyre

**CLAIM Bookshop**
PO Box 503, Blantyre
*Tel:* 620839; 673091
*Key Personnel*
Manager: J T Matenje

Sales Manager: E C Mtumbati
*Owned by:* Christian Literature Association in
Malawi

# Malaysia

**S Abdul Majeed & Co**
No 7, Jalan 3/82B, Bangsar Utama, Off Jalan
Bangsar, 59200 Kuala Lumpur
*Tel:* (03) 2832230 *Fax:* (03) 28225670
*E-mail:* peer@pc.jaring.my
*Key Personnel*
Man Dir: A M S Alaudeen
Type of Business: Distributor, Wholesaler
*Branch Office(s)*
35 Jalan Sekarat, Penang

**Antara Publications (M) Sdn Bhd**
10th floor, Wisma Muisan, 300 Jalan Raja Laut,
50350 Kuala Lumpur
*Tel:* (03) 2913188 *Fax:* (03) 2913299
*Key Personnel*
Man Dir: Kevin Sugumaran
Type of Business: Distributor, Importer, Whole-
saler
*Owned by:* Antara Publications (M) S/B, Singa-
pore
*Bookshop(s):* BBC English Shop, Lot 2.52, 2nd
floor, Mall Complex, 100 Jalan Putra, Kuala
Lumpur

**Badan Bookstore Sdn Bhd**
28 Tingkat Bawah, Kompleks Tun Abdul Razak,
80000 Johur Bahru, Johor
*Tel:* (07) 2234796; (07) 2377562; (07) 2330241;
(07) 330241 *Fax:* (07) 2238188
*Key Personnel*
Dir: Encik Saadon
*Branch Office(s)*
63, Jalan Perang, Taman Pelangi, Johor Bahru

**Flo Enterprise Sdn Bhd**
24 Lorong PJS 1/2A Taman Perangsang Batu 7,
Jalan Kelang Lama, 46000 Petaling Jaya
*Tel:* (03) 77833118 *Fax:* (03) 77831066
*Key Personnel*
Man Dir: Johnny Leong
Type of Business: Distributor, Importer

**IBS Buku Sdn Bhd**
B3-06, P J Industrial Park, Jalan Kemajuan,
46200 Petaling Jaya, Selangor, Darul Ehsan
*Tel:* (03) 79579282; (03) 79579470 *Fax:* (03)
79576026
*E-mail:* info@ibsbuku.com; ibsbuku@po.janing.
my; hibs@tm.net.my
*Web Site:* www.ibsbuku.com
*Key Personnel*
Man Dir: Mohamed Mustafa
Founded: 1971
Type of Business: Distributor, Exporter, Importer,
Wholesaler
*U.S. Office(s):* 6102 Gardenia Court, Alexandria,
VA 22310, United States *Tel:* 703-313-8334
*Fax:* 703-295-4352 *E-mail:* agil@ibsbuku.com

**International Book Service**, see IBS Buku Sdn
Bhd

**Mahir Marketing Services Sdn Bhd**
7 Jl 3/82B, Bangsar Utama, Off Jalan Bangsar,
59000 Kuala Lumpur
*Tel:* (088) 2827372 *Fax:* (088) 718067
*Telex:* MA 30226 MAHIR
*Key Personnel*
President: Tham Ban Hing
*Owned by:* Mahir Holdings Sdn Bhd

*Branch Office(s)*
Stadrum Shah Alam, Arasi, Quadran B Seksyen
13, Shah Alam Selangor *Tel:* (03) 5501755
(03) 5501442 *Fax:* (03) 5501826

**Marican Sdn Bhd**
321 Jalan Tuanku Abdul Rahman, 50100 Kuala
Lumpur
*Tel:* (03) 2981133
*Telex:* MA 31697 Manews *Cable:* Maricanews
*Key Personnel*
General Manager: C C Lo
Also publisher.
Type of Business: Wholesaler
*Branch Office(s)*
171 Middle Rd, Singapore 0718, Singapore
4th floor, Ruby Warehouse Complex, 8 Kaki
Bukit Rd 2, Singapore 1441, Singapore

**Mawaddah Enterprise Sdn Bhd**
75 Jalan Kapitan Tam Yeong, 70000 Seremban,
Negeri Sembilan Darul Khusus
*Tel:* (06) 7611062 *Fax:* (06) 7633062
*E-mail:* azhari@mawadah.pc.my
*Key Personnel*
Man Dir: Haji Azhari Hamzah
Founded: 1977
Type of Business: Distributor, Exporter, Importer,
Wholesaler

**MPH Bookstores SDN BHD**
15 Jalan Tandang, 5th floor, Petaling Jaya, Selan-
gor 46710
*Tel:* (03) 7781 1800; (03) 2398 3817 (customer
service) *Fax:* (03) 7782 1800
*E-mail:* customerservice@mph.com.my
*Web Site:* www.mph.com.my
*Telex:* RS 35853 Mphmag *Cable:* EMPRESS
SINGAPORE
*Key Personnel*
Marketing Manager: Lawrence Geoffrey
Founded: 1906
*Bookshop(s):* 71-77 Stamford Rd, Singapore
178895, Singapore

**MPH Distributors Sdn Bhd**
Unit JA1, Ground Floor, Mid Valley Megamall,
Mid Valley City, 58000 Kuala Lumpur
*Tel:* (03) 2938 3800; (03) 2938 3818 *Fax:* (03)
2938 3811; (03) 2938 3817
*E-mail:* customerservice@mph.com.my
*Web Site:* www.mph.com.my
*Telex:* Jcm MA 37402
*Key Personnel*
General Manager: Francis Heng Siang Goh
Group Financial Controller: Wong Paw
Manager: Tai Kwai Meng
Founded: 1963
Type of Business: Distributor, Importer, Major
Book Chain Headquarters, Wholesaler
*Owned by:* MPH Group Malaysia Sdn Bhd
*Bookshop(s):* Pelangi Leisure Mall, Lot 2.01,
Level 2, No 148, Jl Serampang, Taman
Pelangi, 80400 Johor Bahru *Tel:* (07) 335 2672
*Fax:* (07) 335 2677; F38, 1st floor, Bukit Raja
Shopping Centre, Persiaran Bukit Raja 2, Ban-
dar Baru Klang, 41150 Klang *Tel:* (03) 3342
8580 *Fax:* (03) 3343 1345; Lot 6A, 1st floor,
Tesco Klang, No 3, Jl Batu Nilam, 6/KS6,
Bandar Bukit Tinggi, 41200 Klang *Tel:* (03)
3324 2650 *Fax:* (03) 3324 8071; F1 & F2,
1st floor, Taman Maluri Shopping Centre, Jl
Jejaka, Taman Maluri, Cheras, 55100 Kuala
Lumpur *Tel:* (03) 9285 1317 *Fax:* (03) 9285
1069; 1st Floor, Banqsar Village Shopping
Centre, No 1, Jl Telawi 1, Bangsar Baru, 59100
Kuala Lumpur *Tel:* (03) 2282 7300 *Fax:* (03)
2282 7293; F11-12, 1st floor, Alpha Angle
Shopping Centre, Jl R1, Section 1, Bandar
Baru Wangsa Maju, 53300 Kuala Lumpur
*Tel:* (03) 4142 1246 *Fax:* (03) 4142 1245; Lots
5 & 6, Level 1, Great Eastern Mall, No 303, Jl

Ampang, 50450 Kuala Lumpur *Tel:* (03) 4253
4835 *Fax:* (03) 4253 4204; GF002, Ground
Floor, B B Plaza, Jl Bukit Bintang, 55100
Kuala Lumpur *Tel:* (03) 2142 8231 *Fax:* (03)
2142 9729; Unit 24, Departure Hall, Level
1, KL City Air Terminal, KL Sentral Station,
50470 Kuala Lumpur *Tel:* (03) 2938-3800
*Fax:* (03) 2938-3811; G73B, Ground Floor,
Mahkota Parade, No 1, Jl Merdeka, 75000
Melaka *Tel:* (06) 283 3050 *Fax:* (06) 283 3003;
Lot 170-3-76/79/81/82, 3rd floor, Gurney Plaza,
Gurney Dr, 10250 Penang *Tel:* (04) 227 4202
*Fax:* (04) 227 4303; Lot 18-1-A, 1st floor,
Gurney Tower, 18 Persiaran Gurney, 10250
Penang *Tel:* (04) 370 2115 *Fax:* (04) 370 2116;
LL2.05, Lower Level 2, Sunway Pyramid, 3
Jl PJS 11/15, Bandar Sunway, 46150 Petal-
ing Jaya *Tel:* (03) 7492 5805 *Fax:* (03) 7492
5806; F319 & S319, 1st & 2nd floor, 1 Utama
Shopping Centre, No 1, Lebuh Bandar Utama,
Bandar Utama Damansara, 47800 Petaling
Jaya *Tel:* (03) 7726 9003 *Fax:* (03) 7725
9005; G26A(1), G26B-C & G26D(1), Ground
Floor, Subang Parade, No 5, Jl SS16/1, Subang
Jaya, 47500 Petaling Jaya *Tel:* (03) 5633 9079
*Fax:* (03) 5637 9729; Lot A22-A24, Giant Hy-
permarket Stadium Shah Alam, Lot 2 Jl Per-
siaran Sukan, Seksyen 13, 40100 Shah Alam
*Tel:* (03) 5511 8978 *Fax:* (03) 5511 8976;
Taman Universiti Shopping Centre, UG18,
Upper Ground Floor, Jl Pendidikan 1, 81300
Skudai, Johor *Tel:* (07) 521 1702 *Fax:* (07) 521
2702; Lot 1, Tesco Sungai Petani, No 300, Jl
Lagenda 1, Lagenda Heights, 08000 Sungai
Petani *Tel:* (04) 425 1250 *Fax:* (04) 425 1150;
LG50A, LG56 & LG57, Lower Ground Floor,
The Summit, Subang USJ, Persiaran Kewaji-
pan, USJ1, 47600 UEP Subang Jaya *Tel:* (03)
8024 2261 *Fax:* (03) 8024 1442

**Parry's Book Center Sdn Bhd**
60 Jalan Negara, 53100 Kuala Lumpur
Mailing Address: PO Box 10960, 50730 Kuala
Lumpur
*Tel:* (03) 4079179; (03) 4087235; (03) 4079176;
(03) 4087528 *Fax:* (03) 4079180
*E-mail:* haja@pop3.jaring.my
*Telex:* Parry's MA *Cable:* PABOKCENT
Founded: 1993
University & library suppliers.

**Pearson Education Malaysia Sdn Bhd**
Lot 2, Jalan 215, Off Jalan Templer, 46050 Petal-
ing Jaya, Selangor Darul Ehsan
*Tel:* (03) 77820466 *Fax:* (03) 77853435
*E-mail:* inquiry@personed.com.my
*Web Site:* www.pearsoned-asia.com/mal; www.
pearson.com
*Key Personnel*
International Business: Wendy Spiegel *Tel:* 212-
782-3482 *E-mail:* wendy.spiegel@pearsoned.
com
Type of Business: Distributor, Exporter

**University of Malaya Co-operative Bookshop
Ltd**
Jalan Pantai Baru, 59700 Kuala Lumpur
Mailing Address: PO Box 1127, 59700 Kuala
Lumpur
*Tel:* (03) 756 5000; (03) 756 5425 *Fax:* (03) 755
4424
*Telex:* Unimal MA 39845
*Key Personnel*
Chairman: Royal Prof Ungku A Aziz
Type of Business: Distributor, Exporter, Importer,
Major Independent Bookseller, Wholesaler

# Mali

**Librairie Deves et Chaumet**
BP 64, Bamako
*Tel:* 222784

# Malta

**Audio Visual Centre Ltd**
Mayflower Mansions, Bisazza St, Sliema SLM 01
Mailing Address: PO Box 58, Sliema SLM 01
*Tel:* 21330886 *Fax:* 21346945
*E-mail:* info@avc.com.mt
*Key Personnel*
Owner: Simon Bonello
Founded: 1972

**The Ideal Bookshop**
Main Gate St, Victoria, Gozo
Mailing Address: PO Box 20, Victoria, Gozo
*Tel:* 553944
*Key Personnel*
Manager: A Vassallo
*Owned by:* A Vassallo and Sons Ltd
*Branch Office(s)*
Bxara T-Tajba, Charity St, Victoria, Gozo
*Tel:* (356) 553944 (Christian Bookshop)

**Merlin Library Ltd**
Mountbatten Str, Blata 1-Badja
*Tel:* (021) 234438; (021) 221205 *Fax:* (021)
221135
*E-mail:* mail@merlinlibrary.com
*Web Site:* www.merlinlibrary.com
*Key Personnel*
Dir: Arthur J Gruppetta
Founded: 1964
Type of Business: Distributor, Importer, Major
Independent Bookseller, Remainder Dealer,
Wholesaler

**Giov Muscat & Co Ltd**
213 St Ursula St, Valletta
Mailing Address: PO Box 348, Valletta
*Tel:* 21237668; 21233879 *Fax:* 21240496
*E-mail:* giovmuscat@waldonet.net.mt
*Key Personnel*
Man Dir: J A Muscat
Founded: 1874
Type of Business: Importer, Major Independent
Bookseller
*Bookshop(s):* 48 Merchants St, Valletta

# Mauritius

**EOI Ltd,** see Editions de l'Ocean Indien Ltd

**Editions de l'Ocean Indien Ltd**
Stanley, Rose Hill
*Tel:* 4646761 *Fax:* 4643445
*E-mail:* eoibooks@intnet.mu
*Telex:* MESYND 4739 IW *Cable:* EOI
MAURITIUS
*Key Personnel*
Chairman: Mr Surendra Bissoondoyal
General Manager: Damie Ramtohul; Mr Samrat C
Servansingh
Senior Marketing Manager: Amritlall Kundun
Founded: 1977
Also acts as publisher.
Branch offices in Curepipe, Flacq, Goodlands,
Port Louis, & Rose Hill.

Type of Business: Distributor, Exporter, Importer, Major Book Chain Headquarters, Major Independent Bookseller, Wholesaler
*Owned by:* EPB, Singapore; Government of Mauritius (60%); Longman, United Kingdom; Macmillan, United Kingdom; Nathan, France
*Bookshop(s):* NPF Shopping Centre, J Koenig S Port Louis; Arcades Rond Point, Rose Hill; Arcades Salaffa, Curepipe; Arcades Virginie, Flacq; Jugadambi Sharma SSS, Goodlands

# Mexico

**Libreria Acuario SA de CV**
Tehuantepec 34, Col Roma Sur, 06760 Mexico, DF
*Tel:* (05) 5742966; (05) 5741137 *Fax:* (05) 2642882
Founded: 1974
Type of Business: Distributor, Exporter, Importer
*Bookshop(s):* Ave Baja California 37-B, Col Roma Sur, 06760 Mexico, DF

**American Book Store SA de CV**
Madero No 25, Mexico 06000
*Tel:* (05) 512-6350; (05) 512-0306 *Fax:* (05) 518-6931
Founded: 1928
Type of Business: Importer, Major Independent Bookseller
*Branch Office(s)*
Av Eugenio Garza Sada No 2404, Col Roma, Monterrey, NL *Tel:* (08) 3588028
Circuito Medicos No 2, Ciudad Satelite, 53100 Edo de Mexico *Tel:* (05) 3930682 *Fax:* (05) 5624692
Insurgentes Sur 1636, Col Credito Constructo, 03940 Mexico, DF *Tel:* (05) 6614611 *Fax:* (05) 6615109
Quintana Roo 861, Las Fuentes, Celaya, Gto *Tel:* (0461) 47301 *Fax:* (0461) 47049

**Libreria Bellas Artes**
Av Juarez No 20, 06050 Cuauhtemoc 06050
*Tel:* (05) 510-2276 *Fax:* (05) 518-3755
*Key Personnel*
Manager: Miguel Noriega
Founded: 1946
*Owned by:* Editorial Limusa SA de CV

**Central de Publicaciones SA**
Ave Juarez No 4-B, 06050 Mexico, DF
*Tel:* (05) 5104231
*Owned by:* Galeria de Arte Misrachi SA, Genova No 20-A, Col Jaurez 06600

**Librerias de Cristal, sa de cv** (Cristal Bookstores)
Tehuantepec No 170, 06760 Mexico
*Tel:* (05) 5644100 *Fax:* (05) 2640983; (05) 5644100 ext 287 (fax on demand)
*E-mail:* biblio10@prodigy.net.mx *Cable:* EDIAPSA
*Key Personnel*
Dir: Benito Zychlinski
Information Bibliography Manager: Gabriel Rodriquez *Tel:* (05) 5644100 ext 210
Founded: 1939
Bookstores.
*Owned by:* Editorial Limusa SA de CV
*Branch Office(s)*
Tehuantepec 170, Col Roma Sur, 06760 Mexico City 49 MX *Tel:* (05) 6008390

**Librerias Gonvill SA de CV**
8 de Julio, No 825, Guadalajara, JAL
*Tel:* (033) 3837-2300 *Fax:* (033) 3837-2309

*E-mail:* librosbooks@gonvill.com.mx
*Web Site:* www.gonvill.com.mx
*Key Personnel*
General Dir: Jorge E Gonzalez Villalobos
Administrative Dir: Tirzo F Gonzaez Letechipia
Founded: 1967
Type of Business: Distributor, Exporter, Importer, Major Book Chain Headquarters, Wholesaler

**Grupo Cultural Especializado, SA**
Av Popocaltepetl 510, Col Xoco, Del Benito Juarez, 03330 Mexico, DF
*Tel:* (05) 6889831 *Fax:* (05) 6889965
*Key Personnel*
Dir: Mr Adrian Garcia Valades
General Manager: Ing Meliton Cross
Type of Business: Distributor, Importer, Wholesaler

**Libreria Hamburgo SA**
Insurgentes Sur 58, Mexico
*Tel:* (05) 5126796; (05) 5218265
*Branch Office(s)*
Insurgentes Sur 317, Mexico 11, DF *Tel:* (05) 5744015
Ribera de San Cosme 133, Mexico 4, DF *Tel:* (05) 5464736

**Libreria Interacademica SA de CV**
Ave Sonora 206, Col Hipodromo, Mexico, DF 06100
*Tel:* (05) 265-1165 *Fax:* (05) 265-1164
*Telex:* 1773596 Aldime *Cable:* LIBINTER
*Key Personnel*
Administrative Manager: Lourdes Reyes

**Librolandia del Centro SA de CV**
Matamoros 83 Retorno Gaston Madrid No 4, 83000-18 Hermosillo, Sonora 83000-18
*Tel:* (062) 135646; (062) 170236 *Fax:* (062) 170236
*Key Personnel*
Dir: Miguel A Castellanos Araujo
Type of Business: Major Independent Bookseller

**MACH,** see Mexican Academic Clearing House (MACH)

**Mexican Academic Clearing House (MACH)**
Apdo 13-319, Deleg Benito Juarez, 03500 Mexico, DF
*Tel:* (05) 674 0779; (05) 674 0567 *Fax:* (05) 673 6209
*E-mail:* machbooks@terra.com.mx
*Web Site:* www.machbooks.com.mx
*Key Personnel*
Dir General: Lic Hugo Padilla Chacon
Technical Consultant: Ario Garza Mercado
Founded: 1969
Type of Business: Exporter

**Libreria Patria**
Renacimiento Room 180, Col San Juan Tlihuaca, Mexico, DF 02400
*Tel:* (05) 5613446
*Key Personnel*
Dir General: Rene Solis
Also Publisher.

**Libreria de Porrua Hermanos y Cia, SA**
Justo Sierra No 36, Col Centro, 06020 Mexico, DF
*Tel:* (05) 7025467 *Fax:* (05) 7026529
*E-mail:* porrua@porrua.com
*Web Site:* www.porrua.com *Cable:* PORRUAS, MEXICO
*Key Personnel*
President & Dir General: Jose Antonio Perez Porrua
Founded: 1900

*Branch Office(s)*
Prisciliano Sanchez No 460, Col Centro, 44100 Guadalajara, Jal *Tel:* (033) 36-14-46-16; (033) 36-14-08-58 *Fax:* (033) 36-14-08-27
Camino Real a San Lorenzo Tezonco No 285, Col El Manto, 09830 Mexico, DF *Tel:* (05) 685-69-00; (05) 68578-99
*Bookshop(s):* Urdaneta No 1 locales 7 y 8, Fracc Hornos, 39355 Acapulco, Gro *Tel:* (0744) 486-69-85 *Fax:* (0744) 486-69-95; Universidad Veracruzana, Av Universidad km 7.5, 76030 Coatzacoalcos, Ver; Av Mexico No 3370, Col Monraz, 45120 Guadalajara, Jal *Tel:* (033) 38-13-13-93; Mariano Otero No 3435, Col Verde Valle, 44550 Guadalajara, Jal *Tel:* (033) 36-47-19-36 *Fax:* (033) 36-47-19-46; Prisciliano Sanchez No 460, Col Centro, 44100 Guadalajara, Jal *Tel:* (033) 36-14-46-16; (033) 36-14-08-58 *Fax:* (033) 36-14-08-27; Universidad de Guadalajara, Facultad de Derecho, Av de los Maestros No 1060, Col Alcalde Barranquitas, 44260 Guadalajara, Jal *Tel:* (033) 38-54-66-45 *Fax:* (033) 38-53-51-74; Alonso No 12, 36000 Guanajuato, Gto *Tel:* (0473) 732-21-53; Via Magna Mz 3 lts 13/16, Col Centro Urbano, San Fernando La Herradura Magnocentro, 52760 Huixquilucan, Edo de Mexico *Tel:* (05) 595-92-82; Plaza Buenaventura, calle 31 No 144-AX40 sobre Circuito, Col Buenavista, 97117 Merida, Yucatan *Tel:* (0999) 926-26-09 *Fax:* (0999) 926-26-11; Argentina 15, Col Centro, 06020 Mexico, DF *Tel:* (05) 702-49-34; Bosques de Duraznos No 39 Primer Nivel, Col Bosques de las Lomas, 11700 Mexico, DF *Tel:* (05) 251-42-95; (05) 251-44-49; Camino Real a San Lorenzo Tezonco No 285, Col El Manto, 09830 Mexico, DF *Tel:* (05) 685-69-00; (05) 68578-99; Donceles No 104, Col Centro, 06020 Mexico, DF *Tel:* (05) 702-49-34 (ext 718); Av Juarez No 16, Col Centro, 06050 Mexico, DF *Tel:* (05) 521-28-30; (05) 512-01-75; 20 de Noviembre No 3, Col Centro, 06060 Mexico, DF *Tel:* (05) 728-99-05 (ext 3049); Durango No 230, Col Roma, 06700 Mexico, DF *Tel:* (05) 442-90-00 (ext 2181/2174); Moliere No 222, Col Los Morales, 11520 Mexico, DF *Tel:* (05) 283-72-00 (ext 7093); Av Coyoacan No 2000, Col Xoco, 03330 Mexico, DF *Tel:* (05) 422-19-00 (ext 5193); Periferico Sur No 4690, Col Jardines del Pedregal de San Angel, 04500 Mexico, DF *Tel:* (05) 447-16-00 (ext 4075); Av Vasco de Quiroga No 3800, Centro Comercial Santa Fe, 05109 Mexico, DF *Tel:* (05) 257-92-00; Av Insurgentes Sur No 2411, Col Tizapan, 01090 Mexico, DF *Tel:* (05) 616-26-60; Av Contreras No 300, Col San Jeronimo Lidice, 01020 Mexico, DF *Tel:* (05) 595-92-82; Canal de Miramontes No 2886, Col Alianza Popular Revolucionaria, 04800 Mexico, DF *Tel:* (05) 679-26-75; Pasaje Zocalo-Pino Suarez, locs 11 y 24, Col Centro, 06020 Mexico, DF *Tel:* (05) 522-10-78; (05) 522-53-93; Padre Mier 501-A Oriente, zona centro, 64000 Monterrey, NL *Tel:* (081) 83-43-42-08 *Fax:* (081) 83-43-42-10; Circuito Centro Comercial No 2251, Cd Satelite, 53100 Naucalpan, Edo de Mexico *Tel:* (05) 366-27-00; Plaza Kryss, locales 6, 7 y 8, Av Revolucion No 405, Col Periodistas, 42060 Pachuca, Hgo *Tel:* (0771) 719-37-55; 4 Norte 604 Centro Historico, Puebla, Puebla; Prolongacion Corregidora Sur No 24, Col Cimatario, 76030 Queretaro, Qro *Tel:* (0442) 224-12-80 *Fax:* (0442) 224-12-79; Blvd del Nino Poblano No 2510, Col Concepcion de la Cruz, 72450 Puebla, Pue *Tel:* (022) 22-73-88-00 (ext 4745); Biblioteca Mons Santiago Mendez Bravo, Av Tepeyac No 4800, Fraccionamiento Prados Tepeyac, 45050 Zapopan, Jalisco *Tel:* (0133) 3134-0800 (ext 2407)

**SCRIPTA - Distribucion y Servicios Editoriales SA de CV**
Copilco 178, Edis 22 Local D, Col Copilco Universidad, 04340 Mexico, DF
*Tel:* (05) 5481716 *Fax:* (05)5500564
*Key Personnel*
President & Dir: Bertha R Alavez Magana
Worldwide to academic libraries of scholarly books published in Latin America.
Type of Business: Distributor, Importer
*U.S. Office(s):* Scripta, 4011 Creek Rd, Youngstown, NY 14174, United States, Book Trade Counsellor: Lyman W Newlin *Tel:* 716-754-8145 *Fax:* 716-754-8145

**Servicio a La Iglesia Catolica AC Edicion y Distribucion de Libros Religiosos**
Viaducto Tlaplan No 20, Col Ejidos de Huipulco, Mexico
Mailing Address: PO Box 22-897, Tlalpan 14370
*Tel:* (05) 6710269 *Fax:* (05) 5441675
*Key Personnel*
President: Mrs Amalia R Pino

**Servicios Especializados y Representacionesen Comercio Exterior SA de CV**
Norte 198 No 691 Esq, Con Av Tahel, 15510 Mexico
*Tel:* (05) 7609129; (05) 7605149
*Key Personnel*
Dir: Filiberto Vargas
Manager: Julia Gutierrez

# Mongolia

**State Book Trading Office**
Leniny gudamch 41, Ulan-Bator
*Tel:* (01) 22312 *Cable:* Mongolbook

# Morocco

**Librairie des Colonnes**
54, rue Pasteur, Tanger
*Tel:* (09) 93 69 55 *Fax:* (099) 936955
*Key Personnel*
Dir: Mrs Rachel Muyal
Founded: 1947
Type of Business: Importer, Major Independent Bookseller
*Owned by:* Nouvelle Societe Kalila wa Dimna

**Librairie des Ecoles**
12 Ave Hassan II, Casablanca
*Tel:* (02) 22 25 22; (02) 26 67 41 *Fax:* (02) 20 10 03
Founded: 1947
Type of Business: Distributor, Exporter, Importer, Wholesaler

**Librairie Internationale**
70 rue T'ssoule, Rabat Maroc
Mailing Address: BP 302, Rabat Maroc
*Tel:* (07) 75 86 61 *Fax:* (07) 75 86 61
*E-mail:* libinter@iam.net.ma
*Key Personnel*
President & Owner: Mohamed Kerouach
Vice President: Brigitte Kerouach
Founded: 1960
Specialize in scientific books, CD-ROMs & multimedia.
Type of Business: Distributor, Exporter, Importer, Major Book Chain Headquarters, Major Independent Bookseller

*Owned by:* Kerouach Mohamed
*Branch Office(s)*
V Continents, 3 rue T'ssoule, Rabat (Souissi)

**Librairie Livre-Service**
11, rue Tata (ex Poincare), Casablanca
*Tel:* (02) 262072 *Fax:* (02) 473089
*Key Personnel*
Executive & General Manager: Faouzi Slaoui
Type of Business: Exporter, Importer, Major Book Chain Headquarters

**SMER Diffusion**
3 rue Ghazza, Rabat
*Tel:* (07) 723725; (07) 725960 *Fax:* (07) 701643
*Telex:* 3274
*Key Personnel*
Dir: Youssef Slaoui
*Branch Office(s)*
13 Ave Alaouyine, Rabat
*Bookshop(s):* Librarie Livre-Service, 11 rue Tata, Casablanca *Tel:* (02) 25975; Librarie de L'Agdal, angle Ave de France, Agdal, Rabat

**Societe Cherifienne de Distribution et de Presse Sochepress**
Angle Rues Rahal Ben Ahmed et St-Saens, Casablanca 21700
Mailing Address: BP 13683, 20300 Casablanca
*Tel:* (02) 22400223 *Fax:* (02) 22404032
*E-mail:* infopresse@sochepress.co.ma
*Telex:* 26660 28019 *Cable:* SOCHEPRESS CASABLANCA
*Key Personnel*
President, Dir General: Abdallah Lahrizi
Dir: Zhor Alaoui Belghiti; Mohamed Gounajjar; Meriem Kabbaj; Hassan Lahrizi; Maati Taimouri
Type of Business: Distributor, Exporter, Importer, Wholesaler

# Myanmar

**Hanthawaddy Bookshop**
157 Bo Aung Gyaw St, Rangoon
*Owned by:* Hanthawaddy Book House

**Knowledge Book House**
130, Bogyoke Aung San St, Pazundaung Tsp
*Tel:* (01) 290927
*Owned by:* Knowledge Printing & Publishing House

**Sabe U**
200 50 St, Rangoon

**Sarpay Beikman Bookshop**
529-531 Merchant St, Kyauktada Tsp, Rangoon
*Tel:* (01) 283277; (01) 16611
*Key Personnel*
Manager: U Tin Gyi
Founded: 1956
*Owned by:* Sarpay Beikman Board

**Sarpay Lawka**
173, 33rd St, KTDA, Yangon
*Tel:* (01) 274391; (01) 285166

**Thwe Thauk**
185 48 St, Rangoon

# Namibia

**Central News Agency (CNA)**
Kaiserstra Be Nord Private Bag 13176, Windhoek 9000
*Tel:* (061) 25625 *Fax:* (061) 227210

**ELCIN Book Depot**
PB 2013, Ondangwa 9000
*Tel:* (065) 240211 *Fax:* (065) 240536
*Key Personnel*
Contact: Anna K Kapenda
Type of Business: Major Book Chain Headquarters
*Owned by:* ELCIN

**Swakopmunder Buchhandlung**
PO Box 500, Kaiser Wilhelm St, Swakopmund
*Tel:* 402613 *Fax:* 404183
*Key Personnel*
Owner: H U Delius
Founded: 1900
Type of Business: Major Independent Bookseller

**Windhoeker Buchhandlung**
Independence Ave 69, Windhoek
Mailing Address: PO Box 1327, Windhoek
*Tel:* (061) 225216 *Fax:* (061) 225011
Type of Business: Distributor, Importer, Major Independent Bookseller
*Owned by:* Bertermann

# Nepal

**National Standards Publisher's & Bookseller's Association Nepal (NASPUBAN)**
Kamabakshee Tole, Gha 3-333, Chowk Bitra, Kathmandu 44601
Mailing Address: PO Box 3000, 15B Kathmandu 44601
*Tel:* (01) 212289; (01) 223036; (01) 224005 *Fax:* (01) 223036
*Telex:* 3000 1-SB-ASS-NP *Cable:* ANTERPRAGATISHEELSAPHOOPASA KATMANDU NEPAL
*Key Personnel*
Secretary General: Ganesh Lall Chhipa
Executive Man Dir: Chandra Lall Ranjitkar
Dir: Ganesh Daas Chhipa
Editorial: Aneeta Shobha Tuladhar
Sales: Padma L Tuladhar; Suneeta D Tuladhar; Parbatee S Ranjitkar
Production: Shanta S Ranjitkar
Publicity: Chandrawatee C Ranjitkar
Rights & Permissions: Renooka S Tuladhar
Founded: 1963
Centre for Central General Selling. Order Supplies, Subscriptions & Publications.
*Branch Office(s)*
09-63-07, Dathwee Chhen Twa Gallee
Chowk Bhitra Purano Bazar, Arniko-Barhabise-9, Arniko Rajmarg-87K M Bagmati Anchal, Barhabise, 45303 Katmandu Mail Centre
*Bookshop(s):* People's Friendship Books & Periodicals Shop, Dathwee Chhen Twa Gallee, Purano Bazar, Arniko Barhabise 9, Barhabise 45303; Nepal Books & Periodicals House, Maisthan Tole, Birganj; People's Books & Periodicals Centre, Datraya Square, Bhaktapur; Banepa Books Depot, Banepa Nayan Bazar, Kavrepalanchok Dist; Jagriti Books Centre, Itahary Sunsary, Koshee Zone; People's Books Centre, Chenpur, Sakhuwa Sabha, Koshee Zone; Janapriya Pustak Bhandar, Patan Dhoka, Lalitpur

**Ratna Book Distributors (Pvt) Ltd**
PO Box 1080, Bagbazaar, Kathmandu
*Tel:* 4242027 *Fax:* 4245421
*E-mail:* rpb@wlink.com.np
*Key Personnel*
Manager: Govinda P Shrestha
Contact: Roshan P Shrestha
Founded: 1945
Type of Business: Distributor, Importer, Wholesaler
*Branch Office(s)*
Saraswati Book Centre, Near UNDP Bldg, Pulchowk, Lalitpur, Kathmandu
Ratna Pustak Bhandar, Bhotahity PO Box 98, Kathmandu *Fax:* (01) 248421 *E-mail:* rpb@wlink.com.np

# Netherlands

**Athenaeum Boekhandel**
Spui 14-16, 1012 XA Amsterdam
*Tel:* (020) 6226248 *Fax:* (020) 6384901
*E-mail:* info@athenaeum.nl
*Web Site:* www.athenaeum.nl
*Key Personnel*
Man Dir: M Asscher *Tel:* (020) 6226210
    *E-mail:* m.asscher@athenaeum.nl
Founded: 1966
Type of Business: Importer, Major Independent Bookseller
*Branch Office(s)*
Athenaeum Boekhandel Haarlem, Gedempte Oude Gracht 70, 2011 GT Haarlem
    *Tel:* (023) 5318755 *Fax:* (023) 5322603
    *E-mail:* haarlem@athenaeum.nl
Athenaeum Boekhandel Hogeschoolboekhandel, Kohnstammhuis DO.31, Wibautstraat 2-4, 1091 GM Amsterdam *Tel:* (020) 5995553 *Fax:* (020) 4686186 *E-mail:* wibaut@athenaeum.nl

**John Benjamins Publishing Co**
Klaprozenweg 105, 1033 NN Amsterdam
Mailing Address: Postbus 36224, 1020 ME Amsterdam
*Tel:* (020) 6304747 *Fax:* (020) 6739773 (publishing); (020) 6792956 (antiquariat)
*E-mail:* customer.services@benjamins.nl
*Web Site:* www.benjamins.com
*Key Personnel*
Dir: John Benjamins
Also publisher & antiquarian.
*Branch Office(s)*
Benjamins North America Inc, PO Box 27519, Philadelphia, PA 19118-0519, United States, Manager: Paul Peranteau *Tel:* 215-836-1200 *Fax:* 215-836-1204 *E-mail:* paul@benjamins.com

**Broese BV**
Stadhuisbrug 5, 3511 KP Utrecht
*Tel:* (030) 2335200 *Fax:* (030) 2314071
*E-mail:* info@broese.net
*Web Site:* www.broese.net
*Telex:* 40411 Boek
*Key Personnel*
Man Dir: Hylco Wijnants
Type of Business: Distributor, Exporter, Importer
*Owned by:* Boekhandels Groep Nederland
*Bookshop(s):* Minrebroederstr 13, 3512 GS Utrecht *Tel:* (030) 2336500 *Fax:* (030) 2316000; Heidelberglaan 2, 3584 CS Utrecht *Tel:* (030) 2155400 *Fax:* (030) 2540303

**Bruna BV**
Croeselaan 15, 3521 BJ Utrecht
Mailing Address: Postbus 30130, 3503 AC Utrecht
*Tel:* (0900) 1200 100

*E-mail:* klantenservice@bruna.com
*Web Site:* www.bruna.nl
*Telex:* 47518
*Key Personnel*
President: J V Hanegem
*Owned by:* Buehrmann-Tetterode NV
*Bookshop(s):* A P Standaard Boekhandel (Delft, Zaandam); Boekhandel Bergmans (Maastricht); Boekhandel H Coebergh Haarlem; Boekhandel Hugo Jonkers (Eindhoven); Moderne Boekhandel (Amsterdam); Boekhandel Mosmans ('s Hertogenbosch); Boekhandel Revers en van Brummen (Dordrecht); Boekhandel F Schoth (Boxmeer); Ten Have en Hoofdstadboekhandel (Amsterdam); Boekhandel Van Broek (Zeist); Boekhandel Van Leeuwen (Roosendaal)

**Dekker v d Vegt**
Marikenstr 29, 6511 PX Nijmegen
*Tel:* (024) 322 10 10 *Fax:* (024) 324 21 11
*E-mail:* mariken@dekker.nl
*Web Site:* www.dekker.nl
*Key Personnel*
Manager: P H M Hooghof
Founded: 1856
Type of Business: Major Independent Bookseller
*Owned by:* Boekhandels Groep Nederland
*Branch Office(s)*
Koningstr 31, 6811 DG Arnhem *Tel:* (026) 445 23 45 *Fax:* (026) 351 10 18 *E-mail:* arnhem@dekker.nl
Thomas van Aquinostr 1a, 6525 GD Nijmegen
    *Tel:* (024) 355 11 27 *Fax:* (024) 356 07 20
    *E-mail:* campus@dekker.nl

**European Book Service**
PO Box 130, 3454 ZJ De Meern
*Tel:* (030) 6660211 *Fax:* (030) 6662674
*Key Personnel*
Man Dir: S Valk
Export Manager: R Puyk

**Boekhandel Gianotten BV**
Emmapassage 17, 5038 XA Tilburg
*Tel:* (013) 465 11 11 *Fax:* (013) 535 59 62
*E-mail:* emma@gianotten.nl
*Web Site:* www.gianotten.nl
*Key Personnel*
Manager: A J H Gunsing
*Owned by:* Boekhandels Groep Nederland
*Branch Office(s)*
De Barones 29 & 63, 4811 XZ Breda
    *Tel:* (076) 514 97 00 *Fax:* (076) 514 15 19
    *E-mail:* breda@gianotten.nl
Warandelaan 2, 5037 AB Tilburg *Tel:* (013) 465 11 11 *Fax:* (013) 463 54 04 *E-mail:* acad@gianotten.nl

**Ginsberg Univ Boekhandel**
Breestr 127-129, 2311 CM Leiden
*Tel:* (071) 5160562 *Fax:* (071) 5127505
*E-mail:* bree127@kooyker.nl
*Key Personnel*
Manager: R Egan
Type of Business: Major Independent Bookseller

**ICOB/Atrium**
Ondernemingsweg 60, 2404 HN Alphen aan den Rijn
Mailing Address: Postbus 392, 2400 AJ Alphen aan den Rijn
*Tel:* (0172) 43 72 31 *Fax:* (0172) 43 93 79
*E-mail:* icobal@xs4all.nl
*Key Personnel*
Man Dir: Hans Meijer
Publisher: Dennis Friedhoff
Founded: 1965
Also publisher.
Type of Business: Remainder Dealer

**Nilsson & Lamm BV, Algemene Import Boekhandel**
Pampuslaan 212, 1382 JS Weesp
Mailing Address: Postbus 195, 1380 AD Weesp
*Tel:* (0294) 49 49 49 *Fax:* (0294) 49 44 55
*E-mail:* info@nilsson-lamm.nl
*Web Site:* www.nilsson-lamm.nl
*Key Personnel*
Man Dir: M Brouwer
Sales & Distribution Dir: W J van Loon
Founded: 1880
Also acts as publisher.
Type of Business: Distributor, Wholesaler

**Pegasus Publishers & Booksellers**
Singel 367, 1012 WL Amsterdam
Mailing Address: PO Box 11470, 1001 GL Amsterdam
*Tel:* (020) 6231138 *Fax:* (020) 6203478
*E-mail:* pegasus@pegasusboek.nl
*Web Site:* www.pegasusboek.nl
*Key Personnel*
Dir: Joop F Yisberg
Founded: 1945
Type of Business: Exporter, Importer, Major Independent Bookseller

**Van Piere Boeken**
Heuvel Galerie 190 & 232, 5611 DK Eindhoven
*Tel:* (040) 244 40 45 *Fax:* (040) 246 39 49
*E-mail:* info@vanpiere.nl
*Web Site:* www.vanpiere.nl
*Key Personnel*
Manager: Chris de Plot
Founded: 1848
Type of Business: Major Independent Bookseller
*Owned by:* Boekhandels Groep Nederland
*Branch Office(s)*
Rachelsmolen 1, 5612 MA Eindhoven *Tel:* (0877) 876277 *Fax:* (0877) 876266 *E-mail:* fontys1@vanpiere.nl
Ds Th Fliednerstr 2, 5631 DN Eindhoven
    *Tel:* (0877) 876211 *Fax:* (0877) 876200
    *E-mail:* fontys2@vanpiere.nl
Den Dolech 2, 5612 AZ Eindhoven
    *Tel:* (040) 244 24 39 *Fax:* (040) 245 41 84
    *E-mail:* tuboek@vanpiere.nl

**Scheltema**
Koningsplein 20, 1017 BB Amsterdam
*Tel:* (020) 5231411 *Fax:* (020) 6227684
*E-mail:* scheltema@scheltema.nl; informatie@scheltema.nl
*Web Site:* www.scheltema.nl
*Key Personnel*
General Manager: H Wijnants
Sales Manager: A Luinstra; C Noordhoek; Mrs T Scholtens
Founded: 1853
Type of Business: Major Independent Bookseller
*Owned by:* Boekhandels Groep Nederland
*Branch Office(s)*
Meibergdreef 9, 1105 AZ Amsterdam *Tel:* (020) 566 27 77 *Fax:* (020) 696 87 90 *E-mail:* amc@scheltema.nl
Roeterstr 41, 1030 BH Amsterdam *Tel:* (020) 420 53 67 *Fax:* (020) 420 64 27 *E-mail:* sarphati@scheltema.nl
Tafelbergweg 51, 1105 BD Amsterdam
    *Tel:* (020) 652 12 94 *Fax:* (020) 652 12 93
    *E-mail:* tafelbergweg@scheltema.nl
Weesperzijde 188, 1097 DZ Amsterdam
    *Tel:* (020) 468 60 68 *Fax:* (020) 468 60 69
    *E-mail:* leeuwenburg@scheltema.nl

**Valeton b v**
Nes 35, Amsterdam
*Tel:* (020) 6201454 *Fax:* (020) 6279209
*Key Personnel*
President: Alexander Valeton
Vice President: Heleen Van Ketwich-Verschuur
Founded: 1990

Type of Business: Distributor, Exporter, Importer, Major Book Chain Headquarters, Wholesaler
Owned by: Alexander Valeton
Bookshop(s): Dam 8, 1012 CG Amsterdam; West-zeeoyk 20, Rotterdam

**H de Vries Boeken**
Gedempte Oude Gracht 27, 2011 GK Haarlem
Mailing Address: Postbus 274, 2000 AG Haarlem
Tel: (023) 5319458 Fax: (023) 5311680
E-mail: boeken@vries-boeken.com
Web Site: www.vries-boeken.com
Key Personnel
Man Dir: R H C de Vries; K de Vries Kuijper
Manager, General Bookshop: G Braaksma
Manager, School Textbooks: A Kroenburg
Founded: 1905
Type of Business: Major Independent Bookseller

# Netherlands Antilles

**De WitAruba Boekhandel**
L G Smith Blvd 110, Oranjestad, Aruba
Mailing Address: PO Box 386, Oranjestad, Aruba
Tel: (0297) 823500 Fax: (0297) 821575
    Cable: DEWITSTORES
Key Personnel
Man Dir: R de Zwart
Stationery, souvenirs, gifts, clothing.
Type of Business: Distributor, Importer, Major Independent Bookseller
Owned by: De Wit Stores NV

# New Zealand

**Arts Centre Bookshop**
28 Worcester Blvd, Christchurch
Tel: (03) 365 5277 Fax: (03) 365 3293
E-mail: info@booksnz.com
Web Site: www.booksnz.com
Type of Business: Major Independent Bookseller

**Bennetts Bookshop Ltd**
Massey University Tritea Campus, Commercial Complex, Palmerston North
Tel: (06) 354 6020 Fax: (06) 354 6716
    Toll Free Fax: 0800 118 333
E-mail: books@bennetts.co.nz; massey@bennetts.co.nz
Web Site: www.bennetts.co.nz Cable: Bennibooks
Key Personnel
Group General Manager: Trevor Day
Owned by: Blue Star Consumer Retailing Ltd
Branch Office(s)
Massey University Albany Campus, Albany, Auckland Tel: (09) 443 9707 Fax: (09) 443 9708 E-mail: aku@bennetts.co.nz
Auckland University of Technology, Commerce House, 360 Queen St, Auckland City Tel: (09) 307 9802 Fax: (09) 307 9927 E-mail: qau@bennetts.co.nz
Auckland University of Technology, Student Plaza Gate 2, Wellesley St, Auckland City Tel: (09) 307 9801 Fax: (09) 307 9986 E-mail: wau@bennetts.co.nz
Christchurch Polytechnic Institute of Technology, Madras St, Christchurch Tel: (03) 365 1394 Fax: (03) 365 7314 E-mail: chp@bennetts.co.nz
University of Waikato, Gate 5, Hillcrest Rd, Hamilton Tel: (07) 856 6813 Fax: (07) 856 2255 E-mail: wku@bennetts.co.nz

Walkato Institute of Technology, Gate 5, Tristram St, Hamilton Tel: (07) 839 0003 Fax: (07) 834 1291 E-mail: wkp@bennetts.co.nz
Manukau Institute of Technology, Gate 11, NP Block, Otara Rd, Manukau City Tel: (09) 274 8627 Fax: (09) 274 8830 E-mail: mkp@bennetts.co.nz
Auckland University of Technology Akoranga Campus, Gate 1, Akoranga Drive, Northcote Tel: (09) 307 9803 Fax: (09) 307 9967 E-mail: aau@bennetts.co.nz
Corner Lambton Quay & Bowen St, Wellington Tel: (04) 499 3433 Fax: (04) 499 3375 E-mail: gbs@bennetts.co.nz
Massey University Wellington, Gate E, Tasman St, Wellington Tel: (04) 384 1407 Fax: (04) 384 1408 E-mail: wgp@bennetts.co.nz

**Blackmore's Booksellers BLA**
284 Trafalgar St, Nelson
Tel: (03) 5489992 Fax: (03) 5466779
Key Personnel
Partner: Tim Blackmore; Jennifer Blackmore
Type of Business: Major Independent Bookseller

**Hedley's Bookshop Ltd**
150 Queen St, Masterton
Tel: (06) 3782875 Fax: (06) 3782570
E-mail: sales@hedleysbooks.co.nz
Web Site: www.hedleysbooks.co.nz
Key Personnel
Manager: David Hedley Tel: (061) 3 9499 2645 E-mail: david@hedleysbooks.com.au
Founded: 1907
Also publisher.
Type of Business: Distributor, Major Independent Bookseller
Branch Office(s)
Hedley Australia, PO Box 1058, Melbourne, Victoria 3079, Australia Tel: (02) 4992645 Fax: (03) 4994060
Bookshop(s): Hedley's Bookshop (BAM), Mezzanine level, Central Library Bldg, 65 Victoria St, Wellington Tel: (04) 4731730 Fax: (04) 4711635

**Janeff Books (JM & MJ Books Ltd)**
16 Te Mata Rd, Havelock North 4230
Tel: (070) 777783
Key Personnel
Owner: Max Dempsey; Margaret Dempsey
Type of Business: Major Independent Bookseller

**JM & MJ Books Ltd**, see Janeff Books (JM & MJ Books Ltd)

**Kydds Paper Plus**
77 Hakiaha St, Taumarunui
Tel: (07) 8957430 Fax: (07) 8957977
E-mail: kyddpp@xtra.co.nz
Web Site: www.middle-of-everywhere.co.nz/kyddspp.htm
Key Personnel
Owner: Mrs J J Kydd
Type of Business: Major Independent Bookseller

**Lincoln University Bookshop**
Lincoln University, Ellesmere Junction Rd/Springs Rd, Lincoln, Canterbury
Mailing Address: PO Box 94, Canterbury 8150
Tel: (03) 3252811 Fax: (03) 3252944
E-mail: info@lincoln.ac.nz
Web Site: www.lincoln.ac.nz
Key Personnel
Supervisor: Bronwyn Mclean E-mail: mcleanb@lincoln.ac.nz
Type of Business: Major Independent Bookseller

**Living Word Distribution**
52 Collingwood St, Hamilton 2001
Tel: (07) 839 5607 Fax: (07) 834 3916

E-mail: livingword.ltd@xtra.co.nz
Key Personnel
Executive Dir: G T Hooper
Founded: 1977
Subjects: Books, gifts, music & video, retailer
Type of Business: Distributor, Exporter, Importer, Major Independent Bookseller, Wholesaler
Parent Company: Living Word Distributors Ltd

**McLeods Booksellers**
1269 Tutanekai St, Rotorua
Mailing Address: PO Box 623, Rotorua
Tel: (07) 3485388 Fax: (07) 3490288
E-mail: mcleods@clear.net.nz
Web Site: www.mcleodsbooks.co.nz
Key Personnel
Manager: D C Thorp
Founded: 1944
Traditional, stock-holding combining selection & service with latest bibliographic technology. Specialise in: Maori books & floral art books.
Type of Business: Major Independent Bookseller

**Omega Distributors Ltd**
10 Andrew Baxter Dr, Mangere, 1701 Auckland
Mailing Address: PO Box 107025, Airport Oaks Mangere, 1730 Auckland
Tel: (09) 2570081 Fax: (09) 2570082
E-mail: books@omegavision.co.nz
Web Site: www.omegavision.co.nz/omega.html
Key Personnel
Executive Dir: Graham Walker
General Manager: M J Frith
Founded: 1958
Christian book/Bible/gift distributors.
Memberships: Booksellers Association of New Zealand; Christian Booksellers Association of New Zealand.
Type of Business: Distributor, Importer
Owned by: Vision Resources Ltd

**Pathfinder Bookshop**
New Gallery Bldg, 38 Lorne St, Auckland Central
Tel: (09) 3790147 Toll Free Tel: 0800 55 44 55 Fax: (09) 3098167
E-mail: Tim@pathfinder.co.nz; Jennifer@pathfinder.co.nz
Web Site: www.pathfinder.co.nz
Founded: 1981
Type of Business: Major Independent Bookseller

**Peaceful Living Publications**
Unit 7B 42 Courtney Rd, Tauranga, BOP
Mailing Address: PO Box 300, Tauranga, BOP
Tel: (071) 5718513 Fax: (071) 5718513
E-mail: books@peaceful-living.co.nz
Key Personnel
Manager: Wayne Morgan
Office Manager: Maria Rawson
Metaphysics, mysticism, health, tarot cards, audio cassettes & CDs, self awareness & New Age literature.
Type of Business: Distributor

**School Supplies (NZ) Ltd**
13 Sir William Ave, East Tamaki, Auckland
Mailing Address: PO Box 58004, Greenmount, Auckland
Tel: (09) 273 9883 Toll Free Tel: 800 577 700 Fax: (09) 273 9881 Toll Free Fax: 800 367 724
E-mail: orders@schoolsupplies.co.nz
Web Site: www.schoolsupplies.co.nz
Telex: NZ 63426
Key Personnel
General Manager: Graham Wadams
Curriculum Resource Manager: Michaela Davis
Type of Business: Distributor, Importer, Wholesaler
Owned by: New Zealand Office Products Ltd
Branch Office(s)
108 Bamford St, PO Box 19645, Woolston,

Christchurch *Tel:* (03) 384-6499 *Fax:* 800-249-850
196-208 Middleton Rd, Churton Park, PO Box 50-384, Johnsonville, Wellington *Tel:* (04) 232 8680 *Fax:* (04) 232 9469

**South Pacific Books Imports Ltd**
PO Box 303 243, North Harbour, Auckland 1330
*Tel:* (09) 649 448 1591 *Fax:* (09) 649 448 1592
*E-mail:* sales@soupacbooks.co.nz
*Web Site:* www.soupacbooks.co.nz
*Key Personnel*
Man Dir: Alan McEldowney
Founded: 1984
Book wholesaler.
*Warehouse:* 6 King St, Grey Lynn, Auckland

**South Sea Books**
37 Holliss Ave, Cashmere, Christchurch
*Tel:* (03) 3317630
*E-mail:* southsea@ihug.co.nz
*Web Site:* www.abebooks.com/home/southsea
*Key Personnel*
Owner: Glenn Haszarde
Founded: 1984
Type of Business: Exporter, Importer, Major Independent Bookseller, Wholesaler

**Techbooks**
378 Broadway, Newmarket, Auckland
Mailing Address: Private Bag 99939, Newmarket, Auckland
*Tel:* (09) 524-0132 *Fax:* (09) 523-3769
*E-mail:* techbooks@techbooks.co.nz
*Web Site:* www.techbooks.co.nz
*Key Personnel*
Man Dir: Colin Greenwood
Founded: 1983
Type of Business: Major Independent Bookseller
*Branch Office(s)*
82 Waring Taylor St, Welington
*Bookshop(s):* 378-380 Broadway, Newmarket

**Unity Books Ltd**
57 Willis St, Wellington
*Tel:* (04) 499 4245 *Fax:* (04) 499 4246
*E-mail:* unity.books@clear.net.nz
*Key Personnel*
Dir: A H Preston
Manager: Tilly Lloyd
Type of Business: Major Independent Bookseller
*Bookshop(s):* Unity Books, 19 High St, Auckland
*Tel:* (09) 3070731 *Fax:* (09) 3734883

**University Book Shop (Auckland) Ltd**
Kate Edgar Bldg, 2 Alfred St, Auckland Central 1001
Mailing Address: PO Box 90944, Auckland Mail Centre, Auckland 1001
*Tel:* (09) 306 2700 *Fax:* (09) 306 2701
*E-mail:* ubsbooks@ubsbooks.co.nz
*Web Site:* www.ubsbooks.co.nz *Cable:* UNIBOOKS
*Key Personnel*
Manager: Ken McIntyre
Founded: 1966
Type of Business: Importer, Major Independent Bookseller
*Owned by:* Whitcoulls Ltd/Auckland University Students Association
*Bookshop(s):* Tamaki Campus, The Hub, Merton Rd, Auckland *Tel:* (09) 3737599 (ext 85295); Waiariki Campus, Mokoia Dr, Auckland *Tel:* (07) 3468806 *Fax:* (07) 3468806 *E-mail:* ubsbooks@ubsbooks.com

**University Book Shop (Canterbury) Ltd**
University of Canterbury, Private Bag 4800, Christchurch
*Tel:* (03) 3667001 *Fax:* (03) 3642999
*E-mail:* info@canterbury.ac.nz

*Web Site:* www.canterbury.ac.nz
*Key Personnel*
Manager: David Ault *E-mail:* david@ubscan.co.nz
Founded: 1971
Type of Business: Exporter, Importer, Major Independent Bookseller

**University Book Shop (Otago) Ltd**
378 Great King St, Dunedin
Mailing Address: PO Box 6060, Dunedin
*Tel:* (03) 4776976 *Fax:* (03) 4776571
*E-mail:* ubs@unibooks.co.nz
*Web Site:* www.unibooks.co.nz
*Key Personnel*
Manager: Bill Noble *Tel:* (03) 474 5401 (ext 888) *E-mail:* billn@unibooks.co.nz
Founded: 1945
Type of Business: Major Independent Bookseller

**Whitcoulls Ltd**
Level 5, Synergy House, 131 Queen St, Auckland
Mailing Address: Private Bag 92098, Auckland
*Tel:* (09) 356 5410 *Fax:* (09) 356 5423
*E-mail:* feedback@whitcoulls.co.nz
*Web Site:* www.whitcoulls.co.nz
*Telex:* NZ 60402
*Key Personnel*
Chief Executive: David Brown
General Manager: David Worley
Contact: Simone Howett
59 Stores nationwide.
*Owned by:* W H Smith

# Nicaragua

**Libreria Tecnologica Universitaria**
Universidad Centroamericana, Pista de la Resistencia, Managua
Mailing Address: Apdo 69, Managua
*Tel:* (02) 773026 *Fax:* (02) 670106

**Libreria Universitaria**
Universidad Nacional Autonoma de Nicaragua, Recinto Universitario-Ruben, Dario, Managua
*Tel:* (0311) 2612; (0311) 2613

# Nigeria

**Ahmadu Bello University Bookshop Ltd**
PMB 1094, Samaru, Zaria, Kaduna State
*Tel:* (069) 550054
*Key Personnel*
General Manager: K A Momoh

**Benin University Bookshop**
Ugbowo-Lagos Rd, Ugobowo, Benin City, Edo State
*Tel:* (052) 600443 *Fax:* (052) 602370
*E-mail:* registra@uniben.edu
*Web Site:* www.uniben.edu
*Telex:* 41365
*Key Personnel*
Manager: S O Ehiede

**Challenge Bookshops**
c/o ECWA Productions Ltd, 10, Kano Rd, Jos
Mailing Address: PMB 2010, Jos
*Tel:* (073) 53897; (073) 52230
*Key Personnel*
General Manager: E C Nwobilo

Type of Business: Wholesaler
*Owned by:* ECWA Productions Ltd

**CSS Bookshops**
Division of CSS Limited
19 Broad St, Lagos
Mailing Address: PO Box 174, Lagos
*Tel:* (01) 2633081; (01) 2637009; (01) 2637023; (01) 2633010 *Fax:* (01) 2637089
*E-mail:* cssbookshops@skannet.com.ng
*Key Personnel*
Chief Executive: Kola Olaitan
Secretary: Dotun Adegboyega
Founded: 1869
Also publisher.
Type of Business: Distributor, Importer, Major Book Chain Headquarters, Wholesaler
*Owned by:* The Church of Nigeria

**Fola Abbey Educational Book Services, Fola Abbey Bookshops Ltd**
One Odulami Lane, off Kakawa St, Lagos, Lagos State
*Tel:* (01) 2636679 *Fax:* (01) 825268
*Key Personnel*
Chief Executive: Hakeem A Sanni
Suppliers of all Nigerian publications to Universities, Libraries & individuals.
Type of Business: Exporter

**Mabrochi International Co Ltd**
143 Moshood Abiola Way, Ebute Metta (West), Lagos, Lagos State
Mailing Address: PO Box 1509, Surulere PO, Lagos, Lagos State
*Tel:* (01) 847603 *Fax:* (01) 2662275
*E-mail:* mabrochiadol@yahoo.com
*Key Personnel*
Sales Executive: Adol C Ofoegbu
Founded: 1976
Specialize in mail order services worldwide. Academic jobber for overseas universities & libraries. Subscription agent for Nigerian publications.
Type of Business: Distributor, Exporter, Importer, Major Independent Bookseller, Wholesaler
*Branch Office(s)*
7 Oyabiyi St, Yaba, Lagos, Lagos State (Tertiary textbooks)

**Nigerian Book Suppliers Ltd**
28, Akinremi St, Ikeja
Mailing Address: PO Box 4440, Ikeja
*Tel:* (01) 22407
*Telex:* 20202 Tds Box 052 Ikeja
*Key Personnel*
Man Dir: B Fatayi-Williams
Bookseller & library supplier specializing in professional books (especially legal, management, banking & accountancy), Africana, mass market paperback fiction & library titles for tertiary level libraries.

**Odusote Bookstores Ltd**
68 Obafemi Awolowo Way, Oke-Ado, Ibadan
Mailing Address: PO Box 244, Ibadan
*Tel:* (02) 2316451 *Fax:* (02) 2316451
*E-mail:* odubooks@infoweb.abs.net
*Telex:* 31215 (Odbook NG) *Cable:* ODBOOK, IBADAN
*Key Personnel*
Man Dir: Ola Odusote
Manager: Olufemi Odusote
Founded: 1964
Type of Business: Distributor, Wholesaler
*Branch Office(s)*
177 Herbert Macaulay St, Yaba, Lagos State
*Tel:* (01) 861248

**University Bookshop Ltd**
Obafemi Awolowo University, Ile-Ife, Osun State

*Tel:* (036) 230290 *Cable:* BOOKSHOP
  IFEVARSITY
*Key Personnel*
Man Dir: Oyeniyi Osundina
Founded: 1964
Type of Business: Major Independent Bookseller
*Owned by:* Obafemi Awolowo University
*Branch Office(s)*
Ado-Ekiti
Osogbo

## University Bookshop (Nigeria) Ltd
University of Ibadan, Ibadan, Oyo State
*Tel:* (02) 400550 (ext 1208); (02) 400550 (ext
  1047); (02) 400614 (ext 1244); (02) 400614
  (ext 1042)
*Key Personnel*
General Manager: Akin Aqbebi
*Branch Office(s)*
University College Hospital

## University of Lagos Bookshop
PMB 1013, University of Lagos, Idiaraba, Lagos
*Tel:* (01) 820279 *Fax:* (01) 822644
*Telex:* 26983 Unilag.NG *Cable:* UNIVERSITY
  OF LAGOS
*Key Personnel*
Manager: Mrs Oluronke Orimalade
Founded: 1966
Type of Business: Importer
*Branch Office(s)*
College of Medicine, University of Lagos, Idi-
  Araba, Surulere, Lagos

## University of Nigeria Bookshop Ltd
Nsukka, Enugu State
*Tel:* (042) 332077; (042) 771911
*Key Personnel*
Manager: B U Ezugwu
Founded: 1963
Books, stationery & related goods.
Membership(s): United Educational Institute Ltd.
Type of Business: Distributor, Major Independent
  Bookseller

## John West Publications Co Ltd
Acme Rd, Lagos
Mailing Address: PO Box 2416, Lagos
*Tel:* (01) 932011
*Telex:* John West Ikeja
*Key Personnel*
Man Dir: Alhaji Lateef Kayode Jakande

# Norway

## A/L Biblioteksentralen (The Norwegian
  Library Bureau)
Malerhaugveien 20, 0661 Oslo
Mailing Address: Postboks 6142, Etterstad, 0602
  Oslo
*Tel:* (022) 08 34 00 *Fax:* (022) 08 39 01
*E-mail:* bs@bibsent.no
*Web Site:* www.bibsent.no
*Key Personnel*
Administrative Dir: Borge Hofset *E-mail:* bho@
  bibsent.no
Head of Book/Media Dept: Toril Anderson
Founded: 1952
Bibliographic products & service; Materials, fur-
  nishings & interior architects for libraries.

## Forlagsentralen ANS
Karihaugveien 22, 1086 Oslo
Mailing Address: Postboks 1, Furuset, 1001 Oslo
*Tel:* (022) 32 96 00 *Fax:* (022) 32 96 01
*E-mail:* firmapost@forlagsentralen.no
*Web Site:* www.forlagsentralen.no

*Key Personnel*
President: Eivind T Skogseide
Founded: 1964
Type of Business: Distributor

## ARK Bokhandel
Posboks 6693, St Olavs Plass, 0129 Oslo
*Tel:* 22 99 07 50 *Fax:* 22 99 07 51
*E-mail:* resepsjon@ark.no
*Web Site:* www.arkbokhandel.no *Cable:*
  BOKBEYER BERGEN
*Key Personnel*
Dir: Arne Henrik Frogh
*Bookshop(s):* Ark Aker Brygge, Fjordalleen
  10, 0250 Oslo *Tel:* 22 83 81 33 *Fax:* 22
  83 82 42 *E-mail:* aker.brygge@ark.no; Ark
  Amanda, Longhammerveien 27, 5536 Hauge-
  sund *Tel:* 52 71 98 11 *Fax:* 52 71 21 19
  *E-mail:* amanda@ark.no; Ark Asker, Stroket
  5, 1383 Asker *Tel:* 66 79 95 70 *Fax:* 66 90
  05 80; 66 79 95 80 *E-mail:* asker@ark.no;
  Ark Bekkestua, Gamle Ringeriksv 37, 1357
  Bekkestua *Tel:* 67 12 02 05 *Fax:* 67 12 30
  42 *E-mail:* bekkestua@ark.no; Ark Berge,
  Prostebakken 3, 4006 Stavanger *Tel:* 51 89
  52 50 *Fax:* 51 89 52 52 *E-mail:* berge@ark.
  no; Ark Berge avd BI, Hesbygt 5, 4014 Stavanger *Tel:* 51 55 02 21 *E-mail:* ark.bi@ark.no;
  Ark Beyer Asane, Asane Senter, 5116 Ulset
  *Tel:* 55 18 26 40 *Fax:* 55 19 49 25 *E-mail:* ark.
  beyer.aasane@ark.no; Ark Beyer Nesttun Senter, Nesttun Senter, Ostre Nesttunv 16, 5221
  Nesttun *Tel:* 55 13 28 95 *Fax:* 55 13 28 96
  *E-mail:* nesttun.senter@ark.no; Ark Beyer
  Strandgaten, Strandgt 4, 5013 Bergen *Tel:* 55
  30 77 00 *Fax:* 55 30 77 10 *E-mail:* beyer@
  ark.no; Ark Beyer Vestkanten, Vestkanten,
  5171 Loddefjord *Tel:* 55 26 90 92 *Fax:* 55
  26 56 84 *E-mail:* vestkanten@ark.no; Ark
  Brundalen, Brundalen Videregaende skole,
  7458 Jakobsli *Tel:* 73 91 37 80 *Fax:* 73 91
  37 80 *E-mail:* brundalen@ark.no; Ark Bruns
  Brunhjornet, Kongensgt 10/14, 7484 Trondheim *Tel:* 73 87 93 00 *Fax:* 73 87 93 05
  *E-mail:* bruns@ark.no; Ark Bruns City Syd,
  City Syd, Ostre Rosten, 7075 Tiller *Tel:* 72
  88 88 84 *Fax:* 72 88 13 50 *E-mail:* citysyd@
  ark.no; Ark Bruns Melhus, Melhus torget,
  7224 Melhus *Tel:* 72 87 09 90 *Fax:* 72 87 28
  68 *E-mail:* melhus@ark.no; Ark Bruns Moholt, Moholt storsenter, Brosetvn 177, 7048
  Trondheim *Tel:* 73 93 15 70 *Fax:* 73 93 15
  65 *E-mail:* moholt@ark.no; Ark Bruns Torget, Trondheim Torg, Tinghusplassen 1, 7013
  Trondheim *Tel:* 73 87 93 27 *Fax:* 73 50 50
  53 *E-mail:* torget@ark.no; Ark City Nord,
  City Nord Stormyra, 8013 Bodo *Tel:* 75 50
  80 40 *Fax:* 75 50 80 41 *E-mail:* citynord@
  ark.no; Ark Dahl, Storgt 29, 6413 Molde
  *Tel:* 71 20 55 00 *Fax:* 71 20 55 01; 71 20 55
  02 *E-mail:* dahl@ark.no; Ark Down Town,
  Storgt 70, 3921 Porsgrunn *Tel:* 35 55 76
  70 *Fax:* 35 55 76 70 *E-mail:* down.town@
  ark.no; Ark Dyring, Storgt 154, 3915 Porsgrunn *Tel:* 35 56 98 50 *Fax:* 35 56 98 60
  *E-mail:* dyring@ark.no; Ark Egertorget, Ovre
  Slottsgt 23/25, 0157 Oslo *Tel:* 22 47 32 00
  *Fax:* 22 47 32 49 *E-mail:* egertorget@ark.no;
  Ark Farris, Yttersovn 2, 3274 Larvik *Tel:* 33
  11 66 00 *Fax:* 33 11 66 05 *E-mail:* farris@
  ark.no; Ark Futura, Industrivn 17, 6517 Kristiansund *Tel:* 71 58 44 80 *Fax:* 71 58 44 81
  *E-mail:* futura@ark.no; Ark Glasshuset, Storgt
  5, 8006 Bodo *Tel:* 75 54 97 00 *Fax:* 75 54
  97 01 *E-mail:* glasshuset@ark.no; Ark Glemmen vgs, Glemmen videregaende skole, Tar-
  aveien 13, 1601 Fredrikstad *Tel:* 69 31 52
  94; Ark Grunerlokka, Thorvald Meyersgt 46,
  0552 Oslo *Tel:* 22 71 85 90 *Fax:* 22 71 85 91
  *E-mail:* grunerlokka@ark.no; Ark Herkules,
  Ulefossvn 32B, 3730 Skien *Tel:* 35 53 41 80
  *Fax:* 35 53 20 22 *E-mail:* herkules@ark.no;
  Ark Holmen, Holmensenteret, Vogellund 6,

1394 Nesbru *Tel:* 66 84 77 24 *Fax:* 66 84 96
  80 *E-mail:* holmen@ark.no; Ark Homansbyen,
  Hegdehaugsveien 32, 0352 Oslo *Tel:* 22 46 53
  35 *Fax:* 22 46 53 15 *E-mail:* homansbyen@
  ark.no; Ark Jessheim, Furusethgt 5, 2050
  Jessheim *Tel:* 63 99 69 30 *Fax:* 63 99 69
  35 *E-mail:* jessheim@ark.no; Ark Just, Torget 1, 3256 Larvik *Tel:* 33 18 44 20 *Fax:* 33
  13 02 24 *E-mail:* just@ark.no; Ark Kilden,
  Gartnervn 16, 4016 Stavanger *Tel:* 51 90 61
  80 *Fax:* 51 90 61 81 *E-mail:* kilden@ark.
  no; Ark Klofta, Trondheimsveien 86, 2040
  Klofta *Tel:* 63 98 12 01 *Fax:* 63 98 24 84
  *E-mail:* klofta@ark.no; Ark Kohns, Torvet 6,
  2000 Lillestrom *Tel:* 63 81 60 05 *Fax:* 63 81
  60 81 *E-mail:* kohns@ark.no; Ark Kvadrat,
  Gamle Stokkav 1, 4313 Sandnes *Tel:* 51 96
  04 90 *Fax:* 51 96 04 91 *E-mail:* kvadrat@
  ark.no; Ark Majorstuen, Valkyriegt 1, 0366
  Oslo *Tel:* 22 93 16 80 *Fax:* 22 93 16 99; 22 93
  16 90 *E-mail:* majorstuen@ark.no; Ark Manglerud, Manglerud senter, Plogveien 6, 0679
  Oslo *Tel:* 22 26 43 35 *E-mail:* manglerud@
  ark.no; Ark Metro, Solheimsvn 85, 1473
  Lorenskog *Tel:* 67 97 14 14 *Fax:* 67 97 48
  78 *E-mail:* metro@ark.no; Ark Nordstrand,
  Ekebergvn 228B, 1112 Oslo *Tel:* 22 28 80 10
  *Fax:* 22 28 80 25 *E-mail:* nordstrand@ark.no;
  Ark Odds, Storgt 7, 8039 Bodo *Tel:* 75 54 99
  00 *Fax:* 75 54 99 01 *E-mail:* odds@ark.no;
  Ark Osteras, Osterassenteret, Otto Rugesv
  80, 1361 Osteras *Tel:* 67 14 48 06 *Fax:* 67
  14 97 10 *E-mail:* ark.osteraas@ark.no; Ark
  Qvist, Drammensveien 16, 0255 Oslo *Tel:* 22
  54 26 00 *Fax:* 22 54 26 11 *E-mail:* qvist@
  ark.no; Ark Roseby, Lingedalsvn 6/10, 6415
  Molde *Tel:* 71 25 92 40 *Fax:* 71 25 92 41
  *E-mail:* roseby@ark.no; Ark Sandvika, Rad-
  mann Halmrastv 7, 1337 Sanvika *Tel:* 67 54 05
  80 *Fax:* 67 54 58 92 *E-mail:* sandvika@ark.no;
  Ark Sartor, Sartor Senter, 5353 Straume *Tel:* 56
  38 19 55 *Fax:* 56 33 26 99 *E-mail:* sartor@
  ark.no; Ark Selbu, 7580 Selbu *Tel:* 73 81
  75 20 *Fax:* 73 81 75 20 *E-mail:* selbu@ark.
  no; Ark Sjolyst, Karenlyst Alle 16, 0278
  Oslo *Tel:* 22 56 09 85 *Fax:* 22 56 09 86
  *E-mail:* sjolyst@ark.no; Ark Solli Plass,
  Drammensvn 20, 0255 Oslo *Tel:* 22 44 17
  50 *Fax:* 22 56 07 04 *E-mail:* solli.plass@ark.
  no; Ark Steinkjer, Globus Storsenter, Sjo-
  fartsgt 2, 7729 Steinkjer *Tel:* 74 13 51 50
  *Fax:* 74 13 51 51 *E-mail:* steinkjer@ark.no;
  Ark Stjordal, Torgkvartalet, Stokmovn 2,
  7500 Stjordal *Tel:* 74 84 03 30 *Fax:* 74 84
  03 31 *E-mail:* stjordal@ark.no; Ark Stord,
  Osen 3, 5411 Stord *Tel:* 53 41 14 11 *Fax:* 53
  41 39 50 *E-mail:* stord@ark.no; Ark Storgata, Storgata 33, 0184 Oslo *Tel:* 22 11 34
  05 *Fax:* 22 11 04 46 *E-mail:* storgata@ark.
  no; Ark Stovner, Stovner Senter 3, 0985
  Oslo *Tel:* 22 10 09 50 *Fax:* 22 10 20 29
  *E-mail:* stovner@ark.no; Ark Strommen,
  Stoperiveien 5, 2010 Strommen *Tel:* 63 81
  66 60 *Fax:* 63 81 93 50 *E-mail:* strommen@
  ark.no; Ark Student Haugesund, Bjornson-
  sgt 45, 5528 Haugesund *Tel:* 52 70 26 91
  *Fax:* 52 70 26 92 *E-mail:* student.haugesund@
  ark.no; Ark Student Rommetveit, Hogskolen,
  5414 Stord *Tel:* 53 49 14 17 *Fax:* 53 49 15
  17 *E-mail:* student.rommetveit@ark.no; Ark
  Sund, Haraldsgt 157, 5527 Haugesund *Tel:* 52
  70 41 50 *Fax:* 52 71 59 66 *E-mail:* sund@
  ark.no; Ark Sverdrup, Nedre Enggt 5, 6509
  Kristiansund *Tel:* 71 57 09 60 *Fax:* 71 57 09
  70 *E-mail:* sverdrup@ark.no; Ark Torvbyen,
  Torvbyen kjopesenter, Brochsgt 7/11, 1607
  Fredrikstad *Tel:* 69 30 14 70 *Fax:* 69 30 14
  79 *E-mail:* torvbyen@ark.no; Ark Tveita,
  Tvetenvn 150, 0617 Oslo *Tel:* 22 75 66 50
  *Fax:* 22 75 66 51 *E-mail:* tveita@ark.no;
  Ark Ulleval, Sognsvn 75, Pb 3863, 0855
  Oslo *Tel:* 23 00 99 50 *Fax:* 22 56 59 83
  *E-mail:* ulleval@arkbokhandel.no; Ark
  Vestnes, 6390 Vestnes *Tel:* 71 18 01 15

*Fax:* 71 18 90 04 *E-mail:* vestnes@ark.no; Ark
Vinterbro, Vinterbrosenteret, Sjoskogvn 7, 1407
Vinterbro *Tel:* 64 96 31 11 *Fax:* 64 96 31 12
*E-mail:* vinterbro@ark.no

**Gardum A/S**
Soregata 22-24, 4002 Stavanger
Mailing Address: Postboks 242 Sentrum, 4002
Stavinger
*Tel:* 51894440 *Fax:* 51894404
*E-mail:* firmapost@gardum.no
*Key Personnel*
Manager: Rein Fridtjot Gardum Gardum
Fantasy & Science Fiction, both in English &
Norwegian.

**Libris Emo AS**
Boks 40, 2013 Skjetten
*Tel:* 63849200 *Fax:* 63849345
*Key Personnel*
President: Torgeir Daal
Chain Dir: Morten Aas
Founded: 1972
Type of Business: Major Book Chain Headquar-
ters
*Owned by:* Aker RGI

**Lyngs Bokhandel A/S**
Var Frue Stretel, 7013 Trondheim
Mailing Address: Postboks 327, 7001 Trondheim
*Tel:* 91806230 *Fax:* 73512544
*Key Personnel*
Manager: Ragnvald C Knudsen
Founded: 1927
Type of Business: Major Independent Bookseller

**Olaf Norlis Bokhandel A/S**
Universitetsgt 20-24, 0162 Oslo
Mailing Address: Postboks 1990 Vika, 0125 Oslo
*Tel:* (022) 004300 *Fax:* (022) 422651
*E-mail:* info@norli.no
*Web Site:* www.norli.no
*Key Personnel*
Manager: Tom Vister
Marketing Manager: Hans Petter Yssen
Founded: 1890
Specialize in medicine, education, business, com-
puters, travel, Scandinavian literature, books
in minority & immigrant languages & library
supplier.
Type of Business: Distributor, Exporter, Importer,
Major Independent Bookseller, Wholesaler
*Owned by:* H Aschehoug & Co W Nygaard A/S

**Norsk Bokdistribusjon**
Vakaasveien 7, Hvalstad (Asker)
Mailing Address: Postboks 203, 1379 Nesbru
*Tel:* 66 84 90 40 *Fax:* 66 84 55 90
*E-mail:* vv@vettviten.no
*Web Site:* www.vettviten.no
*Key Personnel*
Publisher: Jan Lien
Sales & Marketing Manager: Jo Lien
Founded: 1987
Specialize in computer science, technology &
medicine.
Type of Business: Distributor, Importer, Whole-
saler
*Ultimate Parent Company:* Forlaget Vett & Viten
AS

**Sentraldistribusjon ANS**
Ostre Akerv 61, 0582 Oslo
*Tel:* (022) 98 57 10 *Fax:* (022) 98 57 20
*E-mail:* sdinfo@sd.no
*Web Site:* www.sd.no
*Key Personnel*
President: Roland Hellberg
Vice President: Jan Erik Stokke
Type of Business: Distributor
*Owned by:* Cappelens Publishing

**SiT Tapir Fagbokhandel**
Nardoveien 12, 7005 Trondheim
*Tel:* 73598420 *Fax:* 73598495
*E-mail:* forlag@tapir.no
*Web Site:* www.campus.tapir.no
*Key Personnel*
Manager: Hans G Auganaes
Founded: 1921
Type of Business: Distributor, Exporter, Importer,
Major Independent Bookseller, Wholesaler
*Branch Office(s)*
Alfred Getz vei 3, Gloshaugen, Manager: Svan-
hild H Karlsen *Tel:* 73593231 *E-mail:* svanhild.
h.karlsen@tapir.no
Gunnerus Gate 1, Kalvskinnet, Manager: Randi
Wist *Tel:* 73559780 *E-mail:* randi.wist@tapir.
no
Leangen Alle 2, 2nd floor, Leangen, Manager:
Inger J Nordvik *Tel:* 7359370 *E-mail:* inger.j.
nordvik@tapir.no
Jonsvannsveien 82, Moholt, Manager: Anne
B Michalsen *Tel:* 73559086 *E-mail:* anne.b.
michalsen@tapir.no
Rotvoll Alle, Rotvoll, Manager: Charlotte
Oiesvold *Tel:* 73559826 *E-mail:* charlotte.
oiesvold@tapir.no
Queen Maud's College of Early Childhood Edu-
cation (DMMH), Thoning Owesens Gate 18,
7044 Trondheim, Manager: Karin Keiseraas
*Tel:* 73805276 *E-mail:* karin.keiseraas@tapir.no
Universitetet Dragvoll, Trondheim, Manager: Ian
Page *Tel:* 73598451 *E-mail:* ian.page@tapir.no

**Tanum Karl Johan A/S**
Karl Johans gate 37-41, 0162 Oslo
Mailing Address: Postboks 1743, Vika, 0121 Oslo
*Tel:* (022) 41 11 00 *Fax:* (022) 33 32 75
*E-mail:* karl.johan@tanum.no; nettservice@
tanum.no
*Web Site:* www.tanum.no
*Telex:* 72427 Tanum N *Cable:* TANUMBOK
*Key Personnel*
Dir: Petter A Knudsen
Manager: Bjorg Andreassen
Type of Business: Exporter, Importer, Wholesaler

**Unipa A/S**
Bredalsmarken 15-17, 5006 Bergen
Mailing Address: Postboks 2607 Mohlenpris, N-
5836 Bergen
*Tel:* (05) 31 84 05 *Fax:* (05) 32 42 70
*E-mail:* unipa@online.no
*Key Personnel*
Man Dir: Terje Bergesen *E-mail:* terje.bergesen@
unipa.com
Type of Business: Major Book Chain Headquar-
ters

**Wennergren-Cappelen A/S**
Ovre Vollgate 15, Sentrum, 0105 Oslo
Mailing Address: Postboks 738 Sentrum, 0105
Oslo
*Tel:* (022) 35 72 50 *Fax:* (022) 33 71 04
*E-mail:* wenca@wenca.no
*Web Site:* www.wenca.no
*Key Personnel*
President: Glenn Andersen
Founded: 1829
Also publishers, stamp dealers & antiquariat.
Type of Business: Distributor, Importer, Whole-
saler
*Parent Company:* Cap AS
*Ultimate Parent Company:* J W Cappelen, Uni-
versitetsgaten 20, 0162 Oslo (also owner)

# Pakistan

**Comprehensive Book Service**
56-New Urdu Bazar, Mohan Rd, Karachi 74200

*Tel:* (021) 214682 *Fax:* (021) 2632131
*E-mail:* shahzad@cbs.khi.sdnpk.undp.org
*Telex:* 23035 Pcokr *Cable:* GOODBOOKS
*Key Personnel*
Proprietor: Shahzad Najmee
Publishers, booksellers & library suppliers.
Type of Business: Distributor, Exporter, Importer,
Major Independent Bookseller, Wholesaler

**Ferozsons (Pvt) Ltd**
60 Shahrah-e-Quaid-e-Azam, Lahore
*Tel:* (042) 6301196; (042) 6301197; (042)
6301198; (042) 111-62-62-62 *Fax:* (042)
6369204
*E-mail:* support@ferozsons.com.pk
*Web Site:* www.ferozsons.com.pk *Cable:*
FEROZSONS
*Key Personnel*
Dir: Mr Zaheer Salam
Man Dir & Publicity: A Salam
Dir, Business Development: Muqeet Salam
Manager, Karachi: Ms Gul Afshan
Manager, Rawalpindi: Aftab A Tariq
Founded: 1894
Also publisher & printer.
Type of Business: Distributor, Exporter, Importer,
Major Independent Bookseller, Wholesaler
*Branch Office(s)*
1st floor, Mehran Heights, Main Clifton Rd,
Karachi, Sindh *Fax:* (042) 5835170
277 Peshawar Rd, Rawalpindi, Punjab *Fax:* (051)
5564273

**Liberty Books (Pvt) Ltd**
3 Rafiq Plaza, M R Kayani Rd, Saddar, Karachi
Mailing Address: PO Box 7427, Saddar, Karachi
*Tel:* (021) 111-311-113; (021) 5671240; (021)
5671244 *Fax:* (021) 5684319
*E-mail:* info@libertybooks.com
*Web Site:* www.libertybooks.com
*Key Personnel*
Man Dir: A Hussein
Sales Dir: Saleem Hussein
Founded: 1948
Type of Business: Distributor, Importer, Whole-
saler
*Branch Office(s)*
Alternate Book Shop, Near Pizza Hut Boat Basin,
Clifton, Karachi *Tel:* (021) 5373443
Book Land, Jinnah Rd, Quetta *Tel:* (081) 824295
Books & More, Shop No 125, Park Towers,
LG 16 Lower Ground floor, Clifton, Karachi
*Tel:* (021) 5832525 (ext 125)
International Book Service, Al-Mustafa Plaza
Chandni Chowk, Room 11, Ground floor,
Rawalpindi *Tel:* (051) 4420924
Liberty Books, Shop No G-1, Plot No GP-5,
Block 5, Clifton, Karachi *Tel:* (021) 5374153
Liberty Books Dolmen Mall, Shop No G 101,
Dolmen Mall, Tariq Rd, PECHS, Karachi
*Tel:* (021) 4387085
Liberty Books Park Towers, Shop No A-11,
Park Towers, Ground floor, Clifton, Karachi
*Tel:* (021) 5832525 (ext 111)
London Book Co, 3, Kohsar Market, F 6/3, Is-
lamabad *Tel:* (051) 2823852
Marriott Book Shop, Lobby Karachi Marriott Ho-
tel, Abdullah Haroon Rd, Karachi *Tel:* (021)
5216532
Pearl Continental Book Shop, Lobby Pearl Conti-
nental Hotel Rd, Karachi *Tel:* (021) 5219829
Sheraton Book Shop, Lobby Karachi Sheraton
Hotel, Club Rd, Karachi *Tel:* (021) 5688374
Variety Books, Liberty Market, Lahore *Tel:* (042)
5758355
Agha's Super Market, Uzma Court DC3 Block 8,
Kehkashan 5, Clifton, Karachi 75600 *Tel:* (021)
5833119; (021) 5833120; (021) 5833121
The Forum, Suite No 123-124, G-20, Block 9,
Clifton, Karachi *Tel:* (021) 5831275; (021)
5831276; (021) 5832687; (021) 5832688

**NGM Communication**
Gulberg Colony, Lahore 54660
Mailing Address: PO Box 3041, Lahore, Punjab 54660
*Tel:* (042) 5713849
*E-mail:* ngm@shoa.net
*Key Personnel*
Editor: Andy Nizami
Founded: 1980
Commercial & Government Booksellers. Dealers in Back issues. International subscription Agents for Pakistani Journals, Periodicals, Serials & Newspapers. Library Suppliers. Publishers' Representatives. Bankers; Habib Bank Limited.
Membership(s): The Pakistan Publishers & Booksellers Association (Karachi Zone).
Type of Business: Distributor, Exporter, Major Book Chain Headquarters, Major Independent Bookseller, Wholesaler
*Owned by:* Fatima Nizami

**Pak American Commercial (Pvt) Ltd**
53/2 Kashmir Rd, Rawalpindi
Mailing Address: PO Box 294, Rawalpindi
*Tel:* (051) 563709 *Fax:* (051) 565190 *Cable:* PAKACINC KARACHI
*Key Personnel*
Dir: Ahsan Jaffri
Retail bookseller & subscription agent; also publisher.
Type of Business: Importer, Major Independent Bookseller, Wholesaler
*Branch Office(s)*
1st floor, Pak Chambers, 5 Temple Rd, Lahore

**Pak Book Corporation**
Aziz Chambers, 21 Queen's Rd, 54000 Lahore
*Tel:* 111-636-636; (042) 6363222 *Fax:* (042) 6362328
*E-mail:* info@pakbook.com
*Web Site:* www.pakbook.com
*Key Personnel*
Man Dir: Khan Akter
Executive Dir: Iqbal Cheema
*E-mail:* iqbalcheema@pakbook.com
Dir: M Shahid Cheema *E-mail:* shahidcheema@pakbook.com
Founded: 1975
Deal with scientific books, journals & films & CD-ROM databases.
Type of Business: Distributor, Exporter, Importer, Wholesaler
*Branch Office(s)*
F J Plaza, Block No. 2, F-7 Markaz, Islamabad
*Tel:* (051) 2654046-8
Star Centre, Main Tariq Rd, PECHS, Karachi
*Tel:* (021) 4536375 *Fax:* (021) 4386809

**Paramount Books (Pvt) Ltd**
PECH Society, 152/0 Block 1, Karachi 75400
*Tel:* (021) 455 0661 *Fax:* (021) 455 3772
*E-mail:* parabks@cyber.net.pk
*Telex:* 25856 PBL PAK *Cable:* PARABOOKS KARACHI
*Key Personnel*
Dir: Iqbal S Mohammad
Manager: Saleem A Latif
Founded: 1947
Type of Business: Distributor, Wholesaler
*Branch Office(s)*
Lahore
Rawalpindi

**Royal Book Co**
232 Saddar Co-operative Market, Abdullah Haroon Rd, Karachi 74400
Mailing Address: PO Box 7737, Karachi 74400
*Tel:* (021) 5684244; (021) 520628 *Fax:* (021) 5683706
*E-mail:* royalbook@hotmail.com
Leading Publisher.

Type of Business: Distributor, Exporter, Importer, Major Independent Bookseller, Wholesaler
*Branch Office(s)*
402 Rehman Centre, Zaibunnisa St, Karachi 74400 *Tel:* (021) 5670628
*Showroom(s):* BE 5 Rex Centre, Zaibunnisa St, Karachi 74400

**West-Pakistan Publishing Co (Pvt) Ltd**
17 Urdu Bazar, Lahore
Mailing Address: GPO Box No 374, Lahore
*Tel:* (042) 52427 *Cable:* WESPUBLISH LAHORE
*Key Personnel*
Chief Executive: Syed Ahsan Shah
Founded: 1932
Also publisher.
Type of Business: Exporter, Importer, Wholesaler

# Panama

**Libreria Cultural Panamena SA**
Via Espana 16, Apdo 2018, Panama
*Tel:* 2235628; 2236267 *Fax:* 2237280 *Cable:* CULPASA
*Key Personnel*
Manager: Amador j Fraguela
Founded: 1955
Type of Business: Distributor, Exporter, Importer, Major Book Chain Headquarters, Wholesaler
*Owned by:* Libreria Cultural Panamena SA, Distribudoira Cultural y Manfer SA

**Libreria Menendez**
Galerias Obarrio, Via Brasil, Panama
*Tel:* 2258996
*Branch Office(s)*
Libreria Menendez Paitilla
Libreria Santa Ana, Plaza Santa Ana
Ave Justo Arosemena y Calle 36

# Papua New Guinea

**University Book Shop Inc**
University Papua New Guinea, Waigani Dr, Waigani
Mailing Address: PO Box 114, University, Waigani
*Tel:* 326 7375 *Fax:* 326 0961
*Telex:* NE 22366
*Key Personnel*
Manager: E Guy

# Paraguay

**Libreria Comuneros**
Cerro Cora 289 C/Iturbe, Casilla de Correos 930, Asuncion
*Tel:* (021) 446-176; (021) 444-667 *Fax:* (021) 444-667
*E-mail:* rolon@conexion.com.py
*Key Personnel*
Proprietor: Oscar R Rolon
Type of Business: Distributor, Exporter, Importer, Major Independent Bookseller, Wholesaler

**Libreria Internacional SA**
Estrella 723, Asuncion
*Tel:* (021) 491 423; (021) 491 424 *Fax:* (021) 449 730
*Key Personnel*
Manager: Victor Buzo
Founded: 1953
Type of Business: Distributor, Importer, Wholesaler
*Bookshop(s):* Casa Central, Estrella 723, Asuncion

**Agencia de Librerias Nizza SA**
Eligio Ayala 1073, Casilla de Correo 2596, Asuncion
*Tel:* (021) 47160
*Owned by:* Ediciones Nizza

# Peru

**Librerias ABC SA**
Sta Catalina 217, Apdo 53, Arequipa
*Tel:* (054) 422900; (054) 422902 *Fax:* (054) 422901 *Cable:* MOLAGENT LIMA
*Key Personnel*
Man Dir: Herbert H Moll
*Branch Office(s)*
Edificio El Pacifico, Miraflores
Centro Comercial Todos, San Isidro

**Adriatica**
Jiron Junin 565, Trujillo
*Tel:* (044) 291569 *Fax:* (044) 294242
*E-mail:* libreria@adriaticaperu.com
*Web Site:* www.adriaticaperu.com
*Key Personnel*
Manager: Adriana Doig Mannucci
Founded: 1994
Type of Business: Distributor, Importer, Major Independent Bookseller
*Branch Office(s)*
Av Larco 857, 2 do Piso, Trujillo

**Distribuidora Importadora Durand SA**
Jr San Pedro 311-313, Lima 34
*Tel:* (014) 4452113 *Fax:* (014) 4463190
*Key Personnel*
General Dir: Arturo Durand Gamero
Type of Business: Distributor, Importer, Wholesaler

**Ediciones Euroamericanas SA**
Av Emancipacion 234, Lima 1
*Tel:* (014) 4274686 *Fax:* (014) 4280545
*Key Personnel*
Manager: Juan Moncayo Larrea
Founded: 1985
Type of Business: Distributor, Importer, Wholesaler

**Liberia Editorial Minerva-Miraflores**
Av Larco No 299, Miraflores, Lima 18
*Tel:* (014) 4475499 *Fax:* (014) 4458583
*E-mail:* minerva@chavin-rcp-net-pe
*Key Personnel*
General Dir: Sandro Mariategui Chiappe
Type of Business: Distributor, Importer, Major Book Chain Headquarters, Major Independent Bookseller, Wholesaler
*Branch Office(s)*
Miraflores, Surquillo San Borja
*Bookshop(s):* Av La Paz Nro 210, Miraflores; Av Primavera 2593, San Borja

**Libreria l'Universidad, Nicolas Ojeda Fierro e Hijos SRL Ltda**
Ave Nicolas de Pierola 639, Lima

*Tel:* (014) 282461; (014) 282036
*Branch Office(s)*
Ave Nicolas de Pierola 681, Lima *Tel:* 282036

**Sociedad Biblica Peruana Asociacion Cultural**
Av Petit Thouars 991, Lima
*Tel:* (014) 4330232 *Fax:* (014) 4336389
*E-mail:* sbpac01@telemail.telematic.edu.pe
*Key Personnel*
General Secretary: Ing P A Quiroz
Founded: 1947
Type of Business: Distributor, Exporter, Importer
*Owned by:* SBP

**Libreria Studium SA**
Pl Francia 1164, Lima 1
Mailing Address: PO Box 2139, Lima 1
*Tel:* (01) 275960; (01) 326278; (01) 325528
    *Fax:* (01) 4325354
*Key Personnel*
Purchasing & Exporting Manager: Sergio Costa B
Also publisher.
*Branch Office(s)*
Calle Moral 107A-107B, Arequipa
Calle Arequipa 110, Ayacucho
Saenz Pena 625, Callao
Elias Aguirre 251, Chiclayo
Meson de la Estrella 144, Cuzco
Calle Real 377, Huancayo
Tacna 145, Ica
Prospero 268-270, Iquitos
Colmena 626, Lima
Jiron de la Union 560, Lima
Ave Larco 720, Miraflores
Tacna 216, Piura
Francisco Pizarro 533, Trujillo

**Libreria y Distribuidora de la Universidad
    Nacional Mayor de San Marcos**
Av Venezuela cdra 34, Ciudad Universitaria-
    costado de la piscina, Lima 1
*Tel:* (01) 464-0560 *Fax:* (014) 464-0560
*E-mail:* libreria@unmsm.edu.pe
*Web Site:* www.unmsm.edu.pe
*Key Personnel*
Administrator: Edilberto Chuchon Huamani
Type of Business: Distributor, Importer

**Ediciones Zeta SCR Ltda**
Pachacutec 1414, Jesus Maria, Lima
Mailing Address: PO Box 4050, Lima
*Tel:* (014) 472-5942; (014) 472-7778 *Fax:* (014)
    472-9890; (014) 472-0781
*E-mail:* jzavaleta@edizeta.com.pe *Cable:*
    EDIZETA LIMA
*Key Personnel*
Manager: Jorge Zavaleta
Founded: 1978
Type of Business: Distributor, Importer, Whole-
    saler
*Bookshop(s):* Zeta Bookstore SRL, Cmdte Es-
    pinar 219, Miraflores, Lima

# Philippines

**Bookmark Inc**
264-A Pablo Ocampo Sr Ave, Makati City
*Tel:* (02) 8958061; (02) 8958062; (02) 8958063;
    (02) 8958064; (02) 8958065 *Fax:* (02) 8970824
*E-mail:* bookmark@info.com.ph
*Web Site:* www.bookmark.com.ph
*Key Personnel*
General Manager: Jose Maria Lorenzo Tan
Founded: 1945
Also publisher & retailer.
Type of Business: Exporter, Major Book Chain
    Headquarters

*Bookshop(s):* Puso ng Baguio Bldg, Session Rd,
    Baguio City *Tel:* (074) 442-4912; T Pinpin
    St, Binondo, Manila *Tel:* (02) 241-5071; 35-
    H Amon Court Gate 1, Salinas Drive, Lahug,
    Cebu City *Tel:* (032) 233-6679 *Fax:* (032) 231-
    0428; 260 Osmena Blvd, Cebu City *Fax:* (032)
    253-1395; The Filipino Bookstore, City Tri-
    angle, C M Recto Ave, Davao City *Tel:* (082)
    224-4000; (082) 224-4180; The Filipino Book-
    store, G-72, Glorietta 1, Ayala Center, Makati
    City *Tel:* (02) 867-2260; (02) 867-2261; 254
    Sen Gil Puyat Ave, Makati City *Tel:* (02)
    843-1126; Bistro Remedios M Adriatico St,
    2nd floor, Remedios Circle, Malate, Manila
    *Tel:* (02) 522-5663; The Filipino Bookstore,
    Unit 123-B, Level 1, Shangri La Plaza, EDSA
    cor Shaw Blvd, Mandaluyong *Tel:* (02) 638-
    4469; (02) 638-4470; Brgy Tambaling, El
    Salvador, Misamis Oriental *Tel:* (08822) 755-
    652; (08822) 755-496; Benmar Bldg 1, Door
    E, Concepcion Grande, Naga City *Tel:* (054)
    472-3665; Lim Bldg Sevilla Norte, Door 6P,
    National Rd, San Fernando City *Tel:* (072)
    242-0640; Brgy Uno, Gen Malvar Ave, Sto
    Tomas, Batangas *Tel:* (043) 778-3723; (043)
    778-3725; University Parkway, Fort Bonifacio
    Global City, Taguig, Metro Manila

**Felta Book Sales Inc**
18 Notre Dame St, Silangan, Cubao, Quezon City
*Tel:* (02) 913-4884 *Fax:* (02) 438-1755
*E-mail:* felta@info.com.ph
*Key Personnel*
President: Felicito Abiva
Founded: 1969
US & UK Publisher's Representative (Educa-
    tional, Children's Books, Mass Paperback); Li-
    censee of Educational Materials (Elem - High
    School); Journal Subscription Agent (Medical
    & Professional).
Type of Business: Distributor, Wholesaler
*Branch Office(s)*
110 Nathan St, White Plains, Quezon City

**Goodwill Bookstore**
Goodwill Bldg, 4th floor, 393 Gil Puyat Ave,
    Makati City
*Tel:* (02) 895-8684 *Fax:* (02) 895-7854
*E-mail:* gbs@goodwillbookstore.net
*Web Site:* www.goodwillbookstore.com
*Telex:* 27302 Gtc Ph *Cable:* Gotrade Manila
*Key Personnel*
President & General Manager: Manuel Cancio
Founded: 1938
*Branch Office(s)*
Pavillion Mall, Barangay San Antonio, BiOan,
    Laguna, Branch Manager: Ethel Mallabo
    *Tel:* (049) 520-8240 *Fax:* (049) 411-7147
SM Southmall, Zapote-Alabang Rd, Brgy Talon,
    Las PiOas City, Branch Manager: Peria Mon-
    dejar *Tel:* (02) 800-4044 *Fax:* (02) 800-4045
49 P del Rosario St, Cebu City, Wholesale Dir:
    Rose Rubio *Tel:* (032) 254-5547 *Fax:* (032)
    255-0826
WVSU, Luna St, La Paz, Iloilo City, Branch
    Manager: Ronnie Bansale *Tel:* (033) 320-8570
    *Fax:* (033) 320-8540
Glorietta 3, Ayala Center, Makati City, Retail
    Sales Dir: Joan L Cruz *Tel:* (02) 813-4956;
    (02) 813-4957 *Fax:* (02) 810-5926; (02) 810-
    9033
SM Megamall, Bldg A, EDSA corner J Vargas
    Ave, Mandaluyong City, Branch Manager:
    Bella Obispo *Tel:* (02) 633-6372 *Fax:* (02) 633-
    6371
513 Rizal Ave, Manila, Branch Manager: Peggy
    Calilong *Tel:* (02) 733-4089 *Fax:* (02) 733-
    4090
380 Quezon Ave, Quezon, Wholesale Dir: Archie
    Abad *Tel:* (02) 732-7433; (02) 732-7436; (02)
    732-7437 *Fax:* (02) 741-4289

SM Annex, SM City, North EDSA, Quezon City,
    Branch Manager: Lorrie Palencia *Tel:* (02) 926-
    4047 *Fax:* (02) 927-0366
2164 Legarda St, Quiapo, Manila, Branch Man-
    ager: Minda Munion *Tel:* (02) 734-7477; (02)
    735-8385 *Fax:* (02) 733-1428

**G Miranda & Sons**
12 UP Shopping Center, Laurel St, UP Diliman,
    Quezon City
*Tel:* (02) 7121620 *Fax:* (02) 7120502 *Cable:*
    MIRANDASONS
*Key Personnel*
Manager: Eloisa D Miranda
*Branch Office(s)*
Miranda Davao, C M Recto Ave, Davao City
Miranda Espana, 1404 Espana St, Manila
Miranda Recto, 1887 C M Recto Ave, Manila
Miranda Morayta, 844 N Reyes St, Morayta,
    Manila
Miranda Cubao, Aurora Blvd, Cubao, Quezon
    City

**National Book Store Inc**
Quad Alpha Centrum, 125 Pioneer St, Mandaluy-
    ong City 1550
*Tel:* (02) 6318061 *Fax:* (02) 6318079
*E-mail:* info@nationalbookstore.com.ph
*Web Site:* www.nationalbookstore.com.ph
*Telex:* 27890 NBS-PH; 41144 NBS-PM
    *Cable:* Nabost Manila
*Key Personnel*
General Manager: Mrs Socorro C Ramos
Also publisher.

**Philippine Education Co Inc**
140 Amorsolo St, 7th floor, Legaspi Village,
    Metro Manila
*Tel:* (02) 487215; (02) 487317
*Telex:* 7222321 *Cable:* Pecoi Manila
*Key Personnel*
General Manager: Antero L Soriano
Also Publisher.
*Branch Office(s)*
Araneta Center, Cubao
Makati Commercial Center, West Drive Arcade,
    Makati
Broadway Centrum, Dona Juana Rodriguez &
    Aurora Blvd, Quezon City

**Popular Book Store**
305 Tomas Morato St, Quezon City
*Tel:* (02) 372-2162 *Fax:* (02) 372-2050
*E-mail:* popular@pworld.net.ph *Cable:* POBOST
*Key Personnel*
President & General Manager: Katherine Ann Po
Type of Business: Distributor, Importer, Major
    Independent Bookseller, Wholesaler
*Owned by:* Popular Trading Corporation

**Rex Book Store Inc**
84 P Florentino St, Santa Mesa Heights, 1008
    Quezon City
*Tel:* (02) 7437688; (02) 4143512; (02) 4146774
    *Fax:* (02) 7437687
*E-mail:* rex@usinc.net
*Key Personnel*
President: Dominador D Buhain
Vice President & General Manager: Mario D
    Buhain
Editorial Manager: Mrs Flor Cabangis
Marketing Dir: Don Timothy I Buhain
*Branch Office(s)*
Rex Miscellaneous & Book Store, Greenhills, San
    Juan
Rex Book Store Cebu
Rex Book Store Davao
Rex Book Store Makati
Rex Book Store Mandaluyong
*Bookshop(s):* Rex Book Store, Recto, 1977 C M
    Recto Ave, Manila

**Reyes Publishing Inc**
Mariwasa Bldg, 717 Aurora Blvd, 1112 Quezon
City
*Tel:* (02) 721-7492 *Fax:* (02) 721-8782
*E-mail:* reyespub@skyinet.net
*Telex:* 63740 Vri pn *Cable:* VERAREYES
MANILA
*Key Personnel*
President: Luis Reyes
Manager: Paolo Reyes
Founded: 1986

# Poland

**ABE Marketing**
ul Grzybowska 37A, 00-855 Warsaw
SAN: 128-0031
*Tel:* (022) 6540675 *Fax:* (022) 6520767
*E-mail:* info@abe.com.pl
*Web Site:* www.abe.com.pl/
*Key Personnel*
President: Marek Nowakowski *E-mail:* marek.
nowakowski@abe.com.pl
Subscription Manager: Irena Ksiezopolska
*E-mail:* irena.ksiezopolska@abe.com.pl
Founded: 1991
Polish sole agent for K G Saur Verlag Munich;
subscription services.
Type of Business: Importer, Major Independent
Bookseller
*Branch Office(s)*
ul Legionow Pilsudskiego 17, 30-509 Krakow
*Tel:* (012) 296 3336 *Fax:* (012) 296 3337
*E-mail:* krakow@abe.pl
ul Wincentego Pola 16, 44-100 Gliwice *Tel:* (032)
3393151 *Fax:* (032) 3393151 *E-mail:* gliwice@
abe.pl
Al Niepodleglosci 767, 81-868 Sopot *Tel:* (058)
5500936 *E-mail:* trojmiasto@abe.pl
*Bookshop(s):* Academic Bookstore Gliwice,
ul Wincentego Pola 16, 44-100 Gliwice
*Tel:* (032) 339 3150 *Fax:* (032) 339 3150
*E-mail:* gliwice@abe.pl; Academic Bookstore
Warsaw

**Centrala Handlu Zagranicznego ARS Polona
SA** (Foreign Trade Enterprise ARS Polona
Joint Stock Company)
25, Obroncow St, 03-933 Warsaw
*Tel:* (022) 509 86 20 *Fax:* (022) 509 86 20
*E-mail:* arspolona@arspolona.com.pl
*Web Site:* www.arspolona.com.pl *Cable:* ARS
POLONA WARSZAWA
*Key Personnel*
President: Magdalena Slusarska
Vice President: Grzegorz Guzowski
Founded: 1953
Export & import of books & periodicals as well
as publish books. Export & import of musical
instruments & philately. Organizer of Warsaw
International & National Book Fairs.
Type of Business: Distributor, Exporter, Importer,
Wholesaler

**Dom Ksiazki, Panstwowe Przedesiebiorstwo**
ul Jasna Nr 26, 00-054 Warsaw
*Tel:* (022) 826 8559 *Fax:* (022) 826 7117
*E-mail:* info@domksiazki.pl
*Web Site:* www.domksiazki.pl
*Key Personnel*
Dir General: Janusz Wojcikowski
Vice Manager: Stanislaw Zahorodny
Founded: 1950
Type of Business: Major Book Chain Headquar-
ters, Wholesaler

**Polish Chamber of Books** (Polska Izba Ksiazki)
ul Oleandrow 8, 00-629 Warsaw

*Tel:* (022) 8759497 *Fax:* (022) 8759496
*E-mail:* biuro@pik.org.pl
*Web Site:* www.pik.org.pl
*Key Personnel*
President: Dorota Malinowska-Grupinska
Vice President: Piotr Marciszuk; Danuta Skora
Founded: 1990

# Portugal

**Centro Antiquar do Alecrim A Trindade**
Rua do Alecrim, 79-81, 1200 Lisbon
*Tel:* (021) 3424660 *Fax:* (021) 3470180
*E-mail:* np75ae@mail.telepac.pt
*Key Personnel*
Contact: Antonio Trindade
Type of Business: Major Independent Bookseller

**Sociedades Livreiras Bertrand**
Rua Anchieta 15, 1249 060 Lisbon
*Tel:* (021) 0305592 *Fax:* (021) 0305596
*E-mail:* info@bertrand.pt
*Web Site:* www.bertrand.pt
*Telex:* 42748
*Key Personnel*
Man Dir: Antero Braga
Assistant Dir: Carlos Vilar
Founded: 1727
*Owned by:* Bertrand Editora Lda
*Branch Office(s)*
Algarveshopping, Lanka Parque Tavagueria, Guia,
8200 Albufeira
Loja 0.079, Estrada Nacional 9, 2645 543 Al-
cabideche *Tel:* (021) 460 70 92
Almada Forum, Loja 1.20, Estrada do Caminho
Municipal 1011, Vale de Morelos, 2800 Al-
mada
CC Continente da Amadora Loja n° 14-A, EN
249/1, 2724 510 Amadora *Tel:* (021) 425 47 42
Av dr Lourenco Peixinho 87 C, 3800 165 Aveiro
*Tel:* (0234) 428 280
Braga Parque, Qt Dos Congregados loja 210,
4710 427 Braga *Tel:* (0253) 257 105
Rua D Diogo de Sousa, 133, 4700 422 Braga
*Tel:* (0253) 218 115
Av Valbom, 19, 2750 508 Cascais
Coimbra Shopping, Loja 0.117, Av Dr Mendes
Silva, 3030 193 Coimbra *Tel:* (0239) 401 933
Largo da Portagem 9, 3000 337 Coimbra
*Tel:* (0239) 823 014
Forum Algarve, Loja 025, Estrada Nacional 125,
Km 103, 8000 Faro *Tel:* (028) 986 51 87
Rua Dr Francisco Gomes 27, 8000 306 Faro
*Tel:* (0289) 828 147
Madeira Shopping, Loja 0016, Caminho de
Sta Quiteria, Sto Ant°, 9000 283 Funchal
*Tel:* (0291) 765 031
Guimaraes Shopping, Quinta das Lameiras,
Creixomil, 4810 058 Guimaraes *Tel:* (0253)
511 909
CC Continente Leiria, loja 19/20, estrada na-
cional, n°1, Alto do Vieiro, 2400 441 Leiria
*Tel:* 244824562 *Fax:* 244833857 *E-mail:* leiria.
livraria@bertrand.pt
Amoreiras Shopping, Loja 2.108, Av Duarte
Pacheco, 1070 103 Lisbon *Tel:* (021) 383 80
34
Centro Colombo, loja 0.135, Av Lusiada, 1500
392 Lisbon *Tel:* (021) 716 71 52
Centro Vasco da Gama, Loja 0.11, Av D Joao II,
Lote 1.05.02, 1990 000 Lisbon *Tel:* (021) 895
13 21
Chiado, Rua Garrett 73-75, 1200 203 Lisbon
*Tel:* (021) 346 86 46
Centro Cultural del Belem, Praca do Imperio,
1449 003 Lisbon *Tel:* (021) 364 56 37
Av de Roma 13B, 1000 261 Lisbon *Tel:* (021)
796 92 71

Olivais Shopping, Loja n° 23, Rua Cidade de Bo-
lama, 1800 079 Lisbon *Tel:* (021) 855 11 61
Picoas Plaza, Loja C 0.9 Rua Tomas Ribeiro,
1050 000 Lisbon
Maia Shopping, Loja n° 139, Lugar de Ardegaes,
4445 000 Maia *Tel:* (022) 975 97 78
Norteshopping, Loja 0.120, Rua Sara Afonso, 105
a 117, 4250 446 Matosinhos *Tel:* (022) 955 97
78
Forum Montijo, loja 0.31, Zona industrial do
Pau, Queimado, Rua da Azinheira, 2870 100
Montijo *Tel:* 212301603 *Fax:* 212301876
*E-mail:* montijo.livraria@bertrand.pt
Shopping Odivelas Parque, loja 1.007, Estrada
da Paia, 2679 461 Odivelas *Tel:* 219316566
*Fax:* 219316582 *E-mail:* odivelas.livraria@
bertrand.pt
Parque Atlantico, Loja 043, Rua da Juventude,
9500 211 Ponta Delgada, Ilha de Sao Miguel
*E-mail:* acores.livraria@bertrand.pt
CC Portimao, Quinta da Malata, lote 1, loja
105/108, 8500 510 Portimao *Tel:* (0282) 418
929 *Fax:* (0282) 483 661 *E-mail:* portimao.
livraria@bertrand.pt
Rua 31 Janeiro 65, 4000 543 Porto *Tel:* (022) 200
43 39
Shopping Brasilia, Piso 4, loja 55, P Mouzinho
de Albuquerque 113, 4100 359 Porto *Tel:* (022)
609 90 18
Shopping Center Cidade do Porto, loja 223,
Rua Goncalo Sampaio, 350, 4150 368 Porto
*Tel:* (022) 600 94 27
Viacatarina Shopping, Piso 1, Loja 1, Rua de
Santa Catarina, 312/350, 4000 443 Porto
*Tel:* (022) 338 97 04
CC Parque Nascente, Loja 534b, Estrada
Exterior da Circunvalacao, 4435 Rio
Tinto *Tel:* 224801575 *Fax:* 224801579
*E-mail:* gondomar.livraria@bertrand.pt
W Shopping, Rua Pedro Santarem, n° 9 Loja
147D, 2000-220 Santarem *Tel:* 243322828
*Fax:* 243325322 *E-mail:* santarem.livraria@
bertrand.pt
Estacao Viana Shopping, loja 1.128,
Av Huberto Delgado, 4900 Viana do
Castelo *Tel:* 258829726 *Fax:* 258829374
*E-mail:* vianaestacao@bertrand.pt
Rua Sacadura Cabral, 32, 4900 517 Viana do
Castelo *Tel:* (0258) 822 838
Gaia Shopping, Av Descobrimentos, 549, 4404
503 Vila Nova de Gaia *Tel:* (022) 372 01 79

**A Tavares de Carvalho**
Av da Republica, 46-3, 1050-195 Lisbon
*Tel:* (021) 797 0377 *Fax:* (021) 795 8880
*Key Personnel*
Owner: A Tavares de Carvalho
Founded: 1959
Medium stock of old rare books in all fields, but
mainly in Portuguese & Spanish 16th Century
books.

**CDL (Central Distribuidora Livreira) Sarl**
Bairro Bela Vista Arm 2 P-30, 2735 Cacem
Agualua-Cacem
*Tel:* (01) 4264422; (01) 769744; (01) 779825
*Key Personnel*
Dir: Mario Lino

**Central Distribuidora Livreira**, see CDL
(Central Distribuidora Livreira) Sarl

**Destarte Lda**
Rua de Santo Antonio da Gloria, 90, 1250-218
Lisbon
*Tel:* (021) 324 2960 *Fax:* (021) 347 5811
*E-mail:* destarte@vianw.pt
*Key Personnel*
Man Dir: Jorge Linhares *Tel:* (021) 347 9164
Founded: 1980
Type of Business: Distributor, Importer

Imprints: Edicoes Destarte
*Branch Office(s)*
Livraria Linhares

**Dinapress**
Largo Dr Antonio de Sousa Macedo, 2, 1200 Lisbon
*Tel:* (021) 608992 *Fax:* (021) 608992
*E-mail:* dinalivro@ip.pt
*Key Personnel*
Marketing: Joel Antero D'Aguiar S Amaro
Founded: 1989
Type of Business: Exporter, Wholesaler
*Owned by:* Sr Silverio Pedroso Amaro
*Bookshop(s):* Centro Cultural Brasi Leiro

**Distri Cultural Lda**
Rua Vasco da Gamma, 4-4A, 2685 Sacavem
*Tel:* (021) 942 53 94 *Fax:* (021) 941 98 93
*E-mail:* cultural@electroliber.pt
*Telex:* 16588 Eliber
*Key Personnel*
Man Dir: Karl-Heinz Petzler
Sales Dir: Carlos Alberto
Marketing & Promotion: Martin E Wragg
Founded: 1980
Main Agencies: Oxford University Press, Hachette, Lanenscheidt, Max Hueber, Kuemmerly & Frey, Berlitz, Pan MacMillan, Harper Collins, RandomHouse, Bantom Doubleday Dell.
Type of Business: Distributor

**Distri Lojas-Sociedade Livreira Lda**
c/o Distri Cultural, Rue Vasco de Gama 4-4A, 2685 Sacavem
*Tel:* (021) 940 65 00 *Fax:* (021) 942 59 90
*Telex:* 62483
*Key Personnel*
Man Dir: Luis Santos
Sales Manager: Luis Alves
Commercial Contact: Jorge Mourao
Founded: 1977
*Owned by:* Grupo Distri
*Bookshop(s):* Algarve; Braga; Cascais; Coimbra; Estoril; Lisbon; Sintra Porto

**Distribuidora Editora Vral, Lda**
Apdo 119, 2745 Queluz Codex
*Tel:* (01) 4393978 *Fax:* (01) 4373558
*Key Personnel*
Contact: Victor Martins
Type of Business: Distributor, Exporter, Importer, Major Independent Bookseller

**Domingos Castro**
Travessa dos Frois, 3-2, 2000 Santarem
*Tel:* (043) 332920 *Fax:* (043) 27406
Founded: 1984
Type of Business: Distributor, Wholesaler
*Branch Office(s)*
Rua da Costa, 14-1 Fre, Lisbon
Rua Nartiags Lizgadade, 190-3, 4000 Porto

**ECL**
Rua D Manuel II, 33-5°, 4050-345 Porto
*Tel:* (022) 600 40 01; (022) 609 01 71 *Fax:* (022) 609 96 15
*E-mail:* ecl@mail.telepac.pt
Founded: 1990
Type of Business: Distributor

**EDC -Empresa De Divulgacao Cultural, SA**
c/o Editorial Verbo, Av August Antonio de Aguiar, 148, 1069-019 Lisbon
*Tel:* (021) 380 1100 *Fax:* (021) 386 5397
*Web Site:* www.editorialverbo.pt
*Telex:* 15177
*Owned by:* Editorial Verbo SA

**Edicoei Tecnicas & Culturais, Lda**, see Domingos Castro

**Edicoes Destarte**, *imprint of* Destarte Lda

**Electroliber Lda**
Rua Vasco da Gama 4, Apdo 164, 2685 Sacavem Codex, Lisbon
*Tel:* (021) 940 6750 *Fax:* (021) 942 52 14
*E-mail:* electrliber@mail.telepac.pt
*Telex:* 16588 *Cable:* TELEGRAMAS ELECTROLIBER
*Key Personnel*
Contact: Pedro R de Vasconcelos; Antonio J Faria
Type of Business: Distributor
*Branch Office(s)*
Porto-Albufeira-Funchal

**Empresa de Comercio Livreiro**, see ECL

**Esquina-Livraria e Papelaria Lda**
Rua Afonso Lopes Vieira, 126 (AO FOCO), 4100-020 Porto
*Tel:* (022) 6065234 *Fax:* (022) 6053878
*E-mail:* livrariaesquina@mail.telepac.pt
*Web Site:* www.esquina-livraria.com
*Key Personnel*
Manager: Luis Barroso *Tel:* (022) 6065314
Also deals in secondhand books.
Type of Business: Wholesaler

**Livraria Ferin Ltda**
Rua Nova do Almada 70-74, 1249-098 Lisbon
*Tel:* (021) 3424422; (021) 3467084 *Fax:* (021) 3471101
*E-mail:* livraria.ferin@ferin.pt
*Key Personnel*
President & General Manager: Margarida Dias Pinheiro
Founded: 1840
Type of Business: Exporter, Importer, Wholesaler

**Julio Logrado de Figueiredo, Lda**
Campo Grande 380, Lote 3C, Escritorio A, 1700-097 Lisbon
*Tel:* (021) 7541600 *Fax:* (021) 7541609
*E-mail:* info@jlf.pt
*Key Personnel*
Contact: Julio Figueiredo
Type of Business: Distributor, Importer

**Figueirinhas Lda**
Rua do Almada 47, 4050 036 Porto
*Tel:* (022) 332 53 00 *Fax:* (022) 332 59 07
*E-mail:* correio@liv-figueirinhas.pt
*Key Personnel*
Contact: Francisco Pimenta
Type of Business: Distributor

**Livraria Guimaraes**
Rua da Misericordia, 68-70, 1200 Lisbon
*Tel:* (021) 3462436 *Fax:* (021) 3462620
*Key Personnel*
Man Dir: Isabel Leao
Founded: 1899
Also publishes under Guimaraes Editores Lda.

**Hipocrates - Livros Tecnicos, Lda**
Av Defensores Chaves 16A, 1000 117 Lisbon
*Tel:* (021) 3571247 *Fax:* (021) 3580902
*E-mail:* info@hipocrates.pt
*Web Site:* www.hipocrates.pt
*Key Personnel*
Contact: Norberto Boletas
Founded: 1976
Subjects: Medical
Type of Business: Importer

**International Book Centre**
c/o Distri Cultural, Rua Vasco de Gama, 4-4A, 2685 Sacavem
*Tel:* (021) 942 53 94 *Fax:* (021) 941 98 93
*Key Personnel*
Man Dir: Karl-Heinz Petzler
Assistant Dir: Beatriz Mestrinho
*Owned by:* Distri Cultural (Grupo Distri)

**Jayantilal Jamnadas, Lda**
Estrada de Benfica, 488A, 2700 Benfica, Lisbon
*Tel:* (021) 4960951
Founded: 1987
Type of Business: Major Independent Bookseller

**Livraria Barata, Antonio D M Barata**
Ave de Roma 11 - A-D, 1000 Lisbon
*Tel:* (021) 848 16 31 *Fax:* (021) 80 33 44
*Key Personnel*
Contact: Graca Didier

**Livraria Buchholz, Lda**
Rua Duque de Palmela, 4, 1250 098 Lisbon
*Tel:* (021) 3170580; (021) 3170589 *Fax:* (021) 3522634
*E-mail:* buchholz@mail.telepac.pt
*Web Site:* www.buchholz.pt
*Key Personnel*
Man Dir: Karin Sousa Ferreira *Tel:* (021) 3170589
Founded: 1943
General & academic titles in Portuguese, English/American, French, German & Spanish language.
Type of Business: Exporter, Importer

**Livraria Caravana**
Rua Jose da Costa Guerreiro, 8100 Loule
*Tel:* (089) 462879 *Fax:* (089) 462871
Founded: 1996
Also tobacco & stationer's shop.
Type of Business: Major Independent Bookseller

**Livraria Latina**
Rua de Sta Catarina, 24000 Porto
*Tel:* (022) 2001294 *Fax:* (022) 2086053
*Key Personnel*
Contact: Henrique Perdigao
Founded: 1941
Also book publisher.
Type of Business: Importer, Major Independent Bookseller, Wholesaler

**Livraria Ler Lda**
Rua Almeida Sousa, 24-E, 1300 Lisbon
*Tel:* (021) 3888371
*Key Personnel*
Dir: Luis Alves Dias
Founded: 1970
Type of Business: Distributor

**Livraria Manuel Ferreira** (Manuel Ferreira Bookshop)
Rua Dr Alves Veiga, 89, 4000 073 Porto
*Tel:* (022) 5363237 *Fax:* (022) 5364406
*E-mail:* livrariaferreira@hotmail.com
*Key Personnel*
Contact: Herculano Ferreira
Founded: 1959
Antiquarian Bookseller, Portuguese Culture.
Membership(s): ILAB-LILA; APLA; AILA.

**Livraria Teorema 1-Cogitum Livrarias Lda**
Shopping Center Massama, Loja 41, 2745 Queluz
*Tel:* (021) 4394912 *Fax:* (021) 4394909
*E-mail:* cogitum@ip.pt
*Key Personnel*
Contact: Joao Nuno Cruz
Founded: 1991
*Owned by:* Cogitum Uvrarias Lda

**Lojas Europa-America**
Apdo 8, Mem Martins Codex
*Tel:* (01) 9211461 *Fax:* (01) 9217940
*Owned by:* Publicacoes Europa-America Lda
*Branch Office(s)*
Ave 25 de Abril 48, Almada
Centro Comercial Pao de Acucar, Lojas 6,7 -
   Estrade a Nacional 6, Cascais
Ave 28 de Maio 61, Castelo Branco
Arcadas do Parque, Estoril
Pr Ferreira de Almeida 21-22, Faro
Rua Jose Relvas 15 B-C, Parede
Ave Antonio Enes 14-B, Queluz
Ave Elias Garcia 104-B, Queluz

**Editorial Noticias**
Rua Cruz Carriera, No 4-B, 1150 Lisbon
*Tel:* (021) 352 2066

**Editorial O Livro Lda**
Rua Major Neutel de Abreu, nº 16 A/B/C, 1500
   Lisbon
*Tel:* (021) 778 35 77 *Fax:* (021) 778 35 36
*E-mail:* prof@editorialolivro.pt
*Web Site:* www.editorialolivro.pt
*Key Personnel*
Man Dir: Carlos de Moura
Also publisher.
*Branch Office(s)*
Rua da Boa Hora, 36 & 68, 4050 Porto *Tel:* (022)
   2005739 *Fax:* (022) 2005736

**Patio-Livraria Inglesa**
Rua da Carreira, 43, 9000 Funchal, Madeira
*Tel:* (0291) 224490 *Fax:* (0291) 232077
*E-mail:* patiolivros@hotmail.com
Founded: 1981
Specialize in exporting books worldwide & in the
   supply of Portuguese/Brazilian publications.
   Carry in stock all available books on Madeira.
Type of Business: Distributor, Exporter, Importer,
   Major Book Chain Headquarters

**Livraria Portugal (Dias e Andrade Lda)**
Rua do Carmo 70-74, Apart 2681, 1200-84 Lis-
   bon Codex
*Tel:* (021) 3474982 *Fax:* (021) 3470264
*E-mail:* liv.portugal@mail.telepac.pt
*Key Personnel*
Manager: Henrique Arronches; Manuel Dias; Jose
   Reis; Jose Simocs
Founded: 1941
Type of Business: Distributor, Exporter, Importer

**Livraria Sa da Costa**
Praca Luis de Camoes 22-4, 1200 Lisbon
*Tel:* (021) 346 07 21
*Key Personnel*
Manager: Manuel F da Costa
*Owned by:* Sa da Costa Editora

**Sodilivros**
Travessa Estevao Pinto 6A, 1000 Lisbon
*Tel:* (021) 658902 *Fax:* (021) 3876281
*E-mail:* sodilivros@mail.telepac.pt
*Key Personnel*
Contact: Jorge De Azevedo
Founded: 1985
Type of Business: Distributor

**Livraria Sousa e Almeida Lda**
Rau da Fabrica 42, 4050-245 Porto
*Tel:* (022) 2050073 *Fax:* (022) 2050073
*E-mail:* sousaealmeida@net.sapo.pt; geral@
   sousaealmeida.com
*Web Site:* www.sousaealmeida.com

# Puerto Rico

**Bookstore, Institute of Puerto Rican Culture**
Apdo 4184, San Juan 00902-4184
*Tel:* 809-723-2115
*Key Personnel*
Owner & Manager, Institute de Cultura Puer-
   toriquena: Rene Grullon Nunez
Stock includes subjects on music, Puerto Rico,
   history, humanities, short stories, poetry & lit-
   erature. Also carry maps & sheet music.

# Qatar

**Arabian Bookshop**
PO Box 7884, Doha
*Tel:* 442648 *Fax:* 449653
*Telex:* 5078 Majed DH

# Reunion

**Cazal SA**
42 Rue Alexis de Villeneuve, Saint-Denis
*Tel:* 213264 *Fax:* 410977
*Telex:* 916453
*Key Personnel*
President: Philippe Baloukjy
Imprints, Printing, Advertising.

**Librairie Universsitaire de la Reunion**
29, Av de la Victoire, Saint Denis 97489
*Tel:* 210758
*Key Personnel*
Manager: Apavou

# Romania

**Artexim - Foreign Trade Co**
Piata Scienteii, No 1, Bucharest
Mailing Address: PO Box 33-16, 70005
   Bucharest
*Tel:* (01) 157672
*Telex:* 011191
Carries out all the commercial operations con-
   nected with book import & export.

**Libraria Universitatii**
Str Universitatii 1, R-3400 Cluj-Napoca
*Tel:* (064) 198 107
Libraria Universitatii belongs to the state & is
   under the rule of the Bookshops' Center, Dos-
   toievski St No 71.

# Russian Federation

**Mezhdunarodnaya Kniga**
39 Bolshaya Yakimanka St, 117049 Moscow
*Tel:* (095) 238-46-89 *Fax:* (095) 230-21-17
*E-mail:* info@mkniga.msk.su
*Web Site:* www.mkniga.msk.su
*Telex:* 411160 MKN RU

*Key Personnel*
Dir: Yuri V Kurenkov
Export organization for books, periodicals, printing equipment, audio & video recordings, &
   other cultural goods. Other services include
   co-editions, copyright, & arranging of fairs &
   exhibitions abroad & in Russia.

# Rwanda

**Librairie Universitaire**
BP 117, Butare
*Tel:* 530330 *Fax:* 530210
*E-mail:* biblio@nur.ac.rw
*Web Site:* www.lib.nur.ac.rw
*Owned by:* Universite Nationale du Rwanda, fac-
   ulte du Droit

# Saudi Arabia

**Dar Al-Ulum Publishers, Booksellers &**
   **Distributors**
PO Box 1050, Riyadh 11431
*Tel:* (01) 4777121 *Fax:* (01) 4793446
*Telex:* 203094 *Cable:* OHALI RIYADH
*Key Personnel*
Proprietor: Abdulla N Al-Ohali; Mohammad S
   Al-Kadi
Manager, Foreign Books: Gaafar I At-Tai
Also publishers.
Type of Business: Distributor
*Bookshop(s):* Sitteen St, Sitteen St

**International Bookshops**
PO Box 22348, Riyadh 11495
*Tel:* (03) 4641851 *Fax:* (03) 4641851
*Key Personnel*
Owner: Said H AlSalah
General Manager: Basim S AlSalah
Also publisher.
Type of Business: Distributor, Importer, Major
   Independent Bookseller
*Branch Office(s)*
Dana Shopping Center, Damman
4 Seasons Center, Rakah
King Fahd St & 28 St

**Tihama Bookstores**
PO Box 8963, Jeddah 21482
*Tel:* (02) 6511100 *Fax:* (02) 6519277
*E-mail:* info@tihama.com
*Web Site:* www.tihama.com/book/book.htm
*Key Personnel*
Manager: Bassam Dayani *Tel:* (02) 651 7164
   *Fax:* (02) 651 6917 *E-mail:* dayani@tihama.
   com
*Owned by:* Tihama Advertising Co

# Senegal

**Librairie Clairafrique**
Place de l'Independance, BP 2005, Dakar
*Tel:* (08) 231261 *Fax:* (08) 218409
*E-mail:* clairaf@telecomplus.sn
*Web Site:* eddefine.net/clairaf
*Telex:* 21403 Clairaf
*Key Personnel*
Manager: Pauline Kemayi
Founded: 1951

Type of Business: Distributor, Major Independent
 Bookseller
*Owned by:* Archdiocese de Dahar

# Serbia and Montenegro

**Forum**
Vojvode Misica 1, 22100 Novi Sad
*Tel:* (021) 57 216 *Fax:* (021) 57 216
Also publisher.
Type of Business: Exporter, Importer

**Nolit Publishing House**
Terazije 27/II, 11000 Belgrade
*Tel:* (011) 3232420; (011) 3228872; (011)
 3231430 *Fax:* (011) 627285
*Telex:* 11-603 *Cable:* NOLIT BGD
*Key Personnel*
General Manager: Radivoje Nesic
Editor-in-Chief: Milos Stambolic
Type of Business: Distributor, Exporter, Importer,
 Major Book Chain Headquarters, Major Inde-
 pendent Bookseller, Wholesaler

**Prosveta**
Cika Ljubina 1, 11000 Belgrade
*Tel:* (011) 629 843; (011) 631 566 *Fax:* (011) 182
 581
*E-mail:* prosveta@eunet.yu
*Web Site:* www.prosveta.co.yu
Also publisher. Over 50 bookshops throughout
 Serbia and Montenegro.
Type of Business: Exporter, Importer

**Vuk Karadzic**
Kraljevica Marka 9, 11000 Belgrade
*Tel:* (011) 628066; (011) 628043 *Fax:* (011)
 623150; (011) 634232
*Key Personnel*
Man Dir: Ancic Vojin
Also publisher.
Type of Business: Exporter, Importer

# Sierra Leone

**Njala University College Bookshop**
PMB, Freetown
*Tel:* (022) 228788
*E-mail:* nuc@sierratel.sl; nuclib@sierratel.sl
*Web Site:* www.nuc-online.com *Cable:*
 Njalunbooks
*Key Personnel*
Manager: J D Kappia

# Singapore

**Info Access & Distribution**
31, Kaki Bukit Rd 3, No 06-07, Techlink, Singa-
 pore 471818
*Tel:* 6741 8422 *Fax:* 6741 8821
*E-mail:* info.sg@igroup.net.com
*Web Site:* www.igroupnet.com
*Key Personnel*
Contact: Mr Lee Pit Teong
Founded: 1990
Type of Business: Remainder Dealer

*Owned by:* iGroup
*Branch Office(s)*
Polly Commercial Bldg, 21-23A Prat Ave, Room
 1007-08, Hong Kong, Hong Kong *Tel:* 2572
 7228 *Fax:* 2575 8822 *E-mail:* info.hk@
 igroupnet.com *Web Site:* hk.igroupnet.com
55A Phan Chu Trinh St, Hoan Kiem District,
 Hanoi, Viet Nam *Tel:* 9435472 *Fax:* 9435475
 *E-mail:* info.vn@igroupnet.com

**Marketasia Distributors (S) Pte Ltd**
Pan-I Complex, 601 Sims Dr, No 04-05, Singa-
 pore 387382
*Tel:* 67448483; 67448486 *Fax:* 67448497;
 67443690
*E-mail:* marketasia@pacific.net.sg
*Web Site:* www.marketasia.com.sg
*Key Personnel*
Dir: Johnson Lee *E-mail:* jl@marketasia.com.sg
Founded: 1987
Specialize in the publishing & distributing of
 books & magazines.
Type of Business: Distributor, Exporter, Importer
*Owned by:* Johnson Lee & Quek Chin Hu

**Masagung Books Pte Ltd**
41 Sixth Ave, Off Bukit Timah Rd, Singapore
 276483
*Tel:* 64683276
*Telex:* rs 34500 A; B Gasing
Also Publisher.

**Pacific Book Centre (S) Pte Ltd**
Blk 73, Ayer Rajah Crescent, 03-01/09 Ayer Ra-
 jah Industrial Estate, Singapore 139952
*Tel:* 6464 0111 *Fax:* 6464 0110
*E-mail:* enquiries@snpcorp.com
*Web Site:* www.snpcorp.com
*Telex:* 36496
*Key Personnel*
Man Dir: Low Tai Ee
Manager: Lawrence Tan
*Owned by:* SNP Corporation Ltd, One Kim Seng
 Promenade, 18-01 Great World City East
 Tower, Singapore 237994
*Branch Office(s)*
Alexandra Branch, Apt Blk 136, 01-155 Alexan-
 dra Rd, Singapore 150136 *Tel:* 4740577
Bras Basah Branch, Bain St, 02-69 Block 231,
 Bras Basah Complex, Singapore 180231
 *Tel:* 3381024
Bukit Batok Branch, Blk 283, Bukit Batok East
 Ave 3 01-275, Singapore 650283 *Tel:* 5674649
Havelock Branch, Apt Blk 22, 01-675 Havelock
 Rd, Singapore 160022 *Tel:* 2724326
Jurong East Branch, Block 130 01-221, Jurong
 East St 13, Singapore 600130 *Tel:* 5666153
Pasir Panjang Branch, 02-02 PSA Bldg, 460
 Alexandra Rd, Singapore 119963 *Tel:* 2781090
Queenstown Branch, Apt Blk 6C, 01-48 Margaret
 Drive, Singapore 142006 *Tel:* 4745701

**Publishers Marketing Services Pte Ltd**
10-C Jalan Ampas, No 07-01, Ho Seng Lee Flat-
 ted Warehouse, Singapore 329513
*Tel:* 62565166 *Fax:* 62530008
*E-mail:* info@pms.com.sg
*Web Site:* www.pms.com.sg
*Key Personnel*
Man Dir: Brian Lim
Office Manager: Nicklaus Tan
Deputy Man Dir: Raymond Lim
Founded: 1980
Type of Business: Distributor, Exporter, Importer,
 Wholesaler
*Owned by:* Brian Lim

**Select Books Pte Ltd**
19 Tanglin Rd No 03-15, Tanglin Shopping Centre, Singapore 247909
*Tel:* 6732 1515 *Fax:* 6736 0855

*E-mail:* info@selectbooks.com.sg
*Web Site:* www.selectbooks.com.sg
*Key Personnel*
Executive Dir: Nancy Chng Way Song
Man Dir: Lena U Wen Lim
Administrative Manager: Mrs Ng San May
Founded: 1976
Distributor & Retailer of books about SE Asia.
Type of Business: Distributor, Exporter, Importer,
 Major Independent Bookseller

**STM Publishers Services Pte Ltd**
Affiliate of i Group Books Asia Pacific
352 Larong Chuan, No 01-05 Laurel Park, Singa-
 pore 556783
*Tel:* 62864998 *Fax:* 62882116
*Key Personnel*
Dir: Tony Poh *E-mail:* tonypoh@pacific.net.sg
Founded: 1993
Subjects: STM, Social Science, Arts, Education,
 Agriculture & Humanities-Publishers represent-
 ing agent for SE & NE Asia Laws.
Type of Business: Distributor
*Branch Office(s)*
Chin Shan Information Service Ltd, 10F-1 No
 166 Jiang Yi Rd, Chong Ho 235, Taipei Hsien,
 Taiwan, Province of China *E-mail:* csis@csis.
 com.tw

**STP Distributors Pte Ltd**
Times Centre, One New Industrial Rd, Singapore
 536196
*Tel:* 6213 9288 *Fax:* 6284 4733; 6288 1186
*E-mail:* tpl@tpl.com.sg
*Web Site:* www.tpl.com.sg
*Telex:* rs 28068 STP *Cable:* STPSALES
 SINGAPORE
*Key Personnel*
Senior Vice President: Michael Kok Pun Liew
*Owned by:* Times Publishing Group

**Times The Bookshop**
Times Centre, One New Industrial Rd, Singapore
 536196
*Tel:* 6213 9288; 6213 9217 (customer service)
 *Fax:* 6382 2571
*E-mail:* ttb@tpl.com.sg
*Web Site:* www.timesone.com.sg
*Telex:* RS 25713 *Cable:* Times Singapore
*Owned by:* Times Publishing Ltd
*Branch Office(s)*
Centerpoint, 176 Orchard Rd, No 04-08/16, Sin-
 gapore 238843 *Tel:* 67349022 *Fax:* 67349313
Plaza Singapura, 68 Orchard Rd, No 04-01, Sin-
 gapore 238839, Manager: Sandy Juraihan Bin
 S *Tel:* 68370552 *Fax:* 68370556
Suntec City Mall, 3 Temasek Blvd, No 02-054/
 056/058/060, Singapore 038983 *Tel:* 63369391
 *Fax:* 63369394
Tampines Mall, 4 Tampines Central 5, No 03-
 26/27, Singapore 529510, Manager: Simon
 Pang *Tel:* 67833106 *Fax:* 67833917
Cold Storage Jelita, 293 Holland Rd, No 02-
 17, Singapore 278628, Manager: Patricia Foo
 *Tel:* 64665702 *Fax:* 64657625
OUB Centre Shopping Podium, 1 Raffles Place,
 Singapore 048616, Manager: Patricia Foo
 *Tel:* 65369124 *Fax:* 65572925

**The World Book Co (Pte) Ltd**
Bras Basah Complex, Block 231, Bain St No 04-
 57, Singapore 180231
*Tel:* 3382323 *Fax:* 3371186
*Telex:* rs 36020 Wbksin
*Key Personnel*
General Manager: H P Foo

# Slovakia

**Slovart Co Ltd**
Pekna cesta 6/b, 830 04 Bratislava 34
Mailing Address: PO Box 14, 830 04 Bratislava 34
*Tel:* (02) 4487 1210 *Fax:* (02) 6541 1375; (02) 4487 1246
*E-mail:* pobox@slovart.sk
*Web Site:* www.slovart.sk; www.slovart.com
*Telex:* 93394 Slov
Type of Business: Exporter, Importer

# Slovenia

**Cankarjeva Zalozba**
Kopitarjeva 2, SI-1512 Ljubljana
*Tel:* (01) 3603 720 *Fax:* (01) 3603 787
*E-mail:* info@cankarjeva-z.si
*Web Site:* www.cankarjeva-z.si
Also publisher & antiquarian bookseller.
Type of Business: Exporter, Importer
*Branch Office(s)*
Miklosiceva 16, Ljubljana
Slovenska 37, Ljubljana
Trg osvoboditve 7, Ljubljana
Trzaska 59, Ljubljana
Zaloska 35, Ljubljana
One junija 27, Trbovlje
Usnjarska stolpic S 15, Vrhnika

**Co Libri**
Dunajska 106, 1000 Ljubljana
*Tel:* (01) 1255111 *Fax:* (01) 224454
*Key Personnel*
Man Dir: Mrs Majda Sikosek
Editor: Mr Vasja Krasevec
Founded: 1946
Also publisher.
Type of Business: Distributor, Exporter, Importer, Wholesaler

**Sraka International**
Valanticevo 17, 8000 Novo Mesto
*Key Personnel*
Dir & Editor: Drago Vovk
Founded: 1990
Type of Business: Distributor, Exporter, Importer
*Owned by:* Drago & Bozica Vovk

**Tehniska Zalozba Slovenije**
Lepi pot 6, PP 541, SI-1000 Ljubljana
*Tel:* (01) 4790211 *Fax:* (01) 4790230
*E-mail:* info@tzs.si
*Web Site:* www.tzs.si
Type of Business: Distributor, Major Independent Bookseller, Wholesaler

# South Africa

**Aloe Educational**
PO Box 4349, Johannesburg 2000
*Tel:* (011) 8393719 *Fax:* (011) 8393720
*Key Personnel*
Chief Executive: Lionel N Schroder
Founded: 1968
Library suppliers & booksellers.
*Owned by:* Aloe Book Agency (Pty) Ltd

**Book Promotions (Pte) Ltd**
PO Box 5, Plumstead 7801
*Tel:* (021) 7060949 *Fax:* (021) 7060940

*E-mail:* enquiries@bookpro.co.za
*Key Personnel*
Man Dir: Roy G Mansell *Tel:* (021) 7060949 (ext 231) *E-mail:* roy@bookpro.co.za
Distributor, Importer.
Type of Business: Distributor, Importer

**Central News Agency Ltd**
PO Box 10799, Johannesburg 2000
*Tel:* (011) 4933200 *Fax:* (011) 4931438
*Branch Office(s)*
PO Box 9, Cape Town 8000 *Tel:* (021) 541261
PO Box 938, Durban 4000 *Tel:* (031) 451875
(also 250 branches throughout the country)

**CNA**, see Central News Agency Ltd

**Faradawn cc**
PO Box 1903, Saxonwold 2132
*Tel:* (011) 885-1847 *Fax:* (011) 885-1829
*E-mail:* faradawn@icon.co.za
*Web Site:* www.faradawn.co.za
*Key Personnel*
Contact: Lorraine Shalekoff; Lesley Thomas
Founded: 1983
Publishers Representatives, Book & Map Distributors.
Type of Business: Distributor, Importer, Wholesaler

**Fogarty's Bookshop**
Shop 20, Walmer Park Shopping Centre, Main St, Walmer-Port Elizabeth 6070
Mailing Address: PO Box 1881, Port Elizabeth 6000
*Tel:* (041) 3681425; (041) 3681454 *Fax:* (041) 3681279
*E-mail:* fogartys@global.co.za
*Key Personnel*
Manager: Teresa Fogarty
Type of Business: Major Independent Bookseller

**Juta & Co Ltd**
Juta House, 55 Wierda Rd E, Corner Albertyn, Wierda Valley, Sandton 2196
Mailing Address: PO Box 14373, Lansdowne 7779
*Tel:* (011) 217-7200 *Fax:* (011) 883-7623
*E-mail:* books@juta.co.za
*Web Site:* www.tmza.co.za/juta
*Key Personnel*
Man Dir: Andrew Cruick Shank
Marketing Manager: Chris Napier
Type of Business: Major Independent Bookseller
*Owned by:* Juta Holdings (Pty) Ltd
*Bookshop(s):* RAU Campus, Shop 21, Entrance 6, 1st floor, Student Center, Akademie Rd, Auckland Park, Johannesburg *Tel:* (011) 482-3566; (011) 489-3463 *Fax:* (011) 482-3565 *E-mail:* raubooks@juta.co.za; Providemus Bldg, Shop 6A, 169 Zastron St, Bloemfontein 9301 *Tel:* (051) 448-6565 *Fax:* (051) 448-9068 *E-mail:* bloembooks@juta.co.za; Shop 10, Corner K90 & N Rand Rd, Boksburg 1460 *Tel:* (011) 823-1539; (011) 823-1530 *Fax:* (011) 823-1506 *E-mail:* bokbooks@juta.co.za; 47 Bree St, PO Box 30, Cape Town 8000 *Tel:* (021) 418-3260 *Fax:* (021) 418-1282 *E-mail:* ctbooks@juta.co.za; 216 Stanger St, PO Box 50197, Durban 4001 *Tel:* (031) 37-3970 *Fax:* (031) 37-1819 *E-mail:* dbnbooks@juta.co.za; Hatfield Plaza, 1122 Burnett St, 1st floor, Private Bag 12, Hatfield 0083 *Tel:* (012) 362-5800 *Fax:* (012) 362-5744 *E-mail:* ptabooks@juta.co.za; Balfour Shopping Centre, Shop 207, 2 Balfour Close, Highlands N Ext 9, Johannesburg 2192 *Tel:* (011) 786-8873; (011) 786-5377 *Fax:* (011) 786-8874 *E-mail:* balbooks@juta.co.za; Mezzanine floor, 111 Commissioner St, PO Box 1010, Johannesburg 2000

*Tel:* (011) 333-5521 *Fax:* (011) 333-4810
*E-mail:* jhbbooks@juta.co.za; Promenade Shopping Centre, Shop 52, Corner Louis Trichardt & Henshall Sts, Nelspruit 1201 *Tel:* (013) 752-2231; (013) 752-6918 *Fax:* (013) 752-7817 *E-mail:* nelbooks@juta.co.za; Shoprite Park, Shop 19/20, 262 Voortrekker Rd, Parow 7500 *Tel:* (021) 418-3260 *Fax:* (021) 930-7962 *E-mail:* pabooks@juta.co.za; Middestad Centre, Shop 39, Corner Rissik & Marshall St, Pietersburg *Tel:* (015) 297-0240 *Fax:* (015) 297-3247 *E-mail:* pietbooks@juta.co.za; Pretoria Church Sq, 225 Church St, Pretoria *Tel:* (012) 3242422 *Fax:* (012) 3242293 *E-mail:* csqbooks@juta.co.za; Renaissance Pl, 444 Jan Smuts Ave, Randburg 2194 *Tel:* (011) 886-8595 *E-mail:* rbgbooks@juta.co.za; Riverside Mall, Upper Ground floor, Shop 36, Main Rd, Rondebosch *Tel:* (021) 686-2094; (021) 686-2095 *Fax:* (021) 686-2096 *E-mail:* rondebooks@juta.co.za; Coetzenberg Gallery, Eikestad Mall, Shop 13A, 43 Andringe St, Stellenbosch *Tel:* (021) 8833378 *Fax:* (021) 8833318 *E-mail:* stelbooks@juta.co.za; Seagate Centre, Shop 2, 7 Torquay St, Summerstrand, Port Elizabeth *Tel:* (041) 583-1732 *Fax:* (041) 583-1854 *E-mail:* pebooks@juta.co.za

**Logans University Bookshop (Pty) Ltd**
39 Gale St, Durban 4001
*Tel:* (031) 3076530 *Fax:* (031) 3073230
*Owned by:* The Literary Group (Pty) Ltd
*Branch Office(s)*
100 Mansfield Rd, Durban *Tel:* 218223 (Technikon)
660 Umbilo Rd, Durban (Medical Books)
Nedbank Plaza, Durban Rd, PMB 301 Pietermaritzburg *Tel:* (0331) 941588

**Maskew Miller Longman**
Corner Logan Way & Forest Dr, Pinelands 7405
Mailing Address: PO Box 396, Cape Town 8000
*Tel:* (021) 531 7750 *Fax:* (021) 531 4049
*E-mail:* firstname@mml.co.za
*Web Site:* www.mml.co.za
*Telex:* 526053 SA *Cable:* MASKEWMILLER
*Key Personnel*
Chief Executive: Fatima Dada
Publishing Dir: J Pienaar
Founded: 1893
Also publisher.
Type of Business: Importer, Wholesaler
*Branch Office(s)*
PO Box 3068, Central Park, Block H, 16 St, Midrand 1685 *Tel:* (011) 315-3647 *Fax:* (011) 315-2757
PO Box 1701, 46 Alexandra Rd, King William's Town 5600 *Tel:* (043) 643-3963 *Fax:* (043) 643-3963
Norlaine, Suite 110, 7-15 Old Main Rd, Pinetown 3610 *Tel:* (031) 701-8813 *Fax:* (031) 702-9627
PO Box 3876, Nelspruit 1200 *Tel:* (083) 633-2917 *Fax:* (013) 753-3073
600 Moolman Bldg, 29 Market St, Pietersburg 0699 *Tel:* (015) 295-9194 *Fax:* (015) 295-6012
Sanlam Plaza, 1st floor, Corner Maitland & East Burger Sts, Bloemfontein 9301 *Tel:* (051) 448-0424 *Fax:* (051) 430-4130
Private Bag X2200, Merlite Bldg, Off 18, Corner Shippard & Warren Sts, Mafikeng 2745 *Tel:* (018) 381-1118 *Fax:* (018) 381-6029

**Media House Publications Pty Ltd**
PO Box 782395, Sandton 2146
*Tel:* (011) 8826237 *Fax:* (011) 8829652
*Key Personnel*
Contact: Kate Everingham
Founded: 1983
Type of Business: Distributor, Exporter, Importer, Wholesaler
*Owned by:* Book Services International SA Pty Ltd

## Nasou Via Afrika
40 Heerengracht, Cape Town 8001
Mailing Address: PO Box 5197, Cape Town 8000
*Tel:* (021) 406-3314 *Fax:* (021) 406-2922; (021) 406-3086
*E-mail:* mdewitt@nasou.com (customer service)
*Web Site:* www.nasou-viaafrika.com
*Key Personnel*
Manager Administration & Retail: Mr G Naude
Type of Business: Distributor, Importer, Major Book Chain Headquarters
*Owned by:* Via Afrika
*Branch Office(s)*
PO Box 1058, Bloemfontein 9300 *Tel:* (051) 448-2345 *Fax:* (051) 448-4544 *E-mail:* bfn@afribooks.com
PO Box 5485, Cape Town 8000 *Tel:* (021) 406-3992 *Fax:* (021) 406-3371 *E-mail:* bvl@afribooks.com
PO Box 279, East London 5200 *Tel:* (043) 735-3888 *Fax:* (043) 735-4200 *E-mail:* el@afribooks.com
PO Box 82, George 6530 *Tel:* (044) 873-2812 *Fax:* (044) 873-2811 *E-mail:* grg@afribooks.com
Private Bag X5022, Kimberley 8300 *Tel:* (082) 254-5382 *Fax:* (082) 832-9475
PO Box 556, Pinetown 3600 *Tel:* (031) 705-2417 *Fax:* (031) 701-8300 *E-mail:* ptn@afribooks.com
PO Box 95, Port Elizabeth 6000 *Tel:* (041) 363-1163 *Fax:* (041) 363-1183 *E-mail:* pe@afribooks.com
PO Box 3626, Randburg 2125 *Tel:* (011) 792-2213 *Fax:* (011) 792-2239 *E-mail:* rbg@afribooks.com

## Shuter & Shooter Publishers (Pty) Ltd
21C Cascades Crescent, Pietermaritzburg 3202
Mailing Address: PO Box 13016, Pietermaritzburg 3202
*Tel:* (033) 347 6100 *Fax:* (033) 347 6120
*Web Site:* www.shuter.co.za
*Key Personnel*
Man Dir: Dave Ryder *E-mail:* dryder@shuters.com
Also Publisher.
*Branch Office(s)*
Teachers Centre, 11 Molteno Rd, Claremont 7700, Agent: Sharifa Mowzer *Tel:* (021) 671 3455
PO Box 618, Ferndale 2194, Regional Manager: Themba Msimanga *Tel:* (011) 792 8363

## The Struik Publishing Group
80 McKenzie St, Gardens 8001
Mailing Address: PO Box 1144, Cape Town 8000
*Tel:* (021) 462 4360 *Fax:* (021) 462 4379
*Web Site:* www.struik.co.za *Cable:* DEKENA
*Key Personnel*
Executive: Gerrit Struik

## Technical Books Ltd
Anreith Corner, 10th floor, Hans Strijdom Ave, Cape Town 8001
Mailing Address: PO Box 2866, Cape Town 8000
*Tel:* (021) 216540 *Fax:* (021) 4216593
*E-mail:* techbkct@mweb.co.za
*Key Personnel*
Chief Executive: Anthony Shapiro *E-mail:* tony@techbooks.co.za
Founded: 1929
STM book specialist.
Type of Business: Distributor, Importer, Major Independent Bookseller, Wholesaler

## Van Schaik Bookstore University Bookshop
On-the-Dot Bldg, Sacks Circle, Bellville South
Mailing Address: PO Box 2355, Bellville 7535
*Tel:* (021) 918 85 00 *Fax:* (021) 951 14 70
*E-mail:* vsblv@vanschaik.com; vsblv@vanschaiknet.com

*Web Site:* www.vsonline.co.za; www.vanschaik.com *Cable:* BOOKSCHAIK
*Key Personnel*
General Manager: Dirk Uys *E-mail:* dirkuys@vanschaik.com
Founded: 1917
*Owned by:* Nasionale Boekhandel Ltd
*Branch Office(s)*
34 Fawley St, PO Box 563, Aucklandpark 2006, Contact: Corina van der Spoel *Tel:* (011) 482-3609 *Fax:* (011) 482-3127 *E-mail:* boekehuis@vanschaik.com
Student Centre of RAU, Auckland Park, Johannesburg 2092, Contact: Tom Hicks *Tel:* (011) 726-1698 *Fax:* (011) 482-1407 *E-mail:* vsrau@vanschaik.com
9 Park Rd, Willows, Bloemfontein 9301, Contact: Elsa Bester *Tel:* (051) 447-6685 *Fax:* (051) 447-7837 *E-mail:* vsbloem@vanschaik.com
University of Free State, Student Center, Shop 19, Bloemfontein 9300, Contact: Rene Schoeman *Tel:* (051) 444-3048 *Fax:* (051) 444-3057 *E-mail:* vsbrand@vanschaik.com
Medical University of SA-Pretoria, PO Box 31361, Braamfontein 2017, Contact: Anos Nkambule *Tel:* (012) 521-4327 *E-mail:* ankambule@vanschaik.com
Wits University (East Campus), Matrix Bldg, Braamfontein 2001, Contact: Thomas Khadaba *Tel:* (011) 339-2775 *Fax:* (011) 339-7180 *E-mail:* vsmatrix@vanschaik.com
Braamfontein Centre, Jorissen Str, Braamfontein, Johannesburg 2000, Contact: Alan Somers *Tel:* (011) 339-1711 *Toll Free Tel:* ‘ *Fax:* (011) 339-7267 *E-mail:* vsbraam@vanschaik.com
Brandwag Shopping Centre, Brandhof, Bloemfontein 9300, Contact: Dave Kok *Tel:* (051) 444-5533 *Fax:* (051) 444-5534 *E-mail:* dkok@vanschaik.com
Cape Technikon, Keizer Gracht Rd, Cape Town 8001, Contact: Stanton Hermanus *Tel:* (021) 465-1697 *Fax:* (021) 465-5121 *E-mail:* kaaptech@vanschaik.com
Naspers Bldg, Ground floor, PO Box 5496, Cape Town 8001, Contact: Susan Parsons *Tel:* (021) 406-2118 *Fax:* (021) 406-2957 *E-mail:* bsentrum@boeksentrum.com
Port Elizabeth Technikon, Hurteria Bldg, York St, George, Contact: Doreen Coetzee *Tel:* (044) 874-2801
Nedbank Forum, Burnett St, Hatfield, Pretoria 0083, Contact: Billy Palk *Tel:* (012) 362-5701 *Fax:* (012) 362-5673 *E-mail:* vshat@vanschaik.com
Wits Medical School, 7 York Rd, Parktown, Johannesburg, Contact: Susannah Mbatha *Tel:* (011) 717-2012 *E-mail:* smbatha@vanschaik.com
Wits University (West Campus), DJ du Plessis Bldg, Johannesburg 2000, Contact: Zoe Marks *Tel:* (011) 339-2828 *Tel:* (011) 403-8087 *E-mail:* zmarks@vanschaik.com
Vaal University of Technology East Rand Campus, Room P014, Process House, c/o Plane & Isando Rd, Kemptonpark 1619, Contact: Elaine Dippenaar *Tel:* (011) 392-4652 *E-mail:* edippenaar@vanschaik.com
Vaal University of Technology, Senpark Bldg, Room 105, c/o Corrie de Kock & Margareth Prinsloo St, Klerksdorp 2520, Contact: Ina Greyvenstein *Tel:* (018) 462-8967 *E-mail:* igreyven@vanschaik.com
Tshwane University of Technology, General Dan Pienaar Rd, Nelspruit, Contact: Lizzy Phiri *Tel:* (013) 745-3552
Sanlam Centre, Voortrekker Rd, Parow 7500, Contact: Erika Burger *Tel:* (021) 930-2480 *Fax:* (021) 939-3767 *E-mail:* vsparow@vanschaik.com
Sanlam Student Village, University Way, Summerstrand, Port Elizabeth 6001, Contact: Seun Gerber *Tel:* (041) 583-3171 *Fax:* (041) 583-2418 *E-mail:* vspe@vanschaik.com

University of Port Elizabeth (Vista Branch), Uitenhage Rd, Missionvale, Port Elizabeth 6001, Contact: Doreen Coetzee *Tel:* (041) 408-3111 *Fax:* (041) 583-2418 *E-mail:* vspe@vanschaik.com
Cachetpark Centre, Tom St, Potchefstroom, Contact: Anne-Marie Viljoen *Tel:* (018) 294-8875 *Fax:* (018) 294-4445 *E-mail:* vspotch@vanschaik.com
Shop 2, Filkem House, c/o Church & Queen Sts, PO Box 724, Pretoria 0001, Contact: Rassie Erasmus *Tel:* (012) 321-2442 *Fax:* (012) 325-7832 *E-mail:* vskerk@vanschaik.com
Tshwane University of Technology, FCM Total Garage, 422 Rebecca St, Pretoria West 0183, Contact: Jaap Kampman *Tel:* (012) 327-1945 *E-mail:* ptatech@vanschaik.com
18 Main Rd, PO Box 279, Rondebosch 7700, Contact: Anand Pillay *Tel:* (021) 689-4112 *Fax:* (021) 686-3404 *E-mail:* vsrbosch@vanschaik.com
Port Elizabeth Technikon, Saasveld, Contact: Doreen Coetzee *Tel:* (044) 801-5111
Officer Commanding, Air Force Base, Langebaan Rd, Saldanha 7395, Contact: Piet Snyman *Tel:* (022) 706-2219
Vaal University of Technology, Vista Campus, Sebokeng, Contact: Gladys Morei *Tel:* (082) 753 4261
University of Stellenbosch, Langenhoven Centre, Stellenbosch 7600, Contact: Ermien Louw *Tel:* (021) 887-2830 *Fax:* (021) 886-6184 *E-mail:* vssbosch@vanschaik.com
Queensmead Mall Shopping Centre, Shop 4, Teigmouth Rd, Umbilo, Contact: Barbara Hoskins *Tel:* (031) 205-5821 *Fax:* (031) 205-5823 *E-mail:* bhoskins@vanschaik.com
North West University, Hendrik v Eck Blvd, PO Box 2850, Vanderbijlpark 1900, Contact: Judy Kuilder *Tel:* (016) 985-1144 *Fax:* (016) 985-1126 *E-mail:* vaalpukke@naspers.com
Vaal University of Technology, Andries Potgieter Blvd, PO Box 5865, Vanderbijlpark 1900, Contact: Magda McClintock *Tel:* (016) 985-2340 *Fax:* (016) 985-1210 *E-mail:* vsvaal@vanschaik.com
19 Swartbos Rd, Witbank 1043, Contact: Celeste Greeff *Tel:* (013) 690-2796 *E-mail:* cgreeff@vanschaik.com

# Spain

## Agencia General de Libreria Internacional SL (AGLI)
Islas Marshall 1, 28035 Madrid
*Tel:* 913769120
*E-mail:* agli@senda.ari.es
*Bookshop(s):* Libreria Jose Ma Padrino Barquillo, 21, 28004 Madrid *Tel:* (091) 5325361 *Fax:* (091) 5328569

**AGLI**, see Agencia General de Libreria Internacional SL (AGLI)

## Alibri Libreria, SL
Balmes 26, 08007 Barcelona
*Tel:* 933170578 *Fax:* 934122702
*E-mail:* books-world@books-world.com
*Cable:* HERDER
*Key Personnel*
General Manager: Gerardo Nahm
Founded: 1925
Academic bookshop.
Type of Business: Exporter, Importer, Major Independent Bookseller
*Owned by:* Andreas Valtl

**Libreria Ancora y Delfin**
Av Diagonal 564, 08021 Barcelona
*Tel:* (093) 2000746 *Fax:* (093) 2000757
*E-mail:* ancoraydelfin@ancoraydelfin.com
*Key Personnel*
Contact: Eulalia Teixidor de Ventos
Founded: 1956
Bookshop.
*Owned by:* Ancora y Delfin SL

**Libreria Bosch**
Ronda Universidad 11, 08007 Barcelona
*Tel:* (093) 394 3600 *Fax:* (093) 412 2764
*E-mail:* info@libreriabosch.es
*Web Site:* www.libreriabosch.es *Cable:*
BOSLIBRI
*Key Personnel*
Manager: Javier Bosch
Founded: 1889
General Bookstore.
Type of Business: Distributor, Exporter, Importer,
Major Independent Bookseller
*Owned by:* Libreria Bosch, SL

**CELESA**, see Centro de Exportacion de Libros
Espanoles SA (CELESA)

**Centro de Exportacion de Libros Espanoles SA
(CELESA)** (Spanish Books Export Center)
Calle Laurel Nº 21, 28005 Madrid
*Tel:* (091) 517 01 70 *Fax:* (091) 517 34 81
*E-mail:* celesa@celesa.com
*Web Site:* www.celesa.es
*Key Personnel*
Dir: D Jose Maria Redondo Suarez
Founded: 1986
Specialize in the export of any book published in
Spain.
Type of Business: Exporter
*Owned by:* 100 Editoriales Espanolas y Ministerio
Cultura

**Libreria DELSA**
Serrano 80, 28006 Madrid
*Tel:* (091) 575 15 41 *Fax:* (091) 575 84 14
*Key Personnel*
Contact: Silvela Sonsoles
21 Branches throughout Spain DELSA de Publi-
caciones SA is also at the above address.

**Diaz de Santos SA - Libreria Cientifico-Tecnica**
Dona Juana I de Castilla, 22, 28027 Madrid
*Tel:* (091) 743 48 90 *Fax:* (091) 743 40 23
*E-mail:* librerias@diazdesantos.es
*Web Site:* www.diazdesantos.es
*Telex:* 45141 Dsan E
*Key Personnel*
Dir General: Joaquin Diaz Gomez
*E-mail:* joaquin.diaz@diazdesantos.es
*Owned by:* Diaz de Santos SA
*Branch Office(s)*
Diaz de Santos SA - Libreria Cientifico-Tecnica,
Calle Balmes 417-419, 08022 Barcelona
*Tel:* (093) 212 86 47 *Fax:* (093) 211 49 91
*E-mail:* barcelona@diazdesantos.es
UPC-Universitaria, Jordi Gironda Salgado, s/n,
Campus Nord, 08034 Barcelona *Tel:* (093)
204 13 24 *Fax:* (093) 204 13 69 *E-mail:* upc@
diazdesantos.es
Diaz de Santos SA - Agropecuaria, Calle La-
gasca 95, 28006 Madrid *Tel:* (091) 576 73
82 *Fax:* (091) 576 73 16 *E-mail:* madrid@
diazdesantos.es
c/ Rosalie de Castro, 36, 15706 Santiago de
Compostela, Galicia *Tel:* (0981) 59 03 00
*Fax:* (0981) 59 03 70 *E-mail:* galicia@
diazdesantos.es
Pl Ruiz de Alda, 11, 41004 Sevilla, Andalucia
*Tel:* (095) 454 26 61 *Fax:* (095) 453 33 78
*E-mail:* andalucia@diazdesantos.es

**EDHASA (Editora y Distribuidora
Hispano-Americana SA)**
Av Diagonal, 519-521, 2º piso, 08029 Barcelona
*Tel:* (093) 4949720 *Fax:* (093) 4194584
*E-mail:* info@edhasa.es
*Web Site:* www.edhasa.es
*Key Personnel*
Editorial Dir: Daniel Fernandez *E-mail:* d.fdez@
edhasa.es
Publisher's Assistant: Virginia Elizondo *E-mail:* v.
elizondo@edhasa.es
Founded: 1946
Subjects: Fine Editions,Illustrated Books, Gen-
eral Trade Books-Hardcover, Juvenile & Young
Adult Books, Translations, Economics, Fiction,
History, How-To, Literature, Literary, Literary
Criticism, Essays, Management, Maritime, Phi-
losophy, Romance, Science Fiction, Fantasy,
Travel
Type of Business: Distributor, Exporter

**Editora y Distribuidora Hispano Americana
SA (EDHASA)**, see EDHASA (Editora y
Distribuidora Hispano-Americana SA)

**Enrique Libreria**
Libreros 8, 28004 Madrid
*Tel:* (091) 522 80 88
*Key Personnel*
Contact: Enrique Bataller Ferrandiz
Founded: 1971
Type of Business: Exporter, Importer, Major Inde-
pendent Bookseller

**Casa del Libro Espasa-Calpe SA**
Complejo Atica, Edificio 4, Via de las Dos Castil-
las, No 33, 28224 Pozuelo de Alarcon, Madrid
*Tel:* (091) 481 13 71
*E-mail:* casadellibro@casadellibro.com
*Web Site:* www.casadellibro.com
*Telex:* 48850 ESPACE *Cable:* ESPACALPE
*Owned by:* Editorial Espasa-Calpe SA
*Branch Office(s)*
Passeig de Gracia, 62, 08007 Barcelona
*Tel:* (093) 272 34 80 *Fax:* (093) 487 14 26
*E-mail:* pgracia@casadellibro.com
Alameda de Urquijo, 9, 48009 Bilbao
*Tel:* (094) 415 32 00 *Fax:* (094) 415 32 22
*E-mail:* alameda@casadellibro.com
Colon de Larreategui, 41, 48009 Bilbao
*Tel:* (094) 424 07 04 *Fax:* (094) 424 38 12
*E-mail:* colon@casadellibro.com
Plaza de Italia, 3, 33206 Gijon *Tel:* (098) 517 65
70 *E-mail:* gijon@casadellibro.com
Alcala, 96, 28009 Madrid *Tel:* (091) 432 26
10 *Fax:* (091) 578 19 90 *E-mail:* alcala@
casadellibro.com
Gran via, 29, 28013 Madrid *Tel:* (091) 524 19
00 *Fax:* (091) 522 77 58 *E-mail:* granvia@
casadellibro.com
Maestro Victoria, 3, 20813 Madrid *Tel:* (091)
521 48 98 *Fax:* (091) 521 91 81
*E-mail:* mvictoria@casadellibro.com
Salud, 17, 28013 Madrid *Tel:* (091) 524 19 39
*Fax:* (091) 522 77 88
Velazquez, 8, 41001 Sevilla *Tel:* (095) 450 29
50 *Fax:* (095) 422 24 96 *E-mail:* sevilla@
casadellibro.com
Passeig Russafa, 11, 46002 Valencia
*Tel:* (096) 353 00 20 *Fax:* (096) 352 84 12
*E-mail:* valencia@casadellibro.com
Velazquez Moreno, 27, 36202 Vigo
*Tel:* (098) 644 16 79 *Fax:* (098) 644 18 53
*E-mail:* vigo@casadellibro.com
Arka, 11, 01005 Vitoria-Gasteiz *Tel:* (094) 515
81 75 *Fax:* (094) 513 36 78 *E-mail:* vitoria@
casadellibro.com

**Hogar del Libro, SA**
Ramelleres, 17, 08001 Barcelona
*Tel:* (093) 3182700 *Fax:* (093) 3010399

*Key Personnel*
Dir: Sebastia Fabregues
*Branch Office(s)*
Pg Placa Major 12, 08202 Sabadell
Pg Placa Major 34, 08202 Sabadell *Tel:* (03)
7255959
Hogar del Libro-Baricentro, Carretera Barcelona a
Sabadell, Local No 135 *Tel:* (03) 7186310
*Bookshop(s):* Elisabets 6, 08001 Barcelona

**Libreria Hispano Americana**
Gran Via de Les Corts Catalanes 594, 08007
Barcelona
*Tel:* (093) 3180079
*E-mail:* info@llibreriaha.com
*Web Site:* www.llibreriaha.com
*Key Personnel*
Manager: Josep M Boixareu Vilaplana
Commercial Manager: Jose Romero Gonzalez
Founded: 1941
Specialize in scientific & technical books.
Type of Business: Importer, Major Independent
Bookseller

**Marcial Pons Librero**
San Sotero, 6, 28037 Madrid
*Tel:* (091) 304 33 03 *Fax:* (091) 327 23 67
*E-mail:* librerias@marcialpons.es
*Web Site:* www.marcialpons.es
Founded: 1948
Type of Business: Distributor, Exporter, Importer,
Major Independent Bookseller, Wholesaler
*Bookshop(s):* Law, Barbara de Braganza, 8, 28004
Madrid; Economics, Plaza de las Salesas, 10,
28004 Madrid; Humanities, Plaza Conde del
Valle de Suchill, 8, 28015 Madrid

**H F Martinez de Murguia SA**
Valverde, 27, 28004 Madrid
*Tel:* (091) 522 66 34; (091) 532 39 71 *Fax:* (091)
531 37 86
*Key Personnel*
Manager: Francisco Gugel
Supplier of books published in Spain.
Type of Business: Distributor, Exporter, Importer,
Wholesaler

**Mundi-Prensa Libros, SA**
Castello, 37, 28001 Madrid
*Tel:* (091) 436 37 00 *Fax:* (091) 575 39 98
*E-mail:* libreria@mundiprensa.es
*Web Site:* www.mundiprensa.com
*Key Personnel*
General Manager: Jose Maria Hernandez
*E-mail:* hernandez@mundiprensa.es
Founded: 1948
Publisher, bookseller & subscription agency.
Type of Business: Distributor, Exporter, Importer,
Major Book Chain Headquarters, Major Inde-
pendent Bookseller, Wholesaler
*Branch Office(s)*
Consell de Cent, 391, 08009 Barcelona *Tel:* (093)
488 3492 *Fax:* (093) 487 7659
Rio Panuco, 141, 06500 Mexico City, Mexico
*Tel:* (05) 5533 5658 *Fax:* (05) 5514 6799
*Bookshop(s):* Libreria Mundi-Prensa

**Libreria Passim SA**
Floridablanca 54-58, Ent 4a B, 08015 Barcelona
*Tel:* (093) 325 03 05 *Fax:* (093) 325 03 05
*E-mail:* passim@intercom.es
*Key Personnel*
Manager: Alex Pujol
Publishes catalogs of new & out-of-print books
about Spain & Latin America published in
Spain. Specialize in sales to universities & li-
braries.
Type of Business: Exporter, Major Independent
Bookseller

**Libreria Pons SL**
Felix Latassa, 33, 50006 Zaragoza
Mailing Address: PO Box 10348, 50006 Zaragoza
*Tel:* (0976) 550 105; (0976) 350 037; (0976) 554
920 *Fax:* (0976) 356 072
*E-mail:* promedit@libreriapons-zaragoza.com;
pedidos@liberiapons-zaragoza.com; admon@
liberiapons-zaragoza.com
*Web Site:* www.libreriapons-zaragoza.com
*Key Personnel*
Dir: Juan F Pons
Founded: 1951
Library supplier.
Type of Business: Distributor, Importer, Major
Independent Bookseller

**PPC Editorial y Distribuidora, SA**
Reus 5-7, 28044 Madrid
*Tel:* (091) 5089224 *Fax:* (091) 5084082
*Telex:* 45051 *Cable:* PEPECE
*Key Personnel*
President: Antonio Montero Moreno
Vice President: Juan Luis Acebal Lujan
Dir: Angel Alos Cortes
Type of Business: Distributor, Exporter, Major
Book Chain Headquarters
*Owned by:* PPC
*Branch Office(s)*
Libreria Pastoral, Velazquez 2, 04002 Almeria
Libreria P P C, Canuda 9, 08002 Barcelona
Libreria Piedelatorre, 29015 Malaga
Libreria Selecta, San Felipe Neri 10, 07002
Palma de Mallorca
Libreria Concilio, Teniente Coronel Segui 1,
41001 Sevilla
Libreria Promocion, c/o Conde de Cardenas 5,
14002 Cordoba

**Promocion Popular Cristiana**, see PPC Editorial
y Distribuidora, SA

**Librcria Rubinos - 1860 SA**
Alcala 98, 28009 Madrid
*Tel:* (091) 435 22 39 *Fax:* (091) 435 32 72
*Key Personnel*
Administrator: Antonio Rubinos Casanueva
Type of Business: Distributor, Exporter, Importer,
Major Book Chain Headquarters, Major Inde-
pendent Bookseller, Wholesaler

# Sri Lanka

**Bright Book Centre (Pvt) Ltd**
S-27, 1st floor, Colombo Central Super Market
Complex, Colombo 11
*Tel:* (0112) 434770 *Fax:* (0112) 333279; (0112)
43470
*Key Personnel*
President: Pon Sakthivel
Founded: 1990
Specialize in book publishing & distributing.
Type of Business: Distributor, Exporter, Importer,
Major Independent Bookseller, Wholesaler
*Branch Office(s)*
77/24 Jampeetta Lane, Colombo 13

**KVG de Silva & Sons**
415 Galle Rd, Colombo 4
*Tel:* (01) 84146 *Fax:* (01) 588875
*Telex:* 22658 GLAXY CE
*Key Personnel*
President: K V J De Silva
Founded: 1898
Dealers in Rare Books & Maps of Sri Lanka &
Sri Lankan Islands & old views of Sri Lanka.
Type of Business: Distributor, Importer, Major
Independent Bookseller

*Branch Office(s)*
Serendib Gallery, 100 Galle Rd, Colombo 4
*Bookshop(s):* K V G's Bookstore, Liberty Plaza,
Colombo 3

**Lake House Bookshop**
40 Hyde Park Corner, Colombo 2
*Tel:* (011) 4712473 *Fax:* (011) 2438704
*E-mail:* sarathi@eureka.lk
*Telex:* 21266 Lakexpo Ce *Cable:* BOOKSALES
*Key Personnel*
Dir & General Manager: Victor Walatara
Founded: 1941
Also publisher.
Type of Business: Distributor, Exporter, Importer,
Major Independent Bookseller, Wholesaler
*Owned by:* Lake House Investments Ltd, 40,
WAD Ramanayake Mawatha, Colombo 2
*Branch Office(s)*
Liberty Plaza, 1/34, 1st floor, New Wing,
Colombo 3 *Tel:* (011) 2574418 *Fax:* (011)
2370736

**Sadeepa Bookshop**
1060, Maradana Rd, Colombo 8
*Tel:* (011) 686114 (hotline); (011) 694289; (011)
678043 *Fax:* (011) 683813; (011) 678044
*E-mail:* sadeepabk@itmin.com
*Web Site:* www.sadeepabooks.com
*Key Personnel*
Man Dir: Sarath Chandra Wanniatchi
Founded: 1987
Also printer & publisher.
Type of Business: Distributor, Importer, Major
Book Chain Headquarters, Major Independent
Bookseller, Wholesaler
*Branch Office(s)*
Sadeepa Print Shop, 1121, Maradana Rd,
Colombo 8 *Tel:* (011) 683813
MBA Shopping Complex, Colombo 8 *Tel:* (011)
684241

**Sarasavi Book Shop Pvt Ltd**
Subsidiary of Sarasavi Group of Companies
30, Stanley Thilakarathna Mawatha, Nugegoda
10250
*Tel:* (01) 2852519; (01) 2820983; (01) 4304546
*Fax:* (01) 2509503; (01) 2821454
*E-mail:* sarasavi@slt.lk
*Web Site:* www.sarasavi.lk
*Key Personnel*
Chairman & Man Dir: Mr H D Premasiri
Founded: 1948
*Membership(s):* Sri Lanka Book Publishers' As-
sociation, Book Sellers Association of Ceylon,
British Book Sellers Association, Sri Lanka
Book Sellers Association.
Type of Business: Importer, Major Independent
Bookseller
Imprints: Sarasavi Publishers
*Branch Office(s)*
Colombo Fort-44/9 YMBA Bldg, Colombo 1
*Tel:* (01) 2326831
Colombo 8-1/50 YMBA Bldg, Borella *Tel:* (01)
2698886
Bakeland Bldg, 87 Minuwangoda Rd, Gampaha
*Tel:* (033) 2222376; (033) 4670236
86 D S Senanayake Veediya, Kandy *Tel:* (0812)
234036
74 Kumaratunga Mawatha, Matara *Tel:* (041)
2228406
74 High Level Rd, Maharagama *Tel:* (01)
2850340
*Warehouse:* 3/1 St John's Church Rd, Nugegoda

**Sarasavi Publishers**, *imprint of* Sarasavi Book
Shop Pvt Ltd

# Sudan

**The Khartoum Bookshop**, see The New
Bookshop

**The New Bookshop**
Zubeir Pasha St, Khartoum
Mailing Address: PO Box 968, Khartoum
*Tel:* (011) 77594
*Telex:* 22159 ds *Cable:* Newstand Khartoum
*Key Personnel*
Owner: P N Flanginis
Founded: 1957
Membership(s): The Sudan Chamber of Com-
merce (Khartoum).
Type of Business: Distributor, Importer, Whole-
saler

**The Nile Bookshop**
New Extension, St 41, Khartoum
Mailing Address: PO Box 8036, Khartoum
*Tel:* (011) 463749 *Fax:* (011) 770821
*E-mail:* mohdelhag@yahoo.com; nilebookshop@
yahoo.com *Cable:* NILE
Type of Business: Distributor, Importer, Major
Independent Bookseller

**The Sudan Bookshop Ltd**
PO Box 156, Khartoum
*Tel:* (011) 74123; (011) 76781
*Telex:* 22480 sisco km *Cable:* Bookshop
Khartoum
*Key Personnel*
Man Dir: Joseph A Tadros

**University of Khartoum Bookshop**
PO Box 321, Khartoum
*Tel:* (011) 80558
*Telex:* 22738 sd
*Key Personnel*
Manager: Dr Khalid El-Mubarak
*Owned by:* Khartoum University Press

# Sweden

**Akademibokhandeln**
Member of Esselte Bokhandel Group
Box 7634, 103 94 Stockholm
*Tel:* (08) 613 61 10 *Fax:* (08) 24 25 43
*E-mail:* bokinfo@akademibokhandeln.se; order@
akademibokhandeln.se
*Web Site:* www.akademibokhandeln.se
*Telex:* 12430
*Key Personnel*
Manager: Wojtek Boguslaw
Type of Business: Exporter, Importer, Major
Book Chain Headquarters

**Akerbloms Universitetsbokhandel**
Affiliate of Bokia
Oestra Radhusgatan 6, Umea
Mailing Address: Box 83, S-90103 Umea
*Tel:* (090) 711250 *Fax:* (090) 711260
*E-mail:* swedish.books@akerbloms.se
*Key Personnel*
Manager: Mats Gyllengahm *E-mail:* mats.
gyllengahm@bokia.se
Founded: 1843
Type of Business: Importer, Major Independent
Bookseller

**Almquist och Wiksell Bokhandeln AB**, see
Akademibokhandeln

**Gleerupska Universitetsbokhandeln**
Box 172, 221 00 Lund
*Tel:* (046) 46 19 60 00 *Fax:* (046) 18 42 47
*Key Personnel*
Manager: Peter Dahl
President: Kjell Dyster-Aas
Contact: Lena Stenlund
Type of Business: Distributor, Importer, Major
Independent Bookseller, Wholesaler

**Soederbokhandeln Hansson och Bruce AB**
Gotgatan 37, Stockholm
*Tel:* (08) 405432; (08) 6405433 *Fax:* (08)
6441315
*Key Personnel*
Manager: Stig Sunnerholm
Founded: 1874

**Samdistribution AB**
Norra Malmvaegen 82, Haeggvik, 191 24 Sollen-
tuna
Mailing Address: Box 449, 191 24 Sollentuna
*Tel:* (08) 696 80 00 *Fax:* (08) 696 83 73
*E-mail:* samdistribution@bok.bonnier.se; magnus.
brundin@samdistribution.se
*Web Site:* www.bok.bonnier.se; samdistribution.se
*Key Personnel*
President: Maria Curman
Man Dir: Eric Johansson
Founded: 1975
Warehousing of books (Book Trade, Book Ser-
vices & Book Club Members).
Type of Business: Distributor
*Owned by:* Bonnierfoerlagen AB

**Wettergrens Bokhandel AB**
Avenyn 21, 411 36 Gothenburg
*Tel:* (031) 706 25 00 *Fax:* (031) 706 25 20
*E-mail:* info@wettergrens.se
*Web Site:* www.wettergrens.se
*Key Personnel*
Contact: Carl Wettergren
Founded: 1882
Type of Business: Major Independent Bookseller

# Switzerland

**H R Balmer AG Buchhandlung Verlag
Verlagauslieferung**
Neugasse 12, Landsgemeindeplatz, 6301 Zug
*Tel:* (041) 726 97 97 *Fax:* (041) 726 97 98
*E-mail:* info@buecher-balmer.ch
*Web Site:* www.buecher-balmer.ch
*Key Personnel*
Contact: Christoph Balmer
Founded: 1864
Type of Business: Distributor, Importer, Major
Independent Bookseller, Wholesaler
*Bookshop(s):* Buches Balmer, Einkaufs-Allee
Metalli, 6304 Zug *Tel:* (041) 726 97 87
*Fax:* (041) 726 97 88

**Brunnen Bibel Panorama**
Wallstr 6, 4002 Basel
*Tel:* (061) 295 60 03 *Fax:* (061) 295 60 68
*E-mail:* info@bibelpanorama.ch
*Web Site:* www.bibelpanorama.ch
*Key Personnel*
Contact: Andreas Walter

**Brunner Buecher AG**, see Buchhandlung zum
Elsasser AG

**Buchhandlung zum Elsasser AG**
Limmatquai 18, 8001 Zurich
*Tel:* (01) 261 08 47; (01) 251 16 12 *Fax:* (01)
261 08 97

*Telex:* 57268
*Key Personnel*
Manager: Mr Hansruedi Brunner

**Fehr'sche Buchhandlung AG**
Schmiedgasse 16, 9001 St Gallen
*Tel:* (075) 222 11 52; (075) 222 53 81
*Key Personnel*
Manager: B Brun

**Huber & Lang**
Schanzenstr 1, 3000 Bern 9
*Tel:* (031) 300 4646 *Fax:* (031) 300 4656
*E-mail:* contact.bern@huberlang.com
*Web Site:* www.huberlang.com
Founded: 1927
Also publisher.
Type of Business: Distributor, Exporter, Importer,
Major Independent Bookseller
*Branch Office(s)*
Stadelhoferstr 28, 8021 Zurich 1 *Tel:* (043)
482 482 *Fax:* (043) 483 483 *E-mail:* contact.
zurich@huberlang.com (Medicine, psychology,
science)
Laenggass-str 76, 3000 Bern 9 *Tel:* (031) 300
4500 *Fax:* (031) 300 4590 *Web Site:* www.
hanshuber.com
Lagerstr 33, 8021 Zurich 1 *Tel:* (043) 317 9451
*Fax:* (013) 317 9452 *E-mail:* sihl@huberlang.
com (High school & college textbooks)

**Buchhaus Meili AG**
Fronwagplatz 13, 8201 Schaffhausen
Mailing Address: PO Box 986, 8201
Schaffhausen
*Tel:* (052) 625 41 44 *Fax:* (052) 625 47 46
*E-mail:* meili@melimedien.ch
*Web Site:* www.books.ch
*Telex:* 76777 Meibuch
*Owned by:* Peter Meili & Co

**No Name Photo Gallery**, see PEP Buchhandlung
& No Name Photo Gallery

**Orell Fuessli Buchhandlungs AG**
Dietzingerstr 3, 8036 Zurich
*Tel:* (0848) 849 848 *Fax:* (01) 455 56 20
*E-mail:* orders@books.ch; info@ofv.ch
*Web Site:* www.ofv.ch; www.books.ch
*Telex:* (01) 813021 orla ch
*Key Personnel*
Manager: Dr Manfred Hiefner *E-mail:* mhiefner@
ofv.ch
Also Publisher.

**PEP Buchhandlung & No Name Photo Gallery**
Unterer Heuberg 2, 4051 Basel
*Tel:* (061) 261 51 61 *Fax:* (061) 261 51 61
*E-mail:* pepnoname@balcab.ch
*Web Site:* www.pepnoname.ch
*Key Personnel*
Vice President: Victor Zwimpfer
Founded: 1980
Bookstore specializing in photo, film, art, tattoo,
Indian literature & photo gallery.
Type of Business: Distributor, Exporter, Importer,
Major Book Chain Headquarters, Major Inde-
pendent Bookseller
*Owned by:* Tobias Toggweiler

**Quellen-Verlag GmbH**
Blumenbergpl 1, 9001 St Gallen
*Tel:* (071) 227 47 77 *Fax:* (071) 227 47 58

**Schweizer Buchzentrum** (Swiss Book Centre)
Postfach 522, 4600 Olten
*Tel:* (062) 476161 *Fax:* (062) 465676
Type of Business: Distributor

**Buchhandlung Staeheli AG**
Bederstr 77, 8021 Zurich 2
*Tel:* (01) 2099111 *Fax:* (01) 2099112
*E-mail:* info@staehelibooks.ch
*Web Site:* www.staehelibooks.ch *Cable:*
STAEHELIBOOKS
*Key Personnel*
Chief Executive Officer: Claus Gretener
*E-mail:* claus.gretener@staehelibooks.ch
Founded: 1934
Booksellers & Subscription Agents
Online Bookshop.
Type of Business: Importer, Major Independent
Bookseller
*Bookshop(s):* 4/5 Am Weinplatz, 8021 Zurich 1

**Staeheli's Bookshops Ltd**, see Buchhandlung
Staeheli AG

**Centre Suisse du Livre**, see Schweizer
Buchzentrum

**Centro Svizzero del Libro**, see Schweizer
Buchzentrum

**Swiss Book Centre**, see Schweizer Buchzentrum

**Wepf & Co AG**
Eisengasse 5, 4001 Basel
*Tel:* (061) 269 85 15 *Fax:* (061) 261 35 97
*E-mail:* wepf@dial.eunet.ch
*Web Site:* www.wepf.ch *Cable:* WEPFCO BASEL
*Key Personnel*
Dir: H U Herrmann
Also publisher & antiquarian bookshop.
*Branch Office(s)*
Freiburgstr 83, 79576 Weil am Rhein - Haltin-
gen, Germany *Tel:* (07621) 75028 *Fax:* (07621)
75992 *E-mail:* info@buchhandlung-wepf.de
5, quai des Bateliers, 67000 Strasbourg, France
*Tel:* (0388) 371327 *Fax:* (0388) 240096

# Syrian Arab Republic

**Avicenne Librairie Internationale**
Rue Tajhiz Imm Karduus, 2456 Damas
*Tel:* (011) 224 44 77 *Fax:* (011) 221 98 33
*E-mail:* avicenne@net.sy
*Telex:* Ortexo 419120 SY
*Key Personnel*
General Manager: Jean-Pierre Dummar
Founded: 1963
Entertainment Articles.
Type of Business: Distributor, Importer, Major
Book Chain Headquarters
*Owned by:* Meridien Bookshop, Kuwatly St, Jean
Pierre Dummar
*Branch Office(s)*
Sheraton Bookshop, Amawiia Sq, Damascus
*Tel:* (011) 2229300
Amir Poloee Bookshop, Aleppo *Tel:* (021)
2246510
Safir Bookshop, Homs *Tel:* (031) 412400

# Taiwan, Province of China

**The Children's Book Store Company Ltd**
10, Lane 144 Section 5, Min Sheng East Rd,
   Taipei 105 ROC
*Tel:* (02) 2762-8222 *Fax:* (02) 2760-4322
*Web Site:* www.tong-nian.com.tw
*Key Personnel*
Chief Exec: Chang Yao-Hwa
Founded: 1955
Type of Business: Wholesaler

**Mei Ya Publications Inc (Sueling Inc)**
10F 82 Fuhsing S Rd, Sec 2, Taipei 106
*Tel:* (02) 7037481 *Fax:* (02) 7033847
*Telex:* 11240 Sueling
*Key Personnel*
Manager: Julia Lee
Specialize in college & university textbook
   reprints (all copyrighted).

# United Republic of Tanzania

**The Dar Es Salaam Bookshop**
PO Box 9030, Dar Es Salaam
*Tel:* (051) 23416
*Key Personnel*
Manager: C Salu

**Readit Books**
PO Box 21100, Dar es Salaam
*Tel:* (022) 2184077 *Fax:* (022) 2181077
*E-mail:* readit@raha.com
Founded: 1993

**University of Dar Es Salaam Bookshop**
Unit of Dar es Salaam University Press Ltd
PO Box 350900, Dar es Salaam
*Tel:* (022) 2410093; (022) 2410500 (ext 2568)
   *Fax:* (022) 2410137
*Key Personnel*
Ag Marketing Manager: Mr A Kanuya *Tel:* (022)
   2410300
Type of Business: Importer, Major Independent
   Bookseller
*Owned by:* University of Dar Es Salaam

# Thailand

**Asia Books Co Ltd**
No 5 Sukhumvit Rd, SOI 61 Wattana, Bangkok
   10110
*Tel:* (02) 715-9000 *Fax:* (02) 391-2299
*E-mail:* information@asiabooks.com
*Web Site:* www.asiabooks.com
*Key Personnel*
Owner: Vinai Suttharoj
Assistant Man Dir: Rachanee Anakepeerasak
   *Tel:* (02) 715-9166 *E-mail:* rachanee@
   asiabooks.com
Founded: 1969

Publisher, Distributor & chain of English lan-
   guage bookshops in Thailand.
Type of Business: Distributor, Importer, Major
   Book Chain Headquarters, Wholesaler
*Showroom(s):* 3rd floor, Central City Plaza, Room
   309, Bangna-Trat Rd, KM 3 Bangkok *Tel:* (02)
   3610743; (02) 3610744 *Fax:* (02) 3610745;
   3rd floor, Emporium Shopping Complex,
   Sukhumvit Rd, Bangkok *Tel:* (02) 6648565-7
   *Fax:* (02) 6648548; 1st floor, Landmark Hotel,
   Sukhumvit Rd, Bangkok *Tel:* (02) 2525839;
   (02) 2525456 *Fax:* (02) 2515993; 3rd floor,
   Landmark Hotel, Sukhumvit Rd, Bangkok
   *Tel:* (02) 2525655; (02) 2529901 *Fax:* (02)
   2515993; 2nd floor, Peninsula Plaza, Rajdamri Rd, Bangkok *Tel:* (02) 2539786; (02)
   2539788 *Fax:* (02) 2540737; 2nd floor, Sea-
   con Sq, Srinakarin Rd, Bangkok *Tel:* (02)
   7218867-8 *Fax:* (02) 7218869; 4th floor,
   Siam Discovery Center, Rama1 Rd, Bangkok
   *Tel:* (02) 6580418-20 *Fax:* (02) 6580421;
   221 Sukhumvit Rd (Between Sois 15-17),
   Bangkok *Tel:* (02) 2527277; (02) 6510428
   *Fax:* (02) 2516042; 3rd floor, Thaniya Plaza
   Bldg, Silom Rd, Bangkok *Tel:* (02) 2312106;
   (02) 2312107 *Fax:* (02) 2312108; 2nd floor,
   Time Square Bldg, Sukhumvit Rd (between
   Sois 12-14), Bangkok *Tel:* (02) 2500162; (02)
   2500163 *Fax:* (02) 2500164; 3rd floor, World
   Trade Centre (Skydome Zone C), Rajdamri
   Rd, Bangkok *Tel:* (02) 2556209; (02) 2556210
   *Fax:* (02) 2556211

**Central Book Distribution Co Ltd**
306 Silom Rd, Bangkok 10500
*Tel:* (02) 229 7556-7 *Fax:* (02) 237-8321
*Telex:* 82768 Cetrac Th *Cable:* CETRAC
   BANGKOK
*Key Personnel*
Owner: Tieng Chirathivat
Man Dir: Ratana Norabhanlobh *E-mail:* ratanan@
   cmg.co.th
Founded: 1948
Type of Business: Distributor, Exporter, Importer,
   Wholesaler

**Christian Bookstore**
14 Pramuan Rd, Bangkok 10500
*Tel:* (02) 234-7991
*Key Personnel*
Manager: Urai Kithpraditkul
Type of Business: Distributor, Importer, Major
   Book Chain Headquarters, Wholesaler

**Nibondh Co Ltd**
PO Box 402, Bangkok GPO
*Tel:* (02) 221-2611; (02) 221-1553 *Fax:* (02) 224-
   6889
*E-mail:* kongsiri@mozart.inet.co
*Web Site:* www.uiowa.edu/~lawlib/vendors/
   nibondh.htm
*Key Personnel*
Manager: Sumetra Kongsiri
English books at the company's main address;
   English, Thai books & magazines at Nibhondh
   (sikak), 40-42 New Rd, Bangkok.

**Odeon Book Store Lp**
Opp Odeon Theatre, Wang Burapha, Bangkok
   10500
*Tel:* (02) 2210742; (02) 2216567 *Fax:* (02)
   2253300; (02) 2548806
*Key Personnel*
Manager: Prasarn Santiwathana
*Branch Office(s)*
218/10-2 soil Siam Sq, Rama I Rd, Bangkok
   10500

**Suksit Siam Co Ltd**
113-115 Fuang Nakhon Rd, Bangkok 10200
*Tel:* (02) 268-7867 *Fax:* (02) 268-6727

*Key Personnel*
Manager, Publicity: Nilchawee Sivaraksa
Also library suppliers.
Type of Business: Importer

**Suriwong Book Centre, Ltd**
54 Sridonchai Rd, Chiang Mai 50100
Mailing Address: PO Box 44, Chiang Mai 50000
*Tel:* (053) 281052 *Fax:* (053) 271902
*E-mail:* suriwong@loxinfo.co.th
*Key Personnel*
Man Dir: Joy Jittidecharaks
Book Retailer in Thai & English, medical jour-
   nals agent.
*Bookshop(s):* 54 Sridonchai Rd, Chiang Mai
   50100 *E-mail:* suriwong@loxinfo.co.th

**Suriyaban Bookstore**
c/o Suriyaban Publishers, 14 Pramuan Rd,
   Bangkok 10500
*Tel:* (02) 2347991; (02) 2347992
*Key Personnel*
Manager: Surapon Byboribankul
*Owned by:* Suriyaban Publishers

**White Lotus Co Ltd**
GPO Box 1141, Bangkok 10501
*Tel:* (02) 332-4915; (02) 741-6288; (02) 741-6289
   *Fax:* (02) 311-4575; (02) 741-6287
*Web Site:* www.thailine.com/lotus
*Key Personnel*
Chief Executive: D Ande *E-mail:* ande@loxinfo.
   ch.th
Founded: 1972
Also publisher.
Type of Business: Distributor, Exporter, Importer,
   Wholesaler

# Togo

**Librairie/Editions Nouvelles Editions
   Africaines du TOGO**
239 Bd du 13 Janvier, Lome
Mailing Address: BP 4862, Lome
*Tel:* 21 67 61 *Fax:* 22 10 03
*Telex:* 5393 NEAOM
*Key Personnel*
Contact: Fatai Joseph Aguiar
Sales Administrator: Takougnadi
*Owned by:* Les Nouvelles Editions Africaines du
   TOGO (NEA-TOGO)
*Bookshop(s):* 239 Blvd du 13 Janvier, Lome;
   Tokoin Doumassesse VB, Lome

**Librairie Walter**
25 rue du Grand Marche, BP 397, Lome

# Trinidad & Tobago

**Campus Corner Ltd**
72 Pembroke St, Port of Spain
*Tel:* 868-623-1678 *Fax:* 868-623-1678
*Key Personnel*
Manager: Hilton S Young
Founded: 1973
Type of Business: Distributor, Importer, Major
   Independent Bookseller, Wholesaler

**Charran's Bookshop (1978) Ltd**
53 Eastern Main Rd, Tunapuna
*Tel:* 868-663-1884

*Key Personnel*
Manager: Betty Charran
*Owned by:* Charran Educational Publishers
*Bookshop(s):* Muir Marshall Ltd, 64a Independence Sq, Port of Spain

# Tunisia

**Librairie Art et Culture**
24 Ave Taieb M'hiri, 7000 Bizerte
*Tel:* 7231072 *Fax:* 72431372
*Key Personnel*
Contact: Mr Limam Nouredine
Type of Business: Distributor

**Editions Bouslama**
15 Av de France, 1000 Tunis
*Tel:* 71245612
Also publisher.
*Branch Office(s)*
53 rue Nahas Pacha, Tunis
7 rue Amilcar, Tunis

**Societe Nationale d'Edition et de Diffusion**
5, ave de Carthage, 1000 Tunis
*Tel:* 71255000; 71261799
Also publisher.

# Turkey

**ABC Kitabevi Sanayi Tic AS**
Tunel Meydani 1, 1 80030 Beyoglu, Istanbul
*Tel:* (0212) 2762404 *Fax:* (0212) 2851860
*Telex:* 46963 Abca Tr
*Key Personnel*
Manager: Hamit Calcskan
*Owned by:* Genclik Kitabevi

**Arkadas Ltd**
Mithatpasa cad 28/C, 06441 Yenisehir, Ankara
*Tel:* (0312) 4344624; (0312) 3548300 *Fax:* (0312) 4356057 *Fax on Demand:* (0312) 3548309
*E-mail:* info@arkadas.com.tr
*Web Site:* www.arkadas.com.tr
*Key Personnel*
Chairman & Owner: Cumhur Ozdemir
    *E-mail:* cumhuro@arkadas.com.tr
Editor: Meltem Ozdemir *E-mail:* meltemo@ arkadas.com.tr
Retail Trade of Book Stationery, Music Cassettes, Compact Discs, Import Diskettes, Poster & Print, Publishing.
Type of Business: Distributor, Importer, Major Independent Bookseller, Wholesaler

**Fen Kitabevi**
Milli Muedafaa Cad 14/7, Ankara
*Tel:* (0312) 425311 *Fax:* (0312) 4185109; (0312) 4171733
Founded: 1975
Type of Business: Importer, Major Independent Bookseller, Wholesaler
*Owned by:* Guellueoglu/Mehmet S

**Redhouse Bookstore**
SEV Matbaacilik ve Yayincilik AS, Rizapasa Yokusu No 50 Mercan, 34450 Istanbul
*Tel:* (0212) 520 7778; (0212) 520 2960; (0212) 520 0090 *Fax:* (0212) 522 1909
*E-mail:* info@redhouse.com.tr
*Web Site:* www.redhouse.com.tr

*Telex:* 23554 Peet Tr *Cable:* PEET ISTANBUL TR
*Key Personnel*
Manager: Charles H Brown
*Owned by:* Redhouse Press

# Uganda

**Uganda Bookshop**
PO Box 7145, Kampala
*Tel:* (077) 464145 *Fax:* (041) 343756 *Cable:* BOOKSHOP
*Key Personnel*
General Manager: Stephen Rostron
Founded: 1927
Type of Business: Distributor, Importer, Major Book Chain Headquarters, Major Independent Bookseller, Wholesaler
*Owned by:* Church of Uganda, PO Box 6246, Kampala

# United Kingdom

**Abbeydale,** *imprint of* Bookmart Ltd

**Africa Book Centre**
38 King St, Covent Garden, London WC2E 8JT
*Tel:* (020) 7240 6649 *Toll Free Tel:* 0845 458 1581 (UK only) *Fax:* (020) 7497 0309
    *Toll Free Fax:* 0845 458 1579 (UK only)
*E-mail:* orders@africabookcentre.com; info@ africabookcentre.com
*Web Site:* www.africabookcentre.com
*Key Personnel*
Man Dir: Anthony W Zurbrugg *Tel:* (020) 7836 3020 *E-mail:* tz@africabookcentre.com
Founded: 1989
Also Publishers' Agent.
Membership(s): Booksellers' Association (UK).
Type of Business: Distributor, Exporter, Importer, Major Independent Bookseller, Wholesaler
*Warehouse:* Central Books Ltd, 99 Wallis Rd, London E9 5LN *Tel:* (020) 8986 4854 *E-mail:* orders@centralbooks.com (Also distribution)

**African Books Collective Ltd**
Kings Meadow, Unit 13, Ferry Hinksey Rd, Oxford OX2 0DP
*Tel:* (01865) 726686 *Fax:* (01865) 793298; (01993) 709265
*E-mail:* abc@africanbookscollective.com
*Web Site:* www.africanbookscollective.com
*Key Personnel*
Head: Mary Jay *E-mail:* mary.jay@ africanbookscollective.com
Marketing: Ejemhen Esangbedo
Customer Services: Krisia Cook *E-mail:* krisia. cook@africanbookscollective.com; Naomi Robertson
Founded: 1989
Marketing & distribution of books published in Africa by 51 publishers from 12 countries. Scholarly, literature & children's, English language titles & Swahiti children's books.
Type of Business: Distributor
*Owned by:* African Publishers Collective
*Warehouse:* Unit 9, Green Farm, Fritwell, Bicester, Oxon OX27 7QU *Tel:* (07719) 792669

**Afterhurst Ltd**
27 Church Rd, Hove, East Sussex BN3 2FA
*Tel:* (01273) 207 411
*E-mail:* book.orders@tandf.co.uk
*Key Personnel*
Sales Manager: Linda Jarrett
Type of Business: Distributor
*Owned by:* Taylor & Francis Ltd, 1 Gunpowder Sq, London EC4A 3DE

**Airlift Book Co**
8 The Arena, Mollison Ave, Enfield, Middx EN3 7NL
*Tel:* (020) 8804 0400 *Fax:* (020) 8804 0044
*E-mail:* customercare@airlift.co.uk
*Web Site:* www.airlift.co.uk
*Key Personnel*
Man Dir: J Bailey
Founded: 1979
Type of Business: Distributor

**Albany Book Co Ltd**
30 Clydeholm Rd, Clydeside Industrial Estate, Glasgow G14 0BJ
*Tel:* (0141) 9542271
*Telex:* 777253
*Key Personnel*
Man Dir: Andrew T Haigh
Dir: Jonathan Ridge; Mike Jones; Joseph Halpin
*Bookshop(s):* Book Services (Scotland) Ltd, 32 Finlas St, Glasgow G22 5DU (School Textbook Supply); College Bookshop, Jordanhill College, Southbrae Dr, Glasgow GI3 1PP (Educational Book Supply)

**Aldington Books Ltd**
Unit 3b, Frith Business Centre, Frith Rd, Aldington, Ashford, Kent TN25 7HJ
*Tel:* (01233) 720123 *Fax:* (01233) 721272
*E-mail:* sales@aldingtonbooks.co.uk
*Web Site:* www.aldingtonbooks.co.uk
*Key Personnel*
Dir: Jan Barker; Ashley Lennox-Kay
Type of Business: Distributor, Importer
*Associate Companies:* Bay Foreign Language Books *Web Site:* baylanguagebooks.co.uk

**The Anglo American Book Company Ltd**
Crown Buildings, Bancyfelin, Carmarthenshire SA33 5ND
*Tel:* (01267) 211880 *Fax:* (01267) 211882
*E-mail:* books@anglo-american.co.uk
*Web Site:* www.anglo-american.co.uk
*Key Personnel*
Man Dir: Dr Martin Roberts
Marketing Dir: David Bowman
Founded: 1992
Mail order book seller & distributor.
Type of Business: Distributor, Exporter, Importer

**Apex Books Concern**
Darus Salaam, 89 Norfolk Rd, Littlehampton, West Sussex BN17 5HE
*Tel:* (01903) 739042 *Fax:* (01903) 734432
*E-mail:* enquiries@apexbooks.co.uk
*Web Site:* www.apexbooks.co.uk
*Key Personnel*
Man Dir: S Dean *Tel:* (01903) 734682
Dir: A Dean; Ms M Hughes
Founded: 1950
Specialist in religious & cultural studies. Books, journals, videos, slides, microforms in all subjects.
Type of Business: Distributor, Exporter, Importer

**Art Books International Ltd**
Unit 14 Groves Business Centre, Shipton Rd Miltonunder-Wychwood, Chipping Norton Oxon OX7 6JP
*Tel:* (01993) 830000 *Fax:* (01993) 830007
*E-mail:* sales@art.bks.com
*Web Site:* www.art-bks.com

*Key Personnel*
Man Dir: Stanley Kekwick *E-mail:* stanley@art-bks.com
Sales Manager: Fiona Smith
Head of Accounts: Stephen Coke
Founded: 1991
Type of Business: Distributor

## Art Data
12 Bell Industrial Estate, 50 Cunnington St, London W4 5HB
*Tel:* (020) 87471061 *Fax:* (020) 87422319
*E-mail:* ibf@artdata.co.uk
*Web Site:* www.artdata.co.uk
*Key Personnel*
Contact: Tim Borton *E-mail:* tim@artdata.co.uk;
    Liana Sperow *E-mail:* liana@artdata.co.uk
Type of Business: Distributor, Wholesaler

## Aspect Marketing Services
Orbital Park, Ashford, Kent TN24 0GA
*Tel:* (01233) 500 800 *Fax:* (01233) 500 700
*E-mail:* mail@aspectmarketing.co.uk
*Web Site:* www.aspectmarketing.co.uk
Founded: 1995
Provides a broad range of Direct Mail, response handling, fulfilment & data services as well as specialist services for publishers to promote new book titles & distribute catalogues to libraries & booksellers.

## Austicks Headrow Bookshop
91 The Headrow, Leeds LS1 6LJ
*Tel:* (0113) 243-9607 *Fax:* (0113) 245-8837
*Key Personnel*
Manager: John Prime

## B McCall Barbour
28 George IV Bridge, Edinburgh EH1 1ES
*Tel:* (0131) 2254816 *Fax:* (0131) 2254816
*Key Personnel*
Partner: Dr T C Danson-Smith
Founded: 1900
Christian Publishers.
Type of Business: Distributor, Exporter, Importer, Major Independent Bookseller, Wholesaler

## Bargain Book Sales
2b Moore Park Rd, London SW6 2JT
*Tel:* (020) 7385 7007 *Fax:* (020) 7385 7007;
    (020) 7385 9727
*Key Personnel*
Owner & Dir: Graham Snell
Founded: 1975
Specialize in high-quality remainders, especially illustrated books on the Fine & Applied Arts, Graphics, Architecture, Photography, the Cinema & Music.
Type of Business: Remainder Dealer

## Bay Foreign Language Books
Unit 3B Frith Business Centre, Frith Rd Aldington, Ashford Kent TN25 7HJ
*Tel:* (01233) 720020 *Fax:* (01233) 721272
*E-mail:* sales@baylanguagebooks.co.uk
*Web Site:* www.baylanguagebooks.co.uk
*Key Personnel*
Partner & Dir: Jan Barker
Dir: A R P Lennox-Kay
Founded: 1990
Publishers, University Library supply; over 480 languages in catalogue.
Membership(s): Bookseller's Association.
Type of Business: Distributor, Exporter, Importer, Major Independent Bookseller, Wholesaler

## George Bayntun Booksellers
Manvers St, Bath BA1 1JW
*Tel:* (01225) 466000 *Fax:* (01225) 482122
*E-mail:* ebc@georgebayntun.com
*Web Site:* www.georgebayntun.com

*Key Personnel*
Proprietor & Owner: Edward Bayntun Coward
Founded: 1894
Rare Books, First Editions & Fine Bindings.

## BEBC Distribution
Albion Close, Newtown Business Park, Parkstone Poole, Dorset BH12 3LL
Mailing Address: PO Box 1496, Parkstone Poole Dorset BH12 3LL
*Tel:* (01202) 712934 *Fax:* (01202) 712913
*E mail:* webenquiry@bebc.co.uk
*Web Site:* www.bebc.co.uk
*Key Personnel*
Distribution Manager: Charles Kipping
    *E-mail:* charlesk@bebc.co.uk
Founded: 1974
Provides order fulfillment service to publishers & book clubs.
*Owned by:* Bournemouth English Book Centre
*Bookshop(s):* BEBC Bookshop, 125 Charminster Rd, Bournemouth Dorset BH8 8UH, Manager: Alice Rowlands *Tel:* (01202) 523103 *Fax:* (01202) 523103 *E-mail:* charminster@bebc.co.uk; BEBC Bookshop at International House, One Yarmouth Pl, London W1V 7DW, Manager: Michael Keenan *Tel:* (020) 7493 5226 *Fax:* (020) 7493 5226 *E-mail:* piccadilly@bebc.co.uk

## Bertrams
One Broadland Business Park, Norwich, Norfolk NR7 0WG
*Tel:* (0870) 4296724 *Fax:* (0870) 4296709
*E-mail:* sales@bertrams.com
*Web Site:* www.bertrams.com
*Key Personnel*
Chairman: Kip Bertram
Chief Executive Officer: Terry Reilly
Dir: Nigel Bertram
Buying Manager: Adrian Stimpson
    *E-mail:* adrian.stimpson@bertrams.com
Sales Dir: Marcus Whewell
Marketing: Tanya DuRose
Founded: 1967
Type of Business: Exporter, Wholesaler

## Bibliophile Books
5 Thomas Rd, London E14 7BN
*Tel:* (020) 7515 9222 *Fax:* (020) 7538 4115
*E-mail:* customercare@bibliophilebooks.com
*Web Site:* www.bibliophilebooks.com
*Key Personnel*
Chief Executive: Anne Quigley
Founded: 1978
Type of Business: Remainder Dealer

## Birmingham Museums & Art Gallery
Chamberlain Sq, Birmingham B3 3DH
*Tel:* (0121) 303 2834; (0121) 303 1966; (0121) 464 9885 (shop) *Fax:* (0121) 303 1394
*E-mail:* info@bmagshop.co.uk
*Web Site:* www.bmag.org.uk; www.bmagshop.co.uk
*Key Personnel*
Senior Assistant Dir: Mr G Allen
Administrator: J Swancutt *Tel:* (0121) 303 3964
    *E-mail:* jackie_swancutt@birmingham.gov.uk
Founded: 1885
Museum & art gallery.

## Blackwell Retail
50 Broad St, Oxford, Oxon OX1 3AJ
*Tel:* (01865) 792792 *Fax:* (01865) 794143
*E-mail:* mail@blackwell.co.uk
*Web Site:* www.blackwell.co.uk
*Telex:* 83118 *Cable:* BOOKS OXFORD
*Key Personnel*
Man Dir: Dominic Myers
Founded: 1879
Booksellers.

Type of Business: Exporter, Major Book Chain Headquarters
*Bookshop(s):* Blackwell's Bookshop, Faculty of Management Bldg, The Robert Gordon University, Garthdee Campus, Garthdee Rd, Aberdeen AB10 7QE *Tel:* (01224) 263987 *Fax:* (01224) 263986 *Web Site:* www.blackwell.co.uk; Blackwell's Medical Bookshop, University Medical School, Polwarth Bldg, Foresterhill, Aberdeen AB25 2ZD *Tel:* (01224) 683431 *Fax:* (01224) 690794 *E-mail:* aberdeen.med@blackwell. co.uk; Blackwell's Reading College, Reading College School of Arts & Design, Kings Rd, Reading, Berkshire RG1 4HU, Manager: Chris Lawson; Alden & Blackwell, Eton College, Windsor, Berkshire SL4 6DF *Tel:* (01753) 863849 *Fax:* (01753) 832453 *E-mail:* eton@ blackwell.co.uk *Web Site:* www.blackwell. co.uk; Blackwell's Business & Law Bookshop, 3 Windsor Arcade, Birmingham B2 5LG *Tel:* (0121) 2334969 *Fax:* (0121) 2363652 *E-mail:* birmingham@blackwell.co.uk *Web Site:* www.blackwell.co.uk; Blackwell's University Bookshop, University of Brighton, Mezzanine Floor, Cockroft Bldg, Moulsecoomb, Brighton BN2 4GJ *Tel:* (01273) 571974 *Fax:* (01273) 620556 *E-mail:* brighton@ blackwell.co.uk *Web Site:* www.blackwell.co. uk; Blackwell's, 89 Park St, Bristol BS1 5PW *Tel:* (0117) 9276602 *Fax:* (0117) 9251854; Blackwell's University Bookshop, The University of the West of England, Coldharbour Lane, Bristol BS16 1QY *Tel:* (0117) 9652573 *Fax:* (0117) 9750437 *E-mail:* uweb@blackwell. co.uk *Web Site:* www.blackwell.co.uk; Blackwell's Map Centre, Unite 3, The Enterprise Centre, 61 Ditton Walk, Cambridge CB5 8QD, Manager: Sarah Copsey *Tel:* (01223) 568417 *Fax:* (01223) 568416 *E-mail:* ordsvy@ blackwell.co.uk; Heffers: Academic + General Books, 20 Trinity St, Cambridge CB2 1TY, Manager: Mary McIntosh *Tel:* (01223) 568568 *Fax:* (01223) 568591 *E-mail:* heffers@heffers. co.uk; Heffers: Art + Graphics, 15-21 King St, Cambridge CB1 1LH, Manager: Michele Thomas *Tel:* (01223) 568495 *Fax:* (01223) 568411 *E-mail:* art@heffers.co.uk; Heffers: Grafton Centre Bookshop, 28B The Grafton Centre, Cambridge CB1 1PS, Manager: Erika McKay *Tel:* (01223) 568573 *Fax:* (01223) 568572 *E-mail:* grafton@heffers.co.uk; Heffers: Plus (Cambridge Paperback), 31 St Andrew's St, CB2 3AX Cambridge, Manager: Terrie Rodgers *Tel:* (01223) 568598 *Fax:* (01223) 568593 *E-mail:* plus@heffers.co.uk; Heffers: Sound, 19 Trinity St, Cambridge CB2 1TB, Manager: Tony McGeorge *Tel:* (01223) 568562 *Fax:* (01223) 568591 *E-mail:* sound@ heffers.co.uk; Blackwell's University Bookshop, University of Wales, College of Cardiff, University Union, Senghennydd Rd, Cardiff CF2 4AZ *Tel:* (01222) 340673 *Fax:* (01222) 382533 *E-mail:* cardiff@blackwell.co.uk *Web Site:* www.blackwell.co.uk; Blackwell's Medical Bookshop, Sir Herbert Duthie Library, University of Wales College of Medicine, Heath Park, Cardiff CF4 4XN *Tel:* (01222) 762878 *E-mail:* cardiff.med@blackwell.co.uk *Web Site:* www.blackwell.co.uk; Blackwell's Medical Bookshop, Ninewells Hospital, Dundee DD1 9SY *Tel:* (01382) 566551 *Fax:* (01382) 669812; Blackwell's Bookshop Edinburgh Academy, Edinburgh Academy, 42 Henderson Row, Edinburgh EH3 5BL, Manager: Robina Brown *Tel:* (0131) 557 9610 *Fax:* (0131) 557 9610 *E-mail:* academy.edinburgh@blackwell. co.uk; Blackwell's Bookshop Fettes College, Fettes College, Comely Bank, Edinburgh EH4 1QX, Manager: Liz Marchant *Tel:* (0131) 332 5657 *Fax:* (0131) 332 5657 *E-mail:* fettes.edinburgh@blackwell.co.uk; Blackwell's Bookshop Heriot Watt University, Heriot Watt University, Hugh Nisbet Bldg, Riccarton Campus, Edinburgh EH14 4AS, Man-

ager: Alistair Millar *Tel:* (0131) 451 5287 *Fax:* (0131) 451 5287 *E-mail:* heriotwatt@ blackwell.co.uk; Blackwell's Bookshop King's Buildings, King's Buildings, University of Edinburgh, West Mains Rd, Edinburgh EH9 3JR, Acting Manager: Tom Tivan *Tel:* (0131) 667 0432 *Fax:* (0131) 667 0432 *E-mail:* kings.edinburgh@blackwell.co.uk; Blackwell's Bookshop Merchiston Castle, Merchiston Castle School, 294 Colinton Rd, Edinburgh EH13 0PU, Manager: Loata Millard *Tel:* (0131) 441 4752 *Fax:* (0131) 441 4752 *E-mail:* merchiston.edinburgh@blackwell.co.uk; Blackwell's Bookshop QMUC, Queen Margaret University College, 36 Clerwood Terrace, Edinburgh EH12 8TS, Manager: Liz Marchant *Tel:* (0131) 334 3818 *Fax:* (0131) 334 3818; Blackwell's Bookshop South Bridge, 53-62 South Bridge, Edinburgh EH1 1YS, Manager: Anne Watson *Tel:* (0131) 622 8222 *Fax:* (0131) 557 8149 *E-mail:* edinburgh@ blackwell.co.uk; Blackwell's Edinburgh Royal Infirmary, Unite GF 319, 51 Little France Crescent, Little France, Edinburgh EH16 4SA, Manager: Bob Carroll *Tel:* (0131) 666 1764 *E-mail:* edinburgh.med@blackwell.co.uk; Blackwell's Napier University Craighouse, c/o Anne Watson, Blackwell's Bookshop South Bridge, 53-62 South Bridge, Edinburgh EH1 1YS; Blackwell's Napier University Merchiston, c/o Anne Watson, Blackwell's Bookshop South Bridge, 53-62 South Bridge, Edinburgh EH1 1YS; Blackwell's Napier University Sighthill, c/o Anne Watson, Blackwell's Bookshop South Bridge, 53-62 South Bridge, Edinburgh EH1 1YS; Blackwell's University Bookshop, University of Exeter, St Luke's College, Stocker Rd, Exeter EX4 4QA *Tel:* (01392) 59456 *Fax:* (01392) 411207 *E-mail:* exeter@ blackwell.co.uk *Web Site:* www.blackwell.co.uk; Blackwell's University Bookshop, School of Education, St Luke's College, University of Exeter, Exeter EX1 2LU *Tel:* (01392) 264956; Blackwell's, Students' Union, St Mary's Pl, St Andrews, Fife KY16 9UZ, Manager: Barbara Dumbleton *Tel:* (01334) 476367 *Fax:* (01334) 476367 *E-mail:* st.andrews@blackwell.co.uk; Blackwell's, 21 Blenheim Terrace, Woodhouse Lane, Leeds LS2 9HJ, Manager: Andrew Lilley *Tel:* (0113) 243 2446 *Fax:* (0113) 243 0661 *E-mail:* leeds@blackwell.co.uk; Blackwell's University Bookshop, University of Liverpool, Alsop Bldg, Brownlow Hill, Liverpool L3 5TX *Tel:* (0151) 7098146 *Fax:* (0151) 7096653 *E-mail:* liverpool@blackwell.co.uk; Blackwell's, 100 Charing Cross Rd, London WC2H 0JG *Tel:* (020) 7292 5100 *Fax:* (020) 7240 9665 *E-mail:* london@blackwell.co.uk *Web Site:* www.blackwell.co.uk; Blackwell's London Business School, 18-22 Park Rd, London NW1 4SH, Manager: Tina Scott *Tel:* (020) 7723 6953 *Fax:* (020) 7723 7017 *E-mail:* lbs@ blackwell.co.uk; Blackwell's Medical Bookshop, 2nd floor, Hunter Wing, Cranmer Terrace, Tooting, London SW15 0RE *Tel:* (020) 8725 0813; Blackwell's University Bookshop, University of North London, 158 Holloway Rd, London N7 8DD *Tel:* (020) 7700 4786 *Fax:* (020) 7700 7687 *E-mail:* unl@blackwell. co.uk *Web Site:* www.blackwell.co.uk; Blackwell's University Bookshop, University of North London, Ladbroke House, 62-66 Highbury Grove, London N5 2AD *Tel:* (020) 7314 4215; Blackwell's University Bookshop, 119-122 London Rd, London SE1 6LF *Tel:* (020) 7928 5378 *Fax:* (020) 7261 9536 *E-mail:* sbu@ blackwell.co.uk *Web Site:* www.blackwell.co. uk; Blackwell's Business & Law Bookshop, 243-244 High Holborn, London WC1V 7DZ *Tel:* (020) 7831 9501 *Fax:* (020) 7405 9412 *E-mail:* holborn@blackwell.co.uk; Blackwell's Academic Bookshop, Union Bldg, Loughborough University, Ashby Rd, Loughborough LE11 3TT *Tel:* (01509) 219788 *Fax:* (01509)

219754 *E-mail:* loughborough@blackwell.co. uk; Blackwell's University Bookshop, Faculty of Agriculture & Food Sciences, Sutton Bonington, Loughborough LE12 5RD *Tel:* (0115) 9516017; Blackwell's University Bookshop, The Precinct Centre, Oxford Rd, Manchester M13 9RN *Tel:* (0161) 2743331 *Fax:* (0161) 2743228 *E-mail:* manchester@ blackwell.co.uk; Blackwell's, University Library, UMIST, Sackville St, Manchester M60 1QD *Tel:* (0161) 2004936 *E-mail:* umist@ blackwell.co.uk; Blackwell's Academic Bookshop, The Elizabeth Gaskell Site, Manchester Metropolitan University, Hathersage Rd, Manchester M13 0JA; Blackwell's, 141 Percy St, Newcastle Upon Tyne NE1 7RS *Tel:* (0191) 232 6421 *Fax:* (0191) 260 2536 *E-mail:* newcastle@blackwell.co.uk; Blackwell's University Bookshop, University of Nottingham, Portland Bldg, University Park, Notts NG7 2RD *Tel:* (0115) 9580272 *Fax:* (0115) 9587063 *E-mail:* nottingham@blackwell.co. uk *Web Site:* www.blackwell.co.uk; Blackwell's Medical Bookshop, Queen's Medical Centre, Clifton Blvd, Notts NG7 2UH *Tel:* (0115) 9780938 *Fax:* (0115) 9709980 *E-mail:* nottingham.med@blackwell.co.uk; Blackwell's University Bookshop, Nottingham Trent University, Chaucer Bldg, Goldsmith St, Notts NG1 5LT *Tel:* (0115) 9417307 *Fax:* (0115) 9417311 *E-mail:* trent@blackwell. co.uk; Blackwell's University Bookshop, Nottingham Trent University, Clifton Campus, Clifton Lane, Clifton, Notts NG11 8NS *Tel:* (0115) 9844474 *Fax:* (0115) 9211410 *E-mail:* clifton@blackwell.co.uk; Blackwell's University Bookshop, 99 High St, Old Aberdeen AB25 3EN *Tel:* (01224) 486102 *Fax:* (01224) 276162 *E-mail:* aberdeen. ub@blackwell.co.uk *Web Site:* blackwell. co.uk; Blackwell's, 48-51 Broad St, Oxford OX1BQ *Tel:* (01865) 792792 *Fax:* (01865) 794143 *E-mail:* oxford@blackwell.co.uk *Web Site:* www.blackwell.co.uk; Blackwell's University Bookshop, Oxford Brookes University, Gipsy Lane, Headington, Oxford OX3 0BP *Tel:* (01865) 483063; (01865) 792792; Blackwell's Medical Bookshop, John Radcliffe Hospital, Headington, Oxford OX3 9DU *Tel:* (01865) 741663 *Fax:* (01865) 741663 *E-mail:* oxford.med@blackwell.co.uk; Blackwell's Art Bookshop, 27 Broad St, Oxford OX1 2AS *Tel:* (01865) 792792 *Fax:* (01865) 794143 *E-mail:* art@blackwell.co.uk *Web Site:* www.blackwell.co.uk; Blackwell's Rare Books, 48-51 Broad St, Oxford OX1 3SW *Tel:* (01865) 333555 *Fax:* (01865) 248833; Blackwell's Music Bookshop, 23-25 Broad St, Oxford OX1 3AX *Tel:* (01865) 333580 *Fax:* (01865) 728020 *E-mail:* music.ox@ blackwell.co.uk; Blackwell's University Bookshop, University of Glamorgan, Llantwit, Treforest, Pontypridd, Mid-Glamorgan CF37 1DL *Tel:* (01443) 401502 *Fax:* (01443) 400791 *E-mail:* glamorgan@blackwell.co. uk; Blackwell's Academic Bookshop, University of Portsmouth, Students Centre, Unit 1, Cambridge Rd, Portsmouth PO1 2EF *Tel:* (023) 92832813 *Fax:* (023) 92851032 *E-mail:* portsmouth@blackwell.co.uk; Blackwell's University Bookshop, University Library Bldg, University of Central Lancashire, 52 St Peter's Square, Preston PR1 2HZ *Tel:* (01772) 254462; (01772) 893990 *Fax:* (01772) 202313 *E-mail:* preston@blackwell.co.uk; The Friar Street Bookshop, 142-143 Friar St, Reading RG1 1EX *Tel:* (0118) 9573082; Blackwell's University Bookshop, University of York, The Market Sq, Vanbrugh Way, Heslington, Yorks YO10 5NM *Tel:* (01904) 432715 *Fax:* (01904) 413420 *E-mail:* york@blackwell.co.uk; Blackwell's University Bookshop, University of Salford, Horlock Court, University Rd, Salford M5 4WT *Tel:* (0161) 7374565 *Fax:* (0161)

7430566 *E-mail:* salford@blackwell.co.uk; Blackwell's University Bookshop, University of Sheffield, Mappin St, Sheffield S1 4DT *Tel:* (0114) 2787211 *Fax:* (0114) 2787629 *E-mail:* sheffield@blackwell.co.uk; Blackwell's University Bookshop, Sheffield Hallam University, City Campus, Pond St, Sheffield S1 1WB *Tel:* (0114) 2752152 *Fax:* (0114) 2798950 *E-mail:* hallam@blackwell.co.uk; Blackwell's, Broomhill, 220 Fulwood Rd, Sheffield S10 3BB *Tel:* (0114) 2660820 *E-mail:* broomhill@blackwell.co.uk; Blackwell's Academic Bookshop, Southampton Institute, Sir James Matthews Bldg, 157-187 Above Bar St, Southampton SO14 7JT *Tel:* (01703) 631806 *Fax:* (01703) 631787 *E-mail:* southampton@blackwell.co.uk

### Roy Bloom Ltd
Fanshaw House, 3-9 Fanshaw St, London N1 6HX
*Tel:* (020) 7729 5373 *Fax:* (020) 7729 2375
*E-mail:* info@roybloom.com
*Web Site:* www.remainder-books.com; www. roybloom.com
*Key Personnel*
Chairman: Roy Bloom *E-mail:* roybloom@ roybloom.com
Man Dir: Adam Bloom
Sales Dir: Paul White *E-mail:* paul.white@ roybloom.com
Founded: 1969
Specialize in publishers' overstocks & remainders.
Type of Business: Remainder Dealer

### Book Representation & Distribution Ltd
Hadleigh Hall, London Rd, Hadleigh, Essex SS7 2DE
*Tel:* (01702) 552912 *Fax:* (01702) 556095
*E-mail:* mail@bookreps.com; info@bookreps.com
*Web Site:* www.bookreps.com
*Key Personnel*
Man Dir: Dan Levey
Secretary: Doreen Mann
Accountant: Richard Foster
Sales Manager: Celia Stocks
Marketing Manager: Don Brown
Founded: 1988
Type of Business: Distributor, Exporter, Importer

### Bookmark Remainders
Rivendell Illand, Launceston, Cornwall PL15 7LS
*Tel:* (01566) 782728 *Fax:* (01566) 782059
*E-mail:* info@book-bargains.co.uk
*Web Site:* book-bargains.co.uk
*Key Personnel*
Man Dir: Andrew Rattray *E-mail:* andrew@book-bargains.co.uk
Founded: 1954
Remainder specialists.
Type of Business: Remainder Dealer

### Bookmart Ltd
Blaby Rd, Wigston, Leicester, Lincs LE18 4SE
*Tel:* (0116) 2759060 *Fax:* (0116) 2759090
*E-mail:* books@bookmart.co.uk
*Key Personnel*
Man Dir: Philip E Parkin
Finance Dir: Andrew Painter
Co-Edition Sales Manager: Linda Williams
Founded: 1989
Publisher & distributor, promotional books.
Imprints: Abbeydale; Silverdale
*Branch Office(s)*
Regent St, London

### Bookpoint Ltd
130 Milton Park, Abingdon, Oxon OX14 4SB
*Tel:* (01235) 827730 *Fax:* (01235) 400454;
  (01235) 821511 (Orders)
*E-mail:* firstname.lastname@bookpoint.co.uk

*Web Site:* www.oxfordshire.co.uk; pubeasy.books.
bookpoint.co.uk
*Telex:* 837091 bookpt g
*Key Personnel*
Man Dir: Tony Bryars *E-mail:* tony.bryars@
bookpoint.co.uk
Founded: 1973
Type of Business: Distributor
*Owned by:* Hodder Headline PLC

**Books for Europe Ltd**
3 Sutton Court, Grange Rd, London W5 3PG
*Tel:* (020) 8840 6672
*Key Personnel*
Man Dir: Juliusz Komarnicki *Tel:* (091) 9671539
*Fax:* (091) 9667865
Type of Business: Exporter

**Books from India (UK) Ltd**
45 Museum St, London WC1A 1LR
*Tel:* (071) 4053784 *Fax:* (071) 8314517
*Key Personnel*
Contact: Shreeram Vidyarthi
Founded: 1978
Also publisher.
Type of Business: Distributor, Exporter, Importer,
Major Independent Bookseller, Wholesaler
*Branch Office(s)*
Asia Publishing House Ltd, Borden Villa, Bor-
den Lane, Sittingbourne, Kent ME10 1BY
*Tel:* (01795) 473149 *Fax:* (01795) 473149

**Bookworld Wholesale Ltd**
Unit 10, Hodfar Rd, Sandy Lane Industrial Estate,
Stourpont-on-Severn, Worcs DY13 9QB
*Tel:* (01299) 823330 *Fax:* (01299) 829970
*Key Personnel*
Dir: Lian Clark; Justin Gainham
Founded: 1988
Specialize in transport, military & modelling
books.
Type of Business: Distributor, Exporter, Importer,
Wholesaler

**Booth-Clibborn Editions,** see Internos Books

**Botes Librair**
Parkhurst Mews, Parkhurst Rd, Bexhill, East Sus-
sex TN40 1DW
Mailing Address: PO Box 22, Bexhill, East Sus-
sex TN40 1DW
*Tel:* (01424) 210871 *Fax:* (01424) 734506;
(01424) 731262
*E-mail:* 100450.3641@compuserve.com
*Key Personnel*
President: David L Gould
Founded: 1964
Library suppliers, educational supplies & special-
ists in medical & scientific publications.
Type of Business: Exporter, Wholesaler
*Branch Office(s)*
Botes Unifoyle Ltd, International School Book
Distributors
*Bookshop(s):* Books Unlimited, PO Box 22, Bex-
hill, East Sussex TN40 1DW

**BPL Remainders**
Princess House, 50 Eastcastle St, Suite 275, Lon-
don W1N 7AP
*Tel:* (020) 7636 5070; (020) 7631 5070
*Fax:* (020) 7580 3001
*Telex:* 22303
*Key Personnel*
General Manager: K Fox
Export Sales Administrator: Francesca Ferguson
Founded: 1982
Type of Business: Remainder Dealer

**Bradt Travel Guides Ltd**
23 High St, Chalfont St Peter, Saint Peter Bucks
SL9 9QE

*Tel:* (01753) 893444 *Fax:* (01753) 892333
*E-mail:* info@bradtguides.com; enquiries@bradt-
travelguides.com
*Web Site:* www.bradtguides.com
*Key Personnel*
President: Hilary Bradt
Office Manager: Debbie Hunter
Founded: 1972
*US Distributor:* Globe Pequot Press.
Type of Business: Exporter

**The Bridge Book Co Ltd**
10 Blenheim Court, Brewery Rd, London N7
9NT
*Tel:* (020) 7697 3000 *Fax:* (020) 7700 4552
*E-mail:* bridgepem@aol.com
*Key Personnel*
Man Dir: Mike Pemberton
Founded: 1962
Type of Business: Distributor, Exporter, Importer,
Remainder Dealer
*Parent Company:* Chrysalis Books Ltd

**Bridge Bookshop Ltd**
Shore Rd, Pt Erin IM9 6HL
*Tel:* (01624) 833378 *Fax:* (01624) 835381
*Key Personnel*
Manager: Joan Hook
Dir: Rosemary Pickard
Founded: 1953
Type of Business: Exporter, Major Independent
Bookseller
*Owned by:* Rosemary & Alan Pickard

**Broomfield Books**
36 De La Warr Rd, East Grinstead, West Sussex
RH19 3BP
*Tel:* (01342) 313 237 *Fax:* (01342) 322 525
*E-mail:* nic@broomfieldbooks.co.uk
*Web Site:* www.broomfieldbooks.co.uk
*Key Personnel*
Sales & Consultancy: Nic Webb *E-mail:* nic@
broomfieldbooks.co.uk
Sales & Public Relations: Andrea Grant-Webb
*E-mail:* andrea@broomfieldbooks.co.uk
Founded: 2003
Publishing consultancy & sales agency for small
& medium publishers of non-fiction & fiction.
The sales agency covers London & the South-
east of England together with UK key accounts
& the export market.
Membership(s): IPG (Independent Publishers
Guild).

**Browne's Bookstore**
56 Mill Rd, Cambridge CB1 2AS
*Tel:* (01223) 350968 *Fax:* (01223) 353456
*E-mail:* brownes_books@msn.com
*Key Personnel*
Contact: Mrs G H Browne
Founded: 1976
Specialize in mail order, library supplies.
Type of Business: Exporter, Major Independent
Bookseller

**Bushwood Books**
6 Marksbury Ave, Kew Gardens, Surrey TW9 4JF
*Tel:* (020) 8392 8585 *Fax:* (020) 8392 9876
*E-mail:* bushwd@aol.com
*Key Personnel*
Contact: Richard Hansen; Victoria Hansen
Founded: 1984
Type of Business: Distributor
*Owned by:* Ultraco Ltd

**Cedar Media**
7-9 Church Hill, Loughton, Essex IG10 1QP
*Tel:* (020) 8508 8856 *Fax:* (020) 8508 8856
*E-mail:* cedarmedia@btinternet.com
*Key Personnel*
Dir: Marie L Barnett; Roger Barnett

Founded: 1987
Marketing, distribution of reference publication
concerning EU & Europe as a whole.
Type of Business: Distributor, Exporter, Importer

**Central Books**
99 Wallis Rd, London E9 5LN
*Tel:* (0845) 458 9911 *Fax:* (0845) 458 9912
*E-mail:* info@centralbooks.com
*Web Site:* www.centralbooks.co.uk; www.
centralbooks.com
*Key Personnel*
Man Dir: William Norris
Sales Manager: Mark Chilver
Accounts: Dave Cope
Founded: 1939
Type of Business: Distributor, Exporter, Importer,
Major Independent Bookseller

**Clarke Associates Ltd**
2-3 Denmark St, 3rd floor, Bristol BS1 5DQ
*Tel:* (0117) 926 8864 *Fax:* (0117) 922 6437
*E-mail:* enq@clarkeassoc.com
*Web Site:* www.clarkeassoc.demon.co.uk
*Key Personnel*
Chairman, Man Dir: Malcolm Clarke
Dir: Susan C Phillips
Founded: 1982
Publishing Consultants.
Type of Business: Distributor, Exporter, Importer
*Owned by:* Clarke Associates Ltd

**Clipper Distribution Services**
Windmill Grove, Portchester, Hants PO16 9HT
*Tel:* (0705) 200080 *Fax:* (0705) 200090
*Key Personnel*
Man Dir: John P C Delieu
Founded: 1988
Type of Business: Distributor

**Colt Associates**
The Old School, Brewhouse Hill, Wheathamp-
stead, St Albans, Herts AL4 8AN
*Tel:* (0158) 2834292 *Fax:* (0158) 825778
*Key Personnel*
President: Roger Lloyd-Taylor
Founded: 1977
Other branch offices located in China, Hong
Kong & Manila.
*Branch Office(s)*
Toyko, Japan

**Combined Book Services**
Units 1/K, Paddock Wood Distribution Center,
Paddock Wood, Tonbridge, Kent TN12 6UU
*Tel:* (01892) 839819 *Fax:* (01892) 837272
*E-mail:* info@combook.co.uk
*Web Site:* www.combook.co.uk
*Key Personnel*
Man Dir: Charles Turner
Mail order book distribution.
Type of Business: Distributor, Exporter, Importer,
Wholesaler

**Commonwealth Education Foundation**
PO Box 367, Edgware, Middx HA8 7AK
*Tel:* (0208) 9312359 *Fax:* (0208) 9592137
*E-mail:* cefoundation@aol.com
*Key Personnel*
Secretary: Nina Novy
Founded: 1989
Suppliers of any book to any country, single vol-
ume to complete libraries, free of charge.

**Computer Bookshops Ltd**
205 Formans Rd, Sparkhill, Birmingham B11
3AX
*Tel:* (0121) 778 3333 *Fax:* (0121) 606 0476
*E-mail:* info@computerbookshops.com
*Web Site:* www.computerbookshops.com

*Key Personnel*
Chairman: Ian Maclean
Man Dir: Donna Jones
Head of Marketing: Paul Savill *E-mail:* pauls@
    compbook.co.uk
Founded: 1978
Type of Business: Distributor, Wholesaler

## Coningsby International Bookshop Services
22 School Lane, Coningsby, Lincoln, Lincolnshire
    LN4 4WX
*Tel:* (01526) 342231 *Fax:* (01526) 344367
*E-mail:* service@coningsby.com
*Web Site:* www.coningsby.com
*Key Personnel*
Owner: Clive Sharples; Ruth Sharples
Founded: 1976
Type of Business: Exporter, Major Independent
    Bookseller

## Cordee Ltd
3a De Montfort St, Leicester, Lincs LE1 7HD
*Tel:* (0116) 2543579 *Fax:* (0116) 2471176
*E-mail:* info@cordee.co.uk
*Web Site:* www.cordee.co.uk
Founded: 1973
Specialize in recreation & travel.
Type of Business: Distributor, Wholesaler

## The Crafts Council
44a Pentonville Rd, Islington, London N1 9BY
*Tel:* (020) 7278 7700 *Fax:* (020) 7837 6891
*Web Site:* www.craftscouncil.org.uk
*Key Personnel*
Manager: Jo Swait *Tel:* (020) 7806 2557
    *E-mail:* j-swait@craftscouncil.org.uk
Contact: Lisa Daniel
Founded: 1971
Government-financed body promoting Britain's
    artist craftsman, craft books & catalogs.
*Bookshop(s):* The Gallery Shop

**Crofthouse Books Ltd**, see Lindsay & Croft

**Cyngor Llyfrau Cymru**, see Welsh Books
    Council

**Cyngor Llyfrau Cymru Canolfan Dosbarthu**,
    see Welsh Books Council

## Cypher Library Books
Elmfield Rd, Morley, Leeds LS27 0NN
*Tel:* (0113) 2012900 *Fax:* (0113) 2012929
*E-mail:* enquiries@cyphergroup.com; library.
    enquiries@bertrams.com
*Web Site:* www.cyphergroup.com
*Key Personnel*
Man Dir: Michael Robinson
Head of Sales & Marketing: Jackie Aspinall
Founded: 1947

## Dawson UK Ltd, Books Division
Foxhills House, Brindley Close, Rushden,
    Northants NN10 6DB
*Tel:* (01933) 417500 *Fax:* (01933) 417501
*E-mail:* bkcustserv@dawsonbooks.co.uk
*Web Site:* www.dawsonbooks.co.uk
*Key Personnel*
Chief Executive: David Blundell
European Book Division Manager: Diane Kerr
European Publisher Relations Manager: Eric Le
    Strat
Marketing Manager: Steven Welch
Sales Manager: George Hammond
    *E-mail:* george.hammond@dawsonbooks.co.uk
Founded: 1809
Subscription Agent.
Type of Business: Distributor, Exporter, Importer

*Owned by:* Dawson Holdings Plc
*Associate Companies:* Dawson UK Subscrip-
    tion & Technology Divisions, Cannon House,
    Folkestone, Kent CT19 5EE

## Delta Books Worldwide
39 Alexandra Rd, Addlestone, Surrey KT15 2PQ
*Tel:* (01932) 854 776 *Fax:* (01932) 849 528
*E-mail:* info@deltabooks.co.uk
*Web Site:* www.deltabooks.co.uk
*Key Personnel*
Contact: Eileen Fryer *E-mail:* eileen.fryer@
    deltabooks.co.uk
Type of Business: Distributor, Exporter, Whole-
    saler

## Dillons, The Bookstore
128 New St, Birmingham B2 4DB
*Tel:* (0121) 6314333 *Fax:* (0121) 6432441
*E-mail:* bhamnew@dillons.eunet.co.uk
Branch offices in Aberdeen, Birmingham, Brom-
    ley, Cambridge, Canterbury, Charing Cross,
    Chichester, Coventry, Crawrey, Croydon,
    Derby, Ealing, Egham, Harrogate, Leicester,
    Liverpool, London, Manchester, Nottingham,
    Oxford, & Wolverhampton.
*Owned by:* THORN EMI Home Electronics (UK)
    Ltd
*Branch Office(s)*
Charing Cross
Chichester
Coventry

## Dillons City Business Book Store
72 Park Rd, London WC2N 5EJ
*Tel:* (020) 7628 7479 *Fax:* (020) 7628 7871
*E-mail:* loncbus@dillons.eunet.co.uk
*Key Personnel*
Manager: Amanda Panedli

## The Economists' Bookshop
Clare Market, Portugal St, London WC2A 2AB
*Tel:* (020) 7405 5531 *Fax:* (020) 7482 4873
*E-mail:* economists@waterstones.co.uk
*Key Personnel*
General Manager: Sue Tarratt
*Owned by:* The EMI Group -Dillons Group,
    Royal House, Prince's Gate House Rd, Soli-
    hull, W Ruplands BG1 3QQ
*Branch Office(s)*
The Barbican Business Book Centre, 9 Moor-
    fields, London *Tel:* (020) 7628 7479
*Bookshop(s):* City Poly Bookshop, Moorgate,
    London EC2; City University Bookshop,
    Northampton Sq, London EC1V 0HB; Queen
    Mary & Westfield College Bookshop, Mile End
    Rd, London E1 4NS; Brunel University Book-
    shop, Cleveland Rd, Uxbridge, Middlesex

## Electronica Books & Media Ltd
Sunbury International Business Center, Brookland
    Close, Sunbury-on-Thames, Middx TW16 7DX
*Tel:* (01932) 765119 *Fax:* (01932) 765429
*Key Personnel*
Dir: Michael Geelan
Founded: 1988
Type of Business: Distributor, Exporter, Importer,
    Wholesaler

## Elstead Maps
Badgery Hookley Lane, Elstead, Godalming, Sur-
    rey GU8 6JE
Mailing Address: PO Box 52, Elstead, Godalm-
    ing, Surrey GU8 6JJ
*Tel:* (01252) 703472 *Fax:* (01252) 703971
*E-mail:* enquiry@elstead.co.uk
*Web Site:* www.elstead.co.uk
*Key Personnel*
Proprietor: Stephen Colebrooke *E-mail:* stephen@
    elstead.co.uk

Founded: 1981
Mail order retailers.

## European Schoolbooks Ltd
The Runnings, Cheltenham GL51 9PQ
*Tel:* (01242) 245252 *Fax:* (01242) 224137
*E-mail:* direct@esb.co.uk
*Web Site:* www.eurobooks.co.uk
*Key Personnel*
Man Dir: Frank A Preiss *E-mail:* fap@esb.co.uk
Founded: 1964
Specialists in major European languages other
    than English.
Type of Business: Distributor, Importer, Whole-
    saler
*Bookshop(s):* The European Bookshop, 5 War-
    wick St, London W1B 5LU *Tel:* (020) 7734
    5259 *Fax:* (020) 7287 1720 *E-mail:* mrg@esb.
    co.uk; The Italian Bookshop, 7 Cecil Court,
    London WC2N 4EZ *Tel:* (020) 7240 1634
    *Fax:* (020) 7240 1635 *E-mail:* italian@esb.co.
    uk; Young Europeans Bookstore, 5 Cecil Court,
    London WC2N 4EZ *Tel:* (020) 7836 6667
    *Fax:* (020) 7240-1635 *E-mail:* yeb@esb.co.uk

## Eurospan Distribution Center Ltd
3 Henrietta St, Covent Garden, London WC2E
    8LU
*Tel:* (0161) 7642296 *Fax:* (0161) 7648213
*E-mail:* info@eurospan.co.uk
*Web Site:* www.eurospan.co.uk
*Key Personnel*
Man Dir: Peter Kershaw Taylor
Founded: 1969
Type of Business: Distributor

## Extenza-Turpin
Stratton Business Park, Pegasus Drive, Big-
    gleswade, Beds SG18 8GB
*Tel:* (01767) 604 806 (sales manager)
    *Fax:* (01767) 601 640
*E-mail:* turpin@turpin-distribution.com
*Web Site:* www.extenza-turpin.com
*Key Personnel*
Man Dir: Lorna M Summers
Operations Manager: Tim Richards
Information Technology Manager: Bill Pease
Accounting: Ruth Campbell
Sales: Kathy Law *E-mail:* lawk@extenza-turpin.
    com
Founded: 1968
Provide worldwide distribution of books & fulfill-
    ment of journals for academic & learned pub-
    lishers from US & UK locations. Customized
    service includes invoicing in the publisher's
    name & using the publisher's own trading
    terms. Management reports are available 24/7
    via internet. Mulilingual customer care & cus-
    tomer stationery. Multiple currencies.
Type of Business: Distributor
*Parent Company:* Royal Swets & Zeitlinger BV
*U.S. Office(s):* Turpin Distribution Services Ltd,
    56 Industrial Park Dr, Pembroke, MA 12359,
    United States *Tel:* 781-829-8973 *Fax:* 781-829-
    9052 *E-mail:* turpin@turpinna.com

## Clive Farahar & Sophie Dupre Booksellers
Horsebrook House, XV The Green, Calne, Wilts
    SN11 8DQ
*Tel:* (01249) 821121 *Fax:* (01249) 821202
*E-mail:* sophie@faraharduprre.co.uk
*Web Site:* www.faraharduprre.co.uk
*Key Personnel*
Contact: Sophie Dupre
Founded: 1981
Antiquarian books on voyages & travels. Auto-
    graph letters, signed photos, signed books,
    photography in all fields especially royalty &
    literature.
Type of Business: Major Independent Bookseller

1341

**T C Farries & Co Ltd**
Irongray Rd, Lochside, Dumfries DG2 0LH
*Tel:* (01387) 720755 *Fax:* (01387) 721105
*Key Personnel*
Chairman: D W N Landale
Sales Dir: Mrs L Bennett
Man Dir: P D R Landale
Finance Dir: J McGrillis
Founded: 1982
Type of Business: Distributor, Exporter, Major
  Independent Bookseller, Wholesaler

**David Flatman Ltd**, see Lomond Books

**FOYLES**
113-119 Charing Cross Rd, London WC2H 0EB
*Tel:* (020) 7437 5660 *Fax:* (020) 7434 1574
*E-mail:* customerservice@foyles.co.uk
*Web Site:* www.foyles.co.uk
*Key Personnel*
Manager: John Cruickshanks

**Walter H Gardner & Co**
16 Chalton Dr, London N2 0QW
*Tel:* (20) 8458 3202 *Fax:* (20) 8458 8499
*E-mail:* walterhgardnerco@aol.com
*Key Personnel*
Man Partner: Walter H Gardner
Sales & Marketing: Mrs D Gardner
Type of Business: Remainder Dealer

**Gardners Books**
One Whittle Dr, Eastbourne, East Sussex BN23
  6QH
*Tel:* (01323) 521666; (01323) 521555
  *Fax:* (01323) 521666
*E-mail:* marketing@gardners.com
*Web Site:* www.gardners.com
*Key Personnel*
Dir, Export Sales: Warwick Bailey
  *E-mail:* wbailey@gardners.com
Contact: Mike Burge
International Book Wholesalers.
Type of Business: Exporter, Wholesaler

**Gazelle Book Services Ltd**
White Cross Mills High Town, Lancaster, Lancs
  LA1 4XS
*Tel:* (01524) 68765 *Fax:* (01524) 63232
*E-mail:* sales@gazellebooks.co.uk
*Web Site:* www.gazellebook.co.uk
*Key Personnel*
Man Dir: Trevor Witcher *E-mail:* trevor.gazelle@
  talk21.com
Dir: Brian Haywood; Mark Trotter
Founded: 1988
Type of Business: Distributor

**George Gregory Bookseller**
Manvers St, Bath BA1 1JW
*Tel:* (01225) 466000 *Fax:* (01225) 482122
*Key Personnel*
President: Mrs C A W Bayntun-Coward
Founded: 1846
Old Books, Maps & Prints.

**William George's Sons Ltd**
89 Park St, Bristol BS1 5PW
*Tel:* (0117) 9276602
*Key Personnel*
Manager: Duncan Dewfall

**Godfrey Cave Associates Ltd**
27 Wrights Lane, London W8 5TZ
*Tel:* (020) 7416 3000 *Fax:* (020) 7416 3289
*Key Personnel*
Man Dir: Kevin Binston
Sales Dir: Deborah Wright
Sales Manager: Patrick Duffin
Publishing, Liason Manager: Roz Scott

Founded: 1972
Type of Business: Remainder Dealer

**Godfrey Cave Holdings Ltd**
27 Wrights Lane, London W8 5TZ
*Tel:* (020) 7416 3000 *Fax:* (020) 7416 3099
Comprised of Godfrey Cave Associates, Blooms-
  bury Editions, Omega Books, Benson Books.
Type of Business: Remainder Dealer

**Gracewing/Fowler Wright**, see Gracewing Ltd

**Gracewing Ltd**
Formerly Gracewing/Fowler Wright
Gracewing House, 2 Southern Ave, Leominster,
  Herefordshire HR6 0QF
*Tel:* (01568) 616835 *Fax:* (01568) 613289
*Web Site:* www.gracewing.co.uk
*Key Personnel*
Man Dir: Tom Longford
Founded: 1958
Type of Business: Distributor, Exporter, Importer,
  Major Independent Bookseller, Wholesaler

**Grange Books PLC**
The Grange, Units 1-6, Kingsnorth Industrial Es-
  tate, Hoo, Nr Rochester, Kent ME3 9ND
*Tel:* (01634) 256 000 *Fax:* (01634) 255 500
*E-mail:* grangebooks@aol.com
*Web Site:* www.grangebooks.co.uk
*Key Personnel*
Man Dir: Michael Ash *E-mail:* michaelash@
  grangebooks.co.uk
Administrative Dir: Heather Staples
  *E-mail:* heather.staples@grangebooks.co.uk
Founded: 1972
Specialize in illustrated adult nonfiction, chil-
  dren's, promotional, reprint & remainder books;
  publisher of promotional books & co-editions.
Type of Business: Remainder Dealer

**Grantham Book Services Ltd**
Isaac Newton Way, Alma Park Industrial Estate,
  Grantham, Lincs NG31 9SD
*Tel:* (01476) 541000; (01476) 541 080 (orders)
  *Fax:* (01476) 541061
*E-mail:* orders@gbs.tbs-ltd.co.uk
*Key Personnel*
Chairman: David Pemberton
Man Dir: Graham Miller
Founded: 1975
Contract Distribution (Publishing).
Type of Business: Distributor
*Owned by:* Random House Group

**Haigh & Hochland Ltd**
Harniman House, 391-401 Oxford Rd, Manch-
  ester M13 9QA
*Tel:* (061) 2734156 *Fax:* (061) 2734340
*Key Personnel*
Man Dir: Michael Beattie
Founded: 1951
Type of Business: Distributor, Exporter, Importer,
  Major Independent Bookseller

**Hatchards Ltd**
187 Piccadilly, London W1J 9LE
*Tel:* (020) 7439 9921 *Fax:* (020) 7494 1313
*E-mail:* books@hatchards.co.uk
*Web Site:* www.hatchards.co.uk
*Key Personnel*
General Manager: Roger Katz
Marketing Assistant: Mark Hammett
Founded: 1797
Booksellers.
*Owned by:* EMI
*Ultimate Parent Company:* HMV Media Group

**Health Sciences Associates International**
15 Roehampton Lane, London SW15 5LS

*Tel:* (020) 8876 2340 *Fax:* (020) 8392 9845
*Key Personnel*
Contact: Neville Mendelson
Founded: 1982
Specialize in marketing, promote & sell by direct
  mail & displays medical veterinary & nursing
  journals, books & electronic publications di-
  rect to doctors & allied professions throughout
  Europe. Also offers US professional medical
  societies & publishers an office address in Eu-
  rope, London, for receipt of orders & inquiries.
Type of Business: Distributor

**Heffers: Academic + General Books**
20 Trinity St, Cambridge CB2 1TY
*Tel:* (01223) 568568 *Fax:* (01223) 568591
*E-mail:* heffers@heffers.co.uk
*Web Site:* www.heffers.co.uk
*Telex:* 81298
*Key Personnel*
Manager: David Robinson
Founded: 1876
Type of Business: Exporter, Major Independent
  Bookseller
*Owned by:* Blackwell's Bookshops
*Branch Office(s)*
Heffers: Grafton Centre Bookshop, 28B The
  Grafton Centre, Cambridge CB1 1PS, Man-
  ager: Erika McKay *Tel:* (01223) 568573
  *Fax:* (01223) 568572 *E-mail:* grafton@heffers.
  co.uk
Heffers: Plus, 31 St Andrews St, Cambridge CB2
  3AX *Tel:* (01223) 568598 *Fax:* (01223) 568593
  *E-mail:* plus@heffers.co.uk (paperbacks, audio
  books, video & DVDs)
Heffers: Sound, 19 Trinity St, Cambridge, Man-
  ager: Tony McGeorge *Tel:* (01223) 568562
  *Fax:* (01223) 568591 *E-mail:* sound@heffers.
  co.uk (recorded music on cassette & compact
  disc, spoken word cassettes, DVDs)

**Hellenic Bookservice**
91 Fortess Rd, Kentish Town, London NW5 1AG
*Tel:* (020) 72679499 *Fax:* (020) 72679498
*E-mail:* info@hellenicbookservice.com
*Web Site:* www.hellenicbookservice.com
*Key Personnel*
Partner: Monica Williams
Founded: 1966
Independent Bookseller.

**Thomas Heneage Art Books**
42 Duke St, St James's, London SW1Y 6DJ
*Tel:* (020) 7930 9223 *Fax:* (020) 7839 9223
*E-mail:* artbooks@heneage.com
*Web Site:* www.heneage.com
*Key Personnel*
Man Dir: Thomas Heneage
Founded: 1977
Sells art books, catalogue raisonnes, monographs
  & exhibition catalogues.
Type of Business: Major Independent Bookseller
*Owned by:* Thomas Heneage

**The Holt Jackson Book Co Ltd**
Preston Rd, Lytham, Lancs FY8 5AX
*Tel:* (01253) 737464 *Fax:* (01253) 733361
*E-mail:* info@holtjackson.co.uk
*Web Site:* www.holtjackson.co.uk
*Key Personnel*
Chairman: Kevin Holden *E-mail:* kholden@
  holtjackson.co.uk
Deputy Chairman: Jonathan Pewtress
Acquisitions Manager: Tom Lee
Sales & Customer Care Dir: Anne Ollier
Finance Dir: Carole Park
Founded: 1932
Suppliers of shelf-ready books to public, business,
  academic & school libraries throughout the UK
  & overseas.
Type of Business: Exporter, Major Independent
  Bookseller, Wholesaler

## Brian Inns Booksales & Services
9 Ashley Crescent, Warwick CV34 6QH
*Tel:* (01926) 498428 *Fax:* (01926) 498428
*Key Personnel*
Man Dir: Brian Inns
Founded: 1989
Sales consultant & sales agency.

## Internos Books
12 Percy St, London W1P 9FB
*Tel:* (020) 7637 4255 *Fax:* (020) 7637 4251
*Key Personnel*
President: E Booth-Clibborn
Editor: M Sutcliffe
Sales Dir: J Booth-Clibborn
Founded: 1987
Type of Business: Distributor, Exporter, Importer, Wholesaler
*Owned by:* Booth-Clibborn Editions

## Richard Joseph Publishers Ltd
PO Box 15, Torrington, Devon EX38 8ZJ
*Tel:* (01805) 625750 *Fax:* (01805) 625376
*E-mail:* info@sheppardsworld.com
*Web Site:* www.sheppardsworld.co.uk
*Key Personnel*
Man Dir: Richard Joseph *E-mail:* rjoe01@aol.com
Founded: 1990
Also acts as print consultant.
Joint owner of Sheppard's Book Search with Nielson Book Data Ltd.

## Kuperard
Division of Bravo Ltd
59 Hutton Grove, London N12 8DS
*Tel:* (020) 8446 2440 *Fax:* (020) 8446 2441
*E-mail:* kuperard@bravo.clara.net; office@kuperard.co.uk
*Web Site:* www.kuperard.co.uk
*Key Personnel*
Man Dir: Joshua Kuperard *E-mail:* joshua@bravo.clara.net
Sales & Marketing Manager: Martin Kaye
Founded: 1986
Publisher.
Type of Business: Distributor, Exporter, Importer

## Lavis Marketing
73 Lime Walk, Headington, Oxford OX3 7AD
*Tel:* (01865) 767575 *Fax:* (01865) 750079
*E-mail:* orders@lavismarketing.co.uk
*Key Personnel*
Contact: James H Lavis *E-mail:* jim@lavismarketing.co.uk
Founded: 1982
Type of Business: Distributor

## The Lexicon Bookshop
63 Strand St, Douglas, Isle of Man IM1 2RL
*Tel:* (01624) 673004 *Fax:* (01624) 661959
*E-mail:* manxbooks@lexiconbookshop.co.im
*Web Site:* www.lexiconbookshop.co.im
*Key Personnel*
Proprietor: D W Ashworth
Founded: 1936
Type of Business: Major Independent Bookseller

## Lindsay & Croft
Formerly Crofthouse Books Ltd
Lake House Woodside Park, Cattleshall Lane, Godalming, Surrey GU7 1LG
*Tel:* (01483) 425 222 *Toll Free Tel:* 866-622-4984 *Fax:* (01483) 425 777
*E-mail:* landc@ybp.com
*Web Site:* lindsayandcroft.co.uk
*Key Personnel*
Dir: David H Smith *E-mail:* david.smith@crofthouse.co.uk
Book supply service for commercial, industrial & academic libraries.

Type of Business: Distributor, Exporter, Importer, Major Independent Bookseller
*Parent Company:* YBP Library Services

## Lister Art Books of Southport
PO Box 31, Southport, Lancs PR9 8BF
*Tel:* (01704) 232033 *Fax:* (01704) 505926
*E-mail:* sales@laboox.demon.co.uk
*Key Personnel*
Contact: Graham Lister
Books on Antiques & Collecting; USA Co represented.
Type of Business: Distributor, Importer

## Littlehampton Book Services Ltd
Faraday Close, Worthing, West Sussex BN13 3RB
*Tel:* (01903) 828500 *Fax:* (01903) 828802
*E-mail:* enquiries@lbsltd.co.uk
*Web Site:* www.lbsltd.co.uk
*Key Personnel*
Man Dir: Martin Evans
Publishing Services Dir: Bridget Radnedge
Finance Dir: Basil May
Type of Business: Distributor
*Owned by:* Orion Publishing Group, 5 Upper St Martin's Lane, London WC2H 9EA

## Chris Lloyd Sales & Marketing Services
Stanley House, 1st floor, 3 Fleets Lane, Poole, Dorset BH15 3AJ
*Tel:* (01202) 649930 *Fax:* (01202) 649950
*E-mail:* chrlloyd@globalnet.co.uk
Founded: 1986
Type of Business: Distributor, Importer

**Lomond**, *imprint of* Lomond Books

## Lomond Books
36 West Shore Rd, Granton, Edinburgh EH5 1QD
*Tel:* (0131) 551 2261 *Fax:* (0131) 559 2042
*E-mail:* info@flatman.co.uk; sales@lomond-books.co.uk
*Web Site:* www.lomond-books.co.uk; www.scottishbookstore.com
*Key Personnel*
Man Dir: David Flatman
Sales & Marketing Dir: Trevor Maher
Sales Manager: Duncan Baxter
Also retailer & publisher.
Type of Business: Remainder Dealer, Wholesaler
Imprints: Lomond

## Mallory International Ltd
Aylesbeare Common Business Park, Exmouth Rd, Aylesbeare, Devon EX5 2DG
*Tel:* (01395) 239199 *Fax:* (01395) 239168
*E-mail:* sales@malloryint.co.uk
*Web Site:* www.malloryint.co.uk
*Key Personnel*
Executive Dir: Norman Guthrie
Dir: Mrs Clare Guthrie *E-mail:* clare@malloryint.co.uk; Julian Hardinge; Mrs Ulrike Hardinge
Founded: 1984
International booksellers.
Type of Business: Distributor, Exporter, Importer, Major Independent Bookseller

## Marston Book Services Ltd
PO Box 269, Abingdon, Oxon OX14 4YN
*Tel:* (01235) 465500 *Fax:* (01235) 465555
*E-mail:* trade.enquiry@marston.co.uk
*Web Site:* www.marston.co.uk
*Telex:* 837515
*Key Personnel*
Chairman: John Holloran
Man Dir: Ross Clayton
Type of Business: Distributor

## Menoshire Ltd
Unit 13, 21 Wadsworth Rd, Perivale, Middx UB6 7LQ
*Tel:* (020) 85667344 *Fax:* (020) 89912439
*E-mail:* sales@menoshire.com
*Web Site:* www.menoshire.com
*Key Personnel*
Man Dir: J M Treacy
Founded: 1975
Type of Business: Exporter, Importer, Wholesaler

## Meresborough Books Ltd
17-25 Station Rd, Rainham, Kent ME8 7RS
*Tel:* (01634) 371591 *Fax:* (01634) 262114
*E-mail:* shop@rainhambookshop.co.uk
*Web Site:* www.rainhambookshop.co.uk
*Key Personnel*
Manager: Hamish Mackay-Miller
Founded: 1977
Independent bookshop & school books supplier.
Type of Business: Major Independent Bookseller, Wholesaler

## Millbank Books Ltd
The Court Yard, The Old Monastery, Windhill, Bishop's Stortford, Herts CM23 2PE
*Tel:* (01279) 655233 *Fax:* (01279) 655244
*E-mail:* caw@millbank.demon.co.uk
*Key Personnel*
Dir: Diana Walsh; Christine Walsh
Founded: 1987
Distributors of General Nonfiction in the UK, Europe & Middle East; Import Specialist Titles from USA, Singapore, Malaysia, Australia & South Africa; Also act as UK agents for overseas publishers to sell the rights of their titles to UK publishers.
Type of Business: Distributor, Exporter, Importer

## Motilal (UK) Books of India
PO Box 324, Borehamwood, Herts WD6 1NB
*Tel:* (020) 8905-1244 *Fax:* (020) 8905-1108
*E-mail:* info@mlbduk.com
*Web Site:* www.mlbduk.com
*Key Personnel*
Owner & Distribution Dir: Ray McLennan
Founded: 1982
Import, Export & Distribution Agency for books published in India.
Type of Business: Distributor, Exporter, Importer
*Parent Company:* Money Savers (London) Ltd

## Music Book Distributors Ltd
44 Station Way, Buckhurst Hill, Essex IG9 6LN
*Tel:* (0181) 559 1522 *Fax:* (0181) 559 1522
*Key Personnel*
Dir: Neil Taylor
Founded: 1988
Type of Business: Wholesaler

## NBN Plymbridge
Plymbridge House, Estover Rd, Plymouth PL6 7PY
*Tel:* (01752) 202300 *Fax:* (01752) 202330
*E-mail:* enquiries@plymbridge.com; orders@plymbridge.com
*Web Site:* www.plymbridge.com
*Key Personnel*
Man Dir: Irv Myers
Type of Business: Distributor
*Owned by:* Rowman & Littlefield Group, Inc

## Nielsen BookData
3rd floor, Midas House, 62 Goldsworth Rd, Woking GU21 6LQ
*Tel:* (0870) 777 8710 *Fax:* (0870) 777 8711
*Web Site:* www.nielsenbookdata.co.uk
Order routing & EDI communication network.
*Parent Company:* VNU Media Measurement & Information

**Northern Map Distributors**
101 Broadfield Rd, Sheffield S8 OXH
*Tel:* (0114) 2582660 *Toll Free Tel:* 800 834920
*Key Personnel*
Partner: David N Smith
Founded: 1975
Map & guide wholesaler.
Subjects: LAM-FORD Maps
Type of Business: Wholesaler

**Orbis Books (London) Ltd**
206 Blythe Rd, London WI4 0HH
*Tel:* (020) 7602 5541 *Fax:* (020) 8742 7686
*E-mail:* bookshop@orbis-books.co.uk
*Key Personnel*
Dir: Jerzy Kulczycki
Specialize in books in English on Central & Eastern Europe. Stockholders of books in Polish, Czech, Slovak & Bulgarian.
Type of Business: Exporter, Importer, Major Independent Bookseller

**Parfitts Book Services**
50 Imber Rd, Warminster, Wilts BA12 0BN
*Tel:* (01985) 216371 *Fax:* (01985) 212982
*E-mail:* parfitts@cix.compulink.co.uk
*Key Personnel*
Dir: J E Parfitt
Type of Business: Distributor, Exporter, Importer, Major Independent Bookseller, Wholesaler

**H Pordes Ltd**
58-60 Charing Cross Rd, London WC2H OBB
*Tel:* (020) 8445 1273 *Fax:* (020) 8445 5510
*Key Personnel*
Dir: Henry Pordes; N Pordes
Manager: Gino Della Ragione
Founded: 1975
Wholesale only-buying & selling of remainders. Also publisher.
Type of Business: Remainder Dealer

**Promotional Reprint Co Ltd**
Kiln House, 210 New Kings Rd, London SW6 4NZ
*Tel:* (020) 7736 5666 *Fax:* (020) 7736 5777
Type of Business: Remainder Dealer

**Rainham Bookshop**, see Meresborough Books Ltd

**Randall & Swift Ltd**
Pioneer Market 4, Winston Way, Ilford, Essex IG1 2RD
*Tel:* (020) 8553 3030 *Fax:* (020) 8559 1522
*Key Personnel*
Dir: Neil Taylor
Founded: 1979
Supplier of printed music & music books to libraries.

**The Richmond Publishing Co Ltd**
PO Box 963, Slough SL2 3RS
*Tel:* (01753) 643104 *Fax:* (01753) 646553
*E-mail:* rpc@richmond.co.uk
*Key Personnel*
Man Dir: Mrs S J Davie
Founded: 1970
Type of Business: Distributor, Exporter, Importer, Major Independent Bookseller, Wholesaler

**RICS Books**
Surveyor Court, Westwood Business Park, Coventry CV4 8JE
*Tel:* (0870) 333 1600 *Fax:* (020) 7334 3851
*E-mail:* mailorder@rics.org.uk
*Web Site:* www.ricsbooks.com
*Key Personnel*
Dir of Operations: Angela Hartland *Tel:* (020)

7222 7000 (ext 744) *Fax:* (020) 7334 3840
*E-mail:* ahartland@rics.org
Managing Editor: Toni Gill *Tel:* (020) 7222 7000 (ext 686) *Fax:* (020) 7334 3840 *E-mail:* tgill@rics.org
Founded: 1981
Distributor for 11 US publishers.
Type of Business: Distributor, Major Independent Bookseller
*Owned by:* Royal Institution of Chartered Surveyors (RICS)
*Bookshop(s):* 7 St Andrews Pl, Cardiff CF10 3BE *Tel:* (029) 2022 4414 *Fax:* (029) 2022 4416; RICS Coventry Bookstall *Tel:* (020) 7222 7000 (ext 698); 12 Great George St, Parliament Sq, London SW1P 3AD *Tel:* (020) 7334 3776 *Fax:* (020) 7222 9430 *E-mail:* bookshop@rics.org

**Louise Ross & Co, Ltd**
Mulberry House, 8 Mount Rd, Lansdown, Bath, Avon BA1 5PW
*Tel:* (0225) 44 87 86 *Fax:* (0225) 44 87 89
*E-mail:* louise.ross@btinternet.com
*Key Personnel*
Man Dir: Louise Ross *E-mail:* louise.ross@btinternet.com
Founded: 1977
Antiquarian & literary books, first editions only; also acts as publisher.
Type of Business: Major Independent Bookseller
*Owned by:* Ross Press

**Roundhouse Group**
Millstone, Limers Lane, Northam, North Devon EX39 2RG
*Tel:* (01237) 474474 *Fax:* (01237) 474774
*E-mail:* roundhouse.group@ukgateway.net
*Web Site:* www.roundhouse.net
*Key Personnel*
President & Chief Executive: Alan T Goodworth
Founded: 1991
Distributor of small/medium publisher lists from USA, Canada & Australia.
Type of Business: Distributor, Exporter, Importer, Wholesaler
*Parent Company:* Roundhouse Publishing Ltd
*Warehouse:* Orca Book Services, Stanley House, 3 Fleets Lane, Poole, Dorset BH15 3AJ *Tel:* (01202) 665 432 *Fax:* (01202) 666 219 *E-mail:* orders@orca-book-services.co.uk

**Royal Institution of Chartered Surveyors**, see RICS Books

**Sandpiper Books Ltd**
24 Langroyd Rd, London SW17 7PL
*Tel:* (020) 8767 7421 *Fax:* (020) 8682 0280
*E-mail:* enquiries@sandpiper.co.uk
*Key Personnel*
Sales Manager: Chris Harley *E-mail:* charley@sandpiper.co.uk
Contact: Juliet Morgan
Founded: 1984
Specializing in scholarly & literary remainders, good quality arts, reprints of academic monographs with Oxford University Press.
Type of Business: Remainder Dealer
*Showroom(s):* 4/5 Academy Buildings, Lower Ground floor, Fanshaw St, London NI 6LQ *Tel:* (020) 7613 4446 *Fax:* (020) 7613 4513

**Saqi Books**
26 Westbourne Grove, London W2 5RH
*Tel:* (020) 7221 9347 *Fax:* (020) 7229 7492
*E-mail:* saqibooks@dial.pipex.com
*Web Site:* www.saqibooks.com
*Key Personnel*
Contact: Mai Ghoussoub
Editorial Manager: Sarah Al-Hamad *E-mail:* sarah@saqibooks.com

Founded: 1979
Type of Business: Exporter, Importer, Major Independent Bookseller
*Owned by:* A & S Gaspard; M Ghoussoub; K & H Makija

**Derek Searle Associates**
The Coach House, Cippenham Lodge, Cippenham Lane, Slough, Berks SL1 5AN
*Tel:* (01753) 539295 *Fax:* (01753) 551863
*E-mail:* dsapublish@aol.com
*Key Personnel*
Contact: Mrs Maureen Corrington
Founded: 1991
Act as Independent Sales & Marketing Agents on behalf of client Publishers.

**Send the Light Ltd**
Kingstown Broadway, Carlisle, Cumbria CA3 OHA
*Tel:* (01228) 512 512 *Fax:* (01228) 514 949
*E-mail:* info@stl.org
*Web Site:* www.stl.org
*Key Personnel*
Chief Executive: Keith Danby
Man Dir, Publishing: Mark Finnie
Founded: 1965
Publish & distribute books to advance the Christian faith.
Type of Business: Distributor, Wholesaler
Subsidiaries: Paternoster Publishing

**Sherratt & Hughes**
c/o WHSmith Retail Ltd, Freepost (sce 4410), Swindon, Wilts SN3 3XS
*Tel:* (01793) 695195
*Key Personnel*
Manager: J D Siverns
Incorporating Bowes & Bowes Books.
*Owned by:* WHSmith & Son Ltd

**Shogun International Ltd**
87 Gayford Rd, London W12 9BY
*Tel:* (020) 8749 2022 *Fax:* (020) 8740 1086
*Key Personnel*
Manager: P Tai
Founded: 1974
Manufactured supply of martial arts equipment, clothing & books (on martial arts only).
Type of Business: Distributor, Exporter, Importer, Wholesaler

**Silverdale**, *imprint of* Bookmart Ltd

**John Smith & Son Booksellers**
Ash House, Headlands Business Park, Ringwood, Hants BH24 3PB
*Tel:* (01425) 471160 *Fax:* (01425) 471718
*Web Site:* www.johnsmith.co.uk
*Telex:* 778881 Jssglw G *Cable:* BOOKS: GLASGOW
*Key Personnel*
Chairman: Peter Gray *E-mail:* pgray@johnsmith.co.uk
Deputy Chairman: Willie Anderson *E-mail:* wtca@johnsmith.co.uk
Man Dir: Terry Field *E-mail:* tfield@johnsmith.co.uk
Business Development Manager: Chris Sugden *E-mail:* crs@johnsmith.co.uk
Founded: 1751

**Springfield Books Ltd**
Norman Rd, Denby Dale, Huddersfield, W Yorks HD8 8TH
*Tel:* (01484) 864955 *Fax:* (01484) 865443
*Key Personnel*
Sales Manager, Publicity: Paula Brennan
Founded: 1984
Type of Business: Distributor

**The Stationery Office**, see TSO (The Stationery Office)

**STL**, see Send the Light Ltd

**THE**, see Total Home Entertainment

**James Thin, Bookseller**
53-62 South Bridge, Edinburgh EH1 1YS
*Tel:* (0131) 622 8222 *Fax:* (0131) 557 8149
*E-mail:* enquiries@jthin.co.uk
*Key Personnel*
Non-Exec Chmn: D Ainslie Thin
Man Dir: Jackie Thin
Dirs: Malcolm Gibson; Ken Lemond; Andrew Thin; James Thin; Graham White
Assistant to Man Dir: Dayle Coltman *Tel:* (0131) 622 8281 *E-mail:* dayle.coltman@jthin.co.uk
Founded: 1848
Specialize in the publication of Scottish interest & outdoor books under the Mercat Press imprint.
Type of Business: Major Independent Bookseller
*Bookshop(s):* James Thin Ltd, Unit 21-23, Sovereign S/Ctr, Weston-Super-Mare, Avon BS23 1HL; James Thin Ltd, 15 Sandgate, Ayr KA7 1BG; The Lanes, 77 Lowther St, Carlisle CA3 8EF; James Thin Ltd, 18/26 Church Crescent, Dumfries DG1 1DQ; James Thin Ltd, 7/8 High St, Dundee DD1 1SS; James Thin Ltd, 53/59 South Bridge, Edinburgh EH1 1YS; James Thin Ltd, 59 George St, Edinburgh EH2 2JQ; James Thin Ltd, 29-31 Buccleuch St, Edinburgh EH8 9LT *Tel:* (0131) 667 6253 *Fax:* (0131) 667 6253 *E-mail:* buccleuchst@jthin.co.uk; James Thin Ltd, Hugh Nisbet Bldg, Heriot-Watt University, Riccarton Campus, Edinburgh EH14 2AS; James Thin Ltd, Kings Bldg Bookshop, University of Edinburgh, W Mains Rd, Edinburgh EH9 3JR *Tel:* (0131) 667 0432 *Fax:* (0131) 667 0432 *E-mail:* kingsbuilding@jthin.co.uk; Gyle, 35 Gyle Ave, South Gyle Broadway, Edinburgh EH12 9JT; James Thin Ltd, 22/24 Thackery Mall, Fareham Shopping Centre, Fareham, Hants PO16 OPQ; James Thin Ltd, Unit SU45, The Lakeside Centre, West Thurrock, Grays, Essex RM16 1ZF; James Thin Ltd, Mid Level, Unit 55-56, The Exchange, Ilford, Essex IGI IAA; James Thin Ltd, 29 Union St, Inverness IVI 1QA; James Thin Ltd, 87 Grampian Rd, Aviemore, Inverness-shire PH22 1RH; James Thin Ltd, Unit LSU 2, Centre Court Shopping Centre, Wimbledon, London SW19 8YE; James Thin Ltd, Unit 26, Treaty Centre, Hounslow, Middlesex TW3 IES; James Thin Ltd, 2A Mercer Walk, The Pavilions, Uxbridge, Middlsex 1LU 1LY; James Thin Ltd, 20/21 Castle Mall, Norwich, Norfolk NR1 3XJ; James Thin Ltd, Unit SU44, The Peacocks Centre, Woking, Surrey GU21 1GD; James Thin Ltd, University Bookshop, Student's Union, St Mary Pl, St Andrews, Fife KY16 9UY, Manager: Barbara Dumbleton *Tel:* (01334) 476367 *Fax:* (01334) 478367 *E-mail:* standrews@jthin.co.uk; James Thin, 176 High St, Perth PH1 5UN; James Thin, 5 New St, Huddersfield, West Yorks HD1 2AX

**Thomson Publishing Services**
Cheriton House, North Way, Andover, Hants SP10 5BE
*Tel:* (01264) 332424 *Fax:* (01264) 364418
*Key Personnel*
General Manager: Barry Hinchmore
Customer Service Dir: Carrie Willicome
Chief Accountant: Jo Jewell
Founded: 1988
Type of Business: Distributor
*Owned by:* The Thomson Corp

**Thornton's of Oxford Ltd**
Wightwick-Boars Hill, Oxford OX1 5DR
*Tel:* (01865) 321126
*E-mail:* thorntons@booknews.demon.co.uk
*Web Site:* www.thorntonsbooks.co.uk
*Key Personnel*
Man Dir: Willem A Meeuws
Founded: 1835
Also Publisher.
Type of Business: Distributor, Exporter, Importer, Major Independent Bookseller

**Tiger Books International PLC**
26A York St, Twickenham, Middx TW1 3LJ
*Tel:* (0181) 8925577 *Fax:* (0181) 8916550
*Key Personnel*
Man Dir: Grahame Parish
Founded: 1985
Type of Business: Remainder Dealer

**Titles Old and Rare Books of Oxford**
15 Turl St, Oxford OX1 3DQ
*Tel:* (01865) 727928 *Fax:* (01865) 727928
*Key Personnel*
Contact: G Stone; R Stone
Founded: 1972
Specialize in literature, general antiquarian & secondhand books.
Subjects: History of Science, Travel, Agriculture
Type of Business: Major Independent Bookseller

**Total Home Entertainment**
Rosevale Business Park, Newcastle-under-Lyme, Staffs ST5 7QT
*Tel:* (01782) 566566 *Fax:* (01782) 565400
*E-mail:* thenews@the.co.uk
*Key Personnel*
Man Dir: Alasdair Ogilvie
Sales & Marketing Dir, Books: Phil Scarlet
Wholesaler for Home Entertainment software including books, videos, music, multimedia products, electronic games & accessories. Multilingual export service & advice centre based in London.
Type of Business: Distributor, Exporter, Wholesaler
*Owned by:* John Menzies (UK) Ltd
*Branch Office(s)*
The International Export Office, Unit 4, Elsinore House, 77 Fulham Palace Rd, London W6 8JA

**Troika**
United House, North Rd, London N7 9DP
*Tel:* (020) 7619 0800 *Fax:* (020) 7619 0801
*E-mail:* troika@sellbooks.demon.co.uk
*Key Personnel*
Man Dir: Aidan Lunn
Founded: 1983
Independent Representatives.

**John Trotter Books**
80 East End Rd, Finchley, London N3 2SY
*Tel:* (020) 8349 9484 *Fax:* (020) 8346 7430
*E-mail:* John.Trotter@bibliophile.net
*Web Site:* www.bibliophile.net/John-Trotter-Books.html
Founded: 1973
Also acts as publisher & remainder dealer.
Type of Business: Major Independent Bookseller

**TSO (The Stationery Office)**
51 Nine Elms Lane, London SW8 5DR
*Tel:* (020) 7873 8787; (0870) 600 5522 (orders) *Fax:* (0870) 600 5533 (orders)
*E-mail:* customer.services@tso.co.uk
*Web Site:* www.theso.co.uk
*Key Personnel*
Chairman: Rupert Pennant-Rea
Chief Executive Officer: Tim Hailstone
Man Dir: Keith Burbage; Jeremy Hook; Dr Shane O'Neill

Chief Financial Officer: Richard Dell
Human Resources Dir: David Orr
Export Manager: Brian Tierney *Tel:* (020) 7873 8211 *Fax:* (020) 7873 8203 *E-mail:* brian.tierney@theso.co.uk
Sales Manager: Rebecca Barley
Publicity Manager: Michelle Brown
Bibliographics Manager: Peter Gutteridge
Editorial: Philip Brooks *Tel:* (01603) 605532 *E-mail:* phil.brooks@theso.co.uk
Contact: Jamie Precious
Founded: 1996
Publishes for UK government departments & a wide variety of public bodies on subjects covering academic & general interests. Also UK distributor for international organizations including UN, UNESCO, FAO, WHO, OECD, EU & IMF.
Type of Business: Distributor, Exporter
*Branch Office(s)*
TSO Ireland, 16 Arthur St, Belfast BT1 4GD, Ireland *Tel:* (02890) 238451
TSO - Norwich, St Crispins, Duke St, Norwich NR3 1PD *Tel:* (01603) 622211
TSO Scotland, 71-73 Lothian Rd, Edinburgh EH3 9AZ *Tel:* (0870) 6065566
TSO Wales, G50, Phase Two, Government Bldgs, Ty-Glas, Llanishen, Cardiff CF14 5ST *Tel:* (02920) 765892
*Bookshop(s):* TSO Scotland Bookshop, 71 Lothian Rd, Edinburgh EH3 9AZ, Manager: Ron Wilson *Tel:* (0870) 606 5566 *Fax:* (0870) 606 5588 *E-mail:* edinburgh.bookshop@tso.co.uk; 16 Arthur St, Belfast BT1 4GD, Ireland, Manager: Sharon Barnes *Tel:* (02890) 238451 *Fax:* (02890) 235401 *E-mail:* belfast.bookshop@tso.co.uk; 68-69 Bull St, Birmingham B4 6AD, Manager: James Furnival *Tel:* (0121) 236 9696 *Fax:* (0121) 236 9699 *E-mail:* birmingham.bookshop@tso.co.uk; 18-19 High St, Cardiff CF10 1PT, Manager: Joanne Fowler *Tel:* (02920) 39 5548 *Fax:* (02920) 38 4347 *E-mail:* cardiff.bookstore@tso.co.uk; 123 Kingsway, London WC2B 6PQ, Manager: Anya Somerville *Tel:* (020) 7242 6393; (020) 7242 6410 *Fax:* (020) 7242 6394 *E-mail:* london.bookshop@tso.co.uk; 9-21 Princess St, Albert Sq, Manchester M60 8AS, Manager: Ian Penney *Tel:* (0161) 834 7201 *Fax:* (0161) 833 0634 *E-mail:* manchester.bookshop@tso.co.uk

**Turnaround Publisher Services Ltd**
Unit 3, Olympia Trading Estate, Coburg Rd, Wood Green, London N22 6TZ
*Tel:* (020) 8829 3000 *Fax:* (020) 8881 5088
*E-mail:* enquires@turnaround-uk.com
*Web Site:* www.turnaround-uk.com
*Key Personnel*
Man Dir: Bill Godber *E-mail:* bill@turnaround-uk.com
Marketing Dir: Claire Thompson *E-mail:* claire@turnaround-uk.com
Founded: 1984
Book distributor of a wide range of US, UK & Irish based publishers to the UK & continental Europe.
Membership(s): Publishers' Association (UK); Bookseller's Association (UK).
Type of Business: Distributor, Exporter, Importer, Wholesaler

**UBS Publishers' Distributors Ltd**
475 N Circular Rd, London NW2 7QG
*Tel:* (020) 8450 8667 *Fax:* (020) 8452 6612
*Key Personnel*
Dir: M K Kalsi *E-mail:* mkkalsi@ubspd.com
Founded: 1937
Represent over 400 Indian publishers, stocks 2 million books in India & has constant liaisons with over 2000 commercial publishers, research institutions & government depts & disseminate information about their new publications

through their weekly bulletins as well as their subject-wise catalogs.
Type of Business: Distributor, Exporter, Importer, Wholesaler

**United Book Suppliers**
689 Antrim Rd, Newtownabbey, Co Antrim BT36 8RN
*Tel:* (01232) 832362 *Fax:* (01232) 848780
*Key Personnel*
Man Dir: John Lindsay
Founded: 1981
Type of Business: Distributor, Exporter, Wholesaler

**University of London**
Central Printing Service, Room P1, Senate House, Malet St, London WC1E 7HU
*Tel:* (020) 7862 8000 *Fax:* (020) 7636 5874
*E-mail:* enquiries@lon.ac.uk
*Web Site:* www.lon.ac.uk
*Key Personnel*
Acting Manager: Allan Kendall
Publications Officer: S M Masters
Type of Business: Major Independent Bookseller

**Robert Vaughan Antiquarian Booksellers**
20 Chapel St, Stratford-Upon-Avon, Warwicks CV37 6EP
*Tel:* (01789) 205312
*Key Personnel*
Contact: Colleen M Vaughan
Founded: 1953
Subjects: Fine & First Editions of English Literature, Theatre & Allied Arts
Type of Business: Major Independent Bookseller

**Vine House Distribution Ltd**
Affiliate of Vine House Book Promotion
Waldenbury, North Common, Chailey, East Sussex BN8 4DR
*Tel:* (01825) 723 398 *Fax:* (01825) 724 188
*E-mail:* sales@vinehouseuk.co.uk
*Web Site:* www.vinehouseuk.co.uk
*Key Personnel*
Man Dir: Richard Squibb
Founded: 1988
International book distributors, including representation & public relations.
Type of Business: Distributor, Exporter, Importer
*Warehouse:* Mullany Business Park, Deanland Rd, Golden Cross, Nr Hailsham, East Sussex BN27 3RP *Tel:* (01825) 873 133

**Peter Ward Book Exports**
Unit 3, Taylors Yard, 67 Alderbrook Rd, London SW12 8AD
*Tel:* (020) 8772 3300 *Fax:* (020) 8772 3309
*E-mail:* pwbookex@dircon.co.uk
*Key Personnel*
Partner & President: Peter Ward
Vice President: Richard Ward
Founded: 1974
Publishers' representatives.
Type of Business: Exporter, Major Independent Bookseller, Wholesaler

**Waterstone & Co Ltd**
Capital Court, Capital Interchange Way, Brentford, Middx TW8 0EX
*Tel:* (020) 8742 3800
*Web Site:* www.waterstones.co.uk

**Welsh Books Council** (Cyngor Llyfrau Cymru)
Castell Brychan, Aberystwyth, Ceredigion SY23 2JB
*Tel:* (01970) 624151 *Fax:* (01970) 625385
*E-mail:* castellbrychan@wbc.org.uk
*Web Site:* www.cllc.org.uk

*Key Personnel*
Manager: Dafydd Charles Jones *E-mail:* dafydd.jones@wbc.org.uk
Founded: 1963
Type of Business: Distributor, Wholesaler

**WHSmith PLC**
Nations House PLC, 103 Wigmore St, London W1U 1WH
*Tel:* (020) 7409 3222 *Fax:* (020) 7514 9633
*E-mail:* customer.relations@whsmith.co.uk
*Web Site:* www.whsmith.co.uk
*Key Personnel*
Chairman: Jeremy Hardie
Corporate Affairs Dir: Tim Blythe
Founded: 1792
There are 553 High Street Stores & 100 airport & station bookstores throughout the UK & 100 specialist bookshops, operating under the name of Waterstones.
Type of Business: Distributor, Major Independent Bookseller

**Wisdom Books**
25 Stanley Rd, Ilford, Essex IG1 1RW
*Tel:* (020) 8553 5020 *Fax:* (020) 8553 5122
*E-mail:* sales@wisdom-books.com
*Web Site:* www.wisdom-books.com
*Key Personnel*
Man Dir: Dennis Heslop
Sales Manager: Mike Gilmore
Title Research: Leigh Wyman
Office Manager: Philip Bradley
Orders: Jonathon Steyn
Founded: 1989
Specialize in all traditions of Buddhism.
Type of Business: Distributor, Importer, Wholesaler

**Witherby & Co Ltd**
Book Dept, 2nd floor, 32-36 Aylesbury St, London EC1R 0ET
*Tel:* (020) 7251 5341 *Fax:* (020) 7251 1296
*E-mail:* books@witherbys.co.uk
*Web Site:* www.witherbys.com
*Key Personnel*
Man Dir & Publisher: Alan Witherby
*E-mail:* alanw@witherbys.co.uk
Founded: 1740
Specialize in insurance & shipping publications.
Subjects: Risk management
Type of Business: Exporter, Major Independent Bookseller
*Bookshop(s):* 20 Aldermanbury, London EC2V 7HY *Tel:* (020) 7417 4431 *Fax:* (020) 7417 4431

**Woodfield & Stanley Ltd**
Broad Lane, Moldgreen, Huddersfield HD5 9BX
*Tel:* (01484) 421467; (01484) 532401
*Fax:* (01484) 510237
*Web Site:* www.woodfield-stanley.co.uk
*Key Personnel*
Man Dir: P G Chadwick
Founded: 1946
Type of Business: Distributor, Major Independent Bookseller, Wholesaler

**World Leisure Marketing**
4 The Old Forge, Ebrington St, Kinsbridge, Devon TQ7 1DE
*Tel:* (01548) 854654 *Fax:* (01548) 857829
*E-mail:* office@wlmsales.co.uk
*Key Personnel*
Man Dir: John Whitby
Sales Dir: John Grundy
Founded: 1991
Type of Business: Distributor, Exporter, Importer

**Roy Yates Books**
Smallfields Cottage, Cox Green, Rudgwick, Horsham, West Sussex RH12 3DE
*Tel:* (01403) 822299 *Fax:* (01403) 823012
*Key Personnel*
Proprietor: Roy Yates
Founded: 1987
Type of Business: Distributor, Exporter, Importer, Major Independent Bookseller, Wholesaler

# Uruguay

**Albe Libros Tecnicos SRL**
Cerrito 564/566, Casilla de Correos 1601, 11000 Montevideo
*Tel:* (02) 95 75 28 *Fax:* (02) 95 75 28
*Key Personnel*
Bookstore & Editorial: Daniel Aljanati
Distributor: Jaime Daniel Aljanati
Founded: 1950
Type of Business: Distributor, Exporter, Importer, Major Independent Bookseller, Wholesaler
*Owned by:* Nuestra Tierra (publishing) & Distribuidora Albe SRL (distribution), Cerrito 566, Montevideo 1100

**America Latina**
18 de Julio 2089, Montevideo
*Tel:* (02) 415127 *Fax:* (02) 495568
*Key Personnel*
Manager: Ismael Munoz
Founded: 1962
Type of Business: Distributor, Importer, Major Independent Bookseller, Wholesaler

**Barreiro y Ramos SA**
25 de Mayo, 604 Montevideo
*Tel:* (02) 95 01 50 *Fax:* (02) 96 23 58
*Key Personnel*
Pres: Dr Gaston Barreiro Zorrilla
Also Publisher.
*Branch Office(s)*
Ave General Artigas 714, Las Piedras
Arocena 1599, Montevideo
Ave 18 de Julio 1852, Montevideo
Ave 18 de Julio 941, Montevideo
Ave 8 de Octubre 3728, Montevideo
Ave Agraciada 3945, Montevideo
Ave Rivera 2684, Montevideo
Calle 21 de Setiembre 2753, Montevideo
Minas 1491, Montevideo

**Feria del Libro**
Ave 18 de Julio 1308, Montevideo
*Tel:* (02) 900 42 48 *Fax:* (02) 900 20 70
*Key Personnel*
Manager: Domingo A Maestro
Type of Business: Distributor, Importer, Major Book Chain Headquarters, Wholesaler

**Libreria Amalio M Fernandez SRL**
25 de Mayo 477, planta baja ofic 2, 11000 Montevideo
*Tel:* (02) 95 26 84 *Fax:* (02) 95 17 82
Founded: 1951
Type of Business: Distributor, Exporter, Importer, Major Independent Bookseller, Wholesaler

**El Galeon**
Juan Carlos Gomez 1327, 11000 Montevideo
*Tel:* (02) 9156139; (02) 9157909 *Fax:* (02) 9157909
*E-mail:* elgaleon@netgate.com.uy *Cable:* GALLEONBOOK MONTEVIDEO
*Key Personnel*
Proprietor: Roberto Cataldo
Founded: 1973

Antiquarian bookseller specializing in history, literature, art, politics; also chart engraving.
Type of Business: Distributor, Exporter, Importer, Major Independent Bookseller, Wholesaler

**Libreria Linardi y Risso**
Juan Carlos Gomez 1435, 11000 Montevideo
*Tel:* (02) 915 7129; (02) 915 7328 *Fax:* (02) 915 7431
*E-mail:* lyrbooks@linardiyrisso.com
*Web Site:* www.linardiyrisso.com
*Key Personnel*
Manager: Andres Linardi; Alvaro J Risso
Founded: 1944
Antiquarian bookseller; Uruguayan Current Books.
Type of Business: Distributor, Exporter, Major Independent Bookseller

**Palacio del Libro**
25 de Mayo 577, Casilla 371, Montevideo
*Tel:* (02) 959019 *Fax:* (02) 957543
*Key Personnel*
Man Dir: Daniel Mussini
Vice President: Liliana Mussini
Editorial Graphic Bindery workshop.
Type of Business: Distributor, Exporter, Importer, Major Independent Bookseller, Wholesaler

# Venezuela

**Libreria del Este**
52 Avda Francisco de Miranda, Edificio Galipan, Caracas 106
Mailing Address: Apdo 60337, Caracas 106
*Tel:* (0212) 951 2307; (0212) 951 1297
*Key Personnel*
Manager: Tomas Pericas
Exclusive distributors of World Bank, United Nations, UNESCO, OIT publications.
Type of Business: Distributor

**Fundacion Kuai-Mare**
c/o Instituto Autonomo Biblioteca Nacional y de Servicios de Bibliotecas, Calla Soledad, Edif Rogi I, Piso 3, Zona Industrial la Trinidad, Apdo 80593, Caracas 1080
*Tel:* (0212) 938535 ext 213; (0212) 9418011 (ext 227) *Fax:* (0212) 9415219
*Telex:* 24621
This is the distribution side of the Instituto Autonomo Biblioteca Nacional y de Servicios de Bibliotecas, specializing in publications by Venezuelan official, cultural & university organizations. There are five other branches.

**Libreria Medica Paris**
Grand Ave, Edif Medica Paris, Caracas 106
*Tel:* (0212) 781-6044 *Fax:* (0212) 7931753
*Telex:* 21420 DISME VC

*Key Personnel*
Manager: Pierre Paneyko
Founded: 1975

**OBE**, see Organizacion de Bienestar Estudiantil (OBE)

**Organizacion de Bienestar Estudiantil (OBE)**
Universidad Central de Venezuela Ciudad Universitaria, Los Chaguaranos, Caracas 1050
*Tel:* (0212) 6054050 (ext 4200); (0212) 6054050 (ext 4201); (0212) 6054050 (ext 4202) *Fax:* (0212) 6930638
*Web Site:* www.ucv.ve/ftproot/obe/obe.htm
*Key Personnel*
Dir: Prof Arelis L Figueroa

**Libreria Tecnica Vega**
Plaza Las Tres Gracias, Edificio Odeon, Los Chagauramos, Caracas 1010-A
Mailing Address: Apdo 51662, Caracas, Los Chaguaramos 1010-A
*Tel:* (0212) 6221397 *Fax:* (0212) 6622092 *Cable:* EDIVEGA
*Key Personnel*
Manager: Lucia Ribas
*Owned by:* Fernando Vega, Ediciones Vega SRL

# Zambia

**Q & B Books**
19 Njoka Rd, Olympia Park, Lusaka
Mailing Address: PO Box 46 unza, Lusaka
*Tel:* (01) 290032; (096) 747187 *Fax:* (01) 290032
*E-mail:* qbbooks@yahoo.com
*Key Personnel*
Dir, Operations: Queen Lutwi Unene
*E-mail:* lutwiunene@yahoo.com
Dir: Bertha Mulowa
Sales Executive: Ashery Mambwe
Membership(s): Booksellers Association of Zambia (BAZA).
Type of Business: Distributor, Exporter, Importer, Major Independent Bookseller

**University Bookshop**
University of Zambia, Lusaka
Mailing Address: PO Box 32379, Lusaka
*Tel:* (01) 294690; (01) 290319 *Fax:* (01) 253952; (01) 294690
*Telex:* ZA 44370
*Key Personnel*
Bookshop Manager: Hudson Unene
*E-mail:* hunene@admin.unza.zm
Accountant: Kenneth Phiri
Bookshop Supervisor: Raphael Makuya
Founded: 1967
Membership(s): Booksellers & Publishers Association of Zambia (BPAZ); Pan African Booksellers Association (PABA).

Type of Business: Distributor, Exporter, Importer, Major Independent Bookseller
*Owned by:* The University of Zambia
*Branch Office(s)*
Pakati Arcade-Lusaka Hotel Outlet, Box 32379, Lusaka

**Zambia Catholic Bookshop (Mission Press)**
Franciscan Centre, Chifubu Rd, Ndola
Mailing Address: PO Box 71581, Ndola
*Tel:* (02) 680456; (02) 680466 *Fax:* (02) 680484
*E-mail:* mpress@zamnet.zm
Type of Business: Distributor, Exporter, Importer, Wholesaler

# Zimbabwe

**Book Centre, Textbook Sales (Pvt) Ltd**
Affiliate of Tutorial Press
4 Conald Rd, Harare
Mailing Address: PO Box 37799, Harare
*Tel:* (04) 790691 *Fax:* (04) 751690 *Cable:* TEXTBOOK
*Key Personnel*
Man Dir: A Wallace
Publisher: Mr G McCullough
Founded: 1956
Branch offices in Bulawayo, Gweru, Masvingo, Mutare, & Rusape.
Type of Business: Distributor, Importer, Major Book Chain Headquarters, Wholesaler
*Bookshop(s):* 16 George Silundika Ave, Harare

**Kingstons Ltd**
Kingstons House, 34 Union Ave, Harare
Mailing Address: PO Box 2374, Harare
*Tel:* (04) 750547; (04) 750548; (04) 750549; (04) 750550 *Fax:* (04) 775533
*Key Personnel*
Man Dir: Elliot Mugamu
Also retailer with 19 branches in Zimbabwe & one in Bobwana.
Type of Business: Wholesaler

**Mambo Bookshop**
Senga Rd, Gweru
Mailing Address: PO Box 779, Gweru
*Tel:* (054) 4016; (054) 4017 *Fax:* (054) 51991
*E-mail:* mambo@icon.co.zw
*Key Personnel*
General Manager: Fr Ron Gentile
Type of Business: Distributor, Exporter, Importer, Major Independent Bookseller, Wholesaler
*Owned by:* Mambo Press
*Bookshop(s):* Speke Ave/First St, Harare
*Tel:* (0154) 705899; Gweru Bookshop, PO Box 779, Gweru *Tel:* (0154) 705899; Mambo Masvingo Bookshop, PO Box 1010, Masvingo *Tel:* (0139) 64566; Bulawago, PO Box 799, Gweru (19) 61162

# Book Trade Reference Books & Journals

Featuring publications for and about the book trade and book publishing industries, titles listed may be relative to one specific country or may be of international relevance. Titles are arranged alphabetically by the country where the publisher is located or the country to which the title relates.

$f$ indicates those publications of international scope.

The type of publication appears in parentheses after the title:

(B) - Book          (J) - Journal          (P) - Periodical

For library-related publications see **Library Reference Books & Journals**.

# Albania

**Bibliografia kombetare e Librit Shqip**
(Albanian National Bibliography of Books) (J)
Published by National Library
Sheshi Skenderbej, Tirana
*Tel:* (042) 23 843; (042) 24 373 *Fax:* (042) 23 843
*Key Personnel*
Dir: Mrs Nermin Basha *E-mail:* BashaN@natlib.tirana.al
Quarterly.

**Drita** (The Light) (P)
Published by Union of Writers & Artists of Albania
Rr Kavajes Nr 4, Tirana
*Tel:* (042) 28229 *Fax:* (042) 27036
*Key Personnel*
Editor: Zija Cela
First published 1960.
Daily.
232 USD (Europe); 297 USD (elsewhere)

**Kultura Popullore** (P)
Published by Academie des Sciences de la RPSA, Institut de Culture Populaire
Sheshi "Fan S NOLI", 7 Tirane
*Tel:* (04) 25 03 69 *Fax:* (04) 22 74 76
*E-mail:* esulstar@akad.edu.al
*Web Site:* www.academyofsciences.net
*Key Personnel*
Editor: Dr Aferdita Onuzi
A scientific review which comprises Albanian ethnographic studies.
First published 1980.
Annually.

**Les Lettres Albanaises** (P)
Published by Union of Writers & Artists of Albania
Rr Kavajes Nr 4, Tirana
*Tel:* (042) 28229 *Fax:* (042) 27036
*Key Personnel*
Editor: Diana Culi
Published in French.
Quarterly.
12 USD

**Libri** (The Book) (J)
Published by National Library
Sheshi Skenderbej, Tirana
*Tel:* (042) 23 843; (042) 24 373 *Fax:* (042) 23 843
*Key Personnel*
Dir: Mrs Nermin Basha *E-mail:* BashaN@natlib.tirana.al

**Nentori** (P)
Published by Union of Writers & Artists of Albania
Rr Kavajes Nr 4, Tirana
*Tel:* (042) 28229 *Fax:* (042) 27036
*Key Personnel*
Editor: Kico Blushi
Text in Albanian.
First published 1954.
Monthly.
20 USD
ISSN: 0548-1600

# Algeria

**Bibliographie de l'Algerie** (J)
Published by Bibliotheque Nationale
One Ave Frantz Fanon, 16000 Algiers
*Tel:* (021) 630632
Published in Arabic & French (Selon lalangue du document).
First published 1964.
Biannually.
40 DZD or 20 USD
ISSN: 0523-2392

# Argentina

**Boletin** (Bulletin) (P)
Published by Sociedad Argentina de Escritores (SADE)
Bartolome Mitre 2815, Piso 2, Of 225 a 230, C1201AAA Buenos Aires
*Tel:* 4864 8101 *Fax:* 4813 0773
*E-mail:* sadecentral@hotmail.com
*Web Site:* www.lasea.org
*Key Personnel*
President: Orlando Guzman
Vice President: Leonardo Tasca
Secretary General: Antonio Las Heras
Treasurer: Abelardo Garcia
Bimonthly.

**Boletin de la Academia Argentina de Letras**
(Bulletin of the Argentine Academy of Letters) (P)
Published by Academia Argentina de Letras (Argentine Academy of Letters)
Sanchez de Bustamente 2663, 1425 Buenos Aires
*Tel:* (011) 4802-3814; (011) 4802-5161
*Fax:* (011) 4-8028340

*E-mail:* aaldespa@fibertel.com.ar; aaladmin@fibertel.com.ar; aalbibl@fibertel.com.ar; despacho@aal.universia.com.ar
*Web Site:* aal.universia.com.ar/aal
*Key Personnel*
Librarian: Alejandro E Parada
Quarterly.
ISSN: 0001-3757

**Criterio** (P)
Published by Kriterion SA
Uruguay 1134 - P 1, Capital Federal, 1016 Buenos Aires
*Tel:* (011) 374 7975 *Fax:* (011) 374 7975
*Key Personnel*
Dir: D Jose Maria Poirier
Text in Spanish.
First published 1928.
21 times/yr.
100 USD
ISSN: 0011-1473

**Davar** (P)
Published by Fundacion Sociedad Hebraica Argentina
Sarmiento 2233, 1044 Buenos Aires
*Tel:* 4952 5886; 4952 5887 *Fax:* 4953 4117
*E-mail:* hebraica@hebraica.org.ar
*Web Site:* www.hebraica.org.ar

# Australia

**APA Directory of Members** (B)
Published by Australian Publishers Association Ltd
60/89 Jones St, Ultimo, NSW 2007
*Tel:* (02) 9281 9788 *Fax:* (02) 9281 1073
*E-mail:* apa@publishers.asn.au
*Web Site:* www.publishers.asn.au
*Key Personnel*
Chief Executive Officer: Susan Bridge
Contains details, key personnel, local & overseas distributors, imprints, ISBN's & agencies.
Annually.
128 pp, 11 AUD members; 29 AUD non-members; 35 AUD overseas

**AUMLA** (P)
Published by Australasian Universities Language & Literature Association
c/o Bruce Parr, EMSAH School, University of Queensland, Brisbane, Qld 4072
*Tel:* (07) 3365 2552 *Fax:* (07) 3365 2799
*Key Personnel*
Managing Editor: Bruce Parr *E-mail:* b.parr@mailbox.uq.edu.au

Editor: Lloyd Davis *E-mail:* lloyd.davis@
mailbox.ug.edu.au
Journal of literary criticism, language & cultural
studies; published in English with occasional
articles in French, German or Spanish.
First published 1951.
Biannually.
170 pp
ISSN: 0001-2793

**The Australian Author** (P)
Published by The Australian Society of Authors
Ltd
PO Box 1566, Strawberry Hills, NSW 2012
*Tel:* (02) 93180877 *Fax:* (02) 93180530
*E-mail:* asa@asauthors.org
*Web Site:* www.asauthors.org
*Key Personnel*
Executive Dir: Jeremy Fisher *E-mail:* jeremy@
asauthors.org
Quarterly.

**Australian Book Review** (J)
Published by Australian Book Review Inc
193A Lennox St, Suite 6, Richmond, Victoria
3121
Mailing Address: PO Box 2320, Richmond,
South Victoria 3121
*Tel:* (03) 9429 6700 *Fax:* (03) 9429 2288
*E-mail:* abr@vicnet.net.au
*Web Site:* home.vicnet.net.au/~abr
*Key Personnel*
Editor: Peter Rose
Deputy Editor: Aviva Tuffield
Publishes reviews & articles on Australian books
& writing.
First published 1962.
10 times/yr.
70 AUD (domestic individuals); 92 AUD (Asia
& Pacific individuals); 120 AUD (individuals
elsewhere); 80 AUD (domestic insitutions); 100
AUD (Asia & Pacific institutions); 132 AUD
(institutions elsewhere)
ISSN: 0155-2864

**Australian Books in Print** (B)
Published by Thorpe-Bowker
85 Turner St, Bldg C3, Port Melbourne, Victoria
3207
*Tel:* (03) 8645 0300; (03) 8645 0389 (customer
service) *Fax:* (03) 8645 0333
*E-mail:* customer.service@thorpe.com.au
*Web Site:* www.thorpe.com.au
*Key Personnel*
Publisher: Andrew Wilkins *Tel:* (03) 8645 0392
*E-mail:* andrew.wilkins@thorpe.com.au
Information on over 100,000 Australian titles in
print as well as publisher & distributor infor-
mation. Other useful book trade related infor-
mation included. Also available on microfiche
& CD-ROM.
First published 1956.
Annually.
2,500 pp
ISBN(s): 1-86452-064-7 (2 vol set)
ISSN: 0067-172X

**Australian Bookseller & Publisher** (P)
Published by Thorpe-Bowker
85 Turner St, Bldg C3, Port Melbourne, Victoria
3207
*Tel:* (03) 8645 0300; (03) 8645 0389 (customer
service) *Fax:* (03) 8645 0333
*E-mail:* customer.service@thorpe.com.au
*Web Site:* www.thorpe.com.au
*Key Personnel*
Publisher: Andrew Wilkins *Tel:* (03) 8645 0392
*E-mail:* andrew.wilkins@thorpe.com.au
News & information about the industry.
First published 1921.
11 times/yr.
ISSN: 0004-8763

**Australian Literary Studies** (P)
Published by University of Queensland Press
The University of Queensland, Brisbane, Qld
4072
Mailing Address: PO Box 6042, Brisbane, Qld
4067
*Tel:* (07) 3365 2452 *Fax:* (07) 3365 7579
*Web Site:* www.uq.edu.au
*Key Personnel*
Publisher: Rosemary Chay *E-mail:* rosiec@uqp.
uq.edu.au
Editor: Dr Leigh Dale
Academic/scholarly publication.
Biannually.
Vol 20, Nos 3 & 4, 2002, 43.80 AUD (domestic
individuals & school libraries); 50 AUD (for-
eign individuals); 82.10 AUD (domestic tertiary
institutions & libraries); 90 AUD (foreign insti-
tutions)
ISSN: 0004-9697

**Australian Society of Indexers Newsletter** (J)
Published by Australian Society of Indexers
GPO Box 2069, Canberra, ACT 2601
*Tel:* (02) 4268-5335
*E-mail:* newsletter@aussi.org
*Web Site:* www.aussi.org/anl
*Key Personnel*
Editor: Peter Judge
Also available in electronic format (ISSN 1326-
2718).
Monthly; excluding Jan & Dec.
ISSN: 0314-3767

ǂ**Bibliographical Society of Australia & New
Zealand Bulletin** (J)
Published by Bibliographical Society of Australia
& New Zealand (BSANZ)
Baillieu Library, University of Melbourne, Mel-
bourne, Victoria 3000
*Tel:* (03) 8344-5366 *Fax:* (03) 9347-8627
*Web Site:* www.csu.edu.au/community/BSANZ
*Key Personnel*
Editor: Ian Morrison *E-mail:* i.morrison@lib.
unimelb.edu.au
First published 1970.
Quarterly.
Free to members
ISSN: 0084-7852

**Biblionews & Australian Notes & Queries** (J)
Published by Book Collectors' Society of Aus-
tralia
16 Edwin St (South), Croydon, NSW 2132
*Tel:* (02) 9798 8984 *Fax:* (02) 9798 8984
*E-mail:* jeff@bcspl.com.au
*Key Personnel*
Ed: Brian Taylor
Secretary: Jeff Bidgood *E-mail:* bidgood@
bigpond.net.au
Quarterly, to members.

**Guide to New Australian Books**, see The A B
& P Book Buyer's Guide

**Introduction to Australian Book Publishing** (B)
Published by Australian Publishers Association
Ltd
60/89 Jones St, Ultimo, NSW 2007
*Tel:* (02) 9281 9788 *Fax:* (02) 9281 1073
*E-mail:* apa@publishers.asn.au
*Web Site:* www.publishers.asn.au
*Key Personnel*
Chief Executive Officer: Susan Bridge
80 pp, 15 AUD members; 20 AUD non-members;
25 AUD overseas
ISBN(s): 0-9599796-8-9

**Island** (P)
Published by Island Magazine Inc
PO Box 210, Sandy Bay, Tas 7006

*Tel:* (03) 6226 2325 *Fax:* (03) 6226 2172
*E-mail:* island@tassie.net.au
*Web Site:* www.islandmag.com
*Key Personnel*
Editor: David Owen
Literary Magazine.
Quarterly.
ISSN: 1035-3127

**New Ceylon Writing** (P)
Published by Macquarie University
Balaclava Rd, North Ryde, NSW
Mailing Address: Macquarie University, NSW
2109
*Tel:* (02) 9850 7111
*E-mail:* mqinfo@mq.edu.au
*Web Site:* www.mq.edu.au
*Key Personnel*
Editor: Yasmine Gooneratne
Creative & critical writing.

**New Zealand Books in Print** (B)
Published by Thorpe-Bowker
85 Turner St, Bldg C3, Port Melbourne, Victoria
3207
*Tel:* (03) 8645 0300; (03) 8645 0389 (customer
service) *Fax:* (03) 8645 0333
*E-mail:* customer.service@thorpe.com.au
*Web Site:* www.thorpe.com.au
*Key Personnel*
Editor: Andrew Wilkins *E-mail:* andrew.wilkins@
thorpe.com.au
Bibliographic data on over 14,000 books in print
from New Zealand & the Pacific Island states.
Includes information on publishers, distributors,
trade associations, as well as information about
booksellers, literary awards & other book trade
related information.
First published 1964.
Annually.
29: 850 pp, 160 AUD
ISBN(s): 1-86452-065-5
ISSN: 0157-7662

**Overland** (P)
Published by The O L Society Ltd
PO Box 14428, Melbourne, Victoria 8001
*Tel:* (03) 9919 4163 *Fax:* (03) 9687 7614
*E-mail:* overland@vu.edu.au
*Web Site:* www.overlandexpress.org
*Key Personnel*
Editor: Nathan Hollier; Katherine Wilson
First published 1954.
Quarterly.
42 AUD (individuals); 45 AUD (institutions); 32
AUD (students); 60 USD (foreign)
ISSN: 0030-7416

**Periodicals in Print & Online: Australia, New
Zealand & Asia Pacific** (B)
Published by Bookman Health
Bookman Health, Level 9, Trak Centre, 443-449
Toorak Rd, Toorak, Victoria 3142
*Toll Free Tel:* 800 060 555 *Fax:* (03) 9826 1744
*E-mail:* bookman@bookman.com.au; sales@
bookman.com.au
*Web Site:* www.bookman.com.au
First published 1981.
ISSN: 1322-3895

**Quadrant** (P)
Published by Quadrant Magazine Co Inc
PO Box 82, Balmain, NSW 2041
*Tel:* (02) 98181155 *Fax:* (02) 98181422
*E-mail:* quadrantmonthly@ozemail.com.au
*Web Site:* www.quadrant.org.au
*Key Personnel*
Editor: P P McGuinness *E-mail:* editor@
quadrant.org.au
Independent review of controversy, ideas, litera-
ture, poetry & the arts.

10 times/yr.
65 AUD (domestic); 58 AUD (student); 90.00
   AUD (New Zealand); 120 AUD (Eastern Asia
   Pacific Islands); 150 AUD (rest of world)

**Reading Time** (P)
Published by Children's Book Council of Aus-
   tralia
PO Box 62, Ashmont, NSW 2650
*Tel:* (02) 6925 4907 *Fax:* (02) 6925 4907
*E-mail:* readingtime@cbc.org.au
*Web Site:* www.cbc.org.au/readtime.htm
*Key Personnel*
Editor & Publisher: Dr John Cohen
   *E-mail:* jcohen@ozemail.com.au
Yearly index to reviews & articles.
Quarterly.
44 pp, 44 AUD (domestic); 55 AUD (Papua New
   Guinea & New Zealand); 65 AUD (other for-
   eign countries)
ISSN: 0155-218X

**Southerly** (P)
Published by English Association, Sydney Branch
Wentworth Bldg, Box 91, University of Sydney,
   Sydney, NSW 2006
*Tel:* (02) 9211 3033
*Web Site:* www.unsw.edu.au/english/EAS
*Key Personnel*
Editor: David G Brooks *Tel:* (02) 9351 2569
   *E-mail:* david.brooks@english.usyd.edu.au;
   Noel Rowe *Tel:* (02) 9351 2270 *E-mail:* noel.
   rowe@english.usyd.edu.au
Short stories, poetry & literary criticism about
   Australian writers.
First published 1939.
Quarterly.
ISSN: 0038-3732

**Sydney Studies in English** (B)
Published by University of Sydney, Department
   of English
Dept of English, A20, University of Sydney,
   NSW 2006
*Tel:* (02) 9351 2349 *Fax:* (02) 9351 2434
*E-mail:* english.enquiries@arts.usyd.edu.au
*Web Site:* www.arts.usyd.edu.au/departs/english
*Key Personnel*
Editor: Prof Margaret Harris *Tel:* (02) 9351 2163
   *E-mail:* margaret.harris@arts.usyd.edu.au
Devoted to criticism & scholarship in English lit-
   erature & drama.
First published 1975.
Annually.
16.50 AUD
ISSN: 0156-5419

**The A B & P Book Buyer's Guide** (P)
Formerly Guide to New Australian Books
Published by Thorpe-Bowker
85 Turner St, Bldg C3, Port Melbourne, Victoria
   3207
*Tel:* (03) 8645 0300; (03) 8645 0389 (customer
   service) *Fax:* (03) 8645 0333
*E-mail:* customer.service@thorpe.com.au
*Web Site:* www.thorpe.com.au
*Key Personnel*
Editor: Andrew Wilkins *E-mail:* andrew.wilkins@
   thorpe.com.au
Listings & descriptions for newly published Aus-
   tralian books, along with information about
   forthcoming titles. Additional information in-
   cludes author & editor.
First published 1990.
6 times/yr.
ISSN: 1449-776X

**Victorian Government Publications (VGP)** (J)
Published by State Library of Victoria
328 Swanston St, Melbourne, Victoria 3000
*Tel:* (03) 8664 7000

*Web Site:* www.slv.vic.gov.au
*Telex:* AA38104
*Key Personnel*
Government Publications Librarian: Dianne Beau-
   mont *E-mail:* dianneb@slv.vic.gov.au
Monthly.

**Weekly Book Newsletter** (P)
Published by Thorpe-Bowker
85 Turner St, Bldg C3, Port Melbourne, Victoria
   3207
*Tel:* (03) 8645 0300; (03) 8645 0389 (customer
   service) *Fax:* (03) 8645 0395
*E-mail:* blue.newsletter@thorpe.com.au;
   yoursay@thorpe.com.au; customer.service@
   thorpe.com.au
*Web Site:* www.thorpe.com.au
*Key Personnel*
Publisher: Andrew Wilkins *Tel:* (03) 8645 0392
   *E-mail:* andrew.wilkins@thorpe.com.au
First published 1972.
Weekly (49 issues/yr).
ISSN: 0812-7042
*Parent Company:* R R Bowker
*Ultimate Parent Company:* Cambridge Informa-
   tion Group

**Westerly** (P)
Published by The Center for Studies in Australian
   Literature
English Communication & Cultural Studies, Uni-
   versity of Western Australia, Crawley, WA
   6009
*Tel:* (08) 9380 2101 *Fax:* (08) 9380 1030
*E-mail:* westerly@cyllene.uwa.edu.au
*Web Site:* westerly.uwa.edu.au
*Key Personnel*
Editor: Delys Bird; Dennis Haskell
Annually.
ISSN: 0043-324X

**Writers and Photographers Marketing Guide:
   Directory of Australian and New Zealand
   Literary and Photo Markets** (B)
Published by Australian Writers' Professional
   Service
Stott House, 140 Flinders St, Melbourne, Victoria
   3000
*Tel:* (03) 6546211; (054) 468275 *Fax:* (03)
   6509648

# Austria

**Adressbuch des oesterreichischen Buchhandels**
   (Directory of Austrian Book Trade) (B)
Published by Hauptverband des Oesterreichischen
   Buchhandels (Austrian Publishers' & Book-
   sellers' Association)
Gruenangergasse 4, 1010 Vienna
*Tel:* (01) 512 15 35 *Fax:* (01) 512 84 82
*E-mail:* hvb@buecher.at
*Web Site:* www.buecher.at

**Anzeiger des oesterreichischen Buchhandels**
   (Austrian Book Trade Gazette) (J)
Published by Hauptverband des Oesterreichischen
   Buchhandels (Austrian Publishers' & Book-
   sellers' Association)
Gruenangergasse 4, 1010 Vienna
*Tel:* (01) 512 15 35 *Fax:* (01) 512 84 82
*E-mail:* hvb@buecher.at
*Web Site:* www.buecher.at
Bimonthly.

**Anzeiger des Verbandes der Antiquare
   Oesterreichs** (Austrian Antiquarian
   Booksellers' Association Gazette) (J)
Published by Verband der Antiquare Oesterreichs
   (Antiquarian Booksellers Association of Aus-
   tria)
Grunangergasse 4, 1010 Vienna
*Tel:* (01) 512 15 35 *Fax:* (01) 512 84 82
*E-mail:* hvb@buecher.at
*Web Site:* www.buecher.at

**Autorensolidaritaet** (Solidarity of Authors) (P)
Published by Interessengemeinschaft oesterre-
   ichischer Autorinnen und Autoren
Literaturhaus, Seidengasse 13, 1070 Vienna
*Tel:* (01) 526204413 *Fax:* (01) 526204455
*E-mail:* ig@literaturhaus.at
*Web Site:* www.literaturhaus.at/lh/ig
*Key Personnel*
Editor: Gerhard Ruiss
Text in German.
Quarterly.

**Die Rampe** (P)
Published by Amt der Ooe Landesregierung, In-
   stitut fuer Kulturfoerderung
Bahn hofplatz 1, 4021 Linz
*Tel:* (0732) 77 20 0 *Fax:* (0732) 77 20116 68
*E-mail:* post@ooe.gv.at
*Web Site:* www.ooe.gv.at
First published 1975.
Biannually.
5.20 EUR

**Die Literatur der oesterreichischen Kunst-,
   Kultur- und Autorenverlage** (Austrian
   Publishing in Arts, Culture & Literature) (B)
Published by Interessengemeinschaft oesterre-
   ichischer Autorinnen und Autoren
Literaturhaus, Seidengasse 13, 1070 Vienna
*Tel:* (01) 526204413 *Fax:* (01) 526204455
*E-mail:* ig@literaturhaus.at
*Web Site:* www.literaturhaus.at/lh/ig
*Key Personnel*
President: Milo Dor

**Literatur und Kritik** (Literature & Criticism) (P)
Published by Otto Mueller Verlag
Josefs Platz 1, 1015 Vienna
*Tel:* (01) 53410 *Fax:* (01) 53410280
*E-mail:* onb@onb.ac.at
*Web Site:* www.onb.ac.at/biblos/omvs/litkrit1.htm
*Key Personnel*
Director General: Dr Rachinger Johanna
Reviews German language literature & literary
   criticism.
First published 1966.
5 times/yr.
28 EUR; 6.80 EUR/issue
ISSN: 0024-466X

**Manuskripte: Zeitschrift fuer Literatur**
   (Manuscripts) (P)
Published by Alfred Kolleritsch Manuskripte
Sackstr 17, 8010 Graz
*Tel:* (0316) 82 56 08 *Fax:* (0316) 82 56 05
*E-mail:* lz@manuskripte.at
*Web Site:* www.manuskripte.at
*Key Personnel*
Editor: Alfred Kolleritsch; Guenter Waldorf
Journal for literature, art & criticism.
Quarterly.
27 EUR (domestic); 32 EUR (foreign)
ISSN: 0025-2638

**Modern Austrian Literature** (P)
Published by International Arthur Schnitzler Research Association
c/o Donald G Daviau, Dept of Comparative Literature, University of California, Riverside, CA
   92521

*Tel:* (909) 787-4314 *Fax:* (909) 787-2160
*E-mail:* austrian@citrus.ucr.edu
*Key Personnel*
Editor: Donald G Daviau
Text & summaries in English & German. Focuses on 19th & 20th century Austrian literature & culture.
Quarterly.
25 USD (individuals); 30 USD (foreign individuals); 35 USD (institutions); 40 USD (foreign institutions)

**Sprachkunst, Beitraege zur Literaturwissenschaft** (Art of Language, Contributions to the Study of Literature) (P)
Published by Verlag der Oesterreichischen Akademie der Wissenschaften (Austrian Academy of Sciences Press)
Dr Ignaz Seipel, Platz 2, 1010 Vienna
*Fax:* (01) 51581-3400
*E-mail:* webmaster@oeaw.ac.at
*Web Site:* www.oeaw.ac.at
Publication of articles particularly on poetical works, on literary history & poetics, reviews in addition. The language is German, English, French & Russian.
Biannually.
ISSN: 0038-8483

**Stueckeboerse Katalog** (J)
Published by Gerhard Ruiss
im Literaturhaus, Seidengasse 13, 1070 Vienna
*Tel:* (01) 526 20 44-13 *Fax:* (01) 526 20 44-55
*E-mail:* ig@literaturhaus.at
*Web Site:* www.literaturhaus.at/lh/ig
*Key Personnel*
President: Milo Dor
Catalogue of unpublished & published Austrian dramatic works.

# Bangladesh

**Bangladesh National Bibliography** (J)
Published by National Library of Bangladesh, Directorate of Archives & Libraries
32 Justice Sayed Mahbub Murshed Sarani, Sher-e-Bangla Nagar (Agargaon), Dhaka 1207
*Tel:* (02) 9129992; (02) 9112733 *Fax:* (02) 9118704
*E-mail:* nab@accesstel.net
*Web Site:* www.infosciencetoday.org/nationallibrary.htm
*Key Personnel*
Dir: Mr Hahashinur Rahman Khan
Text in Bengali & English.
First published 1972.
Annually.

# Barbados

**National Bibliography of Barbados** (B)
Published by National Library Service
Culloden Farm, Culloden Rd, St Michael
*Tel:* 429-5704 *Fax:* 436-1501
*E-mail:* natlib1@caribsurf.com
*Key Personnel*
Senior Librarian, Technical Services: Loleta Herbert *Tel:* 429-5716
Text in English.
First published 1975.
Biannually.
10 USD
ISSN: 0256-7709

# Belarus

**Letopis Pechati Belarusi** (Byelorussian National Bibliography) (J)
Published by Nationalnaya Knizhnaya Palata Belarus (National Book Chamber of Belarus)
ul v Karuzhai, 31a, 220002 Minsk
*Tel:* (0172) 289-33-96 *Fax:* (0172) 289-33-96
*E-mail:* palata@palata.beipak.mihsk.BY
ISSN: 0130-9218

**Neman** (P)
Published by Ministry of Culture
Dom Pravitelstva, ul Sovetskaia, 9, 220010 Minsk
*Tel:* (0172) 236548
*Telex:* 252 267 HOTA
Literary, artistic, socio-political magazine. Text in Russian.
First published 1952.
Monthly.
120 USD (foreign)

# Belgium

**Adresgids Voor Het Boekenvak** (B)
Published by Boek.be
Hof ter Schrieklaan 17, 2600 Berchem, Antwerp
*Tel:* (03) 230 89 23 *Fax:* (03) 281 22 40
*E-mail:* info@boek.be
*Web Site:* www.boek.be
A list of Dutch booksellers & publishers.
First published 1929.
Annually.

**Annuaire** (B)
Published by Commission Belge de Bibliographie et de Bibliologie (Belgian Commission of Bibliography & Bibliology)
4 blvd de l'Empereur, 1000 Brussels
*Tel:* (02) 80510464 *Fax:* (02) 5195610; (02) 5131503
Annually.

**Belgische Bibliografie** (J)
Published by Koninklijke Bibliotheek Alber I
Keizerslaan 4, 1000 Brussels
*Tel:* (02) 519 57 15; (02) 519 53 11; (02) 519 53 05; (02) 519 53 08 *Fax:* (02) 519 55 33
*E-mail:* contacts@kbr.be
*Web Site:* www.kbr.be
*Key Personnel*
Contact: Willy Vanderpijpen *E-mail:* vdpijpen@kbr.be
Monthly.

**Dietsche Warande en Belfort** (P)
Published by Uitgeverij Peeters Leuven (Belgie) (Peeters Publishers & Booksellers)
Bondgenotenlaan 153, 3000 Leuven
*Tel:* (016) 235170 *Fax:* (016) 228500
*E-mail:* peeters@peeters-leuven.be
*Web Site:* www.peeters-leuven.be
Journal for literature, art & spiritual life.

**Gulden Passer** (Golden Compass) (P)
Published by Vereeniging der Antwerpsche Bibliophielene (Association of Antwerp Bibliophiles)
Museum Plantin-Moretus, Vrijdagmarkt 22, 2000 Antwerp
*Tel:* (03) 2330294; (03) 2322455 *Fax:* (03) 2262516
*Key Personnel*
Editor: Francine de Nave; Marcus de Schepper
Text in Dutch, English, French & German.

First published 1878.
Annually.
ISSN: 0777-5067

**Le Livre et l'Estampe** (The Book & The Print) (P)
Published by Societe Royale des Bibliophiles et Iconophiles de Belgique
blvd de l'Empereur 4, 1000 Brussels
*Key Personnel*
Editor: A Grisay
Text in French.
First published 1954.
Biannually.
50 EUR (European Union); 55 EUR (elsewhere)
ISSN: 0024-533X

**Neerlandia** (P)
Published by Algemeen-Nederlands Verbond
Gallaitstraat 86, 1030 Brussels
*Tel:* (02) 241 31 64 *Fax:* (02) 241 31 64
*E-mail:* anv.vlaanderen@edpnet.be
*Web Site:* www.algemeennederlandsverbond.org
5 times/yr.

**Revue generale** (General Review) (P)
Published by De Boeck et Larcier SA
Fond Jean-Paques 4, 1348 Louvain-la-Neuve
*Tel:* (010) 48 26 19 *Fax:* (010) 48 27 50
*E-mail:* info@editions.larcier.com
*Web Site:* www.deboeck.be
*Key Personnel*
Editorial Dir: Anne Knops
Publication includes general information on Belgian politics, economics, literature, etc.
First published 1865.
6 times/yr.
ISSN: 0777-2287

**Steven** (P)
Prinsstraat 15, 2000 Antwerp
*Tel:* (03) 212 10 20 *Fax:* (03) 212 10 22
*E-mail:* streven@skynet.be
*Web Site:* www.come.to/streven
Magazine on culture & society.
First published 1933.
Monthly (except Aug).
96 pp
ISSN: 0039-2324

# Bolivia

**Bio Bibliografia Boliviana** (Bolivian Bibliography) (J)
Published by Los Amigos del Libro
Casilla de Correo 450, Cochabamba 15
*Tel:* (04) 2504150 *Fax:* (04) 115128
*Key Personnel*
Owner: Werner T Guttentag *E-mail:* gutten@amigol.bo.net
Text in Spanish.
First published 1962.
Annually.
170 USD

**Bolivian Booknews** (B)
Published by Los Amigos del Libro Ediciones
Calle Heroinas, No E-0311, esquina Espana, Cochabamba
Mailing Address: Apdo Aereo 450, Cochabamba
*Tel:* (04) 254114; (04) 251140 *Fax:* (04) 0411-5128

## Bosnia and Herzegovina

**Izraz** (P)
Published by SOUR Svjetlost
Petra Preradovica 3, 71000 Sarajevo
Mailing Address: PO Box 129, 71000 Sarajevo
*Key Personnel*
Editor: Dzevad Karahasan
Journal of literary & artistic criticism.
First published 1957.
Monthly.
15 USD
ISSN: 0021-3381

## Botswana

**National Bibliography of Botswana** (P)
Published by Botswana National Library Service
Private Bag 0036, Gaborone
*Tel:* 352-397 *Fax:* 301-149
*E-mail:* natlib@global.bw; automate@global.bw
*Web Site:* www.gov.bw
*Key Personnel*
Dir: Mrs Constance B Modise
  *E-mail:* cbmodise@gov.bw
Editor: Gertrude Kayaga Mulindwa
First published 1969.
Triannually.
6 USD
ISSN: 0027-8777

## Brazil

**Bibliografia Brasileira** (Brazilian Bibliography)
  (J)
Published by Biblioteca Nacional
Av Rio Branco, 219, 22040-008 Rio de Janeiro-
  RJ
*Tel:* (021) 2220-9433 *Fax:* (021) 2220-4173
*E-mail:* inter@bn.br
*Web Site:* www.bn.br
*Key Personnel*
President: Affonso Romano De Sant'Anna
Quarterly.

**Jornal do SNEL/Producao Editorial Brasileira**
  (SNEL Newspaper/Brazilian Editorial
  Production) (B)
Published by Sindicato Nacional dos Editores de
  Livros (SNEL)
Ruada Ajuda, 35, 18° Andar, 20040-000 Rio de
  Janeiro-RJ
*Tel:* (021) 2533-0399 *Fax:* (021) 2533-0422
*E-mail:* snel@snel.org.br
*Web Site:* www.snel.org.br
*Telex:* (021) 37063

**Veritas** (P)
Published by Editora da PUCRS
c/o Antoninho M Naime, Partenon, 90651-970
  Porto Alegre-RS
Mailing Address: CP 12001, 90651-970 Porto
  Alegre-RS

*Tel:* (051) 3391511 *Fax:* (051) 3391564
*Telex:* (051) 3349
Education, Human Sciences, Philosophy. Text in
  Portuguese.
First published 1955.
Quarterly.
15 BRL; 16 USD
ISSN: 0042-3955

## Bulgaria

**Balgarski disertacii** (Bulgarian Dissertations) (P)
Published by Saints Cyril & Methodius National
  Library (Narodna Biblioteka Sv sv Kiril i
  Metodii)
88 Vasil Levski Blvd, 1504 Sofia
*Tel:* (02) 9882811
*E-mail:* nbkm@nationallibrary.bg
*Web Site:* www.nationallibrary.bg
*Key Personnel*
Editor-in-Chief: Alexandra Dipchikova *Tel:* (02)
  9882811 (ext 206) *E-mail:* dipchikova@
  nationallibrary.bg
First published 1973.
Annually.
ISSN: 0323-9411

**Balgarski knigopis, Seria 1** (B)
Published by Saints Cyril & Methodius National
  Library (Narodna Biblioteka Sv sv Kiril i
  Metodii)
88 Vasil Levski Blvd, 1504 Sofia
*Tel:* (02) 9882811
*E-mail:* nbkm@nationallibrary.bg
*Web Site:* www.nationallibrary.bg
*Key Personnel*
Editor-in-Chief: Alexandra Dipchikova *Tel:* (02)
  9882811 (ext 206) *E-mail:* dipchikova@
  nationallibrary.bg
First published 1969.
Annually.
ISSN: 0323-9713

**Balgarski periodichen Pechat, Seria 4**
  (Bulgarian Periodicals, Series 4) (P)
Published by Saints Cyril & Methodius National
  Library (Narodna Biblioteka Sv sv Kiril i
  Metodii)
88 Vasil Levski Blvd, 1504 Sofia
*Tel:* (02) 9882811
*E-mail:* nbkm@nationallibrary.bg
*Web Site:* www.nationallibrary.bg
*Key Personnel*
Editor-in-Chief: Alexandra Dipchikova *Tel:* (02)
  9882811 (ext 206) *E-mail:* dipchikova@
  nationallibrary.bg
Part of *Bulgarska Nacionalna Bibliografija.*
First published 1967.
Annually.
ISSN: 0032-9764

**Bibliographia na Balgarskata Bibliographia**
  (Bibliography of Bulgarian Bibliographies) (B)
Published by Saints Cyril & Methodius National
  Library (Narodna Biblioteka Sv sv Kiril i
  Metodii)
88 Vasil Levski Blvd, 1504 Sofia
*Tel:* (02) 9882811
*E-mail:* nbkm@nationallibrary.bg
*Web Site:* www.nationallibrary.bg
*Key Personnel*
Editor-in-Chief: Alexandra Dipchikova *Tel:* (02)
  9882811 (ext 206) *E-mail:* dipchikova@
  nationallibrary.bg
First published 1965.
Annually.
ISSN: 0204-7373

**Bulgarski knigopis, Seria 1** (The National
  Bibliography) (P)
Published by Saints Cyril & Methodius National
  Library (Narodna Biblioteka Sv sv Kiril i
  Metodii)
88 Vasil Levski Blvd, 1504 Sofia
*Tel:* (02) 9882811
*E-mail:* nbkm@nationallibrary.bg
*Web Site:* www.nationallibrary.bg
*Key Personnel*
Editor-in-Chief: Alexandra Dipchikova *Tel:* (02)
  9882811 (ext 206) *E-mail:* dipchikova@
  nationallibrary.bg
First published 1897.
Monthly.
ISSN: 0323-9616

**Diskographia** (B)
Published by Saints Cyril & Methodius National
  Library (Narodna Biblioteka Sv sv Kiril i
  Metodii)
88 Vasil Levski Blvd, 1504 Sofia
*Tel:* (02) 9882811
*E-mail:* nbkm@nationallibrary.bg
*Web Site:* www.nationallibrary.bg
*Key Personnel*
Editor-in-Chief: Alexandra Dipchikova *Tel:* (02)
  9882811 (ext 206) *E-mail:* dipchikova@
  nationallibrary.bg
Annually.
ISSN: 1310-9154

**Letopis na Statiite ot Balgarskite Spisania i
  Sbornici** (Articles from Bulgarian Journals &
  Collections) (P)
Published by Saints Cyril & Methodius National
  Library (Narodna Biblioteka Sv sv Kiril i
  Metodii)
88 Vasil Levski Blvd, 1504 Sofia
*Tel:* (02) 9882811
*E-mail:* nbkm@nationallibrary.bg
*Web Site:* www.nationallibrary.bg
*Key Personnel*
Editor-in-Chief: Alexandra Dipchikova *Tel:* (02)
  9882811 (ext 206) *E-mail:* dipchikova@
  nationallibrary.bg
First published 1952.
Monthly.
ISSN: 0324-0398

**Letopis na statiite ot balgarskite vestnici**
  (Articles from Bulgarian Newspapers) (P)
Published by Saints Cyril & Methodius National
  Library (Narodna Biblioteka Sv sv Kiril i
  Metodii)
88 Vasil Levski Blvd, 1504 Sofia
*Tel:* (02) 9882811
*E-mail:* nbkm@nationallibrary.bg
*Web Site:* www.nationallibrary.bg
*Key Personnel*
Editor-in-Chief: Alexandra Dipchikova *Tel:* (02)
  9882811 (ext 206) *E-mail:* dipchikova@
  nationallibrary.bg
First published 1952.
Monthly.
ISSN: 0324-0347

**Literaturen Forum** (P)
Published by Literaturen Forum OOD
136 Rakovski Str, Sofia 1000
*Tel:* (02) 870293 *Fax:* (02) 988 10 69
*E-mail:* forum@isoc.bg
*Web Site:* www.bol.bg/forum
*Key Personnel*
Editor-in-Chief: Marin Georgiev
First published 1991.
Weekly (except July & Aug).

**Literaturna Misal** (Literary Thought) (P)
Published by Bulgarian Academy of Sciences,
  Institute of Literature

15 Noemuri St 1, 1040 Sofia
*Tel:* (02) 987-89-66 *Fax:* (02) 986-25-00
*E-mail:* library@cl.bas.bg
*Web Site:* www.cl.bas.bg
*Key Personnel*
Dir, Associate Prof: Raya Kuncheva *Tel:* (02) 979-29-90
Text in Bulgarian. Contents page in English & French.
First published 1957.
Monthly.

# Chile

**Bibliografia chilena** (Chilean Bibliographies) (J)
Published by Biblioteca Nacional de Chile
Alameda 651, Piso 2, Santiago
*Tel:* (02) 3605271
*E-mail:* prensa@dibam.cl
*Web Site:* www.dibam.cl/biblioteca_nacional
*Key Personnel*
Secretary: Pedro Pablo Zegers
First published 1976.
Annually.

**Efimeros** (Ephemerals) (P)
Published by Biblioteca del Congreso Nacional
Compania 1175 & Huerfanos 1117-2° piso, Santiago
*Tel:* (02) 2701700 *Fax:* (02) 2701766
*E-mail:* contacto@bcn.cl
*Web Site:* www.bcn.cl

**Mapocho** (P)
Published by Biblioteca Nacional de Chile
Alameda 651, Piso 2, Santiago
*Tel:* (02) 3605271
*E-mail:* prensa@dibam.cl
*Web Site:* www.dibam.cl
*Key Personnel*
Dir: Alfonso Calderon Squadritto
Distributor Editorial University.
First published 1998.
Irregularly.
ISSN: 0716-2510

**Revista Chilena de Literatura** (Chilean Review of Literature) (P)
Published by Universidad de Chile Facultad de Filosofia y Humanidades, Departamento de Literatura
Ignacio Carrera Pinto 1025, Santiago
*Fax:* (02) 2716823
*E-mail:* rchilite@uchile.cl
*Web Site:* www.uchile.cl/facultades/filosofia/revista_literaria/
*Key Personnel*
Dir: Hugo Montes
Biannually.
ISSN: 0048-7651

# China

**China Today** (P)
Published by China Welfare Institute
24 Baiwanzhuang Rd, Beijing 100037
*Tel:* (010) 68996217 *Fax:* (010) 68997796
*E-mail:* wandi@china.org.cn
*Web Site:* www.china.org.cn
Published in English, French, Arabic, German, English braille & Chinese.
Monthly.

◊**Communications in Theoretical Physics** (J)
Published by International Academic Publishers (IAP)
137 Chaonei Dajie, Beijing 100010
*Tel:* (010) 64077944 *Fax:* (010) 64014877
*E-mail:* wgxs@public3.bta.net.cn
*Web Site:* www.itp.ac.cn/eng/journal.html
*Key Personnel*
Editor: T H Ho
Presents important new developments in the area of theoretical physics. Papers published in this journal are devoted mainly to the fields of atomic & molecular physics, condensed matter & theory of statistical physics, nuclear theory, fluid theory & plasmas, elementary particle physics & quantum field theory, quantum mechanics & quantum optics, theoretical astrophysics, cosmology & relativity. Text in English.
First published 1981.
8 times/yr.
128 pp, 768 EUR or 769 USD (institutions for print or online edition); 921.60 EUR or 922.80 USD (institutions for both print & online editions)
ISSN: 0253-6102

**Directory of Publishers in China** (B)
Published by Foreign Languages Press (FLP)
24 Baiwanzhuanglu Rd, Beijing 100037
*Tel:* (010) 8320579 *Fax:* (010) 8317390
*E-mail:* flpcn@public3.bta.net.cn
*Web Site:* www.flp.com.cn

**Zhongguo jia shu mu** (Chinese National Bibliography) (B)
Published by Beijing Library Press
7 Wenjin St, Xicheng District, Beijing 100034
*Tel:* (010) 66126146; (010) 66174391 *Fax:* (010) 66174391
*E-mail:* btsfxb@publicf.gov.cn
*Web Site:* www.nlcpress.com
*Telex:* 222211 NLC CN *Cable:* 0848

# Colombia

**Anuario Bibliografico Colombiano** (Colombian Bibliographical Annual) (J)
Published by Instituto Caro y Cuervo
Carrera 11 No 64-37, Apdo Aereo 51502, Bogota DC
*Tel:* (01) 2558289 *Fax:* (01) 2170243
*Web Site:* www.caroycuervo.gov.co
Annually.

◊**Boletin Informativo CERLALC** (J)
Published by Centro Regional para el Fomento del Libro en America Latina y el Caribe (Regional Center for the Promotion of Books in Latin America & the Caribbean)
Calle 70 No 9-52, Bogota DC
*Tel:* (01) 540 2071
*E-mail:* libro@cerlalc.org
*Web Site:* www.cerlalc.org
*Key Personnel*
Sub Dir: Julian David Correa

**Directorio Latinoamericano de Editoriales, Distribuidoras y Librerias** (B)
Published by Centro Regional para el Fomento del Libro en America Latina y el Caribe (Regional Center for the Promotion of Books in Latin America & the Caribbean)
Calle 70 No 9-52, Bogota DC
*Tel:* (01) 540 2071
*E-mail:* libro@cerlalc.org
*Web Site:* www.cerlalc.org

*Key Personnel*
Dir: Carmen Barvo
Dos nuevos publicaciones en Dd-Rom, anexo folletos. Para titulos no en inges, favor de proveer traduccion en Asimismo, el libro Manual de edicio.

**Tinta Fresca** (ISBN Bibliographical Bulletin/Editorial Mail) (J)
Published by Camara Colombiana del Libro
Carrera 17A No 37-27, Bogota
*Tel:* (01) 288 6188 *Fax:* (01) 287 3320
*E-mail:* camlibro@camlibro.com.co
*Web Site:* www.camlibro.com.co
Quarterly.

# The Democratic Republic of the Congo

**Bibliographie Nationale** (B)
Published by Bibliotheque Nacionale
BP 3090, Kinshasa-Gombe
*Telex:* 21216 CAU ZR
Zaire Bibliography. Text in French.
First published 1971.
Irregularly.

# Costa Rica

**Anuario bibliografico costarricense** (Annual Costa Rican Bibliography)
Published by Asociacion Costarricense de Bibliotecarios (Costa Rican Association of Librarians)
Apdo 3308, San Jose
Text in Spanish.
First published 1956.
Irregularly.
Free
ISSN: 0066-5010

**Catalogo Nacional ISBN** (National ISBN Catalog) (J)
Published by Direccion General de Bibliotecas y Biblioteca Nacional
Ap 10008, 1000 San Jose
*Tel:* 2331706; 2212436; 2212479 *Fax:* 2235510
*Key Personnel*
Contact: Marco A Chacon Monge

**Indice de Revistas Nacionales** (Catalog of National Periodicals) (J)
Published by Direccion General de Bibliotecas y Biblioteca Nacional
Apdo 10008-1000, San Jose
*Tel:* 2212436; 2212479 *Fax:* 2235510

# Cote d'Ivoire

**Bibliographie de la Cote-d'Ivoire** (Ivory Coast Bibliography) (J)
Published by Bibliotheque Nationale

BP V180, Abidjan
*Tel:* 32 38 72
Text in French.
First published 1969.
Annually.
2 vols, 3,000 XOF
ISSN: 0084-7860

**Revue de Litterature de l'esthetique
negre-africaines & edition de livres
Scolaires, de litterature Jenerale et
d'encyclopedie** (P)
Published by Les Nouvelles Editions Ivoiriennes
One blvd de Marseille, Abidjan 01
Mailing Address: BP 1818, Abidjan 01
*Tel:* 21 24 07 66; 21 24 08 25 *Fax:* 21 24 24 56
*E-mail:* edition@nei-ci.com
*Web Site:* www.nei-ci.com
*Telex:* Cote d Ivoire 22564

# Croatia

**Forum** (J)
Published by Hrvatska Akademija Zhanosti i Um-
jetnosti, Razred Za Suvremenu knjizevnost
Zrinski trg 11, 10000 Zagreb
*Tel:* (01) 48 95 111 *Fax:* (01) 481 99 79
*E-mail:* kabpred@hazu.hr
*Web Site:* www.hazu.hr
*Key Personnel*
Editor: Slavko Mihalic
Journal of the Section for Contemporary Litera-
ture of the Croatian Academy of Sciences &
Arts. Text in Croatian.

# Cuba

**Taller Literario** (Literary Workshop) (P)
Published by Universidad de Oriente, Escuela de
Letras
Avda Patricio Lumumba s-n, CP 90500 Santiago
de Cuba Oriente
*Tel:* (0226) 31973
*Key Personnel*
Dir: Dr Bayardo Dupotey Rivas
Librarian: Caridad Velaquez Alazar
Text in Spanish.
First published 1971.
Quarterly.

**Union** (P)
Published by Ediciones Union, Union de Es-
critores y Artistas de Cuba
Calle 17 No 351 e/H, Plaza de la Revolucion,
Havana
*Tel:* (07) 324551; (07) 324571 *Fax:* (07) 333158
*E-mail:* editora@uneac.co.cu
*Web Site:* www.uneac.com
*Key Personnel*
Dir: Jorge Lois Arcos

# Czech Republic

**Casopis Narodniho muzea Rada historicka**
(Journal of the National Museum Series:
History) (P)
Published by Narodni Muzeum
Vaclavske namesti 68, 115 79 Prague 1

*Tel:* (02) 24497111; (02) 24497212; (02)
24497352; (02) 2449376 *Fax:* (02) 22246047;
(02) 24226488
*Web Site:* www.nm.cz
*Key Personnel*
Dir: Michal Lukes *Tel:* (02) 4497310
*E-mail:* michal.lukes@nm.cz
Secretary: Eva Klickova
Summaries in English, French, German & Rus-
sian.
Quarterly.

**Casopis Narodniho muzea Rada prirodovedna**
(Journal of the National Museum Series:
Natural Science) (P)
Published by Narodni Muzeum
Vaclavske namesti 68, 115 79 Prague 1
*Tel:* (02) 24497111; (02) 24497212; (02)
24497352; (02) 2449376 *Fax:* (02) 22246047;
(02) 24226488
*Web Site:* www.nm.cz
*Key Personnel*
Dir: Michal Lukes *Tel:* (02) 4497310
*E-mail:* michal.lukes@nm.cz
Secretary: Eva Klickova
Summaries in English, French, German & Rus-
sian.
Quarterly.

**Czech Books For You** (J)
Published by Artia Pegas Press Co Ltd
Palac Metro, Narodnitrida 25, 111 21 Prague
Mailing Address: PO Box 825, 110 00 Prague
*Tel:* (02) 266568; (02) 262081 *Fax:* (02) 266568
*Telex:* 121065 ARTA C *Cable:* ARTIASPOL
PRAHA
Bulletin with annotations & prices of approxi-
mately 200 of the most interesting books pub-
lished in the Czech Republic during the previ-
ous quarter. Text in Czech.
First published 1974.
Quarterly.
Free

**Muzejni a vlastivedna prace** (Museum & Local
History) (P)
Published by Narodni Muzeum
Vaclavske namesti 68, 115 79 Prague 1
*Tel:* (02) 24497111; (02) 24497212; (02)
24497352; (02) 2449376 *Fax:* (02) 22246047;
(02) 24226488
*Web Site:* www.nm.cz
*Key Personnel*
Dir: Michal Lukes *Tel:* (02) 4497310
*E-mail:* michal.lukes@nm.cz
Secretary: Eva Klickova
Summaries in English, French, German & Rus-
sian.
Quarterly.

**Numismaticke listy** (Numismatics Journal) (P)
Published by Narodni Muzeum
Vaclavske namesti 68, 115 79 Prague 1
*Tel:* (02) 24497111; (02) 24497212; (02)
24497352; (02) 2449376 *Fax:* (02) 22246047;
(02) 24226488
*Web Site:* www.nm.cz
*Key Personnel*
Dir: Michal Lukes *Tel:* (02) 4497310
*E-mail:* michal.lukes@nm.cz
Secretary: Eva Klickova
Summaries in English, French, German & Rus-
sian.
6 times/yr.

**Sbornik Narodniho muzea Rada A: Historie**
(Collection of the National Museum Series A:
History) (P)
Published by Narodni Muzeum
Vaclavske namesti 68, 115 79 Prague 1

*Tel:* (02) 24497111; (02) 24497212; (02)
24497352; (02) 2449376 *Fax:* (02) 22246047;
(02) 24226488
*Web Site:* www.nm.cz
*Key Personnel*
Dir: Michal Lukes *Tel:* (02) 4497310
*E-mail:* michal.lukes@nm.cz
Secretary: Eva Klickova
Summaries in English, French, German & Rus-
sian.
Quarterly.

**Sbornik Narodniho muzea Rada B: Prirodni
vedy** (Collection of the National Museum
Series B: Natural Science) (P)
Published by Narodni Muzeum
Vaclavske namesti 68, 115 79 Prague 1
*Tel:* (02) 24497111; (02) 24497212; (02)
24497352; (02) 2449376 *Fax:* (02) 22246047;
(02) 24226488
*Web Site:* www.nm.cz
*Key Personnel*
Dir: Michal Lukes *Tel:* (02) 4497310
*E-mail:* michal.lukes@nm.cz
Secretary: Eva Klickova
In English or German, also in Czechoslovakian
with English & German summaries.
Quarterly.

**Sbornik Narodniho muzea Rada C: Literarni
historie** (Magazine of the National Museum of
Prague, Series C: Literary History) (P)
Published by Narodni Muzeum
Vaclavske namesti 68, 115 79 Prague 1
*Tel:* (02) 24497111; (02) 24497212; (02)
24497352; (02) 2449376 *Fax:* (02) 22246047;
(02) 24226488
*Web Site:* www.nm.cz
*Key Personnel*
Dir: Michal Lukes *Tel:* (02) 4497310
*E-mail:* michal.lukes@nm.cz
Secretary: Eva Klickova
Summaries in English, French, German & Rus-
sian.
Quarterly.

**Svetova Literatura** (P)
Published by Spolecnost pro Svetovou Literaturu
Masarykovo nabr 26, 110 00 Prague 1
*Tel:* 422912999 *Fax:* (02) 422912999
*E-mail:* furek@ius.prf.cuni.cz
*Web Site:* www.ff.cuni.cz/~furek/www4.htm
Review of Foreign Literature.
First published 1956.
Irregular.
240 CZK; 50 USD
ISSN: 0039-7075

# Denmark

**Bogormen** (J)
Published by Danske Boghandler Medhjaelper-
forening (The Bookworm, Journal for Book
Trade Employees)
Siljangade 6-8, 2300 Copenhagen S
*Tel:* 31542255 *Fax:* 31572422
*Key Personnel*
Editor: Arvid Honore
For booksellers' assistants as well as other mem-
bers of the book trade.
First published 1903.
Quarterly.
100 DKK
ISSN: 0006-5706

**Born og Boger** (Children & Books) (P)
Published by Danmarks Skolebiblioteksforening
Krimsvej 29 B 1, 2300 Copenhagen S

*Tel:* 33 11 1391 *Fax:* 33 11 1390
*E-mail:* komskolbib@ksbf.dk
*Web Site:* www.ksbf.dk
*Key Personnel*
Editor: Niels Jacobsen
English Summary. Periodical concerning books
& other cultural values for children & young
adults.

**Danish Literary Magazine** (P)
Published by The Danish Arts Agency-The Liter-
ature Center
Kongens Nytorv 3, 1050 Copenhagen K
*Tel:* (033) 74 45 00 *Fax:* (033) 74 45 45
*E-mail:* kontakt@danlitportal.dk
*Web Site:* www.danlit.dk
*Key Personnel*
Dir: Marianne Krukow
Consultant: Annette Bach *E-mail:* annette.bach@
danlit.dk
Excerpts from new Danish books, in addition to
news about Danish books being published in
other countries.
Biannually.

**Dansk Bogfortegnelse** (Danish National
Bibliography, Books) (J)
Published by Danish Bibliographic Centre
Tempovej 7-11, 2750 Ballerup
*Tel:* 44 86 77 77 *Fax:* 44 86 78 91
*E-mail:* dbc@dbc.dk
*Web Site:* www.dbc.dk
*Key Personnel*
Information Officer: Suzanne H Christofferson

**Grafisk Handbog** (Graphical Handbook) (B)
Published by Forlaget Nye Medier
Alhambravej 5, 1826 Frederiksberg C
*Tel:* 38 88 32 22 *Fax:* 38 88 30 38
*Web Site:* www.nyemedier.dk
*Key Personnel*
Contact: Kim Odderskjaer Hansen *Tel:* 70 20
98 38 *E-mail:* kh@nyemedier.dk; Birgit Wal-
tenburg *Tel:* 70 20 98 38 *E-mail:* birgitw@
nyemedier.dk
Directory of prepress, printing & print-finishing
companies in Denmark. Text in Danish.
Annually.
ISSN: 1398-1617

**Hvedekorn** (P)
Published by Borgens Forlag A/S
Valbygardsvej 33, 2500 Valby
*Tel:* 36153615 *Fax:* 36153616
*E-mail:* kunst@hvedekorn.dk
*Web Site:* www.hvedekorn.dk
Magazine for poetry & graphics.

**Nordisk Exlibris Tidsskrift** (Scandinavian
Bookplate Periodical) (P)
Published by Dansk Exlibris Selskab
PO Box 1519, 2700 Copenhagen
*Tel:* 46769166 *Fax:* 46769167
*E-mail:* 113071.3716@compuserve.com
*Key Personnel*
Editor: Klaus Roedel
Text in Danish, English & German.
First published 1946.
Quarterly.
250 DKK
ISSN: 0029-1323

**Orbis Litterarum** (P)
Published by Blackwell
One Rosenorns Alle, 1502 Copenhagen V
Mailing Address: PO Box 227, 1502 Copenhagen
V
*Tel:* 7733 3333 *Fax:* 7733 3377
*E-mail:* info@mks.blackwellpublishing.com
*Web Site:* www.blackwellmunksgaard.com

*Key Personnel*
Editor: Neil Blair Christensen
International Review of literary studies; text
mainly in English, occasionally in French &
German.
Bimonthly.
60 pp
ISSN: 0105-7510

# Egypt (Arab Republic of Egypt)

**Lotus: Afro-Asian Writings** (P)
Published by Permanent Bureau of Afro-Asian
Writers
104 Sharia Kasr El-Aini, Cairo
*Key Personnel*
Editor: Youssef El Sebal
Important quarterly review published for the Per-
manent Bureau of Afro-Asian Writers. Text in
Arabic.
First published 1968.
Quarterly.

# Ethiopia

**Ethiopian Publications: Books, Pamphlets,
Annuals & Periodical Articles** (P)
Published by Addis Ababa University, Institute of
Ethiopian Studies
PO Box 1176, Addis Ababa
*Tel:* (01) 119469 *Fax:* (01) 552688
*E-mail:* ics@padis.gn.apc.org
*Web Site:* www.ies-ethiopia.org
Ethiopian National Bibliography.
Annually.

**List of Ethiopian Authors** (B)
Published by Addis Ababa University, Institute of
Ethiopian Studies
PO Box 1176, Addis Ababa
*Tel:* (01) 119469 *Fax:* (01) 552688
*E-mail:* IES@padis.gn.apc.org
*Web Site:* www.ies-ethiopia.org
ISSN: 0071-1772

# Fiji

**Publications Bulletin** (J)
Published by Fiji Government Printing Depart-
ment
Government Buildings, PO Box 2353, Suva
*Tel:* 3211 201 *Fax:* 3306 034
*E-mail:* info@fiji.gov.fj
*Web Site:* www.fiji.gov.fj
*Key Personnel*
President: Ratu Josefa
Biannually.

⨍**South Pacific Bibliography** (J)
Published by University of the South Pacific Li-
brary
Suva
*Tel:* 331 3900 *Fax:* 330 0830

*E-mail:* library@usp.ac.fj
*Web Site:* www.usp.ac.fj/library/
Biennially.

⨍**South Pacific Periodicals Index** (B)
Published by University of the South Pacific Li-
brary
Suva
*Tel:* 331 3900 *Fax:* 323 1528
*E-mail:* library@usp.ac.fj
*Web Site:* www.usp.ac.fjl~library

# Finland

**Bokvaennen** (The Bibliophile) (J)
Published by Boknoje, Barnens
Box 1253, 251-12 Helsinki
*Tel:* (042) 136415 *Fax:* (042) 147132
*Key Personnel*
Editor: Lars Forsberg

**Books from Finland** (J)
Published by Helsinki University Library
University of Helsinki, Unioninkatu 36, FIN-
00014 Helsinki
Mailing Address: University of Helsinki, PO Box
15, FIN-00014 Helsinki
*Tel:* (09) 1357942 *Fax:* (09) 1357942
*E-mail:* bff@helsinki.fi
*Web Site:* www.lib.helsinki.fi/bff
*Key Personnel*
Editor-in-Chief: Kristina Carlson
Editor: Soila Lehtonen
Editor (London): Hildi Hawkins
A literary journal published in English of books
from & about Finland.
First published 1967.
Quarterly.
80 pp, Annual subscription: 20 EUR (Finland &
Scandinavia); 27 EUR (elsewhere)
ISSN: 0006-7490

**The Finnish National Bibliography** (P)
Published by Helsinki University Library
Slavonic Library, PB 15, Helsingin Yliopisto,
00014 Unioninkatu 36
*Tel:* (09) 191 23196 *Fax:* (09) 191 22719
*E-mail:* hyk-palvelu@helsinki.fi
*Web Site:* www.lib.helsinki.fi
Also on microfiche; monthly with annual cumula-
tion.

**Horisont** (P)
Published by Svenska Osterbottens Litteratur-
forening
Valsbergsvagen 599, 64610 Overmark
*Tel:* (040) 549 7605
*E-mail:* authors_against_literature@msn.com
*Web Site:* www.kulturfonden.fi/sol/horisont.htm
*Key Personnel*
Chief Editor: Oscar Rossi
Literary magazine.
First published 1954.
Quarterly.
35 EUR/yr
ISSN: 0439-5530

**Kirjakauppalehti** (Book Trade Journal) (J)
Published by Kirjamedia Oy
Eerikinkatu 15-17 D 43, 00100 Helsinki
*Tel:* (09) 6859 9110; (09) 6859 9111 *Fax:* (09)
6859 9119
*E-mail:* toimisto@kirjakauppaliitto.fi
*Web Site:* www.kirjakauppalehti.net/; www.
kirjakauppaliitto.fi
*Key Personnel*
Editor-in-Chief: Annika Asvik *Tel:* (09) 6859
9114 *E-mail:* annika.asvik@kirjakauppalehti.net

**Parnasso** (P)
Published by Yhtyneet Kuvalehdet Oy
Maistraatinportti 1, 00015 Helsinki
*Tel:* (09) 15 661; (09) 156 665 *Fax:* (09) 145
  650; (09) 156 6511
*Web Site:* www.kuvalehdet.fi
*Key Personnel*
President: Ilkka Seppala
*Branch Office(s)*
Esterinportti 1, 00015 Helsinki


**Virittaejae** (The Kinder) (J)
Published by Society for the Study of Finnish
Castrenianum, PO Box 3, 00014 University of
  Helsinki
*Tel:* (09) 191 24342 *Fax:* (09) 191 3329
*Web Site:* www.helsinki.fi/jarj/kks/virittaja
*Key Personnel*
Editor: Marja-Liisa Helasvuo *E-mail:* mlhelas@
  utu.fi; Susanna Shore *E-mail:* susanna.shore@
  helsinki.fi
Linguistic journal with summaries in English,
  French & German.
First published 1897.
Quarterly (4 numbers per vol).
54 EUR (47 EUR if paid through a Finnish bank)
ISSN: 0042-6806


# France

**Annales de la Recherche Urbaine** (P)
Published by Plan Urbanisme Contruction Archi-
  tecture (PUCA)
Arche de la Defense-Paroi Nord, 92055 Paris la
  Defense Cedex
*Tel:* (01) 40 81 63 71 *Fax:* (01) 40 81 63 78
*Web Site:* www.equipement.gouv.fr
*Key Personnel*
Editor: Pierre Lassave *Tel:* (01) 40 81 63 70
  *E-mail:* pierre.lassave@equipement.gouv.
  fr; Anne Querrien *Tel:* (01) 40 81 24 46
  *E-mail:* anne.querrien@equipement.gouv.fr
First published 1979.
ISSN: 0180-930X
*Parent Company:* Ministere de l'Equipement, des
  Transports, du Logement, du Tourisme et de la
  Mer
Distributed by Lavoisier Abonnements


ƒ**Bibliotheques et Musees des Arts du
  Spectacle dans le Monde** (Performing Arts
  Libraries & Museums of the World) (B)
Published by Societe Internationale des
  Bibliotheques-Musees des Arts du Spectacle
Centre National de la Recherche Scientifique
  (CNRS), 3-5 rue Michel-Ange, 75794 Paris
*Tel:* (01) 44964000 *Fax:* (01) 44965000


ƒ**Bulletin du Bibliophile** (J)
Published by Electre-Editions du Cercle de la Li-
  brarie
35 rue Gregoire-de-Tours, 75006 Paris
*Tel:* (01) 44 41 28 00 *Fax:* (01) 43 29 68 95
*Key Personnel*
Secretary/Administration: Annie Charon
  *E-mail:* abcharon@club-internet.fr
Published in English, French & German.
First published 1834.
Biannually (June & Dec).
ISSN: 0399-9742


**Choisir** (P)
Published by Centre National de Documentation
  Pedagogique (CNDP)
29 rue d'Ulm, 75230 Paris Cedex 05
*Tel:* (01) 46 34 90 00 *Fax:* (01) 46 34 55 44
*E-mail:* webmaster@cndp.fr

*Web Site:* www.cndp.fr
*Key Personnel*
Editor: J Lanfranchi


ƒ**Copyright Bulletin** (J)
Published by UNESCO
Division of Art & Cultural Enterprise
Unit of Creativity & Copyright
7, Place de Fontenoy, 75352 Paris 07-SP
*Tel:* (01) 45 68 10 00; (01) 45 68 11 78 *Fax:* (01)
  45 67 16 90; (01) 45 68 55 40
*E-mail:* publishing.promotion@unesco.org;
  natcom.ncp@unesco.org; m.e.guerassimos@
  unesco.org
*Web Site:* www.unesco.org/publications; www.
  unesco.org/culture/copyright
*Key Personnel*
Dir General: Kochiro Matsuura
Articles & recent news on international conven-
  tions & developments in the field of copyright.
  Published in English, French, Spanish, Chinese
  & Russian.
Quarterly.
80 pp


ƒ**Copyright Laws & Treaties of the World** (B)
Published by UNESCO Publishing
7 Place de Fontenoy, 75352 Paris 07-SP
*Tel:* (01) 45 68 10 00; (01) 45 68 11 78 *Fax:* (01)
  45 67 16 90; (01) 45 68 55 40
*E-mail:* publishing.promotion@unesco.org;
  natcom.ncp@unesco.org
*Web Site:* www.unesco.org/publications
*Telex:* 204461
*Key Personnel*
Dir General: Koichiro Matsuura
Dir, UNESCO Publishing: Chandran Nair
Editorial Dir: Michiko Tanaka
Rights & Permissions: Georgina Almeida
Promotion & Sales: Cristina Laje
Annually.


**Critique** (P)
Published by Les Editions de Minuit SA
7 rue Bernard-Palissy, 75006 Paris
*Tel:* (01) 44 39 39 20 *Fax:* (01) 45 44 82 36
*E-mail:* contact@leseditionsdeminuit.fr
*Web Site:* www.leseditionsdeminuit.fr
*Key Personnel*
Contact: Isabelle Chave
General review of publications in France &
  abroad.


ƒ**Directory of Documentation, Libraries &
  Archives Services in Africa** (B)
Published by UNESCO Publishing
Office of Public Information, 7 Place de
  Fontenoy, 75352 Paris 07-SP
*Tel:* (01) 45 68 10 00; (01) 45 68 11 78 *Fax:* (01)
  45 67 16 90; (01) 45 68 55 40
*E-mail:* publishing.promotion@unesco.org
*Web Site:* www.unesco.org/publications
*Telex:* 204461
*Key Personnel*
Dir General: Koichiro Matsuura


**Documentation, technique scientifique et
  commerciale** (J)
Published by Librairie Lavoisier
11 rue Lavoisier, 75384 Paris Cedex 08
*Tel:* (01) 47 40 67 00 *Fax:* (01) 47 40 67 88
*E-mail:* edition@lavoisier.fr
*Web Site:* www.lavoisier.fr
Documentation - Technical, Scientific & Commer-
  cial. Text & summaries in English, French &
  German.


**Donnees statistiques sur l'edition du Livre en
  France** (French Book Production Statistics) (B)
Published by Syndicat National de l'Edition (Na-
  tional Union of Publishers)

115 Blvd Saint Germain, 75006 Paris
*Tel:* (01) 44 41 40 50 *Fax:* (01) 44 41 40 77
*Web Site:* www.snedition.fr
*Key Personnel*
President: Serge Eyrolles


**Les Editeurs et Diffuseurs de Langue francaise**
  (International List of French Language
  Publishers & Distributors) (B)
Published by Editions du Cercle de la Librairie
35, rue Gregoire-de-Tours, 75279 Paris Cedex 06
*Tel:* (01) 44 41 28 61 *Fax:* (01) 44 41 28 65
*Telex:* lifran 270838
Text in French.
First published 1975.
Annually.
ISSN: 0245-1875


ƒ**Index Translationum, International
  Bibliography of Translations** (B)
Published by UNESCO
7, Place de Fontenoy, 75352 Paris 07-SP
*Tel:* (01) 45684310; (01) 45684311 *Fax:* (01)
  45685591
*E-mail:* index@unesco.org
*Web Site:* www.unesco.org/culture/xtrans
*Key Personnel*
Dir General: Kochiro Matsuura
Cumulative bibliography available on CD-ROM
  & Internet only.
Annually.
8, 45 USD
ISBN(s): 92-3-003809-1
ISSN: 1020-1386


ƒ**International Association of Literary Critics
  Review** (J)
Published by International Association of Literary
  Critics
Hotel de Massa, 38 rue du Faubourg, St Jacques,
  75014 Paris
*Tel:* (01) 40513300 *Fax:* (01) 43549299
*Web Site:* www.aicl.org
*Key Personnel*
Founder & President: Yves Gandon


ƒ**Lettre Internationale (Revue)** (International
  Letter Review) (J)
41, rue Bobillot, 75013 Paris
Mailing Address: 27, rue St Ambroise, 75011
  Paris
*Tel:* (01) 42470200; (01) 42470734 *Fax:* (01)
  42338324
Published in 9 languages.


**L'Information litteraire** (P)
Published by Societe d'Edition Les Belles Lettres
95 Blvd Raspail, 75006 Paris
*Tel:* (01) 44398420 *Fax:* (01) 45449288
*E-mail:* courrier@lesbelleslettres.com
*Web Site:* www.lesbelleslettres.com
*Key Personnel*
Founder: Paul Mazon
Dir: Michel Desgranges


**Litterature** (P)
Published by Editions Larousse
21 rue du Montparnasse, 75283 Paris Cedex 06
*Tel:* (01) 44 39 44 00 *Fax:* (01) 44 39 43 43
*E-mail:* tleridon@larousee.fr
*Web Site:* www.larousse.fr
*Key Personnel*
Editor: Francois Tremollieres
Text in French.
First published 1971.
Quarterly.
55 EUR (domestic individuals); 65 EUR (foreign
  individuals); 70 EUR (domestic institutions);
  80 EUR (foreign institutions)
ISSN: 0047-4800

**Livres au Format de Poche** (Paperback Books)
(B)
Published by Electre
35, rue Gregoire-de-Tours, 75279 Paris Cedex 06
*Tel:* (01) 44 41 28 00 *Fax:* (01) 44 41 28 65
*E-mail:* commercial@electre.com
*Web Site:* www.electre.com
Annually.
$43.61 F
ISBN(s): 2-7654-0590-5

**Livres de France** (Books of France) (J)
Published by Electre
35 rue Gregoire-de-Tours, 75279 Paris
*Tel:* (01) 44 41 28 62 *Fax:* (01) 44 41 28 64
*E-mail:* commercial@electre.com; mjvillainne@
electre.com
*Web Site:* www.imaginet.fr/electre
*Key Personnel*
Chief Editor: Jean-Marie Doublet
Guide to published books & trade information.
First published 1982.
11 times/yr.
88 EUR
ISSN: 0294-0019

**Livres Disponibles** (B)
Published by Editions du Cercle de la Librairie
35, rue Gregoire-de-Tours, 75279 Paris Cedex 06
*Tel:* (01) 44 41 28 00 *Fax:* (01) 43 29 68 95
French Books in Print. Also available on mi-
crofiche, from database (Electre), & CD-ROM.
First published 1972.
Annually.
ISSN: 0240-6608

**Livres Hebdo** (Weekly Books) (J)
Published by Electre
35 rue Gregoire-de-Tours, 75279 Cedex 06, Paris
*Tel:* (01) 44412862 *Fax:* (01) 44412864
*E-mail:* livreshebdo@electre.com
*Web Site:* www.electre.com
*Key Personnel*
Dir: Jean-Marie Doublet
Editor: Pierre Louis Rozynes
Book market trade journal.
44 issues/year.
ISSN: 0294-0000

**Magazine litteraire** (Literary Magazine) (P)
Published by Magazine-Expansion
4, rue du Texel, 75014 Paris
*Tel:* (01) 40 47 44 90 *Fax:* (01) 40 47 44 98
*E-mail:* magazine@magazine-litteraire.com
*Web Site:* www.magazine-litteraire.com
*Key Personnel*
Dir: Jean Louis Hue
Monthly.
108 pp
ISSN: 0024-9807

**La Nouvelle Revue francaise** (P)
Published by Editions Gallimard
5 rue Sebastien-Bottin, 75328 Paris Cedex 07
*Tel:* (01) 49 54 42 00 *Fax:* (01) 45 44 94 03
*Web Site:* www.gallimard.fr
*Key Personnel*
Editor: Michel Braudeau
First published 1909.
Quarterly.
352 pp
ISSN: 0029-4802

**Quinzaine litteraire** (Literary Fortnightly) (P)
Published by Selis la Quinzaine Litteraire
34092 Montpelier, 84184 Paris Cedex 05
*Tel:* (01) 48 87 75 87 *Fax:* (01) 48 87 13 01
*Web Site:* www.quinzaine-litteraire.presse.fr
Reviews & summaries of recently published
books.

Bimonthly.
30 pp

**Revue de Litterature comparee** (Review of
Comparative Literature) (P)
Published by Editions Klincksieck
6 rue de la Sorbonne, 75005 Paris
*Tel:* (01) 43 54 47 57 *Fax:* (01) 40 51 73 85
*E-mail:* livre@klincksieck.com
*Web Site:* www.klincksieck.com/revues/RLC/
RLCgeneral.html
*Key Personnel*
Dir: Pierre Brunel
Quarterly.
ISSN: 0035-1466

**Revue des Etudes Italiennes** (Review of Italian
Studies) (P)
Published by Societe des Etudes Italiennes (Paris)
Centre Malesherbes, 108, Blvd Malesherbes,
75850 Paris Cedex 17
*Tel:* (01) 43 18 41 69 *Fax:* (01) 43 18 41 71
*Web Site:* www.rivistasinestesie.it/revue
*Key Personnel*
Dir: Francois Livi *E-mail:* francois.livi@paris4.
sorbonne.fr
Text in French.
First published 1936.
Biannually.
160 pp, 40 EUR
ISSN: 0035-2047

**La Revue des Livres pour Enfants** (Children's
Books Review Magazine) (P)
Published by La Joie par les Livres
8 rue St-Bon, 75004 Paris
*Tel:* (01) 48 87 61 95 *Fax:* (01) 48 87 08 52
*E-mail:* cnle@lajoieparleslivres.com
*Web Site:* www.cockpit.fr/lajoie
*Key Personnel*
Contact: Jacques Vidal-Naquet

# Gambia

**National Bibliography of the Gambia** (B)
Published by Gambia National Library
Reg Pye Lane, Banjul
*Tel:* 26 491; 28 312 *Fax:* 23 776
*E-mail:* national.library@qanet.gm
*Key Personnel*
Dir: Abdou W Mbye

# Georgia

**Sakmatsvilo Literaturis Moambe** (Bulletin of
Children's Literature) (J)
Published by Nakaduli
Ketskhoveli 5, 380007 Tbilisi

# Germany

**∮Adressbuch fuer den deutschsprachigen
Buchhandel** (B)
Published by Buchhaendler-Vereinigung Verlag
GmbH
Weichert Str 20, 63741 Aschaffenburg
*Tel:* (06021) 396471 *Fax:* (06021) 396155
*E-mail:* info@buchhandel.de

*Web Site:* www.buchhandel.de
*Telex:* 413573 buchvd
*Key Personnel*
Dir: Eric Dauphin
Directory of the German-language Book Trade.

**The African Book Publishing Record (ABPR)**
(P)
Published by K G Saur Verlag GmbH, A Gale/
Thomson Learning Company
Unit of Thomson Learning
Ortlerstr 8, 81373 Munich
Mailing Address: Postfach 70 16 20, 81316 Mu-
nich
*Tel:* (089) 76902-172 *Fax:* (089) 76902-250
*E-mail:* info@saur.de
*Web Site:* www.saur.de
*Telex:* 5212067
*Key Personnel*
Contact: Gisela Hochgeladen
Bibliographical tool which offers systematic &
comprehensive coverage of new & forthcoming
African publications in a single source, provid-
ing full bibliographic & acquisitions data. Also
includes an extensive book review section &
features news, reports & articles about African
book trade activities & developments.
Quarterly.
*Parent Company:* Gale
*Ultimate Parent Company:* The Thomson Corpo-
ration

**African Books in Print/Livres Africains
Desponibles (5th ed)** (B)
Published by K G Saur Verlag GmbH, A Gale/
Thomson Learning Company
Unit of Thomson Learning
Ortlerstr 8, 81373 Munich
Mailing Address: Postfach 70 16 20, 81316 Mu-
nich
*Tel:* (089) 76902-172 *Fax:* (089) 76902-250
*E-mail:* info@saur.de
*Web Site:* www.saur.de
*Telex:* 5212067
*Key Personnel*
Contact: Gisela Hochgeladen
Major reference work containing full biblio-
graphic details on 24,000 books, published in
45 African countries by more than 700 pub-
lishers & research institutions with publishing
programs.
5th edition
ISBN(s): 3-598-07684-3
*Parent Company:* Gale
*Ultimate Parent Company:* The Thomson Corpo-
ration

**African Studies Abstracts** (J)
Published by K G Saur Verlag GmbH, A Gale/
Thomson Learning Company
Unit of Thomson Learning
Ortlerstr 8, 81373 Munich
Mailing Address: Postfach 70 16 20, 81316 Mu-
nich
*Tel:* (089) 76902-172 *Fax:* (089) 76902-250
*E-mail:* info@saur.de
*Web Site:* www.saur.de
*Key Personnel*
Contact: Gisela Hochgeladen
Abstracting journal providing coverage of all the
leading journals in the field of African Stud-
ies, Third World countries & development is-
sues. Each issue contains approximately 450
abstracts. Published on behalf of the African
Studies Centre, Leiden, Netherlands.
*Parent Company:* Gale
*Ultimate Parent Company:* The Thomson Corpo-
ration

**Akzente** (P)
Published by Carl Hanser Verlag
Kolbergerstr 22, 81679 Munich
*Tel:* (089) 998300 *Fax:* (089) 984809

*E-mail:* info@hanser.de
*Web Site:* www.hanser.de/verlag

## Archiv fuer Geschichte des Buchwesens
(Archive for History Books) (J)
Published by Buchhaendler-Vereinigung Verlag
GmbH
Weichert Str 20, 63741 Aschaffenburg
*Tel:* (06021) 396471 *Fax:* (06021) 396155
*E-mail:* info@buchhandel.de
*Web Site:* www.buchhandel.de
*Telex:* 413573 buchvd
*Key Personnel*
Dir: Eric Dauphin
First published 1958.
Biannually.
ISBN(s): 3-7657-2187-5
ISSN: 0066-6327

## Besprechungen Annotationen (P)
Published by Einkaufszentrale fur offentliche Bib-
liotheken BmbH
Bismarckstr 3, 72764 Reutlingen
*Tel:* (07121) 144-0 *Fax:* (07121) 144-280
*E-mail:* info@ekz.de
*Web Site:* www.ekz.de

## Boersenblatt fuer den Deutschen Buchhandel/Frankfurt am Main und Leipzig
(Official Journal of the German Book Trade)
(J)
Published by Borsenverein des Deutschen Buch-
handels eV
Grosser Hirschgraben 17-21, 60313 Frankfurt am
Main
*Tel:* (069) 1306 363 *Fax:* (069) 2899 86
*E-mail:* boersenblatt@mvb-online.de
*Web Site:* www.boersenblatt.net
*Telex:* 413573 buchvd
*Key Personnel*
Chief Editor: Dr Hendrik Markgraf
   *E-mail:* markgraf@mvb-online.de
First published 1834.
ISSN: 0940-0044

## Buch Aktuell (Topical Book) (P)
Published by Harenberg Kommunikation Verlags-
und Medien GmbH & Co KG
Koenigswall 21, 44137 Dortmund
*Tel:* (0231) 9056-0 *Fax:* (0231) 9056-110
*E-mail:* post@harenberg.de
*Web Site:* www.harenberg.de

## Buch und Buchhandel in Zahlen (Books & the
Book Trade in Figures) (B)
Published by Borsenverein des Deutschen Buch-
handels eV
Grosser Hirschgraben 17-21, 60313 Frankfurt am
Main
*Tel:* (069) 1306 363 *Fax:* (069) 2899 86
*E-mail:* info@mvb-online.de
*Web Site:* www.buchhandel.de
*Telex:* 413573 buchvd
*Key Personnel*
Contact: Eva Martin
ISBN(s): 3-7657-2357-6

## Buchhaendler heute (The Bookseller Today) (J)
Published by Vereinigten Verlagsanstalten GmbH
VVA Kommunikation, Hoeherweg 278, 40231
Duesseldorf
*Tel:* (0211) 7357-0 *Fax:* (0211) 7357-123
*E-mail:* info@vva.de
*Web Site:* www.vva.de
*Key Personnel*
Editor: Stefan Meutsch
Book Trade.
Monthly.

## BuchJournal (J)
Published by Borsenverein des Deutschen Buch-
handels eV
Grosser Hirschgraben 17/21, 60311 Frankfurt am
Main
*Tel:* (069) 1306 363 *Fax:* (069) 2899 86
*E-mail:* info@mvb-online.de
*Web Site:* www.buchhandel.de
*Key Personnel*
Management: Dr Michael Schoen; Peter Schuck
General magazine for booksellers' customers.
Quarterly.

## BuchMarkt (Book Market) (J)
Published by Verlag K Werner GmbH
Sperberweg 4a, 40668 Meerbusch
*Tel:* (02150) 9191-0 *Fax:* (02150) 919191
*E-mail:* redaktion@buchmarkt.de
*Web Site:* www.buchmarkt.de
*Key Personnel*
Publisher, Man Dir & Editor-in-Chief: Chris-
tian von Zittwitz *Tel:* (02150) 9191-19
   *E-mail:* cvz@buchmarkt.de
Journal for the book trade in German-speaking
areas.

## Buchreport (Book Report) (J)
Published by Harenberg Kommunikation Verlags-
und Medien-GmbH & Co KG
Koenigswall 21, 44137 Dortmund
*Tel:* (0231) 9056-0 *Fax:* (0231) 9056-110
*E-mail:* post@harenberg.de
*Web Site:* www.harenberg.de
*Key Personnel*
Publisher: Bodo Harenberg *Tel:* (0231) 9056-104
   *Fax:* (0231) 9056-112
Magazine for booksellers in German-speaking
areas.
First published 1970.
Weekly.
ISSN: 1615-0732

## Buecherkarren (Book Cart) (J)
Published by Verlag Volk & Welt GmbH
Oranienstr 164/165, 10969 Berlin
*Tel:* (030) 61689530 *Fax:* (030) 61689540 *Cable:*
VOLKWELT BERLIN
*Key Personnel*
Editor: Matthias Kotyrba
List of company publications to the general
reader.
Quarterly.
Free

## Buecherkommentare (Book Commentaries) (P)
Published by Rombach GmbH Druck und Ver-
lagshaus & Co
Unterwerkstr 5, 79115 Freiburg
*Tel:* (0761) 4500-2135 *Fax:* (0761) 4500-2125
*E-mail:* info@buchverlag.rombach.de
*Web Site:* www.rombach.de/buchverlag
*Telex:* uber 772728
*Key Personnel*
Management: Andreas Hodeige
Sales: Melanie Panzer *Tel:* (0761) 4500-2135
   *E-mail:* panzer@buchverlag.rombach.de

## Bulletin Jugend und Literatur (Youth &
Literature Bulletin) (P)
Published by Neuland-Verlagsgesellschaft mbH
PO Box 1422, 21496 Geesthacht
*Tel:* (04152) 81342 *Fax:* (04152) 81343
*E-mail:* vertrieb@neuland.com
*Web Site:* www.neuland.com
*Key Personnel*
Editor: Frank Lindermann
First published 1969.
Monthly.
36 pp
ISSN: 0045-351X

## Deutsche Nationalbibliographie (German
National Bibliography) (J)
Published by MVB Marketing- und Verlagsser-
vice des Buchhandels GmbH
Grosser Hirschgraben 17/21, 60311 Frankfurt am
Main
Mailing Address: Postfach 1004 42, 60004 Frank-
furt am Main
*Tel:* (069) 1306-0 *Fax:* (069) 1306255
*E-mail:* info@mvb-online.de
*Web Site:* www.mvb-online.de; www.mvb-
boersenblatt.de
*Key Personnel*
Contact: Marlies Ney

## ∮Dictionnaire pratique de l'Edition en 20
Langues (Woerterbuch des Verlagswesens in
20 Sprachen) (Publishers Practical Dictionary
in Twenty Languages) (B)
Published by K G Saur Verlag GmbH, A Gale/
Thomson Learning Company
Unit of Thomson Learning
Ortlerstr 8, 81373 Munich
Mailing Address: Postfach 70 16 20, 81316 Mu-
nich
*Tel:* (089) 76902-172 *Fax:* (089) 76902-250
*E-mail:* info@saur.de
*Web Site:* www.saur.de
*Telex:* 5212067
*Key Personnel*
Contact: Gisela Hochgeladen
*Parent Company:* Gale
*Ultimate Parent Company:* The Thomson Corpo-
ration

## Directory of Special Collections in Western
Europe (B)
Published by K G Saur Verlag GmbH, A Gale/
Thomson Learning Company
Unit of Thomson Learning
Ortlerstr 8, 81373 Munich
Mailing Address: Postfach 70 16 20, 81316 Mu-
nich
*Tel:* (089) 76902-172 *Fax:* (089) 76902-250
*E-mail:* info@saur.de
*Web Site:* www.saur.de
*Key Personnel*
Contact: Gisela Hochgeladen
*Parent Company:* Gale
*Ultimate Parent Company:* The Thomson Corpo-
ration

## Flugpost - Informationsdienst Luftfahrt
(Airmail-Aviation Information Service) (P)
Published by Flugpost Verlag Peter Pletschacher
Kolpingring 16, 82041 Oberhaching
*Tel:* (089) 613890-0 *Fax:* (089) 613890-10
*E-mail:* aviatic@aviatic.de
*Web Site:* www.aviatic.de
*Key Personnel*
Man Dir: Peter Pletschacher
Newsletter.
First published 1989.
Weekly.
ISSN: 0938-3883

## ∮Frankfurter Book Fair (Frankfurt Book Fair)
(B)
Published by Ausstellungs-und Messe-GmbH des
Borsenvereins des Deutschen Buchhandels
Reineckstr 3, 63013 Frankfurt am Main
Mailing Address: Postfach 100116, 60001 Frank-
furt am Main
*Tel:* (069) 2102-0 *Fax:* (069) 2102-227; (069)
2102-277
*E-mail:* info@book-fair.com
*Web Site:* www.frankfurter-buchmesse.de
*Key Personnel*
President & Chief Executive Officer: Volker Neu-
mann
Vice President: Joachim Kehl
Chief Financial Officer: Gabriele Teucher

∮**Gesamtverzeichnis des deutschsprachigen Schrifttums** (Bibliography of German Language Publications) (B)
Published by K G Saur Verlag GmbH, A Gale/ Thomson Learning Company
Unit of Thomson Learning
Ortlerstr 8, 81373 Munich
Mailing Address: Postfach 70 16 20, 81316 Munich
*Tel:* (089) 76902-172 *Fax:* (089) 76902-250
*E-mail:* info@saur.de
*Web Site:* www.saur.de
*Telex:* 5212067
*Key Personnel*
Contact: Gisela Hochgeladen
Covers 1700-1965.
*Parent Company:* Gale
*Ultimate Parent Company:* The Thomson Corporation

∮**Gesamtverzeichnis des deutschsprachigen Schrifttums ausserhalb des Buchhandels** (Bibliography of German Language Publications Outside the Booktrade) (B)
Published by K G Saur Verlag GmbH, A Gale/ Thomson Learning Company
Unit of Thomson Learning
Ortlerstr 8, 81373 Munich
Mailing Address: Postfach 70 16 20, 81316 Munich
*Tel:* (089) 76902-172 *Fax:* (089) 76902-250
*E-mail:* info@saur.de
*Web Site:* www.saur.de
*Telex:* 5212067
*Key Personnel*
Contact: Gisela Hochgeladen
Covers 1966-1980.
*Parent Company:* Gale
*Ultimate Parent Company:* The Thomson Corporation

∮**Gesamtverzeichnis Deutschsprachiger Hochschulschriften 1966-1980** (Bibliography of German Language Academic Publications 1966-1980) (B)
Published by K G Saur Verlag GmbH, A Gale/ Thomson Learning Company
Unit of Thomson Learning
Ortlerstr 8, 81373 Munich
Mailing Address: Postfach 70 16 20, 81316 Munich
*Tel:* (089) 76902-172 *Fax:* (089) 76902-250
*E-mail:* info@saur.de
*Web Site:* www.saur.de
*Telex:* 5212067
*Key Personnel*
Contact: Gisela Hochgeladen
*Parent Company:* Gale
*Ultimate Parent Company:* The Thomson Corporation

∮**Guide to Microforms in Print** (B)
Published by K G Saur Verlag GmbH, A Gale/ Thomson Learning Company
Unit of Thomson Learning
Ortlerstr 8, 81373 Munich
Mailing Address: Postfach 70 16 20, 81316 Munich
*Tel:* (089) 76902-172 *Fax:* (089) 76902-250
*E-mail:* info@saur.de
*Web Site:* www.saur.de
*Telex:* 5212067
*Key Personnel*
Contact: Gisela Hochgeladen
*Parent Company:* Gale
*Ultimate Parent Company:* The Thomson Corporation

**Guide to Microforms in Print: Author/Title** (P)
Published by K G Saur Verlag GmbH, A Gale/ Thomson Learning Company
Unit of Thomson Learning

Ortlerstr 8, 81373 Munich
Mailing Address: Postfach 70 16 20, 81316 Munich
*Tel:* (089) 76902-172 *Fax:* (089) 76902-250
*E-mail:* info@saur.de
*Web Site:* www.saur.de
*Telex:* 5212067
*Key Personnel*
Contact: Gisela Hochgeladen
Cumulative alphabetical list of books, journals & other materials available from US & foreign publishers in microform.
Annual.
1999: 2,100 pp, 430 USD
ISBN(s): 3-598-11392-7
*Parent Company:* Gale
*Ultimate Parent Company:* The Thomson Corporation

**Hebbeljahrbuch** (Hebbel Year Book) (P)
Published by Westholsteinische Verlagsanstalt und Verlagsdruckerei Boyens & Co
Wulf-Isebrand-Platz, 25767 Heide
*Tel:* (0481) 6886-0 *Fax:* (0481) 6886-469
*E-mail:* boyens@boyens-medien.de
*Web Site:* www.sh-nordsee.de
*Key Personnel*
Dir: Inken Boyens; Sonke Boyens
ISSN: 0073-1560

**Die Horen** (P)
Published by Wirtschaftsverlag NW, Verlag Fuer neue Wissenschaft GmbH
Buergermeister-Smidtstr 74-76, 27568 Bremerhaven
Mailing Address: Postfach 101110, 27511 Bremerhaven
*Tel:* (0471) 945440 *Fax:* (0471) 9454477
*E-mail:* info@nw-verlag.de
*Web Site:* www.nw-verlag.de
First published 1955.
Quarterly.
31 EUR & postage/yr
ISSN: 0018-4942

**Imprimatur** (J)
Published by Gesellschaft der Bibliophilen
Kreuzberger Ring 7b-d, 65205 Wiesbaden
*Tel:* (0611) 530 0 *Fax:* (0611) 530 560
*E-mail:* service@harrassowitz.de
*Web Site:* www.harrassowitz.de
Among other things history of books, printers, bookmindedness.
ISSN: 0073-5620

**International African Bibliography** (J)
Published by K G Saur Verlag GmbH, A Gale/ Thomson Learning Company
Unit of Thomson Learning
Ortlerstr 8, 81373 Munich
Mailing Address: Postfach 70 16 20, 81316 Munich
*Tel:* (089) 76902-172 *Fax:* (089) 76902-250
*E-mail:* info@saur.de
*Web Site:* www.saur.de
*Telex:* 5212067
*Key Personnel*
Contact: Gisela Hochgeladen
Indexes the latest books, articles & papers published internationally on Africa.
Quarterly.
*Parent Company:* Gale
*Ultimate Parent Company:* The Thomson Corporation

∮**International Book Trade Directory** (B)
Published by K G Saur Verlag GmbH, A Gale/ Thomson Learning Company
Unit of Thomson Learning
Ortlerstr 8, 81373 Munich

Mailing Address: Postfach 70 16 20, 81316 Munich
*Tel:* (089) 76902-172 *Fax:* (089) 76902-250
*E-mail:* info@saur.de
*Web Site:* www.saur.de
*Telex:* 5212067
*Key Personnel*
Contact: Gisela Hochgeladen
Listing details of booksellers in 134 countries outside the USA & Canada.
*Parent Company:* Gale
*Ultimate Parent Company:* The Thomson Corporation

∮**International Cataloguing & Bibliographic Control (ICBC)** (J)
Published by IFLA UBCIM Programme
c/o Die Deutsche Bibliothek, Adickesallee 1, 60322 Frankfurt am Main
*Tel:* (069) 15251063 *Fax:* (069) 15251010
*Web Site:* www.ifla.org/vi/3/admin/icbc.htm
*Key Personnel*
President: Alex Byrne
International forum for the exchange of views & research results by members of the library & information management profession.
Quarterly.

∮**Jahrbuch der Auktionspreise fuer Buecher, Handschriften und Autographen** (German Book Prices Current) (B)
Published by Dr Ernst Hauswedell & Co
Haldenstr 30, 70376 Stuttgart
Mailing Address: Postfach 140155, 70071 Stuttgart
*Tel:* (0711) 54 99 71-11 *Fax:* (0711) 54 99 71-21
*E-mail:* hiersemann.hauswedell.verlage@t-online.de
*Web Site:* www.hauswedell.de
*Key Personnel*
Contact: Reinhold Busch
Publication contains Book auction prices in Germany, Austria, Switzerland & the Netherlands.

**LiteraturNachrichten** (Literary News) (P)
Published by Society for the Promotion of African, Asian & Latin American Literature
Reineckstr 3, 60313 Frankfurt am Main
Mailing Address: Postfach 10 01 16, 60001 Frankfurt am Main
*Tel:* (069) 2102247 *Fax:* (069) 2102227
*E-mail:* litprom@book-fair.com
*Web Site:* www.litprom.de
*Key Personnel*
Editor: Peter Ripken
The only quarterly in Germany to report about literary developments in the Southern hemisphere.
First published 1983.
Quarterly.
36 pp, 15 EUR
ISSN: 0935-7807

∮**Microform & Imaging Review** (J)
Published by K G Saur Verlag GmbH, A Gale/ Thomson Learning Company
Unit of Thomson Learning
Ortlerstr 8, 81373 Munich
Mailing Address: Postfach 70 16 20, 81316 Munich
*Tel:* (089) 76902-172 *Fax:* (089) 76902-250
*E-mail:* info@saur.de
*Web Site:* www.saur.de
*Telex:* 5212067
*Key Personnel*
Contact: Gisela Hochgeladen
*Parent Company:* Gale
*Ultimate Parent Company:* The Thomson Corporation

**Neue deutsche Literatur** (New German
   Literature) (P)
Published by Aufbau-Verlag GmbH
Neue Promenade 6, 10178 Berlin
*Tel:* (030) 283940 *Fax:* (030) 28394100
*E-mail:* info@aufbau-verlag.de
*Web Site:* www.aufbau-verlag.de
*Key Personnel*
Editor: Claudia Gehre
Periodical for German literature & reviews.
First published 1953.
Bimonthly.
192 pp, 10 GBP; 15.37 USD
ISSN: 0028-3150

**Neue Rundschau** (New Review) (P)
Published by Martin Bauer
Hedderichstr 114, 60596 Frankfurt am Main
*Tel:* (069) 6062-222 *Fax:* (069) 6062-214
*E-mail:* bauersfv@aol.com
*Web Site:* www.fischerverlage.de
First published 1890.
Quarterly.
ISBN(s): 3-10-809045-3
ISSN: 0028-3347
*Parent Company:* S Fischer Verlag, Berlin

∮**Publishers' International ISBN Directory** (B)
Published by K G Saur Verlag GmbH, A Gale/
   Thomson Learning Company
Unit of Thomson Learning
Ortlerstr 8, 81373 Munich
Mailing Address: Postfach 70 16 20, 81316 Mu-
   nich
*Tel:* (089) 76902-172 *Fax:* (089) 76902-250
*E-mail:* info@saur.de
*Web Site:* www.saur.de
*Telex:* 5212067
*Key Personnel*
Contact: Gisela Hochgeladen
*Parent Company:* Gale
*Ultimate Parent Company:* The Thomson Corpo-
   ration

**Quickborn** (P)
Published by Quickborn, Vereinigung fuer
   Niederdeutsche Sprache und Literatur eV
Alexanderstr 16, 20099 Hamburg
*Tel:* (040) 24 08 09 *Fax:* (040) 3603 0767 15
*E-mail:* info@quickborn-ev.de
*Key Personnel*
Editor: Dirk Roemmer
Magazine for low-German language & literature,
   theatre & radio. Text in German.
First published 1907.
Quarterly.
ISSN: 0170-7558

**Schriften und Zeugnisse zur Buchgeschichte**
   (B)
Published by Harrassowitz Verlag
Kreuzberger Ring 7 b-c, 65174 Wiesbaden
*Tel:* (0611) 5300 *Fax:* (0611) 530560
*E-mail:* service@harrassowitz.de
*Web Site:* www.harrassowitz.de
*Key Personnel*
Library Services: Knut Dorn
History of books, the booktrade, publishers &
   printers. Text in German.
First published 1992.
Irregularly.
ISSN: 0942-4709

**Sinn und Form** (Contents & Form) (P)
Published by Akademie der Kunste, Aufbau-
   Verlag Berlin-Brandenburg
Tucholskystr 2, 10117 Berlin
*Tel:* (030) 28884880 *Fax:* (030) 28884884
*E-mail:* sinnform@adk.de
*Web Site:* www.sinn-und-form.de

*Key Personnel*
Chief Editor: Sebastian Kleinschmidt
Contributions to literature. Articles on literature
   & humanities.
First published 1949.
Bimonthly.
144 pp, 9 EUR
ISSN: 0037-5756

∮**Subject Guide to Microforms in Print** (B)
Published by K G Saur Verlag GmbH, A Gale/
   Thomson Learning Company
Unit of Thomson Learning
Ortlerstr 8, 81373 Munich
Mailing Address: Postfach 70 16 20, 81316 Mu-
   nich
*Tel:* (089) 76902-172 *Fax:* (089) 76902-250
*E-mail:* info@saur.de
*Web Site:* www.saur.de
*Telex:* 5212067
*Key Personnel*
Contact: Gisela Hochgeladen
*Parent Company:* Gale
*Ultimate Parent Company:* The Thomson Corpo-
   ration

**Der Uebersetzer** (The Translator) (J)
Published by Verband Deutschsprachiger Ue-
   bersetzer Literarischer und Wissenschaftlicher
   Werke eV (VDU)
Fuerststr 17, 72072 Tuebingen
*Tel:* (089) 2710994 *Fax:* (089) 2718272
*Key Personnel*
Editor: Klaus Birkenhauer; Eva Bornemann
Text in German.
First published 1964.
Monthly.

**Verlage 2002/2003, Deutschland, Oesterreich,
   Schweiz und auslaendischer Verlage mit
   deutschen Auslieferungen** (Publishers
   2002/2003 Germany, Austria, Switzerland &
   Foreign Publishers with German Distributions)
   (B)
Published by Verlag der Schillerbuchhandlung
   Hans Banger OHG
Guldenbachstr 1, 50935 Cologne
*Tel:* (0221) 46014-0 *Fax:* (0221) 46014-25
*E-mail:* banger@banger.de
*Web Site:* www.banger.de
*Key Personnel*
Editor: Ruth Jepsen
Available on CD-ROM.
Annually.
1,008 pp
ISBN(s): 3-87856-096-6
ISSN: 1439-0736

**Verlagsventretungen 2002/2003, Deutschland,
   Oesterreich, Schweiz** (B)
Published by Verlag der Schillerbuchhandlung
   Hans Banger OHG
Guldenbachstr 1, 50935 Cologne
*Tel:* (0221) 46014-0 *Fax:* (0221) 46014-25
*E-mail:* banger@banger.de
*Web Site:* www.banger.de
*Key Personnel*
Editor: Ruth Jepsen
Annually.
448 pp
ISBN(s): 3-87856-098-2
ISSN: 0944-3754

**Verzeichnis Lieferbarer Buecher** (German
   Books in Print) (B)
Published by K G Saur Verlag GmbH, A Gale/
   Thomson Learning Company
Unit of Thomson Learning
Ortlerstr 8, 81373 Munich
Mailing Address: Postfach 70 16 20, 81316 Mu-
   nich

*Tel:* (089) 76902-172 *Fax:* (089) 76902-250
*E-mail:* info@saur.de
*Web Site:* www.saur.de
*Telex:* 5212067
Editor, Buchhaendler-Verinigung, Frankfurt.
*Parent Company:* Gale
*Ultimate Parent Company:* The Thomson Corpo-
   ration

∮**Who's Who at the Frankfurt Book Fair** (B)
Published by K G Saur Verlag GmbH, A Gale/
   Thomson Learning Company
Unit of Thomson Learning
Ortlerstr 8, 81373 Munich
Mailing Address: Postfach 70 16 20, 81316 Mu-
   nich
*Tel:* (089) 76902-172 *Fax:* (089) 76902-250
*E-mail:* info@saur.de
*Web Site:* www.saur.de
*Telex:* 5212067
An international publishers' guide. A listing of
   publishers at the Frankfurt Book Fair, their ad-
   dresses & the representatives chosen to attend
   the fair & their functions.
*Parent Company:* Gale
*Ultimate Parent Company:* The Thomson Corpo-
   ration

**Wolfenbuetteler Notizen zur Buchgeschichte**
   (Wolfenbuetteler Notes on the History of
   Books) (J)
Published by Harrassowitz Verlag
Kreuzberger Ring 7b-d, 65205 Wiesbaden
*Tel:* (0611) 530-0 *Fax:* (0611) 530-560 (orders)
*E-mail:* service@harrassowitz.de
*Web Site:* www.harrassowitz.de
Biannually.
ISSN: 0341-2253

**Zeitschriften 2002
   Deutserland-Oesterreich-Schweiz** (German
   Language Periodical) (B)
Published by Verlag der Schillerbuchhandlung
   Hans Banger OHG
Guldenbachstr 1, 50935 Cologne
*Tel:* (0221) 46014-0 *Fax:* (0221) 46014-25
*E-mail:* banger@banger.de
*Web Site:* www.banger.de
*Key Personnel*
Editor: Ruth Jepsen
Available on CD-ROM.
Annually.
1,427 pp
ISBN(s): 3-87856-094-X
ISSN: 1439-0728

# Ghana

**Asemka** (J)
Published by University of Cape Coast
University Post Office, Cape Coast
*Tel:* (042) 32483; (042) 32480 (ext 220)
   *Fax:* (042) 32485
*E-mail:* ucclib@ucc.gn.apc.org
*Telex:* 2552
*Key Personnel*
Editor: Y S Boafo
Publishes studies in literature (mostly African) &
   languages.
First published 1974.
Annually.
10 USD (individuals); 20 USD (institutions)
ISSN: 0855-000X

**Ghana National Bibliography** (J)
Published by George Padmore Research Library
   on African Affairs
PO Box 2970, Accra

*Tel:* (021) 223526
*E-mail:* padmoreslib@yahoo.com
*Key Personnel*
Librarian: O M Tenkorang
First published 1965.
Biannually with annual cummulation.
60 USD
ISSN: 0855-0993

# Greece

**Nea Hestia** (P)
Published by G C Eleftheroudakis SA
Nikis 4, 105 63 Athens
*Tel:* 2103222255 *Fax:* 2103239821
*Key Personnel*
Editor: P Charis
Text in Greek.
First published 1927.
Bimonthly.
324 USD
ISSN: 0028-1735

# Guatemala

**Alero** (Eaves) (P)
Published by Universidad de San Carlos de
   Guatemala
Ciudad Universitaria, Zona 12, Edificio de Recto-
   ria Of 307, 01012 Guatemala
*Tel:* (02) 760790 *Fax:* (02) 767221
*Key Personnel*
Editor: Rafael Cuevas del Cid
Text in Spanish.
First published 1973.
Bimonthly.
3.50 GTQ
ISSN: 0252-8711

# Guyana

**Guyanese National Bibliography** (B)
Published by National Library
76-77 Main & Church St, Georgetown
Mailing Address: PO Box 10240, Georgetown
*Tel:* (02) 227-4053; (02) 226-2690; (02) 226-
   2699; (02) 227-4052 *Fax:* (02) 227-4053
*E-mail:* natlib@sdnp.org.gy
*Web Site:* www.landofsixpeoples.com/gynewsjs.
   htm
*Key Personnel*
Editor: Karen Sills
Text in English.
First published 1973.
Quarterly.
100 GYD or 30 USD

# Hong Kong

**PEN News** (P)
Published by Hong Kong PEN Centre (Chinese-
   Speaking)
Mongkok Post Office, Kowloon
Mailing Address: PO Box 78521, Mongkok Post
   Office, Kowloon
Text in Chinese.

# Hungary

ƒ**Helikon Irodalomtudomanyi Szemle** (Helikon
   Review of General & Comparative Literature)
   (J)
Published by Magyar Tudomanyos Akademia
   Irodalomtudomanyi Intezete (Institute of Lit-
   erary Studies of the Hungarian Academy of
   Sciences)
Menesi ut 11-13, 1118 Budapest
*Tel:* (01) 1665938
Summaries published in French, Russian & Ger-
   man.

**The Hungarian Quarterly** (P)
Published by The Hungarian Quarterly Society
Naphegy Tier 8, Budapest 1016
*Tel:* (01) 3756722 *Fax:* (01) 3188297
*E-mail:* hungq@hungary.com
*Web Site:* www.hungarianquarterly.com
*Telex:* 224371; 225859
*Key Personnel*
Editor: Miklos Vajda
Text in English.
4 issues/yr.
160 pp
ISBN(s): 963-7262; 963-7560
ISSN: 0028-5390

**Literatura** (P)
Published by Akademiai Kiado
Prielle Kornelia u 19/D, 1117 Budapest
Mailing Address: PO Box 245, 1516 Budapest
*Tel:* (01) 4648282 *Fax:* (01) 464 8251
*E-mail:* info@akkrt.hu
*Web Site:* www.akkrt.hu
*Telex:* 226228 aknyoh
*Warehouse:* Szentendrei str 89-93, 1033 Budapest
   *Tel:* (01) 437-2443
*Orders to: Fax:* (01) 464 8221 *E-mail:* journals@
   akkrt.hu

# Iceland

**Arsskyrsla** (B)
Published by Borgarbokasafn
Tryggvagotu 15, 101 Reykjavik
*Tel:* 563 1750 *Fax:* 563 1705
*E-mail:* borgarbokasafn@borgarbokasafn.is
*Web Site:* www.borgarbokasafn.is
ISBN(s): 9979-9326

**Skirnir: Journal of the Icelandic Literary
   Society** (J)
Published by Hid Islenzka Bokmenntafelag (Ice-
   landic Literary Society)
Skeifan 3B, 128 Reykjavik
Mailing Address: PO Box 8935, 128 Reykjavik
*Tel:* 5889060 *Fax:* 5889095
*E-mail:* hib@islandia.is
*Web Site:* www.hib.is
*Key Personnel*
Editor: Sveinn Yngvi Egilsson; Svavar H Svavars-
   son
Icelandic cultural studies.
First published 1827.
Biannually.
41 USD
ISSN: 0256-8446

# India

ƒ**African Books Newsletter** (J)
Published by K K Roy (Pvt) Ltd
55 Gariahat Rd, Kolkata 700019
Mailing Address: PO Box 10210, Kolkata 700019
*Tel:* (033) 475-4872; (033) 475-5069
*Key Personnel*
Editor: K K Roy
Check list of recent books published in English,
   arranged according to subject.
First published 1965.
Monthly.
52 USD
ISSN: 0001-9941

ƒ**Akavita** (Blank Verse) (P)
Published by Samkaleen Prakashan
2762, Rajguru Marg, Paharganj, New Delhi
   110055
*Tel:* (011) 3523520; (011) 3518197
Text in Hindi.
First published 1976.
Quarterly.
Inland: 80 INR/yr; Overseas: 24 USD/yr (sea-
   mail); 32 USD/yr (airmail)
ISSN: 0970-096X

ƒ**Art & Poetry Today** (P)
Published by Samkaleen Prakashan
2762, Rajguru Marg, Paharganj, New Delhi
   110055
*Tel:* (011) 3523520; (011) 3518197
Text in English.
First published 1976.
Quarterly.
Inland: 80 INR/yr; $24 USD/yr (foreign, sea-
   mail); $32 USD/yr (foreign, airmail)
ISSN: 0970-1001

ƒ**Asian Books Newsletter** (J)
Published by K K Roy (Pvt) Ltd
55 Gariahat Rd, Kolkata 700019
Mailing Address: PO Box 10210, Kolkata 700019
*Tel:* (033) 475-4872; (033) 475-5069
*Key Personnel*
Editor: K K Roy
Checklist of recent books published in English,
   arranged according to subject.
First published 1966.
Monthly.
48 USD
ISSN: 0004-4547

**Creative Forum** (P)
Published by Bahri Publications
997A/9 Gobindpuri, Kalkaji, New Delhi 110019
Mailing Address: PO Box 4453, Kalkaji, New
   Delhi 110019
*Tel:* (011) 6445710; (011) 6448606 *Fax:* (011)
   6445710
*E-mail:* bahrius@vsnl.com
*Web Site:* business.vsnl.com/bahripublications
*Key Personnel*
Publisher & Editor: Ujjal Singh Bahri
A journal of current literary practices.
First published 1989.
Quarterly.
400 INR or 90 USD (institutions); 300 INR or 60
   USD (individuals)

**D K Fortnight** (J)
Published by D K Publishers' Distributors (P) Ltd
4834/24, Ansari Rd, Darya Ganj, New Delhi 110
   002
*Tel:* (011) 23278368; (011) 23278584; (011)
   23279215; (011) 23261465 *Fax:* (011)
   23264368
*E-mail:* info@dkpd.com; order@dkpd.com
   (orders)

*Web Site:* www.dkpdindia.com
*Telex:* 31-66778
*Key Personnel*
Editor: Praveen Mittal
Lists the new books released during each fortnight in the market by various publishers to
reach the information to the target audience as
early as possible; also contains an editorial on
book industry.

**⨍D K Yearbook** (B)
Published by D K Publishers' Distributors (P) Ltd
4834/24, Ansari Rd, Darya Ganj, New Delhi 110
002
*Tel:* (011) 23278368; (011) 23278584; (011)
23279215; (011) 23261465 *Fax:* (011)
23264368
*E-mail:* info@dkpd.com; order@dkpd.com
(orders)
*Web Site:* www.dkpdindia.com
*Telex:* 31-66778
*Key Personnel*
Chief Editor: Parmil Mittal
Published in English; covers social sciences, hu-
manities & sciences.
Annually.

**Directory of Indian Publishers & Distributors**
(B)
Published by Indian Bibliographic Centre
76 Chandrika Colony, Sigra, Varanasi 221 001
*Tel:* (0542) 221337 *Fax:* (0542) 221337
*E-mail:* rishipub@satyam.net.in
Reference book for librarians, publishers, distribu-
tors & booksellers.
ISBN(s): 81-85131-05-8

**Indian Author** (P)
Published by Authors Guild of India
F-12 Jangpura Ext, New Delhi 110014
*Tel:* (011) 4315063; (011) 6847950 *Fax:* (011)
3321189
Newsletter.
First published 1976.
Quarterly.
30 INR; 5 USD

**Indian Book Industry** (J)
Published by Federation of Indian Publishers
18/6 Institutional Area, near JNU, New Delhi 110
067
*Tel:* (011) 6964847; (011) 6852263 *Fax:* (011)
6864054
*E-mail:* fip1@satyam.net.in
*Web Site:* www.fiponweb.com
Publication devoted to production, promotion &
distribution of books. There are six issues per
year & every issue has a focus on a particular
subject.
Bimonthly.

**Indian Books & Foreign Books** (B)
Published by Researchco Reprints
25-B/2, New Rohtak Rd, New Delhi 110005
*Tel:* (011) 5781565 *Fax:* (011) 7276256
*Telex:* 31-79055 *Cable:* SEARCHBOOK
Annual bibliography of books in English.

**Indian Books in Print** (J)
Published by Indian Bibliographies Bureau
219 Kadambari, 19 IX Rohini, Delhi 110085
*Tel:* (011) 7564112; (011) 7553211 *Fax:* (011)
7256502
*E-mail:* ibb_indian_bibliographies@hotmail.com
*Key Personnel*
Editor: Bhawna Singh; Sher Singh
Assistant Manager: Ms Bimla Rawat
Bibliography of Indian books published in En-
glish.
First published 1969.
Annually.

21st: 3,400 pp, 188 USD
ISSN: 0971-1589

**Indian Horizons** (J)
Published by Indian Council for Cultural Rela-
tions
Azad Bhavan, Indraprastha Estate, New Delhi
110002
*Tel:* (011) 3379309; (011) 3379310 *Fax:* (011)
3778639
*E-mail:* iccr@giasdl01.vsnl.net.in
*Telex:* 31-61860
*Key Personnel*
Editor: Amit Dasgupta
A journal in English on Indian Culture & the arts
& of cultural relations past & present between
India & the world. Contents include articles,
fiction & review.
First published 1952.
Quarterly.
40 USD
ISBN(s): 0019-7203
ISSN: 0378-2964

**Indian Journal of Applied Linguistics** (P)
Published by Bahri Publications
997A/9 Gobindpuri, Kalkaji, New Delhi 110019
Mailing Address: PO Box 4453, Kalkaji, New
Delhi 110019
*Tel:* (011) 6445710; (011) 6448606 *Fax:* (011)
6445710
*E-mail:* bahrius@vsnl.com
*Key Personnel*
Editor: Mr Ujjal Singh Bahri
New theoretical & methodologist ideas & re-
search from several disciplines engaged in Ap-
plied Linguistics.
First published 1975.
Biannually.
160 pp, 400 INR or 90 USD
ISSN: 0379-0037

**Indian Literary Review** (P)
Published by Indian Literary Review Editions
T-58 D C M School Marg, New Rohtak Rd, New
Delhi 110005
*Key Personnel*
Editor: Devindra Kohli; Suresh Kohli
First published 1978.
Triannually.
60 INR (individuals); 75 INR (institutions)

**Indian Literature** (P)
Published by National Academy of Letters:
Sahitya Akademi
Rabindra Bhavan, 35, Ferozeshah Rd, New Delhi
110001
*Tel:* (011) 3386626; (011) 3386627; (011)
3386628; (011) 3386629; (011) 3387386; (011)
3386088 *Fax:* (011) 3382428
*E-mail:* secy@sahitya-akademi.org
*Web Site:* www.sahitya-akademi.org
*Telex:* 31; 65445 SAND IN
Text in English.
Bimonthly.

**Indian National Bibliography** (J)
Published by Central Reference Library
Dept of Culture, Belvedere, Kolkata 700027
*Tel:* (033) 4791722 *Fax:* (033) 4791722
*E-mail:* crlinb@cal3.vsnl.net.in
*Web Site:* www.crlindia.org
*Key Personnel*
Contact: K K Kochukoshy
Index Indiana: journal for Indian language period-
icals, published quarterly in Roman script.
Monthly with annual cumulation.

**The Indian PEN** (P)
Published by Indian PEN Centre

Theosophy Hall, 40 New Marine Lines, Mumbai
400 020
*Tel:* (022) 2032175
*Key Personnel*
Editor: Mr Nissim Ezekiel
Text in English.
First published 1934.
Quarterly.
42 INR or 9 USD
ISSN: 0019-6053

**Indian Publishers' Directory** (B)
Published by Mukherjee & Co Pvt Ltd
P-27B, CIT Rd, Scheme 52, Kolkata WB 700014
*Tel:* (033) 341606

**International Journal of Communication** (P)
Published by Bahri Publications
997A/9 Gobindpuri, Kalkaji, New Delhi 110019
Mailing Address: PO Box 4453, Kalkaji, New
Delhi 110019
*Tel:* (011) 6445710; (011) 6448606 *Fax:* (011)
6445710
*E-mail:* bahrius@vsnl.com
*Key Personnel*
Publisher & Editor: Ujjal Singh Bahri
First published 1991.
Biannually.
240 pp, 400 INR or 90 USD

**International Journal of Translation** (P)
Published by Bahri Publications
997A/9 Gobindpuri, Kalkaji, New Delhi 110019
Mailing Address: PO Box 4453, Kalkaji, New
Delhi 110019
*Tel:* (011) 6445710; (011) 6448606 *Fax:* (011)
6445710
*E-mail:* bahrius@vsnl.com
*Key Personnel*
Publisher & Editor: Ujjal Singh Bahri
A review of translation studies.
First published 1989.
Biannually.
160 pp, 400 INR or 90 USD
ISSN: 0970-9819

**Katha-Sahitya** (J)
Published by Mitra & Ghosh Publishers Pvt Ltd
10 Shyama Charan Dey St, Kolkata 700073
*Tel:* (033) 2241 26420
*Key Personnel*
Contact: Roy Sabitendranath *Tel:* (033) 415 5889;
415 4597
Literary journal. Regular features: editorial, book
review, magazine news, news about authors.
Special issues: Puja issue, published on the eve
of Durga Puja & book fair issue published on
the eve of Kolkata Book Fair.
First published 1949.
Monthly.
128 pp, 6 IRS per copy. Annual subscriptions 145
IRS for India
ISSN: 0971-7137

**Lalit Kala** (P)
Published by Lalit Kala Akademi
c/o National Academy of Art, Rabindra Bhavan,
New Delhi 110001
*Tel:* (011) 23387241
*Web Site:* www.lalitkala.org.in
Ancient arts.

**Language Forum** (P)
Published by Bahri Publications
997A/9 Gobindpuri, Kalkaji, New Delhi 110019
Mailing Address: PO Box 4453, Kalkaji, New
Delhi 110019
*Tel:* (011) 6445710; (011) 6448606 *Fax:* (011)
6445710
*E-mail:* bahrius@vsnl.com
*Key Personnel*
Editor: Mr Ujjal Singh Bahri

Journal of language & literature. Publishes papers on curriculum planning, linguistic analyses of Indian languages & dialects, comparative literature & linguistics & literature in general.
First published 1975.
Biannually.
200 pp, 400 INR or 90 USD
ISSN: 0253-9071

**∮Latin American Books Newsletter** (J)
Published by K K Roy (Pvt) Ltd
55 Gariahat Rd, Kolkata 700019
Mailing Address: PO Box 10210, Kolkata 700019
*Tel:* (033) 475-4872; (033) 475-5069
*Key Personnel*
Editor: John A Gillard
Text in English.
First published 1970.
Monthly.
58 USD
ISSN: 0023-8740

**Literary Criterion** (P)
c/o English Dept, Bangalore University, Jnana Bharathi, Bangalore, Karnataka 560056
*Tel:* (080) 3215299
*Key Personnel*
Editor: Prof C D Narasimhaiah; C N Srinath
Text in English.
First published 1952.
Quarterly.
250 INR or 40 USD
ISSN: 0024-452X

**Literary Half-Yearly** (P)
Published by Literary Press
c/o The Institute of Commonwealth & American Studies & English Language, Literary Press, Anjali 96, 7th Main, Jayalakshmipuram, Mysore, Karnataka 570012
*Tel:* 513030
*Key Personnel*
Editor: H H Anniah Gowda
Text in English.
First published 1960.
Biannually.
80 INR; 20 USD
ISSN: 0024-4554

**∮Marg** (P)
Published by Marg Publications
Army & Navy Bldg, 3rd floor, 148 Mahatma Gandhi Rd, Fort Mumbai 400001
*Tel:* (022) 842520; (022) 821151; (022) 045947; (022) 045948; 56657828 *Fax:* (022) 047102
*E-mail:* margpub@tata.com
*Web Site:* www.marg-art.org
*Key Personnel*
Business Development Manager: Baptist Sequeira
Administration & Circulation Manager: Asha Shiralikar
Publication on Indian art, culture & related civilizations.
First published 1946.
Quarterly.
140 pp
ISSN: 0972-1444

**Miscellany** (P)
Published by Writers Workshop
162-92 Lake Gardens, Kolkata 700045
*Tel:* (033) 4734325; (033) 4732683
*Key Personnel*
Editor: P Lal
First published 1960.
Bimonthly.
18 USD
ISSN: 0026-5896

**MIWA: Major Indian Works Annual** (J)
Published by D K Agencies (P) Ltd

Mohan Garden, A/15-17, DK Ave, Najafgarh Rd, New Delhi 110059
*Tel:* (011) 2535-7104; (011) 2535-7105
*Fax:* (011) 2535-7103; (011) 2564 8053 (orders)
*E-mail:* information@dkagencies.com
*Web Site:* www.dkagencies.com
A bibliography of significant English language works from India.
Annually.
ISSN: 0971-4669

**∮Pacific Islands Books Newsletters** (J)
Published by K K Roy (Pvt) Ltd
55 Gariahat Rd, Kolkata 700019
Mailing Address: PO Box 10210, Kolkata 700019
*Tel:* (033) 475-4872; (033) 475-5069
Text in English.
First published 1981.
Monthly.
71 USD

**Pustak Parichaya** (J)
Published by Indian Publishing House
93 A Lenin Sarani, Kolkata 700013
*Tel:* (033) 3275267
Text in Hindi.

**Recent Indian Books** (J)
Published by Federation of Indian Publishers & Booksellers Associations
Federation H S C, 18/1-C Institutional Area, Aruna Asif Ali Marg, New Delhi 110067
*Key Personnel*
Editor: J C Mehta
First published 1975.
Quarterly.

**∮Samkaleen Kala Aur Kavita** (Contemporary Art & Poetry) (P)
Published by Samkaleen Prakashan
2762, Rajguru Marg, Paharganj, New Delhi 110055
*Tel:* (011) 3523520; (011) 3518197
*Key Personnel*
Editor: Krishan Khullar
Text in Hindi.
First published 1976.
Quarterly.
32 pp
ISBN(s): 81-7083
ISSN: 0970-0986

**Samkalin Bharatiya Sahitya** (Contemporary Indian Literature) (P)
Published by National Academy of Letters: Sahitya Akademi
Rabindra Bhavan, 35, Ferozeshah Rd, New Delhi 110001
*Tel:* (011) 3386626; (011) 3386627; (011) 3386628; (011) 3386629; (011) 3386088; (011) 3387386 *Fax:* (011) 3382428
*E-mail:* secy@sahitya-akademi.org
*Web Site:* www.sahitya-akademi.org
*Telex:* SAHITYAKAR
Creative & critical writings in Hindi & translation into Hindi from all the Indian languages.
First published 1980.
Bimonthly.
200 pp, 10 USD or 6 GBP; 50 USD or 30 GBP (airmail)
ISSN: 0970-8367
*Branch Office(s)*
YA-4 Sahvikas, 68 Patparganj, I P Extension, Delhi 10092

**Samskrit Pratibha** (P)
Published by National Academy of Letters: Sahitya Akademi
Rabindra Bhavan, 35, Ferozeshah Rd, New Delhi 110001

*Tel:* (011) 3386088; (011) 3386626; (011) 3386627; (011) 3386628; (011) 3386629; (011) 3387386 *Fax:* (011) 3382428
*E-mail:* secy@sahitya-akademi.org
*Web Site:* www.sahitya-akademi.org
*Telex:* 31; 65445 SAND IN *Cable:* SAHITYAKAR
Journal of creative & critical writing in Sanskrit. Also publishes scholarly articles on Sanskrit literature of medieval & ancient periods.
First published 1964.
Biennially.

**∮Yuva Kavi** (Young Poets) (P)
Published by Samkaleen Prakashan
2762, Rajguru Marg, Paharganj, New Delhi 110055
*Tel:* (011) 3523520 *Fax:* (011) 3518197
Text in Hindi.
First published 1976.
Quarterly.
32 pp
ISBN(s): 81-7083
ISSN: 0970-0978

# Islamic Republic of Iran

**Bibliography of Customs & Manners in Isphahan** (B)
Published by National Library & Archives of Iran
Anahita Alley, Africa St, PO Box 11365/9597, 19176 Tehran
Mailing Address: Shahid Bahonar St, 19548 Tehran
*Tel:* (021) 8881966 *Fax:* (021) 8786859
*E-mail:* nli@nlai.ir
*Web Site:* www.nlai.ir
*Key Personnel*
Senior Research Librarian: Mrs Poori Soltani
   *E-mail:* poorisoltani@yahoo.com
Author: Ms Nahid Habibi Azad
20 USD

**A Bibliography of Mathematics** (B)
Published by National Library & Archives of Iran
Anahita Alley, Africa St, PO Box 11365/9597, 19176 Tehran
Mailing Address: Shahid Bahonar St, 19548 Tehran
*Tel:* (021) 8881966 *Fax:* (021) 8786859
*E-mail:* nli@nlai.ir
*Web Site:* www.nlai.ir
*Key Personnel*
Senior Research Librarian: Mrs Poori Soltani
   *E-mail:* poorisoltani@yahoo.com
Compiler: M Rahbari
30 USD

**Bibliography of the Medical Manuscripts in Iran** (B)
Published by National Library & Archives of Iran
Anahita Alley, Africa St, PO Box 11365/9597, 19176 Tehran
Mailing Address: Shahid Bahonar St, 19548 Tehran
*Tel:* (021) 8088971 *Fax:* (021) 8786859
*E-mail:* nli@nlai.ir
*Web Site:* www.nlai.ir
*Key Personnel*
Senior Research Librarian: Mrs Poori Soltani
   *E-mail:* poorisoltani@yahoo.com
First published 1992.
1st: 325 pp, 36001 IRR

**Catalogue de Precieux Ouvrages Scientifiques Francais de la Bibliotheque National de la Republique Islamique d'Iran** (Catalog of Valuable French Works in the National Library of Iran) (B)
Published by National Library & Archives of Iran
Anahita Alley, Africa St, PO Box 11365/9597, 19176 Tehran
Mailing Address: Shahid Bahonar St, 19548 Tehran
*Tel:* (021) 8881966 *Fax:* (021) 8786859
*E-mail:* nli@nlai.ir
*Web Site:* www.nlai.ir
*Key Personnel*
Senior Research Librarian: Mrs Poori Soltani
   *E-mail:* poorisoltani@yahoo.com
Compiler: Ms Shohreh Taravatil
First published 1993.
25 USD

**Catalogue of Newspapers in the National Library of Iran** (Directory of Iranian Newspapers) (B)
Published by National Library & Archives of Iran
Anahita Alley, Africa St, PO Box 11365/9597, 19176 Tehran
Mailing Address: Shahid Bahonar St, 19548 Tehran
*Tel:* (021) 8088971 *Fax:* (021) 8786859
*E-mail:* nli@nlai.ir
*Web Site:* www.nlai.ir
First published 1977.
1st: 3,341 pp

**Class PQ: French Literature, Individual Authors 18, 19, 20th Centuries: Based on the Library of Congress Classification** (B)
Published by National Library & Archives of Iran
Anahita Alley, Africa St, PO Box 11365/9597, 19176 Tehran
Mailing Address: Shahid Bahonar St, 19548 Tehran
*Tel:* (021) 8088971 *Fax:* (021) 2288680
*E-mail:* nli@nlai.ir
*Web Site:* www.nlai.ir
*Key Personnel*
Senior Research Librarian: Mrs Poori Soltani
   *E-mail:* poorisoltani@yahoo.com
First published 1994.
1st: 185 pp, 25 USD

**Directory of Documentation Centres, Special Libraries & University Libraries of Iran, 2nd Edition** (B)
Published by National Library & Archives of Iran
Anahita Alley, Africa St, PO Box 11365/9597, 19176 Tehran
Mailing Address: Sh Bahonar Str, 19548 Tehran
*Tel:* (021) 8088971 *Fax:* (021) 8786859
*E-mail:* nli@nlai.ir

**A Directory of Iranian Periodicals & Newspapers** (B)
Published by National Library & Archives of Iran
Anahita Alley, Africa St, PO Box 11365/9597, 19176 Tehran
Mailing Address: Shahid Bahonar St, 19548 Tehran
*Tel:* (021) 8881966 *Fax:* (021) 8786859
*E-mail:* nli@nlai.ir
*Web Site:* www.nlai.ir
*Key Personnel*
Senior Research Librarian: Mrs Poori Soltani
   *E-mail:* poorisoltani@yahoo.com
First published 1994.
Annually.
50 USD
ISBN(s): 964-446-040-5
ISSN: 1028-7035

**The Iranian National Bibliography** (P)
Published by National Library & Archives of Iran

Anahita Alley, Africa St, PO Box 11365/9597, 19176 Tehran
Mailing Address: Shahid Bahonar St, 19548 Tehran
*Tel:* (021) 8088971 *Fax:* (021) 2288680
*E-mail:* nli@nlai.ir
*Web Site:* www.nlai.ir
*Key Personnel*
Senior Research Librarian: Mrs Poori Soltani
   *E-mail:* poorisoltani@yahoo.com
First published 1963.
Biannually.
ISSN: 0075-0522

**Pahlavi Text: Transcript, Translation** (B)
Published by National Library & Archives of Iran
Anahita Alley, Africa St, PO Box 11365/9597, 19176 Tehran
Mailing Address: Sh Bahonar Str, 19548 Tehran
*Tel:* (021) 8088971 *Fax:* (021) 2288680
*E-mail:* nli@nlai.ir
*Key Personnel*
Senior Research Librarian: Mrs Poori Soltani
   *E-mail:* poorisoltani@yahoo.com
First published 1992.
1st edition: 563 pp

**Political Life of Imam Khomeini** (B)
Published by National Library & Archives of Iran
Anahita Alley, Africa St, PO Box 11365/9597, 19176 Tehran
Mailing Address: Shahid Bahonar St, 19548 Tehran
*Tel:* (021) 8088971 *Fax:* (021) 8786859
*E-mail:* nli@nlai.ir

**Rules & Standards for Publishing Books** (B)
Published by National Library & Archives of Iran
Anahita Alley, Africa St, PO Box 11365/9597, 19176 Tehran
Mailing Address: Shahid Bahonar St, 19548 Tehran
*Tel:* (021) 8881966 *Fax:* (021) 8786859
*E-mail:* nli@nlai.ir
*Key Personnel*
Senior Research Librarian: Mrs Poori Soltani
   *E-mail:* poorisoltani@yahoo.com
2nd (1988): 42 pp, 10 USD

**Ruznameye Dowlat-e Alliyah Iran** (B)
Published by National Library & Archives of Iran
Anahita Alley, Africa St, PO Box 11365/9597, 19176 Tehran
Mailing Address: Shahid Bahonar St, 19548 Tehran
*Tel:* (021) 8088971 *Fax:* (021) 2288680
*E-mail:* nli@nlai.ir
*Web Site:* www.nli.ir
This is a reprint of an old newspaper.
1st, 50 USD

# Iraq

**Iraqi National Bibliography** (J)
Published by National Library
Bab-el-Muaddum, Baghdad
*Tel:* (01) 4164190
Triannually.

# Ireland

**Books Ireland** (J)
Published by Jeremy Addis

11 Newgrove Ave, Dublin 4
*Tel:* (01) 2692185 *Fax:* (01) 2604927
*E-mail:* booksi@eircom.net
The trade journal & review medium of the Irish publishing industry.
First published 1976.
9 times/yr.
3 EUR
ISSN: 0376-6039

**Comhar** (Cooperation) (P)
5 Rae Mhuirfean, Baile Atha Cliath 2
*Tel:* (01) 678 5443 *Fax:* (01) 678 5443
*E-mail:* eolas@comhar-iris.ie
*Web Site:* www.comhar-iris.ie
Text in Irish, covering current affairs, the arts & literature.
Monthly.

**Journal of the Irish Colleges of Physicians & Surgeons**, see The Surgeon Journal of the Royal Colleges of Edinburgh & Ireland

**The Surgeon Journal of the Royal Colleges of Edinburgh & Ireland** (J)
Formerly Journal of the Irish Colleges of Physicians & Surgeons
Published by Royal College of Surgeons in Edinburgh & Irish Colleges of Physicians & Surgeons
Edinburgh University Press, 22 George's Square, Edinburgh EH8 9LF
*Web Site:* www.thesurgeon.net; www.eup.ed.ac.uk
*Key Personnel*
Editor-in-Chief: Prof O Eremin; Prof A Leahy
Bimonthly.
195 GBP (UK & Europe); 198 GBP (elsewhere); 338 USD (US & Canada)

# Israel

**Ariel: The Israel Review of Arts & Letters** (P)
Published by The Israel Foreign Ministry
9 Yitzhak Rabin Blvd, Kiryat Ben-Gurion, 91035 Jerusalem
*Tel:* (02) 530 3111 *Fax:* (02) 530 3367
*E-mail:* ask@israel-info.gov.il
*Web Site:* www.mfa.gov.il
*Key Personnel*
Editor: Asher Weill
Published in six separate language editions - English, French, German, Spanish, Russian & Arabic - with occasional issues in other languages (i.e., Chinese & Japanese).
First published 1962.
Quarterly.
96 pp
ISSN: 0004-1343

**Israel Book Trade Directory** (B)
PO Box 7705, Jerusalem 91076
*Tel:* (02) 6432147 *Fax:* (02) 6437502
*E-mail:* debasher@netvision.net.il
Text in English.
First published 1967.
Biennially.
12 USD
ISSN: 0333-6018

**Jerusalem Report** (P)
PO Box 1805, 91017 Jerusalem
*Tel:* (02) 531-5440 *Fax:* (02) 537-9489; (02) 531-5425 (advertising)
*E-mail:* jrep@jreport.co.il (editorial); jsubs@jrport.co.il (subscriptions)
*Web Site:* www.jrep.com
*Key Personnel*
Editor-in-Chief: Sharon Ashley

**Kiryat Sefer** (P)
Published by Jewish National & University Library
Edmond J Safra Campus, Givat Ram, 91904 Jerusalem
Mailing Address: PO Box 39105, 91341 Jerusalem
*Tel:* (02) 658-5974 *Fax:* (02) 658-6315
*E-mail:* bityab@savion.huji.ac.il
*Web Site:* jnul.huji.ac.il/rambi
*Telex:* 25307
Database which catalogs documents acquired by the Library, including bibliographic descriptions for books, dissertations, periodicals & non-printed publications.
National bibliography of the State of Israel & the Jewish people.
First published 1925.

**Modern Hebrew Literature** (P)
Published by The Institute for the Translation of Hebrew Literature
23 Baruch Hirsch St, Bnei Brak
Mailing Address: PO Box 1005 1, 52001 Ramat Gan
*Tel:* (03) 579 6830 *Fax:* (03) 579 6832
*E-mail:* hamachon@inter.net.il
*Web Site:* www.ithl.org.il
*Telex:* 341118 BXTV IL ext 1272 *Cable:* TARGUM TELAVIV
*Key Personnel*
Man Dir: Mrs Nilli Cohen
English-language journal of contemporary Hebrew literature.
Biennially.

# Italy

**Andersen-Il Mondo dell'Infanzia** (Andersen-The Newspaper of Books for Boys) (J)
Published by Feguagiskia' Studios
via Crosa di Vergagni 3, R16124 Genova
*Tel:* (010) 2510829; (010) 2757544 *Fax:* (010) 2510838
*E-mail:* info@andersen.it
*Web Site:* www.andersen.it
Text in Italian. Contains articles on CYL, teaching, theatre & film as well as literary competitions. Includes reviews & news.

**Belfagor** (P)
Published by Casa Editrice Leo S Olschki
Viuzzo del Pozzetto, 50126 Florence
*Tel:* (055) 6530684 *Fax:* (055) 6530214
*E-mail:* celso@olschki.it
*Web Site:* www.olschki.it
*Key Personnel*
Publisher: Leo S Olschki
Review of literature & information.
First published 1946.
6x/yr.
128 pp
ISSN: 0005-8351

**La Bibliofilia** (P)
Published by Casa Editrice Leo S Olschki
Viuzzo del Pozzetto, 50126 Florence
*Tel:* (055) 6530684 *Fax:* (055) 6530214
*E-mail:* celso@olschki.it
*Web Site:* www.olschki.it
*Key Personnel*
Publisher: Leo S Olschki
Text in English, French, German & Italian. Bibliophily, History of Printing.
First published 1899.
Triannually.
110 pp
ISSN: 0006-0941

**Bibliografia Nazionale Italiana** (Italian National Bibliography) (J)
Published by Central Institute of the Union Catalog of Italian Libraries & Bibliographical Information
Piazza dei Cavalleggeri, 1, 50122 Florence
*Tel:* (055) 24919 1 *Fax:* (055) 2342 482
*E-mail:* info@itcaspur.caspur.it
*Web Site:* www.bncf.firenze.sbn.it

**Catalogo dei Libri in Commercio** (Catalog of Books in Print) (B)
Published by Editrice Bibliografica SpA
Via Bergonzoli, 1/5, 20127 Milan
*Tel:* (02) 28315996 *Fax:* (02) 28315906
*E-mail:* bibliografica@bibliografica.it
*Web Site:* www.bibliografica.it
Sponsored by Associazone Italiana Editori, listing 325,000 Italian titles.
ISBN(s): 88-7075-552-5

**Catalogo del Periodici Italiani** (Catalogue of Italian Periodicals) (B)
Published by Editrice Bibliografica SpA
Via Bergonzoli, 1/5, 20127 Milan
*Tel:* (02) 28315996 *Fax:* (02) 28315906
*E-mail:* bibliografica@bibliografica.it
*Web Site:* www.bibliografica.it
ISBN(s): 88-7075-558-4

**Cenobio** (P)
Published by Ignazio Bonoli, Flavio Catenazzi, Franco Lanza, Carlo Monti, Marcello Ostinelli
via Streccia 4, 6943 Vezia
Mailing Address: PO Box 174, 6903 Lugano 3, Switzerland
*Tel:* (091) 966 85 08 *Fax:* (091) 966 51 56
*Web Site:* www.culturactif.ch/revues/cenobio.htm
*Cable:* CH-6943 VEZIA
*Key Personnel*
Editor: Ignazio Bonoli; Flavio Catenazzi; Marcello Ostinelli; Manuel Rossello
Text in French & Italian.

**Giornale della Libreria** (Book Trade Journal) (J)
Published by Editrice Bibliografica SpA
Via Bergonzoli, 1/5, 20127 Milan
*Tel:* (02) 28315996 *Fax:* (02) 28315906
*E-mail:* bibliografica@bibliografica.it
*Web Site:* www.bibliografica.it
Monthly.
102.30 EUR

**Giornale Storico della Letteratura Italiana** (Historical Journal of Italian Literature) (P)
Published by Loescher Editore SRL
Via Vittorio Amedeo II, 18, 10121 Turin
*Tel:* (011) 5654111 *Fax:* (011) 56 25822
*E-mail:* mail@loescher.it
*Web Site:* www.loescher.it

**Gli Editori Italiani** (The Italian Publishers) (B)
Published by Editrice Bibliografica SpA
Via Bergonzoli, 1/5, 20127 Milan
*Tel:* (02) 28315996 *Fax:* (02) 28315906
*E-mail:* bibliografica@bibliografica.it
*Web Site:* www.bibliografica.it
3,200 Italian publisher listings.

**Lettere Italiane** (P)
Published by Casa Editrice Leo S Olschki
Viuzzo del Pozzetto, 50126 Florence
*Tel:* (055) 6530684 *Fax:* (055) 6530214
*E-mail:* celso@olschki.it
*Web Site:* www.olschki.it
*Key Personnel*
Publisher: Leo S Olschki
History of Italian Literature.
First published 1949.
Quarterly.

170 pp
ISSN: 0024-1334

**Letture: Mensile di Informazione Culturale, Letteratura e Spettacolo** (P)
Published by Periodici San Paolo srl
Via Giotto 36, 20145 Milan
*Tel:* (02) 48071 *Fax:* (02) 48072568
*E-mail:* letture@stpauls.it
*Web Site:* www.stpauls.it/letture
*Key Personnel*
Dir: Antonio Rizzolo *Tel:* (02) 48072518 *Fax:* (02) 48072515
First published 1946.
ISSN: 0024-144X

**Libri e Riviste d'Italia** (Italian Books & Periodicals) (J)
Published by Instituto Poligrafico Dello Stato SpA
Piazza Verdi 10, 00198 Rome
*Tel:* (06) 85081 *Fax:* (06) 85082517
*E-mail:* gestionegu@ipzs.it
*Web Site:* www.ipzs.it
Available in Italian editions & international editions in English, French, German & Spanish.
Biannually.

**Nuova Corrente** (New Current) (J)
Published by Tilgher-Genova sas
Via Assarotti 31/15, 16122 Genova
*Tel:* (010) 8391140 *Fax:* (010) 870653
*E-mail:* tilgher@tilgher.it
*Web Site:* www.tilgher.it
*Key Personnel*
Editor: Tiziana Arvigo; Pierfrancesco Fiorato; Santino Mele; Luigi Surdich; Enrico Tacchella; Stefano Verdino; Luisa Villa
Literary/philosophical topics. Text in Italian, but occasional issues in French & English.
First published 1954.
Biennially.

**Paideia** (P)
Published by Carlo Cordie-Giuseppe Scarpat
Via Corsica 130, 25125 Brescia
*Tel:* (030) 222094 *Fax:* (030) 223269
*E-mail:* paideiaeditrice@tin.it
*Key Personnel*
Dir: Giuseppe Scarpat
Literary review with bibliographical information; text in English, French, German & Italian.
First published 1946.
ISSN: 0030-9435

**La Rassegna della Letteratura Italiana** (Italian Literature Review) (P)
Published by Casa Editrice le Lettere
Costa San Giorgio 28, 50125 Florence
*Tel:* (055) 2342710; (055) 2476319 *Fax:* (055) 2346010
*E-mail:* staff@lelettere.it
*Web Site:* www.lelettere.it
*Key Personnel*
Dir: E Ghidetti
First published 1883.
ISSN: 0033-9423

**Rivista di Letteratura Moderne e Comparate** (Review of Modern & Comparative Literature) (P)
Published by Pacini Editore Srl
Via Gherardesca, 56121 Ospedaletto, Pisa
*Tel:* (050) 313011 *Fax:* (050) 3130300
*E-mail:* info@pacinieditore.it
*Web Site:* www.pacinieditore.it
Text in English, French & Italian.
First published 1946.
4 times/yr.
21 EUR (one issue); 57 EUR (domestic-4 issues); 77 EUR (foreign-4 issues)

**Uomini e Libri** (Men and Books) (P)
Published by Edizioni Effe Emme
Viale E Caldara 8, 20122 Milan
*Key Personnel*
Editor: Mario Miccinesi; Fiora Vincenti
Text in Italian.
First published 1965.
Bimonthly.
ISSN: 0042-0654

# Jamaica

**Book Production in Jamaica: A Select List of Jamaican Publications** (B)
Published by Jamaica Library Service
2 Tom Redcam Dr, Cross Roads, Kingston 5
Mailing Address: PO Box 58, Kingston 5
*Tel:* (876) 926-3310 *Fax:* (876) 926-2188
*E-mail:* jamlibs@cwjamaica.com
*Web Site:* www.jamlib.org.jm

∯**Caribbean Quarterly** (J)
Published by Cultural Studies Initiative, Vice
   Chancellery
University of the West Indies, Mona, Kingston 7
*Tel:* (876) 977 1689 *Fax:* (876) 977 6105
*Key Personnel*
Managing Editor: Dr Veronica Salter
   *E-mail:* vsalter@uwimona.edu.jm
Editor: Rex Nettleford
First published 1949.
Quarterly.
120 pp
ISSN: 0008-6495

**Jamaican National Bibliography** (J)
Published by National Library of Jamaica
12 East St, Kingston
*Tel:* (876) 967-1526; (876) 967-2516; (876) 967-
   2496 *Fax:* (876) 922-5567
*E-mail:* nlj@infochan.com
*Web Site:* www.nlj.org.jm *Cable:* NALIBJAM
*Key Personnel*
Editor: Byron Palmer *Tel:* (876) 967-2494
Lists all material published in Jamaica, works by
   Jamaicans published outside of the country, as
   well as works about Jamaica.

# Japan

**Asian/Pacific Book Development (ABD)** (J)
Published by Asia/Pacific Cultural Centre for UN-
   ESCO (ACCU)
Japan Publishers Bldg, 6 Fukuromachi, Shinjuku-
   ku, Tokyo 162-8484
*Tel:* (03) 3269-4435 *Fax:* (03) 3269-4510
*E-mail:* general@accu.or.jp
*Web Site:* www.accu.or.jp *Cable:*
   ASCULCENTRE
*Key Personnel*
Editor-in-Chief: Shigeo Miyamoto
Provides information, news items relating to
   books, publishing & promotional activities in
   Asia & the Pacific contributed by 25 national
   correspondents.
First published 1969.
Quarterly.

**Biblia** (J)
Published by Tenri University Press
Tenri Central Library, Tenri-SHI Nara 632-8577
*Tel:* (0743) 631515 *Fax:* (0743) 637728
*E-mail:* info@tcl.gr.jp

*Web Site:* www.tcl.gr.jp
Text in Japanese.
ISSN: 0006-0860

**Bulletin of Japan Book Publishers Association**
   (J)
Published by Japan Book Publishers Association
6 Fukuro-machi, Shinjuku-ku 162-0828
*Tel:* (03) 3268-1303 *Fax:* (03) 3268-1196
*E-mail:* rd@jbpa.or.jp
*Web Site:* www.jbpa.or.jp
*Key Personnel*
President: Mr Kunizo Asakura
Monthly.

**The Catalog of Books in the Near Future**
   **(Korekara deru Hon)** (P)
Published by Japan Book Publishers Association
6 Fukuro-machi, Shinjuku-ku, Tokyo 162-0828
*Tel:* (03) 3268-1303 *Fax:* (03) 3268-1196
*E-mail:* rd@jbpa.or.jp
*Web Site:* www.jbpa.or.jp
*Key Personnel*
President: Mr Kunizo Asakura
Bimonthly.

**A Comprehensive Bibliography of Japanese**
   **Periodicals** (P)
Published by The Shuppan News Co Ltd
3-2-4 Misaki-cho 3 chome, Chiyoda-ku, Tokyo
   101
*Tel:* (03) 32622076

**A Comprehensive Catalog of Collected Works,**
   **Publishers in Japan** (J)
Published by The Shuppan News Co Ltd
3-2-4 Misaki-cho 3 chome, Chiyoda-ku, Tokyo
   101
*Tel:* (03) 32622076

**Directory of Japanese Publishing Industry** (J)
Published by Publishers' Association for Cultural
   Exchange (PACE) Japan
1-2-1, Sarugaku-cho, Chiyoda-ku, Tokyo 101-
   0064
*Tel:* (03) 3291-5685 *Fax:* (03) 3233-3645
*Web Site:* www.pace.or.jp
Statistics of the Japanese publishing world.
Free

**Doitsu Bungaku** (P)
Published by Nippon Dokubungakkai
c/o Ikubundo, Hongo 5-30-21, Bunkyo-ku, Tokyo
   113-0033
*Key Personnel*
President: Prof Takao Tsunekawa
German Literature.
First published 1947.
ISSN: 0387-2831

**Doshisha Literature** (J)
Published by Doshisha University, English Liter-
   ary Society
Karasuma-Higashi-iru, Imadegawa-dori, Kamigyo-
   ku, Kyoto 602-8580
*Tel:* (075) 251 3260 *Fax:* (075) 251 3057
*E-mail:* ji-koho@mail.doshisha.ac.jp
*Web Site:* www.doshisha.ac.jp/english
Journal of English literature & philology; text in
   English.

**An Introduction to Publishing in Japan** (B)
Published by Japan Book Publishers Association
6 Fukuro-machi, Shinjuku-ku, Tokyo 162-0828
*Tel:* (03) 3268-1303 *Fax:* (03) 3268-1196
*E-mail:* rd@jbpa.or.jp
*Web Site:* www.jbpa.or.jp *Cable:* SHOSEKIKYO
   TOKOYO 1
*Key Personnel*
President: Mr Kunizo Asakura

**Japan Directory of Professional Associations**
   (B)
Published by Intercontinental Marketing Corp
Centre Bldg, 2nd floor, 1-14-13 Taitoku, Tokyo
   110-0013
Mailing Address: IPO Box 5056, Tokyo 100-3191
*Tel:* (03) 3876-3073 *Fax:* (03) 3876-3627
*E-mail:* imcbook@attglobal.net; kunikoi@
   attglobal.net
*Web Site:* jpgsonline.com; imcbook.net
*Key Personnel*
Editor: Warren E Ball
Lists important associations, societies & institu-
   tions, many of which are significant publishers
   or otherwise valuable information sources.
Annually.
ISBN(s): 4-900178-16-0

**Japan English Publications in Print** (B)
Published by Intercontinental Marketing Corp
Centre Bldg, 2nd floor, 1-14-13 Taitoku, Tokyo
   110-0013
Mailing Address: IPO Box 5056, Tokyo 100-3191
*Tel:* (03) 3876-3073 *Fax:* (03) 3876-3627
*E-mail:* imcbook@attglobal.net; kunikoi@
   attglobal.net
*Web Site:* jpgsonline.com; imcbook.net
*Key Personnel*
Editor: Warren E Ball
English journals, books, directories & other publi-
   cations, published in Japan.
Annually.
ISBN(s): 4-900178-15-2

**Japanese Books in Print** (B)
Published by Japan Book Publishers Association
6 Fukuro-machi, Shinjuku-ku, Tokyo 162-0828
*Tel:* (03) 3268-1303 *Fax:* (03) 3268-1196
*E-mail:* rd@jbpa.or.jp
*Web Site:* www.jbpa.or.jp
*Key Personnel*
President: Mr Kunizo Asakura

**Japanese Literature Today** (P)
Published by Japanese PEN Centre
Akasaka Residential Hotel-265, 9-1-7 Akaska,
   Minato-ku, Tokyo 107-0052
*Tel:* (03) 3402-1171 *Fax:* (03) 3402-5951
*E-mail:* penclub@asahi-net.email.ne.jp; japan-
   pen@asahi-net.email.ne.jp
*Web Site:* www.jinjapan.org; www.mmjp.or.
   jp/japan-penclub
Annually.

**Japanese Publications News and Reviews** (J)
Published by Shuppan News Co Ltd
3-2-4 Masaki-cho 3 Chome, Chiyoda-ku, Tokyo
   101
*Tel:* (03) 32622076

**JPG Letter** (J)
Published by Intercontinental Marketing Corp
Centre Bldg, 2nd floor, 1-14-13 Taitoku, Tokyo
   110-0013
Mailing Address: IPO Box 5056, Tokyo 100-3191
*Tel:* (03) 3876-3073 *Fax:* (03) 3876-3627
*E-mail:* imcbook@attglobal.net; kunikoi@
   attglobal.net
*Web Site:* jpgsonline.com; imcbook.net
*Key Personnel*
Editor: Warren E Ball
Newsletter containing information on new English
   publications (periodicals & books) that are pub-
   lished in Japan & other southeast & east Asian
   countries.
Monthly.

**Practical Guide to Publishing in Japan** (B)
Published by Publishers' Association for Cultural
   Exchange (PACE) Japan

1-2-1, Sarugaku-cho, Chiyoda-ku, Tokyo 101-0064
*Tel:* (03) 3291-5685 *Fax:* (03) 3233-3645
*Web Site:* www.pace.or.jp

**Shinkan News** (Shinkan Nyusu) (J)
Published by Tokyo Shuppan Hanbai Co Ltd
6-24 Higashi-Goken-cho, Shinjuku-ku, Tokyo 162-8710
*Tel:* (03) 3269-6111 *Fax:* (03) 3267-3781
*Key Personnel*
Editor: Hiromasa Kohtaki
First published 1959.
Monthly.
ISSN: 0037-3788

**Shuppan Nenkan** (J)
Published by Shuppan News Co Ltd
3-2-4 Masaki-cho 3 Chome, Chiyoda-ku, Tokyo 101
*Tel:* (03) 32622076
Information on publishing for the previous year.
Annually.

**Shuppan Nyusu** (Publishers' News) (J)
Published by Shuppan News Co Ltd
3-2-4 Masaki-cho 3 Chome, Chiyoda-ku, Tokyo 101
*Tel:* (03) 32622076
Text in Japanese.
Trimonthly.
ISSN: 0386-2003

**Studies in English Literature** (P)
Published by Nihon Eibungakkai (English Literary Society of Japan)
501 Kenkyusha Bldg, 9 Surugadai 2-chome, Kanda, Chiyoda-ku, Tokyo 101-0062
*Tel:* (03) 32937528 *Fax:* (03) 32937539
Published annually in Japanese & English.

**Umi** (P)
Published by Chuokoron-Shinsha Inc
2-8-7 Kyobashi, Chuo-ku, Tokyo 104
*Tel:* (03) 3563-1261 *Fax:* (03) 3561-5920
*E-mail:* k.sato@chuko.co.jp
*Web Site:* www.chuko.co.jp
*Key Personnel*
President: Jin Nakamura

# Jordan

**Palestinian Bibliography: A List of Books Published by the Arabs in Palestine 1948-1980** (B)
Published by Jordan Library Association (Message of the Library)
PO Box 6289, Amman
*Tel:* (06) 462 9412 *Fax:* (06) 462 9412

# Kazakstan

**Prostor** (The Expose) (P)
Published by Kazakh Writers' Union
Dr Albai Khana, 105, 480091 Almaty
*Tel:* (03272) 696319 *Fax:* (03272) 691058
*E-mail:* info@prstr.samal.kz
*Web Site:* prostor.samal.kz
Literary, artistic, socio-political magazine.
Monthly.

# Kenya

**African Journal of Health Sciences** (J)
Published by African Forum for Health Sciences
PO Box 54840, Nairobi
*Tel:* (02) 722541 *Fax:* (02) 720030
*E-mail:* afhes@nairobi.mimcom.net; kemri-hq@nairobi.mimcom.net
*Web Site:* www.kemri.org
*Key Personnel*
Editor-in-Chief: Dr Davy Koech
First published 1994.
ISSN: 1022-9272

**African Urban Quarterly** (J)
Published by African Urban Quarterly Ltd, Centre for Urban Research
PO Box 51366, Nairobi
*Tel:* (02) 216574 *Fax:* (02) 444110
International & interdisciplinary journal that covers all aspects of urbanization & regional planning from the most theoretical to the most imperical. AUQ serves as a central clearing house for research with analytical, descriptive, evaluative & prescriptive problems concerned with comparative urbanization & regional planning in Africa with the rest of the world. Topics covered include agriculture, demography, transportation, medicine, politics, geography, history, sociology, economics, mathematics, urbanization, anthropology, archeology, education, law & environmental studies as they affect the quality of human life in both rural as well as in urban areas.
Quarterly.
130 USD
ISSN: 0747-6108

**Kenya National Bibliography** (B)
Published by Kenya National Library Service
PO Box 30573, Nairobi
*Tel:* (02) 725550; (02) 725551; (02) 718177, (02) 718012; (02) 718013 *Fax:* (02) 721749
*E-mail:* knls@nbnet.co.ke
*Web Site:* www.knls.or.ke
*Key Personnel*
Dir: S K Ng'anga

# Republic of Korea

**Books from Korea** (B)
Published by Korean Publishers Association
105-2 Sagan-Dong, Chongno-Gu, Seoul 110-190
*Tel:* (02) 735-2701 *Fax:* (02) 738-5414
*E-mail:* kpa@kpa21.or.kr
*Web Site:* www.kpa21.or.kr
*Key Personnel*
Secretary General: Jong Jin Jung
Text in English.
First published 1971.
Annually.

**Catalog of Government Publications** (B)
Published by National Assembly Library
Yoido-dong 1, Youngdeungpo-gu, Seoul 150-703
*Tel:* (02) 788-4143 (English assistance); (02) 788-3961 *Fax:* (02) 7884193
*E-mail:* question@nanet.go.kr
*Web Site:* www.nanet.go.kr
*Telex:* 25849
Includes university publications.

**Korean National Bibliography** (J)
Published by The National Library of Korea

San 60-1, Banpo-dong, Seocho-gu, Seoul 137-702
*Tel:* (02) 590-0517 *Fax:* (02) 590-0530
*E-mail:* nlkpc@sun.nl.or.kr
*Web Site:* www.nl.go.kr
Annually.

**Korean Publication Yearbook** (B)
Published by Korean Publishers Association
105-2 Sagan-Dong, Chongno-Gu, Seoul 110-190
*Tel:* (02) 735-2701 *Fax:* (02) 738-5414
*E-mail:* kpa@kpa21.or.kr
*Web Site:* www.kpa21.or.kr
*Key Personnel*
Secretary General: Jong Jin Jung
Text in Korean.
Annually.

**Korean Publishers Directory** (B)
Published by Korean Publishers Association
105-2 Sagan-Dong, Chongno-Gu, Seoul 110-190
*Tel:* (02) 735-2701 *Fax:* (02) 738-5414
*E-mail:* kpa@kpa21.or.kr
*Web Site:* www.kpa21.or.kr
*Key Personnel*
Secretary General: Jong Jin Jung
Published annually; text in English.

**KPA Journal** (J)
Published by Korean Publishers Association
105-2 Sagan-Dong, Chongno-Gu, Seoul 110-190
*Tel:* (02) 735-2701 *Fax:* (02) 738-5414
*E-mail:* kpa@kpa21.or.kr
*Web Site:* www.kpa21.or.kr
*Key Personnel*
Secretary General: Jong Jin Jung
Published monthly, in Korean.

# Latvia

**Daugava** (P)
Published by Daugava Ltd
Balasta dambis 3, Riga LV-1081
*Tel:* 7280290
*E-mail:* ravdin@mailbox.riga.lv
*Key Personnel*
Editor: Zhanna Ezit
Literary magazine.
Bimonthly.
47 USD
ISSN: 0207-4001

# Luxembourg

**Bibliographie Luxembourgeoise** (Luxembourg Bibliography) (J)
Published by Bibliotheque Nationale du Grand-Duche de Luxembourg
37 blvd F D Roosevelt, 2450 Luxembourg
*Tel:* 22 97 55-1 *Fax:* 47 56 72
*E-mail:* bib.nat@bi.etat.lu
*Web Site:* www.bibnatlux.etat.lu

**Kritikon Litterarum** (P)
Published by Thesen Verlag Vowinckel
3 pl de la Gare, 6674 Mertert
*Tel:* 748715 *Fax:* 26740429
*E-mail:* schirm.vow@pt.lu
*Key Personnel*
Editor: Kirby Farrell; Gerhard Giesemann; Alain Niderst; Manfred Putz
First published 1972.
Biannually.

# The Former Yugoslav Republic of Macedonia

173 EUR/vol
ISSN: 0340-9767

**Macedonian Review** (P)
Published by Macedonian Scientific Institute
5 Pirotska Str, Sofia 1301
*Tel:* (02) 878 708
*E-mail:* info@macedoniainfo.com
*Web Site:* www.macedoniainfo.com
Cultural Life.
Quarterly.

**Razgledi** (P)
Ul Ivo Ribar-Lola 66, 91000 Skopje
Mailing Address: PO Box 345, 91000 Skopje
*Key Personnel*
Editor: Danilo Kocevski
Review of literature, art & culture; text in Macedonian.
First published 1958.
Monthly.
ISSN: 0034-0227

**Stremez** (P)
Published by Interesna Zaednica na Kulturata Pri Lep
Joska Jordanoski 2, 97500 Prilep
*Tel:* 27308; 21703 *Fax:* 21703
*Key Personnel*
Editor: Branko Olievski
Journal for literature & culture; text in Macedonian.
First published 1957.
10 times/yr.
ISSN: 0039-2294

# Madagascar

**Bibliographie annuelle de Madagascar**
(Madagascar Annual Bibliography) (B)
Published by Bibliotheque Universitarie, Campus Universitaire
Universite de Madagascar, Bibliotheque Universitaire, BP 908, Tananrive
*Tel:* (02) 23228
*E-mail:* buunivtanamg@minitel.refer.org
Annual.
ISSN: 0067-6926

**Bibliographie Nationale de Madagascar**
(Madagascar National Bibliography) (B)
Published by Bibliotheque Nationale (Sous la Direction de Ralaisaholimanana Louis)
Bibliotheque Nationale, BP 257, Anosy, Tananrive
*Tel:* (02) 258 72 *Fax:* (02) 29448

# Malaysia

**Bibliografi Negara Malaysia** (Malaysian National Bibliography) (J)
Published by Perpustakaan Negara Malaysia, Technical Services Div
232, Jalan Tun Razak, 50572 Kuala Lumpur
*Tel:* (03) 26871700 *Fax:* (03) 26942490
*E-mail:* pnmweb@pnm.my
*Web Site:* www.pnm.my
*Telex:* 30092
*Key Personnel*
Editor: Nafisah Ahmad
40 MYR or 50 USD
ISSN: 0126-5210

**Malay Literature** (P)
Published by Dewan Bahasa dan Pustaka
Peti Surat 10803, 50926 Kuala Lumpur
*Tel:* (03) 21481011; (03) 21447269 *Fax:* (03) 2482726
*Web Site:* www.dbp.gov.my
*Key Personnel*
Head, Comparative Literature Dept: Mrs Zalila Shariff *E-mail:* zalila@dbp.gov.my
National Language & Literary Agency of Malaysia.
First published 1967.
June & Dec.
RM 10.00
ISSN: 0128-1186

ƒ**Southeast Asian Archives** (J)
Published by Southeast Asian Regional Branch of the International Council on Archives (SAR-BICA)
c/o National Archives of Malaysia, Jalan Duta, 50568 Kuala Lumpur
*Tel:* (03) 62010688 *Fax:* (03) 62015679
*E-mail:* query@arkib.gov.my
*Web Site:* www.arkib.gov.my

# Malta

**Malta National Bibliography** (B)
Published by Malta National Library
36 Old Treasury St, Valletta CMR 02
*Tel:* 22 43 38; 23 65 85 *Fax:* 23 59 92
*E-mail:* philip.borg@gov.mt
*Web Site:* www.libraries-archives.gov.mt
*Key Personnel*
Contact: M Mallia
Annually.

# Mauritius

**Memorandum of Books Printed in Mauritius & Registered in the Archives** (J)
Published by Mauritius Archives
Development Bank of Mauritius Complex, Petite Riviere
*Tel:* 233-7341; 233-4469 *Fax:* 233-4299
*Key Personnel*
Deputy Chief Archivist: Mr Gheeandut Suneechur
Acting Chief Archives Officer: Pierre Roland Chung Sam Wan
First published 1894.
Quarterly.
Free

# Mexico

**Bibliografia Mexicana** (Mexican Bibliography) (B)
Published by Biblioteca Nacional de Mexico
Centro Cultural Universitario, CU, Delegacion Coyoacan, 04510 Mexico, DF
*Tel:* (055) 5622-6827 *Fax:* (055) 5665-0951
*E-mail:* libros@biblional.bibliog.unam.mx
*Web Site:* biblional.bibliog.unam.mx
*Key Personnel*
Contact: Roxana L Mejia Murillo

**Boletin Bibliografico Mexicano** (Mexican Bibliographical Bulletin) (J)
Published by Libreria de Porrua Hermanos y Cia, SA
Av Republica De Argentina No 15, Col Centro, 06020 Mexico, DF
*Tel:* (05) 7025467 *Fax:* (05) 7024574
*Web Site:* www.porrua.com *Cable:* PORRAUS MEXICO
*Key Personnel*
Ed: Jose Antonio Perez Porrua
Text in Spanish.
Monthly.
ISSN: 0185-2027

**Boletin del Instituto de Investigaciones Bibliograficas** (Bulletin of the Institute of Bibliographic Research) (J)
Published by Instituto de Investigaciones Bibliograficas (Institute of Bibliographic Research)
Hemeroteca Nacional de Mexico, Centro Cultural Universitario, 04510 Mexico, DF
*Tel:* (055) 5622-6827 *Fax:* (055) 5665-0951
*E-mail:* libros@biblional.bibliog.unam.mx
*Web Site:* biblional.bibliog.unam.mx
Book review & historic articles on Mexico & Latin America.

**Como Comprar Libros y Publicaciones Periodicas de Mexico** (How to Obtain Mexican Books & Periodicals) (B)
Published by Camara Nacional de la Industria Editorial Mexicana
Holanda numero 13, col San Diego Churubusco, Del Coyoacan, 04120 Mexico, DF
*Tel:* (055) 5688-2434; (055) 5688-2221; (055) 5688-2011 *Toll Free Tel:* (800) 714-5352 *Fax:* (055) 5604-4347; (055) 5604-3147
*E-mail:* cepromex@caniem.com
*Web Site:* www.caniem.com
Information on the Mexican publishing industry, including a list of principal exporters of Mexican books.
ISBN(s): 968-6276-01-7

**Cuadernos Americanos** (American Notebooks) (P)
Published by Universidad Nacional Autonoma de Mexico Centro (National University of Mexico)
Torre II de Humanidades, Piso 8, Ciudad Universitaria, 04510 Mexico, DF
*Tel:* (055) 662-1902 *Fax:* (055) 616-2515
*E-mail:* cuadamer@servidor.unam.mx
*Web Site:* www.libros.unam.mx; www.ccydel.unam.mx
Our America, Monograph; Our America, Permanent collection; 500 Years After, Commemorative collection of the 500 years of the arrival of Columbus to America; Annual Latin America, permanent collection.
Bimonthly.
200 MXP or 133 USD/yr
ISSN: 0011-2356

**Libros de Mexico** (Books of Mexico) (J)
Published by Camara Nacional de la Industria Editorial Mexicana

Holanda numero 13, col San Diego Churubusco, Del Coyoacan, 04120 Mexico, DF
*Tel:* (055) 5688-2434; (055) 5688-2221; (055) 5688-2011 *Fax:* (055) 5604-4347; (055) 5604-3147
*E-mail:* ciecprom@inetcorp.net.mx
*Web Site:* www.caniem.com
Review of book trade.
Quarterly.

# Morocco

**Bibliographie Nationale Marocaine** (Moroccan National Bibliography) (B)
Published by Bibliotheque Generale et Archives du Maroc
5, Ave Ibn Battouta, Rabat
Mailing Address: CP 1003, Rabat
*Tel:* (07) 77 21 52; (07) 77 60 62
*E-mail:* biblio1@onpt.net.ma
*Key Personnel*
Librarian: Ahmed Toufiq
Biannually.
ISSN: 9981-1818

# Nepal

**Nepalese National Bibliography** (B)
Published by Tribhuvan University Central Library
Kirtipur, Kathmandu
*Tel:* (01) 331317 *Fax:* (01) 331964
*E-mail:* tucl@healthnet.org.np
*Web Site:* www.tucl.org.np
*Key Personnel*
Chief: Mr Krishna Mani Bhandari
First published 1981.
Annually.
3rd: 120 pp, 20 USD
ISBN(s): 99933-51-00-8

# Netherlands

**Amsterdamer Publikationen zur Sprache und Literatur** (P)
Published by Rodopi
Tijnmuiden 7, 1046 AK Amsterdam
*Tel:* (020) 611 48 21 *Fax:* (020) 447 29 79
*E-mail:* info@rodopi.nl
*Web Site:* www.rodopi.nl
Germanic Languages & Literatures.
ISSN: 0169-0221

ƒ**Babel (International Journal of Translation)** (J)
Published by Federation Internationale des Traducteurs (FIT)
John Benjamins Publishing Co, Klaprozenweg 105, 1033 NN Amsterdam
Mailing Address: PO Box 36224, 1020 ME Amsterdam
*Tel:* (020) 6304747 *Fax:* (020) 6739773
*Web Site:* www.benjamins.nl
*Key Personnel*
Journal Subscriptions: Mr Timo Taal
    *E-mail:* subscription@benjamins.nl
Scholarly journal concerned with current issues & events in the field of translation.
Quarterly.
ISSN: 0521-9744

ƒ**Bibliotheca Orientalis** (J)
Published by Nederlands Instituut voor Het Nabije Oosten (Netherlands Institute for the Near East)
PB 9515, 2300 RA Leiden
*Tel:* (071) 527 20 36 *Fax:* (071) 527 20 38
*E-mail:* ninopublications@let.leidenuniv.nl
*Web Site:* www.leidenuniv.nl/nino/ninopubs/publ.html
*Key Personnel*
Editor: R E Kon; A van der Kooij; D J W Meijer; H J A de Meulenaere; J J Roodenberg; J de Roos; M Stol
International bibliographical & reviewing journal for Near Eastern & Mediterranean studies, published in English, French & German.
Bimonthly.
ISSN: 0006-1913

**Boekblad** (J)
Published by Koninklijke Vereeniging ter bevordering van de belangen des Boekhandels/Boekblad bv
Frederiksplein 1, 1017 XK Amsterdam
Mailing Address: Postbus 15007, 1001 MA Amsterdam
*Tel:* (020) 625 31 31 *Fax:* (020) 622 09 08
*E-mail:* redactie@boekblad.kvb.nl
*Web Site:* www.boekblad.nl
News-sheet for the book trade.
Daily, weekly, monthly.

**Brinkman's Cumulatieve Catalogus** (Brinkman's Cumulative Book Catalog) (J)
Published by Uitgeverij Bohn Stafleu Van Loghum BV
PO Box 4, 2400 MA Alphen aan den Rijn
*Tel:* (0172) 466811 *Fax:* (0172) 466770
*Web Site:* www.kb.nl/kb
Netherlands national bibliography.

**Castrum Peregrini** (P)
Published by Castrum Peregrini Presse
PO Box 645, 1000 AP Amsterdam
*Tel:* (020) 623 52 87 *Fax:* (020) 624 70 96
*E-mail:* mail@castrumperegrini.nl
*Web Site:* www.castrumperegrini.nl
Journal for literature & art. Text in German.

**Deutsche Buecher** (The German Books) (J)
Published by Rodopi
Tijnmuiden 7, 1046 AK Amsterdam
*Tel:* (020) 611 48 21 *Fax:* (020) 447 29 79
*E-mail:* info@rodopi.nl
*Web Site:* www.rodopi.nl
*Key Personnel*
Publisher & Editor: Ferdinand van Ingen; Hartmut Laufhuette; Hendrik Meijering
Editor: Andrea Kunne; Achim Nuber
Text in German.
ISSN: 0167-2185

**Forum der Letteren**, see Tijdschrift voor Literatuurwetenschap

**Gids voor de Informatiesector** (B)
Published by NBLC
Platinaweg 10, 2544 EZ The Hague
Mailing Address: Postbus 43300, 2504 AH The Hague
*Tel:* (070) 30 90 100 *Fax:* (070) 30 90 200
*E-mail:* infolijn@nblc.nl
*Web Site:* www.nblc.nl
(Boekenvakboek, 1991) Publishing Industry Statistics.

**Het Nederlandse Boek** (The Dutch Book) (J)
De Lairessestr 108, 1071 PK Amsterdam
Mailing Address: PO Box 10576, Amsterdam 1001 EN
*Tel:* (020) 6264971 *Fax:* (020) 6231696

*E-mail:* info@cpnb.nl
*Web Site:* www.cpnb.nl/index2.html
New Pocket-Books & Paperbacks included.
First published 1852.
Bimonthly.
24 pp, 10 EUR
ISSN: 0166-0586

**Hollands Maandblad** (Holland Monthly) (P)
Published by Stichting Hollands Maandblad
Herengracht 481, 1017 BT Amsterdam
*Tel:* (020) 5249800 *Fax:* (020) 6276851
*E-mail:* hollandsmaandblad@contact-bv.nl
*Web Site:* www.hollandsmaandblad.nl
*Key Personnel*
Editor: Bastiaan Bommelje

ƒ**IFLA Directory** (J)
Published by International Federation of Library Associations & Institutions
c/o Koninklijke Bibliothek, Prins Willem-Alexanderhof 5, The Hague
Mailing Address: PO Box 95312, 2509 The Hague
*Tel:* (070) 3140884 *Fax:* (070) 3834827
*E-mail:* ifla@ifla.org
*Web Site:* www.ifla.org
Biennially.
ISSN: 0074-6002

ƒ**International Information & Library Review** (J)
Published by Academic Press Ltd
PO Box 211, Amsterdam 1000
*Tel:* (020) 485 3757 *Fax:* (020) 485 3432
*E-mail:* nlinfo-f@elsevier.com
*Web Site:* www.elsevier.com/locate/issn/1057-2317
Quarterly.
ISSN: 1057-2317
*Ultimate Parent Company:* Elsevier Science

**LIBER Quarterly: The Journal of European Research Libraries** (J)
Published by Igitur, Utrecht Publishing & Archiving Services
Heidelberglaan 3, 3508 TC Amsterdam
*Tel:* (030) 253 6635 *Fax:* (030) 253 6959
*E-mail:* info@igitur.uu.nl
*Web Site:* liber.library.uu.nl; www.igitur.nl
*Key Personnel*
Managing Editor: Trix Bakker *E-mail:* t.bakker@ubvu.vu.nl
Promotes cooperation among European research libraries. Mainly in English.
First published 1991.
Quarterly.
215 EUR/yr; 59 EUR/issue
ISSN: 1435-5205

**De negentiende EEUW** (The Nineteenth Century) (P)
Published by Maatschappij der Nederlandse Letterkunde, Werkgroep Negentiende Eeuw
Groothertoginnelaan 260, 2517 EZ The Hague
*Tel:* (70) 3106455
*Web Site:* www.leidenuniv.nl/host/mnl/wkgrp19/
*Key Personnel*
Contact: Dr A van Kalmthout *E-mail:* a.b.g.m.van.kalmthout@let.rug.nl
First published 1977.
240 pp
ISSN: 1381-8546

**Quaerendo** (P)
Published by Brill Academic Publishers
Plantijnstr 2, 2321 JC Leiden
Mailing Address: PO Box 9000, 2300 PA Leiden
*Tel:* (071) 53 53 500 *Fax:* (071) 53 17 532
*E-mail:* cs@brill.nl
*Web Site:* www.brill.nl

*Key Personnel*
Editor: A R A Croiset van Uchelen
Journal from the Low Countries devoted to
 manuscripts & printed books; text mainly in
 English, occasionally in French & German.
 Also available online.
First published 1971.
Quarterly.
ISSN: 0014-9527

**De Revisor** (P)
Published by Em Querido's Uitgeverij BV
Singel 262, 1016 AC Amsterdam
*Tel:* (020) 55 11 262 *Fax:* (020) 63 91 968
*Web Site:* www.revisor.nl
*Key Personnel*
President: Ary T Langbroek *E-mail:* b.
 langbroek@querido.nl
Editor-in-Chief: Jacques Dohmen *E-mail:* j.
 dohmen@querido.nl
Publisher: Baerbel Dorweiler *E-mail:* b.
 dorweiler@querido.nl
Foreign Rights: Lucienne van der Leije *E-mail:* l.
 van.der.leije@querido.nl
First published 1971.

**Speurwerk Boeken Omnibus (SBO)** (The Dutch
 Book Market) (J)
Published by Stichting Speurwerk betreffende het
 Boek
Frederiksplein 1, 1017 XK Amsterdam
*Tel:* (020) 625 49 27 *Fax:* (020) 620 88 71
*E-mail:* info@speurwerk.kvb.nl
*Web Site:* www.speurwerk.nl
Quarterly.

**Tijdschrift voor Literatuurwetenschap** (P)
Formerly Forum der Letteren
Published by Amsterdam University Press
Prinsengracht 747-751, 1017 JX Amsterdam
*Tel:* (020) 420-0050 *Fax:* (02) 420-3214
*E-mail:* info@aup.nl
*Web Site:* www.aup.nl
Text in Dutch.
First published 1893.
Quarterly.
ISSN: 1383-7567

# New Zealand

**Te Rarangi Pukapuka Matua o Aotearoa** (New
 Zealand National Bibliography) (J)
Published by National Library of New Zealand
 (Te Puna Matauranga o Aotearoa)
Corner Molesworth & Aitken Streets, Wellington
Mailing Address: PO Box 1467, Wellington 6001
*Tel:* (04) 474 3000 *Fax:* (04) 474 3035
*E-mail:* information@natlib.govt.nz
*Web Site:* www.natlib.govt.nz
First published 1961.
Monthly online version; cumulative on CD-ROM.
830 NZD or 405.29 USD for 1 CD-ROM an-
 nually; 1200 NZD or 585.96 USD for 2 CD-
 ROMs annually; monthly website version free
 & free on CD-ROM for international clients
ISSN: 0028-8497

# Nigeria

∮**African Journal of Academic Librarianship**
 (P)
Published by Standing Conference of African
 University Libraries (SCAUL)

University of Lagos Akoka, PO Box 46, Akoka,
 Yaba, Lagos
*Tel:* (01) 524968
*Key Personnel*
Editor: E B Bankole
Text in English.
First published 1983.
Biannually.
25 NGN; 50 USD
ISSN: 0189-6709

**Benin Review** (J)
Published by Ethiope Publishing Corporation
34 Murtala Mohammed St, Benin City
Mailing Address: PMB 1332, Benin City, Bendel
 State
*Tel:* (052) 253036
*Telex:* 41110
*Key Personnel*
Editor: Abiola Irele; Pius Oleghe
Covers traditional & modern arts in Africa as
 well as cultural life in the Black World.
First published 1974.
Biannually.
3 NGN or 6 USD/yr
ISSN: 0331-0213

∮**Heritage** (J)
Published by Heritage Books
2-8 Calcutta Crescent, Gate 1, 101251 Apapa,
 Lagos
Mailing Address: PO Box 610, 101251 Apapa,
 Lagos
*Tel:* (01) 5871333
*E-mail:* obw@infoweb.abs.net
*Key Personnel*
Editor: Naiwu Osahon
African arts & letters.
First published 1970.
Quarterly.
150 USD/yr
ISSN: 0794-3415

**The Muse** (P)
Published by English Association at Nsukka
University of Nigeria, Dept of English, Nsukka
*Tel:* 771911 *Fax:* 77 0644 *Toll Free Fax:* 77 1500
*Web Site:* www.unnportal.com
*Telex:* 51496
*Key Personnel*
Editor: Onyedika L Okwuonu
Irregularly.

**National Bibliography of Nigeria** (J)
Published by National Library of Nigeria-
 Research & Development Dept
4, Wesley St, PMB 12626, Lagos
Mailing Address: Sanusi Dantata House, Plot 274
 Central Business Area, PMB 1, Garki District,
 Abuja
*Tel:* (01) 2600220 *Fax:* (01) 63 1563
*Web Site:* www.nlbn.org
Cumulations before 1971 published by the Ibadan
 University Press.
First published 1950.
Annually, also available as a weekly service.

**Northern Nigerian Publications** (J)
Published by Ahmadu Bello University Press Ltd
PMB 1094, Zaria, Kaduna State
*Tel:* (069) 50581-5 *Fax:* (069) 50563
*E-mail:* abupl@abu.edu.ng
*Telex:* 75241
Annually.

**Publishing in Nigeria** (B)
Published by Ethiope Publishing Corporation
34 Murtala Mohammed St, Benin City, Bendel
 State
Mailing Address: PMB 1332, Benin City, Bendel
 State

*Tel:* (052) 253036
*Telex:* 41110

**Serials in Print in Nigeria** (B)
Published by National Library of Nigeria-
 Research & Development Dept
4, Wesley St, PMB 12626, Lagos
Mailing Address: Sanusi Dantata House, Plot 274
 Central Business Area, PMB 1, Garki District,
 Abuja
*Tel:* (01) 2600220 *Fax:* (01) 63 1563
*Web Site:* www.nlbn.org

# Norway

**Bok Og Samfunn** (J)
Published by Norwegian Booksellers Association
Ovre Vollgate 15, 0158 Oslo
*Tel:* (22) 40 45 40 *Fax:* (22) 41 12 89
*E-mail:* post@bokogsamfunn.no
*Web Site:* www.bokogsamfunn.no
Trade journal for the Norwegian book trade.

**Edda** (P)
Published by Scandinavian University Press
Universitetsforlaget AS, Sehesteds gate 3, 0105
 Oslo
Mailing Address: Postboks 508 sentrum, 0105
 Oslo
*Tel:* (024) 14 75 00 *Fax:* (024) 14 75 01
*E-mail:* post@universitetsforlaget.no
*Web Site:* www.universitetsforlaget.no
*Key Personnel*
Man Dir: Arne Magnus
Literary research.
Scandinavian.
745 NOK
ISSN: 0013-0818

**The Norseman** (P)
Published by Nordmanns-Forbundet (The Norse
 Federation)
Raadhusgate 23B, 0158 Oslo
*Tel:* (023) 35 71 70 *Fax:* (023) 35 71 75
*E-mail:* norseman@norseman.no
*Web Site:* www.norseman.no
*Key Personnel*
Editor-in-Chief: Kjetil A Flatin
Editor: Gunnar Gran
5 times/yr.
64 pp
ISSN: 0029-1846

**Norsk Bokhandlermatrikkel** (Norwegian
 Booksellers Membership List) (B)
Published by Bok Og Papiransattes Forening
Ovre Vollgate 15, 0158 Oslo
*Tel:* 22205197 *Fax:* 22420033

**Samtiden** (J)
Published by H Aschehoug & Co (W Nygaard)
Sehstedsgt 3, Oslo
Mailing Address: PB 363, Sentrum, 0102 Oslo
*Tel:* (022) 40 04 06 *Fax:* (022) 20 63 95
*E-mail:* knut.olav.amas@samtiden.no
*Web Site:* www.samtiden.no
*Key Personnel*
Editor: Knut Olav Amas *E-mail:* knut.olav.amas@
 samtiden.no
Journal for politics, literature & other social ques-
 tions.

∮**Scandinavian Public Library Quarterly**
 **(SPLQ)** (J)
Published by Statens Bibliotektilsyn
Kronprinsens gate 9, 0033 Oslo
Mailing Address: PO Box 8145 Dep, 0033 Oslo

*Tel:* (021) 02 17 00 *Fax:* (021) 02 17 01
*E-mail:* splq@bs.dk
*Web Site:* www.splq.info
*Key Personnel*
Editor: Jens Thorhauge
First published 1968.

**Syn og Segn** (Vision & Tradition) (P)
Published by Det Norske Samlaget
Postboks 4672 Sofienberg, 0506 Oslo
*Tel:* (022) 70 78 00 *Fax:* (022) 68 75 02
*E-mail:* syn.og.segn@samlaget.no
*Web Site:* www.samlaget.no
Major Norwegian review on political & cultural affairs.
Quarterly.

**Vinduet** (The Window) (P)
Published by Gyldenal Norsk Forlag
Postboks 6860, St Olavs plass, 0164 Oslo
*Tel:* (022) 03 42 44; (022) 034100 *Fax:* (022) 034105
*E-mail:* vinduet@vinduet.no; gnf@gyldendal.no
*Web Site:* www.vinduet.no
*Telex:* 72 880 gyldn n
First published 1947.
Triannually.
ISSN: 0042-6288

# Pakistan

**Ham Qalam** (P)
Published by Pakistan Writers' Guild
11 Abbok Rd Anarkali/ One Mentgomrey Rd, Lahore
*Tel:* 6367124
Monthly.

**Pakistan Library & Information Science Journal** (J)
Published by Library Promotion Bureau
Karachi University Campus, Dastagir Society, Federal B Area, Karachi 75270
Mailing Address: PO Box 8421, Karachi 75270
*Tel:* (021) 479001 *Fax:* (021) 473226
*E-mail:* gsabzwari@yahoo.com
*Key Personnel*
Chief Editor: Mr Adil Usmani
First published 1966.
Quarterly.
150 PKR; 80 USD

**Pakistan National Bibliography** (Qaumi Kitabiaat-E-Pakistan) (J)
Published by Department of Libraries, National Library of Pakistan
Constitution Ave, Islamabad
*Tel:* (051) 9214523; (051) 92026436 *Fax:* (051) 9221375
*E-mail:* nlpiba@isb.paknet.com.pk
*Web Site:* www.nlp.gov.pk
*Key Personnel*
Editor: Muhammad Abas Khan Sherwani
First published 1962.
Annually.
1996: 300 pp, 60 USD

# Papua New Guinea

**Bikmaus** (P)
Published by National Research Institute of Papua New Guinea

PO Box 5854, Boroko, NCD
*Tel:* 326 0061; 326 0079; 326 0083 *Fax:* 326 0213
*E-mail:* nri@global.net.pg
*Web Site:* www.nri.org.pg
First published 1980.
Quarterly.
ISSN: 0255-7231

**Office of Libraries and Archives, Papua, New Guinea** (J)
Published by National Library Service of Papua New Guinea
PO Box 734, Waigani NCD
*Tel:* 3256200 *Fax:* 3251331
*E-mail:* ceminoni@online.net.ps
*Telex:* NE 22234
*Key Personnel*
Dir General: Daniel Paraide *Tel:* 3258013
    *E-mail:* paraide@daltron.com.ps
Annually.

# Peru

**Bibliografia Peruana** (Peruvian National Bibliography) (J)
Published by Biblioteca Nacional del Peru
Av Abancay 4ta cuadra, Lima
*Tel:* (01) 428-7690; (01) 428-7696 *Fax:* (01) 427-7331
*E-mail:* dn@binape.gob.pe
*Web Site:* www.binape.gob.pe
*Key Personnel*
Dir: Sinesio Lopez Jimenez
First published 1943.
Annually.
2000, 50 PEN

**Textual: Revista del Instituto Nacional de Cultura** (P)
Published by Instituto Nacional de Cultura
Av Javier Prado Este 2465, Lima 41
*Tel:* (01) 476-9933 *Fax:* (01) 476-9888
*Web Site:* inc.perucultural.org.pe
*Key Personnel*
Dir: Dr Fernando Silva Santisteban

# Philippines

**Diliman Review** (P)
Published by University of the Philippines, Sciences, Arts, & Letters, & Social Sciences & Philosophy
College of Science, Velasquez St, Diliman, 1101 Quezon City
*Tel:* (02) 924-7392 *Fax:* (02) 929-1266
*Web Site:* www.upd.edu.ph
*Key Personnel*
Editor: Eddie E Eswetura

**Philippine Studies** (P)
Published by Ateneo de Manila University Press
Ground floor, Bellarmine Hall, Katipunan Ave, Loyola Heights, 1109 Quezon City
*Tel:* (02) 4265984; (02) 4266001 (ext 4613); (02) 4266001 (ext 4614 or 4615, editorial); (02) 4266001 (ext 4612 or 4616, business & marketing) *Fax:* (02) 4265909
*E-mail:* unipress@admu.edu.ph
*Web Site:* www.ateneopress.com
Publishes articles, notes & reviews in the humanities, literature, history, social sciences, philosophy & Philippine arts.

First published 1953.
Quarterly.
140 pp, 600 PHP or 40 USD/yr; 50 PHP per back issue
ISSN: 0031-7837

# Poland

**Ksiegarz** (The Bookseller) (J)
Published by Stowarzyszenie Ksiegarzy Polskich (Association of Polish Booksellers)
ul Batorego 24, 43-100 Tychy
*Tel:* (022) 252-874
*E-mail:* sklep@ksiegarz.com
*Web Site:* www.ksiegarz.com.pl

**Pamietnik Teatralny** (The Atrical Diary) (P)
Published by Polish Academy of Sciences, Institute of Art
ul Dluga 26/28, 00-950 Warsaw
*Tel:* (022) 50 48 218 *Fax:* (022) 831 31 49
*E-mail:* ispan@ispan.pl
*Web Site:* www.ispan.uw.edu.pl
History of Polish Theatre.
First published 1952.
Quarterly.

**Polish Publishers & Booksellers** (B)
Published by Panstwowy Instytut Wydawniczy (PIW) (National Publishing Institute)
ul Foksal 17, 00-372 Warsaw
*Tel:* (022) 826-02-01; (022) 826-02-05 *Fax:* (022) 826-15-36
*E-mail:* piw@piw.pl
*Web Site:* www.piw.pl
*Telex:* 814306
Text in English.

**Ruch Wydawniczy w Liczbach** (Polish Publishing in Figures) (B)
Published by Biblioteka Narodowa w Warszawie (The National Library in Warsaw)
al Niepodleglosci 213, 02 086 Warsaw 22
*Tel:* (022) 608-2639 *Fax:* (022) 825-5251
*E-mail:* biblnar@bn.org.pl
*Web Site:* www.bn.org.pl
*Key Personnel*
Editor: Krystyna Bankowska-Bober
First published 1955.
Annually.
102 pp
ISSN: 0511-1196

**Soon to Appear** (J)
Published by AGPOL (Przedsiebiorstwo Reklamy i Wydawnictw Handlu Zagranicznego)
ul Kerbedzia 4, 00-957 Warsaw
*Tel:* (022) 416061 *Fax:* (022) 405607
*Telex:* 813364
*Key Personnel*
Editor: Ryszard Salinger
French, German & Russian editions.
First published 1953.
Monthly.
ISSN: 0239-0345

# Portugal

**Livros de Portugal** (Portuguese Books) (J)
Published by Associacao Portuguesa de Editores e Livreiros
Av Dos Estados Unidos da America, 97-6° Esq, 1700-167 Lisbon
*Tel:* (021) 843 51 80 *Fax:* (021) 848 93 77

*E-mail:* adm@apel.pt
*Web Site:* www.apel.pt
*Telex:* 62735
First published 1940.
Monthly.
50 USD
ISSN: 0870-5259

**Livros Disponiveis** (B)
Published by Associacao Portuguesa de Editores e
    Livreiros
Av Estados Unidos da America, 97 6 Esq, 1700-
    004 Lisbon
*Tel:* (021) 843 51 80 *Fax:* (021) 848 93 77
*E-mail:* adm@apel.pt
*Web Site:* www.apel.pt
Portuguese Books in Print (CD-ROM).
Annually.
36.41 EUR
ISSN: 0870-6093

**O Mundo do Edicao Luso-Brasileira** (B)
Published by Publicacoes Europa-America Lda
Apdo 8, Mem Martins Cedex
*Tel:* (01) 9211461 *Fax:* (01) 9217940
*E-mail:* secretariado@europa-america.pt
*Telex:* 42255 peap
The World of Publishing, Portugal & Brazil.

# Puerto Rico

**Atenea** (P)
Published by University of Puerto Rico at
    Mayaguez, College of Arts & Sciences
Dept of English, Chardon 323, Mayaguez 00680
Mailing Address: Dept of English, Box 9042,
    Mayaguez 00681
*Tel:* (787) 832-4040 (ext 3090) *Fax:* (787) 265-
    3847
*E-mail:* atenea@uprm.edu
*Web Site:* mayaweb.upr.clu.edu/artssciences/
    atenea/atenea.htm
*Key Personnel*
Editor: Nandita Batra
Text in Spanish & English.
Biannually.
ISSN: 0885-6079

**ƒGuide to Review of Books From & About
    Hispanic America** (B)
Published by AMM Editions
c/o Pontifical Catholic University of Puerto Rico,
    Ponce 00732
Mailing Address: Box 151, Sta 6, Ponce 00732
*Tel:* (787) 841-2000 *Fax:* (787) 840-4295
*Key Personnel*
Editor: Antonio Matos
Bibliography.
First published 1965.
Annually.
165 USD/yr

# Romania

**Bibliografia Romaniei** (J)
Published by National Library
Str Ion Ghica 4, Sec 3, 79708 Bucharest
*Tel:* (01) 3157063; (01) 3142434 (ext 232)
    *Fax:* (01) 312 33 81
*E-mail:* go@bibnat.ro
*Web Site:* www.bibnat.ro
Romanian National Bibliography.
First published 1952.
Bimonthly.

156 pp
ISSN: 1221-9126

**Convorbiri Literare** (Literary Conversations) (P)
Published by Uniunea Scriitorilor din Romania
Calea Victoriei 115, Bucharest
*Tel:* (01) 650 72 45 *Fax:* (01) 312 96 34
*E-mail:* romlit@romlit.ro
*Web Site:* www.romlit.ro
*Telex:* 11796
*Key Personnel*
Editor-in-Chief: Cassian Maria Spiridon
First published 1867.
Monthly.
ISSN: 0010-8243

**Euresis - Cahiers Roumains d'Etudes
    Litteraires** (P)
Published by Editura Univers SA
Piata Presei Libere 1, Casa Presei Libere, corp
    central, et 4, sec 1, 79739 Bucharest
*Tel:* (01) 224 32 86 *Fax:* (01) 222 56 52
*E-mail:* univers@rnc.ro
Text in French & English, occasionally in Ger-
    man, Russian, Spanish & Italian.
Biannually.
ISSN: 1223-1193

**Manuscriptum** (P)
Published by Muzeul Literaturii Romane
B-dul Dacia, nr 12, sector 1, Cod 71116
    Bucharest
*Tel:* (004) 021-2125845 *Fax:* (004) 021-2125846
*E-mail:* edit@mlr.ro
*Web Site:* www.mlr.ro
Manuscripts, Literary documents in Romanian, or
    bilingual, if necessary; Summaries in French,
    English, German & Russian.
First published 1970.
Triannually.

**Revista de Istorie si Teorie Literara** (Review of
    Literary History & Theory) (P)
Published by Academia Romana
Str 13 Septembrie nr 13, sector 5, 76117
    Bucharest
*Tel:* (01) 411 90 08 *Fax:* (01) 410 39 83
*E-mail:* edacad@ear.ro
*Web Site:* www.ear.ro
Summaries in French & Russian.
Annually.

**Romania Literara** (Literary Romania) (P)
Published by Uniunea Scriitorilor din Romania
Calea Victoriei 115, Bucharest
*Tel:* (01) 650 72 45 *Fax:* (01) 312 96 34
*E-mail:* romlit@romlit.ro
*Web Site:* www.romlit.ro
*Telex:* 11796
*Key Personnel*
Dir: Nicolae Manolescu
First published 1954.
Weekly.
ISSN: 1584-9465

**Romanian Review** (P)
Published by Foreign Languages Press Romania
PO Box 33-28, Bucharest 71341
*Tel:* (01) 2228481 *Fax:* (01) 3110526
*E-mail:* rps@dialkappa.ro
*Web Site:* www.wsp.ro/rps
Text in English, French & German (monthly),
    Russian (quarterly).
First published 1946.
Monthly.
ISSN: 0035-8088

**Secolul XX** (Twentieth Century) (P)
Published by Uniunea Scriitorilor din Romania
Calea Victoriei 115, Bucharest
*Tel:* (01) 650 72 45 *Fax:* (01) 312 96 34

*E-mail:* romlit@romlit.ro
*Web Site:* www.romlit.ro
*Telex:* 11796
*Key Personnel*
Editor: Don Haulica
First published 1961.
Monthly.
ISSN: 0037-0517

**Steaua** (P)
Published by Uniunea Scriitorilor din Romania
Calea Victoriei 115, Bucharest
*Tel:* (01) 650 72 45 *Fax:* (01) 312 96 34
*E-mail:* romlit@romlit.ro
*Web Site:* www.romlit.ro
*Telex:* 11796
*Key Personnel*
Editor-in-Chief: Aurel Rau
First published 1953.
Monthly.
ISSN: 0039-0852

# Russian Federation

**Avrora** (Aurora) (J)
Published by Russian Federation Union of Writ-
    ers
Ul Millionnaya 4, 191186 St Petersburg
*Tel:* (0812) 3121323
*E-mail:* sekretar@avrora.ru
*Web Site:* www.avrora.ru
*Key Personnel*
Editor: E Shevelyov
Contact: Mrs Marina Zurzumija
Literary, artistic & socio-political journal.
First published 1969.
Monthly.
ISSN: 0320-6858

**Bibliografiia** (Bibliography) (J)
Published by Rossiiskaya Knizhnaya Palata (Rus-
    sian Book Chamber)
Ostogenka, 4, Moscow
*Tel:* (095) 291-12-78 *Fax:* (095) 291-96-30
*E-mail:* bookch@postman.ru
*Web Site:* www.bookchamber.ru
Contains articles on history, theory, methods &
    organization of bibliography, tells about the in-
    teresting experience of bibliographical work
    in libraries, & helps in work with catalogues,
    bibliographical aids & documents.
First published 1929.
Bimonthly.
ISSN: 0869-6020

**Druzhba Narodov** (People's Friendship) (P)
Published by Aspext Press Ltd
Povarskaya ul, 52, 121827 Moscow
*Tel:* (095) 291-62-27; (095) 291-62-49 *Fax:* (095)
    291-63-54
*Web Site:* www.russia.agama.com
*Key Personnel*
Editor: A L Ebanoidze
Literary, artistic, socio-political magazine.
First published 1938.
Monthly.
114 USD
ISSN: 0012-6756

**Ezhemesyachnyi
    Literaturno-Khudozhestvennyi Zhurnal** (P)
Published by Novyi Mir
Maly Putinkovsky per, 1/2, 103806 Moscow
*Tel:* (095) 209-57-02 *Fax:* (095) 200-08-29
*E-mail:* novy-mir@mtu.net.ru
*Web Site:* magazines.russ.ru/novyi_mi

*Key Personnel*
Editor: Andrei Vasilevskii
Literary, artistic & socio-political illustrated journal.
First published 1925.
Monthly.
235 USD/yr
ISSN: 0130-7673

**Knizhnaya Letopis'** (Book Chronicle) (J)
Published by Rossiiskaya Knizhnaya Palata (Russian Book Chamber)
Ostogenka, 4, Moscow
*Tel:* (095) 291-12-78 *Fax:* (095) 291-96-30
*E-mail:* bookch@postman.ru
*Web Site:* www.bookchamber.ru
Book Annals; published by Book Chamber International.
First published 1907.
Weekly.
160 pp, 520 USD
ISSN: 0869-5962

**Knizhnaya Moskva: Putevoditel'-Spravochnik**
(Books in Moscow A Guide and Handbook)
(B)
Published by Reklama
ul Cajkouskogo 7, 121099 Moscow
*Tel:* (095) 2052101

**Knizhnoe Obozrenie** (J)
Published by Ministerstvo Pechati i Informatsii Rossii
Sushchevskiival, 64, 129272 Moscow
*Tel:* (095) 2816266 *Fax:* (095) 2816266
*Web Site:* www.rusf.ru/ko
*Telex:* 411167 GBLSU
*Key Personnel*
Editor-in-Chief: Dmitriy Vatolin
Book Reviews.
First published 1966.
Weekly
132 USD/yr
ISSN: 0023-2378

**Letopis' Periodicheskikh i
Prodolzhaiushchikhsya Izdanii** (Chronicle of Periodical & Continual Editions) (J)
Published by Rossiiskaya Knizhnaya Palata (Russian Book Chamber)
ul Ostozhenka, d ya, 119034 Moscow
*Tel:* (095) 291-12-78 *Fax:* (095) 291-96-30
*E-mail:* bookch@postman.ru
*Web Site:* www.bookchamber.ru
Contains information about magazines & newspapers which have changed their name or which have ceased publication in Russia, in addition to other changes in periodicals.
First published 1933.
Annually.
ISSN: 0201-6265

**Literaturnaya Rossiya** (Literary Russia) (P)
Published by Izdatel'sko-Poligraficheskoe Ob'edinenie Pisatelei Rossii
Tsvetnoi Blvd, 30, 103662 Moscow
*Tel:* (095) 200-4005; (095) 200-2309 (advertising); (095) 200-2467 (advertising) *Fax:* (095) 200-2755
*E-mail:* litrossia@litrossia.ru; info@periodicals.ru
*Web Site:* www.litrossia.ru; www.mkniga.ru
*Key Personnel*
Editor-in-Chief: Vladmir Yeryomenko
*E-mail:* eremenko@litrossia.ru
First published 1958.
Weekly.
126 USD/yr
ISSN: 1560-6856

**Molodaya Gvardiya** (The Young Guards) (P)
Published by Redaktsiya Molodaya Gvardiya

Novodmitrovskaya ul 5-a, 125015 Moscow
*Tel:* (095) 2858829 *Fax:* (095) 285-56-90
*Key Personnel*
Editor: Evgeny Yushin
Literary, artistic, socio-political magazine.
First published 1922.
Monthly.
120 USD /yr
ISSN: 0131-2251

**Moskva** (Moscow) (P)
Published by Soyuz Pisatelei Rossii, Moskovskoe Otdelenie
Arbat 20, 121918 Moscow
*Tel:* (095) 921-96-26 *Fax:* (095) 291-07-32
*E-mail:* moskva@jurmos.msk.ru
*Key Personnel*
Editor: L I Borodin
Literary, artistic, socio-political illustrated magazine.
First published 1957.
Monthly.
165 USD
ISSN: 0131-2332

**Nash Sovremennik** (Our Contemporary) (P)
Tsvetnoi bul, 32, 103750 Moscow
*Tel:* (095) 200-24-24 *Fax:* (095) 200-23-05
*E-mail:* info@periodicals.ru
*Web Site:* www.friends-partners.org/partners/rpiac/nashsovr; www.mkniga.ru
Literary, artistic, socio-political magazine.
First published 1963.
Monthly.
126 USD/yr
ISSN: 0027-8238

**Neva** (P)
Published by NEVA Magazin Ltd
Nevskii prospekt, 3, 191186 St Petersburg
*Tel:* (0812) 312-70-35 *Fax:* (0812) 312-65-37
*E-mail:* redaktion@nevajournal.spb.ru
*Web Site·* www.nevajournal.spb.ru
Literary, artistic, socio-political illustrated magazine, black & white photos.
First published 1955.
Monthly.
106 USD/yr
ISSN: 0130-741X

**Russkaya Literatura** (Russian Literature) (P)
Published by Institut Russkoi Literatury
Makarova nab 4, 199034 Saint-Petersburg
*Tel:* (0812) 218-16-01
*Key Personnel*
Dir: Prof Nikolaj N Skatov *Tel:* (0812) 218-19-01
Historical & literary journal.
First published 1958.
Quarterly.
99 USD/yr
ISSN: 0131-6095

**Slovo** (P)
Published by Slovo (Moscow)
Sushchevskii val 64, 129272 Moscow
*Tel:* (095) 2815098 *Fax:* (095) 2384634
*Telex:* 411 169 GBLSU
*Key Personnel*
Editor-in-Chief: A V Larionov
Now Word.
First published 1936.
Bimonthly.
118 USD/yr

**Staroe Literaturnoe Obozrenie** (P)
Published by Literaturnoe Obozrenie
ul Dobroljubova, 9/11, 127254 Moscow
*Tel:* (095) 219-9263 *Fax:* (095) 218-0398
*E-mail:* info@mkniga.msk.su
*Web Site:* www.rema.ru/komment/litoboz/litoboz.htm; www.mkniga.ru

*Key Personnel*
Editor-in-Chief: Viktor Kulle
Journal of critics & bibliography.
First published 1973.
Bimonthly.
99.95 USD/yr
ISSN: 1680-6077

**Voprosy Literatury** (Questions of Literature) (P)
Published by Fond Literaturnaya Mysl
B Gnezdnikovskii per, 10, 103009 Moscow
*Tel:* (095) 229-49-77 *Fax:* (095) 229-64-71
*E-mail:* voplit@dionis.iasnet.ru
*Web Site:* magazine.russ.ru/voplit
*Telex:* 411950POEMA SU *Cable:* 103009
*Key Personnel*
Editor-in-Chief: L Lazarev
First published 1957.
Bimonthly.
162 RUB/6 months
ISSN: 0042-8795

**Znamya** (The Banner) (P)
ul Nikolskaya ul, 8/1, 103863 Moscow
*Tel:* (095) 924-13-46 *Fax:* (095) 921-32-72
*E-mail:* znamlit@dialup.ptt.ru
*Key Personnel*
Editor: S I Chuprinin
Literary, artistic, socio-political magazine. Contains short stories, archives, memoirs, fiction, documentaries & criticism.
First published 1931.
Monthly.
149.95 USD/yr
ISSN: 0130-1616

**Zvezda** (The Star) (P)
Mokhovaya ul, 20, D28, 191028 St Petersburg
*Tel:* (095) 272-89-48 *Fax:* (0812) 273-52-56
*E-mail:* arjev@zveza.spb.su; gordin@zvezda.spb.su
*Key Personnel*
Editor: G F Nikolaev
Literary, artistic, socio-political magazine.
First published 1924.
Monthly.
123 USD/yr
ISSN: 0321-1878

# Senegal

**Bibliographie du Senegal** (Bibliographies of Senegal) (J)
Published by Archives Nationales du Senegal
Bldg Administratif, Ave Leopold Sedar Senghor, Dakar
*Tel:* (0221) 8217021 *Fax:* (0221) 8225578
*E-mail:* bdas@telecomplus.sn
*Web Site:* www.archivesdusenegal.gouv.sn
First published 1962.
Semiannually.
ISSN: 0378-9942

ʃ**Bibliographie nationale courante de l'
Annee...des pays d' Afrique d' expression
francaise** (National Bibliography for the Year...of Francophone African Countries) (B)
Published by Ecole de Bibliothecaires, Archivistes, et Documentalistes de Dakar
EBAD/UCAD, BP 3252, Dakar
*Tel:* 825 76 60; 864 21 22 *Fax:* 824 05 42
*E-mail:* ebad@ebad.ucad.sn
*Web Site:* www.ebad.ucad.sn
*Key Personnel*
Dir: Mbaye Thiam
Bibliography covering books & other materials published in Francophone Africa.

First published 1967.
Annually.

# Serbia and Montenegro

**Bibliografija Jugoslavije** (Bibliography of
  Yugoslavia) (J)
Published by Jugoslovenski Bibliografsko Infor-
  macijski Institut (Yugoslav Institute for Bibli-
  ography & Information)
Terazije 26, 11000 Belgrade
*Tel:* (011) 687 836; (011) 687 760 *Fax:* (011) 687
  760; (011) 688 840
*E-mail:* yubin@jbi.bg.ac.yu
*Web Site:* www.yugoslavia.com/culture/yubin
*Key Personnel*
Dir: Dr Radomir Glavicki
First published 1950.
Bimonthly.
80 pp
ISSN: 0523-2201

**Catalogue of Books Published by Yugoslav
  Publishers** (B)
Published by Association of Serbia & Montene-
  gro Publishers & Booksellers
Kneza Milosa 25, 11000 Belgrade
*Tel:* (011) 2642-533; (011) 2642-248 *Fax:* (011)
  2686-539; (011) 2646-339
*E-mail:* uikj@eunet.yu
*Web Site:* www.beobookfair.co.yu
*Key Personnel*
General Dir: Mr Zivadin Mitrovic
Book Fairs, Department Manager: Marina Radoji-
  cic

**Knjizevne Novine** (Literary News) (P)
Published by Serbian Unity Congress
Vasina 20, 11000 Belgrade
*Tel:* (011) 3282 893; (011) 3282 960 *Fax:* (011)
  3282 893
*E-mail:* webmaster@bgd.serbianunity.net
*Web Site:* www.serbianunity.net
*Key Personnel*
Editor: Dragan M Jeremic

**Lumina** (P)
Published by Libertatea
str Z Zrenjanina nr 7, 26000 Panciova
*Tel:* 13 353 401; 13 346 447 *Fax:* 21 51 897
*E-mail:* lumina@libertatea.co.yu
*Web Site:* www.libertatea.co.yu
*Key Personnel*
Editor: Ion Balan
Literary & cultural review.
First published 1947.

**Savremenik** (P)
Published by Knjizevne Novine
Francuska 7, 11000 Belgrade
*Tel:* (011) 637-518; (011) 638-159; (011) 639-631
  *Fax:* (011) 637-518; (011) 638-168
*Key Personnel*
Editor: Pavle Zoric
Text in Serbo-Croatian.
First published 1955.
Monthly.
ISSN: 0036-519X

# Sierra Leone

**Sierra Leone Publications** (J)
Published by Sierra Leone Library Board
PO Box 326, Freetown
*Tel:* (022) 226 993; (022) 223 848 *Fax:* (022) 224
  439
*Key Personnel*
Editor: Marian Liek
National bibliography.
First published 1964.
Quarterly.

# Singapore

**Books about Singapore** (B)
Published by National Reference Library
91 Stamford Rd, Singapore 178896
*Tel:* 6332-3255 *Fax:* 6332-3248
*E-mail:* ref@nlb.gov.sg
*Web Site:* www.lib.gov.sg
*Key Personnel*
Chief Executive: Dr N Varaprasad
Biennially.
ISSN: 0068-0176
*Parent Company:* National Library Board

**NBDCS News** (J)
Published by National Book Development Coun-
  cil of Singapore
Geylang East Community Library, National Li-
  brary Board, 50 Geylang East Ave 1, Singapore
  389777
*Tel:* 6848 8290 *Fax:* 6742 9466
*E-mail:* info@bookcouncil.sg
*Web Site:* www.nbdcs.org.sg
First published 1981.
Quarterly.
ISSN: 0129-9239

**Singapore Book World** (J)
Published by National Book Development Coun-
  cil of Singapore
Geylang East Community Library, National Li-
  brary Board, 50 Geylang East Ave 1, Singapore
  389777
*Tel:* 6848 8290 *Fax:* 6742 9466
*E-mail:* info@bookcouncil.sg
*Web Site:* www.nbdcs.org.sg
Reviews of Singapore published books & articles
  on the book trade & reading trends.
First published 1970.
Annually.
ISSN: 0080-9659

**Singapore National Bibliography (SNB)** (J)
Published by National Library Board Singapore,
  Library Support Services
No 3, Changi South St 2, Tower B, Level 3, Sin-
  gapore 486548
*Tel:* 6546-7275 *Fax:* 6546-7262
*E-mail:* gifts_exchanges@nlb.gov.sg
*Web Site:* www.nlb.gov.sg
*Telex:* RS 26620 NATLIB
Annual accumulation.
Biannually.
ISSN: 0129-315X

**Singapore Periodicals Index** (B)
Published by National Reference Library
91 Stamford Rd, Singapore 178896
*Tel:* 6332-3255 *Fax:* 6332-3248
*E-mail:* ref@nlb.gov.sg
*Web Site:* www.lib.gov.sg
*Telex:* RS 26620 NATLIB

*Key Personnel*
Chief Executive: Dr N Varaprasad
Annually.

# Slovakia

**Kniha** (The Book) (P)
Published by Slovenska Narodna Kniznica, Mar-
  tin (Slovak National Library, Martin)
Nam J C Hronskeho 1, 036 01 Martin
*Tel:* (043) 422 07 20; (043) 430 18 02 *Fax:* (043)
  422 07 20; (043) 430 18 02
*E-mail:* snk@snk.sk
*Web Site:* www.snk.sk

**Literatura** (Slovak Literature) (P)
Published by Veda Publishing House of the Slo-
  vak Academy of Sciences
Stefanikova 3, 811 06 Bratislava
*Tel:* (02) 5245 0153 *Fax:* (02) 5245 0153
*E-mail:* ebor@centrum.sk
*Web Site:* www.veda-sav.sk
Contents page & summaries in German & Rus-
  sian.

**Slovak Books in Print** (J)
Published by Slovart Co Ltd
Pekna cesta 6/b, 830 04 Bratislava 34
Mailing Address: PO Box 14, 830 04 Bratislava
  34
*Tel:* (02) 44 87 12 10 *Fax:* (02) 44 87 12 46
*E-mail:* pobox@slovart.sk
*Web Site:* www.slovart.sk; www.slovart.com
*Telex:* 93394 slov c

**Slovenske pohlady na literaturu a umenie**
  (Slovak View on Literature & Art) (P)
Published by Asociacia Slovenskych Spisovatelov
Laurinska 2, 81308 Bratislava
*Tel:* (07) 334316; (07) 334374; (07) 332334; (07)
  5332671 *Fax:* (07) 335411
*Key Personnel*
Editor: Jan Strasser
First published 1846.
Monthly.
ISSN: 0037-7007

# Slovenia

**Slovenska Bibliografija** (Slovene Bibliography)
  (J)
Published by Narodna in Univerzitetna Knjiznica,
  Ljubljana (National & University Library)
Narodna in Univerzitetna Knjiznica, Turjaska 1,
  1001 Ljubljana
*Tel:* (01) 2001 110 *Fax:* (01) 4257 293
*E-mail:* info@nuk.uni-lj.si
*Web Site:* www.nuk.uni-lj.si/vstop.cgi
Quarterly.
ISSN: 0353-1716

# South Africa

**Acta Classica** (P)
Published by Classical Association of South
  Africa
c/o The Managing Editor, Acta Classica, Dept of
  Greek & Latin Studies, Rand Africkaans Uni-
  versity, PO Box 524, 2006 Aucland Park
*Tel:* (021) 808-4490 *Fax:* (021) 808-3714

*E-mail:* wjh@lw.rau.ac.za
*Web Site:* www.sun.ac.za/as/casa
*Key Personnel*
Managing Editor: W J Henderson
Treasurer: J Christoff Zietsman
Annually.
100 ZAR/yr subscription
ISSN: 0065-1141

**Akroterion** (P)
Published by University of Stellenbosch Dept of
   Ancient Studies
Private Bag X1, Matieland 7602
*Tel:* (021) 808-3203 *Fax:* (021) 808-3480
*E-mail:* jct@maties.sun.ac.za
*Web Site:* www.sun.ac.za/AS/journals/akro
Publishes articles in English or Afrikaans aimed
   at the non-specialist, covering all aspects of
   ancient Greek & Roman civilization, but fo-
   cussing especially on the influence & reception
   of the Classics.
First published 1956.
Annually.
ISSN: 0303-1896

**Catalog of Books (English) Published in
   Southern Africa, Still in Print (1970)** (B)
Published by Struik Publishers (Pty) Ltd
80 McKenzie St, Gardens, Cape Town 8001
Mailing Address: PO Box 1144, Cape Town 8000
*Tel:* (021) 462-4360 *Fax:* (021) 462-4379
*Web Site:* www.struik.co.za

**English in Africa** (P)
Published by Institute for the Study of English in
   Africa, Rhodes University
St Peter's Bldg (off Somerset St), Grahamstown
   6140
Mailing Address: PO Box 94, Grahamstown 6140
*Tel:* (046) 603 8111 *Fax:* (046) 622 5049
*E-mail:* j.king@ru.ac.za
*Web Site:* www.ru.ac.za
*Key Personnel*
Managing Editor: Prof Laurence Wright
Editor: Craig Mackenzie
Editorial Assistant: Marion Baxter
Primary source material: critical articles & book
   reviews on all aspects of African literature
   written in English.
First published 1974.
Semiannually in May & Oct.
60 ZAR (individuals); 100 ZAR (institutions);
   16 GBP or 25 USD (elsewhere, individuals &
   institutions)
ISSN: 0376-8902

**Journal of Literary Studies** (P)
Published by University of South Africa, Depart-
   ment of Literary Theory
PO Box 392, Pretoria 0003
*Tel:* (012) 429 6401; (012) 429 6700; (012) 429
   6058 *Fax:* (012) 429 3221
*E-mail:* unisa-press@unisa.ac.za
*Web Site:* www.unisa.ac.za
*Key Personnel*
Editor: Ina Grabe *E-mail:* graberc@alpha.unisa.
   ac.za
Journal to provide a forum for the discussion of
   literary theory, methodology, research & related
   matters, features articles, commentary, book
   reviews & general announcements.
First published 1985.
Vol 17, 100 ZAR
ISSN: 0256-4718

**New Coin Poetry** (P)
Published by Institute for the Study of English in
   Africa, Rhodes University
St Peter's Bldg (off Somerset St), Grahamstown
   6140
Mailing Address: PO Box 94, Grahamstown 6140

*Tel:* (046) 603 8111 *Fax:* (046) 622 5049
*E-mail:* j.king@ru.ac.za
*Web Site:* www.ru.ac.za
*Key Personnel*
Managing Editor: Prof Laurence Wright
Editor: Joan Metelerkamp
Editorial Assistant: Marion Baxter
Collection of South African poetry, reviews &
   interviews.
Biannually in June & Dec.
90 pp, 50 ZAR (Africa); 8.50 GBP or 15 USD
   (elsewhere)
ISSN: 0028-4459

**New Contrast** (J)
Published by South African Literary Journal Ltd
PO Box 3841, Cape Town 8000
*E-mail:* newcontrast@mailbox.co.za
Publishes South African poetry, short fiction, es-
   says, criticisms, book reviews, graphic art &
   general cultural commentary. Does not dis-
   criminate on the basis of race, gender, political
   persuasion or religious creed.
First published 1960.
Quarterly.
70 ZAR; 50 USD
ISSN: 1017-5415

**scrutiny2: issues in English studies in Southern
   Africa** (P)
Published by University of South Africa Press
Dept of English, PO Box 392, Pretoria 0003
*Tel:* (012) 429 6702 *Fax:* (012) 429 3221
*E-mail:* unisa-press@unisa.ac.za
*Web Site:* www.unisa.ac.za/dept/press/onjourn.
   html
*Telex:* 3777 *Cable:* UNISA
*Key Personnel*
Editor: Prof Leon de Kock *Tel:* (012) 429 6294
   *E-mail:* dkockl@unisa.ac.za
Literary articles & reviews.
First published 1996.
Biannually in May & Sept.
80 pp, 30 USD
ISSN: 0041-5359

∫**Shakespeare in Southern Africa** (P)
Published by Shakespeare Society of Southern
   Africa
c/o ISEA, Rhodes University, Grahamstown 6140
Mailing Address: PO Box 94, Grahamstown 6140
*Tel:* (0461) 6038111 *Fax:* (0461) 6225049
*E-mail:* b.cummings@ru.ac.za
*Web Site:* www.ru.ac.za/affiliates/isea/shake
*Key Personnel*
Editor: Prof Brian Pearce *E-mail:* brianp@dit.ac.
   za
Managing Editor: Prof Laurence Wright
   *E-mail:* l.wright@ru.ac.za
Articles, commentary & reviews on all aspects of
   Shakesperean studies & performance, with a
   particular emphasis on the response to Shake-
   speare in Southern Africa.
First published 1987.
Annually.
100 pp, 120 USD/yr
ISSN: 1011-582X

**South African Journal of African Languages**
   (P)
Published by African Language Association of
   Southern Africa
Dept of African Languages, UNISA, PO Box
   392, Pretoria 0003
*Tel:* (012) 429 8070 *Fax:* (012) 429 3355
*E-mail:* unisa-press@unisa.ac.za
*Web Site:* www.unisa.ac.za
*Key Personnel*
Editor: L J Lowrens
Quarterly.

**Staffrider** (P)
Published by Cosaw Publishing (Pty) Ltd
PO Box 421007, Fordsburg 2033
*Tel:* 833 2530 *Fax:* 833 2532
Text in English.
First published 1978.
Quarterly.
12 ZAR/yr
ISSN: 0258-7211

# Spain

**Bibliografia Espanola Monografias** (Spanish
   Bibliography) (J)
Published by Biblioteca Nacional de Espana
Paseo De Recoletos 20, Madrid 28071
*Tel:* (01) 5807706 *Fax:* (01) 5807712
*E-mail:* info.publicaciones@bne.es
*Web Site:* www.bne.es
Monthly.
ISSN: 0214-2694

**Bibliografia Espanola: Suplemento de
   Publicaciones Periodicas** (Periodical
   Publications Supplement to Spanish
   Bibliography) (J)
Published by Biblioteca Nacional de Espana
Paseo de Recoletos 20, Madrid 28071
*Tel:* (091) 5807706 *Fax:* (091) 5807712
*E-mail:* info.publicaciones@bne.es
*Web Site:* www.bne.es

**Catalan Review** (P)
Published by North American Catalan Society,
   Publicacions de L'Abadia de Montseriat
Ausias March 92-98 interior, 08013 Barcelona
*Tel:* (093) 2450303; (093) 2314001 *Fax:* (093)
   247-3594
*E-mail:* pamsa@pamsa.com
*Web Site:* cr.middlebury.edu/catalan/CReview.htm;
   www.pamsa.com
Current & past issues of Catalan Review can be
   purchased from: Merce Vidal Tibbits, Dept of
   Modern Languages & Literatures, Howard Uni-
   versity, Washington, DC 20059.

**Delibros** (J)
Published by Delibros SA
RDM, SL, Eloy Gonzalo, 27-3°, 28010 Madrid
*Tel:* (091) 591 4258 (subscriptions) *Fax:* (091)
   594 3053
*E-mail:* info@delibros.com
*Web Site:* www.delibros.com
*Key Personnel*
Publisher: Jaime Brull
Dir: Teresa M Peces *E-mail:* direccion@delibros.
   com
Publicity Dir: Monica Lizana
   *E-mail:* publicidad@delibros.com
Editor: Virginia de Pablo *E-mail:* redaccion@
   delibros.com
Design: Jose Maria Cerezo
   *E-mail:* maquetacion@delibros.com
Illustration: Blanca Ortega
Subscriptions Coordinator: Nuria Garcia
   *E-mail:* suscripciones@delibros.com
Monthly.
ISSN: 0214-2694

**Libros Espanoles en Venta: Repertorio Anual**
   (Spanish Books in Print) (B)
Published by Agencia Espanola del ISBN
Santiago Rusinol, 8, 28040 Madrid
*Tel:* (091) 536 88 00 *Fax:* (091) 553 99 90
*Web Site:* www.mcu.es/bases/spa/isbn/ISBN.html

Annual three volume compilation of over 266,000 in-print titles from over 10,000 publishers. Also included are 23,000 recent out-of-print titles.
518.52 USD for print edition, 1,112 USD for CD-ROM

**Litoral** (P)
Published by Visor Libros
Isacc Peral, 18, 28015 Madrid
*Tel:* (091) 549 34 09 *Fax:* (091) 544 86 95
*E-mail:* visor-libros@visor-libros.com
*Web Site:* www.visor-libros.com
Poetry review.
Monthly.

**Nuestro Tiempo** (Our Time) (P)
Published by Servicio de Publicaciones de la Universidad de Navarra, SA
Carretera del Sadar, s/n, Campus Universitario, 31080 Pamplona-Navarra
*Tel:* (048) 425 600 *Fax:* (048) 425 718
*E-mail:* nuestrot@unav.es; cbulnes@unav.es
*Web Site:* www.unav.es/nt
50 EUR (subscription)
ISSN: 0029-5795

**Razon y Fe** (Reason & Faith) (P)
Published by Centro Loyola de Estudios y Comunicacion Social
Pablo Aranda, 3, 28006 Madrid
*Tel:* (091) 5624930 *Fax:* (091) 5634073
*E-mail:* celomad@jesuitas.es
*Web Site:* www.jesuitas.es/razonyfe.htm
Spanish-American review.

**Revista de Occidente** (Review of the West) (P)
Published by Instituto Universitario Ortega y Gasset
C/Fortuny, 53, 28010 Madrid
*Tel:* (091) 700 4100 *Fax:* (091) 700 3530
*E-mail:* fogrocci@accessnet.es
*Web Site:* www.ortegaygasset.edu
*Key Personnel*
Dir: Soledad Ortega
First published 1923.

**Serra d'Or** (P)
Published by Publicacions de l'Abadia de Montserrat
Ausias March 92-98, interior, 08013 Barcelona
*Tel:* (093) 245 03 03; (093) 2314001 *Fax:* (093) 247 35 94
*E-mail:* pamsa@pamsa.com
*Web Site:* www.pamsa.com/rev/serrador.asp
*Key Personnel*
Dir: Josep Massot i Muntaner
Editor: Maur M Boix
First published 1955.
80 pp
ISSN: 0037-2501

# Sri Lanka

**Sri Lanka ISBN Publishers Directory** (B)
Published by National Library & Documentation Centre
No 14, Independence Ave, Colombo 07
*Tel:* (01) 698847; (01) 685197 *Fax:* (011) 2685201
*E-mail:* natlib@slt.lk
*Web Site:* www.natlib.lk
*Key Personnel*
Dir General: Mr M S U Amarasiri *E-mail:* dg@mail.natlib.lk
Deputy Dir: Mr G G Upasena *E-mail:* ddadmin@mail.natlib.lk

Assistant Librarian: Ms D Daniel
*E-mail:* libdev@mail.natlib.lk
This directory includes 1,080 Sri Lankan Publishers. It is divided into two parts: namely, Alphabetical Section & Numerical Section. In each section, the publishers are categorized into three groups: Commercial, Governmental & Non-Governmental Institutions & Author/Private Publishers. The ISBN Publishers Directory is computerized & the database is updated monthly.

**Sri Lanka National Bibliography** (J)
Published by National Library & Documentation Centre
No 14, Independence Ave, Colombo 07
Mailing Address: PO Box 1764, Colombo 07
*Tel:* (011) 2698847 *Fax:* (01) 685201
*E-mail:* natlib@slt.lk
*Web Site:* www.natlib.lk
*Key Personnel*
Dir General: Mr M S U Amarasiri *E-mail:* dg@mail.natlib.lk
Deputy Dir: Mr G G Upasena *E-mail:* ddadmin@mail.natlib.lk
Text in English, Sinhala & Tamil. Contains information of the latest publications in Sri Lanka.
First published 1962.
Monthly.
420 LKR or 50 USD

**Vidyodaya Journal of Social Sciences** (J)
Published by University of Sri Jayewardenepura
Gangodawila, Nugegoda
*Tel:* (01) 802695; (01) 802696; (01) 803191; (01) 803192 *Fax:* (01) 852604
*E-mail:* unisjay@sjp.ac.lk
*Web Site:* www.sjp.ac.lk *Cable:* UNISJAY
*Key Personnel*
Editor-in-Chief: Winston E Ratnayake
Librarian/Coordinating Editor: Mr P Vidanapathirana
First published 1968.
Biannually.
ISSN: 1391-1937

# Swaziland

**Swaziland National Bibliography** (J)
Published by University of Swaziland Library
Private Bag 4, Kwaluseni
*Tel:* 518-5108; 518-4011; 518-5356 *Fax:* 518-5276
*E-mail:* kwaluseni@uniswa.sz
*Web Site:* www.uniswa.sz
*Telex:* 222087WD
Irregularly.

# Sweden

**Bonniers Litteraera Magasin** (Bonniers Literary Magazine) (P)
Published by Albert Bonniers Forlag AB
Box 3159, 103 63 Stockholm
*Tel:* (08) 696 86 20 *Fax:* (08) 696 83 61
*E-mail:* info@abforlag.bonnier.se
*Web Site:* www.bok.bonnier.se/new/albertbonniersforlag.htm

**Svensk Bokfoerteckning** (Swedish National Bibliography) (J)
Published by Kungliga Biblioteket, Tidnings AB Svensk Bokhandel
PO Box 5039, 102 41 Stockholm

*Tel:* (08) 463 40 00 *Fax:* (08) 463 40 04
*E-mail:* kungl.biblioteket@kb.se
*Web Site:* www.kb.se
ISSN: 0039-6443

**Svensk Bokhandel** (Swedish Book Trade) (J)
Published by Tidnings AB Svensk Bokhandel
Birkagatan 16 C, 113 86 Stockholm
Mailing Address: PO Box 6888, 113 86 Stockholm
*Tel:* (08) 545 417 70 *Fax:* (08) 545 417 75
*Web Site:* www.svb.se
Published jointly with Swedish Booksellers' Association.

**Svenska Bokfoerlaeggarefoereningen** (B)
Published by Swedish Publishers' Association
Drottninggatan 97 2tr, 11360 Stockholm
*Tel:* (08) 736 19 40 *Fax:* (08) 736 19 44
*E-mail:* svf@forlagskansli.se
*Web Site:* www.forlagskansli.se
*Key Personnel*
Dir: Kristina Ahlinder *E-mail:* kristina.ahlinder@forlagskansli.se
Swedish Publishers Association list of members & agents, together with book trade associates & organizations.
First published 1843.

**Svenska Litteratursaellskapet i Finland Skrifter** (P)
Published by Bokfoerlaget Atlantis
Sturegatan 24, 114 36 Stockholm
*Tel:* (08) 54566070 *Fax:* (08) 54566071
*E-mail:* info@atlantisbok.se
*Web Site:* www.atlantisbok.se
*Key Personnel*
Editor: Nina Edgren-Henrichson *E-mail:* nina.edgren-henrichson@sls.fi
Scholarly publications in history, literature, ethnology, Scandinavian languages, social & political sciences.
First published 1886.
Irregular.
ISSN: 0039-6842

**Text: Svensk Tidskrift foer Bibliografi** (Text Swedish Journal of Bibliography) (J)
Published by Dahlia Books, International Publishers & Booksellers
Box 1025, 751 40 Uppsala
*Tel:* (018) 101098 *Fax:* (018) 100525
*E-mail:* dahlia@telia.com
Bibliographical journal, in English & Swedish.
First published 1974.
Irregularly.
ISSN: 0345-0112

# Switzerland

**Bookbird: A Journal of International Children's Literature** (J)
Published by International Board on Books for Young People (IBBY)
Nonnenweg 12, 4003 Basel
*Tel:* (061) 272 29 17 *Fax:* (061) 272 27 57
*E-mail:* ibby@ibby.org
*Web Site:* www.ibby.org
*Key Personnel*
President: Peter Schneck
Executive Dir: Kimete Basha
Editor: Evelyn B Freeman; Barbara A Lehman; Lilia Ratcheva-Stratieva; Patricia L Scharer
Covers many facets of international children's literature & includes news from IBBY & the IBBY National Sections.
Quarterly.
11.50 USD (back issues)
ISSN: 0006-7377

**Drehpunkt** (Pivot) (P)
Published by Lenos Verlag
Spalentorweg 12, 4051 Basel
*Tel:* (061) 261 34 14 *Fax:* (061) 261 35 18
*E-mail:* lenos@lenos.ch
*Web Site:* www.lenos.ch

**Etudes de Lettres** (Literary Studies) (P)
Published by Universite de Lausanne
Faculte des Lettres, BFSH2 bureau 2050, Univer-
site' de Lausanne Dorigny, 1015 Lausanne
*Tel:* (021) 692-2978; (021) 692-2905 *Fax:* (021)
692-3045
*E-mail:* lidia.peytrignet@dlett.unil.ch
*Web Site:* www.unil.ch
*Key Personnel*
Editor: Johannes Bronkhorst
First published 1960.
Quarterly.
170 pp, 18 CHF (single vol), 26 CHF (double
vol)
ISSN: 0014-2026

ʃ**International Publishers Association
Proceedings of Congress** (B)
Published by International Publishers Association
Av de Miremont 3, 1206 Geneva
*Tel:* (022) 346 3018 *Fax:* (022) 347 5717
*E-mail:* secretariat@ipa-uie.org
*Web Site:* www.ipa-uie.org
*Telex:* 3421883 *Cable:* INPUBLASS
*Key Personnel*
Secretary-General: J Alexis Koutchoumow

**Jugendliteratur** (J)
Published by Schweizerischer Bund fuer Ju-
gendliteratur (Swiss Federation for Youth Liter-
ature)
Gewerbestr 8, 6330 Cham
*Tel:* (041) 741 31 40 *Fax:* (041) 740 01 59
*E-mail:* sbj@bluewin.ch
*Key Personnel*
Chief Editor: Jutta Radel
First published 1975.
Quarterly.
ISSN: 0256-6532

**Librarium** (J)
Published by Schweizerische Bibliophilen -
Gesellschaft
Foundation Martin Bodmer, 19-12 Rt du Guig-
nard, CH-1223 Geneva
*Tel:* (022) 707 4433 *Fax:* (022) 707 4430
*Key Personnel*
Editor: Martin Bircher
Text in German, French, Italian & English.
Triannually.
ISSN: 0024-2152

**orte** (P)
Published by orte-Verlag
Wirtschaft Kreuz, 9427 Wolfhaden
*Tel:* (071) 888 15 56
*E-mail:* info@orteverlag.ch
*Web Site:* www.orteverlag.ch

ʃ**La Propriete industrielle et le droit d'auteur**
(Industrial Property & Copyright) (P)
Published by World Intellectual Property Organi-
zation (WIPO)
34, chemin des Colombettes, 1211 Geneva 20
Mailing Address: PO Box 18, 1211 Geneva 20
*Tel:* (022) 338 91 11 *Fax:* (022) 733 54 28
*E-mail:* info@wipo.int
*Web Site:* www.wipo.org
*Telex:* 412912 ompi ch
*Key Personnel*
Head Information Section: Laurent Manderieux
Monthly, English & French; Bimonthly, Spanish.

**Pruefen & Handeln** (P)
Published by Pruefen & Handeln/Examiner et
Agir
8215 Hallau
*Tel:* (052) 6813144 *Fax:* (052) 6814014
*E-mail:* memopress@klettgau.ch
*Web Site:* www.klettgau.ch/pruefen&handeln
*Cable:* MEMOPRESS; Prufen & Handeln;
Aktion Volk & Parlament
Journalism & literature; text in German. Short
information on politics, economics & religion
with commentary. Summary in French.
*Parent Company:* Aktion Volk und Parlament

**Schweizer Buch** (The Swiss Book) (J)
Published by Schweizerischer Buchhaendler- und
Verleger-Verband SBVV (Swiss Booksellers' &
Publishers' Association (German Language))
Hallwylstr 15, 3003 Bern
*Tel:* (031) 322 89 11 *Fax:* (031) 322 84 63
*E-mail:* slb-bns@slb.admin.ch
*Web Site:* www.snl.ch
Bibliographical bulletin. Cosponsored by
Schweizerische Landesbibliothek.
First published 1943.
Bimonthly.
ISSN: 0036-732X

**Schweizer Buchhandel** (The Swiss Book Trade)
(J)
Published by Schweizerischer Buchhaendler- und
Verleger-Verband SBVV (Swiss Booksellers' &
Publishers' Association (German Language))
Alderstr 40, 8034 Zurich
*Tel:* (01) 421 28 00 *Fax:* (01) 421 28 18
*E-mail:* sbvv@swissbooks.ch
*Web Site:* www.swissbooks.ch

**Schweizer Buchhandels-Adressbuch** (B)
Published by Schweizerischer Buchhaendler- und
Verleger-Verband SBVV (Swiss Booksellers' &
Publishers' Association (German Language))
Alderstr 40, 8034 Zurich
*Tel:* (01) 421 28 00 *Fax:* (01) 421 28 18
*E-mail:* sbvv@swissbooks.ch
*Web Site:* www.swissbooks.ch
Directory of the Swiss book trade, containing lists
of publishers, booksellers, distributors, trade
organizations & cross-reference indexes.
First published 1966.
Annually.
ISSN: 0080-7230

**Schweizer Monatshefte** (Swiss Monthly
Magazine) (P)
Published by Gesellschaft Schweizer Monatshefte
Vogelsangstr 52, 8006 Zurich
*Tel:* (01) 361 26 06 *Fax:* (01) 363 70 05
*E-mail:* info@schweizermonatshefte.ch
*Web Site:* www.schweizermonatshefte.ch
Monthly.
110 CHF

# Taiwan, Province of China

**Chinese National Bibliography** (J)
Published by National Central Library
20 Chung-shan South Rd, Taipei
*Tel:* (02) 2361 9132 *Fax:* (02) 382 1489
*E-mail:* reader@msg.ncl.edu.tw
*Web Site:* www.ncl.edu.tw
Text in Chinese.

**The Chinese PEN** (P)
Published by International PEN, Taipei Chinese
Center
33 Lane 180, 5th floor, Kwang Fu South Rd,
10553 Taipei
*Tel:* (02) 7219101 *Fax:* (02) 7219101
*E-mail:* taipen@tpts5.seed.net.tw
*Key Personnel*
Editor: Pang Yuan Chi
Text in Chinese.
First published 1972.
Quarterly.
600 TWD or 20 USD

**Counter Attack** (P)
Published by National Institute for Compilation &
Translation
247 Chou Shan Rd, Taipei
*Tel:* (02) 33225558 *Fax:* (02) 33225559
*Web Site:* www.nict.gov.tw
*Key Personnel*
Dir: Chi-chun Tseng
First published 1932.

**Shu mo chi kan** (J)
Published by Student Book Co Ltd
198, Sec 1, Ho-ping East Rd, Taipei 10610
*Tel:* (02) 23631097 *Fax:* (02) 23636334
*E-mail:* studentbook@web66.com.tw
*Web Site:* studentbook.web66.com.tw
Bibliography, text in Chinese.
First published 1966.
Quarterly.
ISSN: 0006-1581

**Tamkang Review** (P)
Published by Tamkang University, Graduate Insti-
tute of Western Languages & Literature
Tamkang University, Ching Sheng Bldg, Room
1101, 25137 Taipei
*Tel:* (02) 6215656 (ext 2329) *Fax:* (02) 6209912
*E-mail:* jwu@mail.tku.edu.tw
*Web Site:* www2.tku.edu.tw/~tfwx/trreview.htm
Journal mainly devoted to comparative studies
between Chinese & foreign literatures; text in
English.
Quarterly.

# United Republic of Tanzania

**Tanzania National Bibliography** (J)
Published by Tanzania Library Services Board
Bibi Titi Mohamed St, Dar es Salaam
Mailing Address: PO Box 9283, Dar es Salaam
*Tel:* (022) 215 00 48; (022) 215 00 49 *Fax:* (022)
215 11 00
*E-mail:* tlsb@africaonline.co.tz
*Key Personnel*
Editor: Irene Minja
Text in English.
First published 1970.
Annually.
9.520 TZS or 90 USD/yr
ISSN: 0856-003X

**Umma** (P)
Published by University of Dar Es Salaam
PO Box 35091, Dar es Salaam
*Tel:* (022) 2410500 *Fax:* (022) 2410078
*E-mail:* vc@admin.udsm.ac.tz
*Web Site:* www.udsm.ac.tz
*Key Personnel*
Editor: Clement L Ndulute

Literary magazine published under the auspices of the Department of Literature, University of Dar Es Salaam.
Biannually.

# Turkey

**Turkiye Bibliyografyasi** (Turkish National Bibliography) (J)
Published by National Library of Turkey
Bahcelievler, 06490 Ankara
*Tel:* (0312) 2126200 *Fax:* (0312) 2230451
*E-mail:* katalog@mkutup.gov.tr
*Web Site:* www.mkutup.gov.tr
*Key Personnel*
Librarian: Nurhan Naneci
First published 1928.
Monthly.
Annual subscription 48 USD foreign countries
ISSN: 0041-4328

**Varlik** (Existence) (P)
Published by Varlik Yayinlari AS
Piyerloti Cad Ayerberk Ap 7-9, Cemberlitas, 34400 Istanbul
*Tel:* (0212) 518-0048 (Direct); (0212) 516-2004; (0212) 516-2013 *Fax:* (0212) 516-2005
*E-mail:* varlik@isbank.net.tr; varlik@varlik.com.tr
*Web Site:* www.varlik.com.tr
*Key Personnel*
Editor-in-Chief: Osman Deniztekin
Editor: Filiz Nayir Deniztekin; Enver Ercan
First published 1933.
Monthly.
2,500,000 TRL or 2 USD
ISSN: 1300-1728

# United Kingdom

ƒ**AAB's British Bibliography of Rare & Out-of-Print Titles** (P)
Published by Magna Graecia's Publishers (UK)
PO Box 342, Oxford OX2 7YF
*Tel:* (01865) 553 653 *Fax:* (01865) 553 653
*E-mail:* orders@magnagraciaspublishers.co.uk
*Web Site:* www.magnagraeciaspublishers.co.uk
*Key Personnel*
Editor: Luigi Gigliotti
General Editor: Louis de Sybaris
First published 1975.
Weekly.
ISBN(s): 0-86340-002-7
ISSN: 1362-8534

ƒ**AAB's British Register of Wanted Publications** (B)
Published by Magna Graecia's Publishers (UK)
PO Box 342, Oxford OX2 7YF
*Tel:* (01865) 553 653 *Fax:* (01865) 553 653
*E-mail:* orders@magnagraciaspublishers.co.uk
*Web Site:* www.magnagraeciaspublishers.co.uk
*Key Personnel*
Editor: Luigi Gigliotti
General Editor: L de Sybaris
First published 1976.
Weekly.
ISBN(s): 0-86340-020-5
ISSN: 0966-2413

ƒ**AAB's Guide to Private English Language Schools in the United Kingdom for Overseas Students** (B)
Published by Magna Graecia's Publishers (UK)
PO Box 342, Oxford OX2 7YF
*Tel:* (01865) 553 653 *Fax:* (01865) 553 653
*E-mail:* orders@magnagraciaspublishers.co.uk
*Web Site:* www.magnagraeciaspublishers.co.uk
*Key Personnel*
Editor: Luigi Gigliotti
General Editor: Louis de Sybaris
First published 1975.
Annually.
ISBN(s): 0-95077-280-1
ISSN: 1363-1993

ƒ**Abstracts in New Technologies & Engineering** (J)
Published by CSA (Cambridge Scientific Abstracts)
4640 Kingsgate, Cascade Way, Oxford Business Park South, Oxford, Oxon OX4 2ST
*Tel:* (0865) 336250 *Fax:* (0865) 336258
*E-mail:* service@csa.com
*Web Site:* www.csa.com
*Key Personnel*
Editor: Irene Nicholas *E-mail:* service@csa.com
An index, with abstracts, to scientific & technical periodicals, published in the UK & US.
Bimonthly (journal); Quarterly (CD-ROM); Monthly (web).
1145 EUR or 1,750 USD; 1170 EUR (elsewhere)
ISSN: 1367-9899
*Parent Company:* Cambridge Information Group

ƒ**Advertiser's Annual 2003-2004** (B)
Published by Hollis Publishing Ltd
Harlequin House, 7 High St, Teddington, Middx TW11 8EL
*Tel:* (020) 8977 7711 *Fax:* (020) 8977 1133
*E-mail:* orders@hollis-pr.co.uk
*Web Site:* www.hollis-pr.com
Annually.
275 GBP (includes p&p)

ƒ**African Publishers Networking Directory** (B)
Published by African Books Collective Ltd
Kings Meadow, Unit 13, Ferry Hinksey Rd, Oxford OX2 0DP
*Tel:* (01865) 726686 *Fax:* (01865) 793298
*E-mail:* abc@africanbookscollective.com
*Web Site:* www.africanbookscollective.com
*Key Personnel*
Head: Mary Jay *E-mail:* mary.jay@africanbookscollective.com
Resource directory of major African publishers.

**The African Publishing Companion: A Resource Guide** (B)
Published by Hans Zell Publishing Consultants
Glais Bheinn, Locharron, Ross-shire IV54 8YB
*Tel:* (01520) 722951 *Fax:* (01520) 722953
*E-mail:* hanszell@hanszell.co.uk
*Web Site:* www.hanszell.co.uk; www.africanpublishingcompanion.com
*Key Personnel*
Publisher & Editor: Hans M Zell *E-mail:* hzell@dial.pipex.com
Concise yet detailed information about many aspects of African publishing & book trade. Over 1,600 entries, extensively cross referenced. Purchase of book includes 24 month access to the online version.
First published 2002.
Biannually.
258 pp, 80 GBP or 130 USD
ISBN(s): 0-9541029-0-8

ƒ**African Research & Documentation** (J)
Published by Standing Conference on Library Materials on Africa (SCOLMA)

Commonwealth Secretariat, Marlborough House, Pall Mall, London SW1Y 5HX
*Tel:* (020) 7747 6164 *Fax:* (020) 7747 6168
*E-mail:* scolma@hotmail.com
*Web Site:* www.lse.ac.uk/library/scolma
*Key Personnel*
Editor: John McIlwaine *E-mail:* j.mcilwaine@ucl.ac.uk
First published 1973.
Triannually.
20 GBP or 48 USD

**Agenda** (P)
Published by The Agenda & Editions Charitable Trust
5 Cranbourne Court, Albert Bridge Rd, London SW11 4PL
*Tel:* (020) 228 0700 *Fax:* (020) 228 0700
*Key Personnel*
Editor: William Cookson
Text in English.
First published 1959.
Quarterly.
Individuals: 26 GBP (UK), 28 GBP (Europe), 30 GBP (elsewhere); Libraries & Institutions: 30 GBP (UK), 32 GBP (Europe), 34 GBP (elsewhere)
ISSN: 0002-0796

ƒ**Alexandria: Journal of National & International Library & Information Issues** (J)
Published by Ashgate Publishing Ltd
Gower House, Croft Rd, Aldershot, Hants GU11 3HR
*Tel:* (01252) 331551 *Fax:* (01252) 344405
*E-mail:* journals@ashgatepub.co.uk
*Web Site:* www.ashgate.com
*Key Personnel*
Editor: Ian McGowan
ISSN: 0955-7490

**Ambit** (P)
Published by Dr Martin Bax
17 Priory Gardens, London N6 5QY
*Tel:* (020) 8340 3566
*Web Site:* www.ambitmagazine.co.uk
*Key Personnel*
Editor: Martin Bax
Poetry, prose, short fiction, illustration & reviews.
First published 1959.
Quarterly.
96 pp, 24 GBP (UK); 26 GBP or 52 USD (USA)
ISSN: 0002-6972

**The Author** (P)
Published by Society of Authors
84 Drayton Gardens, London SW10 9SB
*Tel:* (020) 7373 6642 *Fax:* (020) 7373 5768
*E-mail:* info@societyofauthors.org
*Web Site:* www.societyofauthors.net
*Key Personnel*
Manager: Kate Pool *E-mail:* kpool@societyofauthors.org
First published 1890.
Quarterly.
30 GBP (UK); 35 GBP (elsewhere)
ISSN: 0005-0628

**Best Book Guide** (B)
Published by BookTrust
Book House, 45 East Hill, Wandsworth, London SW18 2QZ
*Tel:* (020) 8516 2977 *Fax:* (020) 8516 2978
*Web Site:* www.booktrust.org.uk; www.booktrusted.co.uk
*Key Personnel*
Contact: Ann Newton *E-mail:* ann@booktrust.org.uk
Young Book Trust selection of paperbacks for children 12 & under.
Annually.

**Book & Magazine Collector** (J)
Published by Diamond Publishing Group Ltd
45 St Mary's Rd, Ealing, London W5 5RQ
*Tel:* (020) 8579 1082 *Fax:* (020) 8566 2024
*Key Personnel*
Editor: Peter Doggett
Text in English.
First published 1984.
Monthly.
35.50 GBP (UK); 40 GBP (Europe)
ISSN: 0952-8601

**The Book Collector** (P)
Published by The Collector Ltd
PO Box 12426, London W11 3GW
*Tel:* (020) 8200 5004 *Fax:* (020) 7792 3492
*E-mail:* info@thebookcollector.co.uk
*Web Site:* www.thebookcollector.co.uk
*Key Personnel*
Editor: Nicolas J Barker *E-mail:* nicolasb@nixnet.
    clara-co.uk
Antiquarian books & bibliography.
First published 1952.
Quarterly.
152 pp

**BookBank** (J)
Published by Nielsen BookData
3rd floor, Midas House, 62 Goldsworth Rd, Wok-
    ing GU21 6LQ
*Tel:* (0870) 777 8710 *Fax:* (0870) 777 8711
*E-mail:* customerservices@nielsenbooknet.co.uk
*Web Site:* www.nielsenbookdata.co.uk
*Key Personnel*
Man Dir: Francis Bennett
CD-ROM containing bibliographic information on
    over 1 million UK published titles, plus details
    of over 35,000 publishers' names & addresses.
Monthly or bimonthly.
*Parent Company:* VNU Media Measurement &
    Information

**BookBank Global** (J)
Published by Nielsen BookData
3rd floor, Midas House, 62 Goldsworth Rd, Wok-
    ing GU21 6LQ
*Tel:* (0870) 777 8710 *Fax:* (0870) 777 8711
*E-mail:* customerservices@nielsenbooknet.co.uk
*Web Site:* www.nielsenbookdata.co.uk
CD-ROM containing bibliographic information on
    over 2 million English language titles from the
    UK, Europe, USA, Australia, New Zealand &
    Southern Africa.
Monthly on 2 CD-ROMs.
*Parent Company:* VNU Media Measurement &
    Information

**BookBank Global Compact** (J)
Published by Nielsen BookData
3rd floor, Midas House, 62 Goldsworth Rd, Wok-
    ing GU21 6LQ
*Tel:* (0870) 777 8710 *Fax:* (0870) 777 8711
*E-mail:* customerservices@nielsenbooknet.co.uk
*Web Site:* www.nielsenbookdata.co.uk
*Key Personnel*
Editorial Dir: Michael Healy *E-mail:* michael.
    healy@nielsenbookdata.co.uk
Senior Manager, Publishing Services: Peter Math-
    ews *E-mail:* peter.mathews@nielsenbookdata.
    co.uk
CD-ROM containing bibliographic information on
    over 2 million English language titles from the
    UK, Europe, USA, Australia, New Zealand &
    Southern Africa.
Monthly on 1 CD-ROM.
*Parent Company:* VNU Media Measurement &
    Information

**BookBank OP** (J)
Published by Nielsen BookData

3rd floor, Midas House, 62 Goldsworth Rd, Wok-
    ing GU21 6LQ
*Tel:* (0870) 777 8710 *Fax:* (0870) 777 8711
*E-mail:* customerservices@nielsenbookdata.co.uk
*Web Site:* www.nielsenbookdata.co.uk
*Key Personnel*
Man Dir: Francis Bennett
CD-ROM containing details of over 1.4 million
    out-of-print titles.
Quarterly.
*Parent Company:* VNU Media Measurement &
    Information

**Books & Publishing in Argentina** (B)
Published by Euromonitor PLC
60-61 Britton St, London EC1M 5UX
*Tel:* (020) 7251 8024 *Fax:* (020) 7608 3149
*E-mail:* info@euromonitor.com
*Web Site:* www.euromonitor.com
Analysis of retail, institutional, mail order & in-
    ternet distribution channels; forecast sales data
    & trends to watch; title output by subject statis-
    tics; investigation into import & export sales.
1,500 USD

**Books & Publishing in Australia** (B)
Published by Euromonitor PLC
60-61 Britton St, London EC1M 5UX
*Tel:* (020) 7251 8024 *Fax:* (020) 7608 3149
*E-mail:* info@euromonitor.com
*Web Site:* www.euromonitor.com
Analysis of retail, institutional, mail order & in-
    ternet distribution channels; forecast sales data
    & trends to watch; title output by subject statis-
    tics; investigation into import & export sales.
1,500 USD

**Books & Publishing in Austria** (B)
Published by Euromonitor PLC
60-61 Britton St, London EC1M 5UX
*Tel:* (020) 7251 8024 *Fax:* (020) 7608 3149
*E-mail:* info@euromonitor.com
*Web Site:* www.euromonitor.com
Analysis of retail, institutional, mail order & in-
    ternet distribution channels; forecast sales data
    & trends to watch; title output by subject statis-
    tics; investigation into import & export sales.
1,500 USD

**Books & Publishing in Belgium** (B)
Published by Euromonitor PLC
60-61 Britton St, London EC1M 5UX
*Tel:* (020) 7251 8024 *Fax:* (020) 7608 3149
*E-mail:* info@euromonitor.com
*Web Site:* www.euromonitor.com
Analysis of retail, institutional, mail order & in-
    ternet distribution channels; forecast sales data
    & trends to watch; title output by subject statis-
    tics; investigation into import & export sales.
1,500 USD

**Books & Publishing in Brazil** (B)
Published by Euromonitor PLC
60-61 Britton St, London EC1M 5UX
*Tel:* (020) 7251 8024 *Fax:* (020) 7608 3149
*E-mail:* info@euromonitor.com
*Web Site:* www.euromonitor.com
Analysis of retail, institutional, mail order & in-
    ternet distribution channels; forecast sales data
    & trends to watch; title output by subject statis-
    tics; investigation into import & export sales.
1,500 USD

**Books & Publishing in Canada** (B)
Published by Euromonitor PLC
60-61 Britton St, London EC1M 5UX
*Tel:* (020) 7251 8024 *Fax:* (020) 7608 3149
*E-mail:* info@euromonitor.com
*Web Site:* www.euromonitor.com
Analysis of retail, institutional, mail order & in-
    ternet distribution channels; forecast sales data

& trends to watch; title output by subject statis-
    tics; investigation into import & export sales.
1,500 USD

**Books & Publishing in China** (B)
Published by Euromonitor PLC
60-61 Britton St, London EC1M 5UX
*Tel:* (020) 7251 8024 *Fax:* (020) 7608 3149
*E-mail:* info@euromonitor.com
*Web Site:* www.euromonitor.com
Analysis of retail, institutional, mail order & in-
    ternet distribution channels; forecast sales data
    & trends to watch; title output by subject statis-
    tics; investigation into import & export sales.
1,500 USD

**Books & Publishing in France** (B)
Published by Euromonitor PLC
60-61 Britton St, London EC1M 5UX
*Tel:* (020) 7251 8024 *Fax:* (020) 7608 3149
*E-mail:* info@euromonitor.com
*Web Site:* www.euromonitor.com
Analysis of retail, institutional, mail order & in-
    ternet distribution channels; forecast sales data
    & trends to watch; title output by subject statis-
    tics; investigation into import & export sales.
1,500 USD

**Books & Publishing in Germany** (B)
Published by Euromonitor PLC
60-61 Britton St, London EC1M 5UX
*Tel:* (020) 7251 8024 *Fax:* (020) 7608 3149
*E-mail:* info@euromonitor.com
*Web Site:* www.euromonitor.com
Analysis of retail, institutional, mail order & in-
    ternet distribution channels; forecast sales data
    & trends to watch; title output by subject statis-
    tics; investigation into import & export sales.
1,500 USD

**Books & Publishing in Italy** (B)
Published by Euromonitor PLC
60-61 Britton St, London EC1M 5UX
*Tel:* (020) 7251 8024 *Fax:* (020) 7608 3149
*E-mail:* info@euromonitor.com
*Web Site:* www.euromonitor.com
Analysis of retail, institutional, mail order & in-
    ternet distribution channels; forecast sales data
    & trends to watch; title output by subject statis-
    tics; investigation into import & export sales.
1,500 USD

**Books & Publishing in Japan** (B)
Published by Euromonitor PLC
60-61 Britton St, London EC1M 5UX
*Tel:* (020) 7251 8024 *Fax:* (020) 7608 3149
*E-mail:* info@euromonitor.com
*Web Site:* www.euromonitor.com
Analysis of retail, institutional, mail order & in-
    ternet distribution channels; forecast sales data
    & trends to watch; title output by subject statis-
    tics; investigation into import & export sales.
1,500 USD

**Books & Publishing in Mexico** (B)
Published by Euromonitor PLC
60-61 Britton St, London EC1M 5UX
*Tel:* (020) 7251 8024 *Fax:* (020) 7608 3149
*E-mail:* info@euromonitor.com
*Web Site:* www.euromonitor.com
Analysis of retail, institutional, mail order & in-
    ternet distribution channels; forecast sales data
    & trends to watch; title output by subject statis-
    tics; investigation into import & export sales.
1,500 USD

**Books & Publishing in Netherlands** (B)
Published by Euromonitor PLC
60-61 Britton St, London EC1M 5UX
*Tel:* (020) 7251 8024 *Fax:* (020) 7608 3149
*E-mail:* info@euromonitor.com
*Web Site:* www.euromonitor.com

Analysis of retail, institutional, mail order & internet distribution channels; forecast sales data & trends to watch; title output by subject statistics; investigation into import & export sales.
1,500 USD

**Books & Publishing in Russia** (B)
Published by Euromonitor PLC
60-61 Britton St, London EC1M 5UX
*Tel:* (020) 7251 8024 *Fax:* (020) 7608 3149
*E-mail:* info@euromonitor.com
*Web Site:* www.euromonitor.com
Analysis of retail, institutional, mail order & internet distribution channels; forecast sales data & trends to watch; title output by subject statistics; investigation into import & export sales.
1,500 USD

**Books & Publishing in Spain** (B)
Published by Euromonitor PLC
60-61 Britton St, London EC1M 5UX
*Tel:* (020) 7251 8024 *Fax:* (020) 7608 3149
*E-mail:* info@euromonitor.com
*Web Site:* www.euromonitor.com
Analysis of retail, institutional, mail order & internet distribution channels; forecast sales data & trends to watch; title output by subject statistics; investigation into import & export sales.
1,500 USD

**Books & Publishing in Switzerland** (B)
Published by Euromonitor PLC
60-61 Britton St, London EC1M 5UX
*Tel:* (020) 7251 8024 *Fax:* (020) 7608 3149
*E-mail:* info@euromonitor.com
*Web Site:* www.euromonitor.com
Analysis of retail, institutional, mail order & internet distribution channels; forecast sales data & trends to watch; title output by subject statistics; investigation into import & export sales.
1,500 USD

**Books & Publishing in Taiwan** (B)
Published by Euromonitor PLC
60-61 Britton St, London EC1M 5UX
*Tel:* (020) 7251 8024 *Fax:* (020) 7608 3149
*E-mail:* info@euromonitor.com
*Web Site:* www.euromonitor.com
Analysis of retail, institutional, mail order & internet distribution channels; forecast sales data & trends to watch; title output by subject statistics; investigation into import & export sales.
1,500 USD

**Books & Publishing in United Kingdom** (B)
Published by Euromonitor PLC
60-61 Britton St, London EC1M 5UX
*Tel:* (020) 7251 8024 *Fax:* (020) 7608 3149
*E-mail:* info@euromonitor.com
*Web Site:* www.euromonitor.com
Analysis of retail, institutional, mail order & internet distribution channels; forecast sales data & trends to watch; title output by subject statistics; investigation into import & export sales.
1,500 USD

**Books & Publishing in United States** (B)
Published by Euromonitor PLC
60-61 Britton St, London EC1M 5UX
*Tel:* (020) 7251 8024 *Fax:* (020) 7608 3149
*E-mail:* info@euromonitor.com
*Web Site:* www.euromonitor.com
Analysis of retail, institutional, mail order & internet distribution channels; forecast sales data & trends to watch; title output by subject statistics; investigation into import & export sales.
1,500 USD

**Books for Keeps** (J)
Published by School Bookshop Association
6 Brightfield Rd, Lee, London SE12 8QF
*Tel:* (020) 8852 4953 *Fax:* (020) 8318 7580
*E-mail:* customerservice@csduk.com
*Web Site:* www.suffolkcc.gov.uk
*Key Personnel*
Man Dir: Richard Hill
Reviews of children's books.
6 times/yr.
18.60 GBP (UK); 22.50 GBP (overseas)
ISSN: 0143-909X

**Books In The Media** (J)
Published by VNU Entertainment Media UK Ltd
Endeavour House, 5th floor, 189 Shaftesbury Ave, London WC2H 8TJ
*Tel:* (020) 7420 6178 *Fax:* (020) 7836 2909
*E-mail:* bimsubs@galleon.co.uk
*Web Site:* www.thebookseller.com
*Key Personnel*
Editor: Neill Denny *E-mail:* neill.denny@bookseller.co.uk
Listings of all National Daily & Sunday Press Reviews, TV & Radio Program Tie-ins, Serializations, Best Seller Lists & some Trade News & Comment, Inc Sales Index.
First published 1979.
Weekly.
128 GBP

**The Bookseller** (P)
Published by VNU Entertainment Media UK Ltd
5th floor, Endeavour House, 189 Shaftesbury Ave, London WC2H 8TJ
*Tel:* (020) 7420 6006 *Fax:* (020) 7836 6781; (020) 7420 6102 (advertising); (020) 7420 6103 (editorial)
*E-mail:* information@bookseller.co.uk
*Web Site:* www.thebookseller.com
*Key Personnel*
Editor: Neill Denny *E-mail:* neill.denny@bookseller.co.uk
Book trade newspaper.
First published 1858.
Weekly.
170 GBP (UK); 311 EUR (Europe); 722 AUD (Australia & New Zealand); 406 USD (USA, Canada & elsewhere)
ISSN: 0006-7539
*Parent Company:* VNU Business Media Inc
*Ultimate Parent Company:* VNU NV

**Bookselling** (J)
Published by Booksellers Association of the United Kingdom & Ireland Ltd
Minster House, 272 Vauxhall Bridge Rd, London SW1V 1BA
*Tel:* (020) 7802 0802 *Fax:* (020) 7802 0803
*E-mail:* mail@booksellers.org.uk
*Web Site:* www.booksellers.org.uk
Quarterly.
ISSN: 0969-4862

**BPIF List of Members** (B)
Published by British Printing Industries Federation (BPIF)
Farringdon Point, 29-35 Farringdon Rd, London EC1M 3JF
*Tel:* (0870) 240 4085 *Fax:* (020) 7405 7784
*E-mail:* info@britishprint.com
*Web Site:* www.britishprint.com
*Key Personnel*
Chief Executive: Michael Johnson
Directory of information on the BPIF & the Printing Industry.

**∫British Humanities Index (BHI)** (J)
Published by CSA (Cambridge Scientific Abstracts)
4640 Kingsgate, Cascade Way, Oxford Business Park South, Oxford, Oxon OX4 2ST
*Tel:* (0865) 336250 *Fax:* (0865) 336258
*E-mail:* service@csa.com
*Web Site:* www.csa.com
Indexes humanities-related articles published by British newspapers & journals.
Quarterly (journal & CD-ROM), Monthly (web).
Print subscription: 750 EUR, 1160 USD, 775 EUR (elsewhere); CD-ROM 1250 EUR; Web 1425 EUR
ISSN: 0007-0815
*Parent Company:* Cambridge Information Group

**British National Bibliography** (J)
Published by The British Library
Boston Spa, Wetherby, W Yorks LS23 7BQ
*Tel:* (01937) 546070 *Fax:* (01937) 546586
*E-mail:* nbs-info@bl.uk
*Web Site:* www.bl.uk
British National Bibliography is available in-print, on-line & on CD-ROM.
First published 1950.
Weekly with 2 interim cumulations for Jan-April & May-Aug; annual volume.
ISSN: 0007-1544

**Carousel - The Guide to Children's Books** (B)
Published by David & Jenny Blanch
The Saturn Centre, 54-76 Bissell St, Birmingham B5 7HX
*Tel:* (0121) 622 7458 *Fax:* (0121) 622 7526
*E-mail:* carousel.guide@virgin.net
*Web Site:* www.carouselguide.co.uk
Triannually.
9.75 GBP (UK); 15 GBP (Europe & Ireland); 16 GBP (elsewhere)

**Cencrastus** (P)
Abbey Mount Techbase, Unit 1, Easter Rd, Edinburgh EH8 8EJ
*Tel:* (0131) 661 5687 *Fax:* (0131) 661 5687
*E-mail:* cencrastus@hotmail.com
*Web Site:* www.applegate.co.uk/company
*Key Personnel*
Editor: Raymond Ross
Scottish & International literature, arts & affairs.
First published 1979.
Triannually.
2.95 GBP

**Chapman** (P)
Published by Chapman Magazine
4 Broughton Pl, Edinburgh EH1 3RX
*Tel:* (0131) 5572207 *Fax:* (0131) 5569565
*E-mail:* admin@chapman-pub.co.uk
*Web Site:* www.chapman-pub.co.uk
*Key Personnel*
Editor: Joy Hendry
Assistant Editor: Gerry Stewart
Literary/magazine publisher.
First published 1970.
Triannually.
94th: 144 pp, One yr, 4 issues (personal): 16 GBP, 35 USD (USA), 21 GBP (overseas); Institutions: 20 GBP (UK), 43 USD (USA), 25 GBP (overseas)
ISSN: 0308-2695

**∫The Clio Montessori Series** (B)
Published by ABC-CLIO
c/o BR&D Ltd, Hadleigh Hall, London Rd, Hadleigh SS7 2DE
*Tel:* (01702) 552912 *Fax:* (01702) 556095
*E-mail:* mail@bookreps.com
*Web Site:* www.abc-clio.com
*Key Personnel*
President: Ron Boehm
Collection of paperbacks, aimed at both teacher & parents, which covers Montessori's teachings & beliefs.

**Critical Quarterly** (P)
Published by Blackwell Publishing Ltd
9600 Garsington Rd, Oxford OX4 2DQ
*Tel:* (01865) 776868 *Fax:* (01865) 714591

*E-mail:* customerservices@oxon.
  blackwellpublishing.com
*Web Site:* www.blackwellpublishers.co.uk
*Telex:* 837022 OXBOOK G
*Key Personnel*
Editor: Colin MacCabe
Publishing Editor: Joanna Jellinek
ISSN: 0011-1562 (print); 1467-8705 (online).
Quarterly.
187 USD (Americas); 110 GBP (Europe); 123
  GBP (elsewhere)

**Current British Directories** (B)
Published by CBD Research Ltd
Chancery House, 15 Wickham Rd, Beckenham,
  Kent BR3 5JS
*Tel:* (0871) 222 3440 *Fax:* (020) 8650 0768
*E-mail:* cbd@cbdresearch.com
*Web Site:* www.cbdresearch.com
Guide to directories published in the UK & Ire-
  land.
First published 1952.
Irregularly.
14
ISBN(s): 0-900-246-936

ƒ**Dictionary of International Biography** (B)
Published by Melrose Press Ltd
St Thomas Pl, Ely, Cambs CB7 4GG
*Tel:* (01353) 646600 *Fax:* (01353) 646601
*E-mail:* info@melrosepress.co.uk
*Web Site:* www.melrosepress.co.uk
General reference publication listing leading indi-
  viduals from all fields of interest.
29th, 199.50 USD, 135 GBP or 219 EUR
ISBN(s): 0-948875-19-4

**Directory of BA Members** (B)
Published by Booksellers Association of the
  United Kingdom & Ireland Ltd
Minster House, 272 Vauxhall Bridge Rd, London
  SW1V 1BA
*Tel:* (020) 7802 0802 *Fax:* (020) 7802 0803
*E-mail:* mail@booksellers.org.uk
*Web Site:* www.booksellers.org.uk
2002, 32 GBP plus 5 GBP overseas delivery
ISBN(s): 0-907972-83-7

**Directory of Publishing in Scotland** (B)
Published by Scottish Publishers Association
Scottish Book Centre, 137 Dundee St, Edinburgh
  EH11 1BG
*Tel:* (0131) 2286866 *Fax:* (0131) 2283220
*E-mail:* info@scottishbooks.org
*Web Site:* www.scottishbooks.org
*Key Personnel*
Administrator: Carol Lothian *E-mail:* carol.
  lothian@scottishbooks.org
Handbook for the Scottish book world, listing
  Scottish publishers, details of related organi-
  zations, the addresses of major Scottish book-
  shops, & information on support services.
Annually.

**Directory of Publishing: United Kingdom,
  Commonwealth & Overseas** (B)
Published by The Continuum International Pub-
  lishing Group Ltd
The Tower Bldg, 11 York Rd, London SE1 7NX
*Tel:* (020) 7922 0880 *Fax:* (020) 7922 0881
*Web Site:* www.continuumbooks.com
*Key Personnel*
Editorial Dir: Philip Law

**Directory of UK & Irish Book Publishers
  including distributors, sales agents &
  wholesalers** (B)
Published by Booksellers Association of the
  United Kingdom & Ireland Ltd
Minster House, 272 Vauxhall Bridge Rd, London
  SW1V 1BA

*Tel:* (020) 7802 0802 *Fax:* (020) 7802 0803
*E-mail:* mail@booksellers.org.uk
*Web Site:* www.booksellers.org.uk
Full details on over 3,000 UK & Irish publishers
  & their UK distributors, including imprints.
First published 1954.
Annually.
2002: 900 pp, 62.50 GBP
ISBN(s): 0-907972-78-0

ƒ**The Europa World Yearbook** (B)
Published by Europa Publications
Member of Taylor & Francis Group
11 New Fetter Lane, London EC4P 4EE
*Tel:* (020) 7842 2110 *Fax:* (020) 7842 2249
*E-mail:* info.europa@tandf.co.uk
*Web Site:* www.europapublications.co.uk
*Key Personnel*
Editorial Dir: Paul Kelly *Fax:* (020) 7842 2391
  *E-mail:* edit.europa@tandf.co.uk
Over 4,000 pages of up-to-date statistics & direc-
  tory information surveying over 250 countries
  & territories & outlines over 1,650 international
  organizations.
First published 1926.
Annually.
44th, 2 vols, 570 GBP
ISBN(s): 185743-175-8
ISSN: 0071-2302

ƒ**European Book World** (B)
Published by Anderson Rand Ltd
10 Willow Walk, Cambridge CB1 1LA
*Tel:* (01223) 566640 *Fax:* (01223) 566643
*E-mail:* info@andrand.com
*Web Site:* www.andrand.com
Detailed information on Publishers, Libraries &
  Booksellers throughout Western & Eastern Eu-
  rope, including former USSR. Details on over
  150,000 organizations. Print & CD-ROM.

**The Good Book Guide** (P)
24 Seward St, London EC1V 3GB
*Tel:* (020) 7490 9900 *Fax:* (020) 7490 9908
*E-mail:* enquiries@gbgdirect.com
*Web Site:* www.thegoodbookguide.com
Book review magazine, subscription only.
Monthly.

**Granta** (P)
Published by Granta Publications Ltd
2-3 Hanover Yard, Noel Rd, London N1 8BE
*Tel:* (020) 7704 9776 *Fax:* (020) 7704 0474
*Web Site:* www.granta.com
*Key Personnel*
Editor: Ian Jack
First published 1979.
Quarterly.
256 pp

**In Scotland** (J)
Published by Ramsay Head Press
15 Gloucester Pl, Edinburgh EH3 6EE
*Tel:* (0131) 225 5646 *Fax:* (0131) 225 5646
*E-mail:* ramsayhead@btinternet.com
*Key Personnel*
Editorial Dir & International Rights: Conrad K
  Wilson
First published 1968.
Quarterly.
9.95 GBP/yr
ISSN: 1468-5167

ƒ**The Indexer** (J)
Published by Society of Indexers
Blades Enterprise Centre, John St, Sheffield S2
  4SU
*Tel:* (0114) 292 2350 *Fax:* (0114) 292 2351
*E-mail:* admin@indexers.org.uk
*Web Site:* www.indexers.org.uk

*Key Personnel*
Executive Editor: Christine Shuttleworth
Journal of Australian, American, Canadian &
  Southern African & British Societies of In-
  dexers.
First published 1958.
Biannually.
72 pp, 40 GBP
ISSN: 0019-4131

ƒ**Information Europe** (J)
Published by Beishon Publications Ltd
15 Micawber St, London N1 7TB
*Tel:* (020) 7336 6650 *Fax:* (020) 7336 6640
*E-mail:* beishon@oxford.com
*Web Site:* www.axford.com/info_europe
First published 1992.
80 EUR
ISSN: 1385-2310

ƒ**Information Research Watch International
  (IRWI)** (J)
Published by CSA (Cambridge Scientific Ab-
  stracts)
4640 Kingsgate, Cascade Way, Oxford Business
  Park South, Oxford, Oxon OX4 2ST
*Tel:* (0865) 336250 *Fax:* (0865) 336258
*E-mail:* service@csa.com; tjones@csa.com
  (sales); support@csa.com (technical support);
  eurosupport@csa.com (support in Europe)
*Web Site:* www.csa.com
*Key Personnel*
Editor: Mrs Pirkko Elliott *E-mail:* pirkko@dial.
  piper.com
Newsletter providing brief reports of research in
  library & information science, electronic publishing & use of the internet, & related fields
  such as publishing, museums, archives, records
  management, & information industry. Also includes an editorial & two articles per issue on
  aspects of research in library & information
  science.
First published 1980.
Bimonthly.
24 pp, Annual subscription includes access to a
  web database. Europe 350 GBP, 1535 USD,
  other nations 360 GBP
ISSN: 1470-1391
*Parent Company:* Cambridge Information Group

ƒ**International Printing Sourcebook** (B)
Published by Pira International
Randalls Rd, Leatherhead, Surrey KT22 7RU
*Tel:* (01372) 802080 *Fax:* (01372) 802238
*E-mail:* publications@pira.co.uk
*Web Site:* www.piranet.com
Covers pulp & paper, packaging, publishing &
  printing.
3rd, 150 GBP

**IRWI**, see Information Research Watch
  International (IRWI)

ƒ**The Journal of Commonwealth Literature** (J)
Published by SAGE Publications Ltd
One Oliver's Yard, 55 City Rd, London EC1Y
  1SP
*Tel:* (020) 7324 8500; (020) 7374 0645 (customer
  service) *Fax:* (020) 7374 8600
*E-mail:* info@sagepub.co.uk; orders@sagepub.co.
  uk
*Web Site:* www.sagepub.co.uk
*Key Personnel*
Man Dir: Stephen Barr
Editorial Dir: Ziyad Marar
Editor: John Thieme; Geraldine Stoneham
Critical & bibliographical forum in the field of
  Commonwealth writing. Published triannually,
  the first two issues contain critical comment on
  all aspects of Commonwealth & related litera-
  tures. The third issue contains a comprehensive
  bibliography of publications in the field.
4 times/yr.

63 GPB/yr (individual), 220 GBP/yr (institutions)
ISSN: 0021-9894

**Learned Publishing** (J)
Published by Association of Learned & Professional Society Publishers
South House, The Street, Clapham, Worthing, West Sussex BN13 3UU
*Tel:* (01903) 871 686 *Fax:* (01903) 871 457
*E-mail:* sec-gen@alpsp.org
*Web Site:* www.alpsp.org/journal.htm
*Key Personnel*
Editor: Robert Welham
US Editor: Alma Wills
First published 1977.
Quarterly.
80 pp, 57 GBP, 92 USD or 92 EUR (individuals); 115 GBP, 185 USD or 185 EUR (institutions)
ISSN: 0953-1513

ʄ**Library & Information Update** (J)
Published by Chartered Institute of Library & Information Professionals (CILIP)
7 Ridgmount St, London WC1E 7AE
*Tel:* (020) 7255 0500 *Fax:* (020) 7255 0501
*E-mail:* update@cilip.org.uk
*Web Site:* www.cilip.org.uk/update
*Key Personnel*
Editor: Elspeth Hyams *E-mail:* elspeth.hyams@cilip.org.uk
News Editor: Matthew Mezey *E-mail:* matthew.mezey@cilip.org.uk
Associate Editor: Christina Brockhurst *E-mail:* christina.brockhurst@cilip.org.uk
Managing Editor, Production: Rachel Middleton *E-mail:* rachel.middleton@cilip.org.uk
Mediawatching: Laura Swaffield *E-mail:* laura.swaffield@cilip.org.uk
Art/Design Editor: Marianne Nyman *E-mail:* marianne.nyman@cilip.org.uk
Book Reviews Editor: Diana Dixon *E-mail:* diana.dixon@cilip.org.uk
Head of Advertising: Andrew Nelson-Cole *Tel:* (020) 7255 0550 *Fax:* (020) 7255 0551 *E-mail:* advertising@cilip.org.uk
Industry news, comment & debate within the library & information profession.
First published 2002.
Monthly.
Non-member subscription: 85 GBP (UK), 180 USD (North America), 98 GBP (outside UK)

**Literary Review** (J)
Published by The Literary Review & Quarto Ltd
44 Lexington St, London W1R 3LW
*Tel:* (020) 7437 9392 *Fax:* (020) 7734 1844
*E-mail:* litrev@dircon.co.uk; lindar@warnes.co.uk
Reviews of the best newly published fiction & nonfiction.
First published 1979.
11 times/yr.
64 pp, 30 GBP (UK); 36 GBP (Europe); 39 GBP (North America); 50 GBP (rest of world)
ISSN: 0144-4360

ʄ**LOGOS** (J)
Published by Whurr Publishers Ltd
19b Compton Terrace, London N1 2UN
*Tel:* (020) 7359 5979 *Fax:* (020) 7226 5290
*E-mail:* info@whurr.co.uk
*Web Site:* www.whurr.co.uk
Quarterly.
Vol 15, 45 GBP (individuals); 120 GBP (institutions)
ISSN: 0957-9656

**London Review of Books** (P)
Published by LRB Ltd
28 Little Russell St, London WC1A 2HN
*Tel:* (020) 7209 1141 *Fax:* (020) 7209 1151
*E-mail:* edit@lrb.co.uk

*Web Site:* www.lrb.co.uk
*Key Personnel*
Editor: Mary-Kay Wilmers
Bimonthly.
63.72 GBP (UK); 72.90 GBP (Europe); 42 USD (USA); 50 USD (Canada); 76.50 GBP (elsewhere)
ISSN: 0260-9592

**New Books in German** (J)
Published by British Centre for Literary Translation
c/o Goethe Institute, 50 Princes Gate, Exhibition Rd, London SW7 2PH
*Tel:* (020) 7596 4023 *Fax:* (020) 7594 0245
*E-mail:* nbg@london.goethe.org
*Web Site:* www.new-books-in-german.com
*Key Personnel*
Editor: Sally-Ann Spencer
Reviews German language literature (Swiss, Austrian & German) in English to promote sales into the British & USA markets.
Biannually.

ʄ**New Review of Academic Librarianship** (J)
Published by Taylor & Francis
4 Park Sq, Milton Park, Abingdon, Oxon OX14 4RN
*Tel:* (020) 7017 6000 *Fax:* (020) 7017 6336
*E-mail:* enquiry@tandf.co.uk
*Web Site:* www.tandf.co.uk
*Key Personnel*
Editor: Colin Harris
First published 1995.
Vol 10, 2004, 195 USD or 112 GBP (Institutional); 41 USD or 25 GBP (individual)
ISSN: 1361-4533

ʄ**New Review of Children's Literature & Librarianship** (J)
Published by Taylor & Francis
4 Park Sq, Milton Park, Abingdon, Oxon OX14 4RN
*Tel:* (020) 7017 6000 *Fax:* (020) 7017 6336
*E-mail:* enquiry@tandf.co.uk
*Web Site:* www.tandf.co.uk
*Key Personnel*
Editor: Dr Sally Maynard
First published 1995.
Biannually.
Vol 10, 2004, 195 USD or 112 GBP (institutional); 41 USD or 25 GBP (individual)
ISSN: 1361-4541

ʄ**New Review of Hypermedia & Multimedia** (J)
Published by Taylor & Francis
4 Park Sq, Milton Park, Abingdon, Oxon OX14 4RN
*Tel:* (020) 7017 6000 *Fax:* (020) 7017 6336
*E-mail:* enquiry@tandf.co.uk
*Web Site:* www.tandf.co.uk
*Key Personnel*
Editor: Douglas Tudhope
First published 1995.
Biannually.
Vol 10, 2004, 224 USD or 136 GBP (institutional); 132 USD or 80 GBP (individual)
ISSN: 1361-4568

ʄ**New Review of Information & Library Research**
Published by Taylor & Francis
4 Park Sq, Milton Park, Abingdon, Oxon OX14 4RN
*Tel:* (020) 7017 6000 *Fax:* (020) 7017 6336
*E-mail:* enquiry@tandf.co.uk
*Web Site:* www.tandf.co.uk
*Key Personnel*
Editor: Peter Brophy
First published 1995.
Biannually.

Vol 10, 2004, 195 USD or 112 GBP (institutional); 41 USD or 25 GBP (individual)
ISSN: 1361-455X

ʄ**New Review of Infornmation Networking** (J)
Published by Taylor & Francis
4 Park Sq, Milton Park, Abingdon, Oxon OX14 4RN
*Tel:* (020) 7017 6000 *Fax:* (020) 7017 6336
*E-mail:* info@tandf.co.uk; enquiry@tandf.co.uk
*Web Site:* www.tandf.co.uk
*Key Personnel*
Editor: Michael Breaks
First published 1995.
Biannually.
Vol 10, 2004, 195 USD or 112 GBP (institutional); 41 USD or 25 GBP (individual)
ISSN: 1361-4576

**Orbis** (P)
17 Greenhow Ave, West Kirby, Wirral CH48 5EL
*Tel:* (0191) 4897055 *Fax:* (0191) 4897055; (0191) 4301297
*Web Site:* www.orbisbooks.com
*Key Personnel*
Editor: Carole Baldock *E-mail:* carolebaldock@hotmail.com
Independent British literary quarterly with international connections; publishes mainly poetry, but uses some prose & letters; also features news, educational & review columns.
Quarterly.
15 GBP; 28 USD (overseas)

**Outlets for Specialist New Books in the UK: A Subject Classified, Descriptive Directory** (B)
Published by Peter Marcan Publications
PO Box 3158, London SE1 4RA
*Tel:* (020) 7357 0368
Entries on some 800 businesses of many kinds (including museum/art gallery shops, periodicals & associations, as well as related directories).
First published 1978.
Triennially.
15 GBP/issue

**Outposts Poetry Quarterly** (P)
Published by Hippopotamus Press
22, Whitewell Rd, Frome, Frome, Somerset BA11 4EL
*Tel:* (01373) 466653 *Fax:* (01373) 466653
*E-mail:* rjhippopress@aol.com
*Key Personnel*
Editor: Roland John
New poetry, translations, essays & reviews.
Quarterly.
32 USD
ISSN: 0950-7264

ʄ**PEN International Bulletin of Selected Books** (J)
Published by International PEN
9-10 Charterhouse Bldgs, Goswell Rd, London EC1M 7AT
*Tel:* (020) 7253 4308 *Fax:* (020) 7253 5711
*E-mail:* intpen@dircon.co.uk
*Web Site:* www.internationalpen.org.uk
*Key Personnel*
Editor: Jane Spender
Published in English & French & issued with the assistance of UNESCO.
First published 1950.
Semiannual.
100 pp, 8 GBP or 13 USD
ISSN: 1010-4534

**Phillip's International Paper Directory** (B)
Published by CMP Data & Information Services
Division of CMP Information Ltd

Riverbank House, Angel Lane, Tonbridge, Kent
TN9 1SE
*Tel:* (01732) 377591 *Fax:* (01732) 367301
*E-mail:* orders@cmpinformation.com
*Web Site:* www.cmpdata.co.uk
*Key Personnel*
Commerical Dir: Duncan Clark
Available in print & on CD-ROM.
First published 1904.
Annually.
2003: 752 pp, 149 GBP
ISBN(s): 0-86382-488-9
ISSN: 0954-8521

**Planet - The Welsh Internationalist** (P)
Published by Berw Cyf
PO Box 44, Aberystwyth, Ceredigion SY23 3ZZ
*Tel:* (01970) 611255 *Fax:* (01970) 611197
*E-mail:* planet.enquiries@planetmagazine.org.uk
*Web Site:* www.planetmagazine.org.uk
*Key Personnel*
Editor: John Barnie
Associate Editor: Helle Michelsen; Dafydd Prys
First published 1970.
6 times/yr.
128 pp
ISSN: 0048-4288

**PN Review** (P)
Published by Carcanet Press Ltd
4th floor, Alliance House, Cross St, Manchester
M2 7AP
*Tel:* (0161) 834 8730 *Fax:* (0161) 832 0084
*E-mail:* info@carcanet.u-net.com
*Web Site:* www.carcanet.co.uk; www.pnreview.co.
uk
*Key Personnel*
Editorial & Man Dir: Michael Schmidt
Features poetry & literary criticism.
First published 1972.
Bimonthly.
29.50 GBP

**Poetry Now** (P)
Published by Forward Press Ltd
Remus House, Coltsfoot Drive, Woodston, Peter-
borough PE2 7BU
*Tel:* (01733) 898101 *Fax:* (01733) 313524
*E-mail:* pnmag@forwardpress.co.uk
*Web Site:* www.forwardpress.co.uk
First published 1991.
Bimonthly.
15 GBP (UK); 25 USD (USA); 21 GBP (over-
seas)
*Parent Company:* Forward Press Ltd

**Poetry Review** (P)
Published by The Poetry Society Inc
22 Betterton St, London WC2H 9BX
*Tel:* (020) 7420 9880 *Fax:* (020) 7240 4818
*E-mail:* info@poetrysociety.org.uk
*Web Site:* www.poetrysociety.org.uk/review/
review.htm
*Key Personnel*
Editor: David Herd; Robert Potts
Poetry & reviews.
Quarterly.

**PR Planner** (J)
Published by Waymaker Ltd
Chess House, 34 Germain St, Chesham, Bucks
HP5 1SJ
*Tel:* (0870) 736 0010 *Fax:* (0870) 736 0011
*E-mail:* info@waymaker.co.uk
*Web Site:* www.waymaker.co.uk/prplanner
*Key Personnel*
Man Dir: Neil Palfreeman
CD-based media directory.
Quarterly.
1,349 GBP (UK & Europe); 789 GBP (UK or
Europe); 999 GBP (any 5 countries)

**Printing Trades Directory** (B)
Published by CMP Data & Information Services
Riverbank House, Angel Lane, Tonbridge, Kent
TN9 1SE
*Tel:* (01732) 377591 *Fax:* (01732) 367301
*E-mail:* orders@cmpinformation.com
*Web Site:* www.cmpdata.co.uk
*Key Personnel*
Commercial Dir: Duncan Clark *Tel:* (01732)
377423 *Fax:* (01732) 368324
Editor: Philip Dury *Tel:* (01732) 377542
*Fax:* (01732) 377483
Marketing Manager: Alison Prangnell
*Tel:* (01732) 377627 *Fax:* (01732) 368324
*E-mail:* aprangnell@cmpinformation.com
Comprehensive directory on the UK print indus-
try. Used by manufacturers, printers & print
buyers.
First published 1960.
2003, 115 GBP
ISBN(s): 0-86382-502-8
ISSN: 0079-5372

**Printing World** (J)
Published by United Business Media International
plc
Sovereign House, Sovereign Way, Tonbridge,
Kent TN9 1RW
*Tel:* (01732) 377329 *Fax:* (01732) 377552
*Web Site:* www.dotprint.com
*Key Personnel*
Editor: Gareth Ward *E-mail:* gward@
cmpinformation.com
The oldest weekly magazine serving the printing
industry in the UK.
Weekly.
94.50 GBP (UK); 142 GBP (rest of world)

ϕ**Private Press Books** (B)
Published by Private Libraries Association (PLA)
49 Hamilton Park W, London N5 1AE
*Web Site:* www.the-old-school.demon.co.uk/pla.
htm
*Key Personnel*
Executive Secretary: James Brown
Editor, Private Press Books: Paul W Nash
Publications Secretary: David Chambers
*E-mail:* dchambers@aol.com
Bibliography of the work of private presses
throughout the world.
Annually.
25 GBP or 40 USD
ISSN: 0079-5402

ϕ**The Rialto** (P)
PO Box 309, Aylsham, Norwich, Norfolk NR11
6LN
*Web Site:* www.therialto.co.uk
*Key Personnel*
Editor: Michael Mackmin
Poetry magazine.
First published 1984.
Triannually.
56 pp, 12 GBP (UK); 14 GBP (Europe); 18 GBP
(USA & Canada); 19 GBP (Australia & Japan)
ISSN: 0268-5981

ϕ**The School Librarian** (P)
Published by School Library Association
Lotmead Business Village, Unit 2, Lotmead
Farm, Wanborough, Swindon SN4 0UY
*Tel:* (01793) 791787 *Fax:* (01793) 791786
*E-mail:* info@sla.org.uk
*Web Site:* www.sla.org.uk
*Key Personnel*
Editor: Ray Lonsdale
Articles relating to school libraries & publish-
ing for children. Reviews of books, websites &
CD-ROMs.
First published 1937.
Quarterly.

56 pp, GBP 45
ISSN: 0036-6595

ϕ**Serials In The British Library** (J)
Published by The British Library
Boston Spa, Wetherby, W Yorks LS23 7BQ
*Tel:* (01937) 546070 *Fax:* (01937) 546586
*E-mail:* nbs-info@bl.uk
*Web Site:* www.bl.uk
List all new serial titles acquired by the British
Library reference departments & all UK seri-
als received through legal deport. Coverage is
worldwide & all subject areas.
Three printed issues, annual cumulation.
245 GBP (domestic); 305 GBP (foreign)
ISSN: 0260-0005

**Sheppard's Book Dealers in Australia & New
Zealand** (B)
Published by Richard Joseph Publishers Ltd
PO Box 15, Torrington, Devon EX38 8ZJ
*Tel:* (01805) 625750 *Fax:* (01805) 625376
*E-mail:* info@sheppardsworld.com
*Web Site:* www.sheppardsdirectories.co.uk
*Key Personnel*
Editor: Richard Joseph *E-mail:* rjoe01@aol.com
Advertising: Claire Brumham
Directory of antiquarian & secondhand book deal-
ers in Australia & New Zealand. E-mail & web
sites included.
4th: 252 pp, 27 GBP or 54 USD
ISBN(s): 1-872699-76-6

ϕ**Sheppard's Book Dealers in Europe** (B)
Published by Richard Joseph Publishers Ltd
PO Box 15, Torrington, Devon EX38 8ZJ
*Tel:* (01805) 625750 *Fax:* (01805) 625376
*E-mail:* info@sheppardsworld.com
*Web Site:* www.sheppardsdirectories.co.uk
*Key Personnel*
Editor: Richard Joseph *E-mail:* rjoe01@aol.com
Advertising: Claire Brumham
Antiquarian & second hand book dealers on the
continent of Europe.
First published 1967.
11th: 318 pp, 27 GBP or 54 USD
ISBN(s): 1-872699-65-0

**Sheppard's Book Dealers in India & the
Orient** (B)
Published by Richard Joseph Publishers Ltd
PO Box 15, Torrington, Devon EX38 8ZJ
*Tel:* (01805) 625750 *Fax:* (01805) 625376
*E-mail:* info@sheppardsworld.com
*Web Site:* www.sheppardsdirectories.co.uk
*Key Personnel*
Editor: Richard Joseph *E-mail:* rjoe01@aol.com
Advertising: Claire Brumham
A directory of antiquarian & secondhand book
dealers in India & oriental countries.
Occasionally.
2nd, 24 GBP or 48 USD
ISBN(s): 1-872699-08-1

**Sheppard's Book Dealers in Japan** (B)
Published by Richard Joseph Publishers Ltd
PO Box 15, Torrington, Devon EX38 8ZJ
*Tel:* (01805) 625750 *Fax:* (01805) 625376
*E-mail:* info@sheppardsworld.com
*Web Site:* www.sheppardsdirectories.co.uk
*Key Personnel*
Editor: Richard Joseph *E-mail:* rjoe01@aol.com
Advertising: Claire Brumham
Directory of antiquarian & secondhand book deal-
ers in Japan.
2nd: 200 pp, 27 GBP or 48 USD
ISBN(s): 1-872699-66-9

**Sheppard's Book Dealers in Latin America &
Southern Africa** (B)
Published by Richard Joseph Publishers Ltd
PO Box 15, Torrington, Devon EX38 8ZJ

*Tel:* (01805) 625750 *Fax:* (01805) 625376
*E-mail:* info@sheppardsworld.com
*Web Site:* www.sheppardsdirectories.co.uk
*Key Personnel*
Editor: Richard Joseph *E-mail:* rjoe01@aol.com
Advertising: Claire Brumham
Directory of antiquarian & secondhand book dealers in South America, South Africa & other countries.
88 pp, 21 GBP or 42 USD
ISBN(s): 1-872699-67-7

**Sheppard's Book Dealers in North America** (B)
Published by Richard Joseph Publishers Ltd
PO Box 15, Torrington, Devon EX38 8ZJ
*Tel:* (01805) 625750 *Fax:* (01805) 625376
*E-mail:* info@sheppardsworld.com
*Web Site:* www.sheppardsdirectories.co.uk
*Key Personnel*
Editor: Richard Joseph *E-mail:* rjoe01@aol.com
Advertising: Claire Brumham
Directory of antiquarian & secondhand book dealers in the USA & Canada. E-mail & web sites included.
15th: 560 pp, 30 GBP or 60 USD
ISBN(s): 1-872699-72-3

**Sheppard's Book Dealers in the British Isles** (B)
Published by Richard Joseph Publishers Ltd
PO Box 15, Torrington, Devon EX38 8ZJ
*Tel:* (01805) 625750 *Fax:* (01805) 625376
*E-mail:* info@sheppardsworld.com
*Web Site:* www.sheppardsdirectories.co.uk
*Key Personnel*
Editor: Richard Joseph *E-mail:* rjoe01@aol.com
Advertising: Claire Brumham
Antiquarian & secondhand book dealers in the British Isles, The Channel Islands, The Isle of Man & the Republic of Ireland.
Annually.
27th: 440 pp, 30 GBP or 60 USD
ISBN(s): 1-872699-78-2

ƒ**Sheppard's Dealers in Collectables (UK)** (B)
Published by Richard Joseph Publishers Ltd
PO Box 15, Torrington, Devon EX38 8ZJ
*Tel:* (01805) 625750 *Fax:* (01805) 625376
*E-mail:* info@sheppardsworld.com
*Web Site:* www.sheppardsdirectories.co.uk
*Key Personnel*
Editor: Richard Joseph *E-mail:* rjoe01@aol.com
Advertising: Claire Brumham
Dealers of new & old collectables.
2nd, 18 GBP or 36 USD
ISBN(s): 1-872699-55-3

ƒ**Sheppard's International Directory of Ephemera Dealers** (B)
Published by Richard Joseph Publishers Ltd
PO Box 15, Torrington, Devon EX38 8ZJ
*Tel:* (01805) 625750 *Fax:* (01805) 625376
*E-mail:* info@sheppardsworld.com
*Web Site:* www.sheppardsdirectories.co.uk
*Key Personnel*
Editor: Richard Joseph *E-mail:* rjoe01@aol.com
Advertising: Claire Brumham
Dealers of Ephemera.
First published 1994.
Every 6 years.
300 pp, 27 GBP or 56 USD

ƒ**Sheppard's International Directory of Print & Map Sellers** (B)
Published by Richard Joseph Publishers Ltd
PO Box 15, Torrington, Devon EX38 8ZJ
*Tel:* (01805) 625750 *Fax:* (01805) 625376
*E-mail:* info@sheppardsworld.com
*Web Site:* www.sheppardsdirectories.co.uk

*Key Personnel*
Editor: Richard Joseph *E-mail:* rjoe01@aol.com
Advertising: Claire Brumham
Antiquarian & second hand print & map sellers.
4th, 27 GBP or 54 USD

ƒ**Slavonica** (J)
Published by Maney Publishing
Hudson Rd, Leeds LS9 7DL
*Tel:* (0113) 249 7481 *Fax:* (0113) 248 6983
*E-mail:* maney@maney.co.uk
*Web Site:* www.maney.co.uk
*Key Personnel*
Editor: Jekaterina Young *E-mail:* katya.young@man.ac.uk
Academic publication on the languages, literature, history & culture of Russia & Central & Eastern Europe.
First published 1983.
Biannually.
120 pp, 28 GBP (individuals); 68 GBP (institutions)
ISSN: 1361-7427

**Stand Magazine** (P)
School of English, Leeds University, Leeds LS2 9JT
*Tel:* (0113) 233 4794 *Fax:* (0113) 233 2791
*E-mail:* stand@leeds.ac.uk
*Web Site:* www.people.vcu.edu/~dlatane/stand.html
*Key Personnel*
Managing Editor: Jon Glover
Literary magazine.
First published 1952.
Quarterly.
25 GBP (individuals); 35 GBP (institutions)

**Swedish Book Review** (P)
Published by Swedish-English Literary Translators Association
85 Ediva Rd, Meopham, Kent DA13 0ND
*Tel:* (01603) 593356 (subscriptions) *Fax:* (01603) 250599 (subscriptions)
*E-mail:* editor@swedishbookreview.com
*Web Site:* www.swedishbookreview.com
*Key Personnel*
Editor: Sarah Death
Translators review, in English, of works written in Swedish, originating from Sweden or Swedish writers in Finland.
First published 1983.
Biannually.
15 GBP, 25 USD or 200 SEK
ISSN: 0265-8119

**The Times Literary Supplement** (P)
Published by The Times Supplements Ltd
Admiral House, 66-68 East Smithfield, London E1W 9BX
*Tel:* (020) 7782 3000 *Fax:* (020) 7782 3100
*Web Site:* www.the-tls.co.uk
First published 1902.
Weekly.

**UK Book Printers** (B)
Published by Book Production Section BPIF
British Printing Industries Federation, Farringdon Point, 29-35 Farringdon Rd, London EC1M 3JF
*Tel:* (020) 7915 8300 *Fax:* (020) 7405 7784
*E-mail:* info@bpif.org.uk
*Web Site:* www.britishprint.com
*Key Personnel*
Editor: Leigh Martins
Biannually.

ƒ**UKBookWorld 2003 CD-ROM** (B)
Published by Clique Ltd
7 Pulleyn Dr, York Y024 1DY
*Tel:* (01904) 631752 *Fax:* (01904) 651325

*E-mail:* cole@clique.co.uk
*Web Site:* www.clique.co.uk
Price guide/reference 1.2 million+ books (second-hand/rare/out of print) on CD.
Annually in April.
36 GBP or 65 USD

**Vigil** (P)
Published by Vigil Publications
17 Vineys Yard, Bruton, Somers BA10 0EU
*Tel:* (01749) 813349
*Key Personnel*
Editor: John Howard-Greaves
Poetry & Prose with the accent on developments in form & structure applied to contemporary themes.
Biannually.
6 GBP; 8 GBP (overseas)
ISSN: 0954-0881

**Walford's Guide to Reference Material** (B)
Published by Facet Publishing
7 Ridgmount St, London WC1E 7AE
*Tel:* (020) 7255 0590 *Fax:* (020) 7255 0591
*E-mail:* info@facetpublishing.co.uk
*Web Site:* www.facetpublishing.co.uk
*Key Personnel*
Production Manager: Kathryn Beecroft *Tel:* (020) 7255 0595 *E-mail:* k.beecroft@facetpublishing.co.uk
First published 1959.
Annually.
8th, 3 vols

**Whitaker's Almanac** (B)
Published by A & C Black Publishers Ltd
37 Soho Sq, London W1D 3QZ
*Tel:* (020) 7758 0200
*E-mail:* wayb@acblack.com
*Web Site:* www.acblack.com
*Key Personnel*
Editor: Lauren Hill
General reference book including information on British government.
First published 1868.
Annually.
135th: 1,300 pp, 40 GBP
ISBN(s): 0-7136-6497-5

ƒ**Whitaker's Books In Print: The Reference Catalogue of Current Literature** (B)
Published by Nielsen BookData
3rd floor, Midas House, 62 Goldsworth Rd, Woking GU21 6LQ
*Tel:* (0870) 777 8710 *Fax:* (0870) 777 8711
*E-mail:* customerservices@nielsenbooknet.co.uk
*Web Site:* www.nielsenbookdata.co.uk
Complete listing (5 volumes) of European English Language books in print. Contains details of over 1,110,000 titles from 41,273 publishers.
Annually.
14,523 pp, 580 GBP
ISBN(s): 0-85021-329-0
*Parent Company:* VNU Media Measurement & Information

**Whitaker's Red Book - The Directory of Publishers** (B)
Published by Nielsen BookData
3rd floor, Midas House, 62 Goldsworth Rd, Woking GU21 6LQ
*Tel:* (0870) 777 8710 *Fax:* (0870) 777 8711
*E-mail:* customerservices@nielsenbooknet.co.uk
*Web Site:* www.nielsenbookdata.co.uk
Complete listing of publishers & book trade organizations in the UK. Lists over 4,000 publishers, including addresses, e-mail, websites & contact details.
150 pp, 16.50 GBP
ISBN(s): 0-85021-328-2
*Parent Company:* VNU Media Measurement & Information

ƒ**Who's Who in Asia & the Pacific Nations** (B)
Published by Melrose Press Ltd
St Thomas Pl, Ely, Cambs CB7 4GG
*Tel:* (01353) 646600 *Fax:* (01353) 646601
*E-mail:* info@melrosepress.co.uk
*Web Site:* www.melrosepress.co.uk
Career profiles of leading achievers from this in-
  creasingly influential region.
First published 1989.
5th, 135 GBP, 219 EUR or 199.50 USD
ISBN(s): 1-903986-01-X

ƒ**Willing's Press Guide** (J)
Published by Waymaker Ltd
Chess House, 34 Germain St, Chesham, Bucks
  HP5 1SJ
*Tel:* (0870) 736 0010 *Fax:* (0870) 736 0011
*E-mail:* info@waymaker.co.uk
*Web Site:* www.willingspressguide.com
Media directory containing over 65,000 entries
  covering publications, organizations & media
  outlets.
Annually.
325 GBP (3 vols), 299 GBP (2 vols), 199 GBP (1
  vol)

**The World Market for Books & Publishing** (B)
Published by Euromonitor PLC
60-61 Britton St, London EC1M 5UX
*Tel:* (020) 7251 8024 *Fax:* (020) 7608 3149
*E-mail:* info@euromonitor.com
*Web Site:* www.euromonitor.com
Global Reports incorporating: analysis of retail,
  institutional, mail order & internet distribution
  channels; forecast sales data & trends to watch;
  title output by subject statistics; investigation
  into import & export sales.
7,900 USD

ƒ**The World of Learning** (B)
Published by Europa Publications
Member of Taylor & Francis Group
11 New Fetter Lane, London EC4P 4EE
*Tel:* (020) 7842 2110 *Fax:* (020) 7842 2249
*E-mail:* info.europa@tandf.co.uk
*Web Site:* www.europapublications.co.uk
Directory lists over 30,000 academic institutions
  world-wide together with more than 150,000
  staff & officials.
Annually.
53rd, 365 GBP
ISBN(s): 1-85743-135-9
ISSN: 0084-2117

ƒ**Writers' & Artists' Yearbook** (B)
Published by A & C Black Publishers Ltd
37 Soho Sq, London W1D 3QZ
*Tel:* (020) 7758 0200
*E-mail:* wayb@acblack.com
*Web Site:* www.acblack.com
*Key Personnel*
Editorial: Christine Robinson
Expert advice on writing techniques, research &
  markets.
Annually in Sept.
96th, 12.99 GBP
ISBN(s): 0-7136-6281-6
*Parent Company:* Bloomsbury Publishing PLC

**Writers' Circles Handbook** (B)
Published by Jill Dick
Oldacre, Horderns Park Rd, Chapel-en-le Frith,
  High Peak SK23 9SY
*Tel:* (01298) 812305
*E-mail:* oldacre@btinternet.com
*Web Site:* www.cix.co.uk/~oldacre
*Key Personnel*
Editor: Jill Dick *E-mail:* jillie@cix.co.uk
5 GBP post free

**Writers News** (P)
Published by Warners Group Publications plc
Victoria House, 1st floor, 143-145 The Headrow,
  Leeds LS1 5RL
*Tel:* (0113) 200 2929 *Fax:* (0113) 200 2928
*E-mail:* letters@writersnews.co.uk
*Web Site:* www.writersnews.co.uk
*Key Personnel*
Editor: Derek Hudson *E-mail:* derek.hudson@
  writersnews.co.uk
Information on Markets, Competitions, Short
  Story Competitions, How-To Articles, for both
  the established & aspiring writer.
27.95 GBP

**Writing Magazine** (J)
Published by Warners Group Publications plc
Victoria House, 1st floor, 143-145 The Headrow,
  Leeds LS1 5RL
*Tel:* (0113) 200 2929 *Fax:* (0113) 200 2928
*E-mail:* letters@writersnews.co.uk
*Web Site:* www.writersnews.co.uk
*Key Personnel*
Editor: Derek Hudson *E-mail:* derek.hudson@
  writersnews.co.uk
Commercial Manager: Janet Davison
Senior Sales Executive: Karen Chambers
Subscriptions: Christine Sheppard
Offers interviews with famous authors, writer pro-
  files, how-to articles on poety, fiction, short
  stories, photojournalism, technology, nonfiction
  writing & more competitions.
Bimonthly.
14.95 GBP/yr

# United States

ƒ**Book Review Index** (B)
Published by Thomson Gale
Unit of The Thomson Corp
27500 Drake Rd, Farmington Hills, MI 48331-
  3535
*Tel:* 248-699-4253 *Toll Free Tel:* 800-347-4253
  *Fax:* 248-699-8074 *Toll Free Fax:* 800-414-
  5043
*E-mail:* galeord@gale.com
*Web Site:* www.gale.com
*Telex:* (313) 961-6637
*Key Personnel*
Editor: Dana Ferguson *Tel:* 248-699-4253 ext
  1345 *E-mail:* dana.ferguson@galegroup.com
Provides access to reviews of books, periodicals,
  books on tape & electronic media respresenting
  a wide range of popular, academic & professional interests. More than 600 publications are
  indexed including journals & national general
  interest publications & newspapers.
First published 1980.
3 issues/yr for the current yr; annual cumulation
  for the past yr.
299 USD/yr for 3-issue subscription or annual
  cumulation
ISBN(s): 0-7876-2267-2 (Cumulative Edition
  2000); 0-7876-3545-6 (Cumulative Edition
  2001); 0-7876-5301-2 (2000 Edition)

ƒ**Bookman's Price Index** (B)
Published by Thomson Gale
Unit of The Thomson Corp
27500 Drake Rd, Farmington Hills, MI 48331-
  3535
*Tel:* 248-699-4253 *Toll Free Tel:* 800-347-4253
  *Fax:* 248-699-8075 *Toll Free Fax:* 800-414-
  5043
*E-mail:* galeord@gale.com
*Web Site:* www.gale.com
*Key Personnel*
Editor: Michael Reade

A guide to the prices & availability of more than
  25,000 rare or out-of-print antiquarian books
  as offered for sale in the catalogs of nearly 200
  leading bookdealers in the US, UK & Canada.
  Each volume lists almost 15,000 titles. Volumes do not supersede previous volumes. Each
  volume covers catalogs from the previous 4-6
  months. Each entry includes title, author, edition, year published, physical description (size,
  binding, illustrations), condition of the book &
  price. Arranged alphabetically by author.
First published 1964.
3-4 times/yr.
Vol 76-79, 2004; Vol 80-81, 2005: 1,300 pp, 415
  USD/vol
ISBN(s): 0-7876-6687-4 (Vol 76); 0-7876-7832-
  5 (Vol 77); 0-7876-7833-3 (Vol 78); 0-7876-
  7834-1 (Vol 79); 0-7876-7835-X (Vol 80); 0-
  7876-7836-8 (Vol 81)

ƒ**Contemporary Authors** (B)
Published by Thomson Gale
Unit of The Thomson Corp
27500 Drake Rd, Farmington Hills, MI 48331-
  3535
*Tel:* 248-699-4253 *Toll Free Tel:* 800-347-4253
  *Fax:* 248-699-8070 *Toll Free Fax:* 800-414-
  5043
*E-mail:* galeord@gale.com
*Web Site:* www.gale.com
Each volume includes biographical information
  on approximately 300 modern writers in fiction, general nonfiction, poetry, journalism,
  drama, motion pictures & television.
10 vols/yr, original vols; 10 vols/yr, new revision
  series.
Vols 221-230, 2004, $195 USD/vol
ISBN(s): 0-7876-6701-3 (Vol 221); 0-7876-6702-
  1 (Vol 222); 0-7876-6703-4 (Vol 223); 0-7876-
  6704-8 (Vol 224); 0-7876-6705-6 (Vol 225);
  0-7876-6706-4 (Vol 226); 0-7876-6707-2 (Vol
  227); 0-7876-6708-0 (Vol 228); 0-7876-6709-9
  (Vol 229); 0-7876-6710-2 (Vol 230)

ƒ**Directory of Special Libraries and
  Information Centers** (B)
Published by Thomson Gale
Unit of The Thomson Corp
27500 Drake Rd, Farmington Hills, MI 48331-
  3535
*Tel:* 248-699-4253 *Toll Free Tel:* 800-347-4253
  *Fax:* 248-699-8075 *Toll Free Fax:* 800-414-
  5043
*E-mail:* galeord@gale.com
*Web Site:* www.gale.com
*Key Personnel*
Editor: Matthew Miskelly *Tel:* 248-699-4253 (ext
  1744)
A key to the holdings, services, electronic re-
  sources & personnel of more than 34,500 spe-
  cial libraries & special collections, information
  centers, documentation centers & similar units.
Annual.
30th, 2005: 2,850 pp, 975 USD (3 vol set)
ISBN(s): 0-7876-6864-8

**The Historical Novels Review** (J)
Published by Historical Novel Society
5239 N Commerce Ave, Moorpark, CA 93066
Mailing Address: Booth Library, Eastern Illinois
  University, 600 Lincoln Ave, Charleston, IL
  61920
*Tel:* 217-581-7538 *Fax:* 217-581-7534
*E-mail:* cfsln@eiu.edu (editorial); timarete@
  earthlink.net (subscription)
*Web Site:* www.historicalnovelsociety.org
*Key Personnel*
Coord Ed (UK): Sarah Bower
  *E-mail:* sarahbower@clara.co.uk
Coord Ed (USA): Sarah Johnson
Reviews of currently published historical fiction
  from the USA & Great Britain.

First published 1997.
Quarterly.
54 pp, 45/yr USD
ISSN: 1471-7492

∮**International Literary Market Place** (B)
Published by Information Today, Inc
630 Central Ave, New Providence, NJ 07974
*Tel:* 908-286-1090 *Toll Free Tel:* 800-409-4929;
    800-300-9868 (cust serv) *Fax:* 908-219-0192
*E-mail:* custserv@infotoday.com
*Web Site:* www.literarymarketplace.com
Directory of companies & individuals in the book
    publishing trade, covering 180 countries outside
    the US & Canada. Entries included for more
    than 10,000 publishers & 4,300 book organi-
    zations, including agents, booksellers & library
    associations. The US & Canada are covered
    by Literary Market Place. Web version, which
    includes Literary Market Place, also available.
Annually.
39th: 1,780 pp, $229.00 USD/print, $399 USD/
    web
ISBN(s): 1-57387-218-0
ISSN: 0074-6827

**Literary Market Place** (B)
Published by Information Today, Inc
630 Central Ave, New Providence, NJ 07974
*Tel:* 908-286-1090 *Toll Free Tel:* 800-409-4929;
    800-300-9868 (cust serv) *Fax:* 908-219-0192
*E-mail:* custserv@infotoday.com
*Web Site:* www.literarymarketplace.com
Directory of over 40,000 companies & individu-
    als US & Canadian publishing. A two volume
    set, each containing two alphabetical names &
    numbers indexes, one for key companies listed
    & one for individuals. The rest of the world is
    covered by International Literary Market Place.
    Web version, which includes International Lit-
    erary Market Place, also available.
Annually.
66th: 2,050 pp, $299.99 USD/print, $399 USD/
    web
ISBN(s): 1-57387-210-0 (2 volume set)
ISSN: 0000-1155

∮**Review - Latin American Literature & Arts**
    (J)
Published by Americas Society
680 Park Ave, 4th floor, New York, NY 10021-
    5009
*Tel:* 212-249-8950 *Fax:* 212-517-6247
*E-mail:* inforequest@as-coa.org
*Web Site:* www.americas-society.org
*Key Personnel*
Managing Editor: Daniel Shapiro *Tel:* 212-
    249-8950 (ext 366) *Fax:* 212-249-5868
    *E-mail:* dshapiro@as-coa.org
Contemporary Latin American literature in En-
    glish translation.
Biannually, mid-May & mid-Nov.
22 USD (domestic individuals); 32 USD (domes-
    tic institutions); 34 USD (foreign)

∮**Scandinavian Review** (J)
Published by American-Scandinavian Foundation
58 Park Ave, New York, NY 10016
*Tel:* 212-879-9779 *Fax:* 212-879-2301; 212-249-
    3444
*E-mail:* info@amscan.org
*Web Site:* www.amscan.org
*Key Personnel*
Editor: Adrienne Gyongy *E-mail:* agyongy@
    amscan.org

Cultural/literary/political magazine.
First published 1913.
Triannually.
15 USD (domestic individuals); 22 USD (foreign)

**Solander**
Published by Historical Novel Society
5239 N Commerce Ave, Moorpark, CA 93066
Mailing Address: Marine Cottage, The Strand,
    Starcross, Devon EX6 8NY, United Kingdom
*Tel:* 217-581-7538 *Fax:* 217-581-7534
*E-mail:* histnovel@aol.com
*Web Site:* www.historicalnovelsociety.org
*Key Personnel*
Ed: Sarah Cuthbertson
Publisher: Richard Lee
US Membership Sec: Debra Tash
Literary magazine for historical fiction, with arti-
    cles, interviews & short fiction.
First published 1997.
Biannually.
38 pp, 45/yr USD
ISSN: 1471-7484

**Ulrich's International Periodicals Directory**,
    see Ulrich's Periodicals Directory

∮**Ulrich's Periodicals Directory** (B)
Published by R R Bowker LLC
Subsidiary of Cambridge Information Group Inc
630 Central Ave, New Providence, NJ 07974
*Tel:* 908-286-1090 *Toll Free Tel:* 800-521-8110;
    888-Bowker2; 888-269-5372 *Fax:* 908-219-
    0812
*E-mail:* ulrichs@bowker.com
*Web Site:* www.bowker.com; www.ulrichsweb.
    com
*Key Personnel*
Dir, Serials: Laurie Kaplan
Dir, Print Sales & Training: Serge Sarkis
Four-volume set, arranged by subject classifica-
    tion, includes periodicals, newsletters, news-
    papers, annuals & irregular serials published
    worldwide. Also available on the Internet, CD-
    ROM & online.
First published 1932.
Annually.
43rd, 2005: 11,529 pp, 799 USD
ISBN(s): 0-8352-4666-3 (4 vol set)
ISSN: 0000-2100

∮**United Nations Publications** (B)
2 United Nations Plaza, Sales Section, Rm DC2-
    853, New York, NY 10017
*Tel:* 212-963-8302 *Toll Free Tel:* 800-253-9646
    *Fax:* 212-963-3489
*E-mail:* publications@un.org
*Web Site:* www.un.org/Pubs/index.html

# Uruguay

**Anuario Bibliografico Uruguayo** (Uruguayan
    Bibliographical Annual 1968-) (B)
Published by Biblioteca Nacional del Uruguay
c/o Director General, Ave 15 de Julio, 1790,
    11210 Montevideo
Mailing Address: CP 11200, Montevido
*Tel:* (02) 48 50 30 *Fax:* (02) 49 69 02
*Key Personnel*
Editor: Luis Alberto Musso
Text in Spanish.

First published 1946.
Annually.
400 pp
ISSN: 0304-8861

# Venezuela

**Bibliografia Venezolana** (Venezuelan
    Bibliography) (B)
Published by Instituto Autonomo Biblioteca Na-
    cional y de Servicios de Bibliotecas
Prados del Este, Apdo 80593, Caracas 1080
*Tel:* (0212) 943-1361 *Fax:* (0212) 941-5219
*Telex:* 24621 VC
Text in Spanish.
First published 1970.
Biannually.
650 VEB or 30 USD
ISSN: 0798-0086

# Zambia

**National Bibliography of Zambia** (B)
Published by National Archives
Government Rd, Ridgeway, 10101 Lusaka
Mailing Address: PO Box 50010, 10101 Lusaka
*Tel:* (01) 254081 */Fax:* (01) 254080
*E-mail:* naz@zamnet.zm
*Key Personnel*
Editor: Christine Kamwana
Text in English.
Annually.
ISSN: 0377-1636

# Zimbabwe

∮**African Publishing Review** (J)
Published by African Publishers' Network (AP-
    NET)
18 Van Praagh Ave, Milton Park, Harare
Mailing Address: PO Box 3773, Harare
*Tel:* (04) 708413; (04) 20211801; (04) 708405
    *Fax:* (04) 20211803
*E-mail:* apnetes@yahoo.com; apnet@harare.
    iafrica.com
*Web Site:* www.africanpublishers.org
*Key Personnel*
Editor: Jenny Waddlington; Lesley Humphrey
Newsletter.
First published 1992.
Bimonthly.
30 USD
ISSN: 1019-5823

**Zimbabwe National Bibliography** (B)
Published by National Archives of Zimbabwe
PB 7729, Causeway, Harare
*Tel:* (04) 792741 *Fax:* (04) 792398
*E-mail:* archives@zim.gov.zw
*Web Site:* www.zim.gov.zw
*Key Personnel*
President: R G Mugabe
Annually.
15 USD

# Literary Associations & Prizes

## Literary Associations & Societies

Listed in this section are literary associations and societies. Listings appear alphabetically under the country in which they are located. Other book trade associations and organizations can be found in the sections **Book Trade Organizations** and **Library Associations**.

# Argentina

**Academia Argentina de Letras** (Argentine Academy of Letters)
Sanchez de Bustamante 2663, 1425 Buenos Aires
*Tel:* (011) 4802-3814; (011) 4802-5161; (011) 4802-7509 *Fax:* (011) 4802-8340
*E-mail:* aaldespa@fibertel.com.ar; aaladmin@ fibertel.com.ar; aalbibl@fibertel.com.ar
*Web Site:* www.aal.universia.com.ar/aal
*Key Personnel*
President: Pedro Luis Barcia
General Secretary: Rodolfo Modern
Treasurer: Federico Peltzer
Founded: 1931
Specialize in philosophy, literature & linguistics.
Publication(s): *Boletin de la Academia Argentina de Letras* (Bulletin of the Argentine Academy of Letters, quarterly); *Serie de acuerdos acerca del Idioma*; *Serie de Clasicos Angentinos*; *Serie Estudios academicos y otras publicaciones*; *Serie Estudios Linguisticos y Filologicos*; *Serie Homenajes*

**Argentinian PEN Centre**
Member of International PEN
Coronel Diaz 2089, 17C, 1425 Buenos Aires
*Key Personnel*
President: Rolando Costa Picazo
Publication(s): *Boletin*

# Australia

**ASAL**, see Association for the Study of Australian Literature Ltd (ASAL)

**Association for the Study of Australian Literature Ltd (ASAL)**
University of Queensland, Michie Bldg, St Lucia, Brisbane, Qld 4072
*Tel:* (07) 3665 1369 *Fax:* (07) 3665 2799
*Web Site:* www.asc.uq.edu.au
*Key Personnel*
President: Chris Lee *Tel:* (07) 4631 1045
*Fax:* (07) 4631 1063 *E-mail:* leec@usq.edu.au
Vice President: Lyn McCredden *Tel:* (03) 9244 3960 *Fax:* (03) 9481 6717 *E-mail:* lynmcr@ deakin.edu.au
Treasurer: Simon Ryan *E-mail:* s.ryan@mcauley. acu.edu.au
Secretary: Paul Genoni *Tel:* (08) 9266 7256
*E-mail:* p.genoni@curtin.edu.au
Dir: Dr David Carter *E-mail:* david.carter@ mailbox.uq.edu.au

Deputy Dir: Dr Martin Crotty *E-mail:* m.crotty@ uq.edu.au
Executive Manager: Kerry Kilner *E-mail:* k. kilner@uq.edu.au
Founded: 1899
Publication(s): *Notes & Furphies*

**Australasian Association for Lexicography (Australex)**
Bond University, Gold Coast, Qld 4229
*Tel:* (07) 5595 2502 *Fax:* (07) 5595 2545
*Web Site:* www.anu.edu.au
*Key Personnel*
President: Bruce Moore
Vice President: Pam Peters
Treasurer: Julia Robinson
Secretary: Dr Pauline Bryant *Tel:* (02) 6125 5134
*Fax:* (02) 6279 8214 *E-mail:* pauline.bryant@ anu.edu.au
Founded: 1990
Publication(s): *Australex* (newsletter)

**Australex**, see Australasian Association for Lexicography (Australex)

**Australian Library Publishers' Society**
Barr Smith Library, University of Adelaide, N Terrace, Adelaide, SA 5005
*Tel:* (08) 8303 5372 *Fax:* (08) 8303 4369
*E-mail:* library@adelaide.edu.au
*Web Site:* www.library.adelaide.edu.au/ual/publ/ alps/
*Key Personnel*
Convener & University Librarian: Ray Choate
*Tel:* (02) 8303 4064 *E-mail:* ray.choate@ adelaide.edu.au
Represents 25 library publishers & markets approximately 300 publications.
Publication(s): *Catalogue of Members' Publications* (5th edition)

**Australian Literature Society**, see Association for the Study of Australian Literature Ltd (ASAL)

**The Australian Society of Authors Ltd**
PO Box 1566, Strawberry Hills, NSW 2012
*Tel:* (02) 93180877 *Fax:* (02) 93180530
*E-mail:* asa@asauthors.org
*Web Site:* www.asauthors.org
*Key Personnel*
Chair: Susan Hayes
Deputy Chair: Georgia Blain
Executive Dir: Jeremy Fisher
Treasurer: Libby Gleeson
Founded: 1963
Publication(s): *Australian Author* (triannually, magazine); *Australian Book Contracts*

**Australian Writers' Guild Ltd**
8/50 Reservoir St, Surrey Hills, NSW 2010
*Tel:* (02) 92811554 *Fax:* (02) 92814321
*E-mail:* admin@awg.com.au
*Web Site:* www.awg.com.au
*Key Personnel*
Executive Dir: Megan Elliott *E-mail:* melliott@ awg.com.au
Helps give access to industry information as well as a wide variety of services.
Publication(s): *A Matter of Cultural Sovereignty*; *The Writers' Directory: Writers for Screen, Stage, Radio & Television in Australia*

**Bibliographical Society of Australia & New Zealand (BSANZ)**
PO Box 1463, Waga Waga, NSW 2650
*Tel:* (03) 96699032 *Fax:* (03) 96699032
*Web Site:* www.csu.edu.au/community/BSANZ
*Key Personnel*
President: Prof Dirk H R Spennemann
*E-mail:* dspennemann@csu.edu.au
Vice President: Prof Ross Harvey
*E-mail:* rharvey@csu.edu.au
Secretary & Treasurer: Rachel Salmond
*E-mail:* rsalmond@pobox.com
Founded: 1969
Publication(s): *Broadsheet* (triannually); *Bulletin* (quarterly)

**BSANZ**, see Bibliographical Society of Australia & New Zealand (BSANZ)

**The Children's Book Council of Australia**
PO Box 765, Rozelle, NSW 2039
*Tel:* (02) 9818 3858 *Fax:* (02) 9810 0737
*E-mail:* office@cbc.org.au
*Web Site:* www.cbc.org.au
*Key Personnel*
President: Mark Macleod *E-mail:* president@cbc. org.au
Secretary: Mary McNally *E-mail:* secretary@cbc. org.au
Treasurer: Tony Horgan *E-mail:* treasurer@cbc. org.au
Awards Coordinator: Myra Lee *E-mail:* awards@ cbc.org.au
Branches in New South Wales, Queensland, South Australia, Tasmania, Victoria, Western Australia, Australian Capital Territory, Northern Territory.
Publication(s): *Reading Time* (quarterly)

**Fellowship of Australian Writers**
PO Box 8411, Armadale, Victoria 3143
*Tel:* (03) 9431 2370
*E-mail:* lynspire@bigpond.net.au
*Web Site:* www.writers.asn.au
*Key Personnel*
President & Treasurer: Philip Rainford

Vice President: Michael Dugan
Vice President & Executive Officer: Marcus Niski
Awards Coordinator: Adrian Peniston-Bird
Twenty-one regional branches in suburbs of Sydney & country towns; 1,000 members.
Publication(s): *The Australian Writer* (bimonthly)

**Fellowship of Australian Writers (Vic) Inc**
PO Box 8411, Armadale, Victoria 3143
*Tel:* (03) 9431 2370
*Web Site:* www.writers.asn.au
*Key Personnel*
President: Philip Rainford *E-mail:* rainfordp@aol.com
Founded: 1928
All awards open the second week of September & close the third week of November each year.
Publication(s): *The Australian Writer* (bimonthly)

**Melbourne PEN Centre**
Member of International PEN
PO Box 2273, Caulfield Junction, Victoria 3161
*Tel:* (03) 95097257 *Fax:* (03) 95097257
*Web Site:* www.pen.org.au
*Key Personnel*
President: Judith Buckrich *E-mail:* buckrich@netspace.net.au
Secretary: Danik Bancilhon
Founded to promote friendship & intellectual co-operation among writers everywhere.

**NSW Writers' Centre**
Rozelle Hospital, Balmain Rd, Rozelle, NSW 2039
Mailing Address: PO Box 1056, Rozelle, NSW 2039
*Tel:* (02) 95559757 *Fax:* (02) 98181327
*E-mail:* nswwc@ozemail.com.au
*Web Site:* www.nswwriterscentre.org.au
*Key Personnel*
Chairman: Angelo Loukakis
Deputy Chair: Pat Woolley
Treasurer: David LePage
Secretary: Alan Russell
Executive Dir: Irina Dunn
Founded: 1991
Resource & information centre for emerging & professional writers.
Publication(s): *Newswrite* (monthly)

**Poetry Society of Australia**
Grosvenor St, Sydney, NSW 2000
Mailing Address: PO Box N110, Sydney, NSW 2000
*Tel:* (02) 423861
*Key Personnel*
Joint Secretary: Robert Adamson; Debra Adamson
Publication(s): *New Poetry* (quarterly; also poems, articles, reviews, notes & comments, interviews)

**Sydney PEN Centre**
Member of International PEN
University of Technology, Sydney, PO Box 123, Broadway, NSW 2007
*Tel:* (02) 9514 2738 *Fax:* (02) 9514 2778
*E-mail:* sydney@pen.org.au
*Web Site:* www.pen.org.au
*Key Personnel*
President: Nicholas Jose
Vice President: Mary Cunnane; Rosie Scott
Honorary Secretary: Wilda Moxham
Honorary Treasurer: Chip Rolley
Founded: 1931
Promotes friendship & intellectual cooperation among writers everywhere.
Publication(s): *Newsletter* (quarterly)

# Austria

**Austrian PEN Centre** (Oesterreichischer PEN-Club)
Member of International PEN
Concordia Haus, Bankgasse 8, 1010 Vienna
*Tel:* (01) 5334459 *Fax:* (01) 5328749
*E-mail:* oepen.club@netway.at
*Web Site:* www.penclub.at
*Key Personnel*
President: Jiri Grusa
Secretary: Dr Peter Marginter
Publication(s): *Pen-Nachrichten* (biannually)

**Institut fuer Oesterreichkunde** (Institute for the Knowledge of Austria)
Hanuschgasse 3/3, 1010 Vienna
*Tel:* (01) 512-79-32 *Fax:* (01) 512-79-32
*E-mail:* loek.wirtschaftsgeschichte@univie.ac.at
*Key Personnel*
President: Prof Ernst Bruckmueller, PhD *Tel:* (01) 4277 41312 *E-mail:* ernst.bruckmueller@univie.ac.at
Secretary General: Bernhard Zimmermann
Founded: 1957
Publication(s): *Oesterreich Archiv* (yearly, book); *Oesterreich in Geschichte und Literatur mit Geographie* (bimonthly, journal); *Schriften des Institutes fuer Oesterreichkunde* (yearly, book); *Schriftenreihe Literatur des Institutes fuer Oesterreichkunde*

**Oesterreichische Gesellschaft fuer Literatur** (Austrian Literary Society)
Herrengasse 5, 1010 Vienna
*Tel:* (01) 5338159 *Fax:* (01) 5334067
*E-mail:* office@ogl.at
*Web Site:* www.ogl.at
*Key Personnel*
President: Marianne Gruber
Vice President: Helmuth A Niederle
Founded: 1961

# Bahrain

**Bahrain Writers & Literators Association**
PO Box 1010, Manama
*Key Personnel*
President: Ali al-Shargawi
Secretary: Fareed Ramadan
Founded: 1969

# Bangladesh

**Society of Arts, Literature & Welfare**
Society Park, K C Dey Rd, Chittagong
*Web Site:* www.bjfao.gov.cn
*Key Personnel*
General Secretary: Nesar Ahmed Chowdhury

# Belgium

**Academie Royale de Langue et de Litterature Francaises** (Royal Academy of French Language & Literature)
Palais des Academies, One rue Ducale, 1000 Brussels

*Tel:* (02) 550-2277 *Fax:* (02) 550-2275
*E-mail:* alf@cfwb.be
*Web Site:* www.academielanguelitteraturefrancaises.be
*Key Personnel*
Dir: Raymond Trousson
Vice Dir: Georges-Henri Dumont
Secretary: Corinne Hoste
Permanent Secretary: Jacques De Decker
Publication(s): *Bulletin, Annuaire, Memoires*

**Academie Royale des Sciences, des Lettres et des Beaux-Arts de Belgique** (Belgian Royal Academy of Sciences, Letters & Fine Arts)
Palais des Academies, rue Ducale, One, 1000 Brussels
*Tel:* (02) 5502211; (02) 5502212; (02) 5502213 *Fax:* (02) 5502205
*E-mail:* arb@cfwb.be
*Web Site:* www.cfwb.be/arb; www.arb.cfwb.be
*Key Personnel*
Secretary: Leo Houziaux *Tel:* (02) 5502203 *E-mail:* leo.houziaux@ulq.ac.be
Founded: 1772
Publication(s): *Bulletins* (biannually); *Memoirs*; *Year Book*

**AEBLF**, see Association des Ecrivains Belges de Langue Francaise (AEBLF)

**Association des Ecrivains Belges de Langue Francaise (AEBLF)** (Association of the Belgian Writers of French Language)
chaussee de Wavre, 150, 1050 Brussels
*Tel:* (02) 512 29 68 *Fax:* (02) 502 43 73
*E-mail:* a.e.b@skynet.be
*Web Site:* www.ecrivainsbelges.be
*Key Personnel*
President: France Bastia *E-mail:* france.bastia@skynet.be
Vice President: Prof Emile Kesteman; Marie Nicolai
Secretary General: Jean Lacroix
Treasurer: Jean Pirlet
Publication(s): *Nos Lettres* (10 times/yr)

**Association of Antwerp Bibliophiles**
c/o Museum Plantin-Moretus, Vrijdagmarkt 22, 2000 Antwerp
*Tel:* (03) 2330294 *Fax:* (03) 2262516
*E-mail:* francine.demav@amtwerpa.be
*Key Personnel*
President: Prof L Voet, PhD
Secretary: Prof G Persoons, PhD; Prof L De Pavw-De Veen, PhD
Founded: 1877
Publication(s): *De Gulden Passer* (annually)

**Belgian PEN Centre (French-Speaking)**
Member of International PEN
10 Ave des Cerfs, 1950 Kraainem (Bx)
*Tel:* (02) 7314847 *Fax:* (02) 7314847
*Web Site:* www.oneworld.org/internatpen/centres.htm
*Key Personnel*
President: Huguette de Broqueville *E-mail:* huguette.db@skynet.be
Founded: 1922
A voice of literature worldwide, bringing together poets, novelists, essayists, historians, critics, translators, editors, journalists & screenwriters. Members are united in a common concern for the craft & art of writing & a commitment to freedom of expression through the written word.

**Commission Belge de Bibliographie et de Bibliologie** (Belgian Commission of Bibliography & Bibliology)
4 blvd de l'Empereur, 1000 Brussels
*Tel:* (02) 5195311 *Fax:* (02) 5195533

*Web Site:* www.kbr.be; opac.kbr.be/ekbr1.htm
(web catalogue)
*Key Personnel*
Contact: Dr Raphael De Smedt
Founded: 1837
Publication(s): *Annuaire* (annually); Coll: *Bibliographia Belgica*

**KANTL**, see Koninklijke Academie voor
Nederlandse Taal- en Letterkunde

**Koninklijke Academie voor Nederlandse Taal-
en Letterkunde** (Royal Academy of Dutch
Language & Literature)
Koningstr 18, 9000 Ghent
*Tel:* (09) 265 93 40 *Fax:* (09) 265 93 49
*E-mail:* info@kantl.be
*Web Site:* www.kantl.be
*Key Personnel*
Permanent Secretary: Prof Dr Georges de Schutter *Tel:* (09) 265 93 42 *E-mail:* secretariaat@kantl.be
Librarian: Marijke de Wit *Tel:* (09) 265 93 43
*E-mail:* mdewit@kantl.be
Founded: 1886
Publication(s): *Jaarboek van de Koninklijke
Academie voor Nederlandse Taal-en Letterkunde* (annually); *Verslagen en Mededelingen van de Koninklijke Academie voor Nederlandse Taal-en Letterkunde* (triannually)

**Koninklijke Academie voor Wetenschappen
Letteren en Schone Kunsten Van Belgie**
(Royal Belgian Academy of Sciences, Letters
& Fine Arts)
Paleis der Academien, Hertogsstr 1, 1000 Brussels
*Tel:* (02) 550 23 23 *Fax:* (02) 550 23 25
*E-mail:* info@kvab.be
*Web Site:* www.kvab.be
*Key Personnel*
Publications Officer: Gilbert Reynderg *Tel:* (02)
550 23 32 *E-mail:* gilbert.reynderg@kvab.be
Permanent Secretary: Niceas Schamp
Dutch-speaking Royal Belgian Academy of Sciences, Letters & Fine Arts.
Publication(s): *Collectanea Biblica et Religiosa
Antiqua*; *Collectanea Hellenistica*; *Collectanea
Maritima*; *Corpus Catalogorum Belgii*; *Fontes
Historiae Artis Neerlandicae*; *Iuris Scripta Historica*; *Iusti Lipsi Epistolae (The Correspondence of J Lipsius)*; *(Memoirs) & Fine Arts*;
*National Biography*; *Proceedings Department
of Letters*; *Studia Europea*; *Studies in Belgian
Economic History*; *Year Book*

**Belgian PEN Centre (French-Speaking)**
Member of International PEN
10 Ave des Cerfs, 1950 Kraainem
*Tel:* (052) 351118 *Fax:* (052) 351119
*Key Personnel*
President: Huguette de Broqueville
*E-mail:* huguettedb@skynet.be
Secretary: M Fernand Auwera
Dutch-speaking.

**SABAM**, see Societe Belge des Auteurs,
Compositeurs et Editeurs (SABAM)

**SLLW**, see Societe de Langue et de Litterature
Wallonnes ASBL

**Societe Belge des Auteurs, Compositeurs et
Editeurs (SABAM)** (Belgian Society of
Authors, Composers & Publishers)
Rue d'Arlon 75-77, 1040 Brussels
*Tel:* (02) 286 8211 *Fax:* (02) 230 0589
*E-mail:* info@sabam.de
*Web Site:* www.sabam.be
*Key Personnel*
Dir General: Jacques Lion

Secretary General: Carine Libert
Dir, Communications: Thierry Dachelet
*E-mail:* thierry.dachelet@sabam.be
Dir, Information: Willy Heyns
Dir, Administration, Finance & Human Resources: Luc Van Oycke
Publication(s): *Bulletin* (quarterly)

**Societe de Langue et de Litterature Wallonnes
ASBL** (Society for Walloon Language &
Literature)
Universite de Liege, 7 place du XX Aout, 4000
Liege
*Tel:* (086) 344432
*E-mail:* sllw.be@skynet.be
*Web Site:* users.skynet.be/sllw
*Key Personnel*
President: Guy Belleflamme *E-mail:* guy.
belleflamme@skynet.be
Vice President & Editor: Marie-Guy Boutier
*E-mail:* marie-guy.boutier@skynet.be
Secretary: Victor George
Publication(s): *Chronique de la Societe de
Langue et de Litterature wallonnes* (Irregularly); *Dialectes de Wallonie* (Irregularly)

# Bolivia

**Bolivian PEN Centre** (PEN Club de Bolivia
(Centro Internacional de Escritores))
Member of International PEN
Casilla Postal 5920, Cochabamba
*Key Personnel*
President: Gaby Vallejo Canedo
*E-mail:* gabyvall@supernet.com.bo

# Brazil

**Academia Amazonense de Letras**
Rua Ramos Ferreira 1009 Terreo, 69010-120
Manaus-AM
*Tel:* (092) 633-1426
*Key Personnel*
President: Djalma Batista
Secretary: Genesino Braga
Librarian: Mario Ypiranga Monteiro
Amazonas Academy of Letters.
Publication(s): *Revista*

**Academia Brasileira de Letras**
Ave Presidente Wilson 203 Castelo, 20030-021
Rio de Janeiro-RJ
*Tel:* (021) 3974-2500 *Fax:* (021) 220-6695
*E-mail:* academia@academia.org.br
*Web Site:* www.academia.org.br
*Key Personnel*
Secretary General: Abgar Renault
Librarian: Barbosa Lima Sobrinho
Publication(s): *Revista*

**Academia Catarinense de Letras** (Santa
Catarina Academy of Letters)
c/o Prof Enrique Da Silva Sources, Integrated
Center of Culture, Av Irineu Bornhausen 5600,
88010-970 Florianopolis SC
*Tel:* 2342166
*Web Site:* www.acle.com.br
*Key Personnel*
President: Doris Becke Machado Freitas
Founded: 1968
Publication(s): *Revista* (annually)

**Academia Cearense de Letras** (Ceara Academy
of Letters)
Rua do Rosarion 1, 60005-590 Fortaleza, CE
*Tel:* (085) 2315669
*E-mail:* acletras@accvia.com.br
*Web Site:* www.secrel.com.br
*Key Personnel*
President: Artur Eduardo Benevides
Vice President: Ribeiro Ramos-Segundo
General Secretary: Cesar Loyal Barros
Founded: 1894
Publication(s): *Colecao Antonio Sales*; *Colecao
Dolor Barreira*; *Revista da Academia Cearense
de Letras*

**Academia de Letras da Bahia** (Bahia Academy
of Letters)
Palacete Goes Calmon, Av Joana Angelica 198,
40050-000 Nazare, Salvador BA
*Tel:* (071) 321-4308 *Fax:* (071) 321-4308
*E-mail:* alb@stn.com.br
*Key Personnel*
President: Claudio Veiga
Vice President: Wilson Lins
Secretary: Edivaldo M Boaventura
Publication(s): *Revista* (annually)

**Academia de Letras de Piaui**
64000-490 Teresina, PI
*Key Personnel*
President: Jose de Arimathea Tito Filho
Piaui Academy of Letters.
Publication(s): *Revista*

**Academia Mineira de Letras** (Minas Gerais
Academy of Letters)
Rua da Bahia 1466, Lourdes, 30160-011 Belo
Horizonte-MG
*Tel:* (031) 3222-5764
*E-mail:* amletras@task.com.br
*Web Site:* www.academiamineiradeletras.org.br
*Key Personnel*
President: Murilo Badaro
Vice President: Miguel Augusto Goncalves; Raul
Machado Horta

**Academia Paraibana de Letras** (Parabia
Academy of Letters)
Rua Duque de Caxias 25, CP 334, 58000 Joao
Pessoa, PB
*E-mail:* fsatiro@openline.com.br
*Web Site:* www.pbnet.com.br/openline/fsatiro/
academia.html
*Key Personnel*
President: Wellington Hermes de Aguiar
Vice President: Claudio Santa Cruz Costa
Secretary: Humberto Cavalcante de Melo
Treasurer: Sergio de Castro Pinto
Founded: 1941
Publication(s): *Revista*

**Academia Paulista de Letras** (Sao Paulo
Academy of Letters)
Largo do Arouche 312/324, 01219-010 Sao
Paulo-SP
*Tel:* (011) 3331-7222 *Fax:* (011) 3331-7401
*E-mail:* acadsp@terra.com.br
*Web Site:* www.academiapaulistadeletras.org.br
*Key Personnel*
President: Erwin Theodor Rosenthal
Founded: 1909
Publication(s): *Biblioteca Academia Paulista de
Letras*; *Revista da Academia Paulista de Letras*

**Academia Pernambucana de Letras**
(Pernambuco Academy of Letters)
Ave Rui Barbosa 1596, Gracias, Barrio da Jaqueira, 52050-000 Recife-PE
*Tel:* (081) 3268-2211
*Key Personnel*
President: Luiz de Magalhaes Melo
Secretary: Dr Lucilo Varejao Filho

Founded: 1901
Publication(s): *Revista*

**Brazilian PEN Centre** (PEN Clube do Brasil
(Associacao Universal de Escritores))
Member of International PEN
Praia do Flamengo 172-11° andar, Rio de Janeiro
2000
*Key Personnel*
President: Prof Marcos Almir Madeira
Secretary: Maria Cecilia Ribas Carneiro
Publication(s): *Boletim*

# Bulgaria

**Bulgarian Academy of Sciences, Institute of
Literature**
1, 15 Noemvri Str, 1040 Sofia
*Tel:* (02) 989-84-46 *Fax:* (02) 981-66-29; (02)
986-25-23; (02) 988-04-48
*Web Site:* www.bas.bg
*Telex:* (067) 224-24 BG
*Key Personnel*
Scientific Secretary General: Prof Naumya Yaki-
moff *Tel:* (02) 987-70-87 *E-mail:* yakimoff@
eagle.cu.bas.bg
Founded: 1869
Publication(s): *Literatourna Missul* (Literary
Thought)

**Bulgarian Writers' Union**
5 Anguel Kanchev, 1000 Sofia
*Tel:* (02) 898346 *Fax:* (02) 835411
*Key Personnel*
President: N Haitov
Publication(s): *Literaturen Front* (weekly); *Pla-
mak* (The Flame, monthly); *Savremennik*
(quarterly); *Septemvri* (monthly); *Slaveiche*
(monthly, for children)

# China

**China PEN Centre**
Member of International PEN
Chinese Writers Activity Centre, 25 Dong-
tuchenglu, Beijing 10013
*Fax:* 8610 64221704
*Key Personnel*
President: Mr Ba Jin
Secretary: Jin Jianfan

**Hong Kong PEN Centre (English-Speaking)**
Member of International PEN
1/F, West, Lok Yen Bldg, 23D Peak Rd, Cheung
Chau, Hong Kong
*Tel:* 25774168 *Fax:* 25774168
*E-mail:* hkpen_eng@yahoo.com
*Key Personnel*
President: Fred S Armentrout
Vice President: Peter Stambler
Secretary: Ruth Barzel
Publication(s): *Vietnamese Writers in Hong
Kong's Camps, A Caselist*

# Colombia

**Colombian PEN Centre** (PEN Internacional de
Colombia)
Member of International PEN

PO Box 101830, Zona 10, Bogota
*Tel:* (01) 2846761; (01) 2561540 *Fax:* (01)
2184236
*E-mail:* pencolombia@hotmail.com
*Key Personnel*
President: Cecilia Balcazar de Bucher, PhD
Secretary: Gloria Guardia

**Instituto Caro y Cuervo**
Carrera 11, No 64-37, Apdo Aereo 51502, Bo-
gota
*Tel:* (01) 3456004 *Fax:* (01) 2170243
*E-mail:* secretariagenera@caroycuervo.gov.co
*Web Site:* www.caroycuervo.gov.co
*Key Personnel*
Dir: Ignacio Chaves Cuevas
Secretary General: Carlos Julio Luque Cagua
Founded: 1942
Linguistics, Philology & Literature.

**Instituto Colombiano de Cultura Hispanica**
Calle 12, No 2-41, Apdo 5454, Bogota
*Tel:* (01) 3413857 *Fax:* (01) 2811051
*Key Personnel*
Dir: William Jaramillo Meja
General Secretary: Clemencia Vallejo de Meja
Publication(s): *Flora de la Real Expedicion
Botanica del Nuevo*

# Congo

**Congolese PEN Centre**
Member of International PEN
BP 2181, Brazzaville
*Tel:* 813601 *Fax:* 813601
*Key Personnel*
President: Emmanuel B Dongala

# Czech Republic

**Czech PEN Centre**
Member of International PEN
28 rijna 9, 11000 Prague 1
*Tel:* (02) 24235546; (02) 24234343 *Fax:* (02)
24221926
*E-mail:* centrum@pen.cz
*Web Site:* www.pen.cz
*Key Personnel*
President: Jiri Stransky *E-mail:* jiri@pen.cz
Secretary: Libuse Ludvikova *E-mail:* libuse@pen.
cz
Founded: 1925

**Matice moravska**
Arne Novaka 1, 60200 Brno
*Tel:* (05) 4949 1511 *Fax:* (05) 4949 1520
*E-mail:* bronek@phil.muni.cz
*Web Site:* www.phil.muni.cz
*Key Personnel*
President: Prof Jan Janak, Jr
Secretary: Dr Jiri Malir
Publication(s): *Casopis Matice moravske* (biannu-
ally)

# Denmark

**Dansk Forfatterforening** (The Danish Writers
Association)
Tordenskjolds Gard, Strandgade 6, Stuen, 1401
Copenhagen K
*Tel:* 32 95 51 00 *Fax:* 32 54 01 15
*E-mail:* danskforfatterforening@
danskforfatterforening.dk
*Web Site:* www.danskforfatterforening.dk
*Key Personnel*
President: Mr Knud Vilby *E-mail:* knud@vilby.dk
Founded: 1894
Professional organization for authors, translators
& illustrators of books for children & young
people.
Publication(s): *Forfatteren* (8 times/yr)

**Det Danske Sprog - og Litteraturselskab**
(Society for Danish Language & Literature)
Christians Brygge 1, 1219 Copenhagen K
*Tel:* 33130660 *Fax:* 33140608
*E-mail:* sekretariat@dsl.dk
*Web Site:* www.dsl.dk
*Key Personnel*
Dir: Jorn Lund *E-mail:* jl@dsl.dk
Secretary: Maria Krogh Langner *E-mail:* mkl@
dsl.dk
Founded: 1911

**Det Kongelige Danske Videnskabernes Selskab**
(The Royal Danish Academy of Sciences &
Letters)
H C Andersens Blvd 35, 1553 Copenhagen V
*Tel:* 33435300 *Fax:* 33435301
*E-mail:* e-mail@royalacademy.dk
*Web Site:* www.royalacademy.dk
*Key Personnel*
President: Prof Tom Fenchel
Secretary: Henrik Breuning-Madsen
*E-mail:* hbm@royalacademy.dk
Editor: Prof Flemming Lundgreen-Nielsen
*E-mail:* fln@royalacademy.dk
Founded: 1742
Publication(s): *Biologiske Skrifter*; *Historisk-
filosofiske Meddelelser*; *Historisk-filosofiske
Skrifter*; *Matematisk-fysiske Meddelelser*; *Over-
sigt* (annually with an English summary, re-
port); *Saerpublikationer*

**Nyt Dansk Literaturselskab** (New Danish
Society for Literature)
Hotelvej 9, 2640 Hedehusene
*Tel:* 4659 5520 *Fax:* 4659 5521
*E-mail:* ndl@ndl.dk
*Web Site:* www.ndl.dk
*Key Personnel*
President: Morten Bagger
*E-mail:* mortenbagger@get2net.dk
Manager: Anne Warming
Aims, Publication/Republication of books in short
supply in libraries. Special activity, Magnaprint
(large print books for partially sighted).

# Ecuador

**Academia Ecuatoriana de la Lengua**
Roca E 960 y Tamayo, Quito
*Tel:* (02) 2901518 *Fax:* (02) 2543234
*Key Personnel*
President: Galo Rene Perez
Secretary: Piedad Larrea Borja
Founded: 1874
Publication(s): *Memorias de la Academia de la
hengua*
*Parent Company:* Association of Academies of
the Spanish Language

**Casa de la Cultura Ecuatoriana Benjamin Carrion**
Av 6 de Diciembre 794, Apdo 67, Quito
*Tel:* (02) 2223391; (02) 2565721 (ext 120)
*Fax:* (02) 2566070
*E-mail:* info@cce.org.ec
*Web Site:* cce.org.ec
*Key Personnel*
President: Raul Perez Torres
Secretary General: Dr Marco Antonio Rodriguez
Founded: 1944

# Egypt (Arab Republic of Egypt)

**Atelier, L**
8 Victor Bassili St, Alexandria
*Tel:* (03) 4820526 *Fax:* (03) 4837662
*Key Personnel*
Honorary President: Prof Naima El-Shishiny
Honorary Secretary: D Farouk Wahba
Society of Artists & Writers.

# Finland

**Finlands Svenska Forfattareforening** (Society of Swedish Authors in Finland)
Uhro Kekkonens gata 8 B 14, 00100 Helsinki
*Tel:* (09) 446266 *Fax:* (09) 446871
*Key Personnel*
President: Thomas Wulff
Vice President: Monika Fagerholm; Nalle Valtiala
Secretary: Merete Jensen
Founded: 1919
Membership(s): The Three Seas Writer's & Translator's Council; European Writer's Congress; Baltic Writer's Council; Nordic Writer's Council.

**Finnish PEN Centre**
Member of International PEN
Kauppakartanonkatu 25 G 86, 00930 Helsinki
Mailing Address: PO Box 84, 00131 Helsinki
*Tel:* (09) 3431186 *Fax:* (09) 3431186
*Key Personnel*
President: Elisabeth Nordgren *E-mail:* elisabeth.
nordgren@pp.inet.fi
Secretary: Sanna Jaatinen

**Kirjallisuudentutkijain Seura** (Finnish Literary Research Society)
Dept of Finnish Literature, University of Helsinki, PL 3, Fabianink 33, 00014 Helsinki
*Tel:* (09) 19122658 *Fax:* (09) 19123008
*Web Site:* www.helsinki.fi/jarj/skts
*Telex:* 124690
*Key Personnel*
President: Prof Kaimikkoven *Tel:* (09) 40 8289924
Secretary: Mirjam Ilvas
Founded: 1929
Publication(s): *Kirjallisuudentutkijain Seuran Vuosikirja* (The Yearbook of the Literary Research Society)

**Suomalainen Tiedeakatemia** (Finnish Academy of Science & Letters)
Mariankatu 5, 00170 Helsinki
*Tel:* (09) 636800 *Fax:* (09) 660117

*E-mail:* acadsci@acadsci.fi
*Web Site:* www.acadsci.fi
*Key Personnel*
President: Mauno Koivisto
Secretary General: Matti Saarnisto *Tel:* (09) 636806 *E-mail:* matti.saarnisto@acadsci.fi
Founded: 1908
Publication(s): *Annales Academiae Scientiarium Gennicae, Geologica; Annales Academiae Scientiarium, Humaniora; Annales Academiae Scientiarum Fennicae, Mathematica; Folklore Fellows' Communications, FFC; Vuosikirja* (Yearbook)

**Suomalaisen Kirjallisuuden Seura** (Finnish Literature Society)
Hallituskatu 1, 00170 Helsinki
Mailing Address: PL 259, 00171 Helsinki
*Tel:* (0201) 131 231 *Fax:* (09) 1312 3220
*E-mail:* sks@finlit.fi
*Web Site:* www.finlit.fi
*Key Personnel*
Secretary-General: Urpo Vento
Publisher: Matti Suurpaeae
Librarian: Henni Ilomaeki
Dir, Finnish Literature Information Centre: Marja-Leena Rautalin
Dir, Folklore Archive: Pekka Laaksonen
Dir, Literature Archive: Kaarina Sala
Specialize in folklore, ethnology, literary research, Finnish language, cultural history.
Publication(s): *Studia Fennica; Suomi; Tietolipas; Toimituksia* (irregular)

**Svenska Litteratursaellskapet i Finland** (Society of Swedish Literature in Finland)
Riddaregatan 5, 00170 Helsinki
*Tel:* (09) 618777 *Fax:* (09) 6187 7277
*E-mail:* info@mail.sls.fi
*Web Site:* www.sls.fi
*Key Personnel*
Editor: Nina Edgren-Henrichson *E-mail:* nina.
edgren-henrichson@sls.fi
Founded: 1885
Swedish Literary Society in Finland.
Publication(s): *Skrifter utgivna av Svenska Litteratursaellskapet i Finland* (Writings)

**Svenska Oesterbottens Litteraturfoerening** (Swedish Oesterbottens Literary Association)
Stagnasvagen 85, 66640 Maxmo
*Tel:* (06) 3450286
*Key Personnel*
Contact: Gun Anderssen
Publication(s): *Horisont*

# France

**Academie Goncourte, Societe de gens de Lettres**
c/o Drouant, Place Gaillon, 75002 Paris
*Key Personnel*
Presidents: Herve Bazin; Francis Nourissier
Responsible for annual prizes-poetry scholarships, best romance novels, biographies.

**CALCRE, Association d'Information et de Defense des Auteurs**
BP 10016, 94404 Vitry Cedex
*E-mail:* commande@calcre.com
*Web Site:* www.calcre.com
*Key Personnel*
President: Roger Gaillard
Secretary: Claude Aubert
Treasurer: Andre Muriel
Founded: 1979
Publication(s): *Arlit - Annuaire des Revues Litteraires & Cie* (triannually); *Audace - Annu-*

*aire a l'Usage des Auteurs Cherchant un Editeur* (triannually); *Ecrire & Editer* (bimonthly, magazine); *Savelivre - Guide des Salons et des Fetes du Livre* (quarterly)

**Centre National du Livre**
Hotel de Avejan, 53 rue de Verneuil, 75343 Paris Cedex 07
*Tel:* (01) 49546868 *Fax:* (01) 45491021
*Web Site:* www.centrenationaldulivre.fr
*Key Personnel*
President: Eric Gross *Tel:* (01) 49 54 68 20
Secretary General: Anne Miller *Tel:* (01) 49 54 68 59
National Literary Centre.

**Maison des Ecrivains** (Writers' House)
Hotel d'Avejan, 53 rue de Verneuil, 75007 Paris
*Tel:* (01) 49546880 *Fax:* (01) 42842087
*E-mail:* courrier@maison-des-ecrivains.asso.fr
*Web Site:* www.maison-des-ecrivains.asso.fr
*Key Personnel*
President: Claude Esteban
Dir: Eric Gross

**French PEN Centre** (PEN Club Francais)
Member of International PEN
6 rue Francois-Miron, 75004 Paris
*Tel:* (01) 42 77 37 87 *Fax:* (01) 42 78 64 87
*E-mail:* penfrancais@aol.com
*Key Personnel*
President: Alexandre Blokh
Secretary: Sylvestre Clancier

**SACD**, see Societe des Auteurs et Compositeurs Dramatiques (SACD)

**SNAC**, see Syndicat National des Auteurs et Compositeurs

**Societe des Auteurs et Compositeurs Dramatiques (SACD)**
11 bis rue Ballu, 75442 Paris Cedex 09
*Tel:* (01) 40 23 44 44 *Fax:* (01) 45 26 74 28
*E-mail:* infosacd@sacd.fr
*Web Site:* www.sacd.fr
*Key Personnel*
Dir General: Pascal Rogard
Dir, Communications: Debora Abramowicz
Publication(s): *SACD*
Subsidiaries:

**Societe des Gens de Lettres de France**
Hotel de Massa, 38, rue du Faubourg Saint-Jacques, 75014 Paris
*Tel:* (01) 53 10 12 00 *Fax:* (01) 53 10 12 12
*E-mail:* depot.sgdlf@wanadoo.fr
*Web Site:* www.sgdl.org
*Telex:* 206 963 F
*Key Personnel*
President: Alain Absire
First Vice President: Marie-France Briselance
Secretary General: Jean Claude Bologne
Treasurer: Francois Taillandier
Founded: 1838
Publication(s): *Journal des Lettres et de l'Audiovisuel; Revue des Lettres et de l'Audiovisuel*

**la Societe des Poetes Francais**
16 Rue Monsieur, Le Prince, 75006 Paris
*Tel:* (01) 40 46 99 82 *Fax:* (01) 40 46 99 11
*E-mail:* poetesfrancais@aol.com
*Web Site:* www.societedespoetesfrancais.asso.fr
*Key Personnel*
President: Vital Heurtebize
Secretary General: Linda Bastide
Founded: 1902
Publication(s): *Bulletin* (triannually)

**Societe d'Etudes Dantesques**
Centre Universitaire Mediterraneen, 65 Promenade des Anglais, 06000 Nice
*Tel:* 497134610; 497134611 *Fax:* 497134640
*E-mail:* cum@ville-nice.fr
*Web Site:* www.cum-nice.org
*Key Personnel*
Secretary General: Simon Lorenzi

**Societe d'Histoire Litteraire de la France**
112 rue Monge, 75005 Paris
Mailing Address: BP 173, 75005 Paris
*Tel:* (01) 45872330 *Fax:* (01) 45872330
*E-mail:* srhlf@aol.com
*Key Personnel*
President: R Pomeau
Founded: 1893
French Literary History Association.
Publication(s): *Revue d'Histoire litteraire de la France* (alternate months)

**Syndicat National des Auteurs et Compositeurs**
80 rue Taitbout, 75442 Paris Cedex 09
*Tel:* (01) 48 74 96 30 *Fax:* (01) 42 81 40 21
*E-mail:* snac.fr@wanadoo.fr
*Web Site:* www.snac.fr
*Key Personnel*
President: Maurice Cury
Publication(s): *Bulletin des Auteurs*

# Germany

**Adalbert Stifter Verein eV** (Adalbert Stifter Association)
Hochstr 8, 81669 Munich
*Tel:* (089) 622 716-30 *Fax:* (089) 4891148
*E-mail:* asv@asv-muen.de
*Web Site:* www.asv-muen.de
*Key Personnel*
Man Dir: Dr Peter Becher
Founded: 1947
Information brochure in German, Czech & English; literature, art, cultural history of Bohemia & Moravia.
Publication(s): *Stifter-Jahrbuch/Neue Folge* (since 1987)

**Bundesverband junger Autoren und Autorinnen eV**
Kannenbaeckerstr 9, 53340 Meckenheim
Mailing Address: Postfach 200303, 53133 Bonn
*Tel:* (02225) 7889 *Fax:* (02225) 7889
*Web Site:* www.bvja-online.de
*Key Personnel*
Chairman: Heike Prassel *E-mail:* heike.prassel@bvja-online.de
Secretary: Michael Graf *E-mail:* michael.graf@bvja-online.de
Manager: Thomas Stichtenoth *E-mail:* thomas.stichtenoth@bvja-online.de
Founded: 1987
Publication(s): *Konzepte*; *LiteraturMagazin*

**Deutsche Akademie fuer Sprache und Dichtung** (German Academy of Language & Poetry)
Glueckert-Haus, Alexandraweg 23, 64287 Darmstadt
*Tel:* (06151) 40920 *Fax:* (06151) 409299
*E-mail:* sekretariat@deutscheakademie.de
*Web Site:* www.deutscheakademie.de
*Key Personnel*
President: Prof Dr Christian Meier
Secretary-General: Dr Bernd Busch
Founded: 1949
Publication(s): *Dichtung & Sprache* (irregularly); *Jahrbuch der Deutschen Akademie fuer*

*Sprache & Dichtung* (annually); *Preisschriften* (annually); *Veroeffentlichungen der Deutschen Akademie fuer Sprache & Dichtung* (irregularly)

**Deutscher Literaturfonds eV**
Alexandraweg 23, 64287 Darmstadt
*Tel:* (06151) 40930 *Fax:* (06151) 409333
*E-mail:* info@deutscher-literaturfonds.de
*Web Site:* www.deutscher-literaturfonds.de
*Key Personnel*
Secretary General: Bernd Busch *E-mail:* busch@deutscher-literaturfonds.de

**Gesellschaft fur Interkulturelle Germanistik eV (GIG)**
c/o Institut fur Literaturwissenschaft der Universitat, Universitat Friderciana-Karlsruhe, Kaiserstr 12, 76128 Karlsruhe
*Tel:* (0721) 6080 *Fax:* (0721) 6084290
*Key Personnel*
President, University Bayreuth: Prof A Wierlacher, PhD
Vice President, University Karlsruhe: Prof B Thum, PhD

**Gesellschaft zur Foerderung der Literatur aus Afrika Asien und Lateinamerika eV** (Society for the Promotion of African, Asian & Latin American Literature)
Reineckstr 3, 60313 Frankfurt am Main
Mailing Address: Postfach 100116, 60001 Frankfurt am Main
*Tel:* (069) 2102 247; (069) 2102 250 *Fax:* (069) 2102 227; (069) 2102 277
*E-mail:* litprom@book-fair.com
*Web Site:* www.litprom.de
*Key Personnel*
President: Peter Weidhaas
Dir: Peter Ripken
The Society seeks to promote German translations of creative writing from Africa, Asia & Latin America. It works as a non-profit agency & as a consultant for German language publishers & Third World publishers who have translation rights to offer. It is organizing reading tours & special promotion campaigns & is also in charge of a special programme for translations grants into German.
Publication(s): *Literaturnachrichten* (quarterly in German)

**Goethe-Gesellschaft in Weimar eV**
Burgplatz 4, 99423 Weimar
Mailing Address: Postfach 2251, 99403 Weimar
*Tel:* (03643) 20 20 50 *Fax:* (03643) 20 20 61
*E-mail:* goetheges@aol.com
*Web Site:* www.goethe-gesellschaft.de
*Key Personnel*
President (Weimar): Dr Jochen Golz
Vice President (Dusseldorf): Dr Volkmar Hansen
Contact: Dr Petra Oberhauser
Founded: 1885
Publication(s): *Goethe-Jahrbuch (yearbook)* (annually)

**Gutenberg-Gesellschaft eV** (Gutenberg Society)
Liebfrauenplatz 5, 55116 Mainz
*Tel:* (06131) 22 64 20 *Fax:* (06131) 23 35 30
*E-mail:* gutenberg-gesellschaft@freenet.de
*Web Site:* www.gutenberg-gesellschaft.uni-mainz.de
*Key Personnel*
President: Jens Beutel
Vice President & Treasurer: Hannetraud Schultheiss
Publishing Manager: Dr Stephan Fuessel *E-mail:* fuessel@mail.uni-mainz.de
Secretary General: Karl Delorme

Founded: 1901
Publication(s): *Gutenberg-Jahrbuch (Gutenberg Yearbook)*: *Kleine Drucke der Gutenberg-Gesellschaft* (annually)

**Internationale Vereinigung fuer Geschichte und Gegenwart der Druckkunst eV**, see Gutenberg-Gesellschaft eV

**Literarischer Verein in Stuttgart eV**
Haldenstr 30, 70376 Stuttgart
Mailing Address: Postfach 140155, 70071 Stuttgart
*Tel:* (0711) 5499710 *Fax:* (0711) 54997121
*Key Personnel*
President: Gerd Hiersemann *E-mail:* hiersemann.hauswedell.verlage@t-online.de
The Society's goal (founded in 1839) is to publish the texts of valuable unpublished manuscripts & old printed texts in a new form - especially with regard to old German literature.
Publication(s): *Bibliothek des Literarischen Vereins in Stuttgart* (Vol 1 1842 - Vol 318 1996)

**Literarisches Colloquium Berlin**
Am Sandwerder 5, 14109 Berlin
*Tel:* (030) 8169960 *Fax:* (030) 81699619
*E-mail:* mail@lcb.de
*Web Site:* www.lcb.de
*Key Personnel*
Contact: Dr Ulrich Janetzki *Tel:* (030) 81699612 *E-mail:* janetzki@lcb.de
Founded: 1963
Publication(s): *Sprache im technischen Zeitalter* (quarterly)

**Maximilian-Gesellschaft eV** (Book Collectors Society)
Haldenstr 30, 70376 Stuttgart
Mailing Address: Postfach 140155, 70071 Stuttgart
*Tel:* (0711) 549971-11 *Fax:* (0711) 549971-21
*E-mail:* hiersemann.hauswedell.verlage@t-online.de
*Web Site:* www.maximilian-gesellschaft.de
*Key Personnel*
Chairman: Prof Horst Gronemeyer, PhD
Producer: Reinhold Busch

**German PEN Centre** (Deutsches PEN-Zentrum)
Member of International PEN
Kasinostr 3, 64293 Darmstadt
*Tel:* (06151) 23120 *Fax:* (06151) 293414
*E-mail:* pen-germany@t-online.de
*Web Site:* www.pen-deutschland.de
*Key Personnel*
President: Johano Strasser
Secretary: Wilfried F Schoeller

# Greece

**Kentron Ekdoseos Ellinon Syngrafeon**
Akadimia Athinon, Odos Anagnostopoulou 14, 106 73 Athens
*Tel:* 2103612541 *Fax:* 2103602691
Centre for the Publication of Ancient Greek Authors.

# Haiti

**Le Bibliophile** (The Book Lover)
Caphaitien

*Key Personnel*
President: Silvio Faschi
Secretary: Louis Toussaint
Publication(s): *La Citadelle* (weekly); *Stella*
(monthly)

# Hong Kong

**Chinese Language Society of Hong Kong**
18/F Kam Chung Bldg, 19-21 Hennessy Rd,
Hong Kong
*Tel:* (02) 5284853
*Key Personnel*
Secretary: Leung Nga Mei

**Hong Kong PEN Centre (Chinese-Speaking)**
Member of International PEN
c/o Patrick Woo Chun Hoi, Chairman, Flat A, 22/
F, Blk 4, Cityone Shatin, Shatin NT
*Key Personnel*
President: Pui Yau Ming
Secretary: Susie Chiang
Publication(s): *PEN News* (weekly in Chinese)

# Hungary

**Magyar Irodalomtoerteneti Tarsasag** (Society
of Hungarian Literary History)
Muzeum Korut 4/a, 3.em.23, 1088 Budapest
*Tel:* (01) 2664903 *Fax:* (01) 3377819
*Key Personnel*
President: Sandor Ivan Kovacs
General Secretary: Praznovszky Mihaly
Founded: 1912
Publication(s): *Irodalomtoertenet*

**Magyar Tudomanyos Akademia
Irodalomtudomanyi Intezete** (Institute of
Literary Studies of the Hungarian Academy of
Sciences)
Menesi ut 11-13, 1118 Budapest
*Tel:* (01) 4665938 *Fax:* (01) 3853876
*Web Site:* www.mta.hu/kutatohelyek/intezetek/iti.
htm
*Key Personnel*
Dir: Prof Laszlo Szorenyi *Tel:* (01) 3858970
Publication(s): *Helikon* (bimonthly); *Irodalomto-
erteneti Fuezetek*; *Irodalomtoerteneti Koenyv-
tar*; *Irodalomtoerteneti Koezlemenyek* (quar-
terly); *Literatura* (quarterly); *Neohelicon* (quar-
terly)
*Ultimate Parent Company:* Hungarian Academy
of Science (HAS)

**Hungarian PEN Centre**
Member of International PEN
Karolyi Mihaly u.16, 1053 Budapest
*Tel:* (01) 3184143 *Fax:* (01) 1171722
*E-mail:* pen.hungary@axelero.hu
*Key Personnel*
Acting President: Sumyoni Papp
Secretary: Eva Toth
Publication(s): *The Hungarian PEN, Le PEN hon-
grois* (annually, bulletin)

# Iceland

**Hid Islenzka Bokmenntafelag** (Icelandic
Literary Society)
Skeifan 3B, 128 Reykjavik
*Tel:* 5889060 *Fax:* 5889095
*E-mail:* hib@islandia.is
*Web Site:* www.hib.is
*Key Personnel*
President: Sigurdur Lindal
Secretary: Reynir Axelsson
Founded: 1816
Publication(s): *Skirnir* (biannually in 2 parts)

**Icelandic PEN Centre**
Member of International PEN
PO Box 33, Reykjavik
*Key Personnel*
President: Thor Vilhjalmsson
Secretary: Einar Karason

**Rithofundasamband Islands** (The Icelandic
Writers' Union)
Dyngjuvegi 8, 104 Reykjavik
*Tel:* 5683190 *Fax:* 5683192
*E-mail:* rsi@rsi.is
*Web Site:* www.rsi.is
*Key Personnel*
Chairman: Adalsteinn Asberg Sigurdsson
Man Dir: Ragnheidur Tryggvadottir
Founded: 1974
Publication(s): *Frettabref* (newsletter)

# India

**All-India PEN Centre**, see Indian PEN Centre

**National Academy of Letters, India**, see Sahitya
Akademi

**Indian PEN Centre**
Formerly All-India PEN Centre
Member of International PEN
Theosophy Hall, 40 New Marine Lines, Mumbai
400020
*Tel:* (022) 2032175 *Cable:* CARE ARYAHATA
BOMBAY
*Key Personnel*
President: Annada Sankar
Acting Secretary & Treasurer: Ranjit Hoskote
*E-mail:* ranjithoskote@yhahoo.co.uk
Honorary Secretary-Treasurer: Prof Nissim
Ezekiel
Member, Executive Committee: Rameshchandra
Sirkar
Publication(s): *Asian Liturature: Poetry, Short
Stories & Essays*; *Assamese Literature*; *Bengali
Literature*; *Drama in Modern India & Writer's
Responsibility in a Rapidly Changing World*;
*India Writers Meet*; *Indian Literature of Today*;
*The Indian PEN* (quarterly); *Indian Writers at
Chidambaram*; *Indian Writers in Conference*;
*Indian Writers in Council*; *Indo-Anglian Lit-
erature*; *The Novel in Modern India*; *Telugu
Literature*; *Writers in Free India*; *Writing in
India*

**Sahitya Akademi** (National Academy of Letters)
Rabindra Bhavan, 35 Ferozeshah Rd, New Delhi
110001
*Tel:* (011) 3386626; (011) 3386627; (011)
3386628; (011) 3386629; (011) 3387386; (011)
3386088 *Fax:* (011) 3382428
*Web Site:* www.sahitya-akademi.org *Cable:*
SAHITYAKAR

*Key Personnel*
President: Ramakanta Rath
Vice President: Gopichand Narang
Secretary: Prof K Satchidanandan *E-mail:* secy@
sahitya-akademi.org
Founded: 1954
Regional offices in Bangalore, Chennai, Kolkata
& Mumbai.
Publication(s): *Indian Literature* (bimonthly);
*Samkaleen Bharateeya Sahitya* (bimonthly);
*Samskrita Pratibha* (biannually)

# Indonesia

**Indonesian PEN Centre**
Member of International PEN
Jalan Camara 6, Jakarta, Pusat
*Tel:* (093) 3905837 *Fax:* (093) 325890
*Key Personnel*
Secretary: Dr Toeti Heraty Noerhadi

# Ireland

**Irish Academy of Letters**
4 Ailesbury Grove, Dundum, Dublin 14
*Key Personnel*
Secretary: Sean J White

**Irish PEN Centre**
Member of International PEN
Dunoon, Oldlucan Rd, Palmerstown, Dublin 20
*E-mail:* irishpen@ireland.com
*Key Personnel*
President: Brian Friel
Secretary: Arthur Flynn

# Israel

**ACUM Ltd (Society of Authors, Composers &
Music Publishers in Israel)**
ACUM House, 9 Tuval St, 52117 Ramat-Gan
Mailing Address: PO Box 1704, 52117 Ramat-
Gan
*Tel:* (03) 6113400 *Fax:* (03) 6122629
*E-mail:* info@acum.org.il
*Web Site:* www.acum.org.il
*Key Personnel*
Chairman: Hana Goldberg
Chief Executive Officer: Yorik Ben-David
Deputy Chief Executive Officer: Reuven Ratson
Head of Finances: Dafna Ramchurn
Manager, Licensing Performing Rights: Daliah
Hadar
Manager, Radio/TV Licensing & Distribution:
Brigitte Rayn
Manager, New Media Licensing: Hany Moshe
Marketing & Business Development: Assaf
Nahum
Founded: 1936
Administration of authors & composers' rights
Membership(s): BIEM & CISAC.

**ELEAS**, see English Language Editors'
Association (ELEAS)

**English Language Editors' Association
(ELEAS)**
PO Box 6925, Jerusalem
*Tel:* (02) 586-5772 *Fax:* (02) 586-6411

*Web Site:* www.geocities.com/athens/stage/4942/8Eleas.html
*Key Personnel*
Contact: David Grossman *E-mail:* davidg@macam.ac.il

**Mekize Nirdamim Society**
PO Box 4344, 91042 Jerusalem
*Tel:* (02) 5617919
*Key Personnel*
President: Prof S Abramson
Secretary: Prof I Tashma
Founded: 1864
International society publishes Hebrew works of the older classical Jewish literature.

**Palestinian PEN Centre**
Member of International PEN
Al Khaldi St No 4, Wadi Joz, Jerusalem
*Tel:* (02) 6262970 *Fax:* (02) 6264620
*E-mail:* palpenc@palnet.com
*Key Personnel*
President: Hanan Awwad *Tel:* (02) 5813698
    *Fax:* (02) 5894620

**Israeli PEN Centre**
Member of International PEN
21 Ha-Sharon St, 47240 Ramat-Hasharon
*Tel:* (03) 6964937 *Fax:* (03) 6964937
*Key Personnel*
President: Efraim Bauch
Secretary: Ms Shulamit Kuriansky
    *E-mail:* shulamit02@bezeqint.net

# Italy

**Accademia Nazionale di Scienze Lettere e Arti Modena** (National Academy of Sciences, Literatures & Arts)
Palazzo Coccapani, Corso Vittorio Emanuele II, 59, 41100 Modena
*Tel:* (059) 225566 *Fax:* (059) 225566
*E-mail:* info@accademiasla-mo.it
*Web Site:* www.accademiasla-mo.it
*Key Personnel*
President: Prof Ferdinando Taddei
Publication(s): *Atti e Memorie* (annually)

**Accademia Nazionale Virgiliana di Scienze, Lettere e Arti**
Via dell'Accademia 47, Mantova 46100
*Tel:* (0376) 320314 *Fax:* (0376) 222774
*Web Site:* www.accademiavirgiliana.it/index.htm
*Key Personnel*
President: Prof Claudio Gallico
Founded: 1863
Publication(s): *Atti di Convegni tenuti presso l'Accademia Virgiliana; Atti e Memorie NS* (annually)

**Accademia Petrarca di Lettere, Arti e Scienze** (Petrarch Academy of Letters, Arts & Science)
Via dell'Orto n 28, 52100 Arezzo
*Tel:* (0575) 24700 *Fax:* (0575) 298846
*E-mail:* info@accademiapetrarca.it
*Web Site:* www.accademiapetrarca.it
*Key Personnel*
President: Prof Giulio Firpo
Secretary: Prof Antonio Batinti
Founded: 1787
Publication(s): *Atti e Memorie della Accademia, Studi Petrarcheschi*

**Istituto Lombardo Accademia di Scienze e Lettere**
Via Borgonuovo, 25, 20121 Milan

*Tel:* (02) 864087 *Toll Free Tel:* (02) 86461388
*E-mail:* istituto.lombardo@unimi.it
*Web Site:* www.istitutolombardo.it
*Key Personnel*
President: Prof Emilio Gatti
Vice President: Prof Alberto Quadrio Curzio

**Italian PEN Centre**
Member of International PEN
Via Daverio 7, 20122 Milan
*E-mail:* penclubitalia@dinet.it
*Key Personnel*
President: Lucio Lami
Secretary General: Federica Mormando

**Societa Dantesca Italiana** (Italian Dante Society)
Palagio dell'Arte della Lana, Via Arte della Lana 1, 50123 Florence FI
Mailing Address: PO Box 739, 50123 Florence FI
*Tel:* (055) 287134 *Fax:* (055) 211316
*E-mail:* sdi@leonet.it; sdi.biblio@leonet.it (library)
*Web Site:* www.danteonline.it
*Key Personnel*
President: Prof Francesco Mazzoni, PhD
Founded: 1888
Publication(s): *Edizione Nazionale delle Opere di Dante Alighieri; Quaderni degli Studi Danteschi; Quaderni del Centro Studi e Documentazione Dantesca e Medievale; Studi Danteschi* (annually)

# Japan

**Nihon Eibungakkai** (English Literary Society of Japan)
501 Kenkyusha Bldg, 9, Surugadai 2-chome, Kanda, Chiyoda-ku, Tokyo 101-0062
*Tel:* (03) 32937528 *Fax:* (03) 32937539
*Key Personnel*
President: Kazuhisa Takahashi
Founded: 1917
Publication(s): *Studies in English Literature* (tri-annually)

**Nippon Dokubungakkai** (Japanese Society of German Literature)
c/o Ikubundo, Hongo 5-30-21, Bunkyo-ku, Tokyo 113-0033
*Tel:* (03) 3813 5861 *Fax:* (03) 3813 5861
*E-mail:* e-mail@jgg.jp
*Key Personnel*
Contact: Prof Takao Tsunekawa
Publication(s): *Doitsu Bungaku* (biannually)

**Nippon Hikaku Bungakukai** (Comparative Literature Society of Japan)
Aoyama Gakuin University, Shibuya-ku, Tokyo
*Key Personnel*
President: K Nakajam
Secretary General: Saburo Ota

**Nippon Rosiya Bungakkai** (Russian Literary Society in Japan)
c/o Baba-ken, Tokyo Institute of Technology, 2-12-1 O-okayama, Meguro-ku, Tokyo 152-8552
*Key Personnel*
President: Togo Masanobu
Secretary General: T Egawa

**Japanese PEN Centre**
Member of International PEN
20-3 Kabuto-cho, Nihon bashi, Chuo-ku, Tokyo 103-0026
*Tel:* (03) 3402-1171; (03) 3402-1172 *Fax:* (03) 3402-5951

*E-mail:* secretariat03@japanpen.or.jp
*Web Site:* www.japanpen.or.jp
*Key Personnel*
President: Hisashi Inoue
Secretary: Nobuhiro Akio
Publication(s): *Japanese Literature Today* (annually since 1976)

# Republic of Korea

**Korean PEN Centre**
Member of International PEN
Rm 1105, Oseong B/D, 13-5 Youido-dong, Yongdungpo-ku, Seoul 150010
*Tel:* (02) 782 1337; (02) 782 1338 *Fax:* (02) 786 1090
*E-mail:* penkon2001@yahoo.co.kr
*Key Personnel*
Secretary: Prof Ki-Jo Song
Publication(s): *Korean Literature Today* (quarterly)

# Liechtenstein

**Liechenstein PEN Centre**
Member of International PEN
Postfach 416, FL-9490 Vaduz
*Tel:* (0423) 2327271 *Fax:* (0423) 2328071
*E-mail:* info@pen-club.li
*Web Site:* www.pen-club.li *Cable:* PEN CLUB
*Key Personnel*
President: Paul Flora
Secretary: Werner Fuld
Publication(s): *Zifferblatt* (annually)

# The Former Yugoslav Republic of Macedonia

**Dru-stvo na Pisatelite na Makedonija** (Macedonian Writers Association)
Maksim Gorki 18, Skopje 1000
*Tel:* (02) 228039
*E-mail:* contact@dpism.org.mk
*Web Site:* www.dpism.org.mk
*Key Personnel*
President: Vele Smilevski *E-mail:* vsmil@dpism.org.mk
Secretary: Paskal Gilovski; Svetlana Hristova-Jocic
Founded: 1947

**Macedonian PEN Centre**
Member of International PEN
Str Maksim Gorki 18, 1000 Skopje
*Tel:* (02) 3130054 *Fax:* (02) 3130054
*E-mail:* macedpen@unet.com.mk
*Web Site:* www.pen.org.mk
*Key Personnel*
President: Dimitar Basevski
Secretary: Ermis Lafazanovski

# Malaysia

**Dewan Bahasa dan Pustaka**
Peti Surat 10803, 50926 Kuala Lumpur
*Tel:* (03) 21481011; (03) 2484211; (03) 2481820
*Fax:* (03) 2482726; (03) 2142005; (03)
21414109; (03) 2148420
*Web Site:* www.dbp.gov.my
*Telex:* MA 32683
*Key Personnel*
Dir General: Haji Jumaat Moho Noor
National Language & Literary Agency.
Publication(s): *Dewan Bahasa*; *Dewan Budaya*;
*Dewan Masyarakat*; *Dewan Pelajar*; *Dewan
Sastera* (monthly); *Dewan Siswa* (monthly);
*Tenggara* (biannually)

# Mexico

**Mexican PEN Centre**
Member of International PEN
Heriberto Frias 1452-407, Col Del Valle, Mexico
03100 DF
*Tel:* (05) 574-4882 *Fax:* (05) 264-0813
*E-mail:* presidencia@penmexico.org.mx
*Web Site:* www.penmexico.org.mx
*Key Personnel*
President: Maria Elena Ruiz Cruz
Publication(s): *Directorio de Escritores* (annually)

# Nepal

**Nepal PEN Centre**
Member of International PEN
PO Box 4490, Kathmandu
*Fax:* (01) 522346
*E-mail:* daman@wlink.com.np
*Key Personnel*
President: Bhuwan Dhungana
Vice President: Nagendra Raj Sharma
Secretary General: Greta Rana
Secretary: Archana Singh Karki
Publication(s): *Jane Eyre (in Nepali)* (With help
from the Bronte Society, Translator-S Rai)

# Netherlands

**Maatschappij der Nederlandse Letterkunde**
(Society of Netherlands Literature)
Universiteitsbibliotheek, Witte Singel 27, 2311
BG Leiden
Mailing Address: Postbus 9501, 2300 RA Leiden
*Tel:* (071) 527 2801; (071) 527 2814 *Fax:* (071)
527 2836
*E-mail:* mnl@library.leidenuniv.nl
*Web Site:* www.leidenuniv.nl/host/mnl
*Key Personnel*
Secretary: Dr Leo L van Maris
Founded: 1766
Publication(s): *Indische Letteren* (quarterly); *Jaar-
boek der Maatschappij* (annually); *De negen-
tiende eeuw* (quarterly); *Tijdschrift voor Neder-
landse Taal- en Letterkunde* (quarterly)

**Netherlands PEN Centre**
Member of International PEN
Reinier Vinkelskade 41-1, 1071 SV Amsterdam
*Tel:* (043) 433498 *Fax:* (043) 433498

*E-mail:* secretariaat@pencentrum.nl
*Key Personnel*
President: Barber van de Pol
Secretary: Daan Cartens

# New Zealand

**New Zealand Book Council**
Old Wool House, 5th floor, 139-141 Featherson
St, Wellington
*Tel:* (04) 499 1569 *Fax:* (04) 499 1424
*E-mail:* admin@bookcouncil.org.nz
*Web Site:* www.bookcouncil.org.nz
*Key Personnel*
President: Sir Kenneth Keith
Vice President: Elizabeth Styron
Executive Dir: Karen Ross *E-mail:* director@
bookcouncil.org.nz
Publication(s): *Book Buyers in New Zealand*;
*Books You Couldn't Buy*; *Landmarks of New
Zealand Writing to 1945*; *Writers in Schools*

**New Zealand Council for Educational
Research**
10th floor, West Block, Education House, 178-
182 Willis St, Wellington
Mailing Address: PO Box 3237, Wellington
*Tel:* (04) 384 7939 *Fax:* (04) 384 7933
*Web Site:* www.nzcer.org.nz
*Key Personnel*
Dir: Robyn Baker *E-mail:* robyn.baker@nzcer.
org.nz
Founded: 1934

**New Zealand Society of Authors (NZSA)**
PO Box 67013, Mount Eden, Auckland 1030
*Tel:* (09) 356 8332 *Fax:* (09) 356 8332
*E-mail:* nzsa@clear.net.nz
*Web Site:* www.authors.org.nz
*Key Personnel*
President: Chris Else
Vice President: Maxine Alterio; Stephen Stratford
Executive Dir: Liz Allen
Membership Secretary: Jan Hughes
Publication(s): *New Zealand Author* (bimonthly)

**New Zealand Writers Guild**
1/243 Ponsonby Rd, Ponsonby, Auckland 1034
Mailing Address: PO Box 47 886, Ponsonby,
Auckland 1034
*Tel:* (09) 360 1408 *Fax:* (09) 360 1409
*E-mail:* info@nzwritersguild.org.nz
*Web Site:* www.nzwritersguild.org.nz
*Key Personnel*
President: Denis Edwards
Vice President: Kathryn Burnett
Secretary: Dominic Sheehan

**NZSA**, see New Zealand Society of Authors
(NZSA)

**PEN NZ Inc**, see New Zealand Society of
Authors (NZSA)

# Norway

**Information Office for Norwegian Literature
Abroad**, see NORLA (Information Office for
Norwegian Literature Abroad)

**NORLA (Information Office for Norwegian
Literature Abroad)**
Victoria terr 11, 0203 Solli, Oslo
Mailing Address: PO Box 2663, 0203 Solli, Oslo
*Tel:* 23 27 63 50 *Fax:* 23 27 63 51
*E-mail:* firmapost@norla.no
*Web Site:* www.norla.no
*Key Personnel*
Man Dir: Kristin Brudevoll
Literary Advisor: Andrine Pollen
Secretary: Ingrid Overwien
Founded: 1978
State supported foundation offering grants to
translations of Norwegian literature.
Publication(s): *Selected Norwegian Fiction*

**Norske Akademi for Sprog og Litteratur**
(Norwegian Academy for Language &
Literature)
Inkognitogaten 24, 0256 Oslo
*Tel:* 22 56 29 50 *Fax:* 22 55 37 43
*E-mail:* ordet@riksmalsforbundet.no
*Web Site:* www.riksmalsforbundet.no
*Key Personnel*
President: Helge Nordahl
Secretary: Prof Sissel Lange-Nielsen

**Det Norske Videnskaps-Akademi** (The
Norwegian Academy of Science & Letters)
Drammensveien 78, 0271 Oslo
*Tel:* 22121090 *Fax:* 22121099
*E-mail:* dnva@online.no
*Web Site:* www.dnva.no
*Key Personnel*
President: Prof Lars Walloe
Vice President: Prof Jan Fridthjof Bernt
Secretary General: Prof Reidun Sirevag
Publication(s): *Arbok*; *Avhandlinger*; *Skrifter*

**Norwegian PEN Centre**
Member of International PEN
Tordenskjoldsgate 6B, 0160 Oslo
*Tel:* 22194551 *Fax:* 22194551
*E-mail:* pen@norskpen.no
*Key Personnel*
President: Kjell Olaf Jensen

# Pakistan

**Anjuman Taraqqi-e-Urdu Pakistan**
Baba-e-Urdu Rd, D-159 Block 7, Gulshan-e
Iqbal, Karachi 75300
*Tel:* (021) 461406; (021) 4973296; (021) 7724023
*Key Personnel*
President: N H Jafarey
Secretary: Jamiluddin A'Ali
Founded: 1903
For the promotion of the Urdu language & litera-
ture.
Publication(s): *Qaumi Zaban* (monthly); *Urdu*
(quarterly)

**Pakistan Writers' Guild**
One Mentgomrey Rd, Lahore
*Tel:* 6367124
*Key Personnel*
Research Officer: Inamul Haq Javeid
Secretary General: Mohamed Tufail
Founded: 1959
Publication(s): *Ham Qalam* (monthly)

**Sindhi Adabi Board**
Station Rd, Sindhi University Campus, Hyderabad
Mailing Address: PO Box 12, Jamshoro, Hyder-
abad
*Tel:* (0221) 771276; (0221) 771465; (0221)
771600
*Key Personnel*
Chairman: Muhammad Ibrahim Joyo

Secretary: Ghulam Rabbani Agro
To promote the language, literature & culture of
the Sind region.

# Panama

**Panamanian PEN Centre**
Member of International PEN
Apdo 6-212, El Dorado 1
*Tel:* 263-8822 *Fax:* 263-9918
*Key Personnel*
President: Rosa Maria Britton *E-mail:* rmbritton@
cwpanama.net
Secretary: Dr Juan David Morgan

# Philippines

**Philippine PEN Centre**
Member of International PEN
531 Padre Faura, 1099 Ermita, Manila
Mailing Address: PO Box 359, 1099 Manila
*Tel:* (02) 5230870 *Fax:* (02) 5255038
*E-mail:* philippinepen@yahoo.com *Cable:*
SOLDAD MANILA
*Key Personnel*
President: Alejandro Roces
National Secretary: Francisco Sionil Jose

# Poland

**Instytut Badan Literackich PAN** (Institute of
Literary Research of the Polish Academy of
Sciences)
ul Nowy Swiat 72, 00-330 Warsaw
*Tel:* (022) 8269945; (022) 6572895 *Fax:* (022)
8269945
*E-mail:* ibadlit@ibl.waw.pl
*Web Site:* www.ibl.waw.pl
*Key Personnel*
Dir: Prof Alina Witkowska; Prof Elzbieta
Sarnawska-Temeriusz
Publication(s): *Kwartalnik Historii Prasy Polskiej*
(Quarterly of the History of the Polish Press);
*Literary Studies in Poland* (biannually); *Pamiet-
nik Literacki* (Literary Journal, quarterly)

**Polish PEN Centre** (Polski PEN Club)
Member of International PEN
Krakowskie Przedmiescie 87/89, 00-079 Warsaw
*Tel:* (022) 8265784; (022) 8282823 *Fax:* (022)
8265784
*E-mail:* penclub@ikp.atm.com.pl
*Web Site:* www.penclub.atomnet.pl
*Key Personnel*
President: Wladyslaw Bartoszewski
Vice President: Adam Pomorski; Kazimierz Tra-
ciewicz
Secretary: Krzysztof Dorosz
Treasurer: Iwona Smolka
Founded: 1925

**Towarzystwo Literackie im Adama
Mickiewicza** (Mickiewicz Literary Society)
ul Nowy Swiat 72, Palac Staszica, 00-330 War-
saw
*Tel:* (022) 265231 (ext 279)
*Key Personnel*
President: Prof Zdzislaw Libera, PhD
Publication(s): *Rocznik* (Yearbook)

# Portugal

**Instituto Portugues da Sociedade Cientifica de
Goerres** (Portuguese Institute of the Goerres
Research Society)
c/o Universidade Catolica Portuguesa, Palm de
Cima, 1600 Lisbon
*Tel:* (021) 7265554 *Fax:* (021) 7260546
*E-mail:* mrato@reitoria.ucp.pt
*Key Personnel*
Contact: Maria Eugenia Rato
Research in Portuguese.
Publication(s): *Portugiesische Forschungen der
Goerres Gesellschaft*

**Portuguese PEN Centre**
Member of International PEN
Rua Embaixador Martins, Janeira, 15-6.Esq, 1200
Lisbon
*Tel:* (021) 7573452 *Fax:* (021) 7573452
*E-mail:* penclube@netcabo.pt
*Key Personnel*
President: Casimiro de Brito
Secretary: Annabel Rita
Founded: 1978
Writers' Association.

**Sociedade Portuguesa de Autores**
Av Duque de Loule 31, 1069-153 Lisbon, Codex
*Tel:* (021) 3594400 *Fax:* (021) 3530257
*E-mail:* geral@spautores.pt
*Web Site:* www.spautores.pt *Cable:* AUTORES
*Key Personnel*
President: Dr Luiz Francisco Rebello
Vice President: Dr Alvaro Salazar
Publication(s): *Autores*

# Puerto Rico

**Puerto Rican PEN Centre** (PEN Club of Puerto
Rico)
Member of International PEN
721 Calle Hernandez, apt 11N, San Juan 00907
*Tel:* (787) 724-0869 *Fax:* (787) 724-2060
*E-mail:* saturno@prtc.net
*Key Personnel*
President: Juan Duchesne-Winter
Secretary: Maria E Ramos

# Romania

**Romanian PEN Centre**
Member of International PEN
Bdul Ferdinand 29 ap 3, 70313 Bucharest
*Tel:* (01) 3111112 *Fax:* (01) 3125854
*E-mail:* univers@rnc.ro
*Key Personnel*
President: Ana Blandiana
Secretary: Denisa Comanescu

**Societatea de Stiinte Filologice din Romania
(SSF)** (Romanian Philological Sciences
Society)
Mendeleev Str, nr 21-25, sector 1, 70761
Bucharest 1
*Tel:* (021) 3123148
*Key Personnel*
President: Paul Cornea
Secretary General: Mircea Franculescu

Contact: Florentina Samihaian
Publication(s): *Buletinul SSF*; *Limba si literatura*
(quarterly, journal); *Limba si Literatura Romania*

**SSF**, see Societatea de Stiinte Filologice din
Romania (SSF)

# Russian Federation

**Russian PEN Centre**
Member of International PEN
Neglinnaya St 18/1 Bldg 2, 103031 Moscow
*Tel:* (095) 2094589; (095) 2093171 *Fax:* (095)
2000293
*E-mail:* penrussian@dol.ru; penrus@aha.ru
*Web Site:* www.penrussia.org
*Key Personnel*
Dir General: Alexandr Tkachenko
Editor: Mikhail Kaminsky
Contact: Y Tutchaninova
Founded: 1921

# Senegal

**Senegal PEN Centre**
Member of International PEN
Rue 1 Prolongee Pointe, Dakar
*Tel:* 8256700; 8258009 *Fax:* 8643375
*E-mail:* memgoree@sonatel.senet.net
*Key Personnel*
President: Ousmane Sembene
Secretary: Alioune Badara Beye

# Serbia and Montenegro

**Serbian PEN Centre**
Member of International PEN
Milutina Bojica 4, 11000 Belgrade
*Tel:* (011) 626081 *Fax:* (011) 635979
*E-mail:* pencent@bitsyu.net
*Key Personnel*
President: Jovan Hristic
Secretary: Dr Kosta Cavoski
Publication(s): *Pismo* (quarterly, published jointly
with "Jovan Popovic" Library, Zemun)

**Sojuz na drustvata za makedonski jazik i
literatura** (Union of Associations for
Macedonian Language & Literature)
Grigor Prlicev 5, 91000 Skopje
*Key Personnel*
President: Elena Bendevska
Secretary: Ljupco Mitrevski
Union of Associations for Macedonian Language
& Literature.
Publication(s): *Literaturen zbor* (biannually)

# Slovenia

**Slovene PEN Centre**
Member of International PEN
Tomsiceva 12, 61000 Ljubljana
*Tel:* (01) 4254847
*E-mail:* slopen@guest.arnes.si
*Key Personnel*
President: Veno Taufer
Secretary: Iztok Ososnik
Publication(s): *Litterae Slovenicae*

# Spain

**Ateneo Cientifico, Literario y Artistico**
(Scientific, Literary & Artistic Athenaeum)
Calle del Prado 21, 28014 Madrid
*Tel:* (09142) 974 42
*Key Personnel*
President: Jose Prat Garcia
General Secretary: David M Rivas Infante
Founded: 1837

**Ateneo Cientifico, Literario y Artistico**
(Scientific, Literary & Artistic Athenaeum)
Sa Rovellada de Dalt, 25, 07701 Mahon, Minorca, Balearic Islands
*Tel:* (071) 360553 *Fax:* (071) 352194
*E-mail:* ateneo@intercom.es
*Web Site:* www.usuarios.intercom.es/ateneo
*Key Personnel*
President: Francesc Tutzo Bennasar
Secretary: Miguel Angel Limon Pons
Founded: 1905
Publication(s): *Revista de Menorca* (quarterly)

**Galician PEN Centre**
Member of International PEN
Rep El Salvador, 14-1° izda, 15701 Santiago de Compostela
*Tel:* (081) 587750
*E-mail:* pengalicia@mundo-r.com
*Key Personnel*
President: Luis G Tosar
Secretary: Helena Villa Maneiro

**Real Academia de Bones Lletres de Barcelona**
(Barcelona Royal Academy of Literature)
Carrer Bisbe Cassador 3, 08002 Barcelona
*Tel:* (093) 3150010 *Fax:* (093) 3102349
*Key Personnel*
President: Eduard Ripoll
Secretary: Frederic Udina
Librarian: Francisco Marsa
Publication(s): *Boletin, Memorias*

**Real Academia Sevillana de Buenas Letras**
(Seville Royal Academy of Literature)
Casa de los Pinelo, Abades, 14, 41004 Seville
*Tel:* (09542) 21198
*E-mail:* insacan@insacan.org
*Web Site:* www.insacan.org
*Key Personnel*
Dir: Dr Rogelio Reyes Cano
Vice Dir: Dr Jose Luis Comellas Garcia-Llera
Secretary: Dr Jacabo Cortines; Enriqueta Vila Vilar
Founded: 1752
Publication(s): *Boletin de Buenas Letras* (quarterly)

**Sociedad de Ciencias, Letras y Artes El Museo Canario**
Dr Verneau, 2 Vegueta, 35001 Las Palmas, Canary Islands

*Tel:* (0928) 336800 *Fax:* (0928) 336801
*E-mail:* info@elmuseocanario.com
*Web Site:* www.elmuseocanario.com
*Key Personnel*
Chairman: Victor Montelongo Parada
Man Dir: Diego Lopez Diaz
Scientific, Literary & Art Society.
Publication(s): *El Museo Canario* (quarterly)

# Sweden

**Kungl Vitterhets Historie och Antikvitets Akademien** (The Royal Academy of Letters, History & Antiquities)
Villagatan 3, 114 86 Stockholm
Mailing Address: PO Box 5622, 114 86 Stockholm
*Tel:* (08) 440 42 80 *Fax:* (08) 440 42 90
*E-mail:* kansli@vitterhetsakad.se
*Web Site:* www.vitterhetsakad.se
*Key Personnel*
President: Prof Anders Jeffner
Secretary-General: Prof Ulf Sporrong *Tel:* (08) 440 42 81 *E-mail:* sekreteraren@vitterhetsakad.se
Founded: 1753
Publication(s): *Arkiv (Archives)* (irregularly); *Arsbok (Yearbook)* (annually); *Fornvaennen (Journal of Swedish Antiquarian Research)* (quarterly); *Handlingar (Proceedings)* (irregularly); *Monografier (Monographs)* (irregularly)

**Samfundet De Nio** (The Academy of the Nine)
Villagatan 14, 114 32 Stockholm
*Tel:* (08) 411 15 42 *Fax:* (08) 21 19 15
*Web Site:* www.samfundetdenio.com
*Key Personnel*
President: Inge Jonsson
Secretary: Anders R Oehman
Founded: 1913

**Swedish PEN Centre** (Svenska Penklubben)
Member of International PEN
c/o Bokforlaget Natur och Kultur, Box 27 323, 102 54 Stockholm
*Tel:* (08) 453 86 80
*E-mail:* info@pensweden.org
*Web Site:* www.pensweden.org
*Key Personnel*
President: Ljiljana Dufgran *E-mail:* dufgran@telia.com

# Switzerland

**Ecrivains Suisses du Groupe d'Olten**, see Schweizer Autorinnen und Autoren Gruppe Olten

**Gesellschaft fur deutsche Sprache und Literatur in Zurich**
Deutsches Seminar der Universitaet Zuerich, Schonberggasseg, CH-8001 Zurich
*Tel:* (01) 6342571 *Fax:* (01) 6344905
*E-mail:* uguenthe@ds.unizh.ch
*Key Personnel*
President: Dr Ulla Gunther
Society for German Language & Literature in Zurich.

**Schweizer Autorinnen und Autoren Gruppe Olten**
Nordstr 9, 8035 Zurich
*Tel:* (01) 350 04 60 *Fax:* (01) 350 04 61

*E-mail:* sekretariat@a-d-s.ch
*Web Site:* www.a-d-s.ch
*Key Personnel*
Dir: Peter A Schmid *E-mail:* paschmid@a-d-s.ch
Secretary: Verena Roethlisberger
*E-mail:* vroethlisberger@a-d-s.ch

**Swiss German PEN Centre** (Deutschweizer PEN Zentrum)
Member of International PEN
Zypressenstr 76, 8004 Zurich
*Tel:* (031) 3724085 *Fax:* (031) 3723032
*E-mail:* infopen@datacomm.ch
*Key Personnel*
President: Brechbuehl Beat
Secretary: Sebastian Hefti
Publication(s): *PEN-Brief*

**Swiss Italian & Reto-Romansh PEN Centre**
Member of International PEN
CP 107, 6903 Lugano
*Tel:* (091) 8039325 *Fax:* (091) 8039300
*E-mail:* p.e.n.lugano@ticino.com
*Key Personnel*
President: Franca Tiberto
Secretary: Attilia F Venturini
Publication(s): *Viceversa PEN International Centro Della Svizzera Italiana e Retoromancia, 1997*

**Schweizerische Bibliophilen-Gesellschaft** (Swiss Society of Bibliophiles)
Had Laubstr 42, 8044 Zuerich
*Key Personnel*
President: Dr Werner G Zimmerman *Tel:* (01) 252 6349
Publication(s): *Librarium* (published triannually since 1958)

**Schweizerischer Bund fuer Jugendliteratur** (Swiss Federation for Youth Literature)
Gewerbestr 8, 6330 Cham
*Tel:* (041) 741 31 40 *Fax:* (041) 740 01 59
*E-mail:* sbj@bluewin.ch
Publication(s): *Autoren und Referenten der Deutschschweiz; Das Buch-Dein Freund* (yearbook for lower & middle grades); *Das Buch fuer Dich* (list of recommended books; yearly); *Information Buch Oberstufe* (yearbook for upper grades); *Jugendliteratur* (quarterly journal)

**Schweizerischer Schriftstellerinnen und Schriftsteller-Verband** (Swiss Writers' Union)
Nordstr 9, 8035 Zurich
*Tel:* (01) 3500460 *Fax:* (01) 3500461
*E-mail:* letter@ch-s.ch
*Web Site:* www.ch-s.ch
*Key Personnel*
Secretary: Peter A Schmid
Founded: 1912
Publication(s): *Neuer Judische Literatur in der Switzerland; Zweifache Eigenheit*

**Suisse Romand PEN Centre** (PEN Club de Suisse romande)
Member of International PEN
14 rue Crespin, 1206 Geneva
*Key Personnel*
President: Alexis Koutchoumow
*E-mail:* jakoutchoumow@bluewin.ch
PEN Club for French-speaking Switzerland.
Publication(s): *PEN Club romand Newsletter* (biannually)

# Taiwan, Province of China

**China National Association of Literature and the Arts**
No 4, Lane 22, Nuigpo St West, Taipei

**Taipei Chinese PEN Centre**
Member of International PEN
4 Lane 68, 4th floor, When Chou St, Taipei
*Tel:* (02) 23693609 *Fax:* (02) 23699948
*E-mail:* taipen@tpts5.seed.net.tw *Cable:* TAIPENCLUB
*Key Personnel*
President: Yu Chen
Secretary: Sarah Jen-Hui Hsiang
Publication(s): *The Chinese PEN* (quarterly)

# Thailand

**Thai PEN Centre**
Member of International PEN
2/49 Ranong 1 Rd, Khet Dusit, Bangkok 10300
Mailing Address: PO Box 81, Dusit Post Office, Bangkok 10300
*Tel:* (02) 6685147; (02) 2792621
*Key Personnel*
President: Srisurang Poolthupya
Secretary: Dr Wareeya Bhavabhutananda Na Mahasarakham *E-mail:* wareeya@hotmail.com
Founded: 1958
Nonprofit literary society.
Publication(s): *Thailand PEN Journal* (journal)

**The Siam Society**
131 Soi Asoke, Sukhumvit 21 Rd, Bangkok 10110
*Tel:* (02) 66164707 *Fax:* (02) 2583491
*E-mail:* info@siam-society.org
*Web Site:* www.siam-society.org
*Key Personnel*
President: Bangkok Chowkwanyun
Publications Coordinator: Kanitha Kasina-ubol
Founded: 1904
Publication(s): *Journal of the Siam Society* (annually); *Natural History Bulletin of the Siam Society* (annually)

# Tunisia

**IBLA**, see Institut des Belles Lettres Arabes (IBLA)

**Institut des Belles Lettres Arabes (IBLA)**
(Arabic Institute of Literature)
12 rue Jamaa El-Haoua, 1008 Tunis
*Tel:* 71560133 *Fax:* 71572683
*E-mail:* ibla@gnet.tn
*Web Site:* www.iblatunis.org
*Key Personnel*
Dir: Jean Fontaine
Founded: 1960
Publication(s): *Revue IBLA*

**Union des Ecrivains Tunisiens** (Tunisian Writers' Union)
Avenue de Paris, Tunis 1000

*Tel:* 71257591 *Fax:* 71257807
*E-mail:* koutteb@planet.tn
*Web Site:* www.alkhadra.com/ittihad-koutteb
*Key Personnel*
President: Midani Ben Salah
Vice President: Mohammed El Kadhi
Secretary General: Souf Abid

# Turkey

**Turkish PEN Centre**
Member of International PEN
General Yazgan Sokak 10/10, Tunel, 80050 Istanbul
*Tel:* (0212) 2526314 *Fax:* (0212) 2526315
*Key Personnel*
President: Nebile Direkcigil *E-mail:* n.direkcigil@iku.edu.tr
Secretary: Suat Karantay

# United Kingdom

**Yr Academi Gymreig** (The Welsh Academy)
Mount Stuart House, 3rd floor, Mount Stuart Sq, Cardiff CF10 5FQ
*Tel:* (029) 20472266 *Fax:* (029) 20492930
*E-mail:* post@academi.org
*Web Site:* www.academi.org
*Key Personnel*
Chief Executive Officer: Peter Finch
Founded: 1959
The Welsh National Literature Promotion Agency & Society of Writers.
Publication(s): *Auto*; *Taliesin*

**The Alliance of Literary Societies**
22 Belmont Grove, Havant, Hants PO9 3PU
*Tel:* (023) 92 475855 *Fax:* (0870) 056 0330
*Web Site:* www.sndc.demon.co.uk/als.htm
*Key Personnel*
President: Aeronwy Thomas
Honorary Secretary: Rosemary Culley
    *E-mail:* rosemary@sndc.demon.co.uk
Founded: 1973
Publication(s): *Open Book* (annually)

**Arts Council of Wales**
9 Museum Pl, Cardiff CF10 3NX
*Tel:* (02920) 376500 *Fax:* (02920) 221447
*Web Site:* www.ccc-acw.org.uk
*Key Personnel*
Chief Executive: Peter Tyndall *E-mail:* peter.tyndall@artswales.org.uk

**Aslib, The Association for Information Management**
Temple Chambers, 3-7 Temple Ave, London EC4Y 0HP
*Tel:* (020) 7583 8900 *Fax:* (020) 7583 8401
*E-mail:* pubs@aslib.com
*Web Site:* www.aslib.co.uk; www.managinginformation.com
*Key Personnel*
Chief Executive: Roger Bowes
Head of Publications: Sarah Blair
Publication(s): *Directory of Information Sources in the UK* (biennially); *Managing Information* (10 times/yr)

**The Association for Information Management**, see Aslib, The Association for Information Management

**Association for Scottish Literary Studies**
c/o Dept of Scottish History, University of Glasgow, 9 University Gardens, Glasgow G12 8QH
*Tel:* (0141) 330 5309 *Fax:* (0141) 330 5309
*Web Site:* www.asls.org.uk
*Key Personnel*
General Manager: Duncan Jones *E-mail:* djones@scothist.arts.gla.ac.uk
Secretary: Jim Alison
Honorary Treasurer: Tom Ralph
Membership Secretary: Isobel McCallum
Founded: 1970
Also publisher.
Publication(s): *New Writing Scotland* (annually); *Scottish Language* (annually); *Scottish Literary Journal* (biannually); *Scottish Studies Review* (biannually)

**Association of Art Historians**
70 Cowcross St, Clerkenwell, London EC1M 6EJ
*Tel:* (020) 7490 3211 *Fax:* (020) 7490 3277
*E-mail:* admin@aah.org.uk
*Web Site:* www.aah.org.uk
*Key Personnel*
Chair: Shearer West *E-mail:* chair@aah.org.uk
Vice Chair: Gen Doy *E-mail:* vice-chair@aah.org.uk
Honorary Secretary: Christiana Payne
    *E-mail:* honsec@aah.org.uk
Honorary Treasurer: Peter Baitup
    *E-mail:* hontreas@aah.org.uk
Administrator: Claire Davies
Founded: 1974
Professional arts organization which promotes the study of art history.
Publication(s): *The Art Book* (quarterly); *Art History* (5 times/yr); *Bulletin* (triannually)

**Association of British Science Writers**
Wellcome Wolfson Bldg, 165 Queen's Gate, London SW7 5HE
*Tel:* (0870) 770 3361
*E-mail:* absw@absw.org.uk
*Web Site:* www.absw.org.uk
*Key Personnel*
Chairman: Pallab Ghosh
Vice Chairman: Peter Wrobel
Secretary: Fabian Acker
Treasurer: Peter Briggs
Publication(s): *Science Reporter* (monthly)

**Francis Bacon Society Inc**
Canonbury Tower, Islington, London N1 2NQ
*Tel:* (020) 7359 6888 *Fax:* (020) 7704 1896
*Web Site:* www.sirbacon.org/links/bmembership.htm
*Key Personnel*
Honorary Vice President: Mary Brameld
Chairman: T D Bokenham, Esq
Designated Chairman: P A Welsford
Librarian: Prof John Spiers
Founded: 1886
Old Established Society; Custodians of the Francis Bacon Tradition.
Publication(s): *Baconiana* (periodically)

**E F Benson**, see The Tilling Society

**E F Benson Society**
The Old Coach House, High St, Rye, East Sussex TN31 7JF
*Tel:* (01797) 223114
*E-mail:* info@efbensonsociety.org
*Web Site:* www.efbensonsociety.org
*Key Personnel*
President: Gwen Watkins
Chair: Keith Cavers

Secretary: Allan Downend
Treasurer: Chris Roby
Founded: 1984
Publication(s): *Bensoniana Onwards Now 3*; *The Benson's*; *The Dodo* (annually, journal)

## BookPower
305-307 Chiswick High Rd, London W4 4HH
*Tel:* (020) 8742 8232 *Fax:* (020) 8747 8715
*E-mail:* bookpower@ibd.uk.net
*Web Site:* www.bookpower.org
*Key Personnel*
Head Administration: Eileen Gillow
Founded: 1996
Charity. Administered by International Book Development Ltd.

## Books Across the Sea
The English-Speaking Union, Dartmouth House, 37 Charles St, London W1X 8AB
*Tel:* (020) 7529 1550 *Fax:* (020) 7495 6108
*E-mail:* esu@mailbox.ulcc.ac.uk
*Web Site:* www.libfl.ru/eng/esu
*Key Personnel*
President: HRH, Prince Philip, The Duke of Edinburgh, KG, KT
Dir General: Valerie Mitchell
Chairman: The Lord Watson
Librarian: Andrea K Wathern
Founded: 1941
Publication(s): *Ambassador Booklist*

## British Fantasy Society (BFS)
201 Reddish Rd, South Reddish, Stockport SK5 7HR
*Tel:* (0161) 6004125
*E-mail:* info@britishfantasysociety.org.uk
*Web Site:* www.britishfantasysociety.org.uk
*Key Personnel*
Chair: Nicki Robson
President: Ramsey Campbell
Secretary & Treasurer: Robert Parkinson
Publication(s): *Chills*; *Dark Horizons Newsletter*; *Mystique*

## The British Science Fiction Association Ltd (BSFA Ltd)
97 Sharp St, Newland Ave, Hull HU5 2AE
*E-mail:* bsfa@enterprise.net
*Web Site:* www.bsfa.co.uk
*Key Personnel*
Membership Secretary: Estelle Roberts
Administrator: Vikki Lee France
Founded: 1948
Publication(s): *Focus* (biannually, magazine); *Matrix* (bimonthly, newsletter); *Vector* (bimonthly, journal)

## The Bronte Society
Bronte Parsonage Museum, Church St, Haworth, Keighley, W Yorks BD22 8DR
*Tel:* (01535) 642323 *Fax:* (01535) 647131
*E-mail:* info@bronte.info
*Web Site:* www.bronte.org.uk
*Key Personnel*
Membership Development Officer: Rebecca Bishop *Tel:* (01535) 640195 *E-mail:* rebecca.bishop@bronte.org.uk
Founded: 1893
Publication(s): *Bronte Studies* (triannually); *Gazette* (biannually)

**BSFA Ltd**, see The British Science Fiction Association Ltd (BSFA Ltd)

## Byron Society (International)
Byron House, 6 Gertrude St, London SW10 0JN
*Tel:* (020) 7352 5112; (020) 7352 7238
*Web Site:* www.byronsociety.com
*Key Personnel*
President: The Lord Byron

Chairman: Lord Gilmour
Honorary Dir: Elma Dangerfield
Publication(s): *The Byron Journal* (annually)

## Randolph Caldecott Society
17 Home Rule Rd, Locks Heath, Southampton SO3 6LH
*Tel:* (01606) 891303
*E-mail:* charles.caldecott@lineone.net
*Web Site:* www.randolphcaldecott.org.uk
*Key Personnel*
Secretary: Kenn N Oultram
Treasurer: Charles Caldecott
Founded: 1983
Publication(s): *Caldecott Sketch*

## Cambridge Bibliographical Society
University Library, West Rd, Cambridge CB3 9DR
*Tel:* (01223) 333000 *Fax:* (01223) 333160
*E-mail:* cbs@ula.cam.ac.uk
*Web Site:* www2.cambridgeshire.gov.uk
*Key Personnel*
Honorary Secretary: N A Smith *E-mail:* nas1000@cam.ac.uk
Founded: 1949
Publication(s): *Monographs* (irregularly); *Transactions* (annually)

## The Centre for Creative Communities
118 Commercial St, London E1 6NF
*Tel:* (020) 7247 5385 *Fax:* (020) 7247 5256
*E-mail:* info@creativecommunities.org.uk
*Web Site:* www.creativecommunities.org.uk
*Key Personnel*
Dir: Jennifer Williams
Research Dir: Cristina Losito
Research Officer: Joanna Cottingham
Information & Communications Manager: Antonio Molina-Vazquez

## Children's Books History Society
25 Field Way, Hoddesdon, Herts EN11 OQN
*Tel:* (01992) 464885 *Fax:* (01992) 464885
*E-mail:* cbhs@abcgarrelt.demon.co.uk
*Key Personnel*
Chairman: Morna Daniels
Secretary: Mrs Pat Garrett
Treasurer: Sarah Jardine-Willoughby
Founded: 1969
In 1990, a biennial Harvey Darton Award was established for a book published in English, which extends our knowledge of some aspect of British children's literature of the past.
Publication(s): *CBHS Newsletter* (triannually, newsletter)

## The John Clare Society
The Stables, 1a West St, Helpston, Peterborough PE6 7DU
*Web Site:* freespace.virgin.net/linda.curry/jclare.htm
*Key Personnel*
President: Ronald Blythe
Vice President: Prof Eric Robinson; Edward Storey; Prof Kelsey Thornton
Chairman: Paul Chirico *Tel:* (01223) 339494 *E-mail:* pac17@cam.ac.uk
Vice Chairman: Emma Trehane
Honorary Secretary: Sue Holgate *Tel:* (01223) 518989 *Fax:* (01223) 509870
Honorary Treasurer & Membership Secretary: Linda Curry *Tel:* (0121) 475 1805 *E-mail:* l.j.curry@bham.ac.uk
Journal Editor & Archivist: Prof John Goodridge *Tel:* (0115) 9418418 *E-mail:* john.goodridge@ntu.ac.uk
Sales Officer: Peter Moyse *Tel:* (01733) 252678 *Fax:* (01733) 252678 *E-mail:* moyse.helpston@talk21.com
Founded: 1981

To promote a wider & deeper knowledge of the poet, John Clare (1793-1864).
Publication(s): *The John Clare Society Journal* (annually)

## The Joseph Conrad Society (UK)
c/o POSK, 238-46 King St, London W6 0RF
*Web Site:* www.bathspa.ac.uk/conrad/
*Key Personnel*
Chairman: Dr Keith Carabine *E-mail:* k.carabine@ukc.ac.uk
President: Philip Conrad
Secretary: Dr Tim Middleton *E-mail:* t.middleton@bathspa.ac.uk
Founded: 1973
Literary society devoted to all aspects of the study of the works & life of Joseph Conrad (1857-1924).
Publication(s): *The Conradian* (biannually)

## Critics' Circle
51 Vartry Rd, London N15 6PS
*Tel:* (020) 7403 1818 *Fax:* (020) 7357 9287
*E-mail:* info@criticscircle.org.uk
*Web Site:* www.criticscircle.org.uk
*Key Personnel*
President: Charles Osborne
Vice President: Mike Dixon
Secretary: Charles Hedges
Treasurer: Peter Cargin
Founded: 1907
Professional association of critics of drama, music, the cinema & dance.

## Daresbury Lewis Carroll Society
Blue Grass, Little Leigh, Northwich, Cheshire CW8 4RJ
*Tel:* (01606) 891303
*Web Site:* lewiscarrollsociety.org.uk
*Key Personnel*
Secretary: Kenneth N Oultram
Founded: 1970
Publication(s): *Stuff & Nonsense*

## The Dickens Fellowship
Dickens House Museum, 48 Doughty St, London WC1N 2LF
*Tel:* (020) 7405 2127 *Fax:* (020) 7831 5175
*E-mail:* dickens.fellowship@btinternet.com
*Web Site:* www.dickens.fellowship.btinternet.co.uk
*Key Personnel*
President: Dr Paul Schlicke
Honorary General Secretary: Thelma Grove *E-mail:* hongensec@aol.com; Dr Tony R Williams *E-mail:* arwilliams33@compuserve.com
Honorary Treasurer: George Wright
Editor: Prof Malcolm Andrews
Founded: 1902
Affiliated to the Alliance of Literary Societies, The Birmingham & Midland Institute, 9 Margaret St, Birmingham, B 3BS.
Publication(s): *The Dickens Magazine* (6 times/yr); *The Dickensian* (triannually); *Mr Dick's Kite* (triannually, newsletter)

## The Dorothy L Sayers Society
Rose Cottage, Malthouse Lane, Hurstpierpoint, West Sussex BN6 9JY
*Tel:* (01273) 833444 *Fax:* (01273) 835988
*E-mail:* info@sayers.org.uk
*Web Site:* www.sayers.org.uk
*Key Personnel*
Chairman: Christopher Dean
Membership Secretary: Lenelle Davis *Tel:* (01252) 626619
Bulletin Secretary: Jasmine Simeone *Tel:* (01248) 714940 *Fax:* (01248) 714940
Publications: Janet Hunt
Founded: 1976
Publication(s): *Poetry of Dorothy L Sayers*; *Sidelights on Sayers* (annually)

**Early English Text Society**
Christ Church, Oxford OX1 1DP
*Web Site:* www.eets.org.uk
*Key Personnel*
Honorary Dir: Prof John Burrow
Executive Secretary: R F S Hamer
    *E-mail:* richard.hamer@chch.ox.ac.uk
Editorial Secretary: Dr H L Spencer
Membership Secretary: Jane Watkinson
Founded: 1864

**Edinburgh Bibliographical Society**
c/o National Library of Scotland, George IV
    Bridge, Edinburgh EH1 1EW
*Tel:* (0131) 226 4531 *Fax:* (0131) 466 2807
*E-mail:* exkb33@srv1.lib.ed.ac.uk
*Web Site:* www.edbibsoc.lib.ed.ac.uk
*Telex:* 727442
*Key Personnel*
President: Dr Murray C T Simpson
Vice President: Prof David Finkelstein; Brenda E
    Moon
Acting Honorary Secretary: Dr Warren Mc-
    Dougall *E-mail:* warrenmcdougall@aol.com
Honorary Treasurer: Peter B Freshwater
Founded: 1890
Publication(s): *Transactions* (biennially)

**The Eighteen Nineties Society**
PO Box 97, High Wycombe, Bucks HP14 4GH
*Tel:* (01869) 248340
*Web Site:* www.1890s.org
*Key Personnel*
Founder: Dr G Krishnamurti
President: Elizabeth The Countess of Longford
Chair: Martyn Goff
Secretary & Treasurer: Steven Halliwell
    *E-mail:* steve@ft-1890s-society.demon.co.uk
Founded: 1963
Publication(s): *The Journal of the Eighteen
    Nineties Societies* (annually); *Keynotes* (quar-
    terly, newsletter)

**The George Eliot Fellowship**
71 Stepping Stones Rd, Coventry, Warwicks CV5
    8JT
*Tel:* (024) 7659 2231
*Web Site:* www.sndc.demon.co.uk/alsdef.htm#e
*Key Personnel*
President: Jonathan G Ouvry
Vice President: A S Byatt; Tenniel Evans; Beryl
    Gray, PhD; Graham Handley, PhD; Prof Bar-
    bara Hardy; F B Pinion; Ann Reader; Harriet
    Williams; Michael Wolff; Margaret Wolfit;
    Gabriel Woolf
Secretary: Hr Kathleen Adams
Founded: 1930
Publication(s): *George Eliot Review* (annually);
    *Pitkin Guide to George Eliot (illustrated);
    Those Of Us Who Loved Her: The Men In
    George Eliot's Life*

**Thomas Ellis Memorial Fund**
University Registry, University of Wales, Cathays
    Park, Cardiff CF10 3NS
*Tel:* (029) 2038 2656 *Fax:* (029) 2039 6040
*E-mail:* awards@wales.ac.uk
*Web Site:* www.wales.ac.uk/newpages/external/
    E5536.asp
*Key Personnel*
Secretary General: Dr Lynn Williams
Grants to assist research into the language, liter-
    ature, history & antiquities of Wales & Mon-
    mouthshire, & the publication of the results of
    such research. Applications should be sent to
    the Secretary General at the University Reg-
    istry.

**The English Association**
University of Leicester, University Rd, Leicester
    LE1 7RH

*Tel:* (0116) 252 3982 *Fax:* (0116) 252 2301
*E-mail:* engassoc@le.ac.uk
*Web Site:* www.le.ac.uk/engassoc
*Key Personnel*
Chair of the Executive Committee: Prof Elaine
    Treharne
Chief Executive & Company Secretary: Helen
    Lucas *Tel:* (0116) 252 2300 *E-mail:* hl11@le.
    ac.uk
President: Martin Blocksidge
Honorary Treasurer: Roger J Claxton
Membership Coordinator: Jeremy Wiltshire
    *E-mail:* jnw4@le.ac.uk
Founded: 1906
Publication(s): *EA Newsletter* (triannually); *En-
    glish* (triannually); *English 4-11* (triannually);
    *Essays & Studies* (annually); *The Use of En-
    glish* (triannually); *The Year's Work in Critical
    & Cultural Theory* (annually); *The Year's Work
    in English Studies* (annually)

**The English-Speaking Union of the
Commonwealth**
Dartmouth House, 37 Charles St, London W1J
    5ED
*Tel:* (020) 7529 1550 *Fax:* (020) 7495 6108
*E-mail:* esu@esu.org
*Web Site:* www.esu.org
*Key Personnel*
Chairman: The Lord Watson of Richmond
Dir General: Valerie Mitchell
Librarian: Gill Hale *E-mail:* gill_hale@esu.org
Membership Secretary: Margaret Garrett
Founded: 1918
Branches worldwide in 52 countries.
Publication(s): *Concord*

**Hakluyt Society**
c/o Map Library, The British Library, 96 Euston
    Rd, London NW1 2DB
*Tel:* (01428) 641850 *Fax:* (01428) 641933
*E-mail:* office@hakluyt.com
*Web Site:* www.hakluyt.com
*Key Personnel*
President: Prof R C Bridges
Administrator: Richard Bateman
Founded: 1846
Publications of scholarly editions of records of
    voyages, travels & other geographical material
    of the past.
Publication(s): *The Hakluyt Society* (3rd series)

**The Thomas Hardy Society**
PO Box 1438, Dorchester, Dorset DT1 1YH
*Tel:* (01305) 251501 *Fax:* (01305) 251501
*E-mail:* info@hardysociety.org
*Web Site:* www.hardysociety.org
*Key Personnel*
Dir: Rosemarie Morgan *E-mail:* rm82@pantheon.
    yale.edu
Founded: 1968
List of publications available.
Publication(s): *The Thomas Hardy Journal* (trian-
    nually)

**Jane Austen Society**
Jane Austen's House, Chawton, Alton, Hants
    GU34 1SD
*Tel:* (01420) 83262 *Fax:* (01420) 83262
*E-mail:* museum@janeausten.demon.co.uk
*Web Site:* www.janeaustensoci.freeuk.com/index.
    htm
*Key Personnel*
Chairman: Patrick Stokes
President: Richard Knight
Honorary Secretary: Maggie Lane
Membership Secretary: Rosemary Culley
    *Tel:* (01705) 475855 *Fax:* (01705) 788842
    *E-mail:* rosemary@sndc.demon.co.uk
Founded: 1940
Publication(s): *Jane Austen's House* (book)

**The Richard Jefferies Society**
Eidsvoll, Bedwells Heath, Boars Hill, Oxford
    OX1 5JE
*Tel:* (01865) 735678
*Web Site:* www.treitel.org/Richard/jefferies.html
*Key Personnel*
President: Prof Jeremy Hooker
Secretary: Phyllis Treitel
Founded: 1950
Publication(s): *The Richard Jefferies Society Jour-
    nal*

**Keats-Shelley Memorial Association (KSMA)**
One Satchwell Walk, Leamington Spa, Warwicks
    CV32 4QE
*Tel:* (01892) 533452 *Fax:* (01892) 519142
*Web Site:* www.keats-shelley.co.uk
*Key Personnel*
Honorary Treasurer: Charles Cary-Elwes
Founded: 1903
Publication(s): *Keats-Shelley Review* (annually)

**Kipling Society**
6 Clifton Rd, London W9 1S5
*Tel:* (020) 7286 0194 *Fax:* (020) 7286 0194
*Web Site:* www.kipling.org.uk
*Key Personnel*
Honorary Secretary: Jane Keskar *E-mail:* jane@
    keskar.fsworld.co.uk
Founded: 1927
Publication(s): *The Kipling Journal* (quarterly)

**Charles Lamb Society**
Guildhall Library, Aldermanbury, London EC2P
    2EJ
*Tel:* (020) 7332 1868; (020) 7332 1870
*Web Site:* users.ox.ac.uk/~scat1492/clsoc.htm
*Key Personnel*
Chairman: N R D Powell
Editor: Richard S Tomlinson
    *E-mail:* romanticism@ameritech.net
Membership Secretary: Robin Healey
Founded: 1935
Publication(s): *The Charles Lamb Bulletin* (quar-
    terly)

**Lancashire Authors' Association**
Heatherslade, 5 Quakerfields, Westhoughton,
    Bolton, Lancs BL5 2BJ
*Tel:* (01254) 56788
*E-mail:* laa@lancs.communigate.co.uk
*Web Site:* www.communigate.co.uk/lancs/laa/
    index.phtml
*Key Personnel*
Chairman & Librarian: George W White
Deputy Chairman & Treasurer: T Halsall
President & General Secretary: Eric Holt
Joint Librarian: B Atkinson
Membership Secretary: B Holt
Founded: 1909
Publication(s): *Lancashire Miscellany* (1987/8/90
    cassette tapes); *The Record* (quarterly)

**Friends of Arthur Machen**
78 Greenwich South St, Greenwich, London
    SE10 8UN
*Tel:* (01633) 422520 *Fax:* (0633) 421055
*Web Site:* www.machensoc.demon.co.uk
*Key Personnel*
Treasurer: Jeremy Cantwell
Publication(s): *Faunus* (biannually, journal);
    *Machenalia* (biannually, newsletter)

**Medical Writers Group**
Society of Authors, 84 Drayton Gardens, London
    SW10 9SB
*Tel:* (020) 7373 6642 *Fax:* (020) 7373 5768
*E-mail:* info@societyofauthors.org
*Web Site:* www.societyofauthors.org
*Key Personnel*
Chairman: Antony Beevor

Secretary: Mark Le Fanu *E-mail:* mlefanu@
societyofauthors.org
Unit of The Society of Authors.
Divisions: The Society of Authors

## William Morris Society
Kelmscott House, 26 Upper Mall, Hammersmith,
London W6 9TA
*Tel:* (020) 8741 3735 *Fax:* (020) 8748 5207
*Web Site:* www.morrissociety.org
*Key Personnel*
President: Linda Parry
Editor: Dr Rosie Miles
Publication(s): *Journal* (quarterly, newsletter)

## The National Centre for Research into
  Children's Literature
40 Dover St, London W1S 4NP
*Tel:* (020) 7408 5092
*Key Personnel*
Secretary: Lucy Jane Tetlow

## Oxford Bibliographical Society
c/o Bodleian Library, Oxford OX1 3BG
*Tel:* (01865) 277069 *Fax:* (01865) 277182
*E-mail:* membership@oxbibsoc.org.uk
*Web Site:* www.oxbibsoc.org.uk
*Telex:* 83656
*Key Personnel*
President: Prof Nigel Palmer
Secretary: Dr Julia Walworth *E-mail:* secretary@
oxbibsoc.org.uk
Treasurer: David Thomas *E-mail:* treasurer@
oxbibsoc.org.uk
Founded: 1922

## English PEN Centre
Member of International PEN
Lancaster House, 33 Islington High St, London
N1 9LH
*Tel:* (020) 7713 0023 *Fax:* (020) 7713 0005
*E-mail:* enquiries@englishpen.org
*Web Site:* www.englishpen.org
*Key Personnel*
President: Dr Alastair Niven
Executive Dir: Susanna Nicklin *E-mail:* susie@
englishpen.org
Programme Dir, Writers in Prison Committee:
Lucy Popescu
Membership Secretary: Simon Burt
Artistic Dir: Diana Reich
Publication(s): *PEN News* (biannually, newsletter)

## The Poetry Society Inc
22 Betterton St, London WC2H 9BX
*Tel:* (020) 7420 9880 *Fax:* (020) 7240 4818
*E-mail:* info@poetrysociety.org.uk
*Web Site:* www.poetrysociety.org.uk
*Key Personnel*
Dir: Jules Mann
Membership Manager: Carl Dhiman
Publications Manager: Janet Phillips
Press & Marketing Manager: Lisa Roberts
Publication(s): *Jumpstart: Poetry in the Secondary
School*; *Poems on the the Underground Posters*;
*The Poetry Book for Primary Schools*; *Poetry
News*; *Poetry Review*

## The Beatrix Potter Society
9 Broadfields, Harpenden, Herts AL5 2HJ
*Tel:* (01625) 267880 *Fax:* (01625) 267879
*E-mail:* info@beatrixpottersociety.org.uk
*Web Site:* www.beatrixpottersociety.org.uk
*Key Personnel*
Chair: Judy Taylor
Founded: 1980
The Society promotes study & appreciation of
Potter's life & works, holds regular talks &
biennial Study Conference in Lake District.
Publication(s): *Books about Beatrix Potter's Life
& Work* (quarterly, newsletter)

## The Arthur Ransome Society Ltd (TARS)
Abbot Hall Museum, Kendal, Cumbria LA9 5AL
*Tel:* (01539) 722464
*E-mail:* tarsinfo@arthur-ransome.org
*Web Site:* www.arthur-ransome.org/ar
*Key Personnel*
President: Norman Willis
Company Secretary: Dr W H Janes
Publication(s): *Literary Transactions* (biannually);
*Mixed Moss* (biannually); *The Outlaw* (biannu-
ally); *Ship's Log* (annually); *Signals* (annually)

**RNA**, see Romantic Novelists' Association
(RNA)

## Romantic Novelists' Association (RNA)
38 Stanhope Rd, Reading, Berks RG2 7HN
*Tel:* (01827) 714776 *Fax:* (01827) 714776
*Web Site:* www.rna-uk.org
*Key Personnel*
President: Diane Pearson
Chairman: Anthea Kenyon
Contact: Trisha Ashley *E-mail:* trisha-ashley@
hotmail.com

## Royal Literary Fund
3 Johnson's Court (off Fleet St), London EC4A
3EA
*Tel:* (020) 7353 7150 *Fax:* (020) 7353 1350
*E-mail:* rlitfund@btconnect.com
*Web Site:* www.rlf.org.uk
*Key Personnel*
President: Sir Stephen Tumim
General Secretary: Eileen Gunn
  *E-mail:* egunnrlf@globalnet.co.uk
Fellowship & Education Officer: Steve Cook
Publication(s): *Archives of the Royal Literary
Fund 1790-1918*

## The Royal Society for the Encouragement of
  Arts, Manufactures & Commerce (RSA)
8 John Adam St, London WC2N 6EZ
*Tel:* (020) 7930 5115 *Fax:* (020) 7839 5805
*E-mail:* general@rsa.org.uk
*Web Site:* www.rsa.org.uk
*Key Personnel*
Dir: Penny Egan *Tel:* (020) 7451 6883
  *E-mail:* director@rsa.org.uk
Encourages the development of a principled, pros-
perous society & the release of human potential
through a program of projects & events with
the support of influential fellows from every
field & every background.
Publication(s): *RSA Journal*

## Royal Society of Literature
Somerset House, Strand, London WC2R 1LA
*Tel:* (020) 7845 4676 *Fax:* (020) 7845 4679
*E-mail:* info@rslit.org
*Web Site:* www.rslit.org
*Key Personnel*
President: Michael Holroyd
Chairman of Council: Maggie Gee
Secretary: Maggie Fergusson
Founded: 1820
Registered charity. Administers & awards three
literary prizes & confers the honor "Companion
of Literature" on selected writers.
Publication(s): *News From the Royal Society of
Literature*

**RSA**, see The Royal Society for the
Encouragement of Arts, Manufactures &
Commerce (RSA)

## The Ruskin Society of London
Subsidiary of The Royal Society of Literature
Affiliate of British Italian Society
351 Woodstock Rd, Oxford OX2 7NX
*Tel:* (01865) 310987; (01865) 515962
  *Fax:* (01865) 240448

*Key Personnel*
Dir: A Hardy
Founded: 1980
Articles & news of Ruskinian interest & 19th
century literary history.
Publication(s): *The Ruskin Gazette* (annually,
journal)

## Scottish PEN Centre
Member of International PEN
Greenleaf Editorial, 15A Lynedoch St, Glasgow
G3 6EF
*Tel:* (01436) 672010
*E-mail:* info@scottishpen.org
*Web Site:* www.scottishpen.org
*Key Personnel*
President: Tessa Ransford
Vice President: Jenni Calder; Douglas Dunn
Secretary: Harry Watson
Treasurer: Mary Baxter

## Shakespearean Authorship Trust
c/o Shakespeare's Globe Theater, 21 New Globe
Walk, London SE1 9DT
*Tel:* (01473) 890264; (020) 7902 1403
  *Fax:* (01473) 890803
*E-mail:* info@shakespeareanauthorshiptrust.org.uk
*Web Site:* www.shakespeareanauthorshiptrust.org.
uk
*Key Personnel*
Chairman: Mark Rylance

## The Shaw Society
6 Stanstead Grove, Catford, London SE6 4UD
*Tel:* (020) 86973619 *Fax:* (020) 86973619
*E-mail:* bernardshawinfo@netscape.net
*Web Site:* www.sndc.demon.co.uk/shawsub.htm
*Key Personnel*
Secretary: Barbara Smoker
Treasurer: A J L Gayfer *E-mail:* anthnyellis@aol.
com
Editor: T F Evans
Publication(s): *The Shavian* (every nine months)

## Society for Editors & Proofreaders
Riverbank House, One Putney Bridge Approach,
Fulham, London SW6 3JD
*Tel:* (020) 7736 3278 *Fax:* (020) 7736 3318
*E-mail:* administration@sfep.org.uk
*Web Site:* www.sfep.org.uk
*Key Personnel*
Chair: Naomi Laredo
Founded: 1988
Professional body providing training, information,
support, electronic resources & newsletters.
Publication(s): *CopyRight* (magazine)

## Society for the Study of Medieval Languages
  & Literature
c/o Dr D G Pattison, Magdalen College, Oxford
OX1 4AU
*Tel:* (01865) 276087 *Fax:* (01865) 276087
*Web Site:* www.mod-langs.ox.ac.uk/ssmll
*Key Personnel*
President: Mr AVC Schmidt
Secretary: Dr Roger Dalrymple *E-mail:* roger.
dalrymple@st-hughs.ox.ac.uk
Treasurer: Dr D G Pattison
Publication(s): *Medium Aevum* (biannually)

## The Society of Women Writers & Journalists
Calvers Farm, Thelveton, Diss, Norfolk IP23
4NG
*Tel:* (01379) 740550 *Fax:* (01379) 741716
*Web Site:* www.swwj.co.uk
*Key Personnel*
Chairman: Jean Hawkes
Vice Chairman: Valerie Dunmore
President: Nina Bawden
Secretary: Zoe King *E-mail:* zoe@zoeking.com

Treasurer: Greg Hawkes
Membership Secretary: Wendy Hughes
  *E-mail:* wendy@stickler.org.uk
Publication(s): *The Woman Writer* (6 times/yr)

**TARS**, see The Arthur Ransome Society Ltd (TARS)

**The Tilling Society**
5 Friars Bank, Guestling, Hastings, East Sussex TN35 4EJ
*Fax:* (01424) 813237
*E-mail:* society@tilling.org.uk
*Web Site:* www.tilling.org.uk/society
*Key Personnel*
Joint Secretary: Cynthia Reavell; Tony Reavell
Founded: 1982
Publication(s): *E F Benson as Mayor of Rye* (book); *Tilling Society Newsletter* (biannually, newsletter)

**The Tolkien Society**
65 Wentworth Crescent, Ash Vale, Surrey GU12 5LF
*Tel:* (01242) 529757
*E-mail:* membership@tolkiensociety.org
*Web Site:* www.tolkiensociety.org
*Key Personnel*
Chairman: Chris Cranshaw
Secretary: Sally Kennett
Membership Secretary: Trevor Reynolds
Publication(s): *Amon Hen* (bimonthly, bulletin); *Mallorn* (annually, journal)

**Translators Association**
c/o Society of Authors, 84 Drayton Gardens, London SW10 9SB
*Tel:* (020) 7373 6642 *Fax:* (020) 7373 5768
*E-mail:* info@societyofauthors.org
*Web Site:* www.societyofauthors.org
*Key Personnel*
Chairman: Antony Beever
Awards Secretary: Dorothy Sym *E-mail:* dsym@societyofauthors.org

The Association is a specialist group representing published literary translators within the Society of Authors.
Publication(s): *In Other Words* (journal); *Quick Guide to Literary Translation*

**Edgar Wallace Society**
84 Ridgefield Rd, Oxford OX4 3DA
*E-mail:* info@edgarwallace.org
*Web Site:* www.edgarwallace.org
*Key Personnel*
President: Penelope Wyrd
Founded: 1969
Publication(s): *The Crimson Circle* (quarterly, magazine)

**H G Wells Society**
Dept of English Literature, Shearwood Mount, Shearwood Rd, Sheffield S10 2TD
*Web Site:* hgwellsusa.50megs.com
*Key Personnel*
Secretary: Steve McLean
Sales Officer: John Green
Founded: 1960
Publication(s): *H G Wells: A Comprehensive Bibliography*; *The Wellsian* (annually, journal)

**The Welsh Academy**, see Yr Academi Gymreig

**West Country Writers' Association**
High Wotton, Wotton Lane, Lympstone, Exmouth, Devon EX8 5AY
*Tel:* (01395) 222749
*E-mail:* wcwa@westcountrywriters.co.uk
*Web Site:* www.author.co.uk/wcwa
*Key Personnel*
Secretary: Judy Joss
Founded: 1951

# Uruguay

**Academia Nacional de Letras** (National Academy of Literature)
Ituziango 1255, 11000 Montevideo 11000
*Tel:* (02) 9152374 *Fax:* (02) 9167460
*E-mail:* academia@montevideo.com.uy
*Telex:* 23133 Mec Ug
*Key Personnel*
President: Antonio Cravotto
Secretary: Carlos Jones
Founded: 1946
Publication(s): *Boletin de la Academia Nacional de Letras*; *Revista Nacional*

# Venezuela

**Venezuelan PEN Centre** (Centro Venezolano del PEN Internacional)
Member of International PEN
10° Transversal con 7° Ave, Residencias Villas Ines, Piso 3, Altamira, Caracas 1010
*Tel:* (0212) 5616691; (0212) 5617589; (0212) 5617287 *Fax:* (0212) 5718064
*Telex:* 26217 Biaya *Cable:* BIAYACUCH
*Key Personnel*
President: Dr Jose Ramon Medina
Secretary: Oswaldo Trejo
Publication(s): *Con Textos*; *Coleccion Plural*

# Zimbabwe

**The Zimbabwe Writers Union**
12 Shurugwi Rd, Gweru
Mailing Address: PO Box 6170, Gweru
*Tel:* (054) 23284
*Key Personnel*
President: D Mungoshi
Secretary General: Pathisa Nyathi

# Literary Prizes

Prizes and awards are listed alphabetically under the country where the sponsor is located. In some instances, recipients are restricted to the country in which the prize or award is presented.

☆ indicates those prizes with no geographical restriction placed upon recipients.

# Argentina

## Concurso Literario Premio Emece
Emece Editores SA
Av Independencia 1668, 1100 Buenos Aires
*Tel:* (011) 4382-4043; (011) 4382-4045
  *Fax:* (011) 4383-3793
*Web Site:* www.emece.com.ar
*Key Personnel*
Editorial Department: Mirta Mallo
  *E-mail:* mmallo@eplaneta.com.ar
Established: 1954
For the best unpublished novel or book of short stories in the Spanish language.
Award: 5,000 ARS

## National Prize for Literature
Argentina Ministry of Education, Science & Technology
Subsecretary of Culture, Pizzurno 935, 1020 Buenos Aires
Awarded triennially for best works of prose & poetry.

## Premio Academia Nacional de la Historia
  (National Academy of History Award)
Academia Nacional de la Historia (National Academy of History)
Balcarce 139, 1064 Buenos Aires
*Tel:* (01) 4343-4416; (01) 4331-4633; (01) 4331-5147 (ext 110) *Fax:* (01) 4331-5147 (ext 0)
*E-mail:* admite@an-historia.org.ar
*Web Site:* www.an-historia.org.ar
*Key Personnel*
Administrative Secretary: Dora B Pinola

# Australia

## The Age Book of the Year Awards
The Age
250 Spencer St, Melbourne, Victoria 3000
Mailing Address: PO Box 257C, Melbourne, Victoria 8001
*Tel:* (03) 9600 4211 *Fax:* (03) 9670 7514
*Web Site:* www.theage.com.au
Two prizes awarded to the two Australian books of outstanding literary merit which best express Australia's identity or character: one prize for a work of imaginative writing, the other for a nonfiction work.
Award: One work to be named 'The Age' Book of the Year & 4,000 AUD; other, best work in its category, 3,000 AUD

## Alexander Henderson Award
Australian Institute of Genealogical Studies Inc
1/41 Railway Rd, Blackburn, Melbourne, Victoria 3130
Mailing Address: PO Box 339, Blackburn, Melbourne, Victoria 3130
*Tel:* (03) 9877 3789 *Fax:* (03) 9877 9066
*E-mail:* info@aigs.org.au

*Web Site:* www.aigs.org.au/
Established: 1973
Best Australian family history book, written & entered for the award.
Award: Certificate & trophy
Closing Date: Nov 30 annually
Presented: Last Friday of May

## The Alice Literary Award
Society of Women Writers (Australia)
73 Church Rd, Carrum, Victoria 3197
*Tel:* (03) 9772 2389
*Web Site:* home.vicnet.net.au/~swwvic
*Key Personnel*
President: Meryl Tobin *Tel:* (03) 5997 6328
  *E-mail:* hmtobin@dcsi.net.au
Established: 1978
Presented biennially for a distinguished & long-term contribution to literature by an Australian woman.

## APA Book Design Awards
Australian Publishers Association Ltd
60/89 Jones St, Ultimo, NSW 2007
*Tel:* (02) 9281 9788 *Fax:* (02) 9281 1073
*E-mail:* apa@publishers.asn.au
*Web Site:* www.publishers.asn.au
*Key Personnel*
Chief Executive Officer: Susan Bridge
Recognizes creativity, excellence & innovation in contemporary Australian book design. Books entered must have been designed in Australia & published for the first time during the preceding calendar year. Entries open in October & close in January.
Award: 20 award categories which feature prizes to the value of 1,000 AUD
Closing Date: April 16
Presented: Book Design Awards, held in conjunction with the Australian Book Fair at Darling Harbour in June

## APA Campus Bookstore of the Year Award
Australian Publishers Association Ltd
60/89 Jones St, Ultimo, NSW 2007
*Tel:* (02) 9281 9788 *Fax:* (02) 9281 1073
*E-mail:* apa@publishers.asn.au
*Web Site:* www.publishers.asn.au
*Key Personnel*
Chief Executive Officer: Susan Bridge

## APA Publisher of the Year Award
Australian Publishers Association Ltd
60/89 Jones St, Ultimo, NSW 2007
*Tel:* (02) 9281 9788 *Fax:* (02) 9281 1073
*E-mail:* apa@publishers.asn.au
*Web Site:* www.publishers.asn.au
*Key Personnel*
Chief Executive Officer: Susan Bridge
Peer-assessment award, acknowledging professional performance by organizations during the previous calendar year.
Presented: Australian Book Industry Awards Dinner at the Australian Book Fair in June, Annually in June

## Arts Queensland Judith Wright Calanthe Award for Poetry
Brisbane Writers Festival Association Inc
PO Box 3453, South Brisbane, Qld 4101
*Tel:* (07) 3255 0254 *Fax:* (07) 3255 0362
*E-mail:* info@brisbanewritersfestival.com.au
*Web Site:* www.brisbanewritersfestival.com.au
*Key Personnel*
Festival Dir: Rosemary Cameron
Festival Manager: Rhiannon Phillips
Chairman: Sallyanne Atkinson
Deputy Chair: Andrew Greenwood
Secretary: Kristy Vernon
Treasurer: Angus Blackwood
Established: 1997
Award for poetry by an Australian author.
Other Sponsor(s): Arts Queensland
Award: 15,000 AUD & certificate
Closing Date: July
Presented: Oct

## Australian Literature Society Gold Medal
Association for the Study of Australian Literature
School of English & European Languages, University of Tasmania, GPO Box 252-82, Hobart, Tas 7001
*Tel:* (03) 6226 2352 *Fax:* (03) 6226 7631
*Web Site:* www.asc.uq.edu.au/asal
*Key Personnel*
President: Lyn McCredden *E-mail:* lynmcr@deakin.edu.au
Vice President: Peter Kirpatrick *Tel:* (02) 4736 0112 *E-mail:* p.kirpatrick@uws.edu.au
Treasurer: Simon Ryan
Secretary: Paul Genoni *Tel:* (08) 9266 7526
  *E-mail:* p.genoni@curtin.edu.au
Award originated by Colonel, the Honourable R A Crouch in 1899 & continued by the Australian Literature Society until 1983 when the ALS incorporated with the Association for the Study of Australian Literature. It is awarded annually for the most outstanding Australian literary work, or for outstanding services to Australian literature.
Award: Gold medal

## Australian Vogel Literary Award
Allen & Unwin Pty Ltd
PO Box 8500, Saint Leonards, NSW 1590
*Tel:* (02) 8425 0100 *Fax:* (02) 99062218
*E-mail:* frontdesk@allenandunwin.com
*Web Site:* www.allenandunwin.com
*Key Personnel*
Contact: Emma Sorensen *E-mail:* emmas@allenandunwin.com
Established: 1980
Literary Award for an unpublished manuscript by Australian authors under 35 years of age.
Other Sponsor(s): The Australian Newspaper; Vogel Breads
Award: 20,000 AUD
Closing Date: May annually
Presented: Sept/Oct

## The Marten Bequest Travelling Scholarships
Trust
35 Clarence St, Sydney, NSW 2001
*Tel:* (01) 300 132 075
*E-mail:* services@trust.com.au

*Web Site:* www.permanentgroup.com.au
*Key Personnel*
Awards Administrator: Petrea Salter
Six scholarships awarded annually for study in the following area(s): singing, instrumental music, painting, ballet, sculpture, architecture, prose, poetry & acting. Entrants must be born in Australia & between the ages of 21-35 (except in the field of ballet: ages 17-35).
Award: Each scholarship 18,000 AUD
Closing Date: Oct/Nov of year previous

## Bronze Swagman Award
Winton Tourist Promotion Association
PO Box 44, Winton, Qld 4735
*Tel:* (07) 4657 1466 *Fax:* (07) 4657 1886
*E-mail:* info@patsopals.com.au
*Web Site:* www.patsopals.com
*Key Personnel*
Contact: M Nowland
Annual award for Bush Verse. Book verse available in December of each year.
Award: 2,500 AUD Bronze statuette of The Swagman, sculpted by Daphne Mayo & a 250 AUD Winton Opal
Closing Date: Jan 31
Presented: Easter

## R Carson Gold Short Story Competition
Fellowship of Australian Writers Queensland Inc (FAWQ)
PO Box 6336, Upper Mountain Gravatt, Qld 4122
*Tel:* (07) 3343 7645 *Fax:* (07) 3343 7645
*Key Personnel*
Receiving Officer: Nancy Cox-Millner
*E-mail:* ncox-mil@bigpond.net.au
Awarded annually for a short story by an Australian with Australian setting. Administered by the Union Fidelity Trust Company of Australia. Open only to persons born in Australia.
Award: 1st prize 1,000 AUD
Closing Date: April 23

## Children's Book of the Year Awards
Children's Book Council of Australia
13 High St, Launceston, Tas 7250
Mailing Address: PO Box 765, Rozelle NSW 2039
*Tel:* (02) 9818-3858 *Fax:* (02) 9810-0737
*E-mail:* office@cbc.org.au
*Web Site:* www.cbc.org.au
*Key Personnel*
Contact: Maureen Mann *Tel:* (03) 6334 2794
*E-mail:* maureen.mann@education.tas.gov.au
Established: 1946
Awarded annually.
(1) Book of the Year, established 1946; (2) Junior Book of the Year, established 1982; (3) Picture Book of the Year, established 1952. $30,000 to be distributed amongst the winners & honor books (possibility of two) in each category.
(4) The Eve Pownall Information Book Award (nonfiction) established 1993. $10,000 to be distributed between winner & up to two honor books.
Closing Date: Dec 31

## The Abbie Clancy Award
Society of Women Writers NSW Inc
GPO Box 1388, Sydney, NSW 2001
*Web Site:* www.womenwritersnsw.org/awards.html
Awarded annually to a needy & deserving English honours student studying at an Australian university.
Award: 1,000 AUD to 1,500 AUD

## Tom Collins Poetry Prize
Western Australia Fellowship of Australian Writers
Tom Collins House, 88 Wood St, Swanbourne, WA 6010

*Tel:* (08) 9384 4771 *Fax:* (08) 9384 4854
*E-mail:* fawwa@iinet.net.au
*Web Site:* members.iinet.net.au/~fawwa
*Key Personnel*
President: Trisha Kotai-Ewers
Established: 1977
Administered by Western Australia FAW & sponsored by J Furphy & Sons, Shepparton, Victoria, since 1984, for a poem of up to 60 lines.
Award: 1st prize 1,000 AUD; 2nd prize 400 AUD; Highly Commended 150 AUD
Closing Date: Dec 31

## C H Currey Memorial Fellowship
State Library of NSW Press
Macquarie St, Sydney, NSW 2000
*Tel:* (02) 9273 1414 *Fax:* (02) 9273 1255
*E-mail:* library@sl.nsw.gov.au
*Web Site:* www.sl.nsw.gov.au
*Key Personnel*
State Librarian: Ms Dagmar Schmidmaier
Established: 1974
For the writing of Australian history from original sources, preferably making use of the State Library's resources.
Award: 20,000 AUD
Closing Date: Sept 1

## Emeritus Awards
Australia Council Literature Board
372 Elizabeth St, Surry Hills, NSW 2010
Mailing Address: PO Box 788, Strawberry Hills, NSW 2012
*Tel:* (02) 9215 9000 *Fax:* (02) 9215 9111
*E-mail:* mail@ozco.gov.au
*Web Site:* www.ozco.gov.au
*Key Personnel*
Administrator: Maggie Joel *E-mail:* m.joel@ozco.gov.au
Open to Australian writers over the age of 65 who must be nominated by other people. They must have produced a critically acclaimed body of work over a long creative life. Nominators must give evidence that the maximum annual income of the nominated writer is less than $40,000.
Award: Up to $40,000
Closing Date: Nomination May 15
Presented: Nov

## FAW Alan Marshall Short Story Award
Fellowship of Australian Writers (Vic) Inc
PO Box 8411, Armadale, Victoria 3143
*Tel:* (03) 9528 7088 *Fax:* (03) 9528 7088
*Web Site:* www.writers.asn.au
*Key Personnel*
Awards Coordinator: Clare Mendes
Award to a young writer (10-14 years of age). One copy of each story is required. No word limit.
Other Sponsor(s): Penguin Books Australia
Award: 150 AUD & 50 AUD
Closing Date: Nov 30

## FAW Anne Elder Poetry Award
Fellowship of Australian Writers (Vic) Inc
PO Box 8411, Armadale, Victoria 3143
*Tel:* (03) 9528 7088 *Fax:* (03) 9528 7088
*Web Site:* www.writers.asn.au
*Key Personnel*
Awards Coordinator: Clare Mendes
Awarded to a first book of poetry. An award is possible where up to four poets contribute to a book, providing it is the first published book-length collection of poetry by the authors concerned. Book must be at least 20 pages. Self-published works are eligible. Publishers & authors can also submit entries. Two copies of each book required & will not be returned. Open to Australia residents only.
Award: 1,000 AUD
Closing Date: Nov 30

## FAW C J Dennis Poetry Award
Fellowship of Australian Writers (Vic) Inc
PO Box 8411, Armadale, Victoria 3143
*Tel:* (03) 9528 7088 *Fax:* (03) 9528 7088
*Web Site:* www.writers.asn.au
*Key Personnel*
Awards Coordinator: Clare Mendes
Award to a young writer (10-14 years of age). Only one copy of poem required. Open to Australia residents only.
Award: 125 AUD & 75 AUD
Closing Date: Nov 30

## FAW Christina Stead Award
Fellowship of Australian Writers (Vic) Inc
PO Box 8411, Armadale, Victoria 3143
*Tel:* (03) 9528 7088 *Fax:* (03) 9528 7088
*Web Site:* www.writers.asn.au
*Key Personnel*
Awards Coordinator: Clare Mendes
For an autobiography, biography or memoir first published after Nov 18, 2001. Books published overseas are ineligible. Two copies of the book required & they will not be returned.
Other Sponsor(s): Merchant of Fairness Bookshop
Award: 500 AUD
Closing Date: Nov 30

## FAW Colin Thiele Poetry Award
Fellowship of Australian Writers (Vic) Inc
PO Box 8411, Armadale, Victoria 3143
*Tel:* (03) 9528 7088 *Fax:* (03) 9528 7088
*Web Site:* www.writers.asn.au
*Key Personnel*
Awards Coordinator: Clare Mendes
Award to a young writer (15-20 years of age). One copy of each poem is required. No word limit.
Other Sponsor(s): Michael Dugan
Award: 200 AUD & 100 AUD
Closing Date: Nov 30

## FAW Jennifer Burbidge Short Story Award
Fellowship of Australian Writers (Vic) Inc
PO Box 8411, Armadale, Victoria 3143
*Tel:* (03) 9528 7088 *Fax:* (03) 9528 7088
*Web Site:* www.writers.asn.au
*Key Personnel*
Awards Coordinator: Clare Mendes
Awarded in honour of Jenny Burbidge for a short story, up to 3,000 words, that deals with any aspect of the lives of those who suffer some form of physical or mental disability &/or its impact on their families in the Australian situation. One copy of each story is required. More than one entry may be submitted.
Other Sponsor(s): Mary Burbidge
Award: 250 AUD
Closing Date: Nov 30

## FAW Jim Hamilton Award
Fellowship of Australian Writers (Vic) Inc
PO Box 8411, Armadale, Victoria 3143
*Tel:* (03) 9528 7088 *Fax:* (03) 9528 7088
*Web Site:* www.writers.asn.au
*Key Personnel*
Awards Coordinator: Clare Mendes
Award honours the contribution Jim Hamilton OAM & his family have made to Australian writers & writing. 1st & 2nd prize will be awarded for a previously unpublished novel or a book-length collection (not less than 30,000 words) of short stories. The manuscript should be aimed at teenage or adult readers.
Other Sponsor(s): Eltham High School; Clare Mendes
Award: 1st prize 1,000 AUD; 2nd prize 500 AUD
Closing Date: Nov 30

## FAW John Morrison Short Story Award
Fellowship of Australian Writers (Vic) Inc

PO Box 8411, Armadale, Victoria 3143
*Tel:* (03) 9528 7088 *Fax:* (03) 9528 7088
*Web Site:* www.writers.asn.au
*Key Personnel*
Awards Coordinator: Clare Mendes
Award to a young writer (15-20 years of age).
    One copy of each story is required. Limit of
    3,000 words per entry.
Other Sponsor(s): Paul Jennings
Award: 1st prize 200 AUD; 2nd prize 100 AUD
Closing Date: Nov 30


**FAW John Shaw Neilson Poetry Award**
Fellowship of Australian Writers (Vic) Inc
PO Box 8411, Armadale, Victoria 3143
*Tel:* (03) 9528 7088 *Fax:* (03) 9528 7088
*Web Site:* www.writers.asn.au
*Key Personnel*
Awards Coordinator: Clare Mendes
For a poem of between 14 & 60 lines (inclusive).
    A suite of poems may be entered as one entry
    provided the individual parts of the suite are
    linked thematically & the total length is not
    more than 60 lines. Thematically separate po-
    ems must be submitted as separate entries. No
    limit to the number of entries.
Other Sponsor(s): Collected Works Bookshop
Award: 1st prize 500 AUD; others may be highly
    commended or commended
Closing Date: Nov 30


**FAW Mary Grant Bruce Story Award for
    Children's Literature**
Fellowship of Australian Writers (Vic) Inc
PO Box 8411, Armadale, Victoria 3143
*Tel:* (03) 9528 7088 *Fax:* (03) 9528 7088
*Web Site:* www.writers.asn.au
*Key Personnel*
Awards Coordinator: Clare Mendes
Award to recognize & honor the contribution by
    Mary Grant Bruce to children's literature &
    to encourage the writing of quality children's
    short stories. The trust is administered by
    Wellington Shire Council. The story should be
    aimed at young readers aged 10-15 years. En-
    tries may be no longer than 5000 words. Two
    copies of the story are required. More than one
    entry may be submitted. 600 AUD award to
    winner of open section. 2nd prize 300 AUD.
    Others may be commended. Writers living in
    the Gippsland area, as described by Municipal
    boundaries, are also eligible for separate 200
    AUD award. Open to Australia residents only.
Closing Date: Nov 30


**FAW Mavis Thorpe Clark Award**
Fellowship of Australian Writers (Vic) Inc
PO Box 8411, Armadale, Victoria 3143
*Tel:* (03) 9528 7088 *Fax:* (03) 9528 7088
*Web Site:* www.writers.asn.au
*Key Personnel*
Awards Coordinator: Clare Mendes
Awarded to postprimary students. Part 1 is for an
    individual submission & Part 2 is for a group
    entry. With the exception of school newspapers,
    all other kinds of creative writing are eligible.
    At least 10 items required, but volume is not
    of great importance. Individual submissions are
    restricted to one per student, but schools may
    submit more than one group entry. All entrants
    must be attending the same postprimary school
    in Australia & the work original & written in
    the current calendar year. Presentation, layout
    & design are not key criteria, but entries should
    be securely bound in some way. Only one copy
    of each entry required. Open to Australia resi-
    dents only.
Award: Individual 350 AUD & framed certificate;
    Group 200 AUD & framed certificate
Closing Date: Nov 30


**The Festival Awards for Literature**
Arts South Australia
West's Coffee Palace, 110 Hindley Street, Ade-
    laide, SA
Mailing Address: GPO Box 2308, Adelaide, SA
    5001
*Tel:* (08) 8463 5444 *Fax:* (08) 8463 5420
*E-mail:* artssa@saugov.sa.gov.au
*Web Site:* www.arts.sa.gov.au
*Key Personnel*
Project Manager: Gail Kovatseff
The awards are offered biennially by the South
    Australian Government & announced during
    Writers' Week of the Adelaide Festival of Arts.
    The seven awards offered are: (1) The National
    Fiction Award for a published novel or a col-
    lection of short stories (15,000 AUD); (2) The
    John Bray Award for Poetry for a published
    collection of poetry (15,000 AUD); (3) The
    National Children's Literature Award for a
    published children's book, fiction or nonfic-
    tion (15,000 AUD); (4) The National Nonfic-
    tion Award for a published work of nonfic-
    tion (16,000 AUD); (5) The Jill Blewett Play-
    wright's Award for a play script performed
    by a professional theatre company or a pro-
    fessional production unit (10,000 AUD); (6)
    Carclew Fellowship, a fellowship of up to 6
    months at Carclew, open to writers resident
    in South Australia (15,000 AUD); (7) South
    Australian Premier's Literary Award for the
    most outstanding published work submitted to
    the Festival for Literature (extra 10,000 AUD
    added to winner's 15,000 AUD category prize).
    Authors of published works must be citizens or
    residents of Australia.
Closing Date: Oct 31, 2005


**The Miles Franklin Literary Award**
Trust
35 Clarence St, Sydney, NSW 2001
*Tel:* (01) 300 132 075
*E-mail:* services@trust.com.au
*Web Site:* www.permanentgroup.com.au
*Key Personnel*
Awards Administrator: Petrea Salter
Established: 1954
Australia's most prestigious literary award. An-
    nual award to the novel or play which is the
    best for its year & which represents Australia's
    life in any of its phases.
Award: 28,000 AUD
Closing Date: Dec 15
Presented: State Library of NSW, May/June


**The Mary Gilmore Award**
Association for the Study of Australian Literature
School of Literary & Communications Studies,
    Deakin University (Burwood Campus), Bur-
    wood, Victoria 3125
*Tel:* (03) 9244 3960 *Fax:* (03) 9481 6717
*Web Site:* www.asc.uq.edu.au/asal
*Key Personnel*
President: Lyn McCredden *E-mail:* lynmcr@
    deakin.edu.au
Established: 1985
Awarded annually for the best first book of poetry
    published in the preceding two calendar years.


**Grants for Writers (New Work & Fellowships)**
Australia Council Literature Board
372 Elizabeth St, Surry Hills, NSW 2010
Mailing Address: PO Box 788, Strawberry Hills,
    NSW 2012
*Tel:* (02) 9215 9000 *Fax:* (02) 9215 9111
*E-mail:* mail@ozco.gov.au
*Web Site:* www.ozco.gov.au
*Key Personnel*
Administrator: Maggie Joel *E-mail:* m.joel@ozco.
    gov.au
New Work & Fellowship categories offer grants
    ranging from 5,000 AUD to 80,000 AUD to

Australian writers. Projects are accepted in the
    following areas: fiction, literary nonfiction, po-
    etry, children's literature, writing for stage or
    radio. Minimum publication/performance re-
    quirements apply. One closing date per year.
Award: 40,000 AUD per year for 2 years
Closing Date: May 15
Presented: Nov


**Greater Dandenong Writing Awards**
City of Greater Dandenong
397-405 Springvale Rd, Springvale, Victoria 3171
Mailing Address: PO Box 200, Dandenong, Vic-
    toria 3175
*Tel:* (03) 9239 5100 *Fax:* (03) 9329 5196
*E-mail:* council@cgd.vic.gov.au
*Web Site:* www.greaterdandenong.com
*Key Personnel*
Project Officer: Sarah Portanier *Tel:* (03) 9239-
    5141
Established: 1979
National competition with categories for short
    stories & poetry.
Award: Up to 6,000 AUD in cash prizes & pub-
    lish winning writers in an anthology
Closing Date: April 30 annually


**Grenfell Henry Lawson Festival of Arts
    Awards**
Henry Lawson Festival of the Arts
Main St, Grenfell, NSW 2810
Mailing Address: PO Box 125, Grenfell, NSW
    2810
*Tel:* (063) 431779 *Fax:* (063) 431548
*E-mail:* grenfelltourism@tpg.com.au
*Web Site:* www.henrylawsonfestival.asn.au
*Telex:* 437156
*Key Personnel*
President: Glenice Clarke *Tel:* (02) 6343 1326
    *Fax:* (02) 6343 1421
Promotions Officer: Fiona Last *Tel:* (063) 431403
    *Fax:* (063) 431421
Coordinator: Marion Knapp *E-mail:* knappdm@
    tpg.com.au
Awards are made for short story up to 5000
    words, verse, art & the words & music of an
    Australian popular song; also a bush ballad.
Award: Cash & engraved bronze statuette created
    by Sydney sculptor Alan Ingham
Closing Date: March
Presented: Annually in June


**Lyndall Hadow/Donald Stuart Short Story
    Award**
Western Australia Fellowship of Australian Writ-
    ers
Tom Collins House, 88 Wood St, Swanbourne,
    WA 6010
*Tel:* (08) 9384 4771 *Fax:* (08) 9384 4854
*E-mail:* fawwa@iinet.net.au
*Web Site:* members.iinet.net.au/~fawwa
*Key Personnel*
President: Trisha Kotai-Ewers
Executive Officer: Alethea Sheehan
Award for a short story not exceeding 3,000
    words. Alternates (even years) with Donald
    Stuart Short Story Award (odd years).
Award: 1st prize 400 AUD; 2nd prize 100 AUD;
    Highly Commended 50 AUD
Closing Date: June 15


**The Grace Leven Prize for Poetry**
Perpetual Trustee Co Ltd
39 Hunter St, Sydney, NSW 2000
*Tel:* (02) 9229 3951 *Toll Free Tel:* 800 501 227
    *Fax:* (02) 9229 3957
*E-mail:* foundations@perpetual.com.au; info@
    perpetual.com.au; giftfund@perpetual.com.au
*Web Site:* www.perpetual.com.au
*Key Personnel*
Chairman: Charles Curran

Instituted under the will of William Bayledridge, the Australian poet, who died in 1942. This prize is offered annually for the best volume of poetry published during the twelve months immediately preceding the year in which the award is made. Competitors must be either Australian born, & writing as Australians, or they must be naturalized in Australia & have lived in that country for at least ten years. The volume chosen may have been published in any country, but copies of it must be freely obtainable in Australia.
Award: 400 AUD

**The Walter McRae Russell Award**
Association for the Study of Australian Literature
School of English, Art History, Film & Media Studies, John Woolley Bldg A20, University of Sydney, Sydney 2006
*Tel:* (02) 9351 8068 *Fax:* (02) 9351 2434
*Web Site:* www.asc.uq.edu.au/asal
*Key Personnel*
Chairman: Ian Henderson *E-mail:* ian. henderson@english.usyd.edu.au
President: Lyn McCredden *E-mail:* lynmcr@ deakin.edu.au
Vice President: Peter Kirpatrick *Tel:* (02) 4736 0112 *E-mail:* p.kirpatrick@uws.edu.au
Treasurer: Simon Ryan
Secretary: Paul Genoni *Tel:* (08) 9266 7526 *E-mail:* p.genoni@curtin.edu.au
Established: 1983
Awarded annually for an outstanding work of literary scholarship by a young or unestablished author on an Australian subject published during the previous calendar year.
Award: 1,000 AUD

**Malvern Newsheet Award**
Fellowship of Australian Writers (Vic) Inc
PO Box 8411, Armadale, Victoria 3143
*Tel:* (03) 9528 7088 *Fax:* (03) 9528 7088
*Web Site:* www.writers.asn.au
*Key Personnel*
Awards Coordinator: Clare Mendes
For a book of short stories &/or poems authored by a Writers' Group. All contributors must be members of the group. Maximum length of book is 30,000 words. Individual contributions to the anthology may not exceed 3,000 words. Each group may only submit one entry & one copy is required. Entries will not be returned.
Other Sponsor(s): Malvern Newsheet; Victorian Community Writers
Award: 1st prize 500 AUD; 2nd prize 200 AUD
Closing Date: Nov 30

**Melbourne University Press Award**
Fellowship of Australian Writers (Vic) Inc
PO Box 8411, Armadale, Victoria 3143
*Tel:* (03) 9528 7088 *Fax:* (03) 9528 7088
*Web Site:* www.writers.asn.au
*Key Personnel*
Awards Coordinator: Clare Mendes
For a nonfiction work of sustained quality & distinction with an Australian theme first published after Nov 18, 2001. Books previously published overseas are ineligible. Two copies of the book are required & they will not be returned. Judges are independent of Melbourne University Press & books published by MUP are eligible.
Other Sponsor(s): Melbourne University Press
Award: 1,000 AUD
Closing Date: Nov 30

**Metcalfe Medallion**
Australian Library & Information Association (ALIA)
ALIA House, 9-11 Napier Close, Deakin, ACT 2600

Mailing Address: PO Box 6335, Kingston, ACT 2604
*Tel:* (02) 6215 8222 *Fax:* (02) 6282 2249
*E-mail:* enquiry@alia.org.au
*Web Site:* www.alia.org.au
*Key Personnel*
Committee Chair: Christine Mackenzie
Recognizes high achievement by a personal financial member in their first five years of practice in libraries & information services. Peer nominations only.
Closing Date: Nominations - Aug 1

**The Kathleen Mitchell Award**
Trust
35 Clarence St, Sydney, NSW 2001
*Tel:* (01) 300 132 075
*E-mail:* services@trust.com.au
*Web Site:* www.permanentgroup.com.au
*Key Personnel*
Awards Administrator: Petrea Salter
Established: 1996
Biannual award for published authors under the age of 30 in the two calendar years preceding the award.
Award: 5,000 AUD

**Angelo B Natoli Short Story Award**
Fellowship of Australian Writers (Vic) Inc
PO Box 8411, Armadale, Victoria 3143
*Tel:* (03) 9528 7088 *Fax:* (03) 9528 7088
*Web Site:* www.writers.asn.au
*Key Personnel*
Awards Coordinator: Clare Mendes
In honour of the late Angelo B Natoli, who for many years served as the Honorary Solicitor to Fellowship of Australian Writers (Vic) Inc. Awarded for a short story, open theme, to a maximum of 3,000 words. Other entries may be highly commended or commended. One copy of each story is required. More than one story may be submitted.
Award: 600 AUD
Closing Date: Nov 30

**New South Wales Premier's Literary Awards**
New South Wales Ministry for the Arts
St James Centre, Level 9, 111 Elizabeth St, Sydney, NSW 2000
Mailing Address: PO Box A226, Sydney South, NSW 1235
*Tel:* (02) 9228 5533 *Toll Free Tel:* 800 358 594 *Fax:* (02) 9228 4722
*E-mail:* ministry@arts.nsw.gov.au
*Web Site:* www.arts.nsw.gov.au
*Key Personnel*
Dir General: Roger B Wilkins
Established: 1979
Presented by the New South Wales Government to honor distinguished achievement by Australian writers. The Ethnic Affairs Commission Award of 10,000 AUD is offered for a work which reflects an aspect of Australia's multicultural society. In addition, the committee judging the book awards may propose that a special award, (usually 5,000 AUD), with or without prize money, be made for a work not readily covered by the existing categories, or in recognition of a writer's achievements generally. Winners in all categories also receive commemorative medallions.
Award: Fiction 20,000 AUD; Nonfiction 20,000 AUD; Poetry 15,000 AUD; A Children's Book 15,000 AUD; Play, film, television or radio script 15,000 AUD; Literary Critism 15,000 AUD; Book of the year an additional 2,000 AUD; Ethnic Affairs Commission Award about Australia's multiculture 10,000 AUD

**New South Wales Writer's Fellowship**
New South Wales Ministry for the Arts

St James Centre, Level 9, 111 Elizabeth St, Sydney, NSW 2000
Mailing Address: PO Box A226, Sydney South, NSW 1235
*Tel:* (02) 9228 5533 *Toll Free Tel:* 800 358 594 *Fax:* (02) 9228 4722
*E-mail:* ministry@arts.nsw.gov.au
*Web Site:* www.arts.nsw.gov.au
*Key Personnel*
Dir General: Roger B Wilkins
Awarded by the New South Wales Government in conjunction with the New South Wales Premier's Literary Awards, to assist the writing of new literary work by a writer living in New South Wales. Applicants must demonstrate their project is likely to result in work of significant quality & be of lasting benefit to the applicant's experience & development as a writer or the advancement of Australian literature in general. Applicants are required to have been resident three years prior to & at the time of application.
Award: 20,000 AUD
Closing Date: June

**Poetry Competition**
Society of Women Writers NSW Inc
GPO Box 1388, Sydney, NSW 2001
*Web Site:* www.womenwritersnsw.org/awards.html
*Key Personnel*
President: Valerie Pybus
Annual competition which, in alternate years, is closed to members only or open to all Australian citizens. In years open to all, it is called the National Poetry Competition. Members only competitions in even-numbered years; National competitions in odd-numbered years.

**Colin Roderick Award**
Foundation for Australian Literary Studies
School of Humanities, James Cook University, Townsville, Qld 4811
*Tel:* (07) 4781 4451; (07) 4781 4426 *Fax:* (07) 4781 5655
*Web Site:* www.faess.jcu.edu.au/soh
*Key Personnel*
Executive Dean: Prof Janet Greeley
Established: 1967
Award to the author of the best book in any field of writing dealing with any aspect of Australian life.
Award: 10,000 AUD & the H T Priestley Medal from the Townsville Foundation for Australian Literary Studies at the James Cook University
Closing Date: Feb 29
Presented: Townsville, Australia, Sept 13

**Society of Women Writers Biennial Book Awards**
Society of Women Writers NSW Inc
GPO Box 1388, Sydney, NSW 2001
*Web Site:* www.womenwritersnsw.org/awards.html
*Key Personnel*
President: Valerie Pybus
Established: 1925
Every second year, members are invited to submit books published over the previous two years. Separate awards are given for fiction, nonfiction, poetry & children's books. Two Children's Book Awards may be given - one for a book for younger readers & one for an adolescent/young adult book. Next award to be given in 2005.

**Victorian Premier's Literary Awards**
State Library of Victoria
328 Swanston St, Melbourne, Victoria 3000
*Tel:* (03) 8664 7000 *Fax:* (03) 9639 7006
*E-mail:* pla@slv.vic.gov.au
*Web Site:* www.statelibrary.vic.gov.au/pla
Established: 1985

Founded in 1985 on the occasion of the centenary of the births of Vance & Nettie Palmer. Open to Australian writers with works first published or performed between May 1 & April 30. The annual awards are (1) Vance Palmer Prize for a work of fiction (30,000 AUD), (2) Nettie Palmer Prize for a work of nonfiction (30,000 AUD), (3) Louis Esson Prize for Drama (15,000 AUD), (4) C J Dennis Prize for Poetry (15,000 AUD), (5) Kraft Foods Prize for Young Adult Fiction (12,000 AUD), (6) Dinny O'Hearn/SBS Book Prize for Literary Translation (15,000 AUD) & (7) Alfred Deakin Prize for an Essay Advancing Public Debate (15,000 AUD). The applications are to be given to the project officer.
Closing Date: April 30
Presented: Mid-Oct

## Patrick White Literary Award
Perpetual Trustee Co Ltd
39 Hunter St, Sydney, NSW 2000
*Tel:* (02) 9229 3951 *Toll Free Tel:* 800 501 227 *Fax:* (02) 9229 3957
*E-mail:* foundations@perpetual.com.au; info@perpetual.com.au; giftfund@perpetual.com.au
*Web Site:* www.perpetual.com.au
*Key Personnel*
Charitable Trusts Manager: Susan Ahmelman
Patrick White applied his Nobel Prize money to establish a trust to make an annual award to an Australian writer who has not been adequately recognized. Submissions are not required.

## Young Australians Best Book Award
Young Australians Best Book Award Council
PO Box 238, Kew, Victoria 3101
*Tel:* (03) 98897749 *Fax:* (03) 9889 3665
*E-mail:* yabbabooks@yahoo.com
*Web Site:* www.vicnet.net.au/~yabba
*Key Personnel*
President: Graham Davey *E-mail:* daveyg@netspace.net.au
Treasurer: Richard Bennett
Established: 1986
Citation from Children.
Awarded annually.
Closing Date: Student nominations are sought in Term 1 (Feb-April)
Presented: Awards Ceremony, November

# Austria

## Austrian Award of Merit for Children's Literature
Bundeskanzleramt-Kunstsektion
Bundeskanzleramt, Ballhausplatz 2, 1014 Vienna
*Tel:* (01) 531-15-0 *Fax:* (01) 531-15-0
*Web Site:* www.art.austria.gv.at
*Key Personnel*
Contact: Franz Morak *E-mail:* franz.morak@bka.gv.at
Established: 1980
Awarded biennially to an author, illustrator & translator in appreciation of his life's work.
Award: 11,000 EUR

## Austrian Children's & Juvenile Book Awards
Bundeskanzleramt-Kunstsektion
Bundeskanzleramt, Ballhausplatz 2, 1014 Vienna
*Tel:* (01) 531-15-0 *Fax:* (01) 531-15-0
*Web Site:* www.art.austria.gv.at
*Key Personnel*
Contact: Franz Morak *E-mail:* franz.morak@bka.gv.at
Established: 1955
Seven categories: four for books for children & young people, an "Austrian Children's &

Young People's Nonfiction Book Prize," "Austrian Children's & Young People's Translation Prize" & an "Austrian Children's & Young People's Prize" for book illustration.
Award: 18,200 EUR to be shared by the prize winners. Prizewinning books are purchased by the Ministry of Education Arts in the amount of 10,200 EUR

## Austrian National Award for Poetry for Children
Bundeskanzleramt-Kunstsektion
Bundeskanzleramt, Ballhausplatz 2, 1014 Vienna
*Tel:* (01) 531-15-0 *Fax:* (01) 531-15-0
*Web Site:* www.art.austria.gv.at
*Key Personnel*
Contact: Franz Morak *E-mail:* franz.morak@bka.gv.at
Established: 1993
For the complete works of an author of poetry for children in German language.
Award: 7,300 EUR biennially

## Austrian Promotional Award for Children's Literature
Bundeskanzleramt-Kunstsektion
Bundeskanzleramt, Ballhausplatz 2, 1014 Vienna
*Tel:* (01) 531-15-0 *Fax:* (01) 531-15-0
*Web Site:* www.art.austria.gv.at
*Key Personnel*
Contact: Franz Morak *E-mail:* franz.morak@bka.gv.at
Established: 1996
Biennial award to an author, illustrator or translator in appreciation of his outstanding contributions to children's literature.
Award: 7,300 EUR

## ☆Austrian State Prize for European Literature
Bundeskanzleramt-Kunstsektion
Bundeskanzleramt, Ballhausplatz 2, 1014 Vienna
*Tel:* (01) 531-15-0 *Fax:* (01) 531-15-0
*Web Site:* www.art.austria.gv.at
*Key Personnel*
Contact: Franz Morak *E-mail:* franz.morak@bka.gv.at
Established: 1965
Presented by the Austrian Minister of Education to a European author (with the exception of an Austrian national) whose work has also been acclaimed outside his own country; this must be demonstrated by translation. No applications; The prize is awarded on the recommendation of an independent jury.
Award: 21,802 EUR & testimonial awarded annually

## Ehrenpreis des oesterreichischen Buchhandels
The Austrian Booksellers & Publishers Association
Gruenangergasse 4, 1010 Vienna
*Tel:* (01) 512 15 35 *Fax:* (01) 512 84 82
*E-mail:* hvb@buecher.at
*Web Site:* www.buecher.at

## Foerderungspreis fuer Literatur (Recognition Prize for Literature)
Bundeskanzleramt-Kunstsektion
Bundeskanzleramt, Ballhausplatz 2, 1014 Vienna
*Tel:* (01) 531-15-0 *Fax:* (01) 531-15-0
*Web Site:* www.art.austria.gv.at
*Key Personnel*
Contact: Franz Morak *E-mail:* franz.morak@bka.gv.at
Awarded by jury. No applications.
Award: 7,267 EUR

## Great Austrian State Prize
Bundeskanzleramt-Kunstsektion
Bundeskanzleramt, Ballhausplatz 2, 1014 Vienna
*Tel:* (01) 531-15-0 *Fax:* (01) 531-15-0

*Web Site:* www.art.austria.gv.at
*Key Personnel*
Contact: Franz Morak *E-mail:* franz.morak@bka.gv.at
Established: 1965
This prize alternates between literature, music & the fine arts. Awarded by Oesterreichischer Kunstsenat. No applications.
Award: 21,802 EUR for life's work

## Grosse Literaturstipendien des Landes Tirol
Amt der Tiroler Landesregierung
Eduard-Wallnofer-, Platz 3, 6020 Innsbruck
*Tel:* (0512) 508-2880 *Fax:* (0512) 508 2245
*E-mail:* j.skamen@tirol.gv.at
*Web Site:* www.tirol.gv.at
*Key Personnel*
Dir: Dr Josef Liener

## Michael Haberlandt Medal
Verein fur Volkskunde
Laudongasse 15-19, 1080 Vienna
*Tel:* (01) 406 89 05 *Fax:* (01) 408 53 42
*E-mail:* office@volkskundemuseum.at
*Web Site:* www.volkskundemuseum.at

## Oesterreichischer Staatspreis fuer literarische Ubersetzungen (Austrian State Prize for Literary Translators)
Bundeskanzleramt-Kunstsektion
Bundeskanzleramt, Ballhausplatz 2, 1014 Vienna
*Tel:* (01) 531-15-0 *Fax:* (01) 531-15-0
*Web Site:* www.art.austria.gv.at
*Key Personnel*
Contact: Franz Morak *E-mail:* franz.morak@bka.gv.at
Award: 7,267 EUR

## Rauriser Encouragement Award
Salzburger Landesregierung
Franziskanergasse 5a, Postafch 527, Salzburg
*Tel:* (0662) 8042-2035; (0662) 8042-2100 *Fax:* (0662) 8042-2919
*E-mail:* kultur@salzburg.gv.at
*Web Site:* www.salzburg.gv.at/kultur
*Key Personnel*
Manager: Dr Monika Kalista
Annual literary award sponsored by the Salzburg provincial government & the village of Rauris. Awarded for a specific topic, as decided by jury.
Award: 3,634 EUR

## Rauriser Literature Prize
Salzburger Landesregierung
Franziskanergasse 5a, Postafch 527, Salzburg
*Tel:* (0662) 8042-2035; (0662) 8042-2100 *Fax:* (0662) 8042-2919
*E-mail:* kultur@salzburg.gv.at
*Web Site:* www.salzburg.gv.at/kultur
*Key Personnel*
Manager: Dr Monika Kalista
For an outstanding first publication in prose, as decided by jury.
Other Sponsor(s): Salzburg Provincial Government
Award: 7,270 EUR annually

## State Scholarship for Literature
Bundeskanzleramt-Kunstsektion
Bundeskanzleramt, Ballhausplatz 2, 1014 Vienna
*Tel:* (01) 531-15-0 *Fax:* (01) 531-15-0
*Web Site:* www.art.austria.gv.at
*Key Personnel*
Contact: Franz Morak *E-mail:* franz.morak@bka.gv.at
Twenty annual awards by jury. Submissions accepted.
Award: Twenty annual awards of 1,090 EUR each month for one year

**Otto Stoessl-Preis**
Otto Stoessl-Stiftung
Seidengasse 13, 1070 Vienna
*Tel:* 526 2044-0 *Fax:* 526 2044-30
*E-mail:* info@literaturhaus.at
*Web Site:* www.literaturhaus.at
*Key Personnel*
Contact: Dr Christoph Binder *E-mail:* christoph.
    binder@stmk.gv.at
Established: 1981
Literature prize for unpublished German stories.
Award: 4,000 EUR
Closing Date: End of every 2nd year (2005,
    2007...)
Presented: Vienna, End of every second year
    (2006, 2008...)

**Georg Trakl Prize**
Salzburger Landesregierung
Franziskanergasse 5a, Postafch 527, Salzburg
*Tel:* (0662) 8042-2035; (0662) 8042-2100
    *Fax:* (0662) 8042-2919
*E-mail:* kultur@salzburg.gv.at
*Web Site:* www.salzburg.gv.at/kultur
*Key Personnel*
Manager: Dr Monika Kalista
An irregular award to a writer of lyric poetry for
    his/her complete poetical works.
Award: 7,270 EUR

**Upper Austria Culture Prize for Literature**
Upper Austria State Government
Klosterstrabe 7, 4021 Linz
*Tel:* (0732) 77 20-114 00 *Fax:* (0732) 77 20-115
    88
*E-mail:* pr.post@ooe.gv.at
*Web Site:* www.ooe.gv.at
*Key Personnel*
Leader: Gerhard Hasenohrl

**City of Vienna Encouragement Prize**
City of Vienna Magistrate
Kulturabteilung Magistratsabteilung 7, 8,
    Friedrich-Schmidt-Platz 5, Mezzanin 1-3 Stock,
    1082 Vienna
*Tel:* (01) 4000-84766 *Fax:* (01) 4000-99-8007
    (national); (01) 4000-7216 (international)
*E-mail:* post@m07.magwien.gv.at
*Web Site:* www.magwien.gv.at/ma07/index.htm
Established: 1951
Awarded annually to talented young writers (un-
    der 40 years of age) whose previous work is
    worthy of recognition & whose development
    shows promise. Candidates must be Austrian
    citizens who have either lived for three years in
    Vienna or who work in the city.
Award: 2,907 EUR

**City of Vienna Prize**
City of Vienna Magistrate
Kulturabteilung Magistratsabteilung 7, 8,
    Friedrich-Schmidt-Platz 5, Mezzanin 1-3 Stock,
    1082 Vienna
*Tel:* (01) 4000-84766 *Fax:* (01) 4000-7216 (inter-
    national); (01) 4000-99-8007 (national)
*E-mail:* post@m07.magwien.gv.at
*Web Site:* www.magwien.gv.at/ma07/index.htm
Established: 1947
Annual award to an author for total literary out-
    put.
Award: 7,267 EUR

**City of Vienna Prize for Books for Children &
Young People**
City of Vienna Magistrate
Kulturabteilung Magistratsabteilung 7, 8,
    Friedrich-Schmidt-Platz 5, Mezzanin 1-3 Stock,
    1082 Vienna
*Tel:* (01) 4000-84766 *Fax:* (01) 4000-7216 (inter-
    national); (01) 4000-99-8007 (national)
*E-mail:* post@m07.magwien.gv.at

*Web Site:* www.magwien.gv.at/ma07/index.htm
Awarded annually by the City of Vienna for dis-
    tinguished books for children & young people,
    including illustration.

**Anton Wildgans Prize of Austrian Industry**
Vereinigung der Oesterreichischen Industrie
Schwarzenbergplatz 4, 1031 Vienna
*Tel:* (01) 711 35-0 *Fax:* (01) 711 35-2910
*E-mail:* iv.office@iv-net.at
*Web Site:* www.iv-net.at
*Key Personnel*
Marketing & Communication: Ilse Steiner
    *E-mail:* i.steiner@iv-net.at
Awarded annually, at the beginning of the au-
    tumn, to an Austrian lyric poet, dramatist, nov-
    elist or essayist, young or middle aged. The
    author must be an Austrian citizen, writing in
    German, who lives either in Austria or abroad.
    Awarded by a committee. No applications.
Award: Maximum prize 7,500 EUR

**Writers Scholarship for Literature**
Bundeskanzleramt-Kunstsektion
Bundeskanzleramt, Ballhausplatz 2, 1014 Vienna
*Tel:* (01) 531-15-0 *Fax:* (01) 531-15-0
*Web Site:* www.art.austria.gv.at
*Key Personnel*
Contact: Franz Morak *E-mail:* franz.morak@bka.
    gv.at
Awarded by jury. Submissions accepted.
Award: 10 annual awards of 291 EUR each
    month for one year

**Wuerdigungspreis (Lower Austria Prize of
Honor)**
AMT der Niederosterreichischen
    Landesregierung-Kulturabteilung
Landhausplatz 1, Haus Franz-Schubert-Platz 3
    (NOE Landesbibliothek), 3109 St Poelten
*Tel:* (02742) 9005-13589 *Fax:* (02742) 9005-
    13610
*E-mail:* lad1euroinfo@noel.gv.at
*Web Site:* www.noe.gv.at

# Bangladesh

**Bangla Academy Literary Awards**
Bangla Academy
Language & Literary Section, Old High Court
    Rd, Dhaka 1000
*Tel:* (02) 861 9577
*Web Site:* www.banglarepublic.com *Cable:*
    ACADEMY, DHAKA
Two awards annually for an overall outstanding
    contribution to Bangla literature.
Award: 100,000 BDT

# Belgium

**Goblet d'Alviella Prize** (Prix Goblet d'Alviella)
Academie Royale de Belgique
Palais des Academies, One rue Ducale, 1000
    Brussels
*Tel:* (02) 550 22 20; (02) 550 22 00 *Fax:* (02)
    550 22 05
*E-mail:* arb@cfwb.be
*Web Site:* www.cfwb.be/arb
*Key Personnel*
Secretary: Leo Houziaux *Tel:* (02) 550 22 03
    *E-mail:* leo.houziaux@ulg.ac.be
Established: 1926

For the best work of a strictly scientific & ob-
    jective character relating to the history of reli-
    gions, published by a Belgian author. Awarded
    every five years.
Award: 1,500 EUR
Closing Date: Dec 31

**Lode Baekelmans Prize**
Koninklijke Academie voor Nederlandse Taal- en
    Letterkunde (Royal Academy of Dutch Lan-
    guage & Literature)
Koningstr 18, 9000 Ghent
*Tel:* (09) 265 93 40 *Fax:* (09) 265 93 49
*E-mail:* info@kantl.be
*Web Site:* www.kantl.be
*Key Personnel*
Librarian: Marijke De Wit *Tel:* (09) 265 93 43
    *E-mail:* mdewit@kantl.be
Established: 1940
For the best literary work in Dutch - novel, po-
    etry, play, radio play, essay, etc - dealing with
    the sea, sailors, navigation, the harbor, inland
    navigation or related topics. Recipients must be
    Belgian nationals. Awarded triennially.
Award: 1,860 EUR

**Internationale Eugene Baie Prijs** (International
    Eugene Baie Prize)
Province of Antwerp/Eugene Baie Foundation
Koningin Elisabethlei 22, 2018 Antwerp
*Tel:* (03) 2405011 *Fax:* (03) 2406470

**Karel Barbier Prize**
Koninklijke Academie voor Nederlandse Taal- en
    Letterkunde (Royal Academy of Dutch Lan-
    guage & Literature)
Koningstr 18, 9000 Ghent
*Tel:* (09) 265 93 40 *Fax:* (09) 265 93 49
*E-mail:* info@kantl.be
*Web Site:* www.kantl.be
*Key Personnel*
Librarian: Marijke De Wit *Tel:* (09) 265 93 43
    *E-mail:* mdewit@kantl.be
Established: 1927
For the best historical novel in Dutch, with a
    national-historical theme. Short stories & ro-
    manticized biographies also taken into consid-
    eration. Recipients must be Belgian nationals.
    Awarded biannually.
Award: 500 EUR

**August Beernaert Prize**
Koninklijke Academie voor Nederlandse Taal- en
    Letterkunde (Royal Academy of Dutch Lan-
    guage & Literature)
Koningstr 18, 9000 Ghent
*Tel:* (09) 265 93 40 *Fax:* (09) 265 93 49
*E-mail:* info@kantl.be
*Web Site:* www.kantl.be
*Key Personnel*
Librarian: Marijke De Wit *Tel:* (09) 265 93 43
    *E-mail:* mdewit@kantl.be
Established: 1912
For the best literary work in Dutch, irrespective
    of the genre, published or unpublished. Re-
    cipients must be Belgian nationals. Awarded
    biennially.
Award: 1,240 EUR

**Prix Auguste Beernaert** (Auguste Beernaert
    Prize)
Academie Royale de Langue et de Litterature
    Francaises (Royal Academy of French Lan-
    guage & Literature)
Palais des Academies, One rue Ducale, 1000
    Brussels
*Tel:* (02) 550 22 77 *Fax:* (02) 550 22 75
*E-mail:* alf@cfwb.be
*Web Site:* www.
    academielanguelitteraturefrancaises.be
*Key Personnel*
Permanent Secretary: Jacques De Decker
Established: 1941

Awarded every four years for the most outstanding work of a Belgian author written in French language. Awarded by a jury.
Award: 1,000 EUR

☆**Anton Bergmann Prize** (Prix Anton Bergmann)
Academie Royale de Belgique
Palais des Academies, One rue Ducale, 1000 Brussels
*Tel:* (02) 550 22 00; (02) 550 22 20 *Fax:* (02) 550 22 05
*E-mail:* arb@cfwb.be
*Web Site:* www.cfwb.be/arb
*Key Personnel*
Secretary: Leo Houziaux *Tel:* (02) 550 22 03
  *E-mail:* leo.houziaux@ulg.ac.be
Established: 1875
For the author of a historical account or monograph, written in Dutch & relating to a Flemish town or community in Belgium. Awarded every five years for a work appearing in print or (provisionally) in manuscript form, during the period. Foreign authors may also compete, provided work is in Dutch & is published in Belgium or the Netherlands.
Award: 1,250 EUR
Closing Date: Dec 31

**Prix Bouvier-Parvillez** (Bouvier-Parvillez Prize)
Academie Royale de Langue et de Litterature Francaises (Royal Academy of French Language & Literature)
Palais des Academies, One rue Ducale, 1000 Brussels
*Tel:* (02) 550 22 77 *Fax:* (02) 550 22 75
*E-mail:* alf@cfwb.be
*Web Site:* www.academielanguelitteraturefrancaises.be
*Key Personnel*
Permanent Secretary: Jacques De Decker
For the entire work of a Belgian author written in French. Awarded every four years.
Award: 850 EUR

**Prix Alix Charlier-Anciaux** (Alix Charlier-Anciaux Prize)
Academie Royale de Langue et de Litterature Francaises (Royal Academy of French Language & Literature)
Palais des Academies, One rue Ducale, 1000 Brussels
*Tel:* (02) 550 22 77 *Fax:* (02) 550 22 75
*E-mail:* alf@cfwb.be
*Web Site:* www.academielanguelitteraturefrancaises.be
*Key Personnel*
Permanent Secretary: Jacques De Decker
Awarded every 5 years to a Belgian author for the whole of their work in the French language.
Award: 1,000 EUR

**Constant de Horion Prize**
Association des Ecrivains Belges de Langue Francaise (AEBLF) (Association of the Belgian Writers of French Language)
Camille Lemonnier-Maison des Ecrivains, 150 Chaussee de Wavre, 1050 Brussels
*Tel:* (02) 512 29 68 *Fax:* (02) 512 29 68
*Web Site:* www.ecrivainsbelges.be
*Key Personnel*
President: France Bastia *E-mail:* france.bastia@skynet.be
Secretary General: Jean Lacroix
Established: 1977
Founded by Baron Jean Constant (the writer Constant de Horion), for recognition of the best essay on literary history or literary criticism by an established Belgian writer, or a literary aspect of French expressionism. Belgian writ-

ers over 40 years of age are eligible. Awarded biennially.
Award: 1,239 EUR

**Prix Henri Cornelus** (Henri Cornelus Prize)
Academie Royale de Langue et de Litterature Francaises (Royal Academy of French Language & Literature)
Palais des Academies, One rue Ducale, 1000 Brussels
*Tel:* (02) 550 22 77 *Fax:* (02) 550 22 75
*E-mail:* alf@cfwb.be
*Web Site:* www.academielanguelitteraturefrancaises.be
*Key Personnel*
Permanent Secretary: Jacques De Decker
Awarded triennially.
Award: 3,000 EUR

**Arthur H Cornette Prize**
Koninklijke Academie voor Nederlandse Taal- en Letterkunde (Royal Academy of Dutch Language & Literature)
Koningstr 18, 9000 Ghent
*Tel:* (09) 265 93 40 *Fax:* (09) 265 93 49
*E-mail:* info@kantl.be
*Web Site:* www.kantl.be
*Key Personnel*
Librarian: Marijke De Wit *Tel:* (09) 265 93 43
  *E-mail:* mdewit@kantl.be
Established: 1950
For the best literary essay, written in Dutch, published or unpublished. Recipients must be Belgian nationals. Awarded every 5 years.
Award: 1,500 EUR
Closing Date: Feb 1, 2006

☆**Prix Albert Counson** (Albert Counson Prize)
Academie Royale de Langue et de Litterature Francaises (Royal Academy of French Language & Literature)
Palais des Academies, One rue Ducale, 1000 Brussels
*Tel:* (02) 550 22 77 *Fax:* (02) 550 22 75
*E-mail:* alf@cfwb.be
*Web Site:* www.academielanguelitteraturefrancaises.be
*Key Personnel*
Permanent Secretary: Jacques De Decker
For a scholarly work on romance languages, in relation to or connected with Belgium. Monetary prize. Awarded every five years.
Award: 1,500 EUR

☆**Franz Cumont Prize** (Prix Franz Cumont)
Academie Royale de Belgique
Palais des Academies, One rue Ducale, 1000 Brussels
*Tel:* (02) 550 22 00; (02) 550 22 20 *Fax:* (02) 550 22 05
*E-mail:* arb@cfwb.be
*Web Site:* www.cfwb.be/arb
*Key Personnel*
Secretary: Leo Houziaux *Tel:* (02) 550 22 03
  *E-mail:* leo.houziaux@ulg.ac.be
Established: 1937
For a work by a Belgian or foreign author dealing with the history of religion or science in antiquity, ie in the Mediterranean area prior to the time of Mohammed. No application necessary. The prize cannot be divided, except where one or more authors have acted in collaboration. Awarded triennially.
Award: 2,500 EUR
Closing Date: Dec 31

**Prix Henri Davignon** (Henri Davignon Prize)
Academie Royale de Langue et de Litterature Francaises (Royal Academy of French Language & Literature)

Palais des Academies, One rue Ducale, 1000 Brussels
*Tel:* (02) 550 22 77 *Fax:* (02) 550 22 75
*E-mail:* alf@cfwb.be
*Web Site:* www.academielanguelitteraturefrancaises.be
*Key Personnel*
Permanent Secretary: Jacques De Decker
Awarded every 5 years to a work of religious inspiration.
Award: 850 EUR

**Nestor de Tiere Prize**
Koninklijke Academie voor Nederlandse Taal- en Letterkunde (Royal Academy of Dutch Language & Literature)
Koningstraat 18, 9000 Ghent
*Tel:* (09) 265 93 40 *Fax:* (09) 265 93 49
*E-mail:* info@kantl.be
*Web Site:* www.kantl.be
*Key Personnel*
Librarian: Marijke De Wit *Tel:* (09) 265 93 43
  *E-mail:* mdewit@kantl.be
Established: 1930
For the best play written in Dutch. Recipients must be Belgian nationals. Awarded biennially.
Award: 500 EUR

**Prix Felix Denayer** (Felix Denayer Prize)
Academie Royale de Langue et de Litterature Francaises (Royal Academy of French Language & Literature)
Palais des Academies, One rue Ducale, 1000 Brussels
*Tel:* (02) 550 22 77 *Fax:* (02) 550 22 75
*E-mail:* alf@cfwb.be
*Web Site:* www.academielanguelitteraturefrancaises.be
*Key Personnel*
Permanent Secretary: Jacques De Decker
For a single work or the entire literary work of a Belgian written in French. Awarded annually.
Award: 850 EUR

☆**Ernest Descailles Prize**
Academie Royale de Belgique
Palais des Academies, One rue Ducale, 1000 Brussels
*Tel:* (02) 550 22 00; (02) 550 22 20 *Fax:* (02) 550 22 05
*E-mail:* arb@cfwb.be
*Web Site:* www.cfwb.be/arb
*Key Personnel*
Secretary: Leo Houziaux *Tel:* (02) 550 22 03
  *E-mail:* leo.houziaux@ulg.ac.be
Established: 1907
Awarded every 5 years for a distinguished literary work written in French, preferably by a poet.
Award: 1,500 EUR
Closing Date: Dec 31

**Jules Duculot Prize** (Prix Jules Duculot)
Academie Royale de Belgique
Palais des Academies, One rue Ducale, 1000 Brussels
*Tel:* (02) 550 22 20; (02) 550 22 00 *Fax:* (02) 550 22 05
*E-mail:* arb@cfwb.be
*Web Site:* www.cfwb.be/arb
*Key Personnel*
Secretary: Leo Houziaux *Tel:* (02) 550 22 03
  *E-mail:* leo.houziaux@ulg.ac.be
Established: 1965
Awarded every 5 years for a work in print or manuscript form, written in French, dealing with the history of philosophy. Awarded only to Belgians, or to foreigners holding an academic grade granted by a Belgian university. Printed work must have been published in the 5 years prior to the end of the relevant period. The prize is awarded for what appears the most

deserving work, irrespective of whether it has been submitted for entry or not.
Award: 3,000 EUR
Closing Date: Dec 31

**Prix Robert Duterne** (Robert Duterne Prize)
Academie Royale de Langue et de Litterature Francaises (Royal Academy of French Language & Literature)
Palais des Academies, One rue Ducale, 1000 Brussels
*Tel:* (02) 550 22 77 *Fax:* (02) 550 22 75
*E-mail:* alf@cfwb.be
*Web Site:* www. academielanguelitteraturefrancaises.be
*Key Personnel*
Permanent Secretary: Jacques De Decker
Awarded every 4 years.
Award: 2,500 EUR

**Charles Duvivier Prize** (Prix Charles Duvivier)
Academie Royale de Belgique
Palais des Academies, One rue Ducale, 1000 Brussels
*Tel:* (02) 550 22 00; (02) 550 22 20 *Fax:* (02) 550 22 05
*E-mail:* arb@cfwb.be
*Web Site:* www.cfwb.be/arb
*Key Personnel*
Secretary: Leo Houziaux *Tel:* (02) 550 22 03
*E-mail:* leo.houziaux@ulg.ac.be
Established: 1905
Awarded triennially for the Belgian author of the best work on the history of Belgian or foreign law, or on the history of Belgian political, judicial or administrative institutions.
Award: 1,250 EUR
Closing Date: Dec 31

**Joris Eeckhout Prize**
Koninklijke Academie voor Nederlandse Taal- en Letterkunde (Royal Academy of Dutch Language & Literature)
Koningstr 18, 9000 Ghent
*Tel:* (09) 265 93 40 *Fax:* (09) 265 93 49
*E-mail:* info@kantl.be
*Web Site:* www.kantl.be
*Key Personnel*
Librarian: Marijke De Wit *Tel:* (09) 265 93 43
*E-mail:* mdewit@kantl.be
Established: 1937
For the best literary essay about an author, written in Dutch, at least 100 pages, published or unpublished. Recipients must be Belgian nationals. Awarded biennially.
Award: 500 EUR

**Leon Elaut Prize** (Leon Elaut Prijs)
Koninklijke Academie voor Nederlandse Taal- en Letterkunde (Royal Academy of Dutch Language & Literature)
Koningstr 18, 9000 Ghent
*Tel:* (09) 265 93 40 *Fax:* (09) 265 93 49
*E-mail:* info@kantl.be
*Web Site:* www.kantl.be
*Key Personnel*
Librarian: Marijke De Wit *Tel:* (09) 265 93 43
*E-mail:* mdewit@kantl.be
Established: 1981
For the best monograph, written in Dutch, about cultural history of Flanders, 1815-1940 in connection with the Flemish movement. Awarded biennially.
Award: 2,480 EUR

**Joseph Gantrelle Prize** (Prix Joseph Gantrelle)
Academie Royale de Belgique
Palais des Academies, One rue Ducale, 1000 Brussels
*Tel:* (02) 550 22 00; (02) 550 22 20 *Fax:* (02) 550 22 05

*E-mail:* arb@cfwb.be
*Web Site:* www.cfwb.be/arb
*Key Personnel*
Secretary: Leo Houziaux *Tel:* (02) 550 22 03
*E-mail:* leo.houziaux@ulg.ac.be
Established: 1890
Awarded biennially to Belgian authors for a work in classical philology.
Award: 1,500 EUR
Closing Date: Dec 31

**Prix Georges Garnir** (Georges Garnir Prize)
Academie Royale de Langue et de Litterature Francaises (Royal Academy of French Language & Literature)
Palais des Academies, One rue Ducale, 1000 Brussels
*Tel:* (02) 550 22 77 *Fax:* (02) 550 22 75
*E-mail:* alf@cfwb.be
*Web Site:* www. academielanguelitteraturefrancaises.be
*Key Personnel*
Permanent Secretary: Jacques De Decker
Awarded triennially.
Award: 850 EUR

**Prix Gaston et Mariette Heux** (Gaston et Mariette Heux Prize)
Academie Royale de Langue et de Litterature Francaises (Royal Academy of French Language & Literature)
Palais des Academies, One rue Ducale, 1000 Brussels
*Tel:* (02) 550 22 77 *Fax:* (02) 550 22 75
*E-mail:* alf@cfwb.be
*Web Site:* www. academielanguelitteraturefrancaises.be
*Key Personnel*
Permanent Secretary: Jacques De Decker
Awarded every 4 years.
Award: 1,800 EUR

**Guido Gezelle Prize**
Koninklijke Academie voor Nederlandse Taal- en Letterkunde (Royal Academy of Dutch Language & Literature)
Koningstr 18, 9000 Ghent
*Tel:* (09) 265 93 40 *Fax:* (09) 265 93 49
*E-mail:* info@kantl.be
*Web Site:* www.kantl.be
*Key Personnel*
Librarian: Marijke De Wit *Tel:* (09) 265 93 43
*E-mail:* mdewit@kantl.be
Established: 1941
Awarded every 5 years for the best volume of Dutch poetry, published or unpublished. Recipients must be Belgian nationals.
Award: 1,240 EUR

**Maurice Gilliams Prize**
Koninklijke Academie voor Nederlandse Taal- en Letterkunde (Royal Academy of Dutch Language & Literature)
Koningstr 18, 9000 Ghent
*Tel:* (09) 265 93 40 *Fax:* (09) 265 93 49
*E-mail:* info@kantl.be
*Web Site:* www.kantl.be
*Key Personnel*
Librarian: Marijke De Wit *Tel:* (09) 265 93 43
*E-mail:* mdewit@kantl.be
Established: 1985
Awarded every 4 years for the best volume of poetry, the best essay about poetry or for a complete poetical work, written in Dutch. Nationality of the recipient is not taken into account.
Award: 2,480 EUR

**Grand Prix de Litterature Francaise Hors de France (Fondation Nessim Habif)**
Academie Royale de Langue et de Litterature Francaises (Royal Academy of French Language & Literature)

Palais des Academies, One rue Ducale, 1000 Brussels
*Tel:* (02) 550 22 77 *Fax:* (02) 550 22 75
*E-mail:* alf@cfwb.be
*Web Site:* www. academielanguelitteraturefrancaises.be
*Key Personnel*
Permanent Secretary: Jacques De Decker
Awarded biennially.
Award: 3,000 EUR

**Prix Nicole Houssa** (Nicole Houssa Prize)
Academie Royale de Langue et de Litterature Francaises (Royal Academy of French Language & Literature)
Palais des Academies, One rue Ducale, 1000 Brussels
*Tel:* (02) 550 22 77 *Fax:* (02) 550 22 75
*E-mail:* alf@cfwb.be
*Web Site:* www. academielanguelitteraturefrancaises.be
*Key Personnel*
Permanent Secretary: Jacques De Decker
Awarded triennially.
Award: 850 EUR

**Prize Joseph Houziaux** (Prix Joseph Houziaux)
Academie Royale de Belgique
Palais des Academies, One rue Ducale, 1000 Brussels
*Tel:* (02) 550 22 00 *Fax:* (02) 550 22 05
*E-mail:* arb@cfwb.be
*Web Site:* www.cfwb.be/arb
*Key Personnel*
Secretary: Leo Houziaux *Tel:* (02) 550 22 03
*E-mail:* leo.houziaux@ulg.ac.be
Established: 1994
Awarded triennially.
Award: 1,500 EUR
Closing Date: Dec 31

**Tobie Jonckheere Prize** (Prix Tobie Jonckheere)
Academie Royale de Belgique
Palais des Academies, One rue Ducale, 1000 Brussels
*Tel:* (02) 550 22 00; (02) 550 22 20 *Fax:* (02) 550 22 05
*E-mail:* arb@cfwb.be
*Web Site:* www.cfwb.be/arb
*Key Personnel*
Secretary: Leo Houziaux *Tel:* (02) 550 22 03
*E-mail:* leo.houziaux@ulg.ac.be
Established: 1957
For a work, in published or manuscript form, devoted to the educational sciences. Awarded triennially.
Award: 1,500 EUR
Closing Date: Dec 31

**Prix Jean Kobs** (Jean Kobs Prize)
Academie Royale de Langue et de Litterature Francaises (Royal Academy of French Language & Literature)
Palais des Academies, One rue Ducale, 1000 Brussels
*Tel:* (02) 550 22 77 *Fax:* (02) 550 22 75
*E-mail:* alf@cfwb.be
*Web Site:* www. academielanguelitteraturefrancaises.be
*Key Personnel*
Permanent Secretary: Jacques De Decker
Awarded triennially.
Award: 1,200 EUR

**Hubert Krains Prize**
Association des Ecrivains Belges de Langue Francaise (AEBLF) (Association of the Belgian Writers of French Language)
Camille Lemonnier-Maison des Ecrivains, 150 Chaussee de Wavre, 1050 Brussels
*Tel:* (02) 512 29 68 *Fax:* (02) 512 29 68
*Web Site:* www.ecrivainsbelges.be

*Key Personnel*
President: France Bastia *E-mail:* france.bastia@
skynet.be
Secretary General: Jean Lacroix
Established: 1950
For the unpublished work of a writer below the
age of 40. Founded by the Association of Belgian Writers in the French Language in memory of one of its presidents.
Award: 500 EUR awarded biennially (alternately
prose & poetry)

**Prize Henri Lavachery**
Academie Royale de Belgique
Palais des Academies, One rue Ducale, 1000
Brussels
*Tel:* (02) 550 22 00; (02) 550 22 20 *Fax:* (02)
550 22 05
*E-mail:* arb@cfwb.be
*Web Site:* www.cfwb.be/arb
*Key Personnel*
Secretary: Leo Houziaux *Tel:* (02) 550 22 03
*E-mail:* leo.houziaux@ulg.ac.be
Established: 1961
Awarded every 5 years to honor a work on eth-
nology. Prize confined to Belgians. Written
work drafted in French only.
Award: 1,500 EUR
Closing Date: Dec 31, 2007

**Rene Lyr Prize for Poetry**
Association des Ecrivains Belges de Langue Fran-
caise (AEBLF) (Association of the Belgian
Writers of French Language)
Camille Lemonnier-Maison des Ecrivains, 150
Chaussee de Wavre, 1050 Brussels
*Tel:* (02) 512 29 68 *Fax:* (02) 512 29 68
*Web Site:* www.ecrivainsbelges.be
*Key Personnel*
President: France Bastia *E-mail:* france.bastia@
skynet.be
Secretary General: Jean Lacroix
Established: 1959
Founded under Friends of Rene Lyr patronage
& awarded triennially to a French-language
poet for published or unpublished, non-prize-
winning work. All poets of French expression-
ism are eligible.
Other Sponsor(s): The Family of Rene Lyr
Award: 875 EUR

**Prix Lucien Malpertuis** (Lucien Malpertuis
Prize)
Academie Royale de Langue et de Litterature
Francaises (Royal Academy of French Lan-
guage & Literature)
Palais des Academies, One rue Ducale, 1000
Brussels
*Tel:* (02) 550 22 77 *Fax:* (02) 550 22 75
*E-mail:* alf@cfwb.be
*Web Site:* www.
academielanguelitteraturefrancaises.be
*Key Personnel*
Permanent Secretary: Jacques De Decker
For an outstanding contribution to Belgian litera-
ture in the field of drama, poetry, short story or
essay written in French. Awarded biennially.
Award: 850 EUR

**Joseph-Edmond Marchal Prize** (Prix
Joseph-Edmond Marchal)
Academie Royale de Belgique
Palais des Academies, One rue Ducale, 1000
Brussels
*Tel:* (02) 550 22 00 *Fax:* (02) 550 22 05
*E-mail:* arb@cfwb.be
*Web Site:* www.cfwb.be/arb
*Key Personnel*
Secretary: Leo Houziaux *Tel:* (02) 550 22 03
*E-mail:* leo.houziaux@ulg.ac.be
Established: 1918

Awarded every 5 years for the Belgian author of
the best work, in print or in manuscript form,
on national antiques or archaeology.
Award: 1,500 EUR
Closing Date: Dec 31, 2007

**Fondation Arthur Merghelynck** (Arthur
Merghelynck Foundation)
Academie Royale de Belgique
Palais des Academies, One rue Ducale, 1000
Brussels
*Tel:* (02) 550 22 00 *Fax:* (02) 550 22 05
*E-mail:* arb@cfwb.be
*Web Site:* www.cfwb.be/arb
*Key Personnel*
Secretary: Leo Houziaux *Tel:* (02) 550 22 03
*E-mail:* leo.houziaux@ulg.ac.be
Established: 1999
Awarded annually.
Award: Subsidy allotted for research or to publi-
cation of works
Closing Date: Dec 31

**Arthur Merghelynck Prize**
Koninklijke Academie voor Nederlandse Taal- en
Letterkunde (Royal Academy of Dutch Lan-
guage & Literature)
Koningstr 18, 9000 Ghent
*Tel:* (09) 265 93 40 *Fax:* (09) 265 93 49
*E-mail:* info@kantl.be
*Web Site:* www.kantl.be
*Key Personnel*
Librarian: Marijke De Wit *Tel:* (09) 265 93 43
*E-mail:* mdewit@kantl.be
Established: 1946
Awarded triennially for the two best literary
works, one prose the other poetry, including
essays about prose or poetry, written in Dutch,
published or unpublished. Recipients must be
Belgian nationals.
Award: 2,480 EUR for each prize

**Prix Auguste Michot** (Auguste Michot Prize)
Academie Royale de Langue et de Litterature
Francaises (Royal Academy of French Lan-
guage & Literature)
Palais des Academies, One rue Ducale, 1000
Brussels
*Tel:* (02) 550 22 77 *Fax:* (02) 550 22 75
*E-mail:* alf@cfwb.be
*Web Site:* www.
academielanguelitteraturefrancaises.be
*Key Personnel*
Permanent Secretary: Jacques De Decker
Awarded biennially.
Award: 850 EUR

**Grand prix de poesie Albert Mockel** (Albert
Mockel Grand Prize for Poetry)
Academie Royale de Langue et de Litterature
Francaises (Royal Academy of French Lan-
guage & Literature)
Palais des Academies, One rue Ducale, 1000
Brussels
*Tel:* (02) 550 22 77 *Fax:* (02) 550 22 75
*E-mail:* alf@cfwb.be
*Web Site:* www.
academielanguelitteraturefrancaises.be
*Key Personnel*
Permanent Secretary: Jacques De Decker
For the best Belgian poet writing in French.
Awarded every five years.
Award: 2,500 EUR

**Gilles Nelod Prize**
Association des Ecrivains Belges de Langue Fran-
caise (AEBLF) (Association of the Belgian
Writers of French Language)
Camille Lemonnier-Maison des Ecrivains, 150
Chaussee de Wavre, 1050 Brussels
*Tel:* (02) 512 29 68 *Fax:* (02) 512 29 68

*Web Site:* www.ecrivainsbelges.be
*Key Personnel*
President: France Bastia *E-mail:* france.bastia@
skynet.be
Secretary General: Jean Lacroix
Established: 1984
Founded by Gilles Nelod & administered by the
Association of Belgian Writers in the French
Language. Awarded biennially for a previously
unpublished work of fiction.
Award: 250 EUR

**Order of the Crown Prize**
Belgium Ministry of Foreign Affairs
Service des Ordres, Rue des Petits, 1000 Brussels
*Tel:* (02) 5018111 *Fax:* (02) 5013669
*E-mail:* info@diplobel.org
*Web Site:* www.belgium-emb.org

**Alex Pasquier Prize**
Association des Ecrivains Belges de Langue Fran-
caise (AEBLF) (Association of the Belgian
Writers of French Language)
Camille Lemonnier-Maison des Ecrivains, 150
Chaussee de Wavre, 1050 Brussels
*Tel:* (02) 512 29 68 *Fax:* (02) 512 29 68
*Web Site:* www.ecrivainsbelges.be
*Key Personnel*
President: France Bastia *E-mail:* france.bastia@
skynet.be
Secretary General: Jean Lacroix
Established: 1972
Established in memory of Association president
Alex Pasquier, by his widow, for recognition
of the best historical novel, published or un-
published, during the preceding five years by a
Belgian writer in the French language.
Award: 625 EUR

**Prix Sander Pierron** (Sander Pierron Prize)
Academie Royale de Langue et de Litterature
Francaises (Royal Academy of French Lan-
guage & Literature)
Palais des Academies, One rue Ducale, 1000
Brussels
*Tel:* (02) 550 22 77 *Fax:* (02) 550 22 75
*E-mail:* alf@cfwb.be
*Web Site:* www.
academielanguelitteraturefrancaises.be
*Key Personnel*
Permanent Secretary: Jacques De Decker
Awarded biennially.
Award: 850 EUR

**Prix Emile Polak** (Emile Polak Prize)
Academie Royale de Langue et de Litterature
Francaises (Royal Academy of French Lan-
guage & Literature)
Palais des Academies, One rue Ducale, 1000
Brussels
*Tel:* (02) 550 22 77 *Fax:* (02) 550 22 75
*E-mail:* alf@cfwb.be
*Web Site:* www.
academielanguelitteraturefrancaises.be
*Key Personnel*
Permanent Secretary: Jacques De Decker
Biennial award to a poet of Belgian nationality.
Award: 850 EUR

**Prix Andre Praga** (Andre Praga Prize)
Academie Royale de Langue et de Litterature
Francaises (Royal Academy of French Lan-
guage & Literature)
Palais des Academies, One rue Ducale, 1000
Brussels
*Tel:* (02) 550 22 77 *Fax:* (02) 550 22 75
*E-mail:* alf@cfwb.be
*Web Site:* www.
academielanguelitteraturefrancaises.be
*Key Personnel*
Permanent Secretary: Jacques De Decker
Biennial award for a Belgian theatrical work.
Award: 850 EUR

**Prix baron de Saint-Genois**
Academie Royale de Belgique
Palais des Academies, One rue Ducale, 1000
  Brussels
*Tel:* (02) 550 22 00; (02) 550 22 20 *Fax:* (02)
  550 22 05
*E-mail:* arb@cfwb.be
*Web Site:* www.cfwb.be/arb
*Key Personnel*
Secretary: Leo Houziaux *Tel:* (02) 550 22 03
  *E-mail:* leo.houziaux@ulg.ac.be
Established: 1867
For the author of the best historical or literary
  work written in Dutch. Awarded every five
  years.
Award: 1,250 EUR
Closing Date: Dec 31

**Prix Georges Lockem** (Georges Lockem Prize)
Academie Royale de Langue et de Litterature
  Francaises (Royal Academy of French Lan-
  guage & Literature)
Palais des Academies, One rue Ducale, 1000
  Brussels
*Tel:* (02) 550 22 77 *Fax:* (02) 550 22 75
*E-mail:* alf@cfwb.be
*Web Site:* www.
  academielanguelitteraturefrancaises.be
*Key Personnel*
Permanent Secretary: Jacques De Decker
Annual award to a French-speaking Belgian, age
  25 or under for a manuscript or work published
  in the preceeding year.
Award: 850 EUR

**Prize for Literature of the Parliament of the
  French Community of Belgium**
Parliament of the French Community of Belgium
  (Prix litteraire de Parlement de la Communaute
  francais de Belgique)
Rue de la Loi 6, 1000 Brussels
*Tel:* (02) 213 35 11 *Fax:* (02) 213 35 13
*E-mail:* cellule-internet@pcf.be
*Web Site:* www.pcf.be
*Key Personnel*
President: Jean-Francois Istasse
Awarded annually.
Award: 1,239 EUR
Closing Date: Feb 1

**Victor Rossel Prize**
Le Soir
rue Royale 112, 1000 Brussels
*Tel:* (02) 225 52 21 *Fax:* (02) 225 59 19
*E-mail:* nathalie.malice@rossel.be
*Web Site:* www.lesoir.be
Established: 1938
Annual award for the best novel or collection of
  short stories published during the year, written
  in French by a Belgian author.
Award: 4,958 EUR

**Prix Leopold Rosy** (Leopold Rosy Prize)
Academie Royale de Langue et de Litterature
  Francaises (Royal Academy of French Lan-
  guage & Literature)
Palais des Academies, One rue Ducale, 1000
  Brussels
*Tel:* (02) 550 22 77 *Fax:* (02) 550 22 75
*E-mail:* alf@cfwb.be
*Web Site:* www.
  academielanguelitteraturefrancaises.be
*Key Personnel*
Permanent Secretary: Jacques De Decker
Awarded triennially.
Award: 750 EUR

**Prix Eugene Schmits** (Eugene Schmits Prize)
Academie Royale de Langue et de Litterature
  Francaises (Royal Academy of French Lan-
  guage & Literature)

Palais des Academies, One rue Ducale, 1000
  Brussels
*Tel:* (02) 550 22 77 *Fax:* (02) 550 22 75
*E-mail:* alf@cfwb.be
*Web Site:* www.
  academielanguelitteraturefrancaises.be
*Key Personnel*
Permanent Secretary: Jacques De Decker
Awarded triennially.
Award: 850 EUR

**Ary Sleeks Prize**
Koninklijke Academie voor Nederlandse Taal- en
  Letterkunde (Royal Academy of Dutch Lan-
  guage & Literature)
Koningstr 18, 9000 Ghent
*Tel:* (09) 265 93 40 *Fax:* (09) 265 93 49
*E-mail:* info@kantl.be
*Web Site:* www.kantl.be
*Key Personnel*
Librarian: Marijke De Wit *Tel:* (09) 265 93 43
  *E-mail:* mdewit@kantl.be
Established: 1974
Triennial award which recognizes the best novel,
  volume of short stories or an essay, published
  or unpublished. Recipients must be Belgian
  nationals.
Award: 620 EUR

**Prix de Stassart**
Academie Royale de Belgique
Palais des Academies, One rue Ducale, 1000
  Brussels
*Tel:* (02) 550 22 00; (02) 550 22 20 *Fax:* (02)
  550 22 05
*E-mail:* arb@cfwb.be
*Web Site:* www.cfwb.be/arb
*Key Personnel*
Secretary: Leo Houziaux *Tel:* (02) 550 22 03
  *E-mail:* leo.houziaux@ulg.ac.be
Established: 1851
Awarded every 5 years.
Award: 1,500 EUR
Closing Date: Dec 31

**Suzanne Tassier Prize** (Prix Suzanne Tassier)
Academie Royale de Belgique
Palais des Academies, One rue Ducale, 1000
  Brussels
*Tel:* (02) 550 22 00; (02) 550 22 20 *Fax:* (02)
  550 22 05
*E-mail:* arb@cfwb.be
*Web Site:* www.cfwb.be/arb
*Key Personnel*
Secretary: Leo Houziaux *Tel:* (02) 550 22 03
  *E-mail:* leo.houziaux@ulg.ac.be
Established: 1956
Biennial award to a Belgian woman who, follow-
  ing study at a Belgian university, has obtained
  at least a Doctorate. The prize is awarded for
  a major scientific work, dealing with a subject
  from history, law, philology or the social sci-
  ences: failing a meritorious work from one of
  these branches, then for a subject from the natural sciences, medicine or mathematics. Preference will be given to a work of an historical
  nature, in its widest sense.
Award: 1,750 EUR
Closing Date: Dec 31

**Auguste Teirlinck Prize** (Prix Auguste Teirlinck)
Academie Royale de Belgique
Palais des Academies, One rue Ducale, 1000
  Brussels
*Tel:* (02) 550 22 00; (02) 550 22 20 *Fax:* (02)
  550 22 05
*E-mail:* arb@cfwb.be
*Web Site:* www.cfwb.be/arb
*Key Personnel*
Secretary: Leo Houziaux *Tel:* (02) 550 22 03
  *E-mail:* leo.houziaux@ulg.ac.be
Established: 1907

For a contribution to Flemish literature. Awarded
  every five years.
Award: 1,250 EUR
Closing Date: Dec 31

**Troubadour de la SABAM**
Belgische Vereniging van Auteurs, Componisten
  en Uitgevers (Socete Belge des Auteurs, Com-
  positeurs et Editeurs
Rue d'Arlon 75-77, 1040 Brussels
*Tel:* (02) 286 82 11 *Fax:* (02) 230 05 89
*E-mail:* info@sabam.be
*Web Site:* www.sabam.be
Established: 1951
Biennial award which recognizes living poets of
  any nationality whose works have significantly
  influenced world poetry.
Award: 2,479 EUR

**Prix Georges Vaxelaire** (Georges Vaxelaire
  Prize)
Academie Royale de Langue et de Litterature
  Francaises (Royal Academy of French Lan-
  guage & Literature)
Palais des Academies, One rue Ducale, 1000
  Brussels
*Tel:* (02) 550 22 77 *Fax:* (02) 550 22 75
*E-mail:* alf@cfwb.be
*Web Site:* www.
  academielanguelitteraturefrancaises.be
*Key Personnel*
Permanent Secretary: Jacques De Decker
Biennial award for a theatrical work by a Belgian
  author represented in Belgium in the theatre or
  on radio/TV.
Award: 850 EUR

**Prix Emmanuel Vossaert** (Emmanuel Vossaert
  Prize)
Academie Royale de Langue et de Litterature
  Francaises (Royal Academy of French Lan-
  guage & Literature)
Palais des Academies, One rue Ducale, 1000
  Brussels
*Tel:* (02) 550 22 77 *Fax:* (02) 550 22 75
*E-mail:* alf@cfwb.be
*Web Site:* www.
  academielanguelitteraturefrancaises.be
*Key Personnel*
Permanent Secretary: Jacques De Decker
Awarded biennially.
Award: 850 EUR

**Prix Frans de Wever** (Frans de Wever Prize)
Academie Royale de Langue et de Litterature
  Francaises (Royal Academy of French Lan-
  guage & Literature)
Palais des Academies, One rue Ducale, 1000
  Brussels
*Tel:* (02) 550 22 77 *Fax:* (02) 550 22 75
*E-mail:* alf@cfwb.be
*Web Site:* www.
  academielanguelitteraturefrancaises.be
*Key Personnel*
Permanent Secretary: Jacques De Decker
Annual award to an author under the age of 40
  for a collection of poems.
Award: 850 EUR

**Prix Carton de Wiart** (Carton de Wiart Prize)
Academie Royale de Langue et de Litterature
  Francaises (Royal Academy of French Lan-
  guage & Literature)
Palais des Academies, One rue Ducale, 1000
  Brussels
*Tel:* (02) 550 22 77 *Fax:* (02) 550 22 75
*E-mail:* alf@cfwb.be
*Web Site:* www.
  academielanguelitteraturefrancaises.be
*Key Personnel*
Permanent Secretary: Jacques De Decker
Awarded every 10 years.
Award: 750 EUR

# Bolivia

**Premios Nacionales de Cultura**
Ministerio de Educacion
Palacio Chico, calle Ayacucho esq Potosi, La Paz
*Tel:* (02) 220 0910; (02) 220 0949 *Fax:* (02) 220
    0948
*E-mail:* administracionvc@cultura.gov.bo
*Web Site:* www.bolivia.com/empresas/cultura
Established: 1969
For recognition of achievements in literature, the
    arts or science. Awarded biannually.
Award: Monetary prizes & a medal

**Concurso Nacional de Novela Erich Guttentag**
    (Erich Guttentag National Novel Competition)
Editorial Los Amigos del Libro
Av Ayacucho S-0156, Casilla 450, Cochabamba
    Casilla 450
*Tel:* (042) 4-504150; (042) 4-504151 *Fax:* (591)
    411 5128
*E-mail:* gutten@amigol.bo.net
*Key Personnel*
President: Werner Guttentag

**Franz Tamayo Prize**
La Paz Municipal Mayor's Office
Oficial Mayor de Cultura, La Paz
For outstanding literary work.
Award: 15,000 & 5000 Bolivian pesos
Presented: Annually

# Brazil

**Afonso Arinos Prize**
Academia Brasileira de Letras
Av Pres Wilson 203, Castelo, 20030-021 Rio de
    Janeiro-RJ
*Tel:* (021) 3974 2500
*E-mail:* academia@academia.org.br
*Web Site:* www.academia.org.br
For the best work of fiction published or writ-
    ten during the two years preceding the year of
    award. Awarded annually.

**Olavo Bilac Prize**
Academia Brasileira de Letras
Av Pres Wilson 203, Castelo, 20030-021 Rio de
    Janeiro-RJ
*Tel:* (021) 3974 2500
*E-mail:* academia@academia.org.br
*Web Site:* www.academia.org.br
For the best book of poetry. Awarded annually.

**Jabuti Prize** (Premio Jabuti)
Camara Brasileira do Livro (Brazilian Book As-
    sociation)
Rua Cristiano Viana 91, 01418-100 Sao Paulo-SP
*Tel:* (011) 3069-1300 *Fax:* (011) 3069-1300
*E-mail:* jabuti@cbl.org.br
*Web Site:* www.cbl.org.br
Established: 1959
Awarded annually for best literary composition
    published in previous year.

**Monteiro Lobato Prize**
Fundacao do Libro Infantil e Juvenil (FNLIJ)
Rua da Imprensa 16/12° andar-Centro, 20030-120
    Rio de Janeiro-RJ
*Tel:* (021) 2262-9130 *Fax:* (021) 2240-6649
*E-mail:* informacao@fnlij.org.br
*Web Site:* www.fnlij.org.br
For children's literature. Awarded annually.

**Julia Lopes de Ameida Prize**
Academia Brasileira de Letras
Av Pres Wilson 203, Castelo, 20030-021 Rio de
    Janeiro-RJ
*Tel:* (021) 3974 2500
*E-mail:* academia@academia.org.br
*Web Site:* www.academia.org.br
For the best unpublished or published literary
    work written by a woman, preferably for a
    novel or collection of short stories. Awarded
    annually.

**Machado de Assis Prize**
Academia Brasileira de Letras
Av Pres Wilson 203, Castelo, 20030-021 Rio de
    Janeiro-RJ
*Tel:* (021) 3974 2500
*E-mail:* academia@academia.org.br
*Web Site:* www.academia.org.br
Established: 1943
Awarded annually to an outstanding Brazilian
    writer for the sum of his work. One of Brazil's
    highest literary honors.

**Odorico Mendes Prize**
Funarte Fudacao Nacional De Arte
Rua da Imprensa, 16, 5° andar Centro, 20030-120
    Rio de Janeiro-RJ
*Tel:* (021) 2279-8003; (021) 2279-8004; (021)
    2279-8005; (022) 2532-7144 *Fax:* (021) 2262-
    5547
*Web Site:* www.funarte.gov.br
For the best translation from foreign literature
    into the Portuguese language. Awarded annu-
    ally.

**National Book Institute Prizes**
Instituto Nacional do Livro
SCRN, 704/705, B1 C, No 40, 2 andaer, 70730
    Brasilia DF
*Tel:* (061) 2742315
For outstanding unpublished literary works of fic-
    tion, poetry, history & essays. In addition, one
    prize is awarded for the best unpublished work
    of children's literature & another for illustra-
    tions of books for children. Awarded annually.

**Luisa Claudio de Sousa Prize**
Brazilian PEN Centre (PEN Clube do Brasil (As-
    sociacao Universal de Escritores))
Praia do Flamengo 172-11° andar, Rio de Janeiro
    2000
*Tel:* (021) 2850491
*E-mail:* penclube@ij.com.br
For the best book published in the previous year.
    Novels, plays, literary history & criticism
    works are considered.

**Jose Verissimo Prize**
Funarte Fudacao Nacional De Arte
Rua da Imprensa, 16, 5° andar Centro, 20030-120
    Rio de Janeiro-RJ
*Tel:* (021) 2279-8005; (021) 2279-8004; (021)
    2279-8003; (022) 2532-7144 *Fax:* (021) 2262-
    5547
*Web Site:* www.funarte.gov.br
For the best essay & a work of scholarship.
    Awarded annually.

# Bulgaria

**International Vaptsarov Prize**
Union of Bulgarian Writers
Angel Kanchev 5, 1040 Sofia
*Tel:* (02) 874711 *Fax:* (02) 874757
*Web Site:* www.art.bg/lit.htm

# Canada

☆**Lorne Pierce Medal**
Royal Society of Canada
283 Sparks St, Ottawa, ON K1R 7X9
*Tel:* 613-991-6990 *Fax:* 613-991-6996
*E-mail:* adminrsc@rsc.ca
*Web Site:* www.rsc.ca
*Key Personnel*
Publications & Awards Coordinator: Genevieve
    Gouin *Tel:* 613-991-5760 *E-mail:* ggouin@rsc.
    ca
Established: 1926
Awarded biennially for achievement & conspicu-
    ous merit in the field of imaginative or critical
    literature, in English or French.
Award: Medal

# Chile

**National Prize for Literature** (Premio Nacional
    de Literatura)
Ministerio de Educacion de Chile
Alameda 1371, Santiago
*Tel:* (02) 3904000
*Web Site:* www.mineduc.cl
Established: 1942
Awarded annually to recognize an author's sum
    of work.
Award: Monetary prize

# Colombia

☆**Felix Restrepo Prize**
Academia Colombiana
Carrera 3A, Numero 17-34, Piso 3, Apdo Aereo
    44763, Bogota, DC
*Tel:* (01) 3414805 *Fax:* (01) 2838552
*E-mail:* accefyn@colciencias.gov.co
*Web Site:* www.accefyn.org.co
For distinguished contributions to philology.
Award: 100,000 Colombian pesos & publication
    of work, awarded annually

# Costa Rica

**Editorial Costa Rica Literary Prize**
Editorial Costa Rica
Apdo 10,010, 1000 San Jose
*Tel:* 253-5354 *Fax:* 253-5091
*E-mail:* difusion@editorialcostarica.com
*Web Site:* www.editorialcostarica.com
*Key Personnel*
Management: Habib Succar *E-mail:* editocr@
    racsa.co.cr
Established: 1973
Annual award is to encourage creative writing
    generally. The prize is rotated in order to be
    open to all genres - fiction, stories, theatre, es-
    says, short stories, poetry, biography, history.
    The most recent winner was Eduardo Oconi-
    trillo.
Award: 700,000 CRC

**Aquileo J Echeverria Prize**
Costa Rican Ministry of Culture, Youth & Sport
Avenidas 3 y 7, calles 11 y 15, frente al parque,
    Espana, San Jose 1000

*Tel:* 255 3188 *Fax:* 255 3252
*E-mail:* info@mcjdcr.go.cr
*Web Site:* www.mcjdcr.go.cr
For Costa Rican citizens who have excelled in
the fields of literature (novel, short story, poetry, essay, scientific literature), history, theatre,
music, fine arts. 40,000 CRC divided between
the selected works. Total sum of awards cannot
exceed 8,000,000 CRC. Awarded annually.
Award: 8,000,000 CRC

### Joven Creacion Literary Prize
Editorial Costa Rica
Apdo 10,010, 1000 San Jose
*Tel:* 253-5354 *Fax:* 253-5091
*E-mail:* difusion@editorialcostarica.com
*Web Site:* www.editorialcostarica.com
*Key Personnel*
Management: Habib Succar *E-mail:* editocr@
racsa.co.cr
Established: 1976
Formed in collaboration with the Associa-
cion de Autores, with the aim of stimulating
young writing in the fields of poetry & narra-
tive/stories.
Award: 350,000 CRC

### Carmen Lyra Literary Prize (Premio Carmen
Lyra - Literatura Infantil)
Editorial Costa Rica
Apdo 10,010, 1000 San Jose
*Tel:* 253-5354 *Fax:* 253-5091
*E-mail:* difusion@editorialcostarica.com
*Web Site:* www.editorialcostarica.com
*Key Personnel*
Management: Habib Succar
Established: 1974
Founded in honour of the writer Maria Isabel
Carvajal (pseudonym Carmen Lyra), this annual
award is to encourage the writing of literature
intended for children & young people.
Award: 450,000 CRC
Closing Date: June 14

### Premio Poesia y Narrativa
Editorial Universitaria Centroamericana (EDUCA)
Ciudad Universitar Rodrigo Facio, Apdo 64,
San Jose 2060
*Tel:* 2243727 *Fax:* 2539141
*E-mail:* educacr@sol.racsa.co.cr
*Key Personnel*
Dir: Sebastian Vaquerano

# Cuba

### ☆Casa de las Americas Literary Award
Casa de las Americas
3ra y G, El Vedado, Havana 10400
*Tel:* (07) 56 2706; (07) 56 2709 *Fax:* (07) 33
4554
*E-mail:* webmaster@casa.cult.cu
*Web Site:* www.casa.cult.cu
*Key Personnel*
Dir: Jorge Fornet
Annual prize awarded to an author for unpublished work in one or other of the following
genres: novels, plays, "testimonial" books, essays on artistic & literary themes - Brazilian &
French Caribbean (or national language) works;
short stories, poetry, essays on historical & social themes, books for children & young people & Anglo-Caribbean (or national language)
works. The winning work will be published.
Award: $3,000 USD (or equivalent in national
currency)

# Czech Republic

### Mlada Fronta Publishing House Prize
Mlada Fronta Publishing House
Radlicka 61, 15000 Prague 5
*Tel:* (02) 2527 6120 *Fax:* (02) 2527 6176
*Key Personnel*
Dir: Martina Hartova *E-mail:* hartova@mf.cz
Awarded annually for literary works of prose,
poetry, journalism, popular science, also trans-
lations, published by them during the preceding
year.

### Jaroslav Seifert Prize
Charta 77 Foundation
Melantrichova 5, 110 00 Prague 1
*Tel:* (02) 24 21 44 52; (02) 24 23 02 16; (02) 24
22 50 92 *Fax:* (02) 24 21 36 47
*Web Site:* www.bariery.cz
*Key Personnel*
Program Dir: Indira Bornova *E-mail:* indira.
bornova@bariery.cz
Established: 1986
For recognition of the best work in Czech & Slo-
vak literature.
Other Sponsor(s): Zivnostenska Banka, Prague
Award: 250,000 CZK & a diploma made by one
of the well known Czechoslovak artists
Closing Date: Spring every year
Presented: Zivnostenska Banka, Prague, Autumn

# Denmark

### Emil Aarestrup Prize (Emil Aarestrup
Medaillen)
Dansk Forfatterforening (The Danish Writers As-
sociation)
Strandgade 6, 1401 Copenhagen K
*Tel:* 32 95 51 00 *Fax:* 32 54 01 15
*E-mail:* danskforfatterforening@
danskforfatterforening.dk
*Web Site:* www.danskforfatterforening.dk
For outstanding poetry. Awarded annually.

### The H C Andersen Prize (H C Andersens
Legat)
Dansk Forfatterforening (The Danish Writers As-
sociation)
Strandgade 6, 1401 Copenhagen K
*Tel:* 32 95 51 00 *Fax:* 32 54 01 15
*E-mail:* danskforfatterforening@
danskforfatterforening.dk
*Web Site:* www.danskforfatterforening.dk
For scientists & writers connected with H C An-
dersen, for outstanding contributions to Danish
literature. Awarded annually.
Award: Prize varies

### Martin Andersen Nexo Prize (Martin Andersen
Nexo Legatet)
Dansk Forfatterforening (The Danish Writers As-
sociation)
Strandgade 6, 1401 Copenhagen K
*Tel:* 32 95 51 00 *Fax:* 32 54 01 15
*E-mail:* danskforfatterforening@
danskforfatterforening.dk
*Web Site:* www.danskforfatterforening.dk
Awarded annually.
Award: 10,000 DKK

### Herman Bang Memorial Prize (Herman Bangs
Mindelegat)
Dansk Forfatterforening (The Danish Writers As-
sociation)
Strandgade 6, 1401 Copenhagen K
*Tel:* 32 95 51 00 *Fax:* 32 54 01 15

*E-mail:* danskforfatterforening@
danskforfatterforening.dk
*Web Site:* www.danskforfatterforening.dk
For works of prose. Awarded annually.
Award: 5,000 DKK

### Danish Academy Prize for Literature
Danish Academy (Danske Akademi)
Vognmagergade 7, 1120 Copenhagen K
*Tel:* 33131112 *Fax:* 33328045
*E-mail:* administrator@danskeakademi.dk
*Web Site:* www.danskeakademi.dk *Cable:*
LAWOFF
*Key Personnel*
Administrator: Prof Allan Philip
Awarded biannually for an outstanding work of
literature.
Award: 300,000 DKK

### Danish Writers' Association Non-Fiction Prize
Dansk Forfatterforening (The Danish Writers As-
sociation)
Strandgade 6, 1401 Copenhagen K
*Tel:* 32 95 51 00 *Fax:* 32 54 01 15
*E-mail:* danskforfatterforening@
danskforfatterforening.dk
*Web Site:* www.danskforfatterforening.dk
Awarded annually.
Award: 30,000 DKK

### Danmarks Skolebibliotekarforenings
Bornebogspris
Danish School Librarian Association
Kaervej 113, 7190 Billund
Mailing Address: Postboks 44, 7190 Billund
*Tel:* 7533 1337
*Web Site:* www.skole-biblioteket.ffw.dk
*Key Personnel*
Contact: Karen Odegaard *E-mail:* karen.
odegaard@skolekom.com

### Dansk Oversaetterforbunds Aerespris
Dansk Forfatterforening (The Danish Writers As-
sociation)
Strandgade 6, 1401 Copenhagen K
*Tel:* 32 95 51 00 *Fax:* 32 54 01 15
*E-mail:* danskforfatterforening@
danskforfatterforening.dk
*Web Site:* www.danskforfatterforening.dk
For the outstanding translation into Danish of one
or more significant works. Awarded annually.
Award: 30,000 DKK

### Johannes Ewald Prize (Johannes Ewald Legatet)
Dansk Forfatterforening (The Danish Writers As-
sociation)
Strandgade 6, 1401 Copenhagen K
*Tel:* 32 95 51 00 *Fax:* 32 54 01 15
*E-mail:* danskforfatterforening@
danskforfatterforening.dk
*Web Site:* www.danskforfatterforening.dk
For prose, poetry & dramatic works. Awarded
annually.
Award: 10,000 DKK

### Soren Gyldendal Prize
Gyldendalske Boghandel - Nordisk Forlag A/S
Klareboderne 3, 1001 Copenhagen K
*Tel:* 33755555 *Fax:* 33755556
*E-mail:* gyldendal@gyldendal.dk
*Web Site:* www.gyldendal.dk
*Telex:* 15887 Gyldal Dk
*Key Personnel*
Man Dir: Stig Andersen
Secretary: Annie Auhagen *Tel:* 33755523
*E-mail:* annie_auhagen@gyldendal.dk
For Danish authors from any field whose work is
of great literary value - Nominations only.
Award: 150,000 DKK

**Holberg Medal** (Holberg-Medaljen)
Dansk Forfatterforening (The Danish Writers Association)
Strandgade 6, 1401 Copenhagen K
*Tel:* 32 95 51 00 *Fax:* 32 54 01 15
*E-mail:* danskforfatterforening@
danskforfatterforening.dk
*Web Site:* www.danskforfatterforening.dk
For outstanding contributions to Danish literature. Awarded annually.
Award: 35,000 DKK & medal

☆**Nordic Council Literature Prize**
Nordic Council, Swedish Delegation
Store Strandstr 18, 1255 Copenhagen
*Tel:* 33 96 04 00 *Fax:* 33 11 18 70
*E-mail:* nordisk-rad@norden.org
*Web Site:* www.norden.org
*Key Personnel*
Secretary General: Eva Smekal *E-mail:* eva.
smekal@riksdagen.se
Established: 1961
Awarded annually for a literary work in the fiction, genre, written in one of the languages of the Nordic countries. It can be a novel, a play, a collection - of poems, short stories or essays - or another work which meets high literary & artistic standards. The aim is to increase interest in Nordic literature & establish a Nordic book marker.
Award: 350,000 DKK
Presented: Nordic Council Conference or a session in Feb or March

**Adam Gottlob Oehlenschlaeger Prize** (Adam Oehlenschlaeger Legatet)
Dansk Forfatterforening (The Danish Writers Association)
Strandgade 6, 1401 Copenhagen K
*Tel:* 32 95 51 00 *Fax:* 32 54 01 15
*E-mail:* danskforfatterforening@
danskforfatterforening.dk
*Web Site:* www.danskforfatterforening.dk
For prose works & poetry. Awarded annually.
Award: 10,000 DKK

**Edvard Pedersens Biblioteksfonds Forfatterpris**
Danish Library Association
c/o Det nordjyske Landsbibliotek, Rendsburggade 2, 9100 Aalborg
Mailing Address: Postboks 839, 9100 Aalborg
*Tel:* 33250935 *Fax:* 33257900
*E-mail:* dkf@dlf.dk
*Web Site:* www.litteraturpriser.dk/pris/epfond.htm; www.edvardp.dk; www.dbf.dk
*Key Personnel*
Secretary: Jane Rasmussen *Tel:* 45858105
*E-mail:* jr-kultur@aalborg.dk

**Henrik Pontoppidan Memorial Prize** (Henrik Pontoppidans Mindefond)
Dansk Forfatterforening (The Danish Writers Association)
Strandgade 6, 1401 Copenhagen K
*Tel:* 32 95 51 00 *Fax:* 32 54 01 15
*E-mail:* danskforfatterforening@
danskforfatterforening.dk
*Web Site:* www.danskforfatterforening.dk
For outstanding contributions to Danish literature. Awarded annually.
Award: 10,000 DKK

# Finland

**Finlandia Junior Prize**
Suomen Kirjasaatio (Finnish Book Foundation)
Lonnrotinkatu 11 A, 00120 Helsinki
Mailing Address: PO Box 177, 00121 Helsinki

*Tel:* (09) 228 77 250 *Fax:* (09) 612 1226
*Web Site:* www.skyry.net
*Key Personnel*
Man Dir: Veikko Sonninen *E-mail:* veikko.
sonninen@skyry.net
Annual award for the outstanding Finnish children's book of the year.
Award: 26,000 EUR

**Rudolf Koivu Prize**
Grafia Ry
Uudenmaankatu 11B9, 00120 Helsinki
*Tel:* (09) 601 941; (09) 601 942 *Fax:* (09) 601 140
*E-mail:* grafia@grafia.fi
*Web Site:* www.grafia.fi
*Key Personnel*
Chairman: Mr Kari Kakko
Biennial award for the illustrator of the year's best Finnish picture-book for children.

**Arvid Lydecken Prize**
Suomen Nuorisokirjailijat ry
Palomaeentie 13 B, 02730 Espoo
*Tel:* (09) 852 2176
*Web Site:* www.nuorisokirjailijat.fi
*Key Personnel*
Chairman: Mrs Tuija Lehtinen *E-mail:* tuija.
lehtinen@nuorisokirjailijat.fi
Established: 1946
Annual award for the writer of the year's best Finnish book for children.

**State Prizes for Literature**
Ministry of Education, Finland
Meritullinkatu 10, Main Bldg, 00171 Helsinki
Mailing Address: PO Box 29, 00023 Helsinki
*Tel:* (09) 160 04; (09) 578 14 *Fax:* (09) 135 9335
*E-mail:* info@minedu.fi
*Web Site:* www.minedu.fi
*Key Personnel*
Minister of Education & Science: Tuula
Haatainen *E-mail:* tuula.haatainen@minedu.fi
Annual prizes for the best literary works.
Award: 13,000 EUR

# France

**Prix de l'Academie des Sciences Arts et Belles Lettres de Dijon** (Dijon Academy of Sciences, Art & Literature Prize)
Academie des Sciences Arts et Belles Lettres de Dijon
Bibliotheque Municipale de Dijon, 5 Rue de l'Ecole de Droit, 21000 Dijon
*Tel:* (080) 44 94 14 *Fax:* (080) 44 94 34
*E-mail:* bmdijon@ville-dijon.fr
*Web Site:* www.ville-dijon.fr
*Key Personnel*
Secretary General: Dr Martine Chauney Bouillot

**Prix de l'Academie Mallarme**
Academie Mallarme
Espace Culturel, 16 rue Monsieur Le Prince, 75006 Paris
*Tel:* (01) 46227125
*Key Personnel*
Secretary General: Charles Dobzynski
Mallarme Academic Prize.

**Prix ALPHA de la Nouvelle** (ALPHA Prize for News)
ALPHA Association
9 Ave Pierre-Curie, 59190 Hazebrouck
*Tel:* 28410744

**Prix Guillaume Apollinaire**
22 rue Felibres, 91600 Savigny-Orge
*Tel:* (01) 6996 3524

**Prix Antonin Artaud**
Association des Ecrivains du Rouergue
BP 307, 12003 Rodez Cedex
*Tel:* (05) 65781307; (05) 65778849 (Secretary)

**Francois-Joseph Audiffred Prize** (Prix Francois-Joseph Audiffred)
Academie des Sciences Morales et Politiques, Institut de France
23 quai de Conti, 75006 Paris
*Tel:* (01) 44 41 43 26 *Fax:* (01) 44 41 43 27
*E-mail:* com@institut-de-france.fr
*Web Site:* www.asmp.fr; www.institut-de-france.fr
*Key Personnel*
Perpetual Secretary: Michel Albert
Annual award for a published work best qualified to inspire love of ethics & virtue & to discourage egoism & envy; or to stimulate knowledge & appreciation of France.

**Prix Baudelaire**
Societe des Gens de Lettres de France
Hotel de Massa, 38 rue du Faubourg Saint-Jacques, 75014 Paris
*Tel:* (01) 53 10 12 00 *Fax:* (01) 53 10 12 12
*Web Site:* www.sgdl.org
*Key Personnel*
President: Alain Absire
First Vice President: Marie-France Briselance
Secretary General: Jean Claude Bologne
Treasurer: Francois Taillandier
Awarded each spring to the best French translation of an English work to which the author is native of the United Kingdom or one of the Commonwealth Countries.
Award: 2,000 EUR
Presented: British Council, Paris

**Prix Bordin**
Academie des Beaux Arts, Institut de France
23 quai Conti, 75006 Paris
*Tel:* (01) 44 41 44 41 *Fax:* (01) 44 41 43 41
*E-mail:* dsa@institut-de-france.fr
*Web Site:* www.academie-des-beaux-arts.fr; www.institut-de-france.fr
*Key Personnel*
Secretaire perpetuel: Arnaud d' Hauterives

**Louis Castex Prize** (Prix Louis Castex)
Academie Francaise, Institut de France
23 quai de Conti, 75006 Paris
*Tel:* (01) 44 41 43 10 *Fax:* (01) 44 41 43 11
*E-mail:* com@institut-de-france.fr
*Web Site:* www.institut-de-france.fr
*Key Personnel*
Administration: Claude-Marie Durix
For a literary work celebrating a major voyage of exploration or archaeological or ethnological discovery. Fictional romance excluded. Awarded annually.

**Honore Chavee Prize**
Academie des Inscriptions et Belles Lettres, Institut de France
23 quai de Conti, 75006 Paris
*Tel:* (01) 44 41 43 10 *Fax:* (01) 44 41 43 11
*E-mail:* com@institut-de-france.fr
*Web Site:* www.aibl.fr; www.institut-de-france.fr
*Key Personnel*
Perpetual Secretary: M Jean Leclant *E-mail:* j.
leclant.aibl@dial.oleane.com
Established: 1821
Biennial award to encourage work in linguistics & in particular, research on romance languages.

**Prix Maurice-Edgar Coindreau**
Societe des Gens de Lettres de France

Hotel de Massa, 38 rue du Faubourg Saint-Jacques, 75014 Paris
*Tel:* (01) 53 10 12 00 *Fax:* (01) 53 10 12 12
*Web Site:* www.sgdl.org
*Key Personnel*
President: Alain Absire
First Vice President: Marie-France Briselance
Secretary General: Jean Claude Bologne
Treasurer: Francois Taillandier
Rewards a literary translation for American work.
Award: 1,000 EUR

**Eve Delacroix Prize** (Eve Delacroix Prize)
Academie Francaise, Institut de France
23 quai de Conti, 75006 Paris
*Tel:* (01) 44 41 43 10 *Fax:* (01) 44 41 43 11
*E-mail:* com@institut-de-france.fr
*Web Site:* www.institut-de-france.fr
*Key Personnel*
Administration: Claude-Marie Durix
Annual award for a literary work, essay or novel combining literary quality, a sense of human dignity & the responsibilities of authorship.
Award: 762 EUR

**Deux Magots Prize** (Prix des Deux Magots)
Cafe des Deux Magots
6 Pl Saint Germain des Pres, 75006 Paris
*Tel:* (01) 45 48 55 25 *Fax:* (01) 45 49 31 29
*E-mail:* cafe.lesdeuxmagots@free.fr
*Web Site:* www.lesdeuxmagots.com
*Key Personnel*
Dir: M J Mathivat
Established: 1933
The prize originated in Paris.
Award: 7,700 EUR

**Alfred Dutens Prize** (Prix Alfred Dutens)
Academie des Inscriptions et Belles Lettres, Institut de France
23 quai de Conti, 75006 Paris
*Tel:* (01) 44 41 43 10 *Fax:* (01) 44 41 43 11
*E-mail:* com@institut-de-france.fr
*Web Site:* www.aibl.fr; www.institut-de-france.fr
*Key Personnel*
Perpetual Secretary: M Jean Leclant *E-mail:* j.leclant.aibl@dial.oleane.com
Awarded every ten years for the most useful work on linguistics.

**Prix Paul Feval de Litterature Populaire**
Societe des Gens de Lettres de France
Hotel de Massa, 38 rue du Faubourg Saint-Jacques, 75014 Paris
*Tel:* (01) 53 10 12 00 *Fax:* (01) 53 10 12 12
*Web Site:* www.sgdl.org
*Key Personnel*
President: Alain Absire
First Vice President: Marie-France Briselance
Secretary General: Jean Claude Bologne
Treasurer: Francois Taillandier
For a translated German work.
Award: 2,000 EUR

**Jean Finot Prize** (Prix Jean Finot)
Academie des Sciences Morales et Politiques, Institut de France
23 quai de Conti, 75006 Paris
*Tel:* (01) 44 41 43 26 *Fax:* (01) 44 41 43 27
*E-mail:* com@institut-de-france.fr
*Web Site:* www.asmp.fr; www.institut-de-france.fr
*Key Personnel*
Perpetual Secretary: Michel Albert
Biennial award for a work of a humanitarian social trend.

**Marshal Foch Prize** (Prix du marechal Foch)
Academie Francaise, Institut de France
23 quai de Conti, 75006 Paris
*Tel:* (01) 44 41 43 10 *Fax:* (01) 44 41 43 11
*E-mail:* com@institut-de-france.fr

*Web Site:* www.institut-de-france.fr
*Key Personnel*
Administration: Claude-Marie Durix
Biennial award for a book on the future of the nation's defence by a French officer, engineer, scholar or philosopher.

**Gegner Prize** (Prix Gegner)
Academie des Sciences Morales et Politiques, Institut de France
23 quai de Conti, 75006 Paris
*Tel:* (01) 44 41 43 26 *Fax:* (01) 44 41 43 27
*E-mail:* com@institut-de-france.fr
*Web Site:* www.asmp.fr; www.institut-de-france.fr
*Key Personnel*
Perpetual Secretary: Michel Albert
Awarded annually to a philosopher-writer whose works contribute to the progress of philosophic science.

**Giles Prize** (Prix Giles)
Academie des Inscriptions et Belles Lettres, Institut de France
23 quai de Conti, 75006 Paris
*Tel:* (01) 44 41 43 10 *Fax:* (01) 44 41 43 11
*E-mail:* com@institut-de-france.fr
*Web Site:* www.aibl.fr; www.institut-de-france.fr
*Key Personnel*
Perpetual Secretary: M Jean Leclant *E-mail:* j.leclant.aibl@dial.oleane.com
Biennial award to a French National for a work on China, Japan or the Far East.

**Goncourt Prize** (Prix Goncourt)
Academie Goncourte, Societe de gens de Lettres
c/o Drouant, Place Gaillon, 75002 Paris
*Tel:* (01) 42651516 *Fax:* (01) 4703498
*Web Site:* www.academic-goncourt.fr
Founded by E de Goncourt, 1914, the annual prize honors a prose work by a younger writer with originality of spirit & form. The novel is the preferred medium. The Academy also awards each year, in various French towns, prizes for short story, biography, historical novel & poetry.
Award: 1,524 EUR to 7,622 EUR

☆**Grand Prix de la Francophonie**
Academie Francaise, Institut de France
23 quai de Conti, 75006 Paris
*Tel:* (01) 44 41 43 10 *Fax:* (01) 44 41 43 11
*E-mail:* com@institut-de-france.fr
*Web Site:* www.institut-de-france.fr
*Key Personnel*
Administration: Claude-Marie Durix
Established: 1986
Annual award established by the Government of Canada in collaboration with the Academie Francaise. The Government of Canada donated 400,000 CAD as a founding sum with the expectation that other countries, organizations & groups would make further contributions. The prize is to reward the work of a French-speaking writer who has contributed in an outstanding manner to the upholding & exemplification of the French language. The prize can also be for literary or philosophical work which individually or collectively has assured the regeneration of the French language in the fields of science, technology or information.
Award: 45,735 EUR

**Grand Prix de la Nouvelle**
Societe des Gens de Lettres de France
Hotel de Massa, 38 rue du Faubourg Saint-Jacques, 75014 Paris
*Tel:* (01) 53 10 12 00 *Fax:* (01) 53 10 12 12
*Web Site:* www.sgdl.org
*Key Personnel*
President: Alain Absire
First Vice President: Marie-France Briselance

Secretary General: Jean Claude Bologne
Treasurer: Francois Taillandier
Award: 3,000 EUR

**Grand Prix de la Societe des Poetes Francais**
(Grand Prize of the French Poet's Society)
la Societe des Poetes Francais
Siege social, 16, rue Monsieur le Prince, 75006 Paris
*Tel:* (01) 40 46 99 82 *Fax:* (01) 40 46 99 11
*E-mail:* poetesfrancais@aol.com
*Web Site:* www.societedespoetesfrancais.asso.fr
*Key Personnel*
President: Vital Heurtebize
Secretary General: Linda Bastide
Established: 1936
Awarded annually for the whole body of a poet's work, as decided by the Committee of the Societe des Poetes (no applications allowed).

**Grand Prix de Litterature de la Societe des Gens de Lettres pour l'ensemble de l'oeuvre**
Societe des Gens de Lettres de France
Hotel de Massa, 38 rue du Faubourg Saint-Jacques, 75014 Paris
*Tel:* (01) 53 10 12 00 *Fax:* (01) 53 10 12 12
*Web Site:* www.sgdl.org
*Key Personnel*
President: Alain Absire
First Vice President: Marie-France Briselance
Secretary General: Jean Claude Bologne
Treasurer: Francois Taillandier
Award: 3,000 EUR

**Grand Prix de Poesie de la Societe des Gens de Lettres**
Societe des Gens de Lettres de France
Hotel de Massa, 38 rue du Faubourg Saint-Jacques, 75014 Paris
*Tel:* (01) 53 10 12 00 *Fax:* (01) 53 10 12 12
*Web Site:* www.sgdl.org
*Key Personnel*
President: Alain Absire
First Vice President: Marie-France Briselance
Secretary General: Jean Claude Bologne
Treasurer: Francois Taillandier
Award: 3,000 EUR

**Grand Prix International de Poesie de la Ville de Grenoble**
Societe des Poetes et Artistes de France
30 CRS-J-Jaures, 38000 Grenoble
*Tel:* (01) 76475483

**Grand Prix Litteraire de l'Afrique Noire**
(Black Africa Literary Prize)
Association des Ecrivains de Langue Francaise (ADELF) (French Language Writers' Association)
14 rue Broussais, 75014 Paris
*Tel:* (01) 43219599 *Fax:* (01) 43201222
*Web Site:* www.ecrivains-nc.org
*Key Personnel*
President: Nicolas Kurtovitch

**Grand Prix SGDL de l'Essai**
Societe des Gens de Lettres de France
Hotel de Massa, 38 rue du Faubourg Saint-Jacques, 75014 Paris
*Tel:* (01) 53 10 12 00 *Fax:* (01) 53 10 12 12
*Web Site:* www.sgdl.org
*Key Personnel*
President: Alain Absire
First Vice President: Marie-France Briselance
Secretary General: Jean Claude Bologne
Treasurer: Francois Taillandier
Established: 1984
For recognition of an outstanding essay.
Award: 3,000 EUR

**Grand Prix SGDL de l'oeuvre Multimedia**
Societe des Gens de Lettres de France

Hotel de Massa, 38 rue du Faubourg Saint-
Jacques, 75014 Paris
*Tel:* (01) 53 10 12 00 *Fax:* (01) 53 10 12 12
*Web Site:* www.sgdl.org
*Key Personnel*
President: Alain Absire
First Vice President: Marie-France Briselance
Secretary General: Jean Claude Bologne
Treasurer: Francois Taillandier
Award: 3,000 EUR

## Grand Prix SGDL du Livre des Arts
Societe des Gens de Lettres de France
Hotel de Massa, 38 rue du Faubourg Saint-
Jacques, 75014 Paris
*Tel:* (01) 53 10 12 00 *Fax:* (01) 53 10 12 12
*Web Site:* www.sgdl.org
*Key Personnel*
President: Alain Absire
First Vice President: Marie-France Briselance
Secretary General: Jean Claude Bologne
Treasurer: Francois Taillandier
For recognition of outstanding works completed
in the past year.
Award: 3,000 EUR

## Grand Prix SGDL du Livre d'Histoire
Societe des Gens de Lettres de France
Hotel de Massa, 38 rue du Faubourg Saint-
Jacques, 75014 Paris
*Tel:* (01) 53 10 12 00 *Fax:* (01) 53 10 12 12
*Web Site:* www.sgdl.org
*Key Personnel*
President: Alain Absire
First Vice President: Marie-France Briselance
Secretary General: Jean Claude Bologne
Treasurer: Francois Taillandier
To recognize the author of an historical work.
Award: 3,000 EUR

## Grand Prix SGDL du Livre Jeunesse
Societe des Gens de Lettres de France
Hotel de Massa, 38 rue du Faubourg Saint-
Jacques, 75014 Paris
*Tel:* (01) 53 10 12 00 *Fax:* (01) 53 10 12 12
*Web Site:* www.sgdl.org
*Key Personnel*
President: Alain Absire
First Vice President: Marie-France Briselance
Secretary General: Jean Claude Bologne
Treasurer: Francois Taillandier
Established: 1982
Annual award to recognize a book intended for
young people by its qualities of invention, writ-
ing & presentation. Works written in French &
published before March of the preceding year
may be submitted by the author or editor.
Award: 3,000 EUR

## Grand Prix SGDL du Roman
Societe des Gens de Lettres de France
Hotel de Massa, 38 rue du Faubourg Saint-
Jacques, 75014 Paris
*Tel:* (01) 53 10 12 00 *Fax:* (01) 53 10 12 12
*Web Site:* www.sgdl.org
*Key Personnel*
President: Alain Absire
First Vice President: Marie-France Briselance
Secretary General: Jean Claude Bologne
Treasurer: Francois Taillandier
For recognition of an outstanding novel. Works
published within the preceding year may be
submitted.
Award: 3,000 EUR

## Grand Prix SGDL du site Internet litteraire
Societe des Gens de Lettres de France
Hotel de Massa, 38 rue du Faubourg Saint-
Jacques, 75014 Paris
*Tel:* (01) 53 10 12 00 *Fax:* (01) 53 10 12 12
*E-mail:* sgdlf@wanadoo.fr

*Web Site:* www.sgdl.org
*Key Personnel*
President: Alain Absire
First Vice President: Marie-France Briselance
Secretary General: Jean Claude Bologne
Treasurer: Francois Taillandier
Award: 3,000 EUR

## Grand Prize for Literature (Grand Prix de Litterature)
Academie Francaise, Institut de France
23 quai de Conti, 75006 Paris
*Tel:* (01) 44 41 43 10 *Fax:* (01) 44 41 43 11
*E-mail:* com@institut-de-france.fr
*Web Site:* www.institut-de-france.fr
*Key Personnel*
Administration: Claude-Marie Durix
Biennial award to a prose-writer for one or more
works noteworthy in form & inspiration.

## Grand Prize for Poetry (Grand prix de Poesie)
Academie Francaise, Institut de France
23 quai de Conti, 75006 Paris
*Tel:* (01) 44 41 43 10 *Fax:* (01) 44 41 43 11
*E-mail:* com@institut-de-france.fr
*Web Site:* www.institut-de-france.fr
*Key Personnel*
Administration: Claude-Marie Durix
Awarded annually.
Award: 7,600 EUR

## ☆Grand Prize for the Influence of the French Language (Prix du Rayonnement de la Langue et de la Litterature Francaises)
Academie Francaise, Institut de France
23 quai de Conti, 75006 Paris
*Tel:* (01) 44 41 43 10 *Fax:* (01) 44 41 43 11
*E-mail:* com@institut-de-france.fr
*Web Site:* www.institut-de-france.fr
*Key Personnel*
Administration: Claude-Marie Durix
For work contributing to the influence of the
French language. Monetary prize awarded an-
nually.

## Grands Prix d'Histoire Chateaubriand - la Vallee-aux-Loups
Maison de Chateaubriand
87 rue Chateaubriand, 92290 Chatenay-Malabry
*Tel:* (01) 55 52 13 00 *Fax:* (01) 55 52 12 98
*E-mail:* chateaubriand@cg92.fr
*Key Personnel*
Dir: M Jean-Paul Clement

## Cardinal Grente Prize (Prix du Cardinal Grente)
Academie Francaise, Institut de France
23 quai de Conti, 75006 Paris
*Tel:* (01) 44 41 43 10 *Fax:* (01) 44 41 43 11
*E-mail:* com@institut-de-france.fr
*Web Site:* www.institut-de-france.fr
*Key Personnel*
Administration: Claude-Marie Durix
Awarded biennially for the entire works of a reg-
ular or secular member of the Roman Catholic
clergy.

## ☆Heredia Prize (Prix Heredia)
Academie Francaise, Institut de France
23 quai de Conti, 75006 Paris
*Tel:* (01) 44 41 43 10 *Fax:* (01) 44 41 43 11
*E-mail:* com@institut-de-france.fr
*Web Site:* www.institut-de-france.fr
*Key Personnel*
Administration: Claude-Marie Durix
Monetary award given in alternate years to (1) a
Latin American writer for a piece of prose or
poetry written in French, (2) the author of a
collection of printed sonnets.

## Grand Prix d'Histoire Nationale Maurice Payard (Maurice Payard National History Grand Prize)
Academie Nationale de Reims
7 rue des Ecoles, 51100 Reims
Mailing Address: 38 rue Gambetta, 51100 Reims
*Tel:* (0326) 910449 *Fax:* (0326) 910449
*Key Personnel*
Secretary General: Patrick Demouy *Tel:* (0326)
479819 *E-mail:* patrick.demouy@laposte.net
Administrative Secretary: Philippe Petit-Stervinou
Established: 1978
Champagne history.
Award: 1,500 EUR
Presented: July

## Interallie Prize
Cercle Interallie
33 rue du Fauborg St Honore, 75008 Paris
*Tel:* (01) 42659600
Awarded since 1930 for a high quality novel,
preferably written by a journalist. Awarded annually.

## ☆Stanislas Julien Prize (Prix Stanislas Julien)
Academie des Inscriptions et Belles Lettres, Insti-
tut de France
23 quai de Conti, 75006 Paris
*Tel:* (01) 44 41 43 10 *Fax:* (01) 44 41 43 11
*E-mail:* com@institut-de-france.fr
*Web Site:* www.aibl.fr; www.institut-de-france.fr
*Key Personnel*
Perpetual Secretary: M Jean Leclant *E-mail:* j.
leclant.aibl@dial.oleane.com
Monetary prize, awarded annually, for the best
work related to China.

## ☆Kalinga Prize for the Popularization of Science
UNESCO Publishing
One rue Miollis, 75015 Paris
*Tel:* (01) 45 68 35 47 *Fax:* (01) 53 69 99 49
*E-mail:* dl.france@unesco.org
*Web Site:* www.unesco.org/science/ips/
science_prizes/kalinga_science_prize.
html; www.unesco.org/science/
unesco_intern_sc_prizes.htm
*Key Personnel*
Contact: Yoslan Nur *E-mail:* y.nur@unesco.org
Established: 1952
Annual award established by the Kalinga Foundation Trust. The recipient must have distin-
guished him or herself in the course of a bril-
liant career as science writer, editor, lecturer,
film producer, radio/TV program director or
presenter. The National Commission for UN-
ESCO within each country forwards a single
nomination to UNESCO on the basis of recommendations from national bodies, including
science journals, national associations for the
advancement of science.
Other Sponsor(s): Kalinga Foundation Trust (India)
Award: 2,000 GBP
Closing Date: May 15
Presented: India in even years; Paris (UNESCO
Headquarters) in odd years, Nov

## Prix Halperine Kaminsky
Societe des Gens de Lettres de France
Hotel de Massa, 38 rue du Faubourg Saint-
Jacques, 75014 Paris
*Tel:* (01) 53 10 12 00 *Fax:* (01) 53 10 12 12
*Web Site:* www.sgdl.org
*Key Personnel*
President: Alain Absire
First Vice President: Marie-France Briselance
Secretary General: Jean Claude Bologne
Treasurer: Francois Taillandier

Composed of two prizes: Le Prix Halperine-
  Kaminsky Consecration & Le Prix Halperine-
  Kaminsky Decouverte.
Award: Le Prix Halperine-Kaminsky Consecra-
  tion 6,000 EUR; Le Prix Halperine-Kaminsky
  Decouverte 1,500 EUR

**Prix Roger Kowalski** (Roger Kowalski Prize)
Ville de Lyon
Universite Lumiere Lyon 2, Faculte des arts, 18
  quai Claude Bernard, 69007 Lyon
Annual prize awarded to a living poet for a
  French language manuscript.

**Prix Valery Larbaud** (Valery Larbaud Prize)
Association International des Amis de Valery Lar-
  baud
Les Eygalades B, 116 rue Edmond-Carrieu,
  30900 Nimes
*Tel:* (01) 04 6664 9402

**Maison de Poesie** (House of Poetry)
Emile Blemont Foundation
11 bis rue Ballu, 75009 Paris
*Tel:* (01) 40234599
Established: 1928

☆**Mandat des Poetes Prize**
Pierre Bearn
60 rue Monsieur-le-Prince, 75006 Paris
*Tel:* (01) 43262273
*Web Site:* pierrebearn.free.fr/pierrebi.htm
Founded in 1950 by Pierre Bearn, to aid a
  French-language poet of talent, young or old,
  in time of need. Awarded annually.

**Medaille de la ville de Avignon** (Medal of the
  Town of Avignon)
la Societe des Poetes Francais
Siege social, 16, rue Monsieur le Prince, 75006
  Paris
*Tel:* (01) 40 46 99 82 *Fax:* (01) 40 46 99 11
*E-mail:* poetesfrancais@aol.com
*Web Site:* www.societedespoetesfrancais.asso.fr
*Key Personnel*
President: Vital Heurtebize
Secretary General: Linda Bastide

**Medaille de la ville de Bayonne** (Medal of the
  Town of Bayonne)
la Societe des Poetes Francais
Siege social, 16, rue Monsieur le Prince, 75006
  Paris
*Tel:* (01) 40 46 99 82 *Fax:* (01) 40 46 99 11
*E-mail:* poetesfrancais@aol.com
*Web Site:* www.societedespoetesfrancais.asso.fr
*Key Personnel*
President: Vital Heurtebize
Secretary General: Linda Bastide

**Medaille de la Ville de Chatcauneuf du Pape**
la Societe des Poetes Francais
Siege social, 16, rue Monsieur le Prince, 75006
  Paris
*Tel:* (01) 40 46 99 82 *Fax:* (01) 40 46 99 11
*E-mail:* poetesfrancais@aol.com
*Web Site:* www.societedespoetesfrancais.asso.fr
*Key Personnel*
President: Vital Heurtebize
Secretary General: Linda Bastide
Instituted by the town of Chatcauneuf-du-Pape &
  other cities in the same area. Awarded annually
  for a poetic work (unpublished, or published
  in previous five years) which, irrespective of
  subject, appears most deserving for its formal
  purity & lofty sentiments. Awarded preferably
  to a young poet.
Award: 152 EUR

**Medaille de la ville de Chatel-Guyon** (Medal of
  the Town of Chatel-Guyon)
la Societe des Poetes Francais
Siege social, 16, rue Monsieur le Prince, 75006
  Paris
*Tel:* (01) 40 46 99 82 *Fax:* (01) 40 46 99 11
*E-mail:* poetesfrancais@aol.com
*Web Site:* www.societedespoetesfrancais.asso.fr
*Key Personnel*
President: Vital Heurtebize
Secretary General: Linda Bastide

**Medaille de la ville de Combo les bains** (Medal
  of the Town of Combo baths)
la Societe des Poetes Francais
Siege social, 16, rue Monsieur le Prince, 75006
  Paris
*Tel:* (01) 40 46 99 82 *Fax:* (01) 40 46 99 11
*E-mail:* poetesfrancais@aol.com
*Web Site:* www.societedespoetesfrancais.asso.fr
*Key Personnel*
President: Vital Heurtebize
Secretary General: Linda Bastide

**Medaille de la ville de Dijon** (Medal of the
  Town of Dijon)
la Societe des Poetes Francais
Siege social, 16, rue Monsieur le Prince, 75006
  Paris
*Tel:* (01) 40 46 99 82 *Fax:* (01) 40 46 99 11
*E-mail:* poetesfrancais@aol.com
*Web Site:* www.societedespoetesfrancais.asso.fr
*Key Personnel*
President: Vital Heurtebize
Secretary General: Linda Bastide

**Medaille de la ville de Douai** (Medal of the
  Town of Douai)
la Societe des Poetes Francais
Siege social, 16, rue Monsieur le Prince, 75006
  Paris
*Tel:* (01) 40 46 99 82 *Fax:* (01) 40 46 99 11
*E-mail:* poetesfrancais@aol.com
*Web Site:* www.societedespoetesfrancais.asso.fr
*Key Personnel*
President: Vital Heurtebize
Secretary General: Linda Bastide

**Medaille de la ville de Gap** (Medal of the Town
  of Gap)
la Societe des Poetes Francais
Siege social, 16, rue Monsieur le Prince, 75006
  Paris
*Tel:* (01) 40 46 99 82 *Fax:* (01) 40 46 99 11
*E-mail:* poetesfrancais@aol.com
*Web Site:* www.societedespoetesfrancais.asso.fr
*Key Personnel*
President: Vital Heurtebize
Secretary General: Linda Bastide

**Medaille de la ville de Melun** (Medal of the
  Town of Melun)
la Societe des Poetes Francais
Siege social, 16, rue Monsieur le Prince, 75006
  Paris
*Tel:* (01) 40 46 99 82 *Fax:* (01) 40 46 99 11
*E-mail:* poetesfrancais@aol.com
*Web Site:* www.societedespoetesfrancais.asso.fr
*Key Personnel*
President: Vital Heurtebize
Secretary General: Linda Bastide

**Medaille de la ville de Metz** (Medal of the Town
  of Metz)
la Societe des Poetes Francais
Siege social, 16, rue Monsieur le Prince, 75006
  Paris
*Tel:* (01) 40 46 99 82 *Fax:* (01) 40 46 99 11
*E-mail:* poetesfrancais@aol.com
*Web Site:* www.societedespoetesfrancais.asso.fr

*Key Personnel*
President: Vital Heurtebize
Secretary General: Linda Bastide

**Medaille de la ville de Pau** (Medal of the Town
  of Pau)
la Societe des Poetes Francais
Siege social, 16, rue Monsieur le Prince, 75006
  Paris
*Tel:* (01) 40 46 99 82 *Fax:* (01) 40 46 99 11
*E-mail:* poetesfrancais@aol.com
*Web Site:* www.societedespoetesfrancais.asso.fr
*Key Personnel*
President: Vital Heurtebize
Secretary General: Linda Bastide

**Medaille de la ville de Reims** (Medal of the
  Town of Rheims)
la Societe des Poetes Francais
Siege social, 16, rue Monsieur le Prince, 75006
  Paris
*Tel:* (01) 40 46 99 82 *Fax:* (01) 40 46 99 11
*E-mail:* poetesfrancais@aol.com
*Web Site:* www.societedespoetesfrancais.asso.fr
*Key Personnel*
President: Vital Heurtebize
Secretary General: Linda Bastide

**Medaille de la ville de Toulon** (Medal of the
  Town of Toulon)
la Societe des Poetes Francais
Siege social, 16, rue Monsieur le Prince, 75006
  Paris
*Tel:* (01) 40 46 99 82 *Fax:* (01) 40 46 99 11
*E-mail:* poetesfrancais@aol.com
*Web Site:* www.societedespoetesfrancais.asso.fr
*Key Personnel*
President: Vital Heurtebize
Secretary General: Linda Bastide

**Medaille de la ville de Vittel** (Medal of the
  Town of Vittel)
la Societe des Poetes Francais
Siege social, 16, rue Monsieur le Prince, 75006
  Paris
*Tel:* (01) 40 46 99 82 *Fax:* (01) 40 46 99 11
*E-mail:* poetesfrancais@aol.com
*Web Site:* www.societedespoetesfrancais.asso.fr
*Key Personnel*
President: Vital Heurtebize
Secretary General: Linda Bastide

**Medaille du Senat** (Medal of the Senate)
la Societe des Poetes Francais
Siege social, 16, rue Monsieur le Prince, 75006
  Paris
*Tel:* (01) 40 46 99 82 *Fax:* (01) 40 46 99 11
*E-mail:* poetesfrancais@aol.com
*Web Site:* www.societedespoetesfrancais.asso.fr
*Key Personnel*
President: Vital Heurtebize
Secretary General: Linda Bastide

**Prix Medicis de l'Essai**
Prix Medicis
25 rue Dombasle, 75015 Paris
*Tel:* (01) 48287690 *Fax:* (01) 48287690
*Key Personnel*
Secretary General: Francine Mallet
  *E-mail:* dominique.larre@wanadoo.fr
Established: 1985
For the best essay in French, including translated
  writing, appearing during the preceding year.
  Monetary prize. Awarded annually.
Presented: Paris, France, Annually in early
  November

**Prix Medicis Etranger**
Prix Medicis
25 rue Dombasle, 75015 Paris
*Tel:* (01) 48287690 *Fax:* (01) 48287690

*Key Personnel*
Secretary General: Francine Mallet
 *E-mail:* dominique.larre@wanadoo.fr
Established: 1970
For the best foreign novel appearing in French
 during the preceding year. Awarded annually.
Presented: Paris, France, November

**Medicis Prize**
Prix Medicis
25 rue Dombasle, 75015 Paris
*Tel:* (01) 48287690 *Fax:* (01) 48287690
*Key Personnel*
Secretary General: Francine Mallet
 *E-mail:* dominique.larre@wanadoo.fr
Established: 1958
Awarded to an avant-garde novel, story or collec-
 tion whose publication has not been accompa-
 nied by the celebrity or fame the author's talent
 deserves.
Presented: Paris, France, Annually in November

**Prix du Meilleur Livre Etranger**
24, rue de Oudinot, 75007 Paris
*Tel:* (01) 45671898 *Fax:* (01) 45447924
Prize for the best foreign book.

**Grand Prix Thyde Monnier de la SGDL**
Societe des Gens de Lettres de France
Hotel de Massa, 38 rue du Faubourg Saint-
 Jacques, 75014 Paris
*Tel:* (01) 53 10 12 00 *Fax:* (01) 53 10 12 12
*Web Site:* www.sgdl.org
*Key Personnel*
President: Alain Absire
First Vice President: Marie-France Briselance
Secretary General: Jean Claude Bologne
Treasurer: Francois Taillandier
Established: 1975
Annual award in recognition of a cycle of novels
 or for a separate work (novel, essay or collec-
 tion of poems) published during the preced-
 ing two years. Writers whose talents have not
 brought them material success are eligible.
Award: 2,000 EUR

**Prix de Poesie Louis Montalte**
Societe des Gens de Lettres de France
Hotel de Massa, 38 rue du Faubourg Saint-
 Jacques, 75014 Paris
*Tel:* (01) 53 10 12 00 *Fax:* (01) 53 10 12 12
*E-mail:* sgdlf@wanadoo.fr
*Web Site:* www.sgdl.org
*Key Personnel*
President: Alain Absire
First Vice President: Marie-France Briselance
Secretary General: Jean Claude Bologne
Treasurer: Francois Taillandier
For recognition of the complete works of a
 known poet.
Award: 3,000 EUR

**Montyon Prize** (Prix Montyon)
Academie Francaise, Institut de France
23 quai de Conti, 75006 Paris
*Tel:* (01) 44 41 43 10 *Fax:* (01) 44 41 43 11
*E-mail:* com@institut-de-france.fr
*Web Site:* www.institut-de-france.fr
*Key Personnel*
Administration: Claude-Marie Durix
Annual award for any work published by a
 French author showing qualities of practical
 idealism.

**Prix Gerard de Nerval**
Societe des Gens de Lettres de France
Hotel de Massa, 38 rue du Faubourg Saint-
 Jacques, 75014 Paris
*Tel:* (01) 53 10 12 00 *Fax:* (01) 53 10 12 12
*E-mail:* sgdlf@wanadoo.fr
*Web Site:* www.sgdl.org

*Key Personnel*
President: Alain Absire
First Vice President: Marie-France Briselance
Secretary General: Jean Claude Bologne
Treasurer: Francois Taillandier
Established: 1989
For recognition of an outstanding translation of a
 German work.
Award: 2,500 EUR

**Grand Prix Poncetton de la SGDL**
Societe des Gens de Lettres de France
Hotel de Massa, 38 rue du Faubourg Saint-
 Jacques, 75014 Paris
*Tel:* (01) 53 10 12 00 *Fax:* (01) 53 10 12 12
*E-mail:* sgdlf@wanadoo.fr
*Web Site:* www.sgdl.org
*Key Personnel*
President: Alain Absire
First Vice President: Marie-France Briselance
Secretary General: Jean Claude Bologne
Treasurer: Francois Taillandier
Established: 1970
For recognition of the total works of a writer
 whose value has not been recognized & whose
 situation has been seriously affected.
Award: 3,000 EUR

**Prix Jeune Poesie**
la Societe des Poetes Francais
Siege social, 16, rue Monsieur le Prince, 75006
 Paris
*Tel:* (01) 40 46 99 82 *Fax:* (01) 40 46 99 11
*E-mail:* poetesfrancais@aol.com
*Web Site:* www.societedespoetesfrancais.asso.fr
*Key Personnel*
President: Vital Heurtebize
Secretary General: Linda Bastide

**Prix Universalis**
Encylopaedia Universalis
18, rue de Tilsitt, 75017 Paris
*Tel:* (01) 45 72 72 72 *Fax:* (01) 45 72 03 43
*Web Site:* www.universalis.fr

**Concours Promethee** (Prix Promethee)
L'Atelier Imaginaire
BP n°2, 65290 Juillan
*Tel:* (0562) 320 370 *Fax:* (0562) 320 370
*E-mail:* contact@atelier-imaginaire.com
*Web Site:* www.atelier-imaginaire.com
*Key Personnel*
President: Guy Rouquet
Annual short story competition.

**Prix de la reedition**
Societe des Gens de Lettres de France
Hotel de Massa, 38 rue du Faubourg Saint
 Jacques, F-75014 Paris
*Tel:* (01) 53 10 12 00 *Fax:* (01) 53 10 12 12
*Key Personnel*
President: Alain Absire
First Vice President: Marie-France Briselance
Secretary General: Jean Claude Bologne
Treasurer: Francois Taillandier
Award: 1,500 EUR

☆**Lucien de Reinach Prize** (Prix Lucien de
 Reinach)
Academie des Sciences Morales et Politiques, In-
 stitut de France
23 quai de Conti, 75006 Paris
*Tel:* (01) 44 41 43 26 *Fax:* (01) 44 41 43 27
*E-mail:* com@institut-de-france.fr
*Web Site:* www.asmp.fr; www.institut-de-france.fr
*Key Personnel*
Perpetual Secretary: Michel Albert
Biennial award for the best original work written
 in French in the most recent two years on an
 overseas subject.

**Prix Tristan Tzara de Traduction**
 **(Franco-Hongrois)**
Societe des Gens de Lettres de France
Hotel de Massa, 38 rue du Faubourg Saint-
 Jacques, 75014 Paris
*Tel:* (01) 53 10 12 00 *Fax:* (01) 53 10 12 12
*E-mail:* sgdlf@wanadoo.fr
*Web Site:* www.sgdl.org
*Key Personnel*
President: Alain Absire
First Vice President: Marie-France Briselance
Secretary General: Jean Claude Bologne
Treasurer: Francois Taillandier
Established: 1986
For recognition of the Hungarian translation of a
 French work.
Award: 1,500 EUR

**Prix de Poesie Charles Vildrac**
Societe des Gens de Lettres de France
Hotel de Massa, 38 rue du Faubourg Saint-
 Jacques, 75014 Paris
*Tel:* (01) 53 10 12 00 *Fax:* (01) 53 10 12 12
*E-mail:* sgdlf@wanadoo.fr
*Web Site:* www.sgdl.org
*Key Personnel*
President: Alain Absire
First Vice President: Marie-France Briselance
Secretary General: Jean Claude Bologne
Treasurer: Francois Taillandier
Established: 1973
Annual award to recognize a writer of a collec-
 tion of poems published during the year pre-
 ceding the award. Writers under 40 years of
 age are eligible.
Award: 1,500 EUR

**Volney Prize** (Prix Volney)
Academie des Inscriptions et Belles Lettres, Insti-
 tut de France
23 quai de Conti, 75006 Paris
*Tel:* (01) 44 41 43 10 *Fax:* (01) 44 41 43 11
*E-mail:* com@institut-de-france.fr
*Web Site:* www.aibl.fr; www.institut-de-france.fr
*Key Personnel*
Perpetual Secretary: M Jean Leclant *E-mail:* j.
 leclant.aibl@dial.oleane.com
For a work in comparative philology.

# Germany

**Adelbert-von-Chamisso-Preis der Robert Bosch**
 **Stiftung**
Bavarian Academy of Fine Arts
Max-Joseph-Platz 3, 80539 Munich
*Tel:* (089) 29 00 77-0 *Fax:* (089) 29 00 77-23
*E-mail:* info@badsk.de
*Web Site:* www.badsk.de
*Key Personnel*
Contact: Dr Oswald Georg Bauer
Annually.
Other Sponsor(s): Robert Bosch Stiftung

**Andreas-Gryphius-Preis**
Art Society
Hafenmarkt 2, 73728 Esslingen
*Tel:* (0711) 3969010 *Fax:* (0711) 39690123
*E-mail:* kuenstlergilde@t-online.de

**Grosser Literaturpreis der Bayerischen**
 **Akademie der Schonen Kunste**
Bavarian Academy of Fine Arts
Max-Joseph-Platz 3, 80539 Munich
*Tel:* (089) 29 00 77-0 *Fax:* (089) 29 00 77-23
*E-mail:* info@badsk.de
*Web Site:* www.badsk.de

*Key Personnel*
Contact: Dr Oswald Georg Bauer
Annually.

## Berlin Art Prizes
Akademie der Kunste, Berlin
Hanseatenweg 10, 10557 Berlin
*Tel:* (030) 390 76-0 *Fax:* (030) 390 76-175
*E-mail:* info@adk.de
*Web Site:* www.adk.de
*Key Personnel*
President: Dr Adolf Muschy
Established: 1948
Major literary award given for a body of work by
the Akademie der Kuenste (Academy of Arts).
The award, Fontane-Preis, is made once every
six years (a similar award being made in other
disciplines in the intervening five years). In ad-
dition, 'encouragement' prizes of 5,000 EUR
are given annually by the Akademie in each of
the six disciplines, including one for literature
& one for film/TV/radio work (which may be
for writing).
Award: 15,000 EUR
Presented: March 18 annually

## Horst Bienek Award for Poetry
Bavarian Academy of Fine Arts
Max-Joseph-Platz 3, 80539 Munich
*Tel:* (089) 29 00 77-0 *Fax:* (089) 29 00 77-23
*E-mail:* info@badsk.de
*Web Site:* www.badsk.de
*Key Personnel*
Contact: Dr Oswald Georg Bauer
Annually.
Other Sponsor(s): Robert Bosch Stiftung

## ☆Bremen Literatur Prize
Bremen City Council
c/o Stadtbibliothek Bremen, Am Wall 201, 28195
Bremen
Mailing Address: Postfach 10 0241, 28002 Bre-
men
*Tel:* (0421) 3614046; (0421) 3614757 *Fax:* (0421)
3616903
*Web Site:* www.stadtbibliothek.bremen.de
*Key Personnel*
Dir: Barbara Lison *E-mail:* barbara.lison@
stadtbibliothek.bremen.de
Established by Senat der Frein Hansestadt Foun-
dation to encourage German-speaking poets &
writers. Awarded annually for a single work.
Award: 15,389 EUR

## ☆Bremen Literature Encouragement Prize
Bremen City Council
c/o Stadtbibliothek Bremeen, Am Wall 201,
28195 Bremen
Mailing Address: Posfach 10 0241, 28002 Bre-
men
*Tel:* (0421) 3614046; (0421) 3614757 *Fax:* (0421)
3616903
*Web Site:* www.stadtbibliothek.bremen.de
*Key Personnel*
Dir: Barbara Lison *E-mail:* barbara.lison@
stadtbibliothek.bremen.de
Established: 1977
Established by Rudolf-Alexander-Schroeder Foun-
dation to encourage young German-speaking
poets & writers. Awarded annually for a single
work.
Award: 5,113 EUR

## Georg-Buechner Preis
Deutsche Akademie fuer Sprache und Dichtung
(German Academy of Language & Poetry)
Alexandraweg 23, 64287 Darmstadt
*Tel:* (06151) 40920 *Fax:* (06151) 409299
*E-mail:* sekretariat@deutscheakademie.de
*Web Site:* www.deutscheakademie.de

*Key Personnel*
Secretary-General: Dr Bernd Busch
Press Officer: Corinna Blattmann *Tel:* (06151)
409216
Established: 1951
Award: 40,000 EUR
Presented: Autumn annually

## Buxtehuder Bulle
Stadt Buxtehude
Postfach 15 55, 21605 Buxtehude
*Tel:* (04161) 5 01-0 *Fax:* (04161) 5 01-3 18
*E-mail:* stadtverwaltung@stadt.buxtehude.de
*Web Site:* www.stadt.buxtehude.de
Established: 1971
Annual literary prize given to the best book
(young readers 14-18 years of age) published
in Germany during the preceding year. By in-
ternal nomination only.
Award: 5,000 EUR & plaque

## Christoph-Martin-Wieland-Preis
Freundeskreis zur Internationalen Forderung Lit-
erarischer und Wissenschaftlicher Uebersetzun-
gen
Implerstr 28, 81371 Munich
*Tel:* (0049) 89 763098
*Key Personnel*
President: Rosemarie Tietze
Established: 1979
Award: Awarded biennially

## Deutscher Jugendliteratur Preis
Arbeitskreis fur Jugendliteratur eV
Metzstr 14c, 81667 Munich
*Tel:* (089) 4580806 *Fax:* (089) 45808088
*E-mail:* info@jugendliteratur.org
*Web Site:* www.jugendliteratur.org
*Key Personnel*
Project Leader: Kristin Bernd
German Section of the International Board on
Books for Young People.

## Alfred-Doeblin Preis
Akademie der Kunste, Berlin
Hanseatenweg 10, 10557 Berlin
*Tel:* (030) 390 76-0 *Fax:* (030) 390 76-175
*E-mail:* info@adk.de
*Web Site:* www.adk.de
*Key Personnel*
President: Dr Adolf Muschy
Established: 1983
This award will generally be made every one or
two years for unpublished work of an epic na-
ture.
Award: Up to 10,226 EUR

## Annette von Droste Huelshoff Preis
Landschaftsverband Westfalen - Lippe Abteilung
Kulturpflege
Warendorfer Str 24, 48133 Muenster
*Tel:* (0251) 591-233 *Fax:* (0251) 591-268
*E-mail:* abt.kulturpflege@lwl.org
*Web Site:* www.lwl.org/kultur
*Key Personnel*
Contact: Prof Karl Teppe
Established: 1946
Biennial award for recognition of special achieve-
ment in poetry written in either high or low
German. Every third time it can be awarded
for creative musical achievement. Recipients
must be natives or residents of the Westfalian -
Lippe region of Germany. Established by Prov-
inzialverband Westfalen in memory of the Ger-
man & Westfalian poetess, Annette von Droste-
Hulshoff (1797-1848). Formerly: Westfaelischer
Literaturpreis.
Award: 12,782 EUR & certificate

## Konrad Duden Prize
Stadt Mannheim, Amt fuer Rats und Oef-
fentlichkeitsarbeit
Rathaus E5, 68159 Mannheim
*Tel:* (0621) 293 0 *Fax:* (0621) 293 9532
*E-mail:* masta@mannheim.de
*Web Site:* www.mannheim.de
*Key Personnel*
Contact: Kirsten Batzler *E-mail:* kirsten.batzler@
mannheim.de
Awarded biennially to personalities who have par-
ticularly contributed to the German language.
The award is noncompetitive.
Award: 12,500 EUR

## Sigmund Freud Preis Fluer Wissenschaftliche Prosa
Deutsche Akademie fuer Sprache und Dichtung
(German Academy of Language & Poetry)
Alexandraweg 23, 64287 Darmstadt
*Tel:* (06151) 40920 *Fax:* (06151) 409299
*E-mail:* sekretariat@deutscheakademie.de
*Web Site:* www.deutscheakademie.de
*Key Personnel*
Secretary-General: Dr Bernd Busch
Press Officer: Corinna Blattmann *Tel:* (06151)
409216
Established: 1964
Award: 12,500 EUR
Presented: Autumn annually

## Friedenspreis des Deutschen Buchhandels
(Peace Prize of the German Book Trade)
Borsenverein des Deutschen Buchhandels eV
Grosser Hirschgraben 17/21, 60311 Frankfurt am
Main
*Tel:* (069) 1306-0 *Fax:* (069) 1306-201
*E-mail:* info@boev.de
*Web Site:* www.boersenverein.de
*Key Personnel*
Acting Man Dir: Dr Harald Heker
Established: 1950
The prize is an amount made up exclusively of
donations from publishers & booksellers. The
Peace Prize is an impressive indication of the
book trade's commitment to serve international
understanding by its activities. According to
tradition, the prize has been awarded annually.
Award: 15,000 EUR
Presented: The Frankfurt Book Fair, Autumn

## Friedrich-Gerstaecker Preis-der Stadt Braunschweig
Stadt Braunschweig-Kulturinstitut
Steintorwall 3, 38100 Braunschweig
*Tel:* (0531) 470 4840 *Fax:* (0531) 470 4809
*E-mail:* kulturinstitut@braunschweig.de
*Web Site:* www.braunschweig.de
Award: 6,000 EUR awarded biennially

## Friedrich Gundolf Preis fuer die Vermittlung Deutscher Kultur im Ausland (Friedrich Gundolf Prize for German Culture in Foreign Countries)
Deutsche Akademie fuer Sprache und Dichtung
(German Academy of Language & Poetry)
Alexandraweg 23, 64287 Darmstadt
*Tel:* (06151) 40920 *Fax:* (06151) 409299
*E-mail:* sekretariat@deutscheakademie.de
*Web Site:* www.deutscheakademie.de
*Key Personnel*
Secretary-General: Dr Bernd Busch
Press Officer: Corinna Blattmann *Tel:* (06151)
409216
Established: 1964
Award: 12,500 EUR
Presented: Spring annually

## Johann-Peter-Hebel-Preis
Ministerium fur Wisserschaft, Forschung und
Kunst Baden-Wurttemberg

Koenigstr 46, 70173 Stuttgart
*Tel:* (0711) 279-3004 *Fax:* (0711) 279-3081
*E-mail:* presse@mwk.bwl.de; poststelle@mwk.
  bwl.de
*Web Site:* www.mwk-bw.de
*Key Personnel*
Publications: Dr Gunter Schanz

### ☆Wilhelm Heinse Medal for Literature in Essay Form (Wilhelm-Heinse-Medaille)
Akademie der Wissenschaften und der Literatur,
  Klasse der Literatur
Geschwister-Scholl-Str 2, 55131 Mainz
*Tel:* (06131) 577-0 *Fax:* (06131) 577-206
*Web Site:* www.adwmainz.de
*Key Personnel*
Contact: Juliane Klein *Tel:* (06131) 577-201
  *E-mail:* juliane.klein@adwmainz.de
Established: 1978
Awarded biennially.

### Ricarda-Huch-Preis
City of Darmstadt
Luisenplatz 5, 64283 Darmstadt 11
*Tel:* (06151) 131 *Fax:* (06151) 133777
*E-mail:* presseamt@darmstadt.de; info@
  darmstadt.de
*Web Site:* www.darmstadt.de
Established: 1978
Award: 10,250 EUR

### ☆Inter Nationes Culture Prize
Inter Nationes eV
Kennedyalle 91-103, 53175 Bonn
*Tel:* (0228) 8800 *Fax:* (0228) 880457
*E-mail:* info@inter-nationes.de
*Web Site:* www.inter-nationes.de
Established: 1968
Biennial award to recognize publishers, historians,
  writers, translators, etc., who have made a valu-
  able contribution to international understanding
  in cultural fields. Awarded to foreign nationals
  only. Formerly Inter Nationes - Preis fur Werke
  der Literatur und bildenden Kunst (1988).
Award: 5,113 EUR & a personally dedicated
  booklet

### International Youth Library, see White Ravens

### Thomas Mann Prize
Hansestadt Lubeck-Bereich Kunst und Kultur
Breite Str 62, 23539 Luebeck
*Tel:* (0451) 12 21 300 *Fax:* (0451) 12 21 331
*E-mail:* kunst-und-kultur@luebeck.de; info@
  luebeck.de
*Web Site:* www.luebeck.de
Established: 1975
Founded in honor of Thomas Mann, to celebrate
  the 100th anniversary of his birth. The prize
  will be awarded to personalities who have,
  through their literary work, shown the human-
  itarian spirit set out in the work of Thomas
  Mann. No application fee. Awarded triennially.
Award: 7,669 EUR

### Johann-Heinrich-Merck-Preis fuer literarische Kritik und Essay (J H Merck Prize for Literary Criticism & Essay)
Deutsche Akademie fuer Sprache und Dichtung
  (German Academy of Language & Poetry)
Alexandraweg 23, 64287 Darmstadt
*Tel:* (06151) 40920 *Fax:* (06151) 409299
*E-mail:* sekretariat@deutscheakademie.de
*Web Site:* www.deutscheakademie.de
*Key Personnel*
Secretary-General: Dr Bernd Busch
  *E-mail:* bernd.busch@deutscheakademie.de
Press Officer: Corinna Blattmann *Tel:* (06151)
  409216 *E-mail:* corinna.blattmann@
  deutscheakademie.de
Established: 1964

Award: 12,500 EUR
Presented: Autumn annually

### Rolandpreis fur Kunst im offentlichen Raum
Senator for Bildung, Wissenschaft, Kunst und
  Sport
Rembertiring 8-12, 28195 Bremen
*Tel:* (0421) 361-4995; (0421) 361-2978
  *Fax:* (0421) 361-15543
Established: 1989
Bremen City Council.

### Schiller Prize
Stadt Mannheim, Amt fuer Rats und Oef-
  fentlichkeitsarbeit
Rathaus E5, 68159 Mannheim
*Tel:* (0621) 293 0 *Fax:* (0621) 293-9532
*E-mail:* masta@mannheim.de
*Web Site:* www.mannheim.de
*Key Personnel*
Contact: Rainer Gluth *E-mail:* rainer.gluth@
  mannheim.de
Prize awarded to persons who have contributed.
  Awarded every four years significantly to cul-
  tural development by their total works or an in-
  dividual work of outstanding quality, or whose
  previous work shows promise in the cultural
  field.
Award: 12,782 EUR

### Literaturpreis der Landeshauptstadt Stuttgart (Stuttgart Literary Prize)
Landeshauptstadt Stuttgart
Rathaus, Marktplatz(M) 1, 70173 Stuttgart
*Tel:* (0711) 216-0 *Fax:* (0711) 216-4773
*E-mail:* post@stuttgart.de
*Web Site:* www.stuttgart.de
*Telex:* 722854 Kult d
*Key Personnel*
Contact: Dr Wolfgang Schuster
Award: 20,000 EUR

### Thaddaeus-Troll-Preis
Foerderkreis Deutscher Schriftsteller in Baden-
  Wurttemberg eV
Gartenstr 58, 76135 Karlsruhe
*Fax:* (0711) 6365364
*E-mail:* info@schriftsteller-in-bawue.de
*Web Site:* www.schriftsteller-in-bawue.de
*Key Personnel*
Chairman: Ulrich Zimmermann
Established: 1981
Applications not accepted for this award.
Award: Foerderpreis

### Johann-Heinrich-Voss-Preis fuer Uebersetzung
Deutsche Akademie fuer Sprache und Dichtung
  (German Academy of Language & Poetry)
Alexandraweg 23, 64287 Darmstadt
*Tel:* (06151) 40920 *Fax:* (06151) 409299
*E-mail:* sekretariat@deutscheakademie.de
*Web Site:* www.deutscheakademie.de
*Key Personnel*
Secretary-General: Dr Bernd Busch
Press Officer: Corinna Blattmann *Tel:* (06151)
  409216
Established: 1958
Award: 15,000 EUR
Presented: Spring annually

### Walter Tiemann Award
Hochschule fuer Grafik und Buchkunst Leipzig
  (Academy of Visual Arts Leipzig)
Waechterstr 11, 04107 Leipzig
*Tel:* (0341) 21 35-0 *Fax:* (0341) 21 35-166
*E-mail:* hgb@hbg-leipzig.de
*Web Site:* www.hgb-leipzig.de
*Key Personnel*
Public Administration & Public Relations: Sibylle
  Schulz Shibru

To recognize independent publishers, small publishers & printing-presses. One to three different titles published within the preceding two
  years may be submitted. Established in honor
  of Walter Tiemann, a teacher & the rector from
  1920 to 1945.
Award: A small sculpture & 1st prize 5,113 EUR;
  2nd prize 1,534 EUR; 3rd prize 1,023 EUR

### White Ravens
Internationale Jugendbibliothek (International
  Youth Library)
Schloss Blutenburg, 81247 Munich
*Tel:* (089) 8912110 *Fax:* (089) 8117553
*E-mail:* bib@ijb.de; information@ijb.de
*Web Site:* www.ijb.de
Established: 1983
Awarded annually to promote high quality chil-
  dren's books of international interest. About
  250 children's books, by authors & illustrators
  from all over the world, are given recognition.
  Children's books submitted by publishers dur-
  ing the year prior to the award are considered.
  White Ravens books are listed in the annual
  international selected bibliography & exhibited
  during the Children's Book Fair in Bologna,
  Italy & thereafter upon request in libraries &
  other institutions. Titles in over 30 languages
  from 50 countries.
Closing Date: Dec
Presented: Bologna Children's Book Fair, Italy,
  April

# Greece

### Book Prizes of the Circle of the Greek Children's Book
Circle of the Greek Children's Book IBBY
  (Greek Section)
Bouboulinas 28, 106 82 Athens
*Tel:* 2108222296 *Fax:* 2108222296
*E-mail:* kyklos@greekibby.gr
*Web Site:* www.greekibby.gr
*Key Personnel*
President: Loty Petrovits *Tel:* 2108223008
  *E-mail:* loty@loty.gr
Established: 1970
Awarded annually for various types of children's
  literature.
Award: 1,000 to 1,500 EUR

### Parnassos Foundation Prize
Parnassos Literary Society
8 George Karytsis Sq, 105 61 Athens
*Tel:* 2103213363 *Fax:* 2103249398
Established: 1980
Annual award to provide recognition for the best
  play of the year.
Award: Monetary prize & honorary recognition

# Haiti

### Prix litteraire Henri Deschamps (Henri Deschamps Literary Prize)
Maison Henri Deschamps, Grand Rue
PO Box 164, Port-au-Prince
*Tel:* (509) 223-2215; (509) 223-2216 *Fax:* (509)
  223-4975
*E-mail:* entdeschamps@gdfhaiti.com
*Key Personnel*
Secretary General: Paulette Poujol Oriol
Established: 1975

Annual award open to unpublished Haitian writers, on any subject.
Award: 1,000 USD & 1,000 free publishing copies

# Hong Kong

**Awards for Creative Writing in Chinese**
Hong Kong Public Libraries
66 Causeway Rd, Causeway Bay, Hong Kong
*Tel:* 2921 0208 *Fax:* 2415 8211
*E-mail:* enquiries@lcsd.gov.hk
*Web Site:* www.hkpl.gov.hk
*Key Personnel*
Assistant Dir: Michael Mak *E-mail:* mklmak@lcsd.gov.hk
Senior Librarian (Extension Activities):
 Sun Tinny YM *Tel:* (02) 2921 2687
 *E-mail:* tymsun@lcsd.gov.hk
Established: 1979
Biennial award to residents of Hong Kong 16 years of age & over, under six categories (prose, poetry, fiction, literary criticism, children's storybook & children's picture book) to cultivate interest in creative writing in Chinese.
Award: 1st prize: 12,000 HKD for each category

**Hong Kong Biennial Award for Chinese Literature**
Hong Kong Public Libraries
66 Causeway Rd, Causeway Bay, Hong Kong
*Tel:* (02) 2921 0208 *Fax:* (02) 2415 8211
*E-mail:* enquiries@lcsd.gov.hk
*Web Site:* www.hkpl.gov.hk
*Key Personnel*
Senior Librarian (Extension Activities):
 Sun Tinny YM *Tel:* (02) 2921 2687
 *E-mail:* tymsun@lcsd.gov.hk
Established: 1991
Award is by open nomination to give recognition to the outstanding achievements of established Hong Kong writers & to encourage them to write quality literary work. Awards presented biennially for fiction, prose, poetry, children's literature & literary criticism, published in Hong Kong in the previous two years & written in Chinese.
Award: 50,000 HKD

# Hungary

**Jozsef Attila Prize**
Ministry of Culture & Education
Szalay-utca 10/14, 1055 Budapest
*Tel:* (01) 473-7000 *Fax:* (01) 473-7001
*E-mail:* info@om.hu
*Web Site:* www.om.hu
For highly significant work in prose or poetry. Given to writers, poets & critics. Since 1950 awarded to 8-10 people a year.

**Robert Graves Prize**
Hungarian Writers' Union
Magyar Iroszovetseg, Bajza utca 18, 1062 Budapest
*Tel:* (01) 322-8840; (01) 322-0631 *Fax:* (01) 321-3419
*Key Personnel*
President: Marton Kalasz

**Kossuth Prize**
Muvelodesi Miniszterium
Kossuth Lajos-Ter 1-3, 1055 Budapest, V
*Tel:* (01) 1120600 *Fax:* (01) 530124
Established: 1948
An irregular award to outstanding artists, including writers.

☆**Hungarian PEN Club Medal**
Hungarian PEN Centre
Karolyi Mihaly u 16, 1053 Budapest
*Tel:* (01) 184143
For translation of Hungarian literary work into foreign languages. Awarded when merited.

**Szakszervezete Muveszeti Kulturalis Dij** (Trade Union's Art & Cultural Prize)
National Confederation of Hungarian Trade Unions (Magyar Szakszervezetek Orszagos Szovetsege)
Magdolna u 5-7, 1086 Budapest
*Tel:* (01) 3232 660 *Fax:* (01) 3232 662
*E-mail:* sajto@mszosz.hu; ikorte@mszosz.hu
*Web Site:* www.mszosz.hu
Established: 1958
Awarded annually. Established by the Central Council of Hungarian Trade Unions, prizes are awarded to artists, scientists, educators, as well as for literary works. Nominees are people who excel in improving worker-artist contacts & in disseminating knowledge. Selection is by public opinion poll.

# India

**Bhai Santokh Singh Award**
Haryana Sahitya Akademi
1563/18-D, Chanaigarh 160018
*Tel:* (0172) 565521; (0172) 563340
*Key Personnel*
Dir: A S Shergill
Awarded annually to an Indian national domiciled in Haryana State for contributions to the development of Panjabi literature. Presented for the life long contribution to the Panjabi writer once in a lifetime.
Award: 21,000 INR

**I C Chacko Award**
Kerala Sahitya Akademi
Town Hall Rd, Thrissur, Kerala 680020
*Tel:* (011) 331069
*Web Site:* www.keralasahityaakademi.org
*Key Personnel*
Secretary: P V Krishnan Nair
Awarded annually for the best book published in Malayalam during the preceding three years in the field of linguistics.
Award: 2,000 INR

**Escorts Book Award**
Delhi Management Association
India Habitat Centre, Core 6A, 1st floor, Lodhi Rd, New Delhi 110003
*Tel:* (011) 4649552; (011) 4649551 *Fax:* (011) 4649553
*E-mail:* dmadelhi@ndb.vsnl.net.in
*Key Personnel*
Program Manager: S Kumar
Established: 1965
Instituted by Escorts Ltd & administered by Delhi Management Association. For original books on management principles & practices by Indian writers. Awarded annually.
Award: 5,000 & 3,000 INR each

**Indian Books Centre Oriental Studies Award**
Sri Satguru Publications
40/5 Shakti Nagar, Delhi 110007
*Tel:* (011) 27434930; (011) 27126497 *Fax:* (011) 27227336
*E-mail:* ibcindia@vsnl.com
*Web Site:* www.indianbookscentre.com
For the best work in Oriental Studies, published in Sanskrit, English, Tibetan or Hindi.
Award: 1,100 INR, a shawl & a citation are awarded on a regular basis

**Jnanpith Award**
Bharatiya Jnanpith
18 Institutional Area, Lodi Rd, New Delhi 110 003
*Tel:* (011) 4626467; (011) 4654196; (011) 4656201; (011) 4698417 *Fax:* (011) 4654197
*E-mail:* jnanpith@satyam.net.in; jnanpith@satyam.com
*Key Personnel*
Dir: Aditya Sharma

**Kerala Sahitya Akademi Awards**
Kerala Sahitya Akademi
Town Hall Rd, Thrissur, Kerala 680020
*Tel:* (011) 331069
*Web Site:* www.keralasahityaakademi.org
*Key Personnel*
Secretary: P V Krishnan Nair
Annual awards for literary works in Malayalam published during the preceding three years, in the following categories: fiction; drama; poetry; short stories; novels; literary criticism; (biography; autobiography; travelogs & humor); scientific & scholarly works (including philosophy; education; sociology).
Award: varies

**C B Kumar Award**
Kerala Sahitya Akademi
Town Hall Rd, Thrissur, Kerala 680020
*Tel:* (011) 331069
*Web Site:* www.keralasahityaakademi.org
*Key Personnel*
Secretary: P V Krishnan Nair
Annual award for the best collection of essays in Malayalam.
Award: 1,500 INR

**Kuttippuzha Award**
Kerala Sahitya Akademi
Town Hall Rd, Thrissur, Kerala 680020
*Tel:* (011) 331069
*Web Site:* www.keralasahityaakademi.org
*Key Personnel*
Secretary: P V Krishnan Nair
Awarded annually for the best book of criticism published in Malayalam during the preceding three years.
Award: 2,000 INR

**Law Books in Hindu Prize**
Indian Law Institute
Bhagwan Das Rd, New Delhi 110 001
*Tel:* (011) 23387526 *Fax:* (011) 23782140
*E-mail:* ili@ilidelhi.org
*Web Site:* www.ilidelhi.org
Awarded annually for law books/manuscripts in Hindi. The first prize is 10,000 INR & prizes up to 100,000 INR may be awarded.

**Mahrishi Vedvyasa Prize**
Haryana Sahitya Akademi
1563/18-D, Chanaigarh 160018
*Tel:* (0172) 565521
Awarded annually to an Indian national domiciled in Haryana State for contribution towards the development of Sanskrit literature.
Award: 15,000 INR

**Meera Award**
Rajasthan Sahitya Akademi
Hiran Magri, Sector 4, Udaipur 313 002

*Tel:* (0294) 583717; (0294) 583629
Established: 1959
Awarded annually for the best literary work in
Hindi.
Award: 11,000 INR

**K R Namboodiri Award**
Kerala Sahitya Akademi
Town Hall Rd, Thrissur, Kerala 680020
*Tel:* (011) 331069
*Web Site:* www.keralasahityaakademi.org
*Key Personnel*
Secretary: P V Krishnan Nair
Awarded annually for the best work on Vedic lit-
erature in Malayalam.
Award: 2,000 INR

**Pandit Lakhmi Chand Prize**
Haryana Sahitya Akademi
1563/18-D, Chanaigarh 160018
*Tel:* (0172) 565521
Awarded annually to an Indian national for out-
standing work on literature, art, history & cul-
ture of Haryana.
Award: 15,000 INR

**Sahitya Akademi Award**
Sahitya Akademi (National Academy of Letters)
Rabindra Bhavan, 35 Ferozshah Rd, New Delhi
110 001
*Tel:* (011) 3386626; (011) 3386627; (011)
3386628; (011) 3386629; (011) 3387386; (011)
3386088 *Fax:* (011) 3382428
*Web Site:* www.sahitya-akademi.org
*Key Personnel*
Secretary: Prof K Satchidanandan *E-mail:* secy@
sahitya-akademi.org
Established: 1955
For outstanding literary works written in each of
the 22 languages of India recognized by the
Indian National Academy of Letters (Sahitya
Akademi). Awarded annually to Indian nation-
als only.
Award: 25,000 INR each
Closing Date: Dec annually
Presented: New Delhi, Feb annually

**Sur Award**
Haryana Sahitya Akademi
1563/18-D, Chanaigarh 160018
*Tel:* (0172) 565521
Awarded annually to an Indian national domiciled
in Haryana State for outstanding contribution to
development of Hindi, Sanskrit & Haryanvi.
Award: 50,000 INR

**Sree Padmanabha Swami Prize**
Kerala Sahitya Akademi
Town Hall Rd, Thrissur, Kerala 680020
*Tel:* (011) 331069
*Web Site:* www.keralasahityaakademi.org
*Key Personnel*
Secretary: P V Krishnan Nair
Awarded annually for the best drama literature
published in Malayalam during the preceding
three years.
Award: 10,000 INR

**Tagore Literacy Award**
Indian Adult Education Association
17-B, I P Estate, New Delhi 110 002
*Tel:* (011) 3319282; (011) 3722206; (011)
3721336 *Fax:* (011) 3366306
*E-mail:* iaea@vsnl.com
*Key Personnel*
President: B S Garg
Recognition of outstanding contribution to promo-
tion of women's literacy & adult education in
India.

**Urdu Akademy Awards**
Urdu Academy Delhi
Ghata Masjid Rd, Darya Ganj, New Delhi 110002
*Tel:* (011) 3276211; (011) 3262693; (011)
3251206
*E-mail:* urduacademy@yahoo.com
Awarded annually to Indian nationals for Urdu
literature.

# Islamic Republic of Iran

**Children's Book Council Award** (Jayezeh
Showraye Ketabe Koodak)
Children's Book Council of Iran
PO Box 13145-133, Tehran 13158
*Tel:* (021) 6408074 *Fax:* (021) 6405878
*E-mail:* anmo@kanoon.net
*Web Site:* www.schoolnet.ir/~cbc
*Key Personnel*
General Secretary: Noushine Ansari
Established: 1963
For recognition of a contribution in the field of
children's literature. Iranian writers, illustrators
& translations are eligible. Established by A
Yamini Sharif.
Award: A plaque or diploma is awarded annually
Presented: CBCI Annual Meeting, Jan annually

# Ireland

**Aosdana Membership**
The Arts Council/An Chomhairle Ealaion
70 Merrion Sq, Dublin 2
*Tel:* (01) 618 0200 *Fax:* (01) 676 1302
*E-mail:* info@artscouncil.ie
*Web Site:* www.artscouncil.ie
*Key Personnel*
Dir: Mary Cloake *Tel:* (01) 618 0225
Special honorary affiliation of creative artists. To
be eligible for membership, the artist must have
been born in Ireland or been a resident of Ire-
land for five years, must not be less than 35
years of age & must have produced a body of
works. Membership is by election.
Award: Annuities up to 11,072 EUR

**The Clo Iar-Chonnacta Literary Award**
Clo Iar-Chonnachta Teo
Indreabhan, Conamara, Co Galway
*Tel:* (091) 593 307 *Fax:* (091) 593 362
*E-mail:* cic@iol.ie
*Web Site:* www.cic.ie
*Key Personnel*
General Manager: Deirdre Thuathail
Presented annually for a newly written & unpub-
lished work in the Irish language.
Award: 5,000 GBP
Closing Date: Dec

**Denis Devlin Memorial Award for Poetry**
The Arts Council/An Chomhairle Ealaion
70 Merrion Sq, Dublin 2
*Tel:* (01) 618 0200 *Fax:* (01) 676 1302
*E-mail:* info@artscouncil.ie
*Web Site:* www.artscouncil.ie
*Key Personnel*
Dir: Mary Cloake *Tel:* (01) 618 0225

Given for the finest collection of poetry in the
English language by an Irish citizen published
in the previous three years.
Award: 1,500 GBP

**Fish Short Story Prize**
Fish Publishing
Durrus, Bantry, Co Cork
*Tel:* (027) 55645 *Fax:* (027) 61246
*E-mail:* info@fishpublishing.com
*Web Site:* www.fishpublishing.com
*Key Personnel*
Dir: Clem Cairns; Jula Walton
Established: 1994
Closing Date: Nov 30 annually

**Fish Unpublished Novel Award**
Fish Publishing
Durrus, Bantry, Co Cork
*Tel:* (027) 55645 *Fax:* (027) 61246
*E-mail:* info@fishpublishing.com
*Web Site:* www.fishpublishing.com
*Key Personnel*
Dir: Clem Cairns; Jula Walton
Closing Date: Sept

**Fish VERY Short Story Prize**
Fish Publishing
Durrus, Bantry, Co Cork
*Tel:* (027) 55645 *Fax:* (027) 61246
*E-mail:* info@fishpublishing.com
*Web Site:* www.fishpublishing.com
*Key Personnel*
Dir: Clem Cairns; Jula Walton
Established: 2003
Closing Date: Feb 14 annually

**Gregory Medal**
Irish Academy of Letters, School of Irish Studies
4 Ailesbury Grove, Dundum, Dublin 14
For distinction in letters or outstanding literary
work in Irish. Awarded periodically.

☆**International Fiction Prize**
Irish Times Ltd
10-16 D'Olier St, Dublin 2
*Tel:* (01) 6758000 *Fax:* (01) 6793910
*E-mail:* services@irish-times.com
*Web Site:* www.ireland.com
Awarded biannually for a work of fiction written
in English & published in Ireland, the United
Kingdom or the United States within a two
year period from August 1 of the previous year
to July 31 of the year of the prize. Four titles
are shortlisted for this prize.

☆**The Irish Literature Prize: Fiction**
Irish Times Ltd
10-16 D'Olier St, Dublin 2
*Tel:* (01) 6758000 *Fax:* (01) 6773282
*E-mail:* services@irish-times.com
*Web Site:* www.ireland.com
Awarded biannually along with the Poetry Prize.
Books can be in either English or Irish & pub-
lished in Ireland, the United Kingdom or the
United States within a two-year time period
from August 1 & July 31 of the year of the
prize. Three books are shortlisted for this prize.

☆**The Irish Literature Prize: Nonfiction**
Irish Times Ltd
10-16 D'Olier St, Dublin 2
*Tel:* (01) 6758000 *Fax:* (01) 6773282
*E-mail:* services@irish-times.com
*Web Site:* www.ireland.com
Awarded biannually along with the First Book
Prize. Books can be in either English or Irish
& published in Ireland, the United Kingdom
or the United States within a two-year period
from August 1 & July 31 of the year of the
prize. Three books are shortlisted for this prize.

## ☆The Irish Literature Prize: Poetry
Irish Times Ltd
10-16 D'Olier St, Dublin 2
*Tel:* (01) 6758000 *Fax:* (01) 6773282
*E-mail:* services@irish-times.com
*Web Site:* www.ireland.com
Awarded biannually along with the Fiction Prize. Books can be in either English or Irish & published in Ireland, the United Kingdom or the United States within a two-year period from August 1 & July 31 of the year of the prize. Three books are shortlisted for this prize.

## Macaulay Fellowship
The Arts Council/An Chomhairle Ealaion
70 Merrion Sq, Dublin 2
*Tel:* (01) 618 0200 *Fax:* (01) 676 1302
*E-mail:* info@artscouncil.ie
*Web Site:* www.artscouncil.ie
*Key Personnel*
Dir: Mary Cloake *Tel:* (01) 618 0225
Triennial award in literature to young Irish writers who are usually under 30 years of age.
Award: 3,500 GBP

## Novel Prize
Irish Academy of Letters, School of Irish Studies
4 Ailesbury Grove, Dundum, Dublin 14
For the best novel written in Irish. Awarded annually.

## ☆The Prize for Poetry in Irish/An Duais don bhFiliiocht in Gaeilge
The Arts Council/An Chomhairle Ealaion
70 Merrion Sq, Dublin 2
*Tel:* (01) 618 0200 *Fax:* (01) 676 1302
*E-mail:* info@artscouncil.ie
*Web Site:* www.artscouncil.ie
*Key Personnel*
Dir: Mary Cloake *Tel:* (01) 618 0225
Established: 1962
Awarded to the author of the best book of poetry in the Irish language (Gaelic) published in the previous three years.
Award: 1,500 GBP

## Rooney Prize for Irish Literature
Rooney Prize Committee
Strathin, Templecarrig, Delgany Co, Wicklow
*Tel:* (01) 2874769 *Fax:* (01) 2872595
*E-mail:* rooneyprize@ireland.com
*Key Personnel*
Chairman: Jim Sherwin *E-mail:* jsherwin@rol.ue
Annual award for Irish Literature. A noncompetitive prize to encourage young Irish creative talent. Enquiries to Jim Sherwin at above address.
Award: 5,000 IRL

## Marten Toonder Award
The Arts Council/An Chomhairle Ealaion
70 Merrion Sq, Dublin 2
*Tel:* (01) 618 0200 *Fax:* (01) 676 1302
*E-mail:* info@artscouncil.ie
*Web Site:* www.artscouncil.ie
*Key Personnel*
Dir: Mary Cloake *Tel:* (01) 618 0225
Triennial literature award.
Award: 7,875 GBP - 10,000 GBP

# Israel

## ACUM Prize for Literature and Music
Society of Authors, Composers and Music Publishers in Israel
PO Box 14220, 61140 Tel Aviv
*Tel:* (03) 6850115 *Fax:* (03) 5620119
Established: 1957
To encourage creative work in the fields of literature & music. Israeli citizens are eligible.
Award: Monetary prizes annually

## Award for Original Hebrew Novel
Mordechai Bernstein Literary Prizes Association
c/o The Book Publishers Association of Israel, 29 Carlebach St, 67132 Tel Aviv
Mailing Address: PO Box 20123, 61201 Tel Aviv
*Tel:* (03) 5614121 *Fax:* (03) 5611996
*E-mail:* info@tbpai.co.il
*Web Site:* www.tbpai.co.il
Established: 1981
To encourage authors under the age 50 who write Hebrew novels. Established to honor Mordechal Bernstein, an Israeli author.
Award: Monetary award, biennially

## Award for Original Hebrew Poetry
Mordechai Bernstein Literary Prizes Association
c/o The Book Publishers Association of Israel, 29 Carlebach St, 67132 Tel Aviv
Mailing Address: PO Box 20123, 61201 Tel Aviv
*Tel:* (03) 5614121 *Fax:* (03) 5611996
*E-mail:* info@tbpai.co.il
Established: 1981
To encourage Hebrew poets under the age of 50. Established in honor of Mordechai Bernstein, an Israeli author.
Award: A monetary prize is awarded biennially

## Bialik Prize for Literature
Tel-Aviv-Yafo Municipality
Dept of Municipal Prizes, Tel Aviv
*Web Site:* www.tel-aviv.gov.il/english/home.asp
The highest literary award of the Tel-Aviv-Yafo Municipality, awarded in two categories: belles-lettres & Jewish studies.
Award: 80,000 shekels awarded annually

## Brenner Prize
Hebrew Writers' Association in Israel
PO Box 7111, Tel Aviv
*Tel:* (03) 253-256
In recognition of outstanding literary works.
Award: 12,000 shekels awarded annually

## Israeli Prize in Humanities and Social Sciences
Israeli Ministry of Education and Culture
Rechov Shivtei Yisrael 34, 91911 Jerusalem
*Tel:* (02) 278211
For the most original, outstanding contribution to the humanities & social sciences. Prize awarded annually in each one of the following areas: (1) Judaica, Modern Hebrew Literature & Education; (2) the Humanities & the Social Sciences; (3) the Arts; (4) Science & Technology; (5) outstanding life-long service to the welfare of Israeli society.
Award: 110,000 shekels

## ☆The Jerusalem Prize For Freedom of the Individual in Society
Jerusalem International Book Fair
PO Box 775, Jerusalem 91007
*Tel:* (02) 629 7922; (02) 629 6412 *Fax:* (02) 624 3144
*E-mail:* jerfairs@jerusalem.muni.il
*Web Site:* www.jerusalembookfair.com
*Key Personnel*
Chairman & Man Dir: Zev Birger
Contact: Annette Aaronson
Established: 1963
Biennial award made to a world-renowned author whose works express the idea of the freedom of the individual in society.
Award: $5,000 cash
Presented: Jerusalem International Book Fair

## Shazar Prize
Israel Ministry of Education & Culture
Rechov Shivtei Yisrael 34, 91911 Jerusalem
*Tel:* (02) 278-211
Awarded to immigrant writers, young authors & writers dealing with the Holocaust.
Award: 5,000 to 12,000 shekels to each author, awarded annually

## Tchernichowsky Prize
Tel-Aviv-Yafo Municipality
Dept of Municipal Prizes, Tel Aviv
*Web Site:* www.tel-aviv.gov.il/english/home.asp
For outstanding translations into Hebrew. 60,000 shekels divided between two translators: one of belles-lettres & one of scientific material. Awarded biennially.
Award: 60,000 shekels divided

# Italy

## Bagutta Prize
Bagutta Restaurant
via Bagutta 14, 20121 Milan
*Tel:* (02) 76000902; (02) 76002767 *Fax:* (02) 799613
*Web Site:* www.bagutta.it; www.acena.it/bagutta
Founded in 1926 for the best book of the year. Annual award given for several literary forms including the novel & poetry.

## ☆BolognaRagazzi Award
Bologna Children's Book Fair
Viale della Fiera 20, 40128 Bologna
*Tel:* (051) 282213; (051) 282111 *Fax:* (051) 6374040
*E-mail:* visitorinfo@art4.it
*Web Site:* www.bookfair.bolognafiere.it
*Key Personnel*
Contact: Marisa del Todesco *E-mail:* marisa.deltodesco@bolognafiere.it
Established: 1966
Annual award aimed to focus attention on publishing houses of emerging countries (Arab world, Latin America, Asia & Africa) where children's literature offers new angles free of well-established traditions.

## Isle of Elba - Rafaello Brignetti Literary Award
Premio Letterario Isola d'Elba - Raffaello Brignetti
c/o Consorzio Elba Promotion, Calata Italia 26, 57037 Portoferraio LI
*Tel:* (056) 5960157 *Fax:* (056) 5917632
*E-mail:* cronaca@elbaoggi.it
*Web Site:* www.elbaexplorer.com
Annual award for recognition of outstanding works of prose, poetry, or literary essays. Works by European authors published in Italy or translated into Italian during the previous year are eligible. Formerly Premio Letterario Isola d'Elba. Renamed in 1984 in honor of Raffaello Brignetti.
Award: 5,165 EUR

## Campiello Prize
Campiello Foundation
Via Torino, 151/c, 30172 Mestre-Venice
*Tel:* (041) 2517511 *Fax:* (041) 2517576
*E-mail:* campiello@industrialiveneto.org
*Web Site:* www.premiocampiello.org
*Telex:* 420380
Established: 1963
Promoted by the seven industrial association founder members of Fondazione Campiello.

Annual award for a previously unpublished work of fiction.
Award: 8,263 EUR

### ☆Giosue Carduccie Prize
Bologna University
via Zamboni 33, 40126 Bologna
*Tel:* (51) 228621
*Web Site:* www.unibo.it
Established: 1950
For poetry, monographs & essays on poetry & poets. Awarded annually.
Award: 775 EUR

### Castello-Sanguinetto Prize
Comune di Sanguinetto
Interno Castello 2, 37058 Sanguinetto VR
*Tel:* (0442) 81036 *Fax:* (0442) 365150
*E-mail:* info@comune.sanguinetto.vr.it
*Web Site:* www.comune.sanguinetto.vr.it
Established: 1951
Awarded annually to encourage the development of novels for young readers between 11 & 14 years of age. The novel must be published in Italy before July 15 of the current year. Established by Professor Giulletto Accordi.
Other Sponsor(s): Cassa di Risparmio di Verona - Vicenza e Belluno
Award: 1st prize 2,066 EUR

### Certamen Capitolinum
Istituto Nazionale di Studi Romani
Piazza dei Cavalieri di Malta, 2, 00153 Rome
*Tel:* (06) 5743442; (06) 5743445 *Fax:* (06) 5743447
*E-mail:* studiromani@studiromani.it
*Web Site:* www.studiromani.it
*Key Personnel*
President: Prof Mario Mazza
Dir: Dr Fernanda Roscetti
Established: 1950
Awarded annually to provide recognition for the best works on the Latin language & literature. Teachers, scholars & students are eligible.
Award: 1st prize 310 EUR & a silver sculpture of a she-wolf; 2nd prize 155 EUR & a silver medallion; 3rd prize 52 EUR & a diploma (to students); Honorable Mentions

### ☆Antonio Feltrinelli Prize
Accademia Nazionale dei Lincei (National Italian Academy of Sciences)
Palazzo Corsini, Via della Lungara 10, 00165 Rome
*Tel:* (06) 68307831 *Fax:* (06) 6893616
*E-mail:* ufficio.premi@lincei.it
*Web Site:* www.lincei.it
Annual prizes for accomplishment in the various branches of sciences, humanities & literature. These prizes were instituted by an Italian businessman who died in 1942 & bequeathed his fortune to the academy for the purpose of "rewarding toil, study, intelligence . . . those men who with greater success distinguished themselves with high achievements in art & science, since they are the true benefactors of their own country as well as of all humanity". The literature award is granted every five years & the amount varies.

### Grinzane Cavour Prize
Grinzane Cavour Prize Association (Premio Grinzane Cavour)
Via Montebello 21, 10124 Turin
*Tel:* (011) 8100111 *Fax:* (011) 8125456
*E-mail:* info@grinzane.it
*Web Site:* www.grinzane.it
Established: 1982
To encourage the diffusion of reading in the Italian school, especially of books of contemporary fiction. Literary critics, scholars, writers,

journalists & people in the world of Italian culture judge the books. Established by Prof. Giuliano Soria. Awarded annually in five categories: contemporary Italian fiction; contemporary foreign fiction translated into Italian; an international prize for the complete works of a foreign writer; young beginning author, aged less than forty; essay writing.
Other Sponsor(s): Fondazione Cassa di Risparmio di Torino; Provincia di Torino; Regione Piemonte; SEAT
Award: International prize for the complete works of a foreign writer - 5,165 EUR; all others 3,615 EUR

### ☆Naples Prize
Fondazione Premio Napoli
Palazzo Reale, Piazza del Plebiscito, 80132 Naples
*Tel:* (081) 403187; (081) 422362 *Fax:* (081) 402023
*E-mail:* fnp@fondazionepremionapoli.it
*Web Site:* www.premionapoli.it
*Key Personnel*
Contact: Carmen Petillo
Established: 1954
Annual award for recognition of an outstanding work of literature in Italian. Italian & non-Italian authors are eligible.
Award: 10,000,000 ITL & plaque

### Laura Orvieto Prize
Fondazione Premio Laura Orvieto
Archivo Contemporaneo del Gabinetto, GP Vieusseux, Via Maggio 42, 50125 Florence
*Tel:* (055) 697877; (055) 697981; (055) 697946
Established: 1954
Monetary prize awarded biennially to provide recognition for the manuscript of a book of fiction for children from 8 to 11 years of age. Italian authors are eligible. Established by Adriana Guasconi Orvieto in memory of Laura Orvieto.

### ☆Premio Langhe Ceretto
Biblioteca Civica G Ferrero
Via Vittorio Emanuele 11, 19, 12051 Alba CN
*Tel:* (0172) 290092 *Fax:* (0173) 282383
*E-mail:* ceretto@ceretto.com
*Web Site:* www.ceretto.com
*Key Personnel*
Secretary: Dr Gianfranco Maggi
Established: 1991
Annual food & wine culture prize.

### Strega Prize
Fondazione Marie e Goffredo Bellonci
via Marciana Marina, 58, 00138 Rome
*Tel:* (06) 88327652 *Fax:* (06) 8109668
*E-mail:* fond.bellonci@flashnet.it
*Web Site:* www.fondazionebellonci.com
*Key Personnel*
President: Antonio Maccanico
Dir: Anna Maria Rimoaldi
Established: 1947
Founded by Maria Bellonci & Guido Alberti for a work of fiction.

### Viareggio Prizes
Premio Viareggio
Via Francesco Borgatti 25, 00191 Rome
*Tel:* (06) 3293736
Established: 1929
Since 1967, the annual award has been divided into three sections: fiction, nonfiction & poetry. Given to foreign writers & poets.
Award: 12,911 EUR

# Japan

### Gunzo for Fiction du Critique Prize
Kodansha Ltd
2-12-21 Otowa, Bunkyo-ku, Tokyo 112-8001
*Tel:* (03) 3946-6201 *Fax:* (03) 3944-9915
*Web Site:* www.kodansha.co.jp; www.kodanclub.com
*Key Personnel*
President: Mitsuru Tomita
Established: 1967
To provide recognition for an outstanding work of fiction by a new writer. Formerly known as the Gunzo Fiction Prize.
Award: 500,000 JPY

### Japan Translation Prize for Publisher
Japan Society of Translators
c/o Orion Press, 1-13 Kanda-Jimbocho, Chiyoda-ku, Tokyo 101
*Tel:* (03) 32943936 *Fax:* (03) 33061251
*E-mail:* jst@orionpress.jp
Awarded annually for outstanding translations.

### Kodansha Cultural Prize in Publishing for Book Design
Kodansha Ltd
2-12-21 Otowa, Bunkyo-ku, Tokyo 112-8001
*Tel:* (03) 3946-6201 *Fax:* (03) 3944-9915
*Web Site:* www.kodansha.co.jp; www.kodanclub.com
*Key Personnel*
President: Mitsuru Tomita
Award: 1,000,000 JPY

### Kodansha Cultural Prize in Publishing for Illustrations
Kodansha Ltd
2-12-21 Otowa, Bunkyo-ku, Tokyo 112-8001
*Tel:* (03) 3946-6201 *Fax:* (03) 3944-9915
*Web Site:* www.kodansha.co.jp; www.kodanclub.com
*Key Personnel*
Contact: Tetsu Shirai
Established: 1970
Awarded annually to the best work of illustration.
Award: 1,000,000 yen

### Kodansha Cultural Prize in Publishing for Photographs
Kodansha Ltd
2-12-21 Otowa, Bunkyo-ku, Tokyo 112-8001
*Tel:* (03) 3946-6201 *Fax:* (03) 3944-9915
*Web Site:* www.kodansha.co.jp; www.kodanclub.com
*Key Personnel*
President: Mitsuru Tomita
Award: 1,000,000 JPY

### Kodansha Cultural Prize in Publishing for Picture Books
Kodansha Ltd
2-12-21 Otowa, Bunkyo-ku, Tokyo 112-8001
*Tel:* (03) 3946-6201 *Fax:* (03) 3944-9915
*Web Site:* www.kodansha.co.jp; www.kodanclub.com
*Key Personnel*
Contact: Tetsu Shirai
Established: 1970
Awarded annually for the most outstanding picture book.
Award: 1,000,000 yen

### Kodansha Essay Prize
Kodansha Ltd
2-12-21 Otowa, Bunkyo-ku, Tokyo 112-8001
*Tel:* (03) 3946-6201 *Fax:* (03) 3944-9915
*Web Site:* www.kodansha.co.jp; www.kodanclub.com

*Key Personnel*
Contact: Tetsu Shirai
Established: 1985
Annual award for the best essay.
Award: 1,000,000 yen

### Kodansha Nonfiction Prize
Kodansha Ltd
2-12-21 Otowa, Bunkyo-ku, Tokyo 112-8001
*Tel:* (03) 3946-6201 *Fax:* (03) 3944-9915
*Web Site:* www.kodansha.co.jp; www.kodanclub.
   com
*Key Personnel*
Contact: Tetsu Shirai
Established: 1979
Annual award for the best nonfiction work.
Award: 1,000,000 yen

### Kodansha Prize for Comics
Kodansha Ltd
2-12-21 Otowa, Bunkyo-ku, Tokyo 112-8001
*Tel:* (03) 3946-6201 *Fax:* (03) 3944-9915
*Web Site:* www.kodansha.co.jp; www.kodanclub.
   com
*Key Personnel*
President: Mitsuru Tomita
Award: 1,000,000 JPY

### Noma Award for Publishing in Africa
Kodansha Ltd
2-12-21 Otowa, Bunkyo-ku, Tokyo 112-8001
*Tel:* (01993) 775235; (03) 3946-6201
   *Fax:* (01993) 709265; (03) 3944-9915
*Web Site:* www.nomaaward.org; www.kodanclub.
   com
*Key Personnel*
Secretary to the NOMA Award Managing Com-
   mittee: Mary Jay *E-mail:* maryljay@aol.com
Established: 1979
Established by the late Shoichi Noma, former
   President of the Japanese publishing company
   Kodansha Ltd, for African writers & scholars
   whose work is published in Africa. The annual
   award is given for an outstanding work in any
   of the following categories: (1) scholarly or
   academic, (2) children's books, (3) literature
   & creative writing (including fiction, drama or
   poetry).
Award: 10,000 USD & commemorative plaque
Closing Date: Feb 28
Presented: Various places, mainly within Africa

### Noma Award for the Translation of Japanese Literature
Kodansha Ltd
2-12-21 Otowa, Bunkyo-ku, Tokyo 112-8001
*Tel:* (03) 3946-6201 *Fax:* (03) 3944-9915
*Web Site:* www.kodansha.co.jp; www.kodanclub.
   com
*Key Personnel*
President: Mitsuru Tomita
Established: 1990
For the best translation of a post-1926 Japanese
   novel or essay.
Award: 10,000 USD

### Noma Concours for Children's Picture Book Illustrations
Kodansha Ltd
2-12-21 Otowa, Bunkyo-ku, Tokyo 112-8001
*Tel:* (03) 3946-6201 *Fax:* (03) 3944-9915
*Web Site:* www.kodansha.co.jp; www.kodanclub.
   com
*Key Personnel*
President: Mitsuru Tomita
Established to promote high standards in chil-
   dren's book illustration.
Award: 2,000 USD

### Noma Juvenile Literature Prize for New Writers
Kodansha Ltd
2-12-21 Otowa, Bunkyo-ku, Tokyo 112-8001
*Tel:* (03) 3946-6201 *Fax:* (03) 3944-9915
*Web Site:* www.kodansha.co.jp; www.kodansha.
   co.jp
*Key Personnel*
Contact: Tetsu Shirai
Established: 1963
Annual award for the best juvenile novel by a
   new writer.
Award: 1,000,000 yen

### Noma Literacy Prize
Kodansha Ltd
2-12-21 Otowa, Bunkyo-ku, Tokyo 112-8001
*Tel:* (03) 3946-6201 *Fax:* (03) 3944-9915
*Web Site:* www.kodansha.co.jp; www.kodanclub.
   com
*Key Personnel*
President: Mitsuru Tomita
Established to honor an individual or group work-
   ing to improve literacy levels in the Third
   World.
Award: 10,000 USD

### Noma Literature Prize for New Writers
Kodansha Ltd
2-12-21 Otowa, Bunkyo-ku, Tokyo 112-8001
*Tel:* (03) 3946-6201 *Fax:* (03) 3944-9915
*Web Site:* www.kodansha.co.jp; www.kodanclub.
   com
*Key Personnel*
Contact: Tetsu Shirai
Established: 1979
Annual award for the best novel by a new writer.
Award: 1,000,000 yen

### Noma Prize for Juvenile Literature
Kodansha Ltd
2-12-21 Otowa, Bunkyo-ku, Tokyo 112-8001
*Tel:* (03) 3946-6201 *Fax:* (03) 3944-9915
*Web Site:* www.kodansha.co.jp; www.kodanclub.
   com
*Key Personnel*
Contact: Tetsu Shirai
Established: 1963
Annual award for the best juvenile novel.
Award: 2,000,000 yen

### Noma Prize for Literature
Kodansha Ltd
2-12-21 Otowa, Bunkyo-ku, Tokyo 112-8001
*Tel:* (03) 3946-6201 *Fax:* (03) 3944-9915
*Web Site:* www.kodansha.co.jp; www.kodanclub.
   com
*Key Personnel*
Contact: Tetsu Shirai
Established: 1941
Annual award for the best Japanese novel of the
   year.
Award: 3,000,000 yen

### Oya Soichi Nonfiction Prize
The Society for the Promotion of Japanese Litera-
   ture
c/o Bungei Shunju Bldg, 3-23 Kioi-cho, Chiyoda-
   ku, Tokyo 102-8008
*Tel:* (03) 3265-1211 *Fax:* (03) 3265-2624
*Key Personnel*
Contact: Kazukiyo Takahashi
Established: 1969
Annual award to encourage new nonfiction writ-
   ers.
Award: 1,000,000 yen

### Printing Culture Prize
Japan Federation of Printing Industries
1-16-8 Shintomi, Chuo-ku, Tokyo 104-0041
*Tel:* (03) 3552-4571

*E-mail:* info@jfpi.or.jp
*Web Site:* www.jfpi.or.jp
Established: 1987
To provide recognition in the field of printing for
   a work that is artistically, historically & aca-
   demically valuable. Formerly, Insatsu Bunka
   Sho. Awarded every 4 years.
Award: Monetary award & plaque

### Yoshikawa Eiji Cultural Prize
Kodansha Ltd
2-12-21 Otowa, Bunkyo-ku, Tokyo 112-8001
*Tel:* (03) 3946-6201 *Fax:* (03) 3944-9915
*Web Site:* www.kodansha.co.jp; www.kodanclub.
   com
*Key Personnel*
President: Mitsuru Tomita
Award: 1,000,000 JPY

### Yoshikawa Eiji Literature Prize
Kodansha Ltd
2-12-21 Otowa, Bunkyo-ku, Tokyo 112-8001
*Tel:* (03) 3946-6201 *Fax:* (03) 3944-9915
*Web Site:* www.kodansha.co.jp; www.kodanclub.
   com
*Key Personnel*
Contact: Tetsu Shirai
Established: 1967
Annual award for a popular novel.
Award: 3,000,000 yen & commemorative plaque

### Yoshikawa Eiji Literature Prize for New Writers
Kodansha Ltd
2-12-21 Otowa, Bunkyo-ku, Tokyo 112-8001
*Tel:* (03) 3946-6201 *Fax:* (03) 3944-9915
*Web Site:* www.kodansha.co.jp; www.kodanclub.
   com
*Key Personnel*
Contact: Tetsu Shirai
Established: 1980
Annual award to recognize the most promising
   work of fiction by a new writer published dur-
   ing the preceding year.
Award: 1,000,000 yen & commemorative plaque

# Kenya

### Jomo Kenyatta Prize for Literature
Kenya Publishers Association
Occidental Plaza, 4th floor, Muthithi Rd, East &
   Central Africa, Nairobi
Mailing Address: PO Box 42767, Nairobi 00100
*Tel:* (02) 375 2344 *Fax:* (02) 375 4076
*E-mail:* kenyapublishers@wananchi.com; info@
   kenyabooks.org
*Web Site:* www.kenyabooks.org
*Key Personnel*
Executive Secretary: Lynnette Kariuki
Established: 1974
Awarded annually to provide recognition for an
   outstanding literary work written in the English
   or Swahili languages. Only Kenyan authors are
   eligible.
Other Sponsor(s): Text Book Centre
Award: Monetary
Closing Date: Mid-year, biannually
Presented: Nairobi International Book Fair, Late
   Sept, biannually

# Republic of Korea

**Korean Literature Translation Award**
Korean Literature Translation Institute
Seojin Bldg, 5th floor, 149-1 Pyeong-dong,
  Jongno-gu, Seoul 110-102
*Tel:* (02) 732-1442 *Fax:* (02) 732-1443
*E-mail:* info@ltikorea.net
*Web Site:* www.ltikorea.net
*Key Personnel*
Contact: Park Eun Young
Established: 1993
Awarded biennially as part of the Korean govern-
  ment's efforts to introduce & promote Korean
  literary works overseas through translation.
Award: $60,000

# Liechtenstein

**Liechtenstein-Preis zur Foerderung**
  **Zeitgenoessischer Literatur** (Liechtenstein
  Prize for the Advancement of Literature)
Liechtenstein PEN Centre
PO Box 416, 9490 Vaduz
*Tel:* (0423) 2327271 *Fax:* (0423) 2328071
*E-mail:* info@pen-club.li
*Web Site:* www.pen-club.li
Established: 1980

# Luxembourg

**Trophee International de la Reliure d'Art** (Art
  of Bookbinding International Trophy)
ARA International
58, Domaine Mehlstrachen, 6942 Niederanven
*Tel:* 34 85 91 *Fax:* 34 85 91
*E-mail:* amisrelart@pt.lu
*Web Site:* www.ara-international.lu

# Madagascar

**Literature Prize**
Malagasy Ministry of Culture, Communication &
  Leisure
Antsahovola, BP 305, 101 Tananrive
*Tel:* (02) 27092
For an outstanding novel. 130,000 Malagasy
  francs. Awarded every two years.

# Malaysia

**Anugerah Sastera Negara Prize**
Dewan Bahasa dan Pustaka
Peti Surat 10803, 50926 Kuala Lumpur
*Tel:* (03) 21481011 *Fax:* (03) 2482726; (03)
  2142005; (03) 21414109; (03) 2148420
*Web Site:* www.dbp.gov.my
*Telex:* 32683 DBP MA
Established: 1980

National Literary Award. The highest governmental award to an author writing in the national
  language, who has made a major contribution
  to the development of the country's literature.
Award: 30,000 MYR, publication facilities &
  other benefits

**Dewan Bahasa Dan Pustaka Prize**
Dewan Bahasa Dan Pustaka
Peti Surat 10803, 50926 Kuala Lumpur
*Tel:* (03) 21481011 *Fax:* (03) 21482726; (03)
  2142005; (03) 21414109; (03) 2148420
*Web Site:* www.dbp.gov.my
Established: 1982
Malaysian Literary Prize. Awarded by the
  Malaysian Government biennially for creative
  writing in the national language, covering short
  story, novel, poetry & drama, & with the aim
  of encouraging new talent & enhancing the
  quality of the national literature.

# Mexico

**Concurso de Cuento de Ciencia Ficcion**
  (Science Fiction Story Competition)
National Autonomous University of Mexico, Ciu-
  dad Universitaria
Delegacion - Coyoacan, 04510 Mexico, DF
*Tel:* (055) 5505215
*Web Site:* www.unam.mx

**Jorge Cuesta National Poetry Prize**
Gobierno del Estado de Veracruz-Llave
Instituto Veracruzano de Cultura Francisco Canal
  s/n esq, 91700 Veracruz
*Tel:* (029) 316994; (029) 316967 *Fax:* (029)
  316962
*Web Site:* www.veracruz.gob.mx

☆**Rafael Heliodoro Valle Prize**
National Library of Mexico
Insurgentes Sur 3000, Centro Cultural Universi-
  tario, 04510 Mexico, DF
*Tel:* (055) 6226801 *Fax:* (055) 650951
Established: 1976
Founded to reward an especially notable writer
  (in odd-numbered years; in even numbered
  years to an historian for research work & syn-
  thesis). The candidate must have been born in
  Latin America, over age 50 & the work written
  in Spanish or Portuguese.
Award: 20,000,000 MXN, plus diploma & gold
  medal

**National Prize for Linguistics & Literature**
Senate of the Republic
Insurgentes Sur No 2387, piso 3, Col San Angel,
  CP 01000 Mexico, DF
*Tel:* (05) 7236620; (05) 7236622
Annual award for the best literary works in the
  fields of the novel, poetry, essay, biography,
  drama & motion picture scriptwriting.
Award: 100,000 pesos

☆**Alfonso Reyes Prize**
Senate of the Republic
Consejo del Premio Nacional de Ciencias y Artes,
  Argentina 28, Oficina 124, 06029 Mexico, DF
*Tel:* (05) 7236620
Established: 1973
Awaded by the Federal Government of Mexico
  to an author of any nationality for his or her
  literary output on the study of the works of Al-
  fonso Reyes or on Mexico.
Award: 20,000,000 pesos

**Jose Ruben Romero (Premio de Novela Jose**
  **Ruben Romero)**
Instituto Nacional de Bellas Artes
Morelos Norte No 485, Centro, Morelia Michoa-
  can, CP 58000 Mexico
*Tel:* (05) 5207241 *Fax:* (05) 5202724
*Web Site:* www.inba.gob.mx
Established: 1978
Annual award to recognize unpublished novels of
  outstanding literary quality by authors in the
  Spanish language who are residents of Mex-
  ico. Works to be considered should be 120-300
  pages in length. Established in memory of the
  Mexican author.
Other Sponsor(s): State of Michoacan
Award: 80,000,000 MXN & certificate
Closing Date: Aug 1

**Juan Rulfo First Novel Prize** (Premio Juan
  Rulfo Para Primera Novela)
Instituto Nacional de Bellas Artes
Av Juarez No 62, Centro, CP 90000 Tlaxcala
*Tel:* (05) 5207241 *Fax:* (05) 5202724
Established: 1980
Annual award to recognize the best first novel
  by an author in the Spanish language residing
  in Mexico. Works to be considered should be
  120-300 pages in length. Established in mem-
  ory of the Mexican author.
Other Sponsor(s): State of Guerrero
Award: 10,000,000 MXN & certificate
Closing Date: Aug 11

**Premio Xavier Villaurrutia de Escritores para**
  **Escritores**
Sociedad Alfonsina Internacional AC
Ave Transmisiones 42, 01790 Mexico, DF
*Tel:* (055) 6831217
Annual prizes for poetry, prose, novel, short story,
  drama or essays by new or young authors.
Award: 50,000 MXN

# Monaco

☆**Prix Litteraire Prince Pierre-de-Monaco**
Foundation Prince Pierre de Monaco
Centre de Presse, 10, quai Antoine-ler, 98000
  Monte Carlo
*Tel:* (093) 15 22 22 *Fax:* (093) 15 22 15
*E-mail:* centre-info@gouv.mc
*Web Site:* www.gouv.mc
*Key Personnel*
Administrator: Beatrice Dunoyer *Tel:* (093)
  158776
Secretary General: Rainier Rocchi
Established: 1951
Restricted to French-speaking writers. Annual
  award for the entire literary work of one au-
  thor. No applications accepted.
Award: 100,000 FRF

# Myanmar

**National Literary Awards**
Sarpay Beikman Public Library
529 Merchant St, Yangon
When the Burma Translation Society (now renamed Sarpay Beikman Board) was founded in
  1947, it established the Best-Published-Novel-
  of-the-Year Prize with prize money of 1000
  MMK. The awards were gradually increased
  & in 1962 Sarpay Beikman was offering nine
  awards.

When Sarpay Beikman was taken over by the
Revolutionary Government in August 1963 the
awards were transformed into National Literary
Awards. More literary awards were gradually
added & there are now 13 awards for the best
published novel of the year, the best collection of short stories, the best belles letters, the
best book of knowledge (arts), the best book
of knowledge (science), the best book of poems, the best translation of a world classic, the
best translation in the general knowledge field,
the best published play, the best book for children, the best book for youth, the best book on
Burmese culture & the best book on political
affairs.
Each national literary award now draws prize
money of 6000 MMK.

# Netherlands

**Henriette de Beaufort-prijs** (Henriette de
Beaufort Prize)
Maatschappij der Nederlandse Letterkunde (Soci-
ety of Netherlands Literature)
Witte Singel 27, Universiteitsbibliotheek Leiden,
2300 RA Leiden
Mailing Address: PO Box 9501, 2300 RA Leiden
*Tel:* (071) 5272832 *Fax:* (071) 5272836
*E-mail:* mnl@library.leidenuniv.nl
*Web Site:* www.leidenuniv.nl/host/mnl
*Key Personnel*
Secretary: Dr Leo L van Maris
Established: 1985
Awarded triennially to recognize the author of a
biographical work. Awarded alternately to a
Dutch & a Flemish author.
Award: 2,500 EUR

**F Bordewijk Prize**
Jan Campert Foundation
PO Box 12654, 2500 DP The Hague
*Tel:* (070) 3533637 *Fax:* (070) 3533058
*Key Personnel*
Secretary: A P Spijkers
For the best Dutch novel.
Award: 10,000 Dutch florins awarded annually

**Jan Campert Prize**
Jan Campert Foundation
PO Box 12654, 2500 DP The Hague
*Tel:* (070) 3533637 *Fax:* (070) 3533058
*Key Personnel*
Secretary: A P Spijkers
For outstanding Dutch poetry.
Award: 10,000 Dutch florins awarded annually

**Hendrik de Vries Award**
City Council of Groningen
Trompsingel 27, 9724 DA Groningen
*Tel:* (050) 3676254 *Fax:* (050) 3676249
Established: 2001
To recognize achievement in or contribution to
literature & the visual arts. The entry must, in
some way, be related to Groningen or to the
work of Hendrik de Vries. Established in honor
of Hendrik de Vries (1896-1989), a poet &
painter.
Award: 5,672 EUR awarded to young artists. The
award has to be used to create some kind of art
project

**Frans Erensprijs**
Stichting Frans Erensprijs
Europalaan 49, 6226 CN Maastricht
*Tel:* (043) 3635340
Established: 1986
Awarded every three years to recognize a Dutch
author for memoirs, essays, or creative liter-
ary works in prose or poetry. Named for Frans
Erens, a Dutch author (1857-1935).
Award: 5,165 EUR

**Dr Wijnaendts Francken Prijs**
Maatschappij der Nederlandse Letterkunde (Soci-
ety of Netherlands Literature)
Universiteitsbibliotheek Leiden, Witte Singel 27,
2300 RA Leiden
Mailing Address: PO Box 9501, 2300 RA Leiden
*Tel:* (071) 5272832 *Fax:* (071) 5272836
*E-mail:* mnl@library.leidenuniv.nl
*Web Site:* www.leidenuniv.nl/host/mnl
*Key Personnel*
Secretary: Dr Leo L van Maris
Established: 1934
Awarded triennially for a work written in Dutch
alternately in one of following categories: (1)
essays & literary criticism, (2) cultural history.
Award: 2,500 EUR

☆**Herman Gorterprijs (Poezie)** (Herman Gorter
Prize (Poetry))
Amsterdams Fonds voor de Kunst (Amsterdam
Funds for the Arts)
Herengracht 609, 1017 CE Amsterdam
*Tel:* (020) 520 0520 *Fax:* (020) 623 8389
*E-mail:* afk@afk.nl
*Web Site:* www.afk.nl
Established: 1972
Subsidies, grants & prizes for the arts. Annual art
awards of the city of Amsterdam; no applica-
tion.

**The G H's-Gravesande Prize**
Jan Campert Foundation
PO Box 12654, 2500 DP The Hague
*Tel:* (070) 3533637 *Fax:* (070) 3533058
*Key Personnel*
Secretary: A P Spijkers
For special services to literature.
Award: 10,000 Dutch florins awarded triennially

**J Greshoff Prize**
Jan Campert Foundation
PO Box 12654, 2500 DP The Hague
*Tel:* (070) 3533637 *Fax:* (070) 3533058
*Key Personnel*
Secretary: A P Spijkers
For the best Dutch essay.
Award: 10,000 Dutch florins awarded biennually

**Nienke van Hichtum Prize**
Jan Campert Foundation
PO Box 12654, 2500 DP The Hague
*Tel:* (070) 3533637 *Fax:* (070) 3533058
*Key Personnel*
Secretary: A P Spijkers
For the best Dutch children's book.
Award: 10,000 Dutch florins awarded every two
years

**P C Hooft Prize for Literature**
Boekblad
Frederiksplein 1, 1017 XK Amsterdam
Mailing Address: Postbus 15007, 1001 MA Ams-
terdam
*Tel:* (020) 625 31 31 *Fax:* (020) 622 09 08
*E-mail:* redactie@boekblad.kvb.nl
*Web Site:* www.boekblad.nl
For important & original literary works in Dutch.
Awarded annually where possible: one year for
poetry, the next year for prose, the next year
for literary essay.

**Lucy B & C W van der Hoogt Prize**
Maatschappij der Nederlandse Letterkunde (Soci-
ety of Netherlands Literature)
Universiteitsbibliotheek Leiden, Witte Singel 27,
2300 RA Leiden
Mailing Address: PO Box 9501, 2300 RA Leiden

*Tel:* (071) 5272832 *Fax:* (071) 5272836
*E-mail:* mnl@library.leidenuniv.nl
*Web Site:* www.leidenuniv.nl/host/mnl
*Key Personnel*
Secretary: Dr Leo L van Maris
Established: 1921
Awarded annually to a promising Dutch or Flem-
ish writer.
Award: 6,000 EUR & a medal

**Busken Huetprijs (Essay/biografie)** (Busken
Huet Prize (Essay/Biography))
Amsterdams Fonds voor de Kunst (Amsterdam
Funds for the Arts)
Herengracht 609, 1017 CE Amsterdam
*Tel:* (020) 520 0520 *Fax:* (020) 623 8389
*E-mail:* afk@afk.nl
*Web Site:* www.afk.nl
Established: 1973
Subsidies, grants & prizes for the arts. Annual art
awards of the city of Amsterdam; award cannot
be applied for.

**Constantijn Huygens Prize**
Jan Campert Foundation
PO Box 12654, 2500 DP The Hague
*Tel:* (070) 3533637 *Fax:* (070) 3533058
*Key Personnel*
Secretary: A P Spijkers
To a distinguished Dutch author for all his works.
Award: 20,000 Dutch florins awarded annually

**Charlotte Kohlerprijs**
Stichting Charlotte Kohler
Postbus 19750, 1000 GT Amsterdam
*Tel:* (020) 5206130 *Fax:* (020) 6238499
*E-mail:* info@cultuurfonds.nl
*Web Site:* www.cultuurfonds.nl
*Key Personnel*
Contact: Mrs A de Boer
Award: 5,000 EUR

**Multatuli Prize**
Amsterdam City Government, Stichting Amster-
dams Fonds voor de Kunst
Herengracht 609, 1017 CE Amsterdam
*Tel:* (020) 5200520 *Fax:* (020) 6238389
*E-mail:* afk@afk.nl
*Web Site:* www.afk.nl
*Key Personnel*
Contact: Desmond Spruyt
Established: 1972
Subsidies, grants & prizes for the arts.

**Prijs der Nederlandse Letteren**
Nederlandse Taalunie (Dutch Language Union)
Lange Voorhout 19, 2514 EB The Hague
Mailing Address: Postbus 10595, 2501 HN The
Hague
*Tel:* (070) 346 95 48 *Fax:* (070) 365 98 18
*E-mail:* info@taalunie.org
*Web Site:* www.taalunie.org
*Key Personnel*
General Secretary: Koen Jaspaert
Established: 1956
Triennial award to the most outstanding prose
writer, essay writer, drama writer or poet in the
Netherlands or in Belgium writing in Dutch.
Award: 16,000 EUR

☆**Martinus Nijhoff Prijs voor Vertalingen**
(Martinus Nijhoff Prize for Translators)
Prince Bernhard Cultural Foundation
Herengracht 476, 1017 CB Amsterdam
Mailing Address: Postbus 19750, 1000 GT Ams-
terdam
*Tel:* (020) 5206130 *Fax:* (020) 6238499
*E-mail:* info@cultuurfonds.nl
*Web Site:* www.cultuurfonds.nl
Established: 1953

Annual award for translation of literary work into & from Dutch.
Award: 50,000 EUR

**Henriette Roland Holst Prijs**
Maatschappij der Nederlandse Letterkunde (Society of Netherlands Literature)
Universiteitsbibliotheek Leiden, Witte Singel 27, 2300 RA Leiden
Mailing Address: PO Box 9501, 2300 RA Leiden
*Tel:* (071) 5272832 *Fax:* (071) 5272836
*E-mail:* mnl@library.leidenuniv.nl
*Web Site:* www.leidenuniv.nl/host/mnl
*Key Personnel*
Secretary: Dr Leo L van Maris
Established: 1957
Awarded triennially for a work written in Dutch & reflecting social concerns.
Award: 2,500 EUR

☆**Jenny Smelik IBBY Prize**
Dutch Section of the International Board on Books for Young People
PO Box 17162, 1001 JD Amsterdam
*Tel:* (071) 527 40 78 *Fax:* (071) 527 39 45
*E-mail:* ibby-nederland@planet.nl
*Web Site:* www.ibby.org
*Key Personnel*
Dir: Toin Duijx
Established: 1983
To recognize alternately an author & an illustrator of children's books who contribute to a better understanding of minorities. Selection is by nomination & application. Established by Klasina Smelik in honor of the children's book author, Jenny Smelik-Kiggen. Formerly: Jenny Smilik-Kiggenprijs.
Award: 2,000 EUR biennial by the Dutch section of IBBY

**Theo Thijssen Prize for Children's & Youth Literature**
Postbus 90515, Prins Willem, Alexanderhof 5, 2595 LM The Hague
*Tel:* (070) 3339666 *Fax:* (070) 3477941
*Key Personnel*
Secretary: Aad Meinderts
For the best author's work for children & young people. Awarded triennially.
Award: 75,000 Dutch florins

# New Zealand

**Bank of New Zealand Essay Award**
Bank of New Zealand
State Insurance Tower, One Willis St, Wellington
Mailing Address: PO Box 2392, Wellington
*Tel:* (04) 801 2400
*Web Site:* www.bnz.co.nz
*Key Personnel*
Sponsorship & Events Consultant: Lyndal McMeeking *E-mail:* lyndal_mcmeeking@bnz.co.nz
Biennial award open to essays on a topic of the writers choice. Entries must not have been published or broadcast. Entrants have to be either born in New Zealand or New Zealand citizens or residents for 3 years. Max length 2,500 words.
Award: 1st prize 1,000 NZD

**Bank of New Zealand Katherine Mansfield Award**
Bank of New Zealand
State Insurance Tower, One Willis St, Wellington
Mailing Address: PO Box 2392, Wellington
*Tel:* (04) 801 2400
*E-mail:* kmawards@bnz.co.nz

*Web Site:* www.bnz.co.nz
*Key Personnel*
Sponsorship & Event Consultant: Lyndal McMeeking *E-mail:* lyndal_mcmeeking@bnz.co.nz
Biennial award for an unpublished short story. Sponsored by the Bank of New Zealand. Entrants to be either born in New Zealand or New Zealand citizens or residents for 3 years. Max length 3000 words.
Award: 1st prize 5,000 NZD; 2nd prize 1,500 NZD

**Bank of New Zealand Novice Writer's Award**
Bank of New Zealand
State Insurance Tower, One Willis St, Wellington
Mailing Address: PO Box 2392, Wellington
*Tel:* (04) 801 2400
*Web Site:* www.bnz.co.nz
*Key Personnel*
Sponsorship & Events Consultant: Lyndal McMeeking *E-mail:* lyndal_mcmeeking@bnz.co.nz
Biennial award open to writers whose works have not previously been published or broadcast for payment. Entrants must be either born in New Zealand, or New Zealand citizens or resident for 3 years. Max length 3000 words.
Award: 1st prize 1,500 NZD

**Bank of New Zealand Young Writers' Award**
Bank of New Zealand
State Insurance Tower, One Willis St, Wellington
Mailing Address: PO Box 2392, Wellington
*Tel:* (04) 801 2400
*Web Site:* www.bnz.co.nz
*Key Personnel*
Sponsorship & Events Consultant: Lyndal McMeeking *E-mail:* lyndal_mcmeeking@bnz.co.nz
Contact: Joy Cowley
Biennial award for an unpublished short story written by a secondary-school pupil (over 13 years). The entrant must be either born in New Zealand or a New Zealand citizen or resident for 3 years. Min length 750 words - max length 2000 words.
Award: 1st prize 1,000 NZD; Prize to school of winning student 500 NZD

**Buckland Literary Award**
Trustees Executors & Agency Company of New Zealand Ltd
24 Water St, Dunedin 9001
*Tel:* (03) 779 466 *Fax:* (03) 799 466
Founded in 1966 by the late Freda M Buckland for the work of the highest literary merit by a New Zealand writer. Awarded annually.

**NZSA Hubert Church Best First Book of Fiction Award**
Booksellers New Zealand
Level 1, Survey House, 21-29 Broderick Rd, Wellington
Mailing Address: PO Box 13 248, Wellington
*Tel:* (04) 478 5511 *Fax:* (04) 478 5519
*E-mail:* enquiries@booksellers.co.nz
*Web Site:* www.booksellers.co.nz
*Key Personnel*
Contact: Beth McGregor *E-mail:* beth.mcgregor@booksellers.co.nz
Established: 1944
Annual prize for the best first book of fiction, 48 pages or more (24 pages if a work of drama), written by a New Zealand citizen or a person resident in New Zealand for the previous five years.
Award: 1,000 NZD

**Russell Clark Award**
Library & Information Association of New Zealand Aotearoa (LIANZA)

Old Wool House, Level 5, 139-141 Featherston St, Wellington 6001
Mailing Address: PO Box 12-212, Wellington 6038
*Tel:* (04) 473 5834 *Fax:* (04) 499 1480
*E-mail:* office@lianza.org.nz
*Web Site:* www.lianza.org.nz
*Key Personnel*
Office Manager: Eve Young *E-mail:* eve@lianza.org.nz
Established: 1975
Annual award for the most distinguished illustrations for a children's book. Illustrator must be a citizen or resident of New Zealand.
Award: Bronze medal & 1,000 NZD

**Esther Glen Award**
Library & Information Association of New Zealand Aotearoa (LIANZA)
Old Wool House, Level 5, 139-141 Featherston St, Wellington 6001
Mailing Address: PO Box 12-212, Wellington 6038
*Tel:* (04) 473 5834 *Fax:* (04) 499 1480
*E-mail:* office@lianza.org.nz
*Web Site:* www.lianza.org.nz
*Key Personnel*
Office Manager: Eve Young *E-mail:* eve@lianza.org.nz
Established: 1944
Annual award for the best children's book of fiction by an author who is a citizen of, or resident in, New Zealand.
Award: 1,000 NZD & Bronze Medal
Presented: Annual Conference

**Elsie Locke Award**
Library & Information Association of New Zealand Aotearoa (LIANZA)
Old Wool House, Level 5, 139-141 Featherston St, Wellington 6001
Mailing Address: PO Box 12-212, Wellington 6038
*Tel:* (04) 473 5834 *Fax:* (04) 499 1480
*E-mail:* office@lianza.org.nz
*Web Site:* www.lianza.org.nz
*Key Personnel*
Office Manager: Eve Young *E-mail:* eve@lianza.org.nz
Established: 1986
Awarded annually for the most distinguished contribution to nonfiction writing for young people. Author(s) must be a citizen or resident of New Zealand.
Award: 1,000 NZD & medal

**NZSA Jessie Mackay Best First Book Award**
Booksellers New Zealand
Level 1, Survey House, 21-29 Broderick Rd, Wellington
Mailing Address: PO Box 13 248, Wellington
*Tel:* (04) 478 5511 *Fax:* (04) 478 5519
*E-mail:* enquiries@booksellers.co.nz
*Web Site:* www.booksellers.co.nz
*Key Personnel*
Contact: Beth McGregor *E-mail:* beth.mcgregor@booksellers.co.nz
Established: 1940
Annual prize for the best first book of published poetry, of 24 pages or more, written by a New Zealand citizen or a person resident in New Zealand for the previous five years.
Award: 1,000 NZD

**Montana New Zealand Book Awards**
Booksellers New Zealand
Level 1, Survey House, 21-29 Broderick Rd, Wellington
Mailing Address: PO Box 13 248, Wellington
*Tel:* (04) 478 5511 *Fax:* (04) 478 5519
*E-mail:* enquiries@booksellers.co.nz
*Web Site:* www.booksellers.co.nz

*Key Personnel*
Contact: Beth McGregor *E-mail:* beth.mcgregor@
booksellers.co.nz
Established: 1967
For the book of the year based on: (1) quality of
writing & illustrations; (2) quality of editing,
design & production; (3) impact on the community. Open only to books by New Zealand
authors produced by New Zealand book publishers.
Other Sponsor(s): Creative New Zealand; Montana Wines
Award: 10,000 NZD
Presented: July

**New Zealand Post Children's Book Awards**
Booksellers New Zealand
Level One, Survey House, 21-29 Broderick Rd,
Wellington
Mailing Address: PO Box 13 248, Wellington
*Tel:* (04) 478 5511 *Fax:* (04) 478 5519
*E-mail:* enquiries@booksellers.co.nz
*Web Site:* www.booksellers.co.nz
*Key Personnel*
Contact: Beth McGregor *E-mail:* beth.mcgregor@
booksellers.co.nz
Sponsored by Aim Toothpaste Division of Lever
Rexona Ltd & awarded annually. The awards
aim to provide recognition & reward to New
Zealand authors & illustrators of high-quality
children's literature & are awarded in four categories:
5,000 NZD to the author of the best junior fiction
book
2,500 NZD each to the author & illustrator of
the best children's picture book (one award of
5,000 NZD where the author & illustrator are
the same person)
5,000 NZD to the author of the best senior fiction
book
5,000 NZD to the author of the best nonfiction
book
1,000 NZD to a promising first children's book.
Other Sponsor(s): Creative New Zealand; New
Zealand Post

**PEN Best First Book Award**
New Zealand Society of Authors (NZSA)
PO Box 67013, Mount Eden, Auckland 1030
*Tel:* (09) 356 8332 *Fax:* (09) 356 8332
*E-mail:* nzsa@clear.net.nz
*Web Site:* www.authors.org.nz
*Key Personnel*
Executive Dir: Liz Allen
Annual award for the best first book of published
nonfiction of 48 pages or more, written by
a New Zealand citizen or a person resident
in New Zealand throughout the previous five
years.
Award: 1,000 NZD
Closing Date: March 13

# Nigeria

**Concord Press Award for Academic Publishing**
Concord Press Board of Trustees
Enuwa Sq, Ile-Ife
Mailing Address: PO Box 845, Ile-Ife
*Tel:* (036) 230190
Established 1984. Sponsored by M K O Abiola
(founder & Chairman of the Concord Press of
Nigeria Ltd). The principal aim of the Award is
to encourage publication of works by Nigerian
authors & scholars which are suitable as text-
books at University level. 25,000 naira awarded
annually.

**Delta Fiction Award**
Delta Publications (Nigeria) Ltd
PO Box 3606, Lagos
*Tel:* (042) 253215
For an unpublished novel on any subject, al-
though theme should have an international fla-
vor.
Award: 10,000 NGN

**Distinguished Authors Award**
University Bookshop Ltd
c/o University Bookshop, Obafemi Awolowo University, Ile-Ife, Osun State
*Tel:* (036) 230290

**Nigerian Book Development Council Book
Prize**
Nigerian Book Development Council
6 Obanta Rd, Apapa, Lagos
*Tel:* (01) 862269; (01) 862272
For the best book of social significance by a
Nigerian author. 200 naira awarded annually.

**Nigerian Book Development Council Literary
Prize**
Nigerian Book Development Council
6 Obanta Rd, Apapa, Lagos
*Tel:* (01) 862269; (01) 962272
For the best book written by a Nigerian & pub-
lished in Nigeria (excluding children's books).
300 naira awarded annually.

# Norway

**Bastianprisen** (Bastian Prize)
The Norwegian Association of Literary Transla-
tors
Postboks 579 Sentrum, 0150 Oslo
*Tel:* 22478090 *Fax:* 22420356
*E-mail:* post@translators.no
*Web Site:* skrift.no/no/english/index.asp
*Key Personnel*
Contact: Hilde Sveinsson *E-mail:* hilde@
translators.no
Established: 1951
Awarded annually for an outstanding translation
to Norwegian.
Closing Date: Jan 15 annually

**N W Damm Children's Book Prize**
N W Damm og Son A/S
Tordenskioldsgate 6B, 0055 Oslo
*Tel:* 22471000 *Fax:* 22471149; 22471142
*E-mail:* marked@damm.no
Established: 1952
Award: 60,000 NOK biennially

**Literature Awards for Children & Young
People**
Ministry of Cultural Affairs Norwegian Direc-
torate for Public Libraries
Apotekergata 8, 0180 Oslo
Mailing Address: PO Box 8145 DEP, 0033 Oslo
*Tel:* 23 11 75 00 *Fax:* 23 11 75 01
*E-mail:* post@abm-utvikling.no
*Web Site:* www.abm-utvikling.no
*Key Personnel*
Librarian: Elin Thomsen *Tel:* 21 02 17 25
*E-mail:* elin.thomsen@bibtils.no
Established: 1949
Annual awards for the best books for children
in the following categories: novel (ca 40,000
NOK), picture book (ca 40,000 NOK), illus-
trations, new-comer, translations (new Norwe-
gian), translations (literary Norwegian), facts &
comics.

**Norske Akademis Pris Til Minne om Thorleif
Dahl**
Norwegian Academy for Language & Literature
Inkognitogaten 24, 0256 Oslo
*Tel:* (022) 56 29 50 *Fax:* (022) 55 37 43
*E-mail:* ordet@riksmalsforbundet.no
*Web Site:* www.riksmalsforbundet.no

**Tarjei Vesaas Debutant Prize**
Den Norske Forfatterforening
Radhusgata 7, Postboks 327, Sentrum, 0103 Oslo
*Tel:* 23357620
*E-mail:* post@forfatterforeningen.no
*Web Site:* skrift.no/dnf
Annual award to a writer under age 30 for the
best first book of prose or poetry.
Award: 14,000 NOK

# Pakistan

**Adamjee Prize**
Pakistan Writers' Guild
One Mentgomrey Rd, Lahore
*Tel:* 6367124
Founded in 1960 for the best book of creative
& progressive poetry, novel, short story,
drama, travelogue or biography. 20,000 ru-
pees. Awarded annually. Administered by the
Pakistan Writers' Guild in Karachi.

**Dawood Prize for Literature**
Pakistan Writers' Guild
One Mentgomrey Rd, Lahore
*Tel:* 6367124
Established: 1963
Founded for the best books on literary research,
literary history, literary criticism; for research
works on the Pakistan movement & for the best
translation. Sponsored by the Dawood Founda-
tion. Awarded annually.
Award: 25,000 rupees

**Habib Bank Prize for Literature**
Pakistan Writers' Guild
One Mentgomrey Rd, Lahore
*Tel:* 6367124
Established: 1968
Founded for the best translation or adaptation of
the year (into English or a Pakistani language)
of a modern or classical work in any Pakistani
language.
Award: 25,000 rupees awarded annually

**National Bank of Pakistan Prize for Literature**
Pakistan Writers' Guild
One Mentgomrey Rd, Lahore
*Tel:* 6367124
Established: 1964
Founded for the best books on economics & sci-
entific, technical & professional subjects.
Award: 25,000 rupees awarded annually

**President's Award for Pride of Performance**
Pakistan Ministry of Education
Block D Pakistan Secretariat, Islamabad
*Tel:* (051) 212020; (051) 821392 *Fax:* (051)
822851
Awarded annually for notable achievements in
literature.

**Prizes for Manuscripts of Juveniles**
Pakistan Writers' Guild
One Mentgomrey Rd, Lahore
*Tel:* 6367124
Six prizes for creative writing in the field of chil-
dren's literature in the Urdu language. Awarded
annually.

**Regional Literature Awards**
Pakistan Writers' Guild
One Mentgomrey Rd, Lahore
*Tel:* 6367124
For the best literary works, including the novel,
short story, drama, poetry, biography, travel,
literary criticism or research work, in each of
the four regional languages of Punjabi, Pushto,
Sindhi & Gujrati. Awarded annually.

**United Bank Prize for Literature**
Pakistan Writers' Guild
One Mentgomrey Rd, Lahore
*Tel:* 6367124
Established: 1967
Founded for books in Urdu & Bengali in the fol-
lowing categories: for children up to 15 years
of age; also poetry or prose, fiction or nonfic-
tion, for young children.
Award: 20,000 rupees awarded annually

# Panama

**Literary Prize**
Revista Nacional de Cultura, Instito Nacional de
Cultura
Apdo 662, Panama 1
*Tel:* 2284362 *Fax:* 2288664
*Key Personnel*
Dir: A Ortega
Established: 1946
Annual award founded by Ricardo Miro to pay
tribute to those who furthered the cause of
learning, arts & sciences. Given in each of five
sections: poetry, short story, fiction, theatre,
essay.
Award: $2,000 Balboas for each section

# Philippines

**Cultural Centre of the Philippines Literary
Awards/Literature Grants**
Cultural Centre of the Philippines
CCP Complex, Roxas Blvd, 1300 Pasay City,
Manila
Mailing Address: PO Box 310, 1004 Metro
Manila
*Tel:* (02) 832-1125 *Fax:* (02) 832-3683
*E-mail:* ccp@culturalcenter.gov.ph
*Web Site:* www.culturalcenter.gov.ph
*Telex:* 40518 CULTURE PM *Cable:* CULTURE
PM
*Key Personnel*
President: Nestor O Jardin
Division Chief, Literature Division: Herminio
S Beltran, Jr *Tel:* (02) 832-1125 (ext 1706);
(02) 832-1125 (ext 1707) *Fax:* (02) 832-3674
*E-mail:* ccplit@hotmail.com
Awarded annually for the best volume of verse,
essay, fiction & best play written in Filipino &
other Philippine languages. Open to resident
Filipino citizens. Winning works are published
in the series of CCP literary quarterly journal,
*Ani.*
Award: 10,000 PHP in each category. Prizes also
for 2nd & 3rd places. CCP Literature Grants
award 25,000 PHP for a novel & 15,000 each
for poetry, short fiction, essay, play & children's literature

**Don Carlos Palanca Memorial Awards for
Literature Contest**
Carlos Palanca Foundation Inc

Ground floor, CPJ Bldg, 105 Carlos Palanca Jr St,
Legaspi Village, Makati, Metro Manila 1229
*Tel:* (02) 8183681 *Fax:* (02) 8174045
*E-mail:* cpawards@info.com.ph; palancaawards@
yahoo.com
*Web Site:* www.viloria.com
Established: 1950
Open to all Philipino citizens except current offi-
cers of the Carlos Palanca Foundation.
Award: Cash, certificate & medals
Closing Date: Jan-April 30

# Poland

**Cracow City Literary Prize**
Zwiazek Literatow Polskich (Union of Polish Let-
ters)
Krakowskie Przedmiescie 87/89, 00-079 Warsaw
*Tel:* (022) 8265785 *Fax:* (022) 8260866
*Cable:* ZLP KRAKOW KRUPNICZA 22 - PL
*Key Personnel*
Vice President, Writer & Journalist: Leszek
Maruta *Tel:* (012) 423 43 55
For the entire work of an author whose life &
writings were connected with Cracow. Awarded
annually.

**Nagroda Literacka SBP**
Stowarzyszenie Bibliotekarzy Polskich (Polish
Librarians Association)
Al Niepodleglosci 213, 02-086 Warsaw
*Tel:* (022) 825-97-05; (022) 825-50-24 (market-
ing) *Fax:* (022) 621-19-68; (022) 825-53-49
(marketing)
*E-mail:* biurozgsbp@wp.pl
*Web Site:* ebib.oss.wroc.pl/sbp
Established: 1983
Awarded annually for recognition of work that
has had an impact on publishing activity. Out-
standing works of fiction & nonfiction are con-
sidered. Opinions of the local branches of PLA
are sought in the selection process.
Award: Plaque, diploma & registration

**Jan Parandowski Prize**
Polish PEN Centre (Polski PEN Club)
Krakowskie Przedmiescie 87/89, 00-079 Warsaw
*Tel:* (022) 8282823 *Fax:* (022) 8265784
*E-mail:* penclub@ikp.atm.com.pl
*Web Site:* www.penclub.atomnet.pl
*Key Personnel*
President: Wladyslaw Bartoszewski
Awarded annually to commemorate Jan
Parandowski's personality & works. Every Pol-
ish author of literary merit is eligible.

**PEN Club Prizes for Editors**
Polish PEN Centre (Polski PEN Club)
Krakowskie Przedmiescie 87/89, 00-079 Warsaw
*Tel:* (022) 8282823 *Fax:* (022) 8265784
*E-mail:* penclub@ikp.atm.com.pl
*Web Site:* www.penclub.atomnet.pl
*Key Personnel*
President: Wladyslaw Bartoszewski
Awarded annually for the best editorial work. Ev-
ery Polish editor of editorial merit is eligible.

**PEN Club Prizes for Essay, Prose & Poetry**
Polish PEN Centre (Polski PEN Club)
Krakowskie Przedmiescie 87/89, 00-079 Warsaw
*Tel:* (022) 8282823 *Fax:* (022) 8265784
*E-mail:* penclub@ikp.atm.com.pl
*Web Site:* www.penclub.atomnet.pl
*Key Personnel*
President: Wladyslaw Bartoszewski
Awarded annually for the best literary works in
the year. Polish essayists, prose writers & poets
are eligible.

**PEN Club Prizes for Translators of Foreign
Literature into Polish**
Polish PEN Centre (Polski PEN Club)
Krakowskie Przedmiescie 87/89, 00-079 Warsaw
*Tel:* (022) 8282823 *Fax:* (022) 8265784
*E-mail:* penclub@ikp.atm.com.pl
*Web Site:* www.penclub.atomnet.pl
*Key Personnel*
President: Wladyslaw Bartoszewski
Annual awards to promote foreign literature in
Poland. Open to all Polish translators of for-
eign literature into Polish.

**PEN Club Prizes for Translators of Polish
Literature into Foreign Languages**
Polish PEN Centre (Polski PEN Club)
Krakowskie Przedmiescie 87/89, 00-079 Warsaw
*Tel:* (022) 8282823 *Fax:* (022) 8265784
*E-mail:* penclub@ikp.atm.com.pl
*Web Site:* www.penclub.atomnet.pl
*Key Personnel*
President: Wladyslaw Bartoszewski
Annual awards to promote Polish literature
abroad. All foreign translators of Polish liter-
ature & poetry are eligible.

**Polish Prime Minister Award for Literature for
Children and Youth**
Polish Prime Minister's Office
Al Ujazdowskie 1/3, 00-583 Warsaw
*Tel:* (022) 841-38-32; (022) 694-69-83 *Fax:* (022)
628-48-21
*E-mail:* cirinfo@kprm.gov.pl
*Web Site:* www.kprm.gov.pl
For the entire work of an author of books for
children & young people. Awards biennially.

☆**Polish Society of Authors (Zaiks) Prizes**
Stowarzyszenie Autorow Zaiks (Nagrody i
Wyrozniania Stowarzyszenia Autorow ZAIKS)
ul Hipoteczna 2, 00 092 Warsaw
*Tel:* (022) 8281705 *Fax:* (022) 8289204
*E-mail:* info@zaiks.org.pl
*Web Site:* www.zaiks.org.pl
Literary award for translators, est 1966, awarded
annually; Award for the promotion of Polish
creativity, est 1990, awarded annually; Varas-
viane Award: for works devoted to Warsaw,
est 1988, awarded biannually; Award for creative achievements in choreography, est 2001,
awarded biannually; Medal of ZAIKS.

**Ksawery Pruszynski Prize**
Polish PEN Centre (Polski PEN Club)
Krakowskie Przedmiescie 87/89, 00-079 Warsaw
*Tel:* (022) 8282823 *Fax:* (022) 8265784
*E-mail:* penclub@ikp.atm.com.pl
*Web Site:* www.penclub.atomnet.pl
*Key Personnel*
President: Wladyslaw Bartoszewski
Annual award to commemorate the personality
& output of Ksawery Pruxzynski. Polish prose
writers & essayists of editorial merit are eligi-
ble.

**Jan Strzelecki Prize**
Polish PEN Centre (Polski PEN Club)
Krakowskie Przedmiescie 87/89, 00-079 Warsaw
*Tel:* (022) 8282823 *Fax:* (022) 8265784
*E-mail:* penclub@ikp.atm.com.pl
*Web Site:* www.penclub.atomnet.pl
*Key Personnel*
President: Wladyslaw Bartoszewski
Awarded annually to commemorate Jan Strz-
elecki's personality & works. Polish authors,
essayists & sociologists are eligible.

**Commander Kazimierz Szczesny Prize**
Polish PEN Centre (Polski PEN Club)
Krakowskie Przedmiescie 87/89, 00-079 Warsaw
*Tel:* (022) 8265784 *Fax:* (022) 8282823

*E-mail:* penclub@ikp.atm.com.pl
*Web Site:* www.penclub.atomnet.pl
*Key Personnel*
President: Wladyslaw Bartoszewski
Triennial award to commemorate Commander
Kazimierz Szczesny. Polish marine writers &
authors whose works are connected with the
sea are eligible.

# Portugal

## Calouste Gulbenkian Translation Prize
Lisbon Academy of Sciences
Rua da Academie das Ciencias, nº 19, 1249-122
Lisbon
*Tel:* (021) 3219730 *Fax:* (021) 3420395
*E-mail:* geral@acad-ciencias.pt; biblioteca@acad-ciencias.pt
*Web Site:* www.acad-ciencias.pt
Annual award recognizes the best translator of
a work of fiction, a play, or a work of poetry
from a foreign language into Portuguese. Aes-
thetic & vernacular qualities of the translation
are considered by the jury. Portuguese transla-
tors whose works are published during the year
of the award are eligible.
Award: Two prizes of 100 EUR each, one for
prose & one for poetry

## Ricardo Malheiros Prize
Acedemia Das Ciencias De Lisboa
Rua da Academia das Ciencias, nº 19, 1249-122
Lisbon
*Tel:* (021) 3219730 *Fax:* (021) 3420395
*E-mail:* geral@acad-ciencias.pt; biblioteca@acad-ciencias.pt
*Web Site:* www.acad-ciencias.pt
Awarded annually to an author for a work of
imaginative literature.
Award: 30 EUR

## National Award for Poetry & the Novel
Associacao Portuguesa de Escritores (Portuguese
Association of Writers)
Rua de S Domingos a Lapa 17, 1200 Lisbon
*Tel:* (021) 7932322 *Fax:* (021) 3972341
Annual award of two prizes, one for the best
book of poetry & the other for the best novel
or book of short stories.
Award: 249 EUR each

## National Essay Award
Associacao Portuguesa de Escritores (Portuguese
Association of Writers)
Rua de S Domingos a Lapa 17, 1200 Lisbon
*Tel:* (021) 7932322 *Fax:* (021) 3972341
Awarded biennially for the best essay written by
a Portuguese author & printed in Portuguese.
Award: 300 EUR

## Revelation Awards (Poetry & Prose)
Associacao Portuguesa de Escritores (Portuguese
Association of Writers)
Rua de S Domingos a Lapa 17, 1200 Lisbon
*Tel:* (021) 7932322 *Fax:* (021) 3972341
Annual award with four prizes, two given for the
best unpublished manuscript of poetry & two
for prose.
Award: 30 EUR

## Revelation Prize for Children's Literature
Associacao Portuguesa de Escritores (Portuguese
Association of Writers)
Rua de S Domingos a Lapa 17, 1200 Lisbon
*Tel:* (021) 7932322 *Fax:* (021) 3972341

Annual award for the best book written for readers between four & sixteen.
Award: 601 EUR

## Aquilino Ribeiro Literary Prize
Lisbon Academy of Sciences
Rua da Academia das Ciencias, nº 19, 1249-122
Lisbon
*Tel:* (021) 3219730 *Fax:* (021) 3420395
*E-mail:* geral@acad-ciencias.pt; biblioteca@acad-ciencias.pt
*Web Site:* www.acad-ciencias.pt

# Romania

## Romanian Writers' Union Prizes
Uniunea Scriitorilor din Romania (Romanian
Writer's Union)
Calea Victoriei 115, 71102 Bucharest
*Tel:* (01) 6502838; (01) 6507817 *Fax:* (01)
2107211
*Key Personnel*
President: Laurentiu Ulici
For an outstanding contribution to Romanian liter-
ature in poetry, prose, drama, literary criticism,
history of literature, literary reportage, literature
for children & youth, translations from world
literature & for a promising new literary work
by a young writer. Awarded annually (separate
prizes are awarded by Bucharest, Cluj, Jassy,
Timisoara, Craiova, Sibiu, Brasov & Tiirgu-
Mures Writers' Associations). Awarded annually. For further information contact the appropriate Associations of the Writers' Union of the
Socialist Republic of Romania.

# Singapore

## National Book Development Council of Singapore Book Awards
National Book Development Council of Singa-
pore
Geylang East Community Library, National Li-
brary Board, 50 Geylang East Ave 1, Singapore
389777
*Tel:* 6848 8290 *Fax:* 6742 9466
*E-mail:* info@bookcouncil.sg
*Web Site:* www.nbdcs.org.sg
*Key Personnel*
Dir: Prof Tommy Koh
Established: 1976
Awarded for outstanding works of creative & non
creative writing by local authors in any of the
four official languages (Malay, English, Chi-
nese & Tamil). The awards are for fiction, po-
etry, drama, nonfiction, children's & young
people's books. Up to 15 prizes awarded biennially.
Award: 500 SGD to 2,000 SGD

# Slovakia

## Mlade Ieta Prize
Young Years Publishing House
Peter Cacko, Nam SNP 12, CS-815 19 Bratislava
*Tel:* (07) 364475 *Fax:* (07) 364563
For existing works or for outstanding achieve-
ments in the field of juvenile literature. The
executive body of the Frano Kral Prize is the
Slovak Literary Fund, the Circle of Friends

of Childrens Books in Slovakia & publishing
house Mlade leta. The prize is awarded annually.

## ☆Pavol Orszagh-Hviezdoslav Prize
Association of Slovak Writers (Spolak Slovenskych Spisovatelov)
Stefanikova 14, 815 08 Bratislava
*Tel:* (07) 43615
Awarded annually by the Union of Slovak Writers to outstanding translators of Slovak literature abroad during the preceding year. 10,000
crowns, plus a fortnight in Slovakia.

# Slovenia

## International Literary Award Vilenica
Slovene Writers' Association
Tomsiceva 12, SI 1000 Ljubljana
*Tel:* (01) 4252340; (01) 2514144 *Fax:* (01)
4216430
*E-mail:* info@drustvo-dsp.si
*Web Site:* www.drustvo-dsp.si; www.vilenica.org
*Key Personnel*
Dir: Iztok Osojnik *E-mail:* iztok.osojnik@guest.
arnes.si
Award for exceptional achievements in the field
of poetry & prose.
Award: 1,500,000 SIT
Presented: International Literary gathering
Vilenica

# South Africa

## Academy Prize for Translated Work
South African Academy for Science & Arts, En-
gelenburghuis
Ziervogelstr 574, Arcadia, Pretoria 0083
Mailing Address: Privaatsak X11, Arcadia 0007
*Tel:* (012) 3285082 *Fax:* (012) 3285091
*E-mail:* akademie@mweb.co.za
*Web Site:* www.akademie.co.za
*Key Personnel*
Contact: Dr D J C Geldenhuys
Established: 1948
For translations into Afrikaans of belletristic work
from any other language. Awarded triennially.
Award: 2,500 ZAR

## Alba Bouwer Prize
South African Academy for Science & Arts, En-
gelenburghuis
Ziervogelstr 574, Arcadia, Pretoria 0083
Mailing Address: Privaatsak X11, Arcadia 0007
*Tel:* (012) 3285082 *Fax:* (012) 3285091
*E-mail:* akademie@mweb.co.za
*Web Site:* www.akademie.co.za
*Key Personnel*
Contact: Dr D J C Geldenhuys
Established: 1989
For recognition of Afrikaans literature for chil-
dren 7-12 years old. A monetary prize donated
by the Akademie is awarded triennially.

## CNA Literary Award
CNA (Central News Agency)
c/o Public Relations, Johannesburg 2000
Mailing Address: PO Box 10799, Johannesburg
2000
*Tel:* (011) 4917902 *Fax:* (011) 4930777
*E-mail:* angelaa@cna.co.za
Established in 1961 for the best original works,
one in English & one in Afrikaans, published
for the first time during the calendar year of

the competition. 15,500 ZAR each for the winner & 3,500 ZAR for the runners-up in both the English & Afrikaans categories, with an additional prize of 3,000 ZAR for the best debut work published in each category. Awarded annually. Books must be in one of following categories: novel, short story, poetry, biography, drama, history, travel. Authors must be South African citizens or registered permanent residents of South Africa.

**English Association (South African Branch) Literary Competition**
English Association
B204 Devonshire Hill, Grotto Rd, Rondebosch, Cape Town 7700
*Tel:* (021) 6854242
For original unpublished manuscripts by residents of Southern Africa. Subject, literary form & amount of award vary from year to year. Three prizes are usually awarded annually according to the standard reached.

**Percy FitzPatrick Prize**
English Academy of Southern Africa
PO Box 124, Wits 2050
*Tel:* (011) 717-9339 *Fax:* (011) 717-9339
*E-mail:* englishacademy@societies.wits.ac.za
*Web Site:* www.englishacademy.co.za
*Key Personnel*
Awards & Prizes: Prof Rosemary Gray
Awarded biennially. Recognizes achievement by Southern African writers publishing in South Africa in the field of children's books between the ages of 10-14 years.
Award: 2,000 ZAR

**Katrine Harries Award**
Library & Information Association of South Africa (LIASA)
PO Box 1598, Pretoria 0001
*Tel:* (012) 481 2870; (012) 481 2876; (012) 481 2875 *Fax:* (012) 481 2873
*E-mail:* liasa@liasa.org.za
*Web Site:* www.liasa.org.za
*Key Personnel*
Executive Dir: Gwenda Thomas
For outstanding illustrations in South African children's books, regardless of language. Awarded biennially.

**Hertzog Prize**
South African Academy for Science & Arts, Engelenburghuis
Ziervogelstr 574, Arcadia, Pretoria 0083
Mailing Address: Private Bag X11, Arcadia, Pretoria 0007
*Tel:* (012) 3285082 *Fax:* (012) 3285091
*E-mail:* akademie@mweb.co.za
*Web Site:* www.akademie.co.za
Established: 1914
A prestige prize for Afrikaans literature. Prizes are awarded in rotation for poetry, drama & prose. Awarded annually.
Award: 17,000 ZAR & 18 ct gold medal

**Louis Hiemstra Prize for Nonfiction**
South African Academy for Science & Arts, Engelenburghuis
Ziervogelstr 574, Arcadia, Pretoria 0083
Mailing Address: Private Bag X11, Arcadia, Pretoria 0007
*Tel:* (012) 3285082 *Fax:* (012) 3285091
*E-mail:* akademie@mweb.co.za
*Web Site:* www.akademie.co.za
Established: 2001
Awarded every three years for nonfiction work in Afrikaans.
Award: 20,000 ZAR

**W A Hofmeyr Prize**
Tafelberg Publishers Ltd
12 de Verdieping, 12th floor, Naspers, Heerengracht 40, Roggebaai 8012
Mailing Address: PO Box 879, Cape Town 8000
*Tel:* (021) 406 3033 *Fax:* (021) 406 3812
*E-mail:* tafelbrg@tafelberg.com
*Web Site:* www.nb.co.za/tafelberg
Established: 1954
Awarded annually for the best literary work published by Nasoek publishers, including Tafelberg, Human & Rousseau, Nasou Via Afrika, JL van Schaik, Jonathan Ball, Kwela, Queillerie, Pharos, Sunbird & Van Schaik Publishers.
Award: 5,000 ZAR & gold medallion (1 ounce pure gold)

**Tienie Holloway Medal**
South African Academy for Science & Arts, Engelenburghuis
Ziervogelstr 574, Arcadia, Pretoria 0083
Mailing Address: Privaatsak X11, Arcadia 0007
*Tel:* (012) 3285082 *Fax:* (012) 3285091
*E-mail:* akademie@mweb.co.za
*Web Site:* www.akademie.co.za
*Key Personnel*
Contact: Dr D J C Geldenhuys
Established: 1969
Established by Dr J E Holloway & awarded triennially to a writer who has produced the best work in Afrikaans literature for infants.
Award: Gold medal

**C P Hoogenhout Award**
Library & Information Association of South Africa (LIASA)
PO Box 1598, Pretoria 0001
*Tel:* (012) 481 2870; (012) 481 2875; (012) 481 2876 *Fax:* (012) 481 2873
*E-mail:* liasa@liasa.org.za
*Web Site:* www.liasa.org.za
*Key Personnel*
Award Chair: G H Haffajee
To encourage the production of outstanding Afrikaans children's books appropriate for ages 7-12 years. Awarded biannually.
Award: Gold medal & certificate

**C J Langenhoven Prize**
South African Academy for Science & Arts, Engelenburghuis
Ziervogelstr 574, Arcadia, Pretoria 0083
Mailing Address: Privaatsak X11, Arcadia 0007
*Tel:* (012) 3285082 *Fax:* (012) 3285091
*E-mail:* akademie@mweb.co.za
*Web Site:* www.akademie.co.za
*Key Personnel*
Contact: Dr D J C Geldenhuys
For outstanding work in field of Afrikaans linguistics. Awarded triennially.

**H Recht Malan Prize**
Tafelberg Publishers Ltd
12 de Verdieping, 12th floor, Naspers, Heerengracht 40, Roggebaai 8012
Mailing Address: PO Box 879, Cape Town 8000
*Tel:* (021) 406 3033 *Fax:* (021) 406 3812
*E-mail:* tafelbrg@tafelberg.com
*Web Site:* www.nb.co.za/tafelberg
Awarded annually for the best nonfiction book published by Nasboek publishers, including Tafelberg, Human & Rousseau, Kwela, Queillerie, Pharos, JL van Schaik, Sunbird, Jonathan Ball, Van Schaik Publishers & Nasou Via Afrika.
Award: 5,000 ZAR & gold medallion (1 ounce pure gold)

**Eugene Marais Prize**
South African Academy for Science & Arts, Engelenburghuis

Ziervogelstr 574, Arcadia, Pretoria 0083
Mailing Address: Privaatsak X11, Arcadia 0007
*Tel:* (012) 3285082 *Fax:* (012) 3285091
*E-mail:* akademie@mweb.co.za
*Web Site:* www.akademie.co.za
*Key Personnel*
Contact: Dr D J C Geldenhuys
Established: 1961
For a first or early work of belletristic publication in Afrikaans. The prize can be awarded only once to any particular writer. Awarded annually.
Award: 11,000 ZAR

**MER Prize**
Tafelberg Publishers Ltd
12 de Verdieping, 12th floor, Naspers, Heerengracht 40, Roggebaai 8012
Mailing Address: PO Box 879, Cape Town 8000
*Tel:* (021) 406 3033 *Fax:* (021) 406 3812
*E-mail:* tafelbrg@tafelberg.com
*Web Site:* www.nb.co.za/tafelberg
*Key Personnel*
Contact: Riellela de Jage *E-mail:* rdejage@tafelberg.com
Awarded annually for the best children's book published by Nasboek publishers, including Tafelberg, Human & Rousseau, Kwela, Queillerie, Pharos, JL van Schaik, Sunbird, Jonathan Ball, Van Schaik Publishers & Nasou Via Afrikay.
Award: 5,000 ZAR & gold medallion (1 ounce pure gold)

**Gustav Preller Prize**
South African Academy for Science & Arts, Engelenburghuis
Ziervogelstr 574, Arcadia, Pretoria 0083
Mailing Address: Privaatsak X11, Arcadia 0007
*Tel:* (012) 3285082 *Fax:* (012) 3285091
*E-mail:* akademie@mweb.co.za
*Web Site:* www.akademie.co.za
*Key Personnel*
Contact: Dr D J C Geldenhuys
For literary science & literary criticism in Afrikaans. Awarded triennially.

**Thomas Pringle Awards**
English Academy of Southern Africa
PO Box 124, Wits 2050
*Tel:* (011) 717-9339 *Fax:* (011) 717-9339
*E-mail:* englishacademy@societies.wits.ac.za
*Web Site:* www.englishacademy.co.za
*Key Personnel*
Awards & Prizes: Prof Rosemary Gray
Awarded every year in three of five categories, including play, book, film & television reviews in newspapers & periodicals; literary articles or substantial book reviews in academic & other journals & in newspapers; articles on language & the teaching of English in academic, teachers' & other journals & in newspapers; short stories & one-act plays in periodicals; & poetry in periodicals.
Other Sponsor(s): FNB Vita
Award: 2,000 ZAR in each category

**Scheepers Prize**
South African Academy for Science & Arts, Engelenburghuis
Ziervogelstr 574, Arcadia, Pretoria 0083
Mailing Address: Privaatsak X11, Arcadia 0007
*Tel:* (012) 3285082 *Fax:* (012) 3285091
*E-mail:* akademie@mweb.co.za
*Web Site:* www.akademie.co.za
*Key Personnel*
Contact: Dr D J C Geldenhuys
Established: 1956
Awarded triennially in recognition of excellence in children's literature to authors of Afrikaans.

**Olive Schreiner Prize for English Literature**
English Academy of Southern Africa
PO Box 124, Wits 2050
*Tel:* (011) 717-9339 *Fax:* (011) 717-9339
*E-mail:* englishacademy@societies.wits.ac.za
*Web Site:* www.englishacademy.co.za
*Key Personnel*
Awards & Prizes: Prof Rosemary Gray
For original literary work in English by a promising South African writer & published in South Africa. Awarded annually in one of the following categories: prose, poetry, drama.
Other Sponsor(s): FNB Vita
Award: 5,000 ZAR

# Spain

**Miguel de Cervantes Prize**
Direccion General del Libro y Bibliotecas, Ministerio de Cultura
Plaza del Rey 1, 28071 Madrid
*Tel:* (091) 7017000 *Fax:* (091) 7017003; (091) 7017004; (091) 7017005
*E-mail:* informa.admini@sqt.mcu.es
*Web Site:* www.mcu.es
Annual award for the work of a writer who has made an outstanding contribution to Spanish Literature.
Award: 90,152 EUR

**☆Premio Destino Infantil-Apel.les Mestres**
(Destino Children's Book Prize)
Ediciones Destino
Diagonal, 662-664, 08034 Barcelona
*Tel:* (093) 496 70 01 *Fax:* (093) 496 70 02
*E-mail:* edicionesdestino@stl.logiccontrol.es
*Web Site:* www.edestino.es
*Key Personnel*
Editor: Joaquim Palau Fau
Established: 1980
Open to all illustrated literary works which have not been published in any form & are intended for children. Works can be in Spanish, Catalan, Basque, Galician, English, French or Italian. Exists to acknowledge creative effort in the world of illustrated books.
Award: 4,500 EUR
Closing Date: Sept
Presented: Oct annually

**Espejo de Espana Prize**
Editorial Planeta SA
C/Corsega, 273-279, 08008 Barcelona
*Tel:* (093) 2283700 *Fax:* (093) 4151265
*Web Site:* www.planeta.es
*Telex:* 93458 EDTPE
Established: 1975
Awarded annually for an essay.
Award: 24,040 EUR

**Fastenrath Prize**
Real Academia Espanola
C/Academia, 28071 Madrid
*Tel:* (091) 4201478 *Fax:* (091) 4200079
*Web Site:* www.rae.es
Established: 1909
Annual award for works of excellence written in the Spanish language. Awarded in rotation for the following categories of writing: poetry; essays, criticism; novel or story; history, biography; drama.
Award: 12,000 EUR

**Lazarillo Prize**
Organizacion Espanola para Libro Infantily Juvenil
Santiago Rusinol 8, 28040 Madrid

*Tel:* (091) 5530821 *Fax:* (091) 5539990
*E-mail:* oepli@arrakis.es
*Web Site:* www.oepli.org
Established: 1982
Awarded for the author of narration, poetry or theater, of a children's or young adult book.
Award: 1st place 6,000 EUR; 2nd place 1,320 EUR

**Ramon Llull Prize**
Editorial Planeta SA
C/Corsega, 273-279, 08008 Barcelona
*Tel:* (093) 2283700 *Fax:* (093) 4151265
*Web Site:* www.planeta.es
*Telex:* 93458 EDTPE
*Key Personnel*
Chairman: Jose Manuel Lara Hernandez
Established: 1968
Founded for the purpose of contributing to the increase & promotion of narrative in Catalan. Since 1995, it has accepted both fictional works (novels, narratives, etc) & nonfictional works (essays, memoirs, biographies, etc).
Award: 60,000 EUR
Presented: Jan annually

**Premio Nadal** (Nadal Prize)
Ediciones Destino
Diagonal, 662-664, 08034 Barcelona
*Tel:* (093) 496 70 01 *Fax:* (093) 496 70 02
*E-mail:* edicionesdestino@stl.logiccontrol.es
*Web Site:* www.edestino.es
*Key Personnel*
Editor: Joaquim Palau Fau
Secretary: Yolanda Bolsa *E-mail:* ybolsa@edestino.es
Established: 1944
The Nadal Prize is the oldest literary prize to be awarded to novels written in Spanish. Starting with the 2001 prize, novels presented for this award will also be competing for the Premio Destino-Guion script award, which will be awarded to the best novel according to its potential for adaptation to a film or audio-visual script.
Award: 18,030 EUR (winner); 4,988 EUR (runner-up)
Presented: Jan annually

**National Prize for Illustration of Children's Literature**
Direccion General del Libro y Bibliotecas, Ministerio de Cultura
Plaza del Rey 1, 28071 Madrid
*Tel:* (091) 7017000 *Fax:* (091) 7017003; (091) 7017004; (091) 7017005
*E-mail:* informa.admini@sqt.mcu.es
*Web Site:* www.mcu.es
Annual award for the best illustrations in a book for children or young people. Awarded in alternate years in each category.
Award: 4,988 EUR

**National Prize for Literature**
Direccion General del Libro y Bibliotecas, Ministerio de Cultura
Plaza del Rey 1, 28071 Madrid
*Tel:* (091) 7017000 *Fax:* (091) 7017003; (091) 7017004; (091) 7017005
*E-mail:* informa.admini@sqt.mcu.es
*Web Site:* www.mcu.es
Established: 1984
Three annual awards for the best books of poetry, fiction & essays published in the previous year in one of the official languages of Spain.
Award: 12,470 EUR each

**National Prize of Spanish Letters**
Direccion General del Libro y Bibliotecas, Ministerio de Cultura
Plaza del Rey 1, 28071 Madrid

*Tel:* (091) 7017000 *Fax:* (091) 7017003; (091) 7017004; (091) 7017005
*E-mail:* informa.admini@sqt.mcu.es
*Web Site:* www.mcu.es
Established: 1986
Awarded in recognition of an author, writing in one of the official Spanish languages, for the whole of his work.
Award: 24,940 EUR

**National Prizes for Children's Literature**
Direccion General del Libro y Bibliotecas, Ministerio de Cultura
Plaza del Rey 1, 28071 Madrid
*Tel:* (091) 7017000 *Fax:* (091) 7017003; (091) 7017004; (091) 7017005
*E-mail:* informa.admini@sqt.mcu.es
*Web Site:* www.mcu.es
Established: 1978
Two annual awards for the best literary works intended for children or young people, written in any of the official languages of Spain. Awarded in alternate years in each category.
Award: 7,482 EUR for original work; 4,988 EUR for a translation

**☆Leopoldo Panero Prize**
Instituto de Cooperacion Iberoamericana
Avda de los Reyes Catolicos 4, Ciudad Universitaria, 28040 Madrid
*Tel:* (091) 5838100 *Fax:* (091) 5838310
For poetry in Spanish, awarded annually.
Award: 7482 EUR

**☆Planeta Prize**
Editorial Planeta SA
C/Corsega, 273-279, 08008 Barcelona
*Tel:* (093) 2283700 *Fax:* (093) 4151265
*Web Site:* www.planeta.es
*Key Personnel*
Chairman: Jose Manuel Lara Hernandez
Established: 1952
Spain: promotes Spanish authors. The award is presented annually in Oct
Argentina: given for previously unpublished works in Spanish, continuing in its objective of promoting the production of novels. Presented annually in Oct
Chile: awarded for the first time in 2000 for journalistic research. May be entered by journalists or writers with works referring to Chilean subject matter in any written journalistic genre: information, report, chronicle, biography, analysis or interview. Pieces may be the work of a single author or of several. Presented annually in Oct
Colombia: prize awarded in recognition of the life & works of, alternately, a journalist & historian. Presented annually in Dec.
Award: Cash

**Premi Josep Pla** (Josep Pla Prize)
Ediciones Destino
Diagonal, 662-664, 08034 Barcelona
*Tel:* (093) 496 70 01 *Fax:* (093) 496 70 02
*E-mail:* edicionesdestino@stl.logiccontrol.es
*Web Site:* www.edestino.es
*Key Personnel*
Editor: Joaquim Palau Fau
Secretary: Yolanda Bolsa *E-mail:* ybolsa@edestino.es
Established: 1969
Awarded for prose in Catalan without limits in terms of genre (novels, short stories, accounts, travel books, memoirs or biographies).
Award: 4,988 EUR
Presented: Jan annually

**Alvarez Quintero Prize**
Real Academia Espanola
C/Academia, 28071 Madrid
*Tel:* (091) 4201478 *Fax:* (091) 4200079
*Web Site:* www.rae.es

Established: 1949
Biennial award for the best work in two categories alternately: novel or story collection & theatrical works.
Award: 600 EUR

## Reading & Writing National Competition
Direccion General del Libro y Bibliotecas, Ministerio de Cultura
Plaza del Rey 1, 28071 Madrid
*Tel:* (091) 7017000 *Fax:* (091) 7017003; (091) 7017004; (091) 7017005
*E-mail:* informa.admini@sqt.mcu.es
*Web Site:* www.mcu.es
Established: 1978
Annual competition for students at COU, BUP or equivalent levels of 'Formacion Profesional'. Prizes are given for literary works, in any of the official languages of Spain, related to an important figure in Spanish literature. Prize winners are selected from 150 qualifying works. A second group of awards is made for students at EGB level for illustrations related to an important figure in Spanish literature. Winners must use the prize money exclusively for the purchase of books.
Award: 1st prize 274 EUR; 2nd prize 249 EUR; 3rd prize 224 EUR for both literary & illustrations; 125 EUR for each additional prize

## Rivadeneyra Prizes
Real Academia Espanola
C/Academia, 28071 Madrid
*Tel:* (091) 4201478 *Fax:* (091) 4200079
*Web Site:* www.rae.es
Established: 1940
Annual award for the best work on Spanish literature & linguistics.
Award: Two prizes: 1,800 EUR & 1,200 EUR

## ☆La Sonrisa Vertical Prize
La Sonrisa Vertical, Tusquets Editores
Cesare Cantu, 8, 08023 Barcelona
*Tel:* (093) 2530400 *Fax:* (093) 4176703
*Web Site:* www.tusquets-editores.es
*Telex:* 99061 TUSQ E
Established: 1978
Founded in homage to Lopez Barbadillo. Awarded annually for the best erotic novel written in Spanish or another language of the Spanish State. The prize is an advance on the work prior to publication, together with an artistic object.
Award: 6,000 EUR

# Sri Lanka

## Literary Prizes for Sinhala Literature
Ministry of Cultural Affairs
Sethsiripaya, 8th floor, Battaramulla
*Tel:* (01) 545777
Awarded annually for the best books published in the previous year in the Sinhala language in the following categories: novels, short stories, poetry, translations, children's literature, scientific literature, drama; also three awards in miscellaneous literary areas & awards for original works in Pali, Sanskrit & Arabic.
Award: 5,000 LKR; Children's literature 2,000 LKR

## D R Wijewardene Memorial Award
Lake House Bookshop
100 Ser Chittampalam, Gardines Mawatha, Colombo 2
*Tel:* (01) 432105; (01) 432104 *Fax:* (01) 432104
*E-mail:* bookshop@sri.lanka.net
*Telex:* 21266 LAKEXPO CE BOOKSALES

*Key Personnel*
Chairman: Mr R S Wijewardena
General Manager: Mr Sarath de Silva
Established: 1984
Established by the Lake House Bookshop, Colombo, for the best unpublished manuscript of a novel or short story collection in Sinhala. Awarded annually.
Award: 50,000 LKR
Closing Date: Nov
Presented: Sri Lanka Foundation, Colombo 7, June

# Sweden

## Carl Akermarks Stipendium
Swedish Academy
PO Box 2118, 103 13 Stockholm
*Tel:* (08) 555 125 00 *Fax:* (08) 555 125 49
*E-mail:* sekretariat@svenskaakademien.se
*Web Site:* www.svenskaakademien.se
Reward for theatre. This award cannot be applied for. Awarded annually.
Award: Five prizes of 20,000 SEK

## Aniara Priset
Svensk Biblioteksforening (Swedish Library Association)
Saltmaetargatan 3A, 103 62 Stockholm
Mailing Address: PO Box 3127, 103 62 Stockholm
*Tel:* (08) 545 132 30 *Fax:* (08) 545 132 31
*E-mail:* info@biblioteksforeningen.org
*Web Site:* www.biblioteksforeningen.org

## Bellman Prize
Swedish Academy
PO Box 2118, 103 13 Stockholm
*Tel:* (08) 555 125 00 *Fax:* (08) 555 125 49
*E-mail:* sekretariat@svenskaakademien.se
*Web Site:* www.svenskaakademien.se
Annual award for poetry. This prize cannot be applied for.
Award: 200,000 SEK

## Blekinge County Council Culture Prize
Blekinge County Council
Karlskrona, 37181 Karlskrona
*Tel:* (0455) 731000 *Fax:* (0455) 80250
*E-mail:* landstinget.blekinge@ltblekinge.se
*Web Site:* www.ltblekinge.se
Established: 1964
Annual prize to recognize a person or organization for a valuable contribution to science, arts, poetry, literature, music, dance, theatre, journalism or free education.
Award: 50,000 SEK

## Gerard Bonnier's Prize
Swedish Academy
PO Box 2118, 103 13 Stockholm
*Tel:* (08) 555 125 00 *Fax:* (08) 555 125 49
*E-mail:* sekretariat@svenskaakademien.se
*Web Site:* www.svenskaakademien.se
Annual prize to a writer active in the fields within the academy's mandate. This award cannot be applied for.
Award: 125,000 SEK

## Dobloug Prize
Swedish Academy
PO Box 2118, 103 13 Stockholm
*Tel:* (08) 555 125 00 *Fax:* (08) 555 125 49
*E-mail:* sekretariat@svenskaakademien.se
*Web Site:* www.svenskaakademien.se

Annual prize for outstanding literary work by two Norwegian & two Swedish writers. This award cannot be applied for.
Award: Two prizes of 80,000 SEK in each category

## Signe Ekblad-Eldh Prize
Swedish Academy
PO Box 2118, 103 13 Stockholm
*Tel:* (08) 555 125 00 *Fax:* (08) 555 125 49
*E-mail:* sekretariat@svenskaakademien.se
*Web Site:* www.svenskaakademien.se
To famous Swedish writers. This award cannot be applied for.
Award: 70,000 SEK annually

## Gun & Olof Engqvist Prize
Swedish Academy
PO Box 2118, 103 13 Stockholm
*Tel:* (08) 555 125 00 *Fax:* (08) 555 125 49
*E-mail:* sekretariat@svenskaakademien.se
*Web Site:* www.svenskaakademien.se
For Swedish Literature & Cultural Journalism. This award cannot be applied for.
Award: 100,000 SEK awarded annually

## Lydia & Herman Eriksson Prize
Swedish Academy
PO Box 2118, 103 13 Stockholm
*Tel:* (08) 555 125 00 *Fax:* (08) 555 125 49
*E-mail:* sekretariat@svenskaakademien.se
*Web Site:* www.svenskaakademien.se
Awarded to a Swedish writer for a work of prose or poetry. This prize cannot be applied for.
Award: 70,000 SEK every second year

## Nils Holgersson Plaque
Svensk Biblioteksforening (Swedish Library Association)
Saltmaetargatan 3A, 103 62 Stockholm
Mailing Address: PO Box 3127, 103 62 Stockholm
*Tel:* (08) 54513230 *Fax:* (08) 54513231
*E-mail:* info@biblioteksforeningen.org
*Web Site:* www.biblioteksforeningen.org
Established: 1950

## Kalleberger Prize
Swedish Academy
PO Box 2118, 103 13 Stockholm
*Tel:* (08) 555 125 00 *Fax:* (08) 555 125 49
*E-mail:* sekretariat@svenskaakademien.se
*Web Site:* www.svenskaakademien.se
An award in memory of Tekla Hansson to a Swedish writer for a work of prose or poetry. This prize cannot be applied for.
Award: 30,000 SEK annually

## Kellgren Prize
Swedish Academy
PO Box 2118, 10313 Stockholm
*Tel:* (08) 555 125 00 *Fax:* (08) 555 125 49
*E-mail:* sekretariat@svenskaakademien.se
*Web Site:* www.svenskaakademien.se
Annual award for important achievements in any of the fields of the academy. This prize cannot be applied for.
Award: 125,000 SEK

## Literary Award
Svenska Dagbladet
Master Samuelsgatan 56, 105 17 Stockholm
*Tel:* (08) 13 50 00 *Fax:* (08) 52 34 97
*E-mail:* nyhetstipset@svd.de
*Web Site:* www.svd.se
Established: 1944
To encourage Swedish theatre design & to recognize contributions during the preceding theatre season. Awarded annually.
Award: 25,000 SEK

## ☆Nobel Prize for Literature
Swedish Academy
PO Box 2118, 103 13 Stockholm
*Tel:* (08) 555 125 00 *Fax:* (08) 555 125 49
*E-mail:* sekretariat@svenskaakademien.se
*Web Site:* www.svenskaakademien.se
Of all the literary prizes, the Nobel Prize for Literature is the biggest in value & in honor bestowed. It is one of the five prizes founded by Alfred Nobel (1833-1896); the other four awards are for physics, chemistry, physiology or medicine, & peace. By the terms of Nobel's will, the prize for literature is to be given to the person "who shall have produced in the field of literature the most distinguished work of an idealistic tendency." No one may apply for the Nobel Prize, there is no competition. It is awarded to an author usually for their total literary output & not for any single work.
Award: A gold medal, a diploma & a sum of money
Presented: Dec 10, the anniversary of Nobel's death

## Margit Pahlson Prize
Swedish Academy
PO Box 2118, 103 13 Stockholm
*Tel:* (08) 555 125 00 *Fax:* (08) 555 125 49
*E-mail:* sekretariat@svenskaakademien.se
*Web Site:* www.svenskaakademien.se
Annual award for achievements of particular significance for the Swedish language. This award cannot be applied for.
Award: 100,000 SEK

## Swedish Academy Nordic Prize
Swedish Academy
PO Box 2118, 103 13 Stockholm
*Tel:* (08) 555 125 00 *Fax:* (08) 555 125 49
*E-mail:* sekretariat@svenskaakademien.se
*Web Site:* www.svenskaakademien.se
Annual award for important achievements in any of the fields of interest of the academy. Citizens of any of the Scandinavian countries are eligible. This award cannot be applied for.
Award: 250,000 SEK

## Swedish Academy Prizes
Swedish Academy
PO Box 2118, 103 13 Stockholm
*Tel:* (08) 555 125 00 *Fax:* (08) 555 125 49
*E-mail:* sekretariat@svenskaakademien.se
*Web Site:* www.svenskaakademien.se
In addition to those fully listed individually, the Swedish Academy awards the following prizes: Ida Baeckman Prize (Literature/Journalism: biennial); Beskow Prize (Literary: biennial); Blom Prize (Swedish Language: annual); Karin Gierow Prizes (for (1) Cultural Information: annual; (2) Promotion of Knowledge: annual); Axel Hirsch Prize (Biographic/Historic: annual); Ilona Kohrtz Prize (Prose/Poetry: annual); Royal Prize (Cultural/Literary: annual); Birger Schoeldstroem Prize (Literary History/Biography: every 4 years); Schueck Prize (Literary History: annual); Swedish Language & Literature Teachers' Prize (annual); Swedish Linguistics Prize (annual); Swedish into Foreign Language Translation Prize (annual); Translation into Swedish Prize (annual); Zibet Prize (Literary/Historic referring to reign of Gustav III: biennial); miscellaneous prizes for work in literary or linguistic fields
These prizes cannot be applied for.

## Swedish Authors' Fund Awards
Swedish Authors'
Klara Norra Kyrkogata 29, Box 1106, 11181 Stockholm
*Tel:* (08) 4404550 *Fax:* (08) 4404565
*E-mail:* svff@svff.se
*Web Site:* www.svff.se

*Key Personnel*
Chairperson: Bengt Westerberg
To recognize authors, translators & illustrators who have made special contributions within their own fields. Main purpose of the fund is to administer the Swedish system of library loan compensation to authors, translators & book illustrators.
Award: 20,000 SEK

## Lena Vendelfelt Prize
Swedish Academy
PO Box 2118, 103 13 Stockholm
*Tel:* (08) 555 125 00 *Fax:* (08) 555 125 49
*E-mail:* sekretariat@svenskaakademein.se
*Web Site:* www.svenskaakademein.se
For a literary work, mainly poetry. This prize cannot be applied for.
Award: 30,000 SEK annually

# Switzerland

## ☆Hans Christian Andersen Awards
International Board on Books for Young People (IBBY)
Nonnenweg 12, Postfach, 4003 Basel
*Tel:* (061) 272 29 17 *Fax:* (061) 272 27 57
*E-mail:* ibby@ibby.org
*Web Site:* www.ibby.org
*Key Personnel*
Administrative Dir: Elizabeth Page
Established: 1956
The International Board on Books for Young People (IBBY) gives these awards every two years to a living author & a living illustrator who, through their works, have made distinguished contributions to international children's & young adult literature. (Until 1966 a prize was awarded for a specific book & to an author only.) A jury of ten members, appointed by the Executive Committee of IBBY, makes the decision from nominations submitted from member countries all over the world.
Other Sponsor(s): Nissan Motor Corp
Award: Biennial, gold medal & diploma

## Anne Frank Literary Award
Anne Frank-Fonds
Steinengraben 18, 4051 Basel
*Tel:* (061) 2741174 *Fax:* (061) 2741175
*E-mail:* info@annefrank.ch
*Web Site:* www.annefrank.ch
*Key Personnel*
President of the Board: Buddy Elias
Established: 1963

## Grand Prix Ramuz
Foundation C F Ramuz
Case Postale 181, 1009 Pully
*Tel:* (021) 721 3643
*Key Personnel*
Contact: Rebetez Maurice
Established: 1955
To recognize a writer for his entire work. Swiss authors writing in the French language are eligible.
Award: 15,000 Swiss francs every five years

## Grosser Schillerpreis
Schweizerische Schillerstiftung, Fondation Schiller Suisse
Mattenway 4, 8126-3270 Aarberg
*Tel:* 032 393 72 64
*Key Personnel*
Secretary: Agnes Aeschlimann
Prizes for Swiss citizens only.

## ☆IBBY-Asahi Reading Promotion Award
International Board on Books for Young People (IBBY)
Nonnenweg 12, 4003 Basel
*Tel:* (061) 272 29 17 *Fax:* (061) 272 27 57
*E-mail:* ibby@ibby.org
*Web Site:* www.ibby.org
*Key Personnel*
Administrative Dir: Elizabeth Page
Established: 1986
Presented annually to a group or institution that is making a significant contribution to book promotion programs for children & young adults.
Other Sponsor(s): Asahi Shimbun
Award: 1,000,000 JPY
Presented: Bologna Children's Book Fair

## ☆IBBY Honour List
International Board on Books for Young People (IBBY)
Nonnenweg 12, 4003 Basel
*Tel:* (061) 272 29 17 *Fax:* (061) 272 27 57
*E-mail:* ibby@ibby.org
*Web Site:* www.ibby.org
*Key Personnel*
Administrative Dir: Elizabeth Page
Biennial selection of outstanding, recently published books, honoring writers, illustrators & translators from IBBY member countries. Titles are selected by the National Sections. The Honor List Diplomas are presented to the recipients at the IBBY Congresses.

## Inner Swiss Literature Award
Inner Swiss Cultural Foundation
Bildungs-und Kulturdepartement des Kantons Luzern, Kulturabteilung, Bahnhofstr 18, 6002 Lucerne
*Tel:* (041) 2285206 *Fax:* (041) 2100573
*Key Personnel*
Contact: Daniel Huber *E-mail:* daniel.huber@lu.ch
Established: 1951
Annual award for recognition of outstanding literary work. Authors living in the central part of Switzerland (Innerschweiz, cantons: Lucerne, Uri, Schwyz, Obwalden, Nidwalden, & Zug) or who originate from those areas are eligible.
Award: 20,000 CHF & certificate

## International Award for the Promotion of Human Understanding
The International Organization for the Elimination of All Forms of Racial Discrimination (EAFORD)
5 Route des Morillons, burea No 475, 1211 Geneva 2
Mailing Address: Case Postale 2100, 1211 Geneva 2
*Tel:* (022) 7886233 *Fax:* (022) 7886245
*E-mail:* info@eaford.org
*Web Site:* www.eaford.org
*Key Personnel*
President: Mr Abdalla Sharafeddin
Secretary General: Dr Anis Al-Qasem
Established: 1978
Annual international award for outstanding published work in English, French, Arabic, Spanish or Portuguese dealing with questions of racism & racial discrimination.
Award: Monetary & certificate

## ☆Gottfried Keller Prize
Martin Bodmer-Stiftung fur einen Gottfried Keller-Preis
PO Box 1425, 8032 Zurich
Established: 1921
Founded by Martin Bodmer for Swiss & other writers who have honored the Swiss spirit. Awarded biennially.
Award: 25,000 CHF

**Prix Liberte Litteraire**
Foundation Armleder
Hotel Richemond, CH-1206 Geneva
*Tel:* (022) 7311400 *Fax:* (022) 7312414
Freedom Literary Prize.

**Prix Litteraire de la Ville de La**
**Chaux-de-Fonds et de la Revue** (Literary
Review Prize of La Chaux de Fronds)
Editions
19-21 Rue du Manege, 2301 La Chaux de Fonds
*Tel:* (032) 9682418 *Fax:* (032) 9682750

**Preis der Schweizerische Schillerstiftung**
Schweizerische Schillerstiftung, Fondation
Schiller Suisse
Mattenway 4, 8126-3270 Aarberg
*Tel:* 032 393 72 64
*Key Personnel*
Secretary: Agnes Aeschlimann
Prize for Swiss citizens, or foreigners living in
Switzerland for a minimum of five years.

**City of Zurich Literary Prize**
Praesidialdepartement der Stadt Zurich
Postfach, 8022 Zurich
*Tel:* (01) 2163125 *Fax:* (01) 2121404
*E-mail:* musik.literatur@prd.stzh.ch
*Key Personnel*
Contact: Roman Hess
Established: 1930
Founded by the city of Zurich to reward an au-
thor for his or her whole literary work. No ap-
plications or nominations accepted.
Award: 50,000 CHF awarded at irregular intervals

# Thailand

**Bangkok Bank Foundation Prize**
Bangkok Bank Foundation
333 Silom Rd, Bangkok 10500
*Tel:* (02) 645-5555; (02) 231-4333 *Fax:* (02) 231-
4742
*E-mail:* info@bangkokbank.com
*Web Site:* www.bangkokbank.com
For prose or poetry in Thai concerning history,
art, culture, religion, social affairs, philosophy
or new creative ideas. Awarded annually.
Award: 50,000 THB

# Turkey

**Award for Literature & Scientific Publications**
Turkish Language Institution (Turk Dil Kurumu)
Ataturk Bulvari, 217, Kavaklidere, 06680 Ankara
*Tel:* (0312) 4286100 *Fax:* (0312) 4285288
*E-mail:* bim@tdk.gov.tr
*Web Site:* www.tdk.gov.tr
*Key Personnel*
President: Dr Hasan Eren
To encourage & sponsor research & studies in
Turkish language literature & linguistics.

# United Kingdom

☆**Academi Cardiff International Poetry**
**Competition**
Academi
Mount Stuart House, 3rd floor, Mount Stuart Sq,
Cardiff CF10 5FQ
*Tel:* (029) 2047 2266 *Fax:* (029) 2049 2930
*E-mail:* post@academi.org
*Web Site:* www.academi.org
*Key Personnel*
Chief Executive Officer: P Finch
Established: 1986
Awarded annually. Poems in the English language
of no more than 50 lines on any subject. Open
to all nationalities.
Other Sponsor(s): Cardiff Council
Award: 1st prize 5,000 GBP; 2nd prize 700 GBP;
3rd prize 300 GBP; five prizes of 200 GBP
Closing Date: Jan 30

**Airey Neave Research Award**
The Airey Neave Trust
40 Bernard St, London WC1N 1WJ
Mailing Address: PO Box 36800, London WC1N
1WJ
*Tel:* (020) 7833 4440 *Fax:* (020) 7491 1118
*E-mail:* info@aireyneavetrust.org.uk
*Web Site:* www.aireyneavetrust.org.uk
*Key Personnel*
Administrative: Hannah Scott
Award: 1-3 year research fellowship
Closing Date: May 1

**Alexander Prize**
The Royal Historical Society
University College London, Gower St, London
WC1E 6BT
*Tel:* (020) 7387 7532 *Fax:* (020) 7387 7532
*E-mail:* royalhistsoc@ucl.ac.uk; rhsinfo@rhs.ac.
uk
*Web Site:* www.rhs.ac.uk
*Key Personnel*
Executive Secretary: Joy McCarthy
For an essay in English on a historical subject:
must be a genuine work of original research.
Candidates must either be under the age of 35
or be registered for a higher degree or have
been registered for such a degree within the
last three years. Must not exceed 8,000 words
including foot-notes & can relate to any historical subject. Candidates are required to state
the total number of words of their entry. It
may be derived from a doctoral thesis (either
in progress or completed) but it should be self-
contained & suitable for reading as a lecture.
No more than one essay submitted per year.
To apply: send one typescript copy of the essay, without identification of the author, with
a cover letter (stating name, address, date of
birth, institution, details of degree registration
where relevant & essay title).
Award: 250 GBP

☆**Arts Council Awards & Bursaries**
Arts Council of England
14 Great Peter St, London SW1P 3NQ
*Tel:* (0845) 300 6200 *Fax:* (020) 7973 6564
*E-mail:* enquiries@artscouncil.org.uk
*Web Site:* www.artscouncil.org.uk
Intended to provide experienced playwrights with
an opportunity to research & develop work
for theater independent of financial pressures
& free from the need to write for a particular
market. Full details of the help given to playwrights is available on request.
Award: Grants 500-5,000 GBP

**The Arts Council of Wales Book of the Year**
**Awards**
Arts Council of Wales
Holst House, 9 Museum Pl, Cardiff CF10 3NX
*Tel:* (02920) 376525 *Fax:* (02920) 221447
*E-mail:* wai@artswales.org.uk
*Web Site:* www.artswales.org
*Key Personnel*
Chief Executive: Peter Tyndall *E-mail:* peter.
tyndall@artswales.org.uk
Contact: Ms Lleucu Siencyn
Since 1968, The Arts Council of Wales has given
awards to Welsh authors (by birth of residence)
whose books are of exceptional literary merit.
The books may be written in English or Welsh.
The prizes are awarded to recognize achieve-
ment, to draw attention to writers of promise &
to encourage the writing of creative literature
in English & Welsh. Two prizes of 3,000 GBP
are awarded annually to winners & 1,000 GBP
to four other short-listed authors.
Other Sponsor(s): Hay-on-Wye Festival of Literature
Presented: Hay-on-Wye Festival of Literature

☆**Arvon Foundation International Poetry**
**Competition**
Arvon Foundation Ltd
42A Buckingham Palace Rd, 2nd floor, London
SW1W 0RE
*Tel:* (020) 7931 7611 *Fax:* (020) 7963 0961
*E-mail:* comps@arvonfoundation.org; london@
arvonfoundation.org
*Web Site:* www.arvonfoundation.org
*Key Personnel*
Dir: Stephanie Anderson
Established: 1980
Entries for the competition must be previously
unpublished poems of any length written in En-
glish. An anthology of winning poems, & those
selected by the judges for special commenda-
tion, are published by the Arvon Foundation.

**Authors' Club Best First Novel Award**
The National Centre for Research into Children's
Literature
40 Dover St, London W1S 4NP
*Tel:* (020) 7499 8581 *Fax:* (020) 7409 0913
*E-mail:* secretary@theartsclub.co.uk
*Web Site:* theartsclub.co.uk
*Key Personnel*
Secretary: Lucy Jane Tetlow
Annual award for the most promising first novel
published in English in the United Kingdom in
the preceding year.
Award: 1,000 GBP
Closing Date: Oct 15

**Authors' Club Sir Banister Fletcher Award**
The National Centre for Research into Children's
Literature
40 Dover St, London W1S 4NP
*Tel:* (020) 7499 8581 *Fax:* (020) 7409 0913
*E-mail:* secretary@theartsclub.co.uk
*Web Site:* theartsclub.co.uk
*Key Personnel*
Secretary: Lucy Jane Tetlow
Annual award for the most deserving book on
architecture or the arts.
Award: 1,000 GBP
Closing Date: April

**Aventis Prizes for Science Books**
The Royal Society
6-9 Carlton House Terrace, London SW1Y 5AG
*Tel:* (020) 7451 2500 *Fax:* (020) 7930 2170
*E-mail:* info@royalsoc.ac.uk
*Web Site:* www.royalsoc.ac.uk
*Key Personnel*
Prize Administrator: Natasha Martineau
*E-mail:* natashamartineau@yahoo.co.uk

Spirit Publicity: Reeta Bhatiani *E-mail:* reeta@
spiritpublicity.com
Established: 1988
Prizes were established to celebrate the best in
popular science writing & are awarded annually to books that make science more accessible to readers of all ages & backgrounds.
Other Sponsor(s): Aventis
Award: Up to 30,000 GBP awarded annually in
two categories: General (10,000 GBP) for a
book with a general readership; Junior (10,000
GBP) for a book for under-14's. Up to 5 shortlisted authors in each category receive 1,000
GBP each

## ☆Benson Medal
Royal Society of Literature
Somerset House, Strand, London WC2R 1LA
*Tel:* (020) 7845 4676 *Fax:* (020) 7845 4679
*E-mail:* info@rslit.org
*Web Site:* www.rslit.org
*Key Personnel*
Chairman: Ronald Harwood
Assistant Secretary: Julia Abel Smith *Tel:* (020)
7845 4677 *E-mail:* julia@rslit.org
Established: 1961
Founded by Dr A C Benson. For a body of mer-
itorious work in poetry, fiction, history, biog-
raphy or belles lettres. A silver medal given
periodically at the discretion of the Council of
the Royal Society of Literature. Applications
are not invited.

## David Berry Prize
The Royal Historical Society
University College London, Gower St, London
WC1E 6BT
*Tel:* (020) 7387 7532 *Fax:* (020) 7387 7532
*E-mail:* royalhistsoc@ucl.ac.uk; rhsinfo@rhs.ac.
uk
*Web Site:* www.rhs.ac.uk
*Key Personnel*
Executive Secretary: Joy McCarthy
For an essay in English on a subject, to be selected by the candidates, dealing with Scottish
history. The essay submitted must be a genuine
work of research based on original (manuscript
or printed) materials. The essay should be between 6,000 & 10,000 words in length (excluding foot-notes & appendices). It must be
submitted in typescript. The author's name
should not appear on the typescript & should
be submitted separately. No person to whom
the prize has been awarded may enter for any
subsequent competition for the prize.
Award: 250 GBP
Closing Date: Oct 31

## Besterman/McColvin Medal
Chartered Institute of Library & Information Professionals (CILIP)
7 Ridgmount St, London WC1E 7AE
*Tel:* (020) 7255 0500 *Fax:* (020) 7255 0501
*E-mail:* info@cilip.org.uk
*Web Site:* www.cilip.org.uk
*Key Personnel*
Marketing Manager: Louisa Myatt *E-mail:* louisa.
myatt@cilip.org.uk
For outstanding works of reference published in
the UK. One for print & one for electronic
formats. The judges will assess the authority,
scope & coverage, arrangement & currency of
the information, quality of indexing, adequacy
of references, physical presentation, originality
& value for money.
Award: 500 GBP & certificate
Presented: Sept

## James Tait Black Memorial Prizes
University of Edinburgh
David Hume Tower, George Sq, Edinburgh EH8
9JX

*Tel:* (0131) 650 3620 *Fax:* (0131) 650 6898
*E-mail:* english.literature@ed.ac.uk
*Web Site:* www.ed.ac.uk/~englitw3/jtbinf.htm
*Key Personnel*
Contact: Sheila Strathdee *E-mail:* s.strathdee@ed.
ac.uk
Established: 1919
These literary prizes were founded by the late
Mrs Janet Coats Black in memory of her hus-
band, a partner in the publishing house of
A&C Black Ltd, London. Mrs Black set aside
11,000 GBP to be used for two prizes of what-
ever income the fund would produce after pay-
ing expenses. The prizes, supplemented by the
Scottish Arts Council, now amount annually to
approximately 3,000 GBP each. Literary Prizes
are awarded to the best biography & to the best
work of fiction published during the calendar
year Oct 1 to Sept 30.
Award: Approximately 3,000 GBP each
Closing Date: Jan 31, 2006

## The K Blundell Trust
Society of Authors
84 Drayton Gardens, London SW10 9SB
*Tel:* (020) 7373 6642 *Fax:* (020) 7373 5768
*E-mail:* info@societyofauthors.org
*Web Site:* www.societyofauthors.net
Provides grants to published British authors un-
der 40 years of age & to published authors
who need additional funding to write their next
book.
Award: Generally 1,000-2,000 GBP (not to ex-
ceed 4,000 GBP)
Closing Date: April 30 & Oct 31

## ☆Boardman Tasker Prize for Mountain Literature
Boardman Tasker Charitable Trust
Pound House, Llangennith, Swansea SA3 1JQ
*Tel:* (01792) 386 215 *Fax:* (01792) 386 215
*Web Site:* www.boardmantasker.com
*Key Personnel*
Contact: Margaret Body *E-mail:* margaretbody@
lineone.net
Established: 1983
Established to commemorate the lives of distin-
guished mountaineers Peter Boardman & Joe
Tasker who died in 1982 on Mount Everest.
Awarded annually to an author of a published
work of nonfiction or fiction, written in the En-
glish language, initially or in translation, which
makes an outstanding contribution to mountain
literature; published between Nov 1 of previous
year & Oct 31 of year of the prize.
Award: 2,000 GBP
Closing Date: Aug 1 of year in which the prize is
offered
Presented: Alpine Club, London, UK, Nov

## The Bridport Prize Poetry & Short Stories
Bridport Arts Centre
South St, Bridport, Dorset DT6 3NR
*Tel:* (01308) 459444 *Fax:* (01308) 459166
*E-mail:* info@bridport-arts.com
*Web Site:* www.bridport-arts.com
Established: 1973
Open writing competition for short stories (5,000
words maximum) & poetry (24 lines maxi-
mum).
Award: Prizes for both categories: 1st prize 3,000
GBP; 2nd prize 1,000 GBP; 3rd prize 500
GBP; 10 supplementary prizes
Closing Date: June 30th annually
Presented: Bridport Arts Centre, Last Saturday of
Oct, annually

## British Book Awards
Publishing News Ltd
7 John St, London WC1N 2ES
*Tel:* (0870) 870 2345 *Fax:* (0870) 870 0385
*E-mail:* rodneyburbeck@publishingnews.co.uk

*Web Site:* www.publishingnews.co.uk
*Key Personnel*
Organizer: Merric Davidson *Tel:* (01580) 212041
*E-mail:* nibbies@mdla.co.uk
Established: 1989
The UK Book Trade 'OSCARS'.
Other Sponsor(s): Activair; Baker Tilly; BCA;
Blackwell's; The Bookseller; Borders (UK)
Ltd; Butler & Tanner; Chrysalis Books; The
Daily Mail; Expert Books; KPMG; Nielsen
BookData; Nielsen BookScan; Oneword;
Reader's Digest; Securicor Omega Express; W
H Smith; The Spoken Word Publishing Asso-
ciation; Stora Enso; The Times; Virgin Books;
VISTA International; Waterstone's
Closing Date: mid-Nov
Presented: Grosvenor House on Park Lane, Feb,
annually

## British Science Fiction Association Awards
The British Science Fiction Association Ltd
(BSFA Ltd)
97 Sharp St, Newland Ave, Hull HU5 2AE
*E-mail:* bsfa@enterprise.net
*Web Site:* www.bsfa.co.uk
*Key Personnel*
Awards Administrator: Claire Brialey
Annual awards in four categories: best novel, best
short fiction, best nonfiction & best artwork.
Novel & nonfiction are for works first pub-
lished in the UK in the previous year.
Closing Date: Jan 31
Presented: Eastercon

## The Calouste Gulbenkian Foundation Prize
Society of Authors - Translators Association
84 Drayton Gardens, London SW10 9SB
*Tel:* (020) 7373 6642 *Fax:* (020) 7373 5768
*E-mail:* info@societyofauthors.org
*Web Site:* www.societyofauthors.org
The triennial prize is for translations of works
from any period by a Portuguese national. The
translation must have been first published in
the UK.
Award: 1,000 GBP
Closing Date: Dec 20

## The Carey Award
Society of Indexers
Blades Enterprise Centre, John St, Sheffield S2
4SU
*Tel:* (0114) 292 2350 *Fax:* (0114) 292 2351
*E-mail:* admin@socind.demon.co.uk
*Web Site:* www.socind.demon.co.uk
*Key Personnel*
Administrator: P W Burrow
The award is made by Council for services to in-
dexing.

## Carnegie Medal
Chartered Institute of Library & Information Pro-
fessionals (CILIP)
7 Ridgmount St, London WC1E 7AE
*Tel:* (020) 7255 0500 *Fax:* (020) 7255 0501
*E-mail:* info@cilip.org.uk
*Web Site:* www.carnegiegreenaway.org.uk/
carnegie/carn.html; www.cilip.org.uk
*Key Personnel*
Marketing Manager: Louisa Myatt *E-mail:* louisa.
myatt@cilip.org.uk
Established: 1936
Established by The Library Association in mem-
ory of Scottish-born philanthropist, Andrew
Carnegie (1835-1919). Awarded annually to the
writer of an outstanding book for children.
Award: Golden medal & 500 GBP worth of
books to donate to a library of their choice

## Cartier Diamond Dagger
Crime Writers' Association
PO Box 63, Wakefield WF2 0YW
*E-mail:* info@theCWA.co.uk

*Web Site:* www.thecwa.co.uk
*Key Personnel*
Chairman: Hilary Bonner
Secretary: Judith Cutler *Tel:* (07227) 709 782
   *E-mail:* judith.cutler@virgin.net
Established: 1986
Annual award for marking a lifetime achievement in crime fiction published in the English language, whether originally or in translation.
Other Sponsor(s): Cartier
Award: Silver book with diamond dagger

**Children's Award**
Arts Council of England
14 Great Peter St, London SW1P 3NQ
*Tel:* (0845) 300 6200 *Fax:* (020) 7973 6564
*E-mail:* enquiries@artscouncil.org.uk
*Web Site:* www.artscouncil.org.uk
Celebrates the accomplishments & raises the profile of theatre for children & most especially, playwrights who work in this field.

**☆Cholmondeley Awards for Poets**
Society of Authors
84 Drayton Gardens, London SW10 9SB
*Tel:* (020) 7373 6642 *Fax:* (020) 7373 5768
*E-mail:* info@societyofauthors.org
*Web Site:* www.societyofauthors.net
Established by the late Dowager Marchioness of Cholmondeley for the benefit & encouragement of poets of any age, sex or nationality. The noncompetitive award is for work generally, not for a specific book & submissions are not accepted. Awarded annually.
Award: Total of 8,000 GBP
Presented: 1966

**Arthur C Clarke Award**
Science Fiction Foundation, British Science Fiction Association, Science Museum
60 Bournemouth Rd, Folkestone, Kent CT 19 5AZ
*Tel:* (01303) 232939 *Fax:* (01303) 252939
*E-mail:* arthurclarkeaward@yahoo.co.uk
*Web Site:* www.clarkeaward.com
*Key Personnel*
Administrator: Paul Kincaid
Established: 1986
For the best science fiction novel published in the United Kingdom. The winner is chosen by a panel of six judges representing the Science Fiction Foundation, the British Science Fiction Association & the International Science Policy Foundation.
Award: Annual award of an engraved bookend & 2,005 GBP. (The amount of the award matches the year)
Presented: The Science Museum, London, Mid-May

**David Cohen British Literature Prize**
Arts Council of England
14 Great Peter St, London SW1P 3NQ
*Tel:* (0845) 300 6200 *Fax:* (020) 7973 6564
*E-mail:* enquiries@artscouncil.org.uk
*Web Site:* www.artscouncil.org.uk
Established: 1993
Administered by the Arts Council in association with Coutts & Co, this prize will be awarded biennially in recognition of the entire body of a writer's work.
Award: 40,000 GBP

**Commonwealth Writers Prize**
Commonwealth Foundation
Booktrust, Book House, 45 East Hill, London SW18 2QZ
*Tel:* (020) 8516 2977 *Fax:* (020) 8516 2978
*E-mail:* geninfo@commonwealth.int; cwp@ cumberlandlodge.ac.uk; info@booktrust.org.uk
*Web Site:* www.commonwealthwriters.com

Established: 1987
Annual award for a work of prose fiction, written by a citizen of the Commonwealth & published the previous year. The work must be in English & of reasonable length. Entries must be made by the publisher & are restricted to four entries per region.
Closing Date: Dec 31
Presented: May

**☆Thomas Cook Travel Book Award**
The Thomas Cook Group
Thomas Cook Business Park, Unit 19-21 Coningsby Rd, Peterborough PE3 8XX
*Tel:* (01733) 416477 *Fax:* (01733) 416688
*Web Site:* www.thetravelbookaward.com
*Key Personnel*
Prize Administrator: Joan Lee *Tel:* (01482) 610707
Established: 1980
Awarded to the travel narrative which most inspires in the reader the desire to travel. Books must be published in English, or translated into English & published between Jan 1 - Dec 31 in the preceding year. Books may only be submitted by publishers & may only be entered once. Minimum 150 pages.
Other Sponsor(s): The Daily Telegraph
Award: 10,000 GBP plus a reproduction picture from the Thomas Cook company archives for the winner & shortlisted author
Closing Date: March 31

**☆Duff Cooper Prize**
Duff Cooper
54 St Maur Rd, London SW6 4DP
*Tel:* (020) 7736 3729 *Fax:* (020) 7731 7638
*Key Personnel*
Prize Administrator: Ms Artemis Cooper
Established: 1956
For a literary work of history, biography, poetry or politics supported by a recognized publisher in English or French. The prize is the interest from a trust fund. Awarded annually.
Award: 4,000 GBP & copy of Duff Cooper's autobiography, Old Men Forget
Closing Date: Nov 30
Presented: Feb

**☆The Rose Mary Crawshay Prize**
British Academy
The British Academy, 10 Carlton House Terrace, London SW1Y 5AH
*Tel:* (020) 7969 5200 *Fax:* (020) 7969 5300
*E-mail:* secretary@britac.ac.uk
*Web Site:* www.britac.ac.uk
*Key Personnel*
Administrator: Angela Pusey *Tel:* (020) 7969 5264 *Fax:* (020) 7969 5414 *E-mail:* a.pusey@ britac.ac.uc
Established: 1888
Awarded by the Council of the British Academy to women writers of any nationality for an historical or critical work of value on any subject concerning English literature published within the preceding three years. Preference is given to works on Byron, Shelley or Keats. Two prizes awarded annually. Applications are not sought.
Award: 500 GBP

**John Creasey Memorial Dagger**
Crime Writers' Association
PO Box 63, Wakefield WF2 0YW
*E-mail:* info@theCWA.co.uk
*Web Site:* www.thecwa.co.uk
*Key Personnel*
Chairman: Danuta Reah
Secretary: Judith Cutler *Tel:* (07227) 709 782
   *E-mail:* judith.cutler@virgin.net
Established: 1973

Award for a first book by an unpublished writer. Submission by publishers only.
Award: Ornamental dagger & 1,000 GBP

**Dagger in the Library**
Crime Writers' Association
PO Box 63, Wakefield WF2 0YW
*Key Personnel*
Chairman: Danuta Reah
Secretary: Judith Cutler *Tel:* (07227) 709 782
   *E-mail:* judith.cutler@virgin.net
Award for the living author whose body of work has given the most pleasure to library users.

**Debut Dagger**
Crime Writers' Association
PO Box 63, Wakefield WF2 0YW
*Key Personnel*
Chairman: Danuta Reah
Secretary: Judith Cutler *Tel:* (07227) 709 782
   *E-mail:* judith.cutler@virgin.net
Award for unpublished authors of fiction.
Award: 250 GBP

**☆Isaac & Tamara Deutscher Memorial Prize**
Lloyds Bank Ltd
Faculty of Law & Social Sciences, SOAS, University of London, Thorhaugh St, Russell Sq, London WC1H 0XG
*Web Site:* www.deutscherprize.org.uk/home.htm
Established: 1968
Awarded annually for a work published or in typescript in any of the main European languages which contributes to the development of Marxist thought.
Award: 250 GBP
Closing Date: May 1
Presented: November

**John Dryden Translation Competition**
British Comparative Literature Association/British Centre for Literary Translation
c/o Penny Brown, BCLA Secretary, Dept of French Studies, University of Manchester, Oxford Rd, Manchester M13 9PL
*Web Site:* www.bcla.org
*Key Personnel*
BCLA Secretary: Penny Brown
   *E-mail:* 101501_560@compuserve.com
Literary translation from any language into English including poetry, fiction or literary prose, from any period; maximum 25 typed pages. Entry fee of 5 GBP.
Award: 1st prize 350 GBP; 2nd prize 200 GBP; 3rd prize 100 GBP. Winning entries will be published in full on the website; extracts from winning entries are eligible for publication in BCLA's journal "Comparative Critical Studies"
Closing Date: Jan 31 annually
Presented: Announced in July on BCLA website; presentation later in the year, July

**Ellis Peters Historical Dagger**
Crime Writers' Association
PO Box 63, Wakefield WF2 0YW
*Key Personnel*
Chairman: Danuta Reah
Secretary: Judith Cutler *Tel:* (07227) 709 782
   *E-mail:* judith.cutler@virgin.net
award of r the best historical crime novel.
Award: 3,000 GBP

**Encore Award**
Society of Authors
84 Drayton Gardens, London SW10 9SB
*Tel:* (020) 7373 6642 *Fax:* (020) 7373 5768
*E-mail:* info@societyofauthors.org
*Web Site:* www.societyofauthors.net
Awarded to a second novel (or novels) judged to be the best first published in the UK during the

year preceding the year in which the award is presented; publisher entry only.
Award: 10,000 GBP
Closing Date: Nov 30
Presented: Spring

## ☆Christopher Ewart-Biggs Memorial Prize
Hugo Arnold
The Secretary to the Judges Committee, Flat 3, 149 Hamilton Terrace, London NW8 9QS
Established: 1977
Awarded in memory of the British Ambassador to Ireland who was assassinated in Dublin in 1976. This award aims to create greater understanding between the peoples of Britain & Ireland, or co-operation between the partners of the European Community. Entries should be in English or French. Awarded biennially.
Award: 5,000 GBP
Closing Date: Dec 31

## ☆The Geoffrey Faber Memorial Prize
Faber & Faber Ltd
3 Queen Sq, London WC1N 3AU
*Tel:* (020) 7465 0045 *Fax:* (020) 7465 0043
*Web Site:* www.faber.co.uk
*Key Personnel*
Prize Administrator: Belinda Matthews
   *E-mail:* belinda.matthews@faber.co.uk
Established: 1963
Established as a memorial to the founder & first chairman of the firm. It is given in alternate years, for a volume of verse & for a volume of prose fiction. It is given to that volume of verse or prose fiction first published originally in the United Kingdom during the two years preceding the year in which the award is given which is, in the opinion of the judges, of the greatest literary merit. To be eligible for the prize the volume of verse or prose fiction in question must be by a writer who is: (a) not more than forty years old at the date of publication, (b) a citizen of the United Kingdom & Colonies, of any other Commonwealth state, of Ireland or of the Republic of South Africa. There are three judges, who are reviewers of poetry or fiction as the case may be, & they are nominated each year by the editors or literary editors of newspapers & magazines which regularly publish such reviews. Faber & Faber invite nominations from such editors & literary editors. No submissions for the prize are to be made.
Award: 1,000 GBP

## Eleanor Farjeon Award
Booktrust
The Children's Book Circle, Hodder Children's Books, 338 Euston Rd, London NW1 3BH
*Tel:* (020) 7739 2929 *Fax:* (020) 7739 2318
*Web Site:* www.booktrusted.com
*Key Personnel*
Contact: Rachel Wade
Established: 1965
Established to commemorate the work of the late children's book author. The Children's Book Circle makes an annual award which may be given to a librarian, teacher, author, artist, publisher, reviewer, bookseller or television producer who, in the judgment of the Awards Committee, is considered to have done outstanding work for children's books.
Other Sponsor(s): Books for Children
Award: 500 GBP

## The Fidler Award
Scottish Book Trust
Sandeman House, Trunk's Close, 55 High St, Edinburgh EH1 1SR
*Tel:* (0131) 524 0160 *Fax:* (0131) 524 0161
*E-mail:* info@scottishbooktrust.com
*Web Site:* www.scottishbooktrust.com
Established: 1983

Awarded to an unpublished novel written for 8-12 year olds. The author may have had previous books published, but this must be the first for this age range. Hodder Children's Books will publish the winning entry.
Other Sponsor(s): Hodder Children's Books
Award: Advance of 1,500 GBP, royalty package & rosewood/silver trophy, to be held for one year
Closing Date: Nov 30 annually

## John Florio Prize
Society of Authors - Translators Association
84 Drayton Gardens, London SW10 9SB
*Tel:* (020) 7373 6642 *Fax:* (020) 7373 5768
*E-mail:* info@societyofauthors.org
*Web Site:* www.societyofauthors.org
Established: 1963
Established under the auspices of the Italian Institute & the British-Italian Society & named after John Florio. For the best translation into English of a 20th Century Italian work of literary merit & general interest, published by a British publisher during the preceding two years.
Award: 1,000 GBP
Closing Date: Dec 20

## Fraenkel Prize in Contemporary History
Institute of Contemporary History & Wiener Library
4 Devonshire St, London W1W 5BH
*Tel:* (020) 7636 7247 *Fax:* (020) 7436 6428
*E-mail:* info@wienerlibrary.co.uk
*Web Site:* www.wienerlibrary.co.uk
*Key Personnel*
Administrative Co-ordinator: Rod Digges
Established: 1989
Inaugurated by Mr Ernst Fraenkel for an outstanding work in the field of contemporary history.
Award: Two awards: 6,000 USD (open to all entrants); 4,000 USD (entrants who have yet to publish a major work)
Closing Date: May 10

## Gibb Memorial Trust
E J W Gibb Memorial Trust
2 Penarth Pl, Cambridge CB3 9LU
*Tel:* (01223) 566630 *Fax:* (01223) 511182
*Web Site:* www.gibbtrust.org
*Key Personnel*
Secretary to the Trustees: Robin Bligh
Established: 1902
Publishers of works about Persian, Turkish & Arabic history & religions.

## The Gladstone History Book Prize
The Royal Society
University College London, Gower St, London WC1E 6BT
*Tel:* (020) 7387 7532 *Fax:* (020) 7387 7532
*E-mail:* royalhistsoc@ucl.ac.uk; rhsinfo@rhs.ac.uk
*Web Site:* www.rhs.ac.uk
*Key Personnel*
Executive Secretary: Joy McCarthy
Established: 1997
Based on any historical subject which is not primarily related to British history. Must be its author's first solely written history book & published in English during the calendar year by a scholar normally resident in the UK. Must be an original & scholarly work of historical research. Author or publisher should submit three copies (non-returnable) of an eligible book by the end of the year.
Award: 1,000 GBP
Closing Date: Dec 31 annually
Presented: Royal Historical Society Annual Reception, July

## Glenfiddich Food & Drink Awards
William Grant & Sons
c/o Grayling Co, 4 Bedford Sq, London WC1B 3RA
*Tel:* (020) 7255 1100 *Fax:* (020) 7436 4164
*E-mail:* lindsay.stewart@grayling.co.uk
*Web Site:* www.glenfiddich.com
*Key Personnel*
Public Relations Manager, William Grant & Sons International: Fiona Coleman *Tel:* (020) 8332 1188
Established: 1970
Established to recognise excellence in writing, publishing & broadcasting on the subjects of food & drink.
Closing Date: January
Presented: January

## Gold Dagger for Fiction
Crime Writers' Association
PO Box 63, Wakefield WF2 0YW
*E-mail:* info@theCWA.co.uk
*Web Site:* www.thecwa.co.uk
*Key Personnel*
Chairman: Danuta Reah
Secretary: Judith Cutler *Tel:* (07227) 709 782
   *E-mail:* judith.cutler@virgin.net
Established: 1955
For the best crime-fiction novel of the year awarded annually by a panel of reviewers. Submission by publishers only.
Other Sponsor(s): The Macallan
Award: Ornamental dagger & 3,000 GBP

## Gold Dagger for Non-Fiction
Crime Writers' Association
PO Box 63, Wakefield WF2 0YW
*E-mail:* info@theCWA.co.uk
*Web Site:* www.thecwa.co.uk
*Key Personnel*
Chairman: Danuta Reah
Secretary: Judith Cutler *Tel:* (07227) 709 782
   *E-mail:* judith.cutler@virgin.net
Established: 1978
Winner is selected by an independent panel. Submission by publishers only.
Award: 2,000 GBP & an ornamental dagger

## Edgar Graham Book Prize
School of Oriental & African Studies
Geography Dept, Thornhaugh St, Russell Sq, London WC1H 0XG
*Tel:* (020) 7637 2388 *Fax:* (020) 7436 3844
*Web Site:* www.soas.ac.uk/
*Key Personnel*
Secretary: C Darfour *E-mail:* cd16@soas.ac.uk
Award is given biennially to a work of original scholarship published in English on agricultural &/or industrial development in Asia &/or Africa.
Award: 1,500 GBP

## Kate Greenaway Medal
Chartered Institute of Library & Information Professionals (CILIP)
7 Ridgmount St, London WC1E 7AE
*Tel:* (020) 7255 0650 *Fax:* (020) 7255 0501
*E-mail:* info@cilip.org.uk
*Web Site:* www.carnegiegreenaway.org.uk/green/green.html; www.cilip.org.uk
*Key Personnel*
Marketing Manager: Louisa Myatt *E-mail:* louisa.myatt@cilip.org.uk
Established: 1955
Offered annually for the most distinguished work in the illustration of children's books first published in the United Kingdom during the preceding year.
Award: Golden medal & 500 GBP worth of books to donate to a library of their choice

## Eric Gregory Trust Fund Awards

Society of Authors
84 Drayton Gardens, London SW10 9SB
*Tel:* (020) 7373 6642 *Fax:* (020) 7373 5768
*E-mail:* info@societyofauthors.org
*Web Site:* www.societyofauthors.org
*Key Personnel*
Administrator: Dorothy Sym
A number of awards are made each year to encourage young British poets. Candidates for awards must be British subjects by birth, ordinarily resident in the United Kingdom & under the age of 30 on March 31 in the year of the award. Candidates must submit a published or unpublished volume of belles lettres, poetry or drama-poems.
Award: 25,000 GBP
Closing Date: Oct 31

## ☆Guardian Children's Fiction Prize

The Guardian
119 Farringdon Rd, London EC1R 3ER
*Tel:* (020) 7278 2332 *Fax:* (020) 7713 4368
*E-mail:* sara@guardian.co.uk
*Web Site:* www.books.guardian.co.uk
*Key Personnel*
Children Books Editor: Stephanie Nettel
Established: 1965
Awarded to an outstanding work of fiction (not picture books) for children written by a British or Commonwealth author, first published in the UK during the calendar year preceding the year in which the award is presented. The winner is chosen by a panel of authors & the review editor for The Guardian's children's books section. Awarded annually.
Award: 1,500 GBP

## ☆The Guardian First Book Award

The Guardian
119 Farringdon Rd, London EC1R 3ER
*Tel:* (020) 7278 2332 *Fax:* (020) 7713 4368
*E-mail:* sara@guardian.co.uk
*Web Site:* www.books.guardian.co.uk
*Telex:* 8811746
This award recognizes & rewards new writings by honouring an author's first book. Its aim is to reflect the breadth of coverage of all genres on The Guardian books pages & underpin the paper's commitment to new quality writing.
Award: 10,000 GBP plus an advertising package within The Guardian & Observer. Also, an endowment of 1,000 GBP worth of books will be made by The Guardian to a UK school of the author's choice

## Francis Head Bequest

Society of Authors
84 Drayton Gardens, London SW10 9SB
*Tel:* (020) 7373 6642 *Fax:* (020) 7373 5768
*E-mail:* info@societyofauthors.org
*Web Site:* www.societyofauthors.org
*Key Personnel*
Administrator: Dorothy Sym
Provides grants to professional authors over 35 years of age whose main source of income is from their writing & who, through accident, illness or other causes, are temporarily unable to write.

## Felicia Hemans Prize for Lyrical Poetry

University of Liverpool
PO Box 147, Liverpool L69 3BX
*Tel:* (0151) 794 2458; (0151) 794 2000
   *Fax:* (0151) 794 3765
*E-mail:* wilder@liv.ac.uk
*Web Site:* www.liv.ac.uk
*Telex:* 627095
Annual prize is open to past & present members & students of the University of Liverpool only, is awarded to a lyrical poem, the subject of which may be chosen by the competitor. Only one poem, either published or unpublished, may be submitted. The prize shall not be awarded more than once to the same competition Poems, endorsed 'Hemans Prize'. Awarded annually.
Award: One year's income from the Felicia Hemans Memorial Fund
Closing Date: May 1

## The Joan Hessayon New Writers' Award

Romantic Novelists' Association (RNA)
16 St Briacway, Exmouth EX8 5RN
*Tel:* (01395) 279659
*E-mail:* enquiries@rna-uk.org
*Web Site:* www.rna-uk.org
*Key Personnel*
President: Diane Pearson
Established: 1960
For an unpublished romantic novel.
Award: Trophy & cash prize
Closing Date: Sept annually
Presented: Party in London, May annually

## William Hill Sports Book of the Year

William Hill Organization
50 Station Rd, London N22 7TP
*Tel:* (020) 8918 3858 *Fax:* (020) 8889 0472
*Key Personnel*
Press Officer: Serena Momberg
Awarded annually to the best sports book published in the year preceding the year in which the prize is awarded. Publisher entry only.
Award: 15,000 GBP
Closing Date: Sept 12
Presented: Nov

## Winifred Holtby Memorial Prize

Royal Society of Literature
Somerset House, Strand, London WC2R 1LA
*Tel:* (020) 7845 4676 *Fax:* (020) 7845 4679
*E-mail:* info@rslit.org
*Web Site:* www.rslit.org
*Key Personnel*
Assistant Secretary: Julia Abel Smith *Tel:* (020) 7845 4677 *E-mail:* julia@rslit.org
Established: 1966
Founded by Vera Brittain in memory of Winifred Holtby. An annual award for the best regional novel of its year; if no suitable work of fiction can be found the jury may consider works of nonfiction. Submissions by publishers, not by individual authors. Award Type is for regional fiction.
Closing Date: Dec 15 (entries are not accepted until mid-Oct)
Presented: St Bride Institute, London, June

## Ian Fleming Steel Dagger

Crime Writers' Association
PO Box 63, Wakefield WF2 0YW
*Key Personnel*
Chairman: Danuta Reah
Secretary: Judith Cutler *Tel:* (07227) 709 782
   *E-mail:* judith.cutler@virgin.net
Award for best adventure/thriller novel in the vein of James Bond.
Award: 2,000 GBP

## The Independent Foreign Fiction Award

Arts Council of England
14 Great Peter St, London SW1P 3NQ
*Tel:* (0845) 300 6200 *Fax:* (020) 7973 6564
*E-mail:* enquiries@artscouncil.org.uk
*Web Site:* www.artscouncil.org.uk
Annual prize for the best contemporary work of prose fiction translated into English from any other tongue, published between Jan 1 & Dec 31 each year. The prize is funded by the Arts Council & promoted by The Independent newspaper.
Award: 10,000 GBP to be divided equally between author & translator

## International Short Story Competition/International Poetry Competition

Stand Magazine
Leeds University, School of English, Leeds LS2 9JT
*Tel:* (0113) 233 4794 *Fax:* (0113) 233 2791
*E-mail:* stand@leeds.ac.uk
*Web Site:* www.people.vcu.edu
*Key Personnel*
Administrator: Linda Goldsmith
Sample copies available for $13 US from David Latane, Dept of English, VCU, Richmond, VA 23284, USA.
Closing Date: March 31

## ☆Kraszna-Krausz Book Awards

Kraszna-Krausz Foundation
122 Fawnbrake Ave, London SE24 0BZ
*Tel:* (020) 7738 6701 *Fax:* (020) 7738 6701
*E-mail:* info@k-k.org.uk
*Web Site:* www.editor.net/k-k
*Key Personnel*
Contact: Andrea Livingstone
International awards made to encourage & recognize outstanding achievements in the publishing & writing of books on the art, history, practice & technology of photography & of the moving image. The Awards are made annually, with prizes for books on still photography alternating with those for books on the moving image (film, television, video). Publisher entry only.
Award: 5,000 GBP for each category winner; 1,000 GBP special commendations

## Lakeland Book of the Year Awards

Cumbria Tourist Board
Ashleigh, Holly Rd, Windermere, Cumbria LA23 2AQ
*Tel:* (015394) 44444 *Fax:* (015394) 44041
*Key Personnel*
Coordinator: Sheila Lindsay
Established: 1984
These annual awards were established by Hunter Davies & Cumbria Tourist Board. The Hunter Davies Award is for a book which best helps visitors or residents to enjoy a greater love or understanding of life in Cumbria - the Lake District. The Tullie House Prize is for a book which best helps develop a greater appreciation of the built &/or natural environment of Cumbria. The Barclays Bank Award is for the best small book on any aspect of Cumbria life, people or culture. The Border Television Prize is for a book which best illustrates the beauty & character of Cumbria.
Award: 100 GBP & a framed certificate

## Lancashire County Library Children's Book of the Year Award

Lancashire County Library
County Library Manager, County Library Headquarters, County Hall, PO Box 61, Preston PR1 8RJ
*Tel:* (01772) 264018 *Fax:* (01772) 264880
*E-mail:* library@lcl.lancscc.gov.uk
*Web Site:* www.lancashire.gov.uk/libraries/
*Key Personnel*
Contact: David G Lightfoot *E-mail:* david. lightfoot@lcl.lancscc.gov.uk
Established: 1986
Annual award, sponsored by The University of Central Lancashire, given for a work of fiction or a collection of short stories by a single author. The book should be suitable for children 11-14 years of age.
Award: 500 GBP & an engraved decanter

## Ralph Lewis Award

University of Sussex Library
Sussex House, Brighton BN1 9QL

*Tel:* (01273) 678163 *Fax:* (01273) 678441
*E-mail:* library@sussex.ac.uk
*Web Site:* www.sussex.ac.uk/library
*Key Personnel*
Contact: Pat Ringshaw *Tel:* (01273) 678158
   *E-mail:* p.a.ringshaw@sussex.ac.uk
Established: 1985
Occasional award for promising manuscripts
   given to a UK-based publisher. No direct ap-
   plications from writers.
Award: Grant

**London Writers' Competition**
Arts Office: Wandsworth Borough Council
Town Hall, Wandsworth High St, London SW18
   2PU
*Tel:* (020) 8871 7380 *Fax:* (020) 8871 7630
*E-mail:* arts@wandsworth.gov.uk
*Web Site:* www.wandsworth.gov.uk/
   wbclondonwriters.htm
The competition is open to London writers only
   & has Poetry, Play, Short Story & Fiction for
   Children. All entries must be in English.
Award: 1st prize 600 GBP; 2nd prize 250 GBP;
   3rd prize 100 GBP; two runners-up of 25 GBP
Closing Date: June 26

☆**Enid McLeod Literary Prize**
Franco-British Society
Room 227 Linen Hall, 162-168 Regent St, Lon-
   don W1R 5TB
*Tel:* (020) 7734 0815 *Fax:* (020) 7734 0815
*Web Site:* www.booktrust.org.uk/prizes/mcleod.
   htm; www.francobritishsociety.org.uk
Established: 1981
Awarded annually to a book that contributes the
   most to Franco-British understanding, written
   in English & published in the UK during the
   calendar year preceding the year in which the
   award is presented.
Closing Date: Dec 31

**The Macmillan Prize for Children's Picture
   Book Illustration**
Macmillan Children's Books
20 New Wharf Rd, London N1 9RR
*Tel:* (020) 7014 6000 *Fax:* (020) 7014 6142
*Web Site:* www.macmillan.co.uk
*Key Personnel*
Contact: Emma Giacon *E-mail:* e.giacon@
   macmillan.co.uk
Established: 1986
Annual award, established in order to stimulate
   new work from young illustrators in British
   art schools. Open to all art students in higher
   education establishments in the UK.
Award: 1000 GBP (1st prize), 500 GBP (2nd
   prize) & 250 GBP (3rd prize)

**Macmillan Silver Pen Award for Short Stories**
English PEN Centre
6-8 Amwell St, London EC1R 1UQ
*Tel:* (020) 7713 0023 *Fax:* (020) 7837 7838
*E-mail:* enquiries@englishpen.org
*Web Site:* www.englishpen.org
*Key Personnel*
President: Victoria Glendinning
Executive Dir: Susanna Nicklin *E-mail:* susie@
   englishpen.org
Presented annually for a collection of short stories
   written in English by an author of British na-
   tionality & published in the UK in the previous
   year.
Other Sponsor(s): Macmillan Publishers; S T
   Dupont; Stern Family (nonfiction award in
   memory of James Stern)
Award: 500 GBP & a silver Dupont pen
Presented: PEN International Writers' Day

☆**The Man Booker Prize**
Man Group plc

Sugar Quay, Lower Thames St, London EC3R
   6DU
*Tel:* (020) 7144 1000 *Fax:* (020) 7220 9984
*Web Site:* www.themanbookerprize.com
*Key Personnel*
Prize Administrator: Martyn Goff
Established: 1969
Annual prize for any full-length novel, written in
   English by a citizen of The Commonwealth,
   or the Republic of Ireland. Any UK publisher
   who publishes works of fiction may enter up
   to two novels, with scheduled publication dates
   between October 1 & September 30. In addition, publishers may enter any current novel by
   an author who has previously been shortlisted
   or won the Booker Prize.
Award: 50,000 GBP

**Marsh Award for Children's Literature in
   Translation**
The National Centre for Research into Children's
   Literature
Digby Stuart College, University of Surrey Roe-
   hampton, Roehampton Lane, London SW15
   5PU
*Tel:* (020) 8392 3008
*Web Site:* www.booktrusted.co.uk
*Key Personnel*
Administration: Gillian Lathey *E-mail:* G.
   Lathey@roehampton.ac.uk
Public Relations: Nicky Potter *E-mail:* nicpot@
   dircon.co.uk
Established: 1995
Awarded biennially to the best translation of a
   childrens book, by a British translator, from a
   foreign language into English, & published in
   the UK by a British publisher. Submissions are
   accepted from publishers for books produced
   for readers from 4-16 years of age. The award
   is made to the translator.
Other Sponsor(s): The Marsh Christian Trust
Award: 1000 GBP
Closing Date: June 30

**Marsh Biography Award**
The English Speaking Union
Dartmouth House, 37 Charles St, London W1X
   8AB
*Tel:* (020) 7493 3328 *Fax:* (020) 7495 6108
*E-mail:* esu@esu.org
*Web Site:* www.booktrust.org.uk/prizes/marshbiog.
   htm
*Key Personnel*
Cultural Affairs Officer: Lucy Passmore
   *E-mail:* lucy_passmore@esu.org
Established: 1986
Awarded biennially to a signficant biography by a
   British author published in the UK in the two
   years prior to the year in which the prize is
   awarded. Publisher entry only.
Other Sponsor(s): B P Marsh & Co Ltd
Award: 3,500 GBP & silver trophy
Closing Date: April 1

☆**MCA Book Prize**
Management Consultancies Association (MCA)
49 Whitehall, London SW1A 2BX
*Tel:* (020) 7321 3990 *Fax:* (020) 7321 3991
*E-mail:* MCA@MCA.org.uk
*Web Site:* www.mca.org.uk
*Key Personnel*
Awards Administrator: Andrea Livingstone
   *Tel:* (020) 7738 6701 *Fax:* (020) 7738 6701
Deputy Dir: Sarah Taylor *Tel:* (020) 7321 3993
   *E-mail:* sarah.taylor@mca.org.uk
Established: 1993
Annual prize aimed to recognize & reward British
   writers of management books & to offer en-
   couragement to writers whose books contribute
   stimulating, original & progressive ideas on
   management issues.
Award: 5,000 GBP

**MIND Book of the Year**
MIND Publications
15-19 Broadway, London E15 4BQ
*Tel:* (020) 8519 2122 *Fax:* (020) 8522 1725
*E-mail:* contact@mind.org.uk
*Web Site:* www.mind.org.uk
*Key Personnel*
Publicity: Anne McCarthy *Tel:* (020) 8522 1743
Established: 1981
Inaugurated by MIND & the National Book
   League in memory of Allen Lane. Awarded
   annually to the author of the book (fiction or
   nonfiction) which outstandingly furthers public
   awareness of mental health problems.
Award: 1,500 GBP

**Scott Moncrieff Prize**
Society of Authors - Translators Association
84 Drayton Gardens, London SW10 9SB
*Tel:* (020) 7373 6642 *Fax:* (020) 7373 5768
*E-mail:* info@societyofauthors.org
*Web Site:* www.societyofauthors.org
*Key Personnel*
Secretary: Dorothy Sym
Established: 1964
Established under the auspices of the Transla-
   tors Association of the Society of Authors to
   be awarded annually for the best translation
   published by a British publisher during the pre-
   vious year. Only translations of French 20th
   Century works of literary merit & general in-
   terest will be considered. The work should be
   entered by the publisher & not the individual
   translator.
Closing Date: Dec 20

☆**The Shiva Naipaul Memorial Prize**
Spectator
56 Doughty St, London WC1N 2LL
*Tel:* (020) 7405 1706 *Fax:* (020) 7242 0603
*E-mail:* syndication@spectator.co.uk
*Web Site:* www.spectator.co.uk
Established: 1985
Awarded annually, this prize is given to an
   English-language writer of any nationality under 35 years of age best able to describe a visit
   to a foreign place or people. The award will
   not be for travel writing in the conventional
   sense, but for the most acute & profound ob-
   servation of cultures &/or scenes (which could
   be within the writer's native country) evidently
   alien to the writer. Submissions should not previously have been published & should not be
   more than 4,000 words.
Award: 3,000 GBP & publication of winning entry in The Spectator
Closing Date: April 30

**National Poetry Competition**
The Poetry Society Inc
22 Betterton St, London WC2H 9BX
*Tel:* (020) 7420 9880 *Fax:* (020) 7240 4818
*E-mail:* competition@poetrysociety.org.uk; info@
   poetrysociety.org.uk
*Web Site:* www.poetrysociety.org.uk
Established: 1978
Awarded annually for a poem written in English.
   Send self-addressed envelope for entry form or
   visit website.
Award: 1st prize 5,000 GBP; 2nd prize 1,000
   GBP; 3rd prize 500 GBP; 10 commendations
   50 GBP
Closing Date: Oct 31

**Natural World Book Prize**
Booktrust
Book House, 45 East Hill, London SW18 2QZ
*Tel:* (020) 8516 2977 *Fax:* (020) 8516 2978
*Web Site:* www.booktrust.org.uk
*Key Personnel*
Prize Administrator: Tarryn McKay *Tel:* (020)
   8516 2977 *E-mail:* tarryn@booktrust.org.uk

Established: 1987

Annual prize awarded to the author(s) of the book which most imaginatively promotes the conservation of the natural environment & all its animals & plants. The judges reserve the right to award a prize of 1,000 GBP for a runner-up. All entries must be published in the UK, by a UK publisher between June 1 & the following May 31. This award is open to any nationality. The author(s) must be alive at the time of submission.

Other Sponsor(s): BP, The Wildlife Trusts & Subbuteo Books

Award: 5,000 GBP

## The Nestle Smarties Book Prize

Booktrust

Book House, 45 East Hill, London SW18 2QZ

*Tel:* (020) 8516 2977 *Fax:* (020) 8516 2978

*Web Site:* www.booktrust.org.uk

*Key Personnel*

Prize Administrator: Tarryn McKay *Tel:* (020) 8516 2977 *E-mail:* tarryn@booktrust.org.uk

Established: 1985

To encourage high standards & stimulate interest in children's books. The prize is only open to works of fiction or poetry for children, written in English by a citizen of the UK, or an author resident in the UK. The author of the book must be living at the time of publication. The adult panel must choose three from each category. The age categories are 5 & under, 6-8 & 9-11. The shortlisted books are then given to the Young Judges, who have to read the books & decide which book gets Gold, Silver & Bronze. The Young Judges are chosen from classes of school children, who have to complete tasks set for their age category. A new Young Judge category was added a couple of years ago, chosen from Kids' Club Networks. They read & judge the 6-8 books.

Other Sponsor(s): Nestle

Award: 2,500 GBP Gold Prize; 1,000 GBP Silver Prize; 500 GBP Bronze Prize

## Observer National Children's Poetry Competition

The Observer

119 Farrington Rd, London EUR 3ER

*Tel:* (020) 7278 2332 *Fax:* (020) 7278 1449

*Web Site:* observer.guardian.co.uk

First awarded in 1986 & sponsored then & in 1987 & 1988 by the Water Authorities Association. The competition is open to three age groups: 10 years & under, 11-14 years & 15-18 years. There is an additional prize for the best group of poems from any school.

## Outposts Poetry Competition

Hippopotamus Press

22 Whitewell Rd, Frome, Somerset BA11 4EL

*Tel:* (0373) 466653 *Fax:* (0373) 466653

*Web Site:* www.jbwb.co.uk/poetpubs

*Key Personnel*

Competition Organizer: M Pargitter

Established: 1991

Awarded annually in the Autumn for new poetry adjudicated by a great poet.

Award: 1st prize 500 GBP; 2nd prize 200 GBP; 3rd prize 100 GBP

## Parker Romantic Novel of the Year

Romantic Novelists' Association (RNA)

38 Stanhope Rd, Reading, Berks RG2 7HN

*Tel:* (01904) 765035

*Web Site:* www.rna-uk.org/awards.html

*Key Personnel*

President: Diane Pearson

Award Organizer: Joan Emery

Established: 1960

Established as the RNA Major Award. For the best romantic novel (modern or historical) published during the year. Open to non-members.

Other Sponsor(s): Parker Pen Co

Award: 10,000 GBP & a set of Parker Duofold pens worth over 400 GBP

Closing Date: Nov 30

Presented: Awards luncheon, London, April annually

## The Michael Powell Book Award

British Film Institute

21 Stephen St, London W1T 1LN

*Tel:* (020) 7255 1444 *Fax:* (020) 7436 7950

*Web Site:* www.bfi.org.uk

Established: 1983

This annual award is given to a book published in Britain dealing with film or television by a UK author. The award takes the form of a specially commissioned plaque.

## Premio Valle Inclan

Society of Authors - Translators Association

84 Drayton Gardens, London SW10 9SB

*Tel:* (020) 7373 6642 *Fax:* (020) 7373 5768

*E-mail:* info@societyofauthors.org

*Web Site:* www.societyofauthors.org

*Key Personnel*

Secretary: Dorothy Sym

This annual prize is for published translations of full length Spanish works of literary merit & general interest (the original must have been written in Spanish but can be from any period & from anywhere in the world). The translation must have been first published in the UK.

Award: 1,000 GBP

Closing Date: Dec 20

## ☆Quadrennial Prize for Bibliography

International League of Antiquarian Booksellers

15 Maze Hill, St Leonards, East Sussex TN38 0HN

*Tel:* (01424) 426146

*E-mail:* info@ilab-lila.com

*Web Site:* www.ilab-lila.com

*Key Personnel*

Prize Secretary: Raymond Kilgariff

General Secretary: Steven Temple

To the author of the best work, published or unpublished, of learned bibliography, of research into the history of the book or typography, or a book of general interest on the subject. The competition is open, without restriction, but entries must be submitted in a language which is universally read. An already published work is eligible only if it has an imprint bearing a date within the four years preceding the closing date for submission. Entries in the form of a specialized catalogue of one or more books destined for sale are not eligible, nor periodicals or public library catalogues. Any further information relating to the prize for Bibliography awarded by ILAB can be obtained from the National Associations of Antiquarian Booksellers.

Award: 10,000 USD every four years

Presented: Summer 2006

## Red House Children's Book Award

Red House

c/o The Federation of Children's Book Groups, 2 Bridge Wood View, Horsforth, Leeds LS18 5PE

*Tel:* (0113) 2588910 *Fax:* (0113) 2588920

*E-mail:* info@fcbg.org.uk

*Web Site:* www.fcbg.org.uk; www.redhousechildrensbookaward.co.uk

*Key Personnel*

Coordinator: Marianne Adey

*E-mail:* marianneadey@aol.com

Established: 1980

Coordinated by the Federation of Children's Book Groups, this award is given annually for the best work of fiction (published in the United Kingdom). Chosen by children for children.

## ☆Trevor Reese Memorial Prize

Institute of Commonwealth Studies

University of London, 28 Russell Sq, London WC1B 5DS

*Tel:* (020) 7862 8844 *Fax:* (020) 7862 8820

*E-mail:* ics@sas.ac.uk

*Web Site:* www.sas.ac.uk/commonwealthstudies/

*Key Personnel*

Events & Publicity Officer: Stephanie Kearins

*Tel:* (020) 7862 8825 *E-mail:* skearins@sas.ac.uk

Established: 1976

The prize was established from a memorial fund to Dr Trevor Reese, Reader in Imperial Studies at the Institute of Commonwealth Studies, who died in 1976. The adjudicators are interested in wide-ranging publications, but the terms of the Prize specifically apply to scholarly works usually by a single author, in the field of Imperial & Commonwealth history. Awarded biennially.

Award: 1,000 GBP

## ☆John Llewellyn Rhys Prize

Booktrust

45 East Hill, London SW18 2QZ

*Tel:* (020) 8516 2977 *Fax:* (020) 8516 2978

*Web Site:* www.booktrust.org.uk/prizes/btprizes/mosjlr.htm

*Key Personnel*

Prize Administrator: Tarryn McKay *Tel:* (020) 8516 2977 *E-mail:* tarryn@booktrust.org.uk

Prize Manager: Susy Behr *Tel:* (020) 8516 2993 *E-mail:* susy@booktrust.org.uk

Established: 1942

Founded by Jane Oliver, the widow of John Llewellyn Rhys, a young writer killed in action in World War II. To be eligible, entries may be any work of literature written by a British or Commonwealth writer under the age of 35 at the time of publication. Books must be written in English & published in the UK during the year of the Prize. Previous winners of the prize may not enter. This prize is open to published works only, entries submitted by UK publisher only & is awarded annually.

Other Sponsor(s): The Mail on Sunday

Award: 5,000 GBP to the winner & 500 GBP to each of the other shortlisted authors

## The Robinson Medal

Chartered Institute of Library & Information Professionals (CILIP)

7 Ridgmount St, London WC1E 7AE

*Tel:* (020) 7255 0650 *Fax:* (020) 7255 0501

*E-mail:* info@cilip.org.uk

*Web Site:* www.cilip.org.uk/practice/awards.html

*Key Personnel*

Marketing Manager: Louisa Myatt *E-mail:* louisa.myatt@cilip.org.uk

Awarded biennially to recognize innovation & excellence in library administration & administrative procedures. It is aimed specifically at attracting submissions from people working at paraprofessional levels in the library & information field.

Other Sponsor(s): Demco Group

Award: Trophy, certificate & 50 GBP book token

Presented: CILIP Awards Gala Ceremony, Landmark Hotel

## Royal Historical Society/History Today Prize

The Royal Society

University College London, Gower St, London WC1E 6BT

*Tel:* (020) 7387 7532 *Fax:* (020) 7387 7532

*E-mail:* royalhistsoc@ucl.ac.uk

*Web Site:* www.rhs.ac.uk

*Key Personnel*
Executive Secretary: Joy McCarthy
For the best third year undergraduate dissertation in History in a higher education institution in the UK.
Award: 250 GBP

**The Royal Society of Medicine Prizes for Medical Writing & Illustration**
The Society of Authors, Medical Writers Group
84 Drayton Gardens, London SW10 9SB
*Tel:* (020) 7373 6642 *Fax:* (020) 7373 5768
*E-mail:* info@societyofauthors.org
*Web Site:* www.societyofauthors.org
*Key Personnel*
Contact: Dorothy Sym

**Saltire History Book of the Year Award**
The Saltire Society
9 Fountain Close, 22 High St, Edinburgh EH1 1TF
*Tel:* (0131) 556 1836 *Fax:* (0131) 557 1675
*E-mail:* saltire@saltiresociety.org.uk
*Web Site:* www.saltiresociety.org.uk
*Key Personnel*
Administrator: Kathleen Munro
Established: 1965
In memory of Dr Agnes Mure Mackenzie, this award is given biennially for a published work of Scottish Historical Research (including intellectual history & the history of science). Editions of texts are not eligible.
Award: A bound & inscribed copy of the winning publication

**Sasakawa Prize**
Society of Authors - Translators Association
84 Drayton Gardens, London SW10 9SB
*Tel:* (020) 7373 6642 *Fax:* (020) 7373 5768
*E-mail:* info@societyofauthors.org
*Web Site:* www.societyofauthors.org
*Key Personnel*
Secretary: Dorothy Sym
This prize is for translations of full length Japanese works of literary merit & general interest, from any period. The translation must have been first published in the UK.
Award: 2,000 GBP

**Schlegel-Tieck Prize**
Society of Authors - Translators Association
84 Drayton Gardens, London SW10 9SB
*Tel:* (020) 7373 6642 *Fax:* (020) 7373 5768
*E-mail:* info@societyofauthors.org
*Web Site:* www.societyofauthors.org
*Key Personnel*
Secretary: Dorothy Sym
Established under the auspices of the Translators Association, a subsidiary organization of the Society of Authors, to be awarded annually for the best translation published by a British publisher during the previous year. Only translations of German 20th Century works of literary merit & general interest will be considered. The work should be entered by the publisher & not the individual translator.
Closing Date: Dec 20

**Scottish Arts Council Book Awards**
The Scottish Arts Council
Literature Dept, 12 Manor Pl, Edinburgh EH3 7DD
*Tel:* (0131) 226 6051 *Fax:* (0131) 225 9833
*E-mail:* help.desk@scottisharts.org.uk
*Web Site:* www.sac.org.uk
*Key Personnel*
Literature Officer: Gavin Wallace *E-mail:* gavin. wallace@scottisharts.org.uk
Ten awards annually. Awarded in Spring & Autumn. Authors must be Scottish, resident in Scotland, or work must be of particular Scot-

tish interest. Preference is given to literary fiction & poetry, but many other types of books are eligible for consideration. Reprints, technical or scientific books, & books that are highly specialized will not be considered. Works should be submitted by publishers on behalf of their authors. Publishers of children's books can submit titles to the SAC Children's Book Awards under separate guidelines.
Award: 1,000 GBP each
Closing Date: Spring Award: Jan 31 for books published between July & Dec; Autumn Award: July 31 for books published between Jan & June
Presented: April (Spring); Nov (Autumn)

**Scottish Book of the Year Award & Scottish First Book of the Year**
The Saltire Society
9 Fountain Close, 22 High St, Edinburgh EH1 1TF
*Tel:* (0131) 556 1836 *Fax:* (0131) 557 1675
*E-mail:* saltire@saltiresociety.org.uk
*Web Site:* www.saltiresociety.org.uk
*Key Personnel*
Administrator: Kathleen Munro
Established: 1982
Award established by The Saltire Society & now funded by The Scotsman. Awarded for a book of a literary nature written by an author of Scottish descent or living in Scotland, or a book which deals with the work or life of a Scot or with a Scottish problem, event or situation. The Scotsman contributes substantial monetary sums to be awarded annually.
Award: Scottish Book of the Year 5,000 GBP, Scottish First Book of the Year 1,500 GBP
Closing Date: Sept 7 for nominations

**Scottish International Open Poetry Competition**
Ayshire Writers & Artists Society
42 Tollerton Drive, Irvine, Ayrshire KA12 0ER
*Tel:* (01294) 276381
*Web Site:* www.irvineayrshire.org/openpoetry.htm
Established: 1972
Longest running poetry competition in UK. Free entry. Open to established & aspiring poets but two IRC's required.
Closing Date: Nov 30

**Short Story Dagger**
Crime Writers' Association
PO Box 63, Wakefield WF2 0YW
*E-mail:* info@theCWA.co.uk
*Web Site:* www.thecwa.co.uk
*Key Personnel*
Chairman: Danuta Reah
Secretary: Judith Cutler *Tel:* (07227) 709 782 *E-mail:* judith.cutler@virgin.net
Established: 1955
Awarded for a short story published in a crime anthology. Submission by publishers only.
Award: 1,500 GBP & gold pin of the CWA's crossed daggers emblem

**Silver Dagger for Fiction**
Crime Writers' Association
PO Box 63, Wakefield WF2 0YW
*E-mail:* info@theCWA.co.uk
*Web Site:* www.thecwa.co.uk
*Key Personnel*
Chairman: Danuta Reah
Secretary: Judith Cutler *Tel:* (07227) 709 782 *E-mail:* judith.cutler@virgin.net
Established: 1955
Runner-up for the top crime novel of the year.
Award: Ornamental dagger & 2,000 GBP

**Andre Simon Fund Book Awards**
Andre Simon Memorial Fund

5 Sion Hill Pl, Bath BA1 5SJ
*Tel:* (01225) 336305 *Fax:* (01225) 421862
*Key Personnel*
Contact: Tessa Hayward *E-mail:* tessa@tantraweb. co.uk
Awards given annually for the best book on food or drinks.
Award: 2,000 GBP

**Somerset Maugham Awards**
Society of Authors
84 Drayton Gardens, London SW10 9SB
*Tel:* (020) 7373 6642 *Fax:* (020) 7373 5768
*E-mail:* info@societyofauthors.org
*Web Site:* www.societyofauthors.org
*Key Personnel*
Administrator: Dorothy Sym
Established: 1946
Founded by Somerset Maugham to encourage young British writers to travel abroad. Given to a promising author of a published work of poetry, fiction, criticism, biography, history, philosophy, belles lettres or travel. Candidates must be British subjects by birth & ordinarily resident in the United Kingdom & under age 35. Awards must be used for foreign travel. Entry by publisher.
Award: Total of 12,000 GBP
Closing Date: Dec 20

☆**Stand Magazine International Short Story Competition**
Stand Magazine
Leeds University, School of English, Leeds LS2 9JT
*Tel:* (0113) 233 4794 *Fax:* (0113) 233 2791
*E-mail:* stand@leeds.ac.uk
*Web Site:* www.people.vcu.edu
*Key Personnel*
Administrator: Linda Goldsmith
Established: 1983
Hosted by the Cheltenham Festival of Literature to encourage & promote the work of new or unknown short-story writers. Awarded biennially. Please send UK stamped-addressed envelope or two international reply coupons.
Award: 1st prize 1,250 GBP; further prizes totaling 1,000 GBP: runners-up prizes of one-year magazine subscriptions to Stand Magazine

**Sunday Times Small Publisher of the Year Award**
The Sunday Times
Independent Publishers Guild, 4 Middle St, Great Gransden, Sandy, Beds SG19 3AD
*Tel:* (01767) 677753 *Fax:* (01767) 677069
*Key Personnel*
Administrator: Sheila Bounford *E-mail:* sheila@ ipg.uk.com
Annual award for the best independent publisher in the UK which produces between 5 & 40 titles in a calendar year, with a maximum turnover of 1.5 million GBP per year.
Award: 1,000 GBP
Closing Date: Jan 31
Presented: London Book Fair

☆**The Times Educational Supplement Information Book Award**
Times Educational Supplement
Admiral House, 66-68 East Smithfield, London E1W 1BX
Mailing Address: PO Box 495, London E1W 2XY
*Tel:* (020) 7782 3000 *Fax:* (020) 7782 3200
*Web Site:* www.tes.co.uk

☆**The Times Educational Supplement Schoolbook Award**
Times Educational Supplement
Admiral House, 66-68 East Smithfield, London E1W 1BX

Mailing Address: PO Box 495, London E1W
2XY
*Tel:* (020) 7782 3000 *Fax:* (020) 7782 3200
*Web Site:* www.tes.co.uk
The Award is administered jointly by the TES &
the Educational Publishers Council. There are
two categories, Primary, for children ages 5-
11 & Secondary, for young people ages 11-16.
Prizes are to be awarded to the authors of the
most outstanding schoolbooks in the subject of
National Curriculum Books (subject decided
each year). The category changes annually.
To be eligible, books must have originated in
Great Britain, final entry date usually Dec 31.
No proof copies can be considered. There is
no limit to the number of entries but the publishers are asked to be selective in their entries
& no books may be entered simultaneously
for the Schoolbook Award & the TES Information Book Awards. One copy of each entry
should be sent directly to TES & to each of the
judges.

**Tom-Gallon Trust Award**
Society of Authors
84 Drayton Gardens, London SW10 9SB
*Tel:* (020) 7373 6642 *Fax:* (020) 7373 5768
*E-mail:* info@societyofauthors.org
*Web Site:* www.societyofauthors.org
*Key Personnel*
Administrator: Dorothy Sym
Established: 1943
Awarded biennially to short story writers of lim-
ited means. Entrants must submit a list of al-
ready published fiction, one published or un-
published short story, & a brief statement of
their financial position & willingness to devote
substantial time to writing fiction as soon as
they are financially able.
Award: 1,000 GBP
Closing Date: Sept 20

☆**The Betty Trask Prize & Awards**
Society of Authors
84 Drayton Gardens, London SW10 9SB
*Tel:* (020) 7373 6642 *Fax:* (020) 7373 5768
*E-mail:* info@societyofauthors.org
*Web Site:* www.societyofauthors.org
*Key Personnel*
Administrator: Dorothy Sym
Established: 1983
Awards are for the benefit of authors under 35
years of age who are Commonwealth citizens
& are given for a first novel (published or un-
published) of a romantic or traditional nature.
All winners are required to use the money for a
period or periods of foreign travel with a view
to increasing their experience & knowledge for
future literary benefit.
Award: Up to 25,000 GBP total value
Closing Date: Jan 31

**Travelling Scholarships**
Society of Authors
84 Drayton Gardens, London SW10 9SB
*Tel:* (020) 7373 6642 *Fax:* (020) 7373 5768
*E-mail:* info@societyofauthors.org
*Web Site:* www.societyofauthors.net
*Key Personnel*
Administrator: Dorothy Sym
Established: 1944
Annual awards to enable British writers to keep
in touch with their colleagues abroad. Honorary
Scholarships are awarded for a body of work &
submissions are not accepted.
Award: 6,000 GBP

**VER Poets Open Competition**
VER Poets
181, Sandridge Rd, St Albans, Herts AL1 4A4
*Tel:* (01727) 867005

*Key Personnel*
Chairman: Ray Badman
President: John Cotton
Vice President: John Mole
Editor & Organiser: May Badman
Established: 1966
Award: Total Prizes 1,000 GBP; 1st prizr 500
GBP; 2nd prize 300 GBP; two 3rd prizes 100
GBP each; plus publication in anthology
Closing Date: April 30
Presented: St Albans, June

**Vondel Translation Prize**
Society of Authors - Translators Association
84 Drayton Gardens, London SW10 9SB
*Tel:* (020) 7373 6642 *Fax:* (020) 7373 5768
*E-mail:* info@societyofauthors.org
*Web Site:* www.societyofauthors.org
*Key Personnel*
Secretary: Dorothy Sym
The biennial prize is for translations of works
into English of Dutch & Flemish works of lit-
erary merit & general interest. The translation
must have been first published in the UK or the
USA.
Award: Approximately 2,000 GBP
Closing Date: Dec 20

**Walford Award**
Chartered Institute of Library & Information Pro-
fessionals (CILIP)
7 Ridgmount St, London WC1E 7AE
*Tel:* (020) 7255 0650 *Fax:* (020) 7255 0501
*E-mail:* info@cilip.org.uk
*Web Site:* www.cilip.org.uk
*Key Personnel*
Marketing Manager: Louisa Myatt *E-mail:* louisa.
myatt@cilip.org.uk
Presented to an individual who has made a sus-
tained & continual contribution to the science
& art of bibliography in the UK. The nominee
need not be a resident in the UK.
Award: 500 GBP & certificate

**The David Watt Prize**
Rio Tinto PLC
6 Saint James's Sq, London SW1Y 4LD
*Tel:* (020) 7930 2399 *Fax:* (020) 7930 3249
*E-mail:* davidwattprize@riotinto.com
*Web Site:* www.riotinto.com
*Key Personnel*
Contact: Celia Beale *E-mail:* celiabeale@
globalnet.co.uk; Andrea Redfern
Established: 1988
Annual journalism prize for outstanding contribu-
tions towards the clarification of political issues
& the promotion of their greater understanding.
Award: 7,500 GBP
Closing Date: March 31

**Wheatley Medal**
Chartered Institute of Library & Information Pro-
fessionals (CILIP)
7 Ridgmount St, London WC1E 7AE
*Tel:* (020) 7255 0650 *Fax:* (020) 7255 0501
*E-mail:* info@cilip.org.uk
*Web Site:* www.cilip.org.uk
*Key Personnel*
Marketing Manager: Louisa Myatt *E-mail:* louisa.
myatt@cilip.org.uk
Established: 1961
Presented in association with The Society of In-
dexers, for an outstanding printed index pub-
lished in the UK between Jan 1 & April 27.
Indexes will be judged on clarity, comprehen-
siveness, choice of terms & headings, use of
cross reference, avoidance of strings of undif-
ferentiated page references, layout, presenta-
tion, overall impact of the index & relevance to
text.
Award: 500 GBP, certificate & gold medal
Presented: Awards ceremony, Sept

**Whitbread Book Awards**
Booksellers Association of the United Kingdom
& Ireland Ltd
Minster House, 272 Vauxhall Bridge Rd, London
SW1V 1BA
*Tel:* (020) 7802 0802 *Fax:* (020) 7802 0803
*E-mail:* mail@booksellers.org.uk
*Web Site:* www.whitbread-bookawards.co.uk
*Key Personnel*
Contact: Denise Bayat
Established: 1971
The awards celebrate & promote the best con-
temporary British writing. The awards are
judged in two stages & open to five categories:
Novel, Biography, Poetry & Children's Book
of the Year. The Novel, First Novel, Biography & Poetry Awards are judged by a panel
of three judges & the winner of each category
receives an award of 5,000 GBP. Three adult
judges & two young judges select a shortlist of
four books for the Whitbread Children's Book
of the Year. The final judges then select the
Whitbread Children's Book of the Year, worth
5,000 GBP & then go on to choose the Whitbread Book of the Year from the winners of
the Novel, First Novel, Biography & Poetry
Awards & the winner of the Whitbread Children's Book of the Year. The winner receives a
check for 25,000 GBP. Writers must have lived
in Great Britain & Ireland for three or more
years. Submissions must be received from publishers.
Award: Total of 50,000 GBP
Closing Date: Early July

**Whitfield Prize**
The Royal Society
University College London, Gower St, London
WC1E 6BT
*Tel:* (020) 7387 7532 *Fax:* (020) 7387 7532
*E-mail:* royalhistsoc@ucl.ac.uk; rhsinfo@rhs.ac.
uk
*Web Site:* www.rhs.ac.uk
*Key Personnel*
Executive Secretary: Joy McCarthy
Established: 1976
Annual prize for a new book on British history.
Award: 1,000 GBP
Closing Date: Dec 31
Presented: Royal Historical Society Annual Re-
ception, July

**John Whiting Award**
Arts Council of England
14 Great Peter St, London SW1P 3NQ
*Tel:* (0845) 300 6200 *Fax:* (020) 7973 6564
*E-mail:* enquiries@artscouncil.org.uk
*Web Site:* www.artscouncil.org.uk
Award is intended to help future careers & en-
hance reputations of British playwrights & to
draw to public attention the importance of writ-
ers in contemporary theatre.

**Meyer Whitworth Award**
Arts Council of England
14 Great Peter St, London SW1P 3NQ
*Tel:* (0845) 300 6200 *Fax:* (020) 7973 6564
*E-mail:* enquiries@artscouncil.org.uk
*Web Site:* www.artscouncil.org.uk
Intended to help further the careers of UK play-
wrights who are not yet established.

☆**WHSmith Literary Award**
WHSmith PLC
Nations House PLC, 103 Wigmore St, London
W1U 1WH
*Tel:* (020) 7514 9623 *Fax:* (020) 7514 9635
*Web Site:* www.whsmith.co.uk; www.whsmithplc.
com
*Key Personnel*
Awards Manager: Elizabeth Walker
Established: 1959

The prize is awarded to a work of fiction or non-fiction that makes an outstanding contribution to English literature & written by an author from The UK, The Commonwealth or The Republic of Ireland. The winner is chosen by nomination; entries are not required.
Award: 10,000 GBP

**WHSmith Young Writers' Competition**
WHSmith PLC
Nations House PLC, 103 Wigmore St, London W1U 1WH
*Tel:* (020) 7514 9623 *Fax:* (020) 7514 9635
*E-mail:* customer.relations@whsmith.co.uk
*Web Site:* www.whsmith.co.uk; www.whsmithplc.com
*Key Personnel*
Contact: Ruth Farrow
Established: 1959
Established as the Children's Literary Competition & previously run by the 'Daily Mirror', the competition aims to encourage creativity in written English. Open to all children in the United Kingdom & of British nationality abroad, up to the age of 16 years. The award-winning work is published in book form.
Award: 93 awards totaling more than 7,000 GBP

**Wolfson History Prize**
The Wolfson Foundation
8 Queen Anne St, London W1M 9LD
*Tel:* (020) 7323 5730 *Fax:* (020) 7323 3241
Established: 1972
Two awards totaling up to 25,000 GBP are made annually to British authors of historical writing which is considered both scholarly & accessible to the general reader.
Award: 15,000 GBP & 10,000 GBP

**Writers' Bursaries**
Arts Council of England
14 Great Peter St, London SW1P 3NQ
*Tel:* (0845) 300 6200 *Fax:* (020) 7973 6564
*E-mail:* enquiries@artscouncil.org.uk
*Web Site:* www.artscouncil.org.uk
*Key Personnel*
Contact: Alex Holdaway
Fifteen awards: open to published writers resident in England who need funds to complete a work in progress.
Award: 7,000 GBP each

☆**Yorkshire Post Book of the Year Award**
Yorkshire Post Newspapers Ltd
Wellington St, Leeds LS1 1RF
Mailing Address: PO Box 168, Leeds LS1 1RF
*Tel:* (0113) 2432701 *Fax:* (0113) 2443430
*Web Site:* www.applegate.co.uk
*Key Personnel*
Organizer: Margaret Brown
Established: 1964
Awarded to the best book published each year in the United Kingdom called 'Book of the Year' Award. Translations, reissues & works of a strictly scientific or technical nature are excluded. In addition, there is a Best First Work Award for a new author. There are also special annual awards for books selected to advance the popular appreciation of art & music. Publisher entry only.
Award: 1,200 GBP

# United States

☆**American-Scandinavian Foundation Translation Prize**
American-Scandinavian Foundation
58 Park Ave, New York, NY 10016

*Tel:* 212-879-9779 *Fax:* 212-879-2301; 212-249-3444
*E-mail:* info@amscan.org
*Web Site:* www.amscan.org
*Key Personnel*
Editor: Adrienne Gyongy *E-mail:* agyongy@amscan.org
Established: 1980
Initiated by 'Scandinavian Review' (three per year) to bring best of contemporary Scandinavian literature to American readers. There is a prize either for poetry or fiction, in addition to publication. Awarded annually for the best translation of work by a Danish, Finnish, Icelandic, Norwegian or Swedish author born after 1800; for more details request rules.
Award: 2,000 USD
Closing Date: Postmark deadline of June 1

☆**Children's Book Award**
International Reading Association
800 Barksdale Rd, Newark, DE 19714
Mailing Address: PO Box 8139, Newark, DE 19714-8139
*Tel:* 302-731-1600 *Toll Free Tel:* 800-336-7323
*Fax:* 302-731-1057
*E-mail:* pubinfo@reading.org
*Web Site:* www.reading.org
*Key Personnel*
Public Information Associate: Janet Butler
*Tel:* 302-731-1600 (ext 293) *E-mail:* jbutler@reading.org
Established: 1974
Awarded annually for a first or second book (any language) to authors who show unusual promise in the children's/young adult book field. There are three categories: Primary (ages preschool - 8), Intermediate (ages 9-13) & Young Adult (ages 14-17). Entries in languages other than English must include a one-page abstract in English & a translation into English of one chapter or similar selection.
Award: Four awards of 500 USD for 1st or 2nd published book
Presented: San Francisco

☆**Hugo Awards**
World Science Fiction Society (WSFS)
PO Box 426159, Kendall Square Station, Cambridge, MA 02142
*Web Site:* worldcon.org/hugos.html
Established: 1953
Established as Science Fiction Achievement Awards for the best science fiction writing in several categories. Chrome-plated rocket ship model awarded annually.

☆**IBC International Book Award**
International Book Committee (IBC)
800 Barksdale Rd, Newark, DE 19714
Mailing Address: PO Box 8139, Newark, DE 19714
*Tel:* 302-731-1600 *Fax:* 302-731-1057
*E-mail:* pubinfo@reading.org
*Web Site:* www.reading.org
*Key Personnel*
Chairman: Alan Farstrup
Vice Chairman: Leena Maissen
Established: 1972
Founded by book professionals as an outgrowth of the Support Committee for the Unesco International Book Year, the award is granted annually to outstanding persons or groups for their contribution to the promotion of books & reading internationally.

☆**The Irish American Cultural Institute Literary Awards**
The Irish American Cultural Institute
One Lackawanna Pl, Morristown, NJ
*Tel:* 973-605-1991 *Fax:* 973-605-8875
*E-mail:* irishway@aol.com

*Web Site:* www.iaci-usa.org
Established: 1966
For writers in the Irish or English language. Butler awards for each language in alternate years & O'Shaughnessy award for poetry. There is also funding to primary research on Irish-American themes. No application procedure.
Award: 10,000 USD for each language; 5,000 USD for poetry
Closing Date: Fall
Presented: Fall of the following year

☆**The Kiriyama Prize**
The Kiriyama Pacific Rim Institute
650 Delancey St, Suite 101, San Francisco, CA 94107-2082
*Tel:* 415-777-1628 *Fax:* 415-422-1646
*E-mail:* admin@pacificrimvoices.org; info@pacificrimvoices.org
*Web Site:* www.kiriyamaprize.org; www.pacificrimvoices.org
*Key Personnel*
Prize Administrator: Peter Coughlan
Prize Manager: Jeannine Cuevas
*E-mail:* jeannine@kiriyamaprize.org
Established: 1996
Annual prize for the book judged to have contributed most to understanding among Pacific Rim countries. Books must be published in English, either originating in English or translated into English. Books must be published during the previous calendar year. Open to nonfiction or fiction of any genre.
Other Sponsor(s): Center for the Pacific Rim, University of San Francisco
Award: 30,000 USD (15,000 USD to winning authors, fiction & nonfiction)
Closing Date: July 3
Presented: Annually in spring

☆**Neustadt International Prize for Literature**
University of Oklahoma
University of Oklahoma, 110 Monnet Hall, Norman, OK 73019-4033
*Tel:* 405-325-4531 *Fax:* 405-325-7495
*Web Site:* www.ou.edu/worldlit/neustadt
*Key Personnel*
Executive Dir: Robert Con Davis-Undiano
Established: 1969
An international prize awarded biennially for distinguished & continuing artistic achievement in the fields of poetry, drama or fiction. A new international jury of 12 is appointed for each successive award by the editor in consultation with the editorial board. Each juror presents one candidate for the prize. A majority (seven) of the jury must be present for the deliberations & the final voting. Representative selections of a candidate's work must be available to the jury in either French or English translation. Announcement of the winner is made in February or March, & the award is officially presented at The University of Oklahoma, Norman, Oklahoma, every other year. 'World Literature Today' dedicates one issue to the recipient. The University of Oklahoma Press will seriously consider the publication of a book by or on the winner. Prize not open to application.
Other Sponsor(s): World Literature Today (literary journal)
Award: Certificate, replica of an eagle's feather in silver & 50,000 USD

# Venezuela

**National Prize for Literature**
Concejo Nacional de la Cultura (CONAC)
Centro Simon Bolivar, Torre Norte, Pisos 13-16, Caracas

*Tel:* (0212) 484 21 72
Awarded annually to the best Venezuelan author. Also includes contestants in narrative prose & essays.
Award: 30,000 VEB

# Zimbabwe

**The Literature Bureau Annual Literary Award**
The Literature Bureau
Ministry of Education, Sport & Culture, Causeway, Harare

Mailing Address: PO Box CY121, Causeway, Harare
*Tel:* (04) 726929; (04) 729120
Award for the best works in Shona & Ndebele. Most genres, including translations, qualify for entry.
Award: 500 ZWD

# Book Trade Calendar

## Calendar of Book Trade & Promotional Events— Alphabetical Index of Sponsors

# Calendar of Book Trade & Promotional Events— Alphabetical Index of Events

# Calendar of Book Trade & Promotional Events

Arranged chronologically by year and month, this section lists book trade events worldwide. Preceding this section are two indexes: the Sponsor Index is an alphabetical list of event sponsors followed by the names and dates of those events they sponsor; the Event Index is an alphabetical list of events along with the dates on which the events are held.

## 2005

### OCTOBER

**Frankfurt Book Fair**
Sponsored by Ausstellungs-und Messe-GmbH des Borsenvereins des Deutschen Buchhandels
Reineckstr 3, 63013 Frankfurt am Main, Germany
Mailing Address: Postfach 100116, 60001 Frankfurt am Main, Germany
*Tel:* (069) 21020 *Fax:* (069) 2102 227
*E-mail:* info@book-fair.com
*Web Site:* www.book-fair.com *Cable:*
BUCHMESSE
*Key Personnel*
CEO & Dir: Juergen Boos
Largest international book & media fair attracting more than 6,700 exhibitors & 280,000 visitors.
Location: Frankfurt Fairgrounds, Frankfurt, Germany
Oct 19-23, 2005

**Latino Book & Family Festival**
Sponsored by Latino Literacy Now
2777 Jefferson St, Suite 200, Carlsbad, CA 92008, United States
*Tel:* 760-434-4484
*Web Site:* www.latinobookfestival.com
*Key Personnel*
Mktg Dir: Jim Sullivan *Fax:* 760-434-7476
*E-mail:* jim@lbff.us
Location: Fairplex, Pomona, CA
Oct 22-23, 2005

**Texas Book Festival**
610 Brazos St, Suite 200, Austin, TX 78701, United States
*Tel:* 512-477-4055 *Fax:* 512-322-0722
*E-mail:* bookfest@texasbookfestival.org
*Web Site:* www.texasbookfestival.org
*Key Personnel*
Exec Dir: Mary Herman *Tel:* 512-320-5451
*E-mail:* maryherman@texasbookfestival.org
Literary Dir: Clay Smith *Tel:* 512-472-3808
*E-mail:* clay@texasbookfestival.org
Off Mgr: Andrea V Prestridge *Tel:* 512-477-4055
*E-mail:* andrea@texasbookfestival.org
The festival is a statewide program that promotes reading & literacy highlighted by a two-day festival featuring authors from Texas & across the country. Money raised from the festival is distributed as grants to public libraries throughout the state.
Location: State Capitol Bldg, Austin, TX, USA
Oct 29-30, 2005

### NOVEMBER

**American Academy of Religion**
Sponsored by American Schools of Oriental Research
825 Houston Mill Rd, Suite 201, Atlanta, GA 30329-4205, United States
*Tel:* 404-727-3049 *Fax:* 404-727-7959
*E-mail:* aar@aarweb.org

*Web Site:* www.aarweb.org
*Key Personnel*
Prog Dir: Aislinn Jones
Location: Pennslyvania Convention Center, Philadelphia, PA, USA
Nov 19-22, 2005

**American Translators Association Annual Conference**
Sponsored by American Translators Association (ATA)
225 Reinekers Lane, Suite 590, Alexandria, VA 22314, United States
*Tel:* 703-683-6100 *Fax:* 703-683-6122
*E-mail:* ata@atanet.org
*Web Site:* www.atanet.org
*Key Personnel*
Exec Dir: Walter Bacak *Tel:* 703-683-6100 ext 3006 *E-mail:* walter@atanet.org
Location: Seattle, WA, USA
Nov 9-12, 2005

**Antwerp Book Fair**
Sponsored by Boek.be
Hof ter Schrieclaan 17, 2600 Berchem/Antwerp, Belgium
*Tel:* (03) 230 89 23 *Fax:* (03) 281 22 40
*E-mail:* info@boek.be
*Web Site:* www.boek.be
Location: Bouwcentrum, Jan van Rijswijcklaan 191, Antwerp, Belgium
November 1-11, 2005

**Cairo International Children's Book Fair**
Sponsored by General Egyptian Book Organization
Corniche el-Nil - Ramlet Boulac, Cairo 11221, Egypt (Arab Republic of Egypt)
*Tel:* (02) 5765436; (02) 5775228; (02) 5775109; (02) 5775367; (02) 5775436; (02) 5775545; (02) 5775000 *Fax:* (02) 5765058
*E-mail:* info@egyptianbook.org
*Web Site:* www.childrensbookfair.org; www.egyptianbook.org; www.egyptianbook.net
*Key Personnel*
Chmn: Dr Nasser El Ansary
VChmn: Dr Waheed Abdel Majeed
Location: Cairo, Egypt
Nov 2005

**Children's Book Week**
Sponsored by The Children's Book Council (CBC)
12 W 37 St, 2nd fl, New York, NY 10118-7480, United States
*Tel:* 212-966-1990 *Toll Free Tel:* 800-999-2160 (orders only) *Fax:* 212-966-2073
*Toll Free Fax:* 888-807-9355 (orders only)
*Web Site:* www.cbcbooks.org
*Key Personnel*
Pres: Paula Quint
Location: Nationwide across the USA
Nov 14-20, 2005

**China Didac/WORLDDIDAC**
Sponsored by Worlddidac
Bollwerk 21, 3001 Bern, Switzerland
Mailing Address: PO Box 8866, 3001 Bern, Switzerland

*Tel:* (031) 311 76 82 *Fax:* (031) 312 17 44
*E-mail:* info@worlddidac.org
*Web Site:* www.worlddidac.org
*Key Personnel*
Proj Mgr: Daniela Leu *E-mail:* leu@worlddidac.org
International exhibition for educational materials, professional training & e-learning.
Location: Shanghai, China
Nov 1-3, 2005

**Color Imaging Conference - Color Science Systems & Applications**
Sponsored by Society for Imaging Science & Technology (IS&T)
7003 Kilworth Lane, Springfield, VA 22151, United States
*Tel:* 703-642-9090 *Fax:* 703-642-9094
*E-mail:* info@imaging.org
*Web Site:* www.imaging.org
*Key Personnel*
Gen Co-chair: Po-Chief Hung; Michael Brill
Location: SunBurst Hotel, Scottsdale, AZ, USA
Nov 7-11, 2005

**Content Management Europe**
Sponsored by VNU Exhibitions Europe
Subsidiary of VNU Business Media Europe
32-34 Broadwick St, London W1A 2HG, United Kingdom
*Tel:* (020) 7316 9000 *Fax:* (020) 7316 9598
*E-mail:* info@vnuexhibitions.co.uk
*Web Site:* www.cme-expo.co.uk
*Key Personnel*
Conference Mgr: Lorna Candy *E-mail:* lorna.candy@vnuexhibitions.co.uk
Held in conjunction with Online Information.
Location: Olympia Grand Hall, London, UK
Nov 28-Dec 1, 2005

**ECPA Publishing University**
Sponsored by Evangelical Christian Publishers Association
4816 S Ash Ave, Suite 101, Tempe, AZ 85282-7735, United States
*Tel:* 480-966-3998 *Fax:* 480-966-1944
*E-mail:* info@ecpa.org
*Web Site:* www.ecpa.org
*Key Personnel*
Pres: Mark Kuyper *E-mail:* mkuyper@ecpa.org
Excellence in Christian publishing through professional instruction, interactive learning & practical training.
Location: Indian Lakes Resort, Bloomingdale, IL, USA
Nov 6-8, 2005

**Feria Internacional del Libro de Guadalajara**
Av Alemania 1370, Colonia Moderna, 44190 Guadalajara Jalisco, Mexico
*Tel:* (033) 3810 0291; (033) 3810 0331
*Fax:* (033) 3810 0379
*E-mail:* fil@fil.com.mx; filny@aol.com
*Web Site:* www.fil.com.mx
*Key Personnel*
Pres: Raul Padilla Lopez
Dir: Nubia Edith Macias Navarro *E-mail:* dirfil@fil.com.mx

Gen Coord, Events & Prizes: Laura Niembro
Diaz *E-mail:* eventosf@fil.com.mx
Location: Guadalajara, Mexico
Nov 26-Dec 4, 2005

**Jewish Book Month**
Sponsored by Jewish Book Council
15 E 26 St, New York, NY 10010-1579, United
States
*Tel:* 212-532-4949 (ext 297) *Fax:* 212-481-4174
*E-mail:* jbc@jewishbooks.org
*Web Site:* www.jewishbookcouncil.org
*Key Personnel*
Exec Dir: Carolyn Starman Hessel
*E-mail:* carolynhessel@jewishbooks.org
Nov 26-Dec 26, 2005

**Karlsruher Buecherschau** (Karlsruhe Book
Exhibition)
Sponsored by Boersenverein des Deutschen Buch-
handels, Landesverband Baden-Wuerttemberg
eV (Association of Publishers & Booksellers in
Baden-Wuerttemberg eV)
Paulinenstr 53, 70178 Stuttgart, Germany
*Tel:* (0711) 61941-0 *Fax:* (0711) 61941-44
*E-mail:* post@buchhandelsverband.de
*Web Site:* www.buchhandelsverband.de
*Key Personnel*
Exhibition Mgr: Lisa Buchhorn *Tel:* (0711) 61941
26 *E-mail:* buchhorn@buchhandelsverband.de
Contact: Andrea Baumann *Tel:* (0711) 61941-23
*Fax:* (0711) 61941-44 *E-mail:* baumann@
buchhandelsverband.de
Location: Landesgewerbeamt Baden-Wurttemberg,
Karl-Friedrich Str 17, Karlsruhe, Germany
Nov 11-Dec 4, 2005

**Latino Book & Family Festival**
Sponsored by Latino Literacy Now
2777 Jefferson St, Suite 200, Carlsbad, CA
92008, United States
*Tel:* 760-434-4484
*Web Site:* www.latinobookfestival.com
*Key Personnel*
Mktg Dir: Jim Sullivan *Fax:* 760-434-7476
*E-mail:* jim@lbff.us
Location: Unity School, Cicero, IL, USA
Nov 12-13, 2005

**Miami Book Fair International**
Subsidiary of The Florida Center for the Literary
Arts at Miami Dade College
300 NE Second Ave, Suite 3704, Miami, FL
33132, United States
*Tel:* 305-237-3258 *Fax:* 305-237-3003
*E-mail:* wbookfair@mdc.edu
*Web Site:* www.miamibookfair.com
*Key Personnel*
Dir of Opers: Judy Schmelzer
Exhibitor Liaison: Giselle Hernandez *Tel:* 305-
237-3315
Miami Book Fair International is the largest &
finest event of its kind in the U.S. For more
than 22 years, the fair has been held over eight
days each November. The 22nd edition will
be held from November 13 to November 20
at the Wolfson Campus of Miami-Dade College in downtown Miami, FL. In addition to
readings by more than 300 authors from all
over the world & the sale of thousands of
books in many languages, the fair offers book-
centered fun for children, panel discussions
& writing classes in English & Spanish. This
year's participating authors include Margaret
Atwood, Joan Didion, Jonathan Safran Foer,
Joe Lelyveld, John Hope Franklin, Marilynne
Robinson, Scott Turow, Andrew Weil & Garry
Wills. For up to date information, please call
305-237-3258, or visit the book fair web site at
www.miamibookfair.com.

Location: Miami-Dade Community College,
Wolfson Campus, Miami FL, USA
Nov 13-20, 2005, Street Fair Nov 18-20, 2005

**Multicultural Children's Book Festival**
Sponsored by Kids Cultural Books
811 Elaine Dr, Stamford, CT 06902, United
States
*Tel:* 203-359-6925 *Fax:* 203-359-3226
*E-mail:* info@kidsculturalbooks.org
*Web Site:* www.kidsculturalbooks.org
Location: Kennedy Center, Washington, DC, USA
Nov 2005

**Online Information**
Sponsored by VNU Exhibitions Europe
Subsidiary of VNU Business Media Europe
32-34 Broadwick St, London W1A 2HG, United
Kingdom
*Tel:* (020) 7316 9000 *Fax:* (020) 7316 9598
*E-mail:* info@vnuexhibitions.co.uk
*Web Site:* www.online-information.co.uk
*Key Personnel*
Conference Mgr: Lorna Candy *E-mail:* lorna.
candy@vnuexhibitions.co.uk
Held in conjunction with Content Management
Europe, the show brings together hundreds of
companies exhibiting the worlds best infor-
mation resources, together with solutions for
information management, knowledge exchange,
content management, intranets & extranets &
epublishing. It attracts thousands of international information managers, knowledge managers, librarians, academics, publishers, information users & IT professionals..
Location: Olympia Grand Hall, London, UK
Nov 28-Dec 1, 2005

**Quod Libet/International Antiquarian Book
Fair & Artists Books**
Sponsored by Luckwaldt Messen
Bruechhorststr 34, 24641 Sievershuetten, Ger-
many
*Tel:* (04) 194 8101 *Fax:* (04) 194 636
*E-mail:* frauke@luckwaldt.de
*Web Site:* www.quod-libet.com
*Key Personnel*
Organizer: Frauke Luckwaldt
Location: Hamburger Boerse in der Handelskam-
mer, Adolphsplatz 1, Hamburg, Germany
Nov 11-13, 2005

**Salon du Livre de Montreal** (Montreal Book
Show)
300 St-Secrement, Suite 430, Montreal, QC H2Y
1X4, Canada
*Tel:* (514) 845-2365 *Fax:* (514) 845-7119
*E-mail:* slm.info@videotron.ca
*Web Site:* www.salondulivredemontreal.com
*Key Personnel*
Gen Mgr: Francine Bois
Location: La Place Bonaventure, Montreal, PQ,
Canada
Nov 17-21, 2005

**Salon du Livre et de la Presse de Jeunesse**
Sponsored by Reed Expositions France
Subsidiary of Reed Exhibition Companies
11 rue du Colonel Pierre Avia, 75726 Paris Cedex
15, France
*Tel:* (01) 41 90 47 47 *Fax:* (01) 41 90 47 49
*E-mail:* info@reedexpo.fr; cplj@ldg.tm.fr;
contact@slpj.fr
*Web Site:* www.salon-livre-presse-jeunesse.net;
www.ldj.tm.fr
*Key Personnel*
Contact: Denis-Luc Panthin *E-mail:* denis-luc.
panthin@slpj.fr
France's leading publishing event dedicated to
children's books, organized by Centre de pro-
motion du livre de jeunesse.

Location: Montreuil Halle d'exposition, Montreuil, France
Nov 30-Dec 5, 2005

**Seybold San Francisco**
Sponsored by MediaLive International
795 Folsom St, 6th fl, San Francisco, CA 94107-
1243, United States
*Tel:* 415-905-2300 *Fax:* 415-905-2329
*Web Site:* www.Seybold365.com
*Key Personnel*
Gen Mgr: Drew Miller
Location: Palace Hotel, San Francisco, CA, USA
Nov 29-Dec 2, 2005

**Stuttgarter Buchwochen (Stuttgart Bookweeks)**
Sponsored by Boersenverein des Deutschen Buch-
handels, Landesverband Baden-Wuerttemberg
eV (Association of Publishers & Booksellers in
Baden-Wuerttemberg eV)
Paulinenstr 53, 70178 Stuttgart, Germany
*Tel:* (0711) 61941-0; (0711) 123 34 99
*Fax:* (0711) 61941-44
*E-mail:* post@buchhandelsverband.de
*Web Site:* www.buchhandelsverband.de
*Key Personnel*
Contact: Andrea Baumann *Tel:* (0711) 61941-23
*Fax:* (0711) 61941-44 *E-mail:* baumann@
buchhandelsverband.de
Location: Haus der Wirtschaft, Willi-Bleicher Str
19, Stuttgart, Germany
Nov 17-Dec 11, 2005

# DECEMBER

**Modern Language Association of America
Annual Convention**
Sponsored by Modern Language Association of
America (MLA)
26 Broadway, 3rd fl, New York, NY 10004-1789,
United States
*Tel:* 646-576-5000 *Fax:* 646-576-9930
*E-mail:* convention@mla.org
*Web Site:* www.mla.org
*Key Personnel*
Dir, Conventions: Maribeth T Kraus
Assoc Dir, Conventions: Karin Bagnall
Location: Marriott Wardham Park, Washington
Hilton & Omni Shoreham, Washington, DC,
USA
Dec 27-30, 2005

**The National Center for Database Marketing
(NCDM)**
Sponsored by Primedia Business Exhibitions
11 River Bend Dr S, Stamford, CT 06907, United
States
Mailing Address: PO Box 4254, Stamford, CT
06907-0254, United States
*Tel:* 203-358-9900 *Toll Free Tel:* 800-927-5007
*Fax:* 203-358-5818
*Web Site:* www.primediabusiness.com; www.
ncdmsummer.com; www.ncdmwinter.com
Location: Walt Disney World Dolphin, Orlando,
FL, USA
Dec 12-14, 2005

**Small Press Book Fair**
Sponsored by Small Press Center
20 W 44 St, New York, NY 10036, United States
*Tel:* 212-764-7021 *Fax:* 212-354-5365
*E-mail:* info@smallpress.org
*Web Site:* www.smallpress.org
*Key Personnel*
Dir: Karin Taylor
Location: Small Press Center, New York, NY,
USA
Dec 3-4, 2005

# 2006

## JANUARY

**Advance 2006: The Strategic Event for the Christian Retail Channel**
Formerly CBA Advance
Sponsored by CBA
9240 Explorer Dr, Colorado Springs, CO 80920-5001, United States
Mailing Address: PO Box 62000, Colorado Springs, CO 80962-2000, United States
*Tel:* 719-265-9895 *Toll Free Tel:* 800-252-1950
*Fax:* 719-272-3510
*E-mail:* info@cbaonline.org
*Web Site:* www.cbaonline.org
*Key Personnel*
Pres: William Anderson *E-mail:* banderson@cbaonline.org
VP & COO: Dorothy Gore
Convention & Expositions Mgr: Scott Graham
Location: Opryland Hotel, Nashville, TN, USA
Jan 23-27, 2006

**American Library Association Mid-Winter Meeting**
Sponsored by American Library Association (ALA)
50 E Huron St, Chicago, IL 60611, United States
*Toll Free Tel:* 800-545-2433 *Fax:* 312-944-6780
*E-mail:* ala@ala.org
*Web Site:* www.ala.org/midwinter
*Key Personnel*
Public Info Dir: Mark Gould
Press Officer: Larra Clark *E-mail:* lclark@ala.org
Location: San Antonio, TX, USA
Jan 20-25, 2006

**Cairo International Book Fair**
Sponsored by General Egyptian Book Organization
Corniche el-Nil - Ramlet Boulac, Cairo 11221, Egypt (Arab Republic of Egypt)
*Tel:* (02) 5765436; (02) 5775228; (02) 5775109; (02) 5775367; (02) 5775436; (02) 5775545; (02) 5775000 *Fax:* (02) 5765058
*E-mail:* info@egyptianbook.org
*Web Site:* www.cibf.org; www.egyptianbook.org
*Key Personnel*
Chmn: Dr Nasser El Ansary
VChmn: Dr Waheed Abdel Majeed
Location: Nasr City Fairground, Cairo, Egypt
Jan 2006

**ECPA Trade Show**
Sponsored by Evangelical Christian Publishers Association
4816 S Ash Ave, Suite 101, Tempe, AZ 85282-7735, United States
*Tel:* 480-966-3998 *Fax:* 480-966-3417
*E-mail:* TradeShows@ecpa.org
*Web Site:* www.ecpa.org
*Key Personnel*
Pres: Mark Kuyper *E-mail:* mkuyper@ecpa.org
Location: Greensboro, NC, USA
Jan 5-6, 2006
Location: Hershey, PA, USA
Jan 9-10, 2006
Location: Chicaco, IL USA
Jan 12-13, 2006
Location: Arlington, TX USA
Jan 17-18, 2006
Location: Riverside, CA, USA
Jan 31-Feb 1, 2006

**Football Writers Association of America Annual Meeting**
Sponsored by Football Writers Association of America
18652 Vista Del Sol, Dallas, TX 75287, United States
*Tel:* 972-713-6198
*E-mail:* tigerfwaa@aol.com
*Web Site:* www.fwaa.com; www.footballwriters.com
*Key Personnel*
Pres, Orlando Sentinel: Alan Schmadtke
1st VP, CBS Sports Line: Dennis Dodd
2nd VP, Knoxville News-Sentinal: Mike Griffith
Location: Beverly Hilton Hotel, Beverly Hills, CA, USA
Jan 3-5, 2006

**IS&T/SPIE Electronic Imaging Science & Technology**
Sponsored by SPIE - The International Society for Optical Engineering
1000 20 St, Bellingham, WA 98225, United States
Mailing Address: PO Box 10, Bellingham, WA 98227-0010, United States
*Tel:* 360-676-3290 *Fax:* 360-647-1445
*E-mail:* info@imaging.org
*Web Site:* www.electronicimaging.org
*Key Personnel*
Symposium Chair: Charles A Bouman; Gabriel G Marcu
Exhibits Coord: Pam Forness
Tech Coord: Jeanne Anderson
Location: San Jose Marriott & San Jose Convention Center, San Jose, CA, USA
Jan 15-19, 2006

**IS&T/SPIE's Electronic Imaging Science & Technology**
Sponsored by Society for Imaging Science & Technology (IS&T)
7003 Kilworth Lane, Springfield, VA 22151, United States
*Tel:* 703-642-9090 *Fax:* 703-642-9094
*E-mail:* info@imaging.org
*Web Site:* www.imaging.org
Location: San Jose Marriott & San Jose Convention Center, San Jose, CA, USA
Jan 15-19, 2006

**Macworld Conference & Expo**
Sponsored by IDG World Expo
Unit of IDG
3 Speen St, Framingham, MA 01701, United States
*Tel:* 508-879-6700 *Toll Free Tel:* 800-645-EXPO
*Fax:* 508-620-6668
*Web Site:* www.macworldexpo.com
*Key Personnel*
VP: Darrell Baker
Location: Moscone Convention Center, San Francisco, CA, USA
Jan 9-13, 2006

**Publishers Winter Conclave**
Sponsored by Publishers Association of the South (PAS)
4412 Fletcher St, Panama City, FL 32405-1017, United States
*Tel:* 850-914-0766 *Fax:* 850-769-4348
*E-mail:* executive@pubsouth.org
*Web Site:* www.pubsouth.org
*Key Personnel*
Pres: Janice Shay
Assn Exec: Pat Sabiston
Location: Maison Dupuy, New Orleans, LA, USA
Jan 27-29, 2006

**Remainder & Promotional Book Fair**
Sponsored by Ciana Ltd
24 Langroyd Rd, London SW17 7PL, United Kingdom
*Tel:* (020) 8682 1969 *Fax:* (020) 8682 1997
*E-mail:* enquiries@ciana.co.uk
*Web Site:* www.ciana.co.uk
Location: Brighton, UK
Jan 15-16, 2006

**Special Libraries Association Leadership Summit**
Sponsored by Special Libraries Association (SLA)
313 S Patrick St, Alexandria, VA 22314, United States
*Tel:* 703-647-4900 *Fax:* 703-647-4901
*E-mail:* sla@sla.org
*Web Site:* www.sla.org
*Key Personnel*
Exec Dir: Janice LaChance *E-mail:* janice@sla.org
Location: Houston, TX, USA
Jan 18-21, 2006

**Technology, Reading & Learning Difficulties (TRLD)**
Sponsored by Don Johnson Inc
26799 W Commerce, Volo, IL 60073, United States
*Toll Free Tel:* 888-594-1249 *Fax:* 847-740-7326
*E-mail:* info@trld.com
*Web Site:* www.trld.com
*Key Personnel*
Contact: Linda Hoening
TRLD is the only conference that integrates technology interventions with expert literacy strategies to ensure student success. The conference brings together educators, experienced literacy leaders & technology experts to share, discuss & work towards a solution to the nationwide concern of bringing literacy success to all students. Through quality speakers & relevant topics, TRLD gives educators ideas & strategies to immediately implement with students with high incidence disabilities.
Location: Hyatt Regency San Francisco, San Francisco, CA, USA
Jan 26-28, 2006

**Westpack**
Sponsored by Canon Communications
11444 W Olympic Blvd, Suite 900, Los Angeles, CA 90064, United States
*Tel:* 310-445-4200 *Fax:* 310-996-9499
*Web Site:* www.cancom.com; www.canontradeshows.com
Location: Anaheim Convention Center, Anaheim, CA, USA
Jan 31-Feb 2, 2006

## FEBRUARY

**Antiques & Fine Arts Exhibition/Luxembourg Book Festival**
Sponsored by LuxExpo
10 circuit de la Foire Internationale, 1347 Luxembourg-Kirchberg, Luxembourg
*Tel:* 43 99 1 *Fax:* 43 99 315
*E-mail:* info@luxexpo.lu
*Web Site:* www.luxexpo.lu
*Key Personnel*
Contact: Francine Scheikin *E-mail:* scheikin@luxexpo.lu
Location: LuxExpo Luxembourg Conference & Exhibition Center, Luxembourg, Luxembourg
Feb 3-6, 2006

**Association of American Publishers Professional & Scholarly Publishing Divison Annual Meeting**
Sponsored by Association of American Publishers (AAP)
71 Fifth Ave, 2nd fl, New York, NY 10003-3004, United States

*Tel:* 212-255-0200 *Fax:* 212-255-7007
*Web Site:* www.publishers.org
*Key Personnel*
Pres & CEO: Patricia S Schroeder *Tel:* 202-347-3375 *Fax:* 202-347-3690
Location: Renaissance Mayflower Hotel, Washington, DC, USA
Feb 6-8, 2006

**Association of American Publishers School Division Annual Meeting**
Sponsored by Association of American Publishers (AAP)
71 Fifth Ave, 2nd fl, New York, NY 10003-3004, United States
*Tel:* 212-255-0200 *Fax:* 212-255-7007
*Web Site:* www.publishers.org
*Key Personnel*
Pres & CEO: Patricia S Schroeder *Tel:* 202-347-3375 *Fax:* 202-347-3690
Location: Summy Isles, FL, USA
Feb 9-10, 2006

**Christian Booksellers' Convention**
Sponsored by Christian Booksellers' Convention (CBC) Ltd
PO Box 148, Uckfield, East Sussex TN22 5GR, United Kingdom
*Tel:* (08125) 840254 *Fax:* (08125) 840068
*E-mail:* cbc@cbcltd.co.uk
*Web Site:* www.cbcltd.co.uk
*Key Personnel*
Conference Organiser: Norman Nibloe
Location: International Centre, Telford, UK
Feb 27-March 1, 2006

**Dog Writers' Association of America Annual Meeting**
Sponsored by Dog Writers' Association of America Inc (DWAA)
173 Union Rd, Coatesville, PA 19320, United States
*Tel:* 610-384-2436 *Fax:* 610-384-2471
*E-mail:* rhydowen@aol.com
*Web Site:* www.dwaa.org
*Key Personnel*
Pres: Ranny Green
Sec: Pat Santi
Location: Southgate Hotel, New York, NY, USA
Feb 12, 2006

**The Federation of Children's Book Groups Annual Conference**
Sponsored by Federation of Children's Book Groups
2 Bridge Wood View, Horsforth, Leeds, W Yorks LS18 5PE, United Kingdom
*Tel:* (0113) 2588910
*E-mail:* info@fcbg.org.uk
*Web Site:* www.fcbg.org.uk
*Key Personnel*
Contact: M Simkin
Theme "Happy Ever After".
Location: The Paragon Hotel, Birmingham, UK
Feb 24-26, 2006

**Graphics of the Americas**
Sponsored by Printing Association of Florida Inc
6095 NW 167 St, Suite D7, Hialeah, FL 33015, United States
*Tel:* 305-558-4855 *Toll Free Tel:* 800-749-4855 *Fax:* 305-823-8965
*E-mail:* tradeshow@pafgraf.org
*Web Site:* www.graphicsoftheamericas.com
*Key Personnel*
VP, Trade Shows: Chris Price *Tel:* 305-558-4855, ext 18 *E-mail:* cprice@pafgraf.org
Location: Miami Beach Convention Center, Miami Beach, FL, USA
Feb 3-5, 2006

**International Book Fair/Los Angeles Book Fair**
Sponsored by Antiquarian Booksellers' Association of America
20 W 44 St, 4th fl, New York, NY 10036-6604, United States
*Tel:* 212-944-8291 *Fax:* 212-944-8293
*E-mail:* hq@abaa.org
*Web Site:* www.abaa.org
*Key Personnel*
Dir: Liane Wade
Co Dir: Susan Dixon
Location: Los Angeles, CA, USA
Feb 2006

**National Press Foundation Annual Awards Dinner**
Sponsored by The National Press Foundation
1211 Connecticut Ave NW, Suite 310, Washington, DC 20036, United States
*Tel:* 202-663-7280 *Fax:* 202-530-2855
*E-mail:* npf@nationalpress.org
*Web Site:* www.nationalpress.org
*Key Personnel*
Pres: Bob Meyers
Dir of Progs: Nolan Walters
Dir of Devt & Mktg: Lisa Peckler
Dir of Opers: Donna Washington
Asst to the Pres: Kashmir Hill
Location: Washington Hilton, Washington, DC, USA
Feb 23, 2006

**PRIMEX 2006 (Print Media Executive Summit)**
Sponsored by IDEAlliance
100 Daingerfield Rd, Alexandria, VA 22314, United States
*Tel:* 703-837-1070 *Fax:* 703-837-1072
*E-mail:* info@idealliance.org
*Web Site:* www.idealliance.org
*Key Personnel*
Dir of Events: Georgia Volakis *Tel:* 703-837-1075 *E-mail:* gvolakis@idealliance.org
Location: Renaissance Vinoy Resort & Golf Club, St Petersburg, FL, USA
Feb 6-8, 2006

**Print Buyers Conference**
Sponsored by Pacific Printing & Imaging Association
1400 SW Fifth Ave, Suite 815, Portland, OR 97201, United States
*Toll Free Tel:* 877-762-7742 *Toll Free Fax:* 800-824-1911
*E-mail:* info@pacprinting.org
*Web Site:* www.pacprinting.org
*Key Personnel*
Exec Dir: Marcus Sassaman
Location: Hyatt Regency San Francisco, San Francisco, CA, USA
Feb 2006

**Southern California Writers' Conference San Diego**
Division of Random Cove, IE
1010 University Ave, Suite 54, San Diego, CA 92103, United States
*Tel:* 619-233-4651 *Fax:* 619-233-4651
*E-mail:* wewrite@writersconference.com
*Web Site:* www.writersconference.com
*Key Personnel*
Exec Dir: Michael Gregory *E-mail:* msg@writersconference.com
Location: Red Lion Hanalei, San Diego, CA, USA
Feb 17-20, 2006

**Winter Conference on Writing & Illustrating for Children**
Sponsored by Society of Children's Book Writers & Illustrators (SCBWI)

8271 Beverly Blvd, Los Angeles, CA 90048, United States
*Tel:* 323-782-1010 *Fax:* 323-782-1892
*E-mail:* conference@scbwi.org
*Web Site:* www.scbwi.org
*Key Personnel*
Pres: Steve Mooser
Always held the beginning of February.
Location: Hilton New York, Avenue of the Americas, New York, NY, USA
Feb 3-5, 2006

**Xplor Global Conference**
Sponsored by Xplor International
24238 Hawthorne Blvd, Torrance, CA 90505-6505, United States
*Tel:* 310-373-3633 *Toll Free Tel:* 800-669-7567 (ext 521) *Fax:* 310-375-4240
*E-mail:* info@xplor.org
*Web Site:* www.xplor.org
Location: Miami Beach Convention Center, Miami Beach, FL, USA
Feb 1-5, 2006

# SPRING

**Binding, Finishing & Distribution Seminar**
Sponsored by Research & Engineering Council of NAPL (National Association for Printing Leadership)
75 W Century Rd, Paramus, NJ 07652-1408, United States
*Tel:* 201-634-9600 *Toll Free Tel:* 800-642-6275 *Fax:* 201-634-0327
*E-mail:* information@napl.org
*Web Site:* www.napl.org
Seminar designed for bindery managers, manufacturing/operations executives & warehouse supervisors.
*Shipping Address:* 816 Rappahannock Dr, White Stone, VA 22578, United States
Location: IL, USA
Spring 2006

**DGI Online Conference & Annual Meeting**
Sponsored by Deutsche Gesellschaft fur Informationswissenschaft und Informationspraxis eV (The Association for Information Science & Practice)
Ostbahnhofstr 13, 60314 Frankfurt am Main, Germany
*Tel:* (069) 43 03 13 *Fax:* (069) 49 09 09 6
*E-mail:* online@dgi-info.de
*Web Site:* www.dgi-info.de
Location: Frankfurt, Germany
Spring 2006

**ECPA Management Conference**
Sponsored by Evangelical Christian Publishers Association
4816 S Ash Ave, Suite 101, Tempe, AZ 85282-7735, United States
*Tel:* 480-966-3998 *Fax:* 480-966-1944
*E-mail:* info@ecpa.org
*Web Site:* www.ecpa.org
*Key Personnel*
Pres: Mark Kuyper *E-mail:* mkuyper@ecpa.org
Spring 2006

**Izmir Book Fair**
Sponsored by Tuyap Fuar ve Kongre Merkezi (Tuyap Fairs & Exhibitions Organization Inc)
E-5 Karayolu Gurpinar Kavsagi, Beylikduzu/Buyukcekmece, 34522 Istanbul, Turkey
*Tel:* (0212) 886 68 43 *Fax:* (0212) 886 62 43
*E-mail:* artlink@tuyap.com.tr
*Web Site:* www.tuyap.com.tr
Annual event organized in co-operation with the Turkish Publishers Association.

Location: Izmir Culture Park Fair Venue, Izmir, Turkey
Spring 2006

## World Book Fair
Sponsored by Times Business Information Pte Ltd
Division of Times Publishing Ltd
Times Centre, One New Industrial Rd, Singapore 536196, Singapore
*Tel:* 6213 9288 *Fax:* 6285 0161
*E-mail:* tceexh@tpl.com.sg
*Web Site:* www.bookfair.com.sg
*Key Personnel*
Contact: Christine Ngor *E-mail:* christineng@tpl.com.sg
9 day event.
Location: Suntec Singapore International Convention & Exhibition Centre, Singapore, Singapore
Spring 2006

# MARCH

## AAAA Media Conference & Trade Show
Sponsored by American Association of Advertising Agencies (AAAA)
405 Lexington Ave, 18th fl, New York, NY 10174-1801, United States
*Tel:* 212-682-2500 *Fax:* 212-573-8968
*E-mail:* aaaaconferences@aaaa.org
*Web Site:* www.aaaa.org
*Key Personnel*
Pres & CEO: O Burtch Drake *E-mail:* obd@aaaa.org
Sr VP, Conferences & Special Events: Karen Proctor *E-mail:* karen@aaaa.org
Conference Mgr: Michelle Montalto *E-mail:* michelle@aaaa.org
Conference Coord: Michelle James *E-mail:* mjames@aaaa.org
Location: Loews Royal Pacific Resort at Universal, Orlando, FL, USA
March 1-3, 2006

## Adelaide Bank Festival of Arts
Sponsored by Adelaide Festival Corp
Level 9, 33 King William St, Adelaide, SA 5000, Australia
Mailing Address: PO Box 8221, Station Arcade, Adelaide, SA 5000, Australia
*Tel:* (08) 8216 4444 *Fax:* (08) 8216 4455
*E-mail:* afa@adelaidefestival.com.au
*Web Site:* www.adelaidefestival.com.au
*Key Personnel*
Artistic Dir: Brett Sheehy
Location: Pioneer Women's Memorial Gardens, King William St, Adelaide, Australia
March 3-19, 2006

## Associated Writing Programs Annual Conference & Bookfair
Sponsored by Association of Writers & Writing Programs (AWP)
George Mason University, MS-1E3, Fairfax, VA 22030-4444, United States
*Tel:* 703-993-4301 *Fax:* 703-993-4302
*E-mail:* awp@awpwriter.org
*Web Site:* www.awpwriter.org
*Key Personnel*
Exec Dir: D W Fenza
Dir of Conferences: Matt Scanlon
Association of writers & writing programs.
Location: Hilton Austin & Austin Convention Center, Austin, TX, USA
March 8-11, 2006

## Association of American Publishers Annual Meeting
Sponsored by Association of American Publishers (AAP)
71 Fifth Ave, 2nd fl, New York, NY 10003-3004, United States
*Tel:* 212-255-0200 *Fax:* 212-255-7007
*Web Site:* www.publishers.org
*Key Personnel*
Pres & CEO: Patricia S Schroeder *Tel:* 202-347-3375 *Fax:* 202-347-3690
Location: New York, NY, USA
March 2006

## Association of American Publishers Annual Meeting for Small & Independent Publishers
Sponsored by Association of American Publishers (AAP)
71 Fifth Ave, 2nd fl, New York, NY 10003-3004, United States
*Tel:* 212-255-0200 *Fax:* 212-255-7007
*Web Site:* www.publishers.org
*Key Personnel*
Pres & CEO: Patricia S Schroeder *Tel:* 202-347-3375 *Fax:* 202-347-3690
Location: New York, NY, USA
March 15, 2006

## Binding Industries Association Executive Leadership Conference
Formerly Binding Industries Association International Spring/Presidents Conference
Sponsored by Binding Industries Association (BIA)
Affiliate of Special Industry Group of Printing Industries of America Inc
100 Daingerfield Rd, Alexandria, VA 22314, United States
*Tel:* 703-519-8137 *Fax:* 703-519-6481
*Web Site:* www.gain.net
*Key Personnel*
Exec Dir: Beth Parrott
Conference for top management held in conjunction with PIA/GATF Presidents Conference. Specially designed educational events & numerous networking activities for BIA members.
Location: Oahu, Hawaii, USA
March 11-16, 2006

## Bologna Children's Book Fair
Sponsored by BolognaFiere SpA
Via della Fiera, 20, 40128 Bologna, Italy
*Tel:* (051) 282 111 *Fax:* (051) 637 40 04
*E-mail:* dir.sogn@bolognafiere.it; bookfair@bolognafiere.it
*Web Site:* www.bookfair.bolognafiere.it
Location: BolognaFiere Exhibition Centre, Bologna, Italy
March 27-30, 2006

## BookTech Conference & Expo
Sponsored by BookTech
401 N Broad St, 5th Fl, Philadelphia, PA 19108, United States
*Toll Free Tel:* 888-627-2630 *Fax:* 215-409-0100
*E-mail:* tradeshows@napco.com
*Web Site:* www.booktechexpo.com
BookTech incorporates the PrintMedia Conference & Expo & the In-Plant Graphics Conference plus a world-class expo on publishing & printing solutions providers.
Location: Hilton New York, 1335 Avenue of the Americas, New York, NY, USA
March 20-22, 2006

## Buch-IBO
Sponsored by Boersenverein des Deutschen Buchhandels, Landesverband Baden-Wuerttemberg eV (Association of Publishers & Booksellers in Baden-Wuerttemberg eV)

Division of Internationale Bodensee-Messe, Friedrichshafen
Paulinenstr 53, 70178 Stuttgart, Germany
*Tel:* (0711) 61941-0 *Fax:* (0711) 61941-44
*E-mail:* post@buchhandelsverband.de
*Web Site:* www.buchhandelsverband.de
March 18-26, 2006

## CAMEX
Sponsored by National Association of College Stores (NACS)
500 E Lorain St, Oberlin, OH 44074, United States
*Tel:* 440-775-7777 *Toll Free Tel:* 800-622-7498 *Fax:* 440-775-4769
*E-mail:* info@nacs.org
*Web Site:* www.nacs.org; www.camex.org
*Key Personnel*
CEO: Brian Cartier
PR Dir: Laura Nakoneczny *Tel:* 440-775-7777, ext 2351 *E-mail:* lnakoneczny@nacs.org
Conference & tradeshow dedicated exclusively to the more than $11 billion collegiate retailing industry.
Location: George R Brown Convention Center, Houston, TX, USA
March 3-7, 2006

## Docugroup 2006
Sponsored by Docucorp International
Lincoln One Centre, 6500 LBJ Freeway, Suite 300, Dallas, TX 75240, United States
*Tel:* 214-891-6500 *Fax:* 214-987-8187
*E-mail:* info@docucorp.com
*Web Site:* www.docucorp.com
*Key Personnel*
Pres & CEO: Michael D Andereck
Location: Hilton Dallas Lincoln Centre, Dallas, TX, USA
March 26-29, 2006

## FOSE
Sponsored by Post Newsweek Tech Media
10 G St NE, Suite 500, Washington, DC 20002-4228, United States
*Tel:* 202-772-2500 *Toll Free Tel:* 866-447-6864 *Fax:* 202-771-2511
*E-mail:* fose.exhibit@postnewsweektech.com
*Web Site:* www.fose.com; www.postnewsweektech.com
*Key Personnel*
VP, Trade Shows: Lorenz Hassenstein *Tel:* 202-772-5738 *E-mail:* lhassenstein@postnewsweektech.com
Dir: Gloria Lombardo *Tel:* 203-381-9245 *E-mail:* glombardo@postnewsweektech.com
Trade Show Opers Mgr: Lauri Nichols *Tel:* 202-772-5750 *E-mail:* lnichols@postnewsweektech.com
Location: Washington Convention Center, Washington, DC, USA
March 7-9, 2006

## Inter American Press Association Mid-Year Meeting
Sponsored by Inter American Press Association (IAPA)
Jules Dubois Bldg, 1801 SW Third Ave, Miami, FL 33129, United States
*Tel:* 305-634-2465 *Fax:* 305-635-2272
*E-mail:* info@sipiapa.org
*Web Site:* www.sipiapa.org
*Key Personnel*
Exec Dir: Julio E Munoz
Location: Quito, Ecuador
March 17-20, 2006

## Leipzig Book Fair
Sponsored by Leipziger Messe GmbH, Projektteam Buchmesse
Messe-Allee 1, 04356 Leipzig, Germany

Mailing Address: Postfach 100 720, 04007
Leipzig, Germany
*Tel:* (0341) 678 8240 *Fax:* (0341) 678 8242
*E-mail:* info@leipziger-buchmesse.de
*Web Site:* www.leipziger-buchmesse.de
*Key Personnel*
Exhibition Dir: Oliver Zille *Tel:* (0341) 678 8241
Held annually in conjunction with The Leipzig
Antiquarian Book Fair.
Location: Neues Messegelande, Leipzig, Germany
March 16-19, 2006

**Literary Festival**
Sponsored by Vystaviste Flora Olomouc as
Wolkerova 17, 771 11 Olomouc, Czech Republic
Mailing Address: PO Box 46, 771 11 Olomouc,
Czech Republic
*Tel:* (0585) 726 111 *Fax:* (0585) 413 370
*E-mail:* info@flora-ol.cz
*Web Site:* www.flora-ol.cz
Location: Olomouc, Czech Republic
March 2006

**London Book Fair**
Sponsored by Reed Exhibitions (UK)
Division of Reed Business
Oriel House, 26 The Quadrant, Richmond, Surrey
TW9 1DL, United Kingdom
*Tel:* (020) 8910 7910 *Fax:* (020) 8910 2171
*E-mail:* esther.camps.linnell@reedexpo.co.uk
*Web Site:* www.lbf-virtual.com
*Telex:* 8951389 ITFLONG
*Key Personnel*
Exhibition Dir: Alistair Burtenshaw
*E-mail:* alistair.burtenshaw@reedexpo.co.uk
Key Acct Mgr: Emma House *E-mail:* emma.
house@reedexpo.co.uk
Sponsored by The Booksellers Association of the
United Kingdom & Ireland Limited. Spring
publishing event attended by publishers, book-
sellers, literary agents. librarians, authors, pro-
duction & content managers & international
rights agents.
Location: ExCel, London, UK
March 5-7, 2006

**National Association of Printing Ink
Manufacturers Annual Convention**
Sponsored by National Association of Printing
Ink Manufacturers (NAPIM)
581 Main St, Woodbridge, NJ 07095, United
States
*Tel:* 732-855-1525 *Fax:* 732-855-1838
*E-mail:* napim@napim.org
*Web Site:* www.napim.org
*Key Personnel*
Exec Dir: James E Coleman
Event Coord: Sue Coleman
Location: La Costa Resort & Spa, Carlsbad, CA,
USA
March 18-22, 2006

**National Newspaper Association Annual
Government Affairs Conference**
Sponsored by National Newspaper Association
PO Box 5737, Arlington, VA 22205-9998, United
States
*Tel:* 703-465-8808 *Fax:* 703-812-4555
*E-mail:* info@nna.org
*Web Site:* www.nna.org
Location: Wyndham Washington Hotel, Washing-
ton, DC, USA
March 8-11, 2006

**Plano Book Festival for Adult Literacy**
Sponsored by Collin County Adult Literacy
Council
PO Box 941802, Plano, TX 75094, United States
*Tel:* 972-633-9603
*Web Site:* www.planobookfestival.com

The purpose of the festival is to increase awareness of & support for adults who do not have
the literacy skills necessary for everyday living.
Location: Downtown Plano, Plano, TX, USA
March 26, 2006

**Salon du Livre de Paris**
Sponsored by Reed Expositions France
Subsidiary of Reed Exhibition Companies
11 rue du Colonel Pierre Avia, 75726 Paris Cedex
15, France
*Tel:* (01) 41 90 47 47 *Fax:* (01) 41 90 47 49
*E-mail:* livre@reedexpo.fr
*Web Site:* www.salondulivreparis.com
*Key Personnel*
Fair Mgr: Taya de Reynies
*E-mail:* taya_reynies@reedexpo.fr
PR Mgr: Catherine Vauselle *E-mail:* catherine.
vauselle@reedexpo.fr
Annual international publishing event for publish-
ers, booksellers, teachers & librarians. Open to
the trade & the public.
Location: Paris Expo, Hall 1, Porte de Versailles,
Paris, France
March 17-22, 2006

**Virginia Festival of the Book**
Sponsored by Virginia Foundation for the Hu-
manities
145 Ednam Dr, Charlottesville, VA 22903, United
States
*Tel:* 434-924-6890 *Fax:* 434-296-4714
*E-mail:* vabook@virginia.edu
*Web Site:* www.vabook.org
*Key Personnel*
Program Dir: Nancy Damon *Tel:* 434-924-7548
*E-mail:* ndamon@virginia.edu
Assoc Program Dir: Kevin McFadden
*E-mail:* kmcfadden@virginia.edu
Annual free public festival for children & adults
featuring authors, illustrators, publishers, pub-
licists, agents & other book professionals in
panel discussions & readings for adults & chil-
dren of all ages. More than 200 authors invited
annually.
Location: Charlottesville, VA, USA
March 22-26, 2006

# APRIL

**AAAA Management Conference**
Sponsored by American Association of Advertis-
ing Agencies (AAAA)
405 Lexington Ave, 18th fl, New York, NY
10174-1801, United States
*Tel:* 212-682-2500 *Fax:* 212-573-8968
*E-mail:* aaaaconferences@aaaa.org
*Web Site:* www.aaaa.org
*Key Personnel*
Pres & CEO: O Burtch Drake *E-mail:* obd@aaaa.
org
Sr VP, Conferences & Special Events: Karen
Proctor *E-mail:* karen@aaaa.org
Conference Mgr: Michelle Montalto
*E-mail:* michelle@aaaa.org
Conference Coord: Michelle James
*E-mail:* mjames@aaaa.org
Location: The Phoenician, Scottsdale, AZ, USA
April 5-7, 2006

**African American Children's Book Festival**
Sponsored by Kids Cultural Books
811 Elaine Dr, Stamford, CT 06902, United
States
*Tel:* 203-359-6925 *Fax:* 203-359-3226
*E-mail:* info@kidsculturalbooks.org
*Web Site:* www.kidsculturalbooks.org

Location: Cathedral of St John the Divine, New
York, NY, USA
April 29, 2006

**Alberta Library Conference**
Sponsored by Library Association of Alberta
80 Baker Crescent NW, Calgary, AB T2L 1R4,
Canada
*Tel:* 403-284-5818 *Toll Free Tel:* 877-522-5550
*Fax:* 403-282-6646
*E-mail:* info@laa.ab.ca
*Web Site:* www.laa.ab.ca
*Key Personnel*
Pres: Judy Moore
Exec Dir: Christine Sheppard *E-mail:* christine.
sheppard@shaw.ca
Location: Jasper Park Lodge, Jasper, AB, Canada
April 27-30, 2006

**Arizona Book Festival**
Sponsored by Arizona Humanities Council
1242 N Central, Phoenix, AZ 85004, United
States
*Tel:* 602-257-0335 *Fax:* 602-257-0392
*Web Site:* www.azbookfestival.org/index.html
*Key Personnel*
Dir: Jill Bernstein
Location: Carnegie Center, Phoenix, AZ, USA
April 1, 2006

**Association of Directory Publishers Annual
Meeting**
Sponsored by Association of Directory Publishers
116 Cass St, Traverse City, MI 49684-2505,
United States
Mailing Address: PO Box 1929, Traverse City,
MI 49685-1929, United States
*Toll Free Tel:* 800-267-9002 *Fax:* 231-486-2182
*E-mail:* hq@adp.org
*Web Site:* www.adp.org
*Key Personnel*
Pres & CEO: R Lawrence Angove *E-mail:* larry.
angove@adp.org
Location: Saddlebrook Resort, Tampa, FL, USA
April 6-8, 2006

**BMI Management Conference**
Sponsored by Book Manufacturers' Institute Inc
(BMI)
2 Armand Beach Dr, Suite 1-B, Palm Coast, FL
32137, United States
*Tel:* 386-986-4552 *Fax:* 386-986-4553
*E-mail:* info@bmibook.com
*Web Site:* www.bmibook.org
*Key Personnel*
Exec VP: Bruce W Smith
Location: The Biltmore Hotel, Coral Gables, FL,
USA
April 29-May 2, 2006

**English Association Centenary Conference**
Sponsored by The English Association
University of Leicester, University Rd, Leicester
LE1 7RH, United Kingdom
*Tel:* (0116) 252 3982 *Fax:* (0116) 252 2301
*E-mail:* engassoc@le.ac.uk
*Web Site:* www.le.ac.uk/engassoc
*Key Personnel*
Chief Exec: Helen Lucas
Asst to Chief Exec: Julia Hughes
Location: St Catherines College, Oxford, UK
April 22, 2006

**Gutenberg & Digital Outlook**
Sponsored by NPES The Association for Sup-
pliers of Printing, Publishing & Converting
Technologies
1899 Preston White Dr, Reston, VA 20191-4367,
United States
*Tel:* 703-264-7200 *Fax:* 703-620-0994
*E-mail:* npes@npes.org

*Web Site:* www.gasc.org
*Key Personnel*
Pres: Regis J Delmontagne
Dir, Communs & Mktg: Carol J Hurlburt
*E-mail:* churlbur@npes.org
Location: Los Angeles Convention Center, Los Angeles, CA, USA
April 20-22, 2006

**Gutenberg Festival**
Sponsored by Graphic Arts Show Company
1899 Preston White Dr, Reston, VA 20191-4367, United States
*Tel:* 703-264-7200 *Fax:* 703-620-9187
*E-mail:* info@gasc.org
*Web Site:* www.gasc.org
*Key Personnel*
Dir, Communs: David Poulos
Annual trade show for graphic design, digital prepress, printing, publishing & converting.
Location: Los Angeles Convention Center, Los Angeles, CA, USA
April 20-22, 2006

**Infosystem**
Sponsored by Poznan International Fair Ltd
ul Glogowska 14, 60-734 Poznan, Poland
*Tel:* (061) 869 2000 *Fax:* (061) 866 5827
*E-mail:* infosystem@mtp.pl
*Web Site:* www.infosystem.pl
*Key Personnel*
Proj Mgr: Jerzy Kaczmarek *Tel:* (061) 869 2138 *Fax:* (061) 869 2956 *E-mail:* jerzy.kaczmarek@mtp.pl
International fair of telecommunications, information technology & electronics.
Location: Poznan International Fairground, Poznan, Poland
April 2006

**International Children's Book Day**
Sponsored by International Board on Books for Young People (IBBY)
Nonnenweg 12, Postfach, 4003 Basel, Switzerland
*Tel:* (061) 272 29 17 *Fax:* (061) 272 27 57
*E-mail:* ibby@ibby.org
*Web Site:* www.ibby.org
*Key Personnel*
Pres: Peter Schneck
Admin Dir: Liz Page
On or around Hans Christian Andersen's birthday, April 2nd, International Children's Book day (ICBD) is celebrated to inspire a love of reading & to call attention to children's books. Each year a different national section has the opportunity to be the international sponsor. It decides upon a theme & invites a prominent author to write a message to the children of the world & a well-known illustrator to design a poster. These materials are used in different ways to promote books & reading around the world.
Location: Slovakia
April 2, 2006

**International Reading Association Annual Convention**
Sponsored by International Reading Association
800 Barksdale Rd, Newark, DE 19714, United States
Mailing Address: PO Box 8139, Newark, DE 19714-8139, United States
*Tel:* 302-731-1600 *Fax:* 302-731-1057
*E-mail:* conferences@reading.org
*Web Site:* www.reading.org
*Key Personnel*
Pres: Dick Allington
Exec Dir: Alan E Farstrup
Great books inspire great teachers & great teachers inspire the world.

Location: McCormick Place Convention Center, Chicago, IL, USA
April 30-May 4, 2006

**Los Angeles Times Festival of Books**
Sponsored by Los Angeles Times
Division of Tribune Co
202 W First St, 6th fl, Los Angeles, CA 90012, United States
*Tel:* 213-237-5000 *Toll Free Tel:* 800-528-4637 *Fax:* 213-237-2335
*Web Site:* www.latimes.com/festivalofbooks
Location: UCLA Campus, Los Angeles, CA, USA
April 29-30, 2006

**MILIA: World Interactive Content Forum**
Sponsored by Reed Midem
Subsidiary of Reed Exhibition Companies
11 rue du Colonnel Pierre Avia, 75015 Paris, France
Mailing Address: BP 572, 75726 Paris Cedex 15, France
*Tel:* (01) 41 90 44 00 *Fax:* (01) 41 90 44 70
*E-mail:* info@milia.com; milia.conferences@reedmidem.com
*Web Site:* www.milia.com
*Key Personnel*
Dir: Ted Baracos *Tel:* (01) 41 90 46 30 *Fax:* (01) 41 90 44 70 *E-mail:* ted.baracos@reedmidem.com
The combination of MIPTV & MILIA, the world's leading audiovisual & digital content market, symbolises the all-important convergence of entertainment & technology around the world..
Location: Palais des Festivals, Cannes, France
April 3-7, 2006

**National Library Week**
Sponsored by American Library Association (ALA)
50 E Huron St, Chicago, IL 60611, United States
*Tel:* 312-944-6780 *Toll Free Tel:* 800-545-2433 *Fax:* 312-944-8520
*E-mail:* pio@ala.org
*Web Site:* www.ala.org/events
*Key Personnel*
Public Info Dir: Mark Gould
Press Officer: Larra Clark *E-mail:* lclark@ala.org
Location: Nationwide throughout the USA
April 2-8, 2006

**Newspaper Association of America Annual Convention**
Sponsored by Newspaper Association of America (NAA)
1921 Gallows Rd, Suite 600, Vienna, VA 22182, United States
*Tel:* 703-902-1600 *Fax:* 703-902-1790
*E-mail:* willa@naa.org
*Web Site:* www.naa.org
*Key Personnel*
Pres & CEO: John Sturm
Meetings Mgr: Kristen Andersen Fleming
Location: Fairmont Chicago, Chicago, IL, USA
April 2-5, 2006

**NEXPO®**
Sponsored by Newspaper Association of America (NAA)
1921 Gallows Rd, Suite 600, Vienna, VA 22182, United States
*Tel:* 703-902-1600 *Fax:* 703-902-1843
*E-mail:* sarns@naa.org
*Web Site:* www.nexpo.com
*Key Personnel*
Dir of Exhibition Sales: Brad Smith
Annual technical exposition & conference for newspapers.

Location: McCormick Place Conference, Chicago, IL, USA
April 1-4, 2006

**North American Agricultural Journalists Spring Meeting**
Sponsored by North American Agricultural Journalists
2604 Cumberland Ct, College Station, TX 77845, United States
*Tel:* 979-845-2872 *Fax:* 979-845-2414
*Web Site:* naaj.tamu.edu
*Key Personnel*
Exec Sec, Treas: Kathleen Phillips *E-mail:* kaphillips@tamu.edu
Location: Washington, DC, USA
April 2006

**Northern Arizona Book Festival**
PO Box 1871, Flagstaff, AZ 86002-1871, United States
*Tel:* 928-380-8682
*E-mail:* rbyrkit@nazbookfestival.org
*Web Site:* www.nazbookfestival.org
*Key Personnel*
Exec Dir: Rebecca Byrkit
The Northern Arizona Book Festival offers a three day weekend of readings, workshops, panel discussions & other literary events for readers & writers of all ages. The festival is held at a variety of venues in historic Flagstaff, AZ.
Location: Flagstaff, AZ, USA
April 21-23, 2006

**Paper Week**
Sponsored by American Forest & Paper Association
1111 19 St NW, Suite 800, Washington, DC 20036, United States
*Tel:* 202-463-2700 *Toll Free Tel:* 800-878-8878 *Fax:* 202-463-4703
*E-mail:* info@afandpa.org
*Web Site:* www.afandpa.org; www.paperweek.org
*Key Personnel*
Pres & CEO: W Henson Moore
Location: Waldorf-Astoria Hotel & Towers, New York, NY, USA
April 9-12, 2006

**Print Distribution Conference 2006**
Sponsored by IDEAlliance
100 Daingerfield Rd, Alexandria, VA 22314, United States
*Tel:* 703-837-1070 *Fax:* 703-837-1072
*E-mail:* info@idealliance.org
*Web Site:* www.idealliance.org
*Key Personnel*
Dir of Events: Georgia Volakis *Tel:* 703-837-1075 *E-mail:* gvolakis@idealliance.org
Location: Renaissance Vinoy Resort & Golf Club, St Petersburg, FL, USA
April 23-26, 2006

**The Quest for Excellence**
Sponsored by American Society for Quality
600 N Plankinton Ave, Milwaukee, WI 53203, United States
Mailing Address: PO Box 3005, Milwaukee, WI 53201-3005, United States
*Tel:* 414-272-8575 *Toll Free Tel:* 800-248-1946 *Fax:* 414-272-1734
*E-mail:* cs@asq.org
*Web Site:* www.asq.org
*Telex:* 31-6567
*Key Personnel*
Exec Dir & Chief Strategic Officer: Paul Borawski
Events Mgmt Mgr: Shirley Krentz
April 2006

## Society of American Business Editors & Writers Annual Convention & Exhibition

Sponsored by Society of American Business Editors & Writers Inc
University of Missouri, School of Journalism, 385 Mcreynolds Hall, Columbia, MO 65211-1200, United States
*Tel:* 573-882-7862 *Fax:* 573-884-1372
*E-mail:* sabew@missouri.edu
*Web Site:* www.sabew.org
*Key Personnel*
Exec Dir: Carrie M Paden *E-mail:* padenc@missouri.edu
Exec Asst: Vicky Edwards
Location: Minneapolis Hyatt Regency, Minneapolis/St Paul, MN, USA
April 30-May 2, 2006

## Southern Kentucky Book Fest

1906 College Heights Blvd, Cravens Library 106, Bowling Green, KY 42101, United States
*Tel:* 270-745-5016 *Fax:* 270-745-6422
*E-mail:* jayne.pelaski@wku.edu
*Web Site:* www.sokybookfest.org
Location: Sloan Convention Center, Bowling Green, KY, USA
April 7-8, 2006

## UK Serials Group Annual Conference & Exhibition

Sponsored by UK Serials Group
Bowman & Hillier Bldg, The Old Brewery, Priory Lane, Burford, Oxon OX18 4SG, United Kingdom
*Tel:* (01635) 254292 *Fax:* (01635) 253826
*E-mail:* alison@uksg.org
*Web Site:* www.uksg.org
*Key Personnel*
Busn Mgr: Alison Whitehorn
Annual 3 day event open to everyone.
Location: University of Warwick, Coventry, UK
April 3-5, 2006

## VUE/POINT Conference

Sponsored by NPES The Association for Suppliers of Printing, Publishing & Converting Technologies
1899 Preston White Dr, Reston, VA 20191-4367, United States
*Tel:* 703-264-7200 *Fax:* 703-620-0994
*E-mail:* npes@npes.org
*Web Site:* www.gasc.org
*Key Personnel*
Pres: Regis J Delmontagne
Dir, Communs & Mktg: Carol J Hurlburt
  *E-mail:* churlbur@npes.org
Trade Association representing companies which manufacture equipment, systems, software & supplies used in printing, publishing & converting.
Location: Orlando, FL, USA
April 10-12, 2006

## Young People's Poetry Week

Sponsored by The Children's Book Council (CBC)
12 W 37 St, 2nd fl, New York, NY 10118-7480, United States
*Tel:* 212-966-1990 *Toll Free Tel:* 800-999-2160 (orders only) *Fax:* 212-966-2073
  *Toll Free Fax:* 888-807-9355 (orders only)
*Web Site:* www.cbcbooks.org
*Key Personnel*
Pres: Paula Quint
Location: Nationwide throughout the USA
April 10-16, 2006

# MAY

## ABA Convention & Trade Exhibit

Sponsored by American Booksellers Association
200 White Plains Rd, Tarrytown, NY 10591, United States
*Tel:* 914-591-2665 *Toll Free Tel:* 800-637-0037
  *Fax:* 914-591-2720
*E-mail:* info@bookweb.org
*Web Site:* www.bookweb.org
*Key Personnel*
Assoc Dir of Programming & Constituent Groups Liaison: Kristen Gilligan
Held in conjunction with BookExpo America.
Location: Washington Convention Center, Washington, DC, USA
May 18-21, 2006

## AIIM 2006 Conference & Exposition

Sponsored by Questex Media Group Inc
275 Grove St, Suite 2-130, Newton, MA 02466, United States
*Tel:* 617-219-8300 *Fax:* 617-219-8310
*E-mail:* aiim@aiim.org
*Web Site:* www.aiim.org
*Key Personnel*
Show Dir: Christina Condos
Location: Pennsylvania Convention Center, Philadelphia, PA, USA
May 16-18, 2006

## ASQ World Conference on Quality & Improvement

Sponsored by American Society for Quality
600 N Plankinton Ave, Milwaukee, WI 53203, United States
*Tel:* 414-272-8575 *Toll Free Tel:* 800-248-1946
  *Fax:* 414-272-1734
*E-mail:* cs@asq.org
*Web Site:* www.asq.org
*Telex:* 31-6567
*Key Personnel*
Exec Dir & Chief Strategic Officer: Paul Borawski
Events Mgmt Mgr: Shirley Krentz
Location: Midwest Airlines Center, Milwaukee, WI, USA
May 1-3, 2006

## BookExpo America (BEA)

Sponsored by Reed Exhibitions
Affiliate of Reed Exhibition Companies
383 Main Ave, Norwalk, CT 06851, United States
*Tel:* 203-840-5614 *Toll Free Tel:* 800-840-5614
  *Fax:* 203-840-5580
*E-mail:* inquiry@bookexpoamerica.com
*Web Site:* bookexpoamerica.com
*Key Personnel*
Industry VP: Chris McCabe *E-mail:* cmccabe@reedexpo.com
Mktg Dir: Tom Kobak *E-mail:* tkobak@reedexpo.com
Dir of Strategic Accts: Steve Rosato
  *E-mail:* srosato@reedexpo.com
Group Sales Dir: Jim Fama *E-mail:* jfama@reedexpo.com
Produced & managed by Reed Exhibitions, BEA is sponsored by American Booksellers Association & Association of American Publishers.
Location: Washington Convention Center, Washington, DC, USA
May 19-21, 2006

## Booksellers Association of the United Kingdom & Ireland Annual Conference

Sponsored by Booksellers Association of the United Kingdom & Ireland Ltd
Minster House, 272 Vauxhall Bridge Rd, London SW1V 1BA, United Kingdom
*Tel:* (020) 7802 0802 *Fax:* (020) 7802 0803
*E-mail:* mail@booksellers.org.uk
*Web Site:* www.booksellers.org.uk
*Key Personnel*
Conference-Events Organiser: Anna O'Kane
  *E-mail:* anna.okane@booksellers.org.uk
Location: Bournemouth International Centre, Exeter Rd, Bournemouth, UK
May 7-9, 2006

## Catholic Press Association of the US and Canada Annual Convention

Sponsored by Catholic Press Association of the US & Canada
3555 Veterans Memorial Hwy, Unit O, Ronkonkoma, NY 11779, United States
*Tel:* 631-471-4730 *Fax:* 631-471-4804
*E-mail:* cathjourn@catholicpress.org
*Web Site:* www.catholicpress.org
*Key Personnel*
Pres: Helen Osman *Tel:* 512-476-4888
  *E-mail:* helen_osman@austindiocese.org
Exec Dir: Owen P McGovern *E-mail:* owen@catholicpress.org
Location: Nashville, TN, USA
May 2006

## Evangelical Press Association Annual Conference

Sponsored by Evangelical Press Association (EPA)
PO Box 28129, Crystal, MN 55428-0129, United States
*Tel:* 763-535-4793 *Fax:* 763-535-4794
*E-mail:* director@epassoc.org
*Web Site:* www.epassoc.org
*Key Personnel*
Exec Dir: Doug Trouten
Location: Orlando Airport Marriott, Orlando, FL, USA
May 7-10, 2006

## EXPOLIT Exposicion de Literatura Cristiana Book Fair

Sponsored by Spanish Evangelical Publishers Association (SEPA)/Associacion de Editores Evangelicos and Editorial Unilit
1360 NW 88 Ave, Miami, FL 33172, United States
*Tel:* 305-503-1191 *Toll Free Tel:* 800-767-7726
  *Fax:* 305-717-6886
*E-mail:* wendy@expolit.com
*Web Site:* www.expolit.com
*Key Personnel*
Pres, EXPOLIT: David Ecklebarger
Program Dir: Marie Tanayo
Spanish Christian Literature Convention.
Location: Sheridan Convention Center, Miami, FL, USA
May 18-23, 2006

## GAA Expo 2006

Sponsored by Gravure Association of America Inc
1200-A Scottsville Rd, Rochester, NY 14624, United States
*Tel:* 585-436-2150 *Fax:* 585-436-7689
*E-mail:* gaa@gaa.org
*Web Site:* www.gaa.org
*Key Personnel*
Meeting Planner: Pamela Schenk
Location: Marriott Richmond, Richmond, VA, USA
May 8-11, 2006

## ICIS '06 International Congress of Imaging Science

Sponsored by Society for Imaging Science & Technology (IS&T)
7003 Kilworth Lane, Springfield, VA 22151, United States
*Tel:* 703-642-9090 *Fax:* 703-642-9094
*E-mail:* info@imaging.org
*Web Site:* www.imaging.org
Held every 4 years.

Location: Hyatt Regency Hotel, Rochester, NY, USA
May 7-12, 2006

**IS&T Archiving Conference**
Sponsored by Society for Imaging Science & Technology (IS&T)
7003 Kilworth Lane, Springfield, VA 22151, United States
*Tel:* 703-642-9090 *Fax:* 703-642-9094
*E-mail:* info@imaging.org
*Web Site:* www.imaging.org
Location: Ottawa, ON, Canada
May 2006

**Nigeria International Book Fair**
Division of Nigerian Book Fair Trust
Literamed Bldg, Plot 45 Oregun Industrial Estate, Alausa Bus-Stop, Ikeja, Lagos State, Nigeria
Mailing Address: PO Box 21068, Ikeja, Lagos State, Nigeria
*Tel:* (01) 4823402; (01) 3451208 *Fax:* (01) 4935258
*E-mail:* info@nibf.org
*Web Site:* www.nibf.org
*Key Personnel*
Exec Secy: Kunle Oyediran
Location: Lagos, Nigeria
May 2006

**ON DEMAND**
Sponsored by Questex Media Group Inc
275 Grove St, Suite 2-130, Newton, MA 02466, United States
*Tel:* 617-219-8300 *Fax:* 617-219-8310
*E-mail:* ondemand@advanstar.com
*Web Site:* www.ondemandexpo.com
*Key Personnel*
Conference Dir: Tom Bliss
Show Dir: Christina Condos
Digital printing & publishing.
Location: Pennsylvania Convention Center, Philadelphia, PA, USA
May 16-18, 2006

**Paper Expo**
Sponsored by Technical Association of the Pulp & Paper Industry (TAPPI)
15 Technology Pkwy S, Norcross, GA 30092, United States
*Tel:* 770-446-1400 *Toll Free Tel:* 800-332-8686 *Fax:* 770-446-6947
*Web Site:* www.tappi.org
*Key Personnel*
Publg Dir: Mary Beth Cornell *E-mail:* mcornell@tappi.org
Corp Rel Dir: Clare Reagan *E-mail:* creagan@tappi.org
Adv Mgr: Vince Saputo *E-mail:* vsaputo@tappi.org
Location: Chattanooga Convention Center, Chattanooga, TN, USA
May 8-10, 2006

**Periodical Writers' Association of Canada Annual General Meeting**
Sponsored by Periodical Writers' Association of Canada
215 Spadina Ave, Suite 123, Toronto, ON M5T 2C7, Canada
*Tel:* 416-504-1645 *Fax:* 416-913-2327
*E-mail:* info@pwac.ca
*Web Site:* www.pwac.ca; www.writers.ca
*Key Personnel*
Exec Dir: John Degan
Location: Ottawa, ON, Canada
May 2006

**Sofia National Book Fair**
Sponsored by Bulgarian Book Association
11 Slaveikov Sq, 1000 Sofia, Bulgaria

Mailing Address: PO Box 1046, 1000 Sofia, Bulgaria
*Tel:* (02) 986 79 93; (02) 986 79 70 *Fax:* (02) 986 79 93
*E-mail:* bba@otel.net; bulgarian.book@gmail.com
*Web Site:* www.bba-bg.org
*Key Personnel*
Sec Gen: Madlena Romanova *E-mail:* bba@otel.net
PR: Dimmo Petrov *E-mail:* bulgarian.book@gmail.com
Location: National Palace of Culture, Sofia, Bulgaria
May 24-28, 2006

**Warsaw International Book Fair**
Sponsored by Ars Polon SA
25 Obroncow St, 03-933 Warsaw, Poland
*Tel:* (022) 509 86 00 *Fax:* (022) 509 86 10
*E-mail:* arspolona@arspolona.com.pl; bookfair@arspolona.com.pl
*Web Site:* www.bookfair.pl
*Key Personnel*
Sec Gen: Ms Joanna Aleksandrowicz *E-mail:* joannaa@arspolona.com.pl
Location: Palace of Culture & Science, Warsaw, Poland
May 18-21, 2006

**Annual Web Offset Association Conference**
Sponsored by Web Offset Association
Division of PIA/GATF
200 Deer Run Rd, Sewickley, PA 15143, United States
*Tel:* 412-741-6860 *Toll Free Tel:* 800-910-4283 *Fax:* 412-259-1800
*Web Site:* www.gain.net
*Key Personnel*
Meetings Asst: Ricardo Vila-Roger *E-mail:* rvilaroger@piagatf.org
Location: Gaylord Palms Resort, Orlando, FL, USA
May 22-24, 2006

## SUMMER

**The National Center for Database Marketing (NCDM)**
Sponsored by Primedia Business Exhibitions
11 River Bend Dr S, Stamford, CT 06907, United States
Mailing Address: PO Box 4254, Stamford, CT 06907-0254, United States
*Tel:* 203-358-9900 *Toll Free Tel:* 800-927-5007 *Fax:* 203-358-5818
*Web Site:* www.primediabusiness.com; www.ncdmsummer.com; www.ncdmwinter.com
Summer 2006

## JUNE

**American Library Association Annual Conference**
Sponsored by American Library Association (ALA)
50 E Huron St, Chicago, IL 60611, United States
*Tel:* 312-280-3200 *Toll Free Tel:* 800-545-2433 *Fax:* 312-944-7841
*E-mail:* ala@ala.org
*Web Site:* www.ala.org
*Key Personnel*
Public Info Dir: Mark Gould
Press Officer: Larra Clark *E-mail:* lclark@ala.org
Dir, Intl Rel: Michael Dowling

Location: New Orleans, LA, USA
June 22-28, 2006

**Association of American University Presses Annual Meeting**
Sponsored by Association of American University Presses (AAUP)
71 W 23 St, Suite 901, New York, NY 10010, United States
*Tel:* 212-989-1010 *Fax:* 212-989-0176; 212-989-0275
*E-mail:* info@aaupnet.org
*Web Site:* www.aaupnet.org
*Key Personnel*
Exec Dir: Peter J Givler
Asst Dir: Timothy Muench
Admin Mgr: Linda McCall
Location: Sheridan Hotel, New Orleans, LA, USA
June 15-18, 2006

**Bibliographical Society of Canada/La Societe bibliographique du Canada Annual Meeting**
Sponsored by Bibliographical Society of Canada/La Societe bibliographique du Canada
PO Box 575, Sta P, Toronto, ON M5S 2T1, Canada
*E-mail:* mcgaughe@yorku.ca
*Web Site:* www.library.utoronto.ca/bsc
*Key Personnel*
Pres: Carl Spadoni
Conference Coord: David McKnight *E-mail:* david.mcknight@mcgill.ca
Location: Toronto, ON, Canada
June 2006

**BookExpo Canada**
Sponsored by Reed Exhibitions Canada
3761 Victoria Park Ave, Unit 1, Toronto, ON M1W 3S2, Canada
*Tel:* 416-491-7565 (Toronto area); 514-845-1125 (Montreal area) *Toll Free Tel:* 888-322-7333 *Fax:* 416-491-7096 (Toronto area); 514-845-8089 (Montreal area) *Toll Free Fax:* 888-633-3376
*Web Site:* www.bookexpo.ca
*Key Personnel*
Show Mgr: Jennifer Sickinger *Tel:* 416-848-1692 *E-mail:* jsickinger@reedexpo.com
Canada's largest book industry event. Sponsored by Canadian Booksellers Association.
Location: Metro Toronto Convention Centre, Toronto, ON, Canada
June 9-12, 2006

**British & Irish Association of Law Librarians Annual Conference**
Sponsored by British & Irish Association of Law Librarians
26 Myton Crescent, Warwick CV34 6QA, United Kingdom
*Tel:* (01926) 491717 *Fax:* (01926) 491717
*Key Personnel*
BIALL Administrator: Susan Frost *E-mail:* susanfrost5@hotmail.com
Location: Brighton, UK
June 15-17, 2006

**The Bronte Society Annual General Meeting**
Sponsored by The Bronte Society
Bronte Parsonage Museum, Church St, Haworth, Keighley, W Yorks BD22 8DR, United Kingdom
*Tel:* (01535) 642323 *Fax:* (01535) 647131
*E-mail:* info@bronte.org.uk
*Web Site:* www.bronte.org.uk
*Key Personnel*
Museum Mgr: Alan Bentley
Location: West Lane Baptist Church, Haworth, W Yorks, UK
June 3, 2006

**Canadian Library Association Annual Convention & Tradeshow**
Sponsored by Canadian Library Association (CLA)
328 Frank St, Ottawa, ON K2P 0X8, Canada
*Tel:* 613-232-9625 *Fax:* 613-563-9895
*E-mail:* info@cla.ca
*Web Site:* www.cla.ca
*Key Personnel*
Pres: Madeleine Lefebvre
Exec Dir: Don Butcher *E-mail:* dbutcher@cla.ca
Location: Ottawa Congress, Ottawa, ON, Canada
June 14-17, 2006

**CGIV 2006: IS&T's Third European Conference on Color in Graphics, Imaging & Vision, including the 6th International Symposium on Multispectral Color Science**
Formerly DPP - International Conference on Digital Production Printing
Sponsored by Society for Imaging Science & Technology (IS&T)
7003 Kilworth Lane, Springfield, VA 22151, United States
*Tel:* 703-642-9090 *Fax:* 703-642-9094
*E-mail:* info@imaging.org
*Web Site:* www.imaging.org
*Key Personnel*
Conference Mgr: Pamela Forness
Location: University of Leeds, Leeds, UK
June 19-22, 2006

**Eastpack: The Power of Packaging**
Sponsored by Canon Communications
11444 W Olympic Blvd, Suite 900, Los Angeles, CA 90064, United States
*Tel:* 310-445-4200 *Fax:* 310-996-9499
*Web Site:* www.cancom.com; www.canontradeshows.com
Location: Jacob K Javits Convention Center, New York, NY, USA
June 6-8, 2006

**European Conference on Managing Directories**
Sponsored by European Association of Directory & Database Publishers (EADP)
127 ave Franklin Roosevelt, 1050 Brussels, Belgium
*Tel:* (02) 646 30 60 *Fax:* (02) 646 36 37
*E-mail:* mailbox@eadp.org
*Web Site:* www.eadp.org
*Key Personnel*
Congress & Conference Officer: Karen Chevalier
*E-mail:* karenchevalier@eadp.org
Location: Hilton Cavalieri, Rome, Italy
June 1-2, 2006

**Gutenberg-Gesellschaft Annual General Meeting**
Sponsored by Gutenberg-Gesellschaft eV (Gutenberg Society)
Liebfrauenplatz 5, 55116 Mainz, Germany
*Tel:* (06131) 22 64 20 *Fax:* (06131) 23 35 30
*E-mail:* gutenberg-gesellschaft@freenet.de
*Web Site:* www.gutenberg-gesellschaft.uni-mainz.de
Location: Mainz, Germany
June 2006

**IEPRC Annual Conference**
Sponsored by International Electronic Publishing Research Centre Ltd (IEPRC)
c/o David Haywood, LCP, Elephant & Castle, London SE1 6SB, United Kingdom
*Tel:* (020) 7514 6938 *Fax:* (020) 7514 6940
*E-mail:* admin@ieprc.org
*Web Site:* www.ieprc.org
June 2006

**International Association of Business Communicators Conference**
Sponsored by International Association of Business Communicators (IABC)
One Hallidie Plaza, Suite 600, San Francisco, CA 94102, United States
*Tel:* 415-544-4700 *Toll Free Tel:* 800-776-4222
*Fax:* 415-544-4747
*E-mail:* conf@iabc.com
*Web Site:* www.iabc.com
*Key Personnel*
Pres: Julie Freeman
Location: Vancouver, BC, Canada
June 2006

**International Association of Music Libraries, Archives & Documentation Centres Conference**
Sponsored by International Association of Music Libraries, Archives & Documentation Centres
c/o National Library of New Zealand, PO Box 1467, Wellington 6001, New Zealand
*Tel:* (04) 474 3039 *Fax:* (04) 474 3035
*Web Site:* www.iaml.info
*Key Personnel*
Secretary General: Roger Flury *E-mail:* roger.flury@natlib.govt.nz
Location: Gothenburg, Sweden
June 18-23, 2006

**International Newsletter & Specialized - Information Conference**
Sponsored by Newsletter & Electronic Publishers Association
1501 Wilson Blvd, Suite 509, Arlington, VA 22209, United States
*Tel:* 703-527-2333 *Toll Free Tel:* 800-356-9302
*Fax:* 703-841-0629
*E-mail:* ncpa@ncwslcttcrs.org
*Web Site:* www.newsletters.org
*Key Personnel*
Exec Dir: Patti Wysocki
Location: Mayflower Hotel, Washington, DC, USA
June 2006

**International Newspaper Financial Executives Annual Conference**
Sponsored by International Newspaper Financial Executives
21525 Ridgetop Circle, Suite 200, Sterling, VA 20166, United States
*Tel:* 703-421-4060
*Web Site:* www.infe.org
*Key Personnel*
VP & Exec Dir: Robert J Kasabian
Location: Del Coronado, Coronado Island, CA, USA
June 17-21, 2006

**International Plate Printers', Die Stampers' & Engravers' Union of North America Mini Meeting**
Sponsored by International Plate Printers', Die Stampers' & Engravers' Union of North America
3957 Smoke Rd, Doylestown, PA 18901, United States
*Tel:* 215-340-2843
*Key Personnel*
Sec & Treas: James Kopernick
Location: Washington, DC, USA
June 2006

**Outdoor Writers Association of America Annual Conference**
Sponsored by Outdoor Writers Association of America
158 Lower Georges Valley Rd, Spring Mills, PA 16875, United States
*Tel:* 814-364-9557 *Fax:* 814-364-9558

*E-mail:* eking4owaa@cs.com
*Web Site:* www.owaa.org
Location: L'auberge du Lac, Lake Charles, LA, USA
June 17-21, 2006

**Print Sales & Marketing Executives Conference**
Sponsored by Printing Industries of America Inc
200 Deer Run Rd, Sewickley, PA 15143, United States
*Tel:* 412-741-6860 *Fax:* 412-741-2311
*E-mail:* piagatf@piagatf.org
*Web Site:* www.gain.net
Location: Stoweflake Resort, Stowe, VT, USA
June 25-28, 2006

**School Library Association Annual Conference**
Sponsored by School Library Association
Unit 2, Lotmead Business Village, Lotmead Farm, Wanborough, Swindon, Wilts SN4 0UY, United Kingdom
*Tel:* (01793) 791787 *Fax:* (01793) 791786
*E-mail:* info@sla.org.uk
*Web Site:* www.sla.org.uk
*Key Personnel*
Chief Executive: Kathy Lemaire *E-mail:* kathy.lemaire@sla.org.uk
Exhibitions & Pubns Sec: Jane Cooper
*E-mail:* jane.cooper@sla.org.uk
Location: University of Bath, Bath, UK
June 23-25, 2006

**Science Fiction Research Association Annual Meeting**
Sponsored by Science Fiction Research Association Inc
University of Guelph, Guelph, ON N1G 2W1, Canada
*Tel:* 519-824-4120
*Web Site:* www.sfra.org
*Key Personnel*
Pres: Dave Mead *E-mail:* dave.mead@iris.tamucc.edu
Organizer: Elizabeth Hull *E-mail:* ehull@harpercollege.edu; Beverly Friend
*E-mail:* friend@oakton.edu
Location: Crowne Plaza Hotel, White Plains, NY, USA
June 22-24, 2006

**Society for Scholarly Publishing Annual Meeting**
Sponsored by Society for Scholarly Publishing
10200 W 44 Ave, Suite 304, Wheat Ridge, CO 80033-2840, United States
*Tel:* 303-422-3914 *Fax:* 303-422-8894
*E-mail:* ssp@resourcecenter.com; info@sspnet.org
*Web Site:* www.sspnet.org
Location: Marriott Crystal Gateway, Crystal City, VA, USA
June 7-9, 2006

**Southwestern Graphics**
Sponsored by Texas Graphic Arts Educational Foundation
13410 Preston Rd, No 1-100, Dallas, TX 75240-5299, United States
*Tel:* 940-763-8370 (Intl only) *Toll Free Tel:* 800-540-8280 *Fax:* 940-763-8395 (Intl Only)
*Toll Free Fax:* 800-540-5019
*E-mail:* info@swgraphics.com
*Web Site:* www.swgraphics.com
*Key Personnel*
Asst Show Mgr: Laura Bates
Location: Gonzales Convention Center, San Antonio, TX, USA
June 1-3, 2006

## Special Libraries Association Annual Conference
Sponsored by Special Libraries Association (SLA)
313 S Patrick St, Alexandria, VA 22314, United States
*Tel:* 703-647-4900 *Fax:* 703-647-4901
*E-mail:* sla@sla.org
*Web Site:* www.sla.org
*Key Personnel*
Exec Dir: Janice LaChance *E-mail:* janice@sla.org
Location: Baltimore, MD, USA
Junc 11-14, 2006

## JULY

### ARLIS/UK & Ireland Annual Conference
Sponsored by ARLIS/UK & Ireland Art Libraries Society
The Courtauld Institute of Art, Somerset House, The Strand, WC2R ORN London, United Kingdom
*Tel:* (020) 7848 2703
*Web Site:* www.arlis.org.uk
*Key Personnel*
Administrator: Anna Mellows *E-mail:* arlis@courtauld.ac.uk
Conference Chair: Deborah Sutherland *E-mail:* d.sutherland@vam.ac.uk
Registration Contact: Chris Fowler
*E-mail:* cbfowler@brookes.ac.uk
Theme: The Baltic & Beyond.
Location: University of Northumbria, Newcastle upon Tyne, UK
July 19-21, 2006

### Buenos Aires Children's Book Fair
Sponsored by Fundacion El Libro
Hipolito Yrigoyen 1628 5º piso, C1089AAF Buenos Aires, Argentina
*Tel:* (011) 4374 3288 *Fax:* (011) 4375 0268
*E-mail:* fundacion@el-libro.com.ar; informes@el-libro.com.ar
*Web Site:* www.el-libro.com.ar
*Key Personnel*
Proj Mgr: Marta Diaz
Location: Centro de Exposiciones de la Ciudad de Buenos Aires, Avdas Figueroa Alcorta y Pueyrredon, Buenos Aires, Argentina
July 2006

### Church & Synagogue Library Association Conference
Sponsored by Church & Synagogue Library Association
PO Box 19357, Portland, OR 97280-0357, United States
*Tel:* 503-244-6919 *Toll Free Tel:* 800-542-2752
*Fax:* 503-977-3734
*E-mail:* csla@worldaccessnet.com
*Web Site:* www.csla.info
Location: Sheridan Hotel, Greensboro, NC, USA
July 29-Aug 1, 2006

### DP: Digital Publishing Fair
Sponsored by Reed Exhibitions Japan Ltd
18F Shinjuku-Nomura Bldg, 1-26-2 Nishishin-juku, Shinjuku-ku, Toyko 163-0570, Japan
*Tel:* (03) 3349 8501 *Fax:* (03) 3349 8599
*E-mail:* digi@reedexpo.co.jp
*Web Site:* www.reedexpo.co.jp/digi
Organized by Reed Exhibitions Japan Ltd, TIBF Executive Committee.
Location: Tokyo Big Sight, Tokyo, Japan
July 6-9, 2006

### Hong Kong Book Fair
Sponsored by Hong Kong Trade Development Council
Unit 13, Expo Galleria, Hong Kong Convention & Exhibition Centre, One Expo Dr, Wanchai, Hong Kong
*Tel:* 2584-4333; 2240-4024 (sales); 1830-668 (visitors) *Fax:* 2824-0026; 2824-0249
*E-mail:* exhibitions@tdc.org.hk
*Web Site:* hkbookfair.com
Location: Hong Kong Convention & Exhibition Center, One Harbour Rd, Wanchai, Hong Kong
July 2006

### International Christian Retail Show
Formerly CBA International Convention
Sponsored by CBA
9240 Explorer Dr, Colorado Springs, CO 80920-5001, United States
Mailing Address: PO Box 62000, Colorado Springs, CO 80962-2000, United States
*Tel:* 719-265-9895 *Toll Free Tel:* 800-252-1950
*Fax:* 719-272-3510
*E-mail:* info@cbaonline.org
*Web Site:* www.cbaonline.org
*Key Personnel*
Pres: William Anderson *E-mail:* banderson@cbaonline.org
VP & COO: Dorothy Gore
Convention & Expositions Mgr: Scott Graham
For almost 50 years, the annual CBA International Convention has been our industry's single-most impacting week. During this week, people of the industry from all over the world meet face-to-face for buying & selling, education, inspiration, fellowship & future planning. Here individuals unite to further the mission of seeing Christian product impact lives for God's kingdom the world over. At this unique gathering, our industry's strength is most evident & our goals are most clearly in focus. It is, in short, the most important week in the ministry of your business & of the industry as a whole.
Location: Colorado Convention Center, Denver, CO, USA
July 9-13, 2006

### RWA Annual National Conference
Sponsored by Romance Writers of America
16000 Stuebner Airline, Suite 140, Spring, TX 77379, United States
*Tel:* 832-717-5200 *Fax:* 832-717-5201
*E-mail:* info@rwanational.org
*Web Site:* www.rwanational.org
*Key Personnel*
Exec Dir: Allison Kelley *E-mail:* akelley@rwanational.org
Location: Atlanta Marriott Marquis, Atlanta, GA, USA
July 26-29, 2006

### TIBF: Tokyo International Book Fair
Sponsored by Reed Exhibitions Japan Ltd
18F Shinjuku-Nomura Bldg, 1-26-2 Nishishin-juku, Shinjuku-ku, Toyko 163-0570, Japan
*Tel:* (03) 3349 8501 *Fax:* (03) 3349 8599
*E-mail:* tibf-eng@reedexpo.co.jp
*Web Site:* www.reedexpo.co.jp/tibf
Organized by Reed Exhibition Japan Ltd, TIBF executive committee.
Location: Tokyo Big Sight, Tokyo, Japan
July 6-9, 2006

### Zimbabwe International Book Fair
Sponsored by Zimbabwe International Book Fair Association
PO Box CY1179, Causeway, Harare, Zimbabwe
*Tel:* (04) 702104 *Fax:* (04) 702129
*E-mail:* information@zibf.org.zw
*Web Site:* www.zibf.org.zw
Annual event the first week of August at the Harare Sculpture Gardens.
Location: Harare Sculpture Gardens, Harare, Zimbabwe
July 30-Aug 5, 2006

## AUGUST

### The Dorothy L Sayers Society Annual Convention
Sponsored by The Dorothy L Sayers Society
Rose Cottage, Malthouse Lane, Hurstpierpoint, West Sussex BN6 9JY, United Kingdom
*Tel:* (01273) 833444 *Fax:* (01273) 835988
*E-mail:* info@sayers.org.uk
*Web Site:* www.sayers.org.uk
*Key Personnel*
Chmn: Christopher Dean
Members only event.
Location: University of York, Heslington, York, UK
Aug 4-7, 2006

### Edinburgh International Book Festival
Scottish Book Centre, 137 Dundee St, Edinburgh EH11 1BG, United Kingdom
*Tel:* (0131) 228 5444 *Fax:* (0131) 228 4333
*E-mail:* admin@edbookfest.co.uk
*Web Site:* www.edbookfest.co.uk
*Key Personnel*
Dir: Catherine Lockerbie
Personal Asst to the Dir: Lyn Trotter
Mktg & PR Mgr: Amanda Barry
The festival takes place in Charlotte Square Gardens (just off the West End of Princes St) over 17 days each August. An extensive program showcases the work of the world's authors & thinkers for people of all ages.
Location: Charlotte Square Gardens, Edinburgh, UK
Aug 12-28, 2006

### Engineering & Pulping Conference
Formerly TAPPI Fall Technical Conference
Sponsored by Technical Association of the Pulp & Paper Industry (TAPPI)
15 Technology Pkwy S, Norcross, GA 30092, United States
*Tel:* 770-446-1400 *Toll Free Tel:* 800-332-8686
*Fax:* 770-446-6947
*Web Site:* www.tappi.org
*Key Personnel*
Publg Dir: Mary Beth Cornell *E-mail:* mcornell@tappi.org
Adv Mgr: Vince Saputo *E-mail:* vsaputo@tappi.org
Corp Rel Dir: Clare Reagan *E-mail:* creagan@tappi.org
Location: Atlanta Marriott, Atlanta, GA, USA
Aug 2006

### Garden Writers Association of America Meeting & Symposium
Sponsored by Garden Writers Association of America
10210 Leatherleaf Ct, Manassas, VA 20111, United States
*Tel:* 703-257-1032 *Fax:* 703-257-0213
*E-mail:* info@gardenwriters.org
*Web Site:* www.gardenwriters.org
*Key Personnel*
Pres: Cathy Wilkerson Barash
Exec Dir: Robert LaGasse
Location: Philadelphia, PA, USA
August 2006

### Society of Professional Journalists National Convention
Sponsored by The Society of Professional Journalists

Eugene S Pulliam National Journalism Ctr, 3909
N Meridian St, Indianapolis, IN 46208, United
States
*Tel:* 317-927-8000 *Fax:* 317-920-4789
*E-mail:* spj@spj.org
*Web Site:* www.spj.org
*Key Personnel*
Exec Dir: Terrance G Harper
Deputy Dir: Julie Grimes
Dir of Programs: Chris Vachon
Location: Hyatt Regency Chicago, Chicago, IL,
USA
Aug 24-26, 2006

### South African Booksellers Association Annual Conference

Sponsored by South African Booksellers Associa-
tion (SABA)
PO Box 870, Bellville 7535, South Africa
*Tel:* (021) 945 1572 *Fax:* (021) 945 2169
*E-mail:* saba@sabooksellers.com
*Web Site:* sabooksellers.com
Location: Durban, South Africa
Aug 2006

### SWANICK: The Writer's Summer School

Sponsored by Writer's Summer School
10 Stag Rd, Lake Sandown, Isle of Wight PO36
8PE, United Kingdom
*Tel:* (07050) 630949 *Fax:* (07050) 630949
*Web Site:* www.wss.org.uk
*Key Personnel*
Sec: Jean Sutton *E-mail:* jean.sutton@lineone.net
A week-long summer school of informal talks
& discussion groups, forums, panels, quizzes,
competition & a lot of fun. Open to everyone,
from absolute beginners to published authors.
Held annually in August.
Location: The Hayes Conference Centre, Swan-
wick, Derbyshire, UK
Aug 2006

### World Library & Information Congress

Sponsored by International Federation of Library
Associations & Institutions (IFLA) (Federation
internationale des associations de bibliothe-
caires et des bibliotheques)
Prins Willem-Alexanderhof 5, 2595 BE The
Hague, Netherlands
Mailing Address: PO Box 95312, 2509 CH The
Hague, Netherlands
*Tel:* (070) 3140884 *Fax:* (070) 3834827
*E-mail:* ifla@ifla.org
*Web Site:* www.ifla.org
*Key Personnel*
Sec Gen: Peter J Lor
Coord of Prof Activities: Sjoerd M J Koopman
*E-mail:* sjoerd.koopman@ifla.org
Location: Seoul, Republic of Korea
Aug 20-24, 2006

## AUTUMN

### Advertising Research Foundation Annual Convention & Trade Show

Sponsored by Advertising Research Foundation
641 Lexington Ave, 11th fl, New York, NY
10022, United States
*Tel:* 212-751-5656 *Fax:* 212-319-5265
*E-mail:* info@thearf.org
*Web Site:* www.thearf.org
*Key Personnel*
VP, Mktg: Lisa Malone *E-mail:* lisa@thearf.org
VP, Conference Brands: Caryn Brown
*E-mail:* caryn@thearf.org
Edit Asst: Zena Pagan *Tel:* 212-751-5656 ext 216
*E-mail:* zena@thearf.org

Location: New York, NY, USA
Autumn 2006

### Antwerp Book Fair

Sponsored by Boek.be
Hof ter Schrieklaan 17, 2600 Berchem/Antwerp,
Belgium
*Tel:* (03) 230 89 23 *Fax:* (03) 281 22 40
*E-mail:* info@boek.be
*Web Site:* www.boek.be
Location: Antwerp, Belgium
Autumn 2006

### Business & Design Conference

Sponsored by American Institute of Graphic Arts
(AIGA)
164 Fifth Ave, New York, NY 10010, United
States
*Tel:* 212-807-1990 (ext 223) *Fax:* 212-807-1799
*E-mail:* aiga@aiga.org; programs@aiga.org
*Web Site:* www.aiga.org
*Key Personnel*
Exec Dir: Richard Grefe
Biennial event.
Autumn 2006

### Great Salt Lake Book Festival

Sponsored by Utah Humanities Council
202 W 300 N, Salt Lake City, UT 84103, United
States
*Tel:* 801-359-9670 *Fax:* 801-531-7869
*Web Site:* www.utahhumanities.org/bookfestival
*Key Personnel*
Dir: Rebecca Batt
Asst Dir & Dir of Progs: Jean Cheney
Free literary event featuring nationally known au-
thors.
Location: Salt Lake City Library, Salt Lake City,
UT, USA
Autumn 2006

### Istanbul Book Fair

Sponsored by Tuyap Fuar ve Kongre Merkezi
(Tuyap Fairs & Exhibitions Organization Inc)
E-5 Karayolu Gurpinar Kavsagi, Beylikduzu/
Buyukcekmece, 34522 Istanbul, Turkey
*Tel:* (0212) 886 68 43 *Fax:* (0212) 886 62 43
*E-mail:* artlink@tuyap.com.tr
*Web Site:* www.tuyap.com.tr
Annual event organized in co-operation with the
Turkish Publishers Association.
Location: Tuyap Fair, Convention & Congress
Center, Beylikduzu, Istanbul, Turkey
Autumn 2006

### NEPA's Annual Fall Conference

Sponsored by Newsletter & Electronic Publishers
Association
1501 Wilson Blvd, Suite 509, Arlington, VA
22209, United States
*Tel:* 703-527-2333 *Toll Free Tel:* 800-356-9302
*Fax:* 703-841-0629
*E-mail:* nepa@newsletters.org
*Web Site:* www.newsletters.org
*Key Personnel*
Exec Dir: Patti Wysocki
Autumn 2006

### Publishers Association of the South Fall Annual Conference & Trade Show

Sponsored by Publishers Association of the South
(PAS)
4412 Fletcher St, Panama City, FL 32405-1017,
United States
*Tel:* 850-914-0766 *Fax:* 850-769-4348
*E-mail:* executive@pubsouth.org
*Web Site:* www.pubsouth.org
*Key Personnel*
Pres: Janice Shay
Association Exec: Pat Sabiston
Autumn 2006

### Remainder & Promotional Book Fair

Sponsored by Ciana Ltd
24 Langroyd Rd, London SW17 7PL, United
Kingdom
*Tel:* (020) 8682 1969 *Fax:* (020) 8682 1997
*E-mail:* enquiries@ciana.co.uk
*Web Site:* www.ciana.co.uk
Location: London, UK
Autumn 2006

### Twin Cities Book Festival

Sponsored by Rain Taxi Review of Books
PO Box 3840, Minneapolis, MN 55403, United
States
*Tel:* 612-825-1528 *Fax:* 612-825-1528
*E-mail:* bookfest@raintaxi.com
*Web Site:* www.raintaxi.com
*Key Personnel*
Dir: Eric Lorberer
Gala celebration of books, featuring large exhi-
bition, author readings & signings, book art
activities, panel discussions, used book sale &
children's events.
Location: Minneapolis Community & Technical
College, Minneapolis, MN, USA
Autumn 2006

## SEPTEMBER

### Beijing International Book Fair

Sponsored by CNPIEC Exhibition Dept
BIBF Management Office, 16 Gongti E Rd,
Chaoyang District, Beijing 100020, China
*Tel:* (010) 6506 3080 *Fax:* (010) 6508 9188
*E-mail:* bibfmo@bibf.nct
*Web Site:* www.bibf.net
*Key Personnel*
Dir: Mr Zhu Zhigang
Mgr: Feng Qiao
Location: China International Exhibition Center,
Beijing, China
Sept 2006

### European Association of Directory & Database Publishers Annual Congress

Sponsored by European Association of Directory
& Database Publishers (EADP)
127 ave Franklin Roosevelt, 1050 Brussels, Bel-
gium
*Tel:* (02) 646 30 60 *Fax:* (02) 646 36 37
*E-mail:* mailbox@eadp.org
*Web Site:* www.eadp.org
*Key Personnel*
Congress & Conference Officer: Karen Chevalier
*E-mail:* karenchevalier@eadp.org
Location: Four Seasons Hotel, Lisbon, Portugal
Sept 27-29, 2006

### Goeteborg Book Fair

Sponsored by Bok & Bibliotek
Maessans Gata 20, 412 94 Goeteborg, Sweden
*Tel:* (031) 708 84 00 *Fax:* (031) 20 91 03
*E-mail:* info@goteborg-bookfair.com
*Web Site:* www.goteborg-bookfair.com
*Key Personnel*
Man Dir: Anna Falck *E-mail:* af@bok-bibliotek.
se
Conference Mgr: Gunilla Sandin *E-mail:* gs@
bok-bibliotek.se
Exhibition Mgr: Lisa Oden *E-mail:* lo@bok-
bibliotek.se
Prog Coord: Anneli Jonasson *E-mail:* aj@bok-
bibliotek.se
Location: Goeteborg, Sweden
Sept 21-24, 2006

### Higher Education Conference

Sponsored by The English Association

University of Leicester, University Rd, Leicester
LE1 7RH, United Kingdom
*Tel:* (0116) 252 3982 *Fax:* (0116) 252 2301
*E-mail:* engassoc@le.ac.uk
*Web Site:* www.le.ac.uk/engassoc
*Key Personnel*
Chief Exec: Helen Lucas
Asst to Chief Exec: Julia Hughes
Location: Wadham College, Oxford, UK
Sept 2, 2006

**Inter American Press Association General
Assembly**
Sponsored by Inter American Press Association
(IAPA)
Jules Dubois Bldg, 1801 SW Third Ave, Miami,
FL 33129, United States
*Tel:* 305-634-2465 *Fax:* 305-635-2272
*E-mail:* info@sipiapa.org
*Web Site:* www.sipiapa.org
*Key Personnel*
Exec Dir: Julio E Munoz
Location: Mexico City, Mexico
Sept 29-Oct 3, 2006

**International Board on Books for Young
People Biennial Congress**
Sponsored by International Board on Books for
Young People (IBBY)
Nonnenweg 12, Postfach, 4003 Basel, Switzerland
*Tel:* (061) 272 29 17 *Fax:* (061) 272 27 57
*E-mail:* ibby@ibby.org
*Web Site:* www.ibby.org
*Key Personnel*
Pres: Peter Schneck
Admin Dir: Liz Page
IBBY's biennial congresses, hosted by differ-
ent countries, are the most important meeting
points for IBBY members & other people in-
volved in children's books & reading devel-
opment. They are wonderful opportunities to
make contacts, exchange ideas & open hori-
zons.
Location: Beijing, China
Sept 20-24, 2006

**LIBER Feria Internacional del Libro**
Sponsored by Federacion de Gremios de Editores
de Espana (FGEE) (Spanish Publishers Associ-
ation)
Cea Bermudez, 44-2º Dche, 2003 Madrid, Spain
*Tel:* (091) 534 51 95 *Fax:* (091) 535 26 25
*E-mail:* fgee@fge.es
*Web Site:* www.federacioneditores.org
*Key Personnel*
Executive Dir: Antonio Ma Avila
Location: Barcelona, Spain
Sept 27-29, 2006

**Montana Festival of the Book**
Sponsored by Montana Committee for the Hu-
manities
311 Brantly Hall, University of Montana, Mis-
soula, MT 59812-8214, United States
*Tel:* 406-243-6022 *Toll Free Tel:* 800-624-6001
(MT only)
*Web Site:* www.bookfest-mt.org
*Key Personnel*
Coord: Kim Anderson
Two day celebration featuring over 70 authors &
50 events.
Location: Downtown Missoula, Missoula, MT,
USA
Sept 2006

**Moscow International Book Fair**
Sponsored by General Directorate of International
Book Exhibitions & Fairs
Malaya Dmitrovka St, 16, Moscow 127006, Rus-
sian Federation
*Tel:* (095) 299 40 34 *Fax:* (095) 973 21 32

*E-mail:* mibf@mibf.ru
*Web Site:* www.mibf.ru
*Key Personnel*
Gen Dir: Mr Nikolay Ph Ovsyannikov
Location: All Russian Exhibition Centre,
Moscow, Russia
Sept 2006

**National Federation of Press Women National
Conference**
Sponsored by National Federation of Press
Women Inc (NFPW)
PO Box 5556, Arlington, VA 22205-0056, United
States
*Tel:* 703-812-9487 *Toll Free Tel:* 800-780-2715
*Fax:* 703-812-4555
*E-mail:* presswomen@aol.com
*Web Site:* www.nfpw.org
*Key Personnel*
Exec Dir: Carol Pierce
Location: Denver, CO, USA
Sept 2006

**NIP 22: The 22nd International Congress on
Digital Printing Technologies**
Sponsored by Society for Imaging Science &
Technology (IS&T)
7003 Kilworth Lane, Springfield, VA 22151,
United States
*Tel:* 703-642-9090 *Fax:* 703-642-9094
*E-mail:* info@imaging.org
*Web Site:* www.imaging.org
Location: Denver Convention Center Hotel, Den-
ver, CO, USA
Sept 17-22, 2006

**PSA International Conference of Photography**
Sponsored by Photographic Society of America
Inc (PSA)
3000 United Founders Blvd, Suite 103, Oklahoma
City, OK 73112-3940, United States
*Tel:* 405-843-1437 *Fax:* 405-843-1438
*E-mail:* hq@psa-photo.org
*Web Site:* www.psa-photo.org
*Key Personnel*
VP, Conventions: Gerald Emmerich, Jr
Location: Hunt Valley Inn, Baltimore, MD, USA
Sept 4-9, 2006

**Southeast Booksellers Association Annual
Meeting & Trade Show**
Sponsored by Southeast Booksellers Association
(SEBA)
2611 Forest Dr, Suite 124, Columbia, SC 29204,
United States
*Tel:* 803-779-0118 *Fax:* 803-779-0113
*E-mail:* sebajewell@aol.com
*Web Site:* www.sibaweb.org
*Key Personnel*
Exec Dir: Wanda Jewell
Location: Gaylord Palms Resort & Convention
Center, Orlando, FL, USA
Sept 8-10, 2006

**Spectrum 2006**
Sponsored by IDEAlliance
100 Daingerfield Rd, Alexandria, VA 22314,
United States
*Tel:* 703-837-1070 *Fax:* 703-837-1072
*E-mail:* info@idealliance.org
*Web Site:* www.idealliance.org
*Key Personnel*
Dir of Events: Georgia Volakis *Tel:* 703-837-1075
*E-mail:* gvolakis@idealliance.org
Location: Fairmont Princess Hotel, Scottsdale,
AZ, USA
Sept 17-20, 2006

## OCTOBER

**American Medical Writers Association Annual
Conference**
Sponsored by American Medical Writers Associa-
tion
40 W Gude Dr, Suite 101, Rockville, MD 20850-
1192, United States
*Tel:* 301-294-5303 *Fax:* 301-294-9006
*E-mail:* amwa@amwa.org
*Web Site:* www.amwa.org
Location: Albuquerque Convention Center, Albu-
querque, NM, USA
Oct 26-28, 2006

**Belgrade International Book Fair**
Sponsored by Association of Serbia & Montene-
gro Publishers & Booksellers
Kneza Milosa 25, 11000 Belgrade, Serbia and
Montenegro
*Tel:* (011) 2642-533; (011) 2642-248 *Fax:* (011)
2646-339; (011) 2686-539
*E-mail:* uikj@eunet.yu
*Web Site:* www.beobookfair.co.yu
*Key Personnel*
Gen Dir: Mr Zivadin Mitrovic
Book Fairs Dept Mgr: Miss Marina Radojicic
Location: Belgrade, Serbia and Montenegro
Oct 2006

**BMI Annual Conference**
Sponsored by Book Manufacturers' Institute Inc
(BMI)
2 Armand Beach Dr, Suite 1-B, Palm Coast, FL
32137, United States
*Tel:* 386-986-4552 *Fax:* 386-986-4553
*E-mail:* info@bmibook.com
*Web Site:* www.bmibook.org
*Key Personnel*
Exec VP: Bruce W Smith
Location: Ritz Carlton Naples, FL, USA
Oct 22-25, 2006

**Chicago Book Festival**
Sponsored by Chicago Public Library
400 S State St, Chicago, IL 60605, United States
*Tel:* 312-747-1194
*E-mail:* info@chicagopubliclibrary.org
*Web Site:* www.chicagopubliclibrary.org
Location: Chicago, IL, USA
Oct 1-31, 2006

**Distripress Annual Congress**
Sponsored by Distripress
Beethovenstr 20, CH-8002 Zurich, Switzerland
*Tel:* (01) 202 41 21 *Fax:* (01) 202 10 25
*E-mail:* info@distripress.ch
*Web Site:* www.distripress.net
*Key Personnel*
Man Dir: Dr Peter Emod *E-mail:* peter.emod@
distripress.ch
Congress Coord: Susanne Jorg *E-mail:* susanne.
joerg@distripress.ch
Non-profit association for the promotion of the
International Press Distribution.
Location: Barcelona, Spain
Oct 15-19, 2006

**DMA Annual Conference & Exhibition**
Sponsored by The Direct Marketing Association
Inc (The DMA)
1120 Avenue of the Americas, New York, NY
10036-6700, United States
*Tel:* 212-768-7277 *Fax:* 212-302-6714
*E-mail:* customerservice@the-dma.org
*Web Site:* www.the-dma.org
*Key Personnel*
Sr VP of Educ & Events: Anne Schaeffer
Oct 2006

**Frankfurt Book Fair**
Sponsored by Ausstellungs-und Messe-GmbH des
   Borsenvereins des Deutschen Buchhandels
Reineckstr 3, 63013 Frankfurt am Main, Germany
Mailing Address: Postfach 100116, 60001 Frank-
   furt am Main, Germany
*Tel:* (069) 21020 *Fax:* (069) 2102 227
*E-mail:* info@book-fair.com
*Web Site:* www.book-fair.com *Cable:*
   BUCHMESSE
*Key Personnel*
CEO & Dir: Juergen Boos
Largest international book & media fair attracting
   more than 6,700 exhibitors & 280,000 visitors.
Location: Frankfurt Fairgrounds, Frankfurt, Ger-
   many
Oct 4-8, 2006

**Graph Expo & Converting Expo**
Sponsored by NPES The Association for Sup-
   pliers of Printing, Publishing & Converting
   Technologies
1899 Preston White Dr, Reston, VA 20191-4367,
   United States
*Tel:* 703-264-7200 *Fax:* 703-620-0994
*E-mail:* npes@npes.org
*Web Site:* www.gasc.org
*Key Personnel*
Pres: Regis J Delmontagne
Dir, Communs & Mktg: Carol J Hurlburt
   *E-mail:* churlbur@npes.org
Location: McCormick Place South & North,
   Chicago IL, USA
Oct 15-18, 2006

**Louisiana Book Festival**
Sponsored by State Library of Louisiana
701 N Fourth St, Baton Rouge, LA 70802,
   United States
*Tel:* 225-219-9503 *Toll Free Tel:* 888-487-2700
   *Fax:* 225-219-9840
*Web Site:* louisianabookfestival.org
Location: Louisana State Capital, State Library &
   State Museum, Baton Rouge, LA, USA
Oct 28, 2006

**Monterrey International Book Fair**
Sponsored by Instituto Tecnologico y de Estudios
   Superiores de Monterrey
Ave Eugenio Garza Sada 2501 SW, 64849 Mon-
   terrey, Nuevo Leon, Mexico
*Tel:* (81) 8328-4328; (81) 8328-4282 *Fax:* (81)
   8359-9623
*E-mail:* fil.mty@itesm.mx
*Web Site:* fil.mty.itesm.mx
*Key Personnel*
Contact: Cecilia Barragan
Oct 2006

**National Association of Science Writers
   Annual Meeting**
Sponsored by National Association of Science
   Writers (NASW)
PO Box 890, Hedgesville, WV 25427, United
   States
*Tel:* 304-754-5077 *Fax:* 304-754-5076
*Web Site:* www.nasw.org
*Key Personnel*
Exec Dir: Diane McGurgan *E-mail:* diane@nasw.
   org
Location: Baltimore, MD, USA
Oct 21, 2006

**National Newspaper Association Annual
   Convention & Trade Show**
Sponsored by National Newspaper Association
PO Box 7540, Columbia, MO 65205-7540,
   United States
Mailing Address: 127-129 Neff Annex, Columbia,
   MO 65211-1200, United States

*Tel:* 573-882-5800 *Toll Free Tel:* 800-829-4662
   *Fax:* 573-884-5490
*E-mail:* info@nna.org
*Web Site:* www.nna.org
*Key Personnel*
Exec Dir: Brian Steffens *E-mail:* briansteffens@
   nna.org
Meeting Planner: Cindy Joy-Rodgers
   *E-mail:* crodgers@nna.org
Location: Oklahoma City, OK, USA
Oct 11-13, 2006

**New Atlantic Independent Booksellers
   Association Annual Trade Show**
Sponsored by New Atlantic Independent Book-
   sellers Association (NAIBA)
2667 Hyacinth St, Westbury, NY 11590, United
   States
*Tel:* 516-333-0681 *Fax:* 516-333-0689
*E-mail:* info@naiba.com; readingent@aol.com
*Web Site:* www.naiba.com
*Key Personnel*
Exec Dir: Eileen Dengler
Location: Tropicana Hotel & Casino, Atlantic
   City, NJ, USA
Oct 15-16, 2006

**PACK EXPO International**
Sponsored by Packaging Machinery Manufactur-
   ers Institute
4350 N Fairfax Dr, Suite 600, Arlington, VA
   22203, United States
*Tel:* 703-243-8555 *Fax:* 703-243-3038
*E-mail:* expo@pmmi.org
*Web Site:* www.packexpo.com
*Key Personnel*
Exhibitor Servs Mgr: Kim Beaulieu
   *E-mail:* kim@pmmi.org
Location: McCormick Center, Chicago, IL, USA
Oct 29-Nov 2, 2006

**SPAN Conference**
Sponsored by Small Publishers Association of
   North America (SPAN)
1618 W Colorado Ave, Colorado Springs, CO
   80904, United States
*Tel:* 719-475-1726 *Fax:* 719-471-2182
*E-mail:* span@spannet.org
*Web Site:* www.spannet.org
*Key Personnel*
Exec Dir: Scott Flora *E-mail:* scott@spannet.org
Busn Mgr: Debi Flora
A meaty, in-depth college for independent
   presses, authors & self-publishers. Emphasis
   is on "can-do" marketing/PR strategies.
Location: Los Angeles, CA, USA
Oct 2006

**Texas Book Festival**
610 Brazos St, Suite 200, Austin, TX 78701,
   United States
*Tel:* 512-477-4055 *Fax:* 512-322-0722
*E-mail:* bookfest@texasbookfestival.org
*Web Site:* www.texasbookfestival.org
*Key Personnel*
Exec Dir: Mary Herman *Tel:* 512-320-5451
   *E-mail:* maryherman@texasbookfestival.org
Literary Dir: Clay Smith *Tel:* 512-472-3808
   *E-mail:* clay@texasbookfestival.org
Off Mgr: Andrea V Prestridge *Tel:* 512-477-4055
   *E-mail:* andrea@texasbookfestival.org
The festival is a statewide program that promotes
   reading & literacy highlighted by a two-day
   festival featuring authors from Texas & across
   the country. Money raised from the festival is
   distributed as grants to public libraries through-
   out the state.
Location: State Capitol Bldg, Austin, TX, USA
Oct 27-29, 2006

**Texas Outdoor Writers Association Annual
   Conference**
Sponsored by Texas Outdoor Writers Association
7503 Bayswater, Amarillo, TX 79119, United
   States
*Tel:* 806-345-3280 *Fax:* 806-372-3717
*Web Site:* www.towa.org
*Key Personnel*
Pres: Greg Berlocher *E-mail:* bigredfish@aol.com
Exec Dir & Treas: Lee Leschper *E-mail:* l.
   leschper@worldnet.att.net
Location: Texas State Capitol, Austin, TX, USA
Oct 27-29, 2006

**WORLDDIDAC Basel 2006**
Sponsored by Worlddidac
Bollwerk 21, 3001 Bern, Switzerland
Mailing Address: PO Box 8866, 3001 Bern,
   Switzerland
*Tel:* (031) 311 76 82 *Fax:* (031) 312 17 44
*E-mail:* info@worlddidac.org
*Web Site:* www.worlddidac.org
International exhibition for educational materials,
   professional training & e-learning.
Location: Basel, Switzerland
Oct 25-27, 2006


# NOVEMBER

**American Academy of Religion**
Sponsored by American Schools of Oriental Re-
   search
825 Houston Mill Rd, Suite 201, Atlanta, GA
   30329-4205, United States
*Tel:* 404-727-3049 *Fax:* 404-727-7959
*E-mail:* aar@aarweb.org
*Web Site:* www.aarweb.org
*Key Personnel*
Prog Dir: Aislinn Jones
Location: Washington, DC, USA
Nov 18-21, 2006

**American Translators Association Annual
   Conference**
Sponsored by American Translators Association
   (ATA)
225 Reinekers Lane, Suite 590, Alexandria, VA
   22314, United States
*Tel:* 703-683-6100 *Fax:* 703-683-6122
*E-mail:* ata@atanet.org
*Web Site:* www.atanet.org
*Key Personnel*
Exec Dir: Walter Bacak *Tel:* 703-683-6100 ext
   3006 *E-mail:* walter@atanet.org
Location: New Orleans, LA, USA
Nov 2-5, 2006

**Cairo International Children's Book Fair**
Sponsored by General Egyptian Book Organiza-
   tion
Corniche el-Nil - Ramlet Boulac, Cairo 11221,
   Egypt (Arab Republic of Egypt)
*Tel:* (02) 5765436; (02) 5775228; (02) 5775109;
   (02) 5775367; (02) 5775436; (02) 5775545;
   (02) 5775000 *Fax:* (02) 5765058
*E-mail:* info@egyptianbook.org
*Web Site:* www.childrensbookfair.org; www.
   egyptianbook.org; www.egyptianbook.net
*Key Personnel*
Chmn: Dr Nasser El Ansary
VChmn: Dr Waheed Abdel Majeed
Location: Cairo, Egypt
Nov 2006

**Children's Book Week**
Sponsored by The Children's Book Council
   (CBC)

12 W 37 St, 2nd fl, New York, NY 10118-7480, United States
*Tel:* 212-966-1990 *Toll Free Tel:* 800-999-2160 (orders only) *Fax:* 212-966-2073 *Toll Free Fax:* 888-807-9355 (orders only)
*Web Site:* www.cbcbooks.org
*Key Personnel*
Pres: Paula Quint
Location: Nationwide across the USA
Nov 13-19, 2006

**Color Imaging Conference - Color Science Systems & Applications**
Sponsored by Society for Imaging Science & Technology (IS&T)
7003 Kilworth Lane, Springfield, VA 22151, United States
*Tel:* 703-642-9090 *Fax:* 703-642-9094
*E-mail:* info@imaging.org
*Web Site:* www.imaging.org
*Key Personnel*
Gen Co-chair: Po-Chief Hung; Michael Brill
Nov 2006

**ECPA Publishing University**
Sponsored by Evangelical Christian Publishers Association
4816 S Ash Ave, Suite 101, Tempe, AZ 85282-7735, United States
*Tel:* 480-966-3998 *Fax:* 480-966-1944
*E-mail:* info@ecpa.org
*Web Site:* www.ecpa.org
*Key Personnel*
Pres: Mark Kuyper *E-mail:* mkuyper@ecpa.org
Excellence in Christian publishing through professional instruction, interactive learning & practical training.
Location: Indian Lakes Resort, Bloomingdale, IL, USA
Nov 5-7, 2006

**Feria Internacional del Libro de Guadalajara**
Av Alemania 1370, Colonia Moderna, 44190 Guadalajara Jalisco, Mexico
*Tel:* (033) 3810 0291; (033) 3810 0331 *Fax:* (033) 3810 0379
*E-mail:* fil@fil.com.mx; filny@aol.com
*Web Site:* www.fil.com.mx
*Key Personnel*
Pres: Raul Padilla Lopez
Dir: Nubia Edith Macias Navarro *E-mail:* dirfil@fil.com.mx
Gen Coord, Events & Prizes: Laura Niembro Diaz *E-mail:* eventosf@fil.com.mx
Location: Guadalajara, Mexico
Nov 25-Dec 3, 2006

**Ghana International Book Fair**
Sponsored by Ghana International Book Fair (GIBF)
PO Box NT601, Accra New Town, Accra, Ghana
*Tel:* (021) 277182; (021) 783421
*E-mail:* info@ghanainternationalbookfair.org
*Web Site:* www.ghanainternationalbookfair.org
Location: National Theatre, Accra, Ghana
Nov 2006

**Hall of Fame Awards & Annual Convention**
Sponsored by Copywriter's Council of America (CCA)
Division of The Linick Group Inc
CCA Bldg, 7 Putter Lane, Middle Island, NY 11953-1920, United States
Mailing Address: PO Box 102, Middle Island, NY 11953-0102, United States
*Tel:* 631-924-8555 (ext 203)
*E-mail:* cca4dmcopy@att.net
*Web Site:* www.lgroup.addr.com/CCA.htm
*Key Personnel*
VP: Roger Dextor
Dir, Spec Proj: Barbara Deal

Location: Orlando, FL, USA
Nov 2006

**Karlsruher Buecherschau** (Karlsruhe Book Exhibition)
Sponsored by Boersenverein des Deutschen Buchhandels, Landesverband Baden-Wuerttemberg eV (Association of Publishers & Booksellers in Baden-Wuerttemberg eV)
Paulinenstr 53, 70178 Stuttgart, Germany
*Tel:* (0711) 61941-0 *Fax:* (0711) 61941-44
*E-mail:* post@buchhandelsverband.de
*Web Site:* www.buchhandelsverband.de
*Key Personnel*
Exhibition Mgr: Lisa Buchhorn *Tel:* (0711) 61941 26 *E-mail:* buchhorn@buchhandelsverband.de
Contact: Andrea Baumann *Tel:* (0711) 61941-23 *Fax:* (0711) 61941-44 *E-mail:* baumann@buchhandelsverband.de
Location: Landesgewerbeamt Baden-Wurttemberg, Karl-Friedrich Str 17, Karlsruhe, Germany
Nov 17-Dec 10, 2006

**Multicultural Children's Book Festival**
Sponsored by Kids Cultural Books
811 Elaine Dr, Stamford, CT 06902, United States
*Tel:* 203-359-6925 *Fax:* 203-359-3226
*E-mail:* info@kidsculturalbooks.org
*Web Site:* www.kidsculturalbooks.org
Location: Kennedy Center, Washington, DC, USA
Nov 2006

**National College Media Convention**
Sponsored by Associated Collegiate Press (ACP)
Subsidiary of National Scholastic Press Assn
2221 University Ave SE, Suite 121, Minneapolis, MN 55414, United States
*Tel:* 612-625-8335 *Fax:* 612-626-0720
*E-mail:* info@studentpress.org
*Web Site:* studentpress.org
*Key Personnel*
Assoc Dir: Ann Akers
Also sponsored by College Media Advisors.
Location: Adams Mark, St Louis, MO, USA
Nov 2-5, 2006

**Salon du Livre de Montreal** (Montreal Book Show)
300 St-Secrement, Suite 430, Montreal, QC H2Y 1X4, Canada
*Tel:* (514) 845-2365 *Fax:* (514) 845-7119
*E-mail:* slm.info@videotron.ca
*Web Site:* www.salondulivredemontreal.com
*Key Personnel*
Gen Mgr: Francine Bois
Location: La Place Bonaventure, Montreal, PQ, Canada
Nov 2006

**Salon du Livre et de la Presse de Jeunesse**
Sponsored by Reed Expositions France
Subsidiary of Reed Exhibition Companies
11 rue du Colonel Pierre Avia, 75726 Paris Cedex 15, France
*Tel:* (01) 41 90 47 47 *Fax:* (01) 41 90 47 49
*E-mail:* info@reedexpo.fr; cplj@ldg.tm.fr; contact@slpj.fr
*Web Site:* www.salon-livre-presse-jeunesse.net; www.ldj.tm.fr
*Key Personnel*
Contact: Denis-Luc Panthin *E-mail:* denis-luc.panthin@slpj.fr
France's leading publishing event dedicated to children's books, organized by Centre de promotion du livre de jeunesse.
Location: Rue de Paris, Montreuil, France
Nov 19-23, 2006

**Seybold San Francisco**
Sponsored by MediaLive International

795 Folsom St, 6th fl, San Francisco, CA 94107-1243, United States
*Tel:* 415-905-2300 *Fax:* 415-905-2329
*Web Site:* www.Seybold365.com
*Key Personnel*
Gen Mgr: Drew Miller
Location: Palace Hotel, San Francisco, CA, USA
Nov 2006

**Stuttgarter Buchwochen (Stuttgart Bookweeks)**
Sponsored by Boersenverein des Deutschen Buchhandels, Landesverband Baden-Wuerttemberg eV (Association of Publishers & Booksellers in Baden-Wuerttemberg eV)
Paulinenstr 53, 70178 Stuttgart, Germany
*Tel:* (0711) 61941-0; (0711) 123 34 99 *Fax:* (0711) 61941-44
*E-mail:* post@buchhandelsverband.de
*Web Site:* www.buchhandelsverband.de
*Key Personnel*
Contact: Andrea Baumann *Tel:* (0711) 61941-23 *Fax:* (0711) 61941-44 *E-mail:* baumann@buchhandelsverband.de
Location: Haus der Wirtschaft, Willi-Bleicher Str 19, Stuttgart, Germany
Nov 9-Dec 3, 2006

# WINTER

**The National Center for Database Marketing (NCDM)**
Sponsored by Primedia Business Exhibitions
11 River Bend Dr S, Stamford, CT 06907, United States
Mailing Address: PO Box 4254, Stamford, CT 06907-0254, United States
*Tel:* 203-358-9900 *Toll Free Tel:* 800-927-5007 *Fax:* 203-358-5818
*Web Site:* www.primediabusiness.com; www.ncdmsummer.com; www.ncdmwinter.com
Winter 2006

# DECEMBER

**Modern Language Association of America Annual Convention**
Sponsored by Modern Language Association of America (MLA)
26 Broadway, 3rd fl, New York, NY 10004-1789, United States
*Tel:* 646-576-5000 *Fax:* 646-576-9930
*E-mail:* convention@mla.org
*Web Site:* www.mla.org
*Key Personnel*
Dir, Conventions: Maribeth T Kraus
Assoc Dir, Conventions: Karin Bagnall
Location: New Orleans, LA, USA
Dec 27-30, 2006

**Small Press Book Fair**
Sponsored by Small Press Center
20 W 44 St, New York, NY 10036, United States
*Tel:* 212-764-7021 *Fax:* 212-354-5365
*E-mail:* info@smallpress.org
*Web Site:* www.smallpress.org
*Key Personnel*
Dir: Karin Taylor
Location: Small Press Center, New York, NY, USA
Dec 2-3, 2006

**Sofia National Book Fair**
Sponsored by Bulgarian Book Association
11 Slaveikov Sq, 1000 Sofia, Bulgaria

Mailing Address: PO Box 1046, 1000 Sofia, Bulgaria
*Tel:* (02) 986 79 93; (02) 986 79 70 *Fax:* (02) 986 79 93
*E-mail:* bba@otel.net; bulgarian.book@gmail.com
*Web Site:* www.bba-bg.org
*Key Personnel*
Sec Gen: Madlena Romanova *E-mail:* bba@otel.net
PR: Dimmo Petrov *E-mail:* bulgarian.book@gmail.com
Location: National Palace of Culture, Sofia, Bulgaria
Dec 13-17, 2006

# 2007

## JANUARY

**Advance 2007: The Strategic Event for the Christian Retail Channel**
Sponsored by CBA
9240 Explorer Dr, Colorado Springs, CO 80920-5001, United States
Mailing Address: PO Box 62000, Colorado Springs, CO 80962-2000, United States
*Tel:* 719-265-9895 *Toll Free Tel:* 800-252-1950 *Fax:* 719-272-3510
*E-mail:* info@cbaonline.org
*Web Site:* www.cbaonline.org
*Key Personnel*
Pres: William Anderson *E-mail:* banderson@cbaonline.org
VP & COO: Dorothy Gore
Convention & Expositions Mgr: Scott Graham
Location: Indiana Convention Center, Indianapolis, IN, USA
Jan 29-Feb 3, 2007

**American Library Association Mid-Winter Meeting**
Sponsored by American Library Association (ALA)
50 E Huron St, Chicago, IL 60611, United States
*Toll Free Tel:* 800-545-2433 *Fax:* 312-944-6780
*E-mail:* ala@ala.org
*Web Site:* www.ala.org/midwinter
*Key Personnel*
Public Info Dir: Mark Gould
Press Officer: Larra Clark *E-mail:* lclark@ala.org
Location: Seattle, WA, USA
Jan 19-24, 2007

**Cairo International Book Fair**
Sponsored by General Egyptian Book Organization
Corniche el-Nil - Ramlet Boulac, Cairo 11221, Egypt (Arab Republic of Egypt)
*Tel:* (02) 5765436; (02) 5775228; (02) 5775109; (02) 5775367; (02) 5775436; (02) 5775545; (02) 5775000 *Fax:* (02) 5765058
*E-mail:* info@egyptianbook.org
*Web Site:* www.cibf.org; www.egyptianbook.org
*Key Personnel*
Chmn: Dr Nasser El Ansary
VChmn: Dr Waheed Abdel Majeed
Location: Nasr City Fairground, Cairo, Egypt
Jan 2007

**Technology, Reading & Learning Difficulties (TRLD)**
Sponsored by Don Johnson Inc
26799 W Commerce, Volo, IL 60073, United States
*Toll Free Tel:* 888-594-1249 *Fax:* 847-740-7326
*E-mail:* info@trld.com
*Web Site:* www.trld.com

*Key Personnel*
Contact: Linda Hoening
TRLD is the only conference that integrates technology interventions with expert literacy strategies to ensure student success. The conference brings together educators, experienced literacy leaders & technology experts to share, discuss & work towards a solution to the nationwide concern of bringing literacy success to all students. Through quality speakers & relevant topics, TRLD gives educators ideas & strategies to immediately implement with students with high incidence disabilities.
Location: Hyatt Regency San Francisco, San Francisco, CA, USA
Jan 25-27, 2007

## FEBRUARY

**International Book Fair/San Francisco Book Fair**
Sponsored by Antiquarian Booksellers' Association of America
20 W 44 St, 4th fl, New York, NY 10036-6604, United States
*Tel:* 212-944-8291 *Fax:* 212-944-8293
*E-mail:* hq@abaa.org
*Web Site:* www.abaa.org
*Key Personnel*
Dir: Liane Wade
Co Dir: Susan Dixon
Location: San Francisco, CA, USA
Feb 2007

**Jerusalem International Book Fair**
PO Box 775, Jerusalem 91007, Israel
*Tel:* (02) 629 7922; (02) 629 6412 *Fax:* (02) 624 3144
*E-mail:* jerfairs@jerusalem.muni.il
*Web Site:* www.jerusalembookfair.com
*Key Personnel*
Man Dir: Zev Birger
Location: Jerusalem Convention Center, Jerusalem, Israel
Feb 11-16, 2007

## SPRING

**Poligrafia**
Sponsored by Poznan International Fair Ltd
ul Glogowska 14, 60-734 Poznan, Poland
*Tel:* (061) 869 2000 *Fax:* (061) 866 5827
*E-mail:* poligrafia@mtp.pl
*Web Site:* poligrafia.mtp.pl
*Key Personnel*
Proj Mgr: Jerzy Kaczmarek *Tel:* (061) 869 2138 *Fax:* (061) 869 2956 *E-mail:* jerzy.kaczmarek@mtp.pl
International fair of printing machines, materials & services.
Location: Poznan, Poland
Spring 2007

**VUE/POINT Conference**
Sponsored by NPES The Association for Suppliers of Printing, Publishing & Converting Technologies
1899 Preston White Dr, Reston, VA 20191-4367, United States
*Tel:* 703-264-7200 *Fax:* 703-620-0994
*E-mail:* npes@npes.org
*Web Site:* www.gasc.org
*Key Personnel*
Pres: Regis J Delmontagne

Dir, Communs & Mktg: Carol J Hurlburt
*E-mail:* churlbur@npes.org
Trade Association representing companies which manufacture equipment, systems, software & supplies used in printing, publishing & converting.
Spring 2007

## MARCH

**CAMEX**
Sponsored by National Association of College Stores (NACS)
500 E Lorain St, Oberlin, OH 44074, United States
*Tel:* 440-775-7777 *Toll Free Tel:* 800-622-7498 *Fax:* 440-775-4769
*E-mail:* info@nacs.org
*Web Site:* www.nacs.org; www.camex.org
*Key Personnel*
CEO: Brian Cartier
PR Dir: Laura Nakoneczny *Tel:* 440-775-7777, ext 2351 *E-mail:* lnakoneczny@nacs.org
Conference & tradeshow dedicated exclusively to the more than $11 billion collegiate retailing industry.
Location: Orlando, FL, USA
March 23-27, 2007

**Inter American Press Association Mid-Year Meeting**
Sponsored by Inter American Press Association (IAPA)
Jules Dubois Bldg, 1801 SW Third Ave, Miami, FL 33129, United States
*Tel:* 305-634-2465 *Fax:* 305-635-2272
*E-mail:* info@sipiapa.org
*Web Site:* www.sipiapa.org
*Key Personnel*
Exec Dir: Julio E Munoz
Location: Cartagena, Colombia
March 2007

**Leipzig Book Fair**
Sponsored by Leipziger Messe GmbH, Projektteam Buchmesse
Messe-Allee 1, 04356 Leipzig, Germany
Mailing Address: Postfach 100 720, 04007 Leipzig, Germany
*Tel:* (0341) 678 8240 *Fax:* (0341) 678 8242
*E-mail:* info@leipziger-buchmesse.de
*Web Site:* www.leipziger-buchmesse.de
*Key Personnel*
Exhibition Dir: Oliver Zille *Tel:* (0341) 678 8241
Held annually in conjunction with The Leipzig Antiquarian Book Fair.
Location: Neues Messegelande, Leipzig, Germany
March 2007

**Virginia Festival of the Book**
Sponsored by Virginia Foundation for the Humanities
145 Ednam Dr, Charlottesville, VA 22903, United States
*Tel:* 434-924-6890 *Fax:* 434-296-4714
*E-mail:* vabook@virginia.edu
*Web Site:* www.vabook.org
*Key Personnel*
Program Dir: Nancy Damon *Tel:* 434-924-7548 *E-mail:* ndamon@virginia.edu
Assoc Program Dir: Kevin McFadden *E-mail:* kmcfadden@virginia.edu
Annual free public festival for children & adults featuring authors, illustrators, publishers, publicists, agents & other book professionals in panel discussions & readings for adults & children of all ages. More than 200 authors invited annually.

Location: Charlottesville, VA, USA
March 21-25, 2007

## APRIL

**Dataprint**
Sponsored by Reed Messe Wien Gesellschaft
mbH
Messeplatz 1, 1020 Vienna, Austria
Mailing Address: Postfach 277, 1021 Vienna,
Austria
*Tel:* (01) 727 20-0 *Fax:* (01) 727 20-443
*E-mail:* info@messe.at; dataprint@reedexpo.at
*Web Site:* www.messe.at; www.dataprint.at
*Key Personnel*
Mgr: Gabriele Lindinger
Fair Coord: Claudia Wrana
International trade fair for print media & digital
production.
Location: Design Center, Linz, Austria
April 2007

**International Children's Book Day**
Sponsored by International Board on Books for
Young People (IBBY)
Nonnenweg 12, Postfach, 4003 Basel, Switzerland
*Tel:* (061) 272 29 17 *Fax:* (061) 272 27 57
*E-mail:* ibby@ibby.org
*Web Site:* www.ibby.org
*Key Personnel*
Pres: Peter Schneck
Admin Dir: Liz Page
On or around Hans Christian Andersen's birth-
day, April 2nd, International Children's Book
day (ICBD) is celebrated to inspire a love of
reading & to call attention to children's books.
Each year a different national section has the
opportunity to be the international sponsor. It
decides upon a theme & invites a prominent
author to write a message to the children of
the world & a well-known illustrator to design
a poster. These materials are used in different
ways to promote books & reading around the
world.
Location: New Zealand
April 2, 2007

**Los Angeles Times Festival of Books**
Sponsored by Los Angeles Times
Division of Tribune Co
202 W First St, 6th fl, Los Angeles, CA 90012,
United States
*Tel:* 213-237-5000 *Toll Free Tel:* 800-528-4637
*Fax:* 213-237-2335
*Web Site:* www.latimes.com/festivalofbooks
Location: UCLA Campus, Los Angeles, CA,
USA
April 28-29, 2007

**National Library Week**
Sponsored by American Library Association
(ALA)
50 E Huron St, Chicago, IL 60611, United States
*Tel:* 312-944-6780 *Toll Free Tel:* 800-545-2433
*Fax:* 312-944-8520
*E-mail:* pio@ala.org
*Web Site:* www.ala.org/events
*Key Personnel*
Public Info Dir: Mark Gould
Press Officer: Larra Clark *E-mail:* lclark@ala.org
Location: Nationwide throughout the USA
April 15-21, 2007

**NEXPO®**
Sponsored by Newspaper Association of America
(NAA)
1921 Gallows Rd, Suite 600, Vienna, VA 22182,
United States

*Tel:* 703-902-1600 *Fax:* 703-902-1843
*E-mail:* sarns@naa.org
*Web Site:* www.nexpo.com
*Key Personnel*
Dir of Exhibition Sales: Brad Smith
Annual technical exposition & conference for
newspapers.
Location: Orange County Convention Center, Or-
lando, FL, USA
April 21-24, 2007

**North American Agricultural Journalists
Spring Meeting**
Sponsored by North American Agricultural Jour-
nalists
2604 Cumberland Ct, College Station, TX 77845,
United States
*Tel:* 979-845-2872 *Fax:* 979-845-2414
*Web Site:* naaj.tamu.edu
*Key Personnel*
Exec Sec, Treas: Kathleen Phillips *E-mail:* ka-
phillips@tamu.edu
Location: Washington, DC, USA
April 2007

**Northprint**
Sponsored by IIR Exhibitions
Member of IIR Group
29 Bressenden Place, London SW1E 5DR, United
Kingdom
*Tel:* (020) 7915 5132 *Fax:* (020) 7915 5021
*Web Site:* www.northprintexpo.co.uk; www.iir-
exhibitions.com
*Key Personnel*
Man Dir: Nicky Mason *E-mail:* newstec@iirx.co.
uk
Event Mgr: Gordon Kirk *E-mail:* gkirk@iirx.co.
uk
Exhibitions Administrator: Katie Morris
*E-mail:* kmorris@iirx.co.uk
National mainstream graphic arts event for com-
mercial printers.
Location: Harrogate Exhibition Centre, Harrogate,
UK
April 24-26, 2007

**SouthPack**
Sponsored by Canon Communications
11444 W Olympic Blvd, Suite 900, Los Angeles,
CA 90064, United States
*Tel:* 310-445-4200 *Fax:* 310-996-9499
*E-mail:* feedback@devicelink.com
*Web Site:* www.cancom.com; www.
canontradeshows.com
Biennial.
Location: Georgia World Congress Center, At-
lanta, GA, USA
April 24-26, 2007

**Annual Web Offset Association Conference**
Sponsored by Web Offset Association
Division of PIA/GATF
200 Deer Run Rd, Sewickley, PA 15143, United
States
*Tel:* 412-741-6860 *Toll Free Tel:* 800-910-4283
*Fax:* 412-259-1800
*Web Site:* www.gain.net
*Key Personnel*
Meetings Asst: Ricardo Vila-Roger
*E-mail:* rvilaroger@piagatf.org
Location: Sheraton Centre Toronto, Toronto, ON,
Canada
April 29-May 2, 2007

**Young People's Poetry Week**
Sponsored by The Children's Book Council
(CBC)
12 W 37 St, 2nd fl, New York, NY 10118-7480,
United States
*Tel:* 212-966-1990 *Toll Free Tel:* 800-999-
2160 (orders only) *Fax:* 212-966-2073
*Toll Free Fax:* 888-807-9355 (orders only)

*Web Site:* www.cbcbooks.org
*Key Personnel*
Pres: Paula Quint
Location: Nationwide throughout the USA
April 16-22, 2007

## MAY

**Canadian Library Association Annual
Convention & Tradeshow**
Sponsored by Canadian Library Association
(CLA)
328 Frank St, Ottawa, ON K2P 0X8, Canada
*Tel:* 613-232-9625 *Fax:* 613-563-9895
*E-mail:* info@cla.ca
*Web Site:* www.cla.ca
*Key Personnel*
Pres: Madeleine Lefebvre
Exec Dir: Don Butcher *E-mail:* dbutcher@cla.ca
Location: St John's, NL, Canada
May 30-June 2, 2007

**EXPOLIT Exposicion de Literatura Cristiana
Book Fair**
Sponsored by Spanish Evangelical Publishers
Association (SEPA)/Associacion de Editores
Evangelicos and Editorial Unilit
1360 NW 88 Ave, Miami, FL 33172, United
States
*Tel:* 305-503-1191 *Toll Free Tel:* 800-767-7726
*Fax:* 305-717-6886
*E-mail:* wendy@expolit.com
*Web Site:* www.expolit.com
*Key Personnel*
Pres, EXPOLIT: David Ecklebarger
Program Dir: Marie Tanayo
Spanish Christian Literature Convention.
Location: Sheridan Convention Center, Miami,
FL, USA
May 17-22, 2007

**Grafivak**
Sponsored by Amsterdam RAI
Europaplein, 1078 GZ Amsterdam, Netherlands
Mailing Address: PO Box 77777, 1070-MS Ams-
terdam, Netherlands
*Tel:* (020) 549 12 12 *Fax:* (020) 549 18 43
*E-mail:* grafivak@rai.nl
*Web Site:* www.grafivak.nl
*Key Personnel*
Prod Mgr: Xander de Bruine *Tel:* (020) 549 22
44 *E-mail:* x.d.bruine@rai.nl
Press & PR Mgr: Pim van Houten *Tel:* (020) 549
12 12 *E-mail:* p.v.houten@rai.nl
Biennial exhibition for communication, pre-media
& print.
Location: Amsterdam RAI Exhibition Center,
Amsterdam, Netherlands
May 8-11, 2007

**Newspaper Association of America Annual
Convention**
Sponsored by Newspaper Association of America
(NAA)
1921 Gallows Rd, Suite 600, Vienna, VA 22182,
United States
*Tel:* 703-902-1600 *Fax:* 703-902-1790
*E-mail:* willa@naa.org
*Web Site:* www.naa.org
*Key Personnel*
Pres & CEO: John Sturm
Meetings Mgr: Kristen Andersen Fleming
Location: New York Marriott Marquis, New York,
NY, USA
May 6-9, 2007

**PrintEx07**
Sponsored by Graphic Arts Merchants Association of Australia Inc (GAMAA)
PO Box 1051, Crows Nest, NSW 2065, Australia
*Tel:* (02) 9417 0500 *Fax:* (02) 9417 0400
*E-mail:* enquire@gamaa.net.au
*Web Site:* www.printex.net.au; www.gamaa.net.au
PrintEx brings the latest printing & graphic communications technologies to the industry. Co-sponsored by the Printing Industries Association of Australia (PIAA).
Location: Sydney Convention & Exhibition Centre, Darling Harbour, Sydney, NSW, Australia
May 24-26, 2007

**Sofia National Book Fair**
Sponsored by Bulgarian Book Association
11 Slaveikov Sq, 1000 Sofia, Bulgaria
Mailing Address: PO Box 1046, 1000 Sofia, Bulgaria
*Tel:* (02) 986 79 93; (02) 986 79 70 *Fax:* (02) 986 79 93
*E-mail:* bba@otel.net; bulgarian.book@gmail.com
*Web Site:* www.bba-bg.org
*Key Personnel*
Sec Gen: Madlena Romanova *E-mail:* bba@otel.net
PR: Dimmo Petrov *E-mail:* bulgarian.book@gmail.com
Location: National Palace of Culture, Sofia, Bulgaria
May 2007

**Southwestern Graphics**
Sponsored by Texas Graphic Arts Educational Foundation
13410 Preston Rd, No 1-100, Dallas, TX 75240-5299, United States
*Tel:* 940-763-8370 (Intl only) *Toll Free Tel:* 800-540-8280 *Fax:* 940-763-8395 (Intl Only)
*Toll Free Fax:* 800-540-5019
*E-mail:* info@swgraphics.com
*Web Site:* www.swgraphics.com
*Key Personnel*
Asst Show Mgr: Laura Bates
Location: Reliant Center, Houston, TX, USA
May 17-19, 2007

# SUMMER

**The Dorothy L Sayers Society Annual Convention**
Sponsored by The Dorothy L Sayers Society
Rose Cottage, Malthouse Lane, Hurstpierpoint, West Sussex BN6 9JY, United Kingdom
*Tel:* (01273) 833444 *Fax:* (01273) 835988
*E-mail:* info@sayers.org.uk
*Web Site:* www.sayers.org.uk
*Key Personnel*
Chmn: Christopher Dean
Members only event.
Location: Wheaton College, Wheaton, IL, USA
Summer 2007

**Umbrella 2007**
Sponsored by Chartered Institute of Library & Information Professionals (CILIP)
7 Ridgmount St, London WC1E 7AE, United Kingdom
*Tel:* (020) 7255 0500; (020) 7255 0544 (conferences) *Fax:* (020) 7255 0501; (020) 7255 0541 (conferences)
*E-mail:* conferences@cilip.org.uk; umbrella@cilip.org.uk
*Web Site:* www.cilip.org.uk
*Key Personnel*
Contact: Joan Thompson

Location: UMIST, Manchester, UK
Summer 2007

# JUNE

**American Library Association Annual Conference**
Sponsored by American Library Association (ALA)
50 E Huron St, Chicago, IL 60611, United States
*Tel:* 312-280-3200 *Toll Free Tel:* 800-545-2433 *Fax:* 312-944-7841
*E-mail:* ala@ala.org
*Web Site:* www.ala.org
*Key Personnel*
Public Info Dir: Mark Gould
Press Officer: Larra Clark *E-mail:* lclark@ala.org
Dir, Intl Rel: Michael Dowling
Location: Washington, DC, USA
June 21-27, 2007

**AsiaPack AsiaPrint**
Sponsored by Reed Tradex Co Ltd
32nd fl, Sathorn Nakorn Tower, 100/68-69, North Sathorn Rd, Silom, Bangkok 10500, Thailand
*Tel:* (02) 636 7272 *Fax:* (02) 636 7282
*E-mail:* printpack@reedtradex.co.th
*Web Site:* www.asiapackasiaprint.com
*Key Personnel*
Sales & Mktg: Ms Kanokwan Thitapanich
Biennial international trade exhibition for printing, packaging & processing machinery, equipment materials, supplies & solutions. Co-organized by the Thai Printing Association.
Location: Bangkok International Trade & Exhibition Centre, Bangkok, Thailand
June 2007

**BookExpo America (BEA)**
Sponsored by Reed Exhibitions
Affiliate of Reed Exhibition Companies
383 Main Ave, Norwalk, CT 06851, United States
*Tel:* 203-840-5614 *Toll Free Tel:* 800-840-5614 *Fax:* 203-840-5580
*E-mail:* inquiry@bookexpoamerica.com
*Web Site:* bookexpoamerica.com
*Key Personnel*
Industry VP: Chris McCabe *E-mail:* cmccabe@reedexpo.com
Mktg Dir: Tom Kobak *E-mail:* tkobak@reedexpo.com
Dir of Strategic Accts: Steve Rosato *E-mail:* srosato@reedexpo.com
Group Sales Dir: Jim Fama *E-mail:* jfama@reedexpo.com
Produced & managed by Reed Exhibitions, BEA is sponsored by American Booksellers Association & Association of American Publishers.
Location: Jacob K Javits Convention Center, New York, NY, USA
June 1-3, 2007

**The Bronte Society Annual General Meeting**
Sponsored by The Bronte Society
Bronte Parsonage Museum, Church St, Haworth, Keighley, W Yorks BD22 8DR, United Kingdom
*Tel:* (01535) 642323 *Fax:* (01535) 647131
*E-mail:* info@bronte.org.uk
*Web Site:* www.bronte.org.uk
*Key Personnel*
Museum Mgr: Alan Bentley
Location: West Lane Baptist Church, Haworth, W Yorks, UK
June 2, 2007

**International Association of Music Libraries, Archives & Documentation Centres Conference**
Sponsored by International Association of Music Libraries, Archives & Documentation Centres
c/o National Library of New Zealand, PO Box 1467, Wellington 6001, New Zealand
*Tel:* (04) 474 3039 *Fax:* (04) 474 3035
*Web Site:* www.iaml.info
*Key Personnel*
Secretary General: Roger Flury *E-mail:* roger.flury@natlib.govt.nz
Location: Sydney, NSW, Australia
June 30-July 6, 2007

**Special Libraries Association Annual Conference**
Sponsored by Special Libraries Association (SLA)
313 S Patrick St, Alexandria, VA 22314, United States
*Tel:* 703-647-4900 *Fax:* 703-647-4901
*E-mail:* sla@sla.org
*Web Site:* www.sla.org
*Key Personnel*
Exec Dir: Janice LaChance *E-mail:* janice@sla.org
Location: Denver, CO, USA
June 3-6, 2007

# JULY

**Church & Synagogue Library Association Conference**
Sponsored by Church & Synagogue Library Association
PO Box 19357, Portland, OR 97280-0357, United States
*Tel:* 503-244-6919 *Toll Free Tel:* 800-542-2752 *Fax:* 503-977-3734
*E-mail:* csla@worldaccessnet.com
*Web Site:* www.csla.info
Location: Hilton Valley Forge, King of Prussia, PA, USA
July 22-24, 2007

**International Christian Retail Show**
Formerly CBA International Convention
Sponsored by CBA
9240 Explorer Dr, Colorado Springs, CO 80920-5001, United States
Mailing Address: PO Box 62000, Colorado Springs, CO 80962-2000, United States
*Tel:* 719-265-9895 *Toll Free Tel:* 800-252-1950 *Fax:* 719-272-3510
*E-mail:* info@cbaonline.org
*Web Site:* www.cbaonline.org
*Key Personnel*
Pres: William Anderson *E-mail:* banderson@cbaonline.org
VP & COO: Dorothy Gore
Convention & Expositions Mgr: Scott Graham
For almost 50 years, the annual CBA International Convention has been our industry's single-most impacting week. During this week, people of the industry from all over the world meet face-to-face for buying & selling, education, inspiration, fellowship & future planning. Here individuals unite to further the mission of seeing Christian product impact lives for God's kingdom the world over. At this unique gathering, our industry's strength is most evident & our goals are most clearly in focus. It is, in short, the most important week in the ministry of your business & of the industry as a whole.
Location: Georgia World Congress, Atlanta, GA, USA
July 8-12, 2007

## RWA Annual National Conference
Sponsored by Romance Writers of America
16000 Stuebner Airline, Suite 140, Spring, TX
77379, United States
*Tel:* 832-717-5200 *Fax:* 832-717-5201
*E-mail:* info@rwanational.org
*Web Site:* www.rwanational.org
*Key Personnel*
Exec Dir: Allison Kelley *E-mail:* akelley@
rwanational.org
Location: Hyatt Regency Dallas, Dallas, TX,
USA
July 11-14, 2007

## AUGUST

### Edinburgh International Book Festival
Scottish Book Centre, 137 Dundee St, Edinburgh
EH11 1BG, United Kingdom
*Tel:* (0131) 228 5444 *Fax:* (0131) 228 4333
*E-mail:* admin@edbookfest.co.uk
*Web Site:* www.edbookfest.co.uk
*Key Personnel*
Dir: Catherine Lockerbie
Personal Asst to the Dir: Lyn Trotter
Mktg & PR Mgr: Amanda Barry
The festival takes place in Charlotte Square Gar-
dens (just off the West End of Princes St) over
17 days each August. An extensive program
showcases the work of the world's authors &
thinkers for people of all ages.
Location: Charlotte Square Gardens, Edinburgh,
UK
Aug 11-27, 2007

### SWANICK: The Writer's Summer School
Sponsored by Writer's Summer School
10 Stag Rd, Lake Sandown, Isle of Wight PO36
8PE, United Kingdom
*Tel:* (07050) 630949 *Fax:* (07050) 630949
*Web Site:* www.wss.org.uk
*Key Personnel*
Sec: Jean Sutton *E-mail:* jean.sutton@lineone.net
A week-long summer school of informal talks
& discussion groups, forums, panels, quizzes,
competition & a lot of fun. Open to everyone,
from absolute beginners to published authors.
Held annually in August.
Location: The Hayes Conference Centre, Swan-
wick, Derbyshire, UK
Aug 2007

### World Library & Information Congress
Sponsored by International Federation of Library
Associations & Institutions (IFLA) (Federation
internationale des associations de bibliothe-
caires et des bibliotheques)
Prins Willem-Alexanderhof 5, 2595 BE The
Hague, Netherlands
Mailing Address: PO Box 95312, 2509 CH The
Hague, Netherlands
*Tel:* (070) 3140884 *Fax:* (070) 3834827
*E-mail:* ifla@ifla.org
*Web Site:* www.ifla.org
*Key Personnel*
Sec Gen: Peter J Lor
Coord of Prof Activities: Sjoerd M J Koopman
*E-mail:* sjoerd.koopman@ifla.org
Location: Durban, South Africa
Aug 2007

## AUTUMN

### National Design Conference
Sponsored by American Institute of Graphic Arts
(AIGA)

164 Fifth Ave, New York, NY 10010, United
States
*Tel:* 212-807-1990 (ext 223) *Fax:* 212-807-1799
*E-mail:* aiga@aiga.org; programs@aiga.org
*Web Site:* www.aiga.org
*Key Personnel*
Exec Dir: Richard Grefe
Biennial event.
Autumn 2007

## SEPTEMBER

### Distripress Annual Congress
Sponsored by Distripress
Beethovenstr 20, CH-8002 Zurich, Switzerland
*Tel:* (01) 202 41 21 *Fax:* (01) 202 10 25
*E-mail:* info@distripress.ch
*Web Site:* www.distripress.net
*Key Personnel*
Man Dir: Dr Peter Emod *E-mail:* peter.emod@
distripress.ch
Congress Coord: Susanne Jorg *E-mail:* susanne.
joerg@distripress.ch
Non-profit association for the promotion of the
International Press Distribution.
Location: Vienna, Austria
Sept 23-37, 2007

### Goeteborg Book Fair
Sponsored by Bok & Bibliotek
Maessans Gata 20, 412 94 Goeteborg, Sweden
*Tel:* (031) 708 84 00 *Fax:* (031) 20 91 03
*E-mail:* info@goteborg-bookfair.com
*Web Site:* www.goteborg-bookfair.com
*Key Personnel*
Man Dir: Anna Falck *E-mail:* af@bok-bibliotek.
se
Conference Mgr: Gunilla Sandin *E-mail:* gs@
bok-bibliotek.se
Exhibition Mgr: Lisa Oden *E-mail:* lo@bok-
bibliotek.se
Prog Coord: Anneli Jonasson *E-mail:* aj@bok-
bibliotek.se
Location: Goeteborg, Sweden
Sept 27-30, 2007

### Graph Expo & Converting Expo
Sponsored by NPES The Association for Sup-
pliers of Printing, Publishing & Converting
Technologies
1899 Preston White Dr, Reston, VA 20191-4367,
United States
*Tel:* 703-264-7200 *Fax:* 703-620-0994
*E-mail:* npes@npes.org
*Web Site:* www.gasc.org
*Key Personnel*
Pres: Regis J Delmontagne
Dir, Communs & Mktg: Carol J Hurlburt
*E-mail:* churlbur@npes.org
Location: McCormick Place South, Chicago, IL,
USA
Sept 9-12, 2007

### PSA International Conference of Photography
Sponsored by Photographic Society of America
Inc (PSA)
3000 United Founders Blvd, Suite 103, Oklahoma
City, OK 73112-3940, United States
*Tel:* 405-843-1437 *Fax:* 405-843-1438
*E-mail:* hq@psa-photo.org
*Web Site:* www.psa-photo.org
*Key Personnel*
VP, Conventions: Gerald Emmerich, Jr
Location: Starr Pass Marriott Resort & Spa, Tuc-
son, AZ, USA
Sept 3-8, 2007

## OCTOBER

### Inter American Press Association General Assembly
Sponsored by Inter American Press Association
(IAPA)
Jules Dubois Bldg, 1801 SW Third Ave, Miami,
FL 33129, United States
*Tel:* 305-634-2465 *Fax:* 305-635-2272
*E-mail:* info@sipiapa.org
*Web Site:* www.sipiapa.org
*Key Personnel*
Exec Dir: Julio E Munoz
Location: Miami, FL, USA
Oct 2007

### National Association of Science Writers Annual Meeting
Sponsored by National Association of Science
Writers (NASW)
PO Box 890, Hedgesville, WV 25427, United
States
*Tel:* 304-754-5077 *Fax:* 304-754-5076
*Web Site:* www.nasw.org
*Key Personnel*
Exec Dir: Diane McGurgan *E-mail:* diane@nasw.
org
Location: Seattle, WA, USA
Oct 2007

### National College Media Convention
Sponsored by Associated Collegiate Press (ACP)
Subsidiary of National Scholastic Press Assn
2221 University Ave SE, Suite 121, Minneapolis,
MN 55414, United States
*Tel:* 612-625-8335 *Fax:* 612-626-0720
*E-mail:* info@studentpress.org
*Web Site:* studentpress.org
*Key Personnel*
Assoc Dir: Ann Akers
Also sponsored by College Media Advisors.
Location: Washington Hilton, Washington, DC,
USA
Oct 25-28, 2007

### PACK EXPO Las Vegas
Sponsored by Packaging Machinery Manufactur-
ers Institute
4350 N Fairfax Dr, Suite 600, Arlington, VA
22203, United States
*Tel:* 703-243-8555 *Fax:* 703-243-3038
*E-mail:* expo@pmmi.org
*Web Site:* www.packexpo.com
*Key Personnel*
Exhibitor Servs Mgr: Kim Beaulieu
*E-mail:* kim@pmmi.org
Location: Las Vegas Convention Center, Las Ve-
gas, NV, USA
Oct 15-17, 2007

### Texas Book Festival
610 Brazos St, Suite 200, Austin, TX 78701,
United States
*Tel:* 512-477-4055 *Fax:* 512-322-0722
*E-mail:* bookfest@texasbookfestival.org
*Web Site:* www.texasbookfestival.org
*Key Personnel*
Exec Dir: Mary Herman *Tel:* 512-320-5451
*E-mail:* maryherman@texasbookfestival.org
Literary Dir: Clay Smith *Tel:* 512-472-3808
*E-mail:* clay@texasbookfestival.org
Off Mgr: Andrea V Prestridge *Tel:* 512-477-4055
*E-mail:* andrea@texasbookfestival.org
The festival is a statewide program that promotes
reading & literacy highlighted by a two-day
festival featuring authors from Texas & across
the country. Money raised from the festival is
distributed as grants to public libraries through-
out the state.

Location: State Capitol Bldg, Austin, TX, USA
Oct 2007

## NOVEMBER

### American Academy of Religion
Sponsored by American Schools of Oriental Research
825 Houston Mill Rd, Suite 201, Atlanta, GA
  30329-4205, United States
*Tel:* 404-727-3049 *Fax:* 404-727-7959
*E-mail:* aar@aarweb.org
*Web Site:* www.aarweb.org
*Key Personnel*
Prog Dir: Aislinn Jones
Location: San Diego, CA, USA
Nov 17-20, 2007

### BMI Annual Conference
Sponsored by Book Manufacturers' Institute Inc
  (BMI)
2 Armand Beach Dr, Suite 1-B, Palm Coast, FL
  32137, United States
*Tel:* 386-986-4552 *Fax:* 386-986-4553
*E-mail:* info@bmibook.com
*Web Site:* www.bmibook.org
*Key Personnel*
Exec VP: Bruce W Smith
Location: St Regis Resort Monarch Beach, Dana
  Point, CA, USA
Nov 3-6, 2007

### Cairo International Children's Book Fair
Sponsored by General Egyptian Book Organization
Corniche el-Nil - Ramlet Boulac, Cairo 11221,
  Egypt (Arab Republic of Egypt)
*Tel:* (02) 5765436; (02) 5775228; (02) 5775109;
  (02) 5775367; (02) 5775436; (02) 5775545;
  (02) 5775000 *Fax:* (02) 5765058
*E-mail:* info@egyptianbook.org
*Web Site:* www.childrensbookfair.org; www.
  egyptianbook.org; www.egyptianbook.net
*Key Personnel*
Chmn: Dr Nasser El Ansary
VChmn: Dr Waheed Abdel Majeed
Location: Cairo, Egypt
Nov 2007

### Children's Book Week
Sponsored by The Children's Book Council
  (CBC)
12 W 37 St, 2nd fl, New York, NY 10118-7480,
  United States
*Tel:* 212-966-1990 *Toll Free Tel:* 800-999-
  2160 (orders only) *Fax:* 212-966-2073
  *Toll Free Fax:* 888-807-9355 (orders only)
*Web Site:* www.cbcbooks.org
*Key Personnel*
Pres: Paula Quint
Location: Nationwide across the USA
Nov 12-18, 2007

### Stuttgarter Buchwochen (Stuttgart Bookweeks)
Sponsored by Boersenverein des Deutschen Buch-
  handels, Landesverband Baden-Wuerttemberg
  eV (Association of Publishers & Booksellers in
  Baden-Wuerttemberg eV)
Paulinenstr 53, 70178 Stuttgart, Germany
*Tel:* (0711) 61941-0; (0711) 123 34 99
  *Fax:* (0711) 61941-44
*E-mail:* post@buchhandelsverband.de
*Web Site:* www.buchhandelsverband.de
*Key Personnel*
Contact: Andrea Baumann *Tel:* (0711) 61941-23
  *Fax:* (0711) 61941-44 *E-mail:* baumann@
  buchhandelsverband.de

Location: Haus der Wirtschaft, Willi-Bleicher Str
  19, Stuttgart, Germany
Nov 2007

## DECEMBER

### Small Press Book Fair
Sponsored by Small Press Center
20 W 44 St, New York, NY 10036, United States
*Tel:* 212-764-7021 *Fax:* 212-354-5365
*E-mail:* info@smallpress.org
*Web Site:* www.smallpress.org
*Key Personnel*
Dir: Karin Taylor
Location: Small Press Center, New York, NY,
  USA
Dec 1-2, 2007

### Sofia National Book Fair
Sponsored by Bulgarian Book Association
11 Slaveikov Sq, 1000 Sofia, Bulgaria
Mailing Address: PO Box 1046, 1000 Sofia, Bul-
  garia
*Tel:* (02) 986 79 93; (02) 986 79 70 *Fax:* (02)
  986 79 93
*E-mail:* bba@otel.net; bulgarian.book@gmail.com
*Web Site:* www.bba-bg.org
*Key Personnel*
Sec Gen: Madlena Romanova *E-mail:* bba@otel.
  net
PR: Dimmo Petrov *E-mail:* bulgarian.book@
  gmail.com
Location: National Palace of Culture, Sofia, Bul-
  garia
Dec 2007

## 2008

## JANUARY

### American Library Association Mid-Winter Meeting
Sponsored by American Library Association
  (ALA)
50 E Huron St, Chicago, IL 60611, United States
*Toll Free Tel:* 800-545-2433 *Fax:* 312-944-6780
*E-mail:* ala@ala.org
*Web Site:* www.ala.org/midwinter
*Key Personnel*
Public Info Dir: Mark Gould
Press Officer: Larra Clark *E-mail:* lclark@ala.org
Location: Philadelphia, PA, USA
Jan 11-16, 2008

## SPRING

### VUE/POINT Conference
Sponsored by NPES The Association for Sup-
  pliers of Printing, Publishing & Converting
  Technologies
1899 Preston White Dr, Reston, VA 20191-4367,
  United States
*Tel:* 703-264-7200 *Fax:* 703-620-0994
*E-mail:* npes@npes.org
*Web Site:* www.gasc.org
*Key Personnel*
Pres: Regis J Delmontagne
Dir, Communs & Mktg: Carol J Hurlburt
  *E-mail:* churlbur@npes.org

Trade Association representing companies which
  manufacture equipment, systems, software &
  supplies used in printing, publishing & converting.
Spring 2008

## MARCH

### Virginia Festival of the Book
Sponsored by Virginia Foundation for the Hu-
  manities
145 Ednam Dr, Charlottesville, VA 22903, United
  States
*Tel:* 434-924-6890 *Fax:* 434-296-4714
*E-mail:* vabook@virginia.edu
*Web Site:* www.vabook.org
*Key Personnel*
Program Dir: Nancy Damon *Tel:* 434-924-7548
  *E-mail:* ndamon@virginia.edu
Assoc Program Dir: Kevin McFadden
  *E-mail:* kmcfadden@virginia.edu
Annual free public festival for children & adults
  featuring authors, illustrators, publishers, pub-
  licists, agents & other book professionals in
  panel discussions & readings for adults & chil-
  dren of all ages. More than 200 authors invited
  annually.
Location: Charlottesville, VA, USA
March 26-30, 2008

## APRIL

### National Library Week
Sponsored by American Library Association
  (ALA)
50 E Huron St, Chicago, IL 60611, United States
*Tel:* 312-944-6780 *Toll Free Tel:* 800-545-2433
  *Fax:* 312-944-8520
*E-mail:* pio@ala.org
*Web Site:* www.ala.org/events
*Key Personnel*
Public Info Dir: Mark Gould
Press Officer: Larra Clark *E-mail:* lclark@ala.org
Location: Nationwide throughout the USA
April 13-19, 2008

### Young People's Poetry Week
Sponsored by The Children's Book Council
  (CBC)
12 W 37 St, 2nd fl, New York, NY 10118-7480,
  United States
*Tel:* 212-966-1990 *Toll Free Tel:* 800-999-
  2160 (orders only) *Fax:* 212-966-2073
  *Toll Free Fax:* 888-807-9355 (orders only)
*Web Site:* www.cbcbooks.org
*Key Personnel*
Pres: Paula Quint
Location: Nationwide throughout the USA
April 14-20, 2008

## MAY

### EXPOLIT Exposicion de Literatura Cristiana Book Fair
Sponsored by Spanish Evangelical Publishers
  Association (SEPA)/Associacion de Editores
  Evangelicos and Editorial Unilit
1360 NW 88 Ave, Miami, FL 33172, United
  States
*Tel:* 305-503-1191 *Toll Free Tel:* 800-767-7726
  *Fax:* 305-717-6886

*E-mail:* wendy@expolit.com
*Web Site:* www.expolit.com
*Key Personnel*
Pres, EXPOLIT: David Ecklebarger
Program Dir: Marie Tanayo
Spanish Christian Literature Convention.
Location: Sheridan Convention Center, Miami,
  FL, USA
May 15-20, 2008

## SUMMER

### IPA Congress
Sponsored by International Publishers Association
Av de Miremont 3, 1206 Geneva, Switzerland
*Tel:* (022) 3463018 *Fax:* (022) 3475717
*E-mail:* secretariat@ipa-uie.org
*Web Site:* www.ipa-uie.org
*Key Personnel*
Secretary General: Jens Bammel
Held every 4 years.
Location: Korea
Summer 2008

## JUNE

### American Library Association Annual Conference
Sponsored by American Library Association
  (ALA)
50 E Huron St, Chicago, IL 60611, United States
*Tel:* 312-280-3200 *Toll Free Tel:* 800-545-2433
  *Fax:* 312-944-7841
*E-mail:* ala@ala.org
*Web Site:* www.ala.org
*Key Personnel*
Public Info Dir: Mark Gould
Press Officer: Larra Clark *E-mail:* lclark@ala.org
Dir, Intl Rel: Michael Dowling
Location: Anaheim, CA, USA
June 26-July 2, 2008

## JULY

### International Christian Retail Show
Formerly CBA International Convention
Sponsored by CBA
9240 Explorer Dr, Colorado Springs, CO 80920-
  5001, United States
Mailing Address: PO Box 62000, Colorado
  Springs, CO 80962-2000, United States
*Tel:* 719-265-9895 *Toll Free Tel:* 800-252-1950
  *Fax:* 719-272-3510
*E-mail:* info@cbaonline.org
*Web Site:* www.cbaonline.org
*Key Personnel*
Pres: William Anderson *E-mail:* banderson@
  cbaonline.org
VP & COO: Dorothy Gore
Convention & Expositions Mgr: Scott Graham
For almost 50 years, the annual CBA International Convention has been our industry's
  single-most impacting week. During this week,
  people of the industry from all over the world
  meet face-to-face for buying & selling, education, inspiration, fellowship & future planning.
  Here individuals unite to further the mission of
  seeing Christian product impact lives for God's
  kingdom the world over. At this unique gathering, our industry's strength is most evident
  & our goals are most clearly in focus. It is, in
  short, the most important week in the ministry
  of your business & of the industry as a whole.
Location: Orange County Convention Center, Orlando, FL, USA
July 13-17, 2008

### RWA Annual National Conference
Sponsored by Romance Writers of America
16000 Stuebner Airline, Suite 140, Spring, TX
  77379, United States
*Tel:* 832-717-5200 *Fax:* 832-717-5201
*E-mail:* info@rwanational.org
*Web Site:* www.rwanational.org
*Key Personnel*
Exec Dir: Allison Kelley *E-mail:* akelley@
  rwanational.org
Location: San Francisco Marriott, San Francisco,
  CA, USA
July 30-Aug 2, 2008

### Special Libraries Association Annual Conference
Sponsored by Special Libraries Association
  (SLA)
313 S Patrick St, Alexandria, VA 22314, United
  States
*Tel:* 703-647-4900 *Fax:* 703-647-4901
*E-mail:* sla@sla.org
*Web Site:* www.sla.org
*Key Personnel*
Exec Dir: Janice LaChance *E-mail:* janice@sla.
  org
Location: Seattle, WA, USA
July 27-30, 2008

## AUGUST

### SWANICK: The Writer's Summer School
Sponsored by Writer's Summer School
10 Stag Rd, Lake Sandown, Isle of Wight PO36
  8PE, United Kingdom
*Tel:* (07050) 630949 *Fax:* (07050) 630949
*Web Site:* www.wss.org.uk
*Key Personnel*
Sec: Jean Sutton *E-mail:* jean.sutton@lineone.net
A week-long summer school of informal talks
  & discussion groups, forums, panels, quizzes,
  competition & a lot of fun. Open to everyone,
  from absolute beginners to published authors.
  Held annually in August.
Location: The Hayes Conference Centre, Swan-
  wick, Derbyshire, UK
August 2008

### World Library & Information Congress
Sponsored by International Federation of Library
  Associations & Institutions (IFLA) (Federation
  internationale des associations de bibliothe-
  caires et des bibliotheques)
Prins Willem-Alexanderhof 5, 2595 BE The
  Hague, Netherlands
Mailing Address: PO Box 95312, 2509 CH The
  Hague, Netherlands
*Tel:* (070) 3140884 *Fax:* (070) 3834827
*E-mail:* ifla@ifla.org
*Web Site:* www.ifla.org
*Key Personnel*
Sec Gen: Peter J Lor
Coord of Prof Activities: Sjoerd M J Koopman
  *E-mail:* sjoerd.koopman@ifla.org
Location: Quebec, Canada
Aug 2008

## SEPTEMBER

### AICC/TAPPI SuperCorrExpo® 2008
Sponsored by Technical Association of the Pulp
  & Paper Industry (TAPPI)
15 Technology Pkwy S, Norcross, GA 30092,
  United States
*Tel:* 770-446-1400 *Toll Free Tel:* 800-332-8686
  *Fax:* 770-446-6947
*Web Site:* www.tappi.org
*Key Personnel*
Publg Dir: Mary Beth Cornell *E-mail:* mcornell@
  tappi.org
Corp Rel Dir: Clare Reagan *E-mail:* creagan@
  tappi.org
Adv Mgr: Vince Saputo *E-mail:* vsaputo@tappi.
  org
Location: Georgia World Congress Center, At-
  lanta, GA, USA
Sept 22-26, 2008

### International Board on Books for Young People Biennial Congress
Sponsored by International Board on Books for
  Young People (IBBY)
Nonnenweg 12, Postfach, 4003 Basel, Switzerland
*Tel:* (061) 272 29 17 *Fax:* (061) 272 27 57
*E-mail:* ibby@ibby.org
*Web Site:* www.ibby.org
*Key Personnel*
Pres: Peter Schneck
Admin Dir: Liz Page
IBBY's biennial congresses, hosted by differ-
  ent countries, are the most important meeting
  points for IBBY members & other people in-
  volved in children's books & reading devel-
  opment. They are wonderful opportunities to
  make contacts, exchange ideas & open hori-
  zons.
Location: Copenhagen, Denmark
Sept 6-10, 2008

## OCTOBER

### American Academy of Religion
Sponsored by American Schools of Oriental Re-
  search
825 Houston Mill Rd, Suite 201, Atlanta, GA
  30329-4205, United States
*Tel:* 404-727-3049 *Fax:* 404-727-7959
*E-mail:* aar@aarweb.org
*Web Site:* www.aarweb.org
*Key Personnel*
Prog Dir: Aislinn Jones
Location: Chicago, IL, USA
Oct 25-28, 2008

### Distripress Annual Congress
Sponsored by Distripress
Beethovenstr 20, CH-8002 Zurich, Switzerland
*Tel:* (01) 202 41 21 *Fax:* (01) 202 10 25
*E-mail:* info@distripress.ch
*Web Site:* www.distripress.net
*Key Personnel*
Man Dir: Dr Peter Emod *E-mail:* peter.emod@
  distripress.ch
Congress Coord: Susanne Jorg *E-mail:* susanne.
  joerg@distripress.ch
Non-profit association for the promotion of the
  International Press Distribution.
Location: Istanbul, Turkey
October 26-30, 2008

### Graph Expo & Converting Expo
Sponsored by NPES The Association for Sup-
  pliers of Printing, Publishing & Converting
  Technologies

1899 Preston White Dr, Reston, VA 20191-4367,
United States
*Tel:* 703-264-7200 *Fax:* 703-620-0994
*E-mail:* npes@npes.org
*Web Site:* www.gasc.org
*Key Personnel*
Pres: Regis J Delmontagne
Dir, Communs & Mktg: Carol J Hurlburt
    *E-mail:* churlbur@npes.org
Location: McCormick Place South, Chicago, IL,
USA
Oct 26-29, 2008

## NOVEMBER

**Children's Book Week**
Sponsored by The Children's Book Council
(CBC)
12 W 37 St, 2nd fl, New York, NY 10118-7480,
United States
*Tel:* 212-966-1990 *Toll Free Tel:* 800-999-
2160 (orders only) *Fax:* 212-966-2073
    *Toll Free Fax:* 888-807-9355 (orders only)
*Web Site:* www.cbcbooks.org
*Key Personnel*
Pres: Paula Quint
Location: Nationwide across the USA
Nov 17-23, 2008

## DECEMBER

**Small Press Book Fair**
Sponsored by Small Press Center
20 W 44 St, New York, NY 10036, United States
*Tel:* 212-764-7021 *Fax:* 212-354-5365
*E-mail:* info@smallpress.org
*Web Site:* www.smallpress.org
*Key Personnel*
Dir: Karin Taylor
Location: Small Press Center, New York, NY,
USA
Dec 6-7, 2008

# 2009
## JANUARY

**American Library Association Mid-Winter
Meeting**
Sponsored by American Library Association
(ALA)
50 E Huron St, Chicago, IL 60611, United States
*Toll Free Tel:* 800-545-2433 *Fax:* 312-944-6780
*E-mail:* ala@ala.org
*Web Site:* www.ala.org/midwinter
*Key Personnel*
Public Info Dir: Mark Gould
Press Officer: Larra Clark *E-mail:* lclark@ala.org
Location: Denver, CO, USA
Jan 23-28, 2009

## SPRING

**VUE/POINT Conference**
Sponsored by NPES The Association for Sup-
pliers of Printing, Publishing & Converting
Technologies

1899 Preston White Dr, Reston, VA 20191-4367,
United States
*Tel:* 703-264-7200 *Fax:* 703-620-0994
*E-mail:* npes@npes.org
*Web Site:* www.gasc.org
*Key Personnel*
Pres: Regis J Delmontagne
Dir, Communs & Mktg: Carol J Hurlburt
    *E-mail:* churlbur@npes.org
Trade Association representing companies which
manufacture equipment, systems, software &
supplies used in printing, publishing & convert-
ing.
Spring 2009

## MARCH

**Virginia Festival of the Book**
Sponsored by Virginia Foundation for the Hu-
manities
145 Ednam Dr, Charlottesville, VA 22903, United
States
*Tel:* 434-924-6890 *Fax:* 434-296-4714
*E-mail:* vabook@virginia.edu
*Web Site:* www.vabook.org
*Key Personnel*
Program Dir: Nancy Damon *Tel:* 434-924-7548
    *E-mail:* ndamon@virginia.edu
Assoc Program Dir: Kevin McFadden
    *E-mail:* kmcfadden@virginia.edu
Annual free public festival for children & adults
featuring authors, illustrators, publishers, pub-
licists, agents & other book professionals in
panel discussions & readings for adults & chil-
dren of all ages. More than 200 authors invited
annually.
Location: Charlottesville, VA, USA
March 18-22, 2009

## APRIL

**National Library Week**
Sponsored by American Library Association
(ALA)
50 E Huron St, Chicago, IL 60611, United States
*Tel:* 312-944-6780 *Toll Free Tel:* 800-545-2433
    *Fax:* 312-944-8520
*E-mail:* pio@ala.org
*Web Site:* www.ala.org/events
*Key Personnel*
Public Info Dir: Mark Gould
Press Officer: Larra Clark *E-mail:* lclark@ala.org
Location: Nationwide throughout the USA
April 12-18, 2009

**Young People's Poetry Week**
Sponsored by The Children's Book Council
(CBC)
12 W 37 St, 2nd fl, New York, NY 10118-7480,
United States
*Tel:* 212-966-1990 *Toll Free Tel:* 800-999-
2160 (orders only) *Fax:* 212-966-2073
    *Toll Free Fax:* 888-807-9355 (orders only)
*Web Site:* www.cbcbooks.org
*Key Personnel*
Pres: Paula Quint
Location: Nationwide throughout the USA
April 13-19, 2009

## MAY

**EXPOLIT Exposicion de Literatura Cristiana
Book Fair**
Sponsored by Spanish Evangelical Publishers
Association (SEPA)/Associacion de Editores
Evangelicos and Editorial Unilit
1360 NW 88 Ave, Miami, FL 33172, United
States
*Tel:* 305-503-1191 *Toll Free Tel:* 800-767-7726
    *Fax:* 305-717-6886
*E-mail:* wendy@expolit.com
*Web Site:* www.expolit.com
*Key Personnel*
Pres, EXPOLIT: David Ecklebarger
Program Dir: Marie Tanayo
Spanish Christian Literature Convention.
Location: Sheridan Convention Center, Miami,
FL, USA
May 14-19, 2009

**Pacprint09**
Sponsored by Graphic Arts Merchants Associa-
tion of Australia Inc (GAMAA)
PO Box 1051, Crows Nest, NSW 2065, Australia
*Tel:* (02) 9417 0500 *Fax:* (02) 9417 0400
*E-mail:* enquire@gamaa.net.au
*Web Site:* www.gamaa.net.au; www.pacprint.com.
au
*Key Personnel*
Chmn: Ron Patterson
Co-sponsored by the Printing Industries Associa-
tion of Australia (PIAA).
Location: Melbourne Exhibition Centre, Mel-
bourne, Victoria, Australia
May 2009

## JUNE

**Special Libraries Association Annual
Conference**
Sponsored by Special Libraries Association
(SLA)
313 S Patrick St, Alexandria, VA 22314, United
States
*Tel:* 703-647-4900 *Fax:* 703-647-4901
*E-mail:* sla@sla.org
*Web Site:* www.sla.org
*Key Personnel*
Exec Dir: Janice LaChance *E-mail:* janice@sla.
org
Location: Washington, DC, USA
June 14-17, 2009

## JULY

**American Library Association Annual
Conference**
Sponsored by American Library Association
(ALA)
50 E Huron St, Chicago, IL 60611, United States
*Tel:* 312-280-3200 *Toll Free Tel:* 800-545-2433
    *Fax:* 312-944-7841
*E-mail:* ala@ala.org
*Web Site:* www.ala.org
*Key Personnel*
Public Info Dir: Mark Gould
Press Officer: Larra Clark *E-mail:* lclark@ala.org
Dir, Intl Rel: Michael Dowling
Location: Chicago, IL, USA
July 9-15, 2009

**International Christian Retail Show**
Formerly CBA International Convention

Sponsored by CBA
9240 Explorer Dr, Colorado Springs, CO 80920-5001, United States
Mailing Address: PO Box 62000, Colorado Springs, CO 80962-2000, United States
*Tel:* 719-265-9895 *Toll Free Tel:* 800-252-1950
*Fax:* 719-272-3510
*E-mail:* info@cbaonline.org
*Web Site:* www.cbaonline.org
*Key Personnel*
Pres: William Anderson *E-mail:* banderson@cbaonline.org
VP & COO: Dorothy Gore
Convention & Expositions Mgr: Scott Graham
For almost 50 years, the annual CBA International Convention has been our industry's single-most impacting week. During this week, people of the industry from all over the world meet face-to-face for buying & selling, education, inspiration, fellowship & future planning. Here individuals unite to further the mission of seeing Christian product impact lives for God's kingdom the world over. At this unique gathering, our industry's strength is most evident & our goals are most clearly in focus. It is, in short, the most important week in the ministry of your business & of the industry as a whole.
Location: Colorado Convention Center, Denver, CO, USA
July 12-16, 2009

**RWA Annual National Conference**
Sponsored by Romance Writers of America
16000 Stuebner Airline, Suite 140, Spring, TX 77379, United States
*Tel:* 832-717-5200 *Fax:* 832-717-5201
*E-mail:* info@rwanational.org
*Web Site:* www.rwanational.org
*Key Personnel*
Exec Dir: Allison Kelley *E-mail:* akelley@rwanational.org
Location: Marriott Wardman Park Hotel, Washington, DC, USA
July 15-18, 2009

## SEPTEMBER

**Print®**
Sponsored by NPES The Association for Suppliers of Printing, Publishing & Converting Technologies
1899 Preston White Dr, Reston, VA 20191-4367, United States
*Tel:* 703-264-7200 *Fax:* 703-620-0994
*E-mail:* npes@npes.org
*Web Site:* www.gasc.org
*Key Personnel*
Pres: Regis J Delmontagne
Dir, Communs & Mktg: Carol J Hurlburt
*E-mail:* churlbur@npes.org
Location: McCormick Place, Chicago. IL, USA
Sept 11-17, 2009

## NOVEMBER

**American Academy of Religion**
Sponsored by American Schools of Oriental Research
825 Houston Mill Rd, Suite 201, Atlanta, GA 30329-4205, United States
*Tel:* 404-727-3049 *Fax:* 404-727-7959
*E-mail:* aar@aarweb.org
*Web Site:* www.aarweb.org
*Key Personnel*
Prog Dir: Aislinn Jones

Location: Montreal, PQ, Canada
Nov 7-10, 2009

**Children's Book Week**
Sponsored by The Children's Book Council (CBC)
12 W 37 St, 2nd fl, New York, NY 10118-7480, United States
*Tel:* 212-966-1990 *Toll Free Tel:* 800-999-2160 (orders only) *Fax:* 212-966-2073
*Toll Free Fax:* 888-807-9355 (orders only)
*Web Site:* www.cbcbooks.org
*Key Personnel*
Pres: Paula Quint
Location: Nationwide across the USA
Nov 16-22, 2009

## DECEMBER

**Small Press Book Fair**
Sponsored by Small Press Center
20 W 44 St, New York, NY 10036, United States
*Tel:* 212-764-7021 *Fax:* 212-354-5365
*E-mail:* info@smallpress.org
*Web Site:* www.smallpress.org
*Key Personnel*
Dir: Karin Taylor
Location: Small Press Center, New York, NY, USA
Dec 5-6, 2009

# 2010

## JANUARY

**American Library Association Mid-Winter Meeting**
Sponsored by American Library Association (ALA)
50 E Huron St, Chicago, IL 60611, United States
*Toll Free Tel:* 800-545-2433 *Fax:* 312-944-6780
*E-mail:* ala@ala.org
*Web Site:* www.ala.org/midwinter
*Key Personnel*
Public Info Dir: Mark Gould
Press Officer: Larra Clark *E-mail:* lclark@ala.org
Location: Boston, MA, USA
Jan 15-20, 2010

## SPRING

**VUE/POINT Conference**
Sponsored by NPES The Association for Suppliers of Printing, Publishing & Converting Technologies
1899 Preston White Dr, Reston, VA 20191-4367, United States
*Tel:* 703-264-7200 *Fax:* 703-620-0994
*E-mail:* npes@npes.org
*Web Site:* www.gasc.org
*Key Personnel*
Pres: Regis J Delmontagne
Dir, Communs & Mktg: Carol J Hurlburt
*E-mail:* churlbur@npes.org
Trade Association representing companies which manufacture equipment, systems, software & supplies used in printing, publishing & converting.
Spring 2010

## APRIL

**National Library Week**
Sponsored by American Library Association (ALA)
50 E Huron St, Chicago, IL 60611, United States
*Tel:* 312-944-6780 *Toll Free Tel:* 800-545-2433
*Fax:* 312-944-8520
*E-mail:* pio@ala.org
*Web Site:* www.ala.org/events
*Key Personnel*
Public Info Dir: Mark Gould
Press Officer: Larra Clark *E-mail:* lclark@ala.org
Location: Nationwide throughout the USA
April 4-10, 2010

**Young People's Poetry Week**
Sponsored by The Children's Book Council (CBC)
12 W 37 St, 2nd fl, New York, NY 10118-7480, United States
*Tel:* 212-966-1990 *Toll Free Tel:* 800-999-2160 (orders only) *Fax:* 212-966-2073
*Toll Free Fax:* 888-807-9355 (orders only)
*Web Site:* www.cbcbooks.org
*Key Personnel*
Pres: Paula Quint
Location: Nationwide throughout the USA
April 12-18, 2010

## MAY

**EXPOLIT Exposicion de Literatura Cristiana Book Fair**
Sponsored by Spanish Evangelical Publishers Association (SEPA)/Asociacion de Editores Evangelicos and Editorial Unilit
1360 NW 88 Ave, Miami, FL 33172, United States
*Tel:* 305-503-1191 *Toll Free Tel:* 800-767-7726
*Fax:* 305-717-6886
*E-mail:* wendy@expolit.com
*Web Site:* www.expolit.com
*Key Personnel*
Pres, EXPOLIT: David Ecklebarger
Program Dir: Marie Tanayo
Spanish Christian Literature Convention.
Location: Sheridan Convention Center, Miami, FL, USA
May 13-18, 2010

## JULY

**RWA Annual National Conference**
Sponsored by Romance Writers of America
16000 Stuebner Airline, Suite 140, Spring, TX 77379, United States
*Tel:* 832-717-5200 *Fax:* 832-717-5201
*E-mail:* info@rwanational.org
*Web Site:* www.rwanational.org
*Key Personnel*
Exec Dir: Allison Kelley *E-mail:* akelley@rwanational.org
Location: Gaylord Opryland Nashville, Nashville, TN, USA
July 28-31, 2010

## OCTOBER

**Graph Expo & Converting Expo**
Sponsored by NPES The Association for Suppliers of Printing, Publishing & Converting Technologies
1899 Preston White Dr, Reston, VA 20191-4367, United States
*Tel:* 703-264-7200 *Fax:* 703-620-0994
*E-mail:* npes@npes.org
*Web Site:* www.gasc.org
*Key Personnel*
Pres: Regis J Delmontagne
Dir, Communs & Mktg: Carol J Hurlburt
  *E-mail:* churlbur@npes.org
Location: McCormick Place South, Chicago, IL, USA
Oct 10-13, 2010

## NOVEMBER

**Children's Book Week**
Sponsored by The Children's Book Council (CBC)

12 W 37 St, 2nd fl, New York, NY 10118-7480, United States
*Tel:* 212-966-1990 *Toll Free Tel:* 800-999-2160 (orders only) *Fax:* 212-966-2073
  *Toll Free Fax:* 888-807-9355 (orders only)
*Web Site:* www.cbcbooks.org
*Key Personnel*
Pres: Paula Quint
Location: Nationwide across the USA
Nov 15-21, 2010

# 2011

## APRIL

**National Library Week**
Sponsored by American Library Association (ALA)
50 E Huron St, Chicago, IL 60611, United States
*Tel:* 312-944-6780 *Toll Free Tel:* 800-545-2433
  *Fax:* 312-944-8520
*E-mail:* pio@ala.org
*Web Site:* www.ala.org/events
*Key Personnel*
Public Info Dir: Mark Gould

Press Officer: Larra Clark *E-mail:* lclark@ala.org
Location: Nationwide throughout the USA
April 10-16, 2011

## JULY

**RWA Annual National Conference**
Sponsored by Romance Writers of America
16000 Stuebner Airline, Suite 140, Spring, TX 77379, United States
*Tel:* 832-717-5200 *Fax:* 832-717-5201
*E-mail:* info@rwanational.org
*Web Site:* www.rwanational.org
*Key Personnel*
Exec Dir: Allison Kelley *E-mail:* akelley@rwanational.org
Location: New York Marriott Marquis, New York, NY, USA
July 27-30, 2011

# Library Resources

## Major Libraries

The majority of the libraries and archives listed are those associated with government or educational institutions. Many are also involved in publishing activities.

# Afghanistan

**Kabul Central Library**
Formerly Public Library
Malik Ashgar Crossroads, Sharh e Nau, Kabul
*Tel:* 23166
*Key Personnel*
Dir: Nilab Rahimi

**Ministry of Education Library**
PO Box 717, Kabul
*Key Personnel*
Chief Officer: Mohamad Quasem Hilaman

**Library of the National Bank**
Ibn Sina Wat, Kabul
*Key Personnel*
Dir: A Aziz

**Public Library**, see Kabul Central Library

**University Library**, see University of Kabul
Library

**University of Kabul Library**
Formerly University Library
Jamal Mina, Kabul
*Tel:* 42594
*Key Personnel*
Dir: Mohammad Sediq Waheed

# Albania

**Biblioteka Kombetare** (National Library of the
Republic of Albania)
Sheshi Skenderbej, Place Scanderbeg, Tirana
*Tel:* 42 23 843 *Fax:* 42 23 843
*Web Site:* www.monitor.albnet.net/mkrs/
institucionet/biblkomb/bk.htm
*Key Personnel*
Dir: Dr Aurel Plasari *E-mail:* plasari@natlib.
tirana.al
Founded: 1922
National Library.
Publication(s): *Bibliografia kombeetare e Repub-
likees see Shipeerisee, Periodiku* (Albanian Na-
tional Bibliography of Periodicals); *Bibliografia
kombeetare e Republikees see Shqipeerise Libri*
(Albanian National Bibliography of Books)

**Shkoder Public Library**
Shkoder

# Algeria

**Agence ISBN**, see Bibliotheque Nationale
d'Algerie

**Bibliotheque Municipale de Constantine**
Hotel de Ville, Constantine

**Bibliotheque Nationale d'Algerie**
One Ave Frantz Fanon, 16000 Algiers
Mailing Address: BP 127 El Hamma Les
Anasser, 16000 Algiers
*Tel:* (021) 679544; (021) 675781 *Fax:* (021)
682300
*E-mail:* contact@biblionat.dz
*Web Site:* www.biblionat.dz
*Key Personnel*
Dir: Mahamed Aissamoussa
Founded: 1835
Total Titles: 350,000 Print
Publication(s): *Bibliographie de l'Algerie* (biannu-
ally, in Arabic & French)

**Bibliotheque Universitaire Centrale (BUC)**
Universite Mentouri, Route d'Ain El-Bey, 25000
Constantine
Mailing Address: BP 325, 25000 Constantine
*Tel:* (031) 61-42-05 *Fax:* (031) 61-21-90
*E-mail:* bucne@hotmail.com
*Web Site:* www.buc-constantine.edu.dz
*Telex:* 92436
*Key Personnel*
Chief Librarian: Noureddine Talhour
Founded: 1969
Publication(s): *Des Catalogues Thematiques*

**Ecole nationale polytechnique, Bibliotheque**
10, Ave Hassen Badi, El Harrach, 16200 Algiers
*Tel:* (021) 52 14 94 *Fax:* (021) 52 29 73
*E-mail:* enp@ist.cerist.dz
*Web Site:* www.enp.edu.dz
*Telex:* 64147 Enp
*Key Personnel*
Librarian: Hamitouche Mourad

**Institut National Agronomique, Bibliotheque**
Ave Pasteur Hassen Badi, El-Harrach, 16200 Al-
giers
*Tel:* (021) 52 19 87 *Fax:* (021) 82 27 29
*Web Site:* www.ina.dz/bibliotheque.htm
*Telex:* 64143 DZ
*Key Personnel*
Chief Librarian: Chaabane Hemina
Publication(s): *Annals de l'INA*

**Institut Pasteur d'Algerie, Bibliotheque**
One rue du Dr Laveran, El-Hamma, 16000 Al-
giers
*Tel:* 21 67 25 02; 21 67 25 11; 21 67 23 44
*Fax:* 267 25 03
*E-mail:* ipa@ibnsima.ands.dz; ipabib@sante.dz
*Web Site:* www.ands.dz/ipa/pageaccueil.htm
*Telex:* 65-337; 65-627
*Key Personnel*
Dir: Prof F Boulahbal
Publication(s): *Archives de l'Institut Pasteur
d'Algerie* (annually)

**Archives Nationales d'Algerie**
BP 61, Algiers Gare
*Tel:* (02) 54-21-60 *Fax:* (02) 54-16-16
*Web Site:* www.archives-dgan.gov.dz
*Telex:* 62524
*Key Personnel*
Dir: Abdelkrim Badjada

**Bibliotheque Centrale, Universite d'Alger**
2 rue Didouche Mourad, 16000 Algiers
*Tel:* (021) 63-71-01 *Fax:* (021) 63-76-29
*E-mail:* bu@univ-alger.dz
*Web Site:* www.univ-alger.dz
*Telex:* 66529
*Key Personnel*
Librarian: Zoulikha Bekaddour

**Universite d'Oran, Bibliotheque**
BP 1524, El M'Naouer, 31000 Oran
*Tel:* (041) 41-69-39; (041) 41-66-44 *Fax:* (041)
41-60-21
*E-mail:* igmo@univ-oran.dz
*Web Site:* www.univ-oran.dz
*Telex:* 22993 UNIRX DZ

# Angola

**Direccao Provincial Servicos de Geologia e
Minas de Angola Biblioteca**
CP 1260, Luanda
*Tel:* (02) 323024 *Fax:* (02) 321655
*Telex:* 3324

**Biblioteca Municipal de Luanda**
CP 1227, Luanda
*Tel:* (02) 392297 *Fax:* (02) 33902
*Key Personnel*
Librarian: Antonio Jose Emidio De Brito

**Biblioteca Nacional de Angola** (Angola National
Library)
Av Norton de Matos, Luanda
Mailing Address: CP 2915, Luanda
*Tel:* (02) 337 317 *Fax:* (02) 323 979
*E-mail:* biblioteca@netangola.com
*Telex:* 4129 Mincult

*Key Personnel*
Dir: Maria Jose Faria Ramos
Founded: 1968
Publication(s): *Novas* (News)

**Universidade Agostinho Neto Biblioteca**
Av 4 de Fevereiro 7, Luanda
Mailing Address: CP 815, Luanda
*Tel:* (02) 330 517 *Fax:* (02) 330 520
*Web Site:* www.uan.ao
*Telex:* 3076
*Key Personnel*
Librarian: Jeronimo Octavio Xavier Belo

# Argentina

**Biblioteca Argentina Dr Juan Alvarez**
Presidente Roca 731, 2000 Rosario
*Tel:* 4802538; 4802539 *Fax:* 4802561
*E-mail:* bibliarghem@rosario.gov.ar
*Web Site:* www.rosario.gov.ar
*Key Personnel*
Contact: Maria del Carmen D'Angelo

**Biblioteca del Banco Central de la Republica**
  **Argentina** (Library of the Central Bank of the
  Argentine Republic)
Reconquista 250, 1004 Buenos Aires
*Tel:* (011) 4348 3772 *Fax:* (011) 4348 3771
*E-mail:* biblio@bcra.gov.ar
*Web Site:* www.bcra.gov.ar
*Telex:* 24031 BCFEXAR
Publication(s): *Boletin Estadistico* (monthly);
  *Boletin Monetario y Financiero* (quarterly);
  *Central de Deudores* (monthly); *Informacion
  de Entidades Financieras* (monthly); *Informe
  Anual del Presidente al Congreso de la Nac*
  (annually); *Resumen de las Regulaciones del
  Sistema Financiero Argentino* (biannually)

**Biblioteca Nacional**
Aguero 2502, 1425 Buenos Aires
*Tel:* (011) 4808-6000 *Fax:* (011) 4806-6157
*E-mail:* bibnal@red.bibnal.edu.ar
*Web Site:* www.bibnal.edu.ar
*Key Personnel*
Dir: Elvio Vitale

**Biblioteca Nacional de Maestros** (National
  Teachers' Library)
Pizzurno 953, 1020 Buenos Aires
*Tel:* (011) 4129-1272 *Fax:* (011) 4129-1268
*E-mail:* bnmsecre@me.gov.ar
*Web Site:* www.bnm.me.gov.ar
*Key Personnel*
Dir: Teresa Perrone
Contact: Dr R Levene
Publication(s): *Historia de la Biblioteca Nacional
  de Maestros*; *La Biblioteca* (monthly)

**Biblioteca del Congreso de la Nacion** (National
  Library of Congress)
Hipolito Yrigoyen 1750, 1089 Buenos Aires
*Tel:* (011) 4010-3000
*E-mail:* drg@bcnbib.gov.ar
*Web Site:* www.bcnbib.gov.ar
*Key Personnel*
Dir of Technical Processes: Liliana Casteran
  Racedo

**Sistema de Bibliotecas y de Informacion**
Azcuenaga 280, 1029 Buenos Aires
*Tel:* (011) 4952-0078 *Fax:* (011) 4952-6557
*E-mail:* webmaster@sisbi.uba.ar
*Web Site:* www.sisbi.uba.ar

*Telex:* 18694-IBUBA-AR
*Key Personnel*
General Coordinator: Elsa Elena Elizalde

**Biblioteca Central, Universidad del Salvador**
Presidente Peron 1818, 1040 Buenos Aires
*Tel:* (011) 4371-0422 *Fax:* (011) 4371-0422
*E-mail:* uds-bibl@salvador.edu.ar
*Web Site:* www.salvador.edu.ar
*Key Personnel*
Dir: Liliana Rega

**Biblioteca Mayor de la Universidad Nacional**
  **de Cordoba** (Principal Library of the National
  University of Cordoba)
Calle Obispo Trejo 242, ler Piso 63, 5000 Cor-
  doba
*Tel:* (351) 4331072; (351) 4331079
*E-mail:* biblio@bmayor.unc.edu.ar
*Web Site:* www.unc.edu.ar
*Key Personnel*
Deputy Dir: Lic Rosa M Bestani
Founded: 1613
Collections from the 16th, 17th & 18th centuries.
Publication(s): *Informativo* (irregularly)

**Biblioteca de la Universidad Nacional de La**
  **Plata**
Plaza Rocha Nº 137, 1900 La Plata
*Tel:* (021) 423-6600; (021) 423-6608; (021) 423-
  6607; (021) 423-6601 *Fax:* (021) 425-5004
*E-mail:* biblio@isis.unlp.edu.ar
*Web Site:* www.unlp.edu.ar
*Telex:* 31151 Bulap
*Key Personnel*
Dir: Prof Javier Fernandez

**Universidad Nacional del Litoral**
Blvd Pellegrini 2750, 3000 Santa Fe
*Tel:* (0342) 4571110 *Fax:* (0342) 4571110
*E-mail:* informes@unl.edu.ar
*Web Site:* www.unl.edu.ar
*Key Personnel*
Dir: Beatriz S Perez Risso de Costa

# Aruba

**Biblioteca Nacional Aruba** (Aruba National
  Library)
George Madurostr 13, Oranjestad
*Tel:* 582-1580 *Fax:* 582-5493
*E-mail:* info@bibliotecanacional.aw
*Web Site:* www.bibliotecanacional.aw
*Telex:* bc 5060
*Key Personnel*
Dir: Astrid J T Britten
System Librarian: Lilian A Semeleer
Founded: 1949
National & Public Library
Membership(s): Acuril; IFLA.
*Branch Office(s)*
Filiaal San Nicolaas, Peter Stuyvesant Straat Z/N,
  San Nicolas *Tel:* 584-5277; 584-3939 *Fax:* 584-
  5004 *E-mail:* sn@setarnet.aw

# Australia

**Archives Office of New South Wales**
2 Globe St, The Rocks, Sydney, NSW 2000
Mailing Address: PO Box 516, Kingswood, NSW
  2747
*Tel:* (02) 9673-1788 *Fax:* (02) 9833-4518
*E-mail:* srecords@records.nsw.gov.au
*Web Site:* www.records.nsw.gov.au

*Key Personnel*
Dir: David Roberts *E-mail:* director@records.nsw.
  gov.au
*Branch Office(s)*
76 Miller Red, Villawood

**Australian National University Library**
Cor Fellows & Garran Rd, RG Menzies Bldg
  (No. 2), Canberra, ACT 0200
*Tel:* (02) 6125 5111 *Fax:* (02) 6125 5931
*E-mail:* library.info@anu.edu.au
*Web Site:* www.anu.edu.au
*Key Personnel*
University Librarian: Vic Elliott *Tel:* (02) 6125
  2003 *E-mail:* librarian@anu.edu.au
Publication(s): *User response to URICA: a cata-
  logue on line*

**Barr Smith Press, University of Adelaide**
  **Library**
Barr Smith Library, The University of Adelaide,
  Adelaide, SA 5005
*Tel:* (08) 8303 5372 *Fax:* (08) 8303 4369
*E-mail:* library-services@library.adelaide.edu.au
*Web Site:* www.library.adelaide.edu.au
*Key Personnel*
University Librarian: Ray Choate *Tel:* (08) 8303
  4064 *E-mail:* ray.choate@adelaide.edu.au
Publication(s): *Joanna & Robert, the Barr Smith's
  Life in Letters, 1853-1919* (1996); *Poems &
  Recollections of the Past* (1996)

**CSIRO**, see CSIRO (Commonwealth Scientific &
  Industrial Research Organization)

**CSIRO (Commonwealth Scientific & Industrial**
  **Research Organization)**
Bag 10, Clayton South, Victoria 3169
*Tel:* (03) 9545 2176 *Fax:* (03) 9545 2175
*E-mail:* enquiries@csiro.au
*Web Site:* www.csiro.au
*Telex:* 30236
*Key Personnel*
Chief Executive: Dr Geoff Garrett
Deputy Chief Executive: Dr Ron Sandlund
Library Network Services provides cost effective,
  specialized library services to CSIRO's Net-
  work of 45 libraries throughout Australia &
  delivery of a complete range of library services
  to staff of the Information Services Branch.

**Monash University Library**
Box 4, Monash University, Victoria 3800
*Tel:* (03) 9905 5054 *Fax:* (03) 9905 2610
*E-mail:* library@lib.monash.edu.au
*Web Site:* www.lib.monash.edu.au
*Key Personnel*
University Librarian: Cathrine Harboe-Ree
  *E-mail:* cathrine.harboe-ree@lib.monash.edu.au

**The State Library of New South Wales**
Macquarie St, Sydney, NSW 2000
*Tel:* (02) 9273 1414 *Fax:* (02) 9273 1255
*E-mail:* library@sl.nsw.gov.au
*Web Site:* www.sl.nsw.gov.au
*Key Personnel*
State Librarian: Dagmar Schmidmaier
Founded: 1826
Publication(s): *Public Library News* (newsletter);
  *Public Library Statistics* (annually)

**State Library of Queensland**
South Bank Bldg, Level 2, South Brisbane, Qld
  4101
Mailing Address: PO Box 3488, South Brisbane,
  Qld 4101
*Tel:* (07) 3840 7666 *Fax:* (07) 3846 2421
*E-mail:* srlenquiries@slq.qld.gov.au
*Web Site:* www.slq.qld.gov.au/
*Key Personnel*
State Librarian: Lea Giles-Peters

Includes the John Oxley Library of Queensland
History.
Publication(s): *Annual Report of the Library
Board of Queensland*; *The Development of
State Libraries & Their Effect on the Public
Library Movement in Australia* (1809-1964);
*Directory of State & Public Library Service
in Queensland* (annually); *North Queensland
Towns & Districts Bibliography* (1975); *Pub-
lic Libraries in Queensland: Statistical Bulletin*
(annually); *Queensland Government Publica-
tions* (quarterly)

**State Library of South Australia**
North Terrace, Adelaide, SA 5000
Mailing Address: GPO Box 419, Adelaide SA
5001
*Tel:* (08) 82077250 *Toll Free Tel:* 800-182-013
*Fax:* (08) 82077247
*E-mail:* info@slsa.sa.gov.au
*Web Site:* www.slsa.sa.gov.au
*Key Personnel*
Chairman: Peter Goldsworthy
Acting Dir: Margaret Allen
Founded: 1884
Publication(s): *Collection Development Policy*;
*Extra Extra* (biannually); *Strategic Plan* (2001-
04)

**State Library of Tasmania**
91 Murray St, Hobart, Tas 7000
*Tel:* (03) 6233 7511 *Fax:* (03) 6231 0927
*E-mail:* state.library@education.tas.gov.au
*Web Site:* www.statelibrary.tas.gov.au
*Key Personnel*
Dir: Siobhan Gaskell *E-mail:* siobhan.gaskell@
education.tas.gov.au
Senior Librarian (Policy Planning): Bridget
Hutton *Tel:* (03) 6233 6815 *E-mail:* bridget.
hutton@education.tas.gov.au
Founded: 1850
State library & public library service.

**State Library of Victoria**
328 Swanston St, Melbourne, Victoria 3000
*Tel:* (03) 8664 7002 *Fax:* (03) 9639 3854
*E-mail:* info@slv.vic.gov.au
*Web Site:* www.statelibrary.vic.gov.au
*Key Personnel*
Chief Executive & State Librarian: Frances Aw-
cock
Publication(s): *La Trobe Library Journal* (bian-
nually); *Victorian Government Publications*
(monthly)

**State Library of Western Australia**
Alexander Library Bldg, Perth Cultural Centre,
Perth, WA 6000
*Tel:* (08) 9427 3111 *Fax:* (08) 9427 3256
*E-mail:* info@liswa.wa.gov.au
*Web Site:* www.liswa.wa.gov.au
*Key Personnel*
Chief Executive Officer & State Librarian: Claire
Forte
Publication(s): *The Genealogy Centre Resource
List: Australasia* (1999); *Katatjin: A guide to
the Indigenous Records in the Baltye Library*
(2003)

**University of Melbourne Baillieu Library**
Parkville Campus, Melbourne, Victoria 3010
*Tel:* (03) 8344 5378; (03) 8344 0444 *Fax:* (03)
9348 1142
*Web Site:* www.lib.unimelb.edu.au/
*Telex:* 30815
Library of arts, humanities & social sciences.

**University of New South Wales Library**
Sydney, NSW 2052
*Tel:* (02) 9385 1000
*Web Site:* www.info.library.unsw.edu.au

*Key Personnel*
University Librarian: Andrew Wells
Founded: 1948

**University of Queensland Library**
Level 1, Duhig North Bldg, Saint Lucia, Qld
4072
*Tel:* (07) 3365 6949 *Fax:* (07) 3365 1737
*E-mail:* universitylibrarian@library.uq.edu.au
*Web Site:* www.library.uq.edu.au
*Key Personnel*
University Librarian: Janine Schmidt *Tel:* (07)
3365 6342

**University of South Australia Library**
Flexible Learning Centre, Holbrooks Rd, Under-
dale, SA 5032
*Tel:* (08) 8302 6661 *Fax:* (08) 8302 6250
*Web Site:* www.library.unisa.edu.au
*Key Personnel*
Dir, Library Services: Helen Livingston
Publisher of library science texts & conference
proceedings.

**University of Sydney Library**
Parramatta Rd, University of Sydney, NSW 2006
*Tel:* (02) 9351 2990 *Fax:* (02) 9351 2890
*Web Site:* www.library.usyd.edu.au
*Key Personnel*
University Librarian: John Shipp *E-mail:* j.
shipp@library.usyd.edu.au

**University of Technology, Sydney Library**
PO Box 123, Broadway, NSW 2007
*Tel:* 9514 2000
*E-mail:* info@uts.edu.au
*Web Site:* www.uts.edu.au
*Key Personnel*
Librarian: Alex Byrne *E-mail:* alex.byrne@uts.
edu.au
Publication(s): *Axis Online* (3-4 times/yr, newslet-
ter); *Library Link* (quarterly, newsletter); *News
& Events*

**University of Western Australia Library**
35 Stirling Highway, Crawley, WA 6009
*Tel:* (08) 9380 1777 *Toll Free Tel:* 1800 263 921
*Fax:* (08) 9380 1012
*E-mail:* uwalibrary@library.uwa.edu.au
*Web Site:* www.library.uwa.edu.au
*Telex:* 92992 Uniwa *Cable:* Uniwest
*Key Personnel*
Librarian: John Arfield *E-mail:* librarian@library.
uwa.edu.au

# Austria

**Amtsbibliothek des Bundesministeriums fur
Unterricht, und Kulturelle Angelegenheiten
und des Bundesministeriums fur
Wissenschaft und Verkehr**
Minoritenplatz 5, 1014 Vienna
*Tel:* (01) 53 120-0 *Fax:* (01) 53 120-3099
*E-mail:* ministerium@bmbwk.gv.at
*Web Site:* www.bmbwk.gv.at/
*Telex:* 115532
*Key Personnel*
Manager: Dr Norbert Neumann
Publication(s): *Euro-Dok: Bildung, Forschung,
Kultur, Kunst, Unterricht, Wissenschaft*;
*Forschungspolitische Dokumentation* (Political
Research Documentation); *Veroeffentlichungen:
Zuwachsverzeichnis*

**Bibliothek der Osterreichischen Akademie der
Wissenschaften** (Library of the Austrian
Academy of Science)
Dr-Ignaz-Seipel-Platz 2, 1010 Vienna
*Tel:* (01) 51581-1262
*E-mail:* webmaster@oeaw.ac.at
*Web Site:* www.oeaw.ac.at
*Telex:* (01) 12628
*Key Personnel*
Contact: Dr Christine Harrauer *E-mail:* christine.
harrauer@oeaw.ac.at
Publication(s): *Kosmos und Mythos*; *Meliouchos*

**Bibliothek des Benediktinerklosters Melk in
Niederoesterreich** (Library of the Melk
Benedictine Monastery in Lower Austria)
Abt Berthold Diemayrstr 1, 3390 Melk
*Tel:* (02752) 555-342 *Fax:* (02752) 555-52
*E-mail:* stiftsbibliothek.melk@nextra.at
*Web Site:* www.stiftmelk.at
*Key Personnel*
Librarian: P Gottfried Glassner
*E-mail:* gglassner@magnet.at
Publication(s): *Die Anfaenge der Melker Biblio-
thek* (1996)

**Bibliothek des Osterreichischen Patentamtes**
(Library of the Austrian Patent Office)
Osterreichisches Patentamt, Dresdner Strasse 87,
PO Box 95, 1200 Vienna
*Tel:* (01) 53424 153; (01) 53424 155 *Fax:* (01)
53424 110
*E-mail:* info@patent.bmvit.gv.at
*Web Site:* www.patentamt.at
*Telex:* 136847 OEPA
*Key Personnel*
President: Dr Friedrich Roedler
Librarian: Dr Ingrid Weidinger
Publication(s): *Oesterreichischer Musteronzeiger*;
*Ostereichisches Gebroiuchsmusterblett*; *Oester-
reichischer Markenanzeiger*; *Oesterreichisches
Patentblatt*; *Patentschriften*

**Universitaetsbibliothek Graz** (University Library
Graz)
Universitaetsplatz 3a, 8010 Graz
*Tel:* (0316) 380 3102 *Fax:* (0316) 384 987
*E-mail:* ub.auskunft@uni-graz.at
*Web Site:* www.ub.uni-graz.at
*Key Personnel*
Librarian: Dr Werner Schlachee
Founded: 1573
Publication(s): *Jahresbericht* (annually, 1973);
*News (Informationsschrift der Universitaetsbib-
liothek Graz)* (booklet, 1987)
*Parent Company:* Karl-Franzens Universitat Graz,
Universitaetsplatz 3, 8010 Graz

**IAEA Library**, see Vienna International Centre
Library

**Universitaetsbibliothek Innsbruck**
Innrain 50, 6010 Innsbruck
*Tel:* (0512) 507 2401 *Fax:* (0512) 507 2893
*E-mail:* ub-hb@uibk.ac.at
*Web Site:* ub.uibk.ac.at
*Telex:* 553708
*Key Personnel*
Dir: Dr Walter Neuhauser
Publication(s): *Vom Codex zum Computer*

**Oberoesterreichische Landesbibliothek**
(Regional Library Upper Austria)
Schillerpl 2, Postfach 129, 4021 Linz 2
*Tel:* (0732) 664071-00 *Fax:* (0732) 664071-44
*E-mail:* landesbibliothek@ooe.gv.at
*Web Site:* www.landesbibliothek.at
*Key Personnel*
Dir: Dr Christian Enichlmayr *Tel:* (0732)
66407722 *E-mail:* christian.enichlmayr@ooe.
gv.at

Founded: 1774
Reference Library.
*Parent Company:* Land Oberoesterreich

**Oesterreichisches Staatsarchiv** (Austrian State
   Archives)
Nottendorfer, Gasse 2, 1030 Vienna
*Tel:* (01) 79540 201 *Fax:* (01) 79540 109
*E-mail:* gdpost@oesta.gv.at
*Web Site:* www.oesta.gv.at
*Key Personnel*
General Dir: Dr Lorenz Mikoletzky
   *E-mail:* lorenz.mikoletzky@oesta.gv.at
Personnel & Administrative Dir: Mag Luzia Owa-
   jko
Dir, Archives of the Republic: Hr Dr Manfred
   Fink
Dir, Finance Archives: Hr Dr Christian Sapper
Dir, War Archive: Hr Dr Christoph Tepperberg
Dir, Courthouse & State Archives: Hr Prof Dr
   Leopold Auer
Provisional Dir, General Adminstrative Archive:
   Dr Gerald Theimer
Founded: 1945
Publication(s): *Mitteilungen des Oesterreichischen
   Staatsarchivs* (Annually)

**Osterreichische Nationalbibliothek** (Austrian
   National Library)
Josefspl 1, 1015 Vienna
Mailing Address: PO Box 308, 1015 Vienna
*Tel:* (01) 534 10 *Fax:* (01) 534˙ 10 280
*E-mail:* onb@onb.ac.at
*Web Site:* www.onb.ac.at
*Telex:* 112624 AOenb
*Key Personnel*
Dir General: Dr Johanna Rachinger
   *E-mail:* johanna.rachinger@onb.ac.at
Publication(s): *Informationsfuehrer Bibliotheken
   und Dokumentations- stellen in Oesterreich*
   (Information Guide to Libraries and Documen-
   tation Centres in Austria)

**Universitaetsbibliothek Salzburg**
Hofstallgasse 2-4, 5020 Salzburg
*Tel:* (0662) 8044 77550 *Fax:* (0662) 8044 103
*E-mail:* info.hb@sbg.ac.at
*Web Site:* www.ubs.sbg.ac.at
*Key Personnel*
Librarian: Dr Ursula Schachl-Raber

**Die Steiermaerkische Landesbibliothek**
Kalchberggasse 2, 8010 Graz
Mailing Address: Postfach 861, 8010 Graz
*Tel:* (0316) 8016-4600 *Fax:* (0316) 8016-4633
*E-mail:* stlbib@stmk.gv.at
*Web Site:* www.stmk.gv.at/verwaltung/stlbib/
*Key Personnel*
Dir: Dr Christoph Binder *Tel:* (0316) 8016-4611
   *E-mail:* christoph.binder@stmk.gv.at
Founded: 1811
Public scientific library.
Publication(s): *Geschichte und Gegenwart* (His-
   tory & the Present, quarterly, 2000, scien-
   tific journal); *Veroeffentlichungen der Steier-
   maerkischen Landesbibliothek 24: Joerg-Martin
   Willnauer: Die Steiermark in Wort und Schild*
   (2000, scientific series concerning Styrian liter-
   ature history & history of culture)

**Universitaetsbibliothek der Technischen
   Universitaet Wien** (Vienna University of
   Technology Library)
Resselgasse 4, 1040 Vienna
*Tel:* (01) 58801 44051 *Fax:* (01) 58801 44099
*E-mail:* info@mail.ub.tuwien.ac.at
*Web Site:* www.ub.tuwien.ac.at
*Key Personnel*
Librarian: Dr Peter Kubalek

Founded: 1815
Focuses on the natural & technical sciences but
   also covers related subjects such as environmental technology.

**Vienna International Centre Library**
Wagramer Str 5, 1400 Vienna
Mailing Address: PO Box 100, 1400 Vienna
*Tel:* (01) 2600-22620 *Fax:* (01) 2600-29584
*E-mail:* iaea.library.infodesk@iaea.org
*Web Site:* www.iaea.or.at
*Telex:* 112645 *Cable:* Inatom Vienna

**Universitaetsbibliothek Wien** (Vienna University
   Library)
D-Karl-Lueger-Ring 1, 1010 Vienna
*Tel:* (01) 427715001 *Fax:* (01) 42779150
*E-mail:* aer.ub@univie.ac.at; info.ub@univie.ac.at
*Web Site:* ub.univie.ac.at
*Key Personnel*
Librarian: Maria Seissl *E-mail:* maria.seissl@
   univie.ac.at
Founded: 1365

**Wiener Stadt- und Landesarchiv**
Gasometer D, Guglgasse 14, 1082 Vienna
Mailing Address: Rathaus, 1082 Vienna
*Tel:* (01) 4000-84815 *Fax:* (01) 4000-7238
*E-mail:* post@m08.magwien.gv.at
*Web Site:* www.magwien.gv.at
*Key Personnel*
Dir: Dr Ferdinand Opll
Vienna Municipal Archives.
Publication(s): *Veroeffentlichungen des Wiener
   Stadt-und Landesarchivs*

**Wiener Stadt- und Landesbibliothek** (Vienna
   Municipal & County Library)
Rathaus, 1082 Vienna
*Tel:* (01) 4000-84920 *Fax:* (01) 4000-7219
*E-mail:* post@m09.magwien.gv.et
*Web Site:* www.stadtbibliothek.wien.at
*Key Personnel*
Man Dir: Gerhard Renner

# Azerbaijan

**Azerbaidzhanskaya respublikanskaya
   biblioteka im M F Akhundova** (M F
   Achudova State Library of Azerbaijan
   Republic)
Ul Khagani 29, 370601 Baku
*Tel:* (012) 934 003
*Key Personnel*
Dir: Leyla Gafurova
Founded: 1923
Publication(s): *Azerbaijan in Foreign Press* (Bibli-
   ographic Indexes); *Scientific Transactions of M
   F Akhundov State Library*

# Bahamas

**The College of the Bahamas Library**
Oakes Field Campus, PO Box N4912, Nassau
*Tel:* 302-4552 *Fax:* 326-7834
*Web Site:* www.cob.edu.bs/library
*Key Personnel*
Dir: Willamae Johnson *E-mail:* wjohnson@cob.
   edu.bs
Founded: 1975
Has branches in Freeport, Grand Bahama & New
   Providence.

Publication(s): *Bahamas Reference Collection:
   a Bibliography* (1980, with irregular supplements); *The Chickcharney Express* (irregular);
   *The Library Informer* (per semester, newsletter)

**Sir Charles Hayward Library**
The Mall, PO Box F-40040, Freeport
*Tel:* 352-7048
*Key Personnel*
Adult Librarian: Elaine B Talma

**Nassau Public Library**
Shirley St, Nassau, New Providence
*Tel:* 3224907; 3285029
Founded: 1837

# Bahrain

**Bahrain Centre for Studies, Research Library
   & Information Dept**
PO Box 496, Manama
*Fax:* (0973) 754678
*E-mail:* bcsr@batelco.com.bh
*Web Site:* www.batelco.com.bh/bcsr/
*Telex:* BCSR 9764 BN
*Key Personnel*
Library Dir: Najim Rashid

**College of Medicine Library, Arabian Gulf
   University**
PO Box 26671, Manama
*Tel:* 239 999 *Fax:* 274 822
*E-mail:* agulibrary@agu.edu.bh
*Web Site:* www.agu.edu.bh
*Telex:* 7319
*Key Personnel*
Librarian: Khushnud Hassan *Tel:* 239 999 ext 606

**Manama Central Library,** see Shaikh Isa
   Library

**Shaikh Isa Library**
Formerly Manama Central Library
PO Box 43, Manama
*Tel:* 258550 *Fax:* 274036
*E-mail:* dolp@batelco.com.bh
*Key Personnel*
Dir of Public Libraries: Mansoor Sarhan
Founded: 1946

**University of Bahrain Library**
PO Box 32038, Sukhair
*Tel:* 17438808 *Fax:* 17449838
*E-mail:* library@admin.uob.bh
*Web Site:* www.uob.edu.bh
*Telex:* 9258
*Key Personnel*
Dir: Hedi Talbi *E-mail:* talbi@admin.uob.bh
Deputy Dir: Tahani Hassan Al-Khalifa
   *E-mail:* tahanikh@admin.uob.bh
Founded: 1986
Membership(s): CILIP; SLA.
Publication(s): *Awan*; *Journal of Educational &
   Psychological Science*; *Journal of Human Sci-
   ences*; *Thaqafat*

# Bangladesh

**Bangladesh Central Public Library,** see Sufia
   Kamel National Public Library

## Bangladesh Institute of Development Studies Library
E-17 Agargaon, Sher-e-Bangla Nagar, Dhaka 1207
Mailing Address: GPO Box 3854, Dhaka 1207
*Tel:* (02) 9118999 *Fax:* (02) 8113023
*E-mail:* secy10bids@sdnbd.org; chieflib@sdnbd. org
*Web Site:* www.bids-bd.org *Cable:* BIDECON DHAKA
*Key Personnel*
Chief Librarian: Nilufar Akhter *E-mail:* nilufar@ sdnbd.org

## National Library of Bangladesh, Directorate of Archives & Libraries
32 Justice Sayed Mahbub Murshed Sarini, Sher-e-Bangla Nagar (Agargaon), Dhaka 1207
*Tel:* (02) 326572; (02) 318704
*Key Personnel*
Dir: Mr Hahashinur Rahman Khan

## British Council Library
5 Fuller Rd, Dhaka 1000
*Tel:* (02) 861 8905-7; (02) 861 8867-8 *Fax:* (02) 861 3375; (02) 861 3255
*E-mail:* library@bd.britishcouncil.org
*Web Site:* www.britishcouncil.org/bangladesh/
*Telex:* 642470 Bric
*Key Personnel*
Dir: Dr June Rollinson
Deputy Dir: Charles Nuttall

## Dhaka University Library
Ramna, Dhaka 1000
*Tel:* (02) 966-1900 *Fax:* (02) 865583
*E-mail:* duregstr@bangla.net
*Web Site:* www.univdhaka.edu
*Key Personnel*
Librarian: Dr Serajul Islam
Founded: 1921

## Sufia Kamel National Public Library
Formerly Bangladesh Central Public Library
Kazi Nazrul Islam Ave, Shahbagh, Dhaka 1000
*Tel:* (02) 50 08 19; (02) 50 08 39; (02) 50 28 16
*Key Personnel*
Librarian: Dr A F M Badiur-Rahman
Founded: 1958

## University of Rajshahi Library
Rajshahi 6205
*Tel:* (0721) 750041; (0721) 750033 *Fax:* (0721) 750064
*E-mail:* rajcc@citechco.net
*Web Site:* www.ugc.org/rajsahai_uni.htm
*Key Personnel*
Administrator: Prof Abaydur Rahman Pramanik
Founded: 1955

# Barbados

## National Library Service
Coleridge St, Bridgetown 2
*Tel:* 426-1744; 426-3981 (adult's Library); 429-9557 (children's library) *Fax:* 436-1501
*E-mail:* natlib1@caribsurf.com
*Web Site:* www.barbados.gov.bb/natlib/
*Key Personnel*
Dir: Annette Smith *Tel:* 436-6081
Founded: 1847
*Publication(s):* National Bibliography of Barbados; West Indian Collection
*Branch Office(s)*
Eagle Hall Branch Library, Eagle Hall, St Michael, Supervisor: John Downes *Tel:* 427-3045

Holetown Branch Library, Holetown, St James, Supervisor: Marva Watson *Tel:* 432-1818
Six Cross Roads Branch Library, Six Cross Roads, St Philip, Supervisor: Nadine Goddard *Tel:* 423-6557
Valley Branch Library, Valley, St George, Supervisor: Avaline Henry *Tel:* 429-4029
Gall Hill Branch Library, Gall Hill, St John, Supervisor: Carl Adamson *Tel:* 433-1522
Oistins Branch Library, Oistins, Christ Church, Supervisor: Jennifer Yarde *Tel:* 428-7666
Speightstown Branch Library, Speightstown, St Peter, Supervisor: Kathy-Anne Latchman *Tel:* 422-2311

## University of the West Indies Library (Barbados)
Cave Hill Campus, PO Box 1334, Bridgetown
*Tel:* (0246) 417-4444 *Fax:* (0246) 425-1327
*E-mail:* webmaster@uwichill.edu.bb
*Web Site:* www.cavehill.uwi.edu
*Telex:* 2257 Univados *Cable:* UNIVADOS BARBADOS
*Key Personnel*
Librarian: Carlisle Best *E-mail:* cbest@uwichill. edu.bb

# Belarus

## National Library of Belarus
Krasnoarmeyskaya St, 9, 220636 Minsk
*Tel:* (017) 227-54-63 *Fax:* (017) 227-54-63
*E-mail:* sol@nacbibl.minsk.by
*Web Site:* kolas.bas-net.by/bla/nb.htm
*Key Personnel*
Dir: Galina Nikolaevna Oleynik
Deputy Dir: Kiruchina Ludmila Gennadyevna *Tel:* (017) 227-53-16; Chernov Sergey Ivanovich *Tel:* (017) 227-56-84; Aksenova Tamara Vladimirovna *Tel:* (017) 227-87-43
Founded: 1922
*Publication(s):* Chernobyl (triannually, bibliographic index); Cultural Life of Belarus (monthly); Current literature on the history of Belarus & its historical science (triannually, bibliographic index); Signal Information on Culture & Arts (weekly); Social Sciences (monthly)

# Belgium

## AMVC-Letterenhuis (AMVC-Literary Centre)
Minderbroedersstraat 22, 2000 Antwerp
*Tel:* (03) 222 9320 *Fax:* (03) 222 9321
*E-mail:* amvc.letterenhuis@stad.antwerpen.be
*Web Site:* museum.antwerpen.be/ amvc_letterenhuis
*Key Personnel*
Curator: Leen Van Dijck *Tel:* (03) 222 9329 *E-mail:* helena.vandijck@cs.antwerpen.be
Founded: 1933
Archives & Museum of Flemish Culture.

## Archives generales du Royaume
Rue de Ruysbroeck 2, 1000 Brussels
*Tel:* (02) 513 76 80 *Fax:* (02) 513 76 81
*E-mail:* archives.generales@arch.be
*Web Site:* arch.arch.be
*Key Personnel*
General State Archivist: Karel Velle
National Archives.

## Bibliotheque Central du Ministere de l'Education Nationale
Rue de Stassart, 43, 1050 Brussels
*Tel:* (02) 511 59 80 *Fax:* (02) 513 43 33
*Key Personnel*
Dir: J M Andrin

## Bibliotheque du Musee Royal de Mariemont
100 chaussee de Mariemont, 7140 Morlanwelz-Mariemont
*Tel:* (064) 21 21 93 *Fax:* (064) 26 29 24
*E-mail:* info@musee-mariemont.be
*Web Site:* www.musee-mariemont.be
*Key Personnel*
Librarian: M B Delattre *E-mail:* marie-blanche. delattre@musee-mariemont.be
*Publication(s):* Bulletin d'Information (quarterly); Cahiers de Mariemont (annually); Catalogues d'Expositions, Monographies, Dossiers Pedagogiques

## Bibliotheque Fonds Quetelet
Rue de Progres 50, 1210 Brussels
*Tel:* (02) 277 55 55 *Fax:* (02) 277 55 53
*E-mail:* quetelet@mineco.fgov.be
*Web Site:* www.mineco.fgov.be
*Key Personnel*
Chief Librarian: Stefaan Jacobs
Founded: 1841
Library of the Federal Public Service Economy, SMEs, Self-employed & Energy.
Scientific library.
*Publication(s):* Accroissements de la Bibliotheque Fonds Quetelet (monthly)

## Bibliotheque Royale Albert Ier
4 Blvd de l'Empereur, 1000 Brussels
*Tel:* (02) 519 53 11 *Fax:* (02) 519 55 33
*E-mail:* contacts@kbr.be
*Web Site:* www.kbr.be
*Telex:* 21157
*Key Personnel*
Dir General: Patrick Lefevre
Koninklijke Bibliotheek Albert I.
*Publication(s):* Bibliograhie de Belgique (Belgisch Bibliographie) (monthly); Bulletin de la BR (KB Bulletin) (quarterly)

## Bibliotheques de l'Universite Libre de Bruxelles
50 Ave Franklin D Roosevelt, 1050 Brussels
*Tel:* (02) 650 36 63 *Fax:* (02) 650 20 07
*E-mail:* mdesb@ulb.ac
*Web Site:* www.bib.ulb.ac.be/
*Key Personnel*
Librarian: Tyana Altounian *E-mail:* taltouni@ admin.ulb.ac.be

## Centre d'Information et de Conservation de l'Universite de Liege
Place du 20-Aout, 9, 4000 Liege
*Tel:* (04) 366 52 18 *Fax:* (04) 366 57 98; (04) 366 44 22
*E-mail:* press@ulg.ac.be
*Web Site:* www.ulg.ac.be/hp.html
*Key Personnel*
Head Librarian: Nicole Haesenne
Chief Librarian: Dr J Denooz *E-mail:* joseph. denooz@ulg.ac.be
*Publication(s):* Bibliotheca Universitatis Leodiensis

## Goethe-Institut
58 rue Belliard Str, 1040 Brussels
*Tel:* (02) 230 39 70 *Fax:* (02) 230 77 25
*E-mail:* info@bruessel.goethe.org
*Web Site:* www.goethe.de/be/bru/deindex.htm
*Key Personnel*
Librarian: Margareta Hauschild
Founded: 1959

**Institut Royal des Sciences Naturelles de Belgique, Bibliotheque** (Royal Belgian Institute of Natural Sciences Library)
KBIN-Library/Documentation Service, Rue Vautier 29, 1000 Brussels
*Tel:* (02) 627 42 52 *Fax:* (02) 627 44 66
*E-mail:* bib@naturalsciences.be
*Web Site:* www.naturalsciences.be
*Telex:* INSNAT
*Key Personnel*
Librarian: Laurent Meese *Tel:* (02) 627 42 16
    *E-mail:* laurent.meese@naturalsciences.be
Head Department Vertebrates: J Govaere
Founded: 1846
Publication(s): *Bulletin de L'Institut Royal des Sciences Naturelles de Belgique - Biology* (annually, 2003); *Bulletin de L Institut Royal des Sciences Naturelles de Belgique - Bulletin Van Het Koninkluk Belgisch Instituut Voor Natuurwetenschappen - Entomology* (annually, 2003); *Bulletin de L'Institut Royal des Sciences Naturelles de Belgique - Earth Sciences* (annually, 2004); *Documents de Travail de L'IR Sc N B*

**Katholieke Universiteit Leuven**
Centrale Bibliotheek, Mgr Ladeuzeplein 21, 3000 Leuven
*Tel:* (016) 32 46 06; (016) 32 46 91 *Fax:* (016) 32 46 32
*E-mail:* centrale.bibliotheek@bib.kuleuven.ac.be
*Web Site:* www.bib.kuleuven.ac.be
*Key Personnel*
Head Librarian: Mel Collier
University Library of Louvain.
Publication(s). *Ex officina* (Bulletin of the Friends of Louvain University Library)

**Bibliotheque Universitaire Moretus Plantin**
    (Moretus Plantin University Library)
Unit of The University of Namur
19 rue Grandgagnage, 5000 Namur
*Tel:* (081) 724646 *Fax:* (081) 724645
*E-mail:* public@fundp.ac.be
*Web Site:* www.fundp.ac.be/bump
*Key Personnel*
Dir General: Jean-Marie Andre *E-mail:* jean-marie.andre@fundp.ac.be
Secretary: Yvette Deherve-Wilquet
    *E-mail:* yvettewilquet@fundp.ac.be
Academic library.

**Bibliotheque Parlement Federal**
Rue de la Loi 13, 1000 Brussels
*Tel:* (02) 5499212 *Fax:* (02) 5499498
*E-mail:* bibliotheque@lachambre.be
*Web Site:* www.lachambre.be
*Key Personnel*
Librarian: Roland Van Nieuwenborgh
Founded: 1831

**Museum Plantin-Moretus**
Vrijdagmarkt 22, 2000 Antwerp
*Tel:* (03) 221 14 50; (03) 221 14 51 *Fax:* (03) 221 14 71
*E-mail:* museum.plantin.moretus@antwerpen.be
*Web Site:* museum.antwerpen.be
*Key Personnel*
Dir: Dr Francine de Nave
Publication(s): *About types, books & prints. Didactic brochure for the Plantin-Moretus Museum & City Prints Gallery* (1989, monograph); *The Illustration of Books Published by the Moretuses* (1996, monograph); *Plantin-Moretus Museum Antwerp (Musea Nostra)* (1995, monograph)

**Stadsbibliotheek**
Hendrik Conscienceplein 4, 2000 Antwerp
*Tel:* (03) 206 87 10 *Fax:* (03) 206 87 75
*E-mail:* stadsbibliotheek@stad.antwerpen.be
*Web Site:* stadsbibliotheek.antwerpen.be

*Key Personnel*
Dir: An Renard *Tel:* (03) 206 87 28 *E-mail:* an.renard@cs.antwerpen.be
Founded: 1481
Reference library of the city of Antwerp concentrating on humanities.

**Bibliotheek Universitair Centrum**
Middelheimlaan 1, 2020 Antwerp
*Tel:* (03) 265 37 94 *Fax:* (03) 265 36 52
*E-mail:* helpdesk@lib.ua.ac.be
*Web Site:* lib.ua.ac.be
*Key Personnel*
Contact: Dr B van Styvendaele *E-mail:* benoni.vanstyvendaele@ua.ac.be

**Universite Catholique de Louvain**
Place de l'Universite 1, 1348 Louvain-la-Neuve
*Tel:* (010) 47 21 11
*E-mail:* sceb@sceb.ucl.ac.be
*Web Site:* www.ucl.ac.be
*Key Personnel*
Chief Librarian: Charles-Henri Nyns
    *E-mail:* nyns@sceb.ucl.ac.be

**Universiteit Antwerpen Bibliotheek UFSIA**
    (University of Antwerp UFSIA Library)
Prinsstr 9, 2000 Antwerp
*Tel:* (03) 2204996 *Fax:* (03) 2204437
*E-mail:* helpdesk@lib.ua.ac.be
*Web Site:* lib.ua.ac.be
*Telex:* 33599 Ufsia
*Key Personnel*
Chief Librarian: Julien Van Borm *Tel:* (03) 2204440 *E-mail:* julien.vanborm@ua.ac.be
Dir: Theo Boeckx *Tel:* (03) 2204448
    *E-mail:* theo.boeckx@ufsia.ac.be
Founded: 1852
Universiteit Antwerpen consists of Universitaire Faculteiten Sint-Ignatius (UFSIA), Universitaire Instelling Antwerpen (UIA), Rijksuniversitair Centrum Antwerpen (RUCA), each with its own library. The above entry details refer to UFSIA.

**University Library of Louvain (Leuven)**, see Katholieke Universiteit Leuven

**University Library of Louvain (Louvain-la-Neuve) Les Bibliotheques de l'Universite Catholique de Louvain**, see Universite Catholique de Louvain

**Vrije Universiteit Brussel Universiteitsbibliotheek**
Campus Oefenplein, Pleinlaan 2, 1050 Brussels
*Tel:* (02) 629 25 05 *Fax:* (02) 629 26 93
*E-mail:* interlib@vub.ac.be
*Web Site:* www.vub.ac.be
*Telex:* 61051
*Key Personnel*
Head Librarian: Patrick Vanouplines

# Belize

**National Library Service of Belize**
Princess Margaret Drive, Belize City
Mailing Address: PO Box 287, Belize City
*Tel:* (02) 34248; (02) 34249 *Fax:* (02) 34246
*E-mail:* nls@btl.net; leo2003@hotmail.com
*Web Site:* www.nlsbze.bz
*Key Personnel*
Chief Librarian: Mrs Trevelee Williams
Committed to the promotion of a more informed, aware & literate society & seeks to provide universal access to information through the

maintenance of a National Library & Public Library service.
Memberships: Comla; ACURIL; ABINIA-AC; IFLA; INFOLAC.
*Parent Company:* Ministry of Education, Government of Belize

# Benin

**Bibliotheque Nationale du Benin**
BP 401, Porto Novo
*Tel:* 22 25 85
*E-mail:* bn.benin@bj.refer.org
*Web Site:* www.bj.refer.org/benin_ct/tur/bnb/Pagetitre.htm
*Key Personnel*
Dir: H N Amoussou
Publication(s): *Les Numeras de la Bibliographie Nationale*

**Bibliotheque Universitaire Centrale**
Campus d'Abomey-Calavy, BP 04 789, Cotonou
*Tel:* 36 01 01 *Fax:* 34 06 42
*E-mail:* bu_unb@bj.refer.org
*Telex:* 5010 *Cable:* Biblionationale
*Key Personnel*
Dir: Pascal Gandaho
Founded: 1970

**Direction des Archives Nationales du Benin**
BP 629, Porto Novo
*Tel:* 21 30 79 *Fax:* 21 30 79
*Telex:* 5347
*Key Personnel*
Dir: Elise R Paraiso *Tel:* 050266; 223497
Chief Archivist: H Paul Deme
Founded: 1913
Memberships: CIA; AIAF; WARBICA.
Publication(s): *Bulletin des Archives*; *Guide de l'usager*; *Memoire du Benin*; *Repertoire Serie E: Affaires politiques*; *Repertoire Serie N: Affaires Militaires*; *Repertoire Serie Q: Affaires Economiques*

# Bermuda

**Bermuda Archives**
Government Administration Bldg, 30 Parliament St, Hamilton HM 13
*Tel:* 295-2007 *Fax:* 295-8751
*Key Personnel*
Dir & Archivist: Karla M Hayward
    *E-mail:* khayward@gov.bm
Publication(s): *A Guide to the Records of Bermuda* (1980)

**Bermuda College Library**
Stonington Ave, South Rd, Paget PG 04
Mailing Address: PO Box 297, Paget PG BX
*Tel:* (0441) 239-4033 *Fax:* (0441) 239-4034
*E-mail:* info@bercol.bm
*Web Site:* www.bercol.bm
*Key Personnel*
Dir: Daurene Aubrey *E-mail:* dva@bercol.bm
Librarian: Annette Lowe

**Bermuda National Library**
13 Queen St, Hamilton HM11
*Tel:* 295-2905 *Fax:* 292-8443
*E-mail:* libraryinfo@gov.bm
*Web Site:* www.bermudanationallibrary.bm
*Telex:* 3775 Modus
*Key Personnel*
Head Librarian: C Joanne Brangman
    *E-mail:* jbrangman@gov.bm

Technical Services Librarian: Patrice A Carvell
 *E-mail:* pcarvell@gov.bm
Adult Services Librarian: Julie Bean
 *E-mail:* jbean@gov.bm
Youth Services Librarian: Marla Smith
 *E-mail:* msmith@gov.bm
Publication(s): *Bermuda National Bibliography*
 (quarterly)
*Branch Office(s)*
Bermuda Youth Library, 74 Church St, Hamilton HM12 *Tel:* 295-0487 *Fax:* 296-0973
 *E-mail:* youthlib@gov.bm
Mobile Library

# Bolivia

**Biblioteca del Congreso Nacional**
Mercado Esquina, Calle Ayacucho, No 308, La
 Paz
*Tel:* (02) 354108; (02) 392658 *Fax:* (02) 392402;
 (02) 341649
*Web Site:* www.congreso.gov.bo
*Telex:* 3204
Publication(s): *Fuentas del Congreso* (bulletin)

**Biblioteca y Archivo Nacional de Bolivia**
Calle Espana 43, Sucre
Mailing Address: Casilla 793, Sucre
*Tel:* (04) 6451481; (04) 6452246; (04) 64528864
 *Fax:* (04) 6461208
*E-mail:* abnb@mara.scr.entelnet.bo
*Key Personnel*
Dir: Marcela Inch Calvimonte
Founded: 1836

**Biblioteca de la Direccion General de Cultura**
Alcaldia Municipal, Casilla 1856, La Paz 1832
Library of Cultural Affairs Administration.

**Universidad Autonoma Tomas Frias,
 Departamento de Bibliotecas**
Av del Maestro, Casilla 36, Potosi
*Tel:* (062) 27300 *Fax:* (062) 27329; (062) 26663
*Web Site:* www.uatf.edu.bo
*Key Personnel*
Dir: Julia B De Lopez
Publication(s): *Boletin del Departamento de Bibliotecas* (& occasional papers)

**Biblioteca Central de la Universidad Mayor de
 San Andres**
Ave Villazon 1995, Monoblock Central, La Paz
*Tel:* (02) 440047; (02) 352232 *Fax:* (02) 442505
*E-mail:* rector@umsanet.edu.bo
*Web Site:* www.umsanet.edu.bo; www.bc.umsanet.
 edu.bo
*Key Personnel*
Dir, Lic: Alberto Crespo Rodas

**Biblioteca Central de la Universidad Mayor de
 San Francisco Xavier de Chuquisaca**
Casilla 232, Sucre
*Tel:* (04) 6453308 *Fax:* (04) 6455308
*Web Site:* www.usfx.edu.bo
*Key Personnel*
Dir: Agar Penaranda

**Biblioteca Central Universitaria 'Jose Antonio
 Arze'**
Campus Universitaria Las Cuadras, Casilla 992,
 Cochabamba
*Tel:* (042) 232540
*E-mail:* biblioteca-c@umss.edu.bo
*Web Site:* www.umss.edu.bo
*Telex:* 6363
*Key Personnel*
Dir: Dr Luis Alberto Ponce

Founded: 1926
Publication(s): *Boletin Bibliografico*; *Notas Bibliotecologicas*

# Bosnia and Herzegovina

**Narodna i univerzitetska biblioteka Bosne i
 Hercegovine**
Zmaja od Bosne 8B, 71000 Sarajevo
*Tel:* (071) 33 275 312 *Fax:* (071) 33 275 431
*E-mail:* nubbih@nub.ba
*Web Site:* www.nub.ba
*Key Personnel*
Dir: Dr Enes Kujundzjc
National & University Library of Bosnia &
 Herzegovina.

# Botswana

**Botswana National Archives & Records
 Services**
PO Box 239, Gaborone
*Tel:* 391 820 *Fax:* 390 545
*Web Site:* www.gov.bw
*Telex:* 2994BD *Cable:* HOMES
*Key Personnel*
Dir: Ms K P Kgabi *E-mail:* kkgabi@gov.bw
Principal Archivist: A S B Akhaabi; C T Nengomasha
Librarian: A R Adekanmbi
Founded: 1967
Provides a national archives services to preserve
 for posterity historically important records &
 data for research, education & reference.
Publication(s): *Botswana National Archives &
 Records Services Library Accessions List* (annually)

**Botswana National Library Service**
Private Bag 0036, Gaborone
*Tel:* 352-397 *Fax:* 301-149
*E-mail:* natlib@global.bw; automate@global.bw
*Web Site:* www.gov.bw *Cable:* Bonalibs
*Key Personnel*
Dir: Ms C B Modise *E-mail:* cbmodise@gov.bw
Publication(s): *The National Bibliography of
 Botswana*

**Geological Survey Department Library**
Private Bag 14, Lobatse
*Tel:* 330327 *Fax:* 332013
*E-mail:* geosurv@global.bw
*Web Site:* www.gov.bw/government/geology.htm
*Telex:* 2293 Geo *Cable:* Rocks Lobatse
*Key Personnel*
Dir: T P Machacha *Tel:* 332495

**University of Botswana Library**
Private Bag 00390, Gaborone
*Tel:* 355-0000; 355-2304; 355-2295 *Fax:* 395-6591; 395-7291
*Web Site:* www.ub.bw
*Telex:* 2429
*Key Personnel*
Dir: H K Raseroka *E-mail:* raseroka@mopipi.ub.
 bw
Founded: 1971

# Brazil

**Arquivo Nacional**
Rua Azeredo Coutinho, 77, Centro, 20230-170
 Rio de Janeiro-RJ
*Tel:* (021) 3806-6171 *Fax:* (021) 2232-8430
*E-mail:* conarq@arquivonacional.gov.br
*Web Site:* www.arquivonacional.gov.br/
*Telex:* 2134103
*Key Personnel*
General Dir: Jaime Antones Da Silva
 *E-mail:* directorialgeral@arquivnacional.gov.br
Publication(s): *ACERVO-Revista do Arquivo Nacional*; *Serie de Publicacoes Historicas*; *Serie
 de Publicacoes Tecnicas*; *Serie Instrumentos de
 Trabalho*; *Serie Publicacoes Avulsas*

**Biblioteca do Ministerio das Relacoes
 Exteriores**
Esplanada dos Ministerios, Bloco H, 70170-900
 Brasilia DF
*Tel:* (061) 2116359 *Fax:* (061) 2237362
*Web Site:* www.mre.gov.br *Cable:* 1319
*Key Personnel*
Dir, Librarian: Maria Salete Carvalho Reis
Publication(s): *Referencia de Periodicos*
 (monthly)

**Biblioteca Municipal Mario de Andrade**
Ave Sao Joao 473, Largo do Paissandu-Centro,
 01035-000 Sao Paulo
*Tel:* (011) 3334-0001 *Fax:* (011) 3224-0009
*E-mail:* smc@prodam.pmsp.sp.gov.br
*Web Site:* www.prefeitura.sp.gov.br
*Key Personnel*
Dir: Lucia Neiza Pereira DaSilva
Contact: Marli Monteiro
Publication(s): *Boletim Bibliografico Biblioteca
 Mario de Andrade* (quarterly)

**Biblioteca Publica do Estado do Rio de Janeiro**
Ave Presidente Vargas 1261, 20071-004 Rio de
 Janeiro-RJ
*Tel:* (021) 2224-6184 *Fax:* (021) 2252-6810
*E-mail:* bibliotecapublica@bperj.rj.gov.br
*Web Site:* www.bperj.rj.gov.br
*Key Personnel*
Dir General: Ana Ligia Silva Medeiros
President: Francisco Paula Freitas

**Centro de Documentacao e Informacao da
 Camara dos Deputados** (House of
 Representatives' Centre of Documentation &
 Information)
Palacio do Congresso Nacional Edificio Principal,
 Praca dos Tres Ponderes, 70160-900 Brasilia-
 DF
*Tel:* (061) 216 0000 *Toll Free Tel:* 800 619 619
*Web Site:* www2.camara.gov.br
*Telex:* 0611164
*Key Personnel*
Dir: Nelda Mendonca Raulino *E-mail:* nelda.
 raulino@camara.gov.br

**Fundacao Biblioteca Nacional**
Ave Rio Branco 219-39, 20040-008 Rio de
 Janeiro-RJ
*Tel:* (021) 22209433 *Fax:* (021) 22204173
*Web Site:* www.bn.br
*Key Personnel*
President: Eduardo Mattos Portella
 *E-mail:* portella@bn.br
Publication(s): *Anais da Biblioteca Nacional*; *Bibliografia Brasileira*; *Brazilian Book Magazine*;
 *revista "Poesia Sempre"*

**SIBi/USP**, see Sistema Integrado de Bibliotecas
 da Universidade de Sao Paulo (SIBi)

**Sociedade Brasileira de Cultura Inglesa -
Biblioteca**
Rua Plinio Moscoso, 945, Rio de Janeiro-RJ
*Tel:* (071) 247-9788 *Fax:* (021) 245-3287
*E-mail:* culturainglesa@br.inter.net
*Web Site:* www.culturainglesa-ba.com.br
*Key Personnel*
Contact: Ma de Fatima B Goncalves
Publication(s): *Library News*

**UFRGS**, see Universidade Federal do Rio Grande
do Sul (UFRGS), Biblioteca Central

**Universidade de Brasilia, Biblioteca Central**
Campus Universitario Darcy Ribeiro Gleba "A"
BCE, 70910-900 Brasilia DF
*Tel:* (061) 307-2417 *Fax:* (061) 274-2412
*E-mail:* informacoes@bce.unb.br
*Web Site:* www.bce.unb.br
*Telex:* 1083
*Key Personnel*
Dir: Clarimar Almeida Valle *Tel:* (061) 307 2400
   *E-mail:* direcao@bce.unb.br

**Sistema Integrado de Bibliotecas da
Universidade de Sao Paulo (SIBi)** (University
of Sao Paulo Integrated Library System)
Av Prof Luciano Gualberto, Trav J, 374/1 andar,
Cidade Universitaria, 05508-010 Sao Paulo-SP
*Tel:* (011) 818 4194; (011) 818 4197 *Fax:* (011)
815 2142
*E-mail:* dtsibi@org.usp.br
*Web Site:* www.usp.br/sibi
*Key Personnel*
Dir: Adriana Cybele Ferrari
Founded: 1981
Membership(s): CRB (Brazilian Regional Librar-
ian Council); FEBAB (Brazilian Federation of
Library Associations); IFLA; OCLC.
Publication(s): *Bibliotheca Universitatis - Acervo
Bibliografico da Universidade de Sao Paulo -
Sec XVII* (annually, book, 2003); *Boletim An-
nual do Departamento do SIBi/USP* (annually,
2003, print & online serial); *Cadernos de Estu-
dos, 9* (irregularly, book, 2003); *Dados Estatis-
ticos do Sistema Integrado de Bibliotecas da
USP* (annually, 2003, print & online serial)

**Biblioteca Central da Universidade Federal do
Parana**
Rua XV de Novembro, 1299, 80060-000 Curitiba,
Parana PR
*Tel:* (041) 360-5000 *Fax:* (041) 262-7784
*E-mail:* bc@ufpr.br
*Web Site:* www.ufpr.br/
*Telex:* 5100
*Key Personnel*
Dir: Elayne Margareth Schloegel

**Centro de Ciencias da Saude da Universidade
Federal do Rio de Janeiro**
Predio do CCS-Bloco L, Cidade Universitaria,
21949-900 Rio de Janeiro-RJ
Mailing Address: CP 68032, 21949-900 Rio de
Janeiro-RJ
*Tel:* (021) 2562 6632; (021) 2562 6716; (021)
2562 6641 *Fax:* (021) 2270 0119
*E-mail:* ccsbib@eagle.ufrj.br
*Web Site:* www.sibi.ufrj.br *Cable:* C P 68032
*Key Personnel*
Dir: Marco Tullio Azevedo Juric
Librarian: Maria de Fatima Gama
Medical School Library of the University of Rio
de Janeiro.

**Universidade Federal do Rio Grande do Sul
(UFRGS), Biblioteca Central**
Av Paulo Gama, 110, Terreo de Reitoria Predio
12107, 90040-060 Porto Alegre, Rio Grande de
Sul

Mailing Address: Cx Postal 2303, 90001-970
Porto Alegre-RS
*Tel:* (051) 3316-3065 *Fax:* (051) 3316-3984
*E-mail:* bcentral@bc.ufrgs.br; biblioteca@bc.
ufrgs.br
*Web Site:* www.biblioteca.ufrgs.br
*Telex:* 0511055
*Key Personnel*
Dir: Viviane Carrion Castanho
Librarian: Veleida Blank; Ana Maria Galvao

# Brunei Darussalam

**Dewan Bahasa dan Pustaka**
Ministry of Culture, Youth & Sports, Old Airport,
Berakas, Negara Brunei Darussalam BB3510
*Tel:* (02) 235501 *Fax:* (02) 224763
*E-mail:* Chieflib@Brunei.bn
*Web Site:* www.kkbs.gov.bn; www.brunei.gov.bn/
index.htm; dbp.gov.bn
*Key Personnel*
Librarian: Hj Abu Bakar Hj Zainal
National Language & Literature Bureau Library.
Publication(s): *Acquis List; Ind Exes*

# Bulgaria

**Bulgarian Academy of Sciences, Central
Library**
1, 15 Noemvri Str, 1040 Sofia
*Tel:* (02) 989-84-46; (02) 878 966; (02) 84 141
(ext 251) *Fax:* (02) 981-66-29; (02) 986-25-23;
(02) 988-04-48; (02) 986 2500
*E-mail:* library@cl.bas.bg
*Web Site:* www.cl.bas.bg
*Telex:* (067) 224-24 BG
*Key Personnel*
Dir: Dincho Krastev *Tel:* (02) 987-89-66; (02)
989-84-46 (ext 250) *Fax:* (02) 986-25-00
   *E-mail:* dincho@cl.bas.bg
Publication(s): *Bulgarian Academic Books* (cata-
log); *Problemi na specialnite biblioteki* (Prob-
lems of Special Libraries, irregularly); *Prob-
lems of Special Libraries; Collected Papers*

**Central Agricultural Library**
125, Tsarigadsko Shosse Blvd, Block 1, 1113
Sofia
*Tel:* (02) 70-55-17

**Central State Archives**
Division of General Department of Archives of
the Republic of Bulgaria
Moskovska 5, 1000 Sofia
*Tel:* (02) 9400101; (02) 9400120; (02) 9400176
   *Fax:* (02) 980 14 43
*E-mail:* gua@archives.government.bg
*Web Site:* www.archives.government.bg
*Key Personnel*
Dir: G Chernev
Founded: 1993
Collecting, registering, handling, preserving, using
& making accessible to the public the archival
holdings of the state agencies, public & private
bodies.
*Ultimate Parent Company:* Council of Ministers

**Central Technical Library**
50, D-r GM Dimitrov Blvd, 1125 Sofia
*Tel:* (02) 8173841; (02) 8173842; (02) 8173850
(Interlibrary loan) *Fax:* (02) 9173120

*E-mail:* ctb@nacid.nat.bg; ctbloan@nacid.nat.bg
(Interlibrary loan)
*Web Site:* www.nacid.nat.bg
*Key Personnel*
Dir: Valentina Slavcheva *E-mail:* vs@nacid.nat.bg
Founded: 1962
*Parent Company:* National Centre for Information
& Documentation (NACID)

**Saints Cyril & Methodius National Library**
(Narodna Biblioteka Sv sv Kiril i Metodii)
88 Vasil Levski Blvd, 1504 Sofia
*Tel:* (02) 9882811 (ext 231); (02) 9882811
(ext 234); (02) 9882811 (ext 235) *Fax:* (02)
8435495
*E-mail:* nl@nationallibrary.bg; cbi@
nationallibrary.bg
*Web Site:* www.nationallibrary.bg
*Key Personnel*
Editor-in-Chief: Alexandra Dipchikova *Tel:* (02)
9882811 (ext 206) *E-mail:* dipchikova@
nationallibrary.bg
Librarian: Prof Boryana Hristova *Tel:* (02)
9881600 *E-mail:* hristova@nationallibrary.bg
Founded: 1878
Publication(s): *Biblioteka* (6 times/yr, journal,
1993, library sciences); *Bulgarska Nacionalna
Bibliografija, Ser 1-8* (Bulgarian National Bibliography); *Bulgarski Knigopis* (monthly, bulletin, books, official, music, prints, maps); *Bulgarski periodicen Pecat* (annually, Bulgarian
periodicals)

**General Department of Archives of the
Republic of Bulgaria**
Moskovska 5, 1000 Sofia
*Tel:* (02) 940 0101; (02) 940 0120 *Fax:* (02) 980
14 43
*E-mail:* gua@archives.government.bg
*Web Site:* www.archives.government.bg
*Key Personnel*
Chairman: Atanas Atanassov *Tel:* (02) 940 0105
Deputy Chairman: Ventsislav Velchev
Secretary: Mr Panto Kolev
Founded: 1951
Administration, coordination, control & publish-
ing of archival records.
Publication(s): *Archival Review* (quarterly,
Archival Reference Book); *Arhivite govoriat*
(The Archives are Speaking); *Arhivni sprav-
ochnitsi* (Archival Finding Aids); *Journal of the
State Archives* (biannually)

**Medical University - Sofia, Central Medical
Library**
One, St G Sofiiski, 1431 Sofia
*Tel:* (02) 92301 (ext 498) *Toll Free Tel:* 888
443348 *Fax:* (02) 952 31 71
*Web Site:* www.medun.acad.bg/
*Key Personnel*
Dir: Dr Lydia Tacheva *E-mail:* lydia@medun.
acad.bg
Deputy Dir: Dr Christo Mutafov *Tel:* (02) 522
342 *Fax:* (02) 52 2393 *E-mail:* mutafov@Sun.
medun.acad.bg
Head Librarian: Pepa Kotsilkova
   *E-mail:* pslavova@medun.acad.bg
Founded: 1918

**National Library 'Ivan Vazov'**
17 Avksentii Veleshki St, 4000 Plovdiv
*Tel:* (032) 62 29 15; (032) 62 50 46 *Fax:* (032)
62 47 25
*E-mail:* nbiv@plovdiv.techno-link.com
*Web Site:* fobos.primasoft.bg/libplovdiv
*Key Personnel*
Dir: Radka Videva Koleva *Tel:* (032) 62 68 46
Deputy Dir: Dimitar T Minev *Tel:* (032) 62 47 25
   *E-mail:* dimin@abv.bg
Founded: 1879
Publication(s): *Plovdivski kraj* (annually)
*Branch Office(s)*
Children's Department, 15, Avksentii Ve-

leshki St, 4000 Plovdiv *Tel:* (032) 622 045
*E-mail:* nbiv@plovdiv.techno-link.com
Vustanicheski Residential District, 49, Dimitar
Talev St, 4004 Plovdiv

**Sofia City & District State Archives**
Moskovska 5, 1000 Sofia
*Tel:* (02) 940 01 06 *Fax:* (02) 980 14 43
*Web Site:* www.archives.government.bg
*Key Personnel*
Dir: Kr Milcheva
Founded: 1952
Collecting, registering, handling, use & making
available to the public the archives about Sofia
& Sofia district.
*Parent Company:* General Department of
Archives of the Republic of Bulgaria
*Ultimate Parent Company:* Council of Ministers

**Sofia University Kliment Ohridski Biblioteka**
Tzar Osvoboditel 15 Blvd, 1043 Sofia
*Tel:* (02) 467584; (02) 9308554; (02) 9308209
*Fax:* (02) 467170
*E-mail:* lsu@libsu.uni-sofia.bg
*Web Site:* www.libsu.uni-sofia.bg
*Telex:* 23296 Suko RBG
*Key Personnel*
Dir: Ivanka Yankova *E-mail:* yankova@libsu.uni-sofia.bg
Founded: 1888

**Technical University of Sofia Library & Information Complex**
8, Kliment Ohridski St, 1000 Sofia
*Tel:* (02) 62 3073 *Fax:* (02) 68 5343
*E-mail:* office_tu@tu-sofia.bg
*Web Site:* www.tu-sofia.bg
*Telex:* 23574
*Key Personnel*
Dir: A Todorova
Founded: 1994

**University of Sofia Library**, see Sofia University
Kliment Ohridski Biblioteka

# Burkina Faso

**Centre National des Archives**
Presidence du Faso, BP 7030, Ouagadougou
*Tel:* 33-61-96; 32-47-12; 32-46-38 *Fax:* 31-49-26
*Telex:* 5221
*Key Personnel*
Dir: Assane Sawadogo *E-mail:* assaned49@yahoo.fr
Founded: 1970

**Universite de Ouagadougou**
BP 7021, Ouagadougou
*Tel:* 30 70 64; 30 70 65 *Fax:* 30 72 42
*E-mail:* info@univ-ouaga.bf
*Web Site:* www.univ-ouaga.bf
*Telex:* 512 BF

# Burundi

**Bibliotheque Nationale du Burundi** (National
Library of Burundi)
BP 1095, Bujumbura
*Tel:* (02) 25051 *Fax:* (02) 26231
*E-mail:* biefbdi@cbinf.com

**Bibliotheque Publique**
BP 960, Bujumbura

**Office National du Tourisme (ONT)**
2, Avenue des Euphorbes, BP 902, Bujumbura
*Tel:* 229 390 *Fax:* 229 390
*E-mail:* ontbur@cbinf.com
*Telex:* Cab Pub BDI 5081, 5082
*Key Personnel*
Dir: Hermenegilde Nimbona
*Branch Office(s)*
7, Boulevard de l'Uprona, Bujumbura
Aeroport International de Bujumbura

**ONT**, see Office National du Tourisme (ONT)

**Bibliotheque de l'Universite du Burundi**
BP 1550, Bujumbura
*Tel:* (022) 2857
*Web Site:* www.ub.edu.bi *Cable:* UNIVARWA
*Key Personnel*
Chief Librarian: Tharlisse Nsabimana
Founded: 1964

# Cameroon

**Archives Bibliotheque nationales du Cameroon**
BP 1053, Yaounde
*Tel:* 220078 *Fax:* 232010
*Key Personnel*
Dir: Emerant Mbon Mekompomb
Founded: 1952

**Universite de Yaounde, Bibliotheque**
BP 337, Yaounde
*Tel:* 222 1320 *Fax:* 222 1320
*E-mail:* rect.uyl@uycdc.uninet.cm
*Web Site:* www.uninet.cm/acceuil.html
*Telex:* 8384
*Key Personnel*
Librarian: Peter Nkangafaok Chateh
Publication(s): *Etudes et Recherches en Bibliotheconomie*

**University of Dschang Central Library**
PO Box 255, Dschang
*Tel:* 451351 *Fax:* 451381
*Telex:* 7013KN
*Key Personnel*
Head Librarian: Tchouamo Micheline

# Central African Republic

**Bibliotheque Universitaire de Bangui**
BP 1450, Bangui
*Tel:* 61 20 00 *Fax:* 61 78 90
*Web Site:* www.univ-bangui.cf
*Telex:* 5283
*Key Personnel*
Dir: Thomas Poussoumandji

# Chad

**CDU**, see Centre De Documentation Universitaire
(CDU)

**Centre De Documentation Universitaire (CDU)**
(University Documentation Center)
Av Mobutu, N'Djamena

Mailing Address: BP 1117, N'Djamena
*Tel:* 5144 44; 5144 44 697 *Fax:* 514 033
*E-mail:* runiv.rectorat@sdnted.undp.org
*Key Personnel*
Chief Librarian: Mr Koulassim Doumtangar
Founded: 1972
*Parent Company:* Universite De N'Djamena

**Centre de Recherche des Archives et de Documentation (CRAD)**
731 Place Fontaine de l'Union, N'Djamena
*Tel:* 514 671 *Fax:* 516 079
*Telex:* 524 SKD UNESCO *Cable:* VNESCO
NDJAMENA
*Key Personnel*
Dir: Dr Khalil Alio
Chief of Center, Librarian: Ngaryaka Neldjita
Contact: Haroun Said
Publication(s): *COMNAT*

**CRAD**, see Centre de Recherche des Archives et
de Documentation (CRAD)

# Chile

**Biblioteca del Congreso Nacional**
Huerfanos 1117, 2° Piso, Santiago
*Tel:* (02) 2701700 *Fax:* (02) 2701766
*Web Site:* www.bcn.cl
*Key Personnel*
Dir: Soledad Ferreiro Serrano *E-mail:* sferreiro@bcn.cl
Library of Congress.
Publication(s): *Boletin Informativo*; *Estudios*; *Serie Estudios*; *Temas de Actualidad* (triannually)
*Branch Office(s)*
3° y 4° piso del Edificio del Congreso Nacional,
Valparaiso *Tel:* (032) 263100

**Biblioteca Nacional de Chile**
Ave Libertador B O'Higgins 651, Santiago
Mailing Address: Clasificador 1400, Santiago
*Tel:* (02) 3605200; (02) 3605239; (02) 3605275
*Fax:* (02) 6380461; (02) 6381975; (02)
6321091; (02) 6381151
*E-mail:* biblioteca.nacional@bndechile.cl
*Web Site:* www.dibam.cl/biblioteca_national
*Key Personnel*
Dir: Gonzalo Catalan Bertoni
National Library of the Office of Libraries,
Archives & Museums.
Publication(s): *Bibliografia chilena* (formerly 'Anuario de la Prensa', 1982); *Referencias Criticas sobre Autores Chilenos* (annually, 1988)

**Pontificia Universidad Catolica de Chile Sistema de Bibliotecas**
Avda Vicuna Mackenna 4860, Santiago
*Tel:* (02) 6864616; (02) 6864762 *Fax:* (02)
6865852
*Web Site:* www.puc.cl
*Key Personnel*
Dir: Maria Luisa Arenas Franco

**Biblioteca de la Universidad Catolica de Valparaiso**
Ave Brasil 2950, Casilla 4059, Valparaiso
*Tel:* (032) 273261; (032) 273000 *Fax:* (032)
273183
*Web Site:* biblioteca.ucv.cl
*Telex:* 230389 Ucv
*Key Personnel*
Dir: Atilio Bustos Gonzalez *E-mail:* abustos@ucu.cl

**Biblioteca Central de la Universidad de Chile**
Av Diagonal Paraguay No 265 of 703, Santiago
*Tel:* (02) 6782583 *Fax:* (02) 6782574
*E-mail:* sisib@uchile.cl
*Web Site:* www.uchile.cl/bibliotecas
*Key Personnel*
Dir: Alamiro de Avila Martel
Founded: 1936

**Universidad de Concepcion Direccion de Bibliotecas**
Edificio Eula, Centro Eula, 2° Piso, Concepcion
*Tel:* (041) 20 41 15; (041) 20 43 93 *Fax:* (041) 24 60 76
*E-mail:* info@udec.cl
*Web Site:* www.bib.udec.cl
*Key Personnel*
Dir: Maria Nieves Alsonso Martinez

**Universidad Technologica Metropolitana (UTEM), Sistema de Bibliotecas**
Avda Jose Pedro Alessandri 1242-Nunoa, Santiago
*Tel:* (02) 272-40-32
*Web Site:* www.bibliotecautem.cl
*Key Personnel*
Dir: Ximena Sanchez *E-mail:* xsanchez@bibliotecautem.cl
Librarian: Antonienta Figueroa *Tel:* (02) 7877163
Founded: 1989
Academic text in Humanities, Social Sciences, Pure & Applied Sciences.

# China

**Chongqing Library**
11 First Section Changjiang Rd, Chongqing 400014
*Tel:* (023) 6362-2596 *Fax:* (023) 6385-1474
*Key Personnel*
Dir: Shao Kangqing *E-mail:* skqcq@21cn.com
Founded: 1947

**Dalian University of Technology Library**
Linggong Rd 2, Ganjingzi District, Dalian City, Liaoning Province 116024
*Tel:* (0411) 84708620 *Fax:* (0411) 84708620; (0411) 84708626
*E-mail:* lib@dlut.edu.cn; libaqui4@dlut.edu.cn
*Web Site:* www.lib.dlut.edu.cn
*Telex:* 86231 DUTCN *Cable:* 7108
*Key Personnel*
Dir: Prof Liu Yuanfang
Founded: 1950
Publication(s): *Chinese Journal of Computational Mechanics* (bimonthly, periodical, 1984); *Journal of Dalian University of Technology* (bimonthly, periodical, 1950); *Journal of Mathematical Research & Exposition* (quarterly, periodical, 1981)

**Fudan University Library**
220 Han Dan Rd, Shanghai 200433
*Tel:* (021) 65642222; (021) 65643168 *Fax:* (021) 65649814
*E-mail:* libref@fudan.edu.cn
*Web Site:* www.library.fudan.edu.cn; www.fudan.edu.cn/english/index_en.html
*Key Personnel*
Professor: Xu Peng; Qin Zeng-Fu
Publication(s): *Mathematical Analysis* (Lectures on Higher Mathematics)

**Liaoning Provincial Library**
111 Wan Liu Tang Dong Ling, Shenyang, Liaoning Province 110015
*Tel:* (024) 2482-2241 *Fax:* (024) 2482-2449

*Web Site:* www.lnlib.com
Founded: 1948

**Library of Chinese Academy of Sciences**
33 Beisihuan Xilu, Haidan Dist, Beijing 100080
*Tel:* (010) 82623303; (010) 82626611-6720 *Fax:* (010) 62566846
*E-mail:* ask@mail.las.ac.cn
*Web Site:* www.las.ac.cn
*Telex:* 83020
*Key Personnel*
Dir: Zhang Xiaolin
Membership(s): IFLA.

**Nanjing tushuguan** (Nanjing Library)
66 Chengxian St, Nanjing, 210018 Jiangsu Province
*Tel:* (025) 3640241; (025) 3370259 *Fax:* (025) 3640241
*E-mail:* ntbgs@sina.com
*Web Site:* www.jslib.org.cn
*Key Personnel*
Executive Dir: Ma Ning *Tel:* (025) 83361845
Deputy Dir: Gong Aidong *Tel:* (025) 83617705; Yuan Dazhi *Tel:* (025) 84543649; Xu Jianye
Founded: 1907
Membership(s): IFLA; China Society for Library Science.
Publication(s): *Xin Shiji Tushuguan* (New Century Library, bimonthly, 2002, Co-sponser: Jiangsu Society for Library Science)

**The National Library of China**
33, Zhongguancun Nandajie, Haidian District, Beijing 100081
*Tel:* (010) 68415566 *Fax:* (010) 68419271
*E-mail:* webmaster@publicf.nlc.gov.cn
*Web Site:* www.nlc.gov.cn
*Telex:* 222211 NLC CN *Cable:* 0848
*Key Personnel*
Dir: Ren Jiyu
Founded: 1916
Zhongguo guojia tushuguan; formerly National Library of Beijing, Beijing Library, Peking Library, National Library of Peking, etc.
Publication(s): *Chinese Classification - A System Used in Chinese Libraries*; *Documentation* (series); *Journal of The National Library of China*; *The National Catalogue of Foreign Periodicals*

**Peking University Library**
Haidian District, Beijing 100871
*Tel:* (010) 62751051; (010) 62757223 *Fax:* (010) 62761008
*E-mail:* office@lib.pku.edu.cn
*Web Site:* www.lib.pku.edu.cn
*Key Personnel*
Dir: Prof Longji Dai *Tel:* (010) 62753503 *E-mail:* dailj@lib.pku.edu.cn
Founded: 1902

**Qinghua daxue tushuguan** (Qinghua University Library)
Tsinghua University Library, Beijing 100084
*Tel:* (010) 62782137 *Fax:* (010) 62781758
*E-mail:* tsg@mail.lib.tsinghua.edu.cn
*Web Site:* www.lib.tsinghua.edu.cn
*Telex:* 22617
*Key Personnel*
Dir: Xue Fangyu *Tel:* (010) 62771838
Founded: 1912

**Library of the Renmin University of China**
175 Haidian Rd, Beijing 100872
*Tel:* (010) 62511014 *Fax:* (010) 62515263; (010) 62515336
*E-mail:* rmdxxb@mail.ruc.edu.cn; leader@mail.ruc.edu.cn
*Web Site:* www.ruc.edu.cn

*Key Personnel*
Contact: Yang Dongliag *E-mail:* yangpj@sun.ihep.ac.cn
Founded: 1937

**Shanghai Academy of Social Sciences Library**
1610 Zhongshan W Rd, Shanghai 200233
*Tel:* (021) 6486 2266 (ext 1304) *Fax:* (021) 6427 6018
*E-mail:* tsg@sass.stc.sh.cn
*Web Site:* www.sass.stc.sh.cn *Cable:* 7306
*Key Personnel*
Dir: Xie-Jun Chen
Librarian: Ms Zhang Jianfen

**Shanghai tushuguan** (Shanghai Library)
1555 Huai Hai Zhong Lu, Shanghai 200031
*Tel:* (021) 64455555 *Fax:* (021) 64455001
*Web Site:* www.libnet.sh.cn
*Key Personnel*
Dir: Shu Qing Zho
Hon Dir: Gu Ting-long

**Xiamen University Library**
422 Siming Rd S, Xiamen, Fujian 361005
*Tel:* (0592) 2085102 *Fax:* (0592) 2182360
*E-mail:* xiaodh@xmu.edu.cn
*Web Site:* www.xmu.edu.cn
*Key Personnel*
Chief Librarian: Dr Mingguang Chen *Tel:* (0592) 2185442
Founded: 1921
Specialize in book borrowing & reading, document, information services.

**Yunnan Provincial Library**
2 Cuihu Nan Rd, Kunming, Yunnan 650031
*Tel:* (0871) 331 3357; (0871) 532 3851
*Web Site:* www.ynu.edu.cn
*Key Personnel*
Dir: Wu Rui

**ZheJiang Provincial Library**
38 Shuguang Rd, Hangzhou, Zhejiang 310007
*Tel:* (0571) 8798 8566 *Fax:* (0571) 8799 5860
*E-mail:* bgs@zlib.net.cn
*Web Site:* ztiii.zjlib.net.cn
*Key Personnel*
Chief Officer: Wang Xiaoliang
Chekiang Library, Hangchow.

**Zhongguo guojia tushuguan**, see The National Library of China

**Zhongshan Library of Guangdong Province**
213 Wen Ming Lu, Guangzhou, Guangdong Province 510110
*Tel:* (020) 83830676; (020) 83810164
*E-mail:* bgs@zslib.com.cn
*Web Site:* www.zslib.com.cn
*Key Personnel*
Dir: Huang Jungui
Also 81 Wende Rd, Guangdong (Canton) Tel: (020) 330349.

# Colombia

**Biblioteca Agropecuaria de Colombia (BAC)**
(Farming & Livestock Library of Colombia)
Centro de Investigacion Tibaitato, KM-14 via a Mosquera, Cundinamarca
Mailing Address: Apdo Aereo 240142, Las Palmas, Bogota DC
*Tel:* (01) 4227373 (ext 1254) *Fax:* (01) 2813088
*E-mail:* bac@corpoica.org.co
*Web Site:* www.corpoica.org.co

*Key Personnel*
Dir: Francisco Salazar Alonso
*Parent Company:* Corpoica-Corporacion Colombiana de Investigacion Agropecuaria

**Biblioteca Luis Angel Arango Banco de la Republica** (Luis Angel Arango Library-Central Bank of Colombia)
Calle 11, No 4-14, Bogota
Mailing Address: CP 12362, Bogota
*Tel:* (01) 3431212 *Fax:* (01) 2863551
*E-mail:* wbiblio@banrep.gov.co
*Web Site:* www.banrep.gov.co *Cable:* REDESBANCO BIBLIOTECA
*Key Personnel*
Dir: Jorge Orlando Melo *E-mail:* jmelogo@banrep.gov.co
Publication(s): *Boletin Cultural y Bibliografico* (quarterly); *Estudios sobre Politica Economica* (biannually)

**Archivo General de la Nacion de Colombia**
Calle 24, 5-60, Bogota
*Tel:* (01) 2431336 *Fax:* (01) 3414030
*E-mail:* bnc@mincultura.gov.co
*Web Site:* www.bibliotecanacional.gov.co
*Key Personnel*
Dir: Lina Espitaleta *Tel:* (01) 3414029
*E-mail:* direccion.binal@mincultura.gov.co
National Archives.

**BAC**, see Biblioteca Agropecuaria de Colombia (BAC)

**Biblioteca Nacional de Colombia**
Calle 24 No 5-60, Bogota
*Tel:* (01) 2431336 *Fax:* (01) 3414030
*E-mail:* bnc@mincultura.gov.co
*Web Site:* www.bibliotecanacional.gov.co
*Key Personnel*
Dir: Lina Espitaleta *Tel:* (01) 3414029
*E-mail:* direccion.binal@mincultura.gov.co
Founded: 1777
Publication(s): *Revista Senderos*

**British Council Library**
Calle 87 No 12-79, Bogota
*Tel:* (01) 618 0118; (01) 618 7680 *Fax:* (01) 218 7754
*E-mail:* info@britishcouncil.org.co
*Web Site:* www2.britishcouncil.org/colombia.htm
*Telex:* 45715 Bcoun
*Key Personnel*
Dir: Joe Docherty
Librarian: Maria Clemencia de Bohorquez

**Centro de Estudios sobre Desarrollo Economico CEDE** (Centre for Studies on Economic Development)
Cra 1 E No 18A-1 0, Bogota
*Tel:* (01) 339499; (01) 3394949 *Fax:* (01) 3324472
*E-mail:* cede@uniandes.edu.co; infocom@uniandes.edu.co
*Web Site:* www.uniandes.edu.co
*Telex:* 42343 Unand
*Key Personnel*
Coordinator: Miguel Angel Guerrero
*E-mail:* miguerre@uniandes.edu.co

**Pontificia Universidad Javeriana, Biblioteca General**
Carrera 7 No 41-00, Bogota
*Tel:* (01) 320 8320 (ext 2135); (01) 320 8320 (ext 2150); (01) 320 8320 (ext 2151) *Fax:* (01) 320 8320 (ext 2131)
*E-mail:* biblioteca@javeriana.edu.co
*Web Site:* www.javeriana.edu.co
*Key Personnel*
Dir: Luz Maria Carbarcas Santoya

**Universidad de los Andes, Biblioteca General, Ramon de Zubiria**
10 Edificio Franco, Bloque G AA, Cra 1 Este No 18 A, 4976 Bogota
*Tel:* (01) 3394999; (01) 3394949 *Fax:* (01) 3324472
*E-mail:* sisbibli@uniandes.edu.co
*Web Site:* biblioteca.uniandes.edu.co
*Telex:* 42343
*Key Personnel*
Librarian: Angela Maria Mejia de Gutierrez
*Tel:* (01) 3394949 (ext 2147) *E-mail:* amejia@uniandes.edu.co

**Universidad de Antioquia, Escuela Interamericana de Bibliotecologia, Biblioteca**
Calle 67, No 53-108, Ciudad Universitaria Bloque 12, Of 324, 1226 Medellin
*Tel:* (04) 2105930; (04) 2105933 *Fax:* (04) 2105946
*E-mail:* dbibliotecologia@arhuaco.udea.edu.co
*Web Site:* nutabe.udea.edu.co/eib
*Key Personnel*
Dir: Maria Teresa Munera Torres
Memberships: FID; ALA; AIBDA; IFLA; SALALM; Asociacion Latinoamericana de Archivos; The Library Association; ACURIL.
Publication(s): *Bibliografia Bibliotecologica*; *Bibliografica y de Obras de Referencia Colombianas* (Bibliography of Library Science, Bibliography & Colombian Works of Reference)

**Universidad de los Andes, Centro de Estudios sobre Desarrollo Economico (CEDE)**, see Centro de Estudios sobre Desarrollo Economico CEDE

**Universidad Externado de Colombia Biblioteca**
Calle 12 N° 1-17 Este, Bogota
*Tel:* (01) 3420288; (01) 3419900 (ext 3350); (01) 3419900 (ext 3351)
*E-mail:* biblioteca@uexternado.edu.co
*Web Site:* www.uexternado.edu.co/biblioteca/
*Key Personnel*
Dir: Lina Espitaleta

**Universidad Nacional de Colombia, Biblioteca Central**
Ciudad Universitaria, Ave Eldorado 44 A 40, Bogota
*Tel:* (01) 3351199
*E-mail:* refer@biblioteca.campus.unal.edu.co
*Web Site:* www.unal.edu.co
*Key Personnel*
Dir: Jorge Aurelio Diaz

# Congo

**Bibliotheque Universitaire, Universite Marien Ngouabi**
BP 69, Brazzaville
*Tel:* 814207; 812436 *Fax:* 814207
*E-mail:* unmgbuco@congonet.cg
*Telex:* 5331 KG
*Key Personnel*
Dir: F Wellot Samba
Librarian: Innocent Mabiala
Publication(s): *Annales*; *Dimi*; *Repertoire d'auteurs congolais*; *Revue d'histoire anthropologie* (Also other lists & catalogs)

**Centre Culturel Francais, Bibliotheque**
BP 2141, Brazzaville
*Tel:* 81 19 00; 81 17 05; 81 38 55 *Fax:* 83 06 18
*Key Personnel*
Contact: Andre Malraux

**Bibliotheque Nationale Populaire**
PB 1489, Brazzaville
*Tel:* 833485
*Key Personnel*
Dir: Pierre Mayola
Publication(s): *Repertorie bibliographique nationale*

# The Democratic Republic of the Congo

**Archives Nationales**
42a Ave de la Justice, Kinshasa-Gombe
Mailing Address: BP 3428, Kinshasa-Gombe
*Tel:* (012) 31 083
*Key Personnel*
Librarian: Kiobe Lumenga-Neso
Founded: 1953
Publication(s): *Kinshasa. Genese et Sites Historiques* (Arnaza-Bief 1995)

**Bibliotheque Centrale, Universite de Kinshasa**
BP 190, Kinshasa 11
*Tel:* (012) 21361; (012) 21362 (ext 320)
*E-mail:* centreinfo@ic.cd
*Web Site:* unikin.sciences.free.fr
Publication(s): *Annales de la Bibliotheque Centrile de Kinshasa*

**Bibliotheque Publique de Kinshasa**
10 bd Tshatshi, BP 410, Kinshasa
*Tel:* (012) 3070
*Key Personnel*
Librarian: B Mongu

**Institut Pedagogique National**
BP 8815, Kinshasa-Binza
*Tel:* (012) 80573

**Institut pour la Recherche Scientifique en Afrique Centrale (IRSAC)**
Bibliotheque Centrale, Bukavu
*Key Personnel*
Chief Librarian: Mburunge Murhagane

**IRSAC**, see Institut pour la Recherche Scientifique en Afrique Centrale (IRSAC)

**Universite de Kisangani Bibliotheque Centrale**
Campus de Kisangani, BP 2012, Kisangani
*Tel:* 215-2
*Key Personnel*
Chief Librarian: Muzila Label Kakes

**Bibliotheque Centrale de l'Universite de Lubumbashi**
BP 1825, Lubumbashi, Katanga
*Tel:* (022) 22-5285
*E-mail:* unilu@unilu.net
*Web Site:* www.unilu.net
*Key Personnel*
Librarian: Mubadi Sule Mwanansuka

# Costa Rica

**Biblioteca Nacional**
Calle 15-17, Av 3 y 3b, San Jose
Mailing Address: Apdo 10008-1000, San Jose
*Tel:* 233 1706; 221 2436; 221 2479 *Fax:* 223
  5510
*Telex:* 3334 Dider
*Key Personnel*
Dir: Guadalupe Rodriguez
Contact: Marco A Chacon Monge
Publication(s): *Catalogo Nacional ISBN*; *Indice
  de Diarios y Semanarios de Costa Rica* (Cat-
  alog of Costa Rican Daily & Weekly Newspa-
  pers); *Indice de Revistas Nacionales* (Catalog
  of National Periodicals)

**Biblioteca Mark Twain, Centro Cultural
  Costarricense-Norteamericano**
Apdo 1489-1000, San Jose
*Tel:* 207-7574; 207-7577 *Toll Free Tel:* 800-207-
  7500 *Fax:* 224-1480
*E-mail:* mercadeo@cccncr.com
*Web Site:* www.cccncr.com
*Key Personnel*
Librarian: Guisella Ruiz

**Universidad de Costa Rica Sistema de
  Bibliotecas, Documentacion e Informacion**
Ciudad Universitaria Rodrigo Facio, Apdo 2060,
  San Jose
*Tel:* 253-6152; 207-5316; 207-4461 *Fax:* 204-
  2809
*E-mail:* marqueda@sibdi.bldt.ucr.ac.cr
*Web Site:* sibdi.bldt.ucr.ac.cr
*Telex:* UNICORI 2544
*Key Personnel*
Dir: Maria E Briceno Meza *Tel:* 207-5316
  *E-mail:* mbriceno@sibdi.bldt.ucr.ac.cr; Maria
  Julia Vargas *Tel:* 207-4208 *E-mail:* mjvargas@
  sibdi.bldt.ucr.ac.cr
Publication(s): *Agronomia Costarricense* (bian-
  nually); *Annario del Cooperativismo en Costa
  Rica*; *Anuario de Estudios Centroamericanos*
  (annually); *Ciencia Y Tecnologia* (biannually);
  *Ciencias Economicas* (biannually); *Ciencias
  Matematicas* (biannually); *Educacion* (bian-
  nually); *Escena: Revista Teatral* (biannually);
  *Herencia* (biannually); *Ingenieria* (biannually);
  *Kanina: Revista de Artes Y Letras* (biannually); *Revista de Biologia Tropical* (biannually);
  *Revista de Filologia Y Linguistica* (biannually); *Revista de Filosofia* (biannually); *Revista
  de Historia* (biannually); *Revista Geologica
  de America Central* (biannually); *Revistas de
  Ciencias Sociales* (quarterly)

# Cote d'Ivoire

**Archives Nationales de Cote d'Ivoire**
BP V126, Abidjan
*Tel:* 32 41 58 *Fax:* 21 50 13
*Telex:* 22296
*Key Personnel*
Dir: Missa Kouassi
Founded: 1957

**Bibliotheque Centrale de la Cote d'Ivoire**
BPV 6243, Abidjan-Treichville
*Tel:* 323872
*Key Personnel*
Librarian: P Zelli Any-Grah
Founded: 1963

**Bibliotheque de l'Universite Nationale de Cote
  d'Ivoire**
BP 859, 08 Abidjan
*Tel:* 439 000 *Fax:* 44 35 31
*Telex:* 3469
*Key Personnel*
Dir: Bakary Toure
Librarian: Francoise N'Goran
Founded: 1963
Publication(s): *Annales de l'Universite d'Abidjan*

**Bibliotheque Municipale**
BP 24, Plateau, Abidjan

**Bibliotheque Nationale**
BPV 180, Abidjan
*Tel:* 32 38 72
*Key Personnel*
Librarian: Ambroise Agnero
Publication(s): *Bibliographie de la Cote-d'Ivoire*

**Centre Culturel Francais, Bibliotheque**
01 BP 3995, 01 Abidjan
*Tel:* (020) 211699; (020) 225628 *Fax:* 227132
*E-mail:* ccf@netafric.ci
*Telex:* 22465 Miscop Ci
*Key Personnel*
Dir: Jean-Marc Fratani
Dir Adjoint: Jean-Michael Neher

**INADES (Institut Africain pour le
  Developpment Economique et Social)**
08 BP 8, Abidjan 08
*Tel:* 22 40 02 16 *Fax:* 22 40 02 30
*E-mail:* ifsiege@inadesfo.ci
*Web Site:* www.inadesfo.org
*Key Personnel*
Dir: Michel Lambotte
Librarian: Nicole Vial
Publication(s): *COURRIER* (trimonthly); *Manuels
  de Bibliotheconomic* (quarterly)

# Croatia

**Nacionalna i Sveucilisna Knjiznica Biblioteka**
  (National & University Library)
Ulica Hrvatske bratske zajednice 4, 10000 Zagreb
*Tel:* (01) 616-4111; (01) 616-4008; (01) 616-4129
  *Fax:* (01) 616-4186
*E-mail:* nsk@nsk.hr; dpsenica@nsk.hr
*Web Site:* www.nsk.hr
*Key Personnel*
Contact: Prof Dubravka Fiala *E-mail:* dfiala@nsk.
  hr
Publication(s): *Bibliografija knjiga tiskanih u SR
  Hrvatskoj*; *Bibliografija rasprava, clanaka i
  knjizevnih radova u casopisima SR Hrvatske*;
  *Grada za hrvatsku retrospektivnu bibliografiju*

# Cuba

**Archivo Nacional de Cuba**
Compostela 906, Esquina San Isidro Habana
  Vieja, Havana 10100
*Tel:* (07) 862 9436; (07) 636 489 *Fax:* (07) 33
  8089
*E-mail:* arnac@ceniainf.cu
*Key Personnel*
Dir Dra: Berarda Salabarra Abraham

**Biblioteca Central de la Universidad de
  Oriente**
Ave Patricio Lumumba, Santiago 90 500

*Tel:* (022) 633013 *Fax:* (022) 633011
*E-mail:* marcosc@rect.uo.edu.cu
*Web Site:* www.uo.edu.cu
*Key Personnel*
Librarian: Maura Gonzalez

**Biblioteca del Instituto Pre-Universitario de la
  Habana**
Zulueta y San Jose, Havana
*Key Personnel*
Dir: Jose Manuel
Library of the Pre-University Institute of Educa-
  tion.

**Biblioteca Historica Cubana y Americana**
Municipio de la Habana, Oficina del Historiador
  de la Ciudad, Havana
Cuban & American Historical Library.

**Biblioteca Nacional Jose Marti** (Jose Marti
  National Library)
Apdo 6881, Havana
*Tel:* (07) 81 6224 *Fax:* (07) 33 5072
*Telex:* 511963 Bnjm
*Key Personnel*
Dir: Eliades Ignacio Acosta Matos
  *E-mail:* eliadesa@jm.lib.cult.cu
Publication(s): *Bibliografia Cubana*; *Bibliografias
  Especializadas*; *Boletines Bibliograficas e In-
  formacion Senal*; *Documentos Extranjeros
  Adquiridos*; *Ediciones Especializadas sobre
  la Cultura y el Arte*; *Indice General de Pub-
  licaciones Periodicas Cubanas*; *Revista de la
  Biblioteca Nacional Jose Marti*
Branch Office(s)
Ninguna

**Biblioteca Jose Antonio Echeverria**
Casa de las Americas, 3a y G, El Vedado, Havana
  10400
*Tel:* (07) 3235 8789 *Fax:* (07) 334 554
*E-mail:* casa@tinored cu
*Telex:* 511019
*Key Personnel*
Dir: Ernest Sierra
Founded: 1959
Specialize in Latin-American literature, history &
  sociology.

**IDICT**, see Instituto de Informacion Cientifica y
  Tecnologica (IDICT)

**Instituto de Informacion Cientifica y
  Tecnologica (IDICT)**
Dept Comercial y de Marketing, Capitolio de la
  Habana, Prado Centre Dragones y San Jose, La
  Habana Vieja, Havana 10200
Mailing Address: Apdo 2213, La Habana Vieja,
  Havana 10200
*Tel:* (07) 862-6531; (07) 860-3411 *Fax:* (07) 862-
  6531
*E-mail:* andresdt@idict.cu; commercial@idict.cu
*Web Site:* www.idict.cu/
*Telex:* 511203 *Cable:* 62-6501 IDICT CU
*Key Personnel*
General Dir: Eduardo Orozco Silva
Dir: Nestor Diaz; Katia Leiva; Carmen Rojas;
  Enrique Zarabozo
Publication(s): *Cubaciencia*; *Directorio Biomundi*
Branch Office(s)
Biblioteca Nacional de Ciencia y Tecnica (BNCT)
Centro de Estudios y Desarollo Profesional en
  Ciencias de la Informacion (PROINFO)
Centro de Intercambio Automatizado (CENIAI)
Consultoria en Biotecnologia e Industria Medico-
  Farmaceutica (BIOMUNDI)

**Instituto de Literatura y Lingueistica**
Av Salvador Allende 710, CP 10300 Havana
*Tel:* (07) 786486; (07) 701310 *Fax:* (07) 335718
*E-mail:* acc@ceniai.cu
*Telex:* 511290 acdcp cu

*Key Personnel*
Dir: Yolanda Ricardo Garcell
Vice Dir: Nuria Gregori Torada
Librarian: Pedro Luis Suarez Sola

**Biblioteca Manuel Sanguily**
Cuchillo de Zanja 19, Primer Piso entre Rayo y
San Nichlas, Centro, Havana
*Tel:* (07) 63 3232
*Key Personnel*
Dir: Estrella Garcia

**Biblioteca Central Ruben Martinez Villena**, see
Universidad de la Habana, Direccion de
Informacion Cientifico Tecnica

**UCLV**, see Biblioteca General de la Universidad
Central "Marta Abreu" de las Villas (UCLV)

**Biblioteca General de la Universidad Central
"Marta Abreu" de las Villas (UCLV)**
(Central Library of Central Marta Abreu
University of Las Villas)
Carretera de Camajuani, Km 5 5, Santa Clara,
Villa Clara 54830
*Tel:* (0422) 81410; (0422) 81618; (0422) 8178
*Fax:* (0422) 81608; (0422) 22113
*E-mail:* luishs@dri.uclv.edu.cu
*Key Personnel*
Lib Inquiries: Jose Rivero Diaz
Founded: 1959
Subdivided into small branches for technical &
social matters regarding careers studied in the
University. Specific reference (eg cybernetics,
economics, etc).

**Universidad de la Habana, Direccion de
Informacion Cientifico Tecnica**
L y San Lazaro, Vedado, Havana
*Tel:* (07) 78-3231 *Fax:* (07) 33-5774
*Telex:* 0512210 Dict Uh
*Key Personnel*
Dir: Dr Maria Christina Santos *E-mail:* cristina@
dict.uh.cu

# Cyprus

**The Library of the Archbishop Makarios III
Foundation**
Archbishopric, Archbishop Kyprianos Sq, 1505
Nicosia
*Tel:* (022) 430008 *Fax:* (022) 346753
*Key Personnel*
Dir: Dr Maria Stavrou

**British Council Library**
3 Museum St, 1097 Nicosia
Mailing Address: PO Box 25654, 1387 Nicosia
*Tel:* (022) 585000 *Fax:* (022) 677257
*E-mail:* enquiries@britishcouncil.org.cy
*Web Site:* www.britcoun.org/cyprus
*Telex:* 3911 Briconic
*Key Personnel*
Deputy Librarian: Joan Georghallides
Founded: 1940

**Cyprus Library**
Eleftherias Sq, 1011 Nicosia
*Tel:* (022) 303180; (022) 676118 *Fax:* (022)
304532
*E-mail:* cypruslibrary@cytanet.com.cy
*Key Personnel*
Librarian: Dr Antonis Maratheftis
*E-mail:* amatheftis@hotmail.com
Founded: 1927

Membership(s): Conference of European National
Librarians (CENL); IFLA.
Publication(s): *Cyprus Bibliography* (annually,
1999)
*Parent Company:* Ministry of Education & Cul-
ture

**Library of the Cyprus Museum - Dept of
Antiquities**
Mouseiou 1, 1516 Lefkosia
Mailing Address: PO Box 22024, 1516 Lefkosia
*Tel:* (022) 865864; (022) 865888 *Fax:* (022)
303148
*E-mail:* roctarch@cytanet.com.cy
*Key Personnel*
Librarian: Maria Economidou
Founded: 1934

**Municipal Library**
PO Box 41, Famagusta
*Key Personnel*
Chief Librarian: Ch Christofides

**Library of the Padagogic Institute Academia
(College of Education)**
c/o Ministry of Education, Tah Case 12720, 2252
Nicosia
*Tel:* (022) 402-300 *Fax:* (022) 480-505
*E-mail:* webmaster@cyearn.pi.ac.cy
*Web Site:* athena.pi.ac.cy/pedagogical/index.html
*Key Personnel*
Librarian: Soula Agdpiou; Maria Demetriou

**Library of Phaneromeni**, see The Library of the
Archbishop Makarios III Foundation

**Sultan's Library**
Evcaf, Nicosia

**Cyprus Turkish Public Library**
Kizilay Ave, Nicosia
*Tel:* (022) 83257
*Key Personnel*
Chief Librarian: Fatma Oenen

# Czech Republic

**Knihovna Narodniho muzea** (The National
Museum Library)
Praha 1, Vaclavske namisti 68, 115 79 Prague
*Tel:* (02) 24497111 *Fax:* (02) 24497331
*E-mail:* nm@nm.cz
*Web Site:* www.nm.cz
*Key Personnel*
Dir: Helga Turkova, PhD *Tel:* (02) 24497343;
(02) 24497344 *E-mail:* helga.turkova@nm.cz
Publication(s): *Sbornik Narodniho muzea, Rada
C: literarni historie* (Journal/Magazine of the
National Museum Prague, series C: Literary
History, annually, journal, 2003, summaries in
English & German)

**Mestska knihovna v Praze** (Municipal Library
in Prague)
Marianske Nam 1, 115 72 Prague 1
*Tel:* (02) 22113111 *Fax:* (02) 22328230
*E-mail:* informace@mlp.cz
*Web Site:* www.mlp.cz
*Key Personnel*
Dir: Tomas Rehak *E-mail:* reditel@mlp.cz

**Moravska Zemska Knihovna** (Moravian
Library)
Kounicova 65a, 601 87 Brno
*Tel:* (05) 41646111 *Fax:* (05) 41646100

*E-mail:* mzk@mzk.cz
*Web Site:* www.mzk.cz
*Key Personnel*
Dir: Dr Jaromir Kubicek *Tel:* (05) 41646110
*E-mail:* kubicek@mzk.cz
Founded: 1808

**Narodni knihovna Ceske republiky** (The
National Library of the Czech Republic)
Klementinum 190, 110 01 Prague 1
*Tel:* (02) 21663111; (02) 21663202 *Fax:* (02)
21663267; (02) 21663277
*E-mail:* public.ur@nkp.cz
*Web Site:* www.nkp.cz
*Key Personnel*
Dir: Vlastimil Jezek
Deputy Dir: Adolf Knoll
Public Relations: Libuse Piherova, PhD
*E-mail:* libuse.piherova@nkp.cz
Founded: 1777
Publication(s): *Ceska narodni bibliografie Knihy*
(The Czech National Bibliography-Books, an-
nually); *Narodni bibliografie Ceske republiky,
Hudebniny* (The National Bibliography of the
Czech Republic-Music, quarterly, Czech Mu-
sic); *Narodni Knihovna* (National Library, quar-
terly)
*Parent Company:* The Ministry of Culture of the
Czech Republic

**Pamatnik narodniho pisemnictvi** (Museum of
Czech Literature)
Division of Ministry of Culture, Czech Rep
Strahovske nadvori 1/132, 118 38 Prague 1
*Tel:* (02) 20516695 *Fax:* (02) 20517277
*E-mail:* post@pamatniknarodnihopisemnictvi.cz
*Web Site:* www.pamatniknarodnihopisemnictvi.cz
*Key Personnel*
Dir: Dr Eva Wolfova *E-mail:* wolfova@
pamatniknarodnihopisemnictvi.cz
Membership(s): ICOM.
Publication(s): *Literarni Archiv-Almanac* (annu-
ally)

**Parlamentni Knihovna** (Parliamentary Library)
Division of Office of the Chamber of Deputies
Snimovni 4, 118 26 Prague 1
*Tel:* (02) 57534 409; (02) 57174 501 *Fax:* (02)
57534 408
*E-mail:* posta@psp.cz
*Web Site:* www.psp.cz
*Key Personnel*
Director: Dr Karel Sosna *E-mail:* sosna@psp.cz
Founded: 1857
Membership(s): IFLA; ECPRD.
*Parent Company:* Chamber of Deputies of the
Czech Parliament

**Statni technicka knihovna** (State Technical
Library)
Marianske namesti 5, 110 01 Prague 1
Mailing Address: PO Box 206, 110 01 Prague 1
*Tel:* (02) 21 663 111 *Fax:* (02) 22 221 340
*E-mail:* techlib@stk.cz
*Web Site:* www.stk.cz
*Key Personnel*
Dir: Martin Svoboda *Tel:* (02) 21 663 402
*E-mail:* m.svoboda@stk.cz
Division Head: Dr Jan Bayer *Tel:* (02) 21 663
480 *E-mail:* j.bayer@stk.cz

**Vedecka knihovna V olomouci** (Research
Library in Olomouc)
Bezrueova 2, 779 11 Olomouc 9
*Tel:* (068) 585223441 *Fax:* (068) 585225774
*E-mail:* info@vkol.cz
*Web Site:* www.vkol.cz
*Key Personnel*
Contact: Dr Marie Nadvornikova, PhD *Tel:* (068)
5222328
Founded: 1573

**Vysoka skola banska - Technicka Univerzita Ostrava** (VSB - Technical University of Ostrava)
17 listopadu 15, 708 33 Ostrava-Poruba
*Tel:* (069) 596 991 111 *Fax:* (069) 596 998 507
*Web Site:* www.vsb.cz
*Key Personnel*
University Librarian: Daniela Tkacikova
    *E-mail:* daniela.tkacikova@vsb.cz

# Denmark

**Aalborg Universitetsbibliotek** (Aalborg University Library)
Langagervej 2, 9220 Aalborg
Mailing Address: Postboxs 8200, 9220 Aalborg
*Tel:* 96359400 *Fax:* 98156859
*E-mail:* aub@aub.aau.dk
*Web Site:* www.aub.aau.dk
*Key Personnel*
Chief Librarian: Niels-Henrik Gylstorff
Information Coordinator: Karen Dissing
    *Tel:* 96359343 *E-mail:* kd@aub.aau.dk

**Arhus Kommunes Biblioteker** (Arhus Public Library)
Mollegade 1, 8000 Aarhus C
*Tel:* 8940 9200 *Fax:* 8940 9393
*Web Site:* www.aakb.dk
*Key Personnel*
Chief Librarian: Rolf Hapel

**Biblioteksstyrelsen** (Danish National Library Authority)
Nyhavn 31 E, 1051 Copenhagen K
*Tel:* 33 73 33 73 *Fax:* 33 73 33 72
*E-mail:* bs@bs.dk
*Web Site:* www.bs.dk
*Key Personnel*
Dir: Jens Thorhauge *E-mail:* jth@bs.dk
Contact: Vibeke Cranfield *E-mail:* vhc@bs.dk
Government agency under the Danish Ministry of Culture.
Publication(s): *Nyt fra Nyhavn* (quarterly, Info on library related matters)

**Danmarks BlindeBibliotek** (The Danish National Library for the Blind)
Teglvaerksgade 37, 2100 Copenhagen O
*Tel:* 39 13 46 00 *Fax:* 39 13 46 01
*E-mail:* dbb@dbb.dk
*Web Site:* www.dbb.dk
*Key Personnel*
Dir: Elsebeth Tank *E-mail:* eta@dbb.dk
Head of Distribution & Projects: Lisbeth Trinskjer
    *E-mail:* lmt@dbb.dk

**Danmarks Natur-og Laegevidenskabelige Bibliotek, Universitet de sbiblioteket** (The Danish National Library of Science & Medicine, University Library)
Norre Alle 49, 2200 Copenhagen N
*Tel:* 3539 6523 *Fax:* 3539 8533
*E-mail:* dnlb@dnlb.dk
*Web Site:* www.dnlb.dk
*Key Personnel*
Advisory Librarian: Torsten Schlichtkrull
    *Tel:* 353-25070 *E-mail:* ts@dnlb.dk
Head Librarian: Mette Stockmarr *Tel:* 353-25001
    *E-mail:* ms@dnlb.dk
Founded: 1482
Publication(s): *Acta Historica Scientiarum Naturalium et Medicinalium*; *Skrifter Udgivet af Danmarks Natur-og Laegevedenskabelige Bibliotek, Kobenhavns Universitets Bibiotek*

**Danmarks Paedagogiske Bibliotek** (National Library of Education)
Emdrupvej 101, 2400 Copenhagen NV
Mailing Address: PO Box 840, 2400 Copenhagen NV
*Tel:* 8888 9300 *Fax:* 8888 9391
*E-mail:* dpb@dpu.dk
*Web Site:* www.dpb.dpu.dk/
*Key Personnel*
Dir: Soren Carlsen *E-mail:* sca@dpu.dk
Deputy Dir: Jakob Andersen *E-mail:* jak@dpu.dk

**Danmarks Statistik Biblioteket** (National Statistical Library)
Sejrogade 11, 2100 Copenhagen O
*Tel:* 3917 3917; 3917 3030 *Fax:* 3917 3999; 3917 3003
*E-mail:* dst@dst.dk; bib@dst.dk
*Web Site:* www.dst.dk/bibliotek
*Key Personnel*
Librarian: Per Knudsen *Tel:* 3917 3001
    *E-mail:* pkn@dst.dk

**Danmarks Tekniske Videncenter (DTV)**
Anker Engelunds Vej 1, 2800 Lyngby
Mailing Address: PO Box 777, 2800 Lyngby
*Tel:* 4525 7200 *Fax:* 4588 3040
*E-mail:* dtv@dtv.dk
*Web Site:* www.dtv.dk
*Key Personnel*
Dir: Annette Winkel Schwarz *E-mail:* aws@dtv.dk
Chief of Library: Frede Morch *Tel:* 4525 7308
    *Fax:* fm@dtv.dk
Technical Knowledge Center & Library of Denmark.

**DBB,** see Danmarks BlindeBibliotek

**DTV,** see Danmarks Tekniske Videncenter (DTV)

**Frederiksberg Kommunes Biblioteker** (Frederiksberg Public Library)
Fanogade 15, 2100 Copenhagen
*Tel:* 39470000 *Fax:* 39470001
*E-mail:* fdb@fkb.dk
*Web Site:* www.fkb.dk
*Telex:* 16548 fkbib
*Key Personnel*
Chief Librarian: Anne Moeller-Rasmussen
    *E-mail:* anra03@frederiksberg.dk
Founded: 1887

**Gentofte Bibliotekerne** (Gentofte Municipal Library)
Ahlmanns Alle 6, 2900 Hellerup
*Tel:* 39487500 *Fax:* 39487507
*E-mail:* bek@gentofte.bibnet.dk; bibliotek@gentofte.bibnet.dk
*Web Site:* www.gentofte.bibnet.dk
*Key Personnel*
Chief Librarian: Laone Gladbo
*Branch Office(s)*
Dyssegard Branch Library, Dyssegardsvej 24, 2900 Hellerup *Tel:* 39 65 58 90
    *E-mail:* dyssegaardbibliotek@gentofte.bibnet.dk
Gentofte Branch Library, Gentoftegade 45, 2820 Gentofte *Tel:* 39 65 03 23
    *E-mail:* gentoftebibliotek@gentofte.bibnet.dk
Jaegersborg Branch Library, Smakkegardsvej 112, 2820 Gentofte *Tel:* 39 65 05 10
    *E-mail:* jaegersborgbibliotek@gentofte.bibnet.dk
Ordrup Branch Library, Ordrupvej 121, 2920 Charlottenlund *Tel:* 39 64 14 40
    *E-mail:* ordrupbibliotek@gentofte.bibnet.dk
Vangede Branch Library, Vangede Bygade 45, 2820 Gentofte *Tel:* 39 65 38 47
    *E-mail:* vangedebibliotek@gentofte.bibnet.dk

**Kobenhavns Kommunes Biblioteker** (Copenhagen Municipal Libraries)
Islands Brygge 37, 2300 Copenhagen S
*Tel:* 33664650 *Fax:* 33667120
*E-mail:* bibliotek@kkb.bib.dk
*Web Site:* www.kkb.bib.dk/
*Telex:* 16648
*Key Personnel*
City Librarian: Jens Ingemann Larsen
Publication(s): *Arsberetning* (annual report)

**Kobenhavns Stadsarkiv** (City Archives of Copenhagen)
Radhus, 1599 Copenhagen
*Tel:* 33662370 *Fax:* 33667039
*E-mail:* stadsarkiv@kff.kk.dk
*Web Site:* www.ksa.kk.dk
*Key Personnel*
Head Archivist: Henrik Gautier
Copenhagen City Archives.
Publication(s): *Historiske Meddelelser om Kobenhavn* (Historical Yearbook)

**Det Kongelige Bibliotek**
Soren Kierkegaards Plads, 1016 Copenhagen K
Mailing Address: Postbox 2149, 1016 Copenhagen K
*Tel:* 33 47 47 47 *Fax:* 33 93 22 18
*E-mail:* kb@kb.dk
*Web Site:* www.kb.dk
*Key Personnel*
Dir-General: Erland Kolding Nielsen
    *E-mail:* ekn@kb.dk
Acquisitions: Jette Hagen
Founded: 1648
Publication(s): *Catalogue of Oriental Manuscript; Xylographs, etc in Danish Collections* (irregularly, 1966); *Fund og Forskning i Det Kongelige Biblioteks Samlinger* (annually, 1961, Discovery & Research in the Collections in the Royal Library)
*Branch Office(s)*
The Royal Library Amager, Njalsgade 80
    *Tel:* 3347 4747 *Fax:* 3393 2218
The Royal Library Fiolstraede, Fiolstraede 1
    *Tel:* 3347 4747 *Fax:* 3393 2218

**Det nordjyske Landsbibliotek**
Hovedbiblioteket, Rendsburggade 2, 9100 Aalborg
Mailing Address: PO Box 839, 9100 Aalborg
*Tel:* 99 31 44 00 *Fax:* 99 31 43 90
*E-mail:* njl@njl.dk
*Web Site:* www.njl.dk
*Key Personnel*
Librarian: Kirsten Boel
Central Library for the County of North Jutland.

**Odense Centralbibliotek** (Odense County Library)
Ostre Stationsvej 15, 5000 Odense C
*Tel:* 66514301 *Fax:* 66137337
*E-mail:* teleservice-bib@odense.dk
*Web Site:* www.odensebib.dk
*Key Personnel*
Chief Librarian: Lene Byrialsen *Tel:* 65514400
    *E-mail:* lby@odense.dk

**Odense Universitetsbibliotek** (University Library of Southern Denmark)
Campusvej 55, 5230 Odens M
*Tel:* 6550 2644 *Fax:* 6550 2601
*E-mail:* sdub@bib.sdu.dk
*Web Site:* www.bib.sdu.dk
*Key Personnel*
Dir & Librarian: Aase Lindahl *Tel:* 6550 2683
    *E-mail:* lindahl@bib.sdu.dk

**Rigsarkivet** (Danish National Archives)
Rigsdagsgarden 9, 1218 Copenhagen K
*Tel:* 33923310 *Fax:* 33153239

*E-mail:* mailbox@ra.sa.dk
*Web Site:* www.sa.dk
*Key Personnel*
National Archivist: Johan Peter Noack
Secretary: Helle Gjellerup *Tel:* 33922336
    *E-mail:* hg@ra.sa.dk
Danish National Archives.
Publication(s): *Siden Saxo*

**Roskilde University Library**
Universitetsvej 1, 4000 Roskilde
Mailing Address: PO Box 258, 4000 Roskilde
*Tel:* 46742207 *Fax:* 46743090
*E-mail:* rub@ruc.dk
*Web Site:* www.rub.ruc.dk
*Key Personnel*
Dir: Niels Senius Clausen *Tel:* 46742235
    *E-mail:* nsc@ruc.dk
Founded: 1971

**Statsbiblioteket** (State & University Library, Aarhus)
Universitetsparken, 8000 Aarhus
*Tel:* 89462022 *Fax:* 89462220
*E-mail:* sb@statsbiblioteket.dk
*Web Site:* www.statsbiblioteket.dk
*Key Personnel*
Chief Executive: Svend Larsen
Publication(s): *Avismikrofilm i Statsbiblioteket*; *Journalism, Media & Communication; Ongoing Research in Denmark, Finland, Norway & Sweden*; *Nordicom; Bibliography of Nordic Mass Communication Literature* (ISSN 0105-1385)

# Dominican Republic

**Biblioteca Dominicana** (Dominican Library)
Chapel of the Dominican Order, Santo Domingo
*Key Personnel*
Dir: Jose Rijo
Founded: 1914

**Biblioteca Nacional** (National Library)
Cesar Nicolas Penson 91, Santo Domingo
*Tel:* 688-4086; 688-4660 *Fax:* 685-8941
*E-mail:* biblioteca.nacional@dominicana.com
*Web Site:* www.bnrd.gov.do
*Key Personnel*
Dir: Roberto DeSoto
Founded: 1971

**Biblioteca de la Camara Oficial de Comercio, Agricultura e Industria del Distrito Nacional** (Library of the Chamber of Commerce, Agriculture and Industry)
Noel 52-Altos, Apdo 815, Santo Domingo
*Tel:* 682-2688; 682-7206 *Fax:* 685-2228

**Universidad Nacional Pedro Henriquez Urena**
Campus 2, Edificio 3, Autopista Duarte km 6 1/2, Santo Domingo
*Tel:* (0809) 542-6888 (ext 2301-2315, 2320 & 2321) *Fax:* (0809) 566-2206; (0809) 540-3803
*E-mail:* biblioteca@unphu.edu.do
*Web Site:* www.unphu.edu.do/unphu/biblioteca
*Key Personnel*
Librarian: Carmen Iris Olivo
Founded: 1966
Publication(s): *Revista Aula 2da Epoca y Campus*; *Revista de Ciencias Juridicas y Politicas*

**Biblioteca Municipal de Santo Domingo**
Padre Billini 18, Santo Domingo
*Key Personnel*
Librarian: Luz Del Carmen Rijo

**Biblioteca de la Secretaria de Estado de Relaciones Exteriores**
752 Independencia Ave, Santo Domingo
*Tel:* 535-6280 *Fax:* 508-6863; 533-5772
*E-mail:* correspondencia@serex.gov.do
*Web Site:* www.serex.gov.do
Library of the Secretariat of Foreign Affairs.

**Biblioteca de la Universidad Autonoma de Santo Domingo**
Av Alma Mater, Ciudad Universitaria, Santo Domingo
*Tel:* 533-1104 *Fax:* 508-7374
*E-mail:* rectoria.uasd@codetel.net.do
*Web Site:* www.uasd.edu.do
*Key Personnel*
Dir: Martha Maria DeCastro Cotes

# Ecuador

**Archivo Nacional de Historia** (National Historical Archives)
Av 10 de Agosto N11-539 y Santa Prisca Casilla 17-12-878, Quito
*Tel:* (02) 2280431 *Fax:* (02) 2280431
*E-mail:* ane@ane.gov.ec
*Web Site:* www.ane.gov.ec
*Key Personnel*
Dir: Grecia Vasco de Escudero
Founded: 1938

**Biblioteca Nacional del Ecuador** (National Library of Ecuador)
Casa de la Cultura Ecuatoriana Benjamin Carrion, 12 de Octobre 555, Patria, Quito
Mailing Address: Casilla 67, Quito
*Tel:* (02) 2528840 *Fax:* (02) 2223391
*E-mail:* benjamincarrion@andinanet.net
*Key Personnel*
Dir: Laura de Crespo

**Biblioteca de la Casa de la Cultura Ecuatoriana**, see Biblioteca Nacional Eugenio Espejo de la Casa de la Cultura Ecuatoriana

**Biblioteca Ecuatoriana Aurelio Espinosa Polit'**
Apdo 17-01-160, Quito
*Tel:* (02) 2491 157; (02) 2491 156 *Fax:* (02) 2493 928
*E-mail:* beaep@uio.satnet.net
*Web Site:* www.beaep.org.ec
*Key Personnel*
Dir: Rev Julian G Bravo *E-mail:* director@beaep. org.ec
Founded: 1928
Publication(s): *Diccionaris Bibliografico Ecuatoriano* (Vols I, II, III & IV)

**Biblioteca Nacional Eugenio Espejo de la Casa de la Cultura Ecuatoriana**
Avs 12 de Octubre 555 y Patria, Quito
Mailing Address: Apdo 67, Quito
*Tel:* (02) 2223391; (02) 2565721 (ext 120)
*E-mail:* info@cce.org.ec
*Web Site:* cce.org.ec
*Key Personnel*
Dir Lic: Ruth Garaicoa Soria
Founded: 1792
Library of Ecuadorian Culture.

**Museo y Biblioteca Municipal**
Ave 10 de Agosto entre Chile y Calle Pedro Carbo Palacio, Municipal Apdo 6069, Guayaquil
*Tel:* (04) 515738
*Key Personnel*
Dir: Patricia De Quevedo

**Biblioteca de la Universidad Central de Ecuador**
Av America y Av Universitaria, Quito
*Tel:* (02) 2234 722 *Fax:* (02) 2236 367; (02) 2521 925
*Web Site:* www.ucentral.edu.ec

**Biblioteca General, Universidad de Guayaquil**
Chile 900 y Av Olmedo, Guayaquil
*Tel:* 2282440 *Fax:* 2391010
*E-mail:* zd@ug.edu.ec
*Web Site:* www.ug.edu.ec
*Telex:* 3179
*Key Personnel*
Dir: Leonor Villao de Santander

# Egypt (Arab Republic of Egypt)

**Alexandria Municipal Library**
18 Sharia Menasce Moharrem Beey, Alexandria
*Key Personnel*
Chief Librarian: Sheikh Beshir Beshir El Shindi

**Alexandria University Central Library**
163 El-Horia Ave, El-Shatby, Alexandria
Mailing Address: PO Box 233, El-Ebrahemia, Alexandria
*Tel:* (03) 4282 928 *Fax:* (03) 4282 927
*E-mail:* auclib@auclib.edu.eg
*Web Site:* www.auclib.edu.eg
*Telex:* 54467
*Key Personnel*
Chief Librarian: Prof Mohamed Khamis Elzouka

**American University in Cairo Library**
113 Sharia Kasr El Aini, Cairo 11511
Mailing Address: PO Box 2511, Cairo 11511
*Tel:* (02) 797-6904 *Fax:* (02) 792-3824
*E-mail:* aucpress@aucegypt.edu; library@ aucegypt.edu
*Web Site:* library.aucegypt.edu
*Telex:* 92224 AUCAI UN EGYPT
*Key Personnel*
Dean, Libraries & Learning Technologies: Shahira El Sawy *Tel:* (02) 797-6901
    *E-mail:* selsawy@aucegypt.edu
Head, ILL/Document Delivery & Electronic Resource Services: Hoda El Ridi *Tel:* (02) 797-6365 *E-mail:* elridhi@aucegypt.edu

**Al- Azhar University Library**
El-Nasr Rd, Cairo
*Tel:* (02) 5881152; (02) 5881153
*E-mail:* info@alazhar.org
*Web Site:* www.alazhar.org
*Key Personnel*
Librarian: M E A Hady

**Egyptian National Library (Dar-ul-Kutub)**
Sharia Corniche El-Nil, Bulaq, Cairo
*Tel:* (02) 900 232

*Key Personnel*
General Dir: Ali Abdul Mohsen
Founded: 1870

**Ein Shams University Library**
Abbasiyah 11566, Cairo
*Tel:* (02) 4820230; (02) 6831474; (02) 6831231;
   (02) 6831492; (02) 6831417; (02) 6831090
   *Fax:* (02) 687824
*E-mail:* info@asunet.shams.edu.eg
*Web Site:* net.shams.edu.eg
*Key Personnel*
Librarian: Nasr El Din Abdel Rahman

**Institute of Arab Research & Studies Arab League Educational, Cultural & Scientific Organization Library**
One Tolombat St, Garden City, Cairo
Mailing Address: PO Box 229, Cairo
*Tel:* (02) 3551648 *Fax:* (02) 3562543
*Telex:* 92642 Alcso *Cable:* IREALEA CAIRO
*Key Personnel*
President: Prof M S Abulezz, PhD
Dir: Prof Ahmed Youssef
Founded: 1953

**Library of the People's Assembly**
Majilis al-Shab St, Cairo
Mailing Address: PO Box 1183, Cairo
*Tel:* (02) 3540279 *Fax:* (02) 3548977
*Telex:* 20054 EGYAS UN

**Ministry of Education Library**
12 El Falaki St, Cairo
*Tel:* (02) 516 9744 *Fax:* (02) 516 9560
*E-mail:* info@mail.emoe.org
*Web Site:* www.emoe.org
*Key Personnel*
Dir: Hassen Abdel Shafi

**Ministry of Justice Library**
Midan Lazoghli, Cairo
*Tel:* (02) 20806 *Fax:* (02) 795 8103
*E-mail:* mojeb@idsc1.gov.eg
*Key Personnel*
Librarian: Fekry Abou-El-Kheir

**National Archives**
Al-Qalcah, Cairo

**National Information & Documentation Centre (NIDOC)**
Al Tahrir St, Dokki, Cairo
*Tel:* (02) 3371696
*Key Personnel*
Dir: Dr Mostaga Esmat El-Sarha
Publication(s): *Directory of Scientific & Technical Libraries*

**NIDOC**, see National Information & Documentation Centre (NIDOC)

**University of Ain Shams Library**, see Ein Shams University Library

**University of Cairo Library**
Gameet el Qahira Street, Giza, Cairo
*Tel:* (02) 5729584 *Fax:* (02) 628884
*Key Personnel*
General Dir: Fatina Ibrahim

# El Salvador

**Biblioteca Nacional**
Calle Delgado y 8A Ave Norte, San Salvador

Mailing Address: Apdo 2455, San Salvador
*Tel:* 221-6312; 221-4373; 271-5661; 272-2886
   *Fax:* 221-8847; 221-4419
*E-mail:* dibiaes@es.com.sv
*Key Personnel*
Dir: Manilo Argueta *E-mail:* manilo_a@yahoo.es
National Dir, Promotion & Diffusion: Silvia Martinez *E-mail:* silviamartinez@salnet.net

**Biblioteca P Florentino Idoate, SJ**, see Biblioteca de la Universidad Centroamericana Jose Simeon Canas

**Biblioteca de la Universidad Centroamericana Jose Simeon Canas**
Blvd Los Proceres, San Salvador
Mailing Address: Apdo 01-168, San Salvador
*Tel:* 210-6600 (ext 278) *Fax:* 210-6657
*E-mail:* ucabib.director@bib.uca.edu.sv
*Web Site:* www.uca.edu.sv
*Key Personnel*
Dir: Katherine Miller *E-mail:* kmiller@bib.uca.edu.sv
Publication(s): *Estudios Centro Americanas (ECA)*

**Biblioteca Central de la Universidad de El Salvador**
Sistema Bibliotecario, Apdo 2923, San Salvador
*Tel:* 503 2250278 *Fax:* 503 2250278
*E-mail:* sb@biblio.ues.edu.sv
*Web Site:* www.ues.edu.sv/biblio.html
*Key Personnel*
Dir: Carlos R Colindres *E-mail:* carlos@biblio.ues.edu.sv
Publication(s): *Boletin* (monthly); *Lista de Acquisiciones Recientes* (monthly)

# Eritrea

**University of Asmara Library**
PO Box 1220, Asmara
*Tel:* (01) 161926; (01) 162553 *Fax:* (01) 162236
*Web Site:* www.uoa.edu.er
*Telex:* 42091 *Cable:* ASMUNIV
*Key Personnel*
Dir & Librarian: Assefaw Abraha
   *E-mail:* assefawa@asmara.uoa.edu.er
*Ultimate Parent Company:* Ministry of Education

# Estonia

**Eesti Rahvusraamatukogu** (National Library of Estonia)
Tonismaegi 2, 15189 Tallinn
*Tel:* 630 7611 *Fax:* 631 1410
*E-mail:* nlib@nlib.ee
*Web Site:* www.nlib.ee
*Key Personnel*
Dir General: Tiiu Valm *Tel:* 630 7600
   *E-mail:* tiiu.valm@nlib.ee
Dir of Library: Ene Loddes *Tel:* 630 7107
   *E-mail:* ene.loddes@nlib.ee
The National Library of Estonia is also the Parliamentary Library of Estonia; it is the central library in the field of humanities & art.
Publication(s): *Eesti Rahvusbibliograafia: Artiklid* (The Estonian National Bibliography: Articles from Serials); *Eesti Rahvusraamatukogu: Raamatud* (The Estonian National Bibliography: Books)

**Tartu University Library** (Tartu Ulikooli Raamatukogu)
One W Struve Str, 50091 Tartu
*Tel:* (07) 375 702 *Fax:* (07) 375 701
*E-mail:* library@utlib.ee
*Web Site:* www.utlib.ee
*Key Personnel*
Library Dir: Toomas Liivamagi *Tel:* (07) 375 700
   *E-mail:* toomas.liivamagi@ut.ee
Founded: 1802
Membership(s): European Information Association (EIA) & its branch for Baltic & Nordic Countries; European Association for Health Information & Libraries Association (EAHIL); Association of Libraries of the Baltic Sea Region *Bibliotheca Baltica*; International Association of Music Libraries, Archives & Documentation Centres (IAML); International Association of Law Libraries (IALL); League of European Research Libraries (LIBER); Consortium of Legal Resource Centres & Legal Information Specialists of Central & Eastern Europe & Asia (CLCLIS CEEA).
Publication(s): *Eksliibrised Tartu Ulikooli Raamatukogus* (Bookplates in Tartu University Library, irregular, 1975, Four publications to introduce the collection); *Publicationes Bibliothecae Universitatis Litterarum Tartuensis* (irregular, 1973, Introduces Tartu University Library collections of manuscripts); *Raamat-aegrestaureerimine* (Book-Time-Restoration, irregular, 1969); *Raamatukogu toeid* (Publications of Tartu University Libary. I-XI, 1968, Papers on the library); *Tartu (Riiklik) Uelikool* (Tartu State University, The Bibliography of Works Published, irregular, Records all the works published by university faculty & students); *Tartu Uelikooli Raamatukogu vanagraafika kogu kataloogid* (Tartu University Library collections of graphic art since 15th centruy, irregular, 1974, Nine publications about English, German, Flemish, Dutch, Italian & French works of graphic art); *Tartu Ulikooli Raamatukogu aastaraamat* (Tartu University Library Yearbook, regular, 1996, Contains annual report, list of donations & research articles)

# Ethiopia

**Addis Adaba University Library**
PO Box 1176, Addis Adaba
*Tel:* (01) 115673; (01) 550844 *Fax:* (01) 550655
*Telex:* 21205 *Cable:* AAUNIV
*Key Personnel*
Librarian: Adhana Mengsteab
Founded: 1950

**African Union Library**
Roosvelt St (Old Airport Area), PO Box 3243, W21 K19 Addis Ababa
*Tel:* (01) 51 77 00 *Fax:* (01) 51 78 44
*Web Site:* www.africa-union.org
*Telex:* 21046 *Cable:* OAU
*Key Personnel*
Chief Librarian: Mrs J C Ranaivoravelo

**Agricultural Institute Library**
PO Box 307, Jimma
*Tel:* (07) 11-00-19
*Key Personnel*
Librarian: Goitom Ghebru

**Alemaya University of Agriculture Library**
PO Box 138, Dire Dawa
*Tel:* (05) 11-14-00 *Fax:* (05) 11-40-08
*Key Personnel*
Assistant Librarian: Tesfaye Salilew

Founded: 1952
Publication(s): *The Alemayan*

**British Council Library**
Artistic Bldg, Adwa Ave, Addis Ababa
Mailing Address: PO Box 1043, Addis Ababa
*Tel:* (01) 55 00 22 *Fax:* (01) 55 25 44
*E-mail:* bc.addisababa@et.britishcouncil.org
*Web Site:* www.britishcouncil.org/ethiopia/index.
htm; www.britishcouncil.org/ethiopia.htm
*Telex:* 21561
*Key Personnel*
Assistant Dir Knowledge & Learning Services:
Hailemelekot Taye *E-mail:* hailemelekot.taye@
et.britishcouncil.org
Specialize in provision of library & information
services.

**Institute of Ethiopian Studies Library**
PO Box 1176, Addis Ababa
*Tel:* (01) 55-05-44; (01) 11-57-72 *Fax:* (01) 55-
26-88
*E-mail:* ies.aau@telecom.net.et
*Web Site:* www.ies-ethiopia.org/indexf.htm; www.
aau.edu.et/research/ies/library.htm
*Telex:* 21205 *Cable:* AA N IV
*Key Personnel*
Librarian: Degife Gabre Tsadik
Founded: 1963
Publication(s): *Ethiopian Publications* (annually);
*List of Current Periodical Publications* (biannu-
ally)
*Parent Company:* Addis Ababa University

**National Archives & Library of Ethiopia**
PO Box 717, Addis Ababa
*Tel:* (01) 516532 *Fax:* (01) 526411
*E-mail:* nale@ethionet.et
*Web Site:* www.nale.gov.et
*Key Personnel*
Librarian: Almaz Mengistu
Founded: 1944

**United Nations Economic Commission for
Africa Library**
PO Box 3001, Addis Ababa
*Tel:* (01) 44 31 14 *Fax:* (01) 51 44 16
*E-mail:* ecainfo@uneca.org; ecalibadmin@uneca.
org
*Web Site:* www.uneca.org
*Telex:* 21029 *Cable:* ECA ADDIS ABABA
*Key Personnel*
Chief Librarian: Ms Petria Amonoo
*E-mail:* pamonoo@uneca.org
Founded: 1958
Publication(s): *Africa Index: Selected articles on
socio-economic development* (quarterly)

# Faroe Islands

**Foroya Landsbokasavn** (National Library of the
Faroe Islands)
J C Svabosgotu 16, 110 Torshavn
Mailing Address: PO Box 61, 110 Torshavn
*Tel:* 31 16 26 *Fax:* 31 88 95
*E-mail:* utlan@flb.fo
*Web Site:* www.flb.fo
*Key Personnel*
National Librarian: Herluf Hansen
*E-mail:* herhan@flb.fo
Founded: 1828
Publication(s): *The Faroese* (book list)

**Standard Book Numbering Agency,** see Foroya
Landsbokasavn

# Fiji

**Library Service of Fiji**
PO Box 2526, Suva
*Tel:* 315 344 *Fax:* 314 994
*Key Personnel*
Chief Librarian: Humesh Prasad
Senior Librarian: Shafig Gafoor
*Parent Company:* Ministry of Education
*Branch Office(s)*
Northern Regional Library, Labasa
Western Regional Library, PO Box 150, Lautoka

**National Archives of Fiji**
25 Carnarvon St, Suva
Mailing Address: PO Box 2125, Suva
*Tel:* 304 144; 304 228 *Fax:* 307 066
*Web Site:* www.fiji.gov.fj *Cable:* ARCHIVIST
*Key Personnel*
Archivist: Setareki Tale *E-mail:* stale@govnet.
gov.fj
Founded: 1958

**Suva City Library**
Victoria Parade, Suva
Mailing Address: PO Box 176, Suva
*Tel:* 313 433 *Fax:* 302 158 *Cable:* TOWN
CLERK SUVA
*Key Personnel*
Chief Librarian: Ms Lalita Sudhakar Lal
Founded: 1909
Publication(s): *Suva City Council* (annual report)

**University of the South Pacific Library**
Suva
*Tel:* 323 1000 *Fax:* 323 1528
*E-mail:* library@usp.ac.fj
*Web Site:* www.usp.ac.fj/library
*Key Personnel*
Dir: Dr Esther Williams *Tel:* 323 2282
*E-mail:* williams_e@usp.ac.fj
Founded: 1969
Coordination Unit for Pacific Islands Marine Re-
sources Information System (PIMRIS), Re-
gional Center for Population Information Net-
work (POPIN).
Publication(s): *PIC Newsletter* (quarterly); *PIM-
RIS Newsletter* (quarterly); *South Pacific Peri-
odicals Index*; *South Pacific Research Register*
(biennially)

# Finland

**Abo Akademis bibliotek** (Abo Akademi
University Library)
Domkyrkogt 2-4, 20500 Abo
*Tel:* (02) 2154180 *Fax:* (02) 2154795
*E-mail:* hblan@abo.fi
*Web Site:* www.abo.fi/library
*Key Personnel*
Librarian: Tore Ahlback *Tel:* (02) 2154182
*E-mail:* ahlback@abo.fi
Financial Secretary: Anders Ekberg *Tel:* (02)
2154190 *E-mail:* anders.ekberg@abo.fi
Publication(s): *Skrifter utgivna av Abo Akademis
bibliotek*

**Eduskunnan Kirjasto** (Library of Parliament,
Finland)
Aurorankatu 6, 00102 Helsinki
*Tel:* (09) 4321 *Fax:* (09) 432 3495
*E-mail:* kirjasto@eduskunta.fi; library@
parliament.fi
*Web Site:* www.eduskunta.fi/kirjasto/
*Key Personnel*
Library Dir: Tuula H Laaksovirta

Secretary: Satu Saarikivi *E-mail:* satu.saarikivi@
eduskunta.fi
Publication(s): *Bibliographia iuridica Fennica*

**Helsingin Kaupunginkirjasto - yleisten
kirjastojen keskuskirjasto** (Helsinki City
Library - Central Library for Public Libraries)
Rautatielaisenkatu 8, 00520 Helsinki
Mailing Address: PO Box 4100, 00099 City of
Helsinki
*Tel:* (09) 3108511 *Fax:* (09) 31085517
*E-mail:* city.library@hel.fi
*Web Site:* www.lib.hel.fi
*Key Personnel*
Library Dir: Ms Maija Berndtson
Executive Assistant: Reita Hamalainen *Tel:* (09)
31085520 *E-mail:* reita.hamalainen@hel.fi

**Helsinki University Library**
Unioninkatu 36, 00014 Helsingin, Yliopisto
Mailing Address: PL 15, 00014 Helsingin,
Yliopisto
*Tel:* (09) 191 23196 *Fax:* (09) 191 22719
*E-mail:* hyk-palvelu@helsinki.fi
*Web Site:* www.lib.helsinki.fi
*Telex:* 121538 Hyk
*Key Personnel*
Dir: Kai Ekholm *Tel:* (09) 191 22721
Founded: 1640
Publication(s): *Books from Finland* (quarterly,
mostly in English, but also in French & Ger-
man); *The Finnish National Bibliography* (CD-
ROM); *Publications of the University Library
at Helsinki*
*Branch Office(s)*
Slavonic Library, PB 15, Helsingin Yliopisto,
00014 Unioninkatu 36 *Tel:* (09) 19123196
American Resource Center, Box 15, Helsingin
Yliopisto, 00014 Unioninkatu 36 *Tel:* (09)
19124048 *Fax:* (09) 652940 *E-mail:* ARC@
usembassy.fi

**Joensuun Yliopisto** (Joensuu University)
Yliopistokatu 2, PO Box 107, 80101 Joensuu
*Tel:* (013) 251 2690 *Fax:* (013) 251 2691
*E-mail:* joyk@joensuu.fi
*Web Site:* www.joensuu.fi/
*Telex:* 46223
*Key Personnel*
Librarian: Helena Hamynen *Tel:* (013) 251 2660
*E-mail:* helena.hamynen@joensuu.fi

**Jyvaskylan Yliopiston Kirjasto** (Jyvaskyla
University Library)
Seminaarinkatu 15, 40014 Jyvaskylan Yliopisto
Mailing Address: PO Box 35 (B), 40014 Jy-
vaskyla
*Tel:* (014) 260 1211 *Fax:* (014) 260 3371
*E-mail:* jyk@Library.jyu.fi
*Web Site:* www.jyu.fi
*Key Personnel*
Dir: Pirjo Vatanen *Tel:* (014) 260 3373
*E-mail:* pirjo.vatanen@library.jyu.fi
Founded: 1863
*Parent Company:* Jyvaskylan Yliopiston (Jy-
vaskyla University)

**Kansallisarkisto Kirjasto** (National Archives of
Finland/Library)
Rauhankatu 17, 00170 Helsinki
Mailing Address: PO Box 258, 00171 Helsinki
*Tel:* (09) 228521 *Fax:* (09) 176302
*E-mail:* kansallisarkisto@narc.fi
*Web Site:* www.narc.fi
*Key Personnel*
Head of Library: Elisa Orrman *E-mail:* elisa.
orrman@narc.fi
Library Assistant: Marjut Nuikka *E-mail:* marjut.
nuikka@narc.fi
Founded: 1869
National Archives of Finland.

**Library of Statistics**, see Statistics Finland
Library

**Oulun Yliopiston Kirjasto** (Oulu University
Library)
PL 7500, 90014 Oulu
*Tel:* (08) 553 1011 *Fax:* (08) 556 9135
*Web Site:* www.kirjasto.oulu.fi/
*Telex:* 32256 Oyk
*Key Personnel*
Dir: Paivi Kytomaki *Tel:* (08) 553 3500
*E-mail:* paivi.kytomaki@oulu.fi
Publication(s): *Acta Universitatis Ouluensis* (pub-
lications of Oulu University Library)

**Sibelius-Akatemian Kirjasto** (Sibelius Academy
Library)
Toeoeloenkatu 28, 00260 Helsinki
Mailing Address: PL 86, 00251 Helsinki
*Tel:* (020) 7539 538 *Fax:* (020) 7539 542
*E-mail:* sibakirjasto@siba.fi
*Web Site:* lib.siba.fi/fin/
*Key Personnel*
Librarian: Irmeli Koskimies

**Statistics Finland Library**
Tyoepajakatu 13B, 00022 Helsinki
Mailing Address: PO Box 2B, 00022 Helsinki
*Tel:* (09) 1734 2220 *Fax:* (09) 1734 2279
*E-mail:* library@stat.fi
*Web Site:* www.stat.fi/tk/kk/index_en.html
*Key Personnel*
Chief Librarian: Hellevi Yrjoelae

**Tampereen Yliopiston Kirjasto** (Tampere
University Library)
Yliopistonkatu 38, 33014 Tampere
Mailing Address: PL 617, 33014 Tampere
*Tel:* (03) 215 6434 *Fax:* (03) 215 7493
*E-mail:* yliopiston.kirjasto@uta.fi
*Web Site:* www.uta.fi/~kimiii
*Telex:* 22263 Tayk
*Key Personnel*
Chief Librarian: Dr Mirja Iivonen *E-mail:* mirja.t.
iivonen@uta.fi
Founded: 1925
Publication(s): *University Publications*

**Teknillisen Korkeakoulun Kirjasto** (Helsinki
University of Technology Library)
Otaniementie 9, 02015 Hut
Mailing Address: PO Box 7000, 02015 Hut
*Tel:* (09) 451 4111 *Fax:* (09) 451 4132
*E-mail:* infolib@tkk.fi
*Web Site:* lib.tkk.fi
*Key Personnel*
Dir of Libraries: Ari Muhonen *E-mail:* ari.
muhonen@hut.fi
Head of Information Services: Irma Pasanen
National Resource Library for Technology in Fin-
land.
Publication(s): *Annual Bibliography of the
Helsinki University of Technology* (online
only); *Research at HUT* (annually, online
only); *Tenttu* (online only)

**TERKKO**, see Terveystieteiden keskuskirjasto
(TERKKO)

**Terveystieteiden keskuskirjasto (TERKKO)**
(National Library of Health Sciences)
Haartmaninkatu 4, 00290 Helsinki
Mailing Address: PL 61, 00014 Helsinki
*Tel:* (09) 191 26643 *Fax:* (09) 241 0385
*E-mail:* terkko-info@helsinki.fi
*Web Site:* www.terkko.helsinki.fi/
*Key Personnel*
Library Dir: Pirjo Rajakiili *Tel:* (09) 191 26646
*E-mail:* pirjo.rajakiili@helsinki.fi
Publication(s): *FINMED/MEDIC* (bibliography &
database)

**Turun Yliopiston Kirjasto** (Turku University
Library)
Hallinto, 20014 Turku
*Tel:* (02) 333 51 *Fax:* (02) 333 5050
*E-mail:* kirjasto@utu.fi
*Web Site:* kirjasto.utu.fi
*Telex:* 62123 Tyk
*Key Personnel*
Librarian: Tuulikki Nurminen
Turku University Library.
Publication(s): *Annales Universitatis Turkuensis*

# France

**American Library in Paris**
10, rue du General-Camou, 75007 Paris
*Tel:* (01) 53 59 12 60 *Fax:* (01) 45 50 25 83
*E-mail:* alparis@noos.fr
*Web Site:* www.americanlibraryinparis.org
*Key Personnel*
Dir: Shirley Lambert *E-mail:* s.lambert@noos.fr
Assistant Dir: Adele Witt
Reference Librarian: Kim LeMinh
Founded: 1920
Special Collections: Gregory Usher Cookbook
Collection; Marlene Dietrich Collection
Specialize in social sciences, humanities, US his-
tory & civilization, literary criticism.

**Bibliothcque Universitaire Antilles-Guyane
(BUAG)**
Campus de Schoelcher, BP 7210, 97275
Schoelcher Cedex
*Tel:* (0596) 727530 *Fax:* (0596) 727527
*Web Site:* www.univ-ag.fr/buag
*Key Personnel*
Dir: Marie-Francoise Bernabe *E-mail:* marie-
francoise.bernabe@martinique.univ-ag.fr
Librarian In-Charge, Martinique Section: Marie-
France Grouvel *E-mail:* marie-france.grouvel@
martinique.univ-ag.fr
Librarian In-Charge, Cayenne Section: Nicole
Clement-Martin *Tel:* (0594) 252155
*Fax:* (0594) 309668 *E-mail:* nicole.
clementmartin@guyane.univ-ag.fr
In-Charge, Guadeloupe Section: Catherine Vas-
silieff *Tel:* (0590) 489001 *Fax:* (0590) 489089
*E-mail:* catherine.vassilieff@univ-ag.fr

**Archives Nationales**
56 Rue des Francs Bourgeois, 75141 Paris Cedex
03
*Tel:* (01) 40 27 64 19 *Fax:* (01) 40 27 66 01
*E-mail:* chan.paris@culture.gouv.fr
*Web Site:* www.archivesnationales.culture.gouv.fr
*Key Personnel*
Dir: H Lerch
*Branch Office(s)*
09/63-02 Dathwee Chhen Twa Gallee, Chowk
Bhitra 2nd floor Purano Bazaar, Arniko-
Barhabise VDC-9, Arniko Rajmarg-87 K M,
Bagmati Anchal, Barhabise Mail PO Code
45303,, Kathmandu, Nepal

**Bibliotheque de l' Arsenal**
Division of Bibliotheque Nationale de France
One Rue de Sully, 75004 Paris
*Tel:* (01) 53 01 25 25 *Fax:* (01) 53 01 25 07
*E-mail:* arsenal@bnf.fr
*Web Site:* www.bnf.fr
*Key Personnel*
Dir: Bruno Blasselle *E-mail:* bruno.blasselle@bnf.
fr

**BDIC**, see Bibliotheque de Documentation
Internationale Contemporaine (BDIC)

**Bibliotheque Centrale du Museum National
d'Histoire Naturelle**
38 rue Geoffry-Saint Hilaire, 75005 Paris
*Tel:* (01) 40 79 36 27 *Fax:* (01) 40 79 36 56
*E-mail:* bcmweb@mnhn.fr
*Web Site:* www.mnhn.fr/mnhn/bcm
*Key Personnel*
Dir: Michele Mauries
Chief Librarian: Monique Duereux
*E-mail:* ducreux@mnhn.fr

**Bibliotheque d'Art et d'Archeologie Jacques
Doucet**
Division of Universites de Paris IV et Paris I
58, rue de Richelieu, Paris
Mailing Address: 2 rue Vivienne, 75002 Paris
Cedex 02
*Tel:* (01) 47037623 *Fax:* (01) 47037630
*E-mail:* bibliotheque@inha.fr
*Web Site:* www.paris4.sorbonne.fr
*Key Personnel*
Dir: Martine Poulain

**Bibliotheque Historique de la Ville de Paris**
(Historical Library of Paris)
24 rue Pavee, 75004 Paris
*Tel:* (01) 44 59 29 40 *Fax:* (01) 42 74 03 16
*Key Personnel*
Curator: Jean Derens

**Bibliotheque Interuniversitaire de Montpellier**
Bibliotheque Interuniversitaire, 60, rue des Etats
Generaux, 34965 Montpellier Cedex 2
*Tel:* (04) 67 13 43 50 *Fax:* (04) 67 13 43 51
*E-mail:* biu.secretariat@univ-montpl.fr
*Web Site:* www.biu.univ-montp1.fr
*Key Personnel*
Chief Librarian: Pierre Gaillard *E-mail:* pierre.
gaillard@univ-montp3.fr

**Bibliotheque Municipale de Besancon**
One rue de la Bibliotheque, 25000 Besancon
Cedex
*Tel:* (03) 81878140 *Fax:* (03) 81619877
*E-mail:* bib.etude@besancon.com
*Web Site:* www.besancon.com/biblio/francais/
*Key Personnel*
Librarian: Helene Richard *E-mail:* helene.
richard@besancon.com
Dir: Marie-Claire Waille *E-mail:* marie-claire.
waille@besancon.com

**Bibliotheque Municipale de Grenoble**
12 blvd Marechal Lyautey, 38021 Grenoble
Cedex 1
*Tel:* (04) 76 86 21 00 *Fax:* (04) 76 86 21 19
*E-mail:* bm.etude@bm-grenoble.fr
*Web Site:* www.bm-grenoble.fr
*Key Personnel*
Librarian: Sylvie Crouzet; Catherine Pouyet
Publication(s): *Bibliotheque municipale de Greno-
ble, Catalogue general auteurs des livres im-
primes jusqu'a 1900* (1980, 12 vols available
from K G Saur, Germany)

**Bibliotheque Municipale de Lyon**
30 blvd Vivier-Merle, 69003 Lyon Cedex 03
*Tel:* (04) 78 62 18 00 *Fax:* (04) 78 62 19 49
*E-mail:* bm@bm-lyon.fr
*Web Site:* www.bm-lyon.fr
*Key Personnel*
Librarian: Patrick Bazin *Tel:* (04) 78 62 19 24
*E-mail:* pbazin@bm-lyon.fr

**Bibliotheque Municipale de Rennes** (Rennes
Public Library)
One rue de la Borderie, 35042 Rennes
*Tel:* (02) 99 63 09 09; (02) 99 87 98 98 *Fax:* (02)
99 36 05 96; (02) 99 87 98 99
*E-mail:* contact@bm-rennes.fr

*Web Site:* www.bm-rennes.fr
*Key Personnel*
Dir: Marie-Therese Pouillias *E-mail:* marie-
therese.pouillias@bm-rennes.fr
Publication(s): *Cing cents ans d'imprimerie en
Bretagne, 1484-1985* (catalog); *Jean Larcher*
(catalog); *Le Femme 1900 dans les collections
Henri Polles* (catalog); *Le Pelletier* (dictionary);
*Le Romantisme breton: collection Henri Polles*;
*L'itinerarie de Kenneth White* (catalog); *Paul
Feval, 1816-1887*

**Bibliotheque Nationale de France** (National
Library of France)
Quai Francois-Mauriac, 75706 Paris Cedex 13
*Tel:* (01) 53 79 59 59 *Fax:* (01) 47 03 77 34
*Web Site:* www.bnf.fr
*Key Personnel*
President: Jean Pierre Angremy
Dir General: Philippe Belaval

**Bibliotheque Nationale et Universitaire de
Strasbourg**
5 rue du Marechal Joffre, BP 1029/F, 67070
Strasbourg Cedex
*Tel:* (03) 88 25 28 00 *Fax:* (03) 88 25 28 03
*E-mail:* contact@bnu.fr
*Web Site:* www-bnus.u-strasbg.fr
*Key Personnel*
Administrator: Bernard Falga *Tel:* (03) 88 25 28
10 *E-mail:* administrateur@bnu.fr
(main address & Management & Legal Section);
6 place de la Republique, BP 1029/F, 67070
Strasbourg cedex (Alsace Region Affairs Sec-
tion); 3 bis rue du Marechal Joffre, BP 1029/F,
67070 Strasbourg Cedex Tel: (03) 88 25 28 46.
Publication(s): *Bibliographie alsacienne*; *Catalogue critique des manuscrits persans*; *Papyrus
grecs de la BNUS*

**Bibliotheque Universitaire Droit-Sciences
Economiques**
11, pl Carnot, 54042 Nancy Cedex
Mailing Address: BP 4232, Nancy Cedex
*Tel:* (03) 83 30 81 57 *Fax:* (03) 83 30 82 38
*Web Site:* www.univ-nancy2.fr/webbib/webbib/
budroit.html
*Key Personnel*
Contact: Annie Kammerer *Tel:* (03) 83 30 82 30
*E-mail:* annie.kammerer@univ-nancy2.fr
*Parent Company:* Universites de Nancy

**Bibliotheque Municipale de Bordeaux**
(Bordeaux Public Library)
85 Cours du Marechal Juin-F, 33000 Bordeaux
*Tel:* (05) 56 10 30 00 *Fax:* (05) 56 10 30 90
*E-mail:* bibli@mairie-bordeaux.fr
*Web Site:* www.bordeaux-city.com/cbiblio.htm
*Key Personnel*
Dir: Pierre Botineau
Founded: 1803

**BUAG**, see Bibliotheque Universitaire
Antilles-Guyane (BUAG)

**La Documentation Francaise**
29 Quai Voltaire, 75007 Paris Cedex 07
*Tel:* (01) 40 15 71 10 *Fax:* (01) 40 15 67 83
*E-mail:* libparis@ladocumentationfrancaise.fr
*Web Site:* www.ladocumentationfrancaise.fr
*Key Personnel*
Man Dir: Sophie Moati
Commercial Dir: Alain-Marie Bassy
Editorial Dir: M Meusy
Chief Sales: Bernard Meunier

**Bibliotheque de Documentation Internationale
Contemporaine (BDIC)**
Centre Universitaire, 6 allee de l'Universite,
92001 Nanterre Cedex
*Tel:* (01) 40 97 79 00 *Fax:* (01) 40 97 79 40

*E-mail:* courrier@bdic.fr
*Web Site:* www.bdic.fr/
*Key Personnel*
Dir: Genevieve Dreyfus-Armand
*E-mail:* genevieve.dreyfus-amand@u-paris10.fr
This is a Paris University library.
Publication(s): *Collection des Publications de la
BDIC*

**Ecole Nationale Superieure des Sciences de
l'information et des bibliotheques (ENSSIB)**
17-21 Blvd du 11 Novembre 1918, 69623 Villeur-
banne Cedex
*Tel:* (04) 72 44 43 43 *Fax:* (04) 72 44 43 44
*E-mail:* com@enssib.fr
*Web Site:* www.enssib.fr
*Key Personnel*
Dir: Francois Dupuigrenet-Desroussilles
*E-mail:* dupuigre@enssib.fr
Dir, Publications: Pierre-Yves Duchemin
Dir, Studies: Raymond Berard *E-mail:* berard@
enssib.fr
Publication(s): *Bulletin des bibliotheques
de France*; *Monographies en sciences de
l'information et des bibliotheques* (travaux
d'etude et de recherche); *Presses de l'Enssib*

**Bibliotheque de Geographie**
191 rue St-Jacques, 75005 Paris
*Tel:* (01) 44 32 14 61; (01) 44 32 14 63 *Fax:* (01)
44 32 14 67
*Web Site:* www.univ-paris1.fr
*Key Personnel*
Librarian: Joseph Maie
*Parent Company:* Universite de Paris

**INIST**, see Institut de l'Information Scientifique
et Technique (INIST)

**Bibliotheque de l'Institut de France**
23 quai Conti, 75006 Paris
*Tel:* (01) 44 41 44 10 *Fax:* (01) 44 41 44 11
*E-mail:* bibliotheque@bif.univ-paris5.fr
*Web Site:* www.institut-de-france.fr/bibliotheques/
institut.htm
*Key Personnel*
Dir & Librarian: Mireille Pastoureau
*E-mail:* mireille.pastoureau@bif.univ-paris5.fr
Founded: 1795

**Institut de l'Information Scientifique et
Technique (INIST)**
Affiliate of CNRS (French National Centre for
Scientific Research)
2 Allee du Parc de Brabois, 54514 Vandoeuvre-
les-Nancy Cedex
*Tel:* (03) 83 50 46 00 *Fax:* (03) 83 50 46 50
*E-mail:* webmaster@inist.fr
*Web Site:* www.inist.fr
*Key Personnel*
Dir: A Pain Chanudet
Founded: 1988
INIST-CNRS, a French scientific & technical
information center, is a service unit of the
French National Centre for Scientific Research
(CNRS). It collects basic & applied research
publications in cooperation with French &
international organizations. Producer of multidisciplinary & multilingual bibliographical
databases - PASCAL, FRANCIS & ARTI-
CLE@INIST - listing documents published in
most areas of science & technology, medicine,
the humanities, social sciences & economics.
Also acts as a scientific & technical document
delivery service.
Publication(s): *Articlesciences* (1990, bibliographic database); *Francis* (1972, bibliographic
database, monthly updates); *Pascal* (1973, bibliographic database, weekly updates)

**Bibliotheque Interuniversitaire des Langues
Orientales**
Universite Sorbonne Nouvelle, 4, rue de Lille,
75007 Paris
*Tel:* (01) 44 77 87 20 *Fax:* (01) 44 77 87 30
*E-mail:* biulo@idf.ext.jussieu.fr
*Web Site:* www.univ-paris3.fr
*Key Personnel*
Dir: Nelly Guillaume *E-mail:* guillaum@idf.ext.
jussieu.fr
Founded: 1868
Paris University library.

**Bibliotheque Mazarine**
23 quai de Conti, 75006 Paris
*Tel:* (01) 44 41 44 06 *Fax:* (01) 44 41 44 07
*Web Site:* www.bibliotheque-mazarine.fr
*Key Personnel*
Chief Curator & Dir: Christian Peligry
*E-mail:* christian.peligry@mazarine.univ-paris5.
fr

**Bibliotheque Interuniversitaire de Medecine**
12 rue de l'Ecole de Medecine, 75270 Paris
Cedex 06
*Tel:* (01) 40461951 *Fax:* (01) 44411020
*Web Site:* www.bium.univ-paris5.fr
*Key Personnel*
Dir & Chief Curator: P Casseyre
This is a Paris University library.
Publication(s): *Catalogue des Periodiques de la
Bibliotheque (1976-1981)*; *Bibliotheque de
l'ancienne Faculte de Medecine de Paris: Cat-
alogue des Livres du XVIe siecle extrait du
catalogue general du fonds ancien*

**Bibliotheque Municipale de Nancy**
43 rue Stanislas, CS 4230, 54042 Nancy Cedex
*Tel:* (03) 83373883 *Fax:* (03) 83379182
*E-mail:* bmnancy@mairie-nancy.fr
*Web Site:* www.nancy.fr
*Key Personnel*
Chief Librarian: Andre Markiewicz
Founded: 1750

**Bibliotheque du Musee de l'Homme**
Palais de Chaillot, 17 Pl du Trocadero, 75116
Paris
*Tel:* (01) 44 05 72 03 *Fax:* (01) 44 05 72 12
*E-mail:* bmhweb@mnhn.fr
*Web Site:* www.mnhn.fr/mnhn/bmh
*Key Personnel*
Dir: Jacqueline Dubois
Contact: Chatherine Breux-Delmas

**Bibliotheque Interuniversitaire de Pharmacie**
4 ave de l'Observatoire, 75270 Paris Cedex 6
*Tel:* (01) 53 73 95 22; (01) 53 73 95 23 *Fax:* (01)
53 73 99 05
*E-mail:* piketty@pharmacie.univ_paris5.fr
*Web Site:* www.biup.univ-paris5.fr
*Key Personnel*
Librarian: Francoise Malet
This is a Paris University library seat of CADIST
for culture (beauty culture: perfumes & cosmet-
ics).

**Bibliotheque Sainte-Genevieve**
10 pl du Pantheon, 75005 Paris
*Tel:* (01) 44 41 97 97 *Fax:* (01) 44 41 97 96
*E-mail:* bsgmail@univ.paris1.fr
*Web Site:* www-bsg.univ-paris1.fr
*Key Personnel*
Librarian: Nathalie Jullian
This is a Paris University library & public library.

**Service commun de la documentation de
l'Universite de Lille III**
Universite de Sciences et Technologies de Lille,
BP 155, 59653 Villeneuve d'Ascq Cedex
*Tel:* (03) 20 43 44 10 *Fax:* (03) 20 33 71 04
*E-mail:* boite-contact-bu@univ.lille1.fr

*Web Site:* ustl.univ-lille1.fr
*Key Personnel*
Dir: M Julien Roche *E-mail:* julien.roche@univ-lille1.fr

**Bibliotheque de la Sorbonne**
17 rue de la Sorbonne, 75257 Paris Cedex 05
Mailing Address: 47 rue des Ecoles, 75257 Paris Cedex 05
*Tel:* (01) 40 46 30 27 *Fax:* (01) 40 46 30 44
*E-mail:* adminst@biu.sorbonne.fr
*Web Site:* www.sorbonne.fr; www.sorbonne.fr/BIU.html
*Key Personnel*
Chief Librarian: Catherine Gaillard *E-mail:* gaillard@biu.sorbonne.fr
Founded: 1762
This is a Paris Interuniversity library.
*Branch Office(s)*
Lettres et Sciences humaines

**Bibliotheque Universite d'Avignon et des Pays du Vaucluse**
74 Rue Louis Pasteur, 84029 Avignon Cedex 1
*Tel:* (04) 90 16 25 00 *Fax:* (04) 90 16 25 10
*E-mail:* bu@univ-avignon.fr
*Web Site:* www.univ-avignon.fr
*Key Personnel*
Dir: Francoise Febvre *Tel:* (04) 90 16 27 60

**Universite de Toulouse-Mirail**
5 allees Antonio Machado, BP 1350, 31106 Toulouse Cedex 09
*Tel:* (0561) 50 40 64 *Fax:* (0561) 50 40 50
*E-mail:* bu-mirail@univ-tlse2.fr
*Web Site:* www.univ-tlse2.fr/bu-centrale
*Key Personnel*
Dir & Chief Librarian: Jean-Claude Annezer *Tel:* (0561) 50 42 25 *E-mail:* jean-claude.annezer@univ-tlse2.fr
Librarian: Valerie Morell *Tel:* (0561) 50 44 63 *E-mail:* valerie.morell@univ-tlse.fr
Publication(s): *Anglophonia; Caravelle; Champs du Signe; Criticon; Litteratures; Pallas*

# French Guiana

**Institut Francais de Recherche Scientifique pour le Developpement en Cooperation**
(French Institute for Scientific Research for Cooperative Development)
Centre de Cayenne, 0,275 Km Rte de Montabo, BP 165, 97323 Cayenne Cedex
*Tel:* 299 292 *Fax:* 319 855
*E-mail:* direction@cayenne.ird.fr
*Web Site:* www.cayenne.ird.fr
*Key Personnel*
Dir: Patrick Sechet
Office of Scientific & Technical Research Overseas.
Publication(s): *La Nature et l'Homme* (irregularly)
*Parent Company:* Institut de Recherche pour le Developpement

# Gabon

**Bibliotheque de l'Universite Omar Bongo**
Blvd Leon M'Ba, Libreville
Mailing Address: BP 13131, Libreville
*Tel:* 732956 *Fax:* 734530
*E-mail:* uob@internetgabon.cm
*Web Site:* www.uob.ga.refer.org
*Telex:* 5336

*Key Personnel*
Dir: Stary Mezeme Be'ndong
Founded: 1976
Publication(s): *Inventaire du fonds documentaire, par discipline* (annually); *Liste des nouvelles acquisitions* (quarterly); *Liste des periodiques en cours* (annually)

**Centre Bibliotheque d'Information**
BP 750, Libreville
*Tel:* 21115

**Direction Generale des Archives Nationales, de la Bibliotheque Nationale et de la Documentation Gabonaise (DGABD)** (Gabon National Archives, National Library)
BP 1188, Libreville
*Tel:* 732543; (0241) 730 239 *Fax:* 730239
*Key Personnel*
Archives Dir: Rene G Sonnet-Azize
Dir: Jean Paul Mifouna

# Gambia

**Gambia College Library**
PO Box 144, Brikama
*Tel:* 484452; 484748; 484812 *Fax:* 483224
*Key Personnel*
Librarian: Rosanna A Jallon Ndaw-Jallow
President: N S Z Njie

**The Gambia National Library**
Reg Pye Lane, Banjul
Mailing Address: PMB 552, Banjul
*Tel:* 226491; 225876; 228312; 223776 *Fax:* 223 776
*E-mail:* national.library@qanet.gm
*Key Personnel*
Dir: Abdou W Mbye
Chief Librarian: Mary E Fye
Founded: 1946

# Georgia

**Gosudarstvennaya Respublikanskaya biblioteka Gruzinskoi SSR im K Marksai**
Kecchoveli ul 5, Tblisi 700078
*E-mail:* navoi@physic.uzsci.net
*Web Site:* www.osi.uz/library
*Key Personnel*
Dir: Zukhriddin Nizomiddinovich *Tel:* (099871) 139 16 58 *Fax:* (099871) 133 09 08
Deputy Dir: Rasulov Khusan *Tel:* (099871) 139 40 36; Maminova Irina Zakirovna *Tel:* (098871) 139 40 20
Founded: 1998
State Republican Karl Marx Library of the Georgian SSR.

# Germany

**Universitaetsbibliothek Georgius Agricola**
Technische Universitaet Bergakademie Freiberg, Agricolastr 10, 09599 Frieberg
*Tel:* (03731) 39 29 59 *Fax:* (03731) 39 32 89
*E-mail:* unibib@ub.tu-freiberg.de
*Web Site:* www.tu-freiberg.de

*Key Personnel*
Dir: Karin Mittenzwei *E-mail:* karin.mittenzwei@ub.tu-freiberg.de
Publication(s): *Veroeffentlichungen der Bibliothek "Georgius Agricola" der TU Bergakademie Freiberg*

**Badische Landesbibliothek**
Erbprinzenstr 15, 76133 Karlsruhe
Mailing Address: Postfach 1429, 76033 Karlsruhe
*Tel:* (0721) 175-20 01; (0721) 175-22 22 *Fax:* (0721) 175-23 33
*E-mail:* informationszentrum@blb-karlsruhe.de
*Web Site:* www.blb-karlsruhe.de
*Key Personnel*
Dir: Dr Peter Michael Ehrle *Tel:* (0721) 175-22 00 *E-mail:* ehrle@blb-karlsruhe.de
Deputy Dir: Dr Ruediger Schmidt *Tel:* (0721) 175-22 10 *E-mail:* schmidt@blb-karlsruhe.de
Founded: 1500

**Staatsbibliothek Bamberg**
Neue Residenz, Domplatz 8, 96049 Bamberg
*Tel:* (0951) 95503-0 *Fax:* (0951) 95503-145
*E-mail:* info@staatsbibliothek-bamberg.de
*Web Site:* www.staatsbibliothek-bamberg.de
*Key Personnel*
Chief Librarian: Dr Bernhard Schemmel *E-mail:* bernhard.schemmel@staatsbibliothek-bamberg.de
Publication(s): *Auserlesene Schrift-Bilder; Bambergische Bildhauerzeichnungen des Rokoko und Klassizismus; Das Allgemeine Krankenhaus Fuerstbischof Franz Ludwig von Erthals in Bamberg von 1789; Der Bamberger Siddur; Die Ingenieur- und Zeichenakademie des Leopold Westen und ihre Entwicklung; Die Neuen Welten in alten Buechern; Duerer und die Literatur; Edler Schatz Holden Erinnerns; Fuers Schoene Geschlecht; Illuminierte Bologneser Handschriften 1260-1340; Johann Lukas Schoenlein; Karl Theodor von Buseck 1803-1860; Vergil 2000 Jahre*

**Bayerische Staatsbibliothek** (Bavarian State Library)
Ludwigstr 16, 80539 Munich, Bavaria
*Tel:* (089) 28638-0; (089) 28638-2322 *Fax:* (089) 28638-2200
*E-mail:* direktion@bsb-muenchen.de; info@bsb-muenchen.de
*Web Site:* www.bsb-muenchen.de
*Key Personnel*
General Director: Dr Hermann Leskien *Tel:* (089) 28638-2206 *E-mail:* leskien@bsb-muenchen.de
Founded: 1558
Publication(s): *Bayerische Staatsbibliothek* (ein Selbstportrait); *Jahresbericht* (annually)

**Bibliothek des Instituts fuer Weltwirtschaft**, see ZBW-Deutsche Zentralbibliothek fuer Wirtschaftswissenschaften/Bibliothek des Instituts fuer Weltwirtschaft

**Bibliothek fur Zeitgeschichte/Library of Contemporary History**
Konrad Adenauerstr 8, 70173 Stuttgart
Mailing Address: Postfach 10 54 41, 70047 Stuttgart
*Tel:* (0711) 212-4454; (0711) 212-4424 *Fax:* (0711) 212-4422
*E-mail:* bfz@wlb-stuttgart.de; information@wlb-stuttgart.de
*Web Site:* www.wlb-stuttgart.de/bfz
*Key Personnel*
Dir: Dr Hannsjoerg Kowark *E-mail:* kowark@wlb-stuttgart.de
Founded: 1915
This library is housed in same building as the Wuerttembergische Landesbibliothek, covering library (approx 310,000 books & approx 650 current periodicals), archives, documentation center for grey literature, research facilities, etc.

Publication(s): *Schriften der Bibliothek fuer Zeit-geschichte NF*; *Stuttgarter Vortraege zur Zeit-geschichte*
*Parent Company:* Wuerttembergische Landse Bib-liothek
*Ultimate Parent Company:* Land Baden-Wuerttemberg

**Bibliotheks und Informationssystem der Universitaet Oldenburg**
Uhlhornsweg 49-55, Oldenburg 26129
Mailing Address: Postfach 2541, Oldenburg 26015
*Tel:* (0441) 798-2023 *Fax:* (0441) 798-4040
*E-mail:* zi@bis.uni-oldenburg.de
*Web Site:* www.bis.uni-oldenburg.de/
*Telex:* 25655 unoldd
*Key Personnel*
Dir: Hans-Joahim Waetjen *Tel:* (0441) 798-4010
*E-mail:* waetjen@bis.uni-oldenburg.de
Founded: 1974
Research library, scientific publishing house, me-dia centre.
*Parent Company:* Carl von Ossietzky University Oldenburg

**Universitaet Bonn**
Universitaets -und Landesbibliothek, Adenaueralle 39-41, 53113 Bonn
Mailing Address: Postfach 2460, 53014 Bonn
*Tel:* (0228) 73-7352 *Fax:* (0228) 73-7546
*E-mail:* ulb@ulb.uni-bonn.de
*Web Site:* www.ulb.uni-bonn.de
*Key Personnel*
Dir: Dr Renate Vogt *E-mail:* renate.vogt@ulb.uni-bonn.de
Publication(s): *Universitaets -und Landesbiblio-thek Bonn*

**Technische Universitaet Braunschweig**
Pockelsstr 13, 38106 Braunschweig
*Tel:* (0531) 391-5018; (0531) 391-5011
*Fax:* (0531) 391-5836
*E-mail:* ub@tu-bs.de
*Web Site:* www.biblio.tu-bs.de
*Key Personnel*
Librarian: Prof Dietmar Brandes, PhD *E-mail:* d.brandes@tu-braunschweig.de
Publication(s): *Veroeffentlichungen der Universi-taetsbibliothek Braunschweig*

**Bucharchiv**, see Deutsches Bucharchiv Muenchen, Institut fur Buchwissenschaften

**Die Deutsche Bibliothek**
Adickesallee 1, 60322 Frankfurt am Main
*Tel:* (069) 1525-0 *Fax:* (069) 1525-1010
*E-mail:* info@dbf.ddb.de
*Web Site:* www.ddb.de
*Key Personnel*
Dir General: Dr Elisabeth Niggemann
Contact: Kathrin Ansorge *Tel:* (069) 1525-1004
*E-mail:* ansorge@dbf.ddb.de
Founded: 1947
National Library & National Bibliographic Agency.
Publication(s): *Deutsche Nationalbibliografie* (brochure)
*Branch Office(s)*
Deutsches Musikarchiv Berlin, Gaertner St 25-32, 12207 Berlin, Acting Representative: Ingo Ko-lasa *Tel:* (030) 770020 *Fax:* (030) 77002299
*E-mail:* info@dma.ddb.de
Deutsche Buecherei Leipzig, Deutscher Platz 1, Leipzig, Deputy: Birgit Schneider *Tel:* (0341) 22710 *Fax:* (0341) 2271444 *E-mail:* info@dbl.ddb.de

**Deutsche Buecherei Leipzig**, see Die Deutsche Bibliothek

**Deutscher Bundestag Bibliothek**
Platz der Republik 1, 11011 Berlin
*Tel:* (030) 227 32626 *Fax:* (030) 227 36087
*E-mail:* bibliothek@bundestag.de
*Web Site:* www.bundestag.de
*Key Personnel*
Head of Library: Marga Coing

**Deutsches Bucharchiv Muenchen, Institut fur Buchwissenschaften**
Salvatorplatz 1, 80333 Munich
Mailing Address: Von-der-Tann-Str 5, 80539 Mu-nich
*Tel:* (089) 29151-0; (089) 790 12 20 *Fax:* (089) 291951-95; (089) 790 14 19
*E-mail:* kontakt@bucharchiv.de
*Web Site:* www.bucharchiv.de
*Key Personnel*
Dir: Prof Ludwig Delp *Tel:* (089) 790 11 90
Founded: 1948
Institute for Book Research.
Publication(s): *Buchwissenschaftliche Beitraege aus dem Deutschen Bucharchiv Muenchen*

**Deutsches Musikarchiv Berlin**, see Die Deutsche Bibliothek

**Die Deutsche Bibliothek/Deutsche Bucherei Leipzig**
Deutscher Platz 1, 04103 Leipzig
*Tel:* (0341) 22710 *Fax:* (0341) 2271444
*E-mail:* info@dbl.ddb.de
*Web Site:* www.ddb.de
*Key Personnel*
Dir: Dr Elisabeth Niggemann
User Services & Archiving: Joerg Raeuber
National Library & National Bibliography Agency.
Publication(s): *Deutsche Nationalbibliographie* (German National Bibliography, weekly)

**Universitaetsbibliothek Erlangen-Nuernberg**
Schuhstr 1a, 91052 Erlangen
*Tel:* (09131) 85-22160 *Fax:* (09131) 85-29309
*E-mail:* direktion@bib.uni-erlangen.de
*Web Site:* www.ub.uni-erlangen.de
*Key Personnel*
Dir: Dr Hans-Otto Keunecke

**Ernst-Moritz-Arndt Universitaet Greifswald, Universitaetsbibliothek**
Friedrich-Ludwig-Jahn-Str 14a, 17487 Greifswald
*Tel:* (03834) 86-1502 *Fax:* (03834) 86-1501
*E-mail:* ub@uni-greifswald.de
*Web Site:* www.ub.uni-greifswald.de
*Key Personnel*
Dir: Dr Peter Wolff *Tel:* (03834) 86-1500
Founded: 1604
Publication(s): *Buchmalerei aus Handschriften und Drucken der Universitaetsbibliothek Greif-swald*; *Die Vitae Pomeranorum*

**Fachhochschule Dortmund Hochschulbibliothek** (University of Applied Sciences Dortmund Library)
Vogelpothsweg 76, 44227 Dortmund
Mailing Address: Postfach 105018, 44047 Dort-mund
*Tel:* (0231) 7554047 *Fax:* (0231) 7554604
*E-mail:* bibliothek@fhb.fh-dortmund.de
*Web Site:* www.fh-dortmund.de
*Key Personnel*
Librarian: Dr Robert Klitzke *E-mail:* klitzke@fhb.fh-dortmund.de
Founded: 1972

**Fachhochschule Stuttgart Hochschule der Medien** (University of Applied Sciences School of Media)
Hochschule der Medien, Nobelstr 10, 70569 Stuttgart

*Tel:* (0711) 257060 *Fax:* (0711) 25706300
*E-mail:* office@hdm-stuttgart.de; friedling@hdm-stuttgart.de
*Web Site:* www.hdm-stuttgart.de
*Key Personnel*
Scientific Dir, Library: Prof Peter Vodosek
*E-mail:* vodosek@hdm-stuggart.de
Library Manager: Friedling Erik *Tel:* (0711) 25706-123 *E-mail:* friedling@hdm-stuttgart.de
Founded: 1942
Information material on demand.
Publication(s): *HDM aktuell* (biannually)

**Hamburgisches Welt-Wirtschafts-Archiv (HWWA) Bibliothek** (Hamburg Institute of International Economics Library)
Neuer Jungfernstieg 21, 20347 Hamburg
*Tel:* (040) 42834-219 *Fax:* (040) 42834-550
*E-mail:* bib.auskunft@hwwa.de
*Web Site:* www.hwwa.de
*Key Personnel*
Head, Library: Hubert-Guenter Striefler
*E-mail:* guenter.striefler@hwwa.de
Founded: 1908
Special library for economy.

**Universitaetsbibliothek Hannover und Technische Informationsbibliothek** (University Library of Hannover & Technical Information Library)
Universitatsbibliothek und TIB Welfengarten 1B, 30167 Hannover
Mailing Address: Postfach 6080, 30167 Hannover
*Tel:* (0511) 762 2268 *Fax:* (0511) 715936
*E-mail:* ubtib@tib.uni-hannover.de
*Web Site:* www.tib.uni-hannover.de
*Key Personnel*
Head Librarian: Uwe Rosemann *E-mail:* uwe.rosemann@tib.uni-hannover.de
Deputy Librarian: Petra Dueren *E-mail:* petra.deuren@tib.uni-hannover.de; Dr Irina Sens
*E-mail:* irina.sens@tib.uni-hannover.de
Founded: 1831 (University Library of Hannover; Technical Information Library founded in 1959)
Document delivery.
Publication(s): *TIBORDER-Document Delivery System* (online catalog on STN International)

**Herzog August Bibliothek**
Lessingplatz 1, 38304 Wolfenbuettel
Mailing Address: Postfach 1364, 38299 Wolfen-buettel
*Tel:* (05331) 808-0 *Fax:* (05331) 808-173
*E-mail:* auskunft@hab.de
*Web Site:* www.hab.de
*Key Personnel*
Dir: Prof Helwig Schmidt-Olintzer
*E-mail:* direktor@hab.de

**Herzogin Anna Amalia Bibliothek**
Platz der Demokratie 1, 99423 Weimar
Mailing Address: Postfach 2012, 99401 Weimar
*Tel:* (03643) 545-200 *Fax:* (03643) 545-220
*E-mail:* haab@swkk.de
*Web Site:* www.swkk.de
*Key Personnel*
Dir: Dr Michael Knoche *E-mail:* michael.knoche@swkk.de
Library is part of the Stiftung Weimarer Klassik und Kunstsammlungen.
Publication(s): *Internationale Bibliographie zur Deutschen Klassik, 1750-1850*
*Parent Company:* Stiftung Weimarer Klassik und Kunstsammlungen

**Humboldt Universitaet zu Berlin**
Universitaetsbibliothek, Dorotheenstr 27, 10099 Berlin
*Tel:* (030) 2093 3212 *Fax:* (030) 2093 3207
*E-mail:* wwwadm.ub@ub.hu-berlin.de
*Web Site:* www.ub.hu-berlin.de

*Key Personnel*
Chief Librarian: Dr Milan Bulaty *Tel:* (030) 2093
3200 *E-mail:* milan.bulaty@ub.hu-berlin.de
Head of Library Administration: Gudrun von Gar-
rel *Tel:* (030) 2093 3208 *E-mail:* gudrun.von.
garrel@ub.hu-berlin.de

**Ibero-Amerikanisches Institut Preussischer**
**Kulturbesitz** (Ibero American Institute)
Potsdamerstr 37, 10785 Berlin
*Tel:* (030) 266 2500 *Fax:* (030) 266 2503
*E-mail:* iai@iai.spk-berlin.de
*Web Site:* www.iai.spk-berlin.de
*Telex:* 183160 staab d
*Key Personnel*
Dir: Dr Gunther Maihold
Library Dir: Peter Altekrueger *Tel:* (030) 266
2533 *E-mail:* altekrueger@iai.spk-berlin.de
Founded: 1930
Research institute & special library for Latin
America, Spain & Portugal
Membership(s): Lasa; Salalm; Redial; Adlaf;
Liber.
Publication(s): *Biblioteca Luso-Brasileira* (book);
*Bibliotheca Iberoamericana* (book); *Ibero-*
*Analysen* (book); *Ibero-Bibliographien* (book);
*Iberoamericana, Indiana* (journal)

**Internationale Jugendbibliothek** (International
Youth Library)
Schloss Blutenburg, 81247 Munich
*Tel:* (089) 891211-0 *Fax:* (089) 8117553
*E-mail:* bib@ijb.de
*Web Site:* www.ijb.de
*Key Personnel*
Public Relations: Carola Gade *Tel:* (089)
89121130
Founded: 1949
International children & youth literature, posters,
original illustrations, manuscripts & handwrit-
ing. 530,000 volumes in over 130 languages &
250 current magazines.
Publication(s): *IJB Report* (biannual report)

**Universitat Konstanz**
Universitaetsstr 10, 78464 Konstanz
Mailing Address: 78457 Konstanz
*Tel:* (07531) 88-0 *Fax:* (07531) 88-3688
*E-mail:* Posteingang@uni-konstanz.de
*Web Site:* www.uni-konstanz.de
*Key Personnel*
Librarian: Klaus Franken *E-mail:* klaus.franken@
uni.konstanz.de

**Library of Contemporary History**, see
Bibliothek fur Zeitgeschichte/Library of
Contemporary History

**Landesbibliothek Mecklenburg-Vorpommern**
Johannes Stelling Str 29, 19053 Schwerin
*Tel:* (0385) 558440 *Fax:* (0385) 5584424
*E-mail:* lb@lbmv.de
*Web Site:* www.lbmv.de
*Key Personnel*
Dir: Dr R Juergen Wegener *E-mail:* wegener@
lbmv.de
Publication(s): *CD-ROM Geschichtliche Bibli-*
*ographie von Mecklenburg von den Anfangen*
*bis 1945* (1998, bibiography); *Mecklenburg-*
*Vorpommersche Bibliographie* (annually,
bibliographical yearbook); *Periodica aus*
*Mecklenburg-Vorpommern* (1996, bibliogra-
phy of in Meckl-Vorp published newspapers,
journals, yearbooks)
*Branch Office(s)*
Musikaliensammlung, Molkereistr 3, 19053
Schwerin, Herr Jedeck *Tel:* (0385) 5584431
*Fax:* (0385) 5584439 *E-mail:* jedeck@lbmv.de

**Niedersaechsische Landesbibliothek** (Lower
Saxony State Library)
Waterloostr 8, 30169 Hannover
*Tel:* (0511) 1267-0 *Fax:* (0511) 1267-202
*E-mail:* information@gwlb.de
*Web Site:* www.nlb-hannover.de
*Key Personnel*
Deputy Dir: Peter Marmein *Tel:* (0511) 1267-341
*E-mail:* peter.marmein@gwlb.de
Dir: Dr Georg Ruppelt *Tel:* (0511) 1267-303
*Fax:* (0511) 1267-207
Founded: 1665

**Niedersaechsische Staats- und**
**Universitaetsbibliothek Goettingen**
(Goettingen State & University Library)
Division of University of Goettingen
Platz der Goettinger Sieben 1, Papendiek 14,
37073 Goettingen
Mailing Address: 37070 Goettingen
*Tel:* (0551) 395212 (Secretariat); (0551) 393079
(chemistry); (0551) 392360 (physics); (0551)
395220 (medicine) *Fax:* (0551) 395222
*E-mail:* sub@sub.uni-goettingen.de
*Web Site:* www.sub.uni-goettingen.de
*Key Personnel*
Dir: Prof Elmar Mittler, PhD *Tel:* (0551) 395210
*E-mail:* mittler@sub.uni-goettingen.de
Assistant Dir: Dr Klaus Ceynowa *Tel:* (0551)
395214 *E-mail:* ceynowa@sub.uni-goettingen.
de
Founded: 1734

**Unlversitatsbibliothek Regensburg**
Universitaetsstr 31, 93053 Regensburg
*Tel:* (0941) 943-3901; (0941) 943-3902
*Fax:* (0941) 943-3285
*Web Site:* www.bibliothek.uni-regensburg.de
*Key Personnel*
Dir: Dr Friedrich Geisselmann
*E-mail:* friedrichgeisselmann@bibliothek.uni-
regensburg.de

**Rheinisch-Westfaelische Technische**
**Hochschule**, see RWTH Aachen
Hochschulbibliotek

**Rheinische Landesbibliothek Koblenz** (Rhenish
Regional Library of the German 'Land'
Rhineland Palatinate)
Bahnofplatz 14, 56068 Koblenz
Mailing Address: PO Box 201352, 56013
Koblenz
*Tel:* (0261) 91500 40 *Fax:* (0261) 91500 91
*E-mail:* info@rlb.de
*Web Site:* www.rlb.de
*Key Personnel*
Dir: Dr Ernst-Ludwig Berz *Tel:* (0261) 91500 14
*Fax:* (0261) 91500 90 *E-mail:* berz@rlb.de
General Research Library.

**Universitaet Rostock Universitaetsbibliothek**
Altbettelmoenschtr 4, 18051 Rostock
*Tel:* (0381) 4 98 22 83 *Fax:* (0381) 4 98 22 70
*E-mail:* ub-sekretariat@ub.uni-rostock.de00.de
*Web Site:* www.uni-rostock.de
*Key Personnel*
Dir: Dr Peter Hoffmann *E-mail:* peter.hoffmann@
ub.uni-rostock.de

**RWTH Aachen Hochschulbibliotek**
Templergraben 61, 52062 Aachen
Mailing Address: Bibliothek-RWTH Aachen,
52056 Aachen
*Tel:* (0241) 80-94445 *Fax:* (0241) 80-92273
*E-mail:* bth@bth.rwth-aachen.de
*Web Site:* www.rwth-aachen.de; www.bth.rwth-
aachen.de
*Telex:* 0832704

*Key Personnel*
Dir: Ulrike Eich *Tel:* (0241) 80-94446
*E-mail:* eich@bth.rwth-aachen.de
Founded: 1870

**Saarlaendische Universitaets und**
**Landesbibliothek** (University & State Library
of the Saarland)
Im Stadtisald, Gebaeude 3, 66123 Saarbruecken
Mailing Address: Postfach 151141, 66041 Saar-
bruecken
*Tel:* (0681) 3022070 *Fax:* (0681) 3022796
*E-mail:* sulb@sulb.uni-saarland.de
*Web Site:* www.sulb.uni-saarland.de
*Key Personnel*
Dir: Prof Bernd Hagenau
Acquisitions: Gabriele Mohrbach *Tel:* (0681)
3022510 *E-mail:* g.mohrbach@sulb.uni-
saarland.de
Founded: 1950
Specialize in academic library.
*Parent Company:* Univsersitaet des Saarlandes
*Branch Office(s)*
Medizinische Bibliothek, 66421 Homburg, Con-
tact: Reinhard Kraemer *Tel:* (0684) 162 6059
*Fax:* (0684) 162 6033 *E-mail:* m.kraemer@
sulb.uni-saarland.de

**Saechsische Landesbibliothek- Staats- und**
**Universitaetsbibliothek Dresden**
Zelleway 18, 01054 Dresden
*Tel:* (0351) 4677-123 *Fax:* (0351) 4677-111
*E-mail:* direktion@slub-dresden.de
*Web Site:* www.tu-dresden.de/slub
*Key Personnel*
Dir General: Prof Juergen Hering
Publication(s): *Aurich, Frank; Die Anfange*
*des Buchdrucks in Dresden; Bibliographie*
*Geschichte der Technik; Saechsische Bibliogra-*
*phie; Schwarze Kopfe; SLUB-Kurier; Tradition*
*und Herausforderung*

**Walther-Schuecking-Institut fuer**
**Internationales Recht an der Universitaet**
**Kiel**
Christian-Albrechts-Universitaet zu Kiel, Westring
400, 24098 Kiel
*Tel:* (0431) 880 2367 *Fax:* (0431) 880 1619
*E-mail:* fb.internat-recht@ub.uni-kiel.de
*Web Site:* www.uni-kiel.de/internat-recht
*Key Personnel*
Dir: Dr Rainer Hofmann *Tel:* (0431) 880-1733
*E-mail:* hofmann-thies@internat-recht.uni-kiel.
de; Dr Andreas Zimmermann *Tel:* (0431) 880-
2152 *E-mail:* azimmermann@internat-recht.uni-
kiel.de
Publication(s): *German Yearbook Of Interna-*
*tional Law; Veroeffentlichungen des Walther-*
*Schuecking-Instituts fuer Internationales Recht*
(series)

**Staats- und Universitaetsbibliothek Hamburg**
**Carl von Ossietzky** (State & University
Library)
Von-Melle Park 3, 20146 Hamburg
*Tel:* (040) 42838-2233 *Fax:* (040) 42838-3352
*E-mail:* auskunft@sub.uni-hamburg.de
*Web Site:* www.sub.uni-hamburg.de
*Key Personnel*
Dir: Prof Peter Rau, PhD *Tel:* (040) 42838-2211
*E-mail:* rau@sub.uni-hamburg.de
Founded: 1479
State & University library. All areas of science;
Special collections: politics & peace research,
science of administration, Spain & Portugal.
Coastal & sea fishing, language & culture of
North American Indians & Eskimos.

**Staats- und Universitatsbibliothek Bremen**
Bibliothekstr, 28359 Bremen
*Tel:* (0421) 2182615 *Fax:* (0421) 2182614

*E-mail:* suub@suub.uni-bremen.de
*Web Site:* www.suub.uni-bremen.de
*Key Personnel*
Library Dir: Annette Rath-Beckmann

**Staatsbibliothek zu Berlin - Preussischer
Kulturbesitz** (Berlin State Library - Prussian
Cultural Foundation)
Unter den Linden 8, 10117 Berlin
Mailing Address: Potsdamer Str 33, 10785 Berlin
*Tel:* (030) 266-0
*Web Site:* www.staatsbibliothek-berlin.de; www.
sbb.spk-berlin.de
*Key Personnel*
General Dir: Dipl Ing Barbara Schneider-Kempf
*E-mail:* barbara.schneider-kempf@sbb.spk-
berlin.de
Founded: 1661
International research library.
Publication(s): *Beitraege aus der Staatsbiblio-
thek zu Berlin - PK* (irregularly); *Interna-
tional ISBN Publishers' Directory* (annually);
*ISBN Newsletter* (irregularly); *ISBN Review*
(annually); *ISMN Newsletter* (irregularly);
*Jahresbericht* (annually); *Kartographische Be-
standsverzeichnisse* (irregularly); *Kataloge der
Handschriftenabteilung, Reihe 1: Handschriften
& Reihe 2: Nachlaesse* (irregularly); *Kataloge der Musikabteilung* (irregularly); *Veroeffentlichungen der Osteuropa-Abteilung* (irregularly)

**Stadt Frankfurt a Main Stadt-und
Universitaetsbibliothek**
Bockenheimer Landstr 134-138, 60325 Frankfurt
am Main
*Tel:* (069) 212-39-205 *Fax:* (069) 212-39-380
*E-mail:* direktion@ub.uni-frankfut.de
*Web Site:* www.ub.uni-frankfurt.de
*Key Personnel*
Dir: Brendt Dugall *Tel:* (069) 212-39-230
*E-mail:* b.dugall@ub.uni-frankfurt.de

**Stadt- und Universitaetsbibliothek**
Bockenheimer Landstr 134-138, 60325 Frankfurt
am Main
*Tel:* (069) 212-39-205; (069) 212-39-256; (069)
212-39-229; (069) 212-39-231 *Fax:* (069) 212-
39-380; (069) 212-39-062
*E-mail:* direktion@uni-frankfurt.com; auskunft@
stub.uni-frankfurt.de
*Web Site:* www.ub.uni-frankfurt.de
*Key Personnel*
Dir: Berndt Dugall *Tel:* (069) 212-39-230
*E-mail:* b.dugall@ub.uni-frankfurt.de

**Stadtbibliothek Leipzig**
Wilhelm-Leuschner-Platz 10/11, 04107 Leipzig
Mailing Address: Postfach 100927, 04009 Leipzig
*Tel:* (0341) 123 53 43 *Fax:* (0341) 123 53 05
*E-mail:* stadtbib@leipzig.de
*Web Site:* www.leipzig.de/stadtbib.htm
*Key Personnel*
Dir: Reinhard Stridde

**Thueringer Universitaets- und
Landesbibliothek**
Bibliotheksplatz 2, 07743 Jena
Mailing Address: Postfach, 07737 Jena
*Tel:* (03641) 9-40000 *Fax:* (03641) 9-40002
*E-mail:* thulb_direktion@thulb.uni-jena.de;
thulb_auskunft@thulb.uni-jena.de
*Web Site:* www.uni-jena.de/thulb
*Key Personnel*
Dir: Dr Sabine Wefers
Publication(s): *Keine Aenderungen*; *Thueringen -
Bibliographic (Online)*

**Universitat Ulm**
89069 Ulm
*Tel:* (0731) 502-01 *Fax:* (0731) 5022038

*E-mail:* post@uni-ulm.de
*Web Site:* www.uni-ulm.de
*Key Personnel*
Dir: S Franke

**Universitaetbibliothek Dortmund**
Vogelpothsweg 76, 44227 Dortmund
*Tel:* (0231) 755-4001 *Fax:* (0231) 755-4007
*Web Site:* www.uni-dortmund.de
*Key Personnel*
Librarian: Marlene Nagelsmeier-Linke
*E-mail:* marlene.nagelsmeier-linke@ub.uni-
dortmund.de

**Universitaets-Bibliothek Osnabrueck**
(University of Osnabrueck Library)
49069 Osnabruck
*Tel:* (0541) 969-0 *Fax:* (0541) 969-4482
*E-mail:* aaa@uni-osnabrueck.de
*Web Site:* www.uni-osnabrueck.de
*Key Personnel*
Library Dir: Felicitas Hundhausen
*E-mail:* felicitas.hundhausen@ub.uni-
osnabrueck.de
Founded: 1974
Publication(s): *Ausstellungs Kataloge*

**Universitaets- und Landesbibliothek Muenster**
(University & Regional Library Muenster)
Krummer Timpen 3-5, 48143 Muenster
*Tel:* (0251) 83 224021 *Fax:* (0251) 83 28398
*E-mail:* sekretariat.ulb@uni-muenster.de
*Web Site:* www.uni-muenster.de/ULB
*Key Personnel*
Editor: Daniel Busse; Dr Stephanie Kloetgen;
Dagmar Klose; Karin Vogel
Contact: Dr Beate Troeger *Tel:* (0251) 83 24022
Founded: 1588

**Universitaets - und Landesbibliothek
Sachsen-Anhalt**
August-Bebel-Str 13, 06108 Halle (Saale)
*Tel:* (0345) 55 22000 *Fax:* (0345) 55 27140
*E-mail:* direktion@bibliothek.uni-halle.de;
auskunft@bibliothek.uni-halle.de
*Web Site:* www.bibliothek.uni-halle.de
*Key Personnel*
Dir: Dr Heiner Schnelling *E-mail:* heiner.
schnelling@bibliothek.uni-halle.de
Founded: 1696

**Universitaets- und Stadtbibliothek Koeln**
(Cologne University & City Library)
Universitaetsstr 33, 50931 Cologne
*Tel:* (0221) 470-2214; (0221) 470-2374; (0221)
470-3316 *Fax:* (0221) 470-5166
*E-mail:* auskunft@ub.uni-koeln.de; sekretariat@
ub.uni-koeln.de
*Web Site:* www.ub.uni-koeln.de
*Key Personnel*
Dir & Professor: Dr Wolfgang Schmitz
*Tel:* (0221) 470-2260 *E-mail:* schmitz@ub.uni-
koeln.de
Founded: 1920

**Universitaetsbibliothek Bamberg**
Feldkirchenstr 21, 96052 Bamberg
*Tel:* (0951) 863-1503; (0951) 863-1501
*Fax:* (0951) 863-1565
*E-mail:* unibibliothek.bamberg@unibib.uni-
bamberg.de
*Web Site:* www.uni-bamberg.de/unibib/

**Universitaetsbibliothek Bochum**
Universitaetsstr 150, 44780 Bochum
*Tel:* (0234) 3222350; (0234) 3222351 *Fax:* (0234)
3214736
*E-mail:* direktion-ub@ruhr-uni-bochum.de
*Web Site:* www.ub.ruhr-uni-bochum.de

*Key Personnel*
Dir: Dr Erdmute Lapp *E-mail:* erda.lapp@rub.de
Deputy Dir: George Sander

**Universitaetsbibliothek Eichstaett - Ingolstadt**
Universitaetsallee 1, 85072 Eichstaett
*Tel:* (08421) 931492 *Fax:* (08421) 931791
*E-mail:* ub-www@ku-eichstaett.de
*Web Site:* www.ku-eichstaett.de
*Key Personnel*
Dir: Hermann Holzbauer *Tel:* (08421) 931331
*E-mail:* ub-direktion@ku-eichstaedtt.de
Founded: 1972

**Universitaetsbibliothek Freiburg**
Werthmannplatz 2, 79098 Freiburg im Breisgau
Mailing Address: Postfach 1629, 79016 Freiburg
im Breisgau
*Tel:* (0761) 203-3918 *Fax:* (0761) 203-3987
*E-mail:* info@ub.uni-freiburg.de
*Web Site:* www.ub.uni-freiburg.de
*Key Personnel*
Dir: Baerbel Schubel *Tel:* (0761) 203-3900
*E-mail:* schubel@ub.uni-freiburg.de
Publication(s): *Festschrift: Tradition-
Organisation-Innovation*; *Reihe: Schriften der
Universitaets Bibliothek Freiburg*

**Universitaetsbibliothek Freie Universitaet
Berlin** (Free University of Berlin)
Garystr 39, 14195 Berlin
*Tel:* (030) 838 54224; (030) 838 54273
*Fax:* (030) 838 53738
*E-mail:* auskunft@ub.fu-berlin.de
*Web Site:* www.ub.fu-berlin.de
*Key Personnel*
Librarian: Ulrich Naumann *E-mail:* naumann@ub.
fu-berlin.de
Founded: 1952
*Parent Company:* Freie Universitaet Berlin

**Universitaetsbibliothek Heidelberg**
Ploeck 107-109, 69117 Heidelberg
Mailing Address: Postfach 10 57 49, 69047 Hei-
delberg
*Tel:* (06221) 54 2380 *Fax:* (06221) 54 2623
*E-mail:* ub@ub.uni-hd.de
*Web Site:* www.ub.uni-heidelberg.de
*Key Personnel*
Dir: Dr Veit Probst *E-mail:* probst@ub.uni-
heidelberg.de
Publication(s): *Bibliothek-Forschung und Praxis*;
*Bibliothek und Wissenschaft*; *Heidelberger Bib-
liothehsschriften*; *Neuerwerbungslisten der
Sondersammelgebiete Aegyptologie, Klassis-
che Archaeologie, Mittlere und Neuere Kun-
stgeschichte*; *Zeitschriftenverzeichnis Aegyp-
tologie, Klassische Archaeologie und Mittlere
und Neuere Kunstgeschichte*; *Heidelberger
Zeitschriftenverzeichnis*
Bookshop(s): Im Neuenheimer Feld 368, 69120
Heidelberg *Tel:* (06221) 544272 *Fax:* (06221)
544204 *Web Site:* ub.uni-hd.de

**Universitaetsbibliothek Kaiserslautern**
(University Library of Kaiserslautern)
Paul-Ehrlich-Str, 67663 Kaiserslautern
Mailing Address: Postfach 2040, 67608 Kaiser-
slautern
*Tel:* (0631) 205-2241 *Fax:* (0631) 205-2355
*E-mail:* unibib@ub.uni-kl.de
*Web Site:* www.uni-kl.de/bibliothek
*Key Personnel*
Dir: Ralf Werner Wildermuth
*E-mail:* wildermuth@ub.uni-kl.de
Founded: 1970
*Parent Company:* Technische Universitaet Kaiser-
slautern

**Universitaetsbibliothek Leipzig**
Beethovenstr 6, 04107 Leipzig

*Tel:* (0341) 97 30577 *Fax:* (0341) 97 30596
*E-mail:* auskunft@ub.uni-leipzig.de
*Web Site:* www.ub.uni-leipzig.de/ubl
*Key Personnel*
Dir: Dr Phil Ekkehard Henschke
Publication(s): *Geschriebenes aber bleibt*

### Universitaetsbibliothek Mannheim
Schloss Ostfluegel und A3, 68131 Mannheim
*Tel:* (0621) 181-2941; (0621) 181-2948; (0621)
181-2989 *Fax:* (0621) 181-2939
*E-mail:* biblubma@bib.uni-mannheim.de
*Web Site:* www.bib.uni-mannheim.de
*Key Personnel*
Dir: Christian Benz *Tel:* (0621) 181-2941

### Universitaetsbibliothek Tuebingen (University
Library)
Wilhelmstr 32, 72016 Tuebingen
Mailing Address: Postfach 2620, 72016 Tuebin-
gen
*Tel:* (07071) 29-72846 *Fax:* (07071) 29-3123
*E-mail:* info-zentrum@ub.uni-tuebingen.de
*Web Site:* www.uni-tuebingen.de/ub
*Key Personnel*
Head Librarian: Dr Ulrich Schapka *Tel:* (07071)
29-72505 *E-mail:* ulrich.schapka@uni-
tuebingen.de
Founded: 1477

### Universitaetsbibliothek Wuppertal
Gauss-Str 20, 42119 Wuppertal
Mailing Address: Postfach 100127, 42001 Wup-
pertal
*Tel:* (0202) 439-2705 *Fax:* (0202) 439-2695
*E-mail:* information@bib.uni-wuppertal.de
*Web Site:* www.bib.uni-wuppertal.de
*Key Personnel*
Dir: Dr Dieter Staeglich *Tel:* (0202) 439-2691

### Universitat Wuerzburg
Universitaetsbibliothek Am Hubland, 97074
Wuerzburg
*Tel:* (0931) 888-5906 *Fax:* (0931) 888-5970
*E-mail:* direktion@bibliothek.uni-wuerzburg.de;
information@bibliothek.uni-wuerzburg.de
*Web Site:* www.bibliothek.uni-wuerzburg.de
*Key Personnel*
Librarian: Karl Suedekum *Tel:* (0931) 888-5942
*E-mail:* suedekum@bibliothek.uni.wuerzburg.de
Publication(s): *Verzeichnis auf Anfrage*

### Universitats und Landesbibliothe Darmstadt
(University & State Library Darmstadt)
Division of Technische Universitat Darmstadt
Schloss, 64283 Darmstadt
*Tel:* (06151) 165850 *Fax:* (06151) 165897
*E-mail:* info@ulb.tu-darmstadt.de
*Web Site:* www.ulb.tu-darmstadt.de
*Key Personnel*
Librarian: Dr Hans Georg Nolte-Fischer
*Tel:* (06151) 165801 *E-mail:* nolte@ulb.tu-
darmstadt.de
Executive Secretary: Doris Michel *Tel:* (06151)
165801 *E-mail:* michel@ulb.tu-darmstadt.de
Founded: 1568
*Branch Office(s)*
Patentinformationszentrum, Schoefferstr 8, 64295
Darmstadt *Tel:* (06151) 165427 *E-mail:* info@
main-piz.de *Web Site:* www.main-piz.de
Zweigbibliothek Lichtwiese, El Lissitzkystr
1, 64287 Darmstadt *Tel:* (06151) 165867
*E-mail:* zweigbib@ulb.tu-darmstadt.de

### Universitatsbibliothek Augsburg
Universitatsstr 22, 86135 Augsburg
*Tel:* (0821) 598 5320; (0821) 598 5306; (0821)
598 5305 *Fax:* (0821) 598 5354
*E-mail:* info@bibliothek.uni-augsburg.de
*Web Site:* www.bibliothek.uni-augsburg.de
*Telex:* 53830

*Key Personnel*
Contact: Eva Schoeppl *Tel:* (0821) 598 5304
*E-mail:* eva.schoeppl@bibliothek.uni-augsburg.
de
Founded: 1970

### Wissenschaftliche Allgemeinbibliothek der
Stadt Erfurt
Dompl 1, 99084 Erfurt
*Tel:* (0361) 562 48 76 *Fax:* (0361) 646 20 71
*Key Personnel*
Contact: Kerstin Weishaeupl

### Wuerttembergische Landesbibliothek
Konrad-Adenauerstr 8, 70173 Stuttgart
Mailing Address: Postfach 105441, 70047
Stuttgart
*Tel:* (0711) 2124424 *Fax:* (0711) 2124422
*E-mail:* direktion@wlb-stuttgart.de; information@
wlb-stuttgart.de
*Web Site:* www.wlb-stuttgart.de
*Key Personnel*
Dir: Dr H Kowark *E-mail:* kowark@wlb-stuttgart.
de
Contact: Horst Hilger *Tel:* (0711) 2124390;
(0711) 2124504 *E-mail:* hilger@wlb-stuttgart.
de
Founded: 1765
Regional library for the state of Baden-
Wurttemberg, currently comprised of 4.65 mil-
lion media items.
Publication(s): *Ausstellungs- und Bestandskata-
loge*

### ZBW-Deutsche Zentralbibliothek fuer
Wirtschaftswissenschaften/Bibliothek des
Instituts fuer Weltwirtschaft (German
National Library of Economics/Library of the
Kiel Institute for World Economics)
Duesternbrooker Weg 120, 24105 Kiel
*Tel:* (0431) 8814-383; (0431) 8814-555
*Fax:* (0431) 8814-520
*E-mail:* info@zbw.ifw-kiel.de
*Web Site:* www.zbw-kiel.de *Cable:*
WELTWIRTSCHAFT KIEL
*Key Personnel*
Dir: Horst Thomsen *Tel:* (0431) 8814-444
*Fax:* (0431) 8814-530 *E-mail:* h.thomsen@
zbw.ifw-kiel.de
Deputy Librarian: Ekkehart Seusing *Tel:* (0431)
8814-436 *E-mail:* e.seusing@zbw.ifw-kiel.de
Worldwide economics special library. Also pro-
vides document delivery services.
Publication(s): *ECONIS* (Database of references
to literature in economics & adjacent subjects);
*Thesaurus der ZBW*

### Zentral- und Landesbibliothek Berlin (ZLB)
(Central & Regional Library of Berlin)
Bluecherplatz 1, 10961 Berlin
*Tel:* (030) 90226-401 *Fax:* (030) 90226-163
*E-mail:* info@zlb.de
*Web Site:* www.zlb.de
*Key Personnel*
General Dir: Dr Claudia Lux *Tel:* (030) 90226-
450 *E-mail:* lux@zlb.de
Founded: 1901
Full library & information services.

**ZLB**, see Zentral- und Landesbibliothek Berlin
(ZLB)

# Ghana

**Balme Library**, see University of Ghana Library

### British Council Library
Bank Rd, Kumasi
Mailing Address: PO Box KS 1996, Kumasi
*Tel:* (051) 23462; (051) 37197 *Fax:* (051) 26725
*E-mail:* infokumasi@gh.britishcouncil.org
*Web Site:* www.britishcouncil.org/ghana
*Telex:* 2369 brico gh
*Key Personnel*
Education Information Officer: Benjamin Addo
*E-mail:* benjaminaddo@bcgha.africainline.com.
gh
Head Libraries & Information Services: Ruth
Osci

### Council for Scientific & Industrial
Research-Institute for Scientific &
Technological Information
PO Box M 32, Accra
*Tel:* (021) 777651-4 *Fax:* (021) 777655
*E-mail:* csir@ghana.com; cemensah@hotmail.com
*Web Site:* www.csir.org.gh
*Telex:* SCIENCES
*Key Personnel*
Acting Dir-General: Prof E Owusu Benoah
Publication(s): *CSIR Newsletter* (quarterly); *Di-
rectory of High Level Manpower* (every 5
years); *Directory of Research Projects (Sci-
ence & Technology) in Ghana (1990)* (every
5 years); *Directory of Special & Research Li-
braries in Ghana*; *Ghana Journal of Agricul-
tural Science* (biannually); *Ghana Journal of
Science* (biannually); *Ghana Science Abstracts*
(annually); *Union List of Scientific Serials in
Ghanaian Libraries (1976)*

**CSIR-INSTI**, see Council for Scientific &
Industrial Research-Institute for Scientific &
Technological Information

### Geological Survey Department Reference
Library
Geological Survey Dept, PO Box M 80, Accra
*Tel:* (021) 228093; (021) 28079 *Fax:* (021)
228063; (021) 224676
*E-mail:* ghgeosur@ghana.com
*Key Personnel*
Librarian: E Hammond

### Ghana Institute of Management & Public
Administration, Library & Documentation
Centre
Greenhill, Achimota, Accra
Mailing Address: PO Box 50, Achimota, Accra
*Tel:* (021) 401681; (021) 401682; (021) 401683
*Fax:* (021) 405805
*E-mail:* gimpa@excite.com
*Telex:* 2551 Gimpa Gh *Cable:* GIMPA
ACHIMOTA
*Key Personnel*
Librarian: Theresa Gyedu

### Ghana Library Board
Thorpe Rd, Accra
Mailing Address: PO Box 663, Accra
*Tel:* (021) 665 083 *Fax:* (021) 678 258 *Cable:*
GHANLIB ACCRA
*Key Personnel*
Dir & Librarian: David Cornelius
The research library on African Affairs, a division
of the Ghana Library Board performs some
functions of a national library for Ghana.
Publication(s): *Ghana National Bibliography, A
Guide to Creative Writing by Africans in En-
glish* (Annual Report)

### Institute of African Studies Library
University of Ghana, Legon, Accra
Mailing Address: PO Box LG 73, Legon, Accra
*Tel:* (021) 500512 *Fax:* (021) 502397
*E-mail:* asofo@ghana.com

*Key Personnel*
Director: Dr Irene Odotei
Assistant Librarian: Mrs Olive Adoah
Founded: 1961
Publication(s): *Research Review* (magazine)

**Kwame Nkrumah University of Science & Technology Library**
Private Post Bag, Kumasi
*Tel:* (051) 60199; (051) 60133 *Fax:* (051) 60358
*E-mail:* ustlib@libr.ug.edu.gh
*Key Personnel*
University Librarian: Mrs H R Asamoah-Hassan
Founded: 1951

**George Padmore Research Library on African Affairs**
PO Box 2970, Accra
*Tel:* (021) 228 402; (021) 223526 *Fax:* (021) 247 768
*Key Personnel*
Librarian: Omari Mensah Tenkorang
Founded: 1961
Publication(s): *Current Ghana Bibliography* (every two months, 1968); *Ghana National Bibliography* (annually)
*Parent Company:* Ghana Library Board

**School of Administration Library**
University of Ghana, PO Box 78, Legon, Accra
*Fax:* (021) 500024
*E-mail:* soa@libr.ug.edu.gh
*Key Personnel*
Librarian: Mr G Odartey-Cofie *Tel:* (021) 500591
   *E-mail:* odarteycofiesoa@libr.ug.edu.gh
Founded: 1960
Publication(s): *Journal of Management Studies* (annually)

**Statistical Service**
PO Box 1098, Accra
*Tel:* (021) 682629 *Fax:* (021) 667069
*E-mail:* baahwadieh@yahoo.com
*Telex:* 2205 MIFAEP GH
*Key Personnel*
Government Statistician: Dr Oti Boateng Daasebre
Deputy Government Statisticians: Dr K A Twum-Baah; Mr K Addomah-Gyabaah
Information Officer: Mr J Y Amankrah
Collection, compilation, analysis, publication & dissemination of statistical information.

**University of Cape Coast Library**
PMB, University Post Office, Cape Coast
*Tel:* (042) 60133 *Fax:* (042) 32485
*E-mail:* Ucclib@ucc.gn.apc.org
*Telex:* 2552 UCC GH
*Key Personnel*
Librarian: Richard Arkaifie

**University of Ghana Library**
PO Box 25, Legon
*Tel:* (021) 502701 *Fax:* (021) 502701
*E-mail:* balme@ug.gn.apc.org
*Web Site:* www.ug.edu.gh *Cable:* UNIVERSITY LEGON
*Key Personnel*
Ag Librarian: Prof A A Alemna
Ag Dept Librarian: Mrs V Dodoo
Assistant Librarian: S K Asiedu
Founded: 1948

# Gibraltar

**Garrison Library**
2 Library Gardens, Gibraltar 77418

Mailing Address: PO Box 374, Gibraltar
*Tel:* 77418 *Fax:* 79927
*Key Personnel*
Secretary: J M Searle
Gibraltor & Western Mediterranean research by arrangement with secretary.

**Gibraltar Library Service,** see John Mackintosh Hall Library

**John Mackintosh Hall Library**
Knightsfield Holdings Ltd, 308 Main St, Gibraltar
*Tel:* 78000 *Fax:* 40843
*Key Personnel*
Dir: Geraldine Finlayson *E-mail:* gfjmh@gibnet. gi
Founded: 1964
Free lending library set up under will of late John Mackintosh, mainly adult fiction & nonfiction. Now incorporating the Gibraltar Library Service.

# Greece

**Athens Academy Library**
Odos Venizelou 28, 106 79 Athens
*Tel:* 2103600209
*Web Site:* www.academyofathens.gr

**British Council Library & Resource Centre**
17 Kolonaki Sq, 106 73 Athens
*Tel:* 2103692333 *Fax:* 2103634769
*E-mail:* general.enquiries@britcoun.gr
*Web Site:* www.britishcouncil.gr/infoexch/greinfll. htm
*Telex:* 218799 Bric Gr
*Key Personnel*
Dir: Desmond Lauder *E-mail:* desmond.lauder@ britishcouncil.gr
*Branch Office(s)*
9 Ethnikis Amnysis str, 540 13 Thessaloniki
   *Tel:* 2310378300 *Fax:* 2310282498

**Ethnikon Idryma Erevnon**
48 Vassileou Voulgaroktonou Ave, 116 35 Athens
*Tel:* 2107210554 *Fax:* 2107246212
*Telex:* 224064 EIE GR
*Key Personnel*
Man Dir: Prof B Maglaris
President: Prof Nikos Athanassiades
National Hellenic Research Foundation.

**Eugenides Foundation Technical Library**
387 Sygrou Ave, 174 65 Athens
*Tel:* 2109411181 *Fax:* 2109417372
*E-mail:* lib@eugenfound.edu.gr
*Web Site:* www.eugenfound.edu.gr *Cable:* FONDATIONEVGE
*Key Personnel*
Librarian: Hara Brindesi

**Gennadius Library**
American School of Classical Studies at Athens, 61 Souidias St, 106 76 Athens
*Tel:* 2107210536 *Fax:* 2107237767
*E-mail:* ascsa@ascsa.edu.gr
*Web Site:* www.ascsa.edu.gr/gennadius
*Key Personnel*
Dir: Dr Haris Kalligas *E-mail:* hkalligas@ascsa. edu.gr
Head Librarian: Sophie Papageorgiou
   *E-mail:* spapageorg@ascsa.edu.gr
Publication(s): *The New Griffon, No 1, 1991* (in Greek)

**National Library of Greece** (Ethnike Bibliotheke tes Hellados)
32 Panepistimiou St, 106 79 Athens
*Tel:* 2103382601 *Fax:* 2103382502
*Web Site:* www.nlg.gr
*Key Personnel*
Dir: Dr George Zachos *E-mail:* gzachos@nlg.gr
Founded: 1828

**Library of the National Technological University of Athens**
Zografou Campus 9 Heroon, Polytechniou Ave, 157 73 Zografos Athens
*Tel:* 2107721471 *Fax:* 2107721565
*E-mail:* pstath@softlab.ntua.gr
*Web Site:* www.lib.ntua.gr
*Key Personnel*
Dir: Prof E Galanis
Founded: 1836

**Library of the Technical Chamber of Greece**
23-25 Lekka Str, 105 62 Athens
*Tel:* 2103291701; 2103245180 *Fax:* 2103237 525
*E-mail:* tee_lib@tee.gr
*Web Site:* www.tee.gr
*Key Personnel*
Head of Documentation & Information Unit: Katerina Toraki

**Library of the University of Crete**
Gallos Campus, 741 00 Rethymnon
*Tel:* 2831077810 *Fax:* 2831077850
*Web Site:* www.libh.uoc.gr
*Telex:* 291145
*Key Personnel*
Dir: Eleni Diamantaki
Acquisitions Librarian: K Karadaki *Tel:* 28310 77808 *E-mail:* karadaki@libr.uoc.gr

**Library of the University of Thessaloniki**
c/o Aristotle University of Thessaloniki, University Campus, 540 06 Thessaloniki
*Tel:* 2310995325; 2310995327 *Fax:* 2310995 322
*E-mail:* syra@ipatia.ccf.auth.gr
*Web Site:* www.lib.auth.gr
*Telex:* 0412181 auth
*Key Personnel*
Dir: Syra Nikolakaki Fotini *E-mail:* syra@ipatia. ccf.auth.gr
Librarian: D Dimitriou
Founded: 1927
Contains resources for the region of Macedonia, from antiquity to the present, in Greek & other languages.
Total Titles: 150,000 Print

# Guatemala

**Archivo General de Centro America**
4ta Av, 7-41, Zona 1, Guatemala City
*Tel:* 232-3037
*Key Personnel*
Dir: Arturo Valdes

**Biblioteca Nacional de Guatemala** (National Library of Guatemala)
5a Av 7-26, Zona 1, Guatemala City
*Tel:* (0502) 2322443 *Fax:* (0502) 2539071
*E-mail:* biblioguatemala@intelnett.com
*Web Site:* www.biblionet.edu.gt
*Key Personnel*
Dir: Victor Castillo Lopez
Founded: 1876

**Biblioteca Central de la Universidad de San Carlos**
Ciudad Universitaria, Zona 12, Guatemala City
*Tel:* (02) 460 611
*E-mail:* usacbibc@usac.edu.gt
*Web Site:* www.usac.edu.gt/dependencias/biblioteca
*Key Personnel*
Acting Dir: Lieda Ofelia Aguilar
Founded: 1974
Publication(s): *Boletin Bibliografico*; *Boletin Contenidos*

# Guinea

**Bibliotheque Nationale** (National Library)
BP 561, Conakry
*Tel:* (01) 461 010
*Key Personnel*
Librarian: Lansana Sylla
Founded: 1958

# Guyana

**Guyana Medical Science Library**
Georgetown Hospital Compound, Georgetown
*Key Personnel*
Librarian: Mrs Jennifer Wilson

**National Library**
76/77 Church & Main St, Georgetown
*Tel:* (02) 227-4053; (02) 227-4052; (02) 226-2690; (02) 227-2699 *Fax:* (02) 227-4053
*E-mail:* natlib@sdnp.org.gy
*Web Site:* www.natlib.gov.gy
*Key Personnel*
Chief Librarian: Karen Sills
Founded: 1909
Publication(s): *Guyanese National Bibliography*

# Haiti

**Bibliotheque du Petit Seminaire**
Port-au-Prince

**Bibliotheque Haitienne des Freres de l'I.C., Saint Louis de Gonzague**
180 Rue du Centre, BP 1758, Port-au-Prince HT 6110
*Tel:* 2232148; 2237508 *Fax:* 2232029
*Key Personnel*
Dir: Br Ernest Even
Founded: 1920
Secteurs les plus importants du fonds documentaire; a) collections de journaux des XIXe et XXe siecles b) histoire de Saint-Domingue et de l'Haiti contemporaine c) litterature haitienne.

**Bibliotheque Nationale d'Haiti** (National Library of Haiti)
193 rue du Centre, Port-au-Prince
*Tel:* 220 236; 220 198 *Fax:* 238 773
*Key Personnel*
Dir: Francoise Beaulieu Thybulle
Founded: 1940

# Holy See (Vatican City State)

**Biblioteca Apostolica Vaticana** (Vatican Apostolic Library)
Cortile del Belvedere, 00120 Vatican City
*Tel:* (06) 6987 9402 *Fax:* (06) 6988 4795
*E-mail:* bav@vatlib.it
*Web Site:* 212.77.1.230/it/v_home_bav/home_bav.shtml
*Telex:* 2024 Dirgental VA
*Key Personnel*
Dir: Raffaele Farina
Prefect: Prof Don Raffaele Farina
Founded: 1451

# Honduras

**Biblioteca Nacional de Honduras** (National Library of Honduras)
Apdo 4563, Tegucigalpa
*Tel:* 228 02 41 *Fax:* 222 85 77
*F-mail:* binah@sdnhon.org.hn; binah@ns.hondunet.net
*Web Site:* www.binah.gob.hn
*Key Personnel*
Dir: Hector Roberto Luna
Founded: 1880

**Sistema Bibliotecario**
c/o Carretera a Suyapa, Ciudad Univeritaria, Tegucigalpa
*Tel:* 232-2204 *Fax:* 232-2204
*E-mail:* webmaster@biblio.unah.edu.hn
*Web Site:* www.biblio.unah.edu.hn
*Telex:* 1289 Unah Ho
*Key Personnel*
Dir: Orfylia S Pinel
Publication(s): *Boletin del Sistema Bibliotecario*

# Hong Kong

**British Council Library**
3 Supreme Court Rd, Admirality, Hong Kong
*Tel:* 2913 5100 *Fax:* 2913 5102
*E-mail:* info@britishcouncil.org.hk
*Web Site:* www.britishcouncil.org.hk
*Telex:* 74141 bcoun hx
*Key Personnel*
Assistant Dir, Information: L J Nairn

**Chinese University of Hong Kong Library System**
Shatin, New Territories
*Tel:* 2609-7306 *Fax:* 2603-6952
*E-mail:* library@cuhk.edu.hk
*Web Site:* www.lib.cuhk.edu.hk
*Telex:* 50301 Cuhk Hx *Cable:* SINOVERSITY
*Key Personnel*
University Librarian: Dr Colin Storey *Tel:* 2609-7318 *E-mail:* storey@cuhk.edu.hk
Publication(s): *Catalogue of the Chinese Rare Books in the Libraries of The Chinese University of Hong Kong*; *History of Medicine: An Annotated Bibliography of Titles at The Chinese University of Hong Kong*; *Newspapers of Hong Kong, 1841-1979*; *Serials of Hong Kong,* *1845*; *Union Catalogue of Asian Fine Arts Collection*
*Branch Office(s)*
Architecture Library *Tel:* 2609 6599 *Fax:* 2603 6584
Chung Chi College Library *Tel:* 2609 6969 *Fax:* 2603 5793
Li Ping Medical Library *Tel:* 2632 2459 *Fax:* 2637 7817
New Asia College Library *Tel:* 2609 7655 *Fax:* 2603 5796
United College Library *Tel:* 2609 7564 *Fax:* 2603 5729

**The Hong Kong Polytechnic University Library**, see Pao Yue-Kong Library

**Hong Kong Public Libraries**
11/F Hong Kong Central Library, 66 Causeway Rd, Hong Kong
*Tel:* 2921 0208 *Fax:* 2415 8211
*E-mail:* enquiries@lcsd.gov.hk
*Web Site:* www.hkpl.gov.hk
*Key Personnel*
Assistant Dir: Michael Mak *E-mail:* mklmak@lcsd.gov.hk
Provide free public library services through a network of 71 libraries.

**Pao Yue-Kong Library**
Formerly The Hong Kong Polytechnic University Library
Hung Hom, Kowloon
*Tel:* 2766 6863
*E-mail:* lbinf@polyu.edu.hk
*Web Site:* www.polyu.edu.hk
*Key Personnel*
University Librarian: Barry Burton *E-mail:* lbbarry@inet.polyu.edu.hk
Publication(s): *Hongkongiana* (index to selected Hong Kong periodicals electronic database)

**Sun Yat-Sen Library**
172-174 Boundary St, Kowloon
*Tel:* 23365291
*Key Personnel*
Librarian: Mrs Megie M L Tong

**University of Hong Kong Libraries**
University of Hong Kong, Main Library, Pokfulam
*Tel:* 2859 7000; 2859 2203 *Fax:* 2858 9420
*E-mail:* libadmin@hkucc.hku.hk
*Web Site:* lib.hku.hk
*Key Personnel*
Librarian: Dr Anthony W Ferguson *Tel:* 2859 2200
Deputy Librarian: Peter Sidorko *Tel:* 2859 8056; Lawrence Wai Hong Tam *Tel:* 2859 8019
Assistant Librarian (Administration): Esther Woo *Tel:* 2859 2206 *E-mail:* emwwoo@hkucc.hku.hk
Founded: 1912
Publication(s): *The University of Hong Kong Libraries Publications Series*

# Hungary

**BME KTK**, see Budapesti Muszaki es Guzdasagtudomanyi Egyetem Orszagos Muszaki Informacios Kozpont es Konyvtar

**Budapesti Kozgazdasagtudomanyi es Allamigazoatasi Luyutemi Egyetem Kozponti Konyvtar** (Budapest University of Economic Sciences & Public Administration-Central Library)

Koezraktar u 18-20, 1093 Budapest
Mailing Address: PF 489, 1828 Budapest 5
*Tel:* (01) 217-6827 *Fax:* (01) 217-4910
*E-mail:* konyvtar@lib.bkae.hu
*Web Site:* www.lib.bke.hu
*Key Personnel*
Dir: Dr Hedvig Huszar *Tel:* (01) 217-5827
  *E-mail:* huszar@lib.bkae.hu

**Budapesti Muszaki es Guzdasagtudomanyi Egyetem Orszagos Muszaki Informacios Kozpont es Konyvtar** (Budapest University of Technology & Economics, National Technical Information Centre & Library)
Budafoki u 4-6, Budapest 1111
Mailing Address: PO Box 91, Budapest 1502
*Tel:* (01) 463-3534; (01) 463-1069 *Fax:* (01) 463-2440
*E-mail:* refposta@omikk.bme.hu
*Web Site:* www.bme.hu; www.omikk.bme.hu
*Key Personnel*
Dir: Ilona Fonyo *E-mail:* ifonyo@omikk.bme.hu

**Foszekesegyhazi Konyvtar** (Cathedral Library)
Pazmany P U 2, 2500 Esztergom
*Tel:* 33411891
*E-mail:* bibliotheca@ehf.hu *Cable:* BIBLIOTHECA ESZTERGOM
*Key Personnel*
Dir: Bela Czekli

**Fovarosi Szabo Ervin Konyvtar** (Ervin Szabo Metropolitan Library)
Szabo Ervin ter 1, 1088 Budapest
*Tel:* (01) 1185815; (01) 411-5000 *Fax:* (01) 1185914
*E-mail:* info@fszek.hu
*Web Site:* www.fszek.hu
*Key Personnel*
Dir: Jenoe Kiss

**Jozsef Attila Tudomanyegyetem Egyetemi Koenyvtar** (University of Szeged University Library)
Dugonics Sq 13, 6720 Szeged
Mailing Address: Postfach 393, 6701 Szeged
*Tel:* (062) 544-036 *Fax:* (062) 544-035
*E-mail:* mader@bibl.u-szeged.hu
*Web Site:* www.bibl.u-szeged.hu
*Key Personnel*
Chief Librarian: Dr Bela Mader
Publication(s): *Acta Bibliothecaria* (irregularly); *Acta Universitatis Szegediensis de Attila Jozsef Nominatae; Dissertationes ex Bibliotheca Universitatis de Attila Jozsef nominatae; Koenyvtartoerteneti Fuezetek* (History of Libraries series, with German summaries)

**Koezponti Statisztikai Hivatal Koenyvtar es Dokumentacios Szolgalat** (Hungarian Central Statistical Office, Library & Documentation Service)
Keleti Karoly Str 5, 1024 Budapest
*Tel:* (01) 3456105 *Fax:* (01) 3456112
*Web Site:* www.ksh.hu; www.lib.ksh.hu
*Key Personnel*
Dir General: Dr Erzebet Nemes
Founded: 1867
Publication(s): *Magyarorszag toerteneti helysegnevtara 1773-1808* (Historical Gazetteer of Hungary, 2000); *Statisztikai modszerek-Temadokumentacio* (Statistical Methods-Surveys of Literature on Various Subjects, 2000); *Szakbibliografiak-Statisztikai adatforrasok bibliografia* (Special Bibliographies-Sources of Statistical Data Bibliography, 2002); *Toerteneti statisztikai fuezetek* (Papers on Historical Statistics, 2000); *Toerteneti statisztikai tanulmanyok* (Studies on Historical Statistics, 2000)

**Kossuth Lajos Tudomanyegyetem Egyetemi Koenyvtar**
Pf 39, 4010 Debrecen
*Tel:* (052) 316-835; (052) 316-666; (052) 512-900 *Fax:* (052) 410-443
*E-mail:* comp@lib.unideb.hu
*Web Site:* www.lib.unideb.hu
*Telex:* 72200
*Key Personnel*
Chief Librarian: Dr Olga Gomba
Dir General: Dr Iren Levay
Lajos Kossuth University Library.

**Magyar Orszagos Leveltar (MOL)** (National Archives of Hungary)
Becsi kapu ter 4, 1014 Budapest 1
Mailing Address: PO Box 3, 1250 Budapest
*Tel:* (01) 225-2800 *Fax:* (01) 225-2817
*E-mail:* info@natarch.hu
*Web Site:* www.natarch.hu
*Key Personnel*
Dir: Prof Lajos Gecsenyi, PhD *Tel:* (01) 225-2803
  *E-mail:* gecsenyi@natarch.hu
Founded: 1756
Publication(s): *Leveltari Kozlemenyek* (Archival Publications, biannually, 1923, academical & scholar); *Magyar Orszagos Leveltar Kiadvanyai* (Publications of National Archives of Hungary, biannually)

**Magyar Tudomanyos Akademia Koenyvtara** (Library of the Hungarian Academy of Sciences)
Arany Janos u l, 1051 Budapest
Mailing Address: PF 1002, 1245 Budapest
*Tel:* (01) 411 6100 *Fax:* (01) 311 6954
*E-mail:* mtak@vax.mtak.hu
*Web Site:* w3.mtak.hu
*Key Personnel*
Deputy Dir General: Dr Karolyne Domsa
  *E-mail:* domsa@vax.mtak.hu
Founded: 1826
Library of the Hungarian Academy of Sciences/Library of the HAS.
Publication(s): *Budapest Oriental Reprints Ser A & Ser B* (irregular, scientific monographs); *Oriental Studies* (irregular, scientific monographs); *Publicationes Bibliothecae Academiae Scientiarum Hungaricae* (irregular, scientific monographs)

**MOL**, see Magyar Orszagos Leveltar (MOL)

**Orszagos Muoszaki, Informacios Koozpont es Koonyvtar (OMIKK)** (National Technical Information Centre & Library)
Budafoki ut 4-6, 1111 Budapest
Mailing Address: Postafiok 91, 1502 Budapest
*Tel:* (01) 463-3534; (01) 463-1069 *Fax:* (01) 463-2440
*E-mail:* kolcsonzes@omikk.bme.hu
*Web Site:* www.omikk.bme.hu
*Key Personnel*
Dir General: Akos Robert Herman, PhD
  *E-mail:* har@omk.omikk.hu
Librarian: Peter Szanto
Translation department, offers translation from Hungarian & other languages.
Publication(s): *Tudomanyos es Muoszaki Tajekoztatas* (scientific & technical information)

**Orszagos Szechenyi Koenyvtar**
Budavari Palota F epuelet, 1827 Budapest
*Tel:* (01) 224-3788 *Fax:* (01) 202-0804; (01) 375-9984
*E-mail:* kint@oszk.hu
*Web Site:* www.oszk.hu
*Key Personnel*
Dir General: Geza Poprady
National Center for Library Science & Methodology, Hungarian national ISBN & ISDS Center.

Publication(s): *A magyar irodalom es irodalomtudomany bibliografaja* (Bibliography of Hungarian Literature & Literary Studies); *Az Orszagos Szechenyi Koenyvtar evkoenyve* (National Szechenyi Library Year Book); *Hungariaka informacio* (Hungarica Information); *Kurrens Kuelfoeldi idoeszaki Kiadvanyok a Magyar Koenyvtarakban* (Current Foreign Periodical Publications in Hungarian Libraries); *Magyar Koenyveszet* (annually, Cumulation of Hungarian National bibliography); *Magyar nemzeti bibliografia Idoszaki kiadvanyok bibliografiaja* (Hungarian National Bibliography of Serials); *Magyar nemzeti bibliografia. Idoszaki kiadvanyok repertoriuma* (Hungarian National Bibliography. Repertory of Periodicals); *Magyar nemzeti bibliografia Koenyvek bibliografiaja* (Hungarian National Bibliography Bibliography of Books); *Magyar nemzeti bibliografia. Zenemuvek bibliografiaja* (Hungarian National Bibliography of Music Scores & Records); *Mikrofilmek cimjegyzeke. Idoszaki kiadvanyok* (List of Microfilm Titles. Periodical Publications); *Mikrofilmek cimjegyzeke. Modern nyomtatvanyok* (List of Microfilm Titles. Modern Printed Matter); *Mikrofilmek cimjegyzeke. Szines grafikai plakatok* (List of Microfilm Titles. Colored Graphic Posters); *Mikrofilmek cimjegyzeke. Zenei gyujtemeny. Zenemukeziratok* (List of Microfilm Titles. Music Collection. Music Manuscripts); *Uj periodikumok* (New Periodicals)

**Sarospataki Reformatus- Kollegium Tudomanyos Gyuejtemenyei Nagykoenyvtar**
Rakoczy ut 1, 3950 Sarospatak
*Tel:* 4111057
*Key Personnel*
Dir: Michael Szentimrel
The Library of Scientific Collections of the Reformed College of Saroapatak.

# Iceland

**Kennarahaskoli Islands** (Iceland University of Education)
v/Stakkahlio, 105 Reykjavik
*Tel:* 5633800 *Fax:* 5633914
*E-mail:* vefur@khi.is
*Web Site:* www.khi.is
*Key Personnel*
Learning Center Dir: Kristin Indridadottir
  *E-mail:* kindr@khi.is
Founded: 1908

**Landsbokasafn Islands-Haskolabokasafn** (National & University Library of Iceland)
Arngrimsgata 3, 107 Reykjavik
*Tel:* 525 5600 *Fax:* 525 5615
*E-mail:* lbs@bok.hi.is
*Web Site:* www.bok.hi.is
*Key Personnel*
National Librarian: Sigrun Klara Hannesdottir
Deputy Librarian: Porsteinn Hallgrimsson
National Library & University Library of Iceland.
Publication(s): *Handritasafn Landsbokasafns* (catalog of manuscripts); *Islensk bokaskra* (Icelandic National Bibliography); *Islensk Hljodritaskra* (Bibliography of Icelandic Sound Recordings, supplement to Islensk bokaskra); *Ritmennf* (annually, journal)

**Borgarbokasafn Reykjavikur** (Reykjavik City Library)
Tryggvatgatu 15, 107 Reykjavik
*Tel:* 5631717 *Fax:* 5631705
*E-mail:* borgarbokasafn@borgarbokasafn.is
*Web Site:* www.borgarbokasafn.is

*Key Personnel*
City Librarian: Erla Kristin Jonasdottir
  *E-mail:* erla@borgarbokasafn.is
Founded: 1923
Publication(s): *Arsskyrsla*
*Branch Office(s)*
Foldasafn, Grafarvogskirkju Church, 112 Reykjavik *Tel:* 5675320 *Fax:* 5675356
Gerduberg, Gerduberg 3-5, 111 Reykjavik
  *Tel:* 5579122 *Fax:* 5579160
Kringlusafn, Borgarleikhus v/Listabraut, 104
  Reykjavik *Tel:* 5806200 *Fax:* 5806219
Seljasafn, Holmascli 4-6, 109 Reykjavik
  *Tel:* 5873320
Solheimasafn, Solheimar 27, 104 Reykjavik
  *Tel:* 5536814 *Fax:* 5813780

# India

## American Information Resource Center
Division of Public Affairs Section, American Embassy
The American Center, 24 Kasturba Gandhi Marg, New Delhi 110001
*Tel:* (011) 2331-6841; (011) 2331-4251
  *Fax:* (011) 2332-9499
*E-mail:* libdel@pd.state.gov
*Web Site:* americanlibrary.in.library.net; newdelhi.usembassy.gov
*Key Personnel*
AIRC Dir: Veena Chawla
Public library.
*Branch Office(s)*
38-A Jawaharlal Nehru Rd, Kolkata 700071
  *Tel:* (033) 2245-1211; (033) 2245-1218
  *Fax:* (033) 2245 2445

## The Asiatic Society of Mumbai
Town Hall, Mumbai 400 023
*Tel:* (022) 2660956 *Fax:* (022) 2665139
*E-mail:* asbl@bom2.vsnl.net.in
*Web Site:* education.vsnl.com/asbl/
*Key Personnel*
President: Mr B G Deshmukh
Vice President: Dr Devangana Desai; Mr Rajan M Jayakar; Dr Mani Kamerkar; Mr Eknath Kshirsagar
Honorary Secretary: Mrs Vimal Shah
Founded: 1804
Publication(s): *Journal of the Asiatic Society of Mumbai & Monographs*

## British Council Libraries
17, Kasturba Gandhi Marg, New Delhi 110001
*Tel:* (011) 371 1401 *Fax:* (011) 371 0717
*E-mail:* delhi.library@in.britishcouncil.org
*Web Site:* www.bclindia.org/library
*Key Personnel*
Head, Library & Info Services: P Jayarajan
  *E-mail:* jayarajan@in.britishcouncil.org
*Branch Office(s)*
Bhaikaka Bhawan, Law Garden, Ellisbridge, 380 006 Ahmedabad, Gujarat *Tel:* (079) 6464693
  *Fax:* (079) 6469493
Prestige Takt 23, Kasturba Rd Cross, Bangalore 560001 *Tel:* (080) 2240763 *Fax:* (080) 2240767
GTB Complex, Roshanpura Naka, Bhopal 462003
  *Tel:* (0755) 553767 *Fax:* (0755) 765211
SCO 36-38, Sector 8C, Madhya Marg, Chandigarh 160008 *Tel:* (0172) 546540; (0172) 546541 *Fax:* (0172) 547540 *E-mail:* bl.chandigarh@in.britishcouncil.org
737 Anna Salai, Chennai 600002 *Tel:* (044) 8525002 *Fax:* (044) 8523234 *E-mail:* library.chennai@in.britishcouncil.org
5-9-22 Secretariat Rd, Sarovar Centre, Hyderabad 560001 *Tel:* (040) 23230774 *Fax:* (040) 23298273

L&T Chambers, 1st floor, 16 Camac St, Kolkata 700071 *Tel:* (033) 2825370 *E-mail:* kolkata.library@in.britishcouncil.org
Mittal Towers "A" Wing, 1st floor, Nariman Point, Mumbai 400021 *Tel:* (022) 2823530 *Fax:* (022) 2852024 *E-mail:* mumbai.library@in.britishcouncil.org
917/1 Ferugusson College Rd, Shivaji Nagar, Pune 411004 *Tel:* (020) 5654352 *Fax:* (020) 5654351
YMCA Bldg, Thiruvananthapuram 695001
  *Tel:* (0471) 330716 *Fax:* (0471) 330717

## Central Library
Vadodara, Gujaat, Baroda 390006
*Tel:* (0265) 540133
*Key Personnel*
State Librarian: Bakulesh Bhuta
Publication(s): *Granth Deep* (quarterly)

## Central Secretariat Library
Dept of Culture, G Wing, Shastri Bhavan, New Delhi 110 001
*Tel:* (011) 338 9684 *Fax:* (011) 338 4846
*E-mail:* root%csl@delnet.ren.nic.in
*Key Personnel*
Dir: Kalpana Dasgupta

## Delhi Public Library
S P Mukherjee Marg, New Delhi 110006
*Tel:* (011) 291 6881 *Fax:* (011) 294 3990
*Key Personnel*
Dir: Dr Banwari Lal
Founded: 1951

## Delhi University Library System
Delhi 110007
*Tel:* (011) 27667725 *Fax:* (011) 27667126
*E-mail:* crl@delnet.ven.nic.in
*Web Site:* www.du.ac.in
*Key Personnel*
University Librarian: M L Saini *Tel:* (011) 27667848 (ext 1127)

## Gujarat Vidyapith Granthalaya
PO Navjivan, Ashram Rd, Ahmedabad, Gujarat 380014
*Tel:* (079) 7541148 *Fax:* (079) 7542547
*E-mail:* guivi@adinet.emet.in; gvpahd@ad1vsnl.net.in
*Telex:* 121-6254 GUVI IN
*Key Personnel*
Librarian: K K Bhausar
Combined university, state central & public library.
Publication(s): *Gujarati Samayik Lekh Suchi* (Gujarati Indexing of Articles from Selected Gujarati Journals); *Tapas Nibandh Suchi* (Gujarati Bibliography of Dissertations)

## Indian Council of World Affairs Library
Sapru House, Barakhamba Rd, New Delhi 110001
*Tel:* (011) 3317246 *Fax:* (011) 3317248
  *Cable:* INTERASIA
*Key Personnel*
Acting Librarian: Man Singh Deora
  *E-mail:* dgicwa@hotmail.com
Publication(s): *Documentation on Asia* (annually)

## Indian Institute of Management
Vikram Sarabhai Library, Vastrapur, Ahmedabad 380 015
*Tel:* (079) 2630 7241 *Fax:* (079) 2630 6896
*E-mail:* director@iimahd.ernet.in
*Web Site:* www.iimahd.ernet.in
*Key Personnel*
Dir: Prof Bakul Dholakia
Founded: 1962

## Indian Institute of Technology Madras Central Library
Central Library IITPO, Chennai 600 036
*Tel:* (044) 2578740 *Fax:* (044) 2350509
*E-mail:* libinfo@iitm.ac.in
*Web Site:* www.cenlib.iitm.ac.in
*Telex:* 418926 *Cable:* TECHNOLOGY
*Key Personnel*
Librarian: Dr Harish Chandra *E-mail:* hchandra@iitm.ac.in

## Institute for Social & Economic Change Library
Nagarabhavi, Bangalore, Karnataka 560072
*Tel:* (080) 23215468; (080) 23215519; (080) 23215592; (080) 23215468 *Fax:* (080) 23217008
*E-mail:* admin@isec.ac.in
*Web Site:* www.isec.ac.in
*Key Personnel*
Librarian: TRB Sarma *Tel:* (080) 23215468 (ext 302) *E-mail:* trbsarma@isec.ac.in
Founded: 1972

## Madras Literary Society Library
College Rd, Chennai 600 006
*Tel:* 827 9666
*Key Personnel*
Manager: P N Balasundaram

## National Archives of India
Janpath, New Delhi 110001
*Tel:* (011) 23383436 *Fax:* (011) 23384127
*E-mail:* archives@ren02.nic.in
*Web Site:* nationalarchives.nic.in
*Key Personnel*
Librarian: R C Puri
Dir General: H D Singh
Founded: 1891

## The National Library, Government of India
Belvedere, Kolkata 700027
*Tel:* (033) 2479 1381; (033) 2479 1384
  *Fax:* (033) 2479 1462
*E-mail:* nldirector@rediffmail.com; nldirector@nlindia.org
*Web Site:* www.nlindia.org
*Telex:* 021 8117 *Cable:* LIBRARIAN
*Key Personnel*
Dir: Dr Ramanuj Bhattacharjee *Tel:* (033) 479 2968
Principal Library & Information Officer: Dr R Ramachandran *Tel:* (033) 479 2467
Publication(s): *India's National Library*; *India's National Library: Systematization & Modernization*; *The National Library & Public Libraries in India*

## Nehru Memorial Museum & Library (NMML)
Teen Murti House, New Delhi 110011
*Tel:* (011) 23017587 *Fax:* (011) 23015026
*Key Personnel*
Dir: Dr O P Kejariwal
Librarian: Mrs Kanwal Verma
Contact: Mrs Indu Jolly
Research center on modern Indian history, with emphasis on Indian Nationalism; large collections of newspapers, microfilms, private papers, institutional records, photographs & oral history recordings.

## Pt Ravishankar Shukla University Library
Raipur, Madhya Pradesh 492010
*Tel:* (0771) 534 356 *Fax:* (0771) 234 283
*E-mail:* info@rsuniversity.com
*Key Personnel*
Librarian: Rameshwar Singh

## Sahitya Akademi Library (National Academy of Letters Library)
Rabindra Bhavan, 35 Ferozeshah Rd, New Delhi 110001

*Tel:* (011) 3386626; (011) 3387386; (011) 3386088 *Fax:* (011) 3382428
*E-mail:* secy@sahitya-akademi.org
*Web Site:* www.sahitya-akademi.org *Cable:* SAHITYAKAR
*Key Personnel*
President: Ramakanta Rath
Librarian: K C Dutt
Publication(s): *Indian Literary Index* (biannually)

**State Central Library**
Afzalgunj, Hyderabad 500012
*Tel:* (040) 4600107; (040) 4615621
*Key Personnel*
Librarian: T V Vedamrutham

**University of Mumbai Library**
Rajabai Tower, Fort Campus, Mumbai 400032
*Tel:* (022) 2652819 *Fax:* (022) 2652832
*Web Site:* members.rediff.com/vidyarthi/mulhome.htm
*Key Personnel*
Librarian: Dr S R Ganpule
Founded: 1879

# Indonesia

**Arsip Nasional Republik Indonesia** (National Archives of the Republic of Indonesia)
Jalan Ampera Raya, Cilandak III, Jakarta 12560
*Tel:* (021) 78 05 851 *Fax:* (021) 78 05 812
*E-mail:* anri@indo.net.id
*Web Site:* www.archivesindonesia.or.id
*Key Personnel*
Reference & Information Service: Dr Noerhadi Magetsari
National Archives.

**British Council Library**
Jakarta Stock Exchange Bldg, 16th floor, Jl Jenderal Sudirman, Jakarta 12190
*Tel:* (021) 515 5561 *Fax:* (021) 515 5562
*E-mail:* information@britishcouncil.or.id
*Web Site:* www.britishcouncil.or.id
*Telex:* 45246 BRICOUN JKT
*Key Personnel*
Librarian: Toosye Damayanti

**CALTD**, see Center for Agricultural Library & Technology Dissemination (CALTD)

**Center for Agricultural Library & Technology Dissemination (CALTD)** (Pusat Perpustakaan dan Penyebaran Teknalogi Pertanian)
Jl Ir Haji Juanda 20, Bogor 16122
*Tel:* (0251) 321746 (ext 66) *Fax:* (0251) 326561
*E-mail:* pustaka@bogor.net
*Web Site:* pustaka.bogor.net *Cable:* Pustaka
*Key Personnel*
Dir: Dr Tjeppy D Soedjana
Founded: 1842
Publication(s): *Indonesian Journal of Agricultural Science (IJAS)*
Parent Company: Agency for Agricultural Research & Development

**Perpustakaan Dewan Perwakilan Rakjat - RI**
Jalan Jenderal Gatot Subroto, Jakarta, Pusat 10270
*Tel:* (021) 5715220; (021) 5715224 *Fax:* (021) 5715884
*Telex:* 65396 RHM DPR-RI
*Key Personnel*
Chief Librarian: Mrs Roemningsih
Parliamentary Library of Indonesia.
Publication(s): *Aquisition List*

**Pusat Dokumentasi dan Informasi Ilmiah**
Jl Jend Gatot Subroto 10, Jakarta 12710
*Tel:* (021) 5733465; (021) 5733466; (021) 5250719 *Fax:* (021) 5733467
*E-mail:* info@pdii.lipi.go.id
*Telex:* 62875 IA *Cable:* PDII
*Key Personnel*
Contact: Mr B Sudarsono
Indonesian Centre for Scientific Documentation & Information.
Publication(s): *Baca* (bimonthly, Read); *Bibliografi Khusus* (Special Bibliographies, irregular); *Direktori Perpustakaan Khusus dan Sumber Informasi di Indonesia* (Directory of Special Libraries and Information Sources in Indonesia irregular); *Indeks Laporan Penelitian dan Survei* (Index of Research and Survey Report, annual, lists of acquisitions, books & microfiches); *Indeks Majalah Ilmiah Indonesia* (Index of Indonesian Learned Periodicals, semi-annual)

**Hasanuddin University Library**
Gedung Perpustakaan UNHAS Lt 2-4, Kampus Tamalanrea, Jl Perintis Kemerdekaan, Ujung Pandang 90245
*Tel:* (0411) 586 026; (0411) 587 027 *Fax:* (0411) 512 027
*Web Site:* www.unhas.ac.id/~perpus
*Telex:* 7179 UNHAS
*Key Personnel*
Head Librarian: Dr Syarifuddin Atjtje

**Hatta Foundation Library**
Perpustakaan, Jl Solo 155, Yogyakarta 55281
*Tel:* (0274) 87747 *Fax:* (0274) 87747
*Key Personnel*
Librarian: R Soedjatmiko
Contact: Fauzie Ridjal
Hatta Foundation Library.
*Branch Office(s)*
Perpustakaan Yayasan Hatta, Jl Adisutjipto 155, Yogyakarta 55281

**Perpustakaan Pusat Institut Teknologi Bandung** (Central Library, Bandung Institute of Technology)
Jl Ganesha 10, Bandung 40132
*Tel:* (022) 250 0089 *Fax:* (022) 250 0089
*E-mail:* library@itb.ac.id
*Web Site:* www.lib.itb.ac.id
*Telex:* ITB BD 28324
*Key Personnel*
Chief Librarian: Dr Adjat Sakri
Librarian: Dr I Nyoman Susila
Publication(s): *Proceedings Institut Teknologi Bandung*

**Perpustakaan Islam** (Islamic Library)
Jl P Mangkubumi 38, Yogyakarta
*Tel:* (0274) 2078
*Web Site:* www.perpustakaan-islam.com
*Key Personnel*
Dir: Dr H Asyhuri Dahlan
Librarian: Moh Amien Mansoer

**National Library of Indonesia**, see Perpustakaan Nasional

**Perpustakaan Nasional**
Jalan Salemba Raya 28A, Jakarta 10002
Mailing Address: PO Box 3624, Jakarta 10002
*Tel:* (021) 315 4863; (021) 315 4864; (021) 315 4870 *Fax:* (021) 310 3554
*E-mail:* pusjasa@rad.net.id; info@pnri.go.id
*Web Site:* www.pnri.go.id/beranda
*Key Personnel*
Dir: Mr Dady Rachmananta
National library of Indonesia.

**Library of Political and Social History**
Medan Merdeka Selatan 11, Jakarta
*Tel:* (021) 360136
*Key Personnel*
Librarian: Dr Soekarman
Publication(s): *Index Pemilu* (Index of General Elections); *Press index; Index Artikel Tentang Negara* (Index of Official Publications)

**Universitas Udayana Library**
Jl PB Sudirman Denpasar, Bukit Jimbaran, Denpasar, Bali
*Tel:* (0361) 702772 *Fax:* (0361) 702-765
*Web Site:* www.unud.ac.id
*Key Personnel*
Librarian: Dr I Gusti Nyeman Tirtayasa
Publication(s): *Bibliografi*

# Islamic Republic of Iran

**Ferdowsi University of Mashhad Central Library & Information Centre**
PO Box 331-91735, 91735 Mashhad
*Tel:* (0511) 8789263-66; (0511) 8796798-9 *Fax:* (0511) 8796822
*E-mail:* info@ferdowsi.um.ac.ir
*Web Site:* c-library.um.ac.ir
*Telex:* 512271
*Key Personnel*
General Dir: Dr M T Eclalati
Founded: 1973

**IRANDOC**, see Iranian Information Documentation Centre

**Iranian Information Documentation Centre**
Affiliate of Ministry of Culture & Higher Education
1188, Enghelab Ave, Tehran
Mailing Address: PO Box 13185-1371, Tehran
*Tel:* (021) 6462548 *Fax:* (021) 6462254
*E-mail:* info@irandoc.ac.ir
*Web Site:* www.irandoc.ac.ir
*Telex:* 6415330 *Cable:* ASNDIRAN
*Key Personnel*
Dir: Prof Hussein Gharibi
International Relations Manager: Mr Mansoor Sheydaee
Contact: Ms Nastaron Sadeghi
Founded: 1968
Engaged in information sciences fields. Main activities include production & dissemination of Iranian scientific information (Persian); research on information science; Iranian dissertion abstracts (students graduated in Iran & abroad); research projects abstracts; Iranian scientific meetings & proceedings; Iranian government reports & other topics available for free online. Researchers can access the materials via the web page, periodicals & connecting to SABA intranet, a local network. They can also apply to search documents by letter or in person to the Search Unit of the library.
Publication(s): *The Abstract of Scientific & Technical Papers* (quarterly, 1993, bibliographic data & in some cases abstracts of the sci-tech articles published in Persian language journals); *Current Research in Iranian Universities and Research Centers* (quarterly, 1993, details with abstracts of the research project carried out in Iran); *Directory of Scientific Meeting Held In Iran* (quarterly, 1993, bibliographic data on the papers & lectures in the seminars held in Iran since 1989); *Dissertion Abstracts of Iranian*

*Graduates Abroad* (quarterly, 1995, abstract of Masters & PhD dissertations of the Iranian graduates abroad since 1994); *Index to Latin periodicals available in Iranian special libraries* (electronic journal (www.irandoc.ac.ir)); *Iranian Dissertion Abstracts* (quarterly, 1973, bibliographic information & abstracts of the dissertation submitted by graduate students & PhD); *Iranian Government Report* (quarterly, 1998, reports gathered from ministries & governmental research organizations); *Iranian Scholars & Experts Database* (quarterly, 1996, name & details of selected Iranian experts holding Masters & PhD)

**The Islamic Republic of Iran Parliament Library, No 1 (Ketab Khane-ye Majles-e Shora-ye Elsami, No 1)** (Library, Museum & Documentation Center of the Islamic Consultative Assembly Number 1)
Baharestan Sq, Parliamentary Library, 11576-11119 Tehran
*Tel:* (021) 3130920 *Fax:* (021) 3124339
*E-mail:* frelations@majlislib.com; irparlib@majlislib.com; info@majlislib.com
*Web Site:* www.majlislib.com
*Key Personnel*
Dir: Seyyed Mohammad Ali Ahmadi Abhari
 *E-mail:* abhari@majlislib.com
Founded: 1923
Library & information services; manuscripts collection; indexing of the manuscripts; publishing; renovation, maintenance, disinfection & antiacidification of old books & manuscripts; making microfilms.
*Ultimate Parent Company:* Majles-e Shora-ye Eslami (The Islamic Consultative Assembly)

**The Islamic Republic of Iran Parliament Library, No 2 (Ketab Khane-ye Majles-e Shora-ye Eslami, no 2)** (Library, Museum & Documentation Center of the Islamic Consultative Assembly, No 2)
Baharestan Sq, Parliament Library, 11576-11119 Tehran
*Tel:* (021) 3130920 *Fax:* (021) 3130919; (021) 3124339
*E-mail:* frelations@majlislib.com
*Web Site:* www.majlislib.com
*Key Personnel*
Dir: Seyyed Mohammad Ali Ahmadi Abhari
 *Tel:* (021) 3130920 *E-mail:* Abhari@majlislib.com
Founded: 1950
Library & Information Services.
*Ultimate Parent Company:* Majles-e Shora-ye Eslami (The Islamic Consultative Assembly)

**Mirzaye Shirazi Library**
Eram Campus, Shiraz 71944
*Tel:* (0711) 6260011 *Fax:* (0711) 6202380
*Web Site:* www.shirazu.ac.ir
*Telex:* 65912; 332169
*Key Personnel*
President: Dr Zouhayr Hayati *E-mail:* zhayati@rose.shirazu.ac.ir; Dr M Ershad Langroodi
Acquisition Librarian: E Emami
*Parent Company:* Shiraz University

**The National Library of the Islamic Republic of Iran**
Anahita Alley, Africa Ave, 19176 Tehran
*Tel:* (021) 2288680 *Fax:* (021) 8088950
*E-mail:* natlibir@neda.net
*Web Site:* www.nlai.ir/new/english; www.nlai.ir
*Key Personnel*
Dir: Dr Mohammed Khatami
Publication(s): *A Bibliography of the Folklore of Isfahan*; *Catalog of Valuable French Works in the National Library of Iran*; *A Catalogue of the manuscripts in the National Library of Iran*; *A Directory of Iranian Periodicals &*

*Newspapers*; *Glossary of Library Terms*; *The Iranian National Bibliography*; *List of Persian Subject Headings*; *The Name Authority List of Authors & Famous People*; *Persian Author Marks*; *Political Life of Imain Khomevni*; *Rules & Standards for Publishing Books*; *Technical Services* (8th ed)

**Organizations of Libraries, Museums & Documentation Centre of Astan Quds**
PO Box 91735-177, Mashhad
*Tel:* (098511) 2216009 *Fax:* (098511) 2220845
*E-mail:* webmaster@aqlibrary.org; info@aqlibrary.org
*Web Site:* www.aqlibrary.org
*Key Personnel*
Dir General: Dr A M Baradaran Rafiei
Publication(s): *Library & Information Science Quarterly* (quarterly)
*Parent Company:* Astan Quds Razavi

**University of Isfahan Library**
Hezar Jerib Ave, Isfahan
*Tel:* (0311) 684799; (0311) 792-2793 *Fax:* (0311) 275145
*Telex:* 312295 IREU IR
*Key Personnel*
Dir of Libraries: M Jamshidian, PhD

**University of Tabriz Central Library**
Central Library & Documentation Center, University of Tabriz, Tabriz
*Tel:* (0411) 3342199 *Fax:* (0411) 3355993
*Web Site:* www.tabrizu.ac.ir/ccntrallibrary/libgeneral.htm
*Telex:* 412045 TBUN-IR
*Key Personnel*
Dir: A Adine Ghahramani; Dr G H Tasbihi

**Central Library & Documentation Centre of University of Teheran**
Enghelab Ave, 16 Azar St, Teheran
*Tel:* (021) 6462699; (021) 6419831; (021) 6405047 *Fax:* (021) 6409348
*E-mail:* publicrel@ut.ac.ir
*Web Site:* pages.ut.ac.ir/library/home.htm
*Telex:* 13944; 222966
*Key Personnel*
Head of Library: Dr Ali Akbar Enayati
Deputy: Dr Ziaee
Public Relations: Jabbar Khodadoost

# Iraq

**Al-Awqaf Central Library**
Bab Al-Muadham, Baghdad
Mailing Address: PO Box 14146, Baghdad
*Tel:* (01) 4169362 *Fax:* (01) 4167790
*Telex:* 2785
*Key Personnel*
Librarian: Jassim M Al-Juboory
Dir: Afaf Abidul Latif
Founded: 1928
Library of Waqfs.
*Branch Office(s)*
Adhamiya, Mosul
Main Mosque, Anbar
A1-Qazzaza Library, Baghdad
Munier A1-Qadhi Library, Baghdad
Amarah
Diala
Kerkuk
Nasiriyah
Sulaymaniyah

**The Diwan Library, Ministry of Education**
PO Box 11317, Baghdad

*Tel:* (01) 8872949
*Telex:* 2259
*Key Personnel*
Librarian: Dr Kadhim G Al-Khazraji

**Library of the Iraq Museum**
Salhiya Quarter, Baghdad West
*Tel:* (01) 8879687
*Key Personnel*
Dir: Dr Muyad Said Damerji; Zounab Sadiq
Founded: 1934

**Library of the Mosul Museum**
Dawassa, Mosul
*Key Personnel*
Dir: Hazmin A Hameed

**Mosul Public Library**
1930 Abdul-Halim Al-Lawand, Mosul
*Tel:* (060) 810162 *Fax:* (060) 814765
*Telex:* 8011
*Key Personnel*
Gen Dir: Adran S Natheev

**National Centre of Archives**
National Library Bldg, 2nd floor, Bab-al-Muaddam, Baghdad
Mailing Address: POB 594, Baghdad
*Tel:* (01) 416 8440 *Cable:* CENTARCHIV
*Key Personnel*
Dir General: Salim Al-Alousi
Founded: 1972

**National Library**
Bab-el-Muaddum, Baghdad
*Tel:* (01) 416 4190
*Key Personnel*
Dir: Abdul Hameed Alwaehi
Founded: 1961
Publication(s): *al-Maktaba al-Arabia Journal*; *Iraqi National Bibliography* (triannually)

**Scientific Documentation Centre**
Central Science Library, Abu Nuas Rd, Baghdad
Mailing Address: PO Box 2441, Baghdad
*Tel:* (01) 7760023
*Telex:* 2187 Bathilmi IK
*Key Personnel*
Dir: Dr Faik Abdul S Razzaq

**Central Library of the University of Baghdad**
PO Box 47303, Baghdad
*Tel:* (01) 776 7819 *Fax:* (01) 776 3592
*Telex:* 2197
*Key Personnel*
Librarian: Dr Zeki Al-Werdi

**Central Library of the University of Basrah**
PO Box 49, Basrah
*Tel:* (01) 8868520 *Fax:* (01) 8868520
*E-mail:* basrahyni@uruklink.net
*Telex:* 207025
*Key Personnel*
Librarian: Dr Tarik Al-Manassir

**Central Library of the University of Mosul**
Mosul
*Tel:* (060) 810162 *Fax:* (060) 8011; (060) 8015
*Telex:* 8011
*Key Personnel*
Dir General: Dr Adnan S Natheev

**Central Library of the University of Salahaddin**
Arbil/Iraqi Kurdistan
*Tel:* 00873762566859 *Fax:* 00873762566861
*Web Site:* www.salun.org
*Telex:* 218510
*Key Personnel*
Dir: Dr Abdull S Abbas

# Ireland

### The Chester Beatty Library
Dublin Castle, Dublin 2
*Tel:* (01) 4070750 *Fax:* (01) 4070760
*E-mail:* info@cbl.ie
*Web Site:* www.cbl.ie
*Key Personnel*
Dir & Librarian: Dr Michael Ryan
Reference Librarian: Celine Ward *Tel:* (01)
4070757 *E-mail:* cward@cbl.ie
Among items on display at the Library is material
showing the development of the written word
from 2700 BC (the date of the Library's earli-
est clay tablet) down to modern times.

**Boole Library**, see University College Cork,
Boole Library

### Central Catholic Library
74 Merrion Sq, Dublin 2
*Tel:* (01) 676 1264
*Key Personnel*
Librarian: Teresa Whitington
*E-mail:* teresawhitington@eircom.net

### Dublin City Public Libraries
Administrative Headquarters, 138-144 Pearse St,
Dublin 2
*Tel:* (01) 674 4800 *Fax:* (01) 674 4879
*E-mail:* dublinpubliclibraries@dublincity.ie
*Web Site:* www.dublincity.ie
*Telex:* 33287
*Key Personnel*
Dublin City Librarian & Dir: Deirdre Ellis-King
Headquarters of the International IMPAC Dublin
Literary Awards.

**James Hardiman Library**, see National
University of Ireland Galway (NUI, Galway)

**Leabharlann Boole**, see University College
Cork, Boole Library

**The Mercer Library**, see Royal College of
Surgeons in Ireland Library

### National Archives
Bishop St, Dublin 8
*Tel:* (01) 4072 300 *Fax:* (01) 4072 333
*E-mail:* mail@nationalarchives.ie
*Web Site:* www.nationalarchives.ie
*Key Personnel*
Dir: Dr David Craig

### National Library of Ireland
Kildare St, Dublin 2
*Tel:* (01) 6030200 *Fax:* (01) 6766690
*E-mail:* info@nli.ie
*Web Site:* www.nli.ie
*Key Personnel*
Dir: Aongus O hAonghusa
Editor: Dr Noel Kissane
Publishes material from its collection in the
medium of folders, facsimile documents, il-
lustrated booklets & books.
Publication(s): *Ex Camera, 1860-1960* (1990);
*The Irish Face* (1987); *The Irish Famine: A
Documentary History* (1995); *The Irish Pub-
lishing Record* (annually); *James Joyce* (1982);
*The James Joyce/Paul Leon Papers* (1992);
*Parnell - A Documentary History* (1991); *Trea-
sures from the National Library of Ireland*
(1994); *Writers, Racouteurs & Notable History*
(1993); *W B Yeats & His Circle* (1989)

### National University of Ireland Galway (NUI, Galway)
University Rd, Galway
*Tel:* (091) 524411 *Fax:* (091) 522394
*E-mail:* library@nuigalway.ie
*Web Site:* www.nuigalway.ie
*Key Personnel*
Chief Librarian: Marie Reddan *E-mail:* marie.
reddan@nuigalway.ie
Founded: 1845

### Oireachtas Library
Leinster House, Kildare St, Dublin 2
*Tel:* (01) 618 3412 *Fax:* (01) 661 5583
*Web Site:* www.irlgov.ie/oireachtas
*Key Personnel*
Librarian: Maura Corcoran *E-mail:* maura.
corcoran@oireachtas.ie
Selective works of parliamentary interest.

### Representative Church Body Library
Braemor Park, Churchtown, Dublin 14
*Tel:* (01) 4923979 *Fax:* (01) 4924770
*E-mail:* library@ireland.anglican.org
*Web Site:* www.ireland.anglican.org
*Key Personnel*
Librarian & Archivist: Raymond Refaussé
Founded: 1932
Publication(s): *A Handlist of Church of Ireland
Parish Registers in the Representative Church
Body Library*; *A Handlist of Church of Ire-
land Vestry Minute Books in the Representative
Church Body Library*; *A Library on the Move.
Twenty Five Years of the Representative Church
Body Library in Churchtown*; *Register of Holy
Trinity Church, Cork, 1643-1668* (1998); *Reg-
ister of the Cathedral Church of St Columb,
Derry, 1703-1732*; *Register of the Cathedral
Church of St Columb, Derry, 1732-1775*; *Reg-
ister of the Church of St Thomas, Lisnagarvey,
Co Antrim, 1637-1646*; *Register of the Parish
of Leixlip, Co Kildare, 1665-1778*; *Register of
the Parish of St Thomas, Dublin, 1750-1791*;
*Registers of the Parish of St John the Evange-
list, Dublin* (book)

### Royal College of Surgeons in Ireland Library
Mercer St Lower, Dublin 2
*Tel:* (01) 402 2407 *Fax:* (01) 402 2457
*E-mail:* library@rcsi.ie
*Web Site:* www.rcsi.ie
*Key Personnel*
Librarian: Beatrice M Doran *E-mail:* bdoran@
rcsi.ie
Deputy Librarian: Paul Murphy *Tel:* (01) 4022406
*E-mail:* pauljmurphy@rcsi.ie
Publication(s): *Journal of the Irish Colleges of
Physicians & Surgeons*
*Branch Office(s)*
Beaumont Hospital Library, Beaumont Rd, Dublin
9 *Tel:* (01) 809 2531 *Fax:* (01) 836 7396
*E-mail:* bhlibrary@rcsi.ie

### Royal Dublin Society Library
Ballsbridge, Dublin 4
*Tel:* (01) 6680866; (01) 2407288 *Fax:* (01)
6604014
*E-mail:* info@rds.ie
*Web Site:* www.rds.ie *Cable:* SOCIETY, DUBLIN
*Key Personnel*
Librarian: Mary Kelleher *E-mail:* mary.kelleher@
rds.ie
Founded: 1731
Private society.

### Trinity College Library Dublin
College St, Dublin 2
*Tel:* (01) 608 1661 *Fax:* (01) 608 3774
*Web Site:* www.tcd.ie/library
*Telex:* 93782

*Key Personnel*
Librarian & College Archivist: Robin Adams
*E-mail:* robin.adams@tcd.ie
Founded: 1592
Academic & legal deposit library.
Publication(s): *Long Room*
*Parent Company:* Trinity College Dublin

### University College Cork, Boole Library
College Rd, Cork
*Tel:* (021) 4902794 *Fax:* (021) 4273428
*E-mail:* library@ucc.ie
*Web Site:* booleweb.ucc.ie
*Telex:* 7605 Unicei
*Key Personnel*
President: Dr Michael Mortell
Librarian: John Fitzgerald
Deputy Librarian: Edward Fahy

### University College Dublin Library
Belfield, Dublin 4
*Tel:* (01) 716 7583; (01) 716 7694 *Fax:* (01) 283
7667
*E-mail:* library@ucd.ie
*Web Site:* www.ucd.ie/library
*Key Personnel*
Librarian: Sean Phillips *E-mail:* sean.phillips@
ucd.ie

# Israel

**Aranne Library**, see Ben-Gurion University of
the Negev Aranne Library

### Bar Ilan University Central Library
c/o Wurzweiler Central Library, PO Box 90000,
52900 Ramat-Gan
*Tel:* (03) 5318486 *Fax:* (03) 5349233
*E-mail:* barmae@mail.biu.ac.il
*Web Site:* www.biu.ac.il/lib
*Key Personnel*
Acting University Librarian: Ms Bina Eiger
*Tel:* (03) 5318357 *E-mail:* eigerb@mail.biu.
ac.il
Founded: 1955
Publication(s): *Hebrew Subject Headings for Use
in Cataloging* (online); *Index to Literary Sup-
plements of the Daily Hebrew Press* (internal
online)

### Ben-Gurion University of the Negev Aranne Library
PO Box 653, 84105 Beer-Sheva
*Tel:* (08) 6461413 *Fax:* (08) 6472940
*E-mail:* asner@bgumail.bgu.ac.il
*Web Site:* www.bgu.ac.il/aranne/
*Key Personnel*
Dir: Avner Shmuelevitz *Tel:* (08) 6461432
*E-mail:* avner@bgumail.bgu.ac.il
Founded: 1965

### The Central Archives for the History of the Jewish People (CAHJP)
46 Jabotinsky St, Jerusalem
Mailing Address: PO Box 1149, 91010 Jerusalem
*Tel:* (02) 5635716 *Fax:* (02) 5667686
*E-mail:* archives@vms.huji.ac.il
*Web Site:* www.sites.huji.ac.il/cahjp/index.htm
*Key Personnel*
Dir: Assouline Hadassah
Formerly Jewish Historical General Archives.

### Central Library for the Blind, Visually Impaired & Handicapped
4 Hahistadrut St, Netanya 42441
*Tel:* (09) 8617874 *Fax:* (09) 8626346
*E-mail:* office@clfb.org.il

*Web Site:* www.clfb.org.il
*Key Personnel*
Dir: Uri Cohen *Tel:* (03) 6315555 *Fax:* (03) 6315577
*Branch Office(s)*
Elinore & Athol Burns, 66 Moshe Dayan St, Yad-Eliyahu, Tel Aviv *Tel:* (03) 6315555 *Fax:* (03) 6315577

**Central Library of Agricultural Science**
PO Box 12, 76100 Rehovot
*Tel:* (08) 9489906 *Fax:* (08) 9361348; (08) 9489399
*E-mail:* szekely@agri.huji.ac.il
*Web Site:* www.agri.huji.ac.il/library/menu.html
*Telex:* 381331
*Key Personnel*
Dir: B Gurrman *E-mail:* gurman@agri.huji.ac.il

**Dvir Bialik Municipal Central Public Library**
14 Hibat-Zion St, Ramat Gan
*Tel:* (03) 786375
*Key Personnel*
Librarian: Hadassah Pelach

**Israel State Archives**
Quiryath Ben-Gurion, Bldg 3, 91919 Jerusalem
*Tel:* (02) 568 06 80 *Fax:* (02) 679 33 75
*Key Personnel*
Dir: M Mossek
Publication(s): *Documents on the Foreign Policy of Israel* (series); *Israel Government Publications* (annually)

**Jerusalem City (Public) Library**
11 Bezalel St, Jerusalem 94591
Mailing Address: PO Box 1409, 94591 Jerusalem
*Tel:* (02) 256 785 *Fax:* (02) 255 785
*Key Personnel*
Dir: A Vilner
Founded: 1964
Specialize in dramatic theatre, music & music performance.

**Jewish National & University Library**
Edmond J Safra Campus, Givat Ram, 91904 Jerusalem
Mailing Address: PO Box 39105, 91341 Jerusalem
*Tel:* (02) 6586315 *Fax:* (02) 6511771
*Web Site:* www.huji.ac.il; jnul.huji.ac.il
*Key Personnel*
Dir: Prof Yoram Tsafrir *Tel:* (02) 6584651
   *E-mail:* yoramt@savion.huji.ac.il
Publication(s): *Kiryat Sefer* (quarterly, bibliographical); *RAMBI: The Index of Articles on Jewish Studies* (online)

**Knesset Library**
The Knesset, Kiryat Ben-Gurion, Hakiryah, 91950 Jerusalem
*Tel:* (02) 6753246; (02) 6496043 *Fax:* (02) 662733
*E-mail:* feedback@knesset.gov.il
*Web Site:* www.knesset.gov.il
*Key Personnel*
Librarian: Sandra Fine
Founded: 1950

**Pevsner Public Library**
54 Pevsner St, 31053 Haifa
Mailing Address: PO Box 5345, 31053 Haifa
*Tel:* (04) 8667766; (04) 8667768 *Fax:* (04) 8666492
*Key Personnel*
Librarian: Dr S Back

**Shaar Zion Library**
Division of Culture
Beit Ariela, Shaul Hamelech Bd, Tel Aviv

*Tel:* (03) 69101410
*Key Personnel*
Library Dir: Ora Nebenzahl
*Ultimate Parent Company:* Tel Aviv Municipality

**Technion - Israel Institute of Technology Libraries**
Elyachar Central Library, Technion City, 32000 Haifa
*Tel:* (04) 8292507 *Fax:* (04) 8295662
*E-mail:* webteam@tx.technion.ac.il
*Web Site:* library.technion.ac.il
*Telex:* 46650
*Key Personnel*
Dir: Nurit Roitberg *E-mail:* roitberg@tx.technion.ac.il

**Tel Aviv University Library, Sourasky Central Library**
PO Box 39038, 61390 Tel Aviv
*Tel:* (03) 640-8745 *Fax:* (03) 640-7833
*E-mail:* tauinfo@post.tau.ac.il
*Web Site:* www.tau.ac.il
*Telex:* 342227 versy1L
*Key Personnel*
Dir: Mira Lipstein *E-mail:* miril@tauex.tau.ac.il

**University of Haifa Library**
Mt Carmel, Haifa, 31905 Israel
*Tel:* (04) 8240289 *Fax:* (04) 8257753
*E-mail:* libmaster@univ.haifa.ac.il
*Web Site:* lib.haifa.ac.il
*Key Personnel*
Dir: Mr Oren Weinberg *E-mail:* oren@univ.haifa.ac.il
Publication(s): *Index to Hebrew Periodicals* (online)

**Weitz Center for Development Study**
PO Box 2355, 76122 Rehovot
*Tel:* (08) 9474111 *Fax:* (08) 9475884
*E-mail:* dsc@netvision.net.il
*Key Personnel*
Dir: Julia Margulis *Tel:* (08) 9474373
   *E-mail:* training@netvision.net.il

**Weizmann Institute of Science Libraries**
PO Box 26, 76100 Rehovot
*Tel:* (08) 9343583 (WIX Central Library); (08) 9343211 (Weizmann Institute) *Fax:* (08) 9344176
*E-mail:* hedva.milo@weizmann.ac.il
*Web Site:* www.weizmann.ac.il/WIS-library
*Key Personnel*
Chief Librarian: Ilana Pollack *Tel:* (08) 9343583
   *E-mail:* ilana.pollack@weizmann.ac.il

# Italy

**Biblioteca Ambrosiana**
Piazza Pio XI 2, 20123 Milan
*Tel:* (02) 80 692 1 *Fax:* (02) 80 692 210
*E-mail:* info@ambrosiana.it
*Web Site:* www.ambrosiana.it
*Key Personnel*
Librarian: Gianfranco Ravasi *E-mail:* gfravasi@ambrosiana.it
Publication(s): *Fontes Ambrosiani*

**Biblioteca Angelica**
Piazza Sant' Agostino 8, 00186 Rome
*Tel:* (06) 6868041; (06) 6875874 *Fax:* (06) 6832312
*E-mail:* angelica.polosbn@inroma.roma.it
*Web Site:* biblioroma.sbn.it/angelica

*Key Personnel*
Dir: Armida Bator *Tel:* (06) 6874113
   *E-mail:* angelica.direzione@librari.beniculturali.it
Paola Munafo e Nicoletta Muratore: La Biblioteca Angelica, Roma, Instituto Poligrafico dello Stato (1989).

**Biblioteca Comunale dell' Archiginnasio**
Piazza Galvani 1, 40124 Bologna
*Tel:* (051) 276811 *Fax:* (051) 261160
*E-mail:* archiginnasio@comune.bologna.it
*Web Site:* www.archiginnasio.it
*Key Personnel*
Dir: Dr Pierangelo Bellettini
Founded: 1801
Publication(s): *L'Archiginnasio: Bollettino della Biblioteca Comunale di Bologna* (annually)

**Archivio Centrale dello Stato**
Piazzale degli Archivi, 27, 00144 Rome
*Tel:* (06) 545481 *Fax:* (06) 5413620
*E-mail:* acs@archivi.beniculturali.it
*Web Site:* www.archiviocentraledellostato.it; archivi.beniculturali.it/ACS
*Key Personnel*
Dir: Maurizio Fallace
Librarian: Eugenia Nieddu
National archives.
Publication(s): *Bollettino Delle Nuove Accessioni*

**Biblioteca dell'Archivio Storico Civico e Biblioteca Trivulziana**
Castello Sforzesco, Piazza Castello, 1, 20121 Milan
*Tel:* (02) 88463690; (02) 88463696 *Fax:* (02) 88463698
*E-mail:* ascb.trivulziana@comune.milano.it
*Web Site:* www.milanocastcllo.it
*Key Personnel*
Librarian: Ivanoe Riboli
Library publications are sent free by request or in exchange for other publications.

**Biblioteca Centrale della Regione Siciliana gia Biblioteca Nazionale di Palermo**
Corso Vittorio Emanuele 429/431, 90134 Palermo
*Tel:* (091) 6967642 *Fax:* (091) 6967644
*E-mail:* bcrs@regione.sicilia.it
*Web Site:* www.regione.sicilia.it/beniculturali/bibliotecacentrale
*Key Personnel*
Dir: Gaetano Gullo *Tel:* (091) 7077601

**Biblioteca Medicea Laurenziana**
Affiliate of Ministero per i Beni e le Attivita Culturali
Piazza San Lorenzo n° 9, 50123 Florence
*Tel:* (055) 210760; (055) 211590; (055) 214443
   *Fax:* (055) 2302992
*E-mail:* medicea@unifi.it
*Web Site:* www.bml.firenze.sbn.it
*Key Personnel*
Chief Librarian: Dr Franca Arduini
   *E-mail:* bmldirezione@unifi.it

**Biblioteca Nazionale Vittorio Emanuele III**
Piazza del Plebiscito 1, 80132 Naples
*Tel:* (081) 7819111 *Fax:* (081) 403820
*E-mail:* Emanuele@librari.beniculturali.it
*Web Site:* www.bnnonline.it
*Key Personnel*
Dir: Mauro Giancaspro
Librarian: Anna Giaccio *Tel:* (081) 7819215
Publication(s): *I Quaderni della Biblioteca Nazionale de Napoli*

**Biblioteca Nazionale Braidense**
Via Brera 28, 20121 Milan
*Tel:* (02) 86460907 *Fax:* (02) 72023910
*E-mail:* info@braidense.it
*Web Site:* www.braidense.it

*Key Personnel*
Dir: Dr Goffredo Dotti
Contact: Dr Arminda Batori

**Biblioteca Nazionale Centrale**
Piazza dei Cavalleggeri 1, 50122 Florence
*Tel:* (055) 24919 1 *Fax:* (055) 2342 482
*E-mail:* info@bncf.firenze.sbn.it
*Web Site:* www.bncf.firenze.sbn.it
*Key Personnel*
Dir: Dr Antonia Ida Fontana

**Biblioteca Nazionale Centrale di Roma**
Viale Castro Pretorio 105, 00185 Rome
*Tel:* (06) 49891 *Fax:* (06) 4457635
*E-mail:* bncrm@bnc.roma.sbn.it
*Web Site:* www.bncrm.librari.beniculturali.it
*Key Personnel*
Dir: Osvaldo Avallone
Publication(s): *Bollettino delle opere moderne straniere acquisite dalle Biblioteche Pubbliche statali Italiane; Quaderni della Biblioteca nazionale centrale di Roma; Studi guide, cataloghi*

**Biblioteca Nazionale Marciana**
Piazzetta San Marco 7, 30124 Venice
*Tel:* (041) 2407211 *Fax:* (041) 5238803
*E-mail:* biblioteca@marciana.venezia.sbn.it
*Web Site:* www.marciana.venezia.sbn.it/
*Key Personnel*
Dir: Dr Marino Zorzi
Publication(s): *Miscellanea Marciana*

**Biblioteca Nazionale Universitaria**
Piazza Carlo Alberto 3, 10123 Turin
*Tel:* (011) 8101111 *Fax:* (011) 8121021
*E-mail:* bnto@librari.benicultural.it
*Web Site:* www.bnto.librari.beniculturali.it
*Key Personnel*
Dir: Aurelio Aghemo

**Biblioteca Universitaria**
Subsidiary of Biblioteca Estense
Biblioteca Estense Universitaria, Largo S Agostino 337, 41100 Modena
*Tel:* (059) 222248 *Fax:* (059) 230195
*E-mail:* biblio.estense@cedoc.mo.it
*Web Site:* www.cedoc.mo.it/estense
*Key Personnel*
Chief Librarian: Dr Ernesto Milano
    *E-mail:* estdir@cedoc.mo.it
Economics, medicine, engineering, mathematics.

**Biblioteca Musicale S Cecilia**
Via dei Greci 18, 00187 Rome
*Tel:* (06) 3609671 *Fax:* (06) 36001800
*Web Site:* www.conservatoriosantacecilia.it/
    Biblioteca./Biblioteca.htm
*Key Personnel*
Librarian: Dr Domenico Carboni

**Biblioteca Estense Universitaria**
Largo S Agostino 337, 41100 Modena
*Tel:* (059) 222248 *Fax:* (059) 230195
*E-mail:* estense@kril.cedoc.unimo.it; biblio.
    estense@cedoc.mo.it
*Web Site:* www.cedoc.mo.it/estense
*Key Personnel*
Dir: Dr Ernesto Milano

**European University Institute Library**
Via dei Roccettini 9, 50016 San Domino
*Tel:* (055) 4685340 *Fax:* (055) 4685283
*E-mail:* library@iue.it
*Web Site:* www.iue.it
*Telex:* 571528 Iue *Cable:* UNIVEUR
*Key Personnel*
Dir: Veerle Deckmyn
Deputy Dir: Tommaso Giordano

**Biblioteca Comunale Malatestiana**
Piazza Bufalini 1, 47023 Cesena (Forli)
*Tel:* (0547) 610 892 *Fax:* (0547) 421237
*E-mail:* malatestiana@sbn.provincia.ra.it
*Web Site:* www.malatestiana.it
*Key Personnel*
Dir: Daniela Savoia
Founded: 1452

**Biblioteca Riccardiana**
Palazzo Medici Riccardi, Via Ginori 10, 50123
    Florence
*Tel:* (055) 212586; (055) 293385 *Fax:* (055)
    211379
*E-mail:* riccardiana@riccardiana.firenze.sbn.it
*Web Site:* www.riccardiana.librari.beniculturali.it
*Key Personnel*
Dir: Dott Giovanna Lazzi *E-mail:* giovanna.
    lazzi@riccardiana.firenze.sbn.it

**Biblioteca Nazionale Sagarriga Visconti Volpi**
Piazza Umberto 1, 70122 Bari, Pugla
*Tel:* (080) 5212534; (080) 5211298 *Fax:* (080)
    5211298
*E-mail:* visconti@librari.beniculturali.it
*Key Personnel*
Dir: Maria Teresa Tafuri di Melignano

**Universita degli Studi di Firenze, Sistema Bibliotecario di Ateneo**
via Cavour 82, 50121 Florence
*Tel:* (055) 2757705; (055) 2757706; (055)
    2757735 *Fax:* (055) 2757702
*E-mail:* cb@biblio.unifi.it
*Web Site:* www.sba.unifi.it
*Key Personnel*
Dir: Floriana Tagliabue *E-mail:* floriana.
    tagliabue@unifi.it

**Universita di Roma 'La Sapienza'**
Division of Uffieio Centrale Per I Beni Librari E
    Istituti Culturali
Piazzale Aldo Moro 5, 00185 Rome
*Tel:* (06) 4474021 *Fax:* (06) 44740222
*E-mail:* alessandrina@librari.beniculturali.it
*Web Site:* www.alessandrina.librari.beniculturali.it;
    www.uniroma1.it
*Key Personnel*
Dir: Maria Concetta Petrollo *E-mail:* petrollo@
    uniromal.it
Publication(s): *Catalogo Del Fondo Leopardiano;
    Inchiostri Per L'Infanzia; Voci Di Roma*
Parent Company: Ministero Per I Beni E Le At-
    tivita Culturali

**Biblioteca Universitaria di Padua**
Via S Biagio 7, 35121 Padua
*Tel:* (049) 8240211; (049) 8240241 *Fax:* (049)
    8762711
*E-mail:* info@cab.unipd.it
*Web Site:* www.unipd.it/bibliotecauniversitaria
*Key Personnel*
Dir: Francesco Aliano
Librarian: Rosalba Suriano *E-mail:* rosalba.
    suriano@unipd.it
Founded: 1629

# Jamaica

**Jamaica Archives**
Corner King & Manchester Sts, Spanish Town, St
    Catherine
*Tel:* (876) 984-2581; (876) 984-5001 *Fax:* (876)
    984-8254
*Key Personnel*
Government Archivist: Elizabeth Williams

**Jamaica Library Service**
2 Tom Redcam Dr, Kingston 5
Mailing Address: PO Box 58, Kingston 5
*Tel:* (876) 926-3315 *Fax:* (876) 926-3354
*E-mail:* jamlibs@cwjamaica.com
*Web Site:* www.jamlib.org.jm
*Key Personnel*
Dir General: Patricia Roberts
Publication(s): *Book Production in Jamaica: A
    Select List of Jamaican Publications; Jamaica:
    A Select Bibliography 1900-1963; Jamaica Li-
    brary Service 21 Years of Progress in Pictures
    1948-1969; Jamaica Poetry: A Checklist, Slav-
    ery to the Present; Reflections on Black River;
    What's New in Librarianship*

**National Library of Jamaica**
12 East St, Kingston
*Tel:* (876) 967-1526; (876) 967-2516; (876) 967-
    2494; (876) 967-2496 *Fax:* (876) 922-5567
*E-mail:* nlj@infochan.com
*Web Site:* www.nlj.org.jm *Cable:* NALIBJAM
*Key Personnel*
Dir: Winsome Hudson
Founded: 1979
The Library is the National Reference Library of
    Jamaica. Its main functions are to collect &
    preserve the national imprint, to serve as the
    bibliographic center for Jamaica & the focal
    point of the national information system.
Publication(s): *Gleaner* (of Jamaica); *Jamaican
    National Bibliography* (Occasional bibliography
    series); *The Gleaner* (Index monthly index to
    the)

**Northern Caribbean University**
Hiram S Walters Resource Center, Mandeville,
    Manchester
*Tel:* (876) 962-2204-7 *Fax:* (876) 962-0075
*E-mail:* info@ncu.edu.jm
*Web Site:* www.ncu.edu.jm
*Key Personnel*
Dir: Heather Rodriguez-James *Tel:* (876) 523-
    2101
Librarian: Hortense Riley; Cordel McFarlane
*Branch Office(s)*
Andrews School of Nursing, Kingston

**United Theological College of the West Indies**
7 Golding Ave, Kingston 7
*Tel:* (876) 927-1724; (876) 977-0810 *Fax:* (876)
    977-0812
*E-mail:* unitheol@cyjamaica.com
*Web Site:* www.utcwi.edu.jm
*Key Personnel*
President: Dr Lewin Williams
Librarian: Rev Gillian Wilson
Founded: 1966
Theological Seminary.
Publication(s): *Caribbean Journal of Religious
    Studies* (biennially)

**University of Technology, Jamaica**
Calvin McKain Library, 237 Old Hope Rd,
    Kingston 6
*Tel:* (876) 927-1680-9 *Fax:* (876) 927-1614
*E-mail:* library@utech.edu.jm
*Web Site:* www.utechjamaica.edu.jm
*Key Personnel*
University Librarian: Hermine C Salmon
Founded: 1958

**University of the West Indies Library
    (Jamaica)**
Main Library, Mona Campus, Kingston 7
*Tel:* (876) 935-8479; (876) 935-8294; (876) 935-
    8296 *Fax:* (876) 927-1926
*E-mail:* main.library@uwimona.edu.jm
*Web Site:* wwwlibrary.uwimona.edu.jm:1104
*Telex:* 2123 *Cable:* UNIVERS

**Key Personnel**
University/Campus Librarian: Dunstan Newman *Tel:* (876) 935-8840 *E-mail:* dunstan.newman02@uwimona.edu.jm
Founded: 1948
Educational Institution.
Publication(s): *Medical Caribbeana: An Index to Caribbean Health Sciences Literature* (Library Annual Report); *Research for Development, Vol 1* (1998, Bibliography of staff publications 1993-1998); *Research for Development: Strengthening Our Tourism Product* (Bibliography)
*Branch Office(s)*
Medical Library
Science Library

# Japan

**Gifu Diagaku Fuzoku Toshokan**
Yanagido 1-1, Gifu 501-1193
*Tel:* (0582) 93-2191 *Fax:* (0582) 30-1107
*E-mail:* lsetsuek@cc.gifu-u.ac.jp
*Web Site:* www.gifu-u.ac.jp

**Hokkaido University Library**
Kita 8, Nishi 5, Kita-ku, Sapporo 060-0808
*Tel:* (011) 706-4998 *Fax:* (011) 747-2855
*E-mail:* bureau@hokudai.ac.jp
*Web Site:* www.lib.hokudai.ac.jp/index_e.html
*Key Personnel*
Dir: Yoshiro Inoue
Lib Prof: T Sanbong
Librarian: Hiroshi Yoshida
Founded: 1876
Publication(s): *Yuin* (Quarterly, The Hokkaido University Library Bulletin, in Japanese)

**International Documentation Center, The University of Tokyo**
7-3-1 General Library, 3rd floor, Hongo, Bunkyo-ku, Tokyo 113-0033
*Tel:* (03) 5841-2645 *Fax:* (03) 5841-2611
*E-mail:* kokusai@lib.u-tokyo.ac.jp
*Web Site:* www.lib.u-tokyo.ac.jp/undepo
*Key Personnel*
Head Librarian: Akira Ohno
Librarian: Ms Kayu Sakata
Publication(s): *Watakushitachi no Kokuren* (1995, Japanese brochure about the United Nations)

**Keio University School of Library & Information Science**
2-15-45 Mita, Minato-ku, Tokyo 108
*Tel:* (03) 3453-4511 *Fax:* (03) 5427-1578
*E-mail:* slis-office@slis.keio.ac.jp
*Web Site:* www.slis.keio.ac.jp
*Key Personnel*
Librarian: Motoko Sekiguchi

**Kokuritsu Kobunshokan** (National Archives of Japan)
Kitanomaru Koen 3-2, Chiyoda-ku, Tokyo 102
*Tel:* (03) 3214-0621 *Fax:* (03) 3212-8806
*Web Site:* www.archives.go.jp/index_e.html
*Key Personnel*
Dir Gen: Kazumasa Iwahashi

**Kyoto Sangyo University Library**
Kamigamo-Motoyama, Kita-Ku, Kyoto 603-8555
*Tel:* (075) 7012151 *Fax:* (075) 7051447
*E-mail:* ksu-lib@star.kyoto-su.ac.jp
*Web Site:* www3.kyoto-su.ac.jp/lib
*Key Personnel*
Dir: Satora Yabunaka
Founded: 1987

**Kyushu University Library**
6-10-1, Hakozaki, Higashi-ku, Fukuoka-shi 812-8581
*Tel:* (092) 6411101; (092) 6422111
*E-mail:* w3-admin@lib.kyushu-u.ac.jp
*Web Site:* www.lib.kyushu-u.ac.jp
*Key Personnel*
Librarian: S Arikana
Founded: 1903

**National Diet Library**
1-10-1 Nagata-cho, Chiyoda ku, Tokyo 100-8924
*Tel:* (03) 3581-2331 *Fax:* (03) 3508-2934
*E-mail:* webmaster@ndl.go.jp
*Web Site:* www.ndl.go.jp
*Key Personnel*
Librarian: Takao Kurosawa
Dir Planning & Cooperation Division: Hiroyuki Taya
Founded: 1948
As the only national library in Japan, provides services for the Diet, for the government & for the general public. As the only depository library in Japan, the library acquires all materials published in Japan, preserves them as national cultural heritage, compiles catalogs of these publications in a database or other format, & with these collections provides library services.
Publication(s): *Annual Report of the National Diet Library*; *Biburosu* (Biblos, quarterly, online (www.ndl.go.jp/jp/publication/biblos/index.html)); *Books on Japan* (quarterly, online (www.ndl.go.jp/en/publication/books_on_japan/boi_top_E.html)); *CDNLAO Newsletter*; *Current Awareness*; *Current Awareness-E*; *Kin gendai nihon seiji kankei jinbutsu bunken mokuroku* (Bibliography of Persons in Modern Japanese Politics, online (refsys.ndl.go.jp/hito.nsf/Internet?OpenFrameset)); *NDL Newsletter* (bimonthly, online (www.ndl.go.jp/en/publication/ndl_newsletter/index.html)); *NDL Research Report*; *Nihon kagakugijutsu kankei chikuji kankobutsu soran* (Directory of Japanese Scientific Periodicals, online (refsys.ndl.go.jp/E001_EP01.nsf/PublicE?OpenFrameset)); *Nihon zenkoku shoshi* (Japanese National Bibliography, weekly, online (www.ndl.go.jp/jp/publication/inbwl/inb_top.html)); *Proceedings*; *Refarensu* (Reference, monthly)

**Osaka Prefectural Nakanoshima Library**
1-2-10 Nakanoshima, Kita-ku, Osaka 530
*Tel:* (06) 6203-0474 *Fax:* (06) 2034914
*Web Site:* www.library.pref.osaka.jp
*Key Personnel*
Head Librarian: Shigemitsu Nakayama
Founded: 1904

**Osaka University Library**
1-4 Machikaneyama, Toyonaka, Osaka 560-0043
*Tel:* (06) 6850-5066 *Fax:* (06) 6850-5069
*Web Site:* www.library.osaka-u.ac.jp
*Key Personnel*
Dir, Library Services: Takeshi Hayashi

**Tenri Central Library**
Tenri University, 1050 Soma-no-uchi, Tenri, Nara 632-8577
*Tel:* (0743) 63-9200 *Fax:* (0743) 63-7728
*E-mail:* info@tcl.gr.jp
*Web Site:* www.tcl.gr.jp
*Key Personnel*
Chief Librarian: Keiichiro Moroi

**Tohoku University Library**
UN Depository Library, Kawauchi, Aoba-ku, Sendai 980-8576
*Tel:* (022) 217 5943; (0221) 217 4844
*Fax:* (0222) 217 5949; (0222) 217846

*E-mail:* fetsu1@library.tohoku.ac.jp
*Web Site:* www.library.tohoku.ac.jp

**Tokyo Metropolitan Central Library**
5-7-13 Minami-Azabu, Minato-ku, Tokyo 106-8575
*Tel:* (03) 3442-8451 *Fax:* (03) 3447-8924
*Web Site:* www.library.metro.tokyo.jp/
*Key Personnel*
Dir: Okabe Kazukuni
Founded: 1973

**The Toyo Bunko**
2-28-21 Honkomagome, Bunkyo-ku, Tokyo 113 0021
*Tel:* (03) 39420121 *Fax:* (03) 39420258
*E-mail:* webmaster@toyo-bunko.or.jp
*Web Site:* www.toyo-bunko.or.jp
*Key Personnel*
Dir: Yoshinobu Shiba
Founded: 1917
Also Centre for East Asian Cultural Studies for UNESCO, for which publications include various directories, bibliographies & monographs.
Publication(s): *Asian Research Trends: A Humanities & Social Science Review* (journal, annually); *Memoirs of the Research Department of the Toyo Bunko* (journal, annually)

**University of Tokyo Library**
7-3-1, Hongo, Bunkyo-ku, Tokyo 113-0033
*Tel:* (03) 5841 2612 *Fax:* (03) 3816 4208
*E-mail:* kikaku@lib.u-tokyo.ac.jp
*Web Site:* www.lib.u-tokyo.ac.jp
*Key Personnel*
Dir: K Rodumoto

**Waseda University Library**
1-6-1 Nishi-waseda, Shinjuku-ku, Tokyo 169-8050
*Tel:* (03) 32034141
*E-mail:* info@wul.waseda.ac.jp
*Web Site:* www.wul.waseda.ac.jp
*Telex:* 2323280
*Key Personnel*
Librarian: T Hamada
Publication(s): *Bulletin of Waseda University Library*

# Jordan

**Amman Public Library**
PO Box 182181, Amman
*Tel:* (06) 637 111 *Fax:* (06) 649420
*Telex:* 21969 Amcity Jo
*Key Personnel*
City Librarian: Abdul-Fattah Al-Homran
Founded: 1960

**British Council Library**
Rainbow St, First Circle, Jebel Amman, Amman 11118
Mailing Address: PO Box 634, Amman 11118
*Tel:* (06) 4636147; (06) 4636148 *Fax:* (06) 4656413
*E-mail:* information@britishcouncil.org.jo
*Web Site:* www.britishcouncil.org.jo
*Key Personnel*
Information Officer: Sonia Kawas *E-mail:* sonia.kawas@britishcouncil.org.jo
Founded: 1950

**The Department of the National Library**
King Talal Circle (3rd Circle) Jabal Amman, Al-Hussein Bin Ali St, Amman
*Tel:* (06) 4610311 *Fax:* (06) 4616832
*E-mail:* nl@nic.net.jo

*Web Site:* www.nl.gov.jo
*Key Personnel*
Dir General: Ousama Mikadi

## Jordan University of Science & Technology Library
PO Box 3030, Irbid 22110
*Tel:* (02) 295111 *Fax:* (02) 295123
*Web Site:* www.just.edu.jo
*Telex:* 21629
*Key Personnel*
Dir: Dr Issa Lallu
Founded: 1986

## Mu'tah University Library
PO Box 5, Al-Karak 61710
*Tel:* (03) 2372380; (03) 2372399 *Fax:* (03) 2375703
*E-mail:* libdir@mutah.edu.jo
*Web Site:* www.mutah.edu.jo
*Telex:* 63003 Mu'tah JO
*Key Personnel*
Dir: Dr AbdelWahab Mobideen *E-mail:* libdir@mutah.edu.jo
Assistant Dir: Mohammad Al-Sarireh
Founded: 1984

## Public Library
PO Box 348, Irbid 1957
*Key Personnel*
Librarian: Anwar Ishaq Al-Nshiwat

## Royal Scientific Society Library
Building Research Centre, PO Box 1438, Amman 11941
*Tel:* (06) 5344701 *Fax:* (06) 5344806
*Web Site:* www.rss.gov.jo
*Telex:* 21276 RAMAH
*Key Personnel*
Dir: Khaled Kahhaleh, PhD *E-mail:* kahhaleh@rss.gov.jo

## University of Jordan Library
University of Jordan, Amman 11942
*Tel:* 5355000 (ext 3135) *Fax:* 5355570
*E-mail:* library@ju.edu.jo
*Web Site:* www.ju.edu.jo
*Telex:* 21629 Unvj jo
*Key Personnel*
Acting Dir: Dr Salah Jarrar
Founded: 1962
Publication(s): *Al-Maktaba* (monthly, newsletter); *Arab References till 1980* (in Arabic); *Jordanian Publications in 1982*; *The Library Guide* (in English & Arabic); *Periodical Holdings* (in English & Arabic)

## Yarmouk University Library
Irbid
*Tel:* (02) 7211111 (ext 2871) *Fax:* (02) 7211124
*E-mail:* yarmouk@yu.edu.jo
*Web Site:* www.yu.edu.jo; library.yu.edu.jo
*Telex:* 51566 Yarmuk Jo *Cable:* Yarmouk Jordan
*Key Personnel*
Dir: Dr Muhammad Saraireh *Tel:* (02) 7211111 (ext 2870) *E-mail:* saraireh@yu.edu.jo
Founded: 1976
Specialize in education/library.

# Kazakstan

## Kazakhstan Academy of Sciences
National Academy of Sciences of the Republic of Kazakhstan, 28 Shevchenko St, Almaty 480021
*Tel:* (03272) 624871 *Fax:* (03272) 62500
*E-mail:* teta@nursat.kz

*Web Site:* www.president.kz
*Key Personnel*
Dir: K K Abugalieva

# Kenya

## Egerton University Library
PO Box 536, Njoro
*Tel:* (051) 62265; (051) 62491; (051) 62389; (051) 62278 *Fax:* (051) 62527
*E-mail:* info@egerton.ac.ke
*Web Site:* www.egerton.ac.ke
*Telex:* 33075
*Key Personnel*
University Librarian: Sylvester C Otenya
Founded: 1939
Publication(s): *Egerton University Journal*

## Kenya Agricultural Research Institute
PO Box 57811, Karihq, Nairobi
*Tel:* (02) 583301-20 *Fax:* (02) 583344
*E-mail:* resource.centre@kari.org
*Web Site:* www.hridir.org
*Key Personnel*
Head Librarian: Vivienne Ochieng
  *E-mail:* vivienneo@kari.org

## Kenya National Archives & Documentation Service
Kenya National Archives Bldg, Moi Ave, Nairobi 00100
Mailing Address: PO Box 49210, Nairobi 00100
*Tel:* (02) 228959 *Fax:* (02) 228020
*E-mail:* knarchives@kenyaweb.com
*Web Site:* www.kenyarchives.go.ke
*Telex:* 228020 *Cable:* ARCHIVES
*Key Personnel*
Dir: Musila Musembi
Librarian: Wekalao Namande
Founded: 1946
Publication(s): *Acquisitions guides*

## Kenya National Library Service
Ngong Rd, Nairobi
Mailing Address: PO Box 30573, Nairobi 60100
*Tel:* (02) 725550; (02) 725551; (02) 718177; (02) 718012; (02) 718013 *Fax:* (02) 721749
*E-mail:* knls@nbnet.co.ke
*Web Site:* www.knls.or.ke *Cable:* KENLIB
*Key Personnel*
Dir: S K Ng'anga
Founded: 1969
Publication(s): *Kenya National Bibliography*; *Kenya Periodicals Directory*

## Kenya Polytechnic Library
Haile Selassie Ave, Nairobi
Mailing Address: PO Box 52428, Nairobi
*Tel:* (02) 338231; (02) 338232 *Fax:* (02) 219689
*Key Personnel*
Librarian: P Okoth

## Kenya School of Law
PO Box 30369, Nairobi
*Tel:* (02) 715895 *Fax:* (02) 714783
*Key Personnel*
Chief Librarian: Peter Okoth

## Kenya Technical Teachers' College Library (KTTC)
Gigiri, PO Box 44600, Nairobi
*Tel:* (02) 520211-5 *Fax:* (02) 520037
*Key Personnel*
Librarian: G M King'ori
Publication(s): *Mwalimu Kenya Education Supplement* (monthly); *Secondary School Library*

*Facilities in Central Province, Kenya*; *Serials Literature, Exploitation & Use in Libraries*; *The Problems of Providing Library Services to School Children in Developing Countries*

## Kenyatta University Library
PO Box 43844, Nairobi
*Tel:* (02) 810901 *Fax:* (02) 811575
*E-mail:* info@ku.ac.ke
*Telex:* 25483
*Key Personnel*
Librarian: Alice R Bulogosi *E-mail:* arbulogosi@avu.org
Publication(s): *Directory of Research in the University*; *Education in Kenya: an Index* (1984); *Education in Kenya since Independence: a bibliography* (1963-1983)

## McMillan Memorial Library
Banda St, Nairobi
*Tel:* (02) 21844
*Key Personnel*
Chief Librarian: A O Esilaba
Founded: 1931

## Mines & Geological Department Library
Ministry of Environment & Natural Resources, Machakos Rd, Nairobi
Mailing Address: PO Box 30009, Nairobi
*Tel:* (02) 229261; (02) 541040 *Fax:* (02) 216951
  *Cable:* Mineralogy
*Key Personnel*
Commissioner: C Y O Owayo

## Ministry of Agriculture & Livestock Development Marketing Library
Kilimo House, Cathedral Rd, Nairobi
Mailing Address: PO Box 30028, Nairobi
*Tel:* (02) 718-870 *Fax:* (02) 725-774
*Telex:* 22766 minag ke
Under the charge of The Library Services Co-ordinator.
Publication(s): *Economic Review of Agriculture*

## Mombasa Polytechnic Library
Tom Mboya Ave, Mombasa
Mailing Address: PO Box 90420, Mombasa
*Tel:* (011) 492222 *Fax:* (011) 495632
*E-mail:* msapoly@africaonline.com
*Key Personnel*
Librarian: R Kasina
Founded: 1972

## National Public Health Laboratory Services (Medical Department)
Ministry of Health, Afya House, Cathedral Rd, Nairobi
Mailing Address: PO Box 30016, Nairobi
*Tel:* (02) 717077
*E-mail:* healthmin@nbnet.co.ke
*Web Site:* www.ministryofhealth.go.ke
*Key Personnel*
Dir: Dr Jack Nyamongo

## University of Nairobi Libraries
PO Box 30197, Nairobi
*Tel:* (02) 318262 *Fax:* (02) 336885
*E-mail:* jkml@uonbi.ac.ke
*Web Site:* library.uonbi.ac.ke
*Telex:* 22095-Varsity KE *Cable:* VARSITY NAIROBI
*Key Personnel*
University Librarian: Salome W Mathangani
  *Tel:* (02) 318262 (ext 28501) *E-mail:* salma@uonbi.ac.ke
Specialize in supporting study, teaching & research needs of the University of Nairobi.
*Branch Office(s)*
Chiromo Library, College of Biological & Physical Sciences, Chiromo, Nairobi *Tel:* (02) 43181-90

Kabete Library, PO Box 30197, College of Agriculture & Veterinary Sciences, Kabete, Nairobi *Tel:* (02) 632211; (02) 631340
ADD, State House Road, Nairobi *Tel:* (02) 724520/5 (Architecture Design & Development)
Kikuyu Library, College of Education & External Studies, PO Box 92, Kikuyu *Tel:* (02) 32021; (02) 32016; (02) 31117-8
Lower Kabete Library, Lower Kabete, Nairobi *Tel:* (02) 732160/5
Parklands Law Library, Parklands Campus, Parklands, Nairobi *Tel:* (02) 340859; (02) 340858; (02) 340477
Medical, Ngong Rd, Nairobi *Tel:* (02) 726300

**Upper Kabete Library**
PO Box 30197, Nairobi
*Tel:* (02) 631353 *Fax:* (02) 336885
*Web Site:* library.uonbi.ac.ke
*Key Personnel*
College Librarian: S N Munavu

# Democratic People's Republic of Korea

**Grand People's Study House**
PO Box 200, Pyongyang
*Tel:* (02) 84 4066
*Key Personnel*
Contact: Mr Choe Gwang Ryol
Founded: 1982

# Republic of Korea

**Dongguk University Central Library**
26, 3-ga, Pil-dong, Chung-gu, Seoul 100-715
*Tel:* (02) 2260-3114 *Fax:* (02) 2277-1274
*E-mail:* dong0104@dongguk.edu
*Web Site:* lib.dgu.ac.kr; www.dongguk.edu

**Ewha Womans University Central Library**
11-1 Daehyun-dong, Seodaemun-gu, Seoul 120-750
*Tel:* (02) 3277-3131 *Fax:* (02) 3277-2856
*E-mail:* infoserv@ewha.ac.kr
*Web Site:* lib.ewha.ac.kr
*Key Personnel*
Librarian: Bong Hee Kim

**Korea Development Institute Library**
207-41, Chongnyangri-Dong, Dongdaemun-gu, Seoul 130-012
Mailing Address: PO Box 113, Chongnyang, Seoul 130-012
*Tel:* (02) 958 4266 *Fax:* (02) 958 4261
*E-mail:* library@kdi.re.kr
*Web Site:* www.kdi.re.kr
*Key Personnel*
Chief Librarian: Hwajin Yoon
Founded: 1971
Economics Research Institution.

**Korea University Library**
1, 5-Ka Anam-dong, Sungbuk-ku, Seoul 136-701
*Tel:* (02) 3290-1499 *Fax:* (02) 3234-763
*E-mail:* unneu@korea.ac.kr; libweb@korea.ac.kr
*Web Site:* library.korea.ac.kr

**Kyungpook National University Central Library**
1370 Sangyeok-dong, Buk-gu, Daegu 702-701
*Tel:* (053) 950-6510 *Fax:* (053) 950-6533
*E-mail:* mspark@kyungpook.ac.kr
*Web Site:* kudos.knu.ac.kr
*Key Personnel*
Dir: Chong-moon Seo *Tel:* (053) 955-5516
    *E-mail:* cmseo@kyungpook.ac.kr

**National Assembly Library**
Youido-dong 1, Yeongdeungpo-gu, Seoul 150-703
*Tel:* (02) 788-4101 (english service available)
    *Fax:* (02) 7884301; (02) 7884193
*E-mail:* question@nanet.go.kr
*Web Site:* www.nanet.go.kr
*Telex:* 25849
*Key Personnel*
Librarian: Bae Yong Soo
Publication(s): *Acquisition List (in Korean)* (bimonthly & annually); *Index to Korean-Language Periodicals (in Korean)* (bimonthly & annually); *Index to Korean Laws and Statutes (in Korean)* (biennially); *Index to National Assembly Debates (in Korean)* (irregularly); *Index to Recent Periodical Articles of Major Interests (in Korean)* (monthly); *Issue Briefs (in Korean)* (irregularly); *Legislative Information Analysis (in Korean)* (quarterly); *List of Theses for Doctors' and Masters' Degrees Awarded in Korea (in Korean)* (annually); *National Assembly Library Review (in Korean)* (bimonthly)

**The National Library of Korea**
San 60-1 Banpo-Dong, Seocho-Gu, Seoul 137-702
*Tel:* (02) 535-4142 *Fax:* (02) 590-0530
*E-mail:* yeolram@www.nl.go.kr
*Web Site:* www.nl.go.kr
*Key Personnel*
Dir: Kim Tae Geun
Librarian: Hyun_Taek Shin
Publication(s): *Bibliographie Index of Korea*; *Korean National Bibliography*
*Branch Office(s)*
635 Yeoksam-dong, Kangnam-gu, Seoul

**Seoul National University Library**
San 56-1, Shillim-dong, Kwanak-gu, Seoul 151-749
*Tel:* (02) 880-8001 *Fax:* (02) 878-2730
*E-mail:* libhelp@snu.ac.kr
*Web Site:* library.snu.ac.kr
*Key Personnel*
Library Dir: Nam-Jin Huh *Tel:* (02) 880-5280
    *E-mail:* libdir@snu.ac.kr

**United Nations Depository Library**
1, 5ka Anam-dong, Sungbuk-gu, Seoul 136-701
*Tel:* 23 290 1499 *Fax:* 29 234 763
*E-mail:* unneu@korea.ac.kr
*Web Site:* library.korea.ac.kr
*Key Personnel*
Chief Librarian: Kim Deoug Hoon

**Yonsei University Library**
134 Shinchon-dong, Seodaemun-gu, Seoul 120-749
*Tel:* (02) 2123-3486 *Fax:* (02) 393-7272
*E-mail:* ewebmaster@yonsei.ac.kr
*Web Site:* library.yonsei.ac.kr
*Key Personnel*
Dir: Prof Young-mee Chung

# Kuwait

**Kuwait University Library**
PO Box 5969, 13060 Safat
*Tel:* 4813182 *Fax:* 4816095
*Web Site:* www.kuniv.edu.kw
*Telex:* 22616
*Key Personnel*
Dir: Dr Husain A Al-Ansari
Publication(s): *The Library Bulletin*

**National Library of Kuwait**
Mubarakiya St, (Opposite) Al-Muzaini Exchange, Kuwait City
Mailing Address: PO Box 26182, 13122 Safat
*Tel:* 2415192 *Fax:* 2415195
*E-mail:* nccalknl@ncc.moc.kw *Cable:* Thaquf
*Key Personnel*
Dir General: Wafa'a H Al-Sane
Founded: 1994
National Depository, ISBN, UN Depository.
*Parent Company:* National Council for Culture, Arts & Letters

**National Scientific & Technical Information Center (NSTIC)**
Kuwait Institute for Scientific Research, 13109 Safat
Mailing Address: PO Box 24885, 13109 Safat
*Tel:* 4836100; 4818630 *Fax:* 4830643
*E-mail:* public_relations@safat.kisr.edu.kw
*Web Site:* www.kisr.edu.kw/nstic_intro.asp
*Telex:* Kisr Kt 22299 *Cable:* SCIENCE KUWAIT
*Key Personnel*
Deputy Dir: Mrs Ferial Al-Freih

**NSTIC**, see National Scientific & Technical Information Center (NSTIC)

# Laos People's Democratic Republic

**Bibliotheque Nationale** (Bibliotheque nationale du Laos)
PO Box 122, Vientiane
*Tel:* (021) 212 452 *Fax:* (021) 212 408
Founded: 1957

# Latvia

**LNB**, see National Library of Latvia

**National Library of Latvia** (Latvijas Nacionala Biblioteka)
Kr Barona 14 Str, Riga LV 1423
*Tel:* 7365 250; 7287 620 *Fax:* 7280 851
*E-mail:* lnb@lnb.lv
*Web Site:* www.lnb.lv
*Key Personnel*
Dir: Mr Andris Vilks *E-mail:* andrisv@lbi.lnb.lv
Founded: 1919
The National Library of Latvia is the keeper of all printed matter of the Republic of Latvia, the developer of national bibliographic resources & the center for development of a system of state libraries. NLL, coordinating with other libraries, forms a depository of national literature

& performs the functions of an interlibrary loan center in Latvia.
Publication(s): *Latviesu zinatne un literatura*; *Latvijas preses hronika*

# Lebanon

**American University of Beirut Libraries**
Bliss St, Riad El Solh, Beirut 1107 2020
Mailing Address: PO Box 11-0236, Riad El Solh, Beirut 1107 2020
*Tel:* (01) 340460 *Fax:* (01) 744703
*E-mail:* library@aub.edu.lb
*Web Site:* www.aub.edu.lb/
*Telex:* 20801 *Cable:* AMUNOB
*Key Personnel*
University Librarian: Helen Bikhazi
  *E-mail:* hb02@aub.edu.lb
Constituent Libraries: Jafet Memorial Library (Central Library), Farm Library; Science & Agriculture Library; Engineering & Architecture Library.

**Library of Beirut Arab University**
PO Box 11-5020, Beirut 1107 2089
*Tel:* (01) 300110 *Fax:* (01) 818402
*E-mail:* bau@inco.com.lb
*Web Site:* www.bau.edu.lb

**Bibliotheque de l'Ecole Superieure des Lettres**
rue de Damas, BP 1931, Beirut

**Bibliotheque des Sciences Medicales**
Campus des Sciences Medicales, Rue de Damas, BP 11-5076 Riyad El-Solh, Beirut
*Tel:* (01) 614001-2 *Fax:* (01) 614054
*E-mail:* csm.biblio@usj.edu.lb
*Web Site:* www.biblio-csm.usj.edu.lb
*Key Personnel*
Librarian: Joseph Chebli
*Parent Company:* Universite Saint Joseph

**Ecole Superieure d'Ingenieurs de Beyrouth (ESIB)**
Universite de St Joseph (USJ), Campus des sciences et technologies, Mar Rou Kos-Mkalles, Beirut 1107 2050
Mailing Address: BP 11-514, Riad El Solh, Beirut 1107 2050
*Tel:* (04) 532661 *Fax:* (04) 532645
*E-mail:* esib@usj.edu.lb
*Web Site:* www.fi.usj.edu.lb
*Key Personnel*
Dir: Wajdi Najem
*Parent Company:* Universite Saint Joseph de Beyrouth

**ESIB**, see Ecole Superieure d'Ingenieurs de Beyrouth (ESIB)

**Library of the Faculty of Law**
Universite St Joseph, Rue Huvelin, Mar Michael, Beirut 1104 2020
Mailing Address: BP 17-5208, Mar Michael, Beirut 1104 2020
*Tel:* (01) 200 625 *Fax:* (01) 215473
*E-mail:* css.biblio@usj.edu.lb
*Web Site:* www.biblio-css.usj.edu.lb
*Key Personnel*
Contact: Georges Chahwan
Publication(s): *Proche-Orient, Etudes Juridiques*

**Bibliotheque de l'Institut Francais d'Archeologie du Proche Orient**
Rue de Damas, Orient, Beirut

*Tel:* (01) 615 844; (01) 615 844 *Fax:* (01) 615 866
*E-mail:* ifapo@lb.refer.org
*Key Personnel*
Dir: Jean-Marie Dentzer
Publication(s): *Bibliotheque Archeologique et Historique* (147 titles); *Syria, Revue d'art oriental et d'archeologie* (annually, 2 vols)

**Nami C Jafet Memorial Library**, see American University of Beirut Libraries

**Bibliotheque Nationale du Liban**
BP 11-945, Beirut
*Tel:* (01) 862957 *Fax:* (01) 374079

**Library of the Near East School of Theology**
PO Box 13-5780, Chouran, Beirut
*Tel:* (01) 354194; (01) 349901 *Fax:* (01) 347129
*E-mail:* nest.lib@inco.com.lb
*Telex:* 44246 NEST LE
*Key Personnel*
Librarian: David A Kerry
Founded: 1932
Publication(s): *Theological Review*

**Library of the Monastery of St-Saviour (Basilian Missionary Order of St-Saviour)**
Saida

**Bibliotheque Orientale** (Oriental Library)
Quartier jesuite, Rue de l'Universite St Joseph, Beirut 1100 2150
Mailing Address: BP 16-6778 - Achrafieh, Beirut 1100 2150
*Tel:* (01) 202 421 *Fax:* (01) 339 287
*E-mail:* bo@usj.edu.lb
*Web Site:* www.usj.edu.lb
*Key Personnel*
Dir: May Seeman Seigneurie
Founded: 1875
University Research Library.
Publication(s): *Melanges de l'Universite Saint-Joseph (1906-)*
*Parent Company:* Compagnie de Jesus-Beyrouth (Beirut)
*Ultimate Parent Company:* Universite Saint-Joseph-Beyrouth

# Lesotho

**British Council Library**
Hobson's Sq, Maseru 100
Mailing Address: PO Box 429, Maseru 100
*Tel:* 312609 *Fax:* 310363
*E-mail:* general.enquiries@bc-lesotho.bcouncil.org
*Key Personnel*
Library Supervisor: Zanedde Nsibirwa

**Lesotho National Library Service**
PO Box 985, Maseru 100
*Tel:* 322 592; 323 100 *Fax:* 323 100
*Telex:* 4228
*Key Personnel*
Librarian: Ms Dikeledi J Setlogelo
Founded: 1976

**National University of Lesotho Library**
PO Roma 180, Maseru
*Tel:* 340601; 213426 *Fax:* 340000
*Web Site:* www.nul.ls/library/default.htm
*Telex:* 4303 10 *Cable:* UNITER

*Key Personnel*
Acting University Librarian: M M Moshoeshoe-Chadzingwa
Acting Department Librarian: Samuel M Mohai
  *E-mail:* s.mohai@nul.ls

# Liberia

**Cuttington University College Library**
Episcopal Church of Liberia, 1000 Monrovia 10
Mailing Address: PO Box 10-0277, 1000 Monrovia 10
*Tel:* 227-413 *Fax:* 226-059
*E-mail:* cuttingtonuniversity@yahoo.com
*Web Site:* www.cuttington.org

**Government Public Library**
Ashmun St, Monrovia

**University of Liberia Libraries**
PO Box 9020, Monrovia
*Tel:* 226 418 *Fax:* 227 033; 226 418
*Web Site:* www.hometown.aol.com/dcronteh/myhomepage/index.html
*Key Personnel*
Dir: Dr C Wesley Armstrong

# Libyan Arab Jamahiriya

**Benghazi Public Library**
Shar a Umar al-Mukhtar, Benghazi
*Tel:* (061) 96379

**Al-Fateh University, The Central Library**
PO Box 13482, Tripoli
*Tel:* (022) 605441 *Fax:* (022) 605460
*Telex:* 20629
*Key Personnel*
University Librarian: Dr Mohamed Abdul Jaleel

**Government Library**
14 Shar'a al-Jazair, Tripoli

**National Archives**
Castello, Tripoli
*Tel:* (021) 40 166
Founded: 1928

**National Library of Libya**
PO Box 9127, Benghazi
*Tel:* (061) 9097074 *Fax:* (061) 9096380
*E-mail:* nat_lib_libya@hotmail.com
*Web Site:* www.nll.8m.com
*Telex:* 40107

**University of Garyounis Library**
PO Box 1308, Benghazi
*Tel:* (061) 2220147 *Fax:* (061) 2229602
*E-mail:* info@garyounis.eu
*Web Site:* www.garyounis.edu
*Telex:* 40175 unigarly
*Key Personnel*
Librarian: Ahmed M Gallal
Founded: 1955

# Liechtenstein

**Liechtensteinische Landesbibliothek**
Gerberweg 5, 9490 Vaduz
Mailing Address: Postfach 385, 9490 Vaduz
*Tel:* 236 63 62 *Fax:* 233 14 19
*E-mail:* info@landesbibliothek.li
*Web Site:* www.lbfl.li
*Key Personnel*
Librarian: Barbara Vogt
Founded: 1961
National Library.
Publication(s): *Liechtensteinische Bibliographie*

# Lithuania

**Martynas Mazvydas National Library of Lithuania (Lietuvos Nacionaline Martyno Mazvydo Biblioteka)**
Gedimino Ave 51, 01504 Vilnius
*Tel:* (5) 2497023 *Fax:* (5) 2496129
*E-mail:* biblio@lnb.lt
*Web Site:* www.lnb.lt
*Key Personnel*
Dir: Vytautas Gudaitis
Deputy Dir: Algirdas Plioplys; Dr Regina Varniene; Genovaite Sablauskiene
Founded: 1919
Library & information services.
Publication(s): *Bibliografijos Zinios* (Bibliographical News, monthly, 1947, Indices of current national bibliography); *Lietuvos Spaudos Statistika* (Lithuanian Press Statistics, annually, 1981, Publishing statistics); *Nacionalines Bibliografijos Duomenu Bankas (NBDB)* (National Bibliographic Data Bank (NBDB), online database); *Tarp Knygu* (In the World of Books, monthly, journal, 1949, Professional journal for librarians)

**Vilnius University Library** (Vilniaus Universiteto Biblioteka)
Universiteto 3, 01122 Vilnius
*Tel:* (5) 2687101 *Fax:* (5) 2687104
*E-mail:* mb@mb.vu.lt
*Web Site:* www.mb.vu.lt
*Key Personnel*
Dir & Librarian: B Butkeviciene *E-mail:* birute.butkeviciene@mb.vu.lt
Founded: 1570
Membership(s): Lithuanian Academic Libraries Association.

# Luxembourg

**Bibliotheque de la Ville**
26, rue Emile Mayrisch, 4240 Esch/Alzette
*Tel:* 54 73 83-496 *Fax:* 55 20 37
*Key Personnel*
Librarian: Fernand Roeltgen

**Bibliotheque nationale de Luxembourg** (National Library of Luxembourg)
37, Bd F D Roosevelt, 2450 Luxembourg
*Tel:* 22 97 55-1 *Fax:* 47 56 72
*E-mail:* bib.nat@bi.etat.lu
*Web Site:* www.bnl.lu
*Key Personnel*
Dir: Dr Monique Kieffer
Publication(s): *Bibliographie d'histoire luxembourgeoise*; *Bibliographie luxembourgeoise*

**Archives Nationales du Grand-Duche de luxembourg** (National Archives)
Plateau du St-Esprit, 2010 Luxembourg
Mailing Address: BP 6, 2010 Luxembourg
*Tel:* 4786660; 4786661 *Fax:* 474692
*E-mail:* archives.nationales@an.etat.lu
*Web Site:* www.etat.lu
*Key Personnel*
Dir: Dr Cornel Meder
Publication(s): *Publications des Anlux, Plusieurs Series* (catalogs, repertories, reprints)

# Macau

**Biblioteca Central de Macau**
Av Conselheiro Ferreira de Almeida No 89A-B, Macao
*Tel:* 567576; 558049 *Fax:* 318756
*Key Personnel*
Chief Librarian: Ophelia Tang
Publication(s): *Boletim Bibliografico de Macau*

# The Former Yugoslav Republic of Macedonia

**Arhiv na Makedonija** (Archives of Macedonia)
Grigor Prlichev, 3, 91000 Skopje
*Tel:* (091) 237-211; (091) 115-783; (091) 115-827 *Fax:* (091) 165-944
*Web Site:* www.arhiv.gov.mk
*Key Personnel*
Dir: Kiro Dojcinovski
Founded: 1951

**Narodna i univerzitetska biblioteka Kliment Ohridski** ('Kliment Ohridski' National & University Library)
bul "Goce Delcev" 6, 91000 Skopje
*Tel:* (02) 3115 177; (02) 3133 418 *Fax:* (02) 3226 846
*E-mail:* kliment@nubsk.edu.mk
*Web Site:* www.nubsk.edu.mk
Publication(s): *Bibliografija KPJ-SKM 1919-1979; Bilten na izdanija od oblasta na samoupravuvanjeto vo Jugoslavija; Katalog na staropecateni i retki knigi vo Narodnata i Univerzitetskata Biblioteka 'Kliment Ohridski' - Skopje; Makedonska Bibliografija*

# Madagascar

**Bibliotheque Universitaire d'Antananarivo**
Campus Universitaire d'Ankatso, PO Box 908, 101 Tananrive
*Tel:* (020) 22 612 28 *Fax:* (020) 22 612 29
*E-mail:* bu@univ-antananarivo.mg
*Web Site:* www.univ-antananarivo.mg
*Key Personnel*
Dir: Jean-Marie Andrianiaina
Founded: 1960
Publication(s): *Bibliographie annuelle de Madagascar*

**Bibliotheque du Centre Culturel Albert Camus**
14 ave de l'Independance, 101 Tananrive
Mailing Address: BP 488, 101 Tananrive
*Tel:* 22 213 75; 22 236 47 *Fax:* 22 213 38
*E-mail:* medccac@dts.ng
*Telex:* 22507
*Key Personnel*
Contact: Singare Reinhard Veionique

**Bibliotheque Nationale Malagasy**
BP 257, Anosy, Tananrive
*Tel:* (02) 25872 *Fax:* (02) 22-9448
*Key Personnel*
Dir: Mr Louis-Dominique Ralaisaholimanana
Contact: Mr Roland Franck Ranaivoson

**Bibliotheque Municipale**
Av du 18 juin, Tananrive
Mailing Address: BP 729, Tananrive
*Tel:* (04) 21176
*Key Personnel*
President: Julien Razafimandimbilaza
Librarian: Albert Denis Rakoto

**Archives Nationales de Madagascar**
23 rue Karija Tsaralalana, 101 Tananrive
Mailing Address: BP 3384, 101 Tananrive
*Tel:* (020) 22 235 34
*E-mail:* rijandriamihamina@malagasy.com
*Key Personnel*
Dir: Mdme Sahondra Andriamihamina

# Malawi

**British Council Library**
PO Box 30222, Lilongwe 3
*Tel:* (01) 773244 *Fax:* (01) 772945
*E-mail:* info@britishcouncil.org.mw
*Web Site:* www.britishcouncil.org/malawi.htm
*Telex:* 44476 Bricoun Ml
*Key Personnel*
Dir: Brendan Barker *E-mail:* brendan.barker@britishcouncil.org.mw

**Bunda College of Agriculture Library**
PO Box 219, Lilongwe
*Tel:* (01) 277222 *Fax:* (01) 277251
*E-mail:* bundalibrary@bunda.sdnp.org.mw
*Web Site:* www.bunda.unima.mw/library.htm
*Telex:* 43622 Bunda MI *Cable:* BUNDAGRIC
*Key Personnel*
College Librarian: Geoffrey F Salanje
*Parent Company:* Bunda College of Agriculture, University of Malawi

**Malawi National Library Service**
PO Box 30314, Lilongwe, Lilongwe Central Region 3
*Tel:* 773 700 *Fax:* 771 616
*E-mail:* nls@malawi.net
*Key Personnel*
National Librarian: R S Mabomba

**National Archives of Malawi**
PO Box 62, Zomba
*Tel:* 525 240 *Fax:* 524 089; 525 240
*E-mail:* archives@sdnp.org.mw
*Web Site:* chambo.sdnp.org.mw/ruleoflaw/archives
*Key Personnel*
Acting Dir/Sr Librarian: O W Ambali
Publication(s): *Malawi National Bibliography*

**University of Malawi Libraries**
PO Box 278, Zomba
*Tel:* (01) 526 622; (01) 524 297
*E-mail:* university.office@unima.mw
*Web Site:* www.unima.mw

*Telex:* 44742
*Key Personnel*
Librarian: Steve S Mwiyeriwa
 *E-mail:* smwiyeriwa@unima.wn.apc.org;
 smwiyeriwa@chirunga.sdnp.org.mw
Founded: 1965
Publication(s): *An Annotated Bibliography of Education in Malawi*; *Directory of Malawi Libraries*; *Library Bulletin*; *Report on University Libraries*
*Branch Office(s)*
Bunda College of Agriculture Library, PO Box 219, Lilongwe, Geoffrey F Salanje *Tel:* (01) 277222 *Fax:* (01) 277251 *E-mail:* gsalanje@bunda.sdnr.org.mw
Chancellor College Library, PO Box 280, Zomba, D B V Phiri *Tel:* (01) 524 222 *Fax:* (01) 524 046 *E-mail:* dbvphiri@chanco.unima.mw
College of Medicine Library, Private Bag 360, Chichiri, Blantyre 3, Ralph Masanjika *Tel:* (01) 677 441, (01) 671 911 *Fax:* (01) 675 313 *E-mail:* registrar@medcol.mw
Kamuzu College of Nursing Library, Private Bag 1, Lilongwe, Godwin Shaba *Tel:* (01) 751 622 *Fax:* (01) 756 424 *E-mail:* kcnll@sdnp.org.mw
Polytechnic Library, PB 303, Chichiri, Blantyre 3, Felix Mussa *Tel:* (01) 670411 *Fax:* (01) 674710

**University of Malawi, Polytechnic Library**
PB 303, Chichiri, Blantyre 3
*Tel:* (01) 670411 *Fax:* (01) 670578
*Web Site:* www.poly.ac.mw
*Telex:* 44613 Polytec
*Key Personnel*
Librarian: Felix Mussa

# Malaysia

**British Council Library**
Ground floor, West Block Wisma Selangor Dredging, 142C Jalan Ampang, 50450 Kuala Lumpur
*Tel:* (03) 2723 7900 *Fax:* (03) 2713 6599
*E-mail:* information@britishcouncil.org.my
*Web Site:* www.britcoun.org/malaysia
*Telex:* MA 31052
*Key Personnel*
Librarian & Information Services Manager: Ms Gaik Sim Khoo
*Branch Office(s)*
3 Weld Quay, 10300 Penang *Tel:* (04) 263 0330 *Fax:* (04) 263 3262 *E-mail:* penang.enquiries@britishcouncil.org.my
PO Box 10746, 88808 Sabah *Tel:* (088) 222 059 *Fax:* (088) 238 059 *E-mail:* sabah@britishcouncil.org.my
PO Box 2963, 97358 Sarawak *Tel:* (082) 256 044 *Fax:* (082) 425 199 *E-mail:* sarawak@britishcouncil.org.my

**Ministry of Agriculture Library**
Wisma Tani, 1st floor, Jalan Sultan Salahuddin, 50624 Kuala Lumpur
*Tel:* (03) 26954215 (ext 4216, 4217or 4298)
*Fax:* (03) 26932220
*E-mail:* dahlia@agri.moa.my; lht@agri.moa.my; fuziah@agri.moa.my
*Web Site:* agrolink.moa.my/library
*Telex:* TANIAN MA 33045 *Cable:* TANI KUALA LUMPUR
Founded: 1905
Publication(s): *Bulletin of the Ministry of Agriculture* (irregular); *Malaysian Agricultural Journal* (biannual)

**Ministry of Environment & Public Health, Library Division**
Tingkat 2, Wisma Masja, Jalan Medan, 93360 Kuching Sarawak
*Tel:* (082) 319614; (082) 319613 *Fax:* (082) 311216
*E-mail:* info@moeswk.gov.my
*Web Site:* www.moeswk.gov.my
*Key Personnel*
Chief Librarian: Johnny Kueh

**National Archives of Malaysia**
Jalan Duta, 50568 Kuala Lumpur
*Tel:* (03) 6510688 *Fax:* (03) 6515679
*E-mail:* query@arkib.gov.my
*Web Site:* arkib.gov.my *Cable:* ARKIB KUALALUMPUR
*Key Personnel*
Dir-Gen: Mrs Zakiah Hanum Nor
Other publications include Acquisitions List, List of Record & Archives Groups available for researchs bibliographies & others.
Publication(s): *Annual Report of the National Archives* (Bulletins)

**National Library of Malaysia (Gift & Exchange Unit)**
232, Jalan Tun Razak, 50572 Kuala Lumpur
*Tel:* (03) 26871700 *Fax:* (03) 26942490
*E-mail:* pnmweb@www1.pnm.my
*Web Site:* www.pnm.my
*Telex:* MA NATLIB 30092
*Key Personnel*
Dir General: Zawiyah binti Baba
Publication(s): *Bibliography of books in Bahasa Malaysia*; *Directory of Librarians in Malaysia*; *Directory of Libraries in Malaysia*; *Index to Malaysian Conferences* (annually); *Malaysian National Bibliography* (quarterly, annually); *Malaysian Newspaper Index* (quarterly); *Malaysian Periodicals Index* (biannually)

**National University of Malaysia Library**
Universiti Kebangsaan Malaysia, 43600 UKM Bangi, Selangor Darul Ehsan
*Tel:* (03) 8921 3446; (03) 8921 5053 *Fax:* (03) 8925 4890
*E-mail:* puspa@pkrisc.cc.ukm.my
*Web Site:* www.ukm.my
*Telex:* MA 31496
*Key Personnel*
Chief Librarian: Muslim Norsham
 *E-mail:* norsham@pkrisc.cc.ukm.my
Holds Malay Library Collection (approx 30,000 titles).
Publication(s): *Katalog Koleksi Melayu, Penerbit Ukm 1990*

**Perpustakaan Negeri Sabah**, see Sabah State Library

**Perpustakaan Sultanah Zanariah**
Universiti Teknologi Malaysia, 81310 UTM Skudai, Johor
*Tel:* (07) 5533333 *Fax:* (07) 5572555
*E-mail:* psz@utm.my
*Web Site:* www.utm.my
*Telex:* MA 60205 *Cable:* UNITEK MA
*Key Personnel*
Chief Librarian: Rosna Binti Mohd Taib *Tel:* (07) 26154596 *E-mail:* rosna@psz.utm.my
Head Administration & Support Services: Kamariah BTE Nor Mohd Desa *Tel:* (07) 5502107 *E-mail:* kamariah@psz.tum.my
Assistant Registrar: Hazara Binti Sulaiman
 *E-mail:* hazara@mel.psz.utm.my
Publication(s): *Berita Unitek, Berita Satelit*; *Jurnal Teknologi*
*Branch Office(s)*
Kuala Lumpur Campus Branch, Universiti Teknologi Malaysia, Jalan Semarak, 54100

Kuala Lumpur *Tel:* (03) 26154100 *Fax:* (03) 26922186 *Web Site:* www.psz.utm.my/pszkl.html

**Rubber Research Institute of Malaysia Library**
260 Jalan Ampang, 50908 Kuala Lumpur
Mailing Address: PO Box 10150, 50908 Kuala Lumpur
*Tel:* (03) 4567033 *Fax:* (03) 4511301
*Web Site:* w3.itri.org.tw/k0000/apec/malaysia/malay-1.htm
*Telex:* Rrim MA 30369 *Cable:* SEARCHING
*Key Personnel*
Librarian: H S Kaw
Publication(s): *Journal Natural Rubber Research* (Planters' Bulletin)

**Sabah State Library**
Locked Bag 2023, 88999 Kota Kinabalu, Sabah
*Tel:* (088) 214828 *Fax:* (088) 270714
*Web Site:* www.ssl.sabah.gov.my
*Key Personnel*
Contact: Mrs Ku Joo Bee *E-mail:* joobee.ku@sabah.gov.my
Founded: 1953

**SEACEN**, see South East Asian Central Banks (SEACEN) Research & Training Centre

**Selangor Public Library**
c/o Perpustakaan Raja Tun Uda, Persiaran, Bandaraya, 40572 Shah Alam, Selangor
*Tel:* (03) 55197667 *Fax:* (03) 55196045
*E-mail:* ppas@sel.lib.edu.my; jothi@ppas.org.my
*Web Site:* www.ppas.org.my
*Key Personnel*
Dir: Mrs Shahaneem Mustafa

**South East Asian Central Banks (SEACEN) Research & Training Centre**
Lorong Universiti A, 59100 Kuala Lumpur
*Tel:* (03) 7958 5600 *Fax:* (03) 7957 4616
*E-mail:* info@seacen.org
*Web Site:* www.seacen.org
*Key Personnel*
Chief Librarian: Zainon Zubir *E-mail:* zzainon@seacen.po.my

**Tun Razak Library**
Jalan Kelab, 3000 lpoh
*Tel:* (05) 508073
Publication(s): *Accession Lists* (in English, Malay, Chinese & Tamil); *Malaysiana Collection* (plus supplement)

**Library Tun Seri Lanang**
43600 UKM Bangi, Selangor DE
*Tel:* (03) 89213446 *Fax:* (03) 89256067
*E-mail:* kpustaka@pkrisc.cc.ukm.my
*Web Site:* www.ukm.my/library
*Telex:* 34196
Founded: 1970
*Parent Company:* Universiti Kebangsaan Malaysia

**Universiti Putra Malaysia Library (UPM)**
43400 UPM Serdang, Selangor Darul Ehsan
*Tel:* (03) 89468642 *Fax:* (03) 89483745
*E-mail:* lib@lib.upm.edu.my
*Web Site:* www.lib.upm.edu.my
*Telex:* Uniper MA 37454 *Cable:* UNIPERTAMA SUNGAI BESI
*Key Personnel*
Acting Chief Librarian: Badilah Saad *Tel:* (03) 894868601 *E-mail:* badilah@lib.upm.edu.my

**University Library, Universiti Sains Malaysia**
11800 Penang
*Tel:* (04) 6533888; (04) 6533700; (04) 6585518 *Fax:* (04) 6571526
*E-mail:* chieflib@notes.usm.my

*Web Site:* www.lib.usm.my *Cable:* UNISAINS
*Key Personnel*
Acting Chief Librarian: Datin Masrah Abidin
  *Tel:* (04) 6533888 (ext 3728)
Founded: 1969
Publication(s): *Bibliography series* (irregularly);
  *Midas Bulletin* (quarterly)

**University of Malaya Library**
Lembah Pantai, 50603 Kuala Lumpur
*Tel:* (03) 7956 7800 *Fax:* (03) 7957 3661
*E-mail:* query_perpustakaan@um.edu.my
*Web Site:* www.umlib.um.edu.my
*Key Personnel*
Librarian: Ismail Azrizal *E-mail:* azrizal@cc.um.
  edu.my
Publication(s): *Kekal Abadi* (quarterly newsletter);
  *Maklumat Semasa* (monthly)

**University of Technology Malaysia Library**, see
  Perpustakaan Sultanah Zanariah

**UPM**, see Universiti Putra Malaysia Library
  (UPM)

# Mali

**Bibliotheque du Centre Culturel Francais de
  Bamako**
Blvd de l'independance, Bamako
Mailing Address: BP 1547, Bamako
*Tel:* 222 40 19 *Fax:* 222 58 28
*E-mail:* dir@ccfbamako.org
*Web Site:* www.ccfbko.org.ml
*Telex:* 2569
*Key Personnel*
Librarian: Veronique Reinhard-Singare

**Bibliotheque Nationale**
BP 159, Bamako
*Tel:* 22 49 63 *Fax:* 23 59 31
*E-mail:* info@culture.gov.ml
*Web Site:* w3.culture.gov.ml
*Key Personnel*
Dir: Bouna Boukary Diouara
Founded: 1962

**Centre francais de Documentation**, see
  Bibliotheque du Centre Culturel Francais de
  Bamako

**Ecole normale superieure**
BP 241, Bamako
*Tel:* 222189

**Faculte de Medecine de Pharmuacie et
  d'Odonto-Stomatologie**
Bibliotheque, BP 1805, Bamako
*Tel:* 22 52 77 *Fax:* 22 96 58
*E-mail:* codiawara@caramail.com
*Key Personnel*
Librarian: M Cheick Oumar Diawara

# Malta

**Gozo Public Library**
Triq Vajringa, Victoria VCT 105
*Tel:* (021) 556200 *Fax:* (021) 560599
*E-mail:* gozo.libraries@gov.mt
*Web Site:* servicecharters.gov.mt

*Key Personnel*
Librarian: George V Borg *Tel:* (021) 561510
  *E-mail:* george.borg@magnet.mt
Founded: 1853

**National Library of Malta** (Bibljoteka
  Nazzjonali ta' Malta)
36, Old Treasury St, Valletta CMR 02
*Tel:* 21243297; 21236585; 21232691; 21245303
  *Fax:* 21235992
*E-mail:* customercare.nlm@gov.mt
*Web Site:* www.libraries-archives.gov.mt
*Key Personnel*
Librarian: Joseph M Boffa *E-mail:* joseph.boffa@
  magnet.mt
Contact: M Vella
Founded: 1555
Publication(s): *Malta National Bibliography*

**University of Malta Library**
Tal-Qroqq, Msida MSD06
*Tel:* 2340 2316 *Fax:* 21 314 306
*Web Site:* www.lib.um.edu.mt
*Telex:* 407 Hieduc *Cable:* UNIVERSITY MALTA
*Key Personnel*
Dir, Library Services: Anthony Mangion *Tel:* 21
  310 239 *E-mail:* librarian@lib.um.edu.mt

# Martinique

**Archives Departementales de la Martinique**
19 Ave Saint-John-Perse, Tartenson, 97263 Fort
  de France Cedex
Mailing Address: BP 649, Tartenson, 97263 Fort
  de France Cedex
*Tel:* 63 88 46 *Fax:* 70 04 50
*E-mail:* archives@cg972.fr
*Key Personnel*
Dir: Dominique Taffin
Founded: 1949
Publication(s): *Declaration des droits de
  l'homme et abolition de l'esclavage* (1998);
  *L'eglise martiniquaise et la piete populaire*
  (2001); *Enfances martiniquaises* (2001);
  *Guide des Archives de la Martinique* (1978);
  *L'immigration indienne a la Martinique* (2003);
  *Inventaire analytique du Conseil souverain de
  la Martinique - Tome 1* (1985); *Inventaire ana-
  lytique du Conseil souverain de la Martinique
  - Tome 2* (1999); *Inventaire des sources de
  l'esclavage* (1998); *La Martinique de Pierre
  Verger* (2000); *1902 et apres* (2002)

**Bibliotheque Schoelcher**
One Rue de la Liberte, 97200 Fort-de-France
Mailing Address: BP 640, 97262 Fort-de-France
  Cedex
*Tel:* 702 667 *Fax:* 724 555
*E-mail:* biblio-schoelcher-dep@cg972.fr
*Key Personnel*
Librarian: Jacqueline Leger *E-mail:* legerbib@
  cg972.fr
Founded: 1883

# Mauritania

**Arab Library**
Chinguetti
*Key Personnel*
Contact: M Abdallahi Ouid Fall

**Bibliotheque Nationale**
BP 20, Nouakchott
*Tel:* 24 35

**Direction des Archives Nationales, Bibliotheque
  Publique et Centre du Documentation**
ave de l'Independenance, Nouakchott
Mailing Address: BP 77, Nouakchott
*Tel:* 2523 1732
*Telex:* Prim 580 Mtn
*Key Personnel*
Dir: Moktar Ould Hemeina
Founded: 1955

# Mauritius

**British Council Library**
Royal Rd, Rose Hill
*Tel:* 4549550; 4549551; 4549552 *Fax:* 4549553
*E-mail:* general.enquiries@mu.britishcouncil.org
*Web Site:* www.britishcouncil.org/mauritius
*Key Personnel*
Dir: Rosalind Burford *E-mail:* rosalind.burford@
  mu.britishcouncil.org

**Carnegie Library**
Queen Elizabeth II Ave, Curepipe
*Tel:* 670 4897; 670 4898 *Fax:* 676 5054
*E-mail:* contact@curepipe.org
*Web Site:* www.curepipe.org
*Key Personnel*
Senior Librarian: T K Ramnauth *Tel:* 674 2278
Founded: 1920
Large collection of material on historical back-
  ground of Mauritius & original manuscripts,
  papers on colonization by French & British.
*Parent Company:* Municipal Council of Curepipe
*Ultimate Parent Company:* Ministry of Local
  Government & Environment

**City Library**
City Hall, Sir Jules Koenig St, Port Louis
Mailing Address: PO Box 422, Port Louis
*Tel:* 212 0831 (ext 163) *Fax:* 212 4258
*E-mail:* mpllib@intnet.mu
*Web Site:* mpl.intnet.mu *Cable:* CERNE/PORT
  LOUIS
*Key Personnel*
Librarian: Gaetan Benoit
Founded: 1851
Publication(s): *Bibliography: Mauritiana in City
  Library*; *Literary Publishing & Bibliographi-
  cal Control in Mauritius*; *Newspapers Index:
  Mauritius*

**Mauritius Archives**
Development Bank of Mauritius Complex, Coro-
  mandel
*Tel:* 233-4469; 233 7341 *Fax:* 233 4299
*Key Personnel*
Deputy Chief Archivist: Mr Gheeandut Suneechur
Publication(s): *Annual Report of the Archives
  Department* (including a bibliographical sup-
  plement); *Quarterly Memorandum of Books
  Printed in Mauritius and Registered in the
  Archives*

**Mauritius Institute Public Library**
Chaussee St, Port Louis
Mailing Address: PO Box 54, Port Louis
*Tel:* 212 06 39 *Fax:* 212 57 17
*Key Personnel*
Head Librarian: Sewannah Ankiah
Founded: 1970

**University Library**
University of Mauritius, Reduit

*Tel:* 454 1041 (ext 1229) *Fax:* 454 0905
*E-mail:* library@uom.ac.mu
*Web Site:* www.uom.ac.mu
*Telex:* 4621
Publication(s): *Journal of the University of Mauritius* (irregular); *University of Mauritius Calendar*; *University of Mauritius Report* (annually)

# Mexico

## Anglo Mexican Foundation Library
Formerly Biblioteca del Instituto Anglo-Mexicano de Cultura
Antonio Caso No 127, Colonia San Rafael, 06470 Mexico, DF
*Tel:* (05) 566-4500 *Fax:* (05) 566-6739
*E-mail:* biblioteca@tamf.org.mx
*Web Site:* www.theanglo.org.mx; www.tamf.org.mx/tamf/biblioteca.htm
*Telex:* 01772938 Brcome
*Key Personnel*
Head Librarian: Aurora P Vela
Anglo-Mexican Cultural Institute.

## Biblioteca Nacional de Antropologia e Historia
Paseo de la Reforma y Calzada Gandhi s/n, Col Polanco, CP 11560, Mexico, DF
*Tel:* (055) 536231; (055) 536342 *Fax:* (055) 861743
*E-mail:* direccion.bnah@inah.gob.mx
*Web Site:* www.bnah.inah.gob.mx/
*Key Personnel*
Dir: Dr Cesar Moheno
Founded: 1888
*Parent Company:* Instituto Nacional de Antropologia e Historia
*Branch Office(s)*
Subireccion de Documentacion

## Archivo General de la Nacion
Eduardo Molina y Albaniles s/n, Col Penitenciaria Ampliacion Deleg Venustiano Carranza, 15350 Mexico, DF
*Tel:* 5133-9900 *Fax:* 5789-5296
*E-mail:* agn@segob.gob.mx
*Web Site:* www.agn.gob.mx
*Key Personnel*
Dir: Jorge Ruiz Duenas *E-mail:* argena@segob.gob.mx
Publication(s): *Boletin*

## Biblioteca Benjamin Franklin (USIS)
Liverpool 31, Col Juarez, Mexico, DF
Mailing Address: CP 06600, Mexico DF
*Tel:* 5080 2801 (ext 2802 & 2803) *Fax:* (055) 5910075
*E-mail:* garciae@state.gov
*Web Site:* www.usembassy-mexico.gov/biblioteca.htm
Publication(s): *Boletin de Seleccion de Adquisiciones Recientes* (quarterly)

## Biblioteca Central
Campus Chapingo, Km 38 5 Carretera Mexico, CP 56230 Texcoco
*Tel:* (0595) 952-15-00 (exts 7111, 4741 & 5440) *Fax:* (0595) 952-15-01
*E-mail:* biblioteca_central@correo.chapingo.mx
*Web Site:* www.chapingo.mx
*Key Personnel*
Head of Library: Blanca Margarita Garcia Ocampo *E-mail:* blmgaro@chapingo.mx
Head of Consultation Office: Ramon Suarez Espinosa *E-mail:* rsuarez@chapingo.mx
Previously named Escuela Nacional de Agricultura Periodicals. Chapingo, Revista de Geografia Agricola, Textual.

## Biblioteca de Mexico
Plaza de la Ciudadela No 4, Col Centro, CP, 06040 Mexico, DF
*Tel:* (055) 7 09 11 01; (055) 7 09 10 85 *Fax:* (055) 7 09 11 73
*Web Site:* www.cnart.mx/cnca/buena/biblioteca
*Key Personnel*
Librarian: Carmen E de Moreno
Founded: 1946

## Biblioteca Nacional de Mexico
Centro Cultural Universitario, 04510 Delegacion Coyoacan
*Tel:* (05) 622 6800 *Fax:* (05) 665 0951
*E-mail:* liceaj@biblional.bibliog.unam.mx
*Web Site:* biblional.bibliog.unam.mx
*Key Personnel*
Dir: Vicente Quirarte Castaneda
*E-mail:* quirarte@biblional.bibliog.unam.mx
Publication(s): *Bibliografia Mexicana*; *Boletin del Instituto de Investigaciones Bibliograficas* (annually)

## Centro de Informacion Cientifica y Humanistica
Universidad Nacional Autonoma de Mexico, Ciudad Universitaria, Apdo 70-392, 04510 Mexico, DF
*Tel:* (055) 6223960 *Fax:* (055) 6162557
*E-mail:* admin@estadistica.unam.mx
*Telex:* 01774523
*Key Personnel*
Dir: Mtro Juan Voutssas Marquez
Unidad de Bibliotecas de Investigacion Cientifica de la UNAM.

## Biblioteca Francisco Xavier Clavigero, see Biblioteca de la Universidad Iberoamericana

## Biblioteca del Congreso de la Union
Tacuba 29, Centro Historico de la Cuidad de Mexico, 06000 Mexico, DF
*Tel:* (05) 5 10 38 66; (05) 5 12 52 05 *Fax:* (05) 5 12 10 85
*E-mail:* emolina@servidor.unam.mx; emolina@cddhcu.gob.mx
*Web Site:* www.cddhcu.gob.mx/bibcongr

## Direccion General de Bibliotecas de la Universidad Nacional Autonoma de Mexico
Ciudad Universitaria, Circuito Interior, 04510 Mexico, DF
*Tel:* (055) 5622 1603 *Fax:* (055) 5616 0664
*E-mail:* webdgb@dgb.unam.mx
*Web Site:* www.dgbiblio.unam.mx
*Key Personnel*
Librarian: Alberto Castro Thompson
*E-mail:* acastro@servidor.unam.mx
Publication(s): *Biblioteca Universitaria Revista de la Direccion General de Bibliotecas de la UNAM* (biannual, journal, 1986, specializes in library & information science); *Directorio de Bibliotecas UNAM* (monthly, directory for the 139 libraries in UNAM's library system); *Librunam* (database of books existing in UNAM's library system); *Seriunam* (database of journals & serial publications existing in UNAM's library system); *Tesiunam* (database of theses from UNAM & other Mexican universities)

## Hemeroteca Nacional de Mexico
Centro Cultural Universitario, CU, Del Coyoacan, 04510 Mexico, DF
*Tel:* (055) 622 6818 *Fax:* (055) 665 0951
*Web Site:* biblional.bibliog.unam.mx
*Key Personnel*
Dir: Dr Vicente Quirate
National Periodicals Library.

## Biblioteca del Instituto Anglo-Mexicano de Cultura, see Anglo Mexican Foundation Library

## Instituto de Investigaciones Electricas
Reforma St, 113, Palmira, 62490 Cuernavaca, Morelos
*Tel:* (777) 3623811 *Fax:* (777) 3189854
*E-mail:* difusion@iie.org.mx
*Web Site:* www.iie.org.mx
*Telex:* 17-76352 IIEMME
*Key Personnel*
Executive Dir: Oswaldo Gangoiti
*E-mail:* gangoiti@iie.org.mx

## Biblioteca del Instituto Panamericano de Geografia e Historia (Library of the Pan American Institute of Geography & History)
Ex-Arzobispado 29, Col Observatorio, 11860 Mexico, DF
*Tel:* (055) 5277 5888; (055) 5277 5791; (055) 5515 1910 *Fax:* (055) 5271 6172
*E-mail:* info@ipgh.org.mx
*Web Site:* www.ipgh.org.mx
*Key Personnel*
Secretary General: Santiago Borrero Mutis
*E-mail:* secretariageneral@ipgh.org.mx
Publications Coordinator: Jaime Curenom
Publication(s): *Ver Informacion Adjunta*

## Instituto Tecnologico y de Estdios Superiores de Monterrey Biblioteca
Ave Eugenio Garza Sada 2501 Sur, 64849 Monterrey, NL
*Tel:* (081) 8328-4096 *Fax:* (081) 8328-4067
*Web Site:* cib.mty.itesm.mx; biblioteca.itesm.mx
*Key Personnel*
Librarian: Miguel A Arreola
*E-mail:* miguel_arreola@itesm.mx
Publication(s): *Transferencia* (Strategic Studies Center monthly)

## ITESM Biblioteca, see Instituto Tecnologico y de Estdios Superiores de Monterrey Biblioteca

## Biblioteca de la Universidad Iberoamericana
Prol Paseo de la Reforma 880, Lomas de Santa Fe, 01210 Mexico, DF
*Tel:* (055) 5950 4000 *Fax:* (055) 5950 4248
*E-mail:* buzon@uiacia.bib.uia.mx
*Web Site:* www.bib.uia.mx
*Key Personnel*
Dir: Mtro Fernando Alvarez Ortega

## Biblioteca Daniel Cosio Villegas El Colegio de Mexico AC
Camino al Ajusco 20, Col Pedregal Sta Teresa, 10740 Mexico, DF
Mailing Address: Apdo 20-671, 01000 Mexico, DF
*Tel:* (055) 5449 3000; (055) 5449 2909; (055) 5449 2936; (055) 5449 2934 *Fax:* (055) 5645 0464; (055) 5645 4584
*E-mail:* biblio@colmex.mx
*Web Site:* biblio.colmex.mx
*Telex:* 1777585 COLME *Cable:* COLME
*Key Personnel*
Library Dir: Micaela Chavez *E-mail:* mch@colmex.mx
Founded: 1940
Graduate institution for research & education in the social sciences & the humanities.
Publication(s): *Boletin de la BDCV*
*Parent Company:* El Colegio de Mexico

# Monaco

**Bibliotheque Louis Notari** (Library Louis Notari)
8 rue Louis-Notari, 98000 Monaco
*Tel:* (093) 30-95-09 *Fax:* (093) 152941
*Key Personnel*
Dir: Herve Barral
Administrative Sectretary: Catherine Notari

# Mongolia

**State Archives**
Ulan-Bator State Public Library of Mongolia, Chinggis Av 3, Ulan-Bator 11
*Tel:* (01) 323100
*Key Personnel*
Dir: M Bayaizul

# Morocco

**Bibliotheque Generale et Archives du Maroc**
5, Ave Ibn Batouta, CP 1003, Rabat
*Tel.* (07) 77 18 90, (07) 77 21 52 *Fax:* (07) 77 60 62
*E-mail:* biblio1@onpt.net.ma
*Key Personnel*
Librarian: Ahmed Toufiq
Publication(s): *Bibliographie nationale marocaine*

**British Council Library**
36, Rue de Tanger, Rabat
Mailing Address: BP 427, Rabat
*Tel:* (037) 76 08 36 *Fax:* (037) 76 08 50
*E-mail:* bc@britishcouncil.org.ma
*Web Site:* www2.britishcouncil.org/morocco
*Telex:* 36293
*Key Personnel*
Dir: Steve McNulty
British Cultural Centre.
*Branch Office(s)*
87, Blvd Nador, Polo, Casablanca *Tel:* (022) 52 09 90 *Fax:* (022) 52 09 64 *E-mail:* casa.info@britishcouncil.org.ma

**Centre National de Documentation**
Ave Al Haj Ahmed Cherkaoui, 10004 Rabat
Mailing Address: BP 826, 10004 Rabat
*Tel:* (037) 77 49 44 *Fax:* (037) 77 31 34
*E-mail:* cnd@mpep.gov.ma
*Web Site:* www.cndportal.net.ma
*Key Personnel*
Dir: Mr Adnan Benchekroun
Contact: Mr Ahmed Idouba *E-mail:* idouba@cnd.mpep.gov.ma
Publication(s): *voir liste jointe*

**Bibliotheque de la Communaute Urbaine de Casablanca**
142, Av des Forces Armees Royales, Casablanca
*Tel:* (02) 314 170
*Key Personnel*
Dir: Haj Mohamed Bouzid

**Bibliotheque Generale et Archives**
32 av Mohammed V, Tetouan
Mailing Address: BP 692, Tetouan
*Tel:* (0996) 3 258
*Key Personnel*
Librarian: M M Dellero

**Institut Scientifique**
Charia lbn Batouta, BP 703, 10106 Agdal-Rabat
*Tel:* (07) 77 45 48; (07) 77 45 49; (07) 77 45 50; (07) 77 45 55 *Fax:* (07) 77 45 70
*Web Site:* www.emi.ac.ma/univ-MdV/IS.html
*Telex:* MADILM 36361M
*Key Personnel*
Dir: Driss Najid
Founded: 1920
Publication(s): *Bulletin de l'Institut Scientifique*; *Documents de l'Institut Scientifique*; *Travaux de l'Institut Scientifique*

**Bibliotheque de l'Universite Quaraouyine**
Place des Seffarines, BP 790, Fes

**Bibliotheque Ben Youssef**
Ave 11 Janvier Hay Mohamadi Daoudiat, Marrakech
*Tel:* (04) 25465
*Web Site:* www.minculture.gov.ma/fr/bibliotheque_bibliobus.htm
*Key Personnel*
Dir: Seddik Bellarbi

# Mozambique

**Biblioteca Municipal**
Pacos de Concelho, Maputo

**Biblioteca Nacional de Mocambique**
PO Box 141, Maputo
*Tel:* (01) 425 676
*Key Personnel*
Librarian: Joaquim Chigogoro Mussassa

**Direccao Nacional de Geologia (Centro de Documentacao)** (National Directorate of Geology (Documentation Center))
PO Box 217, Praca 25 de Junho, Maputo
*Tel:* (01) 305399 *Fax:* (01) 429216
*E-mail:* geologia@zebra.uem.mz
*Telex:* 6-584 GEOMI MO
*Key Personnel*
National Dir: Elias XF Daudi *E-mail:* exfdaudi@teledate.mz
National Deputy Dir: Fatima Momade
Founded: 1928
Publication(s): *Boletim Geologico* (Geological Bulletin, annually, report of activities of DNG)
*Parent Company:* Ministry of Mineral Resources & Energy
*Branch Office(s)*
Beira
Gaza
Manica
Nampula
Niassa
Tete

**Arquivo Historico de Mocambique** (Mozambique Historical Archives)
Division of Eduardo Mondlane University
Ave Filipe Magaia, 715, Maputo
Mailing Address: CP 2033, Maputo
*Tel:* (01) 321177; (01) 321178 *Fax:* (01) 323428
*E-mail:* jneves@zebra.uem.mz
*Web Site:* www.ahm.uem.mz
*Key Personnel*
Dir: Maria Ines Nogueira da Costa
Editor: J P Borges Coelho
Librarian: Antonio Sopa

Specialize in administrative & colonial archives 19th & 20th centuries. Bibliographic, cartographic, photographic & poster collectives.
Publication(s): *Arquivo* (Archive, every six weeks, bulletin, 1987); *Documentos* (annually, series); *Estudos* (Studies, 7 times/yr, series)

**Bibliotecas da Universidade Eduardo Mondlane**
Campus Universitario, Av Julius Nyerere, Maputo
Mailing Address: CP 257, Maputo
*Tel:* (01) 492875 *Fax:* (01) 493174
*Web Site:* www.uem.mz/reitoria/dsd/bibdsd.htm
*Telex:* 6-718 UEM MO
*Key Personnel*
Head of Services: Wanda do Amaral
*E-mail:* wanda@nambu.uem.mz
The University Eduardo Mondlane does not have a Central Library, but controls 15 departmental libraries; Direccao id responsible for all library & documentation services throughout the University.

# Myanmar

**Institute of Economics Library**
Pyay Rd, Yangon
*Tel:* (01) 530376 *Fax:* (01) 664889
*Web Site:* www.aun.chula.ac.th/u_iey_mm.htm
Founded: 1964

**Institute of Education Library**
Pyay Rd, Yangon
*Tel:* (01) 31345

**Magwe Degree College Library**
University Campus, Magwe
*Tel:* (63) 21030
*Key Personnel*
Dir: Khin Myint Myint

**Mandalay University Library**
University Estate, Mandalay
*Tel:* (02) 21211
*Key Personnel*
Librarian: U Myint Thein
Founded: 1958

**National Library**
Six-Storeyed Bldg, Strand Rd, Yangon
*Tel:* (01) 283332; (01) 275997 *Fax:* (01) 212367
*Web Site:* www.myanmar.com/culture/text/P001.htm
*Key Personnel*
Dir: U Kyaw Oo
Founded: 1952

**Universities' Central Library**
Yangon University, PO 11041, Yangon
*Tel:* (01) 545 750 *Fax:* (01) 545 750
*E-mail:* ucl@mptmail.net.mm
Founded: 1929

# Namibia

**National Archives of Namibia**
340 Mandume Ndemufayo Ave, Pioneers Park, Windhoek
Mailing Address: Private Bag 13301, Windhoek
*Tel:* (061) 2063874 *Fax:* (061) 2063876
*E-mail:* library@unam.na

*Web Site:* www.unam.na/ilrc/library/archives.html
*Key Personnel*
Head Archivist: Everon Kloppers *Tel:* (061)
	2063692 *E-mail:* ekloppers@unam.na

**National Library of Namibia**
PO Box 13349, Windhoek 9000
*Tel:* (061) 2934203; (061) 2934204 *Fax:* (061)
	229808
*E-mail:* postmstr@natlib.mec.gov.na
*Web Site:* yaotto.natlib.mec.gov.na
*Key Personnel*
Chief, National Library: Mr J Loubser
	*E-mail:* johan@yaotto.natlib.mec.gov.na
Librarian: M K Hoffmann
Founded: 1926

**Windhoek Public Library**
4 Luederitz St, Private Bag 13183, Windhoek
*Tel:* (061) 224899 *Fax:* (061) 212169
*E-mail:* rviljoen@unam.na
*Key Personnel*
Librarian: Mrs L Hansmann

# Nepal

**British Council Library**
PO Box 640, Kathmandu
*Tel:* (01) 4410 798 *Fax:* (01) 4410 545
*E-mail:* general.enquiry@britishcouncil.org.np
*Web Site:* www.britishcouncil.org/nepal
*Key Personnel*
Information Services Manager: Raju Shakya
	*E-mail:* raju.shakya@britishcouncil.org.np

**Madan Puraskar Library**
PO Box 42, Lalitpur 44702
*Tel:* (01) 5521014 *Fax:* (01) 5536390
*E-mail:* kmldxt@wlink.com.np
*Key Personnel*
Librarian: Kamalmani Dixit
	*E-mail:* kamalmanidixit@hotmail.com
Founded: 1956

**Nepal National Library**
Harihar Bhawan, PO Box 182, Lalitpur
*Tel:* (01) 5521132 *Fax:* (01) 5536461
*E-mail:* nnl@nnl.wlink.com.np
*Web Site:* www.natlib.gov.np
*Key Personnel*
Chief Librarian: Dasharath Thapa
Founded: 1957

**Tribhuvan University Central Library**
Kirtipur, Katmandu
*Tel:* (01) 331317; (01) 330834 *Fax:* (01) 226964
*E-mail:* tucl@healthnet.org.np
*Web Site:* www.tucl.org.np
*Key Personnel*
Chief: Mr Krishna Mani Bhandari
Founded: 1959
Serves the university, government, ministries,
	foreign diplomatic missions, local & foreign
	researchers & the general public. Also is a
	depository for 11 international organizations
	including UN publications since 1965. The
	library has nearly 245,000 books at present.
	There are about 500 titles of learned peri-
	odicals, newspapers & valuable manuscripts.
	Nepal ISBN Agency is located here. Nepal Na-
	tional coordinating agency for the International
	Networking for the Availability of Scientific
	Publication. Depository Library of the voice
	records of the works of prominent Naplese au-
	thors in the Library of Congress website.
Publication(s): *Bibliography of non-alignment,
	1982*; *Bibliography of Population & Family*

*Planning, 1981*; *Nepalese National Bibliog-
	raphy* (annually, 1981, books published from
	Nepal, all subjects); *Nepal's Foreign Affaires*
	(bibliographical guide to resources in the Tucl,
	1974); *Research on Nepal, a Bibliography
	of PhD Thesis* (2003, submitted by research
	scholars engaged in various fields of Nepal)

# Netherlands

**Bibliotheek van het Centraal Bureau voor de
	Statistiek** (Statistics Netherlands Library)
Prinses Beatrixlaan 428, 2273 XZ Voorburg
Mailing Address: PO Box 4000, 2270 JM Voor-
	burg
*Tel:* (070) 337 51 51 *Fax:* (070) 337 59 84
*E-mail:* bibliotheek@cbs.nl
*Web Site:* www.cbs.nl
*Key Personnel*
Librarian: Ms M F Wijngaarden *Tel:* (070) 337
	51 49 *E-mail:* mwei@cbs.nl
*Branch Office(s)*
Kloosterweg 1, PO Box 4481, 6401 CZ Heerlen
	*Tel:* (045) 5707187; (045) 5707188 *Fax:* (045)
	5706280

**Bibliotheek Wageningen UR** (Wageningen
	University & Research Centre Library)
Generaal Foulkesweg 19, 6703 BK Wageningen
Mailing Address: PO Box 9100, 6700 HA Wa-
	geningen
*Tel:* (0317) 484440 *Fax:* (0317) 484761
*E-mail:* helpdesk.library@wur.nl
*Web Site:* library.wur.nl
*Key Personnel*
Head of Library: G Naber *Tel:* (0317) 484106

**Bibliotheekvoorziening van de Radboud
	Universiteitsbibliotheek Nijmegen** (Radboud
	University Nijmegen Library)
Erasmuslaan 36, 6525 GG Nijmegen
Mailing Address: PO Box 9100, 6500 HA Ni-
	jmegen
*Tel:* (024) 3612428 *Fax:* (024) 3615944
*E-mail:* info@ubn.kun.nl
*Web Site:* www.kun.nl/ubn/
*Key Personnel*
Chief Librarian: Mrs H P A Smith

**DBA**, see Dienst Bibliotheek en Archief

**Dienst Bibliotheek en Archief**
Spui 68, 2511 BT The Hague
*Tel:* (070) 353 4401; (070) 353 4479 *Fax:* (070)
	353 4479
*Web Site:* www.bibliotheekdenhaag.nl/dob/
*Key Personnel*
Librarian: W M Renes
Public library.

**Bibliotheek Technische Universiteit Eindhoven**
	(Eindhoven University of Technology Library)
De Hal Bldg, Het Kranenveld, 5612 AZ Eind-
	hoven
Mailing Address: Postbus 90159, 5600 RM Eind-
	hoven
*Tel:* (040) 2472381 *Fax:* (040) 2447015
*E-mail:* helpdesk.bib@tue.nl
*Web Site:* www.tue.nl/bib
*Key Personnel*
Head Librarian: L Osinski *E-mail:* l.osinski@tue.
	nl

**EVD eenheid Bibliotheek**
Juliana Van Stolberglaan 148, 2595 CL The
	Hague

Mailing Address: Postbus 20105, 2500 EC The
	Hague
*Tel:* (070) 778 8888 *Fax:* (070) 778 8889
*E-mail:* evd@info.evd.nl
*Web Site:* www.evd.nl
*Telex:* 31099 Ecza nl *Cable:* ECONINF
*Key Personnel*
Librarian: G P van der Sluys

**Internationaal Instituut voor Sociale
	Geschiedenis** (International Institute of Social
	History)
Cruquiusweg 31, 1019 AT Amsterdam
*Tel:* (020) 6685866; (020) 6928810 *Fax:* (020)
	6654181; (020) 6630349; (020) 4680505
*E-mail:* info@iisg.nl; user.service@iisg.nl
*Web Site:* www.iisg.nl
*Key Personnel*
General Dir: Jaap Kloosterman *E-mail:* jkl@iisg.
	nl
Publication(s): *Catalogs & Monograph Series*;
	*International Review of Social History*

**Koninklijke Bibliotheek** (Royal Library)
Prins Willem Alexanderhof 5, 2595 BE The
	Hague
Mailing Address: PO Box 90407, 2509 LK The
	Hague
*Tel:* (070) 3140911 *Fax:* (070) 3140450
*E-mail:* info@kb.nl
*Web Site:* www.kb.nl
*Telex:* 34402 KB NL
Publication(s): *Bibliography of Translations* (from
	the Dutch); *Dutch Bibliography - Brinkman's
	Cumulatieve Catalogues*

**Museum Meermanno-Westreenianum**
Prinsessegracht 30, 2514 AP The Hague
*Tel:* (070) 3462700 *Fax:* (070) 3630350
*E-mail:* info@meermanno.nl
*Web Site:* www.meermanno.nl/
*Key Personnel*
Dir: Dr Leo Voogt
Founded: 1848
National book museum.

**Nederlands Instituut voor Wetenschappelijke
	Informatiediensten** (Library of Royal
	Netherlands Academy of Arts & Sciences)
Joan Muyskenweg 25, 1096 CJ Amsterdam
Mailing Address: PO Box 95110, 1090 HC Ams-
	terdam
*Tel:* (020) 462 8600 *Fax:* (020) 665 8013
*E-mail:* info@niwi.knaw.nl
*Web Site:* www.niwi.knaw.nl
Founded: 1997

**NIWI**, see Nederlands Instituut voor
	Wetenschappelijke Informatiediensten

**Openbare Bibliotheek/Gemeentearchief**, see
	Dienst Bibliotheek en Archief

**Rijksmuseum Research Library**
Frans van Mierisstr 92, 1071 RZ Amsterdam
Mailing Address: PO Box 74888, 1070 DN Ams-
	terdam
*Tel:* (020) 67 47 267 *Fax:* (020) 6747001
*E-mail:* library@rijksmuseum.nl
*Web Site:* library.rijksmuseum.nl
*Key Personnel*
Contact: G J Koot *Tel:* (020) 6747250 *E-mail:* g.
	koot@rijksmuseum.nl
Founded: 1885
Specializes in art history.
Membership(s): International Federation of Li-
	brary Associations & Institutions (IFLA).

**Bibliotheek der Rijksuniversiteit Groningen**
	(University of Groningen Library)
Oude Boteringestr 44, 9712 GL Groningen

Mailing Address: Postbus 72, 9700 AB Gronin-
gen
*Tel:* (050) 363 5445; (050) 363 5446 *Fax:* (050)
363 6300
*E-mail:* info@ub.rug.nl
*Web Site:* www.rug.nl/bibliotheek
*Key Personnel*
Librarian: A C Klugkist

**Gemeentebibliotheek Rotterdam** (Rotterdam
Municipal Library)
Hoogstr 110, 3011 PV Rotterdam
Mailing Address: Postbus 22140, 3003 DC Rot-
terdam
*Tel:* (010) 281 61 00 *Fax:* (010) 2816181
*E-mail:* communicatie@bibliotheek.rotterdam.nl
*Web Site:* www.bibliotheek.rotterdam.nl
*Telex:* 25221 gbr nl
*Key Personnel*
Librarian: F H Meijer

**Stichting Arnhemse Openbare en Gelderse
Wetenschappelijke Bibliotheek**
Koningstr 26, 6811 DG Arnhem
*Tel:* (026) 3543111 *Fax:* (026) 4458616
*Web Site:* www.biblioarnhem.nl
*Key Personnel*
Head: Dr Marc Wingens
Librarian: A J Hovy *E-mail:* j.hovy@
biblioarnhem.nl
Founded: 1853
Public library.

**Bibliotheek van de Universiteit van
Amsterdam** (Amsterdam University Library)
Singel 425, 1012 WP Amsterdam
Mailing Address: Po Box 19185, 1000 GD Ams-
terdam
*Tel:* (020) 525 2301 *Fax:* (020) 525 2311
*E-mail:* secr-uba@uva.nl
*Web Site:* www.uba.uva.nl
*Key Personnel*
Librarian: Dr N Verhagen
Founded: 1578

**Universiteitsbibliotheek Leiden**
WSD-Gebouw 1169, Witte Singel 27, 2311 BG
Leiden
Mailing Address: Postbus 9501, 2300 RA Leiden
*Tel:* (071) 527 2814 *Fax:* (071) 527 2836
*E-mail:* secretariaat@library.leidenuniv.nl;
helpdesk@library.leidenuniv.nl
*Web Site:* ub.leidenuniv.nl
*Key Personnel*
Librarian: P W J L Gerretsen

**Universiteitsbibliotheek Utrecht** (University
Library Utrecht)
Heidelberglaan 3, 3524 CS Utrecht
Mailing Address: PO Box 80.124, 3508 TC
Utrecht
*Tel:* (030) 2536600; (030) 2536601 (central
lending desk); (030) 2537262 (renewals)
*Fax:* (030) 2538398
*E-mail:* info@library.uu.nl; uitleen@library.uu.nl
(central lending desk)
*Web Site:* www.library.uu.nl
*Key Personnel*
Librarian: J S M Savenije *Tel:* (030) 2536502
*Fax:* (030) 2539292 *E-mail:* b.savenije@library.
uu.nl
*Publication(s): Handschriften en Qude Drukken
van de Utrechtse Universiteits bibliothek*
(Manuscripts & Old Books of Utrecht Uni-
versity Library); *Illuminated & Decorated
Medieval Manuscripts in the University Li-
brary Utrecht* (catalog, illustrated); *The Utrecht
Psalter, Picturing the Psalms of David* (CD-
ROM); *Vier eeuwen Universiteitsbibliotheek
Utrecht (Four Centuries University Library,
Utrecht: Part 1 1584-1878)* (summary in En-
glish)

**Universiteit Wageningen,** see Bibliotheek
Wageningen UR

# Netherlands Antilles

### Openbare Bibliotheek
Abraham M Chumaceiro Blvd 17, Willemstad,
Curacao
*Tel:* (09) 434 5200 *Fax:* (09) 465 6247
*E-mail:* publiclibrary@curinfo.an
*Web Site:* www.curacaopubliclibrary.an
*Key Personnel*
Librarian: Rose Marie de Paula
Founded: 1922
*Branch Office(s)*
Barber Branch, St Janschool, Barber 6, Curacao
*Tel:* (09) 8641606

**Universiteits-Bibliotheek, Universiteit van de
Nederlandse Antillen**
Jan Noorduyweg 111, Curacao, NA
Mailing Address: PO Box 3059, Curacao, NA
*Tel:* (09) 8442222 *Fax:* (09) 8442200
*E-mail:* bibliotheek@una.an
*Web Site:* www.una.net
*Telex:* 110111
*Key Personnel*
Librarian: Dr Stanley R Criens *E-mail:* s.criens@
una.an

# New Caledonia

**Bibliotheque Bernheim, Bibliotheque
territoriale de la Nouvelle-Caledonie**
BP G1, 98848 Noumea
*Tel:* 24 20 90 *Fax:* 27 65 88
*E-mail:* bibbern@canl.nc
*Web Site:* www.bernheim.nc
*Key Personnel*
Librarian: Jean-Francois Carrez-Corral

**Secretariat of the Pacific Community Library**
BPD5, 98848 Noumea Cedex
*Tel:* 26 20 00 *Fax:* 26 38 18
*E-mail:* library@spc.int
*Web Site:* www.spc.int/library
*Telex:* 3139NM Sopacom *Cable:* SOUTH
PACOM
*Key Personnel*
Librarian: Rachele Oriente
Founded: 1947
To support development in the Pacific via SPC
programs.
*Ultimate Parent Company:* Pacific Community
*Branch Office(s)*
Suva, Fiji, Contact: Christina Tuitubou

# New Zealand

**Archives New Zealand** (Te Whare Tohu
Tohituhinga O Aotearoa)
10 Mulgrave St, Thorndon, Wellington
Mailing Address: PO Box 12-050, Wellington
*Tel:* (04) 4995595; (04) 4956226 (reference)
*Fax:* (04) 4956210
*E-mail:* wellington@archives.govt.nz
*Web Site:* www.archives.govt.nz

*Key Personnel*
Chief Archivist: Dianne Macaskill
Specialize in the preservation of government
records.
*Branch Office(s)*
Auckland Regional Office, 525 Mt Wellington
Highway, PO Box 91-220, Auckland, Re-
gional Archivist: Mark Stoddart *Tel:* (09) 270-
1100 *Fax:* (09) 276-4472 *E-mail:* auckland@
archives.govt.nz
Christchurch Regional Office, 90 Peterborough St,
PO Box 642, Christchurch, Regional Archivist:
Chris Adam *Tel:* (03) 377-0760 *Fax:* (03) 377-
2662 *E-mail:* christchurch@archives.govt.nz
Dunedin Regional Offices, 556 George St, PO
Box 6183, Dunedin North, Regional Archivist:
Peter Miller *Tel:* (03) 477-0404 *Fax:* (03) 477-
0422 *E-mail:* dunedin@archives.govt.nz

**Auckland City Libraries**
44-46 Lorne St, Auckland
Mailing Address: PO Box 4138, Auckland 1030
*Tel:* (09) 377 0209 *Fax:* (09) 307 7741
*E-mail:* library_reference@aucklandcity.govt.nz
*Web Site:* www.aucklandcitylibraries.com
*Telex:* 2750
*Key Personnel*
City Librarian: Barbara Birkbeck

**Canterbury University Library**
Private Bag 4800, Christchurch 8020
*Tel:* (03) 364 2987 (ext 8723) *Fax:* (03) 364 2055
*E-mail:* lending@libr.canterbury.ac.nz; helpdesk@
libr.canterbury.ac.nz
*Web Site:* library.canterbury.ac.nz/
*Telex:* 4144 unicant
*Key Personnel*
University Librarian: Gail Pattie *Tel:* (03) 364
2987 (ext 8740) *E-mail:* gail.pattie@canterbury.
ac.nz

**Christchurch City Libraries**
PO Box 1466, Christchurch
*Tel:* (03) 941 7923 *Fax:* (03) 941 7848
*E-mail:* library@ccc.govt.nz
*Web Site:* library.christchurch.org.nz
*Key Personnel*
Library Manager: Sue Sutherland
Promotions & Publications Coordinator: Sasha
Bowers *E-mail:* sasha.bowers@govt.nz
Marketing & Development Manager: Glenda Ful-
ten *Tel:* (03) 372 7840 *E-mail:* glenda.fulten@
ccc.govt.nz
*Publication(s): Bookmark* (monthly); *Connect*
(monthly)

**Dunedin Public Libraries**
Moray Pl, Dunedin
Mailing Address: PO Box 5542, Dunedin
*Tel:* (03) 4743690 *Fax:* (03) 4743660
*E-mail:* library@dcc.govt.nz
*Key Personnel*
Library Services Manager: Bernie Hawke
*Tel:* (03) 4743657 *E-mail:* bhawke@dcc.govt.
nz
Collection Development Librarian: Barbara Frame
*Tel:* (03) 4743620 *E-mail:* bframe@dcc.govt.nz
Founded: 1908
*Parent Company:* Dunedin City Council

**Napier Public Library**
Station St, Napier
Mailing Address: PO Box 940, Napier
*Tel:* (06) 834 4180 *Fax:* (06) 834 4138
*E-mail:* library@napier.govt.nz
*Web Site:* www.napier.govt.nz/inlib.php
*Key Personnel*
Manager: Leslie Clague *Tel:* (06) 834 4142
*E-mail:* lesliec@napier.govt.nz
*Branch Office(s)*
Taradale Library, PO Box 7056, Taradale, Napier,

Team Leader: Chrissy Arnold *Tel:* (06) 845 9005 *Fax:* (06) 844 7462 *E-mail:* carnold@ napier.govt.nz

## National Library of New Zealand (Te Puna Matauranga o Aotearoa)
Corner Molesworth & Aitken Streets, Wellington
Mailing Address: PO Box 1467, Wellington 6001
*Tel:* (04) 474 3000 *Fax:* (04) 474 3035
*E-mail:* information@natlib.govt.nz; reference@ natlib.govt.nz
*Web Site:* www.natlib.govt.nz
*Telex:* NZ (04) 4730-080
*Key Personnel*
Chief Executive: Penny Carnaby
    *E-mail:* carnabyp@natlib.govt.nz
National Librarian: Christopher Blake
Dir, Collection Services: Allison Elliott
    *E-mail:* elliotta@natlib.govt.nz
Founded: 1965

## North Shore City Libraries
PO Box 93-508, Takapuna, North Shore City
*Tel:* (09) 4868460 *Fax:* (09) 4868519
*Web Site:* www.shorelibraries.govt.nz
*Key Personnel*
City Librarian: Geoff Chamberlain *Tel:* (09) 4868461 *E-mail:* geoffc@shorelibraries.govt.nz
Founded: 1879
*Branch Office(s)*
Albany Village Library, 30 Kell Dr, Albany Village North Shore City, Manager: Ann Hill *E-mail:* annh@shorelibraries.govt.nz
Birkenhead Library, PO Box 34-370, Birkenhead, North Shore City, Manager: Sue Parr *Tel:* (09) 486-8559 *E-mail:* suep@shorelibraries.govt.nz
Devonport Library, PO Box 32-003, Devonport, North Shore City, Manager: Megan Hayward *Tel:* (09) 486-8527 *E-mail:* meganh@ shorelibraries.govt.nz
East Coast Bays Library, PO Box 35-017, Browns Bay, North Shore City, Manager: Ann Hill *Tel:* (09) 486-8577 *E-mail:* annh@ shorelibraries.govt.nz
Glenfield Library, PO Box 40-099, Glenfield, North Shore City, Manager: Eileen O'Loan *Tel:* (09) 486-8554 *E-mail:* eileeno@ shorelibraries.govt.nz
Northcote Library, PO Box 36-001, Northcote, North Shore City, Manager: Kim Sipeli *Tel:* (09) 486-8490 *E-mail:* kims@ shorelibraries.govt.nz

## Palmerston North City Library
4 The Square, Palmerston North
Mailing Address: PO Box 1948, Palmerston North
*Tel:* (06) 351 4100 *Fax:* (06) 351 4102
*E-mail:* pncl@pncc.govt.nz
*Web Site:* citylibrary.pncc.govt.nz
*Key Personnel*
City Librarian: Anthony Lewis *E-mail:* anthony. lewis@pncc.govt.nz
Administration Manager: Sarah Palmer
Advisory Services Manager: Brendon Brookie
    *E-mail:* brendon.brookie@pncc.govt.nz
Technical Services Manager: Mary Holmes
    *Fax:* mary.holmes@pncc.govt.nz
Founded: 1876

## Parliamentary Library
Parliament Bldg, Wellington 6001
*Tel:* (04) 471 9611 *Fax:* (04) 472 8206
*E-mail:* intdoc@parliament.govt.nz
*Web Site:* www.ps.parliament.govt.nz/library.htm
*Key Personnel*
Parliamentary Librarian: Moira Fraser

## Alexander Turnbull Library
Division of National Library of New Zealand/Te Puna Matauranga o Aotearoa

National Library of New Zealand, National Library Bldg, Corner of Aitken & Molesworth Sts, Wellington
Mailing Address: PO Box 1467, 6001 Wellington
*Tel:* (04) 474 3000 *Fax:* (04) 474 3035
*E-mail:* atl@natlib.govt.nz
*Web Site:* www.natlib.govt.nz
*Key Personnel*
Chief Librarian: Margaret Calder
    *E-mail:* margaret.calder@natlib.govt.nz
Founded: 1918
Research library for New Zealand & the Pacific; John Milton's life & work; the history of the book.
Publication(s): *Off the Record* (annually, series); *Turnbull Library Record* (annually, series)

## University of Auckland Library
2 Alfred St, Auckland
Mailing Address: PO Box 92019, Auckland
*Tel:* (09) 3737599 (ext 88044) *Fax:* (09) 3737565
*E-mail:* library@auckland.ac.nz
*Web Site:* www.library.auckland.ac.nz
*Key Personnel*
University Librarian: Janet Copsey *Tel:* (09) 3737599 (ext 87352) *E-mail:* jl.copsey@ auckland.ac.nz

## University of Otago Library
65 Albany St, Dunedin
Mailing Address: PO Box 56, Dunedin
*Tel:* (03) 479 8910 *Fax:* (03) 479 8947
*E-mail:* library@otago.ac.nz; reference.central@ library.otago.ac.nz
*Web Site:* www.library.otago.ac.nz
*Key Personnel*
Senior Librarian: Mark Hughes *Tel:* (03) 479 8916 (ext 5028) *E-mail:* mark.hughes@library. otago.ac.nz
Founded: 1869

## Wellington City Libraries
65 Victoria St, Wellington
Mailing Address: PO Box 1992, Wellington
*Tel:* (04) 801 4040 *Fax:* (04) 801 4047
*E-mail:* central@wcl.govt.nz
*Web Site:* www.wcl.govt.nz
*Key Personnel*
Manager, Libraries: Jane Hill *Tel:* (04) 801 4101
    *E-mail:* jane.hill@wcc.govt.nz
*Branch Office(s)*
Brooklyn Library, Corner of Harrison St & Cleveland St, Brooklyn, Wellington *Tel:* (04) 384 6814 *Fax:* (04) 384 2857 *E-mail:* brooklyn@ wcl.govt.nz
Cummings Park Library, 1a Ottawa Rd, Ngaio, Wellington *Tel:* (04) 479 2344 *Fax:* (04) 479 4186 *E-mail:* cummingspark@wcl.govt.nz
Ruth Gotlieb (Kilbirnie) Library, 101 Kilbirnie Crescent, Kilbirnie *Tel:* (04) 387 1480 *Fax:* (04) 387 1490 *E-mail:* ruthgotlieb@wcl. govt.nz
Island Bay Library, 167 The Parade, Island Bay *Tel:* (04) 383 7216 *Fax:* (04) 383 7215 *E-mail:* islandbay@wcl.govt.nz
Johnsonville Library, 5 Broderick Rd, Wellington *Tel:* (04) 477 6151 *Fax:* (04) 477 6153 *E-mail:* johnsonville@wcl.govt.nz
Karori Library, 253 Karori Rd, Wellington *Tel:* (04) 476 7585 *Fax:* (04) 476 2265 *E-mail:* karori@wcl.govt.nz
Mervyn Kemp (Tawa) Library, Corner of Cambridge & Main Rd, Wellington *Tel:* (04) 232-1690 *Fax:* (04) 232-1699 *E-mail:* mervynkemp@wcl.govt.nz
Khandallah Library, 8 Ganges Rd, Wellington *Tel:* (04) 479 7535 *Fax:* (04) 479 2573 *E-mail:* khandallah@wcl.govt.nz
Miramar Library, 68 Miramar Ave, Wellington *Tel:* (04) 388 8005 *Fax:* (04) 388 4187 *E-mail:* miramar@wcl.govt.nz
Mobile Library *Tel:* (04) 801-4089

Newtown Library, 13 Constable St, Newtown, Wellington *Tel:* (04) 389 2830 *Fax:* (04) 389 2827 *E-mail:* newtown@wcl.govt.nz
Wadestown Library, Corner of Moorehouse St & Lennel Rd, Wellington *Tel:* (04) 473 5211 *Fax:* (04) 473 5389 *E-mail:* wadestown@wcl. govt.nz

# Nicaragua

## Archivo Nacional de Nicaragua
Del Cine Cabrera 2 1/2 C al lago, Managua
*Tel:* (02) 223 240 *Fax:* (02) 22722
*E-mail:* binanic@tmx.com.nic
*Key Personnel*
Dir: Alfredo Gonzalez Vilchez
Publication(s): *Boletin*

## Biblioteca Nacional
C del Triunfo 302, Managua
Mailing Address: Apdo 101, Managua
*Tel:* (02) 897 517 *Fax:* (02) 894 387

**INCAE**, see Instituto Centroamericano de Administracion de Empresas (INCAE) Library

## Instituto Centroamericano de Administracion de Empresas (INCAE) Library
Campus Francisco de Sola, Montefresco, Km 15 1/2 Carretera Sur, Managua
Mailing Address: Apdo 2485, Managua
*Tel:* (02) 65 8141; (02) 65 8149; (02) 65 8272
    *Fax:* (02) 65 8617; (02) 65 8630
*E-mail:* biblioteca@mail.incae.edu.ni; incaeni@ mail.incae.edu.ni
*Web Site:* www.incae.ac.cr/biblioteca
*Telex:* 2360
*Key Personnel*
Associate Dir: Antonio Acevedo
Publication(s): *Revista INCAE*

**Ruben Dario**, see Biblioteca Nacional

## Universidad Centroamericana (Central American University)
Avenida Universitaria, Managua
Mailing Address: Apdo 69, Managua
*Tel:* (02) 278-3923 *Fax:* (02) 267-0106
*E-mail:* comsj@ns.uca.edu.ni
*Web Site:* www.uca.edu.ni
*Telex:* 2296
*Key Personnel*
Librarian: Conny Mendez R

# Niger

## Centre d'Enseignement Superieur de Niamey
Bibliotheque, BP 237, Niamey
*Tel:* 732713 *Fax:* 733862
*Telex:* uninim 5258 hi
University Education Centre.

## Bibliotheqe l'Ecole nationale d'administration du Niger
Rue Martin Luther King Jr, Niamey
Mailing Address: BP 542, Niamey
*Tel:* 723183 *Fax:* 724383
*Key Personnel*
Librarian: Mme Yacouba Halimatou

## Institut de Recherche en Sciences Humaines
BP 318, Niamey
*Tel:* 73-51-41

*Telex:* 5258
*Key Personnel*
Director: Zakari Maikorema
Publication(s): *Etudes Nigeriennes*

**Bibliotheque de l'Universite de Niamey**
BP 10 896, Niamey
*Tel:* 74-12-73 *Fax:* 73-38-62
*Telex:* 5258
*Key Personnel*
Contact: M Saidou Harouna

# Nigeria

**Ahmadu Bello University Library**
Ahmadu Bello University, PMB 1044, Zaria
*Tel:* (069) 505-71; (069) 505-72; (069) 505-73;
(069) 505-74 *Fax:* (069) 505-63
*Telex:* 75241 Zarabu Ng *Cable:* AGRICSEARCH,
ZARIA
Founded: 1922
Publication(s): *Agroclimatological Atlas of North-
ern States of Nigeria*; *NOMA* (magazine,
news); *Samaru Journal of Agricultural Re-
search*; *Soil Survey Bulletin*

**Anabra State Library Board**
PMB 01026, Market Rd, Enugu
*Tel:* (042) 334 103 *Cable:* LIBRARIES ENUGU
*Key Personnel*
Librarian: C N Ekweozoh

**Bendel State Library**
PMB 1127, 17 James Watt Rd, Benin City, Ben-
del State
*Tel:* (052) 200 810 *Cable:* LIBRARY BENIN
*Key Personnel*
Dir: D O Oboro
Founded: 1971
Publication(s): *Bendel Library Journal*

**Benin University Library**
PMB 1154, Ugbowo-Lagos Rd, Ugbowo, Benin
City, Edo State
*Tel:* (052) 600443 *Fax:* (052) 602370
*E-mail:* registra@uniben.edu; registra@uniben.
edu.ng; library@uniben.edu
*Web Site:* www.uniben.edu
*Telex:* 41365 *Cable:* Uniben; Benin
*Key Personnel*
University Librarian: S A Ogunrombi
Publication(s): *List of Serials*

**IAR**, see Institute for Agricultural Research
(IAR)

**Institute for Agricultural Research (IAR)**
PMB 1044, Samaru-Zaria
*Tel:* (069) 550571; (069) 550572; (069) 550573;
(069) 550574; (069) 550681 *Fax:* (069) 50563
*E-mail:* iar.abu@kaduna.rcl.ng.com
*Key Personnel*
Dir: Prof J P Voh
Publication(s): *KWIC Index to the Abstracting
& Indexing*; *Library Accession List* (monthly);
*List of Current Serials in the Library* (annu-
ally); *Subject Bibliographies on Nigeria Agri-
culture*

**International Institute of Tropical Agriculture
(IITA) Library**
PMB 5320, Ibadan, Oyo State
*Tel:* (02) 241 2626 *Fax:* (02) 241 2221
*E-mail:* iita@cgiar.org
*Web Site:* www.iita.org/info/libsrv.htm

*Telex:* 31417; 31159 Tropib Ng *Cable:*
TROPFOUND IKEJA
*Key Personnel*
Head, Library & Documentation: Y Adedigba
*E-mail:* y.adedigba@cgiar.org
Publication(s): *IITA Annual Report*; *IITA Re-
search*

**Library Board of Kaduna State**
PMB 2061, Kaduna
*Tel:* (062) 242590
*Key Personnel*
Dir: J A Maigari
Publication(s): *Biographies of Governors of For-
mer Northern Nigeria & Kaduna State, 1960-
1990*; *Meet Our Friends*; *Proceedings of the
First Kaduna State Book Fair*; *Proceedings of
the First Northern States Book Fair*; *Proceed-
ings of the Second Kaduna State Book Fair*

**Kano State Library Board**
PMB 3094, Kano
*Tel:* (064) 645614
*Web Site:* www.library.unt.edu/nigeria/Kano/Kano.
htm
*Key Personnel*
Executive Director: Sanusi A Nassarawa
*E-mail:* nassarawa2001@yahoo.com
Publication(s): *Library Guide*

**Lagos City Council Libraries**
48 Broad St, Lagos
Mailing Address: PMB 2025, Lagos
*Tel:* (01) 50246

**National Archives of Nigeria Library**
University of Ibadan, Chapel Rd, Ibadan
*Tel:* (022) 415000 *Cable:* DARCHNES
*Key Personnel*
Dir: Comfort Aina Ukwu

**National Library of Nigeria-Research &
Development Dept**
Sanusi Dantata House, Plot 274 Central Business
Area, PMB 1, Garki District, Abuja
*Tel:* (09) 2646773; (09) 2346774 *Fax:* (09)
2646772
*E-mail:* info@nlbn.org
*Web Site:* www.nlbn.org
*Telex:* 21746 Nat Lib Ng *Cable:* BIBLIOS
*Key Personnel*
National Librarian: Mrs O O Omolayde
Publication(s): *Afribiblios* (biannually); *Libraries
in Nigeria, a Directory*; *National Bibliography
of Nigeria*; *Nigerbiblios* (quarterly); *Nigerian
Books in Print*; *Nominal List of Practicing Li-
brarians in Nigeria*; *Serials in Print in Nigeria*

**Nnamdi Azikiwe Library**
University of Nigeria, Nsukka, Enugu State
*Tel:* (042) 771444 *Fax:* (042) 770644
*E-mail:* misunn@aol.com
*Telex:* Ulions 51496 *Cable:* NIGERSITY
LIBRARY
*Key Personnel*
Acting Librarian: C C Uwechie
Collection includes 9000 items in microform;
CD-ROM facilities available.
Publication(s): *Nsukka Library Notes*; *Readers'
Guide* (Annual Report); *UNLAN* (University of
Nigeria Library Accessions and News)

**Obafemi Awolowo University Library**
c/o Hezekiah Oluwasanmi Library, Ile-Ife, Osun
State
*Tel:* (036) 230291 ext 2287; (036) 230290
*Fax:* (036) 230291 (ext 2287)
*E-mail:* ul@libraryoauife.edu.ng
*Key Personnel*
Librarian: Adedeji Adelabu

**University of Ibadan, Kenneth Dike Library**
Ibadan
*Tel:* (02) 810 3118 *Fax:* (02) 810 3118
*E-mail:* library@kdl.ui.edu.ng
*Key Personnel*
Librarian: Joseph Ezenwani Ikem
Founded: 1948
Publication(s): *Library Record* (monthly)

**University of Jos Library**
PMB 2084, Jos, Plateau State
*Tel:* (073) 610514; (073) 53724; (073) 44952
*Fax:* (073) 610514
*Web Site:* 128.255.135.155/libraries
*Telex:* 81136 Unijos NG *Cable:* LIBRARIAN
UNIJOS
*Key Personnel*
University Librarian: Dr A Ochai
Publication(s): *JULIA (Jos University Library In-
formation & Accessories)* (bimonthly); *Know
Your Library: Readers' Guide to the Library*

**University of Lagos Library**
Akoka, Lagos
*Tel:* (01) 41 361 *Fax:* (01) 822644
*Web Site:* www.unilag.edu/library/index.asp
*Telex:* 26983
*Key Personnel*
Librarian: S A Orimoloye
Founded: 1962

**University of Nigeria**
Nnamdi Azikiwe Library, Enugu
Mailing Address: University of Nigeria, Nsukka
*Tel:* (042) 771444 *Fax:* (042) 770644
*E-mail:* unnlibrary@yahoo.com
*Web Site:* www.unn-edu.net
*Telex:* 51496 ULIONS NG
*Key Personnel*
University Librarian: Emenike Ikeqbune
Founded: 1960

# Norway

**Bergen offentlige Bibliotek** (Bergen Public
Library)
Stromgaten 6, 5015 Bergen
*Tel:* 55 56 85 60; 55 56 85 50 *Fax:* 55 56 85 65
*Web Site:* www.bergen.folkebibl.no
*Key Personnel*
Dir: Trine Kolderup Flaten *E-mail:* trine@bergen.
folkebib.no
Founded: 1872

**Deichmanske Bibliotek**
Henrik Ibsensgt 1, 0179 Oslo
*Tel:* 23 43 29 00 *Fax:* 22 11 33 89
*E-mail:* deichman@deichman.no
*Web Site:* www.deich.folkebibl.no
*Key Personnel*
Chief Librarian: Liv Saeteren
City library of Oslo.

**Drammen Folkebibliotek**
Gl Kirkeplass 7, Postboks 136-Bragernes, 3001
Drammen
*Tel:* 32046303 *Fax:* 32046453
*E-mail:* drm@drammen.folkebibl.no
*Web Site:* www.drammen.kommune.no/bibliotek
*Key Personnel*
Librarian: Solvi Tellefsen *E-mail:* solvi.tellefsen@
drammen.folkebibl.no
Public library of Drammen; county library of
Buskerud.

**Styret for det Industrielle Rettsvern**, see
Patentstyret - Styret for det Industrielle
Rettsvern Infosenteret

**Kristiansand Folkebibliotek**
Radhusgt 11, 4611 Kristiansand
Mailing Address: Postboks 476, 4664 Kris-
tiansand
*Tel:* (038) 12 49 10 *Fax:* (038) 12 49 49
*E-mail:* post.folkebibliotek@kristiansand.
kommune.no
*Web Site:* www.kristiansand.folkebibl.no
*Key Personnel*
Chief Librarian: Oddhild Hildre
Municipal library.

**Nobelinstituttet** (Nobel Institute)
Biblioteket, Drammensveien 19, 0255 Oslo
*Tel:* 22 12 93 00 *Fax:* 22 12 93 10
*E-mail:* library@nobel.no
*Web Site:* www.nobel.no
*Key Personnel*
Head Librarian: Anne C Kjelling *Tel:* 22 12 93
21 *E-mail:* ack@nobel.no
Founded: 1904
Library covers following fields: international rela-
tions, international law, peace, & international
economics.

**Norges Landbrukshogskoles Bibliotek**
(Agricultural University of Norway Library)
Postboks 5003, 1432 As
*Tel:* (064) 96 55 00 *Fax:* (064) 94 76 70
*E-mail:* biblutl@umb.no
*Web Site:* www.nlh.no/biblioteket
*Key Personnel*
Librarian: Gerd Antonsen *E-mail:* gerd.
antonsen@umb.no

**Patentstyret - Styret for det Industrielle
Rettsvern Infosenteret** (Norwegian Patent
Office Information Center)
Formerly Styret for det Industrielle Rettsvern
Kobenhavngaten 10, Postboks 8160 Dep, 0033
Oslo
*Tel:* (022) 38 73 33 *Fax:* (022) 38 73 31
*E-mail:* infosenteret@patentstyret.no
*Web Site:* www.patentstyret.no
*Telex:* 19152 nopat n
*Key Personnel*
Dir: Jorgen Smith
Library of the Norwegian Patent Office.

**Riksarkivet**
Folke Bernadottes vei 21, Oslo
Mailing Address: Postboks 4013, Ulleval Stadion,
0806 Oslo
*Tel:* (022) 02 26 00 *Fax:* (022) 23 74 89
*E-mail:* riksarkivet@riksarkivaren.dep.no
*Web Site:* www.riksarkivet.no; www.arkivverket.
no
National archives of Norway.

**Statistisk sentralbyras bibliotek og
informasjonssenter** (Statistics Norway-
Library & Information Centre)
Kongens gate 6, 0033 Oslo
Mailing Address: Postboks 8131 Dep, 0033 Oslo
*Tel:* 21 09 46 42 *Fax:* 21 09 45 04
*E-mail:* biblioteket@ssb.no
*Web Site:* www.ssb.no/biblioteket
*Key Personnel*
Head of Division: Lars Rogstad *Tel:* 21 09 44 95
*E-mail:* rog@ssb.no
Founded: 1917

**Universitetsbiblioteket i Bergen** (University of
Bergen Library)
Stein Rokkans hus, Nygardsgt 5, 5015 Bergen
*Tel:* 55 58 25 32 *Fax:* 55 58 97 03
*E-mail:* post@ub.uib.no

*Web Site:* www.ub.uib.no
*Telex:* 42690 ubb n
*Key Personnel*
Dir: Kari Garnes *Tel:* 55 58 25 01 *E-mail:* kari.
garnes@ub.uib.no
Founded: 1948

**Universitetsbiblioteket i Oslo**
Georg Sverdrups Hus, 4th floor, 0317 Oslo
Mailing Address: PB 1085, Blindern, Oslo 0317
*Tel:* 22 84 40 01 *Fax:* 22 84 41 50
*E-mail:* informasjon@uio.no
*Web Site:* www.ub.uio.no
*Key Personnel*
Dir: Jan Erik Roed *E-mail:* j.e.roed@ub.uio.no
Founded: 1811
Publication(s): *Bibliografi over Norges offentlige
publikasjoner 1956-1990; Helse-NOTA 1992-
; Kataloger pa mikrofilm kort; Maskinles-
bare data; Mikrofilmer* (35mm Norske aviser,
Norske tidsskrifter, Norske og utenlandske
boker); *Nansen bilde data base pa CD-ROM;
Nasjonalbibliografiske data NBDATA 1962-
(CD-ROM); Nordisk samkatalog for peri-
odika CDNOSP; Norsk bokfortegnelse; Norsk
bokfortegnelse: Musikktrykk; Norsk lokalhis-
torisk litteratur 1946-1970; Norsk lokalhis-
torisk litteratur 1971-1990; Norsk musikkfortegnelse: lydfestinger; Norsk musikkfortegnelse:
notetrykk; Norsk periodikafortegnelse 1993-
(annually); Norsk samkatalog for boker CD-
SAM 1981; Norsk samkatalog for boker CD-
SAM 1983-; Norske tidsskriftartikler 1980-;
Norske tidsskrifter 1971-1983; NOSP adres-
seliste* (annually); *UBO: Brosjyrer; UBO: Diverse publikasjonerk; UBO: Skrifter; UBO:
Veiledninger*

**Universitetsbiblioteket i Trondheim**
NTNU, 7491 Trondheim
*Tel:* 73 59 51 10 *Fax:* 73 59 51 03
*E-mail:* ubit@adm.ntnu.no
*Web Site:* www.ub.ntnu.no
*Key Personnel*
Dir: Ingar Lomheim
Founded: 1768
University library of Trondheim, incorporating
libraries of the College of Arts & Sciences
& of the museum (formerly Library of the
Royal Norwegian Society of Sciences & Let-
ters, DKNVS).

**University of Oslo Library**, see
Universitetsbiblioteket i Oslo

# Pakistan

**British Council Library**
House 1, St 61, F-6/3, PO Box 1135, Islamabad
44000
*Tel:* (051) 111 424 424 *Toll Free Tel:* 0800 22000
*Fax:* (051) 111 425 425
*E-mail:* info@britishcouncil.org.pk
*Web Site:* www.britishcouncil.org.pk
*Telex:* 54644
*Key Personnel*
Acting Dir: Andrew Picken
Deputy Dir: John Payne

**Ewing Memorial Library**
Forman Christian College, Ferezepur Rd, Lahore
54600
*Key Personnel*
Librarian: Jacob Lal Din
Founded: 1866

**Dr Mahmud Husain Library**
Karachi University, Karachi 32
*Tel:* (021) 474953 *Fax:* (021) 473226
*E-mail:* librarian@library.ku.edu.pk
*Key Personnel*
In Charge: Ms Syeda Arjumand Bano
Founded: 1952
Publication(s): *Guide to Bibliographical Sources*
(Catalog of rare books)

**Islamic Research Institute Library**
PO Box 1035, Islamabad 44000
*Tel:* (051) 9261761; (051) 2252816
*Web Site:* www.iiu.edu.pk
*Telex:* 54068 IIU Pak *Cable:* ISLAMSERCH
*Key Personnel*
Rector: Dr Khalil-ur-Rehman Khan
*Ultimate Parent Company:* International Islamic
University, Islamabad 44000

**National Archives of Pakistan**
Administrative Block Area, N Block, Pakistan
Secretariat, Islamabad 44000
*Tel:* (051) 9202044 *Fax:* (051) 9206349
*Web Site:* www.pakistan.gov.pk
*Telex:* ARCHIVES
*Key Personnel*
Dir General: Raja Muhammad Ikram-ul-Haq
Dir: Mr Mond Ramzan
Founded: 1951
Storage & presentation of historical & public
records.
Membership(s): International Council on Archives
(ICA).
Publication(s): *Pakistan Archives* (biannually,
journal)
*Branch Office(s)*
Frere Market Rd, Karachi *Tel:* (021) 7765232

**National Library of Pakistan**
Constitution Ave, Islamabad 44000
*Tel:* (051) 9214523; (051) 92026436; (051)
9206440 *Fax:* (051) 9221375
*E-mail:* nlpiba@isb.paknet.com.pk
*Web Site:* www.nlp.gov.pk
*Key Personnel*
Dir General: Muhammad Nazir *Tel:* (051)
9214523 (ext 237)
Founded: 1993

**Pakistan Institute of Development Economics
(PIDE)**
Quaid-i-Azam University Campus, PO Box 1091,
Islamabad 44000
*Tel:* (051) 9206616 *Fax:* (051) 9210886
*E-mail:* pide@pide.org.pk
*Web Site:* www.pide.org.pk
*Key Personnel*
Deputy Chief, Library & Documentation:
Zafar Jared Naqvi *Tel:* (051) 9214041
*E-mail:* naqvi2j@hotmail.com
Founded: 1957
Research organization.
Publication(s): *Pakistan Development Review*
(quarterly)

**Pakistan Institute of Nuclear Science &
Technology Library, Science Information
Division**
Nilore, Islamabad
*Tel:* (051) 452350 *Fax:* (051) 429533
*E-mail:* ctc@shell.portal.com
*Telex:* 5725 Atcom Pk
*Key Personnel*
Head, Scientific Information Division: Dr Abdul-
lah Sadiq
Principal Librarian: Mohammad Shafique

**Pakistan Scientific & Technological
Information Centre (PASTIC)**
Quaid-I-Azam University Campus, Pastic Bldg,
Islamabad

*Tel:* (051) 9201340; (051) 9201341; (051)
9207641 *Fax:* (051) 9207211
*E-mail:* pastic@isb.pol.com.pk
*Web Site:* www.pastic.gov.pk
*Key Personnel*
Dir: Ms Nageen Ainuddin *E-mail:* nainuddin61@
yahoo.com
Founded: 1974
Publication(s): *Directory of Scientific Periodicals
of Pakistan*; *Pakistan Science Abstracts* (quar-
terly)
*Parent Company:* Pakistan Science Foundation
(PSF)
*Ultimate Parent Company:* Ministry of Science &
Technology

**PASTIC**, see Pakistan Scientific & Technological
Information Centre (PASTIC)

**Punjab Public Library**
Library Rd, Lahore 54000
*Tel:* (042) 325487
*E-mail:* zilpk@yahoo.com
*Key Personnel*
Librarian: Hafiz Khuda Bakhsh
Founded: 1884

**Punjab University Library**
Quaid-Azam Campus, Lahore 54590
*Tel:* (042) 9230834; (042) 9231126 *Fax:* (042)
9230892
*E-mail:* info@library.pu.edu.pk
*Web Site:* www.pulibrary.edu.pk
*Key Personnel*
Chief Librarian: Abdul Waheed
*E-mail:* chieflibrarian@pu.edu.pk
Founded: 1882

**Sind University Central Library**
Allama ll Kazi Campus, Jamshoro, Sind
*Tel:* (0221) 771188
*Key Personnel*
Librarian: Mohammad IshaqueI Laghari

**University of Baluchistan Library**
Sariab Rd, Quetta
*Tel:* (081) 41770
*Key Personnel*
Librarian: Brohi Ghulam Murtaza
Founded: 1971

**University of Engineering & Technology
Central Library (UET)**
Grand Trunk Rd, Lahore 54890
*Tel:* (042) 6829243 *Fax:* (042) 6822566
*E-mail:* central_library@yahoo.com
*Web Site:* www.uet.edu.pk *Cable:*
UNIVENGTECH
*Key Personnel*
Librarian: Abdul Hameed
Assistant Librarian: Muhammad Saeed *Tel:* (042)
6822667
Founded: 1961
Publication(s): *Central Library Bulletin* (bi-
monthly)

# Panama

**Biblioteca Bio-Medica del Laboratorio
Conmemorativo Gorgas**
Av Justo Arosemena 35-30, Apdo 6991, Panama
5
*Tel:* (02) 274111 *Fax:* (02) 254366
*E-mail:* igorgas@sin.fonet
*Telex:* 3433 *Cable:* GOMELA
*Key Personnel*
Dir: Dr Rolando E Saenz

Librarian: Nora E Osses; Gloria O de Cano
*Branch Office(s)*
PO Box 935, APO, Miami, FL, United States
Gorgas Memorial Laboratory
Bio-medical Research Library

**Biblioteca Nacional**
Parque Recreativo y Cultural Omar, Via Porras,
San Francisco, Ciudad de Panama
Mailing Address: Apdo 7906, Panama 9
*Tel:* 224-9466 *Fax:* 224-9988
*E-mail:* referencia@binal.ac.pa
*Web Site:* www.binal.ac.pa
*Key Personnel*
Dir: Algeria Pimentel S
Founded: 1942
Publication(s): *Bibliografias nacionales*

**Universidad de Panama, Biblioteca
Interamericana Simon Bolivar**
Estafeta Universitaria, Apdo 3277, Panama
*Tel:* 2636133
*Key Personnel*
Librarian: Nuria F de Gonzalez
Publication(s): *Boletin Bibliografico*

# Papua New Guinea

**Office of Libraries and Archives, Papua, New
Guinea**
PO Box 734, Waigani
*Tel:* 325-6200 *Fax:* 325-1331
*E-mail:* ola@datec.com.pg *Cable:* PNG LIB
BOROKO
*Key Personnel*
Dir General: Daniel Paraide
Founded: 1975
Publication(s): *Ola Nius (formerly National Li-
brary Nius)*; *Papua New Guinea National
Bibliography*; *Selective Index to the Times of
Papua New Guinea*

**Papua New Guinea Institute of Public
Administration Library (PNGIPA)**
PO Box 1216, Boroko
*Tel:* 3260433; 3267345; 3267163 *Fax:* 3261654
*E-mail:* gaudichn@upng.ac.pg
*Telex:* 23011 *Cable:* PNGIPA
*Key Personnel*
Contact: Lewis Kusso-Alles
Publication(s): *Administration for Development*
(college journal)
*Branch Office(s)*
Papua New Guinea Institute of Public Adminis-
tration, Boroko

**PNGIPA Library**, see Papua New Guinea
Institute of Public Administration Library
(PNGIPA)

**Michael Somare Library**
PO Box 319, University Post Office, Waigani 134
NCD
*Tel:* 326 7280 *Fax:* 326 7187
*E-mail:* Library@upng.ac.pg
*Web Site:* www.theatrelibrary.org
*Telex:* ne 22366
*Key Personnel*
Contact: Florence J Griffin
Founded: 1966
Publication(s): *Guide to Manuscripts in the New
Guinea Collection* (by Nancy Lutton 1980);
*New Guinea Periodical Index* (quarterly)

# Paraguay

**Biblioteca y Archivo Nacionales** (National
Library & Archives)
Mariscal Estigarriba 95, Asuncion

**Biblioteca de la Sociedad Cientifica del
Paraguay** (Library of the Paraguayan Scientific
Society)
Avda Espana 505, Asuncion
*Tel:* (021) 24832

# Peru

**ALIDE**, see Asociacion Latinoamericana de
Instituciones Financieras Para El Desarrollo
(ALIDE)

**Archivo General de la Nacion del Peru**
Jr Manuel Cuadros s/n Palacio de Justicia, Lima
*Tel:* (01) 427-5930; (01) 427-5939 *Fax:* (01) 428-
2829
*Web Site:* agn.perucultural.org.pe
*Key Personnel*
Chief Librarian & Dir: Aida Mendoza Navarro

**Asociacion Latinoamericana de Instituciones
Financieras Para El Desarrollo (ALIDE)**
(Latin American Association of Development
Financing Institutions)
Paseo de la Republica, Lima, San Isidro 3211
Mailing Address: Apartado Postal 3988, Lima
100
*Tel:* (01) 442 2400 *Fax:* (01) 442 8105
*E-mail:* sg@alide.org.pe
*Web Site:* www.alide.org.pe
*Key Personnel*
Secretary General: Rommel Acevedo
*E-mail:* racevedo@alide.org.pe
Head, Institutional Relations Division: Eduardo
Vasquez *E-mail:* dri@alide.org.pe
Founded: 1968
Represents institutions that finance development
in Latin America & the Caribbean. Provides
information & documentation related to devel-
opment banking fields of interest, as well as
having information on materials relative to spe-
cific economic sectors & technological aspects.
Collects specialized documentation concerned
with banking & financing development.
Membership(s): World Federation of Development
Financing Institutions (WFDFI).
Publication(s): *Boletin Alide* (Alide Bulletin, 6
times/yr, dedicated to the provision of articles
& analytical information, in depth studies &
documents of a technical & legal nature related
to banking & financing development); *Memoria
Annual* (annually, report)

**Biblioteca Central de la Universidad Nacional
de San Agustin**
Apdo 23, Arequipa
*Tel:* (054) 229 719
*E-mail:* sisbiblio@unmsm.edu.pe
*Web Site:* sisbib.unmsm.edu.pe/sbweb
Founded: 1828

**Biblioteca Central de la Universidad Nacional
Mayor de San Marcos**
Simon Rodriquez 681, Apdo 454, Lima 1
*Tel:* (01) 4285210 *Fax:* (01) 4285210
*E-mail:* ogeibl@sanfer.edu.pe

**Biblioteca Nacional**
Av Abancay, 4ta cuadra, Lima
*Tel:* (01) 428-7690; (01) 428-7696 *Fax:* (01) 427-7331
*E-mail:* sg@binape.gob.pe
*Web Site:* www.binape.gob.pe
*Key Personnel*
Dir: Sinesio Lopez Jimenez
Publication(s): *Anuario Bibliografico Peruano* (Bibliographical Annual of Peru, annually); *Bibliografia Nacional* (annually, 2000, Peruvian monthly Bibliographical Information); *Boletin de la Biblioteca Nacional* (Bulletin of the National Library); *Gaceta Bibliotecaria* (Library Gazette, irregularly); *Revista Fenix* (Phoeniz Magazine, magazine)

**ESAN - Escuela de Administracion de Negocios para Graduados, Direccion de Investigacion**
Alonso de Molina 1652, Monterrico, Surco, Lima
Mailing Address: Apdo 1846, Lima 100
*Tel:* (01) 317-7226 *Fax:* (01) 345-1328; (01) 345-1276
*E-mail:* cendoc@esan.edu.pe
*Web Site:* www.esan.edu.pe
*Key Personnel*
Dir: Santiago Roca, PhD

**Fondo Editorial de le Pontificia Universidad Catolica del Peru**
Plaza Francis 1164, Lima 1
Mailing Address: Apdo 1761, Lima 32
*Tel:* (01) 3307410; (01) 3307411 *Fax:* (01) 3307405
*E-mail:* feditor@pucp.edu.pe
*Web Site:* www.pucp.edu.pe
*Key Personnel*
Contact: Annie Ordonez *E-mail:* aordonez@pucp.edu.pe
Also publisher of books & 13 academic journals.

**Universidad del Pacifico Libreria**
Av Salaverry 2020, Jesus Maria, Lima 100
*Tel:* (01) 219-0100; (01) 472-9635 *Fax:* (01) 470-6121
*E-mail:* biblioteca@up.edu.pe
*Web Site:* www.up.edu.pe/biblioteca
*Telex:* 25650
*Key Personnel*
Dir: Maria C Bonilla de Gaviria
   *E-mail:* mbonilla@up.edu.pe
Publication(s): *Apuntes*; *Counterbalance Points* (monthly); *Intercampus*

**Universidad Nacional San Antonio Abad del Cusco (UNSAAC)**
Av De la Cultura, Nro 733, Cusco
Mailing Address: Apdo 921, Cusco
*Tel:* (084) 222271 *Fax:* (084) 238156
*Web Site:* www.unsaac.edu.pe

# Philippines

**Far Eastern University Library**
Nicanor Reyes St, St Sampaloc, Manila
*Tel:* (02) 735-5649 *Fax:* (02) 732-0232
*Web Site:* www.feu.edu.ph/library.asp
*Key Personnel*
Chief Librarian: Zenaida M Galang
Founded: 1991
Publication(s): *Far Eastern University Journal*

**Manila City Library**
Alvarez St, Santa Cruz, Manila
Mailing Address: City Hall, Room 501, Manila
*Tel:* (02) 711-98-40

*E-mail:* info@cityofmanila.com.ph
*Web Site:* www.cityofmanila.com.ph
*Key Personnel*
City Librarian: Paz C Gagolinan

**National Library of the Philippines**
TM Kalaw St, Ermita, 1000 Manila
*Tel:* (02) 525-3196 (Filipiniana); (02) 582271 (Reference); (02) 582660 (Public Documents); (02) 525-1748 *Fax:* (02) 524-2329
*E-mail:* amb@nlp.gov.ph
*Web Site:* www.nlp.gov.ph
*Telex:* (02) 505143 (Filipiniana); 582271 (Reference); 582660; 582511 (Public Documents)
   *Cable:* NALIBPHILS
*Key Personnel*
Dir: Prudenciana C Cruz
Founded: 1901

**Philippine Normal College Library & Library Science Departments**
Taft Ave, Manila
*Tel:* (02) 5270372 *Fax:* (02) 5270372
*Key Personnel*
Contact: Calixta Aquirre

**Rizal Library**
Katipunan Rd, Loyola Heights, 1108 Quezon City, Metro Manila
Mailing Address: PO Box 154, 1099 Manila
*Tel:* (02) 426-6001; 5800-5816 (Local) *Fax:* (02) 426-5961
*Web Site:* rizal.lib.admu.edu.ph
*Key Personnel*
Dir: Mrs Lourdes T David *E-mail:* ltdavid@ateneo.edu
Founded: 1921
Educational institution.
*Parent Company:* Ateneo de Manila University

**Science & Technology Information Institute Department of Science & Technology**
DOST Complex, Bicutan, Taguig, Metro Manila
Mailing Address: PO Box 3596, Manila
*Tel:* (02) 837-2191 *Fax:* (02) 837-7520
*Web Site:* www.stii.dost.gov.ph
*Key Personnel*
Chief: Dr Irene D Amores
Publication(s): *Philippine Science & Technology Abstracts*; *R & D Philippines*; *SEA Abstracts*; *Series of Philippine Scientific Bibliographies*; *Union Catalogue of NISST*; *Union List of Serials of NSTA and its Agencies*

**Silliman University Library**
Dumaguete City, 6200 Negros Oriental
*Tel:* (035) 4227208; (035) 4226002 *Fax:* (035) 4227208
*E-mail:* sulib@su.edu.ph
*Web Site:* su.edu.ph
*Key Personnel*
President: Agustin A Pulido *E-mail:* pres@su.edu.ph
University Librarian: Lorna T Yso *E-mail:* lty@su.edu.ph
Founded: 1901
Publication(s): *Convergence* (annually, journal, 1994, multidisciplinary journal of the arts & sciences); *Sands & Coral* (annually, journal, 1948, student literary journal); *Silliman Journal* (biannually, journal, 1954, humanities, sciences & social sciences); *Silliman University Library Bulletin* (bimonthly, newsletter, 1971, contains news about the library personnel, resources, services & facilities)

**Ramona S Tirona Memorial Library**
The Philippine Women's University, Taft Ave, 1004 Manila
*Tel:* (02) 5268421 (loc 176) *Fax:* (02) 5266935

*Key Personnel*
Librarian: Dionisia M Angeles
Publication(s): *Administrative Bulletin*; *Philippine Educational Forum*; *PWU Bulletin/FTB Bulletin*; *The Alumni Link and Philippine Women's University Forum*; *The Link*

**University of Manila Central Library**
546 MV delos Santos St, Sampaloc, Manila
*Tel:* (02) 7355256 *Fax:* (02) 7355089
*E-mail:* um@univman.edu.ph
*Web Site:* www.univman.edu.ph

**University of San Carlos Library System**
P del Rosario St, 6000 Cebu City
*Tel:* (032) 2531000 *Fax:* (032) 2540432
*E-mail:* direklib@usc.edu.ph
*Web Site:* www.usc.edu.ph *Cable:* STEYL CEBU
*Key Personnel*
Dir, Libraries: Dr Marilou P Tadlip

**University of Santo Tomas Library**
Espana St, Sampaloc, Manila
*Tel:* (02) 731-3034 *Fax:* (02) 740-9709
*E-mail:* library@ust.edu.ph
*Web Site:* www.ust.edu.ph
*Key Personnel*
Chief Librarian: Estrella S Majuelo
Prefect of Libraries: Fr Angel A Aparicio
Founded: 1611

**University of the East Library**
2219 C M Recto Ave, Manila
*Tel:* (02) 7358544 *Fax:* (02) 7356976
*E-mail:* webmaster@uec.edu.ph
*Web Site:* www.ue.edu.ph
*Key Personnel*
Dir: Sarah C De Jesus
Chief Librarian: Narcisa F Tioco

**University of the Philippines Diliman University Library**
Gonzalez Hall, cor Apacible St, Diliman, 1101 Quezon City
*Tel:* (02) 981-8500, Local 2852 *Fax:* (02) 926-1876
*Web Site:* www.mainlib.upd.edu.ph
*Key Personnel*
University Librarian: Salvacion M Arlante
   *E-mail:* salvacion.arlante@up.edu.ph
Founded: 1922
Publication(s): *Index to Philippine Periodicals (IPP)* (quarterly)

# Poland

**Naczelna Dyrekcja Archiwow Panstwowych**
ul Dluga 6, 00-238 Warsaw
Mailing Address: PO Box 1005, 00-950 Warsaw
*Tel:* (022) 635-68-22 *Fax:* (022) 831-75-63
*E-mail:* coia-info@archiwa.gov.pl
*Web Site:* www.archiwa.gov.pl
*Key Personnel*
Contact: Doc dr hab Daria Nalecz
Main directorate of the Polish state archives.
Publication(s): *Archeion, Teki archiwalne*

**Archiwum Glowne Akt Dawnych**
ul Dluga 7, 00-263 Warsaw
*Tel:* (022) 831-54-91 *Fax:* (022) 831-16-08
*Web Site:* www.piasa.org/polisharchives/warsawhr.html
*Key Personnel*
Dir: Dr Hubert Wajs
Founded: 1808
Central archives for historical documents.
Publication(s): *Miscellanea Historico-archivistica*

**Biblioteka Jagiellonska** (Jagiellonian Library)
al Mickiewicza 22, 30-059 Krakow
*Tel:* (012) 633 63 77; (012) 634 59 45 (ext
354, 355, 359, 360 & 361); (012) 633 09 03
*Fax:* (012) 633 09 03
*Web Site:* www.bj.uj.edu.pl
*Key Personnel*
Dir: Zdislaw Pietrzyk, PhD *E-mail:* pietrzyk@if.
uj.edu.pl
Deputy Dir: Ryszard Juchniewicz; Teresa Malik
*Tel:* (012) 633 98 82 *E-mail:* malikter@
if.uj.edu.pl; Dr Andrzej Obrebski
*E-mail:* obrebski@if.uj.edu.pl
Founded: 1364
Publication(s): *Katalog drukow XVI Wieku ze
Biblioteki Jagiellonskiej; Biuletyn Biblioteki
Jagiellonskiej* (The Jagiellonian Library Bul-
letin, annually); *In wentarz rekopisow Bib-
lioteki Jagiellonskiej* (Inventory of Manuscripts
of the Jagiellonian Library); *Katalog drukow
XVI Wieku ze zbiorow Biblioteki Jagiellonskiej*
(Catalogue of XVI Century Publications from
the Jagiellonian Library Collections)
*Parent Company:* Uniwersytet Jagiellonski
(Jagiellonian University)

**Biblioteka Narodowa w Warszawie** (The
National Library in Warsaw)
al Niepodleglosci 213, 02-086 Warsaw
*Tel:* (022) 452-2999 *Fax:* (022) 825-5251
*E-mail:* biblnar@bn.org.pl
*Web Site:* www.bn.org.pl
*Key Personnel*
Dir: Prof Adam Manikowski
The National Library. See also Instytut Bibli-
ograficzny, a division of the National Library.
Publication(s): *Biuletyn Informacyjny Biblioteki
Narodowej* (The National Library Information
Bulletin); *Rocznik Biblioteki Narodowej* (The
National Library Yearbook)

**Biblioteka Publiczna m st Warszawy -
Biblioteka Glowna Wojewodztwa
Mazowieckiego** (The Warsaw Public
Library-The Central Library of Masovia
Province)
ul Koszykowa 26/28, 00-553 Warsaw
Mailing Address: PO Box 365, 00-950 Warsaw
*Tel:* (022) 6217852 *Fax:* (022) 6211968
*E-mail:* biblioteka@biblpubl.waw.pl
*Web Site:* www.biblpubl.waw.pl
*Key Personnel*
Manager: Michal Strak
Founded: 1907
Publication(s): *Prace Biblioteki Publicznej m
st Warszawy* (The Works of Warsaw Public
Library, irregularly); *Sesje varsavianistyczne*
(Varsaviana Sessions, irregularly)

**Biblioteka Uniwersytecka w Poznaniu** (Poznan
University Library)
ul Ratajczaka 38/40, 61-816 Poznan
*Tel:* (061) 829-3800 *Fax:* (061) 829-3824
*E-mail:* library@amu.edu.pl
*Web Site:* lib.amu.edu.pl
*Telex:* 412714 Bup
*Key Personnel*
Dir: Dr Artur Jazdon *Tel:* (061) 852-2955
*E-mail:* jazar@amu.edu.pl
Founded: 1919
Publication(s): *Biblioteka* (annually); *Zeszyty
Naukowe Biblioteki Uniwersyteckiej w Poznaniv*
(irregularly)
*Parent Company:* Uniwersytek im Adama Mick-
iewicza w Poznaniu (UAM)

**Biblioteka Gdanska PAN**
Walowa 15, 80-858 Gdansk
*Tel:* (058) 312251-54 *Fax:* (058) 312970
*E-mail:* bgpan@task.gda.pl

*Key Personnel*
Librarian: Zbigniew Nowak
Publication(s): *Libri Gedanenses* (annually)

**Politechnika Gdanska**
ul Narutowicza 11/12, 80-952 Gdansk Wrzeszcz
*Tel:* (058) 347-25-75 *Fax:* (058) 347-27-58
*E-mail:* mainlibr@sunrise.pg.gda.pl; library@pg.
gda.pl
*Web Site:* www.pg.gda.pl
*Telex:* 415821
*Key Personnel*
Manager: Miroslaw Komendecki
Publication(s): *Bibliografia publikacji pracown-
ikow Politechniki Gdanskiej* (Bibliographic
Publication of the Employees of the Techni-
cal University of Gdansk); *Raporty Wydzialow
PG* (annually, Berichte der Fakultaten der TU
Gdansk); *Wykaz nabytkow BG PG* (monthly,
Directory of New Recruting of the Central Li-
brary of Gdansk); *Zhistorii Politechniki Gdan-
skiej* (The History of the Technical University
of Gdansk, quarterly)

**Glowna Biblioteka Lekarska**
Chocimska 22, 00-791 Warsaw
*Tel:* (022) 849-78-51 *Fax:* (022) 849-78-02
*E-mail:* gbl@gbl.waw.pl
*Web Site:* www.gbl.waw.pl
*Telex:* 814820
*Key Personnel*
Dir: Prof Janusz Kapuscik
Central medical library.
Publication(s): *Biuletyn GBL; Polska Bibliografia
Lekanska*

**Biblioteka Glowna Politechniki Warszawskiej**
Pl Politechniki 1, 00-661 Warsaw
*Tel:* (022) 621 13 70 *Fax:* (022) 621 13 70
*E-mail:* bgpw@bg.pw.edu.pl
*Web Site:* www.bg.pw.edu.pl
Library of the Technical University of Warsaw.

**Instytut Bibliograficzny** (Bibliographical
Institute)
Division of National Library - Biblioteka Naro-
dowa
Biblioteka Narodowa, al Niepodleglosci 213, 02-
086 Warsaw
*Tel:* (022) 452-2999 *Fax:* (022) 825-5251
*E-mail:* biblnar@bn.org.pl
*Web Site:* www.bn.org.pl
*Telex:* 816761 Bn Pl
*Key Personnel*
Librarian: Jadwiga Sadowska, PhD
Publication(s): *Bibliografia Bibliografii Polskich*
(Bibliography of Polish Bibliographies, An-
nually); *Bibliografia Wydawnictw Ciagych*
(Bibliography of Serials, Quarterly); *Bibli-
ografia Zawartosci Czasopism* (Index to Pe-
riodicals, Monthly); *Polonica Zagraniczne*
(Foreign Polonica, Annually); *Polska Bibli-
ografia Bibliologiczna* (Polish Bibliography of
Library Science, Annually); *Przewodnik Bib-
liograficzny* (Bibliographical Guide, Weekly);
*Ruch Wydawniczy w Liczbach* (Polish Publishing in Figures, Annually)

**Politechnika Krakowska im Tadeusza
Kosciuszki** (Cracow University of Technology)
ul Warszawska 24, 31-155 Krakow
*Tel:* (012) 628-20-14 *Fax:* (012) 628-20-14
*E-mail:* listy@biblos.pk.edu.pl
*Web Site:* www.pk.edu.pl
*Key Personnel*
Librarian: Dorota Buzdygan *E-mail:* buzdygan@
biblos.pk.edu.pl; Marek M Gorski
*E-mail:* gorski@biblos.pk.edu.pl
Membership(s): International Association of Tech-
nological University Libraries (IATUL).

**Politechnika Slaska** (The Silesian Technical
University)
Biblioteka Glowna, ul Kaszubska 23, 44-100 Gli-
wice
*Tel:* (032) 237-12-69 *Fax:* (032) 237-15-51
*E-mail:* rjo1@polsl.pl
*Web Site:* www.polsl.gliwice.pl/alma.mater/
biblioteka.html
*Key Personnel*
Manager: Halina Baluka
Founded: 1945

**Politechnika Wroclawskiej/Biblioteka Glowna i
OINT** (Wroclaw University of
Technology/Main Library & Scientific
Information Centre)
Wybrzeze Wyspianskiego 27, 50-370 Wroclaw
*Tel:* (071) 328-27-07; (071) 320-23-05; (071)
320-23-31 *Fax:* (071) 328-29-60
*E-mail:* bg@pwr.wroc.pl
*Web Site:* www.bg.pwr.wroc.pl
*Key Personnel*
Dir: Henryk Szarski *E-mail:* bibl.gi@bg.pwr.
wroc.pl
Deputy Dir: Lucja Talarczyk-Malcher
Publication(s): *Acta of Bioengineering and
Biomechanics; Architectus; Badania Opera-
cyjne i Decyzje; Environment Protection En-
gineering; Fizykochemiczne Problemy Miner-
alurgii; Inzynieria Chemiczna i Procesowa;
Optica Applicata; Studia Geotechnica and Me-
chanica; Systems Science*

**Polska Fundacja Spraw Miedzynarodowych**
(Polish Foundation of International Affairs)
ul Warecka 1a, PL 00-950 Warsaw
Mailing Address: PO Box 1000, PL00-950 War-
saw
*Tel:* (022) 523 90 12; (022) 523 90 86 *Fax:* (022)
523 90 27
*E-mail:* warecka@qdnet.pl
*Web Site:* www.sprawymiedzynarodowe.pl
*Key Personnel*
Head of Publications: Aleksandra Zieleniec
*Tel:* (022) 523 90 25 *E-mail:* aleksandra.
zieleniec@msz.gov.pl
Publication(s): *The Polish Quarterly of Interna-
tional Affairs* (quarterly); *Yearbook of Polish
Foreign Policy* (annually)

**Biblioteka Slaska** (Silesian Library)
Plac Rady Europy 1, 40-021 Katowice
*Tel:* (032) 20-83-700 *Fax:* (032) 20-83-720
*E-mail:* bsl@bs.katowice.pl
*Web Site:* www.bs.katowice.pl
*Key Personnel*
Dir: Prof Jan Malicki *Tel:* (032) 206-06-875
Research library. Main special collections cov-
ering: literature, history, law, religion, social
science & economy, special Silesian collection.
Publication(s): *Bibliografia Slaska* (annually);
*Ksiaznica Slaska* (irregularly, bulletin, informa-
tion on the Silesian Library activites & articles
on the history of Silesian books)

**Uniwersytet Szczecinski**
ul Mickiewicza 16, 70-384 Szczecin
*Tel:* (091) 444-23-61 *Fax:* (091) 444-23-62
*E-mail:* info@bg.univ.szczecin.pl
*Web Site:* www.univ.szczecin.pl/us/biblioteka.html
*Cable:* 422719
*Key Personnel*
Rector of University: Prof Tadeusz Wierzabicki
Dir: Jolanta Goc
Publication(s): *Przeglad Zachodniopomorski*
(quarterly)

**Biblioteka Uniwersytecka w Warszawie**
(Warsaw University Library)
Ul Dobra 56/66, 00-312 Warsaw

*Tel:* (022) 5525660; (022) 5525178 *Fax:* (022) 5525659
*E-mail:* buw@uw.edu.pl
*Web Site:* www.buw.uw.edu.pl
*Key Personnel*
Dir: Ewa Kobierska-Maciuszko *Tel:* (022) 552566
   *E-mail:* e.maciuszko@uw.edu.pl
Founded: 1817
Publication(s): *Prace Biblioteki Uniwersyteckiej w Warszawie - Acta Bibliothecae* (irregularly)

**Biblioteka Uniwersytecka we Wroclawiu**
   (Library of the University of Wroclaw)
ul Karola Szajnochy 10, 50-076 Wroclaw
*Tel:* (071) 346 31 10 *Fax:* (071) 346 31 66
*E-mail:* infnauk@bu.uni.wroc.pl
*Web Site:* www.bu.uni.wroc.pl
*Key Personnel*
Dir: Grazyna Piotrowicz
Founded: 1945
Publication(s): *Bibliothecalia Wratislaviensia* (irregular, newspaper, 1995)

**Uniwersytet Gdanski**
Biblioteka Glowna UG, ul Armii Krajowej 110, 81-824 Sopot
*Tel:* (058) 550-94-13 *Fax:* (058) 551-52-21
*E-mail:* bib@bg.univ.gda.pl; info@bg.univ.gda.pl
*Web Site:* www.bg.univ.gda.pl/library/
*Key Personnel*
Dir: Urszula Sawicka
Founded: 1970

**Biblioteka Uniwersytecka w Toruniu**
   (University Library in Torun)
ul Gagarina 13, 87-100 Torun
*Tel:* (056) 611-44-08 *Fax:* (056) 652-04-19
*E-mail:* sekretariat@bu.uni.torun.pl
*Web Site:* www.bu.uni.torun.pl/en
*Key Personnel*
Dir: Miroslaw Adam Supruniuk, PhD
Founded: 1945
Library of the Mikolaj Kopernik University in Torun.
*Parent Company:* Uniwersytet Mikolaja Kopernika w Toruniu

# Portugal

**Biblioteca da Academia das Ciencias de Lisboa**
   (Library of the Academy of Sciences of Lisbon)
Rua da Academia das Ciencias, nº 19, 1249-122 Lisbon
*Tel:* (021) 321 97 30 *Fax:* (021) 342 03 95
*E-mail:* biblioteca@acad-ciencias.pt
*Web Site:* www.acad-ciencias.pt

**Biblioteca da Ajuda**
Palacio Nacional da Ajuda, 1349-021 Lisbon
*Tel:* (021) 363 85 92 *Fax:* (021) 363 85 92
*Key Personnel*
Dir: Francisco Delfim Cunha Leao

**Biblioteca Geral da Universidade de Coimbra**
   (University of Coimbra General Library)
Largo da Porta Ferrea, 3000-447 Coimbra
*Tel:* (0239) 859800; (0239) 859900; (0239) 859831 *Fax:* (0239) 827135
*E-mail:* bguc@uc.pt
*Web Site:* www.uc.pt
*Telex:* (039) 52275
*Key Personnel*
Dir: Carlos Manuel Baptista Fiolhais
Publication(s): *Acta Universitatis Conimbrigensis*; *Biblioteca da Universidade de Coimbra*; *Biblioteca Geral da Universidade de Coimbra* (an-

nually); *Divulgacao Bibliografica*; *Revista da Universidade de Coimbra* (annually); *Sumarios das Publicacoes Periodicas Portuguesas* (10 times/yr)

**Biblioteca Nacional** (National Library)
Campo Grande 83, 1749-081 Lisbon
*Tel:* (021) 7982000 *Fax:* (021) 7982138
*E-mail:* bn@bn.pt
*Web Site:* www.bn.pt
*Key Personnel*
Deputy Dir: Fernanda Maria Fields *Tel:* (021) 7982022 *E-mail:* fcampos@bn.pt
Founded: 1796
Publication(s): *Leituras: Revista da Biblioteca Nacional* (2 times/yr)

**Biblioteca Popular de Lisboa**
R Academia Ciencias 19, 1200 Lisbon
*Tel:* (021) 346 98 83
*Key Personnel*
Contact: Belkiss Pousao Lopes

**Biblioteca Publica de Evora** (Public Library of Evora)
Largo Conde de Vila Flor, 7000 804 Evora
*Tel:* (0266) 769 330 *Fax:* (0266) 769 331
*E-mail:* bpevora@ptnetbiz.pt
*Key Personnel*
Dir: Jose Antonio Calixto *E-mail:* jac.bpe@ptnetbiz.pt
Public library.
Publication(s): *Evora, BPADE, 1988*; *Isabel Cid-Incunabulos da Biblioteca Publica e Arquivo Distrital de Evora-Catalogo Abreviado*; *Isabel Cid-Incunabulos E Seus Possuidores, Estudo das marcas de posse dos incunabulos da Biblioteca Publica e Arquivo Distrital de Evora, Lisboa INIC, 1988*; *Isabel Cid-Lil Vicente e asua Epoca, Evora, 1992*
*Parent Company:* Instituto dos Arquivos Nacionais/Torre do Tombo

**Biblioteca Publica Municipal do Porto**
Jardim de Sao Lazaro, 4099 Porto
*Tel:* (02) 572147 *Fax:* (022) 5193488
*Key Personnel*
Dir: L Cabral
Municipal library of Porto.

**Fundacao para a Ciencia e a Tecnologia/Servico de Informacao e Documentacao(SID)**
Av D Carlos I, 126, 1249-074 Lisbon
*Tel:* (01) 3924300 *Fax:* (01) 3907481
*Web Site:* www.fct.mct.pt
*Telex:* 12290 junic
*Key Personnel*
Dir: Dr Gabriela Lopes da Silva *E-mail:* g.l.silva@fct.mct.pt
Centre of Scientific & Technical Information, a branch of the Junta Nacional de Investigacao Cientifica e Technologia (National Council for Scientific & Technological Research).
Publication(s): *Guia de servicos di Documentacao e di Bibliotecas em Portugal*

**Instituto dos Arquivos Nacionais/Torre do Tombo**
Alameda da Universidade, 1600 Lisbon
*Tel:* (01) 7811500 *Fax:* (01) 7937230
*E-mail:* dc@iantt.pt
*Telex:* 65729 ANTTP
*Key Personnel*
Head of Division: Dr Maria de Lurdes Henriques

**Biblioteca do Palacio Nacional de Mafra**
Terreiro de D Joao V, 2640 Mafra
*Tel:* (0261) 817 550 *Fax:* (0261) 811947
*Key Personnel*
Dir: Maria Margarida Montenegro

**Universidade do Minho** (Minho University)
Campus de Gualtar, 4710-057 Braga
*Tel:* (0253) 604150 *Fax:* (0253) 604159
*E-mail:* sdum@sdum.uminho.pt
*Web Site:* www.uminho.pt; www.sdum.uminho.pt/site/home.asp
*Telex:* 132135
*Key Personnel*
Dir Documentation Services: Eloy Rodrigues
   *E-mail:* eloy@sdum.uminho.pt
Founded: 1973

# Puerto Rico

**Archivo General de Puerto Rico** (Puerto Rican General Archive)
Apdo 9024184, San Juan 00902-4184
*Tel:* (787) 724-0700 *Fax:* (787) 724-8393
*Web Site:* www.icp.gobierno.pr
*Key Personnel*
Dir: Karin O Cardona
National archives of Puerto Rico.

**Conrad F Asenjo Library**, see University of Puerto Rico, Medical Sciences Campus Library

**Biblioteca General de Puerto Rico** (General Library of Puerto Rico)
Convento de los Dominicos No 98, San Juan 00902
Mailing Address: Apdo 9024184, San Juan 00902-4184
*Tel:* (787) 722-2299 *Fax:* (787) 724-0470
*E-mail:* biblioteca@icp.gobierno.pr
*Web Site:* www.icp.gobierno.pr/bge/index.htm
*Key Personnel*
Dir: Ada T Rodriguez
Founded: 1967

**Caribbean & Latin American Studies Library**
PO Box 21927, San Juan 00931-1927
*Tel:* (787) 764-0000 (ext 3319) *Fax:* (787) 763-5685
*Key Personnel*
Chief Librarian: Almaluces Figueroa
   *E-mail:* afiguer@upracd.upr.clu.edu
Research collection open to the general public.

**Inter American University of Puerto Rico Library**
Bo San Daniel Sector Las Canelas Carretera 2, Arecibo 00613
*Tel:* (787) 878-5475 (ext 320) *Fax:* (787) 880-1624
*E-mail:* sabreu@uiprl.inter.edu

**Universidad de Puerto Rico Recinto de Rio Piedras Sistema de Bibliotecas** (University of Puerto Rico, Library System, Rio Piedras Campus)
PO Box 23302, San Juan 00931-3302
*Tel:* (787) 764-0000 (ext 3311); (787) 764-0000 (ext 5085); (787) 764-0000 (ext 5089) *Fax:* (787) 772-1479
*Web Site:* biblioteca.uprrp.edu
*Key Personnel*
Acting Dir: Prof Evangelina Perez
   *E-mail:* evperez@rrpac.upr.clu.edu
Acting Associate Dir: Prof Thrown Amilcar
   *E-mail:* atirado@rrpac.upr.clu.edu
Publication(s): *Al Dia, Entorno*; *Biblionotas*; *Boletines de Divulgacion*; *Lumbre*; *Perspectiva*; *Servicio de Alerta*

**University of Puerto Rico, General Library, Mayaguez Campus**
PO Box 9022, Mayaguez 00681-9022
*Tel:* (787) 265-3810; (787) 832-4040 (ext 3810, 2151, 2155) *Fax:* (787) 265-5483
*E-mail:* library@rumlib.uprm.edu
*Web Site:* www.uprm.edu/library
*Key Personnel*
Library Dir: Prof Irma N Ramirez Aviles
 *E-mail:* irma@rumlib.uprm.edu

**University of Puerto Rico, Medical Sciences Campus Library**
PO Box 365067, San Juan 00936-5067
*Tel:* (787) 758-2525; (787) 751-8199 *Fax:* (787) 759-6713
*E-mail:* zgarcia@rcmaca.upr.clu.edu
*Web Site:* www.rcm.upr.edu
*Telex:* 3859173
*Key Personnel*
Dir: Prof Francisca Corrada del Rio
 *E-mail:* f_corrada@rcmaca.upr.clu.edu
Circulation & Reserve: Mrs Luz Evelyn Acevedo
 *E-mail:* e_acevedo@rcmaca.upr.clu.edu
Special Collections: Prof Aura Jiminez
 *E-mail:* a_jiminez@rcmaca.upr.clu.edu
Technical Services: Prof Nilca Parrilla Diaz
 *E-mail:* n_parrilla@rcmaca.upr.clu.edu
Reference: Prof Margarita Gonzalez Perez
 *E-mail:* m_gonzalez@rcmaca.upr.clu.edu
Serials: Prof Leticia Perez Guzman
 *E-mail:* l_perez@rcmaca.upr.clu.edu

# Qatar

**Qatar National Library**
PO Box 205, Doha
*Tel:* 442 9955 *Fax:* 442 9976
*E-mail:* qanaly@qatar.net.qa
*Telex:* 4743 Qanali DH
*Key Personnel*
Dir: Mohammed Hamad Al-Nassr
*Branch Office(s)*
Al-Khansa
Al-Shekh Ali
Al-Khore
Al-Rayyan
Al-Shamal
Al-Wakra

**Qatar University Library**
University St, Al-Dafana, Doha
Mailing Address: Libraries Administration, PO Box 2713, Doha
*Tel:* 4852405 *Fax:* 4835092
*E-mail:* postmaster@qu.edu.qa
*Web Site:* www.qu.edu.qa/english/library/libraries.htm
*Telex:* 4630 Unvsty DH
*Key Personnel*
Dir: Dr Ahmed M Al-Qattan *Tel:* 4852629
 *E-mail:* alqattan@qu.edu.qa

# Reunion

**Archives Departementales**
rue Marcel Pagnol-Champ Fleuri, 97490 Sainte-Clotilde
*Tel:* 94 04 14 *Fax:* 94 04 21
*E-mail:* archives@cg974.fr
*Key Personnel*
Archivist: Nadine Rouayroux

**Bibliotheque Departemental de Pret**
One, place Joffre, 97400 Saint Denis
*Tel:* 21 03 24 *Fax:* 21 41 30
*Key Personnel*
Librarian: Marie-Colette Maujean

**Mediatheque de Saint Pierre**
7, rue du College Arthur, 97458 St-Pierre Cedex
Mailing Address: BP 396, 97458 St-Pierre, Cedex
*Tel:* (02) 62967196 *Fax:* (02) 62257410
*E-mail:* mediasp@mediatheque-saintpierre.fr
*Web Site:* www.mediatheque-saintpierre.fr
*Key Personnel*
Librarian: Linda Koo Seen Lin *E-mail:* ksl@mediatheque-saintpierre.fr

**SCD,** see Universite de la Reunion, Service Commun de la Documentation

**Universite de la Reunion, Service Commun de la Documentation**
15, ave Rene Cassin, 97715 Saint-Denis messag cedex 9
Mailing Address: BP 7152, 97715 Saint-Denis messag cedex 9
*Tel:* 93 83 83 *Fax:* 93 83 64
*Web Site:* www.univ-reunion.fr
*Key Personnel*
Dir: Lefe Bure
Conservateur General: Anne-Marie Blanc

# Romania

**Academia de Studii Economice, Biblioteca Centrala**
Piata Romana nr 6, sector 1, Bucharest 10374
*Tel:* (01) 319 19 00; (01) 319 19 01 *Fax:* (01) 312 95 49
*Web Site:* www.biblioteca.ase.ro
*Telex:* Asero 11863

**Arhivele Nationale ale Romaniei** (National Archives of Romania)
Bulevardul Elisabeta, nr 49, sector 5, Bucharest
*Tel:* (01) 3152503 *Fax:* (01) 3125841
*E-mail:* webmaster@mai.gov.ro
*Web Site:* www.mai.gov.ro
*Key Personnel*
General Dir: Dr Costin Fenesan
Membership(s): International Association of Francopone Archives; International Council of Archives.
Publication(s): *Historical Abstract & America-History & Life* (article abstracts & index)

**Biblioteca Centrala Universitara din Bucuresti** (Central University Library of Bucharest)
Str Boteanu, nr 1, sector 1, 010027 Bucharest
*Tel:* (021) 313 16 05; (021) 313 16 06 *Fax:* (021) 312 01 08
*Web Site:* www.bcub.ro
*Key Personnel*
Dir: Dr Mircea Regneala *E-mail:* regneala@bcub.ro
Deputy Dir: Robert Coravu; Voichita Dragomir
Publication(s): *Literatura romana; Ghid bibliografic Partea I: Surse. Partea a II-a: Scriitori. Vol.I: A-L. Vol.II: M-Z. 1979, 1982, 1983*

**Biblioteca Nationala a Romaniei** (National Library of Romania)
Str Ion Ghica 4, 030046 Bucharest
*Tel:* (01) 3157063 *Fax:* (01) 3123381
*E-mail:* go@bibnat.ro
*Key Personnel*
Dir: Mrs Rodica Maiorescu
Founded: 1955

**Biblioteca Centrala Universitara Mihail Eminescu** (Central University Library)
Str Pacurari, nr 4, 700511 Iasi
*Tel:* (0232) 264245 *Fax:* (0232) 261796
*E-mail:* bcuis@bcu-iasi.ro
*Web Site:* www.bcu-iasi.ro
*Key Personnel*
Dir: Prof Al Calinescu *E-mail:* alcalinescu@bcu-iasi.ro
*Parent Company:* Ministry of Education & Research

**INID,** see Institutul National de Informare si Documentare (INID)

**Institutul National de Informare si Documentare (INID)** (National Institute for Information & Documentation)
Str I D Mendeleev nr 21-25, 010362 Bucharest
*Tel:* (01) 315 87 65 *Fax:* (01) 312 67 34
*E-mail:* inid@home.ro
*Web Site:* www.inid.ro
*Key Personnel*
General Dir: Ana-Eugenia Negulescu, MA
Publication(s): *Asigurarea si Promovarea Calitatii* (quarterly); *Informarea si Documentarea Moderna* (quarterly); *Management si Marketing Conpemporan* (quarterly)

**Biblioteca Municipala Mihail Sadoveanu**
Str Take Ionescu nr 4, 79711 Bucharest
*Tel:* (01) 2113625 *Fax:* (01) 2113625
*Key Personnel*
Assistant Dir: Rodica Cosmaciuc
Founded: 1935
Memberships: EBLIDA; IFLA; IMTAMEL.
Publication(s): *The Bibliography of Bucharest City* (1996); *Biblioteca Bucurestilor* (Bucharest's Library Review, monthly, 1998); *Foaia Cartierului* (Neighborhood's Review, monthly)

**Universitatea Transilvania Din Brasov Biblioteca Centrala** (Transylvania University of Brasov Central Library)
Bd Eroilor 29, 2200 Brasov
*Tel:* (068) 413 000 *Fax:* (068) 150 474
*E-mail:* libr@vega.unitbv.ro
*Key Personnel*
Dir: Aurel Negrutiu
Head, Library Service: Andrea Deaconescu
 *E-mail:* deacon@vega.unitbv.ro
Founded: 1948
Specialize in academic library, engineering, forestry, wood industry, humanities, sciences, medicine, music & economy.
*Parent Company:* Transilvania University of Brasov

**Universitatea de Medicina si Farmacie Biblioteca Centrala** (Central Library of the Univeristy of Medicine and Pharmacy)
Division of Government of Romania
Avram Iancu 31, 3400 Cluj-napoca
*Tel:* (064) 192629 *Fax:* (064) 190832
*Web Site:* www.bib.umfcluj.ro
*Key Personnel*
Dir: Iona Robu *E-mail:* irobu@umfcluj.ro
Founded: 1948
*Parent Company:* University of Medicine & Pharmacy Ministry of Education

**Biblioteca Universitatii Politehnica Bucuresti**
Calea Grivitei, nr 132, corp I, etaj 2, camera 210, Bucharest
*Tel:* (021) 402 3982 *Fax:* (021) 312 70 44
*Web Site:* www.library.pub.ro
*Telex:* 10252 ipolb
*Key Personnel*
Dir: Dan-Radu Popescu *E-mail:* dr_popescu@library.pub.ro

# Russian Federation

**Fundamental Library of the Academy of Medical Sciences**
Baltiiskaya Ul 8, 125874 Moscow
*Tel:* (095) 155-17-93
*Key Personnel*
Contact: G I Bakhereva

**Biblioteka Akademii Nauk Rossii** (Russian Academy of Sciences Library)
Birzevaja linija 1, 199034 St Petersburg
*Tel:* (0812) 3283592 *Fax:* (0812) 3287436
*E-mail:* ban@info.rasl.spb.ru
*Web Site:* www.ban.ru
*Key Personnel*
Contact: Dr Valerij Leonov
Founded: 1714

**All-Russian Patent Technical Library**
Berezhkovskaya naberezhnaya 24, 121857
Moscow
*Tel:* (095) 2406425 *Fax:* (095) 2404437
*E-mail:* vptb@aha.ru
*Telex:* 411774 bipat SU
*Key Personnel*
Library Dir: V I Amelkina
Deputy Dir: O I Kosolapov

**Central State Archives**
Vyborgskaya 3, 125212 Moscow
*Tel:* (095) 1597383
*Key Personnel*
Dir: A Prokopenko

**Gosudarstvennaya publichnaya nauchno-tekhnicheskaya biblioteka SSSR**
Kuznetskij most, 12, 103919 Moscow
*Tel:* (095) 9259288 *Fax:* (095) 9219862
*E-mail:* root@gpntb.msk.su
*Telex:* 411180
*Key Personnel*
Editor: A I Zemskov
Manager: N P Pavlova
State Public Scientific and Technical Library of the USSR.

**Gosudarstvennaya publichnaya istoricheskaya biblioteka Rossii** (State Public Historical Library of Russia)
Starosadskiy per 9, 101990 Moscow
*Tel:* (095) 928-46-82 *Fax:* (095) 928-02-84
*E-mail:* stru@shpl.ru
*Web Site:* www.shpl.ru
*Key Personnel*
Dir: Dr Mikhail Dmitriyevich Afanasiev

**Institut Nauchnoy Informatsii po Obschestvennym Naukam, Rossijskoj Akademii Nauk RF**
Nakhimovskii Prospeckt, d 51/21, 117997
Moscow
*Tel:* (095) 128-88-81; (095) 128-89-30 *Fax:* (095) 420-22-61
*E-mail:* info@inion.ru
*Web Site:* www.inion.ru
Institute of Scientific Information in the Social Sciences of the Russian Academie of Sciences, Russian Federation.

**Nauchnaya biblioteka im M Gor'kogo Sankt-Peterburgskogo** (Scientific Library of St Petersburg University)
Universitetskaya nab 7/9, 199034 Saint-Petersburg
*Tel:* (0812) 328-27-41; (0812) 328-95-46
  *Fax:* (0812) 328-27-41

*E-mail:* info@mail.lib.pu.ru
*Web Site:* www.lib.pu.ru
*Key Personnel*
Dir: Natalja A Sheshina
Vice Dir: Marina Karpova
M Gor'kii Scientific Library of the State University of St Petersburg.

**Petrozavodskij Gosudarstvennyj Universitet**
prospekt Lenina 33, 185640 Petrozavodsk
*Tel:* (08142) 74-28-65 *Fax:* (08142) 71-10-00
*E-mail:* lib@mainpgu.karelia.ru
*Web Site:* www.karelia.ru
*Key Personnel*
Dir: Marina P Otlivanchik *E-mail:* otl@pgu.karelia.ru
Assistant Dir: Klaudia P Shirshina *Tel:* (08142) 71-10-44
Editor: Natalya V Markova

**Rossiiskaya Nacionalnaya biblioteka** (National Library of Russia)
18, Sadovaya, 191069 St Petersburg
*Tel:* (0812) 310-2856; (0812) 110-6253
  *Fax:* (0812) 310-6148
*E-mail:* office@nlr.ru; english@nlr.ru
*Web Site:* www.nlr.ru
*Key Personnel*
Dir: Vladimir Zaitsev *Tel:* (0812) 118-85-00
  *E-mail:* v.zaitsev@nlr.ru

**Gosudarstvennaya publichnaya nauchno-tekhnicheskaya biblioteka Sibirskogo otdeleniya Rossiiskoi Akademii Nauk** (State Public Scientific Technological Library of the Siberian Branch Academy of Sciences of Russia)
Voskhod 15, 200 Novosibirsk
*Tel:* (0382) 66-18-60 *Fax:* (0382) 66-33-65
*E-mail:* root@libr.nsk.su
*Web Site:* www.gpntb.ru
*Telex:* 133220 *Cable:* 1023 LIBRO
*Key Personnel*
Dir: Prof Boris Stepanovich Yelepov
Deputy Dir: Yelena Borisovna Soboleva
Secretary, International Ties: Vera Nicolaevna Cabanova
Founded: 1918

**Russian State Historical Archives**
Angliyskaya Embankment 4, 190000 St Petersburg
*Tel:* (0812) 311-09-26 *Fax:* (0812) 311-22-52
*Key Personnel*
Dir: V G Gerasimov

**Sankt-Peterburgskogo Gosudarstvennogo Universiteta**
7-9, Universitetskaya nab, 199034 St Petersburg
*Tel:* (0812) 3262000 *Fax:* (0812) 2182741
*E-mail:* office@inform.pu.ru
*Web Site:* www.spbu.ru
*Key Personnel*
Vice Dir: M Karpova

**Scientific Library of St Petersburg University**, see Nauchnaya biblioteka im M Gor'kogo Sankt- Petersburgskogo

**Scientific Library Voronezh State University**
prospekt Revoljucii 24, 394000 Voronezh
*Tel:* (0732) 55-35-59 *Fax:* (0732) 208-258
*E-mail:* root@lib.vsu.ru
*Web Site:* www.lib.vsu.ru
*Key Personnel*
Librarian: Svetlana Yants *E-mail:* yants@lib.vsu.ru
Founded: 1918

**State Archives of the Russian Federation**
Bolshaya Pirogovskaya ul 17, 119817 Moscow
*Tel:* (095) 245-81-41 *Fax:* (095) 245-12-87
*E-mail:* garf@online.ru
*Web Site:* www.rusarchives.ru/federal/garf-or-gard.narod.ru
*Key Personnel*
Dir: Sergei Vladimirovich Mironenko

**Vserossijskaja gosudarstvennaja biblioteka inostrannoj literatury im M I Rudomino** (M I Rudomino All-Russia State Library for Foreign Literature)
Nikolojamskaya ul, 1, 109189 Moscow
*Tel:* (095) 9153621 *Fax:* (095) 9153637
*E-mail:* vgbil@libfl.ru
*Web Site:* www.libfl.ru
*Key Personnel*
Dir General: Ekaterina Genieva
Founded: 1922
General research & public library; an international cultural center.
Membership(s): International Federation of Library Associations & Institutions (IFLA); Russian Library Association.

# Rwanda

**Bibliotheque de l'Institut National de la Recherche Scientifique**
BP 192, Butare
*Tel:* 30395 *Fax:* 30939
*Telex:* 22605

**Service de l'Information et des Archives Nationales**
Presidence de la Republique, BP 15, Kigali
*Tel:* 76 995 *Fax:* 82 162
*Telex:* 517 PRESIREP RW
*Key Personnel*
Dir: Charles Uyisenga

**Bibliotheque de l'Universite Nationale du Rwanda**
BP 117, Butare
*Tel:* 530272 *Fax:* 530210
*E-mail:* biblio@nur.ac.rw
*Telex:* 22605
*Key Personnel*
Dir: Serugendo Emmanuel

# Samoa

**Nelson Memorial Public Library**
PO Box 598, Apia
*Tel:* (0685) 21028 *Fax:* (0685) 21028
*Key Personnel*
Chief Librarian: Ms Jacinta P Godinet
  *E-mail:* jpgodinet@lesamoa.net
Founded: 1960

# Saudi Arabia

**Imam Mohamed Bin Saud University Library**
PO Box 5701, Riyadh 11432
*Tel:* (01) 258 0000 *Fax:* (01) 259 0271
*Telex:* 401166 Univer SJ
*Key Personnel*
Acting Dean of Library Affairs: Dr Mohamed Al Zeer

**Institute of Public Administration Library**
PO Box 205, Riyadh 11141
*Tel:* (01) 476 1600 *Fax:* (01) 479 2136
*E-mail:* library@ipa.edu.sa
*Web Site:* www.ipa.edu.sa
*Telex:* 404360 SJ *Cable:* IPADMIN
*Key Personnel*
Dir of Libraries: Mostafa M Sadhan
Publication(s): *Maktabat Al Idarah* (Library Administration, quarterly)

**Islamic University Central Library**
PO Box 170, Medina
*Tel:* (04) 847 4080 *Fax:* (04) 847 4560
*Telex:* 570022 Islami SJ
*Key Personnel*
University Rector: Dr Abdullah Saleh Alobeid
Dean & Library Affairs & Man Dir: Dr Mohammad Yakub Turkustani
Editor in Chief: Dr Ali Sultan Alhakamy
Founded: 1961

**King Abdul Aziz Public Library**
PO Box 86486, Riyadh 11622
*Tel:* (01) 4911300; (01) 4911304 *Fax:* (01) 4911949
*E-mail:* kapl@anet.net.sa
*Web Site:* www.kapl.org.sa
*Telex:* 406444 KAPL
*Key Personnel*
Dir General: Faisal A Al-Muammar

**King Abdulasiz University Library**
PO Box 80213, Jeddah 21589
*Tel:* (02) 695 2562 *Fax:* (02) 640 0169
*E-mail:* library@kaau.edu.sa
*Web Site:* www.kaau.edu.sa
*Telex:* 401141 Kauni SJ
*Key Personnel*
Dean, Library Affairs: Dr Faisal I Iskanderani
   *E-mail:* eng-vicedean2@kaau.edu.sa
Administrator: Mohammed Ahmed Basager
   *Tel:* (02) 695 2481 *E-mail:* lia3003@kaau.edu.sa
A central library with 10 branches in various faculties.
Publication(s): *Annual Index of Umm Al-Qura* (Arabic); *Catalogue of MSS in the Central Library* (Arabic); *Dissertations on Saudi Arabia* (English)

**King Fahad National Library**
King Fahad Rd, Riyadh 11472
*Tel:* (01) 462 4888 *Fax:* (01) 462 5892
*Web Site:* www.kfnl.gov.sa

**King Faisal University Library**
PO Box 1758, Al-Hasa 31982
*Tel:* (03) 5801247 *Fax:* (03) 8576748
*E-mail:* library@kfu.edu.sa
*Web Site:* www.kfu.edu.sa/library/lib.asp
*Telex:* 870020 FAISAL SJ
*Key Personnel*
Dean of Library Affairs: Dr Mohammed Nassir Al-Dasari *Tel:* (03) 5801247 *E-mail:* mdosari@kfu.edu.sa
Vice Dean of Libraries: Dr Fares A Al-Faredi
   *E-mail:* vdean_library@damman.kfu.edu.sa

**King Saud University Library**
PO Box 2454, Riyadh 11451
*Tel:* (01) 4676148 *Fax:* (01) 4676162
*E-mail:* info@ksu.edu.sa
*Web Site:* www.ksu.edu.sa
*Telex:* 201019 Ksu SJ *Cable:* University
*Key Personnel*
Dean: Dr Sulaiman S Al-Ogla *E-mail:* sfalogla@.ksu.edu.sa
Founded: 1979
Publication(s): *Directory of Libraries in Saudi Arabia* (1979)

**Umm al Qura University Library**
PO Box 1629, Azizia, Makkah
*Tel:* (02) 5565621; (02) 5501000 (ext 5562) *Fax:* (02) 5501000 (ext 5562)
*E-mail:* lib@uqu.edu.sa
*Web Site:* www.uqu.edu.sa
*Telex:* 540026 Jammka SJ
*Key Personnel*
Dean of Library Affairs: Dr Hammad M Ae-Thomaly

# Senegal

**L'Alliance francaise, Bibliotheque**
2, rue Assane Ndoye, Dakar
Mailing Address: BP 1777, Dakar
*Tel:* 21 0822

**Archives du Senegal**
Immeuble administratif, ave Leopold Sedar Senghor, Dakar
*Tel:* 8217021; 8231088 (ext 595) *Fax:* 8217021
*E-mail:* bdas@telecomplus.sn
*Web Site:* www.archivesdusenegal.sn
*Key Personnel*
Dir: Saliou Mbaye *E-mail:* pmarchi@primature.sn
National Archives of Senegal.
Publication(s): *Bibliographie du Senegal* (annual report); *Dictionnaire de sigles et acronymes en usage au Senegal* (1990, monographic); *Guide de Archives de l'AOF* (monographic); *Histoire des institutions coloniales Francaise en Afrique de l'ouest (1816-1960)* (1991, monographic)

**Ecole des Bibliothecaires, Archivistes et Documentalistes de l'Universite Cheikh Anta Diop de Dakar**
BP 3252, Dakar
*Tel:* 825 76 60; 864 21 22 *Fax:* 824 05 42
*E-mail:* ebad@ebad.ucad.sn
*Web Site:* www.ebad.ucad.sn
*Telex:* 51-262 UNIVDAK SG
*Key Personnel*
Dir: Mbaye Thiam *E-mail:* mbaye.thiam@ebad.ucad.sn

**IDEP**, see Institut Africain de Developpement Economique et de Planification (IDEP), Bibliotheque

**Institut Africain de Developpement Economique et de Planification (IDEP), Bibliotheque**
BP 3186, Dakar
*Tel:* 823 10 20 *Fax:* 822 29 64
*E-mail:* idep@sonatel.senet.net
*Telex:* 51579 Idep *Cable:* IDEP
*Key Personnel*
Dir: Dr Jeggan C Senghor

**Institut Fondamental d'Afrique Noire, Bibliotheque**
BP 206, Campus universitaire Dakar, Dakar
*Tel:* 825 00 90; 825 98 90; 825 71 24 *Fax:* 24 49 18
*E-mail:* bifan@telecomplus.sn
*Telex:* 51262
*Key Personnel*
Librarian: Gora Dia

**Universite Cheikh Anta Diop de Dakar, Bibliotheque Universitaire**
BP 2006, Dakar
*Tel:* 825 02 79; 824 69 81 *Fax:* 824 23 79
*Web Site:* www.bu.ucad.sn
*Telex:* 5126256 UNIVDAK

*Key Personnel*
Dir: Mr Henri Sene *E-mail:* hsene@bu.ucad.sn
Founded: 1957
University library.
Publication(s): *Collective Catalogue of Memoires*; *Collective Catalogue of Periodicals*; *Collective National Catalogue of Periodical Publications*

# Serbia and Montenegro

**Centralna Narodna Biblioteka SR Crne Gore**
   (Central National Library of Montenegro)
Bulevar Crnogorskih junaka 163, 81250 Cetinje
*Tel:* (086) 231 143 *Fax:* (086) 231 726
*E-mail:* cnb@cg.yu
*Key Personnel*
Dir: Dr Cedomir Draskovic
Founded: 1946
Central National Library of Montenegro, national depository, general scientific library; special collection of Montenegrina, old & rare books.
Publication(s): *Bibliografski vjesnik* (Bibliographic Courier, 3 times/yr)

**Biblioteka Matice Srpske** (Matica Srpska Library)
Ul Matice Srpska 1, 21000 Novi Sad
*Tel:* (021) 420 271; (021) 528 747 *Fax:* (021) 28 574; (021) 420 271; (021) 25 859
*E-mail:* bms@bms.ns.ac.yu
*Web Site:* www.bms.ns.ac.yu
*Key Personnel*
Dir: Miro Vuksanovic *Tel:* (021) 528 910
   *E-mail:* miro@bms.ns.ac.yu
Founded: 1826
Library & information work.
Membership(s): International Federation of Library Associations & Institutions (IFLA).
Publication(s): *Matica Srpska Library Guide*

**Narodna Biblioteka Srbije** (National Library of Serbia)
Skerliceva 1, 11000 Belgrade
*Tel:* (011) 451-242; (011) 451-281; (011) 451-287 *Fax:* (011) 451-289; (011) 452-952
*Web Site:* www.nbs.bg.ac.yu
*Telex:* 12 208 NB SRB YU
*Key Personnel*
Dir: Milomar Petrovic; Mr Sreten Ugricic
   *Tel:* (011) 434-091 *E-mail:* sugricic@nbs.bg.ac.yu
Dir for International Relations: Vesna Injac
   *Tel:* (011) 453-843 *E-mail:* injac@nbs.bg.ac.yu
Head, Publishing & Editor: Djurdjic Ljiljana
Founded: 1832
Publishing department of the National Library of Serbia.

**Arhiv Srbije** (Archives of Serbia)
Karnegijeva 2, 11000 Belgrade
*Tel:* (011) 33-70-781; (011) 33-70-782; (011) 33-70-879; (011) 33-70-880 *Fax:* (011) 33-70-246
*E-mail:* office@archives.org.yu
*Web Site:* www.archives.org.yu
*Key Personnel*
Dir: Vjera Mitrovic
Librarian: Tatjana Jovanovic
Founded: 1900
Publication(s): *Arhivski Pregled*

**Biblioteka Srpske Akademije Nauka i Umetnosti** (Library of the Serbian Academy of Sciences & Arts)
Knez Mihailova 35, 11000 Belgrade
*Tel:* (011) 33-42-400 *Fax:* (011) 639-120

*E-mail:* admin@bib.sanu.ac.yu
*Web Site:* www.bib.sanu.ac.yu
*Key Personnel*
Exchange Librarian (English-speaking Countries):
  Prof Spomenka Ninic *Tel:* (011) 33-42-400, ext
  233 *E-mail:* ninic@bib.sanu.ac.yu
Dir, Library of SASA & Librarian: Prof Mr Niksa
  Stipcevic
Founded: 1842
Publication(s): *Izdanja Biblioteke Srske Akademije
  Nauka i Umetnosti*

**Univerzitet u Beogradu biblioteka 'Svetozar
  Markovic'**
Bulevar Kralja Aleksandra 71, 11000 Belgrade
*Tel:* (011) 3370-509 *Fax:* (011) 3370-354
*Web Site:* ns.unilib.bg.ac.yu
*Key Personnel*
Librarian: Ivan Gadjanski

# Sierra Leone

**British Council Library**
Tower Hill, Freetown
Mailing Address: PO Box 124, Freetown
*Tel:* (022) 222223; (022) 222227; (022) 2224683
  *Fax:* (022) 224123
*E-mail:* enquiry@sl.britishcouncil.org
*Web Site:* www.britishcouncil.org/sierraleone
*Telex:* 3453 Bricon SL
*Key Personnel*
Contact: Abator Thomas

**Fourah Bay College Library**
University of Sierra Leone, Mount Aureol, Free-
  town
Mailing Address: PO Box 87, Freetown
*Tel:* (022) 227924; (022) 224260 *Fax:* (022)
  224260
*E-mail:* fbcadmin@sierratel.sl
*Web Site:* fbcusl.8k.com
*Telex:* 3210 BOOTH SL *Cable:* FOURAH BAY
*Key Personnel*
Librarian: Deanna Thomas Lnm'jamtu-Sie
Founded: 1827

**Milton Margai Teachers' College Library**
Goderich hr, Freetown
*Tel:* (022) 024305

**Njala University College Library (University of
  Sierra Leone)**
PMB, Freetown
*Tel:* (022) 228788
*E-mail:* nuc@sierratel.sl; nuclib@sierratel.sl
*Web Site:* www.nuc-online.com
*Key Personnel*
Librarian: A N T Deen

**Public Archives of Sierra Leone**
University of Sierra Leone, Mount Aureol, Free-
  town
Mailing Address: PO Box 87, Mount Aureol,
  Freetown
*Tel:* (022) 229 471
*Key Personnel*
Hon Govt Archivist Prof: Akintola J G Wyse

**Sierra Leone Library Board**
PO Box 326, Freetown
*Tel:* (022) 226 993
*Key Personnel*
Chief Librarian: Mrs I O'Brien-Coker
Publication(s): *Sierra Leone Publications* (annu-
  ally)

**United States Information Service Library**
c/o American Embassy, 8 Walpole, Freetown
*Tel:* 226481 *Fax:* 225471
*Telex:* 3509
*Key Personnel*
Librarian: Florence Nylander

**University of Sierra Leone,** see Njala University
College Library (University of Sierra Leone)

# Singapore

**National Archives of Singapore**
One Canning Rise, Singapore 179868
*Tel:* 6332 7909
*Web Site:* www.nhb.gov.sg/NAS/nas.shtml
Founded: 1968

**National University of Singapore Library**
12 Kent Ridge Crescent, Singapore 119275
*Tel:* 6874-2028 *Fax:* 6777-8581
*E-mail:* clbsec@nus.edu.sg
*Web Site:* www.lib.nus.edu.sg
*Telex:* RS 33943 UNISPO
*Key Personnel*
Dir: Sylvia Yap *Tel:* 6874-2069 *Fax:* 6777-1272
  *E-mail:* clbyapsb@nus.edu.sg
Senior Librarian: Mrs Kim-Chew Ah Too
  *Tel:* 6874-2060
Publication(s): *LINUS Newsletter of the NUS
  Library*; *NUS Library Guide*; *SMC Ondisc
  CD-ROM* (contains PERIND database: In-
  dex to Periodical Articles relating to Singa-
  pore, Malaysia, Brunei & ASEAN; Singa-
  pore/Malaysia Collection database; NUS The-
  ses Collection database)
*Branch Office(s)*
Central Library
Chinese Library
Hon Sui Sen Memorial Library
C J Koh Law Library
Medical Library
Science Library

# Slovakia

**Centrum Vedecko-Technickych Informacii SR**
  (Slovak Centre of Scientific & Technical
  Information)
Slovak Centre of Scientific & Technical Informa-
  tion, Namestie slobody 19, 81223 Bratislava
*Tel:* (02) 5292 3527 *Fax:* (02) 5292 3527; (02)
  5727 6236
*E-mail:* cvti@tbb1.cvtisr.sk
*Web Site:* www.cvtisr.sk
*Key Personnel*
Dir: Dipl Ing Jan Kurak
Deputy Dir: Vlasta Cikatricisova
Publication(s): *Bulletin Centra VTI SR* (Signale
  informacie); *EURO-info*; *Infotrend*

**Univerzitna Kniznica**
Michalska 1, 814 17 Bratislava
*Tel:* (02) 54 434 981 *Fax:* (02) 54 434 246
*E-mail:* ill@ulib.sk
*Web Site:* www.ulib.sk
*Key Personnel*
Manager: Peter Tausche
Librarian: Emil Vontorcik, PhD
Diplomat: Julius Balogh

**Univerzita Pavla Jozefa Safarika**
Srobarova 2, 041 80 Kosice

*Tel:* (055) 622 26 08 *Fax:* (055) 766 959
*E-mail:* kancelar@upjs.sk; rektor@upjs.sk
*Web Site:* www.upjs.sk
*Key Personnel*
Dir: Darina Kozuchova

**Slovenska Narodna Kniznica, Martin** (Slovak
  National Library, Martin)
Nam J C Hronskeho 1, 036 01 Martin
*Tel:* (043) 422 07 20 *Fax:* (043) 430 18 02
*E-mail:* snk@snk.sk
*Web Site:* www.snk.sk
*Key Personnel*
General Dir: Dusan Katuscak
Publication(s): *Hudobny archiv* (Music Archive);
  *Kniha* (The Book); *Kniznica* (monthly, Li-
  braries & scientific information); *Literarny
  archiv* (Literary Archive); *Slovenska narodna
  bibliografia* (Print, CD-ROM, monthly, Slovak
  National Bibliography)

**Ustredna kniznica Slovenskej akademie vied**
  (Central Library of the Slovak Academy of
  Sciences)
Klemensova 19, 814 67 Bratislava
*Tel:* (02) 52926 321; (02) 52926 325 *Fax:* (02)
  52921 733
*E-mail:* knizhorv@klemens.savba.sk
*Web Site:* www.uk.sav.sk/
*Key Personnel*
Dir: Andrea Doktorova *E-mail:* andrea.
  doktorova@savba.sk
Publication(s): *Informacny Bulletin UK SAV* (Bul-
  letin)
*Parent Company:* Slovak Academy of Sciences

# Slovenia

**Arhiv Republike Slovenije** (Archives of the
  Republic of Slovenia)
Zvezdarska 1, pp 21, 1127 Ljubljana
*Tel:* (01) 24 14 200 *Fax:* (01) 24 14 269
*E-mail:* ars@gov.si
*Web Site:* www.sigov.si/ars
*Key Personnel*
Dir: Dragan Matic *Tel:* (01) 24 14 240
  *E-mail:* dragan.matic@gov.si
Librarian: Alenka Hren *Tel:* (01) 24 12 218
  *E-mail:* alenka.hren@gov.si
Founded: 1859
Publication(s): *Arhivi* (Archives); *Inventarji* (In-
  ventories); *Katalogi* (Catalogs); *Viri* (Sources);
  *Vodniki* (Guides)

**Narodna in Univerzitetna Knjiznica, Ljubljana**
  (National & University Library)
Turjaska 1, 1000 Ljubljana
*Tel:* (01) 2001 110 *Fax:* (01) 4257 293
*E-mail:* info@nuk.uni-lj.si
*Web Site:* www.nuk.uni-lj.si/vstop.cgi
*Telex:* 32285 *Cable:* NUK LJUBLJANA
*Key Personnel*
Man Dir: Mr Lenart Setinc
Secretary: Mr Borut Abram
Publication(s): *Knjiznicarske novice*; *Signalne in-
  formacije*; *Slovenska bibliografija*
*Branch Office(s)*
Leskoskova 12, 1000 Ljubljana *Tel:* (01) 5861
  300 *Fax:* (01) 5861 311

**Univerza Ljubljana**
Kongresni trg 12, 1000 Ljubljana
*Tel:* (01) 241 85 00 *Fax:* (01) 241 86 60
*E-mail:* info@nuk.uni-lj.si
*Web Site:* www.uni-lj.si
*Telex:* 32285 NUK-LJB-YU *Cable:* NUK
  LJUBLJANA
*Key Personnel*
Librarian: Lenart Setinc

# Somalia

**Biblioteca dell'Universita Nazionale della Somalia**
PO Box 15, Mogadishu
*Tel:* (01) 20535

**National Library of Somalia**
PO Box 1754, Mogadishu
*Tel:* (01) 227 58

# South Africa

**Bloemfontein Public Library**
PO Box 1029, Bloemfontein 9300
*Tel:* (051) 405 8248 *Fax:* (051) 405 8604
*E-mail:* pat@dux.bfncouncil.co.za
*Key Personnel*
City Librarian: P J van der Walt

**Cape Provincial Library Service**
c/o Chiappini & Alfred St, Cape Town 8001
Mailing Address: PO Box 2108, Cape Town 8000
*Tel:* (021) 483 2241 *Fax:* (021) 419 7541
*E-mail:* capelib@pgwc.gov.za
*Web Site:* www.capegateway.gov.za
*Key Personnel*
Contact: Stefan Wehmeyer

**Cape Town City Libraries**
PO Box 3541, Cape Town 8000
*Tel:* (021) 467 15 67; (021) 467-15-68 *Fax:* (021) 461 5732
*Key Personnel*
Contact: Mrs M Raymond

**The College of Education at Wits, Harold Holmes Library**
27 St Andrews Rd, Parktown, Johannesburg 2193
Mailing Address: PB X1, Johannesburg 2050
*Tel:* (011) 717-3242; (011) 717-3240 *Fax:* (011) 717-3046
*Web Site:* www.wits.ac.za/library/campuslib/edulib.htm
*Key Personnel*
Librarian: Mark Sandham *Tel:* (011) 717-3239
  *E-mail:* marks@library.wits.ac.za
Deputy Librarian: Alison Chisholm
  *E-mail:* alisonc@library.wits.ac.za

**Council for Scientific & Industrial Research**, see CSIR Information Services

**CSIR Information Services**
Meiring Naude Rd, Brummeria, Pretoria
Mailing Address: PO Box 395, Pretoria 0001
*Tel:* (012) 841-2911 *Fax:* (012) 349-1153
*Web Site:* www.csir.co.za
*Telex:* 32043
*Key Personnel*
Dir: Roy Page-Shipp *Tel:* (012) 841-3070
Manager: Colleen Mogane *Tel:* (012) 841-2557
  *E-mail:* cmogane@csir.co.za
Scientific, technological & business information, decision support value-added services, electronic real-time access to local & international databases.

**Department of Science & Technology**
Oranje Nassau Bldg, 188 Schoeman St, Pretoria
Mailing Address: Private Bag X894, Pretoria 0001
*Tel:* (012) 317 4300 *Fax:* (012) 323 8308
*Web Site:* www.dst.gov.za

*Key Personnel*
General Dir: Dr Robert Martin Adam
Publication(s): *Library News*

**East London Municipal Library**
Unisa Library Depot, PO Box 652, East London 5200
*Tel:* (043) 724991; (043) 724992 *Fax:* (043) 7431729
*Web Site:* www.unisa.ac.za/library
*Key Personnel*
Manager: Mrs M M Davidson

**Education Library & Information Services**, see EDULIS (Education Library & Information Services)

**EDULIS (Education Library & Information Services)**
15 Kruskal Ave, Bellville 7530
Mailing Address: Private Bag X9099, Cape Town 8000
*Tel:* (021) 957-9600 *Fax:* (021) 948-0748
*E-mail:* edulis@pgwc.gov.za
*Web Site:* wced.wcape.gov.za
*Key Personnel*
Head: Mrs Lyne Metcalfe *E-mail:* lmetcalf@pgwc.gov.za
Publication(s): *RESENSIONES: RECOMMENDED CURRICULUM RESOURCE MATERIAL FOR SECONDARY PRIMARY PREPRIMA* (annually)
*Parent Company:* Western Cape Education Department
*Ultimate Parent Company:* Western Cape Provincial Administration

**Ethekwini Municipal Libraries**
PO Box 917, Durban 4000
*Tel:* (031) 311 1111 *Fax:* (031) 311 2203
*Key Personnel*
Acting Dir Libraries: Ms Reigneth Nyongwana

**Free State Provincial Library & Information Services**
Private Bag X20606, Bloemfontein 9300
*Tel:* (051) 4054681 *Fax:* (051) 4033567
  *Cable:* ORANVRY
*Key Personnel*
Senior Manager: Ms J J Schimper
  *E-mail:* jacomien@sac.fs.gov.za
Founded: 1948
Publication(s): *Free State Libraries* (quarterly, journal)

**Harold Holmes Library**, see The College of Education at Wits, Harold Holmes Library

**Johannesburg Public Library**
Library Gardens, Corner of Fraser & Market Streets, Johannesburg 2001
Mailing Address: PB X93, Marshalltown 2107
*Tel:* (011) 836 3787 *Fax:* (011) 836 6607
*E-mail:* library@mj.org.za
*Key Personnel*
Librarian: E J Bevan *E-mail:* jbevan@mj.org.za
Founded: 1890
Publication(s): *Local Government Library Bulletin* (irregular)

**Kempton Park Public Library**
CR Swart Dr/Pretoria Rd, Kempton Park 1620
*Tel:* (011) 9212173 *Fax:* (011) 9750921
*Key Personnel*
Chief Librarian: J H van der Walt

**Kimberley Public Library**
Chapel St, Kimberley 8300
Mailing Address: PO Box 627, Kimberley 8300
*Tel:* (053) 8306241 *Fax:* (053) 8331954

*E-mail:* fritz@kbymun.org.za
*Key Personnel*
City Librarian: Mr F H van Dyke
Founded: 1878
City Public Libraries including 6 branches & 18 depots.
*Parent Company:* Sol Plaatje Municipality
*Branch Office(s)*
Africana Library *E-mail:* afrilib@global.co.za
Judy Scott Library

**Kwa-Zulu Natal Provincial Library Service**
PB X9016, Pietermaritzburg 3200
*Tel:* (033) 3940241 *Fax:* (033) 3942237
*E-mail:* daviess@plho.kzntl.gov.za
*Telex:* 643030
*Key Personnel*
Deputy Dir: Dr Rookaya Bawa
Contact: Janet Hart *E-mail:* hartj@natalia.kzntl.gov.za
Publication(s): *KZN Librarian* (Journal of Kwa-Zulu Natal Provincial Library Service)

**KwaZulu-Natal Law Society Library**
200 Berg St, Pietermaritzburg 3201
Mailing Address: PO Box 1454, Pietermaritzburg 3200
*Tel:* (033) 345 1304 *Fax:* (033) 394 9544
*E-mail:* info@lawsoc.co.za
*Web Site:* www.lawlibrary.co.za
*Key Personnel*
Dir: Mr J C Morrison
Librarian: Lucky Mosia *E-mail:* lucky@lawlibrary.co.za
Founded: 1851
South African journals, legal books & pamphlets, South African trade & commercial directories. Information produced by & about the South African government.
Publication(s): *Aids Bibliography* (5 vols); *Natalia* (historical journal)

**Library of Parliament**
NCOP Wing, Ground floor, Parliament St, Cape Town
Mailing Address: PO Box 18, Cape Town 8000
*Tel:* (021) 403 2140; (021) 403 2141; (021) 403 2142 *Fax:* (021) 461 4331
*E-mail:* library@parliament.gov.za
*Web Site:* www.parliament.gov.za
*Key Personnel*
Chief Librarian: Albert Ntunja *Tel:* (021) 403 2126 *E-mail:* antunja@parliament.gov.za
Founded: 1854

**Natal Archives Depot**, see State Archives Service: Natal Archives Depot

**National Archives of South Africa, Orange Free State Archives Repository, Library/Free State Provincial Archives**
29 Badenhorst St, Bloemfontein
Mailing Address: Private Bag X20504, Bloemfontein 9300
*Tel:* (051) 522 6762 *Fax:* (051) 522 6765
  *Fax on Demand:* (051) 522 6765
*E-mail:* fsarch@sac.fs.gov.za
*Web Site:* www.national.archives.gov.za
*Key Personnel*
Contact: Mr P F Wheeler

**National Archives Repository Library**
24 Hamilton St, Arcadia, Pretoria 0001
Mailing Address: Private Bag X236, Pretoria 0001
*Tel:* (012) 323 5300 *Fax:* (012) 323 5287
*E-mail:* enquiries@dac.gov.za
*Web Site:* www.national.archives.gov.za
*Key Personnel*
National Archivist: Dr G A Dominy *E-mail:* jo.pretorius@dac.gov.za

Founded: 1909
*Parent Company:* National Archives & Record
Services

**National Library of South Africa**
5 Queen Victoria St, Cape Town
Mailing Address: PO Box 496, Cape Town 8000
*Tel:* (021) 424 6320 *Fax:* (021) 423 3359
*E-mail:* macmahon@salib.ac.za
*Web Site:* www.nlsa.ac.za
*Key Personnel*
Dir: P E Westra
Founded: 1818

**National Library of South Africa**
239 Vermeulen St, Pretoria
Mailing Address: PO Box 397, 0001 Pretoria
*Tel:* (012) 321 8931 *Fax:* (012) 325 5984
*E-mail:* andrew.malotle@nlsa.ac.za
*Web Site:* www.nlsa.ac.za
*Key Personnel*
Dir: Dr Peter J Lor
Publication(s): *Directory of South African Pub-
lishers*; *Index to South African Periodicals
(ISAP)*; *Micrographic Series Indexes*; *Period-
icals in Southern African Libraries (PISAL)*;
*Public & Community Libraries Inventory of
South Africa*; *SANB (South African National
Bibliography)*
*Parent Company:* National Department of Arts &
Culture

**Rhodes University Library**
PO Box 184, Grahamstown 6140
*Tel:* (046) 603 8436 *Fax:* (046) 6223487
*E-mail:* library@ru.ac.za
*Web Site:* www.rhodes.ac.za/library/
*Key Personnel*
Chief Librarian: Margaret Kenyon *Tel:* (046)
6038079 *E-mail:* m.kenyon@ru.ac.za

**Royal Society of South Africa Library**
P D Hahn Bldg, UCT, Cape Town 8000
Mailing Address: PO Box 594, Cape Town 8000
*Tel:* (021) 650 2543 *Fax:* (021) 650 2710
*E-mail:* roysoc@science.uct.ac.za
*Web Site:* www.rssa.uct.ac.za
*Telex:* 5-214-39 SA
*Key Personnel*
President: L R Nassimbeni
Editor: J D Skinner
Honorary Librarian: D E Rawlings
Publication(s): *Transactions of the Royal Society
of South Africa* (irregular)

**South African Library for the Blind**
PO Box 115, Grahamstown 6140
*Tel:* (046) 622 7226 *Fax:* (046) 622 4645
*E-mail:* blindlib@iafrica.com
*Web Site:* www.blindlib.org.za
*Key Personnel*
Dir: Johan Roos *E-mail:* director@blindlib.org.za
Founded: 1918

**State Archives Service: Natal Archives Depot**
Private Bag X9012, Pietermaritzburg 3200
*Tel:* (033) 342 4712 *Fax:* (033) 394 4352
*Key Personnel*
Chief Archivist: J N Hawley

**Transvaal Museum Library**
432 Paul Kruger St, Pretoria 0001
Mailing Address: PO Box 413, Pretoria 0001
*Tel:* (012) 322 7632 *Fax:* (012) 322 7939
*Web Site:* www.nfi.org.za
*Telex:* 30302 *Cable:* TRANSATOR
*Key Personnel*
Manager: C Malherbe
Head Librarian: Tersia Perregil *E-mail:* perregil@
nfi.co.za
Librarian: Jakkie Luus

Founded: 1937
Publication(s): *Annals of the Transvaal Museum,
Vol 41*; *Overvaal Musea, Book parade*

**Tshwane Community Library & Information
Service**
Sammy Marks Sq, Pretoria 0002
Mailing Address: PO Box 2673, Pretoria 0001
*Tel:* (012) 3088837 *Fax:* (012) 3088873
*Key Personnel*
Library Manager: Johannes Magoro
Founded: 1964

**University of Cape Town Libraries**
Upper Campus, Library Rd, Rondebosch 7701
*Tel:* (021) 650-3134 *Fax:* (021) 689-7568
*E-mail:* selref@uctlib.uct.ac.za
*Web Site:* www.lib.uct.ac.za/
*Telex:* 5720327
*Key Personnel*
Library Head: Ingrid Thomson
Librarian: A S C Hooper
Publication(s): *Bibliographical series* (irregu-
larly); *Jagger Journal* (annually); *Varia series*
(irregularly)

**University of Port Elizabeth Library**
Private Bag X6058, Port Elizabeth 6000
*Tel:* (041) 504 2281 *Fax:* (041) 504 2280
*E-mail:* library@upe.ac.za
*Web Site:* www.upe.ac.za/library *Cable:* UNIPE
*Key Personnel*
Scientific Editor: Mr S J Gerber *Tel:* (041) 504
2298
Publication(s): *UPE Publication Series*

**University of Pretoria Academic Information
Services**
Hillcrest, Pretoria 0002
*Tel:* (012) 420 2241 *Fax:* (012) 362 5100
*Web Site:* www.ais.up.ac.za *Cable:* PUNIV
*Key Personnel*
Acting Dir: Prof J A Boon *E-mail:* jaboon@up.
ac.za

**University of South Africa Library**
PO Box 392, Pretoria 0003
*Tel:* (012) 4293206 *Fax:* (012) 4292925
*E-mail:* willej@alpha.unisa.ac.za
*Web Site:* www.unisa.ac.za *Cable:* UNISA
PRETORIA
*Key Personnel*
Executive Dir: Prof J Willemse
Publication(s): *Mousaion* (in collaboration with
the University of South Africa's Dept of Infor-
mation Science)

**University of Stellenbosch Library**
Private Bag X5036, Stellenbosch 7599
*Tel:* (021) 808 4385 *Fax:* (021) 808 4336
*Web Site:* www.sun.ac.za/library
*Telex:* 526661
*Key Personnel*
Acting Senior Dir: Johan Engelbrecht *Tel:* (021)
808 4878 *E-mail:* jpe@sun.ac.za
Central library of the US Library Service.

**University of the Western Cape Library**
Modderdam Rd, Bellville 7535
Mailing Address: Private Bag X17, Bellville 7535
*Tel:* (021) 959 2947; (021) 959 2209 *Fax:* (021)
959 2659
*Web Site:* www.uwc.ac.za/library
*Telex:* 576661
*Key Personnel*
University Librarian: Ms E R Tise *E-mail:* etise@
uwc.ac.za
Deputy University Librarian: Mr J S Andrea; Ms
K Kekana

**University of the Witwaterstrand Library**
One Jan Smuts Ave, Johannesburg 2001
Mailing Address: Private Bag 31550, Braam-
fontein
*Tel:* (011) 716-2400 *Fax:* (011) 403-1421
*E-mail:* 056heath@libris.wwl.wits.ac.za
*Telex:* 422460 *Cable:* UNIWITS
*Key Personnel*
Librarian: H M Edwards
Founded: 1934

# Spain

**Biblioteca de la Agencia Espanola de
Cooperacion Internacional**
Ave de Reyes Catolicos 4, 28040 Madrid
*Tel:* (091) 5838175 *Fax:* (091) 5838525
*E-mail:* biblioteca.hispanica@aeci.es
*Web Site:* www.aeci.es
Library of the Institute of Spanish-American Fel-
lowship.

**Archivo de la Corona de Aragon**
Calle Almogaveres 77, 08018 Barcelona
*Tel:* (093) 4854 318; (093) 4854 285; (093) 3153
928 *Fax:* (093) 3001 252
*E-mail:* aca@cult.mec.es
*Web Site:* www.cultura.mecd.es/archivos/index.
html
*Key Personnel*
Dir: Rafael Conde y Delgado de Molina
Royal Archives of Aragon.
Publication(s): *Coleccion de Documentos Inedi-
tos del Archivo de la Corona de Aragon (from
1847)*

**Archivo General de Indias**
Avda de la Constitucion 3, 41071 Seville
Mailing Address: Edificio de la Cilla, Calle Santo
Tomas 5, 41071 Seville
*Tel:* (05) 954 500 530; (05) 954 500 528
*Fax:* 954 219 485
*E-mail:* agi1@cult.mec.es
*Web Site:* www.cultura.mecd.es; www.mcu.es
*Key Personnel*
Contact: Rosario Parra Cala
Archives of the Indies.
*Parent Company:* Ministerio de Educacion, Cul-
tura y Deporte

**Archivo Historico Nacional** (National Historical
Archives)
Calle Serrano 115, 28006 Madrid
*Tel:* (091) 7688 500 *Fax:* (091) 5631 199
*Web Site:* www.mcu.es/archivos
Founded: 1866
Indexed genealogical records from the 15th to the
19th century.
*Parent Company:* Ministerio de Educacion, Cul-
tura y Deporte

**Archivo y Biblioteca Capitulares**
Catedral de Toledo, Hombre de Palo, 2, 45001
Toledo
*Tel:* (0925) 21 24 23 *Fax:* (0925) 21 24 23
*E-mail:* archicapto@terra.es
*Web Site:* www.architoledo.org/catedral/archivos/
textoarchivo.htm
*Key Personnel*
Dir: Dr Angel Fernandez Collado; Dr Ramon
Gonzalvez
Archives & library of the cathedral chapter.

**Biblioteca Bergnes de las Casas - Bibioteca de
Catalunya**
Carrer de l'Hospital, 56, 08001 Barcelona
*Tel:* (093) 270 23 00 *Fax:* (093) 270 23 04

*E-mail:* bustia@bnc.es
*Web Site:* www.gencat.es/bc
*Key Personnel*
Librarian: Maria Artal
Library attached to Biblioteca de Catalunya.

**The British Council Library**
P° General Martinez Campos 31, 28010 Madrid
*Tel:* (091) 337 3500 *Fax:* (091) 337 3573
*E-mail:* madrid@britishcouncil.es
*Web Site:* www.britishcouncil.es
*Key Personnel*
Contact: Antonia Dominguez

**Biblioteca de Catalunya** (National Library of
Catalonia)
Carrer de l'Hospital, 56, 08001 Barcelona
*Tel:* (093) 270 23 00 *Fax:* (093) 270 23 04
*E-mail:* infocat@gencat.net
*Web Site:* www.gencat.es/bc
*Key Personnel*
Dir: Mrs Vinyet Panyella
Chief of Difussion Area: Montserrat Fonoll
*E-mail:* mfonoll@bnc.es
Publication(s): *Nota Bene* (bimonthly, information
bulletin of the biblioteca de Catalunya)

**Biblioteca General de Humanidades Consejo
Superior de Investigaciones Cientificas**
(Spanish Council for Scientific Research)
Duque de Medinaceli, 6 planta baja, 28014
Madrid
*Tel:* (091) 360 18 10; (091) 360 18 12 *Fax:* (091)
369 09 40
*E-mail:* bghpre@bib.csic.es
*Web Site:* www.csic.es/cbic/BGH/bgh.htm
*Key Personnel*
Library Dir: Carmela M Perez-Montes Salmeron
*E-mail:* carmela@bib.csic.es
Library of the Council for Scientific Research.
*Parent Company:* Ministerio de Educacion y
Ciencia

**Fundacion Esade**
Marques de Mulhacen, 40-42, 08034 Barcelona
*Tel:* (093) 280 61 62 *Fax:* (093) 204 81 05
*Web Site:* www.esade.es/biblio
*Telex:* 98286
*Key Personnel*
Head Librarian: Francisca Buxo *E-mail:* buxo@
esade.edu

**Hemeroteca Municipal de Madrid**
Calle Conde Duque 9-11, 28015 Madrid
*Tel:* (091) 588 57 71
*Key Personnel*
Dir: Carlos Dorado Fernandez
Madrid periodical library.

**Biblioteca y Casa - Museo de Menendez Pelayo**
Rubio 6, 39001 Santander
*Tel:* (042) 23 45 34
*E-mail:* xjagenjo@sarenet.es
*Web Site:* www.turcantabria.com
*Key Personnel*
Librarian: Manuel Revuelta Sanudo
Publication(s): *La Biblioteca de Menendez
Pelayo*; *Boletin de la Biblioteca de Menen-
dez Pelayo* (annually); *Estudios de literatura y
pensamiento hispanicos* (series)

**Biblioteca Nacional**
Paseo de Recoletos 20, 28071 Madrid
*Tel:* (091) 580 7800
*Web Site:* www.bne.es; www.mec.es
*Key Personnel*
Dir: Alicia Giron Garcia
*Parent Company:* Ministerio de Education, Cul-
tura y Deporte

**Patrimonio Nacional, Real Biblioteca**
Palacio Real, Calle Bailen s/n, 28071 Madrid
*Tel:* (091) 454 87 00; (091) 454 87 32 *Fax:* (091)
454 87 21
*E-mail:* realbiblioteca@patrimonionacional.es
*Web Site:* www.patrimonionacional.es
*Key Personnel*
Dir: Maria Luisa Lopez-Vidriero
*E-mail:* lvidriero@patrimonionacional.es
Library of the Royal Palace.

**Servei de Biblioteques de la UAB**
Universitat Autonoma de Barcelona, Edifici N,
08193 Bellaterra, Cerdanyola del Valles
*Tel:* (093) 581 1015 *Fax:* (093) 581 3219
*E-mail:* bib.utp@uab.es; s.biblioteques@uab.es
*Web Site:* www.bib.uab.es; www.uab.es
*Telex:* 52040 EDVCIE
*Key Personnel*
Dir: Joan Gomez Escofet *Tel:* (093) 581 10 71
*E-mail:* joan.gomez.escofet@uab.es
Deputy Librarian: Nuria Balague *E-mail:* nuria.
balague@uab.es
Publication(s): *Biblioteca Informacions*

**Servicio de Biblioteca de Ciencias de la Salud**
Hospital de Cruces, Apdo 69, 48080 Bilbao
*Tel:* (04) 6006125 *Fax:* (04) 6006049
*E-mail:* biblioteca.cruces@hcru.osakidetza.net
*Web Site:* www.hospitalcruces.com/
informacioncientifica/biblioteca.asp
Service in information & scientific documentation
in health sciences.
Publication(s): *Catalogo de Publicaciones y Se-
ries Periodicas de Ciencias de la Salud*

**Universidad Autonoma - Biblioteca
Universitaria**
Carretera de Colmenar Viejo, Km 15, 28049
Madrid
*Tel:* (091) 3974399 *Fax:* (091) 3975058
*E-mail:* servicio.biblioteca@uam.es
*Web Site:* www.uam.es
*Key Personnel*
President: Jesus Matilla Quiza
*E-mail:* vicerrectorado@investigacion@uam.es
Dir of Library: D Santiago Fernandez Conti
*E-mail:* santiago.conti@uam.es
Contact: Maria Sintes *E-mail:* msintes@uam.es

**Biblioteca de la Universidad Complutense**
Cuidad Universitaria, 28040 Madrid
*Tel:* (091) 394 69 25; (091) 394 69 39 *Fax:* (091)
394 69 26
*E-mail:* bucweb@buc.ucm.es
*Web Site:* www.ucm.es/BUCM
*Key Personnel*
Dir: Jose Antonio Magan Wals *E-mail:* magan@
buc.ucm.es
Head Librarian: Ana Delgado Perez

**Universidad de Cantabria Biblioteca**
Ave de Los Castros s/n, 39005 Santander
*Tel:* (0942) 201 180 *Fax:* (0942) 201 183
*E-mail:* infobuc@gestion.unican.es
*Web Site:* www.buc.unican.es
*Key Personnel*
Dir: Maria Jesus Saiz *E-mail:* maria.saiz@
gastion.unican.es

**Universidad Pontificia de Salamanca,
Biblioteca**
Compania 5, 37002 Salamanca
*Tel:* (0923) 277 118 *Fax:* (0923) 277 101
*E-mail:* bibliotecario.general@upsa.es; bibliot.
maribel@upsa.es
*Web Site:* www.upsa.es/biblioteca.html

**Biblioteca de la Universitat de Barcelona**
Baldiri Reixac 2, 08028 Barcelona
*Tel:* (093) 403 45 89 *Fax:* (093) 403 45 92

*E-mail:* sbib@org.ub.es
*Web Site:* www.bib.ub.es
*Key Personnel*
Dir: Jane Neus *Tel:* (093) 402 90 66 *Fax:* (093)
403 44 91
Publication(s): *Memoria*; *Red de Bibliothecas
Universitarias*

# Sri Lanka

**British Council Information Resource Centre**
49 Alfred House Gardens, Colombo 3
Mailing Address: PO Box 753, Colombo 3
*Tel:* (01) 581171 *Fax:* (01) 587079
*E-mail:* enquiries@britishcouncil.lk
*Web Site:* www.britishcouncil.lk
*Key Personnel*
Dir: Tony O'Brien
Deputy Dir: Anna Searle
Library & Information Services Manager: Ran-
mali de Silva *E-mail:* library@britishcouncil.uk
Founded: 1949
*Branch Office(s)*
88/3 Kotugodella Veediya, Kandy, Branch
Manager: Alison Markwick *Tel:* (081)
2222410; (081) 2234634 *Fax:* (081) 2234284
*E-mail:* bckandy@britishcouncil.lk

**Colombo National Museum Library**
Sir Marcus Fernando Mawatha, Colombo 07
Mailing Address: PO Box 854, Colombo 07
*Tel:* (01) 692092; (01) 693314 *Fax:* (01) 695366
*E-mail:* cnmid@sltnet.lk
*Key Personnel*
Dir: Mrs N A Wikramasingha
See also Department of National Museums (Pub-
lisher).
Publication(s): *Spolia Zeylanica: Bulletin of the
National Museums of Sri Lanka*; *Sri Lanka Pe-
riodicals Index*; *Ceylon Periodiocals Directory
(Annual Supplements)*
*Parent Company:* Ministry of Cultural Affairs

**Colombo Public Library**
No 15, Sir Marcus Fernando Mawatha, Colombo
07
*Tel:* (011) 2691968; (011) 2695156; (011)
2696530 *Fax:* (011) 2691968
*E-mail:* info@cmc.lk
*Web Site:* www.cmc.lk/library.asp
*Key Personnel*
Chief Librarian: Mr M D H Jayawardana
Founded: 1925
Publication(s): *Libraries & People: A Manual for
Public Libraries in Sri Lanka*; *Road to Wis-
dom*; *Glimpses of Colombo*
*Parent Company:* Colombo Municipal Council

**Department of National Archives**
7 Reid Ave, Colombo 7
Mailing Address: PO Box 1414, Colombo 7
*Tel:* (01) 694523; (01) 696917 *Fax:* (01) 694419
*E-mail:* narchive@slt.lk *Cable:* ARCHIVES
*Key Personnel*
Dir: Dr K D G Wimalaratne
*Parent Company:* Ministry of Cultural Affairs

**Industrial Technology Institute Information
Services Centre**
363 Bauddhaloka Mawatha, Colombo 7
*Tel:* (01) 693807; (01) 693808; (01) 693809;
(01) 698621; (01) 698622; (01) 698623
*Fax:* (01) 686567
*E-mail:* info@iti.lk
*Web Site:* www.iti.lk *Cable:* CISIR
*Key Personnel*
Dir: Dr A M Mubarak *Tel:* (01) 691614
*E-mail:* dir_ceo@iti.lk

Manager, Information Services: Dilmani Warnasuriya *E-mail:* dilmani@iti.lk
Founded: 1955

**National Library & Documentation Centre**
No 14, Independence Ave, Colombo 07
*Tel:* (011) 2698847; (011) 2685197 *Fax:* (011) 2685201
*E-mail:* nldc@mail.natlib.lk
*Web Site:* www.natlib.lk
*Key Personnel*
Dir General: Mr M S U Amarasiri *Tel:* (011) 2687581 *E-mail:* dg@mail.natlib.lk
Founded: 1970
Publication(s): *Directory of Social Science Libraries, Information Centres & Data Bases in Sri Lanka*; *International Standard Book Numbering in Sri Lanka* (brochure); *Library News* (quarterly); *Sri Lanka Conference Index, 1976-1986, 1987-1990, 1991-1992* (Sri Lanka Newspaper article Index-1993); *Sri Lanka (ISBN) Publishers Directory, 1991 edition*; *Sri Lanka National Bibliography* (monthly)

**University of Peradeniya Library**
University Park, 20400 Peradeniya
Mailing Address: PO Box 35, Peradeniya
*Tel:* (081) 2386004 *Fax:* (081) 2388678
*E-mail:* lib@mail.pdn.ac.lk
*Web Site:* www.pdn.ac.lk/library/main
*Key Personnel*
Librarian: Harrison Perera *E-mail:* librarian@pdn.ac.lk
Founded: 1921
Publication(s): *Ceylon Journal of Science: Biological Sciences* (irregularly, academic journal); *Ceylon Journal of Science: Physical Sciences* (irregularly, academic journal); *Modern Sri Lanka Studies* (irregularly, academic journal); *Sri Lanka Journals of the Humanities* (irregularly, academic journal)

# Sudan

**ACADI**, see Arab Organization for Agricultural Development

**Al-Neelain University**
Affiliate of Ministry of Higher Education & Scientific Research
PO Box 12702, Khartoum
*Tel:* (011) 880055 *Fax:* (011) 776338
*E-mail:* neelain@an.mail.com
*Telex:* 23027 NILUN SD B
Founded: 1992
Academic teaching & lecturing.

**AOAD**, see Arab Organization for Agricultural Development

**Arab Center for Agricultural Documentation**, see Arab Organization for Agricultural Development

**Arab Organization for Agricultural Development**
St No 7, Al Alamarat, Khartoum
Mailing Address: PO Box 474, Khartoum
*Tel:* (011) 472176; (011) 472183 *Fax:* (011) 471402; (011) 471050
*E-mail:* info@aoad.org
*Web Site:* www.aoad.org
*Telex:* 22554 AOAD SD *Cable:* AOAD KHARTOUM
*Key Personnel*
Dir General: Dr Yahia Bakour

**British Council Library**
14 Abu Sinn St, Khartoum
Mailing Address: PO Box 1253, Khartoum
*Tel:* (0183) 780817; (0183) 777310 *Fax:* (0183) 774935
*E-mail:* info@sd.britishcouncil.org
*Web Site:* www.britishcouncil.org/sudan
*Telex:* 23114 Bckht Sd
*Key Personnel*
Dir: Paul Doubleday *E-mail:* paul.doubleday@sd.britishcouncil.org
Librarian: Ali Hassan Salih

**Khartoum Polytechnic Library**
PO Box 407, Khartoum
*Tel:* 78922
*Key Personnel*
Librarian: Mohammad Bakheit

**National Records Office Library**
PO Box 1914, Khartoum
*Tel:* (011) 784135; (011) 784255 *Fax:* (011) 778 603
*Key Personnel*
Librarian: Abdel Aziz Gabir Mohamed
Founded: 1949

**Omdurman Islamic University**
PO Box 382, Omdurman 14415
*Tel:* 784348; 784365; 554272 *Fax:* 775253
*Web Site:* www.sudanembassy.org/contemporarylooks/umdurman.htm
*Telex:* 22527
Founded: 1921

**University of Khartoum Library**
PO Box 321, Khartoum
*Web Site:* www.sudan.net/uk
*Key Personnel*
Librarian: Dr Mohammed Nouri Al/Amin
Assistant Librarian: Asma Ibrahim Al-Iman

# Suriname

**Bibliotheek Cultureel Centrum Suriname**
(Library of the Cultural Centre Suriname)
Gravenstr 112-114, Paramaribo
Mailing Address: PO Box 1241, Paramaribo
*Tel:* 472369; 473309 *Fax:* 476516
*E-mail:* sccs@sr.net; stgccs1947@hotmail.com
*Key Personnel*
Dir: Johan Roozer
Founded: 1947

# Swaziland

**Swaziland College of Technology Library**
PO Box 69, Mbabane 14100
*Tel:* (040) 42681; (040) 43539 *Fax:* (040) 44521
*E-mail:* scotlibrary@africaonline.co.sz
Founded: 1946
*Parent Company:* Ministry of Education

**Swaziland National Library Service**
PO Box 1461, Mbabane
*Tel:* 42633 *Fax:* 43863
*E-mail:* snlssz@realnet.co.sz
*Web Site:* www.library.ohiou.edu/subjects/swaziland/snls.htm
*Telex:* 2270 Wd
*Key Personnel*
Dir: D Kunene *E-mail:* dijkunene@realnet.co.sz

Senior Librarian: Nomsa V Mkhwanazi *Tel:* 404 2633; 404 2757 *E-mail:* nomkhwa@realnet.co.sz
Librarian: N Fakudze *E-mail:* nqfakudze@realnet.co.sz

**University of Swaziland Library**
Private Bag 4, Kwaluseni
*Tel:* (051) 84011; (051) 85108 *Fax:* (051) 85276
*E-mail:* kwaluseni@uniswa.sz
*Web Site:* library.uniswa.sz
*Telex:* 2087 WD
*Key Personnel*
Librarian: Ms Makana R Mavuso *E-mail:* mmavuso@uniswacc.uniswa.sz
Publication(s): *Serials in Swaziland University Libraries* (irregularly); *Swaziland National Bibliography* (irregularly)

# Sweden

**Goteborgs Stadsbibliotek**
PO Box 5404, SE-40227 Gothenburg
*Tel:* (031) 61-65-00 *Fax:* (031) 61-66-93
*Key Personnel*
Contact: Anna Petren-Kihlstrom
City & county library.

**Goeteborgs Universitetsbibliotek**
Centralbiblioteket, Renstroemsgatan 4, 405 30 Gothenburg
Mailing Address: Box 222, 40530 Gothenburg
*Tel:* (031) 7731000 *Fax:* (031) 16 37 97
*E-mail:* library@ub.gu.se
*Web Site:* www.ub.gu.se
*Key Personnel*
Librarian: Jon Erik Nordstrand *Tel:* (031) 773 1760
Publication(s): *Acta Bibliothecae Universitatis Gothoburgensis* (irregularly); *New Literature on Women. A Bibliography* (quarterly)

**Kungl Tekniska Hoegskolan Biblioteket (Royal Institute of Technology Library)**
Osquars backe 31, 100 44 Stockholm
*Tel:* (08) 790 7088 *Fax:* (08) 790 7122
*E-mail:* loandept@lib.kth.se
*Web Site:* www.lib.kth.se
Publication(s): *Stockholm Papers in History & Philosophy of Science & Technology*

**Kungliga Biblioteket**
Box 5039, 102 41 Stockholm
*Tel:* (08) 463 40 00 *Fax:* (08) 463 40 04
*E-mail:* kungl.biblioteket@kb.se
*Web Site:* www.kb.se
*Key Personnel*
National Librarian: Gunnar Sahlin *Tel:* (08) 463 40 01 *E-mail:* gunnar.sahlin@kb.se
The Royal Library - National Library of Sweden.
Publication(s): *Acta Bibliothecae Regiae Stockholmiensis*; *Bibliography of Swedish Sheet Music* (On Line only); *Kungl Bibliotekets Utstaellningskatalog*; *Rapport*; *Suecana Extranea* (On Line only); *Svensk Bokfoerteckning* (On Line only); *Svensk Musikfoerteckning* (On Line only); *Svensk Periodicafoerteckning* (On Line only)

**Lunds Universitets Bibliotek**
Tornavaegen 9B, Lund
Mailing Address: PO Box 117, 221 00 Lund
*Tel:* (046) 222 00 00 *Fax:* (046) 222 47 20
*E-mail:* webmaster@lub.lu.se
*Web Site:* www.lub.lu.se
*Key Personnel*
Dir: Lars Bjornshauge *E-mail:* lars.bjornshauge@lub.lu.se

Senior Administrative Officer: Berit Nilsson
*Tel:* (046) 222 92 04 *E-mail:* berit.nilsson@
lub.lu.se
Publication(s): *Scripta Academica*

**Malmoe Stadsbibliotek**
Kung Oscars vaeg, 211 33 Malmoe
*Tel:* (040) 660 85 00 *Fax:* (040) 660 86 81
*E-mail:* info@mail.stadsbibliotek.org
*Web Site:* www2.malmo.stadsbibliotek.org
*Key Personnel*
Librarian: Ulla Brohed *Tel:* (040) 660 86 80
  *E-mail:* ulla.brohed@mail.stadsbibliotek.org;
  Gunilla Konradsson Mortin *E-mail:* gunilla.
  konradsson@mail.stadsbibliotek.org
City library & lending centre for southern &
  western Sweden.

**Riksarkivet**
Fyrverkarbacken 13-17, 102 29 Stockholm
Mailing Address: PO Box 125 41, 102 29 Stock-
  holm
*Tel:* (08) 737 63 50 *Fax:* (08) 737 64 74
*E-mail:* registry@riksarkivet.ra.se
*Web Site:* www.ra.se
National record office, national archives of Swe-
  den.

**Statistics Sweden Library**
Karlavaegen 100, 104 51 Stockholm
Mailing Address: Box 24 300, 104 51 Stockholm
*Tel:* (08) 506 948 01; (08) 506 950 66 *Fax:* (08)
  506 940 45
*E-mail:* information@scb.se
*Web Site:* www.scb.se
*Key Personnel*
Chief Librarian: Rolf-Allan Norrmosse
Publication(s): *Statistics from Individual Coun-
  tries; National Statistics from Sweden and
  other Countries; Statistics from International
  Organizations and other (issuing) Bodies*

**Stockholms Stadsbibliotek** (Stockholm Public
  Library)
Sveavaegen 73, 113 80 Stockholm
*Tel:* (08) 508 31 060 *Fax:* (08) 508 31 007
*E-mail:* info.ssb@kultur.stockholm.se
*Web Site:* www.ssb.stockholm.se
*Telex:* 19478
*Key Personnel*
City Librarian: Inga Lunden *E-mail:* inga.
  lunden@kultur.stockholm.se

**Stockholms Universitetsbibliotek**
Universitetsvaegen 10, 106 91 Stockholm
*Tel:* (08) 16 28 00 *Fax:* (08) 15 77 76
*Web Site:* www.sub.su.se
*Key Personnel*
Head of Information & IT Department: Gunilla
  Lilie Bauer *Tel:* (08) 162747 *E-mail:* gunilla.
  lilie.bauer@sub.swe
Librarian: Gunnar Sahlin
This library incorporates the Library of the Royal
  Swedish Academy of Sciences (Kungliga Sven-
  ska Vetenskapsakademiens Bibliotek) covering
  humanities, law, social sciences, mathematics
  & natural sciences, psychology & education.
Publication(s): *Stockholms universitetsbibliotek
  Rapport*

**Svenska Barnboksinstitutet**
Odengatan 61, 113 22 Stockholm
*Tel:* (08) 54 54 20 50 *Fax:* (08) 54 54 20 54
*E-mail:* info@sbi.kb.se; biblioteket@sbi.kb.se
*Web Site:* www.sbi.kb.se
*Key Personnel*
Dir: Sonja Svensson *E-mail:* sonja.svensson@sbi.
  kb.se
Head Librarian: Cecilia Ostlund *E-mail:* cecilia.
  ostlund@sbi.kb.se
Founded: 1965

Swedish institute for children's books.
Publication(s): *Barnboken: Svenska Barnboksin-
  stitutets Tidskrift (ISSN 0347-772X)* (biennually,
  1978, English Summary)

**Sveriges Lantbruksuniversitets Bibliotek**
Undervisningsplan 10, 750 07 Uppsala
Mailing Address: Box 7070, 750 07 Uppsala
*Tel:* (018) 67 10 00 *Fax:* (018) 67 20 00
*E-mail:* registrator@slu.se
*Web Site:* www.bib.slu.se
*Telex:* 76062
*Key Personnel*
Dir: Ulf Heyman
Librarian: Bruno Johnsson *Tel:* (090) 786 82 79
  *Fax:* (090) 786 59 25 *E-mail:* bruno.johnsson@
  bibum.slu.se
Libraries of the Swedish University of Agricul-
  tural Sciences.

**Umea University Library**
Samhaellsvetarhuset, 901 74 Umea
*Tel:* (090) 786 5693 *Fax:* (090) 786 6677
*E-mail:* laneexp@ub.unu.se; www.
  bibliotekschefen@ub.umu.se
*Web Site:* www.ub.umu.se
*Key Personnel*
Librarian: Lars-Ake Idahl *Tel:* (090) 786 9680
  *E-mail:* lars-ake.idahl@ub.umu.se

**Uppsala Universitetsbibliotek**
Dag Hammarskjoelds vaeg 1, 751 20 Uppsala
Mailing Address: Box 510, 751 20 Uppsala
*Tel:* (018) 471 39 00 *Fax:* (018) 471 39 13
*E-mail:* info@ub.uu.se
*Web Site:* www.ub.uu.se
*Key Personnel*
Chief Librarian: Ulf Goranson *Tel:* (018) 471 39
  10
Publication(s): *Acta Bibliothecae R Universitatis
  Upsaliensis; Scripta Minora Bibliothecae R
  Universitatis Upsaliensis; Uppsala Universitets-
  biblioteks Utstaellningskataloger*

# Switzerland

**Archives Economiques Suisses**, see
  Schweizerisches Wirtschaftsarchiv

**Bibliotheca Bodmeriana** (Fondation Martin
  Bodmer)
19-21, route du Guignard, 1223 Cologny
*Tel:* (022) 707 44 33 *Fax:* (022) 707 44 30
*E-mail:* info@fondationbodmer.ch
*Web Site:* www.fondationbodmer.org
*Key Personnel*
Dir: Dr Martin Bircher
Founded: 1972

**Bibliotheque Cantonale et Universitaire de
  Lausanne**
Pl de la Riponne 6, 1015 & 1003 Lausanne
*Tel:* (021) 3167880 *Fax:* (021) 3167870
*Web Site:* www.unil.ch/BCU
*Key Personnel*
Dir: Hubert Villard
Vice Dir: Silvia Kimmeier

**Bibliotheque Cantonale et Universitaire
  (Kantons- und Universitatsbibliothek)**
Rue Joseph Piller 2, 1700 Fribourg
*Tel:* (026) 305 13 33 *Fax:* (026) 305 13 77
*E-mail:* bcu@fr.ch
*Web Site:* www.fr.ch/bcu/
*Key Personnel*
Dir: Martin Good *Tel:* (026) 305 13 05
  *E-mail:* goodm@fr.ch

**Bibliotheque de la Ville**, see Bibliotheque
  Publique et Universitaire de Neuchatel

**Bibliotheque nationale suisse**, see
  Schweizerische Landesbibliothek

**Bibliotheque Publique et Universitaire de
  Geneve** (Geneva Public & University Library)
Promenade des Bastions, PO Box, 1211 Geneva 4
*Tel:* (022) 418 28 00 *Fax:* (022) 418 28 01
*E-mail:* info.bpu@ville-ge.ch
*Web Site:* www.ville-ge.ch/bpu/
*Key Personnel*
Dir: Alain L Jacquesson *Tel:* (022) 418 28 28
  *E-mail:* alain.jacquesson@bpu.ville-ge.ch
Founded: 1562
Publication(s): *Compte rendu* (annually)

**Bibliotheque Publique et Universitaire de
  Neuchatel**
rue Numa-Droz 3, Case postale 1916, 2000
  Neuchatel
*Tel:* (032) 717-73-02; (032) 717 73 20 *Fax:* (032)
  717-73-09
*Web Site:* bpun.unine.ch
*Key Personnel*
Dir: Michel Schlup *E-mail:* michael.schlup@
  unine.ch
Publication(s): *Ville de Neuchatel: Bibliotheques
  et Musees* (annually)

**Bureau International du Travail**, see
  International Labour Office, Bureau of Library
  & Information Services

**ETH- Bibliothek (Eidgenossische Technische
  Hochschule Bibliothek)**
Raemistr 101, 8092 Zurich
Mailing Address: Post Box, 8092 Zurich
*Tel:* (01) 632 21 35 *Fax:* (01) 632 10 87
*E-mail:* info@library.ethz.ch
*Web Site:* www.ethbib.ethz.ch
*Key Personnel*
Dir: Dr Wolfram Neubauer *Tel:* (01) 632 25 49
  *E-mail:* neubauer@library.ethz.ch
Head, Collection Development: Dr Karin Ass-
  mann *Tel:* (01) 632 21 24 *E-mail:* assmann@
  library.ethz.ch
Library of the Swiss Federal Institute of Technol-
  ogy Zurich.
*Parent Company:* ETH Zurich (Swiss Federal In-
  stitute of Technology Zurich)

**ILO**, see International Labour Office, Bureau of
  Library & Information Services

**International Labour Office, Bureau of
  Library & Information Services**
4, route des Morillons, 1211 Geneva 22
*Tel:* (022) 799 8675 *Fax:* (022) 799 6516
*E-mail:* inform@ilo.org
*Web Site:* www.ilo.org/inform
Publication(s): *ILO Manual for Labour Infor-
  mation Centers (1992)* (available in English,
  French or Spanish); *ILO Thesaurus 1998:
  Labour, Employment & Training Terminology*
  (in English, French & Spanish); *Labordoc* (data
  base in English, French & Spanish)

**Oeffentliche Bibliothek der Universitaet Basel**
  (Public Library of Basel University)
Schoenbeinstr 18-20, 4056 Basel
*Tel:* (061) 267 3100 *Fax:* (061) 267 3103
*E-mail:* sekretariat-ub@unibas.ch
*Web Site:* www.ub.unibas.ch
*Key Personnel*
Dir: Hannes Hug *Tel:* (061) 267 3131
Founded: 1471

Publication(s): *Jahresbericht* (Occasional Papers & Indexes in the Series Publikationen der Universitaetsbibliothek)
*Branch Office(s)*
Medizinbibliothek, Hebelstr 20, 4031 Basel
WWZ-Bibliothek, Petersgraben 51, 4051 Basel

**Schweizerische Landesbibliothek** (Swiss National Library)
Division of Federal Office of Culture
Hallwylstr 15, 3003 Bern
*Tel:* (031) 322 89 11; (031) 3228979 (Lending Dept); (031) 3228935 (Information)
*Fax:* (031) 322 84 63
*E-mail:* IZ-Helvetica@slb.admin.ch
*Web Site:* www.snl.ch
*Key Personnel*
Dir: Dr Jean-Frederic Jauslin
Publication(s): *Das Schweizer Buch* (national bibliography); *The Swiss National Library*

**Schweizerisches Bundesarchiv** (Swiss Federal Archives)
Archivstr 24, 3003 Bern
*Tel:* (031) 322 89 89 *Fax:* (031) 322 78 23
*E-mail:* bundesarchiv@bar.admin.ch
*Web Site:* www.bundesarchiv.ch
*Key Personnel*
Contact: Hans von Ruette *E-mail:* hans.vonruette@bar.admin.ch
Founded: 1798

**Schweizerisches Wirtschaftsarchiv** (Swiss Economic Archives)
Petersgraben 51, 4003 Basel
*Tel:* (061) 267 32 19 *Fax:* (061) 267 32 08
*E-mail:* info-wwzb@unibas.ch
*Web Site:* www.ub.unibas.ch/wwz
*Key Personnel*
Dir: Johanna Gisler *E-mail:* johanna.gisler@unibas.ch
Founded: 1910

**Stadt- und Universitaetsbibliothek** (Municipal & University Library of Berne)
Munstergasse 61, 3011 Berne
Mailing Address: Postfach, 3000 Berne
*Tel:* (031) 320 32 11 *Fax:* (031) 320 32 99
*E-mail:* info@stub.unibe.ch
*Web Site:* www.stub.unibe.ch
*Key Personnel*
Dir: Susanna Bliggenstorfer *Tel:* (031) 320 32 01 *E-mail:* susanna.bliggenstorfer@stub.unibe.ch
Vice Dir: Christian Luethi *Tel:* (031) 320 32 87 *E-mail:* christian.luethi@stub.unibe.ch
Founded: 1528

**Stiftsbibliothek** (Abbey Library of St Gall)
Klosterhof 6d, 9004 St Gallen
Mailing Address: Postfach, 9004 St Gallen
*Tel:* (071) 227 34 16 *Fax:* (071) 227 34 18
*E-mail:* stibi@stibi.ch
*Web Site:* www.stibi.ch
*Key Personnel*
Librarian: Theres Flury *Tel:* (071) 227 34 17 *E-mail:* theres.flury@kk-stibi.sg.ch; Prof Ernst Tremp *E-mail:* ernst.tremp@kk-stibi.sq.ch
Historical library with a unique collection of early medieval manuscripts.

**United Nations Library**
Palais des Nations, 1211 Geneva 10
*Tel:* (022) 917 41 81 *Fax:* (022) 917 04 18
*E-mail:* library@unog.ch
*Web Site:* www.unog.ch/library
*Telex:* 412962

**Universitat Zentralbibliothek Zuerich**
Zaehringerplatz 6, 8001 Zurich
*Tel:* (01) 2683100 *Fax:* (01) 2683290
*E-mail:* zb@zb.unizh.ch

*Web Site:* www.zb.unizh.ch
*Key Personnel*
Dir: Dr Hermann Koestler *E-mail:* hermann.koestler@zb.unizh.ch
Vice-Dir: Christoph Meyer *E-mail:* christoph.meyer@zb.unizh.ch

# Syrian Arab Republic

**Al Maktabah Al Wataniah**
Bab El-Faradj, Aleppo
*Key Personnel*
Librarian: Younis Roshdi
Founded: 1924
National Library.

**Assad National Library**
Malki St, Damascus
Mailing Address: PO Box 3639, Damascus
*Tel:* (011) 3320803 *Fax:* (011) 3320804
*E-mail:* contact@alassad-library.com
*Web Site:* www.alassad.library.com
*Telex:* 419134
*Key Personnel*
Librarian: Ghassan Lahham
Founded: 1984
Publication(s): *Analytical Index to Syrian Periodicals*; *List of Syrian Dissertations*; *Syrian National Bibliography*

**Damascus University Library**
Damascus University Library, Damascus, Baramkah
*Tel:* (011) 2215104; (011) 2215101 *Fax:* (011) 2236010
*E-mail:* info@damascus-online.com
*Web Site:* www.damascus-online/university.htm
*Telex:* 411971
*Key Personnel*
Contact: Nizar Oyoun El-Soud
Publication(s): *Bibliography of the Middle East*

**Public Library of Latakia**
Latakia, Syria
*Key Personnel*
Dir: Mohamad Ali Nitayfi

**Al Zahiriah**
Damascus
*Tel:* (011) 112813
National Library.

# Taiwan, Province of China

**Bureau of International Exchange of Publications**
National Central Library, 20 Chungshan South Rd, Taipei
*Tel:* (02) 23169132 *Fax:* (02) 23110155
*E-mail:* shiny@msg.ncl.edu.tw
*Web Site:* www.ncl.edu.tw
*Key Personnel*
Bureau Chief: Teresa Wang Chang *E-mail:* teresa@msg.ncl.edu.tu
Publication(s): *Chinese Cultural Organizations Directory*; *National Central Library Newsletter*

**Fu Ssu-Nien Library, Institute of History & Philology, Academia Sinica**
Nankang, Taipei 11529
*Tel:* (02) 27829555 *Fax:* (02) 27868834
*E-mail:* fsndb@pluto.ihp.sinica.edu.tw
*Web Site:* lib.ihp.sinica.edu.tw
*Key Personnel*
Dir: Juei-hsiu Wu

**National Central Library**
20 Chung Shan S Rd, Taipei 100-01
*Tel:* (02) 2361 9132 *Fax:* (02) 382 1489
*Web Site:* www.ncl.edu.tw
*Key Personnel*
Dir: Dr Juang Fang-Rung
Founded: 1933
Publication(s): *Index to Chinese Periodical Literature*; *National Bibliography of the Republic of China*; *National Union List of Chinese Periodicals of the Republic of China*; *Union Catalog of Books in the Republic of China*; *Yearbook of Libraries in the Republic of China*

**National Taiwan University Library**
One Sec 4, Roosevelt Rd, Taipei 106
*Tel:* (02) 3366-2326 *Fax:* (02) 2362 7383
*E-mail:* tul@ntu.edu.tw
*Web Site:* www.lib.ntu.edu.tw
*Key Personnel*
Dir: Jieh Hsiang
Founded: 1915
Publication(s): *An Atlas of Plants from the Tanaka Collection at National Taiwan Univeristy Library*; *Bibliography of the Works of Dr Tyozaburo Tanaka*; *Catalog of Chinese Stitched Binding Books in the National Taiwan University*; *Catalog of National Taiwan University Publications (1946-1985)*; *Catalog of the Tanaka Collection at National Taiwan University Library*; *Ino Kanori & Taiwan Studies* (a special exhibition of Ino Collections); *List of Publications of the Faculty & Staff of the National Taiwan University Theses & Dissertations (1959-1985)*; *National Taiwan University Catalog of Old Japanese Materials on Taiwan Studies*; *National Taiwan University Catalog of Rare Books Title Index*; *National Taiwan University Catalog of Rare Rooks*; *National Taiwan University College of Law Catalog of Old Japanese Materials on Taiwan Studies*; *National Taiwan University Library Newsletter* (monthly, newsletter); *National Taiwan University List of Serials in Chinese, Japanese & Korean Languages*; *National Taiwan University Union List of Collected Mainland Periodicals*; *Supplement & Index Report on the Present Status of Documents on Taiwanese History at the National Taiwan University*; *University Library Journal* (semiannually)

**National War College Library**
Yangmingshan, Taipei
*Tel:* (02) 3619132 *Fax:* (02) 3110155
*Key Personnel*
Contact: Lo Mou-pin

**Sun Yat-sen Library**
2F, 505 Jen-ai Rd, Sec 4, Taipei
*Tel:* (02) 2758 2045 *Fax:* (02) 2729 7030

**Taiwan Branch Library, National Central Library**
One Hsinshen S Rd, Section 1, Taipei 106
Mailing Address: PO Box 106, Taipei 106
*Tel:* (02) 771 8528
*Key Personnel*
Library Dir: Wei-jei Lin
Librarian: Hui-Hsien Jill Yu
Founded: 1915

List of non-Chinese serials of National Central Library Taiwan branch.
Publication(s): *Catalog on China in Western Languages*; *N C L Taiwan Branch Bulletin*; *Southeast Asia Catalog*

# Tajikistan

**Gousudarstvennaja Biblioteka Respublika Tadzkistan im Firdousi**
Rudaki 36, 734025 Dushanbe
*Tel:* (03772) 274 726
*Key Personnel*
Librarian: S Goibnazarov
Founded: 1933

# United Republic of Tanzania

**British Council Library**
Samora Ave, Ohio St, Dar Es Salaam
Mailing Address: PO Box 9100, Dar Es Salaam
*Tel:* (022) 2116574; (022) 2118255; (022) 2138303; (022) 2116575; (022) 2116576
*Fax:* (022) 2112669; (022) 2116577
*E-mail:* info@britishcouncil.or.tz
*Web Site:* www.britishcouncil.org/tanzania
*Telex:* 41719 *Cable:* BRICO
*Key Personnel*
Librarian: Oreste Makafu

**Eastern & Southern African Management Institute (ESAMI)**
PO Box 3030, Arusha
*Tel:* (027) 250-8384; (027) 250-8388 *Fax:* (027) 250-8285
*E-mail:* esamihq@esamihq.ac.tz
*Web Site:* www.esami-africa.org
*Telex:* 42076
*Key Personnel*
Assistant Serials Librarian: Grace Lema
Publication(s): *African Management Development Forum* (biannual); *ESAMI Newsletter* (quarterly)
*Branch Office(s)*
Harare
Kampala
Lilongwe
Lusaka
Maputo
Mbabane
Nairobi

**Kivukoni College Library**
PO Box 9193, Dar Es Salaam
*Tel:* (051) 820047
*Telex:* 41390
*Key Personnel*
Librarian: George M Gwahemba

**Makumira Lutheran Theological College Library**
Box 55, Usa River
*Tel:* (027) 255-3634; (027) 255-3635 *Fax:* (027) 255-3493
*E-mail:* library@makumira.ac.tz
*Web Site:* www.makumira.ac.tz
*Telex:* 42054

*Key Personnel*
Chief Librarian: Ismael Mbise *Tel:* 255 057 8599
*E-mail:* mbise@makumira.ac.tz
Founded: 1947
Theology, East Africana.
Publication(s): *Africa Theological Journal & Larida la Uchungagi*

**Mzumbe University Library**
Mzumbe
Mailing Address: PO Box 1, Mzumbe
*Tel:* (023) 260-4380; (023) 260-4381; (023) 260-4383; (023) 260-4384 *Fax:* (023) 260-4382
*E-mail:* idm@raha.com
*Telex:* idm morogoro
*Key Personnel*
Dir: Matilda Kuzilwa *E-mail:* matildakuz@yahoo.co.uk
Founded: 1964
Academic library.
*Parent Company:* Ministry of Science, Technology & Higher Education

**Sokoine University of Agriculture Library**
PO Box 3000, Morogoro
*Tel:* (056) 3510; (056) 3514
*E-mail:* usa@hnettan.gri.apc.org
*Telex:* 55308 Univmo Tz *Cable:* Uniagric Morogoro
*Key Personnel*
Librarian: Ms E V Chiduo
Publication(s): *Annual Record of Research*; *Bibliography of Higher Degree Theseses & Dissertations held by the Library of the Sokoine University of Agriculture*; *Library Accessions List* (quarterly); *The Green Revolution: A Bibliography*
*Branch Office(s)*
Mazimbu Library

**Standard Book Numbering Agency**, see Tanzania Library Service

**Tanzania Library Service**
PO Box 9283, Dar es Salaam
*Tel:* (022) 215 09 23; (022) 215 00 48 *Fax:* (022) 215 11 00
*E-mail:* tlsb@africaonline.co.tz
*Telex:* Tanlis
*Key Personnel*
Dir: E A Mwinyimvua
Publication(s): *Tanzania National Bibliography*; *Directory of Libraries in Tanzania* (1984)

**University of Dar es Salaam Library**
PO Box 35092, Dar Es Salaam
*Tel:* (022) 2410241 *Fax:* (022) 2410241
*E-mail:* libdirec@udsm.ac.tz; director@libis.udsm.ac.tz
*Web Site:* www.udsm.ac.tz/library
*Telex:* 41561
*Key Personnel*
Senior Librarian & Dir: E Kiondo
Publication(s): *East Africana Accessions Bulletin*; *Tanzania Regional Bib Series*; *University of Dar Es Salaam Library Journal*

# Thailand

**British Council Library**
254 Chulalongkorn Soi 64, Siam Sq, Phyathai Rd, Pathumwan, Bangkok 10330
*Tel:* (02) 652 5480; (02) 652 5489 *Fax:* (02) 253 5312
*E-mail:* bc.bangkok@britcoun.or.th
*Web Site:* www.britishcouncil.or.th/en/index.asp
*Telex:* 72058

*Key Personnel*
Dir: Bhaskar Chakravarti
British education information provider.

**Center of Academic Resources Chulalongkorn University**
Phya Thai Rd, Pathumwan, Bangkok 10330
*Tel:* (02) 218-2929; (02) 218-2903 *Fax:* (02) 215-3617; (02) 215-2907
*Web Site:* www.car.chula.ac.th
*Key Personnel*
Dir: Dr Pimrumpai Premsmit, PhD
*E-mail:* pimrumpai.p@chula.ac.th
Includes Central Library, Thailand Information Center & Audiovisual Center.
Publication(s): *Academic Resources Journal*; *Union Catalog of Chulalongkorn University Libraries*; *Union List of Serials in Thailand* (online database)

**Main Library, Kasetsart University**
Phahonyothin Rd, Chatuchak, Bangkok 10903
Mailing Address: PO Box 1084, Chatuchak, Bangkok 10903
*Tel:* (02) 9428615 *Fax:* (02) 5611369; (02) 9428614
*E-mail:* libspn@ku.ac.th
*Web Site:* www.lib.ku.ac.th
*Key Personnel*
Librarian: Mrs Piboonsin Watanapongse
*E-mail:* upvp@ku.ac.th

**National Archives Division**
Fine Arts Dept Samsen Rd, Bangkok 10300
*Tel:* (02) 281 1599; (02) 281 0263; (02) 281 5450
*Fax:* (02) 281 1599; (02) 281 0263; (02) 281 5450

**The National Library of Thailand**
Samsen Rd, Bangkok 10300
*Tel:* (02) 2810263; (02) 281 5999; (02) 281 5450
*Fax:* (02) 281 0263; (02) 281 5999; (02) 282 5450
*E-mail:* suwaksir@emisc.moe.go.th
*Telex:* 84189 DEPFIAR TH
*Key Personnel*
Dir: Mrs Kullasap Gesmankit

**Siriraj Medical Library**
Mahidol University, Siriraj Hospital, 2 Prannok Rd, Bangkoknoi, Bangkok 10700
*Tel:* (02) 411 3112; (02) 419 7635; (02) 419 7637
*Fax:* (02) 412 8418
*E-mail:* silib@diamond.mahidol.ac.th
*Web Site:* www.medlib.si.mahidol.ac.th
*Key Personnel*
Chief Librarian: Porntip Anaprayot
*E-mail:* lipan@mahidol.ac.th

**Srinakharinwirot University, Central Library**
Sukhumvit 23 Rd, Watthana, Bangkok 10110
*Tel:* (02) 2584002 (ext 160, 161, 162); (02) 2584003 (ext 160, 161, 162); (02) 6641000 (ext 5382) *Fax:* (02) 2604514; (02) 2584002
*E-mail:* library@swu.ac.th
*Web Site:* www.swu.ac.th/lib
*Telex:* 72270 Unisirin Th
*Key Personnel*
Dir: Mr Chaleo Pansida

**Thai National Documentation Centre (TNDC)**
Thailand Institute of Scientific & Technological Research, 196 Phaholyothin Rd, Chatuchak, Bangken, Bangkok 10900
*Tel:* 0-2579-1121; (02) 579 1130; (02) 579 5515; (02) 579 0160 *Fax:* (02) 561 4771
*Telex:* 21392 TISTR TH *Cable:* TISTR/BANGKOK
*Key Personnel*
Contact: Mrs Nongphanga Chitrakorn
Publication(s): *Abstracts of TISTR Technical Reports*; *List of Scientific and Technical Literature*

*Relating to Thailand; Scientific Serials in Thai Libraries; Thai Abstracts; TISTR Bibliographical Series*

**Thammasat University Libraries**
2 Prachan Rd, Pranakorn, Bangkok 10200
*Tel:* (02) 613-3544 *Fax:* (02) 623-5173
*E-mail:* tulib@alpha.tu.ac.th
*Web Site:* library.tu.ac.th
*Telex:* 72432 TAMSAT TH
*Key Personnel*
Dir: Ms Prapaiphan Jaruthavee *Tel:* (02) 623-5171
    *E-mail:* prapai@alpha.tu.ac.th
Librarian: Mrs Chooman Thirakit *Tel:* (02) 613-3518
Founded: 1934
Academic libraries.
Publication(s): *Dom Thad* (biennial, journal)

**TNDC**, see Thai National Documentation Centre (TNDC)

# Togo

**Bibliotheque Nationale**
Ave de la Victoire, PO Box 1002, Lome
*Tel:* 21 63 67; 21 04 10; 22 21 16 *Fax:* 22 19 67
*Telex:* 5322 Minedue
*Key Personnel*
Dir: Moussa Senghor
Founded: 1960
Publication(s): *Bibliographie Nationale*

**Bibliotheque de l'Universite du Benin**
BP 1515, Lome
*Tel:* 21 30 27 *Fax:* 21 85 95
*E-mail:* cafmicro@ub.tg
*Web Site:* www.ub.tg
*Telex:* 52 - 58

# Trinidad & Tobago

**Central Library of Trinidad & Tobago**, see National Library & Information System Authority (NALIS)

**National Archives**
Unit of Ministry of Public Administration & Information
The Government Archivist, 105 St Vincent St, Port of Spain
Mailing Address: PO Box 763, Port of Spain
*Tel:* (868) 625-2689 *Fax:* (868) 625-2689
*E-mail:* natt@tstt.net.tt
*Key Personnel*
Government Archivist: Helena Leonce
Founded: 1960
Preserves the documentary heritage of Trinidad & Tobago.

**National Library & Information System Authority (NALIS)**
Hart & Abercromby Sts, Port of Spain
*Tel:* (868) 623-6962; (868) 624-4466 *Fax:* (868) 625-6096 *Fax on Demand:* 624-3120
*E-mail:* nalis@nalis.gov.tt
*Web Site:* www.nalis.gov.tt; library2.nalis.gov.tt
    *Cable:* Centralib Trinidad
*Key Personnel*
Executive Dir: Pamella Benson

Founded: 1998
National Library System.
Publication(s): *Trinadad & Tobago National Bibliography* (annually)

**Trinidad Public Library**, see National Library & Information System Authority (NALIS)

**University of the West Indies Library (Trinidad & Tobago)**
The Main Library, St Augustine
*Tel:* 868-662 2002 (ext 2132) *Fax:* 868-662-9238
*E-mail:* mainlib@library.uwi.tt
*Web Site:* www.mainlib.uwi.tt
*Telex:* 24520 Uwi-Wg *Cable:* STOMATA, PORT OF SPAIN
*Key Personnel*
Librarian: Dr Margaret D Rouse-Jones *Tel:* (0868) 662 2002, ext 2008
Publication(s): *CARINDEX: Science & Technology; CARINDEX: Social Sciences & Humanities; Directory of Publishers, Printers & Booksellers in Trinidad & Tobago; OPreP Newsletter*

# Tunisia

**Archives nationales**
Le Premier Ministere, La Casbah, 1020 Tunis
*Tel:* 71560556 *Fax:* 71569175
*Key Personnel*
Dir: Moncef Fakhfakh
Founded: 1874

**Bibliotheque Nationale**
20 Souk el Attarine, Tunis
Mailing Address: BP 42, Tunis
*Tel:* 71245338 *Fax:* 71342700
*Key Personnel*
Librarian: Ibrahim M Chabbouh
Publication(s): *Bibliographie Nationale: Publications en serie; Bibliographie nationale: Publications officielles et non officielles; Bibliographies Specialisees (Themes tunisiens notamment); Fahras al-Makhtuetat (catalogue des manuscrits); Informations bibliographiques; Repertoire des Unites de Documentation en Tunisie*

**British Council Library**
c/o British Embassy, 141/143 Avenue de la Liberte, 1002 Tunis
Mailing Address: BP 96, 1002 Tunis
*Tel:* 71 353 568 *Fax:* 71 353 985
*E-mail:* info@tn.britishcouncil.org
*Web Site:* www.britishcouncil.org/tunisia

**Centre de Recherches et d'Etudes Administratives**
24, av docteur Calmette, Mutuelleville, 1002 Tunis
*Tel:* 71848435; 71848300 *Fax:* 71794188
*E-mail:* webmaster@ena.nat.tn
*Web Site:* www.ena.nat.tn
*Telex:* Ena 13198
*Key Personnel*
Dir: Mohamed Hedi Touati
Founded: 1964
Publication(s): *Revue tunisienne d'Administration Publique* (biannually)

**CREA**, see Centre de Recherches et d'Etudes Administratives

**Bibliotheque de la Faculte des Sciences de Tunis**
University, El Manar-Tunis, 1060 Tunis
*Tel:* 71872600 *Fax:* 71885073

**Institut de Presse & des Sciences de l'Information**
7, impasse Mohamed Bachrouch, Montfluery, 1008 Tunis
*Tel:* 71335216 *Fax:* 71348596
*Telex:* 15254 IPSI.TN
*Key Personnel*
Director: Mustapha Hassen *E-mail:* mustapha.hassen@ipsi.rau.tn
Publication(s): *Revue Tunisienne de Communication*

# Turkey

**Ankara University Library**
Tandogan, 06100 Ankara
*Tel:* (0312) 212 60 40 *Fax:* (0312) 212 60 49
*Web Site:* www.ankara.edu.tr
*Key Personnel*
Librarian: Dr Sekine Karakas
Founded: 1933

**The Beyazit State Library**
Imaret Sok 18, Istanbul-Beyazit
*Tel:* (0212) 522 2488 *Fax:* (0212) 526 1133
*Key Personnel*
Librarian: Yusuf Tavacl
Founded: 1882

**Bilkent University Library**
Bilkent, 06800 Ankara
*Tel:* (0312) 2664472 *Fax:* (0312) 2664391
*Web Site:* library.bilkent.edu.tr
*Key Personnel*
University Librarian: Dr Phyllis L Erdogan
    *Tel:* (0312) 266 4472 (ext 1418 & 1291)
    *E-mail:* librdirector@bilkent.edu.tr
Founded: 1986
Membership(s): IFLA; LIBER; ALA; LA (UK); IATUL; MELA; IAML.
*Branch Office(s)*
Bilkent University East Campus Library, 06800 Ankara *Tel:* (312) 266-5117
    *E-mail:* eastlibrary@bilkent.edu.tr

**Bogazici University Library**
Bebek, 34342 Istanbul
*Tel:* (0212) 3595400 *Fax:* (0212) 2575016
*Web Site:* www.library.boun.edu.tr
*Telex:* 26411
*Key Personnel*
Dir: Guen Kut *E-mail:* kut@boun.edu.tr

**The Grand National Assembly of Turkey Library & Documentation TBMM** (TBMM Kutuephane Dokuemantasyon ve Tercueme Mueduerluegue)
Bakanliklar, 06543 Ankara
*Tel:* (0312) 420 68 35 *Fax:* (0312) 420 75 48
*E-mail:* library@tbmm.gov.tr
*Web Site:* www.tbmm.gov.tr
*Key Personnel*
Dir: Ali Riza Cihan *E-mail:* acihan@tbmm.gov.tr
Membership(s): APLAP; ECPRD; IFLA; LIBER.

**Istanbul Universitesi Merkez Kuetuephanesi**
Beyazit, 34452 Istanbul
*Tel:* (0212) 455 57 83 *Fax:* (0212) 455 57 84
*E-mail:* bilgi@library.istanbul.edu.tr
*Web Site:* www.istanbul.edu.tr; www.kutuphane.istanbul.edu.tr

## Key Personnel
Librarian: Guelguen Sayari
Istanbul University central library.

## Library of the Mineral Research & Exploration General Directorate
MTA, 06520 Ankara
*Tel:* (0312) 287 34 30 *Fax:* (0312) 287 91 88
*E-mail:* mta@mta.gov.tr
*Web Site:* www.mta.gov.tr
*Telex:* 42741 42060mta tr *Cable:* METEA/
  ANKARA
*Key Personnel*
Librarian: Gonul Kocer
Founded: 1935
Specialize in books on mining exploration, geological investigation, earth investigations.
*Publication(s): Bulletin of the Mineral Reserch & Exploration* (bulletin)
*Parent Company:* Bureau of Mines, USA
*Ultimate Parent Company:* BROM, France

## Middle East Technical University Library
Inonu Bulvari, 06531 Ankara
*Tel:* (0312) 210 27 80; (0312) 210 27 82
  *Fax:* (0312) 210 11 19
*E-mail:* lib-hot-line@metu.edu.tr
*Web Site:* ww2.lib.metu.edu.tr
*Telex:* 42761
*Key Personnel*
Dir: Buelent Karasoezen *E-mail:* bulent@metu.
  edu.tr
Membership(s): IATUL (International Association
  of Technological University Libraries).

## Milli Kuetuephane
Baskanligi Bahcelievler Son Durak, 06490
  Ankara
*Tel:* (0312) 212 62 00 *Fax:* (0312) 223 04 51
*Web Site:* www.mkutup.gov.tr
*Key Personnel*
President: Tuncel Acar *E-mail:* tuncel@mkutup.
  gov.tr
Librarian: Sahika Unal
National library.
Publication(s): *Turkiye Bibliyografyasi*

## National Library of Izmir
Mill Kuetuephane Caddesi, no 39, Konak, Izmir
*Tel:* (0232) 4842002 *Fax:* (0232) 4821703
*Key Personnel*
Dir: Ali Riza Atay
Founded: 1912
Publication(s): *Izmir Milli Kuetuphanesi, Yazma Eserler Katalogu, Vol 1 ve 2* (manuscript catalogue of Izmir National Library Vol I & Vol II)

## Sueleymaniye Kuetuephanesi
Aysekadin Hamami Sokak 35 Beyazit, Istanbul
*Tel:* (0212) 520 64 60 *Fax:* (0212) 520 64 62
*Key Personnel*
Librarian: Muammer Ulker
Library of the Sueleymaniye.
Publication(s): *Nail Bayraktar* (1984, catalog of the important Arabic manuscripts in Bagdatli Vehbi Efendi Library, Istanbul); *The Union Catalogue Islamic Medical Manuscripts in Turkish Library* (1984); *Turkiye Yazmalari Toplu Katalogiu (TUYATOK)* (The union catalogue of manuscripts in Turkey)

## Technical University Library
Ayazaga Campus, 34469 Maslak/Istanbul
*Tel:* (0212) 285 35 96 *Fax:* (0212) 285 33 02
*E-mail:* kutuphane@itu.edu.tr
*Web Site:* www.library.itu.edu.tr
*Key Personnel*
Dir: Ayhan Kaygusuz *E-mail:* kaygusuz@itu.edu.
  tr
Contact: Nurten Atalik

## Tuerdok (Turkish Scientific & Technical Documentation Centre)
Atatuerk Bulvari 221, Kavaklidere, 06100 Ankara
*Tel:* (0312) 468 5300 *Fax:* (0312) 427 2672
*E-mail:* www-adm@tubitak.gov.tr
*Web Site:* www.tubitak.gov.tr
*Telex:* 43186 Btak Tr *Cable:* TUBITAK,
  ANKARA

# Turkmenistan

## National Library of Turkmenistan
Pl K Marksa, 744000 Aschabad
*Tel:* (07) 3632 25 3254 *Fax:* (012) 257 481
*Key Personnel*
Dir: Nazar Atabaevich Kurbanov
Founded: 1895

# Uganda

## Central Reference Library
c/o Public Libraries Board Headquarters, 11-13
  Buganda Rd, Kampala
Mailing Address: PO Box 4262, Kampala
*Tel:* (041) 233633 *Fax:* (041) 348625
*E-mail:* library@imul.com
*Key Personnel*
Dir: P Birungi
Founded: 1972

## Albert Cook Medical Library
Makerere University Medical School, Kampala
Mailing Address: PO Box 7072, Kampala
*Tel:* (041) 534149 *Fax:* (041) 530024
*E-mail:* acook@uga.healthnet.org *Cable:*
  MAKUNIKA KAMPALA
*Key Personnel*
Deputy University Librarian: Maria Musoke
  *E-mail:* mmusoke@uga.healthnet.org
Publication(s): *East African Medical Bibliography* (bimonthly); *The Uganda Health Information Digest* (3 times/yr)

## Makerere Institute of Social Research Library
PO Box 7062, Kampala
*Tel:* (041) 55 45 82; (041) 53 28 30; (041) 53 28
  37; (041) 53 28 38; (041) 53 28 39 *Fax:* (041)
  53 28 21
*E-mail:* jmugasha@mulib.mak.ac.ug
*Web Site:* www.makerere.ac.ug/research/misr.htm

## Makerere University Library
PO Box 7062, Kampala
*Tel:* (041) 531041 *Fax:* (041) 540374
*E-mail:* info@mulib.mak.ac.ug;
  universitylibrarian@mulib.mak.ac.ug
*Web Site:* www.makerere.ac.ug/mulib *Cable:*
  MAKUNIKA
*Key Personnel*
Librarian: James Mugasha *E-mail:* jmugasha@
  mulib.mak.ac.ug
Founded: 1957

## National Library of Uganda
11-13 Buganda Rd, 11 Bombo Rd, Kampala
Mailing Address: PO Box 4262, Kampala
*Tel:* (041) 233633 *Fax:* (041) 348625
*E-mail:* library@imul.com *Cable:* LIBRARY,
  KAMPALA
*Key Personnel*
Dir: Ms G K Mulindwa
Founded: 1964 (as Public Libraries Board, established 2003 as National Library of Uganda)

Nationwide public library service & preservation
  of national heritage.
*Parent Company:* Ministry of Gender, Labour &
  Social Development

## Uganda Polytechnic Library at Uganda Technical College
PO Box 7181, Kampala
*Tel:* (041) 28 5211 *Cable:* TECHNICAL
*Key Personnel*
Chief Librarian: R Nganwa
Founded: 1954

# Ukraine

## Vernadsky Central Scientific Library of the National Academy of Sciences of Ukraine
Prospekt 40-richja Snavtnja 3, UA-252650 Kiev
  34
*Tel:* (044) 285 81 64 *Fax:* (044) 264 33 98
*E-mail:* nlu@csl.freenet.kiev.ua
*Key Personnel*
Dir: Aleksei Semenovich Onischenko

# United Arab Emirates

## Centre for Documentation & Research
Abu Dhabi
Mailing Address: PO Box 5884, Abu Dhabi
*Tel:* (02) 444 5400 *Fax:* (02) 444 5811
*Web Site:* www.gebcad.com
Founded: 1988
Archival collections.
Publication(s): *Documents of UAE* (annually)
*Ultimate Parent Company:* Abu Dhabi Government

## National Library
Zayed 1st St, Abu Dhabi
Mailing Address: PO Box 2380, Abu Dhabi
*Tel:* (02) 215300 *Fax:* (02) 217472
*E-mail:* nlibrary@ns1.cultural.org.ae
*Web Site:* www.cultural.org.ae
*Telex:* 22414 Culcen Em
*Key Personnel*
Dir: Jumaa Alqubaisi *E-mail:* jqubaisi@nsl.
  cultural.org.ae
Total Titles: 800,000 Print

# United Kingdom

## Belfast Public Library
Royal Ave, Belfast BT1 1EA
*Tel:* (01232) 243 233 *Fax:* (01232) 332 819
*Telex:* 747359
*Key Personnel*
Chief Librarian: J N Montgomery
Founded: 1888

## Birmingham Library Information Services
University of Birmingham, Edgbaston, Birmingham B15 2TT
*Tel:* (0121) 414 5828 *Fax:* (0121) 471 4691
*E-mail:* library@bham.ac.uk

*Web Site:* www.is.bham.ac.uk/mainlib
*Telex:* 337655
*Key Personnel*
Contact: Mrs Marjorie Westley *Tel:* (0121) 303 2868 *E-mail:* marje.westley@birmingham.gov.uk
Assistant Dir: V M Griffiths
Publication(s): *Birmingham Between the Wars*; *Briefing* (bimonthly); *Bygone Bartley Green*; *Directory of the Irish in Birmingham*; *In the Midst of Life*; *Lost Railways of Birmingham*; *National Socialist Literature in Birmingham Reference Library*; *News Review* (5 issues a week); *The Nine Days in Birmingham*; *Statistics & Market Research* (monthly); *Struggling Manor*

### Bodleian Library
Broad St, Oxford OX1 3BG
*Tel:* (01865) 277183 *Fax:* (01865) 277182
*E-mail:* secretary@bodley.ox.ac.uk
*Web Site:* www.bodley.ox.ac.uk
*Telex:* 83656
*Key Personnel*
Librarian: Reginald P Carr *Tel:* (01865) 277166
*E-mail:* bodleys.librarian@bodley.ox.ac.uk

### The British Library
St Pancras, 96 Euston Rd, London NW1 2DB
*Tel:* (0870) 444 1500
*Web Site:* www.bl.uk
Also publisher of books of interest to the general reader & collector, including facsimiles of items in the collection & works of general bibliography.
Publication(s): *British National Bibliography* (weekly); *Serials in the British Library* (quarterly); *The UKMARC Exchange Record Format* (1997); *UKMARC Manual: A Cataloguer's Guide to the Bibliographic Format* (1996)

### British Library Document Supply Centre
Document Supply Centre, Boston Spa, Wetherby, W Yorks LS23 7BQ
*Tel:* (01937) 546060 *Fax:* (01937) 546333
*E-mail:* dsc-customer-services@bl.uk
*Web Site:* www.bl.uk/services/document/contact.html
*Key Personnel*
Publishing Officer: Dr Dorothy Dryden
Publications Officer: Andrea Seed
Also publisher.
Publication(s): *Alphanumeric Reports Publications Index*; *Books at Boston Spa* (on microfiche); *Boston Spa Books* (on CD-ROM); *Boston Spa Conferences* (on CD-ROM); *Boston Spa Serials* (on CD-ROM); *British Reports, Translations & Theses*; *Current Serials Received*; *Directory of Acronyms*; *Focus on British Biological & Medical Research*; *Focus on British Business & Management Science Research*; *Focus on British Engineering & Computer Sciences Research*; *East-West Links*; *Index of Conference Proceedings* (monthly with annual cumulations); *Index of Conference Proceedings 1964-1988*; *Inside Conferences* (on CD-ROM); *Inside Information* (on CD-ROM); *Keyword Index to Serial Titles* (on microfiche); *POPSI-The Popular Song Index*

### British Library, Newspaper Library
Colindale Ave, London NW9 5HE
*Tel:* (020) 7412 7353 *Fax:* (020) 7412 7379
*E-mail:* newspaper@bl.uk
*Web Site:* www.bl.uk
*Telex:* 21462
*Key Personnel*
Newspaper Librarian: Edmund King *Tel:* (020) 7412 7362 *E-mail:* ed.king@bl.uk

Editor of the Newsletter: Christopher Skelton-Foord
The national collection of British & overseas newspapers.

### British Library of Political & Economic Science
London School of Economics, 10 Portugal St, London WC2A 2HD
*Tel:* (020) 7955 7229 *Fax:* (020) 7955 7454
*E-mail:* library@lse.ac.uk
*Web Site:* www.lse.ac.uk/library
*Key Personnel*
Librarian & Dir Information Services: Jean Sykes
Not a British Library division.
Publication(s): *The International Bibliography of the Social Sciences*

### British Library Oriental & India Office Collections
96 Euston Rd, London NW1 2DB
*Tel:* (020) 7412 7873 *Fax:* (020) 7412 7641
*E-mail:* oioc-prints@bl.uk
*Web Site:* www.bl.uk
*Key Personnel*
Dir: G W Shaw
Publication(s): *Calcutta: City of Palaces* (1990); *Catalogue of the Nevill Collection of Sinhalese Mss* (4 vols, 1987-1990); *Catalogue of the Urdu, Panjabi, Pashto and Kashmiri Documents in the India Office Library and Records* (1990); *Descriptive Catalogue of the Batala Collection of Mughal Documents 1527-1757* (1990); *General Guide to the India Officer Records* (1988); *The Life of the Buddha* (1992); *Oriental Gardens* (1991)
*Orders to:* Turpin Distribution Services Ltd, Blackhorse Rd, Letchworth, Herts SG6 1HN *Tel:* (01462) 672555 *Fax:* (01462) 480947

### The British Library, Science Technology & Business Collections
Science Technology & Business Collections, 96 Euston Rd, London NW1 2DB
*Tel:* (020) 7412 7288; (020) 7412 7494
*E-mail:* scitech@bl.uk
*Web Site:* www.bl.uk
*Key Personnel*
Head of Library: Julia Stocken
List of seminars & publications available upon request. The national library for science, technology, business, patents & the social sciences, is the most comprehensive reference collection in Western Europe of such literature from the whole world. Inquiries are also handled by telephone, fax & e-mail. The library has inquiry & referral services (especially in business information, the environment, industrial property, health care & the social sciences); online database search, photocopy & linguistic aid services; runs courses & seminars & provides a wide range of publications from newsletters to definitive bibliographies.

### Cambridge University Library
West Rd, Cambridge CB3 9DR
*Tel:* (01223) 333000 *Fax:* (01223) 333160
*E-mail:* library@lib.cam.ac.uk
*Web Site:* www.lib.cam.ac.uk
*Key Personnel*
Librarian: Mr P K Fox *Tel:* (01223) 333045
Deputy Librarian: Mr D J Hall *Tel:* (01223) 333047; Ms A E Murray *Tel:* (01223) 333083
Founded: 1400
List of publications available on request from the library offices or online.
*Branch Office(s)*
Medical Library, Addenbrooke's Hospital, Hills Rd, Cambridge CB2 2SP *Tel:* (01223) 336750 *Fax:* (01223) 331918 *E-mail:* library@medschl.cam.ac.uk

Betty & Gordon Moore Library, Wilberforce Rd, Cambridge CB3 0WD *Tel:* (01223) 765670 *Fax:* (01223) 765678 *E-mail:* moore-library@lib.cam.ac.uk
Central Science Library, Bene't St, Cambridge CB2 3PY *Tel:* (01223) 334742 *Fax:* (01223) 334748 *E-mail:* lib-csl-inquiries@lists.cam.ac.uk
Squire Law Library, 10 West Rd, Cambridge CB3 9DZ *Tel:* (01223) 330077 *Fax:* (01223) 330048 *E-mail:* squire@law.cam.ac.uk

### Durham Chapter Library
The College, Durham DH1 3EH
*Tel:* (0191) 386 2489 *Fax:* (0191) 386 4267
*E-mail:* library@durhamcathedral.co.uk
*Web Site:* www.durhamcathedral.co.uk/
*Key Personnel*
Canon Librarian: Prof David Brown
Assistant Librarian: Joan Williams

### Durham University Library
Stockton Rd, Durham DH1 3LY
*Tel:* (0191) 334 2968 *Fax:* (0191) 334 2971
*E-mail:* main.library@durham.ac.uk
*Web Site:* www.dur.ac.uk/library
*Key Personnel*
University Librarian: Dr John T D Hall *Tel:* (0191) 334 2960 *E-mail:* j.t.d.hall@durham.ac.uk

### Edinburgh City Library & Information Services
Central Library, George IV Bridge, Edinburgh EH1 1EG
*Tel:* (0131) 242 8020 *Fax:* (0131) 242 8009
*E-mail:* central.lending.library@edinburgh.gov.uk
*Web Site:* www.edinburgh.gov.uk/libraries
*Key Personnel*
Head, Lib & Info Servs: W Wallace
Founded: 1890
Public library service.
*Parent Company:* Culture & Leisure Dept
*Ultimate Parent Company:* City of Edinburgh Council

### Edinburgh University Library
George Sq, Edinburgh EH8 9LJ
*Tel:* (0131) 650 3384; (0131) 650 3374 (reference & information services) *Fax:* (0131) 667 9780; (0131) 650 3380 (administration); (0131) 650 6863 (special collections)
*E-mail:* library@ed.ac.uk
*Web Site:* www.lib.ed.ac.uk
*Key Personnel*
Dir Library Services: Sheila E Cannell *E-mail:* sheila.cannell@ed.ac.uk
Founded: 1580
Publication(s): *Catalogue of Printed Books* (1988, microfiche); *Catalogue of the Library of The Rev James Nairn* (guides, leaflets, exhibition catalogs); *Collection of Historical Essays* (1982); *Edinburgh University Library, 1580-1980*; *Manuscript Treasures of Edinburgh University Library* (1980)

### Glasgow City Libraries & Archives, the Mitchell Library
North St, Glasgow G3 7DN
*Tel:* (0141) 287 2999; (0141) 287 2876 *Fax:* (0141) 287 2815
*E-mail:* lil@cls.glasgow.gov.uk
*Web Site:* www.mitchelllibrary.org; www.glasgowlibraries.org
*Key Personnel*
Commercial Manager: Verina Litster
Publication(s): *West of Scotland Census Returns & Old Parochial Registers* (a directory of public library holdings in the West of Scotland)

**Guildhall Library**
Aldermanbury, London EC2P 2EJ
*Tel:* (020) 7332 1868; (020) 7332 1870; (020)
7332 1863; (020) 7332 1839 *Fax:* (020) 7600
3384
*E-mail:* printedbooks.guildhall@corpoflondon.gov.
uk; manuscripts.guildhall@corpoflondon.gov.uk
*Web Site:* www.corpoflondon.gov.uk
*Key Personnel*
Librarian: Melvyn Barnes
Total Titles: 189,000 Print

**Institute of Development Studies**
University of Sussex, Brighton BN1 9RE
*Tel:* (01273) 606261 *Fax:* (01273) 621202;
(01273) 691647
*E-mail:* blds@ids.ac.uk
*Web Site:* www.ids.ac.uk
*Telex:* 877997 IDSBTN G
*Key Personnel*
Head, Communications: Geoff Barnard *E-mail:* g.
barnard@ids.ac.uk
Founded: 1966

**Leeds University Library**
Leeds LS2 9JT
*Tel:* (0113) 343 5663 *Fax:* (0113) 233 5561
*E-mail:* libraryenquiries@leeds.ac.uk
*Web Site:* www.leeds.ac.uk/library
*Key Personnel*
University Librarian: Margaret Coutts *Tel:* (0113)
343 5501 *E-mail:* m.m.coutts@leeds.ac.uk
Founded: 1874
Publication(s): *The Brotherton Collection*; *Catalogue of German Literature Printed in the 17th
& 18th Centuries*; *A Catalogue of the Icelandic
Collection*; *Catalogue of the Romany Collection*

**Liverpool Libraries & Information Services**
Central Library, William Brown St, Liverpool L3
8EW
*Tel:* (0151) 233 5829 *Fax:* (0151) 233 5886
*E-mail:* refbt.central.library@liverpool.gov.uk
*Key Personnel*
Head of Library & Information Services: Joyce
Little *Tel:* (0151) 233 6346 *E-mail:* joyce.
little@liverpool.gov.uk
Publication(s): *Liverpool-Capital of the Slave
Trade*; *Liverpool Women at War*; *The Battle
of the Atlantic* (personal memories)

**The Mitchell Library**, see Glasgow City
Libraries & Archives, the Mitchell Library

**The National Archives**
Formerly Public Record Office
Kew, Richmond, Surrey TW9 4DU
*Tel:* (020) 8876 3444 *Fax:* (020) 8392 5286
*E-mail:* enquiry@nationalarchives.gov.uk
*Web Site:* www.nationalarchives.gov.uk
*Key Personnel*
Head of Enterprises: Anne Kilminster *Tel:* (020)
8392 5206 *E-mail:* anne.kilminster@pro.gov.uk
Founded: 1838
National archive for the records of the British
courts of law & central departments of state.

**National Library for the Blind**
Far Cromwell Rd, Bredbury, Stockport SK6 2SG
*Tel:* (0161) 355 2000 *Fax:* (0161) 355 2098
*E-mail:* enquiries@nlbuk.org
*Web Site:* www.nlb-online.org
*Key Personnel*
Chief Executive: Helen Brazier
Chairman: Dr Gillian Burrington
Dir, External Relations: Phil Robertshaw
Dir, ICT & Operations: Carol Pollitt
Dir, Library & Information Services: Pat Beech
Resources Dir: Susan Cohen
Founded: 1882

A leading national agency in the provision of library services for visually impaired people &
Europe's largest lending library for people who
cannot read print.
Publication(s): *Annual Review*; *Focus* (triannually,
newsletter); *New Reading* (quarterly, catalog);
*Read On* (quarterly, magazine)

**National Library of Scotland**
George IV Bridge, Edinburgh EH1 1EW
*Tel:* (0131) 623 3700 *Fax:* (0131) 623 3701
*E-mail:* enquiries@nls.uk
*Web Site:* www.nls.uk
*Key Personnel*
National Librarian: Martyn Wade *Tel:* (0131) 623
3700 (ext 3730) *E-mail:* m.wade@nls.uk
Publication(s): *Special & Named Printed Collections in the National Library of Scotland, Ed G
Hogg* (1999)

**National Library of Wales**
Aberystwyth, Ceredigion, Cymru SY23 3BU
*Tel:* (01970) 632 800 *Fax:* (01970) 615 709
*E-mail:* holi@llgc.org.uk
*Web Site:* www.llgc.org.uk
*Key Personnel*
Librarian: Andrew M W Green
Also publisher.
Publication(s): *Llyfryddiaeth Cymru - A Bibliography of Wales* (no longer published on paper, available only as an online service on the
web catalog); *The National Library of Wales
Journal* (semiannually, academic, based on the
library's holdings)

**The Natural History Museum Library**
Cromwell Rd, London SW7 5BD
*Tel:* (020) 7942 5000 *Fax:* (020) 7942 5559
*E-mail:* genlib@nhm.ac.uk
*Web Site:* www.nhm.ac.uk/library
*Key Personnel*
Head of Library & Information Services: Ray
Lester
Founded: 1881

**NLB**, see National Library for the Blind

**Oxford University, Taylor Institution Library**
St Giles', Oxford OX1 3NA
*Tel:* (01865) 2-78154; (01865) 2-78158 (book enquiries) *Fax:* (01865) 2-78165
*E-mail:* enquiries@taylib.ox.ac.uk
*Web Site:* www.taylib.ox.ac.uk
*Key Personnel*
Librarian in Charge: Ms A J Peters *Tel:* (01865)
2-78160 *E-mail:* amanda.peters@taylib.ox.ac.uk
Contact: Mrs E A C Baird *Tel:* (01865) 2-78162
*E-mail:* liz.baird@taylib.ox.ac.uk
Founded: 1845
Graduate research library for modern languages.

**PRONI (Public Record Office of Northern
Ireland)**
66 Balmoral Ave, Belfast BT9 6NY
*Tel:* (02890) 255905 *Fax:* (02890) 255999
*E-mail:* proni@dcalni.gov.uk
*Web Site:* www.proni.gov.uk
*Key Personnel*
Deputy Keeper & Chief Executive: Dr Gerry
Slater *E-mail:* slaterg.proni@doeni.gov.uk

**Public Record Office**, see The National Archives

**Public Record Office of Northern Ireland**, see
PRONI (Public Record Office of Northern
Ireland)

**John Rylands University Library of
Manchester**
Oxford Rd, Manchester M13 9PP

*Tel:* (0161) 275 3751 (Main Library Bldg);
(0161) 834 5343 (Deansgate Bldg) *Fax:* (0161)
273 7488 (Main Library Bldg); (0161) 834
5574 (Deansgate Bldg)
*E-mail:* libtalk@man.ac.uk
*Web Site:* rylibweb.man.ac.uk
*Key Personnel*
Dir & University Librarian: Bill Simpson
*Tel:* (0161) 275 3700 *E-mail:* bill.simpson@
man.ac.uk
Assistant Dir & Deputy Librarian: Dr Diana
Leitch *Tel:* (0161) 275 3737 *E-mail:* diana.
leitch@man.ac.uk
General Administration: Peter Wadsworth
*Tel:* (0161) 275 3760 *E-mail:* peter.
wadsworth@man.ac.uk
Publication(s): *The Bulletin of the John Rylands
University Library of Manchester*

**School of Oriental & African Studies Library**
University of London, Thornhaugh St, Russell Sq,
London WC1H 0XG
*Tel:* (020) 7898 4163 *Fax:* (020) 7436 3844
*E-mail:* libenquiry@soas.ac.uk
*Web Site:* www.soas.ac.uk/library/home.html
*Key Personnel*
Head of Library Services: Anne Poulson
*Tel:* (020) 7898 4161 *E-mail:* ap45@soas.ac.uk
Publication(s): *Library Catalogue* (1978-1984
supplement on microfiche); *Library Guide*

**Scottish Poetry Library**
5 Crichton's Close, Canongate, Edinburgh EH8
8DT
*Tel:* (031) 557 2876 *Fax:* (031) 557 8393
*E-mail:* inquiries@spl.org.uk
*Web Site:* www.spl.org.uk
*Key Personnel*
Dir: Robyn Marsack *E-mail:* rmarsack@spl.org.
uk
Librarian: Iain Young *E-mail:* librarian1@spl.org.
uk
Founded: 1984
Free lending & reference library specializing in
Scottish & international poetry of mainly 20th
century. Computer index to poetry now available online. Travelling van service provided.
Stock includes books, audio & video tapes,
periodicals, news cuttings. Workshops for children organized in term-time & holidays.
Publication(s): *Index to Scottish Poetry Magazines*
(forthcoming, Vols 1-9 published)

**Senate House Library University of London**
Senate House, Malet St, London WC1E 7HU
*Tel:* (020) 7862 8500 *Fax:* (020) 7862 8480
*E-mail:* enquiries@shl.lon.ac.uk
*Web Site:* www.ull.ac.uk
*Key Personnel*
Dir: David Pearson *Tel:* (020) 7862 8410
*E-mail:* dpearson@shl.lon.ac.uk
Founded: 1837
Academic research library.
Publication(s): *Catalogue of Goldsmiths' Library of Economic Literature, Vol I-V* (Guides;
Brochures)

**Trinity College Library**
Cambridge CB2 1TQ
*Tel:* (01223) 338488 *Fax:* (01223) 338532
*E-mail:* trin-lib@lists.cam.ac.uk
*Web Site:* library.trin.cam.ac.uk
*Key Personnel*
Librarian: D J McKitterick

**ULL**, see Senate House Library University of
London

**University of Aberdeen**
Queen Mother Library, Meston Walk, Old Aberdeen AB24 3UE
*Tel:* (01224) 273600 *Fax:* (01224) 273956

*E-mail:* library@abdn.ac.uk
*Web Site:* www.abdn.ac.uk/diss/library
*Key Personnel*
Manager, Library Division: Ms Carole Munro
*Tel:* (01224) 273321 *E-mail:* lib229@abdn.ac.uk
Contact: Christine A Miller *Tel:* (01224) 272572
*E-mail:* c.a.miller@abdn.ac.uk
Founded: 1495
University library.
Publication(s): *George Washington Wilson Photographic Series* (irregular, Based on the Library's archive of Victorian glass plate negatives)
*Branch Office(s)*
Education Library (agriculture & forestry)
Medical Library
Taylor Library (law & European documentation centre)

## University of Exeter Library
Stocker Rd, Exeter EX4 4PT
*Tel:* (01392) 263867 *Fax:* (01392) 263871
*E-mail:* library@exeter.ac.uk
*Web Site:* www.ex.ac.uk/library/
*Key Personnel*
Librarian: Alasdair T Paterson

## University of Glasgow Library
Hillhead St, Glasgow G12 8QE
*Tel:* (0141) 330 6704 *Fax:* (0141) 330 4952
*E-mail:* library@lib.gla.ac.uk
*Web Site:* www.lib.gla.ac.uk
*Key Personnel*
Dir, Library Services: Chris Bailey
Founded: 1451
Specialize in university higher education.

## University of Leicester Library
University Rd, Leicester LE1 9QD
Mailing Address: PO Box 248, Leicester LE1 9QD
*Tel:* (0116) 252 2043 *Fax:* (0116) 252 2066
*E-mail:* libdesk@le.ac.uk
*Web Site:* www.le.ac.uk/library
*Key Personnel*
Librarian: Christine Fyfe *Tel:* (0116) 252 2031
*E-mail:* c.fyfe@le.ac.uk

## The University of Reading Library
Whiteknights, PO Box 223, Reading RG6 6AE
*Tel:* (0118) 378 8770 *Fax:* (0118) 378 6636
*E-mail:* library@reading.ac.uk
*Web Site:* www.library.rdg.ac.uk
*Key Personnel*
Librarian: Julia Munro *Tel:* (0118) 378 8774
*E-mail:* j.h.munro@rdg.ac.uk
Founded: 1892
Publication(s): *Beckett at Reading: Catalogue of the Beckett Manuscript Collection at the University of Reading* (catalog, 1998); *The Samuel Beckett Collection* (catalog, 1978); *Beckett's Dream Notebook* (1999); *Catalogue of the Collection of Children's Books 1617-1939 in the Library of the University of Reading* (catalog, 1988); *W M Childs: An Account of His Life & Work* (1976); *The Cole Library of Early Medicine & Zoology, Part 1: 1472-1800* (catalog, 1969); *The Cole Library of Early Medicine & Zoology, Part 2, 1800 to Present Day & Supplement* (catalog, 1975); *The Finzi Book Room at the University of Reading* (catalog, 1981); *Robert Gibbings 1889-1958* (1989); *Historical Farm Records: A Summary Guide to Manuscripts & Other Material Collected by the Institute of Agricultural History & Museum of English Rural Life* (1973); *The Ideal Core of the Onion: Reading Beckett Archives* (1992); *The Kingsley Read Alphabet Collection* (catalog, 1983); *Records Management in British Universities: A Survey with Some Suggestions* (1978)

## University of Southampton Library
University Rd, Highfield, Southampton SO17 1BJ
*Tel:* (01703) 22180 *Fax:* (01703) 23007
*E-mail:* libenqs@soton.ac.uk
*Web Site:* www.library.soton.ac.uk
*Telex:* 47661
*Key Personnel*
Librarian: Dr Mark Brown *Tel:* (0173) 22677
*E-mail:* m.l.brown@soton.ac.uk

## Wellcome Library for the History & Understanding of Medicine
Affiliate of Welcome Trust Centre for the History of Medicine at UCL
210 Euston Rd, London NW1 2BE
*Tel:* (020) 7611 8722 *Fax:* (020) 7611 8369
*E-mail:* library@wellcome.ac.uk
*Web Site:* library.wellcome.ac.uk
*Key Personnel*
Librarian: Frances Norton
Provides insight & information to anyone seeking to understand medicine & its role in society, past & present.
*Parent Company:* Wellcome Trust

## Westminster Abbey Library
E Cloister, London SW1P 3PA
*Tel:* (020) 7654 4830 *Fax:* (020) 7654 4827
*E-mail:* library@westminster-abbey.org
*Web Site:* westminster-abbey.org
*Key Personnel*
Librarian: Dr Tony A Trowles

# Uruguay

## Biblioteca Nacional del Uruguay
18 de Julio 1790, Casilla de Correo 452, 11200 Montevideo
*Tel:* (02) 48 50 30 *Fax:* (02) 49 69 02
*E-mail:* bibna@adinet.com.uy
*Web Site:* www.bibna.gub.uy
*Key Personnel*
Dir: Prof Rafael Gomensoro
Founded: 1816
Publication(s): *Anuario Bibliografico Uruguayo 1968-*; *Directorio de Servicios de Informacion y Documentacion en el Uruquay, 1988-*; *Revista Archivo, 1987-*; *Revista Biblioteca Nacional 1966-*; *Uruquay: Indice de publicaciones periodicas en ciencia y tecnologia 1981-1983, 1986-*
*Branch Office(s)*
Oficina de Ventas, Instituto Nacional del Libro, San Jose, 1116 Montevideo *Tel:* (02) 986740

## Centro Nacional de Documentacion Cientifica, Tecnica y Economics (CNDCTE)
18 de Julio 1790, Cassilla de Correo 452, Montevideo
*Tel:* (02) 484172 *Fax:* (02) 496902
*Key Personnel*
Dir: Elena Castro
Part of the National Library (Biblioteca National del Uruguay).
Publication(s): *Directorio de Servicios de Informacion y Documentacion en el Uruguay*; *Indice de publicaciones periodicas en ciencia y tecnologia 1981-1983*

## Biblioteca Central y Publicaciones del Consejo de Educacion Secundaria
Eduardo Acevedo 1427, Planta Alta, 11200 Montevideo
*Tel:* (02) 408 42 73; (02) 408 30 51; (02) 408 12 52 *Fax:* (02) 408 12 52
*Key Personnel*
Dir: Juana Alekandronicius

## Biblioteca Facultad de Humanidades y Ciencias de la Educacion
Magallanes 1577, Montevideo 11200
*Tel:* (02) 49 11 04; (02) 49 11 05; (02) 49 11 06 *Fax:* (02) 48 43 03
*E-mail:* biblio@fhudec.edu.uy
*Web Site:* www.rau.edu.uy/universidad/fhcet.htm
*Key Personnel*
Librarian: Margarita Llado

## Biblioteca del Museo Historico Nacional
Rincon 437, CP 11000 Montevideo
*Tel:* (02) 95 10 51; (02) 915 33 16 *Fax:* (02) 915 68 63
*Key Personnel*
Contact: Luis Segarra

## Biblioteca del Palacio Legislativo, see Biblioteca del Poder Legislativo

## Biblioteca del Poder Legislativo (Library of the Legislative Power)
Av de las Leyes, s/n, 11800 Montevideo
*Tel:* (02) 208937 *Fax:* (02) 949162
*Telex:* 23203 CARE UY
*Key Personnel*
Librarian: Luis H Boions Pombo; Mazzeo Condenanza
Founded: 1928
Publication(s): *Anales Parlamentarios* (semestrial); *Bibliografia Uruguaya* (irregularly); *Boletin Bibliografico* (monthly); *Fichas Analiticas de Articulos de Publicaciones Periodicos* (monthly)

## Biblioteca Municipal Dr Joaquin de Salterain
Solis 1456 y 25 de Mayo, Montevideo 11000
*Tel:* (02) 95 62 82
*Web Site:* www.mec.gub.uy/biblo.htm
*Key Personnel*
Contact: Graciela Fernandez Ribeiro

# Uzbekistan

## Alisher Navoi National Library of Uzbekistan
5 Mustakillik Sq, 700078 Tashkent
*Tel:* (099871) 139 16 58 *Fax:* (099871) 133 09 08
*E-mail:* navoi@physic.uzsci.net
*Web Site:* www.rsl.ru/sonegos/e_son4_17.htm
*Key Personnel*
Dir: A A Umarov
Founded: 1870

# Venezuela

## Archivo General de la Nacion (AG)
Esquinas de Santa Capilla y Carmelitas n° 15, Avenida Urdanata (Apdo 5935), Caracas 101
Mailing Address: PO Box 3910, Caracas 1010
*Tel:* (0212) 862-99-07 *Fax:* (0212) 81-93-28
*Web Site:* www.ucab.edu.ve/biblioteca
*Key Personnel*
Dir: Prof Emilio Piriz Perez *E-mail:* epiriz@ucab.edu.ve

## Biblioteca de la Universidad Catolica 'Andres Bello'
Montalban, La Vega Apdo 29068, Caracas 1020
*Tel:* (0212) 4074190

*Web Site:* www.ucab.edu.ve/biblioteca
*Key Personnel*
Librarian: Emilio Piriz Perez *E-mail:* epiriz@
ucab.edu.ve

**Biblioteca del Congreso**
Servicio Autonomo de Informacion Legislativa
  (SAIL), 3er piso, oficina 37, Caracas 1010
*Tel:* (0212) 5645327 *Fax:* (0212) 5636696
*Telex:* 21252 CCASSVC
*Key Personnel*
Contact: Bertha Pina Montes

**Biblioteca Nacional**
Final Av Panteon Foro Libertador, Edificio Sede,
  Caracas 1010
*Tel:* (0212) 505 91 25 *Fax:* (0212) 505 91 24
*E-mail:* dir.general@bnv.bib.ve
*Web Site:* www.bnv.bib.ve
*Telex:* 24621 IASBN
*Key Personnel*
Dir: Virginia Betancourt *E-mail:* vbetanc@
reaccium.ve

**Instituto Autonomo, Biblioteca Nacional y de
  Servicios de Bibliotecas**
Final Av Panteon Esq Fe a Remedios, Apdo
  6525, Caracas 1010-DL
*Tel:* (0212) 5059141 *Fax:* (0212) 5059159
*Web Site:* www.bnv.bib.ve
*Telex:* 24621 Iabn Vc
*Key Personnel*
Dir Lic: Virginia Betancourt
National Library, Public Library Services, Audio-
  visual Archive of Venezuela.
Publication(s): *Anuarios Bibliograficos* (to 1977);
  *Bibliografia Venezolana* (from 1978); *Catalogo
  de Publicaciones Oficiales*; *Informe Anual*

**Biblioteca Marcel Roche del Instituto
  Venezolano de Investigaciones Cientificas**
  (Marcel Roche Library of the Venezuelan
  Institute for Scientific Research)
Altos de Pipe, Km 11 Carretera Panamericana,
  Apdo 21827, Caracas 1020-A
*Tel:* (0212) 504 12 36 *Fax:* (0212) 504 14 23
*E-mail:* bibliotk@ivic.ivic.ve
*Web Site:* biblioteca.ivic.ve
*Telex:* 21657 *Cable:* IVICSAS
*Key Personnel*
Librarian: Xiomara Jayaro *E-mail:* xjayaro@ivic.
ve

**Biblioteca Central de la Universidad Central
  de Venezuela**
Biblioteca Central, Universidad Central de
  Venezuela, Caracas 1051
*Tel:* (0212) 605-29-09; (0212) 605-29-10
  *Fax:* (0212) 6622486
*E-mail:* bibcentral@sicht.ucv.ve
*Web Site:* www.ucv.ve
*Telex:* 28479
*Key Personnel*
Dir: Elsi Jimenez *E-mail:* jimeneze@sicht.ucv.ve

**Servicios Bibliotecarios Universidad de los
  Andes (Serbiula)**
Edif Administrativo piso 5, Merida 5101
*Tel:* (0274) 2402731; (0274) 2402729 *Fax:* (0274)
  2402507; (0274) 2402748
*E-mail:* adquisi@serbi.ula.ve
*Web Site:* www.serbi.ula.ve
*Telex:* 74206 BMULA-VC
*Key Personnel*
Coordinator: Jesus Rivero M
Head of Acquisitions: Crisalida Fuentes
  *Tel:* (0274) 2401227 *E-mail:* cfuentes@ula.ve
Founded: 1980
University library services.

**Biblioteca Central de la Universidad de Zulia**
Nucleo Humanistico, Maracaibo
*Tel:* (061) 596701 *Fax:* (061) 596700
*Web Site:* www.serbi.luz.ve
*Key Personnel*
Librarian: Elga Ortega
Publication(s): *Boletin* (biennially)

# Viet Nam

**General Sciences Library of Ho Chi Minh City**
69 Ly Tu Trong, Ho Chi Minh City
*Tel:* (08) 822 5055 *Fax:* (08) 829 5632
*Key Personnel*
Dir: Nguyen Thi Bac
Founded: 1976

**National Library of Vietnam**
31 Trang Hi St, Hanoi
*Tel:* (04) 8248051 *Fax:* (04) 8253357
*E-mail:* info@nlv.gov.vn
*Web Site:* www.nlv.gov.vn
*Key Personnel*
Dir: Mr Pham The Khang
Founded: 1917
Publication(s): *Cong tac Thu' vien-Thu' muc*
  (Journal of Library & Bibliography); *Thu' muc
  quoc gia Viet nam* (National Bibliography)

**Social Sciences Library**
34 Ly Tu Trong, Ho Chi Minh City
*Tel:* (08) 20644 *Fax:* (08) 223735
*Key Personnel*
Dir: Tran Minh Duc

# Yemen

**British Council Library**
Algiers St, Administrative Tower, 3rd floor,
  Sana'a Trade Centre, Sana'a
Mailing Address: PO Box 2157, Sana'a
*Tel:* (01) 448 356; (01) 448 357; (01) 448 358;
  (01) 448 359 *Fax:* (01) 448 360
*E-mail:* britishcouncil@ye.britishcouncil.org
*Web Site:* www.britishcouncil.org/yemen.htm
*Telex:* 2748 Brcoun Ye

**Library of the Great Mosque of Sana'a**
Al Jamia al Kabir, Sana'a

# Zambia

**CBU Library**, see The Copperbelt University
  Library

**The Copperbelt University Library**
Division of Ministry of Education
c/o Copperbelt University, Box 21692, Kitwe
*Tel:* (02) 222066; (02) 225155 *Fax:* (02) 222469;
  (02) 223972
*E-mail:* library@cbu.ac.zm
*Web Site:* www.cbu.edu.zm
*Telex:* ZA 53270
*Key Personnel*
Librarian: Charles B M Lungu
  *E-mail:* cbmlungu@cbu.ac.zm
Assistant Librarian: Nellie C Chiinza; Charles
  Maambo *E-mail:* maambo@cbu.ac.zm; Mwala

Sheba *E-mail:* shebamk@cbu.ac.zm; Hamaton
  Sitwala
Founded: 1987
Membership(s): Association of African Universi-
  ties.
*Ultimate Parent Company:* Government of the
  Republic of Zambia

**Hammarskjold Memorial Library**
PO Box 21493, Kitwe
*Tel:* (02) 214572; (02) 219012; (02) 211488
  *Fax:* (02) 211001
*E-mail:* daglib@zamnet.zm
*Telex:* 52050 Za *Cable:* MINCEN KITWE
*Key Personnel*
Librarian: Dunstan Chikonka
Founded: 1963
Information provision to the foundation's par-
  ticipant's & many other copperbelt residents
  interested in various research programs.
Publication(s): *Mindolo Weekly* (newsletter); *Min-
  dolo World* (biannually, various reports of con-
  ferences & research programs)
*Parent Company:* Mindolo Ecumenical Founda-
  tion

**Evelyn Hone College Library**
PO Box 30029, Lusaka
*Tel:* (01) 225127 *Fax:* (01) 225127
*Key Personnel*
Librarian: Regina Shula

**Kitwe City Library**
PO Box 20070, Kitwe
*Tel:* (02) 226162; (02) 221001; (02) 222927
  *Fax:* (02) 224698

**Lusaka City Library**
PO Box 31304, Lusaka
*Tel:* (01) 227282
*Telex:* 40157 Za
*Key Personnel*
City Librarian: J C Nkole

**National Archives**
PO Box 50010, 10101 Lusaka
*Tel:* (01) 254080 *Fax:* (01) 254081
*E-mail:* naz@zamnet.zm
*Key Personnel*
Acting Dir: Chrispin Hamooya
Publication(s): *List of Periodicals in the National
  Archives of Zambia*; *National Archives of Zam-
  bia Annual Reports*; *National Bibliography of
  Zambia*

**National Institute of Public Administration
  Library**
PO Box 31990, 10101 Lusaka
*Tel:* (01) 228802 *Fax:* (01) 27213
*Telex:* 40523
*Key Personnel*
Librarian: A G Kasonso

**Natural Resources Development College
  Library**
PO Box 310099, Lusaka
*Tel:* (01) 224610 *Fax:* (01) 224639 *Cable:*
  NATIVE LUSAKA
*Key Personnel*
Deputy Principal: Francis K Sinyangwe
Founded: 1964

**Ndola Public Library**
PO Box 70388, Ndola
*Tel:* (02) 620599
*Telex:* 30270
*Key Personnel*
Librarian: K Mumba Chisaka

**Northern Technical College Library**
Chela Rd, Ndola
Mailing Address: PO Box KJ250093, Ndola

*Tel:* (02) 680141 *Fax:* (02) 680423
*E-mail:* nortec@zamtel.zm
*Key Personnel*
Librarian: P Nabombe

## University of Zambia Press (UNZA Press)
PO Box 32379, 10101 Lusaka
*Tel:* (01) 290740; (01) 290409 *Fax:* (01) 253952
*Telex:* 44370 Za *Cable:* UNZA-Press
*Key Personnel*
Publisher: Samuel Kasankha *E-mail:* skasankha@
admin.unza.zm
Membership(s): Book Sellers & Publishers Association of Zambia.
Publication(s): *Six Scholarly & Academic Journals* (biannually)
*Parent Company:* University of Zambia

## Zambia Library Service
Division of Ministry of Education
PO Box 30802, Lusaka
*Tel:* (01) 254993 *Fax:* (01) 254993
*E-mail:* zamlibs@zamnet.zm *Cable:* ZAMLIBS
*Key Personnel*
Deputy Chief Librarian: E M Msadabwe
Publication(s): *Annual Report*; *Teacher/Librarians* (biannually, newsletter)

# Zimbabwe

## Bulawayo Public Library
100 Fort St, Bulawayo
Mailing Address: Private Bag 586, Bulawayo
*Tel:* (09) 60965 *Fax on Demand:* (09) 60965
*E-mail:* bpl@gatorzw.com
*Web Site:* www.angelfire.com/ky/bpl
*Key Personnel*
Librarian & Secretary: Robin W Doust
Founded: 1896
Public library & legal deposit (archive) collection.

## Geological Survey of Zimbabwe
Box CY210, Causeway
*Tel:* (04) 726342; (04) 726343; (04) 252016; (04) 252017 *Fax:* (04) 739601
*E-mail:* zimgeosv@africaonline.co.zw
*Web Site:* www.geosurvey.co.zw
*Telex:* 22416 MINESZW *Cable:* MINES
*Key Personnel*
Dir: S M N Ncube

## Harare City Library
PO Box 1087, Harare
*Tel:* (04) 751834; 751835
*Key Personnel*
Librarian: Mrs M Ross-Smith

## Harare Polytechnic Library
Herbert Chitepo Ave, Harare
Mailing Address: PO Box CY-407, Causeway, Harare
*Tel:* (04) 752311
*Key Personnel*
Head: Mr P Chimanda
Founded: 1924
*Ultimate Parent Company:* Ministry of Higher Education

## National Archives of Zimbabwe
Borrowdale Rd, Gunhill, Causeway, Harare
Mailing Address: Private Bag 7729, Causeway, Harare
*Tel:* (04) 792741; (04) 792742; (04) 792743 *Fax:* (04) 792398
*E-mail:* archives@gta.gov.zw
*Web Site:* www.gta.gov.zw
*Key Personnel*
Editor: O Wytete
Founded: 1935
Publication(s): *Guides to the National Archives collections* (series); *Zimbabwe National Bibliography*; *Directory of Libraries in Zimbabwe* (1986)

## National Free Library of Zimbabwe
Dugald Niven Library, 12 Ave S Park, Bulawayo
Mailing Address: PO Box 1773, Bulawayo
*Tel:* (09) 69827; (09) 62359 *Fax:* (09) 77662
*Telex:* 33128
*Key Personnel*
Chief Librarian: D E Barron
Founded: 1944

**NAZ**, see National Archives of Zimbabwe

## Library of Parliament
PO Box CY 298, Causeway, Harare
*Tel:* (04) 729722 *Fax:* (04) 795548
*Telex:* 24064
*Key Personnel*
Librarian: Mr Nelson Masawi
Founded: 1923

## Turner Memorial Library
Queensway Civic Complex, Kingsway, POB 48, Mutare
*Tel:* (0120) 63412 *Fax:* (0120) 61002
*Key Personnel*
Head, Library Services: Mr Darlington Mandowo
Founded: 1936
Membership(s): Zimbabwe Library Association; United Nations Associated Libraries (UNAL).
*Parent Company:* City of Mutare (Municipality)
*Branch Office(s)*
Dangamvura Public Library & Sakubva Public Library, PO Box 448, Mutare

## University of Zimbabwe Library
PO Box MP45, Mount Pleasant, Harare
*Tel:* (04) 303211 *Fax:* (04) 335383
*E-mail:* mainlib@uzlib.uz.zw; infocentre@uzlib.uz.ac.zw
*Web Site:* uzweb.uz.ac.zw/library
*Telex:* 26580 Univ Z Zw *Cable:* UNIVERSITY
*Key Personnel*
Librarian: Dr B Mbambo *E-mail:* bmbambo@uzlib.uz.ac.zw

# Library Associations

Listed below are library or library-related associations. Other book trade associations and organizations can be found in **Literary Associations & Societies** and **Book Trade Organizations**.

# Albania

**Council of Libraries**
Ruga Abdi Toptani, no 3, Tirana
*Tel:* (042) 7984; (042) 7823
*Key Personnel*
President: M Domi

# Algeria

**Institut de Bibliotheconomie et des Sciences Documentaires** (Institute of Library Economics & Documentation)
Universite d'Alger, 2 rue Didouche Mourad, Algiers
*Tel:* 6377101 *Fax:* 637629
*Web Site:* www.univ-alger.dz
*Key Personnel*
Faculty: Annexe Bouzareah

# Argentina

**ABGRA (Asociacion de Bibliotecarios Graduados de la Republica Argentina)**
(Association of Graduate Librarians of Argentina)
Tucuman 1424, 8° piso, Dpto D, C1050AAB Buenos Aires
*Tel:* (011) 4371 5269; (011) 4373 0571
*Fax:* (011) 4371 5269
*E-mail:* info@abgra.org.ar
*Web Site:* www.abgra.org.ar
*Key Personnel*
President: Ana Maria Peruchena Zimmermann
Vice President: Claudia Ataulfo Rodriguez
Executive Secretary: Rosa Emma Monfasani
Founded: 1953
Publication(s): *Referencias*

**Asociacion Argentina de Bibliotecas y Centros de Informacion Cientificos y Tecnicos**
Ave Santa Fe 1145, 1059 Buenos Aires
*Tel:* (011) 3938406
*Key Personnel*
President: Abilio Bassets
Technical Secretary: Ernesto G Gietz
Argentian Association of Scientific & Technical Libraries & Information Centres.

**Asociacion de Bibliotecarios Graduados de la Republica Argentina**, see ABGRA
(Asociacion de Bibliotecarios Graduados de la Republica Argentina)

**Centro de Documentacion Bibliotecologica**
Universidad Nacional del Sur, Avda Alem 1253, 8000 Bahia Blanca
*Tel:* (0291) 4595132
*Web Site:* www.uns.edu.ar
*Telex:* 81712 ARDUIOR

*Key Personnel*
Dir: Atilio Peralta
Centre for Library Science Documentation.
Publication(s): *Bibliografia Bibliotecologica Argentina* (Argentine Library Science Bibliography); *Documentacion Bibliotecologica*; *Guia de las Bibliotecas Universitarias Argentinas* (Guide to Argentine University Libraries); *Junta de Bibliotecas Universitarias Nacionales Argentinas* (National Joint of Argentine University Libraries); *Quien es Quien en la Bibliotecologia Argentina* (Who's Who in Argentine Library Science)

**Instituto de Bibliografia del Ministerio de Educacion de la Provincia de Buenos Aires**
Calle 47 No 510 - 6 piso, 1900 La Plata
*Tel:* (021) 35915
*Key Personnel*
Dir: Maria del Carmen Crespi de Bustos
Publication(s): *Bibliografia Argentina de Historia*; *Boletin de Informacion Bibliografica*

# Australia

**ALIA**, see Australian Library & Information Association

**Australian Law Librarians' Group Inc**
Law Courts Library, Level 15, Queens Sq, Sydney, NSW
*Tel:* (02) 9230 8675 *Fax:* (02) 9233 7952
*Web Site:* www.allg.asn.au
*Key Personnel*
National President: Dorothy Shea
  *E-mail:* dorothy.shea@justice.tas.gov.au
National Vice President: James Butler
  *E-mail:* james.butler@supremecourt.vic.gov.au
National Secretary: Merrilyn Evans
  *E-mail:* merrilyn.evans@fedcourt.gov.au
National Treasurer: Alison Jekimovics
  *E-mail:* alison.jekimovics@justice.tas.gov.au
National Publishers' Liaison Coordinator: Sue Woodman *E-mail:* swoodman@liv.asn.au
Founded: 1969
Publication(s): *Australian Law Librarian* (quarterly)

**Australian Library & Information Association**
PO Box 6335, Kingston, ACT 2604
*Tel:* (02) 6215 8222 *Fax:* (02) 6282 2249
*E-mail:* enquiry@alia.org.au
*Web Site:* www.alia.org.au
*Key Personnel*
President: Christine Mackenzie
Executive Dir: Jennifer Nicholson
Founded: 1937
Publication(s): *Australian Academic & Research Libraries* (quarterly); *Australian Library Journal* (quarterly); *Australian Special Libraries News*; *Cataloguing Australia*; *Conference Proceedings* (biennially); *Directory of Special Libraries in Australia*; *inCite* (newsletter); *Library Services in Distance Education*; *Orana* (journal, school & children's librarianship & related issues); *Periodicals for School Libraries*

**Australian Society of Archivists**
Queensland State Archives, 435 Compton Rd, Runcorn, Qld 4113
Mailing Address: PO Box 1397, Sunnybank Hills, Qld 4109
*Tel:* (07) 3131 7777 *Fax:* (07) 3131 7764
*E-mail:* info@archives.qld.gov.au
*Web Site:* www.archives.qld.gov.au
*Key Personnel*
President: Kathryn Dan
Secretary: Fiona Burn
Man Editor: Shauna Hicks
Publication(s): *Archives and Manuscripts* (biannually); *ASA Bulletin* (6 times/yr); *Debates & Discourses: Selected Australian Writings in Archival Theory, 1951-1990*; *Directory of Archives in Australia*

**CAVAL**, see Cooperative Action by Victorian Academic Libraries (CAVAL)

**Cooperative Action by Victorian Academic Libraries (CAVAL)**
4 Park Dr, Bundoora, Victoria 3083
*Tel:* (03) 9459 2722 *Fax:* (03) 9459 2733
*E-mail:* caval@caval.edu.au
*Web Site:* www.caval.edu.au
*Key Personnel*
Chief Executive Officer: Steve O' Connor
  *Tel:* (03) 9450 5501 *E-mail:* steveo@caval.edu.au
Education & Business Development Manager: Sue Henczel *Tel:* (03) 9450 5505
  *E-mail:* sueh@caval.edu.au
Information Services Manager: Cathie Jilovsky
  *Tel:* (03) 9450 5504 *E-mail:* cathiej@caval.edu.au
Administrative Services Coordinator: David Noble
  *Tel:* (03) 9450 5528 *E-mail:* davidn@caval.edu.au
Publication(s): *CAVAL* (newsletter)

**Council of Australian State Libraries**
State Library of Victoria, 328 Swanston St, Melbourne, Victoria 3000
*Tel:* (03) 8664 7512 *Fax:* (03) 9639 4737
*E-mail:* casl@slv.vic.gov.au
*Web Site:* www.casl.org.au
*Telex:* 92231
*Key Personnel*
Chief Executive Officer & State Librarian: Anne-Marie Schwirtlich

**National Library of Australia**
Parkes Pl, Canberra, ACT 2600
*Tel:* (02) 6262 1111 *Fax:* (02) 6257 1703
*E-mail:* www@nla.gov.au
*Web Site:* www.nla.gov.au
*Telex:* 62100
*Key Personnel*
Dir General: Jan Fullerton
Assistant Dir General: Jasmine Cameron
Publications Dir: Dr Paul Hetherington *Tel:* (02) 6262 1474 *E-mail:* phetheri@nla.gov.au
Editorial & Production Coordinator: Heather Clark *Tel:* (02) 6262 1253 *E-mail:* hclark@nla.gov.au

# Austria

### Dokumentationsstelle fur neuere Osterreichische Literatur
Seidengasse 13, 1070 Vienna
*Tel:* (01) 526 20 44-0 *Fax:* (01) 526 20 44-30
*E-mail:* info@literaturhaus.at
*Web Site:* www.literaturhaus.at
*Key Personnel*
Dir: Dr Heinz Lunzer *E-mail:* hl@literaturhaus.at
Founded: 1965
Documentation Centre for Modern Austrian Literature.
Publication(s): *Zirkular* (quarterly)

### Oesterreichische Gesellschaft fuer Dokumentation und Information (OGDI)
(Austrian Documentation Society)
c/o Wirtschaftuniversitaet Wien, Augasse 9, 1090 Vienna
*Tel:* (01) 31336 5107 *Fax:* (01) 31336 905107
*E-mail:* oegdi@termnet.at
*Web Site:* www.oegdi.at
*Key Personnel*
Chairman: Dr Gerhard Richter *E-mail:* gerhard.r.richter@gmx.at
Secretary: Hermann Huemer *E-mail:* hermann.huemer@academicus.info
Founded: 1951
Membership(s): Austrian Society for Documentation & Information; FID.
Publication(s): *Oegdi Aktuell*

### Oesterreichisches Institut fuer Bibliotheksforschung, Dokumentations- und Informationswesen
Resselgasse 4, 1040 Vienna
*Key Personnel*
Chairman: J Wawrosch
Austrian Institute for Library Research, Documentation and Information.

### Vereinigung Oesterreichischer Bibliothekarinnen und Bibliothekare
(VOEB) (Association of Austrian Librarians)
Voralberger Federal State Library, Fluherstr 4, 6900 Bregenz
*E-mail:* voeb@uibk.ac.at
*Web Site:* voeb.uibk.ac.at
*Key Personnel*
President: Dr Harald Weigel *E-mail:* harald.weigel@vorarlberg.at
Vice President: Dr Sigrid Reinitzer *Tel:* (0316) 380-3101; (0316) 380-3102; (0316) 380-3103 *Fax:* (0316) 38 49 87 *E-mail:* sigrid.reinitzer@kfunigraz.ac.at; Maria Seissl *E-mail:* maria.seissl@univie.ac.at
Secretary: Dr Werner Schlacher *E-mail:* werner.schlacher@kfunigraz.ac.at
Treasurer: Dr Gerhard Zechner *E-mail:* gerhard.zechner@voralberg.at
Founded: 1945
Publication(s): *Biblos* (quarterly, bulletin); *Mitteilungen* (quarterly, bulletin); *Verleger-Publisher: Gesellschaft der Freunde der Oesterreichischen National-bibliothek* (published in German)

VOEB, see Vereinigung Oesterreichischer Bibliothekarinnen und Bibliothekare (VOEB)

# Bangladesh

### National Library of Bangladesh, Directorate of Archives & Libraries
32 Justice Sayed Mahbub Murshed Sarani, Sher-e-Bangla Nagar (Agargaon), Dhaka 1207
*Tel:* (02) 326572 *Fax:* (02) 318704
*E-mail:* ifla@ifla.org
*Web Site:* www.ifla.org
*Key Personnel*
Dir: Mr Hahashinur Rahman Khan
Founded: 1972
Collection, preservation & reproduction of books & other documents; reference & readers service. ISBN Agency of all publications. Hold seminars, exhibitions & workshops to create awareness of library services.
Membership(s): IFLA (International Federation of Library Associations & Institutions).
Publication(s): *Artical Index* (annually); *Bangladesh National Bibliography* (annually); *Public Library Directory* (annually)
*Parent Company:* Ministry of Cultural Affairs

LAB, see The Library Association of Bangladesh (LAB)

### The Library Association of Bangladesh (LAB)
c/o Central Public Library Bldg, Shahbagh, Ramma, Dhaka 1000
*Tel:* (02) 8631471; (02) 0189258564 (mobile)
*E-mail:* msik@icddrb.org
*Key Personnel*
President: M Shamsul Islam Khan
Vice President: Kazi Abdul Mazed; Dr Md Abdul Matir; Md Harun-ar-Rashid
General Secretary: Kh Fazlur Rahman
Treasurer: Md Abdul Latif
Founded: 1956
Work for the professional development in Bangladesh & offers training courses.
Publication(s): *The Eastern Librarian* (twice a year); *Upatta* (newsletter, quarterly, text in Bengali)

# Barbados

### Library Association of Barbados
PO Box 827E, Bridgetown
*Key Personnel*
President: Shirley Yearwood
Secretary: Hazelyn Devonish
Publication(s): *Bulletin* (irregularly); *Update* (irregularly, newsletter)

# Belgium

APBD, see Association Professionnelle des Bibliothecaires et Documentalistes (APBD)

### Archief- en Bibliotheekwezen in Belgie (Belgian Association of Archivists & Librarians)
Ruisbroekstr 2-10, 1000 Brussels
*Tel:* (02) 5195351 *Fax:* (02) 5195533
*Telex:* 21157
*Key Personnel*
General Secretary: Wim De Vos *E-mail:* wim.devos@kbr.be
Publication(s): *Archives et Bibliotheques de Belgique* (text in Dutch, English, French, German, Italian, Latin & Spanish)

### Association Belgium de Documentation
(Belgian Association for Documentation)
Highwaye de Wavre 1683, Waversesteenweg, 1160 Brussels
*Tel:* (02) 675 58 62 *Fax:* (02) 672 74 46
*E-mail:* info@abd-bvd.be
*Web Site:* www.abd-bvd.be
*Key Personnel*
President: Philippe Laurent *Tel:* (010) 474262 *Fax:* (010) 474603 *E-mail:* laurent@spri.ucl.ac.be
Vice President: Paul Heyvaert *Tel:* (02) 519 56 41 *E-mail:* paul.heyvaert@kbr.be
Secretary: Vincent Maes *Tel:* (02) 246 45 31 *Fax:* (02) 246 39 58 *E-mail:* v.maes@advalvas.be
Treasurer: Guy Delsaut *Tel:* (02) 678 37 95 *E-mail:* guy.delsaut@heidelbergcement.com
Founded: 1947
Membership(s): EBLIDA; ECIA.
Publication(s): *ABD-BVD Info* (newsletter); *Cahiers de la Documentation - Bladen voor Documentatie* (quarterly, text in Dutch, English & French)

### Association des Archivistes et Bibliotheques, see Archief- en Bibliotheekwezen in Belgie

### Association des Bibliothecaires Belges d'Expression Francaise
39 Emile Vandevandel Str, 1470 Genappe
Mailing Address: BP 20, 1470 Genappe
*Tel:* (067) 771477; (067) 790683 *Fax:* (067) 771477
*E-mail:* abbef.be@gate71.be; abbef@freeworld.be
*Key Personnel*
President: Michel Dagneau *E-mail:* dagneau.m@swing.be
Association of French-speaking Librarians from Belgium.
Publication(s): *Le Bibliothecaire: Revue d'Information culturelle et bibliographique*

### Association Professionnelle des Bibliothecaires et Documentalistes (APBD)
Ave Reve d'or, 30, 7100 La Louviere
*Tel:* (071) 61 43 35 *Fax:* (071) 61 16 34
*E-mail:* biblio.hainaut@skynet.be
*Web Site:* www.apbd.be
*Key Personnel*
President: Jean-Claude Trefois *Tel:* (071) 21 55 18 *E-mail:* jean_claude.trefois@hainaut.be
Secretary: Laurence Hennaux *Tel:* (064) 45 87 76
Publication(s): *Bloc-notes*; *Un cadeau, un livre* (annual selection of children's books)

### Scientific & Technical Information Service
Keizerslaan 4 Bld de l'Empereur, 1000 Brussels
*Tel:* (02) 519 56 40 *Fax:* (02) 519 56 45
*E-mail:* info@stis.fgov.be
*Web Site:* www.stis.fgov.be
*Key Personnel*
Dir: Dr Jean Moulin *Tel:* (02) 519 56 56 *E-mail:* jean.moulin@stis.fgov.be
Publication(s): *The Electronic Information Services Industry in Belgium 1997-1999*
*Parent Company:* Federal Office for Scientific, Technical & Cultural Affairs

SIST-DWTI, see Scientific & Technical Information Service

### Vereniging van Religieus-Wetenschappelijke Bibliothecarissen (Association of Religious Academic Librarians)
Sint-Michielsstr 6, 3000 Leuven
*Tel:* (016) 323807 *Fax:* (016) 323862
*Web Site:* www.theo.kuleuven.ac.be/vrb
*Key Personnel*
President: Etienne D'hondt *E-mail:* etienne.dhondt@theo.kuleuven.ac.be

Secretary: Kris van de Casteele *Tel:* (03) 2873563 *Fax:* (03) 2873562 *E-mail:* kris.vandecasteele@ ua.ac.be
Founded: 1965
Membership(s): Bibliotheques Europeennes de Theologie (BETH).
Publication(s): *VRB-Informatie* (quarterly)

**Vlaamse Vereniging voor Bibliotheek- Archief-en Documentatiewezen (VVBAD)** (Flemish Association for Libraries, Archives & Documentation Centres)
Statiestr 179, 2600 Berchem Antwerp
*Tel:* (03) 2814457 *Fax:* (03) 2188077
*E-mail:* vvbad@vvbad.be
*Web Site:* www.vvbad.be
*Key Personnel*
President: Geert Puype
Executive Dir: Marc Storms *E-mail:* marc. storms@vvbad.be
Secretary: Marc Engels
Founded: 1921
Publication(s): *Archiefkunde* (monographs); *Bibliotheek- en Archiefgids* (Library & Archive Guide, 6 times/yr); *Bibliotheekkunde* (monographs); *INFO* (monthly, membership journal); *Vlaamse Archief-, Bibliotheek- en Documentatiegids* (biennially, address guide to archives, libraries & documentation centers in Dutch-speaking part of Belgium)

**VRB**, see Vereniging van Religieus-Wetenschappelijke Bibliothecarissen

# Belize

**Belize Library Association**
c/o Bliss Institute, PO Box 287, Belize City
*Tel:* (02) 7267; (02) 34248; (02) 34249 *Fax:* (02) 34246
*Web Site:* www.ambergriscaye.com
*Key Personnel*
President: H W Young
Secretary: Robert Hulse
Publication(s): *Belize Library Association Bulletin*

# Bolivia

**Asociacion Boliviana de Bibliotecarios (ABB)** (Bolivia Association of Librarians)
c/o Efrain Virreira Sanchez, Casilla 992, Cochabamba
*Tel:* (064) 1481
*Key Personnel*
Dir: Gunnar Mendoza
Founded: 1836

**Centro Nacional de Documentacion Cientifica y Tecnologica - Universidad Mayor De S an Andres**
Av Mariscal Santa Cruz N° 1175, esquina c, Ayacucho
*Tel:* (02) 359583 *Fax:* (02) 359586
*E-mail:* iiicndct@huayna.umsa.edu.bo
*Web Site:* www.bolivian.com/industrial/cndct
*Telex:* 3438 UMSA-BV
*Key Personnel*
Contact: Ruben Valle Vera
National Scientific & Technological Documentation Centre.
Publication(s): *Bibliography Series* (3-5 times/ year); *Boletin Accesos* (quarterly); *Current Events* (annually)

# Bosnia and Herzegovina

**Drustvo Bibliotekara Bosne i Hercegovine** (National & University Library of Bosnia & Herzegovina)
Zmaja od Bosne 8b, 71000 Sarajevo
*Tel:* (033) 275 312 *Fax:* (033) 218 431
*E-mail:* nubbih@nub.ba
*Web Site:* www.nub.ba
*Key Personnel*
President: Nevenka Hajdarovic *E-mail:* nevenka@ nub.ba
Publisher: Emina Memija
Dir: Dr Enes Kujundzic *E-mail:* bedita@nub.ba
Founded: 1945
Publication(s): *Bibliotekarstvo* (annually)

# Botswana

**Botswana Library Association**
PO Box 1310, Gaborone
*Tel:* (031) 3552295 *Fax:* (031) 357291
*Web Site:* www.bla.0catch.com
*Telex:* 2429BD
*Key Personnel*
Chairperson: Ms Bobana Badisang
Secretary: Peter Tshukudu
Founded: 1978
Publication(s): *Botswana Library Association Journal*

# Brazil

**Associacao dos Arquivistas Brasileiros** (Association of Brazilian Archivists)
Av Presidente Vargas, 1733, Sala 903, 20210-030 Rio de Janeiro-RJ
*Tel:* (021) 2507-2239 *Fax:* (021) 3852-2541
*E-mail:* aab@aab.org.br
*Web Site:* www.aab.org.br
*Key Personnel*
President: Lucia Maria Vellosode Oliveira
Secretary: Laura Regina Xavier
Publication(s): *Associacao dos Arquivistas Brasileiros* (Association of Brazilian Archivists, bulletin); *Revista Arquivo & Administracao* (biannually)

**Instituto Brasileiro de Informacao em Ciencia e Tecnologia**
SAS Quadra 5 Lote 6 Bloco H, 70070-914 Brasilia DF
*Tel:* (061) 217-6360; (061) 217-6350 *Fax:* (061) 226-2677
*E-mail:* webmaster@ibict.br
*Web Site:* www.ibict.br
*Telex:* (061) 2481
*Key Personnel*
Dir: Nilson Lemos Lage *E-mail:* lage@ibict.br
Publication(s): *Bibliografia Brasileira de Ciencia da Informacao* (Brazilian Bibliography of Information Science, annually); *Bibliografic Brasileira de Politica Cientifica e Tecnologica* (Brazilian Bibliography of Political Science & Technology); *Boletim Qualidade & Produtividade* (Quality & Productivity Bulletin, quarterly); *Calendario de Eventos em C&T* (Calendar of Events in C&I, quarterly); *Ciencia*
*da Informacao* (Information Science, biannually); *Informativo IBICT* (Informative IBICT, biannually)

**Federacao Brasileira de Associacoes de Bibliotecarios - Comissao Brasileira de Documentacao Juridica (FEBAB/CBDJ)** (Brazilian Federation of Library Associations - Brazilian Committee of Legal Documentation)
Rua Avanhandava, 40, cj 110, 01306-001 Sao Paulo-SP
*Tel:* (011) 3257-9979 *Fax:* (011) 3257-9979
*E-mail:* febab@febab.org.br
*Web Site:* www.febab.org.br
*Key Personnel*
President: Marcia Rosetto
Vice President: Carminda Nogueira de Castro Ferreira
Publication(s): *Noticias* (News)

**IBICT**, see Instituto Brasileiro de Informacao em Ciencia e Tecnologia

# Brunei Darussalam

**Persatuan Perpustakaan Kebangsaan Negara Brunei Darussalam (PPKNBD)** (National Library Association of Brunei)
Perpustakaan Universiti Brunei Darussalam, Jalan Tungku Link Gadong BE 1410
*Tel:* (02) 223060 *Fax:* (02) 235472; (02) 241817
*Web Site:* www.ppknbd.org.bn
*Key Personnel*
President: Puan Nellie bte Dato Paduka Haji Sunny *Tel:* (02) 249001 *Fax:* (02) 249504 *E-mail:* chieflib@lib.ubd.edu.bn
Vice President: Pg Haji Mohd Shahminan bin Pg Haji Sulaiman *Tel:* (02) 380318 *Fax:* (02) 38200
Chief Librarian: Haji Abu Bakar Haji Zainal *Tel:* (02) 235501 *Fax:* (02) 224763 *E-mail:* chieflib@brunet.bn
Publication(s): *Wadah Pustaka* (newsletter, 1994)

**PPKNBD**, see Persatuan Perpustakaan Kebangsaan Negara Brunei Darussalam (PPKNBD)

# Cameroon

**Association des Bibliothecaires, Archivistes, Documentalistes et Museographes du Cameroon (ABADCAM)** (Association of Librarians, Archivists, Documentalists & Museum Curators of Cameroon)
BP 4609, Nlongkak Centre Province
*Tel:* 222 6362 *Fax:* 222 4785; 222 6262
*E-mail:* abadcam@yahoo.fr
*Telex:* 8384
*Key Personnel*
President: Hilaire Omokolo
Librarian: P N Chateh
Works in collaboration with the Ministry of Culture in formulating policies for librarians, archivists, documentalists & museographers in Cameroon.
Publication(s): *Newsletter*

# Chile

**Colegio de Bibliotecarios de Chile AG**
Diagonal Paraguay 383, Torre 11 Oficina 122,
6510017 Santiago
*Tel:* (02) 222 56 52 *Fax:* (02) 635 50 23
*E-mail:* cdc@bibliotecarios.cl
*Web Site:* www.bibliotecarios.cl
*Key Personnel*
President: Marcia Marinovic Simunovic *Tel:* (02)
231 38 46 *E-mail:* mmarinovic@vtr.cl
Vice President: Claudia Cuevas Saavedra
*Tel:* (02) 270 17 43 *Fax:* (02) 270 17 47
*E-mail:* ccuevas@bcn.cl
Secretary: Ana Maria Pino Yanez *Tel:* (02) 270
17 51 *Fax:* (02) 270 17 47 *E-mail:* apino@bcn.
cl
Chilean Library Association.
Publication(s): *Indices de Publicaciones Periodi-
cas en Bibliotecologia* (Catalogue of Periodical
Publications on Librarianship); *Micronoticias*

**Comision Nacional de Investigacion Cientifica
y Technologica**, see CONICYT

**CONICYT** (National Commission for Science &
Technology)
Departamento de Informacion, Canada 308, Prov-
idencia, Santiago
*Tel:* (02) 3654400 *Fax.* (02) 6551396
*E-mail:* info@conicyt.cl
*Web Site:* www.conicyt.cl
*Key Personnel*
President: Sr Eric Goles Chacc
Head of Dept: Ana Maria Prat *Tel:* (02) 3654450
*E-mail:* amprat@conicyt.cl
Founded: 1967
Publication(s): *Serie Directorios*; *Serie Informa-
cion y Documentacion*

# China

**China Society for Library Science**
33 Zhongguancun (S), Beijing 100081
*Tel:* (010) 6841 9270 *Fax:* (010) 6841 9271
*E-mail:* ztxhmsc@publicf.nlc.gov.cn
*Web Site:* www.nlc.gov.cn
*Telex:* 222211
*Key Personnel*
President: Liu Deyou
Secretary General: Gulian Li
Dir: Mr Ren Jiyu
Founded: 1979
Publication(s): *Journal of China Library Science*

# Colombia

**Asociacion Colombiana de Bibliotecologos y
Documentalistas**
Carrera 50, 27-70, modulo 1 nivel 4, bloque C-
Colceincias, Bogota
*Tel:* (01) 3603077 (ext 326)
*Web Site:* www.ascolbi.org/acerca.htm
*Key Personnel*
President: Carlos Alberto Zapata
Vice President: Edgar Allan Delgado
Colombian Library Association.
Publication(s): *Boletin*

# Congo

**Direction Generale des Services de
Bibliotheques, Archives et Documentation**
(General Management of Library, Archives &
Documentation Services)
Bibliotheque Nationale Populaire, BP 1489, Braz-
zaville
*Tel:* 833 485 *Fax:* 832 253

# The Democratic Republic of the Congo

**Association Zairoise des Archivistes,
Bibliothecaires et Documentalistes**
BP 805, Kinshasa X1
*Tel:* (012) 30123; (012) 30124
*Key Personnel*
Executive Secretary: E Kabeba-Bangasa
Zaire Association of Archivists, Librarians and
Documentalists.
Publication(s): *Mukanda*

# Costa Rica

**Asociacion Costarricense de Bibliotecarios**
(Costa Rican Association of Librarians)
Apdo 3308, San Jose
*Tel:* 234-9889
*E-mail:* info@cesdepu.com
*Web Site:* www.cesdepu.com
*Key Personnel*
Secretary-General: Dr Rodolfo Saborio Valverde
Publication(s): *Anuario bibliografico costarri-
cense* (bulletin)

# Cote d'Ivoire

**ADBACI**, see Association pour le Developpement
de la Documentation, des Bibliotheques et
Archives de la Cote d'Ivoire (ADBACI)

**Association pour le Developpement de la
Documentation, des Bibliotheques et
Archives de la Cote d'Ivoire (ADBACI)**
c/o Bibliotheque Nationale, BPV 180, Abidjan
*Tel:* 32 38 72
*Key Personnel*
Dir: Ambroise Agnero
Secretary General: Cangah Guy

# Croatia

**HKD**, see Hrvatsko knjiznicarsko drustvo

**Hrvatsko knjiznicarsko drustvo** (Croatian
Library Association)
c/o Nacionalna i sveucilisna knjiznica, Hrvatske
bratske zajednice 4, 10 000 Zagreb
*Tel:* (01) 615 93 20 *Fax:* (01) 615 93 20
*E-mail:* hkd@nsk.hr
*Web Site:* www.hkdrustvo.hr
*Key Personnel*
President: Alemka Belan-Simic
Secretary: Ana-Marija Dodigovic
Founded: 1940
Membership(s): IFLA (International Federation of
Library Associations); EBLIDA (European Bu-
reau of Library, Information & Documentation
Associations): UNESCO (United Nations Edu-
cational, Scientific & Cultural Organization).
Publication(s): *Vjesnik bibliotekara Hrvatske*
(biannually, scientific magazine)

# Cuba

**Library Association of Cuba**
c/o Direccion de Relaciones Internacionales, Min-
isterio de Culture, Calle 4 e/m 11y13, Vedado,
Havana
Mailing Address: Apdo 6881, Havana
*Tel·* (07) 552244 *Fax:* (07) 662053
*Telex:* 0571963
*Key Personnel*
Dir: Marta Terry Gonzalez
Vice President: Elisa Masiques; Blanca Mercedes
Mesa

# Cyprus

**Library Association of Cyprus**
PO Box 1039, 1434 Nicosia
*Tel:* (022) 404849
*Key Personnel*
President: Costas D Stephanov
Secretary: Paris G Rossos
Publication(s): *Deltion Vivliothikarion* (Library
Bulletin)

# Czech Republic

**Svaz knihovniku informacnich pracovniku
Ceske republiky (SKIP)** (Association of
Library & Information Professionals of the
Czech Republic)
National Library, Klementinum 190, 11001
Prague
*Tel:* (02) 21663111 *Fax:* (02) 21663261
*Web Site:* www.nkp.cz
*Key Personnel*
President: Vit Richter *E-mail:* vit.richter@nkp.cz
Honorary President: Dr Jarmila Burgetova
*Tel:* (02) 3115030 *E-mail:* jarmila.burgetova@
seznam.cz
Founded: 1968
Membership(s): IFLA.
Publication(s): *SKIP* (quarterly, bulletin)

# Denmark

**Arkivarforeningen**
c/o Landsarkivet for Sjaelland, Jagtvej 10, 22
Copenhagen N
*Tel:* 31393520 *Fax:* 33153239
*Key Personnel*
President: Tyge Krogh
Secretary: Charlotte Steinmark
Archives Society.
Publication(s): *Kommunal opgavelosning 1842-1970* (Odense University Press, 1990)

**Danmarks Biblioteksforening** (Danish Library
Association)
Vesterbrogade 20, 5 sal, 1620 Copenhagen V
*Tel:* 33 25 09 35 *Fax:* 33 25 79 00
*Web Site:* www.dbf.dk
*Key Personnel*
Dir: Winnie Vitzansky *Tel:* 33 26 0072
*E-mail:* wv@dbf.dk
Publication(s): *Biblioteksvejviser* (Library Guide);
*Bogens Verden* (Library Journal); *Danmarks
Biblioteker* (Members Magazine)

**Danmarks Forskningsbiblioteksforening**
c/o Statsbiblioteket, Universitetsparken, 8000
Arhus C
*Tel:* (045) 89 46 22 07 *Fax:* (045) 89 46 22 20
*E-mail:* df@statsbiblioteket.dk
*Web Site:* www.dfdf.dk
*Key Personnel*
President: Erland Kolding Nielsen
Secretary: Hanne Dahl
Danish Research Library Association: Section 1
Research Libraries; Section 2 Staff members of
Danish Research Libraries.
Publication(s): *DF-Revy*

**Dansk Musikbiblioteks Forening (DMBF)**
(Danish Music Library Association)
Nordjysk Musikkonservatorium, Ryesgade 52,
9000 Aalborg
*Tel:* 33 47 43 16 *Fax:* 33 47 47 10
*E-mail:* dmbf@kb.dk
*Web Site:* www.dmbf.nu
*Key Personnel*
President: Ole Bisbjerg *Tel:* 89 46 21 33
*E-mail:* ob@statsbiblioteket.dk
Vice President: Kirsten Husted *Tel:* 75 82 32 00,
ext 135 *Fax:* 75 82 32 13 *E-mail:* kh@vejlebib.
dk
Secretary General: Jane Mariegaard *Tel:* 96 31 31
61 *E-mail:* jane@hordkons.dk
Treasurer: Erling Dujardin *Tel:* 38 21 19
00 *Fax:* 38 21 19 99 *E-mail:* erdu01@
frederiksberg.dk
Membership(s): Association of Danish Music Li-
braries (Danish section of AIBM/IAML).
Publication(s): *MusikBIB* (Journal for Music Libraries, quarterly, 2000, text in Danish)

**Kommunernes Skolebiblioteksforening**
(Association of Danish School Libraries)
Krimsvej 29 B 1, 2300 Copenhagen S
*Tel:* 33111391 *Fax:* 33111390
*E-mail:* komskolbib@ksbf.dk
*Web Site:* www.ksbf.dk
*Key Personnel*
Chief Executive: Paul Erik Sorensen
Editor: Niels Jacobsen
Publication(s): *Born og Boger* (Children &
Books); *Skolebiblioteksarbogen* (School Li-
braries Annual)

# Dominican Republic

**Asociacion Dominicana de Bibliotecarios
(ASODOBI)** (Dominican Association of
Librarians)
c/o Biblioteca Nacional, Cesar Nicolas Penson 91,
Plaza de la Cultura, Santo Domingo
*Tel:* 6884086; 6884660 *Fax:* 685841
*E-mail:* biblioteca.nacional@dominicana.com;
intec.biblioteca@codetel.net.do
*Key Personnel*
President: Prospero J Mella-Chavier
Secretary-General: Ms V Regus
Founded: 1971
Publication(s): *El Papiro*

**ASODOBI**, see Asociacion Dominicana de
Bibliotecarios (ASODOBI)

**Departamento de Documentacion y Bibliotecas**
Galeria Nacional de Bellas Artes y Cultos, Santo
Domingo
*Key Personnel*
Dir: Dr Jose de J Alvarez Valverde
Library and Documentation Service.

**Grupo Bibliografico Nacional de la Republica
Dominicana**
Archivo General de la Nacion, Calle ME Diaz,
Santo Domingo

# Ecuador

**Asociacion Ecuatoriana de Bibliotecarios
(AEB)** (Ecuadorian Library Association)
c/o Casa de la Cultura Ecuatoriana Benjamin Car-
rion, Av 12 de Octubre 555, Quito
*Tel:* 2528-840 *Fax:* 2223-391
*E-mail:* asoebfp@hotmail.com
*Web Site:* www.reicyt.org.ec/aeb
*Key Personnel*
President: Wilson Vega *Tel:* 446-233 (ext 132)
*E-mail:* wilson_vega@ecuabox.com
Vice President: Eugenia Lopez *Tel:* 504-692 (ext
42)
Dir: Laura de Crespo
Secretary: Rosario Moreno E *Tel:* 502-456; 502-
262
Treasurer: Cesar Calero *Tel:* 509-753; 509-754
Publication(s): *Unidad Bibliotecaria*

# Egypt (Arab Republic of Egypt)

**Egyptian Association for Library &
Information Science**
c/o Dept Archives, Librarianship & Information
Science, Faculty of Arts, University of Cairo,
Cairo
*Tel:* (02) 5676365 *Fax:* (02) 5729659
*Key Personnel*
President: Dr S Khalifa
Secretary: M Hosam El-Din
Publication(s): *Alam al-Maktabat* (Library World)

# El Salvador

**Asociacion de Bibliotecarios de El Salvador** (El
Salvador Library Association)
Apdo 2923, San Salvador
*Tel:* 216312 *Fax:* 225-02 78
*Web Site:* www.ues.edu.sv/abes
*Key Personnel*
President: Carmen Salinas de Salinas
Vice President: Blanca Handal de Colorado
Publication(s): *Informa* (monthly, newsletter)

**Asociacion General de Archivistas de El
Salvador (AGAES)** (Association of Archivists
of El Salvador)
Edificio Comercial San Francisco N 214, C Ote
Y 2a Ave Nte, San Salvador
*Tel:* 222 94 18 *Fax:* 281 58 60
*E-mail:* agnes@agn.gob.sv
*Web Site:* www.agn.gob.sv

# Ethiopia

**Ethiopian Library & Information Association**
PO Box 30530, Addis Ababa
*Tel:* (01) 511344 *Fax:* (01) 552544
*Key Personnel*
President: Mulugeta Hunde
Secretary: Girma Makonnen
Founded: 1961
Publication(s): *Directory of Ethiopian Libraries*;
*Ethiopian Library Association* (biannually, bul-
letin)

# Finland

**BMF**, see Bibliothecarii Medicinae Fenniae
(BMF)

**Finnish Library Association**, see Suomen
Kirjastoseura

**Bibliothecarii Medicinae Fenniae (BMF)**
(Finnish Medical Librarians' Association)
PL 61, 00014 Helsingin Yliopisto
*Tel:* (09) 191 26645 *Fax:* (09) 191 26652
*E-mail:* etunimi.sukunimi@helsinki.fi
*Web Site:* www.terkko.helsinki.fi/bmf
*Key Personnel*
Chairman: Ulla Neuvonen
Founded: 1980
Membership(s): IFLA (International Federation
of Library Associations & Institutions); EAHIL
(European Association for Health Information
& Libraries); NAMHI (Nordic Association for
Medical & Health Information).

**Suomen Kirjastoseura** (Finnish Library
Association)
Kansakoulukatu 10 A 19, 00100 Helsinki
*Tel:* (09) 694 1858 *Fax:* (09) 694 1859
*E-mail:* fla@fla.fi
*Web Site:* www.kaapeli.fi/~fla/presentation.html
*Key Personnel*
Secretary General: Tuula Haavisto
President: Mirja Ryynanen
Founded: 1910
Publication(s): *Kirjastolehti* (monthly, journal)

**Suomen Tieteellinen Kirjastoseura ry** (Finnish
Research Library Association)
PO Box 217, 00171 Helsinki

*Tel:* (017) 34 22 25 *Fax:* (017) 34 22 79
*E-mail:* meri.kuula@arcada.fi
*Web Site:* pro.tsv.fi/stks
*Key Personnel*
Chairperson & President: Tuula Ruhanen
 *Tel:* (09) 191 280 51 *Fax:* (09) 191 280 86
 *E-mail:* tuula.ruhanen@helsinki.fi
Secretary: Meri Kuula-Bruun *Tel:* (09) 52532
 465 *Fax:* (09) 52532 444 *E-mail:* meri.kuula-
 bruun@arcada.fi
Publication(s): *Guide to Research Libraries &
 Information Services in Finland*; *Signum* (8
 times/yr, text in Finnish)

### Tietohuollon Neuvottelukunta
c/o Ministry of Education, Meritullinkatu 10,
 00170 Helsinki
Mailing Address: PO Box 29, 00023 Helsinki
*Tel:* (09) 13 41 71 *Fax:* (09) 65 67 65
*E-mail:* jylha@csc.fi
*Web Site:* www.csc.fi
*Telex:* 122109 Mined
*Key Personnel*
Chairman: Juhani Hakkarainen
Secretary General: Annu Jylhae-Pyykoenen
Finnish Council for Information Provision.

# France

**ABEF**, see Association des Bibliotheques
 Chretiennes France (ABEF)

**ADBS**, see L'Association des Professionnels de
 l'Information et de la Documentation (ADBS)

**ADEBD**, see Association des Diplomes de
 l'Ecole de Bibliothecaires-Documentalistes

### Association des Archivistes Francais
 (Association of French Archivists)
9 rue Montcalm, 75018 Paris
*Tel:* (01) 46 06 39 44 *Fax:* (01) 46 06 39 52
*E-mail:* secretariat@archivistes.org
*Web Site:* www.archivistes.org
*Key Personnel*
President: Henri Zuber
Vice President: Vincent Doom; Pierre Fournie;
 Elisabeth Verry
Secretary: Agnes Dejob
Treasurer: Didier Bondue
Publication(s): *La Gazette des Archives*
*Branch Office(s)*
Centre de Formation, 9 rue Rodier, 75009 Paris

### Association des Bibliothecaires Francais
 (Association of French Librarians)
31 rue de Chabrol, 75010 Paris
*Tel:* (01) 55 33 10 30 *Fax:* (01) 55 33 10 31
*E-mail:* abf@abf.asso.fr
*Web Site:* www.abf.asso.fr
*Key Personnel*
President: Gerard Briand
General Secretary: Jan-Francois Jacques
Founded: 1906
Publication(s): *Bulletin d'informations de l'ABF*

### Association des Bibliotheques Chretiennes
 France (ABEF) (Association of Ecclesiastical
 Libraries in France)
6 rue du Regard, 75006 Paris
*Tel:* (01) 42 22 44 11 *Fax:* (01) 42 22 37 90
*E-mail:* agmd.bibliotheque@wanadoo.fr
*Key Personnel*
President: Paul de Crombrugghe
Vice President: Jerome Rousse-Lacordaire

Secretary: Colette Moron
Publication(s): *Bulletin de liaison de l'ABEF*
 (ISSN 0066-8958)

### Association des Diplomes de l'Ecole de
 Bibliothecaires-Documentalistes (Association
 of Graduates of the School of Librarians and
 Documentalists)
c/o Bibliotheque du Saulchoir, 43 bis, rue de la
 Glaciere, 75013 Paris
*Tel:* (01) 45 87 05 33 *Fax:* (01) 43 31 07 56
*E-mail:* adbs@adbs.fr
*Web Site:* www.adbs.fr
*Key Personnel*
President: Marie-Cecile Comerre *Tel:* (01) 48 00
 20 70
Secretary: M Potier
Publication(s): *Bulletin d'Information* (annually,
 text in French)

**F A D B E N**, see Federation des Enseignants
 Documentalistes de l'Education nationale

### Federation des Enseignants Documentalistes de
 l'Education nationale (Federation of
 Associations of National Educational Record
 Clerks & Librarians)
25, rue Claude Tillier, 75012 Paris
*Tel:* (01) 43 72 45 60 *Fax:* (01) 43 72 45 60
*E-mail:* fadben@wanadoo.fr
*Web Site:* www.fadben.asso.fr
*Key Personnel*
President: Isabelle Fructus *Tel:* (01) 44 07 80 40
 *E-mail:* fructus@univ-paris1.fr
Vice President: Isabelle Laudin *Tel:* (03) 29 45 32
 00 *E-mail:* isabelle.laudin@ac-nancy-metz.fr;
 Marcelle Taffonneau *Tel:* (05) 62 66 82 25
 *E-mail:* marcelle.taffonneau@worldonline.fr
Publication(s): *La Lettre* (quarterly); *Mediadoc*
 (triannually)

### L'Association des Professionnels de
 l'Information et de la Documentation
 (ADBS) (French Association of Information &
 Documentation Professionals)
25, rue Claude Tillier, 75012 Paris
*Tel:* (01) 43 72 25 25 *Fax:* (01) 43 72 30 41
*E-mail:* adbs@adbs.fr
*Web Site:* www.adbs.fr
*Key Personnel*
President: Florence Wilhelm
Delegated General: Laurence Dapon
Delegated General Assistant: Claudine Masse
Publication(s): *Documentaliste - Sciences de
 l'Information et ouvrages Specialises*

# Germany

**A Sp B**, see Arbeitsgemeinschaft der
 Spezialbibliotheken eV (ASpB)

### Arbeitsgemeinschaft der Archive und
 Bibliotheken in der evangelischen Kirche
 (Joint Association of Archives & Libraries in
 the Evangelical Church)
Veilhofstr 28, 90489 Nuremberg
Mailing Address: Postfach 250429, 90129
 Nuremburg
*Tel:* (0911) 58869-0 *Fax:* (0911) 58869-69
*E-mail:* LKANuernberg@t-online.de
*Web Site:* www.ekd.de/archive/deutsch/arbeitsg.
 htm
*Key Personnel*
President: Dr Helmut Baier

Publication(s): *Aus Evangelischen Archiven,
 Neue Folge der Allgemeinen Mitteilungen der
 AABevk*; *Veroeffentlichungen der AABevK* (Pub-
 lications of the AABevK)

### Arbeitsgemeinschaft der Regionalbibliotheken
 (Joint Association of Regional Libraries)
Konrad-Adenauer-Str 8, 70173 Stuttgart
*Tel:* (0711) 212-4423 *Fax:* (0711) 212-4422
*Web Site:* www.regionalbibliotheken.de
*Key Personnel*
Dir: Dr Hannsjoerg Kowark *E-mail:* kowark@
 wlb-stuttgart.de
Founded: 1983
German library federation.

### Arbeitsgemeinschaft der Spezialbibliotheken
 eV (ASpB) (Association of Special Libraries,
 Germany)
c/o Forschungszentrum, Julich GmbH, Zentralbib-
 liothek, 52425 Julich
*Tel:* (02461) 612907; (02461) 615368
 *Fax:* (02461) 616103
*Web Site:* www.aspb.de
*Key Personnel*
Chairman: Dr Rafael Ball, PhD *E-mail:* r.ball@
 fz-juelich.de
Project Manager & Secretary Dir: Edith Salz
 *E-mail:* e.salz@fz-juelich.de
Founded: 1946
Membership(s): International Federation of Li-
 brary Associations & Institutions (IFLA).
Publication(s): *Bericht ueber elte Tagungi
 elekrouischer* (biennially, newsletter, conference
 report)

### Arbeitsgemeinschaft fur juristisches
 Bibliotheks- und Dokumentationswesen
 (Joint Association for Law Libraries & Legal
 Documentation)
Bibliot, Ismaninger Str 109, 81675 Munich
*Tel:* (089) 9231 358 *Fax:* (089) 9231 201
*Web Site:* www.ajbd.de
*Key Personnel*
Chairman: Dr Hans-Peter Ziegler *E-mail:* hans-
 peter.ziegler@bfh.bund.de
Vice Chairman: Dr Wolfgang Schwab
 *Tel:* (0316) 3801270 *Fax:* (0316) 3809160
 *E-mail:* wolfgang.schwab@uni-graz.at
Secretary: Gerda Graf *Tel:* (0331) 9773571
 *Fax:* (0331) 9773816 *E-mail:* ggraf@rz.uni-
 potsdam.de
Treasurer: Annette Schlag *Tel:* (030) 2025-9715
 *Fax:* (030) 2025-9660 *E-mail:* kassenwartin@
 ajbd.de
Editor: Heinz-Guenther Black *Tel:* (0941)
 943 2497 *Fax:* (0941) 943 3285
 *E-mail:* herausgeber@ajbd.de; Cornelie Butz
 *Tel:* (0341) 2007 1600 *Fax:* (0341) 2007 1000
 *E-mail:* butz@bverwg.bund.de
Publication(s): *Arbeitshefte* (irregularly); *Mit-
 teilungen der Arbeitsgemeinschaft fuer juris-
 tisches Bibliotheks- und Dokumentationswesen*
 (triannually)

### Arbeitsgemeinschaft fur medizinisches
 Bibliothekswesen
c/o Deutsche Zentralbibliothek fuer Medi-
 zin (DZM), Joseph-Stelzmann-Str 9, 50924
 Cologne
*Tel:* (0621) 7592376 *Fax:* (0621) 7594419
*E-mail:* agmb@agmb.de
*Web Site:* www.agmb.de
*Key Personnel*
Chairman: Ulrich Korwitz
Founded: 1970

### Berufsverband Information Bibliothek (BIB)
Gartenstr 18, 72764 Reutlingen
*Tel:* (07121) 3491-0 *Fax:* (07121) 300433
*E-mail:* mail@bib-info.de

*Web Site:* www.bib-info.de
*Key Personnel*
President: Klaus-Peter Boettger *Tel:* (0208) 455-4141 *Fax:* (0208) 455-4125 *E-mail:* klaus.peter.boettger@sdadt-mh.de
Secretary: Katharina Boulanger
Association of Librarians.
Publication(s): *BuB-Forum for Bibliothek und Information*

**BIB**, see Berufsverband Information Bibliothek (BIB)

**Bibliothek & Information Deutschland (BID) - The Federal Union of German Library & Information Associations**
Str des 17, Juni 114, 10623 Berlin
*Tel:* (030) 39 00 14 80; (030) 39 00 14 81
*Fax:* (030) 39 00 14 84
*E-mail:* bid@bideutschland.de
*Web Site:* www.bideutschland.de/index2.html
*Key Personnel*
Speaker: Dr Georg Ruppelt *Tel:* (0511) 1267 303 *Fax:* (0511) 1267 207 *E-mail:* nlb@mail.nlb-hannover.de
Contact: Elke Daempfert *E-mail:* gs@bdb-dachverband.de
Formed by the joining of the German Association for Information Science & Practice (DGI) with the Federal Union of German Library Associations (BDB).
Publication(s): *Ausbildung im Europaeischen Rahmen-Abschlussbericht; BDB-Jahresbericht 1989/90; Bibkliotheken '93; Bibliotheken in der Informationsgesellschaft; Bibliotheksdienst* (monthly, journal, Official publication of BDB; Edited by Zentral- and Landesbibliothek Berlin); *Drehscheibe der Information; Menschen, Buecher und Computer; Umsetzung der EG-Richtlinien zum Vermiet-und Verleihrecht*
*Branch Office(s)*
Fadbodsdule Hamburg, Griudellof 30, 20146 Hamburg

**BID**, see Bibliothek & Information Deutschland (BID) - The Federal Union of German Library & Information Associations

**DBV**, see Deutscher Bibliotheksverband eV (DBV)

**Deutsche Exlibris Gesellschaft ev** (German Bookplate Society)
Fliednerstr 27, 65191 Wiesbaden
*Tel:* (0611) 502907 *Fax:* (0611) 503021
*Web Site:* www.exlibris-gesellschaft.de
*Key Personnel*
President: Dr Gernot Blum *E-mail:* info@exlibris-blum.de
Secretary: Birgit M A Goebel-Stiegler *E-mail:* birgit.goebel@t-online.de
Membership(s): FISAE (Federation International des Societes Amateurs d Exlibris).
Publication(s): *Jahrbuch Exlibriskunst und Graphik* (annually)

**Deutsche Gesellschaft fur Informationswissenschaft und Informationspraxis eV** (The Association for Information Science & Practice)
Ostbahnhofstr 13, 60314 Frankfurt am Main
*Tel:* (069) 43 03 13 *Fax:* (069) 49 09 09 6
*E-mail:* mail@dgi-info.de
*Web Site:* www.dgd.de
*Key Personnel*
President: Dr Gabriele Beger *E-mail:* beger@dgi-info.de
Vice President: Dieter Mewes *E-mail:* mewes@dgi-info.de; Dr Ralph Schmidt *E-mail:* schmidt@dgi-info.de

Treasurer: Dr Klaus Steffen Dittrich *E-mail:* dittrich@dgi-info.de
Publication(s): *nfd-Information Wissenschaft und Praxis* (Documentation)

**Deutscher Bibliotheksverband eV (DBV)**
(Association of German Libraries)
Str des 17, Juni 114, 10623 Berlin
*Tel:* (030) 39 00 14 80; (030) 39 00 14 81
*Fax:* (030) 39 00 14 84
*E-mail:* dbv@bibliotheksverband.de
*Web Site:* www.bibliotheksverband.de
*Key Personnel*
Chairman: Dr Georg Ruppelt
President: Brigitte soot Scherer
Contact: Elke Daempfert *E-mail:* daempfert@bdbibl.de
Publication(s): *D B V-Info* (annually)

**Deutscher Verband Evangelischer Buchereien eV** (German Association of Protestant Libraries)
Buergerstr 2a, 37073 Goettingen
*Tel:* (0551) 500759-0 *Fax:* (0551) 704415
*E-mail:* dveb@dveb.info
*Web Site:* www.dveb.info
*Key Personnel*
Chairman: Dr Eckart V Vietinghoff
Manager: Gabriele Kassenbrock
Publication(s): *Der Evangelische Buchberater* (quarterly); *Handwoerterbuch der evangelischen Buechereiarbeit 1980*

**Deutsches Bibliotheksinstitut** (German Library Institute)
Kurt-Schumacher-Damm 12-16, 13405 Berlin
*Tel:* (030) 410 34-0 *Fax:* (030) 410 34-100
*E-mail:* dbilink@dbi-berlin.de
*Web Site:* www.dbi-berlin.de
*Key Personnel*
Dir: Prof Gunter Beyersdorff
Also several reference books, monographs, bibliographical & statistical services.
Publication(s): *Bibliotheks Info* (monthly); *Bibliotheksdienst* (monthly, journal)
*Branch Office(s)*
Luisenstr 57, 10117 Berlin

**GBDL**, see Gesellschaft fur Bibliothekswesen und Dokumentation des Landbaues (GBDL)

**Gesellschaft fur Bibliothekswesen und Dokumentation des Landbaues (GBDL)**
(Society for Librarianship & Documentation in Agriculture)
Affiliate of Arbcitsgemeinschaft der Specialbibliotheken e v (ASpB)
c/o TU Muenchen, Informations- und Dokumentationszentrum Weihenstephan, 85350 Freising
*Tel:* (08161) 71 34 26 *Fax:* (08161) 71 44 09
*Web Site:* www.weihenstephan.de
*Key Personnel*
President: Prof W Laux, PhD
Secretary: Dr Birgid Schlindwein *E-mail:* schlind@weihenstephan.de
Publication(s): *Mitteilungen der Gesellschaft fuer Bibliothekswesen und Dokumentation des Landbaues*
*Shipping Address:* Voettingerstr 47, 85354 Freising

**Informationszentrum fuer Informationswissenschaft und -praxis (IZ)**
Fachhochschule Potsdam, Friedrich-Ebert-Str 4, 14467 Potsdam
Mailing Address: Postfach 600608, Pappelallee 8-9, 14469 Potsdam
*Tel:* (0331) 580-2210; (0331) 580-2230
*Fax:* (0331) 580-2229
*E-mail:* iz@fh-potsdam.de
*Web Site:* forge.fh-potsdam.de

*Key Personnel*
Manager: Karen Falke *E-mail:* falke@fh-potsdam.de
Documentation & Information Society.

**IZ**, see Informationszentrum fuer Informationswissenschaft und -praxis (IZ)

**NABD**, see Normenausschuss Bibliotheks- und Dokumentationswesen (NABD) im DIN Deutsches Institut fuer Normung eV

**Normenausschuss Bibliotheks- und Dokumentationswesen (NABD) im DIN Deutsches Institut fuer Normung eV**
Burggrafenstr 6, 10787 Berlin
*Tel:* (030) 2601-0 *Fax:* (030) 2601-1231
*E-mail:* postmaster@din.de
*Web Site:* www.nabd.din.de *Cable:* DEUTSCHNORMEN BERLIN
*Key Personnel*
Contact: Dr Winfried Hennig *E-mail:* winfried.hennig@din.de

**VdA - Verband deutscher Archivarinnen und Archivare e V** (Association of German Archivists)
Marstallstr 2, 99423 Weimar 99423
Mailing Address: Postfach 2119, 99402 Weimar
*Tel:* (03643) 870-235 *Fax:* (03643) 870-164
*E-mail:* info@vda.archiv.net
*Web Site:* www.vda.archiv.net
*Key Personnel*
Chairman: Dr Volker Wahl *E-mail:* wahl@vda.archiv.net
Man Dir: Thilo Bauer *E-mail:* bauer@vda.archiv.net
Founded: 1946
Publication(s): *Archive in der Bundesrepublik Deutschland, Oesterreich & der Schweiz* (Register of Archives in Germany, Austria & Switzerland, at irregular intervals of several years)

**Verein der Diplom-Bibliothekare an wissenschaftlichen Bibliotheken eV**
c/o Stadtbuecherei Muelheim an der Ruhr, Friedrich-Ebert-Str 47, 45468 Muelheim an der Ruhr
*Tel:* (0221) 5747161 *Fax:* (0221) 5747110
*Web Site:* www.bibliothek.uni-regensburg.de/vddb
*Key Personnel*
Chairman: Klaus-Peter Boettger *Tel:* (0208) 455-4141 *Fax:* (0208) 455-4125 *E-mail:* klaus-peter.boettger@stadt-mh.de
Deputy Chairman: Kerstin Cevajka *Tel:* (07431) 579-179 *Fax:* (07431) 579-181 *E-mail:* kcevajka@fh-albsig.de; Sabine Stummeyer *Tel:* (0511) 762-19870 *Fax:* (0511) 762-4075; (0511) 762-4076 *E-mail:* sabine.stummeyer@tib.uni-hannover.de
Association of Certified Librarians at Academic Libraries.
Publication(s): *Rundschreiben*

**Verein Deutscher Bibliothekar eV (VDB)**
(Association of German Librarians)
Unter den Linden 8, 10117 Berlin
*Tel:* (030) 266-1728 *Fax:* (030) 266-1717
*E-mail:* olaf.hanann@sbb.spk-berlin.de; info@vdb_online.de
*Web Site:* www.vdb-online.org
*Key Personnel*
Chairman: Annette Rath-Beckmann *Tel:* (0421) 218-2601; (0421) 218-2602 *E-mail:* rathb@uni-bremen.de
President: Dr Daniela Luelfing
1st Vice President: Dr Wilfried Suehl-Strohmenger
2nd Vice President: Dr Ulrich Hohoff

Secretary: Dr Thomas Elsmann
  *E-mail:* elsmann@uni-bremen.de
Founded: 1900
Publication(s): *Jahrbuch der deutschen Biblio-theken* (Yearbook of German Libraries, biennial); *Zeitschrift fuer Bibliothekswesen und Bibliographie* (Journal of Library Science & Bibliography)

**Wuerttembergische Bibliotheksgesellschaft**
Konrad-Adenauer-Str 8, 70173 Stuttgart
Mailing Address: Postfach 10 54 41, 70047 Stuttgart
*Tel:* (0711) 212-4454; (0711) 212-4424
  *Fax:* (0711) 212-4422
*E-mail:* information@wlb-stuttgart.de
*Web Site:* www.wlb-stuttgart.de
*Key Personnel*
Dir: Dr Hannsjorg Kowark
Secretary: Christine Demmier; Verena Hoser
Society of Friends of the Wuerttemberg State Library.

# Ghana

**Ghana Library Association**
PO Box 5015, Accra
*Tel:* (021) 764822 *Fax:* (021) 763523
*Key Personnel*
President: E S Asiedo
Secretary: A W K Insaidoo
Founded: 1962
Publication(s): *Ghana Library Journal* (irregularly)

# Greece

**Enosis Hellinon Bibliothekarion** (Greek Library Association)
4 Skoulenion St, 105 61 Athens
*Tel:* 2103226625
*Key Personnel*
President: K Xatzopoulou
General Secretary: E Kalogeraky
Publication(s): *Greek Library Association Bulletin*

# Guinea

**Direction de la Recherche Scientifique et Techniques** (National Research & Documentation Institute)
Bibliothelique Nationale, BP 561, Conakry
*Tel:* 46 10 10
*Key Personnel*
Dir: Lansana Sylla

# Guyana

**Guyana Library Association**
c/o National Library, 76-77 Church & Main Sts, Georgetown
*Tel:* (0226) 2690; (0226) 2699; (0227) 4052
  *Fax:* (0227) 4053
*E-mail:* natlib@sdnp.org.gy
*Web Site:* www.natlib.gov.gy

*Key Personnel*
President: Ivor Rodrigues
Secretary: Gwyneth George

# Holy See (Vatican City State)

**Biblioteca Apostolica Vaticana** (Vatican Apostolic Library)
Cortile del Belvedere, 00120 Vatican City
*Tel:* (06) 6987 9402 *Fax:* (06) 6988 4795
*E-mail:* bav@librs6k.vatlib.it
*Web Site:* www.vatican.va
*Telex:* 2024 Dirgental VA
*Key Personnel*
Dir: Prof Don Raffaele Farina *Tel:* (06) 6987 9400 *Fax:* (06) 6988 5327 *E-mail:* prefetto@vatlib.it

# Honduras

**Asociacion de Bibliotecarios y Archivistas de Honduras** (Association of Librarians & Archivists of Honduras)
11a Calle, Pritnera y Segunda Ave, No 105, Comayaguela DC, Tegucigalpa
*Key Personnel*
President: Francisca de Escoto Espinoza
Secretary General: Juan Angel R Ayes
Publication(s): *Catalogo de Prestamo*

# Hong Kong

**Hong Kong Library Association**
GPO 10095, Hong Kong
*E-mail:* hkla@hkla.org
*Web Site:* www.hkla.org
*Key Personnel*
President: Julia Chan
Honorary Secretary: Annabelle Pau *Tel:* 2241-5898
Publication(s): *Journal of the Hong Kong Library Association* (irregularly)

# Hungary

**Magyar Koenyvtarosok Egyesuelete** (Association of Hungarian Librarians)
Hold u 6, 1054 Budapest
*Tel:* (01) 311 8634 *Fax:* (01) 311 8634
*E-mail:* mke@oszk.hu
*Web Site:* www.mke.oszk.hu
*Key Personnel*
President: Bakos Klara *E-mail:* bakos@zmne.hu
Executive Secretary: Eva Jaki
Founded: 1935

# Iceland

**Upplysing - Felag bokasafns- og upplysingafraeoa** (Information - the Icelandic Library & Information Science Association)
Lagmuli 7, 108 Reykjavik
*Tel:* 553-7290; 862-8627 *Fax:* 588-9239
*E-mail:* upplysing@bokis.is
*Web Site:* www.bokis.is
*Key Personnel*
President: H A Hardarson
Secretary: A Agnarsdottir
Publication(s): *Bokasafnid* (journal, yearbook of library & information science); *Fregnir* (3 times/yr, newsletter)

# India

**Documentation Research & Training Centre (DRTC)**
Indian Statistical Institute, Eighth Mile Mysore Rd, RVCE Post, Bangalore 560 059
*Tel:* (080) 8483002 (ext 490); (080) 8483003 (ext 490); (080) 8483004 (ext 490); (080) 8483006 (ext 490) *Fax:* (080) 8484265
*E-mail:* drtc@isibang.ac.in
*Web Site:* www.drtc.isibang.ac.in
*Telex:* 8458376 Isib In *Cable:* STATISTICA
*Key Personnel*
Head of Dept: I K Ravichandra Rao
Founded: 1962
Indian statistical institute.
Publication(s): *Annual Seminar, DRTC* (annually); *Refresher Seminar, DRTC* (annually)

**DRTC**, see Documentation Research & Training Centre (DRTC)

**IASLIC**, see Indian Association of Special Libraries & Information Centres (IASLIC)

**Indian Association of Special Libraries & Information Centres (IASLIC)**
P291, CIT Scheme 6M, Kankurgachi, Kolkata 700054
*Tel:* (033) 334 9651; (033) 2354 9066
*E-mail:* iaslic@vsnl.net
*Web Site:* www.iaslic.org
*Key Personnel*
Publisher: J M Das
Publication(s): *Directory of Special & Research Libraries in India* (12 times/yr, newsletter); *Indian Library Science Abstracts* (quarterly)

**Indian Association of Academic Librarians**
c/o Jawaharlal Nehru University Library, New Mehrauli Rd, New Delhi 110067
*Tel:* (011) 6831717
*Key Personnel*
Secretary: M M Kashyap

**Indian Library Association**
A/40-1, Flat No 201, Ansal Bldg, Mukerjee Nagar, Delhi 110009
*Tel:* (011) 326 4748; (011) 765 1743
*E-mail:* ilanet1@nda.vsnl.net.in
*Web Site:* www.delhiindia.com
*Key Personnel*
President: Ms Kalpana Dasgsupta

# Indonesia

**Ikatan Pustakawan Indonesia** (Indonesian
  Library Association)
Jalan Merdeka Selatan No 11, 10110 Jakarta,
  Pusat
*Tel:* (021) 3855729 *Fax:* (021) 3855729
*E-mail:* mahmudin@lib.itb.ac.id
*Web Site:* ipi.pnri.go.id
*Key Personnel*
President: S Kartosdono
Publication(s): *Majalah Ikatan Pustakawan In-
  donesia*

# Iraq

**Arab Archivists Institute**
c/o National Centre of Archives, National Library
  Bldg, 2nd floor, Bab-Al-Muaddum, Baghdad
Mailing Address: PO Box 594, Baghdad
*Tel:* (01) 416 8440
*Key Personnel*
Dir: Salim Al-Alousi
Founded: 1972

# Ireland

**Central Catholic Library Association Inc**
74 Merrion Sq, Dublin 2
*Tel:* (01) 676 1264
*E-mail:* catholicresearch@eircom.net
*Key Personnel*
Librarian: Teresa Whitington
  *E-mail:* teresawhitington@eircom.net

**An Chomhairle Leabharlanna** (Library Council)
53/54 Upper Mount St, Dublin 2
*Tel:* (01) 6761963; (01) 6761167 *Fax:* (01)
  6766721
*E-mail:* info@librarycouncil.ie
*Web Site:* www.librarycouncil.ie
*Key Personnel*
Dir: Mrs Norma McDermott
Research & Information Officer: Alun Bevan
  *E-mail:* abevan@librarycouncil.ie
Development agency for public libraries in Ire-
  land.
Publication(s): *Annual Report*; *Irish Library News*
  (monthly)

**Cumann Leabharlann na h-Eireann** (Library
  Association of Ireland)
53 Upper Mount St, Dublin 2
*Tel:* (01) 61202193 *Fax:* (01) 61213090
*Web Site:* www.libraryassociation.ie
*Key Personnel*
President: Ruth Flanagan *E-mail:* president@
  libraryassociation.ie
Honorary Secretary: Denis Murphy
Founded: 1928
Membership(s): IFLA; EBLIDA.
Publication(s): *An Leabharlann* (published jointly
  with CILIP-Northern Ireland); *The Library
  Association of Ireland* (4 per year, published
  jointly with CILIP-Northern Ireland)

**National Library of Ireland Society**
Kildare St, Dublin 2
*Tel:* (01) 603 02 00 *Fax:* (01) 676 66 90
*E-mail:* info@nli.ie
*Web Site:* www.nli.ie

*Key Personnel*
Library Administration Officer: Kevin Browne
Executive Officer: Margaret Toomey

# Israel

**Israel Librarians & Information Specialists
  Association**
The Isreal Center for Libraries, 9 Beit Hadfus St,
  Givaat Shaul, Jerusalem
*Tel:* (02) 6589515 *Fax:* (02) 6251628
*E-mail:* icl@icl.org.il
*Web Site:* www.icl.org.il
*Key Personnel*
President: Benjamin Schachter
Founded: 1965
Publication(s): *The Reader's Aid (Yad Lakore)-
  Israel Journal for Libraries and Archives*

**Israel Society of Libraries & Information
  Centers (ASMI)**
PO Box 28273, 91282 Jerusalem
*Tel:* (02) 6249421 *Fax:* (02) 6249421
*E-mail:* asmi@asmi.org.il
*Web Site:* www.asmi.org.il
*Key Personnel*
Chairperson: Shoshana Langerman *Tel:* (02)
  5632756 *Fax:* (02) 5630640 *E-mail:* shala@
  barak-online.net
Founded: 1966
Membership(s): International Federation of Li-
  brary Associations & Institutions (IFLA).
Publication(s): *Information & Librarianship* (ir-
  regularly, 2002, 2 issues per volume)

**The Israeli Center for Libraries**
28 Baruch Hirsh St, Benei-Berak 51131
Mailing Address: PO Box 3251, Bnei-Berak
  51131
*Tel:* (03) 6180151 *Fax:* (03) 5798048
*E-mail:* icl@icl.org.il
*Web Site:* www.icl.org.il
*Key Personnel*
Chairman: Jacob Agmon
Dir: Orly Onn
Contact: Ariella Barrett
Founded: 1965
Publication(s): *Basifriot* (newspaper); *Yad-la-Kore*
  (The Reader's Aid Library Quarterly & Library
  Monographs)

# Italy

**Associazione Italiana Biblioteche** (Italian
  Library Association)
c/o Biblioteca Nazionale Centrale, Viale Castro
  Pretorio 105, 00185 Rome
Mailing Address: CP 2461, 00100 Rome
*Tel:* (06) 4463532 *Fax:* (06) 4441139
*E-mail:* aib@aib.it
*Web Site:* www.aib.it
*Key Personnel*
President: Mauro Guerrini
Secretary: Gianfranco Crupi
Editorial Office: Maria Teresa Natale
  *E-mail:* natale@aib.it
Publication(s): *AIB Notizie* (monthly); *Bollettino
  AIB* (quarterly); *Rapporti AIB* (irregularly)

**Istituto Centrale per il Catalogo Unico delle
  Biblioteche Italiane e per le Informazioni
  Bibliografiche** (Central Institute of the Union

Catalog of Italian Libraries & Bibliographical
  Information)
Viale del Castro Pretorio, 105-00185 Rome
*Tel:* (06) 4989484 *Fax:* (06) 4959302
*Web Site:* www.iccu.sbn.it
*Key Personnel*
Dir: Dr Luciano Scala
Publication(s): *Bibliografia di Inventari e Cata-
  loghi a Stampa dei Manoscritti*; *Bibliografia
  Nazionale Italiana*; *Catalogo Collettivo di
  Periodici - Archivio ISRDS/CNR*; *I Emilia
  Romagna - Il Friuli Venezia Giulia*; *Le Edi-
  zioni Italiane del XVI sec, Guida alla Cata-
  logazione per Autori delle Stampe, Inventari
  Non a Stampa di Manoscritti*; *Periodici Italiani
  1886-1981*; *Quaderno RICA*; *Regole Italiane
  di Catalogazione per Autori*; *Soggettario per i
  Cataloghi delle Biblioteche Italiane*

# Jamaica

**Jamaica Library Association**
PO Box 125, Kingston 5
*Tel:* (876) 927-1614 *Fax:* (876) 927-1614
*E-mail:* liajapresident@yahoo.com
*Web Site:* www.liaja.org.jm
*Key Personnel*
President: Byron Palmer
Secretary: F Salmon
Honorary Secretary: Yulande Lindsay
Founded: 1949
Publication(s): *JLA Bulletin* (bulletin, 2002); *LI-
  AJA Annual Report* (annually, report); *LIAJA
  News* (newsletter); *LIAJA Newslink* (2002)

# Japan

**Gakujutsu Bunken Fukyu-Kai** (Association for
  Science Documents Information)
c/o Tokyo Institute of Technology, 2-12-1 Oh-
  Okayama, Meguro-Ku, Tokyo 152-8550
*Tel:* (03) 5734-3443 *Fax:* (03) 5734-2053
*E-mail:* gakujyutubunken@mvd.biglobe.ne.jp
*Web Site:* www.titech.ac.jp
*Key Personnel*
President: Shu Kanbara

**Joho Kagaku Gijutsu Kyokai** (Information
  Science & Technology Association
  (INFOSTA))
Sasaki Bldg, 2-5-7 Koishikawa, Bunkyo-ku,
  Tokyo 112-0002
*Tel:* (03) 3813-3791 *Fax:* (03) 3813-3793
*E-mail:* infosta@infosta.or.jp
*Web Site:* www.infosta.or.jp
*Key Personnel*
President: T Gondoh
General Manager: Yukio Ichikawa
Founded: 1950
Publication(s): *Journal of Information Science &
  Technology Association* (biannually, microfiche)

**Joho Shori Gakkai** (Information Processing
  Society of Japan)
Kagaku-Kaikan (Chemistry Hall) 4F, 1-5 Kanda-
  Surugadai, Chiyoda-ku, Tokyo 101-0062
*Tel:* (03) 3518-8374 *Fax:* (03) 3518-8375
*E-mail:* intl@ipsj.or.jp
*Web Site:* www.ipsj.or.jp
*Key Personnel*
President: Takashi Masuda
Founded: 1960
Publication(s): *Joho-shori* (monthly, journal);
  *Transactions of IPSJ* (monthly)

**Mita Toshokan Joho Gakkai** (Mita Society for Library & Information Science)
c/o School of Library & Information Science, Keio University, 2-15-45 Mita, Minato-ku, Tokyo 108-8345
*Tel:* (03) 5427-1654
*Web Site:* www.mita.lib.keio.ac.jp
*Key Personnel*
President: Kimio Hosono
Secretary: Satoko Suzuki *E-mail:* mslis@slis.keio.ac.jp
Publication(s): *Library & Information Science* (biannually)

**Nihon Igaku Toshokan Kyokai** (Japan Medical Library Association)
Gakkai Center Bldg, 5F, 2-4-16 Yayoi, Bunkyo-ku, Tokyo 113-0032
*Tel:* (03) 38151942 *Fax:* (03) 38151608
*E-mail:* imlahq@nisiq.net; jmlajimu@sirius.ocn.ne.jp
*Web Site:* wwwsoc.nii.ac.jp/jmla
*Key Personnel*
Secretary: Junzo Tsuno
Founded: 1927
Publication(s): *Igakutoshokan*; *List of current periodicals acquired by the Japanese Medical, Dental & Pharmaceutical Libraries*; *Union Catalogue of Foreign Books in the Libraries of Japan Medical Schools*

**Nihon Toshokan Joho Gakkai Shi** (Japan Society of Library & Information Science)
c/o Aichi Shukutoku University, 9 Katahira Nagakute, Nagakute-cho, Aichi-gun, Aichi 480-1197
*Tel:* (0561) 62-4111 *Fax:* (0561) 63-9308
*E-mail:* muransky@asu.aasa.ac.jp
*Web Site:* www.soc.nii.ac.jp/jslis/
*Key Personnel*
President: Maso Nagasawa
Executive Secretary: Tomohide Muranushi
Contact: Shinichi Toda *Tel:* (03) 3945 7444
*E-mail:* toda@hakusrv.toyo.ac.jp
Founded: 1953
Publication(s): *Nihon Toshokan Joho Gakkaishi* (Journal of Japan Society of Library & Information Science, quarterly)

**Nihon Toshokan Kyokai** (Japan Library Association)
1-11-14 Shinkawa, Chuo-ku, Tokyo 104-0033
*Tel:* (03) 3523-0811 *Fax:* (03) 3523-0841
*E-mail:* info@jla.or.jp
*Web Site:* www.jla.or.jp
*Key Personnel*
Secretary-General: Reiko Sakagawa
Founded: 1892
Publication(s): *Basic Subject Headings (BSH)* (1983); *JLA Library & Information Science Text Series* (1999); *Librarianship in Japan* (1994); *Nihon No Sankotosho* (Guide to Japanese Reference Books, 1980); *Nihon no Toshokan* (Statistics on Libraries in Japan, annually); *Nippon Cataloging Rules (NCR)* (1987); *Nippon Decimal Classification (NDC)* (1996); *Sentei Tosho Somokuroku* (Standard Catalog of Selected Books, annually, catalog); *Toshokan Handobukku* (Librarian's Handbook, 1990); *Toshokan Nenkan* (Library Yearbook, annually); *Toshokan No Shigoto* (Library Work); *Toshokan Yogoshu* (Librarian's Glossary, 1988); *Toshokan'in No Tame No Eikaiwa Handobukku* (English Conversation Handbook for Librarians, 1991); *Toshokan'in Sensho* (Selective Books for Librarians)

**Nippon Yakugaku Toshokan Kyogikai** (Japan Pharmaceutical Library Association)
c/o Library, Faculty of Pharmaceutical Sciences, University of Tokyo, 7-3-1 Hongo, Bunkyo-ku, Tokyo 113-0033

*Tel:* (03) 38122111
*Web Site:* wwwsoc.nii.ac.jp/jpla
Publication(s): *Yakugaku Toshokan* (Pharmaceutical Library Bulletin)

**Senmon Toshokan Kyogikai (SENTOKYO)**
c/o Japan Library Association, Bldg F6, 1-11-14 Shinkawa, Chuo-ku, Tokyo 104-0033
*Tel:* (03) 3537-8335 *Fax:* (03) 3537-8336
*E-mail:* jsla@jsla.or.jp
*Web Site:* www.jsla.or.jp
*Key Personnel*
President: Kousaku Inaba
Executive Dir: Fumihisa Nakagawa
Japan Special Libraries Association.
Publication(s): *Hakusho: Nihon no Senmon Toshokan*; *Senmon Joho Kikan Soran* (triennially); *Senmon Toshokan* (6 times/yr, bulletin)

**SENTOKYO**, see Senmon Toshokan Kyogikai (SENTOKYO)

# Jordan

**Jordan Library Association** (Message of the Library)
PO Box 6289, Amman
*Tel:* (06) 462 9412 *Fax:* (06) 462 9412
*E-mail:* info@jorla.org
*Web Site:* www.jorla.org
*Key Personnel*
President: Anwar Akroush
Secretary: Yousra Abu Ajamieh
Contact: Fadil Klayb
Publication(s): *Anglo-American Cataloguing Rules* (1983, 2nd ed, in Arabic); *Directory of Jordanian Periodicals* (1982); *Directory of Libraries & Librarians in Jordan* (1984); *Directory of Libraries in Jordan 1976*; *Introduction to Librarianship & Information Science* (1982, in Arabic); *Jordanian National Bibliography* (annually); *The Palestinian Bibliography: A List of Books Published by the Arabs in Palestine 1948-1980*; *Palestinian-Jordanian Bibliography 1900-1970 & 1971-1975*; *Rissalat al-Maktaba* (The Message of the Library, quarterly); *Technical Processing of Information* (in Arabic)

# Kenya

**Kenya Library Association**
PO Box 46031, Nairobi
*Tel:* (02) 334244 *Fax:* (02) 336885
*Key Personnel*
Chairman: Jacinta Were *E-mail:* jwere@ken.healthnet.org
Secretary: Alice Bulogosi
Publication(s): *Kelias News* (bimonthly); *Maktaba Journal* (biannually, text in English & Swahili)

# Republic of Korea

**Hanguk Seoji Hakhoe** (Korean Bibliographical Society)
One Yoido-dong, Youngdeungpo-gu, Seoul 150-703

*Tel:* (02) 788-4143 *Fax:* (02) 788-3385
*E-mail:* w3@nanet.go.kr
*Web Site:* www.nanet.go.kr

**Hanguk Tosogwan Hakhoe**
c/o Dept of Library Science, Sung Kyun Kwan University, 53, 3-ga, Myungryun-dong, Chongro-ku, Seoul 110-745
*Tel:* (02) 7600114 *Fax:* (02) 7442453
Korean Library Science Society.
Publication(s): *Tosogwan Hak* (Journal of the Korean Library Science Society, Korean with English abstracts)

**Korean Library Association (KLA)**
1-KA, Hoehyun-Dong, Choong-ku, Seoul 100-177
*Tel:* (02) 5354868 *Fax:* (02) 5355616
*E-mail:* klanet@hitel.net
*Web Site:* www.korla.or.kr
*Key Personnel*
President: Ki Nam Shin
Executive Dir: Won Ho Jo
Publication(s): *KLA Bulletin* (bimonthly, text in Korean); *Korean Cataloguing Rules*; *Korean Decimal Classification*; *The Patterns of Book Cover Design in Korea (1392-1945)*; *Statistics on Libraries in Korea* (annually)

**Korean Research & Development Library Association (KORDELA)**
Room 0411 KIST Library, Cheongryang, Seoul
Mailing Address: POB 131, Cheongryang, Seoul
*Tel:* (02) 9673692 *Fax:* (02) 29634013
*Telex:* 27380 Kistrok K
*Key Personnel*
President: Ke Hong Park
Secretary: Keon Tak Oh

# Kuwait

**Kuwait University Library**
PO Box 17140, 92452 Khaldiya
*Tel:* 4816497
*Web Site:* www.kuniv.edu.kw
*Key Personnel*
Dir: Dr Husain A Al-Ansari
Publication(s): *The University Library*

# Laos People's Democratic Republic

**Association des Bibliothecaires Laotiens** (Association of Laos Librarians)
c/o Direction de la Bibliotheque Nationale, Ministry of Information & Culture, PO Box 122, Vientiane
*Tel:* 212452 *Fax:* 212408
*E-mail:* pfd-mill@pan.laos.net.la

# Latvia

**Library Association of Latvia**
Latvian National Library, Kr Barona 14, 2 Stavs, 205 telpa, 1423 Riga
*Tel:* (0371) 7287620 *Fax:* (0371) 7280851

*E-mail:* lnb@lbi.lnb.lv
*Web Site:* www.lnb.lv
*Telex:* TEMA SU
*Key Personnel*
President: Aldis Abele
Dir: Andris Vilks *E-mail:* andrisv@lbi.lnb.lv
Vice President: Silvia Linina
Editor: Antra Purina
Publication(s): *Nota Bene* (quarterly, journal)

# Lebanon

**The Lebanese Library Association**
c/o American University of Beirut, University Library/Serials Dept, Beirut
Mailing Address: PO Box 11-0236, Beirut 1107 2020
*Tel:* (01) 350000; (01) 340460 *Fax:* (01) 351706
*Web Site:* www.aub.edu.lb
*Telex:* 20801
*Key Personnel*
President: Mr Fawz Abdalleh
Executive Secretary: Rudaynah Shoujah
Publication(s): *Al-Nashrah* (triannually, bulletin)

# Lesotho

**Lesotho Library Association**
Private Bag A26, Maseru
*Tel:* 340 601 *Fax:* 340 601
*E-mail:* mmc@doc.isas.nul.ls
*Web Site:* www.sn.apc.org *Cable:* Lelia Maseru
*Key Personnel*
Chairman: S M Mohai
Secretary: N Taole
Publication(s): *Lesotho Library Association Newsletter* (annually)

# Lithuania

**Lithuanian Librarians Association**
Sv Ignoto 6-108, 2600 Vilnius
*Tel:* (02) 750340 *Fax:* (02) 750340
*E-mail:* lbd@vpu.lt
*Web Site:* www.lbd.lt
*Key Personnel*
President: Vida Garunkstyte
Vice President: Emilija Banionyte *E-mail:* emilija.banionyte@vpu.lt
Founded: 1935

# The Former Yugoslav Republic of Macedonia

**Bibliotekarsko Drustvo na Makedonija**
(Macedonian Library Association)
Bul Goce Delcev 6, 91000 Skopje
Mailing Address: PO Box 566, 91000 Skopje
*Tel:* (091) 226846 *Fax:* (091) 232649

*E-mail:* mile@nubsk.edu.mk; bmile47@yahoo.com
*Web Site:* www.nubsk.edu.mk
*Key Personnel*
President: Mile Boseski
Secretary: Poliksena Matkovska
Union of Librarians' Associations of Macedonia Official titles: Savez drustava biblioteckih radnika Jugoslavije (Serbo-Croatian), Sojuz na drustvata na bibliotecnite rabotnici na Yugoslavija (Macedonian), Zveza durstev bibliotecnih delavcev Jugoslavije (Slovene). The headquarters of the League is situated in each of the six republics & two provinces of Serbia & Montenegro in turn & changes every two years.
Publication(s): *Bibliotekarska iskra*

# Malawi

**The Malawi Library Association**
PO Box 429, Zomba
*Tel:* (050) 522222 *Fax:* (050) 523225
*E-mail:* d.b.v.phiri@unima.wn.apc.org
*Key Personnel*
Chairman: Joseph J Uta
Secretary: Vote D Somba
Publication(s): *Libraries in Malawi: Textbook for Library Assistants*; *MALA Bulletin* (biannually); *Manual for Small Libraries*

# Malaysia

**Persatuan Perpustakaan Malaysia** (Library Association of Malaysia)
c/o Perpustakaan Negara Malaysia, 232 Jalan Tun Razak, 50572 Kuala Lumpur
*Tel:* (03) 26871700 *Fax:* (03) 26942490
*E-mail:* pnmweb@pnm.my
*Web Site:* www.pnm.my
*Key Personnel*
President: Chew Wing Foong
Secretary: Leni Abdul Latif
Honorary Secretary: Ahmad Ridzuan Wan Chik
Publication(s): *Berita PPM* (bimonthly); *Majallah Perpustakaan Malaysia* (annually); *Sumber Pustaka* (newsletter)

# Mali

**AMBAD,** see Association Malienne des Bibliothecaires, Archivistes et Documentalistes (AMBAD)

**Association Malienne des Bibliothecaires, Archivistes et Documentalistes (AMBAD)**
Rue Kasse Keita, Bamako
*Tel:* 22 49 63
*Key Personnel*
Dir: Mamadou Konoba Keiita

# Malta

**MaLIA,** see Malta Library & Information Association (MaLIA)

**Malta Library & Information Association (MaLIA)**
c/o University of Malta Library, Tal-Qroqq, Msida MSD 06
*Tel:* 21322054
*E-mail:* mpar1@lib.um.edu.mt
*Web Site:* www.malia-malta.org
*Key Personnel*
Chairperson: Robert Mizzi *E-mail:* robmiz@mail.global.net.mt
Deputy Chairperson: Laurence Zerafa
Honorary Secretary: Ruth Muscat
Treasurer: Josephine Spiteri
Founded: 1969
Publication(s): *Directory of Libraries & Information Units in Malta* (1996); *Directory of Maltese Publishers, Printers, Book Designers & Book Dealers* (1981); *MaLIA Newletter* (quarterly)

# Mauritania

**Association Mauritanienne des Bibliothecaires, Archivistes et Documentalistes**
c/o Bibliotheque Nationale BP 20, Nouakchott
*Key Personnel*
President: O Diouwara
Secretary: Sid'Ahmed Fall dit Dah

# Mauritius

**Mauritius Library Association**
c/o The British Council, Royal Rd, Rose Hill
Mailing Address: POB 111, Rose Hill
*Tel:* 4549550; 4549551; 4549552 *Fax:* 4549553
*E-mail:* ielts@mu.britishcouncil.org
*Web Site:* www.britishcouncil.org/mauritius/
*Key Personnel*
President: K Appadoo
Secretary: S Rughoo
Publication(s): *Mauritius Library Association Newsletter* (quarterly)

# Mexico

**AMBAC,** see Asociacion Mexicana de Bibliotecarios AC (AMBAC)

**Asociacion Mexicana de Bibliotecarios AC (AMBAC)**
Angel Urraza 817-A, Col Del Valle, 03100 Mexico, DF
Mailing Address: Apdo 80-065, Administracion de correos 80, 06001 Mexico, DF
*Tel:* (055) 55 75 33 96 *Fax:* (055) 55-75-11-35
*E-mail:* correo@ambac.org.mx
*Web Site:* www.ambac.org.mx
*Key Personnel*
President: Felipe Becerril Torres
*E-mail:* becerrilf@state.gov
Secretary: Elias Cid Ramirez
Publication(s): *Memorias de Jornadas*; *Noticiero* (bulletin)

**Escuela Nacional de Biblioteconomia y Archivonomia** (National School of Librarianship & Archives)
Calz Ticoman No 645, Col Santa Maria Ticoman Del Gustavo A Madero, 07330 Mexico, DF
*Tel:* (055) 5329 7176; (055) 5329 7181
*Web Site:* www.enba.sep.gob.mx

*Key Personnel*
Dir: Prof Eduardo Salas Estrada
Publication(s): *Bibliotecas y Archivos* (irregularly)

**Instituto de Investigaciones Bibliograficas**
(Institute of Bibliographic Research)
Centro Cultural Universitario, Delagacion Coyoa-
can, 04510 Mexico, DF
*Tel:* (055) 5622-6827 *Fax:* (055) 5665-0951
*Web Site:* biblional.bibliog.unam.mx
*Key Personnel*
Dir: Vicente Quirarte
Coordinator: Aurora Cano Andaluz; Judith Licea
de Arenas
Institute of Bibliographic Research.
Publication(s): *Bibliografia Mexicana*

# Myanmar

**Myanmar Library Association (MLA)**
c/o National Library, Strand Rd, Yangon
*Key Personnel*
President: U Khin Maung Tin

# Nepal

**Nepal National Library**
GPO 2773, Kathmandu
*Tel:* (01) 5521132
*E-mail:* info@nla.org.np
*Web Site:* www.nla.org.np
*Key Personnel*
Contact: Rudra Prasad Dulal
Founded: 1980
Science & technology membership.
Publication(s): *Encyclopedia of Library & Infor-
mation Science* (2nd ed, print & online)

# Netherlands

**Koninklijke Vereniging van Archivarissen in
Nederland** (Royal Association of Archivists in
the Netherlands)
Cruquisweg 31, 1019 AT Amsterdam
*Tel:* (020) 462 77 27 *Fax:* (020) 462 77 28
*E-mail:* bureau@kvan.nl
*Web Site:* www.kvan.nl
*Key Personnel*
Office Dir: Mrs Marjoke de Roos
Publication(s): *Almanak van het Nederlands
archiefwezen*; *Archievenblad*

**FOBID**, see Stichting Federatie van Organisaties
van Bibliotheek-, Informatie-,
Dokumentatiewezen (FOBID)

**IFLA**, see International Federation of Library
Associations & Institutions (IFLA)

**International Federation of Library
Associations & Institutions (IFLA)**
(Federation internationale des associations de
bibliothecaires et des bibliotheques)
PO Box 95312, 2509 CH The Hague
*Tel:* (070) 3140884 *Fax:* (070) 3834827
*E-mail:* ifla@ifla.org
*Web Site:* www.ifla.org

*Key Personnel*
Secretary General: Peter J Lor
See also under International Organizations sec-
tion.

**NBBI**, see Nederlands Bureau voor
Bibliotheekwezen en Informatieverzorging
(NBBI)

**NBLC Vereniging van Openbare Bibliotheken**
(NBLC, Netherlands Public Library
Association)
Grote Markstr 43, 1st floor, 2500 BC The Hague
Mailing Address: PO Box 16146, 2500 BC The
Hague
*Tel:* (070) 30 90 100 *Fax:* (070) 30 90 200
*E-mail:* info@debibliotheken.nl
*Web Site:* www.debibliotheken.nl
*Telex:* nblc nl
*Key Personnel*
Executive Dir: J E van der Putten
Contact: Marian Koren *Tel:* (070) 3090115
   *E-mail:* koren@nblc.nl
Founded: 1972
Membership(s): National Association of Public
Libraries; IFLA; EBLIDA.
Publication(s): *Bibliotheek Blad* (biweekly, jour-
nal)

**Nederlands Bureau voor Bibliotheekwezen en
Informatieverzorging (NBBI)**
Burg Van Karnebeeclaan 19, 2585 The Hague
Mailing Address: PO Box 80544, 2585 The
Hague
*Tel:* (070) 3607833 *Fax:* (070) 3615011
*Web Site:* www.stb.tno.nl
*Key Personnel*
Dir: Dr J DeVuyst
Contact: W Leys
Library & information science.

**Nederlandse Vereniging voor
beroepsbeoefenaren in de
bibliotheeck-informatie-en kennissector
(NVB)** (The Netherland Association of
Librarians, Documentalists & Information
Specialists)
NVB-Nieuwegracht 15, 3512 LC Utrecht
*Tel:* (030) 2311263 *Fax:* (030) 2311830
*E-mail:* nvbinfo@wxs.nl
*Web Site:* www.nvb-online.nl
*Key Personnel*
President: Dr J S M Savenije *E-mail:* b.savenije@
ubu.ruu.nl

**Stichting Federatie van Organisaties van
Bibliotheek-, Informatie-,
Dokumentatiewezen (FOBID)** (Federation of
Organizations for Libraries, Information &
Documentation)
Leidseveer 35, 3500 GG Utrecht
Mailing Address: Postbus 2290, 3500 GG Utrecht
*Tel:* (030) 234 66 00 *Fax:* (030) 233 29 60
*E-mail:* info@surf.nl
*Web Site:* www.surf.nl
*Key Personnel*
Chairman: Dr J H de Swart
Secretary: G M Van Westrienen
   *E-mail:* vanwestrienen@surf.nl
Founded: 1974
National umbrella organization for cooperation
between the national library organizations.
Publication(s): *Cataloguing Rules* (parts 1-8); *Li-
brary & Documentation Centres in the Nether-
lands*; *Library & Documentation Guide*

# Netherlands Antilles

**Antillion Library Association**
c/o Openbare Bibliotheek Curacao, Abr M Chu-
maceiro Blvd, Willemstad, Curacao
*Tel:* (09) 4345200 *Fax:* (09) 4656247
*Web Site:* www.curacaopubliclibrary.an
*Key Personnel*
Secretary: Ms Marvis Amerikaan
Publication(s): *APLA Newsletter*

# New Zealand

**IAML**, see International Association of Music
Libraries, Archives & Documentation Centres

**International Association of Music Libraries,
New Zealand Branch, Inc**
Christchurch City Libraries, Christchurch
Mailing Address: PO Box 1466, Christchurch
*Tel:* (03) 941 7923 *Fax:* (03) 941 7848
*E-mail:* library@ccc.govt.nz
*Web Site:* library.christchurch.org.nz
*Key Personnel*
President: Lisa Allcott *Tel:* (09) 524 3860
   *E-mail:* lisa.allcott@natlib.govt.nz
Secretary: Marilyn Hayr *Tel:* (09) 307 7751
   *E-mail:* hayrm@akcity.govt.nz
Treasurer: Freda Blanchard *Tel:* (09) 372 5645
   *E-mail:* f.blanchard@internet.co.nz
Publication(s): *Bibliography of Writings about
New Zealand Music Published to end of 1983*;
*Crescendo*; *Directory of New Zealand Musical
Organizations*; *Orchestral Scores* (performing
editions list); *Sing!* (choral scores Catalogue)

**International Association of Music Libraries,
Archives & Documentation Centres**
National Library of New Zealand, PO Box 1467,
Wellington
*Tel:* (04) 474 3039 *Fax:* (04) 474 3035
*Web Site:* www.iaml.info
*Key Personnel*
President: Massimo Gentili-Tedeschi
   *E-mail:* gentili@mail.cilea.it
Secretary General: Roger Flury *E-mail:* roger.
flury@natlib.govt.nz
Treasurer: Martie Severt *E-mail:* m.severt@mco.
nl
Founded: 1951
Publication(s): *Fontes Artis Musicae* (quarterly,
journal); *IAML-L Newsletter* (irregularly, elec-
tronic)

**LIANZA**, see Library & Information Association
of New Zealand Aotearoa (LIANZA)

**Library & Information Association of New
Zealand Aotearoa (LIANZA)**
Old Wool House, Level 5, 139-141 Featherston
St, Wellington 6001
Mailing Address: PO Box 12-212, Wellington
6038
*Tel:* (04) 473 5834 *Fax:* (04) 499 1480
*E-mail:* office@lianza.org.nz
*Web Site:* www.lianza.org.nz
*Key Personnel*
President: Steven Lulich
Editor & Office Assistant: Anna O'Keeffe
   *E-mail:* anna@lianza.org.nz
Founded: 1910
Professional association.

Publication(s): *DILSINZ* (Directory of Information & Library Services in New Zealand); *Library Life* (11 per year, magazine); *New Zealand Libraries* (biannually); *Public Libraries of New Zealand* (1995); *Public Library Statistics* (1999); *Valuing the Economic Costs & Benefits of Libraries* (1996); *Who's Who in New Zealand Libraries* (1990)

# Nicaragua

**Asociacion Nicaraguense de Bibliotecarios y Profesionales a Fines** (Nicaraguan Association of Librarians)
Apdo 3257, Managua
*Key Personnel*
Executive Secretary: Susana Morales Hernandez

# Nigeria

**Anambra State School Libraries Association**
c/o University of Nigeria, Enugu Campus Library, Enugu
*Tel:* (042) 252080; (042) 332091
*Web Site:* www.universityofnigeria.com *Cable:* Nigersity Enugu
*Key Personnel*
Honorary Secretary: Virginia W Dike
Publication(s): *Manual for School Libraries on Small Budgets*; *School Libraries Bulletin* (triannually)

**Nigerian Library Association**
c/o National Library Association, Sanusi Dantata House, Business Central District, Garki District, Abuja 900001
*Tel:* 8055365245 *Fax:* (09) 234-6773
*E-mail:* info@nla-ng.org
*Web Site:* www.nla-ng.org
*Telex:* 21746
*Key Personnel*
President: A O Banjo
Secretary: D D Bwayili
There are also regional associations in the various states under the umbrella of the Nigerian Library Association.
Publication(s): *Nigerian Libraries* (triannually); *NLA Newsletter*

# Norway

**Arkivarforeningen** (The Association of Archivists)
Postboks 4015, Ulleval Station, 0806 Oslo
*Tel:* 22022657 *Fax:* 22237489
*E-mail:* synne.stavheim@riksarkivaren.dep.no
*Web Site:* www.forskerforbundet.no
Publication(s): *Norsk arkivforum*

**Norsk Bibliotekforening** (Norwegian Library Association)
Malerhaugveien 20, 0661 Oslo
*Tel:* 2324 3430 *Fax:* 2267 2368
*E-mail:* nbf@norskbibliotekforening.no
*Web Site:* www.norskbibliotekforening.no
*Key Personnel*
Dir: Berit Aaker
Publication(s): *Internkontakt*

**Riksbibliotektjenesten**
Apotekergata 8, Vika, Oslo
Mailing Address: Postboks 8145 Dep, 0033 Oslo
*Tel:* 23 11 75 00 *Fax:* 23 11 75 01
*E-mail:* post@abm-utvikling.no
*Web Site:* www.abm-utvikling.no
*Key Personnel*
Acting Dir General: Kirsten Engelstad
National Office for Research & Documentation, Academic & Professional Libraries.
Publication(s): *Handbook of Research & Special Libraries* (irregularly); *Skrifter fra Riksbibliotektjenesten* (irregularly); *Synopsis* (6 times/yr)

# Pakistan

**Government of Pakistan Department of Libraries**
National Library of Pakistan, Constitution Ave, Islamabad 44000
*Tel:* (051) 9214523; (051) 92026436; (051) 9206440 *Fax:* (051) 9221375
*E-mail:* nlpiba@isb.paknet.com.pk
*Web Site:* www.nlp.gov.pk
*Key Personnel*
Dir General: Muhammad Nazir
Editor: Amjad Majeed
Publication(s): *Accessions List Pakistan* (monthly); *Pakistan National Bibliography* (annually)

**Karachi University Library Science Alumni Association**
c/o University of Karachi, Dept of Library Science, Karachi 75270
*Tel:* (021) 479001 *Fax:* (021) 473226
*E-mail:* vc@ku.edu.pk
*Web Site:* www.ku.edu.pk
*Key Personnel*
Chairperson: Dr Nasim Fatima

**Library Promotion Bureau**
Karachi University Campus, Karachi 75270
Mailing Address: PO Box 8421, Karachi 75270
*Tel:* (021) 6321959; (021) 6977737 *Fax:* (021) 6321959
*E-mail:* vc@ku.edu.pk
*Web Site:* www.ku.edu.pk
*Key Personnel*
Vice Chancellor: Dr Pirzada Qasim; Raza Siddiqui
Founded: 1965
Publication(s): *Bibliographical Services Throughout Pakistan* (2nd Edition); *Documents Procurement Service*; *Libraries of Pakistan*; *Pakistan Book Trade Directory*; *Pakistan Library Bulletin* (quarterly); *Secondary School Library Resources & Services in Pakistan*; *University Librarianship in Pakistan*; *Who's Who in Library & Information Science*

**Pakistan Library Association (PLA)**
Constitution Ave, Islamabad 44000
Mailing Address: c/o Institute of Development Economics, PO Box 1091, Islamabad 44000
*Tel:* (051) 921-4523; (051) 920-2544; (051) 920-2549 *Fax:* (051) 922-1375
*E-mail:* nlpiba@isb.paknet.com.pk
*Web Site:* www.nlp.gov.pk
*Key Personnel*
President: Sain Malik
Secretary General: Atta Ullah
Vice President, Federal Branch: Zafar Javed Naqvi *E-mail:* pide@ish.paknet.com.pk
Founded: 1957
Professional body of Library & Information Managers of Pakistan.

Publication(s): *Code of Ethics for Librarians*; *PLA Newsletter* (bimonthly, text in English); *Public Libraries Facilities in Pakistan*; *Standards of College Libraries*; *Standards of Special Libraries*; *Standards of University Libraries*

**PLA**, see Pakistan Library Association (PLA)

# Panama

**Asociacion de Bibliotecarios Graduados del Istmo de Panama**
c/o Director de la Biblioteca Bio-Medica de Laboratorio Conmemorativo Gorgas, Avda Justo Arosemena No 35-30, Apdo 6991, Panama 5
*Tel:* 2227411 *Fax:* 2254366
*Key Personnel*
President: Prof Manuel Victor De Las Casas
Secretary: Iris de Espinosa
Association of Graduate Librarians of the Isthmus of Panama (AGLIP).

**Asociacion Panamena de Bibliotecarios**
c/o Biblioteca Interamericana Simon Bolivar, Estafeta Universitaria, Panama City
*Key Personnel*
President: Bexie Rodriguez de Leon
Panama Library Association.
Publication(s): *Boletin*

# Paraguay

**Asociacion de Bibliotecarios Universitarios del Paraguay** (Paraguayan Association of University Librarians)
c/o Prof Yoshiko M de Freundorfer, Head, Escuela de Bibliotecologia, Universidad Nacional de Asuncion, Asuncion Casilla 910, 2064 Asuncion
*Tel:* (021) 507080 *Fax:* (021) 213734
*Web Site:* www.una.py
*Key Personnel*
President: Prof Gloria Ondina Ortiz C
Secretary: Celia Villamayor de Diaz

# Peru

**ADAP**, see Asociacion de Archiveros del Peru (ADAP)

**Asociacion de Archiveros del Peru (ADAP)** (Peruvian Association of Archivists)
Archivo Central Salaverry 2020 Jesus Mario, Universidad del Pacifico, 11 Lima 11
*Tel:* (01) 219-0100 *Fax:* (01) 472-9635
*E-mail:* dri@u8p.edu.pe
*Web Site:* www.up.edu.pe
*Key Personnel*
President: Jose Luis Abanto Arrelucea
1a Vocal: Yolanda Auqui Chayez
2a Vocal: Denise Ballivian Seminario

**Asociacion Peruana de Bibliotecarios (APB)**
Bellavista 561 Miraflores Apdo 995, Lima 18
*Tel:* (01) 474869
*Key Personnel*
President: Martha Fernandez de Lopez

Secretary: Luzmila Tello de Medina
Peruvian Association of Librarians.

# Philippines

ASLP, see Association of Special Libraries of the
Philippines (ASLP)

**Association of Special Libraries of the
Philippines (ASLP)**
The National Library Bldg, Room 301, T M
Kalaw St, 2801 Ermita, Manila
*Tel:* (02) 893-9590 *Fax:* (02) 893-9589
*E-mail:* vvt126_ph@yahoo.com
*Key Personnel*
President: Valentina Tolentino
Secretary: Socorro G Elevera
Publication(s): *ASLP Bulletin* (annually); *Directory of Special Library Resources & Research
Facilities in the Philippines*

**Bibliographical Society of the Philippines**
National Library of the Philippines, T M Kalaw
St, 1000 Ermita, Manila
*Tel:* (02) 583-252 *Fax:* (02) 502-329
*E-mail:* amb@nlp.gov.ph
*Web Site:* www.nlp.gov.ph
*Key Personnel*
Chief: Leonila D A Tominez *Fax:* (02) 524-1011

**Philippine Librarians Association Inc**
c/o National Library, T M Kalaw St, Room 301,
1000 Manila, Ermita
*Tel:* (02) 523-00-68
*Web Site:* www.dlsu.edu.ph/library/plai
*Key Personnel*
President: Fe Angelo Verzosa *E-mail:* libfamv@
mail.dlsu.edu.ph
Vice President: Teresita C Moran
*E-mail:* tmoran@pusit.admu.edu.ph
Secretary: Shirley L Nava
Treasurer: Mona Lisa P Leguiab
Publication(s): *PLAI Bulletin* (annually); *PLAI
Newsletter* (biannually)

# Poland

**Stowarzyszenie Bibliotekarzy Polskich** (Polish
Librarians Association)
al Niepodleglosci 213, 02-086 Warsaw
*Tel:* (022) 6082256 *Fax:* (022) 8259157
*E-mail:* biurozgsbp@wp.pl
*Web Site:* ebib.oss.wroc.pl/sbp/
*Key Personnel*
Chairman: Jan Wolosz *E-mail:* bnwolosz@bn.org.
pl
Vice Chairman: Piotr Bierczynski
*E-mail:* biercz@hiacynt.wimbp.lodz.pl; Jerzy
Krawczyk *E-mail:* jurek@bg.agh.edu.pl; Stanislaw Krzywicki *E-mail:* ksiaznica@ksiaznica.
szczecin.pl
Secretary General: Elzbieta Stefanczyk
*E-mail:* bngroma@bn.org.pl
Treasurer: Andrzej Jopkiewicz *E-mail:* k.kruk@
stat.gov.pl
Founded: 1946
Publication(s): *Bibliotekarz* (The Librarian); *Poradnik Bibliotekarza* (The Librarian's Adviser);
*Przeglad Biblioteczny* (Library Review)

# Portugal

**Associacao Portuguesa de Bibliotecarios,
Arquivistas e Documentalistas** (The
Portuguese Association of Librarians Archivists
& Documentalists)
R Morais Soares, 43C-1 DTD, 1900-341 Lisbon
Codex
*Tel:* (021) 816 19 80 *Fax:* (021) 815 45 08
*E-mail:* bad@apbad.pt; formacao@apbad.pt;
contabilidade@apbad.pt
*Web Site:* www.apbad.pt
*Key Personnel*
President: Antonio Jose de Pina Falcao
Contact: Sandrine Jercaeret
Portuguese Association of Librarians, Archivists
& Documentalists.
Publication(s): *Cadernos de Biblioteconomia, Arquivistica e Documentacao* (biannually)

# Puerto Rico

**Sociedad de Bibliotecarios de Puerto Rico**
(Society of Librarians of Puerto Rico)
PO Box 22898, San Juan 00931-2898
*Tel:* (787) 764-0000 (ext 5205) *Fax:* (787) 764-
0000 (ext 5204)
*E-mail:* vtorres@upracd.upr.clu.edu
*Web Site:* www.geocities.com/sociedadsbpr
*Key Personnel*
President: Victor Federico Torres
Secretary: Doris E Rivera Marrero
Publication(s): *Boletin, Informa* (newsletter);
*Cuadernos Bibliotecologicos, Cuadernos Bibliograficos*

# Senegal

ASBAD, see Association Senegalaise des
Bibliothecaires, Archivistes et Documentalistes
(ASBAD)

**Association Senegalaise des Bibliothecaires,
Archivistes et Documentalistes (ASBAD)**
c/o Ecole des Bibliothecaires, Archivistes et Documentalistes, Universite Cheikh Anta Diop de
Dakar, BP 3252, Dakar
*Tel:* (0221) 864 27 73 *Fax:* (0221) 824 23 79
*E-mail:* ebad@ebad.ucad.sn
*Web Site:* www.ebad.ucad.sn
*Key Personnel*
President: Ndiaye Djibril
Publication(s): *Canal-ist*

# Serbia and Montenegro

**Jugoslovenski Bibliografsko Informacijski
Institut** (Yugoslav Institute for Bibliography &
Information)
Terazije 26, 11000 Belgrade
*Tel:* (011) 687 836; (011) 687 760 *Fax:* (011) 687
760; (011) 688 840
*E-mail:* yubin@jbi.bg.ac.yu
*Web Site:* www.yu-yubin.org

*Key Personnel*
Dir: Dr Radomir Glavicki
Publication(s): *Belgrade; Bibliografija Jugoslavije*
(Bibliography of Yugoslavia, includes books,
pamphlets, music scores & articles of literary,
scientific interest, philology, art & sport); *Universal Decimal Classification, International*
(Serbocroatian version)

YUBIN, see Jugoslovenski Bibliografsko
Informacijski Institut

# Sierra Leone

**Sierra Leone Association of Archivists,
Librarians & Information Scientists
(SLAALIS)**
7 Percival St, Freetown
*Tel:* (022) 220758
*Key Personnel*
President: Deanna Thomas
Founded: 1987
Publication(s): *SLAALIS Bulletin* (quarterly)

SLAALIS, see Sierra Leone Association of
Archivists, Librarians & Information Scientists
(SLAALIS)

# Singapore

**Library Association of Singapore**
Geylang East Community Library, 50 Geylang
East Ave 1, 3rd floor, Singapore 389777
*Tel:* 6749 7990 *Fax:* 6749 7480
*Web Site:* www.las.org.sg
Publication(s): *Directory of Information
Databases in Singapore; Directory of Libraries
in Singapore; Singapore Libraries* (annually);
*Singapore Libraries Bulletin* (quarterly)

# Slovenia

ZBDS, see Zveza bibliotekarskih drustev
Slovenije (ZBDS)

**Zveza bibliotekarskih drustev Slovenije
(ZBDS)** (Union of Associations of Slovene
Librarians)
Turjaska 1, 1000 Ljubljana
*Tel:* (01) 20 01 193 *Fax:* (01) 42 57 293
*E-mail:* zveza-biblio.ds-nuk@quest.arnes.si
*Web Site:* www.zbds-zveza.si
*Key Personnel*
President: Melita Ambrozic *Tel:* (01) 20 01 207
*E-mail:* melita.ambrozic@nuk.uni-lj.si
Founded: 1947
Publication(s): *Knjiznica* (Library, quarterly,
1957)

# South Africa

LIASA, see Library & Information Association
of South Africa (LIASA)

**Library & Information Association of South Africa (LIASA)**
PO Box 1598, Pretoria 0001
*Tel:* (012) 481 2870; (012) 481 2875; (012) 481 2876 *Fax:* (012) 481 2873
*E-mail:* liasa@liasa.org.za
*Web Site:* www.liasa.org.za
*Key Personnel*
President: Robert Moropa *E-mail:* moropar@ais.up.ac.za
Deputy President: Naomi Haasbroek *E-mail:* naomi@tlabs.ac.za
Secretary: Kalien DeKlerk *E-mail:* kdeklerk@mandelametro.ac.za
Publication(s): *LIASA-IN-Touch* (quarterly, magazine); *LIASA News* (quarterly, newsletter); *South African Journal of Library & Information Science* (biannually, journal)

# Spain

**Asociacion Espanola de Archiveros, Bibliotecarios, Museologos y Documentalistas** (Spanish Association of Archivists, Librarians, Curators & Documentalists)
Recoletos 5, 28001 Madrid
*Tel:* (091) 5751727 *Fax:* (091) 5781615
*E-mail:* anabad@anabad.org
*Web Site:* www.anabad.org
*Key Personnel*
President: Julia M Rodrigez Barrero
Publication(s): *Boletin* (with bibliography section)

# Sri Lanka

**National Library & Documentation Services Board (NLDSB)**
No 14, Independence Ave, Colombo 07
Mailing Address: PO Box 1764, Colombo 07
*Tel:* (01) 698847 *Fax:* (01) 685201
*E-mail:* nldsb@mail.natlib.lk
*Web Site:* www.natlib.lk
*Key Personnel*
Dir General: Mr M S U Amarasiri *Tel:* (01) 687581 *E-mail:* dg@mail.natlib.lk
Publication(s): *Directory of Social Science Libraries, Information Centres & Databases in Sri Lanka*; *International Standard Book Numbering in Sri Lanka* (brochure); *Library News* (quarterly); *Pustakala Dave Bhanda*; *Sri Lanka (ISBN) Publishers Directory*; *Sri Lanka National Bibliography* (monthly); *Sri Lanka Newspaper Article Index-1993* (conference index)

**NLDSB**, see National Library & Documentation Services Board (NLDSB)

**Sri Lanka Library Association**
Professional Center, 275/75 Bauddhaloka Mawatha, Colombo 7
*Tel:* (011) 2589103 *Fax:* (011) 2589103
*E-mail:* slla@operamail.com
*Web Site:* www.naresa.ac.lk/slla; www.nsf.ac.lk/slla
*Key Personnel*
President: Ms Deepali Talagala
Vice President: Ms D I D Andradi
Secretary: Gayathri Amarasekera
Publication Officer: Mr J S K Weerawardane
Assistant Secretary: Ms Jayanthi Weerathunge
Education Officer: Ms R H I S Ranasinghe

Assistant Education Officer: Ms Padma Bandaranayake
Treasurer: Mr Anton D Nallathamby
Publication(s): *SLLA News Letter* (quarterly); *Sri Lanka Library Review* (biannually)

# Swaziland

**Swaziland Library Association**
PO Box 2309, Mbabane H100
*Tel:* 404-2633 *Fax:* 404-3863
*E-mail:* sdnationalarchives@realnet.co.sz
*Web Site:* www.swala.sz
*Key Personnel*
Chairperson: Mrs Nomsa Mkhwanazi *E-mail:* nomkhwa@realnet.co.sz
Secretary: Sibongile Nxumalo *E-mail:* sdnationalarchives@realnet.co.sz
Founded: 1984

# Sweden

**Svensk Biblioteksforening** (Swedish Library Association)
Saltmaetargatan 3A, 103 62 Stockholm
Mailing Address: PO Box 3127, 103 62 Stockholm
*Tel:* (08) 54513230 *Fax:* (08) 54513231
*E-mail:* info@biblioteksforeningen.org
*Web Site:* www.biblioteksforeningen.org
*Key Personnel*
Secretary General: Niclas Lindberg *Tel:* (08) 54513233 *E-mail:* ni@biblioteksforeningen.org
Editor & Chief: Marianne Steinsaphir *E-mail:* ms@bbl.sab.se
Publication(s): *Biblioteksbladet* (The Library Journal, 10 times/yr)

**Svenska Arkivsamfundet** (Swedish Society of Archivists)
c/o Landsarkivet i Lund, Anna-Christina Ulfsparre, Box 2016, 22002 Lund
*Tel:* (046) 197000 *Fax:* (046) 197070
*E-mail:* info@arkivsamfundet.org
*Web Site:* www.arkivsamfundet.org
*Key Personnel*
President: Berndt Fredriksson *E-mail:* berndt.fredriksson@foreign.ministry.se
Vice President: Carina Sjogren *E-mail:* carina.sjogren@srf.se
Secretary: Julia Aslund *E-mail:* julia.aslund@ssa.stockholm.se
Treasurer: Peter Nordstrom *E-mail:* peter.nordstrom@krigsarkivet.ra.se
Publication(s): *Arkiv, Samhaelle, Forskning* (Archives, Society, Research, biannually)

**Tekniska Litteratursaellskapet** (The Swedish Society for Technical Documentation)
Box 55580, 102 04 Stockholm
*Tel:* (08) 678 23 20 *Fax:* (08) 678 23 01
*E-mail:* kansliet@tls.se
*Web Site:* www.tls.se
*Key Personnel*
President: L Lindskog
Secretary: K Wahl
Publication(s): *Tidskrift foer Dokumentation* (quarterly)

# Switzerland

**Association des Bibliotheques et Bibliothecaires Suisses** (Association of Swiss Librarians & Libraries)
Hallerstr 58, 3012 Bern
*Tel:* (031) 3824240 *Fax:* (031) 3824648
*E-mail:* bbs@bbs.ch
*Web Site:* www.bbs.ch
*Key Personnel*
General Secretary: Rosemarie Simmen
Publication(s): *Arbido* (monthly, jointly with Swiss Association for Documentation & Swiss Association of Archivists)

**Schweizerische Vereinigung fur Dokumentation**
Schmidgasse 4, 6301 Zug
*Tel:* (041) 726 45 05 *Fax:* (041) 726 45 09
*E-mail:* svd-asd@hispeed.ch
*Web Site:* www.svd-asd.org
*Key Personnel*
President: Dr Urs Naegeli
Secretary: H Schweuk

**Verband der Bibliotheken und der Bibliothekarinnen/Bibliothekare der Schweiz (BBS)**, see Association des Bibliotheques et Bibliothecaires Suisses

**Verein Schweizerischer Archivarinnen und Archivare** (Association of Swiss Archivists)
Schweizerisches Bundesarchiv, Aarchivsor 24, 3003 Bern
*Tel:* (031) 322 89 89; (031) 322 92 85
*Web Site:* www.staluzern.ch/vsa
*Key Personnel*
President: Andreas Kellerhals *E-mail:* andreas.kellerhals@bar.admin.ch
Founded: 1922
Membership(s): ICA.
Publication(s): *Arbido*

# Taiwan, Province of China

**LAC**, see Library Association of China (LAC)

**Library Association of China (LAC)**
National Central Library, 20 Chung Shan S Rd, Taipei 100-01
*Tel:* (02) 2331-2475 *Fax:* (02) 2370-0899
*E-mail:* lac@msg.ncl.edu.tw
*Web Site:* lac.ncl.edu.tw
*Key Personnel*
President: Huang Shih-wson
Secretary General: Teresa Wang Chang
Publication(s): *Library Association of China Bulletin* (biannually); *Library Association of China Newsletter* (quarterly)

# United Republic of Tanzania

**Tanzania Library Association**
PO Box 33433, Dar Es Salaam

*Tel:* (022) 2775411
*E-mail:* tla_tanzania@yahoo.com
*Web Site:* www.tlatz.org
*Key Personnel*
Chairman: Dr Alli Mcharazo
   *E-mail:* amcharazo@hotmail.com
Secretary: Matilda Kazilwa *E-mail:* kuz.idm@
   raha.com
Treasurer: Hermenegild Haule
Editor: Sam Kasulwa
Founded: 1975
Publication(s): *Matukio* (Events, biannually);
   *Someni* (Read, journal)

# Thailand

**Thai Library Association**
1346 Akarnsongkrau Rd 5, Klongchan, Bangkapi,
   Bangkok 10240
*Tel:* (02) 734-8022; (02) 734-8023 *Fax:* (02) 734-
   8024
*Web Site:* tla.or.th
*Key Personnel*
President: Khunying Maenmas Chawalit
Executive Secretary: Mrs Vorrarat Srinamngern
Foreign Relations: Yupin Chancharoensin
   *E-mail:* yupin@car.chula.ac.th
Founded: 1954

# Togo

**Association Togolaise pour le Developpement
de la Documentation des Bibliotheques,
Archives et Musees**
c/o Bibliotheque de l'Universite du Benin, BP
   1515, Lome
*Tel:* 21 30 27 *Fax:* 21 85 95
*E-mail:* cafmicro@ub.tg
*Web Site:* www.ub.tg
*Key Personnel*
Secretary: E E Amah

**ATODBAM,** see Association Togolaise pour le
   Developpement de la Documentation des
   Bibliotheques, Archives et Musees

# Trinidad & Tobago

**Library Association of Trinidad & Tobago**
PO Box 1275, Port of Spain
*Tel:* (0868) 687 0194
*E-mail:* secretary@latt.org.tt
*Web Site:* www.latt.org.tt/cms/
*Key Personnel*
President: Lillibeth S V Ackbarali
   *E-mail:* lackbara@yahoo.com
Secretary: Sally Anne Montserin
   *E-mail:* smontserin@tatt.org.tt
Founded: 1960
Publication(s): *Blatt* (annually, Bulletin of the Li-
   brary Association of Trinidad & Tobago)

# Tunisia

**Association Tunisienne des Documentalistes,
Bibliothecaires et Archivistes**
Centre de Documentation Nationale, Rue 8004,
   Rue Sidi El Benna R P, 1000 Tunis
*Tel:* 651924
*Key Personnel*
President: Ahmed Ksibi
Tunisian Association of Record-Keepers, Librari-
   ans and Archivists.
Publication(s): *L'Enfant et la Lecture*; *RASSID*

# Turkey

**Tuerk Kueuephaneciler Dernegi** (Turkish
   Librarians' Association)
Elguen Sok-8/8, 06442 Kizilay/Ankara
*Tel:* (0312) 230 13 25 *Fax:* (0312) 232 04 53
*E-mail:* tkd-o@tr.net
*Web Site:* www.kutuphaneci.org.tr
*Key Personnel*
President: A Berberoglu
Secretary: A Kaygusuz
Publication(s): *Tuerk Kuetuiphaneciligi* (quarterly)

# Uganda

**Uganda Library Association (ULA)**
PO Box 8147, Kampala
*Tel:* (0141) 256-77-467698
*Web Site:* www.ou.edu/cas/slis/ULA/ula_index.
   htm
*Key Personnel*
Editor: Matthew Lubuulwa *E-mail:* mlubuulaw@
   yahoo.com
Founded: 1972
Discussing the usage of libraries & their informa-
   tion resources in Uganda.
Publication(s): *Uganda Information Bulletin*
   (quarterly, newsletter); *Ugandan Libraries*
   (biannually)

**ULA,** see Uganda Library Association (ULA)

# United Kingdom

**ALCL,** see Association of London Chief
   Librarians (ALCL)

**ARLIS/UK & Ireland Art Libraries Society**
18 College Rd, Bromsgrove, Worcs B60 2NE
*Tel:* (01527) 579298 *Fax:* (01527) 579298
*Web Site:* www.arlis.org.uk
*Key Personnel*
Chair: Sue Price *Tel:* (020) 7848 2887
   *E-mail:* sue.price@courtauld.ac.uk
Founded: 1969
Professional body for librarians & all concerned
   with the documentation of virtual art.
Publication(s): *ARLIS News-sheet* (6 times/yr);
   *Art Libraries Journal* (quarterly); *Directory*
   (annually)

**Aslib, The Association for Information
Management**
Holywell Centre, One Phipp St, London EC2A
   4PS
*Tel:* (020) 7613 3031 *Fax:* (020) 7613 5080
*E-mail:* aslib@aslib.com
*Web Site:* www.aslib.co.uk
*Key Personnel*
Dir: R B Bowes
Head of Publications: Sarah Blair
Publication(s): *Aslib Book Guide* (monthly); *Aslib
   Proceedings* (monthly); *Current Awareness Ab-
   stracts* (monthly); *Forthcoming International
   Scientific & Technical References* (quarterly);
   *International Journal of Electronic Library Re-
   seach* (quarterly); *IT Link* (monthly); *Journal of
   Documentation* (annually); *Managing Informa-
   tion* (monthly); *Program* (quarterly)

**The Association for Information Management,**
   see Aslib, The Association for Information
   Management

**Association of British Theological &
Philosophical Libraries**
Dr Williams's Library, 14 Gordon Sq, London
   WC1H 0AR
*Tel:* (020) 7387 3727
*Web Site:* www.newman.ac.uk/abtapl/
*Key Personnel*
Chairman: Judith Powles *E-mail:* j.powles@
   spurgeons.ac.uk
Honorary Secretary: Judith Shiel
   *E-mail:* jbshiel@fs1.li.man.ac.uk
Publication(s): *Bulletin of ABTAPL* (triannually)

**Association of London Chief Librarians
(ALCL)**
Hall Place, Bourne Rd, Bexley DA5 1PQ

**Bibliographical Society**
Institute of English Studies, Senate House, Room
   304, Malet St, London WC1E 7HU
*Tel:* (020) 7611 7244 *Fax:* (020) 7611 8703
*E-mail:* secretary@bibsoc.org.uk
*Web Site:* www.bibsoc.org.uk/bibsoc.htm
*Key Personnel*
President: John Flood
Vice President: John Barnard; Christine Ferdi-
   nard; Lotte Hellinga; Mervyn Jannetta; Elisa-
   beth Leedham-Green; David Pearson
Honorary Secretary: Meg Ford
   *E-mail:* secretary@bibsoc.org.uk
Founded: 1892
Publication(s): *The Library* (quarterly, various
   books on bibliographical subjects)

**Book Aid International**
39-41 Coldharbour Lane, Camberwell, London
   SE5 9NR
*Tel:* (020) 7733 3577 *Fax:* (020) 7978 8006
*E-mail:* info@bookaid.org
*Web Site:* www.bookaid.org
*Key Personnel*
Chairman: Tim Rix
Dir: Sara Harrity
Deputy Dir: David Membrey *E-mail:* david.
   membrey@bookaid.org
Book aid charity sending about 750,000 new &
   used books a year to partners in developing
   world countries & supporting development of
   local publishing.

**British & Irish Association of Law Librarians**
26 Myton Crescent, Warwick CV34 6QA
*Tel:* (01926) 491717 *Fax:* (01926) 491717
*E-mail:* holborn@linclib.sonnet.co.uk
*Web Site:* www.biall.org.uk
*Key Personnel*
Chairman: Susan Doe
Administrator: Susan Frost

Treasurer: Catherine Bowl
Founded: 1969
Publication(s): *The Law Librarian*

## Chartered Institute of Library & Information Professionals (CILIP)
7 Ridgmount St, London WC1E 7AE
*Tel:* (020) 7255 0500; (020) 7255 0505 (text-phone) *Fax:* (020) 7255 0501
*E-mail:* info@cilip.org.uk
*Web Site:* www.cilip.org.uk
*Key Personnel*
Chief Executive: Bob McKee
Member Services: Sue Brown
Founded: 2002
Professional body for librarians & information managers.
Publication(s): *Update* (monthly, magazine)
Imprints: Facet Publishing

**CILIP**, see Chartered Institute of Library & Information Professionals (CILIP)

## Circle of State Librarians
Home Office Library, ISU Resources, Queen Anne's Gate, Room 1004, London SW1H 9AT
*Tel:* (020) 7273 4463 *Fax:* (020) 7273 3957
*Web Site:* www.circleofstatelibrarians.co.uk
*Key Personnel*
Chairperson: Ms Maewyn Cumming *Tel:* (020) 7276 3098 *E-mail:* maewyn.cumming@e-envoy.gsi.gov.uk
Vice Chairperson: Jan Parry *Tel:* (020) 7273 3883 *Fax:* (020) 7273 3957 *E-mail:* jan.parry@homeoffice.gsi.gov.uk
Treasurer: Diane Murgatroyd *Tel:* (020) 7008 5943 *Fax:* (020) 7008 5935 *E-mail:* diane.murgatroyd@fco.gov.uk
Membership Secretary: Gillian Harrison *E-mail:* gillian.harrison2@homeoffice.gsi.gov.uk
Minutes Secretary: Lynda A Cooper *E-mail:* lynda.cooper@homeoffice.gsi.gov.uk
Editor State Librarian: Pat Bell *Tel:* (0161) 827 0243 *Fax:* (0161) 827 0491 *E-mail:* pat.bell@hmce.gsi.gov.uk
Business Manager: Peter Harvey *Tel:* (0870) 785 3621 *E-mail:* peter.harvey1@hmce.gsi.gov.uk
Publication(s): *State Librarian* (triannually)

**CSL**, see Circle of State Librarians

**Facet Publishing**, *imprint of* Chartered Institute of Library & Information Professionals (CILIP)

## Facet Publishing
Imprint of Chartered Institute of Library & Information Professionals (CILIP)
7 Ridgmount St, London WC1E 7AE
*Tel:* (020) 7255 0590 *Fax:* (020) 7255 0591
*E-mail:* info@facetpublishing.co.uk
*Web Site:* www.facetpublishing.co.uk
*Key Personnel*
Man Dir: Janet Liebster
Publisher: Helen Carley
Marketing Executive: Mark O'Loughlin *Tel:* (020) 7255 0597 *E-mail:* mark.o'loughlin@facetpublishing.co.uk
Professional body for librarians & information managers.
Publication(s): *A Directory of Libraries in the UK & Ireland*; *A Directory of Rare Books & Special Collections in the UK & Ireland*; *A Guide to World Language Dictionaries*; *The Successful LIS Professional Series*; *Walfords Guide to Reference Material* (3 vols)

## Friends of the National Libraries
Dept of Manuscripts, The British Library, 96 Euston Rd, London NW1 2DB
*Tel:* (020) 7412 7559

*Web Site:* www.bl.uk/about/cooperation/friends2.html
*Key Personnel*
Chairman: Lord Egremont
Honorary Secretary: Michael Borrie
Founded: 1931

## Impact
c/o The Library Association, 7 Ridgmount St, London WC1E 7AE
Mailing Address: Engineering Employer's Federation, Broadway House, Tothill St, London SW1H 9NQ
*Tel:* (020) 7222 7777; (020) 7636 7543 *Fax:* (020) 7222 2782; (020) 7436 7218
*Key Personnel*
President: Peter Loewenstein
Publication(s): *Adult Sequels*; *Children's Sequels*; *EU Information Sources*; *Counter Point Series*; *Cumulated Fiction Index*; *Fiction Index*; *Junior Fiction Index*; *Picture Book Index*

## International Association of Music Libraries, Archives & Documentation Centres (UK & Ireland Branch)
Edinburgh City Libraries, 9 George IV Bridge, Edinburgh EH1 1EG
*Tel:* (0131) 242 8053 *Fax:* (0131) 242 8009
*Web Site:* www.iaml-uk-irl.org
*Key Personnel*
President: Kathryn Adamson *E-mail:* k.adamson@ram.ac.uk
Treasurer: Peter Linnitt *E-mail:* peter.linnitt@bbc.co.uk
Membership Secretary: Almut Boehme *E-mail:* a.boehme@nls.uk
Publications Officer: Ann Keith *E-mail:* eak12@cam.ac.uk
General Secretary: Geoff Thomason *E-mail:* geoff.thomason@rncm.ac.uk
Founded: 1953
Publication(s): *Brio* (biannually)

## School Library Association
Unit 2, Lotmead Business Village, Lotmead Farm, Wanborough, Swindon, Wilts SN4 0UY
*Tel:* (01793) 791787 *Fax:* (01793) 791786
*E-mail:* info@sla.org.uk
*Web Site:* www.sla.org.uk
*Key Personnel*
President: Aidan Chambers
Chief Executive: Kathy Lemaire *E-mail:* kathy.lemaire@sla.org.uk
Founded: 1937
Promote the development of effective school libraries through advocacy, publishing & training.
Publication(s): *The School Librarian* (quarterly)

**SCONUL**, see Society of College, National & University Libraries (SCONUL)

## Scottish Library Association
1st floor, Bldg C, Brandon Gate, Leechlee Rd, Hamilton ML3 6AU
*Tel:* (01698) 458888 *Fax:* (01698) 283170
*E-mail:* slic@slainte.org.uk
*Web Site:* www.slainte.org.uk
*Key Personnel*
Dir: Elaine Fulton *E-mail:* e.fulton@slainte.org.uk
Publication(s): *Scottish Libraries* (bimonthly)

## SHINE-Scottish Health Information Network
c/o Margaret Forrest, Health Promotion Library Scotland, Health Education Board for Scotland, The Priory, Canaan Lane, Edinburgh EH10 4SG
*Tel:* (0131) 536 5582 *Fax:* (0131) 536 5502
*E-mail:* mdg@ednet.co.uk
*Web Site:* www.shinelib.org.uk

*Key Personnel*
Chair: Cathy Smith *Tel:* (01592) 226839 *E-mail:* catherinesmith@nhs.net
Publication(s): *Directory of Health Information Resources in Scotland*
*Branch Office(s)*
Erskine Medical Library, Hugh Robson Bldg, George Sq, Edinburgh EH8 9XE *Tel:* (031) 650-3692

## Society of Archivists
Prioryfield House, 20 Canon St, Taunton, Somerset TA1 1SW
*Tel:* (01823) 327030 *Fax:* (01823) 371719
*E-mail:* offman@archives.org.uk
*Web Site:* www.archives.org.uk
*Key Personnel*
Chairman: Peter Anderson *Tel:* (0131) 535 1406 *Fax:* (0131) 535 1430 *E-mail:* peter.anderson@nas.gov.uk
Vice Chairman: David Thomas
Executive Secretary: Patrick Cleary *Tel:* (0115) 962 6499 *Fax:* (0115) 962 6499 *E-mail:* execsec@archives.org.uk
Publication(s): *Careers Opportunities* (monthly); *Journal of the Society of Archivists* (biannually, newsletter)

## Society of College, National & University Libraries (SCONUL)
102 Euston St, London NW1 2HA
*Tel:* (020) 7387 0317 *Fax:* (020) 7383 3197
*E-mail:* info@sconul.ac.uk
*Web Site:* www.sconul.ac.uk
*Key Personnel*
Executive Secretary: A J C Bainton *E-mail:* toby.bainton@sconul.ac.uk
Founded: 1950

## The Society of County Librarians
c/o Northamptonshire Libraries & Information Service, Wellingborough, Northants NN8 1BP
*Tel:* (01933) 231971 *Fax:* (01933) 231762
*E-mail:* enquiries@c2portal.com
*Web Site:* www.connect2northamptonshire.com
*Key Personnel*
Secretary: Keith Crawshaw; Derek Jones; Treyor Knight
Aim is to further the position of public libraries across England, Northern Ireland & Wales to influence decision makers.

## Welsh Library Association
c/o Publications Office, Dept of Information & Library Studies, Llanbadarn Fawr, Aberystwyth Dyfed SY23 3AS
*Tel:* (01970) 622174 *Fax:* (01970) 622190
*E-mail:* hle@aber.ac.uk
*Web Site:* www.dil.aber.ac.uk/holi/wla/wla.htm
*Key Personnel*
President: Andrew Green *E-mail:* andrew.green@llgc.org.uk
Professional assocation.
Publication(s): *Y Ddolen* (journal); *The Festiniog Railway 1954-1994: A Bibliography*; *Mynegai-Y Cylchgrawn Efengylaidd 1948-1999*; *Newyddion* (newsletter); *Pwy yw Pwy yn Llyfrgelly-ddiaeth Cymru* (Who's Who In Welsh Librarianship); *Rhestr o Fynegeion: Gylchgronau a Phapurau Newydd Cymreig* (A List of Indexes to Welsch Periodicals & Newspapers, online); *Service Delivery Plans in Welsh Unitary Authorities for the Financial Year 1996/97 & their Relevance to Public Library Services* (1996); *The Teifi Library Project: An Investigation of the Library & Information Requirements of Mobile Library Users in South Ceredigion* (report); *Wales Unitary Public Library Authorities* (directory, 1996)

# Uruguay

**Agrupacion Bibliotecologica del Uruguay**
(Group Librarian of Uruguay)
Cerro Largo 1666, Montevideo 11200
*Tel:* (02) 400 57 40
*Key Personnel*
President: Luis Alberto Musso
Founded: 1964
Uruguayan Library & Archive Science Association.
Publication(s): *Anales del Senado del Uruguay*
(Annals of the Senate of Uruguay, 1971);
*Aportes para la historia de la bibliotecologia
en el Uruguay* (Library Proffesion story, 1969);
*Archivos del Uruguay* (Uruguay archives,
1974); *Bibliografia bibliografica y biblioteca-
cologica* (Bibliography, 1964); *Bibliografia
de Historia del Uruguay* (Bibliography His-
tory, 1977); *Bibliografia uruguaya sobre Brasil*
(Brasil Bibliography, 1973); *La Estrella del
sur-Indice* (The Southern Star, 1968); *Colo-
nizacion Canaria en la Banda Oriental del
Uruguay* (Canary of Uruguay Colonization,
1997); *El Dia - Indice General Alfabetico* (The
Day - Indice General Alfabetico); *Fernandez
Saldana, relacion de su obra bibliografica* (Fernandez Saldana Bibliography, 1989); *El Rio
de la Plata en el Archivo de Indias* (The River
Plate in Archive General of Indias, 1997); *De
Libros y lectores* (Books and Readers, 2000);
*Uruguay-Brasil y sus medallas* (Uruguay Brasil
Medals, 1976)

**Asociacion de Bibliotecologos del Uruguay**
(Uruguayan Library Association)
Eduardo V Haedo 2255, 11200 Montevideo

Mailing Address: PO Box 1315, 11000 Montev-
ideo
*Tel:* (02) 4099989 *Fax:* (02) 4099989
*E-mail:* ABU@adinet.com.uy
*Key Personnel*
President: Eduardo Correa
Founded: 1978
Professional Association.
Publication(s): *Panel de Noticias* (News Board,
monthly; free to members only)

# Venezuela

**Colegio de Bibliotecologos y Archivologos de
Venezuela**, see Venezuelan Library & Archives
Association

**Venezuelan Library & Archives Association**
Apdo 6283, Caracas
*Tel:* (0212) 5721858
*Key Personnel*
President: Elsi Jimenez de Diaz

# Viet Nam

**Hoi Thu-Vien Vietnam** (Vietnamese Library
Association)
National Library of Vietnam, 31 Trang Thi,
10000 Hanoi
*Tel:* (04) 824 8051 *Fax:* (04) 825 3357
*E-mail:* info@nlv.gov.vn

*Web Site:* www.nlv.gov.vn
Publication(s): *Thu'-Vien Tap-san* (Library Bulletin)

# Zambia

**Zambia Library Association**
PO Box 32839, 10101 Lusaka
*Key Personnel*
Chairman: Benson Njobvu
*E-mail:* bensonnjobvu@hotmail.com
Publication(s): *Zambia Library Association Jour-
nal* (quarterly); *Zambia Library Association
Newsletter*

# Zimbabwe

**Library & Information Science Society**
PO Box CY 407, Causeway, Harare
*Tel:* (04) 752311 *Fax:* (04) 720955
*Key Personnel*
Contact: Dakarai Mashava

**Zimbabwe Library Association (ZLA)**
PO Box 3133, Harare
*Tel:* (04) 692741
*Key Personnel*
Chairman: Driden Kunaka
Honorary Secretary: Albert Masheka
Publication(s): *The Zimbabwean Librarian*

**ZLA**, see Zimbabwe Library Association (ZLA)

# Library Reference Books & Journals

The publications in this section are library related and are listed alphabetically under the country of the publisher.

The type of publication appears in parentheses after the title:

(B) - Book          (J) - Journal          (P) - Periodical

For information on reference books, journals and periodicals relating to the book publishing industry see **Book Trade Reference Books & Journals**.

# Argentina

**Guia de las Bibliotecas Universitarias Argentinas** (Guide to Argentine University Libraries) (B)
Published by Centro de Documentacion Bibliotecologica, Universidad Nacional del Sur
Av Alem 1253, 8000 Bahia Blanca
*Tel:* (091) 4595111 *Fax:* (091) 4595110
*E-mail:* unsbc@criba.edu.ar
*Web Site:* bc.uns.edu.ar
*Key Personnel*
Chief Librarian: Marta Ibarlucca

**Referencias** (References) (J)
Published by AGBRA (Asociacion de Bibliotecarios Graduados de la Republica Argentina)
Tucuman 1424, 8° piso, D, 1050 Buenos Aires
*Tel:* (011) 4373 5269 *Fax:* (011) 4371 0571
*E-mail:* info@abgra.org.ar
*Web Site:* www.abgra.org.ar
*Key Personnel*
President: Ana Maria Peruchena Zimmermann
Vice President: Claudia Rodriguez
ISSN: 0328-1507

# Australia

**ABN Catalogue** (J)
Published by Australian Bibliographic Network, National Library of Australia
Canberra, ACT 2600
*Tel:* (02) 6262 1111; 800 026 372 (TTY)
   *Fax:* (02) 6257 1703
*E-mail:* www@nla.gov.au
*Web Site:* www.nla.gov.au
*Key Personnel*
Dir General: Jan Fullerton *E-mail:* jfullert@nla.gov.au
Deputy Dir Gen: David Toll
Bimonthly.

**Access** (J)
Published by Australian School Library Association Inc
PO Box 155, Zillmere, Qld 4034
*Tel:* (617) 3633-0510 *Fax:* (617) 3633-0570
*E-mail:* asla@asla.org.au
*Web Site:* www.asla.org.au
*Key Personnel*
Executive Officer: Karen Bonanno
   *E-mail:* kbonanno@bigpond.com
Editor: Margaret Butterworth *E-mail:* margaret@iinet.net.au
Quarterly.

**Australian Academic & Research Libraries** (J)
Published by Australian Library & Information Association

PO Box E441, Kingston, ACT 2604
*Tel:* (02) 6285 1877 *Fax:* (02) 6282 2249
*E-mail:* aarl@alia.org.au
*Web Site:* www.alia.org.au
*Key Personnel*
Editor: Dr Peter Clayton *Tel:* (02) 6201 5431
Quarterly.
106 AUD (Overseas air)
ISSN: 0004-8623

**Australian Libraries: the Essential Directory** (B)
Published by Auslib Press Pty Ltd
PO Box 622, Blackwood, SA 5051
*Tel:* (08) 8278 4363 *Fax:* (08) 8278 4000
*E-mail:* info@auslib.com.au
*Web Site:* www.auslib.com.au
*Key Personnel*
Executive Dir: Alan Bundy
Man Dir: Judith Bundy
Biennially.
7th: 300 pp, 70 AUD plus 8 AUD P&H
ISBN(s): 1-875145-55-9
ISSN: 1031-5187

**Australian Library Journal** (J)
Published by Australian Library & Information Association
9-11 Napier Close, Deakin, ACT 2600
Mailing Address: PO Box E441, Kingston, ACT 2604
*Tel:* (02) 6215 8222 *Fax:* (02) 6282 2249
*E-mail:* enquiry@alia.org.au
*Web Site:* www.alia.org.au/alj
*Key Personnel*
Editor: John Levett *Tel:* (03) 6292 1699
   *E-mail:* alj@alia.org.au
Academic/scholarly publication.
First published 1951.
Quarterly.
106 AUD (Overseas air)

**inCite** (P)
Published by Australian Library & Information Association
9-11 Napier Close, Deakin, ACT 2600
Mailing Address: PO Box E441, Kingston, ACT 2604
*Tel:* (02) 6285 1877 *Fax:* (02) 6282 2249
*E-mail:* incite@alia.org.au
*Web Site:* www.alia.org.au
*Key Personnel*
Editor: Emma Davis
Managing Editor: Ivan Trundle
Magazine.
First published 1980.
Monthly.
129 AUD (Overseas air)
ISSN: 0158-0876

**Orana** (J)
Published by Australian Library & Information Association
9-11 Napier Close, Deakin, ACT 2600
Mailing Address: PO Box 6335, Kingston 2604

*Tel:* (02) 6215 8222 *Fax:* (02) 6282 2249
*E-mail:* enquiry@alia.org.au
*Web Site:* www.alia.org.au
*Key Personnel*
Editor: Margaret Steinberger *E-mail:* margste@telpacific.com.au
Production Editor: Shirley Campbell
   *E-mail:* shirley.campbell@alianet.alia.org.au
Children's, youth services & school libraries journal.
Triannually.
ISSN: 0045-6705

**Our Heritage: A Directory to Archives and Manuscript Repositories in Australia** (B)
Published by Australian Society of Archivists
PO Box 77, Dickson, ACT 2602
*Toll Free Tel:* 800 622 251 *Fax:* (06) 2093931
*E-mail:* ozarch@velocitynet.com.au
*Web Site:* www.archivists.org.au
*Key Personnel*
Dir General: G E Nichols
Editor: Maggie Shapley
   *E-mail:* asajournaleditor@emailme.com.au
Provides archivists & other record keeping & information professionals with up to date material on professional issues & practice.
First published 1955.
Biannually.
ISSN: 0157-6895

**La Trobe Journal** (P)
Published by State Library of Victoria
328 Swanston St, Melbourne, Victoria 3000
*Tel:* (03) 8664 7000; (03) 9639 7006 (TTY)
   *Fax:* (03) 9639-4737
*E-mail:* webinfo@slv.vic.gov.au
*Web Site:* www.slv.vic.gov.au
*Key Personnel*
Editor: Prof John Barnes *E-mail:* r.j.barnes@latrobe.edu.au
First published 1968.
Biannually.
ISSN: 1441-3760

# Austria

**Biblos** (J)
Published by Boehlau Verlag GmbH & Co KG
Wiesingerstr 1, 1010 Vienna
Mailing Address: Postfach 87, 1201 Vienna
*Tel:* (01) 330 24 27 *Fax:* (01) 330 24 32
*E-mail:* boehlau@boehlau.at
*Web Site:* www.boehlau.at
*Key Personnel*
Man Dir: Dr Peter Rauch *E-mail:* peter.rauch@boehlau.at
Austrian journal for book & library personnel, documentation, bibliography & bibliophily; published in English & German.

First published 1952.
Biannually.

**Scrinium** (J)
Published by Verband Oesterreichischer Archivare
(Association of Austrian Archivists)
Postfach 164, 1014 Vienna
*Tel:* (01) 79540450 *Fax:* (01) 79540109
*Key Personnel*
Editor: Rainer Egger
Text in German.
First published 1969.
Biannually.
ISSN: 1012-0327

**Vereinigung Oesterreichischer
Bibliothekarinnen und Bibliothekare
Mitteilungen** (Bulletin of the Association of
Austrian Librarians) (J)
Published by Vereinigung Oesterreichischer Bib-
liothekarinnen und Bibliothekare (VOEB) (As-
sociation of Austrian Librarians)
Fluherstr 4, 6900 Bregenz
*Tel:* (042) 771-5011 *Fax:* (0512) 507-2893
*E-mail:* voeb@uibk.ac.at
*Web Site:* www.uibk.ac.at/sci-org/voeb/vm
*Key Personnel*
Contact: Renate Klepp *E-mail:* renate.klepp@
univie.ac.at
Text in German.
First published 1948.
Quarterly.
40 EUR
ISSN: 1022-2588

# Bangladesh

**Eastern Librarian** (J)
Published by The Library Association of
Bangladesh (LAB)
c/o Institute of Library & Information Science,
Bangladesh Central Public Library Bldg, Shah-
bagh, Dhaka 1000
*Tel:* (02) 504269
*Key Personnel*
Editor: M Shamsul Islam Khan *E-mail:* msik@
icddrb.org
Research articles, case studies & short reports on
library & information science & documenta-
tion. Text in English.
First published 1966.
Biannually.
30 USD
ISSN: 1021-3651

# Belgium

**Archives et Bibliotheques de Belgique** (Library
Archives of Belgium) (J)
Published by Archives et Bibliotheques de Bel-
gique a s b l
Blvd de l'Empereur 4, 1000 Brussels
*Tel:* (02) 5195393 *Fax:* (02) 5195533
*Key Personnel*
Chairman & Rights & Permissions: Frank Daele-
mans *E-mail:* frank.daelemans@klr.be
Text in Dutch, English, French, German, Italian,
Latin & Spanish.
First published 1923.
Annually.
30 USD
ISSN: 0003-9748

**Bibliotheek- & archiefgids** (Library & Archive
Guide) (J)
Published by Vlaamse Vereniging voor
Bibliotheek- Archief-en Documentatiewezen
(VVBAD) (Flemish Association for Libraries,
Archives & Documentation Centres)
Statiestr 179, 2600 Antwerp
*Tel:* (03) 2814457 *Fax:* (03) 2188077
*Web Site:* www.vvbad.be
*Key Personnel*
Editor: Peter Van den Broeck
Editorial Secretary: Marijke Hoflack
*E-mail:* marijke.hoflack@vvbad.be
First published 1922.
Bimonthly.
48 pp
ISSN: 0772-7003

**Les Cahiers de la Documentation** (J)
Published by Association Belgium de Documenta-
tion (Belgian Association for Documentation)
Chaussee de Wavre 1683, 1160 Brussels
*Tel:* (02) 675 58 62 *Fax:* (02) 672 74 46
*E-mail:* info@abd-bvd.be
*Web Site:* www.abd-bvd.be
*Key Personnel*
Contact: Mrs Simone Jerome
Text in Dutch, English & French.
First published 1947.
Quarterly.
49.58 EUR per year
ISSN: 0007-9804

# Bosnia and Herzegovina

**Bibliotekarstvo** (Librarianship) (J)
Published by Drustvo Bibliotekara Bosne i Herce-
govine (National & University Library of
Bosnia & Herzegovina)
Zmaja od Bosne 8b, 71000 Sarajevo
*Tel:* 33 218 431 *Fax:* 33 218 431
*E-mail:* nubbih@nub.ba
*Web Site:* www.nub.ba
*Key Personnel*
President: Nevenka Hajdarovic *E-mail:* nevenka@
nub.ba
Dir: Dr Enes Kujundzic *E-mail:* bedita@nub.ba
First published 1956.
ISSN: 0006-1832

# Brazil

**Ciencia da Informacao** (Information Science) (J)
Published by Instituto Brasileiro de Informacao
em Ciencia e Tecnologia
SAS Qd 5, Lote 6, Bloco H - 5° andar, 70070-
914 Brasilia-DF
*Tel:* (061) 217-6360; (061) 217-6350 *Fax:* (061)
226-2677
*E-mail:* webmaster@ibict.br
*Web Site:* www.ibict.br; www.ibict.br/cionline/
inicio.htm
*Key Personnel*
Dir: Nilson Lemos Lage *E-mail:* lage@ibict.br
Triannually.

# Bulgaria

**Biblioteca Journal** (The Library Journal) (J)
Published by St Cyril & St Methodius National
Library
88 Vasil Levski Blvd, 1037 Sofia
*Web Site:* www.nationallibrary.bg/press.html
*Key Personnel*
Editor-in-Chief: Dr Alexandra Dipchikova
*Tel:* (02) 988 28 11 (ext 206)
*E-mail:* dipchikova@nationallibrary.bg
First published 1954.
Bimonthly.
12 BGN (domestic); 48 USD (foreign)
ISSN: 0861-847X

# China

**Library & Information Service** (J)
Published by Library of Chinese Academy of Sci-
ences
33 Beisihuan xilu, Zhongguancum, Beijing
100080
*Tel:* (010) 8262-6611 *Fax:* (010) 8262-5255
*E-mail:* journal@mail.las.ac.cn; menggj@mail.las.
ac.cn
*Web Site:* www.las.ac.cn
*Key Personnel*
Dir: Zhang Xiaolin
Monthly.
96 pp, $142

# Colombia

**ASCOLBI Revista** (J)
Published by Asociacion Colombiana de Bibliote-
cologos y Documentalistas
Calle 10 No 3-16, Apdo 30883, Bogota
*Tel:* (01) 3603077 (ext 326) *Fax:* (01) 3600885
*E-mail:* lbecerra@panamerica.com.co
Text in Spanish.
Quarterly.
ISSN: 0121-0203

**Boletin Cultural y Bibliografico** (Cultural &
Bibliographical Bulletin) (J)
Published by Biblioteca Luis Angel Arango
Banco de la Republica (Luis Angel Arango
Library-Central Bank of Colombia)
Calle 11 No 4-14, Bogota 12362
*Tel:* (01) 3431202; (01) 2827840 *Fax:* (01)
2863551
*E-mail:* wbiblio@banrep.gov.co
*Web Site:* www.banrep.gov.co/blaa
*Key Personnel*
Contact: Romero E Astrid
Quarterly.

# Croatia

**Vjesnik bibliotekara Hrvatske** (Croatian
Librarians' Report) (J)
Published by Hrvatsko knjiznicarsko drustvo
(Croatian Library Association)
c/o Nacionalna i sveucilisna knjiznica, Hrvatske
bratske zajednice 4, 10 000 Zagreb
*Tel:* (01) 615 93 20 *Fax:* (01) 616 41 86
*E-mail:* hkd@nsk.hr

*Web Site:* jagor.srce.hr/hkd; www.hkdrustvo.hr
*Key Personnel*
President: Dubravka Stancin-Rosic *Tel:* (01) 616 40 37
Editor-in-Chief: Tinka Katic *E-mail:* tkatic@nsk. hr
Text in Croatian, English, German; summaries in Croatian & English. Back issues available. Cumulative index every 5 years.
First published 1950.
Quarterly.
200 pp, 300 HRK or 50 USD
ISSN: 0507-1925

# Cuba

**Biblioteca Nacional Jose Marti Revista** (Jose Marti National Library Review) (J)
Published by Biblioteca Nacional Jose Marti
Independence Ave y 20 de Mayo, Plaza de la Revolucion, Havana City 10600
*Tel:* (537) 555442 *Fax:* (537) 816224; (537) 335938
*E-mail:* publiweb@bnjm.cu
*Web Site:* www.bnjm.cu
*Telex:* 511963
*Key Personnel*
Dir: Eliades Acosta Matos
Editor: Julio Le Riverend
Text in Spanish.
First published 1909.
Triannually.
15 USD
ISSN: 0006-1727

# Denmark

**Bibliotekspressen** (The Library Press) (J)
Published by Bibliotekarforbundet
Lindevangs Alle 2, 2000 Frederiksberg
*Tel:* 38 88 22 33 *Fax:* 38 88 32 01
*E-mail:* bibliotekspressen@bf.dk
*Web Site:* www.bibliotekspressen.dk
*Key Personnel*
Editor: Per Nyeng *E-mail:* pn@bf.dk; Hanne Folmer Schade *E-mail:* hfs@bf.dk
ISSN: 1395-0401

**Biblioteksvejviser** (Guide to Danish Libraries) (B)
Published by Danmarks Biblioteksforening (Danish Library Association)
Vesterbrogade 20, 5 sal, 1620 Copenhagen V
*Tel:* 33 25 09 35 *Fax:* 33 25 79 00
*E-mail:* dbf@dbf.dk
*Web Site:* www.dbf.dk
*Key Personnel*
Dir: Winnie Vitzansky *Tel:* 33 26 0072
   *E-mail:* wv@dbf.dk
Editor: Hanne Klemmed *E-mail:* hk@dbf.dk
Text in Danish; index in English.
First published 1970.
Annually.
385 DKK per year
ISSN: 0420-1108

**Bogens Verden** (Book Magazine) (J)
Published by Danmarks Biblioteksforening (Danish Library Association)
Vesterbrogade 20, 5 sal, 1620 Copenhagen V
*Tel:* 33 25 09 35 *Fax:* 33 25 79 00
*E-mail:* dbf@dbf.dk
*Web Site:* www.dbf.dk

*Key Personnel*
Dir: Winnie Vitzansky *Tel:* 33 26 0072
   *E-mail:* wv@dbf.dk
Editor: Bruno Svindborg
Magazine for Danish & foreign literature & culture.
First published 1918.
6 times/yr.
ISSN: 0006-5692

**Danmarks Biblioteker** (J)
Published by Danmarks Biblioteksforening (Danish Library Association)
Vesterbrogade 20, 5 sal, 1620 Copenhagen V
*Tel:* 33 25 09 35 *Fax:* 33 25 79 00
*E-mail:* dbf@dbf.dk
*Web Site:* www.dbf.dk
*Key Personnel*
Dir: Winnie Vitzansky *Tel:* 33 26 0072
   *E-mail:* wv@dbf.dk
Newsletter from the Danish Library Association.
First published 1987.
10 times/yr.
ISSN: 1397-1026

**DF-Revy** (J)
Published by Danmarks Forskningsbiblioteks-forening
Handelshojskolens Bibliotek, Fuglesangs Alle 4, 8210 Aarhus V
*Tel:* 89 48 65 23 *Fax:* 86 15 96 27
*E-mail:* nap@asb.dk
*Web Site:* www.dfdf.dk/dfrevy.shtml
*Key Personnel*
President: Erland Kolding Nielsen
Editor: Naja Porsild *E-mail:* nap@asb.dk

**Over Broen - Library Student's Journal** (J)
Published by Danmarks Biblioteksskole/Royal School of Library & Information Science
Birketinget 6, 2300 Copenhagen S
*Tel:* 32 58 60 66 *Fax:* 32 84 02 01
*E-mail:* db@db.dk; dbilaan@db.dk
*Web Site:* www.db.dk
*Key Personnel*
Librarian: Ivar A L Hoel *E-mail:* ialh@db.dk
ISSN: 0904-3853

**Skolebiblioteksaarbog** (School Libraries Annual) (B)
Published by Danmarks Skolebiblioteksforening
Vesterbrogade 20, 5 sal, 1620 Copenhagen V
*Tel:* 33 25 09 35 *Fax:* 33 25 79 00
*E-mail:* dbf@dbf.dk
*Web Site:* www.dbf.dk
First published 1969.
ISSN: 0900-9582

# Ethiopia

**Bulletin** (J)
Published by Ethiopian Library & Information Association
PO Box 30530, Addis Ababa
*Tel:* (01) 511344
*Key Personnel*
Editor: Kebreab W Giorgis
First published 1969.
Biannually.
ISSN: 0014-1747

**Bulletin** (J)
Published by Ethiopian Manuscript Microfilm Library
PO Box 30274, Addis Ababa
*Tel:* (01) 110844

First published 1974.
Quarterly.

# Fiji

**Journal** (P)
Published by Fiji Library Association (FLA)
Government Buildings, PO Box 2292, Suva
*Tel:* 304144 *Fax:* 304144
*Telex:* FJ2276 *Cable:* UNIVERSITY SUVA
First published 1979.
Biannually (June & Dec).
7 FJD per issue
ISSN: 1016-9989

# Finland

**Kirjastolehti** (Bulletin) (J)
Published by Suomen Kirjastoseura (Finnish Library Association)
Vuorikatu 22 A18, 00100 Helsinki
*Tel:* (09) 6221 340 *Fax:* (09) 6221 466
*E-mail:* fla@fla.fi
*Web Site:* www.fla.fi/kirjastolehti
*Key Personnel*
President: Tarja Cronberg
First published 1908.
8 times/yr.
40 pp
ISSN: 0023-1843

**Signum** (J)
Published by Suomen Tieteellinen Kirjastoseura (Finnish Research Library Association)
Library of Parliament, Aurorankatu 6, 00102 Helsinki
*Tel:* (050) 466 0778 *Fax:* (09) 432 3495
*Web Site:* www.pro.tsv.fi/stks
*Key Personnel*
Editor: Paivikki Karhula *E-mail:* paivikki. karhula@eduskunta.fi
First published 1968.
8 times/yr.

# France

**Documentaliste - Sciences de l'Information** (Documentalist - Information Sciences) (J)
Published by L'Association des Professionnels de l'Information et de la Documentation (ADBS) (French Association of Information & Documentation Professionals)
25 rue Claude Tillier, 75012 Paris
*Tel:* (01) 43 72 25 25 *Fax:* (01) 43 72 30 41
*E-mail:* adbs@adbs.fr
*Web Site:* www.adbs.fr
*Key Personnel*
President: Florence Wilhelm
Director of the Review: Jean-Claude Le Moal
Editor: Jean Michel Rauzier *E-mail:* jean-michel. rauzier@adbs.fr
General Manager: David Cayre
French review devoted to techniques, professions, services & policies in the information & library fields & to research in information sciences, with particular focus on European & French-speaking countries. Abstracts in English.
First published 1964.
5 times/yr.
80 pp
ISSN: 0395-3858

**INTER BCD** (J)
Published by Centre d'Etude de la Documentation
　et de l'Information Scolaires
16, rue des Belles-Croix, 91150 Etampes
*Tel:* (01) 64 94 39 51 *Fax:* (01) 64 94 49 35
*E-mail:* redaction-intercdi@wanadoo.fr
*Web Site:* www.ac-versailles.fr/cedis
*Key Personnel*
Publisher: Michel Mouillet
Editor: Marie Noelle Michaut
Journal for specialist librarians.
Biannually.
ISSN: 1270-1467

**INTER CDI** (J)
Published by Centre d'Etude de la Documentation
　et de l'Information Scolaires
16, rue des Belles-Croix, 91150 Etampes
*Tel:* (01) 64 94 39 51 *Fax:* (01) 64 94 49 35
*E-mail:* redaction-intercdi@wanadoo.fr
*Web Site:* www.ac-versailles.fr/cedis
*Key Personnel*
Publisher: Michel Mouillet
Journal for Specialist Librarians (second level).
First published 1972.
Bimonthly.
108 pp
ISSN: 0242-2999

# Germany

**Beitraege zum Buch-und Bibliothekswesen** (B)
Published by Harrassowitz Verlag
Kreuzberger Ring 7b-d, 65205 Wiesbaden
*Tel:* (0611) 530-0 *Fax:* (0611) 530999
*E-mail:* verlag@harrassowitz.de; service@
　harrassowitz.de
*Web Site:* www.harrassowitz.de
*Key Personnel*
Editor: Michael Knoche
Rights & Permissions: Michael Langfeld
　*E-mail:* mlangfeld@harrassowitz.de
This book series deals with, among other things,
　library science, bibliographies & the history of
　books, libraries & publishing houses.
First published 1965.
Irregularly.
ISSN: 0408-8107

**Bibliothek und Wissenschaft** (Libraries &
　Science) (J)
Published by Harrassowitz Verlag
Kreuzberger Ring 7b-d, 65205 Wiesbaden
*Tel:* (0611) 530-0 *Fax:* (0611) 530999
*E-mail:* verlag@harrassowitz.de; service@
　harrassowitz.de
*Web Site:* www.harrassowitz.de
*Key Personnel*
Publicity Dir: Robert Gietz *Tel:* (0611) 530-551
　*E-mail:* rgietz@harrassowitz.de
History of books, libraries & science.
First published 1964.
Annually.
99 EUR or 168 CHF per vol
ISSN: 0067-8236

**Buchprofile** (J)
Published by Borromausverein eV
Wittelsbacherring 9, 53115 Bonn
*Tel:* (0228) 7258-0 *Fax:* (0228) 7258-189
*E-mail:* lektorat@borro.de
*Web Site:* www.buchprofile.de
*Key Personnel*
Dir:　Rolf Pitsch
Editor: Herbert Stangl
Book profile for Catholic library work.

**Buchwissenschaftliche Beitraege aus dem
　Deutschen Bucharchiv Muenchen** (Articles of
　the German Archives in Munich) (B)
Published by Harrassowitz Verlag
Kreuzberger Ring 7b-d, 65205 Wiesbaden
*Tel:* (0611) 530-0 *Fax:* (0611) 530999
*E-mail:* verlag@harrassowitz.de; service@
　harrassowitz.de
*Web Site:* www.harrassowitz.de
*Key Personnel*
Rights & Permissions: Robert Gietz
Editor: Ludwig Delp; Ursula Neumann
This book series deals, among other things, with
　the history of books, libraries, literature & pub-
　lishing houses.
First published 1950.
Irregularly.
ISSN: 0724-7001

**Erwerbung in Deutschen Bibliotheken**
　(Acquisitions Departments of German
　Libraries) (J)
Published by Harrassowitz Verlag
Kreuzberger Ring 7b-d, 65205 Wiesbaden
*Tel:* (0611) 530-0 *Fax:* (0611) 530999
*E-mail:* verlag@harrassowitz.de; service@
　harrassowitz.de
*Web Site:* www.harrassowitz.de
*Key Personnel*
Rights & Permissions: Robert Gietz
First published 1994.
Biennially.
20 EUR or 35.20 CHF per year
ISSN: 1434-792X

**Geschichte des Buchhandels** (History of the
　Book Trade) (B)
Published by Harrassowitz Verlag
Kreuzberger Ring 7b-d, 65205 Wiesbaden
*Tel:* (0611) 530-0 *Fax:* (0611) 530999
*E-mail:* verlag@harrassowitz.de; service@
　harrassowitz.de
*Web Site:* www.harrassowitz.de
*Key Personnel*
Rights & Permissions: Robert Gietz
The series deals with the history of the interna-
　tional booktrade. Presently the following vol-
　umes are available Germany, Netherlands, Hun-
　gary, Norway, Russia & Soviet Union.
First published 1975.
Irregularly.
ISSN: 0941-7877

**Gesellschaft fuer das Buch** (Society for the
　Book) (J)
Published by Harrassowitz Verlag
Kreuzberger Ring 7b-d, 65205 Wiesbaden
*Tel:* (0611) 530-0 *Fax:* (0611) 530999
*E-mail:* verlag@harrassowitz.de; service@
　harrassowitz.de
*Web Site:* www.harrassowitz.de
*Key Personnel*
Rights & Permissions: Robert Gietz
First published 1995.
Irregularly.
ISSN: 0948-5007

**Handbuch der Bibliotheken** (Directory of
　Libraries) (B)
Published by K G Saur Verlag GmbH, A Gale/
　Thomson Learning Company
Unit of Thomson Learning
Ortlerstr 8, 81373 Munich
Mailing Address: Postfach 70 16 20, 81316 Mu-
　nich
*Tel:* (089) 76902-0 *Fax:* (089) 76902-150
*E-mail:* saur.info@thomson.com
*Web Site:* www.saur.de
*Telex:* 5212067
*Key Personnel*
Man Dir: Gregor D Dalrymple; Christoph Hahne

Bundesrepublik Deutschland, Oesterreich,
　Schweiz, Germany, Austria, Switzerland.
*Parent Company:* Gale
*Ultimate Parent Company:* The Thomson Corpo-
　ration

**IFLA Journal** (J)
Published by K G Saur Verlag GmbH, A Gale/
　Thomson Learning Company
Unit of Thomson Learning
Ortlerstr 8, 81373 Munich
Mailing Address: Postfach 70 16 20, 81316 Mu-
　nich
*Tel:* (089) 76902-0 *Fax:* (089) 76902-150
*E-mail:* saur.info@thomson.com
*Web Site:* www.saur.de
*Telex:* 5212067
*Key Personnel*
Man Dir: Gregor D Dalrymple; Christoph Hahne
*Parent Company:* Gale
*Ultimate Parent Company:* The Thomson Corpo-
　ration

**IFLA Publications** (B)
Published by K G Saur Verlag GmbH, A Gale/
　Thomson Learning Company
Unit of Thomson Learning
Ortlerstr 8, 81373 Munich
Mailing Address: Postfach 70 16 20, 81316 Mu-
　nich
*Tel:* (089) 76902-0 *Fax:* (089) 76902-150
*E-mail:* saur.info@thomson.com
*Web Site:* www.saur.de
*Telex:* 5212067
*Key Personnel*
Man Dir: Gregor D Dalrymple; Christoph Hahne
A series of publications related to the Interna-
　tional Federation of Library Associations &
　Institutions.
*Parent Company:* Gale
*Ultimate Parent Company:* The Thomson Corpo-
　ration

**Jahrbuch der Deutschen Bibliotheken**
　(Yearbook of German Libraries) (B)
Published by Harrassowitz Verlag
Kreuzberger Ring 7b-d, 65205 Wiesbaden
*Tel:* (0611) 530-0 *Fax:* (0611) 530999
*E-mail:* verlag@harrassowitz.de; service@
　harrassowitz.de
*Web Site:* www.harrassowitz.de
Information about German Scientific Libraries.
First published 1902.
Biennially.
79 EUR
ISSN: 0075-2223

**Leipziger Jahrbuch zur Buchgeschichte** (J)
Published by Harrassowitz Verlag
Kreuzberger Ring 7b-d, 65205 Wiesbaden
*Tel:* (0611) 530-0 *Fax:* (0611) 530999
*E-mail:* verlag@harrassowitz.de; service@
　harrassowitz.de
*Web Site:* www.harrassowitz.de
*Key Personnel*
Editor: Thomas Keiderling; Lothar Poethe; Volker
　Titel
History of books, the booktrade, publishers &
　printers.
First published 1991.
Annually.
59 EUR
ISSN: 0940-1954

**Librarianship and Information Work
　Worldwide** (B)
Published by K G Saur Verlag GmbH, A Gale/
　Thomson Learning Company
Unit of Thomson Learning
Ortlerstr 8, 81373 Munich
Mailing Address: Postfach 70 16 20, 81316 Mu-
　nich
*Tel:* (089) 76902-0 *Fax:* (089) 76902-150

*E-mail:* saur.info@thomson.com
*Web Site:* www.saur.de
*Parent Company:* Gale
*Ultimate Parent Company:* The Thomson Corporation

**Marginalien Zeitschrift fuer Buchkunst und Bibliophilie** (Marginal Notes - Journal for Book Art & Bibliophilic) (J)
Published by Harrassowitz Verlag
Kreuzberger Ring 7b-d, 65205 Wiesbaden
*Tel:* (0611) 530-0 *Fax:* (0611) 530999
*E-mail:* verlag@harrassowitz.de; service@harrassowitz.de
*Web Site:* www.harrassowitz.de
First published 1948.
Quarterly.
69 EUR
ISSN: 0025-2948

**Schulbibliothek aktuell** (School Library Today) (J)
Published by Deutsches Bibliotheksinstitut (German Library Institute)
Kurt-Schumacher-Damm 12-16, 13405 Berlin
*Tel:* (030) 410 34-0 *Fax:* (030) 410 34-100
*E-mail:* publikationen@dbi-berlin.de
*Web Site:* www.dbi-berlin.de
*Key Personnel*
Dir: Prof Gunter Beyersdorff
First published 1975.
Quarterly.
ISSN: 0341-471X

**Wolfenbuetteler Schriften zur Geschichte des Buchwesens** (J)
Published by Harrassowitz Verlag
Kreuzberger Ring 7b-d, 65205 Wiesbaden
*Tel:* (0611) 530-0 *Fax:* (0611) 530999
*E-mail:* verlag@harrassowitz.de; service@harrassowitz.de
*Web Site:* www.harrassowitz.de
*Key Personnel*
Rights & Permissions: Robert Gietz
This journal series deals with the history of books, libraries & publishing houses. Published in cooperation with Herzog August Bibliothek.
First published 1977.
Irregularly.
ISSN: 0724-9586

**World Guide to Libraries** (B)
Published by K G Saur Verlag GmbH, A Gale/Thomson Learning Company
Ortlerstr 8, 81373 Munich
Mailing Address: Postfach 70 16 20, 81316 Munich
*Tel:* (089) 76902-0 *Fax:* (089) 76902-150
*E-mail:* saur.info@thomson.com
*Web Site:* www.saur.de
*Telex:* 5212067
Furnishes details on 47,000 libraries in 167 countries. Covers national, general research, university, school, government, corporate, ecclesiastical, special & public libraries with over 30,000 volumes. Alphabetical index.
1,200 pp
ISBN(s): 3-598-20725-5
*Parent Company:* Gale
*Ultimate Parent Company:* The Thomson Corporation
*U.S. Office(s):* Thomson Learning

**World Guide to Special Libraries** (B)
Published by K G Saur Verlag GmbH, A Gale/Thomson Learning Company
Unit of Thomson Learning
Ortlerstr 8, 81373 Munich
Mailing Address: Postfach 70 16 20, 81316 Munich
*Tel:* (089) 76902-0 *Fax:* (089) 76902-150

*E-mail:* saur.info@thomson.com
*Web Site:* www.saur.de
*Telex:* 5212067
*Parent Company:* Gale
*Ultimate Parent Company:* The Thomson Corporation

**Zeitschrift fuer Bibliothekswesen und Bibliographie** (Journal of Library Science & Bibliography) (J)
Published by Vittorio Klostermann GmbH
Frauenlobstr 22, 60487 Frankfurt am Main
Mailing Address: Postfach 90 06 01, 60446 Frankfurt am Main
*Tel:* (069) 97 08 16-0 *Fax:* (069) 70 80 38
*E-mail:* verlag@klostermann.de
*Web Site:* www.klostermann.de
*Key Personnel*
Editor: Dr Elisabeth Niggemann
Publisher: Vittorio E Klostermann *Tel:* (069) 97 08 16-0 (ext 11) *E-mail:* vek@klostermann.de
Marketing: Martin Warny *Tel:* (069) 97 08 16-12 *E-mail:* m.warny@klostermann.de
6 times/yr.
ISSN: 0044-2380

# Ghana

**Directory of Research & Special Libraries in Ghana** (B)
Published by Council for Scientific & Industrial Research
PO Box M32, Accra
*Tel:* (021) 778808; (021) 780708; (021) 780709 *Fax:* (021) 777655
*E-mail:* cemensah@hotmail.com
*Web Site:* www.csir.org.gh
*Key Personnel*
Acting Dir General: Prof E Owusu Benoah

# Guyana

**Bulletin** (J)
Published by Guyana Library Association
c/o National Library, 76-77 Church & Main Sts, Georgetown
*Tel:* (02) 227-4053; (02) 227-4052; (02) 226-2690; (0226) 2699 *Fax:* (02) 227-4053
*E-mail:* natlib@sdnp.org.gy
*Web Site:* www.natlib.gov.gy
*Key Personnel*
Editor: Wenda Stevenson
First published 1970.
Biannually.
ISSN: 1023-3385

# Hungary

**Hungarian Library & Information Science Abstracts** (J)
Published by Orszagos Szechenyi Konyvtar (National Szechenyi Library)
Budavari Palota F Bldg, Room 801, 1827 Budapest
*Tel:* (01) 224-3700; (01) 224-3845 (reference); (01) 224-3848 (reference) *Fax:* (01) 202-0804
*E-mail:* racz@oszk.hu; fazokas@oszk.hu
*Web Site:* www.oszk.hu
*Telex:* 224226 bibln h

*Key Personnel*
Editor: Laszlo Nagypal *E-mail:* lnagypal@oszk.hu
Text in English.
First published 1972.
Biannually.
17 EUR
ISSN: 0046-8304

**Koenyvtartoerteneti Fuezetek** (History of Libraries series) (J)
Published by Jozsef Attila Tudomanyegyetem Egyetemi Koenyvtar
6720 Szeged, Dugonics Sq 13, 6720 Szeged
Mailing Address: PO Box 393, 6701 Szeged
*Tel:* (062) 544036 *Fax:* (062) 544035
*E-mail:* mader@bibl.u-szeged.hu
*Web Site:* www.bibl.u-szeged.hu

**Konyvtari Figyelo Uj folyam** (Library Review) (J)
Published by Orszagos Szechenyi Konyvtar (National Szechenyi Library)
Buda Royal Palace Wing F, 1827 Budapest
*Tel:* (01) 224-3788 *Fax:* (01) 202-0804
*E-mail:* racz@oszk.hu; fazokas@oszk.hu
*Web Site:* www.oszk.hu
*Telex:* 224226 bibln h
*Key Personnel*
Editor-in-Chief: Dr Peter Dippold *E-mail:* dippold@oszk.hu
Text in Hungarian; summaries in English & German.
First published 1955.
Quarterly.
51 EUR
ISSN: 0023-3773

**Magyar Konyvtari Szakirodalom Bibliografiaja** (Bibliography on Hungarian Library Literature) (J)
Published by Orszagos Szechenyi Konyvtar (National Szechenyi Library)
Budavari Palota F Bldg, Room 801, 1827 Budapest
*Tel:* (01) 224-3793 *Fax:* (01) 375-9984
*E-mail:* racz@oszk.hu; fazokas@oszk.hu
*Web Site:* www.oszk.hu
*Telex:* 224226 bibln h
*Key Personnel*
Editor: Ferencne Javori *E-mail:* javori@oszk.hu
Text in Hungarian.
First published 1965.
Quarterly.
ISSN: 0133-736X

# Iceland

**Bokasafnid**
Published by Upplysing - Felag bokasafns- og upplysingafraeoa (Information - the Icelandic Library & Information Science Association)
Lagmuli 7, 108 Reykjavik
Mailing Address: Borgarbokasafn Reykjavikur, Tryggvagoetu 15, 101 Reykjavik
*Tel:* 553-7290; 862-8627 *Fax:* 588-9239
*E-mail:* upplysing@bokis.is
*Web Site:* www.bokasafnid.is
*Key Personnel*
President: H A Hardarson
Yearbook of library & information science.
Annually.
ISSN: 1670-0066

**Fregnir** (J)
Published by Upplysing - Felag bokasafns- og upplysingafraeoa (Information - the Icelandic Library & Information Science Association)

Lagmuli 7, 108 Reykjavik
*Tel:* 553-7290; 862-8627 *Fax:* 588-9239
*E-mail:* upplysing@bokis.is
*Web Site:* www.bokis.is
*Key Personnel*
President: H A Hardarson
Newsletter.
Triannually.
ISSN: 1605-4415

# India

**Annals of Library & Information Studies** (J)
Published by National Institute of Science Com-
munication & Information Resources (NIS-
CAIR)
14 Satsang Vihar Marg, Spl Institutional Area
New Mehrauli Rd, New Delhi 110067
*Tel:* (011) 26560141; (011) 26560143; (011)
26560165; (011) 26560189 *Fax:* (011)
26862228
*E-mail:* sales@niscair.res.in
*Web Site:* www.niscair.res.in
*Telex:* 031-73099
*Key Personnel*
Dir: Mr V K Gupta *E-mail:* vkg@niscair.res.in
Text in English.
First published 1954.
Quarterly.
400 INR or 75 USD
ISSN: 0972-5423

**Books of the Week Bulletin** (J)
Published by D K Agencies (P) Ltd
Mohan Garden, A/15-17, DK Ave, Najafgarh Rd,
New Delhi 110059
*Tel:* (011) 2535-7104; (011) 2535-7105
*Fax:* (011) 2535-7103
*E-mail:* information@dkagencies.com
*Web Site:* www.dkagencies.com
Source for bibliographical details of English lan-
guage publications published from India.
Weekly.

**Bulletin** (J)
Published by Indian Library Association
A/40-41, Flat No 201, Ansal Bldg, Mukherjee
Nagar, Delhi 110009
*Tel:* 27651743 *Fax:* 27651743
*E-mail:* info@ilaindia.org
*Web Site:* www.ilaindia.org
*Key Personnel*
President: Dr C R Karisiddappa
Editor: S Ansari
Text in English.
First published 1965.
Quarterly.
750 INR or 55 USD
ISSN: 0019-5782

**D K Newsletter** (J)
Published by D K Agencies (P) Ltd
Mohan Garden, A/15-17, DK Ave, Najafgarh Rd,
New Delhi 110059
*Tel:* (011) 2535-7104; (011) 2535-7105
*Fax:* (011) 2535-7103
*E-mail:* information@dkagencies.com
*Web Site:* www.dkagencies.com
News & reviews of Indian publications in En-
glish.
First published 1975.
Quarterly.
ISSN: 0971-4448

**IASLIC Bulletin** (J)
Published by Scientific Publishers
P291, CIT Scheme 6M, Kankurgachi, Kolkata
700054

*Tel:* (033) 334 9651; (033) 2354 9066
*E-mail:* iaslic@vsnl.net
*Web Site:* www.iaslic.org
*Key Personnel*
Honorary Editor: Dr Arjun Dasgupta
Corporate author: Indian Association of Special
Libraries & Information. Text in English.
First published 1956.
Quarterly.
20 USD individuals, 80 USD institutions
ISSN: 0018-8441

**Indian Library Science Abstracts** (J)
Published by Scientific Publishers
P291, CIT Scheme 6M, Kankurgachi, Kolkata
700054
*Tel:* (033) 334 9651
*E-mail:* iaslic@vsnl.net
*Web Site:* www.iaslic.org
*Key Personnel*
President: Dr Prithvish Nag
First published 1967.
Annually.
35 USD
ISSN: 0019-5790

**Journal of Library & Information Science** (J)
Published by University of Delhi, Department of
Library & Information Science
University Rd, Delhi 110007
*Tel:* (011) 27666656
*Web Site:* www.du.ac.in
*Key Personnel*
Editor: Dr S R Gupta
First published 1976.
Biannually.
80 INR or 14 USD
ISSN: 0970-714X

**MIWA-Major Indian Works Annual** (B)
Published by D K Agencies (P) Ltd
Mohan Garden, A/15-17, DK Ave, Najafgarh Rd,
New Delhi 110059
*Tel:* (011) 2535-7104; (011) 2535-7105
*Fax:* (011) 2535-7103
*E-mail:* information@dkagencies.com
*Web Site:* www.dkagencies.com
Bibliographic guide to carefully chosen, gen-
uinely significant works of higher aca-
demic/research/general value.
Annually.

**The National Library & Public Libraries in
India** (B)
Published by The National Library
Belvedere, Kolkata 700027
*Tel:* (033) 24791381; (033) 24791384 *Fax:* (033)
24791462
*E-mail:* nldirector@rediffmail.com; nldirector@
nlindia.org
*Web Site:* nlindia.org
*Telex:* 021-8117
*Key Personnel*
Dir: Sri K K Banerjee
Principal Library & Information: Dr R Ra-
machandran

**Special List** (J)
Published by D K Agencies (P) Ltd
Mohan Garden, A/15-17, DK Ave, Najafgarh Rd,
New Delhi 110059
*Tel:* (011) 2535-7104; (011) 2535-7105
*Fax:* (011) 2535-7103
*E-mail:* information@dkagencies.com
*Web Site:* www.dkagencies.com
Information by subject on books & back numbers
of Indian periodicals.

**Subscribers' Guide to Indian
Periodicals/Serials** (J)
Published by D K Agencies (P) Ltd

Mohan Garden, A/15-17, DK Ave, Najafgarh Rd,
New Delhi 110059
*Tel:* (011) 2535-7104; (011) 2535-7105
*Fax:* (011) 2535-7103
*E-mail:* information@dkagencies.com
*Web Site:* www.dkagencies.com
Biennially.

# Indonesia

**Baca** (Read) (J)
Published by Indonesian Institute of Sciences,
Centre for Scientific Documentation & Infor-
mation
PO Box 4298, 12042 Jakarta
*Tel:* (021) 573 34 65; (021) 573 34 66 *Fax:* (021)
573 34 67
*E-mail:* admin@pdii.lipi.go.id
*Web Site:* www.pdii.lipi.go.id
*Key Personnel*
Editor: Antari Wahyuning Mawarti
*E-mail:* Antari_s@hotmail.com
First published 1974.
Quarterly.
ISSN: 0125-9008

**Majalah Ikatan Pustakawan Indonesia** (J)
Published by Indonesian Library Association
Jl Medan Merdeka Selatan No 11, Jakarta 10110
*Tel:* (021) 3855729 *Fax:* (021) 3855729
*Web Site:* ipi.pnri.go.id
*Key Personnel*
President: Mr Dady P Rachmananta *Tel:* (021)
3101472 *Fax:* (021) 3101472 *E-mail:* dady@
pnri.go.id
Secretary-General: Mrs Zurniaty Nasrul
*Tel:* (021) 5733465 *Fax:* (021) 5733467
*E-mail:* zurniaty@pdii.lipi.go.id
Indonesian Library Association Journal.
Irregularly.

# Islamic Republic of Iran

**A Catalog of the Manuscripts in the National
Library of Iran** (B)
Published by National Library & Archives of Iran
Anahita Alley, Africa St, PO Box 11365/9597,
19176 Tehran
Mailing Address: Sh Bahonar Str, 19548 Tehran
*Tel:* (021) 8881966 *Fax:* (021) 8786859
*E-mail:* nli@nlai.ir
*Web Site:* www.nlai.ir
*Key Personnel*
Manuscript Dept: H Aximi

**Class DSR: History of Iran** (B)
Published by National Library & Archives of Iran
Anahita Alley, Africa St, PO Box 11365/9597,
19176 Tehran
Mailing Address: Sh Bahonar Str, 19548 Tehran
*Tel:* (021) 8881966 *Fax:* (021) 8786859
*E-mail:* nli@nlai.ir
*Web Site:* www.nlai.ir
*Key Personnel*
Author & Research Librarian: Kamran Fani
An adaptation of Library of Congress Classifica-
tion.
First published 1980.
3rd (2000): 198 pp, 50 USD
ISBN(s): 964-446-056-1

## Class PIR: Iranian Languages & Literature (B)
Published by National Library & Archives of Iran
Anahita Alley, Africa St, PO Box 11365/9597, 19176 Tehran
Mailing Address: Sh Bahonar Str, 19548 Tehran
*Tel:* (021) 8088971 *Fax:* (021) 8786859
*E-mail:* nli@nlai.ir
*Web Site:* www.nlai.ir
Based on the Library of Congress Classification.
2nd

## Dewey Decimal Classification: Geography of Iran (B)
Published by National Library & Archives of Iran
Anahita Alley, Africa St, PO Box 11365/9597, 19176 Tehran
Mailing Address: Shahid Bahonar St, 19548 Tehran
*Tel:* (021) 8088971 *Fax:* (021) 8786859
*E-mail:* nli@nlai.ir
*Web Site:* www.nlai.ir
3rd

## Dewey Decimal Classification: History of Iran (B)
Published by National Library & Archives of Iran
Anahita Alley, Africa St, PO Box 11365/9597, 19176 Tehran
Mailing Address: Shahid Bahonar St, 19548 Tehran
*Tel:* (021) 8881966 *Fax:* (021) 8786859
*E-mail:* nli@nlai.ir
*Web Site:* www.nlai.ir
*Key Personnel*
Author & Research Librarian: Kamran Fani
Senior Research Librarian: Mrs Poori Soltani
   *E-mail:* poorisoltani@yahoo.com
First published 1982.
3rd (1999), 20 USD
ISBN(s): 964-446-037-5

## Dewey Decimal Classification: Iranian Languages (B)
Published by National Library & Archives of Iran
Anahita Alley, Africa St, PO Box 11365/9597, 19176 Tehran
Mailing Address: Shahid Bahonar St, 19548 Tehran
*Tel:* (021) 8088971 *Fax:* (021) 8786859
*E-mail:* nli@nlai.ir
*Web Site:* www.nlai.ir
*Key Personnel*
Senior Research Librarian: Mrs Poori Soltani
   *E-mail:* poorisoltani@yahoo.com
First published 1988.
3rd (1998), 15 USD
ISBN(s): 964-446-031-6

## Dewey Decimal Classification: Iranian Literature (B)
Published by National Library & Archives of Iran
Anahita Alley, Africa St, PO Box 11365/9597, 19176 Tehran
Mailing Address: Shahid Bahonar St, 19548 Tehran
*Tel:* (021) 8881966 *Fax:* (021) 8786859
*E-mail:* nli@nlai.ir
*Web Site:* www.nlai.ir
*Key Personnel*
Senior Research Librarian: Mrs Poori Soltani
   *E-mail:* poorisoltani@yahoo.com
Text in Persian.
First published 1972.
2nd (1998), 50 USD
ISBN(s): 964-446-032-4

## A Directory of Iranian Newspapers (B)
Published by National Library & Archives of Iran
Anahita Alley, Africa St, PO Box 11365/9597, 19176 Tehran

Mailing Address: Shahid Bahonar St, 19548 Tehran
*Tel:* (021) 8881966 *Fax:* (021) 8786859
*E-mail:* nli@nlai.ir
*Web Site:* www.nlai.ir
Annually.

## Farsi Author Numbers, to be used with the Library of Congress Classification Schedules (B)
Published by National Library & Archives of Iran
Anahita Alley, Africa St, PO Box 11365/9597, 19176 Tehran
Mailing Address: Shahid Bahonar St, 19548 Tehran
*Tel:* (021) 8088971 *Fax:* (021) 8786859
*E-mail:* nli@nlai.ir
*Web Site:* www.nlai.ir
*Key Personnel*
Senior Research Librarian: Mrs Poori Soltani
   *E-mail:* poorisoltani@yahoo.com
First published 1997.
3rd: 34 pp

## Faslname-ye Ketab (J)
Published by National Library & Archives of Iran
Shahid Bahonar St, 19548 Tehran
*Tel:* (021) 8088971 *Fax:* (021) 8088950
*E-mail:* nli@nlai.ir
*Web Site:* www.nlai.ir
*Key Personnel*
Editor: Abbas Horri
Journal of The National Library of Iran.
First published 1990.
Quarterly.
ISSN: 1022-6451

## List of Persian Subject Headings (B)
Published by National Library & Archives of Iran
Anahita Alley, Africa St, PO Box 11365/9597, 19176 Tehran
Mailing Address: Shahid Bahonar St, 19548 Tehran
*Tel:* (021) 8088971 *Fax:* (021) 8786859
*E-mail:* nli@nlai.ir
*Web Site:* www.nlai.ir
*Key Personnel*
Senior Research Librarian: Mrs Poori Soltani
   *E-mail:* poorisoltani@yahoo.com
3 vols.
First published 1993.
3rd (2002), 50 USD
ISBN(s): 964-446-070-7

## Technical Services (B)
Published by National Library & Archives of Iran
Anahita Alley, Africa St, PO Box 11365/9597, 19176 Tehran
Mailing Address: Shahid Bahonar St, 19548 Tehran
*Tel:* (021) 8088971 *Fax:* (021) 8786859
*E-mail:* nli@nlai.ir
*Web Site:* www.nlai.ir
8th, 501 USD
ISBN(s): 964-446-029-4

# Ireland

## Directory of Libraries & Information Services in Ireland (B)
Published by Library Association of Ireland & CILIP (Northern Ireland)
53 Upper Mount St, Dublin 2
*Tel:* (061) 202193
*E-mail:* laisec@iol.ie
*Web Site:* www.libraryassociation.ie

*Key Personnel*
President: Ruth Flanagan *E-mail:* president@libraryassociation.ie
Available online only.
5th

## Irish Library News (J)
Published by An Chomhairle Leabharlanna (Library Council)
53/54 Upper Mount St, Dublin 2
*Tel:* (01) 6761963; (01) 6761167 *Fax:* (01) 6766721
*E-mail:* info@librarycouncil.ie
*Web Site:* www.librarycouncil.ie
*Key Personnel*
Dir: Norma McDermott *E-mail:* nmcdermott@librarycouncil.ie
Editor: Alun Bevan *E-mail:* abevan@librarycouncil.ie
Newssheet issued free to libraries.
First published 1977.
Monthly.
ISSN: 0332-0049

## An Leabharlann (Irish Library) (J)
Published by Library Association of Ireland & CILIP-Northern Ireland
53 Upper Mount St, Dublin 2
*Tel:* (091) 562471 *Fax:* (091) 565039
*Web Site:* www.libraryassociation.ie
*Key Personnel*
President: Ruth Flanagan *E-mail:* president@libraryassociation.ie
Editor: Pat McMahon *E-mail:* pmm@eircom.net
First published 1930.

## Long Room (J)
Published by Friends of the Library
Trinity College, College St, Dublin 2
*Tel:* (01) 6081673; (01) 6772125 *Fax:* (01) 6719003
*E-mail:* infoserv@tcd.ie
*Web Site:* www.tcd.ie
*Telex:* 93782
*Key Personnel*
Editor: Vincent Kinane *E-mail:* vkinane@lib1.tcd.ie
Information Service Librarian: Deirdre Allen
Ireland's Journal for the History of the Book.
Annually.

# Israel

## Bibliography of Modern Hebrew Literature in Translation (B)
Published by The Institute for the Translation of Hebrew Literature
23 Baruch Hirsch St, Bnei Brak
Mailing Address: PO Box 1005 1, 52001 Ramat Gan
*Tel:* (03) 579 6830 *Fax:* (03) 579 6832
*E-mail:* hamachon@inter.net.il; litscene@ithl.org.il
*Web Site:* www.ithl.org.il
*Key Personnel*
Man Dir: Mrs Nilli Cohen
First published 1979.
Annually.
ISSN: 0334-309X

## Index to Hebrew Periodicals (P)
Published by University of Haifa Library
Mount Carmel, PO Box 242, Jerusalem 31905
*Tel:* (04) 8240289 *Fax:* (04) 8257753
*E-mail:* amira@univ.haifa.ac.il; libmaster@univ.haifa.ac.il
*Web Site:* lib.haifa.ac.il

*Key Personnel*
Chairman: Jacob Agmon
Available online only. http://libnet.ac.il/
libnet/ihp.
First published 1977.
Annually.
ISSN: 0334-2921

**Yad La-Kore** (Reader's Aid) (P)
Published by The Israeli Center for Libraries
5 Hachavatzelet St, 91002 Jerusalem
Mailing Address: PO Box 242, 91002 Jerusalem
*Tel:* (02) 6252949 *Fax:* (02) 3250620
*E-mail:* rochelle@actcom.co.il
*Web Site:* www.icl.org.il
*Key Personnel*
Dir: Dr Martin Weyl
Israel Journal for Libraries & Archives.
First published 1946.
Quarterly.
ISSN: 0334-200X

# Italy

**Accademie e Biblioteche d'Italia** (Academies &
Libraries of Italy) (J)
Published by Ministero per i Beni Culturali e
Ambientali
Via Michele Mercati 4, 00100 Rome
*Tel:* (06) 362161 *Fax:* (06) 3214752
*E-mail:* uclibrari@librari.beniculturali.it
*Web Site:* www.beniculturali.it; www.librari.
beniculturali.it
Quarterly.
96 pp
ISSN: 0001-4451

**Bollettino AIB** (AIB Bulletin) (J)
Published by Italian Library Association (Associ-
azione Italiana Biblioteche)
Castro Pretorio 105, 00185 Rome
*Tel:* (06) 4463532 *Fax:* (06) 4441139
*E-mail:* bollettino@aib.it
*Web Site:* www.aib.it/aib/boll/boll.htm
*Key Personnel*
Editor: Giovanni Solimine
Contact: Maria Teresa Natale
Quarterly.
ISSN: 1121-1490

**Catalogo Collettivo di Periodici - Archivio
ISRDS/CNR** (Catalog of Collective
Periodicals) (B)
Published by Istituto Centrale per il Catalogo
Unico delle Biblioteche Italiane e per le In-
formazioni Bibliografiche (Central Institute of
the Union Catalog of Italian Libraries & Bibli-
ographical Information)
Viale del Castro Pretorio, 105-00185 Rome
*Tel:* (06) 4989484 *Fax:* (06) 4959302
*Web Site:* www.iccu.sbn.it
*Key Personnel*
Dir: Dr Luciano Scala
Contains listings of over 46,000 periodicals in
1500 libraries.

**Periodici Italiani 1966-1981** (Italian Periodicals
1966-1981) (B)
Published by Istituto Centrale per il Catalogo
Unico delle Biblioteche Italiane e per le Informazioni Bibliografiche (Central Institute of
the Union Catalog of Italian Libraries & Bibliographical Information)
Viale del Castro Pretorio, 105-00185 Rome
*Tel:* (06) 4989484 *Fax:* (06) 4959302

*Web Site:* www.iccu.sbn.it
*Key Personnel*
Dir: Dr Luciano Scala

**Regole Italiane di Catalogazione per Autori**
(Italian Rules of Cataloging by Author) (B)
Published by Istituto Centrale per il Catalogo
Unico delle Biblioteche Italiane e per le In-
formazioni Bibliografiche (Central Institute of
the Union Catalog of Italian Libraries & Bibli-
ographical Information)
Viale del Castro Pretorio, 105-00185 Rome
*Tel:* (06) 4989484 *Fax:* (06) 4959302
*Web Site:* www.iccu.sbn.it
*Key Personnel*
Dir: Dr Luciano Scala

**Soggettario per i Cataloghi delle Biblioteche
Italiane** (Subject Collections in Italian
Libraries) (J)
Published by Istituto Centrale per il Catalogo
Unico delle Biblioteche Italiane e per le In-
formazioni Bibliografiche (Central Institute of
the Union Catalog of Italian Libraries & Bibli-
ographical Information)
Viale del Castro Pretorio, 105-00185 Rome
*Tel:* (06) 4989484 *Fax:* (06) 4959302
*Web Site:* www.iccu.sbn.it
*Key Personnel*
Dir: Dr Luciano Scala

# Jamaica

**JLA Bulletin** (J)
Published by Jamaica Library Association
PO Box 125, Kingston 5
*Tel:* (876) 927-1614 *Fax:* (876) 927-1614
*E-mail:* liajapresident@yahoo.com
*Web Site:* www.liaja.org.jm
*Key Personnel*
President: Byron Palmer
Contact: Mrs Ouida Lewis *E-mail:* ouida.lewis@
uwimona.edu.jm
First published 1950.
Annually.
300 JMD

**JLA News** (B)
Published by Jamaica Library Association
PO Box 125, Kingston 5
*Tel:* (876) 927-1614 *Fax:* (876) 927-1614
*E-mail:* liajapresident@yahoo.com
*Web Site:* www.liaja.org.jm
*Key Personnel*
President: Byron Palmer
News of current events in the libraries of Ja-
maica.
Quarterly.

# Japan

**Biblos** (J)
Published by National Diet Library
1-10-1 Nagata-cho, Chiyoda-ku, Tokyo 100-8924
*Tel:* (03) 3581-2331 *Fax:* (03) 3508-2934
*E-mail:* kokusai@ndl.go.jp
*Web Site:* www.ndl.go.jp
*Key Personnel*
Dir, Planning & Cooperation Dept: Yukiko Saito
Online magazine for branch, executive, judicial &
other special libraries.
ISSN: 1344-8412

**Bulletin of the Japan Special Libraries
Association** (J)
Published by Japan Special Libraries Association
c/o Japan Library Association Bldg F6, 1-11-14
Shinkawa, Chuo-ku, Tokyo 104-0033
*Tel:* (03) 35378335 *Fax:* (03) 35378336
*E-mail:* jsla@jsla.or.jp
*Web Site:* www.jsla.or.jp
Abstracts in English.
Bimonthly.
50 pp, 13,000 JPY/yr

**Directory of Special Information Institutions**
(B)
Published by Japan Special Libraries Association
c/o Japan Library Association Bldg F6, 1-11-14
Shinkawa, Chuo-ku, Tokyo 104-0033
*Tel:* (03) 35378335 *Fax:* (03) 35378336
*E-mail:* jsla@jsla.or.jp
*Web Site:* www.jsla.or.jp
Entry names also in English.
Triennially.
32,000 JPY
ISBN(s): 4-88130-020-2

**Gendai no Toshokan** (Libraries Today) (J)
Published by Japan Library Association
1-11-14 Shinkawa, Chuo-ku, Tokyo 104-0033
*Tel:* (03) 3523 0811 *Fax:* (03) 3523 0841
*E-mail:* info@jla.or.jp
*Web Site:* www.jla.or.jp
First published 1963.
Quarterly.
ISSN: 0016-6332

**Journal of Information Science & Technology
Association** (J)
Published by Information Science and Technoloy
Association Japan (INFOSTA)
Sasaki Bldg, 2-5-7- Koishikawa, Bunkyo-ku,
Tokyo 112-0002
*Tel:* (03) 38133791 *Fax:* (03) 38133793
*E-mail:* infosta@infosta.or.jp
*Web Site:* www.infosta.or.jp
*Key Personnel*
Chairman: Zepher Tachibara
Features articles which review new technologies
in the global information world.
Monthly.

**Nihon no Sankotosho Shikiban** (Guide to
Japanese Reference Books) (J)
Published by Japan Library Association
1-11-14 Shinkawa, Chuo-ku, Tokyo 104-0033
*Tel:* (03) 3523 0811 *Fax:* (03) 3523 0841
*E-mail:* info@jla.or.jp
*Web Site:* www.jla.or.jp
First published 1962.
Irregularly.

**Nihon no Toshokan** (Statistics on Libraries in
Japan) (B)
Published by Japan Library Association
1-11-14 Shinkawa, Chuo-ku, Tokyo 104-0033
*Tel:* (03) 3523 0811 *Fax:* (03) 3523 0841
*E-mail:* info@jla.or.jp
*Web Site:* www.jla.or.jp
Statistics & directory of public & university li-
braries.
First published 1952.
Annually.

**Refarensu** (Reference) (J)
Published by National Diet Library
1-10-1 Nagata-cho, Chiyoda-ku, Tokyo 100-8924
*Tel:* (03) 3581-2331 *Fax:* (03) 3508-2934
*E-mail:* kokusai@ndl.go.jp
*Web Site:* www.ndl.go.jp
*Key Personnel*
Dir, Planning & Cooperation Dept: Yukiko Saito
First published 1951.

Monthly.
ISSN: 0034-2912

**Toshokan Zasshi** (Library Journal) (J)
Published by Japan Library Association
1-11-14 Shinkawa, Chuo-ku, Tokyo 104-0033
*Tel:* (03) 3523 0811 *Fax:* (03) 3523 0841
*E-mail:* info@jla.or.jp
*Web Site:* www.jla.or.jp
First published 1907.
Monthly.

# Jordan

**Jordanian National Bibliography** (B)
Published by Jordan Library Association
King Talal Circle (3rd Circle) Jabal Amman, Al-
  Hussein Bin Ali St, Amman
Mailing Address: PO Box 6289, Amman
*Tel:* 629-412
*E-mail:* nl@amra.nic.gov.jo
*Web Site:* www.nis.gov.jo/english/index.html
Text in Arabic, English.
First published 1979.
Annually.

**Rissalat al-Maktaba** (J)
Published by Jordan Library Association (Mes-
  sage of the Library)
PO Box 6289, Amman
*Tel:* (06) 4629412 *Fax:* (06) 4629412
*Key Personnel*
President: Anwar Akroush
Text in Arabic, summaries in English.
First published 1965.
Quarterly.
ISSN: 0257-7739

# Kenya

**Accessions List of the Library of Congress
  Office, Nairobi, Kenya** (P)
Published by US Library of Congress Office
PO Box 30598, 00100 Nairobi GPO
*Tel:* (02) 363 6300; (02) 363 6146; (02) 363 6153
  *Fax:* (02) 363 6321
*E-mail:* nairobi@libcon-kenya.org
*Web Site:* www.loc.gov/acq/ovop/nairobi/
*Key Personnel*
Field Dir: Paul J Steere
Bimonthly.
ISSN: 1527-5396

**Maktaba** (J)
Published by Kenya Library Association
PO Box 46031, Nairobi
*Tel:* (02) 811-622 *Fax:* (02) 811-455
*E-mail:* arbulogosi@avu.org
*Key Personnel*
Chairman: Jacinta Were *E-mail:* jwere@ken.
  healthnet.org
Official journal of the Kenya Library Association.
Biannually.
ISSN: 0070-7988

# Republic of Korea

**Bibliographic Index of Korea** (B)
Published by The National Library of Korea
San 60-1, Banpo-dong, Seocho-gu, Seoul 137-702
*Tel:* (02) 535-4142 *Fax:* (02) 590-0530
*E-mail:* nlkpc@sun.nl.or.kr
*Web Site:* www.nl.go.kr
*Key Personnel*
Dir: Gi-Young Jeong
Annually.

**Journal of the Korean Society for Library &
  Information Science** (J)
Published by Korean Society for Library & Infor-
  mation Science
Sungkyunkwan University, 53, 3-ga, Myungnyun-
  dong, Chongno-gu, Seoul 110-745
*Tel:* (02) 760-0330 *Fax:* (02) 760-0326
*Web Site:* www.kliss.or.kr
*Key Personnel*
President: Eun-Chul Lee *E-mail:* eclee@skku.ac.
  kr
Text in Korean with English abstracts.
First published 1970.
Quarterly.
300 pp
ISSN: 1225-598X

**KLA Bulletin** (J)
Published by Korean Library Association (KLA)
60-1, Banpo-dong, Seocho-gu, Seoul 137-702
*Tel:* (02) 5354868 *Fax:* (02) 5355616
*E-mail:* klanet@hitel.net
*Web Site:* www.korla.or.kr
*Key Personnel*
Editor: Dae Kwon Park
Bimonthly.
20 USD/yr
ISSN: 0022-7358

**Kukhoe Tosogwanbo** (National Assembly
  Library Review) (J)
Published by National Assembly Library
One Yoido-dong, Yongdungpo-ku, Seoul 150-703
*Tel:* (02) 7884143 (english service); (02) 7883961
  *Fax:* (02) 7884291
*E-mail:* intlcoop@nanet.go.kr
*Web Site:* www.nanet.go.kr
*Telex:* 25849
*Key Personnel*
Librarian: Bae Yong Soo
Bimonthly.
ISSN: 0027-8572

**Statistics on Libraries in Korea** (J)
Published by Korean Library Association (KLA)
60-1, Banpo-dong, Seocho-gu, Seoul 137-702
*Tel:* (02) 5354868 *Fax:* (02) 5355616
*E-mail:* klanet@hitel.net
*Web Site:* www.korla.or.kr
*Key Personnel*
President: Shin Ki Nam
Annually.
ISSN: 1225-5521

# Kuwait

**The Library Bulletin** (P)
Published by Kuwait University Library
PO Box 17140, 92452 Khaldiya
*E-mail:* info@kuniv.edu

*Web Site:* www.kuniv.edu
*Key Personnel*
Dir: Dr Husain A Al-Ansari

**The University Library** (P)
Published by Kuwait University Library
PO Box 17140, 92452 Khaldiya
*E-mail:* info@kuniv.edu
*Web Site:* www.kuniv.edu
*Key Personnel*
Dir: Dr Husain A Al-Ansari

# Lebanon

**Newsletter** (J)
Published by The Lebanese Library Association
c/o American University of Beirut, University Li-
  brary, Beirut
*Tel:* (01) 350000 *Fax:* (01) 351706
*Telex:* 2080
*Key Personnel*
President: Marouf Rafi

# Malawi

**Directory of Malawi Libraries** (B)
Published by University of Malawi Libraries
Central Library, Box 280, Zomba
*Tel:* 522 222; 523 225 *Fax:* 523 225; 524 046
*Web Site:* www.sdnp.org.mw/webwshp/schinyamu
*Key Personnel*
Librarian: Mr S S Mwiyeriwa

**MALA Bulletin** (J)
Published by Malawi Library Association
PO Box 429, Zomba
*Tel:* (050) 522222 *Fax:* (050) 523225
*Key Personnel*
Editor: D B Vuwa Phiri *E-mail:* d.b.v.phiri@
  unima.wn.apc.org
First published 1978.
Biannually.
300 MWK or 20 USD/yr

# Malaysia

**Directory of Libraries in Malaysia** (B)
Published by National Library of Malaysia (Gift
  & Exchange Unit)
232 Jalan Tun Razak, 50572 Kuala Lumpur
*Tel:* (03) 26871700; (03) 26943234 *Fax:* (03)
  26942490
*E-mail:* pnmweb@pnm.my
*Web Site:* www.pnm.my
*Telex:* 30092
*Key Personnel*
Dir-General: Mariam Abdul Kadir

**Majallah Perpustakaan Malaysia** (J)
Published by Persatuan Perpustakaan Malaysia
  (Library Association of Malaysia)
c/o Perpustakaan Negara Malaysia, 232 Jalan Tun
  Razak, 50572 Kuala Lumpur
*Tel:* (03) 2694 7390 *Fax:* (03) 2694 7390
*E-mail:* ppm55@po.jaring.my
*Web Site:* www.pnm.my/ppm/
Official journal, text in English & Malay.

**Sumber Pustaka** (J)
Published by Persatuan Perpustakaan Malaysia
   (Library Association of Malaysia)
c/o Perpustakaan Negara Malaysia, 232 Jalan Tun
   Razak, 50572 Kuala Lumpur
*Tel:* (03) 2694 7390 *Fax:* (03) 2694 7390
*E-mail:* ppm55@po.jaring.my
*Web Site:* www.pnm.my/ppm/
Malaysian Library Association official newsletter,
   text in English & Malay.

# Malta

**A Bibliography of Maltese Bibliographies** (B)
Published by University of Malta Library
c/o University of Malta, Tal Qroqq MSD 06
*Tel:* 2340 2316 *Fax:* 21 314 306
*E-mail:* librarian@lib.um.edu.mt
*Web Site:* www.lib.um.edu.mt
*Key Personnel*
Chancellor: Prof J Rizzo Naudi
Dir, Library Services: Anthony Mangion *Tel:* 21
   310 239 *E-mail:* librarian@lib.um.edu.mt
Librarian: Dr Paul Xuereb *E-mail:* paul.m.
   xuereb@um.edu.mt
First published 1993.

**Malia Newsletter** (J)
Published by Malta Library & Information Asso-
   ciation
c/o University of Malta Library, Tal-Qroqq, Msida
   MSD 06
*E-mail:* mpar1@lib.um.edu.mt
*Web Site:* www.malia-malta.org
*Key Personnel*
Chairman: Robert Mizzi
Honorary Secretary: Ruth Muscat
Quarterly.

# Mauritius

**Mauritius Library Association Newsletter** (J)
Published by Mauritius Library Association
c/o Ministry of Education Public Library, Moka
   Rd, Rose Hill
*Tel:* 4549550; 4549551; 4549552 *Fax:* 4549553
*E-mail:* general.equiries@mu.britishcouncil.org
*Web Site:* www.britishcouncil.org/mauritius/
Quarterly.

**Memorandum of Books printed in Mauritius
   & Registered in the Archives Office** (B)
Published by Mauritius Archives
Development Bank of Mauritius Complex, Petite
   Riviere
*Tel:* 233-4469 *Fax:* 233-4299
First published 1894.
Quarterly.
Free

# Mexico

**Boletin** (Bulletin) (J)
Published by Instituto de Investigaciones Bibli-
   ograficas (Institute of Bibliographic Research)
Ciudad Universitaria, Coyoacan, 04510 Mexico,
   DF
*Tel:* (055) 6226807 *Fax:* (05) 6650951
*E-mail:* libros@biblional.bibliog.unam.mx
*Web Site:* biblional.bibliog.unam.mx

*Key Personnel*
Editor: Jose G Moreno de Alba
First published 1969.
Biannually.
300 MXN or 90 USD
ISSN: 0006-1719

**Centro de Bibliotecologia, Archivologia e
   Informacion Anuario** (Annual of Library
   Science, Archives & Information Science) (B)
Published by Universidad Nacional Autonoma de
   Mexico Centro (National University of Mexico)
Torre 1 de Humanidades PB 20 piso, Ciudad Uni-
   versitaria, 04510 Mexico, DF
*Tel:* (05) 6221603 *Fax:* (05) 6160664
*Web Site:* www.unam.mx
*Key Personnel*
Dir: Adolfo Rodriquez Gallardo

**Noticiero de la AMBAC** (News of the Mexican
   Association of Librarians) (J)
Published by Asociacion Mexicana de Bibliote-
   carios AC (AMBAC)
Angel Urraza 817-A, Col Del Valle, 03100 Mex-
   ico, DF
Mailing Address: Apdo 80-065, Administracion
   de correos 80, 06001 Mexico, DF
*Tel:* (055) 55 75 33 96 *Fax:* (055) 55-75-11-35
*E-mail:* correo@ambac.org.mx
*Web Site:* www.ambac.org.mx
*Key Personnel*
President: Saul Armendariz Sanchez
   *E mail:* asaul@xcaret.iqeofcu.unam.mx
Vice President: Felipe Becerril Torres

# Netherlands

**BibliotheckBlad** (Library Journal) (J)
Published by Vereniging NBLC
Platinaweg 10, 2544 EZ The Hague
Mailing Address: PO Box 43300, 2504 AH The
   Hague 5
*Tel:* (070) 30 90 100 *Fax:* (070) 30 90 200
*E-mail:* bibliotheckblad@nblc.nl
*Web Site:* www.nblc.nl

**Brinkman's Cumulative Catalog** (B)
Published by Uitgeverij Bohn Stafleu Van
   Loghum BV
2400 MA Alphen aan den Rijn, PO Box 4, Hol-
   land
*Tel:* (0172) 466811 *Fax:* (0172) 466770
*E-mail:* klantenservice@bsl.nl
*Web Site:* www.kb.nl
Dutch National Bibliography.
Quarterly.

**Informatie Professional** (J)
Published by Nederlandse Vereniging voor
   beroepsbeoefenaren in de bibliotheeck-
   informatie-en kennissector (NVB) (The Nether-
   land Association of Librarians, Documentalists
   & Information Specialists)
c/o NVB-Verenigingsbureau Plompetorengracht
   11, Nieuwegracht 15, 3512 LC Utrecht
*Tel:* (030) 2311263 *Fax:* (030) 2311830
*E-mail:* info@nvbonline.nl
*Web Site:* www.nvb-online.nl
*Key Personnel*
President: Dr J S M Savenije *E-mail:* b.savenije@
   ubu.ruu.nl
Professional journal for librarians, researchers &
   documentalists (joint publication).
Monthly.

**Nederlands Archievenblad** (Netherlands) (J)
Published by Vereniging van Archivaissen in
   Nederland
Cruquiusweg 31, 1019 AT Amsterdam
*Tel:* (020) 462 77 27 *Fax:* (020) 462 77 28
*E-mail:* bureau@kvan.nl
*Web Site:* www.kvan.nl
*Key Personnel*
Contact: Mathilda van Geem

# New Zealand

**Library Life** (J)
Published by Library & Information Association
   of New Zealand Aotearoa (LIANZA)
Old Wool House, Level 5, 139-141 Featherston
   St, Wellington 6001
Mailing Address: PO Box 12-212, Wellington
   6038
*Tel:* (04) 473 5834 *Fax:* (04) 499 1480
*E-mail:* editor@lianza.org.nz
*Web Site:* www.lianza.org.nz
*Key Personnel*
President: Mirla Edmundson
   *E-mail:* edmundsonm@hermes.cpit.ac.nz
Managing Editor: Corin Pearce-Haines *E-mail:* c.
   pearce-haines@massey.ac.nz
Editor & Office Assistant: Anna O'Keeffe
   *E-mail:* anna@lianza.org.nz
11 times/yr (not Janualry).
ISSN: 0110-4373

**New Zealand Libraries** (J)
Published by Library & Information Association
   of New Zealand Aotearoa (LIANZA)
Old Wool House, Level 5, 139-141 Featherston
   St, Wellington 6001
Mailing Address: PO Box 12-212, Wellington
   6038
*Tel:* (04) 473 5834 *Fax:* (04) 499 1480
*E-mail:* office@lianza.org.nz
*Web Site:* www.lianza.org.nz
*Key Personnel*
Editor: Barbara Frame *E-mail:* frame@xtra.co.nz
Biannually.
ISSN: 0028-8381

# Nigeria

**Afribiblios** (J)
Published by National Library of Nigeria-
   Research & Development Dept
Sanusi Dantata House, Plot 274 Central Business
   Area, PMB 1, Garki District, Abuja
*Tel:* (09) 2347714; (09) 2347900
*E-mail:* nln@nlbn.org
*Web Site:* www.nlbn.org
*Key Personnel*
Chairman: Francis Z Gana
Dir: Mr E N O Adimorah
Biannually.

**Bendel Library Journal** (J)
Published by Edo State Library
PMB 1127, Benin City
*Tel:* (052) 200810
*E-mail:* info@edostatelibrary.com
*Web Site:* www.edostatelibrary.com
*Key Personnel*
Dir: J O U oDiase

**Libraries in Nigeria: A Directory** (B)
Published by National Library of Nigeria-
    Research & Development Dept
Sanusi Dantata House, Plot 274 Central Business
    Area, PMB 1, Garki District, Abuja
*Tel:* (09) 2347714; (09) 2347900
*E-mail:* nln.rusd@nlbn.org
*Web Site:* www.nlbn.org
*Telex:* 21746
*Key Personnel*
Dir: Mr E N O Adimorah
National Librarian: Mrs O O Omolayole

**Library Forum** (J)
Published by Nigerian Library Association
c/o National Library Association, Sanusi Dantata
    House, Business Central District, Garki Dis-
    trict, Abuja 900001
*Tel:* 8055365245 *Fax:* (09) 234-6773
*E-mail:* info@nla-ng.org
*Web Site:* www.nla-ng.org
*Telex:* 21746
*Key Personnel*
Chairman: Francis Z Gana
Quarterly.

**Library Record** (J)
Published by University of Ibadan, Kenneth Dike
    Library
Ibadan
*Tel:* (02) 810 3118 *Fax:* (02) 810 3118
*E-mail:* library@kdl.ui.edu.ng
*Web Site:* www.ui.edu.ng/unitslibrary.htm
*Key Personnel*
Librarian: Ola Christopher Olumuyiwa
    *E-mail:* co.ola@mail.ui.edu.ng
Monthly.
ISSN: 0046-8436

**Nigerian Libraries** (J)
Published by Nigerian Library Association
c/o National Library Association, Sanusi Dantata
    House, Business Central District, Garki Dis-
    trict, Abuja 900001
*E-mail:* nigerianlibraries@nla-ng.org
*Web Site:* www.nla-ng.org
*Telex:* 21746
*Key Personnel*
Editor-in-Chief: Dr S Olajire Olanlokun
Biannually.
300 NGN/yr; 65 USD/yr (OAU countries) or 60
    USD/yr (other countries)
ISSN: 0029-0122

**Nigerian Periodicals Review** (J)
Published by ABIC Books & Equipment Ltd
18 Kenyatta St, Nsukka Enugu
Mailing Address: PO Box 13740, Nsukka Enugu
*Tel:* (042) 331827 *Fax:* (042) 334811
First published 1986.
Quarterly.
ISSN: 0794-3865

**Nominal List of Practicing Librarians in
    Nigeria** (B)
Published by National Library of Nigeria-
    Research & Development Dept
Sanusi Dantata House, Plot 274 Central Business
    Area, PMB 1, Garki District, Abuja
*Tel:* (09) 2347714; (09) 2347900
*E-mail:* nln@nlbn.org
*Web Site:* www.nlbn.org
*Telex:* 21746
*Key Personnel*
Chairman: Francis Z Gana
Dir: Mr E N O Adimorah
Names & addresses of practicing librarians at 59
    libraries in Nigeria.
Annually.

**Nsukka Library Notes** (J)
Published by Nnamdi Azikiwe Library
University of Nigeria, Nsukka, Enugu State
*Tel:* (042) 770 709 *Fax:* (042) 770 644
*E-mail:* misunn@aol.com
*Telex:* ULIONS NG 51496
*Key Personnel*
Librarian: C C Uwechie

# Norway

**Bok og Bibliotek** (Books & Libraries) (J)
Published by Statens bibliotektilsyn
Postboks 8145 Dep, 0033 Oslo
*Tel:* 23 11 75 00 *Fax:* 23 11 75 01
*E-mail:* post@abm-utvikling.no
*Web Site:* www.abm-utvikling.no
*Key Personnel*
Dir: Jon Birger Ostby *Tel:* 957 40 863
Contact: Chris Erichsen

# Pakistan

**Libraries of Pakistan** (B)
Published by Library Promotion Bureau
Karachi University Campus, PO Box 8421,
    Karachi 75270
*Tel:* (021) 6321959; (021) 6977737 *Fax:* (021)
    6321959
*Web Site:* www.ku.edu.pk
*Key Personnel*
Dir: Dr Manzoor Ahmed

**Pakistan Library & Information Science
    Journal** (J)
Formerly Pakistant Library Bulletin
Published by Library Promotion Bureau
Karachi University Campus, PO Box 8421,
    Karachi 75270
*Key Personnel*
Editor-in-Chief: Ghaniul Akram Sabzwari
    *Tel:* (021) 6321959 *E-mail:* gsabzwari@yahoo.
    com
First published 1966.
Quarterly.
150 PKR or 80 USD

**Pakistant Library Bulletin,** see Pakistan Library
    & Information Science Journal

**Plan for Development of Libraries in Pakistan**
    (B)
Published by Library Promotion Bureau
Karachi University Campus, PO Box 8421,
    Karachi 75270
*Tel:* (021) 6321959; (021) 6977737 *Fax:* (021)
    6321959
*Web Site:* www.ku.edu.pk
*Key Personnel*
President: Dr Ghaniul Akram Sabzwari
    *E-mail:* gsabzwari@yahoo.com
Librarian: Dr Manzoor Ahmed

# Papua New Guinea

**Directory of Libraries in Papua New Guinea**
    (B)
Published by National Library Service of Papua
    New Guinea
131 National Capital District, Waigani
Mailing Address: PO Box 734, Waigani
*Tel:* 325 6200 *Fax:* 325 1331
*E-mail:* ola@datec.com.pg
*Web Site:* www.pngbuai.com
*Telex:* 23472
*Key Personnel*
Dir: Daniel Paraide

**Guide to Manuscripts in the New Guinea
    Collection** (B)
Published by University of Papua New Guinea
    Library
POB 320, Waigani NCD 134
*Tel:* 326 0900 *Fax:* 326 7187
*E-mail:* library@upng.ac.pg
*Web Site:* www.upng.ac.pg
*Key Personnel*
Librarian: Florence Griffin
By Nancy Lutton (1980).

# Peru

**Boletin Bibliografico** (Bibliographical Bulletin)
    (J)
Published by Biblioteca Central de la Universidad
    Nacional Mayor de San Marcos
Pje Simon Rodriguez N°697, Lima
Mailing Address: Apdo 454, Lima 1
*Tel:* (014) 4285210 *Fax:* (014) 336337
*Key Personnel*
Dir: Dr Oswaldo Salaverry Garcia

**Boletin de la Biblioteca Nacional del Peru**
    (National Library of Peru Bulletin) (J)
Published by Biblioteca Nacional del Peru
Avda Abancay 4ta cuadra, Lima
*Tel:* (01) 428-7690; (01) 428-7696 *Fax:* (01) 427-
    7331
*E-mail:* jefatura@binape.gob.pe
*Web Site:* binape.perucultural.org.pe/
*Key Personnel*
Dir: Sinesio Lopez Jimenez
First published 1943.
Irregularly.

**FENIX Revista de la Biblioteca Nacional del
    Peru** (FENIX National Library of Peru
    Review) (J)
Published by Biblioteca Nacional del Peru
Avda Abancay 4ta cuadra, Lima 1
*Tel:* (01) 428-7690; (01) 428-7696 *Fax:* (01) 427-
    7331
*E-mail:* jefatura@binape.gob.pe
*Web Site:* binape.perucultural.org.pe/
*Key Personnel*
Dir: Sinesio Lopez Jimenez
First published 1944.
Annually.
44 (2003), 10 PEN (domestic); 25 USD (foreign)
ISSN: 0015-0002

# Philippines

**ASLP Bulletin** (J)
Published by Association of Special Libraries of
the Philippines (ASLP)
National Library of the Philippines, TM Kalaw
St, 1000 Ermita, Manila
*Tel:* (02) 525-3196; (02) 525-1748 *Fax:* (02) 524-
2324
*E-mail:* director@nlp.gov.ph
*Web Site:* www.nlp.gov.ph
*Key Personnel*
President: Lilia F Echiverri
Dir: Adoracion B Mendoza
Editor: Angelica A Carbanero
Text in English.
First published 1954.
Quarterly.
30 PHP or 15 USD per year to members
ISSN: 0001-2548

**Bulletin** (J)
Published by Philippine Librarians Association
Inc
The National Library Bldg, TM Kalaw St, Manila
1000
*Tel:* (02) 523-00-68 *Fax:* (02) 524-23-29
*E-mail:* amb@max.ph.net
*Web Site:* www.dlsu.edu.ph/library/plai
*Key Personnel*
President: Fe Angela Verzosa *Tel:* (02) 524-4611
*Fax:* (02) 524-8835 *E-mail:* libfamv@mail.
dlsu.edu.ph

**Index to Philippine Periodicals (IPP)** (B)
Published by University of the Philippines Li-
brary, Indexing Section
Gonzalez Hall Cor Apacible St, Diliman, 1101
Quezon City
*Tel:* (02) 981-8500 *Fax:* (02) 926-1876
*E-mail:* salvacion.arlante@up.edu.ph
*Web Site:* www.mainlib.upd.edu.ph
*Key Personnel*
University Librarian: Salvacion M Arlante
First published 1946.
Quarterly.

**Journal of Philippine Librarianship** (J)
Published by University of the Philippines, Insti-
tute of Library Science
Diliman, Quezon City 1101
*Tel:* (02) 920 5367 *Fax:* (02) 920 5367
*Web Site:* www.upd.edu.ph
*Key Personnel*
Business Manager: Nathalie N de la Torre
*E-mail:* nathalie8_4@yahoo.com
Text in English.
Annually.
150 PHP; 15 USD
ISSN: 0022-359X

**Newsletter** (J)
Published by University of the Philippines, Insti-
tute of Library Science
Diliman, Gonzalez Hall, 1101 Quezon City
*Tel:* (02) 920 5367 *Fax:* (02) 920 5367
*Web Site:* www.upd.edu.ph
*Key Personnel*
Business Manager: Nathalie N de la Torre
*E-mail:* nathalie8_4@yahoo.com
Text in English.
ISSN: 0300-3612

**Philippine National Bibliography** (J)
Published by National Library of the Philippines
T M Kalaw St, 1000 Ermita, Manila
*Tel:* (02) 583 252 *Fax:* (02) 502 329
*E-mail:* director@nlp.gov.ph; bibliography@nlp.
gov.ph

*Web Site:* www.nlp.gov.ph
*Key Personnel*
Chief: Leonila D A Tominez
First published 1974.
Quarterly with annual cumulation.
ISSN: 971-556
*Parent Company:* National Commission for Cul-
ture & the Arts

# Poland

**Bibliografia Wydawnictw CIAGLYCH**
(Bibliography of Polish Serials) (J)
Published by Biblioteka Narodowa w Warszawie
(The National Library in Warsaw)
al Niepodleglosci 213, 02-086 Warsaw
*Tel:* (022) 608-2999 *Fax:* (022) 825-5251
*E-mail:* biblnar@bn.org.pl
*Web Site:* www.bn.org.pl
*Telex:* 813702 BNPL; 816761 *Cable:* AL
NIEPODLEGLOSCI
*Key Personnel*
Dir: Michael Jagiello
Librarian: Ewa Krysiak *E-mail:* ekrysiak@biblnar.
bn.org.pl
Available in CD-ROM or online only.
Annually.

**Bibliotekarz** (The Librarian) (J)
Published by Polish Librarians' Association
al Niepodleglosci 213, 02-086 Warsaw
*Tel:* (022) 825-50-24 *Fax:* (022) 825-53-49
*E-mail:* wyd.sbp-portal@wp.pl
*Web Site:* ebib.oss.wroc.pl/sbp/wydaw.htm
*Key Personnel*
President: Stanislaw Czajka
Dir: Janusz Nowicki
Editor-in-Chief: Jan Wolosz
Text in Polish. Summaries in English & Russian.
Weekly.

**Biblioteki Publiczne w Liczbach** (Public
Libraries in Figures) (B)
Published by Biblioteka Narodowa w Warszawie
(The National Library in Warsaw)
al Niepodleglosci 213, 02-086 Warsaw
*Tel:* (022) 608-2999 *Fax:* (022) 825-5251
*E-mail:* biblnar@bn.org.pl
*Web Site:* www.bn.org.pl
*Telex:* 816761
*Key Personnel*
Dir: Prof Adam Manikowski
ISSN: 0137-2726

**Informator Adresowy Podstawowych Placowek
Informacji Naukowej i Technicznej** (B)
Published by Centralne Laboratorium Przemyslu
Ziemniacanego (Starch & Potato Products Re-
search Laboratory)
ul Armii Poznari 49, 62-030 Lubon
*Tel:* (061) 8934605 *Fax:* (061) 8934608
*E-mail:* clpz@man.poznan.pl
*Web Site:* www.clpz.poznan.pl
ISBN(s): 83-907889
ISSN: 83-907889

**Informator Biblioteczny** (Library Guide) (B)
Published by Polish Librarians' Association
ul Konopczynskiego 5/7, 00-335 Warsaw
*Tel:* (022) 827-52-96
*E-mail:* biurozqsbp@wp.pl
*Web Site:* ebib.oss.wroc.pl/sbp/english/index_en.
html
*Key Personnel*
President: Stanislaw Czajka
Dir: Janusz Nowicki

**Informator Nauki Polskiej** (Polish Research
Directory) (B)
Published by Osrodek Przetwarzania Informacji
Al Niepodleglosci 188 B, 00-950 Warsaw
*Tel:* (022) 825 12 40 *Fax:* (022) 825 33 19
*E-mail:* opi@opi.org.pl
*Web Site:* www.opi.org.pl
*Key Personnel*
Dir: Pawel Gierycz *Tel:* (022) 825 61 78
*E-mail:* gierycz@opi.org.pl
Available in Polish & English language versions,
four volumes.

**Informator o Bibliotekach Wspolpracujacych
w Ramach Specjalizacji Zbiorow**
(Information About Modern Libraries Working
on Group Specializations) (B)
Published by Biblioteka Glowna Politechniki
Warszawskiej
Plac Politechniki 1, 00-661 Warsaw
*Tel:* (022) 621-13-70 *Fax:* (022) 621-13-70
*Web Site:* www.bg.pw.edu.pl
*Key Personnel*
Dir: Elzbieta Dudzinska *E-mail:* dudz@bg.pw.
edu.pl

**Katalog Rozpraw Doktorskich i
Habilitacyjnych** (Science, Information,
Business-Catalogue of Doctoral &
Habilitational Dissertations) (P)
Published by Osrodek Przetwarzania Informacji
Al Niepodleglosci 188 B, 00-950 Warsaw
Mailing Address: PO Box 355, 00-950 Warsaw
*Tel:* (022) 825 12 40 *Fax:* (022) 825 33 19
*E-mail:* opi@opi.org.pl
*Web Site:* www.opi.org.pl
*Key Personnel*
Dir: Pawel Gierycz *Tel:* (022) 825 61 78
*E-mail:* gierycz@opi.org.pl
Annually.

**Komputerowe Bazy Danych o Nauce i Technice**
(Computerized Databases on Science &
Technology) (B)
Published by Osrodek Przetwarzania Informacji
Al Niepodleglosci 188 B, 00-950 Warsaw
Mailing Address: PO Box 355, 00-950 Warsaw
*Tel:* (022) 825 12 40 *Fax:* (022) 825 33 19
*E-mail:* opi@opi.org.pl
*Web Site:* www.opi.org.pl
*Key Personnel*
Dir: Pawel Gierycz *Tel:* (022) 825 61 78
*E-mail:* gierycz@opi.org.pl

**Nauka, Informacja, Biznes** (Science,
Information, Business) (P)
Published by Osrodek Przetwarzania Informacji
Al Niepodleglosci 188 B, 00-950 Warsaw
Mailing Address: PO Box 355, 00-950 Warsaw
*Tel:* (022) 825 12 40 *Fax:* (022) 825 33 19
*E-mail:* opi@opi.org.pl
*Web Site:* www.opi.org.pl
*Key Personnel*
Dir: Pawel Gierycz *Tel:* (022) 825 61 78
*E-mail:* gierycz@opi.org.pl
Seven mathematical series.
Quarterly.

**Placowki Informacji Naukowej i Technicznej w
Polsce** (Scientific & Technical Information
Centres in Poland) (B)
Published by Osrodek Przetwarzania Informacji
Al Niepodleglosci 188 B, 00-950 Warsaw
Mailing Address: PO Box 355, 00-950 Warsaw
*Tel:* (022) 825 12 40 *Fax:* (022) 825 33 19
*E-mail:* opi@opi.org.pl
*Web Site:* www.opi.org.pl
*Key Personnel*
Dir: Pawel Gierycz *Tel:* (022) 825 61 78
*E-mail:* gierycz@opi.org.pl

**Polska Bibliografia Bibliologiczna** (Polish
Bibliography of Library Science) (B)
Published by Biblioteka Narodowa w Warszawie
(The National Library in Warsaw)
al Niepodleglosci 213, 02-086 Warsaw
*Tel:* (022) 608-2999 *Fax:* (022) 825-5251
*E-mail:* biblnar@bn.org.pl
*Web Site:* www.bn.org.pl
*Telex:* 816761
*Key Personnel*
Dir: Prof Adam Manikowski

**Poradnik Bibliotekarza** (The Librarian's
Adviser) (J)
Published by Polish Librarians' Association
al Niepodleglosci 213, 02-086 Warsaw
*Tel:* (022) 825-50-24 *Fax:* (022) 825-53-49
*E-mail:* sbp@ceti.pl
*Web Site:* ebib.oss.wroc.pl/sbp/wydaw.htm
*Key Personnel*
President: Stanislaw Czaja
Editor-in-Chief: Jadwiga Chruscinska *Tel:* (022)
822-99-78
Monthly.

**Rocznik Biblioteki Narodowej** (National Library
Yearbook) (B)
Published by Biblioteka Narodowa w Warszawie
(The National Library in Warsaw)
al Niepodleglosci 213, 02-086 Warsaw
*Tel:* (022) 608-2999; (022) 452-2999 *Fax:* (022)
825 5349
*E-mail:* biblnar@bn.org.pl
*Web Site:* www.bn.org.pl
*Telex:* 816761
Covers scientific library science with text in Pol-
ish with English summaries.
Annually.
ISSN: 0083-7261

# Portugal

**Boletim de Bibliografia Portuguesa** (J)
Published by Instituto da Biblioteca Nacional e
do Livro
Campo Grande 83, 1751 Lisbon
*Tel:* (021) 7967639; (021) 7950134; (021)
7982000 *Fax:* (021) 7982138
*E-mail:* bn@bn.pt
*Web Site:* www.bn.pt
*Key Personnel*
Assistant Dir: Fernanda Maria Fields *Tel:* (021)
7982022 *E-mail:* fcampos@bn.pt
Portuguese Bibliographic Bulletin.

**Cadernos de Biblioteconomia, Arquivistica e
Documentacao** (Library Management,
Archives & Documentation) (J)
Published by Associacao Portuguesa de Bibliote-
carios, Arquivistas e Documentalistas (The Por-
tuguese Association of Librarians Archivists &
Documentalists)
R Morais Soares, 43-C, 1° Dto, 1900-341 Lisbon
*Tel:* (021) 816 19 80 *Fax:* (021) 815 45 08
*E-mail:* apbad@apbad.pt
*Web Site:* www.apbad.pt
*Key Personnel*
President: Antonio Jose de Pina Falcao
Coordinator: Jose Manuel Felix Correia
Triannually.

**Guia de Servicos de Documentacao e de
Bibliotecas em Portugal** (List of Portuguese
Libraries & Documentation Services) (B)
Published by Fundacao para a Ciencia e a Tec-
nologia/Servico de Informacao e Documenta-
cao(SID)

Av D Carlos I, 126, 1249-074 Lisbon
*Tel:* (021) 3924440 *Fax:* (021) 3957284
*E-mail:* sid@fct.mces.pt
*Web Site:* www.fct.mct.pt
*Key Personnel*
President: Prof Fernando Ramoa Ribeiro
Dir: Dr Gabriela Lopes da Silva *E-mail:* g.l.
silva@fct.mct.pt
Internet database only at www.fct.mct.pt, option:
Bibliotecas com Revistas de C&T.

**Sumarios das Publicacoes Periodicas
Portuguesas** (Current Contents of Portuguese
Periodicals) (J)
Published by Biblioteca Geral da Universidade
de Coimbra (University of Coimbra General
Library)
Largo da Porta Ferrea, 3000-447 Coimbra
*Tel:* (0239) 859800; (0239) 859800/15
*Fax:* (0239) 827135
*E-mail:* bguc@uc.pt
*Web Site:* www.uc.pt
*Key Personnel*
Dir: Carlos Manuel Baptista Fiolhais

# Romania

**ABSI - Abstracte in bibliologie si stiinta
informarii** (ABSI - Abstracts in Library &
Information Science) (J)
Published by National Library
Str Ion Ghica nr 4, 79708 Bucharest
*Tel:* (01) 314 24 34; (01) 314 24 33; (01) 315 70
63 *Fax:* (01) 312 33 81
*E-mail:* go@bibnat.ro
*Web Site:* www.bibnat.ro
*Key Personnel*
Dir General: Ion Dan Erceanu *Tel:* (021) 310 08
60
Chief Editor: Ioana Varlan
Contact: Dina Paladi *Tel:* (021) 314 24 34 ext
131 *E-mail:* dina.paladi@bibnat.ro
First published 1960.
Monthly.
51 pp
ISSN: 1220-3092

**Biblioteconomie Culegere de Traduceri
Prelucrate** (Librarianship: Collected Adapted
Translations) (J)
Published by National Library
Str Ion Ghica nr 4, Sector 3, 79708 Bucharest
*Tel:* (01) 314 24 34; (01) 314 24 33; (01) 315 70
63 *Fax:* (01) 312 33 81
*E-mail:* go@bibnat.ro
*Web Site:* www.bibnat.ro
*Key Personnel*
Dir General: Ion Dan Erceanu *Tel:* (021) 310 08
60
Chief Editor: Anca Moraru
Librarianship: Collected adapted translations.
First published 1964.
Quarterly.
95 pp
ISSN: 1220-3076

**Probleme de Informare si Documentare**
(Information & Documentation Problems) (J)
Published by National Institute for Information &
Documentation
21-25 Mendeleev St, Sector 1, Bucharest 70141
*Tel:* (01) 315 87 65 *Fax:* (01) 312 67 34
*E-mail:* inid@home.ro
*Key Personnel*
Editor: Viorica Prodan
About 500 different publications in Romanian,
periodicals (science, know-hows, machines,
products, works, etc).

First published 1967.
Quarterly.
ISSN: 0032-924X

# Russian Federation

**Bibliotechnoe delo i Bibliografiya
Bibliografieheskaya informatsiya** (Library
Science & Theory of Bibliography,
Bibliographic Information) (B)
Published by Russian State Library
3/5 Vozdvizhenka St, 119019 Moscow
*Tel:* (095) 202-5790 (inquiries); (095) 202-7607
(administration) *Fax:* (095) 290-6062
*E-mail:* mbs@rsl.ru
*Web Site:* www.rsl.ru
*Telex:* 411167 GBL SU
*Key Personnel*
Dir: Viktor Vasilyevich Fedorov, PhD

**Biblioteka** (The Librarian) (J)
Published by Tovarishchestvo Libedeya
Prospekt Marksa ll-1, 121019 Moscow
*Tel:* (095) 9258387 *Fax:* (095) 2029716
*E-mail:* biblio@gpntb.ru
*Telex:* 411167 GBLSU
*Key Personnel*
Editor: S I Samsonov
Co-Sponsor: Ministry of Culture.
First published 1923.
Monthly.
130 USD/yr
ISSN: 0869-4915

**Biblioteka v epohu peremen, Informatsionnyj
sbornik** (J)
Published by Russian State Library
3/5 Vozdvizhenka St, 119019 Moscow
*Tel:* (095) 202-5790 (inquiries); (095) 202-7607
(administration) *Fax:* (095) 290-6062
*E-mail:* mbs@rsl.ru
*Web Site:* www.rsl.ru
*Key Personnel*
Dir: Viktor Vasilyevich Fedorov, PhD
First published 1999.
Quarterly.
160 pp, 50 USD

**Bibliotekovedenie** (Library Science) (J)
Published by Russian State Library
3/5 Vozdvizhenka St, 119019 Moscow
*Tel:* (095) 202-5790 (inquiries); (095) 202-7607
(administration) *Fax:* (095) 290-6062
*E-mail:* mbs@rsl.ru
*Web Site:* www.rsl.ru
*Key Personnel*
Dir: Viktor Vasilyevich Fedorov, PhD

**Bibliotekovedenie i Bibliografiya za
Rubezhom-Librarianship & Bibliography
Abroad** (Librarianship & Bibliography
Abroad) (B)
Published by Russian State Library
3/5 Vozdvizhenka St, 119019 Moscow
*Tel:* (095) 202-5790 (inquiries); (095) 202-7607
(administration) *Fax:* (095) 290-6062
*E-mail:* mbs@rsl.ru
*Web Site:* www.rsl.ru
*Telex:* 411167 GBL SU
*Key Personnel*
Dir: Viktor Vasilyevich Fedorov, PhD

**Esteticheskoe vospitanie
Referativno-Bibliograficheskaya informatsiya**
(Aesthetic Education Bibliographic
Information) (B)

Published by Russian State Library
3/5 Vozdvizhenka St, 119019 Moscow
*Tel:* (095) 202-5790 (inquiries); (095) 202-7607
   (administration) *Fax:* (095) 290-6062
*E-mail:* mbs@rsl.ru
*Web Site:* www.rsl.ru
*Telex:* 411167 GBL SU
*Key Personnel*
Dir: Viktor Vasilyevich Fedorov, PhD

**Izobrazitelnoye Iskustvo, Bibliograficheskaya
   Informatsiya** (Fine Art, Bibliographic
   Information) (B)
Published by Russian State Library
3/5 Vozdvizhenka St, 119019 Moscow
*Tel:* (095) 202-5790 (inquiries); (095) 202-7607
   (administration) *Fax:* (095) 290-6062
*E-mail:* mbs@rsl.ru
*Web Site:* www.rsl.ru
*Telex:* 411167 GBL SU
*Key Personnel*
Dir: Viktor Vasilyevich Fedorov, PhD
Theory & practice of fine art in Russia & abroad.

**Kultura, Kulturologiya,
   Referativno-bibliograficheskaya informatsiya**
   (Culture, Culturology, Bibliographic
   Information) (J)
Published by Russian State Library
3/5 Vozdvizhenka St, 119019 Moscow
*Tel:* (095) 202-5790 (inquiries); (095) 202-7607
   (administration) *Fax:* (095) 290-6062
*E-mail:* mbs@rsl.ru
*Web Site:* www.rsl.ru
*Key Personnel*
Dir: Viktor Vasilyevich Fedorov, PhD

**Kultura v Sovremennom Mire, Informatsionni
   Sbornik** (Culture in the Modern World, Serial
   Information) (B)
Published by Russian State Library
3/5 Vozdvizhenka St, 119019 Moscow
*Tel:* (095) 202-5790 (inquiries); (095) 202-7607
   (administration) *Fax:* (095) 290-6062
*E-mail:* mbs@rsl.ru
*Web Site:* www.rsl.ru
*Telex:* 411167 GBL SU
*Key Personnel*
Dir: Viktor Vasilyevich Fedorov, PhD
The world cultural process, cultural policy, views
   & analyses, innovation in culture & art.

**Massovaya Biblioteca, Teoriya i Practica**
   (Public Library, Theory & Practice) (B)
Published by Russian State Library
3/5 Vozdvizhenka St, 119019 Moscow
*Tel:* (095) 202-5790 (inquiries); (095) 202-7607
   (administration) *Fax:* (095) 290-6062
*E-mail:* mbs@rsl.ru
*Web Site:* www.rsl.ru
*Key Personnel*
Dir: Viktor Vasilyevich Fedorov, PhD
Serial information publication.

**Materialnaya Baza Sfery Kulturi,
   Informatsionni Sbornik** (Material Base of the
   Cultural Sphere, Serial Information) (B)
Published by Russian State Library
3/5 Vozdvizhenka St, 119019 Moscow
*Tel:* (095) 202-5790 (inquiries); (095) 202-7607
   (administration) *Fax:* (095) 290-6062
*E-mail:* mbs@rsl.ru
*Web Site:* www.rsl.ru
*Telex:* 411167 GBL SU
*Key Personnel*
Dir: Viktor Vasilyevich Fedorov, PhD
Material & technical facilities, economy, manage-
   ment in culture.

**Mir Bibliotek Segodnya** (Library World Today)
   (J)
Published by Russian State Library
3/5 Vozdvizhenka St, 119019 Moscow
*Tel:* (095) 202-5790 (inquiries); (095) 202-7607
   (administration) *Fax:* (095) 290-6062
*E-mail:* mbs@rsl.ru
*Web Site:* www.rsl.ru
*Key Personnel*
Dir: Viktor Vasilyevich Fedorov, PhD
Original & abstract information on Russian &
   world libraries. Serial information publication.

**Muzeynoe delo i ohrana pamyatnikov,
   Referativno-bibliograficheskaya informatsiya**
   (Museums & Protection of Monuments,
   Bibliographic Information) (J)
Published by Russian State Library
3/5 Vozdvizhenka St, 119019 Moscow
*Tel:* (095) 202-5790 (inquiries); (095) 202-7607
   (administration) *Fax:* (095) 290-6062
*E-mail:* mbs@rsl.ru
*Web Site:* www.rsl.ru
*Key Personnel*
Dir: Viktor Vasilyevich Fedorov, PhD

**Muzika, Bibliograficheskaya Informatsiya**
   (Music, Bibliographic Information) (B)
Published by Russian State Library
3/5 Vozdvizhenka St, 119019 Moscow
*Tel:* (095) 202-5790 (inquiries); (095) 202-7607
   (administration) *Fax:* (095) 290-6062
*E-mail:* mbs@rsl.ru
*Web Site:* www.rsl.ru
*Telex:* 411167 GBL SU
*Key Personnel*
Dir: Viktor Vasilyevich Fedorov, PhD
Theory, history & genres of music.

**Narodnoie Tvorchestvo: Sociokulturnaya
   Deyatelnost v Sfere Dosuga, Informatsionni
   Sbornik** (Sociocultural Activity in the Sphere
   of Leisure, Serial Information) (B)
Published by Russian State Library
3/5 Vozdvizhenka St, 119019 Moscow
*Tel:* (095) 202-5790 (inquiries); (095) 202-7607
   (administration) *Fax:* (095) 290-6062
*E-mail:* mbs@rsl.ru
*Web Site:* www.rsl.ru
*Key Personnel*
Dir: Viktor Vasilyevich Fedorov, PhD
Folk art, amateur activity & national traditional
   art.

**Nauchnye i tekhnicheskie biblioteki** (Scientific
   & Technical Libraries) (J)
Published by GPNTB Rossii
Kuznetskii Most 12, 103031 Moscow
*Tel:* (095) 9259288 *Fax:* (095) 9219862
*E-mail:* info@gpntb.ru; gpntb@gpntb.ru
*Web Site:* www.gpntb.ru
*Telex:* 411167 GBLSU
*Key Personnel*
Dir & Editor-in-Chief: Dr A I Zemskov
Professional journal on library science & the
   practice of regional & metropolitan libraries
   of all types, sci-tech information centers, LIS
   colleges & universities.
First published 1961.
Monthly.
140 pp, 129.95 USD per year
ISSN: 0130-9765

**Nauka o Kulture, Itogi i perspektivy,
   Informatsionnyj sbornik** (Culture Science,
   Results & Perspectives, Serial Information) (J)
Published by Russian State Library
3/5 Vozdvizhenka St, 119019 Moscow
*Tel:* (095) 202-5790 (inquiries); (095) 202-7371
   (administration) *Fax:* (095) 290-6062
*E-mail:* nbros@rsl.ru

*Web Site:* www.rsl.ru
*Key Personnel*
Dir: Viktor Vasilyevich Fedorov, PhD

**Panorama kulturnoi zhizni Rossiyskoi
   Federatsii, Informatsionnyj sbornik**
   (Panorama of Cultural Life in Russian
   Federation, Serial Information) (J)
Published by Russian State Library
3/5 Vozdvizhenka St, 119019 Moscow
*Tel:* (095) 202-5790 (inquiries); (095) 202-7371
   (administration) *Fax:* (095) 290-6062
*E-mail:* nbros@rsl.ru
*Web Site:* www.rsl.ru
*Key Personnel*
Dir: Viktor Vasilyevich Fedorov, PhD

**Panorama kulturnoi zhizni stran SNG i Baltii,
   Informatsionnyj sbornik** (Panorama of
   Cultural Life in the States of the CIS & in the
   Baltic States, Serial Information) (J)
Published by Russian State Library
3/5 Vozdvizhenka St, 119019 Moscow
*Tel:* (095) 202-5790 (inquiries); (095) 202-7371
   (administration) *Fax:* (095) 290-6062
*E-mail:* nbros@rsl.ru
*Web Site:* www.rsl.ru
*Key Personnel*
Dir: Viktor Vasilyevich Fedorov, PhD

**Panorama kulturnoi zhizni zarubezhnyh stran
   Informatsionnyj sbornik** (Panorama of
   Cultural Life Abroad. Serial Information) (J)
Published by Russian State Library
3/5 Vozdvizhenka St, 119019 Moscow
*Tel:* (095) 202-5790 (inquiries); (095) 202-7371
   (administration) *Fax:* (095) 290-6062
*E-mail:* nbros@rsl.ru
*Web Site:* www.rsl.ru
*Key Personnel*
Dir: Viktor Vasilyevich Fedorov, PhD

**Russkaya Kultura Vne Granits** (Russian
   Culture Beyond Frontiers) (B)
Published by Russian State Library
3/5 Vozdvizhenka St, 119019 Moscow
*Tel:* (095) 202-5790 (inquiries); (095) 202-7371
   (administration) *Fax:* (095) 290-6062
*E-mail:* nbros@rsl.ru
*Web Site:* www.rsl.ru
*Key Personnel*
Dir: Viktor Vasilyevich Fedorov, PhD
Serial Information Culture, History & Policy.

**Sociokulturnaya Deyatelnost v Sfere Dosuga,
   Referativno-Bibliograficheskaya
   Informatsiya** (Sociocultural Activities in the
   Sphere of Leisure, Bibliographic Information)
   (B)
Published by Russian State Library
3/5 Vozdvizhenka St, 119019 Moscow
*Tel:* (095) 202-5790 (inquiries); (095) 202-7371
   (administration) *Fax:* (095) 290-6062
*E-mail:* nbros@rsl.ru
*Web Site:* www.rsl.ru
*Telex:* 411167 GBL SU
*Key Personnel*
Dir: Viktor Vasilyevich Fedorov, PhD
Problems of outdoor recreation.

**Zrelischnie Iskustva
   Referativno-Bibliograficheskaya
   Informatsiya** (Performing Arts, Bibliographic
   Information) (B)
Published by Russian State Library
3/5 Vozdvizhenka St, 119019 Moscow
*Tel:* (095) 202-5790 (inquiries); (095) 202-7371
   (administration) *Fax:* (095) 290-6062
*E-mail:* nbros@rsl.ru
*Web Site:* www.rsl.ru
*Telex:* 411167 GBL SU

*Key Personnel*
Dir: Viktor Vasilyevich Fedorov, PhD
Theatre, circus, dance & music hall art.

# Saudi Arabia

**Bulletin** (J)
Published by King Fahad National Library
PO Box 7572, Riyadh 11472
*Tel:* (01) 462 4888 *Fax:* (01) 464 5341
*Web Site:* www.kfnl.gov.sa
*Key Personnel*
Dir: Abdur Rahman Al Sarra

**Directory of Libraries in Saudi Arabia** (B)
Published by King Saud University Library
al-Jami'ah St, Riyadh 11495
Mailing Address: PO Box 22480, Riyadh 11495
*Tel:* (01) 4676148; (01) 4676 6149 *Fax:* (01) 467 6162
*E-mail:* sfalogia@ksu.edu.sa
*Web Site:* www.ksu.edu.sa
*Key Personnel*
Dean: Dr Sulaiman S Al-Agla
First published 1979.
215 pp

# Senegal

**Repertoire des Bibliotheques et Organismes de Documentation au Senegal** (Catalogue of the Libraries and Documentation Centres of Senegal) (B)
Published by Ecole des Bibliothecaires, Archivistes et Documentalistes de l'Universite Cheikh Anta Diop de Dakar
Faculty of Arts & Social Sciences, BP 3252 Dakar
*Tel:* 825 76 60; 864 21 22 *Fax:* 824 05 42
*E-mail:* ebad@ebad.ucad.sn
*Web Site:* www.ebad.ucad.sn
*Key Personnel*
Dir: Mbaye Thiam *E-mail:* mbaye.thiam@ebad.ucad.sn
Archives & documentation centres throughout Senegal. Information on 124 libraries.

# Serbia and Montenegro

**Biblioteke u Jugoslaviji** (Libraries in Yugoslavia) (B)
Published by Jugoslovenski Bibliografsko-informacijski institut, Yubin, Agencija za ISBN (Yugoslav Institute for Bibliography & Information)
Terazije 26, 11000 Belgrade
*Tel:* (011) 687 836 *Fax:* (011) 687 760
*E-mail:* yubin@jbi.jbi.bg.ac.yu
*Web Site:* www.jbi.bg.ac.yu
*Key Personnel*
Contact: Vera Stojadinovic

**Biblioteke u SR Srbiji** (Libraries in Serbia) (B)
Published by Narodna Biblioteka Srbije (National Library of Serbia)
Skerliceva 1, 11000 Belgrade
*Tel:* (011) 2451 242

*Web Site:* www.nbs.bg.ac.yu
*Key Personnel*
Dir: Milomir Petrovic

# Sierra Leone

**SLAALIS Bulletin** (J)
Published by Sierra Leone Association of Archivists, Librarians & Information Scientists (SLAALIS)
7 Percival St, Freetown
*Tel:* (022) 23848
*Key Personnel*
Chief Librarian: Irene O'Brien-Coker
First published 1987.
Quarterly.
1.50 SLL per year

# Singapore

**Directory of Libraries in Singapore** (B)
Published by Library Association of Singapore
Geylang East Community Library, 50 Geylang East Ave 1, 3rd floor, Singapore 389777
*Tel:* 6749 7990 *Fax:* 6749 7480
*Web Site:* www.las.org.sg
*Key Personnel*
President: Mr Choy Fatt Cheong *Tel:* 780 5289
  *E-mail:* choyfc@tp.edu.sg
Administrative Officer: Ms Azian Mohammad
  *E-mail:* lassec@singnet.com.sg
80 SGD plus postage & admin

**Singapore Journal of Library Information Management** (B)
Published by Library Association of Singapore
Geylang East Community Library, 50 Geylang East Ave 1, 3rd floor, Singapore 389777
*Tel:* 6749 7990 *Fax:* 6749 7480
*Web Site:* www.las.org.sg
*Key Personnel*
President: Mr Choy Fatt Cheong *Tel:* 780 5289
  *E-mail:* choyfc@tp.edu.sg
Administrative Officer: Ms Azian Mohammad
  *E-mail:* lassec@singnet.com.sg
Annually.
40 SGD (local & Malaysia); 60 SGD (other countries)

**Singapore Libraries Bulletin** (P)
Published by Library Association of Singapore
Geylang East Community Library, 50 Geylang East Ave 1, 3rd floor, Singapore 389777
*Tel:* 6749 7990 *Fax:* 6749 7480
*Web Site:* www.las.org.sg
*Key Personnel*
Editor: Ms Zarinah Mohamed *E-mail:* zarinah@las.org.sg
Quarterly.

**Singapore Periodicals Index** (P)
Published by National Library Board Singapore, Library Supply Services
91 Stamford Rd, Singapore 178896
*Tel:* 6546 7225 *Fax:* 6546 7262
*Web Site:* www.nlb.gov.sg *Cable:* RS 26620 NATLIB
Serial (CD-ROM).
First published 1969.
Annually.
ISSN: 0377-7928

# Slovenia

**Knjiznica: Revija za Podrocje Bibliotekarstva in Informacijske Znanosti** (Library: Journal for Library & Information Science) (J)
Published by Zveza bibliotekarskih drustev Slovenije (ZBDS) (Union of Associations of Slovene Librarians)
Turjaska 1, 1000 Ljubljana
*Tel:* (01) 2001 193 *Fax:* (01) 4257 293
*E-mail:* zveza-biblio.ds-nuk@quest.arnes.si
*Web Site:* www.zbds-zveza.si
*Key Personnel*
President: Melita Ambrozic *Tel:* (01) 20 01 207
  *E-mail:* melita.ambrozic@nuk.uni-lj.si
Text in Slovenian; summaries in English. Library & information sciences.
First published 1957.
Quarterly.
150 pp, 7,100 SIT/yr (domestic); 62 EUR/yr (foreign)
ISSN: 0023-2424

# South Africa

**Cape Librarian** (P)
Published by Cape Provincial Library Service
PO Box 2108, Cape Town 8000
*Tel:* (021) 4102 446 *Fax:* (021) 419 7541
*E-mail:* capelib@pawc.wcape.gov.za
*Web Site:* www.westerncape.gov.za
*Key Personnel*
Dir: N F Van Der Merwe
Text in Afrikaans & English.
First published 1957.
Monthly (except July & Dec).
ISSN: 0008-5790

**Free State Libraries** (J)
Published by Department of Sport, Arts, Culture, Science & Technology Library, Information & Technology Services Directorate
Private Bag X20606, Bloemfontein 9300
*Tel:* (051) 4054681 *Fax:* (051) 4033567
*E-mail:* loader@majuba.ofs.gov.za; jacomien@majuba.ofs.gov.za
*Telex:* 267056t
*Key Personnel*
Editor: Adri Smuts
First published 1958.
Quarterly.
ISSN: 0016-0458

**Index to South African Periodicals (ISAP)** (J)
Published by National Library of South Africa
239 Vermeulen St, Pretoria
Mailing Address: PO Box 397, 0001 Pretoria
*Tel:* (012) 321 8931 *Fax:* (012) 325 5984
*E-mail:* askotze@statelib.pwv.gov.za
*Web Site:* www.nlsa.ac.za
*Key Personnel*
Dir: Dr Peter J Lor
First published 1940.

**Kwaznaplis** (J)
Published by Kwazulu Natal Provincial Library Services
PB X9016, Pietermaritzbur, Kwazulu-Natal 3200
*Tel:* (0331) 940241 *Fax:* (0331) 942237
*Key Personnel*
Editor: J R Hart *E-mail:* hartj@natalia.kzntl.gov.za
First published 1971.
6 times/yr.
Free to libraries in South Africa

**LIASA News** (J)
Published by Library & Information Association
   of South Africa (LIASA)
PO Box 1598, Pretoria 0001
*Tel:* (012) 481 2870; (012) 481 2875; (012) 481
   2876 *Fax:* (012) 481 2873
*E-mail:* liasa@liasa.org.za
*Web Site:* www.liasa.org.za
*Key Personnel*
Executive Dir: Gwenda Thomas
Quarterly.

**Local Government Library Bulletin** (J)
Published by Johannesburg Public Library
Library Gardens, Corner Fraser & Market Sts,
   Johannesburg 2001
Mailing Address: PB X93, Marshalltown 2107
*Tel:* (011) 836 3787 *Fax:* (011) 836 6607
*E-mail:* library@mj.org.za
*Key Personnel*
Librarian: E J Bevan *E-mail:* jbevan@mj.org.za
Monthly.
Free

**Mousaion** (P)
Published by Unisa Press
Unisa Main Campus, Preller St, Nieu Muck-
   leneuk, Pretoria 0003
Mailing Address: PO Box 392, Unisa 0003
*Tel:* (012) 429-4111 *Fax:* (012) 429-4111
*E-mail:* kempg@alpha.unisa.ac.za
*Web Site:* www.unisa.ac.za
*Telex:* 350068 *Cable:* UNISA
*Key Personnel*
Editor: Prof J A Kruger
Biannually.
20 USD

**Periodicals in Southern African Libraries**
   **(PISAL)** (J)
Published by National Library of South Africa
239 Vermeulen St, Pretoria
Mailing Address: PO Box 397, 0001 Pretoria
*Tel:* (012) 321 8931 *Fax:* (012) 325 5984
*Web Site:* www.nlsa.ac.za
*Key Personnel*
Dir: Dr Peter J Lor

**Quarterly Bulletin of the South African**
   **Library** (J)
Published by National Library of South Africa
5 Queen Victoria St, Cape Town 8000
Mailing Address: PO Box 496, Cape Town 8000
*Tel:* (021) 424 6320 (ext 238) *Fax:* (021) 423
   3359
*E-mail:* docdel@nlsa.ac.za
*Web Site:* www.nlsa.ac.za

**South African Journal of Library &**
   **Information Science** (J)
Published by Library & Information Association
   of South Africa (LIASA)
PO Box 1598, Pretoria 0001
*Tel:* (012) 481 2870; (012) 481 2875; (012) 481
   2876 *Fax:* (012) 481 2873
*E-mail:* liasa@liasa.org.za
*Web Site:* www.liasa.org.za
*Key Personnel*
Executive Dir: Gwenda Thomas
Biannually.

**South African Journal of Library &**
   **Information Science** (J)
Published by Bureau for Scientific Publications
PO Box 11663, Pretoria, Hatfield 0028
*Tel:* (012) 3226404 *Fax:* (012) 3207803
*E-mail:* bspman@icon.co.za
*Telex:* 350068
*Key Personnel*
Editor: C M Walker
First published 1933.

Quarterly.
330 ZAR/yr (institutions)
ISSN: 0256-8861

**South African National Bibliography (SANB)**
   (J)
Published by National Library of South Africa
239 Vermeulen St, Pretoria
Mailing Address: PO Box 397, 0001 Pretoria
*Tel:* (012) 321 8931 *Fax:* (012) 325 5984
*Web Site:* www.nlsa.ac.za
Annual cumulation.
ISSN: 0085-5677

# Spain

**Biblioteca Hispana** (Spanish Library) (B)
Published by Consejo Superior de Investigaciones
   Cientificas
Vitruvio, 8, 28006 Madrid
SAN: 001-1347
*Tel:* (091) 562 96 33 *Fax:* (091) 562 96 34
*E-mail:* publ@orgc.csic.es
*Web Site:* www.csic.es/publica
*Key Personnel*
Pres: Cesar Nombela Cano

# Sri Lanka

**Directory of Social Science Libraries,**
   **Information Centres and Data Bases in Sri**
   **Lanka 1990** (B)
Published by National Library & Documentation
   Centre
No 14, Independence Ave, Colombo 07
*Tel:* (01) 698847; (01) 685197 *Fax:* (011)
   2685201
*E-mail:* nldsb@mail.natlib.lk; nldsb@mail.natlib.
   lk
*Web Site:* www.natlib.lk
*Key Personnel*
Dir General: Mr M S U Amarasiri *E-mail:* dg@
   mail.natlib.lk
Other publications relevent to Social Sciences,
   Conference Index; Selected Bibliography on
   SAARC; Sri Lanka Pustakala Namawaliya; Sri
   Lanka Rajaye Prakashana Namawaliya; Direc-
   tory of Libraries in Sri Lanka; Directory of So-
   cial Scientists in Sri Lanka Part I; Bibliography
   on Kataragama; Bibliography on Mahindaga-
   manaya; Lama Grantha Namawaliaya; Pustakala Dave Bhanda; Sri Lanka Newspaper article index.

**Library News** (J)
Published by National Library & Documentation
   Centre
No 14, Independence Ave, Colombo 07
*Tel:* (011) 2698847; (011) 2685197 *Fax:* (01)
   685201
*E-mail:* nldsb@mail.natlib.lk; nldsb@mail.natlib.
   lk
*Web Site:* www.natlib.lk
*Key Personnel*
Dir General: Mr M S U Amarasiri *E-mail:* dg@
   mail.natlib.lk
Quarterly.
ISSN: 1391-0000

**Sri Lanka Library Review** (J)
Published by Sri Lanka Library Association
275/75 Bauddhaloka Mawatha, Colombo 7

*Tel:* (011) 2589103; (011) 2556990 *Fax:* (011)
   2589103
*E-mail:* slla@operamail.com
*Web Site:* www.naresa.ac.lk/slla
*Key Personnel*
President: Mrs Daya Ratnayake
General Secretary: Ms Deepali Talagala

**Sri Lanka Periodicals Index** (P)
Published by Sri Lanka Department of National
   Museums
Sir Marcus Fernando Mawatha, PO Box 854,
   Colombo 07
*Tel:* (01) 695 366 *Fax:* (01) 695 366
*Key Personnel*
Contact: Lionel R Amarakoon
First published 1969.
Biannually.

# Swaziland

**Directory of Swaziland Libraries** (B)
Published by University of Swaziland Library
Private Bag 4, Kwaluseni
*Tel:* 518-4011; 518-5108 *Fax:* 518-5276
*E-mail:* kwaluseni@uniswa.sz
*Web Site:* www.uniswa.sz
*Key Personnel*
Librarian: M R Mavuso *E-mail:* librarian@
   uniswa.sz
Irregularly.

**Serials in Swaziland University Libraries** (B)
Published by University of Swaziland Library
Private Bag 4, Kwaluseni
*Tel:* 518-4011; 518-5108 *Fax:* 518-5276
*E-mail:* kwaluseni@uniswa.sz
*Web Site:* www.uniswa.sz
*Telex:* 2087
*Key Personnel*
Librarian: M R Mavuso *E-mail:* librarian@
   uniswa.sz
Irregularly.

# Sweden

**Biblioteksbladet** (Library Journal) (J)
Published by Svensk Biblioteksforening (Swedish
   Library Association)
Saltmaetargatan 3 A, 111 60 Stockholm
Mailing Address: PO Box 3127, 103 62 Stock-
   holm
*Tel:* (08) 545 132 30 *Fax:* (08) 545 132 31
*E-mail:* info@biblioteksforeningen.org
*Web Site:* www.biblioteksforeningen.org
Text in Scandinavian languages with summaries
   in English.

**Svensk periodicafoerteckning** (Current Swedish
   Periodicals) (B)
Published by Kungliga Biblioteket, Bibliografiska
   avdelningen
Box 5039, 102 41 Stockholm
*Tel:* (08) 463 40 00 *Fax:* (08) 463 40 04
*E-mail:* kungl.biblioteket@kb.se
*Web Site:* www.kb.se
*Telex:* 19640 KBS S
*Key Personnel*
Contact: Eva Crantz *Tel:* (08) 463-42 22
   *E-mail:* eva.crantz@kb.se
ISSN: 1104-1102

**Tidskrift foer Dokumentation** (Documentation Periodical) (J)
Published by Tekniska Litteratursaellskapet (The Swedish Society for Technical Documentation)
Grev Turegatan 14, Stockholm
Mailing Address: Box 55580, 102 04 Stockholm
*Tel:* (08) 678 23 20 *Fax:* (08) 678 23 01
*E-mail:* kansliet@tls.se
*Web Site:* www.tls.se
Text in Swedish, with summaries & occasional articles in English Nordic Journal of Documentation.
Quarterly.
ISSN: 0040-6872

# Switzerland

**Arbido** (J)
Published by Association des Bibliotheques et Bibliothecaires Suisses (Association of Swiss Librarians & Libraries)
Hallerstr 58, 3008 Bern
*Tel:* (031) 382 42 40 *Fax:* (031) 382 46 48
*E-mail:* bbs@bbs.ch
*Web Site:* www.bbs.ch
*Key Personnel*
President: Dr Peter Wille

# Syrian Arab Republic

**Damascus University Library Review** (J)
Published by Damascus University Press
Damascus University Library, Damascus, Baramkah
*Tel:* (011) 2215104; (011) 2215101 *Fax:* (011) 2236010
*E-mail:* info@damascus-online.com
*Web Site:* www.damascus-online/university.htm
*Telex:* 411971

# Taiwan, Province of China

**Chung-hua min-kuo t'u-shu-kuan nien-chien** (B)
Published by National Central Library
20 Chung Shan S Rd, Taipei 100-01
*Tel:* (02) 2361 9132 (ext 250); (02) 2314 7322 *Fax:* (02) 382 1489
*Web Site:* www.ncl.edu.tw
*Key Personnel*
Dir: Dr Tseng Chi-Chun
Yearbook of Libraries in the Republic of China.

**Chung-kuo t'u-shu-kuan hsueh-hui hui-pao** (J)
Published by Library Association of China (LAC)
20 Chungshan S Rd, Taipei 10010
*Tel:* (02) 2331-2675; (02) 2361-9132 *Fax:* (02) 2370-0899
*E-mail:* lac@msg.ncl.edu.tw
*Web Site:* www.ncl.edu.tw
*Key Personnel*
President: James HC Hu

Secretary General: Teresa Wang Chang
Bulletin of the Library Association of China.

**Journal of Library & Information Science** (J)
Published by Department of Adult & Continuing Education, National Taiwan Normal University
162 Hoping East Rd, sec 1, Taipei 10610
*Tel:* (02) 321-8457; (02) 391-4248 *Fax:* (02) 341-8431
*E-mail:* mtc@mtc.ntnu.edu.tw
*Web Site:* www.mtc.ntnu.edu.tw
*Key Personnel*
President: Hsi-Muh Leu
CALA Editor: Wilfred W Fong *Tel:* (0414) 229-5421 *Fax:* (0414) 229-4848 *E-mail:* wfong@csd.uwm.edu
First published 1975.
Biannually.
ISSN: 0363-3640

**Tseng-pu hsiu-ting Chung-hua min-kuo Chung-wen ch'i-k'an lien-ho mu-lu** (B)
Published by National Central Library
20 Chung Shan S Rd, Taipei 100-01
*Tel:* (02) 2361 9132 (ext 250); (02) 2314 7322 *Fax:* (02) 382 1489
*Web Site:* www.ncl.edu.tw
*Key Personnel*
Dir: Tseng Chi-Chun
National Union List of Chinese Periodicals of the Republic of China.

# United Republic of Tanzania

**Directory of Libraries, Museums & Archives in Tanzania** (B)
Published by Tanzania Library Service
PO Box 33433, Dar es Salaam
*Tel:* (022) 2775411 *Fax:* (022) 2775411
*E-mail:* tla_tanzania@yahoo.com
*Web Site:* www.tlatz.org
*Key Personnel*
Dir General: Ellezer A Mwinyimvua
First published 1979.

**Matukio** (J)
Published by Tanzania Library Association
PO Box 33433, Dar es Salaam
*Tel:* (022) 2775411 *Fax:* (022) 2775411
*E-mail:* tla_tanzania@yahoo.com
*Web Site:* www.tlatz.org
*Key Personnel*
Chairman: Dr Alli Mcharazo
   *E-mail:* amcharazo@hotmail.com

# Thailand

**An Annotated Bibliography of Librarianship in Thailand** (B)
Published by Department of Library Science, Chulalongkorn University, Faculty of Arts
c/o Chulalongkorn University, 254 Phyathai Rd Patumwan, Bangkok 10330
*Tel:* (02) 215-0871-3 *Fax:* (02) 215-4804
*E-mail:* info@chula.ac.th
*Web Site:* www.chula.ac.th
*Telex:* 20217
*Key Personnel*
Prof: Dr Boonrod Binson

**Bulletin** (J)
Published by Thai Library Association
1346 Akarnsongkrau Rd 5, Klongchan, Bangkapi Bangkok 10240
*Tel:* (0662) 734-8022-3 *Fax:* (02) 734-8024
*Web Site:* tla.or.th
*Key Personnel*
President: Khunying Maenmas Chawalit
Foreign Relations: Yupin Chancharoensin
   *E-mail:* yupin@car.chula.ac.th
Executive Secretary: Mrs Vorrarat Srinamngern
Quarterly.

**List of Scientific Libraries in Thailand** (B)
Published by Thai National Documentation Centre (TNDC)
196 Phahonyothin Rd, Chatuchak, Bangkok 10900
*Tel:* 0-2579-1121 *Fax:* 0-2579-8594
*E-mail:* tndc@tistr.or.th
*Web Site:* tndc.tistr.or.th
*Telex:* 21392
*Key Personnel*
Dir: Mrs Nongphanga Chitrakorn

# Trinidad & Tobago

**Bulletin** (J)
Published by Library Association of Trinidad & Tobago
PO Box 1275, Port of Spain
*Tel:* (868) 687-0194
*E-mail:* latt@mailcity.com
*Web Site:* www.latt.org.tt
*Key Personnel*
President: Ernesta Greenidge
   *E-mail:* egreenidge@library.uwi.tt
Secretary: Sheryl Washington
   *E-mail:* swashington@ag.gov.tt
First published 1964.
ISSN: 0521-9590

# United Kingdom

**Archives** (J)
Published by British Records Association
c/o Finsbury Library, 245 St John St, London EC1V 4NB
*Tel:* (020) 7833 0428 *Fax:* (020) 7833 0416
*E-mail:* britrecassoc@hotmail.com
*Web Site:* www.hmc.gov.uk/bra
ISBN(s): 0-900222

**Art Libraries Journal** (J)
Published by ARLIS/UK & Ireland Art Libraries Society
18 College Rd, Bromsgrove, Wores B60 2NE
*Tel:* (01527) 579298 *Fax:* (01527) 579298
*E-mail:* info@arlis.org.uk
*Web Site:* www.arlis.org.uk
*Key Personnel*
Editor: Gillian Varley *E-mail:* g.varley@arlis2.demon.co.uk
First published 1976.
Quarterly.
52 GBP
ISSN: 0307-4722

**Aslib Book Guide** (J)
Published by Aslib, The Association for Information Management
Holywell Centre, One Phipp St, London EC2A 4PS
*Tel:* (020) 7613 3031 *Fax:* (020) 7613 5080
*E-mail:* aslib@aslib.com
*Web Site:* www.aslib.co.uk
*Telex:* 23667
Monthly.

**Aslib Directory of Information Sources in the UK** (B)
Published by Aslib, The Association for Information Management
Holywell Centre, One Phipp St, London EC2A 4PS
*Tel:* (020) 7613 3031 *Fax:* (020) 7613 5080
*E-mail:* aslib@aslib.com
*Web Site:* www.aslib.co.uk
*Telex:* 23667
Listing of over 9,000 organizations in the UK.
First published 1928.
1,577 pp
ISBN(s): 0-85142-472-4

**Bibliography of Printed Works on London History to 1939** (B)
Published by Facet Publishing
7 Ridgmount St, London WC1 7AE
*Tel:* (020) 7255 0590 *Fax:* (020) 7255 0591
*E-mail:* info@facetpublishing.co.uk
*Web Site:* www.facetpublishing.co.uk
*Key Personnel*
Editor: Heather Creaton
First bibliography on London History.
First published 1994.
895 pp, 89.95 GBP
ISBN(s): 1-85604-074-7

**The Bibliotheck** (P)
Published by Scottish Cente for the Book, Napier University
c/o Scottish Centre for the Book, Napier University, Craighouse Rd, Edinburgh EH10 5LG
*Tel:* (0131) 455-6150 *Fax:* (0131) 455-6193
*E-mail:* scob@napier.ac.uk
*Web Site:* www.pmpc.napier.ac.uk/scob/bibliothek.html
*Key Personnel*
Editor: Dr William A Kelly; Prof Alistair Mc-Cleery
A Scottish journal of bibliography & allied topics.
15 GBP

**Brio** (J)
Published by International Association of Music Libraries Archives & Documentation Centres: UK & Ireland Branch
County Library HQ, Walton St, Aylesbury, Bucks HP20 1UU
*Web Site:* www.iaml-uk-irl.org
*Key Personnel*
Publications Officer: Margaret Roll
    *E-mail:* mroll@buckscc.gov.uk
Editor: Rupert Ridgewell
Articles relevant to the music library profession, reviews of books & scores & news from music libraries.
First published 1964.
Biannually, May & Nov.
27 GBP or 56 USD; free with membership
ISSN: 0007-0173

**Chartered Institute of Library & Information Professionals Yearbook**, see CILIP Yearbook

**CILIP Yearbook** (B)
Published by Facet Publishing
7 Ridgmount St, London WC1E 7AE

*Tel:* (020) 7255 0590 *Fax:* (020) 7255 0591
*E-mail:* info@facetpublishing.co.uk
*Web Site:* www.facetpublishing.co.uk
*Key Personnel*
Production Manager: K A Beecroft
    *E-mail:* kathryn.beecroft@facetpublishing.co.uk
Listing of officers, members, Royal Charter & bylaws.
Annually.
464 pp, 39.95 GBP
ISBN(s): 1-85604-476-9

**Directory of Acquisitions Librarians in the UK & Republic of Ireland** (B)
Published by National Acquisitions Group
12 Holm Oak Dr, Madeley, Nr Crewe CW3 9HR
*Tel:* (01782) 750462 *Fax:* (01782) 750462
*E-mail:* nag@btconnect.com
*Web Site:* www.nag.org.uk
*Key Personnel*
Chair: Jo Grocott
Administration: Marie Hackett; Diane Roberts
Publications: Jonathan Earl
8th

**Directory of Rare Book & Special Collections in the UK & Republic of Ireland** (B)
Published by Facet Publishing
7 Ridgmount St, London WC1E 7AE
*Tel:* (020) 7255 0590 *Fax:* (020) 7255 0591
*E-mail:* info@facetpublishing.co.uk
*Web Site:* www.facetpublishing.co.uk
*Key Personnel*
Editor: Barry Bloomfield
Details of the rare & special collections of over 1200 libraries.

**Impact: Journal of the Career Development Group** (J)
Published by Chartered Institute of Library & Information Professionals (CILIP)
Music Library, University of Reading, 35 Upper Redlands Rd, Reading RG1 5JE
*Tel:* (0118) 931 8413
*E-mail:* editor@careerdevelopmentgroup.org.uk
*Web Site:* www.careerdevelopmentgroup.org.uk
*Key Personnel*
Publisher: Jayne Hickton *E-mail:* jaynehickton@yahoo.com
Bimonthly.
20 pp
ISSN: 1468-1625

**Information Scotland** (J)
Published by Scottish Library Association
Bldg C, 1st floor, Brandon Gate, Leechlee Rd, Hamilton ML3 6AU
*Tel:* (01698) 458888 *Fax:* (01698) 283170
*E-mail:* slic@slainte.org.uk
*Web Site:* www.slainte.org.uk
*Key Personnel*
Dir: Elaine Fulton *E-mail:* e.fulton@slainte.org.uk
Assistant Dir: Rhona Arthur *E-mail:* r.arthur@slainte.org.ok

**Interlending & Document Supply** (J)
Published by Emerald
60/62 Toller Lane, Bradford, W Yorks BD8 9BY
*Tel:* (01274) 777700 *Fax:* (01274) 785201
*E-mail:* gcrawford@emeraldinsight.com
*Web Site:* www.emeraldinsight.com
*Key Personnel*
Man Dir: Dr Keith Howard
ISSN: 0264-1615

∮**Journal of Documentation** (J)
Published by Emerald
60/62 Toller Lane, Bradford, W Yorks BD8 9BY
*Tel:* (01274) 777700 *Fax:* (01274) 785201
*E-mail:* gcrawford@emeraldinsight.com
*Web Site:* www.emeraldinsight.com

*Key Personnel*
Man Dir: Dr Keith Howard
Managing Editor: Diane Heath *E-mail:* dheath@emeraldinsight.com
First published 1944.
6 times/yr.
Vol 60, 2004: 720 pp
ISSN: 0022-0418

**Journal of Information Science** (J)
Published by SAGE Publications Ltd
One Oliver's Yard, 55 City Rd, London EC1Y 1SP
*Tel:* (020) 7324 8500; (020) 7374 0645 (customer service) *Fax:* (020) 7374 8600
*E-mail:* info@sagepub.co.uk; orders@sagepub.co.uk
*Web Site:* www.sagepub.co.uk
*Key Personnel*
Man Dir: Stephen Barr
Editorial Dir: Ziyad Marar
Editor: Adrian Dale
Published in association with Chartered Institute of Library & Information Professionals.
Bimonthly.
241 GBP/yr (institutional)
ISSN: 0165-5515

**Journal of the Society of Archivists** (J)
Published by Routledge
4 Park Sq, Milton Park, Abingdon, Oxon OX14 4RN
*Tel:* (01235) 828600 *Fax:* (01235) 829000
*E-mail:* info@routledge.co.uk
*Web Site:* www.routledge.co.uk
*Key Personnel*
Editor: Cressida Annesley; Susan Corrigall; Andrew Flinn; Kate Manning
Journal for archivists, record managers & conservators worldwide.
First published 1955.
Biannually.
ISSN: 0037-9816

**Legal Information Management**
Published by Cambridge University Press
The Edinburgh Bldg, Shaftesbury Rd, Cambridge CB2 2RU
*Tel:* (01223) 312393 *Fax:* (01223) 315052
*E-mail:* journals@cambridge.com
*Web Site:* www.cup.cam.ac.uk; www.biall.org.uk
*Key Personnel*
Editor: Christine Miskin
Corporate author: British & Irish Association of Law Libraries.
First published 1970.
Quarterly.
ISSN: 1472-6696

**The Libraries Directory** (B)
Published by James Clarke & Co Ltd
PO Box 60, Cambridge CB1 2NT
*Tel:* (01223) 350865 *Fax:* (01223) 366951; 209-671-8124 (US fax)
*E-mail:* publishing@jamesclarke.co.uk
*Web Site:* www.jamesclarke.co.uk
*Key Personnel*
Man Dir: Adrian Brink
Editor: Iain Walker
Directory of Public Libraries, Special Libraries, Record Offices, Archives & Library Organizations in the UK & Ireland.
First published 1890.
Biennially.
2000-2002: 510 pp
ISBN(s): 0-227-67956-3 (Hardcover 99 GBP); 0-227-67957-1 (CD-ROM Reference Edition (Stand Alone) 99 GBP+VAT); 0-227-67958-X (CD-ROM Marketing Edition (Stand Alone) 175 GBP+VAT); 0-227-67959-8 (CD-ROM Reference Edition (Network) 150 GBP+VAT);

0-227-67960-1 (CD-ROM Marketing Edition
(Network) 250 GBP+VAT)
ISSN: 0961-4575

**Libraries in The United Kingdom & The
Republic of Ireland** (B)
Published by Facet Publishing
7 Ridgmount St, London WC1E 7AE
*Tel:* (020) 7255 0590 *Fax:* (020) 7255 0591
*E-mail:* info@facetpublishing.co.uk
*Web Site:* www.facetpublishing.co.uk
Listing of public library services & a select list of
academic & other library addresses.
Annually.
29th: 464 pp, 39.95 GBP
ISBN(s): 1-85604-450-5

**The Library** (P)
Published by Bibliographical Society
Institute of English Studies, Senate House, Room
304, Malet St, London WC1E 7HU
*Web Site:* www.bibsoc.org.uk/library.htm
*Key Personnel*
Editor: Dr Oliver Pickering *Tel:* (01132) 336 377
*E-mail:* o.s.pickering@leeds.ac.uk
Bibliography.
Quarterly.

**Library & Information Science Abstracts
(LISA)** (J)
Published by CSA (Cambridge Scientific Ab-
stracts)
4640 Kingsgate, Cascade Way, Oxford Business
Park South, Oxford, Oxon OX4 2ST
*Tel:* (0865) 336250 *Fax:* (0865) 336258
*E-mail:* sales@csa.com; support@csa.com
(technical support)
*Web Site:* www.csa.com
*Key Personnel*
Editor: Lilian Lincoln *E-mail:* llincoln@csa.com
Monthly publication. Indexes & abstracts 500
periodicals from over 65 countries in over 20
languages. Current awareness & search service
for information about library & information
science & related areas including the inter-
net & information industry. Also available as
a CD-ROM, searchable database & as a web
database.
First published 1969.
Monthly.
100 pp, Subscription for 11 issues plus cumulated annual index: Europe 650 GBP/yr, $1,175
USD/yr
ISSN: 0024-2179
*Parent Company:* Cambridge Information Group

**Library Review** (J)
Published by Emerald
60/62 Toller Lane, Bradford, W Yorks BD8 9BY
*Tel:* (01274) 777700 *Fax:* (01274) 785201
*E-mail:* gcrawford@emeraldinsight.com
*Web Site:* www.emeraldinsight.com
*Key Personnel*
Man Dir: Dr Keith Howard
ISSN: 0024-2535

**LISA,** see Library & Information Science
Abstracts (LISA)

**Managing Information** (J)
Published by Aslib, The Association for Informa-
tion Management
Holywell Centre, One Phipp St, London EC2A
4PS
*Tel:* (020) 7613 3031 *Fax:* (020) 7613 5080
*E-mail:* pubs@aslib.com
*Web Site:* www.aslib.com
Biennially.

**New Library World** (J)
Published by Emerald
60/62 Toller Lane, Bradford, W Yorks BD8 9BY
*Tel:* (01274) 777700 *Fax:* (01274) 785201
*E-mail:* information@emeraldinsight.com
(academic sales & enquiries)
*Web Site:* www.emeraldinsight.com
*Key Personnel*
Managing Editor: Diane Heath *E-mail:* dheath@
emeraldinsight.com
Editor: Linda Ashcroft *E-mail:* l.s.ashcroft@livjm.
ac.uk
Assistant Editor: Stephanie McIvor *E-mail:* s.
mcivor@ntlworld.com
Incorporates Information & Library Manager.
ISSN: 0307-4803

**The Private Library** (J)
Published by Private Libraries Association (PLA)
49 Hamilton Park W, London N5 1AE
*Tel:* (020) 7503 9827
*Web Site:* www.the-old-school.demon.co.uk/pla.
htm
*Key Personnel*
Executive Secretary: James Brown
Editor, Private Press Books: Paul W Nash
Publications Secretary: David Chambers
*E-mail:* dchambers@aol.com
Concerned with book collecting.
First published 1957.
Quarterly.
48 pp, 25 GBP or 40 USD
ISSN: 0032-8898

**Reference Reviews** (J)
Published by Emerald
60/62 Toller Lane, Bradford, W Yorks BD8 9BY
*Tel:* (01274) 777700 *Fax:* (01274) 785201
*E-mail:* information@emeraldinsight.com
(academic sales & enquiries)
*Web Site:* www.emeraldinsight.com
*Key Personnel*
Managing Editor: Diane Heath *E-mail:* dheath@
emeraldinsight.com
Editor: Anthony Chalcraft *E-mail:* a.chalcraft@
yorksj.ac.uk
Reviews of current reference materials, electronic
version only.
ISSN: 0950-4125

**The SLG Directory to Children's and School
Library Services in the British Isles** (B)
Published by Library Association, School Li-
braries Group
% CILIP, 7 Ridgmount St, London WC1E 7AE
*Tel:* (020) 7255 0500 *Fax:* (020) 7255 0501
*E-mail:* lapublishing@la-hq.org.uk
*Web Site:* www.la-hq.org.uk/directory/about/slg.
html
*Key Personnel*
Chief Executive: Bob McKee
Publisher: Helen Carley
Man Dir: Janet Liebster
2nd
ISBN(s): 0-85365; 0-948933

**State Librarian** (J)
Published by Circle of State Librarians
HM Customs & Excise, 4th floor West, Ralli
Quays, Salford M60 9LA
*Tel:* (0161) 827 0243 *Fax:* (0161) 827-0491
*E-mail:* mags.griffin@hmce.gsi.gov.uk
*Web Site:* www.circleofstatelibrarians.co.uk
*Key Personnel*
Editor: Pat Bell *E-mail:* pat.bell@hmce.gsi.gov.uk
Contact: Gareth Vaughan

# Uruguay

**Bibliografia y documentacion en el Uruguay**
(Bibliography and Documentation in Uruguay)
(B)
Published by Agrupacion Bibliotecologica del
Uruguay (Group Librarian of Uruguay)
Cerro Largo 1666, Montevideo 11200
*Tel:* (02) 400 57 40
*Key Personnel*
Pres: Luis Alberto Musso

**Revista de la Biblioteca Nacional** (National
Library Review) (J)
Published by Biblioteca Nacional del Uruguay
c/o Director General, Ave 15 de Julio, 1790,
11210 Montevideo
*Tel:* (02) 48 50 30 *Fax:* (02) 49 69 02
*Key Personnel*
Dir: Prof Rafael Gomensoro
Bimonthly.
ISSN: 0797-9061

# Zambia

**Directory of Libraries in Zambia** (B)
Published by Zambia Library Association
PO Box 32839, 10101 Lusaka
*Key Personnel*
Chairman: Benson Njobvu
*E-mail:* bensonnjobvu@hotmail.com
Provides details on all the major libraries in the
country.

**Zambia Library Association Journal** (J)
Published by Zambia Library Association
PO Box 32839, 10101 Lusaka
*Key Personnel*
Editor: W D Sweeney
First published 1969.
Quarterly.

# Zimbabwe

**Directory of Libraries** (B)
Published by National Archives of Zimbabwe
Borrowdale Rd, Gun Hill, Harare
Mailing Address: PB 7729, Causeway, Harare
*Tel:* (04) 792741 *Fax:* (04) 792398
*E-mail:* archives@gta.gov.zw
*Web Site:* sdrc.lbi.ulowa.edu/ejab/1/zimbabwe.
html
*Key Personnel*
Dir: M I Murambiwa

**The Zimbabwe Librarian** (P)
Published by Zimbabwe Library Association
(ZLA)
PO Box 3133, Harare
*Tel:* (04) 788694 *Fax:* (04) 738693
*Key Personnel*
Editor: Sabelo Mapasure
Newsletter with text in English.
First published 1969.
Biannually.
30 ZWD; 30 USD to non-members

# NOTES

# NOTES

# NOTES

# NOTES

# NOTES

# NOTES

# NOTES

# NOTES

# Industry Yellow Pages

Arranged alphabetically by company/organization name, the industry yellow pages include the page number(s) where the listing can be found as well as the organization's country, telephone, fax, e-mail address and web address. Companies/organizations listed in the following sections are excluded from the yellow pages: **Book Trade Reference Books and Journals; Literary Prizes; Calendar of Book Trade & Promotional Events** and **Library Reference Books & Journals.**

A A Publishing (United Kingdom) *Tel:* (01256) 491522 *Fax:* (0191) 235 5111 *E-mail:* aapublish@theaa.com *Web Site:* www.theaa.com; www.aanewsroom.com, pg 650

A & A (Italy) *Tel:* (02) 876 999 *Fax:* (02) 877 928, pg 370

A & A & A Edicoes e Promocoes Internacionais Ltda (Brazil) *Tel:* (024) 221-3359 *Fax:* (024) 221-2740 *E-mail:* aaaipe@compuland.com.br, pg 76

A & A Farmar (Ireland) *Tel:* (01) 4963625 *Fax:* (01) 4970107 *E-mail:* afarmar@iol.ie *Web Site:* www. farmarbooks.com, pg 354

A & B Personal Management Ltd (United Kingdom) *Tel:* (020) 7839 4433 *Fax:* (020) 7930 5738, pg 1128

A Francke Verlag (Tubingen und Basel) (Germany) *Tel:* (089) 718 747 *Fax:* (089) 7142039 *E-mail:* info@ iudicium.de *Web Site:* www.geist.de, pg 190

A/L Biblioteksentralen (The Norwegian Library Bureau) (Norway) *Tel:* (022) 08 34 00 *Fax:* (022) 08 39 01 *E-mail:* bs@bibsent.no *Web Site:* www.bibsent.no, pg 1323

A L Publishers (India) *Tel:* (040) 7611600, pg 323

A-Mail Academic (United Kingdom) *Tel:* (020) 7871 9139 *Fax:* (020) 7871 9140 *E-mail:* a-mail@djlb.co.uk *Web Site:* www.a-mail.co.uk, pg 650

A-R Editions Inc (United States) *Tel:* 608-836-9000 *Toll Free:* 800-736-0070 (US book orders only) *Fax:* 608-831-8200 *E-mail:* info@areditions.com *Web Site:* www.areditions.com, pg 1155, 1176, 1238

A R T Dialog (Czech Republic) *Tel:* (0420) 24148 2808 *Fax:* (0420) 24148 1442 *E-mail:* artdialog@mybox.cz *Web Site:* www.artdialog-literary.wz.cz, pg 1119

Aache Ediciones (Spain) *Tel:* (0949) 220 438 *Fax:* (0949) 220 438 *E-mail:* ediciones@aache.com *Web Site:* aache.iberlibro.net, pg 566

Aafzam Ltd (Zambia) *Tel:* (01) 223261, pg 775

Aalborg Universitetsbibliotek (Denmark) *Tel:* 96359400 *Fax:* 98156859 *E-mail:* aub@aub.aau.dk *Web Site:* www.aub.aau.dk, pg 1500

Aarachne Verlag (Austria) *Tel:* (01) 2855353 *Fax:* (01) 2855353 *E-mail:* spinne@aarachne.at *Web Site:* www. aarachne.at, pg 47

Aardvark Enterprises (Canada) *Tel:* 403-256-4639, pg 1143, 1165, 1205

Aare-Verlag (Switzerland) *Tel:* (062) 836 86 86 *Fax:* (062) 836 86 20 *E-mail:* bildung@sauerlaender. ch *Web Site:* www.sauerlaender.ch, pg 612

Aarhus Universitetsforlag (Denmark) *Tel:* 89425370 *Fax:* 89425380 *E-mail:* unipress@au.dk *Web Site:* www.unipress.dk, pg 128

The AB Book Club (BAB) (Iceland) *Tel:* 522 2138 *Fax:* 522 2026 *Web Site:* www.ab.is, pg 1243

AB Svenska Laromedel-Editum (Finland) *Tel:* (09) 88704017 *Fax:* (09) 8043257 *E-mail:* jjohnson@ schildts.fi, pg 141

ABA Books (New Zealand) *Tel:* (07) 8549360 *Fax:* (07) 8549361 *Web Site:* www.ababooks.co.nz, pg 489

Editorial Abaco de Rodolfo Depalma SRL (Argentina) *Tel:* (011) 4371-1675 *Fax:* (011) 4371-5802 *E-mail:* info@abacoeditorial.com.ar *Web Site:* www. abacoeditorial.com.ar, pg 2

Mandira Jaya Abadi (Indonesia) *Tel:* (024) 3519547; (024) 3519548 *Fax:* (024) 3542189, pg 349

Publicacions de l'Abadia de Montserrat (Spain) *Tel:* (093) 2450303; (093) 2314001 *Fax:* (093) 2473594 *E-mail:* pamsa@pamsa.com *Web Site:* www. pamsa.com, pg 566

Abagar Pablioing (Bulgaria) *Tel:* (02) 702826 *Fax:* (02) 702926 *E-mail:* abagar@gti.bg, pg 92

Abagar, Veliko Tarnovo (Bulgaria) *Tel:* (062) 43936; (062) 47814 *Fax:* (062) 46993 *E-mail:* abagar@dir.bg, pg 92

Abakus Musik Barbara Fietz (Germany) *Tel:* (06478) 2250 *Fax:* (06478) 1355 *E-mail:* hotline@abakus-musik.de *Web Site:* www.abakus-musik.de, pg 190

Abakus Verlag GmbH (Austria) *Tel:* (0662) 632076 *Fax:* (0662) 8044137, pg 47

Abbotsford Publishing (United Kingdom) *Tel:* (01543) 255749; (01543) 258903 *Web Site:* www. abbotsfordpublishing.com, pg 650

ABC Books (Australian Broadcasting Corporation) (Australia) *Tel:* (02) 8333 3959 *Fax:* (02) 8333 3999 *E-mail:* abcbooks@abc.net.au *Web Site:* abcshop.com. au, pg 10

ABC-CLIO (United Kingdom) *Tel:* (01865) 311350 *Fax:* (01865) 311358 *E-mail:* oxford@abc-clio.ltd.uk *Web Site:* www.abc-clio.com, pg 650

ABC der Deutschen Wirtschaft, Verlagsgesellschaft mbH (Germany) *Tel:* (06151) 38920 *Fax:* (06151) 33164; (06151) 389280 *E-mail:* info@abconline.de *Web Site:* www.abconline.de, pg 190

ABC Kitabevi AS (Turkey) *Tel:* (0212) 27 62 404; (0212) 28 51 860, pg 644

ABC Kitabevi Sanayi Tic AS (Turkey) *Tel:* (0212) 2762404 *Fax:* (0212) 2851860, pg 1337

Librerias ABC SA (Argentina) *Tel:* (011) 4314-8106 *Fax:* (011) 4314-8106 *E-mail:* libabcc@datamarkets. com.ar *Web Site:* www.libreriasabc.com.ar, pg 1287

Librerias ABC SA (Peru) *Tel:* (054) 422900; (054) 422902 *Fax:* (054) 422901, pg 511, 1325

Ben Abdallah Editions (Tunisia) *Tel:* 71237011 *Fax:* 71786290, pg 643

S Abdul Majeed & Co (Malaysia) *Tel:* (03) 283-2230 *Fax:* (03) 282-5670, pg 451

S Abdul Majeed & Co (Malaysia) *Tel:* (03) 2832230 *Fax:* (03) 28225670 *E-mail:* peer@pc.jaring.my, pg 1316

ABE Marketing (Poland) *Tel:* (022) 6540675 *Fax:* (022) 6520767 *E-mail:* info@abe.com.pl *Web Site:* www. abe.com.pl/, pg 1327

Gruppo Abele (Italy) *Tel:* (011) 3841066 *E-mail:* segreteria@gruppabele.it *Web Site:* www. gruppoabele.it, pg 370

Abeledo-Perrot SAE e I (Argentina) *Tel:* (011) 4124-9750 *Fax:* (011) 4371-5156 *E-mail:* editorial@ abeledo-perrot.com, pg 2

Edizioni Abete (Italy) *Tel:* (06) 225821 *Fax:* (06) 2282960, pg 371

ABGRA (Asociacion de Bibliotecarios Graduados de la Republica Argentina) (Argentina) *Tel:* (011) 4371 5269; (011) 4373 0571 *Fax:* (011) 4371 5269 *E-mail:* info@abgra.org.ar *Web Site:* www.abgra.org. ar, pg 1557

Abhinav Publications (India) *Tel:* (011) 26566387; (011) 26524658 *Fax:* (011) 26857009 *Web Site:* www. abhinavexports.com, pg 323

Abhishek Publications (India) *Tel:* (0172) 707562 *Fax:* (0172) 704668, pg 323

ABIC Books & Equipment Ltd (Nigeria) *Tel:* (042) 331827 *Fax:* (042) 334811, pg 498

Universite d'Abidjan (Cote d'Ivoire) *Tel:* 441285 *Fax:* 434254 *E-mail:* puci@africaonline.co.ci, pg 116

Abimo (Belgium) *Tel:* (052) 462407 *Fax:* (052) 461962 *E-mail:* info@abimo-uitgeverij.com *Web Site:* www. abimo-uitgeverij.com, pg 62

Abisega Publishers (Nigeria) Ltd (Nigeria) *Tel:* (022) 415802, pg 498

Editrice Abitare Segesta (Italy) *Tel:* (02) 210581 *Fax:* (02) 21058316 *Web Site:* www.abitare.it, pg 371

Abiva Publishing House Inc (Philippines) *Tel:* (02) 7120245 *Fax:* (02) 7320308 *E-mail:* info@abiva. ph *Web Site:* www.abiva.com.ph, pg 513

Libraira-Papeterie ABM (Benin) *Tel:* 330690 (voice & fax), pg 1292

Abo Akademis bibliotek (Finland) *Tel:* (02) 2154180 *Fax:* (02) 2154795 *E-mail:* hblan@abo.fi *Web Site:* www.abo.fi/library, pg 1503

Abo Akademis forlag - Abo Akademi University Press (Finland) *Tel:* (02) 215 3292 *Fax:* (02) 215 4490 *E-mail:* forlaget@abo.fi *Web Site:* www.abo. fi/stiftelsen/forlag, pg 141

Aboriginal Studies Press (Australia) *Tel:* (02) 6246 1183 *Fax:* (02) 6261 4285 *E-mail:* sales@aiatsis.gov.au *Web Site:* www.aiatsis.gov.au, pg 10

Editorial Abril SA (Argentina) *Tel:* (011) 4331-0112, pg 2

Abril SA (Brazil) *Tel:* (011) 877-1319 *Fax:* (011) 877-1437 *Web Site:* abril.com.br, pg 76

Absolute Press (United Kingdom) *Tel:* (01225) 316 013 *Fax:* (01225) 445 836 *E-mail:* info@absolutepress.co. uk *Web Site:* www.absolutepress.co.uk, pg 650

Absolutt Kontroll (Norway) *Tel:* 24051010 *Fax:* 24051099 *E-mail:* post@damm.no *Web Site:* www.dammbokklubb.no, pg 1244

Ediciones Abya-Yala (Ecuador) *Tel:* (02) 2506251; (02) 2506247 *Fax:* (02) 2506255 *E-mail:* editorial@ abyayala.org *Web Site:* www.abyayala.org, pg 136

Yr Academi Gymreig (United Kingdom) *Tel:* (029) 20472266 *Fax:* (029) 20492930 *E-mail:* post@ academi.org *Web Site:* www.academi.org, pg 1400

Academia (Czech Republic) *Tel:* (02) 24 941 976 *Fax:* (02) 24 212 582 *E-mail:* academia@academia.cz *Web Site:* www.academia.cz, pg 121

Academia Amazonense de Letras (Brazil) *Tel:* (092) 633-1426, pg 1391

Academia Argentina de Letras (Argentina) *Tel:* (011) 4802-3814; (011) 4802-7509; (011) 4802-5161 *Fax:* (011) 4-8028340 *E-mail:* aaldespa@fibertel.com. ar; aaladmin@fibertel.com.ar; aalbibl@fibertel.com.ar, pg 2

Academia Argentina de Letras (Argentina) *Tel:* (011) 4802-3814; (011) 4802-5161; (011) 4802-7509 *Fax:* (011) 4802-8340 *E-mail:* aaldespa@fibertel.com. ar; aaladmin@fibertel.com.ar; aalbibl@fibertel.com.ar *Web Site:* www.aal.universia.com.ar/aal, pg 1389

Academia Brasileira de Letras (Brazil) *Tel:* (021) 3974-2500 *Fax:* (021) 220-6695 *E-mail:* academia@academia.org.br *Web Site:* www.academia.org.br, pg 1391

Academia-Bruylant (Belgium) *Tel:* (010) 45 23 95 *Fax:* (010) 45 44 80 *E-mail:* academia.bruylant@skynet.be *Web Site:* www.academia-bruylant.be, pg 62

Academia Catarinense de Letras (Brazil) *Tel:* 2342166 *Web Site:* www.acle.com.br, pg 1391

Academia Cearense de Letras (Brazil) *Tel:* (085) 2315669 *E-mail:* acletras@accvia.com.br *Web Site:* www.secrel.com.br, pg 1391

Academia das Ciencias de Lisboa (Portugal) *Tel:* (021) 346-3866 *Fax:* (021) 342-0395, pg 523

Biblioteca da Academia das Ciencias de Lisboa (Portugal) *Tel:* (021) 321 97 30 *Fax:* (021) 342 03 95 *E-mail:* biblioteca@acad-ciencias.pt *Web Site:* www.acad-ciencias.pt, pg 1537

Academia de Centro America (Costa Rica) *Tel:* 283-1847 *Fax:* 283-1848 *E-mail:* info@academiaca.or.cr; rherrera@acedmiaca.or.cr, pg 114

Academia de la Llingua Asturiana (Spain) *Tel:* (0985) 211837 *Fax:* (0985) 226816 *E-mail:* alla@asturnet.es *Web Site:* www.asturnet.es/alla, pg 566

Academia de Letras da Bahia (Brazil) *Tel:* (071) 321-4308 *Fax:* (071) 321-4308 *E-mail:* alb@stn.com.br, pg 1391

Academia de Letras de Piaui (Brazil), pg 1391

Academia de Studii Economice, Biblioteca Centrala (Romania) *Tel:* (01) 319 19 00; (01) 319 19 01 *Fax:* (01) 312 95 49 *Web Site:* www.biblioteca.ase.ro, pg 1538

Academia Ecuatoriana de la Lengua (Ecuador) *Tel:* (02) 2901518 *Fax:* (02) 2543234, pg 1392

Academia Mineira de Letras (Brazil) *Tel:* (031) 3222-5764 *E-mail:* amletras@task.com.br *Web Site:* www.academiamineiradeletras.org.br, pg 1391

Academia Nacional de la Historia (Venezuela) *Tel:* (0212) 481-34-13; (0212) 483-94-35; (0212) 482-67-20; (0212) 486720 *Fax:* (0212) 481-75-47 *E-mail:* informacion@anhvenezuela.org *Web Site:* www.anhvenezuela.org, pg 773

Academia Nacional de Letras (Uruguay) *Tel:* (02) 9152374 *Fax:* (02) 9167460 *E-mail:* academia@montevideo.com.uy, pg 1404

Academia Nicaraguense de la Lengua (Nicaragua) *Tel:* 2495389 *Fax:* 2495389, pg 498

Academia Paraibana de Letras (Brazil) *E-mail:* fsatiro@openline.com.br *Web Site:* www.pbnet.com.br/openline/fsatiro/academia.html, pg 1391

Academia Paulista de Letras (Brazil) *Tel:* (011) 3331-7222 *Fax:* (011) 3331-7401 *E-mail:* acadsp@terra.com.br *Web Site:* www.academiapaulistadeletras.org.br, pg 1391

Academia Pernambucana de Letras (Brazil) *Tel:* (081) 3268-2211, pg 1391

Academia Press (Belgium) *Tel:* (09) 233 80 88 *Fax:* (09) 233 14 09 *E-mail:* info@academiapress.be *Web Site:* www.academiapress.be, pg 62

Academia Publications P Ltd (Malaysia) *Tel:* (03) 572455, pg 451

Academia Scientific Book Inc (Japan) *Tel:* (03) 3819805 *Fax:* (03) 38128509, pg 1311

Academic & General Bookshop (Australia) *Tel:* (03) 9663 3231 *Fax:* (03) 9663 7234 *E-mail:* info@academicbooks.com.au, pg 1287

Academic Book Corporation (India) *Tel:* (0522) 418421; (0522) 416584 *Fax:* (0522) 22061; (0522) 210376, pg 324

Academic Books (Pvt) Ltd (Zimbabwe) *Tel:* (04) 755034; (04) 754224 *Fax:* (04) 781913, pg 777

Academic Library of Tallinn Pedagogical University (Estonia) *Tel:* (02) 6659 401 *Fax:* (02) 6659 400 *E-mail:* ear@ear.ee *Web Site:* www.ear.ee, pg 138

The Academic Press (India) *Tel:* (0124) 6322779; (0124) 6322005 *Fax:* (0124) 6324782 *E-mail:* indoc@indiatimes.com, pg 324

Academic Publishers (Bangladesh) *Tel:* (02) 507355; (02) 507366 *Fax:* (02) 863060, pg 60

Academic Publishers (India) *Tel:* (033) 241-4857 *Fax:* (033) 241-3702 *E-mail:* acabooks@cal.vsnl.net.in, pg 324

Academie Goncourt, Societe de gens de Lettres (France), pg 1393

Academie Nationale de Reims (France) *Tel:* (0326) 910449 *Fax:* (0326) 910449 *E-mail:* academie.nationale.reims@wanadoo.fr, pg 145

Academie Royale de Langue et de Litterature Francaises (Belgium) *Tel:* (02) 550-2277 *Fax:* (02) 550-2275 *E-mail:* alf@cfwb.be *Web Site:* www.academielanguelitteraturefrancaises.be, pg 1390

Academie Royale des Sciences, des Lettres et des Beaux-Arts de Belgique (Belgium) *Tel:* (02) 5502211; (02) 5502212; (02) 5502213 *Fax:* (02) 5502205 *E-mail:* arb@cfwb.be *Web Site:* www.cfwb.be/arb; www.arb.cfwb.be, pg 1390

Academie Tunisienne des Sciences, des Lettres et des Arts Beit El Hekma (Tunisia) *Tel:* 71277275; 71731696; (71) 731 824 *Fax:* 71731204, pg 643

Editura Academiei Romane (Romania) *Tel:* (0410) 411 90 08; (0410) 410 32 00 *Fax:* (0410) 410 39 83 *E-mail:* edacad@ear.ro *Web Site:* www.ear.ro, pg 533

Academon Publishing House (Israel) *Tel:* (02) 5882163 *Fax:* (02) 5815558, pg 361

Academon Publishing House (Israel) *Tel:* (02) 5811326 *Fax:* (02) 5811329 *Web Site:* www.academon.co.il, pg 1309

Academy of Education Planning & Management (AEPAM) (Pakistan) *Tel:* (051) 926-1096 *Fax:* (051) 926-1353; (051) 926-1359 *E-mail:* webinfo@aepam.gov.pk *Web Site:* www.aepam.gov.pk, pg 507

Fundamental Library of the Academy of Medical Sciences (Russian Federation) *Tel:* (095) 155-17-93, pg 1539

Academy of the Hebrew Language (Israel) *Tel:* (02) 6493555 *Fax:* (02) 5617065 *E-mail:* acad2u@vms.huji.ac.il *Web Site:* hebrew-academy.huji.ac.il, pg 361

Academy Science Publishers (Kenya) *Tel:* (020) 884401; (020) 884405 *Fax:* (020) 884406 *E-mail:* aas@africaonline.co.ke; asp@africaonline.co.ke *Web Site:* www.aasciences.org, pg 429

Academy of Sciences Publishing House (Democratic People's Republic of Korea) *Tel:* (02) 51956, pg 433

Acair Ltd (United Kingdom) *Tel:* (01851) 703 020 *Fax:* (01851) 703 294 *E-mail:* enquiries@acairbooks.com *Web Site:* www.acairbooks.com, pg 650

Acantilado (Spain) *Tel:* (093) 4144906 *Fax:* (093) 4147107 *E-mail:* correo@elacantilado.com *Web Site:* www.elacantilado.com, pg 566

Editorial Acanto SA (Spain) *Tel:* (093) 4189093 *Fax:* (093) 4189088 *E-mail:* acantocb@dtinf.net, pg 566

Libreria All'Accademia di Randi Lorenzo & Elena snc (Italy) *Tel:* (049) 8760306 *Fax:* (049) 8751825 *E-mail:* libreria@libreriadraghi.it, pg 1310

Accademia Nazionale di Scienze Lettere e Arti Modena (Italy) *Tel:* (059) 225566 *Fax:* (059) 225566 *E-mail:* info@accademiasla-mo.it *Web Site:* www.accademiasla-mo.it, pg 1396

Accademia Nazionale Virgiliana di Scienze, Lettere e Arti (Italy) *Tel:* (0376) 320314 *Fax:* (0376) 222774 *Web Site:* www.accademiavirgiliana.it/index.htm, pg 1396

Accademia Petrarca di Lettere, Arti e Scienze (Italy) *Tel:* (0575) 24700 *Fax:* (0575) 298846 *E-mail:* info@accademiapetraca.it *Web Site:* www.accademiapetrarca.it, pg 1396

Editions Accarias L'Originel (France) *Tel:* (01) 43 48 73 07 *Fax:* (01) 43 48 73 07 *E-mail:* originel-accarias@club-internet.fr, pg 145

Accedo Verlagsgesellschaft mbH (Germany) *Tel:* (089) 935714 *Fax:* (089) 9294109 *E-mail:* accedoverlag@web.de *Web Site:* www.accedoverlag.de, pg 191

Access International Services (Morocco) *Tel:* (02) 316068 *Fax:* (02) 304685, pg 470

Access Press (Australia) *Tel:* (08) 9328 9188 *Fax:* (08) 9379 3199, pg 10

Uitgeverij Acco (Belgium) *Tel:* (016) 62 80 41 *Fax:* (016) 62 80 01 *E-mail:* uitgeverij@acco.be *Web Site:* www.acco.be, pg 62

Uitgeverij Acco (Belgium) *Tel:* (016) 29 11 00 *Fax:* (016) 20 73 89 *E-mail:* papierhandel@acco.be *Web Site:* www.acco.be, pg 1291

Acento Editorial (Spain) *Tel:* (091) 5088996; (091) 5085145; (091) 4228976 *Fax:* (091) 5089927; (091) 5084974 *E-mail:* informa@acento-editorial.com, pg 566

ACER Agencia Literaria (Spain) *Tel:* (091) 3692061 *Fax:* (091) 3692052, pg 1126

ACER Press (Australia) *Tel:* (03) 9277 5555; (03) 9835 7447 (customer service) *Toll Free Tel:* (800) 338 402 (customer service) *Fax:* (03) 9277 5500; (02) 9835 7499 (customer service) *E-mail:* sales@acer.edu.au *Web Site:* www.acer.edu.au, pg 10

Editorial Acervo SL (Spain) *Tel:* (093) 2122664 *Fax:* (093) 4174425 *E-mail:* acervo25@hotmail.com, pg 566

Ach Publishing House (Israel) *Tel:* (04) 8727227 *Fax:* (04) 8417839, pg 361

Achiasaf Publishing House Ltd (Israel) *Tel:* (09) 8851390 *Fax:* (09) 8851391 *E-mail:* info@achiasaf.co.il *Web Site:* www.achiasaf.co.il, pg 361

Achiever Ltd (Israel) *Tel:* (02) 6253627 *Fax:* (02) 6255740, pg 361

ACHPER Inc (Australian Council for Health, Physical Education & Recreation) (Australia) *Tel:* (08) 8340 3388 *Fax:* (08) 8340 3399 *E-mail:* achper@achper.org.au *Web Site:* www.achper.org.au, pg 10

Achterbahn AG Buch (Germany) *Tel:* (0431) 7028-209 *Fax:* (0431) 7028-228 *E-mail:* info@achterbahn.de *Web Site:* www.achterbahn.de, pg 191

ACI International Ltd (Australia) *Tel:* (03) 6058555, pg 1143

Joh van Acken GmbH & Co KG (Germany) *Tel:* (02151) 44 00-0 *Fax:* (02151) 44 00-11 *E-mail:* verlag@van-acken.de *Web Site:* www.www.van-acken.de, pg 191

F A Ackermanns Kunstverlag GmbH (Germany) *Tel:* (089) 78580826 *Fax:* (089) 78580828 *E-mail:* info@ackermann-kalender.de *Web Site:* www.ackermann-kalender.de, pg 191

Editions ACLA (France) *Tel:* (01) 48 04 00 75 *Fax:* (01) 42 77 72 98, pg 145

Editorial Acme SA (Argentina) *Tel:* (011) 4328-1508; (011) 4328-1662 *Fax:* (011) 4328-9345 *E-mail:* acme@redynet.com.ar, pg 2

Aconcagua Ediciones y Publicaciones SA (Mexico) *Tel:* (05) 555223120 *Fax:* (05) 5432280, pg 458

Acorn Books (South Africa) *Tel:* (011) 8805768 *Fax:* (011) 8805768 *E-mail:* acorbook@iafrica.com, pg 558

ACP Publishing Pty Ltd (Australia) *Tel:* (02) 9282 8000 *Fax:* (02) 9267 4361, pg 10

ACR Edition (France) *Tel:* (01) 47 88 14 92 *Fax:* (01) 43 33 38 81 *E-mail:* acredition@acr-edition.com *Web Site:* www.acr-edition.com, pg 145

Editorial Acribia SA (Spain) *Tel:* (0976) 232089 *Fax:* (0976) 219212 *E-mail:* acribia@editorialacribia. com *Web Site:* www.editorialacribia.com, pg 566

Act 3 Publishing (United Kingdom) *Tel:* (020) 7402 5321, pg 650

Acta Universitatis Gothoburgensis (Sweden) *Tel:* (031) 7731000 *Fax:* (031) 163797 *E-mail:* library@ub.gu.se *Web Site:* www.ub.gu.se, pg 604

Actes-Graphiques (France) *Tel:* (04) 77 21 23 80; (06) 09 42 21 13 *Fax:* (04) 77 25 39 28 *Web Site:* www. actes-graphiques.com, pg 145

Editions Actes Sud (France) *Tel:* (04) 90 49 86 91 *Fax:* (04) 90 96 95 25 *E-mail:* contact@actes-sud.fr *Web Site:* www.actes-sud.fr, pg 145

Actinic Press Ltd (United Kingdom) *Tel:* (01684) 540154 *Fax:* (01684) 540154, pg 650

Action Artistique de la Ville de Paris (France) *Tel:* (01) 43 25 30 30 *Fax:* (01) 43 25 17 69 *E-mail:* aavp@ club-internet.fr; edition@aavp.com *Web Site:* www. aavp.com, pg 145

Action Editora Ltda (Brazil) *Tel:* (021) 3325-7229 *Fax:* (021) 3325-7229 *E-mail:* action@plugue.com.br *Web Site:* www.editora.com.br, pg 76

Action Magazine (Zimbabwe) *Tel:* (04) 747217 *Fax:* (04) 747409 *E-mail:* action@action.co.zw *Web Site:* www. action.co.zw, pg 777

Action Publications (Cyprus) *Tel:* (022) 818884 *Fax:* (022) 873634, pg 121

Action Publishers (Kenya) *Tel:* (020) 608-810 *Fax:* (020) 753-227 *E-mail:* actonpublishersinfo@acton.co.ke *Web Site:* www.acton.co.ke, pg 429

Actualquarto (Belgium) *Tel:* (071) 21 61 53 *Fax:* (071) 21 77 13, pg 62

Libreria Acuario SA de CV (Mexico) *Tel:* (05) 5742966; (05) 5741137 *Fax:* (05) 2642882, pg 1318

ACUM Ltd (Society of Authors, Composers & Music Publishers in Israel) (Israel) *Tel:* (03) 6113400 *Fax:* (03) 6122629 *E-mail:* info@acum.org.il *Web Site:* www.acum.org.il, pg 1395

Acumen Publishing Ltd (United Kingdom) *Tel:* (01494) 794398 *Fax:* (01494) 784850 *Web Site:* www. acumenpublishing.co.uk, pg 651

ACURIL (Puerto Rico) *Tel:* (787) 790-8054; (787) 764-0000 (ext 3319) *Fax:* (787) 764-2311 *E-mail:* acuril@ rrpac.upr.clu.edu; acuril@coqui.net *Web Site:* acuril. rrp.upr.edu, pg 1272

Editions Ad Solem (Switzerland) *Tel:* (022) 321 19 30 *Fax:* (022) 321 19 31 *E-mail:* office@adsolem.ch *Web Site:* www.ad-solem.com, pg 612

ADA Edita Tokyo Co Ltd (Japan) *Tel:* (03) 3403-1581 *Fax:* (03) 3497-0649 *E-mail:* info@ga-ada.co.jp *Web Site:* www.ga-ada.co.jp, pg 411

Ada Korn Editora SA (Argentina) *Tel:* (011) 4374-6199 *Fax:* (011) 4374-9699 *E-mail:* adakorn@datamarkets. com.ar, pg 2

Ada Press Publishers (Turkey) *Tel:* (0212) 243 1778; (0212) 243 1779 *Fax:* (0212) 249 3545, pg 644

Adaex Educational Publications Ltd (Ghana) *Tel:* (024) 367145; (021) 854188; (021) 854189 *E-mail:* epublication@yahoo.com, pg 300

ADAGP (Societe des Auteurs dans les Arts Grarphiques et Plastiques) (France) *Tel:* (01) 43590979 *Fax:* (01) 45634489 *E-mail:* adagp@adagp.fr *Web Site:* www. adagp.fr, pg 1257

Adalbert Stifter Verein eV (Germany) *Tel:* (089) 622 716-30 *Fax:* (089) 4891148 *E-mail:* asv@asv-muen.de *Web Site:* www.asv-muen.de, pg 1394

Adam Matthew Publications (United Kingdom) *Tel:* (01672) 511921 *Fax:* (01672) 511663 *E-mail:* info@ampltd.co.uk *Web Site:* www.adam-matthew-publications.co.uk, pg 651

Adamantine Press Ltd (United Kingdom), pg 651

Centro de Estudios Adams-Ediciones Valbuena SA (Spain) *Tel:* (093) 4465000; (0902) 333 543 *Fax:* (093) 4465004 *E-mail:* info@adams.es *Web Site:* www.adams.es, pg 566

Mario Adda Editore SNC (Italy) *Tel:* (080) 5539502 *Fax:* (080) 5539502 *E-mail:* info@addaeditore.it *Web Site:* www.addaeditore.it, pg 371

Addis Ababa University Press (Ethiopia) *Tel:* (01) 239746; (01) 239800 (ext 227) *Fax:* (01) 239729 *E-mail:* aau.pres@telecom.net.et, pg 140

Addis Ababa University Library (Ethiopia) *Tel:* (01) 115673; (01) 550844 *Fax:* (01) 550655, pg 1502

Addison-Wesley Pte Ltd (India) *Tel:* (011) 214 6067 *Fax:* (011) 214 6071 *E-mail:* info@pearsoned.co.in *Web Site:* www.pearsonedindia.com, pg 324

Adea Edizioni (Italy) *Tel:* (0372) 430402 *Fax:* (0372) 43363 *E-mail:* info@adea.it *Web Site:* www.adea. it/edizioni.html, pg 371

Adebara Publishers Ltd (Nigeria), pg 498

Adelphi Edizioni SpA (Italy) *Tel:* (02) 725731 *Fax:* (02) 89010337 *E-mail:* info@adelphi.it *Web Site:* www. adelphi.it, pg 371

ADEVA (Akademische Druck-u Verlagsanstalt) (Austria) *Tel:* (0316) 3644 *Fax:* (0316) 364424 *E-mail:* info@ adeva.com *Web Site:* www.adeva.com, pg 1143, 1165, 1205

Adeyle Brothers & Co (Bangladesh) *Tel:* (02) 233508, pg 60, 1291

ADIRA (Switzerland) *Tel:* (022) 312 25 43 *Fax:* (022) 312 26 13 *E-mail:* adira@adira.net *Web Site:* www. adira.net, pg 612

Adivinar y Multiplicar, SA de CV (Mexico) *Tel:* (055) 91164450; (055) 11349065 *Fax:* (055) 5604-1583 *E-mail:* multiplimx@msn.com, pg 458

Deborah Adlam (United Kingdom) *Tel:* (0131) 6676048, pg 1139

Adlard Coles Nautical (United Kingdom) *Tel:* (020) 7758 0200 *Fax:* (020) 7758 0222 *E-mail:* acn@ acblack.com *Web Site:* www.adlardcoles.com, pg 651

ADMICAL (Association pour le Developpement du Mecenat Industriel et Commercial) (France) *Tel:* (01) 42552001 *Fax:* (01) 42557132 *E-mail:* contact@ admical.org *Web Site:* www.admical.org, pg 1257

Adobe Systems GmbH (Germany) *Tel:* (0180) 2304316 *Fax:* (089) 31705-777 *E-mail:* cic@adobe.de *Web Site:* www.adobe.de, pg 1145

Adonia-Verlag (Switzerland) *Tel:* (01) 7207712 *Fax:* (01) 9800622 *Web Site:* www.libroplus.ch, pg 612

ADPF Publications (France) *Tel:* (01) 43 13 11 00 *Fax:* (01) 43 13 11 25 *E-mail:* adpfpublications@adpf. asso.fr *Web Site:* www.france.diplomatie.fr; www.adpf. asso.fr, pg 145

ADR/BookPrint Inc (United States) *Tel:* 316-522-5599 *Toll Free Tel:* 800-767-6066 *Fax:* 316-522-5445 *E-mail:* info@adrbookprint.com *Web Site:* www. adrbookprint.com, pg 1155, 1176, 1217

Adrian (France) *Tel:* (01) 42 36 44 29 *Fax:* (01) 42 36 44 29, pg 145

Adriatica (Peru) *Tel:* (044) 291569 *Fax:* (044) 294242 *E-mail:* libreria@adriaticaperu.com *Web Site:* www. adriaticaperu.com, pg 1325

Adroit Birmingham Ltd (United Kingdom) *Tel:* (0121) 3596831 *Fax:* (0121) 3593974, pg 1173

Adsale Publishing Co Ltd (Hong Kong) *Tel:* 2811 8897 *Fax:* 2516 5024 *E-mail:* publicity@adsale.com.hk *Web Site:* www.adsale.com.hk, pg 312

Advaita Ashrama (India) *Tel:* (033) 22440898; (033) 22452383; (033) 22164000 *Fax:* (033) 22450050 *E-mail:* advaita@vsnl.com *Web Site:* www. advaitaonline.com, pg 324

The Advancement Centre (Australia) *Tel:* (02) 9896 2311 *Fax:* (02) 9368 323, pg 10

Advent Indonesia Publishing (Indonesia) *Tel:* (022) 630392; (022) 642006 *Fax:* (022) 630588, pg 349

Advent Kiado (Hungary) *Tel:* (01) 256-5205 *Fax:* (01) 2565205 *E-mail:* advent12@matavnet.hu, pg 317

The Advent Press (Ghana) *Tel:* (021) 777861 *Fax:* (021) 2119, pg 300

Adverbum SARL (France) *Tel:* (04) 92 81 28 81 *Fax:* (04) 92 81 37 11 *E-mail:* info@adverbum.fr *Web Site:* www.adverbum.fr, pg 145

Advisory Unit: Computers in Education (United Kingdom) *Tel:* (01707) 266714 *Fax:* (01707) 273684 *E-mail:* sales@advisory-unit.org.uk *Web Site:* www. advisory-unit.org.uk, pg 651

Adwinsa Publications (Ghana) Ltd (Ghana) *Tel:* (021) 221654; (021) 21577, pg 300

AE Expaideftikon Vivlion Kai Diskon (Greece) *Tel:* 210 7239474 *Fax:* 2107239483, pg 302

AE Technical Translation Services (United Kingdom) *Tel:* (01286) 650667; (01286) 650555 *Fax:* (01286) 650500, pg 1139

Editorial AEDOS SA (Spain) *Tel:* (093) 488 34 92 *Fax:* (093) 487 76 59 *Web Site:* www.mundiprensa.es, pg 566

Aeneas Verlagsgesellschaft GmbH (Austria) *Tel:* (02236) 25422, pg 47

AENOR (Asociacion Espanola de Normalizacion y Certificacion) (Spain) *Tel:* (091) 4 32 60 00; (0902) 102 201 *Fax:* (091) 3 10 36 95 *E-mail:* info@aenor.es *Web Site:* www.aenor.es, pg 566

Aeolian Press (Australia) *Tel:* (08) 9761 2772 *Fax:* (08) 9761 4151, pg 10

Centre Aequatoria (Belgium) *Tel:* (016) 46 44 84 *E-mail:* info@abbol.com *Web Site:* www.aequatoria. be; www.abbol.com, pg 62

Aerogie-Verlag (Germany) *Tel:* (030) 6 76 32 00 *Fax:* (030) 6 76 32 00, pg 191

Aerospace Publications Pty Ltd (Australia) *Tel:* (02) 6280 0111 *Fax:* (02) 6280 0007 *E-mail:* mail@ ausaviation.com.au *Web Site:* www.ausaviation.com.au, pg 11

AEskan (Iceland) *Tel:* 530-5400 *Fax:* 530-5407 *E-mail:* aeskan@aeskan.is *Web Site:* www.aeskan.is, pg 322

Aesthetica (Italy) *Tel:* (091) 308290 *Fax:* (091) 308290 *E-mail:* aesthetica@unipa.it, pg 371

Afa Yayincilik Sanayi Tic AS (Turkey) *Tel:* (0212) 276 27 67 *Fax:* (0212) 2444362, pg 644

Editorial Afers, SL (Spain) *Tel:* (0961) 26 86 54 *Fax:* (0961) 27 25 82 *E-mail:* afers@provicom.com *Web Site:* www.provicom.com/afers, pg 566

Affiliated East West Press Pvt Ltd (India) *Tel:* (011) 23315398; (011) 23279113; (011) 23264180 *Fax:* (011) 23260538 *E-mail:* aewp.newdel@axcess. net.in; affiliat@vsnl.com, pg 324

Affiliated East West Press Pvt Ltd (India) *Tel:* (011) 23279113; (011) 23264180 *Fax:* (011) 23260538 *E-mail:* affiliat@vsnl.com, pg 1305

Affonso & Reichmann Editores Associados (Brazil) *Tel:* (021) 507-1270 *Fax:* (021) 507-1270 *E-mail:* correio@ra.inf.br, pg 76

A4 Publications Ltd (United Kingdom) *Tel:* (01384) 440591 *Fax:* (01384) 440582, pg 651

Afram Publications (Ghana) Ltd (Ghana) *Tel:* (021) 412561; (021) 406060 *E-mail:* aframpub@punchgh. com, pg 300

Africa Book Centre (United Kingdom) *Tel:* (020) 7240 6649 *Toll Free Tel:* 0845 458 1581 (UK only) *Fax:* (020) 7497 0309 *Toll Free Tel:* 0845 458 1579 (UK only) *E-mail:* orders@africabookcentre. com; info@africabookcentre.com *Web Site:* www. africabookcentre.com, pg 1337

Africa Book Services (EA) Ltd (Kenya) *Tel:* (020) 223641 *Fax:* (020) 330272 *E-mail:* abs@mref.co.ke, pg 429

Africa Christian Press (Ghana) *Tel:* (021) 220271 *Fax:* (021) 220271; (021) 6681155 *E-mail:* acpbooks@ghana.com, pg 300

Africa Literatura Arte Cultura - ALAC (Portugal) *Tel:* (021) 4192274, pg 523

Books for Africa Publishing House (Zimbabwe) *Tel:* (04) 794329 *Fax:* (04) 61881, pg 777

Nouvelles Editions Africaines du Senegal (NEAS) (Senegal) *Tel:* 8211381; 8221580 *Fax:* 8223604, pg 546

African Association for Literacy & Adult Education (AALAE) (Kenya) *Tel:* (020) 222-391; (020) 331-512 *Fax:* (02) 340-849, pg 429

African Books Collective Ltd (United Kingdom) *Tel:* (01865) 726686 *Fax:* (01865) 793298 *E-mail:* abc@africanbookscollective.com *Web Site:* www.africanbookscollective.com, pg 1279

African Books Collective Ltd (United Kingdom) *Tel:* (01865) 726686 *Fax:* (01865) 793298; (01993) 709265 *E-mail:* abc@africanbookscollective.com *Web Site:* www.africanbookscollective.com, pg 1337

African Centre for Technology Studies (ACTS) (Kenya) *Tel:* (020) 7224700; (020) 7224000 *Fax:* (020) 7224701; (020) 7224001 *E-mail:* acts@cgiar.org *Web Site.* www.acts.or.ke, pg 429

African Council for Communication Education (Kenya) *Tel:* (020) 215270-33424 (ext 2068, 2328); (020) 227043 *Fax:* (020) 216135; (020) 750329; (020) 229168 *E-mail:* acceb@arcc.or.ke; acceb@form-net. com, pg 429

African Publishers' Network (APNET) (Cote d'Ivoire) *Tel:* 20211801; 20211802 *Fax:* 20211803 *E-mail:* apnetes@yahoo.com *Web Site:* www.freewebs. com/africanpublishers, pg 1255

African Union Library (Ethiopia) *Tel:* (01) 51 77 00 *Fax:* (01) 51 78 44 *Web Site:* www.africa-union.org, pg 1502

African Universities Press (Nigeria) *Tel:* (022) 317218, pg 499

Africana-FEP Publishers Ltd (Nigeria) *Tel:* (046) 210669, pg 499

Afro-Asian Book Council (AABC) (India) *Tel:* (011) 3261487 *Fax:* (011) 3267437 *E-mail:* sdas@ubspd. com, pg 1263

Edicoes Afrontamento (Portugal) *Tel:* (02) 507 42 20 *Fax:* (02) 507 42 29 *E-mail:* afrontamento@mail. telepac.pt, pg 523

Afterhurst Ltd (United Kingdom) *Tel:* (01273) 207 411 *E-mail:* book.orders@tandf.co.uk, pg 1337

Agalma Psicanalise Editora Ltda (Brazil) *Tel:* (071) 332-8776 *Fax:* (071) 245-7883 *E-mail:* pedidos@agalma. com.br *Web Site:* www.agalma.com.br, pg 76

Agam Kala Prakashan (India) *Tel:* (011) 713395 *Fax:* (011) 7401485, pg 324

AGAPE (Serbia and Montenegro) *Tel:* (021) 469-474 *Fax:* (021) 469-382 *E-mail:* agape@eunet.yu *Web Site:* www.agape.yu, pg 547

Agape Ferences Nyomda es Konyvkiado Kft (Hungary) *Tel:* (062) 444-002; (062) 323-002 *Fax:* (062) 442-592 *E-mail:* agape@tiszanet.hu, pg 317

Editorial AGATA SA de CV (Mexico) *Tel:* (033) 614-4902; (03) 614-4909 *Fax:* (033) 613-8429, pg 458

Age Concern Books (United Kingdom) *Tel:* (020) 8765 7200 *Fax:* (020) 8765 7211 *E-mail:* infodep@ace.org. uk *Web Site:* www.ageconcern.org.uk, pg 651

Editions L'Age d'Homme - La Cite (Switzerland) *Tel:* (021) 312 00 95 *Fax:* (021) 320 84 40 *E-mail:* agedhomme@iprolink.ch, pg 612

Agence Bibliographique de l'Enseignement Superieur (France) *Tel:* (04) 67 54 84 10 *Fax:* (04) 67 54 84 14 *E-mail:* nom@abes.fr *Web Site:* www.abes.fr, pg 145

Agence de Distribution de Presse (ADP) (Senegal) *Tel:* (08) 310052 *Fax:* (08) 324915 *E-mail:* adpresse@ sentoo.sn, pg 546

Agence de l'Est (France) *Tel:* (01) 46334816; (06) 6546 7928 *Fax:* (01) 46334816 *E-mail:* agencedelest1@ wanadoo.fr, pg 1120

Agence et Menageries de la Prense (Belgium) *Tel:* (02) 52 51 641 *Fax:* (02) 52 34 863, pg 1291

Agence Francophone pour la Numerotation Internationale du Livre (AFNIL) (France) *Tel:* (01) 44 41 29 19 *Fax:* (01) 44 41 29 03 *E-mail:* afnil@electre.com *Web Site:* www.afnil.org; www.afnil.com, pg 1257

Agence Hoffman (Germany) *Tel:* (089) 3084807; (089) 3087469 *Fax:* (089) 3082108 *E-mail:* info@ agencehoffman.de *Web Site:* www.agencehoffman.de, pg 1121

Agence Marocaine de l'ISBN (Morocco) *Tel:* (07) 771 890; (07) 772 152 *Fax:* (07) 776 062 *E-mail:* biblio1@onpt.net.ma, pg 1268

Agence Tunisienne de l'ISBN (Tunisia) *Tel:* 71572706 *Fax:* 71572887 *E-mail:* bibliotheque.nationale@email. ati.tn *Web Site:* www.bibliotheque.nat.tn, pg 1279

Agencia Brasileira do ISBN (Brazil) *Tel:* (021) 2220-9367 *Fax:* (021) 2220-4173 *E-mail:* isbn@bn.br *Web Site:* www.bn.br, pg 1253

Agencia Colombiana del ISBN, Camara Colombiana del Libro (Colombia) *Tel:* (01) 288-6188 *Fax:* (01) 287-3320 *E-mail:* agenciaisbn@camlibro.com.co *Web Site:* www.camlibro.com.co, pg 1254

Agencia Espanola de Cooperacion (Spain) *Tel:* (091) 5838100; (091) 5838254; (091) 5838101; (091) 5838102 *Fax:* (091) 5838310; (091) 5838311; (091) 5838313 *Web Site:* www.aeci.es, pg 566

Biblioteca de la Agencia Espanola de Cooperacion Internacional (Spain) *Tel:* (091) 5838175 *Fax:* (091) 5838525 *E-mail:* biblioteca.hispanica@aeci.es *Web Site:* www.aeci.es, pg 1543

Agencia Espanola del ISBN (Spain) *Tel:* (091) 536 88 00 *Fax:* (091) 553 99 90 *Web Site:* www.mcu. es/bases/spa/isbn/ISBN.html, pg 1274

Agencia General de Libreria Internacional SL (AGLI) (Spain) *Tel:* 913769120 *E-mail:* agli@senda.ari.es, pg 1332

Agencija Za Ikonomicesko Programirane i Razvitie (Bulgaria) *Tel:* (02) 9816597 *Fax:* (02) 466110 *E-mail:* aecd@sf.cit.bg, pg 92

The Agency (London) Ltd (United Kingdom) *Tel:* (020) 7727 1346 *Fax:* (020) 7727 9037 *E-mail:* info@ theagency.co.uk *Web Site:* www.writersservices. com/wrhandbook/agency_london.htm, pg 1128

Agens-Werk, Geyer & Reisser, Druck und Verlagsgesellschaft mbH (Austria) *Tel:* (01) 5445641-46 *Fax:* (01) 5445641-46 *E-mail:* prepress@agens-werk.at, pg 47

Agentur des Rauhen Hauses Hamburg GmbH (Germany) *Tel:* (040) 53 53 88-0 *Fax:* (040) 53 53 88-43 *E-mail:* kundenservice@agentur-rauhes-haus.de *Web Site:* www.agentur-rauhes-haus.de, pg 191

Agenzia ISBN per l'Area di Lingua Italiana (Italy) *Tel:* (02) 28315996 *Fax:* (02) 28315906 *E-mail:* bibliografica@bibliografica.it *Web Site:* www. aie.it/ISBN/intro.asp, pg 1264

Agenzia Letteraria Internazionale (Italy) *Tel:* (02) 865445; (02) 861572 *Fax:* (02) 876222 *E-mail:* alidmb@tin.it, pg 1123

Agertofts Forlag A/S (Denmark) *Tel:* 4615 1248 *Fax:* 4615 2404, pg 128

AGIR S/A Editora (Brazil) *Tel:* (021) 221-6424 *Fax:* (021) 252-0410 *E-mail:* info@agireditora.com.br *Web Site:* www.visualnet.com.br/cmaya/cm-ft-01.htm, pg 76

AGIS Verlag GmbH (Germany) *Tel:* (07221) 95 75-0 *Fax:* (07221) 6 68 10 *E-mail:* info@agis-verlag.de *Web Site:* www.agis-verlag.de, pg 191

AGM doo (Croatia) *Tel:* (01) 4856309; (01) 4856307 *Fax:* (01) 4856316 *E-mail:* agm@agm.hr *Web Site:* www.agm.hr, pg 117

Edizioni della Fondazione Giovanni Agnelli (Italy) *Tel:* (011) 6500500 *Fax:* (011) 6502777 *E-mail:* staff@fga.it *Web Site:* www.fondazione-agnelli.it, pg 371

Agni Publishing House (Russian Federation) *Tel:* (08462) 70-32-87; (08462) 70-23-87 (ext 445 - Orders) *Fax:* (08462) 70-23-85 *E-mail:* cdk@transit. samara.ru *Web Site:* www.agni.samara.ru, pg 538

Uitgeversmaatschappij Agon B V (Netherlands) *Tel:* (020) 521 97 77 *Fax:* (020) 622 49 37 *E-mail:* info@boekboek.nl *Web Site:* www.boekboek. nl, pg 473

Agora bvba (Belgium) *Tel:* (053) 78-87-00 *Fax:* (053) 78-26-91 *E-mail:* info@agorabooks.com *Web Site:* www.agorabooks.com, pg 1291

Agora Editorial (Spain) *Tel:* (095) 2228699; (095) 2221847 *Fax:* (095) 2226411, pg 566

Editora Agora Ltda (Brazil) *Tel:* (011) 38723322 *Fax:* (011) 38727476 *E-mail:* agora@editoraagora. com.br *Web Site:* www.gruposummus.com.br/agora, pg 76

De Agostini Scolastica (Italy) *Tel:* (02) 380861 *Fax:* (02) 38086448 *Web Site:* www.scuola.com, pg 371

AGPOL (Przedsiebiorstwo Reklamy i Wydawnictw Handlu Zagranicznego) (Poland) *Tel:* (022) 416061 *Fax:* (022) 405607, pg 1271

Agrargazdsagi Kutato es Informatikai Intezet (Hungary) *Tel:* (01) 2171011 *Fax:* (01) 1177037, pg 317

Universitaetsbibliothek Georgius Agricola (Germany) *Tel:* (03731) 39 29 59 *Fax:* (03731) 39 32 89 *E-mail:* unibib@ub.tu-freiberg.de *Web Site:* www.tu-freiberg.de, pg 1506

Agricole Publishing Academy (India) *Tel:* (011) 692703, pg 324

Agricultural Institute Library (Ethiopia) *Tel:* (07) 11-00-19, pg 1502

Agrivet Publishers (Namibia) *Tel:* (061) 228909 *Fax:* (061) 230619 *E-mail:* agrivet@iafrica.com.na, pg 472

Biblioteca Agropecuaria de Colombia (BAC) (Colombia) *Tel:* (01) 4227373 (ext 1254) *Fax:* (01) 2813088 *E-mail:* bac@corpoica.org.co *Web Site:* www.corpoica. org.co, pg 1496

Ediciones Agrotecnicas, SL (Spain) *Tel:* (091) 5473515 *Fax:* (091) 5474506 *E-mail:* agrotecnicas@ agrotecnica.com *Web Site:* www.agrotecnica.com, pg 566

Agrupacion Bibliotecologica del Uruguay (Uruguay) *Tel:* (02) 400 57 40, pg 1574

AGT Editor SA (Mexico) *Tel:* (05) 273-9228 *Fax:* (05) 2771696, pg 458

Editorial Aguaclara (Spain) *Tel:* 965 240064 *Fax:* 965 259302 *E-mail:* edit.aguaclara@natural.es, pg 567

Agudat Sabah (Israel) *Tel:* (09) 8620544 *Fax:* (09) 8620546, pg 361

Aguilar Altea Taurus Alfaguara SA de CV (Mexico) *Tel:* (05) 688 89 66; (05) 688 82 77; (05) 688 75 66 *Fax:* (05) 6042304; (05) 6886538 *E-mail:* info@ editorialaguilar.com *Web Site:* www.alfaguara.com.mx, pg 458

Aguilar Altea Taurus Alfaguara SA de Ediciones (Argentina) *Tel:* (011) 4912-7220 *Fax:* (011) 4912-7440 *E-mail:* info@alfaguara.com.ar *Web Site:* www. alfaguara.com.ar, pg 2

Aguilar SA de Ediciones (Spain) *Tel:* (091) 7449060 *Fax:* (091) 7449224 *E-mail:* limarquezes@santillana.es *Web Site:* www.gruposantillana.com, pg 567

Libreria Aguirre (Colombia) *Tel:* (04) 2220336, pg 1296

Agyra (Greece) *Tel:* 2102693800 *Fax:* 2102693805 *E-mail:* info@agyra.gr *Web Site:* www.agyra.gr, pg 1302

AHB Publications (Australia), pg 11

Ahmadu Bello University Bookshop Ltd (Nigeria) *Tel:* (069) 550054, pg 1322

Ahmadu Bello University Library (Nigeria) *Tel:* (069) 505-71; (069) 505-72; (069) 505-73; (069) 505-74 *Fax:* (069) 505-63, pg 1532

Ahmadu Bello University Press Ltd (Nigeria) *Tel:* (069) 550054 *E-mail:* abupl@abu.edu.ng, pg 499

Ahn Graphics (Republic of Korea) *Tel:* (02) 743 8065; (02) 743 8066; (02) 743 4154; (02) 743 3353 *Fax:* (02) 743 3352 *E-mail:* ask@ag.co.kr *Web Site:* www.ag.co.kr, pg 433

Al Ahram Establishment (Egypt (Arab Republic of Egypt)) *Tel:* (02) 748248 *Fax:* (02) 745888 *E-mail:* ahram@ahram.org.eg, pg 137

Al Ahram Establishment (Egypt (Arab Republic of Egypt)) *Tel:* (02) 5786500; (02) 5786200; (02) 5786300; (02) 5786400 *Fax:* (02) 3941866; (02) 5786126; (02) 5786833 *E-mail:* ahram@ahram.org.eg *Web Site:* www.ahram.org.eg, pg 1137

Ahriman-Verlag GmbH (Germany) *Tel:* (0761) 502303 *Fax:* (0761) 502247 *E-mail:* ahriman@t-online.de *Web Site:* www.ahriman.com, pg 191

Ai Chih Book Co Ltd (Taiwan, Province of China) *Tel:* (07) 8121571 *Fax:* (07) 8121534, pg 634

Ai Interactive Ltd (United Kingdom) *Tel:* (01235) 529595 *Fax:* (01865) 736917 *E-mail:* medical@ andromeda-interactive.co.uk *Web Site:* www. andromeda-interactive.co.uk, pg 651

AIB Associazione Italiana Bibliotheche (Italy) *Tel:* (06) 4463532 *Fax:* (06) 4441139 *E-mail:* aib@aib.it *Web Site:* www.aib.it, pg 371

AIBDA (Costa Rica) *Tel:* (0506) 2160222 *Fax:* (0506) 2294741; (0506) 2160233 *E-mail:* iicahq@iica.ac.cr *Web Site:* www.iica.int/, pg 1254

Aichinger, Bernhard & Co GmbH (Austria) *Tel:* (01) 5128853 *Fax:* (01) 5128853-13, pg 1289

aid infodienst - Verbraucherdienst, Ernaehrung, Landwirtschaft eV (Germany) *Tel:* (0228) 8499-0 *Fax:* (0228) 8499-177 *E-mail:* aid@aid.de *Web Site:* www.aid.de, pg 191

Aide Editora e Comercio de Livros Ltda (Brazil) *Tel:* (021) 2589-9926 *Fax:* (021) 2589-9926 *E-mail:* aideeditora@radnet.com.br *Web Site:* www. radnet.com.br/aideeditora, pg 76

Aikamedia Oy (Finland) *Tel:* (020) 7619 800 *Fax:* (014) 7514 757 *E-mail:* asiakaspalvelu@aikamedia.fi *Web Site:* www.aikamedia.fi, pg 1242

Aiki News (Japan) *Tel:* (042) 748-1240 *Fax:* (042) 748-2421 *Web Site:* aikinews.com, pg 411

Aina-e-Adab (Pakistan) *Tel:* (042) 54069, pg 507

Aion Verlag (Romania) *Tel:* (059) 147595, pg 533

Air Gallery Edition, Helmut Kreuzer (Germany) *Tel:* (08122) 84487 *Fax:* (08122) 84487, pg 191

Air Larko Panorama ALP (Cyprus) *Tel:* (06) 236181 *Fax:* (06) 245046, pg 121

Airis Press (Russian Federation) *Tel:* (095) 9561684; (095) 7852925 *Fax:* (095) 9561684; (095) 7852925 *E-mail:* rolf@airis.ru *Web Site:* www.airis.ru, pg 539

Airlife Publishing Ltd (United Kingdom) *Tel:* (01743) 235651 *Fax:* (01743) 232944 *E-mail:* info@ airlifebooks.com *Web Site:* www.crowoodpress.co.uk, pg 651

Airlift Book Co (United Kingdom) *Tel:* (020) 8804 0400 *Fax:* (020) 8804 0044 *E-mail:* customercare@airlift.co. uk *Web Site:* www.airlift.co.uk, pg 1337

L'Airone Editrice (Italy) *Tel:* (06) 6570758 *Fax:* (06) 65740509 *E-mail:* gremese@gremese.com *Web Site:* www.gremese.com, pg 371

Aisthesis Verlag (Germany) *Tel:* (0521) 172604 *Fax:* (0521) 172812 *E-mail:* aisthesis@bitel.net *Web Site:* www.aisthesis.de, pg 191

Aithra Scientific Bookstore (Greece) *Tel:* 2103301269 *Fax:* 2103302622, pg 1302

AITI (Associazione Italiana Traduttori e Interpreti) (Italy) *Tel:* (081) 7645362 *Fax:* (081) 7645362 *E-mail:* segreteria@aiti.org *Web Site:* www.aiti.org, pg 1138

AITIM (Asociacion de Investigacion Tecnica de las industrias de la Madera y Corcho) (Spain) *Tel:* (091) 5425864 *Fax:* (091) 5590512 *E-mail:* informame@ aitim.es *Web Site:* www.aitim.es, pg 567

Gillon Aitken Associates Ltd (United Kingdom) *Tel:* (020) 7373 8672 *Fax:* (020) 7373 6002 *E-mail:* reception@gillonaitken.co.uk, pg 1128

Editura Aius (Romania) *Tel:* (051) 196136 *Fax:* (051) 196135 *E-mail:* aius@euroweb.ro, pg 533

Ajanta Books International (India) *Tel:* (011) 23856182 *Fax:* (011) 23856182 *E-mail:* ajantabi@vsnl.com *Web Site:* ajantabooksinternational.com, pg 1122

Ajanta Publications (India) (India) *Tel:* (011) 2917375; (011) 2926182 *Fax:* (011) 741 5016; (011) 713 2908; (011) 7213076, pg 324

Ajstan Publishers (Armenia) *Tel:* (01) 528520, pg 10

Biblioteca da Ajuda (Portugal) *Tel:* (021) 363 85 92 *Fax:* (021) 363 85 92, pg 1537

AK Press & Distribution (United Kingdom) *Tel:* (0131) 5555165 *Fax:* (0131) 5555215 *E-mail:* ak@akedin. demon.co.uk *Web Site:* www.akuk.com, pg 651

Akademiai Kiado (Hungary) *Tel:* (01) 4648220; (01) 4648282; (01) 4648221; (01) 4648231, pg 317

Akademibokhandeln (Sweden) *Tel:* (08) 613 61 10 *Fax:* (08) 24 25 43 *E-mail:* bokinfo@ akademibokhandeln.se; order@akademibokhandeln.se *Web Site:* www.akademibokhandeln.se, pg 1334

Akademie Verlag GmbH (Germany) *Tel:* (030) 4 22 00 60 *Fax:* (030) 422 00 657 *E-mail:* info@akademie-verlag.de *Web Site:* www.akademie-verlag.de, pg 191

Akademiforlaget Corona AB (Sweden) *Tel:* (040) 286161 *Fax:* (040) 286162 *E-mail:* kundservice@cor. se *Web Site:* www.cor.se, pg 604

Biblioteka Akademii Nauk Rossii (Russian Federation) *Tel:* (0812) 3283592 *Fax:* (0812) 3287436 *E-mail:* ban@info.rasl.spb.ru *Web Site:* www.ban.ru, pg 1539

Akademische Druck-u Verlagsanstalt Dr Paul Struzl GmbH (Austria) *Tel:* (0316) 3644 *Fax:* (0316) 3644-24 *E-mail:* info@adeva.com *Web Site:* www.adeva. com, pg 47

Akademisk Forlag A/S (Denmark) *Tel:* 33 43 40 80 *Fax:* 33 43 40 99 *E-mail:* akademisk@akademisk.dk *Web Site:* www.akademisk.dk, pg 128

Libreria Akadia Editorial (Argentina) *Tel:* (011) 4961-8614; (011) 4964-2230 *Fax:* (011) 4961-8614 *E-mail:* akadia@arnet.com.ar, pg 2

Akadoma CV (Indonesia) *Tel:* (021) 3904323, pg 350

Akajase Enterprises (United Republic of Tanzania) *Tel:* (051) 26121, pg 638

Ediciones Akal SA (Spain) *Tel:* (091) 8061996 *Fax:* (091) 6564911; (091) 8044028 *E-mail:* pedidos. akal@akal.com; edicion@akal.com; universidad@akal.com; educacion@akal.com; prensa@ akal.com *Web Site:* www.akal.com, pg 567

Akateeminen Kirjakauppa (Finland) *Tel:* (09) 121 4252 *Fax:* (09) 121 4322 *E-mail:* tilaukset@akateeminen. com *Web Site:* www.akateeminen.com, pg 1299

Akateeminen Kustannusliike Oy (Finland) *Tel:* (09) 434 2320 *Fax:* (09) 43423234 *Web Site:* www.spes.fi, pg 141

Akcali Copyright Agency (Turkey) *Tel:* (0216) 3388771; (0216) 3485160 *Fax:* (0216) 3490778; (0216) 4142265 *E-mail:* akcali@attglobal.net, pg 1128

Akdeniz Yayincilik (Turkey) *Tel:* (0212) 629-0026 *Fax:* (0212) 629-0027, pg 644

Akerbloms Universitetsbokhandel (Sweden) *Tel:* (090) 711250 *Fax:* (090) 711260 *E-mail:* swedish.books@ akerbloms.se, pg 1334

akg-images gmbh (Germany) *Tel:* (030) 80485200 *Fax:* (030) 80485500 *E-mail:* info@akg.de; info@akg-images.com *Web Site:* www.akg-images.com, pg 191

Akita Shoten Publishing Co Ltd (Japan) *Tel:* (03) 3264-7011 *Fax:* (03) 3265-5906 *E-mail:* license@ akitashoten.co.jp *Web Site:* www.akitashoten.co.jp, pg 411

Akohi Editions (Cote d'Ivoire) *Tel:* 24 39 54 79 *Fax:* 24 39 75 58, pg 116

Editions Akpagnon (Togo) *Tel:* 220244 *Fax:* 220244, pg 642

Akritas (Greece) *Tel:* 2109314968; 2109334554 *Fax:* 2109311436, pg 302

M Akselrad (Germany) *Tel:* (06221) 183030 *Fax:* (06221) 181223 *E-mail:* makselrad@gmx.net, pg 191

Akshat Publications (India) *Tel:* (011) 7247234; (011) 7114425; (011) 7240483 *Fax:* (011) 7254734; (011) 7218836, pg 324

Akson Charerntat (S/B Akson) (Thailand) *Tel:* (02) 2214587 *Fax:* (02) 2255356, pg 640

Akti-Oxy Publications (Greece) *Tel:* 2108658502; 2108676125 *Fax:* 2103802030 *E-mail:* info@ oxy.gr *Web Site:* www.oxy.gr, pg 1302

Al-Fateh University (Libyan Arab Jamahiriya) *Tel:* (02133) 621988, pg 444

Editions Al-Fourkane (Morocco) *Tel:* (02) 983351 *Fax:* (02) 983351, pg 470

Editions Al Liamm (France) *Tel:* (0298) 02 10 84, pg 146

Al Maktabah Al Wataniah (Syrian Arab Republic), pg 1547

Al-Neelain University (Sudan) *Tel:* (011) 880055 *Fax:* (011) 776338 *E-mail:* neelain@an.mail.com, pg 1545

Al-Tanwir Al Ilmi (Scientific Enlightenment Publishing House) (Jordan) *Tel:* (026) 4899619 *Fax:* (026) 4899619, pg 428

Aladdin Books Ltd (United Kingdom) *Tel:* (020) 7323 3319 *Fax:* (020) 7323 4829 *E-mail:* kerry.mciver@ aladdinbooks.co.uk *Web Site:* www.aladdinbooks.co. uk, pg 651

Alamire vzw, Music Publishers (Belgium) *Tel:* (011) 610 510 *Fax:* (011) 610 511 *E-mail:* info@alamire.com *Web Site:* www.alamire.com, pg 62

Alamo Ellas (Greece) *Tel:* 2102280027 *Fax:* 210 2280027, pg 302

Editorial 'Alas' (Spain) *Tel:* (093) 4537506; (093) 3233445 *Fax:* (093) 4537506 *E-mail:* sala@editorial-alas.com *Web Site:* www.editorial-alas.com, pg 567

Alba (Italy) *Tel:* (0532) 249854 *Fax:* (0532) 249854 *E-mail:* alba_editrice@virgilio.it, pg 371

Alba Fachverlag GmbH & Co KG (Germany) *Tel:* (0211) 5 20 13-0 *Fax:* (0211) 5 20 13-28 *E-mail:* oepnv@alba.verlag.de *Web Site:* www.alba-verlag.de, pg 191

Albah Publishers (Nigeria), pg 499

J H Goehre Albanus Verlag (Switzerland) *Tel:* (052) 293503, pg 612

Albany Book Co Ltd (United Kingdom) *Tel:* (0141) 9542271, pg 1337

Albarello Verlag GmbH (Germany) *Tel:* (02058) 8279 *Fax:* (02058) 80534 *E-mail:* email@albarello.de *Web Site:* www.albarello.de, pg 192

Albatros (Poland) *Tel:* (022) 842-9867 *Fax:* (022) 842-9867, pg 517

Albatros AS (Czech Republic) *Tel:* (02) 34633261 *Fax:* (02) 34633262 *E-mail:* albatros@bonton.cz *Web Site:* www.albatros.cz, pg 121

Editura Albatros (Romania) *Tel:* (01) 2228493 *Fax:* (01) 2228493, pg 533

Editorial Albatros SACI (Argentina) *Tel:* (011) 4807-2030 *Fax:* (011) 4807-2010 *E-mail:* info@edalbatros.com.ar *Web Site:* www.edalbatros.com.ar, pg 3

Albe Libros Technicos (Uruguay) *Tel:* (02) 915 75 28; (02) 915 74 85 *Fax:* (02) 915 75 28 *Web Site:* www.bosch.es/puntos_internacional.asp, pg 771

Albe Libros Tecnicos SRL (Uruguay) *Tel:* (02) 95 75 28 *Fax:* (02) 95 75 28, pg 1346

Verlag Karl Alber GmbH (Germany) *Tel:* (0761) 27 17-436 *Fax:* (0761) 27 17-212 *E-mail:* info@verlag-alber.de *Web Site:* www.verlag-alber.de, pg 192

Alberdania SL (Spain) *Tel:* (0943) 63 28 14 *Fax:* (0943) 63 80 55 *E-mail:* alberdania@ctv.es, pg 567

Libreria Eduardo Albers Ltda (Chile) *Tel:* (02) 218 5371 *Fax:* (02) 218 1458 *Web Site:* www.albers.cl, pg 1295

Albert Nauck & Co (Germany) *Tel:* (030) 3980640, pg 192

Ermanno Albertelli Editore (Italy) *Tel:* (0521) 290387 *Fax:* (0521) 290387 *E-mail:* info@tuttostoria.it *Web Site:* www.tuttostoria.it, pg 371

Alberti Libraio Editore (Italy) *Tel:* (0323) 402534 *Fax:* (0323) 401074 *E-mail:* info@albertilibraio.it *Web Site:* www.albertilibraio.it, pg 371

Alberts XII (Latvia) *Tel:* (02) 7205286 *Fax:* (02) 7205284 *E-mail:* alberts@internet.lv, pg 441

E Albrecht Verlags-KG (Germany) *Tel:* (089) 85853-0 *Fax:* (089) 85853199 *E-mail:* av@albrecht.de, pg 192

Verlag und Antiquariat Frank Albrecht (Germany) *Tel:* (06203) 65713 *Fax:* (06203) 65311 *E-mail:* albrecht@antiquariat.com *Web Site:* www.antiquariat.com, pg 192

Albyn Press (United Kingdom) *Tel:* (020) 7351 4995 *Fax:* (020) 7351 4995, pg 651

Librairie Francaise Alcheh (Israel) *Tel:* (03) 5604173 *Fax:* (03) 6 994526 *E-mail:* alcheh@zahav.net.il, pg 1309

Alcor-Edimpex (Verlag) Ltd (Romania) *Tel:* (01) 665-34-40 *Fax:* (01) 665 34 40 *E-mail:* ed_alcor@yahoo.com *Web Site:* www.rotravel.com/alcor, pg 533

The Alden Group Ltd (United Kingdom) *Tel:* (01865) 253 200 *Fax:* (01865) 249 070 *E-mail:* information@alden.co.uk *Web Site:* www.alden.co.uk, pg 1173, 1214

Aldington Books Ltd (United Kingdom) *Tel:* (01233) 720123 *Fax:* (01233) 721272 *E-mail:* sales@aldingtonbooks.co.uk *Web Site:* www.aldingtonbooks.co.uk, pg 1337

Aldwych Press Ltd (United Kingdom) *Tel:* (020) 7240 0856 *Fax:* (020) 7379 0609 *E-mail:* info@europspan.co.uk *Web Site:* www.eurospan.co.uk, pg 651

Centro Antiquar do Alecrim A Trindade (Portugal) *Tel:* (021) 3424660 *Fax:* (021) 3470180 *E-mail:* np75ae@mail.telepac.pt, pg 1327

Aleks Print Publishing House (Bulgaria) *Tel:* (052) 823147 *Fax:* (052) 823147 *E-mail:* dstankov@ultranet.bg, pg 92

Aleks Soft (Bulgaria) *Tel:* (02) 328855 *Fax:* (02) 328855 *E-mail:* info@alexsoft.net, pg 92

Alekto Verlag GmbH (Austria) *Tel:* (0463) 591180 *Fax:* (0463) 593217 *E-mail:* bali@bali.co.at, pg 47

Livraria Alema Buecherstube Brooklin Ltda (Brazil) *Tel:* (011) 5543 3829 *Fax:* (011) 5041 4315 *E-mail:* buchlbb@uol.com.br *Web Site:* www.buchlbb.com/, pg 1293

Livraria Alema Ltda Brasileitura (Brazil) *Tel:* (047) 3260499 *Fax:* (0473) 3263062 *E-mail:* alemaeko@nutecnet.com.br, pg 76

Alemar's Best Sellers Club (Philippines) *Tel:* (02) 592617, pg 1245

Alemaya University of Agriculture Library (Ethiopia) *Tel:* (05) 11-14-00 *Fax:* (05) 11-40-08, pg 1502

El Aleph Editores (Spain) *Tel:* (093) 443 71 00 *Fax:* (093) 443 71 30 *E-mail:* correu@grup62.com *Web Site:* www.grup62.com, pg 567

Aletheia Publishing (Australia) *Tel:* (07) 3855 2056 *E-mail:* aletheia@powerup.com.au, pg 11

Alexander Verlag Berlin (Germany) *Tel:* (030) 3021826 *Fax:* (030) 3029408 *E-mail:* info@alexander-verlag.com *Web Site:* www.alexander-verlag.com, pg 192

Alexandria Municipal Library (Egypt (Arab Republic of Egypt)), pg 1501

Alexandria University Central Library (Egypt (Arab Republic of Egypt)) *Tel:* (03) 4282 928 *Fax:* (03) 4282 927 *E-mail:* auclib@auclib.edu.eg *Web Site:* www.auclib.edu.eg, pg 1501

Alexiadou Vefa (Greece) *Tel:* 2102848086 *Fax:* 210 2849689 *E-mail:* vefaeditions@ath.forthnet.gr *Web Site:* www.addgr.com/comp/vefa/index.htm, pg 1302

Vefa Alexiadou Editions (Greece) *Tel:* 2102848086 *Fax:* 2102849689 *E-mail:* vefaeditions@ath.forthnet.gr *Web Site:* www.addgr.com/comp/vefa/index.htm, pg 302

ALFA dd za izdavacke, graficke i trgovacke poslove (Croatia) *Tel:* (01) 4666 066, (01) 4666 077 *Fax:* (01) 4666 258 *E-mail:* alfa-zg@zg.tel.hr, pg 117

Alfa-Narodna Knjiga (Serbia and Montenegro) *Tel:* (011) 3221-484; (011) 3227-426; (011) 3223-910 *Fax:* (011) 3227-946 *E-mail:* alfankkl@eunet.yu *Web Site:* www.narodnaknjiga.co.yu, pg 547

Editora Alfa Omega Ltda (Brazil) *Tel:* (011) 3062-6400; (011) 3062-6690 *Fax:* (011) 3083-0746 *E-mail:* alfaomega@alfaomega.com.br *Web Site:* www.alfaomega.com.br, pg 76

Publicacoes Alfa SA (Portugal) *Tel:* (021) 7587320, pg 523

Alfabeta Bokforlag AB (Sweden) *Tel:* (08) 714 36 30 *Fax:* (08) 643 24 31 *E-mail:* info@alfamedia.se *Web Site:* www.alfamedia.se, pg 604

Alfabeta Impresores Ltda (Chile) *Tel:* (02) 6397765 *Fax:* (02) 6391752, pg 98

Alfadil Ediciones (Venezuela) *Tel:* (0212) 762-3036; (0212) 761-3576; (0212) 763-5676 *Fax:* (0212) 762-0210 *E-mail:* contacto@alfagrupo.com *Web Site:* www.alfagrupo.com, pg 773

Alfagrama SRL ediciones (Argentina) *Tel:* (011) 4342-2452; (011) 4345-2299 *Fax:* (011) 4345-5411 *E-mail:* libros@alfagrama.com.ar *Web Site:* www.alfagrama.com.ar, pg 3

Alfaguara Ediciones SA - Grupo Santillana (Spain) *Tel:* (091) 744 90 60 *Fax:* (091) 744 92 24 *E-mail:* loboan@santillana.es *Web Site:* www.santillana.es, pg 567

Libreria Alfani Editrice SRL (Italy) *Tel:* (055) 2398800 *Fax:* (055) 218251 *E-mail:* info@librerialfani.it *Web Site:* www.librerialfani.it, pg 371

Alfaomega Grupo Editor SA de CV (Mexico) *Tel:* (05) 5755022 (ext 126); (05) 5755022 (ext 222) *Fax:* (052) 5752490 *E-mail:* universitaria@alfaomega.com.mx *Web Site:* www.alfaomega.com.mx, pg 458

Ediciones Alfar SA (Spain) *Tel:* (095) 4406100; (095) 4406366; (095) 4406614 *Fax:* (05) 4402580, pg 567

Edicions Alfons el Magnanim, Institucio Valenciana d'Estudis i Investigacio (Spain) *Tel:* (096) 3883756; (096) 3883751 *Web Site:* www.alfonselmagnanim.com, pg 567

Algarve (Lithuania) *Tel:* (02) 725910; (02) 721635 *Fax:* (02) 721462, pg 445

Editorial Algazara (Spain) *Tel:* (095) 2358284 *Fax:* (095) 2333175, pg 567

Sheikh Shaukat Ali & Sons (Pakistan) *Tel:* (021) 214585; (021) 212289 *Fax:* (021) 2637877, pg 507

Alianza Editorial de Argentina SA (Argentina) *Tel:* (011) 4342-4426; (011) 4342-9029 *Fax:* (011) 4342-4426; (011) 4342-9025 *E-mail:* gconosur@satlink.com, pg 3

Alianza Editorial Mexicana, SA de CV (Mexico) *Tel:* (05) 5670-4887; (05) 5670-4712 *Fax:* (05) 5619797, pg 458

Alianza Editorial SA (Spain) *Tel:* (091) 3938888 *Fax:* (091) 3207480 *E-mail:* alianza@anaya.es; mmorales@anaya.es *Web Site:* www.alianzaeditorial.es, pg 567

Alibri Libreria, SL (Spain) *Tel:* 933170578 *Fax:* 934122702 *E-mail:* books-world@books-world.com, pg 1332

Edizioni Alice (Italy) *Tel:* (02) 83 61 347 *E-mail:* info@hod.it *Web Site:* www.hod.it, pg 371

Alice-Kan (Japan) *Tel:* (03) 3293 9755 *Fax:* (03) 3293 9756, pg 411

Alinari Fratelli SpA Istituto di Edizioni Artistiche (Italy) *Tel:* (055) 23951 *Fax:* (055) 2382857 *E-mail:* info@alinari.it *Web Site:* www.alinari.com, pg 371

Alinco SA - Aura Comunicacio (Spain) *Tel:* (093) 2172054 *Fax:* (093) 2373469, pg 567

Alinea (Italy) *Tel:* (055) 333428 *Fax:* (055) 331013 *E-mail:* ordini@alinea.it; info@alinea.it *Web Site:* www.alinea.it, pg 372

Alinea A/S (Denmark) *Tel:* 33 69 46 66 *Fax:* 33 69 46 60 *E-mail:* alinea@alinea.dk; skoleservice@alinea.dk *Web Site:* www.alinea.dk, pg 128

Alisher Navoi National Library of Uzbekistan (Uzbekistan) *Tel:* (099871) 139 16 58 *Fax:* (099871) 133 09 08 *E-mail:* navoi@physic.uzsci.net *Web Site:* www.rsl.ru/sonegos/e_son4_17.htm, pg 1553

ALITHIA Publishing Co (Cyprus) *Tel:* (022) 463040 *Fax:* (022) 463945, pg 121

Alkem Company (S) Pte Ltd (Singapore) *Tel:* 6265 6666 *Fax:* 6261 7875 *E-mail:* enquiry@alkem.com.sg *Web Site:* www.alkem.com.sg, pg 1150, 1171, 1227

Alkim Kitapcilik-Yayimcilik (Turkey), pg 644

Alkor-Edition Kassel GmbH (Germany) *Tel:* (0561) 3105-282 *Fax:* (0561) 37755 *E-mail:* alkor-edition@baerenreiter.com *Web Site:* www.alkor-edition.com, pg 192

Editora All (Romania) *Tel:* (01) 402 26 00 *Fax:* (01) 402 26 10 *E-mail:* info@all.ro *Web Site:* www.all.ro, pg 533

All'Insegna del Giglio (Italy) *Tel:* (055) 451593 *Fax:* (055) 450030 *E-mail:* ins.giglio@dada.it, pg 372

All-Russian Patent Technical Library (Russian Federation) *Tel:* (095) 2406425 *Fax:* (095) 2404437 *E-mail:* vptb@aha.ru, pg 1539

Ian Allan Publishing (United Kingdom) *Tel:* (01932) 266600 *Fax:* (01932) 266601 *E-mail:* info@ianallanpub.co.uk *Web Site:* www.ianallan.com, pg 652

Umberto Allemandi & Co Publishing (United Kingdom) *Tel:* (020) 7735 3331 *Fax:* (020) 7735 3332 *E-mail:* contact@theartnewspaper.com *Web Site:* www.theartnewspaper.com, pg 652

Umberto Allemandi & C SRL (Italy) *Tel:* (011) 8199111 *Fax:* (011) 8193090 *E-mail:* info@allemandi.com *Web Site:* www.allemandi.com, pg 372

Allen & Unwin Pty Ltd (Australia) *Tel:* (02) 8425 0100 *Fax:* (02) 9906 2218 *E-mail:* frontdesk@allenandunwin.com *Web Site:* www.allenandunwin.com, pg 11

Allert de Lange BV (Netherlands) *Tel:* (020) 6246744 *Fax:* (020) 6384975, pg 473

L'Alliance francaise, Bibliotheque (Senegal) *Tel:* 21 0822, pg 1540

The Alliance of Literary Societies (United Kingdom) *Tel:* (023) 92 475855 *Fax:* (0870) 056 0330 *Web Site:* www.sndc.demon.co.uk/als.htm, pg 1400

Alliance West African Publishers & Co (Nigeria) *Tel:* (085) 230798, pg 499

Allied Book Centre (India) *Tel:* (0135) 656526; (0135) 650949; (0135) 9837066875 *Fax:* (0135) 656554 *E-mail:* abc_book@rediffmail.com, pg 324

Allied Mouse Ltd (United Kingdom) *Tel:* (01349) 865400 *Fax:* (01349) 866066 *E-mail:* info@heartstone. co.uk *Web Site:* www.heartstone.co.uk, pg 652

Allied Publishers Pvt Ltd (India) *Tel:* (011) 3239001; (011) 3233002; (011) 5402792 *Fax:* (011) 3235967 *E-mail:* allied.delhi@vsnl.com; delhi.allied@excess. net.in *Web Site:* www.alliedpublishers.com, pg 325

Allied Publishers Pvt Ltd (India) *Tel:* (011) 3239001; (011) 3233002; (011) 3233004; (011) 3233006667 *Fax:* (011) 3235967 *E-mail:* aplcmd@ndf.vsnl.net.in *Web Site:* www.alliedpublishers.com, pg 1305

Allison & Busby (United Kingdom) *Tel:* (020) 7738 7888 *Fax:* (020) 7733 4244 *E-mail:* all@allisonbusby. com *Web Site:* www.allisonandbusby.com, pg 652

Allt om Hobby AB (Sweden) *Tel:* (08) 99 93 33 *Fax:* (08) 99 88 66 *E-mail:* order@hobby.se *Web Site:* www.hobby.se, pg 604

Allt om Hobbys Publishing Co (Sweden) *Tel:* (08) 99 93 33 *Fax:* (08) 99 88 66 *E-mail:* order@hobby.se *Web Site:* www.hobby.se, pg 1246

Alma (Denmark) *Tel:* 48 25 54 41 *Fax:* 48 25 20 41, pg 128

Alma Littera (Lithuania) *Tel:* (05) 263 88 77 *Fax:* (05) 272 80 26 *E-mail:* post@almali.lt *Web Site:* www. almalittera.lt, pg 445

Alma'Arif PT (Indonesia) *Tel:* (022) 4207177; (022) 4203708 *Fax:* (022) 439194, pg 350

Livraria Almedina (Portugal) *Tel:* 239 851 903 *E-mail:* editora@almedina.net *Web Site:* www. almedina.net, pg 523

Almenna Bokafelagid (Iceland) *Tel:* 522-2000 *Fax:* 522-2025 *Web Site:* www.edda.is, pg 322

Almqvist och Wiksell International (Sweden) *Tel:* (08) 613 61 00 *Fax:* (08) 24 25 43 *E-mail:* scand.mongr@ awi.se *Web Site:* www.akademibokhandeln.se, pg 604

Aloe Educational (South Africa) *Tel:* (011) 8393719 *Fax:* (011) 8393720, pg 1331

Forlaget alokke AS (Denmark) *Tel:* 75671119 *Fax:* 75671074 *E-mail:* alokke@get2net.dk, pg 128

Alouette Verlag (Germany) *Tel:* (040) 712 23 53 *Fax:* (040) 713 41 88 *E-mail:* webmaster@alouette-verlag.de *Web Site:* www.alouette-verlag.de, pg 192

Ediciones Alpe (Mexico) *Tel:* (05) 2114523, pg 458

Alpha-Delta (Greece) *Tel:* 2102280027 *Fax:* 210 2280027, pg 1302

Alpha Literatur Verlag/Alpha Presse (Germany) *Tel:* (069) 555325 *Fax:* (069) 955130-99, pg 192

Editions Alphee (Monaco) *Tel:* (093) 30-40-06 *Fax:* (099) 99-67-18, pg 470

Alpina Color Graphics Inc (United States) *Tel:* 212-285-2700 *Fax:* 212-285-2704 *E-mail:* info@alpina.net *Web Site:* www.alpina.net, pg 1176

AlpnetCompuType Ltd (United Kingdom) *Tel:* (01895) 440791 *Fax:* (01895) 441500 *E-mail:* computype@ computype.co.uk, pg 1173

ALS-Verlag GmbH (Germany) *Tel:* (06074) 82 16-0; (06074) 82 16-50 (orders) *Fax:* (06074) 2 73 22 *E-mail:* info@als-verlag.de *Web Site:* www.als-verlag. de, pg 192

Alsatia SA (France) *Tel:* (03) 89 45 21 53; (03) 89 56 97 60 *Fax:* (03) 89 45 18 98; (03) 89 56 97 63 *Web Site:* www.forum-alsatia.com, pg 146

Alta Fulla Editorial (Spain) *Tel:* (093) 4590708 *Fax:* (093) 2075203 *E-mail:* altafulla@altafulla.com *Web Site:* www.altafulla.com, pg 567

Altberliner Verlag GmbH (Germany) *Tel:* (089) 2101 1913 *Fax:* (089) 2101 1923 *E-mail:* info@altberliner. de *Web Site:* www.altberliner.de, pg 192

Altea,.Taurus, Alfaguara SA (Spain) *Tel:* (091) 744 90 60 *Fax:* (091) 744 92 24 *E-mail:* clientes@santillana. es *Web Site:* www.alfaguara.santillana.es, pg 568

Ediciones Altera SL (Spain) *Tel:* (093) 4519537 *Fax:* (093) 4517441 *E-mail:* editorial@altera.net, pg 568

Altera Forlag A/S (Norway) *Tel:* 22569590 *Fax:* 22565088, pg 503

Alternative Editura (Romania) *Tel:* (021) 2234966; (021) 2229468 *Fax:* (021) 6756074; (021) 2234971, pg 533

Editions Alternatives (France) *Tel:* (01) 43 29 88 64 *Fax:* (01) 43 29 02 70 *E-mail:* info@ editionsalternatives.com *Web Site:* www. editionsalternatives.com, pg 146

Editions ALTESS (France) *Tel:* (01) 47 70 78 79 *Fax:* (01) 47 70 78 77 *E-mail:* eliaur@club-internet.fr *Web Site:* www.ifrance.com/3eMillenaire/altess/index. htm, pg 146

Altin Kitaplar Yayinevi (Turkey) *Tel:* (0212) 5206246; (0212) 5201588; (0212) 5268010 *Fax:* (0212) 5120266 *E-mail:* info@altinkitaplar.com.tr *Web Site:* www. altinkitaplar.com.tr, pg 644

Altina (Belgium) *Tel:* (059) 80-16-51 *Fax:* (059) 51-27-17, pg 62

Altiora Averbode Uitgeverij nv (Belgium) *Tel:* (013) 780 182 *Fax:* (013) 780 179 *E-mail:* averbode.publ@ verbode.be *Web Site:* www.averbode.be, pg 1291

Aluminium-Verlag Marketing & Kommunikation GmbH (Germany) *Fax:* (0211) 15 91-379 *E-mail:* info@alu-verlag.de *Web Site:* www.alu-verlag.de, pg 192

Alumni PT (Indonesia) *Tel:* (022) 2501251; (022) 2503039; (022) 2503038 *Fax:* (022) 2503044, pg 350

Alun Books (United Kingdom) *Tel:* (01639) 886186 *E-mail:* enquiries@alunbooks.co.uk *Web Site:* www. alunbooks.co.uk, pg 652

Biblioteca Argentina Dr Juan Alvarez (Argentina) *Tel:* 4802538; 4802539 *Fax:* 4802561 *E-mail:* bibliarghem@rosario.gov.ar *Web Site:* www. rosario.gov.ar, pg 1488

Livraria Francisco Alves Editora SA (Brazil) *Tel:* (021) 221-3198 *Fax:* (021) 242-3438, pg 77

Alyssa Editions (Tunisia) *Tel:* 740989 *Fax:* 733659, pg 643

Editions Alzieu (France) *Tel:* (04) 76 51 09 51 *Fax:* (04) 76 51 09 51 *E-mail:* admin@editions-alzieu.com *Web Site:* www.editions-alzieu.com, pg 146

Am Oved Publishers Ltd (Israel) *Tel:* (03) 6291526 *Fax:* (03) 6298911 *E-mail:* info@am-oved.co.il *Web Site:* www.am-oved.co.il, pg 361

AMA nakladatelstvi (Czech Republic) *Tel:* (0618) 265 84 *Fax:* (0618) 228 31 *E-mail:* rstudio@login.cz, pg 122

Armenio Amado Editora de Simoes, Beirao & Ca Lda (Portugal) *Tel:* (039) 92150 *Fax:* (039) 851901, pg 523

Amalthea-Verlag (Austria) *Tel:* (01) 712 35 60 *Fax:* (01) 713 89 95 *E-mail:* amalthea.verlag@amalthea.at *Web Site:* www.amalthea.at, pg 48

Pustaka Aman Press Sdn Bhd (Malaysia) *Tel:* (09) 7443681 *Fax:* (09) 7487064, pg 451

Amanda (Denmark) *Tel:* 3379-0110 *Fax:* 33790011 *E-mail:* forlag@dansklf.dk, pg 128

Amar Prakashan (India) *Tel:* (011) 713182, pg 325

Editions de l'Amateur (France) *Tel:* (01) 56 77 06 20, pg 146

Amazonas Editores Ltda (Colombia) *Tel:* (091) 6180256; (091) 2182760 *Fax:* (091) 6180326, pg 109

Ambar Prakashan (India) *Tel:* (011) 2362 5528 *Fax:* (011) 2574 3569 *E-mail:* pitambar@bol.net.in, pg 325

Amber Books Ltd (United Kingdom) *Tel:* (020) 7520 7600 *Fax:* (020) 7520 7606; (020) 7520 7607 *E-mail:* enquiries@amberbooks.co.uk *Web Site:* www. amberbooks.co.uk, pg 652

Amber Lane Press Ltd (United Kingdom) *Tel:* (01608) 810024 *Fax:* (01608) 810024 *E-mail:* info@ amberlanepress.co.uk *Web Site:* www.amberlanepress. co.uk, pg 652

Amberwood Publishing Ltd (United Kingdom) *Tel:* (01634) 290115 *Fax:* (01634) 290761 *E-mail:* books@amberwoodpublishing.com *Web Site:* www.amberwoodpublishing.com, pg 652

Ambit Serveis Editorials, SA (Spain) *Tel:* (093) 4881342 *Fax:* (093) 4874772, pg 568

Uitgeverij Ambo BV (Netherlands) *Tel:* (020) 5245411 *Fax:* (020) 4200422 *E-mail:* info@amboanthos.nl *Web Site:* www.amboanthos.nl, pg 473

Amboss-Verlag E Widmer (Switzerland) *Tel:* (071) 711236; (071) 7444590 *Fax:* (071) 714590, pg 612

Editions Ambozontany (Madagascar) *Tel:* (07) 50027; (07) 51441, pg 450

Librairie Ambozontany (Madagascar) *Tel:* (07) 50027; (07) 51441, pg 450

Biblioteca Ambrosiana (Italy) *Tel:* (02) 80 692 1 *Fax:* (02) 80 692 210 *E-mail:* info@ambrosiana.it *Web Site:* www.ambrosiana.it, pg 1518

Amebo Book Club (Nigeria), pg 1244

America Latina (Uruguay) *Tel:* (02) 415127 *Fax:* (02) 495568, pg 1346

American Book Store SA de CV (Mexico) *Tel:* (05) 512-6350; (05) 512-0306 *Fax:* (05) 518-6931, pg 1318

The American Chamber of Commerce in Hong Kong (Hong Kong) *Tel:* 2526-0165 *Fax:* 2810-1289 *E-mail:* amcham@amcham.org.hk *Web Site:* www. amcham.org.hk, pg 1145

The American Chamber of Commerce in Japan (Japan) *Tel:* (03) 3433-5381 *Fax:* (03) 3433-8454 *E-mail:* info@accj.or.jp *Web Site:* www.accj.or.jp, pg 411

American Chamber of Commerce of Jamaica (Jamaica) *Tel:* 876-929-7866 *Fax:* 876-929-8597 *E-mail:* info@ amchamjamaica.org *Web Site:* www.amchamjamaica. org, pg 409

American Information Resource Center (India) *Tel:* (011) 2331-6841; (011) 2331-4251 *Fax:* (011) 2332-9499 *E-mail:* libdel@pd.state.gov *Web Site:* americanlibrary. in.library.net; newdelhi.usembassy.gov, pg 1514

American Library in Paris (France) *Tel:* (01) 53 59 12 60 *Fax:* (01) 45 50 25 83 *E-mail:* alparis@noos.fr *Web Site:* www.americanlibraryinparis.org, pg 1504

American Pizzi Offset Corp (United States) *Tel:* 212-986-1658 *Fax:* 212-286-1887 *E-mail:* info@ americanpizzi.com, pg 1155, 1176

American-Scandinavian Foundation (United States) *Tel:* 212-879-9779 *Fax:* 212-879-2301 *E-mail:* info@ amscan.org; asf@amscan.org *Web Site:* www.amscan. org, pg 1284

American Technical Publishers (United Kingdom) *Tel:* (01462) 437933 *Fax:* (01462) 433678 *E-mail:* atp@ameritech.co.uk *Web Site:* www. ameritech.co.uk, pg 652

American University in Cairo Library (Egypt (Arab Republic of Egypt)) *Tel:* (02) 797-6904 *Fax:* (02) 792-3824 *E-mail:* aucpress@aucegypt.edu; library@ aucegypt.edu *Web Site:* library.aucegypt.edu, pg 1501

American University in Cairo Press (Egypt (Arab Republic of Egypt)) *Tel:* (02) 797 6926; (02) 797 6895 (orders) *Fax:* (02) 794 1440 *E-mail:* aucpress@ aucegypt.edu *Web Site:* aucpress.com, pg 137

American University of Beirut Libraries (Lebanon) *Tel:* (01) 340460 *Fax:* (01) 744703 *E-mail:* library@ aub.edu.lb *Web Site:* www.aub.edu.lb/, pg 1523

Amerindian Research Unit (Guyana) *Tel:* (02) 4930 *Fax:* (02) 54885 *Web Site:* www.wisard.org, pg 311

Editions d'Amerique et d'Orient, Adrien Maisonneuve (France) *Tel:* (01) 43 26 86 35 *Fax:* (01) 43 54 59 54 *E-mail:* maisonneuve@maisonneuve-adrien.com *Web Site:* www.maisonneuve-adrien.com, pg 146

Editions Amez (France) *Tel:* (03) 88 84 56 56 *Fax:* (03) 88 84 56 84, pg 146

Amichai Publishing House Ltd (Israel) *Tel:* (09) 8859099 *Fax:* (09) 8853464, pg 361

Libreria los Amigos del Libro (Bolivia) *Tel:* (04) 4504150; (04) 4504151 *Fax:* (04) 4115128 *E-mail:* gutten@amigol.bo.net, pg 1292

Los Amigos del Libro Ediciones (Bolivia) *Tel:* (04) 254114 *Fax:* (04) 251140 *Web Site:* www. librosbolivia.com, pg 75

Amir Kabir Book Publishing & Distribution Co (Islamic Republic of Iran) *Tel:* (021) 3933996; (021) 3933997; (021) 3900751-2; (021) 3112118 *Fax:* (021) 3903747, pg 354

L'Amitie par le Livre (France) *Tel:* (03) 81820894 *Fax:* (03) 81820894, pg 146, 1242

Amiza Associate Malaysia Sdn Bhd (Malaysia) *Tel:* (03) 78036100 *Fax:* (03) 78036100, pg 451

AMK Interaksi Sdn Bhd (Malaysia) *Tel:* (03) 215306 *Fax:* (03) 718067, pg 451

Amman Public Library (Jordan) *Tel:* (06) 637 111 *Fax:* (06) 649420, pg 1520

Ammann Verlag & Co (Switzerland) *Tel:* (01) 268 10 40 *Fax:* (01) 268 10 50 *E-mail:* info@ammann.ch *Web Site:* www.ammann.ch, pg 612

Amnesty International Publications (United Kingdom) *Tel:* (020) 7814 6200 *Fax:* (020) 7833 1510 *E-mail:* information@amnesty.org.uk *Web Site:* www. amnesty.org.uk, pg 653

Amnesty International VZW (Belgium) *Tel:* (03) 271 16 16 *Fax:* (03) 235 78 12 *E-mail:* amnesty@aivl.be *Web Site:* www.aivl.be, pg 62

Amnistia Internacional Editorial SL (Spain) *Tel:* (091) 315 2851 *Fax:* (091) 323 2158 *E-mail:* amnistia. internacional@a-i.es, pg 568

Amorrortu Editores SA (Argentina) *Tel:* (011) 4816-5812; (011) 4816-5869 *Fax:* (011) 4816-3321 *E-mail:* info@amorrortueditores.com *Web Site:* www. amorrortueditores.com, pg 3

Amosium Servis (Czech Republic) *Tel:* (069) 624 55 01, pg 122

Editions Amphora SA (France) *Tel:* (01) 43 26 10 87 *Fax:* (01) 40 46 85 76 *E-mail:* sports@ed-amphora.fr *Web Site:* www.ed-amphora.fr, pg 146

Editions Amrita SA (France) *Tel:* (05) 53 50 79 54 *Fax:* (05) 53 50 80 20 *E-mail:* amrita.editions@ perigord.com, pg 146

Amtsbibliothek des Bundesministeriums fur Unterricht, und Kulturelle Angelegenheiten und des Bundesministeriums fur Wissenschaft und Verkehr (Austria) *Tel:* (01) 53 120-0 *Fax:* (01) 53 120-3099 *E-mail:* ministerium@bmbwk.gv.at *Web Site:* www. bmbwk.gv.at/, pg 1489

AMV Ediciones (Spain) *Tel:* (091) 5336926; (091) 5349368 *Fax:* (091) 5530286 *Web Site:* www. amvediciones.com, pg 568

AMVC-Letterenhuis (Belgium) *Tel:* (03) 222 9320 *Fax:* (03) 222 9321 *E-mail:* amvc.letterenhuis@ stad.antwerpen.be *Web Site:* museum.antwerpen. be/amvc_letterenhuis, pg 1491

An Gum (Ireland) *Tel:* (01) 8734700 *Fax:* (01) 8731104 *E-mail:* gum@educ.irlgov.ie, pg 354

Anabas-Verlag Guenter Kaempf GmbH & Co KG (Germany) *Tel:* (069) 94 21 98 71 *Fax:* (069) 94 21 98 72 *E-mail:* info@anabas-verlag.de, pg 192

L'Anabase (France) *Tel:* (04) 67 56 13 38; (01) 30 41 07 47 *Fax:* (01) 34 85 80 73, pg 146

Anabra State Library Board (Nigeria) *Tel:* (042) 334 103, pg 1532

Editorial Anagrama SA (Spain) *Tel:* 93 203 76 52 *Fax:* 93 203 77 38 *E-mail:* anagrama@anagrama-ed.es *Web Site:* www.anagrama-ed.es, pg 568

Anako Editions (France) *Tel:* (01) 43 94 92 88 *Fax:* (01) 43 94 02 45 *E-mail:* anako.editions@anako.com *Web Site:* www.anako.com, pg 146

Anam Publishing Co (Republic of Korea) *Tel:* (02) 22380491 *Fax:* (02) 22524334, pg 433

Anambra State School Libraries Association (Nigeria) *Tel:* (042) 252080; (042) 332091 *Web Site:* www. universityofnigeria.com, pg 1569

Anand Book Club (India) *Tel:* (011) 5550-2222 *E-mail:* customerservice@vsnl.com *Web Site:* www. vsnl.in, pg 1243

Ananda Publishers Pvt Ltd (India) *Tel:* (033) 2241 4352; (033) 2241 3417 *Fax:* (033) 2253240; (033) 2253241 *E-mail:* ananda@cal3.vsnl.net.in *Web Site:* www. anandapub.com, pg 325

Anansi Publishers/Uitgewers (South Africa) *Tel:* (021) 968411 *Fax:* (021) 969698 *E-mail:* anansi@global.co. za, pg 558

Anastasiadis Publications (Greece) *Tel:* 2102284013 *Fax:* 2102236442, pg 1302

Ediciones Anaya SA (Spain) *Tel:* (091) 393 86 00 *Fax:* (091) 320 91 29; (091) 742 66 31 *E-mail:* cga@ anaya.es *Web Site:* www.anaya.es, pg 568

Anaya Educacion (Spain) *Tel:* (091) 393 86 00 *Fax:* (091) 320 91 29; (091) 742 66 31 *E-mail:* cga@ anaya.es *Web Site:* www.anaya.es, pg 568

Anaya-Touring Club (Spain) *Tel:* (091) 393 86 00 *Fax:* (091) 742 66 31; (091) 320 91 29 *E-mail:* cga@ anaya.es *Web Site:* www.anaya.es, pg 568

Editrice Ancora (Italy) *Tel:* (02) 3456081 *Fax:* (02) 34560866 *E-mail:* editrice@ancora-libri.it *Web Site:* www.ancora-libri.it, pg 372

Libreria Ancora y Delfin (Spain) *Tel:* (093) 2000746 *Fax:* (093) 2000757 *E-mail:* ancoraydelfin@ ancoraydelfin.com, pg 1333

Editions l'Ancre de Marine (France) *Tel:* (02) 32 25 45 97 *E-mail:* service-clients@ancre-de-marine.com *Web Site:* www.ancre-de-marine.com, pg 146

Andersen Press Ltd (United Kingdom) *Tel:* (020) 7840 8701 *Fax:* (020) 7233 6263 *E-mail:* andersenpress@ randomhouse.co.uk *Web Site:* www.andersenpress.co. uk, pg 653

Robert Andersen & Associates Pty Ltd (Australia) *Tel:* (03) 9489 3968 *Fax:* (03) 9482 2416 *E-mail:* 100357.354@compuserve.com, pg 11

Darley Anderson Literary TV & Film Agency (United Kingdom) *Tel:* (020) 7385 6652 *Fax:* (020) 7386 5571; (020) 7386 9689 *E-mail:* enquiries@ darleyanderson.com *Web Site:* www.darleyanderson. com, pg 1129

Michelle Anderson Publishing (Australia) *Tel:* (03) 9826 9028 *Fax:* (03) 9826 8552 *E-mail:* mapubl@bigpond. net.au *Web Site:* www.michelleandersonpublishing. com, pg 11

Anderson Rand Ltd (United Kingdom) *Tel:* (01223) 566640 *Fax:* (01223) 316144; (01223) 566643 *E-mail:* info@andrand.com *Web Site:* www.andrand. com, pg 653

Andi Offset (Indonesia) *Tel:* (0274) 561881 *Fax:* (0274) 588282 *E-mail:* andi_pub@indo.net.id, pg 350

Andina Publishing House (Bulgaria) *Tel:* (052) 630902, pg 92

Andorran Standard Book Numbering Agency (Andorra) *Tel:* 826445 *Fax:* 829445 *E-mail:* bncultura.gov@ andorra.ad *Web Site:* bibnac.andorra.ad, pg 1249

Andreas und Andreas Verlagsbuchhandel (Austria) *Tel:* (0662) 6575-0 *Fax:* (0662) 6575-5, pg 48

Andrena Publishers (Lithuania) *Tel:* (02) 703834; (02) 627015 *E-mail:* andrena@takas.lt, pg 445

Andreou Chr Publishers (Cyprus) *Tel:* (022) 666877 *Fax:* (022) 666878 *E-mail:* andzeou2@cytanet.com.cy, pg 121

Andresen & Butenschon AS (Norway) *Tel:* (047) 23139240 *Fax:* (047) 22335805 *E-mail:* abforlag@ abforlag.no, pg 503

Chris Andrews Publications (United Kingdom) *Tel:* (01865) 723404 *Fax:* (01865) 725294 *E-mail:* enquiries@cap-ox.com *Web Site:* www.cap-ox.com, pg 653

Andromeda Oxford Ltd (United Kingdom) *Tel:* (01235) 550 296 *Fax:* (01235) 550 330 *E-mail:* mail@ andromeda.co.uk, pg 653

K C Ang Publishing Pte Ltd (Singapore) *Tel:* 4741680 *Fax:* 2542002, pg 550

Angel Publications (Australia) *Tel:* (02) 4821 1463, pg 11

Angeletos Sokzates (Greece) *Tel:* 2109928100 *Fax:* 210 9940530, pg 1302

Franco Angeli SRL (Italy) *Tel:* (02) 28 37 141 *Fax:* (02) 26 14 47 93 *E-mail:* redazioni@francoangeli.it *Web Site:* www.francoangeli.it, pg 372

Biblioteca Angelica (Italy) *Tel:* (06) 6868041; (06) 6875874 *Fax:* (06) 6832312 *E-mail:* angelica. polosbn@inroma.roma.it *Web Site:* biblioroma.sbn. it/angelica, pg 1518

Angelika und Lothar Binding (Germany) *Tel:* (06221) 20955 *Fax:* (06221) 181846 *E-mail:* Angelika. Binding@gmx.net *Web Site:* www.binding-singles.de, pg 193

Angkasa CV (Indonesia) *Tel:* (022) 4208955; (022) 4204795 *Fax:* (022) 439183, pg 350

The Anglo American Book Company Ltd (United Kingdom) *Tel:* (01267) 211880 *Fax:* (01267) 211882 *E-mail:* books@anglo-american.co.uk *Web Site:* www. anglo-american.co.uk, pg 1337

Anglo-Didactica, SL Editorial (Spain) *Tel:* (091) 3780188 *Fax:* (091) 3780188 *E-mail:* anglodidac@ aregen.net, pg 568

Anglo-German Foundation for the Study of Industrial Society (United Kingdom) *Tel:* (020) 7823 1123 *Fax:* (020) 7823 2324 *E-mail:* info@agf.org.uk *Web Site:* www.agf.org.uk, pg 653

Anglo Mexican Foundation Library (Mexico) *Tel:* (05) 566-4500 *Fax:* (05) 566-6739 *E-mail:* biblioteca@ tamf.org.mx *Web Site:* www.theanglo.org.mx; www. tamf.org.mx/tamf/biblioteca.htm, pg 1527

Angus & Robertson Bookshops (Australia) *Tel:* (03) 8623 1111 *Fax:* (03) 8623 1150 *E-mail:* info@ angusrobertson.com.au *Web Site:* www.angusrobertson. com.au, pg 1287

Anhui Children's Publishing House (China) *Tel:* (0551) 2849301; (0551) 2849306 *E-mail:* ahsebwsh@ mail.hf.ah.cn *Web Site:* www.ahse.cn, pg 100

Anhui People's Publishing House (China) *Tel:* (0551) 257134; (0551) 2653673, pg 100

Anixis Publications (Greece) *Tel:* 2106205436 *Fax:* 210 8079357, pg 303

Anjuman Taraqqi-e-Urdu Pakistan (Pakistan) *Tel:* (021) 461406; (021) 4973296; (021) 7724023, pg 1397

Ankara University Library (Turkey) *Tel:* (0312) 212 60 40 *Fax:* (0312) 212 60 49 *Web Site:* www.ankara.edu. tr, pg 1549

Ankh-Hermes BV (Netherlands) *Tel:* (0570) 678911
*Fax:* (0570) 624632 *E-mail:* info@ankh-hermes.nl
*Web Site:* www.ankh-hermes.com, pg 473

Ankur Prakashani (Bangladesh) *Tel:* (02) 250132
*Fax:* (02) 9567730 *E-mail:* ankur@bangla.net, pg 60

Ankur Publishing Co (India) *Tel:* (022) 543 2817; (022)
536 9907 *Fax:* (022) 543 2817 *E-mail:* ankur@
bom3.vsnl.net.in *Web Site:* www.satyamplastics.
com/ankurpublishing/, pg 325

Anmol Publications Pvt Ltd (India) *Tel:* (011) 3255577;
(011) 3261597; (011) 3278000 *Fax:* (011) 3280289
*E-mail:* anmol@nde.vsnl.net.in, pg 325

Editions d'Annabelle (France) *Tel:* (01) 47 42 01 61
*Fax:* (01) 47 42 42 14, pg 146

Anowuo Educational Publications (Ghana) *Tel:* (021)
669961, pg 300

Anrich Verlag GmbH (Germany) *Tel:* (06201) 6007-0
*Fax:* (06201) 17464, pg 193

Forlagsentralen ANS (Norway) *Tel:* (022) 32 96
00 *Fax:* (022) 32 96 01 *E-mail:* firmapost@
forlagsentralen.no *Web Site:* www.forlagsentralen.no,
pg 1323

Ansay Pty Ltd (Australia) *Tel:* (02) 95602044 *Fax:* (02)
95694585, pg 11

Antara Publications (M) Sdn Bhd (Malaysia) *Tel:* (03)
2913188 *Fax:* (03) 2913299, pg 1316

Pustaka Antara (Malaysia) *Tel:* (03) 26980044 *Fax:* (03)
26917997, pg 451

PT Pustaka Antara Publishing & Printing (Indonesia)
*Tel:* (021) 3156994; (021) 3156995 *Fax:* (021) 322745
*E-mail:* nacelod@indo.net.id, pg 350

Antenna Edicoes Tecnicas Ltda (Brazil) *Tel:* (021) 2223-
2442 *Fax:* (021) 2263-8840 *E-mail:* antenna@anep.
com.br *Web Site:* www.anep.com.br, pg 77

Antex Verlag-Hans Joachin Schuhmacher (Germany)
*Tel:* (033603) 40410 *Fax:* (033603) 40400, pg 193

Edition Anthese (France) *Tel:* (01) 46 56 06 67 *Fax:* (01)
49 85 09 92, pg 147

Uitgeverij Anthos (Netherlands) *Tel:* (020) 5245411
*Fax:* (020) 4200422 *E-mail:* info@amboanthos.nl
*Web Site:* www.amboanthos.nl, pg 474

Editorial Anthropos del Hombre (Spain) *Tel:* (093)
6972296 *Fax:* (093) 6972296, pg 568

Edicoes Antigona (Portugal) *Tel:* (021) 749483
*Fax:* (021) 749483, pg 523

Bibliotheque Universitaire Antilles-Guyane (BUAG)
(France) *Tel:* (0596) 727530 *Fax:* (0596) 727527
*Web Site:* www.univ-ag.fr/buag, pg 1504

Antillion Library Association (Netherlands Antilles)
*Tel:* (09) 4345200 *Fax:* (09) 4656247 *Web Site:* www.
curacaopubliclibrary.an, pg 1568

Antiqua-Verlag GmbH (Germany) *Tel:* (07746) 2273
*Fax:* (07746) 2260, pg 193

Antiquarian Booksellers' Association (United Kingdom)
*Tel:* (020) 7439 3118 *Fax:* (020) 7439 3119
*E-mail:* admin@aba.org.uk *Web Site:* www.aba.org.uk,
pg 1279

Antiquarian Booksellers' Association of Japan
(Japan) *Tel:* (03) 3357-1411 *Fax:* (03) 3351-5855
*E-mail:* kikuo@sc4.so-net.ne.jp *Web Site:* www.abaj.
gr.jp, pg 1265

Antiquariats-Union Vertriebs GmbH & Co KG
(Germany) *Tel:* (04131) 983504 *Fax:* (04131) 9835595
*Web Site:* www.restauflagen.de, pg 193

Antique Collectors' Club Ltd (United Kingdom)
*Tel:* (01394) 389950 *Fax:* (01394) 389999
*E-mail:* peter.hawk@antique-acc.com; sales@antique-
acc.com *Web Site:* www.antique-acc.com, pg 653

Antiques & Collectors Guides Ltd (United Kingdom)
*Tel:* (0141) 8480880 *Fax:* (0141) 8892063, pg 653

Librairies Antoine SAL/Librairie Antoine, A. Naufal &
Freres (Lebanon) *Tel:* (01) 48 10 72; (01) 48 35 13
*Fax:* (01) 49 26 25, pg 1315

Antonius-Verlag (Switzerland) *Tel:* (032) 6253742,
pg 612

Biblioteca Nacional de Antropologia e Historia (Mexico)
*Tel:* (055) 536231; (055) 536342 *Fax:* (055) 861743
*E-mail:* direccion.bnah@inah.gob.mx *Web Site:* www.
bnah.inah.gob.mx/, pg 1527

Editora Antroposofica Ltda (Brazil) *Tel:* (011) 5687-
9714; (011) 5686-4550 *Fax:* (011) 2479714
*E-mail:* editora@antroposofica.com.br *Web Site:* www.
sab.org.br/edit; www.antroposofica.com.br, pg 77

Editrice Antroposofica SRL (Italy) *Tel:* (02) 7491197
*Fax:* (02) 70103173 *E-mail:* libri@rudolfsteiner.it
*Web Site:* www.rudolfsteiner.it/editrice/index.htm,
pg 372

Antroposofsko Izdatelstvo Dimo R Daskalov OOD
(Bulgaria) *Tel:* (042) 54481, pg 92

Maison d'Edition Protestante ANTSO (Madagascar)
*Tel:* (020) 20886 *Fax:* (022) 26372 *E-mail:* fjkm@
dts.mg, pg 450

Anvil Books Ltd (United Kingdom) *Tel:* (020) 8829-
3000 *Fax:* (020) 8881-5088, pg 653

Anvil Press (Zimbabwe) *Tel:* (04) 73-9681; (04) 78-
1770; (04) 78-1771; (04) 792551 *Fax:* (04) 75-1202,
pg 777

Anvil Press Poetry Ltd (United Kingdom) *Tel:* (020)
8469 3033 *Fax:* (020) 8469 3363 *E-mail:* info@
anvilpresspoetry.com *Web Site:* www.anvilpresspoetry.
com, pg 654

Anvil Publishing Inc (Philippines) *Tel:* (02) 671888
*Fax:* (02) 6719235 *E-mail:* anvil@fc.emc.com.ph;
pubdept@anvil.com.ph, pg 513

Any Photo Type (United States) *Tel:* 212-244-1130
*Fax:* 212-594-4697, pg 1176

Anzea Publishers Ltd (Australia) *Tel:* (02) 7631211
*Fax:* (02) 7643201, pg 11

Ao Livro Tecnico Industria e Comercio Ltda (Brazil)
*Tel:* (021) 580-6230; (021) 580-1168 *Fax:* (021) 580-
9955 *E-mail:* contatos@editoraaolivrotecnico.com.br
*Web Site:* www.editoraaolivrotecnico.com.br, pg 77

Aoki Shoten Co Ltd (Japan) *Tel:* (03) 3219 2341
*Fax:* (03) 3219 2585 *Web Site:* www.aokishoten.co.jp,
pg 411

AOL-Verlag Frohmut Menze (Germany) *Tel:* (07227)
95 88-0 *Fax:* (07227) 95 88-95 *E-mail:* info@aol-
verlag.de; bestellung@aol-verlag.de *Web Site:* www.
aol-verlag.de, pg 193

Aoraki Press Ltd (New Zealand) *Tel:* (04) 3858528
*Fax:* (03) 3858528 *E-mail:* aoraki@actrix.gen.nz,
pg 489

AP Information Services Ltd (United Kingdom)
*Tel:* (020) 8349 9988 *Fax:* (020) 8349 9797
*E-mail:* info@apinfo.co.uk *Web Site:* www.apinfo.co.
uk, pg 654

APA (Academic Publishers Associated) (Netherlands)
*Tel:* (020) 626 5544 *Fax:* (020) 528 5298
*E-mail:* info@apa-publishers.com *Web Site:* www.apa-
publishers.com, pg 474

APA Production Pte Ltd (Singapore) *Tel:* 8651600;
8651601 *Fax:* 8616438 *E-mail:* apasin@singnet.com.
sg, pg 550

APAC Publishers Services Pte Ltd (Singapore) *Tel:* 6844
7333 *Fax:* 6747 8916 *E-mail:* service@apacmedia.
com.sg, pg 550

Apaginastantas - Cooperativa de Servicos Culturais
(Portugal) *Tel:* (021) 668987, pg 523

Editions APESS ASBL (Luxembourg) *Tel:* 80 8358
*Fax:* 80 2813 *E-mail:* apess@ci.edu.lu *Web Site:* www.
restena.lu/apess, pg 447

Apex Books Concern (United Kingdom) *Tel:* (01903)
739042 *Fax:* (01903) 734432 *E-mail:* enquiries@
apexbooks.co.uk *Web Site:* www.apexbooks.co.uk,
pg 1337

Apex Press & Publishing (Oman) *Tel:* 799388
*Fax:* 793316 *E-mail:* apexoman@gto.net.om
*Web Site:* www.apexstuff.com, pg 507

Apex Publishing Ltd (United Kingdom) *Tel:* (01255)
428500 *Fax:* (0870) 046 6536 *E-mail:* enquiry@
apexpublishing.co.uk *Web Site:* www.apexpublishing.
co.uk, pg 654

Verlag Der Apfel (Austria) *Tel:* (01) 52 661 52 *Fax:* (01)
52 287 18, pg 48

APH Publishing Corp (India) *Tel:* (011) 5100581;
(011) 5410924; (011) 3285807 *Fax:* (011) 3274050
*E-mail:* aph@mantrasonline.com, pg 325

Verlag APHAIA Svea Haske, Sonja Schumann GbR
(Germany) *Tel:* (030) 813 39 98 *Fax:* (030) 813 39 98
*E-mail:* info@aphaia-verlag.de *Web Site:* www.aphaia-
verlag.de, pg 193

Apimondia (Italy) *Tel:* (06) 6852286 *Fax:* (06) 6852287
*E-mail:* apimondia@mclink.it *Web Site:* www.
apimondia.org, pg 372

Apocalipis Digital (Cuba) *Tel:* (07) 816625
*E-mail:* adigital@tinored.cu; adigital@colombus.cu,
pg 119

Apogeo srl - Editrice di Informatica (Italy) *Tel:* (02)
289981 *Fax:* (02) 26116334 *E-mail:* apogeo@
apogeonline.com *Web Site:* www.apogeonline.com,
pg 372

Apollo-Verlag Paul Lincke GmbH (Germany)
*Tel:* (06131) 246300 *Fax:* (06131) 246861
*E-mail:* apollo@schott-musik.de, pg 193

Apollo's Reklame en Uitgeversburo (Suriname), pg 603

Apostolado da Oracao Secretariado Nacional (Portugal)
*Tel:* (053) 22485 *Fax:* (053) 201221, pg 524

Apostolato della Preghiera (Italy) *Tel:* (06) 697
607 1 *Fax:* (06) 67 81 063 *E-mail:* adp@adp.it
*Web Site:* www.adp.it, pg 372

Biblioteca Apostolica Vaticana (Holy See (Vatican City
State)) *Tel:* (06) 6987 9402 *Fax:* (06) 6988 4795
*E-mail:* bav@vatlib.it, pg 311

Biblioteca Apostolica Vaticana (Holy See (Vatican City
State)) *Tel:* (06) 6987 9402 *Fax:* (06) 6988 4795
*E-mail:* bav@vatlib.it *Web Site:* 212.77.1.230/it/
v_home_bav/home_bav.shtml, pg 1512

Biblioteca Apostolica Vaticana (Holy See (Vatican City
State)) *Tel:* (06) 6987 9402 *Fax:* (06) 6988 4795
*E-mail:* bav@librs6k.vatlib.it *Web Site:* www.vatican.
va, pg 1564

Apostoliki Diakonia tis Ekklisias tis Hellados (Greece)
*Tel:* 2107239417; 2107248681-9 *Fax:* 210723
8149 *E-mail:* editions@apostoliki-diakoria.gr
*Web Site:* www.apostoliki-diakonia.gr, pg 303

Forlaget Apostrof ApS (Denmark) *Tel:* 3920 8420
*Fax:* 3920 8453 *E-mail:* info1@apostrof.dk
*Web Site:* www.apostrof.dk, pg 128

Apotekarsocietetens Forlag (Sweden) *Tel:* (08) 7235000
*Fax:* (08) 205511, pg 604

Apple Books (Zambia) *Tel:* (01) 211216 *Fax:* (01)
224855, pg 775

Apple Press (United Kingdom) *Tel:* (01273) 727268
*Fax:* (01273) 727269 *E-mail:* information@quarto.com
*Web Site:* www.quarto.com, pg 654

Appleby's Bindery Ltd (Canada) *Tel:* 506-488-2086 *Toll
Free:* 800-561-2005 (Canada only) *Fax:* 506-488-
2086 *E-mail:* applbind@nbnet.nb.ca, pg 1205, 1225,
1235

Appletree Press Ltd (United Kingdom) *Tel:* (028) 9024
3074 *Fax:* (028) 9024 6756 *E-mail:* reception@
appletree.ie *Web Site:* www.appletree.ie, pg 654

Appropriate Technology Development Group (Inc) WA
(Australia) *Tel:* (08) 9336 1262 *Fax:* (08) 9430 5729
*E-mail:* apace@argo.net.au *Web Site:* www.argo.net.
au/apace, pg 11

Archivio Centrale dello Stato (Italy) *Tel:* (06) 545481 *Fax:* (06) 5413620 *E-mail:* acs@archivi.beniculturali.it *Web Site:* www.archiviocentraledellostato.it; archivi. beniculturali.it/ACS, pg 1518

Archivio Guido Izzi Edizioni (Italy) *Tel:* (06) 39735580 *Fax:* (06) 39734433 *E-mail:* agizzi@iol.it, pg 372

Archivio Segreto Vaticano (Holy See (Vatican City State)) *Tel:* (06) 69883314 *Fax:* (06) 69885574, pg 311

Biblioteca dell'Archivio Storico Civico e Biblioteca Trivulziana (Italy) *Tel:* (02) 88463690; (02) 88463696 *Fax:* (02) 88463698 *E-mail:* ascb.trivulziana@comune. milano.it *Web Site:* www.milanocastello.it, pg 1518

Archivio Storico Ticinese (Switzerland) *Tel:* (091) 820 0101 *Fax:* (091) 825 1874 *E-mail:* casagrande@ casagrande-online.ch *Web Site:* www.casagrande-online.ch, pg 612

Archivo de la Corona de Aragon (Spain) *Tel:* (093) 4854 318; (093) 4854 285; (093) 3153 928 *Fax:* (093) 3001 252 *E-mail:* aca@cult.mec.es *Web Site:* www.cultura. mecd.es/archivos/index.html, pg 1543

Archivo General de Centro America (Guatemala) *Tel:* 232-3037, pg 1511

Archivo General de Indias (Spain) *Tel:* (05) 954 500 530; (05) 954 500 528 *Fax:* 954 219 485 *E-mail:* agi1@cult.mec.es *Web Site:* www.cultura. mecd.es; www.mcu.es, pg 1543

Archivo General de la Nacion (Mexico) *Tel:* 5133-9900 *Fax:* 5789-5296 *E-mail:* agn@segob.gob.mx *Web Site:* www.agn.gob.mx, pg 1527

Archivo General de la Nacion (AG) (Venezuela) *Tel:* (0212) 862-99-07 *Fax:* (0212) 81-93-28 *Web Site:* www.ucab.edu.ve/biblioteca, pg 1553

Archivo General de la Nacion de Colombia (Colombia) *Tel:* (01) 2431336 *Fax:* (01) 3414030 *E-mail:* bnc@ mincultura.gov.co *Web Site:* www.bibliotecanacional. gov.co, pg 1497

Archivo General de la Nacion del Peru (Peru) *Tel:* (01) 427-5930; (01) 427-5939 *Fax:* (01) 428-2829 *Web Site:* agn.perucultural.org.pe, pg 1534

Archivo General de Puerto Rico (Puerto Rico) *Tel:* (787) 724-0700 *Fax:* (787) 724-8393 *Web Site:* www.icp. gobierno.pr, pg 1537

Archivo Historico Nacional (Spain) *Tel:* (091) 7688 500 *Fax:* (091) 5631 199 *Web Site:* www.mcu.es/archivos, pg 1543

Archivo Nacional de Cuba (Cuba) *Tel:* (07) 862 9436; (07) 636 489 *Fax:* (07) 33 8089 *E-mail:* arnac@ ceniainf.cu, pg 1498

Archivo Nacional de Historia (Ecuador) *Tel:* (02) 2280431 *Fax:* (02) 2280431 *E-mail:* ane@ane.gov.ec *Web Site:* www.ane.gov.ec, pg 1501

Archivo Nacional de Nicaragua (Nicaragua) *Tel:* (02) 223 240 *Fax:* (02) 22722 *E-mail:* binanic@tmx.com. nic, pg 1531

Archivo y Biblioteca Capitulares (Spain) *Tel:* (0925) 21 24 23 *Fax:* (0925) 21 24 23 *E-mail:* archicapto@terra. es *Web Site:* www.architoledo.org/catedral/archivos/ textoarchivo.htm, pg 1543

L'Archivolto (Italy) *Tel:* (02) 29010444; (02) 29010424 *Fax:* (02) 29001942 *E-mail:* info@archivolto.com *Web Site:* www.archivolto.com, pg 372

Naczelna Dyrekcja Archiwow Panstwowych (Poland) *Tel:* (022) 635-68-22 *Fax:* (022) 831-75-63 *E-mail:* coia-info@archiwa.gov.pl *Web Site:* www. archiwa.gov.pl, pg 1535

Archiwum Glowne Akt Dawnych (Poland) *Tel:* (022) 831-54-91 *Fax:* (022) 831-16-08 *Web Site:* www.piasa. org/polisharchives/warsawhr.html, pg 1535

Arcipelago Edizioni di Chiani Marisa (Italy) *Tel:* (02) 36525177 *Fax:* (02) 36553002 *E-mail:* info@ arcipelagoedizioni.com *Web Site:* www. arcipelagoedizioni.com, pg 372

Arco Libros SL (Spain) *Tel:* (091) 4153687; (091) 4161371 *Fax:* (091) 4135907 *E-mail:* arcolibros@ arcomuralla.com *Web Site:* www.arcomuralla.com, pg 569

Arcs Editions (Tunisia) *Tel:* 71351617, pg 643

Arcturus Publishing Ltd (United Kingdom) *Tel:* (020) 7407 9400 *Fax:* (020) 7407 9444 *E-mail:* info@arcturuspublishing.com *Web Site:* www. arcturuspublishing.com, pg 654

ARCult Media (Germany) *Tel:* (0228) 211059 *Fax:* (0228) 217493 *E-mail:* info@arcultmedia.de *Web Site:* www.arcultmedia.de; www.kulturforschung. de; www.ericarts.org, pg 193

Ardey-Verlag GmbH (Germany) *Tel:* (0251) 4132-0 *Fax:* (0251) 4132-20 *E-mail:* ardey@muenster.de *Web Site:* www.ardey-verlag.de, pg 194

Publications Aredit (France) *Tel:* (03) 20 26 79 81, pg 147

Uitgeverij Arena BV (Netherlands) *Tel:* (020) 55 40 500 *Fax:* (020) 42 16 868 *E-mail:* info@boekenarena.nl *Web Site:* www.meulenhoff.nl; www.boekenarena.nl, pg 474

Arena Verlag GmbH (Germany) *Tel:* (0931) 79 644-0 *Fax:* (0931) 79 644-13, pg 194

Edizioni ARES (Italy) *Tel:* (02) 29514202; (02) 29526156 *Fax:* (02) 29520163 *E-mail:* aresed@tin.it; info@ares.mi.it *Web Site:* www.ares.mi.it, pg 373

Arevik (Armenia) *Tel:* (02) 524561 *Fax:* (02) 520536 *E-mail:* arevikp@freenet.am; arevick@netsys.am *Web Site:* www.arevik.am, pg 10

Argalia (Italy) *Tel:* (0722) 328733 *Fax:* (0722) 328756, pg 373

Editorial Argentina Plaza y Janes SA (Argentina) *Tel:* (011) 4862-6769; (011) 4862-6785 *Fax:* (011) 4864-4970, pg 3

Argentine Bible Society (Argentina) *Tel:* (011) 4312-5787; (011) 4312-8558 *Fax:* (011) 4312-3400 *E-mail:* socbiblicaarg@biblica.org *Web Site:* www. biblesociety.org, pg 3

Argentinian PEN Centre (Argentina), pg 1389

Argo (United Kingdom) *Tel:* (020) 8910 5000 *Fax:* (020) 8910 5400, pg 654

ARGO-RISK Publisher (Russian Federation) *Tel:* (095) 4768538 *Fax:* (095) 2926511 *E-mail:* zayats@glas. apc.org, pg 539

Argon Verlag GmbH (Germany) *Tel:* (030) 25 37 38-0 *Fax:* (030) 25 37 38-99 *E-mail:* info.argon@ fischerverlage.de *Web Site:* www.fischerverlage.de, pg 194

Argosy Press (Zimbabwe) *Tel:* (04) 704715; (04) 704766 *Fax:* (04) 752162, pg 777

Argument-Verlag (Germany) *Tel:* (040) 401800-0 *Fax:* (040) 401800-20 *E-mail:* verlag@argument.de *Web Site:* www.argument.de, pg 194

Arguval Editorial SA (Spain) *Tel:* (095) 2318784; (095) 2360213 *Fax:* (095) 2323715 *E-mail:* editorial@ arguval.com *Web Site:* www.arguval.com, pg 569

Argyll Publishing (United Kingdom) *Tel:* 08702402182; (0141) 558 1366 *Fax:* (0141) 557 0189 *E-mail:* customerservices@booksource.net, pg 654

Arhiv na Makedonija (The Former Yugoslav Republic of Macedonia) *Tel:* (091) 237-211; (091) 115-783; (091) 115-827 *Fax:* (091) 165-944 *Web Site:* www.arhiv.gov. mk, pg 1524

Arhiv Republike Slovenije (Slovenia) *Tel:* (01) 24 14 200 *Fax:* (01) 24 14 269 *E-mail:* ars@gov.si *Web Site:* www.sigov.si/ars, pg 1541

Arhivele Nationale ale Romaniei (Romania) *Tel:* (01) 3152503 *Fax:* (01) 3125841 *E-mail:* webmaster@mai. gov.ro *Web Site:* www.mai.gov.ro, pg 1538

Arhus Kommunes Biblioteker (Denmark) *Tel:* 8940 9200 *Fax:* 8940 9393 *Web Site:* www.aakb.dk, pg 1500

Editorial Ariel SA (Spain) *Tel:* (093) 496 70 30 *Fax:* (093) 496 70 32 *E-mail:* editorial@ariel.es *Web Site:* www.ariel.es, pg 569

Ariel Lydbokforlag (Norway) *Tel:* 64943510 *Fax:* 64943510, pg 503

Ariel Publishing House (Israel) *Tel:* (02) 6434540 *Fax:* (02) 6436164, pg 361

Aries-Verlag Paul Johannes Muller (Germany) *Tel:* (08661) 8209 *Fax:* (08661) 985980, pg 194

Arihant Publishers (India) *Tel:* (0141) 515192, pg 325

Ario Company Ltd (Republic of Korea) *Tel:* (02) 7122001; (02) 7122003 *Fax:* (02) 7023156, pg 433

Ariston Editions (Switzerland) *Tel:* (071) 6771190 *Fax:* (071) 6771191 *E-mail:* 106420.3235@ compuserve.com, pg 612

Uitgevirj Aristos (Netherlands) *Tel:* (010) 243 73 70 *Fax:* (010) 243 76 00 *E-mail:* aristos@xs4all.nl *Web Site:* www.xs4all.nl/~feico/aristos, pg 474

Aritbus et Historiae, Rivista Internationale di arti visive ecinema, Institut IRSA - Verlagsanstatt (Poland) *Tel:* (012) 421 90 30; (012) 421 91 55 *Fax:* (012) 421 48 07 *E-mail:* irsa@irsa.com.pl *Web Site:* www.irsa. com.pl, pg 517

Ark Boeken (Netherlands) *Tel:* (020) 6114847 *Fax:* (020) 6114864 *E-mail:* arkboeken@wxs.nl, pg 474

ARK Bokhandel (Norway) *Tel:* 22 99 07 50 *Fax:* 22 99 07 51 *E-mail:* resepsjon@ark.no *Web Site:* www. arkbokhandel.no, pg 1323

Edizioni Arka SRL (Italy) *Tel:* (02) 4818230 *Fax:* (02) 4816752 *E-mail:* arka.edizioni@tin.it, pg 373

Arkadas Ltd (Turkey) *Tel:* (0312) 434 46 24 *Fax:* (0312) 435 60 57, pg 644

Arkadas Ltd (Turkey) *Tel:* (0312) 4344624; (0312) 3548300 *Fax:* (0312) 4356057 *E-mail:* info@arkadas. com.tr *Web Site:* www.arkadas.com.tr, pg 1337

Wydawnictwo Arkady (Poland) *Tel:* (022) 8268980; (022) 8267079; (022) 8269316; (022) 635 83 44 *Fax:* (022) 827 41 94 *E-mail:* arkady@arkady.com.pl *Web Site:* arkady.com.pl, pg 517

Arkana Verlag Tete Boettger Rainer Wunderlich GmbH (Germany) *Tel:* (0551) 41709 *Fax:* (0551) 43868, pg 194

Uitgeverij Jan van Arkel (Netherlands) *Tel:* (030) 2731840 *Fax:* (030) 2733614 *E-mail:* i-books@ antenna.nl *Web Site:* www.antenna.bl/i-books, pg 474

Arkeoloji Ve Sanat Yayinlari (Turkey) *Tel:* (212) 293 0378 *Fax:* (212) 245 6877 *E-mail:* info@ arkeolojisanat.com *Web Site:* www.arkeolojisanat.com, pg 644

Arkin Kitabevi (Turkey) *Tel:* (0212) 522 92 24; (0212) 541 36 20 *Fax:* (0212) 512 19 01, pg 644

Arkitektens Forlag (Denmark) *Tel:* 32836970 *Fax:* 32836940 *E-mail:* eksp@arkfo.dk; red@arkfo.dk *Web Site:* www.arkfo.dk, pg 128

Arkitektur Forlag AB (Sweden) *Tel:* (08) 7027850 *Fax:* (08) 6115270 *E-mail:* redaktionen@arkitektur.se *Web Site:* www.arkitektur.se, pg 604

Arkivarforeningen (Denmark) *Tel:* 31393520 *Fax:* 33153239, pg 1561

Arkivarforeningen (Norway) *Tel:* 22022657 *Fax:* 22237489 *E-mail:* synne.stavheim@riksarkivaren. dep.no *Web Site:* www.forskerforbundet.no, pg 1569

Arktos (Italy) *Tel:* (011) 9773941 *Fax:* (011) 9715340 *E-mail:* arktos@cometacom.it, pg 373

Arlekin-Wydawnictwo Harlequin Enterprises sp zoo (Poland) *Tel:* (022) 8499557; (022) 8499498; (022) 8498630 *Fax:* (022) 8499557, pg 517

ARLIS/UK & Ireland Art Libraries Society (United Kingdom) *Tel:* (01527) 579298 *Fax:* (01527) 579298 *Web Site:* www.arlis.org.uk, pg 1572

Armada Publishing House (Russian Federation) *Tel:* (095) 4544301; (095) 45431526 *Fax:* (095) 4542481 *E-mail:* riv@armada.msk.ru, pg 539

Editions de l'Armancon (France) *Tel:* (03) 80 64 41 87 *Fax:* (03) 80 64 46 96 *E-mail:* info@editions-armancon.fr *Web Site:* www.editions-armancon.fr, pg 147

Editore Armando SRL (Italy) *Tel:* (06) 5894525 *Fax:* (06) 5818564 *E-mail:* info@armandoeditore.com *Web Site:* www.armando.it, pg 373

Armenia Editions (Switzerland) *Tel:* (022) 794474593, pg 613

Gruppo Editoriale Armenia SpA (Italy) *Tel:* (02) 683911 *Fax:* (02) 6684884 *E-mail:* armenia@armenia.it *Web Site:* www.armenia.it, pg 373

Armitano Editores CA (Venezuela) *Tel:* (0212) 2342565; (0212) 2340870; (0212) 2340865 *Fax:* (0212) 2341647 *E-mail:* armiedit@telcel.net.ve *Web Site:* www.armitano.com, pg 773

Grupo Editorial Armonia (Mexico) *Tel:* 54 42 96 00 *E-mail:* corporativo@grupoarmonia.com.mx *Web Site:* www.grupoarmonia.com.mx, pg 458

Arms & Armour Press (United Kingdom) *Tel:* (020) 7420 5555 *Fax:* (020) 7420 7261, pg 654

Livraria Arnado Lda (Portugal) *Tel:* (0239) 27573 *Fax:* (0239) 22598, pg 524

Arnaud Editore SRL (Italy) *Tel:* (055) 216485 *Fax:* (055) 260466, pg 373

Arnette Blackwell SA (France) *Tel:* (01) 45 49 65 00 *Fax:* (01) 45 49 12 88, pg 147

Arnkrone Forlaget A/S (Denmark) *Tel:* 31507000 *Fax:* 32522652, pg 128

Arnold (United Kingdom) *Tel:* (020) 7873 6000 *Fax:* (020) 7873 6325 *E-mail:* feedback.arnold@hodder.co.uk *Web Site:* www.arnoldpublishers.com, pg 654

Edward Arnold (Australia) Pty Ltd (Australia) *Tel:* (03) 9859 9011 *Fax:* (03) 9859 9141, pg 11

Arnoldsche Verlagsanstalt GmbH (Germany) *Tel:* (0711) 645618-0 *Fax:* (0711) 645618-79 *E-mail:* art@arnoldsche.com *Web Site:* www.arnoldsche.com, pg 194

Aromolaran Publishing Co Ltd (Nigeria) *Tel:* (02) 24392, pg 499

Arpoador (Uruguay) *Tel:* (02) 707826 *Fax:* (02) 717278, pg 771

Arquivo Nacional (Brazil) *Tel:* (021) 232-6938 *Fax:* (021) 224-4525 *E-mail:* arqnacdg@rio.com.br, pg 77

Arquivo Nacional (Brazil) *Tel:* (021) 3806-6171 *Fax:* (021) 2232-8430 *E-mail:* conarq@arquivonacional.gov.br *Web Site:* www.arquivonacional.gov.br/, pg 1493

Arquivo Universidade de Coimbra (Portugal) *Tel:* (0239) 25422 *Fax:* (0239) 25841 *Web Site:* www.uc.pt, pg 524

Arrayan Editores (Chile) *Tel:* (02) 4314200 *Fax:* (02) 2741041 *E-mail:* web@arrayan.cl *Web Site:* www.arrayan.cl, pg 98

Arris Publishing Ltd (United Kingdom) *Tel:* (01608) 659328 *Fax:* (01608) 659345 *E-mail:* info@arrisbooks.com *Web Site:* ww.arrisbooks.com, pg 655

J W Arrowsmith Ltd (United Kingdom) *Tel:* (0117) 966 7545 *Fax:* (0117) 963 7829 *E-mail:* jw@arrowsmith.co.uk *Web Site:* www.arrowsmith.co.uk, pg 1152, 1173, 1214, 1237

Ars Edition GmbH (Germany) *Tel:* (089) 3810060 *Fax:* (089) 381006-58, pg 194

Ars Longa Publishing House (Romania) *Tel:* (0232) 215078 *Fax:* (0232) 215078 *E-mail:* arslonga@mail.dntis.ro, pg 534

Ars Poetica Editora Ltda (Brazil) *Tel:* (011) 2405598 *Fax:* (011) 5312648, pg 77

Ars Scribendi bv Uitgeverij (Netherlands) *Tel:* (0348) 443998 *Fax:* (0348) 444076 *E-mail:* info@arsscribendi.com *Web Site:* www.arsscribendi.com, pg 474

Ars Vivendi Verlag (Germany) *Tel:* (09103) 719 29 0 *Fax:* (09103) 719 59 19 *E-mail:* ars@arsvivendi.com *Web Site:* www.arsvivendi.com, pg 194

Bibliotheque de l' Arsenal (France) *Tel:* (01) 53 01 25 25 *Fax:* (01) 53 01 25 07 *E-mail:* arsenal@bnf.fr *Web Site:* www.bnf.fr, pg 1504

Arsenale Editrice SRL (Italy) *Tel:* (04) 5545166 *Fax:* (04) 5545057 *E-mail:* arsenale@arsenale.it *Web Site:* www.arsenale.it, pg 373

D I Arsenidis Publications (Greece) *Tel:* 210 3629538; 2103633923 *Fax:* 2103618707 *Web Site:* www.arsenidis.gr, pg 303

Arsip Nasional Republik Indonesia (Indonesia) *Tel:* (021) 78 05 851 *Fax:* (021) 78 05 812 *E-mail:* anri@indo.net.id *Web Site:* www.archivesindonesia.or.id, pg 1515

Arsorigo Co Ltd (Taiwan, Province of China) *Tel:* (02) 2735-1274 *Fax:* (02) 2725-2387, pg 634

Art Book Co Ltd (Taiwan, Province of China) *Tel:* (02) 23620578 *Fax:* (02) 23623594 *E-mail:* artbook@ms43.hinet.net, pg 634

Art Books International Ltd (United Kingdom) *Tel:* (020) 7720 1503; (020) 7578 1222 *Fax:* (020) 7720 3158 *E-mail:* sales@art-bks.com *Web Site:* www.artbooksinternational.co.uk, pg 655

Art Books International Ltd (United Kingdom) *Tel:* (01993) 830000 *Fax:* (01993) 830007 *E-mail:* sales@art.bks.com *Web Site:* www.art-bks.com, pg 1337

Art Data (United Kingdom) *Tel:* (020) 87471061 *Fax:* (020) 87422319 *E-mail:* ibf@artdata.co.uk *Web Site:* www.artdata.co.uk, pg 1338

Art Directors Club Verlag GmbH (Germany) *Tel:* (030) 59 00 31 0 *Fax:* (030) 59 00 31 0 *E-mail:* adc@adc.de *Web Site:* www.adc.de, pg 194

Librairie Art et Culture (Tunisia) *Tel:* 7231072 *Fax:* 72431372, pg 1337

Art Gallery of South Australia Bookshop (Australia) *Tel:* (08) 8207 7029 *Fax:* (08) 8207 7069 *E-mail:* agsa.bookshop@saugov.sa.gov.au *Web Site:* www.artgallery.sa.gov.au, pg 11

Art Gallery of Western Australia (Australia) *Tel:* (08) 9492 6600 *Fax:* (08) 9492 6655 *E-mail:* admin@artgallery.wa.gov.au *Web Site:* www.artgallery.wa.gov.au, pg 12

Art House Group (Finland) *Tel:* (09) 9800 2500 *Fax:* (09) 693 3762 *Web Site:* www.arthouse.fi, pg 141

Art on the Move (Australia) *Tel:* (08) 9227 7505 *Fax:* (08) 9227 5304 *E-mail:* artmoves@highwayl.com.au, pg 12

Art Sales Index Ltd (United Kingdom) *Tel:* (01784) 451145 *Fax:* (01784) 451144 *E-mail:* sales@art-sales-index.com *Web Site:* www.art-sales-index.com, pg 655

The Art Trade Press Ltd (United Kingdom) *Tel:* (023) 9248 4943, pg 655

Artava Ltd (Latvia) *Tel:* (02) 7222472 *Fax:* (02) 7830254 *E-mail:* arta@com.latnet.lv, pg 441

Artech House (United Kingdom) *Tel:* (020) 7596 8750 *Fax:* (020) 7630 0166 *E-mail:* artech-uk@artechhouse.com *Web Site:* www.artechhouse.com, pg 655

Artel SC (Belgium) *Tel:* (081) 21 37 00 *Fax:* (081) 21 23 72 *E-mail:* erasme@skynet.be, pg 62

Artema (Italy) *Tel:* (011) 3853656 *Fax:* (011) 3853244 *E-mail:* cse@estorinese.inet.it, pg 373

Artemis Verlag (Romania) *Tel:* (01) 2226661, pg 534

Artes de Mexico y del Mundo SA de CV (Mexico) *Tel:* (05) 208 3684; (05) 525 4036; (05) 525 5905 *Fax:* (05) 525 5925 *E-mail:* artesmex@internet.com.mx; artesdemexico@artesdemexico.com *Web Site:* www.artesdemexico.com, pg 458

Artes e Oficios Editora Ltda (Brazil) *Tel:* (051) 311 0832; (051) 311 5442 *Fax:* (051) 311 0832 *E-mail:* artesofi@pro.via-rs.com.br, pg 77

Edi.Artes srl (Italy) *Tel:* (02) 70209917 *Fax:* (02) 70209919, pg 373

Editora Artes Medicas Ltda (Brazil) *Tel:* (011) 221-9033 *Fax:* (011) 223-6635 *E-mail:* artesmedicas@artesmedicas.com.br *Web Site:* www.artesmedicas.com.br, pg 77

Artetech Publishing Co (United Kingdom) *Tel:* (01225) 862482 *Fax:* (01225) 865601, pg 655

Artex (Costa Rica) *Tel:* 2373144 *Fax:* 2379568, pg 114

Artexim - Foreign Trade Co (Romania) *Tel:* (01) 157672, pg 1329

Arthur James Ltd (United Kingdom) *Tel:* (01962) 736880 *Fax:* (01962) 736881 *E-mail:* office@johnhunt-publishing.com *Web Site:* www.johnhunt-publishing.com, pg 655

Artibus et Literis (Germany) *Tel:* (0211) 388-10 *Fax:* (0211) 3881280 *E-mail:* webmaster@artibus.de *Web Site:* www.artibus.de, pg 1300

Artioli Editore (Italy) *Tel:* (059) 827181 *Fax:* (059) 826819 *E-mail:* artiolip@pianeta.it, pg 373

Artis-Historia (Belgium) *Tel:* (02) 2409200 *Fax:* (02) 2480818 *E-mail:* info@artis-historia.be *Web Site:* www.artis-historia.be, pg 63

Artis-Historia (Belgium) *Tel:* (02) 2409200 *Fax:* (02) 2480818 *E-mail:* info@artis-historia.be, pg 1291

Artisjus (Hungary) *Tel:* (01) 488 2600 *Fax:* (01) 212 1544 *E-mail:* info@artisjus.com *Web Site:* www.artisjus.hu, pg 1122

The Artist Publishing Co (Taiwan, Province of China) *Tel:* (02) 23932780 *Fax:* (02) 23932012 *E-mail:* artvenue@tpts6.seed.net.tw, pg 634

ARTMED Editora (Brazil) *Tel:* (051) 33303444 *Fax:* (051) 3302378 *E-mail:* artmed@artmed.com.br *Web Site:* www.artmed.com.br, pg 77

Artmoves Inc (Australia) *Tel:* (03) 9882 8116 *Fax:* (03) 9882 8162 *E-mail:* artmoves@bigpond.com, pg 12

Artprice (France) *Tel:* (04) 72 421 706 *Fax:* (04) 78 220 606 *Web Site:* www.artprice.com, pg 147

ArTresor naklada (Croatia) *Tel:* (01) 487 2917 *Fax:* (01) 487 2916 *E-mail:* artresor@zg.tel.hr, pg 117

Arts Centre Bookshop (New Zealand) *Tel:* (03) 365 5277 *Fax:* (03) 365 3293 *E-mail:* info@booksnz.com *Web Site:* www.booksnz.com, pg 1321

Arts Council of England (United Kingdom) *Tel:* (020) 7333 0100 *Fax:* (020) 7973 6590 *E-mail:* enquiries@artscouncil.org.uk *Web Site:* www.artscouncil.org.uk, pg 655

Arts Council of Wales (United Kingdom) *Tel:* (02920) 376500 *Fax:* (02920) 221447 *Web Site:* www.ccc-acw.org.uk, pg 1400

Wydawnictwa Artystyczne i Filmowe (Poland) *Tel:* (022) 8455301; (022) 8455584; (022) 8455465; (022) 8453936 *Fax:* (022) 8455584; (022) 8455465; (022) 8453936, pg 517

Arun-Verlag (Germany) *Tel:* (036743) 233-0 *Fax:* (036743) 233-17 *E-mail:* info@arun-verlag.de *Web Site:* www.arun-verlag.de, pg 194

Arvore Coop de Actividades Artisticas, CRL (Portugal) *Tel:* (02) 383867 *Fax:* (02) 2002684, pg 524

Arya Medi Publishing House (India) *Tel:* (011) 5717012 *Fax:* (011) 5715850, pg 325

AS Narbuto Leidykla (AS Narbutas' Publishers) (Lithuania) *Tel:* (041) 429335, pg 445

ASA Editions (France) *Tel:* (01) 47 70 42 90 *Fax:* (01) 47 70 42 98 *E-mail:* info@asaeditions.fr *Web Site:* www.asaeditions.fr, pg 147

Asahiya Shoten Ltd (Booksellers) (Japan) *Tel:* (06) 3131191; (06) 3727251; (06) 3727253 *Fax:* (06) 3755650, pg 1312

Asahiya Shuppan (Japan) *Tel:* (03) 3267-0861 *Fax:* (03) 3267-0875, pg 411

Asakura Publishing Co Ltd (Japan) *Tel:* (03) 3260 0141 *Fax:* (03) 3260 0180 *E-mail:* edit@asakura.co.jp *Web Site:* www.asakura.co.jp, pg 412

Asam Establishment for Publishing & Distribution (Saudi Arabia) *Tel:* (01) 4453732 *Fax:* (01) 4412583, pg 545

Asamblea Legislativa, Biblioteca Monsenor Sanabria (Costa Rica) *Tel:* 223-2396 *Fax:* 243-2400 *E-mail:* jvolio@congreso.aleg.go.cr; vvargas@ congreso.aleg.go.cr; epaniagu@congreso.aleg.go.cr, pg 114

Roland Asanger Verlag GmbH (Germany) *Tel:* (08744) 7262 *Fax:* (08744) 967755 *E-mail:* verlag@asanger.de *Web Site:* www.asanger.de, pg 194

The Asano Agency, Inc (Japan) *Tel:* (03) 39434171 *Fax:* (03) 39437637, pg 1124

Aschehoug Dansk Forlag A/S (Denmark) *Tel:* 33305522; 33305822 *Fax:* 33305823 *E-mail:* info@ash.egmont. com *Web Site:* www.aschehoug.dk, pg 128

Aschehoug Forlag (Norway) *Tel:* 22400400 *Fax:* 22206395 *E-mail:* epost@aschehoug.no *Web Site:* www.aschehoug.no, pg 503

H Aschehoug & Co (W Nygaard) A/S (Norway) *Tel:* 22400400 *Fax:* 22206395 *E-mail:* epost@ aschehoug.no *Web Site:* www.aschehoug.no, pg 503

Aschendorffsche Verlagsbuchhandlung GmbH & Co KG (Germany) *Tel:* (0251) 690136 *Fax:* (0251) 690143 *E-mail:* buchverlag@aschendorff.de *Web Site:* www. aschendorff.de/buch, pg 194

Asclepios Edition Lothar Baus (Germany) *Tel:* (06841) 71863 *Web Site:* www.asclepiosedition.de, pg 195

Ascona Presse (Switzerland) *Tel:* (091) 791 13 34 *Fax:* (091) 791 13 34 *E-mail:* info@rmeuter.ch *Web Site:* www.rmeuter.ch, pg 613

Asempa Publishers (Ghana) *Tel:* (021) 221706 *E-mail:* asempa@ghana.com, pg 300

ASFORED (Association Nationale pour la Formation et le Perfectionnement Professionnels dans les Metiers de l'Edition) (France) *Tel:* (01) 45883981 *Fax:* (01) 45815492 *E-mail:* info@asfored.org *Web Site:* www. asfored.org, pg 1257

Asgard Publishing Services (United Kingdom) *Tel:* (0113) 262 8373 *Fax:* (0113) 262 8373 *Web Site:* www.asgardpublishing.co.uk, pg 1140

Asgard-Verlag Dr Werner Hippe GmbH (Germany) *Tel:* (02241) 3164-0 *Fax:* (02241) 316436 *E-mail:* service@asgard.de, pg 195

Ashanti Publishing (South Africa) *Tel:* (011) 8032506 *Fax:* (011) 8035094, pg 558

Ashgate Publishing Ltd (United Kingdom) *Tel:* (01252) 331551 *Fax:* (01252) 344405 *E-mail:* info@ashgate. com *Web Site:* www.ashgate.com, pg 655

Ashgrove Publishing (United Kingdom) *Tel:* (020) 7831 5013 *Fax:* (020) 7831 5011 *Web Site:* www. ashgrovepublishing.com, pg 656

Ashling Books (Australia) *Tel:* (02) 6259 1027, pg 12

Ashmolean Museum Publications (United Kingdom) *Tel:* (01865) 278010 *Fax:* (01865) 278018 *E-mail:* publications@ashmus.ox.ac.uk *Web Site:* www.ashmol.ox.ac.uk/ash/publications, pg 656

Sheikh Muhammad Ashraf Publishers (Pakistan) *Tel:* (042) 353171; (042) 353489 *Fax:* (042) 353489, pg 507

Ashton & Denton Publishing Co (CI) Ltd (United Kingdom) *Tel:* (01534) 735461; (01534) 727976 *Fax:* (01534) 875805, pg 656

Asia Books Co Ltd (Thailand) *Tel:* (02) 715-9000 *Fax:* (02) 391-2299 *E-mail:* information@asiabooks. com *Web Site:* www.asiabooks.com, pg 1336

Asia Pacific Business Press Inc (India) *Tel:* (011) 23845886; (011) 23845654; (011) 23843955; (011) 23844729 *Fax:* (011) 23841561 *E-mail:* niir@vsnl. com *Web Site:* www.niir.org, pg 325

Asia Pacific Communications Ltd (Hong Kong) *Tel:* 2861 0102 *Fax:* 2529 6816 *E-mail:* asiapac@ attglobal.net, pg 312

Asia/Pacific Cultural Centre for UNESCO (ACCU) (Japan) *Tel:* (03) 3269-4435 *Fax:* (03) 3269-4510 *E-mail:* general@accu.or.jp *Web Site:* www.accu.or.jp, pg 1265

Asia Pacific Offset Inc (United States) *Tel:* 202-462-5436 *Toll Free Tel:* 800-756-4344 *Fax:* 202-986-4030 *Web Site:* www.asiapacificoffset.com, pg 1155, 1176, 1217

Asia 2000 Ltd (Hong Kong) *Tel:* 2530 1409 *Fax:* 2526 1107 *E-mail:* info@asia2000.com.hk; editor@ asia2000.com.hk *Web Site:* www.asia2000.com.hk, pg 312

Asian Culture Co Ltd (Taiwan, Province of China) *Tel:* (02) 2507-2606 *Fax:* (02) 2507-4260 *E-mail:* cas@seed.net.tw *Web Site:* www.asianculture. com.tw, pg 634

Asian Educational Services (India) *Tel:* (011) 661493 *Fax:* (011) 6852805; (011) 6855499 *E-mail:* asianeds@nda.vsnl.net.in, pg 325

The Asian Productivity Organization (Japan) *Tel:* (03) 5226 3920 *Fax:* (03) 5226 3950 *E-mail:* apo@apo-tokyo.org *Web Site:* www.apo-tokyo.org, pg 1265

Asian Trading Corporation (India) *Tel:* (080) 5487444; (080) 5490444 *Fax:* (080) 5479444 *E-mail:* mail@ atcbooks.net; sales@atcbooks.net *Web Site:* www. atcbooks.net, pg 326

Asiapac Books Pte Ltd (Singapore) *Tel:* 63928455 *Fax:* 63926455 *E-mail:* asiapacbooks@pacific.net.sg *Web Site:* www.asiapacbooks.com, pg 550

The Asiatic Society of Mumbai (India) *Tel:* (022) 2660956 *Fax:* (022) 2665139 *E-mail:* asbl@bom2. vsnl.net.in *Web Site:* education.vsnl.com/asbl/, pg 1514

ASK Ltd (Ukraine) *Tel:* (044) 241-94-96; (044) 456-72-51 *Fax:* (044) 455-58-89 *E-mail:* ask.sale@i.com.ua, pg 648

Aslib, The Association for Information Management (United Kingdom) *Tel:* (020) 7583 8900 *Fax:* (020) 7583 8401 *E-mail:* aslib@aslib.com; pubs@aslib.com *Web Site:* www.aslib.co.uk, pg 656

Aslib, The Association for Information Management (United Kingdom) *Tel:* (020) 7583 8900 *Fax:* (020) 7583 8401 *E-mail:* pubs@aslib.com *Web Site:* www. aslib.co.uk; www.managinginformation.com, pg 1400

Aslib, The Association for Information Management (United Kingdom) *Tel:* (020) 7613 3031 *Fax:* (020) 7613 5080 *E-mail:* aslib@aslib.com *Web Site:* www. aslib.co.uk, pg 1572

Asociacion de Bibliotecarios Graduados del Istmo de Panama (Panama) *Tel:* 2227411 *Fax:* 2254366, pg 1569

Asociacion Argentina de Bibliotecas y Centros de Informacion Cientificos y Tecnicos (Argentina) *Tel:* (011) 3938406, pg 1557

Asociacion Bautista Argentina de Publicaciones (Argentina) *Tel:* (011) 4863-8924 *Fax:* (011) 4863-6745, pg 3

Asociacion Boliviana de Bibliotecarios (ABB) (Bolivia) *Tel:* (064) 1481, pg 1559

Asociacion Colombiana de Bibliotecologos y Documentalistas (Colombia) *Tel:* (01) 3603077 (ext 326) *Web Site:* www.ascolbi.org/acerca.htm, pg 1560

Asociacion Costarricense de Bibliotecarios (Costa Rica) *Tel:* 234-9889 *E-mail:* info@cesdepu.com *Web Site:* www.cesdepu.com, pg 1560

Asociacion de Archiveros del Peru (ADAP) (Peru) *Tel:* (01) 219-0100 *Fax:* (01) 472-9635 *E-mail:* dri@ u8p.edu.pe *Web Site:* www.up.edu.pe, pg 1569

Asociacion de Bibliotecarios de El Salvador (El Salvador) *Tel:* 216312 *Fax:* 225-02 78 *Web Site:* www. ues.edu.sv/abes, pg 1561

Asociacion de Bibliotecarios Universitarios del Paraguay (Paraguay) *Tel:* (021) 507080 *Fax:* (021) 213734 *Web Site:* www.una.py, pg 1569

Asociacion de Bibliotecarios y Archivistas de Honduras (Honduras), pg 1564

Asociacion de Bibliotecologos del Uruguay (Uruguay) *Tel:* (02) 4099989 *Fax:* (02) 4099989 *E-mail:* ABU@ adinet.com.uy, pg 1574

Asociacion de Escritores y Artistas Espanoles (Spain) *Tel:* (091) 5599067 *Fax:* (091) 5599067, pg 1274

Asociacion Dominicana de Bibliotecarios (ASODOBI) (Dominican Republic) *Tel:* 6884086; 6884660 *Fax:* 685841 *E-mail:* biblioteca.nacional@dominicana. com; intec.biblioteca@codetel.net.do, pg 1561

Asociacion Ecuatoriana de Bibliotecarios (AEB) (Ecuador) *Tel:* 2528-840 *Fax:* 2223-391 *E-mail:* asoebfp@hotmail.com *Web Site:* www.reicyt. org.ec/aeb, pg 1561

Asociacion Espanola de Archiveros, Bibliotecarios, Museologos y Documentalistas (Spain) *Tel:* (091) 5751727 *Fax:* (091) 5781615 *E-mail:* anabad@anabad. org *Web Site:* www.anabad.org, pg 1571

Asociacion General de Archivistas de El Salvador (AGAES) (El Salvador) *Tel:* 222 94 18 *Fax:* 281 58 60 *E-mail:* agnes@agn.gob.sv *Web Site:* www.agn.gob. sv, pg 1561

Asociacion Latinoamericana de Instituciones Financieras Para El Desarrollo (ALIDE) (Peru) *Tel:* (01) 442 2400 *Fax:* (01) 442 8105 *E-mail:* sg@alide.org.pe *Web Site:* www.alide.org.pe, pg 1534

Asociacion Instituto Linguistico de Verano (Colombia) *Tel:* (01) 2821047; (01) 3416185 *E-mail:* sil_colombia@sil.org *Web Site:* www.sil. org/americas/colombia, pg 109

Asociacion Mexicana de Bibliotecarios AC (AMBAC) (Mexico) *Tel:* (055) 55 75 33 96 *Fax:* (055) 55-75-11-35 *E-mail:* correo@ambac.org.mx *Web Site:* www. ambac.org.mx, pg 1567

Asociacion Nicaraguense de Bibliotecarios y Profesionales a Fines (Nicaragua), pg 1569

Asociacion Panamena de Bibliotecarios (Panama), pg 1569

Asociacion para el Progreso de la Direccion (APD) (Spain) *Tel:* (094) 423 22 50 *Fax:* (094) 423 62 49 *E-mail:* apd@bil.apd.es *Web Site:* www.apd.es, pg 569

Asociacion Peruana de Bibliotecarios (APB) (Peru) *Tel:* (01) 474869, pg 1569

Editores Asociados Mexicanos SA de CV (EDAMEX) (Mexico) *Tel:* (05) 5598588 *Fax:* (05) 5757035; (05) 5750555 *Web Site:* www.edamex.com, pg 459

Aspect (Japan) *Tel:* (03) 5281-2550 *Fax:* (03) 5281-2552 *E-mail:* takahira@aspect.co.jp *Web Site:* www.aspect. co.jp, pg 412

Aspect Marketing Services (United Kingdom) *Tel:* (01233) 500 800 *Fax:* (01233) 500 700 *E-mail:* mail@aspectmarketing.co.uk *Web Site:* www. aspectmarketing.co.uk, pg 1338

Aspect Press (New Zealand) *Tel:* (06) 368-2887, pg 489

Aspect Press Ltd (Russian Federation) *Tel:* (095) 3094062 *Fax:* (095) 3091166 *E-mail:* info@ aspectpress.ru *Web Site:* www.aspectpress.ru, pg 539

ASR Publications (Pakistan) *Tel:* (042) 877613; (042) 877496 *Fax:* (042) 5711575, pg 507

Assad National Library (Syrian Arab Republic) *Tel:* (011) 3320803 *Fax:* (011) 3320804 *E-mail:* contact@alassad-library.com *Web Site:* www. alassad.library.com, pg 1547

Association Togolaise pour le Developpement de la Documentation des Bibliotheques, Archives et Musees (Togo) *Tel:* 21 30 27 *Fax:* 21 85 95 *E-mail:* cafmicro@ub.tg *Web Site:* www.ub.tg, pg 1572

Association Tunisienne des Documentalistes, Bibliothecaires et Archivistes (Tunisia) *Tel:* 651924, pg 1572

Association Zairoise des Archivistes, Bibliothecaires et Documentalistes (The Democratic Republic of the Congo) *Tel:* (012) 30123; (012) 30124, pg 1560

Associazione Carmelo Teresiano Italiano, OCD (Italy) *Tel:* (06) 7989081 *Fax:* (06) 79890840 *Web Site:* www.edizioniocd.it, pg 373

Associazione Internazionale di Archeologia Classica (Italy) *Tel:* (06) 6798798 *Fax:* (06) 69789119 *E-mail:* info@aiac.org; segreteria@aiac.org *Web Site:* www.aiac.org, pg 373

Associazione Italiana Biblioteche (Italy) *Tel:* (06) 4463532 *Fax:* (06) 4441139 *E-mail:* aib@aib.it *Web Site:* www.aib.it, pg 1565

Associazione Italiana Editori (Italy) *Tel:* (02) 86463091 *Fax:* (02) 89010863 *E-mail:* aie@aie.it *Web Site:* www.aie.it, pg 1264

Associazione Librai Antiquari d'Italia (Italy) *Tel:* (055) 282635 *Fax:* (055) 214831 *E-mail:* alai@alai.it *Web Site:* www.alai.it, pg 1264

Astor-Verlag, Willibald Schlager (Austria) *Tel:* (01) 9144281 *Fax:* (01) 9144281, pg 48

Editorial Astrea de Alfredo y Ricardo Depalma SRL (Argentina) *Tel:* (011) 4382-1880 *Toll Free Tel:* 800-345-278732 *Fax:* (011) 4382-4203 *E-mail:* info@astrea.com.ar *Web Site:* www.astrea.com.ar, pg 3

Editorial Astri SA (Spain) *Tel:* (034) 936 801 207 *Fax:* (034) 936 803 194 *E-mail:* astri@astri.es *Web Site:* www.astri.es, pg 569

Astrodata AG (Switzerland) *Tel:* (043) 343 33 33 *Fax:* (043) 343 33 43 *E-mail:* info@astrodata.ch *Web Site:* www.astrodata.ch, pg 613

Casa Editrice Astrolabio-Ubaldini Editore (Italy) *Tel:* (06) 855 21 31 *Fax:* (06) 855 27 56, pg 373

Astrolog Publishing House (Israel) *Tel:* (09) 7412044 *Fax:* (09) 7442044, pg 361

AT Verlag (Switzerland) *Tel:* (062) 836 6666 *Fax:* (062) 836 6667 *E-mail:* at-verlag@azag.ch *Web Site:* www. at-verlag.ch, pg 613

Editrice Atanor SRL (Italy) *Tel:* (06) 7024595 *Fax:* (06) 7014422, pg 373

Ataturk Kultur, Dil ve Tarih, Yusek Kurumu Baskanligi (Turkey) *Tel:* (0312) 428 61 00 *Fax:* (0312) 428 52 88 *E-mail:* bim@tdk.gov.tr *Web Site:* www.tdk.gov.tr, pg 644

Ataturk Universitesi (Turkey) *Tel:* (0442) 231 11 11 *Fax:* (0442) 236 10 14 *E-mail:* ata@atauni.edu.tr *Web Site:* www.atauni.edu.tr/, pg 645

Atelier Books (United Kingdom) *Tel:* (0131) 5574050 *Fax:* (0131) 5578382 *E-mail:* mail@bournefineart. co.uk *Web Site:* www.bournefineart.co.uk/books.html, pg 657

Editions de l'Atelier (France) *Tel:* (01) 44 08 95 15 *Fax:* (01) 44 08 95 00, pg 147

Verlag Atelier im Bauernhaus Fischerhude Wolf-Dietmar Stock (Germany) *Tel:* (04293) 491; (04293) 493 *Fax:* (04293) 1238, pg 195

Atelier, L (Egypt (Arab Republic of Egypt)) *Tel:* (03) 4820526 *Fax:* (03) 4837662, pg 1393

Atelier National de Reproduction des Theses (France) *Tel:* (03) 20 30 86 73 *Fax:* (03) 20 54 21 95 *E-mail:* anrt@univ-lille3.fr *Web Site:* www.anrtheses. com.fr, pg 147

Atelier Publishing Co Ltd (Japan) *Tel:* (03) 3357-2741 *Fax:* (03) 3357-2194, pg 412

Atelier Verlag Andernach (AVA) (Germany) *Tel:* (02632) 44432 *Fax:* (02632) 31383 *E-mail:* info@atelierverlag-andernach.de *Web Site:* www.atelierverlag-andernach. de, pg 195

Editura si Atelierele Tipografice Metropol SRL (Romania) *Tel:* (01) 2104593; (01) 2108433 *Fax:* (01) 2106987, pg 1150

Ateliers et Presses de Taize (France) *Tel:* (03) 85 50 30 50 *Fax:* (03) 85 50 30 55 *E-mail:* editions@taize.fr *Web Site:* www.taize.fr, pg 148

Atena (Poland) *Tel:* (061) 228685 *Fax:* (061) 524082 *E-mail:* atena@poz1.commet.pl, pg 517

Atena Kustannus Oy (Finland) *Tel:* (014) 620192 *Fax:* (014) 620190 *E-mail:* atena@atenakustannus.fi *Web Site:* www.atenakustannus.fi, pg 141

Sociedad de Educacion Atenas SA (Spain) *Tel:* (091) 5480127 *Fax:* (091) 5591771, pg 569

Ateneo Cientifico, Literario y Artistico (Spain) *Tel:* (09142) 974 42, pg 1399

Ateneo Cientifico, Literario y Artistico (Spain) *Tel:* (071) 360553 *Fax:* (071) 352194 *E-mail:* ateneo@intercom. es *Web Site:* www.usuarios.intercom.es/ateneo, pg 1399

Editorial Ateneo de Caracas (Venezuela) *Tel:* (0212) 5734622; (0212) 5734400; (0212) 5734600 *Fax:* (0212) 5754475 *E-mail:* webmaster@ateneo.org. ve, pg 773

Ateneo de Manila University Press (Philippines) *Tel:* (02) 4265984; (02) 4261238 *Fax:* (02) 4265909 *E-mail:* unipress@pusit.admu.edu.ph (business/ operations) *Web Site:* www.admu.edu.ph, pg 513

Ateneo Puertorriqueno (Puerto Rico) *Tel:* (787) 722-4839; (787) 721-3877 *Fax:* (809) 725-3873 *E-mail:* ateneopr@caribe.net *Web Site:* www.ateneopr. com, pg 1272

Athenaeum Boekhandel (Netherlands) *Tel:* (020) 6226248 *Fax:* (020) 6384901 *E-mail:* info@ athenaeum.nl *Web Site:* www.athenaeum.nl, pg 1320

Athenaeum Verlag AG (Switzerland) *Tel:* (091) 571536, pg 613

Editora Atheneu Ltda (Brazil) *Tel:* (011) 220-9186 *Fax:* (011) 221-3389 *E-mail:* atheneau@nutecnet.com. br *Web Site:* www.atheneu.com.br, pg 78

Atheneum Forlag A/S (Norway) *Tel:* 23292072; 23291900 *Fax:* 23291901, pg 504

Athens Academy Library (Greece) *Tel:* 2103600209 *Web Site:* www.academyofathens.gr, pg 1511

Athesia Buchhandlung (Italy) *Tel:* (0471) 927111 *Fax:* (0471) 927215 *E-mail:* buch@athesia.it *Web Site:* www.athesiabuch.it, pg 1310

Athesia Verlag Bozen (Italy) *Tel:* (0471) 92 72 03 *Fax:* (0471) 92 72 07 *E-mail:* buchverlag@athesia.it, pg 374

Athina (Greece) *Tel:* 2109341166, pg 1302

Ekdoseis Athina-Mavrogianni (Greece) *Tel:* 210 3821308; 2103304628 *Fax:* 2103838228, pg 303

The Athlone Press Ltd (United Kingdom) *Tel:* (020) 7922 0880 *Fax:* (020) 7922 0881 *E-mail:* athlonepress@btinternet.com *Web Site:* www. transcomm.ox.ac.uk/wwwroot/athlone_press.htm, pg 657

Editora Atica SA (Brazil) *Tel:* (011) 278 93 22 *Fax:* (011) 279 2185, pg 78

Atica, SA Editores e Livreiros (Portugal) *Tel:* (021) 8153220 *Fax:* (021) 8153219, pg 524

Atlantic Transport Publishers (United Kingdom) *Tel:* (01326) 373656 *Fax:* (01326) 378309; (01326) 373656, pg 657

Atlantica Editrice SARL (Italy), pg 374

Editions Atlantica Seguier (France) *Tel:* (05) 59 52 84 00 *Fax:* (05) 59 52 84 01 *E-mail:* atlantica@atlantica.fr *Web Site:* www.atlantica.fr, pg 148

Editorial Atlantida SA (Argentina) *Tel:* (011) 4331-4591; (011) 4331-4599 *Fax:* (011) 4331-3341 *E-mail:* info@ atlantida.com.ar *Web Site:* www.atlantida.com.ar, pg 3

Bokforlaget Atlantis AB (Sweden) *Tel:* (08) 7830440 *Fax:* (08) 6617285 *E-mail:* mail@atlantis-publishers. se, pg 604

Atlantis M Pechlivanides & Co SA (Greece) *Tel:* 210 9220071; 2109220073 *Fax:* 2109025773, pg 303

Atlantis Musikbuch (Switzerland) *Tel:* (01) 305 7068 *Fax:* (01) 305 7069, pg 613

Atlantis sro (Czech Republic) *Tel:* (05) 422 132 21 *Fax:* (05) 422 132 21 *E-mail:* atlantis-brno@volny.cz *Web Site:* www.volny.cz/atlantis/, pg 122

Atlantis-Verlag AG (Switzerland) *Tel:* (01) 2622717 *Fax:* (01) 2512615, pg 613

Atlantisz Kiado (Hungary) *Tel:* (01) 4065645 *Fax:* (01) 4065645 *E-mail:* atlantis@budapest.hu, pg 317

Atlas (Greece) *Tel:* 2103627342 *Fax:* 2103300257 *E-mail:* c_poulos@hotmail.com, pg 303

Editions Atlas (France) *Tel:* (01) 40 74 38 38 *Fax:* (01) 45 61 19 85 *E-mail:* contact@editionsatlas.fr *Web Site:* www.editionsatlas.fr, pg 148

Editora Atlas SA (Brazil) *Tel:* (011) 3357-9144 *E-mail:* edatlas@editora-atlas.com.br *Web Site:* www. edatlas.com.br; www.atlasnet.com.br, pg 78

Atlas Press (United Kingdom) *Tel:* (020) 7490 8742 *Fax:* (021) 7490 8742 *E-mail:* enquiries@atlaspress. co.uk *Web Site:* www.atlaspress.co.uk, pg 657

Atma Ram & Sons (India) *Tel:* (011) 223092 *E-mail:* yogesh2@ndf.vsnl.net.in, pg 326

Atma Ram & Sons (India) *Tel:* (011) 223092, pg 1305

ATP - Packager (France) *Tel:* (0473) 19 58 80 *Fax:* (0473) 195899 *E-mail:* atp.chamalieres@ wanadoo.fr, pg 148

Atrium Group (Spain) *Tel:* (093) 2540099 *Fax:* (093) 2118139 *E-mail:* atrium@atriumgroup.org *Web Site:* www.atriumbooks.com, pg 569

Atrium Verlag AG (Switzerland) *Tel:* (01) 7603171 *Fax:* (01) 7603171, pg 613

Attic Press (Ireland) *Tel:* (021) 490 2980 *Fax:* (021) 431 5329 *E-mail:* corkuniversitypress@ucc.ie *Web Site:* www.corkuniversitypress.com, pg 354

Atuakkiorfik A/S Det Greenland Publishers (Denmark) *Tel:* 32 21 22 *Fax:* 32 25 00 *E-mail:* henri@ atuakkiorfik.gl *Web Site:* www.atuakkiorfik.gl, pg 128

Scoop/Au Vent des Iles (French Polynesia) *Tel:* 50 95 95 *Fax:* 50 95 97 *E-mail:* mail@auventdesiles.pf *Web Site:* www.auventdesiles.pf, pg 190

Aubanel Editions (France) *Tel:* (01) 53 03 31 00 *Fax:* (01) 45 49 17 00 *Web Site:* www.lamartiniere. fr/groupe/aubanel.htm, pg 148

Editions de l'Aube (France) *Tel:* (04) 90 07 46 60 *Fax:* (04) 90 07 53 02 *Web Site:* www.aube-editions. com/, pg 148

Editions Aubier-Montaigne SA (France) *Tel:* (01) 40 51 31 00 *Fax:* (01) 43 29 21 48, pg 148

Auckland City Libraries (New Zealand) *Tel:* (09) 377 0209 *Fax:* (09) 307 7741 *E-mail:* library_reference@ aucklandcity.govt.nz *Web Site:* www. aucklandcitylibraries.com, pg 1530

Auckland University Press (New Zealand) *Tel:* (09) 373 7528 *Fax:* (09) 373 7465 *E-mail:* aup@auckland.ac.nz *Web Site:* www.auckland.ac.nz/aup/, pg 489

Audio-Forum - The Language Source (United Kingdom) *Tel:* (020) 586 4499 *Fax:* (020) 722 1068 *E-mail:* microworld@ndirect.co.uk *Web Site:* www. microworld.ndirect.co.uk, pg 657

Audio Visual Centre Ltd (Malta) *Tel:* 21330886 *Fax:* 21346945 *E-mail:* info@avc.com.mt, pg 1317

Audivox (Belgium) *Tel:* (03) 470 1784 *E-mail:* info@audivox.net, pg 1291

AUE-Verlag GmbH (Germany) *Tel:* (06298) 1328 *Fax:* (06298) 4298 *E-mail:* info@aue-verlag.com *Web Site:* www.aue-verlag.com, pg 195

Ludwig Auer GmbH (Germany) *Tel:* (0906) 73-0 *Fax:* (0906) 73-130 (management); (0906) 73-184 (sales) *E-mail:* org@auer-medien.de *Web Site:* www.auer-medien.de, pg 1145

Auer Verlag GmbH (Germany) *Tel:* (0906) 73-240 *Fax:* (0906) 73177; (0906) 73178 *E-mail:* info@auer-verlag.de *Web Site:* www.auer-verlag.de, pg 195

Aufbau Taschenbuch Verlag GmbH (Germany) *Tel:* (030) 283 94-0 *Fax:* (030) 283 94 100 *E-mail:* info@aufbau-verlag.de *Web Site:* www.aufbau-verlag.de, pg 195

Aufbau-Verlag GmbH (Germany) *Tel:* (030) 28 394-0 *Fax:* (030) 28 394-100 *E-mail:* info@aufbau-verlag.de *Web Site:* www2.aufbauverlag.de, pg 195

Aufstieg-Verlag GmbH (Germany) *Tel:* (0871) 54112 *Fax:* (0871) 54112 *Web Site:* www.aufstieg-verlag.de, pg 195

August Guese Verlag GmbH (Germany) *Tel:* (06039) 48 01 10 *Fax:* (06039) 48 01 48 *E-mail:* info@guese.de www.guese.de, pg 195

J J Augustin Verlag GmbH (Germany) *Tel:* (04124) 20 44-46 *Fax:* (04124) 47 09, pg 195

Augustin-Verlag (Switzerland) *Tel:* (052) 649 31 31 *Fax:* (052) 649 31 94 *E-mail:* info@augustin.ch *Web Site:* www.augustin.ch, pg 613

Augustinus-Verlag Wurzburg Inh Augustinerprovinz (Germany) *Tel:* (0931) 3097-400 *Fax:* (0931) 3097-401 *E-mail:* verlag@augustiner.de *Web Site:* www.augustiner.de, pg 195

Augustus Verlag (Germany) *Tel:* (089) 9271-0 *Fax:* (089) 9271-168 *Web Site:* www.droemer-weltbild.de, pg 195

Editions d'Aujourd'hui (Les Introuvables) (France) *Tel:* (01) 43 54 79 10 *Fax:* (01) 43 29 86 20, pg 148

Aulis Publishers (United Kingdom) *Tel:* (01672) 539 041 *Fax:* (01373) 452 888 *E-mail:* info@aulis.com *Web Site:* www.aulis.com, pg 657

Aulis Verlag Deubner & Co KG (Germany) *Tel:* (0221) 9514540 *Fax:* (0221) 518443 *E-mail:* info@aulis.de *Web Site:* www.aulis.de, pg 196

AULOS sro (Czech Republic) *Tel:* (02) 536863 *Fax:* (02) 90004536 *E-mail:* aulos@volny.cz, pg 122

Aurelia Books PVBA (Belgium) *Tel:* (091) 82 55 82 *Fax:* (091) 82 72 47, pg 63

Aurora (Czech Republic) *Tel:* (02) 24 21 43 26; (02) 24 21 46 24 *Fax:* (02) 24 21 43 26 *E-mail:* eaurora@eaurora.cz *Web Site:* www.eaurora.cz, pg 122

Aurora (Indonesia) *Tel:* (021) 5810413, pg 350

Aurora Art Publishers (Russian Federation) *Tel:* (0812) 312-3753 *Fax:* (0812) 312-5460, pg 539

Aurora Semanario Israeli de Actualidad (Israel) *Tel:* (03) 5462785; (03) 5463297 *Fax:* (03) 5625082 *E-mail:* aurorail@netvision.net.il, pg 361

Aurum Press Ltd (United Kingdom) *Tel:* (020) 7637 3225 *Fax:* (020) 7580 2469 *Web Site:* www.aurumpress.co.uk, pg 657

Auslib Press Pty Ltd (Australia) *Tel:* (08) 8278 4363 *Fax:* (08) 8278 4000 *E-mail:* info@auslib.com.au *Web Site:* www.auslib.com.au, pg 12

Ausmed Publications Pty Ltd (Australia) *Tel:* (03) 9375 7311 *Fax:* (03) 9375 7299 *E-mail:* ausmed@ausmed.com.au *Web Site:* www.ausmed.com.au, pg 12

Aussaat Verlag (Germany) *Tel:* (02845) 392222 *Fax:* (02845) 33689 *E-mail:* info@neukirchener-verlag.de *Web Site:* www.aussaat-verlag.de, pg 196

Aussie Books (Australia) *Tel:* (07) 3345 4253 *Fax:* (07) 3344 1582 *E-mail:* sildale@yahoo.com *Web Site:* www.treasureenterprises.com, pg 12

Aussies Afire Publishing (Australia) *Tel:* (02) 6581 0654 *Fax:* (02) 6581 0745 *Web Site:* www.gracechurchpm.org.au, pg 12

Austed Publishing Co (Australia) *Tel:* (08) 9203 6044 *Fax:* (08) 9203 6055 *E-mail:* net@austed.com.au *Web Site:* www.austed.com.au, pg 12

Austicks Headrow Bookshop (United Kingdom) *Tel:* (0113) 243-9607 *Fax:* (0113) 245-8837, pg 1338

Austin's Book Services (Guyana) *Tel:* (02) 277 395; (02) 267 350 *Fax:* (02) 277 369 *E-mail:* austins@guyana.net.gy, pg 1304

Australasian Association for Lexicography (Australex) (Australia) *Tel:* (07) 5595 2502 *Fax:* (07) 5595 2545 *Web Site:* www.anu.edu.au, pg 1389

Australasian Medical Publishing Company Ltd (AMPCO) (Australia) *Tel:* (02) 9562 6666 *Fax:* (02) 9562 6699 *E-mail:* medjaust@ampco.com.au *Web Site:* www.mja.com.au, pg 12

Australasian Textiles & Fashion Publishers (Australia) *Tel:* (03) 5261 3966 *Fax:* (03) 5261 6950 *Web Site:* www.atfmag.com, pg 12

Australia Council Literature Board (Australia) *Tel:* (02) 9215 9000 *Toll Free Tel:* 800 226 912 *Fax:* (02) 9215 9111 *E-mail:* mail@ozco.gov.au *Web Site:* www.ozco.gov.au, pg 1249

Australian Academic Press Pty Ltd (Australia) *Tel:* (07) 3257 1176 *Fax:* (07) 3252 5908 *E-mail:* info@australianacademicpress.com.au *Web Site:* www.australianacademicpress.com.au, pg 12

Australian Academy of Science (Australia) *Tel:* (02) 6247 5777 *Fax:* (02) 6257 4620 *E-mail:* eb@science.org.au, aas@science.org.au *Web Site:* www.science.org.au, pg 12

The Australian & New Zealand Association of Antiquarian Booksellers (Australia) *Tel:* (03) 9525 1649 *Fax:* (03) 9529 1298 *E-mail:* admin@anzaab.com; bookshop@hincebooks.com.au *Web Site:* www.anzaab.com, pg 1249

Australian Booksellers Association Inc (Australia) *Tel:* (03) 9859 7322 *Fax:* (03) 9859 7344 *E-mail:* mail@aba.org.au *Web Site:* www.aba.org.au, pg 1250

Australian Broadcasting Authority (Australia) *Tel:* (02) 9344 7700 *Toll Free Tel:* 800 22 6667 (Australia only) *Fax:* (02) 9334 7799 *E-mail:* info@aba.gov.au *Web Site:* www.aba.gov.au, pg 13

Australian Chart Book Pty Ltd (Australia) *Tel:* (02) 9489 4786 *Fax:* (02) 9487 2089 *Web Site:* www.austchartbook.com.au, pg 13

Australian Copyright Council (Australia) *Tel:* (02) 9318 1788 (copyright); (02) 9699 3247 (sales) *Fax:* (02) 9698 3536 *E-mail:* info@copyright.org.au *Web Site:* www.copyright.org.au, pg 1250

Australian Film Television & Radio School (Australia) *Tel:* (02) 9805 6611 *Fax:* (02) 9805 1275 *E-mail:* info_nsw@aftrs.edu.au *Web Site:* www.aftrs.edu.au, pg 13

Australian Government Information Management Office (Australia) *Tel:* (02) 6215 2222 *Fax:* (02) 6215 1609 *Web Site:* www.agimo.gov.au/information/publishing, pg 13

Australian Institute of Criminology (Australia) *Tel:* (02) 6260 9200 *Fax:* (02) 6260 9201 *E-mail:* aicpress@aic.gov.au *Web Site:* www.aic.gov.au, pg 13

Australian Institute of Family Studies (AIFS) (Australia) *Tel:* (03) 9214 7888 *Fax:* (03) 9214 7839 *E-mail:* publications@aifs.org.au *Web Site:* www.aifs.org.au, pg 13

Australian Law Librarians' Group Inc (Australia) *Tel:* (02) 9230 8675 *Fax:* (02) 9233 7952 *Web Site:* www.allg.asn.au, pg 1557

Australian Library & Information Association (Australia) *Tel:* (02) 6215 8222 *Fax:* (02) 6282 2249 *E-mail:* enquiry@alia.org.au *Web Site:* www.alia.org.au, pg 1557

Australian Library Publishers' Society (Australia) *Tel:* (08) 8303 5372 *Fax:* (08) 8303 4369 *E-mail:* library@adelaide.edu.au *Web Site:* www.library.adelaide.edu.au/ual/publ/alps/, pg 1389

Australian Licensing Corp (Australia) *Tel:* (02) 9280 2220 *Fax:* (02) 9280 2223 *E-mail:* rodhare@alc-online.com *Web Site:* www.alc-online.com, pg 1119

Australian Marine Conservation Society Inc (AMCS) (Australia) *Tel:* (07) 3848 5235 *Toll Free Tel:* 800 066 299 *Fax:* (07) 3892 5814 *E-mail:* amcs@amcs.org.au *Web Site:* www.amcs.org.au, pg 13

Australian National University Library (Australia) *Tel:* (02) 6125 5111 *Fax:* (02) 6125 5931 *E-mail:* library.info@anu.edu.au *Web Site:* www.anu.edu.au, pg 1488

Australian Press Council (Australia) *Tel:* (02) 9261 1930 *Toll Free Tel:* 800-02-5712 *Fax:* (02) 9267 6826 *E-mail:* presscouncil@presscouncil.org.au *Web Site:* www.presscouncil.org.au, pg 1250

Australian Publishers Association Ltd (Australia) *Tel:* (02) 9281 9788 *Fax:* (02) 9281 1073 *E-mail:* apa@publishers.asn.au *Web Site:* www.publishers.asn.au, pg 1250

Australian Rock Art Research Association (Australia) *Tel:* (03) 9523 0549 *Fax:* (03) 9523 0549 *E-mail:* auraweb@hotmail.com *Web Site:* mc2.vicnet.net.au/home/aura/web/index.html, pg 13

Australian Scholarly Publishing (Australia) *Tel:* (03) 98175208 *Fax:* (03) 8176431 *E-mail:* aspic@ozemail.com.au, pg 13

Australian Society of Archivists (Australia) *Tel:* (07) 3131 7777 *Fax:* (07) 3131 7764 *E-mail:* info@archives.qld.gov.au *Web Site:* www.archives.qld.gov.au, pg 1557

The Australian Society of Authors Ltd (Australia) *Tel:* (02) 93180877 *Fax:* (02) 93180530 *E-mail:* office@asauthors.org *Web Site:* www.asauthors.org/cgi-bin/asa/information.cgi, pg 1250

The Australian Society of Authors Ltd (Australia) *Tel:* (02) 93180877 *Fax:* (02) 93180530 *E-mail:* asa@asauthors.org *Web Site:* www.asauthors.org, pg 1389

Australian Society of Indexers (Australia) *Tel:* (02) 4268-5335 *Web Site:* www.aussi.org, pg 1250

Australian Writers' Guild Ltd (Australia) *Tel:* (02) 92811554 *Fax:* (02) 92814321 *E-mail:* admin@awg.com.au *Web Site:* www.awg.com.au, pg 1389

Austrian PEN Centre (Austria) *Tel:* (01) 5334459 *Fax:* (01) 5328749 *E-mail:* oepen.club@netway.at *Web Site:* www.penclub.at, pg 1390

Authors' Licensing & Collecting Society (United Kingdom) *Tel:* (020) 7395 0600 *Fax:* (020) 7395 0660 *E-mail:* alcs@alcs.co.uk *Web Site:* www.alcs.co.uk, pg 1279

Authorspress (India) *Tel:* (011) 22436299; (011) 22460145 *Fax:* (011) 22460145 *E-mail:* authorspress@yahoo.com, pg 326

Automobilia srl (Italy) *Tel:* (02) 4802 1671 *Fax:* (02) 4819 4968 *E-mail:* automobilia@tin.it, pg 374

Autoren- und Verlags-Agentur GmbH (AVA) (Germany) *Tel:* (08152) 925883 *Fax:* (08152) 3076 *E-mail:* avagmbh@aol.com, pg 1121

Verlag der Autoren GmbH & Co KG (Germany) *Tel:* (069) 23 85 74-0 *Fax:* (069) 24 27 76 44 *E-mail:* buch@verlag-der-autoren.de *Web Site:* www.verlag-der-autoren.de, pg 196

Autorensolidaritat - Verlag der Interessengemeinschaft osterreichischer Autorinnen und Autoren (Austria) *Tel:* (01) 526 20 44-13 *Fax:* (01) 526 20 44-55 *E-mail:* ig@literaturhaus.at, pg 48

Biblioteca de Autores Cristianos (Spain) *Tel:* (091) 3090862; (091) 3090973 *Fax:* (091) 3091980 *E-mail:* bac@planalfa.es, pg 569

Autorinnen und Autoren der Schweiz AdS (Switzerland) *Tel:* (01) 350 04 60 *Fax:* (01) 350 04 61 *E-mail:* sekretariat@a-d-s.ch *Web Site:* www.a-d-s.ch, pg 1152

Autovision Verlag Guenther & Co (Germany) *Tel:* (040) 810327 *Fax:* (040) 87932995 *E-mail:* mail@ autovision.de *Web Site:* www.autovision-verlag.de, pg 196

Autrement Editions (France) *Tel:* (01) 44 73 80 00 *Fax:* (01) 44 73 00 12 *E-mail:* contact@autrement. com *Web Site:* www.autrement.com, pg 148

Autres Temps (France) *Tel:* (0491) 26 80 33 *Fax:* (0491) 41 11 01 *E-mail:* editions.autrestemps@free.fr, pg 148

Autumn Publishing Ltd (United Kingdom) *Tel:* (01243) 531660 *Fax:* (01243) 774433 *E-mail:* autumn@ autumnpublishing.co.uk *Web Site:* www. autumnpublishing.co.uk, pg 657

Editions Philippe Auzou (France) *Tel:* (01) 40 33 84 00 *Fax:* (01) 47 97 20 08 *E-mail:* editions@auzou.fr *Web Site:* www.auzoueditions.com, pg 148

AV Studio Reklamno-vydavatel 'ska agentura (Slovakia) *Tel:* (02) 65426297 *Fax:* (02) 65429750, pg 554

Editions l'Avant-Scene Theatre (France) *Tel:* (01) 46 34 28 20 *Fax:* (01) 43 54 50 14 *Web Site:* www.avant-scene-theatre.com, pg 148

Editorial Avante SA de Cv (Mexico) *Tel:* (05) 5214548; (05) 5217563; (05) 5127634; (05) 5127563 *Fax:* (05) 5215245 *E-mail:* editorialavante@infosel.net.mx *Web Site:* www.editorialavante.com.mx, pg 459

AVCR Historicky ustav (Czech Republic) *Tel:* (02) 868 821 21; (02) 838 813 73 *Fax:* (02) 887 513 *E-mail:* panek@hiu.cas.cz, pg 122

Aventinum Nakladatelstvi spol sro (Czech Republic) *Tel:* (02) 41770660; (02) 441770616; (02) 41767949 *Fax:* (02) 44402405, pg 122

Avero Publications Ltd (United Kingdom) *Tel:* (0191) 2615790 *Fax:* (0191) 2611209 *E-mail:* nstc@ newcastle.ac.uk, pg 657

Avgvstinvs (Spain) *Tel:* (091) 5342070 *Fax:* (091) 5544801 *E-mail:* revista@avgvstinvs.org *Web Site:* www.avgvstinvs.org, pg 569

Aviatic Verlag GmbH (Germany) *Tel:* (089) 613890-0 *Fax:* (089) 613890-10 *E-mail:* aviatic@aviatic.de *Web Site:* www.aviatic.de, pg 196

Aviation Industry Press (China) *Tel:* (010) 64918417 *Fax:* (010) 64922217, pg 100

Avicenne Librairie Internationale (Syrian Arab Republic) *Tel:* (011) 224 44 77 *Fax:* (011) 221 98 33 *E-mail:* avicenne@net.sy, pg 1335

Monte Avila Editores Latinoamericana CA (Venezuela) *Tel:* (0212) 265-6020; (0212) 265-9871 *E-mail:* maelca@telcel.net.ve, pg 773

Avinash Reference Publications (India) *Tel:* (0231) 21024 *Fax:* (0231) 27262, pg 326

AvivA Britta Jurgs GmbH (Germany) *Tel:* (030) 39 73 13 72 *Fax:* (030) 39 73 13 71 *E-mail:* aviva@txt.de *Web Site:* www2.txt.de, pg 196

Avoca Publications (Ireland) *Tel:* (01) 889218, pg 354

Avots (Latvia) *Tel:* (02) 7211394 *Fax:* (02) 7225824 *E-mail:* avots@apollo.lv *Web Site:* www.vardnicas.lv, pg 441

Award Publications Ltd (United Kingdom) *Tel:* (020) 7388 7800 *Fax:* (020) 7388 7887 *E-mail:* info@award. abel.co.uk, pg 657

Al-Awqaf Central Library (Iraq) *Tel:* (01) 4169362 *Fax:* (01) 4167790, pg 1516

AWT World Trade (United States) *Tel:* 773-777-7100 *Fax:* 773-777-0909 *E-mail:* sale@awt-gpi.com *Web Site:* www.awt-gpi.com, pg 1238

Axel Juncker Verlag Jacobi KG (Germany) *Tel:* (089) 360960 *Fax:* (089) 36096432; (089) 36096258, pg 196

Axicon Auto ID Ltd (United Kingdom) *Tel:* (01869) 351155 *Fax:* (01869) 351205 *E-mail:* sales@axicon. com *Web Site:* www.axicon.com, pg 1173

Axiom Publishers & Distributors (Australia) *Tel:* (08) 83627052 *Fax:* (08) 83629430 *E-mail:* axiompub@ camtech.net.au, pg 13

Axiotelis G (Greece) *Tel:* 2103610091; 210 3636264; 2103634264, pg 303

Bokforlaget Axplock (Sweden) *Tel:* (0152) 150 60 *Fax:* (0152) 151 40 *E-mail:* post@axplock.se *Web Site:* www.axplock.se, pg 605

Biblioteca Ayacucho (Venezuela) *Tel:* (0212) 5644402; (0212) 5643583 *Fax:* (0212) 5634223, pg 773

Al-Ayam Press Co Ltd (Sudan) *E-mail:* kalhashmi@ alayam.com *Web Site:* www.alayam.com, pg 603

Aydin Yayincilik (Turkey) *Tel:* (0312) 2873402; (0312) 2873403 *Fax:* (0312) 2873402, pg 645

Editorial Ayuso (Spain) *Tel:* (091) 2228080, pg 569

AZ Bertelsmann Direct GmbH (Germany) *Tel:* (05241) 805438 *Fax:* (05241) 8066962 *E-mail:* az@ bertelsmann.de *Web Site:* www.az.bertelsmann.de, pg 196

AZ Editora SA (Argentina) *Tel:* (011) 4961-4036; (011) 4961-4037; (011) 4961-4038; (011) 4961-0088 *Fax:* (011) 4961-0089 *E-mail:* correo@az-editora.com *Web Site:* www.az-editora.com.ar, pg 3

Grupo Azabache Sa de CV (Mexico) *Tel:* (05) 543-2786 *Fax:* (05) 543-2949, pg 459

Azerbaidzhanskaya respublikanskaya biblioteka im M F Akhundova (Azerbaijan) *Tel:* (012) 934 003, pg 1490

Azernesr (Azerbaijan) *Tel:* (012) 925015, pg 60

Al- Azhar University Library (Egypt (Arab Republic of Egypt)) *Tel:* (02) 5881152; (02) 5881153 *E-mail:* info@alazhar.org *Web Site:* www.alazhar.org, pg 1501

La Azotea Editorial Fotografica SRL (Argentina) *Tel:* (011) 4811-0931 *Fax:* (011) 4811-0931 *E-mail:* azotea@laazotea.com.ar *Web Site:* www. laazotea.com.ar, pg 3

Editorial Azteca SA (Mexico) *Tel:* (05) 5261157, pg 459

B & B (Republic of Korea) *Tel:* (02) 540-4425 *Fax:* (02) 517-8793 *E-mail:* bbpress-98@hanmail.net, pg 433

Ediciones B, SA (Spain) *Tel:* (093) 484 66 00 *Fax:* (093) 232 46 60 *Web Site:* www.edicionesb.es; www. edicionesb.com, pg 569

B I Publications Pvt Ltd (India) *Tel:* (011) 3274443; (011) 3259352; (011) 3255118 *Fax:* (011) 3261290 *E-mail:* bigroup@del3.vsnl.net.in, pg 326

B M Israel BV (Netherlands) *Tel:* (020) 624 70 40 *Fax:* (020) 507 20 32 *E-mail:* bmisrael@xs4all.nl *Web Site:* www.nvva.nl/israelbm, pg 474

b small publishing (United Kingdom) *Tel:* (020) 8974 6851 *Fax:* (020) 8974 6845 *E-mail:* info@bsmall. co.uk *Web Site:* homepage.ntlworld.com/codework/ welcome.htm, pg 657

Ba-reunsa Publishing Co (Republic of Korea) *Tel:* (031) 792-0185, pg 434

Baader Buch- u Offsetdruckerei GmbH & Co KG CL (Germany) *Tel:* (07381) 791 *Fax:* (07381) 411412, pg 1145

Baader Buch- u Offsetdruckerei GmbH & Co KG CL (Germany) *Tel:* (07381) 791 *Fax:* (07371) 4114, pg 1166

Baader Buch- u Offsetdruckerei GmbH & Co KG CL (Germany) *Tel:* (07381) 791, pg 1206

Baader Buch- u Offsetdruckerei GmbH & Co KG CL (Germany) *Tel:* (07381) 791 *Fax:* (07381) 411412, pg 1226, 1235

BAAF Adoption & Fostering (United Kingdom) *Tel:* (020) 7593 2000 *Fax:* (020) 7593 2001 *E-mail:* mail@baaf.org.uk *Web Site:* www.baaf.org.uk, pg 658

Auteursbureau Greta Baars-Jelgersma (Netherlands) *Tel:* (024) 6963336 *Fax:* (024) 6963293 *E-mail:* 6963336@hetnet.nl *Web Site:* home.hetnet. nl/~jelgersma696, pg 1125

Bernard Babani (Publishing) Ltd (United Kingdom) *Tel:* (020) 7603 2581; (020) 7603 7296 *Fax:* (020) 7603 8203 *E-mail:* enquiries@babanibooks.com *Web Site:* www.babanibooks.com, pg 658

Babel Verlag Kevin Perryman (Germany) *Tel:* (08243) 961691 *Fax:* (08243) 961614 *E-mail:* info@babel-verlag.de *Web Site:* www.babel-verlag.de, pg 196

Baberu Inc (Japan) *Tel:* (03) 5530-2205 *Fax:* (03) 5530-2204 *E-mail:* buc@babel.co.jp *Web Site:* www.babel. co.jp, pg 412

Babtext Nakladatelska Spolecnost (Czech Republic) *Tel:* (02) 435 992 *Fax:* (02) 768992; (02) 61221868, pg 122

Joan Bacchus-Xavier (Trinidad & Tobago) *Tel:* (868) 6420244 *Fax:* (868) 6251330, pg 642

Bacharakis (Greece) *Tel:* 2310220160 *Fax:* 2310263776, pg 1302

J P Bachem Verlag GmbH (Germany) *Tel:* (0221) 1619-0 *Fax:* (0221) 1619-159 *E-mail:* info@bachem-verlag.de *Web Site:* www.bachem-verlag.de, pg 196

Dr Bachmaier Verlag GmbH (Germany) *Tel:* (089) 685120 *Fax:* (089) 685120 *E-mail:* contact@verlag-drbachmaier.de *Web Site:* www.verlag-drbachmaier.de, pg 196

Backhuys Publishers BV (Netherlands) *Tel:* (071) 5170208 *Fax:* (071) 5171856 *E-mail:* info@backhuys. com *Web Site:* www.backhuys.com, pg 474

Francis Bacon Society Inc (United Kingdom) *Tel:* (020) 7359 6888 *Fax:* (020) 7704 1896 *Web Site:* www. sirbacon.org/links/bmembership.htm, pg 1400

Editions de la Baconniere SA (Switzerland) *Tel:* (022) 8690029 *Fax:* (022) 8690015 *E-mail:* DEB@ medecinehygiene.ch, pg 613

Badan Bookstore Sdn Bhd (Malaysia) *Tel:* (07) 2234796; (07) 2377562; (07) 2330241; (07) 330241 *Fax:* (07) 2238188, pg 1316

Badan Penerbit Kristen Gunung Mulia (Indonesia) *Tel:* (021) 3901208 *Fax:* (021) 3901633 *E-mail:* corp. off@bpkgm.com *Web Site:* www.bpkgm.com, pg 350

Badenia Verlag und Druckerei GmbH (Germany) *Tel:* (0721) 95 45-0 *Fax:* (0721) 95 45-125 *E-mail:* verlag@badeniaverlag.de *Web Site:* www. badeniaverlag.badeniaonline.de, pg 196

Badische Landesbibliothek (Germany) *Tel:* (0721) 175-20 01; (0721) 175-22 22 *Fax:* (0721) 175-23 33 *E-mail:* informationszentrum@blb-karlsruhe.de *Web Site:* www.blb-karlsruhe.de, pg 1506

Badischer Landwirtschafts-Verlag GmbH (Germany) *Tel:* (0761) 271330 *Fax:* (0761) 2713372 *E-mail:* redaktion@blv-freiburg.de, pg 196

Buchhandlung G D Baedeker (Germany) *Tel:* (0201) 20680 *Fax:* (0201) 2068-100 *E-mail:* service.gdb. essen@baedeker.de *Web Site:* www.baedeker.de, pg 1300

U Baer Verlag (Switzerland) *Tel:* (01) 3835500 *Fax:* (01) 3836883, pg 613

Barenreiter Verlag Basel AG (Switzerland) *Tel:* (061) 3105-0 *Fax:* (061) 3105-176 *E-mail:* info@ baerenreiter.com *Web Site:* www.baerenreiter.com, pg 613

Buchhandlung Baeschlin (Switzerland) *Tel:* (055) 6401125 *Fax:* (055) 6406594 *E-mail:* office@ baeschlin.ch *Web Site:* www.baeschlin.ch, pg 613

K P Bagchi & Co (India) *Tel:* (033) 267474; (033) 269496 *Fax:* (033) 2482973, pg 326

Baha'i (Italy) *Tel:* (06) 9334334 *Fax:* (06) 9334335 *E-mail:* ceb@bahai.it *Web Site:* www.bahai.it, pg 374

Baha'i Publishing Trust (United Kingdom) *Tel:* (01572) 722780 *Fax:* (01572) 724280 *E-mail:* sales@ bahaibooks.co.uk *Web Site:* www.bahai-publishing-trust.co.uk, pg 658

Baha'i Publishing Trust of India (India) *Tel:* (011) 26819391; (011) 26818990 *Fax:* (011) 26812703 *E-mail:* publisher@bahaindia.org; bptindia@del3. vsnl.net.in; nsaindia@bahaindia.org *Web Site:* www. bahaindia.org, pg 326

Baha'i Verlag GmbH (Germany) *Tel:* (06192) 22921 *Fax:* (06192) 22936 *E-mail:* info@bahai-verlag.de *Web Site:* www.bahaipublishers.org, pg 196

Maison d'Editions Baha'ies ASBL (Belgium) *Tel:* (02) 647 07 49 *Fax:* (02) 646 21 77 *E-mail:* meb@swing. be *Web Site:* www.adeb.irisnet.be, pg 63

Bahnsport Aktuell Verlag GmbH (Germany) *Tel:* (06184) 9233-30 *Fax:* (06184) 9233-50 *E-mail:* mce-aktuell@ mce-online.de, pg 196

Bahrain Centre for Studies, Research Library & Information Dept (Bahrain) *Fax:* (0973) 754678 *E-mail:* bcsr@batelco.com.bh *Web Site:* www.batelco. com.bh/bcsr/, pg 1490

Bahrain Writers & Literators Association (Bahrain), pg 1390

Baifukan Co Ltd (Japan) *Tel:* (03) 3262-5270 *Fax:* (03) 3262-5276 *E-mail:* bfkeigyo@mx7.mesh.ne.jp *Web Site:* www.baifukan.co.jp/, pg 412

Baile del Sol, Colectivo Cultural (Spain) *Tel:* 676438253; 922570196 *E-mail:* baile@idecnet.com *Web Site:* www.bailedelsol.com, pg 569

Bill Bailey Publishers' Representatives (United Kingdom) *Tel.* (01626) 331079 *Fax:* (01626) 331080 *E-mail:* billbailey.pubrep@eclipse.co.uk, pg 658

Bailey Brothers & Swinfen Ltd (United Kingdom) *Tel:* (01797) 366905 *Fax:* (01797) 366638, pg 658

Editions J B Bailliere (France) *Tel:* (01) 55 33 69 00 *Fax:* (01) 55 33 68 07, pg 148

W & G Baird Ltd (United Kingdom) *Tel:* (028) 9446 3911 *Fax:* (028) 9446 6250 *E-mail:* wgbaird@ wgbaird.com *Web Site:* www.wgbaird.org, pg 1173, 1214

Bakalar spol sro (Slovakia) *Tel:* (019) 36258105, pg 554

Baken-Verlag Walter Schnoor (Germany) *Tel:* (04822) 1671; (04192) 1784, pg 197

Bakermat NV (Belgium) *Tel:* (015) 42 05 08 *Fax:* (015) 42 05 73 *E-mail:* info@bakermat.com *Web Site:* www. bakermat.com, pg 63

Bakyoung Publishing Co (Republic of Korea) *Tel:* (02) 7336771 *Fax:* (02) 7364818 *E-mail:* psy@pakyoungsa. co.kr, pg 434

Bal-eon (Republic of Korea) *Tel:* (02) 293546; (02) 293547 *Fax:* (02) 293548, pg 434

Balai Pustaka (Indonesia) *Tel:* (021) 3447003; (021) 3447006 *Fax:* (021) 3446555 *E-mail:* mail@ balaiperaga.com *Web Site:* www.balaiperaga.com, pg 350

Uitgeverij Balans (Netherlands) *Tel:* (020) 524 75 80 *Fax:* (020) 524 75 89 *E-mail:* balans@uitgeverijbalans. nl *Web Site:* www.uitgeverijbalans.nl, pg 475

Balassi Kiado Kft (Hungary) *Tel:* (01) 3518075; (01) 3518343 *E-mail:* balassi@mail.datanet.hu, pg 317

Carmen Balcells Agencia Literaria SA (Spain) *Tel:* (093) 2008565; (093) 2008933 *Fax:* (093) 2007041 *E-mail:* ag-balcells@ag-balcells.com, pg 1126

A A Balkema Uitgevers BV (Netherlands) *Tel:* (0252) 435111 *Fax:* (0252) 435447 *E-mail:* orders@swets.nl *Web Site:* www.balkema.nl, pg 475

Jonathan Ball Publishers (South Africa) *Tel:* (011) 622-2900 *Fax:* (011) 622-7610, pg 558

Editions Balland (France) *Tel:* (01) 43 25 74 40 *Fax:* (01) 46 33 56 21 *E-mail:* info@balland.fr *Web Site:* www.balland.fr, pg 148

Ballinakella Press (Ireland) *Tel:* (061) 927030 *Fax:* (061) 927418 *E-mail:* info@ballinakella.com, pg 355

H R Balmer AG Verlag (Switzerland) *Tel:* (041) 726 9797 *Fax:* (041) 726 9798 *E-mail:* info@buecher-balmer.ch *Web Site:* www.buecher-balmer.ch, pg 613

H R Balmer AG Buchhandlung Verlag Verlagsauslieferung (Switzerland) *Tel:* (041) 726 97 97 *Fax:* (041) 726 97 98 *E-mail:* info@buecher-balmer.ch *Web Site:* www.buecher-balmer.ch, pg 1335

Baltos Lankos (Lithuania) *Tel:* (05) 240 86 73; (05) 240 79 06 *Fax:* (05) 240 74 46 *E-mail:* leidykla@ baltoslankos.lt *Web Site:* www.baltoslankos.lt, pg 445

Staatsbibliothek Bamberg (Germany) *Tel:* (0951) 95503-0 *Fax:* (0951) 95503-145 *E-mail:* info@ staatsbibliothek-bamberg.de *Web Site:* www. staatsbibliothek-bamberg.de, pg 1506

Editorial Banca y Comercio SA de CV (Mexico) *Tel:* (05) 2089692; (05) 2081785; (05) 2081705 *Fax:* (05) 2081803 *E-mail:* ventas@edbyc.com.mx *Web Site:* www.edbyc.com.mx, pg 459

Bancaria Editrice SpA (Italy) *Tel:* (06) 6767222; (06) 6767475 *Fax:* (06) 6767250 *Web Site:* www. bancariaeditrice.it, pg 374

Bandansan (Thailand) *Tel:* (02) 825511, pg 640

Bandicoot Books (Australia) *Tel:* (03) 6267 2530 *Fax:* (03) 6267 1223 *Web Site:* www.bandicootbooks. com, pg 14

Bang Printing Co Inc (United States) *Tel:* 218-829-2877 *Toll Free Tel:* 800-328-0450 *Fax:* 218-829-7145 *Web Site:* www.bangprinting.com, pg 1176, 1229

The Bangalore Printing & Publishing Co Ltd (India) *Tel:* (080) 6709638; (080) 6709027 *Fax:* (080) 6704053 *E-mail:* marketing@bangalorepress.com *Web Site:* www.bangalorepress.com, pg 326

C Bange GmbH & Co KG (Germany) *Tel:* (09274) 94130 *Fax:* (09274) 94132 *E-mail:* service@bange-verlag.de *Web Site:* www.bange-verlag.de, pg 197

Bangladesh Books International Ltd (Bangladesh) *Tel:* (02) 232252 (ext 31); (02) 232229; (02) 256071 (ext 19), pg 1291

Bangladesh Government Press, Ministry of Establishment, Government of the Peoples Republic of Bangladesh (Bangladesh) *Tel:* (02) 606 316 *Fax:* (02) 8113095 *E-mail:* adab@bdonline.com, pg 60

Bangladesh Institute of Development Studies Library (Bangladesh) *Tel:* (02) 9118999 *Fax:* (02) 8113023 *E-mail:* secy10bids@sdnbd.org; chieflib@sdnbd.org *Web Site:* www.bids-bd.org, pg 1491

National Library of Bangladesh, Directorate of Archives & Libraries (Bangladesh) *Tel:* (02) 326572; (02) 318704, pg 1491

National Library of Bangladesh, Directorate of Archives & Libraries (Bangladesh) *Tel:* (02) 326572 *Fax:* (02) 318704 *E-mail:* ifla@ifla.org *Web Site:* www.ifla.org, pg 1558

Bangladesh Publishers (Bangladesh) *Tel:* (02) 233135, pg 60

Bani Mandir, Book-Sellers, Publishers & Educational Suppliers (India) *Tel:* (0361) 520241; (0361) 513886 *E-mail:* utpal@gwl.vsnl.net.in *Web Site:* www. banimandir.cjb.net, pg 326

Bank-Verlag GmbH (Germany) *Tel:* (0221) 54 90-0 *Fax:* (0221) 54 90-120 *E-mail:* bank-verlag@bank-verlag.de *Web Site:* www.bank-verlag.de, pg 197

Bannakhan (Thailand) *Tel:* (02) 227796, pg 640

Bannakit Trading (Thailand) *Tel:* (02) 2825520; (02) 2827537; (02) 2814213 *Fax:* (02) 2820076, pg 640

The Banner of Truth Trust (United Kingdom) *Tel:* (0131) 337 7310 *Fax:* (0131) 346 7484 *E-mail:* info@ banneroftruth.co.uk *Web Site:* www.banneroftruth.co. uk, pg 658

Banson (United Kingdom) *Tel:* (020) 7613 1388 *Fax:* (020) 7729 7870 *E-mail:* banson@ourplanet.com, pg 658

The Banton Press (United Kingdom) *Tel:* (01770) 820231 *Fax:* (01770) 820231 *E-mail:* bantonpress@ btinternet.com *Web Site:* www.bantonpress.co.uk, pg 658

Banyan Tree Book Distributors (Australia) *Tel:* (07) 3279 1877 *Fax:* (07) 3279 2871 *E-mail:* enquiries@ banyantreebooks.com.au; orders@banyantreebooks. com.au *Web Site:* www.banyantreebooks.predelegation. com.au, pg 1287

Dr Richard Bar di animali (Germany) *Tel:* (0911) 951 9490 *Fax:* (0911) 951 9489 *E-mail:* di.animali@web. de *Web Site:* www.zivilist.it, pg 197

Bar Ilan University Central Library (Israel) *Tel:* (03) 5318486 *Fax:* (03) 5349233 *E-mail:* barmae@mail. biu.ac.il *Web Site:* www.biu.ac.il/lib, pg 1517

Bar Ilan University Press (Israel) *Tel:* (03) 5318111 *Fax:* (03) 5353446 *E-mail:* press@mail.biu.ac.il *Web Site:* www.biu.ac.il/Press, pg 362

Editorial Barath SA (Spain) *Tel:* (091) 4496049, pg 569

Baraza la Kiswahili la Taifa (United Republic of Tanzania) *Tel:* (051) 23452; (051) 24139, pg 1139

The Barbados National Trust (Barbados) *Tel:* 246-426-2421 *Fax:* 246-429-9055 *E-mail:* natrust@sunbeach. net *Web Site:* trust.funbarbados.com, pg 1119

Barbianx de Garve (Belgium) *Tel:* (050) 380707 *Fax:* (050) 388099 *E-mail:* info@degarve.be *Web Site:* www.varin.be/degarve, pg 63

B McCall Barbour (United Kingdom) *Tel:* (0131) 2254816 *Fax:* (0131) 2254816, pg 1338

McCall Barbour (United Kingdom) *Tel:* (0131) 225-4816 *Fax:* (0131) 225-4816 *E-mail:* ashbethany43@hotmail. com, pg 658

Editorial Barcanova SA (Spain) *Tel:* (093) 2172054 *Fax:* (093) 2373469 *E-mail:* barcanova@barcanova.es *Web Site:* www.barcanova.es, pg 569

Editorial Barcino SA (Spain) *Tel:* (093) 2186888 *Fax:* (093) 2186888 *E-mail:* ebarcino@ editorialbarcino.com *Web Site:* www.editorialbarcino. com, pg 569

Barcode Graphics Inc (Canada) *Tel:* 905-770-1154 *Toll Free Tel:* 800-263-3669 *Fax:* 905-787-1575 *E-mail:* info@barcodegraphics.com *Web Site:* www. barcodegraphics.com, pg 1165

Hjalmar. R Bardarson (Iceland) *Tel:* 555-0729, pg 322

Bardi Editore srl (Italy) *Tel:* (06) 4817656 *Fax:* (06) 48912574 *E-mail:* bardied@tin.it *Web Site:* www. bardieditore.com, pg 374

Bardon-Chinese Media Agency (Taiwan, Province of China) *Tel:* (02) 33932585 *Fax:* (02) 23929577 *Web Site:* www.bardonchinese.com, pg 1128

Barefoot Books (United Kingdom) *Tel:* (01225) 322400 *Fax:* (01225) 322499 *E-mail:* info@barefootbooks.co. uk *Web Site:* www.barefootbooks.com, pg 658

Barenreiter-Verlag Karl-Votterle GmbH & Co KG (Germany) *Tel:* (0561) 3105-0 *Fax:* (0561) 3105-176 *E-mail:* info@baerenreiter.com *Web Site:* www. baerenreiter.com, pg 197

Bargain Book Sales (United Kingdom) *Tel:* (020) 7385 7007 *Fax:* (020) 7385 7007; (020) 7385 9727, pg 1338

Bargezzi-Verlag AG (Switzerland) *Tel:* (031) 221380; (031) 211434, pg 613

Barkfire Press (New Zealand) *Tel:* (09) 3031039 *Fax:* (09) 3031059 *E-mail:* info@barkfire.com *Web Site:* www.barkfire.com, pg 489

Barmarick Publications (United Kingdom) *Tel:* (01964) 630033 *Fax:* (01964) 631716 *Web Site:* www. barmarick.co.uk, pg 658

Barn Dance Publications Ltd (United Kingdom) *Tel:* (020) 8657 2813 *Fax:* (020) 8651 6080 *E-mail:* barndance@pubs.co.uk *Web Site:* www. barndancepublications.co.uk, pg 658

Barnens Bokklubb (Sweden) *Tel:* (08) 506 304 00 *Fax:* (08) 506 304 01 *E-mail:* redaktionen@ barnensbokklubb.se *Web Site:* www.barnensbokklubb. se, pg 1246

Baronet (Czech Republic) *Tel:* (02) 22310115 *Fax:* (02) 22310118 *E-mail:* baronet.odbyt@volny.cz *Web Site:* www.baronet-knihy.cz; www.baronet.cz, pg 122

Barr Smith Press, University of Adelaide Library (Australia) *Tel:* (08) 8303 5372 *Fax:* (08) 8303 4369 *E-mail:* library-services@library.adelaide.edu.au *Web Site:* www.library.adelaide.edu.au, pg 1488

Barreiro y Ramos SA (Uruguay) *Tel:* (02) 98 66 21 *Fax:* (02) 96 23 58, pg 771

Barreiro y Ramos SA (Uruguay) *Tel:* (02) 96 23 58 *Fax:* (02) 96 23 58, pg 1157

Barreiro y Ramos SA (Uruguay) *Tel:* (02) 986621 *Fax:* (02) 962358, pg 1221

Barreiro y Ramos SA (Uruguay) *Tel:* (02) 96 23 58 *Fax:* (02) 96 23 58, pg 1231, 1240

Barreiro y Ramos SA (Uruguay) *Tel:* (02) 95 01 50 *Fax:* (02) 96 23 58, pg 1346

Barrister & Principal (Czech Republic) *Tel:* (05) 45211015 *Fax:* (05) 45210607 *E-mail:* barrister@ barrister.cz *Web Site:* www.barrister.cz, pg 122

La Bartavelle (France) *Tel:* (04) 77 69 01 50 *Fax:* (04) 77 60 11 94, pg 148

Verlag Dr Albert Bartens KG (Germany) *Tel:* (030) 803 56 78 *Fax:* (030) 803 20 49 *E-mail:* info@bartens.com *Web Site:* www.bartens.com, pg 197

Otto Wilhelm Barth-Verlag KG (Germany) *Tel:* (089) 9271-0 *Fax:* (089) 9271-168, pg 197

Editions A Barthelemy (France) *Tel:* (04) 90 03 60 00 *Fax:* (04) 90036009 *E-mail:* infos@editions-barthelemy.com *Web Site:* www.editions-barthelemy. com, pg 149

Bartkowiaks Forum Book Art (Germany) *Tel:* (040) 2793674 *Fax:* (040) 2704397 *E-mail:* info@ forumbookart.de *Web Site:* www.forumbookart.com, pg 197

Bartleby & Co (Belgium) *Tel:* (02) 538 10 51 *E-mail:* bartleby@skynet.be, pg 63

Bartschi Publishing (Switzerland) *Tel:* (01) 7372518 *Fax:* (01) 7372556, pg 613

BAS Printers Ltd (United Kingdom) *Tel:* (01722) 411711 *Fax:* (01722) 411727 *E-mail:* sales@basprint.co.uk *Web Site:* www.basprint.co.uk, pg 1152, 1173, 1214

Basam Books Oy (Finland) *Tel:* (09) 7579 3839 *Fax:* (09) 7579 3838 *E-mail:* bs@basambooks.com *Web Site:* www.basambooks.com, pg 141

Baseball Magazine-Sha Co Ltd (Japan) *Tel:* (03) 3238-0081 *Fax:* (03) 3238-0106 *Web Site:* www.bbm-japan. com, pg 412

Baseline Creative Ltd (United Kingdom) *Tel:* (0117) 962 0006 *Fax:* (0117) 962 5006 *E-mail:* contact@base.co. uk *Web Site:* www.base.co.uk, pg 1173

Basica Editora (Portugal) *Tel:* (021) 779273, pg 524

Basileia Verlag und Basler Missionsbuchhandlung (Switzerland) *Tel:* (061) 251766 *Fax:* (061) 2688321; (061) 232523, pg 614

Basilisken-Presse Marburg (Germany) *Tel:* 06421 15188, pg 197

Basilius Presse AG (Switzerland) *Tel:* (061) 228004; (061) 228005 *Fax:* (061) 232523, pg 614

BasisDruck Verlag GmbH (Germany) *Tel:* (030) 445 76 80 *Fax:* (030) 445 95 99 *E-mail:* basisdruck@ onlinehome.de *Web Site:* www.basisdruck.de, pg 197

Bassermann Verlag (Germany) *Tel:* (089) 41 360 *E-mail:* vertrieb.verlagsgruppe@randomhouse.de *Web Site:* www.randomhouse.de/bassermann, pg 197

Bastei Luebbe Taschenbuecher (Germany) *Tel:* (02202) 121-293; (02202) 121-544 *Fax:* (02202) 121-927 *E-mail:* bastei.luebbe@luebbe.de *Web Site:* www. luebbe.de, pg 197

Bastei Verlag (Germany) *Tel:* (02202) 121-0 *Fax:* (02202) 121-936 *E-mail:* info@bastei.de *Web Site:* www.bastei.de, pg 197

Bastogi (Italy) *Tel:* (0881) 725070 *Fax:* (0881) 728119 *E-mail:* bastogi@tiscali.it *Web Site:* www.bastogi.it, pg 374

Ediciones Bat (Chile) *Tel:* (02) 2743171 *Fax:* (02) 2250261, pg 98

David Bateman Ltd (New Zealand) *Tel:* (09) 415 7664 *Fax:* (09) 415 8892 *E-mail:* bateman@bateman.co.nz *Web Site:* www.bateman.co.nz, pg 489

The Bath Press (United Kingdom) *Tel:* (01225) 428101 *Fax:* (01225) 312418 *E-mail:* bath@cpi-group.co. uk *Web Site:* www.cpi-group.net/eng/fichebath.htm, pg 1152

The Bath Press (United Kingdom) *Tel:* (01225) 428101 *Fax:* (01225) 312418 *E-mail:* bath@cpi-group.co.uk *Web Site:* www.cpi-group.net, pg 1173, 1237

Batsford Ltd (United Kingdom) *Tel:* (020) 7221 2213; (020) 7314 1469 (sales) *Fax:* (020) 7221 6455; (020) 7314 1594 (sales) *E-mail:* enquiries@chrysalis.com *Web Site:* www.chrysalisbooks.co.uk/books/publisher/ batsford, pg 658

Casa Editrice Luigi Battei (Italy) *Tel:* (0521) 233733 *Fax:* (0521) 231291, pg 374

Battre Ledarskap (Sweden) *Tel:* (08) 690 93 30 *Fax:* (08) 690 93 01; (08) 690 93 02 *E-mail:* kundtjanst. liberab@liber.se *Web Site:* www.battreledarskap.net, pg 1246

Wydawnictwo Baturo (Poland) *Tel:* (033) 81 25 086; (033) 81 40 955; (033) 81 62 703 *Fax:* (033) 81 40 955 *E-mail:* baturo@baturo.com.pl *Web Site:* www. baturo.com.pl, pg 517

Societe Nouvelle Rene Baudouin (France) *Tel:* (01) 43290050 *Fax:* (01) 43257241, pg 149

N E Bauman Moscow State Technical University Publishers (Russian Federation) *Tel:* (095) 263-67-98; (095) 263-60-45; (095) 265-37-97 *Fax:* (095) 265-42-98 *E-mail:* press@bmstu.ru *Web Site:* www.bmstu.ru, pg 539

Baumann GmbH & Co KG (Germany) *Tel:* (09221) 949-0 *Fax:* (09221) 949-378 *E-mail:* info@ bayerische_rundschau.de, pg 197

Dr Wolfgang Baur Verlag Kunst & Alltag (Germany) *Tel:* (08171) 217514 *Fax:* (08171) 217515 *E-mail:* verlag@kunstalltag.de *Web Site:* www. kunstalltag.de, pg 198

Bautz Traugott (Germany) *Tel:* (05521) 57 00; (05521) 55 88 *Fax:* (05521) 16 73; (05521) 57 80 *E-mail:* bautz@bautz.de *Web Site:* www.bautz.de, pg 198

Bauverlag GmbH (Germany) *Tel:* (05241) 802119 *Fax:* (05241) 809582 *E-mail:* info@bauverlag.de *Web Site:* www.bauverlag.de, pg 198

Colin Baxter Photography Ltd (United Kingdom) *Tel:* (01479) 873999 *Fax:* (01479) 873888 *E-mail:* sales@colinbaxter.co.uk *Web Site:* www. colinbaxter.co.uk; www.worldlifelibrary.co.uk, pg 659

Bay Foreign Language Books (United Kingdom) *Tel:* (01233) 720020 *Fax:* (01233) 721272 *E-mail:* sales@baylanguagebooks.co.uk *Web Site:* www.baylanguagebooks.co.uk, pg 1338

Bay View Books Ltd (United Kingdom) *Tel:* (01237) 479225; (01237) 421285 *Fax:* (01237) 421286, pg 659

Bayard Presse (France) *Tel:* (01) 44 35 60 60; (01) 44 35 64 20 *Fax:* (01) 44 35 61 61; (01) 44 35 60 73 *E-mail:* communication@bayard-presse.com *Web Site:* www.bayardpresse.com, pg 149

Bayda Books (Australia) *Tel:* (0613) 9387-2799 *Fax:* (0613) 9387-2799 *Web Site:* www.bayda.com.au, pg 14

Buchhandlung Bayer (Austria) *Tel:* (05522) 74770 *Fax:* (05522) 74770 *E-mail:* bayer.buch@utanet.at, pg 1289

Bayerische Akademie der Wissenschaften (Germany) *Tel:* (089) 23031-0 *Fax:* (089) 23031-100 *E-mail:* info@badw.de *Web Site:* www.badw.de, pg 198

Bayerische Staatsbibliothek (Germany) *Tel:* (089) 28638-0; (089) 28638-2322 *Fax:* (089) 28638-2200 *E-mail:* direktion@bsb-muenchen.de; info@bsb-muenchen.de *Web Site:* www.bsb-muenchen.de, pg 1506

Bayerischer Schulbuch-Verlag GmbH (Germany) *Tel:* (089) 450510 *Fax:* (089) 45051-200 *E-mail:* info@oldenbourg-bsv.de *Web Site:* www. oldenbourg-bsv.de, pg 198

Ebenezer Baylis & Son Ltd (United Kingdom) *Tel:* (01905) 357979 *Fax:* (01905) 354919 *E-mail:* theworks@ebaylis.demon.co.uk, pg 1214

Joycelyn Bayne (Australia) *Tel:* (08) 8356 1748, pg 14

George Bayntun Booksellers (United Kingdom) *Tel:* (01225) 466000 *Fax:* (01225) 482122 *E-mail:* ebc@georgebayntun.com *Web Site:* www. georgebayntun.com, pg 1338

BBC Audiobooks (United Kingdom) *Tel:* (01225) 325336 *Fax:* (01225) 310771 *E-mail:* bbc@ covertocover.co.uk *Web Site:* www.bbcaudiobooks. com, pg 659

BBC English (United Kingdom) *Tel:* (020) 8576 2221 *Fax:* (020) 8576 3040 *Web Site:* www.bbcenglish.com, pg 659

BBC Worldwide Publishers (United Kingdom) *Tel:* (020) 8433 2000 *Fax:* (020) 8749 0538 *E-mail:* bbcsales@ bbc.co.uk *Web Site:* www.bbcworldwide.com, pg 659

BCA - Book Club Associates (United Kingdom) *Tel:* (020) 7760 6500 *Fax:* (020) 7760 6501 *Web Site:* www.bca.co.uk, pg 659

BCM Media Inc (Republic of Korea) *Tel:* (02) 567-0644; (02) 533-0089 *Fax:* (02) 552-9169 *E-mail:* bcmpub@ nuri.net *Web Site:* www.bcm.co.kr, pg 434

BCS Publishing Ltd (United Kingdom) *Tel:* (01869) 324423 *Fax:* (01869) 324385, pg 1152, 1173

be.bra verlag GmbH (Germany) *Tel:* (030) 440 23-810 *Fax:* (030) 440 23-819 *E-mail:* post@bebraverlag.de *Web Site:* www.bebraverlag.de, pg 198

Beaconsfield Publishers Ltd (United Kingdom) *Tel:* (01494) 672118 *Fax:* (01494) 672118 *E-mail:* books@beaconsfield-publishers.co.uk *Web Site:* www.beaconsfield-publishers.co.uk, pg 659

Ruth Bean Publishers (United Kingdom) *Tel:* (01234) 720356 *Fax:* (01234) 720590 *E-mail:* ruthbean@ onetel.net.uk, pg 659

Beas Ediciones SRL (Argentina) *Tel:* (011) 4923-4030; (011) 4924-5337 *Fax:* (011) 4924-0217, pg 3

Beascoa SA Ediciones (Spain) *Tel:* (093) 3660300 *Fax:* (093) 3660449 *E-mail:* info@beascoa.com *Web Site:* www.plaza.es, pg 569

Editions des Beatitudes, Pneumatheque (France) *Tel:* (02) 54 88 21 18 *Fax:* (02) 54 88 97 73 *E-mail:* infos2@ editions-beatitudes.fr *Web Site:* www.editions-beatitudes.fr, pg 149

Beatriz Viterbo Editora (Argentina) *Tel:* (0341) 4487521 *Fax:* (0341) 4261919, pg 3

The Chester Beatty Library (Ireland) *Tel:* (01) 4070750 *Fax:* (01) 4070760 *E-mail:* info@cbl.ie *Web Site:* www.cbl.ie, pg 1517

Beauchesne Editeur (France) *Tel:* (01) 53 10 08 18 *Fax:* (01) 53 10 85 19 *E-mail:* beauchesne2@ wanadoo.fr *Web Site:* www.editions-beauchesne.com, pg 149

Beazer Publishing Company Pty Ltd (Australia) *Tel:* (03) 5156 0556 *Fax:* (03) 5156 0556 *E-mail:* info@beazerpublishing.com *Web Site:* www. beazerpublishing.com, pg 14

Mitchell Beazley (United Kingdom) *Tel:* (020) 7531 8400; (020) 7531 8480 (UK sales); (020) 7531 8481 (special sales); (020) 7531 8479 (marketing); (020) 7531 8488 (publicity); (020) 7531 8482 (export sales); (020) 7531 8484 (foreign rights); (020) 7531 8476 (US sales) *Fax:* (020) 7531 8650 *E-mail:* enquiries@ mitchell-beazley.co.uk *Web Site:* www.mitchell-beazley.com, pg 659

BEBC Distribution (United Kingdom) *Tel:* (01202) 712934 *Fax:* (01202) 712913 *E-mail:* webenquiry@ bebc.co.uk *Web Site:* www.bebc.co.uk, pg 1338

Ludwig Bechauf Verlag (Germany) *Tel:* (05204) 888776 *Fax:* (05204) 888775, pg 198

Bechtermuenz Verlag (Germany) *Tel:* (089) 9271 312 *Fax:* (0821) 70 04-179, pg 198

Bechtle Graphische Betriebe und Verlagsgesellschaft GmbH und Co KG (Germany) *Tel:* (0711) 9310-0, pg 198

Verlag C H Beck oHG (Germany) *Tel:* (089) 38189-0 *Fax:* (089) 38189-402 *E-mail:* kundenservice@beck-shop.de *Web Site:* www.beck.de, pg 198

Edition Monika Beck (Germany) *Tel:* (06848) 72152 *Fax:* (06848) 72159 *E-mail:* info@mathbeck.de *Web Site:* www.mathbeck.de/edmb, pg 198

Barbara Beckett Publishing Pty Ltd (Australia) *Tel:* (02) 93312871 *Fax:* (02) 93603106, pg 14

Bedout Editores SA (Colombia) *Tel:* (04) 5112900 *Fax:* (04) 2517946, pg 110

Bokklubben Bedre Ledelse (Norway) *Tel:* 24051010 *Fax:* 24051099 *E-mail:* post@damm.no *Web Site:* www.dammbokklubb.no, pg 1244

Beerenverlag (Germany) *Tel:* (069) 61009551 *Fax:* (069) 61009560, pg 198

Beginners Publishers (Ghana) *Tel:* (021) 503040 *Fax:* (051) 772642 Attn: Beginners Publishers, pg 300

Beijing Ancient Books Publishing House (China) *Tel:* (010) 2016699 313; (010) 2013122 *Fax:* (010) 2012339 *E-mail:* geo@bph.com.cn, pg 100

Beijing Arts & Crafts Publishing House (China) *Tel:* (010) 65230677; (010) 4031811, pg 101

Beijing Education Publishing House (China) *Tel:* (010) 2016699-268; (010) 62013122 *Fax:* (010) 2012339 *E-mail:* geo@bph.com.cn, pg 101

Beijing Fine Arts & Photography Publishing House (China) *Tel:* (010) 2016699; (010) 62016699-315 *Fax:* (010) 2012339 *E-mail:* geo@bph.com.cn, pg 101

Beijing Juvenile & Children's Books Publishing House (China) *Tel:* (010) 2016699-350; (010) 62013122 *Fax:* (010) 2012339 *E-mail:* geo@bph.com.cn, pg 101

Beijing Medical University Press (China) *Tel:* (010) 62092249 *Fax:* (010) 62029848 *E-mail:* bmupress@ public.fhnet.cn.net *Web Site:* www.bjmu.edu.cn, pg 101

Beijing Publishing House (China) *Tel:* (010) 62003964 *Fax:* (010) 62012339; (010) 62016699 *E-mail:* geo@ bph.com.cn; public@bphg.com.cn *Web Site:* www.bph. com.cn, pg 101

Beijing University Press (China) *Tel:* (010) 62752033 *Fax:* (010) 2564095 *E-mail:* psj@pup.pku.edu.cn, pg 101

Dr Ivanka Beil, Internationale Handelsvermittlung im Medien- und Verlagswesen (Germany) *Tel:* (06201) 14611 *Fax:* (06201) 17280, pg 1121

Library of Beirut Arab University (Lebanon) *Tel:* (01) 300110 *Fax:* (01) 818402 *E-mail:* bau@inco.com.lb *Web Site:* www.bau.edu.lb, pg 1523

Belarus Vydavectva (Belarus) *Tel:* (017) 2 238742 *Fax:* (017) 2 238731, pg 61

Verlag Beleke KG (Germany) *Tel:* (0201) 8130-0 *Fax:* (0201) 8130-108 *E-mail:* info@beleke.de *Web Site:* www.beleke.de, pg 198

Belfast Public Library (United Kingdom) *Tel:* (01232) 243 233 *Fax:* (01232) 332 819, pg 1550

Belforte Editore Libraio srl (Italy) *Tel:* (0586) 210919 *Fax:* (0586) 210349 *E-mail:* belforte@librinformatica. it *Web Site:* www.librinformatica.it, pg 374

Belgian PEN Centre (French-Speaking) (Belgium) *Tel:* (02) 7314847 *Fax:* (02) 7314847 *Web Site:* www. oneworld.org/internatpen/centres.htm, pg 1390

Editions Belin (France) *Tel:* (01) 55 42 84 00 *Fax:* (01) 43 25 18 29 *E-mail:* contact@edition-belin.fr *Web Site:* www.editions-belin.com, pg 149

Belitha Press Ltd (United Kingdom) *Tel:* (020) 7221 2213; (020) 7314 1469 (sales) *Fax:* (020) 7221 6455; (020) 7314 1594 (sales) *E-mail:* enquiries@chrysalis. com *Web Site:* www.chrysalis.co.uk, pg 660

Belize Library Association (Belize) *Tel:* (02) 7267; (02) 34248; (02) 34249 *Fax:* (02) 34246 *Web Site:* www. ambergriscaye.com, pg 1559

Bell & Bain Ltd (United Kingdom) *Tel:* (0141) 649 5697 *Fax:* (0141) 632 8733 *E-mail:* info@bell-bain.demon. co.uk *Web Site:* www.bell-bain.co.uk, pg 1152, 1173

Bell & Bain Ltd (United Kingdom) *Tel:* (0141) 649 5697 *Fax:* (0141) 632 8733 *E-mail:* info@bell-bain.co.uk *Web Site:* www.bell-bain.co.uk, pg 1214

Bell & Bain Ltd (United Kingdom) *Tel:* (0141) 649 5697 *Fax:* (0141) 632 8733 *E-mail:* info@bell-bain.demon. co.uk *Web Site:* www.bell-bain.co.uk, pg 1228

Libreria Bellas Artes (Mexico) *Tel:* (05) 510-2276 *Fax:* (05) 518-3755, pg 1318

Ediciones Bellaterra SA (Spain) *Tel:* (093) 3499786 *Fax:* (093) 3520851 *E-mail:* bellaterra@retermail.es, pg 570

Bellcourt Books (Australia) *Tel:* (03) 5572 1310 *Fax:* (03) 5572 1310 *E-mail:* bellcourt@ansonic.com. au, pg 14

Editions Belle Riviere (Switzerland) *Tel:* (024) 498 40 49 *Fax:* (024) 498 40 46, pg 614

Societe d'Edition Les Belles Lettres (France) *Tel:* (01) 44398420 *Fax:* (01) 45449288 *E-mail:* courrier@ lesbelleslettres.com *Web Site:* www.lesbelleslettres. com, pg 149

Bellew Publishing Co Ltd (United Kingdom) *Tel:* (020) 8673 5611 *Fax:* (020) 8675 2142 *E-mail:* bellewsubs@hotmail.com, pg 660

Biblioteca de la Universidad Catolica 'Andres Bello' (Venezuela) *Tel:* (0212) 4074190 *Web Site:* www.ucab. edu.ve/biblioteca, pg 1553

Editorial Andres Bello/Editorial Juridica de Chile (Chile) *Tel:* (02) 2049900; (02) 4619500 *Fax:* (02) 2253600 *Web Site:* www.editorialjuridica.cl, pg 98

Clubs de Lectores Andres Bello (Chile) *Tel:* (02) 2049900; (02) 2049901 *Fax:* (02) 2253600, pg 1241

Libreria Andres Bello (Chile) *Tel:* (02) 2049900 *Fax:* (02) 2253600, pg 1295

Belaruskaya Encyklapedyya (Belarus) *Tel:* 2840600; 2841767 *Fax:* 2840983, pg 61

Belser GmbH & Co KG - Wissenschaftlicher Dienst (Germany) *Tel:* (07054) 2475 *E-mail:* belser@ compuserve.com, pg 199

Julius Beltz GmbH & Co KG (Germany) *Tel:* (06201) 60070 *E-mail:* info@beltz.de *Web Site:* www.beltz.de, pg 199

BeMa (Italy) *Tel:* (02) 252071 *Fax:* (02) 27000692 *E-mail:* segreteria@bema.it *Web Site:* www.bema.it, pg 374

Bemrose Booth (United Kingdom) *Tel:* (01332) 294242; (01332) 267245 *Fax:* (01332) 295848; (01332) 290367 *Web Site:* www.bemrose.co.uk, pg 1214

Bemust (Bosnia and Herzegovina) *Tel:* (033) 414-050; (061) 173780 *Fax:* (033) 414-050 *E-mail:* bemust@ bih.net.ba, pg 75

Ben & Company Ltd (United Republic of Tanzania) *Tel:* (051) 67407 *Fax:* (511) 12440 *E-mail:* siggers@ pearsoned.ema.com, pg 638

Ben-Gurion University of the Negev Aranne Library (Israel) *Tel:* (08) 6461413 *Fax:* (08) 6472940 *E-mail:* asner@bgumail.bgu.ac.il *Web Site:* www.bgu. ac.il/aranne/, pg 1517

Ben-Zvi Institute (Israel) *Tel:* (02) 5398844; (02) 5398848 *Fax:* (02) 5612329 *E-mail:* mahonzvi@h2. hum.huji.ac.il *Web Site:* www.ybz.org.il, pg 362

Bendel State Library (Nigeria) *Tel:* (052) 200 810, pg 1532

James Bendon Ltd (Cyprus) *Fax:* (025) 632352 *E-mail:* books@jamesbendon.com *Web Site:* www. jamesbendon.com, pg 121

Imprimerie Bene (France) *Tel:* (04) 66294897 *Fax:* (04) 66382146, pg 1144, 1206

Benefit Publishing Co (Hong Kong), pg 312

Benghazi Public Library (Libyan Arab Jamahiriya) *Tel:* (061) 96379, pg 1523

Benin University Bookshop (Nigeria) *Tel:* (052) 600443 *Fax:* (052) 602370 *E-mail:* registra@uniben.edu *Web Site:* www.uniben.edu, pg 1322

Benin University Library (Nigeria) *Tel:* (052) 600443 *Fax:* (052) 602370 *E-mail:* registra@uniben. edu; registra@uniben.edu.ng; library@uniben.edu *Web Site:* www.uniben.edu, pg 1532

Eliane Benisti Literary Agency (France) *Tel:* (01) 42228533 *Fax:* (01) 45441817 *E-mail:* benisti@ elianebenisti.com, pg 1120

Biblioteca Benjamin Franklin (USIS) (Mexico) *Tel:* 5080 2801 (ext 2802 & 2803) *Fax:* (055) 5910075 *E-mail:* garciae@state.gov *Web Site:* www.usembassy-mexico.gov/biblioteca.htm, pg 1527

John Benjamins BV (Netherlands) *Tel:* (020) 6304747 *Fax:* (020) 6739773 *E-mail:* customer.services@ benjamins.nl *Web Site:* www.benjamins.com, pg 475

John Benjamins Publishing Co (Netherlands) *Tel:* (020) 6304747 *Fax:* (020) 6739773 (publishing); (020) 6792956 (antiquariat) *E-mail:* customer.services@ benjamins.nl *Web Site:* www.benjamins.com, pg 1320

Petra Bornhauber Benleo Verlag (Germany) *Tel:* (02271) 4782-0 *Fax:* (02271) 4782-20 *Web Site:* www.benleo. de, pg 199

David Bennett Books (United Kingdom) *Tel:* (020) 7221 2213; (020) 7314 1469 (sales) *Fax:* (020) 7221 6455; (020) 7314 1594 (sales) *E-mail:* enquiries@ chrysalis.com *Web Site:* www.chrysalisbooks.co. uk/childrens/publisher/davidbennett, pg 660

James Bennett Pty Ltd (Australia) *Tel:* (02) 9986 7000 *Fax:* (02) 9986 7031 *E-mail:* customerservice@ bennett.com.au *Web Site:* www.bennett.com.au, pg 1287

Bennetts Bookshop Ltd (New Zealand) *Tel:* (06) 354 6020 *Fax:* (06) 354 6716 *Toll Free Fax:* 0800 118 333 *E-mail:* books@bennetts.co.nz; massey@bennetts.co.nz *Web Site:* www.bennetts.co.nz, pg 1321

E F Benson Society (United Kingdom) *Tel:* (01797) 223114 *E-mail:* info@efbensonsociety.org *Web Site:* www.efbensonsociety.org, pg 1400

Benteli Verlag (Switzerland) *Tel:* (031) 9608484 *Fax:* (031) 9617 *E-mail:* info@benteliverlag.ch *Web Site:* www.benteliverlag.ch, pg 614

John Bentley Book Agencies (New Zealand) *Tel:* (09) 4736920 *Fax:* (09) 4736920 *E-mail:* sjsb@zip.co.nz, pg 1125

Benziger Verlag AG (Switzerland) *Tel:* (01) 2527050 *Fax:* (01) 2624792, pg 614

Beobachter Buchverlag (Switzerland) *Tel:* (01) 043 444 53 07 *Fax:* (01) 043 444 53 09 *E-mail:* buchverlag@ beobachter.ch *Web Site:* www.beobachter.ch, pg 614

Beogradski Izdavacko-Graficki Zavod (Serbia and Montenegro) *Tel:* (011) 650-235; (011) 651-666 *Fax:* (011) 651-841 *Web Site:* www.suc.org/biz/BIGZ/, pg 547

Berchtold Haller Verlag (Switzerland) *Tel:* (031) 3111145 *Fax:* (031) 3112583 *Web Site:* www.egw.ch, pg 614

Berenguer Editorial (Chile), pg 1295

Berg International Editeur (France) *Tel:* (01) 43267273 *Fax:* (01) 46339499, pg 149

Berg Publishers (United Kingdom) *Tel:* (01865) 245104 *Fax:* (01865) 791165 *E-mail:* enquiry@bergpublishers. com *Web Site:* www.bergpublishers.com, pg 660

Bergadis (Greece) *Tel:* 2103614263, pg 303

Bergen offentlige Bibliotek (Norway) *Tel:* 55 56 85 60; 55 56 85 50 *Fax:* 55 56 85 65 *Web Site:* www.bergen. folkebibl.no, pg 1532

Berger-Levrault Editions SAS (France) *Tel:* (03) 83 38 83 83 *Fax:* (03) 83 38 86 10; (03) 83 38 37 12 *E-mail:* ble@berger-levrault.fr *Web Site:* www.berger-levrault.fr, pg 149

Berghahn Books Ltd (United Kingdom) *Tel:* (01865) 250011 *Fax:* (01865) 250056 *E-mail:* info@ berghahnbooks.com *Web Site:* www.berghahnbooks. com, pg 660

Berghs (Sweden) *Tel:* (08) 31 65 59 *Fax:* (08) 32 77 45 *E-mail:* info@berghsforlag.se *Web Site:* www. berghsforlag.se, pg 605

Bergli Books AG (Switzerland) *Tel:* (061) 373 27 77 *Fax:* (061) 373 27 78 *E-mail:* info@bergli.ch *Web Site:* www.bergli.ch, pg 614

Bergmoser & Holler Verlag AG (Germany) *Tel:* (0241) 93888-10 *Fax:* (0241) 93888-134 *E-mail:* kontakt@ buhv.de *Web Site:* www.buhv.de, pg 199

Biblioteca Bergnes de las Casas - Bibioteca de Catalunya (Spain) *Tel:* (093) 270 23 00 *Fax:* (093) 270 23 04 *E-mail:* bustia@bnc.es *Web Site:* www.gencat.es/bc, pg 1543

Bergverlag Rother GmbH (Germany) *Tel:* (089) 608669-0 *Fax:* (089) 608669-69 *E-mail:* bergverlag@rother.de *Web Site:* www.rother.de, pg 199

Beri Publishing (Australia) *Tel:* (03) 9809 1434 *Fax:* (03) 9809 1434 *E-mail:* beripub@ozemail.com. au, pg 14

Berichthaus Verlag, Dr Conrad Ulrich (Switzerland) *Tel:* (01) 2526349 *Fax:* (01) 2526426, pg 614

Berita Publishing Sdn Bhd (Malaysia) *Tel:* (03) 7620 8111 *Fax:* (03) 7620 8026 *Web Site:* www. beritapublishing.com.my, pg 451

Berkeley Brasil Editora Ltda (Brazil) *Tel:* (011) 839-5525 *Fax:* (011) 261-1342 *E-mail:* berkeley@siciliano. com.br, pg 78

The Berlin Agency (Jung-Lindemann & Olechnowitz) (Germany) *Tel:* (030) 88702888 *Fax:* (030) 88702889 *E-mail:* junglindemann@berlinagency.de *Web Site:* www.berlinagency.de, pg 1121

Berliner Debatte Wissenschafts Verlag, GSFP-Gesellschaft fur Sozialwissen-schaftliche Forschung und Publizistik mbH & Co KG (Germany) *Tel:* (030) 44651355 *Fax:* (030) 44651358 *E-mail:* web@ berlinerdebatte.de *Web Site:* www.berlinerdebatte.de, pg 199

Berliner Handpresse Wolfgang Joerg und Erich Schonig (Germany) *Tel:* (030) 6148728; (030) 6142605, pg 199

Berliner Wissenschafts-Verlag GmbH (BWV) (Germany) *Tel:* (030) 84 17 70-0 *Fax:* (030) 84 17 70-21 *E-mail:* bwv@bwv-verlag.de *Web Site:* www.bwv-verlag.de, pg 199

Berlitz (UK) Ltd (United Kingdom) *Tel:* (020) 7611 9640 *Fax:* (020) 7611 9656 *E-mail:* publishing@ berlitz.co.uk *Web Site:* www.berlitz.co.uk; languagecenter.berlitz.com/holborn, pg 660

David Berman Developments Inc (Canada) *Tel:* 613-728-6777 *Fax:* 613-728-2867 *E-mail:* info@timewise.net *Web Site:* www.timewise.net, pg 1165

Bermuda Archives (Bermuda) *Tel:* 295-2007 *Fax:* 295-8751, pg 1492

Bermuda College Library (Bermuda) *Tel:* (0441) 239-4033 *Fax:* (0441) 239-4034 *E-mail:* info@bercol.bm *Web Site:* www.bercol.bm, pg 1492

Bermuda National Library (Bermuda) *Tel:* 295-2905 *Fax:* 292-8443 *E-mail:* libraryinfo@gov.bm *Web Site:* www.bermudanationallibrary.bm, pg 1492

The Bermudian Publishing Co (Bermuda) *Tel:* 295-0695 *Fax:* 295-8616 *E-mail:* info@thebermudian.com *Web Site:* www.thebermudian.com, pg 74

Luigi Bernabo Associates SRL (Italy) *Tel:* (02) 45473700 *Fax:* (02) 45473577 *E-mail:* bernabo.luigi@ tin.it, pg 1123

Bernal Publishing (Australia) *Tel:* (0613) 9808-3775 *Fax:* (0613) 9888-7572 *E-mail:* sales@ bernalpublishing.com *Web Site:* www.bernalpublishing. com, pg 14

Bernan Associates, Div of Kraus Organization, Ltd (United States) *Tel:* 301-459-7666 *Toll Free Tel:* 800-274-4888 (USA); 800-233-0504 (Canada) *Fax:* 301-459-0056 *E-mail:* query@berman.com *Web Site:* www. eurunion.org/publicat/sales.htm, pg 1284

Bernard und Graefe Verlag (Germany) *Tel:* (0228) 64830 *Fax:* (0228) 6483109 *E-mail:* 101336.245@ compuserve.com, pg 199

Bernecker Mediagruppe (Germany) *Tel:* (05661) 731-0 *Fax:* (05661) 731-111 *Web Site:* www.bernecker.de, pg 199

Verlag Alexander Bernhardt (Austria) *Tel:* (05242) 62131-0 *Fax:* (05242) 72801, pg 48

Bibliotheque Bernheim, Bibliotheque territoriale de la Nouvelle-Caledonie (New Caledonia) *Tel:* 24 20 90 *Fax:* 27 65 88 *E-mail:* bibbern@canl.nc *Web Site:* www.bernheim.nc, pg 1530

Beroa-Verlag (Switzerland) *Tel:* (01) 4801313 *Fax:* (01) 4801312, pg 614

Bertello Edizioni (Italy) *Tel:* (0171) 699002 *Fax:* (0171) 697729, pg 374

Bertelsmann AG (Germany) *Tel:* (05241) 80-0 *Fax:* (05421) 80-9662; (05421) 80-9663; (05421) 80-9664 *E-mail:* info@bertelsmann.de *Web Site:* www. bertelsmann.de, pg 1145

C Bertelsmann Verlag GmbH (Germany) *Tel:* (089) 41360; (1805) 990505 (hotline for literature & nonfiction) *Fax:* (089) 4372-2812 *E-mail:* vertrieb. verlagsgruppe@randomhouse.de *Web Site:* www. randomhouse.de, pg 199

Bertelsmann Club (Germany) *Tel:* (05) 415 233 *Fax:* (05) 415 744 *E-mail:* service@derclub.de *Web Site:* www.bertelsmann-club.de, pg 1242

Bertelsmann de Mexico SA (Mexico) *Tel:* (05) 5501620; (05) 5489048, pg 1244

Bertelsmann Distribution GmbH (Germany) *Tel:* (05241) 805 718 *Fax:* (05241) 46970 *Web Site:* www. bertelsmann-distribution.de, pg 1300

Bertelsmann Lexikon Verlag GmbH (Germany) *Tel:* (05241) 802286 *Fax:* (05241) 73075 *E-mail:* info@wissenmediaverlag.de *Web Site:* www. lexiconverlag.de/lexiconverlag.html, pg 199

Verlag Bertelsmann Stiftung (Germany) *Tel:* (05241) 81-81175 *Fax:* (05241) 81-81931 *Web Site:* www. bertelsmann-stiftung.de/verlag, pg 200

W Bertelsmann Verlag GmbH & Co KG (Germany) *Tel:* (0521) 911-01-0 *Fax:* (0521) 911 01-79 *E-mail:* service@wbv.de *Web Site:* www.wbv.de; www.berufsbildung.de; www.berufe.net, pg 200

Robert Berthold Photography (Australia) *Tel:* (02) 9887 3986 *Fax:* (02) 9887 3986, pg 14

Editions Bertout (France) *Tel:* (02) 35 04 69 68 *Fax:* (02) 35 04 69 65 *Web Site:* www.editionsbertout. com, pg 149

Bertrams (United Kingdom) *Tel:* (0870) 4296724 *Fax:* (0870) 4296709 *E-mail:* sales@bertrams.com *Web Site:* www.bertrams.com, pg 1338

Editora Bertrand Brasil Ltda (Brazil) *Tel:* (021) 2585 2000 *Fax:* (021) 2585 2085 *E-mail:* record@record. com.br *Web Site:* www.record.com.br, pg 78

Bertrand Editora Lda (Portugal) *Tel:* (021) 320084 *Fax:* (021) 3468286, pg 524

Editions Bertrand-Lacoste (France) *Tel:* (01) 53 40 53 53 *Fax:* (01) 42 33 82 47 *E-mail:* contact@bertrand-lacoste.fr *Web Site:* www.bertrand-lacoste.fr, pg 149

Sociedades Livreiras Bertrand (Portugal) *Tel:* (021) 0305592 *Fax:* (021) 0305596 *E-mail:* info@bertrand.pt *Web Site:* www.bertrand.pt, pg 1327

Verlag Beruf und Schule Belz KG (Germany) *Tel:* (04821) 40140 *Fax:* (04821) 4941 *E-mail:* info@ vbus.de *Web Site:* www.verlag-beruf-schule.de, pg 200

Berufsverband Information Bibliothek (BIB) (Germany) *Tel:* (07121) 3491-0 *Fax:* (07121) 300433 *E-mail:* mail@bib-info.de *Web Site:* www.bib-info.de, pg 1562

Beta Editorial SA (Spain) *Tel:* (093) 2804640 *Fax:* (093) 2806320, pg 570

Beta Medical Publishers (Greece) *Tel:* 210 6714340; 2106714371 *Fax:* 2106715015 *E-mail:* betamedarts@hol.gr *Web Site:* www. betamedarts.gr, pg 303

Editora Betania S/C (Brazil) *Tel:* (031) 3451-1122 *Fax:* (031) 3451-1638 *E-mail:* betanhdv@prover.com. br *Web Site:* www.editorabetania.com.br, pg 78

Bethania Verlag (Austria) *Tel:* (01) 6672216, pg 48

Editions Medicales Roland Bettex (Switzerland) *Tel:* (022) 7029311 *Fax:* (022) 7029355, pg 614

Annette Betz Verlag im Verlag Carl Ueberreuter (Austria) *Tel:* (01) 40 444-172 *Fax:* (01) 40 444-5 *Web Site:* www.annettebetz.com; www.ueberreuter.at, pg 48

Betzel Verlag GmbH (Germany) *Tel:* (05021) 91 48 69 *Fax:* (05021) 914868 *E-mail:* betzelverlag@ proximedia.de, pg 200

Beust Verlag GmbH (Germany) *Tel:* (089) 230895-0 *Fax:* (089) 230895-131 *E-mail:* mail@beustverlag.de *Web Site:* www.beustverlag.de, pg 200

Beuth Verlag GmbH (Germany) *Tel:* (030) 26010 *Fax:* (030) 26011260 *E-mail:* info@beuth.de *Web Site:* www.beuth.de; www.mybeuth.de, pg 200

The Beyazit State Library (Turkey) *Tel:* (0212) 522 2488 *Fax:* (0212) 526 1133, pg 1549

Editions Beyeler (Switzerland) *Tel:* (061) 235412 *Fax:* (061) 229691, pg 614

Joachim Beyer Verlag (Germany) *Tel:* (09274) 95051 *Fax:* (09274) 95053 *E-mail:* info@beyerverlag.de *Web Site:* www.derschachladen.de, pg 200

Bezalel Academy of Arts & Design (Israel) *Tel:* (02) 589 3333 *Fax:* (02) 582 3094 *E-mail:* mail@bezalel.ac.il *Web Site:* www.bezalel.ac.il, pg 362

Bezerr-Editorae e Distribuidora de Abel Antonio Bezerra (Portugal) *Tel:* (0253) 22604 *Fax:* (0253) 617105, pg 524

De Bezige Bij B V Uitgeverij (Netherlands) *Tel:* (020) 3059810 *Fax:* (020) 3059824 *E-mail:* info@ debezigebij.nl *Web Site:* www.debezigebij.nl, pg 475

BFI Publishing (United Kingdom) *Tel:* (020) 7957 4789 *Fax:* (020) 74367950; (020) 76362516 *E-mail:* publishing@bfi.org.uk *Web Site:* www.bfi.org. uk, pg 660

BBT Bhaktivedanta Book Trust (Sweden) *Tel:* (08) 530 257 72 *E-mail:* p.huy@t-online.de, pg 605

Bharat Law House Pvt Ltd (India) *Tel:* (011) 791 0001; (011) 791 0002; (011) 791 0003 *Fax:* (011) 791 0004 *E-mail:* blh@nda.vsnl.net.in, pg 327

Bharat Publishing House (India) *Tel:* (011) 25757081; (011) 23670067 *Fax:* (011) 23676058 *E-mail:* pitambar@bol.net.in, pg 327

Bharatiya Vidya Bhavan (India) *Tel:* (022) 3631261; (022) 8118261; (022) 8118262 *Fax:* (022) 3630058, pg 327

Bhawan Book Service, Publishers & Distributors (India) *Tel:* 2258836; 271559; 612-67-2506 *Fax:* 265315; 612-67-0010 *E-mail:* bbpdpat@glascl01.vsnl.net.in, pg 327

Mauritius Bhojpuri Institute (Mauritius) *Tel:* 2082956 *Fax:* 4643445, pg 457

Bhratara Karya Aksara (Indonesia) *Tel:* 021 81858, pg 350

Bi-bong Publishing Co (Republic of Korea) *Tel:* (02) 3142-6555 *Fax:* (02) 3142-6556 *E-mail:* beebook@ hitel.net, pg 434

The Bialik Institute (Israel) *Tel:* (02) 6783554; (02) 6797942 *Fax:* (02) 6783706 *E-mail:* bialik@actcom. co.il *Web Site:* www.bialik-publishing.com, pg 362

Bianco (Italy) *Tel:* (06) 8554962 *Fax:* (06) 8844703, pg 374

Bianco Lunos Bogtrykkeri AS (Denmark) *Tel:* (03) 615 3300 *Fax:* (03) 615 3301 *E-mail:* direktionen@aller.dk *Web Site:* www.aller.dk, pg 1166

Bianco Lunos Bogtrykkeri AS (Denmark) *Tel:* 33140781 *Fax:* 33913808, pg 1206

Bianco Lunos Bogtrykkeri AS (Denmark) *Tel:* 36 15 33 00 *Fax:* 36 15 33 01, pg 1225

Bibellesbund Verlag (Switzerland) *Tel:* (052) 245 14 45 *Fax:* (052) 245 14 46 *E-mail:* info@bibellesebund.ch *Web Site:* www.bibellesebund.ch, pg 614

Bible Reading Fellowship (United Kingdom) *Tel:* (01865) 319700 *Fax:* (01865) 319701 *E-mail:* enquiries@brf.org.uk *Web Site:* www.brf.org. uk, pg 661

Bible Society (United Kingdom) *Tel:* (01793) 418100 *Fax:* (01793) 418118 *E-mail:* info@bfbs.org.uk *Web Site:* www.biblesociety.org.uk, pg 661

Bible Society in Australia National Headquarters (Australia) *Tel:* (02) 6248 5188 *Fax:* (02) 6288 6168 *E-mail:* customer.service@bible.org.au; bsadm@bible. com.au *Web Site:* www.biblesociety.com.au, pg 14

Bible Society of Namibia (Namibia) *Tel:* (061) 235090 *Fax:* (061) 228663 *E-mail:* bsn@nambible.org.na *Web Site:* www.biblesociety.org, pg 472

Bible Society of South Africa (South Africa) *Tel:* (021) 421-2040 *Fax:* (021) 419-4846 *E-mail:* biblia@ biblesociety.co.za *Web Site:* www.biblesociety.co.za, pg 558

Biblia Impex Pvt Ltd (India) *Tel:* (011) 23278034; (011) 23262515 *Fax:* (011) 2328-2047 *E-mail:* info@ bibliaimpex.com *Web Site:* www.bibliaimpex.com, pg 327

Biblia Impex Pvt Ltd (India) *Tel:* (011) 327-8034; (011) 326-2515 *Fax:* (011) 328-2047 *E-mail:* info@ bibliaimpex.com *Web Site:* www.bibliaimpex.com, pg 1305

Biblio Verlag (Germany) *Tel:* (05402) 641720 *Fax:* (05402) 641722 *E-mail:* info@militaria-biblio.de *Web Site:* www.militaria-biblio.de, pg 200

Bibliografica Internacional SA (Chile) *Tel:* (02) 6394057 *Fax:* (02) 6397693 *E-mail:* bibliograf@entelchile.net, pg 98

Editrice Bibliografica SpA (Italy) *Tel:* (02) 28315996 *Fax:* (02) 28315906 *E-mail:* bibliografica@ bibliografica.it *Web Site:* www.bibliografica.it, pg 374

Bibliographical Society (United Kingdom) *Tel:* (020) 7611 7244 *Fax:* (020) 7611 8703 *E-mail:* secretary@ bibsoc.org.uk *Web Site:* www.bibsoc.org.uk/bibsoc. htm, pg 1572

Bibliographical Society of Australia & New Zealand (BSANZ) (Australia) *Tel:* (02) 6931 8669 *Fax:* (02) 6931 8669 *E-mail:* rsalmond@pobox.com *Web Site:* www.csu.edu.au/community/BSANZ/, pg 1250

Bibliographical Society of Australia & New Zealand (BSANZ) (Australia) *Tel:* (03) 96699032 *Fax:* (03) 96699032 *Web Site:* www.csu.edu.au/community/ BSANZ, pg 1389

Bibliographical Society of the Philippines (Philippines) *Tel:* (02) 583-252 *Fax:* (02) 502-329 *E-mail:* amb@ nlp.gov.ph *Web Site:* www.nlp.gov.ph, pg 1570

Bibliographisches Institut & F A Brockhaus AG (Germany) *Tel:* (0621) 3901-01 *Fax:* (0621) 3901-3 91 *Web Site:* www.brockhaus.de, pg 200

Bibliographisches Institut & F A Brockhaus AG (Switzerland) *Tel:* (041) 7108375 *Fax:* (041) 7108325 *Web Site:* www.bifab.de, pg 614

Bibliographisches Institut GmbH (Germany) *Tel:* (0341) 97 86-30 *Fax:* (0341) 97 86-5 60 *Web Site:* www. bifab.de, pg 200

Bibliography Institute of the National Library of Latvia (Latvia) *Tel:* (02) 7289874 *Fax:* (02) 7280851 *E-mail:* lnb@com.latnet.lv; lnb@lbi.lnb.lv *Web Site:* www.lnb.lv, pg 441

Bibliomed - Medizinische Verlagsgesellschaft mbH (Germany) *Tel:* (05661) 73440 *Fax:* (05661) 8360 *E-mail:* info@bibliomed.de *Web Site:* www.bibliomed. de, pg 200

Le Bibliophile (The Book Lover) (Haiti), pg 1394

Bibliophile Books (United Kingdom) *Tel:* (020) 7515 9222 *Fax:* (020) 7538 4115 *E-mail:* customercare@ bibliophilebooks.co.uk; orders@bibliophilebooks.co.uk *Web Site:* www.bibliophilebooks.com, pg 1246

Bibliophile Books (United Kingdom) *Tel:* (020) 7515 9222 *Fax:* (020) 7538 4115 *E-mail:* customercare@ bibliophilebooks.com *Web Site:* www.bibliophilebooks. com, pg 1338

Verlag Bibliophile Drucke von Josef Stocker AG (Switzerland) *Tel:* (01) 7404444, pg 614

Bibliopolis - Edizioni di Filosofia e Scienze Srl (Italy) *Tel:* (081) 664606 *Fax:* (081) 7616273 *E-mail:* info@ bibliopolis.it *Web Site:* www.bibliopolis.it, pg 374

Biblioteca Central (Mexico) *Tel:* (0595) 952-15-00 (exts 7111, 4741 & 5440) *Fax:* (0595) 952-15-01 *E-mail:* biblioteca_central@correo.chapingo.mx *Web Site:* www.chapingo.mx, pg 1527

Biblioteca Central de la Universidad de Oriente (Cuba) *Tel:* (022) 633013 *Fax:* (022) 633011 *E-mail:* marcosc@rect.uo.edu.cu *Web Site:* www.uo. edu.cu, pg 1498

Biblioteca Central de la Universidad Nacional de San Agustin (Peru) *Tel:* (054) 229 719 *E-mail:* sisbiblio@ unmsm.edu.pe *Web Site:* sisbib.unmsm.edu.pe/sbweb, pg 1534

Biblioteca Central de la Universidad Nacional Mayor de San Marcos (Peru) *Tel:* (01) 4285210 *Fax:* (01) 4285210 *E-mail:* ogeibl@sanfer.edu.pe, pg 1534

Biblioteca Central de Macau (Macau) *Tel:* 567576; 558049 *Fax:* 318756, pg 1524

Biblioteca Centrala Universitara din Bucuresti (Romania) *Tel:* (021) 313 16 05; (021) 313 16 06 *Fax:* (021) 312 01 08 *Web Site:* www.bcub.ro, pg 1538

Biblioteca Centrale della Regione Siciliana gia Biblioteca Nazionale di Palermo (Italy) *Tel:* (091) 6967642 *Fax:* (091) 6967644 *E-mail:* bcrs@regione.sicilia. it *Web Site:* www.regione.sicilia.it/beniculturali/ bibliotecacentrale, pg 1518

Biblioteca de Mexico (Mexico) *Tel:* (055) 7 09 11 01; (055) 7 09 10 85 *Fax:* (055) 7 09 11 73 *Web Site:* www.cnart.mx/cnca/buena/biblioteca, pg 1527

Biblioteca del Banco Central de la Republica Argentina (Argentina) *Tel:* (011) 4348 3772 *Fax:* (011) 4348 3771 *E-mail:* biblio@bcra.gov.ar *Web Site:* www.bcra. gov.ar, pg 1488

Biblioteca del Congreso (Venezuela) *Tel:* (0212) 5645327 *Fax:* (0212) 5636696, pg 1554

Biblioteca del Congreso Nacional (Bolivia) *Tel:* (02) 354108; (02) 392658 *Fax:* (02) 392402; (02) 341649 *Web Site:* www.congreso.gov.bo, pg 1493

Biblioteca del Congreso Nacional (Chile) *Tel:* (02) 2701700 *Fax:* (02) 2701766 *Web Site:* www.bcn.cl, pg 1495

Biblioteca del Instituto Pre-Universitario de la Habana (Cuba), pg 1498

Biblioteca dell'Universita Nazionale della Somalia (Somalia) *Tel:* (01) 20535, pg 1542

Biblioteca do Ministerio das Relacoes Exteriores (Brazil) *Tel:* (061) 2116359 *Fax:* (061) 2237362 *Web Site:* www.mre.gov.br, pg 1493

Biblioteca Dominicana (Dominican Republic), pg 1501

Biblioteca General de Puerto Rico (Puerto Rico) *Tel:* (787) 722-2299 *Fax:* (787) 724-0470 *E-mail:* biblioteca@icp.gobierno.pr *Web Site:* www. icp.gobierno.pr/bge/index.htm, pg 1537

Biblioteca Geral da Universidade de Coimbra (Portugal) *Tel:* (0239) 859800; (0239) 859900 *Fax:* (0239) 827135 *E-mail:* bguc@uc.pt *Web Site:* www.uc.pt, pg 524

Biblioteca Geral da Universidade de Coimbra (Portugal) *Tel:* (0239) 859800; (0239) 859900; (0239) 859831 *Fax:* (0239) 827135 *E-mail:* bguc@uc.pt *Web Site:* www.uc.pt, pg 1537

Biblioteca Historica Cubana y Americana (Cuba), pg 1498

Biblioteca Medicea Laurenziana (Italy) *Tel:* (055) 210760; (055) 211590; (055) 214443 *Fax:* (055) 2302992 *E-mail:* medicea@unifi.it *Web Site:* www. bml.firenze.sbn.it, pg 1518

Biblioteca Municipal (Mozambique), pg 1528

Biblioteca Municipal Mario de Andrade (Brazil) *Tel:* (011) 3334-0001 *Fax:* (011) 3224-0009 *E-mail:* smc@prodam.pmsp.sp.gov.br *Web Site:* www. prefeitura.sp.gov.br, pg 1493

Biblioteca Nacional (Argentina) *Tel:* (011) 4808-6000 *Fax:* (011) 4806-6157 *E-mail:* bibnal@red.bibnal.edu. ar *Web Site:* www.bibnal.edu.ar, pg 1488

Biblioteca Nacional de Colombia (Colombia) *Tel:* (01) 2431336 *Fax:* (01) 3414030 *E-mail:* bnc@mincultura. gov.co *Web Site:* www.bibliotecanacional.gov.co, pg 1497

Biblioteca Nacional (Costa Rica) *Tel:* 233 1706; 221 2436; 221 2479 *Fax:* 223 5510, pg 1498

Biblioteca Nacional (Dominican Republic) *Tel:* 688-4086; 688-4660 *Fax:* 685-8941 *E-mail:* biblioteca. nacional@dominicana.com *Web Site:* www.bnrd.gov. do, pg 1501

Biblioteca Nacional (El Salvador) *Tel:* 221-6312; 221-4373; 271-5661; 272-2886 *Fax:* 221-8847; 221-4419 *E-mail:* dibiaes@es.com.sv, pg 1502

Biblioteca Nacional (Nicaragua) *Tel:* (02) 897 517 *Fax:* (02) 894 387, pg 1531

Biblioteca Nacional (Peru) *Tel:* (01) 4287690; (01) 4287696 *Fax:* (01) 4277331 *E-mail:* dn@binape.gob. pe *Web Site:* www.binape.gob.pe, pg 511

Biblioteca Nacional (Peru) *Tel:* (01) 428-7690; (01) 428-7696 *Fax:* (01) 427-7331 *E-mail:* sg@binape.gob.pe *Web Site:* www.binape.gob.pe, pg 1535

Biblioteca Nacional (Portugal) *Tel:* (021) 7982000 *Fax:* (021) 7982138 *E-mail:* bn@bn.pt *Web Site:* www.bn.pt, pg 1537

Biblioteca Nacional (Venezuela) *Tel:* (0212) 505 91 25 *Fax:* (0212) 505 91 24 *E-mail:* dir.general@bnv.bib.ve *Web Site:* www.bnv.bib.ve, pg 1554

Biblioteca Nacional Aruba (Aruba) *Tel:* 582-1580 *Fax:* 582-5493 *E-mail:* info@bibliotecanacional.aw *Web Site:* www.bibliotecanacional.aw, pg 1488

Biblioteca Nacional de Angola (Angola) *Tel:* (02) 322 070 *Fax:* (02) 323 979, pg 2

Biblioteca Nacional de Chile (Chile) *Tel:* (02) 3605200; (02) 3605239; (02) 3605275 *Fax:* (02) 6380461; (02) 6381975; (02) 6321091; (02) 6381151 *E-mail:* biblioteca.nacional@bndechile.cl *Web Site:* www.dibam.cl/biblioteca_national, pg 1495

Biblioteca Nacional de Guatemala (Guatemala) *Tel:* (0502) 2322443 *Fax:* (0502) 2539071 *E-mail:* biblioguatemala@intelnett.com *Web Site:* www.biblionet.edu.gt, pg 1511

Biblioteca Nacional de Honduras (Honduras) *Tel:* 228 02 41 *Fax:* 222 85 77 *E-mail:* binah@sdnhon.org.hn; binah@ns.hondunet.net *Web Site:* www.binah.gob.hn, pg 1512

Biblioteca Nacional de Maestros (Argentina) *Tel:* (011) 4129-1272 *Fax:* (011) 4129-1268 *E-mail:* bnmsecre@ me.gov.ar *Web Site:* www.bnm.me.gov.ar, pg 1488

Biblioteca Nacional de Mexico (Mexico) *Tel:* (05) 622 6800 *Fax:* (05) 665 0951 *E-mail:* liceaj@biblional. bibliog.unam.mx *Web Site:* biblional.bibliog.unam.mx, pg 1527

Biblioteca Nacional de Mocambique (Mozambique) *Tel:* (01) 425 676, pg 1528

Biblioteca Nacional del Ecuador (Ecuador) *Tel:* (02) 2528840 *Fax:* (02) 2223391 *E-mail:* benjamincarrion@andinanet.net, pg 1501

Biblioteca Nacional del Uruguay (Uruguay) *Tel:* (02) 48 50 30 *Fax:* (02) 49 69 02 *E-mail:* bibna@adinet.com. uy *Web Site:* www.bibna.gub.uy, pg 1553

Biblioteca Nacional Jose Marti (Cuba) *Tel:* (07) 81 6224 *Fax:* (07) 33 5072, pg 1498

Biblioteca Nationala a Romaniei (Romania) *Tel:* (01) 3157063 *Fax:* (01) 3123381 *E-mail:* go@bibnat.ro, pg 1538

Biblioteca Nazionale Vittorio Emanuele III (Italy) *Tel:* (081) 7819111 *Fax:* (081) 403820 *E-mail:* Emanuele@librari.beniculturali.it *Web Site:* www.bnnonline.it, pg 1518

Biblioteca Nazionale Braidense (Italy) *Tel:* (02) 86460907 *Fax:* (02) 72023910 *E-mail:* info@ braidense.it *Web Site:* www.braidense.it, pg 1518

Biblioteca Nazionale Centrale (Italy) *Tel:* (055) 24919 1 *Fax:* (055) 2342 482 *E-mail:* info@bncf.firenze.sbn.it *Web Site:* www.bncf.firenze.sbn.it, pg 1519

Biblioteca Nazionale Centrale di Roma (Italy) *Tel:* (06) 49891 *Fax:* (06) 4457635 *E-mail:* bncrm@bnc.roma. sbn.it *Web Site:* www.bncrm.librari.beniculturali.it, pg 1519

Biblioteca Nazionale Marciana (Italy) *Tel:* (041) 2407211 *Fax:* (041) 5238803 *E-mail:* biblioteca@ marciana.venezia.sbn.it *Web Site:* www.marciana. venezia.sbn.it/, pg 1519

Biblioteca Nazionale Universitaria (Italy) *Tel:* (011) 8101111 *Fax:* (011) 8121021 *E-mail:* bnto@librari. benicultural.it *Web Site:* www.bnto.librari.beniculturali. it, pg 1519

Editorial Biblioteca Nueva SL (Spain) *Tel:* (091) 3100436 *Fax:* (091) 3198235 *E-mail:* editorial@ bibliotecanueva.com *Web Site:* www.bibliotecanueva. es, pg 570

Biblioteca Popular de Lisboa (Portugal) *Tel:* (021) 346 98 83, pg 1537

Biblioteca Publica de Evora (Portugal) *Tel:* (0266) 769 330 *Fax:* (0266) 769 331 *E-mail:* bpevora@ptnetbiz. pt, pg 1537

Biblioteca Publica do Estado do Rio de Janeiro (Brazil) *Tel:* (021) 2224-6184 *Fax:* (021) 2252-6810 *E-mail:* bibliotecapublica@bperj.rj.gov.br *Web Site:* www.bperj.rj.gov.br, pg 1493

Biblioteca Publica Municipal do Porto (Portugal) *Tel:* (022) 5193480 *Fax:* (022) 5193488 *E-mail:* bpmp@em-porto.pt, pg 524

Biblioteca Publica Municipal do Porto (Portugal) *Tel:* (02) 572147 *Fax:* (022) 5193488, pg 1537

Biblioteca Universitaria (Italy) *Tel:* (059) 222248 *Fax:* (059) 230195 *E-mail:* biblio.estense@cedoc.mo.it *Web Site:* www.cedoc.mo.it/estense, pg 1519

Biblioteca y Archivo Nacional de Bolivia (Bolivia) *Tel:* (04) 6451481; (04) 6452246; (04) 64528864 *Fax:* (04) 6461208 *E-mail:* abnb@mara.scr.entelnet.bo, pg 1493

Biblioteca y Archivo Nacionales (Paraguay), pg 1534

Bibliotech International Pty Ltd (Australia) *Tel:* (03) 9502 3056 *Fax:* (03) 9502 3057 *E-mail:* bibliotech@ bibliotech.com.au *Web Site:* www.bibliotech.com.au, pg 1287

Biblioteka Jagiellonska (Poland) *Tel:* (012) 633 63 77; (012) 634 59 45 (ext 354, 355, 359, 360 & 361); (012) 633 09 03 *Fax:* (012) 633 09 03 *Web Site:* www.bj.uj.edu.pl, pg 1536

Biblioteka Kombetare (Albania) *Tel:* 42 23 843 *Fax:* 42 23 843 *Web Site:* www.monitor.albnet.net/mkrs/ institucionet/biblkomb/bk.htm, pg 1487

Biblioteka Narodowa w Warszawie (Poland) *Tel:* (022) 608-2999; (022) 452-2999 *Fax:* (022) 825-7751 *E-mail:* biblnar@bn.org.pl *Web Site:* www.bn.org.pl, pg 517

Biblioteka Narodowa w Warszawie (Poland) *Tel:* (022) 452-2999 *Fax:* (022) 825-5251 *E-mail:* biblnar@bn. org.pl *Web Site:* www.bn.org.pl, pg 1536

Biblioteka Publiczna m st Warszawy - Biblioteka Glowna Wojewodztwa Mazowieckiego (Poland) *Tel:* (022) 6217852 *Fax:* (022) 6211968 *E-mail:* biblioteka@biblpubl.waw.pl *Web Site:* www. biblpubl.waw.pl, pg 1536

Biblioteka Uniwersytecka w Poznaniu (Poland) *Tel:* (061) 829-3800 *Fax:* (061) 829-3824 *E-mail:* library@amu.edu.pl *Web Site:* lib.amu.edu.pl, pg 1536

Bibliotekarsko Drustvo na Makedonija (The Former Yugoslav Republic of Macedonia) *Tel:* (091) 226846 *Fax:* (091) 232649 *E-mail:* mile@nubsk.edu.mk; bmile47@yahoo.com *Web Site:* www.nubsk.edu.mk, pg 1567

Biblioteksstyrelsen (Denmark) *Tel:* 33 73 33 73 *Fax:* 33 73 33 72 *E-mail:* bs@bs.dk *Web Site:* www.bs.dk, pg 1500

Bibliotekstjaenst AB (Sweden) *Tel:* (046) 18 00 00 *Fax:* (046) 18 01 25 *E-mail:* btj@btj.se *Web Site:* www.btj.se, pg 605

Bibliotheca Bodmeriana (Switzerland) *Tel:* (022) 707 44 33 *Fax:* (022) 707 44 30 *E-mail:* info@ fondationbodmer.ch *Web Site:* www.fondationbodmer. org, pg 1546

Bibliotheek van het Centraal Bureau voor de Statistiek (Netherlands) *Tel:* (070) 337 51 51 *Fax:* (070) 337 59 84 *E-mail:* bibliotheek@cbs.nl *Web Site:* www.cbs.nl, pg 1529

Bibliotheek Wageningen UR (Netherlands) *Tel:* (0317) 484440 *Fax:* (0317) 484761 *E-mail:* helpdesk.library@ wur.nl *Web Site:* library.wur.nl, pg 1529

Bibliotheekvoorziening van de Radboud Universiteitsbibliotheek Nijmegen (Netherlands) *Tel:* (024) 3612428 *Fax:* (024) 3615944 *E-mail:* info@ ubn.kun.nl *Web Site:* www.kun.nl/ubn/, pg 1529

Bibliothek & Information Deutschland (BID) - The Federal Union of German Library & Information Associations (Germany) *Tel:* (030) 39 00 14 80; (030) 39 00 14 81 *Fax:* (030) 39 00 14 84 *E-mail:* bid@ bideutschland.de *Web Site:* www.bideutschland. de/index2.html, pg 1563

Bibliothek der Osterreichischen Akademie der Wissenschaften (Austria) *Tel:* (01) 51581-1262 *Fax:* (01) 51581-400 *E-mail:* webmaster@oeaw.ac.at *Web Site:* www.oeaw. ac.at, pg 1489

Bibliothek des Benediktinerklosters Melk in Niederoesterreich (Austria) *Tel:* (02752) 555-342 *Fax:* (02752) 555-52 *E-mail:* stiftsbibliothek.melk@ nextra.at *Web Site:* www.stiftmelk.at, pg 1489

Bibliothek des Osterreichischen Patentamtes (Austria) *Tel:* (01) 53424 153; (01) 53424 155 *Fax:* (01) 53424 110 *E-mail:* info@patent.bmvit.gv.at *Web Site:* www. patentamt.at, pg 1489

Bibliothek fur Zeitgeschichte/Library of Contemporary History (Germany) *Tel:* (0711) 212-4454; (0711) 212-4424 *Fax:* (0711) 212-4422 *E-mail:* bfz@wlb-stuttgart. de; information@wlb-stuttgart.de *Web Site:* www.wlb-stuttgart.de/bfz, pg 1506

Bibliotheks und Informationssystem der Universitaet Oldenburg (Germany) *Tel:* (0441) 798-2023 *Fax:* (0441) 798-4040 *E-mail:* zi@bis.uni-oldenburg.de *Web Site:* www.bis.uni-oldenburg.de/, pg 1507

Bibliotheque Cantonale et Universitaire de Lausanne (Switzerland) *Tel:* (021) 3167880 *Fax:* (021) 3167870 *Web Site:* www.unil.ch/BCU, pg 1546

Bibliotheque Cantonale et Universitaire (Kantons-und Universitatsbibliothek) (Switzerland) *Tel:* (026) 305 13 33 *Fax:* (026) 305 13 77 *E-mail:* bcu@fr.ch *Web Site:* www.fr.ch/bcu/, pg 1546

Bibliotheque Central du Ministere de l'Education Nationale (Belgium) *Tel:* (02) 511 59 80 *Fax:* (02) 513 43 33, pg 1491

Bibliotheque Centrale de la Cote d'Ivoire (Cote d'Ivoire) *Tel:* 323872, pg 1498

Bibliotheque Centrale du Museum National d'Histoire Naturelle (France) *Tel:* (01) 40 79 36 27 *Fax:* (01) 40 79 36 56 *E-mail:* bcmweb@mnhn.fr *Web Site:* www. mnhn.fr/mnhn/bcm, pg 1504

Bibliotheque Centrale, Universite de Kinshasa (The Democratic Republic of the Congo) *Tel:* (012) 21361; (012) 21362 (ext 320) *E-mail:* centreinfo@ic.cd *Web Site:* unikin.sciences.free.fr, pg 1497

Bibliotheque d'Art et d'Archeologie Jacques Doucet (France) *Tel:* (01) 47037623 *Fax:* (01) 47037630 *E-mail:* bibliotheque@inha.fr *Web Site:* www.paris4. sorbonne.fr, pg 1504

Bibliotheque de l'Institut National de la Recherche Scientifique (Rwanda) *Tel:* 30395 *Fax:* 30939, pg 1539

Bibliotheque de l'Universite Omar Bongo (Gabon) *Tel:* 732956 *Fax:* 734530 *E-mail:* uob@internetgabon. cm *Web Site:* www.uob.ga.refer.org, pg 1506

Bibliotheque de la Ville (Luxembourg) *Tel:* 54 73 83-496 *Fax:* 55 20 37, pg 1524

Bibliotheque de l'Ecole Superieure des Lettres (Lebanon), pg 1523

Bibliotheque de l'Universite Nationale de Cote d'Ivoire (Cote d'Ivoire) *Tel:* 439 000 *Fax:* 44 35 31, pg 1498

Bibliotheque Departemental de Pret (Reunion) *Tel:* 21 03 24 *Fax:* 21 41 30, pg 1538

La Bibliotheque des Arts (France) *Tel:* (01) 46331818 *Fax:* (01) 40469596, pg 149

La Bibliotheque des Arts (Switzerland) *Tel:* (021) 3123667 *Fax:* (021) 3123615 *E-mail:* archinf@ archinform.de *Web Site:* www.archinform.net, pg 614

Bibliotheque des Sciences Medicales (Lebanon) *Tel:* (01) 614001-2 *Fax:* (01) 614054 *E-mail:* csm.biblio@usj. edu.lb *Web Site:* www.biblio-csm.usj.edu.lb, pg 1523

Bibliotheque du Centre Culturel Francais de Bamako (Mali) *Tel:* 222 40 19 *Fax:* 222 58 28 *E-mail:* dir@ ccfbamako.org *Web Site:* www.ccfbko.org.ml, pg 1526

Bibliotheque du Musee Royal de Mariemont (Belgium) *Tel:* (064) 21 21 93 *Fax:* (064) 26 29 24 *E-mail:* info@musee-mariemont.be *Web Site:* www. musee-mariemont.be, pg 1491

Bibliotheque du Petit Seminaire (Haiti), pg 1512

Bibliotheque Fonds Quetelet (Belgium) *Tel:* (02) 277 55 55 *Fax:* (02) 277 55 53 *E-mail:* quetelet@mineco. fgov.be *Web Site:* www.mineco.fgov.be, pg 1491

Bibliotheque Generale et Archives du Maroc (Morocco) *Tel:* (07) 77 18 90; (07) 77 21 52 *Fax:* (07) 77 60 62 *E-mail:* biblio1@onpt.net.ma, pg 1528

Bibliotheque Haitienne des Freres de l'I.C., Saint Louis de Gonzague (Haiti) *Tel:* 2232148; 2237508 *Fax:* 2232029, pg 1512

Bibliotheque Historique de la Ville de Paris (France) *Tel:* (01) 44 59 29 40 *Fax:* (01) 42 74 03 16, pg 1504

Bibliotheque Interuniversitaire de Montpellier (France) *Tel:* (04) 67 13 43 50 *Fax:* (04) 67 13 43 51 *E-mail:* biu.secretariat@univ-montpl.fr *Web Site:* www.biu.univ-montp1.fr, pg 1504

Bibliotheque Municipale (Cote d'Ivoire), pg 1498

Bibliotheque Municipale de Besancon (France) *Tel:* (03) 81878140 *Fax:* (03) 81619877 *E-mail:* bib.etude@besancon.com *Web Site:* www.besancon.com/biblio/francais/, pg 1504

Bibliotheque Municipale de Constantine (Algeria), pg 1487

Bibliotheque Municipale de Grenoble (France) *Tel:* (04) 76 86 21 00 *Fax:* (04) 76 86 21 19 *E-mail:* bm.etude@bm-grenoble.fr *Web Site:* www.bm-grenoble.fr, pg 1504

Bibliotheque Municipale de Lyon (France) *Tel:* (04) 78 62 18 00 *Fax:* (04) 78 62 19 49 *E-mail:* bm@bm-lyon.fr *Web Site:* www.bm-lyon.fr, pg 1504

Bibliotheque Municipale de Rennes (France) *Tel:* (02) 99 63 09 09; (02) 99 87 98 98 *Fax:* (02) 99 36 05 96; (02) 99 87 98 99 *E-mail:* contact@bm-rennes.fr *Web Site:* www.bm-rennes.fr, pg 1504

Bibliotheque Nationale (Cote d'Ivoire) *Tel:* 32 38 72, pg 1498

Bibliotheque Nationale (Guinea) *Tel:* (01) 461 010, pg 1512

Bibliotheque Nationale (Mali) *Tel:* 22 49 63 *Fax:* 23 59 31 *E-mail:* info@culture.gov.ml *Web Site:* w3.culture.gov.ml, pg 1526

Bibliotheque Nationale (Mauritania) *Tel:* 24 35, pg 1526

Bibliotheque Nationale (Togo) *Tel:* 21 63 67; 21 04 10; 22 21 16 *Fax:* 22 19 67, pg 1549

Bibliotheque Nationale (Tunisia) *Tel:* 71245338 *Fax:* 71342700, pg 1549

Bibliotheque Nationale d'Algerie (Algeria) *Tel:* (021) 671967; (021) 675781; (021) 671867 *Fax:* (021) 672999, pg 1249

Bibliotheque Nationale d'Algerie (Algeria) *Tel:* (021) 679544; (021) 675781 *Fax:* (021) 682300 *E-mail:* contact@biblionat.dz *Web Site:* www.biblionat.dz, pg 1487

Bibliotheque Nationale de France (France) *Tel:* (01) 53 79 59 59; (01) 53 79 81 75; (01) 53 79 87 94 *Fax:* (01) 53 79 81 72 *E-mail:* commercial@bnf.fr *Web Site:* www.bnf.fr, pg 149

Bibliotheque Nationale de France (France) *Tel:* (01) 53 79 59 59 *Fax:* (01) 47 03 77 34 *Web Site:* www.bnf.fr, pg 1505

Bibliotheque nationale de Luxembourg (Luxembourg) *Tel:* 22 97 55-1 *Fax:* 47 56 72 *E-mail:* bib.nat@bi.etat.lu *Web Site:* www.bnl.lu, pg 1524

Bibliotheque Nationale d'Haiti (Haiti) *Tel:* 220 236; 220 198 *Fax:* 238 773, pg 1512

Bibliotheque Nationale du Benin (Benin) *Tel:* 22 25 85 *E-mail:* bn.benin@bj.refer.org *Web Site:* www.bj.refer.org/benin_ct/tur/bnb/Pagetitre.htm, pg 1492

Bibliotheque Nationale du Burundi (Burundi) *Tel:* (02) 25051 *Fax:* (02) 26231 *E-mail:* biefbdi@cbinf.com, pg 1495

Bibliotheque Nationale et Universitaire de Strasbourg (France) *Tel:* (03) 88 25 28 00 *Fax:* (03) 88 25 28 03 *E-mail:* contact@bnu.fr *Web Site:* www-bnus.u-strasbg.fr, pg 1505

Bibliotheque Publique (Burundi), pg 1495

Bibliotheque Publique de Kinshasa (The Democratic Republic of the Congo) *Tel:* (012) 3070, pg 1497

Bibliotheque Publique et Universitaire de Geneve (Switzerland) *Tel:* (022) 418 28 00 *Fax:* (022) 418 28 01 *E-mail:* info.bpu@ville-ge.ch *Web Site:* www.ville-ge.ch/bpu/, pg 1546

Bibliotheque Publique et Universitaire de Neuchatel (Switzerland) *Tel:* (032) 717-73-02; (032) 717 73 20 *Fax:* (032) 717-73-09 *Web Site:* bpun.unine.ch, pg 1546

Bibliotheque Royale Albert Ier (Belgium) *Tel:* (02) 519 53 11 *Fax:* (02) 519 55 33 *E-mail:* contacts@kbr.be *Web Site:* www.kbr.be, pg 1491

Bibliotheque Universitaire Centrale (Benin) *Tel:* 36 01 01 *Fax.* 34 06 42 *E-mail:* bu_unb@bj.refer.org, pg 1492

Bibliotheque Universitaire Centrale (BUC) (Algeria) *Tel:* (031) 61-42-05 *Fax:* (031) 61-21-90 *E-mail:* bucne@hotmail.com *Web Site:* www.buc-constantine.edu.dz, pg 1487

Bibliotheque Universitaire d'Antananarivo (Madagascar) *Tel:* (020) 22 612 28 *Fax:* (020) 22 612 29 *E-mail:* bu@univ-antananarivo.mg *Web Site:* www.univ-antananarivo.mg, pg 1524

Bibliotheque Universitaire Droit-Sciences Economiques (France) *Tel:* (03) 83 30 81 57 *Fax:* (03) 83 30 82 38 *Web Site:* www.univ-nancy2.fr/webbib/webbib/budroit.html, pg 1505

Bibliotheque Universitaire, Universite Marien Ngouabi (Congo) *Tel:* 814207; 812436 *Fax:* 814207 *E-mail:* unmgbuco@congonet.cg, pg 1497

Bibliotheques de l'Universite Libre de Bruxelles (Belgium) *Tel:* (02) 650 36 63 *Fax:* (02) 650 20 07 *E-mail:* mdesb@ulb.ac *Web Site:* www.bib.ulb.ac.be/, pg 1491

Societe Biblique Francaise (France) *Tel:* (01) 39945051 *Fax:* (01) 39905351 *E-mail:* contacts@alliance-biblique-fr.org *Web Site:* www.la-bible.net, pg 149

Biblos srl (Italy) *Tel:* (049) 5975236 *Fax:* (049) 9409875 *E-mail:* info@biblos.it *Web Site:* www.biblos.it, pg 374

Biddles Ltd (United Kingdom) *Tel:* (01553) 764 728 *Fax:* (01553) 764 633 *E-mail:* enquiries@biddles.co.uk *Web Site:* www.biddles.co.uk, pg 1152

Biddles Ltd (United Kingdom) *Tel:* (01553) 764 728 *Fax:* (01553) 764 633 *E-mail:* enquiries@biddles.co.uk *Web Site:* www.biddlesbooks.co.uk, pg 1214

Biddles Ltd (United Kingdom) *Tel:* (01553) 764 728 *Fax:* (01553) 764 633 *E-mail:* sales@biddles.co.uk; enquiries@biddles.co.uk *Web Site:* www.biddles.co.uk, pg 1228

Joseph Biddulph Publisher (United Kingdom) *Tel:* (01443) 662559, pg 661

Der Baum Wolfgang Biedermann Verlag (Austria) *Tel:* (01) 526 2720, pg 48

Bielefelder Verlagsanstalt GmbH & Co KG Richard Kaselowsky (Germany) *Tel:* (0521) 595 514 *Fax:* (0521) 595 518 *E-mail:* kontakt@bva-bielefeld.de *Web Site:* www.bva-bielefeld.de, pg 201

Bierman og Bierman I/S (Denmark) *Tel:* 75 32 02 88 *Fax:* 75 32 15 48 *E-mail:* mail@bierman.dk *Web Site:* www.bierman.dk, pg 129

Biermann Verlag GmbH (Germany) *Tel:* (02236) 376-0 *Fax:* (02236) 376-999 *E-mail:* info@biermann.net *Web Site:* www.biermann-online.de, pg 201

Bifrost hf Bokaforlag, Bokaklubbur Birtings (Iceland) *Tel:* 562-7700 *Fax:* 562-7710, pg 322

Big Apple Tuttle-Mori Agency Inc (Taiwan, Province of China) *Tel:* (02) 8990-1238 *Fax:* (02) 8990-1129 *E-mail:* bigapple1@worldnet.att.net *Web Site:* www.bigapple1.info, pg 1128

Big Balloon BV (Netherlands) *Tel:* (023) 5176620 *Fax:* (023) 5176630 *E-mail:* info@bigballoon.nl *Web Site:* www.bigballoon.nl, pg 475

Big Database Publishing Pvt Ltd (India), pg 327

Big Tree Publishing (Republic of Korea) *Tel:* (031) 290-7802 *Fax:* (031) 290-7891 *E-mail:* khkang@skku.ac.kr, pg 434

The Big Word (United Kingdom) *Tel:* (0870) 748 8000 *Fax:* (0870) 748 8001 *E-mail:* production@thebigword.com *Web Site:* www.thebigword.com, pg 1140

Bihar Hindi Granth Akademi (India) *Tel:* (0612) 50390, pg 327

Erven J Bijleveld (Netherlands) *Tel:* (030) 2310800 *Fax:* (030) 2311774 *E-mail:* info@bijleveldbooks.nl *Web Site:* www.bijleveldbooks.nl, pg 475

Bijutsu Shuppan-Sha, Ltd (Japan) *Tel:* (03) 32342159 *Fax:* (03) 32349451 *E-mail:* shoseki@bijutsu.co.jp; artmedia@bijutsu.co.jp *Web Site:* www.bijutsu.co.jp, pg 412

Bilal Muslim Mission of Tanzania (United Republic of Tanzania) *Tel:* (051) 30345; (051) 50924 *Fax:* 2116550 *E-mail:* bilal@raha.com, pg 638

Bilblioteka Nov den - Sajuz na Svobodnite Demokrati (Union of Free Democrats) (Bulgaria) *Tel:* (02) 773982; (02) 9814280 *Fax:* (02) 327972, pg 93

BILD Publications (United Kingdom) *Tel:* (01562) 723010 *Fax:* (01562) 723029 *E-mail:* enquiries@bild.org.uk *Web Site:* www.bild.org.uk, pg 661

Bild und Heimat Verlagsgesellschaft GmbH (Germany) *Tel:* (03765) 78 15-0 *Fax:* (03765) 1 22 45, pg 201

Bildarchiv Preussischer Kulturbesitz bpk (Germany) *Tel:* (030) 278 792 0 *Fax:* (030) 278 792 39 *E-mail:* bildarchiv@bpk.spk-berlin.de *Web Site:* www.bildarchiv-bpk.de, pg 201

Bilden Bilgisayar (Turkey) *Tel:* (0216) 449 52 50 *Fax:* (0216) 449 52 51 *E-mail:* bilden@bilden.com.tr *Web Site:* www.bilden.com.tr, pg 645

BW Bildung und Wissen Verlag und Software GmbH (Germany) *Tel:* (0911) 96 76-175 *Fax:* (0911) 96 76-189 *E-mail:* info@bwverlag.de *Web Site:* www.bwverlag.de, pg 201

Bilkent University Library (Turkey) *Tel:* (0312) 2664472 *Fax:* (0312) 2664391 *Web Site:* library.bilkent.edu.tr, pg 1549

Bina Aksara Parta (Indonesia) *Tel:* (361) 95240, pg 350

Bina Cipta PT (Indonesia) *Tel:* (022) 2504319 *Fax:* (022) 2504319, pg 350

Bina Ilmu (Indonesia) *Tel:* (031) 5323214; (031) 5340076 *Fax:* (031) 5315421, pg 350

Bina Rena Pariwara (Indonesia) *Tel:* (021) 7901938 *Fax:* (021) 7901939, pg 350

Bind-It Corp (United States) *Tel:* 631-234-2500 *Toll Free Tel:* 800-645-5110 *Web Site:* www.bindit.com, pg 1217

Bindernagelsche Buchhandlung (Germany) *Tel:* (06031) 7323-0 *Fax:* (06031) 734949, pg 201

Guy Binsfeld & Co Sarl (Luxembourg) *Tel:* 49 68 68-1 *Fax:* 40 76 09; 48 87 70 *E-mail:* editions@binsfeld.lu *Web Site:* www.editionsguybinsfeld.lu, pg 447

Bio Concepts Publishing (Australia) *Tel:* (07) 3868 0699 *Fax:* (07) 3868 0600 *E-mail:* info@bioconcepts.com.au *Web Site:* www.bioconcepts.com.au, pg 14

Biblioteca Bio-Medica del Laboratorio Conmemorativo Gorgas (Panama) *Tel:* (02) 274111 *Fax:* (02) 254366 *E-mail:* igorgas@sin.fonet, pg 1534

Biocommerce Data Ltd (United Kingdom) *Tel:* (020) 8332 4660 *Fax:* (020) 8332 4666 *E-mail:* biocom@pjbpubs.com; custserv@biocom.com (orders) *Web Site:* www.pjbpubs.com/bcd, pg 661

Editoriale Bios (Italy) *Tel:* (0984) 854149 *Fax:* (0984) 854038 *E-mail:* info@edibios.it *Web Site:* www.edibios.it, pg 374

BIOS Scientific Publishers Ltd (United Kingdom) *Tel:* (01235) 828600 *Fax:* (01235) 829011 *E-mail:* sales@bios.co.uk *Web Site:* www.bios.co.uk, pg 661

Editorial Biosfera CA (Venezuela) *Tel:* (0212) 751 9119; (0212) 753 8892 *Fax:* (0212) 751 9320, pg 774

BIR Publishing Co (Republic of Korea) *Tel:* (02) 3443-4318; (02) 3443-4319 *Fax:* (02) 3442-4661 *Web Site:* www.bir.co.kr, pg 434

Biramo Book Distributors (Australia) *Tel:* (02) 49542626 *Fax:* (02) 49565398 *E-mail:* biramobooks@tpg.com. au, pg 1288

Birchalls (Australia) *Tel:* (03) 63313011 *Toll Free Tel:* 800 806867 *Fax:* (03) 63317165 *E-mail:* enquiry@birchalls.com.au *Web Site:* www. birchalls.com.au, pg 1288

Birchgrove Books (Australia) *Tel:* (02) 9810 5040 *Fax:* (02) 9810 6040 *E-mail:* 100406.343@ compuserve.com, pg 14

Birkhauser Verlag AG (Switzerland) *Tel:* (061) 2050707 *Fax:* (061) 2050799 *E-mail:* info@birkhauser.ch; sales@birkhauser.ch *Web Site:* www.birkhauser.ch, pg 614

Birkner & Co Zweigniederlassung Mecklenburg-Vorpommern (Germany) *Tel:* (040) 85308502 *Fax:* (040) 85308381, pg 201

Birlinn Ltd (United Kingdom) *Tel:* (0131) 668 4371 *Fax:* (0131) 668 4466 *E-mail:* info@birlinn.co.uk *Web Site:* www.birlinn.co.uk, pg 661

Birmingham Books (United Kingdom) *Tel:* (0121) 235 2868; (0121) 235 4511 *Fax:* (0121) 233 9702; (0121) 233 4458, pg 661

Birmingham Library Information Services (United Kingdom) *Tel:* (0121) 414 5817 *Fax:* (0121) 471 4691 *E-mail:* library@bham.ac.uk *Web Site:* www.is.bham. ac.uk, pg 661

Birmingham Library Information Services (United Kingdom) *Tel:* (0121) 414 5828 *Fax:* (0121) 471 4691 *E-mail:* library@bham.ac.uk *Web Site:* www.is.bham. ac.uk/mainlib, pg 1550

Birmingham Museums & Art Gallery (United Kingdom) *Tel:* (0121) 303 2834; (0121) 303 1966; (0121) 464 9885 (shop) *Fax:* (0121) 303 1394 *E-mail:* info@ bmagshop.co.uk *Web Site:* www.bmag.org.uk; www. bmagshop.co.uk, pg 1338

Adam Biro Editions (France) *Tel:* (01) 44 59 84 59 *Fax:* (01) 44 59 87 17 *E-mail:* edibiro@freesurf.fr, pg 150

Biro Penyediaan Teks Itm (Biroteks) (Malaysia) *Tel:* (03) 55164548 *Fax:* (03) 55163453, pg 451

Biro Pusat Statistik (Indonesia) *Tel:* (021) 3507057 *Fax:* (021) 3857046 *E-mail:* bpsha@bps.go.id *Web Site:* www.bps.go.id, pg 351

Birsen Yayinevi (Turkey) *Tel:* (0212) 5278578; (0212) 5220829 *Fax:* (0212) 5270895 *Web Site:* www. geocities.com/birsen2us; www.birsenyayin.com, pg 645

BIS Publishers (Netherlands) *Tel:* (020) 524 75 60 *Fax:* (020) 524 75 57 *E-mail:* bis@bispublishers.nl *Web Site:* www.bispublishers.nl, pg 475

Bishopsgate Press Ltd (United Kingdom) *Tel:* (01732) 833778 *Fax:* (01732) 833090, pg 661

Bitan Publishers Ltd (Israel) *Tel:* (03) 6040089; (054) 664575 *Fax:* (03) 5404792, pg 362

BKV-Brasilienkunde Verlag GmbH (Germany) *Tel:* (05452) 4598 *Fax:* (05452) 4357 *E-mail:* brasilien@T-Online.de *Web Site:* www. brasilienkunde.de, pg 201

BLA Publishing Ltd (United Kingdom) *Tel:* (01342) 318980 *Fax:* (01342) 410980, pg 661

A & C Black Publishers Ltd (United Kingdom) *Tel:* (020) 7758 0200 *Fax:* (020) 7758 0222 *E-mail:* enquiries@acblack.co.uk *Web Site:* www. acblack.co.uk, pg 662

Black Academy Press (Nigeria) *Tel:* (083) 230606; (083) 232606, pg 499

Black Ace Books (United Kingdom) *Tel:* (01307) 465096 *Fax:* (01307) 465494 *Web Site:* www. blackacebooks.com, pg 662

Black Bear Press Ltd (United Kingdom) *Tel:* (01223) 424571 *Fax:* (01223) 426877 *E-mail:* enquiries@ black-bear-press.com *Web Site:* www.black-bear-press. com, pg 1173, 1214

Black Dog Books (Australia) *Tel:* (03) 9419 9406 *Fax:* (03) 9419 1214 *E-mail:* dog@bdb.com.au *Web Site:* www.bdb.com.au, pg 14

Black Mask Ltd (Ghana) *Tel:* (021) 500178 *Fax:* (021) 667701 *E-mail:* balme@ug.gn.apc.org, pg 300

Black Spring Press Ltd (United Kingdom) *Tel:* (020) 7613 3066 *Fax:* (020) 7613 0028 *E-mail:* blackspring@dexterhaven.demon.co.uk, pg 662

Blackbooks Co-operative for Aborigines Ltd (Australia) *Tel:* (0612) 9660 2396 *Fax:* (0612) 9660 1924 *E-mail:* tranby@tranby.com.au *Web Site:* www.tranby. com.au, pg 14

Blackie Children's Books (United Kingdom) *Tel:* (020) 7010 3000 *Fax:* (020) 7010 6060, pg 662

Blackmore Ltd (United Kingdom) *Tel:* (01747) 853034 *Fax:* (01747) 854500 *E-mail:* sales@blackmore.co.uk *Web Site:* www.blackmore.co.uk, pg 1173, 1214

Blackmore's Booksellers BLA (New Zealand) *Tel:* (03) 5489992 *Fax:* (03) 5466779, pg 1321

Blackstaff Press (United Kingdom) *Tel:* (028) 9045 5006 *Fax:* (028) 9046 6237 *E-mail:* info@blackstaffpress. com *Web Site:* www.blackstaffpress.com, pg 662

Blackstone Press Pty Ltd (Australia) *Tel:* (02) 9389 7677 *Fax:* c.l.e.@laams.com.au, pg 14

Blackwell & Hadwiger GesmbH British Bookshop (Austria) *Tel:* (01) 5121945; (01) 5132933 *Fax:* (01) 5121026 *E-mail:* britbook@netway.at, pg 1290

Blackwell Publishing Asia (Australia) *Tel:* (03) 8359 1011 *Fax:* (03) 8359 1120 *E-mail:* info@ blackwellpublishingasia.com.au *Web Site:* www. blacksci.co.uk, pg 14

Blackwell Publishing Ltd (United Kingdom) *Tel:* (01865) 791100 *Fax:* (01865) 791347 *Web Site:* www. blackwellpublishers.co.uk, pg 662

Blackwell Retail (United Kingdom) *Tel:* (01865) 792792 *Fax:* (01865) 794143 *E-mail:* mail@blackwell.co.uk *Web Site:* www.blackwell.co.uk, pg 1338

Blackwell Science Ltd (United Kingdom) *Tel:* (01865) 206206 *Fax:* (01865) 721205 *E-mail:* shona. macdonald@blacksci.co.uk, pg 662

Blackwell Wissenschafts-Verlag GmbH (Germany) *Tel:* (030) 32 79 06-0 *Fax:* (030) 32 79 06-10 *E-mail:* verlag@blackwell.de *Web Site:* www.blackwis. de, pg 201

Bladkompaniet A/S (Norway) *Tel:* 24 14 68 00 *Fax:* 24 14 68 01 *E-mail:* bladkompaniet@bladkompaniet.no *Web Site:* www.bladkompaniet.no, pg 504

Horst Blaich Pty Ltd (Australia) *Tel:* (03) 9720 2658 *Fax:* (03) 9762 4225, pg 15

Joan Blair (Australia) *Tel:* (02) 4232 1642, pg 15

John Blake Publishing Ltd (United Kingdom) *Tel:* (020) 7381 0666 *Fax:* (020) 7381 0626 *E-mail:* words@ blake.co.uk *Web Site:* www.blake.co.uk, pg 663

William Blake & Co (France) *Tel:* (05) 56 31 42 20 *Fax:* (05) 56 31 45 47 *E-mail:* editions.william. blake@wanadoo.fr *Web Site:* www.editions-william-blake-and-co.com, pg 150

Blaketon Hall Ltd (United Kingdom) *Tel:* (01392) 210 602 *Fax:* (01392) 421 165 *E-mail:* sales@blaketonhall. co.uk *Web Site:* www.blaketonhall.co.uk, pg 663

Editions Gerard Blanchart & Cie SA (Belgium) *Tel:* (02) 4783706 *Fax:* (02) 4786429, pg 63

Editions Blanco SA (Belgium) *Tel:* (02) 7720320 *Fax:* (02) 7706429, pg 63

Blandford Publishing Ltd (United Kingdom) *Tel:* (020) 7420 5555, pg 663

Blanvalet Verlag GmbH (Germany) *Tel:* (089) 41360; (089) 990505 (literature hotline) *Fax:* (089) 4372-2812 *E-mail:* vertrieb.verlagsgruppe@randomhouse.de *Web Site:* www.blanvalet-verlag.de, pg 201

Verlag Die Blaue Eule (Germany) *Tel:* (0201) 8 77 69 63 *Fax:* (0201) 8 77 69 64 *E-mail:* info@die-blaue-eule.de *Web Site:* www.die-blaue-eule.de, pg 201

Blaukreuz-Verlag Bern (Switzerland) *Tel:* (031) 300 58 60 *Fax:* (031) 300 58 69 *E-mail:* ifbc.bern@bluewin. ch *Web Site:* www.blaueskreuz.ch, pg 615

Blaukreuz-Verlag Wuppertal (Germany) *Tel:* (0202) 6200370 *Fax:* (0202) 6200381 *E-mail:* bkv@ blaukreuz.de *Web Site:* www.blaukreuz.de, pg 201

Blay Foldex (France) *Tel:* (01) 49 88 92 10 *Fax:* (01) 49 88 92 09, pg 150

Blazek und Bergmann (Germany) *Tel:* (069) 152003-0 *Fax:* (069) 152003-44 *E-mail:* info@blazek-und-bergmann.de *Web Site:* www.blazek-und-bergmann.de, pg 1300

Bleicher Verlag GmbH (Germany) *Tel:* (07156) 43 08-0 *Fax:* (07156) 43 08-27 *E-mail:* info@bleicher-verlag. de *Web Site:* www.bleicher-verlag.de, pg 202

BLIC, russko-Baltijskij informaciionnyj centr, AO (Russian Federation) *Tel:* (0812) 3112252 *Fax:* (0812) 3112252; (0812) 1135896 *E-mail:* blitz@blitz.spb.ru, pg 539

Blitzprint Inc (Canada) *Tel:* 403-253-5151 *Toll Free Tel:* 866-479-3248 *Fax:* 403-253-5642 *E-mail:* blitzprint@blitzprint.com *Web Site:* www. blitzprint.com, pg 1205

Bloch Editores SA (Brazil) *Tel:* (021) 555-4167 *Fax:* (021) 555-4069 *E-mail:* blocheditores@ieg.com. br, pg 78

Blockfoil Ltd (United Kingdom) *Tel:* (01473) 721701 *Fax:* (01473) 270705 *E-mail:* info@blockfoil.com *Web Site:* www.blockfoil.com, pg 1214

Bloemfontein Public Library (South Africa) *Tel:* (051) 405 8248 *Fax:* (051) 405 8604 *E-mail:* pat@dux. bfncouncil.co.za, pg 1542

H W Blok Uitgeverij BV (Netherlands) *Tel:* (020) 5159222 *Fax:* (020) 5159100, pg 475

Blondel La Rougery SARL (France) *Tel:* (01) 48 94 94 52 *Fax:* (01) 48 94 94 38, pg 150

Bloodaxe Books Ltd (United Kingdom) *Tel:* (01434) 240 500 *Fax:* (01434) 240 505 *E-mail:* editor@ bloodaxebooks.demon.co.uk *Web Site:* www. bloodaxebooks.com, pg 663

Roy Bloom Ltd (United Kingdom) *Tel:* (020) 7729 5373 *Fax:* (020) 7729 2375 *E-mail:* info@roybloom.com *Web Site:* www.roybloom.com, pg 1152

Roy Bloom Ltd (United Kingdom) *Tel:* (020) 7729 5373 *Fax:* (020) 7729 2375 *E-mail:* info@roybloom.com *Web Site:* www.remainder-books.com; www.roybloom. com, pg 1339

Bloomings Books (Australia) *Tel:* (03) 9427 1234 *Fax:* (03) 9427 9066 *E-mail:* sales@bloomings.com.au *Web Site:* www.bloomings.com.au, pg 15

Bloomsbury Publishing PLC (United Kingdom) *Tel:* (020) 7494 2111 *Fax:* (020) 7434 0151 *E-mail:* csm@bloomsbury.com *Web Site:* www. bloomsburymagazine.com, pg 663

Blorenge Books (United Kingdom) *Tel:* (01873) 856114, pg 663

Eberhard Blottner Verlag GmbH (Germany) *Tel:* (06128) 2 36 00 *Fax:* (06128) 21180 *E-mail:* blottner@ blottner.de *Web Site:* www.blottner.de, pg 202

Blubber Head Press (Australia) *Tel:* (03) 6223 8644 *Fax:* (03) 6223 8644 *E-mail:* books@astrolabebooks. com.au *Web Site:* www.astrolabebooks.com.au, pg 15

Editora Edgard Blucher Ltda (Brazil) *Tel:* (011) 852-5366 *Fax:* (011) 852 2707 *E-mail:* eblucher@uol.com. br, pg 78

Bonsignori Editore SRL (Italy) *Tel:* (06) 5881496 *Fax:* (06) 5882839 *E-mail:* redazione@bonsignori.it, pg 375

Bonum Editorial SACI (Argentina) *Tel:* (011) 4554-1414 *Fax:* (011) 4554-1414 *E-mail:* produccion@ editorialbonum.com.ar *Web Site:* www.editorialbonum. com.ar, pg 3

Boobook Publications (Australia) *Tel:* (02) 4997 0811 *Fax:* (02) 4997 1089, pg 15

Book Agencies of Tasmania (Australia) *Tel:* (03) 6247 7405 *Fax:* (03) 6247 1116 *E-mail:* bookagencies@ trump.net.au, pg 15

Book Aid International (United Kingdom) *Tel:* (020) 7733 3577 *Fax:* (020) 7978 8006 *E-mail:* info@ bookaid.org *Web Site:* www.bookaid.org, pg 1572

Book & Printing Center - Israel Export Institute (Israel) *Tel:* (03) 514 2830 *Fax:* (03) 514 2902; (03) 514 2815 *E-mail:* export-institute@export.gov.il; pama@export. gov.il *Web Site:* www.export.gov.il; duns100.dundb.co. il/1483, pg 1264

Book Centre, Textbook Sales (Pvt) Ltd (Zimbabwe) *Tel:* (04) 790691 *Fax:* (04) 751690, pg 1347

Book Chamber of Kazakhstan ISBN Agency (Kazakstan) *Tel:* (03272) 306 421 *Fax:* (03272) 304 265 *E-mail:* rntb@kaznet.kz *Web Site:* www.isbn-international.org, pg 1265

Book Chamber of Ukraine, National ISBN Agency (Ukraine) *Tel:* (044) 552-0134; (044) 573-0184 *Fax:* (044) 552-0143 *E-mail:* office@ukrbook.net *Web Site:* www.ukrbook.net, pg 1279

Book Circle (India) *Tel:* (011) 23266258; (011) 23288283; (011) 23257798 *Fax:* (011) 23263050 *E-mail:* info@meditechbooks.com *Web Site:* www. meditechbooks.com, pg 327

Book Club Associates (United Kingdom) *Tel:* (0870) 165 0292; (020) 7760 6500 *Fax:* (0870) 165 0222; (044) 1793 567711 *E-mail:* e-support@booksdirect.co.uk *Web Site:* www.bca.co.uk, pg 1246

Book Collectors' Society of Australia (Australia) *Tel:* (02) 9807 5489 *Fax:* (02) 9807 5489, pg 15

The Book Company Publishing Pty Ltd (Australia) *Tel:* (02) 94863711 *Fax:* (02) 94863722 *E-mail:* sales@thebookcompany.com.au *Web Site:* www.thebookcompany.com.au, pg 15

Book Creation Services Ltd (United Kingdom) *Tel:* (020) 7287 0214 *Fax:* (020) 7583 9439 *Web Site:* www. bookcreation.com, pg 1152

Book Creation Services Ltd (United Kingdom) *Tel:* (020) 7583 0553 *Fax:* (020) 7583 9439 *E-mail:* info@ librios.com *Web Site:* www.librios.com, pg 1173

Book Creation Services Ltd (United Kingdom) *Tel:* (01223) 424571 *Fax:* (01223) 426877, pg 1215

Book Creation Services Ltd (United Kingdom) *Tel:* (020) 7583 0553 *Fax:* (020) 7583 9439 *E-mail:* info@ librios.com *Web Site:* www.librios.com, pg 1228

Book Development Council International (BDCI) (United Kingdom) *Tel:* (020) 7691 9191 *Fax:* (020) 7691 9199 *E-mail:* mail@publishers.org.uk *Web Site:* www. publishers.org.uk, pg 1279

Book Editore (Italy) *Tel:* (051) 71 47 20 *Fax:* (051) 71 12 16 *E-mail:* bookeditore@libero.it *Web Site:* web. tiscali.it/bookeditore, pg 375

Book Faith India (India) *Tel:* (011) 713-2459 *Fax:* (011) 724-9674 *E-mail:* pilgrim@del2.vsml.net.in, pg 327

The Book Guild Ltd (United Kingdom) *Tel:* (01273) 472534 *Fax:* (01273) 476472 *E-mail:* info@bookguild. co.uk *Web Site:* www.bookguild.co.uk, pg 664

The Book House (Pakistan) *Tel:* (042) 61212; (042) 232415 *Fax:* (042) 6360955, pg 507

Book Industry Communication (United Kingdom) *Tel:* (020) 7607 0021 *Fax:* (020) 7607 0415 *Web Site:* www.bic.org.uk, pg 1279

Book Lovers Club (India) *Tel:* (011) 26387070; (011) 26386209 *Fax:* (011) 26383788 *E-mail:* ghai@nde. vsnl.net.in *Web Site:* www.sterlingpublishers.com, pg 1243

Book Lovers' Club (Serbia and Montenegro) *Tel:* (011) 651666; (011) 650399, pg 1245

Book Marketing Ltd (Hong Kong) *Tel:* (02) 5620121 *Fax:* (02) 5650187, pg 312

Book Marketing Ltd (United Kingdom) *Tel:* (020) 7440 8930 *Fax:* (020) 7242 7485 *E-mail:* bml@ bookmarketing.co.uk *Web Site:* www.bookmarketing. co.uk, pg 664, 1279

Book Production Consultants PLC (United Kingdom) *Tel:* (01223) 352790 *Fax:* (01223) 460718 *E-mail:* enquiries@bpccam.co.uk *Web Site:* www. bpccam.co.uk, pg 1129

Book Production Consultants PLC (United Kingdom) *Tel:* (01223) 352790 *Fax:* (01223) 460718 *Web Site:* www.bpccam.co.uk, pg 1152

Book Production Consultants PLC (United Kingdom) *Tel:* (01223) 352790 *Fax:* (01223) 460718 *E-mail:* bpc@bpccam.co.uk *Web Site:* www.bpccam. co.uk, pg 1173

Book Production Consultants PLC (United Kingdom) *Tel:* (01223) 352790; (01223) 323092 (ISDN) *Fax:* (01223) 460718 *E-mail:* enquiries@bpccam.co.uk *Web Site:* www.bpccam.co.uk, pg 1237

Book Promotions (Pte) Ltd (South Africa) *Tel:* (021) 7060949 *Fax:* (021) 7060940 *E-mail:* enquiries@ bookpro.co.za, pg 1331

The Book Publishers Association of Israel (Israel) *Tel:* (03) 5614121 *Fax:* (03) 5611996 *E-mail:* info@ tbpai.co.il *Web Site:* www.tbpai.co.il, pg 362

Book Publishers' Association of Israel (Israel) *Tel:* (03) 5614121 *Fax:* (03) 5611996 *E-mail:* info@tbpai.co.il *Web Site:* www.tbpai.co.il, pg 1264

The Book Publishers' Association of Israel, International Promotion & Literary Rights Department (Israel) *Tel:* (03) 5614121 *Fax:* (03) 5611996 *E-mail:* hamol@ tbpai.co.il *Web Site:* www.tbpai.co.il, pg 1123

Book Publishing Institute (Afghanistan), pg 1

Book Representation & Distribution Ltd (United Kingdom) *Tel:* (01702) 552912 *Fax:* (01702) 556095 *E-mail:* mail@bookreps.com; info@bookreps.com *Web Site:* www.bookreps.com, pg 1339

Book Representation & Publishing Co Ltd (Nigeria) *Tel:* (022) 710242, pg 499

Book Sales (K) Ltd (Kenya), pg 429

Book Sales (K) Ltd (Kenya) *Tel:* (02) 221031; (02) 226543, pg 1314

The Book Source (Barbados) *Tel:* 4310379 *Fax:* 4261855 *E-mail:* bksource@caribsurf.com *Web Site:* www. booksourceonline.com, pg 1291

Book Stop (Ireland) *Tel:* (01) 2809917 *Fax:* (01) 2844863 *E-mail:* bookstop@indigo.ie, pg 1308

Book Tokens Ltd (United Kingdom) *Tel:* (020) 7802 0802 *Fax:* (020) 7802 0803 *E-mail:* mail@booksellers. org.uk *Web Site:* www.booksellers.org.uk, pg 1279

The Book Trade Benevolent Society (United Kingdom) *Tel:* (01923) 263128 *Fax:* (01923) 270732 *E-mail:* btbs@booktradecharity.demon.co.uk *Web Site:* www.booktradecharity.demon.co.uk, pg 1280

Bookbank SA (Spain) *Tel:* (091) 3733539 *Fax:* (091) 3165591 *E-mail:* bookbank@nexo.es, pg 1126

Bookbank SL Agencia Literaria (Spain) *Tel:* (091) 3733539 *Fax:* (091) 3165591 *E-mail:* bookbank@ nexo.es, pg 570

Bookbuilders Ltd (Hong Kong) *Tel:* 27968123 *Fax:* 27968267; 27968690 *E-mail:* lph@netvigator. com, pg 1167, 1207

BookBuilders New York Inc (United States) *Tel:* 386-447-8692 *Fax:* 386-447-8746 *Web Site:* www. mcabooks.com, pg 1155

BookBuilders New York Inc (United States) *Tel:* 845-639-5316 *Fax:* 845-639-5318 *Web Site:* www. mcabooks.com, pg 1176

BookBuilders New York Inc (United States) *Tel:* 845-639-5316 *Fax:* 845-639-5318 *E-mail:* mcanewcity@ aol.com *Web Site:* www.mcabooks.com, pg 1218

BookBuilders New York Inc (United States) *Tel:* 845-639-5316 *Fax:* 845-639-5318 *Web Site:* www. mcabooks.com, pg 1229, 1238

Bookionics (India) *Tel:* (040) 593654 *Fax:* (040) 595678 *E-mail:* bookionics@yahoo.com, pg 327

Booklink (United Kingdom) *Tel:* (01923) 828612 *Fax:* (01923) 828455 *E-mail:* info@booklink.co.uk *Web Site:* www.booklink.co.uk, pg 1129

Booklinks Corporation (India) *Tel:* (0842) 65021; (0842) 62282; (0842) 65550, pg 327

Bookmaker (France) *Tel:* (01) 43 54 84 34 *Fax:* (01) 43 54 71 02 *E-mail:* bookmake@club-internet.fr, pg 150

Bookman Books Ltd (Taiwan, Province of China) *Tel:* (02) 2368-7226; (02) 2365-8617 *Fax:* (02) 2363-6630; (02) 2365-3548 *E-mail:* bk@bookman.com.tw *Web Site:* www.bookman.com.tw, pg 634

Bookman Consultants Ltd (Kenya) *Tel:* (020) 245146 *Fax:* (020) 336771 *E-mail:* bookman@wananchi.com, pg 430

Bookman Health (Australia) *Tel:* (03) 9521 3250 *Toll Free Tel:* 800 060 555 *Fax:* (03) 9826 1744 *E-mail:* sales@bookman.com.au *Web Site:* www. bookman.com.au, pg 15

Bookman Literary Agency (Denmark) *Tel:* 45892520 *Fax:* 45892501 *Web Site:* www.bookman.dk, pg 1120

Bookman Printing & Publishing House Inc (Philippines) *Tel:* (02) 712-4813; (02) 712-4818; (02) 712-4843; (02) 740-8108; (02) 740-8107; (02) 712-3587 *Fax:* (02) 712-4843 *E-mail:* bookman@info.com.ph, pg 513

Bookman's & Co Ltd (Japan) *Tel:* (06) 6371-4164 *Fax:* (06) 6371-4174 *E-mail:* info@bookmans.co.jp *Web Site:* www.bookmans.co.jp, pg 1312

Bookmark Inc (Philippines) *Tel:* (02) 8958061; (02) 8958062; (02) 8958063; (02) 8958064; (02) 8958065 *Fax:* (02) 8970824; (02) 8994248 *E-mail:* bookmark@ info.com.ph; bookmktg@info.com.ph *Web Site:* www. bookmark.com.ph, pg 513

Bookmark Inc (Philippines) *Tel:* (02) 8958061; (02) 8958062; (02) 8958063; (02) 8958064; (02) 8958065 *Fax:* (02) 8970824 *E-mail:* bookmark@info.com.ph *Web Site:* www.bookmark.com.ph, pg 1326

Bookmark Remainders (United Kingdom) *Tel:* (01566) 782728 *Fax:* (01566) 782059 *E-mail:* info@book-bargains.co.uk *Web Site:* book-bargains.co.uk, pg 1339

Bookmarks Club (United Kingdom) *Tel:* (020) 7536 9696 *Fax:* (020) 7538 0018 *E-mail:* bookmarks@ internationalsocialist.org *Web Site:* www. internationalsocialist.org, pg 1247

Bookmarks Publications (United Kingdom) *Tel:* (020) 7637 1848 *Fax:* (020) 7637 3416 *E-mail:* mailorder@ bookmarks.uk.com *Web Site:* www.bookmarks.uk.com, pg 664

Bookmart Ltd (United Kingdom) *Tel:* (0116) 2759060 *Fax:* (0116) 2759090 *E-mail:* books@bookmart.co.uk, pg 1339

Bookpoint Ltd (Kenya) *Tel:* (02) 211156; (02) 220221; (02) 226680 *Fax:* (02) 211029 *E-mail:* books@ africaonline.co.ke, pg 1314

Bookpoint Ltd (United Kingdom) *Tel:* (01235) 827730 *Fax:* (01235) 400454; (01235) 821511 (Orders) *E-mail:* firstname.lastname@bookpoint.co.uk *Web Site:* www.oxfordshire.co.uk; pubeasy.books. bookpoint.co.uk, pg 1339

BookPower (United Kingdom) *Tel:* (020) 8742 8232 *Fax:* (020) 8747 8715 *E-mail:* bookpower@ibd.uk.net *Web Site:* www.bookpower.org, pg 1401

Bookprint Consultants Ltd (New Zealand) *Tel:* (04) 381 3071 *Fax:* (04) 381 3067 *E-mail:* gstewart@iconz.co. nz, pg 1150, 1211, 1227, 1236

Books Across the Sea (United Kingdom) *Tel:* (020) 7529 1550 *Fax:* (020) 7495 6108 *E-mail:* esu@mailbox. ulcc.ac.uk *Web Site:* www.libfl.ru/eng/esu, pg 1401

Books & Books (India) *Tel:* (011) 551252, pg 328

Books & Periodicals Agency (India) *Tel:* (011) 205624 *Fax:* 801-881-6189 (US Fax) *E-mail:* bpage@del2. vsnl.net.in *Web Site:* www.bpagency.com, pg 1305

Books Exports (United Kingdom) *Tel:* (020) 8931 2359; (020) 8959 2137 *Fax:* (0181) 9592137 *E-mail:* roshanbp@aol.com, pg 1247

Books for Children (United Kingdom) *Tel:* (020) 7911 8000 *Fax:* (020) 7911 8100 *E-mail:* uk@twbg.co.uk *Web Site:* www.twbg.co.uk, pg 1247

Books for Europe Ltd (United Kingdom) *Tel:* (020) 8840 6672, pg 1340

Books for Keeps (United Kingdom) *Tel:* (020) 8852 4953 *Fax:* (020) 8318 7580 *E-mail:* enquiries@ booksforkeeps.co.uk *Web Site:* www.booksforkeeps. co.uk, pg 1280

Books for Pleasure Inc (Philippines) *Tel:* (02) 771807 *Fax:* (02) 7275240 *E-mail:* vromance@compass.com. ph, pg 513

Books from India (UK) Ltd (United Kingdom) *Tel:* (071) 4053784 *Fax:* (071) 8314517, pg 1340

Books in the Attic Publishers Ltd (Israel) *Tel:* (03) 248324 *Fax:* (03) 623630, pg 362

Books India (India) *Tel:* (011) 327 7463 *Fax:* (011) 241 2912, pg 1305

Books International (Israel) *Tel:* (08) 633 0205 *Fax:* (08) 633 0204 *E-mail:* info@booksinternational.com *Web Site:* www.booksinternational.com, pg 1309

Books of Zimbabwe Publishing Co (Pvt) Ltd (United Kingdom) *Tel:* (01444) 455549 *E-mail:* info@ booksofzimbabwe.com *Web Site:* www. booksofzimbabwe.com, pg 664

Books on African Studies (Germany) *Tel:* (06221) 411861 *Fax:* (06221) 411861, pg 203

Books Registration Office (Hong Kong) *Tel:* 218 09 145; 218 09 146 *Fax:* 218 09 841 *E-mail:* bro@lcsd.gov.hk *Web Site:* www.lcsd.gov.hk, pg 1262

Booksellers' & Publishers' Association of Zambia (BPAZ) (Zambia) *Tel:* (01) 225282 *Fax:* (01) 225195 *E-mail:* bpaz@zamnet.zm; longman@zamnet.zm, pg 1285

Booksellers' Association of Jamaica (Jamaica) *Tel:* (876) 922-5883 *Fax:* (876) 922-4743, pg 1264

Booksellers New Zealand (New Zealand) *Tel:* (04) 4478-5511 *Fax:* (04) 4478-5519, pg 1270

Booksellers New Zealand (New Zealand) *Tel:* (04) 478 5511 *Fax:* (04) 478 5519 *E-mail:* enquiries@ booksellers.co.nz *Web Site:* www.booksellers.co.nz, pg 1270

Bookservice (Italy) *Tel:* (0771) 744350 *Fax:* (0771) 744350, pg 375

Bookstore, Institute of Puerto Rican Culture (Puerto Rico) *Tel:* 809-723-2115, pg 1329

Booktrust (United Kingdom) *Tel:* (020) 8516 2977 *Fax:* (020) 8516 2978 *Web Site:* www.booktrust.org. uk, pg 1280

Bookwise International (Australia) *Tel:* (08) 8268 8222 *Fax:* (08) 8268 8704 *E-mail:* customer.service@ bookwise.com.au *Web Site:* www.bookwise.com.au, pg 1288

Bookworld Ltd (Zambia) *Tel:* (01) 225 282 *Fax:* (01) 225 195 *E-mail:* bookwld@zamtel.zm, pg 776

Bookworld Wholesale Ltd (United Kingdom) *Tel:* (01299) 823330 *Fax:* (01299) 829970, pg 1340

The Bookworm Club (United Kingdom) *Tel:* (01223) 568650 *Fax:* (01223) 568591 *E-mail:* clubs@heffers. co.uk *Web Site:* www.heffers.co.uk, pg 1247

Boolarong Press (Australia) *Tel:* (07) 3848 8200 *Fax:* (07) 3848 8077 *E-mail:* mail@boolarongpress. com.au *Web Site:* www.boolarongpress.com.au, pg 15

Boom Uitgeverij (Netherlands) *Tel:* (020) 625 33 27 *Fax:* (020) 625 33 27 *E-mail:* info@uitgeverijboom.nl *Web Site:* www.uitgeverijboom.nl, pg 475

Boombana Publications (Australia) *Tel:* (07) 3289 8106 *Fax:* (07) 3289 8107 *Web Site:* www. boombanapublications.com, pg 15

Richard Boorberg Verlag GmbH & Co (Germany) *Tel:* (0711) 73 85-0 *Fax:* (0711) 73 85-100 *Web Site:* www.boorberg.de, pg 203

Boosey & Hawkes Music Publishers Ltd (United Kingdom) *Tel:* (020) 7580 2060 *Fax:* (020) 7291 7199 *E-mail:* information@boosey.com *Web Site:* www. boosey.com/publishing, pg 664

Boosey & Hawkes Music Publishers LTD, London (Germany) *Tel:* (030) 25001300 *Fax:* (030) 25001399 *E-mail:* musikverlag@boosey.com *Web Site:* www. boosey.com/publishing, pg 203

Boostan Publishing House (Israel) *Tel:* (03) 9221821 *Fax:* (03) 9221299, pg 362

Edizioni Bora SNC di E Brandani & C (Italy) *Tel:* (051) 356133 *Fax:* (051) 4159651 *E-mail:* daniele. brandani@mailbox.dsnet.it, pg 375

Borba (Serbia and Montenegro) *Tel:* (011) 3243-437 *Fax:* (011) 3244-913 *Web Site:* www.borba.co.yu, pg 547

Bord na Gaeilge (Ireland) *Tel:* (01) 716 8208 *Web Site:* www.ucd.ie/bnag, pg 355

Bord na Gaeilge (Ireland) *Tel:* (01) 6616522 *Fax:* (01) 6612378, pg 1308

Editions Bordas (France) *Tel:* (01) 72 36 40 00 *Fax:* (01) 72 36 40 10 *Web Site:* www.editions-bordas.fr, pg 150

Pierre Bordas & Fils, Editions (France) *Tel:* (01) 43 25 04 51 *Fax:* (01) 43 25 47 84 *E-mail:* pierre.bordas. filsd@wanadoo.fr, pg 150

Bibliotheque Municipale de Bordeaux (France) *Tel:* (05) 56 10 30 00 *Fax:* (05) 56 10 30 90 *E-mail:* bibli@ mairie-bordeaux.fr *Web Site:* www.bordeaux-city. com/cbiblio.htm, pg 1505

Presses Universitaires de Bordeaux (PUB) (France) *Tel:* (05) 57 12 44 22 *Fax:* (05) 57 12 45 34 *E-mail:* pub@u-bordeaux3.fr *Web Site:* www.pub. montaigne.u-bordeaux.fr, pg 150

Borgens Forlag A/S (Denmark) *Tel:* 36 15 36 15 *Fax:* 36 15 36 16 *E-mail:* post@borgen.dk *Web Site:* www. borgen.dk, pg 129

Borim Publishing Co (Republic of Korea) *Tel:* (02) 3141-2222 *Fax:* (02) 3141-8474 *E-mail:* namu@ borimplc.co.kr *Web Site:* www.borimplc.co.kr, pg 434

Edizioni Borla SRL (Italy) *Tel:* (06) 39376728 *Fax:* (06) 39376620 *E-mail:* borla@edizioni-borla.it *Web Site:* www.edizioni-borla.it, pg 375

Born-Verlag (Germany) *Tel:* (0561) 4095107 *Fax:* (0561) 4095112 *E-mail:* info.born@ec-jugend.de *Web Site:* www.born-buch.de, pg 203

Bornegudstjeneste-Forlaget (Denmark) *Tel:* 75934455 *Fax:* 75924275 *E-mail:* lohse@imh.dk, pg 129

Editions Bornemann (France) *Tel:* (01) 42 82 08 16 *Fax:* (01) 48 74 14 88 *Web Site:* www.sangdelaterre. com, pg 150

Borromausverein eV (Germany) *Tel:* (0228) 7258-0 *Fax:* (0228) 7258-189 *E-mail:* info@borro.de *Web Site:* www.borro.de, pg 1260

Editions Emile Borschette (Luxembourg) *Tel:* 87177 *Fax:* 879599, pg 447

Borsen Forlag (Denmark) *Tel:* 33 32 01 02 *Fax:* 33 12 24 45 *E-mail:* redaktionen@borsen.dk *Web Site:* www. borsen.dk, pg 129

Borthwick Institute Publications (United Kingdom) *Tel:* (01904) 321160 *Web Site:* www.york.ac.uk/ borthwick, pg 664

Antoni Bosch Editor SA (Spain) *Tel:* (093) 206 07 30 *Fax:* (093) 206 07 31 *E-mail:* info@antonibosch.com *Web Site:* www.antonibosch.com, pg 570

Bosch Casa Editorial SA (Spain) *Tel:* (093) 4548437; (093) 4544629; (093) 4521050 *Fax:* (093) 3236736 *E-mail:* bosch@boschce.es *Web Site:* www.boschce.es, pg 570

Bosch en Keuning grafische bedrijven (Netherlands) *Tel:* (035) 5412050 *Fax:* (035) 2202446, pg 1150

Bosch en Keuning grafische bedrijven (Netherlands) *Tel:* (035) 5417979, pg 1171

Bosch en Keuning grafische bedrijven (Netherlands) *Tel:* (035) 5412050 *Fax:* (035) 2202446, pg 1211

J M Bosch Editor (Spain) *Tel:* (093) 2654466 *Fax:* (093) 2659031 *E-mail:* info@nexica.com *Web Site:* www. libreriabosch.es/jmb, pg 570

Libreria Bosch (Spain) *Tel:* (093) 394 3600 *Fax:* (093) 412 2764 *E-mail:* info@libreriabosch.es *Web Site:* www.libreriabosch.es, pg 1333

Editorial Maria Jesus Bosch SL (Spain) *Tel:* (093) 4539717 *E-mail:* mjbosch@colon.net, pg 570

Gustav Bosse GmbH & Co KG (Germany) *Tel:* (0561) 31 05-0 *Fax:* (0561) 31 05-2 40 *E-mail:* info@bosse-verlag.de *Web Site:* www.bosse-verlag.de, pg 203

BOSZ scp (Poland) *Tel:* (013) 469 90 00 *Fax:* (013) 469 61 88 *E-mail:* biuro@ks.onet.pl *Web Site:* www.bosz. com.pl, pg 517

Botanisch-Zoologische Gesellschaft (Liechtenstein) *Tel:* (00423) 2324819 *Fax:* (00423) 2332819 *E-mail:* renat@pingnet.li, pg 444

Libreria y Ediciones Botas SA (Mexico) *Tel:* (05) 5702-4083; (05) 5702-5403 *Fax:* (02) 55101788 *E-mail:* botas@mail.nextgeninter.net.mx, pg 459

Bote & Bock Musikalienhandelsgesellschaft mbH (Germany) *Tel:* (030) 2500-1300 *Fax:* (030) 2500-1399 *E-mail:* musikverlag@boosey.com *Web Site:* www.boosey.com, pg 203

Ediciones Botella al Mar (Argentina) *Tel:* (011) 4803-8246 *E-mail:* edicionesbotellaalmar@hotmail.com, pg 4

Botes Librair (United Kingdom) *Tel:* (01424) 210871 *Fax:* (01424) 734506; (01424) 731262 *E-mail:* 100450.3641@compuserve.com, pg 1340

Botimpex Publications Import-Export Agency (Albania) *Tel:* (042) 34023 *Fax:* (042) 26886 *E-mail:* botimpex@albaniaonline.net; botimpex@ icc-al.org; ebega@albmail.com *Web Site:* pages. albaniaonline.net/botimpex/, pg 1

Botswana Book Centre (Botswana) *Tel:* 3974315 *E-mail:* pulapress@botsnet.bw, pg 1293

Botswana Library Association (Botswana) *Tel:* (031) 3552295 *Fax:* (031) 357291 *Web Site:* www.bla. 0catch.com, pg 1559

Botswana National Archives & Records Services (Botswana) *Tel:* 391 820 *Fax:* 390 545 *Web Site:* www.gov.bw, pg 1493

Botswana National Library Service (Botswana) *Tel:* 352-397 *Fax:* 301-149 *E-mail:* natlib@global.bw; automate@global.bw *Web Site:* www.gov.bw, pg 1493

The Botswana Society (Botswana) *Tel:* 3919673 *Fax:* 3919745 *E-mail:* botsoc@botsnet.bw *Web Site:* www.botswanasociety.com, pg 75

Bottin SA (France) *Tel:* (01) 47 48 75 75 *Fax:* (01) 47 48 75 50, pg 150

Boukoumanis' Editions (Greece) *Tel:* 2103618502; 2103637436 *Fax:* 2103630669 *E-mail:* info@ boukoumanis.gr *Web Site:* www.boukoumanis.gr, pg 303

Boulevard Books UK/The Babel Guides (United Kingdom) *Tel:* (01865) 712931 *Fax:* (01865) 712931 *E-mail:* raybabel@dircon.co.uk *Web Site:* www. babelguides.com, pg 664

Bounty Books (United Kingdom) *Tel:* (020) 7531 8600 *Fax:* (020) 7531 8607 *Web Site:* www.bounty-publishing.co.uk, pg 664

Librairie Bourbon (Luxembourg) *Tel:* 40 30 30-21 *Fax:* 40 30 30-45 *E-mail:* librairies@isp.lu *Web Site:* www.librairie.lu, pg 1316

Bourdeaux-Capelle SA (Belgium) *Tel:* (082) 222283; (082) 222277 *Fax:* (082) 226378, pg 63

Christian Bourgois Editeur (France) *Tel:* (01) 45 44 09 13 *Fax:* (01) 45 44 87 86 *E-mail:* bourgois-editeur@wanadoo.fr *Web Site:* www.christianbourgois-editeur.fr, pg 150

Editions Bouslama (Tunisia) *Tel:* 71245612 *Fax:* 71381100, pg 643

Editions Bouslama (Tunisia) *Tel:* 71245612, pg 1337

Bouvier GmbH & Co KG (Germany) *Tel:* (0228) 72901-0; (01803) 258940 (orders) *Fax:* (0228) 72901-178 *E-mail:* bouvier@books.de *Web Site:* www.books.de, pg 1300

Bouvier Verlag (Germany) *Tel:* (0228) 72901124 *Fax:* (0228) 637909 *E-mail:* verlag@books.de *Web Site:* www.bouvier-online.de, pg 203

Bovolenta (Italy) *Tel:* (0532) 259386 *Fax:* (0532) 259387, pg 375

M J Bowen (Australia) *Tel:* (03) 9561 3425 *Fax:* (03) 9882 9405, pg 16

Bowerdean Publishing Co Ltd (United Kingdom) *Tel:* (020) 8788 0938 *Fax:* (020) 8788 0938 *E-mail:* 101467.1264@compuserve.com, pg 664

Boxtree Ltd (United Kingdom) *Tel:* (020) 7014 6000 *Fax:* (020) 7014 6001 *Web Site:* www.panmacmillan. com/imprints/boxtree.html, pg 665

Marion Boyars Publishers Ltd (United Kingdom) *Tel:* (020) 8788 9522 *Fax:* (020) 8789 8122 *Web Site:* www.marionboyars.co.uk, pg 665

David Boyce Publishing & Associates (Australia) *Tel:* (02) 6997484, pg 16

Boydell & Brewer Ltd (United Kingdom) *Tel:* (01394) 610 600 *Fax:* (01394) 610 316 *E-mail:* boydell@boydell.co.uk *Web Site:* www.boydell.co.uk, pg 665

BPB Publications (India) *Tel:* (011) 3281723; (011) 3254990; (011) 3254991 *Fax:* (011) 3266427 *E-mail:* admin@bpbonline.com *Web Site:* www.bpbonline.com, pg 328

BPL Remainders (United Kingdom) *Tel:* (020) 7636 5070; (020) 7631 5070 *Fax:* (020) 7580 3001, pg 1340

BPP Publishing Ltd (United Kingdom) *Tel:* (020) 8740 2222 *Fax:* (020) 8740 1111 *E-mail:* info@bpp.com *Web Site:* www.bpp.com, pg 665

BPS Books (British Psychological Society) (United Kingdom) *Tel:* (0116) 254 9568 *Fax:* (0116) 247 0787 *E-mail:* enquiry@bps.org.uk *Web Site:* www.bps.org.uk, pg 665

BR Publishing Corporation (India) *Tel:* (011) 7430113; (011) 7143353, pg 328

Bokforlaget Bra Bocker AB (Sweden) *Tel:* (040) 665 46 00 *Fax:* (040) 665 46 22 *E-mail:* kundservice@bbb.se *Web Site:* www.bbb.se, pg 605

Brabys Brochures (South Africa) *Tel:* (031) 717 4000 *Fax:* (031) 717 4001 *E-mail:* brabys@brabys.com *Web Site:* www.brabys.com, pg 558

Dr Barry Bracewell-Milnes (United Kingdom) *Tel:* (01737) 350736 *Fax:* (01737) 371415, pg 665

Bradt Travel Guides Ltd (United Kingdom) *Tel:* (01753) 893444 *Fax:* (01753) 892333 *E-mail:* info@bradt-travelguides.com *Web Site:* www.bradtguides.com, pg 665

Bradt Travel Guides Ltd (United Kingdom) *Tel:* (01753) 893444 *Fax:* (01753) 892333 *E-mail:* info@bradtguides.com; enquiries@bradt-travelguides.com *Web Site:* www.bradtguides.com, pg 1340

Bragelonne (France) *Tel:* (01) 48 18 19 70; (01) 48 18 19 71 *Fax:* (01) 48 18 02 47 *E-mail:* info@bragelonne.fr *Web Site:* www.bragelonne.fr, pg 150

Louis Braille Audio (Australia) *Tel:* (03) 9864 9645 *Fax:* (03) 9864 9646 *E-mail:* lba.sales@visionaustralia.org.au *Web Site:* www.louisbrailleaudio.com, pg 16

Braintrust Marketing Services Ges mbH Verlag (Austria) *Tel:* (01) 40416-0 *Fax:* (01) 40416-33 *E-mail:* braintrust@magnet.at *Web Site:* www.braintrust.at, pg 48

J W Braithwaite & Son Ltd (United Kingdom) *Tel:* (01902) 452209 *Fax:* (01902) 352918, pg 1215

Verlag Brandenburger Tor GmbH (Germany) *Tel:* (030) 8557511 *Fax:* (030) 85605332 *E-mail:* info@verlag-brandenburger-tor.de, pg 203

Brandenburgisches Verlagshaus in der Dornier Medienholding GmbH (Germany) *Tel:* (0711) 78803-0 *Fax:* (0711) 78803-0 *E-mail:* info@dornier-verlage.de *Web Site:* www.dornier-verlage.de, pg 203

Brandes & Apsel Verlag GmbH (Germany) *Tel:* (069) 957 301 86 *Fax:* (069) 957 301 87 *E-mail:* brandes-apsel@doodees.de *Web Site:* www.brandes-apsel-verlag.de, pg 203

Brandon Book Publishers Ltd (Ireland) *Tel:* (066) 9151463 *Fax:* (066) 9151234 *Web Site:* www.brandonbooks.com, pg 355

Christian Brandstaetter Verlagsgesellschaft mbH (Austria) *Tel:* (01) 512 15 43 *Fax:* (01) 512 15 43-231 *E-mail:* cbv@oebv.co.at *Web Site:* www.brandstaetter-verlag.at, pg 48

Oscar Brandstetter Verlag GmbH & Co KG (Germany) *Tel:* (0611) 9 91 20-0 *Fax:* (0611) 3 08 37 85 *E-mail:* brandstetter-verlag@t-online.de *Web Site:* www.brandstetter-verlag.de, pg 203

Editora Brasil-America (EBAL) SA (Brazil) *Tel:* (021) 5800303 *Fax:* (021) 5801637, pg 78

Editora do Brasil SA (Brazil) *Tel:* (011) 222 0211 *Fax:* (011) 222 5583 *E-mail:* edbrasil@uol.com.br, pg 78

Instituto Brasileiro de Informacao em Ciencia e Tecnologia (Brazil) *Tel:* (061) 217-6360; (061) 217-6350 *Fax:* (061) 226-2677 *E-mail:* webmaster@ibict.br *Web Site:* www.ibict.br, pg 78, 1559

Brasilia Editora (J Carvalho Branco) (Portugal) *Tel:* (02) 315854 *Fax:* (02) 2055854, pg 524

Editora Brasiliense SA (Brazil) *Tel:* (011) 6198-1488 *Fax:* (011) 6198-1488 *E-mail:* brasilienseedit@uol.com.br *Web Site:* www.editorabrasiliense.com.br, pg 78

Livraria Brasiliense Editora SA (Brazil) *Tel:* (011) 8250122 *Fax:* (011) 673024, pg 1293

Brasilivros Editora e Distribuidora Ltda (Brazil) *Tel:* (011) 3284-8155; (011) 3371-5140 *Fax:* (011) 3371-5166 *Toll Free Fax:* 800 555-546 *E-mail:* vendas@brasilivros.com.br *Web Site:* www.brasilivros.com.br, pg 78

Brassey's UK Ltd (United Kingdom) *Tel:* (020) 7221 2213; (020) 7314 1469 (sales) *Fax:* (020) 7221 6455; (020) 7314 1594 (sales) *E-mail:* enquiries@chrysalis.com *Web Site:* www.chrysalis.co.uk, pg 665

G Braun GmbH & Co KG (Germany) *Tel:* (0721) 1607320 *Fax:* (0721) 1607321 *E-mail:* info@gbraun-immo.de *Web Site:* www.gbraun.de, pg 204

Technische Universitaet Braunschweig (Germany) *Tel:* (0531) 391-5018; (0531) 391-5011 *Fax:* (0531) 391-5836 *E-mail:* ub@tu-bs.de *Web Site:* www.biblio.tu-bs.de, pg 1507

Brazilian PEN Centre (Brazil), pg 1392

Breakthrough Ltd - Breakthrough Publishers (Hong Kong) *Tel:* 2632 0257 *Fax:* 2632 0288 *Web Site:* www.teachlikethis.com, pg 312

Editions Breal (France) *Tel:* (01) 48 12 22 22 *Fax:* (01) 48 12 22 39 *E-mail:* infos@editions-breal.fr *Web Site:* www.editions-breal.fr, pg 151

Nicholas Brealey Publishing (United Kingdom) *Tel:* (020) 7239 0360 *Fax:* (020) 7239 0370 *E-mail:* sales@nbrealey-books.com *Web Site:* www.nbrealey-books.com, pg 666

Bredero (Belgium) *Tel:* (014) 31-84-61 *Fax:* (014) 70-02-05 *Web Site:* www.bredero.be, pg 1292

Breedon Books Publishing Company Ltd (United Kingdom) *Tel:* (01332) 384235 *Fax:* (01332) 292755 *E-mail:* sales@breedonpublishing.co.uk *Web Site:* www.breedonbooks.co.uk, pg 666

Breitkopf & Hartel (Germany) *Tel:* (0611) 450080 *Fax:* (0611) 4500859; (0611) 4500860; (0611) 4500861 *E-mail:* info@breitkopf.com *Web Site:* www.breitkopf.com; www.breitkopf.de, pg 204

Emgleo Breiz (France) *Tel:* (02) 98 44 89 42 *Fax:* (02) 98 02 68 17 *E-mail:* andrelemercier@hotmail.com; brud.nevez@wanadoo.fr *Web Site:* emgleo.breiz.online.fr, pg 151

Breklumer Buchhandlung und Verlag (Germany) *Tel:* (04671) 910020 *Fax:* (04671) 910030 *E-mail:* verlag@breklumer.de *Web Site:* www.breklumer.de, pg 204

Editions Jacques Bremond (France) *Tel:* (04) 66 57 45 61; (06) 78 51 48 15 *Fax:* (04) 66 37 27 40 *E-mail:* editions-jacques-bremond@wanadoo.fr, pg 151

Joh & Sohn Brendow Verlag GmbH (Germany) *Tel:* (02841) 809-0 *Fax:* (02841) 809-291 *E-mail:* info@brendow-verlag.de *Web Site:* www.brendow.de, pg 204

Edizioni Brenner (Italy) *Tel:* (0984) 74537 *Fax:* (0984) 74537, pg 375

Verlag Das Brennglas (Germany) *Tel:* (09342) 915843 *Fax:* (09342) 915843 *E-mail:* info@brennglas.com *Web Site:* www.brennglas.com, pg 204

The Brenthurst Press (Pty) Ltd (South Africa) *Tel:* (011) 6466024 *Fax:* (011) 4861651 *E-mail:* orders@brenthurst.co.az *Web Site:* www.brenthurst.org.za, pg 558

Brepols Publishers NV (Belgium) *Tel:* (014) 448020 *Fax:* (014) 428919 *E-mail:* info@brepols.net *Web Site:* www.brepols.net, pg 63

Breslich & Foss Ltd (United Kingdom) *Tel:* (020) 7819 3990 *Fax:* (020) 7819 3998 *E-mail:* sales@breslichfoss.com, pg 666

Breslov Research Institute (Israel) *Tel:* (02) 5824641 *Fax:* (02) 5825542 *E-mail:* info@breslov.org *Web Site:* www.breslov.org/catalog.html, pg 362

Alain Brethes Editions (France) *Tel:* (02) 40 77 35 11; (02) 51 13 04 55, pg 151

Editore Giorgio Bretschneider (Italy) *Tel:* (06) 6879361 *Fax:* (06) 6864543 *E-mail:* info@bretschneider.it *Web Site:* www.bretschneider.it, pg 375

Brewin Books Ltd (United Kingdom) *Tel:* (01527) 854228 *Fax:* (01527) 852746 *E-mail:* enquiries@brewinbooks.com *Web Site:* www.brewinbooks.com, pg 666

Editions BRGM (France) *Tel:* (02) 38 64 30 28 *Fax:* (02) 38 64 36 82 *E-mail:* editions@brgm.fr *Web Site:* editions.brgm.fr, pg 151

Brick Row Publishing Co Ltd (New Zealand) *Tel:* (09) 4106993 *Fax:* (09) 4106993, pg 489

The Bridge Book Co Ltd (United Kingdom) *Tel:* (020) 7697 3000 *Fax:* (020) 7700 4552 *E-mail:* bridgepem@aol.com, pg 1340

Bridge Books (United Kingdom) *Tel:* (01978) 358661 *Fax:* (01978) 262377, pg 666

Bridge Bookshop Ltd (United Kingdom) *Tel:* (01624) 833378 *Fax:* (01624) 835381, pg 1340

Bridge To Peace Publications (Australia) *Tel:* (02) 9875 1912 *E-mail:* books@bridgetopeace.com.au; adesso@ bridgetopeace.com.au *Web Site:* www.bridgetopeace. com.au, pg 16

Bridgeway Publications (Australia) *Tel:* (07) 3390 4323 *Fax:* (07) 3390 4323 *E-mail:* info@bridgeway.org.au *Web Site:* www.bridgeway.org.au, pg 16

Brigg Verlag Franz-Joset Buchler KG (Germany) *Tel:* (0821) 78094660 *Fax:* (0821) 78094661, pg 204

Bright Arts Hong Kong Ltd (Hong Kong) *Tel.* 25620119 *Fax:* 25657031 *E-mail:* william@brightartshk.com *Web Site:* www.brightartshk.com, pg 1167

Bright Book Centre (Pvt) Ltd (Sri Lanka) *Tel:* (0112) 434770 *Fax:* (0112) 333279; (0112) 43470, pg 1334

Bright Concepts Printing House (Philippines) *Tel:* (0917) 627-3803 *E-mail:* dawnphilatelics@yahoo.com, pg 513

Bright Future Printing Co Ltd (Hong Kong) *Tel:* 2515 1776 *Fax:* 2897 2799; 2558 1717, pg 1145, 1167

Brijbasi Printers Pvt Ltd (India) *Tel:* (011) 6914115; (011) 6841897 *Fax:* (011) 6837835, pg 328

Brill Academic Publishers (Netherlands) *Tel:* (071) 53 53 500 *Fax:* (071) 53 17 532 *E-mail:* cs@brill.nl *Web Site:* www.brill.nl, pg 476

E J Brill, Robert Brown & Associates (Australia) *Tel:* (063) 318577 *Fax:* (063) 321273, pg 16

Brilliant Publications (United Kingdom) *Tel:* (01525) 229720 *Fax:* (01525) 229725 *E-mail:* sales@ brilliantpublications.co.uk *Web Site:* www. brilliantpublications.co.uk, pg 666

Brimax Books (United Kingdom) *Tel:* (01243) 792 489 *Fax:* (020) 7531 8607, pg 666

Brinque Book Editora de Livros Ltda (Brazil) *Tel:* (011) 8428142 *Fax:* (011) 8432235 *E-mail:* brinquebook@ infantil.net, pg 78

The British Academy (United Kingdom) *Tel:* (020) 7969 5200 *Fax:* (020) 7969 5300 *E-mail:* secretary@britac. ac.uk *Web Site:* www.britac.ac.uk, pg 666

British & Irish Association of Law Librarians (United Kingdom) *Tel:* (01926) 491717 *Fax:* (01926) 491717 *E-mail:* holborn@linclib.sonnet.co.uk *Web Site:* www. biall.org.uk, pg 1572

British Association of Communicators in Business Ltd (CIB) (United Kingdom) *Tel:* (0870) 121 7606 *Fax:* (0870) 121 7601 *E-mail:* enquiries@cib.uk.com *Web Site:* www.cib.uk.com, pg 1280

British Copyright Council (United Kingdom) *Tel:* (020) 788 122 *Fax:* (020) 788 847 *E-mail:* secretary@ britishcopyright.org *Web Site:* www.britishcopyright. org, pg 1280

The British Council, Design, Publishing & Print Department (United Kingdom) *Tel:* (020) 7930 8466 *Fax:* (020) 7389 6347 *E-mail:* general.enquiries@ britishcouncil.org *Web Site:* www.britishcouncil.org, pg 666

British Council Information Resource Centre (Sri Lanka) *Tel:* (01) 581171 *Fax:* (01) 587079 *E-mail:* enquiries@britishcouncil.lk *Web Site:* www. britishcouncil.lk, pg 1544

British Council Libraries (India) *Tel:* (011) 371 1401 *Fax:* (011) 371 0717 *E-mail:* delhi.library@in. britishcouncil.org *Web Site:* www.bclindia.org/library, pg 1514

British Council Library (Bangladesh) *Tel:* (02) 861 8905-7; (02) 861 8867-8 *Fax:* (02) 861 3375; (02) 861 3255 *E-mail:* library@bd.britishcouncil.org *Web Site:* www. britishcouncil.org/bangladesh/, pg 1491

British Council Library (Colombia) *Tel:* (01) 618 0118; (01) 618 7680 *Fax:* (01) 218 7754 *E-mail:* info@ britishcouncil.org.co *Web Site:* www2.britishcouncil. org/colombia.htm, pg 1497

British Council Library (Cyprus) *Tel:* (022) 585000 *Fax:* (022) 677257 *E-mail:* enquiries@britishcouncil. org.cy *Web Site:* www.britcoun.org/cyprus, pg 1499

British Council Library (Ethiopia) *Tel:* (01) 55 00 22 *Fax:* (01) 55 25 44 *E-mail:* bc.addisababa@et. britishcouncil.org *Web Site:* www.britishcouncil.org/ ethiopia/index.htm; www.britishcouncil.org/ethiopia. htm, pg 1503

British Council Library (Ghana) *Tel:* (051) 23462; (051) 37197 *Fax:* (051) 26725 *E-mail:* infokumasi@ gh.britishcouncil.org *Web Site:* www.britishcouncil. org/ghana, pg 1510

British Council Library (Hong Kong) *Tel:* 2913 5100 *Fax:* 2913 5102 *E-mail:* info@britishcouncil.org.hk *Web Site:* www.britishcouncil.org.hk, pg 1512

British Council Library (Indonesia) *Tel:* (021) 515 5561 *Fax:* (021) 515 5562 *E-mail:* information@ britishcouncil.or.id *Web Site:* www.britishcouncil.or.id, pg 1515

British Council Library (Jordan) *Tel:* (06) 4636147; (06) 4636148 *Fax:* (06) 4656413 *E-mail:* information@ britishcouncil.org.jo *Web Site:* www.britishcouncil.org. jo, pg 1520

British Council Library (Lesotho) *Tel:* 312609 *Fax:* 310363 *E-mail:* general.enquiries@bc-lesotho. bcouncil.org, pg 1523

British Council Library (Malawi) *Tel:* (01) 773244 *Fax:* (01) 772945 *E-mail:* info@britishcouncil.org.mw *Web Site:* www.britishcouncil.org/malawi.htm, pg 1524

British Council Library (Malaysia) *Tel:* (03) 2723 7900 *Fax:* (03) 2713 6599 *E-mail:* information@ britishcouncil.org.my *Web Site:* www.britcoun.org/ malaysia, pg 1525

British Council Library (Mauritius) *Tel:* 4549550; 4549551; 4549552 *Fax:* 4549553 *E-mail:* general. enquiries@mu.britishcouncil.org *Web Site:* www. britishcouncil.org/mauritius, pg 1526

British Council Library (Morocco) *Tel:* (037) 76 08 36 *Fax:* (037) 76 08 50 *E-mail:* bc@britishcouncil.org.ma *Web Site:* www2.britishcouncil.org/morocco, pg 1528

British Council Library (Nepal) *Tel:* (01) 4410 798 *Fax:* (01) 4410 545 *E-mail:* general.enquiry@ britishcouncil.org.np *Web Site:* www.britishcouncil. org/nepal, pg 1529

British Council Library (Pakistan) *Tel:* (051) 111 424 424 *Toll Free Tel:* 0800 22000 *Fax:* (051) 111 425 425 *E-mail:* info@britishcouncil.org.pk *Web Site:* www.britishcouncil.org.pk, pg 1533

British Council Library (Sierra Leone) *Tel:* (022) 222223; (022) 222227; (022) 2224683 *Fax:* (022) 224123 *E-mail:* enquiry@sl.britishcouncil.org *Web Site:* www.britishcouncil.org/sierraleone, pg 1541

The British Council Library (Spain) *Tel:* (091) 337 3500 *Fax:* (091) 337 3573 *E-mail:* madrid@britishcouncil.es *Web Site:* www.britishcouncil.es, pg 1544

British Council Library (Sudan) *Tel:* (0183) 780817; (0183) 777310 *Fax:* (0183) 774935 *E-mail:* info@ sd.britishcouncil.org *Web Site:* www.britishcouncil. org/sudan, pg 1545

British Council Library (United Republic of Tanzania) *Tel:* (022) 2116574; (022) 2118255; (022) 2138303; (022) 2116575; (022) 2116576 *Fax:* (022) 2112669; (022) 2116577 *E-mail:* info@britishcouncil.or.tz *Web Site:* www.britishcouncil.org/tanzania, pg 1548

British Council Library (Thailand) *Tel:* (02) 652 5480; (02) 652 5489 *Fax:* (02) 253 5312 *E-mail:* bc. bangkok@britcoun.or.th *Web Site:* www.britishcouncil. or.th/en/index.asp, pg 1548

British Council Library (Tunisia) *Tel:* 71 353 568 *Fax:* 71 353 985 *E-mail:* info@tn.britishcouncil.org *Web Site:* www.britishcouncil.org/tunisia, pg 1549

British Council Library (Yemen) *Tel:* (01) 448 356; (01) 448 357; (01) 448 358; (01) 448 359 *Fax:* (01) 448 360 *E-mail:* britishcouncil@ye.britishcouncil.org *Web Site:* www.britishcouncil.org/yemen.htm, pg 1554

British Council Library & Resource Centre (Greece) *Tel:* 2103692333 *Fax:* 2103634769 *E-mail:* general.enquiries@britcoun.gr *Web Site:* www. britishcouncil.gr/infoexch/greinfll.htm, pg 1511

British Educational Communication & Technology Agency (BECTA) (United Kingdom) *Tel:* (024) 7641 6994 *Fax:* (024) 7641 1418 *E-mail:* becta@becta.org. uk *Web Site:* www.becta.org.uk, pg 667

British Fantasy Society (BFS) (United Kingdom) *Tel:* (0161) 6004125 *E-mail:* info@ britishfantasysociety.org.uk *Web Site:* www. britishfantasysociety.org.uk, pg 1401

British Guild of Travel Writers (United Kingdom) *Tel:* (020) 8749 1128 *Fax:* (020) 8749 1128 *E-mail:* bgtw@garlandintl.co.uk *Web Site:* www.bgtw. org, pg 1280

British Horse Society (United Kingdom) *Tel:* (08701) 202 244 *Fax:* (01926) 707 800 *E-mail:* enquiry@bhs. org.uk *Web Site:* www.bhs.org.uk, pg 667

British Institute in Eastern Africa (Kenya) *Tel:* (02) 4343190; (02) 4343330 *Fax:* (02) 43365 *E-mail:* britinst@insightkenya.com *Web Site:* www. britac.ac.uk/institutes/eafrica, pg 430

The British Library (United Kingdom) *Tel:* (0870) 444 1500 *E-mail:* nbs-info@bl.uk *Web Site:* www.bl.uk, pg 667

The British Library (United Kingdom) *Tel:* (0870) 444 1500 *Web Site:* www.bl.uk, pg 1551

British Library Document Supply Centre (United Kingdom) *Tel:* (01937) 546060 *Fax:* (01937) 546333 *E-mail:* dsc-customer-services@bl.uk *Web Site:* www. bl.uk, pg 667

British Library Document Supply Centre (United Kingdom) *Tel:* (01937) 546060 *Fax:* (01937) 546333 *E-mail:* dsc-customer-services@bl.uk *Web Site:* www. bl.uk/services/document/contact.html, pg 1551

British Library, Newspaper Library (United Kingdom) *Tel:* (020) 7412 7353 *Fax:* (020) 7412 7379 *E-mail:* newspaper@bl.uk *Web Site:* www.bl.uk, pg 1551

British Library of Political & Economic Science (United Kingdom) *Tel:* (020) 7955 7229 *Fax:* (020) 7955 7454 *E-mail:* library@lse.ac.uk *Web Site:* www.lse. ac.uk/library, pg 1551

British Library Oriental & India Office Collections (United Kingdom) *Tel:* (020) 7412 7873 *Fax:* (020) 7412 7641 *E-mail:* oioc-prints@bl.uk *Web Site:* www. bl.uk, pg 1551

British Library Publications (United Kingdom) *Tel:* (020) 7412 7000 *Fax:* (020) 7412 7768 *E-mail:* enquiries@ bl.uk *Web Site:* www.bl.uk, pg 667

The British Library, Science Technology & Business Collections (United Kingdom) *Tel:* (020) 7412 7288; (020) 7412 7494 *E-mail:* scitech@bl.uk *Web Site:* www.bl.uk, pg 1551

British Museum Press (United Kingdom) *Tel:* (020) 7637 1292 *Fax:* (020) 7436 7315 *E-mail:* customerservices@bmcompany.co.uk; information@thebritishmuseum.ac.uk *Web Site:* www. britishmuseum.co.uk, pg 667

British Printing Industries Federation (BPIF) (United Kingdom) *Tel:* (0870) 240 4085 *Fax:* (020) 7405 7784 *E-mail:* info@bpif.org.uk *Web Site:* www.britishprint. com, pg 1280

The British Science Fiction Association Ltd (BSFA Ltd) (United Kingdom) *E-mail:* bsfa@enterprise.net *Web Site:* www.bsfa.co.uk, pg 1401

British Sisalkraft Ltd (United Kingdom) *Tel:* (01634) 292700 *Fax:* (01634) 291029 *E-mail:* sales@bsk-laminating.com *Web Site:* www.bsk-laminating.com, pg 1153

British Tourist Authority (United Kingdom) *Tel:* (020) 8846 9000 *Fax:* (020) 8846 0302 *Web Site:* www. visitbritain.com, pg 667

Brockhaus Commission GmbH (Germany) *Tel:* (07154) 1327-33 *Fax:* (07154) 1327-13 *E-mail:* bro@ brockhaus-commission.de, pg 204

Butterworths New Zealand Ltd (New Zealand) *Tel:* (04) 385 1479 *Fax:* (04) 385 1598 *E-mail:* Customer. Relations@butterworths.co.nz *Web Site:* www. butterworths.co.nz; www.lexisnexis.com/au/nz, pg 490

Butterworths Tolley (United Kingdom) *Tel:* (020) 8686 9141; (020) 8662 2000 (customer service) *Fax:* (020) 8686 3155; (020) 8662 2012 (customer service) *E-mail:* customer-services@butterworths.com, pg 668

Butzon & Bercker GmbH (Germany) *Tel:* (02832) 929-0 *Fax:* (02832) 929-112 *E-mail:* service@butzonbercker. de *Web Site:* www.butzonbercker.de, pg 206

BV Uitgevery NZV (Nederlandse Zondagsschool Vereniging) (Netherlands) *Tel:* (033) 460 60 11 *Fax:* (035) 460 60 20 *E-mail:* info@nzv.nl *Web Site:* www.nzv.nl, pg 476

Bwrdd Croeso Cymru (United Kingdom) *Tel:* (029) 2047 5214 *Fax:* (029) 2048 5031 *E-mail:* info@visitwales. com *Web Site:* www.visitwales.com, pg 668

Forlaget By och Bygd (Sweden) *Tel:* (08) 652 09 55, pg 605

Bycornute Books (United Kingdom) *Tel:* (01323) 649053, pg 1129

Byggforlaget (Sweden) *Tel:* (08) 665 36 50 *Fax:* (08) 667 39 49 *Web Site:* www.byggforlaget.se, pg 605

Byron Society (International) (United Kingdom) *Tel:* (020) 7352 5112; (020) 7352 7238 *Web Site:* www.byronsociety.com, pg 1401

BZZTOH Publishers (Netherlands) *Tel:* (070) 3632934 *Fax:* (070) 3631932 *E-mail:* info@bzztoh.nl *Web Site:* www.bzztoh.nl, pg 476

C & C Offset Printing Co Ltd (Hong Kong) *Tel:* 2666-4988 *Fax:* 2666-4938 *E-mail:* offsetprinting@ candcprinting.com *Web Site:* www.ccoffset.com, pg 1145, 1167, 1207

C & C Offset Printing Co Ltd (United States) *Tel:* 503-233-1834 *Fax:* 503-233-7815 *E-mail:* portlandinfo@ ccoffset.com *Web Site:* www.ccoffset.com, pg 1155, 1176, 1218

C&S Publications (New Zealand) *Tel:* (0812) 56807 *Fax:* (0812) 8966583, pg 490

C V Toko Buku Tropen (Indonesia) *Tel:* (021) 381 1669; (021) 381 3543; (021) 380 5938 *Fax:* (021) 380 0566 *E-mail:* tropen@cbn.net.id, pg 1308

Ca Luna Forlaget (Denmark) *Tel:* 86 82 86 88; 26 20 24 68 *Fax:* 86 82 86 64 *E-mail:* caluna@caluna.dk *Web Site:* www.caluna.dk, pg 129

Caann Verlag, Klaus Wagner (Germany) *Tel:* (08121) 9 32 71 *Fax:* (08121) 9 32 78 *E-mail:* info@caann-verlag.de *Web Site:* www.caann-verlag.de, pg 206

CAB International (United Kingdom) *Tel:* (01491) 832111 *Fax:* (01491) 833508 *E-mail:* corporate@cabi. org *Web Site:* www.cabi.org, pg 1280

Ediciones el Caballito SA (Mexico) *Tel:* (05) 5849-2533; (05) 5963400, pg 459

CABI Publishing (United Kingdom) *Tel:* (01491) 832111 *Fax:* (01491) 833508 *E-mail:* publishing@cabi.org *Web Site:* www.cabi-publishing.org, pg 668

Cabildo Insular de Gran Canaria Departamento de Ediciones (Spain) *Tel:* (0928) 219421 *Fax:* (0928) 381627 *E-mail:* webadmin@grancanaria.com *Web Site:* www.grancanaria.com, pg 570

Cabinet Conseil CCMLA (Morocco) *Tel:* (07) 770229; (07) 770264 *Fax:* (07) 770264, pg 470

Cacho Publishing House, Inc (Philippines) *Tel:* (02) 783011-13 *Fax:* (02) 6315244 *E-mail:* cacho@s.com. ph, pg 514

Cacho Publishing inc (Philippines) *Tel:* (02) 6318362; (02) 6318363; (02) 6318364; (02) 6318365 *Fax:* (02) 6315244 *E-mail:* cacho@mozcom.com, pg 1150

Cacho Publishing inc (Philippines) *Tel:* (02) 783011-13 *Fax:* (02) 6315244 *E-mail:* cacho@mozcom.com, pg 1212

Cacucci Editore (Italy) *Tel:* (080) 521 42 20 *Fax:* (080) 523 47 77 *E-mail:* info@cacucci.it *Web Site:* www. cacucci.it, pg 376

Cadans (Netherlands) *Tel:* (020) 6206263 *Fax:* (020) 4288540 *E-mail:* post@sjaloom.nl *Web Site:* www. sjaloom.com, pg 476

Cadence Publicacoes Internacionais Ltda (Brazil) *Tel:* (021) 2637885 *Fax:* (021) 2830812 *E-mail:* cadence@mtecnet.com.br, pg 79

Edizioni Cadmo SRL (Italy) *Tel:* (055) 50 18 1 *Fax:* (055) 50 18 201 *E-mail:* info@casalini.it *Web Site:* www.casalini.it, pg 376

Cadmos Verlag GmbH (Germany) *Tel:* (04107) 8517-0 *Fax:* (041307) 8517-0 *E-mail:* info@cadmos.de *Web Site:* www.cadmos.de, pg 206

Cadogan Guides (United Kingdom) *Tel:* (020) 8740 2050 *Fax:* (020) 8740 2059 *E-mail:* info@cadoganguides. com; editorial@cadoganguides.com; advertising@ cadoganguides.com; publicity@cadoganguides.com; marketing@cadoganguides.com *Web Site:* www. cadoganguides.com, pg 668

Editions du Cadratin (France) *Tel:* (03) 25 38 60 24 *Fax:* (03) 25 38 60 24, pg 151

Caglayan Kitabevi (Turkey) *Tel:* (0212) 2454433 *Fax:* (0212) 1491794 *E-mail:* info@caglayan.com, pg 645

Editions des Cahiers Bourbonnais (France) *Tel:* (0470) 568 061 *Fax:* (0470) 568 080 *Web Site:* www.cahiers-bourbonnais.com, pg 151

Editions Cahiers d'Art (France) *Tel:* (01) 45487673 *Fax:* (01) 45449850 *E-mail:* cahiersart@aol.com, pg 151

Cahiers de la Renaissance Vaudoise (Switzerland) *Tel:* (021) 3121914 *Fax:* (021) 3126714 *E-mail:* courrier@ligue-vaudoise.ch *Web Site:* www. ligue-vaudoise.ch, pg 615

Cahiers du Cinema (France) *Tel:* (01) 53 44 75 77 *Fax:* (01) 43 43 95 04 *E-mail:* cducinema@lemonde.fr *Web Site:* www.cahiersducinema.com, pg 151

Les Cahiers Fiscaux Europeens (France) *Tel:* (04) 93 53 89 39 *Fax:* (04) 93 53 66 28 *E-mail:* auteurs@ fontaneau.com *Web Site:* www.cahiers-fiscoux.com, pg 151

Cahiers Luxembourgeois (Luxembourg) *Tel:* 338885 *Fax:* 336513, pg 447

Cairns Art Society Inc (Australia) *Tel:* (07) 4032 1506, pg 16

Cairo University Press (Egypt (Arab Republic of Egypt)) *Tel:* (02) 846144, pg 137

Caja de Ahorros del Mediterraneo-Obras Sociales (Spain) *Tel:* (06) 5906363; (06) 5905785 *Fax:* (06) 5905828 *E-mail:* cam@cam.es *Web Site:* www.cam.es, pg 570

Calambur Editorial, SL (Spain) *Tel:* (091) 913553033 *Fax:* (091) 913553033 *E-mail:* calambur@ calumbureditorial.com *Web Site:* www. calumbureditorial.com, pg 570

Calamo Editorial (Spain) *Tel:* (096) 5130581 *Fax:* (096) 5115345 *E-mail:* calamo@lobocom.es *Web Site:* www. lobocom.es/~calamo, pg 570

CALCRE, Association d'Information et de Defense des Auteurs (France) *E-mail:* commande@calcre.com *Web Site:* www.calcre.com, pg 1393

Randolph Caldecott Society (United Kingdom) *Tel:* (01606) 891303 *E-mail:* charles.caldecott@ lineone.net *Web Site:* www.randolphcaldecott.org.uk, pg 1401

Calder Publications Ltd (United Kingdom) *Tel:* (020) 7633 0599 *E-mail:* info@calderpublications.com *Web Site:* www.calderpublications.com, pg 669

Calderini SRL (Italy) *Tel:* (051) 6226822 *Fax:* (051) 549329 *E-mail:* comm@calderini.agriline.it *Web Site:* www.calderini.it, pg 1149

Caledonian International Book Manufacturing (United Kingdom) *Tel:* (0141) 7623000 *Fax:* (0141) 7620922 *E-mail:* 101622.235@compuserve.com, pg 1174, 1215

Calesa SA Editorial La (Spain) *Tel:* (0983) 548 102 *Fax:* (0983) 548 024 *E-mail:* editorial@la-calesa.com *Web Site:* www.la-calesa.com, pg 570

Callenbach BV (Netherlands) *Tel:* (038) 3392555 *Fax:* (038) 3311776 *E-mail:* algemeen@kok.nl, pg 476

Callis Editora Ltda (Brazil) *Tel:* (011) 3842-2066 *Fax:* (011) 3849-5882 *E-mail:* editorial@callis.com. br; callis@callis.com.br *Web Site:* www.callis.com.br, pg 79

Verlag Georg D W Callwey GmbH & Co (Germany) *Tel:* (089) 436005-0 *Fax:* (089) 436005-117 *E-mail:* info@callwey.de *Web Site:* www.callwey.de, pg 206

Editions Calmann-Levy SA (France) *Tel:* (01) 49 54 36 00 *Fax:* (01) 45 44 86 32 *E-mail:* editions@calmann-levy.fr *Web Site:* www.editions-calmann-levy.com, pg 151

Calosci (Italy) *Tel:* (0575) 678282 *Fax:* (0575) 678282 *E-mail:* info@calosci.com *Web Site:* www.calosci.com, pg 376

Calvary Press (Sri Lanka) *Tel:* (01) 553110, pg 601

Calwer Verlag GmbH (Germany) *Tel:* (0711) 167 22-0 *Fax:* (0711) 167 22 77 *E-mail:* info@calwer.com *Web Site:* www.calwer.com, pg 206

Edicions Camacuc (Spain) *Tel:* (096) 357 28 56 *Fax:* (096) 357 28 56, pg 570

Camara Argentina del Libro (Argentina) *Tel:* (011) 4381-8383 *Fax:* (011) 4381-9253 *E-mail:* cal@editores.org. ar *Web Site:* www.editores.org.ar, pg 1249

Camara Boliviana del Libro (Bolivia) *Tel:* (02) 44 4239; (02) 44 4077 *Fax:* (02) 44 1523 *E-mail:* cabolib@ ceibo.entelnet.bo, pg 1253

Camara Brasileira do Livro (Brazil) *Tel:* (011) 3069-1300 *Fax:* (011) 3069-1300 *E-mail:* cbl@cbl.org.br *Web Site:* www.cbl.org.br, pg 1253

Camara Chilena del Libro AG (Chile) *Tel:* (02) 6989519; (02) 6724088 *Fax:* (02) 6989226 *E-mail:* prolibro@tie. cl *Web Site:* www.camlibro.cl, pg 1254

Camara Colombiana del Libro (Colombia) *Tel:* (01) 288 6188 *Fax:* (01) 287 3320 *E-mail:* camlibro@camlibro. com.co *Web Site:* www.camlibro.com.co, pg 1254

Camara Dos Deputados Coordenacao De Publicacoes (Brazil) *Tel:* (061) 216-0000 *Fax:* (061) 318-2190 *E-mail:* publicacoes.cedi@camara.gov.br *Web Site:* www.camara.gov.br, pg 79

Camara Ecuatoriana del Libro (Ecuador) *Tel:* (02) 553311; (02) 553314 *Fax:* (02) 222150 *E-mail:* celnp@hoy.net *Web Site:* www.celibro.org.ec, pg 1256

Camara Municipal de Castelo (Portugal) *Tel:* (058) 809300 *Fax:* (058) 809347, pg 524

Camara Nacional de la Industria Editorial Mexicana (Mexico) *Tel:* (05) 6 88 24 34; (05) 6 88 22 21; (05) 6 88 2011 *Toll Free Tel:* (800) 714-5352 *Fax:* (055) 5604-4347; (05) 6 04 31 47 *E-mail:* cepromex@ caniem.com *Web Site:* www.caniem.com, pg 1267

Biblioteca de la Camara Oficial de Comercio, Agricultura e Industria del Distrito Nacional (Dominican Republic) *Tel:* 682-2688; 682-7206 *Fax:* 685-2228, pg 1501

Camara Peruana del Libro (Peru) *Tel:* (01) 428 7690; (01) 428 7696 *Fax:* (01) 427 7331 *E-mail:* dn@ binape.gob.pe *Web Site:* www.binape.gob.pe, pg 1271

Camara Uruguaya del Libro (Uruguay) *Tel:* (082) 41 57 32 *Fax:* (082) 41 18 60 *E-mail:* camurlib@adinet.com. uy, pg 1285

Camara Venezolana del Libro (Venezuela) *Tel:* (0212) 7931347; (0212) 7931368 *Fax:* (0212) 7931368 *E-mail:* cavelibro@cantv.net, pg 1285

Caribbean & Latin American Studies Library (Puerto Rico) *Tel:* (787) 764-0000 (ext 3319) *Fax:* (787) 763-5685, pg 1537

Caribbean Authors Publishing (Jamaica) *Tel:* 876-929-6163 *Fax:* 876-929-1226, pg 409

Caribbean Community Secretariat (Guyana) *Tel:* (02) 26-9280; (02) 26-9281; (02) 26-9282; (02) 26-9283; (02) 26-9284; (02) 26-9285; (02) 26-9286; (02) 26-9287; (02) 26-9288; (02) 26-9289 *Fax:* (02) 26-7816; (02) 25-7341; (02) 25-8031 *E-mail:* carisec1@caricom.org; carisec2@caricom.org; carisec3@caricom.org *Web Site:* www.caricom.org, pg 311

Caribbean Epidemiology Centre (Trinidad & Tobago) *Tel:* (868) 622-4261; (868) 622-4262 *Fax:* (868) 622-2792 *E-mail:* postmaster@carec.paho.org *Web Site:* www.carec.org, pg 642

Caribbean Food & Nutrition Institute (Jamaica) *Tel:* 876-927-1540; 876-927-1927 *Fax:* 876-927-2657 *E-mail:* e-mail@cfni.paho.org, pg 409

Caribbean Telecommunications Union (Trinidad & Tobago) *Tel:* (868) 627-0281; (868) 627-0347 *Fax:* (868) 623-1523 *E-mail:* ctunion@c-t-u.org; secgen@c-t-u.org *Web Site:* www.c-t-u.org, pg 642

Carinthia Verlag (Austria) *Tel:* (0463) 50 12 20-220 *Fax:* (0463) 50 12 20-214 *Web Site:* www.verlag.carinthia.com, pg 49

Carit Andersens Forlag A/S (Denmark) *Tel:* 35436222 *Fax:* 35435151 *E-mail:* info@caritandersen.dk *Web Site:* www.caritandersen.dk, pg 129

Caritas Printing Training Centre (Hong Kong) *Tel:* 2526 1148 *Fax:* 2537 1231 *E-mail:* info@caritas.org.hk *Web Site:* www.caritas.hk, pg 1145

Caritas Printing Training Centre (Hong Kong) *Tel:* 25261148 *Fax:* 25371231 *E-mail:* info@caritas.org.hk *Web Site:* www.caritas.hk, pg 1167

Caritas Printing Training Centre (Hong Kong) *Tel:* 2526 1148 *Fax:* 2537 1231, pg 1207

Caritas Printing Training Centre (Hong Kong) *Tel:* 2524 2701 (ext 647) *Fax:* 2530 3065 *Web Site:* vtes.caritas.org.hk, pg 1226

Carl-Auer-Systeme Verlag (Germany) *Tel:* (06221) 64380 *Fax:* (06221) 643822 *E-mail:* info@carl-auer.de *Web Site:* www.carl-auer.de, pg 207

Fachverlag Hans Carl GmbH (Germany) *Tel:* (0911) 95285-0 (0911) 95285-48; (0911) 95285-71; (0911) 95285-61 *E-mail:* info@hanscarl.com *Web Site:* www.hanscarl.com, pg 207

Fachverlag Hans Carl GmbH (Germany) *Tel:* (0911) 95285-0 *Fax:* (0911) 95285-48 *E-mail:* info@hanscarl.com *Web Site:* www.hanscarl.com, pg 1300

Carl Link Verlag-Gesellschaft mbH Fachverlag fur Verwaltungsrecht (Germany) *Tel:* (09261) 969 4000 *Fax:* (09261) 969 4111 *E-mail:* info@carllink.de *Web Site:* www.carllink.de, pg 207

Carlong Publishers (Caribbean) Ltd (Jamaica) *Tel:* (876) 923-7008 *Fax:* (876) 923-7003 *E-mail:* sales@carlpub.com, pg 410

Forlaget Carlsen A/S (Denmark) *Tel:* 4444 3233 *Fax:* 4444 3633 *E-mail:* carlsen@carlsen.dk *Web Site:* www.carlsen.dk, pg 129

Carlsen Verlag GmbH (Germany) *Tel:* (040) 39 804 0 *Fax:* (040) 39 804 390, pg 207

Carlsson Bokfoerlag AB (Sweden) *Tel:* (08) 411 23 49 *Fax:* (08) 796 84 57, pg 605

Carlton Publishing Group (United Kingdom) *Tel:* (020) 7612 0400 *Fax:* (020) 7612 0401 *E-mail:* enquires@carltonbooks.co.uk; sales@carltonbooks.co.uk; editorial@carltonbooks.co.uk *Web Site:* www.carltonint.co.uk, pg 670

Carmelitana VZW (Belgium) *Tel:* (09) 225.48.36 *Fax:* (09) 224.06.01 *E-mail:* boekhandel@carmelitana.be *Web Site:* www.carmelitana.be, pg 64

Edizioni Carmelitane (Italy) *Tel:* (06) 68100886 *Fax:* (06) 68100887 *E-mail:* edizioni@ocarm.org *Web Site:* www.carmelites.info/edizioni, pg 376

Carnegie Library (Mauritius) *Tel:* 670 4897; 670 4898 *Fax:* 676 5054 *E-mail:* contact@curepipe.org *Web Site:* www.curepipe.org, pg 1526

Carnell Literary Agency (United Kingdom) *Tel:* (01279) 723626 *Fax:* (01279) 600308, pg 1129

Jon Carpenter Publishing (United Kingdom) *Tel:* (01608) 811969 *Fax:* (01608) 811969, pg 670

Editions Didier Carpentier (France) *Tel:* (01) 48 78 85 81 *Fax:* (01) 42 82 91 99, pg 152

Alzira Chagas Carpigiani (Brazil) *Tel:* (011) 849-0189 *Fax:* (011) 227-3384 *E-mail:* kerredit@uol.com.br, pg 79

Carre d'Art Edition Archigraphie (Switzerland) *Tel:* (022) 311 57 50 *Fax:* (022) 312 21 21, pg 615

Carrick Media (United Kingdom) *Tel:* (01563) 530830 *Fax:* (01563) 549503 *E-mail:* cm@carrickmedia.demon.co.uk, pg 670

Edizioni Carroccio (Italy) *Tel:* (049) 700568 *Fax:* (049) 700568, pg 376

Carroggio SA de Ediciones (Spain) *Tel:* (093) 4949922 *Fax:* (093) 4949923 *E-mail:* carroggio@carroggio.com *Web Site:* www.carroggio.es, pg 571

Carroll & Brown Ltd (United Kingdom) *Tel:* (020) 7372 0900 *Fax:* (020) 7372 0460 *E-mail:* carbro.prod@virgin.net, pg 670

The Lewis Carroll Society (United Kingdom) *E-mail:* aztec@compuserve.com *Web Site:* lewiscarrollsociety.org.uk, pg 1280

Carta, The Israel Map & Publishing Co Ltd (Israel) *Tel:* (02) 678 3355 *Fax:* (02) 678 2373 *E-mail:* carta@carta.co.il *Web Site:* www.holyland-jerusalem.com, pg 362

Editura Cartea Moldovei (Republic of Moldova) *Tel:* (02) 244022 *Fax:* (02) 246411, pg 469

Editura Cartea Romaneasca (Romania) *Tel:* (01) 3123733; (01) 6148802 *Fax:* (01) 3110025, pg 534

Edizioni Cartedit SRL (Italy) *Tel:* (0373) 277410 *Fax:* (0373) 277405, pg 376

Carter's (Antiques & Collectibles) P/L (Australia) *Tel:* (02) 8850 4600 *Fax:* (02) 8850 4100 *E-mail:* info@carters.com.au *Web Site:* www.carters.com.au, pg 17

Carto BVBA (Belgium) *Tel:* (02) 2680345 *Fax:* (02) 2680345, pg 64

Cartoeristiek (Federatie van Belgische Autobus- en Autocarondernemers) (BAAV) (Belgium) *Tel:* (051) 226060 *Fax:* (051) 229273, pg 64

Edizioni Cartografiche Milanesi (Italy) *Tel:* (02) 9101649 *Fax:* (02) 9101118 *E-mail:* info@ortelio-ecm.it *Web Site:* www.ortelio-ecm.it, pg 376

Cartographia Ltd (Hungary) *Tel:* (01) 222-6727 *Fax:* (01) 222-6728 *E-mail:* mail@cartographia.hu *Web Site:* www.cartographia.hu, pg 318

Cartoon-Caricature-Contor (CCC) (Germany) *Tel:* (089) 3233669 *Fax:* (089) 3226859 *E-mail:* ccc@c5.net *Web Site:* www.c5.net, pg 1121

The Cartoon Cave (United Kingdom) *Tel:* (01780) 460689; (01780) 460757 *Fax:* (01780) 460689 *Web Site:* www.cartooncave.co.uk, pg 670

CartoTravel Verlag GmbH & Co KG (Germany) *Tel:* (06196) 6096-0 *Fax:* (06196) 27450 *E-mail:* info@cartotravel.de *Web Site:* www.cartotravel.de, pg 207

Carvajal SA (Peru) *Tel:* (01) 440 9685; (01) 440 9618 *Fax:* (01) 440 5871 *E-mail:* carvajal@correo.dnet.com.pe *Web Site:* www.carvajal.com.co, pg 512

Carvajal International Inc (United States) *Tel:* 305-448-6875 *Toll Free Tel:* 800-622-6657 *Fax:* 305-448-9942 *E-mail:* info@cargraphics.com *Web Site:* www.carvajal.com.co, pg 1218

A Tavares de Carvalho (Portugal) *Tel:* (021) 797 0377 *Fax:* (021) 795 8880, pg 1327

Casa de la Cultura Ecuatoriana Benjamin Carrion (Ecuador) *Tel:* (02) 2223391; (02) 2565721 (ext 120) *Fax:* (02) 2566070 *E-mail:* info@cce.org.ec *Web Site:* cce.org.ec, pg 1393

Casa de las Americas (Cuba) *Tel:* (07) 55 2706; (07) 55 2709 *Fax:* (07) 33 4554; (07) 32 7272 *E-mail:* revista@casa.cult.cu *Web Site:* www.casadelasamericas.com, pg 119

Casa de Velazquez (Spain) *Tel:* (091) 5433605 *Fax:* (091) 5446870 *E-mail:* bcv@bibli.cvz.es, pg 571

Casa Editora Abril (Cuba) *Tel:* (07) 8627871; (07) 8624359 *Fax:* (07) 335282 *E-mail:* eabril@jcc.org.cu *Web Site:* www.almamater.cu, pg 120

Casa Editoriala Independenta Europa (Romania) *Tel:* (051) 153487; (051) 425801 *Fax:* (051) 153487, pg 534

Casa Editrice Giuseppe Principato Spa (Italy) *Tel:* (02) 312025; (02) 3315309 *Fax:* (02) 33104295 *E-mail:* info@principato.it *Web Site:* www.principato.it, pg 377

Casa Editrice Libraria Ulrico Hoepli SpA (Italy) *Tel:* (02) 864871 *Fax:* (02) 864322 *E-mail:* hoepli@hoepli.it *Web Site:* www.hoepli.it, pg 377

Casa Editrice Lint Srl (Italy) *Tel:* (040) 360396 *Fax:* (040) 361354 *Web Site:* www.linteditoriale.com, pg 377

Casa Musicale Edizioni Carrara SRL (Italy) *Tel:* (035) 243618 *Fax:* (035) 270398 *E-mail:* info@edizionicarrara.it *Web Site:* www.edizionicarrara.it, pg 377

Casa Musicale G Zanibon SRL (Italy) *Tel:* (02) 88811 *Fax:* (02) 88814317, pg 377

Edizioni Casagrande SA (Switzerland) *Tel:* (091) 820 0101 *Fax:* (091) 825 1874 *E-mail:* casagrande@casagrande-online.ch *Web Site:* www.casagrande-online.ch, pg 615

Casalini Libri (Italy) *Tel:* (055) 5018 1 *Fax:* (055) 5018 201 *E-mail:* info@casalini.it *Web Site:* www.casalini.it, pg 377, 1310

Editorial Casals SA (Spain) *Tel:* (093) 2449550 *Fax:* (093) 2656895 *E-mail:* casals@editorialcasals.com *Web Site:* www.editorialcasals.com, pg 571

Editorial Casariego (Spain) *Tel:* (091) 4424339; (091) 4425178; (091) 4411330; (091) 4416829 *Fax:* (091) 4426224 *E-mail:* casariego@infonegocio.com *Web Site:* www.casariego.com, pg 571

Casarotto Ramsay & Associates Ltd (United Kingdom) *Tel:* (020) 7287 4450 *Fax:* (020) 7287 9128 *E-mail:* agents@casarotto.uk.com *Web Site:* www.casarotto.uk.com, pg 1129

Casket Publications (Australia) *Tel:* (02) 9805 8878; (02) 9481 9145 *Fax:* (02) 9875 5382, pg 17

Frank Cass Publishers (United Kingdom) *Tel:* (020) 8920 2100 *Fax:* (020) 8447 8548 *E-mail:* info@frankcass.com *Web Site:* www.frankcass.com, pg 670

Cassell & Co (United Kingdom) *Tel:* (020) 7420 5555 *Fax:* (020) 7240 7261; (020) 7240 8531, pg 671

Casset Ediciones SL (Spain) *Tel:* (091) 5043584 *Fax:* (091) 2508841, pg 571

Editorial Castalia (Spain) *Tel:* (091) 3195857 *Fax:* (091) 3102442 *E-mail:* castalia@infornet.es *Web Site:* www.castalia.es, pg 571

Casa Editrice Castalia (Italy) *Tel:* (011) 4342621 *Fax:* (011) 4342621, pg 377

Editions Casteilla (France) *Tel:* (01) 30 14 19 30 *Fax:* (01) 34 60 31 32 *E-mail:* info@casteilla.fr *Web Site:* www.casteilla.fr, pg 152

Il Castello srl (Italy) *Tel:* (02) 48401629 *Fax:* (02) 4453617 *E-mail:* il_castello@tin.it, pg 377

Editions Casterman SA (Belgium) *Tel:* (02) 209 83 00 *Fax:* (02) 209 83 01 *E-mail:* info@casterman.com *Web Site:* www.casterman.com, pg 64

Casterman NV (Belgium) *Tel:* (02) 2409320 *Fax:* (02) 2163598, pg 64

Castle House Publications Ltd (United Kingdom) *Tel:* (01892) 39606 *Fax:* (01892) 39609, pg 671

Castle Publications SA (Switzerland) *Tel:* (022) 511036 *Fax:* (022) 7511111; (022) 7884240, pg 615

Castle Translations (United Kingdom) *Tel:* (01524) 841169 *Fax:* (01524) 381721 *E-mail:* info@ castletranslations.co.uk *Web Site:* ukpetsearch.freeuk. com/castletrans, pg 1140

Castlemead Publications (United Kingdom) *Tel:* (01920) 465525 *Fax:* (01920) 465545 *E-mail:* sales@ castlemeadpublications.fsnet.co.uk, pg 671

Le Castor Astral (France) *Tel:* (01) 48 40 14 95 *Fax:* (01) 48 45 97 52 *E-mail:* swproduction@magic. fr, pg 152

Editrice Il Castoro (Italy) *Tel:* (02) 29513529 *Fax:* (02) 29529896 *E-mail:* editrice.castoro@iol.it *Web Site:* www.castoro-on-line.it, pg 377

Edicios do Castro (Spain) *Tel:* (0981) 621494; (0981) 620937; (0981) 620200 *Fax:* (0981) 623804 *E-mail:* edicios.ocastro@sargadelos.com *Web Site:* www.sargadelos.com, pg 571

Castrum Peregrini Presse (Netherlands) *Tel:* (020) 235287 *Fax:* (020) 6247096 *E-mail:* mail@ castrumperegrini.nl *Web Site:* castrumperegrini.nl, pg 477

Biblioteca de Catalunya (Spain) *Tel:* (093) 270 23 00 *Fax:* (093) 270 23 01 *E-mail:* infocat@gencat.net *Web Site:* www.gencat.es/bc, pg 571, 1544

Catchfire Press Inc (Australia) *Tel:* (02) 4951 8859 *E-mail:* catchfire@idl.com.au *Web Site:* www.cust. idl.com.au/catchfire, pg 17

Ediciones Catedra SA (Spain) *Tel:* (091) 3200119; (091) 3938800; (091) 3938787 *Fax:* (091) 7426631; (091) 7412118 *E-mail:* catedra@catedra.com *Web Site:* www.catedra.com, pg 571

Cathedral Books Ltd (Ireland) *Tel:* (01) 8787372 *Fax:* (01) 8787704 *E-mail:* cathedra@indigo.ie, pg 355

Kyle Cathie Ltd (United Kingdom) *Tel:* (020) 7692 7215 *Fax:* (020) 7692 7260 *E-mail:* general.enquiries@kyle-cathie.com *Web Site:* www.kylecathie.co.uk, pg 671

Catholic Institute for International Relations (United Kingdom) *Tel:* (020) 7354 0883 *Fax:* (020) 7359 0017 *E-mail:* ciir@ciir.com *Web Site:* www.ciir.org, pg 672

Catholic Institute of Sydney (Australia) *Tel:* (02) 9752 9500 *Fax:* (02) 9746 6022 *E-mail:* cisinfo@cis. catholic.edu.au *Web Site:* www.cis.catholic.edu.au, pg 17

The Catholic Truth Society (United Kingdom) *Tel:* (020) 7640 0042 *Fax:* (020) 7640 0046 *E-mail:* info@cts-online.org.uk *Web Site:* www.cts-online.org.uk, pg 671

Imprimerie Catholique (Madagascar) *Tel:* (02) 22304, pg 1149

Catia Monser Eggcup-Verlag (Germany) *Tel:* (0211) 215122 *Fax:* (0211) 215122 *E-mail:* cmonserev@aol. com *Web Site:* members.aol.com/CMonserEV, pg 207

Causeway Press Ltd (United Kingdom) *Tel:* (01695) 576048; (01695) 577360 *Fax:* (01695) 570714 *E-mail:* davidalcorn.causewaypress@btinternet.com, pg 671

Caux Books (Switzerland) *Tel:* (021) 9629469 *Fax:* (021) 9629465 *E-mail:* info@caux.ch *Web Site:* www.caux. ch, pg 615

Caux Edition SA (Switzerland) *Tel:* (021) 963 94 69 *Fax:* (021) 962 94 65 *E-mail:* info@caux.ch *Web Site:* www.caux.ch, pg 615

Paul Cave Publications Ltd (United Kingdom) *Tel:* (01703) 223591; (01703) 333457 *Fax:* (01703) 227190 *E-mail:* lanksmag@zone.co.uk, pg 672

Verlag Bo Cavefors (Switzerland) *Tel:* (01) 2017200, pg 615

Marshall Cavendish Books (Singapore) *Tel:* (065) 2848844 *Fax:* (065) 2854871 *E-mail:* te@corp.tpl. com.sg *Web Site:* www.timesone.com.sg/te, pg 550

Marshall Cavendish Partworks Ltd (United Kingdom) *Tel:* (020) 7565 6000 *Fax:* (020) 7734 6221 *E-mail:* info@marshallcavendish.co.uk *Web Site:* www.marshallcavendish.co.uk, pg 672

Cavendish Publishing Pty Ltd (Australia) *Tel:* (02) 9664 0909 *Fax:* (02) 9664 5420 *E-mail:* info@ cavendishpublishing.com *Web Site:* www. cavendishpublishing.com.au, pg 17

Cavendish Publishing Ltd (United Kingdom) *Tel:* (020) 7278 8000 *Fax:* (020) 7278 8080 *E-mail:* info@ cavendishpublishing.com *Web Site:* www. cavendishpublishing.com, pg 672

The Caxton Press (New Zealand) *Tel:* (03) 366 8516 *Fax:* (03) 365 7840 *E-mail:* print.design@caxton.co.nz *Web Site:* www.caxton.co.nz, pg 490

The Caxton Press (New Zealand) *Toll Free Tel:* 800 229 866 *Fax:* (03) 365 7840 *E-mail:* print.design@caxton. co.nz *Web Site:* www.caxton.co.nz, pg 1150

Editorial Caymi SACI (Argentina) *Tel:* (011) 4304-2474 *Fax:* (011) 4304-2474, pg 4

Cazal SA (Reunion) *Tel:* 213264 *Fax:* 410977, pg 1329

CB Print Finishers Ltd (United Kingdom) *Tel:* (0191) 2150101 *Fax:* (0191) 2701651 *E-mail:* sales@cbprint. co.uk *Web Site:* www.cbprint.co.uk, pg 1215

CBA Translations (United Kingdom) *Tel:* (01404) 822284 *Fax:* (01404) 823136 *E-mail:* info@ cbatranslations.co.uk *Web Site:* www.cbatranslations. co.uk, pg 1140

CBD Research Ltd (United Kingdom) *Tel:* (020) 8650 7745 *Fax:* (020) 8650 0768 *E-mail:* cbd@cbdresearch. com *Web Site:* www.cbdresearch.com, pg 672

CCH Editions Ltd (United Kingdom) *Tel:* (020) 8547 3333 *Fax:* (020) 8547 1124 *E-mail:* customerservices@cch.co.uk *Web Site:* www. cch.co.uk, pg 672

CCH New Zealand Ltd (New Zealand) *Tel:* (09) 488 2760 *Toll Free Tel:* 800 500224 (New Zealand only) *Fax:* (09) 488 6911 *E-mail:* nzsales@cch.co.nz *Web Site:* www.cch.co.nz, pg 490

CD Remain Cia Ltda (Ecuador) *Tel:* (02) 224973; (02) 239328 *Fax:* (02) 505760, pg 1298

CDL (Central Distribuidora Livreira) Sarl (Portugal) *Tel:* (01) 4264422; (01) 769744; (01) 779825, pg 1327

Ediciones CEAC (Spain) *Tel:* (093) 2545300 *Fax:* (093) 2545315 *E-mail:* edicionesceac@de-deusto.com; info@ ceacedit.com *Web Site:* www.editorialceac.com, pg 571

Editorial la Cebra (Mexico) *Tel:* (05) 2779529; (05) 2779797; (05) 2737717; (05) 2737888 *Fax:* (05) 2737866 *E-mail:* info@adcebra.com, pg 459

CEC-Cosmic Energy Connections (Switzerland) *Tel:* (0761) 7059 632 *Fax:* (0761) 7059 633, pg 615

Biblioteca Musicale S Cecilia (Italy) *Tel:* (06) 3609671 *Fax:* (06) 36001800 *Web Site:* www. conservatoriosantacecilia.it/Biblioteca./Biblioteca.htm, pg 1519

Ced-Samsom Wolters Kluwer Belgie (Belgium) *Tel:* (02) 7231111 *Fax:* (02) 7231288, pg 64

CEDAM (Casa Editrice Dr A Milani) (Italy) *Tel:* (049) 8239111 *Fax:* (049) 8752900 *E-mail:* info@cedam. com *Web Site:* www.cedam.com, pg 377

Cedar Media (United Kingdom) *Tel:* (020) 8508 8856 *Fax:* (020) 8508 8856 *E-mail:* cedarmedia@btinternet. com, pg 1340

Cedel, Ediciones Jose O Avila Monteso ES (Spain) *Tel:* (093) 4211880 *Fax:* (093) 4228971 *E-mail:* cedel@kadex.com *Web Site:* www.kadex. com/cedel, pg 571

CEEBA Publications Antenne d'Autriche (Austria) *Tel:* (02236) 803115 *Fax:* (02236) 8033 *E-mail:* svd@ steyler.at *Web Site:* www.ceeba.at, pg 49

Editions du CEFAL (Belgium) *Tel:* (04) 254 25 20 *Fax:* (04) 254 24 40 *E-mail:* cefal.celes@skynet.be *Web Site:* www.cefal.com, pg 64

CEIC Alfons El Vell (Spain) *Tel:* (06) 2876551 *Fax:* (06) 2875286, pg 572

Cekit SA (Colombia) *Tel:* (06) 3253033; (06) 3348179; (06) 3348189 *Fax:* (06) 3348020 *E-mail:* comercial@ cekit.com.co *Web Site:* www.cekit.com.co, pg 110

Celebrity Educational Publishers (Singapore) *Tel:* 6785 7274 *Fax:* 6748 9108, pg 550

Celeluck Co Ltd (Hong Kong) *Tel:* 2893 9197; 2893 9147 *Fax:* 2891 5591 *E-mail:* open@open.com.hk *Web Site:* www.open.com.hk, pg 313

Celeste Ediciones (Spain) *Tel:* (091) 6749221 *Fax:* (091) 6557101 *E-mail:* info@celesteediciones.com, pg 572

CELID (Italy) *Tel:* (011) 447 47 74 *Fax:* (011) 447 47 59 *E-mail:* edizioni@celid.it *Web Site:* www.celid.it, pg 377

Celta Editora, Lda (Portugal) *Tel:* (021) 4417433 *Fax:* (021) 4467304 *E-mail:* mail@celtaeditora. pt; celtaeditora@mail.telepac.pt *Web Site:* www. celtaeditora.pt, pg 524

Celuc Libri (Italy) *Tel:* (02) 86 45 07 76 *Fax:* (02) 86 45 14 24, pg 377

CEM Publishers Ltd (Nigeria), pg 499

Cemagref Editions (France) *Tel:* (01) 4096 61 21 *Fax:* (01) 4096 60 36 *E-mail:* info@cemagref.fr *Web Site:* www.cemagref.fr, pg 152

Sociedad Fondo Editorial Cenamec (Venezuela) *Tel:* (0212) 563-2591; (0212) 563-3542; (0212) 563-5597; (0212) 563-8155; (0212) 563-9997; (0212) 563-8244 *E-mail:* cenamec@reacciun.ve *Web Site:* www. cenamec.org.ve/, pg 774

Editions Cenomane (France) *Tel:* (02) 43242157 *Fax:* (02) 43771916, pg 152

Department of Census & Statistics (Sri Lanka) *Tel:* (01) 324348 *E-mail:* colombo@statistics.gov.lk *Web Site:* www.statistics.gov.lk, pg 601

Cent Pages (France) *Tel:* (04) 38 12 16 20 *Fax:* (04) 38 12 16 29 *E-mail:* editions@editions-centpages.fr *Web Site:* www.editions-centpages.fr, pg 152

Centaur Press (1954) (United Kingdom) *Tel:* (020) 7431 4391 *Fax:* (020) 7431 5129 *E-mail:* books@ opengatepress.co.uk *Web Site:* www.opengatepress.co. uk, pg 672

Centaurus-Verlagsgesellschaft GmbH (Germany) *Tel:* (07643) 93 39-0 *Fax:* (07643) 93 39-11 *E-mail:* info@centaurus-verlag.de *Web Site:* www. centaurus-verlag.de, pg 207

Centenary of Technical Education in Bairnsdale (Australia) *Tel:* (03) 5152-4556, pg 17

Centenary Publishing House Ltd (Uganda) *Tel:* (041) 241599 *Fax:* (041) 250427, pg 648

Center for Advanced Welsh & Celtic Studies (United Kingdom) *Tel:* (01970) 626717 *Fax:* (01970) 627066 *E-mail:* cawcs@wales.ac.uk *Web Site:* www.aber.ac. uk/~awcwww/s/cyflwyniad.html, pg 672

Center for Agricultural Library & Technology Dissemination (CALTD) (Indonesia) *Tel:* (0251) 321746 (ext 66) *Fax:* (0251) 326561 *E-mail:* pustaka@bogor.net *Web Site:* pustaka.bogor. net, pg 1515

The Center for Romanian Studies (Romania) *Tel:* (032) 219000 *Fax:* (032) 219010, pg 534

Center of Academic Resources Chulalongkorn University (Thailand) *Tel:* (02) 218-2929; (02) 218-2903 *Fax:* (02) 215-3617; (02) 215-2907 *Web Site:* www. car.chula.ac.th, pg 1548

Center Print Ltd (United Kingdom) *Tel:* (0115) 961 2277 *Fax:* (0115) 938 1424, pg 1153

Center Print Ltd (United Kingdom) *Tel:* (0115) 961 2277 *Fax:* (0115) 938 1424 *E-mail:* cprint@besharapress.co. uk *Web Site:* www.besharapress.com, pg 1174

Center Print Ltd (United Kingdom) *Tel:* (0115) 961 2277 *Fax:* (0115) 938 1424 *E-mail:* cprint@besharapress.co. uk, pg 1215

Centraal Boekhuis BV (Netherlands) *Tel:* (0345) 47 59 11 *Fax:* (0345) 47 56 90 *E-mail:* info@centraal. boekhuis.nl *Web Site:* www.centraalboekhuis.nl, pg 1268

Central Library (India) *Tel:* (0265) 540133, pg 1514

Central Africana Ltd (Malawi) *Tel:* 631509; 243595 *Fax:* 622236 *E-mail:* africana@sdwp.org.mw, pg 451

Central Agricultural Library (Bulgaria) *Tel:* (02) 70-55-17, pg 1494

The Central Archives for the History of the Jewish People (CAHJP) (Israel) *Tel.* (02) 5635/16 *Fax:* (02) 5667686 *E-mail:* archives@vms.huji.ac. il *Web Site:* www.sites.huji.ac.il/cahjp/index.htm, pg 1517

Central Book Distribution Co Ltd (Thailand) *Tel:* (02) 229 7556-7 *Fax:* (02) 237-8321, pg 1336

Central Books (United Kingdom) *Tel:* (0845) 458 9911 *Fax:* (0845) 458 9912 *E-mail:* info@centralbooks.com *Web Site:* www.centralbooks.co.uk; www.centralbooks. com, pg 1340

Central Bookshop Ltd (Malawi) *Tel:* 621 447 *Fax:* 633 863, pg 1316

Central Catequistica Salesiana (CCS) (Spain) *Tel:* (091) 7252000 *Fax:* (091) 7262570 *E-mail:* apedidos@editorialccs.com; sei@editorialccs. com *Web Site:* www.editorialccs.com, pg 572

Central Catholic Library (Ireland) *Tel:* (01) 676 1264, pg 1517

Central Catholic Library Association Inc (Ireland) *Tel:* (01) 676 1264 *E-mail:* catholicresearch@eircom. net, pg 1565

Central de Publicaciones SA (Mexico) *Tel:* (05) 5104231, pg 1318

Central European University Press (Hungary) *Tel:* (01) 327 3000 *Fax:* (01) 327 3183 *E-mail:* ceupress@ ceupress.com *Web Site:* www.ceupress.com, pg 318

Central Library for the Blind, Visually Impaired & Handicapped (Israel) *Tel:* (09) 8617874 *Fax:* (09) 8626346 *E-mail:* office@clfb.org.il *Web Site:* www. clfb.org.il, pg 1517

Central Library of Agricultural Science (Israel) *Tel:* (08) 9489906 *Fax:* (08) 9361348; (08) 9489399 *E-mail:* szekely@agri.huji.ac.il *Web Site:* www.agri. huji.ac.il/library/menu.html, pg 1518

Central News Agency (CNA) (Namibia) *Tel:* (061) 25625 *Fax:* (061) 227210, pg 1319

Central News Agency Ltd (South Africa) *Tel:* (011) 4933200 *Fax:* (011) 4931438, pg 1331

Central Reference Library (Uganda) *Tel:* (041) 233633 *Fax:* (041) 348625 *E-mail:* library@imul.com, pg 1550

Central Secretariat Library (India) *Tel:* (011) 338 9684 *Fax:* (011) 338 4846 *E-mail:* root%csl@delnet.ren.nic. in, pg 1514

Central State Archives (Bulgaria) *Tel:* (02) 9400101; (02) 9400120; (02) 9400176 *Fax:* (02) 980 14 43 *E-mail:* gua@archives.government.bg *Web Site:* www. archives.government.bg, pg 1494

Central State Archives (Russian Federation) *Tel:* (095) 1597383, pg 1539

Central Tanganyika Press (United Republic of Tanzania) *Tel:* (061) 22140 *Fax:* (061) 324565, pg 638

Central Technical Library (Bulgaria) *Tel:* (02) 8173841; (02) 8173842; (02) 8173850 (Interlibrary loan) *Fax:* (02) 9173120 *E-mail:* ctb@nacid. nat.bg; ctbloan@nacid.nat.bg (Interlibrary loan) *Web Site:* www.nacid.nat.bg, pg 1494

Central Tibetan Secretariat (India) *Tel:* (01892) 22467 *Fax:* (01892) 23723 *E-mail:* ltwa@ndf.vsnl.net.in, pg 328

Centrala Handlu Zagranicznego ARS Polona SA (Poland) *Tel:* (022) 509 86 20 *Fax:* (022) 509 86 20 *E-mail:* arspolona@arspolona.com.pl *Web Site:* www. arspolona.com.pl, pg 1327

Biblioteca Centrala Universitara Mihail Eminescu (Romania) *Tel:* (0232) 264245 *Fax:* (0232) 261796 *E-mail:* bcuis@bcu-iasi.ro *Web Site:* www.bcu-iasi.ro, pg 1538

Istituto Centrale per il Catalogo Unico delle Biblioteche Italiane e per le Informazioni Bibliografiche (Italy) *Tel:* (06) 4989484 *Fax:* (06) 4959302 *Web Site:* www. iccu.sbn.it, pg 377, 1565

Centralna Narodna Biblioteka SR Crne Gore (Serbia and Montenegro) *Tel:* (086) 231 143 *Fax:* (086) 231 726 *E-mail:* cnb@cg.yu, pg 1540

Centre Africain d'Animation et d'Echanges Culturels Editions Khoudia (CAEC) (Senegal) *Tel:* 211023 *Fax:* 215109, pg 546

Centre Africain de Formation et de Recherche Administratives pour le Developpement, Centre de Documentation (Morocco) *Tel:* (061) 30 72 69 *Fax:* (039) 32 57 85 *E-mail:* cafrad@cafrad.org *Web Site:* www.cafrad.org, pg 1268

Centre Bibliotheque d'Information (Gabon) *Tel:* 21115, pg 1506

Centre Culturel De Differdange (Luxembourg) *Tel:* 587045 *Fax:* 580295, pg 447

Centre Culturel Francais, Bibliotheque (Congo) *Tel:* 81 19 00; 81 17 05; 81 38 55 *Fax:* 83 06 18, pg 1497

Centre Culturel Francais, Bibliotheque (Cote d'Ivoire) *Tel:* (020) 211699; (020) 225628 *Fax:* 227132 *E-mail:* ccf@netafric.ci, pg 1498

Centre De Documentation Universitaire (CDU) (Chad) *Tel:* 5144 44; 5144 44 697 *Fax:* 514 033 *E-mail:* runiv.rectorat@sdnted.undp.org, pg 1495

Centre de Librairie et d'Editions Techniques (CLET) (France) *Tel:* (01) 40926500 *Fax:* (01) 40926550, pg 152

Centre de Linguistique Appliquee (Senegal) *Tel:* 230126, pg 546

Centre de Publications Evangeliques (Cote d'Ivoire) *Tel:* 444805 *Fax:* 445817, pg 117

Centre de Recherche des Archives et de Documentation (CRAD) (Chad) *Tel:* 514 671 *Fax:* 516 079, pg 1495

Centre de Recherche, et Pedagogie Appliquee (The Democratic Republic of the Congo), pg 113

Centre de Recherches et d'Etudes Administratives (Tunisia) *Tel:* 71848435; 71848300 *Fax:* 71794188 *E-mail:* webmaster@ena.nat.tn *Web Site:* www.ena.nat. tn, pg 1549

Centre de Vulgarisation Agricole (The Democratic Republic of the Congo) *Tel:* (012) 71165 *Fax:* (012) 21351, pg 114

Centre d'Edition et de Diffusion Africaines (Cote d'Ivoire) *Tel:* 21 24 65 10; 21 24 65 11 *Fax:* 21 25 05 67 *E-mail:* infos@ceda-ci.com *Web Site:* www.ceda-ci.com, pg 117

Centre d'Edition et de Diffusion Africaines (Cote d'Ivoire) *Tel:* 22 24 42; 22 20 55 *Fax:* 21 72 62 *Web Site:* www.mbendi.co.za/orgs/cg01.htm, pg 1297

Centre d'Edition et de Production pour l'Enseignement et la Recherche (CEPER) (Cameroon) *Tel:* (023) 221323, pg 97

Centre d'Enseignement Superieur de Niamey (Niger) *Tel:* 732713 *Fax:* 733862, pg 1531

Centre d'Etudes et Documentation Economique Juridique et Sociale (CEDEJ) (Egypt (Arab Republic of Egypt)) *Tel:* (02) 392 87 11; (02) 392 87 16; (02) 392 87 39; (02) 704641 *Fax:* (02) 392 87 91 *E-mail:* cedej@idsc. net.eg *Web Site:* www.cedej.org.eg, pg 137

Centre d'Information et de Conservation de l'Universite de Liege (Belgium) *Tel:* (04) 366 52 18 *Fax:* (04) 366 57 98; (04) 366 44 22 *E-mail:* press@ulg.ac.be *Web Site:* www.ulg.ac.be/hp.html, pg 1491

Centre Europeen pour l'Enseignement Superieur (CEPES) (Romania) *Tel:* (01) 3130839; (01) 3130698; (01) 3159956 *Fax:* (01) 3123567 *E-mail:* cepes@ cepes.ro *Web Site:* www.cepes.ro, pg 1272

Centre for Alternative Technology (United Kingdom) *Tel:* (01654) 705980; (01654) 705959 (mail order); (01654) 705993 (CAT shop) *Fax:* (01654) 702782; (01654) 705999 (mail order); (01654 703605 (education & courses) *E-mail:* pubs@cat.org.uk *Web Site:* www.cat.org.uk, pg 672

Centre for Basic Research (Uganda) *Tel:* (041) 231228; (041) 235533; (041) 342987 *Fax:* (041) 235413 *E-mail:* cbr@cbr-ug.org *Web Site:* www.cbr-ug.org, pg 648

Centre for Comparative Literature & Cultural Studies (Australia) *Tel:* (03) 9905 4000; (03) 9905 3059 *Fax:* (03) 9905 4007 *Web Site:* www.arts.monash. edu/au/cclcs, pg 17

Centre for Conflict Resolution (South Africa) *Tel:* (021) 6502503; (021) 6502750 *Fax:* (021) 6852142; (021) 6504053 *E-mail:* ccr@uctvax.uct.ac.za *Web Site:* www.uct.ac.za, pg 558

The Centre for Creative Communities (United Kingdom) *Tel:* (020) 7247 5385 *Fax:* (020) 7247 5256 *E-mail:* info@creativecommunities.org.uk *Web Site:* www.creativecommunities.org.uk, pg 1401

Centre for Documentation & Research (United Arab Emirates) *Tel:* (02) 444 5400 *Fax:* (02) 444 5811 *Web Site:* www.gebcad.com, pg 1550

Centre for Educational Technology (Israel) *Tel:* (03) 6460183 *Fax:* (03) 6460821, pg 362

Centre for European Policy Studies (Belgium) *Tel:* (02) 2293911 *Fax:* (02) 2194151; (02) 2293971 *E-mail:* info@ceps.be *Web Site:* www.ceps.be, pg 1252

Centre for South Asian Studies (Pakistan) *Tel:* (042) 864014 *Fax:* (042) 5867206, pg 507

Centre International de Recherches 'Primitifs Flamands' ASBL (Belgium) *Tel:* (02) 7396866 *Fax:* (02) 7320105, pg 64

Centre National des Archives (Burkina Faso) *Tel:* 33-61-96; 32-47-12; 32-46-38 *Fax:* 31-49-26, pg 1495

Centre National de Documentation (Morocco) *Tel:* (037) 77 49 44 *Fax:* (037) 77 31 34 *E-mail:* cnd@mpep.gov. ma *Web Site:* www.cndportal.net.ma, pg 1528

Centre National de Documentation Pedagogique (CNDP) (France) *Tel:* (01) 55 43 60 00 *Fax:* (01) 55 43 60 01 *Web Site:* www.cndp.fr/cndp_reseau, pg 152

Centre National de Production de Materiel Didactique (CNAPMAD) (Madagascar) *Tel:* (02) 289-54 *Fax:* (02) 200-53, pg 450

Centre National du Livre (France) *Tel:* (01) 49546868 *Fax:* (01) 45491021 *Web Site:* www. centrenationaldulivre.fr, pg 1393

Centre National Infor-Jeunes (CNIJ) (Belgium) *Tel:* (081) 22 08 72 *Fax:* (081) 22 82 64, pg 64

Centre of Legal Information (Lithuania) *Tel:* (02) 61 75 29; (02) 62 36 50 *Fax:* (02) 62 15 23 *E-mail:* webadm@utic.tm.lt, pg 445

Centre pour l'Innovation et la Recherche en Communication de l'Entreprise (CIRCE) (France) *Tel:* (01) 49 24 96 76, pg 152

Centre Protestant d'Editions et de Diffusion (CEDI) (The Democratic Republic of the Congo), pg 114

Centre Publications (Australia) *Tel:* (03) 8700149, pg 17

Centre Regional pour la Promotion du Livre en Afrique (CREPLA) (Cameroon) *Tel:* 224782; 2936, pg 1253

CentrePolygraph Traders & Publishers Co (Russian Federation) *Tel:* (095) 2817411 *Fax:* (095) 2844074, pg 539

Centro Agronomico Tropical de Investigacion y Ensenanza (CATIE) (Costa Rica) *Tel:* 556-6431 *Fax:* 556-1533 *E-mail:* comunicacion@catie.ac.cr *Web Site:* www.catie.ac.cr, pg 114

Centro Ambrosiano di Documentazione e Studi Religiosi (Italy) *Tel:* (02) 83.75.476 *Fax:* (02) 58.10.09.49 *E-mail:* cadr@cadr.it *Web Site:* www.cadr.it, pg 377

Centro Biblico (Italy) *Tel:* (081) 3340532 *Fax:* (081) 3340877 *Web Site:* www.centrobiblico.it, pg 377

Centro de Cultura Tradicional (Spain) *Tel:* (0923) 293255 *Fax:* (0923) 293256 *E-mail:* cultura@lasalina.es; cctl@lasalina.es *Web Site:* www.dipsanet.es/cultura/culturatradicional, pg 572

Centro de Documentacao e Informacao da Camara dos Deputados (Brazil) *Tel:* (061) 216 0000 *Toll Free Tel:* 800 619 619 *Web Site:* www2.camara.gov.br, pg 1493

Centro de Documentacao e Informao para o Desenvolvimento (Cape Verde) *Tel:* 613969 *Fax:* 1527, pg 98

Centro de Documentacion Bibliotecologica (Argentina) *Tel:* (0291) 4595132 *Web Site:* www.uns.edu.ar, pg 1557

Centro De Educacion Popular (Ecuador) *Tel:* (02) 525 521 *Fax:* (02) 542 818 *E-mail:* cedep@fmlaluna.com *Web Site:* www.jacomenet.com/laluna/cedep.html, pg 136

Centro de Estudios Avanzados en Ciencias Sociales (CEACS) del Instituto Juan March de Estudios e Investigaciones (Spain) *Tel:* (091) 4354240 *Fax:* (091) 5763420 *E-mail:* webmast@mail.march.es *Web Site:* www.march.es, pg 572

Centro de Estudios Mexicanos y Centroamericanos (Mexico) *Tel:* (05) 5 40 59 21; (05) 5 40 59 22 *Fax:* (05) 2 02 77 94 *E-mail:* cemca.lib@francia.org.mx *Web Site:* www.francia.org.mx/cemca, pg 459

Centro de Estudios Politicos Y Constitucionales (Spain) *Tel:* (091) 5401950 *Fax:* (091) 5419574 *E-mail:* cepc@cepc.es *Web Site:* www.cepc.es, pg 572

Centro de Estudios sobre Desarrollo Economico CEDE (Colombia) *Tel:* (01) 339499; (01) 3394949 *Fax:* (01) 3324472 *E-mail:* cede@uniandes.edu.co; infocom@uniandes.edu.co *Web Site:* www.uniandes.edu.co, pg 1497

Centro de Estudos Juridicosdo Para (CEJUP) (Brazil) *Tel:* (091) 225-0355 *Fax:* (091) 241-3184 *E-mail:* cejup@expert.com.br, pg 79

Centro de Exportacion de Libros Espanoles SA (CELESA) (Spain) *Tel:* (091) 517 01 70 *Fax:* (091) 517 34 81 *E-mail:* celesa@celesa.com *Web Site:* www.celesa.es, pg 1333

Centro de Informacion Cientifica y Humanistica (Mexico) *Tel:* (055) 6223960 *Fax:* (055) 6162557 *E-mail:* admin@estadistica.unam.mx, pg 1527

Centro de la Mujer Peruana Flora Tristan (Peru) *Tel:* (01) 433-2765; (01) 433-1457; (01) 433-9060 *Fax:* (01) 433-9500 *E-mail:* postmast@flora.org.pe *Web Site:* www.flora.org.pe, pg 512

Centro de Planificacion y Estudios Sociales (CEPLAES) (Ecuador) *Tel:* (02) 548-547 *Fax:* (02) 566-207 *E-mail:* ceplaes@ceplaes.ec, pg 136

Centro de Traducciones y Terminologia Especializada (CTTE) (Cuba) *Tel:* (07) 862-6531; (07) 860-3411 *Fax:* (07) 862-6531 *E-mail:* comercial@idict.cu *Web Site:* www.cubaciencia.cu/, pg 1137

Centro Di (Italy) *Tel:* (055) 2342668 *Fax:* (055) 2342667 *E-mail:* edizioni@centrodi.it *Web Site:* www.centrodi.it, pg 377

Centro Documentazione Alpina (Italy) *Tel:* (011) 7720444 *Fax:* (011) 7732170 *Web Site:* www.cda.it, pg 378

Centro Editor de America Latina SA (Argentina) *Tel:* (011) 4371-2411, pg 4

Centro Editorial Mexicano Osiris SA (Mexico) *Tel:* (05) 5406902; (05) 2027185 *Fax:* (05) 2027185, pg 459

Centro Editoriale Valtortiano SRL (Italy) *Tel:* (0776) 807032 *Fax:* (0776) 809789 *E-mail:* cev@mariavaltorta.com *Web Site:* www.mariavaltorta.com, pg 378

Centro Estudos Geograficos (Portugal) *Tel:* (021) 778883 *Fax:* (021) 7938690 *E-mail:* ceg@mail.telepac.pt, pg 524

Centro Italiano Studi Alto Medioevo (Italy) *Tel:* (0743) 225630 *Fax:* (0743) 49902 *E-mail:* cisam@cisam.org *Web Site:* www.cisam.org, pg 378

Centro Latinoamericano de Demografia (CELADE) (Chile) *Tel:* (02) 4712000; (02) 2102000; (02) 2085051 *Fax:* (02) 2080252; (02) 2081946 *E-mail:* secepal@eclac.cl *Web Site:* www.eclac.org, pg 1254

Centro Nacional de Documentacion Cientifica, Tecnica y Economics (CNDCTE) (Uruguay) *Tel:* (02) 484172 *Fax:* (02) 496902, pg 1553

Centro Nacional de Documentacion Cientifica y Tecnologica - Universidad Mayor De S an Andres (Bolivia) *Tel:* (02) 359583 *Fax:* (02) 359586 *E-mail:* iiicndct@huayna.umsa.edu.bo *Web Site:* www.bolivian.com/industrial/cndct, pg 1559

Centro Nacional de Informacion, Agencia Nacional ISBN (Mexico) *Tel:* (0555) 230 7632 *Fax:* (0555) 230 7634 *Web Site:* www.sep.gob.mx, pg 1267

Centro Programmazione Editoriale (CPE) (Italy) *Tel:* (059) 908065 *Fax:* (059) 908271 *Web Site:* www.cpe-oggiscuola.com, pg 378

Centro Psicologia Clinica (Portugal) *Tel:* (085) 4211986 *Fax:* (085) 4211986 *E-mail:* cdibera@tin.it *Web Site:* www.centro-psicologia.it, pg 525

Centro Regional para el Fomento del Libro en America Latina y el Caribe (Colombia) *Tel:* (01) 212 6056; (01) 249 5141; (01) 321 7501; (01) 540 2071; (01) 312 5690 *Fax:* (01) 255 4614 *E-mail:* cerlalc@impsat.net.co; info@cerlalc.org; libro@cerlalc.org *Web Site:* www.cerlalc.org, pg 110

Centro Regional para el Fomento del Libro en America Latina y el Caribe (Colombia) *Tel:* (01) 212-6056; (01) 249-5141 *Fax:* (01) 255-4614; (01) 321-7503 *E-mail:* libro@cerlalc.org *Web Site:* www.cerlalc.org, pg 1254

Centro Scientifico Torinese (Italy) *Tel:* (011) 3853656 *Fax:* (011) 3853244 *E-mail:* cse@estorinese.inet.it, pg 378

Edizioni Centro Studi Erickson (Italy) *Tel:* (0461) 950690 *Fax:* (0461) 950698 *E-mail:* info@erickson.it *Web Site:* www.erickson.it, pg 378

Centro Studi Terzo Mondo (Italy) *Tel:* (02) 29409041 *Fax:* (02) 29409041 *E-mail:* cstm@libero.it, pg 378

Centro UNESCO de San Sebastian (Spain) *Tel:* (0943) 427003 *Fax:* (0943) 427003 *E-mail:* unescoeskola@retemail.es *Web Site:* www.servicom.es/unesco, pg 572

Centrul National de Numerotare Standardizata Biblioteca Nationala (Romania) *Tel:* (021) 3112635 *Fax:* (021) 3124990 *E-mail:* isbn@bibnat.ro; issn@bibnat.ro *Web Site:* www.bibnat.ro, pg 1272

Forlaget Centrum (Denmark) *Tel:* 33 32 12 06 *Fax:* 33 32 12 07 *E-mail:* info@forlaget-centrum.dk *Web Site:* www.forlaget-centrum.dk, pg 129

Centrum Vedecko-Technickych Informacii SR (Slovakia) *Tel:* (02) 5292 3527 *Fax:* (02) 5292 3527; (02) 5727 6236 *E-mail:* cvti@tbb1.cvtisr.sk *Web Site:* www.cvtisr.sk, pg 1541

CEP Editions (France) *Tel:* (01) 40 13 30 05 *Fax:* (01) 48 24 34 89, pg 152

Cep Kitaplari AS (Turkey) *Tel:* (0212) 516 20 04 *Fax:* (0212) 516 20 05 *Web Site:* www.varlik.com.tr, pg 645

CEPA - Centro Editor de Psicologia Aplicada Ltda (Brazil) *Tel:* (021) 2220-6545 *Fax:* (021) 2262-2717 *E-mail:* psicocepa@psicocepa.com.br, pg 79 *Web Site:* www.psicocepa.com.br, pg 79

Cepadues Editions SA (France) *Tel:* (05) 61 40 57 36 *Fax:* (05) 61 41 79 89 *E-mail:* cepadues@cepadues.com *Web Site:* www.cepadues.com, pg 152

il Cerchio Iniziative Editoriali (Italy) *Tel:* (0541) 21158; (0541) 708190 *Fax:* (0541) 799173 *E-mail:* info@ilcerchio.it *Web Site:* www.ilcerchio.it, pg 378

Editions Cercle d'Art SA (France) *Tel:* (01) 48 87 92 12 *Fax:* (01) 48 87 47 79 *E-mail:* info@officieldesarts.com *Web Site:* www.officieldesarts.com/cercledart/, pg 153

Cercle de la Librairie (France) *Tel:* (01) 44 41 28 00 *Fax:* (01) 44 41 28 65 *E-mail:* commercial@electre.com *Web Site:* www.electre.com, pg 1257

CERDIC-Publications (France) *Tel:* (0388) 877107 *Fax:* (0388) 877125 *E-mail:* cerdic@wanadoo.fr, pg 153

Editura Ceres (Romania) *Tel:* (01) 2224836, pg 534

Editions du Cerf (France) *Tel:* (01) 44 18 12 12 *Fax:* (01) 45 56 04 27 *Web Site:* www.editionsducerf.fr, pg 153

Cesarini Hermanos (Argentina) *Tel:* (011) 4861-1152 *Fax:* (011) 4861-1152 *E-mail:* cesarinihnos@movi.com.ar, pg 4

Ceska Biblicka Spolecnost (Czech Republic) *Tel:* 284 693 925 *Fax:* 284 693 933 *E-mail:* cbs@dumbible.cz *Web Site:* www.dumbible.cz, pg 122

Ceska Expedice (Czech Republic) *Tel:* (02) 727 612 04, pg 122

Ceske Narodni Stredisko ISSN (Czech Republic) *Tel:* (02) 21 663 440 *Fax:* (02) 2222 1340 *E-mail:* issn@stk.cz *Web Site:* www.stk.cz/en/issn/index.htm, pg 1255

Cesoc Ltda (Chile) *Tel:* (02) 6391081; (02) 6336992 *Fax:* (02) 6325382 *E-mail:* cesoc@bellsouth.cl, pg 98

Cetal Ediciones (Chile) *Tel:* (032) 213360 *Fax:* (032) 214851, pg 98

Edicoes Cetop (Portugal) *Tel:* (021) 926 3222 *Fax:* (021) 921 7940, pg 525

The Ceylon Chamber of Commerce (Sri Lanka) *Tel:* (01) 2452183; (01) 2421745; (01) 2329143 *Fax:* (01) 2437477; (01) 2449352 *E-mail:* info@chamber.lk *Web Site:* www.chamber.lk, pg 601

CFM Publications (Jamaica) *Tel:* 876-927-1660; 876-927-1669 *Fax:* 876-927-0997 *E-mail:* helpdesk@uwimona.edu.jm *Web Site:* www.uwimona.edu.jm, pg 410

CFW Publications Ltd (Hong Kong) *Tel:* 2554 3004 *Fax:* 2543 8007, pg 313

CG Ediz Medico-Scientifiche (Italy) *Tel:* (011) 338507 *Fax:* (011) 3852750 *Web Site:* www.cgems.it, pg 378

CGT Total Exploration-Production (France) *Tel:* (05) 59 83 65 80 *Fax:* (05) 59 83 57 88 *E-mail:* contact.ep@cgt-total.org *Web Site:* www.cgt-total.org/ncgt-ep/, pg 153

Chadwyck-Healey France (CHF) (France) *Tel:* (01) 44 83 81 81 *Fax:* (01) 44 83 81 83, pg 153

Chadwyck-Healey Ltd (United Kingdom) *Tel:* (01223) 215512 *Fax:* (01223) 215513 *E-mail:* marketing@proquest.co.uk *Web Site:* www.proquest.co.uk, pg 672

Chalantika Boighar (Bangladesh) *Tel:* (02) 257345 *Fax:* (02) 7115691, pg 60

Editions du Chalet (France) *Tel:* (01) 53 26 33 35 *Fax:* (01) 53 26 33 36, pg 153

Chalkface Press Pty Ltd (Australia) *Tel:* (08) 9385 1923 *Fax:* (08) 9385 1923 *E-mail:* info@chalkface.net.au; sales@wooldridges.com.au (orders) *Web Site:* www.chalkface.net.au, pg 17

Challenge Bookshops (Nigeria) *Tel:* (073) 53897; (073) 52230, pg 1322

Challenge Machinery Co (United States) *Tel:* 231-799-8484 *Fax:* 231-798-1275 *E-mail:* info@ challengemachinery.com *Web Site:* www. challengemachinery.com, pg 1238

Chamaeleon Verlag AG (Switzerland) *Tel:* (01) 2525497 *Fax:* (01) 2725282, pg 616

Chambers Harrap Publishers Ltd (United Kingdom) *Tel:* (0131) 5565929 *Fax:* (0131) 5565313 *E-mail:* admin@chambers.co.uk; webmanager@ chambers.co.uk *Web Site:* www.chambersharrap.co.uk, pg 672

Editions Jacqueline Chambon (France) *Tel:* (01) 44 27 01 16 *Fax:* (01) 43 54 30 05, pg 153

Editions de la Chambre de Commerce et d'Industrie SA (ECCI) (Belgium) *Tel:* (04) 344-50-88 *Fax:* (04) 343-05-53 *E-mail:* lvenanzi@ecci.be *Web Site:* www.ecci. be, pg 64

Chambre des Employes Prives (Luxembourg) *Tel:* 44 40 91-1 *Fax:* 44 40 91-250 *E-mail:* info@cepl.lu *Web Site:* www.cepl.lu, pg 447

Chambre Nationale du Livre Agence ISBN (Republic of Moldova) *Tel:* (02) 24 65 42 *Fax:* (02) 24 65 11 *E-mail:* cncm@moldova.cc *Web Site:* www.iatp. md/cnc, pg 1268

Editions Champ Vallon (France) *Tel:* (04) 50 56 15 51 *Fax:* (04) 50 56 15 64 *E-mail:* info@champ-vallon. com *Web Site:* www.champ-vallon.com, pg 153

Librairie des Champs-Elysees/Le Masque (France) *Tel:* (01) 44 41 74 50; (01) 44 41 74 00 *Fax:* (01) 43 26 91 04 *Web Site:* www.lemasque.com, pg 153

Chanakya Publications (India) *Tel:* (011) 711976, pg 328

Chancellor Publications (United Kingdom) *Tel:* (020) 7269 9150 *Fax:* (020) 7269 9151 *E-mail:* mail@ chancellorpublication.com *Web Site:* www. chancellorpublication.com, pg 673

Chancerel International Publishers Ltd (Germany) *Tel:* (049711) 6672 5728 *Fax:* (049711) 6672 2004 *E-mail:* tvandree@klett-mail.de *Web Site:* www. chancerel.com, pg 207

Philippe Chancerel Editeur (France) *Tel:* (01) 39 65 69 18, pg 153

Nem Chand & Bros (India) *Tel:* (01332) 272258; (01332) 272752; (01322) 264343 *Fax:* (01332) 273258 *E-mail:* ncb_rke@rediffmail.com, pg 1305

S Chand & Co Ltd (India) *Tel:* (011) 3672080; (011) 3672081; (011) 3672082 *Fax:* (011) 3677446 *E-mail:* schand@vsnl.com, pg 328

Chang-josa Publishing Co (Republic of Korea) *Tel:* (02) 7380393, pg 434

Editions Chanlis (Belgium) *Tel:* (071) 326394, pg 65

Editions Chantecler (Belgium) *Tel:* (03) 8 70 44 00 *Fax:* (03) 8 77 21 15, pg 65

Chapman (United Kingdom) *Tel:* (0131) 5572207 *Fax:* (0131) 5569565 *E-mail:* admin@chapman-pub. co.uk *Web Site:* www.chapman-pub.co.uk, pg 673

Chapter Two (United Kingdom) *Tel:* (020) 8316 5389 *Fax:* (020) 8854 5963 *E-mail:* chapter2UK@aol.com *Web Site:* www.chaptertwo.org.uk, pg 673

Editions Chardon Bleu (France) *Tel:* (02) 31 94 49 59 *Fax:* (02) 31 93 23 92 *E-mail:* chardonbleued@aol. com *Web Site:* www.chardonbleu.com, pg 153

Editions du Chariot (France) *Tel:* (02) 37258989 *Fax:* (02) 37258900 *E-mail:* edchariot@aol.com *Web Site:* members.aol.com/edchariot/, pg 153

Deborah Charles Publications (United Kingdom) *Tel:* (0151) 724 2500 *Fax:* (0151) 729 0371 *E-mail:* dcp@legaltheory.demon.co.uk *Web Site:* www. legaltheory.demon.co.uk, pg 673

Editions Charles-Lavauzelle SA (France) *Tel:* (05) 55 58 45 45 *Fax:* (05) 55 58 45 25 *Web Site:* lavauzelle.com, pg 153

The Charlesworth Group (United Kingdom) *Tel:* (01924) 204830 *Fax:* (01924) 332637 *E-mail:* sales@ charlesworth.com *Web Site:* www.charlesworth.com, pg 1174

The Charlesworth Group (United Kingdom) *Tel:* (01924) 204830 *Fax:* (01924) 332637; (01924) 339107 *E-mail:* sales@charlesworth.com *Web Site:* www. charlesworth.com, pg 1215

Charotar Publishing House (India) *Tel:* (02692) 256237 *Fax:* (02692) 240089 *E-mail:* charotar@icenet.net; charotar@cphbooks.com *Web Site:* www.cphbooks. com, pg 328

Charran's Bookshop (1978) Ltd (Trinidad & Tobago) *Tel:* 868-663-1884, pg 1336

Charran's Educational Publishers (Trinidad & Tobago) *Tel:* (868) 622-3832 *Fax:* (868) 623-5829, pg 642

La Charte Editions juridiques (Belgium) *Tel:* (02) 512 29 49 *Fax:* (02) 512 26 93 *E-mail:* info@lacharte.be *Web Site:* www.lacharte.be, pg 65

The Chartered Institute of Building (United Kingdom) *Tel:* (01344) 630700 *Fax:* (01344) 630777 *E-mail:* reception@ciob.org.uk *Web Site:* www.ciob. org.uk, pg 673

Chartered Institute of Journalists (CIJ) (United Kingdom) *Tel:* (020) 7252 1187 *Fax:* (020) 7232 2302 *E-mail:* memberservices@ioj.co.uk *Web Site:* www.ioj. co.uk, pg 1280

Chartered Institute of Library & Information Professionals (CILIP) (United Kingdom) *Tel:* (020) 7255 0500; (020) 7255 0505 (textphone) *Fax:* (020) 7255 0501 *E-mail:* info@cilip.org.uk *Web Site:* www. cilip.org.uk, pg 1573

Chartered Institute of Library & Information Professionals in Scotland (United Kingdom) *Tel:* (01698) 458888 *Fax:* (01698) 283170 *E-mail:* slic@slainte.org.uk *Web Site:* www.slainte. org.uk, pg 673

Chartered Institute of Personnel & Development (United Kingdom) *Tel:* (020) 8971 9000 *Fax:* (020) 8263 3333 *E-mail:* publish@cipd.co.uk *Web Site:* www.cipd.co. uk, pg 673

The Chartered Institute of Public Finance & Accountancy (United Kingdom) *Tel:* (020) 7543 5600 *Fax:* (020) 7543 5607 *E-mail:* publications@cipfa.org *Web Site:* www.cipfa.org.uk/shop, pg 673

Chase Publishing Services (United Kingdom) *Tel:* (01395) 514709 *Fax:* (01395) 514709 *E-mail:* r. addicott@btinternet.com, pg 1153

Chase Publishing Services (United Kingdom) *Tel:* (01395) 514709 *Fax:* (01395) 514709, pg 1174

Chasse Maree (France) *Tel:* (02) 98 92 66 33 *Fax:* (02) 98 92 04 34 *E-mail:* chasse-maree@glenat.com *Web Site:* www.chasse-maree.com, pg 153

Chatham Publishing (United Kingdom) *Tel:* (020) 8458 6314 *Fax:* (020) 8905 5245 *E-mail:* info@ chathampublishing.com *Web Site:* www. chathampublishing.com, pg 673

Chemical Industry Press (China) *Tel:* (010) 64918054; (010) 4213641; (010) 4234411 *Fax:* (010) 64918054 *Web Site:* www.cip.com.cn, pg 101

Verlag fur chemische Industrie H Ziolkowsky GmbH (Germany) *Tel:* (0821) 325-830 *Fax:* (0821) 325-8323 *E-mail:* info@kosmet.com, pg 207

Editions du Chene (France) *Tel:* (01) 43 92 30 00 *Fax:* (01) 43 92 33 81 *Web Site:* www. editionsduchene.fr, pg 153

Cheng Chung Book Co, Ltd (Taiwan, Province of China) *Tel:* (02) 2382-2815 *Fax:* (02) 2389-3571 *Web Site:* www.ccbc.com.tw, pg 634

Cheng Wen Publishing Company (Taiwan, Province of China) *Tel:* (02) 2362-8032 *Fax:* (02) 2366-0806 *E-mail:* ccicncwp@ms17.hinet.net, pg 634

Cheng Yun Publishing Company Ltd (Taiwan, Province of China) *Tel:* (02) 28117798 *Fax:* (02) 28123041 *E-mail:* toybook@ms3.hinet.net *Web Site:* www. toybook.com.tw, pg 634

Chengdu Maps Publishing House (China) *Tel:* (028) 485 2177; (028) 445 3030 *E-mail:* ccph@public.cd.sc.cn, pg 101

Cheong-mun-gag Publishing Co (Republic of Korea) *Tel:* (02) 9851451; (02) 9897423; (02) 9897421 *Fax:* (02) 9828679 *E-mail:* CMGbook@hitel.kol.co.kr, pg 434

Cheong-rim Publishing Co Ltd (Republic of Korea) *Tel:* (02) 546-4341 *Fax:* (02) 546-8053, pg 434

Le Cherche Midi Editeur (France) *Tel:* (01) 42 22 71 20 *Fax:* (01) 45 44 08 38 *E-mail:* infos@cherche-midi.com *Web Site:* www.cherche-midi.com, pg 154

Cherokee Literary Agency (South Africa) *Tel:* (021) 671-4508 *Fax:* (021) 761-4329, pg 1126

Cherrytree Books (United Kingdom) *Tel:* (020) 7487 0920 *Fax:* (020) 7487 0921 *E-mail:* sales@ evansbrothers.co.uk *Web Site:* www.evansbooks.co.uk, pg 674

Chetana Private Ltd Publishers & International Booksellers (India) *Tel:* (022) 228 81159; (022) 282 4983 *Fax:* (022) 262 4316 *E-mail:* orders@chetana. com; chetana1946@chetana.com *Web Site:* www. chetana.com, pg 328

Chiang Mai University Library (Thailand) *Tel:* (053) 944501 *Fax:* (053) 222766 *E-mail:* prasit@lib.cmunet. edu *Web Site:* www.lib.cmu.ac.th, pg 640

Chien Chen Bookstore Publishing Company Ltd (Taiwan, Province of China) *Tel:* (07) 3820363 *Fax:* (07) 3892816, pg 634

Chihab (Algeria) *Tel:* (021) 97 54 53; (021) 85 95 01; (021) 85 01 75 *Fax:* (021) 97 64 77; (021) 97 51 91; (021) 85 01 75 *E-mail:* chihab.dz@caramail.com, pg 2

Chijin Shokan Co Ltd (Japan) *Tel:* (03) 3235-4422 *Fax:* (03) 3235-8984 *E-mail:* chijinshokan@nifty.com *Web Site:* www.chijinshokan.co.jp, pg 412

Chikuma Shobo Publishing Co Ltd (Japan) *Tel:* (048) 651-0053 *Fax:* (048) 666-4648 *Web Site:* www. chikumashobo.co.jp, pg 412

Chikyu-sha Co Ltd (Japan) *Tel:* (03) 3585-0087 *Fax:* (03) 3589-2902, pg 412

Child Honsha Co Ltd (Japan) *Tel:* (03) 3813-3781 *Fax:* (03) 3818-3765 *E-mail:* ehon@childbook.co.jp *Web Site:* www.childbook.co.jp, pg 412

Childerset Pty Ltd (Australia) *Tel:* (074) 425510 *Fax:* (074) 425512 *E-mail:* tessgsp@ozemail.com.au, pg 17

Children's Book Circle (United Kingdom) *Tel:* (020) 7416 3130 *Fax:* (020) 7739 2318 *Web Site:* www. booktrusted.com/handbook/journals/bookskeeps.html, pg 1280

The Children's Book Council of Australia (Australia) *Tel:* (02) 9818 3858 *Fax:* (02) 9810 0737 *E-mail:* office@cbc.org.au *Web Site:* www.cbc.org.au, pg 1389

The Children's Book Store Company Ltd (Taiwan, Province of China) *Tel:* (02) 2762-8222 *Fax:* (02) 2760-4322 *Web Site:* www.tong-nian.com.tw, pg 1336

Children's Book Trust (India) *Tel:* (011) 23316974; (011) 23316970 *Fax:* (011) 23721090 *E-mail:* cbtnd@vsnl. com *Web Site:* www.childrensbooktrust.com, pg 329

Children's Books History Society (United Kingdom) *Tel:* (01992) 464885 *Fax:* (01992) 464885 *E-mail:* cbhs@abcgarrelt.demon.co.uk, pg 1401

Children's Literature Association of Nigeria (Nigeria) *Tel:* (022) 400550; (022) 400614 *Fax:* (022) 711254, pg 1270

Children's Literature Documentation & Research Centre, Ibadan (Nigeria) *Fax:* (022) 711254, pg 1270

The Children's Press (Ireland) *Tel:* (01) 497-3628 *Fax:* (01) 496-8263 *E-mail:* cle@iol.ie *Web Site:* www.irelandseye.com, pg 355

Children's Writers & Illustrators Group (United Kingdom) *Tel:* (020) 7373 6642 *Fax:* (020) 7373 5768 *Web Site:* www.booktrusted.com/booklists/listindex. html; www.societyofauthors.net, pg 1280

Child's Play (International) Ltd (United Kingdom) *Tel:* (01793) 616286 *Fax:* (01793) 512795 *E-mail:* allday@childs-play.com *Web Site:* www. childs-play.com, pg 674

Child's World Education Ltd (United Kingdom) *Tel:* (01753) 647060 *Fax:* (01753) 645522, pg 674

Chin Chin Publications Ltd (Taiwan, Province of China) *Tel:* (02) 25084331 *Fax:* (02) 25074902 *E-mail:* wcfl768@giga.net.tw *Web Site:* www. weichuan.org.tw, pg 634

China National Association of Literature and the Arts (Taiwan, Province of China), pg 1400

China Agriculture Press (China) *Tel:* (010) 5005665 *Fax:* (010) 5005894 *E-mail:* fcap@bj.col.com.cn, pg 101

China Books (Australia) *Tel:* (03) 9663 8822 *Fax:* (03) 9663 8821 *E-mail:* info@chinabooks.com.au *Web Site:* www.chinabooks.com.au, pg 17

China Braille Publishing House (China) *Tel:* (010) 6382 5214; (010) 6381 7417 *Fax:* (010) 6383 3585, pg 101

China Cartographic Publishing House (China) *Tel:* (010) 6356 4947 *Fax:* (010) 6352 9403 *E-mail:* fanyi@ chinamap.com, pg 101

China Express Media Ltd (Hong Kong) *Tel:* 2575 7288 *Fax:* 2575 7088 *E-mail:* kcchan@ossima.com, pg 313

China Film Press (China) *Tel:* (010) 4217845; (010) 4219917 *Fax:* (010) 4216415, pg 101

China Foreign Economic Relations & Trade Publishing House (China) *Tel:* (010) 64248236; (010) 64219742; (010) 64245686 *Fax:* (010) 64219392 *E-mail:* cfertph@263.net *Web Site:* www.caitec.org. cn/cfertph/indexv3.htm, pg 101

China Forestry Publishing House (China) *Tel:* (010) 6013117; (010) 661884477 *Fax:* (010) 66180373 *E-mail:* cfph@public3.bta.net.cn, pg 102

China International Book Trading Corporation (CIBTC) (China) *Tel:* (010) 684133078; (010) 68413849 *Fax:* (010) 68412166 *E-mail:* sinda@mail.cnokay.com *Web Site:* chinabooks.cnokay.com; www.cnokay.com, pg 1295

China ISBN Agency (China) *Tel:* (010) 65127806; (010) 65212832 *Fax:* (010) 65127875, pg 1254

China Knowledge Press (Singapore) *Tel:* 6310 8737 *Fax:* 6310 8738 *E-mail:* info@chinaknowledge-press.com *Web Site:* www.chinaknowledge-press.com, pg 550

China Labour Publishing House (China) *Tel:* (010) 64911180; (010) 4910488, pg 102

China Law Magazine Ltd (Taiwan, Province of China) *Tel:* (02) 231 46871 *Fax:* (02) 23814211 *E-mail:* chinals@hk.china.com, pg 634

China Light Industry Press (China) *Tel:* (010) 65271562 *Fax:* (010) 65121371, pg 102

China Machine Press (CMP) (China) *Tel:* (010) 88379973 *Fax:* (010) 68320405 (orders) *E-mail:* cjhui@mail.machineinfo.gov.cn *Web Site:* www.cmpbook.com; www.machineinfo.gov. cn, pg 102

China Materials Management Publishing House (China) *Tel:* (010) 68392913; (010) 68392825 *Fax:* (010) 8392911, pg 102

China National Publications Import & Export (Group) Corp (China) *Tel:* (010) 65082324; (010) 65086873; (010) 65086874 *Fax:* (010) 65086860 *E-mail:* info-center@cnpeak.com *Web Site:* www.cnpiec.com.cn, pg 1295

China Ocean Press (China) *Tel:* (010) 62112880-888 *Fax:* (010) 62112880-617 *E-mail:* zbs@oceanpress. com.cn *Web Site:* www.oceanpress.com.cn, pg 102

China Oil & Gas Periodical Office (China) *Tel:* (010) 64219111, pg 102

China PEN Centre (China) *Fax:* 8610 64221704, pg 1392

China Pictorial Publishing House (China) *Tel:* (010) 68412392; (010) 68414896; (010) 68412665 *Fax:* (010) 68413023 *E-mail:* wangjingtang@hotmail. com *Web Site:* www.china-pictorial.com, pg 102

China Social Sciences Publishing House (China) *Tel:* (010) 64031534 *Fax:* (010) 64074509, pg 102

China Society for Library Science (China) *Tel:* (010) 6841 9270 *Fax:* (010) 6841 9271 *E-mail:* ztxhmsc@ publicf.nlc.gov.cn *Web Site:* www.nlc.gov.cn, pg 1560

China Textile Press (China) *Tel:* (010) 64168240 *Fax:* (010) 64168225 *Web Site:* www.c-textilep.com, pg 102

China Theatre Publishing House (China) *Tel:* (010) 62244207; (010) 62244208, pg 102

China Tibetology Publishing House (China) *Tel:* (010) 64917618; (010) 64932942 *Fax:* (010) 4917619, pg 102

China Times Publishing Co (Taiwan, Province of China) *Tel:* (02) 23087111 *Fax:* (02) 23027844 *Web Site:* www.chinatimes.com.tw, pg 634

China Translation & Publishing Corp (China) *Tel:* (010) 66168196; (010) 66168647 *Fax:* (010) 6022734 *E-mail:* ctpc@public.bta.net.cn, pg 102

China Youth Publishing House (China) *Tel:* (010) 64033812; (010) 64032266 *Fax:* (010) 4031803, pg 103

Chinese Christian Literature Council Ltd (Hong Kong) *Tel:* 2367 8031, pg 313

Chinese Christian Literature Council Taiwan Ltd (Taiwan, Province of China) *Tel:* (02) 86676796 *Fax:* (02) 86676795, pg 634

Chinese Language Society of Hong Kong (Hong Kong) *Tel:* (02) 5284853, pg 1395

Chinese Literature Press (China) *Tel:* (010) 68326678 *Fax:* (010) 68326678 *E-mail:* chinalit@public.east.cn. net, pg 103

Chinese Marketing & Communications (United Kingdom) *Tel:* (0161) 237 3821 *Fax:* (0161) 236 7558 *E-mail:* support@chinese-marketing.com *Web Site:* www.chinese-marketing.com, pg 1140

Chinese Pedagogics Publishing House (China) *Tel:* (010) 68326333 *Fax:* (010) 8317390, pg 103

Chinese University of Hong Kong Library System (Hong Kong) *Tel:* 2609-7306 *Fax:* 2603-6952 *E-mail:* library@cuhk.edu.hk *Web Site:* www.lib.cuhk. edu.hk, pg 1512

The Chinese University Press (Hong Kong) *Tel:* 2609 6508 *Fax:* 2603 6692; 2603 7355 *E-mail:* cup@cuhk. edu.hk *Web Site:* www.cuhk.edu.hk/cupress.w1.htm; www.chineseupress.com, pg 313

Chingchic Publishers (Australia) *E-mail:* chingchic@ winshop.com.au *Web Site:* www.chingchic.com, pg 17

Editions Chiron (France) *Tel:* (01) 30141930 *Fax:* (01) 34603132 *E-mail:* info@editionschiron.com *Web Site:* www.editionschiron.com/fr/, pg 154

Chiron Media (Australia) *Tel:* (074) 947311 *Fax:* (074) 947890 *E-mail:* chiron@acslink.net.au, pg 17

Chiron-Verlag Reinhardt Stiehle (Germany) *Tel:* (07071) 8884150 *Fax:* (07071) 8884151 *E-mail:* info@ chironverlag.de *Web Site:* www.chironverlag.de, pg 207

Cedric Chivers Ltd (United Kingdom) *Tel:* (0117) 9371910 *Fax:* (0117) 9371920 *E-mail:* info@ cedricchivers.co.uk *Web Site:* www.cedricchivers.co.uk, pg 1215

Chmielorz GmbH Verlag (Germany) *Tel:* (0611) 360980 *Fax:* (0611) 36098-17 *E-mail:* tme@chmielorz.de *Web Site:* www.chmielorz.de, pg 207

CHOICE Magazine (Australia) *Tel:* (02) 9577 3399 *Fax:* (02) 9577 3377 *E-mail:* ausconsumer@choice. com.au *Web Site:* www.choice.com.au, pg 17

Chokechai Theues Shop (Thailand) *Tel:* (02) 2226660, pg 640

An Chomhairle Leabharlanna (Ireland) *Tel:* (01) 6761963; (01) 6761167 *Fax:* (01) 6766721 *E-mail:* info@librarycouncil.ie *Web Site:* www. librarycouncil.ie, pg 1565

Chong Moh Offset Printing Ltd (Singapore) *Tel:* 8622701 *Fax:* 8624335 *E-mail:* chongmoh@ singnet.com.sg, pg 1150, 1171, 1212

Chong No Books Publishing Co Ltd (Republic of Korea) *Tel:* (02) 7325381 *Fax:* (02) 7326202, pg 434

Chongqing Library (China) *Tel:* (023) 6362-2596 *Fax:* (023) 6385-1474, pg 1496

Chongqing University Press (China) *Tel:* (023) 65111125 *Fax:* (023) 65106879 *E-mail:* chenxy@cqup.com.cn *Web Site:* www.cqup.com.cn, pg 103

Chopsons Pte Ltd (Singapore) *Tel:* 64483634 *Fax:* 64481071 *E-mail:* chopsons@singnet.com.sg, pg 551

Chopsticks Publications Ltd (Hong Kong) *Tel:* 2336-8433 *Fax:* 2338-1462 *E-mail:* chopsticks1971@ netvigator.com, pg 313

Chorion IP (United Kingdom) *Tel:* (020) 7434 1880 *Fax:* (020) 7434 1882 *E-mail:* info@enidblyton.co.uk *Web Site:* www.chorion.co.uk, pg 674

Chorus-Verlag (Germany) *Tel:* (089) 634 999 60 *Fax:* (089) 634 999 61 *Web Site:* www.chorus-verlag. de, pg 208

The Chosun Ilbo Co, Ltd (Republic of Korea) *Tel:* (02) 724-5114 *Fax:* (02) 724-6199, pg 434

Chotard et Associes Editeurs (France) *Tel:* (01) 41 29 96 05 *Fax:* (01) 41 29 98 15, pg 154

Chowkhamba Sanskrit Series Office (India) *Tel:* (0542) 2333458 *Fax:* (0542) 2333458 *E-mail:* cssoffice@ satyam.net.in *Web Site:* www.chowkhambaseries.com, pg 329

Chr Belser AG fur Verlagsgeschaefte und Co KG (Germany) *Tel:* (0711) 2191-0 *Fax:* (0711) 2191-330, pg 208

Christchurch City Libraries (New Zealand) *Tel:* (03) 941 7923 *Fax:* (03) 941 7848 *E-mail:* library@ccc.govt.nz *Web Site:* library.christchurch.org.nz, pg 1530

Christian Audio-Visual Action (CAVA) (Zimbabwe) *Tel:* (04) 752233 *Fax:* (04) 727030 *E-mail:* cava@ mango.zw, pg 777

The Christian Book Centre (Papua New Guinea) *Tel:* 852 2043 *Fax:* 852 3376, pg 510

Christian Book Service (Guyana) *Tel:* (02) 52521 *Fax:* (02) 54039, pg 1304

Christian Booksellers Association (United Kingdom) *Tel:* (0161) 434 7000 *Fax:* (0161) 445 2911 *E-mail:* info@cba-ukeurope.org *Web Site:* www.cba-ukeurop.org, pg 1280

Christian Booksellers' Association (NZ Chapter) (New Zealand) *Tel:* (07) 888 6010 *E-mail:* info@cbaonline. org *Web Site:* www.cbaonline.org, pg 1270

Christian Booksellers Association of Nigeria (Nigeria) *Tel:* (073) 452387 *E-mail:* cban@bwave.net *Web Site:* www.cbaonline.org, pg 1270

Christian Bookselling Association of Australia Inc (Australia) *Tel:* (02) 9524 3347 *Fax:* (02) 9540 3001 *E-mail:* info@cbaa.com.au *Web Site:* www.cbaa.com. au, pg 1250

Christian Bookstore (Thailand) *Tel:* (02) 234-7991, pg 1336

Christian Communications Ltd (Hong Kong) *Tel:* 2725-8558 *Fax:* 2386-1804 *Web Site:* www.ccfellow.org, pg 313

Christian Education (United Kingdom) *Tel:* (0121) 472 4242 *Fax:* (0121) 472 7575 *E-mail:* enquiries@ christianeducation.org.uk *Web Site:* www. christianeducation.org.uk/cep/cep_about.htm, pg 674

Christian Focus Publications Ltd (United Kingdom) *Tel:* (01862) 871 011 *Fax:* (01862) 871 699 *E-mail:* info@christianfocus.com *Web Site:* www. christianfocus.com, pg 674

Christian Literature Association in Malawi (Malawi) *Tel:* 620839; 673091, pg 451

Christian Literature Crusade (Australia) *Tel:* (02) 9875 1330 *Fax:* (02) 9481 8304, pg 17

Christian Literature Crusade (Barbados) *Tel:* 429-5630 *Fax:* 426-9254, pg 1291

The Christian Literature Society (India) *Tel:* (044) 25354296; (044) 25354297 *Fax:* (044) 25354297, pg 329

The Christian Literature Society of Korea (Republic of Korea) *Tel:* (02) 553-0870 *Fax:* (02) 555-7721, pg 435

Christian Research Association (United Kingdom) *Tel:* (020) 8294 1989 *Fax:* (020) 8294 0014 *E-mail:* admin@christian-research.org.uk *Web Site:* www.christian-research.org.uk, pg 674

Christian Verlag GmbH (Germany) *Tel:* (089) 381803-17; (089) 381803-31 *Fax:* (089) 38180381 *E-mail:* info@christian-verlag.de *Web Site:* www. christian-verlag.de, pg 208

Christiana-Verlag (Switzerland) *Tel:* (052) 741 41 31 *Fax:* (052) 741 20 92 *E-mail:* orders@christiana.ch *Web Site:* www.christiana.ch, pg 616

Hans Christians Druckerei und Verlag GmbH & Co KG (Germany) *Tel:* (040) 35 60 06-0 *Fax:* (040) 35 60 06-26 *E-mail:* verlag@christians.de *Web Site:* www. christians.de, pg 208

Christliche Verlagsgesellschaft mbH (Germany) *Tel:* (02771) 8302-0 *Fax:* (02771) 8302-30 *E-mail:* info@cv-dillenburg.de *Web Site:* www.cb-buchshop.de, pg 208

Christliches Verlagshaus GmbH (Germany) *Tel:* (0711) 830000 *Fax:* (0711) 830010, pg 208

Uitgeverij Christofoor (Netherlands) *Tel:* (030) 692 39 74 *Fax:* (030) 691 48 34 *E-mail:* info@christofoor.nl, pg 477

Christoph Merian Verlag (Switzerland) *Tel:* (061) 226 33 25 *Fax:* (061) 226 33 45 *E-mail:* verlag@ merianstiftung.ch *Web Site:* www.christoph-merian-verlag.ch; pg 616

Christophorus-Verlag GmbH (Germany) *Tel:* (0761) 27170 *Fax:* (0761) 2717352, pg 208

Christusbruderschaft Selbitz ev, Abt Verlag (Germany) *Tel:* (09280) 68-34 *Fax:* (09280) 68-68 *E-mail:* info@ verlag-christusbruderschaft.de *Web Site:* www.verlag-christusbruderschaft.de, pg 208

Chroma Graphics (Overseas) Pte Ltd (Singapore) *Tel:* 67423706 *Fax:* 67484097, pg 1171

Chronicles Publishers Ltd (Israel) *Tel:* (03) 5615052 *Fax:* (03) 5624104 *E-mail:* chronicl@inter.net.il, pg 1148

Chronique Sociale (France) *Tel:* (04) 78372212 *Fax:* (04) 78420318 *E-mail:* chroniquesociale@wanadoo.fr *Web Site:* www.chroniquesociale.com, pg 154

Chronos Verlag (Switzerland) *Tel:* (01) 265 4343 *Fax:* (01) 265 4344 *E-mail:* info@chronos-verlag.ch *Web Site:* www.chronos-verlag.ch, pg 616

The Chrysalis Press (United Kingdom) *Tel:* (01926) 855223 *E-mail:* chrysalis@margaretbuckley.com, pg 674

Chrysi Penna - Golden Pen Books (Greece) *Tel:* 210 3805672 *Fax:* 2103825205 *E-mail:* info@ chrissipenna.com *Web Site:* www.chrissipenna.com, pg 303

Chrysopolitissa Publishers (Cyprus) *Tel:* (022) 353929 *Fax:* (022) 353929, pg 121

Chryssos Typos AE Ekodeis (Greece) *Tel:* 2103637945 *Fax:* 2103824417, pg 303

Chu Liu Book Company (Taiwan, Province of China) *Tel:* (02) 236 95 250 *Fax:* (02) 836 913 93 *E-mail:* chuliu@ms13.hinet.net, pg 634

Chugh Publications (India) *Tel:* (0532) 623561, pg 329

Chung Hwa Book Co (HK) Ltd (Hong Kong) *Tel:* 2715 0176 *Fax:* 2713 8202; 2713 4675 *E-mail:* info@ chunghwabook.com.hk; pub-dept@chunghwabook. com.hk *Web Site:* www.chunghwabook.com.hk, pg 313

Chung Hwa Book Co Ltd (Taiwan, Province of China) *Tel:* (02) 8797 8669 *Fax:* (02) 8797 8909, pg 634

Chuo-Tosho Co Ltd (Japan) *Tel:* (075) 441-2174 *Fax:* (075) 441-3300, pg 413

Chuokoron-Shinsha Inc (Japan) *Tel:* (03) 3563-1431 *Fax:* (03) 3561-5922 *E-mail:* honyaku-irie@chuko. co.jp *Web Site:* www.chuko.co.jp, pg 413

Church Archivists Press (Australia) *Tel:* (07) 3865 0466 *Fax:* (07) 3865 0458, pg 18

Church House Publishing (United Kingdom) *Tel:* (020) 7898 1451 *Fax:* (020) 7898 1449 *E-mail:* sales@c-of-e.org.uk *Web Site:* www.chpublishing.co.uk, pg 674

Church Mouse Press (New Zealand) *Tel:* (063) 357-2445 *Fax:* (063) 357-2445, pg 490

Church Society (United Kingdom) *Tel:* (01923) 235111 *Fax:* (01923) 800362 *E-mail:* enquiries@ churchsociety.org *Web Site:* www.churchsociety.org, pg 675

Church Union (United Kingdom) *Tel:* (020) 7222 6952 *Fax:* (020) 7976 7180 *E-mail:* churchunion@care4free. net *Web Site:* www.churchunion.care4free.net, pg 675

Chvojkova nakladatelstvi (Czech Republic) *Tel:* (02) 96202095; (02) 71743023 *Fax:* (02) 96202095, pg 122

Cia Editora Nacional (Brazil) *Tel:* (011) 66926985 *Fax:* (011) 66926985 *E-mail:* nacional@uol.com.br, pg 79

CIACO (Belgium) *Tel:* (018) 213700 *Fax:* (018) 212372, pg 65

CIAT - Centro Internacional de Agricultura Tropical (Colombia) *Tel:* (02) 445-0000 *Fax:* (02) 445-0073 *E-mail:* ciat@cgiar.org *Web Site:* www.ciat.cgiar.org, pg 110

CIC Edizioni Internazionali (Italy) *Tel:* (06) 8412673 *Fax:* (06) 8412688; (06) 8412687 *E-mail:* info@ gruppocic.it *Web Site:* www.gruppocic.it, pg 378

Cicada Press (New Zealand) *Tel:* (09) 4180890 *Fax:* (09) 4181142, pg 490

CICC Book House, Leading Publishers & Booksellers (India) *Tel:* (0484) 353557; (0484) 355658, pg 329

Cicero-Chr Erichsens (Denmark) *Tel:* 3316-0308 *Fax:* 33160307 *E-mail:* info@cicero.dk *Web Site:* www.cicero.dk, pg 129

Cicero Editeurs (France) *Tel:* (01) 43544757 *Fax:* (01) 40517385, pg 154

Cicero Presse Verlag & Antiquariat (Germany) *Tel:* (04651) 890305 *Fax:* (04651) 890885 *E-mail:* ciceropresse@t-online.de *Web Site:* www.zvab. com, pg 208

Cicerone Press (United Kingdom) *Tel:* (01539) 562 069 *Fax:* (01539) 563 417 *E-mail:* info@cicerone.co.uk *Web Site:* www.cicerone.co.uk, pg 675

Editora Cidade Nova (Brazil) *Tel:* (011) 4158-2252 *Fax:* (011) 4158-2252 *E-mail:* editora@cidadenova. org.br *Web Site:* www.cidadenova.org.br, pg 79

Cidade Nova Editora (Portugal) *Tel:* (01) 2478734 *Fax:* (01) 2476369 *Web Site:* perola.net-rubi.com.br, pg 525

CIDAP (Ecuador) *Tel:* (07) 829-451; (07) 828-878 *Fax:* (07) 831-450 *E-mail:* ciesa@pi.pro.ec, pg 136

Cideb Editrice SRL (Italy) *Tel:* (0185) 60241 *Fax:* (0185) 230100 *E-mail:* info@cideb.com *Web Site:* www.cideb.it, pg 378

CIE (International Commission on Illumination Central Bureau) (Austria) *Tel:* (01) 714 31 87 0 *Fax:* (01) 713 08 38 18 *E-mail:* ciecb@ping.at *Web Site:* www.cie. co.at/cie, pg 1251

Ciela Publishing House (Bulgaria) *Tel:* (02) 951 63 76; (02) 954 93 97; (02) 951 66 97 *Fax:* (02) 954 93 97 *E-mail:* ciela@bulnet.bg *Web Site:* www.ciela.net, pg 93

Publicacoes Ciencia e Vida Lda (Portugal) *Tel:* (021) 3427989 *Fax:* (021) 3460224, pg 525

Instituto de Ciencias de la Computacion (NCR) (Paraguay) *Tel:* (021) 490076 *Fax:* (021) 497849, pg 511

Editorial de Ciencias Sociales (Cuba) *Tel:* (07) 2036090; (07) 333441 *Fax:* (07) 2304801 *E-mail:* nuevomil@icl. cult.cu, pg 120

Libreria Cientifica SA (Ecuador) *Tel:* (02) 12556, pg 1298

Livraria Cientifica Ernesto Reichmann Ltda (Brazil) *Tel:* (011) 3255-1342; (011) 3214-3167 *Fax:* (011) 3255-7501 *E-mail:* rrr@erdl.com *Web Site:* www. ernestoreichmann.com.br, pg 1293

Cientifica Interamericana SACI, Editorial (Argentina) *Tel:* (011) 4822-8883 *Fax:* (011) 4827-0486 *E-mail:* edit@interame.satlink.net, pg 4

Editora Cientifica Medica Latinoamerican SA de CV (Mexico) *Tel:* (05) 5206135; (05) 5405600 *Fax:* (05) 52020926, pg 459

Editorial Cientifico Tecnica (Cuba) *Tel:* (07) 2036090 *Fax:* (07) 333441 *E-mail:* nuevomil@icl.cult.cu, pg 120

Ediciones Cieplan (Chile) *Tel:* (02) 2323212; (02) 2324558; (02) 6333836 *Fax:* (02) 3340312 *E-mail:* cieplan@ctcreuna.cl, pg 98

Verlag Marianne Cieslik (Germany) *Tel:* (0203) 30527-0 *Fax:* (0203) 30527-820 *Web Site:* www.verlag-cieslik. de, pg 208

CIESPAL (Centro Internacional de Estudios Superiores de Comunicacion para America Latina) (Ecuador) *Tel:* (02) 2524177 *Fax:* (02) 2502487 *E-mail:* publicaciones@ciespal.net *Web Site:* www. ciespal.net, pg 136

Il Cigno Galileo Galilei-Edizioni di Arte e Scienza (Italy) *Tel:* (06) 6865493; (06) 6873842 *Fax:* (06) 6892109 *E-mail:* info@ilcigno.org, pg 378

CILT, the National Centre for Languages (United Kingdom) *Tel:* (020) 7379 5101; (020) 7379 5110 (resources library & information services) *Fax:* (020) 7379 5082 *E-mail:* publications@cilt.org.uk; library@ cilt.org.uk (library information); info@cilt.org.uk *Web Site:* www.cilt.org.uk, pg 675

Libreria Cima (Ecuador) *Tel:* (02) 571218; (02) 571318, pg 1298

Cimaise sarl (France) *Tel:* (01) 45437045 *Fax:* (01) 45437045, pg 154

Editorial Cincel Kapelusz Ltda (Colombia) *Tel:* (01) 2442035; (01) 3350031 *Fax:* (01) 3350042, pg 110

Cinema (Czech Republic) *Tel:* (02) 627 83 95-6 *Fax:* (02) 627 72 39 *E-mail:* schur@comp.cz, pg 122

Cirad (France) *Tel:* (04) 67 61 58 00 *Fax:* (04) 67 61 55 47 *Web Site:* www.cirad.fr, pg 154

Ciranna e Ferrara (Italy) *Tel:* (0362) 230849 *Fax:* (0362) 326213, pg 378

Ciranna - Roma (Italy) *Tel:* (091) 224499 *Fax:* (091) 311064 *E-mail:* info@ciranna.it *Web Site:* www. ciranna.it, pg 378

Circe Ediciones, SA (Spain) *Tel:* (093) 2040990 *Fax:* (093) 2041183 *E-mail:* circe@oceano.com, pg 572

Circle of State Librarians (United Kingdom) *Tel:* (020) 7273 4463 *Fax:* (020) 7273 3957 *Web Site:* www. circleofstatelibrarians.co.uk, pg 1573

Circle of Wine Writers (United Kingdom) *Tel:* (01225) 783007 *Fax:* (01225) 783152 *E-mail:* administrator@ winewriters.org *Web Site:* www.winewriters.org, pg 1281

Editions Circonflexe (France) *Tel:* (01) 46 34 77 77 *Fax:* (01) 43 25 34 67 *E-mail:* info@circonflexe.fr *Web Site:* www.circonflexe.fr, pg 154

Circulo de Lectores SA (Colombia) *Tel:* (01) 2173211; (01) 2177720 *Fax:* (01) 2178157, pg 1296

Circulo de Lectores SA (Colombia) *Tel:* 2173211; 2177720 *Fax:* 2178157 *Web Site:* www.comercial-eltiempo.com, pg 1241

Circulo de Lectores SA (Spain) *Tel:* (0902) 22 33 55 *E-mail:* atencion-socios@circulo.es *Web Site:* www. circulo.es, pg 1245

Circulo de Leitores (Portugal) *Tel:* 217 626 100 *Fax:* 217 607 149 *E-mail:* correio@circuloleitores.pt *Web Site:* www.circuloleitores.pt, pg 1245

Circulo do Livro SA (Brazil) *Tel:* (011) 8513644 *Fax:* (011) 2827273, pg 1241

CIRIA (United Kingdom) *Tel:* (020) 7549 3300 *Fax:* (020) 7253 0523 *E-mail:* enquiries@ciria.org.uk *Web Site:* www.ciria.org.uk, pg 675

CIS Publishers (Australia) *Tel:* (03) 92467131 *Fax:* (03) 3470175 *E-mail:* samone.underwood@reeducation. com.au, pg 18

CISAC (Confederation Internationale des Societes d'Auteurs et de Compesiteurs) (France) *Tel:* (01) 55 62 08 50 *Fax:* (01) 55 62 08 60 *E-mail:* cisac@cisac. org *Web Site:* www.cisac.org, pg 1257

Cisalpino (Italy) *Tel:* (02) 2040 4031 *Fax:* (02) 2040 4044 *Web Site:* www.monduzzi.com/cisalpino, pg 379

CISAM (Italy) *Tel:* (0743) 225630 *Fax:* (0743) 49902 *E-mail:* cisam@cisam.org *Web Site:* www.cisam.org, pg 379

Cisneros (Spain) *Tel:* (091) 5619900 *Fax:* (091) 5613990, pg 572

Editions Citadelles & Mazenod (France) *Tel:* (01) 53043060 *Fax:* (01) 45220427 *E-mail:* info@ citadelles-mazenod.com *Web Site:* www.citadelles-mazenod.com, pg 154

CITIC Publishing House (China) *Tel:* (010) 85323366 *Fax:* (010) 85322508 *E-mail:* g-office@citic.com.cn; mail@citicpub.com *Web Site:* www.citic.com.cn; www. publish.citic.com, pg 103

Citta Nuova Editrice (Italy) *Tel:* (06) 3216212 *Fax:* (06) 3207185 *E-mail:* segr.rivista@cittanuova.it *Web Site:* www.cittanuova.it, pg 379

Cittadella Editrice (Italy) *Tel:* (075) 813595 *Fax:* (075) 813719 *E-mail:* amministrazione@cittadellaeditrice. com *Web Site:* www.cittadellaeditrice.com, pg 379

City Bookshop Ltd (Kenya) *Tel:* (011) 313 149; (011) 225548 *Fax:* (011) 314815, pg 1314

City Library (Mauritius) *Tel:* 212 0831 (ext 163) *Fax:* 212 4258 *E-mail:* mpllib@intnet.mu *Web Site:* mpl.intnet.mu, pg 1526

Editorial Ciudad Nueva de la Sefoma (Argentina) *Tel:* (011) 4981-4885 *Fax:* (011) 4981-4885 *E-mail:* ciudadnueva@ciudadnueva.org.ar *Web Site:* www.ciudadnueva.org.ar, pg 4

Editorial Ciudad Nueva (Spain) *Tel:* (091) 725 95 30; (091) 356 96 12 *Fax:* (091) 713 04 52 *E-mail:* editorial@ciudadnueva.com *Web Site:* www. ciudadnueva.com, pg 572

Livraria Civilizacao (Americo Fraga Lamares & Ca Lda) (Portugal) *Tel:* (022) 20002286 *Fax:* (022) 312382, pg 525

Civitas SA Editorial (Spain) *Tel:* (091) 902 011 787 *Fax:* (091) 725 26 73 *E-mail:* clientes@civitas.es *Web Site:* www.civitas.es, pg 572

Claassen Verlag GmbH (Germany) *Tel:* (030) 23456-300 *Fax:* (030) 23456-303 *Web Site:* www.claassen-verlag.de, pg 208

CLAIM Bookshop (Malawi) *Tel:* 620839; 673091, pg 1316

Librairie Clairafrique (Senegal) *Tel:* (08) 231261 *Fax:* (08) 218409 *E-mail:* clairaf@telecomplus.sn *Web Site:* eddefine.net/clairaf, pg 1329

Clairefontaine, Editions (Switzerland) *Tel:* (021) 323 08 79, pg 616

The John Clare Society (United Kingdom) *Web Site:* freespace.virgin.net/linda.curry/jclare.htm, pg 1401

Editorial Claret SA (Spain) *Tel:* (093) 3010887 *Fax:* (093) 3174830 *E-mail:* editorial@claret.es; admin@claret.es *Web Site:* www.claret.es, pg 572

Claretian Communications Inc (Philippines) *Tel:* (02) 9213984 *Fax:* (02) 9217429 *E-mail:* cci@claret.org; claret@info.com.ph *Web Site:* www.bible.claret.org, pg 514

Editorial Claretiana (Argentina) *Tel:* (011) 4305-9597; (011) 4305-9510 *Fax:* (011) 4305-6552 *E-mail:* editorial@editorialclaretiana.com.ar *Web Site:* www.editorialclaretiana.com.ar, pg 4

Editorial Claridad SA (Argentina) *Tel:* (011) 4371-5546 *Fax:* (011) 4375-1659 *E-mail:* editorial@heliasta.com. ar *Web Site:* www.heliasta.com.ar, pg 4

Clarke Associates Ltd (United Kingdom) *Tel:* (0117) 926 8864 *Fax:* (0117) 922 6437 *E-mail:* enq@clarkeassoc. com *Web Site:* www.clarkeassoc.demon.co.uk, pg 1340

James Clarke & Co Ltd (United Kingdom) *Tel:* (01223) 350865 *Fax:* (01223) 366951 *E-mail:* publishing@ jamesclarke.co.uk *Web Site:* www.jamesclarke.co.uk, pg 675

Clasicos Roxsil Editorial SA de CV (El Salvador) *Tel:* 2228-1832; 2288-2646; 2229-6742 *Fax:* 2228-1212, pg 138

Clasicos Roxsil Editorial SA de CV (El Salvador) *Tel:* 228 1832; 229 3621 *Fax:* 228 1212, pg 1299

Class Publishing (United Kingdom) *Tel:* (020) 7371 2119 *Fax:* (020) 7371 2878 *E-mail:* post@class.co.uk *Web Site:* www.class.co.uk, pg 675

Werner Classen Verlag (Switzerland) *Tel:* (01) 4916362 *Fax:* (01) 4916362, pg 616

E W Classey Ltd (United Kingdom) *Tel:* (01367) 244700 *Fax:* (01367) 244800 *E-mail:* info@classeybooks.com *Web Site:* www.abebooks.com/home/bugbooks; www. classeybooks.com, pg 675

Classic (Pakistan) *Tel:* (042) 323963; (042) 312977 *Fax:* (042) 7238236, pg 507

Editora Classica (Portugal) *Tel:* (021) 372386 *Fax:* (021) 3474729, pg 525

Classical Publishing Co (India) *Tel:* (011) 563689, pg 329

Classikaletet (Israel) *Tel:* (03) 5616996 *Fax:* (03) 5615526 *E-mail:* kimbooks@netvision.net.it, pg 362

Claudiana Editrice (Italy) *Tel:* (011) 6689804 *Fax:* (011) 6504394 *E-mail:* info@claudiana.it *Web Site:* www. claudiana.it, pg 379

Claudius Verlag (Germany) *Tel:* (089) 12172-123 *Fax:* (089) 12172-138 *E-mail:* info@claudius.de *Web Site:* www.claudius.de, pg 209

Uitgeverij Clavis (Belgium) *Tel:* (011) 28 68 68 *Fax:* (011) 28 68 69 *E-mail:* info@clavis.be *Web Site:* www.clavis.be, pg 65

Clays Ltd (United Kingdom) *Tel:* (01986) 893211 *Fax:* (01986) 895293 *E-mail:* sales@clays.co.uk *Web Site:* www.clays.co.uk, pg 1153, 1215

Clays Ltd (United Kingdom) *Tel:* (01986) 893211 *Fax:* (01986) 89529 *E-mail:* sales@clays.co.uk *Web Site:* www.st-ives.co.uk; www.clays.co.uk, pg 1228

Clays Ltd (United Kingdom) *Tel:* (01986) 893211 *Fax:* (01986) 895293 *E-mail:* sales@clays.co.uk *Web Site:* www.clays.co.uk, pg 1237

CLD (France) *Tel:* (02) 47282068 *Fax:* (02) 47288548, pg 154

Editions CLE (Cameroon) *Tel:* (0237) 22-35-54 *Fax:* (0237) 23-27-09 *E-mail:* edition@iccnet.cm, pg 97

Cle International (France) *Tel:* (01) 45 87 44 00 *Fax:* (01) 45 87 44 10 *E-mail:* cle@cle-inter.com *Web Site:* www.cle-inter.com, pg 154

CLE: The Irish Book Publishers' Association (Ireland) *Tel:* (01) 670-7393 *Fax:* (01) 670-7642 *E-mail:* info@publishingireland.com *Web Site:* www. publishingireland.com, pg 1264

R J Cleary Publishing (Australia) *Tel:* (02) 2643750, pg 18

Clerestory Press (New Zealand) *Tel:* (03) 3553588 *Fax:* (03) 3553588 *E-mail:* young.writers@xtra.co.nz, pg 490

CLEUP - Cooperative Libraria Editrice dell 'Universita di Padova (Italy) *Tel:* (049) 8753496 *Fax:* (049) 650261 *E-mail:* redazione@cleup.it, pg 379

The Cleveland Vibrator Co (United States) *Tel:* 216-241-7157 *Toll Free Tel:* 800-221-3298 *Fax:* 216-241-3480 *Web Site:* www.clevelandvibrator.com, pg 1238

Clever Books (South Africa) *Tel:* (012) 3424715 *Fax:* (012) 4302376 *E-mail:* inl0631@mweb.co.za, pg 558

Editorial Clie (Spain) *Tel:* (093) 7884262; (093) 7885722 *Fax:* (093) 7800514 *E-mail:* libros@clie.es *Web Site:* www.clie.es, pg 572

Editions Climats (France) *Tel:* (04) 99 58 30 91; (04) 67 45 37 90 *Fax:* (04) 99 58 30 92 *E-mail:* contact@ editions-climats.com *Web Site:* www.editions-climats. com, pg 154

Climent, Eliseau Editor (Spain) *Tel:* (06) 3516492 *Fax:* (06) 3529872 *E-mail:* 3i4@arrakis.es, pg 572

Clipper Distribution Services (United Kingdom) *Tel:* (0705) 200080 *Fax:* (0705) 200090, pg 1340

De Clivo Press (Switzerland) *Tel:* (01) 8201124, pg 616

Clo Iar-Chonnachta Teo (Ireland) *Tel:* (091) 593 307 *Fax:* (091) 593 362 *E-mail:* cic@iol.ie *Web Site:* www.cic.ie, pg 355

Clodhanna Teoranta (Ireland), pg 355

Cloister Bookstore Ltd (Barbados) *Tel:* (246) 426-2662 *Fax:* (246) 429-7269 *E-mail:* cloisterbookstore@ caribsurf.com, pg 1291

Jonathan Clowes Ltd (United Kingdom) *Tel:* (020) 7722 7674 *Fax:* (020) 7722 7677, pg 1129

William Clowes Ltd (United Kingdom) *Tel:* (01502) 712884 *Fax:* (01502) 717003 *E-mail:* william@ clowes.co.uk *Web Site:* www.clowes.co.uk, pg 1153, 1174, 1215, 1228, 1237

Club de Lectores (Argentina) *Tel:* (011) 4382-2798 *E-mail:* libreriaaccion@uolsinectis.com.ar, pg 4

Club de Lectores Extemporaneos (Mexico) *Tel:* (05) 5875424; (05) 5878785, pg 1244

Club du Livre SA (France) *Tel:* (01) 47638055 *Fax:* (01) 44404865, pg 1242

CLUEB (Cooperativa Libraria Universitaria Editrice Bologna) (Italy) *Tel:* (051) 220736 *Fax:* (051) 237758 *E-mail:* clueb@clueb.com; info@clueb.com *Web Site:* www.clueb.com, pg 379

Editura Clusium (Romania) *Tel:* (064) 196940 *Fax:* (064) 196940 *E-mail:* clusium@codec.ro, pg 534

CLUT Editrice (Italy) *Tel:* (011) 5647980 *Fax:* (011) 542192 *E-mail:* informazioni@clut.it *Web Site:* www. clut.it, pg 379

CMA Edition (Germany) *Tel:* (0941) 23939; (0941) 34003; (08458) 8960 *Fax:* (08458) 8960; (0941) 34003, pg 209

CMC Publishing Co Ltd (Japan) *Tel:* (03) 3293-2065 *Fax:* (03) 3293-2069 *E-mail:* info@cmcbooks.co.jp *Web Site:* www.cmcbooks.co.jp, pg 413

CMP Information Ltd (United Kingdom) *Tel:* (01732) 377591 *Fax:* (01732) 377440 *Web Site:* www.cmpdata. co.uk, pg 675

CNRS Editions (France) *Tel:* (01) 53 10 27 00 *Fax:* (01) 53 10 27 27 *E-mail:* cnrseditions@cnrseditions.fr *Web Site:* www.cnrseditions.fr, pg 154

Co-Fine Promotions (Hong Kong) *Tel:* 2518 0383 *Fax:* 2518 0361 *E-mail:* cofine@netvigator.com, pg 1235

Co Libri (Slovenia) *Tel:* (01) 1255111 *Fax:* (01) 224454, pg 1331

Coach House Printing (Canada) *Tel:* 416-979-2217 *Fax:* 416-977-1158 *E-mail:* mail@chbooks.com *Web Site:* www.chbooks.com, pg 1165, 1205

Coachwise Ltd (United Kingdom) *Tel:* (0113) 2311310 *Fax:* (0113) 2319606 *E-mail:* enquiries@coachwise. ltd.uk *Web Site:* www.coachwise.ltd.uk, pg 676

La Coccinella Editrice SRL (Italy) *Tel:* (0332) 224690 *Fax:* (0332) 222025, pg 379

Elspeth Cochrane Agency (United Kingdom) *Tel:* (020) 7622 0314 *Fax:* (020) 7622 5815 *E-mail:* info@ elspethcochrane.co.uk, pg 1129

Cockatoo Press (Schweiz), Thailand-Publikationen (Switzerland) *Tel:* (044) 984 17 25 *Fax:* (044) 984 34 20 *E-mail:* books@thailine.com, pg 616

Cockbird Press (United Kingdom) *Tel:* (01435) 830430 *Fax:* (01435) 830027, pg 676

CODE - Europe (United Kingdom) *Tel:* (01865) 202438 *Fax:* (01865) 2024390 *E-mail:* code_europe@ compuserve.com *Web Site:* www.oneworld.org/ code_europe/code_news10.html, pg 1281

Codes Rousseau (France) *Tel:* (02) 51 23 11 00 *Fax:* (02) 51 21 31 02 *E-mail:* info@codes-rousseau.fr *Web Site:* www.codesrousseau.fr, pg 155

CODESRIA (Council for the Development of Social Science Research in Africa) (Senegal) *Tel:* 8259814; 8259822 *Fax:* 8241289; 8640143 *E-mail:* codesria@ sonatel.senet.net *Web Site:* www.cordesria.org, pg 546

Codice Comercio Distribuicao e Casa Editorial Ltda (Brazil) *Tel:* (011) 5031-8033 *E-mail:* codice@ codicenet.com.br, pg 79

Codra Enterprises Inc (United States) *Tel:* 714-891-5652 (ext 30) *Fax:* 714-891-5642 *E-mail:* codra@codra. com; sales@codra.com *Web Site:* www.codra.com, pg 1155

Rene Coeckelberghs Bokfoerlag AB (Sweden) *Tel:* (08) 7230880 *Fax:* (08) 7230311, pg 605

Rene Coeckelberghs Editions (Switzerland) *Tel:* (041) 515060 *Fax:* (041) 516645, pg 616

Coffee Industry Corporation (Papua New Guinea) *Tel:* 732 1266; 732 2466 *Fax:* 732 1431 *E-mail:* cicgka@daltron.com.pg *Web Site:* www. coffeecorp.org.pg, pg 511

Eric Cohen Books Ltd (Israel) *Tel:* (09) 747 8000 *Fax:* (09) 747 8001 *E-mail:* info@ecb.co.il *Web Site:* www.ecb.co.il, pg 1309

Coimbra Editora Lda (Portugal) *Tel:* (0239) 85 2650 *Fax:* (0239) 85 2651 *E-mail:* sede@mail. coimbraeditora.pt; revistas@mail.coimbraeditora.pt *Web Site:* www.coimbraeditora.pt, pg 525

Cole Publications (Australia) *Tel:* (03) 9830 4242 *Fax:* (03) 9830 4242, pg 18

Colegial Bolivariana CA (Venezuela) *Tel:* (0212) 2391055; (0212) 2391244; (0212) 2391377; (0212) 2391166; (0212) 2391944; (0212) 2391433; (0212) 2391777; (0212) 2391555 *Fax:* (0212) 2396502; (0212) 2379942 *Web Site:* co-bo.com, pg 774

Colegio de Bibliotecarios de Chile AG (Chile) *Tel:* (02) 222 56 52 *Fax:* (02) 635 50 23 *E-mail:* cdc@ bibliotecarios.cl *Web Site:* www.bibliotecarios.cl, pg 1560

Ediciones Colegio De Espana (ECE) (Spain) *Tel:* (023) 21 47 88 *Fax:* (023) 21 87 91 *E-mail:* info@colesp. eurart.es *Web Site:* www.eurart.es/emp/colesp, pg 572

El Colegio de Mexico AC (Mexico) *Tel:* (05) 54953080 *Fax:* (05) 54493083 *E-mail:* fgomez@colmex.mx *Web Site:* www.colmex.mx, pg 459

Colegio de Postgraduados en Ciencias Agricolas (Mexico) *Tel:* (0595) 95 2 02 00; (055) 58 04 59 00 *E-mail:* seia@colpos.mx *Web Site:* www.colpos.mx, pg 459

Libreria del Colegio SA (Argentina) *Tel:* (011) 4300-5400; (011) 4362-1222 *Fax:* (011) 4362-7364 *E-mail:* edsudame@satlink.com, pg 4

Charles Coleman Verlag GmbH & Co KG (Germany) *Tel:* (0221) 5497-0 *Fax:* (0221) 5497-326 *E-mail:* coleman@rudolf.mueller.de *Web Site:* www. coleman-verlag.de; www.rudolf-mueller.de, pg 209

Edicoes Colibri (Portugal) *Tel:* (021) 7964038 *Fax:* (021) 7964038 *E-mail:* colibri@edi-colibri.pt *Web Site:* www.edi-colibri.pt, pg 525

Armand Colin, Editeur (France) *Tel:* (01) 44395447 *Fax:* (01) 44394343 *E-mail:* infos@armand-colin.com *Web Site:* www.armand-colin.com, pg 155

Rosica Colin Ltd (United Kingdom) *Tel:* (020) 7370 1080 *Fax:* (020) 7244 6441, pg 676, 1129

COLIVRO - Comercio e Distribuicao de Livros Ltda (Brazil) *Tel:* (021) 2243177 *Fax:* (021) 2424517, pg 1293

Collectieve Propaganda van het Nederlandse Boek (CPNB) (Netherlands) *Tel:* (020) 626 49 71 *Fax:* (020) 623 16 96 *E-mail:* info@cpnb.nl *Web Site:* www.cpnb. nl, pg 1150, 1268

College International des Traducteurs Litteraires (CITL) (France) *Tel:* (04) 90 52 05 50 *Fax:* (04) 90 93 43 21 *E-mail:* citl@provnet.fr, pg 1257

The College of Education at Wits, Harold Holmes Library (South Africa) *Tel:* (011) 717-3242; (011) 717-3240 *Fax:* (011) 717-3046 *Web Site:* www.wits. ac.za/library/campuslib/edulib.htm, pg 1542

College of Medicine Library, Arabian Gulf University (Bahrain) *Tel:* 239 999 *Fax:* 274 822 *E-mail:* agulibrary@agu.edu.bh *Web Site:* www.agu. edu.bh, pg 1490

The College of the Bahamas Library (Bahamas) *Tel:* 302-4552 *Fax:* 326-7834 *Web Site:* www.cob.edu. bs/library, pg 1490

College Press Publishers (Pvt) Ltd (Zimbabwe) *Tel:* (04) 754145; (04) 773231; (04) 773236; (04) 757153; (04) 754255 *Fax:* (04) 754256 *E-mail:* nellym@ collegepress.co.zw, pg 777

Peter Collin Publishing Ltd (United Kingdom) *Tel:* (020) 7494 2111 *Fax:* (020) 7434 0151 *E-mail:* order@ petercollin.com *Web Site:* www.petercollin.com, pg 676

Collins Booksellers Pty Ltd (Australia) *Tel:* (03) 96629472 *Fax:* (03) 96622527 *E-mail:* enquiries@ collinsbooks.com.au *Web Site:* www.collinsbooks.com. au, pg 1288

The Collins Press (Ireland) *Tel:* (021) 4347717 *Fax:* (021) 4347720 *E-mail:* enquiries@collinspress.le *Web Site:* www.collinspress.com, pg 355

Colmegna Libreria y Editorial (Argentina) *Tel:* (042) 423102; (042) 4557345 *Fax:* (042) 4557345, pg 4

Colombian PEN Centre (Colombia) *Tel:* (01) 2846761; (01) 2561540 *Fax:* (01) 2184236 *E-mail:* pencolombia@hotmail.com, pg 1392

Colombo Book Association (Sri Lanka) *Tel:* (01) 686878; (01) 072270652 *Fax:* (01) 696578, pg 601

Colombo National Museum Library (Sri Lanka) *Tel:* (01) 692092; (01) 693314 *Fax:* (01) 695366 *E-mail:* cnmid@sltnet.lk, pg 1544

Colombo Public Library (Sri Lanka) *Tel:* (011) 2691968; (011) 2695156; (011) 2696530 *Fax:* (011) 2691968 *E-mail:* info@cmc.lk *Web Site:* www.cmc.lk/library. asp, pg 1544

Librairie des Colonnes (Morocco) *Tel:* (09) 93 69 55 *Fax:* (099) 936955, pg 1319

Colonnese Editore (Italy) *Tel:* (081) 293900 *Fax:* (081) 455420 *E-mail:* info@colonnese.it *Web Site:* www. colonnese.it, pg 379

Colorcraft Ltd (Hong Kong) *Tel:* 25909033 *Fax:* 25909005; 25909271 *E-mail:* info.cc@colorcraft. com.hk *Web Site:* www.colorcraft.com.hk, pg 1235

Colorprint Offset (Hong Kong) *Tel:* 2896-7777 *Fax:* 2889-6606 *E-mail:* info@cpo.com.hk *Web Site:* www.cpo.com.hk, pg 1146, 1167, 1207

Colorprint Offset Inc (United States) *Tel:* 212-681-9400 *Fax:* 212-681-9362 *E-mail:* ny@cpo.com.hk *Web Site:* www.hq.cpo.bz, pg 1155, 1177, 1218

Colour Library Direct (United Kingdom) *Tel:* (01483) 426777 *Fax:* (01483) 426947 *E-mail:* prod@quad-pub.co.uk, pg 676

Colourpoint Books (United Kingdom) *Tel:* (028) 9182 0505 *Fax:* (028) 9182 1900 *E-mail:* info@colourpoint. co.uk; sales@colourpoint.co.uk *Web Site:* www. colourpoint.co.uk, pg 676

Colt Associates (United Kingdom) *Tel:* (0158) 2834292 *Fax:* (0158) 825778, pg 1340

The Columba Bookservice Ltd (Ireland) *Tel:* (01) 2942556 *Fax:* (01) 2942564 *E-mail:* info@columba.ie *Web Site:* www.columba.ie, pg 1308

The Columba Press (Ireland) *Tel:* (01) 2942556 *Fax:* (01) 2942564 *E-mail:* info@columba.ie *Web Site:* www.columba.ie, pg 355

Columbia Overseas Marketing Pte Ltd (Singapore) *Tel:* 7478607 *Fax:* 7458668, pg 1212

Columbus (Czech Republic) *Tel:* (02) 683 10 17; (02) 683 47 65; (02) 74771407 *Fax:* (02) 683 10 17; (02) 683 08 28 *E-mail:* columbus@alpha-net.cz, pg 122

Columbus Cultural Editora Comercial Importacao e Exporta (Brazil) *Tel:* (011) 8648777 *Fax:* (011) 8646531, pg 1293

Columbus Verlag Paul Oestergaard GmbH (Germany) *Tel:* (07576) 96 03-0 *Fax:* (07576) 96 03-29 *E-mail:* info@columbus-verlag.de *Web Site:* www. columbus-verlag.de, pg 209

Columna Edicions, Libres i Comunicacio, SA (Spain) *Tel:* (093) 4967061 *Fax:* (093) 4967065 *E-mail:* rmaymo@grupcolumna.com *Web Site:* www. columnaedicions.com, pg 572

Combel Editorial SA (Spain) *Tel:* (093) 2449550 *Fax:* (093) 2656895 *E-mail:* casals@editorialcasals. com, pg 572

Combined Academic Publishers (United Kingdom) *Tel:* (01494) 581601 *Fax:* (01494) 581602 *Web Site:* www.combinedacademic.co.uk, pg 676

Combined Book Services (United Kingdom) *Tel:* (01892) 839819 *Fax:* (01892) 837272 *E-mail:* info@combook. co.uk *Web Site:* www.combook.co.uk, pg 1340

Comhairle nan Leabhraichean - The Gaelic Books Council (United Kingdom) *Tel:* (0141) 337 6211 *Fax:* (0141) 341 0515 *E-mail:* fios@gaelicbooks.net *Web Site:* www.gaelicbooks.net, pg 1281

Los Libros del Comienzo (Spain) *Tel:* (091) 5481079 *Fax:* (091) 5400378 *E-mail:* buzon@libroscomienzo. com *Web Site:* www.libroscomienzo.com, pg 572

Comision Nacional Forestal (Mexico) *Tel:* (05) 5349707; (05) 5247862, pg 460

Comissao Nacional de Energia Nuclear (CNEN) (Brazil) *Tel:* (021) 2295-9596 *Fax:* (021) 2295-8696 *E-mail:* macedo@cnen.gov.br *Web Site:* www.cnen. gov.br, pg 80

Biblioteca Central y Publicaciones del Consejo de Educacion Secundaria (Uruguay) *Tel:* (02) 408 42 73; (02) 408 30 51; (02) 408 12 52 *Fax:* (02) 408 12 52, pg 1553

Consejo Episcopal Latinoamericano (CELAM) (Colombia) *Tel:* (01) 6670050; (01) 6706416 *E-mail:* editora@celam.org; celam@celam.org; itepal@celam.org *Web Site:* www.celam.org, pg 110

Consejo Interamericano de Archiveros (CITA) (Mexico) *Tel:* (05) 51 33 99 00 (ext 19327); (05) 57 95 70 80 (ext 19424) *Fax:* (05) 57 89 52 96 *Web Site:* www. agn.gob.mx, pg 1268

Consejo Superior de Investigaciones Científicas (Spain) *Tel:* (091) 561-2833; (091) 5629633 *Fax:* (091) 5629634 *E-mail:* publ@orgc.csic.es *Web Site:* www. csic.es/publica, pg 573

Biblioteca General de Humanidades Consejo Superior de Investigaciones Científicas (Spain) *Tel:* (091) 360 18 10; (091) 360 18 12 *Fax:* (091) 369 09 40 *E-mail:* bghpre@bib.csic.es *Web Site:* www.csic. es/cbic/BGH/bgh.htm, pg 1544

Consello da Cultura Galega - CCG (Spain) *Tel:* (0981) 957202 *Fax:* (0981) 957205 *E-mail:* consello.cultura. galega@xunta.es *Web Site:* www.consellodacultura.org, pg 573

Conservart SA (Belgium) *Tel:* (02) 3322538 *Fax:* (02) 3322840 *E-mail:* conservart@skynet.be, pg 65

Conservation Resources International Inc (United States) *Tel:* 703-321-7730 *Toll Free Tel:* 800-634-6932 *Fax:* 703-321-0629 *E-mail:* crisales@ conservationresources.com *Web Site:* www. conservationresources.com, pg 1230

Conservative Policy Forum (United Kingdom) *Tel:* (020) 7222 9000 *E-mail:* cpf@conservatives.com *Web Site:* www.conservatives.com, pg 678

Uitgeverij Conserve (Netherlands) *Tel:* (072) 5093693 *Fax:* (072) 5094370 *E-mail:* info@conserve.nl *Web Site:* www.conserve.nl, pg 477

Consiglio Nazionale delle Ricerche Rep Pubblicazioni e Informazioni Scientifiche (Italy) *Tel:* (06) 49932019 *Fax:* (06) 49933077 *E-mail:* pgiugni@dcire.cnr.it *Web Site:* www.urp.cnr.it, pg 380

Consolidated Printers Inc (United States) *Tel:* 510-843-8524; 510-843-8565 *Fax:* 510-486-0580 *E-mail:* cpi@ consoprinters.com *Web Site:* www.consoprinters.com, pg 1155, 1218

Constable & Robinson Ltd (United Kingdom) *Tel:* (020) 8741 3663 *Fax:* (020) 8748 7562 *E-mail:* enquiries@constablerobinson.com *Web Site:* www.constablerobinson.com, pg 678

Constancia Editores, SA (Portugal) *Tel:* (021) 4246901; (021) 4246902 *E-mail:* info@constancia-editores. pt; prosa@santillana.pt *Web Site:* www.constancia-editores.pt; www.santillana.pt, pg 525

Editorial Constitucion y Leyes SA - COLEX (Spain) *Tel:* (091) 5813485 *Fax:* (091) 5813490 *E-mail:* colexeditor@interbook.net *Web Site:* www. colex.es, pg 573

Constitutional Publishing Co Pty Ltd (Australia) *Tel:* (08) 9421 6216 *Fax:* (08) 9221 1572, pg 18

Consultor Assessoria de Planejamento Ltda (Brazil) *Tel:* (021) 5893030 *Fax:* (021) 580-2163, pg 80

Ediciones Contables y Administrativas SA (Mexico) *Tel:* (05) 6040140; (05) 6041998; (05) 6040260 *Fax:* (05) 6056730, pg 460

Uitgeverij Contact NV (Belgium) *Tel:* (03) 4572024 *Fax:* (03) 4581327, pg 65

Contex Corporation (Japan) *Tel:* (03) 42-522-0051 *Fax:* (03) 42-526-2345; (03) 42-548-2400 *E-mail:* contex@jade.dt.ne.jp *Web Site:* contex.co.jp/, pg 413

Contexto Editora (Portugal) *Tel:* (021) 347 97 69 *Fax:* (021) 347 97 70 *E-mail:* context-editora@clix.pt, pg 525

Editora Contexto (Editora Pinsky Ltda) (Brazil) *Tel:* (011) 3832-5838 *Fax:* (011) 3832-1043 *E-mail:* contexto@editoracontexto.com.br *Web Site:* www.editoracontexto.com.br, pg 80

Continental Bookshop (Australia) *Tel:* (03) 98247711 *Fax:* (03) 98247855, pg 1288

Continental SRL Editrice (Italy) *Tel:* (035) 237088 *Fax:* (035) 237039, pg 380

The Continuum International Publishing Group Ltd (United Kingdom) *Tel:* (020) 7922 0880 *Fax:* (020) 7922 0881 *E-mail:* info@continuum-books.com *Web Site:* www.continuumbooks.com, pg 678

Jane Conway-Gordon (United Kingdom) *Tel:* (020) 7494 0148 *Fax:* (020) 7287 9264, pg 1129

Conway Maritime Press (United Kingdom) *Tel:* (020) 7221 2213; (020) 7314 1469 (sales) *Fax:* (020) 7221 6455; (020) 7314 1594 (sales) *E-mail:* enquiries@ chrysalis.com *Web Site:* www.chrysalisbooks.co.uk, pg 678

Albert Cook Medical Library (Uganda) *Tel:* (041) 534149 *Fax:* (041) 530024 *E-mail:* acook@uga. healthnet.org, pg 1550

Martin Cook Associates Inc (United States) *Tel:* 386-447-8692 *Fax:* 386-447-8746 *E-mail:* mcanewcity@ aol.com *Web Site:* www.mcabooks.com, pg 1155, 1177, 1218, 1230, 1238

Cookery Book (Australia) *Tel:* (02) 9439 3144 *Fax:* (02) 9439 3405 *E-mail:* answers@cookerybook.com.au *Web Site:* www.cookerybook.com.au, pg 18

Coolabah Publishing (Australia) *Tel:* (02) 6766 4420 *Fax:* (02) 6766 1058 *E-mail:* narnia@mpx.com.au, pg 18

Cooper Dale (United Kingdom) *Tel:* (020) 8995 3157 *Fax:* (020) 8748 5689 *Web Site:* www.cooperdale.com, pg 1174

Leo Cooper (United Kingdom) *Tel:* (01226) 734555 *Fax:* (01226) 734438 *E-mail:* enquiries@pen-sword. co.uk *Web Site:* www.pen-and-sword.co.uk, pg 678

Cooperative Action by Victorian Academic Libraries (CAVAL) (Australia) *Tel:* (03) 9459 2722 *Fax:* (03) 9459 2733 *E-mail:* caval@caval.edu.au *Web Site:* www.caval.edu.au, pg 1557

Cooperative Regionale de l'Enseignement Religieux (CRER) (France) *Tel:* (02) 41689140 *Fax:* (02) 41689141 *E-mail:* crer49@wanadoo.fr, pg 155

Edizioni Cooperative Scarl (Italy) *Tel:* (06) 844391 *Fax:* (06) 84439406 *E-mail:* info@legacoop.it *Web Site:* www.legacoop.it, pg 380

Copenhagen Business School Press (Denmark) *Tel:* 38153960 *Fax:* 38153962 *E-mail:* cbspress@cbs. dk *Web Site:* www.cbspress.dk, pg 129

Editions Copernic (France) *Tel:* (01) 40 61 97 67 *Fax:* (01) 40 61 96 33, pg 155

Coppenrath Verlag (Germany) *Tel:* (0251) 41411-0 *Fax:* (0251) 4141120 *E-mail:* info@coppenrath.de *Web Site:* www.coppenrath.de, pg 209

Copper Beech Publishing Ltd (United Kingdom) *Tel:* (01342) 314734 *Fax:* (01342) 314794 *E-mail:* sales@copperbeechpublishing. co.uk *Web Site:* www.btinternet.com/ ~copperbeechpublishing, pg 678

The Copperbelt University Library (Zambia) *Tel:* (02) 222066; (02) 225155 *Fax:* (02) 222469; (02) 223972 *E-mail:* library@cbu.ac.zm *Web Site:* www.cbu.edu. zm, pg 1554

Copress Verlag (Germany) *Tel:* (089) 1257414 *Fax:* (089) 12162282 *E-mail:* verlag@stiebner.com *Web Site:* www.stiebner.com, pg 209

Editions Coprur (France) *Tel:* (03) 88 14 72 41 *Fax:* (03) 88 14 72 39 *E-mail:* coprur@editions-coprur.fr, pg 155

Copyright Agency Ltd (Australia) *Tel:* (02) 93947600 *Fax:* (02) 93947601 *E-mail:* info@copyright.com.au *Web Site:* www.copyright.com.au, pg 1250

Copyright International Agency Corina GmbH (Germany) *Tel:* (030) 80902386 *Fax:* (030) 80902388 *E-mail:* info@corina.com *Web Site:* www.corina.com, pg 1121

Copyright Licensing Agency (United Kingdom) *Tel:* (020) 7631 5555 *Fax:* (020) 7631 5500 *E-mail:* cla@cla.co.uk *Web Site:* www.cla.co.uk, pg 1281

Copytrain (United Kingdom) *Tel:* (01844) 279345 *Fax:* (01844) 279345, pg 1129

Casa Editrice Corbaccio srl (Italy) *Tel:* (02) 80206338 *Fax:* (02) 804067 *E-mail:* info@corbaccio.it *Web Site:* www.corbaccio.it, pg 380

Cordee Ltd (United Kingdom) *Tel:* (0116) 2543579 *Fax:* (0116) 2471176 *E-mail:* info@cordee.co.uk *Web Site:* www.cordee.co.uk, pg 678, 1341

Bokforlaget Cordia AB (Sweden) *Tel:* (019) 333850 *Fax:* (019) 333859 *F-mail:* forlaget@cordia.se *Web Site:* www.cordia.se, pg 605

Editorial Cordillera Inc (Puerto Rico) *Tel:* 787-767-6188 *Fax:* 787-767-8646 *E-mail:* info@editorialcordillera. com *Web Site:* www.editorialcordillera.com, pg 532

Cordinata Ltd (Holy Land 2000) (Israel) *Tel:* (03) 5226885 *Fax:* (03) 5276661 *E-mail:* cordinata@isdn. net.il, pg 362

Coresi SRL (Romania) *Tel:* (01) 6386045; (01) 6386158; (01) 6386164; (00) 3127115; (00) 6154781 *Fax:* (01) 2230177, pg 534

Corian-Verlag Heinrich Wimmer (Germany) *Tel:* (08271) 5951 *Fax:* (08271) 6931 *E-mail:* 082716941-0001@t-online.de; 101374.1022@compuserve.com, pg 209

Corint Publishing Group (Romania) *Tel:* (0212) 11 97 66 *Fax:* (0212) 10 70 86 *E-mail:* corint@dnt.ro, pg 534

Cork University Press (Ireland) *Tel:* (021) 490 2980 *Fax:* (021) 431 5329 *E-mail:* corkuniversitypress@ ucc.ie *Web Site:* www.corkuniversitypress.com, pg 355

Cornelsen und Oxford University Press GmbH & Co (Germany) *Tel:* (030) 897 850 *Fax:* (030) 897 85 499 *E-mail:* c-mail@cornelsen.de *Web Site:* www. cornelsen.de, pg 209

Cornelsen Verlag GmbH & Co OHG (Germany) *Tel:* (030) 897 85-0 *Fax:* (030) 897 85-299 *E-mail:* c-mail@cornelsen.de *Web Site:* www.cornelsen.com, pg 209

Cornelsen Verlag Scriptor GmbH & Co KG (Germany) *Tel:* (030) 89 7858700 *Fax:* (030) 89 7858799 *E-mail:* c-mail@cornelsen.de *Web Site:* www. cornelsen.de, pg 210

Cornford Press (Australia) *Tel:* (03) 6331 9658 *Fax:* (03) 6331 9658 *E-mail:* info@cornfordpress.com *Web Site:* www.cornfordpress.com, pg 18

Cornucopia Press (Australia) *Tel:* (08) 9388 1965 *Fax:* (09) 3817341 *E-mail:* cornucop@aoi.com.au, pg 18

Corona Publishing Co Ltd (Japan) *Tel:* (03) 3941-3131 *Fax:* (03) 3941-3137 *E-mail:* info@coronasha.co.jp *Web Site:* www.coronasha.co.jp, pg 413

Corona Verlag (Germany) *Tel:* (040) 6424144 *Fax:* (040) 64221023, pg 210

Corporacion de Estudios y Publicaciones (Ecuador) *Tel:* (02) 221-711 *Fax:* (02) 226-256 *E-mail:* cep@ accessinter.net, pg 136

Corporacion de Promocion Universitaria (Chile) *Tel:* (02) 2749022 *Fax:* (02) 2741828, pg 99

Ediciones Corregidor SAICI y E (Argentina) *Tel:* (011) 4374-5000; (011) 4374-4959 *Fax:* (011) 4374-5000 *E-mail:* corregidor@corregidor.com *Web Site:* www. corregidor.com, pg 4

Corsaire Editions (France) *Tel:* (02) 38 53 15 00 *Fax:* (02) 38 54 08 92 *E-mail:* corsaire.editions@ wanadoo.fr *Web Site:* www.corsaire-editions.com, pg 156

Critiques Livres Distribution SAS (France) *Tel:* (01) 43603910 *Fax:* (01) 48973706 *E-mail:* critiques. livres@wanadoo.fr, pg 1299

Croatian ISBN Agency (Croatia) *Tel:* (01) 6164087; (01) 6164288 *Fax:* (01) 6164371 *E-mail:* isbn@nsk.hr *Web Site:* www.nsk.hr, pg 1255

Studia Croatica (Argentina) *Tel:* (011) 4771-4954 *Fax:* (011) 4771-4954 *E-mail:* webmasters@ studiacroatica.com, pg 4

Comite international de la Croix-Rouge (Switzerland) *Tel:* (022) 734 60 01 *Fax:* (022) 733 20 57; (022) 730 27 68 *Web Site:* www.icrc.org, pg 616

Paul H Crompton Ltd (United Kingdom) *Tel:* (020) 88040400 *Fax:* (020) 88040044 *E-mail:* cromptonph@ aol.com, pg 679

Croner CCH Group Ltd (United Kingdom) *Tel:* (020) 85473333 *Fax:* (020) 85472637 *E-mail:* info@croner. co.uk *Web Site:* www.croner.co.uk, pg 679

Editura Cronos SRL (Romania) *Tel:* (044) 262245; (044) 7690952 *Fax:* (01) 2231025 *E-mail:* cronos@dial. kappa.ro, pg 534

Cross Continent Press Ltd (Nigeria) *Tel:* (01) 862437 *Fax:* (01) 685679, pg 499

Crossbridge Books (United Kingdom) *Tel:* (0121) 447 7897 *Fax:* (0121) 445 1063 *E-mail:* crossbridgebooks@btinternet.com *Web Site:* www.crossbridgebooks.com, pg 679

Crossroad Distributors Pty Ltd (Australia) *Tel:* (02) 8845 7744 *Fax:* (02) 8845 7755 *E-mail:* custserv@ crossroad.com.au, pg 18

Crown House Publishing Ltd (United Kingdom) *Tel:* (01267) 211345 *Fax:* (01267) 211882 *E-mail:* books@crownhouse.co.uk *Web Site:* www. crownhouse.co.uk, pg 679

The Crowood Press Ltd (United Kingdom) *Tel:* (01672) 520320 *Fax:* (01672) 520280 *E-mail:* enquiries@ crowood.com *Web Site:* www.crowood.com, pg 679

G L Crowther (United Kingdom) *Tel:* (01772) 257126, pg 680

Crucible Publishers (United Kingdom) *Tel:* (01373) 834900 *Fax:* (01373) 834900 *E-mail:* sales@ cruciblepublishers.com *Web Site:* www. cruciblepublishers.com, pg 680

Ediciones Cruilla SA (Spain) *Tel:* (093) 2376344; (093) 2922172 *Fax:* (093) 2380116 *Web Site:* www.cruilla. com, pg 573

Publicaciones Cruz O SA (Mexico) *Tel:* (055) 56-80-61-22 *Fax:* (055) 56-80-61-22 *E-mail:* infolibros@ libros.com.mx; atencionaclienteslibros@libros.com.mx *Web Site:* www.libros.com.mx, pg 460

Crystal Publishing (Australia) *Tel:* (03) 9525 4549 *E-mail:* minx@alphalink.com.au, pg 18

CS Graphics Pte Ltd (Singapore) *Tel:* 861-0100 *Fax:* 861-0190, pg 1150

CS Graphics Pte Ltd (Singapore) *Tel:* 6865 2010 *Fax:* 6861 0190 *Web Site:* ourworld.compuserve. com/homepages/csgraphics, pg 1171

CS Graphics Pte Ltd (Singapore) *Tel:* 861-0100 *Fax:* 861-0190 *Web Site:* www.csgraphics.us, pg 1212

CS Graphics Pte Ltd (Singapore) *Tel:* 6865 2010 *Fax:* 6861 0190 *E-mail:* rick@csgraphics.us *Web Site:* www.csgraphics.us, pg 1227

CS Graphics USA Inc (United States) *Tel:* 916-791-9066 *Fax:* 916-791-9112, pg 1155, 1177, 1218, 1230

CSA (Cambridge Scientific Abstracts) (United Kingdom) *Tel:* (0865) 336250 *Fax:* (0865) 336258 *E-mail:* service@csa.com; marketing@bowker.uk.co *Web Site:* www.csa.com, pg 680

CSIR Information Services (South Africa) *Tel:* (012) 841-2911 *Fax:* (012) 349-1153 *Web Site:* www.csir.co. za, pg 1542

CSIRO (Commonwealth Scientific & Industrial Research Organization) (Australia) *Tel:* (03) 9545 2176 *Fax:* (03) 9545 2175 *E-mail:* enquiries@csiro.au *Web Site:* www.csiro.au, pg 1488

CSIRO Publishing (Commonwealth Scientific & Industrial Research Organisation) (Australia) *Tel:* (03) 9662 7500 *Fax:* (03) 9662 7555 *E-mail:* publishing@ csiro.au *Web Site:* www.publish.csiro.au, pg 18

CSS Bookshops (Nigeria) *Tel:* (01) 2633081; (01) 2637009; (01) 2637023; (01) 2633010 *Fax:* (01) 2637089 *E-mail:* cssbookshops@skannet.com.ng, pg 499, 1322

CTBI Publications (United Kingdom) *Tel:* (020) 7654 7254 *Fax:* (020) 7654 7222 *E-mail:* info@ctbi.org.uk *Web Site:* www.ctbi.org.uk, pg 680

CTE-Centro de Tecnologia Educativa SA (Spain) *Tel:* (093) 217 74 00 *Fax:* (093) 217 62 53 *Web Site:* www.centrocte.com, pg 573

CTIF (Center Technique Industriel de la Fonderie) (France) *Tel:* (01) 41 14 63 00 *Fax:* (01) 45 34 14 34 *E-mail:* contact@ctif.com *Web Site:* www.ctif.com, pg 156

CTL-Presse Clemens-Tobias Lange (Germany) *Tel:* (040) 39902223 *Fax:* (040) 39902224 *E-mail:* ctl@europe. com *Web Site:* www.ctl-presse.de, pg 210

CTNERHI - Centre Technique National d'Etudes et de Recherches sur les Handicaps et les Inadaptations (France) *Tel:* (01) 45 65 59 00 *Fax:* (01) 45 65 44 94 *E-mail:* ctnerhi@club-internet.fr *Web Site:* perso.club-internet.fr/ctnerhi, pg 156

CTP Book Printers (Pty) Ltd (South Africa) *Tel:* (011) 8890600 *Fax:* (011) 8890922 *E-mail:* ctpjhb@iafrica. com, pg 1172

CTP Book Printers (Pty) Ltd (South Africa) *Tel:* (021) 930 8820 *Fax:* (021) 939 1559 *E-mail:* ctp@ctpbooks. co.za, pg 1213

Editorial Cuarto Propio (Chile) *Tel:* (02) 204 7645 *Fax:* (02) 204 7622 *E-mail:* cuartopropio@ cuartopropio.cl *Web Site:* www.cuartopropio.cl, pg 99

Editorial Cuatro Vientos (Chile) *Tel:* (02) 2258381; (02) 269 5343 *Fax:* (02) 3413107 *E-mail:* 4vientos@ netline.cl *Web Site:* www.cuatrovientos.net, pg 99

Agencia Cubana del ISBN (Cuba) *Tel:* (07) 36034 *Fax:* (07) 333441 *E-mail:* cclfilh@ceniai.cu, pg 1255

Ediciones Cubanas (Cuba) *Tel:* (07) 63 1981; (07) 33 8942; (07) 63 1989 *Fax:* (07) 338 943 *E-mail:* edicuba@artsoft.cult.cu, pg 1297

Cuernavaca Editorial S A (Mexico) *Tel:* (05) 5113619; (05) 5142529; (05) 2867794 *Fax:* (05) 2117112, pg 460

Editions Cujas (France) *Tel:* (01) 44 24 24 36; (01) 44 24 24 37 *Fax:* (01) 44 24 24 38 *E-mail:* cujas@cujas. fr *Web Site:* www.cujas.com, pg 156

Cultur Prospectiv, Edition (Switzerland) *Tel:* (01) 260 69 29 *Fax:* (01) 260 69 29 *E-mail:* cpinstitut@smile.ch *Web Site:* www.culturprospectiv.ch, pg 616

Cultura (Belgium) *Tel:* (032) 093691595 *Fax:* (032) 093695925 *E-mail:* info@cultura-net.com *Web Site:* www.cultura-net.com; www.cultura.be, pg 65

Edizioni Cultura della Pace (Italy) *Tel:* (055) 576149 *Fax:* (055) 5088003, pg 380

Livraria Cultura Editora Ltda (Brazil) *Tel:* (011) 3170-4033 *Fax:* (011) 3285-4457 *E-mail:* livros@ livrariacultura.com.br, pg 1293

Editorial Cultura (Guatemala) *Tel:* (02) 692080 *Fax:* (02) 346135, pg 310

Editora Cultura Medica Ltda (Brazil) *Tel:* (021) 2567-3888 *Fax:* (021) 2569-5443 *E-mail:* atendimento@ culturamedica.com.br *Web Site:* www.culturamedica. com.br, pg 80

Instituto de Cultura Puertorriquena (Puerto Rico) *Tel:* 787-724-0700 *Fax:* 787-724-8393 *E-mail:* www@ icp.gobierno.pr *Web Site:* www.icp.gobierno.pr, pg 532

La Cultura Sociologica (Italy) *Tel:* (02) 29409041 *Fax:* (02) 29409041, pg 380

Ediciones Cultural Colombiana Ltda (Colombia) *Tel:* (01) 2116090 *Fax:* (01) 2176570, pg 110

Editorial Cultural Inc (Puerto Rico) *Tel:* 787-765-9767 *Fax:* 787-765-9767 *E-mail:* cultural@coqui.net *Web Site:* www.editorialcultural.com, pg 532

Cultural Relics Publishing House (China) *Tel:* (010) 64048057 *Fax:* (010) 64010698 *E-mail:* web@wenwu. com *Web Site:* www.wenwu.com, pg 103

Ediciones Culturales Ver Ltda (Colombia) *Tel:* (01) 2859362; (01) 2859204 *Fax:* (01) 2859362, pg 110

Ediciones Culturales Internacionales SA de CV Edicion Compra y Venta de Libros, Casetes, Videos (Mexico) *Tel:* (05) 2508099 (ext 200) *Fax:* (05) 55311597, pg 460

Culture et Bibliotheque pour Tous (France) *Tel:* (01) 45 33 07 07 *Fax:* (01) 45 33 45 76 *E-mail:* uncbpt. services@wanadoo.fr, pg 156

Bibliotheek Cultureel Centrum Suriname (Suriname) *Tel:* 472369; 473309 *Fax:* 476516 *E-mail:* sccs@sr. net; stgccs1947@hotmail.com, pg 1545

Cumann Leabharlann na h-Eireann (Ireland) *Tel:* (01) 61202193 *Fax:* (01) 61213090 *Web Site:* www. libraryassociation.ie, pg 1565

The Mary Cunnane Agency Pty Ltd (Australia) *Tel:* (02) 438599922 *Fax:* (02) 43651093 *E-mail:* info@ cunnaneagency.com *Web Site:* www.cunnaneagency. com, pg 1119

Ediciones CUPSA, Centro de Comunicacion Cultural CUPSA, AC (Mexico) *Tel:* (05) 5925252; (05) 5662307; (05) 5462100, pg 460

Ediciones la Cupula SL (Spain) *Tel:* (093) 268 28 05 *Fax:* (093) 268 07 65 *E-mail:* lacupula@eix.intercom. es *Web Site:* www.lacupula.com, pg 573

Cura Verlag GmbH (Austria) *Tel:* (01) 7136480 *Fax:* (01) 7126258; (01) 7126219, pg 49

Edizioni Curci SRL (Italy) *Tel:* (02) 760361 *Fax:* (02) 76014504 *E-mail:* info@edizionicurci.it *Web Site:* www.edizionicurci.it, pg 380

Curiad (United Kingdom) *Tel:* (01286) 882166 *Fax:* (01286) 882692 *E-mail:* curiad@curiad.co.uk *Web Site:* www.curiad.co.uk, pg 680

Curial Edicions Catalanes SA (Spain) *Tel:* (093) 4588101 *Fax:* (093) 2077427 *E-mail:* curial@lix. intercom.es, pg 573

Currency Press Pty Ltd (Australia) *Tel:* (02) 9319 5877 *Fax:* (02) 9319 3649 *E-mail:* enquiries@currency.com. au *Web Site:* www.currency.com.au, pg 19

Current Books (India) *Tel:* (0487) 2444322 *E-mail:* info@dcbooks.com *Web Site:* www.dcbooks. com/currentbooks.htm, pg 329

Current Pacific Ltd (New Zealand) *Tel:* (09) 480-1388 *Fax:* (09) 480-1387 *E-mail:* info@cplnz.com *Web Site:* www.cplnz.com, pg 491

Current Science Group (United Kingdom) *Tel:* (020) 7323 0323 *Fax:* (020) 7580 1938 *E-mail:* info@ current-science.com *Web Site:* www.current-science-group.com, pg 680

Current Technical Literature Co (Pvt) Ltd (India) *Tel:* (022) 2611045 *Fax:* (022) 2679786, pg 1305

James Currey Ltd (United Kingdom) *Tel:* (01865) 244 111 *Fax:* (01865) 246 454 *E-mail:* editorial@ jamescurrey.co.uk *Web Site:* www.jamescurrey.co.uk, pg 680

Curriculum Corporation (Australia) *Tel:* (03) 9207 9600 *Fax:* (03) 9639 1616 *E-mail:* sales@curriculum.edu.au *Web Site:* www.curriculum.edu.au, pg 19

Eleanor Curtain Publishing (Australia) *Tel:* (03) 9826 3222 *Fax:* (03) 9826 9699 *E-mail:* enquiries@ ecpublishing.com.au *Web Site:* www.ecpublishing. com/au, pg 19

Curtis Brown Group Ltd (United Kingdom) *Tel:* (020) 7393 4400 *Fax:* (020) 7393 4401 *E-mail:* cb@ curtisbrown.co.uk, pg 1129

Cuspide Libros SA (Argentina) *Tel:* (011) 43228868 *Fax:* (011) 43223456 *E-mail:* ventas@cuspide.com *Web Site:* www.cuspide.com, pg 1287

Custom Services (United States) *Tel:* 845-365-0414 *Fax:* 845-365-0864, pg 1177

Cuttington University College Library (Liberia) *Tel:* 227-413 *Fax:* 226-059 *E-mail:* cuttingtonuniversity@ yahoo.com *Web Site:* www.cuttington.org, pg 1523

CyberClub (United Kingdom) *Tel:* (020) 8731 6161 *Fax:* (020) 8905 5050 *Web Site:* www.astorlaw.com, pg 680

Cyhoeddiadau Barddas (United Kingdom) *Tel:* (01792) 792 829, pg 680

Cyhoeddiadau'r Gair (United Kingdom) *Tel:* (01248) 382947 *Fax:* (01248) 383954 *E-mail:* eds00e@bangor. ac.uk, pg 680

Cymdeithas Lyfrau Ceredigion (United Kingdom) *Tel:* (01970) 617776 *Fax:* (01970) 624049; (01970) 625844 *E-mail:* clc.gyf@talk21.com, pg 680

Cynosure Publishing Inc (Taiwan, Province of China) *Tel:* 8862 2657 3275 *Fax:* (02) 2657 5300 *E-mail:* cynobook@tpts4.seed.net.tw *Web Site:* www. books.com.tw, pg 635

Cypher Library Books (United Kingdom) *Tel:* (0113) 2012900 *Fax:* (0113) 2012929 *E-mail:* enquiries@ cyphergroup.com; library.enquiries@bertrams.com *Web Site:* www.cyphergroup.com, pg 1341

Cyprus Library (Cyprus) *Tel:* (022) 303180; (022) 676118 *Fax:* (022) 304532 *E-mail:* cypruslibrary@ cytanet.com.cy, pg 1499

Library of the Cyprus Museum - Dept of Antiquities (Cyprus) *Tel:* (022) 865864; (022) 865888 *Fax:* (022) 303148 *E-mail:* roctarch@cytanet.com.cy, pg 1499

Cyprus Telecommunications Authority (CYTA) (Cyprus) *Tel:* (022) 701000 *Fax:* (022) 497155 *E-mail:* enquiries@cyta.com.cy *Web Site:* www.cyta. com.cy, pg 121

Saints Cyril & Methodius National Library (Bulgaria) *Tel:* (02) 9882811 (ext 231); (02) 9882811 (ext 234); (02) 9882811 (ext 235) *Fax:* (02) 8435495 *E-mail:* nl@nationallibrary.bg; cbi@nationallibrary.bg *Web Site:* www.nationallibrary.bg, pg 1494

Czech PEN Centre (Czech Republic) *Tel:* (02) 24235546; (02) 24234343 *Fax:* (02) 24221926 *E-mail:* centrum@pen.cz *Web Site:* www.pen.cz, pg 1392

Czernin Verlag Ltd (Austria) *Tel:* (01) 403 35 63 *Fax:* (01) 403 35 63-15 *E-mail:* office@czernin-verlag. com *Web Site:* www.czernin-verlag.com, pg 49

Spoldzielnia Wydawnicza 'Czytelnik' (Poland) *Tel:* (022) 6281441 *Fax:* (022) 6283178 *E-mail:* sekretariat@ czytelnik.pl *Web Site:* www.czytelnik.pl, pg 517

D&B Ltd (United Kingdom) *Tel:* (01494) 422000 *Fax:* (01494) 422260 *E-mail:* custserv@dnb.com *Web Site:* www.dnb.com, pg 681

D&B Marketing Pty Ltd (Australia) *Tel:* (03) 9828 3333 *Fax:* (03) 9828 3300 *E-mail:* csc.austral@dnb.com.au *Web Site:* www.dnb.com.au, pg 19

D & K Group (United States) *Tel:* 847-956-0160 *Toll Free Tel:* 800-632-2314 *Fax:* 847-956-8214 *E-mail:* info@dkgroup.net *Web Site:* www.dkgroup. com, pg 1219, 1230, 1238

DA Information Services Pty Ltd (Australia) *Tel:* (03) 9210-7777 *Fax:* (03) 9210-7788 *E-mail:* service@ dadirect.com.au *Web Site:* www.dadirect.com.au, pg 1288

DA-Izdatelstvo Publishers (Bulgaria) *Tel:* (02) 988 1208 *Fax:* (02) 986 6290, pg 93

Ediciones Dabar, SA de CV (Mexico) *Tel:* (05) 6550396 *Fax:* (05) 6033674 *E-mail:* dabar@data.net.mx, pg 460

Dabill Publications (Australia) *Tel:* (02) 4228 8836 *Fax:* (02) 4226 9367 *Web Site:* www.dabill.com.au, pg 19

DachsVerlag GmbH (Austria) *Tel:* (01) 285 22 05-0 *Fax:* (01) 285 22 05-15 *E-mail:* office@dachs.at *Web Site:* www.dachs.at, pg 49

Editura Dacia (Romania) *Tel:* (0264) 452178 *Fax:* (0264) 452178 *E-mail:* office@edituradacia.ro *Web Site:* www.edituradacia.ro; www.cjnet.ro, pg 534

Daco Verlag Guenter Blase oHG (Germany) *Tel:* (0711) 96421-0 *Fax:* (0711) 96421-10 *E-mail:* info@daco-verlag.de *Web Site:* www.daco-verlag.de, pg 210

Les Editions Roger Dacosta (France) *Tel:* (01) 45 44 14 91, pg 156

Edizioni Armando Dado, Tipografia Stazione (Switzerland) *Tel:* (091) 751 48 02 *Fax:* (091) 752 10 26, pg 616

Dae Won Sa Co Ltd (Republic of Korea) *Tel:* (02) 7576717 *Fax:* (02) 7758043, pg 435

Daedalus Verlag (Germany) *Tel:* (0251) 231355 *Fax:* (0251) 232631 *E-mail:* info@daedalus-verlag.de *Web Site:* www.daedalus-verlag.com, pg 210

Daehan Printing & Publishing Co Ltd (Republic of Korea) *Tel:* (031) 730-3850 *Fax:* (031) 735-8104 *E-mail:* mschung@daehane.com; james@daehane.com; sabrachili@daehane.com *Web Site:* www.daehane.com, pg 435

Daehan Printing & Publishing Co Ltd (Republic of Korea) *Tel:* (031) 730-3850 *Fax:* (031) 735-8104 *E-mail:* mschung@daehane.com *Web Site:* www. daehane.com, pg 1149

Daehan Printing & Publishing Co Ltd (Republic of Korea) *Tel:* (0822) 34 75 3800 *Fax:* (0822) 541 8158 *E-mail:* mschung@daehane.com *Web Site:* www. daehane.com, pg 1170

Daehan Printing & Publishing Co Ltd (Republic of Korea) *Tel:* (031) 730-3850; (031) 730-3813 *Fax:* (031) 735-8104 *Web Site:* www.dhpop.com; www.daehane.com, pg 1211

Daehan Printing & Publishing Co Ltd (Republic of Korea) *Tel:* (031) 730-3850 *Fax:* (031) 735-8104 *Web Site:* www.daehane.com, pg 1227

Daejon Trading Co Ltd (Republic of Korea) *Tel:* (02) 536-9555 *Fax:* (02) 536-0025, pg 1315

Daeyoung Munhwasa (Republic of Korea) *Tel:* (02) 716-3883 *Fax:* (02) 703-3839 *E-mail:* spotto29@hotmail. com, pg 435

Dafolo Forlag (Denmark) *Tel:* 9620 6666 *Fax:* 9842 9711 *E-mail:* dafolo@dafolo.dk *Web Site:* www. dafolo.dk; www.dafaloforlag.dk, pg 130

DAFSA (France) *Tel:* (01) 55 45 26 00 *Fax:* (01) 55 45 26 35 *E-mail:* dorra.medjani@dri-wefa.com *Web Site:* www.dafsa.fr, pg 156

Institut Dagang Muchtar (Indonesia) *Tel:* (031) 42973, pg 351

Klub-Dagbreek (South Africa) *Tel:* (011) 6736725 *Fax:* (011) 6736719, pg 1245

Dagmar Dreves Verlag (Germany) *Tel:* (04131) 248100 *Fax:* (04131) 248102, pg 210

Dagraja Press (Australia) *Tel:* (02) 6247 0782; (02) 6262 7533 *E-mail:* granorab@ozemail.com.au, pg 19

Dahlgaard Media BV (Denmark) *Tel:* 3537 3533 *Fax:* 3537 3299, pg 130

Dahlia Books, International Publishers & Booksellers (Sweden) *Tel:* (018) 133511 *E-mail:* dahlia@comhem. se, pg 606

Dai Hak Publishing Co (Republic of Korea) *Tel:* (02) 364-9788 *Fax:* (02) 393-9045, pg 435

Dai Nippon Printing Co (Hong Kong) Ltd (Hong Kong) *Tel:* 2408-0188 *Fax:* 2408-8479 *E-mail:* info@mail. dnp.co.jp *Web Site:* www.dnp.co.jp, pg 1146, 1167

Dai Nippon Printing Co (Hong Kong) Ltd (Hong Kong) *Tel:* 2408-0188 *Fax:* 2614-7585; 2407-6201 *E-mail:* info@mail.dnp.co.jp *Web Site:* www.dnp.co.jp, pg 1207

Dai Nippon Printing Co (Hong Kong) Ltd (Hong Kong) *Tel:* 2408-0188 *Fax:* 2614-7585; 2407-6201 *Web Site:* www.dnp.co.jp, pg 1226

Dai Nippon Printing Co Ltd (Japan) *Tel:* (03) 3266 2111 *E-mail:* info@mail.dnp.co.jp *Web Site:* www.dnp.co.jp, pg 1211

Daiichi Media Pte Ltd (Singapore) *Tel:* 6849 8666 *Fax:* 6256 5922 *E-mail:* info@daiichimedia.com. sg; sales@daiichimedia.com.sg *Web Site:* www. daiichimedia.com, pg 551

Daiichi Shuppan Co Ltd (Japan) *Tel:* (03) 3291-4576 *Fax:* (03) 3291-4579 *Web Site:* www.daiichi-shuppan. co.jp, pg 413

Le Daily-Bul (Belgium) *Tel:* (064) 222973 *Fax:* (064) 222973, pg 65

Daily Times of Nigeria Ltd (Publication Division) (Nigeria) *Tel:* (01) 4977280 *Fax:* (01) 4977284 *Web Site:* www.dailytimesofnigeria.com, pg 499

Daimon Verlag AG (Switzerland) *Tel:* (055) 412 2266 *Fax:* (055) 412 2231 *E-mail:* daimon@compuserve. com *Web Site:* www.daimon.ch, pg 616

Dainippon Tosho Publishing Co, Ltd (Japan) *Tel:* (03) 3561-8672 *Fax:* (03) 3563-5596 *Web Site:* www. dainippon-tosho.co.jp, pg 413

Dalia Peled Publishers, Division of Modan (Israel) *Tel:* (08) 4221821 *Fax:* (08) 4221299, pg 362

Dalian Maritime University Press (China) *Tel:* (0411) 84729480; (0411) 84728394 *Fax:* (0411) 84727996 *E-mail:* dmup@dmupress.com; cbs@dmupress.com *Web Site:* www.dmupress.com, pg 103

Dalian University of Technology Library (China) *Tel:* (0411) 84708620 *Fax:* (0411) 84708620; (0411) 84708626 *E-mail:* lib@dlut.edu.cn; libaqui4@dlut.edu. cn *Web Site:* www.lib.dlut.edu.cn, pg 1496

Editions Dalloz Sirey (France) *Tel:* (01) 40 64 54 54 *Fax:* (01) 40 64 54 60 *E-mail:* ventes@dalloz.fr *Web Site:* www.dalloz.fr, pg 156

Rafael Dalmau, Editor (Spain) *Tel:* (093) 3173338 *Fax:* (093) 3173338, pg 573

Izdatel'stovo Dal'nevostonogo Gosudarstvennogo Universite (Russian Federation) *Fax:* 257200, pg 539

Terence Dalton Ltd (United Kingdom) *Tel:* (01787) 249290 *Fax:* (01787) 248267 *E-mail:* tdl@ lavenhamgroup.cp.uk *Web Site:* www.terencedalton. co.uk, pg 681

Daltons Books (Australia) *Tel:* (02) 62491844 *Fax:* (02) 62475753 *E-mail:* daltons@daltons.com.au *Web Site:* www.daltons.com.au, pg 1288

Ediciones Daly S L (Spain) *Tel:* (095) 2582569 *Fax:* (095) 2583619 *E-mail:* daly@edicionesdaly.com *Web Site:* edicionesdaly.com, pg 573

Damanhur Edizioni (Italy) *Tel:* (0124) 512213 *Fax:* (0124) 512213 *E-mail:* dhbooks@ damanhurbooks.com *Web Site:* www.damanhurbooks. com, pg 380

Damascus University Library (Syrian Arab Republic) *Tel:* (011) 2215104; (011) 2215101 *Fax:* (011) 2236010 *E-mail:* info@damascus-online.com *Web Site:* www.damascus-online/university.htm, pg 1547

Damascus University Press (Syrian Arab Republic) *Tel:* (011) 2215104; (011) 2215101 *Fax:* (011) 2236010 *E-mail:* info@damascus-online.com *Web Site:* www.damascus-online/university.htm, pg 633

Dami Editore SRL (Italy) *Tel:* (02) 76006533 *Fax:* (02) 784010 *E-mail:* damieditore@damieditore.it *Web Site:* www.damieditore.it, pg 380

N W Damm og Son A/S (Norway) *Tel:* 24 05 10 00 *Fax:* 24 05 10 99 *E-mail:* post@egmont.no *Web Site:* www.damm.no, pg 504

Dana Verlag (Germany) *Tel:* (05468) 1813 *Fax:* (05468) 239, pg 210

Dance Books Ltd (United Kingdom) *Tel:* (01420) 86138 *Fax:* (01420) 86142 *E-mail:* dl@dancebooks.co.uk *Web Site:* www.dancebooks.co.uk, pg 681

Dangaroo Press (Australia) *Tel:* (02) 49545938 *Fax:* (02) 49546531, pg 19

Editions Dangles SA-Edilarge SA (France) *Tel:* (02) 38864180 *Fax:* (02) 38837234 *E-mail:* info@editions-dangles.com *Web Site:* www.editions-dangles.com, pg 157

The C W Daniel Co Ltd (United Kingdom) *Tel:* (01799) 521909; (01799) 526216 *Fax:* (01799) 513462 *E-mail:* cwdaniel@dial.pipex.com *Web Site:* www.cwdaniel.com, pg 681

Ann-Christine Danielsson Agency (Sweden) *Tel:* (040) 482380 *Fax:* (040) 482190 *E-mail:* acd.agency@swipnet.se, pg 1127

The Danish Literature Centre (Denmark) *Tel:* 33744500 *Fax:* 33744565 *E-mail:* danlit@danlit.dk *Web Site:* www.literaturenet.dk, pg 130

DanKook University Press (Republic of Korea) *Tel:* (02) 793-5034 *Fax:* (02) 709-5814 *E-mail:* omslit@dankook.ac.kr; pencil58@yahoo.com *Web Site:* www.dankook.ac.kr, pg 435

Danmar Publishers (Kenya) *Tel:* (020) 600431; (020) 600432, pg 430

Danmarks Biblioteksforening (Denmark) *Tel:* 33 25 09 35 *Fax:* 33 25 79 00 *Web Site:* www.dbf.dk, pg 1561

Danmarks BlindeBibliotek (Denmark) *Tel:* 39 13 46 00 *Fax:* 39 13 46 01 *E-mail:* dbb@dbb.dk *Web Site:* www.dbb.dk, pg 1500

Danmarks Forskningsbiblioteksforening (Denmark) *Tel:* (045) 89 46 22 07 *Fax:* (045) 89 46 22 20 *E-mail:* df@statsbiblioteket.dk *Web Site:* www.dfdf.dk, pg 1561

Danmarks Forvaltningshojskole Forlaget (Denmark) *Tel:* 38 14 52 00 *Fax:* 38 14 53 45 *E-mail:* dhf@dhfnet.dk; dspa@dspa.dk *Web Site:* www.dkdfh.dk, pg 130

Danmarks Natur-og Laegevidenskabelige Bibliotek, Universitet de sbiblioteket (Denmark) *Tel:* 3539 6523 *Fax:* 3539 8533 *E-mail:* dnlb@dnlb.dk *Web Site:* www.dnlb.dk, pg 1500

Danmarks Paedagogiske Bibliotek (Denmark) *Tel:* 8888 9300 *Fax:* 8888 9391 *E-mail:* dpb@dpu.dk *Web Site:* www.dpb.dpu.dk/, pg 1500

Danmarks Statistik Biblioteket (Denmark) *Tel:* 3917 3917; 3917 3030 *Fax:* 3917 3999; 3917 3003 *E-mail:* dst@dst.dk; bib@dst.dk *Web Site:* www.dst.dk/bibliotek, pg 1500

Danmarks Tekniske Videncenter (DTV) (Denmark) *Tel:* 4525 7200 *Fax:* 4588 3040 *E-mail:* dtv@dtv.dk *Web Site:* www.dtv.dk, pg 1500

D'Anna (Italy) *Tel:* (055) 2335513 *Fax:* (055) 225932 *E-mail:* gdanna@tin.it; gdanna@mbox.vol.it, pg 380

Hristo G Danov State Publishing House (Bulgaria) *Tel:* (032) 632552; (032) 265421 *Fax:* (032) 260560, pg 93

Dansk Biblioteks Center (Denmark) *Tel:* 44 86 77 77 *Fax:* 44 86 78 91 *E-mail:* dbc@dbc.dk *Web Site:* www.dbc.dk, pg 130

Dansk Forfatterforening (Denmark) *Tel:* 32 95 51 00 *Fax:* 32 54 01 15 *E-mail:* danskforfatterforening@danskforfatterforening.dk *Web Site:* www.danskforfatterforening.dk, pg 1392

Dansk Historisk Handbogsforlag ApS (Denmark) *Tel:* 45 93 48 00 *Fax:* 45 93 47 47 *E-mail:* genos@worldonline.dk, pg 130

Dansk ISBN - Kontor (the Danish ISBN Agency) (Denmark) *Tel:* 44867725 *Fax:* 44867853 *E-mail:* isbn@dbc.dk *Web Site:* www.isbn-kontoret.dk, pg 1255

Dansk Musikbiblioteks Forening (DMBF) (Denmark) *Tel:* 33 47 43 16 *Fax:* 33 47 47 10 *E-mail:* dmbf@kb.dk *Web Site:* www.dmbf.nu, pg 1561

Dansk Psykologisk Forlag (Denmark) *Tel:* 3538 1665 *Fax:* 3538 1655 *E-mail:* salg@dpf.dk; dk-psych@dpf.dk *Web Site:* www.dpf.dk, pg 130

Dansk Teknologisk Institut, Forlaget (Denmark) *Tel:* 42 99 66 11 *Fax:* 42 99 54 36 *E-mail:* info@teknologisk.dk, pg 130

Den Danske Boghandlerforening (Denmark) *Tel:* 32542255 *Fax:* 32540041 *E-mail:* ddb@bogpost.dk *Web Site:* www.bogguide.dk, pg 1255

Den Danske Forlaeggerforening (Denmark) *Tel:* 33 15 66 88 *Fax:* 33 15 65 88 *E-mail:* publassn@webpartner.dk; jh@carlsen.dk, pg 1256

Det Danske Sprog - og Litteraturselskab (Denmark) *Tel:* 33130660 *Fax:* 33140608 *E-mail:* sekretariat@dsl.dk *Web Site:* www.dsl.dk, pg 1392

Libreria Dante di A M Longo (Italy) *Tel:* (0544) 217026 *Fax:* (0544) 217554 *E-mail:* longo-ra@linknet.it *Web Site:* www.longo-editore.it, pg 1310

Danubia Werbung und Verlagsservice (Austria) *Tel:* (01) 792666 *Fax:* (01) 792666443, pg 49

Danubiaprint (Slovakia) *Tel:* (02) 309167 *Fax:* (02) 362613, pg 555

Danuma Prakashakayo (Sri Lanka) *Tel:* (01) 686878 *Fax:* (01) 696578, pg 601

Daphne Diffusion SA (Belgium) *Tel:* (09) 221 45 91 *Fax:* (09) 220 16 12 *E-mail:* info@daphne.be, pg 65

Daphnis-Verlag (Switzerland) *Tel:* (01) 202 52 71 *Fax:* (01) 201 42 31, pg 616

Dar Al-Kitab Al-Loubnani (Lebanon) *Tel:* 861563; (01) 735732 *Fax:* (01) 351433 *E-mail:* info@daralkitab-online.com, pg 442

Dar Al-Kitab Al-Masri (Egypt (Arab Republic of Egypt)) *Tel:* (02) 742168; (02) 754301; (02) 744657 *Fax:* (02) 3924657 *E-mail:* info@daralkitab-online.com, pg 137

Dar Al-Maaref-Liban Sarl (Lebanon) *Tel:* (01) 931243, pg 442

Dar Al Maarifah (Syrian Arab Republic) *Tel:* (011) 44670278 *Fax:* (011) 2241615 *E-mail:* info@easyquran.com *Web Site:* www.dar-al-maarifah.com; www.easyquran.com, pg 633

Dar Al-Matbo at Al-Gadidah (Egypt (Arab Republic of Egypt)) *Tel:* (03) 4825508 *Fax:* (03) 4833819, pg 137

Dar Al-Mirrikh (Mars Publishing House) (Saudi Arabia) *Tel:* (01) 464 7531; (01) 465 7939; (01) 4658523 *Fax:* (01) 465 7939, pg 546

Dar al-Nahda al Arabia (Egypt (Arab Republic of Egypt)), pg 137

Dar Al-raed Al-Loubani (Lebanon) *Tel:* (01) 450757; (01) 451581, pg 442

Dar Al-Rayah for Publishing & Distribution (Saudi Arabia) *Tel:* (01) 4931869 *Fax:* (01) 4911985, pg 546

Dar Al-Shareff for Publishing & Distribution (Saudi Arabia) *Tel:* (01) 4779491, pg 546

Dar Al-Thakafia Publishing (Egypt (Arab Republic of Egypt)) *Tel:* (02) 42718 *Fax:* (02) 4034694 *E-mail:* nassar@hotmail.com, pg 137

Dar Al-Ulum Publishers, Booksellers & Distributors (Saudi Arabia) *Tel:* (01) 4777121 *Fax:* (01) 4793446, pg 1329

Dar An-Nahar Sal (Lebanon) *Tel:* (01) 561 687 *Fax:* (01) 561 693, pg 442

Dar Arabia Lil Kitab (Tunisia) *Tel:* 71888255, pg 643

Dar El Afaq (Tunisia) *Tel:* 71265904 *Fax:* 71569035, pg 643

Dar El Ilm Lilmalayin (Lebanon) *Tel:* (09611) 306666 *Fax:* (09611) 701657 *E-mail:* info@malayin.com *Web Site:* www.malayin.com, pg 442

Dar El Kitab (Morocco) *Tel:* (02) 304581; (02) 305419 *Fax:* (02) 304581, pg 470

Dar El Shorouk (Egypt (Arab Republic of Egypt)) *Tel:* (02) 4023399; (02) 4037567 *Fax:* (02) 3934814 *E-mail:* dar@shorouk.com *Web Site:* www.shorouk.com, pg 137

The Dar Es Salaam Bookshop (United Republic of Tanzania) *Tel:* (051) 23416, pg 1336

Dar Nachr Al Maarifa Pour L'Edition et La Distribution (Morocco) *Tel:* (07) 795702; (07) 796914 *Fax:* (07) 790343, pg 470

Typothito G Dardanos (Greece) *Tel:* 2103642003 *Fax:* 2103642030 *E-mail:* info@dardanosnet.gr *Web Site:* www.dardanosnet.gr, pg 1302

Daresbury Lewis Carroll Society (United Kingdom) *Tel:* (01606) 891303 *Web Site:* lewiscarrollsociety.org.uk, pg 1401

Dareschta Consulting und Handels GmbH (Germany) *Tel:* (0611) 9310992 *Fax:* (0611) 3082096, pg 210

Darf Publishers Ltd (United Kingdom) *Tel:* (020) 7431 7009 *Fax:* (020) 7431 7655 *E-mail:* darf@freeuk.com *Web Site:* home.freeuk.net/darf, pg 681

Dargaud (France) *Tel:* (01) 53 26 32 32 *Fax:* (01) 53 26 32 00 *E-mail:* contact@dargaud.fr *Web Site:* www.dargaud.fr, pg 157

Dargenis Publishers (Lithuania) *Tel:* (037) 205241 *Fax:* (037) 205241 *E-mail:* dargenis@kaunas.omnitel.net, pg 445

Ediciones de Juan Darien (Uruguay) *Tel:* (02) 2090223 *E-mail:* dayraq@chasque.apc.org, pg 771

Verlag Darmstaedter Blaetter Schwarz und Co (Germany) *Tel:* (06151) 48196, pg 210

D'Artagnan Publishing (Australia) *Tel:* (08) 3493425, pg 19

Darton, Longman & Todd Ltd (United Kingdom) *Tel:* (020) 8875 0155; (020) 8875 0134 *Fax:* (020) 8875 0133 *E-mail:* tradesales@darton-longman-todd.co.uk *Web Site:* www.darton-longman-todd.co.uk, pg 681

Darulfikir (Malaysia) *Tel:* (03) 2981636; (03) 26913892 *Fax:* (03) 26928757 *E-mail:* e-mel@darulfikir.com.my *Web Site:* www.darulfikir.com.my, pg 451

Darzhavno Izdatelstvo Zemizdat (Bulgaria) *Tel:* (02) 9867895 *Fax:* (02) 9875454, pg 93

Das Arsenal, Verlag fuer Kultur und Politik GmbH (Germany) *Tel:* (030) 3441827; (030) 34651360 *Fax:* (030) 34651362, pg 210

D'Assis Books (Australia) *Tel:* (07) 5448 2145 *Fax:* (07) 5447 5200, pg 19

Dastane Ramchandra & Co (India) *Tel:* (020) 447 8193; (020) 448 5950; (020) 551 1964 *Fax:* (020) 4478193, pg 330

DAT Publications (Israel) *Tel:* (03) 5071239 *Fax:* (03) 5070458 *E-mail:* dat@y-dat.co.il *Web Site:* www.y-dat.co.il, pg 363

Data Becker GmbH & Co KG (Germany) *Tel:* (0211) 9331 800; (0211) 9334 900 (orders) *Fax:* (0211) 9331 444; (0211) 9334 999 (orders) *E-mail:* info@databecker.de *Web Site:* www.databecker.de, pg 210

DATAMAP - Europe (Bulgaria) *Tel:* (02) 510090 *Fax:* (02) 510090 *E-mail:* datamap@mail.techno-linek.com, pg 93

Datanews (Italy) *Tel:* (06) 70450318/9 *Fax:* (06) 70450320 *E-mail:* info@datanews.it *Web Site:* www.datanews.it, pg 380

Datapage Technologies International Inc (United States) *Tel:* 636-278-8888 *Toll Free Tel:* 800-876-3844 *Fax:* 636-278-2180 *Web Site:* www.datapage.com, pg 1177

Editions du Dauphin (France) *Tel:* (01) 43 27 79 00 *Fax:* (01) 43 27 76 31, pg 157

M d'Auria Editore SAS (Italy) *Tel:* (081) 5518963 *Fax:* (081) 5493827; (081) 5518963 *E-mail:* info@ dauria.it *Web Site:* www.dauria.it, pg 381

Davaco Publishers (Netherlands) *Tel:* (0525) 661823 *Fax:* (0525) 662153 *E-mail:* main@davaco.com *Web Site:* www.davaco.com, pg 477

David & Charles Ltd (United Kingdom) *Tel:* (01626) 323200 *Fax:* (01626) 323319 *E-mail:* postermaster@ davidandcharles.co.uk *Web Site:* www.davidandcharles. co.uk, pg 681

David Godwin Associates (United Kingdom) *Tel:* (020) 7240 9992 *Fax:* (020) 7395 6110 *E-mail:* assistant@ davidgodwinassociates.co.uk, pg 1129

David's Marine Books (New Zealand) *Tel:* (09) 303 1459 *Toll Free Tel:* 508 242 787; 800 422 427 *Fax:* (09) 307 8170 *E-mail:* sales@transpacific.co.nz *Web Site:* www.transpacific.co.nz, pg 491

Davidsfonds Uitgeverij NV (Belgium) *Tel:* (016) 310600 *Fax:* (016) 310608 *E-mail:* informatie@davidsfonds.be *Web Site:* www.davidsfonds.be, pg 65

Christopher Davies Publishers Ltd (United Kingdom) *Tel:* (01792) 648825 *Fax:* (01792) 648825 *E-mail:* sales@cdaviesbookswales.com *Web Site:* www.cdaviesbookswales.com, pg 682

Dawson Books (United Kingdom) *Tel:* (01933) 417500 *Fax:* (01933) 417501 *E-mail:* contactus@dawson. co.uk; bksales@dawsonbooks.co.uk *Web Site:* www. dawson.co.uk, pg 682

Dawson UK Ltd, Books Division (United Kingdom) *Tel:* (01933) 417500 *Fax:* (01933) 417501 *E-mail:* bkcustserv@dawsonbooks.co.uk *Web Site:* www.dawsonbooks.co.uk, pg 1341

Daya Publishing House (India) *Tel:* (011) 23245578; (011) 23244987 *Fax:* (011) 23244987 *E-mail:* dayabooks@vsnl.com *Web Site:* www. dayabooks.com, pg 330

Dayi Information Co (Taiwan, Province of China) *Tel:* (02) 8792 4088 *Fax:* (02) 8792 4089 *Web Site:* www.dayi.com, pg 635

Daystar Press (Publishers) (Nigeria) *Tel:* (022) 412670, pg 499

dbv-Druck Beratungs-und Verlags GmbH Verlag fur die Technische Universitaet Graz (Austria) *Tel:* (0316) 38 30 33 *Fax:* (0316) 38 30 43 *E-mail:* office@dbv.at *Web Site:* www.dbv.at, pg 49

DC Book Club (India) *Tel:* (0481) 2563114; (0481) 2563226; (0481) 2578214 *Fax:* (0481) 2564758 *E-mail:* info@dcbooks.com *Web Site:* www.dcbooks. com, pg 1243

DC Books (India) *Tel:* (0481) 2563114; (0481) 2301614 *Web Site:* www.dcbooks.com, pg 330

Editions De Boeck-Larcier SA (Belgium) *Tel:* (02) 548 07 11 *Fax:* (02) 513 90 09 *Web Site:* www.deboeck. be, pg 65

G De Bono Editore (Italy) *Tel:* (055) 576022 *Fax:* (055) 5001665, pg 381

De Cervantes Ediciones SA (Ecuador) *Tel:* (02) 522 956 *Fax:* (02) 523 452; (02) 223 062, pg 1298

Maria Esther De Fleischmann (Mexico) *Tel:* (05) 5852698 *Fax:* (05) 5854296 *E-mail:* fleischmann1@ compuserve.com.mx, pg 460

De Graaf Publishers (Netherlands) *Tel:* (0172) 57 1461 *Fax:* (0172) 57 2231 *E-mail:* degraaf.books@wxs.nl *Web Site:* www.antiqbook.nl/degraafbooks, pg 477

Ediciones de la Flor SRL (Argentina) *Tel:* (011) 4963-7950 *Fax:* (011) 4963-5616 *E-mail:* edic-flor@ datamarkets.com.ar *Web Site:* www.edicionesdelaflor. com.ar, pg 4

De La Salle University (Philippines) *Tel:* (02) 741-9271; (046) 416-0338; (046) 416-3878 *Fax:* (02) 5264237 *E-mail:* mcovatg@dlsu.edu.ph *Web Site:* www.dasma. dlsu.edu.ph, pg 514

Michel De Maule Editions (France) *Tel:* (01) 42 97 93 56; (01) 42 97 93 48 *Fax:* (01) 42 97 94 90, pg 157

De Plukvogel nv (Belgium) *Tel:* (02) 253-06-58 *Fax:* (02) 253-06-58, pg 1292

De Vecchi Editions SA (France) *Tel:* (01) 69 34 12 01; (01) 44 76 88 88 *Fax:* (01) 64 48 24 97; (01) 44 76 88 89, pg 157

Giovanni De Vecchi Editore SpA (Italy) *Tel:* (02) 66984851 *Fax:* (02) 6701548, pg 381

De Walburg Pers (Netherlands) *Tel:* (0575) 510522 *Fax:* (0575) 542289 *E-mail:* info@walburgpers.nl *Web Site:* www.walburgpers.nl, pg 477

De Wit Stores NV (Netherlands Antilles) *Tel:* (0297) 823500 *Fax:* (0297) 821575 *E-mail:* dewitstores@ sctarnet.aw, pg 488

De WitAruba Boekhandel (Netherlands Antilles) *Tel:* (0297) 823500 *Fax:* (0297) 821575, pg 1321

DEA Diffusione Edizioni Anglo-Americane (Italy) *Tel:* (06) 8551441 *Fax:* (06) 8543228 *E-mail:* info@ deanet.it *Web Site:* www.deanet.com, pg 381

DEA Diffusione Edizioni Anglo-Americane (Italy) *Tel:* (06) 852121 *Fax:* (06) 8543228 *E-mail:* deanet@ deanet.it; info@deanet.it *Web Site:* www.deanet.it, pg 1310

Deakin University Press (Australia) *Tel:* (03) 5227 8144 *Fax:* (03) 5227 2020 *E-mail:* lynnew@deakin.edu.au *Web Site:* www.deakin.edu.au, pg 19

Nouvelles Editions Debresse (France) *Tel:* (01) 45481047, pg 157

Debrett's Ltd (United Kingdom) *Tel:* (020) 7915 9633 *Fax:* (020) 7753 4212 *E-mail:* people@debretts.co.uk *Web Site:* www.debretts.co.uk, pg 682

Decanord (France) *Tel:* (03) 20 09 90 60 *Fax:* (03) 20 09 92 75 *E-mail:* decanord@wanadoo fr *Web Site:* www. decanord.fr, pg 157

Editions La Decouverte (France) *Tel:* (01) 44 08 84 01 *Fax:* (01) 44 08 84 17 *E-mail:* ladecouverte@ editionsladecouverte.com *Web Site:* www. editionsladecouverte.fr, pg 157

Edizioni Dedalo SRL (Italy) *Tel:* (080) 5311413; (080) 5311400; (080) 5311401 *Fax:* (080) 5311414 *E-mail:* info@edizionidedalo.it *Web Site:* www. edizionidedalo.it, pg 381

Dedalo Litostampa SRL (Italy) *Tel:* (080) 531 14 13; (080) 531 14 00; (080) 531 14 01 *Fax:* (080) 531 14 14 *E-mail:* info@edizionidedalo *Web Site:* www. edizionidedalo.it, pg 1149

Dedalo Litostampa SRL (Italy) *Tel:* (080) 531 14 13; (080) 531 1400 *Fax:* (080) 531 14 14 *E-mail:* info@ edizionidedalo.it *Web Site:* www.edizionidedalo.it, pg 1170

Dedalo Litostampa SRL (Italy) *Tel:* (080) 531 14 13; (080) 531 14 00; (080) 531 14 01 *Fax:* (080) 531 14 14 *E-mail:* info@edizionidedalo.it *Web Site:* www. edizionidedalo.it, pg 1210

Dedalo Litostampa SRL (Italy) *Tel:* (080) 531 14 13; (080) 531 14 01; (080) 531 14 00 *Fax:* (080) 531 14 14 *E-mail:* info@edizionidedalo.it *Web Site:* www. edizionidedalo.it, pg 1227

Dedalus Ltd (United Kingdom) *Tel:* (01487) 832382 *Fax:* (01487) 832382 *E-mail:* info@dedalusbooks.com *Web Site:* www.dedalusbooks.com, pg 682

Dee-Jay Publications (Ireland) *Tel:* (0402) 39125 *Fax:* (0402) 39064, pg 356

DEF (De Blauwe Vogel) NV/SA (Belgium) *Tel:* (011) 685751-2 *Fax:* (011) 67-21-70, pg 66

Defiant Publications (United Kingdom) *Tel:* (0121) 745 8421 *E-mail:* info@defiantpublications.co.uk, pg 682

Degener & Co, Manfred Dreiss Verlag (Germany) *Tel:* (09161) 886039 *Fax:* (09161) 886057 *E-mail:* degener@degener-verlag.com *Web Site:* www. degener-verlag.com, pg 210

Edizioni Dehoniane Bologna (EDB) (Italy) *Tel:* (051) 4290011 *Fax:* (051) 4290099 *E-mail:* webmaster@ dehoniane.it *Web Site:* www.dehoniane.it, pg 381

Edizioni Dehoniane (Italy) *Tel:* (06) 624996 *Fax:* (06) 6628326 *E-mail:* webmaster@dehoniane.it *Web Site:* www.dehoniane.it, pg 381

Editorial DEI (Departamento Ecumenico de Investigaciones) (Costa Rica) *Tel:* 253-0229; 253-9124 *Fax:* 2531541 *E-mail:* publicaciones@dei-cr.org *Web Site:* www.dei-cr.org, pg 115

DEI Tipographia del Genio Civile (Italy) *Tel:* (06) 44163792 *Fax:* (06) 4403307 *E-mail:* dei@build.it *Web Site:* www.build.it, pg 381

Deichmanske Bibliotek (Norway) *Tel:* 23 43 29 00 *Fax:* 22 11 33 89 *E-mail:* deichman@deichman.no *Web Site:* www.deich.folkebibl.no, pg 1532

Verlag Horst Deike KG (Germany) *Tel:* (07531) 81550 *Fax:* (07531) 815581 *E-mail:* info@deike-verlag.de *Web Site:* www.deike-verlag.de, pg 210

Editorial Deimos, SL (Spain) *Tel:* (091) 479-23-42 *Fax:* (091) 5438214 *E-mail:* editorial@deimos-es.com *Web Site:* www.deimos-es.com, pg 574

Editions Claude Dejaie (Belgium) *Tel:* (081) 460748, pg 66

Dekel Publishing House (Israel) *Tel:* (03) 6045379 *Fax:* (03) 5440824 *E-mail:* dekelpbl@netvision.net.il *Web Site:* www.dekelpublishing.com, pg 363

Marcel Dekker AG (Switzerland) *Tel:* (061) 260 63 00 *Fax:* (061) 260 63 33 *E-mail:* intlcustserv@dekker. com *Web Site:* www.dekker.com, pg 616

Dekker v d Vegt (Netherlands) *Tel:* (024) 322 10 10 *Fax:* (024) 324 21 11 *E-mail:* mariken@dekker.nl *Web Site:* www.dekker.nl, pg 1320

Instituto del Tercer Mundo (Uruguay) *Tel:* (02) 419 6192 *Fax:* (02) 411 9222 *E-mail:* item@chasque.apc. org, itcm@item.org.uy *Web Site:* www.chasque.apc. org/item/, pg 771

Del Verbo Emprender SA de CV (Mexico) *Tel:* (05) 294-1160; (05) 294-8633 *Fax:* (05) 294-8633, pg 460

Guy Delabergerie Editions Sarl (French Guiana) *Tel:* 311162 *Fax:* 311759, pg 189

Delabie Europrint SA (Belgium) *Tel:* (056) 84 10 00, pg 1205

Editions Delachaux et Niestle SA (Switzerland) *Tel:* (021) 8110711 *Fax:* (021) 8110712 *E-mail:* contact@delachaux-niestle.com, pg 617

Delancey Press Ltd (United Kingdom) *Tel:* (020) 7387 3544 *Fax:* (020) 8383 5314 *E-mail:* delanceypress@ aol.com *Web Site:* www.delanceypress.com, pg 682

Editions Andre Delcourt & Cie (Switzerland) *Tel:* (021) 6479772 *Fax:* (021) 6478831, pg 617

Editions Delcourt (France) *Tel:* (01) 56 03 92 20 *Fax:* (01) 56 03 92 30 *Web Site:* www.editions-delcourt.fr, pg 157

Delectus Books (United Kingdom) *Tel:* (020) 8963 0979 *Fax:* (020) 8963 0502 *Web Site:* abebooks. com/home/delectus; www.delectusbooks.co.uk, pg 682

Delft University Press (Netherlands) *Tel:* (015) 2785706 *Fax:* (015) 2785678 *E-mail:* info@library.tudelft.nl *Web Site:* www.library.tudelft.nl, pg 477

Delhi Public Library (India) *Tel:* (011) 291 6881 *Fax:* (011) 294 3990, pg 1514

Delhi State Booksellers' & Publishers' Association (India) *Tel:* (011) 231867; (011) 2515726 *Fax:* (011) 2936758, pg 1263

Delhi University Library System (India) *Tel:* (011) 27667725 *Fax:* (011) 27667126 *E-mail:* crl@delnet. ven.nic.in *Web Site:* www.du.ac.in, pg 1514

La Delirante (France) *Tel:* (01) 43 54 47 97 *Fax:* (01) 43 54 06 97, pg 157

Delius, Klasing und Co (Germany) *Tel:* (0521) 55 90 *Fax:* (0521) 55 91 13 *E-mail:* info@delius-klasing.de *Web Site:* www.delius-klasing.de, pg 210

Delius Klasing Verlag GmbH (Germany) *Tel:* (0521) 55 90 *Fax:* (0521) 55 91 13 *E-mail:* info@delius-klasing. de *Web Site:* www.delius-klasing.de, pg 210

Casa Editrice Istituto della Santa (Italy) *Tel:* (0321) 22371, pg 381

Edizioni Della Torre di Salvatore Fozzi & C SAS (Italy) *Tel:* (070) 270507 *Fax:* (070) 270507 *E-mail:* info@ librisardi.it *Web Site:* www.librisardi.it, pg 381

Dellasta Publishing Pty Ltd (Australia) *Tel:* (03) 9888 9188 *Fax:* (03) 9888 7806 *E-mail:* dellasta@ publishaust.net.au, pg 19

Edizioni dell'Orso (Italy) *Tel:* (0131) 252349 *Fax:* (0131) 257567 *E-mail:* direzione.commerciale@ ediorso.it *Web Site:* www.ediorso.it, pg 381

Editions Delmas (France) *Tel:* (08) 20 80 00 17 *Fax:* (01) 40 64 89 90 *E-mail:* delmas@dalloz.fr *Web Site:* www.editions-delmas.com, pg 157

Delphin Verlag GmbH (Germany) *Tel:* (02236) 39990 *Fax:* (02236) 399997, pg 211

Delp'sche Verlagsbuchhandlung (Germany) *Tel:* (09841) 9030 *Fax:* (09841) 90315, pg 211

Libreria DELSA (Spain) *Tel:* (091) 575 15 41 *Fax:* (091) 575 84 14, pg 1333

Delta Books (Pty) Ltd (United Kingdom) *Tel:* (01865) 304059 *Fax:* (01865) 304035 *E-mail:* mail@ premierbookmarketing.com, pg 682

Delta Books Worldwide (United Kingdom) *Tel:* (01932) 854 776 *Fax:* (01932) 849 528 *E-mail:* info@ deltabooks.co.uk *Web Site:* www.deltabooks.co.uk, pg 1341

Editions Delta SA (Belgium) *Tel:* (02) 217 55 55 *Fax:* (02) 217 93 93 *E-mail:* editions.delta@skynet.be, pg 66

Pustaka Delta Pelajaran Sdn Bhd (Malaysia) *Tel:* (03) 7570000 *Fax:* (03) 7570001, pg 452

Delta Publications (Nigeria) Ltd (Nigeria) *Tel:* (042) 3606, pg 499

Delta Science Fiction Bok Klubb (Sweden) *Tel:* (08) 254781, pg 1246

Jean-P Delville Editions (France) *Tel:* (01) 42 22 72 90 *Fax:* (01) 42 22 65 62 *E-mail:* editions.delville@ wanadoo.fr, pg 157

Demeter (Tunisia) *Tel:* 71 94 52 42; 71 94 52 46 *Fax:* 71 94 51 99, pg 643

Demetra SRL (Italy) *Tel:* (045) 6159711 *Fax:* (045) 6159700, pg 381

Editions du Demi-Cercle (France) *Tel:* (01) 42330685 *Fax:* (01) 42330862, pg 157

Demonvamp Publications (Australia) *Tel:* (03) 9802 3875, pg 19

Den Norske Bokhandlerforening (Norway) *Tel:* 22 00 75 80 *Fax:* 22 33 38 30 *E-mail:* dfn@ forleggerforeningen.no *Web Site:* www. forleggerforeningen.no, pg 1271

Fundacion Omar Dengo (Costa Rica) *Tel:* 257 6263 *Fax:* 2221654 *E-mail:* info@fod.ac.cr *Web Site:* www. fod.ac.cr, pg 115

Denkmayr GmbH Druck & Verlag (Austria) *Tel:* (0732) 654511 *Fax:* (0732) 65451117 *E-mail:* denkmayr. linz@magnet.at, pg 49

Dennik Smena (Slovakia) *Tel:* (02) 491455; (02) 497171, pg 555

Editions Denoel (France) *Tel:* (01) 44 39 73 73 *Fax:* (01) 44 39 73 90 *E-mail:* denoel@denoel.fr, pg 157

Denor Press (United Kingdom) *Tel:* (020) 8343 7368 *Fax:* (020) 8446 4504 *E-mail:* denor@dial.pipex.com *Web Site:* www.xhf37.dial.pipex.com, pg 682

Verlag Harald Denzel, Auto- und Freizeitfuehrer (Austria) *Tel:* (0512) 586880 *Fax:* (0512) 586880 *E-mail:* denzel-verlag@web.de *Web Site:* members. telering.at/denzel-verlag, pg 49

Depalma SRL (Argentina) *Tel:* (011) 5382-8806 *Fax:* (011) 5382-8888 *E-mail:* info@depalma.ssdnet. com.ar, pg 4

Departamento de Documentacion y Bibliotecas (Dominican Republic), pg 1561

Departamento Nacional do Livro (Brazil) *Tel:* (021) 2220-1707; (021) 2220-1683 *Fax:* (021) 2220-1702 *E-mail:* dnl@bn.br *Web Site:* www.bn.br, pg 1253

Departemento de Publicaciones de la Universidad de la Republica (Uruguay) *Tel:* (02) 408 2906; (02) 408 5714 *Fax:* (02) 408 0303 *E-mail:* infoed@edic.edu.uy *Web Site:* www.rau.edu.uy, pg 772

Book Club of the Dept of Cultural Affairs of Sri Lanka (Sri Lanka) *Tel:* (01) 872035 *Fax:* (01) 872035 *E-mail:* pltm1950@sltnet.lk; gsk@sltnet.lk *Web Site:* www.mca.gov.lk, pg 1246

Department of Culture & Information Government of Sharjah (United Arab Emirates) *Tel:* (06) 5671116; (06) 5673139 *Fax:* (06) 5662126; (06) 5660535 *E-mail:* shjbookfair@hotmail.com; cultural@emirates. net.ae *Web Site:* shjbookfair.gov.ae, pg 649

Department of Energy (NSW) (Australia) *Tel:* (02) 8281 7777 *Fax:* (02) 8281 7799 *E-mail:* information@deus. nsw.gov.au *Web Site:* www.doe.nsw.gov.au, pg 20

Department of National Archives (Sri Lanka) *Tel:* (01) 694523; (01) 696917 *Fax:* (01) 694419 *E-mail:* narchive@slt.lk, pg 1544

Department of Primary Industries, Queensland (Australia) *Tel:* (07) 3239 3772 *Fax:* (07) 3239 6509 *E-mail:* books@dpi.qld.gov.au *Web Site:* www.dpi.qld. gov.au, pg 20

Department of Science & Technology (South Africa) *Tel:* (012) 317 4300 *Fax:* (012) 323 8308 *Web Site:* www.dst.gov.za, pg 1542

The Department of the National Library (Jordan) *Tel:* (06) 4610311 *Fax:* (06) 4616832 *E-mail:* nl@ nic.net.jo *Web Site:* www.nl.gov.jo, pg 1520

Dervy Editions (France) *Tel:* (01) 42 79 25 21 *Fax:* (01) 42 78 25 39 *E-mail:* contact@dervy.fr, pg 157

Derzhavne Naukovo-Vyrobnyche Pidpryemstro Kartografia (Ukraine) *Tel:* (044) 5524033 *Fax:* (044) 2388314 *E-mail:* admin@ukrmap.com.ua *Web Site:* www.ukrmap.com.ua, pg 649

Editorial Desarrollo SA (Peru) *Tel:* (01) 428-5380 *Fax:* (01) 428-6628, pg 512

Desbooks Pty Ltd (Australia) *Tel:* (03) 9484 2465 *Fax:* (03) 9484 3877 *E-mail:* desb@alphalink.com.au, pg 20

Imprimerie Carlo Descamps SA (France) *Tel:* (03) 27400208 *Fax:* (03) 27405683, pg 1144

Deschamps Imprimerie (Haiti) *Tel:* 2461 905; 2501 474; 56-3853; 56-2253 *Fax:* 2491 225 *E-mail:* henrid@ acn2.net, pg 311

Desclee de Brouwer SA (France) *Tel:* (01) 45 49 61 92 *Fax:* (01) 42 22 61 41 *E-mail:* direction@ descleedebrouwer.com *Web Site:* www. descleedebrouwer.com, pg 157

Espanola Desclee De Brouwer SA (Spain) *Tel:* (094) 4233045; (094) 4246843 *Fax:* (094) 4237594 *E-mail:* info@desclee.com *Web Site:* www.desclee. com, pg 574

Desclee Editions (France) *Tel:* (01) 53 26 33 35 *Fax:* (01) 53 26 33 36, pg 158

Desert Research Foundation of Namibia (DRFN) (Namibia) *Tel:* (061) 229855 *Fax:* (061) 228286 *E-mail:* info@drfn.org.na *Web Site:* www.drfn.org.na, pg 472

Design & Artists Copyright Society (DACS) (United Kingdom) *Tel:* (020) 7336 8811 *Fax:* (020) 7336 8822 *E-mail:* info@dacs.co.uk *Web Site:* www.dacs.co.uk, pg 1281

Design Human Resources Training & Development (Hong Kong) *Tel:* 29877018 *Fax:* 29877018, pg 314

Designer Publisher Inc (Taiwan, Province of China) *Tel:* (02) 236 56268 *Fax:* (02) 236 76500 *E-mail:* dpgcmg@ms18.hinet.net, pg 635

Desktop Miracles Inc (United States) *Tel:* 802-253-7900 *Fax:* 802-253-1900 *Web Site:* www.desktopmiracles. com, pg 1177, 1230, 1238

Ediciones Desnivel, SL (Spain) *Tel:* (091) 3602242 *Fax:* (091) 3602264 *E-mail:* edicionesdesnivel@ desnivel.com *Web Site:* www.desnivel.com, pg 574

Dessain - Departement de De Boeck & Larcier SA (Belgium) *Tel:* (02) 548 07 11 *Fax:* (02) 513 90 09 *E-mail:* adeb@adeb.be *Web Site:* www.adeb.irisnet.be, pg 66

Dessain et Tolra SA (France) *Tel:* (01) 44 39 44 00 *Fax:* (01) 44 39 43 43, pg 158

Destarte Lda (Portugal) *Tel:* (021) 324 2960 *Fax:* (021) 347 5811 *E-mail:* destarte@vianw.pt, pg 1327

Ediciones Destino SA (Spain) *Tel:* (093) 496 70 01 *Fax:* (093) 496 70 02 *E-mail:* edicionesdestino@stl. logiccontrol.es *Web Site:* www.edestino.es, pg 574

Editions Desvigne (France) *Tel:* (01) 30 14 19 30 *Fax:* (01) 34 60 31 32 *E-mail:* info@casteilla.fr *Web Site:* www.casteilla.fr, pg 158

Det Danske Bibelselskab (Denmark) *Tel:* 33 12 78 35 *Fax:* 33 93 21 50 *E-mail:* bibelselskabet@ bibelselskabet.dk *Web Site:* www.bibelselskabet.dk, pg 130

Det Norske Samlaget (Norway) *Tel:* (022) 70 78 00 *Fax:* (022) 68 75 02 *E-mail:* det.norske@samlaget.no *Web Site:* www.samlaget.no, pg 504

Detska radost (The Former Yugoslav Republic of Macedonia) *Tel:* (091) 112394; (091) 213059 *Fax:* (091) 225830; (091) 213059 *E-mail:* detskaradost@yahoo.com *Web Site:* www. detskaradost.com, pg 449

Izdatelstvo Detskaya Literatura (Russian Federation) *Tel:* (095) 9280803 *Fax:* (095) 9213007, pg 539

Ediciones Deusto SA (Spain) *Tel:* (094) 4356177 *Fax:* (094) 4356173 *E-mail:* edicio01@sarenet.es *Web Site:* www.e-deusto.com, pg 574

Deuticke im Paul Zsolnay Verlag (Austria) *Tel:* (01) 505 76 61-0 *Fax:* (01) 505 76 61-10 *E-mail:* info@ deuticke.at *Web Site:* www.deuticke.at, pg 49

Andre Deutsch Ltd (United Kingdom) *Tel:* (020) 7612 0400 *Fax:* (020) 7612 0401 *Web Site:* www.carlton. com, pg 682

Verlag Harri Deutsch (Switzerland) *Tel:* (033) 2223975 *Fax:* (033) 2223950 *E-mail:* verlag@harri-deutsch.de *Web Site:* www.harri-deutsch.de, pg 617

Verlag Harri Deutsch (Germany) *Tel:* (069) 77015860 *Fax:* (069) 77015869 *E-mail:* verlag@harri-deutsch.de *Web Site:* www.harri-deutsch.de/verlag, pg 211

Deutsche Akademie fuer Sprache und Dichtung (Germany) *Tel:* (06151) 40920 *Fax:* (06151) 409299 *E-mail:* sekretariat@deutscheakademie.de *Web Site:* www.deutscheakademie.de, pg 1394

Deutsche Bibelgesellschaft (Germany) *Tel:* (0711) 7181-0 *Fax:* (0711) 7181-250 *E-mail:* infoabt@dbg.de *Web Site:* www.dbg.de, pg 211

Die Deutsche Bibliothek (Germany) *Tel:* (069) 1525-0 *Fax:* (069) 1525-1010 *E-mail:* postfach@dbf.ddb.de *Web Site:* www.ddb.de, pg 211

Die Deutsche Bibliothek (Germany) *Tel:* (069) 1525-0 *Fax:* (069) 1525-1010 *E-mail:* info@dbf.ddb.de *Web Site:* www.ddb.de, pg 1507

Deutsche Blinden-Bibliothek (Germany) *Tel:* (06421) 6060 *Fax:* (06421) 606259 *E-mail:* info@blista.de *Web Site:* www.blista.de, pg 211

Deutsche Buch-Gemeinschaft C A Koch's Verlag Nachfolger (Austria) *Tel:* (01) 8123730 *Fax:* (01) 811024, pg 1241

Deutsche Exlibris Gesellschaft ev (Germany) Tel: (0611) 502907 Fax: (0611) 503021 Web Site: www.exlibris-gesellschaft.de, pg 1563

Deutsche Gesellschaft fuer Eisenbahngeschichte eV (Germany) Tel: (02922) 84970 Fax: (02922) 84927 E-mail: info@dgeg.de Web Site: www.dgeg.de, pg 211

Deutsche Gesellschaft fuer Luft-und Raumfahrt Lilienthal Oberth eV (Germany) Tel: (0228) 30 80 5-0 Fax: (0228) 30 80 5-24 E-mail: geschaeftsstelle@ dglr.de Web Site: www.dglr.de, pg 211

Deutsche Gesellschaft fur Informationswissenschaft und Informationspraxis eV (Germany) Tel: (069) 43 03 13 Fax: (069) 49 09 09 6 E-mail: mail@dgi-info.de Web Site: www.dgd.de, pg 1563

Deutsche Landwirtschafts-Gesellschaft VerlagsgesGmbH (Germany) Tel: (069) 24 788-451 Fax: (069) 24 788-484 E-mail: dlg-verlag@dlg-frankfurt.de Web Site: www.dlg-verlag.de, pg 211

Verlag Deutsche Unitarier (Germany) Tel: (0751) 625 96 Fax: (0751) 672 01 E-mail: verlag@unitarier.de Web Site: www.unitarier.de, pg 211

Deutsche Verlags-Anstalt GmbH (DVA) (Germany) Tel: (089) 45554-0 Fax: (089) 45554-100; (089) 45554-111 E-mail: info@dva.de; buch@dva.de Web Site: www.dva.de, pg 211

Deutscher Aerzte-Verlag GmbH (Germany) Tel: (02234) 7011-0 Fax: (02234) 7011-398; (02234) 7011-475 E-mail: zielinka@aerzteverlag.de Web Site: www. aerzteverlag.de, pg 212

Deutscher Apotheker Verlag Dr Roland Schmiedel GmbH & Co (Germany) Tel: (0711) 2582-0 Fax: (0711) 2582-290 E-mail: service@deutscher-apotheker-verlag.de Web Site: www.deutscher-apotheker-verlag.de, pg 212

Deutscher Betriebswirte-Verlag GmbH (Germany) Tel: (07224) 9397-151 Fax: (07224) 9397-905 E-mail: info@betriebswirte-verlag.de Web Site: www. betriebswirte-verlag.de, pg 212

Deutscher Bibliotheksverband eV (DBV) (Germany) Tel: (030) 39 00 14 80; (030) 39 00 14 81 Fax: (030) 39 00 14 84 E-mail: dbv@bibliotheksverband.de Web Site: www.bibliotheksverband.de, pg 1563

Deutscher Buchkreis (Germany) Tel: (07071) 4070-0 Fax: (07071) 4070-26 E-mail: info@grabertverlag.de Web Site: www.hohenrain.de, pg 1242

Deutscher Bundestag Bibliothek (Germany) Tel: (030) 227 32626 Fax: (030) 227 36087 E-mail: bibliothek@ bundestag.de Web Site: www.bundestag.de, pg 1507

Deutscher Drucker Verlagsgesellschaft mbH & Co KG (Germany) Tel: (0711) 448170 Fax: (0711) 442099 E-mail: info@publish.de Web Site: www.publish.de, pg 212

Deutscher EC-Verband (Germany) Tel: (0561) 40950 Fax: (0561) 4095112 E-mail: info.dv@ec-jugend.de Web Site: www.ec-jugend.de, pg 212

Deutscher Fachverlag GmbH (Germany) Tel: (069) 7595-01 Fax: (069) 75952999 E-mail: info@dfv.de Web Site: www.dfv.de, pg 212

Deutscher Gemeindeverlag GmbH (Germany) Tel: (0711) 78630 Fax: (0711) 7863400, pg 212

Deutscher Instituts-Verlag GmbH (Germany) Tel: (0221) 49 81-0 Fax: (0221) 49 81 E-mail: div@iwkoeln.de Web Site: www.divkoeln.de, pg 212

Deutscher Klassiker Verlag (Germany) Tel: (069) 75601-0 Fax: (069) 75601-522 Web Site: www.suhrkamp.de, pg 212

Deutscher Komponisten-Interessenverband eV (Germany) Tel: (030) 84 31 05 80 Fax: (030) 84 31 05 82 E-mail: info@komponistenverband.org Web Site: www.dkiv.allmusic.de, pg 1260

Deutscher Kunstverlag GmbH (Germany) Tel: (089) 121516-0 Fax: (089) 121516-10; (089) 121516-16 E-mail: vertrieb@deutscher-kunstverlag.ccn.de, pg 212

Deutscher Literaturfonds eV (Germany) Tel: (06151) 40930 Fax: (06151) 409333 E-mail: info@ deutscher-literaturfonds.de Web Site: www.deutscher-literaturfonds.de, pg 1394

Deutscher Psychologen Verlag GmbH (DPV) (Germany) Tel: (0228) 987310 Fax: (0228) 641023 E-mail: service@bdp-verband.org Web Site: www.bdp-verband.org, pg 212

Deutscher Sparkassenverlag GmbH (Germany) Tel: (0711) 782-0 Fax: (0711) 782-16 35 E-mail: webredaktion@dsv-gruppe.de Web Site: www. dsv-gruppe.de, pg 212

Deutscher Studien Verlag (Germany) Tel: (06201) 60070 E-mail: info@beltz.de Web Site: www.beltz.de, pg 213

Deutscher Taschenbuch Verlag GmbH & Co KG (dtv) (Germany) Tel: (089) 38167-0 Fax: (089) 346428 E-mail: verlag@dtv.de Web Site: www.dtv.de, pg 213

Deutscher Universitats-Verlag (Germany) Tel: (0611) 7878-0 Fax: (0611) 7878-400 Web Site: www.duv.de; www.gwv-fachverlage.de, pg 213

Deutscher Verband Evangelischer Buchereien eV (Germany) Tel: (0551) 500759-0 Fax: (0551) 704415 E-mail: dveb@dveb.info Web Site: www.dveb.info, pg 1563

Deutscher Verlag fur Grundstoffindustrie GmbH (Germany) Tel: (0711) 8931-0 Fax: (0711) 8931-298 E-mail: kunden.service@thieme.de Web Site: www. thieme.de, pg 213

Deutscher Verlag fur Kunstwissenschaft GmbH (Germany) Tel: (030) 259173589 Fax: (030) 25913537, pg 213

Deutscher Wanderverlag Dr Mair & Schnabel & Co (Germany) Tel: (0711) 455005 Fax: (0711) 4569952, pg 213

Deutscher Wirtschaftsdienst John von Freyend GmbH (Germany) Tel: (0221) 93763-0 Fax: (0221) 93763-99 E-mail: box@dwd-verlag.de Web Site: www.dwd-verlag.de, pg 213

Deutsches Bibliotheksinstitut (Germany) Tel: (030) 410 34-0 Fax: (030) 410 34-100 E-mail: dbilink@dbi-berlin.de Web Site: www.dbi-berlin.de, pg 1563

Deutsches Bucharchiv Muenchen, Institut fur Buchwissenschaften (Germany) Tel: (089) 291951-90; (089) 291951-91 Fax: (089) 291951-95 E-mail: kontakt@bucharchiv.de Web Site: www. bucharchiv.de, pg 213

Deutsches Bucharchiv Muenchen, Institut fur Buchwissenschaften (Germany) Tel: (089) 29151-0; (089) 790 12 20 Fax: (089) 291951-95; (089) 790 14 19 E-mail: kontakt@bucharchiv.de Web Site: www. bucharchiv.de, pg 1507

Deutsches Jugendinstitut (DJI) (Germany) Tel: (089) 62306-0 Fax: (089) 62306-265 E-mail: dji@dji.de Web Site: www.dji.de, pg 213

Les Editions des Deux Coqs d'Or (France) Tel: (01) 43 92 34 55 Fax: (01) 43 92 33 38, pg 158

Deva Wings Publications (Australia) Tel: (03) 5348 1414 Fax: (03) 5348 1414 E-mail: devawings@netconnect. com.au Web Site: www.spacountry.net.au/devawings, pg 20

Development News Ltd (Austria) Tel: (0222) 3880324 Toll Free Tel: (0222) 3880324, pg 49

Institut pour le Developpement Forestier (France) Tel: (01) 40622280 Fax: (01) 45559854 E-mail: paris@association-idf.com, pg 158

Les Devenirs Visuels (France) Tel: (01) 47 70 60 02 Fax: (01) 47 70 60 03, pg 158

Librairie Deves et Chaumet (Mali) Tel: 222784, pg 1317

Perpustakaan Dewan Perwakilan Rakjat - RI (Indonesia) Tel: (021) 5715220; (021) 5715224 Fax: (021) 5715884, pg 1515

Dewan Bahasa dan Pustaka (Brunei Darussalam) Tel: (02) 235501 Fax: (02) 224763 E-mail: Chieflib@ Brunei.bn Web Site: www.kkbs.gov.bn; www.brunei. gov.bn/index.htm; dbp.gov.bn, pg 1494

Dewan Bahasa dan Pustaka (Malaysia) Tel: (03) 21481011 Fax: (03) 21447248 Web Site: www.dbp. gov.my, pg 452

Dewan Bahasa dan Pustaka (Malaysia) Tel: (03) 21481011; (03) 2484211; (03) 2481820 Fax: (03) 2482726; (03) 2142005; (03) 21414109; (03) 2148420 Web Site: www.dbp.gov.my, pg 1397

Dewan Pustaka Islam (Malaysia) Tel: (03) 755 7225 Fax: (03) 755 7871, pg 452

Dexia Bank (Belgium) Tel: (02) 222 54 89 Fax: (02) 222 57 52 E-mail: cultureline@dexia.be Web Site: www. dexia.be/culture, pg 66

Dhaka Book Mart (Bangladesh) Tel: (02) 259173, pg 1291

Dhaka University Library (Bangladesh) Tel: (02) 966-1900 Fax: (02) 865583 E-mail: duregstr@bangla.net Web Site: www.univdhaka.edu, pg 1491

Dharma Edition, Tibetisches Zentrum (Germany) Tel: (040) 6443585 Fax: (040) 6443515 E-mail: tz@ tibet.de Web Site: www.tibet.de, pg 213

The Dharmasthiti Buddist Institute Ltd (Hong Kong) Tel: 2760 8878 Fax: 2760 1223, pg 314

Dhillon Publishers Ltd (Kenya) Tel: (020) 552566; (020) 537533 Fax: (020) 537553 E-mail: dhillon@wananchi. com, pg 430

Di Baio Editore SpA (Italy) Tel: (02) 6692254 Fax: (02) 6709257 Web Site: www.dibaio.com, pg 381

Edition Dia (Germany) Tel: (030) 6235021; (030) 6235022 Fax: (030) 6235023 E-mail: info@editiondia. de Web Site: www.editiondia.de, pg 213

Diachronikes Ekdoseis (Greece) Tel: 2107213225; 2107213387 Fax: 2107246180, pg 303

Editorial Diagonal del grup 62 (Spain) Tel: (093) 4437100 Fax: (093) 4437129, pg 574

Diagonal-Verlag GbR Rink-Schweer (Germany) Tel: (06421) 681936 Fax: (06421) 681944 E-mail: info@diagonal-verlag.de Web Site: www. diagonal-verlag.de, pg 213

The Diagram Group (United Kingdom) Tel: (020) 7482 3633 Fax: (020) 7482 4932 E-mail: diagramuis@aol. com, pg 1174

Diagram Visual Information Ltd (United Kingdom) Tel: (020) 7482 3633 Fax: (020) 7482 4932 E-mail: diagramvis@aol.com, pg 682, 1130

Dialog-Verlag GmbH (Germany) Tel: (040) 7111424 Fax: (040) 7101267, pg 213

Diamond Comics (P) Ltd (India) Tel: 9810003062 (Mobile) Fax: (0120) 2401093; (0120) 2401094; (0120) 2401095; (0120) 2401073 E-mail: comicsdiamond@mantraonline.com Web Site: www.comicsdiamond.com, pg 330

Diamond Inc (Japan) Tel: (03) 5778-7232 Fax: (03) 5778-6612 Web Site: www.diamond.co.jp, pg 413

PT Dian Rakyat (Indonesia) Tel: (021) 460-4444, pg 351

Diana Argentina SA, Editorial (Argentina) Tel: (011) 4922-5035; (011) 4922-5036 Fax: (011) 4922-5035; (011) 4922-5036 E-mail: to_dianaarg@sinectis.com.ar, pg 5

Editorial Diana SA de CV (Mexico) Tel: (055) 5089-1220 Fax: (052) 5089-1230 E-mail: 4sales@diana. com.mx; editors@diana.com.mx Web Site: www.diana. com.mx, pg 460

Diario la Voz del Interior (Argentina) Tel: (011) 4382-2267 Fax: (011) 3822508 E-mail: info@nueva.com.ar, pg 5

Diavlos (Greece) Tel: 2103631169 Fax: 210 3617473 E-mail: info@diavlos-books.gr Web Site: www.diavlos-books.gr, pg 303

Diavlos (Greece) Tel: 2103631169; 2103625315 Fax: 2103617473 E-mail: info@diavlos-books.gr Web Site: www.diavlos-books.gr, pg 1302

Ediciones Diaz de Santos SA (Spain) *Tel:* (091) 7434890 *Fax:* (091) 7434023 *E-mail:* librerias@diazdesantos.es *Web Site:* www.diazdesantos.es, pg 574

Diaz de Santos SA - Libreria Cientifico-Tecnica (Spain) *Tel:* (091) 743 48 90 *Fax:* (091) 743 40 23 *E-mail:* librerias@diazdesantos.es *Web Site:* www.diazdesantos.es, pg 1333

Editorial Ruy Diaz SAEIC (Argentina) *Tel:* (011) 4567-4918; (011) 4567-2865 *Fax:* (011) 4567-4918 *E-mail:* editorial@ruydiaz.com.ar *Web Site:* www.ruydiaz.com.ar, pg 5

The Dickens Fellowship (United Kingdom) *Tel:* (020) 7405 2127 *Fax:* (020) 7831 5175 *E-mail:* dickens.fellowship@btinternet.com *Web Site:* www.dickens.fellowship.btinternet.co.uk, pg 1401

Dickson Price Publishers Ltd (United Kingdom) *Tel:* (01795) 597800 *Fax:* (01795) 597800, pg 683

Didaco Comunicacion y Didactica, SA (Spain) *Tel:* (093) 237 64 00 *Fax:* (093) 218 92 77 *E-mail:* didaco@cambrabcn.es *Web Site:* www.didaco.es, pg 574

Didactica Editora (Portugal) *Tel:* (021) 301 17 31 *Fax:* (021) 273 04 23 *E-mail:* didacticaeditora@mail.telepac.pt; info@didactica.pt *Web Site:* viriato.viatecla.pt/didactica, pg 525

Editura Didactica si Pedagogica (Romania) *Tel:* (01) 3150043 *Fax:* (01) 3122885 *E-mail:* edpdirector@mail.codecnet.ro, pg 534

Organizzazione Didattica Editoriale Ape (Italy) *Tel:* (055) 572584 *Fax:* (055) 578243, pg 381

Diderot sro (Czech Republic) *Tel:* (02) 55707711; (02) 55707703 *Fax:* (02) 55707700 *E-mail:* redakce@diderot.cz; obchod@bp.diderot.cz *Web Site:* www.diderot.cz, pg 123

Die Deutsche Bibliothek/Deutsche Bucherei Leipzig (Germany) *Tel:* (0341) 22710 *Fax:* (0341) 2271444 *E-mail:* info@dbl.ddb.de *Web Site:* www.ddb.de, pg 1507

Die Verlag H Schafer GmbH (Germany) *Tel:* (06172) 95830 *Fax:* (06172) 71288 *E-mail:* dieverlag@t-online.de, pg 213

Dienst Bibliotheek en Archief (Netherlands) *Tel:* (070) 353 4401; (070) 353 4479 *Fax:* (070) 353 4479 *Web Site:* www.bibliotheekdenhaag.nl/dob/, pg 1529

Diesterweg, Moritz Verlag (Germany) *Tel:* (069) 42081-0 *Fax:* (069) 42081-200 *Web Site:* www.diesterweg.de, pg 214

Sammlung Dieterich Verlagsgesellschaft mbH (Germany) *Tel:* (0341) 9954600 *Fax:* (0341) 9954620 *E-mail:* info@aufbau-verlag.de *Web Site:* www.aufbau-verlag.de, pg 214

Dieterichsche Verlagsbuchhandlung Mainz (Germany) *Tel:* (06131) 573276 *Fax:* (06131) 571061 *E-mail:* DVB-mainz@t-online.de *Web Site:* www.dvb-mainz.de, pg 214

Maximilian Dietrich Verlag (Germany) *Tel:* (08331) 2853 *Fax:* (08331) 490364 *E-mail:* dietrich-verlag@freenet.de *Web Site:* www.maximilian-dietrich-verlag.de/index.htm, pg 214

Dietrich zu Klampen Verlag (Germany) *Tel:* (5041) 801133 *Fax:* (5041) 801336 *E-mail:* info@zuklampen.de *Web Site:* www.dan4u.de/zuklampen, pg 214

Dietz GmbH (Austria) *Tel:* (02236) 22596 *Fax:* (02236) 47127, pg 1290

Verlag J H W Dietz Nachf GmbH (Germany) *Tel:* (0228) 23 80 83 *Fax:* (0228) 23 41 04 *E-mail:* info@dietz-verlag.de *Web Site:* www.dietz-verlag.de, pg 214

Dietz Verlag Berlin GmbH (Germany) *Tel:* (030) 24 00 92 90 *Fax:* (030) 24 00 95 90 *E-mail:* info@dietzverlag.de *Web Site:* www.dietzverlag.de, pg 214

DIFEL - Difusao Editorial SA (Portugal) *Tel:* (021) 537677 *Fax:* (021) 545886 *E-mail:* difel.as@mail.telepac.pt, pg 525

Editions de la Difference (France) *Tel:* (01) 53 38 85 38 *Fax:* (01) 42 45 34 94 *E-mail:* editions-de-la-difference@wanadoo.fr *Web Site:* www.ladifference.fr, pg 158

Edition Diffusion de Livre au Maroc (Morocco) *Tel:* (02) 442375; (02) 442376; (02) 445986 *Fax:* (02) 313565 *E-mail:* info@eddif.net.ma, pg 471

Difros Publications (Greece) *Tel:* 2103610811, pg 303

Difusao Cultural (Portugal) *Tel:* (021) 7599364 *Fax:* (021) 7594418, pg 525

Wydawnictwo DiG (Poland) *Tel:* (022) 839 0838 *Fax:* (022) 828-00-96 *E-mail:* biuro@dig.com.pl *Web Site:* www.dig.com.pl, pg 517

Digital Publishing (Germany) *Tel:* (089) 747482-0 *Fax:* (089) 74792308 *E-mail:* info@digitalpublishing.de *Web Site:* www.digitalpublishing.de, pg 214

Digma Publications (South Africa) *Tel:* (011) 8834854 *Fax:* (011) 8836540, pg 559

Dilagro SA (Spain) *Tel:* (0973) 24 51 00; (0973) 23 34 80 *Fax:* (0973) 23 64 13 *Web Site:* www.dilagro.com, pg 574

Le Dilettante (France) *Tel:* (01) 43 37 98 98 *Fax:* (01) 43 37 06 10 *E-mail:* info@ledilettante.com *Web Site:* www.ledilettante.com, pg 158

DILIA (Czech Republic) *Tel:* (02) 83891587 *Fax:* (02) 826348; (02) 83893599; (02) 83890598; (02) 83890597 *E-mail:* chabr@dilia.cz *Web Site:* www.dilia.cz, pg 1119

Dilicom (France) *Tel:* (01) 43254335 *Fax:* (01) 43297688 *E-mail:* contact@dilicom.net *Web Site:* www.dilicom.net, pg 158

Dilicom (France) *Tel:* (01) 43 25 43 35 *Fax:* (01) 43 29 76 88 *E-mail:* contact@dilicom.net *Web Site:* www.dilicom.net, pg 1258

Diligentia-Uitgeverij (Belgium) *Tel:* (052) 44 45 11 *Fax:* (052) 44 45 22 *E-mail:* diligentia.book@planetinternet.be, pg 66

Dillons, The Bookstore (United Kingdom) *Tel:* (0121) 6314333 *Fax:* (0121) 6432441 *E-mail:* bhamnew@dillons.eunet.co.uk, pg 1341

Dillons City Business Book Store (United Kingdom) *Tel:* (020) 7628 7479 *Fax:* (020) 7628 7871 *E-mail:* loncbus@dillons.eunet.co.uk, pg 1341

Editorial Dimensao Ltda (Brazil) *Tel:* (021) 233-2764 *Fax:* (021) 233-2570 *E-mail:* memoria@ig.com.br, pg 80

Dimenze 2 Plus 2 Praha (Czech Republic) *Tel:* (02) 231 11 41 *Fax:* (02) 231 11 41 *Web Site:* www.dub.cz/dimenze.html, pg 123

Dinalivro (Portugal) *Tel:* (021) 670 348 *Fax:* (021) 60 84 89 *E-mail:* dinalivro@ip.pt, pg 526

Dinapress (Portugal) *Tel:* (021) 608992 *Fax:* (021) 608992 *E-mail:* dinalivro@ip.pt, pg 1328

Dinastindo (Indonesia) *Tel:* (021) 7250002; (021) 72799307 *Fax:* (021) 7262145 *E-mail:* dinastindo@yahoo.com, pg 351

Dinsic Publicacions Musicals (Spain) *Tel:* (093) 318 06 05 *Fax:* (093) 412 05 01 *E-mail:* dinsic@dinsic.com *Web Site:* www.dinsic.com/, pg 574

Diogenes Verlag AG (Switzerland) *Tel:* (01) 2548511 *Fax:* (01) 2528407 *E-mail:* info@diogenes.ch *Web Site:* www.diogenes.ch, pg 617

Dion (Greece) *Tel:* 2310265042 *Fax:* 2310 265083 *E-mail:* info@psarasbooks.gr *Web Site:* www.psarasbooks.gr, pg 1303

Dioptra Publishing (Greece) *Tel:* 2103302828 *Fax:* 2103302882 *E-mail:* info@dioptra.gov *Web Site:* www.dioptra.gr, pg 303

Diotima Presse (Austria) *Tel:* (043) 2747-8528 *Fax:* (043) 2747-8528 *E-mail:* buecher4web@diotimapresse.com *Web Site:* www.diotimapresse.com, pg 50

Dipak Kumar Guha (India) *Tel:* 9810094052 *Fax:* (011) 2-550-0998 *E-mail:* dkguha@eth.net; dkginfo@hgcbroadband.com (Hong Kong office), pg 1122

Diponegoro CV (Indonesia) *Tel:* (022) 5201215 *Fax:* (022) 5201215, pg 351

Ediciones Diputacion de Salamanca (Spain) *Tel:* (0923) 29 31 00 *Fax:* (0923) 29 31 29 *E-mail:* informacion@dipsanet.es *Web Site:* www.dipsanet.es, pg 574

Diputacion Provincial de Cordoba (Spain) *Tel:* (0957) 211392; (0957) 211323 *Fax:* (0957) 211387, pg 574

Diputacion Provincial de Malaga (Spain) *Tel:* (0952) 069 207 *Fax:* (0952) 069 215 *E-mail:* cedma@cedma.com *Web Site:* cedma.com, pg 574

Diputacion Provincial de Sevilla, Servicio de Publicaciones (Spain) *Tel:* (095) 4550029 *Fax:* (095) 4550050 *E-mail:* caba174@dipusevilla.es *Web Site:* www.dipusevilla.es, pg 574

Direccao Geral Familia (Portugal) *Tel:* (021) 8470430 *Fax:* (021) 8491516, pg 526

Direccao Nacional de Geologia (Centro de Documentacao) (Mozambique) *Tel:* (01) 305399 *Fax:* (01) 429216 *E-mail:* geologia@zebra.uem.mz, pg 1528

Direccao Provincial Servicos de Geologia e Minas de Angola Biblioteca (Angola) *Tel:* (02) 323024 *Fax:* (02) 321655, pg 1487

Direccion General de Bibliotecas de la Universidad Nacional Autonoma de Mexico (Mexico) *Tel:* (055) 5622 1603 *Fax:* (055) 5616 0664 *E-mail:* webdgb@dgb.unam.mx *Web Site:* www.dgbiblio.unam.mx, pg 1527

Biblioteca de la Direccion General de Cultura (Bolivia), pg 1493

Direccion General de Publicaciones CNCA Coordinacion Juridica (Mexico) *Tel:* (05) 605-85-89 (ext 5127-149) *Fax:* (05) 605-87-31, pg 460

Direction de la Recherche Scientifique et Techniques (Guinea) *Tel:* 46 10 10, pg 1564

Direction des Archives Nationales, Bibliotheque Publique et Centre du Documentation (Mauritania) *Tel:* 2523 1732, pg 1526

Direction des Archives Nationales du Benin (Benin) *Tel:* 21 30 79 *Fax:* 21 30 79, pg 1492

Direction Generale des Archives Nationales, de la Bibliotheque Nationale et de la Documentation Gabonaise (DGABD) (Gabon) *Tel:* 732543; (0241) 730 239 *Fax:* 730239, pg 1506

Direction Generale des Services de Bibliotheques, Archives et Documentation (Congo) *Tel:* 833 485 *Fax:* 832 253, pg 1560

Directory & Database Publishers Association (United Kingdom) *Tel:* (020) 7405 0836 *Fax:* (020) 7404 4167 *Web Site:* www.directory-publisher.co.uk, pg 1281

Direzione Generale Archivi (Italy) *Tel:* (06) 4742177 *Fax:* (06) 4742177 *E-mail:* studi@archivi.beniculturali.it *Web Site:* www.archivi.beniculturali.it, pg 382

Editions Dis Voir (France) *Tel:* (01) 48 87 07 09 *Fax:* (01) 48 87 07 14 *E-mail:* disvoir@aol.com *Web Site:* www.disvoir.com, pg 158

Disal S/A Distribuidores Associados de Livros (Brazil) *Tel:* (011) 3226-3111 *Fax:* (011) 0800-7707106 *E-mail:* disal@disal.com.br *Web Site:* www.disal.com.br, pg 1293

Discordia Verlagsgesellschaft mbH (Germany) *Tel:* (02291) 911024 *Fax:* (02291) 911925, pg 214

Discovery Walking Guides Ltd (United Kingdom) *Tel:* (01604) 244869 *Fax:* (01604) 752576 *Web Site:* www.walking.demon.co.uk, pg 683

Diseno Editorial SA (Spain) *Tel:* (091) 5533168, pg 574

Disha Prakashan (India) *Tel:* 7108832, pg 330

Edition Diskord (Germany) *Tel:* (07071) 40102 *Fax:* (07071) 44710 *E-mail:* ed.diskord@t-online.de *Web Site:* www.edition-diskord.de, pg 214

1647

Editorial Dismar (Uruguay) *Tel:* (02) 407946, pg 772

Disney Hachette Edition (France) *Tel:* (01) 43 92 38 50 *Fax:* (01) 43 92 38 61, pg 158

Distique (France) *Tel:* (02) 3730 5700 *Fax:* (02) 3730 5712, pg 1299

Distri Cultural Lda (Portugal) *Tel:* (021) 942 53 94 *Fax:* (021) 941 98 93; (021) 942 52 14, pg 526

Distri Cultural Lda (Portugal) *Tel:* (021) 942 53 94 *Fax:* (021) 941 98 93 *E-mail:* cultural@electroliber.pt, pg 1328

Distri Lojas-Sociedade Livreira Lda (Portugal) *Tel:* (021) 940 65 00 *Fax:* (021) 942 59 90, pg 1328

Distribuidora Editora Vral, Lda (Portugal) *Tel:* (01) 4393978 *Fax:* (01) 4373558, pg 1328

Distribuidora Importadora Durand SA (Peru) *Tel:* (014) 4452113 *Fax:* (014) 4463190, pg 1325

Editora e Distribuidora Irradiacao Cultural Ltda (Brazil) *Tel:* (021) 5773522 *Fax:* (021) 5771249 *E-mail:* irradcult@ax.apc.org, pg 80

Distribuidoras Unidas SA (Colombia) *Tel:* 413 8079 *Fax:* 413 8502 *E-mail:* ibernal@disunidas.com.co *Web Site:* www.disunidas.com.co, pg 1296

Distripress (Switzerland) *Tel:* (01) 202 41 21 *Fax:* (01) 202 10 25 *E-mail:* info@distripress.ch *Web Site:* www.distripress.ch, pg 1275

Divadelni Ustav (Czech Republic) *Tel:* (02) 24809111 *Fax:* (02) 24811452 *E-mail:* divadelni.ustav@czech-theatre.cz *Web Site:* www.divadelni-ustav.cz, pg 123

Diversity Management (Australia) *Tel:* (02) 9130 4305 *Fax:* (02) 9365 1426, pg 1119

Divyanand Verlags GmbH (Germany) *Tel:* (07764) 93 97-0 *Fax:* (07764) 93 97-39 *E-mail:* info@sandila.de *Web Site:* www.sandila.de, pg 214

The Diwan Library, Ministry of Education (Iraq) *Tel:* (01) 8872949, pg 1516

Dix (United States) *Tel:* 315-478-4700 *Fax:* 315-703-0119 *Web Site:* www.dixtype.com, pg 1219

DIY Publishing (United Kingdom) *Tel:* (020) 7586 4499 *Fax:* (020) 7722 1068 *E-mail:* info@diypublishing.com *Web Site:* www.diypublishing.com, pg 683

Djambatan PT (Indonesia) *Tel:* (021) 7203199 *Fax:* (021) 7208562, pg 351

Djof Publishing Jurist-og Okonomforbundets Forlag (Denmark) *Tel:* 39 13 55 00 *Fax:* 39 13 55 55 *E-mail:* fl@djoef.dk *Web Site:* www.djoef-forlag.dk, pg 130

DK Agencies (P) Ltd (India) *Tel:* (011) 2535-7104; (011) 2535-7105 *Fax:* (011) 2535-7103 *E-mail:* custserv@dkagencies.com *Web Site:* www.dkagencies.com, pg 1305

DK Book House Co Ltd (Thailand) *Tel:* (02) 721-9190 *Fax:* (02) 247-1033, pg 640

DK Printworld (P) Ltd (India) *Tel:* (011) 25453975; (011) 25466019 *Fax:* (011) 25465926 *E-mail:* dkprintworld@vsnl.net, pg 330

DLV Deutscher Landwirtschaftsverlag GmbH (Germany) *Tel:* (0511) 678 06-0 *Fax:* (0511) 678 06-110 *E-mail:* dlv.hannover@dlv.de *Web Site:* www.dlv.de, pg 214

DMG Business Media Ltd (United Kingdom) *Tel:* (01737) 768611 *Fax:* (01737) 855477 *Web Site:* www.dmg.co.uk, pg 683

Dnipro (Ukraine) *Tel:* (044) 224-31-82 *Fax:* (044) 224-41-57, pg 649

DNP America LLC (United States) *Tel:* 212-503-1060 *Fax:* 212-286-1505 *Web Site:* www.dnp.co.jp/, pg 1156, 1177

DNP America LLC (United States) *Tel:* 212-503-1074 *Fax:* 212-286-1505 *Web Site:* www.dnp.co.jp/, pg 1219

DNP America LLC (United States) *Tel:* 212-503-1060 *Fax:* 212-286-1505 *Web Site:* www.dnp.co.jp/, pg 1230

Doaba Publications (India) *Tel:* (011) 3274669; (011) 3259753, pg 330

Ludwig Doblinger (Bernhard Herzmansky) Musikverlag KG (Austria) *Tel:* (01) 515 03-0 *Fax:* (01) 515 03-51 *E-mail:* music@doblinger.at *Web Site:* www.doblinger.at, pg 50

Dobraya Kniga Publishers (Russian Federation) *Tel:* (095) 200 2078; (095) 200 1681 *Fax:* (095) 200 2094 *E-mail:* mail@dkniga.ru *Web Site:* www.dkniga.ru, pg 539

Dobro Publishing (United Kingdom) *Tel:* (020) 8346 4010 *E-mail:* dobropublishing@aol.com *Web Site:* www.drsandradelroy.com, pg 683

Dobunshoin Publishers Co (Japan) *Tel:* (03) 3812-7777 *Fax:* (03) 3812-7792 *E-mail:* dobun@dobun.co.jp *Web Site:* www.dobun.co.jp, pg 413

DOC 6, SA (Spain) *Tel:* (093) 215 43 13 *Fax:* (093) 488 36 21 *E-mail:* mail@doc6.es *Web Site:* www.doc6.es, pg 575

Ediciones Doce Calles SL (Spain) *Tel:* (091) 8924201; (091) 8924218 *Fax:* (091) 925 137 060 *E-mail:* docecalles@infonegocio.com, pg 575

Docendo Finland Oy (Finland) *Tel:* (014) 339 7700 *Fax:* (014) 339 7755 *E-mail:* info@docendo.fi *Web Site:* www.docendo.fi, pg 141

Documenta CV (Belgium) *Tel:* (02) 5102313 *Fax:* (02) 5102497, pg 66

La Documentation Francaise (France) *Tel:* (01) 40 15 70 00 *Fax:* (01) 40 15 67 83 *E-mail:* contact@ladocumentationfrancaise.fr *Web Site:* www.ladocfrancaise.gouv.fr, pg 158

La Documentation Francaise (France) *Tel:* (01) 40 15 71 10 *Fax:* (01) 40 15 67 83 *E-mail:* libparis@ladocumentationfrancaise.fr *Web Site:* www.ladocumentationfrancaise.fr, pg 1505

Bibliotheque de Documentation Internationale Contemporaine (BDIC) (France) *Tel:* (01) 40 97 79 00 *Fax:* (01) 40 97 79 40 *E-mail:* courrier@bdic.fr *Web Site:* www.bdic.fr/, pg 1505

Documentation Research & Training Centre (DRTC) (India) *Tel:* (080) 8483002 (ext 490); (080) 8483003 (ext 490); (080) 8483004 (ext 490); (080) 8483006 (ext 490) *Fax:* (080) 8484265 *E-mail:* drtc@isibang.ac.in *Web Site:* www.drtc.isibang.ac.in, pg 1564

Dodoni Publications (Greece) *Tel:* 210 3636312; 2103637973 *Fax:* 2103637067 *E-mail:* dodoni@elea.gr, pg 303

Doecker Verlag GmbH & Co KG (Austria) *Tel:* (01) 7159200 *Fax:* (01) 715920076 *E-mail:* doecker@ping.at, pg 50

Dogakusha Inc (Japan) *Tel:* (03) 3816-7011 *Fax:* (03) 3816-7044 *E-mail:* eigyoubu@dogakusha.co.jp *Web Site:* www.dogakusha.co.jp, pg 413

Daniel Doglioli (Italy) *Tel:* (0382) 529317 *Fax:* (0382) 529317 *Web Site:* www.filastrocche.it/contempo/daniele/daniele.asp, pg 1123

Dohosha Publishing Co Ltd (Japan) *Tel:* (03) 5276 0831 *Fax:* (03) 5276 0840, pg 413

Christoph Dohr (Germany) *Tel:* (0221) 70 70 02 *Fax:* (0221) 70 43 95 *E-mail:* info@dohr.de *Web Site:* www.dohr.de, pg 214

Doin Editeurs (France) *Tel:* (01) 41 29 99 99 *Fax:* (01) 41 29 77 05, pg 158

Editura DOINA SRL (Romania) *Tel:* (01) 3228107 *Fax:* (01) 3227541, pg 534

Doko Video Ltd (Israel) *Tel:* (03) 5753555 *Fax:* (03) 5753189 *E-mail:* dokoa@ibm.net, pg 363

Pusat Dokumentasi dan Informasi Ilmiah (Indonesia) *Tel:* (021) 5733465; (021) 5733466; (021) 5250719 *Fax:* (021) 5733467 *E-mail:* info@pdii.lipi.go.id, pg 1515

Dokumentationsstelle fur neuere Osterreichische Literatur (Austria) *Tel:* (01) 526 20 44-0 *Fax:* (01) 526 20 44-30 *E-mail:* info@literaturhaus.at *Web Site:* www.literaturhaus.at, pg 1558

Dokumente Verlag Versandbuchhandlung Librairie (Germany) *Tel:* (0781) 923699-0 *Fax:* (0781) 923699-70 *E-mail:* info@dokumente-verlag.de *Web Site:* www.dokumente-verlag.de, pg 1300

Dokuz Eylul Universitesi (Turkey) *Tel:* (0232) 498 5050-51 *Fax:* (0232) 464 8135 *E-mail:* hukuk@deu.edu.tr *Web Site:* www.deu.edu.tr, pg 645

Dolling und Galitz Verlag GmbH (Germany) *Tel:* (040) 3893515 *Fax:* (040) 38904945 *E-mail:* doellingundgalitzverlag@compuserve.com *Web Site:* www.doellingundgalitz.com, pg 215

Wydawnictwo Dolnoslaskie (Poland) *Tel:* (071) 328 89 54; (071) 328 89 52; (071) 328 89 51; (071) 328 82 06 *Fax:* (071) 328 89 54 *E-mail:* sekretariat@wd.wroc.pl; wyd-dol@mikrozet.wroc.pl, pg 517

Dolphin Books (China) *Tel:* (010) 68326332 *Fax:* (010) 8317390, pg 103

Dolphin Press Group Ltd (Bulgaria) *Tel:* (056) 844 044 *Fax:* (056) 844 077 *E-mail:* postmaster@dolphin-press.com *Web Site:* www.dolphin-press.com, pg 93

Dolphin Publications (India) *Tel:* (022) 6490184 *Fax:* (022) 6233674, pg 330

Dom, Izdatel'stvo sovetskogo deskkogo fonda im & I Lenina (Russian Federation) *Tel:* (095) 9236661 *Fax:* (095) 9285322, pg 539

Dom Ksiazki, Panstwowe Przedesiebiorstwo (Poland) *Tel:* (022) 826 8559 *Fax:* (022) 826 7117 *E-mail:* info@domksiazki.pl *Web Site:* www.domksiazki.pl, pg 1327

Dom Techniky Zvazu Slovenskych Vedeckotechnickych Spolocnosti Ltd (Slovakia) *Tel:* (037) 7721102; (037) 7721103 *Fax:* (037) 7721102 *E-mail:* zsvts@rainslde.sk, pg 555

Dom Wydawniczy Bellona (Poland) *Tel:* (022) 620 42 71; (022) 652 2765; (022) 45 70 306 *Fax:* (022) 620 42 71; (022) 652 2765; (022) 45 70 306 *E-mail:* handel@bellona.pl *Web Site:* ksiegarnia.bellona.pl, pg 518

Ekdoseis Domi AE (Greece) *Tel:* 2103637389; 2103672056 *Fax:* 2103601782, pg 303

Domingos Castro (Portugal) *Tel:* (043) 332920 *Fax:* (043) 27406, pg 1328

Dominican Publications (Ireland) *Tel:* (01) 872-1611; (01) 873-1355 *Fax:* (01) 873-1760 *E-mail:* sales@dominicanpublications.com *Web Site:* www.dominicanpublications.com, pg 356

Dominie (Australia) *Tel:* (02) 9050201 *Fax:* (02) 9055209, pg 1288

agenda Verlag Thomas Dominikowski (Germany) *Tel:* (0251) 79 96 10 *Fax:* (0251) 79 95 19 *E-mail:* info@agenda.de *Web Site:* www.agenda.de, pg 215

Domino Verlag, Guenther Brinek GmbH (Germany) *Tel:* (089) 179130 *E-mail:* info@domino-verlag.de *Web Site:* www.domino-verlag.de, pg 215

Domowina Verlag GmbH (Germany) *Tel:* (03591) 5770 *Fax:* (03591) 577243 *E-mail:* domowinaverlag@t-online.de *Web Site:* www.buchhandel.de/domowinaverlag, pg 215

Domus Academy (Italy) *Tel:* (02) 42414001 *Fax:* (02) 4222525 *E-mail:* info@domusacademy.it *Web Site:* www.domusacademy.com, pg 382

Editoriale Domus SpA (Italy) *Tel:* (02) 82472 1 *E-mail:* editorialedomus@edidomus.it *Web Site:* www.edidomus.it, pg 382

Editorial Don Bosco (Bolivia) *Tel:* (02) 357755; (02) 371149 *Fax:* (02) 362822, pg 75

Ediciones Don Bosco Argentina (Argentina) *Tel:* (011) 4981-7314; (011) 4981-1388 *Fax:* (011) 4958-1506 *E-mail:* e.d.b.sofrasa@interlink.com.ar, pg 5

Ediciones Don Bosco SA de C (Mexico) *Tel:* (05) 3963349, pg 460

Don Bosco Verlag (Germany) *Tel:* (089) 48008300 *Fax:* (089) 48008309 *Web Site:* www.donbosco.de, pg 215

Donald Duck's Bokklubb (Norway) *Tel:* 24051010 *Fax:* 24051099 *E-mail:* post@damm.no *Web Site:* www.dammbokklubb.no, pg 1245

John Donald Publishers Ltd (United Kingdom) *Tel:* (0131) 668 4371 *Fax:* (0131) 668 4466 *E-mail:* info@birlinn.co.uk *Web Site:* www.birlinn.co.uk, pg 683

Donat Verlag (Germany) *Tel:* (0421) 274886 *Fax:* (0421) 275106 *E-mail:* donatverlag@excite.de, pg 215

Buchgemeinschaft Donauland Kremayr & Scheriau (Austria) *Tel:* (01) 811 02 348 *Fax:* (01) 811 02 680 *E-mail:* donauland@donauland.at *Web Site:* www.donauland.at, pg 1241

Dong-A Publishing & Printing Co Ltd (Republic of Korea) *Tel:* (02) 866-8800 *Fax:* (02) 862-0410, pg 435

Dong Hwa Publishing Co (Republic of Korea) *Tel:* (02) 7135411; (02) 7135415 *Fax:* (02) 7017041, pg 435

Dongguk University Central Library (Republic of Korea) *Tel:* (02) 2260-3114 *Fax:* (02) 2277-1274 *E-mail:* dong0104@dongguk.edu *Web Site:* lib.dgu.ac.kr; www.dongguk.edu, pg 1522

Donhead Publishing Ltd (United Kingdom) *Tel:* (01747) 828422 *Fax:* (01747) 828522 *E-mail:* sales@donhead.com *Web Site:* www.donhead.com, pg 683

Ad Donker (Pty) Ltd (South Africa) *Tel:* (011) 622-2900 *Fax:* (011) 622-7610, pg 559

Uitgeversmaatschappij Ad Donker BV (Netherlands) *Tel:* (010) 4363009 *Fax:* (010) 4362963 *E-mail:* donker@bart.nl *Web Site:* www.uitgeverijdonker.nl, pg 477

R R Donnelley (United Kingdom) *Tel:* (01423) 796100; (01423) 866132 (ISDN) *Fax:* (01423) 796101 *E-mail:* gms.sales@rrd.com *Web Site:* www.rrdonnelley.co.uk, pg 1215

Editorial Donostiarra SA (Spain) *Tel:* (0943) 215 737; (0943) 213 011 *Fax:* (0943) 219 521 *E-mail:* info@donostiarra.com *Web Site:* www.donostiarra.com, pg 575

Doplnek (Czech Republic) *Tel:* (05) 452-424-55 *Fax:* (05) 452-424-55 *E-mail:* doplnek@doplnek.cz *Web Site:* www.doplnek.cz, pg 123

Dorikos Publishing House (Greece) *Tel:* 2106454726 *Fax:* 2103301866, pg 304

Dorleta SA (Spain) *Tel:* (094) 427 3880 *Fax:* (094) 427 4512 *E-mail:* dorletoi@sarenet.es, pg 575

Dorling Kindersley Ltd (United Kingdom) *Tel:* (020) 7010 3000 *Fax:* (020) 7010 6060 *E-mail:* customer.service@dk.com *Web Site:* www.dk.com, pg 683

Verlagsgruppe Dornier GmbH (Germany) *Tel:* (0711) 78803-0 *Fax:* (0711) 78803-10 *E-mail:* info@verlagsgruppe-dornier.de *Web Site:* www.verlagsgruppe-dornier.de, pg 215

The Dorothy L Sayers Society (United Kingdom) *Tel:* (01273) 833444 *Fax:* (01273) 835988 *E-mail:* info@sayers.org.uk *Web Site:* www.sayers.org.uk, pg 1401

Dorriston Publishers Ltd (United Kingdom) *Tel:* (020) 7272 2722 *Fax:* (020) 7272 2774, pg 1153

Dosmil Editora (Colombia) *Tel:* (01) 2694800, pg 110

Editorial Dossat SA (Spain) *Tel:* (091) 3694011 *Fax:* (091) 3691398, pg 575

Les Dossiers d'Aquitaine (France) *Tel:* (05) 56 91 84 98 *Fax:* (05) 56 91 64 92 *E-mail:* ddabx@wanadoo.fr *Web Site:* www.ddabordeaux.com, pg 159

Dost Kitabevi Yayinlari (Turkey) *Tel:* (0312) 418 8772 *Fax:* (0312) 419 9397, pg 645

Dost Yayinlari (Turkey) *Tel:* (0212) 245 31 41 *Fax:* (0212) 243 02 78, pg 645

Doubleday New Zealand Ltd, Book Club Division (New Zealand) *Tel:* (09) 4782846 *Fax:* (09) 4781609 *Web Site:* www.doubleday.com.au, pg 1244

Doubleday New Zealand Ltd (New Zealand) *Tel:* (09) 4782846; (09) 4792200 (member service hotline) *E-mail:* membercare@doubledayclubs.co.nz, pg 491

Doyle Graphics (Ireland) *Tel:* (0506) 21970 *Fax:* (0506) 51323, pg 1170

Ediciones Doyma SA (Spain) *Tel:* (093) 2000 711 *Fax:* (093) 2091 136 *Web Site:* www.doyma.es, pg 575

Drake Educational Associates Ltd (United Kingdom) *Tel:* (029) 2056 0333 *Fax:* (029) 2056 0313 *E-mail:* info@drakeav.com *Web Site:* www.drakegroup.co.uk, pg 683

Drake Educational Associates Ltd (United Kingdom) *Tel:* (029) 2056 0333 *Fax:* (029) 2055 4909 *E-mail:* info@drakeav.com *Web Site:* www.drakegroup.co.uk; www.drakeed.com, pg 1130

Dramatic Lines Publishers (United Kingdom) *Tel:* (020) 8296 9502 *Fax:* (020) 8296 9503 *E-mail:* mail@dramaticlinespublishers.co.uk *Web Site:* www.dramaticlines.co.uk, pg 683

Drammen Folkebibliotek (Norway) *Tel:* 32046303 *Fax:* 32046453 *E-mail:* drm@drammen.folkebibl.no *Web Site:* www.drammen.kommune.no/bibliotek, pg 1532

Dreamland Editeur (France) *Tel:* (01) 53 20 46 66 *Fax:* (01) 53 20 46 67 *E-mail:* dreamland@nous.fr, pg 159

Dreamland Publications (India) *Tel:* (011) 25106050; (011) 25435657 *Fax:* (011) 25428283 *E-mail:* dreamland@vsnl.com *Web Site:* www.dreamlandpublications.com, pg 330

Drei Brunnen Verlag GmbH & Co (Germany) *Tel:* (0711) 86020 *Fax:* (0711) 860229 *E-mail:* mail@drei-brunnen-verlag.de *Web Site:* www.drei-brunnen-verlag.de, pg 215

Drei-D-World und Foto-World Verlag und Vertrieb (Switzerland) *Tel:* (061) 3013081 *Fax:* (094) 3133862 *E-mail:* gah@swissonline.ch, pg 617

Drei Eichen Verlag Manuel Kissener (Germany) *Tel:* (09732) 9142-0 *Fax:* (09732) 9142-20 *E-mail:* info@drei-eichen.de *Web Site:* www.drei-eichen.de, pg 215

Drei Ulmen Verlag GmbH (Germany) *Tel:* (089) 3087911; (089) 3088343, pg 215

Dreisam Ratgeber in der Rutsker Verlag GmbH (Germany) *Tel:* (0221) 921635-0 *Fax:* (0221) 921635-24 *E-mail:* kontakt@hayit.com *Web Site:* www.hayit.com, pg 215

Cecilie Dressler Verlag GmbH & Co KG (Germany) *Tel:* (040) 607909-03 *Fax:* (040) 6072326 *E-mail:* dressler@vsg-hamburg.de *Web Site:* www.cecilie-dressler.de, pg 215

De Driehoek BV, Uitgeverij (Netherlands) *Tel:* (020) 624 64 26 *Fax:* (020) 638 71 55 *E-mail:* driehoek.uitgeverij@planet.nl, pg 477

Verlagsgruppe Droemer Knaur GmbH & Co KG (Germany) *Tel:* (089) 9271-0 *Fax:* (089) 9271-168 *E-mail:* info@droemer-knaur.de *Web Site:* www.droemer-knaur.de, pg 216

Editions Droguet et Ardant (France) *Tel:* (01)53 26 33 35 *Fax:* (01) 53 26 33 36, pg 159

Literature Verlag Droschl (Austria) *Tel:* (0316) 32-64-04 *Fax:* (0316) 32-40-71 *E-mail:* droschl@droschl.com; literaturverlag@droschl.com *Web Site:* www.droschl.com, pg 50

Droste Verlag GmbH (Germany) *Tel:* (0211) 8605220 *Fax:* (0211) 3230098, pg 216

Librairie Droz SA (Switzerland) *Tel:* (022) 3466666 *Fax:* (022) 3472391 *E-mail:* droz@droz.org *Web Site:* www.droz.org, pg 617

Dru-stvo na Pisatelite na Makedonija (The Former Yugoslav Republic of Macedonia) *Tel:* (02) 228039 *E-mail:* contact@dpism.org.mk *Web Site:* www.dpism.org.mk, pg 1396

Druck & Verlagshaus Fromm GmbH & Co KG (Germany) *Tel:* (0541) 310-0 *Fax:* (0541) 310315 *E-mail:* info@fromm-os.de *Web Site:* www.fromm-os.de, pg 1145

Karl Elser Druck GmbH (Germany) *Tel:* (07041) 805-41 *Fax:* (07041) 805-50 *E-mail:* info@elserdruck.de *Web Site:* www.elserdruck.de, pg 216

Druckerei u Verlagsanstalt Bayerland GmbH (Germany) *Tel:* (08131) 7 20 66 *Fax:* (08131) 73 53 99 *E-mail:* zentrale@bayerland-amperbote.de *Web Site:* www.bayerland.de, pg 216

Druffel-Verlag (Germany) *Tel:* (08143) 992160 *Fax:* (08143) 992241; (08143) 992161, pg 216

Drukarnia I Ksiegarnia Swietego Wojciecha, Dziat Wydawniczy (Poland) *Tel:* (061) 8529186 *Fax:* (061) 8523746 *E-mail:* wydawnictwo.ksw@archpoznan.org.pl, pg 518

The Drummond Agency (Australia) *Tel:* (03) 5427 3644 *Fax:* (03) 5427 3655, pg 1119

Drustvo Bibliotekara Bosne i Hercegovine (Bosnia and Herzegovina) *Tel:* (033) 275 312 *Fax:* (033) 218 431 *E-mail:* nubbih@nub.ba *Web Site:* www.nub.ba, pg 1559

Druzhba Narodov (Russian Federation) *Tel:* (095) 9258671, pg 539

DRW-Verlag Weinbrenner-GmbH & Co (Germany) *Tel:* (0711) 75 91-0 *Fax:* (0711) 75 91-333 *E-mail:* info@weinbrenner.de *Web Site:* www.drw-verlag.de; www.weinbrenner.de, pg 216

Dryden Press (Australia) *Tel:* (02) 331-4571 *Fax:* (02) 398-9782, pg 20

Drzavna Uprava za Zastitu Prirode i Okolisa (State Directorate for the Protection of Nature & Environment) (Croatia) *Tel:* (01) 613 3444 *Fax:* (01) 611 2073 *E-mail:* duzo@ring.net *Web Site:* www.mzopu.hr, pg 117

DSI Data Service & Information (Germany) *Tel:* (049) 2843 3220 *Fax:* (049) 2843 3230 *E-mail:* dsi@dsidata.com *Web Site:* www.dsidata.com, pg 216

Du May (France) *Tel:* (01) 41 31 80 50 *Fax:* (01) 41 31 80 51, pg 159

Duang Kamon Co Ltd (Thailand) *Tel:* (02) 251-6335; (02) 253-1766, pg 640

Livraria Duas Cidades Ltda (Brazil) *Tel:* (011) 220 5134 *Fax:* (011) 220-5813 *E-mail:* livraria@duascidades.com.br *Web Site:* www.duascidades.com.br, pg 80

Livraria Duas Cidades Ltda (Brazil) *Tel:* (011) 3331-5134 *Fax:* (011) 3331-4702, pg 1293

Dublin City Public Libraries (Ireland) *Tel:* (01) 674 4800 *Fax:* (01) 674 4879 *E-mail:* dublinpubliclibraries@dublincity.ie *Web Site:* www.dublincity.ie, pg 1517

Dublin Institute for Advanced Studies (Ireland) *Tel:* (01) 6140100 *Fax:* (01) 6680561 *Web Site:* www.dias.ie, pg 356

Dubois Publishing (Australia) *Tel:* (02) 6567 1407 *Fax:* (02) 9211 1865, pg 20

Duboux Editions SA (Switzerland) *Tel:* (033) 2256060 *Fax:* (033) 2256066 *E-mail:* duboux@duboux.ch *Web Site:* www.duboux.ch, pg 617

Gerald Duckworth & Co Ltd (United Kingdom) *Tel:* (020) 7490 7300 *Fax:* (020) 7490 0080 *E-mail:* info@duckworth-publishers.co.uk *Web Site:* www.ducknet.co.uk, pg 683

Verlag Duerr & Kessler GmbH (Germany) *Tel:* (0180) 304 14 20 *Fax:* (02241) 39 76 190 *E-mail:* info@wolfverlag.de *Web Site:* www.wolfverlag.de, pg 216

Dumara Distribuidora de Publicacoes Ltda (Brazil) *Tel:* (021) 5646869 *Fax:* (021) 2750294 *E-mail:* relume@re-dumara.com.br, pg 80

Dumjahn Verlag (Germany) *Tel:* (06131) 330810 *Fax:* (06131) 330811 *E-mail:* railway@dumjahn.de *Web Site:* www.dumjahn.de, pg 216

DuMont monte Verlag GmbH & Co KG (Germany) *Tel:* (0221) 224-1823 *Fax:* (0221) 224-1812 *E-mail:* info@dumontmonte.de *Web Site:* www. dumontmonte.de, pg 216

DuMont Reiseverlag GmbH & Co KG (Germany) *Tel:* (0221) 224-1839 *Fax:* (0221) 224-1855 *E-mail:* info@dumontreise.de *Web Site:* www. dumontreise.de, pg 216

Dorothy Duncan Braille Library & Transcription Library (Zimbabwe) *Tel:* (04) 251116; (04) 251117 *Fax:* (04) 251117 *E-mail:* chiedza@samara.co.zw, pg 777

Duncker und Humblot GmbH (Germany) *Tel:* (030) 79 00 06-0 *Fax:* (030) 79 00 06-31 *E-mail:* info@ duncker-humblot.de *Web Site:* www.duncker-humblot. de, pg 216

Dunedin Academic Press (United Kingdom) *Tel:* (0131) 473 2397 *Fax:* (01250) 870920 *E-mail:* mail@ dunedinacademicpress.co.uk *Web Site:* www. dunedinacademicpress.co.uk, pg 684

Dunedin Public Libraries (New Zealand) *Tel:* (03) 4743690 *Fax:* (03) 4743660 *E-mail:* library@dcc.govt. nz, pg 1530

Dunia Pustaka Jaya PT (Indonesia) *Tel:* (021) 3909322; (021) 3909284 *Fax:* (021) 3909320, pg 351

Dunmore Press Ltd (New Zealand) *Tel:* (06) 3579242 *Fax:* (06) 3579242 *E-mail:* books@dunmore.co.nz *Web Site:* www.dunmore.co.nz, pg 491

Dunod Editeur (France) *Tel:* (01) 40 46 35 00 *Fax:* (01) 40 46 49 95 *E-mail:* infos@dunod.com *Web Site:* www.dunod.com, pg 159

Kustannus Oy Duodecim (Finland) *Tel:* (09) 618851 *Fax:* (09) 61885400 *E-mail:* etunimi.sukunimi@ duodecim.fi *Web Site:* www.duodecim.fi, pg 141

DUP (1996) Ltd (United Republic of Tanzania) *Tel:* (051) 410300 *Fax:* (051) 410137 *E-mail:* director@dup.udsm.ac.tz, pg 638

Editions Dupuis SA (Belgium) *Tel:* (071) 600 500 *Fax:* (071) 600 599 *E-mail:* info@dupuis.com *Web Site:* www.dupuis.com, pg 66

Editions J Dupuis (France) *Tel:* (01) 44 84 40 80 *Fax:* (01) 44 84 40 99 *E-mail:* info@dupuis.com *Web Site:* www.dupuis.com, pg 159

Durham Chapter Library (United Kingdom) *Tel:* (0191) 386 2489 *Fax:* (0191) 386 4267 *E-mail:* library@ durhamcathedral.co.uk *Web Site:* www. durhamcathedral.co.uk/, pg 1551

Durham University Library (United Kingdom) *Tel:* (0191) 334 2968 *Fax:* (0191) 334 2971 *E-mail:* main.library@durham.ac.uk *Web Site:* www. dur.ac.uk/library, pg 1551

Durieux d o o (Croatia) *Tel:* (01) 23 00 337; (01) 23 21 178 *Fax:* (01) 23 00 337 *E-mail:* durieux@durieux.hr *Web Site:* www.durieux.hr, pg 117

Durvan SA de Ediciones (Spain) *Tel:* (094) 4230777 *Fax:* (094) 4243832 *E-mail:* editorial@durvan.com *Web Site:* www.durvan.com, pg 575

Dustri-Verlag Dr Karl Feistle (Germany) *Tel:* (089) 61 38 61-0 *Fax:* (089) 613 54 12 *E-mail:* info@dustri.de *Web Site:* www.dustri.de, pg 217

Duta Wacana University Press (Indonesia) *Tel:* (0274) 563929 *Fax:* (0274) 513235 *E-mail:* humas@ukdw.ac. id *Web Site:* www.ukdw.ac.id, pg 351

Dutch Connection (United Kingdom) *Tel:* (01625) 610613 *Fax:* (01625) 610613 *E-mail:* dutchconnection@aol.com, pg 1140

Dutta Publishing Co Ltd (India) *Tel:* (0361) 543995, pg 330

Gottlieb Duttweiler Institute for Trends & Futures (Switzerland) *Tel:* (01) 7246111 *Fax:* (01) 7246262 *E-mail:* info@gdi.ch *Web Site:* www.gdi.ch, pg 617

Klaus D Dutz (Germany) *Tel:* (0251) 65514; (0251) 661692 *Fax:* (0251) 661692 *E-mail:* dutz.nodus@t-online.de, pg 217

DVG-Deutsche Verlagsgesellschaft mbH (Germany) *Tel:* (08031) 15643 *Fax:* (08031) 380662, pg 217

Dvir Bialik Municipal Central Public Library (Israel) *Tel:* (03) 786375, pg 1518

Dvir Publishing Ltd (Israel) *Tel:* (08) 9246565 *Fax:* (08) 9251770 *E-mail:* info@zmora.co.il, pg 363

Gwasg Dwyfor (United Kingdom) *Tel:* (01286) 831111 *Fax:* (01286) 831497 *E-mail:* argraff@gwasgdwyfor. demon.co.uk, pg 684

Dykinson SL (Spain) *Tel:* (091) 544 28 46; (091) 544 28 69 *Fax:* (091) 544 60 40 *E-mail:* info@dykinson. com *Web Site:* www.dykinson.es; www.dykinson.com, pg 575

Dymocks Pty Ltd (Australia) *Tel:* (02) 9224 0411 *Toll Free Tel:* 800 805 711 *Fax:* (02) 9224 9401 *E-mail:* feedback@dymocks.com.au; service@ dymocks.com.au *Web Site:* www.dymocks.com.au, pg 1288

Dynamo House P/L (Australia) *Tel:* (03) 9427 0955; (03) 9428 3636 *Fax:* (03) 9429 8036 *E-mail:* info@ dynamoh.com.au *Web Site:* www.dynamoh.com.au, pg 20

Dyonon/Papyrus Publishing House of the Tel-Aviv (Israel) *Tel:* (03) 6408111 *Fax:* (03) 6423149, pg 363

Dyonon/Papyrus Publishing House of the Tel-Aviv (Israel) *Tel:* (03) 6410351; (03) 6410352; (03) 6427545 (head office); (03) 6422667 (import office) *Fax:* (03) 6423149, pg 1309

Dzuka Publishing Co Ltd (Malawi) *Tel:* (01) 672548; (01) 670637 *Fax:* (01) 671114, (01) 670021 *E-mail:* dzuka@malawi.net, pg 451

E D Galgotia & Sons (India) *Tel:* (011) 3322876 *Fax:* (011) 3755150 *E-mail:* galgotia@ndf.vsnl.net.in, pg 1305

Edizioni E - Elle SRL (Italy) *Tel:* (040) 566821 *Fax:* (040) 566819, pg 382

E Mokas - Morfotiki (Greece) *Tel:* 2105227830 *Fax:* 2105200534, pg 304

Edizioni E/O (Italy) *Tel:* (06) 3722829 *Fax:* (06) 37351096 *E-mail:* info@edizionieo.it *Web Site:* www. edizioni-eo.it, pg 382

E P U Editora Pedagogica e Universitaria Ltd (Brazil) *Tel:* (011) 3168-6077 *Fax:* (011) 3078-5803 *E-mail:* epu@epu.com.br *Web Site:* www.epu.com.br, pg 80

EA AD (Bulgaria) *Tel:* (064) 822827 *Fax:* (064) 822528 *E-mail:* ea@famahold.com, pg 93

EA Books (Australia) *Tel:* (02) 9438 1533 *Fax:* (02) 9438 5934 *E-mail:* eabooks@engaust.com.au *Web Site:* www.engaust.com.au, pg 20

Toby Eady Associates Ltd (United Kingdom) *Tel:* (020) 7792 0092 *Fax:* (020) 7792 0879 *E-mail:* toby@tobyeady.demon.co.uk *Web Site:* www. tobyeadyassociates.co.uk, pg 1130

Eagle/Inter Publishing Service (IPS) Ltd (United Kingdom) *Tel:* (01483) 306309 *Fax:* (01483) 579196 *E-mail:* eagle_indeprint@compuserve.com, pg 684

Eagle Press (United Kingdom) *Tel:* (0115) 9552335 *Fax:* (0115) 9552336, pg 1215

Eaglemoss Publications Ltd (United Kingdom) *Tel:* (020) 7590 8300 *Fax:* (020) 7590 8301 *E-mail:* genenq@ eaglemoss.co.uk *Web Site:* www.eaglemoss.co.uk, pg 684

EAIS Literary Agents (France) *Tel:* (01) 47 88 08 40 *Fax:* (01) 47 88 08 40, pg 1120

Early English Text Society (United Kingdom) *Web Site:* www.eets.org.uk, pg 1402

Earthscan /James & James (Science Publishers) Ltd (United Kingdom) *Tel:* (020) 7387 8558 *Fax:* (020) 7387 8998 *E-mail:* jxj@jxj.com *Web Site:* www.jxj. com, pg 684

Earthscan Publications Ltd (United Kingdom) *Tel:* (020) 7387 8558 *Fax:* (020) 7387 8998 *E-mail:* earthinfo@ earthscan.co.uk *Web Site:* www.earthscan.co.uk, pg 684

Eason & Son Ltd (Ireland) *Tel:* (01) 873 3811 *Fax:* (01) 873 3545 *E-mail:* info@eason.ie *Web Site:* www. eason.ie, pg 356

Eason & Son Ltd (Ireland) *Tel:* (01) 858-3800 *Fax:* (01) 858-3806 *E-mail:* info@eason.ie *Web Site:* www. eason.ie, pg 1309

East African Publishing House (United Republic of Tanzania) *Tel:* (02) 557417; (02) 557788, pg 638

East & West Publishing Co (Pakistan) *Tel:* (021) 212036 *Fax:* (021) 7784362, pg 507

East China Normal University Press (China) *Tel:* (021) 62232613 *Fax:* (021) 62864922 *E-mail:* lxb@ecnu. edu.cn *Web Site:* www.ecnu.edu.cn, pg 103

East China University of Science & Technology Press (China) *Tel:* (021) 64132885 *Fax:* (021) 64250735 *E-mail:* ies@ecust.edu.cn *Web Site:* www.ecust.edu.cn, pg 103

East London Municipal Library (South Africa) *Tel:* (043) 724991; (043) 724992 *Fax:* (043) 7431729 *Web Site:* www.unisa.ac.za/library, pg 1542

East West Operation (EWO) Ltd (Slovenia) *Tel:* (01) 4256 272 *Fax:* (01) 2517 348 *E-mail:* ewo-arkadna@ siol.net, pg 557

East-West Publications Fonds BV (Netherlands) *Tel:* (70) 364 45 90 *Fax:* (70) 361 48 64 *E-mail:* epublica@ packardbell.org, pg 477

East-West Publications (UK) Ltd (United Kingdom) *Tel.* (01621) 782466 *Fax:* (01621) 782466, pg 684

Eastern Africa Publications Ltd (United Republic of Tanzania) *Tel:* (057) 3176; (057) 26708, pg 638

Eastern & Southern Africa Regional Branch of the International Council on Archives (ESARBICA) (Kenya) *Tel:* (02) 228959 *Fax:* (02) 240059 *E-mail:* knarchives@form-net.com *Web Site:* www. kenyarchives.go.ke, pg 1265

Eastern & Southern African Management Institute (ESAMI) (United Republic of Tanzania) *Tel:* (027) 250-8384; (027) 250-8388 *Fax:* (027) 250-8285 *E-mail:* esamihq@esamihq.ac.tz *Web Site:* www. esami-africa.org, pg 1548

Eastern Book Centre (India) *Tel:* (011) 3314191, pg 330

Eastern Book Co (India) *Tel:* (0522) 2223171; (0522) 2226517 *Fax:* (0522) 2224328 *E-mail:* sales@ebc-india.com *Web Site:* www.ebc-india.com, pg 330

Eastern Law House Pvt Ltd (India) *Tel:* (033) 237 4989; (033) 237 2301 *Fax:* (033) 215 0491 *E-mail:* elh@cal. vsnl.net.in *Web Site:* easternlawhouse.com, pg 331

Eastview Productions Sdn Bhd (Malaysia) *Tel:* (03) 89438866 *Fax:* (03) 89435675, pg 452

Eastword (United Kingdom) *Tel:* (020) 7582 9349 *Fax:* (020) 7793 0474 *E-mail:* info@eastword.uk.com, pg 1140

Easy Computing NV (Belgium) *Tel:* (02) 346 52 52 *Fax:* (02) 346 01 20 *E-mail:* info@easycomputing.com *Web Site:* www.easycomputing.com, pg 66

Easy Finder Ltd (Hong Kong) *Tel:* 2990 7100 *Fax:* 2623 9315 *E-mail:* easybook@nextmedia.com.hk *Web Site:* www.nextmedia.com.hk, pg 314

Editions l'Eau Vive (Switzerland) *Tel:* (022) 7329847 *Fax:* (022) 7410482, pg 617

Edizioni EBE (Italy) *Tel:* (0766) 858878 *Fax:* (0766) 858877, pg 382

Ediciones Ebenezer (Spain) *Tel:* (093) 2133515 *Fax:* (093) 2131684 *E-mail:* 101745.1635@ compuserve.com, pg 575

EBG Verlags GmbH (Germany) *Tel:* (07154) 1340, pg 1242

Eboris-Coda-Bompiani (Switzerland) *Tel:* (022) 7188820 *Fax:* (022) 7079199, pg 617

ECA Bookshop Co-op Society (Ethiopia) *Tel:* (01) 517200 *Fax:* (01) 510365; (212) 963-4957 (New York) *E-mail:* ecainfo@uneca.org *Web Site:* www.uneca.org, pg 1299

Ediciones Eca SA de CV (Mexico) *Tel:* (055) 5787325; (055) 5549-3477; (055) 5689-1244; (055) 5689-3074 *Fax:* (055) 5689-9935 *Web Site:* www. centroescolareca.edu.mx, pg 461

Biblioteca Jose Antonio Echeverria (Cuba) *Tel:* (07) 3235 8789 *Fax:* (07) 334 554 *E-mail:* casa@tinored cu, pg 1498

Echo Publishing Company Ltd (Taiwan, Province of China) *Tel:* (02) 763-1452 *Fax:* (02) 27568712 *E-mail:* hrmdh@mail.echogroup.com.tw *Web Site:* www.chinesebooks.net, pg 635

Echo Verlag (Germany) *Tel:* (0551) 796824 *Fax:* (0551) 74035 *E-mail:* clages.echoverlag@t-online.de *Web Site:* www.echoverlag.de, pg 217

Echter Wurzburg Frankische Gesellschaftsdruckerei und Verlag GmbH (Germany) *Tel:* (0931) 66068-0 *Fax:* (0931) 66068-23 *E-mail:* info@echterverlag.de *Web Site:* www.echter-verlag.de, pg 217

ECI voor Boeken en platen BV (Netherlands) *Tel:* (0347) 379214 *Fax:* (0347) 379380 *E-mail:* service@eci.nl *Web Site:* www.eci.nl, pg 477

ECI voor Boeken en platen BV (Netherlands) *Tel:* (0347) 379214 *Fax:* (0347) 379380 *Web Site:* www.nbc-club. nl, pg 1244

ECIG (Italy) *Tel:* (010) 2512399 *Fax:* (010) 2512398, pg 382

ECL (Portugal) *Tel:* (022) 600 40 01; (022) 609 01 71 *Fax:* (022) 609 96 15 *E-mail:* ecl@mail.telepac.pt, pg 1328

Editions de l'Eclat (France) *Tel:* (01) 45 77 04 04 *Fax:* (01) 45 75 92 51 *E-mail:* eclat@lyber-eclat.net *Web Site:* www.lyber-eclat.net, pg 159

Ediciones del Eclipse (Argentina) *Tel:* (011) 4771-3583 *Fax:* (011) 4771-3583 *E-mail:* info@deleclipse.com *Web Site:* www.deleclipse.com, pg 5

Eco Verlags AG (Switzerland) *Tel:* (01) 440400, pg 617

Ecobooks (Belgium) *Tel:* (052) 37 11 38 *Fax:* (052) 37 11 51 *E-mail:* ecobooks@ping.be, pg 66

Ecoe Ediciones Ltda (Colombia) *Tel:* (01) 2889821; (01) 2889871 *Fax:* (01) 3201377 *E-mail:* correo@ ecoeediciones.com *Web Site:* www.ecoeediciones.com, pg 110

Editions de l'Ecole (France) *Tel:* (01) 42 22 94 10 *Fax:* (01) 45 48 04 99 *E-mail:* edl@ecoledesloisirs. com *Web Site:* www.ecoledesloisirs.fr, pg 159

Ecole de Traducteurs et d'Interpretes de Beyrouth-Universite Saint-Joseph (ETIB) (Lebanon) *Tel:* (01) 611 456 (ext 5512) *Fax:* (01) 611 360 *E-mail:* etib@ usj.edu.lb *Web Site:* www.usj.edu.lb, pg 1139

Ecole des Bibliothecaires, Archivistes et Documentalistes de l'Universite Cheikh Anta Diop de Dakar (Senegal) *Tel:* 825 76 60; 864 21 22 *Fax:* 824 05 42 *E-mail:* ebad@ebad.ucad.sn *Web Site:* www.ebad.ucad. sn, pg 1540

Editions de l'Ecole des Hautes Etudes en Sciences Sociales (EHESS) (France) *Tel:* (01) 49 54 25 25 *Fax:* (01) 45 44 93 11 *E-mail:* editions@ehess.fr *Web Site:* www.ehess.fr, pg 159

Ecole francaise d'Athenes (Greece) *Tel:* 21036 79900 *Fax:* 2103632101 *E-mail:* efa@efa.gr *Web Site:* www.efa.gr, pg 304

Ecole Francaise de Rome (Italy) *Tel:* (06) 68 60 11 *Fax:* (06) 687 48 34 *E-mail:* publ@ecole-francaise.it *Web Site:* www.ecole-francaise.it, pg 382

Editions et Publications de l'Ecole Lacanienne (EPEL) (France) *Tel:* (01) 45 44 24 00 *Fax:* (01) 45 44 22 85 *E-mail:* contact@epel-edition.com *Web Site:* 60gp.ovh. net/~sartorio/epel/site/, pg 159

Bibliotheqe l'Ecole nationale d'administration du Niger (Niger) *Tel:* 723183 *Fax:* 724383, pg 1531

Ecole nationale polytechnique, Bibliotheque (Algeria) *Tel:* (021) 52 14 94 *Fax:* (021) 52 29 73 *E-mail:* enp@ist.cerist.dz *Web Site:* www.enp.edu.dz, pg 1487

Ecole Nationale Superieure des Beaux-Arts (France) *Tel:* (01) 47035000 *Fax:* (01) 47035080 *E-mail:* info@ ensba.fr *Web Site:* www.ensba.fr, pg 159

Ecole Nationale Superieure des Sciences de l'information et des bibliotheques (ENSSIB) (France) *Tel:* (04) 72 44 43 43 *Fax:* (04) 72 44 43 44 *E-mail:* com@enssib. fr *Web Site:* www.enssib.fr, pg 1505

Ecole normale superieure (Mali) *Tel:* 222189, pg 1526

Ecole Superieure d'Ingenieurs de Beyrouth (ESIB) (Lebanon) *Tel:* (04) 532661 *Fax:* (04) 532645 *E-mail:* esib@usj.edu.lb *Web Site:* www.fi.usj.edu.lb, pg 1523

Librairie des Ecoles (Morocco) *Tel:* (02) 22 25 22; (02) 26 67 41 *Fax:* (02) 20 10 03, pg 1319

Ecomed Verlagsgesellschaft AG & Co KG (Germany) *Tel:* (08191) 1250 *Fax:* (08191) 125492 *E-mail:* info@ ecomed.de *Web Site:* www.ecomed.de, pg 217

Econ Taschenbuchverlag (Germany) *Tel:* (0211) 43596, pg 217

Econ Verlag GmbH (Germany) *Tel:* (030) 23456-300 *Fax:* (030) 23456-303 *Web Site:* www.econ-verlag.de, pg 217

Economic & Business Research (Trinidad & Tobago) *Tel:* (868) 624-5064 *Fax:* (868) 623-4137 *E-mail:* maxifill@opus.co.tt *Web Site:* www.opus.co.tt. /maxifill, pg 642

The Economic & Social Research Institute (Ireland) *Tel:* (01) 6671525 *Fax:* (01) 6686231 *E-mail:* admin@ esri.ie *Web Site:* www.esri.ie, pg 356

The Economist Books (United Kingdom) *Tel:* (020) 7404 3001 *Fax:* (020) 7404 3003 *E-mail:* info@ profilebooks.co.uk, pg 684

The Economist Intelligence Unit (United Kingdom) *Tel:* (020) 7830 1007 *Fax:* (020) 7830 1023 *E-mail:* london@eiu.com *Web Site:* www.eiu.com, pg 684

The Economists' Bookshop (United Kingdom) *Tel:* (020) 7405 5531 *Fax:* (020) 7482 4873 *E-mail:* economists@waterstones.co.uk, pg 1341

Economy and Press (Hong Kong) *Tel:* 28917556, pg 314

Association des Ecrivains de Langue Francaise (ADELF) (France) *Tel:* (01) 43 21 95 99 *Fax:* (01) 43 20 12 22, pg 1258

Biblioteca Ecuatoriana Aurelio Espinosa Polit' (Ecuador) *Tel:* (02) 2491 157; (02) 2491 156 *Fax:* (02) 493928 *E-mail:* beaep@uio.satnet.net *Web Site:* www.beaep. org.ec, pg 136

Biblioteca Ecuatoriana Aurelio Espinosa Polit' (Ecuador) *Tel:* (02) 2491 157; (02) 2491 156 *Fax:* (02) 2493 928 *E-mail:* beaep@uio.satnet.net *Web Site:* www.beaep. org.ec, pg 1501

Ecuazeta De Publicaciones Cia Ltda (Ecuador) *Tel:* (02) 2546 149 *Fax:* (02) 2902 693 *E-mail:* ecuazeta@ interactive.net.ec, pg 1298

ECWA Productions Ltd (Nigeria) *Tel:* (073) 53897; (073) 52230, pg 500

Verlag ED Emmentaler Druck AG (Switzerland) *Tel:* (035) 21911 *Fax:* (035) 0524642, pg 617

Editorial EDAF SA (Spain) *Tel:* (091) 435 82 60 *Fax:* (091) 431 52 81 *E-mail:* edaf@edaf.net *Web Site:* www.edaf.es, pg 575

Edagricole - Edizioni Agricole (Italy) *Tel:* (051) 65751 *Fax:* (051) 6575800 *E-mail:* sede@gce.it *Web Site:* www.edagricole.it, pg 382

Edamex SA de CV (Mexico) *Tel:* (05) 55598588 *Toll Free Tel:* 800 024 8588 *Fax:* (05) 55750555; (05) 55757035 *E-mail:* info@edamex.com *Web Site:* www. edamex.com, pg 461

Edanim Publishers Ltd (Israel) *Tel:* (03) 688-8466 *Fax:* (03) 537-7820, pg 363

EDAS (Italy) *Tel:* (090) 675653 *Fax:* (090) 675653 *E-mail:* info@edas.it *Web Site:* www.edas.it, pg 382

EDC -Empresa De Divulgacao Cultural, SA (Portugal) *Tel:* (021) 380 1100 *Fax:* (021) 386 5397 *Web Site:* www.editorialverbo.pt, pg 1328

Eddison Sadd Editions Ltd (United Kingdom) *Tel:* (020) 7837 1968 *Fax:* (020) 7837 6844 *E-mail:* reception@ eddisonsadd.co.uk *Web Site:* www.eddisonsadd.co.uk, pg 685

Ede Vau Verlag GmbH (Germany) *Tel:* (02154) 490080 *Fax:* (02154) 490081 *E-mail:* evvgmbh@t-online.de, pg 217

Edebe (Spain) *Tel:* (093) 2037408 *Fax:* (093) 2054670 *E-mail:* informacion@edebe.com *Web Site:* www. edebe.com, pg 575

Edelsa Group Didascalia SA (Spain) *Tel:* (091) 4165511; (091) 4165218 *Fax:* (091) 4165411 *E-mail:* edelsa@ edelsa.es *Web Site:* www.edelsa.es, pg 575

EDERSA (Editoriales de Derecho Reunidas SA) (Spain) *Tel:* (091) 5477961 *Fax:* (091) 5478001 *E-mail:* dijusa@dijusa.es, pg 575

Edeval (Universidad de Valparaiso) (Chile) *Tel:* (02) 250792 *Fax:* (02) 252125 *E-mail:* rrpp@uv.cl *Web Site:* www.uv.cl, pg 99

Edex, Centro de Recursos Comunitarios (Spain) *Tel:* (094) 442 57 84 *Fax:* (094) 441-7512 *E-mail:* edex@edex.es *Web Site:* www.edex.es, pg 575

EDHASA (Editora y Distribuidora Hispano-Americana SA) (Spain) *Tel:* (093) 4949720 *Fax:* (093) 4194584 *E-mail:* info@edhasa.es *Web Site:* www.edhasa.es, pg 576, 1333

Edi-Liber Irlan SA (Spain) *Tel:* (093) 4160641 *Fax:* (093) 4160774 *E-mail:* ediliber@mx3.redestb.es, pg 576

Ediart Editrice (Italy) *Tel:* (075) 8943594 *Fax:* (075) 8942411 *E-mail:* ediart@ediart.it *Web Site:* www. ediart.it, pg 382

Ediblanchart sprl (Belgium) *Tel:* (02) 4783706 *Fax:* (02) 4786429, pg 66

Edicart (Italy) *Tel:* (0331) 74291 *Fax:* (0331) 74292 *E-mail:* info@edicart.it *Web Site:* www.edicart.it, pg 382

EDICEP (Spain) *Tel:* (096) 395 20 45; (096) 395 72 93 *Fax:* (096) 395 22 97 *E-mail:* edicep@edicep.com *Web Site:* www.edicep.com, pg 576

Edicial SA (Argentina) *Tel:* (011) 4342-8481; (011) 4342-8482; (011) 4342-8483 *Fax:* (011) 4342-8481 *E-mail:* edicial@edicial.com.ar, pg 5

Ediciclo Editore SRL (Italy) *Tel:* (0421) 74475 *Fax:* (0421) 282070 *E-mail:* posta@ediciclo.it *Web Site:* www.ediciclo.it, pg 382

Ediciones Ekare (Venezuela) *Tel:* (02) 263 00 80; (02) 263 61 70 *Fax:* (02) 263 00 91, pg 774

Ediciones El Almendro de Cordoba SL (Spain) *Tel:* (0957) 082 789; (0957) 274 692 *Fax:* (0957) 274 692 *E-mail:* ediciones@elalmendro.org *Web Site:* www.elalmendro.org, pg 576

Ediciones Euroamericanas SA (Peru) *Tel:* (014) 4274686 *Fax:* (014) 4280545, pg 1325

Ediciones l'Isard, S L (Spain) *Tel:* (093) 436 81 18 *Fax:* (093) 436 03 41 *E-mail:* isard@isard.net *Web Site:* www.isard.net, pg 576

Institut d'Edicions de la Diputacio de Barcelona (Spain) *Tel:* (093) 4022116 *E-mail:* diputacio@diba.es *Web Site:* www.diba.es, pg 66

Editorial Edicol SA (Mexico) *Tel:* (05) 5636990 *Fax:* (05) 5981512, pg 461

Edicomunicacion SA (Spain) *Tel:* (093) 3590866 *Fax:* (093) 3590004 *Web Site:* www.edicomunicacion. com, pg 576

Edicon Editora e Consultorial Ltda (Brazil) *Tel:* (011) 3255-1002 *Fax:* (011) 3255-9822 *E-mail:* edicon@ edicon.com.br *Web Site:* www.edicon.com.br, pg 80

EDIFIR SRL (Italy) *Tel:* (055) 289639 *Fax:* (055) 289478 *E-mail:* edizioni-firenze@edifir.it *Web Site:* www.edifir.it, pg 382

Edigol Ediciones SA (Spain) *Tel:* (093) 372 63 04 *Fax:* (093) 371 76 32 *E-mail:* info@edigol.com *Web Site:* www.edigol.com, pg 576

Edika-Med, SA (Spain) *Tel:* (093) 454 96 00 *Fax:* (093) 323 48 03 *E-mail:* info@edikamed.com *Web Site:* www.edikamed.com, pg 576

Edilesa-Ediciones Leonesas SA (Spain) *Tel:* (0987) 80 11 16 *Fax:* (0987) 84 00 28 *E-mail:* edilesa@edilesa. es *Web Site:* www.edilesa.es, pg 576

Edilux (Spain) *Tel:* (0958) 08 20 00; (0958) 184056 *Fax:* (0958) 184056; (0958) 082472 *E-mail:* ediluxsl@ supercable.es, pg 576

EDIM SA (Mali) *Tel:* 225522 *Fax:* 238503, pg 456

Edimecien Cia Ltda (Ecuador) *Tel:* (02) 2502 427; (02) 2502 428; (02) 2502 431 *Fax:* (02) 2502 429, pg 1298

EDIMSA - Editores Medicos SA (Spain) *Tel:* (091) 376 81 40 *Fax:* (091) 373 99 07 *E-mail:* edimsa@edimsa. es *Web Site:* www.edimsa.es, pg 576

Edinburgh Bibliographical Society (United Kingdom) *Tel:* (0131) 226 4531 *Fax:* (0131) 466 2807 *E-mail:* exkb33@srv1.lib.ed.ac.uk *Web Site:* www. edbibsoc.lib.ed.ac.uk, pg 1402

Edinburgh City Libraries (United Kingdom) *Tel:* (0131) 242 8000 *Fax:* (0131) 242 8009 *E-mail:* elis@ cityedin.demon.co.uk *Web Site:* www.edinburgh.gov. uk/libraries, pg 685

Edinburgh City Library & Information Services (United Kingdom) *Tel:* (0131) 242 8020 *Fax:* (0131) 242 8009 *E-mail:* central.lending.library@edinburgh.gov.uk *Web Site:* www.edinburgh.gov.uk/libraries, pg 1551

Edinburgh University Library (United Kingdom) *Tel:* (0131) 650 3384; (0131) 650 3374 (reference & information services) *Fax:* (0131) 667 9780; (0131) 650 3380 (administration); (0131) 650 6863 (special collections) *E-mail:* library@ed.ac.uk *Web Site:* www. lib.ed.ac.uk, pg 1551

Edinburgh University Press Ltd (United Kingdom) *Tel:* (0131) 650 4223 *E-mail:* marketing@eup.ed.ac. uk; journals@eup.ed.ac.uk (Orders) *Web Site:* www. eup.ed.ac.uk, pg 685

Ediciones Edinford SA (Spain) *Fax:* (095) 254689, pg 576

Edipro-Edicoes Profissionais Ltda (Brazil) *Tel:* (014) 232-3753 *Fax:* (014) 232-4684 *E-mail:* edipro@vol. com.br, pg 80

Edipuglia (Italy) *Tel:* (080) 5333056 *Fax:* (080) 5333057 *E-mail:* edipuglia@tin.it *Web Site:* www.edipuglia.it, pg 382

Edirisooriya & Company (Sri Lanka) *Tel:* (01) 522555; (01) 523216 *Fax:* (01) 446380; (01) 074618905, pg 601

Editrice Edisco (Italy) *Tel:* (011) 54 78 80 *Fax:* (011) 51 75 396 *E-mail:* info@edisco.it *Web Site:* www.edisco. it, pg 382

Edisport Editoriale SpA (Italy) *Tel:* (02) 380851 *Fax:* (02) 38010393 *E-mail:* edisport@edisport.it *Web Site:* www.edisport.it, pg 383

Edistudio (Italy) *Tel:* (050) 48670; (050) 2208745 *Fax:* (050) 500585 *E-mail:* edistudio@edistudio.it, pg 383

Editions Edisud (France) *Tel:* (04) 42 21 61 44 *Fax:* (04) 42 21 56 20 *E-mail:* info@edisud.com *Web Site:* www.edisud.com, pg 159

Edit (Edizioni Italiane) (Croatia) *Tel:* (051) 672 119; (051) 672 153 *Fax:* (051) 672 151 *E-mail:* edit@edit. hr *Web Site:* www.edit.hr, pg 117

Editions Edita (Switzerland) *Tel:* (021) 6251392 *Fax:* (021) 6254291, pg 617

Edita Publishing Oy (Finland) *Tel:* (020) 450 00 *Fax:* (020) 450 2396 *E-mail:* etunimi.sukunimi@edita. fi *Web Site:* www1.edita.fi, pg 141

Editalia (Edizioni d'Italia) (Italy) *Tel:* (06) 85081 *Toll Free Tel:* 800 01 4858 *Fax:* (06) 85085165 *Web Site:* www.editalia.it, pg 383

Editest, SPRL (Belgium) *Tel:* (02) 6476284 *Fax:* (02) 7325629, pg 66

Institute Editeur (France) *Tel:* (01) 40 87 17 17 *Fax:* (01) 40 87 17 18, pg 159

Editeurs et Libraires Catholiques d'Europe ELCE (Switzerland) *Tel:* (071) 279580 *Fax:* (071) 279580 *E-mail:* hawas@mhs.ch, pg 617

Les Editeurs Reunis (France) *Tel:* (01) 43 54 74 46; (01) 43 54 43 81 *Fax:* (01) 43 25 34 79, pg 160

Editorial Editex SA (Spain) *Tel:* (091) 7992040 *Fax:* (091) 7150444 *E-mail:* correo@editex.es *Web Site:* www.editex.es, pg 577

Edition (United Kingdom) *Tel:* (01683) 220808 *Fax:* (01683) 220012 *E-mail:* sales@cameronbooks. co.uk *Web Site:* www.cameronbooks.co.uk, pg 1153

Edition (United Kingdom) *Tel:* (01683) 220808 *Fax:* (01683) 220012 *E-mail:* editorial@ cameronbooks.co.uk; sales@cameronbooks.co.uk *Web Site:* www.cameronbooks.co.uk, pg 1174

Edition Epoca (Switzerland) *Tel:* (01) 4511717 *Fax:* (01) 4511717 *E-mail:* info@epoca.ch *Web Site:* www. epoca.ch, pg 617

Edition1 (France) *Tel:* (01) 49 54 36 00 *Fax:* (01) 45 44 86 32, pg 160

Edition S der OSD (Austria) *Tel:* (01) 61077-315 *Fax:* (01) 61077-419 *E-mail:* office@verlagoesterreich. at, pg 50

Edition XII (United Kingdom) *Tel:* (020) 7229 6471; (020) 7833 0120 *Fax:* (020) 7229 5239; (020) 7923 5500; (020) 7923 5505 *E-mail:* info@editionxii.co.uk *Web Site:* www.editionxii.co.uk, pg 685

Les Editions de Minuit SA (France) *Tel:* (01) 44 39 39 20 *Fax:* (01) 45 44 82 36 *E-mail:* contact@ leseditionsdeminuit.fr *Web Site:* www. leseditionsdeminuit.fr, pg 160

Editions d'Organisation (France) *Tel:* (01) 44 41 11 11 *Fax:* (01) 44 41 11 85 *E-mail:* service-lecteurs@ editions-organisation.com *Web Site:* www.editions-organisation.com, pg 160

Les Editions du CFPJ (Centre de Formation et de Perfectionnement des Journalistes) - Sarl Presse et Formation (France) *Tel:* (01) 44 82 20 00 *Fax:* (01) 44 82 20 01 *E-mail:* cfpj@cfpj.com *Web Site:* www.cfpj. com, pg 160

Editions ELOR (France) *Tel:* (02) 99 91 22 80 *Fax:* (02) 99 91 34 45 *E-mail:* edit.elor@wanadoo.fr *Web Site:* www.elor.com, pg 160

Les Editions ESF (France) *Tel:* (02) 37 29 69 20 *Fax:* (02) 37 29 69 35 *E-mail:* info@esf-editeur.fr *Web Site:* www.esf-editeur.fr, pg 160

Editions Grund (France) *Tel:* (01) 53103600 *Fax:* (01) 43294986 *E-mail:* grund@grund.fr *Web Site:* www. grund.fr, pg 160

Editions Recherche sur les Civilisations (ERC) (France) *Tel:* (01) 43 13 11 00 *Fax:* (01) 43 13 11 25 *E-mail:* erc.edit@adpf.asso.fr *Web Site:* www.france. diplomatie.fr; www.adpf.asso.fr/edition/, pg 160

Editions rue d'Ulm (France) *Tel:* (01) 44 32 30 29 *Fax:* (01) 44 32 36 86 *E-mail:* ulm-editions@ens.fr *Web Site:* www.presses.ens.fr, pg 160

Editions Terrail/Finest SA (France) *Tel:* (01) 56 77 06 20 *Fax:* (01) 56 77 06 26, pg 160

Editions Unes (France) *Tel:* (04) 94673158 *Fax:* (04) 94673175, pg 160

Editogo (Togo) *Tel:* (08) 21-37-18 *Fax:* (08) 21-14-89, pg 642

Companhia Editora Forense (Brazil) *Tel:* (021) 2533-5537 *Fax:* (021) 2533-5537 *E-mail:* forense@forense. com.br *Web Site:* www.forense.com.br, pg 80

Editora Letraviva Importacao Distribuidora Livros Ltd (Brazil) *Tel:* (011) 3088 7992; (011) 3088 7832 *Fax:* (011) 3088 7780 *E-mail:* letraviva@letraviva. com.br *Web Site:* www.letraviva.com.br, pg 1293

Corporacion Editora Nacional (Ecuador) *Tel:* (02) 554358; (02) 554558; (02) 554658 *Fax:* (02) 566340 *E-mail:* cen@accessinter.net, pg 136

Editora Universidade De Brasilia (Brazil) *Tel:* (061) 3035-4200 *Fax:* (061) 323-1017 *E-mail:* editora@unb. br *Web Site:* www.livrariauniversidade.unb.br, pg 1241

Editorama SA (Dominican Republic) *Tel:* 596-6669; 596-4274 *Fax:* 594-1421 *E-mail:* editorama@codetel. net.do *Web Site:* www.editorama.com, pg 135

Editori Laterza (Italy) *Tel:* (06) 3218393 *Fax:* (06) 3223853 *E-mail:* laterza@laterza.it *Web Site:* www. laterza.it, pg 383

Editorial Everest SA (Spain) *Tel:* (0987) 844200 *Fax:* (0987) 844202 *E-mail:* publicaciones@everest.es *Web Site:* www.everest.es, pg 577

Editorial Francesa Espanola SA (Chile) *Tel:* (02) 235-0911; (02) 235-9734 *Fax:* (02) 236-0900, pg 1295

Editpress (Luxembourg) *Tel:* 547131 *Fax:* 547130 *E-mail:* tageblatt@tageblatt.lu, pg 447

Edizioni Associate/Editrice Internazionale Srl (Italy) *Tel:* (06) 44'/04513 *Fax:* (06) 44704513 *E-mail:* easso@tin.it, pg 383

Edizioni d'Arte Antica e Moderna EDAM (Italy) *Tel:* (055) 2298578 *Fax:* (055) 220837, pg 383

Edizioni del Centro Camuno di Studi Preistorici (Italy) *Tel:* (0364) 42091 *Fax:* (0364) 42572 *E-mail:* ccspreist@tin.it *Web Site:* www.rockart-ccsp. com, pg 383

Edizioni di Storia e Letteratura (Italy) *Tel:* (06) 39670307 *Fax:* (06) 39671250 *E-mail:* info@ storiaeletteratura.it *Web Site:* www.storiaeletterature.it, pg 383

Edizioni Il Punto d'Incontro SAS (Italy) *Tel:* (0444) 239189 *Fax:* (0444) 239266 *E-mail:* ordini@ edizionilpuntocontro.it *Web Site:* www. edizionilpuntodincontro.it, pg 383

Edizioni la Scala (Italy) *Tel:* (080) 4975838 *Fax:* (080) 4975839 *E-mail:* lascala@abbazialascala.com *Web Site:* www.abbazialascala.com, pg 383

Edizioni l'Arciere SRL (Italy) *Tel:* (0171) 905566 *Fax:* (0171) 905730 *E-mail:* info@arciere.com *Web Site:* www.arciere.com, pg 383

Edizioni Qiqajon (Italy) *Tel:* (015) 679115 *Fax:* (015) 6794949 *E-mail:* acquisti@qiqajon.it *Web Site:* www. qiqajon.it, pg 383

Edizioni Studio Domenicano (ESD) (Italy) *Tel:* (051) 582034 *Fax:* (051) 331583 *E-mail:* esd@alinet.it *Web Site:* www.esd-domenicani.it, pg 383

EDP Sciences (France) *Tel:* (01) 69 18 75 75 *Fax:* (01) 69 28 84 91 *E-mail:* edps@edpsciences.org *Web Site:* www.edpsciences.org, pg 160

EDT Edizioni di Torino (Italy) *Tel:* (011) 5591816 *Fax:* (011) 2307034 *E-mail:* edt@edt.it *Web Site:* www.edt.it, pg 384

Educatieve Uitgeverij Edu'Actief BV (Netherlands) *Tel:* (0522) 235235 *Fax:* (0522) 235222 *E-mail:* info@ edu-actief.nl *Web Site:* www.edu-actief.nl, pg 477

Educatieve Partners Nederland bv (Netherlands) *Tel:* (030) 6383001 *Fax:* (030) 6383004 *E-mail:* info@ epn.nl *Web Site:* www.epn.nl, pg 478

Education Science Publishing House (China) *Tel:* (010) 62102454; (010) 62013803 *Fax:* (010) 62012454 *E-mail:* esph@public.net.china.com.cn, pg 103

Educational Advantage (Australia) *Tel:* (03) 5480 9466 *Fax:* (03) 5480 9462 *E-mail:* joe@mathsmate.net *Web Site:* www.mathsmate.net, pg 20

Educational Books Publishing House (Democratic People's Republic of Korea), pg 433

The Educational Company of Ireland (Ireland) *Tel:* (01) 4500611 *Fax:* (01) 4500993 *E-mail:* info@edco.ie *Web Site:* www.edco.ie, pg 356

Educational Distributors Ltd (New Zealand) *Tel:* (09) 818 4473 *Fax:* (09) 836 2399 *E-mail:* ed.nz@xtra.co. nz, pg 491

Educational Explorers (Publishers) Ltd (United Kingdom) *Tel:* (0118) 987 3101 *Fax:* (0118) 987 3103 *E-mail:* explorers@cuisenaire.co.uk *Web Site:* www. cuisenaire.co.uk, pg 685

Educational Press & Manufacturers Ltd (Ghana) *Tel:* (051) 5003; (051) 5845 *Fax:* (051) 227572, pg 301

Educational Publishers Council (United Kingdom) *Tel:* (020) 7691 9191 *Fax:* (020) 7691 9199 *E-mail:* mail@publishers.org.uk *Web Site:* www. publishers.org.uk, pg 1281

Educational Publishers Ltd (Ghana) *Tel:* (021) 220395 *Fax:* (021) 227572, pg 301

The Educational Publishing House Ltd (Hong Kong) *Tel:* 24088801 *Fax:* 2810 4201, pg 314

Educational Research & Study Group (Nigeria), pg 500

Educational Supplies Pty Ltd (The Dominie Group) (Australia) *Tel:* (02) 99050201 *Fax:* (02) 99055209, pg 20

Educational Writers' Group (United Kingdom) *Tel:* (020) 7373 6642 *Fax:* (020) 7373 5768 *E-mail:* info@ societyofauthors.org *Web Site:* www.societyofauthors. org, pg 1281

Educum Publishers Ltd (South Africa), pg 559

EDULIS (Education Library & Information Services) (South Africa) *Tel:* (021) 957-9600 *Fax:* (021) 948-0748 *E-mail:* edulis@pgwc.gov.za *Web Site:* wced. wcape.gov.za, pg 1542

EDUSC - Editora da Universidade do Sagrado Coracao (Brazil) *Tel:* (014) 3235-7111 *Fax:* (014) 3235-7219 *E-mail:* edusc@usc.br *Web Site:* www.edusc.com.br, pg 81

Eduskunnan Kirjasto (Finland) *Tel:* (09) 4321 *Fax:* (09) 432 3495 *E-mail:* kirjasto@eduskunta.fi; library@ parliament.fi *Web Site:* www.eduskunta.fi/kirjasto/, pg 1503

Edwina Publishing (Australia) *Tel:* (03) 9836 3810 *Fax:* (03) 9830 1356 *Web Site:* www. edwinapublishing.com, pg 20

Eekhoorn BV Uitgeverij (Netherlands) *Tel:* (036) 610577 *Fax:* (036) 620982 *E-mail:* info@weton-wesgram.nl *Web Site:* www.eekhoorn.com, pg 478

Uitgeverij de Eenhoorn (Belgium) *Tel:* (056) 60 54 60 *Fax:* (056) 61 69 81 *E-mail:* info@eenhoorn.be *Web Site:* www.eenhoorn.be, pg 66

Eesti Entsuklopeediakirjastus (Estonia) *Tel:* 6999 620 *Fax:* 6999 621 *E-mail:* ene@ene.ee *Web Site:* www. ene.ee, pg 139

Eesti Piibliselts (Estonia) *Tel:* 631 1671 *Fax:* 631 1438 *E-mail:* eps@eps.ee *Web Site:* www.eps.ee, pg 139

Eesti Rahvusraamatukogu (Estonia) *Tel:* 630 7611 *Fax:* 631 1410 *E-mail:* nlib@nlib.ee *Web Site:* www. nlib.ee, pg 139, 1502

EFE Tres D-Pub Juridicas Ltda (Brazil) *Tel:* (084) 2233394 *Fax:* (084) 2232263 *E-mail:* f3dsat@ truenetrn.com.br, pg 81

eFeF-Verlag/Edition Ebersbach (Switzerland) *Tel:* (056) 4260618 *Fax:* (056) 4270461 *E-mail:* info@efefverlag. ch *Web Site:* www.efefverlag.ch, pg 618

Effata Editrice (Italy) *Tel:* (0121) 353452 *Fax:* (0121) 353839 *E-mail:* info@effata.it *Web Site:* www.effata.it, pg 384

Effective Publishing (United Kingdom) *Tel:* (01926) 812110, pg 1281

Effendi Harahap Bookstore (Indonesia) *Tel:* (024) 3544694, pg 1308

EFR-Editrici Francescane (Italy) *Tel:* (049) 8225702 *Fax:* (049) 8225713 *E-mail:* info@ bibliotecafrancescana.it *Web Site:* www.biblia.it, pg 384

Efstathiadis Group SA (Greece) *Tel:* 2105154650 *Fax:* 2105154657 *E-mail:* info@efgroup.gr *Web Site:* www.efgroup.gr, pg 1303

Ediciones Ega (Spain) *Tel:* (04) 4216787 *Fax:* (04) 4213010, pg 577

Egales (Editorial Gai y Lesbiana) (Spain) *Tel:* (093) 4127283 *Fax:* (093) 4127283 *E-mail:* egales@auna. com *Web Site:* www.editorialegales.com, pg 577

Egan Publishing Pty Ltd (Australia) *Tel:* (03) 5923451 *Fax:* (03) 95931026, pg 20

Egan-Reid Ltd (New Zealand) *Tel:* (09) 3784100 *Fax:* (09) 3784300 *E-mail:* publishing@eganreid.com *Web Site:* www.egan-reid.com, pg 1171

Egan-Reid Ltd (New Zealand) *Tel:* (09) 3784100 *Fax:* (09) 3784300 *E-mail:* publishing@eganreid.co.nz *Web Site:* www.egan-reid.com, pg 1236

Editions EGC (Monaco) *Tel:* (093) 97984006 *Fax:* (093) 92052422 *E-mail:* multip@webstore.mc, pg 470

EGEA (Edizioni Giuridiche Economiche Aziendali) (Italy) *Tel:* (02) 58365751 *Fax:* (02) 58365753 *E-mail:* egea.edizioni@egea.uni-bocconi.it, pg 384

Egerton University (Kenya) *Tel:* (051) 61620; (051) 61031; (051) 61032 *Fax:* (051) 62527 *Web Site:* www. egerton.ac.ke, pg 430

Egerton University Library (Kenya) *Tel:* (051) 62265; (051) 62491; (051) 62389; (051) 62278 *Fax:* (051) 62527 *E-mail:* info@egerton.ac.ke *Web Site:* www. egerton.ac.ke, pg 1521

Egmont EHAPA Verlag GmbH (Germany) *Tel:* (030) 24008-0 *Fax:* (030) 24008-599 *Web Site:* www.ehapa. de, pg 217

Egmont Franz Schneider Verlag GmbH (Germany) *Tel:* (089) 3 58 11-6 *Fax:* (089) 3 58 11-7 55 *E-mail:* postmaster@schneiderbuch.de *Web Site:* www. schneiderbuch.de, pg 217

Egmont International Holding A/S (Denmark) *Tel:* 33 30 55 50 *Fax:* 33 32 19 02 *E-mail:* egmont@egmont.com *Web Site:* www.egmont.com, pg 130

Egmont Lademann A/S (Denmark) *Tel:* 3615 6600 *Fax:* 3644 1162 *Web Site:* www.egmontbogklub.dk, pg 1241

Egmont Latvia SIA (Latvia) *Tel:* (07) 244066; (07) 467931; (07) 468671 *Fax:* (07) 860049 *E-mail:* egmont@egmont.lv *Web Site:* www.egmont.lv, pg 441

Egmont Lietuva (Lithuania) *Tel:* (02) 231265; (02) 231266; (02) 231267 *Fax:* (02) 231269 *E-mail:* egmont@egmont.com *Web Site:* www.egmont. com, pg 445

Egmont Pestalozzi-Verlag (Germany) *Tel:* (089) 35811 *Fax:* (089) 5811-869, pg 218

Egmont Serieforlaget A/S (Denmark) *Tel:* 70 20 50 35 *Fax:* 33 30 57 60; 36 18 58 90 *E-mail:* abonnement@ tsf.egmont.com *Web Site:* www.serieforlaget.dk, pg 130

Egmont Serieforlaget (Sweden) *Tel:* (040) 6939400 *Fax:* (040) 6939498 *E-mail:* info@egmont.com *Web Site:* www.egmont.com, pg 606

Egmont, SRO (Slovakia) *Tel:* (02) 4333 8064; (02) 4333 3933 *Fax:* (02) 43338755 *E-mail:* egmont@netlab.sk, pg 555

Egmont vgs verlagsgesellschaft mbH (Germany) *Tel:* (0221) 20811-0 *Fax:* (0221) 20811-66 *E-mail:* info@vgs.de *Web Site:* www.vgs.de, pg 218

Egyptian Association for Library & Information Science (Egypt (Arab Republic of Egypt)) *Tel:* (02) 5676365 *Fax:* (02) 5729659, pg 1561

Egyptian National Library (Dar-ul-Kutub) (Egypt (Arab Republic of Egypt)) *Tel:* (02) 900 232, pg 1501

The Egyptian Society for the Dissemination of Universal Culture & Knowledge (ESDUCK) (Egypt (Arab Republic of Egypt)) *Tel:* (02) 35425079; (02) 3542 0295 *Fax:* (02) 3540295, pg 137

The Egyptian Society for the Dissemination of Universal Culture & Knowledge (ESDUCK) (Egypt (Arab Republic of Egypt)) *Tel:* (02) 7940295; (02) 7945079 *Fax:* (02) 7940295, pg 1120

The Egyptian Society for the Dissemination of Universal Culture & Knowledge (ESDUCK) (Egypt (Arab Republic of Egypt)) *Tel:* (02) 3542 0295; (02) 35425079 *Web Site:* www.worldwatch.org, pg 1137

Ehrenwirth Verlag (Germany) *Tel:* (02202) 121-330 *Fax:* (02202) 121-920 *E-mail:* ehrenwirth@luebbe.de *Web Site:* www.luebbe.de, pg 218

Ehrenwirth Verlag GmbH (Germany) *Tel:* (02202) 121-0 *Fax:* (02202) 121 928 *Web Site:* www.ehrenwirth.de, pg 218

Eichborn AG (Germany) *Tel:* (069) 256003-0 *Fax:* (069) 256003-30 *E-mail:* rights@eichborn.de; vertrieb@ eichborn.de *Web Site:* www.eichborn.de, pg 218

Eichosha Company Ltd (Japan) *Tel:* (03) 3263-1641 *Fax:* (03) 3263-6174 *E-mail:* info@eichosha.co.jp *Web Site:* www.eichosha.co.jp, pg 413

J W Eides Forlag A/S (Norway) *Tel:* (05) 32 90 40 *Fax:* (05) 31 90 18 *Web Site:* www.eideforlag.no, pg 504

Drei Eidgenossen Verlag (Switzerland) *Tel:* (061) 475166 *Fax:* (061) 475166, pg 618

Eiffes Romain (Luxembourg) *Tel:* 23651052 *E-mail:* rend@pt.lu, pg 447

The Eighteen Nineties Society (United Kingdom) *Tel:* (01869) 248340 *Web Site:* www.1890s.org, pg 1402

The Eihosha Ltd (Japan) *Tel:* (03) 5206-6020 *Fax:* (03) 5206-6022 *E-mail:* e@eihosha.co.jp *Web Site:* www. eihosha.co.jp, pg 413

Eike-Boekklub (South Africa) *Tel:* (012) 401 0700 *Fax:* (012) 3255498 *E-mail:* lapa@atkv.org.za, pg 1245

Eiland-Verlag Sylt Frank Roseman (Germany) *Tel:* (04651) 936212 *Fax:* (04651) 936214 *E-mail:* info@eiland-verlag.de *Web Site:* www.eiland-verlag.de, pg 218

Ein Shams University Library (Egypt (Arab Republic of Egypt)) *Tel:* (02) 4820230; (02) 6831474; (02) 6831231; (02) 6831492; (02) 6831417; (02) 6831090 *Fax:* (02) 687824 *E-mail:* info@asunet.shams.edu.eg *Web Site:* net.shams.edu.eg, pg 1502

Giulio Einaudi Editore SpA (Italy) *Tel:* (011) 56561 *Fax:* (011) 542903 *Web Site:* www.einaudi.it, pg 384

Bibliotheek Technische Universiteit Eindhoven (Netherlands) *Tel:* (040) 2472381 *Fax:* (040) 2447015 *E-mail:* helpdesk.bib@tue.nl *Web Site:* www.tue.nl/bib, pg 1529

EinfallsReich Verlagsgesellschaft MbH (Germany) *Tel:* (05533) 2017, pg 218

Eironeia-Verlag (Germany) *Tel:* (0761) 581617 *Fax:* (0761) 3603474529, pg 218

Editions Eisele SA (Switzerland) *Tel:* (024) 4531149 *Fax:* (024) 4531901 *E-mail:* pied.du.jura@vtx.ch *Web Site:* www.eisele.ch, pg 618

Christian Ejlers' Forlag aps (Denmark) *Tel:* 3312 2114 *Fax:* 3312 2884 *E-mail:* liber@ce-publishers.dk *Web Site:* www.ejlers.dk, pg 130

EK-Verlag GmbH (Germany) *Tel:* (0761) 70310-31 *Fax:* (0761) 70310-50, pg 218

Ekab Business Ltd (Ghana) *Tel:* (021) 225318, pg 301

Ekdoseis Kazantzaki (Kazantzakis Publications) (Greece) *Tel:* 2103642829 *Fax:* 2103642830, pg 304

Ekdoseis Thetili (Greece) *Tel:* 2103302229; 210 7511300, pg 304

Ekdotike Athenon SA (Greece) *Tel:* 2103608911 *Fax:* 2103606157, pg 304

Ekdotikos Oikos Adelfon Kyriakidi A E (Greece) *Tel:* 2310208540 *Fax:* 2310245541 *E-mail:* johnkyr@the.forthnet.gr, pg 304

Ekelunds Forlag AB (Sweden) *Tel:* (08) 821320 *Fax:* (08) 832956 *E-mail:* education@ekelunds.se, pg 606

Ekenas Tryckeri AB (Finland) *Tel:* (019) 222 800 *Fax:* (019) 222 815 *E-mail:* leif.rex@eta.fi, pg 141

Izdatelstvo Ekologija (Russian Federation) *Tel:* (095) 9287860, pg 540

Ekonomibok Forlag AB (Sweden) *Tel:* (042) 929 50 *Fax:* (042) 929 50, pg 606

Polskie Wydawnictwo Ekonomiczne PWE SA (Poland) *Tel:* (022) 827 80 01 *Fax:* (022) 827 55 67 *E-mail:* pwe@pwe.com.pl *Web Site:* www.pwe.com.pl, pg 518

Izdatelstvo 'Ekonomika' (Russian Federation) *Tel:* (095) 240-4877; (095) 240-4848 *Fax:* (095) 240-4817 *E-mail:* info@economizdat.ru *Web Site:* www. economizdat.ru, pg 540

El Ancora Editores (Colombia) *Tel:* (01) 283 9040; (01) 342 6224; (01) 283 9235 *Fax:* (01) 283 9235 *E-mail:* ancoraed@elancoraeditores.com *Web Site:* www.elancoraeditores.com, pg 110

EL Ciervo 96 (Spain) *Tel:* (093) 200 51 45; (093) 201 00 96 *Fax:* (093) 201 10 15 *E-mail:* redaccion@elciervo.es *Web Site:* www.elciervo.es, pg 577

El Colegio de Michoacan AC (Mexico) *Tel:* (0351) 515 71 00 *Fax:* (0351) 5157100 (ext 1742) *E-mail:* publica@colmich.cmich.udg.mx; publica@colmich.edu.mx *Web Site:* www.colmich.edu.mx, pg 461

El Hogar y la Moda SA (Spain) *Tel:* (093) 508 70 00 *Fax:* (093) 454 87 72 *E-mail:* hymsa@hymsa.com *Web Site:* www.hymsa.com, pg 577

Dar-El-Machreq Sarl (Lebanon) *Tel:* (01) 202423; (01) 202424 *Fax:* (01) 329348 *E-mail:* machreq@cyberia.net.lb *Web Site:* www.darelmachreq.com, pg 442

Editorial El Manual Moderno SA de CV (Mexico) *Tel:* (055) 2651100; (055) 2651124; (055) 2651121 *Fax:* (055) 2651175 *E-mail:* mmoderno@compuserve.com.ux *Web Site:* www.manualmoderno.com.mx, pg 461

El Viso, SA Ediciones (Spain) *Tel:* (091) 5196576; (091) 5196583 *Fax:* (091) 5196583 *E-mail:* lvisoh@anexo.es, pg 577

Eland Publishing Ltd (United Kingdom) *Tel:* (020) 7833 0762 *Fax:* (020) 7833 4434 *E-mail:* info@travelbooks.co.uk *Web Site:* www.travelbooks.co.uk, pg 685

Elanders Publishing AS (Norway) *Tel:* 22636400 *Fax:* 22636594, pg 504

ELC International (United Kingdom) *Tel:* (01865) 513186; (01865) 26520284 *Fax:* (01865) 513186; (01865) 26530180 *E-mail:* snyderpub@aol.com, pg 685

ELCIN Book Depot (Namibia) *Tel:* (065) 240211 *Fax:* (065) 240536, pg 1319

NV Drukkerij Eldorado (Suriname) *Tel:* 472362, pg 603

Electa (Italy) *Tel:* (02) 21563426 (ext 406) *Fax:* (02) 21563350 *Web Site:* www.electaweb.it, pg 384

Electre (France) *Tel:* (01) 44 41 28 00 *Fax:* (01) 44 41 28 65 *E-mail:* biblio@electre.com *Web Site:* www.electre.com, pg 161

Electroliber Lda (Portugal) *Tel:* (021) 940 6750 *Fax:* (021) 942 52 14 *E-mail:* electrliber@mail.telepac.pt, pg 1328

Electronic Publishing Services Ltd (EPS) (United Kingdom) *Tel:* (020) 7837 3345 *Fax:* (020) 7837 8901 *E-mail:* eps@epsltd.com *Web Site:* www.epsltd.com, pg 685

Electronic Technology Publishing Co Ltd (Hong Kong) *Tel:* 2342 8298; 2342 8299; 2342 9845 *Fax:* 2341 4247 *E-mail:* info@electronictechnology.com *Web Site:* www.electronictechnology.com, pg 314

Electronica Books & Media Ltd (United Kingdom) *Tel:* (01932) 765119 *Fax:* (01932) 765429, pg 1341

Electronics Industry Publishing House (China) *Tel:* (010) 68159318; (010) 68159020 *Fax:* (010) 68159032 *Web Site:* www.phei.com.cn, pg 104

Edizioni dell'Elefante (Italy) *Tel:* (06) 4423 4315; (06) 9784 0709 *Fax:* (06) 9784 0052 *E-mail:* info@edelefante.it *Web Site:* www.edelefante.it, pg 384

Eleftheri Skepsis (Greece) *Tel:* 2103614736; 2103630697 *E-mail:* info@eleftheriskepsis.gr *Web Site:* www.eleftheriskepsis.gr, pg 1303

G C Eleftheroudakis Co Ltd (Greece) *Tel:* 2103222255; 2103229388 *Fax:* 2103231401; 2103229388, pg 1303

Eleftheroudakis, GCSA International Bookstore (Greece) *Tel:* 2103229388 *E-mail:* elebooks@netor.gr, pg 304

Elegance Finance Printing Services Ltd (Hong Kong) *Tel:* 2283 2222 *Fax:* 2521 3616 *E-mail:* saledept@elegancefinptg.com, pg 1168

Elegance Finance Printing Services Ltd (Hong Kong) *Tel:* 2283 2222 *Fax:* 2283 2283; 2521 3616 *Web Site:* www.eleganceholdings.com, pg 1235

Elegance Printing & Book Binding (USA) (United States) *Tel:* 516-676-5941 *Fax:* 516-676-5973 *Web Site:* www.elegancebooks.com, pg 1156, 1177, 1219, 1230

Elektor-Verlag GmbH (Germany) *Tel:* (0241) 889090 *Fax:* (0241) 8890988 *E-mail:* redaktion@elektor.de *Web Site:* www.elektor.de, pg 218

Elektrowirtschaft Verlag (Switzerland) *Tel:* (01) 2994141 *Fax:* (01) 2994140 *E-mail:* redaktion@infel.ch *Web Site:* www.infel.ch, pg 618

Element Books Ltd (United Kingdom) *Tel:* (01747) 851448 *Fax:* (01747) 855721, pg 685

Element Uitgevers (Netherlands) *Tel:* (035) 6941750 *Fax:* (035) 6945824 *E-mail:* element@wxs.nl, pg 478

Elephas Books Pty Ltd (Australia) *Tel:* (08) 9370 1461 *Fax:* (08) 9341 8952, pg 20

Editora Elevacao (Brazil) *Tel:* (011) 3358-6868; (011) 3358-6875; (011) 3358-6869 *Fax:* (011) 3331-5803 *E-mail:* info@elevacao.com.br *Web Site:* www.elevacao.com.br, pg 81

Elfande Ltd (United Kingdom) *Tel:* (01372) 220330 *Fax:* (01372) 220340 *E-mail:* sales@contact-uk.com *Web Site:* www.contact-uk.com, pg 685

Ediciones Elfos SL (Spain) *Tel:* (093) 4069479 *Fax:* (093) 4069006 *E-mail:* eltos-ed@teleline.es *Web Site:* www.edicioneselfos.com, pg 577

Edward Elgar Publishing Ltd (United Kingdom) *Tel:* (01242) 226934 *Fax:* (01242) 262111 *E-mail:* info@e-elgar.co.uk *Web Site:* www.e-elgar.co.uk, pg 685

Elgin Consultants Ltd (Hong Kong) *Tel:* 2815 1680 *Fax:* 2815 1706, pg 1146

Elias Modern Publishing House (Egypt (Arab Republic of Egypt)) *Tel:* (02) 5903756; (02) 5939544 *Fax:* (02) 5880091 *E-mail:* eliasmph@gega.net *Web Site:* www.eliaspublishing.com, pg 138

The George Eliot Fellowship (United Kingdom) *Tel:* (024) 7659 2231 *Web Site:* www.sndc.demon.co.uk/alsdef.htm#e, pg 1402

Elitc Printing Co Ltd (Hong Kong) *Tel:* 2558 0119 *Fax:* 2897 2675 *E-mail:* sales@elite.com.hk *Web Site:* www.elite.com.hk, pg 1146

Elkar, Euskal Liburu eta Kantuen Argitaldaria, SL (Spain) *Tel:* (943) 310327 *Fax:* (943) 310345, pg 577

David Ell Press Pty Ltd (Australia) *Tel:* (02) 5551634 *Fax:* (02) 5557067, pg 21

Elle Di Ci - Libreria Dottrina Cristiana (Italy) *Tel:* (011) 9552111 *Fax:* (011) 9574048 *E-mail:* editoriale@elledici.org *Web Site:* www.elledici.org, pg 384

Ellebore Editions (France) *Tel:* (01) 40 01 09 49 *Fax:* (01) 40 01 09 94 *E-mail:* ellebore@wfi.fr; info@ellebore.fr *Web Site:* www.wfi.fr/ellebore, pg 161

Verlag Heinrich Ellermann GmbH & Co KG (Germany) *Tel:* (040) 607909-08 *Fax:* (040) 607909-59 *E-mail:* ellermann@vsg-hamburg.de *Web Site:* www.ellermann.de, pg 218

Ellerstroms (Sweden) *Tel:* (046) 323295 *Fax:* (046) 323295 *E-mail:* info@ellerstroms.se *Web Site:* www.ellerstroms.se, pg 606

Ellert & Richter Verlag GmbH (Germany) *Tel:* (040) 39 84 77-0 *Fax:* (040) 39 84 77-23 *E-mail:* info@ellert-richter.de *Web Site:* www.ellert-richter.de, pg 218

Elliniki Etaireia Metafraston Logotechnias (Greece) *Tel:* 2106717466 *Fax:* 2106717466, pg 1138

Elliniki Leschi Tou Vivliou (Greece) *Tel:* 2106463888 *Fax:* 2106463263 *E-mail:* elli@gezmanosnet.gr, pg 304

Elliot Right Way Books (United Kingdom) *Tel:* (01737) 832202 *Fax:* (01737) 830311 *E-mail:* info@right-way.co.uk *Web Site:* www.right-way.co.uk, pg 686

Elliott & Thompson (United Kingdom) *Tel:* (020) 7831 5013 *Fax:* (020) 7831 5011 *E-mail:* gmo73@dial.pipex.com *Web Site:* elliottthompson.com, pg 686

Ellipses - Edition Marketing SA (France) *Tel:* (01) 45 67 74 19 *Fax:* (01) 47 34 67 94 *E-mail:* infos@editions-ellipses.com *Web Site:* www.editions-ellipses.fr, pg 161

Aidan Ellis Publishing (United Kingdom) *Tel:* (01548) 842755 *E-mail:* mail@aidanellispublishing.co.uk *Web Site:* www.demon.co.uk/aepub, pg 686

Thomas Ellis Memorial Fund (United Kingdom) *Tel:* (029) 2038 2656 *Fax:* (029) 2039 6040 *E-mail:* awards@wales.ac.uk *Web Site:* www.wales.ac.uk/newpages/external/E5536.asp, pg 1402

ELLUG (Editions Litteraires et Linguistiques de l'Universite de Grenoble III) (France) *Tel:* (04) 76 82 43 72; (04) 76 82 77 74 *Fax:* (04) 76 82 41 85 *E-mail:* ellug@u-grenoble3.fr *Web Site:* www-ellug.u-grenoble3.fr/ellug, pg 161

Elm Publications (United Kingdom) *Tel:* (01487) 773254; (01487) 773238 *E-mail:* elm@elm-training.co.uk *Web Site:* www.elm-training.co.uk, pg 686

Elmar BV (Netherlands) *Tel:* (015) 215 32 32 *Fax:* (015) 215 32 30 *E-mail:* elmar@elmar.nl *Web Site:* 212.83.197.79, pg 478

Edicoes ELO (Portugal) *Tel:* (061) 812 143; (061) 812 344 *Fax:* (061) 81 28 20 *E-mail:* eloag@elografica.pt *Web Site:* www.elografica.pt, pg 526

Elpis Verlag GmbH (Germany) *Tel:* (06221) 165789, pg 219

Buchhandlung zum Elsasser AG (Switzerland) *Tel:* (01) 261 08 47; (01) 251 16 12 *Fax:* (01) 261 08 97, pg 1335

Elsevier Advanced Technology (United Kingdom) *Tel:* (01865) 843000 *Fax:* (01865) 843010 *E-mail:* eatsales@elsevier.co.uk (sales) *Web Site:* www.elsevier.com, pg 686

Elsevier Australia (Australia) *Tel:* (029) 5178999 *Toll Free Tel:* 1-800 263 951 (within Australia); 0-800 170 165 (to Australia from New Zealand) *Fax:* (029)

5172249 *Toll Free Fax:* 0-800 170 160 (from Australia to New Zealand) *E-mail:* service@elsevier.com.au *Web Site:* www.elsevier.com.au, pg 21

Elsevier GmbH/Urban & Fischer Verlag (Germany) *Tel:* (089) 5383-0 *Fax:* (089) 5383-939 *E-mail:* info@ elsevier-deutschland.de *Web Site:* www.elsevier.de, pg 219

Elsevier Ltd (United Kingdom) *Tel:* (01865) 843000 *Fax:* (01865) 843010 *E-mail:* initial.surname@elsevier. com *Web Site:* www.elsevier.com, pg 686

Elsevier SAS (Editions Scientifiques et Medicales Elsevier) (France) *Tel:* (01) 71 72 46 50 *Fax:* (01) 71 72 46 50 *Web Site:* www.elsevier.fr, pg 161

Elsevier Science (Japan) *Tel:* (03) 5561-5033 *Toll Free Tel:* (0120) 383-608 (within Japan) *Fax:* (03) 5561-5047 *E-mail:* info@elsevier.co.jp *Web Site:* www. elsevier.co.jp, pg 413

Elsevier Science BV (Netherlands) *Tel:* (020) 5862560 *Fax:* (020) 4852457 *E-mail:* nlinfo-f@elsevier.nl, pg 478

Elstead Maps (United Kingdom) *Tel:* (01252) 703472 *Fax:* (01252) 703971 *E-mail:* enquiry@elstead.co.uk *Web Site:* www.elstead.co.uk, pg 1341

Elton Publications (Australia) *Tel:* (08) 9 446 1328 *Fax:* (08) 9 445 8229 *E-mail:* elton@iinet.net.au *Web Site:* www.elton.iinet.net.au, pg 21

Elvetica Edizioni SA (Switzerland) *Tel:* (091) 6835056 *Fax:* (091) 6837605 *E-mail:* info@swissfinance.com, pg 618

N G Elwert Verlag (Germany) *Tel:* (06421) 17090 *Fax:* (06421) 15487 *E-mail:* elwertmail@elwert.de *Web Site:* www.elwert.de, pg 219

Uitgeverij Elzenga (Netherlands) *Tel:* (020) 55 11 262, pg 478

Gholam Emami (Germany) *Tel:* (0911) 288356 *Fax:* (0911) 288356, pg 219

Emece Editores SA (Argentina) *Tel:* (011) 4382-4045; (011) 4382-4043 *Fax:* (011) 4383-3793 *E-mail:* info@eplaneta.com.ar; pasiusis@planeta.com. ar *Web Site:* www.emece.com.ar, pg 5

Emerald (United Kingdom) *Tel:* (01274) 777700 *Fax:* (01274) 785201 *E-mail:* info@emeraldinsight. com; information@emeraldinsight.com (academic sales & enquiries); editorial@emeraldinsight.com (editorial) *Web Site:* www.emeraldinsight.com, pg 686

Emerald City Books (Australia) *Tel:* (02) 7641115 *Fax:* (02) 7641115 *E-mail:* emeraldcitybooks@ hotmail.com, pg 21

Emerald Publications (Ireland) *Tel:* (021) 962853 *Fax:* (021) 310983 *E-mail:* alongk@iol.ie, pg 356

Editura Eminescu (Romania) *Tel:* (01) 2228540, pg 534

Emirates Printing Press (LLC) (United Arab Emirates) *Tel:* (04) 347 5550; (04) 347 5544 *Fax:* (04) 347 5959 *E-mail:* eppdubai@emirates.net.ae *Web Site:* www. eppdubai.com, pg 1214

Emmaus Bible School (United Republic of Tanzania) *Tel:* (061) 354500 *Fax:* (061) 350911 *E-mail:* CMML-Dodoma@maf.org, pg 639

Emons Verlag (Germany) *Tel:* (0221) 56977-0 *Fax:* (0221) 524937 *E-mail:* info@emons-verlag.de *Web Site:* www.emons-verlag.de, pg 219

Emperor Publishing (Australia) *Tel:* (02) 9261 4055 *Fax:* (02) 9264 9435 *E-mail:* pa@oxfordsquare.com. au, pg 21

Empire Printing Ltd (Hong Kong) *Tel:* 2665 5193 *Fax:* 2661 7722, pg 1146

Emporio de Promocoes Artistica Cultural e Editora Ltda (Brazil) *Tel:* (011) 8262992 *Fax:* (011) 661135, pg 81

Empresa Brasileira de Pesquisa Agropecuaria (Brazil) *Tel:* (061) 348-4113 *Fax:* (061) 347-1041 *E-mail:* webmaster@sct.embrapa.br *Web Site:* www. embrapa.br, pg 81

Empresa Moderna Lda (Mozambique) *Tel:* (01) 424594, pg 471

Empresas Editoriales SA (Mexico) *Tel:* (05) 5288979; (05) 5288417 *Fax:* (05) 5288417, pg 461

Editorial Empuries (Spain) *Tel:* (093) 4870062 *Fax:* (093) 4874147, pg 577

Enalios (Greece) *Tel:* 2102531614 *Fax:* 210 02184854, pg 1303

Enciclopedia Catalana, SA (Spain) *Tel:* (093) 412 0030 *Fax:* (093) 301 4863 *Web Site:* www.enciclopedia-catalana.com, pg 577

Encres Vives (France) *Tel:* (05) 62740787 *E-mail:* encres@mygale.org, pg 161

Ediciones Encuentro SA (Spain) *Tel:* (091) 532 26 07 *Fax:* (091) 532 23 46 *E-mail:* encuentro@ediciones-encuentro.es *Web Site:* www.ediciones-encuentro.es, pg 577

Encyclopaedia Britannica (Australia) Inc (Australia) *Tel:* (02) 9923 5600 *Fax:* (02) 9929 3758 *E-mail:* sales@britannica.com.au *Web Site:* www. britannica.com.au, pg 21

Encyclopaedia Britannica (UK) International Ltd (United Kingdom) *Tel:* (020) 7500 7800; (0845) 075 700 (orders CD or DVD inside UK); (0177) 901 3948 (orders CD or DVD outside UK); (0845) 075 8000 (order books inside UK); (0845) 901 3948 (order books outside UK) *Fax:* (020) 7500 7878 *E-mail:* enquiries@britannica.co.uk *Web Site:* www. britannica.co.uk, pg 687

Encyclopedia Britannica (Germany) *Tel:* (0251) 48 227-0 *Fax:* (0251) 48 227-27 *E-mail:* lexikadienst@aol.com *Web Site:* www.britannica.de, pg 219

Encyclopedia Judaica (Israel) *Tel:* (02) 6557822 *Fax:* (02) 6528962 *E-mail:* info@keter-books.co.il *Web Site:* www.keter-books.co.il, pg 363

Encyclopedia of China Publishing House (China) *Tel:* (010) 68315610 *Fax:* (010) 68316510 *E-mail:* ygh@bj.col.com.cn, pg 104

Encyclopedia Universalis France SA (France) *Tel:* (01) 45 72 72 72 *Fax:* (01) 45 72 03 43 *E-mail:* contact@ universalis.fr *Web Site:* www.universalis.fr, pg 161

Les Encyclopedies du Patrimoine (France) *Tel:* (01) 42 60 66 63 *Fax:* (01) 42 60 66 73, pg 161

Enda Tiers Monde (Senegal) *Tel:* (0221) 821-60-27; (0221) 822-42-29 *Fax:* (0221) 822-26-95 *E-mail:* enda@enda.sn *Web Site:* www.enda.sn, pg 546

Ediciones Endymion (Spain) *Tel:* (01) 5223668; (01) 5222210, pg 577

EnEffect, Center for Energy Efficiency (Bulgaria) *Tel:* (02) 963 17 14; (02) 963 07 23; (02) 963 21 69 *Fax:* (02) 963 25 74 *E-mail:* eneffect@mail.orbitel.bg *Web Site:* www.eneffect.bg, pg 93

Energeia sp zoo Wydawnictwo (Poland) *Tel:* (022) 847 00 53 *Fax:* (022) 847-00-53, pg 518

Energica Foerlags AB/Halsabocker (Sweden) *Tel:* (0250) 55 20 00 *Fax:* (0250) 43191 *Web Site:* www.energica. com, pg 606

Energoatomizdat (Russian Federation) *Tel:* (095) 9259993 *Fax:* (095) 2356585, pg 540

The Energy Information Centre (United Kingdom) *Tel:* (01638) 751 400 *Fax:* (01638) 751 801 *E-mail:* info@eic.co.uk *Web Site:* www.eic.co.uk, pg 687

Engel & Bengel Verlag (Germany) *Tel:* (06353) 8107 *Fax:* (06353) 507057 *E-mail:* verlag@engelundbengel. de *Web Site:* www.engelundbengel.de, pg 219

Engelhorn Verlag GmbH (Germany) *Tel:* (089) 45554-0 *Fax:* (089) 45554-111, pg 219

Englisch Verlag GmbH (Germany) *Tel:* (0611) 9 427 2-0 *Fax:* (0611) 9 42 72 30 *E-mail:* info@englisch-verlag.de *Web Site:* www.englisch-verlag.de, pg 219

The English Agency (Japan) Ltd (Japan) *Tel:* (03) 3406 5385 *Fax:* (03) 3406 5387 *E-mail:* info@eaj.co.jp, pg 1124

The English Association (United Kingdom) *Tel:* (0116) 252 3982 *Fax:* (0116) 252 2301 *E-mail:* engassoc@le. ac.uk *Web Site:* www.le.ac.uk/engassoc, pg 1402

English Book Store (India) *Tel:* (011) 332 9126 *Fax:* (011) 332 1731, pg 1305

English Language Editors' Association (ELEAS) (Israel) *Tel:* (02) 586-5772 *Fax:* (02) 586-6411 *Web Site:* www.geocities.com/athens/stage/4942/ 8Eleas.html, pg 1395

The English-Speaking Union of the Commonwealth (United Kingdom) *Tel:* (020) 7529 1550 *Fax:* (020) 7495 6108 *E-mail:* esu@esu.org *Web Site:* www.esu. org, pg 1402

English Teaching Professional (United Kingdom) *Tel:* (020) 7222 1155 *Fax:* (020) 7222 1551 *E-mail:* info@etprofessional.com *Web Site:* www. etprofessional.com, pg 687

Verlag Peter Engstler (Germany) *Tel:* (09774) 858490 *Fax:* (09774) 858491 *E-mail:* engstler-verlag@t-online. de *Web Site:* www.engstler-verlag.de, pg 219

Enkay Publishers Pvt Ltd (India) *Tel:* (011) 301-6994; (011) 301-2314 *Fax:* (011) 301-2314, pg 331

Enna (Italy) *Tel:* (0935) 500368 *Fax:* (0935) 500568, pg 384

Enne (Italy) *Tel:* (0874) 412357 *Fax:* (0874) 412357 *E-mail:* ed.enne@virgilio.it, pg 384

Ennsthaler GesmbH & Co KG (Austria) *Tel:* (07252) 52053-10 *Fax:* (07252) 52053-16 *E-mail:* buero@ ennsthaler.at *Web Site:* www.ennsthaler.at, pg 50

Enosis Hellinon Bibliothekarion (Greece) *Tel:* 2103226 625, pg 1564

Enrique Libreria (Spain) *Tel:* (091) 522 80 88, pg 1333

Johan Enschede Amsterdam BV (Netherlands) *Tel:* (020) 585 86 00 *Fax:* (020) 585 86 01 *E-mail:* info@jea.nl *Web Site:* www.jea.nl, pg 478

Ensslin und Laiblin Verlag GmbH & Co KG (Germany) *Tel:* (07121) 98 98 0 *Fax:* (07121) 98 98 44 *E-mail:* ensslin-verlag@t-online.de *Web Site:* www. ensslin-verlag.de, pg 219

Editions Entente (France) *Tel:* (01) 55 42 84 00 *Fax:* (01) 40 49 01 02, pg 161

Enterprise International (Hong Kong) *Tel:* 25734161 *Fax:* 28383469, pg 1304

Enterprise Nationale du Livre (ENAL) (Algeria) *Tel:* (021) 737494; (021) 735841 *Fax:* (021) 735841, pg 2

Enterprise Publications (Australia) *Tel:* (08) 8261 9528 *Fax:* (08) 8261 9528, pg 21

Entretenlibro SA de CV (Mexico) *Tel:* (09183) 425570, pg 461

Envirobook (Australia) *Tel:* (02) 9518 6154 *Fax:* (02) 9518 6156 *E-mail:* trekaway@sia.net.au, pg 21

Environmental Research Unit (Ireland) *Tel:* (01) 660 25 11 *Fax:* (01) 668 00 09, pg 356

Enzyklopadie Verlag (Romania) *Tel:* (01) 2243667; (01) 2244014 *Fax:* (01) 2243667, pg 535

EOS Gabinete de Orientacion Psicologica (Spain) *Tel:* (091) 554 12 04 *Fax:* (091) 554 12 03 *E-mail:* eos@eos.es *Web Site:* www.eos.es, pg 577

EOS Verlag der Benefiktiner der Erzabtei St. Ottilien (Germany) *Tel:* (08193) 71261 *Fax:* (08193) 6844 *E-mail:* mail@eos-verlag.de *Web Site:* www.eos-verlag.de, pg 219

EP Graphics (United States) *Tel:* 260-589-2145 *Toll Free Tel:* 877-589-2145 *Fax:* 260-589-2810 *Web Site:* www. epgraphics.com, pg 1219

EPA (Editions Pratiques Automobiles) (France) *Tel:* (01) 43 92 30 00 *Fax:* (01) 43 92 33 81 *Web Site:* www. editionsduchene.fr, pg 161

Editions de l'Epargne (France) *Tel:* (01) 44 16 95 80 *Fax:* (01) 44 16 95 99, pg 161

EPB Publishers Pte Ltd (Singapore) *Tel:* 278 0881 *Fax:* 278 2456 *E-mail:* epb@sbg.com.sg, pg 551

EPER (United Kingdom) *Tel:* (0131) 650 6200 *Fax:* (0131) 667 5927 *E-mail:* ials.enquiries@ed.ac.uk *Web Site:* www.ials.ed.ac.uk, pg 687

Editions les Eperonniers (Belgium) *Tel:* (010) 813614 *Fax:* (010) 815386, pg 66

Epikerotita (Greece) *Tel:* 2103636083; 210 3607382 *Fax:* 2103636083, pg 304

EPO Publishers, Printers, Booksellers (Belgium) *Tel:* (03) 2396874 *Fax:* (03) 2184604 *E-mail:* publishers@epo.be, www.epo.be, pg 66

EPP Books Services (Ghana) *Tel:* (021) 778853; (021) 778347 *Fax:* (021) 779099 *E-mail:* info@eppbooks. com *Web Site:* www.eppbooks.com, pg 301

Eppinger-Verlag OHG (Germany) *Tel:* (0791) 95061-0 *Fax:* (0791) 95061-41 *E-mail:* info@eppinger-verlag. de, pg 219

Epworth Press (United Kingdom) *Tel:* (01733) 325002 *Fax:* (01733) 384180 *Web Site:* www.mph.org.uk, pg 687

Era Books (India) *Tel:* (011) 473993; (022) 5741764, pg 331

Era Publications (Australia) *Tel:* (08) 8352 4122 *Fax:* (08) 8234 0023 *E-mail:* admin@erapublications. com; service@erapublications.com *Web Site:* www. erapublications.com, pg 21

Ediciones Era SA de CV (Mexico) *Tel:* (055) 55 28 1221 *Fax:* (055) 56 06 2904 *E-mail:* edicionesera@ edicionesera.com.mx *Web Site:* www.edicionesera. mx, pg 461

ERA Technology Ltd (United Kingdom) *Tel:* (01372) 367000 *Fax:* (01372) 367099 *E-mail:* info@era.co.uk *Web Site:* www.era.co.uk, pg 687

Editrice Eraclea (Italy) *Tel:* (02) 8693635 *Fax:* (02) 86453613 *E-mail:* cinquevie@libero.it, pg 384

Erasmus Grasser-Verlag GmbH (Germany) *Tel:* (08861) 241900 *Fax:* (08861) 241901 *Web Site:* www.eg-v.de, pg 219

ERB (Czech Republic) *Tel:* 224 810 053 *Fax:* 224 811 566 *Web Site:* www.prace.cz, pg 1241

L'Ere Nouvelle (France) *Tel:* (04) 93 99 30 13 *E-mail:* lerenouvelle@wanadoo.fr *Web Site:* assoc. wanadoo.fr/lerenouvelle/pub, pg 161

Erein (Spain) *Tel:* (0943) 218300; (0943) 218211 *Fax:* (0943) 218311 *E-mail:* erein@erein.com *Web Site:* www.erein.com, pg 577

Eremiten-Presse und Verlag GmbH (Germany) *Tel:* (0211) 66 05 90 *Fax:* (0211) 698 94 70, pg 220

Eren Yayincilik ve Kitapcilik Ltd Sti (Turkey) *Tel:* (0212) 251-2858; (0212) 252-0560 *Fax:* (0212) 243-3016 *E-mail:* eren@turk.net, pg 645

Editions Eres (France) *Tel:* (05) 61 75 15 76 *Fax:* (05) 61 73 52 89 *E-mail:* eres@edition-eres.com *Web Site:* www.edition-eres.com, pg 161

Eres Editions-Horst Schubert Musikverlag (Germany) *Tel:* (04298) 1676 *Fax:* (04298) 5312 *E-mail:* info@ eres-musik.de *Web Site:* www.eres-musik.de, pg 220

Eresco PT (Indonesia) *Tel:* (022) 5205985 *Fax:* (022) 5205984, pg 351

Eretz Hemdah Institute for Advanced Jewish Studies (Israel) *Tel:* (02) 537-1485 *Fax:* (02) 537-9626 *E-mail:* eretzhem@netvision.net.il *Web Site:* www. eretzhemdah.org, pg 363

Erevnites (Greece) *Tel:* 2105234415; 2105234232 *Fax:* (2210) 5241 863 *E-mail:* erevnite@otenet.gr *Web Site:* www.erevnites.gr, pg 1303

ERF-Verlag GmbH (Germany) *Tel:* (06441) 9570 *Fax:* (06441) 957120 *E-mail:* info@erf.de *Web Site:* www.erf.de, pg 220

ERGA SNC di Carla Ottino Merli & C (Edizioni Realizzazioni Grafiche - Artigiana) (Italy) *Tel:* (010) 8328441 *Fax:* (010) 8328799 *Web Site:* www.erga.it, pg 384

Ergebnisse Verlag GmbH (Germany) *Tel:* (040) 4801027 *Fax:* (040) 4801592, pg 220

Edition Ergo Sum (Austria) *Tel:* (02238) 77078 *Fax:* (02238) 77076 *E-mail:* apverlag@magnet.at, pg 50

Ergon Verlag Dr H J Dietrich (Germany) *Tel:* (0931) 280084 *Fax:* (0931) 282872 *E-mail:* service@ergon-verlag.de *Web Site:* www.ergon-verlag.de, pg 220

Erich-Weinert Universitatsbuchhandlung (Germany) *Tel:* (0391) 568590 *Fax:* (0391) 5685923 *E-mail:* e. angerer@weinert.de *Web Site:* www.weinert.de, pg 1300

Erika spol sro (Czech Republic) *Tel:* (02) 71913890 *Fax:* (02) 71913890, pg 123

Eriksson & Lindgren Bokforlag (Sweden) *Tel:* (08) 6523226; (08) 6523227 *Fax:* (08) 6523223 *E-mail:* info@eriksson-lindgren.se, pg 606

Erker-Verlag (Switzerland) *Tel:* (071) 227979 *Fax:* (071) 227919, pg 618

Universitaetsbibliothek Erlangen-Nuernberg (Germany) *Tel:* (09131) 85-22160 *Fax:* (09131) 85-29309 *E-mail:* direktion@bib.uni-erlangen.de *Web Site:* www. ub.uni-erlangen.de, pg 1507

Erlanger Verlag Fuer Mission und Okumene (Germany) *Tel:* (09874) 9 17 00 *Fax:* (09874) 9 33 70 *E-mail:* verlagsleitung@erlanger-verlag.de *Web Site:* www.erlanger-verlag.de, pg 220

L'Erma di Bretschneider SRL (Italy) *Tel:* (06) 6874127 *Fax:* (06) 6874129 *E-mail:* edizioni@lerma.it *Web Site:* www.lerma.it, pg 385

Edi.Ermes srl (Italy) *Tel:* (02) 7021121 *Fax:* (02) 70211283 *E-mail:* eeinfo@eenet.it, pg 385

Ernest Press (United Kingdom) *Tel:* (0141) 637 5492 *Fax:* (0141) 637 5492 *E-mail:* sales@ernest-press.co. uk *Web Site:* www.ernest-press.co.uk, pg 687

Ernst & Young (United Kingdom) *Tel:* (020) 7951 2000 *Fax:* (020) 7951 1345 *Web Site:* www.ey.com, pg 687

Ernst Kabel Verlag GmbH (Germany) *Tel:* (089) 381801-0 *Fax:* (089) 338704 *E-mail:* info@piper.de *Web Site:* www.piper.de, pg 220

Ernst Klett Verlag Gmbh (Germany) *Tel:* (0711) 6151790 *Fax:* (0711) 6151791 *Web Site:* www.klett-verlag.de, pg 220

Ernst-Moritz-Arndt Universitaet Greifswald, Universitaetsbibliothek (Germany) *Tel:* (03834) 86-1502 *Fax:* (03834) 86-1501 *E-mail:* ub@uni-greifswald.de *Web Site:* www.ub.uni-greifswald.de, pg 1507

Ernst, Wilhelm & Sohn, Verlag Architektur und technische Wissenschaft GmbH & Co (Germany) *Tel:* (030) 47031-200 *Fax:* (030) 47031-270 *E-mail:* info@ernst-und-sohn.de *Web Site:* www.wiley. vch.de/ernstsohn, pg 220

Ernster Sarl (Luxembourg) *Tel:* 22 50 77-1 *Fax:* 22 50 73 *E-mail:* librairie@ernster.com *Web Site:* www. ernster.com, pg 1316

Edition Hans Erpf Edition (Switzerland) *Tel:* (037) 711385 *Fax:* (037) 711968, pg 618

Editions Errance (France) *Tel:* (01) 43 26 85 82 *Fax:* (01) 43 29 34 88, pg 161

Errepar SA (Argentina) *Tel:* (011) 4370-2002 *Fax:* (011) 4307-9541 *E-mail:* clientes@errepar.com *Web Site:* www.errepar.com, pg 5

The Erskine Press (United Kingdom) *Tel:* (01953) 88 72 77 *Fax:* (01953) 88 83 61 *E-mail:* erskpres@aol.com *Web Site:* www.erskine-press.com, pg 687

Verlagsgesellschaft des Erziehungsvereins GmbH (Germany) *Tel:* (02845) 392-0 *Fax:* (02845) 392392 *E-mail:* info@neukirchener-verlag.de *Web Site:* www. neukirchener-verlag.de, pg 220

ESA Publications (NZ) Ltd (New Zealand) *Tel:* (09) 579 3126 *Toll Free Tel:* (0800) 372-266 *Fax:* (09) 579 4713 *Toll Free Fax:* (0800) 329-372 *E-mail:* info@ esa.co.nz *Web Site:* www.esa.co.nz, pg 491

ESAN - Escuela de Administracion de Negocios para Graduados, Direccion de Investigacion (Peru) *Tel:* (01) 317-7226 *Fax:* (01) 345-1328; (01) 345-1276 *E-mail:* cendoc@esan.edu.pe *Web Site:* www.esan.edu. pe, pg 1535

Escala Ltda (Colombia) *Tel:* (01) 2878200 *Fax:* (01) 2325148, pg 110

Verlag am Eschbach GmbH (Germany) *Tel:* (07634) 1088 *Fax:* (07634) 3796 *E-mail:* vertrieb@verlag-am-eschbach.de *Web Site:* www.verlag-am-eschbach.de, pg 220

Esco BVBA (Belgium) *Tel:* (03) 2223800 *Fax:* (03) 2223838, pg 67

Escrituras Editora e Distribuidora de Livros Ltda (Brazil) *Tel:* (011) 5082-4190 *Fax:* (011) 5082-4190 *E-mail:* escrituras@escrituras.com.br *Web Site:* www. escrituras.com.br, pg 81

Escuela Nacional de Biblioteconomia y Archivonomia (Mexico) *Tel:* (055) 5329 7176; (055) 5329 7181 *Web Site:* www.enba.sep.gob.mx, pg 1567

Fundacion Escuela Para Todos (Costa Rica) *Tel:* 2255438; 2255338; 2340530; 2341339 *Fax:* 2243014, pg 115

Escutcheon Press (Australia) *Tel:* (02) 4344 2304 *Fax:* (02) 4341 1248, pg 21

Ediciones Escuve SA (Spain) *Tel:* (091) 539-01-03 *Fax:* (091) 528-87-59, pg 578

Editorial Esfinge SA de CV (Mexico) *Tel:* (05) 3591313; (05) 3591111; (05) 3591515 *Fax:* (05) 5761343 *E-mail:* editorial@esfinge.com.mx *Web Site:* www. esfinge.com.mx, pg 461

Eshkol Books Publishers & Printing Ltd (Israel) *Tel:* (02) 5370451; (02) 5370179 *Fax:* (02) 5372732, pg 363

Esic Editorial (Spain) *Tel:* (091) 3527716 *Fax:* (091) 3528534 *E-mail:* editorial.mad@esic.es *Web Site:* www.esic.es, pg 578

Editorial Esin, SA (Spain) *Tel:* (093) 244 95 50 *Fax:* (093) 265 68 95 *E-mail:* combel@editorialcasals. com *Web Site:* www.editorialcasals.com, pg 578

Editions Eska (France) *Tel:* (01) 42 86 55 93 *Fax:* (01) 42 60 45 35 *E-mail:* eska@eska.fr *Web Site:* www. eska.fr, pg 162

Eska Interactive-Sybex France (France) *Tel:* (01) 42 86 55 73 *Fax:* (01) 42 60 45 35 *E-mail:* eska@eska.fr *Web Site:* www.sybex.fr, pg 162

Esogetics GmbH (Germany) *Tel:* (07251) 8001-40 *Fax:* (07251) 8001-55 *E-mail:* info-de@esogetics.com *Web Site:* www.esogetics.com, pg 220

Esoptron (Greece) *Tel:* 2103236852 *Fax:* 210 3210472, pg 1303

Libreria Esoterica (Chile) *Tel:* (02) 6338430 *Fax:* (02) 6397933 *E-mail:* wzzdarmd@entelchile.net, pg 1295

Verlag Esoterische Philosophie GmbH (Germany) *Tel:* (0511) 755331 *Fax:* (0511) 755334 *E-mail:* info@ esoterische-philosophie.de *Web Site:* www.esoterische-philosophie.de, pg 220

Espace de Libertes (Belgium) *Tel:* (02) 6276860 *Fax:* (02) 6266861, pg 67

Editions Espaces 34 (France) *Tel:* (04) 67 84 11 23 *Fax:* (04) 67 84 00 74 *E-mail:* chesp34@club-internet. fr *Web Site:* www.editions-espaces34.fr, pg 162

Espasa-Calpe Argentina SA (Argentina) *Tel:* (011) 4382-4043; (011) 4382-4045 *Fax:* (011) 4383-3793 *E-mail:* info@eplaneta.com.ar, pg 5

Casa del Libro Espasa-Calpe SA (Spain) *Tel:* (091) 481 13 71 *E-mail:* casadellibro@casadellibro.com *Web Site:* www.casadellibro.com, pg 1333

Editorial Espasa-Calpe SA (Spain) *Tel:* (091) 3589689 *Fax:* (091) 3589364; (091) 3589505 *E-mail:* sagerencias@espasa.es *Web Site:* www.espasa. com, pg 578

Espasa-Calpe Mexicana SA (Mexico) *Tel:* (05) 5758585 *Fax:* (05) 5758980, pg 461

Editorial Espaxs SA (Spain) *Tel:* (093) 253 0706 *Fax:* (093) 4510149 *E-mail:* espax-adm@stl. logiccontrol.es, pg 578

Universala Esperanto-Asocio (Netherlands) *Tel:* (010) 4361044 *Fax:* (010) 4361751 *E-mail:* info@uea.org *Web Site:* www.uea.org, pg 1269

Esperanto Translating Service (United Kingdom) *Tel:* (020) 84282829 *Fax:* (020) 84282829 *E-mail:* espero@moose.co.uk, pg 1140

Espiritualidad (Spain) *Tel:* (091) 350-49-22 *Fax:* (091) 350-49-22 *E-mail:* ede@edespiritualidad.org *Web Site:* www.edespiritualidad.org, pg 578

Espresso Verlag GmbH (Germany) *Tel:* (030) 5333 4444 *Fax:* (030) 5333 4159 *E-mail:* info@espresso-verlag. de *Web Site:* www.espresso-verlag.de, pg 221

L'Esprit Du Temps (France) *Tel:* (0556) 02 84 19 *Fax:* (0556) 02 91 31 *E-mail:* espritemp@aol.com *Web Site:* www.psy-book.net, pg 162

Editions Esprit Ouvert (Switzerland) *Tel:* (022) 3639240 *Fax:* (022) 3639242, pg 618

Esquina-Livraria e Papelaria Lda (Portugal) *Tel:* (022) 6065234 *Fax:* (022) 6053878 *E-mail:* livrariaesquina@ mail.telepac.pt *Web Site:* www.esquina-livraria.com, pg 1328

Ess Ess Publications (India) *Tel:* (011) 3260807 *Fax:* (011) 3274173 *E-mail:* sumitsethi@vsnl.com *Web Site:* www.essess.8m.oom, pg 331

Essay und Zeitgeist Verlag (Luxembourg) *Fax:* 425227, pg 447

Essegi (Italy) *Tel:* (0544) 499203 *Fax:* (0544) 499076 *E-mail:* essegi_libri@libero.it, pg 385

Esselibri (Italy) *Tel:* (081) 5757255 *Fax:* (081) 5757944 *E-mail:* info@simone.it *Web Site:* www.simone.it, pg 385

Esslinger Verlag J F Schreiber GmbH (Germany) *Tel:* (0711) 310594-6 *Fax:* (0711) 310594-77; (0711) 310594-65 *E-mail:* esslinger@klett-mail.de, pg 221

Editions de L'Est (France) *Tel:* (03) 88 15 77 27 *Fax:* (03) 88 75 16 21 *E-mail:* nueebleue@dna.fr, pg 162

estamp (United Kingdom) *Tel:* (020) 8994 2379 *Fax:* (020) 8994 2379 *E-mail:* st@estamp.demon.co. uk, pg 687

Editorial Estampa, Lda (Portugal) *Tel:* (021) 355 56 63 *Fax:* (021) 314 19 11 *E-mail:* estampa@mail.telepac. pt *Web Site:* www.browser.pt/estampa, pg 526

Estates Gazette (United Kingdom) *Tel:* (020) 8652 3500; (020) 7411 2540 (edit); (020) 7411 2626 (advertising); (01444) 445335 (subscriptions) *Fax:* (020) 7437 2432; (020) 7437 0294 (edit); (020) 7437 2432 (advertising); (01444) 445567 (subscriptions), pg 687

Libreria del Este (Venezuela) *Tel:* (0212) 951 2307; (0212) 951 1297, pg 1347

Biblioteca Estense Universitaria (Italy) *Tel:* (059) 222248 *Fax:* (059) 230195 *E-mail:* estense@kril.cedoc.unimo. it; biblio.estense@cedoc.mo.it *Web Site:* www.cedoc. mo.it/estense, pg 1519

Estonian Academy Publishers (Estonia) *Tel:* 645 4504 *Fax:* 646 6026 *E-mail:* niine@kirj.ee *Web Site:* www. kirj.ee, pg 139

Estonian ISBN Agency (Estonia) *Tel:* 630 7372 *Fax:* 631 1200 *E-mail:* eraamat@nlib.ee *Web Site:* www.nlib.ee, pg 139

Estonian Publishers Association (Estonia) *Tel:* (02) 6449866 *Fax:* (02) 6411443 *E-mail:* astat@eki.ee, pg 1256

Angel Estrada y Cia SA (Argentina) *Tel:* (011) 4344-5500 *Fax:* (011) 4331-6527 *E-mail:* editocom@ estrada.com.ar *Web Site:* www.estrada.com.ar, pg 5

Estragon Press Ltd (Ireland) *Tel:* (027) 61186 *Fax:* (027) 61186 *E-mail:* estragon@iol.ie, pg 356

Estrella Publishing (Philippines), pg 514

Estudio de Bioinformacion, S L (Spain) *Tel:* (096) 351 46 27 *Fax:* (096) 394 37 27 *E-mail:* bioinformacion@ bioinformacion.com *Web Site:* www.bioinformacion. com, pg 578

Instituto de Estudios Fiscales (Spain) *Tel:* (091) 5063740 (ext 51307) *Fax:* (091) 5273951 *E-mail:* ventas. campillo@minhac.es *Web Site:* www.minhac.es/ief, pg 578

Centro de Estudios Monetarios Latinoamericanos (CEMLA) (Mexico) *Tel:* (05) 533-0300 *Fax:* (05) 525-4432 *E-mail:* cemlasub@mail.internet.com.mx *Web Site:* www.cemla.org, pg 461

Instituto de Estudios Peruanos (Peru) *Tel:* (01) 332-6194; (01) 332-2156; (01) 332-6173; (01) 431-3167 *Fax:* (01) 432-4981 *E-mail:* libreria@iep.org.pe *Web Site:* iep.perucultural.org.pe, pg 512

Instituto de Estudios Riojanos (Spain) *Tel:* (0941) 262064; (0941) 262065 *Fax:* (0941) 246667, pg 578

Institut d'Estudis Metropolitans de Barcelona (Spain) *Tel:* (093) 691 83 61; (093) 691 97 97; (093) 691 91 82 *Fax:* (093) 580 65 72 *E-mail:* iermb@uab.es *Web Site:* www.uab.es/iemb/, pg 578

Centro De Estudos Africanos (Mozambique) *Tel:* (01) 490828; (01) 499876 *Fax:* (01) 491896 *E-mail:* ceadid@zebra.uem.mz *Web Site:* www.cea. uem.mz, pg 471

Etaireia Spoudon Neoellinikou Politismou Kai Genikis Paideias (Greece) *Tel:* 2106795000 *Fax:* 2106795090 *E-mail:* admin@moraitis.edu. gr *Web Site:* www.moraitis.edu.gr, pg 304

Etas Libri (Italy) *Tel:* (02) 50951 *Fax:* (02) 50952309 *E-mail:* etaslab@rcs.it *Web Site:* www.etaslab.it, pg 385

Publicaciones Etea (Spain) *Tel:* (0957) 222100 *Fax:* (0957) 222182 *E-mail:* comunica@etea.com *Web Site:* www.etea.com, pg 578

ETH- Bibliothek (Eidgenossische Technische Hochschule Bibliothek) (Switzerland) *Tel:* (01) 632 21 35 *Fax:* (01) 632 10 87 *E-mail:* info@library.ethz.ch *Web Site:* www.ethbib.ethz.ch, pg 1546

Ethekwini Municipal Libraries (South Africa) *Tel:* (031) 311 1111 *Fax:* (031) 311 2203, pg 1542

Ethics International Press Ltd (United Kingdom) *Tel:* (01223) 357458 *Fax:* (01223) 303598 *E-mail:* info@ethicspress.com *Web Site:* www. ethicspress.com, pg 687

Ethiope Publishing Corporation (Nigeria) *Tel:* (052) 253036, pg 500

Ethiopian Library & Information Association (Ethiopia) *Tel:* (01) 511344 *Fax:* (01) 552544, pg 1561

Ethiopian Nutrition Institute (ENI) (Ethiopia) *Tel:* (01) 151600 *Fax:* (01) 754744, pg 140

Ethnikon Idryma Erevnon (Greece) *Tel:* 2107210554 *Fax:* 2107246212, pg 1511

Institut d'Ethnologie du Museum National d'Histoire Naturelle (France) *Tel:* (01) 40 79 48 38 *Fax:* (01) 40 79 38 58 *E-mail:* diff.pub@mnhn.fr *Web Site:* www. mnhn.fr/publication, pg 162

Eton Press (Auckland) Ltd (New Zealand) *Tel:* (09) 4183635 *Fax:* (09) 4806488 *E-mail:* info@eton.co.nz *Web Site:* www.eton.co.nz, pg 491

ETR (Editrice Trasporti su Rotaie) (Italy) *Tel:* (03) 6541092 *Fax:* (03) 6541092 *E-mail:* etr@itreni.com *Web Site:* www.itreni.com, pg 385

Etu Ediciones SL (Spain) *Tel:* (093) 2741671 *Fax:* (093) 2741671 *E-mail:* etu@arrakis.es, pg 578

Institut d'Etudes Augustiniennes (France) *Tel:* (01) 43 54 80 25 *Fax:* (01) 43 54 39 55 *E-mail:* iea@wanadoo.fr, pg 162

Institut d'Etudes Slaves IES (France) *Tel:* (01) 43 26 50 89; (01) 43 26 79 18 *Fax:* (01) 43 26 16 23; (01) 55 42 14 66 *E-mail:* etudes.slaves@paris4.sorbonne. fr *Web Site:* www.etudes-slaves.paris4.sorbonne.fr, pg 162

EUDEBA (Editorial Universitaria de Buenos Aires) (Argentina) *Tel:* (011) 4383-8025 *Fax:* (011) 4383-2202 *E-mail:* eudeba@eudeba.com *Web Site:* www. eudeba.com.ar, pg 5

Eugenides Foundation Technical Library (Greece) *Tel:* 2109411181 *Fax:* 2109417372 *E-mail:* lib@ eugenfound.edu.gr *Web Site:* www.eugenfound.edu.gr, pg 1511

Biblioteca Nacional Eugenio Espejo de la Casa de la Cultura Ecuatoriana (Ecuador) *Tel:* (02) 2223391; (02) 2565721 (ext 120) *E-mail:* info@cce.org.ec *Web Site:* cce.org.ec, pg 1501

Eugrimas (Lithuania) *Tel:* 52 733 955; 52 754 754 *Fax:* 52 733 955 *E-mail:* info@eugrimas.lt *Web Site:* www.eugrimas.lt, pg 445

Eulama Literary Agencies (Italy) *Tel:* (06) 5407309 *Fax:* (06) 5408772 *E-mail:* eulama@tiscalinet.it, pg 1123

Eular Verlag (Switzerland) *Tel:* (061) 251317 *Fax:* (061) 251286 *E-mail:* eular@reinhardt.ch, pg 618

Eulen Verlag (Germany) *Tel:* (089) 47 07 77 44 *Fax:* (089) 47 07 77 42 *E-mail:* info@eulenverlag.de *Web Site:* www.eulen-verlag.de, pg 221

Eulenhof-Verlag Wolfgang Ehrhardt Heinold (Germany) *Tel:* (040) 490005-14 *Fax:* (040) 490005-15 *E-mail:* w.e.heinold@eulenhof.de *Web Site:* www. eulenhof.de, pg 221

Eulyu Publishing Co Ltd (Republic of Korea) *Tel:* (02) 7338151; (02) 7338152; (02) 7338153 *Fax:* (02) 7329154, pg 435

Eumo Editorial (Spain) *Tel:* (093) 889 28 18; (093) 889 29 61 *Fax:* (093) 889 35 41 *E-mail:* eumoeditorial@ eumoeditorial.com *Web Site:* www.eumoeditorial.com, pg 578

EUNSA (Ediciones Universidad de Navarra SA) (Spain) *Tel:* (0948) 256850 *Fax:* (0948) 256854 *E-mail:* eunsa@ibernet.com *Web Site:* www.eunsa.es, pg 578

Eurasia Academic Publishers (Bulgaria) *Tel:* (02) 241523 *E-mail:* eurasia@realsci.com *Web Site:* www.biblio.hit. bg, pg 93

Eurasia Press (Offset) Pte Ltd (Singapore) *Tel:* 2805522 *Fax:* 2800593; 3825458 *E-mail:* eurasia@mbox3. singnet.com.sg, pg 1151, 1171

Eurasia Press (Offset) Pte Ltd (Singapore) *Tel:* 2805522 *Fax:* 2800593, pg 1212

Eurasia Press (Offset) Pte Ltd (Singapore) *Tel:* 2805522 *Fax:* 2800593 *E-mail:* eurasia@mbox3.singnet.com.sg, pg 1227

Eurasia Press (Offset) Pte Ltd (Singapore) *Tel:* 2805522 *Fax:* 2800593, pg 1236

Eurasia Publishing House Private Ltd (India) *Tel:* (011) 7779891 *Fax:* (011) 7777446 *E-mail:* schandco@ giasdl01.vsnl.net.in, pg 331

Eureka Press Ltd (Jamaica) *Tel:* 876-962-3947 *Fax:* 876-961-5383 *E-mail:* eurekapr@cwjamaica.com, pg 410

Euro Print Verlag (Romania) *Tel:* (021) 0781-3716, pg 535

Euro Translations (United Kingdom) *Tel:* (020) 8668 6133 *Fax:* (020) 8668 6133 *E-mail:* info@euro-translations.net *Web Site:* www.euro-translations.net, pg 1140

Ediciones Euroamericanas (Mexico) *Tel:* (05) 56 10 01 33 *Fax:* (05) 56 10 01 33 *E-mail:* thielemedina@ prodigy.net.mx, pg 461

Eurobook Ltd (United Kingdom) *Tel:* (01865) 858333 *Fax:* (01865) 858263; (01865) 340087 *E-mail:* eurobook@compuserve.com, pg 687

Eurodiastasi (Greece) *Tel:* 2103844695 *Fax:* 210 3844888 *E-mail:* eurodiastasi@internet.gr; eurodiastasi@galaxynet.gr *Web Site:* www.eurodiastasi. gr, pg 1303

EuroGeoGrafiche Mencattini (Italy) *Tel:* (0575) 900010 *Fax:* (0575) 911161 *E-mail:* eurogeo@egm.it *Web Site:* www.egm.it, pg 385

Eurohueco SA (Spain) *Tel:* (093) 7730700 *Fax:* (093) 7730708 *Web Site:* www.eurohueco.es, pg 1213

Eurolibros (Colombia) *Tel:* (01) 2886400 *Fax:* (01) 2450291; (01) 3401811; (01) 3401830; (01) 2886400, pg 1296

Eurolibros Ltda (Colombia) *Tel:* (01) 2886400; (01) 3401837 *Fax:* (01) 2886400, pg 110

Euromedia Group-Odeon (Czech Republic) *Fax:* (02) 241 623 28 *E-mail:* odeon@euromedia.cz, pg 123

Euromonitor PLC (United Kingdom) *Tel:* (020) 7251 8024 *Fax:* (020) 7608 3149 *E-mail:* info@ euromonitor.com *Web Site:* www.euromonitor.com, pg 688

Europ Export Edition GmbH (Germany) *Tel:* (06151) 38920 *Fax:* (06151) 38 92 80 *E-mail:* info@abconline. de *Web Site:* www.abconline.de, pg 221

Publicacoes Europa-America Lda (Portugal) *Tel:* (01) 9211461; (01) 9211462 *Fax:* (01) 9217846, pg 526

Edizioni Europa (Italy) *Tel:* (06) 8419124, pg 385

Europa Konyvkiado (Hungary) *Tel:* (01) 331-2700 *Fax:* (01) 331-4162 *E-mail:* info@europakiado.hu *Web Site:* www.europakiado.hu, pg 318

Verlag Europa-Lehrmittel GmbH & Co KG (Germany) *Tel:* (02104) 6916-0 *Fax:* (02104) 6916-27 *E-mail:* info@europa-lehrmittle.de *Web Site:* www. europa-lehrmittel.de, pg 221

Europa Publications (United Kingdom) *Tel:* (020) 7842 2110; (020) 7842 2133 (marketing & sales) *Fax:* (020) 7842 2249 (marketing & sales) *E-mail:* info.europa@ tandf.co.uk *Web Site:* www.europapublications.com, pg 688

Europa Union Verlag GmbH (Germany) *Tel:* (0228) 7 29 00 0 *E-mail:* Service@euverlag.de *Web Site:* www. europa-union-verlag.de, pg 221

Europa Verlag AG (Switzerland) *Tel:* (01) 2611629; (01) 2516081, pg 618

Europa Verlag GmbH (Germany) *Tel:* (040) 355434-0 *Fax:* (040) 355434-66 *E-mail:* info@europaverlag.de *Web Site:* www.europaverlag.de, pg 221

Europaeische Verlagsanstalt GmbH & Rotbuch Verlag GmbH & Co KG (Germany) *Tel:* (040) 450194-0 *Fax:* (040) 450194-50 *E-mail:* info@rotbuch.de *Web Site:* www.rotbuch.de; www.europaeische-verlagsanstalt.de, pg 221

Verlag Europaeische Wehrkunde (Germany) *Tel:* (0228) 340884 *Fax:* (040) 79713304, pg 221

Europaring der Buch- und Schallplattenfreunde (Switzerland) *Tel:* (031) 584466, pg 1246

European Association for Health Information & Libraries (Netherlands) *Tel:* (030) 2619663 *Fax:* (030) 2311830 *E-mail:* EAHIL-secr@nic.surfnet.nl *Web Site:* www. eahil.org, pg 1269

European Association of Directory & Database Publishers (Belgium) *Tel:* (02) 6463060 *Fax:* (02) 6463637 *E-mail:* mailbox@eadp.org *Web Site:* www. eadp.be, pg 1252

European Book Service (Netherlands) *Tel:* (030) 6660211 *Fax:* (030) 6662674, pg 1320

European Booksellers Federation (EBF) (Belgium) *Tel:* (02) 223 49 40 *Fax:* (02) 223 49 38 *E-mail:* eurobooks@skynet.be *Web Site:* www.ebf-eu.org, pg 1252

European Foundation for the Improvement of Living & Working Conditions (Ireland) *Tel:* (01) 2043100 *Fax:* (01) 2826456 *E-mail:* postmaster@eurofound.eu. int *Web Site:* www.eurofound.ie, pg 356

European Healthcare Management Association (Ireland) *Tel:* (01) 283 9299 *Fax:* (01) 283 8653 *E-mail:* office@ehma.org *Web Site:* www.ehma.org, pg 356

European Information Association (United Kingdom) *Tel:* (0161) 228 3691 *Fax:* (0161) 236 6547 *E-mail:* eia@libraries.manchester.gov.uk *Web Site:* www.eia.org.uk/, pg 1281

European Schoolbooks Ltd (United Kingdom) *Tel:* (01242) 245252 *Fax:* (01242) 224137 *E-mail:* direct@esb.co.uk *Web Site:* www.eurobooks. co.uk, pg 688, 1341

European Society for Opinion & Marketing Research (Netherlands) *Tel:* (020) 664 21 41 *Fax:* (020) 664 29 22 *E-mail:* email@esomar.nl *Web Site:* www.esomar. org, pg 1269

European University Institute Library (Italy) *Tel:* (055) 4685340 *Fax:* (055) 4685283 *E-mail:* library@iue.it *Web Site:* www.iue.it, pg 1519

Europhone Language Institute (Pte) Ltd (Singapore) *Tel:* 3373617; 3363992 *Fax:* 3374506, pg 551

Europress Editores e Distribuidores de Publicacoes Lda (Portugal) *Tel:* (01) 9387180; (01) 9387190; (01) 9387317; (01) 9877560; (01) 9381450 *Fax:* (01) 9381452; (01) 9877560 *E-mail:* europress@mail. telepac.pt, pg 526

Eurospan Distribution Center Ltd (United Kingdom) *Tel:* (0161) 7642296 *Fax:* (0161) 7648213 *E-mail:* info@eurospan.co.uk *Web Site:* www. eurospan.co.uk, pg 1341

The Eurospan Group (United Kingdom) *Tel:* (020) 7240 0856 *Fax:* (020) 7379 0609 *E-mail:* info@eurospan. co.uk *Web Site:* www.eurospan.co.uk, pg 688

EUSIDIC (European Association of Information Services) (Netherlands) *Tel:* (020) 589 32 32 *Fax:* (020) 589 32 30 *E-mail:* eusidic@caos.nl *Web Site:* www.eusidic.org, pg 1269

Evagean Publishing (New Zealand) *Tel:* (07) 884-8783 *Fax:* (07) 884-8783 *E-mail:* alison.honeyfield@clear. net.nz *Web Site:* www.evagean.co.nz, pg 491

Evangel Publishing House (Kenya) *Tel:* (020) 8560839; (020) 8562047 *Fax:* (020) 8562050 *E-mail:* evanglit@ maf.or.ke; publisher@evangelpublishing.org *Web Site:* www.evangelpublishing.org, pg 430

Evangelical Press & Services Ltd (United Kingdom) *Tel:* (01325) 380232 *Toll Free Tel:* 866-588-6778 (US only) *Fax:* (01325) 466153 *Toll Free Fax:* 866-588-6778 (US only) *E-mail:* sales@evangelicalpress.org *Web Site:* www.evangelicalpress.org, pg 688

Evangelische Haupt-Bibelgesellschaft und von Cansteinsche Bibelanstalt (Germany) *Tel:* (030) 28878850-0 *Fax:* (030) 28878850-8 *E-mail:* kontakt@ ehbg.de *Web Site:* www.ehbg.de, pg 221

Evangelische Verlagsanstalt GmbH (Germany) *Tel:* (0341) 71141-0 *Fax:* (0341) 7114150 *E-mail:* info@eva-leipzig.de *Web Site:* www.eva-leipzig.de, pg 221

Evangelischer Presseverband fuer Baden eV (Germany) *Tel:* (0721) 93 27 50 *Fax:* (0721) 9 32 75 20, pg 222

Evangelischer Presseverband fuer Bayern eV (Germany) *Tel:* (089) 121 72-0 *Fax:* (089) 121 72-138 *E-mail:* info@epv.de *Web Site:* www.epv.de, pg 222

Evangelischer Presseverband in Osterreich (Austria) *Tel:* (01) 712 54 61 *Fax:* (01) 712 54 75 *E-mail:* epv@evang.at, pg 50

Evans Brothers Ltd (United Kingdom) *Tel:* (020) 7487 0920 *Fax:* (020) 7487 0921 *E-mail:* sales@ evansbrothers.co.uk *Web Site:* www.evansbooks.co.uk, pg 688

Evans Brothers (Nigeria Publishers) Ltd (Nigeria) *Tel:* (022) 417570; (022) 417601; (022) 407626, pg 500

Faith Evans Associates (United Kingdom) *Tel:* (020) 8340 9920 *Fax:* (020) 8340 9910, pg 1130

EVD eenheid Bibliotheek (Netherlands) *Tel:* (070) 778 8888 *Fax:* (070) 778 8889 *E-mail:* evd@info.evd.nl *Web Site:* www.evd.nl, pg 1529

Everbest Printing Co Ltd (Hong Kong) *Tel:* 2727 4433 *Fax:* 2772 7687 *E-mail:* sales@everbest.com.hk *Web Site:* www.everbest.com, pg 1146, 1168, 1208, 1226

Everest Editora (Portugal) *Tel:* (021) 9152483; (021) 9152510 *Fax:* (021) 9152525 *E-mail:* everesteditora@ mail.telepac.pt *Web Site:* www.everest.pt, pg 526

Evrodiastasi (Greece) *Tel:* 2108611303 *Fax:* 210 8611303, pg 304

EVT Energy Video Training & Verlag GmbH (Germany) *Tel:* (069) 431575 *Fax:* (069) 4950974, pg 222

Ewha Womans University Central Library (Republic of Korea) *Tel:* (02) 3277-3131 *Fax:* (02) 3277-2856 *E-mail:* infoserv@ewha.ac.kr *Web Site:* lib.ewha.ac.kr, pg 1522

Ewha Womans University Press (Republic of Korea) *Tel:* (02) 3277-2114 *Fax:* (02) 393-5903 *Web Site:* www.ewha.ac.kr/, pg 435

Ewing Memorial Library (Pakistan), pg 1533

Ex Libris Forlag A/S (Norway) *Tel:* (022) 47 11 00 *Fax:* (022) 47 11 49 *E-mail:* nwd@egmont.no, pg 504

Ex Libris Press (United Kingdom) *Tel:* (01225) 863595 *Fax:* (01225) 863595 *Web Site:* www.ex-librisbooks. co.uk, pg 689

Exandas Publishers (Greece) *Tel:* 2103822064; 2103084885 *Fax:* 2103873065 *Web Site:* www. exandasbooks.gr, pg 304

Editura Excelsior Art (Romania) *Tel:* (0256) 201078 *Fax:* (0256) 201078 *E-mail:* edituraelcelsior@rdslink. ro, pg 535

Ediciones Exclusivas SA (Mexico) *Tel:* (05) 815878, pg 461

Exhibitions International NV/SA (Belgium) *Tel:* (016) 296900 *Fax:* (016) 296129 *E-mail:* orders@ exhibitionsinternational.be *Web Site:* www. exhibitionsinternational.be, pg 1292

Exil Verlag (Germany) *Tel:* (069) 751102 *Fax:* (069) 751547 *E-mail:* fs7a020@uni-hamburg.de, pg 222

Exisle Publishing Ltd (New Zealand) *Tel:* (09) 817 9192 *Fax:* (09) 817 2295 *E-mail:* admin@exisle.co.nz *Web Site:* www.exisle.co.nz, pg 491

Helen Exley Giftbooks (United Kingdom) *Tel:* (01923) 250505 *Fax:* (01923) 818733 *Toll Free Fax:* 800-440 *E-mail:* enquiry@exleypublications.co.uk, pg 689

Edition Exodus (Switzerland) *Tel:* (01) 2041774 *Fax:* (01) 2024933 *E-mail:* editionexodus@ compuserve.com *Web Site:* www.kath.ch/exodus, pg 618

L'Expansion Scientifique Francaise (France) *Tel:* (01) 45 48 42 60 *Fax:* (01) 45 44 81 55 *E-mail:* expansionscientifiquefrancaise@wanadoo.fr *Web Site:* www.expansionscientifique.com, pg 162

Experimental Art Foundation (Australia) *Tel:* (08) 8211 7505 *Fax:* (08) 8211 7323 *E-mail:* eaf@eaf.asn.au *Web Site:* www.eaf.asn.au, pg 21

expert verlag GmbH, Fachverlag fuer Wirtschaft & Technik (Germany) *Tel:* (07159) 92 65-0 *Fax:* (07159) 92 65-20 *E-mail:* expert@expertverlag.de *Web Site:* www.expertverlag.de, pg 222

Expolibri GmbH (Germany) *Tel:* (0341) 2113 231 *Fax:* (0341) 2115 996, pg 222

Export Booksellers Group (United Kingdom) *Tel:* (020) 7802 0802 *Fax:* (020) 7802 0803 *E-mail:* mail@ booksellers.org.uk *Web Site:* www.booksellers.org.uk, pg 1153

Exportradet Spraktjanst AB (Sweden) *Tel:* (08) 783 85 00 *Fax:* (08) 662 90 93 *E-mail:* infocenter@ swedishtrade.se *Web Site:* www.swedishtrade.se, pg 1139

Groupe Express-Expansion (France) *Tel:* (01) 53 91 11 11 *Fax:* (01) 53 91 10 06 *Web Site:* www.groupe-expansion.com, pg 162

Express Media Corp (United States) *Tel:* 615-360-6400 *Toll Free Tel:* 800-336-2631 *Fax:* 615-360-3140 *E-mail:* info@expressmedia.com *Web Site:* www. expressmedia.com, pg 1156, 1177, 1219, 1238

Express Newspapers (United Kingdom) *Tel:* (020) 7928 8000 *Fax:* (020) 7922 7966, pg 689

Editora Expressao e Cultura-Exped Ltda (Brazil) *Tel:* (021) 444 06 00 *Fax:* (021) 440700 *E-mail:* exped@embratel.net.br, pg 81

Editorial Extemporaneos SA (Mexico) *Tel:* (05) 5875424 *Fax:* (05) 5878785, pg 462

Extent Verlag und Service Wolfgang M Flamm (Germany) *Tel:* (030) 3279805-0; (030) 3279805-11 *Fax:* (030) 3279805-35 *E-mail:* extent@t-online.de, pg 222

Extenza-Turpin (United Kingdom) *Tel:* (01767) 604 806 (sales manager) *Fax:* (01767) 601 640 *E-mail:* turpin@turpin-distribution.com *Web Site:* www.extenza-turpin.com, pg 1341

Universidad Externado de Colombia (Colombia) *Tel:* (01) 3428984; (01) 3420288 (ext 3151) *Fax:* (01) 3424948 *E-mail:* publicaciones@uexternado.edu.co *Web Site:* www.uexternado.edu.co, pg 110

Extraordinary People Press (Australia) *Tel:* (02) 9326 6609 *Fax:* (02) 9399 6587 *E-mail:* info@ extraordinarypeoplepress.com *Web Site:* www. extraordinarypeoplepress.com, pg 21

Eye Books (United Kingdom) *Tel:* (020) 8743 3276 *Fax:* (020) 8743 3276 *E-mail:* info@eye-books.com *Web Site:* www.eye-books.com, pg 689

Editions Eyrolles (France) *Tel:* (01) 44 41 11 11 *Fax:* (01) 44 41 11 85 *E-mail:* service-lecteurs@ editions-eyrolles.com *Web Site:* www.editions-eyrolles. com, pg 162

Ezel Erverdi (Dergah Yayinlari AS) Muessese Muduru (Turkey) *Tel:* (0212) 519 04 21; (0212) 516 00 47 *Fax:* (0212) 519 04 21 *E-mail:* bilgi@dergahyayinlari. com *Web Site:* www.dergahyayinlari.com, pg 645

Fabbri (GE) Ltd (United Kingdom) *Tel:* (020) 7836 0519; (020) 7468 5600 *Fax:* (020) 7836 0280 *E-mail:* mailbox@gefabbri.co.uk *Web Site:* www. gefabbri.co.uk, pg 689

Fabel-Verlag Gudrun Liebchen (Germany) *Tel:* (09701) 1463 *Fax:* (09701) 1463, pg 222

Faber & Faber Ltd (United Kingdom) *Tel:* (020) 7465 0045 *Fax:* (020) 7465 0034 *Web Site:* www.faber.co. uk, pg 689

Fabian Society (United Kingdom) *Tel:* (020) 7227 4900 *Fax:* (020) 7976 7153 *E-mail:* info@fabian-society. org.uk *Web Site:* www.fabian-society.org.uk, pg 689

Fabylon-Verlag (Germany) *Tel:* (0172) 8211847 *Fax:* (089) 8110882 *E-mail:* fabylon@t-online.de *Web Site:* www.fabylonzeitspur.de, pg 222

Facet NV (Belgium) *Tel:* (03) 227 40 28 *Fax:* (03) 227 37 92 *E-mail:* facet@village.uunet.be *Web Site:* www. mijnweb.nu/be021988, pg 67

Facet Publishing (United Kingdom) *Tel:* (020) 7255 0590 *Fax:* (020) 7255 0591 *E-mail:* info@facetpublishing. co.uk *Web Site:* www.facetpublishing.co.uk; www. cilip.org.uk, pg 689

Facet Publishing (United Kingdom) *Tel:* (020) 7255 0590 *Fax:* (020) 7255 0591 *E-mail:* info@facetpublishing. co.uk *Web Site:* www.facetpublishing.co.uk, pg 1573

Fachbuchhandlung fur Wirtschaft und Recht Dr Karl Stropek GmbH (Austria) *Tel:* (01) 4795495 *Fax:* (01) 4796230, pg 1290

Fachbuchverlag Leipzig GmbH (Germany) *Tel:* (0341) 4 90 34-0 *Fax:* (0341) 4 80 62 20 *E-mail:* voigt@ hanser.de *Web Site:* www.hanser.de, pg 222

Fachbuchverlag Pfanneberg & Co (Germany) *Tel:* (02104) 6916-0 *Fax:* (02104) 6916-27 *E-mail:* info@pfanneberg.de *Web Site:* www. pfanneberg.de, pg 222

Fachhochschule Dortmund Hochschulbibliothek (Germany) *Tel:* (0231) 7554047 *Fax:* (0231) 7554604 *E-mail:* bibliothek@fhb.fh-dortmund.de *Web Site:* www.fh-dortmund.de, pg 1507

Fachhochschule Stuttgart Hochschule der Medien (Germany) *Tel:* (0711) 257060 *Fax:* (0711) 25706300 *E-mail:* office@hdm-stuttgart.de; friedling@hdm-stuttgart.de *Web Site:* www.hdm-stuttgart.de, pg 1507

Fachhochschule Stuttgart - Hochschule der Medien (HdM) (Germany) *Tel:* (0711) 685 2807 *Fax:* (0711) 685 6650 *E-mail:* info@hdm-stuttgart.de *Web Site:* www.hdm-stuttgart.de, pg 1166, 1206

Fachmedien Verlag Winfried Ruf (FMV) (Germany) *Tel:* (08233) 4924 *Fax:* (08233) 4789, pg 222

Fachverband der Buch und Medienwirtschaft (Austria) *Tel:* (01) 50105 DW 3331; (01) 50105 DW 3333 *Fax:* (01) 50105 DW 3043 *E-mail:* buchwirtschaft@ wko.at *Web Site:* www.buchwirtschaft.at, pg 1251

Fachverlag fur das graphische Gewerbe GmbH (Germany) *Tel:* (089) 33036131 *Fax:* (089) 33036100, pg 222

Fachverlag Schiele & Schoen GmbH (Germany) *Tel:* (030) 253 75 20 *Fax:* (030) 251 72 48 *E-mail:* service@schiele-schoen.de *Web Site:* www. schiele-schoen.de, pg 222

Fackeltrager-Verlag GmbH (Germany) *Tel:* (0441) 980 66-0 *Fax:* (0441) 980 66-34 *E-mail:* info@lappan.de *Web Site:* www.lappan.de, pg 222

The Factory Shop Guide (United Kingdom) *Tel:* (020) 7622 3722 *Fax:* (020) 7720 3536 *E-mail:* factshop@ macline.co.uk, pg 689

Biblioteca Facultad de Humanidades y Ciencias de la Educacion (Uruguay) *Tel:* (02) 49 11 04; (02) 49 11 05; (02) 49 11 06 *Fax:* (02) 48 43 03 *E-mail:* biblio@ fhudec.edu.uy *Web Site:* www.rau.edu.uy/universidad/ fhcet.htm, pg 1553

Faculte de Medecine de Pharmuacie et d'Odonto-Stomatologie (Mali) *Tel:* 22 52 77 *Fax:* 22 96 58 *E-mail:* codiawara@caramail.com, pg 1526

Bibliotheque de la Faculte des Sciences de Tunis (Tunisia) *Tel:* 71872600 *Fax:* 71885073, pg 1549

Faculte des Sciences Humaines et Sociales de Tunis (Tunisia) *Tel:* 71560950; 71560840 *Fax:* 71567551, pg 643

Facultes Catoliques de Kinshasa (The Democratic Republic of the Congo) *Tel:* (088) 46 965 *Fax:* (088) 46 965 *E-mail:* facakin@ic.cd *Web Site:* www.cenco. cd/facultescath/, pg 114

Library of the Faculty of Law (Lebanon) *Tel:* (01) 200 625 *Fax:* (01) 215473 *E-mail:* css.biblio@usj.edu.lb *Web Site:* www.biblio-css.usj.edu.lb, pg 1523

FADL's Forlag A/S (Denmark) *Tel:* 35 35 62 87 *Fax:* 35 36 62 29 *E-mail:* forlag@fadl.dk *Web Site:* forlag.fadl. dk, pg 130

Forlaget Fag og Kultur (Norway) *Tel:* (022) 23 30 24 00 *Fax:* (022) 23 30 24 04 *E-mail:* firmapost@ fagogkultur.no *Web Site:* www.fagogkultur.no, pg 504

Olaiya Fagbamigbe Ltd (Publishers) (Nigeria) *Tel:* (034) 2075, pg 500

Forlaget for Faglitteratur A/S (Denmark) *Tel:* 33137900 *Fax:* 33145156, pg 130

Fairfield Marketing Group Inc (United States) *Tel:* 203-261-5585; 203-261-5568 *Fax:* 203-261-0884 *E-mail:* ffldmktgrp@aol.com *Web Site:* www. fairfieldmarketing.com, pg 1177, 1219

Fairfield Marketing Group Inc (United States) *Tel:* 203-261-5585; 203-261-5568 *Fax:* 203-261-0884 *E-mail:* ffijmktgrp@aol.com *Web Site:* www. fairfieldmarketing.com, pg 1238

Faksimile Verlag AG (Switzerland) *Tel:* (041) 429 08 20 *Fax:* (041) 429 08 40 *E-mail:* faksimile@faksimile.ch *Web Site:* www.faksimile.ch, pg 618

Christa Falk-Verlag (Germany) *Tel:* (08667) 14 13 *Fax:* (08667) 14 17 *E-mail:* email@chfalk-verlag.de *Web Site:* www.chfalk-verlag.de, pg 223

Falken-Verlag GmbH (Germany) *Tel:* (01805) 990505 *Fax:* (04136) 3333 *E-mail:* vertrieb.verlagsgruppe@ bertelsmann.de *Web Site:* www.randomhouse.de/falken, pg 223

Editions Fallois (France) *Tel:* (01) 42669195 *Fax:* (01) 49240637, pg 162

C J Fallon (Ireland) *E-mail:* sales@cjfallon.ie *Web Site:* www.cjfallon.ie, pg 356

Fama (Bulgaria) *Tel:* (02) 881175; (02) 657006 *Fax:* (02) 657006, pg 93

Famedram Publishers Ltd (United Kingdom) *Tel:* (01651) 842429 *Fax:* (01651) 842180 *E-mail:* adetola@ristol.co.uk *Web Site:* www.artwork. co.uk, pg 689

Family Health Publications (Australia) *Tel:* (08) 9389 8777 *Fax:* (08) 9389 8444 *Web Site:* www. familyhealth.info, pg 22

Family Reading Publications (Australia) *Tel:* (03) 5334 3244 *Fax:* (03) 5334 3299 *E-mail:* info@ familyreading.com.au *Web Site:* www.familyreading. com.au, pg 22

Fan Noli (Albania) *Tel:* (04) 244 399, pg 1

Editions Pierre Fanlac (France) *Tel:* (05) 53-53-41-90 *Fax:* (05) 53-08-05-85 *E-mail:* info@fanlac.com *Web Site:* www.fanlac.com, pg 162

Fanucci (Italy) *Tel:* (06) 639366384 *Fax:* (06) 6382998 *E-mail:* info@fanucci.it *Web Site:* www.fanucci.it, pg 385

Far East Book Co Ltd (Taiwan, Province of China) *Tel:* (02) 2311 8740 *Fax:* (02) 2311 4184 *E-mail:* service@mail.fareast.com.tw *Web Site:* www. fareast.com.tw, pg 635

Far Eastern University Library (Philippines) *Tel:* (02) 735-5649 *Fax:* (02) 732-0232 *Web Site:* www.feu.edu. ph/library.asp, pg 1535

Faradawn cc (South Africa) *Tel:* (011) 885-1847 *Fax:* (011) 885-1829 *E-mail:* faradawn@icon.co.za *Web Site:* www.faradawn.co.za, pg 1331

Clive Farahar & Sophie Dupre Booksellers (United Kingdom) *Tel:* (01249) 821121 *Fax:* (01249) 821202 *E-mail:* sophie@farahardupre.co.uk *Web Site:* www. farahardupre.co.uk, pg 1341

Editions Farel (France) *Tel:* (01) 64 68 46 44 *Fax:* (01) 64 68 39 90 *E-mail:* lire@editionsfarel.com *Web Site:* www.editionsfarel.com, pg 163

Farm-level Applied Methods for East & Southern Africa (FARMESA) (Zimbabwe) *Tel:* (04) 758051-4 *Fax:* (04) 758055 *E-mail:* fspzim@internet.co.zw; fspzim@harare.iafrica.com *Web Site:* www.farmesa.co. zw, pg 777

T C Farries & Co Ltd (United Kingdom) *Tel:* (01387) 720755 *Fax:* (01387) 721105, pg 1342

Farseeing Publishing Company Ltd (Taiwan, Province of China) *Tel:* (02) 23921167 *Fax:* (02) 23567448 *E-mail:* fars@msb.hinet.net *Web Site:* www.farseeing. com.tw, pg 635

Farsight Press (United Kingdom) *Tel:* (020) 8675 1693, pg 689

Fassbaender Verlag (Austria) *Tel:* (01) 8923546 *Fax:* (01) 8923546-22 *E-mail:* mail@fassbaender.com *Web Site:* www.fassbaender.com, pg 50

Editions Fata Morgana (France) *Tel:* (04) 67 54 40 40 *Fax:* (04) 67 04 14 91 *E-mail:* davidini@wanadoo.fr *Web Site:* perso.wanadoo.fr/fatamorgana, pg 163

Editorial Fata Morgana SA de CV (Mexico) *Tel:* (055) 52 80 08 29 *Fax:* (055) 52 80 81 37 *E-mail:* editorial@fatamorgana.com.mx *Web Site:* www.fatamorgana.com.mx, pg 462

Fatatrac (Italy) *Tel:* (055) 6810124 *Fax:* (055) 6810260 *E-mail:* info@fatatrac.com *Web Site:* www.fatatrac. com/, pg 385

Al-Fateh University, The Central Library (Libyan Arab Jamahiriya) *Tel:* (022) 605441 *Fax:* (022) 605460, pg 1523

Editions Faton (France) *Tel:* (03) 80 40 41 00 *Fax:* (03) 80 30 15 37 *E-mail:* infos@faton.fr *Web Site:* www. art-metiers-du-livre.com, pg 163

Ekkehard Faude Verlag (Germany) *Tel:* (041 71) 6883555 *Fax:* (041 71) 6883565, pg 223

Faust Vrancic (Croatia) *Tel:* (01) 4817-123; (01) 4558-469 *Fax:* (01) 4817-123 *E-mail:* fv@faust-vrancic.com *Web Site:* 90-stupnjeva.com; www.faust-vrancic.com, pg 117

Ediciones Librerias Fausto (Argentina) *Tel:* (011) 4372-4919 *Fax:* (011) 4372-3914 *E-mail:* fausto@fausto. com *Web Site:* www.fausto.com, pg 5

Favorit-Verlag Huntemann und Markus & Co GmbH (Germany) *Tel:* (07222) 2 22 54 *Fax:* (07222) 2 98 38 *E-mail:* info@favorit-verlag.de *Web Site:* www.favorit-verlag.de, pg 223

Librairie Artheme Fayard (France) *Tel:* (01) 45498200 *Fax:* (01) 42224017 *Web Site:* www.editions-fayard.fr, pg 163

Fazlee Sons (Pvt) Ltd (Pakistan) *Tel:* (021) 214585; (021) 212289 *Fax:* (021) 6640522 *E-mail:* fazlee@ tarique.khi.sdnpk.undp.org, pg 507

FBT de R Editions (France) *Tel:* (01) 41 15 19 69; (06) 07 68 33 71 *Fax:* (01) 41 15 19 69, pg 163

FCA Editora de Informatica (Portugal) *Tel:* (021) 3151218 *Fax:* (021) 577827, pg 526

Editora FCO Ltda (Brazil) *Tel:* (031) 2131288 *Fax:* (031) 2243825 *E-mail:* editorafco@ig.com.br, pg 81

Feakle Press (Australia) *Tel:* (02) 9557 3248, pg 22

Feather Books (United Kingdom) *Tel:* (01743) 872177 *Fax:* (01743) 872177 *E-mail:* john@waddysweb. freeuk.com *Web Site:* www.waddysweb.com, pg 690

FEDA SA (Switzerland) *Tel:* (091) 9235677 *Fax:* (091) 9220171, pg 618

Federacao Brasileira de Associacoes de Bibliotecarios - Comissao Brasileira de Documentacao Juridica (FEBAB/CBDJ) (Brazil) *Tel:* (011) 3257-9979 *Fax:* (011) 3257-9979 *E-mail:* febab@febab.org.br *Web Site:* www.febab.org.br, pg 1559

Federacion de Gremios de Editores de Espana (FGEE) (Spain) *Tel:* (091) 534 51 95 *Fax:* (091) 535 26 25 *E-mail:* fgee@fge.es *Web Site:* www. federacioneditores.org, pg 1274

Federal Publications (S) Pte Ltd (Singapore) *Tel:* 62139288 *Fax:* 62844733 *E-mail:* tpl@tpl.com.sg *Web Site:* www.tpl.com.sg, pg 551

Federal Publications Sdn Bhd (Malaysia) *Tel:* (03) 7351511 *Fax:* (03) 73 64620 *E-mail:* kesoon@pc. jaring.my, pg 452

Federation d'Activities Culturelles, Fac Editions (France) *Tel:* (01) 45 48 76 51 *Fax:* (01) 42 22 22 31, pg 163

Federation de l'Imprimerie et de la Communaute Graphique-FICG (France) *Tel:* (01) 46 34 21 15 *Fax:* (01) 46 33 73 34 *E-mail:* ficg@ficg.fr *Web Site:* www.ficg.fr, pg 1258

Federation des Enseignants Documentalistes de l'Education nationale (France) *Tel:* (01) 43 72 45 60 *Fax:* (01) 43 72 45 60 *E-mail:* fadben@wanadoo.fr *Web Site:* www.fadben.asso.fr, pg 1562

Federation Francaise de la Randonnee Pedestre (France) *Tel:* (01) 44 89 93 90 *Fax:* (01) 40 35 85 48 *E-mail:* info@ffrp.asso.fr *Web Site:* www.ffrp.asso.fr, pg 163

Federation Internationale des Traducteurs (FIT) (Austria) *Tel:* (01) 4403607; (01) 4709819 *Fax:* (01) 4403756; (01) 4708194 *E-mail:* info@fit.org *Web Site:* www.fit-ift.org/, pg 1251

Federation Luxembourgeoise des Editeurs de Livres, ASBL (Luxembourg) *Tel:* 439444 *Fax:* 439450 *E-mail:* promoculture@ibm.net, pg 1266

Federation of Children's Book Groups (United Kingdom) *Tel:* (0113) 2588910 *Fax:* (0113) 2588920 *E-mail:* info@fcbg.org.uk *Web Site:* www.fcbg.org.uk, pg 1281

Federation of European Publishers (FEP) (Belgium) *Tel:* (02) 7701110 *Fax:* (02) 7712071 *Web Site:* www. fep-fee.be, pg 1252

Federation of Indian Publishers (India) *Tel:* (011) 26964847; (011) 26852263 *Fax:* (011) 26864054 *E-mail:* fip1@satyam.net.in *Web Site:* www.fiponweb. com, pg 1263

The Federation Press (Australia) *Tel:* (02) 9552-2200 *Fax:* (02) 9552-1681 *E-mail:* info@federationpress. com.au *Web Site:* www.federationpress.com.au, pg 22

Federico Motta Editore SpA (Italy) *Tel:* (02) 300761; (02) 30076231 *Fax:* (02) 38010046; (02) 33403275 *E-mail:* info@mottaeditore.it *Web Site:* www. mottaeditore.it, pg 385

Libreria Universal Carlos Federspiel (Costa Rica), pg 1297

Feguagiskia' Studios (Italy) *Tel:* (010) 2757544 *Fax:* (010) 2510838, pg 385

Frank Fehmers Productions (Netherlands) *Tel:* (020) 6238766 *Fax:* (020) 6246262 *Web Site:* www.fbg. nl/34927, pg 478

Fehr'sche Buchhandlung AG (Switzerland) *Tel:* (075) 222 11 52; (075) 222 53 81, pg 1335

Editions Francois Feij (Switzerland) *Tel:* (021) 8254675, pg 618

Felag Islenskra Bokautgefenda (Iceland) *Tel:* 511 8020 *Fax:* 511 5020 *E-mail:* baekur@mmedia.is, pg 1263

Feldheim Publishers Ltd (Israel) *Tel:* (02) 6513947 *Fax:* (02) 6536061 *E-mail:* sales@feldheim.com *Web Site:* www.feldheim.com, pg 363

Fellowship of Australian Writers (Australia) *Tel:* (03) 9431 2370 *E-mail:* lynspire@bigpond.net.au *Web Site:* www.writers.asn.au, pg 1389

Fellowship of Australian Writers (Vic) Inc (Australia) *Tel:* (03) 9431 2370 *Web Site:* www.writers.asn.au, pg 1390

Felta Book Sales Inc (Philippines) *Tel:* (02) 913-4884 *Fax:* (02) 438-1755 *E-mail:* felta@info.com.ph, pg 1326

Giangiacomo Feltrinelli SpA (Italy) *Tel:* (02) 725721 *Fax:* (02) 72572500 *Web Site:* www.feltrinelli.it, pg 385

Librerie Feltrinelli SpA (Italy) *Tel:* (02) 7529151; (02) 748151 *Fax:* (02) 74815339 *E-mail:* info@lafeltrinelli. it *Web Site:* www.lafeltrinelli.it, pg 1310

Feltron-Elektronik Zeissler & Co GmbH (Germany) *Tel:* (02241) 48670 *Fax:* (02241) 404241, pg 223

Editions Des Femmes (France) *Tel:* (01) 42 22 60 74 *Fax:* (01) 42 22 62 73 *E-mail:* info@desfemmes.fr *Web Site:* www.desfemmes.fr, pg 163

Fen Kitabevi (Turkey) *Tel:* (0312) 425311 *Fax:* (0312) 4185109; (0312) 4171733, pg 1337

Fenda Edicoes (Portugal) *Tel:* (021) 8823650 *Fax:* (021) 8823659 *E-mail:* info@fenda.pt, pg 526

Fenice 2000 (Italy) *Tel:* (02) 66984638; (02) 67075155 *Fax:* (02) 67074283, pg 385

Fenix-Kustannus Oy (Finland) *Tel:* (09) 420 8190 *Fax:* (09) 420 8045, pg 141

Editions Le Fennec (Morocco) *Tel:* (02) 220519; (02) 268008; (02) 264380 *Fax:* (02) 264941 *E-mail:* fennec@techno.net.ma, pg 471

FEP International Pvt Ltd (Singapore) *Tel:* 4743135 *Fax:* 4752389, pg 551

FEP International Sdn Bhd (Malaysia) *Tel:* (03) 7036150; (03) 7036152; (03) 7036154 *Fax:* (03) 7036989, pg 452

Ferd Dummler's Verlag (Germany) *Tel:* (02203) 3029-0 *Fax:* (02203) 3029-40, pg 223

Ferdinand Berger und Sohne (Austria) *Tel:* (02982) 4161-332 *Fax:* (02982) 4161-382 *E-mail:* druckerei. office@berger.at *Web Site:* www.berger.at, pg 50

Ferdowsi University of Mashhad Central Library & Information Centre (Islamic Republic of Iran) *Tel:* (0511) 8789263-66; (0511) 8796798-9 *Fax:* (0511) 8796822 *E-mail:* info@ferdowsi.um.ac.ir *Web Site:* c-library.um.ac.ir, pg 1515

Feria Chilena del Libro Ltda (Chile) *Tel:* (02) 632 7334; (02) 639 6758 *Fax:* (02) 633 9374 *E-mail:* ventas@feriachilenadellibro.cl *Web Site:* www. feriachilenadellibro.cl, pg 1295

Feria del Libro (Uruguay) *Tel:* (02) 900 42 48 *Fax:* (02) 900 20 70, pg 1346

Livraria Ferin Ltda (Portugal) *Tel:* (021) 3424422; (021) 3467084 *Fax:* (021) 3471101 *E-mail:* livraria.ferin@ ferin.pt, pg 1328

Fern House (United Kingdom) *Tel:* (01353) 740222 *Fax:* (01353) 741987 *E-mail:* info@fernhouse.com *Web Site:* www.fernhouse.com, pg 1174

Editorial Libreria Amalio M Fernandez (Uruguay) *Tel:* (02) 9151/82; (02) 295 26 84 *Fax:* (02) 295 17 82, pg 772

Libreria Amalio M Fernandez SRL (Uruguay) *Tel:* (02) 95 26 84 *Fax:* (02) 95 17 82, pg 1346

Fernandez Editores SA de CV (Mexico) *Tel:* (05) 6056557 *Fax:* (05) 6889173 *Web Site:* www. fernandezeditores.com.mx, pg 462

Fernfawn Publications (Australia) *Tel:* (07) 3202 6157 *Fax:* (07) 3202 6157, pg 22

Fernhurst Books (United Kingdom) *Tel:* (01903) 882277 *Fax:* (01903) 882715 *E-mail:* sales@fernhurstbooks. co.uk *Web Site:* www.fernhurstbooks.co.uk, pg 690

Fernwood Press (Pty) Ltd (South Africa) *Tel:* (021) 7948636 *Fax:* (021) 7948339 *E-mail:* ferpress@iafrica. com *Web Site:* www.fernwoodpress.co.za, pg 559

Ferozsons (Pvt) Ltd (Pakistan) *Tel:* (042) 6301196; (042) 6301197; (042) 6301198 *Fax:* (042) 6369204 *E-mail:* ferozsons@showroom.edunet.sdnpk.undp.org, pg 507

Ferozsons (Pvt) Ltd (Pakistan) *Tel:* (042) 6301196; (042) 6301197; (042) 6301198; (042) 111-62-62-62 *Fax:* (042) 6369204 *E-mail:* support@ferozsons. pk *Web Site:* www.ferozsons.com.pk, pg 1324

Chaves Ferreira Publicacoes SA (Portugal) *Tel:* (021) 3871373 *Fax:* (021) 7161396 *E-mail:* chavesferreira@ mail.telepac.pt, pg 526

Franz Ferzak World & Space Publications (Germany) *Tel:* (09446) 1403, pg 223

Festina Lente Edizioni (Italy) *Tel:* (055) 292612 *Fax:* (055) 292612, pg 385

Festland Verlag GmbH (Germany) *Tel:* (0228) 36 20 21-23 *Fax:* (0228) 35 17 71 *E-mail:* verlag@festland-verlag.de *Web Site:* www.oeckl-online.de, pg 223

Festo Didactic GmbH & Co KG (Germany) *Tel:* (0711) 3467-1253 *Toll Free Tel:* 800 560-0967 (orders) *Fax:* (0711) 34754-1253 *Toll Free Fax:* 800 560-0843 (orders) *E-mail:* did@festo.com *Web Site:* www.festo. com/didactic, pg 223

Editions du Feu Nouveau (France) *Tel:* (01) 44844797, pg 163

FF Press (Romania) *Tel:* (01) 6191544 *Fax:* (01) 3129694, pg 535

FFSL (Federation francaise des syndicats de libraires) (France) *Tel:* (01) 42 82 00 03 *Fax:* (01) 42 82 10 51, pg 1258

FGUP Izdatelstvo Mashinostroenie (Russian Federation) *Tel:* (095) 2683858 *Fax:* (095) 2694897 *E-mail:* mashpubl@mashin.ru *Web Site:* www.mashin. ru, pg 540

FHB Exporter (Egypt (Arab Republic of Egypt)) *Tel:* (02) 2358329 *Fax:* (02) 2358329 *E-mail:* fhb@ link.net, pg 1299

FHG Publications Ltd (United Kingdom) *Tel:* (0141) 8870428 *Fax:* (0141) 8897204 *E-mail:* fhg@ipcmedia. com *Web Site:* www.holidayguides.com, pg 690

FIAF (International Federation of Film Archives) (Belgium) *Tel:* (02) 538 3065 *Fax:* (02) 534 4774 *E-mail:* info@fiafnet.org *Web Site:* www.fiafnet.org, pg 1252

Fiantsorohana NY Boky Malagasy, Office du Livre Malgache (Madagascar) *Tel:* (02) 24449, pg 1267

FiberMark Red Bridge International Ltd (United Kingdom) *Tel:* (01204) 556900 *Fax:* (01204) 384754 *E-mail:* sales@redbridge.co.uk *Web Site:* www. redbridge.co.uk, pg 1228

Fibre Leather Manufacturing Corp (United States) *Tel:* 508-997-4557 *Toll Free Tel:* 800-358-6012 *Fax:* 508-997-7268 *E-mail:* fibreleather@earthlink.net, pg 1230

Fibre Verlag (Germany) *Tel:* (0541) 431838 *Fax:* (0541) 432786 *E-mail:* info@fibre-verlag.de *Web Site:* www. fibre-verlag.de, pg 223

Fiction Factory International Ltd (Denmark) *Tel:* (043) 33 75 55 60 *Fax:* (043) 33 75 55 22 *E-mail:* information@gyldendal.dk *Web Site:* www. gyldendal-uddannelse.dk, pg 1241

Sadie Fields Productions Ltd (United Kingdom) *Tel:* (020) 8996 9970 *Fax:* (020) 8996 9977 *E-mail:* edith@tangobooks.co.uk, pg 690

Wolfgang Fietkau Verlag (Germany) *Tel:* (033203) 71 105 *Fax:* (033203) 71 109 *E-mail:* post@fietkau.de *Web Site:* www.fietkau.de, pg 223

Julio Logrado de Figueiredo, Lda (Portugal) *Tel:* (021) 7541600 *Fax:* (021) 7541609 *E-mail:* info@jlf.pt, pg 1328

Figueirinhas Lda (Portugal) *Tel:* (022) 332 53 00 *Fax:* (022) 332 59 07 *E-mail:* correio@liv-figueirinhas.pt, pg 1328

Livraria Editora Figueirinhas Lda (Portugal) *Tel:* (022) 324985 *Fax:* (022) 3325907 *E-mail:* correio@liv-figueirinhas.pt, pg 526

Filadelfia forlag (Iceland) *Tel:* 552-5155; 552-0735 *Fax:* 562-0735 *E-mail:* filadelfia-forlag@gospel.is, pg 322

Editions Filipacchi-Sonodip (France) *Tel:* (01) 41 34 90 69; (01) 41 34 90 55 *Fax:* (01) 41 34 90 70 *E-mail:* sonodip@hfp.fr, pg 163

Filistor Publishing (Greece) *Tel:* 2103818457, pg 1303

Ekdoseis Filon (Greece) *Tel:* 2103618705 *Fax:* 210 3618705, pg 304

Filozofski Fakultet Sveucilista u Zagrebu (Croatia) *Tel:* (01) 6120111 *Fax:* (01) 6156879 *E-mail:* tajnik_fakultet@ffzg.hr *Web Site:* www.ffzg.hr, pg 117

Financial Training Co (FTC) (United Kingdom) *Tel:* (020) 7481 6050 *Fax:* (020) 7265 0337 *E-mail:* finmkts@financial-training.com *Web Site:* www.financial-training.com, pg 690

Finansy i Statistika Publishing House (Russian Federation) *Tel:* (095) 925-47-08; (095) 925-35-02 *Fax:* (095) 925-09-57 *E-mail:* mail@finstat.ru *Web Site:* www.finstat.ru, pg 540

Finch Publishing (Australia) *Tel:* (02) 9418 6247 *Fax:* (02) 9418 8878 *E-mail:* info@finch.com.au *Web Site:* www.finch.com.au, pg 22

Findhorn Press Inc (United Kingdom) *Tel:* (01309) 690582 *Fax:* (01309) 690036 *E-mail:* info@ findhornpress.com *Web Site:* www.findhornpress.com, pg 690

Fine Art Publishing Pty Ltd (Australia) *Tel:* (02) 99668400 *Fax:* (02) 99660355 *E-mail:* info@gbpub. com.au *Web Site:* www.gbpub.com.au, pg 22

Bokforlaget Fingraf AB (Sweden) *Tel:* (08) 550 300 23 *Fax:* (08) 550 695 70, pg 606

Emil Fink Verlag (Germany) *Tel:* (0711) 814646 *Fax:* (0711) 8106070 *E-mail:* info@fink-verlag.de *Web Site:* www.fink-verlag.de, pg 223

Verlagsgruppe J Fink GmbH & Co KG (Germany) *Tel:* (0711) 81 4646 *Fax:* (0711) 81 06070 *E-mail:* info@fink-verlag.de *Web Site:* www.fink-verlag.de, pg 223

Wilhelm Fink GmbH & Co Verlags-KG (Germany) *Tel:* (05251) 127-5; (05251) 127-842 *Fax:* (05251) 127-860 *E-mail:* kontakt@fink.de *Web Site:* www.fink. de, pg 223

Finken Verlag GmbH (Germany) *Tel:* (06171) 6388-0 *Fax:* (06171) 6388-44 *E-mail:* info@finken.de *Web Site:* www.finken.de, pg 224

The Arnold & Leona Finkler Institute of Holocaust Research (Israel) *Tel:* (03) 5340333 *Fax:* (03) 5351233 *E-mail:* michmad@mail.biu.ac.il *Web Site:* www.biu. ac.il, pg 363

Finlands Svenska Forfattareforening (Finland) *Tel:* (09) 446266 *Fax:* (09) 446871, pg 1393

Finnish ISBN Agency (Finland) *Tel:* (09) 19144327 *Fax:* (09) 19144341 *E-mail:* isbn-keskus@helsinki.fi *Web Site:* www.lib.helsinki.fi, pg 1256

Finnish PEN Centre (Finland) *Tel:* (09) 3431186 *Fax:* (09) 3431186, pg 1393

Firebird Books Ltd (United Kingdom) *Tel:* (01202) 715349 (sales); (01258) 454675 (editorial) *Fax:* (01202) 736191 *E-mail:* skboorh@bournemouth-net.co.uk, pg 690

Firma KLM Privatee Ltd, Publishers & International Booksellers (India) *Tel:* (033) 274391; (033) 4681209 *Fax:* (033) 276544, pg 331

First & Best in Education Ltd (United Kingdom) *Tel:* (01536) 399004 (editorial); (01536) 399005 (accounts) *Fax:* (01536) 399012 *E-mail:* anne@ firstandbest.co.uk *Web Site:* www.firstandbest.co.uk, pg 690

First Edition Translations Ltd (United Kingdom) *Tel:* (01223) 356733 *Fax:* (01223) 321488 *E-mail:* info@firstedit.co.uk *Web Site:* www.firstedit. co.uk, pg 1140

Editions First (France) *Tel:* (01) 45 49 60 00 *Fax:* (01) 45 49 60 01 *E-mail:* firstinfo@efirst.com *Web Site:* www.efirst.com, pg 163

Librairie Fischbacher (France) *Tel:* (01) 43 26 84 87 *Fax:* (01) 43 26 48 87 *E-mail:* info@ librairiefischbacher.fr *Web Site:* www. librairiefischbacher.fr, pg 163

F Fischer Book Service (Israel) *Tel:* (04) 255830 *Fax:* (04) 244970, pg 1309

Fischer & Co (Sweden) *Tel:* (08) 242160 *Fax:* (08) 247825 *E-mail:* bokforlaget@fischer-co.se *Web Site:* www.fischer-co.se, pg 606

Harald Fischer Verlag GmbH (Germany) *Tel:* (09131) 205620 *Fax:* (09131) 206028 *E-mail:* info@ haraldfischerverlag.de *Web Site:* www. haraldfischerverlag.de, pg 224

Verkehrs-Verlag J Fischer GmbH & Co KG (Germany) *Tel:* (0211) 99193-0 *Fax:* (0211) 6801544; (0211) 9919327 *E-mail:* vvf@verkehrsverlag-fischer.de *Web Site:* www.verkehrsverlag-fischer.de, pg 224

Karin Fischer Verlag GmbH (Germany) *Tel:* (0241) 960 90 90 *Fax:* (0241) 960 90 99 *E-mail:* info@karin-fischer-verlag. de, pg 224

Fischer Media AG fur Verlag und Publishing (Switzerland) *Tel:* (031) 7205111 *Fax:* (031) 7205112 *E-mail:* info@fischerprint.ch *Web Site:* www. fischergroup.ch, pg 618

Verlag Reinhard Fischer (Germany) *Tel:* (089) 791 88 92 *Fax:* (089) 791 83 10 *E-mail:* verlagfischer@ compuserve.de *Web Site:* www.verlag-reinhard-fischer. de, pg 224

Rita G Fischer Verlag (Germany) *Tel:* (069) 941942-0 *Fax:* (069) 941942-99; (069) 941942-98 *E-mail:* r.g. fischer.verlag@t-online.de *Web Site:* www.buchhandel. de/r.g.fischer/, pg 224

S Fischer Verlag GmbH (Germany) *Tel:* (069) 6062-0 *Fax:* (069) 6062-214 *Web Site:* www.fischerverlage.de, pg 224

S Fischer Verlag GmbH (Germany) *Tel:* (069) 6062-0 *Fax:* (069) 6062-319 *Web Site:* www.s-fischer.de, pg 224

Anne Louise Fisher & Suzy Lucas (United Kingdom) *Tel:* (020) 7494 4609 *Fax:* (020) 7494 4611, pg 1130

Fishing News Books Ltd (United Kingdom) *Tel:* (01865) 206206 *Fax:* (01865) 721205 *E-mail:* fishing. newsbooks@oxon.blackwellpublishing.com *Web Site:* www.fishknowledge.com, pg 691

Fitzwilliam Publishing Co Ltd (Ireland) *Tel:* (01) 614575 *Fax:* (01) 614575, pg 356

The Five Mile Press Pty Ltd (Australia) *Tel:* (03) 8756 5500 *Fax:* (03) 8756 5588 *E-mail:* publishing@ fivemile.com.au *Web Site:* www.fivemile.com.au, pg 22

Editions Fivedit (France) *Tel:* (04) 50 66 33 78 *Fax:* (04) 50 23 33 08 *E-mail:* fivedit.sa@wanadoo.fr, pg 163

Izdatelstvo Fizkultura i Sport (Russian Federation) *Tel:* (095) 2582690 *Fax:* (095) 2001217, pg 540

Fizmatlit Publishing Co (Russian Federation) *Tel:* (095) 3347151 *Fax:* (095) 3360666, pg 540

Fjolvi (Iceland) *Tel:* 5688433 *Fax:* 5588142 *E-mail:* fjolvi@fjolvi.is *Web Site:* www.fjolvi.is, pg 322

Flaccovio Dario (Italy) *Tel:* (091) 202533 *Fax:* (091) 227702 *E-mail:* press@darioflaccovio.com *Web Site:* www.darioflaccovio.com, pg 386

Flaccovio Editore (Italy) *Tel:* (091) 589442 *Fax:* (091) 331992 *E-mail:* info@flaccovio.com *Web Site:* www. flaccovio.com, pg 386

Libreria S F Flaccovio (Italy) *Tel:* (091) 589442 *Fax:* (091) 331992 *E-mail:* info@flaccovio.com *Web Site:* www.flaccovio.com, pg 1311

Werner Flach Internationale Fachbuchhandlung (Germany) *Tel:* (069) 9591750 *Fax:* (069) 95917522 *E-mail:* fachbuch@flachbuch.com *Web Site:* www. flachbuch.com, pg 1300

Ediciones FLACSO Costa Rica (Costa Rica) *Tel:* 2248059; 2346890 *Fax:* 2256779 *E-mail:* libros@ flacso.or.cr *Web Site:* www.flacso.or.cr, pg 115

Flactem (Australia) *Tel:* (03) 9889 6855 *Fax:* (03) 98888948, pg 22

Flambard Press (United Kingdom) *Tel:* (01434) 674360 *Fax:* (01434) 674178 *Web Site:* www.flambardpress.co. uk, pg 691

Les Editions du Flamboyant (Benin) *Tel:* 310220 *Fax:* 312079 *E-mail:* IPEC@leland.bj, pg 74

Flame Tree Publishing (United Kingdom) *Tel:* (020) 7386 4700 *Fax:* (020) 7386 4700 *E-mail:* info@ flametreepublishing.com *Web Site:* www. flametreepublishing.com, pg 691

Flammarion (France) *Tel:* (01) 40 51 31 00; (01) 40 51 30 41 *Fax:* (01) 43 29 21 48 *Web Site:* www. flammarion.com/, pg 1299

Flammarion Groupe (France) *Tel:* (01) 40 51 31 00 *Fax:* (01) 43 29 43 43 *Web Site:* www.flammarion. com, pg 163

Flechsig Buchvertrieb (Germany) *Tel:* (0931) 385235 *Fax:* (0931) 385305 *E-mail:* info@verlagshaus.com *Web Site:* www.verlagshaus.com, pg 224

Erich Fleischer Verlag (Germany) *Tel:* (04202) 517-0 *Fax:* (04202) 517-41 *E-mail:* info@efv-online.de *Web Site:* www.efv-online.de, pg 224

Fleischhauer & Spohn GmbH & Co (Germany) *Tel:* (07142) 596161 *Fax:* (07142) 596280 *E-mail:* info@verlag-fleischhauer.de *Web Site:* www. verlag-fleischhauer.de, pg 224

Flensburger Hefte Verlag GmbH (Germany) *Tel:* (0461) 2 63 63; (0461) 2 14 72 *Fax:* (0461) 2 69 12 *E-mail:* flensburgerhefte@t-online.de *Web Site:* www. flensburgerhefte.de, pg 224

Flesch WJ & Partners (South Africa) *Tel:* (021) 4617472 *Fax:* (021) 4613758 *E-mail:* sflesch@iafrica.com, pg 559

Editions Fleurus (France) *Tel:* (01) 53 26 33 35 *Fax:* (01) 53 26 33 36, pg 164

Flicks Books (United Kingdom) *Tel:* (01225) 767 728 *Fax:* (01225) 760 418 *E-mail:* flicks.books@pipex. com, pg 691

Flo Enterprise Sdn Bhd (Malaysia) *Tel:* (03) 77833118 *Fax:* (03) 77831066, pg 1316

The Floating Gallery & Advanced Self Publishing (United States) *Toll Free Tel:* 877-822-2500 *E-mail:* floatingal@aol.com *Web Site:* www. thefloatinggallery.com, pg 1156, 1177, 1219

La Flor del Itapebi (Uruguay) *Tel:* (02) 710 92 67 *Fax:* (02) 710 92 67 *E-mail:* itapebi@itapebi.com.uy *Web Site:* www.itapebi.com, pg 772

Flora Publications International Pty Ltd (Australia) *Tel:* (07) 3229 6366 *Fax:* (07) 3378 7102 *E-mail:* info@flora.com.au, pg 22

Florilegium (Australia) *Tel:* (02) 95558589 *Fax:* (02) 98184409 *E-mail:* florileg@ozemail.com.au, pg 22

Floris Books (United Kingdom) *Tel:* (0131) 337 2372 *Fax:* (0131) 347 9919 *E-mail:* floris@floris.books.co. uk *Web Site:* www.florisbooks.co.uk, pg 691

Flugzeug Publikations GmbH (Germany) *Tel:* (07303) 964220 *Fax:* (07303) 964141, pg 224

Empresa Literaria Fluminense, Lda (Portugal) *Tel:* (021) 601138 *Fax:* (021) 3963371, pg 527

Flyleaf Press (Ireland) *Tel:* (01) 2845906 *Fax:* (01) 2831693 *E-mail:* flyleaf@indigo.ie *Web Site:* www. flyleaf.ie, pg 356

Libreria FMR (Italy) *Tel:* (081) 5802279 *Fax:* (081) 5802279 *E-mail:* commerciale@fmrnapoli.it *Web Site:* www.fmrnapoli.it, pg 1311

FN-Verlag der Deutschen Reiterlichen Vereinigung GmbH (Germany) *Tel:* (02581) 63 62-115 *Fax:* (02581) 63 31 46 *Web Site:* www.fnverlag.de, pg 224

FNPS (Federation nationale depresse d'information specialisee) (France) *Tel:* (01) 44 90 43 60 *Fax:* (01) 44 90 43 72 *E-mail:* contact@fnps.fr *Web Site:* www. fnps.fr, pg 1258

Focus Publications International SA (Panama) *Tel:* 225 6638 *Fax:* 225 0466 *E-mail:* focusint@sinfo.net *Web Site:* focuspublicationsint.com, pg 510

Focus Publishers Ltd (Kenya) *Tel:* (020) 600737 *E-mail:* focus@africaonline.co.ke, pg 430

Focus-Verlag Gesellschaft mbH (Germany) *Tel:* (0641) 76031; (0641) 68225 (orders) *Fax:* (0641) 76031; (0641) 68331 (orders) *E-mail:* info@focus-verlag.de *Web Site:* www.focus-verlag.de, pg 225

Foldmuvelesugyi Miniszterium Muszaki Intezet (Hungary) *Tel:* (028) 320-644 *Fax:* (028) 320-960 *E-mail:* dekani@eng.gau.hu, pg 318

Foereningen Auktoriserade Translatorer (Sweden) *E-mail:* info@eurofat.se *Web Site:* www.eurofat.se, pg 1139

Forlagshuset Norden AB (Sweden) *Tel:* (040) 93 42 50 *Fax:* (040) 93 01 56, pg 606

Foszekesegyhazi Konyvtar (Hungary) *Tel:* 33411891 *E-mail:* bibliotheca@ehf.hu, pg 1513

Maurice et Pierre Foetisch SA (Switzerland) *Tel:* (021) 3239444; (021) 3239445 *Fax:* (021) 3115011, pg 618

Fovarosi Szabo Ervin Konyvtar (Hungary) *Tel:* (01) 1185815; (01) 411-5000 *Fax:* (01) 1185914 *E-mail:* info@fszek.hu *Web Site:* www.fszek.hu, pg 1513

Fogarty's Bookshop (South Africa) *Tel:* (041) 3681425; (041) 3681454 *Fax:* (041) 3681279 *E-mail:* fogartys@ global.co.za, pg 1331

Fogola Editore (Italy) *Tel:* (011) 535897 *Fax:* (011) 530305 *E-mail:* info@fogola.com *Web Site:* www. fogola.com, pg 386

Foi-Commerce (Bulgaria) *Tel:* (02) 227116 *Fax:* (02) 227116 *E-mail:* foi@nlcv.net, pg 93

Foibe Filan-Kevitry NY Mpampianatra (FOFIPA) (Madagascar) *Tel:* (02) 27500 *Fax:* (02) 35788, pg 450

Fola Abbey Educational Book Services, Fola Abbey Bookshops Ltd (Nigeria) *Tel:* (01) 2636679 *Fax:* (01) 825268, pg 1322

Folens Ltd (United Kingdom) *Tel:* (0870) 609 1237 *Fax:* (0870) 609 1236 *E-mail:* folens@folens.com *Web Site:* www.folens.com, pg 691

Folens Publishers (Ireland) *Tel:* (01) 4137200 *Fax:* (01) 4137280 *E-mail:* info@folens.ie *Web Site:* www. folens.ie, pg 356

Editoriale Fernando Folini (Italy) *Tel:* (0131) 807001 *Fax:* (0131) 807001 *E-mail:* edifolini@edifolini.com *Web Site:* www.edifolini.com, pg 386

The Folio Society (United Kingdom) *Tel:* (020) 7400 4200 *Fax:* (020) 7400 4242 *E-mail:* enquiries@ foliosoc.co.uk *Web Site:* www.foliosoc.co.uk, pg 1247

Folio Verlagsgesellschaft mbH (Austria) *Tel:* (01) 5813708-0 *Fax:* (01) 5813708-20 *E-mail:* office@ folioverlag.com; folio@thing.at; folio@dialogon.at *Web Site:* www.folioverlag.com/books.php, pg 50

Folklore Comtois (France) *Tel:* (03) 81 55 29 77 *Fax:* (03) 81 55 23 97 *E-mail:* musee@maisons-comtoises.org *Web Site:* www.maisons-comtoises.org, pg 164

The Folklore Society (United Kingdom) *Tel:* (020) 7862 8564; (020) 7862 8562 *E-mail:* folklore.society@ talk21.com *Web Site:* www.folklore-society.com, pg 1281

Folkuniversitetets foerlag (Sweden) *Tel:* (046) 148720 *Fax:* (046) 132904 *E-mail:* info@ folkuniversitetetsforlag.se *Web Site:* www. folkuniversitetetsforlag.se, pg 606

Editions Foma SA (Switzerland) *Tel:* (021) 6351361 *Fax:* (021) 6351704, pg 618

Fondacija Zlatno Kljuce (Bulgaria) *Tel:* (02) 760-671; (02) 623517 *Fax:* (02) 623517 *E-mail:* ynfirst@mat. bg, pg 94

Institut Fondamental d'Afrique Noire (IFAN) (Senegal) *Tel:* 825 00 90; 825 98 90; 825 71 24 *Fax:* 24 49 18 *E-mail:* bifan@telecomplus.sn *Web Site:* www.refer. sn/ifan, pg 546

Fondation de l'Encyclopedie de Geneve (Switzerland) *Fax:* (022) 3120960; (022) 3120963, pg 618

Fondazzjoni Patrimonju Malti (Malta) *Tel:* 21231515 *Fax:* 21250118 *E-mail:* patrimonju@keyworld.net *Web Site:* www.patrimonju.org.mt, pg 456

Fondo de Cultura Economica SA (Chile) *Tel:* (02) 695 4843 *E-mail:* fcechile@ctcinternet.cl, pg 1295

Fondo de Cultura Economica (Mexico) *Tel:* (05) 2274672 *Fax:* (05) 2274640 *E-mail:* adiezc@ fce.com.mx (editorial) *Web Site:* www. fondodeculturaeconomica.com, pg 462

Fondo de Cultura Economica de Espana SL (Spain) *Tel:* (091) 7632800; (091) 7632766 *Fax:* (091) 7635133 *E-mail:* fcevent@interbook.es, pg 579

Fondo Editorial de la Plastica Mexicana (Mexico) *Tel:* (05) 5549-4291 *Fax:* (05) 5688-1168, pg 462

Fondo Editorial de la Pontificia Universidad Catolica del Peru (Peru) *Tel:* (01) 4602870 *Fax:* (01) 4626390 *Web Site:* www.pucp.edu.pe, pg 512

Fondo Educativo Interamericano SA (Colombia) *Tel:* (01) 3382577; (01) 3382877 *Fax:* (01) 2852891; (01) 2320191 *E-mail:* eeducativa@epm.net.co; educapyv@multi.net.co, pg 110

Fondo Educativo Interamericano (Panama) *Tel:* 2691511; 2230210, pg 510

Fong & Sons Printers Pte Ltd (Singapore) *Tel:* 2663688 *Fax:* 2664988, pg 1212

Fonna Forlag L/L (Norway) *Tel:* 22201303 *Fax:* 22201201, pg 504

Fono Forlag (Norway) *Tel:* 66846490 *Fax:* 66847507 *E-mail:* mail@fonoforlag.no *Web Site:* www. fonoforlag.no, pg 504

The Font Bureau Inc (United States) *Tel:* 617-423-8770 *Fax:* 617-423-8771 *E-mail:* info@fontbureau.com *Web Site:* www.fontbureau.com, pg 1177

Miguel Font Editor (Spain) *Tel:* (071) 477300 *Fax:* (071) 476805 *E-mail:* miquel@globalnet.es, pg 579

Uitgeverij De Fontein BV (Netherlands) *Tel:* (035) 5486311 *Fax:* (035) 5423855 *E-mail:* info@ defonteinbaarn.nl *Web Site:* www.veenboschenkeuning. nl/pages/fontein.htm, pg 478

Livraria Martins Fontes Editora Ltda (Brazil) *Tel:* (011) 3241-3677 *Fax:* (0800) 11-3619 *E-mail:* info@ martinsfontes.com.br *Web Site:* www.martinsfontes. com.br, pg 81

Food & Agriculture Organization of the United Nations (FAO) (Italy) *Tel:* (06) 57054350 *Fax:* (06) 57053360 *E-mail:* telex-room@fao.org *Web Site:* www.fao.org, pg 1264

Food Trade Press Ltd (United Kingdom) *Tel:* (01959) 563944 *Fax:* (01959) 561285 *E-mail:* ftpbooks@aol. com *Web Site:* foodtradepress.net, pg 691

Forbes Publications Ltd (United Kingdom) *Tel:* (020) 7836 5888 *Fax:* (020) 7836 7349 *E-mail:* editorial@ rapportgroup.com, pg 691

Foreign Language Bookshop (Australia) *Tel:* (03) 96542883 *Fax:* (03) 96507664 *E-mail:* flb@ozonline. com.au *Web Site:* www.languages.com.au, pg 1288

The Foreign Language Press Group (Democratic People's Republic of Korea) *Tel:* (02) 841342 *Fax:* (02) 812100, pg 433

Foreign Language Teaching & Research Press (China) *Tel:* (010) 8881-7788 ext 3507 *Fax:* (010) 8881-7889 *E-mail:* international@fltrp.com *Web Site:* www.fltrp. com, pg 104

Foreign Languages Press (China) *Tel:* (010) 68995852; (010) 68996188 *E-mail:* flpcn@public3.bta.net.cn *Web Site:* www.flp.com.cn, pg 104

Foreign Languages Publishing House (Democratic People's Republic of Korea) *Tel:* (02) 51-863, pg 433

Forening for Boghaandvaerk, Nordjysk afdeling (Denmark) *Tel:* 32 95 85 15 *Web Site:* www. boghaandvaerk.dk, pg 1256

Foreningen Svenska Laromedelsproducenter (The Swedish Association of Educational Publishers (Sweden) *Tel:* (08) 736 19 40 *Fax:* (08) 736 19 44 *E-mail:* fsl@fsl.se *Web Site:* www.fsl.se, pg 1275

Foreningen Svenska Laromedelsproducenter (The Swedish Association of Educational Publishers) (Sweden) *Tel:* (08) 736 19 40 *Fax:* (08) 736 19 44 *E-mail:* fsl@fsl.se *Web Site:* www.fsl.se, pg 606

Editora Forense Universitaria Ltda (Brazil) *Tel:* (011) 580-0776 *Fax:* (011) 589-2084 *E-mail:* foruniv@ unisys.com.br, pg 81

Forensic Science Society (United Kingdom) *Tel:* (01423) 506068 *Fax:* (01423) 566391 *E-mail:* tracey@forensic-science-society.org.uk *Web Site:* www.forensic-science-society.org.uk, pg 691

Forlagid (Iceland) *Tel:* 522-2000 *Fax:* 522-2022 *E-mail:* edda@edda.is *Web Site:* www.edda.is, pg 322

Forma Edkotiki E P E (Greece) *Tel:* 2108327008, pg 304

FormAsia Books Ltd (Hong Kong) *Tel:* (02) 2525 8572 *Fax:* (02) 2522 4234 *E-mail:* formasia@hkstar.com *Web Site:* www.formasiabooks.com, pg 314

Formato Editorial ltda (Brazil) *Tel:* (011) 3613-3000 *Fax:* (011) 3611-3308 *E-mail:* falecom@ formatoeditorial.com.br *Web Site:* www. formatoeditorial.com.br, pg 81

Arnaldo Forni Editore SRL (Italy) *Tel:* (051) 6814142; (051) 6814198 *Fax:* (051) 6814672 *E-mail:* info@ fornieditore.com *Web Site:* www.fornieditore.com, pg 386

Foroya Landsbokasavn (Faroe Islands) *Tel:* (031) 311626 *Fax:* (031) 318895 *E-mail:* utlan@flb.fo *Web Site:* www.flb.fo, pg 1256

Foroya Landsbokasavn (Faroe Islands) *Tel:* 31 16 26 *Fax:* 31 88 95 *E-mail:* utlan@flb.fo *Web Site:* www. flb.fo, pg 1503

Forsamlingsforbundets Forlags AB (Finland) *Tel:* (09) 61261546 *Fax:* (09) 603963 *E-mail:* bokhandel@ff-forlag.fi, pg 141

Bengt Forsbergs Foerlag AB (Sweden) *Tel:* (040) 763 20 *Fax:* (040) 303939 *E-mail:* info@forsbergsforlag.se *Web Site:* www.forsbergsforlag.se, pg 606

Forth Naturalist & Historian (United Kingdom) *Tel:* (01786) 467755 *Fax:* (01786) 464994 *Web Site:* www.stir.ac.uk/departments/naturalsciences/ forth_naturalist, pg 691

Fortuna Finanz-Verlag AG (Switzerland) *Tel:* (01) 9803622 *Fax:* (01) 9103353 *E-mail:* info@goldseiten. de *Web Site:* www.goldseiten.de, pg 618

Fortunajaya (Indonesia) *Tel:* (0272) 22030 *Fax:* (0272) 22543, pg 351

Forum (Serbia and Montenegro) *Tel:* (021) 57 286 *Fax:* (021) 57 691, pg 547

Forum (Serbia and Montenegro) *Tel:* (021) 57 216 *Fax:* (021) 57 216, pg 1330

Forum Artis, SA (Spain) *Tel:* (091) 4353180; (091) 4350548 *Fax:* (091) 4355124 *E-mail:* forum@adenet. es, pg 579

Bokforlaget Forum AB (Sweden) *Tel:* (08) 696 84 40; (08) 6968410 (Orders) *Fax:* (08) 696 83 67, pg 606

Forlaget Forum (Denmark) *Tel:* 33411830 *Fax:* 33411831 *E-mail:* kontakt@forlagetforum.dk *Web Site:* www.forlagetforum.dk, pg 130

Forum Publications (Malaysia) *Tel:* (03) 7554007 *Fax:* (03) 7561879 *E-mail:* g2jomo@umcsd.um.edu. my, pg 452

Forum Verlag GmbH & Co (Germany) *Tel:* (0711) 76727-0 *Fax:* (0711) 76727-28 *E-mail:* info@ forumverlag.de *Web Site:* www.forumverlag.de, pg 225

Forum Verlag Leipzig Buch-Gesellschaft mbH (Germany) *Tel:* (0341) 9 80 50 08 *Fax:* (0341) 9 80 50 07 *E-mail:* info@forumverlagleipzig.de *Web Site:* www.forumverlagleipzig.de, pg 225

Fostering Network (United Kingdom) *Tel:* (020) 7620 6400 *Fax:* (020) 7620 6401 *E-mail:* nfca@fostercare. org.uk, pg 691

Editions Foucher (France) *Tel:* (01) 41 23 65 60 *Fax:* (01) 41 23 65 03 *E-mail:* contact@editions-foucher.fr *Web Site:* www.editions-foucher.fr, pg 164

Foulsham Publishers (United Kingdom) *Tel:* (01256) 329242 *Fax:* (01256) 812558; (01256) 812521 *E-mail:* mdl@macmillan.co.uk, pg 692

Foundation Books Ltd (Kenya) *Tel:* (020) 765485, pg 430

Foundation for the Production & Translation of Dutch Literature (Netherlands) *Tel:* (020) 6206261 *Fax:* (020) 6207179 *E-mail:* office@nlpvf.nl *Web Site:* www. nlpvf.nl, pg 1125

The Foundational Book Company (United Kingdom) *Tel:* (016) 7256 4343, pg 692

Lora Fountain & Associates Literary Agency (France) *Tel:* (01) 43 56 21 96 *Fax:* (01) 43 48 22 72 *E-mail:* agence@fountlit.com *Web Site:* www.lora-fountain.com, pg 1120

Fountain Publishers Ltd (Uganda) *Tel:* (041) 259163; (041) 251112; (031) 263041; (031) 263042 *Fax:* (041) 251160 *E-mail:* fountain@starcom.co.ug *Web Site:* www.fountainpublishers.co.ug, pg 648

Four Courts Press Ltd (Ireland) *Tel:* (01) 453-4668 *Fax:* (01) 453-4672 *E-mail:* info@four-courts-press.ie *Web Site:* www.four-courts-press.ie, pg 356

Four Seasons Publishing Ltd (United Kingdom) *Tel:* (020) 8942 4445 *Fax:* (020) 8942 4446 *E-mail:* info@fourseasons.net, pg 692

Fourah Bay College Library (Sierra Leone) *Tel:* (022) 227924; (022) 224260 *Fax:* (022) 224260 *E-mail:* fbcadmin@sierratel.sl *Web Site:* fbcusl.8k. com, pg 1541

Naipes Heraclio Fournier SA (Spain) *Tel:* (0945) 465525 *Fax:* (0945) 465543 *E-mail:* fournier@nhfournier.es *Web Site:* www.nhfournier.es, pg 579

Fourth Dimension Publishing Co Ltd (Nigeria) *Tel:* (042) 459969 *Fax:* (042) 456904 *E-mail:* info@fdpbooks. com; fdpbook@aol.com *Web Site:* www.fdpbooks.com, pg 500

Fourth Estate (United Kingdom) *Tel:* (01206) 256000; (01206) 255678 *Fax:* (01206) 255715; (01206) 255930 *E-mail:* general@4thestate.co.uk *Web Site:* www. 4thestate.co.uk, pg 692

FOYLES (United Kingdom) *Tel:* (020) 7437 5660 *Fax:* (020) 7434 1574 *E-mail:* orders@foyles.co.uk *Web Site:* www.foyles.co.uk, pg 692

FOYLES (United Kingdom) *Tel:* (020) 7437 5660 *Fax:* (020) 7434 1574 *E-mail:* customerservice@ foyles.co.uk *Web Site:* www.foyles.co.uk, pg 1342

Editions Fragments (France) *Tel:* (01) 47 00 76 48 *Fax:* (01) 47 00 22 04 *E-mail:* art@fragmentseditions. com *Web Site:* www.fragmentseditions.com, pg 164

Fragua Editorial (Spain) *Tel:* (091) 544 22 97; (091) 549 18 06 *Fax:* (091) 549 18 06 *E-mail:* fragua@fragua. com *Web Site:* www.fragua.com, pg 579

Franc-Franc podjetje za promocijo kulture Murska Sobota d o o (Slovenia) *Tel:* (02) 5141 841 *Fax:* (02) 5141 841 *E-mail:* franc.franc@siol.net, pg 557

Institut Francais de Recherche pour l'Exploitation de la Mer (IFREMER) (France) *Tel:* (02) 98 22 40 13 *Fax:* (02) 98 22 45 86 *E-mail:* editions@ifremer.fr *Web Site:* www.ifremer.fr, pg 164

Institut Francais d'Etudes Arabes de Damas (Syrian Arab Republic) *Tel:* (011) 3330214; (011) 3331692 *Fax:* (011) 3327887 *E-mail:* ifead@net.sy *Web Site:* www.lb.refer.org/ifead, pg 633

Association Francaise de Normalisation (France) *Tel:* (01) 41 62 80 00 *Fax:* (01) 49 17 90 00 *E-mail:* info.formation@afnor.fr *Web Site:* www.afnor. fr, pg 164

Edition Francaise pour le Monde Arabe (EDIFRAMO) (Lebanon) *Tel:* (01) 862437; (01) 341650; (01) 341614, pg 442

France Edition (France) *Tel:* (01) 44 41 13 13 *Fax:* (01) 46 34 63 83 *E-mail:* info@franceedition.org *Web Site:* www.franceedition.org, pg 1258

France Edition Office de Promotion Internationale (France) *Tel:* (01) 44 41 13 13 *Fax:* (01) 46 34 63 83 *E-mail:* info@franceedition.com *Web Site:* bief.org, pg 164

Editions France-Empire (France) *Tel:* (01) 45 00 33 00 *Fax:* (01) 45 00 20 77 *E-mail:* france-empire@france-empire.fr *Web Site:* www.france-empire.fr, pg 164

France-Loisirs (France) *Tel:* (01) 45 68 60 00 *Fax:* (01) 42 73 14 38 *E-mail:* serviceclub@france-loisirs.com *Web Site:* www.franceloisirs.com, pg 164

France Tosho (Japan) *Tel:* (03) 3346-0396 *Fax:* (03) 3346-9154 *E-mail:* frtosho@blue.ocn.ne.jp *Web Site:* www.francetosho.com, pg 1312

Instituto Frances de Estudios Andinos, IFEA (Peru) *Tel:* (01) 447-6070 *Fax:* (01) 445-7650 *E-mail:* postmaster@ifea.org.pe *Web Site:* www. ifeanet.org, pg 512

Biblioteca Francescana (Italy) *Tel:* (02) 29002736 *Fax:* (02) 29002736 *E-mail:* info@ bibliotecafrancescana.it *Web Site:* www. bibliotecafrancescana.it, pg 386

Francis Balsom Associates (United Kingdom) *Tel:* (01970) 636400 *Fax:* (01970) 636414 *E-mail:* info@fbagroup.co.uk *Web Site:* www. fbagroup.co.uk, pg 692

Les Editions Franciscaines SA (France) *Tel:* (01) 45407351 *Fax:* (01) 40447504 *E-mail:* editions-franciscaines@wanadoo.fr, pg 164

Editorial Franciscana (Portugal) *Tel:* (0253) 22490 *Fax:* (0253) 619735, pg 527

Verlag der Francke Buchhandlung GmbH (Germany) *Tel:* (06421) 17 25-0 *Fax:* (06421) 17 25-30 *E-mail:* info@francke-buch.de *Web Site:* www.francke-buch.de, pg 225

Franckh-Kosmos Verlags-GmbH & Co (Germany) *Tel:* (0711) 2191-0 *Fax:* (0711) 2191-422 *E-mail:* info@kosmos.de *Web Site:* www.kosmos.de, pg 225

Association Frank (France) *Tel:* (01) 43656405 *Fax:* (01) 48596668, pg 164

Frank Brothers & Co Publishers Ltd (India) *Tel:* (011) 263393; (011) 279936; (011) 278150; (011) 260796 *Fax:* (011) 3269032 *E-mail:* fbros@ndb.vsnl.net.in, pg 331

Frank Publishing Ltd (Ghana) *Tel:* (021) 240711, pg 301

Frankfurter Literaturverlag GmbH (Germany) *Tel:* (069) 40894-0 *Fax:* (069) 40894-194 *E-mail:* info@haensel-hohenhausen.de *Web Site:* www.cgl-verlag.de, pg 225

FVA-Frankfurter Verlagsanstalt GmbH (Germany) *Tel:* (069) 96220610 *Fax:* (069) 96220630 *E-mail:* info@frankfurter-verlagsanstalt.de *Web Site:* www.frankfurter-verlagsanstalt.de, pg 225

Franklin Book Programs Inc (Afghanistan), pg 1

Rodney Franklin Agency (Israel) *Tel:* (03) 5600724 *Fax:* (03) 5600479 *E-mail:* rodneyf@netvision.net.il, pg 363

Leanne Franson (Canada) *Tel:* 514-526-4236 *Fax:* 514-526-0972 *E-mail:* inksports@videotron.ca *Web Site:* www.theispot.com/artist/LFranson, pg 1165

Franz-Sales-Verlag (Germany) *Tel:* (08421) 9 34 89-31 *Fax:* (08421) 9 34 89-35 *E-mail:* info@franz-sales-verlag.de *Web Site:* www.franz-sales-verlag.de, pg 225

Verlag Franz Vahlen GmbH (Germany) *Tel:* (089) 38189-381 *Fax:* (089) 38189-402 *E-mail:* info@vahlen.de *Web Site:* www.vahlen.de, pg 225

Franzis-Verlag GmbH (Germany) *Tel:* (08121) 95 0 *Fax:* (08121) 95 16 96 *E-mail:* info@franzis.de *Web Site:* www.franzis.de, pg 225

Fraser Books (New Zealand) *Tel:* (06) 3771359 *Fax:* (06) 3771359, pg 492

The Fraser Press (United Kingdom) *Tel:* (0141) 3331992 *Fax:* (0141) 3331992, pg 692

Fraser Publications (Australia) *Tel:* (018) 039845 *Fax:* (057) 261775 *E-mail:* fraspub@albury.net.au, pg 22

Fundacao Cultural Avatar (Brazil) *Tel:* (021) 621-0217 *Fax:* (021) 2621-0217 *E-mail:* fcavatar@nitnet.com.br *Web Site:* www.nitnet.com.br/~fcavatar, pg 82

Fundacao de Assistencia ao Estudante (Brazil) *Tel:* (061) 223-9329 *Fax:* (061) 226-6270, pg 82

Fundacao Instituto Brasileiro de Geografia e Estatistica (IBGE - CDDI/DECOP) (Brazil) *Tel:* (021) 569-2043 *Fax:* (021) 234-6189 *E-mail:* marisa@ibge.gov.br *Web Site:* www.ibge.gov.br, pg 82

Fundacao Joaquim Nabuco-Editora Massangana (Brazil) *Tel:* (081) 3441-5500 *Fax:* (081) 3441-5600 *E-mail:* editora@fundaj.gov.br *Web Site:* www.fundaj.gov.br, pg 82

Fundacao para a Ciencia e a Tecnologia/Servico de Informacao e Documentacao(SID) (Portugal) *Tel:* (01) 3924300 *Fax:* (01) 3907481 *Web Site:* www.fct.mct.pt, pg 1537

Fundacao Sao Paulo, EDUC (Brazil) *Tel:* (011) 3873-3359 *Fax:* (011) 38733359 *E-mail:* educsp@puc001.pucsp.ansp.br, pg 82

Fundacio La Caixa (Spain) *Tel:* (093) 404 6079 *Fax:* (093) 3395703 *E-mail:* info@lacaixa.es *Web Site:* portal1.lacaixa.es, pg 579

Fundacion Biblioteca Alemana Gorres (Spain) *Tel:* (091) 3668508; (091)3668509, pg 579

Fundacion Centro de Investigacion y Educacion Popular (CINEP) (Colombia) *Tel:* (01) 2456181 *Fax:* (01) 2879089 *E-mail:* info@cinep.org.co *Web Site:* www.cinep.org.co, pg 111

Fundacion Centro Gumilla (Venezuela) *Tel:* (0212) 564 98 03; (0212) 564 58 71; (0212) 562 75 31 *Fax:* (0212) 564 75 57 *E-mail:* comunicacion@gumilla.org.ve; centro@gumilla.org.ve *Web Site:* www.gumilla.org.ve, pg 774

Fundacion Coleccion Thyssen-Bornemisza (Spain) *Tel:* (091) 420 39 44 *Fax:* (091) 4202780 *E-mail:* umseo.thyssen-bornemisza@offcampus.es, pg 579

Fundacion de Cultura Universitaria (Uruguay) *Tel:* (02) 9152532; (02) 959038; (02) 9168360 *Fax:* (02) 9152549 *E-mail:* administrador@fcu.com.uy *Web Site:* www.fcu.com.uy, pg 772

Fundacion de Estudios Libertarios Anselmo Lorenzo (Spain) *Tel:* (091) 7970424 *Fax:* (091) 5052183 *E-mail:* fal@cnt.es *Web Site:* www.cnt.es/fal, pg 579

Fundacion de los Ferrocarriles Espanoles (Spain) *Tel:* (091) 1511 071 *Fax:* (091) 5284822; (091) 5391415 *E-mail:* fuccu20@ffe.es *Web Site:* www.ffe.es, pg 579

Fundacion Editorial de Belgrano (Argentina) *Tel:* (011) 4772-4014 *Fax:* (011) 4775-8788, pg 6

Fundacion El Libro (Argentina) *Tel:* (011) 43743288 *Fax:* (011) 43750268 *E-mail:* fundacion@el-libro.com.ar *Web Site:* www.el-libro.com.ar, pg 1249

Fundacion Esade (Spain) *Tel:* (093) 280 61 62 *Fax:* (093) 204 81 05 *Web Site:* www.esade.es/biblio, pg 1544

Fundacion Gratis Date (Spain) *Tel:* (0948) 123612 *Fax:* (0948) 123612 *E-mail:* fundacion@gratisdate.org *Web Site:* www.gratisdate.org, pg 579

Fundacion Juan March (Spain) *Tel:* (091) 435 42 40 *Fax:* (091) 576 34 20 *E-mail:* webmast@mail.march.es *Web Site:* www.march.es, pg 579

Fundacion Kuai-Mare (Venezuela) *Tel:* (0212) 938535 ext 213; (0212) 9418011 (ext 227) *Fax:* (0212) 9415219, pg 1347

Fundacion Marcelino Botin (Spain) *Tel:* (0942) 226072 *Fax:* (0942) 226045 *E-mail:* fmabotin@fundacionmbotin.org *Web Site:* www.fundacionmbotin.org, pg 579

Fundacion para la Cultura y el Desarrollo (Guatemala) *Tel:* (02) 500216 *Fax:* (02) 325508, pg 310

Fundacion Rosacruz (Spain) *Tel:* (076) 589100 *Fax:* (076) 589161 *E-mail:* correo@fundacionrosacruz.org *Web Site:* www.fundacionrosacruz.org, pg 579

Fundacion Servicio para el Agricultor (Venezuela) *Tel:* (0212) 2843089; (0212) 2841134; (0212) 2852016 *Fax:* (0212) 2853946 *E-mail:* izamora@etheron.net, pg 774

Fundacion Universidad de la Sabana Ediciones INSE (Colombia) *Tel:* (01) 6760867 *E-mail:* susabana@col1.telcom.com.co, pg 111

Editorial Fundamentos (Spain) *Tel:* (091) 319 96 19 *Fax:* (091) 319 55 84 *E-mail:* fundamentos@editorialfundamentos.es *Web Site:* www.editorialfundamentos.es, pg 579

Funfax Ltd (United Kingdom) *Tel:* (020) 7836 5411 *Fax:* (020) 7836 7570 *E-mail:* clairrey@dk-uk.com, pg 693

Furco Ltd (United Kingdom) *Tel:* (04) 726795 *Fax:* (04) 726796 *E-mail:* info@africafilmtv.com *Web Site:* www.africafilmtv.com, pg 694

Furnival Press (United Kingdom) *Tel:* (020) 7274 2067 *Fax:* (020) 7274 6984 *E-mail:* furnprint@aol.com, pg 1215, 1228

Futerman, Rose & Associates (United Kingdom) *Tel:* (020) 8947 0188 *Fax:* (020) 8605 2162 *Web Site:* www.futermanrose.co.uk, pg 1130

Editorial Futura (Portugal) *Tel:* (021) 7155848 *Fax:* (021) 155848, pg 527

Futuribles SARL (France) *Tel:* (01) 53 63 37 70 *Fax:* (01) 42 22 65 54 *E-mail:* revue@futuribles.com *Web Site:* www.futuribles.com, pg 164

Edizioni Futuro SRL (Italy) *Tel:* (045) 915622 *Fax:* (045) 8300261, pg 386

Fuzambo Publishing Co (Japan) *Tel:* (03) 3291-2171 *Fax:* (03) 3291-2179, pg 414

G+B Arts International (Switzerland) *Tel:* (061) 2610138 *Fax:* (061) 2610173, pg 619

G Braun (vormals G Braun'sche Hofbuchdruckerei und Verlag) (Germany) *Tel:* (0721) 1607320 *Fax:* (0721) 1607321 *E-mail:* info@gbraun-immo.de *Web Site:* www.gbraun.de; www.gbraun-immo.de, pg 1206

Gaanetgetal Books (Australia) *Tel:* (02) 4234-0865 *Fax:* (02) 4234-0875 *E-mail:* enquiries@books-on-rugs.com, pg 1288

Gaba Publications Amecea, Pastoral Institute (Kenya) *Tel:* (0321) 61218; (0321) 62153 *Fax:* (0321) 62570 *E-mail:* gabapubs@africaonline.co.ke *Web Site:* www.amecea.org, pg 430

Gabal-Verlag GmbH (Germany) *Tel:* (069) 84 000 66-0 *Fax:* (069) 84 000 66-66 *E-mail:* support@gabal-verlag.de *Web Site:* www.gabal-verlag.de, pg 227

Les Editions Gabalda et Cie (France) *Tel:* (01) 43 26 53 55 *Fax:* (01) 43 25 04 71 *E-mail:* editions@gabalda.com *Web Site:* www.gabalda.com, pg 165

Editions Jacques Gabay (France) *Tel:* (01) 43 54 64 64 *Fax:* (01) 43 54 87 00 *E-mail:* infos@gabay.com *Web Site:* www.gabay.com, pg 165

Gaberbocchus Press (Netherlands) *Tel:* (020) 6245181 *Fax:* (020) 6230672 *E-mail:* info@deharmonie.nl *Web Site:* www.gaberbocchus.nl, pg 478

Betriebswirtschaftlicher Verlag Dr Th Gabler (Germany) *Tel:* (0611) 7878470 *Fax:* (0611) 787878400 *Web Site:* www.gwv-fachverlage.de, pg 227

Verlag Gachnang & Springer, Bern-Berlin (Switzerland) *Tel:* (031) 351 83 83 *Fax:* (031) 351 83 85 *E-mail:* verlag@gachnang-springer.com *Web Site:* www.gachnang-springer.com, pg 619

Editions Victor Gadoury (Monaco) *Tel:* (093) 251296 *Fax:* (093) 501339 *E-mail:* contact@gadoury.com *Web Site:* www.gadoury.com, pg 470

Gads Forlag (Denmark) *Tel:* 7766 6000 *Fax:* 7766 6001 *E-mail:* kuneservice@gads-forlag.dk *Web Site:* www.gads-forlag.dk, pg 131

Gads Forlag (Denmark) *Tel:* 77 66 60 00 *Fax:* 77 66 60 01 *E-mail:* kundeservice@gads-forlag.dk.ell *Web Site:* www.gads-forlag.dk, pg 1298

Ediciones de Arte Gaglianone (Argentina) *Tel:* (011) 4923-2579; (011) 4923-0150 *Fax:* (011) 4923-0150; (011) 4923-2579 *E-mail:* ediciones@gaglianone.com.ar, pg 6

Gaia Books Ltd (United Kingdom) *Tel:* (020) 7323 4010 *Fax:* (020) 7323 0435 *E-mail:* info@gaiabooks.com *Web Site:* www.gaiabooks.co.uk, pg 694

Editora Gaia Ltda (Brazil) *Tel:* (011) 2777999 *Fax:* (011) 2778141 *E-mail:* gaia@dialdata.com.br, pg 82

Gaia Media AG/Literary & Media Agency (Switzerland) *Tel:* (061) 2619119 *Fax:* (061) 2619117 *E-mail:* gaiamediaag@access.ch *Web Site:* www.gaiamedia.org, pg 1127

Imprimerie Gaignault (France), pg 1206

Gairm Publications (United Kingdom) *Tel:* (0141) 221 1971 *Fax:* (0141) 221 1971, pg 694

Gakken Co Ltd (Japan) *Tel:* (03) 3726-8111 *Fax:* (03) 3493-3338 *Web Site:* www.gakken.co.jp, pg 414

Gakujutsu Bunken Fukyu-Kai (Japan) *Tel:* (03) 5734-3443 *Fax:* (03) 5734-2053 *E-mail:* gakujyutubunken@mvd.biglobe.ne.jp *Web Site:* www.titech.ac.jp, pg 1565

GakuseiSha Publishing Co Ltd (Japan) *Tel:* (03) 3857-3031 *Fax:* (03) 3857-3037 *E-mail:* info@gakusei.co.jp *Web Site:* www.gakusei.co.jp, pg 414

Galago Publishing Pty Ltd (South Africa) *Tel:* (011) 9072029 *Fax:* (011) 8690890 *E-mail:* lemur@mweb.co.za *Web Site:* www.galago.co.za, pg 559

Galaktika Publishing House (Bulgaria) *Tel:* (052) 225077; (052) 241132; (052) 241156; (052) 604716; (052) 604715 *Fax:* (052) 234750, pg 94

Izdatelstvo Galart (Russian Federation) *Tel:* (095) 1512502; (095) 1514513 *Fax:* (095) 1513761, pg 540

Galaxia SA Editorial (Spain) *Tel:* (0986) 432100; (0986) 433238 *Fax:* (0986) 223205 *E-mail:* galaxia@editorialgalaxia.es *Web Site:* www.editorialgalaxia.es, pg 579

Galaxie, vydavatelstvi a nakladatelstvi (Czech Republic) *Tel:* (02) 2317801; (02) 2317875 *Fax:* (02) 2311351, pg 123

El Galeon (Uruguay) *Tel:* (02) 9156139; (02) 9157909 *Fax:* (02) 9157909 *E-mail:* elgaleon@netgate.com.uy, pg 1346

La Galera, SA Editorial (Spain) *Tel:* (093) 4120030 *Fax:* (093) 3014863 *Web Site:* www.enciclopedia-catalana.com, pg 580

Galerie Der Spiegel-Dr E Stunke Nachfolge GmbH (Germany) *Tel:* (0221) 25 55 52 *Fax:* (0221) 25 55 53 *E-mail:* der-spiegel@galerie.de *Web Site:* www.galerie.de/der-spiegel, pg 227

Galerie Editions Kutter (Luxembourg) *Tel:* 22 35 71 *Fax:* 47 18 84 *E-mail:* kuttered@pt.lu *Web Site:* www.kutter.lu, pg 447

Editorial Galerna SRL (Argentina) *Tel:* (011) 4867-1661 *Fax:* (011) 4862-5031 *E-mail:* gventas@hg.com.ar, pg 6

Galgotia Publications Pvt Ltd (India) *Tel:* (011) 589334 *Fax:* (011) 3281909; (011) 321909 *E-mail:* gppl.galgtia@axcess.net.in, pg 331

Editions Galilee (France) *Tel:* (01) 43 31 23 84 *Fax:* (01) 45 35 53 68 *E-mail:* editions.galilee@free.fr, pg 165

Galleon Publications (Philippines) *Tel:* (02) 592-519; (02) 523-1825 *Fax:* (02) 525-6129, pg 514

The Gallery Press (Ireland) *Tel:* (049) 8541779 *Fax:* (049) 8541779 *E-mail:* gallery@indigo.ie *Web Site:* www.gallerypress.com, pg 357

Galley Press Publishing (Australia) *Tel:* (02) 9698 9262 *Fax:* (02) 9360 1968 *E-mail:* isbin@ozemail.com.au, pg 23

Editions Gallimard (France) *Tel:* (01) 49 54 42 00
*Fax:* (01) 45 44 94 03 *Web Site:* www.gallimard.fr,
pg 165

Adriano Gallina Editore sas (Italy) *Tel:* (081) 5496730
*Fax:* (081) 5448747, pg 386

Galrev Druck-und Verlagsgesellschaft Hesse & Partner
OHG (Germany) *Tel:* (030) 44 65 01 83 *Fax:* (030) 44
65 01 84 *E-mail:* galrev@galrev.com *Web Site:* www.
galrev.com, pg 227

Galzerano Editore (Italy) *Tel:* (0974) 62028 *Fax:* (0974)
62028, pg 386

Gamberetti Editrice SRL (Italy) *Tel:* (06) 3728394
*Fax:* (06) 3728394 *E-mail:* gamberetti@gamberetti.it
*Web Site:* www.gamberetti.it, pg 386

The Gambia Methodist Bookshop Ltd (Gambia)
*Tel:* 28179, pg 1300

Gambia College Library (Gambia) *Tel:* 484452; 484748;
484812 *Fax:* 483224, pg 1506

The Gambia National Library (Gambia) *Tel:* 226491;
225876; 228312; 223776 *Fax:* 223 776
*E-mail:* national.library@qanet.gm, pg 1506

Ediciones Gamma (Colombia) *Tel:* (01) 6227054; (01)
6227076 *Fax:* (01) 6227129 *E-mail:* diners@cable.net.
co, pg 111

Editions Gamma (France) *Tel:* (03) 44 80 68 63
*Fax:* (03) 44 80 68 60 *E-mail:* contact@editions-
gamma.com *Web Site:* www.editions-gamma.com,
pg 165

Gamma Medya Agency (Turkey) *Tel:* (0212) 663 96 80
*Fax:* (0212) 663 96 81 *E-mail:* web@gammamedya.
net *Web Site:* www.gammamedya.net, pg 1128

Gammaprim (France) *Tel:* (01) 49959492 *Fax:* (01)
40230134 *E-mail:* fgosselin@gammaprim.fr, pg 165

Gamsberg Macmillan Publishers (Pty) Ltd (Namibia)
*Tel:* (061) 232165 *Fax:* (061) 233538 *E-mail:* gmp@
iafrica.com.na *Web Site:* www.macmillan-africa.com,
pg 472

Gandon Editions (Ireland) *Tel:* (021) 770830 *Fax:* (021)
770755, pg 357

Ganesh & Co (India) *Tel:* (044) 4344519 *Fax:* (044)
4342009 *E-mail:* ksm@md2.vsnl.net.in; service@
kkbooks.com, pg 331

Gangan Publishing (Australia) *Tel:* (02) 9280 2120
*Fax:* (02) 9280 2130 *E-mail:* books@gangan.com
*Web Site:* www.gangan.com, pg 23

Gangan Verlag (Austria) *Tel:* (0316) 670 4090
*Fax:* (0316) 670 4096 *Web Site:* www.gangan.com,
pg 50

Gangemi Editore spa (Italy) *Tel:* (06) 6872774; (06)
68806189 (orders) *Fax:* (06) 68806189 *E-mail:* info@
gangemieditore.it *Web Site:* www.gangemieditore.it,
pg 386

A R Gantner Verlag KG (Liechtenstein) *Tel:* 377 1808
*Fax:* 377 1802 *E-mail:* bgc@adon.li *Web Site:* www.
gantner-verlag.com, pg 444

Editions Ganymede (France) *Tel:* (01) 64 25 83 01
*Fax:* (01) 64 42 86 68 *E-mail:* rozeille.hatem@
wanadoo.fr *Web Site:* www.hatem.com/librairie.htm,
pg 165

Garant Publishers Ltd (Belgium) *Tel:* (03) 231 29 00
*Fax:* (03) 233 26 59 *E-mail:* uitgeverij@garant.be
*Web Site:* www.garant.be, pg 67

Garcia Hermanos Imprenta y Litografia (Costa Rica)
*Tel:* 2202003; 2212223 *Fax:* 2310675 *E-mail:* info@
novanet.co.cr *Web Site:* www.novanet.co.cr, pg 115

Vicent Garcia Editores, SA (Spain) *Tel:* (096) 361 9559;
(096) 3691589; (096) 369 3246 *Fax:* (096) 393 00 57
*E-mail:* vgesa@combios.es *Web Site:* www.vgesa.com,
pg 580

Editions du Garde-Temps (France) *Tel:* (01) 44788477
*Fax:* (01) 44788479 *E-mail:* studio-magnet@calva.net,
pg 165

Garden Art Press Ltd (United Kingdom) *Tel:* (01394)
385501 *Fax:* (01394) 384434, pg 694

Gardenhouse Editions Ltd (United Kingdom) *Tel:* (020)
7622 1720 *Fax:* (020) 7720 9114, pg 1153

Imprimerie Librairie Gardet (France) *Tel:* (04) 50 53
67 47 *Fax:* (04) 50 53 67 47 *E-mail:* edimontagne@
wanadoo.fr, pg 165

Walter H Gardner & Co (United Kingdom)
*Tel:* (20) 8458 3202 *Fax:* (20) 8458 8499
*E-mail:* walterhgardnerco@aol.com, pg 694, 1342

Gardners Books (United Kingdom) *Tel:* (01323)
521666; (01323) 521555 *Fax:* (01323) 521666
*E-mail:* marketing@gardners.com *Web Site:* www.
gardners.com, pg 1342

Gardum A/S (Norway) *Tel:* 51894440 *Fax:* 51894404
*E-mail:* firmapost@gardum.no, pg 1324

Editrice Garigliano SRL (Italy) *Tel:* (0776) 21869
*Fax:* (0776) 21869, pg 386

Garnet Publishing Ltd (United Kingdom) *Tel:* (0118) 959
7847 *Fax:* (0118) 959 7356 *E-mail:* enquiries@garnet-
ithaca.demon.co.uk (general enquiries); orders@garnet-
ithaca.demon.co.uk (ordering) *Web Site:* www.garnet-
ithaca.co.uk, pg 694

Garolla (Italy) *Tel:* (02) 48005574 *Fax:* (02) 48003915,
pg 387

Garotech (Philippines) *Tel:* (02) 993286, pg 514

Garr Publishing (Australia) *Tel:* (02) 4367 7223
*Fax:* (02) 4367 7762 *E-mail:* garrpublishing@digisurf.
net.au *Web Site:* www.garrpublishing.com.au, pg 23

Garradunga Press (Australia) *Tel:* (0409) 320 619
(mobile) *Fax:* (07) 4032 5918 *E-mail:* bolton@iig.
com.au, pg 23

John Garratt Publishing (Australia) *Tel:* (03) 9545 3111
*Toll Free Tel:* 300 650 878 *Fax:* (03) 9545 3222
*E-mail:* sales@johngarratt.com.au *Web Site:* www.
johngarratt.com.au, pg 23

Garrison Library (Gibraltar) *Tel:* 77418 *Fax:* 79927,
pg 1511

Gartaganis D (Greece) *Tel:* 2310209680, pg 304

Garuda-Verlag (Switzerland) *Tel:* (056) 6401014
*Fax:* (056) 6401012 *E-mail:* garuda@bluewin.ch,
pg 619

Garzanti Libri (Italy) *Tel:* (02) 674171 *Fax:* (02)
67417323 *Web Site:* www.garzanti.it, pg 387

Verlag HP Gassner AG (Liechtenstein) *Tel:* (075)
2327253 *Fax:* (075) 2323720, pg 444

Gaston Renard Pty Ltd (Australia) *Tel:* (03) 9459 5040
*Fax:* (03) 9459 6787 *E-mail:* books@gastonrenard.
com.au *Web Site:* www.gastonrenard.com.au, pg 1288

Gateway Books (United Kingdom) *Tel:* (01225) 835 127
*Fax:* (01225) 840 012 *E-mail:* sales@gatewaybooks.
com, pg 694

Gatidhara (Bangladesh) *Tel:* (02) 7392077 (press); (02)
7113117 (res); (02) 7115630 (res); (02) 7117515
(showroom); (02) 7118273 (showroom fax); (02)
9134617; (02) 9566456 *E-mail:* akter@aitlbd.net;
gatidara@bdonline.com, pg 60

Gatzanis Verlags GmbH (Germany) *Tel:* (0711) 9640570
*Fax:* (0711) 9640572 *E-mail:* info@gatzanis.de
*Web Site:* www.gatzanis.de, pg 227

Gaulitana (Malta) *Tel:* 2155-4212 *Fax:* 2155-4598
*E-mail:* joseph.bezzina@um.edu.mt, pg 456

Ediciones Gaviota SA (Spain) *Tel:* (091) 358 01 08
*Fax:* (091) 729 38 58 *E-mail:* publicaciones@
ediciones-gaviota.es *Web Site:* www.everest.es, pg 580

Gaya Favorit Press (Indonesia) *Tel:* (021) 513816
*Fax:* (021) 5209366; (021) 4609115 *E-mail:* ptgfp1@
rad.net.id, pg 351

Gazelle Book Services Ltd (United Kingdom)
*Tel:* (01524) 68765 *Fax:* (01524) 63232
*E-mail:* sales@gazellebooks.co.uk *Web Site:* www.
gazellebook.co.uk, pg 1342

Edizioni GB (Italy) *Tel:* (049) 8647834 *Fax:* (049)
8647834, pg 387

Gbabeks Publishers Ltd (Nigeria) *Tel:* (062) 217976,
pg 500

GCL Publishing (1997) Ltd (New Zealand) *Tel:* (09)
3092444 *Fax:* (09) 3092449 *E-mail:* info@gcl.co.nz
*Web Site:* www.gcl.co.nz; www.auto.co.nz, pg 492

Biblioteka Gdanska PAN (Poland) *Tel:* (058) 312251-
54 *Fax:* (058) 312970 *E-mail:* bgpan@task.gda.pl,
pg 1536

Politechnika Gdanska (Poland) *Tel:* (058) 347-25-75
*Fax:* (058) 347-27-58 *E-mail:* mainlibr@sunrise.pg.
gda.pl; library@pg.gda.pl *Web Site:* www.pg.gda.pl,
pg 1536

Gdanskie Wydawnictwo Psychologiczne SC (Poland)
*Tel:* (058) 551-61-04; (058) 550-16-04; (058) 551-
11-01 *Fax:* (058) 551-61-04; (058) 550-16-04
*Web Site:* www.gwp.pl, pg 518

Gea-Libris Publishing House (Bulgaria) *Tel:* (02) 986678
*Fax:* (02) 9866900 *E-mail:* emilgea@techno-link.com;
info@gealibris.com *Web Site:* www.gealibris.com,
pg 94

Gebrueder Borntraeger Science Publishers (Germany)
*Tel:* (0711) 3514560 *Fax:* (0711) 35145699
*E-mail:* mail@schweizerbart.de *Web Site:* www.
schweizerbart.de, pg 227

GECTI (Gabinete de Especializacao e Cooperacao
Tecnica Internacional L) (Portugal) *Tel:* (021)
7968877; (021) 7971940; (021) 7972154
*Fax:* (021) 7963465 *E-mail:* gecti@mail.telepac.pt
*Web Site:* www.inedita.com/gecti, pg 527

Geddes & Grosset (United Kingdom) *Tel:* (01555)
665000 *Fax:* (01555) 665694 *E-mail:* info@gandg.
sol.co.uk, pg 694

Gedins Forlag (Sweden) *Tel:* (08) 662 15 51 *Fax:* (08)
6637073 *E-mail:* gedins@perigab.se, pg 606

Editorial Gedisa SA (Spain) *Tel:* (093) 253 09 04
*Fax:* (093) 253 09 05 *E-mail:* gedisa@gedisa.com
*Web Site:* www.gedisa.com, pg 580

Gee & Son (Denbigh) Ltd-Gwasg Gee-Gee's Press
(United Kingdom) *Tel:* (01745) 812020 *Fax:* (01745)
812825, pg 1153

Geeta Prakashan (India) *Tel:* (0821) 33589, pg 331

Geetha Publishers Sdn Bhd (Malaysia) *Tel:* (03)
40417073 *Fax:* (03) 40417073, pg 452

Gefen Publishing House Ltd (Israel) *Tel:* (02) 5380247
*Fax:* (02) 5388423 *E-mail:* info@gefenpublishing.com
*Web Site:* www.israelbooks.com, pg 363

Konkursbuch Verlag Claudia Gehrke (Germany)
*Tel:* (07071) 78779 *Fax:* (07071) 763780
*E-mail:* office@konkursbuch.com *Web Site:* www.
konkursbuch.com, pg 227

SK-Gehrmans Musikforlag AB (Sweden) *Tel:* (08)
6100610 *Fax:* (08) 6100627 *E-mail:* sales@gehrmans.
se *Web Site:* www.sk-gehrmans.se, pg 606

Geiser Productions (United Kingdom) *Tel:* (020) 8579
4653 *Fax:* (020) 8567 6593 *E-mail:* geiser@gxn.
co.uk *Web Site:* www.geiserproductions.com; www.
sidsjournal.com, pg 694

Uitgevery Gelbis NV (Belgium) *Tel:* (03) 2410202
*Fax:* (03) 2410200 *E-mail:* gelbis.boeken@lequana.
com, pg 67

Caroline van Gelderen Literary Agency (Netherlands)
*Tel:* (020) 6126475 *Fax:* (020) 6180843, pg 1125

Gembooks (United Kingdom) *Tel:* (01202) 399729
*Fax:* (01202) 399729 *E-mail:* readbooks@onmail.co.
uk, pg 694

Verlag Junge Gemeinde E Schwinghammer GmbH &
Co KG (Germany) *Tel:* (0711) 99078-0 *Fax:* (0711)
99078-25, pg 227

General Book Depot (India) *Tel:* (011) 2326 3695; (011) 2325 0635 *Fax:* (011) 2394 0861 *E-mail:* contact@ goyalbookshop.com *Web Site:* www.goyalbookshop. com, pg 331

General Book Depot (India) *Tel:* (011) 3263695; (011) 3250635 *Fax:* (011) 2394 0861, pg 1305

General Department of Archives of the Republic of Bulgaria (Bulgaria) *Tel:* (02) 940 0101; (02) 940 0120 *Fax:* (02) 980 14 43 *E-mail:* gua@archives. government.bg *Web Site:* www.archives.government. bg, pg 1494

General Egyptian Book Organization (Egypt (Arab Republic of Egypt)) *Tel:* (02) 5765436; (02) 5775228; (02) 5775109; (02) 5775367; (02) 5775436; (02) 5775545; (02) 5775000 *Fax:* (02) 5765058 *E-mail:* info@egyptianbook.org *Web Site:* www. egyptianbook.org, pg 138

General Egyptian Book Organization (Egypt (Arab Republic of Egypt)) *Tel:* (02) 5775436; (02) 5775228; (02) 5775109; (02) 5775367; (02) 5775436; (02) 5775545; (02) 5775000 *Fax:* (02) 5765058 *E-mail:* info@egyptianbook.org *Web Site:* www. egyptianbook.org, pg 1256

General Printers & Publishers (India) *Tel:* (022) 2387 3113; (022) 2382 6854 *Fax:* (022) 2382 7197, pg 332

General Publications Ltd (United Republic of Tanzania) *Tel:* (0741) 6195 85; (0741) 6231 82, pg 639

General Sciences Library of Ho Chi Minh City (Viet Nam) *Tel:* (08) 822 5055 *Fax:* (08) 829 5632, pg 1554

Bibliotheque Generale et Archives (Morocco) *Tel:* (0996) 3 258, pg 1528

Librairie Generale Francaise SA (France) *Tel:* (01) 43 92 30 00 *Fax:* (01) 43 92 35 90, pg 165

Generalitat de Catalunya Diari Oficial de la Generalitat vern (Spain) *Tel:* (093) 302 64 62 *Fax:* (093) 318 62 21 *E-mail:* llibrbcn@gencat.net *Web Site:* www.gencat. net/diari, pg 580

Genesis Forlag (Norway) *Tel:* (022) 31 02 40 *Fax:* (022) 31 02 05 *E-mail:* genesis@genesis.no *Web Site:* www. genesis.no, pg 504

Genesis Publications Ltd (United Kingdom) *Tel:* (01483) 540970 *Fax:* (01483) 304709 *E-mail:* info@genesis-publications.com *Web Site:* www.genesis-publications. com, pg 694

Genius Verlag (Germany) *Tel:* (08386) 960401 *Fax:* (08386) 960402 *E-mail:* contact@genius-verlag. de *Web Site:* www.genius-verlag.de, pg 227

Genko-Sha (Japan) *Tel:* (03) 3263-3515 *Fax:* (03) 3239-5886 *E-mail:* gks@genkosha.co.jp *Web Site:* www. genkosha.co.jp, pg 414

Gennadius Library (Greece) *Tel:* 2107210536 *Fax:* 2107237767 *E-mail:* ascsa@ascsa.edu.gr *Web Site:* www.ascsa.edu.gr/gennadius, pg 1511

Uitgeverij en boekhandel Van Gennep BV (Netherlands) *Tel:* (20) 6247033 *Fax:* (20) 6247035 *E-mail:* vangennep@wxs.nl, pg 478

Editora Gente Livraria e Editora Ltda (Brazil) *Tel:* (011) 3675 2505 *Fax:* (011) 3675 0430 *E-mail:* gentedit@ mandic.com.br, pg 82

Editorial Gente Nueva (Cuba) *Tel:* (07) 833-7676 *Fax:* (07) 33-8187 *E-mail:* gentenueva@icl.cult, pg 120

Alfons W Gentner Verlag GmbH & Co KG (Germany) *Tel:* (0711) 63672-0 *Fax:* (0711) 63672747 *E-mail:* gentner@gentnerverlag.de *Web Site:* www. gentnerverlag.de, pg 227

Gentofte Bibliotekerne (Denmark) *Tel:* 39487500 *Fax:* 39487507 *E-mail:* bek@gentofte.bibnet.dk; bibliotek@gentofte.bibnet.dk *Web Site:* www.gentofte. bibnet.dk, pg 1500

Geocart Uitg Cartogr AG Claus BVBA (Belgium) *Tel:* (03) 760 14 60 *Fax:* (03) 760 15 28 *E-mail:* site@geocart.be *Web Site:* www.geocart.be, pg 67

Geocarto International Centre (Hong Kong) *Tel:* 2546-4262 *Fax:* 2559-3419 *E-mail:* geocarto@geocarto.com *Web Site:* www.geocarto.com, pg 314

Istituto Geografico de Agostini SpA (Italy) *Tel:* (0321) 4241 *Fax:* (0321) 471286 *E-mail:* info@deagostini.it *Web Site:* www.deagostini.it, pg 387

Instituto Geografico Militar (Chile) *Tel:* (02) 4606863 *Fax:* (02) 4608294 *E-mail:* clientes@igm.cl *Web Site:* www.igm.cl, pg 99

Geographers' A-Z Map Company Ltd (United Kingdom) *Tel:* (01732) 781000 *Fax:* (01732) 780677 *E-mail:* tradesales@a-zmaps.co.uk *Web Site:* www. azmaps.co.uk, pg 694

The Geographical Association (United Kingdom) *Tel:* (0114) 296 0088 *Fax:* (0114) 296 7176 *E-mail:* ga@geography.org.uk *Web Site:* www. geography.org.uk, pg 695

Bibliotheque de Geographie (France) *Tel:* (01) 44 32 14 61; (01) 44 32 14 63 *Fax:* (01) 44 32 14 67 *Web Site:* www.univ-paris1.fr, pg 1505

Geological Publishing House (China) *Tel:* (010) 62351944 *Fax:* (010) 6024523, pg 104

Geological Society Publishing House (United Kingdom) *Tel:* (01225) 445046 *Fax:* (01225) 442836 *E-mail:* rebecca.toop@geolsoc.org.uk *Web Site:* www. geolsoc.org.uk, pg 695

Geological Survey Department (Zimbabwe) *Tel:* (04) 790701; (04) 726342; (04) 726343; (04) 252016; (04) 252017 *Fax:* (04) 739601 *E-mail:* zimeosv@ africaonline.co.zw; zgs@samara.co.zw *Web Site:* www. geosurvey.co.zw, pg 777

Geological Survey Department Library (Botswana) *Tel:* 330327 *Fax:* 332013 *E-mail:* geosurv@global. bw *Web Site:* www.gov.bw/government/geology.htm, pg 1493

Geological Survey Department Reference Library (Ghana) *Tel:* (021) 228093; (021) 28079 *Fax:* (021) 228063; (021) 224676 *E-mail:* ghgeosur@ghana.com, pg 1510

Geological Survey of Zimbabwe (Zimbabwe) *Tel:* (04) 726342; (04) 726343; (04) 252016; (04) 252017 *Fax:* (04) 739601 *E-mail:* zimgeosv@africaonline.co. zw *Web Site:* www.geosurvey.co.zw, pg 1555

Wydawnictwa Geologiczne (Poland) *Tel:* (022) 495351 (ext 518), pg 518

GEOprojects Sarl (Lebanon) *Tel:* (01) 350721 *Fax:* (01) 353000, pg 443

Georeto-Geogidsen (Belgium) *Tel:* (011) 37 52 54 *Fax:* (011) 37 52 54 *E-mail:* georeto@pandora.be *Web Site:* www.geogidsen.be, pg 67

Georg Editeur SA (Switzerland) *Tel:* (022) 8690029 *Fax:* (022) 8690015 *E-mail:* livres@medecinehygiene. ch *Web Site:* www.medecinehygiene.ch, pg 619

George Gregory Bookseller (United Kingdom) *Tel:* (01225) 466000 *Fax:* (01225) 482122, pg 1342

George Mann Publications (United Kingdom) *Tel:* (01622) 759591 *Fax:* (01622) 209193 *Web Site:* www.gmp.co.uk, pg 695

William George's Sons Ltd (United Kingdom) *Tel:* (0117) 9276602, pg 1342

Georgi GmbH (Germany), pg 227

Editions Gerard de Villiers (France) *Tel:* (01) 43 92 30 00 *Fax:* (01) 43 92 35 80 *Web Site:* www. editionsgerarddevilliers.com, pg 165

Gerhard Wolf Janus-Press GmbH (Germany) *Tel:* (030) 47535220 *Fax:* (030) 47533790, pg 227

German Book Centre (India) *Tel:* (044) 2434-6244; (044) 2434-6266 *Fax:* (044) 2434-6529 *E-mail:* germanbk@ vsnl.com *Web Site:* germanbookcentre.com, pg 1305

Germanisches Nationalmuseum (Germany) *Tel:* (0911) 13310 *Fax:* (0911) 1331 200 *E-mail:* info@gnm.de *Web Site:* www.gnm.de, pg 227

Germinal Press (Australia), pg 23

Gerold & Co (Austria) *Tel:* (01) 532 0102 *Fax:* (01) 532 01 02-15; (01) 532 01 02-22 *E-mail:* office@gerold.at *Web Site:* www.gerold.at, pg 50

Gerold & Co (Austria) *Tel:* (01) 5335014-0 *E-mail:* office@gerold.at *Web Site:* www.gerold.at, pg 1290

Gerstenberg Verlag (Germany) *Tel:* (05121) 1060 *Fax:* (05121) 106498 *E-mail:* verlag@gerstenberg-verlag.de *Web Site:* www.gerstenberg-verlag.de, pg 228

Klaus Gerth Musikverlag (Germany) *Tel:* (06443) 68-0 *Fax:* (06443) 68-34 *E-mail:* info@gerth.de *Web Site:* www.gerth.de, pg 228

Gerth Medien GmbH (Germany) *Tel:* (06443) 68-0 *Fax:* (06443) 68-34 *E-mail:* info@gerth.de *Web Site:* www.gerth.de, pg 228

Verlag fuer Geschichte der Naturwissenschaften und der Technik (Germany) *Tel:* (05441) 92 71 29 *Fax:* (05441) 92 71 27 *E-mail:* info@gnt-verlag.de *Web Site:* www.gnt-verlag.de, pg 228

Verlag fuer Geschichte und Politik (Austria) *Tel:* (01) 712 62 58 *Fax:* (01) 712 62 58 19 *E-mail:* office@ oldenbourg.at, pg 51

Gesellschaft fur Bibliothekswesen und Dokumentation des Landbaues (GBDL) (Germany) *Tel:* (08161) 71 34 26 *Fax:* (08161) 71 44 09 *Web Site:* www. weihenstephan.de, pg 1563

Gesellschaft fur deutsche Sprache und Literatur in Zurich (Switzerland) *Tel:* (01) 6342571 *Fax:* (01) 6344905 *E-mail:* uguenthe@ds.unizh.ch, pg 1399

Gesellschaft fuer Organisationswissenschaft e V (Germany) *Tel:* (09206) 480 *Fax:* (09206) 628, pg 228

Gesellschaft fur Interkulturelle Germanistik eV (GIG) (Germany) *Tel:* (0721) 6080 *Fax:* (0721) 6084290, pg 1394

Verlag Lynkeus/H Hakel Gesellschaft (Austria) *Tel:* (01) 7342294, pg 51

Gesellschaft zur Foerderung der Literatur aus Afrika Asien und Lateinamerika eV (Germany) *Tel:* (069) 2102 247; (069) 2102 250 *Fax:* (069) 2102 227; (069) 2102 277 *E-mail:* litprom@book-fair.com *Web Site:* www.litprom.de, pg 1394

Ediciones Gestio 2000 SA (Spain) *Tel:* (093) 4106767 *Fax:* (093) 4109645 *E-mail:* bustia@gestion2000.com *Web Site:* www.gestion2000.com, pg 580

Gesundheits-Dialog Verlag GmbH (Germany) *Tel:* (089) 6 13 40 24 *Fax:* (089) 6 13 37 87 *E-mail:* dialog. top@t-online.de *Web Site:* www.gesundheits-dialog.de, pg 228

Uitgeverij De Geus BV (Netherlands) *Tel:* (076) 522 81 51 *Fax:* (076) 522 25 99 *E-mail:* email@degeus.nl *Web Site:* www.degeus.nl, pg 478

Paul Geuthner Librairie Orientaliste (France) *Tel:* (01) 46 34 71 30 *Fax:* (01) 43 29 75 64 *E-mail:* geuthner@ geuthner.com *Web Site:* www.geuthner.com, pg 165

Ghana Academy of Arts & Sciences (Ghana) *Tel:* (021) 777651 *E-mail:* gaas@ghastinet.gn.apc.org, pg 301

Ghana Institute of Linguistics Literacy & Bible Translation (GILLBT) (Ghana) *Tel:* (021) 777525, pg 301

Ghana Institute of Management & Public Administration, Library & Documentation Centre (Ghana) *Tel:* (021) 401681; (021) 401682; (021) 401683 *Fax:* (021) 405805 *E-mail:* gimpa@excite.com, pg 1510

Ghana Library Association (Ghana) *Tel:* (021) 764822 *Fax:* (021) 763523, pg 1564

Ghana Library Board (Ghana) *Tel:* (021) 665 083 *Fax:* (021) 678 258, pg 1510

Ghana Publishing Corporation (Ghana) *Tel:* (021) 812921 *Fax:* (021) 664330 *E-mail:* asspcom@ africaonline.com.gh, pg 301

Ghana Publishing Corporation, Distribution and Sales Division (Ghana) *Tel:* (022) 812921, pg 1302

Ghana Universities Press (GUP) (Ghana) *Tel:* (021) 22532, pg 301

Bruno Ghigi Editore (Italy) *Tel:* (0541) 791727 *Fax:* (0541) 791727, pg 387

Ghisetti e Corvi Editori (Italy) *Tel:* (02) 76006232 *Fax:* (02) 76009468 *E-mail:* sedes.spa@gpa.it *Web Site:* www.ghisetticorvi.it, pg 387

Giampiero Casagrande Editore (Switzerland) *Tel:* (091) 9235677 *Fax:* (091) 9220171, pg 619

Giancarlo Politi Editore (Italy) *Tel:* (02) 6887341 *Fax:* (02) 66801290 *E-mail:* politi@interbusiness.it *Web Site:* politi.undo.net, pg 387

Boekhandel Gianotten BV (Netherlands) *Tel:* (013) 465 11 11 *Fax:* (013) 535 59 62 *E-mail:* emma@gianotten. nl *Web Site:* www.gianotten.nl, pg 1320

Giao Duc Publishing House (Viet Nam) *Tel:* (04) 262011 *Fax:* (04) 262010, pg 775

G Giappichelli Editore SRL (Italy) *Tel:* (011) 8153111 *Fax:* (011) 8125100 *E-mail:* spedizioni@giappichelli. com *Web Site:* www.giappichelli.it, pg 387

E J W Gibb Memorial Trust (United Kingdom) *Tel:* (01985) 213409 *Fax:* (01985) 212910 *Web Site:* www.arisandphillips.com, pg 695

Stanley Gibbons Publications (United Kingdom) *Tel:* (01425) 472363 *Fax:* (01425) 470247 *E-mail:* sales@stangib.demon.co.uk *Web Site:* www. stanleygibbons.com, pg 695

Gibraltar Bookshop (Gibraltar) *Tel:* 71894 *Fax:* 75554, pg 1302

Gidlunds Bokforlag (Sweden) *Tel:* (0225) 77 11 55 *Fax:* (0255) 77 11 65 *E-mail:* hedemora@gidlunds.se *Web Site:* www.gidlunds.se, pg 607

Gidrometeoizdat (Russian Federation) *Tel:* (0812) 3520815 *Fax:* (0812) 3522688, pg 540

Gieck-Verlag GmbH (Germany) *Tel:* (089) 8415906 *Fax:* (089) 8403310, pg 228

Verlag Ernst und Werner Gieseking GmbH (Germany) *Tel:* (0521) 1 46 74 *Fax:* (0521) 14 37 15 *E-mail:* gieseking-verlag@t-online.de *Web Site:* www. gieseking-verlag.de, pg 228

H Gietl Verlag & Publikationsservice GmbH (Germany) *Tel:* (09402) 93 37-0 *Fax:* (09402) 93 37-24 *Web Site:* www.gietl-verlag.de, pg 228

Michael Gifkins & Associates (New Zealand) *Tel:* (09) 5235032 *Fax:* (09) 5235033 *E-mail:* michael.gifkins@ xtra.co.nz, pg 1125

Gifu Diagaku Fuzoku Toshokan (Japan) *Tel:* (0582) 93-2191 *Fax:* (0582) 30-1107 *E-mail:* lsetsuek@cc.gifu-u.ac.jp *Web Site:* www.gifu-u.ac.jp, pg 1520

Gihan Book Shop (Sri Lanka), pg 601

Instituto de Cultura Juan Gil-Albert (Spain) *Tel:* (096) 5121 214 *Fax:* (096) 5921 824 *E-mail:* galbert@dip-alicante.es *Web Site:* www.dip-alicante.es/galbert/, pg 580

Gildefachverlag GmbH & Co KG (Germany) *Tel:* (05181) 8004-0 *Fax:* (05181) 8004-90, pg 228

Ediciones Gili SA de CV (Mexico) *Tel:* (05) 373-1744; (05) 5606011 *Fax:* (05) 3601453, pg 462

Editorial Gustavo Gili SA (Spain) *Tel:* (093) 3228161 *Fax:* (093) 3229205 *E-mail:* info@ggili.com *Web Site:* www.ggili.com, pg 580

Giliukas Ltd (Lithuania) *Tel:* (07) 709560 *Fax:* (07) 709560 *E-mail:* giliukas@isi.kvn.lt, pg 1315

Gill & Macmillan Distribution (Ireland) *Tel:* (01) 500 9500 *Fax:* (01) 500 9596 *E-mail:* sales@ gillmacmillan.ie *Web Site:* www.gillmacmillan.ie, pg 1309

Gill & Macmillan Ltd (Ireland) *Tel:* (01) 500 9500 *Fax:* (01) 500 9599 *E-mail:* sales@gillmacmillan.ie *Web Site:* www.gillmacmillan.ie, pg 357

Gilles und Francke Verlag (Germany) *Tel:* (0203) 362787 *Fax:* (0203) 355520 *E-mail:* verlag@gilles-francke.de *Web Site:* www.gilles-francke.de, pg 228

Gim-Yeong Co (Republic of Korea) *Tel:* (02) 7454823; (02) 7454825 *Fax:* (02) 7454826, pg 435

Gina Schlenz Literatur-Agentur Koln (Germany) *Tel:* (02206) 81125 *Fax:* (02206) 81125 *E-mail:* litschlenz@aol.com, pg 1121

Ginn & Co (United Kingdom) *Tel:* (01865) 888000 *Fax:* (01865) 314222 *E-mail:* enquiries@ginn.co.uk *Web Site:* www.myprimary.co.uk, pg 695

A Van Ginneken (France) *Tel:* (0380) 789595 *Fax:* (0380) 740700 *E-mail:* hexalivre@axnet.fr, pg 1299

Ginninderra Press (Australia) *Tel:* (02) 6258 9060 *Fax:* (02) 6258 9069 *Web Site:* www.ginninderrapress. com.au, pg 23

Ginsberg Univ Boekhandel (Netherlands) *Tel:* (071) 5160562 *Fax:* (071) 5127505 *E-mail:* bree127@ kooyker.nl, pg 1320

Giourdas Moschos (Greece) *Tel:* 2103624947; 210 3630219 *Fax:* 2103624947 *E-mail:* mgiurdas@ acci.gr *Web Site:* www.mgiurdas.gr, pg 304

Giovanis Publications, Pangosmios Ekdotikos Organismos (Greece) *Tel:* 2103825798; 210 3301511 *Fax:* 2103824417 *E-mail:* giovani1@ otenet.gr *Web Site:* www.geocities.com/giovanis_pub/ en_main1.htm, pg 304

Edizioni del Girasole srl (Italy) *Tel:* (0544) 212830 *Fax:* (0544) 38432 *E-mail:* info@europart.it, pg 387

Girassol Edicoes, LDA (Portugal) *Tel:* (021) 41 43942 *Fax:* (021) 41 43518 *E-mail:* girassol@mail.telepac.pt, pg 527

Girault Gilbert bvba (Belgium) *Tel:* (02) 2171430; (02) 2175880 *Fax:* (02) 2173375, pg 67

Giri Trading Agency Pvt Ltd (India) *Tel:* (044) 24943551; (044) 24953817; (044) 24953823 *Fax:* (044) 24953823 *E-mail:* giritrading@vsnl.com *Web Site:* www.giritrading.com, pg 1305

Girol Books Inc (Canada) *Tel:* 613-233-9044 *Fax:* 613-233-9044 *E-mail:* info@girol.com *Web Site:* www. girol.com, pg 1165

Gisbert y Cia SA (Bolivia) *Tel:* (02) 20 26 26 *Fax:* (02) 20 29 11 *E-mail:* libgis@ceibo.entelnet.bo, pg 75

Gisbert y Cia SA (Bolivia) *Tel:* (02) 220 26 26 *Fax:* (02) 220 29 11 *E-mail:* libgis@ceibo.entelnet.bo, pg 1292

Editions Jean Paul Gisserot (France) *Tel:* (01) 43 31 80 04 *Fax:* (01) 43 31 88 15 *E-mail:* editions@editions-gisserot.com *Web Site:* www.editions-gisserot.com, pg 165

Gitanjali Publishing House (India) *Tel:* (011) 621991; (011) 6237555, pg 332

Promociones Culturales Gitral SA (Ecuador) *Tel:* (02) 510510; (02) 532060; (02) 32644 *Fax:* (02) 510510; (02) 326733, pg 1298

A Giuffre Editore SpA (Italy) *Tel:* (02) 380891 *Fax:* (02) 38009582 *E-mail:* giuffre@giuffre.it *Web Site:* www. giuffre.it, pg 387

Giunti Gruppo Editoriale (Italy) *Tel:* (055) 5062376 *Fax:* (055) 5062397 *E-mail:* informazioni@giunti.it *Web Site:* www.giunti.it, pg 387

Editrice la Giuntina (Italy) *Tel:* (055) 268684 *Fax:* (055) 219718 *E-mail:* giuntina@fol.it *Web Site:* www. giuntina.it, pg 387

Edizioni Giuridico Scientifiche (SRL) (Italy) *Tel:* (02) 55192219 *Fax:* (02) 76009444, pg 387

Gius Laterza e Figli SpA (Italy) *Tel:* (080) 5281211 *Fax:* (080) 5243461 *E-mail:* laterza@laterza.it *Web Site:* www.laterza.it, pg 387

Giuseppe Laterza Editore (Italy) *Tel:* (080) 5237936 *Fax:* (080) 5237360 *Web Site:* www.giuseppelaterza.it, pg 388

Gjurgja Journalistic & Publishing Firm (The Former Yugoslav Republic of Macedonia) *Tel:* (02) 228076, pg 449

Glad Sounds Sdn Bhd (Malaysia) *Tel:* (03) 7562901; (03) 7556442 *Fax:* (03) 7560528 *E-mail:* gladsnd@po. jaring.my, pg 452

Glas New Russian Writing (Russian Federation) *Tel:* (095) 441 9157 *Fax:* (095) 441 9157 *Web Site:* www.russianpress.com/glas/, pg 540

Glasgow City Libraries & Archives, the Mitchell Library (United Kingdom) *Tel:* (0141) 287 2999; (0141) 287 2876 *Fax:* (0141) 287 2815 *E-mail:* lil@cls.glasgow. gov.uk *Web Site:* www.mitchelllibrary.org; www. glasgowlibraries.org, pg 1551

Glasgow City Libraries Publications (United Kingdom) *Tel:* (0141) 287 2846 *Fax:* (0141) 287 2815 *Web Site:* www.glasgowlibraries.org, pg 696

Eric Glass Ltd (United Kingdom) *Tel:* (020) 7229 9500 *Fax:* (020) 7229 6220, pg 1130

GLB Parkland Verlags-und Vertriebs GmbH (Germany) *Tel:* (0221) 96493-0 *Fax:* (0221) 964933, pg 228

Gleaner Co Ltd (Jamaica) *Tel:* 876-922-3400 *Fax:* 876-922-2319; 876-922-6297; 876-922-6223, pg 410

Gleerupska Universitetsbokhandeln (Sweden) *Tel:* (046) 46 19 60 00 *Fax:* (046) 18 42 47, pg 1335

Verlag Gleitschirm (Switzerland) *Tel:* (081) 235241 *Fax:* (081) 221452, pg 619

Glenat Benelux SA (Belgium) *Tel:* (02) 7612640 *Fax:* (02) 7612645 *E-mail:* glenat@glenat.be *Web Site:* www.glenat.com, pg 67

Editions Glenat (France) *Tel:* (04) 76 88 75 75 *Fax:* (04) 76 88 75 70 *Web Site:* www.glenat.com, pg 166

Gloatz, Hille GmbH & Co KG fur Mehrfarben und Zellglasdruck (Germany) *Tel:* (030) 721 99 12; (030) 723 254 93 *Fax:* (030) 721 95 65 *E-mail:* gloatz.hille. gmbh@gmx.de; info@gloatz-hille.de *Web Site:* www. gloatz-hille.de, pg 228

Global Editora e Distribuidora Ltda (Brazil) *Tel:* (011) 2777999 *Fax:* (011) 2778141 *E-mail:* global@dialdata. com.br, pg 82

Global Editora e Distribuidora Ltda (Brazil) *Tel:* (011) 3277-7999, pg 1293

Global Educational Services Pte Ltd (Singapore) *Tel:* 7585086 *Fax:* 7586172 *E-mail:* global@signet. com.sg, pg 551

Global Interprint (United States) *Tel:* 707-545-1220 *Fax:* 707-545-1210 *Web Site:* www.globalinterprint. com, pg 1219

Global Kontakts Balgarija (Bulgaria) *Tel:* (02) 540636 *Fax:* (02) 528790, pg 94

Global Oriental Ltd (United Kingdom) *Tel:* (01303) 226799 *Fax:* (01303) 243087 *E-mail:* info@ globaloriental.co.uk *Web Site:* www.globaloriental.co. uk, pg 696

Globi Verlag AG (Switzerland) *Tel:* (01) 4552130 *Fax:* (01) 4552188 *E-mail:* info@globi.ch *Web Site:* www.globi.ch, pg 619

Editora Globo SA (Brazil) *Tel:* (011) 3767-7886 *Fax:* (011) 3767-7870 *E-mail:* wcarelli@edglobo.com. br *Web Site:* www.editoraglobo.com.br, pg 82

Globus Buchvertrieb (Austria) *Tel:* (01) 513 96 92 0 *Fax:* (01) 513 96 92 9, pg 51

Casa de editura Globus (Romania) *Tel:* (01) 2231510; (01) 2231530 *Fax:* (01) 6664265, pg 535

Globus-Nakladni zavod DOO (Croatia) *Tel:* (01) 462 8400 *Fax:* (01) 462 8400, pg 118

Glossa (Italy) *Tel:* (02) 877609 *Fax:* (02) 72003162 *E-mail:* informazioni@glossaeditrice.it *Web Site:* www.glossaeditrice.it, pg 388

Government of Pakistan Department of Libraries (Pakistan) *Tel:* (051) 9214523; (051) 92026436; (051) 9206440 *Fax:* (051) 9221375 *E-mail:* nlpiba@isb. paknet.com.pk *Web Site:* www.nlp.gov.pk, pg 1569

Government Press (Afghanistan) *Tel:* 26851, pg 1

Government Press (Kenya) *Tel:* (020) 334075, pg 430

Government Printer (Ethiopia), pg 140

Government Printer (Gambia) *Tel:* 227399, pg 190

The Government Printer (Israel) *Tel:* (02) 5685111; (02) 5685200 *Fax:* (02) 5685226, pg 1149

Government Printer (Lesotho) *Tel:* 313023, pg 444

Government Printer (South Africa) *Tel:* (012) 3344500 *Fax:* (012) 3239574, pg 559

Government Printer (United Republic of Tanzania), pg 639

Government Printer (Zambia) *Tel:* (01) 215401; (01) 215805; (01) 215685; (01) 216972, pg 776

Government Printer (Imprimerie National du Rwanda) (Rwanda) *Tel:* 75350 *Fax:* 75820, pg 545

Government Printer (Imprimerie National Du Tchad) (Chad), pg 98

Government Printer (Imprimerie Nationale) (Madagascar) *Tel:* (02) 23675, pg 450

Government Printer (Imprimerie Nationale) (Malawi) *Tel:* (050) 525155 *Fax:* (050) 52230133, pg 451

Government Printer (Imprimerie Nationale) (Mauritius) *Tel:* 2345284; 2345295, pg 457

Government Printer (Imprimerie Officielle) (Morocco) *Tel:* (077) 65024, pg 471

Government Printer (Imprimerie Officielle de la Republique Tunisienne - IORT) (Tunisia) *Tel:* 71299914, pg 643

Government Printer (Societe De L'Imprimerie Nationale Du Niger) (Niger) *Tel:* 734798, pg 498

Government Publications Ireland (Ireland) *Tel:* (01) 6476000 *Fax:* (01) 6610747 *E-mail:* info@opw.ie *Web Site:* www.opw.ie, pg 357

Govi-Verlag Pharmazeutischer Verlag GmbH (Germany) *Tel:* (06196) 9 28-2 50 *Fax:* (06196) 9 28-2 59 *E-mail:* service@govi.de *Web Site:* www.govi.de, pg 229

Govinda-Verlag (Switzerland) *Tel:* (052) 6726677 *Fax:* (052) 6726678 *E-mail:* info@govinda.ch *Web Site:* www.govinda.ch, pg 619

Govostis Publishing SA (Greece) *Tel:* 2103815433; 2103822251 *Web Site:* www.govostis.gr, pg 305

Gower Publishing Ltd (United Kingdom) *Tel:* (01252) 331551 *Fax:* (01252) 344405 *E-mail:* info@gowerpub. com *Web Site:* www.gowerpub.com, pg 697

Gozo Press (Malta) *Tel:* 551534; 564395 *Fax:* 560857 *E-mail:* gozopress@orbit.net.mt, pg 456

Gozo Public Library (Malta) *Tel:* (021) 556200 *Fax:* (021) 560599 *E-mail:* gozo.libraries@gov.mt *Web Site:* servicecharters.gov.mt, pg 1526

Edicoes Graal Ltda (Brazil) *Tel:* (011) 2236522 *Fax:* (011) 2236290 *E-mail:* producao@pazeterra.com. br, pg 82

Ordem do Graal na Terra (Brazil) *Tel:* (011) 4781-0006 *Fax:* (011) 4781-0006 (ext 217) *E-mail:* graal@graal. org.br *Web Site:* www.graal.org.br, pg 82

Grabert-Verlag (Germany) *Tel:* (07071) 40700 *Fax:* (07071) 407026, pg 229

Gracewing Ltd (United Kingdom) *Tel:* (01568) 616835 *Fax:* (01568) 613289 *Web Site:* www.gracewing.co.uk, pg 1342

Gracewing Publishing (United Kingdom) *Tel:* (01568) 616835 *E-mail:* gracewingx@aol.com *Web Site:* www. gracewing.co.uk, pg 697

Grada Publishing (Czech Republic) *Tel:* (02) 20386401; (02) 20386402 *Fax:* (02) 20386400 *E-mail:* info@ gradapublishing.cz; obchod@gradapublishing.cz *Web Site:* www.gradapublishing.cz; www.grada.cz, pg 123

Gradevinska Knjiga (Serbia and Montenegro) *Tel:* (011) 323 35 65; (011) 324 76 62 *Fax:* (011) 323 32 34, pg 547

Izdavacka preduzece Gradina (Serbia and Montenegro) *Tel:* (018) 25 864; (018) 25 456 *Fax:* (018) 25 456 *E-mail:* gradinar@bankerinter.net, pg 547

Gradiva-Publicacnoes Lda (Portugal) *Tel:* (021) 397 40 67; (021) 397 40 68; (021) 397 13 57 *Fax:* (021) 395 34 71 *E-mail:* geral@ip.pt *Web Site:* www.gradiva.pt, pg 527

Graduate Institute of International Studies (Switzerland) *Tel:* (022) 9085700 *Fax:* (022) 9085710 *E-mail:* info@ hei.unige.ch *Web Site:* www.hei.unige.ch, pg 619

Graefe und Unzer Verlag GmbH (Germany) *Tel:* (089) 4 19 81-0 *Fax:* (089) 4 19 81-113 *E-mail:* leserservice@ graefe-und-unzer.de *Web Site:* www.graefe-und-unzer. de, pg 229

Graf Editions (Germany) *Tel:* (089) 27 159 57 *Fax:* (089) 27 159 97 *E-mail:* info@graf-editions.de *Web Site:* www.graf-editions.de, pg 230

Graff Buchhandlung (Germany) *Tel:* (0531) 480 89-0 *Fax:* (0531) 480 89-89 *E-mail:* infos@graff.de *Web Site:* www.graff.de, pg 1300

Graffiti Publications (Australia) *Tel:* (03) 5472 3805 *E-mail:* graffiti@netcon.net.au *Web Site:* www. graffitipub.com.au, pg 23

Editora e Grafica Carisio Ltda, Minas Editora (Brazil) *Tel:* (034) 2413557 *Fax:* (034) 2413310, pg 82

Grafica e Arte srl (Italy) *Tel:* (035) 255014 *Fax:* (035) 250164 *E-mail:* info@graficaearte.it *Web Site:* www. graficaearte.it, pg 388

Grafica Editora Primor Ltda (Brazil) *Tel:* (021) 4744966, pg 82

Marchesi Grafiche Editoriali SpA (Italy) *Tel:* (06) 331359 *Fax:* (06) 3336505 *Web Site:* www.vol. it/marchesi.index.htm, pg 388

Graficki zavod Hrvatske (Croatia) *Tel:* (01) 430 300; (01) 240 7166 *Fax:* (01) 430 331, pg 118

Grafit Verlag GmbH (Germany) *Tel:* (0231) 7214650 *Fax:* (0231) 7214677 *E-mail:* info@grafit.de *Web Site:* www.grafit.de, pg 230

Grafo (Italy) *Tel:* (030) 393221 *Fax:* (030) 3701411 *Web Site:* www.grafo.it, pg 388

Grafos SA Arte Sobre Papel (Spain) *Tel:* (093) 261 87 50 *Fax:* (093) 263 10 04 *E-mail:* info@grafos-barcelona.com *Web Site:* www.grafos-barcelona.com, pg 1213, 1228

Graham Brash Pte Ltd (Singapore) *Tel:* 6262 4843 *Fax:* 6262 1519 *E-mail:* graham_brash@giro.com.sg *Web Site:* www.grahambrash.com.sg, pg 551

Graham-Cameron Publishing & Illustration (United Kingdom) *Tel:* (01263) 821 333 *Fax:* (01263) 821 334 *E-mail:* enquiry@graham-cameron-illustration. com *Web Site:* www.graham-cameron-illustration.com, pg 697

The Graham Publishing Company (Pvt) Ltd (Zimbabwe) *Tel:* (04) 706207 *Fax:* (04) 752439, pg 777

W F Graham (Northampton) Ltd (United Kingdom) *Tel:* (01604) 645537 *Fax:* (01604) 648414, pg 697

Grahames Bookshop (Australia) *Tel:* (02) 9296144 *Fax:* (02) 9571814, pg 1288

Grainger Museum (Australia) *Tel:* (03) 8344 5270 *Fax:* (03) 9349 1707 *E-mail:* grainger@unimelb.edu.au *Web Site:* www.lib.unimelb.edu.au/collections/grainger, pg 23

Verlag der Stiftung Gralsbotschaft GmbH (Germany) *Tel:* (0711) 294355 *Fax:* (07156) 18663 *E-mail:* info@ gral.de *Web Site:* www.gral.de, pg 230

Gram Editora (Argentina) *Tel:* (011) 4304-4833; (011) 4305-8397 *Fax:* (011) 4304-5692 *E-mail:* grameditora@infovia.com.ar *Web Site:* www. grameditora.com.ar, pg 6

Gramedia (Indonesia) *Tel:* (021) 5483008; (021) 5490666 *Fax:* (021) 5300545 *Web Site:* www. gramedia.co.id, pg 351

Gramedia Bookshop (Indonesia) *Tel:* (021) 5300545 *Fax:* (021) 5486085, pg 1308

Gran Enciclopedia-Asturiana Silverio Canada (Spain) *Tel:* (0985) 170921; (0985) 349684 *Fax:* (0985) 349542 *E-mail:* gea.edi@teleline.es; gea_edi@yahoo. es *Web Site:* www.enciclopediaasturiana.com, pg 580

Editions Jacques Grancher (France) *Tel:* (01) 42 22 64 80 *Fax:* (01) 45 48 25 03 *E-mail:* info@grancher.com *Web Site:* www.grancher.com, pg 166

The Grand National Assembly of Turkey Library & Documentation TBMM (Turkey) *Tel:* (0312) 420 68 35 *Fax:* (0312) 420 75 48 *E-mail:* library@tbmm.gov. tr *Web Site:* www.tbmm.gov.tr, pg 1549

Grand People's Study House (Democratic People's Republic of Korea) *Tel:* (02) 34 40 66 *Fax:* (02) 381-4427; (02) 381-2100, pg 433

Grand People's Study House (Democratic People's Republic of Korea) *Tel:* (02) 84 4066, pg 1522

Editions du Grand-Pont (Switzerland) *Tel:* (021) 3123222 *Fax:* (021) 3113222, pg 619

Grande Loge de Luxembourg (Luxembourg) *Tel:* 463-566 *Fax:* 463566, pg 447

Grandi & Associati SRL (Italy) *Tel:* (02) 4695541; (02) 4818962 *Fax:* (02) 48195108 *E-mail:* agenzia@ grandieassociati.it, pg 1123

Editions Grandir (France) *Tel:* (04) 66 84 01 19 *Fax:* (04) 66 26 14 50, pg 166

Grandreams Ltd (United Kingdom) *Tel:* (020) 7724 5333 *Fax:* (020) 7724 5777 *E-mail:* wrrake@robert-frederick.co.uk, pg 697

Grange Books PLC (United Kingdom) *Tel:* (01634) 256 000 *Fax:* (01634) 255 500 *E-mail:* grangebooks@aol. com *Web Site:* www.grangebooks.co.uk, pg 697, 1342

Granit Editions (France) *Tel:* (01) 42 54 08 00 *Fax:* (01) 42 54 73 04, pg 166

Granit sro (Czech Republic) *Tel:* (02) 27 018 361 *Fax:* (02) 27 018 361 *E-mail:* info@granit-publishing. cz *Web Site:* www.granit-publishing.cz, pg 123

Granrott Press (Australia) *Tel:* (08) 383 6081 *Fax:* (08) 383 6067, pg 23

Grant & Cutler Ltd (United Kingdom) *Tel:* (020) 7734 2012 *Fax:* (020) 7734 9272 *E-mail:* contactus@ grantandcutler.com *Web Site:* www.grantandcutler.com, pg 697

Granta Books (United Kingdom) *Tel:* (020) 7704 9776 *Fax:* (020) 7704 0474 *E-mail:* info@granta.com *Web Site:* www.granta.com, pg 697

Grantham Book Services Ltd (United Kingdom) *Tel:* (01476) 541000; (01476) 541 080 (orders) *Fax:* (01476) 541061 *E-mail:* orders@gbs.tbs-ltd.co. uk, pg 1342

Grantham House Publishing (New Zealand) *Tel:* (04) 3813071 *Fax:* (04) 3813067 *E-mail:* gstewart@iconz. co.nz, pg 492

Grao Editorial (Spain) *Tel:* (093) 4080464 *Fax:* (093) 3524337 *E-mail:* grao@grao.com *Web Site:* www.grao. com, pg 580

Grao Editorial (Spain) *Tel:* (093) 4080464; (093) 4050455 *Fax:* (093) 3524337 *E-mail:* grao@grao.com *Web Site:* www.grao.com, pg 580

Graphic Art (28) Co Ltd (Thailand) *Tel:* (02) 2330302, pg 640

Graphic Educational Publications (New Zealand) *Tel:* (09) 6300488 *Fax:* (09) 6234196, pg 492

Graphic Reproductions Ltd (Ireland) *Tel:* (01) 6230101 *Fax:* (01) 6166598; (01) 6166599, pg 1170

Graphic Services Corp (United States) *Tel:* 203-426-0399 *Fax:* 203-270-1578 *Web Site:* www.independentcartongroup.com, pg 1230

Edition Graphischer Zirkel (Austria) *Tel:* (01) 0277346615, pg 51

GRASPO CZ AS - Druckerei und Buchbinderei (Czech Republic) *Tel:* (0577) 606111 *Fax:* (0577) 104052 *E-mail:* graspo@graspo.com *Web Site:* www.graspo.com, pg 1206

Grass Roots Publishing (Australia) *Tel:* (03) 5794 7256 *Fax:* (03) 5794 7285, pg 23

Grass-Verlag (Germany) *Tel:* (02173) 51305 *Fax:* (02224) 770515, pg 230

Sarl Editions Jean Grassin (France) *Tel:* (02) 97 52 93 63 *Fax:* (02) 97 52 83 90 *E-mail:* j.grassin@wanadoo.fr *Web Site:* www.editions-grassin.com, pg 166

Graton Editeur NV (Belgium) *Tel:* (02) 6756 666 *Fax:* (02) 6756 363 *E-mail:* graton.sa@skynet.be, pg 67

Graz Stadtmuseum (Austria) *Tel:* (0316) 822580-0 *Fax:* (0316) 822580-6, pg 51

Universitaetsbibliothek Graz (Austria) *Tel:* (0316) 380 3102 *Fax:* (0316) 384 987 *E-mail:* ub.auskunft@uni-graz.at *Web Site:* www.ub.uni-graz.at, pg 1489

Great China Book Company (Taiwan, Province of China) *Tel:* (02) 822 63341 *Fax:* (02) 822 65906, pg 635

Library of the Great Mosque of Sana'a (Yemen), pg 1554

Great Wall Graphics Ltd (Hong Kong) *Tel:* 2524 0014 *Fax:* 2845 3588, pg 1146

Great Western Press Pty Ltd (Australia) *Tel:* (02) 4124 394 *Fax:* (02) 9144 5566, pg 24

Greater Glider Productions Australia Pty Ltd (Australia) *Tel:* (07) 5494 3000 *Fax:* (07) 5494 3284, pg 24

Editorial Gredos SA (Spain) *Tel:* (091) 7444920 *Fax:* (091) 5192033 *E-mail:* comercial@editorialgredos.com *Web Site:* www.editorialgredos.com, pg 580

The Greek Bookshop (United Kingdom) *Tel:* (020) 8446 1986 *Fax:* (020) 8446 1985 *E-mail:* info@thegreekbookshop.com *Web Site:* www.thegreekbookshop.com, pg 698

Greek Institute (United Kingdom) *Tel:* (020) 8360 7968 *Fax:* (020) 8360 7968, pg 1140

Green Books Ltd (United Kingdom) *Tel:* (01803) 863260 *Fax:* (01803) 863843 *E-mail:* greenbooks@gn.apc.org *Web Site:* www.greenbooks.co.uk, pg 698

Christine Green Authors' Agent (United Kingdom) *Tel:* (020) 7401 8844 *Fax:* (020) 7401 8860 *E-mail:* info@christinegreen.co.uk *Web Site:* www.christinegreen.co.uk, pg 1130

The Green Pagoda Press Ltd (Hong Kong) *Tel:* 2561 1924 *Fax:* 2811 0946 *E-mail:* gpinfo@gpp.com.hk *Web Site:* www.greenpagoda.com, pg 1168

The Green Pagoda Press Ltd (Hong Kong) *Tel:* 2561 1924 *Fax:* 2811 0946 *E-mail:* gpinfo@gpp.com.hk *Web Site:* www.gpp.com.hk, pg 1208

The Green Pagoda Press Ltd (Hong Kong) *Tel:* 2561 1924 *Fax:* 2811 0946 *E-mail:* gpinfo@gpp.com.hk *Web Site:* www.greenpagoda.com, pg 1226

Green Street Bindery (United Kingdom) *Tel:* (01865) 243297 *Fax:* (01865) 791329, pg 1215

W Green The Scottish Law Publisher (United Kingdom) *Tel:* (0131) 225 4879 (orders); (0131) 225 4879 (marketing); (020) 7449 1104 (trade customers); (0264) 342 828 (international book orders & information); (0264) 342 766 (international subscription orders & information) *Fax:* (0131) 225 2104 (orders); (0131) 225 2104 (marketing); (020) 7449 1144 (trade customers); (0264) 342

761 (international book orders & information); (0264) 342 761 (international subscription orders & information) *E-mail:* enquiries@thomson.com; trade.sales@sweetandmaxwell.co.uk (trade customers) *Web Site:* www.wgreen.co.uk, pg 698

Greene & Heaton Ltd (United Kingdom) *Tel:* (020) 8749 0315 *Fax:* (020) 8749 0318 *Web Site:* www.greeneheaton.co.uk, pg 1130

Greene's Bookshop Ltd (Ireland) *Tel:* (01) 6762554 *Fax:* (01) 6789091 *E-mail:* info@greenesbookshop.com *Web Site:* www.greenesbookshop.com, pg 1309

Greenhill Books/Lionel Leventhal Ltd (United Kingdom) *Tel:* (020) 8458 6314 *Fax:* (020) 8905 5245 *E-mail:* info@greenhillbooks.com; sales@greenhillbooks.com *Web Site:* www.greenhillbooks.com, pg 698

Greger-Delacroix (Hungary) *Tel:* (01) 608936 *E-mail:* gregerdelacroix@compuserve.com; greger@elender.hu, pg 318

Gregg Publishing Co (United Kingdom) *Tel:* (01444) 445070 *Fax:* (01444) 445050 *E-mail:* Rdowling@gowerpub.com, pg 698

Libreria Editrice Gregoriana (Italy) *Tel:* (049) 657493 *Fax:* (049) 659777, pg 388

Gregoriana Libreria Editrice (Italy) *Tel:* (049) 657493 *Fax:* (049) 8786435 *E-mail:* seicom@mclink.it, pg 1311

Gregory & Company Authors' Agents (United Kingdom) *Tel:* (020) 7610 4676 *Fax:* (020) 7610 4686 *E-mail:* info@gregoryandcompany.co.uk *Web Site:* www.gregoryandcompany.co.uk, pg 1130

Ernesto Gremese Editore srl (Italy) *Tel:* (06) 65740507 *Fax:* (06) 65740509 *E-mail:* gremese@gremese.com *Web Site:* www.gremese.com, pg 388

Gremese International srl (Italy) *Tel:* (06) 65740507 *Fax:* (06) 65740509 *E-mail:* gremese@gremese.com *Web Site:* www.gremese.com, pg 388

Gresham Books Ltd (United Kingdom) *Tel:* (01865) 513582 *Fax:* (01865) 512718 *E-mail:* info@gresham-books.co.uk *Web Site:* www.gresham-books.co.uk, pg 698

Greuthof Verlag und Vertrieb GmbH (Germany) *Tel:* (07681) 6025 *Fax:* (07681) 6027, pg 230

Grevas Forlag (Denmark) *Tel:* 86997065 *Fax:* 86997265 *E-mail:* info@grevas.dk; skrodhoj@worldonline.dk *Web Site:* www.grevas.dk, pg 131

Greven Verlag Koeln GmbH (Germany) *Tel:* (0221) 20 33-161 *Fax:* (0221) 20 33-162 *E-mail:* greven.verlag@greven.de *Web Site:* www.greven-verlag.de, pg 230

Piero Gribaudi Editore (Italy) *Tel:* (02) 89302244 *Fax:* (02) 89302376 *E-mail:* info@gribaudi.it *Web Site:* www.gribaudi.it, pg 388

John Grieg Forlag AS (Norway) *Tel:* 55213181 *Fax:* 55218180, pg 505

Editions du Griffon (Neuchatel) (Switzerland) *Tel:* (032) 7252204, pg 619

Grijalbo SA (Venezuela) *Tel:* (0212) 238 15 42; (0212) 238 17 32 *Fax:* (0212) 239 03 08 *E-mail:* griven@etheron.net, pg 774

Grijalbo Mondadon SA Junior (Spain) *Tel:* (093) 4767100 *Fax:* (093) 4767121 *Web Site:* www.grijalbo.com, pg 580

Grijalbo Mondadori SA (Chile) *Tel:* (02) 782-8200 *Fax:* (02) 782-8210 *E-mail:* editorial@randomhouse-mondadori.cl *Web Site:* www.grijalbo.com, pg 99

Grijalbo Mondadori SA (Spain) *Tel:* (093) 4767100 *Fax:* (093) 4767121 *E-mail:* marketing@grijalbo.com *Web Site:* www.grijalbo.com, pg 580

Editorial Grijalbo SA de CV (Mexico) *Tel:* (05) 5545 1620 *Web Site:* www.randomhousemondadori.com.mx, pg 462

Grimm Press Ltd (Taiwan, Province of China) *Tel:* (02) 23965698 *Fax:* (02) 23570954 *E-mail:* ishbel@cite.com.tw *Web Site:* www.cite.com.tw, pg 635

Grivas Publications (Greece) *Tel:* 2105573470 *Fax:* 2105573076 *E-mail:* info@grivas.gr *Web Site:* www.grivas.gr, pg 1303

Groeninghe NV (Belgium) *Tel:* (056) 22 40 77 *Fax:* (056) 22 82 86 *Web Site:* www.groeninghe.com, pg 67

David Grossman Literary Agency Ltd (United Kingdom) *Tel:* (020) 7221 2770 *Fax:* (020) 7221 1445, pg 1130

Grote'sche Verlagsbuchhandlung GmbH & Co KG (Germany) *Tel:* (02234) 1060 *Fax:* (02234) 106284, pg 230

Groto Publikasi (Suriname) *Tel:* 493569, pg 603

Editions Francois Grounauer (Switzerland) *Tel:* (022) 447948, pg 619

Editora Ground Ltda (Brazil) *Tel:* (011) 5031-1500 *Fax:* (011) 5031-3462 *E-mail:* editora@ground.com.br; vendas@ground.com.br; marketing@ground.com.br *Web Site:* www.ground.com.br, pg 83

Groupe de Recherche et d'Echanges Technologiques (GRET) (France) *Tel:* (01) 40 05 61 61 *Fax:* (01) 40 05 61 10 *E-mail:* gret@gret.org; librairie@gret.org *Web Site:* www.gret.org, pg 166

Groupe Hatier International (France) *Tel:* (01) 44 39 28 00 *Fax:* (01) 45 44 84 54 *E-mail:* hatier@intl.com, pg 166

Groupe Revue Fiduciaire (France) *Tel:* (01) 47 70 42 42 *Fax:* (01) 48 24 12 93 *E-mail:* courrier@grouperf.com *Web Site:* www.grouperf.com, pg 166

Groupement d'Information Promotion Presse Edition (GIPPE) (France) *Tel:* (01) 45 32 12 75 *E-mail:* gippe@frec.fr *Web Site:* gippe.free.fr, pg 166

Groupements Francais des Fabricants de Papiers d'Impression-Ecriture (COPACEL) (France) *Tel:* (01) 53 89 24 00 *Fax:* (01) 53 89 24 01 *E-mail:* info@copacel.fr *Web Site:* www.copacel.fr, pg 1258

Grub Street (United Kingdom) *Tel:* (020) 7924 3966; (020) 7738 1008 *Fax:* (020) 7738 1009 *E-mail:* post@grubstreet.co.uk *Web Site:* www.grubstreet.co.uk, pg 698

Verlag Grundlagen und Praxis GmbH & Co (Germany) *Tel:* (0491) 6 18 86 *Fax:* (0491) 36 34 *E-mail:* info@grundlagen-praxis.de *Web Site:* www.grundlagen-praxis.de, pg 230

Gruner + Jahr AG & Co (Germany) *Tel:* (040) 37030 *Fax:* (040) 37036000 *E-mail:* oeffentlichkeiharbeit@guj.de *Web Site:* www.guj.de, pg 230

Grupo Bibliografico Nacional de la Republica Dominicana (Dominican Republic), pg 1561

Editorial Grupo Cero (Spain) *Tel:* (091) 758 19 40; (091) 542 33 49 *Fax:* (091) 758 19 41 *E-mail:* pedidos@editorialgrupocero.com *Web Site:* www.editorialgrupocero.com, pg 581

Grupo Comunicar (Spain) *Tel:* (0959) 248380 *Fax:* (0959) 248380 *E-mail:* info@grupocomunicar.com *Web Site:* www.grupo-comunicar.com, pg 581

Grupo Cultural Especializado, SA (Mexico) *Tel:* (05) 6889831 *Fax:* (05) 6889965, pg 1318

Grupo Editorial CEAC SA (Spain) *Tel:* (093) 2472424 *Fax:* (093) 2315115 *E-mail:* atencioncliente@ceacedit.com *Web Site:* www.ceacedit.com; www.editorialceac.com, pg 581

Grupo Editorial Iberoamerica, SA de CV (Mexico) *Tel:* (05) 5111267; (05) 5116760, pg 462

Grupo Editorial Iberoamerica de Colombia SA (Colombia) *Tel:* (01) 3106553 *Fax:* (01) 3106553 *E-mail:* geicol@colomsat.net.co, pg 1296

Grupo Editorial RIN-78 (Guatemala) *Tel:* (02) 692080 *Fax:* (02) 601834, pg 310

Grupo Editorial Z Zeta SA de CV (Mexico) *Tel:* (05) 6705627; (05) 5817929 *Fax:* (05) 5758280, pg 462

Grupo Noriega Editores de Colombia Ltda (Colombia) *Tel:* (01) 3689036 *Fax:* (01) 3377788 *E-mail:* gnoriega@unete.com.co, pg 1296

Grupo Santillana de Ediciones SA (Spain) *Tel:* (091) 7449060 *Fax:* (091) 3224475 *E-mail:* grupo@ santillana.es *Web Site:* www.gruposantillana.com, pg 581

Schweizer Autorinnen und Autoren Gruppe Olten (Switzerland) *Tel:* (01) 350 04 60 *Fax:* (01) 350 04 61 *E-mail:* sekretariat@a-d-s.ch *Web Site:* www.a-d-s.ch, pg 1399

Gruppe 21 GmbH (Germany) *Tel:* (02054) 10489-0 *Fax:* (02054) 10489-29 *E-mail:* redaktion@info21.de *Web Site:* www.gruppe21.de, pg 230

Verlag Gruppenpaedagogischer Literatur (Germany) *Tel:* (06081) 5 67 40 *Fax:* (06081) 5 74 38 *E-mail:* info@vglw.de *Web Site:* www.vglw.de, pg 230

Gruppo Editoriale Faenza Editrice SpA (Italy) *Tel:* (0546) 670411 *Fax:* (0546) 660440 *E-mail:* info@ faenza.com *Web Site:* www.faenza.com, pg 388

Gruppo Editorialeil Saggiatore (Italy) *Tel:* (02) 202301 *Fax:* (02) 29513061 *Web Site:* www.saggiatore.it, pg 388

Walter de Gruyter GmbH & Co KG (Germany) *Tel:* (030) 260 05-0 *Fax:* (030) 260 05-251 *E-mail:* wdg-info@degruyter.de *Web Site:* www. degruyter.de, pg 230

Editura Gryphon (Romania) *Tel:* (0268) 313 642; (0268) 312 888 *Fax:* (0268) 312 888 *E-mail:* gryphon@ gryphon.ro *Web Site:* www.gryphon.ro, pg 535

GSB (Ghana Standards Board) (Ghana) *Tel:* (021) 662942; (021) 665461, pg 301

GSMBA, Edition Bruno Gasser (Switzerland) *Tel:* (061) 6811103; (061) 6816698 *Fax:* (061) 6811103 *E-mail:* gasser@dial-switch.ck, pg 619

Guadalquivir SL Ediciones (Spain) *Tel:* (095) 422 19 76; (095) 422 19 17 *Fax:* (095) 421 33 20 *E-mail:* guadalquivir.ed@svq.servicom.es *Web Site:* www.guadalquivirediciones.com, pg 581

Editora Guadalupe Ltda (Colombia) *Tel:* (01) 2690788; (01) 2690211 *Fax:* (01) 2685308, pg 111

Editorial Guadalupe (Argentina) *Tel:* (011) 4826-8587 *Fax:* (011) 4826-8587 *E-mail:* ventas@ editorialguadalupe.com.ar *Web Site:* www. editorialguadalupe.com.ar, pg 6

Editora Guanabara Koogan SA (Brazil) *Tel:* (021) 3970-9450 *Fax:* (021) 2252-2732 *E-mail:* gbk@ editoraguanabara.com.br *Web Site:* www. editoraguanabara.com.br, pg 83

Ugo Guanda Editore (Italy) *Tel:* (02) 80206322 *Fax:* (02) 72000306 *E-mail:* info@guanda.it *Web Site:* www. guanda.it, pg 388

Guangdong Science & Technology Press (China) *Tel:* (020) 87768688; (020) 87618770 (Directorial Office); (020) 87769412 (Foreign Cooperation Editorial Office) *Fax:* (020) 87764169 *E-mail:* gdkjwb@ns.guangzhou.gb.com.cn *Web Site:* www.xwcbj.gd.gov.cn, pg 104

Guarro Casas SA (Spain) *Tel:* (093) 7767676 *Fax:* (093) 7767677 *E-mail:* guarro@guarro.com *Web Site:* www. guarro.com, pg 1228

Editorial Guaymuras (Honduras) *Tel:* 237 54 33 *Fax:* 238 45 78 *E-mail:* editorial@sigmanet.hn, pg 312

Librairie Guenegaud (France) *Tel:* (01) 43260791 *Fax:* (01) 40468872 *E-mail:* libraire.guenegaud@ wanadoo.fr, pg 166

Gunter Olzog Verlag GmbH (Germany) *Tel:* (089) 71 04 66 60 *Fax:* (089) 71 04 66 61 *E-mail:* olzog.verlag@t-online.de *Web Site:* www.olzog.de, pg 230

Guenther Butkus (Germany) *Tel:* (0521) 69689 *Fax:* (0521) 174470 *E-mail:* pendragon.verlag@t-online.de *Web Site:* www.pendragon.de, pg 230

Edizioni Guerini e Associati SpA (Italy) *Tel:* (02) 582980 *Fax:* (02) 58298030 *E-mail:* info@guerini.it *Web Site:* www.guerini.it, pg 388

The Guernsey Press Co Ltd (United Kingdom) *Tel:* (01481) 240240; (01481) 243657 (ISDN) *Fax:* (01481) 240282 *E-mail:* books@guernsey-press. com *Web Site:* www.guernsey-press.com, pg 1153

The Guernsey Press Co Ltd (United Kingdom) *Tel:* (01481) 240240; (01481) 243657 (ISDN) *Fax:* (01481) 240290; (01481) 240275 *E-mail:* books@guernsey-press.com *Web Site:* www. guernsey-press.com, pg 1174

The Guernsey Press Co Ltd (United Kingdom) *Tel:* (01481) 240240; (01481) 243657 (ISDN) *Fax:* (01481) 240282 *E-mail:* books@guernsey-press. com *Web Site:* www.guernsey-press.com, pg 1215

The Guernsey Press Co Ltd (United Kingdom) *Tel:* (01481) 240240; (01481) 243657 (ISDN) *Fax:* (01481) 240275 *E-mail:* books@guernsey-press. com *Web Site:* www.guernsey-press.com, pg 1228

Guerra Edizioni GURU srl (Italy) *Tel:* (075) 5289090 *Fax:* (075) 5288244 *E-mail:* geinfo@guerra-edizioni. com *Web Site:* www.guerra-edizioni.com, pg 388

Verlag Klaus Guhl (Germany) *Tel:* (030) 3213062 *Fax:* (030) 30823868, pg 231

Guildhall Library (United Kingdom) *Tel:* (020) 7332 1868; (020) 7332 1870; (020) 7332 1863; (020) 7332 1839 *Fax:* (020) 7600 3384 *E-mail:* printedbooks. guildhall@corpoflondon.gov.uk; manuscripts. guildhall@corpoflondon.gov.uk *Web Site:* www. corpoflondon.gov.uk, pg 1552

Editions d'Art Albert Guillot (France) *Tel:* (04) 78521026, pg 166

Livraria Guimaraes (Portugal) *Tel:* (021) 3462436 *Fax:* (021) 3462620, pg 1328

Guimaraes Editores, Lda (Portugal) *Tel:* (021) 324 3120 *Fax:* (021) 324 3129 *E-mail:* guimaraes.ed@mail. telepac.pt *Web Site:* www.guimaraes-ed.pt, pg 527

Guinness World Records Ltd (United Kingdom) *Tel:* (020) 7891 4567 *Fax:* (020) 7891 4501, pg 699

Guizhou Education Publishing House (China) *Tel:* (0851) 627904; (0851) 524211, pg 104

Gujarat Book Trade Federation (India) *Tel:* (079) 447 634; (079) 447 635, pg 1263

Gujarat Vidyapith Granthalaya (India) *Tel:* (079) 7541148 *Fax:* (079) 7542547 *E-mail:* guivi@adinet. emet.in; gvpahd@ad1vsnl.net.in, pg 1514

Editorial Gulaab (Spain) *Tel:* (091) 6170867 *Fax:* (091) 6170867 *E-mail:* alfaomega@sew.es, pg 581

Gulur Raudur Grenn og Blar Childrens Bookclub (Iceland) *Tel:* 5102525 *Fax:* 5102525 *E-mail:* malogmenning@edda.is *Web Site:* www. malogmenning.is, pg 1243

Gummerus Printing (Finland) *Tel:* (014) 683 525 *Fax:* (014) 685 166 *E-mail:* printing@gummerus.fi *Web Site:* www.gummerus.fi, pg 1166, 1206

Gummerus Publishers (Finland) *Tel:* (09) 584 301 *Fax:* (09) 5843 0200 *Web Site:* www.gummerus.fi, pg 142

M D Gunasena & Co Ltd (Sri Lanka) *Tel:* (01) 323981; (01) 323982; (01) 323983; (01) 323984 *Fax:* (01) 323336 *E-mail:* mdgunasena@mail.ewisl.net *Web Site:* www.mdgunasena.com, pg 601

Gunnar Lie & Associates Ltd (United Kingdom) *Tel:* (020) 8487 9020 *Fax:* (020) 8878 2832 *E-mail:* gunnarlie@compuserve.com, pg 1130

PT BPK Gunung Mulia (Indonesia) *Tel:* (021) 3901208 *Fax:* (021) 3901633 *E-mail:* corp.off@bpkgm.com *Web Site:* www.bpkgm.com, pg 351, 1308

Guru Publishers Ltd (Kenya) *Tel:* (020) 764146, pg 430

Verlag des Gustav-Adolf-Werks (Germany) *Tel:* (0341) 490 62 0 *Fax:* (0341) 4770505 *E-mail:* info@gustav-adolf-werk.de *Web Site:* www.gustav-adolf-werk.de, pg 231

Th Gut Verlag (Switzerland) *Tel:* (01) 9285211 *Fax:* (01) 9285200 *Web Site:* www.gutverlag.ch/, pg 619

Gutenberg-Gesellschaft eV (Germany) *Tel:* (06131) 22 64 20 *Fax:* (06131) 23 35 30 *E-mail:* gutenberg-gesellschaft@freenet.de *Web Site:* www.gutenberg-gesellschaft.uni-mainz.de, pg 231, 1260, 1394

Gutenberg Publications (Greece) *Tel:* 2103642003; 2103800798; 2103843511 *Fax:* 210 3642030; 2103800127; 2103829402 *E-mail:* gutenberg@internet.gr, pg 305

Gutersloher Verlaghaus GmbH /Chr Kaiser/Kiefel/Quell (Germany) *Tel:* (05241) 74050 *Fax:* (05241) 740548 *E-mail:* info@gtvh.de *Web Site:* www.gtvh.de, pg 231

Guthmann & Peterson Liber Libri, Edition (Austria) *Tel:* (01) 877 04 26 *Fax:* (01) 876 40 04 *E-mail:* verlag@guthmann-peterson.de *Web Site:* www. guthmann-peterson.de, pg 51

Guyana Community Based Rehabilitation Progeamme (Guyana) *Tel:* (022) 64004 *Fax:* (022) 62615, pg 311

Guyana Library Association (Guyana) *Tel:* (0226) 2690; (0226) 2699; (0227) 4052 *Fax:* (0227) 4053 *E-mail:* natlib@sdnp.org.gy *Web Site:* www.natlib.gov. gy, pg 1564

Guyana Medical Science Library (Guyana), pg 1512

GVA Publishers Ltd (Switzerland) *Tel:* (022) 3112424 *Fax:* (022) 3112556, pg 619

Gvanim Publishing House (Israel) *Tel:* (03) 5281044; (03) 5283648 *Fax:* (03) 5283648 *E-mail:* traklinm@ zahav.net.il, pg 364

Gwasg Carreg Gwalch (United Kingdom) *Tel:* (01492) 642 031 *Fax:* (01492) 641 502 *E-mail:* llyfrau@ carreg-gwalch.co.uk *Web Site:* www.carreg-gwalch. co.uk, pg 699

Gwasg Gwenffrwd (United Kingdom) *Tel:* (01490) 420 560; (0845) 330 6754, pg 699

Gwasg y Dref Wen (United Kingdom) *Tel:* (01222) 617860 *Fax:* (01222) 610507 *E-mail:* gwil-drefwen@ btinternet.com, pg 699

Gyan Publishing House (India) *Tel:* (011) 23261060; (011) 23282060 *Fax:* (011) 23285914 *E-mail:* gyanbook@del2.vsnl.net.in *Web Site:* www. gyanbooks.com, pg 332

Gyeom-jisa (Republic of Korea) *Tel:* (02) 3351985 *Fax:* (02) 3351986, pg 435

Gyldendal Norsk Forlag A/S (Norway) *Tel:* 22034100 *Fax:* 22034105 *E-mail:* gnf@gyldendal.no *Web Site:* www.gyldendal.no, pg 505

Gyldendals Babybogklubben (Denmark) *Tel:* 70 11 00 33 *Fax:* 70 11 01 33 *E-mail:* boernebogklub@ gyldendal.dk *Web Site:* www.gyldendal.dk, pg 1241

Gyldendals Bogklubben (Denmark) *Tel:* 70 11 00 33 *Fax:* 70 11 01 33 *E-mail:* gyldendals-bogklub@ gyldendal.dk *Web Site:* www.gyldendal.dk, pg 1241

Gyldendals Borne Bogklubben (Denmark) *Tel:* 70 11 00 33 *Fax:* 70 11 01 33 *E-mail:* boernebogklub@ gyldendal.dk *Web Site:* www.gyldendal.dk, pg 1242

Gyldendals Junior Bogklubben (Denmark) *Tel:* 70 11 00 33 *Fax:* 70 11 01 33 *E-mail:* boernebogklub@ gyldendal.dk *Web Site:* www.gyldendal.dk, pg 1242

Gyldendalske Boghandel - Nordisk Forlag A/ S (Denmark) *Tel:* 33755555 *Fax:* 33755556 *E-mail:* gyldendal@gyldendal.dk *Web Site:* www. gyldendal.dk, pg 131

Gylym, Izd-Vo (Kazakstan) *Tel:* (03272) 618005; (03272) 618845 *Fax:* (03272) 618845; (03272) 618005, pg 429

Gyosei Corporation (Japan) *Tel:* (03) 5349-6666 *Fax:* (03) 5349-6655 *E-mail:* eigyo1@gyosei.co.jp *Web Site:* www.gyosei.co.jp, pg 414

H & Y Printing Ltd (Hong Kong) *Tel:* 2870 2379 *Fax:* 2555 0028 *E-mail:* hyphk@netvigator.com, pg 1146

H B Verlags und Vertriebs-Gesellschaft mbH (Germany) *Tel:* (040) 4151-04 *Fax:* (040) 41513231, pg 231

H K Scanner Arts International Ltd (Hong Kong) *Tel:* 29760289 *Fax:* 29760292 *E-mail:* hksagp@ netvigator.com, pg 1168

H L Schlapp Buch- und Antiquariatshandlung GmbH und Co KG Abt Verlag (Germany) *Tel:* (06151) 17 90-0 *Fax:* (06151) 17 90 40 *E-mail:* darmstadt@schlapp. de *Web Site:* www.schlapp.de, pg 231

Verlag H M Hauschild GmbH (Germany) *Tel:* (0421) 1785-0 *Fax:* (0421) 1785-285 *E-mail:* info@hauschild-werbedruck.de *Web Site:* www.hauschild.werbedruck. de, pg 231

Haag und Herchen Verlag GmbH (Germany) *Tel:* (069) 550911-13 *Fax:* (069) 552601; (069) 554922 *E-mail:* verlag@haagundherchen.de *Web Site:* www. haagundherchen.de, pg 231

C W Haarfeld GmbH & Co (Germany) *Tel:* (0201) 720950 *Fax:* (0201) 7209533, pg 231

Wolfgang G Haas - Musikverlag Koeln ek (Germany) *Tel:* (02203) 98 88 3-0 *Fax:* (02203) 98 88 3-50 *E-mail:* info@haas-koeln.de *Web Site:* www.haas-koeln.de, pg 231

P Haase & Sons Forlag A/S (Denmark) *Tel:* 33 18 10 80 *Fax:* 33 11 59 59 *E-mail:* haase@haase.dk *Web Site:* www.haase.dk, pg 131

Dr Rudolf Habelt GmbH (Germany) *Tel:* (0228) 9 23 83-0 *Fax:* (0228) 9 23 83-6 *E-mail:* info@habelt.de *Web Site:* www.habelt.de, pg 231

Habermann Institute for Literary Research (Israel) *Tel:* (08) 9244569; (08) 9241160 *Fax:* (08) 9249466 *E-mail:* zmalachi@post.tau.ac.il, pg 364

Hachette Education (France) *Tel:* (01) 43 92 30 00; (01) 43 92 31 12 *Fax:* (01) 43 92 30 30 *Web Site:* www. hachette-education.com, pg 166

Hachette francais langue etrangere - FLE (France) *Tel:* (01) 43 92 30 00 *Fax:* (01) 43 92 39 20 *E-mail:* fle@hachette-livre.fr *Web Site:* www.fle. hachette-livre.fr, pg 166

Hachette Jeunesse (France) *Tel:* (01) 43923000 *Fax:* (01) 43923338 *Web Site:* www.hachettejeunesse.com, pg 167

Hachette Jeunesse Roman (France) *Tel:* (01) 43 92 30 00 *Fax:* (01) 443 92 33 38, pg 167

Hachette Livre (France) *Tel:* (01) 43 92 30 00 *Fax:* (01) 43 92 30 30 *Web Site:* www.hatchette-livre.fr, pg 167

Hachette Livre Australia (Australia) *Tel:* (02) 8248 0800; (02) 4390 1300 (customer service) *Fax:* (02) 8248 0810 *E-mail:* aspub@hachette.com.au (Australian publishing); hsales@alliancedist.com.au; adscs@ alliancedist.com.au (customer service) *Web Site:* www. hachette.com.au, pg 24

Hachette Livre International (France) *Tel:* (01) 55 00 11 00 *Fax:* (01) 55 00 11 60, pg 167

Hachette Livre SA - H E D (France) *Tel:* (01) 43923000 *Fax:* (01) 43923030 *Web Site:* www.hachette.com, pg 1300

Hachette Pratiques (France) *Tel:* (01) 43 92 30 00 *Fax:* (01) 43 92 30 39, pg 167

Hachmeister Verlag (Germany) *Tel:* (0251) 51210 *Fax:* (0251) 57217 *E-mail:* hachmeister.galerie@t-online.de *Web Site:* www.hachmeister-galerie.de, pg 231

Hadar Publishing House Ltd (Israel) *Tel:* (03) 6812244 *Fax:* (03) 6826138 *E-mail:* info@zmora.co.il, pg 364

Peter Haddock Ltd (United Kingdom) *Tel:* (01262) 678121 *Fax:* (01262) 400043 *E-mail:* enquiries@ peterhaddock.com *Web Site:* www.phpublishing.co.uk, pg 699

Walter Haedecke Verlag (Germany) *Tel:* (07033) 138080 *Fax:* (07033) 1380813 *E-mail:* haedecke_vlg@t-online.de, pg 231

Haedong (Republic of Korea) *Tel:* (02) 953707 *Fax:* (02) 953707, pg 435

Dr Curt Haefner-Verlag GmbH (Germany) *Tel:* (06221) 6446-0 *Fax:* (06221) 6446-40 *E-mail:* info@haefner-verlag.de *Web Site:* www.haefner-verlag.de, pg 231

Haenssler Verlag GmbH (Germany) *Tel:* (07031) 7414-177 *Fax:* (07031) 7414-119 *E-mail:* info@haenssler.de *Web Site:* www.haenssler.de, pg 231

Haere Po Editions (French Polynesia) *Tel:* 582636 *Fax:* 582333 *E-mail:* haerepotahiti@mail.pf, pg 190

Heinz-Jurgen Hausser (Germany) *Tel:* (06151) 22824 *Fax:* (06151) 26854, pg 232

Haffmans Verlag AG (Switzerland) *Tel:* (01) 386 4000 *Fax:* (01) 386 4001 *E-mail:* verlag@haffmans.ch, pg 620

Hagaberg AB (Sweden) *Tel:* (08) 690 90 00 *Fax:* (08) 7021940, pg 607

Lehrmittelverlag Wilhelm Hagemann GmbH (Germany) *Tel:* (0211) 17 92 70-0 *Fax:* (0211) 17 92 70-70 *E-mail:* aktuell@hagemann.de *Web Site:* www. hagemann.de, pg 232

Hagen & Stam Uitgeverij Ten (Netherlands) *Tel:* (070) 3045700 *Fax:* (070) 3045800, pg 479

Hagenbach & Bender GMBH (Switzerland) *Tel:* (031) 3816666 *Fax:* (031) 3816677 *E-mail:* rights@ hagenbach-bender.com *Web Site:* www.hagenbach-bender.com, pg 620

Hahner Verlagsgesellschaft mbH (Germany) *Tel:* (02408) 55 05 *Fax:* (02408) 58081 *E-mail:* office@hvg.de, pg 232

Mary Hahn's Kochbuchverlag (Germany) *Tel:* (089) 2 90 88-0 *E-mail:* l.eggs@herbig.nct *Web Site:* www.herbig. net, pg 232

Hahnsche Buchhandlung (Germany) *Tel:* (0511) 80 71 80 40 *Fax:* (0511) 36 36 98 *E-mail:* verlag@ hahnsche-buchhandlung.de *Web Site:* www.hahnsche-buchhandlung.de, pg 232

Chu Hai Publishing (Taiwan) Co Ltd (Taiwan, Province of China) *Tel:* (02) 7080290 *Fax:* (02) 7084804, pg 635

Haifa University Press (Israel) *Tel:* (04) 8240111 *Fax:* (04) 8342245 *Web Site:* www.haifa.ac.il, pg 364

Haigh & Hochland Ltd (United Kingdom) *Tel:* (061) 2734156 *Fax:* (061) 2734340, pg 1342

Hainaim Publishing Co Ltd (Republic of Korea) *Tel:* (02) 326-1600 *Fax:* (02) 326-1625 *Web Site:* www.hainaim.com, pg 435

Hak Won Publishing Co (Republic of Korea) *Tel:* (02) 741-4621; (02) 741-4623 *Fax:* (02) 765-1877 *E-mail:* ccnstar@hanmail.net, pg 435

Hakgojae Publishing Inc (Republic of Korea) *Tel:* (02) 7361713 *Fax:* (02) 7398592 *E-mail:* hkjass@hitel.kol. co.kr, pg 435

Hakibbutz Hameuchad Publishing House Ltd (Israel) *Tel:* (03) 5785810 *Fax:* (03) 5785811, pg 364

Hakluyt Society (United Kingdom) *Tel:* (01428) 641850 *Fax:* (01428) 641933 *E-mail:* office@hakluyt.com *Web Site:* www.hakluyt.com, pg 699, 1402

Hakmunsa Publishing Co (Republic of Korea) *Tel:* (02) 738-5118 *Fax:* (02) 733-8998 *E-mail:* hakmun@ hakmun.co.kr *Web Site:* www.hakmun.co.kr, pg 435

Hakubunkan-Shinsha Publishers Ltd (Japan) *Tel:* (03) 3811-4721; (03) 3811-6693 *Fax:* (03) 3818-1431 *Web Site:* www.hakubunkan.co.jp, pg 414

Hakusui-Sha Co Ltd (Japan) *Tel:* (03) 3291-7811 *Fax:* (03) 3291-8448 *E-mail:* hpmaster@hakusuisha. co.jp *Web Site:* www.hakusuisha.co.jp, pg 414

Hakutei-Sha (Japan) *Tel:* (03) 3986-3271 *Fax:* (03) 3986-3272 *E-mail:* LDX00227@nifty.ne.jp, pg 414

Hakuyo-Sha (Japan) *Tel:* (03) 5281-9772 *Fax:* (03) 5281-9886 *E-mail:* hakuyo@mars.dti.ne.jp *Web Site:* www. hakuyo-sha.co.jp, pg 414

Hakuyu-Sha (Japan) *Tel:* (03) 3268-8271 *Fax:* (03) 3268-8273 *Web Site:* www.hakubunkan.co.jp, pg 414

Peter Halban Publishers Ltd (United Kingdom) *Tel:* (020) 7437 9300 *Fax:* (020) 7431 9512 *E-mail:* books@halbanpublishers.com *Web Site:* www. halbanpublishers.com, pg 699

Halbooks Publishing (Australia) *Tel:* (02) 9326 4250 *Fax:* (02) 9326 4250 *E-mail:* sean@iotaproductions. com.au, pg 24

Halcyon Publishing Ltd (New Zealand) *Tel:* (09) 4895337 *Fax:* (09) 4442399 *E-mail:* info@ halcyonpublishing.co.nz, pg 492

Haldane Mason Ltd (United Kingdom) *Tel:* (020) 8459 2131 *Fax:* (020) 8728 1216 *E-mail:* haldane.mason@ dial.pipex.com, pg 699

Hale & Iremonger Pty Ltd (Australia) *Tel:* (02) 9560 0470 *Fax:* (02) 9550 0097 *E-mail:* info@ haleiremonger.com *Web Site:* www.haleiremonger.com, pg 24

Robert Hale Ltd (United Kingdom) *Tel:* (020) 7251 2661 *Fax:* (020) 7490 4958 *E-mail:* enquire@halebooks. com *Web Site:* www.halebooks.com, pg 699

Robert Hale Ltd (United Kingdom) *Tel:* (020) 7251 2661 *Fax:* (020) 7490 4958 *E-mail:* webmistress@ halebooks.com *Web Site:* www.halebooks.com, pg 1153

Herbert von Halem Verlag (Germany) *Tel:* (0221) 92 58 29 0 *Fax:* (0221) 92 58 29 29 *E-mail:* info@halem-verlag.de *Web Site:* www.halem-verlag.de; www. inpunkto.de, pg 232

Halldale Publishing & Media Ltd (United Kingdom) *Tel:* (01252) 532000 *Fax:* (01252) 512714 *Web Site:* www.halldale.com, pg 699

Hallgren och Fallgren Studieforlag AB (Sweden) *Tel:* (018) 50 71 00 *Fax:* (018) 12 72 70 *E-mail:* info@hallgren-fallgren.se *Web Site:* www. hallgren-fallgren.se, pg 607

Hallwag Kummerly & Frey AG (Switzerland) *Tel:* (031) 423131 *Fax:* (031) 414133, pg 620

Hallwag Kummerly & Frey AG (Switzerland) *Tel:* (031) 332 31 31 *Fax:* (031) 850 31 00 *E-mail:* info@ swisstravelcenter.ch *Web Site:* www.swisstravelcenter. ch, pg 1152

Hallwag Kummerly & Frey AG (Switzerland) *Tel:* (031) 850 31 31 *Fax:* (031) 850 31 00 *E-mail:* info@ swisstravelcenter.ch *Web Site:* www.swisstravelcenter. ch; www.hallwag.com, pg 1172

Hallwag Kummerly & Frey AG (Switzerland) *Tel:* (031) 850 31 31 *Fax:* (031) 850 31 00 *E-mail:* info@swisstravelcenter.com *Web Site:* www. swisstravelcenter.ch, pg 1213

F H Halpern (Australia) *Tel:* (03) 9596 1436 *Fax:* (03) 9596 1436, pg 24

Hambledon & London Ltd (United Kingdom) *Tel:* (020) 7586 0817 *Fax:* (020) 7586 9970 *E-mail:* office@ hambledon.co.uk *Web Site:* www.hambledon.co.uk, pg 699

Hamburger Lesehefte Verlag Iselt & Co Nfl mbH (Germany) *Tel:* (04841) 8352-0 *Fax:* (04841) 8352-10 *E-mail:* verlagsgruppe.husum@t-online.de *Web Site:* www.verlagsgruppe.de, pg 232

The Hamburgh Register (Guyana) *Tel:* (02) 258486 *Fax:* (02) 258511 *E-mail:* wrma@sdup.org.gy, pg 311

Hamburgisches Welt-Wirtschafts-Archiv (HWWA) Bibliothek (Germany) *Tel:* (040) 42834-219 *Fax:* (040) 42834-550 *E-mail:* bib.auskunft@hwwa.de *Web Site:* www.hwwa.de, pg 1507

Libreria Hamburgo SA (Mexico) *Tel:* (05) 5126796; (05) 5218265, pg 1318

Hamdard Foundation Pakistan (Pakistan) *Tel:* (021) 6616001; (021) 6616002; (021) 6616003; (021) 6616004; (021) 6620945 *Fax:* (021) 6611755 *E-mail:* hamdard@khi.paknet.com.pk *Web Site:* www. hamdard.com.pk, pg 508

Liselotte Hamecher (Germany) *Tel:* (0561) 16611
*Fax:* (0561) 775262, pg 232

Kerri Hamer (Australia) *Tel:* (02) 9349 5170 *Fax:* (02)
9349 5170, pg 24

Hamilton Printing Co (United States) *Tel:* 518-732-
4491 *Toll Free Tel:* 800-242-4222 *Fax:* 518-732-7714,
pg 1156, 1219, 1239

Hamish Hamilton Ltd (United Kingdom) *Tel:* (020)
7010 3000 *Fax:* (020) 7010 6060 *E-mail:* customer.
service@penguin.co.uk *Web Site:* www.penguin.co.uk,
pg 700

Hamlyn (United Kingdom) *Tel:* (020) 7531 8400
*Fax:* (020) 7531 8650 *Web Site:* www.hamlyn.co.uk,
pg 700

Geoffrey Hamlyn-Harris (Australia) *Tel:* (076) 811450
*Fax:* (018) 63662, pg 24

Hammarskjold Memorial Library (Zambia) *Tel:* (02)
214572; (02) 219012; (02) 211488 *Fax:* (02) 211001
*E-mail:* daglib@zamnet.zm, pg 1554

Alfred Hammer (Germany) *Tel:* (06078) 71622
*Fax:* (06078) 71655, pg 232

Peter Hammer Verlag GmbH (Germany) *Tel:* (0202)
505066; (0202) 505067 *Fax:* (0202) 509252
*E-mail:* info@peter-hammer-verlag.de *Web Site:* www.
peter-hammer-verlag.de, pg 232

Maison d'Edition Mohamed Ali Hammi (Tunisia)
*Tel:* 74407440 *Fax:* 74407441 *E-mail:* caeu@gnet.tn,
pg 643

Hammond Bindery Ltd (United Kingdom)
*Tel:* (01924) 204830 *Fax:* (01924) 339107; (01924)
332637 *E-mail:* sales@hammond-bindery.co.uk
*Web Site:* www.hammond-bindery.co.uk, pg 1215

Hammond Bindery Ltd (United Kingdom)
*Tel:* (01924) 204830 *Fax:* (01924) 332637; (01924)
339107 *E-mail:* sales@hammond-bindery.co.uk
*Web Site:* www.hammond-bindery.co.uk, pg 1229

Hammond Bindery Ltd (United Kingdom)
*Tel:* (01924) 204830 *Fax:* (01924) 339107; (01924)
332637 *E-mail:* sales@hammond-bindery.co.uk
*Web Site:* www.hammond-bindery.co.uk, pg 1237

Hammond Packaging Ltd (United Kingdom)
*Tel:* (01924) 204830 *Fax:* (01924) 332637; (01924)
339107 *E-mail:* sales@hammond-bindery.co.uk
*Web Site:* www.hammond-bindery.co.uk, pg 1174

Hammond Packaging Ltd (United Kingdom)
*Tel:* (01924) 204830 *Fax:* (01924) 339107; (01924)
332637 *E-mail:* sales@hammond-bindery.co.uk
*Web Site:* www.hammond-bindery.co.uk, pg 1216

Hammonia-Verlag GmbH Fachverlag der
Wohnungswirtschaft (Germany) *Tel:* (040) 520103-
0 *Fax:* (040) 520103-30 *E-mail:* info@hammonia.de
*Web Site:* www.hvh.de, pg 232

Otzar Hamore (Israel) *Tel:* (03) 6922983 *Fax:* (03)
6922903, pg 364

Hampden Press (Australia) *Tel:* (02) 9351 9070
*Fax:* (02) 9351 9323 *E-mail:* j.higgs@cchs.usyd.edu.
au, pg 24

Editions Viviane Hamy (France) *Tel:* (01) 53171600
*Fax:* (01) 53171609 *E-mail:* information@viviane-
hamy.fr *Web Site:* www.viviane-hamy.fr/0000.html,
pg 167

Hanjin Publishing Co (Republic of Korea) *Tel:* (02)
7137453 *Fax:* (02) 7135510, pg 435

Hand-Presse (Austria) *Tel:* (0512) 87975, pg 51

H&H Publishing (Australia) *Tel:* (03) 98774428
*Fax:* (03) 98774222, pg 24

The Handsel Press (United Kingdom) *Tel:* (01202)
665432 *Fax:* (01202) 666219 *E-mail:* orders@
orcabookservices.co.uk *Web Site:* www.handselpress.
co.uk, pg 700

Verlag Handwerk und Technik GmbH (Germany)
*Tel:* (040) 5 38 08-0 *Fax:* (040) 5 38 08-101
*E-mail:* info@handwerk-technik.de *Web Site:* www.
handwerk-technik-shop.de, pg 232

Hangil Art Vision (Republic of Korea) *Tel:* (02)
5154811; (02) 5154813 *Fax:* (02) 5154816, pg 435

Hanguk Seoji Hakhoe (Republic of Korea) *Tel:* (02) 788-
4143 *Fax:* (02) 788-3385 *E-mail:* w3@nanet.go.kr
*Web Site:* www.nanet.go.kr, pg 1566

Hanguk Tosogwan Hakhoe (Republic of Korea) *Tel:* (02)
7600114 *Fax:* (02) 7442453, pg 1566

Hanitzotz A-Sharara Publishing House (Israel) *Tel:* (03)
6839145 *Fax:* (03) 6839148 *E-mail:* oda@netvision.
net.il *Web Site:* www.odaction.org; www.hanitzotz.
com/challenge, pg 364

Hannibal-Verlag (Germany) *Tel:* (089) 24 245 415
*Fax:* (089) 24 245 294 *E-mail:* info@hannibal-verlag.
de *Web Site:* www.hannibal-verlag.de, pg 232

The Hannon Press (Ireland) *Tel:* (0405) 46089
*Fax:* (0405) 46089, pg 357

Universitaetsbibliothek Hannover und Technische
Informationsbibliothek (Germany) *Tel:* (0511) 762
2268 *Fax:* (0511) 715936 *E-mail:* ubtib@tib.uni-
hannover.de *Web Site:* www.tib.uni-hannover.de,
pg 1507

Hans Furstelberger (Austria) *Tel:* (0732) 773177
*Fax:* (0732) 784485, pg 1290

Hans Prakashan (India) *Tel:* (0532) 623077 *E-mail:* ar@
nde.vsnl.net.in, pg 332

Hansa Verlag Ingwert Paulsen Jr (Germany) *Tel:* (04841)
8352-0 *Fax:* (04841) 8352-10 *E-mail:* verlagsgruppe.
husum@t-online.de *Web Site:* www.verlagsgruppe.de,
pg 232

Edition Wilhelm Hansen AS (Denmark) *Tel:* 33 11
78 88 *Fax:* 33 14 81 78 *E-mail:* ewh@ewh.dk
*Web Site:* www.ewh.dk; www.wilhelm-hansen.dk,
pg 131

Hanseproduktion AB (Sweden) *Tel:* (0498) 24 93 18
*Fax:* (0498) 24 93 18, pg 607

Carl Hanser Verlag (Germany) *Tel:* (089) 9 98 30
0 *Fax:* (089) 98 48 09 *E-mail:* info@hanser.de
*Web Site:* www.hanser.de/verlag, pg 233

Soederbokhandeln Hansson och Bruce AB (Sweden)
*Tel:* (08) 405432; (08) 6405433 *Fax:* (08) 6441315,
pg 1335

Hanthawaddy Bookshop (Myanmar), pg 1319

Hanthawaddy Book House (Myanmar), pg 472

Hanul Publishing Co (Republic of Korea) *Tel:* (02)
3260095; (02) 3366183 *Fax:* (02) 3337543
*E-mail:* newhanul@nuri.net, pg 436

Happy Cat Books (United Kingdom) *Tel:* (020)
7745 2370 *Fax:* (020) 7745 2372 *E-mail:* sales@
bouncemarketing.co.uk, pg 700

Happy Mental Buch- und Musik Verlag (Germany)
*Tel:* (08158) 993303 *Fax:* (08158) 993305, pg 233

Har-El Printers & Publishers (Israel) *Tel:* (03) 681 6834
*Fax:* (03) 681 3563 *Web Site:* www.harelart.com,
pg 1149

Har-El Printers & Publishers (Israel) *Tel:* (03) 681 6834
*Fax:* (03) 681 3563 *E-mail:* mharel@harelart.co.il
*Web Site:* www.harelart.com, pg 1170, 1210

Hara Shobo (Japan) *Tel:* (03) 5212-7801 *Fax:* (03) 3230-
1158 *E-mail:* toshi@harashobo.com *Web Site:* www.
harashobo.com, pg 414

Harare City Library (Zimbabwe) *Tel:* (04) 751834;
751835, pg 1555

Harare Polytechnic Library (Zimbabwe) *Tel:* (04)
752311, pg 1555

Editora Harbra Ltda (Brazil) *Tel:* (011) 5084-2403; (011)
5084-2482; (011) 5571-1122; (011) 5549-2244; (011)
5571-0276 *Fax:* (011) 5575-6876; (011) 5571-9777
*E-mail:* editorial@harbra.com.br *Web Site:* www.
harbra.com.br, pg 83

Harcourt Assessment Inc (United Kingdom) *Tel:* (01865)
888188 *Fax:* (01865) 314348 *E-mail:* info@harcourt-
uk.com *Web Site:* www.harcourt-uk.com, pg 700

Harcourt Education Australia (Australia) *Tel:* (03) 9245
7188 *Toll Free Tel:* 800-810-372 *Fax:* (03) 9245 7333
*E-mail:* customerservice@harcourteducation.com.au
*Web Site:* www.harcourteducation.com.au, pg 24

Harcourt Education International (United Kingdom)
*Tel:* (01865) 311366 *Fax:* (01865) 314641 *E-mail:* uk.
schools@harcourteducation.co.uk *Web Site:* www.
harcourteducation.co.uk, pg 700

Harden's Ltd (United Kingdom) *Tel:* (020) 7839 4763
*Fax:* (020) 7839 7561 *E-mail:* mail@hardens.com
*Web Site:* www.hardens.com, pg 700

Hardt und Worner Marketing fur das Buch (Germany)
*Tel:* (06172) 7005 *Fax:* (01672) 71547 *E-mail:* hardt.
woerner@t-online.de, pg 233

Norman Hardy Printing Group (United Kingdom)
*Tel:* (020) 7378 1579 *Fax:* (020) 7378 6422
*E-mail:* info@thehardygroup.co.uk, pg 1216

Patrick Hardy Books (United Kingdom) *Tel:* (01223)
350865 *Fax:* (01223) 366951 *E-mail:* sales@
lutterworth.com; publishing@lutterworth.com
*Web Site:* www.lutterworth.com, pg 700

The Thomas Hardy Society (United Kingdom)
*Tel:* (01305) 251501 *Fax:* (01305) 251501
*E-mail:* info@hardysociety.org *Web Site:* www.
hardysociety.org, pg 1402

Harenberg Kommunikation Verlags- und Medien-GmbH
& Co KG (Germany) *Tel:* (0231) 9056-0 *Fax:* (0231)
9056-110 *E-mail:* post@harenberg.de *Web Site:* www.
harenberg.de, pg 233

Hargreen Publishing Co (Australia) *Tel:* (03) 9329 9714
*Fax:* (03) 9329 5295 *E-mail:* em@execmedia.com.au,
pg 24

Siegfried Haring Literatten-Verlag Ulm (Germany)
*Tel:* (0731) 9806040 *Fax:* (0731) 9806042
*E-mail:* ratart.edition@t-online.de, pg 233

Harlenic Hellas Publishing SA (Greece) *Tel:* 210
3610218 *Fax:* 2103614846 *E-mail:* info@harlenic.
gr *Web Site:* www.harlenic.gr, pg 305

Harlequin Iberica SA (Spain) *Tel:* (091) 4358623
*Fax:* (091) 4310484 *E-mail:* atencionalcliente@
harlequiniberica.com *Web Site:* www.harlequiniberica.
com, pg 581

Harlequin SA (France) *Tel:* (01) 42166363 *Fax:* (01)
45828694, pg 167

Harley Books (United Kingdom) *Tel:* (01206) 271216
*Fax:* (01206) 271182 *E-mail:* harley@keme.co.uk
*Web Site:* www.harleybooks.com, pg 700

L'Harmattan (France) *Tel:* (01) 40 46 79 11; (01) 40
46 79 20 *Fax:* (01) 43 25 82 03 *E-mail:* harmat@
worldnet.fr *Web Site:* www.editions-harmattan.fr,
pg 167

De Harmonie Uitgeverij (Netherlands) *Tel:* (020)
6245181 *Fax:* (020) 6230672 *E-mail:* info@
deharmonie.nl *Web Site:* www.deharmonie.nl, pg 479

Harmonie Verlag (Germany) *Tel:* (0761) 709667
*Fax:* (0761) 709662 *E-mail:* harmonieverlag@aol.com,
pg 233

HarperCollins UK (United Kingdom) *Tel:* (020) 8741
7070 *Toll Free Tel:* (0870) 900 2050 (customer
service) *Fax:* (020) 8307 4813 *Toll Free Fax:* (0141)
306 3767 (customer service) *E-mail:* contact@
harpercollins.co.uk *Web Site:* www.harpercollins.co.uk,
pg 701

HarperCollinsPublishers (Australia) Pty Ltd (Australia)
*Tel:* (02) 9952 5000 *Fax:* (02) 9952 5555
*Web Site:* www.harpercollins.com.au, pg 24

HarperCollinsPublishers (New Zealand) Ltd (New
Zealand) *Tel:* (09) 443 9400 *Fax:* (09) 443 9403
*E-mail:* editors@harpercollins.co.nz *Web Site:* www.
harpercollins.co.nz, pg 492

Heffers: Academic + General Books (United Kingdom) *Tel:* (01223) 568568 *Fax:* (01223) 568591 *E-mail:* heffers@heffers.co.uk *Web Site:* www.heffers. co.uk, pg 1342

Bokforlaget Hegas AB (Sweden) *Tel:* (042) 330 340 *Fax:* (042) 330 141 *E-mail:* kom.litt@helsingborg.se, pg 607

June Heggenhougen (Norway) *Tel:* 32832125 *Fax:* 32832125, pg 1125

Heibonsha Ltd, Publishers (Japan) *Tel:* (03) 3818-0873; (03) 3818-0874 (sales) *Fax:* (03) 3818-0857 *E-mail:* shop@heibonsha.co.jp *Web Site:* www. heibonsha.co.jp, pg 414

Heideland-Orbis NV (Belgium) *Tel:* (03) 3600211 *Fax:* (03) 3600212, pg 67

Joh Heider Verlag GmbH (Germany) *Tel:* (02202) 95 40-35 *Fax:* (02202) 2 15 31 *E-mail:* anzeigen@ marburger-bund.de *Web Site:* www.heider-verlag. de/mb/mediadaten/, pg 234

Heigl Verlag, Horst Edition (Germany) *Tel:* (07554) 283 *Fax:* (07552) 938756 *E-mail:* info@heigl-verlag.de *Web Site:* www.heigl-verlag.de, pg 234

Yozmot Heiliger Ltd (Israel) *Tel:* (03) 5284851 *Fax:* (03) 5285397 *E-mail:* books@yozmot.com *Web Site:* www. yozmot.com, pg 1309

Heilongjiang Science & Technology Press (China) *Tel:* (0451) 3635613 *Fax:* (0451) 3642127, pg 104

Institut fuer Heilpaedagogik (Switzerland) *Tel:* (041) 3170033 *Fax:* (041) 3170034 *E-mail:* info@ihpl.ch *Web Site:* www.ihpl.ch, pg 620

Heima er Bezt Book Club (Iceland) *Tel:* 5531599; 5882400 *Fax:* 5888994, pg 1243

Max Heindel Verlag Rosenkreuzer Philosophie (Switzerland) *Tel:* (081) 834 20 03 *Fax:* (081) 834 20 04 *E-mail:* info@max-heindel.ch *Web Site:* www. heindel-verlag.ch, pg 620

Heinemann Education Botswana (Botswana) *Tel:* 372305 *Fax:* 371832, pg 75

Heinemann Educational Publishers Southern Africa (South Africa) *Tel:* (011) 322 8600 *Fax:* (011) 322 8716 *E-mail:* customerliaison@heinemann.co.za *Web Site:* www.heinemann.co.za, pg 560

Heinemann Kenya Ltd (EAEP) (Kenya) *Tel:* (020) 4445700; (020) 4445200 (020) 448753; (020) 226286, pg 430

Heinemann Library (Australia) *Tel:* (03) 9245 7188 *Fax:* (03) 9245 7265 *E-mail:* int.schools@ harcourteducation.com.au *Web Site:* www. heinemannlibrary.com.au, pg 25

Heinemann Publishers (Pty) Ltd (South Africa) *Tel:* (011) 3228621 *Fax:* (011) 3228717 *E-mail:* customerliaison@heinemann.co.za *Web Site:* www.heinemann.co.za, pg 560

William Heinemann Ltd (United Kingdom) *Tel:* (020) 7840 8400 *Fax:* (020) 7828 6681, pg 702

Verlag Otto Heinevetter Lehrmittel GmbH (Germany) *Tel:* (040) 25 90 19 *Fax:* (040) 251 2128 *E-mail:* info@heinevetter-verlag.de *Web Site:* www. heinevetter-verlag.de, pg 234

Arnold Heinman Publishers (India) Pvt Ltd (India) *Tel:* (011) 6383422; (011) 60780; (011) 664256 *Fax:* (011) 6877571, pg 332

Heinrich Hugendubel AG (Switzerland) *Tel:* (071) 67711-90 *Fax:* (071) 67711-91, pg 620

Heinrichshofen's Verlag GmbH & Co KG (Germany) *Tel:* (04421) 9267-0 *Fax:* (04421) 9267-99 *E-mail:* info@heinrichshofen.de *Web Site:* www. heinrichshofen.de, pg 234

Heinz-Theo Gremme Verlag (Germany) *Tel:* (02592) 984200 *E-mail:* theo@gremme-verlag.de *Web Site:* www.gremme-verlag.de, pg 234

Heinze GmbH (Germany) *Tel:* (01805) 339833 *Fax:* (01805) 119877 *E-mail:* info@heinze.de; kundenservice@heinze.de *Web Site:* www.heinze.de/; www.heinzebauoffice.de, pg 234

Hekla Forlag (Denmark) *Tel:* 36 15 36 15 *Fax:* 36 15 36 16 *E-mail:* post@borgen.dk *Web Site:* www.borgen.dk, pg 131

Helbing und Lichtenhahn Verlag AG (Switzerland) *Tel:* (061) 2289070 *Fax:* (061) 2289071 *E-mail:* info@ helbing.ch *Web Site:* www.helbing.ch, pg 620

Helbling Verlagsgesellschaft mbH (Austria) *Tel:* (0512) 262333-0 *Fax:* (0512) 262333-111 *E-mail:* office@ helbling.co.at *Web Site:* www.helbling.com, pg 51

HelfRecht Verlag und Druck (Germany) *Tel:* (09232) 6010 *Fax:* (09232) 601280 *E-mail:* info@helfrecht.de *Web Site:* www.helfrecht.de, pg 234

Editorial Heliasta SRL (Argentina) *Tel:* (011) 4371-5546 *Fax:* (011) 4375-1659 *E-mail:* editorial@heliasta.com. ar *Web Site:* www.heliasta.com.ar, pg 6

Helicon Publishing Ltd (United Kingdom) *Tel:* (08709) 200200 *Fax:* (01235) 826999 *E-mail:* helicon@rm. com *Web Site:* www.helicon.co.uk, pg 702

Helikon Kiado (Hungary) *Tel:* (01) 428-9450; (01) 428-9429 *Fax:* (01) 428-9481 *E-mail:* helikon@helikon.hu *Web Site:* www.helikon.hu, pg 318

Helion & Co (United Kingdom) *Tel:* (0121) 705 3393 *Fax:* (0121) 711 4075 *E-mail:* info@helion.co.uk *Web Site:* www.helion.co.uk, pg 703

Heliopol (Bulgaria) *Tel:* (02) 746850; (02) 718513 *E-mail:* heliopol@heliopol.bg, pg 94

Heliopolis-Verlag (Germany) *Tel:* (07473) 5427 *Fax:* (07473) 5427, pg 234

Uitgeverij Helios NV (Belgium) *Tel:* (03) 6645320, pg 67

Hellenic Bookservice (United Kingdom) *Tel:* (020) 72679499 *Fax:* (020) 72679498 *E-mail:* info@ hellenicbookservice.com *Web Site:* www. hellenicbookservice.com, pg 1342

Hellenic Federation of Publishers & Booksellers (Greece) *Tel:* 2103300924; 2103200926 *Fax:* 213301617 *E-mail:* poev@otenet.gr, pg 1262

Hellerau-Verlag Dresden GmbH (Germany) *Tel:* (0351) 803 5293 *Fax:* (0351) 826 0130 *E-mail:* info@ hellerau-verlag.de *Web Site:* www.hellerau-verlag.de/, pg 235

Christopher Helm (Publishers) Ltd (United Kingdom) *Tel:* (020) 7758 0200 *Fax:* (020) 7758 0222 *E-mail:* customerservice@acblack.com; ornithology@ acblack.com, pg 703

Helm Information Ltd (United Kingdom) *Tel:* (01580) 880 561 *Fax:* (01580) 880 541 *Web Site:* www.helm-information.co.uk, pg 703

Helsingin Kaupunginkirjasto - yleisten kirjastojen keskuskirjasto (Finland) *Tel:* (09) 3108511 *Fax:* (09) 31085517 *E-mail:* city.library@hel.fi *Web Site:* www. lib.hel.fi, pg 1503

Helsinki University Library (Finland) *Tel:* (09) 191 23196 *Fax:* (09) 191 22719 *E-mail:* hyk-palvelu@ helsinki.fi *Web Site:* www.lib.helsinki.fi, pg 1503

Verlag Helvetica Chimica Acta (Switzerland) *Tel:* (01) 3602434 *Fax:* (01) 3602435 *E-mail:* info@wiley-vch.de; vhca@vhca.ch *Web Site:* www.wiley-vch.de, pg 620

Helyode Editions (SA-ADN) (Belgium) *Tel:* (02) 3444934 *Fax:* (02) 3475534, pg 67

Hema Maps Pty Ltd (Australia) *Tel:* (07) 3340 0000 *Fax:* (07) 3340 0099 *E-mail:* manager@hemamaps. com.au *Web Site:* www.hemamaps.com, pg 25

Hemco Publications (Mauritius) *Tel:* 4643141, pg 457

Van Hemeldonck NV (Belgium) *Tel:* (014) 611034 *Fax:* (014) 620288 *E-mail:* booksell@innet.be, pg 67

Hemeroteca Municipal de Madrid (Spain) *Tel:* (091) 588 57 71, pg 1544

Hemeroteca Nacional de Mexico (Mexico) *Tel:* (055) 622 6818 *Fax:* (055) 665 0951 *Web Site:* biblional. bibliog.unam.mx, pg 1527

Hemisferio Sur Edicion Agropecuaria (Uruguay) *Tel:* (02) 916 45 15; (02) 916 45 20 *Fax:* (02) 916 45 20 *E-mail:* librperi@adinet.com.uy, pg 772

Editorial Hemisferio Sur SA (Argentina) *Tel:* (011) 49529825 *Fax:* (011) 49528454 *E-mail:* informe@ hemisferiosur.com.ar *Web Site:* www.hemisferiosur. com.ar, pg 6

Editions Hemma (Belgium) *Tel:* (086) 43 01 01 *Fax:* (086) 43 36 40 *Web Site:* www.hemma.be, pg 68

Hemma Holland BV (Netherlands) *Tel:* (020) 675 53 26 *Fax:* (020) 679 62 54, pg 479

Hemming Information Services (United Kingdom) *Tel:* (020) 7973 6694 *Fax:* (020) 7233 5052 *E-mail:* customer@hqluk.com *Web Site:* www.h-info. co.uk, pg 703

Hemus Co Inc (Bulgaria) *Tel:* (02) 981 1769 *Fax:* (02) 981 3341 *E-mail:* hemusb@pbitex.com, pg 1294

Hemus Editora Ltda (Brazil) *Tel:* (011) 55219058 *Fax:* (011) 55219058, pg 83

Henan Science & Technology Publishing House (China) *Tel:* (0371) 5727616; (0371) 5721756-643 *Fax:* (0371) 5727616 *E-mail:* hnkj565@public2.zz.ha.cn, pg 104

Hendon Publishing Co Ltd (United Kingdom) *Tel:* (01282) 613129; (01282) 697725 *Fax:* (01282) 870215, pg 703

Thomas Heneage Art Books (United Kingdom) *Tel:* (020) 7930 9223 *Fax:* (020) 7839 9223 *E-mail:* artbooks@heneage.com *Web Site:* www. heneage.com, pg 1342

G Henle Verlag (Germany) *Tel:* (089) 759820 *Fax:* (089) 7598240 *E-mail:* info@henle.de *Web Site:* www.henle. de, pg 235

Ian Henry Publications Ltd (United Kingdom) *Tel:* (01708) 736213 *Fax:* (01621) 850862, pg 703

Edition Hentrich Druck & Verlag Gebr Hentrich und Tank GmbH & Co KG (Germany) *Tel:* (030) 84410001 *Fax:* (030) 84410002, pg 235

Heraldry Today (United Kingdom) *Tel:* (01672) 520617 *Fax:* (01672) 520183 *E-mail:* heraldry@heraldrytoday. co.uk *Web Site:* www.heraldrytoday.co.uk, pg 703

Herattaja-yhdistys Ry (Finland) *Tel:* (06) 438 8911 *Fax:* (06) 438 7430 *E-mail:* jormakka@nic.fi, pg 142

Editions Herault (France) *Tel:* (02) 41554590 *Fax:* (02) 41554590, pg 167

Herbert Press Ltd (United Kingdom) *Tel:* (020) 7758 0200 *Fax:* (020) 7758 0222 *E-mail:* customerservices@acblack.com *Web Site:* www.acblack.com, pg 703

F A Herbig Verlagsbuchhandlung GmbH (Germany) *Tel:* (089) 2 90 88-0 *E-mail:* l.eggs@herbig.net *Web Site:* www.herbig.net, pg 235

Herbita Editrice di Leonardo Palermo (Italy) *Tel:* (091) 6167732 *Fax:* (091) 6167716 *Web Site:* www. herbitaeditrice.it, pg 389

Hercegtisak doo (Croatia) *Tel:* (021) 320 663 *Fax:* (021) 320 663 *E-mail:* nakladnistvo@hercegtisak.ba *Web Site:* www.hercegtisak.ba, pg 118

Hans-Alfred Herchen & Co Verlag KG (Germany) *Tel:* (069) 550911-13 *Fax:* (069) 552601; (069) 554922, pg 235

Hercules de Ediciones, SA (Spain) *Tel:* (0981) 220585; (0981) 226443 *Fax:* (0981) 220717 *E-mail:* empg05052@empresas-galicia.com, pg 581

Editorial y Libreria Herder Ltda (Colombia) *Tel:* (01) 3344853 *Fax:* (01) 2832272, pg 1296

Herder AG Basel (Switzerland) *Tel:* (061) 8279060 *Fax:* (061) 8279067 *E-mail:* verkauf@herder.ch, pg 620

Herder-Buchgemeinde (Germany) *Tel:* (0761) 2717440 *Fax:* (0761) 2717360 *E-mail:* kundenservice@herder. de *Web Site:* www.herder.de, pg 1242

Editorial Herder SA (Spain) *Tel:* (093) 476 26 26 *Fax:* (093) 207 34 48 *E-mail:* herder@herdereditorial. com *Web Site:* www.herder-sa.com, pg 581

Herder Editrice e Libreria (Italy) *Tel:* (06) 679 53 04; (06) 679 46 28 *Fax:* (06) 678 47 51 *E-mail:* distr@ herder.it *Web Site:* www.herder.it, pg 389

Herder Editrice e Libreria (Italy) *Tel:* (06) 679 53 04; (06) 679 46 28 *Fax:* (06) 678 47 51 *E-mail:* distr@ herder.it; distr@herder.it *Web Site:* www.herder.it, pg 1311

Verlag Herder GmbH & Co KG (Germany) *Tel:* (0761) 2717440 *Fax:* (0761) 2717360 *E-mail:* kundenservice@herder.de *Web Site:* www. herder.de/, pg 235

Heritage Books (Nigeria) *Tel:* (01) 5871333; (01) 5871333 *E-mail:* obw@infoweb.abs.net, pg 500

Heritage House Group Ltd (United Kingdom) *Tel:* (01332) 347087 *Fax:* (01332) 290688 *E-mail:* sales@hhgroup.co.uk *Web Site:* www.hhgroup. co.uk, pg 703

Heritage Press (United Kingdom) *Tel:* (01273) 731296 *Fax:* (01273) 731296, pg 703

Heritage Press Ltd (New Zealand) *Tel:* (09) 4137503; (09) 4139343 *Fax:* (09) 4137503; (09) 4139343 *E-mail:* heritagepressltd@xtra.co.nz *Web Site:* www. heritagepress.co.nz, pg 492

Heritage Publishers (India) *Tel:* (011) 23266258 *Fax:* (011) 23263050 *E-mail:* heritage@nda.vsnl.net. in; info@meditechbooks.com, pg 332

Heritage Publishing Co (Cote d'Ivoire) *Tel:* 433056 *Fax:* 433056, pg 117

Hermagoras/Mohorjeva (Austria) *Tel:* (0463) 56515 21 *Fax:* (0463) 514189 *E-mail:* office@mohorjeva.at *Web Site:* www.mohorjeva.at, pg 51

Hermann editeurs des Sciences et des Arts SA (France) *Tel:* (01) 45 57 45 40 *Fax:* (01) 40 60 12 93 *E-mail:* hermann.sa@wanadoo.fr, pg 167

Editorial Hermes SA (Mexico) *Tel:* (05) 6741425 (ext 171); (05) 6741894; (05) 6744385 *Fax:* (05) 6743949, pg 462

Hermes Edizioni SRL (Italy) *Tel:* (06) 3235433 *Fax:* (06) 3236277 *E-mail:* info@ediz-mediterranee. com *Web Site:* www.ediz-mediterranee.com, pg 389

Hermes Publishing House (Bulgaria) *Tel:* (032) 630630 *Fax:* (032) 634095 *E-mail:* hermes@plovdiv.techno-link.com *Web Site:* www.hermesbooks.com, pg 94

Editions Hermes Science Publications (France) *Tel:* (01) 47 40 67 00 *Fax:* (01) 47 40 67 02 *E-mail:* livres@ lavoisier.fr *Web Site:* www.hermes-science.com; www. editions-hermes.fr, pg 168

Hermess Ltd (Latvia) *Tel:* (02) 7112743 *Fax:* (02) 7313130 *E-mail:* hermess@binet.lv, pg 441

Hermetische Truhe Buchhandlung fuer Esoterische Literatur Barbara Dethlefsen (Germany) *Tel:* (089) 2710650 *Fax:* (089) 2724627, pg 235

Nick Hern Books Ltd (United Kingdom) *Tel:* (020) 8749 4953 *Fax:* (020) 8735 0250 *E-mail:* info@ nickhernbooks.demon.co.uk *Web Site:* www. nickhernbooks.co.uk, pg 704

Editions de l'Herne (France) *Tel:* (01) 42 61 25 06 *Fax:* (01) 42 60 10 00 *E-mail:* lherne@freesurf.fr, pg 168

Hernovs Forlag (Denmark) *Tel:* 32963314 *Fax:* 32960446 *E-mail:* admin@hernov.dk *Web Site:* www.hernov.dk, pg 131

Herodotus Press (Ireland) *Tel:* (01) 4540120 *Fax:* (01) 4541134, pg 357

Herold Business Data AG (Austria) *Tel:* (02236) 401-0 *Fax:* (02236) 401-8 *E-mail:* kundendienst@herold.at *Web Site:* www.herold.co.at, pg 51

Herold Druck-und Verlagsgesellschaft mbH (Austria) *Tel:* (01) 512350331 *Fax:* (01) 795 94-115, pg 51

Herold Verlag Dr Wetzel (Germany) *Tel:* (089) 7915774 *E-mail:* wetzel@herold-verlag.de *Web Site:* www. herold-verlag.de, pg 235

Heron Press Publishing House (Bulgaria) *Tel:* (02) 443368 *Fax:* (02) 443368 *E-mail:* heron_press@ attglobal.net, pg 94

Editorial Herrero SA (Mexico) *Tel:* (05) 5664900 *Fax:* (05) 5664900, pg 463

Herscher (France) *Tel:* (08) 25 82 01 11 *Fax:* (01) 43 25 18 29 *E-mail:* contact@editions-belin.fr *Web Site:* www.editions-belin.fr, pg 168

Axel Hertenstein, Hertenstein-Presse (Germany) *Tel:* (07231) 2 70 84 *Fax:* (07231) 2 70 84, pg 235

Editions Hervas (France) *Tel:* (01) 43 79 10 95 *Fax:* (01) 43 79 77 10, pg 168

Herzog August Bibliothek (Germany) *Tel:* (05331) 808-0 *Fax:* (05331) 808-173 *E-mail:* auskunft@hab.de *Web Site:* www.hab.de, pg 1507

Herzogin Anna Amalia Bibliothek (Germany) *Tel:* (03643) 545-200 *Fax:* (03643) 545-220 *E-mail:* haab@swkk.de *Web Site:* www.swkk.de, pg 1507

HES & De Graaf Publishers BV (Netherlands) *Tel:* (030) 6011955 *Fax:* (030) 6011813 *E-mail:* info@ hesdegraaf.com *Web Site:* www.hesdegraaf.com, pg 479

Hessischer Verleger- und Buchhandler-Verband eV (Germany) *Tel:* (0611) 166 600 *Fax:* (0611) 166 6059 *E-mail:* briefe@hessenbuchhandel.de *Web Site:* www. hessenbuchhandel.de, pg 1260

Hessisches Ministerium fuer Umwelt, Landwirtschaft und Forsten (Germany) *Tel:* (0611) 8150 *Fax:* (0611) 8151941 *Web Site:* www.mulf.hessen.de, pg 235

Hestia-I D Hestia-Kollaros & Co Corporation (Greece) *Tel:* 2103635970; 2103615077; 210360574 *Fax:* 2103606758; 2103606759 *Web Site:* www. ianos.gr, pg 305

Hestra-Verlag Hernichel & Dr Strauss GmbH & Co KG (Germany) *Tel:* (06151) 39070 *Fax:* (06151) 390777, pg 235

Uitgeverij Het-Volk (Belgium) *Tel:* (09) 2656424; (09) 2656420 *Fax:* (09) 2258406, pg 1292

Heuff Amsterdam Uitgever (Netherlands) *Tel:* (020) 620 46 25 *Fax:* (020) 620 46 25, pg 479

Uitgeverij Heureka (Netherlands) *Tel:* (0294) 480 000 *Fax:* (0294) 415 183 *E-mail:* heureka@belboek.com *Web Site:* www.belboek.com/heureka; www.belboek. com/index.html, pg 479

Hexaglot Holding GmbH (Germany) *Tel:* (040) 514560 *Fax:* (040) 51456991 *E-mail:* info@hexaglot.de *Web Site:* www.hexaglot.de/, pg 235

Friedrich W Heye Verlag GmbH (Germany) *Tel:* (089) 6653201 *Fax:* (089) 66532210 *E-mail:* verlag@heye. de *Web Site:* www.heye-verlag.de, pg 235

Carl Heymanns Verlag KG (Germany) *Tel:* (0221) 94373-0 *Fax:* (0221) 94373-901 *E-mail:* marketing@ heymanns.com *Web Site:* www.heymanns.com, pg 235

Johannes Heyn GmbH & Co KG (Austria) *Tel:* (0463) 54 2 49 *Fax:* (0463) 54 2 49-41 *E-mail:* buch@heyn.at *Web Site:* www.heyn.at, pg 51

Verlag Johannes Heyn (Austria) *Tel:* (0463) 54249 *Fax:* (0463) 5424941 *E-mail:* buch@heyn.at; technik@ heyn.at *Web Site:* www.heyn.at, pg 1290

Wilhelm Heyne Verlag (Germany) *Tel:* (089) 41 36 0 *Fax:* (089) 51 48 2229 *E-mail:* heyne-suedwest@ randomhouse.de *Web Site:* www.heyne.de, pg 236

Monica Heyum Agency (Sweden) *Tel:* (08) 7451934 *Fax:* (08) 7771470, pg 1127

Hid Islenzka Bokmenntafelag (Iceland) *Tel:* 5889060 *Fax:* 5889095 *E-mail:* hib@islandia.is *Web Site:* www. hib.is, pg 322, 1395

Max Hieber KG (Germany) *Tel:* (089) 29008023 *Fax:* (089) 229782 *E-mail:* info@eminent-orgeln. de *Web Site:* www.eminent-orgeln.de/kontakte.htm, pg 236

Anton Hiersemann, Verlag (Germany) *Tel:* (0711) 54 99 71-0; (0711) 54 99 71-11 *Fax:* (0711) 54 99 71-21 *E-mail:* verlag@hiersemann.de *Web Site:* www. hiersemann.de, pg 236

Anton Hiersemann, Verlag (Germany) *Tel:* (0711) 5499710; (0711) 5499711 *Fax:* (0711) 54997121 *E-mail:* hiersemann.hauswedell.verlage@t-online.de *Web Site:* www.hiersemann.de, pg 1301

Higginbothams Ltd (India) *Tel:* (044) 852 1841 *Fax:* (044) 852 8101, pg 1306

David Higham Associates Ltd (United Kingdom) *Tel:* (020) 7434 5900 *Fax:* (020) 7437 1072 *E-mail:* dha@davidhigham.co.uk *Web Site:* www. davidhigham.co.uk, pg 1131

Higher Education Press (China) *Tel:* (010) 58581862 *Fax:* (010) 82085552 *Web Site:* www.hep.edu.cn; www.hep.com.cn, pg 105

Highland Books Ltd (United Kingdom) *Tel:* (01483) 424560 *Fax:* (01483) 424388 *E-mail:* info@ highlandbks.com *Web Site:* www.highlandbks.com, pg 704

Hihorse Publishing Pty Ltd (Australia) *Tel:* (03) 9397 3084 *Fax:* (03) 9397 3084 *E-mail:* hihorse@c031. aone.net.au, pg 25

Hikarinokuni Ltd (Japan) *Tel:* (06) 6768-1151 *Fax:* (06) 6768-6795 *E-mail:* hikari@skyblue.ocn.ne.jp *Web Site:* www.hikarinokuni.co.jp, pg 415

Al Hilal Publications (Bahrain) *Tel:* 231122, pg 60

Dar Al Hilal Publishing Institution (Egypt (Arab Republic of Egypt)) *Tel:* (02) 362 5450 *Fax:* (02) 362 5469, pg 138

AIG I Hilbinger Verlag GmbH (Germany) *Tel:* (0611) 4190088; (0611) 7239233 *Fax:* (0611) 7239209, pg 236

Edition E Hilger (Austria) *Tel:* (01) 512 53 15-0 *Fax:* (01) 513 91 26 *E-mail:* hilger@hilger.at, pg 51

Hilit Publishing Co Ltd (Taiwan, Province of China) *Tel:* (02) 2362-6602 *Fax:* (02) 2365-2552 *E-mail:* hilit. publish@msa.hinet.net *Web Site:* www.hilit.com.tw, pg 635

Hill & Knowlton Asia Ltd (Hong Kong) *Tel:* 2894 6321 *Fax:* 2576 3551 *E-mail:* dmaguire@hillandknowlton. com *Web Site:* www.hillandknowlton.com, pg 1146

Hillelforlaget (Sweden) *Tel:* (08) 587 858 04 *Fax:* (08) 587 858 58, pg 607

Hillview Publications Pte Ltd (Singapore) *Tel:* 334 8996 *Fax:* 334 8997, pg 551

Hilmarton Manor Press (United Kingdom) *Tel:* (01249) 760208 *Fax:* (01249) 760379 *E-mail:* mailorder@ hilmartonpress.co.uk *Web Site:* www.hilmartonpress. co.uk, pg 704

Hilt & Hansteen A/S (Norway) *Tel:* (022) 38 40 10 *Fax:* (022) 37 40 15 *Web Site:* hilt-hansteen.no, pg 505

Himalaya Publishing House (India) *Tel:* (011) 3270392; (011) 652225 *Fax:* (022) 3956286, pg 332

Himalayan Books (India) *Tel:* (011) 352126; (011) 351731 *Fax:* (011) 332-1731 *E-mail:* ebs@vsnl.com, pg 332

Himmelsturmer Verlag (Germany) *Tel:* (040) 48061717 *Fax:* (040) 48061799 *E-mail:* himmelstuermer@gmx. de, pg 236

Himpunan Masyarakat Pencinta Buku (Indonesia) *Tel:* (022) 470821; (022) 470287, pg 1243

Hind Pocket Books Private Ltd (India) *Tel:* (011) 202046; (011) 202332; (011) 202467 *Fax:* (011) 2282332, pg 332

Verlag Hinder und Deelmann (Germany) *Tel:* (06462) 1301 *Fax:* (06462) 3307 *Web Site:* www. hinderunddeelmann.de/, pg 236

Hindi Book Centre (India) *Tel:* (011) 23286757; (011) 23258993; (011) 23261696; (011) 23268651 *Fax:* (011) 23273335; (011) 26481565 *E-mail:* info@ hindibook.com *Web Site:* www.hindibook.com, pg 1306

Hindi Pracharak Sansthan (India) *Tel:* (0542) 54470; (0542) 52425; (0542) 52670; (0542) 355168; (0542) 56850; (0542) 361452, pg 333

Hindustan Book Agency (India) *Tel:* (011) 6163294; (011) 6163296 *Fax:* (011) 6193297 *E-mail:* hindbook@nda.vsnl.net.in *Web Site:* www. hindbook.com, pg 1306

Hindy's Enterprise Co Ltd (Hong Kong) *Tel:* 25166318 *Fax:* 25165161, pg 1168, 1208

Hing Yip Printing Co Ltd (Hong Kong) *Tel:* 25532432; 25532828 *Fax:* 28147887, pg 1208

Hinoki Publishing Co Ltd (Japan) *Tel:* (03) 32912488 *Fax:* (03) 32953554 *E-mail:* info@hinoki-shoten.co.jp *Web Site:* www.hinoki-shoten.co.jp, pg 415

Hinstorff Verlag GmbH (Germany) *Tel:* (0381) 49 69-0 *Fax:* (0381) 49 69-103 *E-mail:* sekretariat@hinstorff. de *Web Site:* www.hinstorff.de, pg 236

Ediciones Hiperion SL (Spain) *Tel:* (091) 577 60 15; (091) 577 60 16 *Fax:* (091) 435 86 90 *E-mail:* info@ hiperion.com *Web Site:* www.hiperion.com, pg 581

Hipocrates - Livros Tecnicos, Lda (Portugal) *Tel:* (021) 3571247 *Fax:* (021) 3580902 *E-mail:* info@hipocrates. pt *Web Site:* www.hipocrates.pt, pg 1328

The Hippogriff Press CC (South Africa) *Tel:* (011) 6464229 *Fax:* (011) 6464229, pg 560

Hippopotamus Press (United Kingdom) *Tel:* (01373) 466653 *Fax:* (01373) 466653, pg 704

Hiralal Printing Works Ltd (India) *Tel:* (022) 7672726; (022) 7683012 *Fax:* (022) 7631191, pg 1148

Hiralal Printing Works Ltd (India) *Tel:* (022) 7672726, pg 1169

Hiralal Printing Works Ltd (India) *Tel:* (022) 7672726; (022) 7683012, pg 1210

Hirmer Verlag GmbH (Germany) *Tel:* (089) 1215160 *Fax:* (089) 12151610; (089) 12151616 (distribution) *E-mail:* vertrieb@hirmerverlag.de *Web Site:* www. hirmerverlag.de; www.weltkunstverlag.de, pg 236

Hirokawa Publishing Co (Japan) *Tel:* (03) 3815 3651 *Fax:* (03) 5684 7030, pg 415

Harro V Hirschheydt (Germany) *Tel:* (05130) 36758 *Fax:* (05130) 36799 *E-mail:* kontakt@hirschheydt-online.de, pg 236

F Hirthammer Verlag GmbH (Germany) *Tel:* (089) 3233360 *Fax:* (089) 3241728 *E-mail:* info@ hirthammerverlag.de *Web Site:* www.hirthammerverlag. de, pg 236

S Hirzel Verlag GmbH und Co (Germany) *Tel:* (0711) 25820 *Fax:* (0711) 2582290 *E-mail:* service@hirzel.de *Web Site:* www.hirzel.de, pg 236

Editorial Hispano Europea SA (Spain) *Tel:* (093) 2013709; (093) 2018500 *Fax:* (093) 4142635 *E-mail:* hispaneuropea@mx3.redestb.es, pg 582

Editorial Hispanoamerica (Colombia) *Tel:* (01) 2216694 *Fax:* (01) 2213020, pg 111

Histec Publications (Australia) *Tel:* (03) 9592 3787 *Fax:* (03) 9592 2823 *Web Site:* www.histec.com, pg 26

Editions d'Histoire Sociale (EDHIS) (France) *Tel:* (01) 42614778, pg 168

Historical Association of Zambia (Zambia), pg 776

Arquivo Historico de Mocambique (Mozambique) *Tel:* (01) 321177; (01) 321178 *Fax:* (01) 323428 *E-mail:* jneves@zebra.uem.mz *Web Site:* www.ahm. uem.mz, pg 1528

Institutum Historicum Societatis Iesu (Italy) *Tel:* (06) 689 77673 *Fax:* (06) 686 1342; (06) 689 77663 *E-mail:* ihsiroma@tin.it *Web Site:* space.tin.it/scuola/ mmorales/ihsi.html, pg 389

Instytut Historii Nauki PAN (Poland) *Tel:* (022) 826 87 54; (022) 65 72 746 *Fax:* (022) 826 61 37 *E-mail:* ihn@ihnpan.waw.pl *Web Site:* www.ihnpan. waw.pl, pg 518

Historische Uitgeverij (Netherlands) *Tel:* (050) 3181700; (050) 3135258 *Fax:* (050) 3146383 *E-mail:* info@ histuitg.nl *Web Site:* www.histuitg.nl, pg 479

Historischer Verein fur das Furstentum Liechtenstein (Liechtenstein) *Tel:* 392 17 47 *Fax:* 392 17 05 *E-mail:* info@hvfl.li *Web Site:* www.hvfl.li, pg 444

History House Publishing (Ireland) *Tel:* (065) 24066 *Fax:* (065) 20388, pg 357

Hjemmenes Forlag (Norway) *Tel:* 22143151 *Fax:* 22920738, pg 505

Forlaget Hjulet (Denmark) *Tel:* 31310900 *Fax:* 31310900 *E-mail:* aloa@gte2net.dk, pg 131

Galerie Hlavniho Mesta Prahy (Czech Republic) *Tel:* (02) 3332 1200 *Fax:* (02) 3332 3664 *E-mail:* ghmp@volny.cz *Web Site:* www. citygalleryprague.cz, pg 123

HLT Publications (United Kingdom) *Tel:* (020) 8317 6161 *Fax:* (020) 8317 6001 *E-mail:* obp@ hltpublications.co.uk *Web Site:* www.holborncollege. ac.uk/OldbaileyPress.cfm, pg 704

HMR Publishing Co (Pakistan) *Tel:* (042) 7588972; (042) 7588967 *Fax:* (042) 7581212, pg 508

Ho-Chi Book Publishing Co (Taiwan, Province of China) *Tel:* (02) 2974-0168 *Fax:* (02) 2792-4702 *E-mail:* hochi@ms12.hinet.net; hochi@email.gcn.net. tw, pg 635

Ho Printing Singapore Pte Ltd (Singapore) *Tel:* 6542 9322 *Fax:* 6542 8322 *E-mail:* marketing@hoprinting. com.sg; sales@hoprinting.com.sg *Web Site:* www. hoprinting.com, pg 1151, 1171, 1212

Ho Printing Singapore Pte Ltd (Singapore) *Tel:* 5429322 *Fax:* 5428322 *E-mail:* marketing@hoprinting.com.sg; sales@hoprinting.com.sg *Web Site:* www.hoprinting. com, pg 1228

Ho Printing Singapore Pte Ltd (Singapore) *Tel:* 6542 9322 *Fax:* 6542 8322 *E-mail:* sales@hoprinting.com. sg; marketing@hoprinting.com.sg *Web Site:* www. hoprinting.com, pg 1236

Hobbs The Printers Ltd (United Kingdom) *Tel:* (023) 8066 4800 *Fax:* (023) 8066 4801 *E-mail:* info@hobbs. uk.com *Web Site:* www.hobbstheprinters.co.uk; www. hobbs.uk.com, pg 1174

Hobbs The Printers Ltd (United Kingdom) *Tel:* (023) 8066 4800 *Fax:* (023) 8066 4801 *E-mail:* info@hobbs. uk.com *Web Site:* www.hobbs.uk.com, pg 1216

Hobbs The Printers Ltd (United Kingdom) *Tel:* (023) 8066 4800 *Fax:* (023) 8066 4801 *E-mail:* info@ hobbs.uk.com *Web Site:* www.hobbs.uk.com; www. hobbstheprinters.co.uk, pg 1229, 1237

Hobbyglede (Norway) *Tel:* 24051010 *Fax:* 24051099 *E-mail:* post@damm.no *Web Site:* www. dammbokklubb.no, pg 1245

Hobsons (United Kingdom) *Tel:* (020) 7336 6633 *Fax:* (020) 7608 1034 *E-mail:* enquiries@hobsons. co.uk *Web Site:* www.hobsons.com, pg 704

Hod-Ami, Computer Books Ltd (Israel) *Tel:* (09) 9541207 *Fax:* (09) 9571582 *E-mail:* info@hod-ami. co.il *Web Site:* www.hod-ami.co.il, pg 364

Hodder & Stoughton General (United Kingdom) *Tel:* (020) 7873 6000 *Fax:* (020) 7873 6024, pg 704

Hodder & Stoughton Religious (United Kingdom) *Tel:* (020) 7873 6000 *Fax:* (020) 7873 6059 *E-mail:* firstname.surname@hodder.co.uk *Web Site:* www.headline.co.uk, pg 704

Hodder Children's Books (United Kingdom) *Tel:* (020) 7873 6000 *Fax:* (020) 7873 6225 *Web Site:* www. hodderheadline.co.uk, pg 704

Hodder Education (United Kingdom) *Tel:* (020) 7873 6272 *Fax:* (020) 7873 6299 *E-mail:* joanne.craik@ hodder.co.uk *Web Site:* www.hodderheadline.co.uk, pg 705

Hodder Headline Ltd (United Kingdom) *Tel:* (020) 7873 6000 *Fax:* (020) 7873 6024 *Web Site:* www. hodderheadline.co.uk, pg 705

Hodder Moa Beckett Publishers Ltd (New Zealand) *Tel:* (09) 4781000 *Fax:* (09) 4781010 *E-mail:* admin@ hoddermoa.co.nz, pg 492

Hodges Figgis & Co (Ireland) *Tel:* (01) 6774754 *Fax:* (01) 6792810; (01) 6793402 *E-mail:* books@ hfiggis.ir, pg 1309

Editions Hoebeke (France) *Tel:* (01) 42 22 83 81 *Fax:* (01) 45 44 04 96 *E-mail:* contact@hoebeke.fr *Web Site:* www.hoebeke.fr, pg 168

Lars Hoekerbergs Bokfoerlag (Sweden) *Tel:* (08) 244360 *Fax:* (08) 6503984 *E-mail:* hokerbook@ebox.tninet.se, pg 607

Verlag Hoelder-Pichler-Tempsky (Austria) *Tel:* (01) 401 36-139 *Fax:* (01) 401 36-128 *E-mail:* hpt@hpt.co.at, pg 51

Verlag Wolfgang Hoelker (Germany) *Tel:* (0251) 414110 *Fax:* (0251) 4141140 *E-mail:* info@coppenrath.de *Web Site:* www.coppenrath.de, pg 236

Verlag Peter Hoell (Germany) *Tel:* (06167) 912220 *Fax:* (06167) 912221 *E-mail:* hoell.verlag@t-online.de *Web Site:* www.hoell.de.vu, pg 237

Hofbauer, Christoph und Trojanow Ilia, Akademischer Verlag Muenchen (Germany) *Tel:* (089) 51616151 *Fax:* (089) 51616199 *E-mail:* avm@druckmedien.de, pg 237

Buchhandlung Karl Hofbauer KG (Austria) *Tel:* (03452) 82793; (03452) 82177 *Fax:* (03452) 71218 *E-mail:* hofbauer.buch@magnet.at, pg 1290

Agence Hoffman (France) *Tel:* (01) 43265694 *Fax:* (01) 43263407 *E-mail:* info@agence-hoffman.com, pg 1120

Edition Hoffmann & Co (Germany) *Tel:* (06031) 2443 *Fax:* (06031) 62965, pg 237

Dieter Hoffmann Verlag (Germany) *Tel:* (06136) 95100 *Fax:* (06136) 951037, pg 237

H Hoffmann GmbH (Germany) *Tel:* (033203) 305810 *Fax:* (033203) 305820 *E-mail:* hhvberlin@t-online.de, pg 237

Hoffmann und Campe Verlag GmbH (Germany) *Tel:* (040) 441880 *Fax:* (040) 44188290 *E-mail:* email@hoca.de *Web Site:* www.hoca.de, pg 237

Verlag Karl Hofmann GmbH & Co (Germany) *Tel:* (07181) 4020 *Fax:* (07181) 402111 *E-mail:* info@ hofmann-verlag.de *Web Site:* www.hofmann-verlag.de, pg 237

Friedrich Hofmeister-Figaro Verlag Grossortiment und Musikalienhandlung GesmbH (Austria) *Tel:* (01) 50576510 *Fax:* (01) 5059185, pg 1290

Friedrich Hofmeister Musikverlag (Germany) *Tel:* (0341) 960 07 50 *Fax:* (0341) 960 30 55 *E-mail:* info@ hofmeister-musikverlag.com *Web Site:* www.friedrich-hofmeister.de; www.hofmeister-musikverlag.com, pg 237

Dr Verena Hofstaetter (Austria) *Tel:* (01) 370 33 02 *Fax:* (01) 370 59 34 *E-mail:* verlag@vh-communications.at, pg 51

Hogar del Libro, SA (Spain) *Tel:* (093) 3182700 *Fax:* (093) 3010399, pg 1333

Hogrefe Verlag GmbH & Co Kg (Germany) *Tel:* (0551) 496090 *Fax:* (0551) 4960988 *E-mail:* verlag@hogrefe. de *Web Site:* www.hogrefe.de/, pg 237

Hohenrain-Verlag GmbH (Germany) *Tel:* (07071) 40700 *Fax:* (07071) 407026, pg 237

Matth Hohner AG Verlag (Germany) *Tel:* (07425) 200 *Fax:* (07425) 249 *E-mail:* info@hohner.de *Web Site:* www.hohner.de, pg 237

Hoi Kwong Printing Co Ltd (Hong Kong) *Tel:* 2562-1641; 2562-1096 *Fax:* 2564-2142 *E-mail:* sales@ hoikwong.com *Web Site:* www.hoikwong.com, pg 1147, 1208

Hoi Thu-Vien Vietnam (Viet Nam) *Tel:* (04) 824 8051 *Fax:* (04) 825 3357 *E-mail:* info@nlv.gov.vn *Web Site:* www.nlv.gov.vn, pg 1574

Hoikusha Publishing Co Ltd (Japan) *Tel:* (06) 932-6601 *Fax:* (06) 933-8577 *Web Site:* www.hoikusha.co.jp, pg 415

Hoja Casa Editorial SA de CV (Mexico) *Tel:* (055) 688-4828; (055) 688-6458; (055) 605-7677; (055) 604-0843 *Fax:* (055) 605-7677 *E-mail:* editorialpax@ editorialpax.com *Web Site:* www.editorialpax.com, pg 463

Ediciones Mil Hojas Ltda (Chile) *Tel:* (02) 2743172 *Fax:* (02) 2250261, pg 99

Hokkaido University Library (Japan) *Tel:* (011) 706-4998 *Fax:* (011) 747-2855 *E-mail:* bureau@hokudai. ac.jp *Web Site:* www.lib.hokudai.ac.jp/index_e.html, pg 1520

Hokkaido University Press (Japan) *Tel:* (011) 747-2308 *Fax:* (011) 736-8605 *E-mail:* hupress_6@hup.gr.jp *Web Site:* www.hup.gr.jp, pg 415

Hokuryukan Co Ltd (Japan) *Tel:* (03) 5449-4591 *Fax:* (03) 5449-4950 *E-mail:* hk-ns@mk1.mqcnet.or. jp, pg 415

The Hokuseido Press (Japan) *Tel:* (03) 38270511 *Fax:* (03) 38270567 *E-mail:* info@hokuseido.com, pg 415

Holbrook Design (United Kingdom) *Tel:* (01865) 459000 *Fax:* (01865) 459006 *E-mail:* info@holbrook-design. co.uk *Web Site:* www.holbrook-design.co.uk, pg 1174

Holguin, Ediciones (Cuba) *Tel:* (024) 424974 *E-mail:* promotoraliteraria@baibrama.cult.cu, pg 120

Holkenfeldt 3 (Denmark) *Tel:* 931221 *Fax:* 938241 *E-mail:* holkenfeldt@mail.dk, pg 131

Buchhandlung Holl & Knoll KG, Verlag Alte Uni (Germany) *Tel:* (07262) 4417 *Fax:* (07262) 7942 *E-mail:* alteuni@aol.com, pg 237

Holland & Josenhans GmbH & Co (Germany) *Tel:* (0711) 6143920 *Fax:* (0711) 6143922 *E-mail:* verlag@huj.03.net *Web Site:* www.holland-josenhans.de/, pg 237

Holland Enterprises Ltd (United Kingdom) *Tel:* (020) 8551 7711 *Fax:* (020) 8551 1266 *E-mail:* sales@ holland-enterprises.co.uk *Web Site:* www.holland-enterprises.co.uk, pg 705

Uitgeverij Holland (Netherlands) *Tel:* (023) 5323061 *Fax:* (023) 5342908 *E-mail:* info@uitgeverijholland.nl *Web Site:* www.uitgeverijholland.nl, pg 479

Holland University Press BV (APA) (Netherlands) *Tel:* (020) 626 5544 *Fax:* (020) 528 5298 *E-mail:* info@apa-publishers.com *Web Site:* www.apa-publishers.com, pg 479

Uitgeverij Hollandia BV (Netherlands) *Tel:* (023) 5257150 *Fax:* (023) 52574404 *E-mail:* gottmer@ x54all.nl *Web Site:* www.hiswa.nl, pg 479

Hollinek Bruder & Co mbH Gesellschaftsdruckerei & Verlagsbuchhandring (Austria) *Tel:* (02231) 67365 *Fax:* (02231) 67365 *E-mail:* hollinek@via.at, pg 51

Hollis Publishing Ltd (United Kingdom) *Tel:* (020) 8977 7711 *Fax:* (020) 8977 1133 *E-mail:* hollis@hollis-pr.co.uk; orders@hollis-pr.co.uk *Web Site:* www.hollis-pr.co.uk, pg 705

Hollym Corporation (Republic of Korea) *Tel:* (02) 735-7551 *Fax:* (02) 730-5149; (02) 730-8192 *E-mail:* hollym@chollian.net; info@hollym.co.kr *Web Site:* www.hollym.co.kr, pg 436

Holnap Kiado Vallalat (Hungary) *Tel:* (01) 666928 *Fax:* (01) 656624, pg 318

Holograms (M) Sdn Bhd (Malaysia) *Tel:* (03) 2824002 *Fax:* (03) 2822751, pg 452

Holos Verlag (Germany) *Tel:* (0228) 263020; (0228) 262332 *Fax:* (0228) 212435, pg 237

Holp Book Co Ltd (Japan) *Tel:* (03) 5285-5011 *Fax:* (03) 3225-1663 *E-mail:* holp@holp.co.jp *Web Site:* www.holp.co.jp, pg 415

The Holt Jackson Book Co Ltd (United Kingdom) *Tel:* (01253) 737464 *Fax:* (01253) 733361 *E-mail:* info@holtjackson.co.uk *Web Site:* www. holtjackson.co.uk, pg 1342

Vanessa Holt Ltd (United Kingdom) *Tel:* (01702) 473787 *Fax:* (01702) 471890 *E-mail:* vanessa@holtlimited. freeserve.co.uk, pg 1131

Verlagsgruppe Georg von Holtzbrinck GmbH (Germany) *Tel:* (0711) 2150-0 *Fax:* (0711) 2150-269 *E-mail:* info@holtzbrinck.com *Web Site:* www. holtzbrinck.com, pg 237

Holyoake Books (United Kingdom) *Tel:* (01509) 852333 *Fax:* (01509) 856500 *E-mail:* info@co-opu.demon.co. uk, pg 705

Hans Holzmann Verlag GmbH und Co KG (Germany) *Tel:* (08247) 35401 *Fax:* (08247) 354170 *E-mail:* info@holzmannverlag.de *Web Site:* www. holzmannverlag.de/, pg 237

Home Health Education Service (United Kingdom) *Tel:* (01476) 591700; (01476) 539900 (orders) *Fax:* (01476) 577144 *E-mail:* stanborg@aol.com, pg 705

Uitgeverij Homeovisie BV (Netherlands) *Tel:* (072) 566 1133 *Fax:* (072) 566 1295 *E-mail:* info@vsm.nl *Web Site:* www2.vsminfo.nl, pg 479

Homestead Books (Australia) *Tel:* (03) 9873 7202 *Fax:* (03) 9873-0542 *E-mail:* service@theruralstore. com.au *Web Site:* www.theruralstore.com.au, pg 26

Libros-Ediciones Homines (Puerto Rico) *Tel:* (787) 250-1912 (ext 2347), pg 532

Evelyn Hone College Library (Zambia) *Tel:* (01) 225127 *Fax:* (01) 225127, pg 1554

Honeyglen Publishing Ltd (United Kingdom) *Tel:* (020) 7602 2876 *Fax:* (020) 7602 2876, pg 705

Hong Kong Book Centre Ltd (Hong Kong) *Tel:* 2522-7064 *Fax:* 2868-5079 *E-mail:* orders@hkbookcentre. com.hk *Web Site:* www.swindonbooks.com, pg 1304

Hong Kong China Tourism Press (Hong Kong) *Tel:* 2561 8001 *Fax:* 2561 8196 *E-mail:* edit-e@hkctp.com.hk *Web Site:* www.hkctp.com.hk, pg 314

Hong Kong Christian Service (Hong Kong) *Tel:* 2731-6316 *Fax:* 2731-6333 *E-mail:* info@hkcs.org *Web Site:* www.hkcs.org, pg 1147, 1236

Hong Kong Library Association (Hong Kong) *E-mail:* hkla@hkla.org *Web Site:* www.hkla.org, pg 1564

Hong Kong PEN Centre (English-Speaking) (China) *Tel:* 25774168 *Fax:* 25774168 *E-mail:* hkpen_eng@ yahoo.com, pg 1392

Hong Kong Public Libraries (Hong Kong) *Tel:* 2921 0208 *Fax:* 2415 8211 *E-mail:* enquiries@lcsd.gov.hk *Web Site:* www.hkpl.gov.hk, pg 1512

Hong Kong Publishing Co Ltd (Hong Kong) *Tel:* 25259053, pg 314

Hong Kong University Press (Hong Kong) *Tel:* 2550 2703 *Fax:* 2875 0734 *E-mail:* upweb@hkucc.hku.hk *Web Site:* www.hkupress.org, pg 314

Hongikdong (Republic of Korea) *Tel:* (02) 704-7500 *Fax:* (02) 703-5695 *E-mail:* hongikcb@soback.kornet. nm.kr, pg 436

Honno Welsh Women's Press (United Kingdom) *Tel:* (01970) 623 150 *Fax:* (01970) 623 150 *E-mail:* post@honno.co.uk *Web Site:* www.honno.co. uk, pg 705

Editions Honore Champion (France) *Tel:* (01) 46340729 *Fax:* (01) 46346406 *E-mail:* champion@ honorechampion.com *Web Site:* www.honorechampion. com, pg 168

Hook & Hatton Ltd (United Kingdom) *Tel:* (01604) 847278 *Fax:* (01604) 821486 *E-mail:* hook_hatton@ compuserve.com, pg 1140

Hoover's Business Press (United Kingdom) *Tel:* (01865) 513186 *Fax:* (01865) 513186 *Web Site:* www.hoovers-europe.com, pg 705

Hopeful Monster Editore (Italy) *Tel:* (011) 4367197; (011) 4358519 *Fax:* (011) 4369025 *E-mail:* info@ hopefulmonster.net *Web Site:* www.hopefulmonster.net, pg 389

Hoppenstedt GmbH & Co KG (Germany) *Tel:* (06151) 380-0 *Fax:* (06151) 380-360 *E-mail:* info@ hoppenstedt.de *Web Site:* www.hoppenstedt.de, pg 238

Hora (Italy) *Tel:* (02) 26412203 *Fax:* (02) 26412203 *Web Site:* www.hora.it, pg 389

Horacek Ladislav-Paseka (Czech Republic) *Tel:* (02) 222 710 751-3; (02) 222 718 886 *Fax:* (02) 22718886 *E-mail:* paseka@paseka.cz *Web Site:* www.paseka.cz, pg 123

Horan Wall & Walker (Australia) *Tel:* (02) 8268 8268 *Fax:* (02) 8268 8267 *E-mail:* info@hww.com.au *Web Site:* www.hww.com.au, pg 26

Pierre Horay Editeur (France) *Tel:* (01) 43 54 53 90 *Fax:* (01) 43 54 63 50 *E-mail:* editions@horay-editeur. fr *Web Site:* www.horay-editeur.fr, pg 168

Kate Hordern (United Kingdom) *Tel:* (0117) 923 9368 *Fax:* (0117) 973 1941 *E-mail:* katehorden@ blueyonder.co.uk, pg 1131

Horitsu Bunka-Sha (Japan) *Tel:* (075) 791-7131 *Fax:* (075) 721-8400 *E-mail:* eigy@hou-bun.co.jp *Web Site:* web.kyoto-inet.or.jp/org/houritu, pg 415

Horizon Scientific Press (United Kingdom) *Tel:* (01953) 601106 *Fax:* (01953) 603068 *E-mail:* mail@ horizonpress.com *Web Site:* www.horizonpress.com, pg 705

Editorial Horizonte (Peru) *Tel:* (01) 427-9364 *Fax:* (01) 427-4341, pg 512

Horlemann Verlag (Germany) *Tel:* (02224) 5589 *Fax:* (02224) 5429 *E-mail:* horlemann@aol.com *Web Site:* www.horlemann-verlag.de/, pg 238

Editorial Horsori SL (Spain) *Tel:* (093) 3461997 *Fax:* (093) 3118498 *E-mail:* horsori@retemail.net *Web Site:* www.horsori.es, pg 582

Horus Editora Ltda (Brazil) *Tel:* (011) 288-7681 *Fax:* (011) 288-7681 *E-mail:* horus@horuseditora. br *Web Site:* www.horuseditora.com.br, pg 83

Hospitality Books (Australia) *Tel:* (02) 9809 5793 *Fax:* (02) 9809 4884 *Web Site:* www.hospitalitybooks. com.au, pg 26

Hospitality Training Foundation (United Kingdom) *Tel:* (020) 8579 2400 *Fax:* (020) 8840 6217 *E-mail:* info@htf.org.uk *Web Site:* www.htf.org.uk, pg 705

Host & Son Publishers Ltd (Denmark) *Tel:* 33382888 *Fax:* 33382898 *E-mail:* host@euroconnect.dk, pg 131

Hotei Publishing (Netherlands) *Tel:* (020) 568 8330 *Fax:* (020) 568 8286 *Web Site:* www.kit.nl/hotei, pg 480

House of Lochar (United Kingdom) *Tel:* (01951) 200232 *Fax:* (01951) 200232 *E-mail:* lochar@colonsay.org.uk *Web Site:* www.houseoflochar.com, pg 705

Uitgeverij Houtekiet (Belgium) *Tel:* (03) 2381296 *Fax:* (03) 2388041 *E-mail:* info@houtekiet.com *Web Site:* www.boekenwereld.com, pg 68

Forlaget Hovedland (Denmark) *Tel:* 86276500 *Fax:* 86276537 *E-mail:* mail@hovedland.dk *Web Site:* www.hovedland.dk, pg 131

How To Books Ltd (United Kingdom) *Tel:* (01865) 793806 *Fax:* (01865) 248780 *E-mail:* info@ howtobooks.co.uk *Web Site:* www.howtobooks.co.uk, pg 706

Tanja Howarth Literary Agency (United Kingdom) *Tel:* (020) 7240 5553 *Fax:* (020) 7379 0969 *E-mail:* tanja.howarth@btinternet.com, pg 1131

Josef Hribal (Czech Republic) *Tel:* (02) 542731, pg 123

Hriker (Bulgaria) *Tel:* (02) 319-217, pg 94

Publishing House Hristo Botev (Bulgaria) *Tel:* (02) 9817017 *Fax:* (02) 9817017, pg 94

Izdavacka Delatnost Hrvatske Akademije Znanosti I Umjetnosti (Croatia) *Tel:* (01) 49 22 373; (01) 48 72 902 *Fax:* (01) 48 19 979 *E-mail:* stross@mahazu.hazu. hr, pg 118

Hrvatsko filozofsko drustvo (Croatia) *Tel:* (01) 612 0156 *Fax:* (01) 617 0682 *E-mail:* filozofska-istrazivanja@ zg.tel.hr, pg 118

Hrvatsko knjiznicarsko drustvo (Croatia) *Tel:* (01) 615 93 20 *Fax:* (01) 615 93 20 *E-mail:* hkd@nsk.hr *Web Site:* www.hkdrustvo.hr, pg 1560

Hsiao Yuan Publication Co, Ltd (Taiwan, Province of China) *Tel:* (02) 23676789 *Fax:* (02) 23628429 *E-mail:* ufaf0130@ms5.hinet.net, pg 635

Hsin Yi Publications (Taiwan, Province of China) *Tel:* (02) 23965303 *Fax:* (02) 23965015 *Web Site:* www.hsin-yi.org.tw, pg 635

Hua Yang Printing Holding Co Ltd (Hong Kong) *Tel:* 24167591 *Fax:* 24110235, pg 1208

Hubei Publications Import & Export Corporation (China) *Tel:* (027) 87825561 *Fax:* (027) 87815557 *E-mail:* hbwwsdjkb@163.com, pg 1296

Verlag Huber & Co AG (Switzerland) *Tel:* (052) 723 5617 *Fax:* (052) 723 5619 *E-mail:* buchverlag@huber. ch *Web Site:* www.huber.ch, pg 620

Huber & Lang (Switzerland) *Tel:* (031) 300 4646 *Fax:* (031) 300 4656 *E-mail:* contact.bern@huberlang. com *Web Site:* www.huberlang.com, pg 1335

Hans Huber (Germany) *Tel:* (031) 3004500 *Fax:* (031) 3004590 *E-mail:* verlag@hanshuber.com *Web Site:* www.hanshuber.com, pg 238

Volker Huber Edition & Galerie (Germany) *Tel:* (069) 814523 *Fax:* (069) 880155 *E-mail:* edition-huber@t-online.de *Web Site:* www.volkerhuber.de, pg 238

Hubsch (Luxembourg) *E-mail:* 101755.3213@ compuserve.com, pg 447

Hudanuda Publishing Co Ltd (Nigeria) *Tel:* (069) 5141, pg 500

Hudson Publishing Services Pty Ltd (Australia) *Tel:* (03) 5476 2795 *Fax:* (03) 5476 2744 *E-mail:* travturf@ bigpond.com *Web Site:* www.hudson-publishing.com, pg 26

Max Hueber Verlag GmbH & Co KG (Germany) *Tel:* (089) 9602-0 *Fax:* (089) 9602-358 *E-mail:* kundenservice@hueber.de *Web Site:* www. hueber.de, pg 238

Felicitas Huebner Verlag (Germany) *Tel:* (05695) 1028 *Fax:* (05695) 1027, pg 238

Verlag Uta Huelsey (Germany) *Tel:* (0281) 27227 *Fax:* (0281) 24682 *E-mail:* uta.hulsey@t-online.de, pg 238

Libreria Huemul SA (Argentina) *Tel:* (011) 4822-1666; (011) 4825-2290 *Fax:* (011) 822-1666, pg 6

Libreria Huemul SA (Argentina) *Tel:* (011) 4822-1666; (011) 4825-2290 *Fax:* (011) 822-1666 *E-mail:* libreriahuemul@arnet.com.ar, pg 1287

Hug & Co (Switzerland) *Tel:* (01) 269 41 40 *Fax:* (01) 269 41 06 *E-mail:* info@hug-musikverlage.ch *Web Site:* www.hug-musikverlage.ch, pg 620

Buchhandlung Heinrich Hugendubel GmbH & Co KG (Germany) *Tel:* (01801) 484484 *Fax:* (01801) 484585 *E-mail:* service@hugendubel.de *Web Site:* www. hugendubel.de, pg 1301

Heinrich Hugendubel Verlag GmbH (Germany) *Tel:* (089) 235586-0 *Fax:* (089) 235586-111 *Web Site:* www.hugendubel.de, pg 238

Hugo's Language Books Ltd (United Kingdom) *Tel:* (020) 7010 3000 *Fax:* (020) 7010 6060 *E-mail:* customerservice@dk.com *Web Site:* uk.dk. com, pg 706

Editions Charles Huguenin Pro Arte (Switzerland) *Tel:* (038) 61 27 27 *Fax:* (038) 61 37 19, pg 620

Huia Publishers (New Zealand) *Tel:* (04) 473-9262 *Fax:* (04) 473-9265 *E-mail:* customer.services@huia. co.nz *Web Site:* www.huia.co.nz, pg 493

Huis Van Het Boek (Belgium) *Tel:* (03) 230 89 23 *Fax:* (03) 281 22 40 *E-mail:* info@boek.be *Web Site:* www.boek.be, pg 68

Human & Rousseau (Pty) Ltd (South Africa) *Tel:* (021) 406 3033 *Fax:* (021) 406 3812 *E-mail:* humanhk@ humanrousseau.com *Web Site:* www.humanrousseau. com, pg 560

Human Sciences Research Council (South Africa) *Tel:* (012) 302 2999 *Fax:* (012) 326 5362 *Web Site:* www.hsrc.ac.za, pg 560

Edition Humanistische Psychologie (EHP) (Germany) *Tel:* (02202) 981236 *Fax:* (02202) 981237 *E-mail:* info@ehp-koeln.com *Web Site:* www.ehp-koeln.com; www.ehp.biz, pg 238

Humanistischer Verband Deutschlands, Landesverband Berlin eV (Germany) *Tel:* (030) 6139040 *Fax:* (030) 61390450 *E-mail:* hvd@humanismus.de *Web Site:* www.humanismus.de, pg 238

Humanitas Ltd (Lithuania) *Tel:* (07) 220333 *Fax:* (07) 423653 *E-mail:* info@humanitas.lt *Web Site:* www. humanitas.lt, pg 1315

Humanitas Publishing House (Romania) *Tel:* (021) 3-17-18-19 *Fax:* (021) 3-17-18-24 *E-mail:* editors@ humanitas.ro *Web Site:* www.humanitas.ro, pg 535

Humboldt-Taschenbuch Verlag Jacobi KG (Germany) *Tel:* (089) 360902 *Fax:* (089) 36096-222 (general); (089) 36096-258 (orders) *E-mail:* redaktion@ humboldt.de, pg 238

Humboldt Universitaet zu Berlin (Germany) *Tel:* (030) 2093 3212 *Fax:* (030) 2093 3207 *E-mail:* wwwadm. ub@ub.hu-berlin.de *Web Site:* www.ub.hu-berlin.de, pg 1507

Edition Hundertmark (Germany) *Tel:* (0221) 237944 *Fax:* (0221) 249146 *E-mail:* info@hundertmark-gallery.com *Web Site:* www.hundertmark-gallery.com, pg 239

Hundskolan i Solleftea AB (Sweden) *Tel:* (0620) 832 00 *Fax:* (0620) 832 29 *E-mail:* gundvald@hundskolan.se *Web Site:* www.humanitydog.se, pg 607

Hung Hing Off-set Printing Co Ltd (Hong Kong) *Tel:* 2664 8682 *Fax:* 2664 2070 *E-mail:* info@hhop. com.hk *Web Site:* www.hhop.com.hk, pg 1147, 1168, 1208

John Hunt Publishing Ltd (United Kingdom) *Tel:* (01962) 736880; (01962) 736888 (orders) *Fax:* (01962) 736881 *E-mail:* office@johnhunt-publishing.com *Web Site:* www.johnhunt-publishing. com, pg 706

Hunter & Foulis Ltd (United Kingdom) *Tel:* (01620) 826379 *Fax:* (01620) 829485 *E-mail:* mail@ hunterfoulis.co.uk *Web Site:* www.hunterfoulis.co.uk, pg 1216

Hunter & Foulis Ltd (United Kingdom) *Tel:* (01620) 826 379 *Fax:* (01620) 829 485 *E-mail:* mail@hunterfoulis. co.uk *Web Site:* www.hunterfoulis.co.uk, pg 1229

Hunter Books (Australia), pg 26

Hunter House Publications (Australia) *Tel:* (02) 4930 5992 *Fax:* (02) 4930 5993 *E-mail:* wf&mc@ hunterlink.net.au, pg 26

Huntsmen Offset Printing Pte Ltd (Singapore) *Tel:* 2650600 *Fax:* 2658575, pg 1212

Ediciones Huracan Inc (Puerto Rico) *Tel:* (787) 763-7407 *Fax:* (787) 753-1486, pg 532

Huron Valley Graphics Inc (United States) *Tel:* 734-477-0448 *Toll Free Tel:* 800-362-9655 *Fax:* 734-477-0393 *E-mail:* custserv@hvg.com *Web Site:* www.hvg.com, pg 1177

C Hurst & Co (Publishers) Ltd (United Kingdom) *Tel:* (020) 7240 2666 *Fax:* (020) 7240 2667 *E-mail:* hurst@atlas.co.uk *Web Site:* www.hurstpub. co.uk, pg 706

Dr Mahmud Husain Library (Pakistan) *Tel:* (021) 474953 *Fax:* (021) 473226 *E-mail:* librarian@library.ku.edu. pk, pg 1533

Huss-Medien GmbH (Germany) *Tel:* (030) 421510 *Fax:* (030) 42151332 *E-mail:* huss.medien@ hussberlin.de *Web Site:* huss-medien.de, pg 239

Huss-Verlag GmbH (Germany) *Tel:* (089) 323910 *Fax:* (089) 32391416 *E-mail:* management@huss-verlag.de *Web Site:* www.huss-verlag.de/, pg 239

Husum Druck- und Verlagsgesellschaft mbH Co KG (Germany) *Tel:* (04841) 83520 *Fax:* (04841) 835210 *E-mail:* verlagsgruppe.husum@t-online.de *Web Site:* www.verlagsgruppe.de/, pg 239

Alan Hutchison Ltd (United Kingdom) *Tel:* (020) 7221 0129, pg 706

Huthig GmbH & Co KG (Germany) *Tel:* (06221) 4890 *Fax:* (06221) 489279 *E-mail:* info@huethig.de *Web Site:* www.huethig.de, pg 239

Hutton Press Ltd (United Kingdom) *Tel:* (01964) 550573 *Fax:* (01964) 550573, pg 706

Hutton-Williams Agency (United Kingdom) *Tel:* (020) 8879 0237 *Fax:* (020) 8879 3831, pg 1131

Hw Moon Publishing Co (Republic of Korea) *Tel:* (02) 724897, pg 436

Hyangmunsa Publishing Co (Republic of Korea) *Tel:* (02) 5385671; (02) 5385672 *Fax:* (02) 5385673, pg 436

Hyden House Ltd (United Kingdom) *Tel:* (01730) 823311 *Fax:* (01730) 823322 *E-mail:* info@ permaculture.co.uk *Web Site:* www.permaculture.co.uk, pg 706

Hyein Publishing House (Republic of Korea) *Tel:* (02) 3836928 *Fax:* (02) 3836929 *E-mail:* vvh103@chollian *Web Site:* www.hyeinbooks.co.kr, pg 436

Hyland House Publishing Pty Ltd (Australia) *Tel:* (03) 9376 4461 *Fax:* (03) 9376 4461 *E-mail:* hyland3@ netspace.net.au, pg 26

Hymns Ancient & Modern Ltd (United Kingdom) *Tel:* (01603) 612914 *Fax:* (01603) 624483 *E-mail:* admin@scm-canterburypress.co.uk *Web Site:* www.scm-canterburypress.co.uk, pg 706

Hyoronsha Publishing Co Ltd (Japan) *Tel:* (03) 3260-9401 *Fax:* (03) 3260-9408 *Web Site:* www.hyoronsha. co.jp, pg 415

Editura Hyperion (Republic of Moldova) *Tel:* (02) 244259, pg 469

HYS Culture Co Ltd (Taiwan, Province of China) *Tel:* (02) 6914310 *Fax:* (02) 6914311 *E-mail:* hysccl@ msl.hinet.net *Web Site:* www.hysbook.com.tw, pg 636

Hyun Am Publishing Co (Republic of Korea) *Tel:* (02) 877-2565 *Fax:* (02) 877-2566, pg 436

I Prooptiki, Ekdoseis (Greece) *Tel:* 2108226254 *Fax:* 2108226254 *E-mail:* info@prooptikibooks.gr *Web Site:* wwws.prooptikibooks.gr, pg 305

IAEA - International Atomic Energy Agency (Austria) *Tel:* (01) 2600-0; (01) 2600-22530 *Fax:* (01) 2600-7 *E-mail:* official.mail@iaea.org *Web Site:* www.iaea. org/worldatom/Books, pg 51

Iaith Cyf (United Kingdom) *Tel:* (01239) 711668 *Fax:* (01239) 711698 *E-mail:* ymhol@cwmni-iaith. com *Web Site:* www.cwmni-iaith.com, pg 706

Iamvlichos (Greece) *Tel:* 2103807180 *Fax:* 210 3807828; 2103807435, pg 1303

Ianos (Greece) *Tel:* 2310284833 *Fax:* 2310284 832 *E-mail:* internet@ianos.gr *Web Site:* www. ianos.gr, pg 305

IBA International Media & Book Agency (Germany) *Tel:* (030) 4437 9155 *Fax:* (030) 4437 9199 *E-mail:* office@iba-berlin.de *Web Site:* www.iba-berlin.de, pg 1121

Ibadan University Press (Nigeria) *Tel:* (022) 400550; (022) 400614 (ext 1244, 1042, 1032, 1093), pg 500

Ibaizabal Edelvives SA (Spain) *Tel:* (094) 6308036 *Fax:* (094) 6308028 *E-mail:* ibaizabal@ibaizabal.biz, pg 582

IBC Publishing Inc (Japan) *Tel:* (03) 5770-2438 *Fax:* (03) 5786-7419 *E-mail:* ibc@ibcpub.co.jp *Web Site:* www.ibcpub.co.jp, pg 415

Ibcon SA (Mexico) *Tel:* (055) 52 55 45 77 *Fax:* (055) 52 55 45 77 *E-mail:* ibcon@ibcon.com.mx; ibcon@ infosel.net.mx *Web Site:* www.ibcon.com.mx, pg 463

IBD Publisher & Distributors (India) *Tel:* (011) 23251094 *Fax:* (011) 23259102 *E-mail:* piyush_gahlot@rediffmail.com, pg 333

Ibera VerlagsgesmbH (Austria) *Tel:* (01) 513 19 72 *Fax:* (01) 513 19 72-28 *E-mail:* presse@ibera.at *Web Site:* www.ibera.at, pg 52

Editorial Iberia, SA (Spain) *Tel:* (093) 2010599; (093) 2013807 *Fax:* (093) 2097362 *E-mail:* omega@ ediciones-omega.es *Web Site:* www.ediciones-omega. es, pg 582

Iberico Europea de Ediciones SA (Spain) *Tel:* (091) 4357243, pg 582

Livro Ibero-Americano Ltda (Brazil) *Tel:* (021) 2221 2026 *Fax:* (021) 2252 8814, pg 83

Livro Ibero-Americano Ltda (Brazil) *Tel:* (021) 252 8814 *Fax:* (021) 232 5248 *E-mail:* livo-ibero@uol.com.br, pg 1293

Ibero-Amerikanisches Institut Preussischer Kulturbesitz (Germany) *Tel:* (030) 266 2500 *Fax:* (030) 266 2503 *E-mail:* iai@iai.spk-berlin.de *Web Site:* www.iai.spk-berlin.de, pg 1508

Iberoamericana Editorial Vervuert (Germany) *Tel:* (069) 5974617 *Fax:* (069) 5978743 *E-mail:* info@ iberoamericanalibros.com *Web Site:* www.ibero-americana.net, pg 1301

IBH Publishing Services (India) *Tel:* (022) 2852-7619 *Fax:* (022) 2852-9473 *Web Site:* www.ibhsolves.com, pg 333, 1169

IBIS (Denmark) *Tel:* 35358788 *Fax:* 35350696 *E-mail:* ibis@ibis.dk *Web Site:* www.ibis.dk, pg 132

Ibis (Italy) *Tel:* (031) 3371367; (031) 306836 *Fax:* (031) 306829 *E-mail:* info@ibisedizioni.it *Web Site:* www. ibisedizioni.it, pg 389

IBRASA (Instituicao Brasileira de Difusao Cultural Ltda) (Brazil) *Tel:* (011) 3107 41 00 *Fax:* (011) 3107 35 13 *E-mail:* editora.ibrasa@uol.com.br *Web Site:* www.ibrasa.com.br, pg 83

IBS Buku Sdn Bhd (Malaysia) *Tel:* (03) 7751763; (03) 775-1566; (03) 7760514 *Fax:* (03) 79576026; (03) 776-8551 *E-mail:* ibsbuku@po.jaring.my, pg 452

IBS Buku Sdn Bhd (Malaysia) *Tel:* (03) 79579282; (03) 79579470 *Fax:* (03) 79576026 *E-mail:* info@ ibsbuku.com; ibsbuku@po.janing.my; hibs@tm.net.my *Web Site:* www.ibsbuku.com, pg 1316

ICA bokforlag (Sweden) *Tel:* (021) 194000 *Fax:* (021) 194283 *E-mail:* bok@forlaget.ica.se *Web Site:* www. forlaget.ica.se/bok, pg 607

Icaria Editorial SA (Spain) *Tel:* (093) 3011723 *Fax:* (093) 3178242 *E-mail:* icario@icariaeditorial.com *Web Site:* www.icariaeditorial.com, pg 582

ICBS/IBIS ApS (Denmark) *Tel:* 33114255 *Fax:* 33911167 *E-mail:* icbs@get2net.dk *Web Site:* www.icbs-ibis.dk, pg 1120

ICC United Kingdom (United Kingdom) *Tel:* (020) 7838 9363 *Fax:* (020) 7235 5447 *E-mail:* katharinehedger@ iccorg.co.uk *Web Site:* www.iccwbo.org; www.iccuk. net, pg 706

Publicaciones ICCE (Spain) *Tel:* (091) 725 72 00 *Fax:* (091) 361 10 52 *E-mail:* info@ciberaula.net *Web Site:* www.ciberaula.net, pg 582

Iceland Review (Iceland) *Tel:* 512-7575 *Fax:* 561-8646 *E-mail:* icelandreview@icelandreview.com *Web Site:* www.icelandreview.com, pg 322

ICG/Holliston (United States) *Tel:* 423-357-6141 *Toll Free:* 800-251-0451 *Fax:* 423-357-8840 *Toll Free Fax:* 800-325-0351 *E-mail:* custserv@icgholliston.com *Web Site:* www.icgholliston.com, pg 1230

ICG Publications BV (Netherlands) *Tel:* (070) 4480203 *Fax:* (070) 4480177, pg 480

Ichiryu-Sha (Japan) *Tel:* (03) 3822-0585 *Fax:* (03) 3821-3964, pg 415

Ichtiar Baru van Hoeve (Indonesia) *Tel:* (021) 7511856; (021) 7511901 *Fax:* (021) 7511855 *E-mail:* redaksi@ ibvh.com *Web Site:* www.ibvh.com, pg 1169

Ichtiar Baru van Hoeve (Indonesia) *Tel:* (021) 7511856; (021) 7511901 *Fax:* (021) 7511855, pg 1210

Ichtiar Baru van Hoeve (Indonesia) *Tel:* (021) 7511901, pg 1227

Ici et Ailleurs-Vents d'Ailleurs (France) *Tel:* (04) 42533087 *Fax:* (04) 42533097 *E-mail:* info@kaona. com *Web Site:* www.kaona.com, pg 168

Icicle/Papercom (Hong Kong) *Tel:* 2235 2880 *Web Site:* www.papercom.com.hk, pg 1147, 1168, 1208

ICOB/Atrium (Netherlands) *Tel:* (0172) 43 72 31 *Fax:* (0172) 43 93 79 *E-mail:* icobal@xs4all.nl, pg 1320

Icon Press (United Kingdom) *Tel:* (01323) 507270 *Fax:* (01323) 507270 *E-mail:* iconpress@philipbrown. screaming.net *Web Site:* www.iconpress.co.uk, pg 706

Icone Editora Ltda (Brazil) *Tel:* (011) 36663095; (021) 826-9510 *Fax:* (011) 36663095, pg 83

ICPC Ltd (Ireland) *Tel:* (01) 8474711 *Fax:* (01) 8474546 *Web Site:* www.icpc.ie, pg 1170

ICSA Publishing Ltd (United Kingdom) *Tel:* (020) 7612 7020 *Fax:* (020) 7323 1132 *E-mail:* icsa.pub@icsa.co. uk *Web Site:* www.icsapublishing.co.uk, pg 707

Edition ID-Archiv/ID-Verlag (Germany) *Tel:* (030) 6947703 *Fax:* (030) 6947808 *E-mail:* id-verlag@mail. nadir.org *Web Site:* www.txt.de/id-verlag/, pg 239

Idara-e-Tehqiqat-e-Islami (Pakistan) *Tel:* (051) 850751-5; (051) 850755, pg 508

Idara Ishaat-E-Diniyat Ltd (India) *Tel:* (011) 26926832; (011) 26926833 (office); (011) 461676; (011) 4631786 (showroom) *Fax:* (011) 26932787; (011) 4632786 *E-mail:* sales@idara.com; idara@yahoo.com *Web Site:* www.idara.com, pg 333

Idara Siqafat-e-Islamia (Pakistan) *Tel:* (042) 53908, pg 508

Idea Books (Italy) *Tel:* (0584) 425410 *Fax:* (178) 609 8685 *E-mail:* info@ideabooks.com *Web Site:* www. ideabooks.com, pg 389

Idea Books, SA (Spain) *Tel:* (093) 4533002 *Fax:* (093) 4541895 *E-mail:* ideabooks@ideabooks.es *Web Site:* www.ideabooks.es, pg 582

Idea Verlag GmbH (Germany) *Tel:* (08141) 80939 *Fax:* (08141) 80939 *E-mail:* info@idea-verlag.de *Web Site:* www.idea-verlag.de, pg 239

The Ideal Bookshop (Malta) *Tel:* 553944, pg 1317

Editorial Idearium de la Universidad de Mendoza (EDIUM) (Argentina) *Tel:* (0261) 420-2017; (0261) 420-0740 *Fax:* (0261) 420-1100 *E-mail:* umimen@um. edu.ar *Web Site:* www.um.edu.ar/um/, pg 6

Idegenforgalmi Propaganda es Kiado Vallalat (Hungary) *Tel:* (01) 633652; (01) 633653 *Fax:* (01) 1837320, pg 318

Idegraf SA, Editions (Switzerland) *Tel:* (022) 792 03 96 *Fax:* (022) 793 63 30 *E-mail:* 101512.3363@ compuserve.com, pg 620

Casa Editrice Libraria Idelson di G Gnocchi (Italy) *Tel:* (081) 5453443 *Fax:* (081) 5464991 *E-mail:* info@ idelson-gnocchi.com *Web Site:* www.idelson-gnocchi. com, pg 389

Idelson-Gnocchi Edizioni Scientifiche (Italy) *Tel:* (081) 5453443 *Fax:* (081) 5464991 *E-mail:* ordini@idelson-gnocchi.com *Web Site:* www.idelson-gnocchi.com, pg 389

Identic Books (Australia) *Tel:* (02) 8901 3466 *Fax:* (02) 8901 3404 *E-mail:* enquiries@identic.com.au *Web Site:* www.identic.com.au, pg 1289

Editions Ides et Calendes SA (Switzerland) *Tel:* (032) 725 38 61 *Fax:* (032) 725 58 80 *E-mail:* info@ idesetcalendes.com; artides@artides.com; ides@livre. net *Web Site:* www.artides.com; www.livre.net/ides, pg 620

Idmon Publications (Greece) *Tel:* 2105015550 *Fax:* 2105015550 *E-mail:* idmon@in.gr, pg 305

Istituto Idrografico della Marina (Italy) *Tel:* (010) 24431 *Fax:* (010) 261400 *E-mail:* iim.sre@marina.difesa.it *Web Site:* www.marina.difesa.it, pg 389

Idryma Meleton Chersonisou tou Aimou (Greece) *Tel:* 2310832143 *Fax:* 2310831429 *E-mail:* imxa@imxa.gr, pg 305

Idunn (Iceland) *Tel:* 522-2000 *Fax:* 522-2022 *E-mail:* idunn@idunn.is *Web Site:* www.idunn.is, pg 322

IDW-Verlag GmbH (Germany) *Tel:* (0211) 45610 *Fax:* (0211) 4561206 *E-mail:* post@idw-verlag.de *Web Site:* www.idw-verlag.de, pg 239

Ie-No-Hikari Association (Japan) *Tel:* (03) 3266-9029 *Fax:* (03) 3266-9053 *E-mail:* hikari@mxd.meshnet.or. jp *Web Site:* www.ienohikari.or.jp, pg 415

Ifjusagi Lap-es Konyvkiado Vallalat (Hungary) *Tel:* (01) 1116660 *Fax:* (01) 1530959, pg 318

IG Autorinnen Autoren (Austria) *Tel:* (01) 526 20 44-13 *Fax:* (01) 526 20 44-55 *E-mail:* ig@literaturhaus.at *Web Site:* www.literaturhaus.at/lh/ig, pg 52

Igaku-Shoin Ltd (Japan) *Tel:* (03) 38175600 *Fax:* (03) 38157791 *E-mail:* info@igaku-shoin.co.jp *Web Site:* www.igaku-shoin.co.jp, pg 415

Igel Verlag Literatur Michael Matthias Schardt (Germany) *Tel:* (0441) 6640262 *Fax:* (0441) 6640263 *E-mail:* igelverlag@t-online.de, pg 239

Editorial Pablo Iglesias (Spain) *Tel:* (091) 104 313 *Fax:* (091) 194 585 *E-mail:* administracion@fpi.es *Web Site:* www.fpabloiglesias.es, pg 582

Iglu Editora Ltda (Brazil) *Tel:* (011) 3873-0227 *Fax:* (011) 3873-0227 *E-mail:* iglueditiora@ig.com.br, pg 83

IHT Gruppo Editoriale SRL (Italy) *Tel:* (02) 794181 *Fax:* (02) 784021 *E-mail:* info@iht.it *Web Site:* www. iht.it, pg 389

Ikaros (Greece) *Tel:* 2103225152 *Fax:* 2103235262, pg 1303

Ikaros Ekdotiki (Greece) *Tel:* 2103225152 *Fax:* 2103235262, pg 305

Ikarus - Buchverlag (Germany) *Tel:* (06682) 919383 *Fax:* (06682) 919385 *E-mail:* ikarus-verlag@t-online. de *Web Site:* www.ikarus-verlag.de, pg 239

Ikatan Penerbit Indonesia (IKAPI) (Indonesia) *Tel:* (021) 3141907; (021) 3146050 *Fax:* (021) 3146050 *E-mail:* sekretariat@ikapi.or.id *Web Site:* www.ikapi. or.id, pg 1263

Ikatan Pustakawan Indonesia (Indonesia) *Tel:* (021) 3855729 *Fax:* (021) 3855729 *E-mail:* mahmudin@ lib.itb.ac.id *Web Site:* ipi.pnri.go.id, pg 1565

IKI Nokta Research Press & Publications Industry & Trade Ltd (Turkey) *Tel:* (0216) 349 01 41 *Fax:* (0216) 337 67 56 *E-mail:* ikinokta@superonline.com; ikinokta@turkinfo.com; ikinokta@gisoturkey.com; ikinokta @turkgis.com; ikinokta@infoturk.com *Web Site:* www.ikinokta.com, pg 645

IKO Verlag fur Interkulturelle Kommunikation (Germany) *Tel:* (069) 784808 *Fax:* (069) 7896575 *E-mail:* info@iko-verlag.de *Web Site:* www.iko-verlag. de, pg 239

Ikon Document Management Services (United Kingdom) *Tel:* (0118) 9770510 *Fax:* (0118) 9770513, pg 1153

Ikon Document Management Services (United Kingdom) *Tel:* (0118) 9770510 *Fax:* (0118) 9770513 *E-mail:* pamh@ikonds.co.uk *Web Site:* www.ikon.com, pg 1174

Ikon Document Management Services (United Kingdom) *Tel:* (0118) 9770510 *Fax:* (0118) 9770513 *Web Site:* www.ikon.com, pg 1216

Ikon Document Management Services (United Kingdom) *Tel:* (020) 7336 6509 *Fax:* (020) 7336 7840 *Web Site:* www.uk.ikon.com, pg 1237

Ikon Publishing Ltd (Hungary) *Tel:* (01) 1764401; (01) 1758183 *Fax:* (01) 1158089, pg 318

Ikubundo Publishing Co Ltd (Japan) *Tel:* (03) 3814-5571 *Fax:* (03) 3814-5576 *E-mail:* webmaster@ikubundo. com *Web Site:* www.ikubundo.com, pg 1312

ILA (International Literary Agency) USA (Italy) *Tel:* (0184) 484048; (0347) 9334966 *Fax:* (0184) 487292 *E-mail:* books@librigg.com, pg 1123

Ila - Palma, Tea Nova (Italy) *Tel:* (091) 6124415 *Fax:* (091) 6259260, pg 390

Iletisim Yayinlari (Turkey) *Tel:* (0212) 516 22 60 *Fax:* (0212) 516 12 58 *E-mail:* iletisim@iletisim.com. tr *Web Site:* www.iletisim.com.tr, pg 645

Ilisso Edizioni di Vanna Fois & CSNC (Italy) *Tel:* (0784) 33033 *Fax:* (0784) 35413 *E-mail:* ilisso@ilisso.it *Web Site:* www.ilisso.it, pg 1311

Iljisa Publishing House (Republic of Korea) *Tel:* (02) 7329320 *Fax:* (02) 7222807, pg 436

Iljo-gag Publishers (Republic of Korea) *Tel:* (02) 7335430; (02) 7335431 *Fax:* (02) 7385857 *E-mail:* ilchokak@hitel.kol.co.kr; ilchokak@chollian. dacom.co.kr, pg 436

Illert Publications (Australia) *Tel:* (02) 4283 3009 *Fax:* (02) 4283 3009 *E-mail:* illert@keira.hotkey.net. au, pg 26

Ilmamaa (Estonia) *Tel:* (07) 427 290 *Fax:* (07) 427 320 *E-mail:* ilmamaa@ilmamaa.ee *Web Site:* www. ilmamaa.ee, pg 139

Iluminuras - Projetos e Producoes Editoriais Ltda (Brazil) *Tel:* (011) 3068-9433; (011) 8678583 *Fax:* (011) 3082-5317 *E-mail:* iluminuras@ ilumunuras.com.br, pg 83

Image & Print Group Ltd (United Kingdom) *Tel:* (0141) 353 1900 *Fax:* (0141) 353 8611 *E-mail:* info@ imageandprint.co.uk *Web Site:* www.imageandprint. co.uk, pg 1175

Image & Print Group Ltd (United Kingdom) *Tel:* (0141) 353 1900; (0141) 353 8620 (ISDN) *Fax:* (0141) 353 8611 *E-mail:* info@imageandprint.co.uk *Web Site:* www.imageandprint.co.uk, pg 1216, 1229

Image/Magie (France) *Tel:* (01) 66 80 34 02 *Fax:* (01) 66 80 34 56, pg 168

Image Printing Company Ltd (Hong Kong) *Tel:* 2897 8046 *Fax:* 2558 3044 *E-mail:* imageprt@pop3.hknet. com, pg 1147

Image Printing Company Ltd (Hong Kong) *Tel:* 2873 2633 *Fax:* 2558 3044 *E-mail:* imageprt@pop3.hknet. com, pg 1168, 1208

Image Printing Company Ltd (Hong Kong) *Tel:* 2897 8046 *Fax:* 2558 3044 *E-mail:* imageprt@pop3.hknet. com, pg 1226

Imagen y Deporte, SL (Spain) *Tel:* (0976) 75 40 00 *Fax:* (0976) 75 40 00 *E-mail:* imadepor@encomix.es *Web Site:* www.imagenydeporte.com, pg 582

The Images Publishing Group Pty Ltd (Australia) *Tel:* (03) 9561 5544 *Fax:* (03) 9561 4860 *E-mail:* books@images.com.au *Web Site:* www. imagespublishinggroup.com, pg 26

Imago (United States) *Tel:* 212-921-4411 *Fax:* 212-921-8226 *E-mail:* sales@imagousa.com *Web Site:* www. imagousa.com, pg 1156, 1219, 1230

Editions Imago (France) *Tel:* (01) 46 33 15 33 *Fax:* (01) 60 23 87 51 *E-mail:* info@editions-imago.fr *Web Site:* www.editions-imago.fr, pg 168

Imago Editora Ltda (Brazil) *Tel:* (021) 2242-0627 *Fax:* (021) 2224-8359 *E-mail:* imago@imagoeditora. com.br *Web Site:* www.imagoeditora.com.br, pg 83

Imago Productions (Far East) Pte Ltd (Singapore) *Tel:* 67484433 *Fax:* 67486082 *E-mail:* enquires@ imago.com.sg *Web Site:* www.imago.co.uk, pg 1236

Imago Publishing Ltd (United Kingdom) *Tel:* (01844) 337000 *Fax:* (01844) 339935 *E-mail:* sales@imago.co. uk *Web Site:* www.imago.co.uk, pg 707

Imago Services (HK) Ltd (Hong Kong) *Tel:* 2811 3316 *Fax:* 2597 5256 *E-mail:* enquiries@imago.com.hk *Web Site:* www.imago.com.hk, pg 1147

Imam Mohamed Bin Saud University Library (Saudi Arabia) *Tel:* (01) 258 0000 *Fax:* (01) 259 0271, pg 1539

IMEC (France) *Tel:* (01) 53 34 23 23 *Fax:* (01) 53 34 23 00 *E-mail:* paris@imec-archives.com *Web Site:* www. imec-archives.com, pg 168

Imge Kitabevi (Turkey) *Tel:* (0312) 419 46 10; (0312) 419 46 11 *Fax:* (0312) 425 65 32 *E-mail:* imge@ www.imge.com.tr *Web Site:* www.imgekitabevi.com, pg 645

Immediate Publishing (United Kingdom) *Tel:* (01273) 207259; (01273) 207411 *Fax:* (01273) 205612, pg 707

Impact (United Kingdom) *Tel:* (020) 7222 7777; (020) 7636 7543 *Fax:* (020) 7222 2782; (020) 7436 7218, pg 1573

Impala (Portugal) *Tel:* (021) 4364401 *Fax:* (021) 4366572, pg 527

Impart Books (United Kingdom) *Tel:* (01686) 623484 *E-mail:* impart@books.mid-wales.net *Web Site:* www. books.mid-wales.net, pg 707

Imparudi (Imprimerie et Papeterie du Burundi) (Burundi) *Tel:* (02) 3125; (02) 7381 *Fax:* (02) 2572, pg 1294

Imperial College Press (United Kingdom) *Tel:* (020) 7836 3954 *Fax:* (020) 7836 2002 *E-mail:* edit@ icpress.co.uk *Web Site:* www.icpress.co.uk, pg 707

IMPF bvba (Belgium) *Tel:* (09) 225 44 29 *Fax:* 058 315 77 *E-mail:* maarten@fotobeurs.com *Web Site:* www. fotobeurs.com, pg 1165

IMPF bvba (Belgium) *Tel:* (09) 225 44 29, pg 1205

IMPF bvba (Belgium) *Tel:* (09) 225 44 29; (09) 265 99 00 *Fax:* (09) 233 13 38 *E-mail:* impf@xs4all.be, pg 1235

Impredisur, SL (Spain) *Tel:* (0958) 202955; (0958) 290577, pg 582

Imprensa Nacional-Casa da Moeda (Portugal) *Tel:* (021) 781 07 00 *Fax:* (021) 781 07 54 *Web Site:* www.incm. pt, pg 527

Imprenta de la Universidad Nacional (Colombia) *Tel:* (01) 2686965; (01) 2699111 *Fax:* (01) 2441035, pg 111

Imprenta y Litografia Trejos SA (Costa Rica) *Tel:* 2242411 *Fax:* 2241528, pg 115

Imprima Korea Agency (Republic of Korea) *Tel:* (02) 325-9155 *Fax:* (02) 334-9160 *E-mail:* imprima@ chollian.net *Web Site:* www.imprima.co.kr, pg 1124

Imprimerie Bietlot Freres SA (Belgium) *Tel:* (071) 283611 *Fax:* (071) 283620 *E-mail:* info@bietlot.be *Web Site:* www.bietlot.be, pg 1225

Imprimerie Commerciale et Administrative de Mauritanie (Mauritania), pg 457

Imprimerie de Kabgayi (Rwanda) *Tel:* 62252; 62877 *Fax:* 62345, pg 545

Imprimerie et Papeterie Commerciale, IPC (Mauritius) *Tel:* 2124190; 2127701; 2127702 *Fax:* 2083523, pg 457

Imprimerie Nationale du Burundi (Burundi) *Tel:* (02) 22214; (02) 24046, pg 97

IMPS Research Ltd (Papua New Guinea) *Tel:* 3213283 *Fax:* 3217360 *E-mail:* imps@online.net.pg, pg 511

IMPS SA (Belgium) *Tel:* (02) 6520220 *Fax:* (02) 6520160, pg 68

Impuls (Poland) *Tel:* (012) 422-41-80 *Fax:* (012) 422-59-47 *E-mail:* impuls@impulsoficyna.com.pl *Web Site:* www.impulsoficyna.com.pl, pg 518

Impuls-Theater-Verlag (Germany) *Tel:* (089) 8597577 *Fax:* (089) 8593044 *E-mail:* info@buschfunk.de *Web Site:* www.buschfunk.de, pg 239

Imrie & Dervis Literary Agency (United Kingdom) *Tel:* (020) 8809 3282 *Fax:* (020) 8880 2086 *E-mail:* info@imriedervis.com, pg 1131

In Dialogo (Italy) *Tel:* (02) 58391342 *Fax:* (02) 58391345 *E-mail:* indial@tin.it, pg 390

In-Tune Books (Australia) *Tel:* (02) 9974 5981 *Fax:* (02) 9974 4552 *Web Site:* www.haywardbooks.com.au, pg 26

INADES (Institut Africain pour le Developpment Economique et Social) (Cote d'Ivoire) *Tel:* 22 40 02 16 *Fax:* 22 40 02 30 *E-mail:* ifsiege@inadesfo.ci *Web Site:* www.inadesfo.org, pg 1498

INADES (Institut Africain pour le Developpment Economique et Social) (Rwanda) *Tel:* (0225) 22404720; (0225) 2244 20 59 *Fax:* (0225) 44 84 38 *E-mail:* inades@africaonline.co.ci; inades@ci.refer.org *Web Site:* www.inades.ci.refer.org, pg 545

Inbal Publishers (Israel) *Tel:* (03) 9030111 *Fax:* (03) 9030888 *E-mail:* inbalpub@internet-zahav.net, pg 364

Inbal Travel Information (Israel) *Tel:* (03) 5753032 *Fax:* (03) 5753130, pg 364

Incafo Archivo Fotografico Editorial, SL (Spain) *Tel:* (091) 4313460; (091) 5780961 *Fax:* (091) 4313589, pg 582

Independence Educational Publishers Ltd (United Kingdom) *Tel:* (01223) 566 130 *Fax:* (01223) 566 131 *E-mail:* issues@independence.co.uk *Web Site:* www. independence.co.uk, pg 707

Independent Publishers Guild (United Kingdom) *Tel:* (01763) 247014 *Fax:* (01763) 246293 *E-mail:* info@ipg.uk.com *Web Site:* www.ipg.uk.com/, pg 1281

Independent Writers Publications Ltd (United Kingdom) *Tel:* (020) 8438 0179 *Fax:* (020) 8438 0179, pg 707

Editora Index Ltda (Brazil) *Tel:* (021) 516 2336 *Fax:* (021) 253 3507 *E-mail:* editoraindex@ax.ibase. org.br, pg 83

India Book House Pvt Ltd (India) *Tel:* (022) 2840165 *Fax:* (022) 2835099, pg 333

Indian Association of Special Libraries & Information Centres (IASLIC) (India) *Tel:* (033) 334 9651; (033) 2354 9066 *E-mail:* iaslic@vsnl.net *Web Site:* www. iaslic.org, pg 1564

Indian Association of Academic Librarians (India) *Tel:* (011) 6831717, pg 1564

Indian Book Depot (India) *Tel:* (011) 3673927; (011) 3523635 *Fax:* (011) 3552096 *E-mail:* ibdmaps@ndb. vsnl.net.in; indiabo@indiabookfair.net, pg 333

Indian Council for Cultural Relations (India) *Tel:* (011) 3370732; (011) 3378647 *Fax:* (011) 3712639 *E-mail:* iccr@vsnl.com *Web Site:* education.vsnl. com/iccr, pg 333

Indian Council of Agricultural Research (India) *Tel:* (011) 388991 (ext 496); (011) 23382306 *Fax:* (011) 387293 *E-mail:* jssamra@icar.delhi.nic.in *Web Site:* www.icar.org.in, pg 333

Indian Council of Social Science Research (ICSSR) (India) *Tel:* (011) 23385959; (011) 26717066 *Fax:* (011) 26179836 *E-mail:* info@icssr.org *Web Site:* www.icssr.org, pg 333

Indian Council of World Affairs Library (India) *Tel:* (011) 3317246 *Fax:* (011) 3317248, pg 1514

Indian Documentation Service (India) *Tel:* (0124) 6322005; (0124) 6322779 *Fax:* (0124) 6324782 *E-mail:* indoc@indiatimes.com, pg 334

Indian Institute of Advanced Study (India) *Tel:* (0177) 72303; (0177) 75139 *Fax:* (0177) 75139 *E-mail:* info@iias.org *Web Site:* www.iias.org, pg 334

Indian Institute of Management (India) *Tel:* (079) 2630 7241 *Fax:* (079) 2630 6896 *E-mail:* director@iimahd. ernet.in *Web Site:* www.iimahd.ernet.in, pg 1514

Indian Institute of Technology Madras Central Library (India) *Tel:* (044) 2578740 *Fax:* (044) 2350509 *E-mail:* libinfo@iitm.ac.in *Web Site:* www.cenlib.iitm. ac.in, pg 1514

Indian Institute of World Culture (India) *Tel:* (080) 6678581 *Web Site:* www.ultindia.org/culture.htm, pg 334

Indian Library Association (India) *Tel:* (011) 326 4748; (011) 765 1743 *E-mail:* ilanet1@nda.vsnl.net.in *Web Site:* www.delhiindia.com, pg 1564

Indian Museum (India) *Tel:* (033) 249 9902; (033) 249 9979; (033) 249 8948; (033) 249 8931 *Fax:* (033) 249 5699 *E-mail:* imbot@cal2.vsnl.net.in *Web Site:* www. indianmuseum-calcutta.org, pg 334

Indian Society for Promoting Christian Knowledge (ISPCK) (India) *Tel:* (011) 23866323 *Fax:* (011) 23865490 *E-mail:* ispck@nde.vsnl.net.in *Web Site:* ispck.org.in, pg 334

Instituto Indigenista Interamericano (Mexico) *Tel:* (05) 5595 8410; (05) 5595 4324 *Fax:* (05) 595 8410 *E-mail:* ininin@data.net.mx, pg 463

Indigo & Cote-Femmes Editions (France) *Tel:* (01) 43 79 74 79 *Fax:* (01) 43 79 46 87 *E-mail:* indigo.cote-femmes.edition@wanadoo.fr *Web Site:* www.indigo-cf.com, pg 168

PT Indira (Indonesia) *Tel:* (021) 3904290; (021) 3148868 *Fax:* (021) 3929373 *E-mail:* indirawb@mweb.co.id, pg 351

PT Indira (Indonesia) *Tel:* (021) 3148868; (021) 3904290 *Fax:* (021) 3929373 *E-mail:* indirawb@mweb.co.id, pg 1308

Indo Lingua Services Ltd (United Kingdom) *Tel:* (020) 7515 3987 *E-mail:* indolingua@compuserve.com, pg 1140

Indonesian ISBN Agency (Indonesia) *Tel:* (021) 3154864; (021) 3154870 *Fax:* (021) 3103554 *E-mail:* info@pnri.go.id *Web Site:* www.pnri.go.id, pg 1263

Indra Publishing (Australia) *Tel:* (03) 9439 7555 *Fax:* (03) 9439 7555 *Web Site:* www.indra.com.au, pg 27

Indrajaya CV (Indonesia) *Tel:* (021) 3457039; (021) 3457041 *Fax:* (021) 3457039, pg 352

Indus Publishing Co (India) *Tel:* (011) 25935289; (011) 25151333 *Fax:* (011) 25922102 *E-mail:* indus@ indusbooks.com *Web Site:* www.indusbooks.com, pg 335

Industria-Verlagsbuchhandlung GmbH (Germany) *Tel:* (02323) 1410 *Fax:* (02323) 141123, pg 239

Industrial Publishing House (Democratic People's Republic of Korea) *Fax:* 3814410; 3814427, pg 433

Industrial Technology Institute Information Services Centre (Sri Lanka) *Tel:* (01) 693807; (01) 693808; (01) 693809; (01) 698621; (01) 698622; (01) 698623 *Fax:* (01) 686567 *E-mail:* info@iti.lk *Web Site:* www. iti.lk, pg 1544

Industrias del Envase SA (Peru) *Tel:* (01) 574-1150 *Fax:* (01) 574-1287 *E-mail:* webmast@envase.com.pe *Web Site:* www.envase.com.pe, pg 1211

Verlag Industrielle Organisation (Switzerland) *Tel:* (01) 4667711 *Fax:* (01) 4667412 *E-mail:* info@ofv.ch *Web Site:* www.ofv.ch, pg 620

Industrieschau Verlagsgesellschaft mbH (Germany) *Tel:* (06151) 38920 *Fax:* (06151) 389280 *E-mail:* info@abconline.de *Web Site:* www.abconline. de, pg 239

Industrilitteratur Vindex, Forlags AB (Sweden) *Tel:* (08) 783 81 00 *Fax:* (08) 660 59 11 *E-mail:* aestan. orstadius@industrilitteratur.se, pg 607

Info Access & Distribution (Singapore) *Tel:* 6741 8422 *Fax:* 6741 8821 *E-mail:* info.sg@igroup.net.com *Web Site:* www.igroupnet.com, pg 1330

Infoa (Czech Republic) *Tel:* (0583) 449 091 *Fax:* (0583) 456 810 *E-mail:* infoa@infoa.cz *Web Site:* www.infoa. cz, pg 123

Infoboek NV (Belgium) *Tel:* (014) 369292 *Fax:* (014) 369293 *E-mail:* info@infoboek.be *Web Site:* www. infoboek.com, pg 68

Informa Publishing Group Ltd (United Kingdom) *Tel:* (020) 7017 5000 *E-mail:* publishing.customers@ informa.com *Web Site:* www.informa.com, pg 707

Instituto de Informacion Cientifica y Tecnologica (IDICT) (Cuba) *Tel:* (07) 862-6531; (07) 860-3411 *Fax:* (07) 862-6531 *E-mail:* andresdt@idict.cu; comercial@idict.cu *Web Site:* www.idict.cu, pg 120

Informatica Cosmos SA de CV (Mexico) *Tel:* (05) 6774868; (05) 6776043 *Fax:* (05) 6793575 *E-mail:* online@cosmos.com.mx *Web Site:* www. cosmos.com.mx, pg 463

Mediteg-Gesellschaft fuer Informatik Technik und Systeme Verlag (Germany) *Tel:* (06081) 5171 *Fax:* (06081) 56017, pg 240

Information Agents Ltd (United Kingdom) *Tel:* (020) 7837 3345 *Fax:* (020) 7837 8901 *E-mail:* eps@epsltd. com *Web Site:* www.epsltd.com, pg 1131

Informationsfoerlaget AB (Sweden) *Tel:* (08) 34 09 15 *Fax:* (08) 31 39 03 *E-mail:* red@informationsforlaget. se *Web Site:* www.informationsforlaget.se, pg 607

Informationsstelle Suedliches Afrika eV (ISSA) (Germany) *Tel:* (0228) 464369 *Fax:* (0228) 468177 *E-mail:* issa@comlink.org *Web Site:* www.issa-bonn. org, pg 240

Informationszentrum fuer Informationswissenschaft und -praxis (IZ) (Germany) *Tel:* (0331) 580-2210; (0331) 580-2230 *Fax:* (0331) 580-2229 *E-mail:* iz@ fh-potsdam.de *Web Site:* forge.fh-potsdam.de, pg 1563

Informator dd (Croatia) *Tel:* (01) 4852 665; (01) 4852 668 *Fax:* (01) 4852 673 *E-mail:* informator@ informator.hr *Web Site:* www.informator.hr, pg 118

Infostelle Industrieverband Massivumformung e V (Germany) *Tel:* (02331) 958828 *Fax:* (02331) 958728 *E-mail:* cpair@imu.wsm-net.de *Web Site:* www. metalform.de, pg 240

Infotex NV (Belgium) *Tel:* (09) 265 64 23 *Fax:* (09) 225 84 06, pg 68

Infotex Scoop NV (Belgium) *Tel:* (09) 2056430 *Fax:* (09) 2056449 *E-mail:* scoop@infotex.be, pg 68

INFRA-M Izdatel 'skij dom (Russian Federation) *Tel:* (095) 4857077; (095) 4855918 *Fax:* (095) 4855318 *E-mail:* books@infra-m.ru *Web Site:* www. infra-m.ru, pg 540

Editions Infrarouge (France) *Tel:* (01) 44 93 45 64 *Fax:* (01) 49 95 08 74 *E-mail:* editionsinfrarouge@ libertysurf.fr; editions.infrarouge@caramail.com *Web Site:* www.chez.com/editinfrarouge, pg 168

Ingenioeren/Boger (Denmark) *Tel:* 63 15 17 00 *Fax:* 63 15 17 33 *E-mail:* info@nyttf.dk *Web Site:* www.nyttf. dk, pg 132

Ingenioeren/Boger (Denmark) *Tel:* 63 15 17 00 *Fax:* 63 15 17 33 *E-mail:* info@nyttf.dk *Web Site:* www.bog. ing.dk; www.nyttf.dk, pg 1144

Ingenjoersforlaget AB (Sweden) *Tel:* (08) 796 66 90 *Fax:* (08) 22 77 44 *E-mail:* redaktionen@ miljorapporten.se, pg 607

Inkilap Publishers Ltd (Turkey) *Tel:* (0212) 5140611; (0212) 5140610 *Fax:* (0212) 5140612 *E-mail:* info@ inkilap.com *Web Site:* www.inkilap.com, pg 646

Inland Publishers (United Republic of Tanzania) *Tel:* (068) 40064, pg 639

Inner Mongolia Science & Technology Publishing House (China) *Tel:* (0476) 82222 942, pg 105

Inno Vatio Verlags AG (Germany) *Tel:* (0228) 93-444-33 *Fax:* (0228) 93-444-93 *E-mail:* medien-tenor@ innovatio.de *Web Site:* www.innovatio.de; www. medien-tenor.de, pg 240

Editrice Innocenti SNC (Italy) *Tel:* (0461) 236521 *Fax:* (0461) 230115, pg 390

Innodata Isogen Inc (United States) *Tel:* 201-488-1200 *Toll Free Tel:* 800-567-4784 *Fax:* 201-488-9099 *E-mail:* solutions@innodata-isogen.com *Web Site:* www.innodata-isogen.com, pg 1177

Brian Inns Booksales & Services (United Kingdom) *Tel:* (01926) 498428 *Fax:* (01926) 498428, pg 1343

Universitaetsbibliothek Innsbruck (Austria) *Tel:* (0512) 507 2401 *Fax:* (0512) 507 2893 *E-mail:* ub-hb@uibk. ac.at *Web Site:* ub.uibk.ac.at, pg 1489

Innverlag + Gatt (Austria) *Tel:* (0512) 34 53 31 *Fax:* (0512) 34 12 90 *E-mail:* innverlag@tirol.com; info@innverlag.at *Web Site:* www.innverlag.at, pg 52

Innverlag + Gatt (Austria) *Tel:* (0512) 34 53 31 *Fax:* (0512) 34 12 90 *E-mail:* info@innverlag.at *Web Site:* www.innverlag.at, pg 1290

Inprint Caribbean Ltd (Trinidad & Tobago) *Tel:* (868) 6271569; (868) 6231711 *Fax:* (868) 6271451, pg 642

Editorial Inquerito Lda (Portugal) *Tel:* (021) 9211 460 *Fax:* (021) 9217 940 *E-mail:* publicidade@iol.pt, pg 527

INRA Editions (Institut National de la Recherche Agronomique) (France) *Tel:* (01) 30 83 34 06 *Fax:* (01) 30 83 34 49 *E-mail:* inra-editions@ versailles.inra.fr *Web Site:* www.inra.fr/editions, pg 168

Insel Verlag (Germany) *Tel:* (069) 75601-0 *Fax:* (069) 75601-522 *Web Site:* www.suhrkamp.de, pg 240

Editions INSERM (France) *Tel:* (01) 44 23 60 82 *Fax:* (01) 44 23 60 69 *Web Site:* www.inserm.fr, pg 169

Insituto Centroamericano de Administracion de Empresas (INCAE) (Costa Rica) *Tel:* 433-9908; 433-9961; 437-2305 *Fax:* 433-9989; 433-9983 *E-mail:* incaecr@mail. incae.ac.cr *Web Site:* www.incae.ac.cr, pg 115

Inspirace (Czech Republic) *Tel:* (02) 7356615, pg 123

Editions l'Instant Durable (France) *Tel:* (04) 73 91 13 87 *Fax:* (04) 73 91 13 87 *E-mail:* art@instantdurable.com *Web Site:* www.instantdurable.com, pg 169

Instauratio Press (Australia) *Tel:* (03) 59666217 *Fax:* (03) 59666447 *E-mail:* catholic@scservnet.com, pg 27

Institucion Fernando el Catolico de la Excma Diputacion de Zaragoza (Spain) *Tel:* (0976) 28 88 78; (0976) 28 88 79 *Fax:* (0976) 28 88 69 *E-mail:* info@ifc.dpz.es *Web Site:* www.dpz.es, pg 582

Editorial Institucional y Desarrollo Humanistico SA de CV Edicion de Libros (Mexico) *Tel:* (05) 5215060; (05) 5215009, pg 463

Institut Africain de Developpement Economique et de Planification (IDEP), Bibliotheque (Senegal) *Tel:* 823 10 20 *Fax:* 822 29 64 *E-mail:* idep@sonatel.senet.net, pg 1540

Institution of Electrical Engineers (United Kingdom)
*Tel:* (01438) 313311 *Fax:* (01438) 742792
*E-mail:* postmaster@iee.org.uk *Web Site:* www.iee.
org.uk/publish, pg 708

Instituto Autonomo, Biblioteca Nacional y de Servicios
de Bibliotecas (Venezuela) *Tel:* (0212) 5059141
*Fax:* (0212) 5059159 *Web Site:* www.bnv.bib.ve,
pg 1554

Instituto Caro y Cuervo (Colombia) *Tel:* (01)
3456004 *Fax:* (01) 2170243; (01) 3422121
*E-mail:* direcciongeneral@caroycuervo.gov.co
*Web Site:* www.caroycuervo.gov.co, pg 111

Instituto Caro y Cuervo (Colombia) *Tel:* (01) 3456004
*Fax:* (01) 2170243 *E-mail:* secretariagenera@
caroycuervo.gov.co *Web Site:* www.caroycuervo.gov.
co, pg 1392

Instituto Centroamericano de Administracion de
Empresas (INCAE) Library (Nicaragua) *Tel:* (02) 65
8141; (02) 65 8149; (02) 65 8272 *Fax:* (02) 65 8617;
(02) 65 8630 *E-mail:* biblioteca@mail.incae.edu.ni;
incaeni@mail.incae.edu.ni *Web Site:* www.incae.ac.
cr/biblioteca, pg 1531

Instituto Colombiano de Cultura Hispanica (Colombia)
*Tel:* (01) 3413857 *Fax:* (01) 2811051, pg 1392

Instituto de Bibliografia del Ministerio de Educacion de
la Provincia de Buenos Aires (Argentina) *Tel:* (021)
35915, pg 1557

Instituto de Estudios Economicos (Spain) *Tel:* (091) 782
05 80 *Fax:* (091) 562 36 13 *E-mail:* iee@ieemadrid.
com *Web Site:* www.ieemadrid.com, pg 583

Instituto de Informacion Cientifica y Tecnologica
(IDICT) (Cuba) *Tel:* (07) 862-6531; (07) 860-
3411 *Fax:* (07) 862-6531 *E-mail:* andresdt@idict.
cu; commercial@idict.cu *Web Site:* www.idict.cu/,
pg 1498

Instituto de Investigaciones Bibliograficas (Mexico)
*Tel:* (055) 5622-6827 *Fax:* (055) 5665-0951
*Web Site:* biblional.bibliog.unam.mx, pg 1568

Instituto de Investigaciones Electricas (Mexico)
*Tel:* (777) 3623811 *Fax:* (777) 3189854
*E-mail:* difusion@iie.org.mx *Web Site:* www.iie.org.
mx, pg 1527

Instituto de Literatura y Lingueistica (Cuba) *Tel:* (07)
786486; (07) 701310 *Fax:* (07) 335718 *E-mail:* acc@
ceniai.cu, pg 1498

Instituto dos Arquivos Nacionais/Torre do Tombo
(Portugal) *Tel:* (01) 7811500 *Fax:* (01) 7937230
*E-mail:* dc@iantt.pt, pg 1537

Instituto Interamericano de Cooperacion para la
Agricultura (IICA) (Costa Rica) *Tel:* (0506) 2160222
*Fax:* (0506) 2160233 *E-mail:* iicahq@iica.ac.cr
*Web Site:* www.iica.int, pg 1254

Instituto Nacional de Administracion Publica (Spain)
*Tel:* (091) 3493115; (091) 3493241 *Fax:* (091)
3493287 *E-mail:* cati.fuente@inap.map.es
*Web Site:* www.inap.map.es, pg 583

Instituto Nacional del Educacion Fisica Madrid (INEF-
Madrid) (Spain) *Tel:* (091) 336 4000 *Fax:* (091) 336
4032 *E-mail:* info@inef.upm.es *Web Site:* www.inef.
upm.es, pg 583

Instituto Nacional de Estadistica (Spain) *Tel:* (091) 583
91 00 *Fax:* (091) 583 91 58 *E-mail:* info@ine.es
*Web Site:* www.ine.es, pg 583

Instituto Nacional de la Salud (Spain) *Tel:* (0901)
400-100 *Fax:* (091) 5964480 *E-mail:* oiac@msc.es
*Web Site:* www.msc.es, pg 583

Biblioteca del Instituto Panamericano de Geografia
e Historia (Mexico) *Tel:* (055) 5277 5888; (055)
5277 5791; (055) 5515 1910 *Fax:* (055) 5271 6172
*E-mail:* info@ipgh.org.mx *Web Site:* www.ipgh.org.
mx, pg 1527

Instituto Portugues da Sociedade Cientifica de Goerres
(Portugal) *Tel:* (021) 7265554 *Fax:* (021) 7260546
*E-mail:* mrato@reitoria.ucp.pt, pg 1398

Instituto Tecnologico y de Estdios Superiores de
Monterrey Biblioteca (Mexico) *Tel:* (081) 8328-4096
*Fax:* (081) 8328-4067 *Web Site:* cib.mty.itesm.mx;
biblioteca.itesm.mx, pg 1527

Instituto Vasco de Criminologia (Spain) *Tel:* (0943)
321411; (0943) 321412 *Fax:* (0943) 321272
*Web Site:* www.sc.ehu.es, pg 583

Editura Institutul European (Romania) *Tel:* (032)
230197; (032) 233731; (032) 233800 *Fax:* (032) 230-
197 *E-mail:* rtvnova@mail.cccis.ro; euroedit@mail.
dntis.ro, pg 535

Institutul National de Informare si Documentare (INID)
(Romania) *Tel:* (01) 315 87 65 *Fax:* (01) 312 67 34
*E-mail:* inid@home.ro *Web Site:* www.inid.ro, pg 1538

Instytut Badan Literackich PAN (Poland) *Tel:* (022)
8269945; (022) 6572895 *Fax:* (022) 8269945
*E-mail:* ibadlit@ibl.waw.pl *Web Site:* www.ibl.waw.pl,
pg 1398

Instytut Bibliograficzny (Poland) *Tel:* (022) 452-2999
*Fax:* (022) 825-5251 *E-mail:* biblnar@bn.org.pl
*Web Site:* www.bn.org.pl, pg 1536

Instytut Meteorologii i Gospodarki Wodnej (Poland)
*Tel:* (022) 56-94-100 *Fax:* (022) 834-54-66
*E-mail:* sekretariat@imgw.pl *Web Site:* www.imgw.pl,
pg 518

Instytut Wydawniczy Pax, Inco-Veritas (Poland)
*Tel:* (022) 625 23 01 *Fax:* (022) 625 68 86
*E-mail:* iwpax@com.pl *Web Site:* www.iwpax.com.pl,
pg 518

INT Press (Australia) *Tel:* (03) 9326 2416 *Fax:* (03)
9326 2413 *E-mail:* sales@intpress.com.au
*Web Site:* www.intpress.com.au, pg 27

Integrated Book Technology Inc (United States)
*Tel:* 518-271-5117 *Fax:* 518-266-9422 *E-mail:* mail@
integratedbook.com *Web Site:* www.integratedbook.
com, pg 1156, 1178, 1219, 1230

Integrated Book Technology Inc (United States)
*Tel:* 518-271-5117 *Fax:* 518-266-9422 *Web Site:* www.
integratedbook.com, pg 1239

Intellect Ltd (United Kingdom) *Tel:* (0117) 9589910
*Fax:* (0117) 9589911 *E-mail:* mail@intellectbooks.
com *Web Site:* www.intellectbooks.com, pg 709

Intellectual Publishing Co (Singapore) *Tel:* 7466025
*Fax:* 7489108, pg 552

Intellectual Publishing House (India) *Tel:* (011) 3275860,
pg 335

Inter American University of Puerto Rico Library
(Puerto Rico) *Tel:* (787) 878-5475 (ext 320)
*Fax:* (787) 880-1624 *E-mail:* sabreu@uiprl.inter.edu,
pg 1537

Inter-Cultural Book Promoters (Sri Lanka) *Tel:* 525359
*Fax:* 525359 *E-mail:* inculture@eureka.lk, pg 601

Inter-India Publications (India) *Tel:* (011) 5441120; (011)
5467082, pg 335

Inter-Medica (Argentina) *Tel:* (011) 4961-9234
*Fax:* (011) 4961-5572 *E-mail:* info@inter-medica.com.
ar *Web Site:* www.inter-medica.com.ar, pg 6

Inter-Parliamentary Union (Switzerland) *Tel:* (022) 919
41 50 *Fax:* (022) 919 41 60 *E-mail:* postbox@mail.
ipu.org *Web Site:* www.ipu.org, pg 1275

Inter-Varsity Press (United Kingdom) *Tel:* (0115) 978
1054 *Fax:* (0115) 942 2694 *E-mail:* sales@ivpbooks.
com *Web Site:* www.ivpbooks.com, pg 709

Libreria Interacademica SA de CV (Mexico) *Tel:* (05)
265-1165 *Fax:* (05) 265-1164, pg 1318

Instituto Interamericano de Cooperacion para la
Agricultura (IICA) (Costa Rica) *Tel:* (0506) 216-
0222 *Fax:* (0506) 216-0233 *E-mail:* iicahq@iica.ac.cr
*Web Site:* www.iica.int, pg 115

Interbook-Business AO (Russian Federation) *Tel:* (095)
2006462; (095) 956-37-52 *Fax:* (095) 956-37-52
*E-mail:* interbook@msk.tsi.ru, pg 540

Intercept Ltd (United Kingdom) *Tel:* (01264) 334748
*Fax:* (01264) 334058 *E-mail:* intercept@andover.co.uk
*Web Site:* www.intercept.co.uk, pg 709

Editora Interciencia Ltda (Brazil) *Tel:* (021) 25819378
*Fax:* (021) 25014760, pg 84

Interconnections Reisen und Arbeiten Georg Beckmann
(Germany) *Tel:* (0761) 700650 *Fax:* (0761) 700688,
pg 240

Intercontinental Editora (Paraguay) *Tel:* (021) 496991;
(021) 449738 *Fax:* (021) 448721 *Web Site:* www.
libreriaintercontinental.com.py, pg 511

Intercontinental Literary Agency (United Kingdom)
*Tel:* (020) 7379 6611 *Fax:* (020) 7379 6790
*E-mail:* ila@ila-agency.co.uk, pg 1131

Intercultural Networking Ltd (ICN) (United Kingdom)
*Tel:* (020) 7628 5876 *Fax:* (020) 7628 9147
*E-mail:* icn@dircon.co.uk *Web Site:* www.users.dircon.
co.uk/~icn/, pg 1141

Interculture (Sweden) *Tel:* (08) 642 78 04 *Fax:* (08) 642
35 91, pg 607

Interdigest Publishing House (Belarus) *Tel:* (017)
2133073 *Fax:* (017) 843778, pg 61

InterEditions (France) *Tel:* (01) 40 46 35 00 *Fax:* (01) 40
46 49 95 *Web Site:* www.intereditions.com, pg 169

Les Editions Interferences (France) *Tel:* (01) 45 67 33
56 *E-mail:* interferences@editions-interferences.com
*Web Site:* www.editions-interferences.com, pg 169

Interfisc Publishing (United Kingdom) *Tel:* (020) 8789
4957 *Fax:* (0845) 330 7249 *E-mail:* aogley@interfisc.
com *Web Site:* www.interfisc.com, pg 709

Interfrom AG Editions (Switzerland) *Tel:* (01) 3065200
*Fax:* (01) 3065205, pg 620

Interlivros Edicoes Ltda (Brazil) *Tel:* (021) 3913134
*Fax:* (021) 3521005 *E-mail:* interlivros@ibm.net,
pg 84

Intermedia Audio, Video Book Publishing Ltd (Israel)
*Tel:* (03) 5608501 *Fax:* (03) 5608513 *E-mail:* freed@
inter.net.il, pg 364

Libreria Internacional Estudio (Chile) *Tel:* (041) 225 533
*Fax:* (041) 244 542, pg 1295

Ediciones Internacionales Universitarias SA
(Spain) *Tel:* (091) 5193907 *Fax:* (091) 4136808
*E-mail:* eiunsa@ibernet.com *Web Site:* www.eunsa.es,
pg 583

Internationaal Instituut voor Sociale Geschiedenis
(Netherlands) *Tel:* (020) 6685866; (020) 6928810
*Fax:* (020) 6654181; (020) 6630349; (020)
4680505 *E-mail:* info@iisg.nl; user.service@iisg.nl
*Web Site:* www.iisg.nl, pg 1529

International Bookshops (Saudi Arabia) *Tel:* (03)
4641851 *Fax:* (03) 4641851, pg 1329

International African Institute (United Kingdom)
*Tel:* (020) 7898 4420 (general); (020) 7898 4435
(publications) *Fax:* (020) 7898 4419 *E-mail:* iai@
soas.ac.uk (general); ed2@soas.ac.uk (publications)
*Web Site:* www.iaionthe.net, pg 1282

International Association for Mass Communication
Research (Denmark) *Tel:* (045) 9635 8080
*Fax:* (045) 9815 6864 *E-mail:* prehn@hum.auc.dk
*Web Site:* www.auc.dk/fak-hum, pg 1256

International Association for the Evaluation of
Educational Achievement (IEA) (Netherlands)
*Tel:* (020) 6253625 *Fax:* (020) 4207136
*E-mail:* department@iea.nl *Web Site:* www.iea.nl,
pg 1269

International Association of Agricultural Information
Specialists (United Kingdom) *Tel:* (01865) 340054
*Web Site:* www.iaald.org, pg 1282

International Association of Law Libraries (IALL)
(United States) *Tel:* 804-924-3384 *Fax:* 804-982-2232
*E-mail:* lbw@virginia.edu *Web Site:* www.iall.org,
pg 1284

International Association of Literary Critics (France)
*Tel:* (01) 40513300 *Fax:* (01) 43549299 *E-mail:* aicl.
org@tiscalinet.it *Web Site:* www.aicl.org, pg 1258

International Association of Music Libraries, New
Zealand Branch, Inc (New Zealand) *Tel:* (03) 941
7923 *Fax:* (03) 941 7848 *E-mail:* library@ccc.govt.nz
*Web Site:* library.christchurch.org.nz, pg 1568

International Association of Music Libraries,
Archives & Documentation Centres (IAML) (New
Zealand) *Tel:* (04) 474 3039 *Fax:* 613-520-2750
*Web Site:* www.iaml.info, pg 1270

International Association of Music Libraries, Archives &
Documentation Centres (New Zealand) *Tel:* (04) 474
3039 *Fax:* (04) 474 3035 *Web Site:* www.iaml.info,
pg 1568

International Association of Music Libraries, Archives
& Documentation Centres (UK & Ireland Branch)
(United Kingdom) *Tel:* (0131) 242 8053 *Fax:* (0131)
242 8009 *Web Site:* www.iaml-uk-irl.org, pg 1573

International Association of Orientalist Librarians
(Russian Federation) *Tel:* (095) 2028852 *Fax:* (095)
2029187 *E-mail:* oricen@mail.ru, pg 1272

International Association of Scholarly Publishers (IASP)
(United States) *Tel:* 517-355-9543 *Fax:* 517-432-2611
*E-mail:* bohm@pilot.msu.edu, pg 1284

International Association of School Librarianship
(Australia) *Fax:* (03) 9428 7612 *E-mail:* iasl@
rockland.com *Web Site:* www.iasl-slo.org, pg 1250

International Association of Scientific, Technical &
Medical Publishers (STM) (Netherlands) *Tel:* (070)
314 09 30 *Fax:* (070) 314 09 40 *E-mail:* info@stm-
assoc.org *Web Site:* www.stm-assoc.org, pg 1269

International Association of Sound & Audiovisual
Archives (Germany) *Tel:* (07221) 9293487
*Fax:* (07221) 9294199 *Web Site:* www.llgc.org.
uk/iasa/, pg 1260

International Association of Technological University
Libraries (IATUL) (United Kingdom) *Tel:* (0131) 449
5111 *Fax:* (0131) 451 3164 *E-mail:* iatul@qut.edu.au
*Web Site:* www.iatul.org, pg 1282

International Association of Universities (France)
*Tel:* (01) 45 68 48 00 *Fax:* (01) 47 34 76 05
*E-mail:* iau@unesco.org *Web Site:* www.unesco.
org/iau, pg 1258

International Atomic Energy Agency (IAEA)
(Austria) *Tel:* (0222) 2600-0 *Fax:* (0222) 2600-
7 *E-mail:* official.mail@iaea.org; info@iaea.org
*Web Site:* www.iaea.org, pg 1251

International Bee Research Association (United
Kingdom) *Tel:* (02920) 372409 *Fax:* (02920) 665522
*E-mail:* mail@cardiff.org.uk *Web Site:* www.cf.ac.
uk/ibra, pg 709

International Bible Society (Sweden) *Tel:* (0513) 219 30
*Fax:* (0513) 215 01, pg 607

International Board on Books for Young People (IBBY)
(Switzerland) *Tel:* (061) 272 29 17 *Fax:* (061) 272 27
57 *E-mail:* ibby@ibby.org *Web Site:* www.ibby.org,
pg 1152, 1275

International Book Centre (Portugal) *Tel:* (021) 942 53
94 *Fax:* (021) 941 98 93, pg 1328

International Book Development (IBD) (United
Kingdom) *Tel:* (0118) 902 1000 *Fax:* (0118) 902 1434
*E-mail:* enquiries@cfbt.com *Web Site:* www.cfbt.com,
pg 1282

International Book Distributors (India) *Tel:* (0135)
2656526; (0135) 2657497; (0135) 2650949
*Fax:* (0135) 2656554 *E-mail:* ibdbooks@sancharnet.in
*Web Site:* ibdbooks.com, pg 335

International Book House Pvt Ltd (India) *Tel:* (022)
22021634; (022) 22020765 *Fax:* (022) 22851109
*E-mail:* ibh@vsnl.com; 1ibh@vsnl.in *Web Site:* www.
intbh.com, pg 1306

International Booksellers Federation (IBF) (Belgium)
*Tel:* (02) 223 49 40 *Fax:* (02) 223 49 38 *E-mail:* ibf.
booksellers@skynet.be *Web Site:* www.ibf-booksellers.
org, pg 1252

International Catholic Organization for Cinema
& Audiovisual (OCIC) (Belgium) *Tel:* (02)
7344294 *Fax:* (02) 7343207 *E-mail:* sg@ocic.org
*Web Site:* www.ocic.org, pg 1252

International Centre for Ethnic Studies (Sri Lanka)
*Tel:* (08) 234892 *Fax:* (08) 234892 *E-mail:* ices@slt.lk
*Web Site:* www.icescolombo.org, pg 601

International Centre for Research in Agroforestry
(ICRAF) (Kenya) *Tel:* (02) 524000 *Fax:* (02)
524001 *E-mail:* icraf@cgiar.org *Web Site:* www.
worldagroforestrycentre.org, pg 431

International Centre Study Preservation & Restoration of
Cultural Property (ICCROM) (Italy) *Tel:* (06) 585531
*Fax:* (06) 58553349 *E-mail:* iccrom@iccrom.org
*Web Site:* www.iccrom.org, pg 1264

International Chamber of Commerce (France) *Tel:* (01)
49 53 28 28 *Fax:* (01) 49 53 28 59 *E-mail:* icclib@
ibnet.com; icc@iccwbo.org *Web Site:* www.iccwbo.
org, pg 1258

International Commission of Jurists (Switzerland)
*Tel:* (022) 979 38 00 *Fax:* (022) 979 38 01
*E-mail:* info@icj.org *Web Site:* www.icj.org, pg 1276

International Communications (United Kingdom)
*Tel:* (020) 7713 7711 *Fax:* (020) 7713 7898;
(020) 7713 7970 *E-mail:* icpubs@africasia.com
*Web Site:* www.africasia.com, pg 709

International Community of Writers' Unions (Russian
Federation) *Tel:* (095) 2916307 *Fax:* (095) 2919760,
pg 1273

International Comparative Literature Association
(United States) *Tel:* 416-487-6727 *Fax:* 416-487-6786
*E-mail:* icla@byu.edu *Web Site:* www.byu.edu/~icla,
pg 1284

International Council on Archives (France) *Tel:* (01)
40 27 63 49; (01) 40 27 63 06; (01) 40 27 61
34 *Fax:* (01) 42 72 20 65 *E-mail:* ica@ica.org
*Web Site:* www.ica.org, pg 1258

International Crops Research Institute for the Semi-
Arid Tropics (ICRISAT) (India) *Tel:* (040) 3296161
*Fax:* (040) 3241239; (040) 3296182 *E-mail:* icrisat@
cgnet.com *Web Site:* www.icrisat.org, pg 1263

International Culture Publishing Corp (China) *Tel:* (010)
64013415 *Fax:* (010) 64013437, pg 105

Institut International de la Marionnette (France) *Tel:* (03)
24 33 72 50 *Fax:* (03) 24 33 72 69 *E-mail:* institut@
marionnette.com *Web Site:* www.marionnette.com,
pg 169

The International Documentary Centre of Arab
Manuscripts (Lebanon), pg 443

International Documentation Center, The University
of Tokyo (Japan) *Tel:* (03) 5841-2645 *Fax:* (03)
5841-2611 *E-mail:* kokusai@lib.u-tokyo.ac.jp
*Web Site:* www.lib.u-tokyo.ac.jp/undepo, pg 1520

International Ediemme (Italy) *Tel:* (06) 39378788
*Fax:* (06) 6380839 *E-mail:* iscd@colosseum.it, pg 390

International Editors' Co (Argentina) *Tel:* (011) 4786-
0888 *Fax:* (011) 4786-0888 *E-mail:* escritores@lvd.
com.ar, pg 1119

International Editors' Co SL (Spain) *Tel:* (093) 2158812
*Fax:* (093) 4873583 *E-mail:* ieco@internationaleditors.
com, pg 1126

International Educational Services (Pakistan) *Tel:* (021)
732-6602 *Fax:* (021) 813-1919, pg 508

International Federation for Information Processing
(IFIP) (Austria) *Tel:* (02236) 73616 *Fax:* (02236)
736169 *E-mail:* ifip@ifip.or.at *Web Site:* www.ifip.
or.at, pg 1251

International Federation of Library Associations
& Institutions (IFLA) (Netherlands) *Tel:* (070)
3140884 *Fax:* (070) 3834827 *E-mail:* ifla@ifla.org
*Web Site:* www.ifla.org, pg 1269, 1568

International Federation of Reproduction Rights
Organisations (IFRRO) (Belgium) *Tel:* (02) 551 08
99 *Fax:* (02) 551 08 95 *E-mail:* iffro@skynet.be;
secretariat@ifrro.be *Web Site:* www.ifrro.org, pg 1252

International Fiction Review (Canada) *Tel:* 506-
453-4636 *Fax:* 506-447-3166 *E-mail:* ifr@unb.ca
*Web Site:* www.lib.unb.ca/Texts/IFR, pg 1254

International Institute for Applied Systems Analysis
(IIASA) (Austria) *Tel:* (02236) 807 433 *Fax:* (02236)
71313 *E-mail:* info@iiasa.ac.at; publications@iiasa.ac.
at *Web Site:* www.iiasa.ac.at, pg 52

International Institute for Children's Literature &
Reading Research (UNESCO category C) (Austria)
*Tel:* (01) 505 03 59; (01) 505 28 31 *Fax:* (01)
505 03 59-17; (01) 505 28 31-17 *E-mail:* office@
jugendliteratur.net *Web Site:* www.jugendliteratur.net,
pg 1251

International Institute for Educational Planning (IIEP)
(France) *Tel:* (01) 45 03 77 00 *Fax:* (01) 40 72 83 66
*E-mail:* information@iiep.unesco.org *Web Site:* www.
unesco.org/iiep, pg 1258

International Institute for Labour Studies (Switzerland)
*Tel:* (022) 799 6111 *Fax:* (022) 798 8685
*E-mail:* ilo@ilo.org *Web Site:* www.ilo.org, pg 1276

International Institute for Strategic Studies (United
Kingdom) *Tel:* (020) 7379 7676 *Fax:* (020) 7836 3108
*E-mail:* iiss@iiss.org *Web Site:* www.iiss.org, pg 709

International Institute for Iberoamerican Literature
(United States) *Tel:* 412-624-5246; 412-624-
6100 *Fax:* 412-624-0829 *E-mail:* iili+@pitt.edu
*Web Site:* www.pitt.edu, pg 1284

International Institute of Islamic Thought (Pakistan)
*Tel:* (051) 229-3734 *Fax:* (051) 228-0489
*E-mail:* ziansari@iiitpak.sdnpk.undp.org
*Web Site:* www.iiit.org, pg 508

International Institute of Tropical Agriculture (IITA)
Library (Nigeria) *Tel:* (02) 241 2626 *Fax:* (02) 241
2221 *E-mail:* iita@cgiar.org *Web Site:* www.iita.
org/info/libsrv.htm, pg 1532

International ISBN Agency, International ISMN Agency
(Germany) *Tel:* (030) 266-2498; (030) 266-2496; (030)
266-2336 *Fax:* (030) 266-2378 *E-mail:* isbn@sbb.spk-
berlin.de; ismn@sbb.spk.berlin.de *Web Site:* isbn-
international.org; ismn-international.org, pg 1260

International ISMN Agency (Germany) *Tel:* (030)
266-2496; (030) 266-2498; (030) 266 2338
*Fax:* (030) 266-2378 *E-mail:* ismn@sbb.spk-berlin.de
*Web Site:* ismn-international.org, pg 1260

International Labour Office (United Kingdom) *Tel:* (020)
7828 6401 *Fax:* (020) 7233 5925 *E-mail:* ipu@
ilo-london.org.uk; london@ilo-london.org.uk
*Web Site:* www.ilo.org/london, pg 709

International Labour Office, Bureau of Library &
Information Services (Switzerland) *Tel:* (022) 799
8675 *Fax:* (022) 799 6516 *E-mail:* inform@ilo.org
*Web Site:* www.ilo.org/inform, pg 1546

International Labour Organization (ILO) (Switzerland)
*Tel:* (022) 799 6111 *Fax:* (022) 798 8685
*E-mail:* ilo@ilo.org *Web Site:* www.ilo.org, pg 1276

International Language & Translation School (United
Kingdom) *Tel:* (020) 8882 3362 *Fax:* (020) 8882
3362, pg 1141

International Law Book Services (Malaysia) *Tel:* (03)
7727 4121; (03) 7727 4122; (03) 7727 3890; (03)
7728-3890 *Fax:* (03) 7727 3884 *E-mail:* gbc@pc.
jaring.my *Web Site:* www.malaysialawbooks.com,
pg 453

International League of Antiquarian Booksellers (ILAB)
(United States) *Tel:* 800-441-0076; 612-290-0700
*Fax:* 612-290-0646 *E-mail:* info@ilab-lila.com
*Web Site:* www.ilab.org, pg 1284

International Literatuur Bureau BV (Netherlands)
*Tel:* (035) 6213500 *Fax:* (035) 6215771 *E-mail:* info@
ilb.nu *Web Site:* www.ilb.nu, pg 1125

International Livestock Research Institute (Kenya)
*Tel:* (020) 630 743 *Fax:* (020) 631 499 *E-mail:* ilri-
kenya@cgiar.org *Web Site:* www.cgiar.org/ilri, pg 1265

International Map Trade Association (United
Kingdom) *Tel:* 01425) 620532 *Fax:* (01425) 620532
*Web Site:* www.maptrade.org, pg 709

International Maritime Organization (IMO) (United Kingdom) *Tel:* (020) 7735 7611 *Fax:* (020) 7587 3210 *E-mail:* publications-sales@imo.org *Web Site:* www. imo.org, pg 1282

The International Molinological Society (United Kingdom) *Tel:* (070) 3460885 *Web Site:* tims.geo. tudelft.nl, pg 1282

International Monetary Fund (United States) *Tel:* 202-623-7000; 202-623-7430 *Fax:* 202-623-4661; 202-623-7201 *E-mail:* publicaffairs@imf.org *Web Site:* www. imf.org, pg 1284

International Organization for Standardization (ISO) (Switzerland) *Tel:* (022) 749 01 11 *Fax:* (022) 733 34 30 *E-mail:* central@iso.org *Web Site:* www.iso.org, pg 1276

International PEN (United Kingdom) *Tel:* (020) 7253 4308 *Fax:* (020) 7253 5711 *E-mail:* info@ internationalpen.org.uk *Web Site:* www. internationalpen.org.uk, pg 1282

The International Press Agency (Pty) Ltd (South Africa) *Tel:* (021) 5311926; (021) 5318197 *Fax:* (021) 5318789 *E-mail:* inpra@iafrica.com *Web Site:* www. inpra.co.za, pg 1126

International Press Softcom Ltd (Singapore) *Tel:* 2983800; 2952437 *Fax:* 2971668, pg 1151, 1212

International Press Softcom Ltd (Singapore) *Tel:* 2983800 *Fax:* 2971668, pg 1228

International Publications Agency (IPA) (Saudi Arabia) *Tel:* (03) 8954925, pg 546

International Publications Service Inc (IPS) (Republic of Korea) *Tel:* (02) 2115-8800 *Fax:* (02) 2273-8048 *Web Site:* www.ipsbook.com, pg 1315

International Publishers Association (Switzerland) *Tel:* (022) 346 3018 *Fax:* (022) 347 5717 *E-mail:* secretariat@ipa-uie.org; info@ipa-uie.org *Web Site:* www.ipa-uie.org, pg 1276

International Publishers Distributor (S) Pte Ltd (Singapore) *Tel:* 741 6933 *Fax:* 741 6922 *E-mail:* ipdmktg@sg.gbhap.com, pg 552

International Publishing & Research Company (Nigeria) *Tel:* (080) 2317-5915 *Fax:* (080) 4213 2351, pg 501

International Reading Association (United States) *Tel:* 302-731-1600 *Toll Free Tel:* 800-336-7323 *Fax:* 302-731-1057 *E-mail:* pubinfo@reading.org *Web Site:* www.reading.org, pg 1284

International Rice Research Institute (IRRI) (Philippines) *Tel:* (02) 845-0563; (02) 845-0569 *Fax:* (02) 845-0606 *E-mail:* irri@cgiar.org *Web Site:* www.irri.org, pg 514

International Road Federation (Switzerland) *Tel:* (022) 306 0260 *Fax:* (022) 306 0270 *E-mail:* info@irfnet. org *Web Site:* www.irfnet.org, pg 1276

International Scripts Ltd (United Kingdom) *Tel:* (020) 8319 8666 *Fax:* (020) 8319 0801, pg 1131

International Society for Educational Information (ISEI) (Japan) *Tel:* (03) 33581138 *Fax:* (03) 33597188 *E-mail:* kaya@isei.or.jp *Web Site:* www.isei.or.jp, pg 416

International Standard Book Numbering Agency (South Africa) *Tel:* (012) 401 9718 *Fax:* (012) 324 2441 *E-mail:* isn@nlsa.ac.za *Web Site:* www.nlsa.ac.za, pg 1274

International Standards Books & Periodicals (P) Ltd (Nepal) *Tel:* (01) 212289; (01) 224005; (01) 223036 *Fax:* (01) 223036, pg 473

International Telecommunication Union (ITU) (Switzerland) *Tel:* (022) 730 5111 *Fax:* (022) 733 7256 *E-mail:* itumail@itu.int *Web Site:* www.itu. int/home/contact/index.html, pg 1276

Uitgevery International Theatre & Film Books (Netherlands) *Tel:* (020) 60 60 911 *Fax:* (020) 60 60 914 *E-mail:* info@itfb.nl *Web Site:* www.itfb.nl, pg 480

International Thomson Publishing (ITP) (Germany) *Tel:* (0228) 970240 *Fax:* (0228) 441342 *E-mail:* info@ vmi-buch.de *Web Site:* www.mitp.de, pg 240

International Translations Ltd (United Kingdom) *Tel:* (0161) 834 7431 *Fax:* (0161) 832 4717 *E-mail:* admin@ititranslations.co.uk; inttrans@ compuserve.com, pg 1141

International Union Against Cancer (Switzerland) *Tel:* (022) 809 18 11 *Fax:* (022) 809 18 10 *E-mail:* info@uicc.org *Web Site:* www.uicc.org, pg 1276

International Union of Geological Sciences (IUGS) (Austria) *Tel:* (01) 712 56 74 (ext 180) *Fax:* (01) 712 56 74 56 *Web Site:* www.iugs.org, pg 1251

International University Press Srl (Italy) *Tel:* (06) 8380067 *Fax:* (06) 8380064, pg 390

The International Water Management Institute (Sri Lanka) *Tel:* (011) 2787404; (011) 2784080 *Fax:* (011) 2786854 *E-mail:* iwmi@cgiar.org *Web Site:* www. iwmi.cgiar.org, pg 1274

Internationale Jugendbibliothek (Germany) *Tel:* (089) 891211-0 *Fax:* (089) 8117553 *E-mail:* bib@ijb.de *Web Site:* www.ijb.de, pg 1260, 1508

Verlag fuer Internationale Politik GmbH (Germany) *Tel:* (030) 254 231 46 *Fax:* (030) 254 231 16 *E-mail:* ip@dgap.org *Web Site:* www. internationalepolitik.de, pg 240

Edizioni Internazionali di Letteratura e Scienze (Italy) *Tel:* (06) 61905463 *Fax:* (06) 61905463, pg 390

Internos Books (United Kingdom) *Tel:* (020) 7637 4255 *Fax:* (020) 7637 4251, pg 1343

Interpet Publishing (United Kingdom) *Tel:* (01306) 881033 *Fax:* (01306) 885009 *E-mail:* publishing@ interpet.co.uk, pg 709

Interpres (Bulgaria) *Tel:* (02) 517915 *Fax:* (02) 517915 *E-mail:* interpres@bis.bg; intrpres@usa.net, pg 94

Interpress (Poland) *Tel:* (022) 6214876; (022) 6289331; (022) 6289202; (022) 6282818; (022) 6291060; (022) 6282225 *Fax:* (022) 6289331; (022) 6289202; (022) 6226850 *E-mail:* paiwydaw@pol.pl, pg 518

Interpress Aussenhandels GmbH (Hungary) *Tel:* (01) 302-7525; (01) 2508267 *Fax:* (01) 302-7530, pg 1148

Interpress Aussenhandels GmbH (Hungary) *Tel:* (01) 302-7525 *Fax:* (01) 302-7530 *E-mail:* office@ interpress.hu *Web Site:* www.interpress.hu, pg 1210, 1227

Interpresse A/S (Denmark) *Tel:* 39160200 *Fax:* 39272402 *Web Site:* www.interpresse.dk, pg 132

Interprint Ltd - Malta (Malta) *Tel:* (021) 240169; (021) 222720 *Fax:* (021) 243780; (021) 238115 *Web Site:* www.interprintmalta.com, pg 1149, 1211

Intersentia Uitgevers NV (Belgium) *Tel:* (03) 680 15 50 *Fax:* (03) 658 71 21 *E-mail:* mail@intersentia.be *Web Site:* www.intersentia.com, pg 68

Intersistemas SA de CV (Mexico) *Tel:* (055) 1107-1903 *Fax:* (055) 1107-0196 *E-mail:* ventas@medikatalogo. com *Web Site:* www.medikatalogo.com, pg 463

Interskol Forlag AB (Sweden) *Tel:* (040) 51 01 95 *Fax:* (040) 15 06 25 *E-mail:* info@interskol.se *Web Site:* www.interskol.se, pg 607

Uitgeverij Intertaal BV (Netherlands) *Tel:* (036) 5471650 *Fax:* (036) 5471582 *E-mail:* int@intertaal.nl *Web Site:* www.intertaal.nl, pg 480

Intertrade Publications Pvt Ltd (India) *Tel:* (033) 474872; (033) 475069, pg 335

Intertrans-Verlag GmbH (Germany) *Tel:* (069) 871500 *Fax:* (069) 852894, pg 240

Intext Book Company Pty Ltd (Australia) *Tel:* (03) 9819-4500 *Fax:* (03) 9819-4511 *E-mail:* customerservice@ intextbook.com.au *Web Site:* www.intextbook.com.au, pg 27

Editions Intore (Burundi), pg 97

Intype Libra Ltd (United Kingdom) *Tel:* (020) 8947 7863 *Fax:* (020) 8947 3652 *E-mail:* intype@btconnect. com *Web Site:* www.intype.co.uk, pg 1153

Intype Libra Ltd (United Kingdom) *Tel:* (020) 8947 7863 *Fax:* (020) 8947 3652 *E-mail:* intype@btconnect. com, pg 1175, 1216, 1229

Invandrarfoerlaget (Sweden) *Tel:* (033) 13 60 70 *Fax:* (033) 13 60 75 *E-mail:* migrant@immi.se *Web Site:* www.immi.se, pg 607

El Inversionista Mexicano SA de CV (Mexico) *Tel:* (05) 5245396; (05) 5349297 *Fax:* (05) 5243794 *E-mail:* elimmbi@iserve.net.mx, pg 463

Instituto de Investigacao Cientifica Tropical (Portugal) *Tel:* (021) 361 63 40 *Fax:* (021) 363 14 60 *E-mail:* iict@iict.pt *Web Site:* www.iict.pt, pg 527

Inwardpath Publishers (Australia) *Tel:* (03) 9499 3405 *Fax:* (03) 9497 5656, pg 27

IOM Communications Ltd (United Kingdom) *Tel:* (020) 7451 7300 *Fax:* (020) 7839 1702 *E-mail:* admin@ materials.org.uk *Web Site:* www.iom3.org.uk, pg 709

IOS Press BV (Netherlands) *Tel:* (020) 688 33 55 *Fax:* (020) 620 3419 *E-mail:* info@iospress.nl *Web Site:* www.iospress.nl, pg 480

IP Oslobodenje (Bosnia and Herzegovina) *Tel:* (033) 276900; (033) 468054 *E-mail:* info@oslobodjenje. com.ba *Web Site:* www.oslobodjenje.com.ba, pg 75

Iperborea (Italy) *Tel:* (02) 781458 *Fax:* (02) 798919 *E-mail:* iperborea@iol.it, pg 390

IPIS vzw (International Peace Information Service) (Belgium) *Tel:* (03) 225 00 22; (03) 225 21 96 *Fax:* (03) 231 0151 *E-mail:* info@ipisresearch.be *Web Site:* www.ipisresearch.be, pg 68

IPL - Istituto Propaganda Libraria (Italy) *Tel:* (02) 58301960 *Fax:* (02) 58301960, pg 1264

IPL Publishing Group (New Zealand) *Tel:* (04) 477 3032 *Fax:* (04) 477 3035 *E-mail:* transpress@paradise.net.nz *Web Site:* www.transpressnz.com, pg 493

IPS Copyright Agency (International Publications Service) (Republic of Korea) *Tel:* (02) 21158800 *Fax:* (02) 22646936 *E-mail:* copyright@ips-korea.com *Web Site:* www.ipsbook.com, pg 1124

IR Indo Edicions (Spain) *Tel:* (0986) 21 48 34 *Fax:* (0986) 21 11 33 *E-mail:* correo@irindo.com *Web Site:* www.irindo.com; irindo.net, pg 583

Iralka Editorial SL (Spain) *Tel:* (0943) 32 30 14 *Fax:* (0943) 32 30 22 *E-mail:* iralka@euskalnet.net *Web Site:* www.euskalnet.net/iralka, pg 583

Iranian Information Documentation Centre (Islamic Republic of Iran) *Tel:* (021) 6462548 *Fax:* (021) 6462254 *E-mail:* info@irandoc.ac.ir *Web Site:* www. irandoc.ac.ir, pg 1515

Library of the Iraq Museum (Iraq) *Tel:* (01) 8879687, pg 1516

IRD Editions (France) *Tel:* (01) 48 03 76 06 *Fax:* (01) 48 02 79 09 *E-mail:* editions@paris.ird.fr *Web Site:* www.editions.ird.fr, pg 169

IRDES - Institut de Recherche et (France) *Tel:* (01) 53 93 43 00 *Fax:* (01) 53 93 43 50 *E-mail:* contact@ irdes.fr *Web Site:* www.credes.fr; www.irdes.fr, pg 169

Ireland Literature Exchange (Ireland) *Tel:* (01) 678 8961; (01) 662 5687 *Fax:* (01) 662 5687 *E-mail:* info@ irelandliterature.com *Web Site:* www.irelandliterature. com, pg 1138

Irfon (Tajikistan) *Tel:* (03772) 33-39-06; (03772) 33-62-54, pg 638

Irini Publishing House - Vassilis G Katsikeas SA (Greece) *Tel:* 2103839259; 21038 10465 *Fax:* 2103800651; 2103805113 *E-mail:* katsikgr@hol.gr *Web Site:* www. infomedacoop.gr, pg 305

Iris Verlag AG (Switzerland) *Tel:* (031) 7473300 *Fax:* (031) 7473301 *E-mail:* polyinfo@rentsch.com *Web Site:* www.poly-laupen.ch, pg 621

Istanbul Universitesi Merkez Kuetuephanesi (Turkey) *Tel:* (0212) 455 57 83 *Fax:* (0212) 455 57 84 *E-mail:* bilgi@library.istanbul.edu.tr *Web Site:* www. istanbul.edu.tr; www.kutuphane.istanbul.edu.tr, pg 1549

Istituto della Enciclopedia Italiana (Italy) *Tel:* (06) 68981 *Fax:* (06) 68982294 *E-mail:* dir.edit@treccani.it *Web Site:* www.treccani.it, pg 390

Istituto Lombardo Accademia di Scienze e Lettere (Italy) *Tel:* (02) 864087 *Toll Free Tel:* (02) 86461388 *E-mail:* istituto.lombardo@unimi.it *Web Site:* www. istitutolombardo.it, pg 1396

Ediciones Istmo SA (Spain) *Tel:* (091) 8061996 *Fax:* (091) 8044028, pg 583

IT-og Telestyrelsen (Denmark) *Tel:* 35 45 00 00 *Fax:* 35 45 00 10; 33 37 92 99 *E-mail:* itst@itst.dk *Web Site:* www.denmark.dk; www.si.dk, pg 132

Itaca (Italy) *Tel:* (02) 48009484 *Fax:* (02) 48009493 *E-mail:* info@editoriale-itaca.it *Web Site:* www. editoriale-itaca.it, pg 390

Istituto Italiano Edizioni Atlas (Italy) *Tel:* (035) 249711 *Fax:* (035) 216047 *E-mail:* edizioniatlas@edatlas.it *Web Site:* www.edatlas.it, pg 390

Istituto Italiano Per Il Medio Ed Estremo Oriente (ISMEO) (Italy) *Tel:* (06) 732741; (06) 732742; (06) 732743 *E-mail:* iias@let.leidenuniv.nl *Web Site:* www. iias.nl, pg 390

Itaria Shobo Ltd (Japan) *Tel:* (03) 3262-1656 *Fax:* (03) 3234-6469 *E-mail:* HQM01271@nifty.ne.jp, pg 416

Edicoes ITAU (Instituto Tecnico de Alimentacao Humana) Lda (Portugal) *Tel:* (01) 9661603 *Fax:* (01) 9661227, pg 528

ITC (United States) *Tel:* 954-623-3101 *Fax:* 954-623-3122 *E-mail:* team@inttype.com *Web Site:* www. inttype.com, pg 1178

ITD (United Kingdom) *Tel:* (01296) 27211 *Fax:* (01296) 392019, pg 1153

ITDG Publishing (United Kingdom) *Tel:* (01926) 634501 *Fax:* (01926) 634502 *E-mail:* marketing@ itpubs.org.uk; itpubs@itpubs.org.uk *Web Site:* www. itdgpublishing.org.uk; www.developmentbookshop. com, pg 710

Ithemba! Publishing (South Africa) *Tel:* (011) 726 6529 *Fax:* (011) 726 6529 *E-mail:* firechildren@icon.co. za *Web Site:* www.icon.co.za/~firechildren/ithemba/ ithemba.htm, pg 560

ITpress Verlag (Germany) *Tel:* (07251) 300575 *Fax:* (07251) 14823 *E-mail:* itpress@acm.org *Web Site:* www.itpress.com, pg 241

IUCN-The World Conservation Union (United Kingdom) *Tel:* (01223) 277894 *Fax:* (01223) 277175 *E-mail:* info@books.iucn.org *Web Site:* www.iucn.org, pg 710

Iudicium Verlag GmbH (Germany) *Tel:* (089) 718747 *Fax:* (089) 7142039 *E-mail:* info@iudicium.de *Web Site:* www.iudicium.de, pg 241

Iustus Forlag AB (Sweden) *Tel:* (018) 693091 *Fax:* (018) 693099 *E-mail:* iustus@iustus.se *Web Site:* www. iustus.se, pg 607

Iuventus (Czech Republic) *Tel:* (02) 7817314, pg 123

Ivrea (France) *Tel:* (01) 43 26 06 21 *Fax:* (01) 43 26 11 68, pg 169

Ivy Publications (South Africa) *Tel:* (012) 218931 *Fax:* (012) 3255984 *E-mail:* therese@statelib-pww. gov.za, pg 560

IWA Publishing (United Kingdom) *Tel:* (020) 7654 5500 *Fax:* (020) 7654 5555 *E-mail:* publications@iwap.co. uk *Web Site:* www.iwapublishing.com, pg 710

Iwanami Shoten, Publishers (Japan) *Tel:* (03) 5210-4115 *Fax:* (03) 3239-9619 *Web Site:* www.iwanami.co.jp, pg 416

Reisebuchverlag Iwanowski GmbH (Germany) *Tel:* (02133) 26030 *Fax:* (02133) 260333 *E-mail:* info@iwanowski.de *Web Site:* www. iwanowski.de, pg 241

Iwasaki Shoten Publishing Co Ltd (Japan) *Tel:* (03) 3812-9131 *Fax:* (03) 3816-6033 *E-mail:* ask@ iwasakishoten.co.jp *Web Site:* www.iwasakishoten.co. jp, pg 416

Izdatelstvo Ja (Bulgaria) *Tel:* (046) 26166; (046) 20077, pg 94

Izdatelstvo Lettera (Bulgaria) *Tel:* (032) 600 930 *Fax:* (032) 600 940 *E-mail:* lettera@plovdiv.techno-link.com; office@lettera.bg *Web Site:* www.lettera.bg, pg 94

Izdatelstvo Literatury i isskustva (Uzbekistan) *Tel:* (0371) 445172, pg 773

Editorial Iztaccihuatl SA (Mexico) *Tel:* (05) 7050938; (05) 7051063 *Fax:* (05) 5352321, pg 463

Izvestia Sovetov Narodnyh Deputatov Russian Federation (RF) (Russian Federation) *Tel:* (095) 2093738 *Fax:* (095) 2095394, pg 541

J C Palabay Enterprises (Philippines) *Tel:* (02) 9424512 *Fax:* (02) 9424513, pg 514

J Ch Mellinger Verlag GmbH (Germany) *Tel:* (0711) 543787 *Fax:* (0711) 556889 *E-mail:* mellinger@ sambo.de, pg 241

J Film Process Co Ltd (Thailand) *Tel:* (02) 248-6888 *Fax:* (02) 247-4719, pg 1152, 1214, 1237

J K Publications (Sri Lanka) *Tel:* (01) 518954, pg 601

J M Pantelides Booksellers Ltd (Greece) *Tel:* 210363 9560 *Fax:* 2103636453, pg 1303

Verlag J P Peter, Gebr Holstein GmbH & Co KG (Germany) *Tel:* (09861) 4 00-3 81 *Fax:* (09861) 4 00-70 *E-mail:* peter-verlag@rotabene.de *Web Site:* www. peter-verlag.de, pg 241

J Story-Scientia BVBA (Belgium) *Tel:* (09) 2255757 *Fax:* (09) 2331409 *E-mail:* bookshop@story.be *Web Site:* www.story.be, pg 1292

Uitgeverij J van In (Belgium) *Tel:* (03) 4805511 *Fax:* (03) 4807664, pg 68

Jabiru Press (Australia) *Tel:* (03) 9609 3535 *Fax:* (03) 9857 9110, pg 27

Jabotinsky Institute in Israel (Israel) *Tel:* (03) 6210611; (03) 5287320 *Fax:* (03) 5285587 *E-mail:* jabo@ actcom.co.il *Web Site:* www.jabotinsky.org, pg 365

Editoriale Jaca Book SpA (Italy) *Tel:* (02) 48561520-29 *Fax:* (02) 48193361 *E-mail:* jacabook@jacabook.it *Web Site:* www.jacabook.it, pg 390

Jacana Education (South Africa) *Tel:* (011) 648 1157 *Fax:* (011) 648 5516 *E-mail:* marketing@jacana.co.za; accounts@jacana.co.za *Web Site:* www.jacana.co.za, pg 560

Jacaranda Designs Ltd (Kenya) *Tel:* (020) 569736; (020) 568353 *Fax:* (020) 740524, pg 431

Jacklin Enterprises (Pty) Ltd (South Africa) *Tel:* (011) 265 4200 *Fax:* (011) 314 2984 *E-mail:* mjacklin@ jacklin.co.za *Web Site:* www.jacklin.co.za, pg 560

Gruppo Editoriale Jackson SpA (Italy) *Tel:* (02) 665261 *Fax:* (02) 66526222 *E-mail:* ordini@futura-ge.com, pg 390

JAD Publishers Ltd (Nigeria), pg 501

H I Jaffari & Co Publishers (Pakistan) *Tel:* (051) 811153, pg 508

Editions du Jaguar (France) *Tel:* (01) 44301970 *Fax:* (01) 44301979 *E-mail:* Jaguar@jeuneafrique.com *Web Site:* www.useditionsdujaguar.com, pg 169

Jahreszeiten-Verlag GmbH (Germany) *Tel:* (040) 2717-0 *Fax:* (040) 2717-2056 *E-mail:* jahreszeitenverlag@ jalag.de *Web Site:* www.jalag.de, pg 241

Editions J'ai Lu (France) *Tel:* (01) 44 39 34 70 *Fax:* (01) 44 39 65 52 *E-mail:* ajasmin@jailu.com *Web Site:* www.jailu.com, pg 169

JAI Press Ltd (United Kingdom) *Tel:* (01235) 465500 *Fax:* (01235) 465555 *Web Site:* www.jaipress.com, pg 710

Jaico Publishing House (India) *Tel:* (022) 2676702; (022) 2676802; (022) 2674501 *Fax:* (022) 2656412 *E-mail:* jaicowbd@vsnl.com *Web Site:* www. jaicobooks.com, pg 335

Jaico Publishing House (India) *Tel:* (022) 267 6702; (022) 267 6802; (022) 267 4501 *Fax:* (022) 265 6412 *E-mail:* jaicowbd@vsnl.com *Web Site:* www. jaicobooks.com, pg 1306

B Jain Publishers Overseas (India) *Tel:* (011) 2358 0800; (011) 5169 8991; (011) 2358 3100 *Fax:* (011) 2358 0471; (011) 5169 8993 *E-mail:* bjain@vsnl.com *Web Site:* www.bjainbooks.com, pg 335

B Jain Publishers Overseas (India) *Tel:* 23581100; 23581300 *Fax:* (011) 23580471 *E-mail:* bjain@ vsnl.com; info@bjainbooks.com *Web Site:* www. bjainbooks.com, pg 1306

B Jain Publishers (P) Ltd (India) *Tel:* (011) 23580800; (011) 23581100; (011) 23583100 *Fax:* (011) 23580471 *E-mail:* bjain@vsnl.com *Web Site:* www.bjainbooks. com, pg 335

Jaipur Publishing House (India) *Tel:* (0141) 319198; (0141) 319094 *E-mail:* jph@indiaresult.com, pg 336

Jamaica Archives (Jamaica) *Tel:* (876) 984-2581; (876) 984-5001 *Fax:* (876) 984-8254, pg 1519

The Jamaica Bauxite Institute (Jamaica) *Tel:* (876) 927-2073; (876) 927-2079 *Fax:* (876) 927-1159 *E-mail:* info@jbi.org.jm, pg 410

Jamaica Bureau of Standards (Jamaica) *Tel:* (876) 926-3140; (876) 926-3145 *Fax:* (876) 929-4736 *E-mail:* info@jbs.org.jm *Web Site:* www.jbs.org.jm/, pg 410

Jamaica Information Service (Jamaica) *Tel:* (876) 926-3740; (876) 926-3749 *Fax:* (876) 926-6715 *E-mail:* jis@jis.gov.jm; research@jis.gov.jm *Web Site:* www.jis.gov.jm, pg 410

Jamaica Library Association (Jamaica) *Tel:* (876) 927-1614 *Fax:* (876) 927-1614 *E-mail:* liajapresident@ yahoo.com *Web Site:* www.liaja.org.jm, pg 1565

Jamaica Library Service (Jamaica) *Tel:* (876) 926-3315 *Fax:* (876) 926-3354 *E-mail:* jamlibs@cwjamaica.com *Web Site:* www.jamlib.org.jm, pg 1519

Jamaica Printing Services (Jamaica) *Tel:* 876-967-2250; 876-967-2253; 876-967-2279; 876-967-2280; 876-922-3957 *Fax:* 876-967-2225 *E-mail:* info@jps1992.com; sales@jps1992.com *Web Site:* www.jps1992.com/, pg 410

Jamaica Publishing House Ltd (Jamaica) *Tel:* (876) 922-1385; (876) 967-3866 *Fax:* (876) 922-5412 *E-mail:* jph@jol.com.jm, pg 410

James & James (Publishers) Ltd (United Kingdom) *Tel:* (020) 7482 8888 *Fax:* (020) 7482 8889 *E-mail:* jxj@jamesxjames.co.uk *Web Site:* www. jamesxjames.co.uk, pg 711

James Nicholas Publishers Pty Ltd (Australia) *Tel:* (03) 9690 5955 (customer service); (03) 9696 5545 (editorial office) *Fax:* (03) 9699 2040 *E-mail:* info@ jamesnicholaspublishers.com.au; info@jnponline.com *Web Site:* www.jamesnicholaspublishers.com.au; www. jnponline.com, pg 27

Jamrite Publications (Jamaica) *Tel:* (876) 926-1180; (876) 926-1181 *Fax:* (876) 968-4519 *E-mail:* blackolive@cwjamaica.com, pg 410

Nakladatelstvi Jan Vasut (Czech Republic) *Tel:* (02) 22319 319 *Fax:* (02) 2481 1059 *E-mail:* vasut@mbox. vol.cz *Web Site:* www.vasut.cz, pg 123

Jandi-Sapi Editori (Italy) *Tel:* (06) 68805515; (06) 6876054 *Fax:* (06) 68218203 *E-mail:* info@jandisapi. com *Web Site:* www.jandisapi.com, pg 391

Jane Austen Society (United Kingdom) *Tel:* (01420) 83262 *Fax:* (01420) 83262 *E-mail:* museum@ janeausten.demon.co.uk *Web Site:* www.janeaustensoci. freeuk.com/index.htm, pg 1402

Johannesburg Art Gallery (South Africa) *Tel:* (011) 7253130; (011) 7253180 *Fax:* (011) 7206000 *Web Site:* www.saevents.co.za/gallery.htm, pg 561

Johannesburg Public Library (South Africa) *Tel:* (011) 836 3787 *Fax:* (011) 836 6607 *E-mail:* library@mj. org.za, pg 1542

Johannis (Germany) *Tel:* (07821) 5810 *Fax:* (07821) 581-26 *E-mail:* johannis-druck@t-online.de *Web Site:* www.johannis-verlag.de, pg 241

John Mackintosh Hall Library (Gibraltar) *Tel:* 78000 *Fax:* 40843, pg 1511

Johnson Publications Ltd (United Kingdom) *Tel:* (020) 7486 6757 *Fax:* (020) 7487 5436, pg 711

Johnston & Streiffert Editions (Sweden) *Tel:* (031) 826160 *Fax:* (031) 825150, pg 608

Joho Kagaku Gijutsu Kyokai (Japan) *Tel:* (03) 3813-3791 *Fax:* (03) 3813-3793 *E-mail:* infosta@infosta.or. jp *Web Site:* www.infosta.or.jp, pg 1565

Joho Shori Gakkai (Japan) *Tel:* (03) 3518-8374 *Fax:* (03) 3518-8375 *E-mail:* intl@ipsj.or.jp *Web Site:* www.ipsj. or.jp, pg 1565

Joint Publishing (HK) Co Ltd (Hong Kong) *Tel:* 2523 0105 *Fax:* 2525 8355 *E-mail:* jpchk@hk.super.net *Web Site:* www.jointpublishing.com, pg 314

Joly Editions (France) *Tel:* (01) 56 54 16 00 *Fax:* (01) 56 54 16 46 *E-mail:* loic.even@eja.fr *Web Site:* www. editions-joly.com, pg 170

Jonas Verlag fuer Kunst und Literatur GmbH (Germany) *Tel:* (06421) 25132 *Fax:* (06421) 210572 *E-mail:* jonas@jonas-verlag.de *Web Site:* www.jonas-verlag.de, pg 241

Jones & Bartlett International (United Kingdom) *Tel:* (01892) 539356 *Fax:* (01892) 614944 *E-mail:* j&b@class.co.uk *Web Site:* www.jbpub.com, pg 711

John Jones Publishing Ltd (United Kingdom) *Tel:* (01824) 707255 *Fax:* (01824) 705272 *E-mail:* johnjonespublishing.ltd@virgin.net *Web Site:* www.johnjonespublishing.ltd.uk, pg 711

Dr Werner Jopp Verlag (Germany) *Tel:* (0611) 547116 *Fax:* (0611) 542762, pg 241

Jordan Book Centre Co Ltd (Jordan) *Tel:* (06) 676-882 *Fax:* (06) 5152016 *E-mail:* jbc@nets.com.jo, pg 428

Jordan Book Centre Co Ltd (Jordan) *Tel:* (06) 5151882; (06) 5155882 *Fax:* (06) 5152016 *E-mail:* jbc@go.com. jo, pg 1314

Jordan Distribution Agency Co Ltd (Jordan) *Tel:* (06) 4630191; (02) 4648949 *Fax:* (06) 4635152 *E-mail:* jda@go.com.jo, pg 428

Jordan Distribution Agency Co Ltd (Jordan) *Tel:* (06) 4630191; (06) 4630192 *Fax:* (06) 4635152 *E-mail:* jda@go.com.jo, pg 1314

Jordan House for Publication (Jordan) *Tel:* (06) 24224 *Fax:* (06) 51062, pg 428

Jordan Library Association (Jordan) *Tel:* (06) 462 9412 *Fax:* (06) 462 9412 *E-mail:* info@jorla.org *Web Site:* www.jorla.org, pg 1566

Jordan Publishing Ltd (United Kingdom) *Tel:* (0117) 918 1491 *Fax:* (0117) 623 0063 *E-mail:* electronic@ jordanpublishing.co.uk *Web Site:* www. jordanpublishing.co.uk, pg 711

Jordan University of Science & Technology Library (Jordan) *Tel:* (02) 295111 *Fax:* (02) 295123 *Web Site:* www.just.edu.jo, pg 1521

Jordanverlag AG (Switzerland) *Tel:* (01) 3023676, pg 621

Jose Alfonso Sandoval Nunez (Costa Rica) *Tel:* 2252331; 8-326-426 *E-mail:* asandova@alpha. emate.ucr.ac.cr; k_sanny@hotmail.com, pg 115

Michael Joseph Ltd (United Kingdom) *Tel:* (020) 7416 3000 *Fax:* (020) 7416 3099, pg 711

Richard Joseph Publishers Ltd (United Kingdom) *Tel:* (01805) 625750 *Fax:* (01805) 625376 *E-mail:* info@sheppardsworld.com *Web Site:* www. sheppardsworld.com, pg 712

Richard Joseph Publishers Ltd (United Kingdom) *Tel:* (01805) 625750 *Fax:* (01805) 625376 *E-mail:* info@sheppardsworld.com *Web Site:* www. sheppardsworld.co.uk, pg 1343

Joszoveg Muhely Kiado (Hungary) *Tel:* (01) 226-5935 *Fax:* (01) 226-5935 *E-mail:* info@joszoveg.hu *Web Site:* www.joszoveg.hu, pg 319

Nakladatelstvi Jota spol sro (Czech Republic) *Tel:* (05) 37 014 203 *Fax:* (05) 37 014 213 *E-mail:* jota@ jota.cz; books@bm.cesnet.cz *Web Site:* www.jota.cz, pg 124

Le Jour, Editeur (France) *Tel:* (01) 49 59 11 89; (01) 49 59 11 91 *Fax:* (01) 49 59 11 96 *Web Site:* www. edjour.com, pg 170

Les Editions du Journal L' Unite Maghrebine (Morocco) *Tel:* 780169 *Fax:* 780169, pg 471

Jouvence (Italy) *Tel:* (06) 3211500 *Fax:* (06) 3202897 *E-mail:* jouvence@flashnet.it *Web Site:* www.jouvence-ed.com, pg 391

Jouvence Editions (France) *Tel:* (04) 50 43 28 60 *Fax:* (04) 50 43 29 24 *E-mail:* info@editions-jouvence.com *Web Site:* www.editions-jouvence.com, pg 170

Editions Jouvence (Switzerland) *Tel:* (022) 794 66 22 *Fax:* (022) 794 67 86 *E-mail:* info@editions-jouvence. com *Web Site:* www.editions-jouvence.com, pg 621

Joval Publications (Australia) *Tel:* (053) 674593, pg 28

Casa Editrice Dott Eugenio Jovene SpA (Italy) *Tel:* (081) 5521019; (081) 5521274; (081) 5523471 *Fax:* (081) 5520687 *E-mail:* info@jovene.it *Web Site:* www. jovene.it, pg 391

Jovis Verlag GmbH (Germany) *Tel:* (030) 2636720 *Fax:* (030) 26367272 *E-mail:* jovis@jovis.de *Web Site:* www.jovis.de, pg 241

Jowi-Verlag (Germany) *Tel:* (09353) 2921, pg 242

Joy Verlag GmbH (Germany) *Tel:* (08376) 97383 *Fax:* (08376) 8845 *E-mail:* joy_verlag@compuserve. com, pg 242

Joyas Bibliograficas SA (Spain) *Tel:* (091) 5470220, pg 583

Jozsef Attila Tudomanyegyetem Egyetemi Koenyvtar (Hungary) *Tel:* (062) 544-036 *Fax:* (062) 544-035 *E-mail:* mader@bibl.u-szeged.hu *Web Site:* www.bibl. u-szeged.hu, pg 1513

JPM Publications SA (Switzerland) *Tel:* (021) 6177561 *Fax:* (021) 6161257 *E-mail:* information@jpmguides. com *Web Site:* www.jpmguides.com, pg 621

Ediciones Jucar (Spain) *Tel:* (098) 5170921; (098) 5349684 *Fax:* (098) 55349545, pg 583

Gerald Judd Sales Ltd (United Kingdom) *Tel:* (020) 7828 8821 *Fax:* (020) 7828 0840, pg 1153

Jane Judd Literary Agency (United Kingdom) *Tel:* (020) 7607 0273 *Fax:* (020) 7607 0623, pg 1131

Juedischer Verlag GmbH (Germany) *Tel:* (069) 75601-0 *Fax:* (069) 75601-522 *Web Site:* www.suhrkamp.de, pg 242

Juegos & Co SRL (Argentina) *Tel:* (011) 4374-7903; (011) 4371-1825 *Fax:* (011) 4372-3829 *E-mail:* juegosyc@impsat1.com.ar *Web Site:* www. demente.com, pg 6

Jugend mit einer Mission Verlag (Switzerland) *Tel:* (032) 418988 *Fax:* (032) 418920, pg 621

Jugoslavijapublik (Serbia and Montenegro) *Tel:* (011) 633 266 *Fax:* (011) 622 858, pg 547

Jugoslovenska Revija (Serbia and Montenegro) *Tel:* (011) 625-829, pg 548

Jugoslovenski Bibliografsko Informacijski Institut (Serbia and Montenegro) *Tel:* (011) 687 836; (011) 687 760 *Fax:* (011) 687 760; (011) 688 840 *E-mail:* yubin@ jbi.bg.ac.yu *Web Site:* www.yu-yubin.org, pg 1570

Jugoslovenski Bibliografsko-informacijski institut, Yubin, Agencija za ISBN (Serbia and Montenegro) *Tel:* (011) 2451 242 *Fax:* (011) 459 444 *E-mail:* yubin@jbi.bg. ac.yu *Web Site:* www.jbi.bg.ac.yu/, pg 1273

Julius Klinkhardt Verlagsbuchhandlung (Germany) *Tel:* (08046) 9304 *Fax:* (08046) 9306 *E-mail:* info@ klinkhardt.de *Web Site:* www.klinkhardt.de, pg 242

Junfermann-Verlag (Germany) *Tel:* (05251) 1 34 40 *Fax:* (05251) 13 44 44 *E-mail:* infoteam@junfermann. de *Web Site:* www.junfermann.de, pg 242

Jung-ang Munhwa Sa (Republic of Korea) *Tel:* (02) 717-2114 *Fax:* (02) 716-1369, pg 436

Verlag Jungbrunnen - Wiener Spielzeugschachtel GesellschaftmbH (Austria) *Tel:* (01) 512-1299 *Fax:* (01) 512-1299-75 *E-mail:* office@jungbrunnen. co.at, pg 52

Editura Junimea (Romania) *Tel:* (032) 117290, pg 535

Vydavatelstvo Junior sro Slovart Print (Slovakia) *Tel:* (02) 44872378; (02) 44872379 *Fax:* (02) 44872133 *E-mail:* obchod@junior.sk *Web Site:* www. junior.sk, pg 555

Junius Verlag GmbH (Germany) *Tel:* (040) 892599 *Fax:* (040) 891224 *E-mail:* info@junius-verlag.de *Web Site:* www.junius-verlag.de, pg 242

Junius Verlags- und Vertriebs GmbH (Austria) *Tel:* (01) 4921272, pg 52

Junod Nicolas (Switzerland) *Tel:* (022) 347 02 42 *Fax:* (022) 347 02 42, pg 621

Junta de Castilla y Leon Consejeria de Educacion y Cultura (Spain) *Tel:* (0983) 411587 *Fax:* (0983) 411527 *E-mail:* publicaciones.cec@pop-in.jcyl.es *Web Site:* www.jcyl.es, pg 583

Junta de Educacao Religiosa e Publicacoes da Convencao Batista Brasileira (JUERP) (Brazil) *Tel:* (021) 2690772 *Fax:* (021) 2690296 *E-mail:* juerp@openlink.com.br *Web Site:* www.juerp. org.br, pg 84

Jupiter Verlagsgesellschaft mbH (Austria) *Tel:* (01) 21422940 *Fax:* (01) 2160720, pg 52

Juricom (Costa Rica) *Tel:* 2836942 *Fax:* 2253800 *E-mail:* juricom@sol.racsa.co.cr, pg 115

Juridica Verlag GmbH (Austria) *Tel:* (01) 533 37 47-0 *Fax:* (01) 533 37 47-196 *E-mail:* juridica@manz.at *Web Site:* www.juridica.at, pg 52

Editions Juridiques Africaines (France) *Tel:* (01) 43370401 *Fax:* (01) 43370401, pg 170

Editions Juridiques et Techniques Lamy SA (France) *Tel:* (01) 44 72 12 00 *Fax:* (01) 44 72 18 26, pg 170

Editions du Juris-Classeur (France) *Tel:* (01) 45 58 92 00 *Fax:* (01) 45 58 94 00 *E-mail:* editorial@juris-classeur.com; relations-clients@juris-classeur.com *Web Site:* www.juris-classeur.fr, pg 170

Juris Druck & Verlag AG (Switzerland) *Tel:* (01) 7409038; (01) 2117747 *Fax:* (01) 7409019 *E-mail:* juris@swissonline.ch, pg 621

Juris Editorial (Argentina) *Tel:* (0341) 4267301; (0341) 4267302 *Fax:* (0341) 4267301; (0341) 4267302 *E-mail:* editorialjuris@arnet.com.ar *Web Site:* www. editorialjuris.com, pg 6

Editions Juris Service (France) *Tel:* (04) 72 98 18 40 *Fax:* (04) 78 28 93 83 *E-mail:* info@editionsjuris.com *Web Site:* www.editionsjuris.com, pg 170

Editorial Jus SA de CV (Mexico) *Tel:* (05) 5260538; (05) 5260540 *Fax:* (05) 5290951 *E-mail:* editjus@ data.net.mx, pg 463

Justus-Liebig-Universitat Giessen (Germany) *Tel:* (0641) 99-0 *Fax:* (0641) 99-12259 *E-mail:* michael.kost@ admin.uni-giessen.de *Web Site:* www.uni-giessen.de, pg 242

Juta & Co (South Africa) *Fax:* (021) 797 5569 (orders only) *E-mail:* books@juta.co.za *Web Site:* www.juta. co.za, pg 561

Juta & Co Ltd (South Africa) *Tel:* (011) 217-7200 *Fax:* (011) 883-7623 *E-mail:* books@juta.co.za *Web Site:* www.tmza.co.za/juta, pg 1331

Jutta Pohl Verlag (Germany) *Tel:* (07232) 2239 *Fax:* (07202) 3879 *E-mail:* jutta@pohlverlag.de *Web Site:* www.pohl-verlag.de, pg 242

Juvenile & Children's Publishing House (China) *Tel:* (021) 62823025 *Fax:* (021) 62526963 *Web Site:* www.jcph.com, pg 105

Juventa Verlag GmbH (Germany) *Tel:* (06201) 9020-0 *Fax:* (06201) 9020-13 *E-mail:* juventa@juventa.de *Web Site:* www.juventa.de, pg 242

Libreria Juventud (Bolivia) *Tel:* (02) 2406248 *Fax:* (02) 2406248, pg 1293

Editorial Juventud Colombiana Ltda (Colombia) *Tel:* (01) 2557485; (01) 2490543 *Fax:* (01) 2557416, pg 111

Editorial Juventud SA (Spain) *Tel:* (093) 444 18 00 *Fax:* (093) 439 83 83 *E-mail:* info@editorialjuventud. es *Web Site:* www.editorialjuventud.es, pg 583

Juventus/Femina Publishers (South Africa) *Tel:* (012) 3284620 *Fax:* (012) 3283809, pg 561

Jyvaskylan Yliopiston Kirjasto (Finland) *Tel:* (014) 260 1211 *Fax:* (014) 260 3371 *E-mail:* jyk@Library.jyu.fi *Web Site:* www.jyu.fi, pg 1503

K Dictionaries Ltd (Israel) *Tel:* (03) 5468102 *Fax:* (03) 5468103 *E-mail:* kd@kdictionaries.com *Web Site:* kdictionaries.com, pg 365

K Publishing & Distributors Sdn Bhd (Malaysia) *Tel:* (03) 5501755; (03) 5501442 *Fax:* (03) 5501826, pg 453

Kaantopiiri Oy (Finland) *Tel:* (09) 622 9970 *Fax:* (09) 135 1372 *E-mail:* like@likekustannus.fi *Web Site:* www.likekustannus.fi, pg 142

Kabardino-Balkarskoye knizhnoye izdatelstvo (Russian Federation) *Tel:* 54184, pg 541

Kabul Central Library (Afghanistan) *Tel:* 23166, pg 1487

Kadena Press (Philippines) *Tel:* (02) 9217429; (02) 9213984, pg 514

Kadokawa Shoten Publishing Co Ltd (Japan) *Tel:* (03) 32388431 *Fax:* (03) 32627733 *E-mail:* K-master@ kadokawa.co.jp *Web Site:* www.kadokawa.co.jp, pg 417

Library Board of Kaduna State (Nigeria) *Tel:* (062) 242590, pg 1532

Kaerntner Druck- und Verlags-GmbH (Austria) *Tel:* (0463) 5866 *Fax:* (0463) 5866-321 *E-mail:* info@ kaerntner-druckerei.at *Web Site:* www.kaerntner-druckerei.at, pg 52

Kahn & Averill (United Kingdom) *Tel:* (020) 8743 3278 *Fax:* (020) 8743 3278, pg 712

Lonnie Kahn Ltd (Israel) *Tel:* (03) 9518418 *Fax:* (03) 9518415; (03) 9518416 *E-mail:* lonikahn@netvision. net.il, pg 1310

Kahurangi Cooperative (New Zealand) *Tel:* (09) 2782731, pg 493

Kaibundo Shuppan (Japan) *Tel:* (03) 3815-3291 *Fax:* (03) 3815-3953 *E-mail:* LED04737@nifty.ne.jp, pg 417

Kaigai Publications Ltd (Kaigai Shuppan Boeki Kabushiki Kaisha) (Japan) *Tel:* (03) 32924271 *Fax:* (03) 32924278 *E-mail:* admin@kaigai-pub.co.jp, pg 1312

Kailash Editions (France) *Tel:* (01) 43.29.52.52 *Fax:* (01) 46.34.03.29 *E-mail:* kailash@imaginet.fr, pg 170

Kairali Children's Book Trust (India) *Tel:* (0481) 563226; (0481) 560918 *Fax:* (0481) 564758 *Web Site:* www.dcbooks.com/kcbt.htm, pg 336

Kairalee Mudralayam (India) *Tel:* (0481) 2563114; (0481) 2301614 *Fax:* (0481) 2564758 *E-mail:* info@ dcbooks.com *Web Site:* www.dcbooks.com/kairali.htm, pg 336

Editorial Kairos SA (Spain) *Tel:* (093) 494 9490 *Fax:* (093) 410 5166 *E-mail:* kairos@sendanet.es, pg 584

Kaisei-Sha Publishing Co Ltd (Japan) *Tel:* (03) 32603229 *Fax:* (03) 32603540 *E-mail:* foreign@ kaiseisha.co.jp *Web Site:* www.kaiseisha.co.jp, pg 417

Kaitakusha (Japan) *Tel:* (03) 5842-8900 *Fax:* (03) 5842-5560 *E-mail:* webmaster@kaitakusha.co.jp *Web Site:* www.kaitakusha.co.jp, pg 417

Kajima Institute Publishing Co Ltd (Japan) *Tel:* (03) 5561-2550 *Fax:* (03) 5561 2560 *E-mail:* info@kajima-publishing.co.jp *Web Site:* www.kajima-publishing.co. jp, pg 417

KaJo Verlag (Germany) *Tel:* (0931) 385235 *Fax:* (0931) 385305 *E-mail:* info@verlagshaus.com *Web Site:* www.verlagshaus.com, pg 242

Kajura Publications (United Republic of Tanzania) *Tel:* (051) 866181, pg 639

Editions Kaleidoscope (France) *Tel:* (01) 45 44 07 08 *Fax:* (01) 45 44 53 71 *E-mail:* infos@ editions-kaleidoscope.com *Web Site:* www.editions-kaleidoscope.com, pg 170

Kaleidoscope Publishers Ltd (Denmark) *Tel:* 33755555 *Fax:* 33755544 *E-mail:* gujbt@gyldendal.dk *Web Site:* www.kaleidoscope.publishers.dk; www. gyldendal.dk, pg 132

Kalentis & Sia (Greece) *Tel:* 2103601551 *Fax:* 2103623553 *E-mail:* kalendis@ath.forthnet. gr, pg 305

Kali For Women (India) *Tel:* (011) 6864497; (011) 6852530 *Fax:* (011) 6864497 *E-mail:* kaliw@del2. vsnl.net.in *Web Site:* www.kalibooks.com, pg 336

Kalich SRO (Czech Republic) *Tel:* (02) 24947505; (02) 24220296 *Fax:* (02) 24947504; (02) 24220296 *E-mail:* kalichpub@volny.cz, pg 124

Kalligram spol sro (Slovakia) *Tel:* (02) 54415028 *Fax:* (02) 54410809 *Web Site:* www.kalligram.sk, pg 555

Kallmeyer'sche Verlagsbuchhandlung GmbH (Germany) *Tel:* (0511) 4 00 04-1 75 *Fax:* (0511) 4 00 04-1 76 *E-mail:* leserservice@kallmeyer.de *Web Site:* www. kallmeyer.de, pg 242

Kalos-Verlag (Switzerland) *Tel:* (01) 3022751 *Fax:* (01) 3022751, pg 621

Kalyani Publishers (India) *Tel:* (011) 3274393; (011) 3271469, pg 336

Ilias Kambanas Publishing Organization, SA (Greece) *Tel:* 2105762791 *Fax:* 2105743988 *E-mail:* kambanas@internet.gr, pg 306

Kamenyar (Ukraine) *Tel:* (0322) 72-19-49 *Fax:* (0322) 72-19-49, pg 649

J Kamphausen Verlag & Distribution GmbH (Germany) *Tel:* (0521) 56052-0 *Fax:* (0521) 56052-29, pg 242

KAMS Information & Publishing Ltd (Hong Kong) *Tel:* 23889172 *Fax:* 27716403 *E-mail:* kamsinfo@ hkstar.com *Web Site:* kamsinfo.com, pg 1138

Kanakis Publications & Bookshop (Greece) *Tel:* 210 3302385 *Fax:* 2103811902, pg 1303

Kanehara & Co Ltd (Japan) *Tel:* (03) 3811-7185; (03) 3811-7184 (sales) *Fax:* (03) 3813-0288 *Web Site:* www.kanehara-shuppan.co.jp, pg 417

Kangaroo Press (Australia) *Tel:* (02) 6541502 *Fax:* (02) 6541338, pg 28

Kanisa la Biblia Publishers (KLB) (United Republic of Tanzania) *Tel:* (026) 2354500 *Fax:* (026) 2350911, pg 639

Kanisius Verlag (Switzerland) *Tel:* (026) 425 87 30 *Fax:* (026) 425 87 38 *E-mail:* info@canisius.ch *Web Site:* www.canisius.ch, pg 621

Kano State Library Board (Nigeria) *Tel:* (064) 645614 *Web Site:* www.library.unt.edu/nigeria/Kano/Kano.htm, pg 1532

Kansai University Press (Japan) *Tel:* (06) 6368-1121 *Fax:* (06) 6389-5162 *Web Site:* www.kansai-u.ac. jp/index.html, pg 417

Kansallisarkisto Kirjasto (Finland) *Tel:* (09) 228521 *Fax:* (09) 176302 *E-mail:* kansallisarkisto@narc.fi *Web Site:* www.narc.fi, pg 1503

Jan Kanzelsberger Praha (Czech Republic) *Tel:* (02) 22 51 42 40; (02) 22 52 02 64 *Fax:* (02) 22 51 15 73 *E-mail:* masarykova@volny.cz, pg 124

Kaos Edizioni SRL (Italy) *Tel:* (02) 39310296 *Fax:* (02) 39325749 *E-mail:* kaosedizioni@kaosedizioni.com *Web Site:* www.kaosedizioni.com, pg 391

Kapelusz Editora SA (Argentina) *Tel:* (011) 5236-5000 *Fax:* (011) 5236-5050 *E-mail:* editorial@kapelusz. com.ar *Web Site:* www.kapelusz.com.ar, pg 6

Editorial Kapelusz Venezolana SA (Venezuela) *Tel:* (0212) 517601; (0212) 526281, pg 774

Kapon Editions (Greece) *Tel:* 2109235098 *Fax:* 21 9214089 *Web Site:* www.homemarket.gr, pg 1303

Karachi University Library Science Alumni Association (Pakistan) *Tel:* (021) 479001 *Fax:* (021) 473226 *E-mail:* vc@ku.edu.pk *Web Site:* www.ku.edu.pk, pg 1569

Karas-Sana Oy (Finland) *Tel:* (09) 6815 5600 *Fax:* (09) 6815 5611 *E-mail:* toimitus@sana.fi *Web Site:* www. karas-sana.fi/sana, pg 142

Dionysuis P Karavias Ekdoseis (Greece) *Tel:* 210 3620465 *Fax:* 2103620465, pg 306

Kardamitsa A (Greece) *Tel:* 2103615156 *Fax:* 2103631100 *E-mail:* info@kardamitsa.gr *Web Site:* kardamitsa.gr, pg 306

S Karger GmbH Verlag fuer Medizin und Naturwissenschaften (Germany) *Tel:* (0761) 45 20 70 *Fax:* (0761) 45 20 714 *E-mail:* information@karger.de *Web Site:* www.karger.com; www.karger.de, pg 242

S Karger AG, Medical & Scientific Publishers (Switzerland) *Tel:* (061) 3061111 *Fax:* (061) 3061234 *E-mail:* karger@karger.ch *Web Site:* www.karger.com, pg 621

Karisto Oy (Finland) *Tel:* (03) 63 151 *Fax:* (03) 616 1565 *E-mail:* kustannusliike@karisto.fi *Web Site:* www.karisto.fi, pg 142

Verlag Karl Baedeker GmbH (Germany) *Tel:* (0711) 4502262 *Fax:* (0711) 4502343 *E-mail:* baedeker@ mairsdumont.com *Web Site:* www.baedecker.de, pg 242

Karl-May-Verlag Lothar Schmid GmbH (Germany) *Tel:* (0951) 98 20 60 *Fax:* (0951) 2 43 67 *E-mail:* info@karl-may.de *Web Site:* www.karl-may.de, pg 243

Karmelitanske Nakladatelstvi (Czech Republic) *Tel:* 384 420 295 *Fax:* 384 420 295 *E-mail:* vydri@ karmelitanske-nakladatelstvi.cz; zasilky@kna.cz *Web Site:* www.karmelitanske-nakladatelstvi.cz; www. kna.cz, pg 124

Karnac Books Ltd (United Kingdom) *Tel:* (020) 8969 4454 *Fax:* (020) 8969 5585 *E-mail:* books@karnac. demon.co.uk *Web Site:* www.karnacbooks.com, pg 712

Karnak House (United Kingdom) *Tel:* (020) 7243 3620 *Fax:* (020) 7243 3620 *E-mail:* connection@ karnakhouse.co.uk *Web Site:* www.karnakhouse.co.uk, pg 712

Karni Publishers Ltd (Israel) *Tel:* (03) 812244 *Fax:* (03) 826138 *E-mail:* info@zmora.co.il, pg 366

Karolinger Verlag GmbH & Co KG (Austria) *Tel:* (01) 4092279 *Fax:* (01) 4092279, pg 52

Karolinum, nakladatelstvi (Czech Republic) *Tel:* (02) 24491276 *Fax:* (02) 24212041 *E-mail:* cupress@ruk. cuni.cz; cupress@cuni.cz *Web Site:* www.cupress.cuni. cz, pg 124

The Harry Karren Institute for the Analysis of Propaganda, Yad Labanim (Israel) *Tel:* (09) 9573736 *Fax:* (09) 9546896, pg 366

Karthala Editions-Diffusion (France) *Tel:* (01) 43 31 15 59 *Fax:* (01) 45 35 27 05 *E-mail:* karthala@wanadoo. fr, pg 170

Karto + Grafik Verlagsgesellschaft (K & G Verlagsgesellschaft) (Germany) *Tel:* (069) 76 20 31 *Fax:* (069) 76 91 06 *E-mail:* info@hildebrunds.de *Web Site:* www.hildebrands.de, pg 243

Kartoen (Netherlands) *Tel:* (050) 3110505 *Fax:* (050) 3112299 *E-mail:* mondria@worldonline.nl, pg 480

Kartografie Praha (Czech Republic) *Tel:* (02) 21969411 *Fax:* (02) 21969428 *E-mail:* info@kartografie.cz *Web Site:* www.kartografie.cz, pg 124

Kartographischer Verlag Reinhard Ryborsch (Germany) *Tel:* (06104) 79039 *Fax:* (06104) 75356, pg 243

Karunaratne & Sons Ltd (Sri Lanka) *Tel:* (071) 229 9860 *Fax:* (071) 229 9860 *E-mail:* info@calcey.com *Web Site:* www.calcey.com, pg 601

Karunia CV (Indonesia) *Tel:* (031) 5344120 *Fax:* (031) 5343409, pg 352

Karya Anda, CV (Indonesia) *Tel:* (031) 5344215; (031) 522580; (031) 5315402 *Fax:* (031) 5310594, pg 352

Main Library, Kasetsart University (Thailand) *Tel:* (02) 9428615 *Fax:* (02) 5611369; (02) 9428614 *E-mail:* libspn@ku.ac.th *Web Site:* www.lib.ku.ac.th, pg 1548

Kastaniotis Editions SA (Greece) *Tel:* 2103301208; 2103301327 *Fax:* 2103822530 *E-mail:* info@ kastaniotis.com *Web Site:* www.kastaniotis.com, pg 306

Kastell Verlag GmbH (Germany) *Tel:* (089) 33 21 75; (089) 399742 *Fax:* (089) 340 11 78 *E-mail:* kastell-verlag@t-online.de, pg 243

Katai & Bolza Irodalmi Ugynokseg (Hungary) *Tel:* (01) 456-0313 *Fax:* (01) 215-4420 *Web Site:* www. kataibolza.hu, pg 1122

Katalis PT Bina Mitra Plaosan (Indonesia) *Tel:* (021) 7510477, pg 352

Kathakali (Bangladesh) *Tel:* (031) 619476; (031) 619006; (031) 612625, pg 1291

Katholieke Bijbelstichting (Netherlands) *Tel:* (073) 6133220 *Fax:* (073) 6910140 *Web Site:* www. willibrordbijbel.nl/kbs, pg 480

Katholieke Universiteit Leuven (Belgium) *Tel:* (016) 32 46 06; (016) 32 46 91 *Fax:* (016) 32 46 32 *E-mail:* centrale.bibliotheek@bib.kuleuven.ac.be *Web Site:* www.bib.kuleuven.ac.be, pg 1492

Verlag Katholisches Bibelwerk GmbH (Germany) *Tel:* (0711) 619200 *Fax:* (0711) 6192044 *E-mail:* verlag@bibelwerk.de *Web Site:* www. bibelwerk.de, pg 243

Katholska kirkjan a Islandi - Landakot Publishers Thorlakssjodur (Iceland) *Tel:* 555-0188, pg 323

Katolicki Uniwersytet Wydawniczo -Redakcja (Poland) *Tel:* (081) 5257151 *Fax:* (081) 541246 *E-mail:* sekret@kul.lublin.pl, pg 518

Katoptro Publications (Greece) *Tel:* 2109244827; 2109244852 *Fax:* 2109244756 *E-mail:* info@ katoptro.gr *Web Site:* www.katoptro.gr, pg 306

Katzmann Verlag KG (Germany) *Tel:* (07473) 5427 *Fax:* (07473) 5427, pg 243

Verlag Ernst Kaufmann GmbH (Germany) *Tel:* (07821) 93 90-0 *Fax:* (07821) 9390-11 *E-mail:* info@kaufman-verlag.de *Web Site:* www.kaufmann-verlag.de, pg 243

Kauppakaari Oyj (Finland) *Tel:* (020) 442 4730 *Fax:* (020) 442 4723 *E-mail:* etunimi.sukunimi@ talentum.fi *Web Site:* www.talentum.fi/kirjat, pg 142

Kavaler Publishers (Belarus) *Tel:* (0172) 2506485; (0172) 548198 *Fax:* (0172) 238041 *E-mail:* Kavaler@ inbox.ru, pg 62

Kavkazskaya Biblioteka Publishing House (Russian Federation) *Tel:* (8652) 32314, pg 541

KAW Krajowa Agencja Wydawnicza (Poland) *Tel:* (022) 6578886 *Fax:* (022) 6578887 *E-mail:* kaw@univcomp. waw.pl *Web Site:* www.polska2000.pl, pg 519

Kawade Shobo Shinsha Publishers (Japan) *Tel:* (03) 3404-1201 *Fax:* (03) 3404-6386 *E-mail:* info@ kawade.co.jp *Web Site:* www.kawade.co.jp, pg 417

Al-Farabi Kazakh National University (Kazakstan) *Tel:* (03272) 471691 *Fax:* (03272) 472609 *E-mail:* anurmag@kazsu.kz *Web Site:* www.kazsu.kz, pg 429

Kazakhstan Academy of Sciences (Kazakstan) *Tel:* (03272) 624871 *Fax:* (03272) 62500 *E-mail:* teta@nursat.kz *Web Site:* www.president.kz, pg 1521

Kazakhstan, Izd-Vo (Kazakstan) *Tel:* (03272) 422929; (03272) 428562 *Fax:* (03272) 422929, pg 429

Kazamashobo Co Ltd (Japan) *Tel:* (03) 3291-5729 *Fax:* (03) 3291-5757 *E-mail:* kazama@wd6.so-net. ne.jp *Web Site:* www.kazamashobo.co.jp, pg 417

Izdatelstvo Kazanskago Universiteta (Russian Federation) *Tel:* 325363 *E-mail:* kacimov@niimm.kazan.su, pg 541

Kazi Publications (Pakistan) *Tel:* (042) 7311359; (042) 7350805 *Fax:* (042) 7117606; (042) 7324003 *E-mail:* kazip@brain.net.pk; kazipublications@ hotmail.com *Web Site:* www.brain.net.pk/~kazip, pg 508

KBV Verlags-und Medien - GmbH (Germany) *Tel:* (06593) 998668 *Fax:* (06593) 998701 *E-mail:* info@kbv-verlag.de *Web Site:* www.kbv-verlag.de, pg 243

KCL Language Consultancy Ltd (Hong Kong) *Tel:* (02) 8811368 *Fax:* (02) 8080389 *E-mail:* kcl@iohk.com *Web Site:* www.iohk.com/userpages/kcl, pg 1138

Ke Mong Sa Publishing Co Ltd (Republic of Korea) *Tel:* (02) 531-5535 *Fax:* (02) 531-5550, pg 436

Keats-Shelley Memorial Association (KSMA) (United Kingdom) *Tel:* (01892) 533452 *Fax:* (01892) 519142 *Web Site:* www.keats-shelley.co.uk, pg 1402

Kedros Publishers (Greece) *Tel:* 2103809712 *Fax:* 2103302655 *E-mail:* books@kedros.gr *Web Site:* www.kedros.gr, pg 306

Gregory Kefalas Publishing (Australia) *Tel:* (02) 9789 6049 *Fax:* (02) 97876181, pg 28

Kegan Paul International Ltd (United Kingdom) *Tel:* (020) 7580 5511 *Fax:* (020) 7436 0899 *E-mail:* books@keganpaul.com *Web Site:* www. keganpaul.com, pg 712

Keigaku Publishing Co Ltd (Japan) *Tel:* (03) 3233-3733 *Fax:* (03) 3233-3730, pg 417

Keil & Keil Literary Agency (Germany) *Tel:* (040) 27166892 *Fax:* (040) 27166896 *E-mail:* anfragen@ keil-keil.com *Web Site:* www.keil-keil.com, pg 1121

Keio University School of Library & Information Science (Japan) *Tel:* (03) 3453-4511 *Fax:* (03) 5427-1578 *E-mail:* slis-office@slis.keio.ac.jp *Web Site:* www.slis.keio.ac.jp, pg 1520

Keip GmbH (Germany) *Tel:* (06021) 59 05 0 *Fax:* (06021) 59 05 42 *E-mail:* info@keip.net *Web Site:* www.keip.net, pg 243

Keisuisha Publishing Company Ltd (Japan) *Tel:* (082) 2467909 *Fax:* (082) 2467876 *E-mail:* info@keisui.co. jp *Web Site:* www.keisui.co.jp, pg 417

Verlag Walter Keller, Dornach (Switzerland) *Tel:* (061) 7015713 *Fax:* (061) 7015716 *E-mail:* info@verlag-walterkeller.ch *Web Site:* www.verlag-walterkeller.ch, pg 243

SachBuchVerlag Kellner (Germany) *Tel:* (0421) 77866 *Fax:* (0421) 704058 *E-mail:* kellner-verlag@t-online. de *Web Site:* kellner-verlag.de, pg 243

Kells Publishing Company Ltd (Ireland) *Tel:* (046) 40117; (046) 40255 *Fax:* (046) 41522, pg 358

The Frances Kelly Agency (United Kingdom) *Tel:* (020) 8549 7830 *Fax:* (020) 8547 0051, pg 1131

Kelly's (United Kingdom) *Tel:* (01342) 326972 *Fax:* (01342) 335825 *E-mail:* kellys.mktg@reedinfo. co.uk *Web Site:* www.kellysearch.com, pg 712

Martin Kelter Verlag GmbH u Co (Germany) *Tel:* (040) 68 28 95-0 *Fax:* (040) 68 28 95 50 *E-mail:* info@ kelter.de *Web Site:* www.kelter.de, pg 243

Kemps Publishing Ltd (United Kingdom) *Tel:* (0121) 765 4144 *Fax:* (0121) 706 1408 *E-mail:* info@ kempsgold.co.uk *Web Site:* www.kempsgold.co.uk, pg 712

Kempton Park Public Library (South Africa) *Tel:* (011) 9212173 *Fax:* (011) 9750921, pg 1542

Kenek Ltd (Cyprus) *Tel:* (022) 365842 *Fax:* (022) 475150, pg 121

The Kenilworth Press Ltd (United Kingdom) *Tel:* (01296) 715101 *Fax:* (01296) 715148 *E-mail:* customer.services@kenilworthpress.co.uk *Web Site:* www.kenilworthpress.co.uk, pg 712

Kenkyusha Ltd (Japan) *Tel:* (03) 3288-7777; (03) 3288-7856 *Fax:* (03) 3288-7799 *Web Site:* www.kenkyusha. co.jp, pg 417

Kennarahaskoli Islands (Iceland) *Tel:* 5633800 *Fax:* 5633914 *E-mail:* vefur@khi.is *Web Site:* www. khi.is, pg 1513

Albertine Kennedy Publishing (Ireland) *Tel:* (01) 6607090 *Fax:* (01) 6607090, pg 358

Kentro Byzantinon Erevnon (Greece) *Tel:* 2310270941 *Fax:* 2310228922, pg 306

Kentron Ekdoseos Ellinon Syngrafeon (Greece) *Tel:* 210 3612541 *Fax:* 2103602691, pg 1394

Kenway Publications Ltd (Kenya) *Tel:* (02) 444700; (02) 445260; (02) 445261 *Fax:* (02) 448753 *E-mail:* eaep@africaonline.co.ke *Web Site:* www. eastafricanpublishers.com, pg 431

Kenya Agricultural Research Institute (Kenya) *Tel:* (02) 583301-20 *Fax:* (02) 583344 *E-mail:* resource.centre@ kari.org *Web Site:* www.hridir.org, pg 1521

Kenya Energy & Environment Organisation, Kengo (Kenya) *Tel:* (020) 749747; (020) 748281 *Fax:* (020) 749382, pg 431

Kenya Library Association (Kenya) *Tel:* (02) 334244 *Fax:* (02) 336885, pg 1566

Kenya Literature Bureau (Kenya) *Tel:* (02) 608305; (02) 608806; (02) 605595; (02) 351196; (02) 351197; (02) 506158 *Fax:* (02) 605600 *E-mail:* klb@onlinekenya. com, pg 431

Kenya Literature Bureau (Kenya) *Tel:* (020) 333763 *Fax:* (020) 340954 *E-mail:* klb@onlinekenya.co.ke, pg 1265

Kenya Medical Research Institute (KEMRI) (Kenya) *Tel:* (02) 722541; (02) 722672; (02) 722532 *Fax:* (02) 720030 *E-mail:* kemrilib@ken.healthnet.org *Web Site:* www.kemri.org, pg 431

Kenya Meteorological Department (Kenya) *Tel:* (02) 567880 *Fax:* (02) 576955 *E-mail:* director@lion. meteo.go.ke; imtr@lion.meteo.go.ke *Web Site:* www. meteo.go.ke, pg 431

Kenya National Archives & Documentation Service (Kenya) *Tel:* (02) 228959 *Fax:* (02) 228020 *E-mail:* knarchives@kenyaweb.com *Web Site:* www. kenyarchives.go.ke, pg 1521

Kenya National Library Service (Kenya) *Tel:* (02) 725550; (02) 725551; (02) 718177; (02) 718012; (02) 718013 *Fax:* (02) 721749 *E-mail:* knls@nbnet.co.ke *Web Site:* www.knls.or.ke, pg 1521

Kenya Polytechnic Library (Kenya) *Tel:* (02) 338231; (02) 338232 *Fax:* (02) 219689, pg 1521

Knihovna Narodniho muzea (Czech Republic) *Tel:* (02) 24497111 *Fax:* (02) 24497331 *E-mail:* nm@nm.cz *Web Site:* www.nm.cz, pg 1499

Izdatelstvo Knizhnaya Palata (Russian Federation) *Tel:* (095) 2889247 *Fax:* (095) 1635827, pg 541

Univerzitna Kniznica (Slovakia) *Tel:* (02) 54 434 981 *Fax:* (02) 54 434 246 *E-mail:* ill@ulib.sk *Web Site:* www.ulib.sk, pg 1541

Tehnicka Knjiga (Serbia and Montenegro) *Tel:* (011) 468 596 *Fax:* (011) 473 442 *E-mail:* tknjiga@eunet.yu *Web Site:* www.tehknjiga.co.yu, pg 548

Knjizevni Krug Split (Croatia) *Tel:* (021) 342 226; (021) 361 081 *Fax:* (021) 342 226 *E-mail:* bratislav.lucin@ public.srce.hr, pg 118

Knockabout Comics (United Kingdom) *Tel:* (020) 8969 2945 *Fax:* (020) 8968 7614 *E-mail:* knockcomic@aol. com *Web Site:* www.knockabout.com, pg 713

Knossos Publications (Greece) *Tel:* 2103810108, pg 306

Knowledge Book House (Myanmar) *Tel:* (01) 290927, pg 1319

Knowledge Media International (Germany) *Tel:* (089) 4136-8433 *Fax:* (089) 4136-8411 *Web Site:* www.k-m-i.com, pg 246

Knowledge Press (China) *Tel:* (010) 68315610 *Fax:* (010) 68316510 *E-mail:* ecphtdb@public3.bta. net.cn, pg 105

Knowledge Press & Bookhouse (Myanmar) *Tel:* (01) 290927, pg 472

Verlag Knut Reim, Jugendpresseverlag (Germany) *Tel:* (040) 34 26 41 *Fax:* (040) 34 46 87, pg 246

Koala-Kustannus Oy (Finland) *Tel:* (050) 408 1590 *Fax:* (09) 6845034 *E-mail:* info@koalakustannus.fi *Web Site:* www.koalakustannus.fi, pg 142

Kobenhavns Kommunes Biblioteker (Denmark) *Tel:* 33664650 *Fax:* 33667120 *E-mail:* bibliotek@kkb. bib.dk *Web Site:* www.kkb.bib.dk/, pg 1499

Kobenhavns Stadsarkiv (Denmark) *Tel:* 33662370 *Fax:* 33667039 *E-mail:* stadsarkiv@kff.kk.dk *Web Site:* www.ksa.kk.dk, pg 1500

Kober Verlag Bern AG (Switzerland) *Tel:* (031) 9714687 *E-mail:* koberpress@mindspring.com, pg 622

Verlagsanstalt Alexander Koch GmbH (Germany) *Tel:* (0711) 7591-0 *Fax:* (0711) 7591-380 *Web Site:* www.koch-verlag.de, pg 246

Koch, Neff und Oetinger & Co (Germany) *Tel:* (0711) 78600 *Fax:* (0711) 78602800 *Web Site:* www. buchkatalog.de, pg 1301

Kochbuch Verlag Olga Leeb (Germany) *Tel:* (089) 58998303; (089) 583094 *Fax:* (089) 560208; (089) 58995303, pg 246

Kodansha Disney Children's Book Club (Japan) *Tel:* (03) 3946-6201 *Fax:* (03) 3944-9915 *Web Site:* www. kodansha.co.jp; www.kodanclub.com, pg 1244

Kodansha International Ltd (Japan) *Tel:* (03) 39446491 *Fax:* (03) 39446394 *E-mail:* sales@kodansha-intl.co.jp *Web Site:* www.thejapanpage.com; www.kodansha-intl.co.jp, pg 418

Kodansha Ltd (Japan) *Tel:* (03) 3944-6493 *E-mail:* sales@kodansha-intl.com *Web Site:* www. kodansha.co.jp, pg 418

Koehler & Amelang Verlagsgesellschaft (Germany) *Tel:* (089) 455 54-0 *Fax:* (089) 455 54-100 *E-mail:* buch@dva.de *Web Site:* www.dva.de, pg 246

Eric Koehler (France) *Tel:* (01) 49 27 06 37; (01) 44 55 37 50 *Fax:* (01) 47 03 39 86; (01) 40 20 99 74, pg 170

K F Koehler Verlag GmbH (Germany) *Tel:* (0711) 7892 130 *Fax:* (0711) 7892 132 *E-mail:* info@kfk.de; sabine.haegele@kfk.de, pg 246

Verlagsgruppe Koehler/Mittler (Germany) *Tel:* (040) 7971303 *Fax:* (040) 79713324 *E-mail:* vertrieb@ koehler-mittler.de *Web Site:* www.koehler-mittler.de, pg 246

Koehlers Verlagsgesellschaft mbH (Germany) *Tel:* (040) 79713-03 *Fax:* (040) 79713324 *E-mail:* vertrieb@ koehler-mittler.de *Web Site:* www.koehler-mittler.de, pg 246

Koelner Universitaets-Verlag GmbH (Germany) *Tel:* (0221) 48 81-1 *Fax:* (0221) 49 81-533 *E-mail:* welcome@iwkoeln.de *Web Site:* www. iwkoeln.de, pg 246

Koenigsfurt Verlag, Evelin Buerger et Johannes Fiebig (Germany) *Tel:* (04334) 18 99 02; (04334) 18 22 010 *Fax:* (04334) 18 22 011 *E-mail:* info@koenigsfurt.com *Web Site:* www.koenigsfurt.com, pg 246

Verlag Koenigshausen und Neumann GmbH (Germany) *Tel:* (0931) 78 40-7 00 *E-mail:* info@koenigshausen-neumann.de *Web Site:* www.koenigshausen-neumann. de/, pg 246

Edition Koenigstein (Austria) *Tel:* (02243) 26046 *Fax:* (02243) 26046 *E-mail:* edition.koenigstein@ aon.at *Web Site:* members.aon.at/edition_koenigstein, pg 52

Koenyveshaz Kft (Hungary) *Tel:* (01) 1311566 *Fax:* (01) 1311566, pg 319

Koepel van de Vlaamse Noord - Zuidbeweging 11.11.11 (Belgium) *Tel:* (02) 536-11-13 *Fax:* (02) 536-19-10 *E-mail:* info@11.be *Web Site:* www.11.be, pg 69

Lucy Koerner Verlag (Germany) *Tel:* (0711) 588472 *Fax:* (0711) 5789634, pg 246

Ute Koerner Literary Agent (Spain) *Tel:* (093) 4550414; (093) 4502588 *Fax:* (093) 4365548 *E-mail:* office@ uklitag.com *Web Site:* www.uklitag.com, pg 1126

Verlag Valentin Koerner GmbH (Germany) *Tel:* (07221) 22423 *Fax:* (07221) 38697 *E-mail:* info@ koernerverlag.de *Web Site:* www.koernerverlag.de/, pg 246

Koesel-Verlag GmbH & Co (Germany) *Tel:* (089) 17801-0 *Fax:* (089) 17801-111 *E-mail:* leserservice@koesel. de *Web Site:* www.koesel.de/, pg 247

Magyar Tudomanyos Akademia Koezponti Fizikai Kutato Intezet Koenyvtara (Hungary) *Tel:* (01) 1382344 (ext 44) *Fax:* (01) 1316954 *E-mail:* kolcs@ sunserv.kfki.hu, pg 319

Koezponti Statisztikai Hivatal Koenyvtar es Dokumentacios Szolgalat (Hungary) *Tel:* (01) 3456105 *Fax:* (01) 3456112 *Web Site:* www.ksh.hu; www.lib. ksh.hu, pg 1513

Kogan Page Ltd (United Kingdom) *Tel:* (020) 7278 0433 *Fax:* (020) 7837 6348 *E-mail:* kpinfo@kogan-page. co.uk; kpsales@kogan-page.co.uk; orders@kogan-page.co.uk *Web Site:* www.kogan-page.co.uk, pg 713

Kogyo Chosakai Publishing Co Ltd (Japan) *Tel:* (03) 3817-4701 *Fax:* (03) 3817-4748 *E-mail:* m-order@po.iijnet.or.jp; rtb87919@mtd.biglobe.ne.jp *Web Site:* www.iijnet.or.jp/kocho, pg 418

W Kohlhammer GmbH (Germany) *Tel:* (0711) 7863-0 *Fax:* (0711) 7863-8204 *E-mail:* redaktion@ kohlhammer.de *Web Site:* www.kohlhammer.de, pg 247

Koinonia Comunidade Edicoes Ltda (Brazil) *Tel:* (061) 3479431 *Fax:* (061) 3470972, pg 84

Uitgeverij J H Kok BV (Netherlands) *Tel:* (038) 3392555 *Fax:* (038) 3311776 *E-mail:* algemeen@kok.nl *Web Site:* www.kok.nl, pg 481

Kok Yayincilik (Turkey) *Tel:* (0312) 434472 *Fax:* (0312) 4350497 *E-mail:* kokbilgi@kokyayincilik.com.tr *Web Site:* www.kokyayincilik.com.tr, pg 646

Kokudo-Sha Co Ltd (Japan) *Tel:* (03) 53483710 *Fax:* (03) 53483765 *Web Site:* www.koutoku.co. jp/kokudosha/index.html, pg 418

Kokuritsu Kobunshokan (Japan) *Tel:* (03) 3214-0621 *Fax:* (03) 3212-8806 *Web Site:* www.archives.go. jp/index_e.html, pg 1520

Kokushokankokai Co Ltd (Japan) *Tel:* (03) 5970-7421 *Fax:* (03) 5970-7427 *E-mail:* info@kokusho.co.jp *Web Site:* www.kokusho.co.jp, pg 418

Kola Sanya Publishing Enterprise (Nigeria) *Tel:* (037) 432638, pg 501

Kolibri Forlag A/S (Norway) *Tel:* (022) 438778 *Fax:* (022) 447740 *E-mail:* post@kolibriforlag.no *Web Site:* www.kolibriforlag.no, pg 505

Kolibri Publishing Group (Bulgaria) *Tel:* (02) 988-87-81; (02) 955-84-81; (02) 955-91-990 *Fax:* (02) 813625 *E-mail:* colibri@inet.bg; colibry@bgnet.bg, pg 94

Kolibri-Verlag GmbH (Germany) *Tel:* (040) 2202243 *Fax:* (040) 2276368 *E-mail:* infos@kolibriverlag.de, pg 247

Kolumbus-Verlag (Switzerland) *Tel:* (064) 7711370, pg 622

Komine Shoten Co Ltd (Japan) *Tel:* (03) 3357-3521 *Fax:* (03) 3357-1027 *E-mail:* info@komineshoten.co.jp *Web Site:* www.komineshoten.co.jp, pg 418

Kommissionsverlag Leobuchhandling (Switzerland) *Tel:* (071) 222917 *Fax:* (071) 220587, pg 622

Kommunernes Skolebiblioteksforening (Denmark) *Tel:* 33111391 *Fax:* 33111390 *E-mail:* komskolbib@ ksbf.dk *Web Site:* www.ksbf.dk, pg 1561

Kompass Fleischmann (Italy) *Tel:* (0461) 961240 *Fax:* (0461) 961203, pg 391

Izdatelskii Dom Kompozitor (Russian Federation) *Tel:* (095) 2092380; (095) 2094105 *Fax:* (095) 2095498 *E-mail:* music@sumail.ru, pg 541

Komputerowa Oficyna Wydawnicza Help (Poland) *Tel:* (022) 723 89 21 *Fax:* (022) 723 87 64 *E-mail:* kowhelp@pol.pl *Web Site:* www.besthelp.pl, pg 519

Wydawnictwa Komunikacji i Lacznosci Co Ltd (Poland) *Tel:* (022) 849 27 51 *Fax:* (022) 849 23 22 *E-mail:* wkl@wkl.com.pl *Web Site:* www.wkl.com.pl, pg 519

Konark Publishers Pvt Ltd (India) *Tel:* (011) 22504101; (011) 22455731; (011) 22507103 *Fax:* (011) 22507103 *E-mail:* kppl23@eth.net; konarkpublishers@hotmail. com, pg 336

Det Kongelige Bibliotek (Denmark) *Tel:* 33 47 47 47 *Fax:* 33 93 22 18 *E-mail:* kb@kb.dk *Web Site:* www. kb.dk, pg 1500

Det Kongelige Danske Videnskabernes Selskab (Denmark) *Tel:* 33435300 *Fax:* 33435301 *E-mail:* e-mail@royalacademy.dk *Web Site:* www.royalacademy. dk, pg 1392

Konias (Czech Republic) *Tel:* (019) 28 06 90 *Fax:* (019) 28 06 90 *E-mail:* konias@literaplzen.cz, pg 124

Koninklijke Academie voor Nederlandse Taal- en Letterkunde (Belgium) *Tel:* (09) 265 93 40 *Fax:* (09) 265 93 49 *E-mail:* info@kantl.be *Web Site:* www. kantl.be, pg 1391

Koninklijke Academie voor Wetenschappen Letteren en Schone Kunsten Van Belgie (Belgium) *Tel:* (02) 550 23 23 *Fax:* (02) 550 23 25 *E-mail:* info@kvab.be *Web Site:* www.kvab.be, pg 1391

Koninklijke Bibliotheek (Netherlands) *Tel:* (070) 3140911 *Fax:* (070) 3140450 *E-mail:* info@kb.nl *Web Site:* www.kb.nl, pg 1529

Koninklijke Vermande bv (Netherlands) *Tel:* (070) 3789880 *Fax:* (070) 3789783 *E-mail:* sdu@sdu.nl *Web Site:* www.sdu.nl/uitg/vermande, pg 481

Koninklijke Vlaamse Academie van Belgie voor Wetenschappen en Kunsten (Belgium) *Tel:* (02) 550 23 23 *Fax:* (02) 550 23 25 *E-mail:* info@kvab.be *Web Site:* www.kvab.be, pg 69

Konkordia Verlag GmbH (Germany) *Tel:* (07223) 98 89-0 *Fax:* (07223) 98 89-45 *E-mail:* verlag@konkordia.de *Web Site:* www.konkordia.de, pg 247

Konkret Literatur Verlag (Germany) *Tel:* (040) 47 52 34 *Fax:* (040) 47 84 15 *E-mail:* info@konkret-literatur-verlag.de *Web Site:* www.konkret-verlage.de, pg 247

Anton H Konrad Verlag (Germany) *Tel:* (07309) 26 57 *Fax:* (07309) 60 69 *E-mail:* info@konrad-verlag.de *Web Site:* www.konrad-verlag.de/, pg 247

Konradin-Verlagsgruppe (Germany) *Tel:* (0711) 7594-0 *Fax:* (0711) 7594-390 *E-mail:* info@konradin.de *Web Site:* www.konradin.de, pg 247

Universitat Konstanz (Germany) *Tel:* (07531) 88-0 *Fax:* (07531) 88-3688 *E-mail:* Posteingang@uni-konstanz.de *Web Site:* www.uni-konstanz.de, pg 1508

Konsultace spol sro (Czech Republic) *Tel:* (02) 2310363 *Fax:* (02) 2310363, pg 124

Konsultforlaget AB (Sweden) *Tel:* (018) 55 50 80 *Fax:* (018) 55 50 81 *E-mail:* info@uppsala-publishing. se *Web Site:* www.uppsala-publishing.se, pg 608

KONTEXTverlag (Germany) *Tel:* (030) 94415444 *Fax:* (030) 94415445 *E-mail:* service@kontextverlag. de *Web Site:* www.kontextverlag.de, pg 247

Kookaburra Technical Publications Pty Ltd (Australia) *Tel:* (03) 9560 0841 *Fax:* (03) 9545 1121 *Web Site:* www.boundy39.com/hkooka/HkookaFSO. htm, pg 28

Koolibri (Estonia) *Tel:* 651 5300 *Fax:* 651 5301 *E-mail:* koolibri@koolibri.ee *Web Site:* www.koolibri. ee, pg 139

Koorong Books Pty Ltd (Australia) *Tel:* (02) 9857 4477 *Fax:* (02) 9857 4499 *E-mail:* west_ryde@koorong. com.au; koorong@koorong.com.au *Web Site:* www. koorong.com.au, pg 1289

kopaed verlagsgmbh (Germany) *Tel:* (089) 68890098 *Fax:* (089) 6891912 *E-mail:* info@kopaed.de *Web Site:* www.kopaed.de, pg 247

Koptisch-Orthodoxes Zentrum (Germany) *Tel:* (06085) 23 17 *Fax:* (06085) 26 66 *E-mail:* jugend@kopten.de *Web Site:* www.kopten.de, pg 247

Editions Buma Kor & Co Ltd (Cameroon) *Tel:* (023) 22 48 99 *Fax:* (023) 23 29 03, pg 97

Korea Britannica Corp (Republic of Korea) *Tel:* (02) 2272-9731; (02) 2264-0924 (sales) *Fax:* (02) 2278-9983 *E-mail:* corporate@britannica.co.kr *Web Site:* www.britannica.co.kr, pg 436

Korea Development Institute Library (Republic of Korea) *Tel:* (02) 958 4266 *Fax:* (02) 958 4261 *E-mail:* library@kdi.re.kr *Web Site:* www.kdi.re.kr, pg 1522

Korea Local Authorities Foundation for International Relations (Republic of Korea) *Tel:* (02) 730 2711; (02) 2170-6098 *Fax:* (02) 737 8970; (02) 737-7903 *E-mail:* others@klafir.or.kr *Web Site:* www.klafir.or.kr/, pg 436

Korea Psychological Testing Institute (Republic of Korea) *Tel:* (02) 784-0990 *Fax:* (02) 784-0993 *E-mail:* KPIT@unitel.co.kr *Web Site:* www.kpti.com, pg 437

Korea Publications Export & Import Corporation (Democratic People's Republic of Korea) *Tel:* (02) 3818536 *Fax:* (02) 3814404; (02) 3814410, pg 1314

Korea Science & Encyclopedia Publishing House (Democratic People's Republic of Korea) *Tel:* (02) 381 8091 (Call between 18 & 21 hours Pyongyang local time, Mon, Wed & Fri only) *Fax:* (02) 381 4550 (24 hours); (02) 381 4410; (02) 381 4427, pg 433

Korea Textbook Co Ltd (Republic of Korea) *Tel:* (02) 465-1341 *Fax:* (02) 464-1318 *E-mail:* kpp0114@ hanmail.net, pg 437

Korea University Library (Republic of Korea) *Tel:* (02) 3290-1499 *Fax:* (02) 3234-763 *E-mail:* unneu@korea. ac.kr; libweb@korea.ac.kr *Web Site:* library.korea.ac. kr, pg 1522

Korea University Press (Republic of Korea) *Tel:* (02) 3290 4231 *Fax:* (02) 923 6311, pg 437

Korean Library Association (KLA) (Republic of Korea) *Tel:* (02) 5354868 *Fax:* (02) 5355616 *E-mail:* klanet@ hitel.net *Web Site:* www.korla.or.kr, pg 1566

Korean Publishers Association (Republic of Korea) *Tel:* (02) 735-2701; (02) 735-2704 *Fax:* (02) 738-5414 *E-mail:* kpa@kpa21.or.kr *Web Site:* www.kpa21.or.kr, pg 437, 1266

Korean Publishing Research Institute (Republic of Korea) *Tel:* (02) 7399040 *Fax:* (02) 7376187 *E-mail:* p715@chollian.net, pg 1266

Korean Research & Development Library Association (KORDELA) (Republic of Korea) *Tel:* (02) 9673692 *Fax:* (02) 29634013, pg 1566

Koreaone Press Inc (Republic of Korea) *Tel:* (02) 739-1156 *Fax:* (02) 734-3512, pg 437

Koren Publishers Jerusalem Ltd (Israel) *Tel:* (02) 5660188 *Fax:* (02) 5666658 *Web Site:* www.koren-publishers.co.il, pg 366

Bergstadtverlag Wilhelm Gottlieb Korn GmbH Wuerzburg (Germany) *Tel:* (0711) 4406-193 *Fax:* (0711) 4406-199, pg 247

Galerie Kornfeld & Co (Switzerland) *Tel:* (031) 381 46 73 *Fax:* (031) 382 18 91 *E-mail:* galerie@kornfeld.ch *Web Site:* www.kornfeld.ch, pg 622

Kosei Publishing Co Ltd (Japan) *Tel:* (03) 5385-2319 *Fax:* (03) 5385-2331 *Web Site:* www.kosei-shuppan.co. jp/english/, pg 418

Koseisha-Koseikaku Co Ltd (Japan) *Tel:* (03) 3359-7371 *Fax:* (03) 3359-7375 *E-mail:* koseisha@po.iijnet.or.jp *Web Site:* www.vinet.or.jp/~koseisha; www.kouseisha. com, pg 418

Kosik (Czech Republic) *Tel:* (311) 670929 *Fax:* (02) 2359403, pg 124

Verlag A F Koska (Austria) *Tel:* (0222) 5874344, pg 52

Livraria Kosmos Editora Ltda (Brazil) *Tel:* (021) 2224-8616 *Fax:* (021) 2221-4582 *E-mail:* livro-rio@kosmos. com.br *Web Site:* www.kosmos.com.br, pg 84

Livraria Kosmos Editora Ltda (Brazil) *Tel:* (021) 224-8616 *Fax:* (021) 221-4582, pg 1253

Livraria Kosmos Editora Ltda (Brazil) *Tel:* (021) 2224-8616 *Fax:* (021) 2221-4582, pg 1293

Kossodo Verlag AG (Switzerland) *Tel:* (022) 962230, pg 622

Kossuth Kiado RT (Hungary) *Tel:* (01) 3700607 *Fax:* (01) 3700602 *E-mail:* rt@kossuted.hu *Web Site:* www.kossuth.hu, pg 319

Kossuth Lajos Tudomanyegyetem Egyetemi Koenyvtar (Hungary) *Tel:* (052) 316-835; (052) 316-666; (052) 512-900 *Fax:* (052) 410-443 *E-mail:* comp@lib. unideb.hu *Web Site:* www.lib.unideb.hu, pg 1513

Kotuku Media Ltd (New Zealand) *Tel:* (04) 2331842 *E-mail:* kotuku.media@xtra.co.nz, pg 493

Dr Anton Kovac Slavica Verlag (Germany) *Tel:* (089) 2725612 *Fax:* (089) 2716594 *E-mail:* 101566.2450@ compuserve.com, pg 247

Roman Kovar Verlag (Germany) *Tel:* (08206) 961977 *Fax:* (08206) 961978 *E-mail:* romankovar@gmx.net *Web Site:* www.kovar-verlag.com, pg 248

Kowhai Publishing Ltd (New Zealand) *Tel:* (09) 5759126 *Fax:* (09) 5753178, pg 493

Koyo Shobo (Japan) *Tel:* (075) 312-0788 *Fax:* (075) 312-7447, pg 418

KPI (Indonesia) *Tel:* (021) 361701; (021) 41701, pg 1243

KPT InfoTrader Inc (Japan) *Tel:* (06) 6479 7160 *Fax:* (06) 6479 7163 *E-mail:* osaka@infotrader.jp *Web Site:* www.infotrader.jp, pg 1312

Verlag Karl Kraemer & Co (Switzerland) *Tel:* (01) 2528454 *Fax:* (0711) 784960 (Germany) *E-mail:* info@kraemerverlag.com *Web Site:* www. kraemerverlag.com, pg 622

Karl Kraemer Verlag GmbH und Co (Germany) *Tel:* (0711) 7 84 96-0 *Fax:* (0711) 7 84 96-20 *E-mail:* info@kraemerverlag.com *Web Site:* www. kraemerverlag.com, pg 248

Reinhold Kraemer Verlag (Germany) *Tel:* (040) 4101429 *Fax:* (040) 455770 *E-mail:* info@kraemer-verlag.de *Web Site:* www.kraemer-verlag.de, pg 248

Adam Kraft Verlag (Germany) *Tel:* (0931) 385235 *Fax:* (0931) 385305 *E-mail:* info@verlagshaus.com *Web Site:* www.verlagshaus.com, pg 248

Krafthand Verlag Walter Schultz GmbH (Germany) *Tel:* (08247) 30070 *Fax:* (08247) 300770 *E-mail:* info@krafthand.de *Web Site:* www.krafthand. de, pg 248

Verlag Edition Kraftpunkt Anton Fedrigotti (Germany) *Tel:* (0821) 705011 *Fax:* (0821) 705008, pg 248

Krajowe Biuro Miedzynarodowego Numeru Ksiazki ISBN (Poland) *Tel:* (022) 608 2432 *Fax:* (022) 825 5729 *Web Site:* www.bn.org.pl, pg 1271

Kraks Forlag AS (Denmark) *Tel:* 95 65 00 *Fax:* 95 65 55 *E-mail:* krak@krak.dk *Web Site:* www.krak.dk, pg 132

Kralica MAB (Bulgaria) *Tel:* (02) 767357 *Fax:* (02) 767357 *E-mail:* mab@slovar.org *Web Site:* www. slovar.org/mab, pg 94

Kramds-reklama Publishing & Advertising (Kazakstan) *Tel:* (03272) 453968 *Fax:* (03272) 696753, pg 429

Karin Kramer Verlag (Germany) *Tel:* (030) 6845055; (030) 6842598 *Fax:* (030) 6858577 *E-mail:* kramer@ virtualitas.com *Web Site:* www.anares.org/kramer/, pg 248

Verlag Rene Kramer AG (Switzerland) *Tel:* (091) 518941, pg 622

Verlag Waldemar Kramer (Germany) *Tel:* (069) 449045 *Fax:* (069) 449064 *E-mail:* info@frankfurtbuecher.de *Web Site:* www.frankfurtbuecher.de, pg 248

Kranich-Verlag, Dres AG & H R Bosch-Gwalter (Switzerland) *Tel:* (01) 3918484 *Fax:* (01) 3920884 *E-mail:* boschag@zik.ch, pg 622

Nara Verlag Josef Krauthaeuser (Germany) *Tel:* (08166) 8530; (08166) 8531 *Fax:* (08166) 8530 *E-mail:* info@ nara-verlag.de *Web Site:* www.nara-international.de; www.nara-verlag.de, pg 248

Kremayr & Scheriau Verlag (Austria) *Tel:* (01) 713 8770-10 *Fax:* (01)713 8770-20 *E-mail:* m.scheriau@ kremayr-scheriau.at, pg 52

Hubert Kretschmar Leipziger Verlagsgesellschaft (Germany) *Tel:* (0341) 2210229 *Fax:* (0341) 2210226, pg 248

Verlag Hubert Kretschmer (Germany) *Tel:* (089) 1234530 *Fax:* (089) 1238638 *E-mail:* hubert.kretschmer@t-online.de *Web Site:* www.verlag-hubert-kretschmer.de, pg 248

Kreuz Verlag GmbH & Co KG (Germany) *Tel:* (0711) 788030 *Fax:* (0711) 7880310 *E-mail:* service@ kreuzverlag.de *Web Site:* www.kreuzverlag.de, pg 1301

Svet Kridel (Slovakia) *Tel:* (0267) 201921; (0267) 201922 *Fax:* (0267) 201910 *E-mail:* casiopisv@press. sk *Web Site:* www.svetkridel.cz, pg 555

Kriebel Verlag GmbH (Germany) *Tel:* (08806) 93 60 *Fax:* (08806) 93 61 *E-mail:* info@kriebelverlag.de *Web Site:* www.kriebel-sat.de; www.kriebelverlag.de, pg 248

Antiquariat Walter Krieg Verlag (Austria) *Tel:* (01) 5121093 *Fax:* (01) 5123266, pg 1290

De Krijger (Belgium) *Tel:* (053) 808449 *Fax:* (053) 808453 *E-mail:* de.krijger@primemedia.be, pg 69

Krishnamurthy K (India) *Tel:* (044) 2434 4519 *Fax:* (044) 2434 2009 *E-mail:* service@kkbooks.com *Web Site:* www.kkbooks.com, pg 1306

Kristen Press (Papua New Guinea) *Tel:* 8522988 *Fax:* 823313, pg 511

Kristiansand Folkebibliotek (Norway) *Tel:* (038) 12 49 10 *Fax:* (038) 12 49 49 *E-mail:* post.folkebibliotek@ kristiansand.kommune.no *Web Site:* www.kristiansand. folkebibl.no, pg 1533

Editura Kriterion SA (Romania) *Tel:* (01) 3366509 *Fax:* (01) 313 11 07 *E-mail:* krit@dnt.ro; kriterion@ mail.dnt.cj.ro, pg 535

Kritiki (Greece) *Tel:* 2103803730 *Fax:* 2103803740 *E-mail:* biblia@kritiki.gr *Web Site:* www.kritiki.gr, pg 1303

Kritiki Publishing (Greece) *Tel:* 2103803730 *Fax:* 2103803740 *E-mail:* biblia@kritiki.gr *Web Site:* www.kritiki.gr, pg 306

Alfred Kroner Verlag (Germany) *Tel:* (0711) 6155363 *Fax:* (0711) 61553646 *E-mail:* kontakt@kroener-verlag.de *Web Site:* www.kroener-verlag.de, pg 248

Krscanska sadasnjost (Croatia) *Tel:* (01) 48 28 219; (01) 48 28 222 *Fax:* (01) 48 28 227 *E-mail:* ks@zg.tel.hr *Web Site:* www.ks.hr, pg 118

Krueger Verlag GmbH (Germany) *Tel:* (069) 6062-0 *Fax:* (069) 6062-214 *Web Site:* www.fischerverlage.de, pg 248

Krug & Schadenberg (Germany) *Tel:* (030) 61625752 *Fax:* (030) 61625751 *E-mail:* info@krugschadenberg. de *Web Site:* www.krugschadenberg.de, pg 248

'Ksiazka i Wiedza' Spotdzielnia Wydawniczo-Handlowa (Poland) *Tel:* (022) 8275401; (022) 8279416 *Fax:* (022) 8279416; (022) 8279423 *E-mail:* publisher@kiw.com.pl *Web Site:* www.kiw. com.pl, pg 519

Ksiaznica Publishing Ltd (Poland) *Tel:* (032) 257 22 16 *Fax:* (032) 257 22 17 *E-mail:* ksiaznica@domnet.com. pl, pg 519

Ktitor (The Former Yugoslav Republic of Macedonia) *Tel:* (092) 21903; (092) 34746 *Fax:* (092) 34746, pg 449

Editora Kuarup Ltda (Brazil) *Tel:* (051) 361-5522 *Fax:* (051) 361-3550 *E-mail:* kuarup@conex.com.br, pg 84

Kubbealti Akademisi Kultur ve Sasat Vakfi (Turkey) *Tel:* (0212) 516 23 56; (0212) 518 92 09 *Fax:* (0212) 517 14 60, pg 646

KUbK Publishing House (Russian Federation) *Tel:* (095) 1640910; (095) 3679473 *Fax:* (095) 1528689, pg 541

Kubon & Sagner Buchexport-Import GmbH (Germany) *Tel:* (089) 54 218-0 *Fax:* (089) 54 218-218 *E-mail:* postmaster@kubon-sagner.de *Web Site:* www. kubon-sagner.de, pg 1301

Kuemmerly & Frey (Geographischer Verlag) (Switzerland) *Tel:* (031) 850 3131 *Fax:* (031) 850 3130 *E-mail:* info@swisstravelcenter.ch *Web Site:* www.swisstravelcenter.ch, pg 622

Kuemmerly und Frey Verlags GmbH (Austria) *Tel:* (01) 545 14 45 *Fax:* (01) 545 10 80-83 *E-mail:* kuemmerly-frey@xpoint.at, pg 52

Imprimerie A Kuendig (Switzerland) *Tel:* (022) 966013, pg 622

Kugler Publications (Netherlands) *Tel:* (070) 33-00253 *Fax:* (070) 33-00254 *E-mail:* kuglerspb@wxs.nl *Web Site:* www.kuglerpublications.com, pg 481

Verlag Ernst Kuhn (Germany) *Tel:* (030) 44342230 *Fax:* (030) 4424732 *E-mail:* ernst-kuhn-verlag@t-online.de *Web Site:* www.vek.de, pg 249

Kuiseb-Verlag (Namibia) *Tel:* (061) 225372 *Fax:* (061) 226846 *E-mail:* nwg@iafrica.com.na, pg 472

Kukmin Doseo Publishing Co Ltd (Republic of Korea) *Tel:* (02) 858-2461; (02) 858-2463 *Fax:* (02) 858-2464 *E-mail:* younhlee@chollian.net, pg 437

Kukminseokwan Publishing Co Ltd (Republic of Korea) *Tel:* (02) 7107722; (02) 7107724 *Fax:* (02) 7155771, pg 437

Kultura (Hungary) *Tel:* (01) 2501194 *Fax:* (01) 2500233, pg 1210

Kultura (The Former Yugoslav Republic of Macedonia) *Tel:* (02) 111-332 *Fax:* (02) 228-608 *E-mail:* ipkultura@unet.com.mk *Web Site:* www. kultura.com.mk/en, pg 1316

Kultura (Serbia and Montenegro) *Tel:* (021) 780-144 *Fax:* (021) 780-291, pg 548

Kul'tura redakcionno-izdatel skij kompleks (Russian Federation) *Tel:* (095) 2481151 *Fax:* (095) 2302180, pg 541

Kulturbuch-Verlag GmbH (Germany) *Tel:* (030) 6618484 *Fax:* (030) 6617828 *E-mail:* kbvinfo@kulturbuch-verlag.de *Web Site:* www.kulturbuch-verlag.de, pg 249

Kulturstiftung der deutschen Vertriebenen (Germany) *Tel:* (0228) 915120 *Fax:* (0228) 218397 *E-mail:* kulturstiftung@t-online.de *Web Site:* www. kulturstiftung-der-deutschen-vertriebenen.de, pg 249

Kumsung Publishing Co Ltd (Republic of Korea) *Tel:* (02) 713-9651 *Fax:* (02) 704-1979; (02) 718-4362 *E-mail:* webmaster@kumsungpub.co.kr *Web Site:* www.kumsungpub.com, pg 437

Kungl Ingenjoersvetenskapsakademien (IVA) (Sweden) *Tel:* (08) 7912900 *Fax:* (08) 6115623 *E-mail:* info@ iva.se *Web Site:* www.iva.se, pg 608

Kungl Tekniska Hoegskolan Biblioteket (Royal Institute of Technology Library) (Sweden) *Tel:* (08) 790 7088 *Fax:* (08) 790 7122 *E-mail:* loandept@lib.kth.se *Web Site:* www.lib.kth.se, pg 1545

Kungl Vitterhets Historie och Antikvitets Akademien (Sweden) *Tel:* (08) 440 42 80 *Fax:* (08) 440 42 90 *E-mail:* kansli@vitterhetsakad.se *Web Site:* www. vitterhetsakad.se, pg 1399

Kungliga Biblioteket (Sweden) *Tel:* (08) 463 40 00 *Fax:* (08) 463 40 04 *E-mail:* kungl.biblioteket@kb.se *Web Site:* www.kb.se, pg 1545

Kunlun Publishing House (China) *Tel:* (010) 6732721 *Fax:* (010) 62183683; (010) 66847703, pg 105

Kunnskapsforlaget ANS (Norway) *Tel:* (022) 03 66 00 *Fax:* (022) 03 66 05 *E-mail:* kundeservice@ kunnskapsforlaget.no *Web Site:* www. kunnskapsforlaget.no, pg 505

Verlag der Kunst/G+B Fine Arts Verlag GmbH (Germany) *Tel:* (0351) 3360742; (0351) 3100052 *Fax:* (0351) 3105245 *E-mail:* verlag-der-kunst@t-online.de *Web Site:* www.verlag-der-kunst.de, pg 249

Verlag Antje Kunstmann GmbH (Germany) *Tel:* (089) 1211930 *Fax:* (089) 12119320 *E-mail:* info@ kunstmann.de *Web Site:* www.kunstmann.de, pg 249

Kunstmuseum Liechtenstein Vaduz (Liechtenstein) *Tel:* 235 03 00 *Fax:* 235 03 29 *E-mail:* mail@ kunstmuseum.li *Web Site:* www.kunstmuseum.li, pg 444

Kunstverlag Maria Laach (Germany) *Tel:* (02652) 59360 *Fax:* (02652) 59383 *E-mail:* verlag@maria_laach.de; versand@maria_laach.de *Web Site:* www.ars-liturgica. de/verlag, pg 249

Kunstverlag Weingarten GmbH (Germany) *Tel:* (0751) 561290 *Fax:* (0751) 5612920 *E-mail:* kunstverlag@ weingarten-verlag.de *Web Site:* www.kv-weingarten.de, pg 249

Edition Kunzelmann GmbH (Switzerland) *Tel:* (01) 7103681 *Fax:* (01) 7103817 *Web Site:* www. kunzelmann.ch, pg 622

Kupar Publishers (Estonia) *Tel:* (02) 628 6173; (02) 628 6175 *Fax:* (02) 646 2076 *E-mail:* kupar@netexpress. ee, pg 139

Kuperard (United Kingdom) *Tel:* (020) 8446 2440 *Fax:* (020) 8446 2441 *E-mail:* kuperard@bravo.clara. net *Web Site:* www.kuperard.co.uk, pg 714

Kuperard (United Kingdom) *Tel:* (020) 8446 2440 *Fax:* (020) 8446 2441 *E-mail:* kuperard@bravo.clara. net; office@kuperard.co.uk *Web Site:* www.kuperard. co.uk, pg 1343

Kupfergraben Verlagsgesellschaft mbH (Germany) *Tel:* (030) 2622097 *Fax:* (030) 2621990, pg 249

Kurlana Publishing (Australia) *Tel:* (08) 3886619, pg 28

Kurnia Esanata (Indonesia) *Tel:* (021) 361974; (021) 3104948, pg 352

Kustannus Oy Kolibri (Finland) *Tel:* (09) 774 5310 *Fax:* (09) 701 9351 *E-mail:* susanna.frankenhaeuser@ kolibrikustannus.fi, pg 142

Rakentajain Kustannus Oy (Building Publications Ltd) (Finland) *Tel:* (09) 142855 *Fax:* (09) 5032542, pg 142

Kustannus Oy Semic (Finland) *Tel:* (03) 273 8111 *Fax:* (031) 243 8287 *E-mail:* minna.alanko@egmont-kustannus.fi, pg 142

Kustannus Oy Uusi Tie (Finland) *Tel:* (019) 77 920 *Fax:* (019) 779 2300 *E-mail:* uusitie@uusitie.com *Web Site:* www.uusitie.com, pg 143

Kustannuskiila Oy (Finland) *Tel:* (017) 303 111 *Fax:* (017) 303 242 *E-mail:* anneli-siimes@ savonsanomat.fi, pg 143

Kustannusosakeyhtio Tammi (Finland) *Tel:* (09) 6937 621 *Fax:* (09) 6937 6266 *E-mail:* tammi@tammi.net *Web Site:* www.tammi.net, pg 143

Kuva ja Sana (Finland) *Tel:* (09) 477 4920 *Fax:* (09) 4774 9250 *E-mail:* kuva.sana@patmos.fi, pg 143

The Kuwait Book Shop Company Ltd (Kuwait) *Tel:* 2424687; 2424266 *Fax:* 2420558 *E-mail:* kbs@ ncc.moc.kw, pg 1315

Kuwait Publishing House (Kuwait) *Tel:* 2414697, pg 440

Kuwait University Library (Kuwait) *Tel:* 4813182 *Fax:* 4816095 *Web Site:* www.kuniv.edu.kw, pg 1522

Kuwait University Library (Kuwait) *Tel:* 4816497 *Web Site:* www.kuniv.edu.kw, pg 1566

KVB Koninklijke Vereeniging van het Boekenvak (Netherlands) *Tel:* (020) 624 02 12 *Fax:* (020) 620 88 71 *E-mail:* info@kvb.nl *Web Site:* www.kvb.nl, pg 1269

KVG de Silva & Sons (Sri Lanka) *Tel:* (01) 84146 *Fax:* (01) 586598, pg 601

KVG de Silva & Sons (Sri Lanka) *Tel:* (01) 84146 *Fax:* (01) 588875, pg 1334

Kerstin Kvint Literary & Co-Production Agency (Sweden) *Tel:* (08) 107014 *Fax:* (08) 107606, pg 1127

Kwa-Zulu Natal Provincial Library Service (South Africa) *Tel:* (033) 3940241 *Fax:* (033) 3942237 *E-mail:* daviess@plho.kzntl.gov.za, pg 1542

Kwame Nkrumah University of Science & Technology Library (Ghana) *Tel:* (051) 60199; (051) 60133 *Fax:* (051) 60358 *E-mail:* ustlib@libr.ug.edu.gh, pg 1511

Kwamfori Publishing Enterprise (Ghana), pg 301

Kwang Fu Book Co Ltd (Taiwan, Province of China) *Tel:* (02) 558 15 678 *Fax:* (02) 558 15 141 *E-mail:* lolatiao@kfgroup.com.tw, pg 636

Kwangmyong Publishing Co (Republic of Korea) *Tel:* (02) 2274-1552 *Fax:* (02) 2264-3309 *E-mail:* kwangmgl@hanmail.net, pg 437

KwaZulu-Natal Law Society Library (South Africa) *Tel:* (033) 345 1304 *Fax:* (033) 394 9544 *E-mail:* info@lawsoc.co.za *Web Site:* www.lawlibrary. co.za, pg 1542

KY KE M (Cyprus) *Tel:* (022) 450302 *Fax:* (022) 463624, pg 121

Kydds Paper Plus (New Zealand) *Tel:* (07) 8957430 *Fax:* (07) 8957977 *E-mail:* kyddp@xtra.co.nz *Web Site:* www.middle-of-everywhere.co.nz/kyddspp. htm, pg 1321

Kyi-Pwar-Ye Book House (Myanmar) *Tel:* (02) 21003, pg 472

Kynos Verlag Dr Dieter Fleig GmbH (Germany) *Tel:* (06594) 653 *Fax:* (06594) 452 *E-mail:* info@ kynos-verlag.de *Web Site:* www.kynos-verlag.de, pg 249

Kyobo Book Centre Co Ltd (Republic of Korea) *Tel:* (02) 3973508; (02) 3973509 *Fax:* (02) 7350030 *E-mail:* eslee@kyobobook.co.kr *Web Site:* www. kyobobook.co.kr, pg 437

Kyobo Book Centre Co Ltd (Republic of Korea) *Tel:* (02) 397-3481; (02) 397-3482; (02) 397-3483; (02) 397-3484; (02) 397-3485 *Fax:* (02) 735-0030 *E-mail:* kyobofbd@kyobobook.co.kr, pg 1315

Kyobunkan Inc (Christian Literature Society of Japan) (Japan) *Tel:* (03) 3561-8449 *Fax:* (03) 5250-5109 *E-mail:* fbooks@kyobunkwan.co.jp *Web Site:* www. kyobunkwan.co.jp, pg 1312

Kyodo-Isho Shuppan Co Ltd (Japan) *Tel:* (03) 3818-2361 *Fax:* (03) 3818-2368 *E-mail:* kyodo-ed@fd5.so-net.ne. jp *Web Site:* www.kyodo-isho.co.jp, pg 418

Kyodo Printing Co (S'pore) Pte Ltd (Singapore) *Tel:* 6265 2955 *Fax:* 6264 4939 *E-mail:* cschong@ kyodoprinting.com.sg *Web Site:* kyodosing.com, pg 1212

Kyohaksa Publishing Co Ltd (Republic of Korea) *Tel:* (02) 7174561; (02) 8592017 *Fax:* (02) 7183976, pg 437

Kyoritsu Shuppan Co Ltd (Japan) *Tel:* (03) 3947-2511 *Fax:* (03) 3944-8182 *E-mail:* general@kyoritsu-pub.co. jp *Web Site:* www.kyoritsu-pub.co.jp, pg 418

Kyoto Sangyo University Library (Japan) *Tel:* (075) 7012151 *Fax:* (075) 7051447 *E-mail:* ksu-lib@star. kyoto-su.ac.jp *Web Site:* www3.kyoto-su.ac.jp/lib, pg 1520

Kyrenia Municipality (Cyprus) *Tel:* (022) 818040 *Fax:* (022) 818228, pg 121

Kyriakidis Brothers sa (Greece) *Tel:* 2310208540 *Fax:* 2310245541 *E-mail:* info@kyriakidis.gr *Web Site:* www.kyriakidis.gr, pg 1303

K P Kyriakou (Books - Stationery) Ltd (Cyprus) *Tel:* (025) 747555 *Fax:* (025) 747047 *E-mail:* cybooks@logos.cy.net *Web Site:* www.logos. cy.net, pg 1297

Kyungnam University Press (Republic of Korea) *Tel:* (055) 245-5000 *Fax:* (055) 246-6184 *Web Site:* www.kyungnam.ac.kr, pg 437

Kyungpook National University Central Library (Republic of Korea) *Tel:* (053) 950-6510 *Fax:* (053) 950-6533 *E-mail:* mspark@kyungpook.ac.kr *Web Site:* kudos.knu.ac.kr, pg 1522

Kyushu University Library (Japan) *Tel:* (092) 6411101; (092) 6422111 *E-mail:* w3-admin@lib.kyushu-u.ac.jp *Web Site:* www.lib.kyushu-u.ac.jp, pg 1520

L B Publishing Co (Israel) *Tel:* (02) 5664637 *Fax:* (02) 5290774 *E-mail:* editorial_lb@yahoo.com, pg 366

Laaber-Verlag GmbH (Germany) *Tel:* (09498) 2307 *Fax:* (09498) 2543 *E-mail:* info@laaber-verlag.de *Web Site:* www.laaber-verlag.de, pg 249

Editorial Labor de Venezuela SA (Venezuela) *Tel:* (0212) 7811398; (0212) 7815819, pg 774

Editions Labor (Belgium) *Tel:* (02) 250-06-70 *Fax:* (02) 217-71-97 *E-mail:* labor@labor.be *Web Site:* www. labor.be, pg 69

Labor et Fides SA (Switzerland) *Tel:* (022) 311 32 69 *Fax:* (022) 781 30 51 *E-mail:* contact@laboretfides. com *Web Site:* www.laboretfides.com, pg 622

Labyrint (Czech Republic) *Tel:* (02) 24 922 422 *Fax:* (02) 24 922 422 *E-mail:* labyrint@wo.cz *Web Site:* www.labyrint.net, pg 124

Labyrinth Verlag Gisela Ottmer (Germany) *Tel:* (0531) 64259 *Fax:* (0531) 681358 *E-mail:* labyrinthbraunschweig@t-online.de *Web Site:* www.frauenart.de/labyrinthbraunschweig, pg 249

LAC - Litografia Artistica Cartografica Srl (Italy) *Tel:* (055) 483 557 *Fax:* (055) 483 690 *E-mail:* info@ lac-cartografia.it *Web Site:* www.lac-cartografia.it, pg 391

Editions Lacour-Olle (France) *Tel:* (04) 66 67 30 30 *Fax:* (04) 66 21 11 23 *E-mail:* c.lacour@editions-lacour.com *Web Site:* www.editions-lacour.com, pg 170

Ambro Lacus, Buch- und Bildverlag Walter A Kremnitz (Germany) *Tel:* (08152) 1332 *Fax:* (08152) 40186, pg 249

Ladomir Publishing House (Russian Federation) *Tel:* (095) 530-9833; (095) 530-8477 *Fax:* (095) 537-4742-7870, pg 541

L'Adret editions (France), pg 170

Ladybird Books Ltd (United Kingdom) *Tel:* (020) 7010 2900 *Fax:* (01509) 234672 *Web Site:* www.ladybird. co.uk, pg 714

Laertes SA de Ediciones (Spain) *Tel:* (093) 2187020; (093) 2185558 *Fax:* (093) 2174751 *E-mail:* laertes@ jet.es, pg 584

Les Editions Jeanne Laffitte (France) *Tel:* (04) 91 59 80 43 *Fax:* (04) 91 54 25 64 *E-mail:* editions@ jeanne-laffitte.com *Web Site:* www.jeanne-laffitte. com/editions/, pg 171

Laffont Ediciones Electronicas SA (Argentina) *Tel:* (011) 4302-8668 *Fax:* (011) 4301-2525 *E-mail:* info@ laffont.com.ar *Web Site:* www.laffont.com.ar, pg 6

Editions Robert Laffont (France) *Tel:* (01) 53 67 14 00 *Fax:* (01) 53 67 14 14 *Web Site:* www.laffont.fr, pg 171

Verlag Lafite (Austria) *Tel:* (01) 5126869 *Fax:* (01) 51268699 *E-mail:* redaktion@musikzeit.at, pg 53

Editions Jacques Lafitte - Who's Who in France (France) *Tel:* (0141) 272 830 *Fax:* (0141) 272 840 *E-mail:* whoswho@whoswho.fr *Web Site:* www. whoswho.fr, pg 171

Michel Lafon Publishing (France) *Tel:* (01) 41 43 85 85 *Fax:* (01) 46 24 00 95, pg 171

Librairie Leonce Laget (France) *Tel:* (01) 43 29 90 04 *Fax:* (01) 43 26 89 68 *E-mail:* contact@ librairieleoncelaget.fr *Web Site:* www. librairieleoncelaget.fr, pg 171

Lagos City Council Libraries (Nigeria) *Tel:* (01) 50246, pg 1532

Lahn-Verlag GmbH (Germany) *Tel:* (02832) 929-0 *Fax:* (02832) 929-211 *E-mail:* service@lahn-verlag.de *Web Site:* www.lahn-verlag.de, pg 249

Editorin Laiovento SL (Spain) *Tel:* (0981) 887570 *Fax:* (0981) 572239 *E-mail:* laiovento@laiovento.com *Web Site:* www.laiovento.com, pg 584

Francisco J Laissue Livros (Brazil) *Tel:* (021) 509-7298, pg 84

Lake House Bookshop (Sri Lanka) *Tel:* (011) 4712473 *Fax:* (011) 2438704 *E-mail:* sarathi@eureka.lk, pg 1334

Lake House Investments Ltd (Sri Lanka) *Tel:* (01) 35175; (01) 33271 *Fax:* (01) 44 7848; (01) 44 9504 *E-mail:* lhl@srilanka.net, pg 602

Lake-Livraria Editora Allan Kardec (Brazil) *Tel:* (011) 229-0526; (011) 229-1227; (011) 227-1396; (011) 229-0937; (011) 229-4592; (011) 229-0514 *Fax:* (011) 229-0935; (011) 227-5714 *E-mail:* lake@lake.com.br *Web Site:* www.lake.com.br, pg 84

Lake Publishers & Enterprises Ltd (Kenya) *Tel:* (057) 42750; (057) 2153, pg 431

Lalit Kala Akademi (India) *Tel:* (011) 23387241; (011) 23387243; (011) 23387242 *Fax:* (011) 23782485 *E-mail:* lka@lalitkala.org.in *Web Site:* www.lalitkala. org.in, pg 336

Lalli Editore SRL (Italy) *Tel:* (0577) 933305 *Fax:* (0577) 983308 *E-mail:* lalli@lallieditore.it *Web Site:* www. lallieditore.it, pg 391

Editions Lamarre SA (France) *Tel:* (01) 41 29 99 99 *Fax:* (01) 41 29 77 05, pg 171

Charles Lamb Society (United Kingdom) *Tel:* (020) 7332 1868; (020) 7332 1870 *Web Site:* users.ox.ac. uk/~scat1492/clsoc.htm, pg 1402

Lambda Edition GmbH (Germany) *Tel:* (040) 312836 *Fax:* (040) 3192096, pg 249

Lambertus Verlag GmbH (Germany) *Tel:* (0761) 368250 *Fax:* (0761) 3682533 *E-mail:* info@lambertus.de *Web Site:* www.lambertus.de, pg 249

Lammar Offset Printing Co (Hong Kong) *Tel:* 25631068 *Fax:* 28113375, pg 1208

Lamuv Verlag GmbH (Germany) *Tel:* (0551) 44024 *Fax:* (0551) 41392 *E-mail:* info@lamuv.de *Web Site:* www.lamuv.de, pg 249

Lancashire Authors' Association (United Kingdom) *Tel:* (01254) 56788 *E-mail:* laa@lancs.communigate. co.uk *Web Site:* www.communigate.co.uk/lancs/laa/ index.phtml, pg 1402

Lancer Publisher's & Distributors (India) *Tel:* (011) 6867339; (011) 6854691 *Fax:* (011) 6862077 *Web Site:* www.geocites.com/TheTropics/3328/lancer. htm, pg 336

Landarc Publications (Australia) *Tel:* (03) 93801276 *Fax:* (03) 93801276 *E-mail:* carmar@bigpond.com, pg 28

Landbuch-Verlagsgesellschaft mbH (Germany) *Tel:* (0511) 27046-153 *Fax:* (0511) 27046-150 *E-mail:* info@landbuch.de *Web Site:* www.landbuch. de, pg 250

Landcare Research NZ (New Zealand) *Tel:* (03) 3256700 *Fax:* (03) 3252127 *E-mail:* mwpress@landcare.cri.nz *Web Site:* www.landcare.cri.nz/mwpress/, pg 493

Institut fuer Landes- und Stadtentwicklungsforschung des Landes Nordrhein-Westfalen (Germany) *Tel:* (0231) 90 51-0 *Fax:* (0231) 90 51-1 55 *E-mail:* postelle@ils.nrw. de *Web Site:* www.ils.nrw.de, pg 250

Jay Landesman (United Kingdom) *Tel:* (020) 7837 7290 *Fax:* (020) 7833 1925, pg 714

Landesverband der Verleger und Buchhaendler Rheinland-Pfalz eV (Germany) *Tel:* (06131) 234035 *Fax:* (06131) 230364, pg 1260

Landmark Education Supplies Pty Ltd (Australia) *Tel:* (056) 251701, pg 1289

Lands Department, Survey & Mapping Office (Hong Kong) *Tel:* 2848 2182 *Fax:* 2521 8726, pg 315

Landsberger (Israel) *Tel:* (03) 5176330 *Fax:* (03) 5222646, pg 1310

Landsbokasafn Islands-Haskolabokasafn (Iceland) *Tel:* 525 5600 *Fax:* 525 5615 *E-mail:* lbs@bok.hi.is *Web Site:* www.bok.hi.is, pg 1513

Landy Publishing (United Kingdom) *Tel:* (01253) 895678 *Fax:* (01253) 895678 *E-mail:* bobdobson@ amserve.com, pg 714

Lanfranchi (Italy) *Tel:* (02) 86465210 *Fax:* (02) 8056083 *E-mail:* info@lanfranchieditore.com *Web Site:* www. lanfranchieditore.com, pg 391

Herbert Lang & Cie AG, Buchhandlung, Antiquariat (Switzerland) *Tel:* (031) 3108484 *Fax:* (031) 3108494, pg 622

Lang Kiado (Hungary) *Tel:* (01) 301-3888 *Fax:* (01) 301-3833 *E-mail:* holding@lang.hu *Web Site:* www. lang.hu, pg 319

Peter Lang AG (Switzerland) *Tel:* (031) 306 17 17 *Fax:* (031) 306 17 27 *E-mail:* info@peterlang.com *Web Site:* www.peterlang.com, pg 622

Peter Lang GmbH Europaeischer Verlag der Wissenschaften (Germany) *Tel:* (069) 7807050 *Fax:* (069) 780705-50 *E-mail:* zentrale.frankfurt@ peterlang.com *Web Site:* www.peterlang.de, pg 250

Lang Syne Publishers Ltd (United Kingdom) *Tel:* (0141) 554 9944 *Fax:* (0141) 554 9955 *E-mail:* enquiries@ scottish-memories.co.uk *Web Site:* www.scottish-memories.co.uk, pg 714

Lange & Springer Antiquariat (Germany) *Tel:* (030) 31504196; (030) 3422011 *Fax:* (030) 3410440; (030) 31504197 *E-mail:* buchladen@lange-springer-antiquariat.de *Web Site:* www.lange-springer-antiquariat.de, pg 1301

Langenscheidt-Verlag GmbH (Austria) *Tel:* (01) 6887133 *Fax:* (01) 68014140, pg 53

Langenscheidt AG Zuerich-Zug (Switzerland) *Tel:* (01) 2115000 *Fax:* (01) 2122149, pg 622

Langenscheidt Fachverlag GmbH (Germany) *Tel:* (089) 36096-0 *Fax:* (089) 36096-222 *E-mail:* kundenservice@langenscheidt.de *Web Site:* www.langenscheidt.de, pg 250

The Langenscheidt Group (Germany) *Tel:* (089) 36096-0; (089) 36096-258 (orders) *Fax:* (089) 36096-222; (089) 36096-258 *E-mail:* kundenservice@langenscheidt.de *Web Site:* www.langenscheidt.de, pg 250

Langenscheidt-Hachette (Germany) *Tel:* (089) 360960 *Fax:* (089) 36096-222; (089) 36096-472 (general); (089) 36096-258 (orders) *E-mail:* kundenservice@ langenscheidt.de *Web Site:* www.langenscheidt.de, pg 250

Langenscheidt KG (Germany) *Tel:* (089) 36096-0; (089) 36096-258 (orders) *Fax:* (089) 36096-222 *E-mail:* kundenservice@langenscheidt.de *Web Site:* www.langenscheidt.de, pg 250

Verlag Langewiesche-Brandt KG (Germany) *Tel:* (08178) 4857 *Fax:* (08178) 7388 *E-mail:* textura@ langewiesche-brandt.de *Web Site:* www.langewiesche-brandt.de, pg 250

Karl Robert Langewiesche Nachfolger Hans Koester KG (Germany) *Tel:* (06174) 7333 *Fax:* (06174) 933-039 *E-mail:* info@langewiesche-verlag.de *Web Site:* www. langewiesche-verlag.de, pg 250

Ingrid Langner (Germany) *Tel:* (04123) 7780 *Fax:* (04123) 7885, pg 250

Language Book Centre (Australia) *Tel:* (02) 92671397 *Toll Free Tel:* 800 802 432 (outside Sydney & within Australia) *Fax:* (02) 92648993 *E-mail:* language@ abbeys.com.au *Web Site:* www.languagebooks.com.au, pg 1289

Language Consultancy Services (United Kingdom) *Tel:* (020) 8450 5344 *Fax:* (020) 8452 9005 *E-mail:* lucifer@ladet.demon.co.uk, pg 1141

Language Publishing House (China) *Tel:* (010) 65130349; (010) 65241766, pg 105

Language Teaching Publications (United Kingdom) *Tel:* (023) 9220 0080 *Fax:* (023) 9220 0090 *E-mail:* ltp@ltpwebsite.com *Web Site:* www. ltpwebsite.com, pg 714

Langues & Mondes-L'Asiatheque (France) *Tel:* (01) 42 62 04 00 *Fax:* (01) 42 62 12 34 *E-mail:* info@ asiatheque.com *Web Site:* www.asiatheque.com, pg 171

Bibliotheque Interuniversitaire des Langues Orientales (France) *Tel:* (01) 44 77 87 20 *Fax:* (01) 44 77 87 30 *E-mail:* biulo@idf.ext.jussieu.fr *Web Site:* www.univ-paris3.fr, pg 1505

Drukkerij Lannoo NV (Belgium) *Tel:* (051) 42 42 11 *Fax:* (051) 40 70 70 *E-mail:* lannoo@lannooprint.be *Web Site:* www.lannooprint.be, pg 1143, 1165, 1205

Uitgeverij Lannoo NV (Belgium) *Tel:* (051) 42 42 11 *Fax:* (051) 40 11 52 *E-mail:* lannoo@lannoo.be *Web Site:* www.lannoo.com, pg 69

Editions Fernand Lanore Sarl (France) *Tel:* (01) 43 25 66 61; (01) 46 33 97 65 *Fax:* (01) 43 29 69 81, pg 171

Lansdowne Publishing Pty Ltd (Australia) *Tel:* (02) 9240 9222 *Fax:* (02) 9241 4818 *E-mail:* sales@lanspub. com.au, pg 28

Lansman Editeur (Belgium) *Tel:* (064) 23-78-40 *Fax:* (064) 44-31-02; (064) 23-78-49 *E-mail:* info@ lansman.org *Web Site:* www.lansman.org, pg 69

Lanzhou University Press (China) *Tel:* (0931) 8843000-3514 *Fax:* (0931) 8615095 *E-mail:* press@lzu.edu.cn, pg 105

Lao Dong (Labor) Publishing House (Viet Nam) *Tel:* (04) 253972, pg 775

Lao-phanit (Laos People's Democratic Republic), pg 441

LAPA Publishers (Pty) Ltd (South Africa) *Tel:* (012) 401 0700 *Fax:* (012) 3255498 *E-mail:* lapa@atkv.org.za, pg 561

Michelle Lapautre (France) *Tel:* (01) 47348241 *Fax:* (01) 47340090 *E-mail:* lapautre@club-internet.fr, pg 1120

Lappan Verlag GmbH (Germany) *Tel:* (0441) 980660 *Fax:* (0441) 9806622; (0441) 9806624; (0441) 9806634 *E-mail:* info@lappan.de *Web Site:* www. lappan.de, pg 251

Editions du Laquet (France) *Tel:* (05) 65 37 43 54 *Fax:* (05) 65 37 43 55 *E-mail:* contact@editions-dulaquet.fr *Web Site:* www.editions-dulaquet.fr, pg 171

Leandro Lara Editor (Spain) *Tel:* (093) 6970036; (093) 6970364 *E-mail:* leandro@covnet.com, pg 584

Larcier-Department of De Boeck & Larcier SA (Belgium) *E-mail:* deboeck.larcier@deboeck.be *Web Site:* www.larcier.be, pg 69

Hans Richter Laromedel (Sweden) *Tel:* (0152) 150 60; (0200) 11 55 30 (orders) *Fax:* (0152) 151 40; (0200) 11 55 31 (orders) *E-mail:* info@richter.d.se *Web Site:* www.richter.d.se, pg 608

Ediciones Larousse Argentina SA (Argentina) *Tel:* (011) 4865-9581; (011) 4865-9582; (011) 4865-9583 *Toll Free Tel:* 800-333-5757 *Fax:* (011) 4865-9581; (011) 4865-9582; (011) 4865-9583 *Toll Free Fax:* 800-333-5757 *E-mail:* editorial@aique.com.ar; comercial@ aique.com.ar *Web Site:* www.larousse.com.ar, pg 7

Editions Larousse (France) *Tel:* (01) 44 39 44 00 *Fax:* (01) 44 39 43 43 *Web Site:* www.larousse.fr, pg 171

Larousse Editorial SA (Spain) *Tel:* (093) 2922666 *Fax:* (093) 2922162; (093) 2922163 *E-mail:* larousse@larousse.es, pg 584

Ediciones Larousse SA de CV (Mexico) *Tel:* (05) 52082005; (05) 2085677 *Fax:* (05) 2086225 *Web Site:* www.larousse.com.mx, pg 463

Larousse (Suisse) SA (Switzerland) *Tel:* (021) 335336, pg 622

Lars Hokerbergs Bokvorlag (Sweden) *Tel:* (08) 24 43 60 *Fax:* (08) 650 39 84, pg 608

Bokforlaget Robert Larson AB (Sweden) *Tel:* (08) 732 84 60 *Fax:* (08) 732 71 76 *E-mail:* info@larsonforlag. se *Web Site:* www.larsonforlag.se, pg 608

Laruffa Editore SRL (Italy) *Tel:* (0965) 814948 *Fax:* (0965) 814954 *E-mail:* laruffa@laruffaeditore. com *Web Site:* www.laruffaeditore.com, pg 391

Editrice LAS (Italy) *Tel:* (06) 87290626 *E-mail:* las@ ups.urbe.it *Web Site:* www.las.ups.urbe.it, pg 391

Roger Lascelles (United Kingdom) *Tel:* (0181) 8470935 *Fax:* (0181) 5683886, pg 714

Lasser Press Mexicana SA de CV (Mexico) *Tel:* (05) 5112312; (05) 5142705 *Fax:* (05) 5112576, pg 463

Michael Lassleben Verlag und Druckerei (Germany) *Tel:* (09473) 205 *Fax:* (09473) 8357 *E-mail:* druckerei@oberpfalzverlag-lassleben.de *Web Site:* www.oberpfalzverlag-lassleben.de, pg 251

L'Association des Professionnels de l'Information et de la Documentation (ADBS) (France) *Tel:* (01) 43 72 25 25 *Fax:* (01) 43 72 30 41 *E-mail:* adbs@adbs.fr *Web Site:* www.adbs.fr, pg 1562

Lasten Keskus Oy (Finland) *Tel:* (09) 6877 450 *Fax:* (09) 6877 4545 *E-mail:* tilaukset@lastenkeskus.fi *Web Site:* www.lastenkeskus.fi, pg 143

The Latchmere Press (United Kingdom) *Tel:* (020) 7639 7282, pg 714

Latin America Bureau (United Kingdom) *Tel:* (020) 7278 2829 *Fax:* (020) 7833 0715 *E-mail:* contactlab@ lab.org.uk *Web Site:* www.lab.org.uk, pg 1282

Latina Livraria Editora (Portugal) *Tel:* (02) 2001294 *Fax:* (02) 2086053, pg 528

J Latka Verlag GmbH (Germany) *Tel:* (0228) 919320 *Fax:* (0228) 9193217 *E-mail:* info@latka.de *Web Site:* www.latka.de, pg 251

Library Association of Latvia (Latvia) *Tel:* (0371) 7287620 *Fax:* (0371) 7280851 *E-mail:* lnb@lbi.lnb.lv *Web Site:* www.lnb.lv, pg 1566

Latvian Publishers Association (Latvia) *Tel:* (0371) 7282392 *Fax:* (0371) 7280549 *E-mail:* lga@ gramatizdeveji.lv *Web Site:* www.gramatizdeveji.lv, pg 1266

Laumann-Polska (Poland) *Tel:* (075) 7617182 *Fax:* (075) 7617192, pg 519

Laureate Book Co Ltd (Taiwan, Province of China) *Tel:* 8862 2219 3338 *Fax:* (02) 2218-2860 *E-mail:* laureate@laureate.com.tw *Web Site:* www. laureate.com.tw, pg 636

Laurel Press (Australia) *Tel:* (03) 6239 1139 *Fax:* (03) 6239 1139, pg 28

Editions Le Laurier (France) *Tel:* (01) 45 51 55 08 *Fax:* (01) 45 51 81 83 *E-mail:* editions@lelaurier.fr *Web Site:* www.lelaurier.fr, pg 171

The Lavenham Press Ltd (United Kingdom) *Tel:* (01787) 247436; (01787) 248046 (ISDN) *Fax:* (01787) 248267 *Web Site:* www.lavenhampress.co.uk, pg 1153

The Lavenham Press Ltd (United Kingdom) *Tel:* (01787) 247436; (01787) 248046 (ISDN) *Fax:* (01787) 248267 *E-mail:* lpl@lavenhamgroup.co.uk *Web Site:* www. lavenhampress.co.uk, pg 1216

Les Presses Lavigerie (Burundi) *Tel:* (02) 22368 *Fax:* (02) 220318 *E-mail:* lpl~bujumbura@cbinf.com, pg 97

Lavis Marketing (United Kingdom) *Tel:* (01865) 767575 *Fax:* (01865) 750079 *E-mail:* orders@lavismarketing. co.uk, pg 1343

Editions Lavoisier (France) *Tel:* (01) 47 40 67 00 *Fax:* (01) 47 40 67 88 *E-mail:* edition@tec-et-doc.com *Web Site:* www.tec-et-doc.com, pg 171

Editions Lavoisier (France) *Tel:* (01) 47 40 67 00 *Fax:* (01) 47 40 67 03 *E-mail:* edition@tec-et-doc.com *Web Site:* www.tec-et-doc.com/fr, pg 1300

Edizioni Lavoro SRL (Italy) *Tel:* (06) 44251174 *Fax:* (06) 44251177 *E-mail:* info@edizionilavoro.it *Web Site:* www.edizionilavoro.it, pg 391

Il Lavoro Editoriale (Italy) *Tel:* (071) 2072210 *Fax:* (071) 2083058 *E-mail:* ilepro@tin.it *Web Site:* www.illavoroeditoriale.com, pg 391

LAW Ltd (Lucas Alexander Whitley) (United Kingdom) *Tel:* (020) 7471 7900 *Fax:* (020) 7471 7910 *E-mail:* law@lawagency.co.uk, pg 1131

Law Publishers (India) *Tel:* (0532) 2622758; (0532) 2420974 *Fax:* (0532) 2622781; (0532) 2609943 *E-mail:* lawpub@vsnl.com; lawpub@sancharnet.in *Web Site:* www.law-publishers.com, pg 337

Law Publishers Association (Sri Lanka) *Tel:* (01) 330363 *Fax:* (01) 436629, pg 602

The Law Publishing House (China) *Tel:* (010) 63266796; (010) 63266790, pg 105

Lawpack Publishing Ltd (United Kingdom) *Tel:* (020) 7394 4040 *Fax:* (020) 7394 4041 *E-mail:* enquiries@ lawpack.co.uk *Web Site:* www.lawpack.co.uk, pg 714

Lawrence & Wishart (United Kingdom) *Tel:* (020) 8533 2506 *Fax:* (020) 8533 7369 *E-mail:* info@lwbooks.co. uk *Web Site:* www.l-w-bks.co.uk, pg 714

Laxmi Publications Pvt Ltd (India) *Tel:* (011) 23262368; (011) 23262370 *Fax:* (011) 23262279 *E-mail:* colaxmi@hotmail.com *Web Site:* www. laxmipublications.com, pg 337

LBC Information Services (Australia) *Tel:* (02) 99366444 *Fax:* (02) 98882229, pg 28

Editions Universitaires LCF (France) *Tel:* (05) 56 51 51 37 *Fax:* (05) 56 51 51 37, pg 171

LCG Malmberg BV (Netherlands) *Tel:* (073) 6288811 *Fax:* (073) 6210512 *Web Site:* www.malmberg.nl, pg 481

LDA Editores Ltda (Brazil) *Tel:* (041) 362-9173 *Fax:* (041) 262-3439 *E-mail:* lda.editores@uol.com.br, pg 84

LDA-Living & Learning (Cambridge) Ltd (United Kingdom) *Tel:* (01223) 357788 *Fax:* (01223) 460557 *E-mail:* internationalsales@mcgraw-hill.com, pg 714

Le'Dory Publishing House (Israel) *Tel:* (03) 9612182, pg 366

Lea Publications Ltd (Hong Kong) *Tel:* 25-620121 *Fax:* 2565 0187, pg 315

Lead Wave Publishing Company Ltd (Taiwan, Province of China) *Tel:* (02) 82281288 *Fax:* (02) 82281207 *E-mail:* customer@liwil.com.tw *Web Site:* www.liwil.com.tw, pg 636

Learners Press Private Ltd (India) *Tel:* (011) 26387070; (011) 26386209 *Fax:* (011) 26383788 *E-mail:* info@sterlingpublishers.com *Web Site:* www.sterlingpublishers.com, pg 337

Learning Development Aids (United Kingdom) *Tel:* (01223) 357788 *Fax:* (01223) 460557 *E-mail:* ldaorders@compuserve.com, pg 715

Learning Guides (Writers & Publishers Ltd) (New Zealand) *Tel:* (04) 239 9400 *Fax:* (04) 239 9400 *E-mail:* learning.guides@xtra.co.nz, pg 493

Learning Matters Ltd (United Kingdom) *Tel:* (01392) 215560 *Fax:* (01392) 215561 *E-mail:* info@learningmatters.co.uk *Web Site:* www.learningmatters.co.uk, pg 715

Learning Media Ltd (New Zealand) *Tel:* (04) 472 5522 *Fax:* (04) 472 6444 *E-mail:* info@learningmedia.co.nz *Web Site:* www.learningmedia.co.nz; www.learningmedia.com, pg 493

Learning Together (United Kingdom) *Tel:* (028) 90402086 *Fax:* (028) 90402086 *E-mail:* info@learningtogether.co.uk *Web Site:* www.learningtogether.co.uk, pg 715

The Lebanese Library Association (Lebanon) *Tel:* (01) 350000; (01) 340460 *Fax:* (01) 351706 *Web Site:* www.aub.edu.lb, pg 1567

Lebenshilfe-Verlag Marburg, Verlag der Bundesvereinigung Lebenshilfe fuer Menschen mit geistiger Behinderung eV (Germany) *Tel:* (06421) 4 91-0 *Fax:* (06421) 4 91-1 67 *E-mail:* bundesvereinigung@lebenshilfe.de *Web Site:* www.lebenshilfe.de, pg 251

Lebensstrom eV (Germany) *Tel:* (030) 3131247 *Fax:* (030) 3121098 *E-mail:* info@lebensstrom.com *Web Site:* www.lebensstrom.com, pg 251

Gerda Leber Buch-Kunst-und Musikverlag Proscenium Edition (Austria) *Tel:* (01) 5332858; (01) 6390025, pg 53

LED - Edizioni Universitarie di Lettere Economia Diritto (Italy) *Tel:* (02) 59902055 *Fax:* (02) 55193636 *E-mail:* led@lededizioni.it *Web Site:* www.lededizioni.it, pg 391

LEDA (Las Ediciones de Arte) (Spain) *Tel:* (093) 2379389; (093) 2155273, pg 584

Lee & Lee Communications (Taiwan, Province of China) *Tel:* (02) 237 83373 *Fax:* (02) 237 82803 *E-mail:* service@leelee.com; culture@leelee.com *Web Site:* www.leelee.com, pg 636

Sandra Lee Agencies (Australia) *Tel:* (03) 9592 5235 *Fax:* (03) 9592 7608 *E-mail:* winston@ozonline.com.au, pg 28

Leeds University Library (United Kingdom) *Tel:* (0113) 343 5663 *Fax:* (0113) 233 5561 *E-mail:* libraryenquiries@leeds.ac.uk *Web Site:* www.leeds.ac.uk/library, pg 1552

Editions Francis Lefebvre (France) *Tel:* (01) 41 05 22 00; (01) 41 05 22 06 *Fax:* (01) 41 05 36 80 *Web Site:* www.efl.fr/, pg 171

Claude Lefrancq Editeur (Belgium) *Tel:* (02) 344-49-34 *Fax:* (02) 347-55-34 *E-mail:* claude.lefrancq@skynet.be, pg 69

Legal Action Group (United Kingdom) *Tel:* (020) 7833 2931 *Fax:* (020) 7837 6094 *E-mail:* lag@lag.org.uk *Web Site:* www.lag.org.uk, pg 715

Legal & Technical Translation Services (United Kingdom) *Tel:* (01622) 751537; (01622) 751189 *Fax:* (01622) 754431 *E-mail:* translation@ltts.co.uk *Web Site:* www.ltts.co.uk, pg 1141

Legal Resources Foundation Publications Unit (Zimbabwe) *Tel:* (04) 251170; (04) 251174 *Fax:* (04) 728213 *E-mail:* lrfhre@mweb.co.zw *Web Site:* site.mweb.co.zw/lrf, pg 777

Ediciones Legales SA (Ecuador) *Tel:* (02) 250-7729 *Fax:* (02) 250-8490 *E-mail:* edicioneslegales@corpmyl.com *Web Site:* www.edicioneslegales.com, pg 136

LEGIS - Editores SA (Colombia) *Tel:* (01) 4255255 *Fax:* (01) 4255317 *E-mail:* scliente@legis.com.co, pg 111

Legislation Direct (New Zealand) *Tel:* (04) 495 2882 *Fax:* (04) 495 2880 *E-mail:* ldorders@legislationdirect.co.nz *Web Site:* gplegislation.co.nz, pg 493

Editions Legislatives (France) *Tel:* (01) 40 92 36 36 *Fax:* (01) 40 92 36 63 *E-mail:* infocom@editions-legislatives.fr *Web Site:* www.editions-legislatives.fr, pg 171

Legprombytizdat (Russian Federation) *Tel:* (095) 2330947, pg 541

Libreria Imprenta y Litografia Lehmann SA (Costa Rica) *Tel:* 2231212, pg 115, 1297

Lehnert & Landrock Bookshop (Egypt (Arab Republic of Egypt)) *Tel:* (02) 3927606 *Fax:* (02) 3934421, pg 138

Lehnert & Landrock Bookshop (Egypt (Arab Republic of Egypt)) *Tel:* (02) 3927606; (02) 3935324 *Fax:* (02) 3934421, pg 1299

Verlag fuer Lehrmittel Poessneck GmbH (Germany) *Tel:* (03647) 425018 *Fax:* (03647) 425020, pg 251

Lehrmittelverlag des Kantons Zurich (Switzerland) *Tel:* (01) 465 85 85 *Fax:* (01) 465 85 89 *E-mail:* lehrmittelverlag@lmv.zh.ch *Web Site:* www.lehrmittelverlag.com, pg 622

Leibniz Verlag (Germany) *Tel:* (06741) 1720 *Fax:* (06741) 1749 *E-mail:* reichl-verlag@telda.net, pg 251

Leibniz-Buecherwarte (Germany) *Tel:* (05042) 15 28 *Fax:* (05042) 15 28 *E-mail:* leibniz-buecherwarte@t-online.de *Web Site:* www.leibniz-buecherwarte.com, pg 251

Leipziger Universitaetsverlag GmbH (Germany) *Tel:* (0341) 9900440 *Fax:* (0341) 9900440 *E-mail:* info@univerlag-leipzig.de *Web Site:* www.univerlag-leipzig.de, pg 251

Leitfadenverlag Verlag Dieter Sudholt (Germany) *Tel:* (08151) 51045 *Fax:* (08151) 50357, pg 251

Anton G Leitner Verlag (AGLV) (Germany) *Tel:* (08153) 9525-22 *Fax:* (08153) 9525-24 *E-mail:* info@aglv.com *Web Site:* www.dasgedicht.de, pg 251

Editora Leitura Ltda (Brazil) *Tel:* (031) 3371-4902 *Fax:* (031) 3714902 *E-mail:* leitura@editoraleitura.com.br *Web Site:* www.editoraleitura.com.br, pg 84

Edicions de l'Eixample, SA (Spain) *Tel:* (093) 4584600 *Fax:* (093) 2076248, pg 584

Leksikografski Zavod Miroslav Krleza (Croatia) *Tel:* (01) 4800 492; (01) 4800 494 *Fax:* (01) 4800 399 *E-mail:* lzmk@lzmk.hr *Web Site:* www.lzmk.hr, pg 118

Lembaga Demografi Fakultas Ekonomi Universitas Indonesia (Indonesia) *Tel:* (021) 3900703; (021) 336434; (021) 336539 *Fax:* (021) 3102457 *E-mail:* demofeui@indo.net.id, pg 352

Verlag Otto Lembeck (Germany) *Tel:* (069) 5970988 *Fax:* (069) 5975742 *E-mail:* verlag@lembeck.de *Web Site:* www.lembeck.de, pg 251

Uitgeverij Lemma BV (Netherlands) *Tel:* (030) 2545652 *Fax:* (030) 2512496 *E-mail:* infodesk@lemma.nl *Web Site:* www.lemma.nl, pg 481

Lemniscaat (Netherlands) *Tel:* (010) 2062929 *Fax:* (010) 4141560 *E-mail:* info@lemniscaat.nl *Web Site:* www.lemniscaat.nl, pg 481

Lemos & Crane (United Kingdom) *Tel:* (020) 8348 8263 *Fax:* (020) 8347 5740 *E-mail:* admin@lemosandcrane.co.uk *Web Site:* www.lemosandcrane.co.uk, pg 715

Edicoes Manuel Lencastre (Portugal) *Tel:* 4688328, pg 528

Izdatelstvo Lenizdat (Russian Federation) *Tel:* (0812) 3111451 *Fax:* (0812) 3151295, pg 541

Lennard Publishing (United Kingdom) *Tel:* (01582) 715866 *Fax:* (01582) 715121 *E-mail:* lennard@lenqap.demon.co.uk, pg 715

Lenos Verlag (Switzerland) *Tel:* (061) 261 34 14 *Fax:* (061) 261 35 18 *E-mail:* lenos@lenos.ch *Web Site:* www.lenos.ch, pg 623

Lentz Verlag (Germany) *Tel:* (089) 290880 *Fax:* (089) 29088-144 *E-mail:* l.eggs@herbig.net *Web Site:* www.herbig.net, pg 251

Gundhild Lenz-Mulligan (United Kingdom) *Tel:* (020) 8543 7846 *Fax:* (020) 8543 8909 *E-mail:* lenzmulligan@btconnect.com, pg 1131

Leo Paper Products Ltd (Hong Kong) *Tel:* 28841374 *Fax:* 25130698 *E-mail:* lpp@leo.com.hk *Web Site:* www.leo.com.hk, pg 1147, 1168, 1208

Leo Paper USA (United States) *Tel:* 425-646-8801 *Fax:* 425-646-8805 *E-mail:* leo@leousa.com; sales@leousa.com *Web Site:* www.leousa.com, pg 1156

Leo Paper USA (United States) *Tel:* 425-646-8801 *Fax:* 425-646-8805 *E-mail:* leo@leousa.com *Web Site:* www.leopaper.com, pg 1178, 1220

Leo Reprographic Ltd (Hong Kong) *Tel:* (02) 25696293 *Fax:* (02) 25138400 *E-mail:* lrg@leo.com.hk *Web Site:* www.leo.com.hk, pg 1168

Leong Brothers (Brunei Darussalam) *Tel:* (03) 22381 *Fax:* (03) 222223, pg 92

Leonhardt & Hoier Literary Agency ApS (Denmark) *Tel:* 33132523 *Fax:* 33134992 *Web Site:* www.leonhardt-hoier.dk, pg 1120

Leonis Verlag (Switzerland) *Tel:* (01) 821 4055 *Fax:* (01) 821 4065, pg 623

Uitgeverij Leopold BV (Netherlands) *Tel:* (020) 5511250 *Fax:* (020) 4204699 *E-mail:* verkoop@leopold.nl *Web Site:* www.leopold.nl, pg 481

Leopold Stocker Verlag (Austria) *Tel:* (0316) 82 16 36 *Fax:* (0316) 83 56 12 *E-mail:* stocker-verlag@stocker-verlag.com *Web Site:* www.stocker-verlag.com, pg 53

Leopold Stocker Verlag (Austria) *Tel:* (0316) 82 16 36 *Fax:* (0316) 83 56 12 *E-mail:* buecherquelle@stocker-verlag.com *Web Site:* www.buecherquelle.at, pg 1290

Dr Gisela Lermann (Germany) *Tel:* (06131) 31149 *Fax:* (06131) 387945 *Web Site:* www.lermann-verlag.de, pg 251

Lerner Ediciones (Colombia) *Tel:* (01) 4200650; (01) 2624224 *Fax:* (01) 2624459, pg 111

Editions Dominique Leroy (France) *Tel:* (03) 86 64 15 24 *Fax:* (03) 86 64 15 24 *Web Site:* www.enfer.com, pg 172

Lesotho Library Association (Lesotho) *Tel:* 340 601 *Fax:* 340 601 *E-mail:* mmc@doc.isas.nul.ls *Web Site:* www.sn.apc.org, pg 1567

Lesotho National Library Service (Lesotho) *Tel:* 322 592; 323 100 *Fax:* 323 100, pg 1523

Editions Lessius ASBL (Belgium) *Tel:* (02) 739 34 90 *Fax:* (02) 739 34 91 *E-mail:* info@editions-lessius.be *Web Site:* www.adeb.irisnet.be/annuaire/lessius.htm, pg 69

P Lethielleux Editions (France) *Tel:* (01) 44 32 05 60 *Fax:* (01) 44 32 05 61, pg 172

Letouzey et Ane Editeurs (France) *Tel:* (01) 45 48 80 14 *Fax:* (01) 45 49 03 43 *E-mail:* letouzey@tree.tr, pg 172

Editorial Letras Cubanas (Cuba) *Tel:* (07) 862-6864 *Fax:* (07) 33-8187 *E-mail:* elc@icl.cult.cu, pg 120

Letterbox Library (United Kingdom) *Tel:* (020) 7503 4801 *Fax:* (020) 7503 4800 *E-mail:* info@ letterboxlibrary.com *Web Site:* www.letterboxlibrary. com, pg 715, 1247

Casa Editrice Le Lettere SRL (Italy) *Tel:* (055) 2342710; (055) 2476319 *Fax:* (055) 2346010 *E-mail:* staff@ lelettere.it *Web Site:* www.lelettere.it, pg 392

Letterland International Ltd (United Kingdom) *Tel:* (01223) 262675 *Fax:* (01223) 264126 *E-mail:* info@letterland.com *Web Site:* www.letterland. com, pg 715

Lettre International Kulturzeitung (Germany) *Tel:* (030) 30870441 *Fax:* (030) 2833128 *E-mail:* lettre@lettre.de *Web Site:* www.lettre.de, pg 252

Lettres Modernes Minard (France) *Tel:* (01) 43 36 25 83 *Fax:* (02) 31 84 48 09 *E-mail:* editorat. lettresmodernes@wanadoo.fr, pg 172

Lettres Vives Editions (France) *Tel:* (04) 95 36 40 93 *Fax:* (04) 95 36 59 92 *E-mail:* lettresvives@mic.fr, pg 172

Charles Letts & Co Ltd (United Kingdom) *Tel:* (0131) 663 1971 *Fax:* (0131) 660 3225 *E-mail:* sales@letts. co.uk; diaries@letts.co.uk *Web Site:* www.letts.co.uk, pg 1153

Charles Letts & Co Ltd (United Kingdom) *Tel:* (0131) 663 1971 *Fax:* (0131) 660 3225 *E-mail:* diaries@letts. co.uk *Web Site:* www.letts.co.uk, pg 1216

Letts Educational (United Kingdom) *Tel:* (0845) 602 1937 *Fax:* (020) 8742 8390 *E-mail:* mail@lettsed.co. uk *Web Site:* www.lettsed.co.uk, pg 715

Bernard Letu Editeur (Switzerland) *Tel:* (022) 204757 *Fax:* (022) 208492, pg 623

LEU-VERLAG Wolfgang Leupelt (Germany) *Tel:* (02204) 981141 *Fax:* (02204) 981143 *E-mail:* info@leu-verlag.net *Web Site:* www.leu-verlag. net, pg 252

Leuchter-Verlag EG (Germany) *Tel:* (06150) 97360 *Fax:* (06150) 9736-36, pg 252

Verlag Gerald Leue (Germany) *Tel:* (030) 7865020 *Fax:* (030) 78913876 *E-mail:* vertrieb@leue-verlag.de *Web Site:* www.leue-verlag.de, pg 252

Leuven University Press (Belgium) *Tel:* (016) 32 53 45 *Fax:* (016) 32 53 52 *E-mail:* info@upers.kuleuven.be *Web Site:* www.lup.be; www.kuleuven.be/upers/, pg 69

Levante Editori (Italy) *Tel:* (080) 5213778 *Fax:* (080) 5213778 *E-mail:* levante@tin.it *Web Site:* www. levantebari.com, pg 392

Levanter Publishing & Associates (Australia) *Tel:* (02) 9371 7824, pg 29

A G Leventis Foundation (Greece) *Tel:* 2106165232 *Fax:* 2106165235 *E-mail:* leventcy@zenon.logos. cy.net; eleni.mariolea@leventis.net *Web Site:* www. leventisfoundation.org, pg 306

Liana Levi Editions (France) *Tel:* (01) 44 32 19 30 *Fax:* (01) 46 33 69 56 *E-mail:* liana.levi@wanadoo.fr *Web Site:* www.lianalevi.fr, pg 172

Levrotto e Bella Libreria Editrice Universitaria SAS (Italy) *Tel:* (011) 8121205 *Fax:* (011) 8124025 *E-mail:* levrotto@ipsnet.it, pg 392

Barbara Levy Literary Agency (United Kingdom) *Tel:* (020) 7435 9046 *Fax:* (020) 7431 2063, pg 1131

The Lexicon Bookshop (United Kingdom) *Tel:* (01624) 673004 *Fax:* (01624) 661959 *E-mail:* manxbooks@ lexiconbookshop.co.im *Web Site:* www. lexiconbookshop.co.im, pg 1343

LexisNexis (Singapore) *Tel:* 6733 1380 *Fax:* 6773 1719 *Web Site:* www.lexisnexis.com.sg, pg 552

LexisNexis Butterworths South Africa (South Africa) *Tel:* (031) 268 3111; (031) 268 3007 (customer service) *Fax:* (031) 268 3108; (021) 268 3109 *Toll Free Fax:* (031) 268 3102 (Marketing) *Web Site:* www.lexisnexis.co.za, pg 561

LexisNexis India (India) *Tel:* (011) 373 9614; (011) 373 9615; (011) 373 9616; (011) 332 6454 customer service; (011) 332 6455 customer service *Fax:* (011) 332 6456 *E-mail:* info@lexisnexis.co.in; customer. care@lexisnexis.co.in *Web Site:* www.lexisnexis.co.in, pg 337

Lexus Ltd (United Kingdom) *Tel:* (0141) 2215266 *Fax:* (0141) 2263139 *Web Site:* www. lexusforlanguages.co.uk, pg 1141

La Ley SA Editora e Impresora (Argentina) *Tel:* (011) 4378-4841 *Fax:* (011) 4372-0953 *E-mail:* atcliente1@ laley.com.ar *Web Site:* www.la-ley.com.ar, pg 7

Leykam Buchverlagsges mbH (Austria) *Tel:* (0316) 8076-531 *Fax:* (0316) 8076-539 *E-mail:* verlag@ leykam.com *Web Site:* www.leykam.com; www. leykamverlag.at, pg 53

Les Editions LGDJ-Montchrestien (France) *Tel:* (01) 56 54 16 00 *Fax:* (01) 56 54 16 49 *Web Site:* www.lgdj. fr/lgdj/accueil.php, pg 172

Lia rumantscha (Switzerland) *Tel:* (081) 258 3222 *Fax:* (081) 258 3223 *E-mail:* liarumantscha@ rumantsch.ch *Web Site:* www.liarumantscha.ch, pg 623

Liang Yu Printing Factory Ltd (Hong Kong) *Tel:* 25604453; 25677563 *Fax:* 28858099 *E-mail:* liangyup@netvigator.com, pg 1208

Liaoning People's Publishing House (China) *Tel:* (024) 3861304 *Fax:* (024) 371472, pg 105

Liaoning Provincial Library (China) *Tel:* (024) 2482-2241 *Fax:* (024) 2482-2449 *Web Site:* www.lnlib.com, pg 1496

Librairie du Liban Publishers (Sal) (Lebanon) *Tel:* (09) 217 944; (09) 217945; (09) 217 946; (09) 217 735 *Fax:* (09) 217734; (09) 217 434 *E-mail:* info@ldlp. com *Web Site:* www.ldlp.com, pg 443

Librairie du Liban Publishers (Sal) (Lebanon) *Tel:* (09) 217 735; (09) 217 944; (09) 217 945; (09) 217 946 *Fax:* (09) 217 734 *E-mail:* info@ldlp.com *Web Site:* www.ldlp.com, pg 1315

Bibliotheque Nationale du Liban (Lebanon) *Tel:* (01) 862957 *Fax:* (01) 374079, pg 1523

John Libbey & Co Ltd (United Kingdom) *Tel:* (023) 8065 0208 *Fax:* (023) 8065 0259 *E-mail:* johnlibbey@ aol.com, pg 715

Editions John Libbey Eurotext (France) *Tel:* (01) 46 73 06 60 *Fax:* (01) 40 84 00 99 *E-mail:* contact@john-libbey-eurotext.fr *Web Site:* www.john-libbey-eurotext. fr, pg 172

Die Libelle Verlag Ag Libellen Haus (Switzerland) *Tel:* (071) 688 35 55 *Fax:* (071) 688 35 65 *E-mail:* info@libelle.ch *Web Site:* www.libelle.ch, pg 623

Liber AB (Sweden) *Tel:* (08) 6909200 *Fax:* (08) 6909458 *E-mail:* export@liber.se; infomaster@liber.se *Web Site:* www.liber.se, pg 608

Liber Ediciones, SA (Spain) *Tel:* (0902) 300 307 *Fax:* (0948) 176 667 *E-mail:* info@arsliber.com *Web Site:* www.arsliber.com, pg 584

Liber Hermods AB (Sweden) *Tel:* (040) 258600 *Fax:* (040) 304600 *Web Site:* www.liberhermods.se, pg 608

Liberia Editorial Minerva-Miraflores (Peru) *Tel:* (014) 4475499 *Fax:* (014) 4458583 *E-mail:* minerva@ chavin-rcp-net-pe, pg 1325

Libreria Libertad SA (Chile) *Tel:* (02) 698 8773 *Fax:* (02) 672 6314, pg 99

Ediciones Libertarias/Prodhufi SA (Spain) *Tel:* (091) 593 33 93 *Fax:* (091) 594 16 96 *E-mail:* libertarias@ libertarias.com *Web Site:* www.libertarias.com, pg 584

Libertas- Europaeisches Institut GmbH (Germany) *Tel:* (07031) 6186-80 *Fax:* (07031) 6186-86 *E-mail:* info@libertas-institut.com *Web Site:* www. libertas-institut.com, pg 252

Libertatea (Serbia and Montenegro) *Tel:* (013) 33-51; 13 346 447 *Fax:* (013) 46-447, pg 548

Liberty (United Kingdom) *Tel:* (020) 7403 3888 *Fax:* (020) 7407 5354 *E-mail:* info@liberty-human-rights.org.uk *Web Site:* www.liberty-human-rights.org. uk, pg 715

Liberty Books (Pvt) Ltd (Pakistan) *Tel:* (021) 111-311-113; (021) 5671240; (021) 5671244 *Fax:* (021) 5684319 *E-mail:* info@libertybooks.com *Web Site:* www.libertybooks.com, pg 1324

Libra Books Pty Ltd (Australia) *Tel:* (03) 6230 2656 *Fax:* (03) 6225 0900, pg 29

Libra Editorial SA de CV (Mexico) *Tel:* (05) 6641454; (05) 6514156 *Fax:* (05) 6641454, pg 464

Libra House Ltd (Ireland) *Tel:* (01) 4542717, pg 358

Ediciones Libra, SA de CV (Mexico) *Tel:* (05) 5651-4156 *Fax:* (05) 5664-1454, pg 464

Librairie Bilingue/The Bilingual Bookshop (Cameroon) *Tel:* 224899 *Fax:* 232903, pg 1244

La Librairie de Madagascar (Madagascar) *Tel:* (020) 222454 *Fax:* (020) 2264395; (020) 224395, pg 1316

Librairie des Presses Universitaires (The Democratic Republic of the Congo) *Tel:* (012) 30652, pg 1297

Librairie des Presses Universitaires de Bruxelles (Belgium) *Tel:* (02) 641 1440 *Fax:* (02) 647 7962 *Web Site:* www.ulb.ac.be, pg 1292

Librairie FNAC (France) *Tel:* (01) 42 70 56 90 *E-mail:* service-clientele@fnac.com *Web Site:* www. fnac.com, pg 1300

Editions Librairie-Galerie Racine (France) *Tel:* (01) 43269724 *Fax:* (01) 43269724 *E-mail:* lgr@librairie-galerie-racine.com, pg 172

Librairie Generale des PUF (France) *Tel:* (01) 44 41 81 20 *Fax:* (01) 43 54 64 81 *E-mail:* puf-lib@puf. worldnet.net *Web Site:* www.puf.com, pg 1300

Librairie Internationale (Morocco) *Tel:* (07) 75 86 61 *Fax:* (07) 75 86 61 *E-mail:* libinter@iam.net.ma, pg 1319

Librairie Kaufmann SA (Greece) *Tel:* 2103236817 *Fax:* 2103230320 *E-mail:* ccaldi@otenet.gr, pg 1303

Librairie la Hune (France) *Tel:* (01) 45 48 35 85, pg 1300

Librairie les Volcans (The Democratic Republic of the Congo) *Tel:* 366, pg 1297

Librairie Luginbuhl (France) *Tel:* (01) 45 51 42 58 *Fax:* (01) 45 56 07 80 *E-mail:* liblug@club-internet.fr, pg 172

Librairie Mixte Sarl (Madagascar) *Tel:* (020) 22 251 30 *Fax:* (020) 22 376 16 *E-mail:* librairiemixte@dts.mg, pg 1316

Librairie Orientale sal (Lebanon) *Tel:* (01) 485793; (01) 485794; (01) 485795 *Fax:* (01) 485796; (01) 216021 *E-mail:* libor@cyberia.net.lb, pg 443

Librairie Scientifique et Technique Albert Blanchard (France) *Tel:* (01) 43 26 90 34 *Fax:* (01) 43 29 97 31 *E-mail:* librairie.blanchard@wanadoo.fr *Web Site:* www.blanchard75.fr, pg 172

Librairie Universitaire (Madagascar) *Tel:* (020) 24114, pg 1316

Librairie Universitaire (Rwanda) *Tel:* 530330 *Fax:* 530210 *E-mail:* biblio@nur.ac.rw *Web Site:* www.lib.nur.ac.rw, pg 1329

Libraria Universitatii (Romania) *Tel:* (064) 198 107, pg 1329

The Librarian, University College of Swaziland (Swaziland) *Tel:* 5184011 *Fax:* 5185276 *E-mail:* pmuswazi@uniswa.sz; paiki@uniswacc. uniswa.sz *Web Site:* www.uniswa.sz, pg 1275

Librarie Maritime Outremer (France) *Tel:* (04) 91 54 79 40 *Fax:* (04) 91 54 79 49 *E-mail:* webmaster@ librairie-outremer.com *Web Site:* www.librairie-outremer.com, pg 172

Librarie Mixte (Madagascar) *Tel:* (02) 25130 *Fax:* (02) 25130, pg 450

Library & Information Association of New Zealand Aotearoa (LIANZA) (New Zealand) *Tel:* (04) 473 5834 *Fax:* (04) 499 1480 *E-mail:* office@lianza.org.nz *Web Site:* www.lianza.org.nz, pg 1568

Library & Information Association of South Africa (LIASA) (South Africa) *Tel:* (012) 481 2870; (012) 481 2875; (012) 481 2876 *Fax:* (012) 481 2873 *E-mail:* liasa@liasa.org.za *Web Site:* www.liasa.org.za, pg 1571

Library & Information Science Society (Zimbabwe) *Tel:* (04) 752311 *Fax:* (04) 720955, pg 1574

The Library Association of Bangladesh (LAB) (Bangladesh) *Tel:* (02) 8631471; (02) 0189258564 (mobile) *E-mail:* msik@icddrb.org, pg 1558

Library Association of Barbados (Barbados), pg 1558

Library Association of China (LAC) (Taiwan, Province of China) *Tel:* (02) 2331-2475 *Fax:* (02) 2370-0899 *E-mail:* lac@msg.ncl.edu.tw *Web Site:* lac.ncl.edu.tw, pg 1571

Library Association of Cuba (Cuba) *Tel:* (07) 552244 *Fax:* (07) 662053, pg 1560

Library Association of Cyprus (Cyprus) *Tel:* (022) 404849, pg 1560

Library Association of Singapore (Singapore) *Tel:* 6749 7990 *Fax:* 6749 7480 *Web Site:* www.las.org.sg, pg 1570

Library Association of Trinidad & Tobago (Trinidad & Tobago) *Tel:* (0868) 687 0194 *E-mail:* secretary@latt.org.tt *Web Site:* www.latt.org.tt/cms/, pg 1572

Library of Australian History (Australia) *Tel:* (02) 9929 5087 *Fax:* (02) 9929 5087 *E-mail:* grdxxx@ozemail.com.au, pg 29

Library of Chinese Academy of Sciences (China) *Tel:* (010) 82623303; (010) 82626611-6720 *Fax:* (010) 62566846 *E-mail:* ask@mail.las.ac.cn *Web Site:* www.las.ac.cn, pg 1496

Library of Parliament (South Africa) *Tel:* (021) 403 2140; (021) 403 2141; (021) 403 2142 *Fax:* (021) 461 4331 *E-mail:* library@parliament.gov.za *Web Site:* www.parliament.gov.za, pg 1542

Library of the Mineral Research & Exploration General Directorate (Turkey) *Tel:* (0312) 287 34 30 *Fax:* (0312) 287 91 88 *E-mail:* mta@mta.gov.tr *Web Site:* www.mta.gov.tr, pg 1550

Library of the Near East School of Theology (Lebanon) *Tel:* (01) 354194; (01) 349901 *Fax:* (01) 347129 *E-mail:* nest.lib@inco.com.lb, pg 1523

Library of the People's Assembly (Egypt (Arab Republic of Egypt)) *Tel:* (02) 3540279 *Fax:* (02) 3548977, pg 1502

Library Promotion Bureau (Pakistan) *Tel:* (021) 6321959 *Fax:* (021) 6321959, pg 508

Library Promotion Bureau (Pakistan) *Tel:* (021) 6321959; (021) 6977737 *Fax:* (021) 6321959 *E-mail:* vc@ku.edu.pk *Web Site:* www.ku.edu.pk, pg 1569

Library Service of Fiji (Fiji) *Tel:* 315 344 *Fax:* 314 994, pg 140, 1503

The Library Shop (Ireland) *Tel:* (01) 608 1000 *Fax:* (01) 6081016 *E-mail:* library.shop@tcd.ie *Web Site:* www.tcd.ie/library/shop/, pg 1309

Libreria Cultural Panamena SA (Panama) *Tel:* 2235628; 2236267 *Fax:* 2237280, pg 1325

Libreria Editora Ltda (Brazil) *Tel:* (011) 608-5411 *Fax:* (011) 948-1615 *E-mail:* portal@libreria.com.br; libreria@libreria.com.br *Web Site:* www.libreria.com.br, pg 84

Libreria Editrice Fiorentina (Italy) *Tel:* (055) 579921 *Fax:* (055) 579921, pg 392

Libreria Hispano Americana (Spain) *Tel:* (093) 3180079 *E-mail:* info@llibreriaha.com *Web Site:* www.llibreriaha.com, pg 1333

Libreria Internacional SA (Paraguay) *Tel:* (021) 491 423; (021) 491 424 *Fax:* (021) 449 730, pg 1325

Libreria la Paz (Bolivia) *Tel:* (02) 353323; (02) 357109 *Fax:* (02) 391513, pg 1293

Libreria l'Universidad, Nicolas Ojeda Fierro e Hijos SRL Ltda (Peru) *Tel:* (014) 282461; (014) 282036, pg 1325

Libreria Nacional Ltda (Colombia) *Tel:* (01) 825829; (01) 833849; (01) 2139842; (01) 2139882 *Fax:* (01) 822404; (01) 2138404, pg 1296

Libreria Parroquial de Claveria SA Edicion Compra y Venta de Libros (Mexico) *Tel:* (05) 3967027; (05) 3967718 *Fax:* (05) 3991243, pg 464

Libreria Tecnologica Universitaria (Nicaragua) *Tel:* (02) 773026 *Fax:* (02) 670106, pg 1322

Libreria Universitaria (Chile) *Tel:* (02) 2234555; (02) 2236980 *Fax:* (02) 2099455; (02) 499455, pg 1295

Libreria Universitaria (Ecuador) *Tel:* (02) 212521, pg 1298

Libreria Universitaria (Nicaragua) *Tel:* (0311) 2612; (0311) 2613, pg 1322

Libreria y Distribuidora Lerner Ltda (Colombia) *Tel:* (01) 243 0567; (01) 334 7826 *Fax:* (01) 281 4319, pg 1296

Libresa S A (Ecuador) *Tel:* (02) 230925; (02) 525581 *Fax:* (02) 502992 *E-mail:* libresa@interactive.net.ec, pg 136

Libretto Forlag (Norway) *Tel:* (022) 443011 *Fax:* (022) 443012, pg 505

Librex (Italy) *Tel:* (02) 58302006, pg 392

Edition Libri Illustri GmbH (Germany) *Tel:* (07141) 84720 *Fax:* (07141) 875117 *E-mail:* info@libri-illustri.de *Web Site:* www.edition-libri-illustri.de, pg 252

Libri spol sro (Czech Republic) *Tel:* (02) 5161 3113; (02) 5161 2302 *Fax:* (02) 5161 1013 *E-mail:* libri@libri.cz *Web Site:* www.libri.cz, pg 124

Libris Bokforlaget (Sweden) *Tel:* (019) 208400 *Fax:* (019) 208430 *E-mail:* info@libris.se *Web Site:* www.libris.se, pg 608

Libris Emo AS (Norway) *Tel:* 63849200 *Fax:* 63849345, pg 1324

Libris Ltd (United Kingdom) *Tel:* (020) 7482 2390 *Fax:* (020) 7485 2730 *E-mail:* libris@onetel.net.uk *Web Site:* www.librislondon.co.uk, pg 715

Libro Ltd (Greece) *Tel:* 2107247116; 2107228647 *Fax:* 2107226648 *E-mail:* libro@hol.gr, pg 306

Librograf Editora (Argentina) *Tel:* (011) 4300-3670; (011) 4300-1466 *Fax:* (011) 4300-3670, pg 7

Librolandia del Centro SA de CV (Mexico) *Tel:* (062) 135646; (062) 170236 *Fax:* (062) 170236, pg 1318

Editorial Libros y Libres SA (Colombia) *Tel:* (01) 2907145; (01) 2907862; (01) 2886188 *Fax:* (01) 2696830 *E-mail:* edilibro@colomsat.net.co, pg 111

Libros y Libros Editorial SA (Colombia) *Tel:* (01) 4117527; (01) 4117659; (01) 2886188 *Fax:* (01) 3124291 *E-mail:* edilibro@colomsat.net.co, pg 111

Libros y Revistas SA de CV (Mexico) *Tel:* (05) 5437295 *Fax:* (05) 5364622, pg 464

Libsa Editorial SA (Spain) *Tel:* (091) 657 25 80 *Fax:* (091) 657 25 83 *E-mail:* libsa@libsa.es *Web Site:* www.libsa.es, pg 584

Licap CVBA (Belgium) *Tel:* (02) 5099672 *Fax:* (02) 5099704; (02) 5099780 *E-mail:* info@licap.be, pg 1292

Licht & Burr Literary Agency (Denmark) *Tel:* 3333 0021 *Fax:* 3333 0521 *E-mail:* mail@licht-burr.de *Web Site:* www.licht-burr.de, pg 1120

LID Editorial Empresarial, SL (Spain) *Tel:* (091) 372 90 03 *Fax:* (091) 372 85 14 *E-mail:* info@lideditorial.com *Web Site:* www.lideditorial.com, pg 584

Editora Lidador Ltda (Brazil) *Tel:* (021) 2569-0594 *Fax:* (021) 2204-0684 *E-mail:* lidador@infolink.com.br, pg 84

Lidel Edicoes Tecnicas, Lda (Portugal) *Tel:* (021) 571288 *Fax:* (021) 577827, pg 528

Lider Verlag (Romania) *Tel:* (01) 337-33-067; (01) 3374881 *Fax:* (01) 337-48-22, pg 535

Lidhja e Shkrimtareve dhe e Artisteve toe Shqiperise (Albania) *Tel:* (042) 23843 *Fax:* (042) 23843 *E-mail:* bashan@natlib.tirana.al, pg 1249

Edition Lidiarte (Germany) *Tel:* (030) 3137420 *Fax:* (030) 3127117 *E-mail:* edition@lidiarte.de *Web Site:* www.lidiarte.de, pg 252

Ediciones Lidiun (Argentina) *Tel:* (011) 4942-9002 *Fax:* (011) 4942-9162 *E-mail:* info@ateneo.com, pg 7

Lidman Production AB (Sweden) *Tel:* (08) 6633615 *Fax:* (08) 6633590 *E-mail:* lidman@canit.se, pg 608

Lidove Noviny Publishing House (Czech Republic) *Tel:* (02) 225 223 50; (02) 222 510 845 *Fax:* (02) 225 240 12; (02) 222 514 012 *E-mail:* nln@nln.cz; nln@iol.cz *Web Site:* www.nln.cz, pg 124

Hildegard Liebaug-Dartmann (Germany) *Tel:* (02225) 909343 *Fax:* (02225) 909345 *E-mail:* liebaug-dartmann@t-online.de *Web Site:* www.liebaug-dartmann.de, pg 252

Liebenzeller Mission, GmbH, Abt. Verlag (Germany) *Tel:* (07052) 17-163 *Fax:* (07052) 17-170 *E-mail:* buch@liebenzell.org *Web Site:* www.liebenzell.org/blm/index.htm, pg 252

Liechtenstein Verlag AG (Liechtenstein) *Tel:* 2396010 *Fax:* 2396019 *E-mail:* flbooks@verlag-ag.lol.li *Web Site:* www.lol.li/verlag_ag, pg 444

Liechtenstein Verlag AG (Liechtenstein) *Tel:* (0423) 2322414 *Fax:* (0423) 2324340 *E-mail:* flbooks@verlag-ag.lol.li, pg 1124

Liechtensteinische Landesbibliothek (Liechtenstein) *Tel:* 236 63 62 *Fax:* 233 14 19 *E-mail:* info@landesbibliothek.li *Web Site:* www.lbfl.li, pg 1524

Verlag der Liechtensteinischen Akademischen Gesellschaft (Liechtenstein) *Tel:* 232 30 28 *Fax:* 233 14 49, pg 444

Lielvards Ltd (Latvia) *Tel:* (050) 71860 *Fax:* (050) 71861 *E-mail:* lielvards@lielvards.lv *Web Site:* www.lielvards.lv, pg 441

Robert Lienau GmbH & Co KG (Germany) *Tel:* (069) 9782866 *Fax:* (069) 97828689 *E-mail:* info@lienau-frankfurt.de *Web Site:* www.lienau-frankfurt.de, pg 252

Lienhard Pallast Verlag (Germany) *Tel:* (02244) 5863 *Fax:* (02244) 5863 *E-mail:* lienhard@pallast-publisher.com *Web Site:* www.pallast-publisher.com, pg 252

Liepman Agency AG (Switzerland) *Tel:* (044) 2617660 *Fax:* (044) 2610124 *E-mail:* info@liepmagency.com, pg 1127

Le Lierre et Le Coudrier (France) *Tel:* (01) 42 55 00 27 *Fax:* (01) 42 57 04 97, pg 172

Lietus Ltd (Lithuania) *Tel:* (02) 312298; (02) 8299 35423; (02) 745720 *Fax:* (02) 312298, pg 445

Lietuvos Mokslu Akademijos Leidykla (Lithuania) *Tel:* (02) 626851 *Fax:* (02) 226351, pg 446

Lietuvos Rasytoju Sajungos Leidykla (Lithuania) *Tel:* (05) 2628945; (05) 2628643 *Fax:* (05) 2628945 *E-mail:* info@rsleidykla.lt *Web Site:* www.rsleidykla.lt, pg 446

Life Challenge AFRICA (Kenya) *Tel:* (02) 561121; (02) 722314 *Fax:* (02) 564030 *E-mail:* lca@umsg.org, pg 431

Literas Universitaetsverlag (Austria) *Tel:* (01) 269 22 07 *Fax:* (01) 269 22 07, pg 53

Literature Academy Publishing (Republic of Korea) *Tel:* (02) 7645057 *Fax:* (02) 7458516 *E-mail:* webmaster@munhakac.co.kr *Web Site: www.* munhakac.co.kr, pg 437

Literature and Art Publishing House (Democratic People's Republic of Korea), pg 433

The Literature Bureau (Zimbabwe) *Tel:* (04) 726929; (04) 729120, pg 778

Literature Ministry Department (Hong Kong) *Tel:* 2725 8558 *Fax:* 2386 2304 *E-mail:* hkccllmd@hkstar.com, pg 1147

Lithuanian ISBN Agency (Lithuania) *Tel:* (05) 2497023 *Fax:* (05) 2496129 *E-mail:* isbnltu@lnb.lt *Web Site:* www.lnb.lt, pg 1266

Lithuanian Librarians Association (Lithuania) *Tel:* (02) 750340 *Fax:* (02) 750340 *E-mail:* lbd@vpu.lt *Web Site:* www.lbd.lt, pg 1567

Lithuanian National Museum Publishing House (Lithuania) *Tel:* (05) 262 77 74 *Fax:* (05) 261 10 23 *E-mail:* info@lnm.lt; muziejus@lnm.lt *Web Site:* www.lnm.lt, pg 446

Lithuanian Publishers' Association (Lithuania) *Tel:* (02) 617740 *Fax:* (02) 617740 *E-mail:* lla@centras.lt *Web Site:* www.lla.lt, pg 446

Lithuanian Publishers' Association (Lithuania) *Tel:* (05) 2617740 *Fax:* (05) 2617740 *E-mail:* lla@centras.lt *Web Site:* www.lla.lt, pg 1266

LITkom Elisabeth Falk Agentur fur Literatur und Kommunikation (Germany) *E-mail:* falk@litkom.de *Web Site:* www.litkom.de, pg 1121

Editions Lito (France) *Tel:* (01) 45161700 *Fax:* (01) 48820085 *E-mail:* annick.cabrelli@editionslito.com, pg 173

Lito Technion Ltda (Colombia) *Tel:* (01) 2443502; (01) 2443177; (01) 2441538, pg 111

Litografia e Imprenta LIL SA (Costa Rica) *Tel:* 2350011; 2213622 *Fax:* 2407814, pg 115

Litopia Corp Ltd (United Kingdom) *Tel:* (020) 7224 1748 *Fax:* (020) 7224 1802 *E-mail:* enquiries@litopia. com *Web Site:* www.litopia.com, pg 1131

Editeurs de Litterature Biblique (Belgium) *Tel:* (02) 384-54-02; (02) 384-52-12 *Fax:* (02) 384-98-66 *E-mail:* elbpub@elbeurope.org *Web Site:* www. elbeurope.org, pg 70

Christopher Little Literary Agency (United Kingdom) *Tel:* (020) 7736 4455 *Fax:* (020) 7736 4490 *E-mail:* info@christopherlittle.net *Web Site:* www. christopherlittle.net, pg 1132

Little Hills Press Pty Ltd (Australia) *Tel:* (02) 9677 9658 *Fax:* (02) 9677 9152 *E-mail:* lhills@bigpond.net.au; sales@littlehills.com *Web Site:* www.littlehills.com, pg 29

Little Red Apple Publishing (Australia) *Tel:* (02) 9430 6867 *E-mail:* littleredapple@hotmail.com, pg 29

Littlehampton Book Services Ltd (United Kingdom) *Tel:* (01903) 828500 *Fax:* (01903) 828802 *E-mail:* enquiries@lbsltd.co.uk *Web Site:* www.lbsltd. co.uk, pg 1343

The Littman Library of Jewish Civilization (United Kingdom) *Tel:* (01865) 514688 *Fax:* (01865) 514688 *E-mail:* info@littman.co.uk *Web Site:* www.littman.co. uk, pg 717

Liverpool Libraries & Information Services (United Kingdom) *Tel:* (0151) 233 5829 *Fax:* (0151) 233 5886 *E-mail:* refbt.central.library@liverpool.gov.uk, pg 1552

Liverpool University Press (United Kingdom) *Tel:* (0151) 794 2233; (0151) 794 2237 *Fax:* (0151) 794 2235 *E-mail:* j.m.smith@liv.ac.uk *Web Site:* www.liverpool-unipress.co.uk, pg 717

Living Literary Agency (Italy) *Tel:* (02) 33100584 *Fax:* (02) 33100618 *E-mail:* living@galactica.it, pg 1123

Living Word Distribution (New Zealand) *Tel:* (07) 839 5607 *Fax:* (07) 834 3916 *E-mail:* livingword.ltd@xtra. co.nz, pg 1321

Livraria Apostolado da Imprensa (Portugal) *Tel:* (0253) 22485 *Fax:* (0253) 201221, pg 528

Livraria Barata, Antonio D M Barata (Portugal) *Tel:* (021) 848 16 31 *Fax:* (021) 80 33 44, pg 1328

Livraria Buchholz, Lda (Portugal) *Tel:* (021) 3170580; (021) 3170589 *Fax:* (021) 3522634 *E-mail:* buchholz@mail.telepac.pt *Web Site:* www. buchholz.pt, pg 1328

Livraria Caravana (Portugal) *Tel:* (089) 462879 *Fax:* (089) 462871, pg 1328

Livraria Dos Advogados Editora Ltda (Brazil) *Tel:* (011) 3107-3979 *Fax:* (011) 3107-6878 *E-mail:* lael@lael. com.br *Web Site:* www.lael.com.br, pg 85

Livraria e Editora Infobook SA (Brazil) *Tel:* (021) 263-3807 *Fax:* (021) 263-3807 *E-mail:* infobook@ibpinet. com.br, pg 85

Livraria Latina (Portugal) *Tel:* (022) 2001294 *Fax:* (022) 2086053, pg 1328

Livraria Ler Lda (Portugal) *Tel:* (021) 3888371, pg 1328

Livraria Luzo-Espanhola Lda (Portugal) *Tel:* (021) 3424917, pg 528

Livraria Manuel Ferreira (Portugal) *Tel:* (022) 5363237 *Fax:* (022) 5364406 *E-mail:* livrariaferreira@hotmail. com, pg 1328

Livraria Minerva (Portugal) *Tel:* (0239) 26259 *Fax:* (0239) 717267 *E-mail:* livrariaminerva@mail. telepac.pt, pg 528

Livraria Teorema 1-Cogitum Livrarias Lda (Portugal) *Tel:* (021) 4394912 *Fax:* (021) 4394909 *E-mail:* cogitum@ip.pt, pg 1328

Le Livre de Paris (France) *Tel:* (01) 41 23 65 00 *Fax:* (01) 41 45 34 42 *E-mail:* ldpsiege@hachette-livre.fr *Web Site:* www.livre-de-paris.com, pg 173

Le Livre de Poche-L G F (Librairie Generale Francaise) (France) *Tel:* (01) 43923000 *Fax:* (01) 43923590 *Web Site:* www.livredepoche.com; www.hachette.com, pg 173

Librairie Livre-Service (Morocco) *Tel:* (02) 262072 *Fax:* (02) 473089, pg 1319

Livres de France (Egypt (Arab Republic of Egypt)) *Tel:* (02) 3935512, pg 1299

Les Livres du Dragon d'Or (France) *Tel:* (01) 53 10 36 37 *Fax:* (01) 53 10 36 39 *E-mail:* dragondor@gruend. fr, pg 173

Editora Livros do Brasil Sarl (Portugal) *Tel:* (021) 3426113 *Fax:* (021) 342 84 87 *E-mail:* livbrasil@clix. pt, pg 528

Livros Do Oriente (Macau) *Tel:* 700320; 700421 *Fax:* 700423 *E-mail:* livros.macau@loriente.com *Web Site:* www.loriente.com, pg 448

Livros Horizonte Lda (Portugal) *Tel:* (021) 346 69 17 *Fax:* (021) 326921 *E-mail:* livroshorizonte@mail. telepac.pt, pg 528

Oficina de Livros Ltda (Brazil) *Tel:* (061) 386-2355 *Toll Free Tel:* 800-644-3002 *Fax:* (061) 386-9248 *E-mail:* nicanorsena2001@aol.com.br, pg 85

LK Litho (United States) *Tel:* 631-924-3888 *E-mail:* linickgrp@att.net *Web Site:* www.lgroup.addr. com/lklitho.htm, pg 1156, 1178, 1220, 1231, 1239

LLB France (Ligue pour la Lecture de la Bible) (France) *Tel:* (04) 75 56 02 68 *Fax:* (04) 75 56 02 97 *E-mail:* contact@llbfrance.com *Web Site:* www. llbfrance.com, pg 173

Llibres del Segle (Spain) *Tel:* (093) 795079; (093) 794023 *Fax:* (093) 210354 *E-mail:* costapau@releline. es, pg 584

Chris Lloyd Sales & Marketing Services (United Kingdom) *Tel:* (01202) 649930 *Fax:* (01202) 649950 *E-mail:* chrlloyd@globalnet.co.uk, pg 1343

LLP Ltd (United Kingdom) *Tel:* (020) 7553 1000 *Fax:* (020) 7553 1109 *E-mail:* info@lloydslist.com *Web Site:* www.lloydslist.com, pg 717

Lluvia Editores Srl (Peru) *Tel:* (01) 3326641 *Fax:* (01) 4320732 *E-mail:* lluviaeditores2002@yahoo.com, pg 512

LMH Publishing Ltd (Jamaica) *Tel:* (876) 938-0005 *Fax:* (876) 759-8752 *E-mail:* lmhbookpublishing@ cwjamaica.com *Web Site:* www.lmhpublishingjamaica. com, pg 410

Vincenzo Lo Faro Editore (Italy) *Tel:* (06) 70451187 *Fax:* (06) 70451641, pg 392

Local Consumption Publications (Australia) *Tel:* (02) 95141960 *Fax:* (02) 95197503, pg 29

Editrice la Locusta (Italy) *Tel:* (0444) 324051 *E-mail:* la_locusta@yahoo.com *Web Site:* space.tin. it/io/pibeltra/lalocust.htm, pg 392

Lodenek Press (United Kingdom) *Tel:* (01208) 880850, pg 717

Wydawnictwo Lodzkie (Poland) *Tel:* (042) 6360331; (042) 6366189 *Fax:* (042) 6368524, pg 519

Loecker Verlag (Austria) *Tel:* (01) 512 02 82 *Fax:* (01) 512 02 82-22 *E-mail:* lverlag@loecker.at *Web Site:* www.loecker.at, pg 53

Uitgeverij Loempia (Belgium) *Tel:* (03) 2184292, pg 70

Loescher Editore SRL (Italy) *Tel:* (011) 5654111 *Fax:* (011) 56 25822 *E-mail:* mail@loescher.it *Web Site:* www.loescher.it, pg 392

Rainer Loessl Verlag (Germany) *Tel:* (089) 362646, pg 253

Antiquariat Oskar Loewe (Germany) *Tel:* (02361) 960813 *Fax:* (02361) 960815 *E-mail:* loewe.bochum@ t-online.de *Web Site:* www.antiquariat.net/loewe, pg 253

Loewe Verlag GmbH (Germany) *Tel:* (09208) 51-0 *Fax:* (09208) 51-309 *E-mail:* presse@loewe-verlag.de *Web Site:* www.loewe-verlag.de, pg 253

Loffredo Editore Napoli SpA® (Italy) *Tel:* (081) 5937073 *Fax:* (081) 5936953 *E-mail:* info@loffredo.it *Web Site:* www.loffredo.it, pg 393

LOG-Internationale Zeitschrift fuer Literatur (Austria) *Tel:* (01) 2313433 *Fax:* (01) 2313433, pg 53

Logans University Bookshop (Pty) Ltd (South Africa) *Tel:* (031) 3076530 *Fax:* (031) 3073230, pg 1331

Logophon Verlag und Bildungsreisen GmbH (Germany) *Tel:* (06131) 71645 *Fax:* (06131) 72596 *E-mail:* verlag@logophon.de *Web Site:* www. logophon.de, pg 253

Logos Consorcio Editorial SA (Mexico) *Tel:* (055) 515-16-33, pg 464

Logos (Divine Word) Publications Inc (Philippines) *Tel:* (02) 7111323 *Fax:* (02) 7322736 *E-mail:* dwpsvd@rp1.net, pg 514

Logos Verlag GmbH (Germany) *Tel:* (05232) 960120; (05232) 960124 *Fax:* (05232) 960121 *E-mail:* info@ logos-verlag.de *Web Site:* www.logos-verlag.de, pg 253

Logos-Verlag Literatur & Layout GmbH (Germany) *Tel:* (06893) 986096 *Fax:* (06893) 986095, pg 253

Editora Logosofica (Brazil) *Tel:* (011) 8851476; (011) 8856574 *Fax:* (011) 8879480, pg 85

Loguez Ediciones (Spain) *Tel:* (0923) 138541 *Fax:* (0923) 138586 *E-mail:* loguezediciones@ eresmas.com, pg 584

Ulla Lohren Literary Agency (Denmark) *Tel:* 44494515 *Fax:* 44493515 *E-mail:* ulla.litag@get2net.dk, pg 1120

Lohse Forlag (Denmark) *Tel:* 7593 4455 *Fax:* 7592 4275 *E-mail:* lohse@imh.dk *Web Site:* www.lohse.dk, pg 132

Lojas Europa-America (Portugal) *Tel:* (01) 9211461 *Fax:* (01) 9217940, pg 1329

Lokrundschau Verlag GmbH (Germany) *Fax:* (40) 69692321 *E-mail:* verlag@lokrundschau.de *Web Site:* www.lokrundschau.de, pg 253

Lokvangmaya Griha Pvt Ltd (India) *Tel:* (022) 4362474 *Fax:* (022) 4313220 *E-mail:* lokvang@bol.net.in, pg 337

Y Lolfa Cyf (United Kingdom) *Tel:* (01970) 832 304 *Fax:* (01970) 832 782 *E-mail:* ylolfa@ylolfa.com *Web Site:* www.ylolfa.com, pg 717

Les Editions du Lombard SA (Belgium) *Tel:* (02) 5266811 *Fax:* (02) 5204405 *E-mail:* info@lombard.be *Web Site:* www.lelombard.com, pg 70

Lomond Books (United Kingdom) *Tel:* (0131) 551 2261 *Fax:* (0131) 559 2042 *E-mail:* info@flatman.co.uk; sales@lomand-books.co.uk *Web Site:* www.lomond-books.co.uk; www.scottishbookstore.com, pg 1343

London Chamber of Commerce & Industry Examinations Board (LCCIEB) (United Kingdom) *Tel:* (020) 8309 3000 *Fax:* (020) 8302 4169 *E-mail:* custserv@lccieb. org.uk *Web Site:* www.lccieb.com, pg 717

London Independent Books (United Kingdom) *Tel:* (020) 7706 0486 *Fax:* (020) 7724 3122, pg 1132

Lonely Planet (France) *Tel:* (01) 55 25 33 00 *Fax:* (01) 55 25 33 01 *E-mail:* bip@lonelyplanet.fr *Web Site:* www.lonelyplanet.fr, pg 173

Lonely Planet Publications Pty Ltd (Australia) *Tel:* (03) 8379 8000 *Fax:* (03) 8379 8111 *E-mail:* talk2us@ lonelyplanet.com.au *Web Site:* www.lonelyplanet.com. au, pg 29

Lonely Planet, UK (United Kingdom) *Tel:* (020) 7841 9000 *Fax:* (020) 7841 9001 *E-mail:* go@lonelyplanet. co.uk *Web Site:* www.lonelyplanet.com, pg 717

Barry Long Books (United Kingdom) *Tel:* (01823) 430061 *E-mail:* contact@barrylongbooks.com *Web Site:* www.barrylongbooks.com, pg 717

Longacre Press (New Zealand) *Tel:* (03) 4772911 *Fax:* (03) 4772911 *E-mail:* longacre.press@clear.net. nz, pg 494

Longanesi & C (Italy) *Tel:* (02) 80206310 *Fax:* (02) 72000306 *E-mail:* info@longanesi.it *Web Site:* www. longanesi.it, pg 393

Longman Italia srl (Italy) *Tel:* (02) 6739761 *Fax:* (02) 673976501 *E-mail:* longman-italia@pearsoned-ema. com *Web Site:* www.longman-elt.com, pg 393

Longman Nigeria Plc (Nigeria) *Tel:* (01) 497 89259 *Fax:* (01) 496 4370 *E-mail:* longman@infoweb.abs. net, pg 501

Longman-Pearson Education Hellas SA (Greece) *Fax:* 2109373206 *E-mail:* publ.pass@longman.gr, pg 306

Longman Zimbabwe (Pvt) Ltd (Zimbabwe) *Tel:* (04) 621 661; (04) 621 667 *Fax:* (04) 621670 *E-mail:* customeralicek@longman.co. zw *Web Site:* www.pearsoned.co.uk/contactus/ worldwideoffices/africa, pg 778

Angelo Longo Editore (Italy) *Tel:* (0544) 217026 *Fax:* (0544) 217554 *E-mail:* longo-ra@linknet.it *Web Site:* www.longo-editore.it, pg 393

La Longue Vue (Belgium) *Tel:* (02) 358 23 93 *Fax:* (02) 358 17 37 *E-mail:* longuevue@skynet.be, pg 70

Stefan Loose Verlag (Germany) *Tel:* (030) 6 91 37 89 *Fax:* (030) 6 93 01 71 *E-mail:* info@loose-verlag.de *Web Site:* www.loose-verlag.de, pg 253

Livraria Lopes Da Silva-Editora de M Moreira Soares Rocha Lda (Portugal) *Tel:* (02) 21678 *Fax:* (02) 2006017, pg 528

Lopez Libreros Editores S R L (Argentina) *Tel:* (011) 4963-9646, pg 7

E Lopfe-Benz AG Rorschach, Graphische Anstalt und Verlag (Switzerland) *Tel:* (071) 8440444 *Fax:* (071) 8440445, pg 623

Lorber-Verlag & Turm-Verlag Otto Zluhan (Germany) *Tel:* (07142) 940843 *Fax:* (07142) 940844 *E-mail:* info@lorber-verlag.de; bestellen@lorber-verlag.de *Web Site:* www.lorber-verlag.de, pg 253

Lorenz Books (United Kingdom) *Tel:* (020) 7401 2077 *Fax:* (020) 7633 9499 *E-mail:* bsp2b@aol.com, pg 718

Carlo Lorenzini Editore (Italy) *Tel:* (0432) 691412 *Fax:* (0432) 691412, pg 393

Lorenzo Editore (Italy) *Tel:* (011) 2485387 *Fax:* (011) 2485387 *E-mail:* info@loredi.it *Web Site:* www.loredi. it, pg 393

Johannes Loriz Verlag der Kooperative Duernau (Germany) *Tel:* (07582) 93000 *Fax:* (07582) 930020 *Web Site:* www.kooperative.de, pg 253

Editorial Losada SA (Argentina) *Tel:* (011) 4373-4006; (011) 4375-5001 *Fax:* (011) 4373-4006; (011) 4375-5001 *E-mail:* administra@editoriallosada.com, pg 7

Thomas C Lothian Pty Ltd (Australia) *Tel:* (03) 9694 4900 *Fax:* (03) 9645 0705 *E-mail:* books@lothian. com.au *Web Site:* www.lothian.com.au, pg 29

Verlag an der Lottbek (Germany) *Tel:* (0241) 873434 *Fax:* (0241) 875577, pg 253

Lotu Pacifika Productions (Fiji) *Tel:* 301314 *Fax:* 301183, pg 140

Editions Loubatieres (France) *Tel:* (05) 61 72 83 53 *Fax:* (05) 61 72 83 50 *E-mail:* loubatieres@club-internet.fr, pg 173

Loughborough University (United Kingdom) *Tel:* (01509) 263171; (01509) 223052 *Fax:* (01509) 223053 *E-mail:* dis@lboro.ac.uk *Web Site:* www.lboro. ac.uk, pg 718

Lowden Publishing Co (Australia) *Tel:* (03) 9873 7202 *Fax:* (03) 9873 0542 *E-mail:* service@theruralstore. com.au *Web Site:* www.theruralstore.com.au, pg 29

Lowfield Printing Co Ltd (United Kingdom) *Tel:* (01322) 522216 *Fax:* (01322) 555362 *E-mail:* lowfield@ compuserve.com, pg 1175

Lowfield Printing Co Ltd (United Kingdom) *Tel:* (01322) 522216 *E-mail:* lowfield@compuserve.com *Web Site:* www.applegate.com, pg 1216

Andrew Lownie Literary Agency Ltd (United Kingdom) *Tel:* (020) 7828 1274 *Fax:* (020) 7828 7608 *E-mail:* lownie@globalnet.co.uk *Web Site:* www. andrewlownie.co.uk, pg 1132

Edicoes Loyola SA (Brazil) *Tel:* (011) 69141922 *Fax:* (011) 61634275 *E-mail:* editorial@loyola.com.br *Web Site:* www.loyola.com.br, pg 85

Ediciones LR SA (Argentina) *Tel:* (011) 4326-3725; (011) 4326-3826, pg 7

LT Editions-Jacques Lanore (France) *Tel:* (01) 44 41 89 30 *Fax:* (01) 44 41 89 39 *E-mail:* lanore@lanore.com *Web Site:* www.lanore.com, pg 173

LTC-Livros Tecnicos e Cientificos Editora S/A (Brazil) *Tel:* (021) 2221-7106; (021) 224-5877 *Fax:* (021) 252-2732; (021) 2221-5744, pg 85

LTR Editora Ltda (Brazil) *Tel:* (011) 3667-1101 *Fax:* (011) 3825-6695 *E-mail:* ltr@ltr.com.br *Web Site:* www.ltr.com.br/web/home.asp, pg 85

Steve Lu Publishing Ltd (Hong Kong) *Tel:* 25210681 *Fax:* 28450492 *E-mail:* ltlahk@netvigator.com, pg 315

Lua Viajante-Edicao e Distribuicao de Livros e Material Audiovisual, Lda (Portugal) *Tel:* (01) 9376180 *Fax:* (01) 9381452; (01) 9377560 *E-mail:* europress@ mail.telepac.pt, pg 528

Luath Press Ltd (United Kingdom) *Tel:* (0131) 225 4326 *Fax:* (0131) 225 4324 *E-mail:* sales@luath.co.uk *Web Site:* www.luath.co.uk, pg 718

Wydawnictwo Lubelskie (Poland) *Tel:* (081) 7442667, pg 519

Lubrina (Italy) *Tel:* (035) 3470139396 *Fax:* (035) 241547 *E-mail:* editorelubrina@lubrina.it *Web Site:* www.lubrina.it, pg 393

Luc vydavatelske druzstvo (Slovakia) *Tel:* (02) 65730331 *Fax:* (02) 65730331, pg 555

Edizioni de Luca SRL (Italy) *Tel:* (06) 32650712 *Fax:* (06) 32650715, pg 393

Lucasville Press (Australia) *Tel:* (03) 9395 1446, pg 29

Luchterhand Literaturverlag GmbH/Verlag Volk & Welt GmbH (Germany) *Tel:* (089) 4136-0; (01805) 990505 *Fax:* (089) 21215250 *E-mail:* vertrieb.verlagsgruppe@ randomhouse.de *Web Site:* www.randomhouse.de/ luchterhand, pg 253

Ediciones Luciernaga (Spain) *Tel:* (093) 443 71 00 *Fax:* (093) 443 71 30 *E-mail:* correu@grup62.com *Web Site:* www.grup62.com, pg 584

Lucis Press Ltd (United Kingdom) *Tel:* (020) 7839 4512; (020) 7839 4513 *Fax:* (020) 7839 5575 *E-mail:* london@lucistrust.org *Web Site:* www. lucistrust.org, pg 718

Lucius & Lucius Verlagsgesellschaft mbH (Germany) *Tel:* (0711) 242060 *Fax:* (0711) 242088 *E-mail:* lucius@luciusverlag.com *Web Site:* www. luciusverlag.com, pg 254

Lucky Duck Publishing Ltd (United Kingdom) *Tel:* (0117) 947 5150 *Fax:* (0117) 947 5152 *E-mail:* publishing@luckyduck.co.uk *Web Site:* www. luckyduck.co.uk, pg 718

Editora Lucre Comercio e Representacoes (Brazil) *Tel:* (019) 287-8593 *Fax:* (019) 287 8593 *E-mail:* lucre@mute.net.br, pg 85

Ludowa Spoldzielnia Wydawnicza (Poland) *Tel:* (022) 6205718; (022) 6205719 *Fax:* (022) 6207277, pg 519

Gustav Luebbe Verlag (Germany) *Tel:* (02202) 121-330 *Fax:* (02202) 121-920 *E-mail:* glv@luebbe.de *Web Site:* www.luebbe.de, pg 254

Verlagsgruppe Luebbe GmbH & Co KG (Germany) *Tel:* (02202) 121-0 *Fax:* (02202) 121-920 *E-mail:* info@luebbe.de *Web Site:* www.luebbe.de, pg 254

Editorial Luis Vives (Edelvives) (Spain) *Tel:* (091) 334 48 83 *Fax:* (091) 334 48 93 *E-mail:* jmarketing@ edelvives.es *Web Site:* www.grupoeditorialluisvives. com, pg 584

Lukas Verlag fur Kunst- und Geistesgeschichte (Germany) *Tel:* (030) 44049220 *Fax:* (030) 4428177 *E-mail:* lukas.verlag@t-online.de *Web Site:* www. lukasverlag.com, pg 254

Josef Lukasik A Spol sro (Czech Republic) *Tel:* (02) 471 22 19; (02) 83 22 84; (0603) 95 52 55, pg 125

Editorial Lumen SA (Spain) *Tel:* (093) 3660300 *Fax:* (093) 3660013 *E-mail:* lumen@editoriallumen. com, pg 585

Editions Lumen Vitae ASBL (Belgium) *Tel:* (02) 3490399; (02) 3490370 *Fax:* (02) 3490385 *E-mail:* international@lumenvitae.be *Web Site:* www. catho.be/lumen, pg 70

Editura Lumina (Republic of Moldova) *Tel:* (02) 246397; (02) 246398 *Fax:* (02) 246395 *E-mail:* lumina@mdl. net, pg 469

La Luna (Italy) *Tel:* (091) 345799 *Fax:* (091) 301650 *E-mail:* laluna@arcidonna.it, pg 393

Lund Humphries (United Kingdom) *Tel:* (01252) 331551 *Fax:* (01252) 344405 *E-mail:* info@lundhumphries. com *Web Site:* www.lundhumphries.com, pg 718

Lunde Forlag AS (Norway) *Tel:* (022) 00 73 50 *Fax:* (022) 00 73 73 *E-mail:* lunde@nlm.no *Web Site:* www.lunde-forlag.no, pg 505

Lunds Universitets Bibliotek (Sweden) *Tel:* (046) 222 00 00 *Fax:* (046) 222 47 20 *E-mail:* webmaster@lub.lu.se *Web Site:* www.lub.lu.se, pg 1545

Lundula Publishing House (Zambia) *Tel:* (01) 96758496, pg 776

Luni (Italy) *Tel:* (02) 89693000 *Fax:* (02) 89693011 *E-mail:* luni.editrice@fastwebnet.it, pg 393

Lunwerg Editores, SA (Spain) *Tel:* (093) 2015933 *Fax:* (093) 2011587 *E-mail:* lunwerg.mad@retemail. es, pg 585

Lusaka City Library (Zambia) *Tel:* (01) 227282, pg 1554

Lusatia Verlag-Dr Stuebner & Co KG (Germany) *Tel:* (03591) 532400; (03591) 532401 *Fax:* (03591) 532400 *E-mail:* lusatiaverlag@t-online.de, pg 254

Lusva Editrice (Italy) *Tel:* (02) 4985386, pg 393

Lutchman, Drs LFS (Suriname) *Tel:* 465558; 453419, pg 603

Luther Forlag A/S (Norway) *Tel:* (022) 33 06 08 *Fax:* (022) 42 10 00 *E-mail:* postkasse@lutherforlag. no *Web Site:* www.lutherforlag.no, pg 505

Luther-Verlag GmbH (Germany) *Tel:* (0521) 94 40-137 *Fax:* (0521) 94 40-136 *E-mail:* vertrieb@luther-verlag. de *Web Site:* www.ekvw.de/pressehaus/lv/, pg 254

Lutherische Verlagsgesellschaft mbH (Germany) *Tel:* (0431) 55779-285 *Fax:* (0431) 55779-292, pg 254

Lutherisches Verlagshaus GmbH (Germany) *Tel:* (0511) 1241-716 *Fax:* (0511) 1241-948 *E-mail:* lvh@lvh.de *Web Site:* www.lvh.de, pg 254

The Lutterworth Press (United Kingdom) *Tel:* (01223) 350865 *Fax:* (01223) 366951 *E-mail:* publishing@ lutterworth.com *Web Site:* www.lutterworth.com, pg 718

Lutyens & Rubinstein (United Kingdom) *Tel:* (020) 7792 4855 *Fax:* (020) 7792 4833, pg 1132

Verlag Waldemar Lutz (Germany) *Tel:* (07621) 88812 *Fax:* (07621) 12599 *E-mail:* wlutz@verlag-lutz.de *Web Site:* www.verlag-lutz.de, pg 254

Lux Verbi (Pty) Ltd (South Africa) *Tel:* (021) 8733851 *Fax:* (021) 8730069 *E-mail:* luxverbi.publ@kinglsey. co.za, pg 561

Luxpress VOS (Czech Republic) *Tel:* (02) 203 972 60 *Fax:* (02) 203 972 60 *E-mail:* ibs.czech@iol.cz, pg 125

Lybid (University of Kyyiv Press) (Ukraine) *Tel:* (044) 228-11-12; (044) 228-11-81 *Fax:* (044) 229-11-71, pg 649

Lybra Immagine (Italy) *Tel:* (02) 48000818 *Fax:* (02) 48012748 *E-mail:* lybra@lybra.it *Web Site:* www. lybra.it, pg 393

Lycabettus Press (Greece) *Tel:* 2106741788 *Fax:* 2106710666 *E-mail:* services@lycabettus. com *Web Site:* lycabettus.com, pg 306

Lyle Publications Ltd (United Kingdom) *Tel:* (01750) 23355 *Fax:* (01750) 23388 *E-mail:* lyle.publications@ talk21.com, pg 718

Lyngs Bokhandel A/S (Norway) *Tel:* 91806230 *Fax:* 73512544, pg 1324

Lynx Edicions (Spain) *Tel:* (093) 594 77 10 *Fax:* (093) 592 09 69 *E-mail:* pruizolalla@hbw.com *Web Site:* www.hbw.com, pg 585

Editions Josette Lyon (France) *Tel:* (01) 40 44 81 60 *Fax:* (01) 45 42 30 99 *E-mail:* editions.josette.lyon@ wanadoo.fr *Web Site:* www.editions-josette-lyon.com, pg 173

Editions Lyonnaises d'Art et d'Histoire (France) *Tel:* (04) 78 72 49 00 *Fax:* (04) 78 69 00 48 *Web Site:* www.achatlyon.com/editionslyonnaises, pg 173

Lyra Libri (Italy) *Tel:* (02) 30 241 311 *Fax:* (02) 30 241 333 *E-mail:* info@red-edizioni.it, pg 393

Lyra Pragensis Obecne Prospelna Spolecnost (Czech Republic) *Tel:* 224 910 787; 261 220 516; 602 683 500 *Fax:* 261 218 570 *E-mail:* info@lyrapragensis.cz *Web Site:* www.lyrapragensis.cz, pg 125

Thomas Lyster Ltd (United Kingdom) *Tel:* (01695) 575112 *Fax:* (01695) 570120 *E-mail:* books@tlyster. co.uk *Web Site:* www.tlyster.co.uk, pg 718

M & M Management & Labour Consultants Ltd (Zambia) *Tel:* (01) 217218 *Fax:* (01) 224495, pg 776

M/S Motilal Banarsidass Publishing (P) Ltd (India) *Tel:* (011) 23851985; (011) 23858335; (011) 23854826; (011) 23852747 *Fax:* (011) 23850689; (011) 25797221 *E-mail:* mail@mlbd.com *Web Site:* www.mlbd.com, pg 337

Maaliyot-Institute for Research Publications (Israel) *Tel:* (02) 5353655 *Fax:* (02) 5353947 *E-mail:* ybm@ virtual.co.il, pg 366

Ma'alot Publishing Company Ltd (Israel) *Tel:* (03) 5614121 *Fax:* (03) 5611996 *E-mail:* maalot@tbpai. co.il *Web Site:* www.tbpai.co.il, pg 366

Dar Al Maaref (Egypt (Arab Republic of Egypt)) *Tel:* (02) 759411; (02) 759552 *Fax:* (02) 5744999 *E-mail:* maaref@idsc.gov.eg, pg 138

El-M'aaref Editions (Tunisia) *Tel:* 73256235 *Fax:* 73256530, pg 643

Ma'ariv Book Guild (Sifriat Ma'ariv) (Israel) *Tel:* (03) 5333333 *Fax:* (03) 5333619, pg 366

Ma'ariv Book Guild (Sifriat Ma'ariv) (Israel) *Tel:* (03) 5383313 *Fax:* (03) 6343205, pg 1243

Maatschappij der Nederlandse Letterkunde (Netherlands) *Tel:* (071) 527 2801; (071) 527 2814 *Fax:* (071) 527 2836 *E-mail:* mnl@library.leidenuniv.nl *Web Site:* www.leidenuniv.nl/host/mnl, pg 1397

The MAB Cookery Book Club (Iceland) *Tel:* 522 2138 *Fax:* 522 2026 *Web Site:* www.ab.is, pg 1243

Mabrochi International Co Ltd (Nigeria) *Tel:* (01) 847603 *Fax:* (01) 2662275 *E-mail:* mabrochiadol@ yahoo.com, pg 1322

Casa Editrice Maccari (CEM) (Italy) *Tel:* (0521) 771268 *Fax:* (0521) 771268, pg 393

Ediciones Macchi (Argentina) *Tel:* (011) 4375-1195 *Fax:* (011) 4375-1870; (011) 4374-2506 *E-mail:* info@macchi.com.ar *Web Site:* www.macchi. com, pg 7

Macedonia Prima Publishing House (The Former Yugoslav Republic of Macedonia) *Tel:* (096) 37-109 *Fax:* (096) 23-172, pg 449

Macedonian PEN Centre (The Former Yugoslav Republic of Macedonia) *Tel:* (02) 3130054 *Fax:* (02) 3130054 *E-mail:* macedpen@unet.com.mk *Web Site:* www.pen.org.mk, pg 1396

Antonio Machado, SA (Spain) *Tel:* (091) 4681398 *Fax:* (091) 4681098 *E-mail:* editorial@visordis.es, pg 585

Machbarot Lesifrut (Israel) *Tel:* (08) 9246565 *Fax:* (08) 9251770 *E-mail:* info@zmora.co.il, pg 366

Friends of Arthur Machen (United Kingdom) *Tel:* (01633) 422520 *Fax:* (0633) 421055 *Web Site:* www.machensoc.demon.co.uk, pg 1402

MacKays of Chatham PLC (United Kingdom) *Tel:* (01634) 864 381 *Fax:* (01634) 867 742 *E-mail:* mackays@cpi-group.co.uk *Web Site:* www.cpi-group.net, pg 1216

MacLean Art (Trinidad & Tobago) *Tel:* (868) 622 8679 *Fax:* (868) 622 7583 *E-mail:* gml@wow.net, pg 642

MacLean Dubois Ltd (Writers & Agents) (United Kingdom) *Tel:* (0131) 445 5885 *Fax:* (0131) 445 5898 *E-mail:* info@whiskymax.co.uk, pg 1132

MacLennan & Petty Pty Ltd (Australia) *Tel:* (02) 9349 5811 *Fax:* (02) 9349 5911 *E-mail:* macpetty@zip.com. au, pg 29

Macmillan Audio Books (United Kingdom) *Tel:* (020) 7373 6070 *Fax:* (020) 7244 6379, pg 718

Macmillan Boleswa Publishers (Pty) Ltd (Swaziland) *Tel:* 84533 *Fax:* 85247 *E-mail:* macmillan@iafrica.sz *Web Site:* www.macmillansa.co.za; www.macmillan-africa.com, pg 604

Macmillan Children's Books (United Kingdom) *Tel:* (020) 7014 6000 *Fax:* (020) 7014 6142 *Web Site:* www.panmacmillan.com, pg 718

Macmillan Editores SA de CV (Mexico) *Tel:* (05) 482 2200 *Fax:* (05) 482 2203 *E-mail:* elt@macmillan.com. mx *Web Site:* www.macmillan.com.mx/, pg 464

Editorial Macmillan de Mexico SA de CV (Mexico) *Tel:* (05) 482 2200 *Fax:* (05) 482 2202 *Toll Free Fax:* 800-00-64-100; 800-71-22-363 *Web Site:* www. macmillan.com.mx, pg 464

Macmillan Education (Sierra Leone) *Tel:* (022) 225683 *Fax:* (022) 229186 *E-mail:* macmillan@sierratel.sl *Web Site:* www.macmillan-africa.com, pg 549

Macmillan Education Australia (Australia) *Tel:* (03) 9825 1025 *Fax:* (03) 9825 1010 *E-mail:* mea@macmillan. com.au *Web Site:* www.macmillan.com.au, pg 30

Macmillan Heinemann ELT (Spain) *Tel:* (091) 517 85 40 *Fax:* (091) 517 85 54 *E-mail:* madrid@mad. heinemann.es *Web Site:* www.heinemann.es, pg 585

Macmillan Heinemann ELT (United Kingdom) *Tel:* (01865) 405700 *Fax:* (01865) 405701 *E-mail:* elt@mhelt.com *Web Site:* www.mhelt.com, pg 719

Macmillan Kenya Publishers Ltd (Kenya) *Tel:* (02) 220 012; (02) 224 485 *Fax:* (02) 212 179 *Web Site:* www. macmillan-africa.com, pg 432

Macmillan Ltd (United Kingdom) *Tel:* (020) 7833 4000 *Fax:* (020) 7843 4640 *Web Site:* www.macmillan.com, pg 719

Macmillan Publishers Australia Pty Ltd (Australia) *Tel:* (03) 9825 1000 *Fax:* (03) 9825 1015 *Web Site:* www.panmacmillan.com.au, pg 30

Macmillan Publishers (China) Ltd (Hong Kong) *Tel:* 2811 8781 *Fax:* 2811 0743 *Web Site:* www. macmillan.com.hk, pg 315

Macmillan Publishers New Zealand Ltd (New Zealand) *Tel:* (09) 414 0350; (09) 414 0356 (customer service); (09) 414 0352 (trade sales); (09) 415 6672 *Fax:* (09) 414 0351 *Web Site:* www.macmillan.co.nz, pg 494

Macmillan Publishers (UK) Ltd (United Kingdom) *Tel:* (01256) 329242 *Fax:* (01256) 812558 *E-mail:* mdl@macmillan.com *Web Site:* www. macmillan.com, pg 719

Macmillan Publishers (Zambia) Ltd (Zambia) *Tel:* (01) 223 669 *Fax:* (01) 223 657; (01) 641 018 *E-mail:* macpub@zamnet.zm *Web Site:* www. macmillan-africa.com, pg 776

Macmillan Reference Ltd (United Kingdom) *Tel:* (01256) 329242 *Fax:* (01256) 812558 *E-mail:* mdl@macmillan.co.uk *Web Site:* www. macmillan.co.uk, pg 719

The Macquarie Library Pty Ltd (Australia) *Tel:* (02) 9805 9800 *Fax:* (02) 9888 2984 *E-mail:* alison@dict. mq.edu, pg 30

Macro Edizioni (Italy) *Tel:* (0547) 346290; (0547) 346317 *Fax:* (0547) 345091; (0547) 345141 *E-mail:* ordini@macroedizioni.it *Web Site:* www. macroedizioni.it, pg 393

Macula (France) *Tel:* (01) 45 48 58 70 *Fax:* (01) 45 44 45 89, pg 173

Mad Dog Design Connection Inc (Canada) *Tel:* 416-467-0090 *Fax:* 416-484-1140 *E-mail:* maddogs9@rogers. com, pg 1143

Mad SL Editorial (Spain) *Tel:* (095) 5635900 *Fax:* (095) 5630713 *E-mail:* info@mad.es *Web Site:* www.mad.es, pg 585

Madagascar Print & Press Company (Madagascar) *Tel:* (02) 22526 *Fax:* (02) 2234534 *E-mail:* roi@dts. mg, pg 450

Madan Puraskar Library (Nepal) *Tel:* (01) 5521014 *Fax:* (01) 5536390 *E-mail:* kmldxt@wlink.com.np, pg 1529

Karin Mader (Germany) *Tel:* (04208) 556 *Fax:* (04208) 3429 *E-mail:* info@mader-verlag.de *Web Site:* www. mader-verlag.de, pg 254

Madju FA (Indonesia) *Tel:* (061) 711990; (061) 710430 *Fax:* (061) 717753, pg 352

Madras Editora (Brazil) *Tel:* (011) 6959-1127
*Fax:* (011) 6959-3090 *E-mail:* editor@madras.com.br
*Web Site:* www.madras.com.br, pg 85

Madras Literary Society Library (India) *Tel:* 827 9666,
pg 1514

Madris (Latvia) *Tel:* 7374000; 7374700 *Fax:* 7374000
*E-mail:* madris@latnet.lv, pg 441

Maeander Verlag GmbH (Germany) *Tel:* (08727) 1657
*Fax:* (08727) 1569, pg 254

Annemarie Maeger (Germany) *Tel:* (040) 8992480
*Fax:* (040) 8994475 *E-mail:* re@a-maeger-verlag.de
*Web Site:* www.a-maeger-verlag.de, pg 254

Maeil Gyeongje (Republic of Korea) *Tel:* (02) 276-
0210; (02) 2760211; (02) 2760212; (02) 2760213;
(02) 2760214; (02) 2760215 *Fax:* (02) 271-0463
*E-mail:* mpd@unitel.co.kv, pg 437

Ediciones Maeva (Spain) *Tel:* (091) 355 95 69
*Fax:* (091) 355 19 47 *E-mail:* maeva@infornet.es
*Web Site:* www.maeva.es, pg 585

Magabala Books Aboriginal Corporation (Australia)
*Tel:* (08) 9192 1991 *Fax:* (08) 9193 5254
*E-mail:* info@magabala.com *Web Site:* www.
magabala.com, pg 30

Magari Publishing (New Zealand) *Tel:* (07) 3770169
*Fax:* (07) 3773134 *E-mail:* frontdesk@magari.co.nz
*Web Site:* www.magari.co.nz, pg 494

Magasin du Nord A/S (Denmark) *Tel:* 33 11 44 33
*Fax:* 33 15 18 40 *E-mail:* kundeservice@magasinkort.
dk *Web Site:* www.magasin.dk, pg 1298

Magdalenen-Verlag GmbH (Germany) *Tel:* (08024) 5051
*Fax:* (08024) 7064 *E-mail:* info@magdalenen-verlag.
de *Web Site:* www.magdalenen-verlag.de, pg 254

Magenta Lithographic Consultants Pte Ltd (Singapore)
*Tel:* 62746288 *Fax:* 62746795 *E-mail:* magenta@
singaporebusinessguide.com, pg 1151

Les Editions Maghrebines, EDIMA (Morocco) *Tel:* (02)
353230; (02) 353249; (02) 351797 *Fax:* (02) 355541,
pg 471

Magi Publications (United Kingdom) *Tel:* (020) 7385
6333 *Fax:* (020) 7385 7333 *E-mail:* info@littletiger.
co.uk *Web Site:* www.littletigerpress.com, pg 719

Editorial Magisterio Espanol SA (Spain) *Tel:* (093)
902107007 *Fax:* (093) 6420086 *Web Site:* www.
editorialcasals.com, pg 585

Magna Large Print Books (United Kingdom)
*Tel:* (01729) 840 225; (01729) 840 526; (01729)
840 251 *Fax:* (01729) 840 683 *E-mail:* enquiries@
ulverscroft.co.uk *Web Site:* www.ulverscroft.co.uk,
pg 719

Magnard (France) *Tel:* (01) 44 08 85 85 *Fax:* (01) 44 08
49 79 *Web Site:* www.magnard.fr, pg 173

The Magnes Press (Israel) *Tel:* (02) 6586656
*Fax:* (02) 5633370 *E-mail:* magnes@vms.huji.ac.il
*Web Site:* www.huji.ac.il, pg 366

Magnum Publishing House Ltd (Poland) *Tel:* (022)
6460085; (022) 8485505 *Fax:* (022) 8485505
*E-mail:* magnum@it.com.pl, pg 519

Magnus Edizioni SpA (Italy) *Tel:* (0432) 800081
*Fax:* (0432) 810071 *E-mail:* info@magnusedizioni.it
*Web Site:* www.magnusedizioni.it, pg 393

Magnus Verlag (Germany) *Tel:* (02054) 5080; (02054)
5094; (02327) 292 0 *Fax:* (02054) 83762, pg 254

Magpie Books (Australia) *Tel:* (0613) 9592 9931
*Fax:* (0613) 9592 2045 *E-mail:* admin01@
magpiebooks.com.au *Web Site:* www.magpiebooks.
com.au, pg 30

Magpie Books (Australia) *Tel:* (03) 95929931 *Fax:* (03)
95922045 *E-mail:* admin01@magpiebooks.com.au
*Web Site:* www.magpiebooks.com.au, pg 1289

Magpie Publications (Australia) *Tel:* (06) 2509442, pg 30

Magpies Magazine Pty Ltd (Australia) *Tel:* (07) 3356
4503 *Fax:* (07) 3356 4649 *E-mail:* james@magpies.
net.au *Web Site:* www.magpies.net.au, pg 30

Edicions de la Magrana SA (Spain) *Tel:* (093) 2170088
*Fax:* (093) 2171174 *E-mail:* magrana@rba.es
*Web Site:* www.rbalibros.com, pg 585

Magveto Koenyvkiado (Hungary) *Tel:* (01) 302 2798;
(01) 302 2799 *Fax:* (01) 302 2800 *E-mail:* magveto@
mail.datanet.hu, pg 319

Magwe Degree College Library (Myanmar) *Tel:* (63)
21030, pg 1528

Magyar Irodalomtoerteneti Tarsasag (Hungary) *Tel:* (01)
2664903 *Fax:* (01) 3377819, pg 1395

Magyar Iroszoevetseg (Hungary) *Tel:* (01) 322-8840;
(01) 322-0631 *Fax:* (01) 321-3419, pg 1262

Magyar Iroszovetseg Konyvtara (Hungary) *Tel:* (01) 322-
8840; (01) 322-0631 *Fax:* (01) 321-3419, pg 1138

Magyar Kemikusok Egyesulete (Hungary) *Tel:* (01)
2016883 *Fax:* (01) 343 25 41 *E-mail:* webinfo@
mtesz.hu *Web Site:* www.mtesz.hu, pg 319

Magyar Koenyvkiadok es Koenyvterjesztoek Egyesuelese
(Hungary) *Tel:* (01) 343 25 40 *Fax:* (01) 343 25 41
*E-mail:* mkke@mkke.hu *Web Site:* www.mkke.hu,
pg 1263

Magyar Koenyvkiadok es Koenyvterjesztoek Egyesuelese
Vereinigung der Ungarischen Buchverlage &
Vertriebsunternehmen (Hungary) *Tel:* (01) 343-25-
40 *Fax:* (01) 343 25 41 *E-mail:* mkke@mkke.hu
*Web Site:* www.mkke.hu, pg 320

Magyar Koenyvtarosok Egyesuelete (Hungary) *Tel:* (01)
311 8634 *Fax:* (01) 311 8634 *E-mail:* mke@oszk.hu
*Web Site:* www.mke.oszk.hu, pg 1564

Magyar Orszagos Leveltar (MOL) (Hungary) *Tel:* (01)
225-2800 *Fax:* (01) 225-2817 *E-mail:* info@natarch.hu
*Web Site:* www.natarch.hu, pg 1513

Magyar Tudomanyos Akademia Irodalomtudomanyi
Intezete (Hungary) *Tel:* (01) 4665938 *Fax:* (01)
3853876 *Web Site:* www.mta.hu/kutatohelyek/
intezetek/iti.htm, pg 1395

Magyar Tudomanyos Akademia Koenyvtara
(Hungary) *Tel:* (01) 411 6100 *Fax:* (01) 311 6954
*E-mail:* mtak@vax.mtak.hu *Web Site:* w3.mtak.hu,
pg 1513

Mahajan Publishers Pvt Ltd (India) *Tel:* 78547
*Fax:* (079) 6589101 *E-mail:* mahajan2000@hotmail.
com, pg 337

Mahir Marketing Services Sdn Bhd (Malaysia) *Tel:* (088)
2827372 *Fax:* (088) 718067, pg 1316

Mahir Publications Sdn Bhd (Malaysia) *Tel:* (03)
56379044 *Fax:* (03) 56379048, pg 453

Karl Mahnke, Dierk Mahnke (Germany) *Tel:* (04231)
3011-0 *Fax:* (04231) 3011-11 *E-mail:* info@mahnke-
verlag.de *Web Site:* www.mahnke-verlag.de, pg 254

Maihof Verlag (Switzerland) *Tel:* (041) 767 76 76
*Fax:* (041) 767 76 77 *E-mail:* info@maihofverlag.ch
*Web Site:* www.maihofdruck.ch, pg 623

Giuseppe Maimone Editore (Italy) *Tel:* (095) 310315
*Fax:* (095) 310315 *E-mail:* maimone@maimone.it
*Web Site:* www.maimone.it, pg 394

Mainstream Publishing Co (Edinburgh) Ltd (United
Kingdom) *Tel:* (0131) 557 2959 *Fax:* (0131) 556
8720 *E-mail:* enquiries@mainstreampublishing.com
*Web Site:* www.mainstreampublishing.com, pg 719

Mairs Geographischer Verlag (Germany) *Tel:* (0711)
45020 *Fax:* (0711) 4502340 *E-mail:* info@mairs.de
*Web Site:* www.mairs.de, pg 254

Mairs Geographischer Verlag, Kurt Mair GmbH & Co
(Germany) *Tel:* (0711) 4502-0 *Fax:* (0711) 4502-340,
pg 255

Mairs Geographischer Verlag Kurt Mair GmbH & Co
(Germany) *Tel:* (0711) 4502-0 *Fax:* (0711) 4502-340,
pg 255

La Maison de la Bible (Switzerland) *Tel:* (021) 867
10 10 *Fax:* (021) 867 10 15 *E-mail:* info@bible.ch
*Web Site:* www.bible.ch, pg 623

Maison de la Revelation (France) *Tel:* (05) 56249381
*Fax:* (05) 56931631, pg 173

Maison d'Edition de la Librairie-Imprimerie Evangelique
du Togo (Togo) *Tel:* (08) 214582 *Fax:* (08) 216967
*E-mail:* ctce@cafe.tg, pg 642

Maison des Ecrivains (France) *Tel:* (01) 49546880
*Fax:* (01) 42842087 *E-mail:* courrier@maison-des-
ecrivains.asso.fr *Web Site:* www.maison-des-ecrivains.
asso.fr, pg 1393

Maison des Langues Vivantes-Intertaal SA (Belgium)
*Tel:* (02) 5117117 *Fax:* (02) 5145820 *E-mail:* mlv.i@
skynet.be *Web Site:* maison-des-langues.com, pg 1292

Editions de la Maison des Sciences de l'Homme, Paris
(France) *Tel:* (01) 49 54 20 30; (01) 49 54 20 31
*Fax:* (01) 49 54 21 33 *E-mail:* public@msh-paris.fr
*Web Site:* www.editions.msh-paris.fr, pg 173

La Maison du Dictionnaire (France) *Tel:* (01) 43 22 12
93 *Fax:* (01) 43 22 01 77 *E-mail:* service-client@
dicoland.com *Web Site:* www.dicoland.com, pg 174

Maison Tunisienne de l'Edition (Tunisia) *Tel:* 71345333
*Fax:* 71353992, pg 643

Editions Adrien Maisonneuve (France) *Tel:* (01) 43 26
19 50 *Fax:* (01) 43 54 59 54 *E-mail:* maisonneuve@
maisonneuve-adrien.com *Web Site:* www.maisonneuve-
adrien.com, pg 174

Maisonneuve Editeur (France) *Tel:* (01) 34 63 33 33
*Fax:* (01) 34 65 39 70, pg 174

Maisonneuve et Larose (France) *Tel:* (01) 44414930
*Fax:* (01) 43257741 *E-mail:* servedit1@wanadoo.fr,
pg 174

Makedonska kniga (The Former Yugoslav Republic of
Macedonia) *Tel:* (02) 1164 73 *Fax:* (02) 1212 77,
pg 1316

Makedonska kniga (Knigoizdatelstvo) (The Former
Yugoslav Republic of Macedonia) *Tel:* (02) 116 473;
(02) 3 1610; (02) 235 524 *Fax:* (02) 1212 77, pg 449

Makerere Institute of Social Research Library (Uganda)
*Tel:* (041) 55 45 82; (041) 53 28 30; (041) 53 28 37;
(041) 53 28 38; (041) 53 28 39 *Fax:* (041) 53 28 21
*E-mail:* jmugasha@mulib.mak.ac.ug *Web Site:* www.
makerere.ac.ug/research/misr.htm, pg 1550

Makerere University Library (Uganda) *Tel:* (041) 531041
*Fax:* (041) 540374 *E-mail:* info@mulib.mak.ac.ug;
universitylibrarian@mulib.mak.ac.ug *Web Site:* www.
makerere.ac.ug/mulib, pg 1550

Maklu (Belgium) *Tel:* (03) 231-29-00 *Fax:* (03) 233-26-
59 *E-mail:* info@maklu.be *Web Site:* www.maklu.be,
pg 70

Makron Books do Brasil Editora Ltda (Brazil) *Tel:* (011)
829-6879 *Fax:* (011) 829-8947 *E-mail:* makron@
books.com.br *Web Site:* www.makron.com.br, pg 85

Makros 2000 - Plovdiv (Bulgaria) *Tel:* (032) 642900
*E-mail:* makros@makros.net *Web Site:* www.makros.
net, pg 95

Makumira Lutheran Theological College Library (United
Republic of Tanzania) *Tel:* (027) 255-3634; (027) 255-
3635 *Fax:* (027) 255-3493 *E-mail:* library@makumira.
ac.tz *Web Site:* www.makumira.ac.tz, pg 1548

MM Mal og menning (Iceland) *Tel:* 522 2000 *Fax:* 522
2022; 522 2026 *E-mail:* malogmenning@edda.is
*Web Site:* www.malogmenning.is, pg 1243

Mal og menning (Iceland) *Tel:* 522 2500 *Fax:* 522 2505
*E-mail:* edda@edda.is *Web Site:* www.edda.is, pg 323

Bibliotheque Nationale Malagasy (Madagascar) *Tel:* (02)
25872 *Fax:* (02) 22-9448, pg 1524

Biblioteca Comunale Malatestiana (Italy) *Tel:* (0547) 610
892 *Fax:* (0547) 421237 *E-mail:* malatestiana@sbn.
provincia.ra.it *Web Site:* www.malatestiana.it, pg 1519

The Malawi Library Association (Malawi) *Tel:* (050)
522222 *Fax:* (050) 523225 *E-mail:* d.b.v.phiri@unima.
wn.apc.org, pg 1567

Malawi National Library Service (Malawi) *Tel:* 773 700
*Fax:* 771 616 *E-mail:* nls@malawi.net, pg 1524

Marcham Manor Press (United Kingdom) *Tel:* (01235) 848319, pg 720

Marcial Pons Librero (Spain) *Tel:* (091) 304 33 03 *Fax:* (091) 327 23 67 *E-mail:* librerias@marcialpons. es *Web Site:* www.marcialpons.es, pg 1333

Marcial Pons Ediciones Juridicas SA (Spain) *Tel:* (091) 304 33 03 *Fax:* (091) 327 23 67; (091) 7541218 *E-mail:* librerias@marcialpons.es; ediciones@ marcialpons.es *Web Site:* www.marcialpons.es, pg 585

Editora Marco Zero Ltda (Brazil) *Tel:* (011) 876-2822 *Fax:* (011) 257-2744 *E-mail:* marcozero@mutecnet. com.br, pg 85

Marcombo SA (Spain) *Tel:* (093) 3180079 (Editor) *Fax:* (093) 3189339 *E-mail:* marcombo.boixareu@ marcombo.es *Web Site:* www.marcombo.es, pg 585, 1126

Editions Marcus (France) *Tel:* (01) 45770404 *Fax:* (01) 45759251, pg 174

Mardaga, Pierre, Editeur (Belgium) *Tel:* (04) 3684242 *Fax:* (04) 3684240, pg 70

Mardev (Australia) *Tel:* (02) 9422 2644 *Fax:* (02) 9422 2633 *E-mail:* mardevlists@reedbusiness.com.au *Web Site:* www.mardevlists.com, pg 1250

Marfiah, CV (Indonesia) *Tel:* (031) 46023, pg 352

Editorial Marfil SA (Spain) *Tel:* (096) 5523311 *Fax:* (096) 5523496 *E-mail:* editorialmarfil@ editorialmarfil.com *Web Site:* www.editorialmarfil.com, pg 586

Marg Publications (India) *Tel:* (022) 2821151; (022) 2045947-8; (022) 842520 *Fax:* (022) 047102 *E-mail:* margpub@tata.com *Web Site:* www.tata. com/marg, pg 338

Margaret Hamilton Books Pty Ltd (Australia) *Tel:* (02) 4328 3555 *Toll Free Tel:* 800-021-233 *Fax:* (02) 4323 3827 *Toll Free Fax:* 800-789- 948 *E-mail:* customer_service@scholastic.com.au *Web Site:* www.scholastic.com.au, pg 30

La Marge (France) *Tel:* (04) 95512367 *Fax:* (04) 95500900, pg 174

Margraf Verlag (Germany) *Tel:* (07934) 3071 *Fax:* (07934) 8156 *E-mail:* info@margraf-verlag.de *Web Site:* www.margraf-verlag.de, pg 255

Librairie-Editions J Marguerat (Switzerland) *Tel:* (021) 3237717 *Fax:* (021) 3126732, pg 623

Mariadan (Czech Republic) *Tel:* (02) 41 40 83 91, pg 125

Mariani Ritti Grafiche SRL (Italy) *Tel:* (02) 58310004 *Fax:* (02) 58310408 *E-mail:* ritti@tiw.it, pg 1210

Marican Sdn Bhd (Malaysia) *Tel:* (03) 2981133, pg 1317

Editions Marie-Noelle (France) *Tel:* (03) 81877500; (03) 84812891 *Fax:* (03) 81875669, pg 174

Casa Editrice Marietti SpA (Italy) *Tel:* (02) 67101053 *Fax:* (02) 67389081 *E-mail:* marietti1820@split.it, pg 394

Marin Drinov Publishing House (Bulgaria) *Tel:* (02) 720- 922; (02) 979-34-49; (02) 979-34-41 *Fax:* (02) 704- 054, pg 95

Editorial Marin SA (Spain) *Tel:* (093) 8468101 *Fax:* (093) 8468107, pg 586

Edition Maritim GmbH (Germany) *Tel:* (040) 3396670 *Fax:* (040) 33966777 *E-mail:* mail@edition-maritim. de, pg 255

Maritime Books (United Kingdom) *Tel:* (01579) 343663 *Fax:* (01579) 346747 *E-mail:* editor@navybooks.com *Web Site:* www.navybooks.com, pg 720

Maritime Information Association (United Kingdom) *Tel:* (020) 7261 9535 *Fax:* (020) 7401 2537 *E-mail:* enq@marine-society.org *Web Site:* www. marine-society.org.uk/, pg 1282

The Market Research Society (United Kingdom) *Tel:* (020) 7490 4911 *Fax:* (020) 7490 0608 *E-mail:* info@mrs.org.uk *Web Site:* www.mrs.org.uk, pg 720

Marketasia Distributors (S) Pte Ltd (Singapore) *Tel:* 67448483; 67448486 *Fax:* 67448497; 67443690 *E-mail:* marketasia@pacific.net.sg *Web Site:* www. marketasia.com.sg, pg 1330

Marketing & Wirtschaft Verlagsges, Flade & Partner mbH (Germany) *Tel:* (089) 27813417 *Fax:* (089) 2710156, pg 255

Marketing Focus (Australia) *Tel:* (08) 92571777 *Fax:* (08) 92571888 *Web Site:* www.marketingfocus. net.au, pg 30

Markono Print Media Pte Ltd (Singapore) *Tel:* 6281- 1118 *Fax:* 6286-6663 *E-mail:* saleslead@markono. com.sg *Web Site:* www.markono.com.sg, pg 1151, 1172, 1212, 1228, 1236

Maro Verlag und Druck, Benno Kaesmayr (Germany) *Tel:* (0821) 416034 *Fax:* (0821) 416036 *E-mail:* info@ maroverlag.de *Web Site:* www.maroverlag.de, pg 255

Tommaso Marotta Editore Srl (Italy) *Tel:* (081) 5758060 *Fax:* (081) 418411, pg 394

Ediciones Marova SL (Spain) *Tel:* (091) 5322606 *Fax:* (091) 5225123 *E-mail:* glanzas@infornet.es, pg 586

Marque Publishing Co Pty Ltd (Australia) *Tel:* (02) 4322 4803 *Fax:* (02) 4329 1475 *E-mail:* books@marque. com.au *Web Site:* www.marque.com.au, pg 30

Marrakech Express Inc (United States) *Tel:* 727-942- 2218 *Toll Free Tel:* 800-940-6566 *Fax:* 727-937-4758 *E-mail:* print@marrak.com *Web Site:* www.marrak. com, pg 1156, 1220, 1239

Marren Publishing House, Inc (Philippines) *Tel:* (02) 7115829 *Fax:* (02) 7115830, pg 514

Adrian Mars (United Kingdom) *Tel:* (020) 7433 1345 *Fax:* (0870) 164 0870 *E-mail:* a_mars@cix.co.uk, pg 1132

Mars Business Associates Ltd (United Kingdom) *Tel:* (01367) 252 506 *Fax:* (01367) 252 506 *E-mail:* sales@marspub.co.uk *Web Site:* www. marspub.co.uk, pg 720

The Marsh Agency (United Kingdom) *Tel:* (020) 7399 2800 *Fax:* (020) 7399 2801 *E-mail:* enquiries@marsh- agency.co.uk *Web Site:* www.marsh-agency.co.uk, pg 1132

Tracy Marsh Publications Pty Ltd (Australia) *Tel:* (08) 8363 1248 *Fax:* (08) 8363 1352 *E-mail:* tracy@ tracymarsh.com *Web Site:* www.tracymarsh.com, pg 30

Marshall Editions Ltd (United Kingdom) *Tel:* (020) 7700 6764 *Fax:* (020) 7700 4191 *E-mail:* info@ marshalleditions.com *Web Site:* www.quarto.com/ group/companies/marshalleditions.htm, pg 721

Marsilio Editori SpA (Italy) *Tel:* (041) 2406511 *Fax:* (041) 5238352 *E-mail:* info@marsilioeditori.it *Web Site:* www.marsilioeditori.it, pg 394

Marston Book Services Ltd (United Kingdom) *Tel:* (01235) 465500 *Fax:* (01235) 465555 *E-mail:* trade.enquiry@marston.co.uk *Web Site:* www. marston.co.uk, pg 1343

Marston House (United Kingdom) *Tel:* (01935) 851331 *Fax:* (01935) 851372, pg 721

Marsu Productions SAM (Monaco) *Tel:* (093) 92056111 *Fax:* (093) 92057660 *E-mail:* info@marsupilami.com; marsuproductions@compuserve.com *Web Site:* www. marsupilami.com, pg 470

Martelle (France) *Tel:* (03) 22 71 54 55 *Fax:* (03) 22 92 89 33, pg 174

Horwitz Martin Education (Australia) *Tel:* (02) 9901 6100 *Fax:* (02) 9901 6166, pg 30

H F Martinez de Murguia SAC y E (Argentina) *Tel:* (011) 4952-1088; (011) 4952-6173 (sales) *Fax:* (011) 4952-1088 *E-mail:* info@murguia.com.ar *Web Site:* www.murguia.com.ar, pg 1287

H F Martinez de Murguia SA (Spain) *Tel:* (091) 522 66 34; (091) 532 39 71 *Fax:* (091) 531 37 86, pg 1333

Ediciones Martinez Roca SA (Spain) *Tel:* (091) 423 0314 *Fax:* (091) 423 0306 *E-mail:* info@ ediciones-martinez-roca.es *Web Site:* www. edicionesmartinezroca.com, pg 586

Editions de la Martiniere (France) *Tel:* (01) 40 51 52 00 *Fax:* (01) 40 51 52 05 *E-mail:* coedition@lamartiniere. fr *Web Site:* www.lamartiniere.fr, pg 174

Livraria Tavares Martins (Portugal) *Tel:* (022) 23459, pg 528

Marton Aron Kiado Publishing House (Hungary) *Tel:* (01) 3689527; (01) 3678415 *Fax:* (01) 1689869 *E-mail:* oli@hcbc.hu, pg 320

Martynas Mazvydas National Library of Lithuania (Lithuania) *Tel:* 52398687 *Fax:* 52639111 *E-mail:* leidyba@lnb.lt *Web Site:* www.lnb.lt, pg 446

Martynas Mazvydas National Library of Lithuania (Lietuvos Nacionaline Martyno Mazvydo Biblioteka) (Lithuania) *Tel:* (5) 2497023 *Fax:* (5) 2496129 *E-mail:* biblio@lnb.lt *Web Site:* www.lnb.lt, pg 1524

Maruzen Asia (Pte) Ltd (Singapore) *Tel:* 7751577 *Fax:* 7351678, pg 552

Maruzen Co Ltd (Japan) *Tel:* (03) 3272-0514 *Fax:* (03) 3272-0527 *E-mail:* webmaster@maruzen.co.jp *Web Site:* www.maruzen.co.jp; www.maruzen.co. jp/home-eng/index.html, pg 419

Maruzen Co Ltd (Japan) *Tel:* (03) 3273-6191 *Fax:* (03) 3273-6192 *E-mail:* sd-data@maruzen.co.jp *Web Site:* www.maruzen.co.jp, pg 1312

Editions Marval (France) *Tel:* (01) 48 07 50 40 *Fax:* (01) 48 07 01 08 *E-mail:* info@marval.com *Web Site:* www.marval.com, pg 174

Blanche Marvin Agency (United Kingdom) *Tel:* (020) 7722 2313 *Fax:* (020) 7722 2313, pg 1132

Institut fuer Marxistische Studien und Forschungen eV (IMSF) (Germany) *Tel:* (069) 7392934, pg 255

Marymar Ediciones SA (Argentina) *Tel:* (011) 4381- 9083, pg 7

Marzorati Editore SRL (Italy) *Tel:* (06) 8546146 *Fax:* (06) 8411225, pg 394

Masagung Books Pte Ltd (Singapore) *Tel:* 4683276 *Fax:* 345000, pg 552

Masagung Books Pte Ltd (Singapore) *Tel:* 64683276, pg 1330

Masbytes (Spain) *Tel:* (0948) 848031 *Fax:* (0948) 848158 *E-mail:* mb@masbytes.es *Web Site:* www. masbytes.es, pg 586

La Mascara, SL Editorial (Spain) *Tel:* (096) 3486500 *Fax:* (096) 3487440 *E-mail:* lamascara@arrakis.es, pg 586

Maskew Miller Longman (Botswana) *Tel:* 322969 *Fax:* 322682 *E-mail:* longman@info.bw, pg 76

Maskew Miller Longman (South Africa) *Tel:* (021) 531 7750 *Fax:* (021) 531 4877 *E-mail:* firstname@mml.co. za *Web Site:* www.mml.com, pg 562

Maskew Miller Longman (South Africa) *Tel:* (021) 531 7750 *Fax:* (021) 531 4049 *E-mail:* firstname@mml.co. za *Web Site:* www.mml.co.za, pg 1331

Veselin Maslesa (Bosnia and Herzegovina) *Tel:* (033) 667735; (033) 667736 *Fax:* (033) 668351; (033) 667738 *E-mail:* sapublishing@bihart.com, pg 75

Veselin Maslesa (Bosnia and Herzegovina) *Tel:* (071) 214633, pg 1293

Masmedia (Croatia) *Tel:* (01) 457-7400 *Fax:* (01) 457 7769 *E-mail:* masmedia@zg.tel.hr; mm@masmedia.hr *Web Site:* www.masmedia.hr, pg 118

Kenneth Mason Publications Ltd (United Kingdom) *Tel:* (01243) 377977; (01243) 377978 *Fax:* (01243) 379136 *E-mail:* boatswain@dial.pipex.com, pg 721

Masons Design & Print (United Kingdom) *Tel:* (01244) 674433 *Fax:* (01244) 674274, pg 1153

Massada Press Ltd (Israel) *Tel:* (02) 6719441 *Fax:* (02) 6719442, pg 367

Massada Publishers Ltd (Israel) *Tel:* (03) 5716659; (03) 5712702 *Fax:* (03) 5716639, pg 367

Editrice Massimo SAS di Crespi Cesare e C (Italy) *Tel:* (02) 55 21 08 00 *Fax:* (02) 55 21 13 15, pg 394

Editions Charles Massin et Cie (France) *Tel:* (01) 45 65 48 55 *Fax:* (01) 45 65 47 00 *E-mail:* info@massin.fr *Web Site:* www.massin.fr, pg 174

Masson Editeur (France) *Tel:* (01) 73 28 16 34 *Fax:* (01) 73 28 16 49 *E-mail:* infos@masson.fr *Web Site:* www.masson.fr; www.e2med.com, pg 174

Masson Editores (Mexico) *Tel:* (05) 6870933, pg 464

Masson SpA (Italy) *Tel:* (02) 574952315 *Fax:* (02) 574952-371 *E-mail:* info@masson.it *Web Site:* www.masson.it, pg 394

Masson-Williams et Wilkins (France) *Tel:* (01) 40466000 *Fax:* (01) 40466126 *E-mail:* pradel@lsicom.fr, pg 175

MAST Verlag (Romania) *Tel:* (01) 7786950 *Fax:* (01) 4104588, pg 536

Izdatelstvo Mastatskaya Litaratura (Belarus) *Tel:* (017) 2235809; (017) 2238664, pg 62

Master Flo Technology Inc (Canada) *Tel:* 613-636-0539 *Fax:* 613-636-0762 *E-mail:* info@mflo.com *Web Site:* www.mflo.com, pg 1235

Matar Publishing House (Israel) *Tel:* (03) 7441199 *Fax:* (03) 7441314 *E-mail:* mtriwaks@netvision.net.il, pg 367

MATEX (Bulgaria) *Tel:* (02) 430177 *E-mail:* mmk_fte@uacg.acad.bg, pg 95

Sri Ramakrishna Math (India) *Tel:* (044) 24621110 *Fax:* (044) 24934589 *E-mail:* srkmath@vsnl.com *Web Site:* www.sriramakrishnamath.org, pg 338

Matica hrvatska (Croatia) *Tel:* (01) 4878-360; (01) 4878-354; (01) 4878-362 *Fax:* (01) 4819-319 *E-mail:* matica@matica.hr *Web Site:* www.matica.hr, pg 118

Matice moravska (Czech Republic) *Tel:* (05) 4949 1511 *Fax:* (05) 4949 1520 *E-mail:* bronek@phil.muni.cz *Web Site:* www.phil.muni.cz, pg 1392

Biblioteka Matice Srpske (Serbia and Montenegro) *Tel:* (021) 420 271; (021) 528 747 *Fax:* (021) 28 574; (021) 420 271; (021) 25 859 *E-mail:* bms@bms.ns.ac.yu *Web Site:* www.bms.ns.ac.yu, pg 1540

Matrice (France) *Tel:* (01) 69 42 13 02 *Fax:* (01) 69 40 21 57, pg 175

Mats Publishers Ltd (Estonia) *Tel:* (O2) 6563589, pg 139

Mattes Verlag GmbH (Germany) *Tel:* (06221) 459321; (06221) 437853 *Fax:* (06221) 459322 *E-mail:* verlag@mattes.de *Web Site:* www.mattes.de, pg 255

Matthaes Verlag GmbH (Germany) *Tel:* (0711) 21 33-0 *Fax:* (0711) 21 33-320 *E-mail:* info@matthaes.de *Web Site:* www.matthaes.de, pg 255

Matthes und Seitz Verlag GmbH (Germany) *Tel:* (089) 1232510 *Fax:* (089) 187534, pg 255

Matthias-Gruenewald-Verlag GmbH (Germany) *Tel:* (06131) 92860 *Fax:* (06131) 928626 *E-mail:* mail@gruenewaldverlag.de *Web Site:* members.aol.com/matthgruen, pg 256

Matthias Media (Australia) *Tel:* (02) 3100813; (02) 9663-1478 (overseas) *Toll Free Tel:* 800 814 360 *Fax:* (02) 9663-3265; (02) 9663-3265 *E-mail:* info@matthiasmedia.com.au *Web Site:* www.matthiasmedia.com.au, pg 31

Matthiesen Verlag Ingwert Paulsen Jr (Germany) *Tel:* (04841) 83520 *Fax:* (04841) 835210 *E-mail:* info@verlagsgruppe.de *Web Site:* www.verlagsgruppe.de, pg 256

Hans K Matussek Buchhandlung & Antiquariat (Germany) *Tel:* (02153) 91 64 30 *Fax:* (02153) 1 33 63 *Web Site:* www.buchkatalog.de/matussek, pg 256

Les Editions la Matze (Switzerland) *Tel:* (027) 3231652 *Fax:* (027) 3231652, pg 623

Matzker Verlag DiA (Germany) *Tel:* (0421) 6207934, pg 256

Wilhelm Maudrich KG (Austria) *Tel:* (01) 4024712 *Fax:* (01) 4085080 *E-mail:* medbook@maudrich.com *Web Site:* www.maudrich.com, pg 53

C Maurer Druck und Verlag (Germany) *Tel:* (07331) 930-0 *Fax:* (07331) 93 0-190 *Web Site:* www.maurer-online.de, pg 1166

C Maurer Druck und Verlag (Germany) *Tel:* (07331) 9300 *Web Site:* www.maurer-online.de, pg 1207

Mauritius Archives (Mauritius) *Tel:* 233-4469; 233 7341 *Fax:* 233 4299, pg 1526

Mauritius Institute Public Library (Mauritius) *Tel:* 212 06 39 *Fax:* 212 57 17, pg 1526

Mauritius Library Association (Mauritius) *Tel:* 4549550; 4549551; 4549552 *Fax:* 4549553 *E-mail:* ielts@mu.britishcouncil.org *Web Site:* www.britishcouncil.org/mauritius/, pg 1567

Mavisu International Co Ltd (Thailand) *Tel:* (02) 2711148 *Fax:* (02) 2711168, pg 1214

Mavrogianni Publications (Greece) *Tel:* 2103304628 *Fax:* 2103304628, pg 1303

Mawaddah Enterprise Sdn Bhd (Malaysia) *Tel:* (06) 7611062 *Fax:* (06) 7633062 *E-mail:* azhari@mawadah.pc.my, pg 1317

Max Schimmel Verlag (Germany) *Tel:* (0931) 27 91 400 *Fax:* (0931) 27 91 444 *E-mail:* info@schimmelverlag.de *Web Site:* www.schimmelverlag.de, pg 256

Maxcess International (United States) *Tel:* 405-755-1600 *Toll Free Tel:* 800-639-3433 *Fax:* 405-755-8425 *E-mail:* sales@maxcessintl.com *Web Site:* www.maxcessintl.com, pg 1239

Maxdorf Ltd (Czech Republic) *Tel:* (02) 444 710 37; (02) 41 011 680; (02) 41 011 681 *Fax:* (02) 41 710 245 *E-mail:* info@maxdorf.cz *Web Site:* www.maxdorf.cz, pg 125

Maxima Laurent du Mesnil Editeur (France) *Tel:* (01) 44 39 74 00 *Fax:* (01) 45 48 46 88 *E-mail:* edition@maxima.fr *Web Site:* www.maxima.fr, pg 175

Maximilian-Gesellschaft eV (Germany) *Tel:* (0711) 549971-11 *Fax:* (0711) 549971-21 *E-mail:* hiersemann.hauswedell.verlage@t-online.de *Web Site:* www.maximilian-gesellschaft.de, pg 1394

Maya Publishers Pvt Ltd (India) *Tel:* (011) 6494878; (011) 6494850; (011) 649 0451; (011) 649 0959 *Fax:* (011) 6491039; (011) 686 4614 *E-mail:* surit@del2.vsnl.net.in, pg 338

Ludwig Mayer Jerusalem Ltd (Israel) *Tel:* (02) 625-2628 *Fax:* (02) 623-2640 *E-mail:* mayerbks@netvision.net.il, pg 1310

J A Mayersche Buchhandlung GmbH & Co KG Abt Verlag (Germany) *Tel:* (0241) 4777 499 *Fax:* (0241) 4777 467 *E-mail:* vertrieb@mayersche.de *Web Site:* www.mayersche.de, pg 256

J A Mayersche Buchhandlung GmbH & Co KG Abt Verlag (Germany) *Tel:* (0241) 4777 499 *Fax:* (0241) 4777 467 *E-mail:* info@mayersche.de *Web Site:* www.mayersche.de, pg 1301

Mayibuye Books (South Africa) *Tel:* (021) 9592529; (021) 9592954 *Fax:* (021) 9593411 *E-mail:* mayibuye@mweb.co.za, pg 562

Mayne Publishing (Australia) *Tel:* (07) 4697 3228 *Fax:* (07) 4697 3228 *E-mail:* sales@maynepublishing.com.au *Web Site:* www.maynepublishing.com.au, pg 31

Mayr Miesbach Druckerei und Verlag GmbH (Germany) *Tel:* (08025) 294-0 *Fax:* (08025) 294-235 *E-mail:* info@mayrmiesbach.de *Web Site:* www.mayrmiesbach.de, pg 256

Bibliotheque Mazarine (France) *Tel:* (01) 44 41 44 06 *Fax:* (01) 44 41 44 07 *Web Site:* www.bibliotheque-mazarine.fr, pg 1505

Mazenod Book Centre (Lesotho) *Tel:* 35 0224 *Fax:* 35 0010, pg 444

Mazenod Book Centre (Lesotho) *Tel:* 35 0224; 35 0465 *Fax:* 35 0010, pg 1315

Mazer Publishing Services (United States) *Tel:* 937-264-2600 *Fax:* 937-264-2624 *E-mail:* info@mazer.com *Web Site:* www.mazer.com, pg 1156, 1178, 1220, 1231, 1239

Edizioni Gabriele Mazzotta SRL (Italy) *Tel:* (02) 8055803 *Fax:* (02) 8693046 *E-mail:* ufficiopromozione@mazzotta.it *Web Site:* www.mazzotta.it, pg 394

MBA Literary Agents Ltd (United Kingdom) *Tel:* (020) 7387 2076 *Fax:* (020) 7387 2042 *E-mail:* agent@mbalit.co.uk *Web Site:* www.mbalit.co.uk, pg 1132

MBMS-Bibliography & Management Service (Germany) *Tel:* (02733) 7657 *Fax:* (02733) 8492, pg 1121

Yvonne McBurney (Australia) *Tel:* (02) 6887 3608, pg 31

McCrimmon Publishing Co Ltd (United Kingdom) *Tel:* (01702) 218956 *Fax:* (01702) 216082 *E-mail:* sales@mccrimmons.com (sales); orders@mccrimmons.com (orders); permissions@mccrimmons.com (permission-related inquiries); clipart@mccrimmons.com (clip art); accounts@mccrimmons.com-accounts *Web Site:* www.mccrimmons.com, pg 721

McGallen & Bolden Associates (Singapore) *Tel:* 63246588 *Fax:* 63246966 *E-mail:* sales@mcgallen.com *Web Site:* www.mcgallen.net, pg 552

McGraw-Hill Asia/India Group (Singapore) *Tel:* 6863-1580 *Fax:* 6861-9296 *E-mail:* mghasia@mcgraw-hill.com.sg *Web Site:* www.asia-mcgraw-hill.com.sg, pg 552

McGraw-Hill Australia Pty Ltd (Australia) *Tel:* (02) 9900 1800; (02) 9900 1806 (customer service); (02) 9900 1802 (customer service) *Fax:* (02) 9878 8280 (customer service) *E-mail:* cservice_sydney@mcgraw-hill.com.au *Web Site:* www.mcgraw-hill.com.au, pg 31

McGraw-Hill Colombia (Colombia) *Tel:* (01) 6003800; (01) 6003854 *Fax:* (01) 6003811 *E-mail:* servicioalcliente.co@mcgraw-hill.com *Web Site:* www.mcgraw-hill.com.co, pg 111

Editora McGraw-Hill de Portugal Lda (Portugal) *Tel:* (021) 355 3180 *Fax:* (021) 355 3189 *E-mail:* servico-clientes@mcgraw-hill.com *Web Site:* www.mcgraw-hill.pt, pg 528

McGraw-Hill de Venezuela (Venezuela) *Tel:* (0212) 238 3494; (0212) 761 8181; (0212) 761 6992 *Fax:* (0212) 238 2374; (0212) 761 6993 *E-mail:* dpmail@attmail.com, pg 774

McGraw-Hill Education Europe, Middle East & Africa Group (United Kingdom) *Tel:* (01628) 502500 *Fax:* (01628) 777342 *Web Site:* www.mcgraw-hill.co.uk, pg 721

McGraw-Hill/Interamericana de Espana SAU (Spain) *Tel:* (091) 1803000 *Web Site:* www.mcgraw-hill.es, pg 586

McGraw-Hill Interamericana Editores, SA de CV (Mexico) *Tel:* 576-73-04; 576-90-44 (ext 156) *E-mail:* mcgraw-hill@infosel.net.mx *Web Site:* www.mcgraw-hill.com.mx, pg 464

McGraw-Hill Intermericana del Caribe, Inc (Puerto Rico) *Tel:* (787) 751-2451; (787) 751-3451 *Fax:* (787) 764-1890 *Web Site:* www.mhschool.com/contactus/international.html, pg 532

McGraw-Hill Libri Italia SRL (Italy) *Tel:* (02) 5357181 *Fax:* (02) 5398775 *E-mail:* editor@mcgraw-hill.it, pg 394

McGraw-Hill Mexico (Mexico) *Tel:* (055) 1500-5000 *Toll Free Tel:* 800 713-4540 *Fax:* (055) 1500-5127 *E-mail:* tele_marketing@mcgraw-hill.com *Web Site:* www.mcgraw-hill.com.mx, pg 465

McGraw-Hill Publishing Company (United Kingdom) *Tel:* (01) 628 502500 *Fax:* (01) 628 635895 *Web Site:* www.mcgraw-hill.co.uk, pg 721

J M McGregor Pty Ltd (Australia) *Tel:* (02) 9135 1923, pg 31

McGregor Publishers (Namibia) *Tel:* (061) 62155 *Fax:* (061) 63059 *E-mail:* gmcgregor@unam.na, pg 472

McLaren Morris & Todd Co (Canada) *Tel:* 905-677-3592 *Fax:* 905-677-3675 *Web Site:* www.mmt.ca, pg 1143, 1205, 1225

McLeods Booksellers (New Zealand) *Tel:* (07) 3485388 *Fax:* (07) 3490288 *E-mail:* mcleods@clear.net.nz *Web Site:* www.mcleodsbooks.co.nz, pg 1321

McMillan Memorial Library (Kenya) *Tel:* (02) 21844, pg 1521

McRae Books (Italy) *Tel:* (055) 264384 *Fax:* (055) 212573, pg 394

MDC Publishers Printers Sdn Bhd (Malaysia) *Tel:* (03) 41086600 *Fax:* (03) 41081506 *E-mail:* mdcpp@ mdcpp.com.my *Web Site:* www.mdcpp.com.my, pg 453

Editions MDI (La Maison des Instituteurs) (France) *Tel:* (01) 45 87 52 11 *Fax:* (01) 45 87 51 97 *E-mail:* serviceclient@mdi-editions.com; mpetit@vuef. fr *Web Site:* www.mdi-editions.com, pg 175

ME Editores, SL (Spain) *Tel:* (091) 3151008 *Fax:* (091) 3230844, pg 586

Meander Uitgeverij BV (Netherlands) *Tel:* (071) 5601040 *Fax:* (071) 5619741 *E-mail:* info@ vierwindstreken.com *Web Site:* www.vierwindstreken. com, pg 481

Meandre (Switzerland) *Tel:* (026) 322174 *Fax:* (026) 323287, pg 623

Editora Meca Ltda (Brazil) *Tel:* (011) 2599049; (011) 2599034; (011) 2575346 *Fax:* (011) 2570312 *E-mail:* editora_meca@uol.com.br *Web Site:* www. editorameca.com.br, pg 85

Landesbibliothek Mecklenburg-Vorpommern (Germany) *Tel:* (0385) 558440 *Fax:* (0385) 5584424 *E-mail:* lb@ lbmv.de *Web Site:* www.lbmv.de, pg 1508

Mecron Sdn Bhd (Malaysia) *Tel:* (016) 280 8772 *Fax:* (03) 6251 9869 *Web Site:* www.mecronbooks. com, pg 453

Med Info Publishing Co (Hong Kong) *Tel:* 2522 2713, pg 315

Medcom Ltd (Israel) *Tel:* (03) 9343853 *Fax:* (03) 9343850, pg 367

Bibliotheque Interuniversitaire de Medecine (France) *Tel:* (01) 40461951 *Fax:* (01) 44411020 *Web Site:* www.bium.univ-paris5.fr, pg 1505

Medecine et Hygiene (Switzerland) *Tel:* (022) 702 93 11 *Fax:* (022) 702 93 55 *E-mail:* direction@ medecinehygiene.dr *Web Site:* www.medhyg.ch, pg 623

Stichting Evangelische Uitgeverij H Medema (Netherlands) *Tel:* (0578) 574995 *Fax:* (0578) 573099 *E-mail:* info@medema.nl *Web Site:* www.medema.nl, pg 481

Media Centre (Malta) *Tel:* 21249005; 21223047; 21244913; 21247460; 25699113; 25699114; 25699115 *Fax:* 25699128, pg 456

Media East Press (Australia) *Tel:* (02) 9349 6683 *Fax:* (02) 9349 6683, pg 31

Media House Publications (South Africa) *Tel:* (011) 8826237 *Fax:* (011) 8829652, pg 562

Media House Publications Pty Ltd (South Africa) *Tel:* (011) 8826237 *Fax:* (011) 8829652, pg 1331

Media Institute of Southern Africa (MISA) (Namibia) *Tel:* (061) 232975 *Fax:* (061) 248016 *E-mail:* postmaster@ingrid.misa.org.na *Web Site:* www.misanet.org, pg 472

Media-Print Informationstechnologie GmbH (Germany) *Tel:* (02941) 2 72-300 *Fax:* (02941) 2 72-540 *E-mail:* kg@mediaprint.de *Web Site:* www.mediaprint. de, pg 1145

Media-Print Informationstechnologie GmbH (Germany) *Tel:* (05251) 522 300 *Fax:* (05251) 522 480 *E-mail:* rings@mediaprint-pb.de *Web Site:* www. mediaprint-pb.de, pg 1166

Media-Print Informationstechnologie GmbH (Germany) *Tel:* (02941) 2 72-300 *Fax:* (02941) 2 72-540 *E-mail:* kg@mediaprint.de *Web Site:* www.mediaprint. de, pg 1207

Media Research Publishing Ltd (United Kingdom) *Tel:* (01934) 644 309 *Fax:* (01934) 644 402, pg 721

Mediabank (Republic of Korea) *Tel:* (02) 7420425 *Fax:* (02) 7452174 *E-mail:* sales@mediabank.biz *Web Site:* www.mediabank.pe.kr, pg 1124

Editions Medianes (France) *Tel:* (02) 35 88 85 71 *Fax:* (02) 35 15 28 44 *E-mail:* medianesconseil@ wanadoo.fr, pg 175

Mediapress GmbH (Germany) *Tel:* (08062) 78770 *Fax:* (08062) 6122, pg 256

Mediaspaul Afrique (The Democratic Republic of the Congo) *E-mail:* diffusion@mediaspaul.org *Web Site:* www.mediaspaul.org, pg 114

Editions Mediaspaul (France) *Tel:* (01) 45 48 71 93 *Fax:* (01) 42 22 47 46 *E-mail:* mediaspaul.com@ wanadoo.fr, pg 175

Mediatheque de Saint Pierre (Reunion) *Tel:* (02) 62967196 *Fax:* (02) 62257410 *E-mail:* mediasp@ mediatheque-saintpierre.fr *Web Site:* www. mediatheque-saintpierre.fr, pg 1538

Editorial Medica JIMS, SL (Spain) *Tel:* (093) 2188800 *Fax:* (093) 2188928, pg 586

Editorial Medica Panamericana SA (Argentina) *Tel:* (011) 4821-5520; (011) 4821-0175 *Fax:* (011) 4821-1214 *E-mail:* info@medicapanamericana.com *Web Site:* www.medicapanamericana.com.ar, pg 7

Libreria Medica Paris (Venezuela) *Tel:* (0212) 781-6044 *Fax:* (0212) 7931753, pg 1347

Medica Publishing-Pavla Momcilova (Czech Republic) *Tel:* 272680919; 602271393 *Fax:* 272680919 *E-mail:* momcilova@volny.cz, pg 125

Medical Sciences International Ltd (Japan) *Tel:* (03) 5804-6050 *Fax:* (03) 5804-6055 *E-mail:* info@medsi. co.jp *Web Site:* www.medsi.co.jp, pg 419

Medical University - Sofia, Central Medical Library (Bulgaria) *Tel:* (02) 92301 (ext 498) *Toll Free Tel:* 888 443348 *Fax:* (02) 952 31 71 *Web Site:* www.medun. acad.bg/, pg 1494

Medical Writers Group (United Kingdom) *Tel:* (020) 7373 6642 *Fax:* (020) 7373 5768 *E-mail:* info@ societyofauthors.org *Web Site:* www.societyofauthors. org, pg 1402

Editura Medicala (Romania) *Tel:* (01) 25 25 186 *Fax:* (01) 25 25 189 *E-mail:* edmedicala@fx.ro *Web Site:* www.ed-medicala.ro, pg 536

Editions Medicales et Paramedicales de Charleroi (EMPC) (Belgium) *Tel:* (071) 324689 *Fax:* (071) 324689, pg 70

Ediciones Medicas SA (Argentina) *Tel:* (011) 4384-0750 *Fax:* (011) 4384-0750 *E-mail:* emsa@havasmedimedia. com.ar, pg 7

Edizioni Medicea SRL (Italy) *Tel:* (055) 416048 *Fax:* (055) 416048 *E-mail:* edizionimedicea@ tiscalinet.it *Web Site:* www.edizionimedicea.it, pg 394

Ediciones Medici SA (Spain) *Tel:* (093) 2 010 599; (093) 2 013 807; (093) 2 012 144 *Fax:* (093) 2 097 362 *E-mail:* omega@ediciones-omega.es *Web Site:* www.ediciones-medici.es; www.ediciones-omega.es, pg 586

The Medici Society Ltd (United Kingdom) *Tel:* (020) 8205 2500 *Fax:* (020) 8205 2552 *E-mail:* info@ medici.co.uk *Web Site:* www.medici.co.uk, pg 721

AS Medicina (Estonia) *Tel:* (06) 567660 *Fax:* (06) 567620 *E-mail:* medicina@hot.ee *Web Site:* medicina. co.ee, pg 139

Medicina i Fizkultura EOOD (Bulgaria) *Tel:* (02) 884068 *Fax:* (02) 871308, pg 95

Izdatelstvo Medicina (Russian Federation) *Tel:* (095) 9248785 *Fax:* (095) 9286003, pg 541

Medicina Koenyvkiado (Hungary) *Tel:* (01) 312-2650 *Fax:* (01) 312-2450, pg 320

Medicina Panamericana Editora Do Brasil Ltda (Brazil) *Tel:* (011) 222-0366 *Fax:* (011) 222-0542, pg 86

Bibliothecarii Medicinae Fenniae (BMF) (Finland) *Tel:* (09) 191 26645 *Fax:* (09) 191 26652 *E-mail:* etunimi.sukunimi@helsinki.fi *Web Site:* www. terkko.helsinki.fi/bmf, pg 1561

Medico International eV (Germany) *Tel:* (069) 94438-0 *Fax:* (069) 436002 *E-mail:* info@medico.de *Web Site:* www.medico.de, pg 256

Medien & Recht (Austria) *Tel:* (01) 5052766 *Fax:* (01) 5052766-15 *E-mail:* verlag@medien-recht.ccom *Web Site:* www.medien-recht.com, pg 53

Medien-Verlag Bernhard Gregor GmbH (Germany) *Tel:* (06625) 5011; (0171) 7723972 *Fax:* (06625) 919743 *E-mail:* gregor-medien@t-online.de; mail@ gregor-medien.de *Web Site:* www.gregor-medien.de, pg 256

Medienbuero Muenchen (Germany) *Tel:* (089) 299975 *Fax.* (089) 299975 *E mail:* info@medienbuero-muenchen.com *Web Site:* www.medienbuero-muenchen.com, pg 1121

Medios Publicitarios Mexicanos SA de CV Editora de Directorios de Medios (Mexico) *Tel:* (05) 523-3346; (05) 523-3342 *Fax:* (05) 523-3379 *E-mail:* suscrip@mpm.com.mx; editorial@mpm.com. mx *Web Site:* www.mpm.com.mx, pg 465

Medios y Medios, Sa de CV (Mexico) *Tel:* (05) 56-01-85-11 *Fax:* (05) 56-88-59-85 *E-mail:* mass+medios@ camoapa.com.mx, pg 465

Medis Informatika (The Former Yugoslav Republic of Macedonia) *Tel:* (091) 222253 *Fax:* (091) 222235 *E-mail:* medis@informa.mk, pg 449

Mediserve SRL (Italy) *Tel:* (081) 5452717 *Fax:* (081) 5462026 *E-mail:* contact@mediserve.it *Web Site:* www.mediserve.it, pg 394

Edizioni Mediterranee SRL (Italy) *Tel:* (06) 3235433 *Fax:* (06) 3236277 *E-mail:* info@ediz-mediterranee. com *Web Site:* www.ediz-mediterranee.com, pg 395

Editorial Mediterrania SL (Spain) *Tel:* (093) 218 34 58; (093) 237 86 65 *Fax:* (093) 237 22 10 *E-mail:* edit. med@retemail.es, pg 586

Medium-Buchmarkt (Germany) *Tel:* (0251) 46 000 *Fax:* (0251) 46 745 *E-mail:* info@mediumbooks.com *Web Site:* www.mediumbooks.com, pg 256

Medius Editions (France) *Tel:* (01) 42 79 25 21 *Fax:* (01) 42 78 25 39 *E-mail:* contact@dervy.fr, pg 175

Medizinisch-Literarische Verlagsgesellschaft mbH (Germany) *Tel:* (0581) 808-151 *Fax:* (0581) 808-158 *E-mail:* mlverlag@mlverlag.de *Web Site:* www. mlverlag.de, pg 256

Medpharm Scientific Publishers (Germany) *Tel:* (0711) 2582-0 *Fax:* (0711) 2582-290 *E-mail:* service@ medpharm.de *Web Site:* www.medpharm.de, pg 256

Medsi - Editora Medica e Cientifica Ltda (Brazil) *Tel:* (021) 5694342 *Fax:* (021) 2646392 *E-mail:* medsi@ism.com.br, pg 86

Medusa/Selas Publishers (Greece) *Tel:* 21036483234 *Fax:* 2103648321, pg 307

Wydawnictwo Medyczne Urban & Partner (Poland) *Tel:* (071) 328 54 87; (071) 328 30 68 *Fax:* (071) 328 43 91 *E-mail:* info@urbanpartner.pl *Web Site:* www. urbanpartner.pl, pg 519

Meerut Publishers' Association (India) *Tel:* (0121) 51 0688; (0121) 51 6080 *Fax:* (0121) 52 1545 *E-mail:* vrastogi@vsnl.com, pg 1263

Willem A Meeuws Publisher (United Kingdom) *Tel:* (01235) 821994 *Fax:* (01235) 821994 *E-mail:* thorntons@booknews.demon.co.uk *Web Site:* www.thorntonsbooks.co.uk, pg 721

Megatrade AG (Liechtenstein) *Tel:* 237 5252 *Fax:* 237 5253 *E-mail:* info@wanger.net *Web Site:* www.wanger.net, pg 444

Mehta Publishing House (India) *Tel:* (020) 24476924; (020) 24463048 *Fax:* (020) 24475462 *E-mail:* mehpubl@vsnl.com *Web Site:* www.mehtapublishinghouse.com, pg 338

Mei Ka Printing & Publishing Enterprise Ltd (Hong Kong) *Tel:* 2540 1131 *Fax:* 2559 8718; 2559 7137 *E-mail:* mkpp@netvigator.com *Web Site:* www.meika-printing.com, pg 1147, 1168, 1226

Mei Ya Publications Inc (Sueling Inc) (Taiwan, Province of China) *Tel:* (02) 7037481 *Fax:* (02) 7033847, pg 1336

Meiji Shoin Co Ltd (Japan) *Tel:* (03) 5292-0117 *Fax:* (03) 5292-6182 *E-mail:* nihongol@oak.ocn.ne.jp *Web Site:* www.meijishoin.co.jp, pg 419

Buchhaus Meili AG (Switzerland) *Tel:* (052) 625 41 44 *Fax:* (052) 625 47 46 *E-mail:* meili@melimedien.ch *Web Site:* www.books.ch, pg 1335

Peter Meili & Co, Buchhandlung (Switzerland) *Tel:* (053) 254144 *Fax:* (053) 254746, pg 623

Uitgeverij Meinema (Netherlands) *Tel:* (079) 3615481 *Fax:* (079) 3615489 *E-mail:* info@boekencentrum.nl *Web Site:* www.boekencentrum.nl, pg 481

Felix Meiner Verlag GmbH (Germany) *Tel:* (040) 298756-0 *Fax:* (040) 298756-20 *E-mail:* info@meiner.de *Web Site:* www.meiner.de, pg 256

Meisenbach Verlag GmbH (Germany) *Tel:* (0951) 861-0 *Fax:* (0951) 861-158 *E-mail:* geschltg@meisenbach.de *Web Site:* www.meisenbach.de, pg 256

Otto Meissner Verlag (Germany) *Tel:* (030) 8249558 *Fax:* (030) 8233338, pg 257

Mejikaru Furendo-sha (Japan) *Tel:* (03) 32646611 *Fax:* (03) 32616602 (distribution); (03) 32640704 (editorial affairs) *E-mail:* mfhensyu@mb.infoweb.ne.jp; mfeigyou@mb.infoweb.ne.jp; mfsoumu@mb.infoweb.ne.jp, pg 419

Mekize Nirdamim Society (Israel) *Tel:* (02) 5617919, pg 1396

Melanesian Institute (Papua New Guinea) *Tel:* 732 1777 *Fax:* 732 1214, pg 511

Melantrich, akc spol (Czech Republic) *Tel:* (02) 24227258 *Fax:* (02) 24213176, pg 125

Pustaka Melayu Baru (Malaysia) *Tel:* (03) 087-413615 *Fax:* (03) 087-412184, pg 453

Melbourne Institute of Applied Economic & Social Research (Australia) *Tel:* (03) 8344 2100 *Fax:* (03) 8344 2111 *E-mail:* melb-inst@unimelb.edu.au *Web Site:* www.melbourneinstitute.com, pg 31

Melbourne PEN Centre (Australia) *Tel:* (03) 95097257 *Fax:* (03) 95097257 *Web Site:* www.pen.org.au, pg 1390

Melbourne University Press (Australia) *Tel:* (03) 9342 0300 *Fax:* (03) 9342 0399 *E-mail:* mup-info@unimelb.edu.au *Web Site:* www.mup.unimelb.edu.au, pg 31

Melhoramentos de Portugal Editora, Lda (Portugal) *Tel:* (021) 3963225 *Fax:* (021) 678254, pg 529

Editora Melhoramentos Ltda (Brazil) *Tel:* (011) 3874 0854 *Fax:* (011) 3874 0855 *E-mail:* blerner@melhoramentos.com.br *Web Site:* melhoramentos.com.br, pg 86

Melissa Publishing House (Greece) *Tel:* 2103611692 *Fax:* 2103600865 *E-mail:* sales@melissabooks.com *Web Site:* www.melissabooks.com, pg 307

Melissa Publishing House (Greece) *Tel:* 210 3611692 *Fax:* 2103600865 *E-mail:* webmaster@melissabooks.com *Web Site:* www.melissabooks.com, pg 1303

Mellemfolkeligt Samvirke (Denmark) *Tel:* 7731 0000 *Fax:* 7731 0101 *E-mail:* ms@ms.dk *Web Site:* www.ms.dk, pg 132

Ediciones Melquiades (Chile) *Tel:* (02) 2731545 *Fax:* (02) 2266602, pg 99

Melrose Press Ltd (United Kingdom) *Tel:* (01353) 646600 *Fax:* (01353) 646601 *E-mail:* tradesales@melrosepress.co.uk; info@melrosepress.co.uk *Web Site:* www.melrosepress.co.uk, pg 721

Melting Pot Press (Australia) *Tel:* (02) 9211 1660 *Fax:* (02) 9211 1868 *E-mail:* books@elt.com.au, pg 32

Melway Publishing Pty Ltd (Australia) *Tel:* (03) 9585 9888 *Fax:* (03) 9585 9800 *E-mail:* melway@ausway.com *Web Site:* www.ausway.com, pg 32

Idime Verlag Inge Melzer (Germany) *Tel:* (07541) 55220 *Fax:* (07541) 55201 *E-mail:* idime@t-online.de *Web Site:* www.idime.de, pg 257

Editions MeMo (France) *Tel:* (02) 40 47 98 19 *Fax:* (02) 40 47 98 21 *E-mail:* contactweb@editionsmemo.fr *Web Site:* www.editionsmemo.fr, pg 175

Editions Memoire des Arts (France) *Tel:* (04) 78 83 22 62 *Fax:* (04) 72 19 48 74, pg 175

Editions Memor (Belgium) *Tel:* (02) 644-04-43 *Fax:* (02) 644-04-43, pg 70

Memorias Futuras Edicoes Ltda (Brazil) *Tel:* (021) 2053549 *Fax:* (021) 2252518 *E-mail:* memorias@br.homeshopping.com.br, pg 86

Memorie Domenicane (Italy) *Tel:* (0573) 22056; (0573) 28158 *Fax:* (0573) 975808 *E-mail:* centroriviste@tiscalinet.it, pg 395

Memory/Cage Editions (Switzerland) *Tel:* (01) 281 35 65 *Fax:* (01) 281 35 66 *E-mail:* mail@memorycage.com *Web Site:* www.memorycage.com, pg 623

Mendelova zemedelska a lesnicka univerzita v Brne (Czech Republic) *Tel:* (05) 4513 1111; (05) 4513 2678 *Fax:* (05) 4513 5008 *Web Site:* www.mendelu.cz, pg 125

Sonny A Mendoza (Philippines) *Tel:* (02) 8691111, pg 514

Libreria Menendez (Panama) *Tel:* 2258996, pg 1325

Biblioteca y Casa - Museo de Menendez Pelayo (Spain) *Tel:* (042) 23 45 34 *E-mail:* xjagenjo@sarenet.es *Web Site:* www.turcantabria.com, pg 1544

Edition Axel Menges GmbH (Germany) *Tel:* (0711) 574759 *Fax:* (0711) 574784, pg 257

Editions Menges (France) *Tel:* (01) 44 55 37 50 *Fax:* (01) 40 20 99 74 *E-mail:* info@editions-menges.com *Web Site:* www.editions-menges.com, pg 175

Casa Editrice Menna di Sinisgalli Menna Giuseppina (Italy) *Tel:* (0825) 24080 *Fax:* (0825) 24080, pg 395

Menora Publishing House (The Former Yugoslav Republic of Macedonia) *Tel:* (02) 458447 *Fax:* (02) 418872 *E-mail:* menora@lotus.mpt.com.mk, pg 449

Menoshire Ltd (United Kingdom) *Tel:* (020) 85667344 *Fax:* (020) 89912439 *E-mail:* sales@menoshire.com *Web Site:* www.menoshire.com, pg 1343

Ediciones Mensajero (Spain) *Tel:* (094) 4 470 358 *Fax:* (094) 4 472 630 *E-mail:* mensajero@mensajero.com *Web Site:* www.mensajero.com, pg 586

Menschenkinder Verlag und Vertrieb GmbH (Germany) *Tel:* (0251) 932520 *Fax:* (0251) 9325290 *E-mail:* info@menschenkinder.de *Web Site:* www.menschenkinder.de, pg 257

mentis Verlag GmbH (Germany) *Tel:* (05251) 687902; (05251) 687904 *Fax:* (05251) 687905 *E-mail:* info@mentis.de *Web Site:* www.mentis.de, pg 257

Mentor Kiado (Romania) *Tel:* (0265) 256975 *Fax:* (0265) 256975, pg 536

Mentor Publications (Ireland) *Tel:* (01) 2952112 *Fax:* (01) 2952114 *E-mail:* admin@mentorbooks.ie *Web Site:* www.mentorbooks.ie, pg 358

Mentor-Verlag Dr Ramdohr KG (Germany) *Tel:* (089) 360960 *Fax:* (089) 36096-222 (general); (089) 36096-258 (orders) *E-mail:* mentor@langenscheidt.de, pg 257

Merani Publishing House (Georgia) *Tel:* (032) 996492; (032) 935396; (032) 935554; (032) 935514 *Fax:* (032) 932996, pg 190

Meravigli, Libreria Milanese (Italy) *Tel:* (02) 2157240 *Fax:* (02) 2157833, pg 395

Merbod Verlag (Austria) *Tel:* (02622) 81724 *Fax:* (02622) 817244, pg 53

Editora Mercado Aberto Ltda (Brazil) *Tel:* (051) 3337-4833 *Fax:* (051) 3337-4905 *E-mail:* mercado@mercadoaberto.com.br *Web Site:* www.mercadoaberto.com.br, pg 86

Mercametrica Ediciones SA Edicion de Libros (Mexico) *Tel:* (055) 56-61-62-93; (055) 56-61-92-86 *Fax:* (055) 56-62-33-08 *E-mail:* mercametrica@mercametrica.com *Web Site:* www.mercametrica.com.mx, pg 465

Mercantila Publishers A/S (Denmark) *Tel:* 35436222 *Fax:* 35435151 *E-mail:* info@mercantila.dk *Web Site:* www.gtft.dk, pg 132

Mercat Press (United Kingdom) *Tel:* (0131) 225 5324 *Fax:* (0131) 226 6632 *E-mail:* enquiries@mercatpress.com *Web Site:* www.mercatpress.com, pg 721

Mercatorfonds NV (Belgium) *Tel:* (03) 2027260 *Fax:* (03) 2311319 *E-mail:* artbooks@mercatorfonds.be *Web Site:* www.mercatorfonds.be, pg 70

Merchandising Muenchen KG (Germany) *Tel:* (089) 95078600 *Fax:* (089) 95078700 *E-mail:* info.line@merchandising-muenchen.de *Web Site:* www.merchandisingmedia.com, pg 1121

Merchiston Publishing (United Kingdom) *Tel:* (0131) 455 2227 *Fax:* (0131) 455 2299, pg 722

Editions Franck Mercier (France) *Tel:* (04) 50 57 16 50 *Fax:* (01) 450579301 *E-mail:* franck@mercier.com.ch, pg 175

Mercier Press Ltd (Ireland) *Tel:* (021) 489 9858 *Fax:* (021) 489 9887 *E-mail:* books@mercierpress.ie *Web Site:* www.mercierpress.ie, pg 358

Mercure de France SA (France) *Tel:* (01) 55 42 61 90 *Fax:* (01) 43 54 49 91 *E-mail:* mercure@mercure.fr *Web Site:* www.mercuredefrance.fr, pg 175

Mercury Press Pvt Ltd (Zimbabwe) *Tel:* (04) 75-1515; (04) 75-1084 *Fax:* (04) 73-7670, pg 778

Editora Mercuryo Ltda (Brazil) *Tel:* (011) 5531-8222 *Fax:* (011) 5093-3265 *E-mail:* diretoraeditorial@mercuryo.com.br *Web Site:* www.mercuryo.com.br, pg 86

Meresborough Books Ltd (United Kingdom) *Tel:* (01634) 371591 *Fax:* (01634) 262114 *E-mail:* shop@rainhambookshop.co.uk *Web Site:* www.rainhambookshop.co.uk, pg 722, 1343

Mergus Verlag GmbH Hans A Baensch (Germany) *Tel:* (05422) 3636 *Fax:* (05422) 1404 *E-mail:* info@mergus.de *Web Site:* www.mergus.com, pg 257

Meriberica/Liber (Portugal) *Tel:* (021) 8583849 *Fax:* (021) 8581536 *E-mail:* geral@meriberica.pt; bd@meriberica.pt; encomendar@meriberica.pt (orders) *Web Site:* www.meriberica.pt, pg 529

Meridian Books (United Kingdom) *Tel:* (016) 3554 3816 *Fax:* (016) 3555 1004 *E-mail:* jennie@countrysidebooks.co.uk, pg 722

Editura Meridiane (Romania) *Tel:* (021) 222-33-93 *Fax:* (021) 222-30-37 *E-mail:* meridiane@fx.ro, pg 536

Merlin Library Ltd (Malta) *Tel:* 221205; 234438 *Fax:* 221135 *E-mail:* mail@merlinlibrary.com *Web Site:* www.merlinlibrary.com, pg 456

Milanostampa SpA (Italy) *Tel:* (0173) 746111
*Fax:* (0173) 746248; (0173) 746249 *E-mail:* info@
milanostampa.com; sales@milanostampa.com
*Web Site:* www.milanostampa.com, pg 1170

Milanostampa SpA (Italy) *Tel:* (0173) 746111
*Fax:* (0173) 746248; (0173) 746249 *E-mail:* info@
milanostampa.com *Web Site:* www.milanostampa.it,
pg 1210

Milanostampa SpA (Italy) *Tel:* (0173) 746111
*Fax:* (0173) 746248; (0173) 746249 *E-mail:* info@
milanostampa.com *Web Site:* www.milanostampa.com,
pg 1227

Milella di Lecce Spazio Vivo srl (Italy) *Tel:* (0832)
241131 *Fax:* (0832) 303057 *E-mail:* leccespaziovivo@
tiscalinet.it, pg 395

Milena Verlag (Austria) *Tel:* (01) 402 59 90 *Fax:* (01)
408 88 58 *E-mail:* frauenverlag@milena-verlag.at,
pg 53

Editorial Milenio Arts Grafiques Bobala, SL
(Spain) *Tel:* (0973) 236 611 *Fax:* (0973) 240
795 *E-mail:* editorial.milenio@cambrescat.es
*Web Site:* www.edmilenio.com, pg 586

Miles Kelly Publishing Ltd (United Kingdom)
*Tel:* (01371) 811309 *Fax:* (01371) 811393
*E-mail:* info@mileskelly.net *Web Site:* www.
mileskelly.net, pg 723

Editura Militara (Romania) *Tel:* (01) 3112191; (01)
6133601 *Fax:* (01) 3237822, pg 536

Militzke Verlag (Germany) *Tel:* (0341) 42643-0
*Fax:* (0341) 42643-99 *E-mail:* info@militzke.de
*Web Site:* www.militzke.de, pg 258

Millbank Books Ltd (United Kingdom) *Tel:* (01279)
655233 *Fax:* (01279) 655244 *E-mail:* caw@millbank.
demon.co.uk, pg 1343

Mille et Une Nuits (France) *Tel:* (01) 45 49 82 00
*Fax:* (01) 45 49 79 96 *E-mail:* info1001nuits@
editions-fayard.fr *Web Site:* www.1001nuits.com,
pg 176

Cathy Miller Foreign Rights Agency (United Kingdom)
*Tel:* (020) 7386 5473 *Fax:* (020) 7385 1774, pg 1132

Harvey Miller Publishers (United Kingdom) *Tel:* (01235)
465500 *Fax:* (01235) 465555 *E-mail:* harvey.miller@
brepols.net, pg 723

J Garnet Miller (United Kingdom) *Tel:* (01684) 540154
*Fax:* (01684) 540154, pg 723

Miller's Publications (United Kingdom) *Tel:* (01933)
273411 *Fax:* (01933) 229330, pg 723

Milli Kuetuephane (Turkey) *Tel:* (0312) 212 62 00
*Fax:* (0312) 223 04 51 *Web Site:* www.mkutup.gov.tr,
pg 1550

Mills Group (New Zealand) *Tel:* (04) 5696744 *Fax:* (04)
5697464 *Web Site:* www.millsonline.com, pg 494

Millwood Press Ltd (New Zealand) *Tel:* (04) 4735176
*Fax:* (04) 4735177, pg 494

Milton Margai Teachers' College Library (Sierra Leone)
*Tel:* (022) 024305, pg 1541

Mimosa Publications Pty Ltd (Australia) *Tel:* (03) 9819
0511 *Fax:* (03) 9819 0524 *E-mail:* info@mimosa.pub.
com.au, pg 32

Min-eumsa Publishing Co Ltd (Republic of Korea)
*Tel:* (02) 515-2000; (02) 515-2005; (02) 515-9108
*Fax:* (02) 515-2007; (02) 3444-5185 *Web Site:* www.
minumsa.com, pg 437

Min Jung Seo Rim Publishing Co (Republic of Korea)
*Tel:* (02) 7036541; (02) 7036547 *Fax:* (02) 7036549
*E-mail:* editmin@minjungdic.co.kr *Web Site:* www.
minjungdic.co.kr, pg 437

Librairie Minard (France) *Tel:* (02) 31844706 *Fax:* (02)
31844809, pg 176

MIND Publications (United Kingdom) *Tel:* (020) 8519
2122 *Fax:* (020) 8522 1725; (020) 8534 6399 (orders)
*E-mail:* contact@mind.org.uk; publications@mind.org.
uk (mail order) *Web Site:* www.mind.org.uk, pg 723

Mindanao State University - Mamitua Saber Research
Center (Philippines) *Tel:* (063) 2214050; (063)
3516151; (063) 3516152; (063) 3516172; (063)
3516174; (063) 3516153; (063) 3516154; (063)
3516155; (063) 3516156 *Fax:* (063) 221405
*Web Site:* www.msumain.edu.ph/units/msrc/, pg 514

Libreria Editrice Minerva (Italy) *Tel:* (075) 812381
*Fax:* (075) 816564, pg 1311

Minerva (Serbia and Montenegro) *Tel:* (024) 28834;
(024) 25712 *Fax:* (024) 23-208, pg 548

Minerva Associates (Publications) Pvt Ltd (India)
*Tel:* (033) 2466 3783, pg 338

Editora Minerva Central (Mozambique) *Tel:* (01) 420198
*Fax:* (01) 423677 *E-mail:* minerva@sortmoz.com,
pg 472

Editions Minerva (France) *Tel:* (01) 44 10 75 75
*Fax:* (01) 44 10 75 80 *Web Site:* www.lamartiniere.fr,
pg 176

Editorial Minerva (Portugal) *Tel:* (021) 3220540
*Fax:* (021) 3220549, pg 529

Editura Minerva (Romania) *Tel:* (01) 3308808;
(01) 3308840 *Fax:* (01) 3308808; (01) 3308840
*E-mail:* desfacere@edituraaramis.ro, pg 536

Minerva Italica SpA (Italy) *Tel:* (02) 21213643
*Fax:* (02) 21213698 *E-mail:* info@minervaitalica.it
*Web Site:* www.minervaitalica.it, pg 395

Minerva KG Internationale Fachliteratur fur
Medizin und Naturwissenschaften Neue Medien
(Germany) *Tel:* (06151) 9880 *Fax:* (06151) 98839
*E-mail:* minerva@minerva.de *Web Site:* www.minerva.
de, pg 1301

Minerva Medica (Italy) *Tel:* (011) 67-82-82 *Fax:* (011)
67-45-02 *E-mail:* minervamedica@minervamedica.it
*Web Site:* www.minervamedica.it, pg 1149, 1210

Minerva Publications (Malaysia) *Tel:* (06) 734439
*Fax:* (06) 734439, pg 453

Minerva Shobo Co Ltd (Japan) *Tel:* (075) 581-5191
*Fax:* (075) 581-0589 *E-mail:* info@minervashobo.co.jp
*Web Site:* www.minervashoboco.jp, pg 419

Minerva Edition Wissen Medizinischer und
Naturwissenschaftlicher Verlag und Vertieb (Germany)
*Tel:* (0700) 96 389 352 *Fax:* (0700) 96 389 353
*E-mail:* info@woetzel.de *Web Site:* www.woetzel.de,
pg 258

Minervaverlag Bern (Switzerland) *Tel:* (031) 3726223
*Fax:* (031) 3726223, pg 624

Mines & Geological Department Library (Kenya)
*Tel:* (02) 229261; (02) 541040 *Fax:* (02) 216951,
pg 1521

Ming Pao Publications Ltd (Hong Kong) *Tel:* 2595 3084
*Fax:* 2898 2646 *E-mail:* geocomm@mingpao.com
*Web Site:* security.mingpao.com/books, pg 315

Uitgeverij Mingus (Netherlands) *Tel:* (0348) 42 55 07
*Fax:* (0348) 42 55 07 *E-mail:* mingus-vk@planet.nl,
pg 482

Ministere de la Culture (Luxembourg) *Tel:* 478-1
*Fax:* 40-24-27, pg 447

Ministere des Affaires Etrangeres Division de L'Ecrit
et des Mediatheques (France) *Tel:* (01) 43 17 53
53 *Fax:* (01) 43 17 88 83 *Web Site:* www.france.
diplomatie.gouv.fr, pg 1258

Ministerie van Verkeer en Waterstaat (Netherlands)
*Tel:* (070) 3517086 *Fax:* (070) 3516430
*E-mail:* venwinfo@postbus51.nl *Web Site:* www.
minvenw.nl, pg 482

Ministerio da Marinha Diretoria de Hidrografia
Navegacao (Brazil) *Tel:* (021) 719-2626 (ext 147)
*Fax:* (021) 719-4989 *E-mail:* 01@dhm.mar.mil.sr,
pg 86

Ministerio de Economia y Hacienda Secretario
General Tecnica Centro de Publicaciones (Spain)
*Tel:* (091) 5063740 (ext 51307) *Fax:* (091) 5273951
*E-mail:* ventas.campillo@sgt.meh.es *Web Site:* www.
minhac.es, pg 587

Ministerio de Educacion Biblioteca Central (Venezuela)
*Tel:* (0212) 5628970 (ext 8149); (0212) 5621767;
(0212) 5640025 *Fax:* (0212) 5641224, pg 774

Ministerio de Educacion y Culture Centro de
Publicaciones (Spain) *Tel:* (091) 453 98 00 *Fax:* (091)
453 98 00 *Web Site:* www.mec.es/mec, pg 587

Editorial del Ministerio de Educacion (Guatemala),
pg 310

Ministerio de Justicia e Interior, Centro de Publicaciones
(Spain) *Tel:* (091) 390 20 87; (091) 390 20
82; (091) 390 20 97 *Fax:* (091) 390 20 92
*E-mail:* publicaciones@sb.mju.es *Web Site:* www.mju.
es, pg 587

Ministerio de Trabajo y Asuntos Sociales (Spain)
*Tel:* (091) 4037000 *Fax:* (091) 4030050
*E-mail:* sugerir@sta.mtas.es *Web Site:* www.mtas.
es/insht/index.htm, pg 587

Ministerstvo Kul 'tury RF (Russian Federation) *Tel:* 220
4560 *E-mail:* rnb@q1as.apc.org, pg 542

Ministerstvo Kultury C R, Oddeleni Tisku Oddeleni
Knizi Kultury (Czech Republic) *Tel:* (02) 57 085
111 *Fax:* (02) 24 318 155 *E-mail:* minkult@mkcr.cz
*Web Site:* www.mkcr.cz, pg 1255

Ministry of Agriculture & Livestock Development
Marketing Library (Kenya) *Tel:* (02) 718-870
*Fax:* (02) 725-774, pg 1521

Ministry of Agriculture Library (Malaysia) *Tel:* (03)
26954215 (ext 4216, 4217or 4298) *Fax:* (03)
26932220 *E-mail:* dahlia@agri.moa.my; lht@agri.
moa.my; fuziah@agri.moa.my *Web Site:* agrolink.moa.
my/library, pg 1525

Ministry of Cultural Affairs (Sri Lanka) *Tel:* (01)
872001; (01) 876586 *Fax:* (01) 872020
*E-mail:* mcasec@sltnet.lk *Web Site:* www.mca.gov.lk,
pg 602

Ministry of Defence Publishing House (Israel) *Tel:* (03)
6917940 *Fax:* (03) 6375509, pg 367

Ministry of Education Library (Afghanistan), pg 1487

Ministry of Education Library (Egypt (Arab Republic
of Egypt)) *Tel:* (02) 516 9744 *Fax:* (02) 516 9560
*E-mail:* info@mail.emoe.org *Web Site:* www.emoe.org,
pg 1502

Ministry of Education (Sri Lanka) *Tel:* 565141-5150,
pg 602

Ministry of Education, Department of Educational
Publications (Afghanistan) *Tel:* (0873) 32076
*Fax:* (0873) 15051, pg 1

Ministry of Environment & Public Health, Library
Division (Malaysia) *Tel:* (082) 319614; (082) 319613
*Fax:* (082) 311216 *E-mail:* info@moeswk.gov.my
*Web Site:* www.moeswk.gov.my, pg 1525

Ministry of Information (Kuwait) *Tel:* 245-1566
*Fax:* 245-9530 *E-mail:* admin@media.gov.kw
*Web Site:* www.moinfo.gov.kw, pg 441

Ministry of Information & Broadcasting (India)
*Tel:* (011) 3387983; (011) 3386879; (011)
3387069; (011) 3386452 *Fax:* (011) 3387341
*E-mail:* indiapub@nda.vsnl.net.in; dpd@sb.nic.in
*Web Site:* mib.nic.in, pg 338

Ministry of Justice Library (Egypt (Arab Republic
of Egypt)) *Tel:* (02) 20806 *Fax:* (02) 795 8103
*E-mail:* mojeb@idsc1.gov.eg, pg 1502

Minjisa Publishing Co (Republic of Korea) *Tel:* (02)
9806382 *Fax:* (02) 9861531 *E-mail:* minjisa@
nownuri.net *Web Site:* www.minjisa.co.kr, pg 438

Editions Minkoff (Switzerland) *Tel:* (022) 310 46 60
*Fax:* (022) 310 28 57 *E-mail:* minkoff@minkoff-
editions.com *Web Site:* www.minkoff-editions.com,
pg 624

Minoas SA (Greece) *Tel:* 2102711222 *Fax:* 210
2711056 *E-mail:* info@minoas.gr *Web Site:* www.
minoas.gr, pg 307

Il Minotauro (Italy) *Tel:* (06) 5591864 *Fax:* (06) 5592337 *E-mail:* ilminotauro@tin.it *Web Site:* www. ilminotauroeditore.it, pg 395

Ediciones Minotauro (Spain) *Tel:* (093) 492 8869 *Fax:* (093) 496 7041 *E-mail:* edicionesminotauro@ arrakis.es *Web Site:* www.edicionesminotauro.com, pg 587

Ediciones Minotauro SA (Argentina) *Tel:* (011) 4382-4043; (011) 4382-4045 *Fax:* (011) 4383-3793 *E-mail:* sansaldi@eplaneta.com.ar *Web Site:* www. edicionesminotauro.com, pg 7

Editorial Minutiae Mexicana SA (Mexico) *Tel:* (052) 55-5535-9488 *Fax:* (052) 722-232-0662, pg 465

Izdatelstvo Mir (Russian Federation) *Tel:* (095) 286-17-83 *Fax:* (095) 288-95-22 *Web Site:* www.mir-pubs.dol. ru, pg 542

Mir Knigi Ltd (Russian Federation) *Tel:* (095) 2083879 *Fax:* (095) 7428579, pg 542

Editores Mira, SA (Spain) *Tel:* (0976) 460505 *Fax:* (0976) 460446 *E-mail:* miraeditores@ctv.es *Web Site:* www.miraeditores.com, pg 587

Mirai-Sha (Japan) *Tel:* (03) 3814-5521 *Fax:* (03) 3814-8600, pg 419

Presses Universitaires du Mirail (France) *Tel:* (05) 61 50 38 10 *Fax:* (05) 61 50 38 00 *E-mail:* pum@univ-tlse2.fr *Web Site:* www.univ-tlse2.fr/pum, pg 176

Mirananda Publishers BV (Netherlands) *Tel:* (070) 358 59 43 *Fax:* (070) 358 68 43 *E-mail:* info@mirananda. nl *Web Site:* www.mirananda.nl, pg 482

G Miranda & Sons (Philippines) *Tel:* (02) 7121620 *Fax:* (02) 7120502, pg 1326

Miranda-Verlag Stefan Ehlert (Germany) *Tel:* (0421) 7943226 *Fax:* (0421) 7943226 *E-mail:* miranda-verlag@t-online.de *Web Site:* www.miranda-verlag.de, pg 258

Mirinae (Republic of Korea) *Tel:* (02) 2279-2669 *Fax:* (02) 2279-2665 *E-mail:* mrn@lycos.co.kr, pg 438

Mirkam Publishers (Israel) *Tel:* (06) 6900967 *Fax:* (06) 6900967, pg 367

Mirran (Netherlands) *Tel:* (013) 5169534 *Fax:* (013) 4684764 *E-mail:* info@mirran.com *Web Site:* www. mirran.com, pg 482

Mirza Book Agency (Pakistan) *Tel:* (042) 7353601 *Fax:* (042) 5763714 *E-mail:* merchant@brain.net.pk, pg 1125

Mirzaye Shirazi Library (Islamic Republic of Iran) *Tel:* (0711) 6260011 *Fax:* (0711) 6202380 *Web Site:* www.shirazu.ac.ir, pg 1516

MiS Sport IGP (Serbia and Montenegro) *Tel:* (011) 3220226; (011) 3225361, pg 548

Misgav Yerushalayim (Israel) *Tel:* (02) 5883962 *Fax:* (02) 5815460 *E-mail:* misgav@h2.hum.huji.ac.il *Web Site:* www.hum.huji.ac.il/misgav, pg 367

Instituto Misionero Hijas De San Pablo (Colombia) *Tel:* (01) 6710992 *Fax:* (01) 6706378, pg 111

Miskal Publishing Ltd (Israel) *Tel:* (03) 9246980 *Fax:* (03) 9246985, pg 367

Misr Bookshop (Egypt (Arab Republic of Egypt)) *Tel:* (02) 908920, pg 1299

Galeria de Arte Misrachi SA (Mexico) *Tel:* (05) 5334551 *Fax:* (05) 55257187 *E-mail:* misrachi@acnet.net, pg 465

Missio eV (Germany) *Tel:* (0241) 75 07-00 *Fax:* (0241) 75 07-336 *E-mail:* info@missio-aachen.de *Web Site:* www.missio-aachen.de, pg 258

Mission Publications of Australia (Australia) *Tel:* (02) 4759 1003 *Fax:* (02) 4759 1101 *E-mail:* missionpublaust@bigpond.com, pg 32

Editrice Missionaria Italiana (EMI) (Italy) *Tel:* (051) 326027 *Fax:* (051) 327552 *E-mail:* sermis@emi.it *Web Site:* www.emi.it, pg 395

Missionshandlung (Germany) *Tel:* (05052) 69-0 *Fax:* (05052) 69-222 *E-mail:* central_de@elm.mission. net *Web Site:* www.missionshandlung.de, pg 259

Pietro Missorini & Co - Libreria Commissionaria (Italy) *Tel:* (0521) 993919 *Fax:* (0521) 993929 *E-mail:* info@ missorini.it *Web Site:* www.rsadvnet.it/missorini/, pg 1123

Misuzu Shobo Ltd (Japan) *Tel:* (03) 3815-9181 *Fax:* (03) 3818-8497 *E-mail:* nakagawa@msz.co.jp *Web Site:* www.msz.co.jp, pg 419

MIT Press Ltd (United Kingdom) *Tel:* (020) 7306 0603 *Fax:* (020) 7306 0604 *E-mail:* info@hup-mitpress.co. uk *Web Site:* mitpress.mit.edu, pg 723

Mita Press, Mita Industrial Co Ltd (Japan) *Tel:* (03) 3817-7200 *Fax:* (03) 3817-7207, pg 419

Mita Toshokan Joho Gakkai (Japan) *Tel:* (03) 5427-1654 *Web Site:* www.mita.lib.keio.ac.jp, pg 1566

Mittal Publications (India) *Tel:* (011) 5163610; (011) 5648028; (011) 3250398 *Fax:* (011) 5648725 *E-mail:* mittalp@ndf.vsnl.net.in, pg 338

Mitteldeutscher Verlag GmbH (Germany) *Tel:* (0345) 23322-0 *Fax:* (0345) 23322-66 *E-mail:* mitteldeutscher.verlag@t-online.de *Web Site:* www.buecherkisten.de, pg 259

E S Mittler und Sohn GmbH (Germany) *Tel:* (040) 7 97 13-03 *Fax:* (040) 79713324, pg 259

Mizan (Indonesia) *Tel:* (022) 7200931 *E-mail:* info@ mizan.com *Web Site:* www.mizan.com, pg 352

M Mizrahi Publishers (Israel) *Tel:* (03) 6870936 *Fax:* (03) 5475399, pg 367

MK Ediciones y Publicaciones (Spain) *Tel:* (091) 4316305 *Fax:* (091) 5754978, pg 587

Mlada fronta (Czech Republic) *Tel:* (02) 49 240 315 *Fax:* (02) 25 276 278 *Web Site:* www.mf.cz, pg 125

Mlade leta Spd sro (Slovakia) *Tel:* (02) 55 56 45 12; (02) 55 56 62 82 *Fax:* (02) 21 57 14 *Web Site:* www. mlade-leta.sk, pg 555

Mladezh IK (Bulgaria) *Tel:* (02) 882137 *Fax:* (02) 876135, pg 95

Mladinska Knjiga International (Slovenia) *Tel:* (01) 2413 284; (01) 2413 288 *Fax:* (01) 4252 294 *E-mail:* intsales@mkz-lj.si *Web Site:* www.emka.si, pg 557

Mladost d d Izdavacku graficku i informaticku djelatnost (Croatia) *Tel:* (01) 215-853; (01) 229-811 *Fax:* (01) 239-5336, pg 118

Thomas Mlakar Verlag (Austria) *Tel:* (03579) 2258 *Fax:* (03579) 2258 *E-mail:* mlakar-media@gmx.at, pg 54

mnemes - Alfieri & Ranieri Publishing (Italy) *Tel:* (091) 588813 *Fax:* (091) 588813 *E-mail:* info@mnemes.com *Web Site:* www.mnemes.com, pg 395

Moby Dick Verlag (Germany) *Tel:* (0431) 640110 *Fax:* (0431) 6401112 *E-mail:* mobybook@aol.com, pg 259

Modan Publishers Ltd (Israel) *Tel:* (08) 9221821 *Fax:* (08) 9221299 *E-mail:* modan@modan.co.il *Web Site:* www.modan.co.il, pg 367

mode information Heinz Kramer GmbH (Germany) *Tel:* (02206) 60070 *Fax:* (02206) 600717 *E-mail:* info@modeinfo.com *Web Site:* www. modeinfo.com, pg 259

Modellsport Verlag GmbH (Germany) *Tel:* (07221) 95 21-0 *Fax:* (07221) 95 21-45 *E-mail:* modellsport@ modellsport.de *Web Site:* www.modellsport.de, pg 259

The Modern Book Depot (India) *Tel:* (033) 2493102; (033) 2490933 *Fax:* (033) 2497455 *E-mail:* modcal@ vsnl.com, pg 1306

Modern Electronic & Computing Publishing Co Ltd (Hong Kong) *Tel:* 2342 8299 *Fax:* 2341 4247 *E-mail:* info@computertoday.com.hk *Web Site:* www. computertoday.com.hk, pg 315

Modern Guides Company (Puerto Rico) *Tel:* (787) 723-9105 *Fax:* (787) 723-4380 *E-mail:* avc1941@attglobal. net, pg 532

Modern Press (China) *Tel:* (010) 4215031-383 *Fax:* (010) 4214540, pg 106

Moderna galerija Ljubljana/Museum of Modern Art (Slovenia) *Tel:* (01) 2416 800 *Fax:* (01) 2514 120 *E-mail:* info@mg-li.si *Web Site:* www.mg-lj.si, pg 557

Editora Moderna Ltda (Brazil) *Tel:* (011) 609-0130 *Fax:* (011) 608-3055 *E-mail:* moderna@moderna.com. br *Web Site:* www.moderna.com.br, pg 86

Moderne Buchkunst und Graphie Wolfgang Tiessen (Germany) *Tel:* (06102) 53335 *Fax:* (06102) 53335, pg 259

Editions Modernes Media (France) *Tel:* (01) 44 54 90 42 *Fax:* (01) 44 54 90 47 *E-mail:* ed.mod.media@ wanadoo.fr, pg 176

modo verlag GmbH (Germany) *Tel:* (0761) 2022875 *Fax:* (0761) 2022876 *E-mail:* info@modoverlag.de *Web Site:* www.modoverlag.de, pg 259

Forlaget Modtryk AMBA (Denmark) *Tel:* 8731 7600 *Fax:* 8731 7601 *E-mail:* forlaget@modtryk.dk *Web Site:* www.modtryk.dk, pg 132

Modulo Editora e Desenvolvimento Educacional Ltda (Brazil) *Tel:* (041) 2530077 *Fax:* (041) 2530103 *E-mail:* moduloed@moduloeditora.com.br *Web Site:* www.moduloeditora.com.br, pg 86

Modulverlag (Austria) *Tel:* (01) 5129892 *Fax:* (01) 5129893, pg 54

Moeck Verlag und Musikinstrumentenwerk, Inhaber Dr Hermann Moeck (Germany) *Tel:* (05141) 88 53-0 *Fax:* (05141) 88 53-42 *E-mail:* info@moeck-music.de *Web Site:* www.moeck-music.de, pg 259

Karl Heinrich Moeseler Verlag (Germany) *Tel:* (05331) 95970 *Fax:* (05331) 9597-20, pg 259

MOHN Media (Germany) *Tel:* (05241) 80-4 04 10 *Fax:* (05241) 2 42 82 *E-mail:* mohnmedia@ bertelsmann.de *Web Site:* www.mohnmedia.de, pg 1145

MOHN Media (Germany) *Tel:* (05241) 80 56 29 *Fax:* (05241) 1 66 92 *E-mail:* mohnmedia@ bertelsmann.de *Web Site:* www.mohnmedia.de, pg 1166

MOHN Media (Germany) *Tel:* (05241) 80-4 04 10 *Fax:* (05241) 2 42 82 *E-mail:* mohnmedia@ bertelsmann.de *Web Site:* www.mohnmedia.de, pg 1207, 1226

Mohr Siebeck (Germany) *Tel:* (07071) 923-0 *Fax:* (07071) 5 11 04 *E-mail:* info@mohr.de *Web Site:* www.mohr.de, pg 259

Mohr-ZA Verlagsauslieferungen Ges mbH (Austria) *Tel:* (01) 5121676; (01) 5125711; (01) 5126994 *Fax:* (01) 111859, pg 1290

MOHRBOOKS AG, Literary Agency (Switzerland) *Tel:* (043) 2448626 *Fax:* (043) 2448627 *E-mail:* info@ mohrbooks.com *Web Site:* www.mohrbooks.de, pg 1127

Moksha Institute of Caribbean Arts & Letters (Trinidad & Tobago) *Tel:* (868) 6374516, pg 642

Mokslo ir enciklopediju leidybos institutas (Lithuania) *Tel:* (02) 45 85 26; (02) 457980; (02) 458528 *Fax:* (02) 45 85 37 *E-mail:* meli@meli.lt *Web Site:* www.meli.lt, pg 446

M Moleiro Editor, SA (Spain) *Tel:* (093) 414 20 10 *Fax:* (093) 201 50 62 *E-mail:* mmoleiro@moleiro.com *Web Site:* www.moleiro.com, pg 587

Editorial Molino (Spain) *Tel:* (093) 226 06 25 *Fax:* (093) 226 69 98 *E-mail:* molino@menta.net *Web Site:* www. editorialmolino.es, pg 587

Editorial Moll SL (Spain) *Tel:* (0971) 72 41 76 *Fax:* (0971) 72 62 52 *E-mail:* info@editorialmoll.es *Web Site:* www.editorialmoll.es, pg 587

Librairie Mollat (France) *Tel:* (0556) 564040 *Fax:* (0556) 564088 *E-mail:* mollat@mollat.com *Web Site:* www. mollat.com, pg 1300

Izdatelstvo Molodaya Gvardia (Russian Federation) *Tel:* (095) 9722288 *Fax:* (095) 9720582, pg 542

Mombasa Polytechnic Library (Kenya) *Tel:* (011) 492222 *Fax:* (011) 495632 *E-mail:* msapoly@africaonline. com, pg 1521

Monarch Books (United Kingdom) *Tel:* (01865) 302750 *Fax:* (01865) 302757 *E-mail:* monarch@lionhudson. com *Web Site:* www.lionhudson.com, pg 724

Monash University Library (Australia) *Tel:* (03) 9905 5054 *Fax:* (03) 9905 2610 *E-mail:* library@lib. monash.edu.au *Web Site:* www.lib.monash.edu.au, pg 1488

Library of the Monastery of St-Saviour (Basilian Missionary Order of St-Saviour) (Lebanon), pg 1523

Arnoldo Mondadori Editore SpA (Italy) *Tel:* (02) 75421 *Fax:* (02) 75422302 *Web Site:* www.mondadori.it, pg 395

Giorgio Mondadori & Associati (Italy) *Tel:* (02) 433 131 *Fax:* (02) 89125880 *E-mail:* edgmonai@tin.it, pg 396

Edizioni del Mondo Giudiziario (Italy) *Tel:* (06) 3721071 *Fax:* (06) 35350961 *E-mail:* info@mguidiziario.it *Web Site:* www.mgiudiziario.it, pg 396

Mondo SA (Editions-Verlag-Edizioni) (Switzerland) *Tel:* (021) 924 12 40 *Fax:* (021) 924 46 62 *E-mail:* info@mondo.ch *Web Site:* www.mondo.ch, pg 624

Mondolibro Editore SNC (Italy) *Tel:* (055) 2658269 *Fax:* (055) 2679522 *E-mail:* info@mondolibroeditore. com *Web Site:* www.mondolibroeditore.com, pg 396

Mondria Publishers (Netherlands) *Tel:* (050) 3110505 *Fax:* (050) 3112299 *E-mail:* post@mondria.nl, pg 482

Monduzzi Editore SpA (Italy) *Tel:* (051) 4151123 *Fax:* (051) 4151125 *Web Site:* www.monduzzi.com, pg 396

Gerard Monfort Editeur Sarl (France) *Tel:* (01) 40 27 95 54 *Fax:* (01) 40 27 95 60 *E-mail:* contact@gerard-monfort.com *Web Site:* www.gerard-monfort.com, pg 176

Mongol Knigotorg (Mongolia), pg 470

Monia Verlag (Germany) *Tel:* (06331) 41425 *Fax:* (06331) 41425, pg 259

Editions du Moniteur (France) *Tel:* (01) 40 13 33 72 *Fax:* (01) 40 41 08 87 *E-mail:* clients@ editionsdumoniteur.com *Web Site:* www. editionsdumoniteur.com, pg 176

Monitor-Projectos e Edicoes, LDA (Portugal) *Tel:* (021) 849-48-93 *Fax:* (021) 793-45-51 *E-mail:* monitor@ esoterica.pt, pg 529

Monitorul Oficial, Editura (Romania) *Tel:* (01) 402-2173; (01) 402-2176; (01) 411-5833 *Fax:* (01) 312-0901; (01) 312-4703; (01) 410-7736 *E-mail:* ramomrk@bx. logicnet.ro, pg 536

Edumond Le Monnier (Italy) *Tel:* (055) 64910 *Fax:* (055) 6491200 *E-mail:* monnier@tin.it, pg 396

Monograma Ediciones (Spain) *Tel:* (071) 754124; (071) 712593 *Fax:* (071) 712593 *E-mail:* totem@atlas-iap. es, pg 587

Monoline Ltd (Israel) *Tel:* (08) 9741456 *Fax:* (08) 9741454, pg 1170, 1210, 1236

Ediciones Monserrat (Ecuador) *Tel:* (02) 2222 567; (02) 2505 685 *Fax:* (02) 2222 567 *E-mail:* claudio@uio. satnet.net, pg 1298

Ediciones Monserrate (Colombia) *Tel:* (01) 253 1347; (01) 253 3033 *Fax:* (01) 253 9517 *E-mail:* comercial@edimonserrate.com *Web Site:* www.edimonserrate.com, pg 112

Editorial Monte Carmelo (Spain) *Tel:* (0947) 25 60 61 *Fax:* (0947) 25 60 62; (0947) 27 32 65 *E-mail:* editorial@montecarmelo.com *Web Site:* www. montecarmelo.com, pg 587

Verlag Monte Verita (Austria) *Tel:* (01) 5487080 *Fax:* (01) 5487081 *Web Site:* www.anares.org, pg 54

Editions Paul Montel (France) *Tel:* (01) 46565266, pg 176

A Monteverde y Cia SA (Uruguay) *Tel:* (02) 915 2012; (02) 915 2939; (02) 915 8748 *Fax:* (02) 915 2012 *E-mail:* monteverde@monteverde.com.uy *Web Site:* www.monteverde.com.uy/, pg 772

The Monthly Magazine for Ceramics Co, Ltd (Republic of Korea) *Tel:* (02) 583-2747 *Fax:* (02) 597-8639, pg 438

Montreal-Contacts/The Rights Agency (France) *Tel:* (01) 43 40 06 10 *Fax:* (01) 43 40 02 12, pg 1120

Moon Jin Media Co Ltd (Republic of Korea) *Tel:* (02) 3453-9800 *Fax:* (02) 3453-4001 *E-mail:* mjmedia@ hitel.kol.co.kr, pg 438

Moon-Ta-Gu Books (Australia) *Tel:* (02) 6336 0317 *Fax:* (02) 6336 1319 *E-mail:* wtba@ozemail.com.au, pg 32

Moonlight Publishing (Australia) *Tel:* (03) 5447 8221 *E-mail:* moonlight@impulse.net.au, pg 32

Moonlight Publishing Ltd (United Kingdom) *Tel:* (020) 7376 0299 *Fax:* (020) 7937 8921, pg 724

Moorley's Print & Publishing Ltd (United Kingdom) *Tel:* (0115) 9320643 *Fax:* (0115) 9320643 *E-mail:* info@moorleys.co.uk *Web Site:* www. moorleys.co.uk, pg 724

Mora Ferenc Ifjusagi Koenyvkiado Rt (Hungary) *Tel:* (01) 320 4740 *Fax:* (01) 320 5328 *E-mail:* mora. kiado@elender.hu, pg 320

Ediciones Morata SL (Spain) *Tel:* (091) 448 09 26 *Fax:* (091) 448 09 25 *E-mail:* morata@edmorata.es *Web Site:* www.edmorata.es, pg 587

Editio Moravia-Moravske hudebni vydavatelstvi (Czech Republic) *Tel:* (05) 41220025 *E-mail:* emdl@vtx.cz, pg 125

Moravska Galerie v Brne (Czech Republic) *Tel:* 532 169 131 *Fax:* 532 169 180 *E-mail:* m-gal@moravska-galerie.cz *Web Site:* www.moravska-galerie.cz, pg 125

Moravska Zemska Knihovna (Czech Republic) *Tel:* (05) 41646111 *Fax:* (05) 41646100 *E-mail:* mzk@mzk.cz *Web Site:* www.mzk.cz, pg 1499

Editrice Morcelliana SpA (Italy) *Tel:* (030) 46451 *Fax:* (030) 2400605 *E-mail:* redazione@morcelliana.it *Web Site:* www.morcelliana.it, pg 396

Izdatelstvo Mordovskogo gosudar stvennogo (Russian Federation) *Tel:* 74771 *Fax:* 74771, pg 542

Editions Moressopoulos (Greece) *Tel:* 2103234217 *E-mail:* hcp@photography.gr, pg 307

Moretti & Vitali Editori srl (Italy) *Tel:* (035) 251300 *Fax:* (035) 4329409 *E-mail:* info@morettievitali.it *Web Site:* www.morettievitali.it, pg 396

Bibliotheque Universitaire Moretus Plantin (Belgium) *Tel:* (081) 724646 *Fax:* (081) 724645 *E-mail:* public@ fundp.ac.be *Web Site:* www.fundp.ac.be/bump, pg 1492

Morfotiko Idryma Ethnikis Trapezas (Greece) *Tel:* 210 3230841; 2103221335 *Fax:* 2103245089, pg 307

Morija Sesuto Book Depot (Lesotho) *Tel:* 360204 *Fax:* 360001, pg 1315

Morikita Shuppan Co Ltd (Japan) *Tel:* (03) 3265-8341 *Fax:* (03) 3264-8709 *E-mail:* hiro@morikita.co.jp *Web Site:* www.morikita.co.jp, pg 419

Moritz Verlag (Germany) *Tel:* (069) 4305084 *Fax:* (069) 4305083 *E-mail:* MoritzVerlag@t-online.de, pg 259

Morning Glory Press (China) *Tel:* (010) 68411973; (010) 68433187 *Fax:* (010) 68412023; (010) 68485739 *E-mail:* zh@mail.cibtc.com.cn; zh1@mail.cibtc. cn, pg 106

Morning Star Publisher Inc (Taiwan, Province of China) *Tel:* (04) 23595820 *Fax:* (04) 23597123 *E-mail:* morning@tcts.seed.net.tw, pg 636

Morrigan Book Co (Ireland) *Tel:* (096) 32555 *Fax:* (096) 32555 *E-mail:* admin@atlanticisland.ie, pg 358

William Morris Agency (UK) Ltd (United Kingdom) *Tel:* (020) 7534 6800 *Fax:* (020) 7534 6900 *Web Site:* www.wma.com, pg 1132

William Morris Society (United Kingdom) *Tel:* (020) 8741 3735 *Fax:* (020) 8748 5207 *Web Site:* www. morrissociety.org, pg 1403

Morsak Verlag (Germany) *Tel:* (08552) 4200 *Fax:* (08552) 42050 *E-mail:* morsak@morsak.de *Web Site:* www.morsak.de, pg 259

E J Morten (Publishers) (United Kingdom) *Tel:* (0161) 445 7629 *Fax:* (0161) 445 7629 *E-mail:* timlovat@aol. com, pg 724

Ernst G Mortensens Forlag A/S (Norway) *Tel:* 22941000 *Fax:* 22113040, pg 505

Morula Press, Business School of Botswana (Botswana) *Tel:* (0267) 353499 *Fax:* (0267) 304809, pg 76

Morus-Verlag GmbH (Germany) *Tel:* (030) 89 79 37-0 *Fax:* (030) 75 70 81 12 *E-mail:* mail@morusverlag.de *Web Site:* www.morusverlag.de, pg 259

Mosaico Editores, LDA (Portugal) *Tel:* (021) 681902 *Fax:* (021) 387-10-81 *E-mail:* mosaico@mail.telepac. pt, pg 529

Mosaik Verlag GmbH (Germany) *Tel:* (089) 4372-0; (089) 4136-0; (01805) 990505 (hot line) *Fax:* (089) 4372-2812 *E-mail:* vertrieb.verlagsgruppe@ randomhouse.de *Web Site:* www.randomhouse.de/ mosaik, pg 259

Mosca Hermanos (Uruguay) *Tel:* (02) 4093141; (02) 4011111 *Fax:* (02) 200 0588 *E-mail:* empresas@ mosca.com.uy *Web Site:* www.mosca.com.uy/, pg 772

Moscow University Press (Russian Federation) *Tel:* (095) 229-50-91; (095) 229-75-41 *Fax:* (095) 203-66-71; (095) 229-75-41 *E-mail:* kd_mgu@df.ru, pg 542

The Moshe Dayan Center for Middle Eastern & African Studies (Israel) *Tel:* (03) 640-9646 *Fax:* (03) 641-5802 *E-mail:* dayancen@post.tau.ac.il *Web Site:* www. dayan.org, pg 367

Izdatelstvo Moskovskii Rabochii (Russian Federation) *Tel:* (095) 2210735 *Fax:* (095) 9254274, pg 542

Moss Associates Ltd (New Zealand) *Tel:* (04) 4728226 *Fax:* (04) 4728226 *E-mail:* moss@xtra.co.nz *Web Site:* www.mossassociates.co.nz, pg 494

K & Z Mostafanejad (Australia) *Tel:* (08) 9923 3741 *Fax:* (08) 9923 3741, pg 32

Mostly Unsung (Australia) *Tel:* (03) 9555 5401 *Fax:* (03) 9555 5401 *E-mail:* milhis@alphalink.com.au, pg 32

Library of the Mosul Museum (Iraq), pg 1516

Mosul Public Library (Iraq) *Tel:* (060) 810162 *Fax:* (060) 814765, pg 1516

Motilal Banarsidass (India) *Tel:* (011) 23851985; (011) 23858335; (011) 23854826; (011) 23852747 *Fax:* (011) 23850689; (011) 25797221 *E-mail:* mlbd@ vsnl.com *Web Site:* www.mlbd.com, pg 1306

Motilal Banarsidass Publishers Pvt Ltd (India) *Tel:* (011) 23911985; (011) 23918335; (011) 23974826 *Fax:* (011) 23930689; (011) 25797221 *E-mail:* mlbd@ vsnl.com *Web Site:* www.mlbd.com, pg 338

Motilal (UK) Books of India (United Kingdom) *Tel:* (020) 8905 1244 *Fax:* (020) 8905 1108 *E-mail:* info@mlbduk.com *Web Site:* www.mlbduk. com, pg 724

Motilal (UK) Books of India (United Kingdom) *Tel:* (020) 8905-1244 *Fax:* (020) 8905-1108 *E-mail:* info@mlbduk.com *Web Site:* www.mlbduk. com, pg 1343

Motivate Publishing (United Arab Emirates) *Tel:* (04) 282 4060 *Fax:* (04) 282 4436 *E-mail:* motivate@ motivate.ae *Web Site:* www.booksarabia.com, pg 649

Michael Motley Ltd (United Kingdom) *Tel:* (01684) 276390 *Fax:* (01684) 297355 *E-mail:* michael. motley@amserve.com, pg 1132

Motor Racing Publications Ltd (United Kingdom) *Tel:* (020) 8654 2711 *Fax:* (020) 8407 0339 *E-mail:* mrp.books@virgin.net *Web Site:* www. motorracingpublications.co.uk, pg 724

Motorbuch-Verlag (Germany) *Tel:* (0711) 210 80 65 *Fax:* (0711) 210 80 70 *E-mail:* versand@motorbuch.de *Web Site:* www.motorbuch-versand.de, pg 260

Motovun Book GmbH (Switzerland) *Tel:* (041) 4109515 *Fax:* (041) 4109516 *E-mail:* motovun@bluewin.ch *Web Site:* www.motovun-group-association.org, pg 624

Motovun Co Ltd, Tokyo (Japan) *Tel:* (03) 32614002 *Fax:* (03) 32641443, pg 1124

Federico Motta Editore (Italy) *Tel:* (02) 300761; (02) 30076231 *Fax:* (02) 38010046; (02) 33403275 *E-mail:* info@mottaeditore.it *Web Site:* www. mottaeditore.it, pg 396

Motta Junior Srl (Italy) *Tel:* (02) 300761; (02) 30076231 *Fax:* (02) 38010046; (02) 33403275 *E-mail:* info@ mottaeditore.it *Web Site:* www.mottaeditore.it, pg 396

Mount Eagle Publications Ltd (Ireland) *Tel:* (066) 9151463 *Fax:* (066) 9151234 *Web Site:* www. brandonbooks.com, pg 358

Mountain House Press (Australia) *Tel:* (02) 6688 6318 *Fax:* (02) 6688 6318, pg 32

Mouse House Press (Australia) *Tel:* (02) 93512612 *Fax:* (02) 93512606 *E-mail:* s.juan@edfac.usyd.edu.au, pg 32

Mouseio Benaki (Greece) *Tel:* 2103626215; 210 3612694 *Fax:* 2103622547 *E-mail:* belesioti@ benaki.gr, pg 307

Movement for Multi-Party Democracy (Zambia) *Tel:* (01) 224850; (01) 224851; (01) 224852; (01) 224853 *Fax:* (01) 224855, pg 776

Moxon Paperbacks (Ghana) *Tel:* (021) 665397, pg 301

MPG Books Ltd (United Kingdom) *Tel:* (01208) 73266; (01208) 72008 (ISDN) *Fax:* (01208) 73603 *E-mail:* print@mpg-books.co.uk *Web Site:* www.mpg-books.com, pg 1153

MPG Books Ltd (United Kingdom) *Tel:* (01208) 73266 *Fax:* (01208) 76515 *E-mail:* print@mpg-books.co.uk *Web Site:* www.mpg-books.com, pg 1216

MPG Ltd (United Kingdom) *Tel:* (01483) 757501 *Fax:* (01483) 724629 *E-mail:* print@mpgltd.co.uk *Web Site:* www.mpgltd.co.uk, pg 1175, 1216

MPH Bookstores SDN BHD (Malaysia) *Tel:* (03) 7781 1800; (03) 2398 3817 (customer service) *Fax:* (03) 7782 1800 *E-mail:* customerservice@mph.com.my *Web Site:* www.mph.com.my, pg 1317

MPH Distributors Sdn Bhd (Malaysia) *Tel:* (03) 2938 3800; (03) 2938 3818 *Fax:* (03) 2938 3811; (03) 2938 3817 *E-mail:* customerservice@mph.com.my *Web Site:* www.mph.com.my, pg 1317

MQ Publications Ltd (United Kingdom) *Tel:* (020) 7359 2244 *Fax:* (020) 7359 1616 *E-mail:* mail@ mqpublications.com *Web Site:* gustocreative.dsvr.co. uk/mqp-site/home.html, pg 724

Mucchi Editore SRL (Italy) *Tel:* (059) 374094 *Fax:* (059) 282628 *E-mail:* info@mucchieditore.it *Web Site:* www.mucchieditore.it, pg 396

Anaya & Mario Muchnik (Spain) *Tel:* (091) 393 86 00 *Fax:* (091) 320 91 29; (091) 742 66 31 *E-mail:* cga@ anaya.es *Web Site:* www.anaya.es, pg 587

Mudgala Trust (India) *Tel:* (044) 837257, pg 338

Mudrak Publishers & Distributors (India) *Tel:* (011) 3730818; (011) 3738319; (011) 6416317, pg 339

Verlag Rudolf Muehlemann (Switzerland) *Tel:* (071) 622 53 51 *Fax:* (071) 622 30 04 *E-mail:* wolfau-druck@ bluewin.ch, pg 624

Mueller & Schindler Verlag ek (Germany) *Tel:* (0711) 233204 *Fax:* (0711) 2369977, pg 260

C F Mueller Verlag, Huethig Gmb H & Co (Germany) *Tel:* (06221) 489 395 *Fax:* (06221) 489623 *E-mail:* cfmueller@huethig.de *Web Site:* www.huethig. de, pg 260

Verlag Karl Mueller GmbH (Germany) *Tel:* (0221) 130 65-0 *Fax:* (0221) 130 65-299 *E-mail:* info@karl-mueller-verlag.de *Web Site:* www.karl-mueller-verlag. de, pg 260

Lars Mueller Publishers (Switzerland) *Tel:* (056) 430-17-40 *Fax:* (056) 430-17-41 *E-mail:* info@lars-mueller-publishers.com *Web Site:* www.lars-mueller-publishers. com, pg 624

Verlag Norbert Mueller AG & Co KG (Germany) *Tel:* (089) 5485201 *Fax:* (089) 54852192 *E-mail:* info@vnm.de *Web Site:* www.vnm.de, pg 260

Otto Mueller Verlag (Austria) *Tel:* (0662) 881974-0 *Fax:* (0662) 872387 *E-mail:* onb@onb.ac.at, pg 54

Mueller Rueschlikon Verlags AG (Switzerland) *Tel:* (041) 443040-42 *Fax:* (041) 417115, pg 624

Mueller-Speiser Wissenschaftlicher Verlag (Austria) *Tel:* (06246) 73166 *Fax:* (06246) 73166 *E-mail:* verlag@mueller-speiser.at *Web Site:* www. mueller-speiser.at, pg 54

Mueller und Steinicke Verlag (Germany) *Tel:* (089) 74 99 156 *Fax:* (089) 74 99 157 *E-mail:* info@mueller-und-steinicke.de *Web Site:* www.mueller-und-steinicke. de, pg 260

Mueszaki Koenyvkiado Ltd (Hungary) *Tel:* (01) 1557122 *E-mail:* bcrczis@muzakikiado.hu, pg 320

Robert Muir Old & Rare Books (Australia) *Tel:* (08) 9386 5842 *Fax:* (08) 9386 8211 *E-mail:* books@ muirbooks.com *Web Site:* www.muirbooks.com, pg 1289

Instituto de la Mujer (Ministerio de Trabajo y Asuntos Sociales) (Spain) *Tel:* (091) 363 80 00 *E-mail:* inmujer@mtas.es *Web Site:* www.mtas. es/mujer, pg 587

A Mukherjee & Co Pvt Ltd (India) *Tel:* (033) 2417406; (033) 2418199 *Fax:* (033) 440-8641, pg 339

Mulavon Press Pty Ltd (Australia) *Tel:* (02) 9808 3662 *Fax:* (02) 9552 1608, pg 32

Mulini Press (Australia) *Tel:* (02) 6251 2519 *Fax:* (02) 6251 2519, pg 32

Societa Editrice Il Mulino (Italy) *Tel:* (051) 256011 *Fax:* (051) 256034 *E-mail:* info@mulino.it *Web Site:* www.mulino.it, pg 396

Muller Edition (France) *Tel:* (01) 40 90 09 65 *Fax:* (01) 47 76 33 97 *E-mail:* courrier@muller-edition.com *Web Site:* www.muller-edition.com, pg 176

Mullick Bros (Bangladesh) *Tel:* (02) 280728, pg 61

Mullick Bros (Bangladesh) *Tel:* (02) 8619125; (02) 507434 *Fax:* (02) 8610562 *E-mail:* mullick@bd.com, pg 1291

Mult es Jovo Kiado (Hungary) *Tel:* (01) 316-70-19; (01) 438-38-06; (01) 438-38-07 *Fax:* (01) 316-70-19 *E-mail:* mandj@multesjovo.hu *Web Site:* www. multesjovo.hu, pg 320

Multi-Disciplinary Research Centre Library (Namibia) *Tel:* (061) 206 3909; (061) 206 3051 *Fax:* (061) 206 3050; (061) 206 3684 *E-mail:* tgases@unam.na *Web Site:* www.unam.na, pg 472

Multi Media Kunst Verlag Dresden (Germany) *Tel:* (0351) 8041291 *Fax:* (0351) 8041291, pg 260

Multi-Media Ltd (Trinidad & Tobago) *Tel:* (868) 6288637; (868) 6226774 *Fax:* (868) 6281903, pg 642

Multilingual Matters Ltd (United Kingdom) *Tel:* (01275) 876519 *Fax:* (01275) 871673 *E-mail:* info@ multilingual-matters.com *Web Site:* www.multilingual-matters.com, pg 724

Multimedia Zambia (Zambia) *Tel:* (01) 253666 *Fax:* (01) 363050, pg 776

Multinova (Portugal) *Tel:* (021) 8481820 *Fax:* (021) 8483436 *E-mail:* geral@multinova.pt *Web Site:* www. multinova.pt, pg 529

Ass Italiana Sclerosi Multipla (Italy) *Tel:* (010) 27131 *Fax:* (010) 2470226 *E-mail:* genesi@genesi.org *Web Site:* www.aism.org, pg 396

Multiplex Medway Ltd (United Kingdom) *Tel:* (01634) 684371 *Fax:* (01634) 683840 *E-mail:* enquiries@ multiplex-medway.co.uk *Web Site:* www.multiplex-medway.co.uk, pg 1175

Multiplex Medway Ltd (United Kingdom) *Tel:* (01634) 684371; (01634) 671687 (ISDN) *Fax:* (01634) 683840 *E-mail:* enquiries@multiplex-medway.co.uk *Web Site:* www.multiplex-medway.co.uk, pg 1217

Multiplex Medway Ltd (United Kingdom) *Tel:* (01634) 684371 *Fax:* (01634) 683840 *E-mail:* enquiries@ multiplex-medway.co.uk *Web Site:* www.multiplex-medway.co.uk, pg 1238

Multitech Publishing Co (India) *Tel:* (022) 5118820; (022) 5154206 *Fax:* (022) 5115904, pg 339

Mun Un Dang (Republic of Korea) *Tel:* (02) 7433504; (02) 7433505 *Fax:* (02) 7450265, pg 438

Mundi-Prensa Libros SA (Spain) *Tel:* (091) 4 36 37 00 *Fax:* (091) 5 75 39 98 *E-mail:* liberia@mundiprensa.es *Web Site:* www.mundiprensa.es, pg 587

Mundi-Prensa Libros, SA (Spain) *Tel:* (091) 436 37 00 *Fax:* (091) 575 39 98 *E-mail:* libreria@mundiprensa.es *Web Site:* www.mundiprensa.com, pg 1333

Mundici - Zanetti (Italy) *Tel:* (051) 325347 *Fax:* (051) 326109 *E-mail:* info@zanetti.co.it, pg 396

Editora Mundo Cristao (Brazil) *Tel:* (011) 5668-1700 *Fax:* (011) 5666-4829 *E-mail:* editora@mundocristao. com.br *Web Site:* www.mundocristao.com.br, pg 86

Mundo Medico SA de CV Edicion y Distribucion de Revistas Medicas (Mexico) *Tel:* (05) 5203-8111 *Fax:* (05) 5601-0815 *E-mail:* info@ grupomundomedico.com *Web Site:* www. grupomundomedico.com, pg 465

Mundo Negro Editorial (Spain) *Tel:* (091) 4158115; (091) 4152412 *Fax:* (091) 5192550 *E-mail:* 100623. 1651@compuserve.com, pg 588

Mundo Verlag GmbH (Germany) *Tel:* (0180) 9216350 *Fax:* (0180) 921635-24 *E-mail:* info@mundo-media.de *Web Site:* www.mundo-text.de, pg 260

Munhag-gwan (Republic of Korea) *Tel:* (02) 7186810 *Fax:* (02) 7062225, pg 438

Munich, Edition, Verlag, Handels-und Dienstleistungskontar GmbH (Germany) *Tel:* (089) 349830 *Fax:* (089) 349834 *E-mail:* bzit99e@benezit. de, pg 260

Municipal Library (Cyprus), pg 1499

Biblioteca Municipal de Luanda (Angola) *Tel:* (02) 392297 *Fax:* (02) 33902, pg 1487

Bibliotheque Municipale (Madagascar) *Tel:* (04) 21176, pg 1524

Bibliotheque Municipale de Nancy (France) *Tel:* (03) 83373883 *Fax:* (03) 83379182 *E-mail:* bmnancy@ mairie-nancy.fr *Web Site:* www.nancy.fr, pg 1505

Munoz Moya Editor (Spain) *Tel:* (05) 5653058 *E-mail:* editorial@mmoya.com; ediextre@mmoya.com *Web Site:* www.mmoya.com, pg 588

James Munro & Co (United Kingdom) *Tel:* (0141) 429 1234 *Fax:* (0141) 420 1694 *E-mail:* enquiry@skipper. co.uk; sales@skipper.co.uk (orders) *Web Site:* www. skipper.co.uk, pg 725

Munshiram Manoharlal Publishers Pvt Ltd (India) *Tel:* (011) 3671668; (011) 3673650 *Fax:* (011) 3612745 *E-mail:* mrml@mantraonline.com *Web Site:* www.mrmlbooks.com, pg 339

Munshiram Manoharlal Publishers Pvt Ltd (India) *Tel:* (011) 513841 *E-mail:* mml@mantraonline.com, pg 1306

Uitgeverij Maarten Muntinga (Netherlands) *Tel:* (020) 521 67 67 *Fax:* (020) 626 05 96 *E-mail:* info@rainbow.nl *Web Site:* www.rainbow.nl, pg 482

Munye Publishing Co (Republic of Korea) *Tel:* (02) 3935681; (02) 3935684 *Fax:* (02) 3935685, pg 438

Munzinger-Archiv GmbH Archiv fuer publizistische Arbeit (Germany) *Tel:* (0751) 76931-0 *Fax:* (0751) 65 24 24 *E-mail:* box@munzinger.de *Web Site:* www.munzinger.de, pg 260

Editorial la Muralla SA (Spain) *Tel:* (091) 415 36 87; (091) 416 13 71 *Fax:* (091) 413 59 07 *E-mail:* arcolibros@arcomuralla.com *Web Site:* www.arcomuralla.com, pg 588

Murchison's Pantheon Ltd (United Kingdom) *Tel:* (020) 7374 2828 *Fax:* (020) 7628 6270 *E-mail:* 100450.1105@compuserve.com, pg 725

Murdoch Books (Australia) *Tel:* (02) 8220 2000 *Fax:* (02) 8220 2020 *Web Site:* www.mm.com.au, pg 32

Murdoch Books UK Ltd (United Kingdom) *Tel:* (020) 8785 5995 *Fax:* (020) 8785 5985, pg 725

Murgorski Zoze (The Former Yugoslav Republic of Macedonia) *Tel:* (091) 241340, pg 449

Les Muriers Editions (Spain) *Tel:* (0971) 484 423 *Fax:* (0971) 484 423 *Web Site:* www.lmeditions.com, pg 1126

John Murray (Publishers) Ltd (United Kingdom) *Tel:* (020) 7873 6000 *Fax:* (020) 7873 6446 *E-mail:* enquiries@johnmurrays.co.uk *Web Site:* www.madaboutbooks.co.uk, pg 725

Gruppo Ugo Mursia Editore SpA (Italy) *Tel:* (02) 67378500 *Fax:* (02) 67378605 *E-mail:* info@mursia.com *Web Site:* www.mursia.com, pg 396

Musa Editora Ltda (Brazil) *Tel:* (011) 62-2586 *Fax:* (011) 62-2586 *E-mail:* musaeditora@vol.com.br, pg 86

Giov Muscat & Co Ltd (Malta) *Tel:* 21237668; 21233879 *Fax:* 21240496 *E-mail:* giovmuscat@waldonet.net.mt, pg 1317

Musee d'Art et d'Archaeologie (Madagascar) *Tel:* (02) 21047 *Fax:* (02) 28218 *E-mail:* musedar@syfed.refer.mg, pg 450

Bibliotheque du Musee de l'Homme (France) *Tel:* (01) 44 05 72 03 *Fax:* (01) 44 05 72 12 *E-mail:* bmhweb@mnhn.fr *Web Site:* www.mnhn.fr/mnhn/bmh, pg 1505

Editions de la Reunion des Musees Nationaux (France) *Tel:* (01) 40 13 49 66 *Fax:* (01) 40 13 49 73 *E-mail:* editions@rmn.fr *Web Site:* www.rmn.fr, pg 176

Museo y Biblioteca Municipal (Ecuador) *Tel:* (04) 515738, pg 1501

Biblioteca del Museo Historico Nacional (Uruguay) *Tel:* (02) 95 10 51; (02) 915 33 16 *Fax:* (02) 915 68 63, pg 1553

Museo Chileno de Arte Precolombino (Chile) *Tel:* (02) 6887078; (02) 6972779 *Fax:* (02) 6972779 *E-mail:* bibmchap@ctcreuna.cl *Web Site:* www.precolombino.cl, pg 99

Museo Historico Cultural Juan Santamaria (Costa Rica) *Tel:* 441-4775; 442-1838 *Fax:* 441-6926 *E-mail:* mhcjscr@racsa.co.cr *Web Site:* www.museojuansantamaria.go.cr, pg 115

Museo storico in Trento (Italy) *Tel:* (0461) 230482 *Fax:* (0461) 237418 *E-mail:* info@museostorico.tn.it *Web Site:* www.museostorico.tn.it/editoria_ricerca, pg 397

Museu Maritimo (Macau) *Tel:* 595481; 595483 *Fax:* 512160 *E-mail:* museumaritimo@marine.gov.mo *Web Site:* www.museumaritimo.gov.mo, pg 448

Museum Meermanno-Westreenianum (Netherlands) *Tel:* (070) 3462700 *Fax:* (070) 3630350 *E-mail:* info@meermanno.nl *Web Site:* www.meermanno.nl/, pg 1529

Museum of Victoria (Australia) *Tel:* (03) 8341 7777 *Fax:* (03) 8341 7778 *Web Site:* www.museum.vic.gov.au, pg 32

Museum Tusculanum Press (Denmark) *Tel:* 35 32 91 09 *Fax:* 35 32 91 13 *E-mail:* mtp@mtp.dk *Web Site:* www.mtp.dk, pg 132

Music Book Distributors Ltd (United Kingdom) *Tel:* (0181) 559 1522 *Fax:* (0181) 559 1522, pg 1343

Music Publishers Association (United Kingdom) *Tel:* (020) 7839 7779 *Fax:* (020) 7839 7776 *E-mail:* info@mpaonline.org.uk *Web Site:* www.mpaonline.org.uk, pg 1282

Editorial Musica Moderna (Spain) *Tel:* (091) 416 91 81; (091) 415 37 78, pg 588

Musica Publishing House Ltd (Bulgaria) *Tel:* (02) 877 963; (02) 892 642 *Fax:* (02) 877 963 *E-mail:* musicaph@abv.bg *Web Site:* www.geocities.com/musicapublishinghouse, pg 95

Editions Musicales De La Schola Cantorum (Switzerland) *Tel:* (024) 485 24 80 *Fax:* (024) 485 34 60 *E-mail:* frochaux-schola@bluewin.ch; labatiaz@bluewin.ch, pg 624

Musicoteca Lda (Portugal) *Tel:* (021) 3462653 *Fax:* (021) 3476637 *E-mail:* musicoteca@mail.telepac.pt, pg 529

Musikantiquariat und Dr Hans Schneider Verlag GmbH (Germany) *Tel:* (08158) 3050; (08158) 6967 *Fax:* (08158) 7636 *E-mail:* musikbuch@aol.com; musikantiquar@aol.com, pg 260

Musikverlag Zimmermann (Germany) *Tel:* (069) 978286-6 *Fax:* (069) 978286-89 *E-mail:* info@zimmermann-frankfurt.de; lektorat@zimmermann-frankfurt.de *Web Site:* www.zimmermann-frankfurt.de, pg 260

Musimed Edicoes Musicais Importacao E Exportacao Ltda (Brazil) *Tel:* (061) 244-9799 *Fax:* (061) 226-0478 *E-mail:* cartas@musimed.com.br *Web Site:* www.musimed.com.br, pg 86

Muslim Architecture Research Program (MARP) (Switzerland) *Tel:* (02) 4711228 *Fax:* (02) 4711228, pg 624

Muster-Schmidt Verlag (Germany) *Tel:* (05551) 908420 *Fax:* (05551) 9084229 *E-mail:* info@muster-schmidt.de *Web Site:* www.muster-schmidt.de, pg 260

Musumeci SpA (Italy) *Tel:* (0165) 761216 *Fax:* (0165) 761296, pg 397

MUT Verlag (Germany) *Tel:* (04253) 566; (04253) 672 *Fax:* (04253) 16 03, pg 261

Mu'tah University Library (Jordan) *Tel:* (03) 2372380; (03) 2372399 *Fax:* (03) 2375703 *E-mail:* libdir@mutah.edu.jo *Web Site:* www.mutah.edu.jo, pg 1521

Mutiara Sumber Widya PT (Indonesia) *Tel:* (021) 3909864; (021) 3909261; (021) 3909247 *Fax:* (021) 3160313, pg 352

Mutual Book Inc (Philippines) *Tel:* (02) 796050, pg 515

Muza SA (Poland) *Tel:* (022) 621-17-75; (022) 621-50-58; (022) 629-50-83 *Fax:* (022) 629-23-49 *E-mail:* muza@muza.com.pl *Web Site:* www.muza.com.pl, pg 519

Muze UK Ltd (United Kingdom) *Tel:* (0870) 7277 256 *Fax:* (0870) 7277 257 *E-mail:* colin@muze.co.uk *Web Site:* www.muze.com, pg 725

Editura Muzicala (Romania) *Tel:* (01) 3129867 *Fax:* (01) 3129867 *E-mail:* editura_muzicala@hotmail.com, pg 536

Muzicka Naklada (Croatia) *Tel:* (01) 424 099; (01) 424 019, pg 118

Polskie Wydawnictwo Muzyczne (Poland) *Tel:* (012) 4227171; (012) 4227044 *Fax:* (012) 4227171 *E-mail:* pwm@pwm.com.pl *Web Site:* www.pwm.com.pl, pg 519

Izdatelstvo Muzyka (Russian Federation) *Tel:* (095) 923-04-97 *Fax:* (095) 928-33-04, pg 542

Franco Muzzio Editore (Italy) *Tel:* (06) 3725748 *Fax:* (06) 6868696 *E-mail:* franco@muzzioeditore.it *Web Site:* www.muzzioeditore.it, pg 397

MVB Marketing- und Verlagsservice des Buchhandels GmbH (Germany) *Tel:* (069) 1306-0; (069) 1306-339 (Boersenblatt); (069) 1306-340 (Boersenblatt) *Fax:* (069) 1306-201 *E-mail:* info@mvb-online.de *Web Site:* www.mvb-online.de, pg 261

MVS Medizinverlage Stuttgart GmbH & Co KG (Germany) *Tel:* (0711) 8931-0 *Fax:* (0711) 8931-706 *Web Site:* www.medizinverlage.de, pg 261

MWH London Publishers (United Kingdom) *Tel:* (020) 7263 3071 *Fax:* (020) 7281 12687 *E-mail:* info@mwht.org.uk *Web Site:* www.mwht.org.uk, pg 725

Myanmar Library Association (MLA) (Myanmar), pg 1568

Myrtos Inc (Japan) *Tel:* (03) 3288-2200 *Fax:* (03) 3288-2225 *E-mail:* pub@myrtos.co.jp *Web Site:* www.myrtos.co.jp, pg 419

Izdatelstvo Mysl (Russian Federation) *Tel:* (095) 2324248; (095) 952-5065; (095) 955-0458, pg 542

Mystetstvo Publishers (Ukraine) *Tel:* (044) 235-43-13; (044) 224-91-01 *Fax:* (044) 229-05-64, pg 649

Mzumbe University Library (United Republic of Tanzania) *Tel:* (023) 260-4380; (023) 260-4381; (023) 260-4383; (023) 260-4384 *Fax:* (023) 260-4382 *E-mail:* idm@raha.com, pg 1548

Biblioteca Nacional (Spain) *Tel:* (091) 580 7800 *Web Site:* www.bne.es; www.mec.es, pg 1544

Biblioteca Nacional (Panama) *Tel:* 224-9466 *Fax:* 224-9988 *E-mail:* referencia@binal.ac.pa *Web Site:* www.binal.ac.pa, pg 1534

Biblioteca Nacional de Angola (Angola) *Tel:* (02) 337 317 *Fax:* (02) 323 979 *E-mail:* biblioteca@netangola.com, pg 1487

Instituto Nacional de Antropologia e Historia (Mexico) *Tel:* (055) 5335246; (055) 5332272; (055) 2074559; (055) 2074584 *Fax:* (055) 2074633 *E-mail:* difusion.cdifus@inah.gob.mx *Web Site:* www.inah.gob.mx, pg 465

Instituto Nacional de Ciencia y Tecnica Hidrica (INCYTH) (Argentina) *Tel:* (011) 4295-1503 *Fax:* (011) 4800094, pg 7

Instituto Nacional de Estadistica, Geographia e Informatica (Mexico) *Tel:* 449 910 5300 (ext 5021) *Fax:* 449 918 2232 *E-mail:* ventas@dgd.inegi.gob.mx *Web Site:* www.inegi.gob.mx, pg 465

Instituto Nacional de Estudos e Pesquisa (INEP) (Guinea-Bissau) *Tel:* 21 17 15; 21 44 97; 21 13 01 *Fax:* 25 11 25 *Web Site:* www.inep.gov.br, pg 310

Editorial Nacional de Salud y Seguridad Social Ednass (Costa Rica) *Tel:* 231-2214 *Fax:* 232-7451 *E-mail:* cendeiss@info.ccss.sa.cr, pg 115

Companhia Editora Nacional (Brazil) *Tel:* (011) 6099-7799 (ext 246) *Fax:* (011) 6694-5338 *Web Site:* www.ibep-nacional.com.br, pg 86

Nacionalna i Sveucilisna Knjiznica Biblioteka (Croatia) *Tel:* (01) 616-4111; (01) 616-4008; (01) 616-4129 *Fax:* (01) 616-4186 *E-mail:* nsk@nsk.hr; dpsenica@nsk.hr *Web Site:* www.nsk.hr, pg 1498

Giorgio Nada Editore SRL (Italy) *Tel:* (02) 27301126 *Fax:* (02) 27301454 *E-mail:* info@giorgionadaeditore.it *Web Site:* www.giorgionadaeditore.it, pg 397

Editions Maurice Nadeau, Les Lettres Nouvelles (France) *Tel:* (01) 48 87 75 87 *Fax:* (01) 48 87 13 01, pg 176

Edito Georges Naef SA (Switzerland) *Tel:* (022) 7315000 *Fax:* (022) 7384224 *E-mail:* naef@kister.ch *Web Site:* www.kister.ch, pg 624

Nafees Academy (Pakistan), pg 509

NAG Press (United Kingdom) *Tel:* (020) 7251 2661 *Fax:* (020) 7490 4958 *E-mail:* enquire@halebooks.com *Web Site:* www.halebooks.com/n_a_g_press_files.html, pg 725

National Archives of Malawi (Malawi) *Tel:* 525 240 *Fax:* 524 089; 525 240 *E-mail:* archives@sdnp.org.mw *Web Site:* chambo.sdnp.org.mw/ruleoflaw/archives, pg 1524

National Archives of Malaysia (Malaysia) *Tel:* (03) 6510688 *Fax:* (03) 6515679 *E-mail:* query@arkib.gov. my *Web Site:* arkib.gov.my, pg 1525

National Archives of Namibia (Namibia) *Tel:* (061) 2063874 *Fax:* (061) 2063876 *E-mail:* library@unam. na *Web Site:* www.unam.na/ilrc/library/archives.html, pg 1528

National Archives of Nigeria Library (Nigeria) *Tel:* (022) 415000, pg 1532

National Archives of Pakistan (Pakistan) *Tel:* (051) 9202044 *Fax:* (051) 9206349 *Web Site:* www.pakistan. gov.pk, pg 1533

National Archives of Scotland (United Kingdom) *Tel:* (0131) 535 1334 *Fax:* (0131) 535 1328 *E-mail:* publications@nas.gov.uk; enquiries@nas.gov. uk *Web Site:* www.nas.gov.uk, pg 725

National Archives of Singapore (Singapore) *Tel:* 6332 7909 *Web Site:* www.nhb.gov.sg/NAS/nas.shtml, pg 1541

National Archives of South Africa, Orange Free State Archives Repository, Library/Free State Provincial Archives (South Africa) *Tel:* (051) 522 6762 *Fax:* (051) 522 6765 *E-mail:* fsarch@sac.fs.gov.za *Web Site:* www.national.archives.gov.za, pg 1542

National Archives of Zimbabwe (Zimbabwe) *Tel:* (04) 792 741 *Fax:* (04) 792 398 *E-mail:* nat.archives@gta. gov.zw *Web Site:* www.gta.gov.zw, pg 778

National Archives of Zimbabwe (Zimbabwe) *Tel:* (04) 792741; (04) 792742; (04) 792743 *Fax:* (04) 792398 *E-mail:* archives@gta.gov.zw *Web Site:* www.gta.gov. zw, pg 1555

National Archives Repository Library (South Africa) *Tel:* (012) 323 5300 *Fax:* (012) 323 5287 *E-mail:* enquiries@dac.gov.za *Web Site:* www.national. archives.gov.za, pg 1542

National Assembly for Wales (United Kingdom) *Tel:* (029) 20 825111 *Fax:* (029) 20 825350 *E-mail:* stats.pubs@wales.gsi.gov.uk *Web Site:* www. wales.gov.uk, pg 725

National Assembly Library (Republic of Korea) *Tel:* (02) 788-4101 (english service available) *Fax:* (02) 7884301; (02) 7884193 *E-mail:* question@nanet.go.kr *Web Site:* www.nanet.go.kr, pg 1522

National Association for the Teaching of English (NATE) (United Kingdom) *Tel:* (0114) 255 5419 *Fax:* (0114) 255 5296 *E-mail:* info@nate.org.uk *Web Site:* www. nate.org.uk, pg 725

National Association of Forest Industries Ltd (Australia) *Tel:* (02) 6285 3833 *Fax:* (02) 6285 3855 *E-mail:* enquiries@nafi.com.au *Web Site:* www.nafi. com.au, pg 33

Library of the National Bank (Afghanistan), pg 1487

National Bibliographic Agency (United Republic of Tanzania) *Tel:* (051) 150048; (051) 110573 *Fax:* (022) 2151100 *E-mail:* tlsb@africaonline.co.tz; library@esrf. or.tz, pg 1278

National Book Chamber of Belarus (Belarus) *Tel:* (172) 235839 *Fax:* (172) 235825 *E-mail:* palata@palata. belpak.minsk.by, pg 1252

National Book Foundation (Pakistan) *Tel:* (051) 9261533; (051) 255572 *Fax:* (051) 2264283; (051) 2264283 *E-mail:* nbf@paknet2.ptc.pk *Web Site:* nbf. org.pk, pg 509

National Book Organization (India) *Tel:* (011) 6518378 *Fax:* (011) 6851795 *E-mail:* nbtindia@ndb.vsnl.net.in *Web Site:* www.nbtindia.com, pg 339

National Book Store Inc (Philippines) *Tel:* (02) 6318061; (02) 6318062; (02) 6318063; (02) 6318064; (02) 6318065; (02) 6318066 *Fax:* (02) 6318079 *E-mail:* info@nationalbookstore.com.ph *Web Site:* www.nationalbookstore.com.ph, pg 515

National Book Store Inc (Philippines) *Tel:* (02) 6318061 *Fax:* (02) 6318079 *E-mail:* info@nationalbookstore. com.ph *Web Site:* www.nationalbookstore.com.ph, pg 1326

National Book Trust India (India) *Tel:* (011) 6518378; (011) 23379868 *Fax:* (011) 6851795 *E-mail:* nbtindia@ndb.vsnl.net.in *Web Site:* www. nbtindia.com, pg 339

National Botanical Institute (South Africa) *Tel:* (021) 799 8800 *Fax:* (021) 761 4687 *E-mail:* rpub@nbipre. nbi.ac.za *Web Site:* www.nbi.ac.za, pg 562

National Central Library (Taiwan, Province of China) *Tel:* (02) 2361 9132 *Fax:* (02) 382 1489 *Web Site:* www.ncl.edu.tw, pg 1547

Centre National de la Photographie (France) *Tel:* (01) 53 76 12 31 *Fax:* (01) 53 76 12 33 *E-mail:* centre.national.de.la.photographie@wanadoo.fr *Web Site:* www.cnp-photographie.com, pg 177

National Centre for Language & Literacy (United Kingdom) *Tel:* (0118) 378 8820 *Fax:* (0118) 378 6801 *E-mail:* ncll@reading.ac.uk *Web Site:* www.ncll.org. uk, pg 725

The National Centre for Research into Children's Literature (United Kingdom) *Tel:* (020) 7408 5092, pg 1403

National Centre of Archives (Iraq) *Tel:* (01) 416 8440, pg 1516

National Childbirth Trust Publishing (United Kingdom) *Tel:* (01223) 352790 *Fax:* (01223) 460718 *E-mail:* bpc@bpccam.co.uk *Web Site:* www.bpccam. co.uk, pg 725

National Children's Educational Foundation (Sri Lanka) *Tel:* 578090 *Fax:* 578090, pg 602

National Council for Voluntary Organisations (NCVO) (United Kingdom) *Tel:* (020) 7713 6161 *Fax:* (020) 7713 6300 *E-mail:* ncvo@ncvo-vol.org.uk *Web Site:* www.ncvo-vol.org.uk, pg 725

National Council of Applied Economic Research, Publications Division (India) *Tel:* (011) 23379861; (011) 23379862; (011) 23379863; (011) 23379865; (011) 23379866; (011) 23379868 *Fax:* (011) 23370164 *E-mail:* infor@ncaer.org *Web Site:* www.ncaer.org, pg 339

National Council of Educational Research & Training, Publication Department (India) *Tel:* (011) 6851070; (011) 662708 *Fax:* (011) 6868419 *E-mail:* crc@ giasdlo1.vsnl.net.in *Web Site:* ncert.nic.in, pg 339

Institut National de Recherche Pedagogique INRP (France) *Tel:* (04) 72 89 83 00 *Fax:* (04) 72 89 83 29 *E-mail:* publica@inrp.fr *Web Site:* www.inrp.fr, pg 177

Office National d'Edition de Presse et d'Imprimerie (ONEPI) (Benin) *Tel:* 300299; 301152 *Fax:* 303463, pg 74

National Defence Industry Press (China) *Tel:* (010) 68412244; (010) 6842577 *Fax:* (010) 68413125; (010) 68427707 *E-mail:* ndip@public3.bta.net.cn, pg 106

National Diet Library (Japan) *Tel:* (03) 3581-2331 *Fax:* (03) 3508-2934 *E-mail:* webmaster@ndl.go.jp *Web Site:* www.ndl.go.jp, pg 1520

National Extension College (United Kingdom) *Tel:* (01223) 400 200 *Fax:* (01223) 400 399 *E-mail:* info@nec.ac.uk *Web Site:* www.nec.ac.uk, pg 726

National Federation of Retail Newsagents (United Kingdom) *Tel:* (020) 7253 4225 *Fax:* (020) 7250 0927 *E-mail:* info@nfrn.org.uk *Web Site:* www.nfrn.org.uk, pg 1282

National Federation of Standard Editor's Association in Nepal (NAFSEEN) (Nepal) *Tel:* (01) 212289; (01) 223036; (01) 224005 *Fax:* (01) 223036, pg 1268

National Federation of Standard Periodicals Publishers Association of Nepal (Nepal) *Tel:* (01) 212289; (01) 223036; (01) 224005 *Fax:* (01) 223036, pg 1268

National Federation of Standard Translator's Association in Nepal (Nepal) *Tel:* (01) 212289; (01) 223036; (01) 224005 *Fax:* (01) 223036 ISB-ASS, pg 1268

National Foundation for Educational Research (United Kingdom) *Tel:* (01753) 574123 *Fax:* (01753) 691632 *E-mail:* enquiries@nfer.ac.uk *Web Site:* www.nfer.ac. uk, pg 726

National Free Library of Zimbabwe (Zimbabwe) *Tel:* (09) 69827; (09) 62359 *Fax:* (09) 77662, pg 1555

National Galleries of Scotland (United Kingdom) *Tel:* (0131) 624 6257; (0131) 624 6261 *Fax:* (0131) 315 2963 *E-mail:* publications@nationalgalleries.org *Web Site:* www.nationalgalleries.org, pg 726

National Gallery of Australia (Australia) *Tel:* (02) 6240 6501; (02) 6240 6502 *Fax:* (06) 6240 6427 *E-mail:* information@nga.gov.au *Web Site:* www.nga. gov.au, pg 33

National Gallery of Victoria (Australia) *Tel:* (03) 8620 2212 *Fax:* (03) 8620 2535 *E-mail:* enquiries@ngv.vic. gov.au *Web Site:* www.ngv.vic.gov.au, pg 33

National Historical Institute (Philippines) *Tel:* (02) 590646; (02) 572644 *Fax:* (02) 5250144, pg 515

National House for Publishing, Distributing & Advertising (Iraq) *Tel:* (01) 4251846, pg 354

National Information & Documentation Centre (NIDOC) (Egypt (Arab Republic of Egypt)) *Tel:* (02) 3371696, pg 1256, 1502

National Institute for Compilation & Translation (Taiwan, Province of China) *Tel:* (02) 33225558 *Fax:* (02) 33225559 *Web Site:* www.nict.gov.tw, pg 1139

National Institute of Adult Continuing Education (NIACE) (United Kingdom) *Tel:* (0116) 204 4200; (0116) 204 4201 *Fax:* (0116) 285-4514 *E-mail:* enquiries@niace.org.uk; niace@niace.org.uk *Web Site:* www.niace.org.uk, pg 726

National Institute of Historical & Cultural Research (Pakistan) *Tel:* (051) 218535, pg 509

National Institute of Industrial Research (NIIR) (India) *Tel:* (011) 3923955; (011) 3935654; (011) 3945886 *Fax:* (011) 3941561 *E-mail:* niir@usnl.com *Web Site:* www.niir.org, pg 339

National Institute of Public Administration Library (Zambia) *Tel:* (01) 228802 *Fax:* (01) 27213, pg 1554

National Institute of Science Communication & Information Resources (NISCAIR) (India) *Tel:* (011) 2650141 *Fax:* (011) 26862228 *E-mail:* webmaster@ niscair.res.in *Web Site:* www.niscom.res.in, pg 1138

National ISBN Agency (Bulgaria) *Tel:* (02) 9882811; (02) 9882362 *Fax:* (02) 435495 *E-mail:* nl@ nationallibrary.bg *Web Site:* www.nationallibrary.bg, pg 1253

National ISBN Agency (Mauritius) *Tel:* (0230) 4646761; (0230) 4643959; (0230) 4643452 *Fax:* (0230) 4643445 *E-mail:* eoibooks@intnet.mu, pg 1267

National Library (Bangladesh) *Tel:* (02) 9129992; (02) 9112733 *Fax:* (02) 9118704, pg 1251

National Library (Guyana) *Tel:* (02) 227-4053; (02) 227-4052; (02) 226-2690; (02) 227-2699 *Fax:* (02) 227-4053 *E-mail:* natlib@sdnp.org.gy *Web Site:* www. natlib.gov.gy, pg 1512

National Library (Iraq) *Tel:* (01) 416 4190, pg 1516

National Library (Myanmar) *Tel:* (01) 283332; (01) 275997 *Fax:* (01) 212367 *Web Site:* www.myanmar. com/culture/text/P001.htm, pg 1528

National Library (Thailand) *Tel:* (02) 2810263; (02) 2815999; (02) 2815450 *Fax:* (02) 2810263; (02) 2815999; (02) 2815450 *E-mail:* suwaksin@emisc.moe. go.th *Web Site:* www.natlib.moe.go.th, pg 1278

National Library (United Arab Emirates) *Tel:* (02) 215300 *Fax:* (02) 217472 *E-mail:* nlibrary@ns1. cultural.org.ae *Web Site:* www.cultural.org.ae, pg 1550

National Library & Documentation Centre (Sri Lanka) *Tel:* (01) 685198; (01) 685199; (01) 698847; (01) 685197 *Fax:* (011) 2685201 *E-mail:* natlib@sltnet.lk *Web Site:* www.natlib.lk, pg 602

National Library & Documentation Centre (Sri Lanka) *Tel:* (011) 2698847; (011) 2685197 *Fax:* (011) 2685201 *E-mail:* nldc@mail.natlib.lk *Web Site:* www.natlib.lk, pg 1545

National Library & Documentation Services Board (NLDSB) (Sri Lanka) *Tel:* (01) 698847 *Fax:* (01) 685201 *E-mail:* nldsb@mail.natlib.lk *Web Site:* www.natlib.lk, pg 1571

National Library & Information System Authority (NALIS) (Trinidad & Tobago) *Tel:* (868) 623-6962; (868) 624-4466 *Fax:* (868) 625-6096 *E-mail:* nalis@nalis.gov.tt *Web Site:* www.nalis.gov.tt; library2.nalis.gov.tt, pg 1549

National Library for the Blind (United Kingdom) *Tel:* (0161) 355 2000 *Fax:* (0161) 355 2098 *E-mail:* enquiries@nlbuk.org *Web Site:* www.nlb-online.org, pg 1552

The National Library, Government of India (India) *Tel:* (033) 2479 1381; (033) 2479 1384 *Fax:* (033) 2479 1462 *E-mail:* nldirector@rediffmail.com; nldirector@nlindia.org *Web Site:* www.nlindia.org, pg 1514

The National Library of the Islamic Republic of Iran (Islamic Republic of Iran) *Tel:* (021) 2288680 *Fax:* (021) 8088950 *E-mail:* natlibir@neda.net *Web Site:* www.nlai ir/new/english; www.nlai.ir, pg 1516

National Library 'Ivan Vazov' (Bulgaria) *Tel:* (032) 62 29 15; (032) 62 50 46 *Fax:* (032) 62 47 25 *E-mail:* nbiv@plovdiv.techno-link.com *Web Site:* fobos.primasoft.bg/libplovdiv, pg 1494

National Library of Australia (Australia) *Tel:* (02) 6262 1111 *Fax:* (02) 6257 1703 *E-mail:* www@nla.gov.au *Web Site:* www.nla.gov.au, pg 33, 1557

National Library of Belarus (Belarus) *Tel:* (017) 227-54-63 *Fax:* (017) 227-54-63 *E-mail:* sol@nacbibl.minsk.by *Web Site:* kolas.bas-net.by/bla/nb.htm, pg 1491

The National Library of China (China) *Tel:* (010) 68415566 *Fax:* (010) 68419271 *E-mail:* webmaster@publicf.nlc.gov.cn *Web Site:* www.nlc.gov.cn, pg 1496

National Library of Greece (Greece) *Tel:* 210 3382601 *Fax:* 2103382502 *Web Site:* www.nlg.gr, pg 1511

National Library of Ireland (Ireland) *Tel:* (01) 603 02 00 *Fax:* (01) 6766690 *E-mail:* info@nli.ie *Web Site:* www.nli.ie, pg 358

National Library of Ireland (Ireland) *Tel:* (01) 6030200 *Fax:* (01) 6766690 *E-mail:* info@nli.ie *Web Site:* www.nli.ie, pg 1517

National Library of Ireland Society (Ireland) *Tel:* (01) 603 02 00 *Fax:* (01) 676 66 90 *E-mail:* info@nli.ie *Web Site:* www.nli.ie, pg 1565

National Library of Izmir (Turkey) *Tel:* (0232) 4842002 *Fax:* (0232) 4821703, pg 1550

National Library of Jamaica (Jamaica) *Tel:* (876) 967-1526; (876) 967-2516; (876) 967-2494; (876) 967-2496 *Fax:* (876) 922-5567 *E-mail:* nlj@infochan.com *Web Site:* www.nlj.org.jm, pg 1519

The National Library of Korea (Republic of Korea) *Tel:* (02) 535-4142 *Fax:* (02) 590-0530 *E-mail:* yeolram@www.nl.go.kr *Web Site:* www.nl.go.kr, pg 1522

National Library of Kuwait (Kuwait) *Tel:* 2415192 *Fax:* 2415195 *E-mail:* nccalknl@ncc.moc.kw, pg 1522

National Library of Latvia (Latvia) *Tel:* 7365 250; 7287 620 *Fax:* 7280 851 *E-mail:* lnb@lnb.lv *Web Site:* www.lnb.lv, pg 1522

National Library of Libya (Libyan Arab Jamahiriya) *Tel:* (061) 9097074 *Fax:* (061) 9096380 *E-mail:* nat_lib_libya@hotmail.com *Web Site:* www.nll.8m.com, pg 1523

National Library of Malaysia (Gift & Exchange Unit) (Malaysia) *Tel:* (03) 26871700 *Fax:* (03) 26942490 *E-mail:* pnmweb@www1.pnm.my *Web Site:* www.pnm.my, pg 1525

National Library of Malta (Malta) *Tel:* 21243297; 21236585; 21232691; 21245303 *Fax:* 21235992 *E-mail:* customercare.nlm@gov.mt *Web Site:* www.libraries-archives.gov.mt, pg 1526

National Library of Namibia (Namibia) *Tel:* (061) 2934203; (061) 2934204 *Fax:* (061) 229808 *E-mail:* postmstr@natlib.mec.gov.na *Web Site:* yaotto.natlib.mec.gov.na, pg 1529

National Library of New Zealand (Te Puna Matauranga o Aotearoa) (New Zealand) *Tel:* (04) 474 3000 *Fax:* (04) 474 3035 *E-mail:* information@natlib.govt.nz; reference@natlib.govt.nz *Web Site:* www.natlib.govt.nz, pg 1531

National Library of Nigeria-Research & Development Dept (Nigeria) *Tel:* (09) 2646773; (09) 2346774 *Fax:* (09) 2646772 *E-mail:* info@nlbn.org *Web Site:* www.nlbn.org, pg 1532

National Library of Pakistan (Pakistan) *Tel:* (051) 9214523; (051) 92026436; (051) 9206440 *Fax:* (051) 9221375 *E-mail:* nlpiba@isb.paknet.com.pk *Web Site:* www.nlp.gov.pk, pg 1533

National Library of Scotland (United Kingdom) *Tel:* (0131) 226 4531 *Fax:* (0131) 622 4803 *E-mail:* enquiries@nls.uk *Web Site:* www.nls.uk, pg 726

National Library of Scotland (United Kingdom) *Tel:* (0131) 623 3700 *Fax:* (0131) 623 3701 *E-mail:* enquiries@nls.uk *Web Site:* www.nls.uk, pg 1552

National Library of Somalia (Somalia) *Tel:* (01) 227 58, pg 1542

National Library of South Africa (South Africa) *Tel:* (012) 321 8931 *Fax:* (012) 325 5984 *E-mail:* andrew.malotle@nlsa.ac.za *Web Site:* www.nlsa.ac.za, pg 1543

National Library of South Africa (South Africa) *Tel:* (021) 424 6320 *Fax:* (021) 423 3359 *E-mail:* macmahon@salib.ac.za *Web Site:* www.nlsa.ac.za, pg 1543

The National Library of Thailand (Thailand) *Tel:* (02) 2810263; (02) 281 5999; (02) 281 5450 *Fax:* (02) 281 0263; (02) 281 5999; (02) 282 5450 *E-mail:* suwaksir@emisc.moe.go.th, pg 1548

National Library of the Philippines (Philippines) *Tel:* (02) 525-3196 (Filipiniana); (02) 582271 (Reference); (02) 582660 (Public Documents); (02) 525-1748 *Fax:* (02) 524-2329 *E-mail:* amb@nlp.gov.ph *Web Site:* www.nlp.gov.ph, pg 1535

National Library of Turkmenistan (Turkmenistan) *Tel:* (07) 3632 25 3254 *Fax:* (012) 257 481, pg 1550

National Library of Uganda (Uganda) *Tel:* (041) 233633 *Fax:* (041) 348625 *E-mail:* library@imul.com, pg 1550

National Library of Vietnam (Viet Nam) *Tel:* (04) 8248051 *Fax:* (04) 8253357 *E-mail:* info@nlv.gov.vn *Web Site:* www.nlv.gov.vn, pg 1554

National Library of Wales (United Kingdom) *Tel:* (01970) 632 800 *Fax:* (01970) 615 709 *E-mail:* holi@llgc.org.uk *Web Site:* www.llgc.org.uk, pg 726, 1552

National Library Service (Barbados) *Tel:* 426-1744; 426-3981 (adult's Library); 429-9557 (children's library) *Fax:* 436-1501 *E-mail:* natlib1@caribsurf.com *Web Site:* www.barbados.gov.bb/natlib/, pg 1491

National Library Service (Botswana) *Tel:* 352288; 352397 *Fax:* 301149 *E-mail:* vmaje@gov.bw, pg 76

National Library Service of Belize (Belize) *Tel:* (02) 34248; (02) 34249 *Fax:* (02) 34246 *E-mail:* nls@btl.net; leo2003@hotmail.com *Web Site:* www.nlsbze.bz, pg 1492

National Museum (India) *Tel:* (011) 3018415; (011) 3019272; (011) 3019237 *E-mail:* rdchoudh@ndf.vsnl.net.in *Web Site:* www.nationalmuseumindia.org, pg 340

National Museum & Gallery (United Kingdom) *Tel:* (029) 2039 7951 *Fax:* (029) 2057 3321 *E-mail:* post@nmgw.ac.uk *Web Site:* www.nmgw.ac.uk, pg 726

National Museum of History (Taiwan, Province of China) *Tel:* (02) 3610270-514 *Fax:* (02) 3610171, pg 636

National Museum of the Philippines (Philippines) *Tel:* (02) 5271215 *Fax:* (02) 5270306 *E-mail:* nmuseum@i-next.net *Web Site:* members.tripod.com/philmuseum/index; nmuseum.tripod.com/index.htm, pg 515

Department of National Museums (Sri Lanka) *Tel:* (01) 595366 *Fax:* (01) 595366, pg 602

National Palace Museum (Taiwan, Province of China) *Tel:* (02) 2881-2021 *Fax:* (02) 2882-1440 *E-mail:* service01@npm.gov.tw *Web Site:* www.npm.gov.tw, pg 636

National Portrait Gallery Publications (United Kingdom) *Tel:* (020) 7306 0055 (ext 266); (020) 7312 2482 *Fax:* (020) 7306 0092 *Web Site:* www.npg.org.uk, pg 726

National Public Health Laboratory Services (Medical Department) (Kenya) *Tel:* (02) 717077 *E-mail:* healthmin@nbnet.co.ke *Web Site:* www.ministryofhealth.go.ke, pg 1521

National Publishing House (India) *Tel:* (011) 3274161; (011) 3275267, pg 340

National Records Office Library (Sudan) *Tel:* (011) 784135; (011) 784255 *Fax:* (011) 778 603, pg 1545

National Research Institute of Papua New Guinea (Papua New Guinea) *Tel:* 326 0061; 326 0079; 326 0083 *Fax:* 326 0213 *E-mail:* nri@global.net.pg *Web Site:* www.nri.org.pg, pg 511

National Scientific & Technical Information Center (NSTIC) (Kuwait) *Tel:* 4836100; 4818630 *Fax:* 4830643 *E-mail:* public_relations@safat.kisr.edu.kw *Web Site:* www.kisr.edu.kw/nstic_intro.asp, pg 1522

National Standards Publisher's & Bookseller's Association Nepal (NASPUBAN) (Nepal) *Tel:* (01) 212289; (01) 223036; (01) 224005 *Fax:* (01) 223036, pg 1319

National Standards Wholesaler's Distributor's & Subscriber's Association of Nepal (NASWDISAN) (Nepal) *Tel:* (01) 212289; (01) 223036; (01) 224005 *Fax:* (01) 223036, pg 1268

National Taiwan University Library (Taiwan, Province of China) *Tel:* (02) 3366-2326 *Fax:* (02) 2362 7383 *E-mail:* tul@ntu.edu.tw *Web Site:* www.lib.ntu.edu.tw, pg 1547

Library of the National Technological University of Athens (Greece) *Tel:* 2107721471 *Fax:* 2107721565 *E-mail:* pstath@softlab.ntua.gr *Web Site:* www.lib.ntua.gr, pg 1511

National Trust (United Kingdom) *Tel:* (0870) 609 5380 *Fax:* (020) 7222 5097 *Web Site:* www.nationaltrust.org.uk, pg 726

National Union of Journalists (Book Branch) (United Kingdom) *Tel:* (020) 7278 7916 *Fax:* (020) 7873 8143 *E-mail:* book_branch@hotmail.com *Web Site:* www.nujbook.org, pg 1282

National University of Ireland Galway (NUI, Galway) (Ireland) *Tel:* (091) 524411 *Fax:* (091) 522394 *E-mail:* library@nuigalway.ie *Web Site:* www.nuigalway.ie, pg 1517

National University of Lesotho Library (Lesotho) *Tel:* 340601; 213426 *Fax:* 340000 *Web Site:* www.nul.ls/library/default.htm, pg 1523

National University of Malaysia Library (Malaysia) *Tel:* (03) 8921 3446; (03) 8921 5053 *Fax:* (03) 8925 4890 *E-mail:* puspa@pkrisc.cc.ukm.my *Web Site:* www.ukm.my, pg 1525

Newman Centre Publications (Australia) *Tel:* (02) 9637 9406 *Fax:* (02) 9637 3351, pg 33

Newpro UK Ltd (United Kingdom) *Tel:* (01367) 242411 *Fax:* (01367) 241124 *E-mail:* sales@newprouk.co.uk, pg 728

Newscom Pte Ltd (Singapore) *Tel:* 6291 9861 *Fax:* 6293 1445 *E-mail:* circulation@newscom-mail.com *Web Site:* www.newscomonline.com, pg 552

Newspread International (India) *Tel:* (011) 2331402 *Fax:* (011) 2607252, pg 340

Newton & Compton Editori (Italy) *Tel:* (06) 65002553 *Fax:* (06) 65002892 *E-mail:* info@newtoncompton.com *Web Site:* www.newtoncompton.com, pg 397

Newton Publishing Company Ltd (Taiwan, Province of China) *Tel:* (02) 2706-0336 *Fax:* (02) 2707 3759 *E-mail:* newton00@m517.hinet.net *Web Site:* www.newton.com.tw, pg 636

Next Magazine Advertising Ltd (Hong Kong) *Tel:* 2990-8588 *Fax:* 2623-9278 *E-mail:* subdesk@appledaily.com *Web Site:* www.nextmedia.com.hk, pg 315

Nexus Special Interests (United Kingdom) *Tel:* (01322) 660070 *Fax:* (01322) 667633, pg 728

The NFER-NELSON Publishing Co Ltd (United Kingdom) *Tel:* (020) 8996 8444; (020) 8996 8445 (international enquiries) *Toll Free Tel:* (0845) 602 1937 (customer service) *Fax:* (020) 8996 3660 (international enquiries) *E-mail:* information@nfer-nelson.co.uk; edu&hsc@nfer-Nelson.co.uk (customer service) *Web Site:* www.nfer-nelson.co.uk, pg 728

NGM Communication (Pakistan) *Tel:* (042) 5713849 *E-mail:* ngm@shoa.net, pg 1325

Nibondh Co Ltd (Thailand) *Tel:* (02) 221-2611; (02) 221-1553 *Fax:* (02) 224-6889 *E-mail:* kongsiri@mozart.inet.co *Web Site:* www.uiowa.edu/~lawlib/vendors/nibondh.htm, pg 1336

Nicolaische Verlagsbuchhandlung Beuermann GmbH (Germany) *Tel:* (030) 253738-0 *Fax:* (030) 253738-39 *E-mail:* info@nicolai-verlag.de *Web Site:* www.nicolai-verlag.de, pg 263

Piergiorgio Nicolazzini Literary Agency (Italy) *Tel:* (02) 48713365 *Fax:* (02) 48713365 *E-mail:* info@pnla.it *Web Site:* www.pnla.it, pg 1123

Editura Niculescu (Romania) *Tel:* (01) 2242898; (01) 2220372 *Fax:* (01) 2242898; (01) 2220372 *E-mail:* edit@niculescu.ro *Web Site:* www.niculescu.ro, pg 536

Nie/Nie/Sagen-Verlag (Germany) *Tel:* (07531) 53570 *Fax:* (07531) 64496 *E-mail:* haberkern-imz@t-online.de *Web Site:* www.nie-nie-sagen-verlag.de, pg 263

Niederland-Verlag Helmut Michel (Germany) *Tel:* (07191) 3277-200 *Fax:* (07191) 3277-15 *E-mail:* micheldruck@t-online.de, pg 263

Niederosterreichisches Pressehaus Druck- und Verlagsgesellschaft mbH (Austria) *Tel:* (02742) 802-1412 *Fax:* (02742) 802-1431 *E-mail:* verlag@np-buch.at *Web Site:* www.np-buch.at, pg 54

Niedersaechsische Landesbibliothek (Germany) *Tel:* (0511) 1267-0 *Fax:* (0511) 1267-202 *E-mail:* information@gwlb.de *Web Site:* www.nlb-hannover.de, pg 1508

Niedersaechsische Staats- und Universitaetsbibliothek Goettingen (Germany) *Tel:* (0551) 395212 (Secretariat); (0551) 393079 (chemistry); (0551) 392360 (physics); (0551) 395220 (medicine) *Fax:* (0551) 395222 *E-mail:* sub@sub.uni-goettingen.de *Web Site:* www.sub.uni-goettingen.de, pg 1508

Niedieck Linder AG (Switzerland) *Tel:* (01) 3816592 *Fax:* (01) 3816513 *E-mail:* info@nlagency.ch *Web Site:* www.nlagency.ch, pg 1127

Nielsen BookData (United Kingdom) *Tel:* (0870) 777 8710 *Fax:* (0870) 777 8711 *E-mail:* customerservices@nielsenbooknet.co.uk; helpdesk@nielsenbooknet.co.uk *Web Site:* www.nielsenbookdata.co.uk, pg 728

Nielsen BookData (United Kingdom) *Tel:* (0870) 777 8710 *Fax:* (0870) 777 8711 *Web Site:* www.nielsenbookdata.co.uk, pg 1343

Nielsen BookData Asia Pacific (New Zealand) *Tel:* (09) 360 3294 *Fax:* (09) 360 8853 *E-mail:* info@nielsenbookdata.co.nz *Web Site:* www.nielsenbookdata.co.nz, pg 495

C W Niemeyer Buchverlage GmbH (Germany) *Tel:* (05151) 200-312 *Fax:* (05151) 200-319 *E-mail:* info@niemeyer-buch.de *Web Site:* www.niemeyer-buch.de, pg 263

Max Niemeyer Verlag GmbH (Germany) *Tel:* (07071) 98 94 0 *Fax:* (07071) 98 94 50 *E-mail:* max@niemeyer.de; info@niemeyer.de *Web Site:* www.niemeyer.de, pg 263

Nieswand-Verlag GmbH (Germany) *Tel:* (0431) 7028 200 *Fax:* (0431) 7028 228 *E-mail:* vertrieb@nieswandverlag.de *Web Site:* www.nieswandverlag.de, pg 263

Hans-Nietsch-Verlag (Germany) *Tel:* (0761) 2966930 *Fax:* (0761) 2966960 *E-mail:* mail@nietsch.de *Web Site:* www.nietsch.de, pg 263

Nieuwe Stad Stichting (Netherlands) *Tel:* (033) 4614615 *Fax:* (033) 4635885, pg 482

Nigensha Publishing Co Ltd (Japan) *Tel:* (03) 5210-4703 *Fax:* (03) 5210-4704 *E-mail:* sales@nigensha.co.jp *Web Site:* www.nigensha.co.jp, pg 420

Nigerian Book Development Council (Nigeria) *Tel:* (01) 862269; (01) 862272, pg 1270

Nigerian Book Suppliers Ltd (Nigeria) *Tel:* (01) 22407, pg 1322

Nigerian Environmental Study Team (Nigeria) *Tel:* (02) 8102644; (02) 8105167 *Fax:* (02) 8102644 *E-mail:* nesting@nest.org.ng, pg 501

Nigerian Institute of Advanced Legal Studies (Nigeria) *Tel:* (01) 821752; (01) 821711; (01) 821753 *Fax:* (01) 497 6076; (01) 825558; (09) 234 6505, pg 501

Nigerian Institute of International Affairs (Nigeria) *Tel:* (01) 61 56 06; (01) 61 56 07; (01) 61 56 09; (01) 61 56 10 *Fax:* (01) 61 64 04; (01) 61 63 60 *E-mail:* niia@ric.nig.com, pg 501

Nigerian ISBN Agency (Nigeria) *Tel:* (01) 5850657; (01) 5850649 *Web Site:* www.nlbn.org, pg 1270

Nigerian Library Association (Nigeria) *Tel:* 8055365245 *Fax:* (09) 234-6773 *E-mail:* info@nla-ng.org *Web Site:* www.nla-ng.org, pg 1569

Nigerian Publishers Association (Nigeria) *Tel:* (02) 2414427 *Fax:* (02) 2413396 *E-mail:* nigpa@skannet.com; nigpa@steineng.net; nigpa@freemail.nig.com, pg 1270

Nigerian Trade Review (Nigeria) *Tel:* (01) 961147, pg 501

Verlag Arthur Niggli AG (Switzerland) *Tel:* (071) 6449111 *Fax:* (071) 6449190 *E-mail:* info@niggli.ch *Web Site:* www.niggli.ch, pg 625

Nihon Bunka Kagakusha Co Ltd (Japan) *Tel:* (03) 39463137 *Fax:* (03) 39450908, pg 420

Nihon-Bunkyo Shuppan (Japan Educational Publishing Co Ltd) (Japan) *Tel:* (06) 6692-1261; (06) 6606-5172; (06) 6692-8927 *E-mail:* webadmin@nichibun-g.co.jp *Web Site:* www.nichibun-g.co.jp, pg 420

Nihon Eibungakkai (Japan) *Tel:* (03) 32937528 *Fax:* (03) 32937539, pg 1396

Nihon Igaku Toshokan Kyokai (Japan) *Tel:* (03) 38151942 *Fax:* (03) 38151608 *E-mail:* imlahq@nisiq.net; jmlajimu@sirius.ocn.ne.jp *Web Site:* wwwsoc.nii.ac.jp/jmla, pg 1566

Nihon Keizai Shimbun Inc Publications Bureau (Japan) *Tel:* (03) 3270-0251 *Fax:* (03) 5201-7505 *Web Site:* www.nikkei.co.jp/pub, pg 420

Nihon Rodo Kenkyu Kiko (Japan) *Tel:* (03) 5903-6111 *Fax:* (03) 3594-1113 *E-mail:* jil@jil.go.jp *Web Site:* www.jil.go.jp, pg 420

Nihon-Shoseki Ltd (Japan) *Tel:* (03) 3813-8111 *Fax:* (03) 3818-5665 *Web Site:* www.nihon-shoseki.co.jp, pg 1313

Nihon Shoten Shogyo Kumiai Rengokai (Japan) *Tel:* (03) 32940388, pg 1265

Nihon Tosho Center Co Ltd (Japan) *Tel:* (03) 3945-6448 *Fax:* (03) 3945-4515 *E-mail:* info@nihontosho.co.jp *Web Site:* www.nihontosho.co.jp, pg 420

Nihon Toshokan Joho Gakkai Shi (Japan) *Tel:* (0561) 62-4111 *Fax:* (0561) 63-9308 *E-mail:* muransky@asu.aasa.ac.jp *Web Site:* www.soc.nii.ac.jp/jslis/, pg 1566

Nihon Toshokan Kyokai (Japan) *Tel:* (03) 3523-0811 *Fax:* (03) 3523-0841 *E-mail:* info@jla.or.jp *Web Site:* www.jla.or.jp, pg 1566

Nihon Vogue Co Ltd (Japan) *Tel:* (03) 5261-5081 *Fax:* (03) 3269-8760 *E-mail:* nvsales@giganet.net *Web Site:* www.tezukuritown.com, pg 420

Nijgh & Van Ditmar Amsterdam (Netherlands) *Tel:* (020) 55 11 262 *Fax:* (020) 6203509 *E-mail:* verkoop@querido.nl; info@querido.nl *Web Site:* www.querido.nl, pg 482

Nikas (Greece) *Tel:* 2103634686; 2103633754, pg 307

Nikkagiren Shuppan-Sha (JUSE Press Ltd) (Japan) *Tel:* (03) 5379-1238 *Fax:* (03) 3356-3419 *E-mail:* sales@juse-p.co.jp *Web Site:* www.juse-p.co.jp, pg 420

The Nikkan Kogyo Shimbun Ltd (Japan) *Tel:* (03) 3222-7131 *Fax:* (03) 3234-8504 *Web Site:* www.nikkan.co.jp, pg 420

Nikoklis Publishers (Cyprus) *Tel:* (022) 452079 *Fax:* (022) 360668, pg 121

Nikolopoulos (Greece) *Tel:* 2103607725 *E-mail:* bkyriakid@otenet.gr, pg 307

Nil Editions (France) *Tel:* (01) 53 67 14 00 *Fax:* (01) 53 67 14 90 *Web Site:* www.laffont.fr; www.nil-editions.fr, pg 177

Nile & Mackenzie Ltd (United Kingdom) *Tel:* (020) 7493 0351 *Fax:* (020) 7495 0128, pg 728

The Nile Bookshop (Sudan) *Tel:* (011) 463749 *Fax:* (011) 770821 *E-mail:* mohdelhag@yahoo.com; nilebookshop@hotmail.com, pg 1334

Nilsson & Lamm BV, Algemene Import Boekhandel (Netherlands) *Tel:* (0294) 49 49 49 *Fax:* (0294) 49 44 55 *E-mail:* info@nilsson-lamm.nl *Web Site:* www.nilsson-lamm.nl, pg 1320

Nimaroo Publishers (Australia) *Tel:* (042) 292297, pg 33

Nimrod Publications (Australia) *Tel:* (02) 4957 5562; (02) 4921 5173 *Fax:* (02) 4957 5562 *E-mail:* nimrod@hunterlink.com.au, pg 33

9-12 Club (United Kingdom) *Tel:* (0845) 6039091 *Fax:* (0845) 6039092 *E-mail:* sbenquiries@scholastic.co.uk *Web Site:* www.scholastic.co.uk, pg 1247

Nio Pobjeda - Oour Izdavacko-Publicisticka Djelatnost (Serbia and Montenegro) *Tel:* (081) 45955; (081) 44433; (081) 44474 *Fax:* (081) 52803, pg 548

Nippon Dokubungakkai (Japan) *Tel:* (03) 3813 5861 *Fax:* (03) 3813 5861 *E-mail:* e-mail@jgg.jp, pg 1396

Nippon Hikaku Bungakukai (Japan), pg 1396

Nippon Hoso Shuppan Kyokai (NHK Publishing) (Japan) *Tel:* (03) 3780-3356 *Fax:* (03) 3780-3348 *E-mail:* webmaster@npb.nhk-grp.co.jp *Web Site:* www.nhk-grp.co.jp, pg 421

Nippon Jitsugyo Publishing Co Ltd (Japan) *Tel:* (03) 3814-5161 *Fax:* (03) 3818-1881 *E-mail:* int@njg.co.jp *Web Site:* www.njg.co.jp, pg 421

Nippon Rosiya Bungakkai (Japan), pg 1396

Nippon Shuppan Hanbai Inc (Japan) *Tel:* (03) 3233-1111 *Fax:* (03) 3292-8521 *E-mail:* info@nippon.co.jp *Web Site:* www.nippon.co.jp, pg 1313

Nippon Yakugaku Toshokan Kyogikai (Japan) *Tel:* (03) 38122111 *Web Site:* wwwsoc.nii.ac.jp/jpla, pg 1566

Niro Decje Novine (Serbia and Montenegro) *Tel:* (032) 712246; (032) 712247; (032) 714970; (032) 711256; (032) 711248; (011) 3221476; (011) 342010 *Fax:* (032) 711248, pg 548

James Nisbet & Co Ltd (United Kingdom) *Tel:* (01462) 438331 *Fax:* (01462) 713444, pg 728

Nishimura Co Ltd (Japan) *Tel:* (025) 223-2388 *Fax:* (025) 224-7165 *E-mail:* office@nishimurashoten.co.jp *Web Site:* www.nishimurashoten.co.jp, pg 421

Nissha Printing Co Ltd (Japan) *Tel:* (075) 811-8111 *Fax:* (075) 801-8250 *E-mail:* print-info@nissha.co.jp *Web Site:* www.nissha.co.jp, pg 1211

Nistri - Lischi Editori (Italy) *Tel:* (050) 563371 *Fax:* (050) 562726 *Web Site:* www.nistri-lischi.it, pg 397

Rainar Nitzsche Verlag (Germany) *Tel:* (0631) 61305 *Fax:* (0631) 61305 *E-mail:* rainar.nitzscheverlag@t-online.de *Web Site:* nitzscheverlag.de.vu; www.nitzscheverlag.homepage.t-online.de, pg 263

Niyo Software (India) *Tel:* (020) 546 7296; (020) 400 1603 *Fax:* (020) 400 1603 *E-mail:* info@niyoindia.com *Web Site:* www.niyoindia.com, pg 340

Niyom Witthaya (Thailand) *Tel:* (02) 217661, pg 640

Librairie A-G Nizet Sarl (France) *Tel:* (02) 47 45 50 41 *Fax:* (02) 47 45 50 15 *E-mail:* librairie-a.g-nizet@wanadoo.fr, pg 177

Izdatel'stvo Nizhegorodskogo Gosudarstvennogo Univ (Russian Federation) *Tel:* (08312) 657825 *Fax:* (08312) 658592 *E-mail:* rector@nnucnit.unn.ac.ru *Web Site:* www.unn.ac.ru, pg 543

Agencia de Librerias Nizza SA (Paraguay) *Tel:* (021) 47160, pg 1325

Njala Educational Publishing Centre (Sierra Leone) *Tel:* (022) 228788 *E-mail:* nuc@sierratel.sl; nuclib@sierratel.sl *Web Site:* www.nuc-online.com, pg 550

Njala University College Bookshop (Sierra Leone) *Tel:* (022) 228788 *E-mail:* nuc@sierratel.sl; nuclib@sierratel.sl *Web Site:* www.nuc-online.com, pg 1330

Njala University College Library (University of Sierra Leone) (Sierra Leone) *Tel:* (022) 228788 *E-mail:* nuc@sierratel.sl; nuclib@sierratel.sl *Web Site:* www.nuc-online.com, pg 1541

NKI Forlaget (Norway) *Tel:* (067) 58 88 00 *Fax:* (067) 53 05 00 *E-mail:* post-fj@nki.no *Web Site:* www.nki.no, pg 505

NL SH (Albania) *Tel:* (042) 34207 *Fax:* (042) 34207, pg 1

NMA Publications (Australia) *Tel:* (03) 9428 2405 *Web Site:* www.rainerlinz.net/NMA/, pg 33

NMS Enterprises Ltd - Publishing (United Kingdom) *Tel:* (0131) 247 4026 *Fax:* (0131) 247 4012 *E-mail:* publishing@nms.ac.uk *Web Site:* www.nms.ac.uk, pg 728

Nnamdi Azikiwe Library (Nigeria) *Tel:* (042) 771444 *Fax:* (042) 770644 *E-mail:* misunn@aol.com, pg 1532

The Maggie Noach Literary Agency (United Kingdom) *Tel:* (020) 8748 2926 *Fax:* (020) 8748 8057 *E-mail:* m-noach@dircon.co.uk, pg 1132

Livraria Nobel S/A (Brazil) *Tel:* (011) 3933-2822; (011) 3933-2811 *Fax:* (011) 3218-2833; (011) 3931-3988 *E-mail:* ary@editoranobel.com.br *Web Site:* www.livnobel.com.br, pg 87

Livraria Nobel S/A (Brazil) *Tel:* (011) 3706 1469 *Fax:* (011) 3218-2833 *E-mail:* ary@editoranobel.com.br *Web Site:* www.livrarianobel.com.br, pg 1294

Nobel-Verlag GmbH Vertrieb Neue Medien (Germany) *Tel:* (0201) 81300 *Fax:* (0201) 8130108 *E-mail:* mplatzkoester@beleke.de *Web Site:* www.gewusst-wo.de; www.nobel.de, pg 263

Librairie F de Nobele (France) *Tel:* (01) 43 26 08 62 *Fax:* (01) 40 46 85 96 *E-mail:* librairie.f.de.nobele@wanadoo.fr, pg 177

Nobelinstituttet (Norway) *Tel:* 22 12 93 00 *Fax:* 22 12 93 10 *E-mail:* library@nobel.no *Web Site:* www.nobel.no, pg 1533

NodoLibri (Italy) *Tel:* (031) 243113 *Fax:* (031) 3306370 *E-mail:* nodo.como@libero.it, pg 397

Florian Noetzel Verlag (Germany) *Tel:* (04421) 4 30 03 *Fax:* (04421) 4 29 85 *E-mail:* florian.noetzel@t-online.de, pg 263

Noguer y Caralt Editores SA (Spain) *Tel:* (093) 280 13 99 *Fax:* (093) 280 19 93 *E-mail:* noguer-caralt@mx2.redestb.es, pg 588

NOI - Verlag (Austria) *Tel:* (0463) 224722 *Fax:* (0463) 224744 *E-mail:* office@noisapil.com, pg 54

Noir Sur Blanc (France) *Tel:* (01) 41 43 72 70 *Fax:* (01) 41 43 72 71 *E-mail:* noirsurblanc@noirsurblanc.com *Web Site:* www.noirsurblanc.com, pg 177

Les Editions Noir sur Blanc (Switzerland) *Tel:* (021) 8645931 *Fax:* (021) 8644026 *E-mail:* noirsurblanc@bluewin.ch, pg 625

Nolit Publishing House (Serbia and Montenegro) *Tel:* (011) 345 017; (011) 355 510 *Fax:* (011) 627285, pg 548

Nolit Publishing House (Serbia and Montenegro) *Tel:* (011) 3232420; (011) 3228872; (011) 3231430 *Fax:* (011) 627285, pg 1330

Nomiki Vibliothiki (Greece) *Tel:* 2103600968 *Fax:* 2103636422 *E-mail:* legalinn@otenet.gr, pg 307

Nomos Verlagsgesellschaft mbH und Co KG (Germany) *Tel:* (07221) 2104-0 *Fax:* (07221) 210427 *E-mail:* nomos@nomos.de *Web Site:* www.nomos.de, pg 263

Non (Thailand) *Tel:* (02) 90130, pg 641

Non-Formal Education Centre (Maldive Islands) *Tel:* 324622 *Fax:* 322231, pg 456

Mavis A Noordwijk (Suriname) *Tel:* 479402, pg 603

Editorial Noray (Spain) *Tel:* (093) 280 59 66 *Fax:* (093) 280 61 90 *E-mail:* info@noray.es *Web Site:* www.noray.es, pg 588

Norbertinum (Poland) *Tel:* (081) 5333895 *Fax:* (081) 5341243 *E-mail:* norbertinum@norbertinum.com.pl *Web Site:* www.norbertinum.com.pl, pg 520

Casa Editrice Nord SRL (Italy) *Tel:* (02) 405708 *Fax:* (02) 4042207 *E-mail:* nord@fantascienza.it *Web Site:* www.nord.fantascienza.it, pg 397

Editions Nord-Sud (France) *Tel:* (01) 39 21 90 40 *Fax:* (01) 39 21 90 42 *E-mail:* nord-sud@editions-nord-sud.com, pg 177

Nord-Sued Verlag (Switzerland) *Tel:* (01) 9366868 *Fax:* (01) 9366800 *E-mail:* info@nord-sued.com, pg 625

Nordan-Comunidad (Uruguay) *Tel:* (02) 305 5609 *Fax:* (02) 308 1640 *E-mail:* nordan@nordan.com.uy; pedidos@nordan.com.uy; info@nordan.com.uy *Web Site:* www.chasque.net/nordan/; www.nordan.com.uy, pg 772

Norddeutscher Verleger- und Buchhaendler-Verband eV (Germany) *Tel:* (040) 22 54 79 *Fax:* (040) 2 29 85 14, pg 1261

Nordic Council of Ministers Publications (Denmark) *Tel:* 33960200 *Fax:* 33960202 *E-mail:* nmr@nmr.dk *Web Site:* www.norden.org, pg 1256

Nordica Printing Co Ltd (Hong Kong) *Tel:* 25648444; 25648446 *Fax:* 25656445, pg 1209

Nordik/Tapals Publishers Ltd (Latvia) *Tel:* (02) 7602672; (02) 7602816 *Fax:* (02) 7602818 *E-mail:* nordik@nordik.lv *Web Site:* www.nordik.lv, pg 441

Bengt Nordin Agency (Sweden) *Tel:* (08) 57168525 *Fax:* (08) 57168524 *E-mail:* info@nordinagency.se *Web Site:* www.nordinagency.se, pg 1127

Nordiska Bokhandelns (Sweden) *Tel:* (08) 26 98 09 *Fax:* (08) 25 42 46, pg 609

Det nordjyske Landsbibliotek (Denmark) *Tel:* 99 31 44 00 *Fax:* 99 31 43 90 *E-mail:* njl@njl.dk *Web Site:* www.njl.dk, pg 1500

Norges Landbrukshogskoles Bibliotek (Norway) *Tel:* (064) 96 55 00 *Fax:* (064) 94 76 70 *E-mail:* biblutl@umb.no *Web Site:* www.nlh.no/biblioteket, pg 1533

NORLA (Information Office for Norwegian Literature Abroad) (Norway) *Tel:* 23 27 63 50 *Fax:* 23 27 63 51 *E-mail:* firmapost@norla.no *Web Site:* www.norla.no, pg 1397

Olaf Norlis Bokhandel A/S (Norway) *Tel:* (022) 004300 *Fax:* (022) 422651 *E-mail:* info@norli.no *Web Site:* www.norli.no, pg 1324

Norma de Chile (Chile) *Tel:* (02) 236 3355 *Fax:* (02) 236 3362 *Web Site:* www.norma.com, pg 99

Editions Norma (France) *Tel:* (01) 45 48 70 96 *Fax:* (01) 45 48 05 84 *E-mail:* norma@freesurf.fr, pg 177

Ediciones Norma SA (Spain) *Tel:* (091) 6370760; (091) 6377414 *Fax:* (091) 5470133; (091) 6370760 *E-mail:* norma-capitel@normacapitel.com *Web Site:* www.norma-capitel.com, pg 588

Editorial Norma SA (Colombia) *Tel:* (02) 660 1901 *Fax:* (02) 661 5278 *Web Site:* www.norma.com, pg 112

Cesky normalizacni institut (Czech Republic) *Tel:* (02) 21 80 21 11 *Fax:* (02) 21 80 23 10 *E-mail:* info@csni.cz *Web Site:* www.csni.cz, pg 126

Wydawnictwa Normalizacyjne Alfa-Wero (Poland) *Tel:* (02) 6218750 *Fax:* (02) 6218750, pg 520

Normenausschuss Bibliotheks- und Dokumentationswesen (NABD) im DIN Deutsches Institut fuer Normung eV (Germany) *Tel:* (030) 2601-0 *Fax:* (030) 2601-1231 *E-mail:* postmaster@din.de *Web Site:* www.nabd.din.de, pg 1563

Norsk Bibliotekforening (Norway) *Tel:* 2324 3430 *Fax:* 2267 2368 *E-mail:* nbf@norskbibliotekforening.no *Web Site:* www.norskbibliotekforening.no, pg 1569

Norsk Bokdistribusjon (Norway) *Tel:* 66 84 90 40 *Fax:* 66 84 55 90 *E-mail:* vv@vettviten.no *Web Site:* www.vettviten.no, pg 1324

Norsk Bokreidingslag L/L (Norway) *Tel:* 55301899 *Fax:* 55320356 *E-mail:* post@bodonihus.no, pg 505

Norsk Musikkforleggerforening (Norway) *Tel:* (022) 42 50 90 *Fax:* (022) 42 55 41 *E-mail:* info@mic.no *Web Site:* www.mic.no, pg 1271

Norske Akademi for Sprog og Litteratur (Norway) *Tel:* 22 56 29 50 *Fax:* 22 55 37 43 *E-mail:* ordet@riksmalsforbundet.no *Web Site:* www.riksmalsforbundet.no, pg 1397

Den Norske Forfatterforening (Norway) *Tel:* 23357620; 22 42 40 77; 22 41 11 97 *Fax:* 22 42 11 07 *E-mail:* post@forfatterforeningen.no; forfatterforeningen@online.no *Web Site:* skrift.no/dnf, pg 1271

Den Norske Forleggerforening (Norway) *Tel:* 22 00 75 80 *Fax:* 22 33 38 30 *E-mail:* dnf@forleggerforeningen.no *Web Site:* www.forleggerforeningen.no, pg 1271

Det Norske Videnskaps-Akademi (Norway) *Tel:* 22121090 *Fax:* 22121099 *E-mail:* dnva@online.no *Web Site:* www.dnva.no, pg 1397

P A Norstedt & Soener AB (Sweden) *Tel:* (08) 769 87 00 *Fax:* (08) 21 40 06, pg 609

Norstedts Akademiska Forlag (Sweden) *Tel:* (08) 769 89 50 *Fax:* (08) 769 89 62 *E-mail:* info@norstedtsakademiska.se *Web Site:* www.norstedtsakademiska.se, pg 609

Norstedts Forlag (Sweden) *Tel:* (08) 769 88 50 *Fax:* (08) 769 88 64 *E-mail:* info.norstedts@liber.se *Web Site:* www.norstedts.se, pg 609

Norstedts Juridik AB (Sweden) *Tel:* (08) 690 9100 *Fax:* (08) 690 9033 *E-mail:* kundservice.njab@liber.se *Web Site:* www.nj.se, pg 609

Editorial Norte SA (Argentina) *Tel:* (011) 4921-1440 *Fax:* (011) 4921-1440, pg 7

North Shore City Libraries (New Zealand) *Tel:* (09) 4868460 *Fax:* (09) 4868519 *Web Site:* www. shorelibraries.govt.nz, pg 1531

North York Moors National Park (United Kingdom) *Tel:* (01439) 770657 *Fax:* (01439) 770691 *E-mail:* j. renney@northyorkmoors-npa.gov.uk *Web Site:* www. moors.uk.net, pg 728

Northcote House Publishers Ltd (United Kingdom) *Tel:* (01822) 810066 *Fax:* (01822) 810034 *E-mail:* northcote.house@virgin.net *Web Site:* www. northcotehouse.com, pg 728

Northern Caribbean University (Jamaica) *Tel:* (876) 962-2204-7 *Fax:* (876) 962-0075 *E-mail:* info@ncu.edu.jm *Web Site:* www.ncu.edu.jm, pg 1519

Northern Map Distributors (United Kingdom) *Tel:* (0114) 2582660 *Toll Free Tel:* 800 834920, pg 1344

Northern Nigerian Publishing Co Ltd (Nigeria) *Tel:* (069) 32087, pg 501

Northern Technical College Library (Zambia) *Tel:* (02) 680141 *Fax:* (02) 680423 *E-mail:* nortec@zamtel.zm, pg 1554

Northland Historical Publications Society (New Zealand) *Tel:* (09) 4028244 *Fax:* (09) 4028296, pg 495

Northwestern Publishers (United Republic of Tanzania), pg 639

W W Norton & Company Ltd (United Kingdom) *Tel:* (020) 7323 1579 *Toll Free Tel:* 800-233-4830 (orders) *Fax:* (020) 7436 4553 *Toll Free Fax:* 800-458-6515 (orders) *E-mail:* office@wwnorton.co.uk *Web Site:* www.wwnorton.co.uk, pg 729

The Norwegian Association of Literary Translators (Norway) *Tel:* 22478090 *Fax:* 22420356 *E-mail:* post@translators.no *Web Site:* skrift.no/no/ english/index.asp; skrift.no/no/index.asp, pg 1139

Norwood Publishers Ltd (United Kingdom) *Tel:* (01274) 602454, pg 729

Nosangyoson Bunka Kyokai (Japan) *Tel:* (03) 35851141 *Fax:* (03) 35891387 *E-mail:* mbk@mail.ruralnet.or.jp, pg 421

Editions Mare Nostrum (France) *Tel:* (04) 68 51 17 50 *Fax:* (05) 61 41 15 43 *E-mail:* mare.nost@wanadoo.fr, pg 177

Bibliotheque Louis Notari (Monaco) *Tel:* (093) 30-95-09 *Fax:* (093) 152941, pg 1528

Editorial Noticias (Portugal) *Tel:* (021) 3552130 *Fax:* (021) 3552168; (021) 3552169 *E-mail:* geral@ editorialnoticias.pt *Web Site:* www.editorialnoticias.pt, pg 529

Editorial Noticias (Portugal) *Tel:* (021) 352 2066, pg 1329

Notos (Greece) *Tel:* 2103636577; 2103629746 *Fax:* 2103636737, pg 307

Nour E-Sham Book Centre (Syrian Arab Republic) *Tel:* (011) 4440575 *Fax:* (011) 3324913 *E-mail:* nouresham@mail.sy, pg 1128

Nouveau Cercle Parisien du Livre (France) *Tel:* (01) 43547195 *Fax:* (01) 40518288 *Web Site:* zalber.free.fr, pg 1242

Les Nouveaux Loisirs (France) *Tel:* (01) 49 54 42 00 *Fax:* (01) 45 44 94 03 *Web Site:* www.gallimard.fr, pg 177

Internationale Nouvelle Acropole (Portugal) *Tel:* (021) 827097 *Web Site:* www.acropolis.org, pg 529

La Nouvelle Agence (France) *Tel:* (01) 43258560 *Fax:* (01) 43254798 *E-mail:* lnaparis@aol.com, pg 1120

Nouvelle Cite (France) *Tel:* (01) 40927085 *Fax:* (01) 40921168, pg 177

Les Nouvelles Editions Africaines du Senegal NEAS (Senegal) *Tel:* (08) 211381; (08) 221580 *Fax:* (08) 223604 *E-mail:* neas@sentoo.sn, pg 547

Librairie/Editions Nouvelles Editions Africaines du TOGO (Togo) *Tel:* 21 67 61 *Fax:* 22 10 03, pg 1336

Les Nouvelles Editions Africaines du TOGO (NEA-TOGO) (Togo) *Tel:* (228) 21 67 61 *Fax:* (228) 22 10 03 *E-mail:* ctce@cafe.tg, pg 642

Nouvelles Editions Fiduciaires (France) *Tel:* (01) 46 39 47 13; (01) 46 39 47 00 *Fax:* (01) 47 58 00 63, pg 177

Nouvelles Editions Francaises (France) *Tel:* (01) 44 74 16 00 *Fax:* (01) 44 04 98 03, pg 177

Les Nouvelles Editions Ivoiriennes (Cote d'Ivoire) *Tel:* 21 24 07 66; 21 24 08 25 *Fax:* 21 24 24 56 *E-mail:* edition@nei-ci.com *Web Site:* www.nei-ci. com, pg 117

Les Nouvelles Editions Ivoiriennes (NEI) (Cote d'Ivoire) *Tel:* 21 24 92 12; 21 24 07 66; 21 24 08 25 *Fax:* 21 24 24 56, pg 117

Nouvelles Editions Latines (France) *Tel:* (01) 43 54 77 42 *Fax:* (01) 43 29 69 81 *E-mail:* info@editions-nel. com *Web Site:* www.editions-nel.com, pg 177

Nov Covek Publishing House (Bulgaria) *Tel:* (02) 9863766 *Fax:* (02) 9863772 *E-mail:* newman@mbox. cit.bg; vogda@stratec.net, pg 95

Nov svet (New World) (The Former Yugoslav Republic of Macedonia) *Tel:* (02) 3078-662, pg 449

Editora Nova Aguilar SA (Brazil) *Tel:* (021) 537-7189; (021) 538-1406 *Fax:* (021) 537-8275, pg 87

Editora Nova Alexandria Ltda (Brazil) *Tel:* (011) 5571-5637 *Fax:* (011) 5571-5637 *E-mail:* novaalexandria@ novaalexandria.com.br *Web Site:* www.novaalexandria. com.br, pg 87

Nova Arrancada Sociedade Editora SA (Portugal) *Tel:* (021) 3468837 *Fax:* (021) 3475122 *E-mail:* novaarrancada@mail.telepac.pt, pg 529

Editora Nova Fronteira SA (Brazil) *Tel:* (021) 25 37 87 70; (021) 22 66 51 84 *Fax:* (021) 22 86 67 55 *Web Site:* www.novafronteira.com.br, pg 87

Nova Grupo Editorial SA de CV (Mexico) *Tel:* (05) 5320946 *Fax:* (05) 6050879, pg 465

Editorial Nova, SA de CV (Mexico) *Tel:* (05) 2 80 60 80 *Fax:* (05) 2 80 31 94 *E-mail:* bolind@viernes.iwm. com.mx, pg 465

Novalis Media AG (Switzerland) *Tel:* (052) 6201490 *Fax:* (052) 6201491 *E-mail:* info@novalis.ch *Web Site:* www.novalis.ch, pg 625

Novecento Editrice Srl (Italy) *Tel:* (091) 587417 *Fax:* (091) 585702 *E-mail:* novedi@mbox.vol.it, pg 397

Novello & Co Ltd (United Kingdom) *Tel:* (020) 7434 0066 *Fax:* (020) 7287-6329 *E-mail:* music@ musicsales.co.uk; media@musicsales.co.uk *Web Site:* www.musicsales.co.uk; www.chesternovello. com, pg 729

Novelty Printers & Publishers (Maldive Islands) *Tel:* 318844 *Fax:* 327039 *E-mail:* novelty@dhivehinet. net.mv, pg 456

Novorg International Szervezo es Kiado kft (Hungary) *Tel:* (01) 603790; (01) 603596; (01) 602300 *Fax:* (01) 495581 *E-mail:* info@hu.inter.net, pg 320

Novosti Izdatelstvo (Russian Federation) *Tel:* (095) 265-5008 *Fax:* (095) 975-2065; (095) 230-2119; (095) 230-2667 *E-mail:* novosty@df.ru *Web Site:* www. novosty.ru, pg 543

Novus Forlag (Norway) *Tel:* 2271 7450 *Fax:* 2271 8107 *E-mail:* novus@novus.no *Web Site:* www.novus.no, pg 505

NPA (Neue Presse Agentur) (Switzerland) *Tel:* (052) 7214374, pg 1128

NPS Educational Publishers Ltd (Nigeria Publishers Services) (Nigeria) *Tel:* (02) 2316006; (803) 370-0838, pg 501

NSB Buch- und Phonoclub (Switzerland) *Tel:* (01) 3833622, pg 1246

NSW Agriculture (Australia) *Tel:* (02) 6391 3100 *Fax:* (02) 6391 3336 *E-mail:* nsw.agriculture@agric. nsw.gov.au *Web Site:* www.agric.nsw.gov.au, pg 33

NSW Writers' Centre (Australia) *Tel:* (02) 95559757 *Fax:* (02) 98181327 *E-mail:* nswwc@ozemail.com.au *Web Site:* www.nswwriterscentre.org.au, pg 1390

NTC Research (United Kingdom) *Tel:* (01491) 411000 *Fax:* (01491) 571188 *E-mail:* info@ntc.co.uk *Web Site:* www.ntc-research.com, pg 729

La Nuee Bleue - Dernieres Nouvelles d'Alsace (France) *Tel:* (03) 88 15 77 27 *Fax:* (03) 88 75 16 21 *E-mail:* nuee-bleue@sdv.fr *Web Site:* www.sdv.fr/nuee-bleue/, pg 177

Nuer Ediciones (Spain) *Tel:* (091) 674 92 21; (091) 902 118 298 *Fax:* (091) 655 71 01 *E-mail:* nuer@ pasadizo.com; correo@pasadizo.com *Web Site:* www. pasadizo.com, pg 588

Editorial Nuestro Tiempo SA (Mexico) *Tel:* (05) 5503165; (05) 5503170, pg 465

Nueva Acropolis (Spain) *Tel:* (091) 5228730 *Fax:* (091) 5312952 *E-mail:* oinaes@jet.es *Web Site:* www. acropolis.org, pg 588

Editora Nueva Generacion (Chile) *Tel:* (02) 2183974 *Fax:* (02) 2182281, pg 99

Editorial Nueva Imagen SA (Mexico) *Tel:* (05) 2711980; (05) 2714524, pg 465

Editorial Nueva Nicaragua (Nicaragua) *Tel:* (02) 666520, pg 498

Editorial Nueva Sociedad (Venezuela) *Tel:* (0212) 2659975; (0212) 2650593 *Fax:* (0212) 2673397 *E-mail:* nuso@nuevasoc.org.ve; nusoven@nuevasoc. org.ve *Web Site:* www.nuevasoc.org.ve, pg 774

Nueva Vision (Argentina) *Tel:* (011) 8631461; (011) 8635980, pg 1287

Ediciones Nueva Vision SAIC (Argentina) *Tel:* (011) 4863-1461; (011) 4864-5050 *Fax:* (011) 4863-5980 *E-mail:* ednuevavision@ciudad.com.ar, pg 7

Editorial Nuevo Continente (Honduras) *Tel:* 22-5073, pg 312

Nuova Alfa Editoriale (Italy) *Tel:* (02) 215631 *Fax:* (02) 26413121, pg 397

Nuova Coletti Editore Roma (Italy) *Tel:* (06) 8557981 *Fax:* (06) 8557981 *E-mail:* materiale.web@futura-ge.com, pg 397

Nuova Ipsa Editore srl (Italy) *Tel:* (091) 6819025 *Fax:* (091) 6816399 *E-mail:* info@nuovaipsa.it *Web Site:* www.nuovaipsa.it, pg 397

La Nuova Italia Editrice SpA (Italy) *Tel:* (02) 50951 *Fax:* (02) 50952309, pg 397

Editrice Nuovi Autori (Italy) *Tel:* (02) 89409338 *Fax:* (02) 58107048 *E-mail:* faglier@tin.it *Web Site:* www.paginegialle.it/ednuoviaut, pg 398

Nuovi Sentieri Editore (Italy) *Tel:* (0437) 590308, pg 398

Nuovo Instituto Italiano d'Arti Grafiche (Italy) *Tel:* (035) 329111 *Fax:* (035) 329346 *E-mail:* artigraf@ bertelsmann.de, pg 1170

Nuovo Instituto Italiano d'Arti Grafiche (Italy) *Tel:* (035) 329111 *Fax:* (035) 329322 *E-mail:* info.niiag@arvato. it *Web Site:* artigrafiche.bergamo.it; www.arvato.it, pg 1210

Il Nuovo Melangolo (Italy) *Tel:* (010) 2514002 *Fax:* (010) 2514037 *E-mail:* info@ilmelangolo.com *Web Site:* www.ilmelangolo.com, pg 398

Nurdan YayinlariSanayi ve Ticaret Ltd Sti (Turkey) *Tel:* (0212) 522 55 04; (0212) 513 86 53 *Fax:* (0212) 512 51 86 *E-mail:* nurdan@nurdan.com.tr *Web Site:* www.nurdan.com.tr, pg 646

Andrew Nurnberg Associates Ltd (United Kingdom) *Tel:* (020) 7417 8800 *Fax:* (020) 7417 8812 *E-mail:* all@nurnberg.co.uk, pg 1132

Nusa Indah (Indonesia) *Tel:* (0381) 21502 *Fax:* (0381) 21645; (0381) 22373, pg 352

Nwamife Publishers Ltd (Nigeria) *Tel:* (042) 338454, pg 502

Bokforlaget Nya Doxa AB (Sweden) *Tel:* (0587) 104 16 *Fax:* (0587) 142 57 *E-mail:* info@nya-doxa.se *Web Site:* www.nya-doxa.se, pg 609

nymphenburger (Germany) *Tel:* (089) 2 90 88-0 *Fax:* (089) 2 90 88-1 44 *E-mail:* nymphenburger@ herbig.net *Web Site:* www.herbig.net, pg 263

Nyota Publishers Ltd (United Republic of Tanzania) *Tel:* (051) 25547; (051) 25549, pg 639

Nyt Dansk Literaturselskab (Denmark) *Tel:* 4659 5520 *Fax:* 4659 5521 *E-mail:* ndl@ndl.dk *Web Site:* www. ndl.dk, pg 1392

Nyt Nordisk Forlag Arnold Busck A/S (Denmark) *Tel:* 33733575 *Fax:* 33733576 *E-mail:* nnf@ nytnordiskforlag.dk *Web Site:* www.nytnordiskforlag. dk, pg 133

NZN Buchverlag AG (Switzerland) *Tel:* (01) 266 12 92 *Fax:* (01) 266 12 93 *E-mail:* nzn@nzn.ch *Web Site:* www.nzn.ch, pg 625

O Gracklauer Verlag und Bibliographische Agentur GmbH (Germany) *Tel:* (030) 825 81 39 *Fax:* (030) 826 20 39 *E-mail:* info@gracklauer.de *Web Site:* www.gracklauer.de, pg 1261

Editorial O Livro Lda (Portugal) *Tel:* (021) 7783577 *Fax:* (021) 7783536 *E-mail:* prof@editorialolivro.pt *Web Site:* www.editorialolivro.pt, pg 529

Editorial O Livro Lda (Portugal) *Tel:* (021) 778 35 77 *Fax:* (021) 778 35 36 *E-mail:* prof@editorialolivro.pt *Web Site:* www.editorialolivro.pt, pg 1329

O Neul Publishing Co (Republic of Korea) *Tel:* (02) 716-2811 *Fax:* (02) 712-7392, pg 438

Oak Tree Press (Ireland) *Tel:* (021) 431 3855 *Fax:* (021) 431 3496 *E-mail:* info@oaktreepress.com *Web Site:* www.oaktreepress.com, pg 359

Oakwood Press (United Kingdom) *Tel:* (01291) 650444 *Fax:* (01291) 650484 *E-mail:* oakwood-press@dial. pipex.com *Web Site:* www.oakwood-press.dial.pipex. com, pg 729

OASIS, Producciones Generales de Comunicacion (Spain) *Tel:* (093) 2372020 *Fax:* (093) 2177378, pg 588

Obafemi Awolowo University Library (Nigeria) *Tel:* (036) 230291 ext 2287; (036) 230290 *Fax:* (036) 230291 (ext 2287) *E-mail:* ul@libraryoauife.edu.ng, pg 1532

Obafemi Awolowo University Press Ltd (Nigeria) *Tel:* (036) 230290-9; (036) 230284, pg 502

Obdeestuo Znanie (Russian Federation) *Tel:* (095) 9281531, pg 543

Obelisco Ediciones S (Spain) *Tel:* (093) 3098525 *Fax:* (093) 3098523 *E-mail:* comercial@ edicionesobelisco.com; obelisco@edicionesobelisco. com *Web Site:* www.edicionesobelisco.com, pg 589

Obelisk-Verlag (Austria) *Tel:* (0512) 58 07 33 *Fax:* (0512) 58 07 33 13 *E-mail:* obelisk-verlag@ utanet.at *Web Site:* www.obelisk-verlag.at, pg 54

Oberbaum Verlag GmbH (Germany) *Tel:* (030) 624 69 21 *Fax:* (030) 624 69 21, pg 264

Oberoesterreichische Landesbibliothek (Austria) *Tel:* (0732) 664071-00 *Fax:* (0732) 664071-44 *E-mail:* landesbibliothek@ooe.gv.at *Web Site:* www. landesbibliothek.at, pg 1489

Edition Objectif Lune (Luxembourg) *Tel:* 335230 *Fax:* 335230 *E-mail:* objectif.lune@cmdnet.lu, pg 447

Editora Objetiva Ltda (Brazil) *Tel:* (021) 2556-7824 *Fax:* (021) 2556-3322 *Web Site:* www.objetiva.com.br, pg 87

Obobo Books (Nigeria) *Tel:* (01) 871333; (01) 875389 *E-mail:* obw@infoweb.abs.net, pg 502

Obod (Serbia and Montenegro) *Tel:* (086) 233-331 *Fax:* (086) 233-951 *E-mail:* ipobod@cg.ju, pg 548

O'Brien Educational (Ireland) *Tel:* (01) 4923333 *Fax:* (01) 4922777 *E-mail:* books@obrien.ie *Web Site:* www.obrien.ie, pg 359

The O'Brien Press Ltd (Ireland) *Tel:* (01) 4923333 *Fax:* (01) 4922777 *E-mail:* books@obrien.ie *Web Site:* www.obrien.ie, pg 359

Observatorio Astronomico de Lisboa (Portugal) *Tel:* (021) 361 6739; (021) 361 6730 *Fax:* (021) 362 1722 *E-mail:* info@oal.ul.pt *Web Site:* www.oal.ul.pt, pg 529

Editions Obsidiane (France) *Tel:* (03) 86965218 *Fax:* (03) 86870112 *E-mail:* genevieve.bigant@ wanadoo.fr, pg 178

Obunsha Co Ltd (Japan) *Tel:* (03) 3266-6487; (03) 3266-6000 *Fax:* (03) 3266-6478 *Web Site:* www.obunsha. jp, pg 421

Vydavatelstvo Obzor (Slovakia) *Tel:* (02) 368395 *Fax:* (02) 368395, pg 555

Editions Ocean (Reunion) *Tel:* 588400 *Fax:* 588410 *E-mail:* ocean@guetali.fr, pg 533

Editions de l'Ocean Indien Ltd (Mauritius) *Tel:* 4646761 *Fax:* 4643445 *E-mail:* eoibooks@intnet.mu, pg 457, 1317

Ocean Press (Australia) *Tel:* (03) 9326 4280 *Fax:* (03) 9329 5040 *E-mail:* edit@oceanpress.com.au; info@ oceanbooks.com.au *Web Site:* www.oceanbooks.com. au, pg 33

Oceanida (Greece) *Tel:* 2103806137 *Fax:* 210 3805531 *E-mail:* oceanida@internet.gr, pg 307

Ediciones Oceano Grupo SA (Spain) *Tel:* (093) 280 20 20 *Fax:* (093) 203 17 91 *E-mail:* info@oceano.com, pg 589

Oceanographic Research Institute (ORI) (South Africa) *Tel:* (031) 3288222; (031) 3288238 *Fax:* (031) 3288188 *E-mail:* ori@saambr.org.za *Web Site:* www. ori.org.za, pg 563

Oceans Enterprises (Australia) *Tel:* (03) 5182 5108 *Fax:* (03) 5182 5823 *Web Site:* www.oceans.com.au, pg 34

OCEI (Oficina Central de Estadistica e Informatica) (Venezuela) *Tel:* (0212) 782 11 33; (0212) 782 12 12; (0212) 782 19 45; (0212) 782 10 31; (0212) 793 71 91; (0212) 782 11 67 *Fax:* (0212) 782 97 55, pg 774

Universitetsko Izdatelstvo 'Kliment Ochridski' (Bulgaria) *Tel:* (02) 71288; (02) 71265; (02) 704271; (02) 71151 *Fax:* (02) 704271 *E-mail:* gzisha@ns.sclg.uni-sofia.bg, pg 95

Octagon Press Ltd (United Kingdom) *Tel:* (020) 8341 5971 *Fax:* (020) 8348 9392 *E-mail:* octagon@ schredds.demon.co.uk *Web Site:* www.octagonpress. com, pg 729

OCTAVO Produzioni Editoriali Associale (Italy) *Tel:* (055) 2346022 *Fax:* (055) 2346109 *Web Site:* www.octavo.it, pg 398

Octopus Publishing Group (United Kingdom) *Tel:* (020) 7531 8400 *Fax:* (020) 7531 8650 *Web Site:* www. octopus-publishing.co.uk, pg 729

Octopus Verlag (Switzerland) *Tel:* (081) 252 10 29 *Fax:* (081) 252 94 66, pg 625

Odense Centralbibliotek (Denmark) *Tel:* 66514301 *Fax:* 66137337 *E-mail:* teleservice-bib@odense.dk *Web Site:* www.odensebib.dk, pg 1500

Odense Universitetsbibliotek (Denmark) *Tel:* 6550 2644 *Fax:* 6550 2601 *E-mail:* sdub@bib.sdu.dk *Web Site:* www.bib.sdu.dk, pg 1500

Odeon Book Store Lp (Thailand) *Tel:* (02) 2210742; (02) 2216567 *Fax:* (02) 2253300; (02) 2548806, pg 1336

Odeon Buch- und Phonoclub (Czech Republic) *Tel:* (02) 264100 *Fax:* (02) 24225254 *E-mail:* odeon@comp.cz *Web Site:* www.odeon.cz, pg 1241

Odeon Store LP (Thailand) *Tel:* (02) 2210742 *Fax:* (02) 2253300, pg 641

Editions Odile Jacob (France) *Tel:* (01) 44 41 64 93 *Fax:* (01) 44 41 46 90; (01) 43 29 88 77 *Web Site:* www.odilejacob.fr, pg 178

Anne O'Donovan Pty Ltd (Australia) *Tel:* (03) 9819 5372 *Fax:* (03) 9818 6849 *E-mail:* odonovan@ netspace.net.au, pg 34

Odusote Bookstores Ltd (Nigeria) *Tel:* (02) 2316451 *Fax:* (02) 2316451 *E-mail:* odubooks@infoweb.abs. net, pg 1322

Odysseas Publications Ltd (Greece) *Tel:* 2103624326; 2103625575 *Fax:* 2103648030, pg 307

Odyssey Press Inc (United States) *Tel:* 603-749-4433 *Fax:* 603-749-1425 *E-mail:* info@odysseypress.com *Web Site:* www.odysseypress.com, pg 1239

oebv & hpt Verlagsgesellschaft mbH & Co KG (Austria) *Tel:* (01) 40136-0 *Fax:* (01) 40136-185 *E-mail:* office@oebvhpt.at *Web Site:* www.oebvhpt.at, pg 54

Oeffentliche Bibliothek der Universitaet Basel (Switzerland) *Tel:* (061) 267 3100 *Fax:* (061) 267 3103 *E-mail:* sekretariat-ub@unibas.ch *Web Site:* www.ub.unibas.ch, pg 1546

Oeko-Test Verlag GmbH & Co KG Betriebsgesellschaft (Germany) *Tel:* (069) 9 77 77-0 *Fax:* (069) 9 77 77-139 *E-mail:* oet.verlag@oekotest.de *Web Site:* www. oekotest.de, pg 264

Oekobuch Verlag & Versand GmbH (Germany) *Tel:* (07633) 50613 *Fax:* (07633) 50870 *E-mail:* oekobuch@t-online.de *Web Site:* www. oekobuch.de, pg 264

Oekotopia Verlag, Wolfgang Hoffman GmbH & Co KG (Germany) *Tel:* (0251) 48198-0 *Fax:* (0251) 48198-29 *E-mail:* info@oekotopia-verlag.de *Web Site:* www. oekotopia-verlag.de, pg 264

Oekumenischer Verlag Dr R-F Edel (Germany) *Tel:* (02351) 51547 *Fax:* (02351) 568908, pg 264

OEMF srl International (Italy) *Tel:* (02) 5749521 *Fax:* (02) 33210200 *E-mail:* info@mason.it *Web Site:* www.oemf.it, pg 398

Martina M Oepping Literary Agency (Germany) *Tel:* (069) 59790011 *Fax:* (069) 59790012 *E-mail:* litag@oepping.de *Web Site:* www.oepping.de, pg 1122

Oertel & Sporer GmbH & Co (Germany) *Tel:* (07121) 302 555; (07121) 302 552 *Fax:* (07121) 302 558, pg 264

Oertel & Sporer GmbH & Co (Germany) *Tel:* (07121) 302555 *Fax:* (07121) 302558, pg 1166, 1207

Oesch Verlag AG (Switzerland) *Tel:* (01) 305 70 60 *Fax:* (01) 305 70 66 *E-mail:* info@oeschverlag.ch *Web Site:* www.oeschverlag.ch, pg 625

Verlag Oesterreich GmbH (Austria) *Tel:* (01) 61077-0 *Fax:* (01) 61077-419 *E-mail:* office@verlagoesterreich. at *Web Site:* www.verlagoesterreich.at, pg 54

Oesterreichische Gesellschaft fuer Dokumentation und Information (OGDI) (Austria) *Tel:* (01) 31336 5107 *Fax:* (01) 31336 905107 *E-mail:* oegdi@termnet.at *Web Site:* www.oegdi.at, pg 1558

Oesterreichische Gesellschaft fuer Literatur (Austria) *Tel:* (01) 5338159 *Fax:* (01) 5334067 *E-mail:* office@ ogl.at *Web Site:* www.ogl.at, pg 1390

Oesterreichische Staatsdruckerei (Austria) *Tel:* (01) 61077-0 *Fax:* (01) 61077-419 *E-mail:* office@ verlagoesterreich.at, pg 54

Oesterreichische Verlagsanstalt GmbH (Austria) *Tel:* (01) 5445641-46 *Fax:* (01) 5445641-46 *E-mail:* prepress@agens-werk.at, pg 55

Verlag der Oesterreichischen Akademie der Wissenschaften (OEAW) (Austria) *Tel:* (01) 512 9050; (01) 51581-3401 *Fax:* (01) 51581-3400 *E-mail:* verlag@oeaw.ac.at *Web Site:* verlag.oeaw.ac.at, pg 55

Verlag des Oesterreichischen Gewerkschaftsbundes GmbH (Austria) *Tel:* (01) 662 32 96 *Fax:* (01) 662 32 96-63 85 *E-mail:* office@oegbverlag.at *Web Site:* www.verlag-oegb.co.at, pg 55

Oesterreichischer Agrarverlag, Druck- und Verlags-GmbH (Austria) *Tel:* (02235) 404-440 *Fax:* (02235) 404-459 *E-mail:* buch@agrarverlag.at *Web Site:* www.agrarverlag.at, pg 55

Oesterreichischer Bundesverlag Gmbh (Austria) *Tel:* (01) 5262091-0 *Fax:* (01) 526209111 *E-mail:* oebz@oebv.co.at *Web Site:* www.oebv.at, pg 55

Oesterreichischer Gewerbeverlag GmbH (Austria) *Tel:* (01) 535 9404 *Fax:* (01) 5330768030 *E-mail:* gewerbeverlag@tbxa.telecom.at, pg 55

Oesterreichischer Jagd -und Fischerei-Verlag (Austria) *Tel:* (01) 405 16 36-39 *Fax:* (01) 405 16 36-36 *E-mail:* verlag@jagd.at *Web Site:* www.jagd.at, pg 55

Oesterreichischer Kunst und Kulturverlag (Austria) *Tel:* (01) 587 85 51 *Fax:* (01) 587 85 52 *E-mail:* office@kunstundkulturverlag.at, pg 55

Oesterreichischer Ueberatzer- und Dolmetscherverband Universitas (Austria) *Tel:* (01) 368 60 60 *Fax:* (01) 368 60 08 *E-mail:* info@universitas.org *Web Site:* www.universitas.org, pg 1137

Oesterreichisches Institut fuer Bibliotheksforschung, Dokumentations- und Informationswesen (Austria), pg 1558

Oesterreichisches Katholisches Bibelwerk (Austria) *Tel:* (02243) 2938 *Fax:* (02243) 2939, pg 55

Oesterreichisches Staatsarchiv (Austria) *Tel:* (01) 79540 201 *Fax:* (01) 79540 109 *E-mail:* gdpost@oesta.gv.at *Web Site:* www.oesta.gv.at, pg 1490

Verlag Friedrich Oetinger GmbH (Germany) *Tel:* (040) 607909-02 *Fax:* (040) 6072326 *E-mail:* oetinger@vsg-hamburg.de *Web Site:* www.oetinger.de, pg 264

Dr Oetker Verlag KG (Germany) *Tel:* (0521) 521 155-0 *Fax:* (0521) 521 155-2995 *E-mail:* presse@oetker.de *Web Site:* www.oetker-gruppe.de, pg 264

Off the Shelf Publishing (Australia) *Tel:* (02) 9560 3058 *Fax:* (02) 9564 0758 *E-mail:* offshelf@ozemail.com.au, pg 34

Verlag Offene Worte (Germany) *Tel:* (040) 79713-03 *Fax:* (040) 79713-324 *E-mail:* vertrieb@koehler-mittler.de *Web Site:* www.koehler-mittler.de, pg 264

Office des Publications Officielles des Communautes Europeennes (Luxembourg) *Tel:* 292942001 *Fax:* 292942700, pg 448

Office des Publications Officielles des Communautes Europeennes (Luxembourg) *Tel:* 2929-1 *Fax:* 292944619 *E-mail:* opoce-info-info@cec.eu.int *Web Site:* www.eur-op.eu.int, pg 1266

Office du Livre SA (Buchhaus AG) (Switzerland) *Tel:* (026) 4675111 *Fax:* (026) 4675466 *E-mail:* information@olf.ch *Web Site:* www.olf.ch, pg 625

Office International de Documentation et Librairie (OFFILIB) (France) *Tel:* (01) 55 42 73 00 *Fax:* (01) 43 29 91 67 *E-mail:* info@offilib.com *Web Site:* www.offilib.com, pg 1300

Office International des Epizooties (France) *Tel:* (01) 44 15 18 88 *Fax:* (01) 42 67 09 87 *E-mail:* oie@oie.int *Web Site:* www.oie.int, pg 1259

Office Marocain D'Annonces-OMA (Morocco) *Tel:* (02) 234891; (02) 232342 *Fax:* (02) 234892, pg 471

Office national des Libraires Populaires (ONLP) (Congo) *Tel:* 833 485 *Fax:* 831 879, pg 1297

Office National du Tourisme (ONT) (Burundi) *Tel:* 229 390 *Fax:* 229 390 *E-mail:* ontbur@cbinf.com, pg 1495

Office of Libraries and Archives, Papua, New Guinea (Papua New Guinea) *Tel:* 325-6200 *Fax:* 325-1331 *E-mail:* ola@datec.com.pg, pg 1534

Office of Libraries & Archives, Papua New Guinea (Papua New Guinea) *Tel:* 325-6200 *Fax:* 325-1331 *E-mail:* ola@datec.com.pg, pg 511

The Office of Public Works, Publications Branch (OPW) (Ireland) *Tel:* (01) 6476000 *Fax:* (01) 6610747 *E-mail:* info@opw.ie *Web Site:* www.opw.ie, pg 1122

Officina Edizioni di Aldo Quinti (Italy) *Tel:* (06) 316336 *Fax:* (06) 65740514 *E-mail:* officinaedizioni@yahoo.com, pg 398

Officina Nova Konyvek (Hungary) *Tel:* (01) 557282 *Fax:* (01) 1686674, pg 320

Ediciones Offo, SA (Spain) *Tel:* (091) 5514214 *Fax:* (091) 5010699, pg 589

Offo SL (Spain) *Tel:* (01) 5514214 *Fax:* (01) 5010699, pg 1151

OGC Michele Broutta Editeur (France) *Tel:* (01) 45779371 *Fax:* (01) 40590432, pg 178

Ogunsanya Press, Publishers and Bookstores Ltd (Nigeria) *Tel:* (022) 310924, pg 502

Oguz Yayinlari (Turkey) *Tel:* (0212) 5264745; (0212) 5113418 *Fax:* (0212) 5114695, pg 646

Ohmsa (Republic of Korea) *Tel:* (02) 776-4868-9 *Fax:* (02) 779-6757 *E-mail:* ohm@ohm.co.kr *Web Site:* www.ohm.co.kr, pg 438

Ohmsha Ltd (Japan) *Tel:* (03) 3233-0641 *Fax:* (03) 3233-2426 *E-mail:* kaigaika@ohmsha.co.jp *Web Site:* www.ohmsha.co.jp, pg 421

Oidium Books (Australia) *Tel:* (052) 757045 *E-mail:* tecnilab@ozemail.com.au, pg 34

Oikos (Argentina) *Tel:* (011) 4951-9489; (011) 4951-8129 *E-mail:* postmaster@atlas.edu.ar, pg 8

Oikos-Tau SA Ediciones (Spain) *Tel:* (093) 7590791 *Fax:* (093) 7506825, pg 589

Oilfield Publications Ltd (United Kingdom) *Tel:* (01531) 634563 *Fax:* (01531) 634239; (01531) 633744 *E-mail:* opl@oilpubs.com *Web Site:* www.oilpubs.com, pg 729

Oireachtas Library (Ireland) *Tel:* (01) 618 3412 *Fax:* (01) 661 5583 *Web Site:* www.irlgov.ie/oireachtas, pg 1517

Editions de l'Oiseau-Lyre SAM (Monaco) *Tel:* (093) 300944 *Fax:* (093) 301915 *E-mail:* oiseaulyre@monaco377.com *Web Site:* www.oiseaulyre.com, pg 470

Ediciones Ojeda (Spain) *Tel:* (093) 2370009 *Fax:* (093) 4159845 *E-mail:* lib.europa@mx3.redestb.es, pg 589

Editions Okad (Morocco) *Tel:* (07) 796970; (07) 796971; (07) 796973 *Fax:* (07) 798556 *E-mail:* okad@wanadoo.net.ma, pg 471

Okapi Centre de Diffusion (The Democratic Republic of the Congo) *Tel:* (012) 31457, pg 1297

OKKER Kiado (Hungary) *Tel:* (01) 3324587, pg 320

Okoshko Ltd Publishers (Izdatelstvo) (Russian Federation) *Tel:* (095) 2450998 *Fax:* (095) 2053424, pg 543

Oktagon Verlagsgesellschaft mbH (Germany) *Tel:* (0221) 2059653-54 *Fax:* (0221) 2059660 *E-mail:* oktagon@buchhandlung-walterkoenig.de, pg 264

Forlaget Oktober A/S (Norway) *Tel:* (022) 23 35 46 20 *Fax:* (022) 23 35 46 21 *E-mail:* oktober@oktober.no *Web Site:* www.oktober.no, pg 505

Old Pond Publishing (United Kingdom) *Tel:* (01473) 238200 *Fax:* (01473) 238201 *E-mail:* info@oldpond.com *Web Site:* www.oldpond.com, pg 729

Old Vicarage Publications (United Kingdom) *Tel:* (01260) 279276 *Fax:* (01260) 298913, pg 729

Oldcastle Books Ltd (United Kingdom) *Tel:* (01582) 761264 *Fax:* (01582) 761264 *E-mail:* info@noexit.co.uk *Web Site:* www.noexit.co.uk, pg 730

Verlag Oldenbourg (Austria) *Tel:* (01) 712 62 58 *Fax:* (01) 712 62 58-19 *E-mail:* office@oldenbourg.at, pg 55

R Oldenbourg Verlag GmbH (Germany) *Tel:* (089) 45 05 10; (089) 45 05 12 04 *Fax:* (089) 45051333 (Zeitschriften); (089) 4505200 (Schulbuch); (089) 4505333 (Fachbuch), pg 264

Ole Brumm (Norway) *Tel:* 24051010 *Fax:* 24051099 *E-mail:* post@damm.no *Web Site:* www.dammbokklubb.no, pg 1245

The Oleander Press (United Kingdom) *Tel:* (01223) 357768 *E-mail:* editor@oleanderpress.com *Web Site:* oleanderpress.com, pg 730

David O'Leary Literary Agents (United Kingdom) *Tel:* (020) 7229 1623 *Fax:* (020) 7727 9624 *E-mail:* d.o'leary@virgin.net, pg 1133

Olho D'Agua Comercio e Servicos Editoriais Ltda (Brazil) *Tel:* (011) 2631287 *Fax:* (011) 2631287 *E-mail:* editora@olhodaguo.com.br, pg 87

Editoriale Olimpia SpA (Italy) *Tel:* (055) 30321 *Fax:* (055) 3032280 *E-mail:* editore@edolimpia.it; moie@edolimpia.it *Web Site:* www.edolimpia.it, pg 398

Ediciones Olimpic, SL (Spain) *Tel:* (093) 2382864 *E-mail:* edolimpic@worldonline.es, pg 589

Olion Publishers (Estonia) *Tel:* 655 0175 *Fax:* 655 0173 *E-mail:* olion@not.ee, pg 139

Edizioni Olivares (Italy) *Tel:* (02) 76001753 *Fax:* (02) 76002579 *E-mail:* olivares@edizioniolivares.com *Web Site:* www.edizioniolivares.com, pg 398

Oliveira Rocha-Comercio e Servics Ltda Dialetica (Brazil) *Tel:* (011) 2845527; (011) 2886440 *Fax:* (011) 2845362; (011) 2842096 *E-mail:* dialetic@virtual.net.com.br, pg 87

Editions Olizane (Switzerland) *Tel:* (022) 328 52 52 *Fax:* (022) 328 57 96 *E-mail:* guides@olizane.ch *Web Site:* www.olizane.ch, pg 625

Olkos Editions (Greece) *Tel:* 2103621379 *Fax:* 2103625576 *Web Site:* www.olkos.gr, pg 1303

Ollif Publishing Co (Australia) *Tel:* (02) 9477-3496, pg 34

Edition Olms AG (Switzerland) *Tel:* (01) 2445030 *Fax:* (01) 2445031 *E-mail:* info@edition-olms.com *Web Site:* www.edition-olms.com, pg 625

Georg Olms Verlag AG (Germany) *Tel:* (05121) 15010 *Fax:* (05121) 150150; (05121) 32007 *E-mail:* info@olms.de *Web Site:* www.olms.de, pg 264

Leo S Olschki (Italy) *Tel:* (055) 6530684 *Fax:* (055) 6530214 *E-mail:* celso@olschki.it *Web Site:* www.olschki.it, pg 398

Nakladatelstvi Olympia AS (Czech Republic) *Tel:* (02) 224 810 146 *Fax:* (02) 222 312 137 *E-mail:* olympia@mbox.vol.cz, pg 126

O'Mahony & Co Ltd (Ireland) *Tel:* (061) 418155 *Fax:* (061) 414558 *E-mail:* info@omahonys.ie *Web Site:* www.omahonys.ie, pg 1309

Michael O'Mara Books Ltd (United Kingdom) *Tel:* (020) 7720 8643 *Fax:* (020) 7627 8953 (Editorial); (020) 7627 4900 (Foreign Sales) *E-mail:* enquiries@michaelomarabooks.com *Web Site:* www.michaelomarabooks.com, pg 730

Omdurman Islamic University (Sudan) *Tel:* 784348; 784365; 554272 *Fax:* 775253 *Web Site:* www.sudanembassy.org/contemporarylooks/umdurman.htm, pg 1545

Omega Boek BV (Netherlands) *Tel:* (020) 690 59 97 *Fax:* (020) 695 74 28 *E-mail:* info@omegaboek.nl, pg 483

Omega Distributors Ltd (New Zealand) *Tel:* (09) 2570081 *Fax:* (09) 2570082 *E-mail:* books@ omegavision.co.nz *Web Site:* www.omegavision.co. nz/omega.html, pg 1321

Ediciones Omega SA (Spain) *Tel:* (093) 2010599; (093) 2013807; (093) 2012144 *Fax:* (093) 2097362 *E-mail:* omega@ediciones-omega.es *Web Site:* www. ediciones-omega.es, pg 589

Omilos Pnevmatikis Ananeoseos (Cyprus) *Tel:* (022) 772898 *Fax:* (022) 311931, pg 121

Omnibus Books (Australia) *Tel:* (08) 8363 2333 *Fax:* (08) 8363 1420 *E-mail:* omnibus@scholastic. com.au, pg 34

Editions Omnibus (France) *Tel:* (01) 44 16 05 00 *Fax:* (01) 44 16 05 18 *E-mail:* omnibus@psb-editions. com *Web Site:* www.omnibus.tm.fr, pg 178

Omnibus Press (United Kingdom) *Tel:* (020) 7434 0066 *Fax:* (020) 7287 6329 *E-mail:* music@musicsales.co. uk *Web Site:* www.musicsales.com, pg 730

Omnicon, SA (Spain) *Tel:* (091) 527 82 49 *Fax:* (091) 528 13 48 *E-mail:* omnicon@skios.es *Web Site:* www. omnicon.es, pg 589

Omnipress Praha (Czech Republic) *Tel:* (02) 61211406 *Fax:* (02) 61211856 *E-mail:* dcf.clock@omnipress.cz *Web Site:* www.omnipress.cz, pg 126

Omsons Publications (India) *Tel:* (011) 5412452 *Fax:* (011) 3289353 *E-mail:* omsons@satyam.net.in, pg 340

Omun Gak (Republic of Korea) *Tel:* (02) 3453-8278 *Fax:* (02) 508-5210, pg 438

On Stream Publications Ltd (Ireland) *Tel:* (021) 4385798 *Fax:* (021) 4385798 *E-mail:* info@onstream.ie *Web Site:* www.onstream.ie, pg 359

On The Stone (Australia) *Tel:* (02) 6334 3442 *Fax:* (02) 6334 3009 *Web Site:* www.onthestone.com.au, pg 34

Oncken Verlag KG (Germany) *Tel:* (02302) 930 93 800 *Fax:* (02302) 930 93 801 *E-mail:* info@brockhaus-verlag.de *Web Site:* www.brockhaus-verlag.de, pg 265

Ondorisha Publishers Ltd (Japan) *Tel:* (03) 3268-3101 *Fax:* (03) 3235-3530, pg 421

Oneindige Verhaal, t bvba (Belgium) *Tel:* (03) 7765225 *Fax:* (03) 7765225 *E-mail:* oneindigeverhaal@ boekenbank.be, pg 1292

Oneworld Publications (United Kingdom) *Tel:* (01865) 310597 *Fax:* (01865) 310598 *E-mail:* info@ oneworld-publications.com *Web Site:* www.oneworld-publications.com, pg 730

Ongaku No Tomo Sha Corporation (Japan) *Tel:* (03) 3235-2091 *Fax:* (03) 3235-2148 *E-mail:* home@ ongakunotomo.co.jp *Web Site:* www.ongakunotomo. co.jp, pg 421

Onibon-Oje Book Club (Nigeria) *Tel:* (022) 313956, pg 1244

Onibon-Oje Publishers (Nigeria) *Tel:* (022) 313956, pg 502

ONK Agency Ltd (Turkey) *Tel:* (0212) 2498602; (0212) 2498603 *Fax:* (0212) 2525153 *E-mail:* karaca@ onkagency.com *Web Site:* www.onkagency.com, pg 1128

Online Information Resources (Australia) *Tel:* (03) 6257 9177 *Fax:* (03) 6257 9030, pg 34

Onlywomen Press Ltd (United Kingdom) *Tel:* (020) 8354 0796 *Fax:* (020) 8960 2817 *E-mail:* onlywomenpress@aol.com *Web Site:* www. onlywomenpress.com, pg 730

Dr C D Ooft (Suriname) *Tel:* 499139, pg 603

Ooievaar (Netherlands) *Tel:* (020) 624 19 34 *Fax:* (020) 622 54 61 *E-mail:* pbo@pbo.nl *Web Site:* www.pbo.nl, pg 483

Op der Lay (Luxembourg) *Tel:* 83 97 42 *Fax:* 89 93 50 *E-mail:* opderlay@pt.lu *Web Site:* webplaza.pt. lu/public/opderlay; www.phi.lu, pg 448

Bokforlaget Opal AB (Sweden) *Tel:* (08) 6571990 *Fax:* (08) 6183470 *E-mail:* opal@opal.se *Web Site:* www.opal.se, pg 609

The Open Book (Australia) *Tel:* (08) 8124 0049 *Fax:* (08) 8223 4552 *E-mail:* openbook@openbook. com.au; service@openbook.com.au *Web Site:* www. openbook.com.au, pg 1289

Open Books Publishing Ltd (United Kingdom) *Tel:* (01460) 52565 *Fax:* (01460) 52565, pg 731

Open Gate Press (United Kingdom) *Tel:* (020) 7431 4391 *Fax:* (020) 7431 5129 *E-mail:* books@ opengatepress.co.uk *Web Site:* www.opengatepress. co.uk, pg 731

Open University of Israel (Israel) *Tel:* (03) 6460460 *Fax:* (03) 6419279 *E-mail:* englishsite@openu.ac.il *Web Site:* www.openu.ac.il, pg 367

Open University Press (United Kingdom) *Tel:* (01628) 502500; (01628) 502720 (customer service) *Fax:* (01628) 635895 (customer service) *E-mail:* enquiries@openup.co.uk; emea_orders@ mcgraw-hill.com (orders); emea_queries@mcgraw-hill.com (customer service) *Web Site:* mcgraw-hill.co. uk/openup, pg 731

Open University Worldwide (United Kingdom) *Tel:* (01908) 858785 *Fax:* (01908) 858787 *E-mail:* ouwenq@open.ac.uk *Web Site:* www.open. ac.uk, pg 731

Openbare Bibliotheek (Netherlands Antilles) *Tel:* (09) 434 5200 *Fax:* (09) 465 6247 *E-mail:* publiclibrary@ curinfo.an *Web Site:* www.curacaopubliclibrary.an, pg 1530

Openbook Publishers (Australia) *Tel:* (08) 8223 5468 *Fax:* (08) 8223 4552 *E-mail:* openbook@peg.apc.org; service@openbook.com.au *Web Site:* www.openbook. com.au, pg 34

Opera (Greece) *Tel:* 2103304546 *Fax:* 210 3303634 *E-mail:* opera@acci.gr, pg 308

Opera Tres Ediciones Musicales (Spain) *Tel:* (091) 542 4320 *Fax:* (091) 541 0580; (091) 680 76 26, pg 589

Editions Ophrys (France) *Tel:* (04) 92 53 85 72 *Fax:* (04) 92 51 78 65 *E-mail:* edition.ophrys@ophrys. fr; infos@ophrys.fr *Web Site:* www.ophrys-editions. com, pg 178

Opinio Verlag AG (Switzerland) *Tel:* (061) 2646450 *Fax:* (061) 2646488 *E-mail:* opinio@reinhardt.ch *Web Site:* www.opinio.ch, pg 625

Opsys Operating System (France) *Tel:* (04) 76 84 34 20; (04) 76 84 34 34 *Fax:* (04) 76 84 34 21 *E-mail:* opsys@opsys.fr *Web Site:* www.opsys.fr, pg 178

Opus Book Publishing Ltd (United Kingdom) *Tel:* (01380) 871354 *Fax:* (01380) 871354 *E-mail:* opus@dmac.co.uk, pg 731

Opus Libri SRL (Italy) *Tel:* (055) 660833 *Fax:* (055) 670604 *E-mail:* opuslib@dada.it, pg 1311

Opus Publishing Ltd (United Kingdom) *Tel:* (020) 7267 1034 *Fax:* (020) 7267 6026 *E-mail:* opuspub@ btconnect.com, pg 731

Opus Records & Publishing House (Slovakia) *Tel:* (02) 222680 *E-mail:* opus@ba.profinet.sk, pg 555

Edicoes Ora & Labora (Portugal) *Tel:* (0252) 94 11 76 *Fax:* (0252) 87 29 47 *E-mail:* msingeverga@net.sapo. pt, pg 529

Verlag Orac im Verlag Kremayr & Scheriau (Austria) *Tel:* (01) 713 87 70 *Fax:* (01) 713 87 70-20 *E-mail:* office@kremayr-scheriau.at *Web Site:* www. kremayr-scheriau.at, pg 55

Or'am Publishers (Israel) *Tel:* (03) 5372277 *Fax:* (03) 5372281 *E-mail:* orampub@netvision.net.il *Web Site:* www.oram.co.il, pg 367

Editions de l'Orante (France) *Tel:* (01) 47 83 55 02 *Fax:* (01) 45 66 00 16, pg 178

Orbis Books (London) Ltd (United Kingdom) *Tel:* (020) 7602 5541 *Fax:* (020) 8742 7686 *E-mail:* bookshop@ orbis-books.co.uk, pg 1344

Ediciones Orbis SA (Spain) *Tel:* (093) 2800512 *Fax:* (093) 2801472 *E-mail:* orbis@edorbis.es, pg 589

Orbis Verlag fur Publizistik GmbH (Germany) *Tel:* (01805) 990 505 *Fax:* (089) 4136-3333, pg 265

Orca Publishing Services Ltd (New Zealand) *Tel:* (03) 377-0370 *Fax:* (03) 377-0390 *E-mail:* info@hazard.co. nz *Web Site:* www.hazardonline.com, pg 495

Orchid Press (Suriname), pg 603

Orchid Press (Thailand) *Tel:* (02) 939-0973; (02) 930-0149 *Fax:* (02) 930-5646 *E-mail:* wop@inet.co.th *Web Site:* d30021575.purehost.com, pg 641

Ordfront Foerlag AB (Sweden) *Tel:* (08) 462 44 00 *Fax:* (08) 4624490 *E-mail:* forlaget@ordfront.se; info@ordfront.se *Web Site:* www.ordfront.se, pg 609

Ordnance Survey (United Kingdom) *Tel:* (08456) 05 05 05 (customer information); (023) 8079 2912 (outside Britain); (023) 8030 5030 (business enquiries) *Fax:* (023) 8079 2615 (trade customer information); (023) 8079 2615 (outside Britain) *E-mail:* customerservices@ordnancesurvey.co.uk *Web Site:* www.ordnancesurvey.co.uk, pg 731

Orell Fuessli Buchhandlungs AG (Switzerland) *Tel:* (01) 466 77 11 *Fax:* (01) 466 74 12 *E-mail:* info@ofv.ch *Web Site:* www.ofv.ch, pg 625

Orell Fuessli Buchhandlungs AG (Switzerland) *Tel:* (0848) 849 848 *Fax:* (01) 455 56 20 *E-mail:* orders@books.ch; info@ofv.ch *Web Site:* www.ofv.ch; www.books.ch, pg 1335

Oreos Verlag GmbH (Germany) *Tel:* (08021) 86 68 *Fax:* (08021) 17 50 *E-mail:* lachenmann@oreos.de *Web Site:* www.oreos.de, pg 265

Orfanidis Publications (Greece) *Tel:* 2103836925 *Fax:* 2103845623, pg 308

Organisation for Economic Co-operation & Development OECD (France) *Tel:* (01) 45 24 82 00 *Fax:* (01) 45 24 85 00 *E-mail:* sales@oecd.org *Web Site:* www.oecd. org/bookshop; www.sourceoecd.org, pg 178

Verlag Organisator AG (Switzerland) *Tel:* (01) 2961030 *Fax:* (01) 2961031 *E-mail:* redaktion@organisator.ch *Web Site:* www.organisator.ch, pg 625

Organizacao Andrei Editora Ltda (Brazil) *Tel:* (011) 223-5111 *Fax:* (011) 221-0246 *E-mail:* diretoria@editora-andrei.com.br *Web Site:* www.editora-andrei.com.br, pg 87

Izdavacka Organizacija Rad (Serbia and Montenegro) *Tel:* (011) 3239-758; (011) 3239-998 *Fax:* (011) 3230-923, pg 548

Organizacion Cultural LP SA de CV (Mexico) *Tel:* (05) 55112312; (05) 147608 *E-mail:* orgcult@mail.internet. com.mx, pg 466

Organizacion de Bienestar Estudiantil (OBE) (Venezuela) *Tel:* (0212) 6054050 (ext 4200); (0212) 6054050 (ext 4201); (0212) 6054050 (ext 4202) *Fax:* (0212) 6930638 *Web Site:* www.ucv.ve/ftproot/obe/obe.htm, pg 1347

Organization for Economic Cooperation & Development (OECD) (France) *Tel:* (01) 45 24 82 00 *Fax:* (01) 45 24 85 00 *E-mail:* news.contact@oecd.org *Web Site:* www.oecd.org, pg 1259

Organizations of Libraries, Museums & Documentation Centre of Astan Quds (Islamic Republic of Iran) *Tel:* (098511) 2216009 *Fax:* (098511) 2220845 *E-mail:* webmaster@aqlibrary.org; info@aqlibrary.org *Web Site:* www.aqlibrary.org, pg 1516

The Organizing Committee of the 11th International Zeolite Conference (Republic of Korea) *Tel:* (042) 69-8161 *Fax:* (042) 69-8170 *E-mail:* skihm@sorak.kaist. ac.kr, pg 438

Orient Book Club (India) *Tel:* (011) 5550-2220 *E-mail:* customerservice@vsnl.com *Web Site:* www. vsnl.in, pg 1243

Orient Paperbacks (India) *Tel:* (011) 2386-2267; (011) 2386-2201 *Fax:* (011) 2386-2935 *E-mail:* orientpbk@ vsnl.com *Web Site:* www.orientpaperbacks.com, pg 341

Oriental Books (Republic of Korea) *Tel:* (02) 334-9404 *Fax:* (02) 334-6624, pg 438

Oriental Press BV (APA) (Netherlands) *Tel:* (020) 626 5544 *Fax:* (020) 528 5298 *E-mail:* info@apa-publishers.com *Web Site:* www.apa-publishers.com, pg 483

Oriental Publications (Australia) *Tel:* (08) 8212 6055 *Fax:* (08) 8410 0863 *E-mail:* oriental@dove.mtx.net. au, pg 34

Bibliotheque Orientale (Lebanon) *Tel:* (01) 202 421 *Fax:* (01) 339 287 *E-mail:* bo@usj.edu.lb *Web Site:* www.usj.edu.lb, pg 1523

Editorial Oriente (Cuba) *Tel:* (0226) 22496; (0226) 28096 *Fax:* (0226) 86111 *E-mail:* edoriente@cultstgo. cult.cu, pg 120

Ediciones del Oriente y del Mediterraneo (Spain) *Tel:* (091) 854 34 28 *Fax:* (091) 854 83 52 *E-mail:* sicamor@teleline.es *Web Site:* www.webdoce. com/orienteymediterraneo, pg 589

Origen Editorial SA (Mexico) *Tel:* (055) 575-07-11 (ext 30); (055) 575-07-11 (ext 31), pg 466

Origo Verlag (Switzerland) *Tel:* (031) 3114480 *Fax:* (031) 3114470, pg 626

Origo Forlag (Norway) *Tel:* 22160769 *Fax:* 22164837, pg 505

Orin Books (Australia) *Tel:* (03) 9534 5680; (03) 9534 4746 *Fax:* (03) 9527 6995, pg 34

Orion Children's Books (United Kingdom) *Tel:* (020) 7240 3444 *Fax:* (020) 7240 4822 *E-mail:* info@ orionbooks.co.uk *Web Site:* www.orionbooks.co.uk, pg 731

Editorial Orion (Mexico) *Tel:* (05) 5200224 *Fax:* (05) 5200224, pg 466

Editura Orion (Romania) *Tel:* (01) 3125250 *Fax:* (01) 2104636, pg 536

Orion Publishing Group Ltd (United Kingdom) *Tel:* (020) 7240 3444 *Fax:* (020) 7240 4822 *E-mail:* info@orionbooks.co.uk *Web Site:* orionbooks. co.uk, pg 731

The Orkney Press Ltd (United Kingdom) *Tel:* (01343) 540844, pg 731

Orlanda Frauenverlag (Germany) *Tel:* (030) 216-3566; (030) 216-2960 *Fax:* (030) 2153958 *E-mail:* post@ orlanda.de *Web Site:* www.orlanda.de, pg 265

Ormstunga (Iceland) *Tel:* 561 0055 *Fax:* 552 4650 *E-mail:* books@ormstunga.is *Web Site:* www. ormstunga.is, pg 323

Oros Verlag (Germany) *Tel:* (02505) 947191 *Fax:* (02505) 3534, pg 265

Orpheus Books Ltd (United Kingdom) *Tel:* (01993) 774949 *Fax:* (01993) 700330 *E-mail:* info@ orpheusbooks.com *Web Site:* www.orpheusbooks.com, pg 731

Orszagos Muoszaki, Informacios Koozpont es Koonyvtar (OMIKK) (Hungary) *Tel:* (01) 463-3534; (01) 463-1069 *Fax:* (01) 463-2440 *E-mail:* kolcsonzes@omikk. bme.hu *Web Site:* www.omikk.bme.hu, pg 1513

Orszagos Szechenyi Koenyvtar (Hungary) *Tel:* (01) 224-3788 *Fax:* (01) 202-0804; (01) 375-9984 *E-mail:* kint@oszk.hu *Web Site:* www.oszk.hu, pg 1513

Orszagos Szechenyi Konyvtar (Hungary) *Tel:* (01) 224-3700 *Fax:* (01) 202-0804 *E-mail:* isbn@oszk.hu *Web Site:* www.oszk.hu, pg 1263

Orte-Verlag (Switzerland) *Tel:* (01) 888 1556 *E-mail:* info@orteverlag.ch *Web Site:* www.orteverlag. ch, pg 626

Editorial Alfredo Ortells SL (Spain) *Tel:* (096) 347 10 00 *Fax:* (096) 347 39 10 *E-mail:* editorial@ortells.com *Web Site:* www.ortells.com, pg 589

Editora Ortiz SA (Brazil) *Tel:* (051) 225-3026 *Fax:* (051) 225-3026, pg 87

Oruem Publishing House (Republic of Korea) *Tel:* (02) 5859122; (02) 5859123 *Fax:* (02) 5847952, pg 438

OS (Organizzazioni Speciali SRL) (Italy) *Tel:* (055) 6236501 *Fax:* (055) 669446, pg 398

Osaka Oviss Inc (Japan) *Tel:* (06) 352 7090 *Fax:* (06) 352 8898 *E-mail:* .ovissbk@osk.3web.ne.jp, pg 1313

Osaka Prefectural Nakanoshima Library (Japan) *Tel:* (06) 6203-0474 *Fax:* (06) 2034914 *Web Site:* www.library. pref.osaka.jp, pg 1520

Osaka University Library (Japan) *Tel:* (06) 6850-5066 *Fax:* (06) 6850-5069 *Web Site:* www.library.osaka-u.ac.jp, pg 1520

Osanna Venosa (Italy) *Tel:* (0972) 35952 *Fax:* (0972) 35723 *E-mail:* osanna@osannaedizioni.it *Web Site:* www.osannaedizioni.it, pg 398

Osborne Books Ltd (United Kingdom) *Tel:* (01905) 748071 *Fax:* (0190) 748952 *E-mail:* books@osborne. u-net.com *Web Site:* www.osbornebooks.co.uk, pg 732

Oscar Book International (Malaysia) *Tel:* (03) 7753515; (03) 7762797 *Fax:* (03) 7762797, pg 453

Osho Verlag GmbH (Germany) *Tel:* (0221) 278 04-0 *Fax:* (0221) 278 04-66 *E-mail:* info@oshoverlag.de *Web Site:* www.oshoverlag.de, pg 265

Osimpam Educational Books (Ghana), pg 301

Osiris Kiado (Hungary) *Tel.* (01) 266-6560 *Fax:* (01) 267-0935 *E-mail:* kiado@osirismail.hu *Web Site:* www.osiriskiado.hu, pg 320

Osnova, Kharkov State University Press (Ukraine) *Tel:* (057) 224647, pg 649

Osnovy Publishers (Ukraine) *Tel:* (044) 295 25 82; (044) 295 86 36 *Fax:* (044) 295 25 82; (044) 295 86 36 *E-mail:* osnovy@ukrnet.net, pg 649

Osprey Publishing Ltd (United Kingdom) *Tel:* (01933) 443863 *Toll Free Tel:* 800-826-6600 *Fax:* (01865) 727017 *E-mail:* info@ospreydirect.co.uk; info@ ospreydirectusa.com (USA & Canada) *Web Site:* www. ospreypublishing.com, pg 732

Ossian Publications (Ireland) *Tel:* (021) 4502040 *Fax:* (021) 4502025 *E-mail:* ossian@iol.ie *Web Site:* www.ossian.ie, pg 359

Ossolineum Zaklad Narodowy im Ossolinskich - Wydawnictwo (Poland) *Tel:* (071) 3436961 *Fax:* (071) 3448103 *E-mail:* wydawnictwo@ossolineum.pl, pg 520

Verlag des Osterr Kneippbundes GmbH (Austria) *Tel:* (03842) 21682; (03842) 21718; (03842) 24094 *Fax:* (03842) 2171832 *E-mail:* office@kneippverlag. com *Web Site:* www.kneippverlag.com, pg 55

Osterreichische Bibelgesellschaft (Austria) *Tel:* (01) 5238240 *Fax:* (01) 5238240-20 *E-mail:* bibelhaus@ bibelgesellschaft.at *Web Site:* www.bibelgesellschaft.at, pg 1290

Osterreichische Nationalbibliothek (Austria) *Tel:* (01) 534 10 *Fax:* (01) 534 10 280 *E-mail:* onb@onb.ac.at *Web Site:* www.onb.ac.at, pg 1490

Osterreichischer Wirtschaftsverlag Druck-und Verlagsgesellschaft mbH (Austria) *Tel:* (01) 546 64-0 *Fax:* (01) 546 64-215 *E-mail:* office@oewv.at, pg 55

Ostfalia-Verlag Jurgen Schierer (Germany) *Tel:* (05171) 41763 *Fax:* (05171) 41769 *E-mail:* juergen.schierer@ t-online.de *Web Site:* www.ostfalia-verlag.de, pg 265

Ostschweiz Druck und Verlag (Switzerland) *Tel:* (071) 2922929 *Fax:* (071) 2922938, pg 626

Vydavatel'stvo Osveta (Verlag Osveta) (Slovakia) *Fax:* (043) 413 5036; (043) 413 5060, pg 555

Osvita (Ukraine) *Tel:* (032) 297 1206 *Fax:* (032) 297 1794 *E-mail:* info@osvita.org *Web Site:* www.osvita. org, pg 649

Otago Heritage Books (New Zealand) *Tel:* (03) 477 1500 *Fax:* (03) 477 1500 *E-mail:* otagoheritagebooks@clear. net.nz, pg 495

Otava Publishing Co Ltd (Finland) *Tel:* (09) 19961 *Fax:* (09) 643 136 *Web Site:* www.otava.fi, pg 143

OTEN (Open Training & Education Network) (Australia) *Tel:* (02) 9715 8000; (02) 9715 8222 (sales) *Fax:* (02) 9715 8111; (02) 9715 8174 (sales) *E-mail:* oten. courseinfo@tafensw.edu.au *Web Site:* www.oten.edu. au, pg 34

Otokar Kersovani (Croatia) *Tel:* (051) 338 558; (051) 338 016 *Fax:* (051) 331 690 *E-mail:* otokar-kersovani@ri.tel.hr *Web Site:* www.o-k.hr, pg 119

Otsuki Shoten Publishers (Japan) *Tel:* (03) 3813-4651 *Fax:* (03) 3813-4656 *E-mail:* otsuki@meibun.or.jp, pg 421

Ott Verlag Thun (Switzerland) *Tel:* (033) 225 39 39 *Fax:* (033) 225 39 33 *E-mail:* info@ott-verlag.ch *Web Site:* www.ott-verlag.ch, pg 626

Ott Verlag Thun (Switzerland) *Tel:* (031) 318 31 33 *Fax:* (031) 318 31 35 *E-mail:* info@hep-verlag.ch *Web Site:* www.ott-verlag.ch, pg 1152

Otto-Friedrich Universitat Bamberg (Germany) *Tel:* (0951) 863-1021 *Fax:* (0951) 863-4021 *E-mail:* presse@uni-bamberg.de *Web Site:* www.uni-bamberg.de/zuv/presse/mitarbeiter, pg 265

Oue Eesti Raamat (Estonia) *Tel:* 658 7885; 658 7886; 658 7887; 658 7889 *Fax:* 658 7889 *E-mail:* helgi. gailit@mail.ee *Web Site:* www.eestiraamat.ee, pg 139

Ouest Editions (France) *Tel:* (01) 39 02 11 82 *Fax:* (01) 39 50 19 44 *E-mail:* contact@ouest-editions.com *Web Site:* www.ouest-editions.com, pg 179

Editions Ouest-France (France) *Tel:* (02) 99 32 58 23 *Fax:* (02) 99 32 58 30 *Web Site:* www.edilarge.com, pg 179

Oulun Yliopiston Kirjasto (Finland) *Tel:* (08) 553 1011 *Fax:* (08) 556 9135 *Web Site:* www.kirjasto.oulu.fi/, pg 1504

Editions Oum (Morocco) *Tel:* (02) 274972; (02) 220454 *Fax:* (02) 208882; (02) 950963, pg 471

Our Lady of Manaoag Publisher (Philippines) *Tel:* (02) 610214; (02) 610219 *Fax:* (06) 610219, pg 515

Outback Books - CQU Press (Australia) *Tel:* (07) 4923 2520 *Fax:* (07) 4923 2525 *E-mail:* cqupress@cqu.edu. au *Web Site:* www.outbackbooks.com, pg 34

Outdoor Press Pty Ltd (Australia) *Tel:* (03) 5790 5226 *Fax:* (03) 5790 5393 *Web Site:* www.goldexpeditions. com.au, pg 34

Outrigger Publishers (New Zealand) *Tel:* (07) 856 6981, pg 495

Outskirts Press (United States) *Toll Free Tel:* 888-672-6657 *E-mail:* info@outskirtspress.com *Web Site:* www. outskirtspress.com, pg 1220

Editorial Oveja Negra Ltda (Colombia) *Tel:* (01) 5309678 *Fax:* (01) 2577900, pg 112

George Over Ltd (United Kingdom) *Tel:* (01788) 573621 *Fax:* (01788) 578738 *E-mail:* xuz23@dial.pinex.com, pg 1217

Overseas Printing Corporation (United States) *Tel:* 415-835-9999 *Fax:* 415-835-9899 *Web Site:* www. overseasprinting.com, pg 1157

Deborah Owen Ltd (United Kingdom) *Tel:* (020) 7987 5119; (020) 7987 5441 *Fax:* (020) 7538 4004 *E-mail:* do@deborahowen.co.uk, pg 1133

Peter Owen Ltd (United Kingdom) *Tel:* (020) 7373 5628; (020) 7370 6093 *Fax:* (020) 7373 6760 *E-mail:* admin@peterowen.com *Web Site:* www. peterowen.com, pg 732

Owl Publishing (Australia) *Tel:* (03) 95966064 *Fax:* (03) 95966942 *E-mail:* owlbooks@bigpond.com, pg 34

Palace Press International (Hong Kong) *Tel:* 2357 9019 *Fax:* 415-532-3007 *E-mail:* palacehk@palacepress.
ecm; ppihk@palacepress.com; info@palacepress.com
*Web Site:* www.palacepress.com, pg 1147

Palace Press International - Corporate Headquarters (United States) *Tel:* 415-526-1370 *Fax:* 415-526-1394 *E-mail:* info@palacepress.com *Web Site:* www.
palacepress.com, pg 1157, 1178, 1220, 1231, 1239

Palacio del Libro (Uruguay) *Tel:* (02) 959019 *Fax:* (02) 957543, pg 1347

Biblioteca do Palacio Nacional de Mafra (Portugal) *Tel:* (0261) 817 550 *Fax:* (0261) 811947, pg 1537

Palas Editores Lda (Portugal) *Tel:* (021) 574903 *Fax:* (021) 795-4019, pg 529

Palatina Editrice (Italy) *Tel:* (0521) 282388 *Fax:* (0521) 282388 *Web Site:* culturitalia.uibk.ac.at, pg 399

Edit Palavra Magica (Brazil) *Tel:* (016) 610-0204 *Fax:* (016) 625-4583 *E-mail:* editora@palavramagica.
com.br *Web Site:* www.palavramagica.com.br, pg 87

Palazzi Verlag GmbH (Germany) *Tel:* (0421) 32 11 00 *Fax:* (0421) 32 13 00 *Web Site:* www.palazzi-kalender.
de, pg 265

Palestinian PEN Centre (Israel) *Tel:* (02) 6262970 *Fax:* (02) 6264620 *E-mail:* palpenc@palnet.com, pg 1396

Palgrave Publishers Ltd (United Kingdom) *Tel:* (01256) 329242 *Fax:* (01256) 479476 *E-mail:* orders@
palgrave.com (ordering online); catalogue@
palgrave.com (catalogue requests); conferences@
palgrave.com (conference & exhibition information); rights@palgrave.com (copyright & permissions); lectureservices@palgrave.com (inspection copy service); reviews@palgrave.com (review copy requests); booksellers@palgrave.com (bookseller queries) *Web Site:* www.palgrave.com, pg 733

Pallas-Akademia Editura (Romania) *Tel:* (066) 171036 *Fax:* (066) 171036 *E-mail:* pallas@nextra.ro, pg 536

Pallas Athene (United Kingdom) *Tel:* (020) 7229 2798 *Fax:* (020) 7792 1067, pg 733

Pallas Editora e Distribuidora Ltda (Brazil) *Tel:* (021) 270-0186 *Fax:* (021) 590-6996; (21) 5618007 *E-mail:* pallas@alternex.com.br *Web Site:* www.
pallaseditora.com.br, pg 87

Vydavatel'stvo SFVU Pallas (Slovakia) *Tel:* (02) 296627 *Fax:* (02) 294229; (02) 292820, pg 555

Palle Fogtdal A/S (Denmark) *Tel:* 3315 3915 *Fax:* 3393 3505 *E-mail:* pallefogtdal@pallefogtdal.dk, pg 133

Pallottinum Wydawnictwo Stowarzyszenia Apostolstwa Katolickiego (Poland) *Tel:* (061) 867-52-33 *Fax:* (061) 867-52-38 *E-mail:* pallottinum@pallottinum.pl
*Web Site:* www.pallottinum.pl, pg 520

Palm Beach Press (Australia) *Tel:* (02) 6646 1622 *Fax:* (02) 9946 1515, pg 35

Palmerston North City Library (New Zealand) *Tel:* (06) 351 4100 *Fax:* (06) 351 4102 *E-mail:* pncl@pncc.
govt.nz *Web Site:* citylibrary.pncc.govt.nz, pg 1531

Palms Press (Australia) *Tel:* (02) 4973 1236, pg 35

Palmyra Verlag (Germany) *Tel:* (06221) 165409 *Fax:* (06221) 167310 *E-mail:* palmyra-verlag@t-online.de *Web Site:* www.palmyra-verlag.de, pg 265

Fratelli Palombi SRL (Italy) *Tel:* (06) 3214150 *Fax:* (06) 3214752 *E-mail:* flli.palombi@mail.stm.it, pg 399

Palphot Ltd (Israel) *Tel:* (09) 9525252 *Fax:* (09) 9525277 *E-mail:* palphot@palphot.com
*Web Site:* www.palphot.com, pg 1310

Joergen Paludan Forlag ApS (Denmark) *Tel:* 4975-1536 *Fax:* 4975-1537 *E-mail:* paludans.forlag@mobilixnet.
dk, pg 133

G B Palumbo & C Editore SpA (Italy) *Tel:* (091) 588850 *Fax:* (091) 6111848 *E-mail:* redazione@
palumboeditore.it *Web Site:* www.palumboeditore.it, pg 399

Pamatnik narodniho pisemnictvi (Czech Republic) *Tel:* (02) 20516695 *Fax:* (02) 20517277
*E-mail:* post@pamatniknarodnihopisemnictvi.cz
*Web Site:* www.pamatniknarodnihopisemnictvi.cz, pg 1499

Pan African Institute for Development (PAID) (Cameroon) *Tel:* 332 28 06 *Fax:* 332 28 06
*E-mail:* info@paid-wa.org *Web Site:* www.irc.nl/page/
6919, pg 1254

Pan Agency (Sweden) *Tel:* (08) 769 87 00 *Fax:* (08) 769 88 04 *Web Site:* www.panagency.se, pg 1127

Pan Korea Book Corporation (Republic of Korea) *Tel:* (02) 733-2011; (02) 733-2018 *Fax:* (02) 736-8696 *E-mail:* info@bumhanbook.co.kr *Web Site:* www.
bumhanbook.co.kr, pg 438

Pan Macmillan (United Kingdom) *Tel:* (020) 7881 8000 *Fax:* (020) 7881 8001 *Web Site:* www.panmacmillan.
com, pg 733

Pan Macmillan Australia Pty Ltd (Australia) *Tel:* (02) 9285 9100 *Fax:* (02) 9285 9100 *E-mail:* pansyd@
macmillan.com.au; panpublicity@macmillan.com.au
(publicity) *Web Site:* www.panmacmillan.com.au, pg 35

Pan Malayan Publishing Co Sdn Bhd (Malaysia) *Tel:* (603) 7910420 *Fax:* (603) 92214333, pg 454

Pan Pacific Publications (S) Pte Ltd (Singapore) *Tel:* 2616288 *Fax:* 2616088 *E-mail:* ppps@pacific.
net.sg, pg 552

Pan Yayincilik (Turkey) *Tel:* (0212) 2618072; (0212) 2275675 *Fax:* (0212) 2275674 *E-mail:* pan@pankitap.
com *Web Site:* www.pankitap.com, pg 646

Panaf Books (United Kingdom) *Tel:* (0870) 333 1192 *E-mail:* zakakembo@yahoo.co.uk *Web Site:* www.
panafbooks.com, pg 733

Editorial Panamericana (Colombia) *Tel:* (01) 360 30 77; (01) 277 01 00; (01) 3649000 (ext 213); (03) 5603831; (03) 5603832; (03) 5603833 *Fax:* (01) 2373805 *E-mail:* panaedit@panamericanaeditorial.com
*Web Site:* www.panamericanaeditorial.com, pg 112

Panamericana Libreria y Papeleria SA (Colombia) *Tel:* (01) 3649000 (ext 213) *Fax:* (01) 3600885 *E-mail:* servicliente@panamericana.com.co
*Web Site:* www.panamericana.com.co, pg 1296

Instituto Panamericano de Geografia e Historia (Mexico) *Tel:* (05) 2775888; (05) 5151910; (05) 2775791 *Fax:* (05) 2716172 *E-mail:* cvasi@ipgh.spin.com.mx, pg 466

Libreria Commissionaria Internazionale di Raffaele Pancaldi (Italy) *Tel:* (051) 229466 *Fax:* (051) 229466, pg 1311

Panchasheel Prakashan (India) *Tel:* (0141) 65072 *Fax:* (0141) 326554, pg 341

Pandani Press (Australia) *Tel:* (03) 6225 1956 *E-mail:* pandani@iprimus.com.au, pg 35

Pandion-Verlag, Ulrike Schmoll (Germany) *Tel:* (06761) 7142 *Fax:* (06761) 77172 *E-mail:* pandion@t-online.
de; info@pandion-verlag.de *Web Site:* www.pandion-verlag.de, pg 265

Petraco-Pandora NV (Belgium) *Tel:* (03) 2338770 *Fax:* (03) 2333399, pg 71

Pandora Publishing House (Romania) *Tel:* (021) 243 3739, pg 537

Panem (Hungary) *Tel:* (01) 460-0273 *Fax:* (01) 460-0274 *E-mail:* panem@mail.datanet.hu *Web Site:* www.
panem.hu, pg 320

Panepistimio Ioanninon (Greece) *Tel:* 26510 97122 *Fax:* 2651097015 *E-mail:* intlrel@uoi.gr
*Web Site:* www.uoi.gr, pg 308

Pangea Editores, Sa de CV (Mexico) *Tel:* (05) 5738684 *Fax:* (05) 5130638 *E-mail:* pangea@data.net.mx, pg 466

Franco Cosimo Panini Editore (Italy) *Tel:* (059) 343572 *Fax:* (059 )344274 *E-mail:* info@fcp.it
*Web Site:* www.fcp.it; www.francopanini.com, pg 399

Pankaj Publications (India) *Tel:* (011) 3363395; (011) 3348805 *Fax:* (011) 5163525; (01) 5511684 *E-mail:* pankajbooks@hotmail.com, pg 341

Panmun Book Co Ltd (Republic of Korea) *Tel:* (02) 953-2451 (ext 5) *Fax:* (02) 953-2456 (ext 7) *E-mail:* pmbtrd2@chollian.net; pmbimp@unitel.co.kr, pg 438

Panmun Book Co Ltd (Republic of Korea) *Tel:* (02) 953-2451-5 *Fax:* (02) 953-2456-7 *E-mail:* panmunex@
unitel.co.kr, pg 1315

Editions du Panorama (Switzerland) *Tel:* (032) 3581665 *Fax:* (032) 3581665, pg 626

Panorama Editorial, SA (Mexico) *Tel:* (05) 5359348; (05) 5359074; (05) 5350377 *Fax:* (05) 5359202; (05) 5351217 *E-mail:* panorama@iserve.net.mx
*Web Site:* www.panoramaed.com.mx, pg 466

Panorama NIJP/ID Grigorije Bozovic (Serbia and Montenegro) *Tel:* (038) 29 090; (038) 21 156; (038) 29 866 *Fax:* (038) 29 809, pg 548

Panorama Publishing House (Russian Federation) *Tel:* (095) 2053707 *Fax:* (095) 2053708, pg 543

Panos Institute (United Kingdom) *Tel:* (020) 7278 1111 *Fax:* (020) 7278 0345 *E-mail:* info@panoslondon.org.
uk *Web Site:* www.panos.org.uk, pg 733

Panstwowe Przedsiebiorstwo Wydawnictw Kartograficznych (Poland) *Tel:* (022) 6283251; (022) 6214850 *Fax:* (022) 6280236; (022) 6214850 *E-mail:* ppwk@pdsox.com, pg 520

Panstwowe Wydawnictwo Rolnicze i Lesne (Poland) *Tel:* (022) 8276338 *Fax:* (022) 8276338, pg 520

Panstwowy Instytut Wydawniczy (PIW) (Poland) *Tel:* (022) 8260201; (022) 8260202; (022) 8260203; (022) 8260204; (022) 826-02-05 *Fax:* (022) 826-15-36 *E-mail:* piw@piw.pl *Web Site:* www.piw.pl, pg 520

Panther Publishing (Malaysia) *Tel:* (03) 2749854, pg 454

Pao Yue-Kong Library (Hong Kong) *Tel:* 2766 6863 *E-mail:* lbinf@polyu.edu.hk *Web Site:* www.polyu.
edu.hk, pg 1512

D Papadimas (Greece) *Tel:* 2103627318 *Fax:* 210 3610271, pg 308

Kyr I Papadopoulos E E (Greece) *Tel:* 2102816134; 2102846074; 2102846075 *Fax:* 2102817127 *E-mail:* info@picturebooks.gr *Web Site:* www.
picturebooks.gr, pg 308

Papazissis Publishers SA (Greece) *Tel:* 2103838020; 2103822496 *Fax:* 2103809150, pg 308

Paper Art Product Ltd (Hong Kong) *Tel:* 2481 2929 *Fax:* 2489 2255 *E-mail:* paperart@netvigator.com, pg 1147, 1209

Paperback Publishers Ltd (Nigeria) *Tel:* (022) 317363, pg 502

Papirus Editora (Brazil) *Tel:* (0192) 3272 4500; (0192) 3272 4534 *Fax:* (0192) 3272 7578 *E-mail:* editora@
papirus.com.br *Web Site:* www.papirus.com.br/, pg 1294

Papua New Guinea Institute of Medical Research (PNGIMR) (Papua New Guinea) *Tel:* 732-2800 *Fax:* 732-1998 *E-mail:* general@pngimr.org.pg
*Web Site:* www.pngimr.org.pg, pg 511

Papua New Guinea Institute of Public Administration Library (PNGIPA) (Papua New Guinea) *Tel:* 3260433; 3267345; 3267163 *Fax:* 3261654 *E-mail:* gaudichn@
upng.ac.pg, pg 1534

PapyRossa Verlags GmbH & Co Kommanditgesellschaft KG (Germany) *Tel:* (0221) 44 85 45 *Fax:* (0221) 44 43 05 *E-mail:* mail@papyrossa.de *Web Site:* www.
papyrossa.de, pg 265

Editions du Papyrus (France) *Tel:* (01) 48 57 27 05 *Fax:* (01) 48 57 26 79 *E-mail:* papyrus@netfly.fr
*Web Site:* www.editions-papyrus.com, pg 179

Papyrus Publishing (Australia) *Tel:* (03) 5342 2394 *Fax:* (03) 5342 2423 *E-mail:* editor@papyrus.com.au
*Web Site:* www.papyrus.com.au, pg 35

Izdatel'stvo Patriot (Russian Federation) *Tel:* (095) 2844904, pg 543

Editorial Patris SA (Chile) *Tel:* (02) 2351343 *Fax:* (02) 2351343 *E-mail:* edit.patris@entelchile.net *Web Site:* www.patris.cl, pg 99

Libreria Internazionale Patron (Italy) *Tel:* (051) 223208 *Fax:* (051) 223208, pg 1311

Patron Editore SrL (Italy) *Tel:* (051) 767003 *Fax:* (051) 768252 *E-mail:* info@patroneditore.com *Web Site:* www.patroneditore.com, pg 399

Pattloch Verlag GmbH & Co KG (Germany) *Tel:* (089) 9271-0 *Fax:* (089) 9271-168 *E-mail:* vertrieb@ droemer-knaur.de *Web Site:* www.droemer-weltbild.de, pg 266

Ediciones Paulinas (Libreria San Pablo) (Colombia) *Tel:* (01) 2444516 *Fax:* (01) 2684288, pg 1296

Paulinas (Portugal) *Tel:* (021) 848 43 55 *Fax:* (021) 847 41 51 *E-mail:* paulinas@mail.telepac.pt, pg 529

Paulinas Editorial (Brazil) *Tel:* (011) 50855199 *Fax:* (011) 50855198 *E-mail:* editora@paulinas.org.br, pg 87

Paulines Publications-Africa (Kenya) *Tel:* (020) 4447202; (020) 4447203 *Fax:* (020) 4442097 *E-mail:* publications@paulinesafrica.org *Web Site:* www.paulinesafrica.org, pg 432

Paulinus Verlag GmbH (Germany) *Tel:* (0651) 4608-0 *Fax:* (0651) 4608-221 *E-mail:* service@paulinus.de *Web Site:* www.paulinus.de, pg 266

Paulinus Verlag GmbH (Germany) *Tel:* (0651) 4608-0; (0651) 4608-121; (0651) 4608-120 *Fax:* (0651) 4608220, pg 266

Paulus Editora (Brazil) *Tel:* (011) 50843066; (011) 5757362 *Fax:* (011) 5703627 *E-mail:* dir.editorial@ paulus.org.br *Web Site:* www.paulus.com.br, pg 87

Pavilion Books Ltd (United Kingdom) *Tel:* (020) 7221 2213; (020) 7314 1469 (sales) *Fax:* (020) 7221 6455; (020) 7314 1594 (sales) *E-mail:* info@chrysalisbooks. co.uk; enquiries@chrysalis.com *Web Site:* www. chrysalisbooks.co.uk/books/publisher/pavilion, pg 734

Pavilion Publishing (Brighton) Ltd (United Kingdom) *Tel:* (01273) 623222 *Fax:* (01273) 625526 *E-mail:* info@pavpub.com *Web Site:* www.pavpub. com, pg 734

Pawel Panpresse (Germany) *Tel:* (06041) 5822, pg 266

John Pawsey (United Kingdom) *Tel:* (01903) 205167 *Fax:* (01903) 205167, pg 1133

Pax Forlag A/S (Norway) *Tel:* (023) 136900 *Fax:* (023) 136919, pg 505

Editorial Pax Mexico (Mexico) *Tel:* 5688-4828; 5604-0843 *Fax:* 5605-7677 *E-mail:* editorialpax@ editorialpax.com *Web Site:* www.editorialpax.com, pg 466

Payel Yayinevi (Turkey) *Tel:* (0212) 511 82 33; (0212) 512 43 53 *E-mail:* shemsa@ttnet.net.tr, pg 646

Payot & Rivages (France) *Tel:* (01) 44413990 *Fax:* (01) 44413969 *E-mail:* editions@payotrivages.com, pg 179

Editions Payot Lausanne (Switzerland) *Tel:* (021) 3290264 *Fax:* (021) 3290266 *E-mail:* ed.payot.nadir@ bluewin.ch, pg 626

Editora Paz e Terra (Brazil) *Tel:* (011) 3337-8399 *Fax:* (011) 223-6290 *E-mail:* vendas@pazeterra.com.br *Web Site:* www.pazeterra.com.br, pg 88

Paz-Editora de Multimedia, LDA (Portugal) *Tel:* (021) 8101282 *Fax:* (021) 8101287 *E-mail:* paz@esoterica. pt, pg 529

PC Publishing (United Kingdom) *Tel:* (01953) 889900 *Fax:* (01953) 889901 *E-mail:* info@pc-publishing.com *Web Site:* www.pc-publishing.co.uk, pg 734

PCE Press (Australia) *Tel:* (07) 3252 1114 *Fax:* (07) 3852 1564 *E-mail:* pcq@gil.com.au *Web Site:* www. pcq.org.au, pg 36

Peace Book Co Ltd (Hong Kong) *Tel:* 2804-6687 *Fax:* 2804-6409, pg 315

Peaceful Living Publications (New Zealand) *Tel:* (071) 5718513 *Fax:* (071) 5718513 *E-mail:* books@ peaceful-living.co.nz, pg 1321

Peak Technologies UK Ltd (United Kingdom) *Tel:* (01344) 290000 *Fax:* (01344) 290001 *E-mail:* info@peakeurope.com *Web Site:* www. peakeurope.com/uk, pg 1217

Peak Translations (United Kingdom) *Tel:* (01663) 732074 *Fax:* (01663) 735499 *E-mail:* info@peak-translations.co.uk *Web Site:* www.peak-translations. co.uk, pg 1141

Peake Associates (United Kingdom) *Tel:* (020) 7267 8033 *Fax:* (020) 7267 8033 *E-mail:* tony@tonypeake. com *Web Site:* www.tonypeake.com/agency/index.htm, pg 1133

Maggie Pearlstine Associates Ltd (United Kingdom) *Tel:* (020) 7828 4212 *Fax:* (020) 7834 5546 *E-mail:* post@pearlstine.co.uk, pg 1133

Pearson Educacion de Argentina (Argentina) *Tel:* (011) 4309 6100 *Fax:* (011) 4309 6199 *Web Site:* www. pearsoneducacion.net, pg 8

Pearson Educacion de Colombia Ltda (Colombia) *Tel:* (01) 4059300 *Fax:* (01) 4059300, pg 112

Pearson Educacion de Mexico, SA de CV (Mexico) *Toll Free Tel:* 800 005 4276 *Fax:* (05) 387-0700 *E-mail:* firstname.lastname@pearsoned.com *Web Site:* www.pearsoned.com.mx, pg 466

Pearson Educacion SA (Spain) *Tel:* (091) 5903432 *Fax:* (091) 5903448 *E-mail:* firstname.lastname@ pearsoned-ema.com, pg 590

Pearson Education (Switzerland) *Tel:* 747 4747 *Fax:* 747 4777 *E-mail:* firstname.lastname@pearson.ch; mailbox@pearson.ch *Web Site:* www.pearson.ch, pg 626

Pearson Education (Taiwan, Province of China) *Tel:* (02) 2370 8168 *Fax:* (02) 2370 8169 *E-mail:* firstname@ pearsoned.com.tw *Web Site:* www.pearsoned.com.tw, pg 636

Pearson Education (United Kingdom) *Tel:* (020) 7447 2000 *Fax:* (020) 7240 5771 *E-mail:* firstname. lastname@pearsoned-ema.com, pg 734

Pearson Education Asia (Philippines) *Tel:* (02) 434 5501 *Fax:* (02) 433466 *E-mail:* custserv@pearsoned.com.ph *Web Site:* www.pearsoned.com, pg 515

Pearson Education Asia Pte Ltd (Singapore) *Tel:* 3199388 *Fax:* 3199175 *E-mail:* asia@pearsoned. com.sg *Web Site:* www.pearsoned-asia.com, pg 553

Pearson Education Australia (Australia) *Tel:* (02) 9454 2200 *Fax:* (02) 9453 0089 *E-mail:* firstname. lastname@pearsoned.com.au *Web Site:* www.pearson. com.au, pg 36

Pearson Education Benelux (Netherlands) *Tel:* (020) 575-5800 *Fax:* (020) 664-5334 *E-mail:* firstname. lastname@mail.aw.nl; amsterdam@pearsoned-ema.com *Web Site:* www.pearsoneducation.nl, pg 483

Pearson Education China Ltd (Hong Kong) *Tel:* 3181 0000 *Fax:* 2565 7440 *E-mail:* info@ilongman.com *Web Site:* www.pearsoned.com.hk, pg 315

Pearson Education Deutschland GmbH (Germany) *Tel:* (089) 46003-0 *Fax:* (089) 46003-120 *E-mail:* firstinitiallastname@pearson.de; info@pearson. de *Web Site:* www.pearsoned.de, pg 266

Pearson Education Do Brasil (Brazil) *Tel:* (011) 3611 0740 *Fax:* (011) 3611 0444 *E-mail:* firstname. lastname@pearsoned.com.br, pg 88

Pearson Education Europe, Mideast & Africa (United Kingdom) *Tel:* (01279) 62 3623 *Fax:* (01279) 41 4130 *E-mail:* firstname.lastname@pearsoned-ema.com *Web Site:* www.pearsoned.co.uk, pg 734

Pearson Education France (France) *Tel:* (01) 7274 9000 *Fax:* (01) 4804 5361 (sales); (01) 4887 7130 (finance); (01) 4205 2217 *E-mail:* infos@pearsoned.fr *Web Site:* www.pearsoneducation.fr, pg 179

Pearson Education Indochina, Ltd (Thailand) *Tel:* (02) 731-7156-57; (02) 731-7150-51 (Hotline) *Fax:* (02) 731-7158 *E-mail:* cserv@pearson-indochina.com *Web Site:* www.pearson-indochina.com, pg 641

Pearson Education Japan (Japan) *Tel:* (03) 3365 9001 *Fax:* (03) 3365 9009 *E-mail:* firstname.lastname@ pearsoned.co.jp; elt@pearsoned.co.jp *Web Site:* www. pearsoned.co.jp, pg 421

Pearson Education Korea Ltd (Republic of Korea) *Tel:* (02) 353 0422 *Fax:* (02) 335 0092 *E-mail:* elt@ pearsoned.co.kr, pg 438

Pearson Education Malaysia Sdn Bhd (Malaysia) *Tel:* (03) 7782 0466; (03) 7782 0659; (03) 7782 0702 *Fax:* (03) 7781 8005 *E-mail:* inquiry@pearsoned.com. my *Web Site:* www.pearson.com, pg 454

Pearson Education Malaysia Sdn Bhd (Malaysia) *Tel:* (03) 77820466 *Fax:* (03) 77853435 *E-mail:* inquiry@personed.com.my *Web Site:* www. pearsoned-asia.com/mal; www.pearson.com, pg 1317

Pearson Education (PENZ) (New Zealand) *Tel:* (09) 444 4968 *Fax:* (09) 444 4957 *E-mail:* firstname.lastname@ pearsoned.co.nz *Web Site:* www.pearsoned.co.nz, pg 495

Pearson Education Polska Sp z oo (Poland) *Tel:* (022) 533 1533 *Toll Free Tel:* 0800 1200 76 *Fax:* (022) 533 1534 *E-mail:* office@longman.com.pl *Web Site:* www. longman.com.pl, pg 520

Pearson Education (Prentice Hall) (South Africa) *Tel:* (021) 686 6356 *Fax:* (021) 686 4590 *E-mail:* firstname@mml.co.za *Web Site:* www. pearsoned.com, pg 563

Pearson Education Turkey (Turkey) *Tel:* (0212) 288 6941 *Fax:* (0212) 267 1851 *E-mail:* firstname.lastname@ pearsoned-ema.com *Web Site:* www.pearsoneduc, pg 646

Peartree Publications (United Kingdom) *Tel:* (01424) 844274, pg 735

Pedagogika Press (Russian Federation) *Tel:* (095) 2465969 *Fax:* (095) 2465969, pg 543

Editions A Pedone (France) *Tel:* (01) 43 54 05 97 *Fax:* (01) 46 34 07 60 *E-mail:* editions-pedone@ wanadoo.fr, pg 179

Pedrazzini Tipografia (Switzerland) *Tel:* (091) 751 7734 *Fax:* (091) 751 5118 *E-mail:* tipedra@webshuttle.ch, pg 626

Universidad Nacional Pedro Henriquez Urena (Dominican Republic) *Tel:* (0809) 542-6888 (ext 2301-2315, 2320 & 2321) *Fax:* (0809) 566-2206; (0809) 540-3803 *E-mail:* biblioteca@unphu.edu. do *Web Site:* www.unphu.edu.do/unphu/biblioteca, pg 1501

Peepal Tree Press Ltd (United Kingdom) *Tel:* (0113) 245 1703 *Fax:* (0113) 246 8368 *E-mail:* contact@ peepaltreepress.com *Web Site:* www.peepaltreepress. com, pg 735

Peeters-France (France) *Tel:* (01) 6 23 51 70 *Fax:* (01) 6 22 85 00 *E-mail:* peeters@peeters-leuven.be *Web Site:* www.peeters-leuven.be, pg 179

Uitgeverij Peeters Leuven (Belgie) (Belgium) *Tel:* (016) 23 51 70 *Fax:* (016) 22 85 00 *E-mail:* peeters@ peeters-leuven.be *Web Site:* www.peeters-leuven.be, pg 71

Editoriale PEG (Italy) *Tel:* (02) 4859181 *Fax:* (02) 485918220 *E-mail:* info@millerfreeman.it, pg 399

Pegasus Publishers & Booksellers (Netherlands) *Tel:* (020) 6231138 *Fax:* (020) 6203478 *E-mail:* pegasus@pegasusboek.nl *Web Site:* www. pegasusboek.nl, pg 1320

Pehuen Editores Ltda (Chile) *Tel:* (02) 2049399 *Fax:* (02) 2049399 *E-mail:* pehuen@cmet.net, pg 99

Ediciones Peisa (Promocion Editorial Inca SA) (Peru) *Tel:* (01) 4404603; (01) 4410473 *Fax:* (01) 4425906 *E-mail:* peisa@terro.com.pe, pg 512

Peking University Library (China) *Tel:* (010) 62751051; (010) 62757223 *Fax:* (010) 62761008 *E-mail:* office@ lib.pku.edu.cn *Web Site:* www.lib.pku.edu.cn, pg 1496

Pelanduk Publications (M) Sdn Bhd (Malaysia) *Tel:* (03) 56386573; (03) 56386885 *Fax:* (03) 56386577; (03) 56386575 *E-mail:* pelpub@tm.net.my *Web Site:* www. pelanduk.com, pg 454

Pelckmans NV, De Nederlandsche Boekhandel (Belgium) *Tel:* (03) 660 27 00 *Fax:* (03) 660 27 01 *E-mail:* uitgeverij@pelckmans.be *Web Site:* www. pelckmans.be, pg 71

Uitgeverij Pelckmans NV (Belgium) *Tel:* (03) 6602700 *Fax:* (03) 66022701 *E-mail:* uitgeverij@pelckmans.be *Web Site:* www.pelckmans.be, pg 71

Pelikan Vertriebsgesellschaft mbH & Co KG (Germany) *Tel:* (0511) 6969-0 *Fax:* (0511) 6969-212 *E-mail:* info@pelikan.de *Web Site:* www.pelikan.de, pg 266

Pelita Masa PT (Indonesia) *Tel:* (022) 50823, pg 353

Luigi Pellegrini Editore (Italy) *Tel:* (0984) 795065 *Fax:* (0984) 792672 *E-mail:* info@pellegrinieditore.it *Web Site:* www.pellegrinieditore.it, pg 399

Pembimbing Masa PT (Indonesia) *Tel:* (021) 367645; (021) 366042, pg 353

Pembimbing Masa PT (Indonesia) *Tel:* (021) 367645, pg 1308

Pen & Sword Books Ltd (United Kingdom) *Tel:* (01226) 734555 *Fax:* (01226) 734438 *E-mail:* enquiries@pen-and-sword.co.uk *Web Site:* www.pen-and-sword.co.uk, pg 735

Belgian PEN Centre (French-Speaking) (Belgium) *Tel:* (052) 351118 *Fax:* (052) 351119, pg 1391

Congolese PEN Centre (Congo) *Tel:* 813601 *Fax:* 813601, pg 1392

English PEN Centre (United Kingdom) *Tel:* (020) 7713 0023 *Fax:* (020) 7713 0005 *E-mail:* enquiries@ englishpen.org *Web Site:* www.englishpen.org, pg 1403

French PEN Centre (France) *Tel:* (01) 42 77 37 87 *Fax:* (01) 42 78 64 87 *E-mail:* penfrancais@aol.com, pg 1393

Galician PEN Centre (Spain) *Tel:* (081) 587750 *E-mail:* pengalicia@mundo-r.com, pg 1399

German PEN Centre (Germany) *Tel:* (06151) 23120 *Fax:* (06151) 293414 *E-mail:* pen-germany@t-online. de *Web Site:* www.pen-deutschland.de, pg 1394

Hong Kong PEN Centre (Chinese-Speaking) (Hong Kong), pg 1395

Hungarian PEN Centre (Hungary) *Tel:* (01) 3184143 *Fax:* (01) 1171722 *E-mail:* pen.hungary@axelero.hu, pg 1395

Icelandic PEN Centre (Iceland), pg 1395

Indian PEN Centre (India) *Tel:* (022) 2032175, pg 1395

Indonesian PEN Centre (Indonesia) *Tel:* (093) 3905837 *Fax:* (093) 325890, pg 1395

Irish PEN Centre (Ireland) *E-mail:* irishpen@ireland. com, pg 1395

Israeli PEN Centre (Israel) *Tel:* (03) 6964937 *Fax:* (03) 6964937, pg 1396

Italian PEN Centre (Italy) *E-mail:* penclubitalia@dinet.it, pg 1396

Japanese PEN Centre (Japan) *Tel:* (03) 3402-1171; (03) 3402-1172 *Fax:* (03) 3402-5951 *E-mail:* secretariat03@japanpen.or.jp *Web Site:* www. japanpen.or.jp, pg 1396

Korean PEN Centre (Republic of Korea) *Tel:* (02) 782 1337; (02) 782 1338 *Fax:* (02) 786 1090 *E-mail:* penkon2001@yahoo.co.kr, pg 1396

Liechtenstein PEN Centre (Liechtenstein) *Tel:* (0423) 2327271 *Fax:* (0423) 2328071 *E-mail:* info@pen-club.li *Web Site:* www.pen-club.li, pg 1396

Mexican PEN Centre (Mexico) *Tel:* (05) 574-4882 *Fax:* (05) 264-0813 *E-mail:* presidencia@penmexico. org.mx *Web Site:* www.penmexico.org.mx, pg 1397

Nepal PEN Centre (Nepal) *Fax:* (01) 522346 *E-mail:* daman@wlink.com.np, pg 1397

Netherlands PEN Centre (Netherlands) *Tel:* (043) 433498 *Fax:* (043) 433498 *E-mail:* secretariaat@pencentrum. nl, pg 1397

Norwegian PEN Centre (Norway) *Tel:* 22194551 *Fax:* 22194551 *E-mail:* pen@norskpen.no, pg 1397

Panamanian PEN Centre (Panama) *Tel:* 263-8822 *Fax:* 263-9918, pg 1398

Philippine PEN Centre (Philippines) *Tel:* (02) 5230870 *Fax:* (02) 5255038 *E-mail:* philippinepen@yahoo.com, pg 1398

Polish PEN Centre (Poland) *Tel:* (022) 8265784; (022) 8282823 *Fax:* (022) 8265784 *E-mail:* penclub@ ikp.atm.com.pl *Web Site:* www.penclub.atomnet.pl, pg 1398

Portuguese PEN Centre (Portugal) *Tel:* (021) 7573452 *Fax:* (021) 7573452 *E-mail:* penclube@netcabo.pt, pg 1398

Puerto Rican PEN Centre (Puerto Rico) *Tel:* (787) 724-0869 *Fax:* (787) 724-2060 *E-mail:* saturno@prtc.net, pg 1398

Romanian PEN Centre (Romania) *Tel:* (01) 3111112 *Fax:* (01) 3125854 *E-mail:* univers@rnc.ro, pg 1398

Russian PEN Centre (Russian Federation) *Tel:* (095) 2094589; (095) 2093171 *Fax:* (095) 2000293 *E-mail:* penrussian@dol.ru; penrus@aha.ru *Web Site:* www.penrussia.org, pg 1398

Senegal PEN Centre (Senegal) *Tel:* 8256700; 8258009 *Fax:* 8643375 *E-mail:* memgoree@sonatel.senet.net, pg 1398

Serbian PEN Centre (Serbia and Montenegro) *Tel:* (011) 626081 *Fax:* (011) 635979 *E-mail:* pencent@bitsyu. net, pg 1398

Slovene PEN Centre (Slovenia) *Tel:* (01) 4254847 *E-mail:* slopen@guest.arnes.si, pg 1399

Swiss German PEN Centre (Switzerland) *Tel:* (031) 3724085 *Fax:* (031) 3723032 *E-mail:* infopen@ datacomm.ch, pg 1399

Swiss Italian & Reto-Romansh PEN Centre (Switzerland) *Tel:* (091) 8039325 *Fax:* (091) 8039300 *E-mail:* p.e.n.lugano@ticino.com, pg 1399

Taipei Chinese PEN Centre (Taiwan, Province of China) *Tel:* (02) 23693609 *Fax:* (02) 23699948 *E-mail:* taipen@tpts5.seed.net.tw, pg 1400

Thai PEN Centre (Thailand) *Tel:* (02) 6685147; (02) 2792621, pg 1400

Turkish PEN Centre (Turkey) *Tel:* (0212) 2526314 *Fax:* (0212) 2526315, pg 1400

Venezuelan PEN Centre (Venezuela) *Tel:* (0212) 5616691; (0212) 5617589; (0212) 5617287 *Fax:* (0212) 5718064, pg 1404

PEN Club-German Speaking Writers Abroad (Germany) *E-mail:* intpen@dircon.co.uk *Web Site:* www.exilpen. de, pg 1261

PEN Club Writers in Exile London Branch (United Kingdom) *Tel:* (020) 8340 5279, pg 1282

Pendo Verlag GmbH (Switzerland) *Tel:* (01) 3897030 *Fax:* (01) 3897035 *E-mail:* info@pendo.ch *Web Site:* www.pendo.ch, pg 626

Pendragon Verlag (Germany) *Tel:* (0521) 69689 *Fax:* (0521) 174470 *E-mail:* pendragon.verlag@t-online.de *Web Site:* www.pendragon.de, pg 266

Penerbit Erlangga (Indonesia) *Tel:* (021) 8717006 *Fax:* (021) 8717011 *E-mail:* erlprom@rad.net.id *Web Site:* www.erlangga.com, pg 353

Penerbit Fajar Bakti Sdn Bhd (Malaysia) *Tel:* (03) 7047011 *Fax:* (03) 7047024, pg 454

Penerbit Jayatinta Sdn Bhd (Malaysia) *Tel:* (03) 7764036, pg 454

Penerbit Prisma Sdn Bhd (Malaysia) *Tel:* (03) 56380541 *Fax:* (03) 56347250, pg 454

Penerbit Universiti Sains Malaysia (Malaysia) *Tel:* (04) 6533888 *Fax:* (04) 6575714 *E-mail:* penerbitusm@ notes.usm.my *Web Site:* www.lib.usm.my/press, pg 454

Penerbitan Jaya Bakti (Malaysia) *Tel:* (03) 62519399 *Fax:* (03) 62519585, pg 454

Penerbitan Pelangi Sdn Bhd (Malaysia) *E-mail:* info@ pelangibooks.com; ppsb@po.jaring.my *Web Site:* www.pelangibooks.com, pg 454

Penguin Books Ltd (United Kingdom) *Tel:* (020) 7416 3000 *Fax:* (020) 7416 3099; (020) 7416 3293 *Web Site:* www.penguin.com, pg 735

Penguin Books Netherlands BV (Netherlands) *Tel:* (020) 6259566 *Fax:* (020) 6258676, pg 483

Penguin Books (NZ) Ltd (New Zealand) *Tel:* (09) 415-4700; (09) 415-4702 (orders) *Fax:* (09) 415-4701; (09) 415-4703 (orders) *E-mail:* marketing@penguin.co.nz *Web Site:* www.penguin.co.nz, pg 495

Penguin Group (Australia) (Australia) *Tel:* (03) 9811 2400 *Fax:* (03) 9811 2620 *Web Site:* www.penguin. com.au, pg 36

The Penguin Group UK (United Kingdom) *Tel:* (020) 7010 3000 *E-mail:* editor@penguin.co.uk *Web Site:* www.penguin.co.uk, pg 735

Ediciones Peninsula (Spain) *Tel:* (093) 443 71 00 *Fax:* (093) 443 71 30 *E-mail:* correu@grup62.com *Web Site:* www.grup62.com, pg 591

Penki Kontinentai (Lithuania) *Fax:* (05) 2664501 *E-mail:* info@5ci.lt *Web Site:* www.5ci.lt, pg 1125

Il Pensiero Scientifico Editore SRL (Italy) *Tel:* (06) 862821 *Fax:* (06) 86282250 *E-mail:* pensiero@ pensiero.it *Web Site:* www.pensiero.it, pg 399

The Pensions Management Institute (United Kingdom) *Tel:* (020) 7247 1452 *Fax:* (020) 7375 0603 *E-mail:* enquiries@pensions-pmi.org.uk *Web Site:* www.pensions-pmi.org.uk, pg 735

Pensoft Publishers (Bulgaria) *Tel:* (02) 716451 *Fax:* (02) 704508 *E-mail:* pensoft@mbox.infotel.bg; orders@ pensoft.net; info@pensoft.net *Web Site:* www.pensoft. net, pg 95

Pensord Press Ltd (United Kingdom) *Tel:* (01495) 223721; (01495) 222020 (customer service) *Fax:* (01495) 220672 *E-mail:* sales@pensord.co.uk *Web Site:* www.pensord.co.uk, pg 1154

Pentalfa Ediciones (Spain) *Tel:* (034) 985 985 386 *Fax:* (034) 985 985 512 *E-mail:* pentalfa@helicon.es *Web Site:* www.helicon.es/pentalfa.htm, pg 591

Pentathol Publishing (United Kingdom), pg 735

Institut Penyelidikan Minyak Kelapa Sawit Malaysia (Malaysia) *Tel:* (03) 8335155; (03) 8259775 *Fax:* (03) 8259446 *E-mail:* pub@porim.gov.my, pg 454

The People's Communications Publishing House (China) *Tel:* (010) 64214479 *Fax:* (010) 64213713, pg 106

People's Education Press (China) *Tel:* (010) 6402 4555 *Fax:* (010) 6401 0370 *E-mail:* yaod@pep. com.cn (English); dongyj@pep.com.cn (Japanese) *Web Site:* www.pep.com.cn/yingwenban; www.pep. com.cn/index.htm, pg 106

People's Fine Arts Publishing House (China) *Tel:* (010) 65122375 *Fax:* (010) 65122370, pg 106

People's Literature Publishing House (China) *Tel:* (010) 65138394 *Fax:* (010) 65138394, pg 106

People's Medical Publishing House (PMPH) (China) *Tel:* (010) 67015812; (010) 67028822 *Fax:* (010) 67025429, pg 106

The People's Posts & Telecommunication Publishing House (China) *Tel:* (010) 65139968; (010) 65138129 *Fax:* (010) 65138139, pg 106

People's Publishing House (P) Ltd (India) *Tel:* (011) 529365, pg 341

People's Sports Publishing House (China) *Tel:* (010) 67117673 *Fax:* (010) 67116129 *E-mail:* cbszbs@sohu. com, pg 106

PEP Buchhandlung & No Name Photo Gallery (Switzerland) *Tel:* (061) 261 51 61 *Fax:* (061) 261 51 61 *E-mail:* pepnoname@balcab.ch *Web Site:* www. pepnoname.ch, pg 1335

The Pepin Press (Netherlands) *Tel:* (020) 420 20 21 *Fax:* (020) 420 11 52 *E-mail:* mail@pepinpress.com *Web Site:* www.pepinpress.com, pg 483

Peramiho Publications (United Republic of Tanzania) *Tel:* (054) 2730 *Fax:* (054) 2917, pg 639, 1152, 1172, 1214, 1237

Perea Ediciones (Spain) *Tel:* (026) 568261 *Fax:* (026) 586386, pg 591

Editorial Peregrino SL (Spain) *Tel:* (0926) 338 245 *Fax:* (0926) 338 042 *E-mail:* editorialperegrino@mac. com *Web Site:* www.editorialperegrino.net, pg 591

Perfect Frontier Sdn Bhd (Malaysia) *Tel:* (03) 7832926 *Fax:* (03) 7816448, pg 455

Editorial Perfils (Spain) *Tel:* (0973) 242160 *Fax:* (0973) 221670 *E-mail:* perfils@arrakis.es, pg 591

Editora Pergaminho Lda (Portugal) *Tel:* (021) 652441 *Fax:* (021) 687543 *E-mail:* pergaminho@mail.telepac. pt, pg 530

Pergamon Flexible Learning (United Kingdom) *Tel:* (01865) 310366; (01865) 388190 *Fax:* (01865) 314290 *E-mail:* bhmarketing@repp.co.uk *Web Site:* www.bh.com/pergamonfl, pg 735

Peribo Pty Ltd (Australia) *Tel:* (02) 9457-0011 *Fax:* (02) 9457-0022 *E-mail:* peribo@bigpond.com, pg 36

Periodical & Book Publishers Association (Malta) *Fax:* (507) 295 9217 *E-mail:* bookpub@cwebdesign. com *Web Site:* www.cwebdesign.com/pbpa, pg 1267

Perioodika (Estonia) *Tel:* 644 1262 *Fax:* 644 2484 *E-mail:* perioodika@hot.ee, pg 140

E Perlinger Naturprodukte Handelsgesellschaft mbH (Austria) *Tel:* (05332) 524 40 *Fax:* (05332) 516 79 *E-mail:* engelberts.naturprodukte@tirol.com, pg 56

Permanyer Publications (Spain) *Tel:* (093) 207 59 20 *Fax:* (093) 457 66 42 *E-mail:* permanyer@permanyer. com *Web Site:* www.dolor.es; www.aidsreviews.com, pg 591

Permskaja Kniga (Russian Federation) *Tel:* (03422) 324245, pg 543

Perpetuity Press (United Kingdom) *Tel:* (0116) 221 7778 *Fax:* (0116) 221 7171 *E-mail:* orders@perpetuitypress. com *Web Site:* www.perpetuitypress.com, pg 736

Editorial El Perpetuo Socorro (Spain) *Tel:* (091) 445 51 26 *Fax:* (091) 445 51 27 *E-mail:* ed-ps@planalfa.es, pg 591

Editorial Perpetuo Socorro (Spain) *Tel:* (091) 445 51 26 *Fax:* (091) 445 51 27 *E-mail:* perso@pseditorial.com *Web Site:* www.pseditorial.com, pg 591

Perpustakaan Nasional (Indonesia) *Tel:* (021) 315 4863; (021) 315 4864; (021) 315 4870 *Fax:* (021) 310 3554 *E-mail:* pusjasa@rad.net.id; info@pnri.go.id *Web Site:* www.pnri.go.id/beranda, pg 1515

Perpustakaan Sultanah Zanariah (Malaysia) *Tel:* (07) 5533333 *Fax:* (07) 5572555 *E-mail:* psz@utm.my *Web Site:* www.utm.my, pg 1525

Perret Edition (Switzerland) *Tel:* (01) 9972717 *Fax:* (01) 9972718, pg 626

Persatuan Perpustakaan Kebangsaan Negara Brunei Darussalam (PPKNBD) (Brunei Darussalam) *Tel:* (02) 223060 *Fax:* (02) 235472; (02) 241817 *Web Site:* www.ppknbd.org.bn, pg 1559

Persatuan Perpustakaan Malaysia (Malaysia) *Tel:* (03) 26871700 *Fax:* (03) 26942490 *E-mail:* pnmweb@pnm. my *Web Site:* www.pnm.my, pg 1567

Verlag Sigrid Persen (Germany) *Tel:* (04163) 81400 *Fax:* (04163) 814050 *E-mail:* info@persen.de *Web Site:* www.persen.de, pg 267

Perskor Books (Pty) Ltd (South Africa) *Tel:* (011) 315-3647 *Fax:* (011) 315-2757 *E-mail:* vlaeberg@icon.co. za, pg 563

Editora Perspectiva (Brazil) *Tel:* (011) 8858388 *Fax:* (011) 3885-8388 *E-mail:* editora@ editoraperspectiva.com.br *Web Site:* www. editoraperspectiva.com.br, pg 88

Perspectivas e Realidades, Artes Graficas, Lda (Portugal) *Tel:* (021) 3471371 *Fax:* (021) 3471372, pg 530

Justus Perthes Verlag Gotha GmbH (Germany) *Tel:* (03621) 385-0 *Fax:* (03621) 385-102; (03621) 385-103 *E-mail:* perthes@klett-mail.de *Web Site:* www.klett-verlag.de/klett-perthes, pg 267

Pet Plus (Bulgaria) *Tel:* (02) 9874188 *E-mail:* editor@ 545plus.com; petplus@bnc.bg *Web Site:* www.545plus. com, pg 96

Peter Pan Publications (Australia) *Tel:* (07) 3848 0350 *Fax:* (07) 3848 4945 *E-mail:* paramountbooks@ optusnet.com.au *Web Site:* www.peterpan.ziby.net, pg 36

Verlag Sankt Peter (Austria) *Tel:* (0662) 842166-82 *Fax:* (0662) 842166-80 *E-mail:* verlag-st.peter@ magnet.at *Web Site:* www.stift-stpeter.at, pg 56

C F Peters Musikverlag GmbH & Co KG (Germany) *Tel:* (069) 6300990 *Fax:* (069) 635401 *E-mail:* vertrieb@musia.de; info@musia.de *Web Site:* www.musia.de, pg 267

Jens Peters Publikationen (Germany) *Tel:* (030) 7847265 *Fax:* (030) 7883127 *E-mail:* jens.peters@usa.net *Web Site:* www.jenspeters.de, pg 267

Heinrich Petersen Hans Buchimport GmbH (Germany) *Tel:* (040) 71003-0 *Fax:* (040) 71003-141 *E-mail:* vertrieb@petersen-buchimport.com *Web Site:* www.petersen-buchimport.com, pg 1301

Petit Editora e Distribuidora Ltda (Brazil) *Tel:* (011) 698 4162; (011) 691 7165 *Fax:* (011) 292 4616 *E-mail:* petit@dialdata.com.br *Web Site:* www.petit. com.br, pg 88

Petrion Verlag (Romania) *Tel:* (01) 3103407; (01) 3152641 *Fax:* (01) 3124525; (01) 3152641 *E-mail:* petrion@stranets.ro, pg 537

Petroleum Information Publishing Co (Taiwan, Province of China) *Tel:* (02) 29996909 *Fax:* (02) 29996746 *E-mail:* pip@oil.net.tw *Web Site:* www.oil.net.tw, pg 637

Petrony Livraria (Portugal) *Tel:* (021) 3423911 *Fax:* (021) 3431602, pg 530

Galousis P Petros (Greece) *Tel:* 2103605004, pg 308

Petrozavodskij Gosudarstvennyj Universitet (Russian Federation) *Tel:* (08142) 74-28-65 *Fax:* (08142) 71-10-00 *E-mail:* lib@mainpgu.karelia.ru *Web Site:* www. karelia.ru, pg 1539

Pevsner Public Library (Israel) *Tel:* (04) 8667766; (04) 8667768 *Fax:* (04) 8666492, pg 1518

Pfaffenweiler Presse (Germany) *Tel:* (07664) 8999 *Fax:* (07664) 8999 *E-mail:* info@pfaffenweiler-presse. de *Web Site:* www.pfaffenweiler-presse.de, pg 267

Pfalzische Verlagsanstalt GmbH (Germany) *Tel:* (06341) 142-0 *Fax:* (06341) 142-265, pg 267

PFD (United Kingdom) *Tel:* (020) 7344 1000 *Fax:* (020) 7836 9539 *E-mail:* postmaster@pfd.co.uk *Web Site:* www.pfd.co.uk, pg 1133

J Pfeiffer Verlag (Germany) *Tel:* (089) 4130010, pg 267

Verlag Dr Friedrich Pfeil (Germany) *Tel:* (089) 7428270 *Fax:* (089) 7242772 *E-mail:* info@pfeil-verlag.de *Web Site:* www.pfeil-verlag.de, pg 267

Richard Pflaum Verlag GmbH & Co KG (Germany) *Tel:* (089) 12607-0 *Fax:* (089) 12607-333 *E-mail:* info@pflaum.de *Web Site:* www.pflaum.de, pg 267

Verlag Die Pforte im Rudolf Steiner Verlag (Switzerland) *Tel:* (061) 706 91 30 *Fax:* (061) 706 91 49 *E-mail:* verlag@rudolf-steiner.com *Web Site:* www. rudolf-steiner.com, pg 626

PG Medical Books (Singapore) *Tel:* 4726339 *Fax:* 4728279, pg 553

Phaidon Press Ltd (United Kingdom) *Tel:* (020) 7843 1234 *Fax:* (020) 7843 1111 *E-mail:* esales@phaidon. com *Web Site:* www.phaidon.com, pg 736

Phantom Publishers (Zimbabwe) *Tel:* (04) 737241, pg 778

Pharmaceutical Press (United Kingdom) *Tel:* (020) 7735 9141 *Fax:* (020) 7572 2509 *E-mail:* pharmpress@ rpsgb.org *Web Site:* www.pharmpress.com, pg 736

Bibliotheque Interuniversitaire de Pharmacie (France) *Tel:* (01) 53 73 95 22; (01) 53 73 95 23 *Fax:* (01) 53 73 99 05 *E-mail:* piketty@pharmacie.univ_paris5.fr *Web Site:* www.biup.univ-paris5.fr, pg 1505

Pharos-Verlag, Hansrudolf Schwabe AG (Switzerland) *Tel:* (061) 541021 *Fax:* (061) 2797972, pg 626

Editions Phebus (France) *Tel:* (01) 46 33 36 36 *Fax:* (01) 43 25 67 69 *E-mail:* phebedit@wanadoo.fr *Web Site:* www.phebus-editions.fr, pg 180

Pheljna Edizioni d'Arte e Suggestione (Italy) *Tel:* (0125) 234114 *Fax:* (0125) 230085, pg 399

Editions Phi (Luxembourg) *Tel:* 541382-220 *Fax:* 541387 *E-mail:* editions.phi@editpress.lu; phi@ phi.lu *Web Site:* www.phi.lu, pg 448

Philip & Tacey Ltd (United Kingdom) *Tel:* (01264) 332171 *Fax:* (01264) 384808 *E-mail:* sales@ philipandtacey.co.uk *Web Site:* www.philipandtacey. co.uk, pg 736

Philipp Reclam Jun Verlag GmbH (Germany) *Tel:* (07156) 163 0 *Fax:* (07156) 163 197 *E-mail:* info@reclam.de *Web Site:* www.reclam.de, pg 267

Philippine Normal College Library & Library Science Departments (Philippines) *Tel:* (02) 5270372 *Fax:* (02) 5270372, pg 1535

Philippine Baptist Mission SBC FMB Church Growth International (Philippines) *Tel:* (02) 526-0264; (02) 526-0265; (02) 526-0266; (02) 526-0267; (02) 599256; (02) 599257 *Fax:* (02) 522-4639 *E-mail:* csm@i-manila.com.ph *Web Site:* www.fsbc.org.ph, pg 515

Philippine Education Co Inc (Philippines) *Tel:* (02) 487215; (02) 487317 *E-mail:* publications@pidsnet. pids.gov.ph *Web Site:* www.pids.gov.ph, pg 515

Philippine Education Co Inc (Philippines) *Tel:* (02) 487215; (02) 487317, pg 1326

Philippine Educational Publishers' Association (Philippines) *Tel:* (02) 7124106 *Fax:* (02) 7313448; (02) 7437687 *Web Site:* nbdb.gov.ph/pubindust.htm, pg 1271

Philippine Graphic Arts Inc (Philippines) *Tel:* (02) 364-4591 *Fax:* (02) 631-9733 *E-mail:* philippinegraphicarts@yahoo.com, pg 1212

Philippine Librarians Association Inc (Philippines) *Tel:* (02) 523-00-68 *Web Site:* www.dlsu.edu.ph/ library/plai, pg 1570

Philippka-Sportverlag (Germany) *Tel:* (0251) 23005-0 *Fax:* (0251) 23005-79 *E-mail:* info@philippka.de *Web Site:* www.philippka.de, pg 267

Philipps-Universitaet Marburg (Germany) *Tel:* (06421) 28-20 *Fax:* (06421) 28-22500 *E-mail:* pressestell@ verwaltung.uni.marburg.de *Web Site:* www.uni-marburg.de, pg 267

Philip's (United Kingdom) *Tel:* (020) 7644 6900 *Fax:* (020) 7644 6987 *E-mail:* philips@philips-maps. co.uk *Web Site:* www.philips-maps.co.uk, pg 736

Phillimore & Co Ltd (United Kingdom) *Tel:* (01243) 787636 *Fax:* (01243) 787639 *E-mail:* bookshop@ phillimore.co.uk *Web Site:* www.phillimore.co.uk, pg 736

Editorial Planeta SA (Spain) *Tel:* (093) 2285800 *Fax:* (093) 2177140; (093) 2177748 *E-mail:* marketing@planeta.es *Web Site:* www. . editorial.planeta.es, pg 591

Editorial Planeta Venezolana (Venezuela) *Tel:* (0212) 913982; (0212) 924872 *Fax:* (0212) 913792 *E-mail:* planeta@viptel.com *Web Site:* www. editorialplaneta.com.ve, pg 774

Planetas Kiadoi es Kereskedelmi Kft (Hungary) *Tel:* (01) 4071018 *Fax:* (01) 4071787, pg 321

Plantagenet Press (Australia) *Tel:* (09) 4304466 *Fax:* (09) 4305217 *E-mail:* rogergarwood@compuserve.com, pg 36

Museum Plantin-Moretus (Belgium) *Tel:* (03) 221 14 50; (03) 221 14 51 *Fax:* (03) 221 14 71 *E-mail:* museum. plantin.moretus@antwerpen.be *Web Site:* museum. antwerpen.be, pg 1492

Plantin Publishers (United Kingdom) *Tel:* (029) 2056 0333 *Fax:* (029) 2056 0313 *E-mail:* drakegroup@ btinternet.com *Web Site:* www.drakeed.com/cap, pg 738

Platano Editora SA (Portugal) *Tel:* (021) 7979278 *Fax:* (021) 7954019 *E-mail:* geral@platanoeditora.pt *Web Site:* www.plantanoeditora.pt, pg 530

Platform 5 Publishing Ltd (United Kingdom) *Tel:* (0114) 255 8000 *Fax:* (0114) 255 2471 *E-mail:* platform5@ platfive.freeserve.co.uk, pg 738

Plawerg Editores SA (Spain) *Tel:* (093) 414 72 26 *Fax:* (093) 209 50 01 *E-mail:* info@plawerg.es *Web Site:* www.plawerg.com, pg 591

Playbox Theatre Co (Australia) *Tel:* (03) 9685 5100 *Fax:* (03) 9685 5112 *E-mail:* playbox@netspace.net.au *Web Site:* www.playbox.com.au, pg 37

Playlab Press (Australia) *Tel:* 3236 1396 *Fax:* 3236 1026 *E-mail:* cluster@thehub.com.au, pg 37

Playmarket (New Zealand) *Tel:* (04) 382 8462 *Fax:* (04) 382 8461 *E-mail:* info@playmarket.org.nz *Web Site:* www.playmarket.org.nz, pg 1125

Editorial Playor SA (Spain) *Tel:* (091) 3690652 *Fax:* (091) 3694441 *E-mail:* playor@attglobal.net, pg 591

The Playwrights Publishing Co (United Kingdom) *Tel:* (01159) 313356 *E-mail:* playwrightspublishingco@yahoo.com *Web Site:* www.geocities.com/playwrightspublishingco, pg 738

Plaza y Janes Editores SA (Spain) *Tel:* (093) 3660340 *Fax:* (093) 3660105 *Web Site:* www.plaza.es, pg 591

Plaza y Valdes SA de CV (Mexico) *Tel:* (05) 5359851; (05) 5664055 *E-mail:* editorial@plazayvaldes.com.mx, pg 466

Editorial Pleamar (Argentina) *Tel:* (011) 485-6597, pg 8

Plein Chant (France) *Tel:* (05) 45 81 93 26 *Fax:* (05) 45 81 92 83 *Web Site:* www.nanga.fr, pg 1144

Plein Chant (France) *Tel:* (05) 45 81 93 26 *Fax:* (05) 45 81 92 83 *Web Site:* www.lelibraire.com, pg 1206

Pleniluni Edicions (Spain) *Tel:* (093) 301 08 87 *Fax:* (093) 3174830, pg 591

Jurriaan Plesman (Australia) *Tel:* (02) 9130 6247 *Fax:* (02) 9130 6202 *E-mail:* jurplesman@hotmail. com, pg 37

Plexus Publishing Ltd (United Kingdom) *Tel:* (020) 7622 2440 *Fax:* (020) 7622 2441 *E-mail:* info@plexusuk. demon.co.uk *Web Site:* www.plexusbooks.com, pg 738

Editorial Pliegos (Spain) *Tel:* (091) 4291545 *Fax:* (091) 4291545, pg 591

Uitgeverij Ploegsma BV (Netherlands) *Tel:* (020) 5511250 *Fax:* (020) 6203504 *E-mail:* info@ploegsma. nl *Web Site:* www.ploegsma.nl, pg 483

Plon-Perrin (France) *Tel:* (01) 44 41 35 00 *Fax:* (01) 44 41 35 02 *Web Site:* www.editions-perrin.fr, pg 180

Plough Publishing House of Bruderhof Communities in the UK (United Kingdom) *Tel:* (01580) 883 344 *Fax:* (01580) 883 317 *Toll Free Fax:* 800-018-3347 *E-mail:* contact@bruderhof.com *Web Site:* www. plough.com, pg 738

Plum Press (Australia) *Tel:* (07) 3870 2964 *Fax:* (07) 3870 2860 *E-mail:* tom@justasktom.com *Web Site:* www.justasktom.com, pg 37

Editions Plume (France) *Tel:* (01) 40 51 31 00 *Fax:* (01) 43 14 02 01, pg 180

Plurigraf SPA (Italy) *Tel:* (05) 5576841 *Fax:* (05) 55000766 *E-mail:* plurigraf@tiscalinet.it, pg 400

Bokforlaget Plus AB (Sweden) *Tel:* (08) 654 74 08, pg 609

Editorial Plus Ultra SA (Argentina) *Tel:* (011) 4374-2973; (011) 4374-5092 *Fax:* (011) 4374-2973 *E-mail:* plus_ultra@epu.virtual.ar.net, pg 8

Pluto Books Ltd (United Kingdom) *Tel:* (020) 8348 2724 *Fax:* (020) 8348 9133 *E-mail:* pluto@plutobooks.com *Web Site:* www.plutobooks.com, pg 738

Pluto Press (United Kingdom) *Tel:* (020) 8348 2724 *Fax:* (020) 8348 9133 *E-mail:* pluto@plutobooks.com *Web Site:* www.plutobooks.com, pg 738

Pluto Press Australia Pty Ltd (Australia) *Tel:* (02) 9692 5111; (03) 9328 3811 *Fax:* (02) 9692 5192; (03) 9329 9939 *E-mail:* pluto@plutoaustralia.com *Web Site:* www.plutoaustralia.com, pg 37

PoChinChai Printing Co Ltd (Republic of Korea) *Tel:* (031) 955-1150; (031) 955-1151 *Fax:* (031) 943-3234 *Web Site:* www.pochinchai.com, pg 439

Pociao's Books (Germany) *Tel:* (0228) 229583 *Fax:* (0228) 219507 *E-mail:* pociao@t-online.de *Web Site:* www.sanssoleil.de, pg 1301

Max Pock, Universitaetsbuchhandlung (Austria) *Tel:* (0316) 825254-0 *Fax:* (0316) 825258; (0316) 825254-8, pg 1290

Biblioteca del Poder Legislativo (Uruguay) *Tel:* (02) 208937 *Fax:* (02) 949162, pg 1553

Podium Uitgeverij (Netherlands) *Tel:* (020) 421 38 30 *Fax:* (020) 421 37 76 *E-mail:* post@uitgeverijpodium. nl *Web Site:* www.uitgeverijpodium.nl, pg 483

Wydawnictwo Podsiedlik-Raniowski i Spolka (Poland) *Tel:* (061) 867 95 46 *Fax:* (061) 867 68 50 *E-mail:* office@priska.com.pl, pg 520

Verlag Walter Podszun Burobedarf-Bucher Abt (Germany) *Tel:* (02961) 2507 *Fax:* (02961) 2508 *E-mail:* verlag.podszun@t-online.de, pg 268

Podzun-Pallas Verlag GmbH (Germany) *Tel:* (06036) 9436 *Fax:* (06036) 6270 *Web Site:* www.podzun-pallas.de, pg 268

Poetes Presents (France) *Tel:* (02) 97 52 93 63 *Fax:* (02) 97 52 83 90 *Web Site:* perso.wanadoo.fr/j.grassin, pg 1242

Poetry Society of Australia (Australia) *Tel:* (02) 423861, pg 1390

The Poetry Book Society Ltd (United Kingdom) *Tel:* (020) 7833 9247 *Fax:* (020) 7833 5990 *E-mail:* info@poetrybooks.co.uk *Web Site:* www. poetrybooks.co.uk, pg 1247

The Poetry Society Inc (United Kingdom) *Tel:* (020) 7420 9880 *Fax:* (020) 7240 4818 *E-mail:* info@ poetrysociety.org.uk *Web Site:* www.poetrysociety.org. uk, pg 1403

Poeziecentrum (Belgium) *Tel:* (09) 225 22 25 *Fax:* (09) 225 90 54 *E-mail:* info@poeziecentrum.be *Web Site:* www.poeziecentrum.be, pg 71

Pohjoinen (Finland) *Tel:* (08) 5377 111 *Fax:* (08) 5377 572 *E-mail:* pohjoinen@kaleva.fi *Web Site:* www. kaleva.fi, pg 143

Point Hors Ligne Editions (France) *Tel:* (01) 43544964 *Fax:* (01) 43253032, pg 180

Les Editions du Point Veterinaire (France) *Tel:* (01) 45 17 02 61 *Fax:* (01) 45 17 02 60 *E-mail:* serviceclients@pointveterinaire.com *Web Site:* www.pointveterinaire.com, pg 180

Pointer Publishers (India) *Tel:* (0141) 2568159 *Fax:* (0141) 2568159 *E-mail:* info@pointerpublishers. com; pointerpub@hotmail.com *Web Site:* www. pointerpublishers.com, pg 342

Editions POL (France) *Tel:* (01) 43 54 21 20 *Fax:* (01) 43 54 11 31 *E-mail:* pol@pol-editeur.fr *Web Site:* www.pol-editeur.fr, pg 180

The Polding Press (Australia) *Tel:* (03) 9639 0844 *Fax:* (03) 9639 0879 *E-mail:* manager@ catholicbookshop.com.au *Web Site:* www. catholicbookshop.com.au, pg 37

Literatur-Agentur Axel Poldner (Germany) *Tel:* (089) 909 558 92 *Fax:* (089) 909 558 91 *E-mail:* info@ poldner.de *Web Site:* www.poldner.de, pg 1122

Le Pole Nord ASBL (Belgium) *Tel:* (02) 2184576 *Fax:* (02) 2184576 *E-mail:* pole.nord@skynet.be, pg 71

Editorial Polemos SA (Argentina) *Tel:* (011) 4383-5291 *Fax:* (011) 4382-4181 *E-mail:* editorial@polemos.com. ar *Web Site:* www.polemos.com.ar, pg 8

Polestar Purnell Ltd (United Kingdom) *Tel:* (01761) 404142 *Fax:* (01761) 404191 *Web Site:* www.polestar-group.com/purnell, pg 1154

Polgart Kft (Hungary) *Tel:* (01) 399 0859 *Fax:* (01) 399 0859 *E-mail:* polgart@elender.hu, pg 321

Police Review Publishing Company Ltd (United Kingdom) *Tel:* (020) 7440 4700 *Fax:* (020) 7405 7167; (020) 7405 7163, pg 739

The Policy Press (United Kingdom) *Tel:* (0117) 331 4054 *Fax:* (0117) 331 4093 *E-mail:* tpp-info@bristol. ac.uk *Web Site:* www.policypress.org.uk, pg 739

Policy Studies Institute (PSI) (United Kingdom) *Tel:* (020) 7468 0468 *Fax:* (020) 7388 0914 *E-mail:* website@psi.org.uk *Web Site:* www.psi.org.uk, pg 739

Polifemo, Ediciones (Spain) *Tel:* (091) 7257101 *Fax:* (091) 3556811 *E-mail:* libros@polifemo.com *Web Site:* www.polifemo.com, pg 592

Il Polifilo (Italy) *Tel:* (02) 6551549 *Fax:* (02) 6598045, pg 400

Istituto Poligrafico e Zecca Dello Stato (Italy) *Tel:* (06) 85081 *Toll Free Tel:* 800 864035 *Fax:* (06) 8508-2517 *E-mail:* infoipzs@ipzs.it *Web Site:* www.ipzs.it, pg 1149

Istituto Poligrafico e Zecca dello Stato (Italy) *Tel:* (06) 85081 *Toll Free Tel:* 800-864035 *Fax:* (06) 85082517 *E-mail:* infoipzs@ipzs.it *Web Site:* www.ipzs.it, pg 400

Il Poligrafo (Italy) *Tel:* (049) 776986 *Fax:* (049) 775328, pg 400

Polirom Verlag (Romania) *Tel:* (032) 214-100; (032) 214-111; (032) 217-440 *Fax:* (032) 214-100; (032) 214-111; (032) 217-440 *E-mail:* office@polirom.ro *Web Site:* www.polirom.ro, pg 537

Polish Chamber of Books (Poland) *Tel:* (022) 826 12 01 *Fax:* (022) 826 78 55 *E-mail:* pik@arspolona.com.pl *Web Site:* www.pik.org.pl, pg 1271

Polish Chamber of Books (Poland) *Tel:* (022) 8759497 *Fax:* (022) 8759496 *E-mail:* biuro@pik.org.pl *Web Site:* www.pik.org.pl, pg 1327

Polish Scientific Publishers PWN (Poland) *Tel:* (022) 6954321; (022) 6954181 *Fax:* (022) 8267163; (022) 6954288 *E-mail:* pwn@pwn.com.pl *Web Site:* www. pwn.pl, pg 520

Politechnika Krakowska im Tadeusza Kosciuszki (Poland) *Tel:* (012) 628-20-14 *Fax:* (012) 628-20-14 *E-mail:* listy@biblos.pk.edu.pl *Web Site:* www.pk.edu. pl, pg 1536

Politechnika Slaska (Poland) *Tel:* (032) 237-12-69 *Fax:* (032) 237-15-51 *E-mail:* rjo1@polsl.pl *Web Site:* www.polsl.gliwice.pl/alma.mater/biblioteka. html, pg 1536

Marilyn Potts International Language Consultants (United Kingdom) *Tel:* (0191) 222 1775 *Fax:* (0191) 261 6426 *E-mail:* info@marilyn-potts.co.uk *Web Site:* www.marilyn-potts.co.uk, pg 1141

Pournaras Panagiotis (Greece) *Tel:* 2310270941 *Fax:* 2310228922 *E-mail:* pournarasbooks@the.forthnet.gr, pg 1304

Editions Pourquoi Pas (Switzerland) *Tel:* (022) 7511031, pg 627

Power Publications (Australia) *Tel:* (02) 9351 6904 *Fax:* (02) 9351 7323 *E-mail:* power.publications@ arts.usyd.edu.au *Web Site:* www.power.arts.usyd.edu.au/institute, pg 37

Shelley Power Literary Agency Ltd (France) *Tel:* (01) 42383649 *Fax:* (01) 40407008, pg 1121

T & AD Poyser Ltd (United Kingdom) *Tel:* (020) 8308 5700 *Fax:* (020) 8308 5702 *E-mail:* cservice@ harcourt.com, pg 740

Neri Pozza Editore (Italy) *Tel:* (0444) 320787; (0444) 323036 *Fax:* (0444) 324613 *Web Site:* www.neripozza.it, pg 400

Edizioni Luigi Pozzi SRL (Italy) *Tel:* (06) 8553548 *Fax:* (06) 8554105 *E-mail:* edizioni_pozzi@tin.it, pg 400

PPC Editorial y Distribuidora, SA (Spain) *Tel:* (091) 4228800 *Fax:* (091) 4226117 *E-mail:* buzonppc@ ppc-editorial.com *Web Site:* www.ppc-editorial.com, pg 592

PPC Editorial y Distribuidora, SA (Spain) *Tel:* (091) 5089224 *Fax:* (091) 5084082, pg 1334

PPP Printers Ltd (New Zealand) *Tel:* (03) 3662727 *Fax:* (03) 3654606, pg 1150, 1171, 1211

Prabhat Prakashan (India) *Tel:* (011) 3264676; (011) 3289555; (011) 3289666 *Fax:* (011) 3253233 *E-mail:* prabhat@indianabooks.com; prabhat1@vsnl.com *Web Site:* www.indianabooks.com, pg 342

Pracha Chang & Co Ltd (Thailand), pg 641

Georg Prachner KG (Austria) *Tel:* (01) 512 85 49-0 *Fax:* (01) 512-01-58, pg 56

Georg Prachner KG (Austria) *Tel:* (01) 5128549-0 *Fax:* (01) 5120158, pg 1290

Pradeepa Publishers (Sri Lanka) *Tel:* (094) 435074; (094) 863261; (071) 735532 *Fax:* (094) 863261, pg 602

Pragma 4 (Czech Republic) *Tel:* 241 768 565; 241 768 566; 603 205 099 *Fax:* 241 768 561 *E-mail:* pragma@ pragma.cz *Web Site:* www.pragma.cz, pg 126

Agamee Prakashani (Bangladesh) *Tel:* (02) 711-1332; (02) 711-0021 *Fax:* (02) 9562018; (02) 7123945 *E-mail:* agamee@bdonline.com *Web Site:* www.agameeprakashani-bd.com, pg 61

Prasan Mit (Thailand) *Tel:* (02) 3915287; (02) 3925230, pg 641

Prasenz Verlag der Jesus Bruderschaft eV (Germany) *Tel:* (06438) 81281 *Fax:* (06438) 81282 *Web Site:* www.uni-giessen.de, pg 269

Pratibha Pratishthan (India) *Tel:* (011) 3289666 *Toll Free Tel:* (011) 3253233, pg 342

Wydawnictwo Prawnicze Co (Poland) *Tel:* (022) 5729500; (022) 5729507 *Fax:* (022) 5729509 *E-mail:* biuro@lexisnexis.pl *Web Site:* sklep.lexpolonica.pl, pg 521

Prazske nakladatelstvi Pluto (Czech Republic) *Tel:* (02) 249 301 89; (02) 43 25 05 *Fax:* (02) 249 301 89, pg 126

PRC Publishing Ltd (United Kingdom) *Tel:* (020) 7700 7799 *Fax:* (020) 7700 0635 *E-mail:* info@ chrysalisbooks.co.uk *Web Site:* www.chrysalisbooks.co.uk/books/publisher/prc, pg 740

Le Pre-aux-clercs (France) *Tel:* (01) 44 16 05 00; (01) 44 16 05 80 *Fax:* (01) 44 16 05 01 *Web Site:* www.horscollection.com, pg 181

Pre-Textos (Spain) *Tel:* (096) 333 32 26 *Fax:* (096) 395 54 77 *E-mail:* info@pre-textos.com *Web Site:* www.pre-textos.com, pg 592

Precision Publishing Papers Ltd (United Kingdom) *Tel:* (01935) 431800; (732) 563-9292 (USA & other) *Fax:* (01935) 431805 *E-mail:* precisionpub@pppl.co.uk *Web Site:* www.hspg.com/precision, pg 1154

Izdavacko Preduzece Matice Srpske (Serbia and Montenegro) *Tel:* (021) 420 199; (021) 420 198 *Fax:* (021) 28 574; (021) 25 859 *E-mail:* bms@bms.ns.ac.yu *Web Site:* www.bms.ns.ac.yu, pg 548

Ediciones Preescolar SA (Argentina) *Tel:* (011) 4581-3182 *Fax:* (011) 4581-3182, pg 8

Premop Verlag GmbH (Germany) *Tel:* (089) 562257 *Fax:* (089) 5803214 *E-mail:* premop@mnet-online.de, pg 269

Preney Print & Litho Inc (Canada) *Tel:* 519-966-3412 *Toll Free Tel:* 877-870-4164 *Fax:* 519-966-4996 *E-mail:* contactus@preneyprint.com *Web Site:* www.preneyprint.com, pg 1165, 1205

Editorial Prensa Espanola (Spain) *Tel:* (091) 4462616, pg 592

Prensa Medica Latinoamericana (Uruguay) *Tel:* (02) 4000 916 *Fax:* (02) 4000 916 *E-mail:* prensmed@ adinet.com.uy, pg 772

Ediciones Cientificas La Prensa Medica Mexicana SA de CV (Mexico) *Tel:* (05) 5504500 *Fax:* (05) 6589193, pg 467

Prensas Universitarias de Zaragoza (Spain) *Tel:* (0976) 761330 *Fax:* (0976) 761063 *E-mail:* spublica@posta.unizar.es *Web Site:* wzar.unizar.es/spub/, pg 592

Prentsmidjan Oddi (Iceland) *Tel:* 5155000 *Fax:* 5155001 *E-mail:* oddi@oddi.is *Web Site:* www.oddi.is, pg 323

PrePress Imaging Inc (United States) *Tel:* 636-940-9146 *Toll Free Tel:* 800-886-6122 *Fax:* 636-896-8107 *E-mail:* mail@ppi-stl.com *Web Site:* www.ppi-stl.com, pg 1178

Casa Editora Presbiteriana SC (Brazil) *Tel:* (011) 270-7099 *Fax:* (011) 279-1255 *E-mail:* cep@cep.org.br *Web Site:* www.cep.org.br, pg 88

Presbyterian Book Depot & Printing Press Ltd (PRESBOOK) (Cameroon) *Tel:* 332114 *Fax:* 332694, pg 1294

Presbyterian Book Depot Ltd (Ghana) *Tel:* (021) 663124 *Fax:* (021) 662415 *E-mail:* pcg@africaonline.com.gh, pg 1302

Editorial Presenca (Portugal) *Tel:* (021) 4347000 *Fax:* (021) 4346502 *E-mail:* info@editpresenca.pt *Web Site:* www.editpresenca.pt, pg 530

Presence Africaine Editions (France) *Tel:* (01) 43 54 13 74; (01) 43 54 15 88 *Fax:* (01) 43 25 96 67 *E-mail:* presaf@club-internet.fr *Web Site:* www.letissu.com, pg 181

Editorial Presencia Gitana (Spain) *Tel:* (091) 373 62 07 *Fax:* (091) 373 44 62 *E-mail:* anpregit@teleline.es, pg 592

Preses Nams (Latvia) *Tel:* (02) 7062270 *Fax:* (02) 7062344 *E-mail:* presesnams@presesnams.lv *Web Site:* www.presesnams.lv, pg 442

President Boekklub (South Africa) *Tel:* (012) 401 0700 *Fax:* (012) 3255498 *E-mail:* lapa@atkv.org.za *Web Site:* www.lapauitgewers.org.za, pg 1245

President Inc (Japan) *Tel:* (03) 32373734 *Fax:* (03) 32373746 *E-mail:* matu-pre@po.iijnet.or.jp *Web Site:* www.president.co.jp; www.president.co.jp/pre/english.html, pg 422

The Press (Jamaica) *Tel:* (876) 977-2659 *Fax:* (876) 977-2660 *E-mail:* uwipress_marketing@cwjamaica.com; cuserv@cwjamaica.com (customer service & orders) *Web Site:* www.uwipress.com, pg 410

Press Agency (Kuwait) *Tel:* 432269; 417732 *Fax:* 411495, pg 441

Press & Publication Administration of the People's Republic of China (China) *Tel:* (010) 5127809 *Fax:* (010) 5127875, pg 1254

Press & Publicity Centre Ltd (United Republic of Tanzania) *Tel:* (051) 127765; (051) 122881; (051) 131078 *Fax:* (051) 113619; (051) 116749, pg 639

The Press & Publishing Engineering Society (Russian Federation) *Tel:* (095) 291 59 43; (095) 291-42-42 *Fax:* (095) 291-85-06 *E-mail:* sitsev@mail.sitek.ru *Web Site:* usea.mailru.com, pg 1273

Press for Success (Australia) *Tel:* (08) 9221 6166 *Fax:* (08) 9221 6166 *E-mail:* press4@press4success.com.au *Web Site:* www.press4success.com.au, pg 37

Press Mark Media Ltd (Hong Kong) *Tel:* 28822230 *Fax:* 2882 3949; 2882 2471 *E-mail:* magazine@ todayliving.com, pg 315

Press Photo Publications (Greece) *Tel:* 2108541400 *Fax:* 2108541485 *E-mail:* photomag@photo.gr *Web Site:* www.photo.gr, pg 1304

Pressa Publishing House (Russian Federation) *Tel:* (095) 2573482 *Fax:* (095) 2505205, pg 543

PressArt Nakladatelstvi (Czech Republic) *Tel:* (048) 29377 *Fax:* (048) 27958, pg 126

Presse-Grosso-Bundesverband Deutscher Buch-, Zeitungs-und Zeitschriften-Grossisten eV (Germany) *Tel:* (0221) 9213370 *Fax:* (0221) 92133744 *E-mail:* bvpg@bvpg.de *Web Site:* www.pressegrosso.de, pg 1261

PIAG Presse Informations AG (Germany) *Tel:* (07221) 301 7560 *Fax:* (07221) 301 7570 *E-mail:* office@piag.de *Web Site:* www.piag.de, pg 269

Presse Verlagsgesellschaft mbH (Germany) *Tel:* (069) 97460 0 *Fax:* (069) 97460-400 *E-mail:* journal@mmg.de *Web Site:* www.journal-frankfurt.de, pg 269

Presses agronomiques de Gembloux ASBL (Belgium) *Tel:* (081) 62 22 42 *Fax:* (081) 62 22 42 *E-mail:* pressesagro@fsagx.ac.be *Web Site:* www.bib.fsagx.ac.be/presses/, pg 71

Presses de la Cite (France) *Tel:* (01) 44160500 *Fax:* (01) 44160505 *Web Site:* www.pressesdelacite.com, pg 181

Presses de la Renaissance (France) *Tel:* (01) 44 16 05 00 *Fax:* (01) 44 16 05 64 *Web Site:* www.presses-renaissance.fr, pg 181

Presses de la Sorbonne Nouvelle/PSN (France) *Tel:* (01) 40 46 48 02 *Fax:* (01) 40 46 48 04 *E-mail:* psn@univ-paris3.fr *Web Site:* www.univ-paris3.fr/recherche/psn/, pg 181

Presses de l'Ecole Nationale des Ponts et Chaussees (France) *Tel:* (01) 44 58 27 40 *Fax:* (01) 44 58 27 44 *Web Site:* www.enpc.fr, pg 181

Presses de Sciences Politiques (France) *Tel:* (01) 44 39 39 60 *Fax:* (01) 45 48 04 41 *E-mail:* info.presses@ sciences-po.fr *Web Site:* www.sciences-po.fr/edition/, pg 181

Les Presses d'Ile-de-France Sarl (France) *Tel:* (01) 44 52 37 24 *Fax:* (01) 42 38 09 87 *E-mail:* contact@presses-idf.fr *Web Site:* www.scouts-france.fr, pg 181

Les Presses du Management (France) *Tel:* (01) 53 00 11 71 *Fax:* (01) 53 00 10 08, pg 181

Presses Polytechniques et Universitaires Romandes, PPUR (Switzerland) *Tel:* (021) 693 41 31 *Fax:* (021) 693 40 27 *E-mail:* ppur@epfl.ch *Web Site:* www.ppur.org, pg 622

Presses Universitaires d'Afrique (Cameroon) *Tel:* (023) 22 00 30 *Fax:* (023) 22 23 25, pg 98

Presses Universitaires de Bruxelles asbl (Belgium) *Tel:* (02) 641 79 62 *Fax:* (02) 647 79 62, pg 72

Presses Universitaires de Caen (France) *Tel:* (02) 31 56 62 20 *Fax:* (02) 31 56 62 25 *E-mail:* puc@mrsh.unicaen.fr *Web Site:* www.unicaen.fr/mrsh/puc, pg 181

Presses Universitaires de France (PUF) (France) *Tel:* (01) 58 10 31 00 *Fax:* (01) 58 10 31 82 *E-mail:* puf.com@ puf.com *Web Site:* www.puf.com, pg 181

Presses Universitaires de Grenoble (France) *Tel:* (04) 76 82 56 51; (04) 76 82 56 52 *Fax:* (04) 76 82 78 35 *E-mail:* pug@pug.fr *Web Site:* www.pug.fr, pg 182

Presses Universitaires de Liege (Belgium) *Tel:* (041) 562218, pg 72

Presses Universitaires de Lyon (France) *Tel:* (04) 78 29 39 39 *Fax:* (04) 78 29 39 41 *Web Site:* sites.univ-lyon2.fr/pul, pg 182

Presses Universitaires de Namur ASBL (Belgium) *Tel:* (081) 72 48 84 *Fax:* (081) 72 49 12 *E-mail:* pun@fundp.ac.be *Web Site:* www.pun.be, pg 72

Presses Universitaires de Nancy (France) *Tel:* (03) 83 96 84 30 *Fax:* (03) 83 96 84 39 *E-mail:* pun@univ-nancy2.fr *Web Site:* www.univ-nancy2.fr, pg 182

Presses Universitaires de Strasbourg (France) *Tel:* (03) 88 25 97 21 *Fax:* (03) 88 35 65 23 *E-mail:* info@pu-strasourg.com *Web Site:* www.pu-strasbourg.com, pg 182

Presses Universitaires du Septentrion (France) *Tel:* (03) 20 41 66 80 *Fax:* (03) 20 41 66 90 *E-mail:* septentrion@septentrion.com *Web Site:* www.septentrion.com, pg 182

Presses Universitaires du Zaiire (PUZ) (The Democratic Republic of the Congo) *Tel:* 30652, pg 114

Pressfoto Vydavatelstvi Ceske Tiskove Kancelare (Czech Republic) *Tel:* (02) 727 700 10 *Fax:* (02) 727 700 10, pg 126

Guido Pressler Verlag (Germany) *Tel:* (02429) 1385; (02408) 929692 *Fax:* (02408) 955931 *E-mail:* info@pressler-verlag.com *Web Site:* www.pressler-verlag.com, pg 269

Prestel Verlag (Germany) *Tel:* (089) 38 17 09 0 *Fax:* (089) 33 51 75 *E-mail:* info@prestel.de *Web Site:* www.prestel.de, pg 269

Prestige Booksellers & Stationers (Kenya) *Tel:* (02) 223515 *Fax:* (02) 2246796 *E-mail:* prest@iconnect.co.ke, pg 1314

Preston Corporation Sdn Bhd (Malaysia) *Tel:* (03) 7563734 *Fax:* (03) 7573607, pg 455

Helmut Preussler Verlag (Germany) *Tel:* (0911) 95478 0 *Fax:* (0911) 542486 *E-mail:* preussler_verlag@t_online.de, pg 269

Mathew Price Ltd (United Kingdom) *Tel:* (01935) 816010 *Fax:* (01935) 816310 *E-mail:* mathewp@mathewprice.com *Web Site:* www.mathewprice.com, pg 740

Price Publishing (Australia) *Tel:* (02) 9904 9811 *E-mail:* pricesys@localnet.com.au, pg 37

Priese GmbH & Co (Germany) *Tel:* (030) 8263024, pg 1145

Priese GmbH & Co (Germany) *Tel:* (030) 8263024 *Fax:* (030) 3249630, pg 1167

Priese GmbH & Co (Germany) *Tel:* (030) 8263024 *Fax:* (030) 8266024, pg 1207

Priese GmbH & Co (Germany) *Tel:* (030) 8263024 *Fax:* (030) 3249630, pg 1226

Priese GmbH & Co (Germany) *Tel:* (030) 8263024 *Fax:* (030) 8266024, pg 1235

Priestley Consulting (Australia) *Tel:* (07) 4937179 *Fax:* (07) 54458288 *E-mail:* adpriestley@ozemail.com.au, pg 37

Prim-Ed Publishing UK Ltd (United Kingdom) *Tel:* (0870) 876 0151 *Fax:* (0870) 876 0152 *E-mail:* sales@prim-ed.com *Web Site:* www.prim-ed.com, pg 740

Primary English Teaching Association (Australia) *Tel:* (02) 9565 1277 *Fax:* (02) 9565 1070 *E-mail:* info@peta.edu.au *Web Site:* www.peta.edu.au, pg 37

Edizioni Primavera SRL (Italy) *Tel:* (055) 50621 *Fax:* (055) 5062298 *E-mail:* d.bascialfarei@giunti.it, pg 401

Editora Primor Ltda (Brazil) *Tel:* (021) 4744966, pg 88

Primrose Hill Press Ltd (United Kingdom) *Tel:* (01869) 277 000 *Fax:* (01869) 277 820 *Web Site:* www.primrosehillpress.co.uk, pg 740

Principato (Italy) *Tel:* (02) 312025 *Fax:* (02) 33104295 *E-mail:* princi.red@comm2000.it, pg 401

Printafoil Ltd (United Kingdom) *Tel:* (020) 8640 3075 *Fax:* (020) 8640 2136, pg 1217

Printafoil Ltd (United Kingdom) *Tel:* (01473) 721701 *Fax:* (01473) 270705 *E-mail:* printafoil@blockfoil.com *Web Site:* www.blockfoil.com, pg 1229

Printcrafters Inc (Canada) *Tel:* 204-633-7117 *Fax:* 204-694-1519 *E-mail:* info@printcraftersinc.com *Web Site:* www.printcraftersinc.com, pg 1165, 1205, 1225, 1235

Editions Le Printemps (Mauritius) *Tel:* 6961017 *Fax:* 6867302 *E-mail:* elp@intnet.mu, pg 458

Printer Industria Grafica SA (Spain) *Tel:* (093) 631 01 23 *Fax:* (093) 631 02 05; (093) 631 02 06 *E-mail:* info.printer@arvato-print.es *Web Site:* www.printer-spain.com, pg 1213

Printer Portuguesa Industria Grafica Lda (Portugal) *Tel:* (01) 9216025 *Fax:* (01) 9218363 *E-mail:* lissabon.printerportuguesa@bertelsmann.de, pg 1212

Printing Corp of the Americas Inc (United States) *Tel:* 954-781-8100 *Fax:* 954-781-8421, pg 1157, 1179, 1220, 1231

Printing Industry Publishing House (China) *Tel:* (010) 68218367 *Fax:* (010) 8214683 *E-mail:* capt@public3.bta.net.cn, pg 106

Printpak (Z) Ltd (Zambia) *Tel:* (01) 611001; (01) 611002; (01) 600113; (01) 612027 *Fax:* (01) 617096, pg 776

Prints India (India) *Tel:* (011) 3268645 *Fax:* (011) 3275542, pg 1307

PrintWest (Canada) *Tel:* 306-525-2304 *Toll Free:* 800-236-6438 *Fax:* 306-757-2439 *E-mail:* general@printwest.com *Web Site:* www.printwest.com, pg 1143, 1165, 1225, 1235

Printworld Services Pte Ltd (Singapore) *Tel:* 7442166 *Fax:* 7460845 *E-mail:* printw@mbox2.singnet.com.sg, pg 553

Prion Books Ltd (United Kingdom) *Tel:* (01256) 329242 *Fax:* (01256) 812558; (01256) 812521 *E-mail:* mdl@macmillan.co.uk, pg 740

Priroda Publishing (Slovakia) *Tel:* (02) 5556 4672 *Fax:* (02) 5556 4669 *E-mail:* priroda@priroda.sk *Web Site:* www.priroda.sk, pg 555

Prism Press Book Publishers Ltd (United Kingdom) *Tel:* (01202) 665432 *Fax:* (01202) 666219 *E-mail:* orders@orcabookservices.co.uk, pg 740

Bokforlaget Prisma (Sweden) *Tel:* (08) 7698900; (08) 7698700 (international rights) *Fax:* (08) 241276; (08) 7698804 (international rights) *E-mail:* prisma@prismabok.se *Web Site:* www.prismabok.se, pg 609

Prismi - Editrice Politecnica (Italy) *Tel:* (081) 7612884 *Fax:* (081) 668339, pg 401

Priuli e Verlucca, Editori (Italy) *Tel:* (0125) 23 99 29 *Fax:* (0125) 23 00 85 *E-mail:* info@priulieverlucca.it *Web Site:* www.priulieverlucca.it, pg 401

Private Equity Media (Australia) *Tel:* (02) 9713 7608 *Fax:* (02) 9713 1004 *E-mail:* info@privateequitymedia.com.au *Web Site:* www.privateequitymedia.com.au, pg 37

Private Libraries Association (PLA) (United Kingdom) *Web Site:* www.the-old-school.demon.co.uk/pla.htm, pg 1283

Privredni Pregled (Serbia and Montenegro) *Tel:* (011) 625522; (011) 628477 *Fax:* (011) 3281473; (011) 3281912 *E-mail:* novinska@hotmail.com; desk@grmec.co.yu *Web Site:* www.grmec.co.yu, pg 548

Pro Juventute Verlag (Switzerland) *Tel:* (01) 2567777 *Fax:* (01) 2567778 *E-mail:* info@projuventute.ch *Web Site:* www.projuventute.ch, pg 627

Pro Media Productions (Suriname) *Tel:* 479355, pg 603

Pro Natur Verlag GmbH (Germany) *Tel:* (069) 9688610 *Fax:* (069) 96886124, pg 269

Pro Natura (Hungary) *Tel:* (01) 1317330 *Fax:* (01) 1117270, pg 321

Editions Pro Schola (Switzerland) *Tel:* (021) 323 66 55 *Fax:* (021) 323 67 77 *E-mail:* benedict@benedict-schools.com *Web Site:* www.benedict-international.com, pg 627

Proa SA (Chile) *Tel:* (02) 633 65 34; (02) 633 98 54 *Fax:* (02) 633 98 54 *E-mail:* proa@eutelchile.net, pg 99

Edicions Proa, SA (Spain) *Tel:* (093) 4120030 *Fax:* (093) 3014863 *E-mail:* enciclo.catalan@bcn.servicom.es, pg 592

Procultura SA (Colombia) *Tel:* (01) 2818254, pg 112

PRODIG (France) *Tel:* (01) 44 32 14 81; (01) 42 34 56 21 *Fax:* (01) 43 29 63 83 *E-mail:* prodig@univ-paris1.fr *Web Site:* prodig.univ-paris1.fr/umr, pg 182

Prodim SPRL (Belgium) *Tel:* (02) 640 59 70 *Fax:* (02) 640 59 91 *E-mail:* prodim.books@prodim.be *Web Site:* www.prodim.be, pg 72

Professional Book Supplies Ltd (United Kingdom) *Tel:* (01235) 861234 *Fax:* (01235) 861601 *E-mail:* probooks@aol.com, pg 740

Professional, Managerial & Healthcare Publications (United Kingdom) *Tel.* (01243) 576444 *Fax:* (01243) 576456 *E-mail:* admin@pmh.uk.com *Web Site:* www.pmh.uk.com, pg 741

Professional Publishing Co (Hong Kong) *Tel:* 25254623 *Fax:* 28453681, pg 1148

Profile Books Ltd (United Kingdom) *Tel:* (020) 7404 3001 *Fax:* (020) 7404 3003 *E-mail:* info@profilebooks.co.uk *Web Site:* www.profilebooks.co.uk, pg 741

Profile Publishing Ltd (New Zealand) *Tel:* (09) 6308940; (09) 3585455 *Fax:* (09) 6302307; (09) 6301046; (09) 3585462 *E-mail:* info@profile.co.nz *Web Site:* www.profile.co.nz, pg 495

Profizdat (Russian Federation) *Tel:* (095) 924-5740; (095) 924-8225 (books); (095) 924-4637 (periodicals) *Fax:* (095) 975-2329 *E-mail:* profizdat@profizdat.ru *Web Site:* www.profizdat.ru, pg 543

Progensa Editorial (Spain) *Tel:* (0954) 186 200 *Fax:* (0954) 186 111 *E-mail:* progensa@progensa.com *Web Site:* www.progensa.es, pg 592

Editorial Progreso SA de CV (Mexico) *Tel:* (05) 547-1780 *Fax:* (05) 541-1189 *E-mail:* editprogresosav@infosel.net.mx, pg 467

Progress Press Co Ltd (Malta) *Tel:* 21241464; 21241469; 21241411; 21241412 *Fax:* 21241171, pg 456

Progress Publishers (Russian Federation) *Tel:* (095) 2469032 *Fax:* (095) 2302403, pg 543

Progress-Verlag Dr Micolini's Witwe (Austria) *Tel:* (0316) 829508 *Fax:* (0316) 829508, pg 56

Prohazka I Kacarmazov (Bulgaria) *Tel:* (02) 654969 *Fax:* (02) 654969 *E-mail:* eto@einet.bg, pg 96

Projektion J Buch- und Musikverlag GmbH (Germany) *Tel:* (06443) 68-0 *Fax:* (06443) 68-34 *E-mail:* info@gerth.de *Web Site:* www.gerth.de, pg 269

Prolog Publishing House (Israel) *Tel:* (03) 9022904 *Fax:* (03) 9022906 *E-mail:* info@prolog.co.il *Web Site:* www.prolog.co.il, pg 368

De Prom (Netherlands) *Tel:* (035) 5482403 *Fax:* (035) 5418221 *E-mail:* info.fontein@defonteinbaarn.nl, pg 483

Promedia Verlagsges mbH (Austria) *Tel:* (01) 405 27 02 *Fax:* (01) 405 71 59 22 *E-mail:* promedia@mediashop.at *Web Site:* www.mediashop.at, pg 56

Ediciones Promesa (Costa Rica) *Tel:* 253-3759; 225-1511; 283-3033 *Fax:* 225-1286 *E-mail:* edicionespromesa@hotmail.com, pg 115

Ediciones Promesa, SA de CV (Mexico) *Tel:* (05) 5623174; (05) 3938707 *Fax:* (05) 5623174 *E-mail:* promesa@mati.net.mx; riveraluisa@hotmail.com, pg 467

Prometej Izdatelstvo (Russian Federation) *Tel:* (095) 2454495, pg 543

Prometheus (Netherlands) *Tel:* (020) 624 19 34 *Fax:* (020) 622 54 61 *E-mail:* pbo@pbo.nl *Web Site:* www.pbo.nl, pg 483

Promilla & Publishers (India) *Tel:* (011) 668720 *Fax:* (011) 6448947, pg 342

Promociones de Mercados Turisticos SA de CV (Mexico) *Tel:* (05) 2771480; (05) 5160162; (05) 2714736 *Fax:* (05) 2725942 *E-mail:* tm@mail.internet.com.mx *Web Site:* www.travelguidemexico.com, pg 467

Editions Promoculture (Luxembourg) *Tel:* 480691 *Fax:* 400950 *E-mail:* promocul@pt.lu *Web Site:* www.promoculture.lu, pg 448

Librairie Promoculture (Luxembourg) *Tel:* 480691 *Fax:* 400950 *E-mail:* info@promoculture.lu *Web Site:* www.promoculture.lu, pg 1316

Promoedition SA (Switzerland) *Tel:* (022) 8099460 *Fax:* (022) 7811414, pg 627

Promotion Litteraire (France) *Tel:* (01) 45004210 *Fax:* (01) 45001018 *E-mail:* promolit@club-internet.fr, pg 1121

Promotional Reprint Co Ltd (United Kingdom) *Tel:* (020) 7736 5666 *Fax:* (020) 7736 5777, pg 1344

Prompter Publications (Republic of Korea) *Tel:* (02) 82 2214 1794, pg 439

Pronaos, SA Ediciones (Spain) *Tel:* (091) 5418199; (091) 5412766 *Fax:* (091) 4203429; (091) 5412766 *E-mail:* pronaos@teleline.es; jaire@teleline.es, pg 592

PRONI (Public Record Office of Northern Ireland) (United Kingdom) *Tel:* (02890) 255905 *Fax:* (02890) 255999 *E-mail:* proni@dcalni.gov.uk *Web Site:* www.proni.gov.uk, pg 1552

Prontaprint Asia Ltd (Hong Kong) *Tel:* 28657525 *Fax:* 28661064 *E-mail:* postmaster@pronta.com.hk, pg 1148, 1209

Prontaprint Asia Ltd (Hong Kong) *Tel:* 28657525 *Fax:* 28661064, pg 1226, 1236

Henri Proost & Co, Pvba (Belgium) *Tel:* (014) 40 08 11 *Fax:* (014) 42 87 94 *Web Site:* www.proost.be, pg 72

Propos 2 Editions (France) *Tel:* (04) 92 73 08 94 *Fax:* (04) 92 73 08 94 *E-mail:* ProposdeC@aol.com *Web Site:* www.propos2editions.net, pg 182

Propylaeen Verlag, Zweigniederlassung Berlin der Ullstein Buchverlage GmbH (Germany) *Tel:* (030) 2591-3570 *Fax:* (030) 2591-3533, pg 269

ProQuest Information & Learning (United Kingdom) *Tel:* (01223) 215512 *Fax:* (01223) 215513 *E-mail:* marketing@proquest.co.uk *Web Site:* www.proquest.co.uk, pg 741

Proskinio Spyros Ch Marinis (Greece) *Tel:* 210 3648170 *Fax:* 2103648033, pg 308

Prospect Media (Australia) *Tel:* (02) 9422 2222 *Fax:* (02) 9422 2444 *Web Site:* www.lexisnexis.com.au, pg 37

Prostor, nakladatelstvi sro (Czech Republic) *Tel:* (02) 224 826 688 *Fax:* (02) 242 441 694 *E-mail:* prostor@ini.cz *Web Site:* www.prostor-nakladatelstvi.cz, pg 126

Izdatelstvo Prosveshchenie (Russian Federation) *Tel:* (095) 789-30-29; (095) 789-30-40 *Fax:* (095) 200-42-66; (095) 289-33-98 *E-mail:* msamodwrova@prosv.ru *Web Site:* www.prosv.ru, pg 543

Prosveta (Serbia and Montenegro) *Tel:* (011) 629 843; (011) 631 566 *Fax:* (011) 182 581, pg 549

Prosveta (Serbia and Montenegro) *Tel:* (011) 629 843; (011) 631 566 *Fax:* (011) 182 581 *E-mail:* prosveta@eunet.yu *Web Site:* www.prosveta.co.yu, pg 1330

Editions Prosveta (France) *Tel:* (04) 94 19 33 33 *Fax:* (04) 94 19 33 34 *E-mail:* international@prosvesta.com *Web Site:* www.prosveta.com, pg 182

Prosveta-Izdavako preduzece (Serbia and Montenegro) *Tel:* (011) 629 843; (011) 631 566; (011) 625760 *Fax:* (011) 627465, pg 1245

Prosveta Publishers AS (Bulgaria) *Tel:* (02) 760651; (02) 9743696; (02) 761182 *Fax:* (02) 764451 *E-mail:* prosveta@intech.bg, pg 96

Prosvetno Delo Publishing House (The Former Yugoslav Republic of Macedonia) *Tel:* (02) 117 255; (02) 2 225 434 *Fax:* (02) 129 402; (02) 225 434 *E-mail:* prodelo@nic.mpt.com.mk *Web Site:* www.prodelo.com.mk, pg 449

Prosvjeta d d Bjelovar (Croatia) *Tel:* (043) 245-222; (043) 245-223 *Fax:* (043) 245-220, pg 119

Prosvjeta doo (Croatia) *Tel:* (01) 4872-477 *Fax:* (01) 4872-481 *E-mail:* redakcija@prosvjeta-zg.hr, pg 119

Protestant Publications (Australia) *Tel:* (02) 9868 4591 *Fax:* (02) 9868 7953, pg 37

Proton Editora Ltda (Brazil) *Tel:* (011) 2103616; (011) 8147922; (011) 8159708 *Fax:* (011) 8159920 *E-mail:* sitaenk@uol.com.br, pg 88

Instituto Provincial de Investigaciones y Estudios Toledanos (IPIET) (Spain) *Tel:* (0925) 259367 *Fax:* (0925) 259348 *E-mail:* diputolepu@diputoledo.es, pg 592

Prozoretz Ltd Publishing House (Bulgaria) *Tel:* (02) 765171; (02) 746053 *Fax:* (02) 746053 *E-mail:* prozor@tea.bg, pg 96

Prugg Verlag (Austria) *Tel:* (02682) 2114, pg 56

Przedsiebiorstwo Wydawniczo-Handlowe Wydawnictwo Siedmiorog (Poland) *Tel:* (071) 341 68 71 *Fax:* (071) 341 68 87 *E-mail:* siedmiorog@siedmiorog.com.pl *Web Site:* www.siedmiorog.pl, pg 521

Wydawnictwa Przemyslowe WEMA (Poland) *Tel:* (022) 8275456; (022) 8272117 *Fax:* (022) 6355779, pg 521

PSAI Press (Ireland) *Tel:* (01) 6081651 *E-mail:* nconnol4@tcd.ie *Web Site:* www.politics.tcd.ie/psai, pg 359

M Psaropoulos & Co EE (Greece) *Tel:* 2103606808 *Fax:* 2103609645, pg 308

Psichogios Publications SA (Greece) *Tel:* 210 3302535; 2103302234 *Fax:* 2103604683; 2103302098 *E-mail:* psicho@otenet.gr, pg 308

Psicologica Editrice (Italy) *Tel:* (06) 35453558 *Fax:* (06) 35341466 *E-mail:* ontonet@tin.it, pg 401

Bookclub Psyche (Japan) *Tel:* (03) 33290031 *Fax:* (03) 53747186 *Web Site:* www.seiwa-pb.co.jp, pg 1244

Psychiatrie-Verlag GmbH (Germany) *Tel:* (0228) 725340 *Fax:* (0228) 7253420 *E-mail:* verlag@psychiatrie.de *Web Site:* www.psychiatrie.de/verlag, pg 269

Psychoanalyticke Nakladatelstvi (Czech Republic) *Tel:* (02) 33340305; (02) 545 97 12; (02) 627 1855 *Fax:* (02) 312 03 05, pg 126

Psychologie Verlags Union GmbH (Germany) *Tel:* (06201) 60070 *E-mail:* info@beltz.de *Web Site:* www.beltz.de, pg 269

Psychosophische Gesellschaft (Switzerland) *Tel:* (071) 59 13 01 *Fax:* (071) 3672301, pg 627

Psychosozial-Verlag (Germany) *Tel:* (0641) 77819 *Fax:* (0641) 77742 *E-mail:* info@psychosozial-verlag.de; bestellung@psychosozial-verlag.de *Web Site:* www.psychosozial-verlag.de, pg 270

Psykologifoerlaget AB (Sweden) *Tel:* (08) 775 09 00; (08) 775 09 10 (orders) *Fax:* (08) 775 09 20 *E-mail:* info@psykologiforlaget.se *Web Site:* www.psykologiforlaget.se, pg 609

PT Bhakti Baru (Indonesia) *Tel:* (0411) 5192 *Fax:* (0411) 7156, pg 353

PT Pradnya Paramita (Indonesia) *Tel:* (021) 8583369 *Fax:* (021) 8504944, pg 353

PT Pradnya Paramita (Indonesia) *Tel:* (021) 8583369 *Fax:* (021) 8583369, pg 1308

PT Pustaka LP3ES Indonesia (Indonesia) *Tel:* (021) 5674211; (021) 5667139; (021) 56967920 *Fax:* (021) 5683785 *Web Site:* www.lp3es.or.id, pg 353

Pt Ravishankar Shukla University Library (India) *Tel:* (0771) 534 356 *Fax:* (0771) 234 283 *E-mail:* info@rsuniversity.com, pg 1514

PTI - Publicacoes Tecnicas Internacionais Ltda (Brazil) *Tel:* (011) 3159 2535 *Fax:* (011) 3159 2450 *E-mail:* info@pti.com.br *Web Site:* www.pti.com.br, pg 1294

Publi-Fusion (France) *Tel:* (05) 65220303 *Fax:* (05) 65220322 *E-mail:* publi-fusion@wanadoo.fr, pg 182

Public Archives of Sierra Leone (Sierra Leone) *Tel:* (022) 229 471, pg 1541

Public Lending Right (United Kingdom) *Tel:* (01642) 604699 *Fax:* (01642) 615641 *E-mail:* registrar@plr.uk.com *Web Site:* www.plr.uk.com, pg 1283

Public Lending Right Scheme (Australia) *Tel:* (02) 6271 1650 *Toll Free Tel:* 800 672 842 (Australia only) *Fax:* (02) 6271 1651 *E-mail:* plr.mail@dcita.gov.au *Web Site:* www.dcita.gov.au, pg 1250

Public Library (Jordan), pg 1521

Public Library of Latakia (Syrian Arab Republic), pg 1547

Publicaciones Cultural SA de CV (Mexico) *Tel:* (05) 55618333; (05) 55619299 *Fax:* (05) 5615231; (05) 55614063 *E-mail:* info@patriacultural.com.mx *Web Site:* www.patriacultural.com.mx, pg 467

Publicaciones de la Universidad de Alicante (Spain) *Tel:* (0965) 909 576 *Fax:* (0965) 909 445 *E-mail:* publicaciones.ventas@ua.es *Web Site:* publicaciones.ua.es, pg 592

Publicaciones de la Universidad Pontificia Comillas-Madrid (Spain) *Tel:* (091) 542 28 00 *Fax:* (091) 734 45 70 *E-mail:* edit@pub.upco.es *Web Site:* www.upco.es, pg 592

Publicaciones Importantes SA (Mexico) *Tel:* (05) 5101884; (05) 5109489 *Fax:* (05) 5129411, pg 467

Publicaciones Lo Castillo SA (Chile) *Tel:* (02) 235 2606 *Fax:* (02) 235 2007, pg 100

Publicaciones Nuevo Extremo (Chile) *Tel:* (02) 698 1523; (02) 697 2337 *Fax:* (02) 697 2545 *E-mail:* nexxtremo@entelchile.net, pg 100

Publicaciones y Ediciones Salamandra SA (Spain) *Tel:* (093) 2151199 *Fax:* (093) 2154636 *E-mail:* derechos@salamandra-info.com, pg 592

Publicacoes Dom Quixote Lda (Portugal) *Tel:* (021) 538079 *Fax:* (021) 574595, pg 530

Ediouro Publicacoes, SA (Brazil) *Tel:* (021) 5606122 *Fax:* (011) 55893300 *E-mail:* ediourolivrosp@openlink.com.br; livros@ediouro.com.br *Web Site:* www.ediouro.com.br, pg 88

Editora de Publicacoes Medicas Ltda (Brazil) *Tel:* (021) 2654047; (021) 2253516 *Fax:* (021) 2613749, pg 88

Publication Bureau (India) *Tel:* (0172) 541782; (0172) 534373, pg 342

Publications & Information Directorate, CSIR (India) *Tel:* (011) 5785359; (011) 5786301 (ext 288) *Fax:* (011) 5787062, pg 342

Publications de la Fondation Temimi pour la Recherche Scientifique et L'Information (Tunisia) *Tel:* 72676446; 72680110 *Fax:* 72676710 *E-mail:* temimi.fond.@gnet.tn *Web Site:* temimi.org (in Arabic); refer.org/6 (in French), pg 644

Publications de l'Ecole Moderne Francaise (PEMF) (France) *Tel:* (04) 92284284 *Fax:* (016) 92921804 *E-mail:* commercial@pemf.fr *Web Site:* www.pemf.fr, pg 1242

Editions Publications de l'Ecole Moderne Francaise sa (PEMF) (France) *Tel:* (04) 92 28 42 84 *Fax:* (04) 92 28 42 99, pg 182

Publications de l'Universite de Rouen (France) *Tel:* (02) 35 14 63 43; (02) 35 14 65 31 *Fax:* (02) 35 14 63 47 *Web Site:* www.univ-rouen.fr, pg 182

Publications des Facultes Universitaires Saint Louis (Belgium) *Tel:* (02) 211 78 94 *Fax:* (02) 211 79 97 *Web Site:* www.fusl.ac.be, pg 72

Publications du Palais de Monaco (Monaco) *Tel:* 093 251831, pg 470

Publications Orientalistes de France (POF) (France) *Tel:* (04) 71 43 23 78 *Fax:* (04) 71 43 23 78 *E-mail:* sieffert@pofjapon.com *Web Site:* www. pofjapon.com, pg 182

Publik-Forum-Verlagsgesellschaft mbH (Germany) *Tel:* (06171) 70030 *Fax:* (06171) 700340, pg 270

Publishers' & Booksellers' Association of Thailand (Thailand) *Tel:* (02) 954-9560-4 *Fax:* (02) 954-9565-6 *E-mail:* info@pubat.or.th *Web Site:* www.pubat.or.th, pg 1278

Publishers Association (Russian Federation) *Tel:* (095) 2021174 *Fax:* (095) 2023989, pg 1273

The Publishers Association (United Kingdom) *Tel:* (020) 7691 9191 *Fax:* (020) 7691 9199 *E-mail:* mail@ publishers.org.uk *Web Site:* www.publishers.org.uk, pg 1283

Publishers' Association for Cultural Exchange (PACE) Japan (Japan) *Tel:* (03) 32915685 *Fax:* (03) 32333645 *E-mail:* office@pace.or.jp *Web Site:* www.pace.or.jp, pg 1265

Publishers' Association of South Africa (PASA) (South Africa) *Tel:* (021) 426 2728; (021) 426 1726 *Fax:* (021) 426 1733 *E-mail:* pasa@publishsa.co.za *Web Site:* www.publishsa.co.za, pg 1274

Publishers' Enterprises Group (PEG) Ltd (Malta) *Tel:* 21440083; 21448539; 21490540 *Fax:* 21488908 *E-mail:* contact@peg.com.mt *Web Site:* www.peg.com. mt, pg 457

Publishers Group South West (Ireland) (Ireland) *Tel:* (027) 73025 *Fax:* (027) 73131 *E-mail:* 73551. 655@compuserve.com, pg 359

Publishers Licensing Society Ltd (United Kingdom) *Tel:* (020) 7299 7730 *Fax:* (020) 7299 7780 *E-mail:* pls@pls.org.uk *Web Site:* www.pls.org.uk, pg 1283

Publishers Marketing Services Pte Ltd (Singapore) *Tel:* 62565166 *Fax:* 62530008 *E-mail:* info@pms. sg *Web Site:* www.pms.com.sg, pg 1330

Publishers United Pvt Ltd (Pakistan) *Tel:* (042) 7352238 *Fax:* (042) 6316015 *E-mail:* smalipub2@hotmail.com; smalipub@wol.net.pk, pg 509

Publishing Council of the Academy of Sciences of the Russian Academy of Sciences (Russian Federation) *Tel:* (095) 952905 *Fax:* (095) 2379107, pg 1273

Publishing Resources Inc (Puerto Rico) *Tel:* (787) 268-8080 *Fax:* 787-774-5781 *E-mail:* publishingresources@att.net, pg 532

Publishing Resources Inc (Puerto Rico) *Tel:* 787-268-8080 *Fax:* 787-774-5781 *E-mail:* pri@tld.net, pg 1171

Publishing Resources Inc (Puerto Rico) *Tel:* 787-268-8080 *Fax:* 787-774-5781 *E-mail:* publishingresources@worldnet.att.net, pg 1212

Publishing Resources Inc (Puerto Rico) *Tel:* (787) 727-1800 *Fax:* (0787) 727-1823 *E-mail:* pri@chevako.net, pg 1236

Publishing Services Suriname (Suriname) *Tel:* 472746; 455792 *Fax:* 410366 *E-mail:* pssmoniz@sr.net *Web Site:* www.parbo.com, pg 603

Publishing Solutions Ltd (New Zealand) *Tel:* (04) 4710582 *Fax:* (04) 4710717 *E-mail:* gen@pubsol.co. nz, pg 496

Publishing Training Centre at BookHouse (United Kingdom) *Tel:* (020) 8874 2718 *Fax:* (020) 8870 8985; (020) 7207 5915 (bookings) *E-mail:* publishing. training@bookhouse.co.uk *Web Site:* www. train4publishing.co.uk, pg 741

Publisud Editions (France) *Tel:* (01) 45 80 78 50 *Fax:* (01) 45 89 94 15 *E-mail:* publisud@compuserve. com; edipublisud@wanadoo.fr, pg 182

Publitec Publications (Lebanon) *Tel:* (01) 495401; (01) 495403 *Fax:* (01) 493330, pg 443

Publitoria Publishers (South Africa) *Tel:* (012) 3790279 *Fax:* (012) 3793464, pg 563

Pudeleco/Publicaciones de Legislacion (Ecuador) *Tel:* (02) 543273 *Fax:* (02) 2543607 *E-mail:* pudeleco@uio.satnet.net, pg 136

Pueblo y Educacion Editorial (PE) (Cuba) *Tel:* (07) 20021490 *Fax:* (07) 2040844 *E-mail:* epe@ceniai.inf. cu, pg 120

Ediciones Puerto (Puerto Rico) *Tel:* 787-721-0844 *Fax:* 787-725-0861 *E-mail:* feriapr@caribe.net, pg 532

Puffin Book Clubs (United Kingdom) *Tel:* (020) 7416 3000 *Toll Free Tel:* (0500) 454 444 *Fax:* (020) 7010 6667 *E-mail:* pbccustomerservice@penguin.co.uk *Web Site:* www.penguin.co.uk; www.puffinbookclub. co.uk, pg 1247

Editions du Puits Fleuri (France) *Tel:* (01) 64 23 61 46 *Fax:* (01) 64 23 69 42 *E-mail:* puitsfleuri@wanadoo.fr *Web Site:* www.puitsfleuri.com, pg 183

Pulp Master Frank Nowatzki Verlag (Germany) *Tel:* (030) 6868292 *Fax:* (030) 6868292 *E-mail:* master@txt.de *Web Site:* www.maasmedia.de, pg 270

Pulso Ediciones, SL (Spain) *Tel:* (0935) 896 264 *Fax:* (0935) 895 077 *E-mail:* pulso@pulso.com *Web Site:* www.pulso.com, pg 592

Puma Editora Lda (Portugal) *Tel:* (021) 9425394 *Fax:* (021) 9425214, pg 530

Punjab Public Library (Pakistan) *Tel:* (042) 325487 *E-mail:* zilpk@yahoo.com, pg 1534

Punjab University Library (Pakistan) *Tel:* (042) 9230834; (042) 9231126 *Fax:* (042) 9230892 *E-mail:* info@ library.pu.edu.pk *Web Site:* www.pulibrary.edu.pk, pg 1534

Punktum AG (Switzerland) *Tel:* (01) 422 45 40, pg 1246

Punktum AG, Buchredaktion und Bildarchiv (Switzerland) *Tel:* (01) 422 45 40 *Fax:* (01) 422 48 13, pg 627

Il Punto D Incontro (Italy) *Tel:* (0444) 239189 *Fax:* (0444) 239266 *E-mail:* ordini@ edizionilpuntodincontro.it *Web Site:* www. edizionilpuntodincontro.it, pg 401

Punto de Encuentro Ediciones (Uruguay) *Tel:* (02) 405167, pg 772

Pursuit Publishing (New Zealand) *Tel:* (09) 4385725 *Fax:* (09) 4382543 *Web Site:* www.pursuit.co.nz, pg 496

Pusat Penelitian Perkebunan Sumbawa (Indonesia) *Tel:* (0711) 312182; (0711) 361793 *Fax:* (0711) 361793, pg 353

Pushtu Toulana, Afghan Academy (Afghanistan) *Tel:* 20350, pg 1

Pustak Mahal (India) *Tel:* (011) 23276539; (011) 23272783; (011) 23272784 *Fax:* (011) 3260518 *E-mail:* pustakmahal@vsnl.net.in *Web Site:* www. pustakmahal.com, pg 342

Pustaka Cipta Sdn Bhd (Malaysia) *Tel:* (03) 2744593 *Fax:* (03) 2749588 *E-mail:* rrapc@pc.jaring.my, pg 455

Pustaka Nasional Pte Ltd (Singapore) *Tel:* 67454321; 67454649 *Fax:* 67452417 *E-mail:* sales@pustaka. com.sg; mohamed@pustaka.com.sg *Web Site:* www. pustaka.com.sg, pg 553

Pustaka Sistem Pelajaran Sdn Bhd (Malaysia) *Tel:* (03) 904-7558; (03) 904-7017; (03) 904-7018 *Fax:* (03) 90747573, pg 455

Pustaka Utama Grafiti, PT (Indonesia) *Tel:* (021) 8567502 *Fax:* (021) 8582430, pg 353

Verlag Anton Pustet (Austria) *Tel:* (0662) 87 35 07-55 *Fax:* (0662) 87 35 07-79 *E-mail:* buch@verlag-anton-pustet.at *Web Site:* www.verlag-anton-pustet.at, pg 56

Verlag Friedrich Pustet GmbH & Co Kg (Germany) *Tel:* (0941) 94 24 105 *Fax:* (0941) 94 24 100 *E-mail:* buecher@pustet.de *Web Site:* www.pustet.de, pg 270

Puthigar Ltd (Bangladesh) *Tel:* (02) 231374; (02) 235333; (02) 259867, pg 1291

Verlag Harry Putz (Czech Republic) *Tel:* (048) 515 21 20; (048) 510 32 75 *Fax:* (048) 510 32 75 *E-mail:* harrputz@mbox.vol.cz, pg 127

PYC Edition (France) *Tel:* (01) 53 26 48 00 *Fax:* (01) 53 26 48 01 *E-mail:* info@pyc.fr *Web Site:* www.pyc.fr, pg 183

Pyeong-hwa Chulpansa (Republic of Korea) *Tel:* (02) 7343341; (02) 7343343 *Fax:* (02) 7392129, pg 439

Editions Pygmalion (France) *Tel:* (01) 45 67 40 77 *Fax:* (01) 47 34 51 52 *E-mail:* pygmalion@pygmalion. fr, pg 183

Pyunghwa Dang Printing Co Ltd (Republic of Korea) *Tel:* (02) 735-4011 *Fax:* (02) 734-5201 *E-mail:* comuser@hitel.kol.co.kr, pg 1170

Pyunghwa Dang Printing Co Ltd (Republic of Korea) *Tel:* (02) 735 4011 *Fax:* (02) 734 5201 *E-mail:* comuser@hitel.kol.co.kr, pg 1211

PZWL Wydawnictwo Lekarskie Ltd (Poland) *Tel:* (022) 6954033; (022) 6954497 *Fax:* (022) 6954032; (022) 6954497 *E-mail:* promocja@pzwl.pl *Web Site:* www. pzwl.pl, pg 521

Q & B Books (Zambia) *Tel:* (01) 290032; (096) 747187 *Fax:* (01) 290032 *E-mail:* qbbooks@yahoo.com, pg 1347

edition q Berlin Edition in der Quintessenz Verlags-GmbH (Germany) *Tel:* (030) 761 80-5 *Fax:* (030) 761 80-680 *E-mail:* editionq@quintessenz.de; info@ quintessenz.de *Web Site:* www.quintessenz.de, pg 270

The Q Group Plc (United Kingdom) *Tel:* (01279) 719070 *Fax:* (01279) 757409 *E-mail:* marketing@ qgroupplc.com; support@qgroupplc.com *Web Site:* www.qgroupplc.com, pg 1154

Qatar National Library (Qatar) *Tel:* 442 9955 *Fax:* 442 9976 *E-mail:* qanaly@qatar.net.qa, pg 1538

Qatar University Library (Qatar) *Tel:* 4852405 *Fax:* 4835092 *E-mail:* postmaster@qu.edu.qa *Web Site:* www.qu.edu.qa/english/library/libraries.htm, pg 1538

Qi Lu Press (China) *Tel:* (0531) 6910055-4920 *Fax:* (0531) 2906811, pg 106

Qingdao Publishing House (China) *Tel:* (0532) 5814611; (0532) 362524 *Fax:* (0532) 515240, pg 107

Qinghua daxue tushuguan (China) *Tel:* (010) 62782137 *Fax:* (010) 62781758 *E-mail:* tsg@mail.lib.tsinghua. edu.cn *Web Site:* www.lib.tsinghua.edu.cn, pg 1496

Quaderns Crema SA (Spain) *Tel:* (093) 4144906 *Fax:* (093) 4147107 *E-mail:* correo@acantilado.es *Web Site:* www.quadernscrema.com, pg 593

Il Quadrante SRL (Italy) *Tel:* (081) 991433 *Fax:* (081) 981672 *E-mail:* info@ilquadrante.com *Web Site:* www. ilquadrante.com, pg 401

Quadrille Publishing Ltd (United Kingdom) *Tel:* (020) 7839 7117 *Fax:* (020) 7839 7118 *Web Site:* www. quadrille.co.uk, pg 741

Quaid-i-Azam University Department of Biological Sciences (Pakistan) *Tel:* (051) 2482513 *Fax:* (051) 2482513 *E-mail:* qau@gmx.net; daud@gmx.net *Web Site:* members.tripod.com/qau, pg 509

Quaker Books (United Kingdom) *Tel:* (020) 7663 1000 *Fax:* (020) 7663 1008; (020) 7663 1001 (orders) *E-mail:* bookshop@quaker.org.uk *Web Site:* www. quaker.org.uk, pg 741

Quakers Hill Press (Australia) *Tel:* (02) 9626 6112 *Fax:* (02) 9626 9846 *E-mail:* dayp@mpx.com.au, pg 37

Qualitymark Editora Ltda (Brazil) *Tel:* (021) 3860-8422 *Fax:* (021) 3860-8424 *E-mail:* quality@qualitymark. com.br *Web Site:* www.qualitymark.com.br, pg 88

Qualum Technical Services (United Kingdom) *Tel:* (0845) 3001 123 *Fax:* (020) 7681 1316 *E-mail:* technical@qualum.com *Web Site:* qualum. com, pg 741

Quantum Colorgraphics (United States) *Tel:* 973-783-0462 *Fax:* 973-783-0637, pg 1179

Quartet Books Ltd (United Kingdom) *Tel:* (020) 7636 3992; (020) 7636 0968 *Fax:* (020) 7637 1866 *E-mail:* quartetbooks@easynet.co.uk, pg 741

Quarto Publishing plc (United Kingdom) *Tel:* (020) 7700 6700 *Fax:* (020) 7700 4191 *E-mail:* quarto@quarto. com *Web Site:* www.quarto.com, pg 741

Quartz Editions (United Kingdom) *Tel:* (020) 8951 5656 *Fax:* (020) 8904 1200 *E-mail:* quartzeditions@ btconnect.com, pg 741

Edizioni Quasar di Severino Tognon SRL (Italy) *Tel:* (06) 84241993; (06) 85358444 *Fax:* (06) 85833591 *E-mail:* qn@edizioniquasar.it *Web Site:* www.edizioniquasar.it, pg 401

Quatro Elementos Editores (Portugal) *Tel:* (021) 703695, pg 530

Edizioni Quattroventi SNC (Italy) *Tel:* (0722) 2588 *Fax:* (0722) 320998 *E-mail:* info@ edizioniquattroventi.it *Web Site:* www. edizioniquattroventi.it, pg 401

Queen Anne Press (United Kingdom) *Tel:* (01582) 715866 *Fax:* (01582) 715121 *E-mail:* queenanne@ lenqap.demon.co.uk, pg 741

Queen Victoria Museum & Art Gallery Publications (Australia) *Tel:* (03) 6323 3777 *Fax:* (03) 6323 3776 *E-mail:* qvmag@qvmag.tas.gov.au *Web Site:* www. qvmag.tas.gov.au, pg 38

Queensland Art Gallery (Australia) *Tel:* (07) 3840 7333; (07) 3840 7303 *Fax:* (07) 3844 8865; (07) 3840 7350 *E-mail:* gallery@qag.qld.gov.au *Web Site:* www.qag. qld.gov.au, pg 38

Queensway Bookshop & Stores Ltd (Ghana) *Tel:* (021) 62707, pg 1302

Editorial Quehacer Politico SA (Mexico) *Tel:* (05) 5414245 *Fax:* (05) 5384855, pg 467

Queillerie Publishers (South Africa) *Tel:* (021) 4232677 *Fax:* (021) 4242510 *E-mail:* rbarnard@quellerie.com, pg 563

Quell Verlag (Germany) *Tel:* (0711) 601000 *Fax:* (0711) 6010076, pg 270

Quelle Press (Germany) *Tel:* (07664) 7016 *Fax:* (07664) 60979 *E-mail:* quellepress.germany@gmx.net, pg 1122

Quelle und Meyer Verlag GmbH & Co (Germany) *Tel:* (06766) 903200 *Fax:* (06766) 903320 *E-mail:* service@humanitas-book.de *Web Site:* www. quelle-meyer.de, pg 270

Quellen-Verlag GmbH (Switzerland) *Tel:* (071) 227 47 77 *Fax:* (071) 227 47 58, pg 1335

Quentin Books Ltd (United Kingdom) *Tel:* (01206) 825433; (01206) 825434 *Fax:* (01206) 822990, pg 742

Em Querido's Uitgeverij BV (Netherlands) *Tel:* (020) 55 11 200 *Fax:* (020) 55 11 256 *E-mail:* info@querido.nl *Web Site:* www.querido.nl, pg 483

Editrice Queriniana (Italy) *Tel:* (030) 2306925 *Fax:* (030) 2306932 *E-mail:* direzione@queriniana.it; redazione@ queriniana.it *Web Site:* www.queriniana.it, pg 401

Querverlag GmbH (Germany) *Tel:* (030) 78 70 23 39; (030) 78702340 *Fax:* (030) 788 49 50 *E-mail:* mail@ querverlag.de *Web Site:* www.querverlag.de, pg 270

Quesire SRL (Italy) *Tel:* (06) 68136068 *Fax:* (06) 68134167 *E-mail:* ristucciad@quesire.it *Web Site:* www.ristucciaadvisors.com, pg 401

Editorial Quetzal-Domingo Cortizo (Argentina) *Tel:* (011) 4641-5639 *E-mail:* profika@ciudad.com.ar, pg 8

Quetzal Editores (Portugal) *Tel:* (021) 3426172 *Fax:* (021) 3426173 *E-mail:* quetzal@ip.pt, pg 530

Quick Service Books Ltd (Ghana) *Tel:* (021) 224236, pg 302

Quid Juris - Sociedade Editora (Portugal) *Tel:* (021) 651946 *Fax:* (021) 3875538 *E-mail:* quidjuris@mail. telepac.pt, pg 530

Quiller Publishing Ltd (United Kingdom) *Tel:* (01939) 261616 *Fax:* (01939) 261606 *E-mail:* info@ quillerbooks.com, pg 742

Quimera Editores Lda (Portugal) *Tel:* (021) 845 59 50 *Fax:* (021) 845 59 51 *E-mail:* quimera@quimera-editores.com *Web Site:* www.quimera-editores.com, pg 530

Quintessence Publishing Co Ltd (United Kingdom) *Tel:* (020) 89496087 *Fax:* (020) 83361484 *E-mail:* info@quintpub.co.uk *Web Site:* www.quintpub. co.uk, pg 742

Quintessenz Verlags-GmbH (Germany) *Tel:* (030) 761805 *Fax:* (030) 76180680 *E-mail:* info@ quintessenz.de *Web Site:* www.quintessenz.de, pg 270

Quintet Publishing Ltd (United Kingdom) *Tel:* (020) 7700 8001 *Fax:* (020) 7700 4191 *E-mail:* quintet@ quarto.com *Web Site:* www.quarto.com, pg 742

R & R Publications Pty Ltd (Australia) *Tel:* (03) 9381 2199 *Toll Free Tel:* 800 063 296 *Fax:* (03) 9381 2689, pg 38

R P L Books (New Zealand) *Tel:* (09) 4437448 *Fax:* (09) 4430147 *E-mail:* rplbooks@rplbooks.co.nz, pg 496

RA-MA, Libreria y Editorial Microinformatica (Spain) *Tel:* (091) 658 42 80 *Fax:* (091) 662 81 39 *E-mail:* editorial@ra-ma.com *Web Site:* www.ra-ma. com, pg 593

Dr Josef Raabe-Verlags GmbH (Germany) *Tel:* (0711) 62900-0 *Fax:* (0711) 6290010 *Web Site:* www.raabe. de, pg 270

Rabe Verlag AG Zuerich (Switzerland) *Tel:* (01) 261 85 40 *Fax:* (01) 261 85 41, pg 627

Raben och Sjoegren Bokforlag (Sweden) *Tel:* (08) 7698800 *Fax:* (08) 7698813 *E-mail:* raben-sjogren@ raben.se *Web Site:* www.raben.se, pg 610

Raben Verlag von Wittern KG (Germany) *Tel:* (089) 3594879 *Fax:* (089) 3596622, pg 271

Raboni Editora Ltda (Brazil) *Tel:* (019) 32428433 *Fax:* (019) 32428505 *E-mail:* raboni@raboni.com.br *Web Site:* www.raboni.com.br, pg 88

RAC Publishing (United Kingdom) *Tel:* (020) 8686 0088 *Fax:* (020) 8688 2882, pg 742

RACC-62 (Spain) *Tel:* (093) 443 71 00 *Fax:* (093) 443 71 30 *E-mail:* correu@grup62.com *Web Site:* www. grup62.com, pg 593

Andre De Rache Editeur (Belgium) *Tel:* (061) 656091 *Fax:* (061) 656091, pg 72

Editions Racine (Belgium) *Tel:* (02) 646 44 44 *Fax:* (02) 646 55 70 *E-mail:* info@racine.be *Web Site:* www. racine.be, pg 72

Radcliffe Medical Press Ltd (United Kingdom) *Tel:* (01235) 528820 *Fax:* (01235) 528830 *E-mail:* contact.us@radcliffemed.com *Web Site:* www. radcliffe-oxford.com, pg 742

Wydawnictwa Radia i Telewizji (Poland) *Tel:* (022) 412264, pg 521

Radiant Publishers (India) *Tel:* (011) 6435477; (011) 6482861 *Fax:* (011) 6479870 *E-mail:* rpbooksind@ yahoo.com, pg 343

Radiating Books (Australia) *Tel:* (066) 536 280 *Fax:* (066) 514 970, pg 38

Radin-Repro I Roto (Croatia) *Tel:* (01) 3869 200 *Fax:* (01) 3862 673 *E-mail:* radin-repro-i-roto@zg. tel.hr *Web Site:* www.odisej.hr, pg 1144

Izdatelstvo Radio i Svyaz (Russian Federation) *Tel:* (095) 2585351, pg 543

Radius-Verlag GmbH (Germany) *Tel:* (0711) 6076666; (0172) 7126573 *Fax:* (0711) 6075555 *E-mail:* radiusverlag@freenet.de, pg 271

Radnicka Stampa (Serbia and Montenegro) *Tel:* (011) 3230-927; (011) 3230-921; (011) 3236-259 *E-mail:* radstamp@sezampro.yu *Web Site:* www. radnickastampa.co.yu/, pg 549

Raduga Publishers (Russian Federation) *Tel:* (095) 265-55-28 *Fax:* (095) 265-55-28 *E-mail:* raduga@pol.ru, pg 543

Robert Raeber, Buchhandlung am Schweizerhof (Switzerland) *Tel:* (041) 512371, pg 627

Edition Raetia Srl-GmbH (Italy) *Tel:* (0471) 976904 *Fax:* (0471) 976908 *E-mail:* info@raetia.com *Web Site:* www.raetia.com, pg 401

Rageot Editeur (France) *Tel:* (01) 45 48 07 31 *Fax:* (01) 42 22 68 01 *E-mail:* rageotediteur@editions-hatier.fr *Web Site:* www.rageotediteur.fr, pg 183

Ragged Bears Ltd (United Kingdom) *Tel:* (01935) 851590 *Fax:* (01935) 851803 *E-mail:* books@ragged-bears.co.uk *Web Site:* www.ragged-bears.co.uk, pg 742

Rahul Publishing House (India) *Tel:* (0121) 2774518, pg 343

RAI-ERI (Italy) *Tel:* (06) 36864418 *Fax:* (06) 36822071 *E-mail:* rai-eri@rai.it *Web Site:* www.eri.rai.it, pg 401

Rainbow Book Agencies Pty Ltd (Australia) *Tel:* (03) 9481 6611 *Fax:* (03) 9481 2371 *E-mail:* rba@ rainbowbooks.com.au; custserv@rainbowbooks.com. au; despatch@rainbowbooks.com.au (warehouse) *Web Site:* www.rainbowbooks.com.au, pg 38

Rainbow Grafics Intl - Baronian Books SC (Belgium) *Tel:* (02) 649 53 91 *Fax:* (02) 649 27 57, pg 72

Rainbow Graphic & Printing Co Ltd (Hong Kong) *Tel:* 27523423 *Fax:* 28974890 *E-mail:* rgarts@ netvigator.com, pg 1169

Raincloud Productions (Australia) *Tel:* (02) 6251 1765, pg 38

Rainforest Publishing (Australia) *Tel:* (02) 93313004 *Fax:* (02) 93805729 *E-mail:* rod.ritchie@sfine.arts.sa. edu.au, pg 38

Rajasthan Hindi Granth Academy (India) *Tel:* (0141) 61410; (0141) 511129, pg 343

Rajendra Publishing House Pvt Ltd (India) *Tel:* (022) 6300741; (022) 6300742; (022) 6301930 *Fax:* (022) 6301940; (022) 6322146 *E-mail:* books@ rajendrabooks.com *Web Site:* www.rajendrabooks.com, pg 343

Rajesh Publications (India) *Tel:* (011) 274550, pg 343

Rajkamal Prakashan Pvt Ltd (India) *Tel:* (011) 3288769; (011) 3274463 *Fax:* (011) 3278144, pg 343

Rajpal & Sons (India) *Tel:* 223904; 229174 *Fax:* (0141) 2967791, pg 343

Rake Verlag GmbH (Germany) *Tel:* (0431) 6611515 *Fax:* (0431) 6611517 *E-mail:* info@rake.de *Web Site:* www.rake.de, pg 271

Rakennusalan Kustantajat RAK (Finland) *Tel:* (09) 503 2540 *Fax:* (09) 503 2542 *E-mail:* info@sarmala.com *Web Site:* www.sarmala.com, pg 143

Rakennustieto Oy (Finland) *Tel:* (09) 549 5570 *Fax:* (09) 5495 5320 *E-mail:* rakennustieto@rakennustieto.fi *Web Site:* www.rakennustieto.fi, pg 143

Rakla (Bulgaria) *Tel:* (02) 580-569 *E-mail:* grigorit@yahoo.com, pg 96

RAM Editores (Colombia) *Tel:* (01) 2623067, pg 112

Ramakrishna Vedanta Centre (United Kingdom) *Tel:* (01628) 526464 *E-mail:* vedantauk@talk21.com *Web Site:* www.ramakrishna.org; www.vedantauk.com, pg 742

Dr Mohan Krischke Ramaswamy Edition RE (Germany) *Tel:* (0171) 8026882 *Fax:* (0171) 5311065 *E-mail:* edition.re@epost.de, pg 271

Ramboro Books Plc (United Kingdom) *Tel:* (020) 7700 7444 *Fax:* (020) 7700 4552 *E-mail:* enquiries@ramboro.co.uk, pg 742

Rams Skull Press (Australia) *Tel:* (07) 4093 7474 *Fax:* (07) 4051 4484 *E-mail:* ramskull@tpg.com.au, pg 38

Editions Ramsay (France) *Tel:* (01) 53 10 02 80 *Fax:* (01) 53 10 02 88, pg 183

Ramsay Head Press (United Kingdom) *Tel:* (0131) 225 5646 *E-mail:* ramsayhead@btinternet.com, pg 742

Randall & Swift Ltd (United Kingdom) *Tel:* (020) 8553 3030 *Fax:* (020) 8559 1522, pg 1344

Ian Randle Publishers Ltd (Jamaica) *Tel:* (876) 978-0739; (876) 978-0745 *Toll Free Tel:* 866-330-5469 (orders) *Fax:* (876) 978-1156 *E mail:* info@ianrandlepublishers.com *Web Site:* www.ianrandlepublishers.com, pg 411

Random House Australia (Australia) *Tel:* (02) 8923 9863 *Fax:* (02) 9753 3944 *E-mail:* randomhouse@randomhouse.com.au, pg 38

Random House UK Ltd (United Kingdom) *Tel:* (020) 7840 8400 *Fax:* (020) 7233 8791 *E-mail:* enquiries@randomhouse.co.uk *Web Site:* www.randomhouse.co.uk, pg 742

Rankin Publishers (Australia) *Tel:* (07) 3376 9115 *Fax:* (07) 3376 9360 *E-mail:* info@rankin.com.au *Web Site:* www.rankin.com.au, pg 38

Ransom Publishing Ltd (United Kingdom) *Tel:* (01491) 613 711 *Fax:* (01491) 613 733 *E-mail:* ransom@ransom.co.uk *Web Site:* www.ransom.co.uk, pg 743

The Arthur Ransome Society Ltd (TARS) (United Kingdom) *Tel:* (01539) 722464 *E-mail:* tarsinfo@arthur-ransome.org *Web Site:* www.arthur-ransome.org/ar, pg 1403

Grupul Editorial RAO (Romania) *Tel:* (01) 224-12-31; (01) 224-14-72; (01) 224-18-47; (01) 224-21-36 *Fax:* (01) 224-12-31; (01) 224-14-72; (01) 224-18-47; (01) 224-21-36 *E-mail:* office@raobooks.com; club@raobooks.com *Web Site:* www.raobooks.com, pg 537

RAO International Publishing Co (Romania) *Tel:* (01) 224-1002; (01) 224-1704 *Fax:* (01) 222-8059 *E-mail:* rao.b@bx.logicnet.ro, pg 537

Raphael, Editions (Switzerland) *Tel:* (021) 9215230 *Fax:* (021) 9215237, pg 627

Rapra Technology Ltd (United Kingdom) *Tel:* (01939) 250383 *Fax:* (01939) 251118 *E-mail:* publications@rapra.net *Web Site:* www.rapra.net; www.polymer-books.com, pg 743

Rara Istituto Editoriale di Bibliofilia e Reprints (Italy) *Tel:* (02) 4983264 *Fax:* (02) 4814676, pg 401

Margi Rastai Publishers (Lithuania) *Tel:* (02) 429526; (02) 429709; (02) 429527; (02) 426705 *Fax:* (02) 426705 *E-mail:* margirastai@takas.lt, pg 446

Rastogi Publications (India) *Tel:* 24142; 24688 *E-mail:* vrastogi@vsnl.com; info@indianbookmart.com, pg 343

F J Ratchford Ltd (United Kingdom) *Tel:* (0161) 4808484 *Fax:* (0161) 4803679 *E-mail:* info@fjratchford.co.uk *Web Site:* www.fjratchford.co.uk, pg 1154

Rationalisierungs-Kuratorium der Deutschen Wirtschaft eV (RKW) (Germany) *Tel:* (0211) 680010 *Fax:* (0211) 68001 68; (0211) 68001 69 *E-mail:* info@rkw-nrw.de *Web Site:* www.rkwnrw.de, pg 271

Rationalist Press Association (United Kingdom) *Tel:* (020) 7436 1151 *Fax:* (020) 7079 3588 *E-mail:* info@rationalist.org.uk *Web Site:* www.rationalist.org.uk, pg 743

Ratna Book Distributors (Pvt) Ltd (Nepal) *Tel:* 4242027 *Fax:* 4245421 *E-mail:* rpb@wlink.com.np, pg 1320

Werner Rau Verlag (Germany) *Tel:* (0711) 7819 4610 *Fax:* (0711) 7819 4654 *E-mail:* info@rau-verlag.de *Web Site:* www.rau-verlag.de, pg 271

Rauhreif Verlag (Switzerland) *Tel:* (061) 851 53 63, pg 627

Gerhard Rautenberg Druckerei und Verlag GmbH & Co KG (Germany) *Tel:* (0931) 385235 *Fax:* (0931) 385305 *E-mail:* info@verlagshaus.com *Web Site:* www.verlagshaus.com, pg 271

Rav Kook Institute (Israel) *Tel:* (02) 6526231 *Fax:* (02) 6526968, pg 368

Rav Kook Institute (Israel) *Tel:* (02) 6526231 *Fax:* (02) 6526968 *E-mail:* mosad-haravkook@neto.bezeqint.net, pg 1310

Ravan Press (Pty) Ltd (South Africa) *Tel:* (011) 4840916 *Fax:* (011) 4842631, pg 563

Ravensburger Buchverlag Otto Maier GmbH (Germany) *Tel:* (0751) 86 1717 *Fax:* (0751) 861818 *E-mail:* info@ravensburger.de *Web Site:* www.ravensburger.de, pg 271

Ravenstein Verlag GmbH (Germany) *Tel:* (06196) 609630 *Fax:* (06196) 63619 *E-mail:* g.koenig@ravenstein-verlag.de, pg 271

Ravette Publishing Ltd (United Kingdom) *Tel:* (01403) 711443 *Fax:* (01403) 711554 *E-mail:* ravettepub@aol.com, pg 743

Rawlhouse Publishing (Australia) *Tel:* (08) 9321 8951 *Fax:* (08) 9481 1914 *E-mail:* info@rawlhouse.com *Web Site:* www.rawlinsons.com, pg 38

RCS Libri SpA (Italy) *Tel:* (02) 50951 *Fax:* (02) 5065361 *Web Site:* www.rcslibri.it, pg 401

RCS Rizzoli Libri SpA (Italy) *Tel:* (02) 50951 *Fax:* (02) 5065361 *Web Site:* www.rcslibri.it, pg 401

RCS Rizzoli Libri SpA (Italy) *Tel:* (02) 50951 *Fax:* (02) 5065361 *Web Site:* www.rcs.it, pg 1123

RDC Agencia Literaria (Spain) *Tel:* (091) 3085585 *Fax:* (091) 3085600 *E-mail:* rdc@idecnet.com, pg 1126

Reach Publications (New Zealand) *Tel:* (09) 376 3235 *Fax:* (09) 376 3250 *E-mail:* giftedednz@xtra.co.nz, pg 496

Read-a-Book Club (Zambia) *Tel:* (01) 222324; (01) 236629 *Fax:* (01) 225073, pg 1248

Oficyna Wydawnicza Read Me (Poland) *Tel:* (022) 8706024 (ext 130) *Fax:* (022) 6771425 *E-mail:* readme@rm.com.pl *Web Site:* www.rm.com.pl, pg 521

Reader's Digest AB (Sweden) *Tel:* (08) 58710900 *Fax:* (08) 58710990 *E-mail:* red@readersdigest.se *Web Site:* www.readersdigest.se, pg 1246

The Reader's Digest Association Ltd (United Kingdom) *Tel:* (020) 7715 8000 *Fax:* (020) 7715 8181 *Web Site:* www.readersdigest.co.uk, pg 743

Reader's Digest (Australia) Pty Ltd (Australia) *Tel:* (02) 96906935 *Fax:* (02) 96906390, pg 39

Reader's Digest Children's Books (United Kingdom) *Tel:* (01225) 312200 *Fax:* (01225) 460942, pg 743

Reader's Digest Deutschland Verlag Das Beste GmbH (Germany) *Tel:* (0711) 66020 *Fax:* (0711) 6602547 *E-mail:* verlag@readersdigest.de *Web Site:* www.readersdigest.de, pg 271

Reader's Digest SA (Belgium) *Tel:* (02) 5268111 *Fax:* (02) 5268112 *E-mail:* service@readersdigest.be *Web Site:* www.rd.com, pg 72

Reader's Digest Southern Africa (South Africa) *Tel:* (021) 670 6100 *Fax:* (021) 670 6200 *E-mail:* customer.sa@readersdigest.com *Web Site:* www.readersdigest.co.za, pg 563

Readers Union (United Kingdom) *Tel:* (020) 7629 8144 *Fax:* (020) 7499 9751, pg 1247

Readit Books (United Republic of Tanzania) *Tel:* (022) 2184077 *Fax:* (022) 2181077 *E-mail:* readit@raha.com, pg 639, 1336

Ready-Ed Publications (Australia) *Tel:* (08) 9349 6111 *Fax:* (08) 9349 7222 *E-mail:* info@readyed.com.au *Web Site:* www.readyed.com.au, pg 39

Reaktion Books Ltd (United Kingdom) *Tel:* (020) 7404 9930 *Fax:* (020) 7404 9931 *E-mail:* info@reaktionbooks.co.uk *Web Site:* www.reaktionbooks.co.uk, pg 743

Real Academia de Bones Lletres de Barcelona (Spain) *Tel:* (093) 3150010 *Fax:* (093) 3102349, pg 1399

Real Academia Sevillana de Buenas Letras (Spain) *Tel:* (09542) 21198 *E-mail:* insacan@insacan.org *Web Site:* www.insacan.org, pg 1399

The Real Estate Institute of Australia (Australia) *Tel:* (02) 6282 4277 *Fax:* (02) 6285 2444 *E-mail:* reia@reiaustralia.com.au *Web Site:* www.reiaustralia.com.au, pg 39

Real Ireland Design (Ireland) *Tel:* (01) 2860799 *Fax:* (01) 2829962 *E-mail:* info@realireland.ie *Web Site:* www.realireland.ie, pg 360

Realisations pour l'Enseignement Multilingue International (REMI) (France) *Tel:* (01) 45 75 78 49 *Fax:* (01) 45 79 06 66, pg 183

Realitatea Casa de Edituri Productie Audio-Video Film (Romania) *Tel:* (01) 6117105; (01) 6517105; (01) 6332468; (01) 6143793 *Fax:* (01) 2105411 *E-mail:* leu@dnt.ro, pg 537

Realizacoes Artis (Portugal) *Tel:* (01) 363796 *Fax:* (01) 9170130, pg 530

Reardon Publishing (United Kingdom) *Tel:* (01242) 231800 *E-mail:* reardon@bigfoot.com *Web Site:* www.reardon.co.uk; www.coltswoldbookshop.com (bookshop), pg 743

Rebel Publishing House Pvt Ltd (India) *Tel:* (0212) 628562 *Fax:* (0212) 624181, pg 343

Rebo Productions BV (Netherlands) *Tel:* (0252) 431 556 *Fax:* (0252) 431 557 *E-mail:* info@rebo-publishers.com *Web Site:* www.rebo-publishers.com, pg 484

Recallmed Oy (Finland) *Tel:* (09) 8797177 *Fax:* (09) 8797088 *E-mail:* recallmed@recallmed.fi, pg 143

Verlag fuer Recht und Gesellschaft AG (Switzerland) *Tel:* (061) 726 26 26 *Fax:* (061) 726 26 27 *E-mail:* info@vrg-verlag.ch *Web Site:* www.vrg-verlag.ch, pg 627

Verlag Recht und Wirtschaft GmbH (Germany) *Tel:* (06221) 9060 *Fax:* (06221) 906259 *E-mail:* verlag@ruw.de; info@ruw.de *Web Site:* www.ruw-ruw.de, pg 271

Reclam Verlag Leipzig (Germany) *Tel:* (0341) 997170 *Fax:* (0341) 9971730 *E-mail:* info@reclam-leipzig.de *Web Site:* www.reclam.de, pg 271

RECOM Verlag (Switzerland) *Tel:* (056) 249224-0; (0700) 20055555 (service) *Fax:* (056) 249224-18 *E-mail:* info@recom-verlag.de *Web Site:* www.recom-verlag.de, pg 627

Distribuidora Record de Servicos de Imprensa SA (Brazil) *Tel:* (021) 2585-2000 *Fax:* (021) 2580-4911 *E-mail:* record@record.com.br *Web Site:* www.record.com.br, pg 88

Red Editorial Iberoamericana Mexico SA de CV (Mexico) *Tel:* (05) 5456860; (05) 5456861 *Fax:* (05) 5619112, pg 467

The Red House Books Ltd (United Kingdom) *Tel:* (0870) 191 99 80 *Fax:* (0870) 6077720 *E-mail:* enquiries@redhouse.co.uk *Web Site:* www. redhouse.co.uk, pg 1247

Red Internacional Del Libro (Chile) *Tel:* (02) 2238100 *Fax:* (02) 2254269 *E-mail:* ril@rileditores.com *Web Site:* www.rileditores.com, pg 100

Red/Studio Redazionale (Italy) *Tel:* (02) 30 241 311 *Fax:* (02) 30 241 333 *E-mail:* info@red-edizioni.it *Web Site:* www.red-edizioni.it, pg 402

Redcliffe Press Ltd (United Kingdom) *Tel:* (01884) 243242 *Fax:* (01884) 243325, pg 743

Rede Das Artes Industria, Comercio, Importacaoe Exportacao Ltda (Brazil) *Tel:* (011) 246-5565 *Fax:* (011) 246-5565, pg 89

Redhouse Bookstore (Turkey) *Tel:* (0212) 520 7778; (0212) 520 2960; (0212) 520 0090 *Fax:* (0212) 522 1909 *E-mail:* info@redhouse.com.tr *Web Site:* www. redhouse.com.tr, pg 1337

Redhouse Press (Turkey) *Tel:* (0212) 520 7778; (0212) 520 2960; (0212) 520 0090 *Fax:* (0212) 522 1909 *E-mail:* info@redhouse.com.tr; sales@redhouse.com.tr *Web Site:* www.redhouse.com.tr, pg 646

Bokforlaget Rediviva, Facsimileforlaget (Sweden) *Tel:* (08) 25 70 07, pg 610

Redstone Press (United Kingdom) *Tel:* (020) 7352 1594 *Fax:* (020) 7352 8749 *Web Site:* www.redstonepress. co.uk, pg 743

Redwood Books Ltd (United Kingdom) *Tel:* (01225) 769979 *Fax:* (01225) 769050 *E-mail:* enquiries@ redwood-books.co.uk *Web Site:* www.cpi-group.net, pg 1175

Redwood Books Ltd (United Kingdom) *Tel:* (01225) 769979 *Fax:* (01225) 769050 *E-mail:* enquiries@ redwood-books.co.uk, pg 1217

Reed Business Information (United Kingdom) *Tel:* (020) 8652 3500 *Fax:* (01342) 335960 *E-mail:* webmaster@ rbi.co.uk *Web Site:* www.reedbusiness.com, pg 744

Reed Elsevier Deutschland GmbH (Germany) *Tel:* (089) 898170 *Fax:* (089) 89817-300 *Web Site:* www. reedbusiness.de, pg 271

Reed Elsevier Group plc (United Kingdom) *Tel:* (020) 7222 8420 *Fax:* (020) 7227 5799 *Web Site:* www.reed-elsevier.com, pg 744

Reed Elsevier Nederland BV (Netherlands) *Tel:* (020) 485 2222 *Fax:* (020) 618 0325 *Web Site:* www. elsevier.com, pg 484

Reed Elsevier, South East Asia (Singapore) *Tel:* 6789 9900 *Fax:* 6789 9966 *Web Site:* www.reed-elsevier. com, pg 553

Reed for Kids (Australia) *Tel:* (03) 5516111 *Fax:* (03) 95517490, pg 39

Reed Publishing (NZ) Ltd (New Zealand) *Tel:* (09) 441 2960 *Fax:* (09) 480 4999 *E-mail:* info@reed.co.nz *Web Site:* www.reedpublishing.co.nz, pg 496

William Reed Directories (United Kingdom) *Tel:* (01293) 613 400 *Fax:* (01293) 610 322 *E-mail:* directories@ william-reed.co.uk *Web Site:* www.william-reed.co.uk, pg 744

References cf (France) *Tel:* (04) 75 27 52 59 *Fax:* (04) 75 27 52 59, pg 183

Regalia 6 Publishing House (Bulgaria) *Tel:* (02) 754111 *Fax:* (02) 566573 *E-mail:* vpruu@dir.bg, pg 96

Regenbogen Verlag (Switzerland) *Tel:* (01) 454 3033 *Fax:* (01) 454 3035 *E-mail:* info@regenbogen-verlag. ch *Web Site:* www.regenbogen-verlag.ch, pg 627

Regency House Publishing Ltd (United Kingdom) *Tel:* (014383) 14488 *Fax:* (014383) 11303 *E-mail:* regencyhouse@btclick.com, pg 744

Regency Press CP Ltd (United Kingdom) *Tel:* (020) 7482 4596 *Fax:* (020) 7485 8353 *E-mail:* info@ regency.org *Web Site:* www.regency.org, pg 744

Regency Publications (India) *Tel:* (011) 5712539; (011) 5740038 *Fax:* (011) 5783571 *E-mail:* regency@ satyam.net.in, pg 343

Regency Publishing (Australia) *Tel:* (08) 8348 4599 *Toll Free Tel:* 800 649 898 (ext 4599) *Fax:* (08) 8348 4400 *E-mail:* regencypublishing@regency.tafe.sa.edu.au *Web Site:* www.regencypublishing.com.au; www.tafe. sa.edu.au/institutes/regency/regency-publishing/main. htm, pg 39

REGENSBERG Druck & Verlag GmbH & Co (Germany) *Tel:* (0251) 749800 *Fax:* (0251) 7498040, pg 272

Universitatsbibliothek Regensburg (Germany) *Tel:* (0941) 943-3901; (0941) 943-3902 *Fax:* (0941) 943-3285 *Web Site:* www.bibliothek.uni-regensburg.de, pg 1508

Editora Regional de Murcia - ERM (Spain) *Tel:* (068) 280246 *Fax:* (068) 298293 *E-mail:* editora.regional@ carm.es *Web Site:* www.carm.es, pg 593

Regional ISBN Agency (CARICOM) (Guyana) *Tel:* (02) 226 9280 *Fax:* (02) 226 7816 *E-mail:* carisec1@ caricom.org; carisec2@caricom.org; carisec3@ caricom.og *Web Site:* www.caricom.org, pg 1262

Regional ISBN Centre The ISBN Officer (Fiji) *Tel:* 3313 900 *Fax:* 3300 830 *E-mail:* mamtora_j@usp.ac.fj; library@usp.ac.fj *Web Site:* www.usp.ac.fj, pg 1256

Verlag fuer Regionalgeschichte (Germany) *Tel:* (05209) 6714; (05209) 980266 *Fax:* (05209) 6519; (05209) 980277 *E-mail:* regionalgeschichte@t-online.de *Web Site:* www.regionalgeschichte.de, pg 272

Regura Verlag (Germany) *Tel:* (0711) 2269835 *Fax:* (0711) 2238829 *Web Site:* www.regura.de, pg 272

Ediciones Rehue Ltda (Chile) *Tel:* (02) 6344653; (02) 6341804 *Fax:* (02) 6351096, pg 100

Konrad Reich Verlag GmbH (Germany) *Tel:* (0381) 693020 *Fax:* (0381) 693021, pg 272

Reich Verlag AG (Switzerland) *Tel:* (041) 4103721 *Fax:* (041) 4103227 *Web Site:* www.terramagica.de, pg 627

Dr Ludwig Reichert Verlag (Germany) *Tel:* (0611) 461851 *Fax:* (0611) 468613 *E-mail:* info@reichert-verlag.de *Web Site:* www.reichert-verlag.de, pg 272

Reichl Verlag Der Leuchter (Germany) *Tel:* (06741) 1720 *Fax:* (06741) 1749 *E-mail:* reichl-verlag@telda. net *Web Site:* www.reichl-verlag.de, pg 272

Ernesto Reichmann Distribuidores de Livros LTDA (Brazil) *Tel:* (011) 61982122 *Fax:* (011) 61982122 *E-mail:* rrr@erdl.com, pg 1294

J R Reid Printing Group Ltd (United Kingdom) *Tel:* (01698) 826000 *Fax:* (01698) 824944 *E-mail:* office@reid-print-group.co.uk *Web Site:* www. reid-print-group.co.uk, pg 1175

J R Reid Printing Group Ltd (United Kingdom) *Tel:* (01698) 826000 *Fax:* (01698) 824944 *E-mail:* printsales@reid-print-group.co.uk *Web Site:* www.reid-print-group.co.uk, pg 1217

J R Reid Printing Group Ltd (United Kingdom) *Tel:* (01698) 826000 *Fax:* (01698) 824944 *E-mail:* info@reid-print-group.co.uk *Web Site:* www. reid-print-group.co.uk, pg 1229

Reimei-Shobo Co Ltd (Japan) *Tel:* (052) 9623045 *Fax:* (052) 9519065 *E-mail:* reimei@mui.biglobe.ne.jp *Web Site:* wwwl.biz.biglobe.ne.jp/~reimei/, pg 422

Dietrich Reimer Verlag GmbH (Germany) *Tel:* (030) 25 91 15 70 *Fax:* (030) 25 91 15 77 *E-mail:* vertrieb-kunstverlage@reimer-verlag.de *Web Site:* www.reimer-verlag.de, pg 272

Ernst Reinhardt Verlag GmbH & Co KG (Germany) *Tel:* (089) 17 80 16 0 *Fax:* (089) 17 80 16 30 *E-mail:* webmaster@reinhardt-verlag.de *Web Site:* www.reinhardt-verlag.de, pg 272

Verlag Friedrich Reinhardt AG (Switzerland) *Tel:* (061) 264 64 50 *Fax:* (061) 264 64 88 *E-mail:* verlag@ reinhardt.ch *Web Site:* www.reinhardt.ch, pg 627

E Reinhold Verlag (Germany) *Tel:* (03447) 311889 *Fax:* (03447) 375611 *E-mail:* erv@querstand.de *Web Site:* www.querstand.de, pg 272

Reinhold Schmidt Verlag (Austria) *Tel:* (02236) 72469 *Fax:* (02236) 73784, pg 56

Reise Know-How (Germany) *Tel:* (06872) 91737 *Fax:* (06872) 91738 *E-mail:* hoff-verlag@reise-know-how.com *Web Site:* www.reise-know-how.com, pg 272

Reise Know-How Verlag-Daerr GmbH (Germany) *Tel:* (0521) 946490 *Fax:* (0521) 441047 *E-mail:* info@ reise-know-how.de *Web Site:* www.reise-know-how.de, pg 272

Reise Know-How Verlag Dr Hans-R Grundmann GmbH (Germany) *Tel:* (04488) 761994 *Fax:* (04488) 761030 *E-mail:* reisebuch@aol.com, pg 272

Reise Know-How Verlag Helmut Hermann (Germany) *Tel:* (07145) 8278 *Fax:* (07145) 26736, pg 272

Reise Know-How Verlag Peter Rump GmbH (Germany) *Tel:* (0521) 94649-0 *Fax:* (0521) 441047 *E-mail:* info@reise-know-how.de *Web Site:* www.reise-know-how.de, pg 273

Reise Know-How Verlag Tondok (Germany) *Tel:* (089) 3514857 *Fax:* (089) 3518485 *E-mail:* rhk@tondok-verlag.de *Web Site:* www.tondok-verlag.de, pg 273

Verlagsgruppe Reise Know-How (Germany) *Tel:* (0521) 946490 *Fax:* (0521) 441047 *E-mail:* info@reise-know-how.de *Web Site:* www.reise-know-how.de, pg 273

C A Reitzel Boghandel & Forlag A/S (Denmark) *Tel:* 33 12 24 00 *Fax:* 33 14 02 70 *E-mail:* info@careitzel.dk *Web Site:* www.careitzel.dk, pg 133

C A Reitzel Boghandel & Forlag A/S (Denmark) *Tel:* 33 12 24 00 *Fax:* 33 14 02 70 *Web Site:* www.careitzel. dk, pg 1298

Hans Reitzel Publishers Ltd (Denmark) *Tel:* 33382800 *Fax:* 33382808 *E-mail:* hrf@hansreitzel.dk *Web Site:* www.hansreitzel.dk, pg 133

Rekha Prakashan (India) *Tel:* (011) 23279907; (011) 23279904 *Fax:* (011) 2321783 *E-mail:* rprakashan@satyam.net.in *Web Site:* www. museumoffolkandtribalart.org, pg 343

RELATE (United Kingdom) *Tel:* (01788) 573241 *Fax:* (01788) 535007 *E-mail:* enquires@relate.org.uk *Web Site:* www.relate.org.uk, pg 744

Relay Books (Ireland) *Tel:* (067) 31734 *Fax:* (067) 31734 *E-mail:* relaybooks@eiscom.net, pg 360

Reliance Publishing House (India) *Tel:* (011) 5852605; (011) 5772768; (011) 5737377 *Fax:* (011) 5786769 *E-mail:* reliance@indiatimes.com, pg 343

Remaja Rosdakarya CV (Indonesia) *Tel:* (022) 5200287, pg 353

Remzi Kitabevi (Turkey) *Tel:* (0212) 522 05 83; (0212) 519 09 81; (0212) 513 94 74; (0212) 513 94 75 *Fax:* (0212) 522 90 55 *E-mail:* post@remzi.com.tr *Web Site:* www.remzi.com.tr, pg 646

La Renaissance du Livre (Belgium) *Tel:* (069) 89 15 55 *Fax:* (069) 89 15 50 *Web Site:* www. larenaissancedulivre.com, pg 72

Les Editions Albert Rene (France) *Tel:* (01) 45 00 41 41 *Fax:* (01) 40 67 95 12 *E-mail:* rene.cominfo@editions-albert-rene.com *Web Site:* www.editions-albert-rene. com, pg 183

Library of the Renmin University of China (China) *Tel:* (010) 62511014 *Fax:* (010) 62515263; (010) 62515336 *E-mail:* rmdxxb@mail.ruc.edu.cn; leader@ mail.ruc.edu.cn *Web Site:* www.ruc.edu.cn, pg 1496

Rentrop & Straton Verlagsgruppe und Wirtschaftsconsulting (Romania) *Tel:* (021) 337.4146 *Fax:* (021) 337.2211 *E-mail:* rs@rs.ro; office@rs.ro *Web Site:* www.rs.ro, pg 537

Verlag Norman Rentrop (Germany) *Tel:* (0228) 36 88 40 *Fax:* (0228) 36 58 75 *E-mail:* jra@rentrop.com *Web Site:* www.normanrentrop.de, pg 273

Editora Replicacao Lda (Portugal) *Tel:* (021) 677058 *Fax:* (021) 396 9808 *E-mail:* replic@mail.telepac.pt, pg 530

Reporter (Bulgaria) *Tel:* (02) 760834; (02) 761084; (02) 769028 *Fax:* (02) 745114 *E-mail:* reporter@techno-link.com, pg 96

Representative Church Body Library (Ireland) *Tel:* (01) 4923979 *Fax:* (01) 4924770 *E-mail:* library@ireland. anglican.org *Web Site:* www.ireland.anglican.org, pg 1517

Republicki Zavod za Unapredivanje Vaspitanja i Obrazovanja (Serbia and Montenegro) *Tel:* (011) 659322, pg 549

Res Polona (Poland) *Tel:* (042) 6363634; (042) 6374587; (042) 6374607 *Fax:* (042) 6373010 *E-mail:* info@ res-polona.com.pl *Web Site:* www.res-polona.com.pl, pg 521

Resch Verlag (Austria) *Tel:* (089) 8 54 65-0 *Fax:* (089) 8 54 65-11 *E-mail:* info@resch-verlag.com *Web Site:* www.resch-verlag.com, pg 56

Research Centre for Translation (Hong Kong) *Tel:* 2609 7399; 2609 7407 *Fax:* 2603 5110; 2603 5195 *E-mail:* rct@cuhk.edu.hk *Web Site:* www.cuhk.edu. hk/rct/home.html, pg 315

Research Signpost (India) *Tel:* (0471) 2460384 *Fax:* (0471) 2573051 *E-mail:* ggcom@vsnl.com *Web Site:* www.researchsignpost.com, pg 344

Research Society of Pakistan (Pakistan) *Tel:* (042) 322542, pg 509

Research Studies Press Ltd (RSP) (United Kingdom) *Tel:* (01462) 895060 *Fax:* (01462) 892546 *E-mail:* info@research-studies-press.co.uk *Web Site:* www.research-studies-press.co.uk, pg 744

Researchco Reprints (India) *Tel:* (011) 28712565; (011) 55150446; (011) 28714057 *Fax:* (011) 28716134, pg 344

Editora Resenha Tributaria Ltda (Brazil) *Tel:* (011) 5772822 *Fax:* (011) 5772526, pg 89

Residenz Verlag GmbH (Austria) *Tel:* (0662) 641986-0 *Fax:* (0662) 643548 *E-mail:* info@residenzverlag.at *Web Site:* www.residenzverlag.at, pg 56

Resource Books Ltd (New Zealand) *Tel:* (09) 5758030 *Fax:* (09) 5758055 *E-mail:* sales@resourcebooks.co.nz *Web Site:* www.resourcebooks.co.nz, pg 496

Respublica Verlag (Germany) *Tel:* (02241) 62925; (02241) 64039 *Fax:* (02241) 53891, pg 273

Respublika (Russian Federation) *Tel:* (095) 251-7956, pg 544

Respublikanskij izdatei skij Kabinet (Kazakstan) *Tel:* (03272) 910703; (03272) 910333 *Fax:* (03272) 631207, pg 429

Retail Entertainment Data Publishing Ltd (United Kingdom) *Tel:* (020) 7566 8216 *Fax:* (020) 7566 8259 (Inquiry); (020) 7566 8316 (Editorial) *E-mail:* info@ redpublishing.co.uk *Web Site:* www.redpublishing.co. uk, pg 744

Luis A Retta Libros (Uruguay) *Tel:* (02) 400-0766 *Fax:* (02) 409-0174 *E-mail:* rettalib@chasque.apc.org, pg 772

Editorial Reus SA (Spain) *Tel:* (091) 2213619; (091) 2223054 *Fax:* (091) 5312408 *E-mail:* reus@ editorialreus.es *Web Site:* www.editorialreus.es, pg 593

Editora Revan Ltda (Brazil) *Tel:* (021) 25027495 *Fax:* (021) 22736873 *E-mail:* editor@revan.com.br *Web Site:* www.revan.com.br, pg 89

Ediciones Luis Revenga (Spain) *Tel:* (091) 5434646 *Fax:* (091) 5434706 *E-mail:* cuadcerv@elr.es, pg 593

Reverdito Edizioni (Italy) *Tel:* (0461) 942285 *Fax:* (0461) 946563 *E-mail:* reverditoedizioni@ virgilio.it *Web Site:* www.culturitalia.uibk.ac.at, pg 402

Editorial Reverte SA (Spain) *Tel:* (093) 419 33 36; (093) 419 32 76 *Fax:* (093) 419 51 89 *E-mail:* istz0125@ tsai.es; prom.reverte@teleline.es *Web Site:* www. ludosoft.net/reverte/present.htm, pg 593

Editorial Reverte Venezolana SA (Venezuela) *Tel:* (0212) 572 44 68; (0212) 572 66 70 *Fax:* (0212) 572 25 98, pg 775

Review Publishing Co Ltd (Hong Kong) *Tel:* 2573 7121 *Fax:* 2503 1530 *E-mail:* service@feer.com *Web Site:* www.feer.com, pg 1148

Livraria Editora Revinter Ltda (Brazil) *Tel:* (021) 2563-9700 *Fax:* (021) 2563-9701 *E-mail:* livraria@revinter. com.br *Web Site:* www.revinter.com.br, pg 89

Editorial Revista Agustiniana (Spain) *Tel:* (091) 550-5000 *Fax:* (091) 550-5225 *E-mail:* revista@ agustiniana.com *Web Site:* www.agustiniana.com, pg 593

Revista Penteado (Portugal) *Tel:* (021) 862963 *Fax:* (021) 870972 *E-mail:* rromano@mail.telepac.pt, pg 530

Editions Revue EPS (France) *Tel:* (01) 41 74 82 82 *Fax:* (01) 43 98 37 38 *E-mail:* revue@revue-eps.com *Web Site:* www.revue-eps.com, pg 183

Revue Espaces et Societes (France) *Tel:* (05) 61 50 35 65 *Fax:* (05) 61 50 49 61 *E-mail:* espacesetsocietes@ msh-paris.fr *Web Site:* www.espacesetsocietes.msh-paris.fr, pg 183

Revue Noire (France) *Tel:* (01) 43 20 92 00 *Fax:* (01) 43 22 92 60 *E-mail:* redaction@revuenoire.com *Web Site:* www.revuenoire.com, pg 183

Rex Book Store Inc (Philippines) *Tel:* (02) 7437688; (02) 4143512; (02) 4146774 *Fax:* (02) 7437687 *E-mail:* rex@usinc.net, pg 1326

Rex Bookstores & Publishers (Philippines) *Tel:* (02) 7437688; (02) 4143512; (02) 4146774 *Fax:* (02) 7437687 *E-mail:* rex@usinc.net, pg 515

Rex Verlag (Switzerland) *Tel:* (041) 4194719 *Fax:* (041) 4194711 *E-mail:* info@rex-freizyt.ch *Web Site:* www. rex-freizyt.ch, pg 628

Libreria Universitaria Jose T Reyes (Honduras) *Tel:* 232-2110 *Fax:* 235-3361 *Web Site:* www.unah.hn, pg 1304

Reyes Publishing Inc (Philippines) *Tel:* (02) 721-8792 *Fax:* (02) 721-8782 *E-mail:* reyesbub@skyinet.net, pg 1150

Reyes Publishing Inc (Philippines) *Tel:* (02) 721-8782 *Fax:* (02) 721-8782 *E-mail:* reyesbub@skyinet.net, pg 1171

Reyes Publishing Inc (Philippines) *Tel:* (02) 721-7492 *Fax:* (02) 721-8782 *E-mail:* reyespub@skyinet.net, pg 1327

Borgarbokasafn Reykjavikur (Iceland) *Tel:* 5631717 *Fax:* 5631705 *E-mail:* borgarbokasafn@ borgarbokasafn.is *Web Site:* www.borgarbokasafn.is, pg 1513

Verlagsgruppe Rhein Main GmbH & Co KG (Germany) *Tel:* (06131) 48-46-94 *E-mail:* info@main-rheiner.de *Web Site:* www.main-rheiner.de, pg 273

Rhein-Trio, Edition/Editions du Fou (Switzerland) *Tel:* (061) 6831635 *Fax:* (061) 6831635 *E-mail:* rhein-trio@usa.net, pg 628

Rheinische Landesbibliothek Koblenz (Germany) *Tel:* (0261) 91500 40 *Fax:* (0261) 91500 91 *E-mail:* info@rlb.de *Web Site:* www.rlb.de, pg 1508

Verlag Rheinischer Merkur GmbH (Germany) *Tel:* (0228) 884-0 *Fax:* (0228) 88 41 70 (sales); (0228) 88 41 99 (editorial); (0228) 88 42 99 (advertising) *E-mail:* abo@merkur.de *Web Site:* www.merkur.de, pg 273

RVBG Rheinland-Verlag-und Betriebsgesellschaft des Landschaftsverbandes Rheinland mbH (Germany) *Tel:* (02234) 9854265 *Fax:* (02234) 82503, pg 273

Rheintal Handelsgesellschaft Anstalt (Liechtenstein) *Tel:* (075) 3921882; (01) 8442786 *Fax:* (075) 3923646; (01) 8442806 *E-mail:* vetsch.p@bluewin.ch, pg 444

RHJ Livros Ltda (Brazil) *Tel:* (031) 3334-1566 *Fax:* (031) 3332-5823 *Web Site:* www.editorarhj.com. br, pg 89

Rhodes University Library (South Africa) *Tel:* (046) 603 8436 *Fax:* (046) 6223487 *E-mail:* library@ru.ac.za *Web Site:* www.rhodes.ac.za/library/, pg 1543

Rhodos, International Science & Art Publishers (Denmark) *Tel:* 32543020 *Fax:* 32543022 *E-mail:* rhodos@rhodos.com *Web Site:* www.rhodos. dk, pg 133

Rhombus Verlag (Austria) *Tel:* (01) 526 61 52 *Fax:* (01) 522 87 18, pg 56

Ediciones Rialp SA (Spain) *Tel:* (091) 3260504 *Fax:* (091) 3261321 *E-mail:* ediciones@rialp.com *Web Site:* www.rialp.com/, pg 593

RIBA Publications (United Kingdom) *Tel:* (020) 7251 0791 *Fax:* (020) 7608 2375 *Web Site:* www. ribabookshop.com; www.ribac.co.uk, pg 745

RIC Publications Pty Ltd (Australia) *Tel:* (09) 9240 9888 *Fax:* (09) 9240 1513 *E-mail:* mail@ricgroup.com.au *Web Site:* www.ricgroup.com.au, pg 39

Biblioteca Riccardiana (Italy) *Tel:* (055) 212586; (055) 293385 *Fax:* (055) 211379 *E-mail:* riccardiana@ riccardiana.firenze.sbn.it *Web Site:* www.riccardiana. librari.beniculturali.it, pg 1519

Franco Maria Ricci Editore (FMR) (Italy) *Tel:* (02) 414101 *Fax:* (02) 48301473 *E-mail:* ricci@ fmrmagazine.it *Web Site:* www.fmrspa.it, pg 402

Riccardo Ricciardi Editore SpA (Italy) *Tel:* (01) 156561 *Web Site:* www.mondadori.it, pg 402

Edizioni del Riccio SAS di G Bernardi (Italy) *Tel:* (0571) 609338 *Fax:* (055) 716362, pg 402

Richardi Helmut Verlag GmbH (Germany) *Tel:* (069) 9708330 *Fax:* (069) 7078400 *E-mail:* kreditwesen@t-online.de, pg 273

Richards Literary Agency (New Zealand) *Tel:* (09) 479 5681 *Fax:* (09) 479 5681 *E-mail:* rla.richards@clear. net.nz, pg 1125

The Richmond Publishing Co Ltd (United Kingdom) *Tel:* (01753) 643104 *Fax:* (01753) 646553 *E-mail:* rpc@richmond.co.uk, pg 745, 1344

Richters Egmont (Sweden) *Tel:* (040) 38 06 00 *Fax:* (040) 933708 *E-mail:* egmont@egmont.com *Web Site:* www.egmont.com, pg 610

Richters Forlag (Sweden) *Tel:* (040) 38 06 80 *Fax:* (040) 29 43 50 *E-mail:* kundservice@richters.se *Web Site:* www.egmontrichter.com, pg 1246

Ricordi Americana SAEC (Argentina) *Tel:* (011) 4371-9841; (011) 4371-9843 *Fax:* (011) 4372-3459 *E-mail:* ricordi@sminter.com.ar, pg 8

RICS Books (United Kingdom) *Tel:* (020) 7222 7000 (ext 698) *Fax:* (020) 7334 3851 *E-mail:* weborders@ rics.org.uk *Web Site:* www.ricsbooks.com, pg 745

RICS Books (United Kingdom) *Tel:* (0870) 333 1600 *Fax:* (020) 7334 3851 *E-mail:* mailorder@rics.org.uk *Web Site:* www.ricsbooks.com, pg 1344

Editora Rideel Ltda (Brazil) *Tel:* (011) 6977-8344 *Fax:* (011) 6976-7415 *E-mail:* rideel@virtual-net.com. br *Web Site:* www.rideel.com.br, pg 89

Rigodon-Verlag Norbert Wehr (Germany) *Tel:* (0201) 77 81 11; (0221) 360 21 92 *Fax:* (0201) 77 81 22; (0221) 360 21 92 *E-mail:* Schreibheft@NetCologne.de *Web Site:* www.schreibheft.de, pg 273

Rigsarkivet (Denmark) *Tel:* 33923310 *Fax:* 33153239 *E-mail:* mailbox@ra.sa.dk *Web Site:* www.sa.dk, pg 1500

The Rihani House Estate (Lebanon) *Tel:* (01) 868384 *Fax:* (01) 868384, pg 443

Rijksmuseum Research Library (Netherlands) *Tel:* (020) 67 47 267 *Fax:* (020) 6747001 *E-mail:* library@ rijksmuseum.nl *Web Site:* library.rijksmuseum.nl, pg 1529

Bibliotheek der Rijksuniversiteit Groningen (Netherlands) *Tel:* (050) 363 5445; (050) 363 5446 *Fax:* (050) 363 6300 *E-mail:* info@ub.rug.nl *Web Site:* www.rug.nl/bibliotheek, pg 1529

Riksarkivet (Norway) *Tel:* (022) 02 26 00 *Fax:* (022) 23 74 89 *E-mail:* riksarkivet@riksarkivaren.dep.no *Web Site:* www.riksarkivet.no; www.arkivverket.no, pg 1533

Riksarkivet (Sweden) *Tel:* (08) 737 63 50 *Fax:* (08) 737 64 74 *E-mail:* registry@riksarkivet.ra.se *Web Site:* www.ra.se, pg 1546

Riksbibliotektjenesten (Norway) *Tel:* 23 11 75 00 *Fax:* 23 11 75 01 *E-mail:* post@abm-utvikling.no *Web Site:* www.abm-utvikling.no, pg 1569

Rimbaud Verlagsgesellschaft mbH (Germany) *Tel:* (0241) 54 25 32; (0241) 9019583 *Fax:* (0241) 514117 *E-mail:* info@rimbaud.de *Web Site:* www.rimbaud.de, pg 273

RIMU Publishing Co Ltd (New Zealand) *Tel:* (07) 8555536 *Fax:* (07) 8555536, pg 496

Ringier Pacific (Hong Kong) *Tel:* 2369-8788 *Fax:* 2869-5919 *E-mail:* thaihoa@ringierasia.com *Web Site:* www.ringierpacific.com, pg 316

Rinsen Book Co Ltd (Japan) *Tel:* (075) 721-7111 *Fax:* (075) 781-6168 *E-mail:* kyoto@rinsen.com *Web Site:* www.rinsen.com, pg 422

Edizioni Ripostes (Italy) *Tel:* (089) 336049 *Fax:* (089) 336049 *Web Site:* web.tiscali.it/ripostes, pg 402

Riquelme y Vargas Ediciones SL (Spain) *Tel:* (053) 270066 *Fax:* (053) 270066, pg 593

Rirea Casa Editrice della Rivista Italiana di Ragioneria e di Economia Aziendale (Italy) *Tel:* (06) 8417690 *Fax:* (06) 8845732 *E-mail:* rirea_@infinito.it, pg 402

Riso-Sha (Japan) *Tel:* (047) 366-8003 *Fax:* (047) 360-7301 *E-mail:* risosha@risosha.co.jp *Web Site:* www.risosha.co.jp, pg 422

Rithofundasamband Islands (Iceland) *Tel:* 5683190 *Fax:* 5683192 *E-mail:* rsi@rsi.is *Web Site:* www.rsi.is, pg 1395

Ritter Druck und Verlags KEG (Austria) *Tel:* (0463) 42631 *Fax:* (0463) 42631-77 *E-mail:* office@ritterbooks.com *Web Site:* www.ritterbooks.com, pg 56

Ritterbach Verlag GmbH (Germany) *Tel:* (02234) 18 66 0 *Fax:* (02234) 18 66 90 *E-mail:* service@ritterbach.de; coeln.ml@ritterbach.de *Web Site:* www.ritterbach.de, pg 273

Ritzau KG Verlag Zeit und Eisenbahn (Germany) *Tel:* (08196) 252 *Fax:* (08196) 1240 *E-mail:* mail@ritzau.kg.de *Web Site:* www.ritzau-kg.de, pg 273

Editori Riuniti (Italy) *Tel:* (06) 68801021 *Fax:* (06) 68392028 *E-mail:* ufficio.stampa@editoririuniti.it *Web Site:* www.editoririuniti.it, pg 402

River Press (New Zealand) *Tel:* (03) 5738383 *Fax:* (03) 5738383, pg 496

Rivers Oram Press (United Kingdom) *Tel:* (020) 7607 0823 *Fax:* (020) 7609 2776 *E-mail:* ro@riversoram.demon.co.uk, pg 745

Riverside Agency SAC (Argentina) *Tel:* (011) 4957-2336 *Fax:* (011) 4956-1985 *E-mail:* riverside@laisla.net, pg 1287

Riverside Communications (Nigeria) *Tel:* (084) 334042 *Fax:* (084) 334042 *E-mail:* isoun@aol.com; rvsdcom@aol.com, pg 502

La Riviere Creatief (Netherlands) *Tel:* (035) 5486600 *Fax:* (035) 5486675, pg 484

Yves Riviere Editeur (France) *Tel:* (01) 42 74 77 84 *Fax:* (01) 42 78 12 65 *E-mail:* yvestri@mail.club.internet.fr, pg 183

Rizal Library (Philippines) *Tel:* (02) 426-6001; 5800-5816 (Local) *Fax:* (02) 426-5961 *Web Site:* rizal.lib.admu.edu.ph, pg 1535

Libreria Rizzoli della Rizzoli Editore SpA (Italy) *Tel:* (02) 50951 *Fax:* (02) 5065361, pg 1311

RMIT Publishing (Australia) *Tel:* (03) 9925 8100 *Fax:* (03) 9925 8134 *E-mail:* info@rmitpublishing.com.au *Web Site:* www.rmitpublishing.com.au, pg 39

Road Editions (Greece) *Tel:* 2103613242 *Fax:* 210 3614681 *E-mail:* roadsales@road.gr *Web Site:* www.road.gr, pg 1304

Roadmaster Publishing (United Kingdom) *Tel:* (01634) 862843 *Fax:* (01634) 201555 *E-mail:* info@roadmasterpublishing.co.uk; sales@roadmasterpublishing.co.uk, pg 745

Editorial Roasa SL (Spain) *Tel:* (058) 0227846 *Fax:* (058) 132530, pg 593

Le Robert (France) *Tel:* (01) 45 87 43 00 *Fax:* (01) 45 35 76 06 *Web Site:* www.lerobert.com, pg 183

Roberts Rinehart Publishers (Ireland) *Tel:* (01) 497-6860 *Fax:* (01) 497-6861 *E-mail:* books@townhouse.ie, pg 360

Tom Roberts (Pat Roberts) (Australia) *Tel:* (08) 8143 7578, pg 39

J Robinson & Co (Israel) *Tel:* (03) 5605461; (03) 5601626 *Fax:* (03) 5660439 *E-mail:* rob_book@netvision.net.il *Web Site:* www.robinson.co.il, pg 1310

The Robinswood Press Ltd (United Kingdom) *Tel:* (01384) 397475 *Fax:* (01384) 440443 *E-mail:* info@robinswoodpress.com *Web Site:* www.robinswoodpress.com, pg 745

Robson Books (United Kingdom) *Tel:* (020) 7221 2213; (020) 7314 1469 (sales) *Fax:* (020) 7221 6455; (020) 7314 1594 (sales) *E-mail:* robson@chrysalisbooks.co.uk *Web Site:* www.chrysalisbooks.co.uk/books/publisher/robson, pg 745

Laurus Robuffo Edizioni (Italy) *Tel:* (06) 5651492 *Fax:* (06) 5651233 *E-mail:* post@laurusrobuffo.it *Web Site:* www.laurusrobuffo.it, pg 402

Ediciones Roca, SA (Mexico) *Tel:* (05) 5758585; (05) 2770946, pg 467

Livraria Roca Ltda (Brazil) *Tel:* (011) 221-8609; (011) 221-6814 *Fax:* (011) 3331-8653 *E-mail:* edroca@uol.com.br *Web Site:* www.editoraroca.com.br, pg 89

Ediciones La Rocca (Argentina) *Tel:* (011) 4382 8526 *Fax:* (011) 4384 5774 *E-mail:* ed-larocca@sinectis.com, pg 8

Editora Rocco Ltda (Brazil) *Tel:* (021) 2507-2000 *Fax:* (021) 2507-2244 *E-mail:* rocco@rocco.com.br *Web Site:* www.rocco.com.br, pg 89

Roce (Consultants) Ltd (Uganda) *Tel:* (041) 106010 *Fax:* (041) 321062 *Web Site:* www.rutaagi.com, pg 648

Editiones Roche (Switzerland) *Tel:* (061) 688 3611 *Fax:* (061) 688 2775 *Web Site:* www.roche.com, pg 628

Editions du Rocher (France) *Tel:* (01) 40 46 54 00 *Fax:* (01) 46 34 64 26 *E-mail:* info@editionsdurocher.net, pg 183

Les Editions du Rocher (Monaco) *Tel:* (093) 40465400 *Fax:* (093) 43293506 *E-mail:* jpb.droits@wanadoo.fr, pg 470

Rodera-Verlag der Cardun AG (Switzerland) *Tel:* (052) 292442 *Fax:* (052) 292592 *E-mail:* info@cardun.ch *Web Site:* www.cardun.ch, pg 628

Rodopi (Netherlands) *Tel:* (020) 6114821 *Fax:* (020) 4472979 *E-mail:* info@rodopi.nl *Web Site:* www.rodopi.nl, pg 484

Ediciones Joaquin Rodrigo (Spain) *Tel:* (091) 555 2728 *Fax:* (091) 556 4334 *E-mail:* ediciones@joaquin-rodrigo.com *Web Site:* www.joaquin-rodrigo.com, pg 593

Libreria Rodriguez SA, Dto Suscripciones (Argentina) *Tel:* (011) 4326-3725; (011) 4326-3826 *Fax:* (011) 4326-1959 *E-mail:* librerod@ssdnet.com.ar, pg 1287

Roehrig Universitaets Verlag Gmbh (Germany) *Tel:* (06894) 8 79 57 *Fax:* (06894) 87 03 30 *E-mail:* info@roehrig-verlag.de *Web Site:* www.roehrig-verlag.de, pg 273

Verlag Roeschnar (Austria) *Tel:* (0463) 740513 *Fax:* (0463) 740817 *E-mail:* roesch@eunet.at *Web Site:* members.eunet.at/roesch, pg 56

Erich Roeth-Verlag (Germany) *Tel:* (039206) 90103 *Fax:* (039206) 90103, pg 273

Roetzer Druck GmbH & Co KG (Austria) *Tel:* (02682) 2473 *Fax:* (02682) 65008 *E-mail:* roetzeredition@wellcom.at, pg 56

Rogan McIndoe Print Ltd (New Zealand) *Tel:* (03) 474 0111 *Toll Free Tel:* 800-477-0355 *Fax:* (03) 477 0116 *E-mail:* quality@rogan.co.nz *Web Site:* www.rogan.co.nz, pg 1150

Rogan McIndoe Print Ltd (New Zealand) *Tel:* (03) 474 0111 *Toll Free Tel:* 800-477-0355 *Fax:* (03) 474 0116 *E-mail:* quality@rogan.co.nz *Web Site:* www.rogan.co.nz, pg 1171

Rogan McIndoe Print Ltd (New Zealand) *Tel:* (03) 474 0111 *Fax:* (03) 474 0116 *E-mail:* quality@rogan.co.nz *Web Site:* www.rogan.co.nz, pg 1211

Rogan McIndoe Print Ltd (New Zealand) *Tel:* (03) 474 0111 *Toll Free Tel:* 800 477 0355 *Fax:* (03) 474 0116 *E-mail:* quality@rogan.co.nz *Web Site:* www.rogan.co.nz, pg 1227

Rogan McIndoe Print Ltd (New Zealand) *Tel:* (03) 474 0111 *Toll Free Tel:* (0800) 477 0355 *Fax:* (03) 474 0116 *E-mail:* production@rogan.co.nz *Web Site:* www.rogan.co.nz, pg 1236

Libreria Editrice Rogate (LER) (Italy) *Tel:* (06) 7023430 *Fax:* (06) 7020767, pg 402

Rogers, Coleridge & White Ltd (United Kingdom) *Tel:* (020) 7221 3717 *Fax:* (020) 7229 9084 *E-mail:* rcwlitagency@rcwlitagency.co.uk, pg 1133

Rogner und Bernhard GmbH & Co Verlags KG (Germany) *Tel:* (069) 420 8000 *Fax:* (069) 420 800 198 *E-mail:* service@zweitausendeins.de *Web Site:* www.zweitausendeins.de, pg 274

Hans Rohr Verlag (Switzerland) *Tel:* (01) 3614846 *Fax:* (01) 3639513 *E-mail:* buchhandlung.hans.rohr@dm.krinfo.ch, pg 628

Ediciones ROL SA (Spain) *Tel:* (093) 200 80 33 *Fax:* (093) 200 27 62 *E-mail:* rol@e-rol.es *Web Site:* www.e-rol.es, pg 593

Roli Books Pvt Ltd (India) *Tel:* (011) 6462782; (011) 6442271; (011) 6460886 *Fax:* (011) 6467185 *E-mail:* roli@vsnl.com *Web Site:* rolibooks.com, pg 344

Edicoes Rolim Lda (Portugal) *Tel:* (021) 526375, pg 531

Verlag und Buchversand Wolfgang Roller (Germany) *Tel:* (06103) 71886 *Fax:* (06103) 929501 *E-mail:* verlag-roller@t-online.de *Web Site:* www.verlag-roller.de, pg 274

Rolnik Publishers (Israel) *Tel:* (03) 6496663 *Fax:* (03) 6478661 *E-mail:* rolknik@attglobal.net *Web Site:* www.rolnik.com; www.bible2000.com, pg 368

Edizioni Universitarie Romane (Italy) *Tel:* (06) 491503; (06) 4940658 *Fax:* (06) 4453438 *E-mail:* eur@eurom.it *Web Site:* www.eurom.it, pg 402

Romantic Cyprus Publications (Cyprus) *Tel:* 22665155, pg 121

Romantic Novelists' Association (RNA) (United Kingdom) *Tel:* (01827) 714776 *Fax:* (01827) 714776 *Web Site:* www.rna-uk.org, pg 1403

Rombach GmbH Druck und Verlagshaus & Co (Germany) *Tel:* (0761) 4500 0 *Fax:* (0761) 4500 2125 *E-mail:* info@buchverlag.rombach.de *Web Site:* www.rombach.de, pg 274

Editions Rombaldi SA (France) *Tel:* (01) 41 23 65 00 *Fax:* (01) 46 45 34 42, pg 183

Romiosini Verlag (Germany) *Tel:* (0531) 336050 *Fax:* (0531) 336049 *E-mail:* romiosini@unisolo. de *Web Site:* www.unisolo.de/pls/romiosini/ griechische_literatur, pg 274

George Ronald Publisher Ltd (United Kingdom) *Tel:* (01235) 529137 *E-mail:* sales@grbooks.com *Web Site:* www.grbooks.com, pg 745

Rondeau Giannipiero a Monaco (Monaco) *Tel:* (093) 303075 *Fax:* (093) 257047, pg 470

Rondo Verlag (Switzerland) *Tel:* (055) 246 39 37 *Fax:* (055) 246 42 93 *E-mail:* info1@rondo-verlag.ch *Web Site:* www.rondo-verlag.ch, pg 628

Rooster Books Ltd (United Kingdom) *Tel:* (01763) 242717 *Fax:* (01763) 243332 *Web Site:* www. solutions-for-books.co.uk/rooster, pg 745

Roraima Publishers Ltd (Guyana) *Tel:* (02) 2-73551; (02) 2-2363; (02) 2-5057 *Fax:* (02) 62319; (02) 58844 *E-mail:* roraima-distributors@solutions2000.net, pg 311

Mercedes Ros Literary Agency (Spain) *Tel:* (093) 5401353 *Fax:* (093) 5401346 *E-mail:* info@ mercedesros.com *Web Site:* www.mercedesros.com, pg 1126

Mercedes Ros Literary Agency (Spain) *Tel:* (093) 540 13 53 *Fax:* (093) 540 13 46 *E-mail:* info@mercedesros. com *Web Site:* www.mercedesros.com, pg 1213

Sean Ros Press (Ireland) *Tel:* (051) 28666, pg 360

Rosda Jaya Putra (Indonesia) *Tel:* (021) 3904984; (021) 3901692; (021) 3904985 *Fax:* (021) 3901703, pg 353

Rosebud Ediciones (Uruguay) *Tel:* (02) 771773 *Fax:* (02) 6287111 *E-mail:* zapican@adinet.com.uy, pg 772

Rosenberg e Sellier SpA (Italy) *Tel:* (011) 812 76 56 *Fax:* (011) 812 77 44, pg 1311

Rosenberg e Sellier Editori in Torino (Italy) *Tel:* (011) 8127820 *Fax:* (011) 8127808 *E-mail:* info@ rosenbergesellier.it *Web Site:* www.rosenbergesellier.it, pg 402

Rosendale Press Ltd (United Kingdom) *Tel:* (020) 7834 1123 *Fax:* (020) 7834 1240 *E-mail:* info@rosendale. demon.co.uk, pg 745

Rosenheimer Verlagshaus GmbH & Co KG (Germany) *Tel:* (08031) 2838 0 *Fax:* (08031) 2838 44 *E-mail:* info@rosenheimer.com *Web Site:* www. rosenheimer.com, pg 274

Rosenkilde & Bagger (Denmark) *Tel:* 33157044 *Fax:* 33937007 *E-mail:* r-b@rosenkilde-bagger.dk *Web Site:* www.rosenkilde-bagger.dk, pg 133

Guide Rosenwald (France) *Tel:* (01) 44 30 81 00 *Fax:* (01) 44 30 81 11 *E-mail:* info@rosenwald.com *Web Site:* www.rosenwald.com, pg 184

Rosie O'Hara German Translations (United Kingdom) *Tel:* (01667) 456 222 *Fax:* (01667) 456 222 *Web Site:* www.rosieohara.co.uk/index1.htm, pg 1141

Rosikon Press (Poland) *Tel:* (022) 7226101; (022) 7226102; (022) 7226666 *Fax:* (022) 7226667 *E-mail:* biuro@rosikonpress.com; office@ rosikompress.com *Web Site:* www.rosikonpress.com, pg 521

Roskilde University Library (Denmark) *Tel:* 46742207 *Fax:* 46743090 *E-mail:* rub@ruc.dk *Web Site:* www. rub.ruc.dk, pg 1501

Louise Ross & Co, Ltd (United Kingdom) *Tel:* (0225) 44 87 86 *Fax:* (0225) 44 87 89 *E-mail:* louise.ross@ btinternet.com, pg 1344

Rossato (Italy) *Tel:* (0455) 411000 *Fax:* (0455) 411550 *E-mail:* grossato@didanet.it, pg 402

Rossi, E Kdoseis Eleni Rossi-Petsiou (Greece) *Tel:* 2103304440; 2103301854 *Fax:* 210 3304410, pg 308

Rossiiskaya Knizhnaya Palata (Russian Federation) *Tel:* (095) 291-12-78; (095) 291-96-30 *Fax:* (095) 291-96-30; (095) 202-67-25 *E-mail:* bookch@postman.ru; bci@aha.ru *Web Site:* www.bookchamber.ru, pg 1273

Rossiiskaya Nacionalnaya biblioteka (Russian Federation) *Tel:* (0812) 310-2856; (0812) 110-6253 *Fax:* (0812) 310-6148 *E-mail:* office@nlr.ru; english@ nlr.ru *Web Site:* www.nlr.ru, pg 1539

Gosudarstvennaya publichnaya nauchno-tekhnicheskaya biblioteka Sibirskogo otdeleniya Rossiiskoi Akademii Nauk (Russian Federation) *Tel:* (0382) 66-18-60 *Fax:* (0382) 66-33-65 *E-mail:* root@libr.nsk.su *Web Site:* www.gpntb.ru, pg 1539

Rossijskoye avtorskoye obshestvo (Russian Federation) *Tel:* (095) 2033777; (095) 2033260 *E-mail:* rao@rao. ru *Web Site:* www.rao.ru, pg 1126

Rossipaul Kommunikation GmbH (Germany) *Tel:* (089) 17 91 06 0 *Fax:* (089) 17 91 06 22 *E-mail:* info@ rossipaul.de *Web Site:* www.rossipaul.de, pg 274

Universitaet Rostock Universitaetsbibliothek (Germany) *Tel:* (0381) 4 98 22 83 *Fax:* (0381) 4 98 22 70 *E-mail:* ub-sekretariat@ub.uni-rostock.de00.de *Web Site:* www.uni-rostock.de, pg 1508

Rotedic SA (Spain) *Tel:* (091) 8031676 *Fax:* (091) 8038316 *Web Site:* www.rotedic.com, pg 1213

Roth et Sauter SA (Switzerland) *Tel:* (021) 801 75 61 *Fax:* (021) 802 32 79, pg 628

Rothschild & Bach (Netherlands) *Tel:* (020) 6389329, pg 484

RotoVision SA (United Kingdom) *Tel:* (01273) 727 268 *Fax:* (01273) 727 269 *E-mail:* sales@rotovision.com *Web Site:* www.rotovision.com, pg 745

Rotpunktverlag (Switzerland) *Tel:* (01) 2418434 *Fax:* (01) 2418474 *E-mail:* info@rotpunktverlag.ch *Web Site:* www.rotpunktverlag.ch, pg 628

Rotten-Verlags AG (Switzerland) *Tel:* (027) 948 30 32 *Fax:* (027) 948 30 33 *E-mail:* rottenverlag@mengis.ch, pg 628

Gemeentebibliotheek Rotterdam (Netherlands) *Tel:* (010) 281 61 00 *Fax:* (010) 2816181 *E-mail:* communicatie@bibliotheek.rotterdam.nl *Web Site:* www.bibliotheek.rotterdam.nl, pg 1530

Editions Roudil SA (France) *Tel:* (01) 43 54 47 97 *Fax:* (01) 43 54 06 97, pg 184

Editions du Rouergue (France) *Tel:* (05) 65.77.73.70 *Fax:* (05) 65.77.73.71 *E-mail:* info@lerouergue.com *Web Site:* www.lerouergue.com, pg 184

Rough Guides Ltd (United Kingdom) *Tel:* (020) 7010 3703 *Fax:* (020) 7010 6767 *E-mail:* mail@ roughguides.com *Web Site:* www.roughguides.com, pg 746

Roularta Books NV (Belgium) *Tel:* (051) 266967 *Fax:* (051) 266680 *E-mail:* info@roularta.be *Web Site:* www.roulartabooks.be, pg 72

Round Hall Sweet & Maxwell (Ireland) *Tel:* (01) 662 5301 *E-mail:* info@roundhall.ie *Web Site:* www. roundhall.ie, pg 360

Roundhouse Group (United Kingdom) *Tel:* (01237) 474 474 *Fax:* (01237) 474 774 *E-mail:* roundhouse. group@ukgateway.net *Web Site:* www.roundhouse.net, pg 746

Roundhouse Group (United Kingdom) *Tel:* (01237) 474474 *Fax:* (01237) 474774 *E-mail:* roundhouse. group@ukgateway.net *Web Site:* www.roundhouse.net, pg 1344

Routledge (United Kingdom) *Tel:* (020) 7583 9855 *Fax:* (020) 7842 2298 *E-mail:* info@routledge.co.uk *Web Site:* www.routledge.com, pg 746

RoutledgeCurzon (United Kingdom) *Tel:* (020) 7583 9855 *Fax:* (020) 7842 2298 *E-mail:* info@routledge. co.uk *Web Site:* www.routledge.com, pg 746

Antony Rowe Ltd (United Kingdom) *Tel:* (01249) 659 705 *Fax:* (01249) 448 900 *E-mail:* sales@antonyrowe. co.uk *Web Site:* www.antonyrowe.co.uk, pg 1154, 1175, 1217

Antony Rowe Ltd (United Kingdom) *Tel:* (01249) 659 705; (01249) 445 535 (ISDN) *Fax:* (01249) 448 900 *E-mail:* sales@antonyrowe.co.uk *Web Site:* www. antonyrowe.co.uk, pg 1229, 1238

Joseph Rowntree Foundation (United Kingdom) *Tel:* (01904) 629241 *Fax:* (01904) 620072 *E-mail:* julia.lewis@jrf.org.uk *Web Site:* www.jrf.org. uk, pg 746

Rowohlt Berlin Verlag GmbH (Germany) *Tel:* (030) 2853840 *Fax:* (040) 28538422 *E-mail:* info@rowohlt. de *Web Site:* www.rowohlt.de, pg 274

Rowohlt Verlag GmbH (Germany) *Tel:* (040) 72720 *Fax:* (040) 7272319 *E-mail:* info@rowohlt.de *Web Site:* www.rowohlt.de, pg 274

Elizabeth Roy Literary Agency (United Kingdom) *Tel:* (01778) 560672 *Fax:* (01778) 560672, pg 1133

Royal Book Co (Pakistan) *Tel:* (021) 5684244 *Fax:* (021) 5683706, pg 509

Royal Book Co (Pakistan) *Tel:* (021) 5684244; (021) 520628 *Fax:* (021) 5683706 *E-mail:* royalbook@ hotmail.com, pg 1325

Royal College of General Practitioners (RCGP) (United Kingdom) *Tel:* (020) 7581 3232 *Fax:* (020) 7225 3047; (020) 7584 6716 (editorial) *E-mail:* info@rcgp. org.uk *Web Site:* www.rcgp.org.uk, pg 746

Royal College of Surgeons in Ireland Library (Ireland) *Tel:* (01) 402 2407 *Fax:* (01) 402 2457 *E-mail:* library@rcsi.ie *Web Site:* www.rcsi.ie, pg 1517

Royal Dublin Society (Ireland) *Tel:* (01) 6680866 *Fax:* (01) 6604014 *E-mail:* info@rds.ie *Web Site:* www.rds.ie, pg 360

Royal Dublin Society Library (Ireland) *Tel:* (01) 6680866; (01) 2407288 *Fax:* (01) 6604014 *E-mail:* info@rds.ie *Web Site:* www.rds.ie, pg 1517

Royal Institute of International Affairs (United Kingdom) *Tel:* (020) 7957 5700 *Fax:* (020) 7957 5710 *E-mail:* contact@riia.org *Web Site:* www.riia.org, pg 746

Royal Irish Academy (Ireland) *Tel:* (01) 6762570 *Fax:* (01) 6762346 *E-mail:* admin@ria.ie *Web Site:* www.ria.ie, pg 360

Royal Literary Fund (United Kingdom) *Tel:* (020) 7353 7150 *Fax:* (020) 7353 1350 *E-mail:* rlitfund@ btconnect.com *Web Site:* www.rlf.org.uk, pg 1403

Royal Nepal Academy (Nepal) *Tel:* (01) 547714; (01) 547715; (01) 547716; (01) 547717; (01) 547718 *Fax:* (01) 547713 *E-mail:* info@ronast.org.np; ronast@mos.com.np *Web Site:* www.ronast.org.np, pg 473

Royal Scientific Society Library (Jordan) *Tel:* (06) 5344701 *Fax:* (06) 5344806 *Web Site:* www.rss.gov.jo, pg 1521

The Royal Society (United Kingdom) *Tel:* (020) 7839 5561 *Fax:* (020) 7930 2170 *E-mail:* info@royalsoc.ac. uk *Web Site:* www.royalsoc.ac.uk, pg 747

The Royal Society for the Encouragement of Arts, Manufactures & Commerce (RSA) (United Kingdom) *Tel:* (020) 7930 5115 *Fax:* (020) 7839 5805 *E-mail:* general@rsa.org.uk *Web Site:* www.rsa.org.uk, pg 1403

The Royal Society of Chemistry (United Kingdom) *Tel:* (020) 7437 8656 *Fax:* (020) 7437 8883 *E-mail:* sales@rsc.org *Web Site:* www.rsc.org, pg 747

Royal Society of Literature (United Kingdom) *Tel:* (020) 7845 4676 *Fax:* (020) 7845 4679 *E-mail:* info@rslit. org *Web Site:* www.rslit.org, pg 1403

Royal Society of Medicine Press Ltd (United Kingdom) *Tel:* (020) 7290 2921 *Fax:* (020) 7290 2929 *E-mail:* publishing@rsm.ac.uk *Web Site:* www. rsmpress.co.uk, pg 747

Royal Society of New South Wales (Australia) *Tel:* (02)9036 5282 *Fax:* (02) 9036 5309 *E-mail:* info@nsw.royalsoc.org.au *Web Site:* nsw. royalsoc.org.au, pg 39

Royal Society of South Africa Library (South Africa) *Tel:* (021) 650 2543 *Fax:* (021) 650 2710 *E-mail:* roysoc@science.uct.ac.za *Web Site:* www.rssa. uct.ac.za, pg 1543

Royal Society of Victoria Inc (Australia) *Tel:* (03) 9663 5259 *Fax:* (03) 9663 2301 *E-mail:* sciencevictoria@ org.au; rsvinc@vicnet.net.au *Web Site:* www. sciencevictoria.org.au, pg 39

RSG Industrial Printing (United States) *Tel:* 760-961-0803 *Toll Free Tel:* 866-743-4066 *Fax:* 760-961-0813 *E-mail:* sales@rsg123.com *Web Site:* www. rsgindustrialprinting.com, pg 1221

RSVP Publishing Co Ltd (New Zealand) *Tel:* (09) 3723480 *Fax:* (09) 3728480 *E-mail:* rsvppub@iconz. co.nz *Web Site:* www.rsvp-publishing.co.nz, pg 496

Wydawnictwo RTW (Poland) *Tel:* (022) 633 70 10; (022) 663 74 74 *Fax:* (022) 633 70 10; (022) 39120123 *E-mail:* rtw@wydawrtw.media.pl, pg 521

Josep Ruaix Editor (Spain) *Tel:* (093) 820 81 36; (093) 830 02 33 *Web Site:* www.ruaix.com/, pg 593

Ruamsarn (1977) Co Ltd (Thailand) *Tel:* (02) 221-6483 *Fax:* (02) 222-2038, pg 641

Rubber Research Institute of Malaysia Library (Malaysia) *Tel:* (03) 4567033 *Fax:* (03) 4511301 *Web Site:* w3.itri.org.tw/k0000/apec/malaysia/malay-1.htm, pg 1525

Rubbettino Editore (Italy) *Tel:* (0968) 662034 *Fax:* (0968) 662035 *E-mail:* info@rubbettino.it *Web Site:* www.rubbettino.it, pg 402

The Rubicon Press (United Kingdom) *Tel:* (020) 7937 6813 *Fax:* (020) 7937 6813, pg 747

Rubin Mass Ltd (Israel) *Tel:* (02) 627-7863 *Fax:* (02) 627-7864 *E-mail:* rmass@barak.net.il *Web Site:* www. rubin-mass.com, pg 368, 1310

Libreria Rubinos - 1860 SA (Spain) *Tel:* (091) 435 22 39 *Fax:* (091) 435 32 72, pg 1334

Rudolf Haufe Verlag GmbH & Co KG (Germany) *Tel:* (0761) 3683-0 *Fax:* (0761) 3683-195 *E-mail:* online@haufe.de *Web Site:* www.haufe.de, pg 274

Rueda, SL Editorial (Spain) *Tel:* (091) 619 27 79; (091) 619 25 64 *Fax:* (091) 610 28 55 *E-mail:* ed_rueda@ infornet.es *Web Site:* www.editorialrueda.es, pg 594

Ruegger Verlag (Switzerland) *Tel:* (01) 4912130 *Fax:* (01) 4931176 *E-mail:* info@rueggerverlag.ch *Web Site:* www.rueggerverlag.ch, pg 628

Ruetten & Loening Berlin GmbH (Germany) *Tel:* (030) 283 94 0 *Fax:* (030) 283 94 100 *E-mail:* info@ aufbau-verlag.de *Web Site:* www.aufbau-verlag.de, pg 274

Dieter Ruggeberg Verlagsbuchhandlung (Germany) *Tel:* (0202) 592811 *Fax:* (0202) 592811 *E-mail:* vrggeberg@aol.com *Web Site:* www.vbdr.de, pg 274

Rugginenti Editore (Italy) *Tel:* (02) 89501283 *Fax:* (02) 89531273 *E-mail:* info@rugginenti.com *Web Site:* www.rugginenti.com, pg 403

Ruh ve Madde Yayinlari ve Saglik Hizmetleri AS (Turkey) *Tel:* (0212) 2431814 *Fax:* (0212) 2520718 *E-mail:* bilyay@bilyay.org.tr *Web Site:* www. ruhvemadde.com, pg 647

Ruhland Verlag Gimblt (Germany) *Tel:* (069) 811768 *Fax:* (069) 811769, pg 274

Verlag an der Ruhr GmbH (Germany) *Tel:* (0208) 4395454 *Fax:* (0208) 4395439 *E-mail:* info@ verlagruhr.de *Web Site:* www.verlagruhr.de, pg 275

Rumsby Scientific Publishing (Australia) *Tel:* (02) 98076184 *Fax:* (02) 98076184 *Web Site:* www. angelfire.com/biz/rumsby, pg 39

Runa Press (Ireland) *Tel:* (01) 2801869, pg 360

Rupa & Co (India) *Tel:* (011) 344821; (011) 346305 *Fax:* (011) 327 7294 *E-mail:* rupa@ndb.vsnl.net.in; del.rupaco@axcess.net.in, pg 344

Rupa & Co (India) *Tel:* (011) 23272161; (011) 23270260 *Fax:* (011) 23277294 *E-mail:* rupa@ndb.vsnl.net.in, pg 1307

Rusconi Libri Srl (Italy) *Tel:* (05) 41326306 *Fax:* (05) 41392344 *E-mail:* relazioniesterne@rusconi.it, pg 403

Ruskin Rowe Press (Australia) *Tel:* (02) 9918-8810 *Fax:* (02) 9918-8884, pg 39

The Ruskin Society of London (United Kingdom) *Tel:* (01865) 310987; (01865) 515962 *Fax:* (01865) 240448, pg 1403

Michael Russell Publishing Ltd (United Kingdom) *Tel:* (01953) 887776 *Fax:* (01953) 887762, pg 747

Russian State Historical Archives (Russian Federation) *Tel:* (0812) 311-09-26 *Fax:* (0812) 311-22-52, pg 1539

Russkaya Kniga Izdatelstvo (Publishers) (Russian Federation) *Tel:* (095) 2053377 *Fax:* (095) 2053424, pg 544

Russkij Jazyk (Russian Federation) *Tel:* (095) 9239705 *Fax:* (095) 9288906 *Web Site:* www.russyaz.ru, pg 544

K Rustem & Bro (Cyprus) *Tel:* (022) 71041; (022) 71418; (022) 52085, pg 1297

The Rutland Press (United Kingdom) *Tel:* (0131) 229 7545 *Fax:* (0131) 228 2188 *E-mail:* info@rias.org.uk *Web Site:* www.rias.org.uk, pg 747

Rux Guru srl (Italy) *Tel:* (075) 5270257; (075) 5270258 *Fax:* (075) 5288244 *E-mail:* ruxinfo@rux-distribuzione.com *Web Site:* www.rux-distribuzione. com, pg 1311

RWS Translations Ltd (United Kingdom) *Tel:* (01753) 480200 *Fax:* (01753) 480280 *E-mail:* rwstrans@rws. com *Web Site:* www.rws.com, pg 1141

RWTH Aachen Hochschulbibliotek (Germany) *Tel:* (0241) 80-94445 *Fax:* (0241) 80-92273 *E-mail:* bth@bth.rwth.rwth-aachen.de *Web Site:* www.rwth-aachen.de; www.bth.rwth-aachen.de, pg 1508

Ryland Peters & Small Ltd (United Kingdom) *Tel:* (020) 7436 9090 *Fax:* (020) 7436 9790 *E-mail:* info@rps.co. uk *Web Site:* www.rylandpeters.com, pg 747

John Rylands University Library of Manchester (United Kingdom) *Tel:* (0161) 275 3751 (Main Library Bldg); (0161) 834 5343 (Deansgate Bldg) *Fax:* (0161) 273 7488 (Main Library Bldg); (0161) 834 5574 (Deansgate Bldg) *E-mail:* libtalk@man.ac.uk *Web Site:* rylibweb.man.ac.uk, pg 1552

Ryosho-Fukyu-Kai Co Ltd (Japan) *Tel:* (03) 3813-1251 *Fax:* (03) 3811-6490 *E-mail:* ryosho@po.iijnet.or.jp, pg 422

Simon Rysavy (Czech Republic) *Tel:* (05) 42 212 052; (05) 42 213 849 *Fax:* (05) 42 216 633 *E-mail:* info@ rysavy.cz *Web Site:* www.itn.cz/rysavy-books; www. rysavy.cz, pg 127

Ryvellus Medienagentur Dopfer (Germany) *Tel:* (0681) 372313 *Fax:* (0681) 3904102, pg 275

S/A Tiesiskas informacijas cerfus (Latvia) *Tel:* (02) 7220422 *Fax:* (02) 7213854 *E-mail:* mariss@date.lv, pg 442

Edicioes Joao Sa da Costa Lda (Portugal) *Tel:* (021) 8400428; (021) 571118; (021) 563603 *Fax:* (021) 534194, pg 531

Sa da Costa Livraria (Portugal) *Tel:* (021) 346 07 21; (021) 346 07 23; (021) 346 07 24; (021) 346 07 25 *Fax:* (021) 346 07 22, pg 531

Livraria Sa da Costa (Portugal) *Tel:* (021) 346 07 21, pg 1329

Saar Publishing House (Israel) *Tel:* (03) 5445292 *Fax:* (03) 5445293, pg 368

Saara Buddhi Publication (Sri Lanka), pg 602

Saarbrucker Druckerei und Verlag GmbH (SDV) (Germany) *Tel:* (0681) 66501-0 *Fax:* (0681) 66501-10 *Web Site:* www.sdv-saar.de, pg 275

Saarlaendische Universitaets und Landesbibliothek (Germany) *Tel:* (0681) 3022070 *Fax:* (0681) 3022796 *E-mail:* sulb@sulb.uni-saarland.de *Web Site:* www. sulb.uni-saarland.de, pg 1508

Saatkorn-Verlag GmbH (Germany) *Tel:* (04131) 98 35-02 *Fax:* (04131) 98 35 505 *E-mail:* info@saatkornverlag. de *Web Site:* www.saatkorn-verlag.de, pg 275

SAB Schweiz Arbeitsgemeinschaft fuer die Berggebiete (Switzerland) *Tel:* (031) 382 1010 *Fax:* (031) 382 1016 *E-mail:* info@sab.ch *Web Site:* www.sab.ch, pg 628

Sabah Kitaplari (Turkey) *Tel:* (0212) 5028410; (0212) 5028319, pg 647

Sabah State Library (Malaysia) *Tel:* (088) 214828 *Fax:* (088) 270714 *Web Site:* www.ssl.sabah.gov.my, pg 1525

SABDA (India) *Tel:* (0413) 2334980; (0413) 2223328 *Fax:* (0413) 2223328 *E-mail:* sabda@ sriaurobindoashram.org *Web Site:* sabda. sriaurobindoashram.org, pg 344

Sabe AG Verlagsinstitut (Switzerland) *Tel:* (062) 8368690 *Fax:* (062) 8368695 *E-mail:* verlag@sabe.ch, pg 628

Sabe U (Myanmar), pg 1319

SACEM (Societe des Auteurs Copositeurs et Editeurs de Musique) (France) *Tel:* (01) 47 15 47 15 *Fax:* (01) 47 15 47 86 *E-mail:* communication@sacem.fr *Web Site:* www.sacem.fr, pg 1259

Verlag Werner Sachon GmbH & Co (Germany) *Tel:* (08261) 999-0 *Fax:* (08261) 999 391 *E-mail:* info@sachon.de *Web Site:* www.sachon.de, pg 275

Sachse & Heinzelmann Kunst- und Buchhandlung GmbH (Germany) *Tel:* (0511) 360240 *Fax:* (0511) 324167 *E-mail:* info@sachse-heinzelmann.de *Web Site:* www.sachse-heinzelmann.de, pg 1301

Sachsenbuch Verlagsgesellschaft Mbh (Germany) *Tel:* (0341) 9784259; (0341) 9784261 *Fax:* (0341) 9784259, pg 275

Sada, Literaturno-Izdatel'skij Centr (Azerbaijan) *Tel:* (012) 927564 *Fax:* (012) 929843, pg 60

Sadan Publishing Ltd (Israel) *Tel:* (03) 6954402 *Fax:* (03) 6953122, pg 368

Sadeepa Bookshop (Sri Lanka) *Tel:* (011) 686114 (hotline); (011) 694289; (011) 678043 *Fax:* (011) 683813; (011) 678044 *E-mail:* sadeepabk@itmin.com *Web Site:* www.sadeepabooks.com, pg 1334

Biblioteca Municipala Mihail Sadoveanu (Romania) *Tel:* (01) 2113625 *Fax:* (01) 2113625, pg 1538

Saechsische Landesbibliothek- Staats- und Universitaetsbibliothek Dresden (Germany) *Tel:* (0351) 4677-123 *Fax:* (0351) 4677-111 *E-mail:* direktion@ slub-dresden.de *Web Site:* www.tu-dresden.de/slub, pg 1508

Saeculum IO (Romania) *Tel:* (021) 2228597 *Fax:* (021) 3452827; (021) 2228597 *E-mail:* saeculum@tcnet.ro *Web Site:* www.saeculum.ro, pg 537

Saela Shobo (Librairie Ca et La) (Japan) *Tel:* (03) 3268-4261 *Fax:* (03) 3268-4264 *E-mail:* info@saela.co.jp *Web Site:* www.saela.co.jp, pg 422

Saendig Reprint Verlag, Hans-Rainer Wohlwend (Liechtenstein) *Tel:* 232 36 27 *Fax:* 232 36 49 *E-mail:* saendig@adon.li *Web Site:* www.saendig.com, pg 445

J.C. Saez Editor (Chile) *Tel:* (02) 3260104 *E-mail:* jcsaezc@jcsaezeditor.cl *Web Site:* www. jcsaezeditor.cl, pg 100

Univerzita Pavla Jozefa Safarika (Slovakia) *Tel:* (055) 622 26 08 *Fax:* (055) 766 959 *E-mail:* kancelar@upjs. sk; rektor@upjs.sk *Web Site:* www.upjs.sk, pg 1541

Klub Saffier (South Africa) *Tel:* (011) 6736725 *Fax:* (011) 6736719, pg 1245

Sagano Shoin (Japan) *Tel:* (075) 391-7686 *Fax:* (075) 391-7321 *E-mail:* sagano@mbox.kyoto-inet.or.jp *Web Site:* www.saganoshoin.co.jp, pg 422

Ratna Sagar Pvt Ltd (India) *Tel:* (011) 7654095; (011) 7654099 *Fax:* (011) 7250787 *E-mail:* rsagar@ giasdlo1.vsnl.net.in; rsagar@nda.vsnl.net.in, pg 344

Biblioteca Nazionale Sagarriga Visconti Volpi (Italy) *Tel:* (080) 5212534; (080) 5211298 *Fax:* (080) 5211298 *E-mail:* visconti@librari.beniculturali.it, pg 1519

SAGE Publications India Pvt Ltd (India) *Tel:* (011) 2649 1290 *Fax:* (011) 2649 2117 *E-mail:* sage@vsnl.com; marketing@indiasage.com; editors@indiasage.com *Web Site:* www.indiasage.com, pg 344

SAGE Publications Ltd (United Kingdom) *Tel:* (020) 7324 8500 *Fax:* (020) 7374 8600 *E-mail:* info@ sagepub.co.uk *Web Site:* www.sagepub.co.uk, pg 747

SAGEP Libri & Comunicazione Srl (Italy) *Tel:* (010) 593355 *Fax:* (010) 581713 *E-mail:* info@sagep.it *Web Site:* www.sagep.it, pg 403

Il Saggiatore (Italy) *Tel:* (02) 202301 *Fax:* (02) 29513061 *E-mail:* stampa@saggiatore.it *Web Site:* www.saggiatore.it, pg 403

Verlag Otto Sagner (Germany) *Tel:* (089) 54 218-0 *Fax:* (089) 54 218-218 *E-mail:* postmaster@kubon-sagner.de *Web Site:* www.kubon-sagner.de, pg 275

Sagra-D C Luzzatto Livreiros, Editores e Distribuidores Ltda (Brazil) *Tel:* (051) 3227 5222 *Fax:* (051) 3227 4438 *E-mail:* atendimento@sagra-luzzatto.com.br *Web Site:* www.sagra-luzzatto.com.br, pg 1294

Sahasrara Publications (India) *Tel:* (011) 2432617 *E-mail:* sahasrarapublications@yahoo.co.in, pg 344

Edition Sahel (Senegal) *Tel:* 212164, pg 547

Sahitya Akademi (India) *Tel:* (011) 3386626; (011) 3735297; (011) 3364207 (sales); (011) 3386629 *Fax:* (011) 3382428; (011) 3364207 *E-mail:* sesy@ ndl.vsnl.net.in, pg 345

Sahitya Akademi (India) *Tel:* (011) 3386626; (011) 3386627; (011) 3386628; (011) 3386629; (011) 3387386; (011) 3386088 *Fax:* (011) 3382428 *Web Site:* www.sahitya-akademi.org, pg 1395

Sahitya Akademi Library (India) *Tel:* (011) 3386626; (011) 3387386; (011) 3386088 *Fax:* (011) 3382428 *E-mail:* secy@sahitya-akademi.org *Web Site:* www. sahitya-akademi.org, pg 1514

Sahitya Pravarthaka Co-operative Society Ltd (India) *Tel:* (0481) 4111; (0481) 4112, pg 345

Saiensu-Sha Co Ltd (Japan) *Tel:* (03) 5474-8500 *Fax:* (03) 5474-8900 *E-mail:* rikei@saiensu.co.jp, pg 422

Saik Wah Press (Pte) Ltd (Singapore) *Tel:* 6292 8759 *Fax:* 6296 0638 *E-mail:* sales@saikwah.com.sg *Web Site:* www.saikwah.com.sg, pg 1151

The Sailor Publishing Co, Ltd (Japan) *Tel:* (03) 3846-2955 *Fax:* (03) 3846-0452, pg 422

Sainsbury Publishing Ltd (United Kingdom) *Tel:* (01636) 830499 *Fax:* (01636) 830175, pg 748

Saint Andrew Press (United Kingdom) *Tel:* (0131) 225 5722 *Fax:* (0131) 220 3113 *E-mail:* standrewpress@ cofscotland.org.uk *Web Site:* www.churchofscotland. org.uk, pg 748

St Andrew's Biblical Theological College (Russian Federation) *Tel:* (095) 2702200 *Fax:* (095) 2707644 *E-mail:* standrews@standrews.ru *Web Site:* www. standrews.ru, pg 544

St Armand Paper Mill (Canada) *Tel:* 514-931-8338 *Fax:* 514-931-5953 *Web Site:* www.st-armand.com, pg 1225

Editions Saint-Augustin (Switzerland) *Tel:* (024) 486 05 04 *Fax:* (024) 486 05 23 *E-mail:* editions@staugustin. ch, pg 628

St Clair Press (Australia) *Tel:* (02) 9818 1942 *Fax:* (02) 9418 1923 *E-mail:* stclair@australis.net.au *Web Site:* www.stclairpress.com.au, pg 40

St Clement of Ohrid National & University Library (The Former Yugoslav Republic of Macedonia) *Tel:* (02) 3115 177; (02) 3133 418 *Fax:* (02) 3226 846 *E-mail:* kliment@nubsk.edu.mk *Web Site:* www.nubsk. edu.mk, pg 449

Verlag St Gabriel (Austria) *Tel:* (02236) 803-225 *Fax:* (02236) 24483 *E-mail:* zeitschriften.stgabriel@ steyler.at@steyler.at *Web Site:* www.steyler.at, pg 56

St George Books (Australia) *Tel:* (08) 9482 9051 *Fax:* (08) 9482 9043, pg 40

St George's Press (United Kingdom) *Tel:* (020) 8504 1199 *Fax:* (020) 8559 0989 *E-mail:* sgp17@aol.com *Web Site:* www.eppingforest.co.uk/stgeorgespress, pg 748

St Jerome Publishing (United Kingdom) *Tel:* (0161) 973 9856 *Fax:* (0161) 905 3498 *E-mail:* stjerome@ compuserve.com *Web Site:* www.stjerome.co.uk, pg 748

St Joseph Publications (Australia) *Tel:* (02) 99297344 *Fax:* (02) 91303678; (02) 99297994 *E-mail:* sosjelt@ internet-australia.com, pg 40

Saint Mary's Publishing Corp (Philippines) *Tel:* (02) 7119730; (02) 7119743 *Fax:* (02) 7350955, pg 516

Saint Michael's Mission Social Centre (Lesotho), pg 444

Editions Saint-Michel SA (France) *Tel:* (04) 75 87 10 50 *Fax:* (04) 75 87 10 61, pg 184

Librairie Saint-Paul (The Democratic Republic of the Congo) *Tel:* 77726, pg 1297

Editions Saint-Paul (Luxembourg) *Tel:* 4993-275 *Fax:* 4993-580 *E-mail:* info@biblioservice.lu *Web Site:* www.biblioservice.lu; www.libo.lu (orders), pg 448

Editions Saint-Paul (Switzerland) *Tel:* (026) 4264331 *Fax:* (026) 4264330 *E-mail:* druckerei@st-paul.ch *Web Site:* www.st-paul.ch, pg 628

Editions Saint-Paul SA (France) *Tel:* (01) 39 67 16 00 *Fax:* (01) 30 21 41 95, pg 184

St Pauls (Republic of Korea) *Tel:* (02) 9861361; (02) 9861364 *Fax:* (02) 984-4622 *E-mail:* miari@paolo.net; felix@paolo.net; stpaul@paolo.net *Web Site:* www. paolo.net, pg 439

St Paul's Bibliographies Ltd (United Kingdom) *Tel:* (0130) 386 2258 *Fax:* (0130) 386 2660 *E-mail:* stpauls@stpaulsbib.com *Web Site:* www. oakknoll.com/spbib.html, pg 748

St Pauls Publications (Australia) *Tel:* (02) 9746 2288 *Fax:* (02) 9746 1140 *E-mail:* publications@stpauls. com.au; info@stpauls.com.au; sales@stpauls.com.au *Web Site:* www.stpauls.com.au, pg 40

St Pauls Publishing (United Kingdom) *Tel:* (020) 7978 4300 *Fax:* (020) 7978 4370 *E-mail:* editions@stpauls. org.uk *Web Site:* www.stpauls.ie, pg 748

Saint Publishing (New Zealand) *Tel:* (09) 623-2510 *Fax:* (09) 623-2890 *E-mail:* info@saintpublish.co.nz, pg 496

Bibliotheque Sainte-Genevieve (France) *Tel:* (01) 44 41 97 97 *Fax:* (01) 44 41 97 96 *E-mail:* bsgmail@univ. paris1.fr *Web Site:* www-bsg.univ-paris1.fr, pg 1505

Sairaanhoitajien Koulutussaatio (Finland) *Tel:* (09) 5666788 *Fax:* (09) 531504, pg 143

Sajha Prakashan, Co-operative Publishing Organization (Nepal) *Tel:* (01) 5521118, pg 473

The Sakai Agency Inc (Japan) *Tel:* (03) 32951405 *Fax:* (03) 32954366 *E-mail:* sakai@sakaiagency.com, pg 1124

Sakartvelo Publishing House (Georgia) *Tel:* 954201; 952927, pg 190

Sakkoulas Publications SA (Greece) *Tel:* 2103387500 *Fax:* 2103390075 *E-mail:* info@sakkoulas.gr *Web Site:* www.sakkoulas.gr, pg 308

Salamander Books Ltd (United Kingdom) *Tel:* (01256) 329242 *Fax:* (01256) 812558; (01256) 812521 *E-mail:* mdl@macmillan.co.uk *Web Site:* www. chrysalisbooks.co.uk/books/publisher/salamander, pg 748

Salamandra Consultoria Editorial SA (Brazil) *Tel:* (021) 2406306 *Fax:* (021) 2404775; (021) 5331622 *E-mail:* salprod@openlink.com.br, pg 89

Adriano Salani Editore srl (Italy) *Tel:* (028) 0206624 *Fax:* (027) 2018806 *E-mail:* info@salani.it, pg 403

The Salariya Book Co Ltd (United Kingdom) *Tel:* (01273) 603 306 *Fax:* (01273) 693 857 *E-mail:* salariya@salariya.com *Web Site:* www. salariya.com, pg 748

Saldo Penzugyi Tanacsado es Informatikai Rt (Hungary) *Tel:* (01) 237-9800 *Fax:* (01) 237-9841 *E-mail:* kiado@saldo.hu *Web Site:* www.saldo.hu, pg 321

Salerno Editrice SRL (Italy) *Tel:* (06) 3608201 *Fax:* (06) 3223132 *E-mail:* info@salernoeditrice.it *Web Site:* www.salernoeditrice.it, pg 403

Salesian Press/Don Bosco Sha (Japan) *Tel:* (03) 3351-7041 *Fax:* (03) 3351-5430, pg 422

Salesiana Publishers Inc (Philippines) *Tel:* (02) 8161506; (02) 889234 *Fax:* (02) 8922154, pg 516

Edicoes Salesianas (Portugal) *Tel:* (022) 565750 *Fax:* (022) 536 58 00 *E-mail:* edisal@clix.pt, pg 531

Salmon Publishing (Ireland) *Tel:* (065) 7081941 *Fax:* (065) 7081941 *E-mail:* info@salmonpoetry.com *Web Site:* www.salmonpoetry.com, pg 360

Biblioteca Municipal Dr Joaquin de Salterain (Uruguay) *Tel:* (02) 95 62 82 *Web Site:* www.mec.gub.uy/biblo. htm, pg 1553

The Saltire Society (United Kingdom) *Tel:* (0131) 556 1836 *Fax:* (0131) 557 1675 *E-mail:* saltire@ saltiresociety.org.uk *Web Site:* www.saltiresociety.org. uk, pg 748

Salto Publishers (Greece) *Tel:* 2310262854 *Fax:* 2310 285879 *E-mail:* saltos@spocrk.net.gr, pg 1304

Saltwater Publications (Australia) *Tel:* (03) 5974 1959 *Fax:* (03) 5974 1959, pg 40

Salvat Editores de Mexico (Mexico) *Tel:* (05) 2034813; (05) 2034393 *Fax:* (05) 5318773 *E-mail:* hachettemex@hachette.ex.com.mx, pg 467

Salvat Editores SA (Spain) *Tel:* (090) 2117547 *Fax:* (093) 4955710 *E-mail:* infosalvat@salvat.com *Web Site:* www.salvat.es, pg 594

Editorial Miguel A Salvatella SA (Spain) *Tel:* (093) 2189026 *Fax:* (093) 2177437 *E-mail:* editorial@ salvatella.com *Web Site:* www.salvatella.com, pg 594

Salvationist Publishing & Supplies Ltd (United Kingdom) *Tel:* (020) 7387 1656 *Fax:* (020) 7383 3420 *E-mail:* mail_order@sp-s.co.uk *Web Site:* www. archive.salvationarmy.org.uk, pg 748

Editions Salvator Sarl (France) *Tel:* (01) 53 10 38 38 *Fax:* (01) 53 10 38 39 *E-mail:* salvator.editions@ wanadoo.fr, pg 184

Salvioni arti grafiche SA (Switzerland) *Tel:* (091) 8211111 *Fax:* (091) 8211112, pg 628

Salvy Editeur (France) *Tel:* (01) 43 25 74 40 *Fax:* (01) 46 33 56 21, pg 184

Universitaetsbibliothek Salzburg (Austria) *Tel:* (0662) 8044 77550 *Fax:* (0662) 8044 103 *E-mail:* info.hb@ sbg.ac.at *Web Site:* www.ubs.sbg.ac.at, pg 1490

Verlag der Salzburger Druckerei (Austria) *Tel:* (0662) 873507-56 *Fax:* (0662) 873507-62 *E-mail:* verlag@ salzburger-druckerei.at, pg 57

Salzburger Kulturvereinigung (Austria) *Tel:* (0662) 845346 *Fax:* (0662) 842665 *E-mail:* kulturvereinigung@salzburg.co.at *Web Site:* www.salzburg.com/kulturvereinigung, pg 57

Salzburger Nachrichten Verlagsgesellschaft mbH & Co KG (Austria) *Tel:* (0662) 8373-0; (0662) 8373-210 *Fax:* (0662) 8373-210 *E-mail:* anzeigen@salzburg.com *Web Site:* www.salzburg.com, pg 57

Sam Woode Ltd (Ghana) *Tel:* (021) 229487 *Fax:* (021) 310482 *E-mail:* samwoode@ghana.com, pg 302

Saman Saha Madara Publishers (Sri Lanka) *Tel:* (01) 2862055 *Fax:* (01) 2868071 *E-mail:* prince@eureka.lk, pg 602

Samaya SRL (Italy) *Tel:* (0789) 750039 *Fax:* (0789) 750081 *E-mail:* info@benesseresardegna.com, pg 403

Samayawardena Printers Publishers & Booksellers (Sri Lanka) *Tel:* (01) 694682 *Fax:* (01) 698977; (01) 683525 *E-mail:* samaya@applestr.lk, pg 602

Sambandet Forlag (Norway) *Tel:* 55317963 *Fax:* 55310944 *E-mail:* vestlandskes.bokhandel@c2i. net, pg 505

Samdistribution AB (Sweden) *Tel:* (08) 696 80 00 *Fax:* (08) 696 83 73 *E-mail:* samdistribution@bok. bonnier.se; magnus.brundin@samdistribution.se *Web Site:* www.bok.bonnier.se; samdistribution.se, pg 1335

Samfundet De Nio (Sweden) *Tel:* (08) 411 15 42 *Fax:* (08) 21 19 15 *Web Site:* www.samfundetdenio. com, pg 1399

Samfundslitteratur (Denmark) *Tel:* 38153880 *Fax:* 35357822 *E-mail:* samfundslitteratur@sl.cbs.dk; slforlag@sl.cbs.dk *Web Site:* www.samfundslitteratur. dk, pg 133

Samho Music Publishing Co Ltd (Republic of Korea) *Tel:* (02) 512-3578 *Fax:* (02) 512-3594 *E-mail:* webmaster@samhomusic.com *Web Site:* www. samhomusic.com, pg 439

Samhwa Publishing Co Ltd (Republic of Korea) *Tel:* (02) 7766687 *Fax:* (02) 7732993, pg 439

Samkaleen Prakashan (India) *Tel:* (011) 3523520; (011) 3518197, pg 345

Samkwang Publishing Co (Republic of Korea) *Tel:* (02) 3237275 *Fax:* (02) 3251153, pg 439

Samlerens Bogklub (Denmark) *Tel:* 70 11 00 33 *Fax:* 70 11 01 33 *E-mail:* samlerens-bogklub@gyldendal.dk *Web Site:* www.samlerens-bogklub.dk; www.gyldendal. dk, pg 1242

Samlerens Forlag A/S (Denmark) *Tel:* 3341 1800 *Fax:* 3341 1801 *E-mail:* samleren@samleren.dk *Web Site:* www.samleren.dk, pg 134

Verlag fuer Sammler (Austria) *Tel:* (0316) 47 22 30 *Fax:* (0316) 67 39 87 *E-mail:* ssu@literaturhaus.at *Web Site:* www.literaturhaus.at/buch/verlagsportraits/ sammler.html, pg 57

Samseong Publishing Co Ltd (Republic of Korea) *Tel:* (02) 3470-6852 *Fax:* (02) 3452-2907, pg 439

Samsom BedrijfsInformatie BV (Netherlands) *Tel:* 0172 466633 *Fax:* 0172 475933 *E-mail:* info@kluwer.nl *Web Site:* www.kluwer.nl, pg 484

Samsprak Forlags AB (Sweden) *Tel:* (019) 13 24 45 *Fax:* (019) 18 72 55 *E-mail:* info@samsprak.se *Web Site:* www.samsprak.se, pg 610

San Carlos Publications (Philippines) *Tel:* (032) 253-1000 *Fax:* (032) 255-4341 *E-mail:* uscjournals@lycos. com, pg 516

Editoriale San Giusto SRL Edizioni Parnaso (Italy) *Tel:* (040) 370200 *Fax:* (040) 3728970 *E-mail:* info@ edizioniparnaso.it *Web Site:* www.edizioniparnaso.it, pg 403

Edizioni San Lorenzo (Italy) *Tel:* (0522) 323140 *Fax:* (0522) 323140 *E-mail:* redazione@edizioni-sanlorenzo.it *Web Site:* www.edizioni-sanlorenzo.it, pg 403

Editrice San Marco SRL (Italy) *Tel:* (035) 940178 *Fax:* (035) 944385 *E-mail:* info@editricesanmarco.it *Web Site:* www.editricesanmarco.it, pg 403

Editorial San Martin (Spain) *Tel:* (091) 8599964 *Fax:* (091) 8599964, pg 594

San Min Book Co Ltd (Taiwan, Province of China) *Tel:* (02) 25006600 *Fax:* (02) 25064000 *E-mail:* editor@sanmin.com.tw *Web Site:* www. sanmin.com.tw, pg 637

San Pablo (Argentina) *Tel:* (011) 5555-2400; (011) 555-2401 *Fax:* (011) 5555-2425 *E-mail:* sobicain@san-pablo.com.ar *Web Site:* www.san-pablo.com.ar, pg 8

San Pablo Ediciones (Spain) *Tel:* (091) 917 425 113 *Fax:* (091) 917 425 723 *E-mail:* dir.editorial@ sanpablo-ssp.es *Web Site:* www.sanpablo-ssp.es, pg 594

Libreria San Pablo (Chile) *Tel:* (02) 698 9145 *Fax:* (02) 671 6884 *E-mail:* alameda@san-pablo.cl *Web Site:* www.san-pablo.cl, pg 1295

Edizioni San Paolo SRL (Italy) *Tel:* (02) 660751 *Fax:* (02) 66075211 *E-mail:* sanpaoloedizioni@stpauls. it, pg 403

Ediciones San Pio X (Spain) *Tel:* (091) 726.28.17; (091) 355 2727 *Fax:* (091) 726.28.17 *E-mail:* espx@ planalfa.es, pg 594

Simone Sanchez (French Polynesia) *Tel:* (0689) 533260, pg 190

Forlaget Sanctus (Metodistkyrkans Forlag) (Sweden) *Tel:* (08) 31 55 70 *Fax:* (08) 31 55 79, pg 610

Editions Sand et Tchou SA (France) *Tel:* (01) 44 55 37 50 *Fax:* (01) 40 20 99 74 *E-mail:* info@editions-menges.com, pg 184

Erik Sandberg (Norway) *Tel:* 22335555 *Fax:* 22413562, pg 506

Sandila Import-Export Handels-GmbH (Germany) *Tel:* (07764) 93970 *Fax:* (07764) 939739 *E-mail:* info@sandila.de *Web Site:* www.sandila.de, pg 1301

Sandpiper Books Ltd (United Kingdom) *Tel:* (020) 8767 7421 *Fax:* (020) 8682 0280 *E-mail:* enquiries@ sandpiper.co.uk, pg 1344

Sandviks Bokforlag (Norway) *Tel:* (051) 44 00 00 *Fax:* (051) 44 00 99 *Web Site:* www.sandviks.com, pg 506

Lennart Sane Agency AB (Spain) *Tel:* (0952) 834180 *Fax:* (0952) 833196 *Web Site:* www.lennartsaneagency. com, pg 1126

Lennart Sane Agency AB (Sweden) *Tel:* (0454) 123 56 *Fax:* (0454) 149 20 *Web Site:* www.lennartsaneagency. com, pg 1127

Sane Toregard Agency (Sweden) *Tel:* (0454) 123 56 *Fax:* (0454) 149 20, pg 1127

Sang Choy International Pte Ltd (Singapore) *Tel:* (065) 6289 0829 *Fax:* (065) 6282 7673 *E-mail:* marketing@ sc-international.com.sg *Web Site:* www.sc-international.com.sg, pg 1172

Editions Sang de la Terre (France) *Tel:* (01) 42 82 08 16 *Fax:* (01) 48 74 14 88 *E-mail:* editeur@sangdelaterre. com *Web Site:* www.sangdelaterre.com, pg 184

Sang-e-Meel Publications (Pakistan) *Tel:* (042) 7220100; (042) 7228143 *Fax:* (042) 7245101 *E-mail:* smp@ sang-e-meel.com *Web Site:* www.sang-e-meel.com, pg 510

Sangam Books Ltd (United Kingdom) *Tel:* (020) 7377-6399 *Fax:* (020) 7375-1230 *E-mail:* goatony@aol.com, pg 749

Sangdad Publishing Company Ltd (Thailand) *Tel:* (02) 5385553; (02) 5387576 *Fax:* (02) 559-2643; (02) 5381499 *E-mail:* sangdad@asianet.co.th, pg 641

Sangster's Book Stores Ltd (Jamaica) *Tel:* 876-922-3648; 876-922-3640 *Toll Free Tel:* 888-269-2665 *Fax:* 876-922-3813 *E-mail:* info@sangstersbooks.com *Web Site:* www.sangstersbooks.com, pg 1311

Sangyo-Tosho Publishing Co Ltd (Japan) *Tel:* (03) 3261-7821 *Fax:* (03) 3239-2178 *E-mail:* info@san-to.co.jp *Web Site:* www.san-to.co.jp, pg 422

Sankt-Johannis-Druckerei (Germany) *Tel:* (07821) 581-0 *Fax:* (07821) 581-26 *E-mail:* fels@johannis-druckerei. de *Web Site:* www.medienverbaende.de, pg 1145

Verlag der Sankt-Johannis-Druckerei C Schweickhardt (Germany) *Tel:* (07821) 5810 *Fax:* (07821) 58126 *E-mail:* johannis-druck@t-online.de *Web Site:* www. johannis-verlag.de, pg 275

Sankt-Peterburgskogo Gosudarstvennogo Universiteta (Russian Federation) *Tel:* (0812) 3262000 *Fax:* (0812) 2182741 *E-mail:* office@inform.pu.ru *Web Site:* www. spbu.ru, pg 1539

Sankyo Publishing Company Ltd (Japan) *Tel:* (03) 3264-5711 *Fax:* (03) 3264-5149 *Web Site:* www. sankyoshuppan.co.jp, pg 423

Sanra Book Trust (Bulgaria) *Tel:* (02) 659594; (02) 9549481 *Fax:* (02) 657252, pg 96

Sanseido Bookstore Ltd (Japan) *Tel:* (03) 3233 3312 *Fax:* (03) 3291 3033 *E-mail:* fbook_stock@mail. books-sanseido.co.jp *Web Site:* www.books-sanseido. co.jp, pg 1313

Sanseido Co Ltd (Japan) *Tel:* (03) 3230-9404 *Fax:* (03) 3230-9569 *Web Site:* www.sanseido-publ.co.jp/, pg 423

Sanshusha Publishing Co, Ltd (Japan) *Tel:* (03) 3842-1711 *Fax:* (03) 3845-3965 *E-mail:* info@sanshusha.co. jp *Web Site:* www.sanshusha.co.jp, pg 423

Sansoni-RCS Libri (Italy) *Tel:* (02) 50951 *Fax:* (02) 5065361 *E-mail:* sansoni@rcs.it, pg 403

Sant Jordi Asociados Agencia (Spain) *Tel:* (093) 2240107 *Fax:* (093) 2254539 *E-mail:* info@santjordi-asociados.com *Web Site:* www.santjordi-asociados. com, pg 1127

Libreria Santa Fe (Argentina) *Tel:* (011) 4824-5005; (011) 4829-2545 (virtual store) *Fax:* (011) 824-7932 *E-mail:* info@lsf.com.ar *Web Site:* www.lsf.com.ar; www.libreriasantafe.com, pg 1287

Editions du Santal (New Caledonia) *Tel:* (0687) 262533 *Fax:* (0687) 262533 *E-mail:* santal@offratel.nc, pg 489

Graficas Santamaria SA (Spain) *Tel:* (0945) 229100 *Fax:* (0945) 246393 *E-mail:* grsantamaria@ graficassantamaria.com *Web Site:* www. graficassantamaria.com, pg 1151

Graficas Santamaria SA (Spain) *Tel:* (0945) 229100 *Fax:* (0945) 246393 *E-mail:* grsantamaria@sea.es; grsantamaria@graficassantamaria.com *Web Site:* www. graficassantamaria.com, pg 1172

Graficas Santamaria SA (Spain) *Tel:* (0945) 229100 *Fax:* (0945) 246393 *E-mail:* grsantamaria@ graficassantamaria.com *Web Site:* www. graficassantamaria.com, pg 1213

Universidad de Santiago de Compostela (Spain) *Tel:* (0981) 593 500 *Fax:* (0981) 593 963 *E-mail:* spublic@usc.es, pg 594

Editorial Santiago Rueda (Argentina) *Tel:* (011) 4825-7337 *E-mail:* esantiruedaediciones@hotmail.com, pg 8

Editorial Santillana SA de CV (Mexico) *Tel:* (05) 6887566; (05) 6888227; (05) 6888966 *Fax:* (05) 6042304 *E-mail:* mexico@santillana.com.mx *Web Site:* www.gruposantillana.com, pg 467

Grupo Santillana (Mexico) *Tel:* (05) 6888966; (05) 6887566; (05) 6888227 *Fax:* (05) 6042304 *E-mail:* mexico@santillana.com.mx *Web Site:* www. gruposantillana.com, pg 467

Editorial Santillana SA (Colombia) *Tel:* (01) 635 12 00 *Fax:* (01) 236 93 82 *E-mail:* alfaquar@latino.net.co *Web Site:* www.santillana.com.co, pg 112

Biblioteca Municipal de Santo Domingo (Dominican Republic), pg 1501

Livraria Santos Editora Comercio e Importacao Ltda (Brazil) *Tel:* (011) 574-1200 *Fax:* (011) 573-8774 *E-mail:* editorasantos@terra.com.br, pg 89

Editora Santuario (Brazil) *Tel:* (012) 3104-2000 *Fax:* (012) 565 2141 *E-mail:* vendas@redemptor.com. br *Web Site:* www.redemptor.com.br, pg 89

Santype International Ltd (United Kingdom) *Tel:* (01722) 334261 *Fax:* (01722) 333171 *E-mail:* info@santype. com *Web Site:* www.santype.com, pg 1175

Sanyo Shuppan Boeki Co Inc (Japan) *Tel:* (03) 5351-3021 *Fax:* (03) 5351-3028 *E-mail:* ssb01@mx1.alpha-web.ne.jp, pg 423

Sanyo Shuppan Boeki Co Inc (Japan) *Tel:* (03) 5351 3021 *Fax:* (03) 5351 3028 *E-mail:* ssb01@mx1.alpha-web.ne.jp, pg 1313

Sapere 2000 SRL (Italy) *Tel:* (06) 4465363 *Fax:* (06) 4465363 *E-mail:* sapere2000@flshnet.it, pg 403

Sapes Trust Ltd (Zimbabwe) *Tel:* (04) 252962; (04) 252963; (04) 252965 *Fax:* (04) 252963 *E-mail:* administrator@sapes.org.zw *Web Site:* www.sapes.co.zw, pg 778

Paul Sappl, Schulbuch- und Lehrmittelverlag (Austria) *Tel:* (05372) 64300 *Fax:* (05372) 64300-17, pg 57

Saqi Books (United Kingdom) *Tel:* (020) 7221 9347 *Fax:* (020) 7229 7492 *E-mail:* info@saqibooks.com *Web Site:* www.saqibooks.com, pg 749

Saqi Books (United Kingdom) *Tel:* (020) 7221 9347 *Fax:* (020) 7229 7492 *E-mail:* saqibooks@dial.pipex.com *Web Site:* www.saqibooks.com, pg 1344

Saraiva SA, Livreiros Editores (Brazil) *Tel:* (011) 861-3344 *Fax:* (011) 861-3308 *E-mail:* diretoria.editora@editorasaraiva.com.br *Web Site:* www.editorasaraiva.com.br, pg 89

Saraiva SA, Livreiros Editores (Brazil) *Tel:* (011) 3933-3300 *Fax:* (011) 3662-2062 *E-mail:* atendimento@livrariasaraiva.com.br *Web Site:* www.livrariasaraiva.com.br; www.saraiva.com.br, pg 1294

Sarasavi Book Shop Pvt Ltd (Sri Lanka) *Tel:* (01) 2852519; (01) 2820983; (01) 4304546 *Fax:* (01) 2509503; (01) 2821454 *E-mail:* sarasavi@slt.lk *Web Site:* www.sarasavi.lk, pg 1334

Saraswati Publishers & Distributors (India), pg 345

Saray Medikal Yayin Tic Ltd Sti (Turkey) *Tel:* (0232) 3394969 *Fax:* (0232) 3733700 *E-mail:* eozkarahan@novell.cs.eng.dev.edu.tr, pg 647

Sardini Editrice (Italy) *Tel:* (030) 7750430 *Fax:* (030) 7254348 *E-mail:* sardini@intelligenza.it *Web Site:* www.sardini.it, pg 403

M C Sarkar & Sons (P) Ltd (India) *Tel:* (033) 2417490, pg 345

Sarment/Editions du Jubile (France) *Tel:* (01) 53 58 06 07 *Fax:* (01) 53 58 06 08 *E-mail:* contact@editionsdujubile.com *Web Site:* www.editionsdujubile.com, pg 184

Saros International Publishers (Nigeria) *Tel:* (084) 331763 *Fax:* (084) 331763, pg 502

Sarpay Beikman Book Club (Myanmar) *Tel:* (01) 283277, pg 1244

Sarpay Beikman Bookshop (Myanmar) *Tel:* (01) 283277; (01) 16611, pg 1319

Sarpay Beikman Public Library (Myanmar) *Tel:* (01) 283277, pg 472

Sarpay Lawka (Myanmar) *Tel:* (01) 274391; (01) 285166, pg 1319

Sarvier - Editora de Livros Medicos Ltda (Brazil) *Tel:* (011) 571-4570 *Fax:* (011) 571-3439, pg 89

Sarvodaya Vishva Lekha (Sri Lanka) *Tel:* (01) 714820; (01) 714829; (01) 731601 *Fax:* (01) 738932 *E-mail:* sarvs101@sri.lanka.net, pg 1151

Sasa Sema Publications Ltd (Kenya) *Tel:* (020) 550400; 722-200544; 734-600887 *E-mail:* sasasema@wananchi.com *Web Site:* www.sasasema.com, pg 432

Sasavona Publishers & Booksellers (South Africa) *Tel:* (011) 4032502; (011) 4034150 *Fax:* (011) 3397274, pg 564

Sassafras Verlag (Germany) *Tel:* (02151) 787770 *Fax:* (02151) 771302, pg 275

Sasta Sahitya Mandal (India) *Tel:* (011) 3310505, pg 345

Sastra Hudaya PT (Indonesia) *Tel:* (021) 3904223, pg 353

Sat Sahitya Prakashan (India) *Tel:* (011) 3276316, pg 345

Sri Satguru Publications (India) *Tel:* (011) 716497; (011) 7434930 *Fax:* (011) 7227336 *E-mail:* ibcindia@vsnl.com *Web Site:* www.indianbookscentre.com, pg 345

Vicki Satlow Literary Agency (Italy) *Tel:* (02) 48015553 *E-mail:* vickisatlow@tin.it, pg 1123

Satprakashan Sanchar Kendra (India) *Tel:* (0731) 475744; (0731) 475637 *Fax:* (0731) 47573 *E-mail:* sskin@sancharnet.in, pg 345

Satrap Publishing & Translation (United Kingdom) *Tel:* (020) 8748 9397 *Fax:* (020) 8748 9394 *E-mail:* satrap@btconnect.com *Web Site:* www.satrap.co.uk, pg 1141

Oy Satusiivet - Sagovingar AB (Lasten Parhaat Kirjat) (Finland) *Tel:* (09) 6937 621 *Fax:* (09) 6937 6266 *Web Site:* www.tammi.net, pg 1299

Satyr-Verlag Dr Humbel (Switzerland) *Tel:* (01) 380 3351 *Fax:* (01) 380 3352, pg 628

Saudi Publishing & Distributing House (Saudi Arabia) *Tel:* (03) 8334158 *Fax:* (03) 8335520 *E-mail:* info@spdh-sa.com *Web Site:* www.spdh-sa.com, pg 546

I H Sauer Verlag GmbH (Germany) *Tel:* (06221) 9060 *Fax:* (06221) 906259 *E-mail:* sauer-verlag@ruw.de *Web Site:* www.ruw-ruw.de, pg 275

Sauerlaender AG (Switzerland) *Tel:* (062) 836 86 86 *Fax:* (062) 836 86 20 *E-mail:* verlag@sauerlaender.ch *Web Site:* www.sauerlaender.ch, pg 628

Verlag Sauerlaender GmbH (Germany) *Tel:* (0211) 16795-0 *Fax:* (0211) 16795-75, pg 275

J D Sauerlaender's Verlag (Germany) *Tel:* (069) 555217 *Fax:* (069) 5964344 *E-mail:* j.d.sauerlaenders.verlag@t-online.de *Web Site:* www.sauerlaender-verlag.com, pg 275

K G Saur Verlag GmbH, A Gale/Thomson Learning Company (Germany) *Tel:* (089) 76902-0 *Fax:* (089) 76902-150 *E-mail:* saur.info@thomson.com *Web Site:* www.saur.de, pg 275

Sauramps Medical (France) *Tel:* (04) 67 63 68 80 *Fax:* (04) 67 52 59 05 *E-mail:* sauramps.medical@livres-medicaux.com *Web Site:* www.livres-medicaux.com, pg 184

Librairie Sauramps Medical (France) *Tel:* (04) 67 63 68 80 *Fax:* (04) 67 52 59 05 *E-mail:* christelle.itasse@livres-medicaux.com *Web Site:* www.livres-medicaux.com, pg 1300

Editions Andre Sauret SA (Monaco) *Tel:* (093) 506794 *Fax:* (093) 307104, pg 470

Steve Savage Publishers Ltd (United Kingdom) *Tel:* (020) 7770 6083 *Fax:* (020) 7770 6083 *E-mail:* mail@savagepublishers.com *Web Site:* www.savagepublishers.com, pg 749

Savannah Editions SARL (New Caledonia) *Tel:* (0687) 252919 *Fax:* (0687) 282470, pg 489

Savannah Publications (United Kingdom) *Tel:* (020) 8244 4350 *Fax:* (020) 8244 2448 *E-mail:* savpub@dircon.co.uk *Web Site:* www.savannah-publications.com, pg 749

Savez Inzenjera i Tehnicara Jugoslavije (Serbia and Montenegro) *Tel:* (011) 3243653; (011) 3243652 *Fax:* (011) 3243652 *E-mail:* internet@eunet.yu, pg 549

Savitri Books Ltd (United Kingdom) *Tel:* (020) 7436 9932 *Fax:* (020) 7580 6330, pg 749

Savremena Administracija (Serbia and Montenegro) *Tel:* (011) 668567; (011) 661913; (011) 667436 *Fax:* (011) 667436, pg 549

Sawan Kirpal Publications (India) *Tel:* (011) 7110722; (011) 7222244 *Fax:* (011) 7210720, pg 345

SAWD Publications (United Kingdom) *Tel:* (01795) 472 262 *Fax:* (01795) 422 633 *E-mail:* wainman@sawd.demon.co.uk, pg 749

Sax-Verlag Beucha (Germany) *Tel:* (034292) 75210 *Fax:* (034292) 75220 *E-mail:* info@sax-verlag.de *Web Site:* www.sax-verlag.de, pg 276

The Sayle Literary Agency (United Kingdom) *Tel:* (01223) 303035 *Fax:* (01223) 301638, pg 1133

Sayrols Editorial SA de CV (Mexico) *Tel:* (05) 660-3535 *Fax:* (05) 687-4699 *E-mail:* ventas@sayrols.com.mx *Web Site:* www.sayrols.com.mx, pg 467

SB Publications (United Kingdom) *Tel:* (01323) 893498 *Fax:* (01323) 893860 *E-mail:* sales@sbpublications.swinternet.co.uk, pg 749

SBT Professional Publications (Malaysia) *Tel:* (03) 80265811; (03) 80235663 *Fax:* (03) 8023566; (03) 80265999 *E-mail:* admin@sbtpp.com *Web Site:* www.sbtpp.com, pg 455

SBW Publishers (India) *Tel:* (011) 3279603, pg 345

Scaillet, SA (Belgium) *Tel:* (071) 516335 *Fax:* (071) 511795, pg 72

Editions Scala (France) *Tel:* (01) 49 29 42 25 *Fax:* (01) 49 29 99 33 *E-mail:* editions.scala@wanadoo.fr, pg 184

Scala Group spa (Italy) *Tel:* (055) 623311 *Fax:* (055) 6233280 *E-mail:* info@scalagroup.com *Web Site:* scalagroup.it, pg 403

Scan-Globe A/S (Denmark) *Tel:* 46 18 54 00 *Fax:* 46 18 52 70 *E-mail:* info@scanglobe.dk, pg 134

Scandinavia Publishing House (Denmark) *Tel:* 35 31 03 30 *Fax:* 35 31 03 34 *E-mail:* info@scanpublishing.dk *Web Site:* www.scanpublishing.dk, pg 134

scaneg Verlag (Germany) *Tel:* (089) 759 33 36 *Fax:* (089) 759 39 14 *E-mail:* verlag@scaneg.de *Web Site:* www.scaneg.de, pg 276

Scanvik Books Import ApS (Denmark) *Tel:* 3312 7766 *Fax:* 33 91 28 82 *E-mail:* mail@scanvik.dk; scanvik@bog.dk *Web Site:* www.scanvik.dk, pg 1120

Scanvik Books Import ApS (Denmark) *Tel:* 33 12 77 66 *Fax:* 33 91 28 82 *E-mail:* mail@scanvik.dk *Web Site:* www.scanvik.dk, pg 1298

Lo Scarabeo Srl (Italy) *Tel:* (011) 283793; (011) 283978 *Fax:* (011) 280756 *E-mail:* info@loscarabeo.com *Web Site:* www.loscarabeo.com, pg 404

Scarthin Books (United Kingdom) *Tel:* (01629) 823272 *Fax:* (01629) 825094 *E-mail:* clare@scarthinbooks.demon.co.uk *Web Site:* www.scarthinbooks.com; www.books.co.uk, pg 749

Scena (Lithuania) *Tel:* (02) 751 828; (02) 614 145 *Fax:* (02) 610 814, pg 446

De Schaar/Geknipt Papier (Belgium) *Tel:* (09) 225 5414 *Fax:* (09) 225 9724 *E-mail:* geknipt@skynet.be, pg 72

Verlag Th Schaefer im Vicentz Verlag KG (Germany) *Tel:* (0511) 87575-075 *Fax:* (0511) 87575-079, pg 276

Verlag Anke Schaefer (Germany) *Tel:* (06439) 7870, pg 276

Schaeffer-Poeschel Verlag fuer Wirtschaft Steuern Recht (Germany) *Tel:* (0711) 2194-0 *Fax:* (0711) 2194-119 *E-mail:* info@schaeffer-poeschel.de *Web Site:* www.schaeffer-poeschel.de, pg 276

Schangrila Verlags und Vertriebs GmbH (Germany) *Tel:* (08343) 581 *Fax:* (08343) 657 *E-mail:* info@schangrila.com *Web Site:* www.schangrila.com, pg 276

Schapen Edition, H W Louis (Germany) *Tel:* (0531) 360921 *Fax:* (0531) 363190 *E-mail:* schapen.edition@t-online.de, pg 276

M & H Schaper GmbH & Co KG (Germany) *Tel:* (05181) 8009-0 *Fax:* (05181) 8009-33 *E-mail:* info@schaper-verlag.de *Web Site:* www.schaper-verlag.de, pg 276

Schattauer GmbH Verlag fuer Medizin und Naturwissenschaften (Germany) *Tel:* (0711) 2 29 87-0 *Fax:* (0711) 2 29 87-50 *E-mail:* info@schattauer.de *Web Site:* www.schattauer.de, pg 276

Guillermo Schavelzon & Asociados, Literary Agency (Spain) *Tel:* 932 011 310 *Fax:* 932 006 886 *E-mail:* info@schavelzon.com, pg 1127

Schawk (Canada) *Tel:* 416-703-1445 *Fax:* 416-703-1494 *Web Site:* www.schawk.com, pg 1166, 1205

Scheffler-Verlag (Germany) *Tel:* (02330) 1743 *Fax:* (02330) 2281, pg 276

Scheltema (Netherlands) *Tel:* (020) 5231411 *Fax:* (020) 6227684 *E-mail:* scheltema@scheltema.nl; informatie@scheltema.nl *Web Site:* www.scheltema.nl, pg 1320

Schelzky & Jeep, Verlag fuer Reisen und Wissen (Germany) *Tel:* (030) 6939495 *Fax:* (030) 6914697 *E-mail:* schelzky.jeep@t-online.de, pg 276

Schena Editore (Italy) *Tel:* (080) 4414681 *Fax:* (080) 4426690 *E-mail:* info@schenaeditore.com *Web Site:* www.schenaeditore.it, pg 404

Dr A Schendl GmbH und Co KG (Austria) *Tel:* (01) 484 17 85-0 *Fax:* (01) 484 17 85-15 *E-mail:* info@schendl.at *Web Site:* www.schendl.at, pg 57

Renate Schenk Verlag (Germany) *Tel:* (0341) 2300825 *Fax:* (0341) 2300826 *E-mail:* schenk-verlag@t-online.de *Web Site:* www.schenk-verlag.de, pg 276

Richard Scherpe Verlag GmbH (Germany) *Tel:* (02151) 539-0 *Fax:* (02151) 505390 *E-mail:* info@scherpe.de *Web Site:* www.scherpe.de, pg 277

Scherz Verlag AG (Switzerland) *Tel:* (031) 3277117 *Fax:* (031) 3277171; (031) 3277169 *E-mail:* scherz@scherzverlag.ch, pg 629

Papierfabrik Scheufelen GmbH & Co KG (Germany) *Tel:* (07026) 66-1 *Fax:* (07026) 66-701 *E-mail:* service@scheufelen.de *Web Site:* www.scheufelen.com, pg 1145

Schibsted Forlagene A/S (Norway) *Tel:* 24 14 68 00 *Fax:* 24 14 68 01 *E-mail:* schibstedforlagene@schibstedforlagene.no *Web Site:* www.schibstedforlagene.no, pg 506

Ulrich Schiefer bahn Verlag (Germany) *Tel:* (089) 89020999 *Fax:* (089) 89020087, pg 277

Schiffahrts-Verlag (Germany) *Tel:* (040) 79713-02 *Fax:* (040) 79713-324; (040) 79713-208; (040) 79713-214 *Web Site:* www.hansa-online.de, pg 277

Schild-Verlag GmbH (Germany) *Tel:* (089) 8 64 1189 *Fax:* (089) 8 63 2310, pg 277

Schildts Forlags AB (Finland) *Tel:* (09) 88 70 400 *Fax:* (09) 804 32 57 *E-mail:* schildts@schildts.fi *Web Site:* www.schildts.fi, pg 144

Verlag der Schillerbuchhandlung Hans Banger OHG (Germany) *Tel:* (0221) 46014-0 *Fax:* (0221) 46014-25; (0221) 46014-26 *E-mail:* banger@banger.de *Web Site:* www.banger.de, pg 277

Schillinger Verlag GmbH (Germany) *Tel:* (0761) 33233 *Fax:* (0762) 39055 *E-mail:* schillingerverlag@t-online.de *Web Site:* schillingerverlag.de, pg 277

Paul Schiltz (Belgium) *Tel:* (087) 553271, pg 72

Karin Schindler (Brazil) *Tel:* (011) 5041-9177 *Fax:* (011) 5041-9077 *E-mail:* kschind@terra.com.br, pg 1119

Karin Schindler Representante de Direitos Autorais (Brazil) *Tel:* (011) 241-9177 *Fax:* (011) 241-9077, pg 89

Schirmer/Mosel Verlag GmbH (Germany) *Tel:* (089) 2126700 *Fax:* (089) 338695 *E-mail:* mail@schirmer-mosel.com *Web Site:* www.schirmer-mosel.com, pg 277

Schirner Verlag (Germany) *Tel:* (06151) 29 39 59 *Fax:* (06151) 29 39 87 *E-mail:* info@schirner.com *Web Site:* www.schirner.com, pg 277

Schlaepfer & Co AG (Switzerland) *Tel:* (071) 354 64 64 *Fax:* (071) 354 64 65 *E-mail:* appenzellerverlag@appon.ch *Web Site:* www.appenzellerverlag.ch, pg 629

Schlesinger Institute (Israel) *Tel:* (02) 655-5266 *Fax:* (02) 655-5266 *E-mail:* medhal@szmc.org.il *Web Site:* www.szmc.org.il, pg 368

Agora Verlag Manfred Schlosser (Germany) *Tel:* (030) 8545372; (030) 8545915 *Fax:* (030) 8545372 *E-mail:* agora2@gmx.net, pg 277

Thomas Schlueck GmbH (Germany) *Tel:* (05131) 4975-60 *Fax:* (05131) 4975-89 *E-mail:* mail@schlueckagent.com *Web Site:* www.schlueckagent.com, pg 1122

Schmetterling Verlag Jorg Hunger und Paul Sander (Germany) *Tel:* (0711) 62 67 79 *Fax:* (0711) 62 69 92 *E-mail:* info@schmetterling-verlag.de *Web Site:* www.schmetterling-verlag.de, pg 277

Schmid Verlag GmbH (Germany) *Tel:* (0941) 21519 *Fax:* (0941) 28766 *E-mail:* schmid-verlag.de *Web Site:* www.schmid-verlag.de, pg 277

Verlag Dr Otto Schmidt KG (Germany) *Tel:* (0221) 9 37 38-01 *Fax:* (0221) 9 37 38 00 *E-mail:* info@otto-schmidt.de *Web Site:* www.otto-schmidt.de, pg 277

Erich Schmidt Verlag GmbH & Co (Germany) *Tel:* (030) 25 00 85-0 *Fax:* (030) 25 00 85-305 *E-mail:* esv@esvmedien.de *Web Site:* www.erich-schmidt-verlag.de, pg 277

Verlag Hermann Schmidt Universitatsdruckerei GmbH & Co (Germany) *Tel:* (06131) 506030 *Fax:* (06131) 506080 *E-mail:* info@typografie.de *Web Site:* www.typografie.de, pg 277

Schmidt Periodicals GmbH (Germany) *Tel:* (08064) 221 *Fax:* (08064) 557 *E-mail:* schmidt@periodicals.com *Web Site:* www.periodicals.com, pg 278

Max Schmidt-Roemhild Verlag (Germany) *Tel:* (0451) 70 31-01 *Fax:* (0451) 70 31-253 *E-mail:* msr-luebeck@t-online.de *Web Site:* www.schmidt-roemhild.de, pg 278

Wilhelm Schmitz Verlag (Germany) *Tel:* (0641) 877 3939 *E-mail:* kontakt@wilhelm-schmitz-verlag.de *Web Site:* www.wilhelm-schmitz-verlag.de, pg 278

Schneekluth Verlag (Germany) *Tel:* (089) 9271-0 *Fax:* (089) 9271-168 *Web Site:* www.schneekluth.de, pg 278

Wolf Schneider (Germany) *Tel:* (089) 8113466 *Fax:* (089) 8110619, pg 278

Verlag Schnell und Steiner GmbH (Germany) *Tel:* (0941) 787850 *Fax:* (0941) 7878516 *E-mail:* susvertrieb@t-online.de, pg 278

Schnellmann-Verlag (Switzerland) *Tel:* (055) 2111472 *Fax:* (055) 2111477 *Web Site:* www.dictionaries.ch, pg 629

Andreas Schnider Verlags-Atelier (Austria) *Tel:* (0316) 471302 *Fax:* (0316) 4713024 *E-mail:* bookstore@net.burger.at, pg 57

Schnitzer GmbH & Co KG (Germany) *Tel:* (07724) 9432-0 *Fax:* (07724) 9432-20, pg 278

Schocken Publishing House Ltd (Israel) *Tel:* (03) 5610130 *Fax:* (03) 5622668 *E-mail:* find@schocken.co.il, pg 368

Schoeffling & Co (Germany) *Tel:* (069) 92 07 87-0 *Fax:* (069) 92 07 87-20 *E-mail:* info@schoeffling.de *Web Site:* www.schoeffling.de, pg 278

Bibliotheque Schoelcher (Martinique) *Tel:* 702 667 *Fax:* 724 555 *E-mail:* biblio-schoelcher-dep@cg972.fr, pg 1526

Verlag fuer Schoene Wissenschaften (Switzerland) *Tel:* (061) 7013911 *Fax:* (061) 7011417 *E-mail:* schoene_wissenschaften@bluewin.ch, pg 629

Verlag Hans Schoener GmbH (Germany) *Tel:* (07232) 4007-0 *Fax:* (07232) 4007-99 *E-mail:* info@verlag-schoener.de *Web Site:* www.verlag-schoener.de, pg 278

Ferdinand Schoeningh Verlag GmbH (Germany) *Tel:* (05251) 1275 *Fax:* (05251) 127860; (05251) 127670 *E-mail:* info@schoeningh.de *Web Site:* www.schoeningh.de, pg 278

Schofield & Sims Ltd (United Kingdom) *Tel:* (01484) 607080 *Fax:* (01484) 606815 *E-mail:* post@schofieldandsims.co.uk *Web Site:* www.schofieldandsims.co.uk, pg 749

Scholastic Australia Pty Ltd (Australia) *Tel:* (02) 4328 3555 *Toll Free Tel:* 800-021-233 *Fax:* (02) 4323 3827 *Toll Free Fax:* 800-789-948 *E-mail:* customerservice@scholastic.com.au *Web Site:* www.scholastic.com.au, pg 40

Scholastic Ltd (United Kingdom) *Tel:* (01926) 887799; (01926) 813910 (warehouse) *Fax:* (01926) 883331 *E-mail:* scholastic@tens.co.uk *Web Site:* www.scholastic.co.uk, pg 749

Scholastic Publications Ltd (United Kingdom) *Tel:* (0845) 6039091; (01993) 893475 (outside UK) *Fax:* (0845) 6039092; (01993) 893424 (outside UK) *E-mail:* sbcenquiries@scholastic.co.uk *Web Site:* www.scholastic.co.uk/schoolbookclub, pg 1247

Kurt Scholl (Germany) *Tel:* (06221) 707661, pg 1301

Det Schonbergske Forlag A/S (Denmark) *Tel:* 33 73 35 85 *Fax:* 33 73 35 76 *E-mail:* Schoenberg@nytnordiskforlag.dk *Web Site:* www.nytnordiskforlag.dk, pg 134

School Library Association (United Kingdom) *Tel:* (01793) 791787 *Fax:* (01793) 791786 *E-mail:* info@sla.org.uk *Web Site:* www.sla.org.uk, pg 1573

School of Administration Library (Ghana) *Fax:* (021) 500024 *E-mail:* soa@libr.ug.edu.gh, pg 1511

School of Oriental & African Studies (United Kingdom) *Tel:* (020) 7637 2388 *Fax:* (020) 7436 3844 *E-mail:* md2@soas.ac.uk; aol@soas.ac.uk *Web Site:* www.soas.ac.uk, pg 749

School of Oriental & African Studies Library (United Kingdom) *Tel:* (020) 7898 4163 *Fax:* (020) 7436 3844 *E-mail:* libenquiry@soas.ac.uk *Web Site:* www.soas.ac.uk/library/home.html, pg 1552

School Supplies (NZ) Ltd (New Zealand) *Tel:* (09) 273 9883 *Toll Free Tel:* 800 577 700 *Fax:* (09) 273 9881 *Toll Free Fax:* 800 367 724 *E-mail:* orders@schoolsupplies.co.nz *Web Site:* www.schoolsupplies.co.nz, pg 1321

SchoolPlay Productions Ltd (United Kingdom) *Tel:* (01206) 540111 *Fax:* (01206) 766944 *E-mail:* schoolplay@inglis-house.demon.co.uk *Web Site:* www.schoolplayproductions.co.uk, pg 749

Schott Freres SA (Editeurs de Musique) (Belgium) *Tel:* (02) 5132742 *Fax:* (02) 5133049 *E-mail:* eric.junne@skynet.be *Web Site:* www.classicalscores.com, pg 72

Schott Musik International GmbH & Co KG (Germany) *Tel:* (06131) 246-0 *Fax:* (06131) 246-211 *E-mail:* info@schott-musik.de *Web Site:* www.schott-online.com, pg 278

Schrader Verlag (Germany) *Tel:* (0711) 210 80 0 *Fax:* (0711) 236 04 15 *E-mail:* verlag@motorbuch.de *Web Site:* www.motorbuch.de, pg 278

Verlag Silke Schreiber (Germany) *Tel:* (089) 2710180 *Fax:* (089) 2716957 *E-mail:* metzel@verlag-Silke-schreiber.de *Web Site:* www.verlag-silke-schreiber.de, pg 279

Verlag und Schriftenmission der Evangelischen Gesellschaft Wuppertal (Germany) *Tel:* (0202) 278500 *Fax:* (0202) 2785040, pg 279

Schroedel Schulbuchverlag GmbH (Germany) *Tel:* (531) 708-0 *Fax:* (0531) 708-209 *E-mail:* sco@schroedel.de *Web Site:* www.schroedel.de, pg 279

Verlag Anton Schroll & Co (Austria) *Tel:* (01) 5445641-46 *Fax:* (01) 544564166 *E-mail:* prepress@agens-werk.at, pg 57

Schubert & Franzke Gesellschaft mbH (Austria) *Tel:* (02742) 78 501-0 *Fax:* (02742) 78 501-15 *E-mail:* office@schubert-franzke.com *Web Site:* www.map2web.cc/schubert-franzke, pg 57

A Schudel & Co AG Verlag (Switzerland) *Tel:* (061) 645 1011 *Fax:* (061) 645 1045 *Web Site:* www.schudeldruck.ch, pg 629

Walther-Schuecking-Institut fuer Internationales Recht an der Universitaet Kiel (Germany) *Tel:* (0431) 880 2367 *Fax:* (0431) 880 1619 *E-mail:* fb.internat-recht@ub.uni-kiel.de *Web Site:* www.uni-kiel.de/internat-recht, pg 1508

Carl Ed Schuenemann KG (Germany) *Tel:* (0421) 369030 *Fax:* (0421) 3690339 *Web Site:* www2.schuenemann-verlag.de, pg 279

Casa Editrice Marietti Scuola SpA (Italy) *Tel:* (011) 2098741; (011) 2098720 *Fax:* (011) 2098765 *E-mail:* redazione@mariettiscuola.it *Web Site:* www.mariettiscuola.it, pg 404

Ediciones Scriba SA (Spain) *Tel:* (093) 215 20 89; (093) 215 19 33 *Fax:* (093) 487 37 66, pg 594

SCRIPTA - Distribucion y Servicios Editoriales SA de CV (Mexico) *Tel:* (05) 5481716 *Fax:* (05) 6161496 *E-mail:* dyse@data.net.mx, pg 468

SCRIPTA - Distribucion y Servicios Editoriales SA de CV (Mexico) *Tel:* (05) 5481716 *Fax:* (05)5500564, pg 1319

Scripta Theofilus Palevratzis-Ashover (Greece) *Tel:* 2105230382 *Fax:* 2105233574, pg 309

Editions Scriptar SA (Switzerland) *Tel:* (021) 7960096 *Fax:* (021) 7914084 *E-mail:* info@jsh.ch, pg 629

Scriptum (Netherlands) *Tel:* (010) 4271022 *Fax:* (010) 4736625 *E-mail:* info@scriptum.nl *Web Site:* www.scriptum.nl, pg 484

Scriptum Forlags AB (Finland) *Fax:* (06) 3242 210 *E-mail:* scriptum@svof.fi *Web Site:* www.svof.fi/scriptum, pg 144

Scripture Union (United Kingdom) *Tel:* (01908) 856000 *Fax:* (01908) 856111 *E-mail:* info@scriptureunion.org.uk *Web Site:* www.scriptureunion.org.uk, pg 750

Editura 'Scrisul Romanesc' (Romania) *Tel:* (051) 419506, pg 537

Scroll Publishers (Australia) *Tel:* (07) 5573 0835 *Fax:* (07) 5529 9155, pg 40

Editrice la Scuola SpA (Italy) *Tel:* (030) 29931 *Fax:* (030) 2993299 *Web Site:* www.lascuola.it, pg 404

Scuola Vaticana Paleografia - Scuola Vaticana di Paleografia Diplomatica e Archivistica (Holy See (Vatican City State)) *Tel:* (06) 69883595 *Fax:* (06) 69881377 *E-mail:* pagano@librs6k.vatlib.it, pg 311

SDL Agency (United Kingdom) *Tel:* (0114) 253 5353 *Toll Free Tel:* 800 917 0044 *Fax:* (0114) 253 5200 *Web Site:* www.sdl.com, pg 1141

SDU Juridische & Fiscale Uitgeverij (Netherlands) *Tel:* (070) 3789880; (070) 3789911 *Fax:* (070) 3854321; (070) 3789783; (070) 3458068 *E-mail:* sdu@sdu.nl *Web Site:* www.sdu.nl, pg 484

Sdu Uitgevers bv (Netherlands) *Tel:* (070) 378 99 11; (070) 378 98 80 *Fax:* (070) 385 43 21; (070) 378 97 83 *E-mail:* sdu@sdu.nl *Web Site:* www.sdu.nl, pg 484

SDX (Shenghuo-Dushu-Xinzhi) Joint Publishing Co (China) *Tel:* (010) 64002730 *Fax:* (010) 64001122, pg 107

Se-Kwang Music Publishing Co (Republic of Korea) *Tel:* (02) 714-0046 *Fax:* (02) 719-2191, pg 439

Seagull Press (New Zealand) *Tel:* (03) 3899338, pg 496

Seanachas Press (Australia) *Tel:* (02) 6299 5434, pg 40

Search Press Ltd (United Kingdom) *Tel:* (01892) 510850 *Fax:* (01892) 515903 *E-mail:* searchpress@searchpress.com *Web Site:* www.searchpress.com, pg 751

Derek Searle Associates (United Kingdom) *Tel:* (01753) 539295 *Fax:* (01753) 551863 *E-mail:* dsapublish@aol.com, pg 1344

Universitas Sebelas Maret (Indonesia) *Tel:* (0271) 646994; (0271) 646761; (0271) 646624 *Fax:* (0271) 46655 *E-mail:* due-uns@slo.mega.net.id; pptk-uns@slo.mega.net.id *Web Site:* www.uns.ac.id, pg 353

SECAP (Ecuador) *Fax:* (02) 2 283-851 *E-mail:* secap@plus.net.ec *Web Site:* www.secap.gov.ec, pg 136

Martin Secker & Warburg (United Kingdom) *Tel:* (020) 7840 8570 *Fax:* (020) 7233 6117 *E-mail:* enquiries@randomhouse.co.uk *Web Site:* www.randomhouse.co.uk, pg 751

Seckin Yayinevi (Turkey) *Tel:* (0312) 4353030 *Fax:* (0312) 4352472 *E-mail:* satis@seckin.com.tr *Web Site:* www.seckin.com.tr, pg 647

Biblioteca de la Secretaria de Estado de Relaciones Exteriores (Dominican Republic) *Tel:* 535-6280 *Fax:* 508-6863; 533-5772 *E-mail:* correspondencia@serex.gov.do *Web Site:* www.serex.gov.do, pg 1501

Secretariado Trinitario (Spain) *Tel:* (0923) 23 56 02 *Fax:* (0923) 23 56 02 *E-mail:* editorialst@secretariadotrinitario.org *Web Site:* www.aecae.es/secretrinitario, pg 594

Secretariat of the Pacific Community Library (New Caledonia) *Tel:* 26 20 00 *Fax:* 26 38 18 *E-mail:* library@spc.int *Web Site:* www.spc.int/library, pg 1530

Seculo XXI Editora e Comercio de Livros (Brazil) *Tel:* (051) 3614459 *Fax:* (051) 3614459 *E-mail:* sewloxxi@poa-online.com.br, pg 90

Securit World Ltd (United Kingdom) *Tel:* (020) 8266 3300 *Fax:* (020) 8203 1027 *E-mail:* sales@securitworld.com *Web Site:* www.securitworld.com, pg 1175

SEDA Publications (United Kingdom) *Tel:* (0121) 415 6801 *Fax:* (0121) 415 6802 *E-mail:* office@seda.ac.uk *Web Site:* www.seda.ac.uk/publications.htm, pg 751

Sedco Publishing Ltd (Ghana) *Tel:* (021) 221332 *Fax:* (021) 220107 *E-mail:* sedco@africaonline.com.gh, pg 302

SEDIT (Societe d'Etudes et de Diffusion des Industries Thermiques et Aerauliques) (France) *Tel:* (01) 30 85 20 10 *Fax:* (01) 30 85 20 38 *E-mail:* sedit@costic.com *Web Site:* www.costic.com, pg 184

See Australia Guides P/L (Australia) *Tel:* (03) 5962 5723 *Fax:* (03) 5962 4718 *E-mail:* sag@minopher.net.au, pg 40

Editions Seghers (France) *Tel:* (01) 53 67 14 00 *Fax:* (01) 53 67 14 14 *Web Site:* www.laffont.fr/seghers, pg 184

Segment BV (Netherlands) *Tel:* (046) 43894444 *Fax:* (046) 4389401; (046) 4370161 *E-mail:* secretariant@segment.nl *Web Site:* www.segment.nl, pg 484

Edizioni Segno SRL (Italy) *Tel:* (0432) 575179 *Fax:* (0432) 575589 *E-mail:* info@edizionisegno.it *Web Site:* www.edizionisegno.it, pg 404

Segretariato Nazionale Apostolato della Preghiera (Italy) *Tel:* (06) 6976071 *Fax:* (06) 6781063 *E-mail:* adp@adp.it *Web Site:* www.adp.it, pg 404

Seibido (Japan) *Tel:* (03) 3291-2261 *Fax:* (03) 3293-5490 *E-mail:* seibido@mua.biglobe.ne.jp *Web Site:* www.seibido.co.jp, pg 423

Seibido Shuppan Company Ltd (Japan) *Tel:* (03) 3814-4351 *Fax:* (03) 3814-4355 *Web Site:* www.seibidoshuppan.co.jp, pg 423

Seibt Verlag GmbH (Germany) *Tel:* (06151) 380-140 *Fax:* (06151) 380-141 *E-mail:* info@seibt.com *Web Site:* www.seibt.de, pg 280

Seibu Time Co Ltd (Japan) *Tel:* (03) 5283-0270 *Fax:* (03) 5283-0234, pg 423

Seibundo (Japan) *Tel:* (03) 3203-9201 *Fax:* (03) 3203-9206 *E-mail:* eigyobu@seibundoh.co.jp *Web Site:* www.seibundoh.co.jp, pg 423

Seibundo Publishing Co Ltd (Japan) *Tel:* (06) 6211-6265 *Fax:* (06) 6211-6492, pg 423

Seibundo Shinkosha Publishing Co Ltd (Japan) *Tel:* (03) 5800-5780 *Fax:* (03) 5800-5781 *Web Site:* www.seibundo.net, pg 423

Seishin Shobo (Japan) *Tel:* (03) 3946-5666 *Fax:* (03) 3945-8880 *Web Site:* www.seishinshobo.co.jp, pg 423

Seiun-Sha (Japan) *Tel:* (03) 3947-1021 *Fax:* (03) 3947-1617 *E-mail:* greatobe@yo.rim.ur.jp, pg 423

Seiwa Shoten Co Ltd (Japan) *Tel:* (03) 3329-0033 *Fax:* (03) 5374-7186 *E-mail:* sales@seiwa-pb.co.jp *Web Site:* www.seiwa-pb.co.jp, pg 423

Seix Barral (Argentina) *Tel:* (011) 4382-4043; (011) 4382-4045; (011) 4381-8285 *Fax:* (011) 4383-3793 *E-mail:* editorial@seix-barral.es *Web Site:* www.seix-barral.es, pg 8

Editorial Seix Barral SA (Spain) *Tel:* (093) 496 7003 *Fax:* (093) 496 7004 *E-mail:* editorial@seix-barral.es *Web Site:* www.seix-barral.es, pg 594

Seizando-Shoten Publishing Co Ltd (Japan) *Tel:* (03) 3357-5861 *Fax:* (03) 3357-5867 *E-mail:* publisher@seizando.co.jp *Web Site:* www.seizando.co.jp, pg 423

Seizmoloska Opservatorija (The Former Yugoslav Republic of Macedonia) *Tel:* (091) 231953 *Fax:* (091) 114042 *E-mail:* ljupco@iunona.pmf.ukim.edu.mk, pg 449

Sejong Daewang Kinyom Saophoe (Republic of Korea), pg 439

Sekai Bunka-Sha (Japan) *Tel:* (03) 3262-5111 *Fax:* (03) 3237-8446 *Web Site:* www.sekaibunka.com, pg 423

Selangor Public Library (Malaysia) *Tel:* (03) 55197667 *Fax:* (03) 55196045 *E-mail:* ppas@sel.lib.edu.my; jothi@ppas.org.my *Web Site:* www.ppas.org.my, pg 1525

Selecoes Eletronicas Editora Ltda (Brazil) *Tel:* (021) 2232442 *Fax:* (021) 2638840 *E-mail:* an-ep@pobox.com, pg 90

Select Books Pte Ltd (Singapore) *Tel:* 6732 1515 *Fax:* 6736 0855 *E-mail:* info@selectbooks.com.sg *Web Site:* www.selectbooks.com.sg, pg 1330

Select Publishing Pte Ltd (Singapore) *Tel:* 6732 1515 *Fax:* 6736 0855 *E-mail:* info@selectbooks.com.sg *Web Site:* www.selectbooks.com.sg, pg 553

Selecta-Catalonia Ed (Spain) *Tel.* (093) 3172331; (093) 3185183 *Fax:* (093) 3024793, pg 594

Selection du Reader's Digest SA (France) *Tel:* (01) 46748484 *Fax:* (01) 46748580 *E-mail:* serviceclients@readersdigest.tm.fr *Web Site:* www.selectionclic.com/srd/; www.rd.com/international/shared/?countryid=fr, pg 184

Editions Selection J Jacobs SA (France), pg 184

Selector SA de CV (Mexico) *Tel:* (055) 588-7272 *Fax:* (055) 761-5716 *E-mail:* info@selector.com.mx *Web Site:* www.selector.com.mx, pg 468

SELF Syndicate of French Language Authors (France) *Tel:* (01) 40600501 *Fax:* (01) 46707395, pg 1259

Selina Publishers (India) *Tel:* (011) 3280711 *Fax:* (011) 3277230, pg 345

Selinunte Editora Ltda (Brazil) *Tel:* (011) 2760318, pg 90

Sellerio Editore (Italy) *Tel:* (091) 6254110 *Fax:* (091) 6258802, pg 404

Dr Arthur L Sellier & Co KG-Walter de Gruyter GmbH & Co KG OHG (Germany) *Tel:* (030) 26005-0 *Fax:* (030) 260 05-251 *E-mail:* wdq-info@degruyter.de *Web Site:* www.degruyter.de, pg 280

Selwood Printing (United Kingdom) *Tel:* (01444) 236060 *Fax:* (01444) 245043 *E-mail:* sales@selwood.com, pg 1217

SEMAR Publishers SRL (Netherlands) *Tel:* (070) 356 04 03; (070) 345 90 38 *Fax:* (070) 360 24 71 *E-mail:* info@semar.org *Web Site:* www.semar.org, pg 484

Semences Africaines (Cameroon) *Tel:* (023) 224058, pg 98

Bokforlaget Semic AB (Sweden) *Tel:* (08) 799 30 50 *Fax:* (08) 799 30 64 *E-mail:* info@semic.se *Web Site:* www.semic.se, pg 610

Semic Bokforlaget International AB (Sweden) *Tel:* (08) 779 30 50 *Fax:* (08) 799 30 64 *E-mail:* info@semic.se *Web Site:* www.semic.se, pg 610

Semic Junior Press (Netherlands) *Tel:* (035) 6944914 *Fax:* (035) 6944909, pg 484

Seminar on the Acquisition of Latin American Library Materials (SALALM) (United States) *Tel:* 505-277-5102 *Fax:* 505-277-0646, pg 1285

Senate Books Co Ltd (Taiwan, Province of China) *Tel:* (02) 23213054 *Fax:* (02) 23214041, pg 637

Senate House Library University of London (United Kingdom) *Tel:* (020) 7862 8500 *Fax:* (020) 7862 8480 *E-mail:* enquiries@shl.lon.ac.uk *Web Site:* www.ull.ac.uk, pg 1552

Sencor (United States) *Tel:* 212-947-5601 *Fax:* 212-947-5604 *E-mail:* sales@sencor.net *Web Site:* www.sencor.net, pg 1179

Send the Light Ltd (United Kingdom) *Tel:* (01228) 512 512 *Fax:* (01228) 514 949 *E-mail:* info@stl.org *Web Site:* www.stl.org, pg 1344

Senmon Toshokan Kyogikai (SENTOKYO) (Japan) *Tel:* (03) 3537-8335 *Fax:* (03) 3537-8336 *E-mail:* jsla@jsla.or.jp *Web Site:* www.jsla.or.jp, pg 1566

Senouhy Publishers (Egypt (Arab Republic of Egypt)), pg 138

Sentraldistribusjon ANS (Norway) *Tel:* (022) 98 57 10 *Fax:* (022) 98 57 20 *E-mail:* sdinfo@sd.no *Web Site:* www.sd.no, pg 1324

Seogwangsa (Republic of Korea) *Tel:* (02) 9246161; (02) 9246165 *Fax:* (02) 9224993, pg 439

Seoul International Publishing House (Republic of Korea) *Tel:* (02) 4698326; (02) 4698327, pg 439

Seoul National University Library (Republic of Korea) *Tel:* (02) 880-8001 *Fax:* (02) 878-2730 *E-mail:* libhelp@snu.ac.kr *Web Site:* library.snu.ac.kr, pg 1522

Seoul National University Press (Republic of Korea) *Tel:* (02) 880-5114 *Fax:* (02) 885-5272 *Web Site:* www.snu.ac.kr, pg 439

Sepia Editions (France) *Tel:* (01) 43 97 22 14 *Fax:* (01) 43 97 32 62 *E-mail:* sepia@editions-sepia.com *Web Site:* www.editions-sepia.com, pg 184

Editions de Septembre (France) *Tel:* (01) 53 68 96 20 *Fax:* (01) 53 68 96 21, pg 185

Serafin (Slovakia) *Tel:* (02) 54432159 *Fax:* (02) 54434342 *E-mail:* vydserafin@orangemail.sk *Web Site:* www.serafin.sk, pg 555

Ediciones del Serbal SA (Spain) *Tel:* (093) 408 08 34 *Fax:* (093) 408 07 92 *E-mail:* serbal@ed-serbal.es *Web Site:* www.ed-serbal.es, pg 594

Seren (United Kingdom) *Tel:* (01656) 663018 *Fax:* (01656) 649226 *E-mail:* general@seren-books.com *Web Site:* www.seren-books.com, pg 751

Serie-pocket-klubben (Sweden) *Tel:* (08) 7993110 *Fax:* (08) 7645764, pg 1246

Serif (United Kingdom) *Tel:* (020) 8981 3990 *Fax:* (020) 8981 3990, pg 751

Editions Le Serpent a Plumes (France) *Tel:* (01) 55 35 95 85 *Fax:* (01) 42 61 17 46 *E-mail:* contact@serpentaplumes.com, pg 185

Serpent's Tail Ltd (United Kingdom) *Tel:* (020) 7354-1949 *Fax:* (020) 7704-6467 *E-mail:* info@serpentstail.com *Web Site:* www.serpentstail.com, pg 751

Servedit (France) *Tel:* (01) 44 41 49 30 *Fax:* (01) 43 25 77 41 *E-mail:* servedit@wanadoo.fr, pg 185

Servei de Biblioteques de la UAB (Spain) *Tel:* (093) 581 1015 *Fax:* (093) 581 3219 *E-mail:* bib.utp@uab.es; s.biblioteques@uab.es *Web Site:* www.bib.uab.es; www.uab.es, pg 1544

Service Central de la Statistique et des Etudes Economiques (STATEC) (Luxembourg) *Tel:* 478-4384 *Fax:* 464289 *E-mail:* info@statec.etat.lu *Web Site:* www.statec.lu; www.statec.public.lu, pg 448

Service Central des Imprimes et des Fournitures de Bureau de l'Etat (Luxembourg) *Tel:* 4988111 *Fax:* 400881 *E-mail:* hotline@scie.etat.lu *Web Site:* www.scie.etat.lu, pg 448

Service commun de la documentation de l'Universite de Lille III (France) *Tel:* (03) 20 43 44 10 *Fax:* (03) 20 33 71 04 *E-mail:* boite-contact-bu@univ.lille1.fr *Web Site:* ustl.univ-lille1.fr, pg 1505

Service de l'Information et des Archives Nationales (Rwanda) *Tel:* 76 995 *Fax:* 82 162, pg 1539

Service des Publications Scientifiques du Museum National d 'Histoire Naturelle (France) *Tel:* (01) 40 79 48 38 *Fax:* (01) 40 79 38 40 *E-mail:* diff.pub@mnhn.fr *Web Site:* www.mnhn.fr/publication, pg 185

Service Hydrographique et Oceanographique de la Marine (SHOM) (France) *Tel:* (01) 44 38 41 16 *E-mail:* cartespa@shom.fr *Web Site:* www.shom.fr, pg 185

Service Technique pour l'Education (France) *Tel:* (01) 45084756, pg 185

Editions Services et Informations pour Etudiants (Morocco) *Tel:* (02) 210163, pg 471

Services for Export & Language (SEL) (United Kingdom) *Tel:* (0161) 7457480 *Fax:* (0161) 2955110 *E-mail:* sales@sel-uk.com *Web Site:* www.scl-uk.com, pg 1141

Servicio a La Iglesia Catolica AC Edicion y Distribucion de Libros Religiosos (Mexico) *Tel:* (05) 6710269 *Fax:* (05) 5441675, pg 1319

Servicio de Biblioteca de Ciencias de la Salud (Spain) *Tel:* (94) 6006125 *Fax:* (94) 6006049 *E-mail:* biblioteca.cruces@hcru.osakidetza.net *Web Site:* www.hospitalcruces.com/informacioncientifica/biblioteca.asp, pg 1544

Servicio de Publicaciones Universidad de Cadiz (Spain) *Tel:* (956) 015268 *Fax:* (956) 015634 *E-mail:* publicacions@uca.es *Web Site:* www.uca.es/serv/publicacions, pg 594

Servicio de Publicaciones Universidad de Cordoba (Spain) *Tel:* (0957) 21 81 25 *Fax:* (0957) 21 81 96; (057) 218666 (Director) *E-mail:* publicaciones@uco.es; pa11gocag@lucano.uco.es (Director) *Web Site:* www.uco.es/organiza/servicios/publica/presenta.htm, pg 594

Servicio de Publicaciones y Produccion Documental de la Universidad de Las Palmas de Gran Canaria (Spain) *Tel:* (0928) 451000; (0928) 451023 *Fax:* (0928) 451022 *E-mail:* universidad@ulpgc.es *Web Site:* www.ulpgc.es, pg 595

Servicios Especializados y Representacionesen Comercio Exterior SA de CV (Mexico) *Tel:* (05) 7609129; (05) 7605149, pg 1319

Servire BV Uitgevers (Netherlands) *Tel:* (030) 2349211 *Fax:* (030) 2349247 *E-mail:* info@kosmoszk.nl *Web Site:* www.servire.nl; www.boekenwereld.com, pg 1125

Servitium (Italy) *Tel:* (035) 4398011 *Fax:* (035) 792030 *E-mail:* servitium@spm.it, pg 404

Forlaget Sesam (Denmark) *Tel:* 3330-5044; 3330-5522 *Fax:* 3391-3878 *E-mail:* aschehoug@ash.egmont.com, pg 134

Sesame Publication Co (Hong Kong) *Tel:* 2508 9920; 2508 9311 *Fax:* 2508 9603 *E-mail:* sesame01@hkstar.hk, pg 316

Setberg (Iceland) *Tel:* 5517667; 552-9150 *Fax:* 5526640, pg 323

Bokforlaget Settern AB (Sweden) *Tel:* (0435) 80070 *Fax:* (0435) 80400 *E-mail:* info@settern.se *Web Site:* www.settern.se, pg 610

Editions du Seuil (France) *Tel:* (01) 40 46 50 50 *Fax:* (01) 40 46 43 00 *E-mail:* contact@seuil.com *Web Site:* www.seuil.com, pg 185

Seven Hills Publishers (Bulgaria) *Tel:* (032) 262235 *Fax:* (032) 262235, pg 96

Klub 707 (South Africa) *Tel:* (011) 6736725 *Fax:* (011) 6736719, pg 1245

Edicoes 70 Lda (Portugal) *Tel:* (021) 319 02 40 *Fax:* (021) 319 02 49 *E-mail:* edi.70@mail.telepac.pt *Web Site:* www.edicoes70.pt, pg 531

Severn House Publishers Inc (United Kingdom) *Tel:* (020) 8770 3930 *Fax:* (020) 8770 3850 *E-mail:* sales@severnhouse.com; editorial@severnhouse.com *Web Site:* www.severnhouse.com, pg 751

Severnside Printers Ltd (United Kingdom) *Tel:* (01452) 720250 *Fax:* (01452) 723012 *E-mail:* info@ssl-uk.net *Web Site:* www.ssl-uk.net, pg 1175, 1217

Ediciones Seyer (Spain) *Tel:* (095) 2320887 *Fax:* (095) 2325511, pg 595

Sh Ghulam Ali & Sons (Pvt) Ltd (Pakistan) *Tel:* (042) 7588979; (042) 7501664 *Fax:* (042) 7583611, pg 510

Shaar Zion Library (Israel) *Tel:* (03) 69101410, pg 1518

Shaibya Prakashan Bibhag (India) *Tel:* (033) 388268; (033) 2411748, pg 345

Shaikh Isa Library (Bahrain) *Tel:* 258550 *Fax:* 274036 *E-mail:* dolp@batelco.com.bh, pg 1490

Shakai Hoken Shuppan-Sha (Japan) *Tel:* (03) 3291-9841 *Fax:* (03) 3291-9847, pg 424

Shakai Shiso-Sha (Japan) *Tel:* (03) 3813-8101 *Fax:* (03) 3813-9061, pg 424

Shakespearean Authorship Trust (United Kingdom) *Tel:* (01473) 890264; (020) 7902 1403 *Fax:* (01473) 890803 *E-mail:* info@shakespeareanauthorshiptrust.org.uk *Web Site:* www.shakespeareanauthorshiptrust.org.uk, pg 1403

Shakti Communications Ltd (United Kingdom) *Tel:* (020) 8903 5442 *Fax:* (020) 8903 4684 *E-mail:* info@shakticom.com *Web Site:* www.shakticom.com, pg 751

Shalem Press (Israel) *Tel:* (02) 566-0601 *Fax:* (02) 566-0590 *E-mail:* shalem@shalem.org.il *Web Site:* www.shalem.org.il, pg 368

Shandong Education Publishing House (China) *Tel:* (0531) 2092661; (0531) 2092663 *Fax:* (0531) 2092661 *E-mail:* sdjys@sjs.com.cn *Web Site:* www.sjs.com.cn, pg 107

Shandong Fine Arts Publishing House (China) *Tel:* (0531) 6910055 *Fax:* (021) 6911563, pg 107

Shandong Friendship Publishing House (China) *Tel:* (0531) 2060055-7302 *Fax:* (0531) 2909354 *E-mail:* friendpub@sina.com *Web Site:* www.sdpress.com.cn, pg 107

Shandong Literature & Art Publishing House (China) *Tel:* (0531) 6910052-7300 *Fax:* (0531) 613584, pg 107

Shandong People's Publishing House (China) *Tel:* (0531) 6910055 *Fax:* (0531) 613584 *Web Site:* www.sd-book.com.cn, pg 107

Shandong Science & Technology Press (China) *Tel:* (0531) 6915110 *Fax:* (0531) 2023898 *E-mail:* li_yujn@sina.com, pg 107

Shandong University Press (China) *Tel:* (0531) 8902601 *E-mail:* hustpub@blue.hust.edu.cn, pg 107

Shanghai Academy of Social Sciences Library (China) *Tel:* (021) 6486 2266 (ext 1304) *Fax:* (021) 6427 6018 *E-mail:* tsg@sass.stc.sh.cn *Web Site:* www.sass.stc.sh.cn, pg 1496

Shanghai Book Co Ltd (Hong Kong) *Tel:* 2548 6160, pg 316

The Shanghai Book Co (Pte) Ltd (Singapore) *Tel:* 336 0144 *Fax:* 336 0490 *E-mail:* shanghaibooks@sbg.com.sg, pg 553

Shanghai Calligraphy & Painting Publishing House (China) *Tel:* (021) 64311905 *Fax:* (021) 3207505 *E-mail:* shcpph@online.sh.cn, pg 107

Shanghai College of Traditional Chinese Medicine Press (China) *Tel:* (021) 64175039 *Fax:* (021) 64175039, pg 107

Shanghai Educational Publishing House (China) *Tel:* (021) 64 37 71 65 *Fax:* (021) 64 33 99 95 *E-mail:* wuyiyang@public2.sta.net.cn, pg 107

Shanghai Far East Publishers (China) *Tel:* (021) 62247733-661 *Fax:* (021) 62414469 *E-mail:* ydbook@ydbook.com *Web Site:* www.ydbook.com, pg 108

Shanghai Foreign Language Education Press (China) *Tel:* (021) 65425300; (021) 65422896 *Fax:* (021) 35051287 *E-mail:* shudfk@online.sh.ca *Web Site:* www.sflep.com, pg 108

Shanghai People's Fine Arts Publishing House (China) *Tel:* (021) 54044520 *Fax:* (021) 54032331 *E-mail:* finearts@shi63.net, pg 108

Shanghai Scientific & Technical Publishers (China) *Tel:* (021) 64736055; (021) 64184881; (021) 64174349 *Fax:* (021) 64730679 *E-mail:* gjb@sstp.cn *Web Site:* www.sstp.com.cn; www.sstp.cn, pg 108

Shanghai Scientific & Technological Literature Press (China) *Tel:* (021) 64370782, pg 108

Shanghai tushuguan (China) *Tel:* (021) 64455555 *Fax:* (021) 64455001 *Web Site:* www.libnet.sh.cn, pg 1496

Sharbain's Bookshop (Jordan) *Tel:* (06) 638709 *Fax:* (06) 699119, pg 1314

Sharda Prakashan (India) *Tel:* (011) 653982, pg 345

Shaw & Sons Ltd (United Kingdom) *Tel:* (01322) 621100 *Fax:* (01322) 550553 *E-mail:* sales@shaws.co.uk *Web Site:* www.shaws.co.uk, pg 751

David Shaw & Associates Ltd (Canada) *Tel:* 416-487-2019 *Fax:* 416-486-1744 *E-mail:* djshaw@simpatico.ca, pg 1166

The Shaw Society (United Kingdom) *Tel:* (020) 86973619 *Fax:* (020) 86973619 *E-mail:* bernardshawinfo@netscape.net *Web Site:* www.sndc.demon.co.uk/shawsub.htm, pg 1403

Shearwater Associates Ltd (New Zealand) *Tel:* (04) 2399024 *Fax:* (04) 2399024, pg 496

Shearwater Press Ltd (United Kingdom) *Tel:* (01624) 627727 *Fax:* (01624) 663627, pg 751

Sheck Wah Tong Printing Press Ltd (Hong Kong) *Tel:* 25628293 *Fax:* 25655431 *Web Site:* www.sheckwahtong.com, pg 1209

Sheed & Ward UK (United Kingdom) *Tel:* (020) 7922 0880 *Fax:* (020) 7922 0881 *E-mail:* info@breathemail.net *Web Site:* www.continuumbooks.com, pg 751

Sheffield Academic Press Ltd (United Kingdom) *Tel:* (01202) 665 432 *Fax:* (01202) 666 219 *E-mail:* orders@orcabookservices.co.uk *Web Site:* www.sheffieldacademicpress.com, pg 751

Sheil Land Associates Ltd (United Kingdom) *Tel:* (020) 7405 9351 *Fax:* (020) 7831 2127 *E-mail:* info@sheilland.co.uk, pg 1133

Caroline Sheldon Literary Agency (United Kingdom) *Tel:* (01983) 760205, pg 1133

Sheldon Press (United Kingdom) *Tel:* (020) 7592 3900 *Fax:* (020) 7592 3939 *E-mail:* director@sheldonpress.co.uk *Web Site:* www.sheldonpress.co.uk, pg 752

Sheldrake Press (United Kingdom) *Tel:* (020) 8675 1767; (01752) 202301 (orders); (01752) 202300 (warehouse) *Fax:* (020) 8675 7736 *E-mail:* mail@sheldrakepress.demon.co.uk *Web Site:* www.sheldrakepress.co.uk, pg 752

Shelfmark Books (United Kingdom) *Tel:* (020) 8986 4854 *Fax:* (020) 8533 5821 *E-mail:* orders@centralbooks.com, pg 752

Sherbourne Publications (United Kingdom) *Tel:* (01691) 657 853 *Fax:* (01691) 657 853, pg 752

The Sheringa Book Committee (Australia) *Tel:* (086) 878750, pg 40

Sherratt & Hughes (United Kingdom) *Tel:* (01793) 695195, pg 1344

Sherwood Publishing (United Kingdom) *Tel:* (01923) 224737 *Fax:* (01923) 210648 *E-mail:* sherwood@adinternational.com *Web Site:* www.sherwoodpublishing.com, pg 752

R R Sheth & Co (India) *Tel:* (022) 2013441 *Fax:* (079) 5321732 *E-mail:* chintan@rrsheth.com *Web Site:* www.rrsheth.com, pg 346

R R Sheth & Co (India) *Tel:* (079) 5356573 *E-mail:* chintan@rrsheth.com *Web Site:* www.rrsheth.com, pg 1307

Shibil Publications (Pvt) Ltd (Pakistan) *Tel:* (021) 533414; (021) 539570; (021) 571488, pg 510

Shibun-Do (Japan) *Tel:* (03) 3268-2441 *Fax:* (03) 3268-3550 *E-mail:* eigy@imail.plala.or.jp, pg 424

Shiko-Sha Co Ltd (Japan) *Tel:* (03) 3400-7151 *Fax:* (03) 3400-7294, pg 424

Shiksha Bharati (India) *Tel:* (011) 386-7791, pg 346

Shimizu-Shoin (Japan) *Tel:* (03) 3260-5261 *Fax:* (03) 3260-5270 *Web Site:* www.shimizushoin.co.jp, pg 424

Shin Won Agency Co (Republic of Korea) *Tel:* (031) 955-2255 *Fax:* (031) 955-2266 *E-mail:* main@shinwonagency.co.kr *Web Site:* www.shinwonagency.co.kr; shinwonagency.com, pg 1124

Shincho-Sha Co Ltd (Japan) *Tel:* (03) 3266 5411 *Fax:* (03) 3266 5534 *E-mail:* matsuie@shinchosha.co.jp *Web Site:* www.shinchosha.co.jp, pg 424

SHINE-Scottish Health Information Network (United Kingdom) *Tel:* (0131) 536 5582 *Fax:* (0131) 536 5502 *E-mail:* mdg@ednet.co.uk *Web Site:* www.shinelib.org.uk, pg 1573

Shing Lee Group Publishers (Singapore) *Tel:* 7601388 *Fax:* 7651506 *E-mail:* kongjing@shinglee.com.sg, pg 553

Shingakusha Co Ltd (Japan) *Tel:* (075) 581-6111 *Fax:* (075) 501-0514 *E-mail:* info@sing.co.jp *Web Site:* www.sing.co.jp, pg 424

Shinkenchiku-Sha Co Ltd (Japan) *Tel:* (03) 38117101 *Fax:* (03) 38128229, pg 424

Shinko Tsusho Co Ltd (Japan) *Tel:* (03) 33531751 *Fax:* (03) 33532205 *E-mail:* shinko@tokyo.e-mail.ne.jp, pg 1313

Shinkwang Publishing Co (Republic of Korea) *Tel:* (02) 9255051; (02) 9255053 *Fax:* (02) 9255054, pg 439

Shire Publications Ltd (United Kingdom) *Tel:* (01844) 344301 *Fax:* (01844) 347080 *E-mail:* shire@shirebooks.co.uk *Web Site:* www.shirebooks.com, pg 752

Shirikon Publishers (Kenya), pg 432

Shiseido Booksellers Ltd (Japan) *Tel:* (075) 431 2345 *Fax:* (075) 432 6588 *E-mail:* shiseido@jd5.so-net.ne.jp *Web Site:* www.shiseido-book.co.jp, pg 1313

Shkoder Public Library (Albania), pg 1487

Shoal Bay Press Ltd (New Zealand) *Tel:* (03) 384 6057 *Fax:* (03) 384 6087 *E-mail:* ros@shoalbay.co.nz, pg 496

Akane Shobo Co Ltd (Japan) *Tel:* (03) 3263-0641 *Fax:* (03) 3263-5440 *E-mail:* mail@akaneshobo.co.jp *Web Site:* www.akaneshobo.co.jp/, pg 424

Shobunsha Publications Inc (Japan) *Tel:* (03) 3556-8154 *Fax:* (03) 3556-5973 *E-mail:* LEH05353@niftyserve.or.jp *Web Site:* www.mapple.co.jp, pg 424

Shogakukan Inc (Japan) *Tel:* (03) 3230-5211 *Fax:* (03) 3234-5660 *E-mail:* info@shogakukan.co.jp *Web Site:* skygarden.shogakukan.co.jp, pg 424

Shogun International Ltd (United Kingdom) *Tel:* (020) 8749 2022 *Fax:* (020) 8740 1086, pg 1344

Mitsumura Suiko Shoin (Japan) *Tel:* (075) 493-8244 *Fax:* (075) 493-6011 *E-mail:* mitsumur@mbox.kyoto-inet.or.jp *Web Site:* www.mitsumura-suiko.co.jp, pg 424

Shokabo Publishing Co Ltd (Japan) *Tel:* (03) 3262-9166 *Fax:* (03) 3262-9130 *E-mail:* shkb-01@cb3.so-net.ne.jp *Web Site:* www.shokabo.co.jp/, pg 424

Shokokusha Publishing Co Ltd (Japan) *Tel:* (03) 3359-3231 *Fax:* (03) 3357-3961 *Web Site:* www.shokokusha.co.jp, pg 424

Shorin-Sha Co ltd (Japan) *Tel:* (03)3815 4921 *Fax:* (03) 3815 4923, pg 424

Shortland Publications Ltd (New Zealand) *Tel:* (09) 687128 *Fax:* (09) 6230143 *E-mail:* heather.peach@mcgraw hill.com, pg 496

Shtepia Botuese Enciklopedike (Albania) *Tel:* (04) 228064 *Fax:* (04) 228064, pg 1

Shueisha Inc (Japan) *Tel:* (03) 3230-6111 *Fax:* (03) 3238 9239 *Web Site:* www.shueisha.co.jp, pg 424

Shufu-to-Seikatsu Sha Ltd (Japan) *Tel:* (03) 3563-5120 *Fax:* (03) 3563-2073 *Web Site:* www.shufu.co.jp, pg 425

Shufunotomo Co Ltd (Japan) *Tel:* (03) 5280-7539 *Fax:* (03) 5280-7587 *E-mail:* international@shufunotomo.co.jp *Web Site:* www.shufunotomo.co.jp, pg 425

Shumawa Publishing House (Myanmar), pg 472

Shunjusha (Japan) *Tel:* (03) 3255-9614 *Fax:* (03) 3253-9370 *E-mail:* main@shunjusha.co.jp *Web Site:* www.shunjusha.co.jp, pg 425

Shuppan News Co Ltd (Japan) *Tel:* (03) 3262-2076 *Fax:* (03) 3261-6817 *E-mail:* snews@snews.net *Web Site:* www.snews.net, pg 425

Oru Shuppan (Japan) *Tel:* (03) 3234-0971 *Fax:* (03) 3261-6602, pg 425

Shuter & Shooter Publishers (Pty) Ltd (South Africa) *Tel:* (033) 394 8881 *Fax:* (033) 342 7419 *Web Site:* www.shuter.co.za, pg 564

Shuter & Shooter Publishers (Pty) Ltd (South Africa) *Tel:* (033) 347 6100 *Fax:* (033) 347 6120 *Web Site:* www.shuter.co.za, pg 1332

Shuttle Multimedia Inc (Taiwan, Province of China) *Tel:* (02) 87924088 *Fax:* (02) 87924089 *E-mail:* school@dayi.com *Web Site:* www.eduplus.com, pg 637

Shwepyidan Printing & Publishing House (Myanmar), pg 472

Shy Mau & Shy Chaur Publishing Co Ltd (Taiwan, Province of China) *Tel:* (02) 2218-3277 *Fax:* (02) 2218-3239 *E-mail:* chien218@ms5.hinet.net, pg 637

The Siam Society (Thailand) *Tel:* (02) 66164707 *Fax:* (02) 2583491 *E-mail:* info@siam-society.org *Web Site:* www.siam-society.org, pg 1400

Siamantas VA A Ouvas (Greece) *Tel:* 2108824960 *Fax:* 2108824960, pg 309

Sibelius-Akatemian Kirjasto (Finland) *Tel:* (020) 7539 538 *Fax:* (020) 7539 542 *E-mail:* sibakirjasto@siba.fi *Web Site:* lib.siba.fi/fin/, pg 1504

Sibi (Bulgaria) *Tel:* (02) 9870141 *Fax:* (02) 9875709 *E-mail:* sibi@ind.interner-bg.bg, pg 96

SIBS Publishing House Inc (Philippines) *Tel:* 687-6164 *Fax:* 687-1716 *E-mail:* sibsbook@info.com.ph; sibs@eyp.ph *Web Site:* www.sibs.com.ph, pg 516

Wydawnictwo SIC (Poland) *Tel:* (022) 8400753 *Fax:* (022) 8400753 *E-mail:* sic@sic.ksiazka.pl, pg 521

Sicania (Italy) *Tel:* (090) 2936373 *Fax:* (090) 2932461 *Web Site:* www.sicania.me.it, pg 404

Sichuan Science & Technology Publishing House (China) *Tel:* (028) 664982; (028) 662 5025 *Fax:* (028) 6654063, pg 108

Sichuan University Press (China) *Tel:* (028) 583875-62529, pg 108

Edizioni Librarie Siciliane (Italy) *Tel:* (091) 8570221 *Fax:* (091) 342670, pg 404

Siciliano SA (Brazil) *Tel:* (011) 36494634; (011) 8319911 *Fax:* (011) 8328616, pg 90

J Sideris OE Ekdoseis (Greece) *Tel:* 2103833434; 2105140627 *Fax:* 2103832294, pg 309

Michalis Sideris (Greece) *Tel:* 2103301165; 210 03301161 (bookstore) *Fax:* 2103301164, pg 309

Sidgwick & Jackson Ltd (United Kingdom) *Tel:* (020) 7014 6000 *Fax:* (020) 7014 6001, pg 752

Siebenberg-Verlag (Germany) *Tel:* (05695) 1028 *Fax:* (05695) 1027 *E-mail:* fh@huebner-books.de *Web Site:* www.huebner-books.de, pg 280

Siebert Verlag GmbH (Germany) *Tel:* (06201) 6007-0 *E-mail:* info@beltz.de *Web Site:* www.beltz.de, pg 280

Siedler Verlag (Germany) *Tel:* (089) 41 36-0 *E-mail:* vertrieb.verlagsgruppe@randomhouse.de *Web Site:* www.randomhouse.de/siedler, pg 280

Siegler & Co Verlag fuer Zeitarchive GmbH (Germany) *Tel:* (02241) 3164-0, pg 280

Georg Siemens Verlagsbuchhandlung (Germany) *Tel:* (030) 769904-0 *Fax:* (030) 769904-18 *E-mail:* gsiemensv@t-online.de, pg 280

Sierra Leone Association of Archivists, Librarians & Information Scientists (SLAALIS) (Sierra Leone) *Tel:* (022) 220758, pg 1570

Sierra Leone Library Board (Sierra Leone) *Tel:* (022) 226 993, pg 1541

Sifrı Ltd (Israel) *Tel:* (03) 5784679, pg 368

Sifriat Poalim Ltd (Israel) *Tel:* (03) 5183143 *Fax:* (03) 5183191 *E-mail:* akantor@inter.net.il, pg 368

Siglo XXI Editores de Colombia Ltda (Colombia) *Tel:* (01) 6110787 *Fax:* (01) 6110757, pg 112

Siglo XXI de Espana Editores SA (Spain) *Tel:* (091) 562 37 23; (091) 561 77 48 *Fax:* (091) 561 58 19 *E-mail:* sigloxxi@sigloxxieditores.com *Web Site:* www.sigloxxieditores.com, pg 595

Siglo XXI Editores SA de CV (Mexico) *Tel:* (05) 6587999; (05) 6587588 *Fax:* (05) 6587599 *E-mail:* sigloxxi@inetcorp.net.mx *Web Site:* www.sigloxxi-editores.com.mx, pg 468

Sigloch Edition Helmut Sigloch GmbH & Co KG (Germany) *Tel:* (07953) 883-0 *Fax:* (07953) 883-320 *E-mail:* info@sigloch.de *Web Site:* www.sigloch.de, pg 280

Sigma (Greece) *Tel:* 2103638941; 2103607667 *Fax:* 2103638941 *E-mail:* sigma@sigmabooks.gr *Web Site:* www.sigmabooks.gr, pg 309

Sigma Press (United Kingdom) *Tel:* (01625) 531035 *Fax:* (01625) 531035 *E-mail:* info@sigmapress.co.uk *Web Site:* www.sigmapress.co.uk, pg 752

Edition Sigma e.Kfm (Germany) *Tel:* (030) 623 23 63 *Fax:* (030) 623 93 93 *E-mail:* verlag@edition-sigma. de *Web Site:* www.edition-sigma.de, pg 280

Editorial Sigmar SACI (Argentina) *Tel:* (011) 4381-2844; (011) 4381-2241 *Fax:* (011) 4383-5633 *E-mail:* editorial@sigmar.com.ar *Web Site:* www. sigmar.com.ar, pg 9

Editions Du Signal Rene Gaillard (Switzerland) *Tel:* (021) 3290194 *Fax:* (021) 3290194, pg 629

Signament I Comunicacio, SL Signament Edicions (Spain) *Tel:* (093) 4516888 *Fax:* (093) 3234417, pg 595

Editura Signata (Romania) *Tel:* (056) 153081, pg 538

Signes du Monde (France) *Tel:* (06) 12 99 73 37 *Fax:* (0561) 575717, pg 1166

Signes du Monde (France) *Tel:* (05) 58 79 54 90, pg 1206

Ediciones Sigueme SA (Spain) *Tel:* (0923) 21 82 03 *Fax:* (0923) 27 05 63 *E-mail:* sigueme@ctv.es, pg 595

Uitgeverij De Sikkel NV (Belgium) *Tel:* (03) 312 86 30 *Fax:* (03) 311 77 39 *E-mail:* informatie@deboeck.be *Web Site:* www.desikkel.be, pg 72

Sila & Zivot (Bulgaria) *Tel:* (056) 20965 *E-mail:* silajivot@bse.bg, pg 96

Edicoes Silabo (Portugal) *Tel:* (021) 525880 *Fax:* (021) 314 58 80 *E-mail:* silabo@mail.telepac.pt, pg 531

Edicoes Silabo (Portugal) *Tel:* (021) 8130345 *Fax:* (021) 8166719 *E-mail:* silabo@silabo.pt *Web Site:* www. silabo.pt, pg 1150

Edicoes Silabo (Portugal) *Tel:* (021) 316 12 81 *Fax:* (021) 314 58 80 *E-mail:* silabo@silabo.pt *Web Site:* www.silabo.pt, pg 1171

Edicoes Silabo (Portugal) *Tel:* (021) 8130345 *Fax:* (021) 8166719 *E-mail:* silabo@silabo.pt *Web Site:* www. silabo.pt, pg 1212, 1236

Silberburg-Verlag Titus Haeussermann GmbH (Germany) *Tel:* (07071) 6885-0 *Fax:* (07071) 6885-20 *E-mail:* info@silberburg.de *Web Site:* www.silberburg. com, pg 280

Die Silberschnur Verlag GmbH (Germany) *Tel:* (02687) 929068 *Fax:* (02687) 929524 *E-mail:* info@ silberschnur.de *Web Site:* www.silberschnur.de, pg 281

Silex Ediciones (Spain) *Tel:* (091) 356.69.09 *Fax:* (091) 361.00.75 *E-mail:* pedidosweb@silexediciones.com *Web Site:* www.silexediciones.com, pg 595

Silkroad Publishers Agency, Ltd (Thailand) *Tel:* (02) 2584798; (02) 2588266 *Fax:* (02) 6620553 *E-mail:* silkroad@ji-net.com, pg 1128

Silkworm Books (Thailand) *Tel:* (053) 271889 *Fax:* (053) 275178 *E-mail:* silkworm@loxinfo.co.th *Web Site:* www.silkwormbooks.info, pg 641

Silliman University Library (Philippines) *Tel:* (035) 4227208; (035) 4226002 *Fax:* (035) 4227208 *E-mail:* sulib@su.edu.ph *Web Site:* su.edu.ph, pg 1535

Editions Siloe (France) *Tel:* (02) 43 53 26 01 *Fax:* (02) 43 53 56 01 *E-mail:* contact@siloe.fr *Web Site:* www. siloe.fr, pg 185

Silsilah Publication (Philippines) *Tel:* (02) 5663, pg 516

Silva (Italy) *Tel:* (0521) 804106 *Fax:* (0521) 804406, pg 404

Editions Andre Silvaire Sarl (France) *Tel:* (01) 43 26 72 34 *Fax:* (01) 55 42 16 69, pg 185

Silvana Editoriale SpA (Italy) *Tel:* (02) 618361 *Fax:* (02) 6172464 *E-mail:* international@silvanaeditoriale.it *Web Site:* www.silvanaeditoriale.it, pg 404

Silver Link Publishing Ltd (United Kingdom) *Tel:* (01536) 330588 *Fax:* (01536) 330469 *E-mail:* sales@nostalgiacollection.com *Web Site:* www.nostalgiacollection.com, pg 752

Dorie Simmonds Agency (United Kingdom) *Tel:* (020) 7569 8686 *Fax:* (020) 7569 8696, pg 1134

Jeffrey Simmons (United Kingdom) *Tel:* (020) 7224 8917 *Fax:* (020) 7224 8918 *E-mail:* jas@london-inc. com, pg 1134

Simon & Schuster (Australia) Pty Ltd (Australia) *Tel:* (02) 9415 9900 *Fax:* (02) 9417 3188 (customer service); (02) 9417 4292 (editorial); (02) 9417 1087 (publicity) *E-mail:* cservice@simonandschuster. com.au; rights.dept@simonandschuster.com. au *Web Site:* www.simonsays.com; www. simonandschuster.com.au, pg 40

Simon & Schuster Ltd (United Kingdom) *Tel:* (020) 7316 1900 *Fax:* (020) 7316 0332 *E-mail:* firstname. surname@simonandschuster.co.uk *Web Site:* www. simonsays.co.uk, pg 752

Buchkonzept Simon KG (Germany) *Tel:* (089) 21939012 *Fax:* (089) 21939014, pg 281

Simon Stevin NV (Belgium) *Tel:* (02) 5121085; (02) 5138295 *Fax:* (02) 5117015, pg 1292

The Simul Press Inc (Japan) *Tel:* (03) 3226-2861 *Fax:* (03) 3226-2860, pg 425

Sin Min Chu Publishing Co (Hong Kong) *Tel:* (02) 2334 9327 *Fax:* (02) 76 58 471, pg 316

Sinag-Tala Publishers Inc (Philippines) *Tel:* (02) 8192681 *Fax:* (02) 8192563, pg 516

Sinai Publishing Co (Israel) *Tel:* (03) 5163672 *Fax:* (03) 5176783, pg 368

Sind University Central Library (Pakistan) *Tel:* (0221) 771188, pg 1534

Sindhi Adabi Board (Pakistan) *Tel:* (0221) 771276; (0221) 771465; (0221) 771600, pg 1397

Sindicato Nacional dos Editores de Livros (SNEL) (Brazil) *Tel:* (021) 2233-6481 *Fax:* (021) 2253-8502 *E-mail:* snel@snel.org.br *Web Site:* www.snel.org.br, pg 1253

Sing Cheong Printing Co Ltd (Hong Kong) *Tel:* 25618801; 25626317 *Fax:* 25659467 *E-mail:* info@singcheong.com.hk, pg 1148, 1209

Singapore Book Publishers' Association (Singapore) *Tel:* (065) 3447801; (065) 4407409 *Fax:* (065) 4470897 *E-mail:* twcsbpa@singnet.com.sg, pg 1273

Singapore University Press Pte Ltd (Singapore) *Tel:* 67761148; 68742382 *Fax:* 67740652 *E-mail:* nusbooks@nus.edu.sg *Web Site:* www.nus. edu.sg/npu, pg 553

Single X Publications (Australia) *Tel:* (08) 8127 0827, pg 41

Sinisukk (Estonia) *Tel:* 656 1872 *Fax:* 656 1872 *E-mail:* sinisukk@vorguvara.ee, pg 140

Sino Publishing House Ltd (Hong Kong) *Tel:* 2884 9963 *Fax:* 2884 9321 *E-mail:* benyan@sinophl.com *Web Site:* www.sinophl.com, pg 1148

Sino Publishing House Ltd (Hong Kong) *Tel:* 2884 9963 *Fax:* 2884 9321 *Web Site:* www.sinophl.com, pg 1209, 1226

Sino Publishing House Ltd (Hong Kong) *Tel:* 2884 9963 *Fax:* 2884 9321 *E-mail:* benyan@sinophl.com *Web Site:* www.sinophl.com, pg 1236

Editora Sinodal (Brazil) *Tel:* (051) 590-2366 *Fax:* (051) 590-2664 *E-mail:* editora@editorasinodal.com.br *Web Site:* www.editorasinodal.com.br, pg 90

Editora Sinodal (Brazil) *Tel:* (051) 590 2366 *Fax:* (051) 590 2664 *E-mail:* editora@editorasinodal.com.br *Web Site:* www.editorasinodal.com.br, pg 1294

Sinodalno Izdatelstvo na Balgarskata pravoslavna carkva (Bulgaria) *Tel:* (02) 875611; (02) 875245, pg 96

Sinorama Magazine Co (Taiwan, Province of China) *Tel:* (02) 2392-2256 *Fax:* (02) 2397-0655 *E-mail:* service@mail.sinorama.com.tw *Web Site:* www.sinorama.com.tw, pg 637

Editorial Sintes SA (Spain) *Tel:* (093) 3182838, pg 595

Editorial Sintesis, SA (Spain) *Tel:* (091) 593 20 98 *Fax:* (091) 445 86 96 *E-mail:* sintesis@sintesis.com *Web Site:* www.sintesis.com, pg 595

Sinwel-Buchhandlung Verlag (Switzerland) *Tel:* (031) 3325205 *Fax:* (031) 3331376 *E-mail:* sinwel@sinwel. ch *Web Site:* www.sinwel.ch, pg 629

Alex Siokis & Co (Greece) *Tel:* 2310230257; 2310287016 *Fax:* 2310281014 *E-mail:* siokis@ spark.net.gr, pg 309

SIPI (Servizio Italiano Pubblicazioni Internazionali) Srl (Italy) *Tel:* (06) 5920509 *Fax:* (06) 5924819 *Web Site:* www.sipi.it, pg 405

SIR Publishing (New Zealand) *Tel:* (04) 472 7421 *Fax:* (04) 473 1841 *E-mail:* sirp@rsnz.govt.nz *Web Site:* www.rsnz.govt.nz/publ, pg 496

Siriraj Medical Library (Thailand) *Tel:* (02) 411 3112; (02) 419 7635; (02) 419 7637 *Fax:* (02) 412 8418 *E-mail:* silib@diamond.mahidol.ac.th *Web Site:* www. medlib.si.mahidol.ac.th, pg 1548

Equipo Sirius SA (Spain) *Tel:* (091) 710 73 49 *Fax:* (091) 705 43 04 *E-mail:* sirius@equiposirius.com *Web Site:* www.equiposirius.com, pg 595

R Sirkis Publishers Ltd (Israel) *Tel:* (03) 7510792 *Fax:* (03) 7513750 *E-mail:* sirkispb@inter.net.il, pg 368

Sirmio (Spain) *Tel:* (093) 2123808 *Fax:* (093) 4182317 *E-mail:* qcrema@mito.ibernet.com, pg 595

Ediciones Siruela SA (Spain) *Tel:* (091) 3555720; (091) 3554605; (091) 3552202 *Fax:* (091) 3552201 *E-mail:* atencionlector@siruela.com *Web Site:* www.siruela.com, pg 595

Sistema Bibliotecario (Honduras) *Tel:* 232-2204 *Fax:* 232-2204 *E-mail:* webmaster@biblio.unah.edu.hn *Web Site:* www.biblio.unah.edu.hn, pg 1512

Sistema de Bibliotecas y de Informacion (Argentina) *Tel:* (011) 4952-0078 *Fax:* (011) 4952-6557 *E-mail:* webmaster@sisbi.uba.ar *Web Site:* www.sisbi.uba.ar, pg 1488

Sistemas Tecnicos de Edicion SA de CV (Mexico) *Tel:* (05) 6559144; (05) 6845220 *Fax:* (05) 5739412, pg 468

Sistemas Universales, SA (Mexico) *Tel:* (05) 705-4568; (05) 705-5937 *Fax:* (05) 705-3421, pg 468

SiT Tapir Fagbokhandel (Norway) *Tel:* 73598420 *Fax:* 73598495 *E-mail:* forlag@tapir.no *Web Site:* www.campus.tapir.no, pg 1324

Sita Books & Periodicals Pvt Ltd (India) *Tel:* (022) 55555589; (022) 5973281; (022) 5973282; (022) 5973283 *Fax:* (022) 5561622 *E-mail:* ssrao@bom5.vsnl.net.in; sitabook@bom7.vsnl.net.in *Web Site:* www.sitabooks.com, pg 346

Sita-MB (Bulgaria) *Tel:* (092) 872285, pg 96

6-9 Club (United Kingdom) *Tel:* (0845) 6039091 *Fax:* (0845) 6039090 *E-mail:* sbcenquiries@scholastic.co.uk *Web Site:* www.scholastic.co.uk, pg 1247

Edicions 62 (Spain) *Tel:* (093) 4437100 *Fax:* (093) 4437130 *E-mail:* correu@grup62.com *Web Site:* www.grup62.com, pg 595

Grup 62 (Spain) *Tel:* (093) 443 71 00 *Fax:* (093) 443 71 30 *E-mail:* correu@grup62.com *Web Site:* www.grup62.com, pg 595

Sjaloom Uitgeverijen (Netherlands) *Tel:* (020) 6206263 *Fax:* (020) 4288540 *E-mail:* post@sjaloom.nl *Web Site:* www.sjaloom.nl, pg 485

Sjoestrands Foerlag (Sweden) *Tel:* (08) 29 99 32 *Fax:* (08) 98 46 45, pg 610

Skandinavia Verlag (Germany) *Tel:* (030) 8137006 *Fax:* (030) 8141029, pg 1122

SKAT (Swiss Centre for Development Cooperation in Technology & Management) (Switzerland) *Tel:* (071) 2285454 *Fax:* (071) 2285455 *E-mail:* info@skat.ch *Web Site:* www.skat.ch, pg 629

A/S Skattekartoteket (Denmark) *Tel:* 33117874 *Fax:* 33938025 *E-mail:* magnus@cddk.dk, pg 134

Skills Publishing (Australia) *Tel:* (02) 4759 2844 *Fax:* (02) 4759 3721 *E-mail:* aww@skillspublish.com.au *Web Site:* www.skillspublish.com.au, pg 41

Charles Skilton Ltd (United Kingdom) *Tel:* (020) 7351 4995 *Fax:* (020) 7351 4995, pg 753

Editions D'Art Albert Skira SA (Switzerland) *Tel:* (022) 906 80 00 *Fax:* (022) 3495535, pg 629

Skjaldborg Ltd (Iceland) *Tel:* 5882400 *Fax:* 5888994 *E-mail:* skjaldborg@skjaldborg.is, pg 323

Skolska Knjiga (Croatia) *Tel:* (01) 48 30 491; (01) 48 30 511 *Fax:* (01) 48 30 506 *E-mail:* skolska@skolskaknjiga.hr *Web Site:* www.skolskaknjiga.hr, pg 119

Skoob Russell Square (United Kingdom) *Tel:* (020) 7278 8760 *E-mail:* books@skoob.com *Web Site:* www.skoob.com, pg 753

SKT's Boghandel (Denmark) *Tel:* 44686662 *Fax:* 44686660 *E-mail:* skt@sktbooks.dk *Web Site:* www.sktbooks.dk, pg 1298

'Slask' Ltd (Poland) *Tel:* (032) 258 07 56; (032) 2581812; (032) 2583222; (032) 2581910 *Fax:* (032) 2583229 *E-mail:* biuro@slaskwn.com.pl *Web Site:* www.slaskwn.com.pl, pg 522

Biblioteka Slaska (Poland) *Tel:* (032) 20-83-700 *Fax:* (032) 20-83-720 *E-mail:* bsl@bs.katowice.pl *Web Site:* www.bs.katowice.pl, pg 1536

Slatkine Reprints (Switzerland) *Tel:* (022) 3100476 *Fax:* (022) 3107101 *E-mail:* librarie@slatkine.ch *Web Site:* www.slatkine.ch, pg 629

Slavena (Bulgaria) *Tel:* (052) 602465; (052) 225935 *Fax:* (052) 225935 *E-mail:* slavena@triada.bg *Web Site:* www.slavena.net, pg 96

Privlacica Slavonska Naklada (Croatia) *Tel:* (032) 306 068; (032) 306 069; (032) 306 070 *Fax:* (032) 331735 *E-mail:* privlacica@vk.tel.hr, pg 119

Verlag Josef Otto Slezak (Austria) *Tel:* (01) 587 02 59 *Fax:* (01) 587 02 59 *E-mail:* verlag.slezak@aon.at *Web Site:* www.byronny.at/index.html, pg 57

SLG Press (United Kingdom) *Tel:* (01865) 721301 *Fax:* (01865) 790860 *E-mail:* editor@slgpress.co.uk; orders@slgpress.co.uk *Web Site:* www.slgpress.co.uk, pg 753

Slo Viet (Slovakia) *Tel:* (02) 52494886, pg 556

Slon Sociologicke Nakladatelstvi (Czech Republic) *Tel:* (02) 222 020 025 *Fax:* (02) 222 220 025 *E-mail:* redakce@slon-knihy.cz *Web Site:* www.slon-knihy.cz, pg 127

Slouch Hat Publications (Australia) *Tel:* (03) 5986-6437 *Fax:* (03) 5986-6312 *E-mail:* slouchat@surf.net.au *Web Site:* www.slouch-hat.com.au, pg 41

Slovart Co Ltd (Slovakia) *Tel:* (02) 4487 1210 *Fax:* (02) 6541 1375; (02) 4487 1246 *E-mail:* pobox@slovart.sk *Web Site:* www.slovart.sk; www.slovart.com, pg 1331

Slovenska matica (Slovenia) *Tel:* (01) 2514 200; (01) 2514 227; (01) 4263 190 *Fax:* (01) 2514 200, pg 557

Slovenska Narodna Kniznica, Martin (Slovakia) *Tel:* (0842) 31861 *Fax:* (0842) 32993 *E-mail:* vms@esix.matica.sk, pg 556

Slovenska Narodna Kniznica, Martin (Slovakia) *Tel:* (043) 422 07 20 *Fax:* (043) 430 18 02 *E-mail:* snk@snk.sk *Web Site:* www.snk.sk, pg 1541

Slovenske pedagogicke nakladateistvo (Slovakia) *Tel:* (02) 55423892 *Fax:* (02) 55571894 *E-mail:* spn@spn.sk *Web Site:* www.spn.sk, pg 556

Slovensky Spisovatel Ltd as (Slovakia) *Tel:* (02) 399790; (02) 399736 *Fax:* (02) 399736, pg 556

Vydavatelstvo Slovensky Tatran spol sro (Slovakia) *Tel:* (02) 54435849 *Fax:* (02) 54435777, pg 556

SLS Legal Publications (NI) (United Kingdom) *Tel:* (028) 9097 3452 *Fax:* (028) 9097 3376; (028) 9097 5040 *E-mail:* law-enquiries@qub.ac.uk *Web Site:* www.law.qub.ac.uk, pg 753

Sluntse Publishing House (Bulgaria) *Tel:* (02) 988 37 97 *Fax:* (02) 987 14 05 *E-mail:* info@sluntse.com *Web Site:* www.sluntse.com, pg 96

Sluzbeni List (Serbia and Montenegro) *Tel:* (011) 3060333; (011) 3060310 *Fax:* (011) 3060393, pg 549

Ediciones SM (Spain) *Tel:* (091) 4228800 *Fax:* (091) 5089927 *E-mail:* jcabrerap@ediciones-sm.com, pg 595

Small Industry Research Institute (SIRI) (India) *Tel:* (011) 23841893; (011) 2916804 *Fax:* (011) 2910805 *E-mail:* siri@ndf.vsnl.net.in; siricon@vsnl.com, pg 346

Smart & Mookerdum (Myanmar), pg 472

SMC Publishing Inc (Taiwan, Province of China) *Tel:* (02) 2362-0190 *Fax:* (02) 3623834 *Web Site:* www.smcbook.com.tw, pg 637

Koninklijke Smeets Offset (Netherlands) *Tel:* (0495) 57 09 11 *Fax:* (0495) 54 29 05 *E-mail:* rswinfo@rotosmeets.com, pg 485

Rudolf G Smend (Germany) *Tel:* (0221) 312047 *Fax:* (0221) 9 32 07 18 *E-mail:* smend@smend.de, pg 281

SMER Diffusion (Morocco) *Tel:* (07) 723725; (07) 725960 *Fax:* (07) 701643, pg 1319

Smith-Gordon & Co Ltd (United Kingdom) *Tel:* (020) 7351 7042 *Fax:* (020) 7351 1250 *E-mail:* publisher@smithgordon.com *Web Site:* www.smithgordon.com, pg 753

John Smith & Son Booksellers (United Kingdom) *Tel:* (01425) 471160 *Fax:* (01425) 471718 *Web Site:* www.johnsmith.co.uk, pg 1344

Smith Settle Ltd (United Kingdom) *Tel:* (01756) 701381 *Fax:* (01524) 251708 *E-mail:* editorial@dalesman.co.uk, pg 753

Smurfit Print (Ireland) *Tel:* (01) 202-7000 *Fax:* (01) 269-4481 *Web Site:* www.smurfit.ie, pg 1170

Smurfit Print (Ireland) *Tel:* (01) 202 7000 *Fax:* (01) 269 4481 *Web Site:* www.smurfit.ie, pg 1210

Colin Smythe Ltd (United Kingdom) *Tel:* (01753) 886000 *Fax:* (01753) 886469 *E-mail:* sales@colinsmythe.co.uk *Web Site:* www.colinsmythe.co.uk, pg 753

Snoeck-Ducaju en Zoon NV (Belgium) *Tel:* (09) 267.04.11 *Fax:* (09) 267.04.60 *E-mail:* sdz@sdz.be *Web Site:* www.sdz.be, pg 73

Snofugl Forlag (Norway) *Tel:* 72872411 *Fax:* 72871013 *E-mail:* snofugl@online.no, pg 506

Snowbooks Ltd (United Kingdom) *Tel:* (020) 7553 4473 *Fax:* (020) 7251 3130 *E-mail:* info@snowbooks.com *Web Site:* www.snowbooks.com, pg 753

SNP Best-Set Typesetter Ltd (Hong Kong) *Tel:* 2897 6033 *Fax:* 2897 5170 *E-mail:* bestset@snpcorp.com *Web Site:* www.bestset-typesetter.com, pg 1169, 1209

SNP Best-Set Typesetter Ltd (United States) *Tel:* 914-693-1565 *Toll Free Tel:* 866-888-8767 *Fax:* 914-674-5923 *Web Site:* www.bestset-typesetter.com, pg 1179

SNP Leefung Holdings Ltd (Hong Kong) *Tel:* 2810 6801 *Fax:* 2810 5612 *Web Site:* www.leefung-asco.com, pg 1148

SNP Panpac Pacific Publishing Pte Ltd (Singapore) *Tel:* 6261 6288 *Fax:* 6261 6088 *Web Site:* www.snp.com/sg, pg 553

SNP SPrint Pte Ltd (Singapore) *Tel:* 6741-2500 *Fax:* 6744-7098; 6743-9661 *E-mail:* enquiries@snpcorp.com *Web Site:* www.snpcorp.com, pg 1151

SNP SPrint Pte Ltd (Singapore) *Tel:* 6826-9600 *Fax:* 6820-3341 *E-mail:* enquiries@snpcorp.com *Web Site:* www.snp-corp.com, pg 1172

SNP SPrint Pte Ltd (Singapore) *Tel:* 6741 2500 *Fax:* 6744 3770 *E-mail:* enquiries@snpcorp.com *Web Site:* www.snpcorp.com, pg 1212

SNP SPrint Pte Ltd (Singapore) *Tel:* 6741-2500 *Fax:* 6744-7098 *E-mail:* enquiries@snpcorp.com *Web Site:* www.snpcorp.com, pg 1228, 1236

SNS Foerlag (Sweden) *Tel:* (08) 507 025 00 *Fax:* (08) 507 025 15 *E-mail:* info@sns.se *Web Site:* www.sns.se, pg 610

William Snyder Publishing Associates (United Kingdom) *Tel:* (01865) 513186 *Fax:* (01865) 513186 *E-mail:* snyderpub@aol.com, pg 753

Sober Foerlags AB (Sweden) *Tel:* (08) 672 6000 *Fax:* (08) 672 6001, pg 610

Sobrindes Linha Grafica E Editora Ltda (Brazil) *Tel:* (061) 2247778; (061) 2247706; (061) 2247756 *Fax:* (061) 2241895 *E-mail:* linhagrafica@conectanet.com.br, pg 90

Sobun-Sha (Japan) *Tel:* (03) 3263-7101 *Fax:* (03) 3263-6789 *E-mail:* info@sobunsha.co.jp *Web Site:* www.sobunsha.co.jp, pg 425

Sociaal en Cultureel Planbureau (Netherlands) *Tel:* (070) 3407000 *Fax:* (070) 3407044 *E-mail:* info@scp.ul *Web Site:* www.scp.nl, pg 485

Social Club Books (Australia) *Tel:* (03) 9473 5555 *Fax:* (03) 9417 5574 *E-mail:* info@scb.com.au *Web Site:* www.scb.com.au, pg 41

Social Science Press (Australia) *Tel:* 800-654-831 *Fax:* 800-641-823 *E-mail:* newtext@thomsonlearning. com.au *Web Site:* www.thomsonlearning.com.au/ higher/index.asp, pg 41

Social Sciences Library (Viet Nam) *Tel:* (08) 20644 *Fax:* (08) 223735, pg 1554

Sociedad Biblica Peruana Asociacion Cultural (Peru) *Tel:* (014) 4330232 *Fax:* (014) 4336389 *E-mail:* sbpac01@telemail.telematic.edu.pe, pg 1326

Biblioteca de la Sociedad Cientifica del Paraguay (Paraguay) *Tel:* (021) 24832, pg 1534

Sociedad de Bibliotecarios de Puerto Rico (Puerto Rico) *Tel:* (787) 764-0000 (ext 5205) *Fax:* (787) 764-0000 (ext 5204) *E-mail:* vtorres@upracd.upr.clu.edu *Web Site:* www.geocities.com/sociedadsbpr, pg 1570

Sociedad de Ciencias, Letras y Artes El Museo Canario (Spain) *Tel:* (0928) 336800 *Fax:* (0928) 336801 *E-mail:* info@elmuseocanario.com *Web Site:* www. elmuseocanario.com, pg 1399

Sociedad Editorial Americana (Dominican Republic) *Tel:* 689 7813 *Fax:* 688 9378 *E-mail:* fco.franco@ codetel.net.do, pg 135

Sociedad General de Autores de la Argentina (SGAA) (Argentina) *Tel:* (011) 4811-2582; (011) 4811-9996 *Fax:* (011) 4812-6954 *E-mail:* info@argentores.org.ar *Web Site:* www.argentores.org.ar, pg 1249

Sociedad General Espanola de Libreria SA - SGEL (Spain) *Tel:* (091) 657 69 00 *Fax:* (091) 657 69 28 *Web Site:* www.sgel.es, pg 596

Sociedade Brasileira de Cultura Inglesa - Biblioteca (Brazil) *Tel:* (071) 247-9788 *Fax:* (021) 245-3287 *E-mail:* culturainglesa@br.inter.net *Web Site:* www. culturainglesa-ba.com.br, pg 1494

Sociedade Distribuidora de Livros Ltda (Sodilivro) (Brazil) *Tel:* (021) 580-1168; (021) 580-6230 *Fax:* (021) 580-9955, pg 90

Sociedade Portuguesa de Autores (Portugal) *Tel:* (021) 3594400 *Fax:* (021) 3530257 *E-mail:* geral@ spautores.pt *Web Site:* www.spautores.pt, pg 1398

Societa Dantesca Italiana (Italy) *Tel:* (055) 287134 *Fax:* (055) 211316 *E-mail:* sdi@leonet.it; sdi.biblio@ leonet.it (library) *Web Site:* www.danteonline.it, pg 1396

Societa Editrice Internazionale (SEI) (Italy) *Tel:* (011) 52271 *Fax:* (011) 5211320 *Web Site:* www.seieditrice. com, pg 405

Societa Editrice la Goliardica Pavese SRL (Italy) *Tel:* (0382) 529570 *Fax:* (0382) 423140 *E-mail:* info@lagoliardicapavese.it *Web Site:* www. lagoliardicapavese.it, pg 405

Societa Napoletana Storia Patria Napoli (Italy) *Tel:* (081) 2536340 *Fax:* (081) 2536509 *E-mail:* snsp@unina.it *Web Site:* www.storia.unina.it, pg 405

Societa Stampa Sportiva (Italy) *Tel:* (06) 5817311 *Fax:* (06) 5806526 *E-mail:* segreteria@stampasportiva. com *Web Site:* www.stampasportiva.com, pg 405

Societa Storica Catanese (Italy) *Tel:* (095) 434782, pg 405

Societa Ziaristilor din Romania (Romania) *Tel:* (01) 222 83 51; (01) 222 38 71; (01) 315 24 82 *Fax:* (01) 222 42 66 *E-mail:* szrpress@moon.ro, pg 1272

Societaets-Verlag (Germany) *Tel:* (069) 75 01-0 *Fax:* (069) 75 01-48 77 *Web Site:* www.societaets-verlag.de, pg 281

Societatea de Stiinte Filologice din Romania (SSF) (Romania) *Tel:* (021) 3123148, pg 1398

Societe Africaine d'Edition (Senegal) *Tel:* 217977; 220284, pg 547

La Societe Africaine d'Edition et de Communication (SAEC) (Guinea) *Tel:* 45 34 44 *Fax:* 45 34 44 *E-mail:* dtniane@eti-bull.net, pg 1262

Societe Belge des Auteurs, Compositeurs et Editeurs (SABAM) (Belgium) *Tel:* (02) 286 8211 *Fax:* (02) 230 0589 *E-mail:* info@sabam.de *Web Site:* www. sabam.be, pg 1391

Societe Cherifienne de Distribution et de Presse Sochepress (Morocco) *Tel:* (02) 22400223 *Fax:* (02) 22404032 *E-mail:* infopresse@sochepress.co.ma, pg 1319

Societe de Langue et de Litterature Wallonnes ASBL (Belgium) *Tel:* (086) 344432 *E-mail:* sllw.be@skynet. be *Web Site:* users.skynet.be/sllw, pg 1391

Societe d'Edition d'Afrique Nouvelle (Senegal) *Tel:* (08) 211381; (08) 221580 *Fax:* (08) 223604, pg 547

Societe des Auteurs et Compositeurs Dramatiques (SACD) (France) *Tel:* (01) 40 23 44 44 *Fax:* (01) 45 26 74 28 *E-mail:* infosacd@sacd.fr *Web Site:* www. sacd.fr, pg 1393

Societe des Editions Grasset et Fasquelle (France) *Tel:* (01) 44392200 *Fax:* (01) 42226418 *E-mail:* editorial@grasset.fr *Web Site:* www.grasset.fr, pg 185

Societe des Editions Privat SA (France) *Tel:* (05) 34 31 81 81; (05) 34 31 81 88 *Fax:* (05) 34 31 64 44 *E-mail:* editionsprivat@wanadoo.fr, pg 185

Societe des Gens de Lettres de France (France) *Tel:* (01) 53 10 12 00 *Fax:* (01) 53 10 12 12 *E-mail:* depot. sgdlf@wanadoo.fr *Web Site:* www.sgdl.org, pg 1393

Societe des Libraires et Editeurs de la Suisse Romande (SLESR) (Switzerland) *Tel:* (021) 319 71 11 *Fax:* (021) 319 79 10 *E-mail:* aself@centrezational. cl *Web Site:* www.culturactif.ch/editions/asef1.htm, pg 1276

la Societe des Poetes Francais (France) *Tel:* (01) 40 46 99 82 *Fax:* (01) 40 46 99 11 *E-mail:* poetesfrancais@ aol.com *Web Site:* www.societedespoetesfrancais.asso. fr, pg 1393

Societe d'Etudes Dantesques (France) *Tel:* 497134610; 497134611 *Fax:* 497134640 *E-mail:* cum@ville-nice.fr *Web Site:* www.cum-nice.org, pg 1394

Societe d'Histoire Litteraire de la France (France) *Tel:* (01) 45872330 *Fax:* (01) 45872330 *E-mail:* srhlf@aol.com, pg 1394

Societe Ennewrasse Service Librairie et Imprimerie (Morocco) *Tel:* (077) 6413 *Fax:* (077) 6413, pg 471

Societe Francaise des Traducteurs (France) *Tel:* (01) 48 78 43 32 *Fax:* (01) 44 53 01 14 *E-mail:* sft@tiscali.fr *Web Site:* www.sft.fr, pg 1137

Societe Internationale des Bibliotheques et des Musees des Arts du Spectacle (SIBMAS) (United Kingdom) *Tel:* (020) 7943 4720 *Fax:* (020) 7943 4777 *Web Site:* www.theatrelibrary.org/sibmas/sibmas.html, pg 1283

Societe Mathematique de France - Institut Henri Poincare (France) *Tel:* (01) 44 27 67 96 *Fax:* (01) 40 46 90 96 *E-mail:* smf@dma.ens.fr *Web Site:* smf. emath.fr, pg 186

Societe Nationale d'Edition et de Diffusion (Tunisia) *Tel:* 71255000; 71261799, pg 1337

Society for Editors & Proofreaders (United Kingdom) *Tel:* (020) 7736 3278 *Fax:* (020) 7736 3318 *E-mail:* administration@sfep.org.uk *Web Site:* www. sfep.org.uk, pg 1403

Society for Endocrinology (United Kingdom) *Tel:* (01454) 642200 *Fax:* (01454) 642222 *E-mail:* info@endocrinology.org; sales@ endocrinology.org *Web Site:* www.endocrinology.org, pg 754

Society for Macedonian Studies (Greece) *Tel:* 2310 268710 *Fax:* 2310971501 *E-mail:* ems@hyper.gr, pg 309

The Society for Promoting Christian Knowledge (SPCK) (United Kingdom) *Tel:* (020) 7592 3900 *Fax:* (020) 7592 3939 *E-mail:* spck@spck.org.uk *Web Site:* www. spck.org.uk, pg 754

Society for the Promotion of African, Asian & Latin American Literature (Germany) *Tel:* (069) 2102247 *Fax:* (069) 2102227 *E-mail:* litprom@book-fair.com *Web Site:* www.litprom.de, pg 1122

Society for the Study of Medieval Languages & Literature (United Kingdom) *Tel:* (01865) 276087 *Fax:* (01865) 276087 *Web Site:* www.mod-langs.ox. ac.uk/ssmll, pg 1403

Society of Archivists (United Kingdom) *Tel:* (01823) 327030 *Fax:* (01823) 371719 *E-mail:* offman@ archives.org.uk *Web Site:* www.archives.org.uk, pg 1573

Society of Arts, Literature & Welfare (Bangladesh) *Web Site:* www.bjfao.gov.cn, pg 1390

Society of Authors (United Kingdom) *Tel:* (020) 7373 6642 *Fax:* (020) 7373 5768 *E-mail:* info@ societyofauthors.org *Web Site:* www.societyofauthors. net, pg 1154, 1283

Society of College, National & University Libraries (SCONUL) (United Kingdom) *Tel:* (020) 7387 0317 *Fax:* (020) 7383 3197 *E-mail:* info@sconul.ac.uk *Web Site:* www.sconul.ac.uk, pg 1573

The Society of County Librarians (United Kingdom) *Tel:* (01933) 231971 *Fax:* (01933) 231762 *E-mail:* enquiries@c2portal.com *Web Site:* www. connect2northamptonshire.com, pg 1573

Society of Indexers (United Kingdom) *Tel:* (0114) 292 2350 *Fax:* (0114) 292 2351 *E-mail:* admin@indexers. org.uk *Web Site:* www.socind.demon.co.uk, pg 1283

The Society of Mctaphysicians Ltd (United Kingdom) *Tel:* (01424) 751577 *Fax:* (01424) 751577 *E-mail:* newmeta@btinternet.com; info@ metaphysicians.org.uk *Web Site:* www.newmeta. btinternet.co.uk; www.metaphysicians.org.uk; metaphysicalresearchgroup.org.uk, pg 754

The Society of Women Writers & Journalists (United Kingdom) *Tel:* (01379) 740550 *Fax:* (01379) 741716 *Web Site:* www.swwj.co.uk, pg 1403

Society of Women Writers NSW Inc (Australia) *Tel:* (03) 63310267 *Web Site:* www.womenwritersnsw.org, pg 1250

SocTip SA (Portugal) *Tel:* (021) 263 00 99 00 *Fax:* (021) 263 00 99 99 *E-mail:* soctip@soctip.pt *Web Site:* www.soctip.pt, pg 531

Edizioni Rosminiane Sodalitas (Italy) *Tel:* (0323) 30091 *Fax:* (0323) 31623 *E-mail:* edizioni@rosmini.it *Web Site:* www.rosmini.it/EdRosminiane.htm, pg 405

Soderstroms Forlag (Finland) *Tel:* (09) 6841 8620 *Fax:* (09) 6841 8621 *E-mail:* soderstrom@soderstrom. fi *Web Site:* www.soderstrom.fi, pg 144

Sodilivros (Portugal) *Tel:* (021) 658902 *Fax:* (021) 3876281 *E-mail:* sodilivros@mail.telepac.pt, pg 1329

Soemwit Bannakhan (Thailand) *Tel:* (02) 214541, pg 641

Soez Yayin/Oyunajans (Turkey) *Tel:* (0212) 2806701 *Fax:* (0212) 2806803 *Web Site:* www.oyunajans.com, pg 647

Sofa (Slovakia) *Tel:* (02) 55422508 *Fax:* (02) 55422508 *E-mail:* sofa@ba.sknet.sk, pg 556

Sofia City & District State Archives (Bulgaria) *Tel:* (02) 940 01 06 *Fax:* (02) 980 14 43 *Web Site:* www. archives.government.bg, pg 1495

Sofia University Kliment Ohridski Biblioteka (Bulgaria) *Tel:* (02) 467584; (02) 9308554; (02) 9308209 *Fax:* (02) 467170 *E-mail:* lsu@libsu.uni-sofia.bg *Web Site:* www.libsu.uni-sofia.bg, pg 1495

Sofiac (Societe Francaise des Imprimeries Administratives Centrales) (France) *Tel:* (01) 40 64 42 42 *Fax:* (01) 40 64 42 40 *E-mail:* ble@berger-levrault.fr *Web Site:* www.editions.berger-levrault.fr, pg 186

Sofiprin (Czech Republic) *Tel:* (0602) 30 87 21 *Fax:* (02) 758280, pg 127

Sogang University Press (Republic of Korea) *Tel:* (02) 705-8213 *Fax:* (02) 705-0797 *E-mail:* chisook@ccs. sogang.ac.kr *Web Site:* www.sogang.ac.kr, pg 439

Sogensha Publishing Co Ltd (Japan) *Tel:* (06) 62319011 *Fax:* (06) 62333112 *E-mail:* sgse@email.msn.com *Web Site:* www.sogensha.co.jp, pg 425

Sohaksa (Republic of Korea) *Tel:* (02) 7967600 *Fax:* (02) 7968700, pg 439

Verlag SOI (Schweizerisches Ost-Institut) (Switzerland) *Tel:* (031) 431212 *Fax:* (031) 3513801, pg 630

Sojuz na drustvata za makedonski jazik i literatura (Serbia and Montenegro), pg 1398

Sokoine University of Agriculture Library (United Republic of Tanzania) *Tel:* (056) 3510; (056) 3514 *E-mail:* usa@hnettan.gri.apc.org, pg 1548

Soldi-Verlag im Drockzentrum Harburg (Germany) *Tel:* (04181) 29 16 22 *Fax:* (04181) 29 16 23 *E-mail:* kontakt@karismaverlag.de *Web Site:* www. karismaverlag.de, pg 281

Il Sole 24 Ore Libri (Italy) *Tel:* (02) 30223944 *Fax:* (02) 3022405 *E-mail:* servizioclienti.libri@ilsole24ore.com *Web Site:* www.ilsole24ore.com, pg 405

Il Sole 24 Ore Pirola (Italy) *Tel:* (02) 30226651 *Fax:* (02) 38011205 *E-mail:* servizio.abbonamenti@ ilsole24ore.com *Web Site:* www.ilsole24ore.com, pg 405

Editions du Soleil (Haiti) *Tel:* (01) 23147, pg 311

Solidaridad Publishing House (Philippines) *Tel:* (02) 586581; (02) 591241 *Fax:* (02) 525-5038, pg 516

Editions Soline (France) *Tel:* (01) 43 33 74 24 *Fax:* (01) 43 33 67 37 *E-mail:* contact@soline.fr *Web Site:* perso.wanadoo.fr/soline, pg 186

Solivros (Portugal) *Tel:* (0252) 42385, pg 531

Solum Forlag A/S (Norway) *Tel:* (022) 50 04 00 *Fax:* (022) 50 14 53 *E-mail:* solumfor@online.no *Web Site:* www.solumforlag.no, pg 506

Somaiya Publications Pvt Ltd (India) *Tel:* (022) 2048272 *Fax:* (022) 2047297 *Web Site:* www.somaiya.com, pg 346

Michael Somare Library (Papua New Guinea) *Tel:* 326 7280 *Fax:* 326 7187 *E-mail:* Library@upng.ac.pg *Web Site:* www.theatrelibrary.org, pg 1534

Somawathi Hewavitharana Fund (Sri Lanka) *Tel:* (01) 698079, pg 602

Somerset Publications (Australia) *Tel:* (07) 3425 1857 *Fax:* (07) 3425 1857 *E-mail:* info@ crabbetarabian.com; crabbetarabian@hotkey.net.au *Web Site:* www.crabbetarabian.com; www.hotkey.net. au/~crabbetarabian, pg 41

Sommer & Sorensen (Denmark) *Tel:* 36153615 *Fax:* 36153616 *E-mail:* post@borgen.dk, pg 134

Somogy editions d'art (France) *Tel:* (01) 48 05 70 10 *Fax:* (01) 48 05 71 70 *E-mail:* somogy@magic.fr, pg 186

Edizioni Sonda (Italy) *Tel:* (0142) 461516 *Fax:* (0142) 461523 *E-mail:* sonda@sonda.it *Web Site:* www.sonda. it, pg 405

Sonnentanz-Verlag Roland Kron (Germany) *Tel:* (0821) 311070 *Fax:* (0821) 158979 *E-mail:* sonnentanz@t-online.de, pg 281

Sonneville Press (Uitgeverij) VTW (Belgium) *Tel:* (050) 321112, pg 73

Johannes Sonntag Verlagsbuchhandlung GmbH (Germany) *Tel:* (0711) 8931-0 *Fax:* (0711) 8931-706 *Web Site:* www.sonntag-verlag.com, pg 281

Sony Magazines Inc (Japan) *Tel:* (03) 3234-5811 *Fax:* (03) 3234-5842 *Web Site:* www.sonymagazines. jp, pg 425

Sonzogno (Italy) *Tel:* (02) 50951 *Fax:* (02) 5065361 *Web Site:* www.sonzogno.rcslibri.it, pg 405

Editorial Sopena Argentina SACI e I (Argentina) *Tel:* (011) 4912-2383 *Fax:* (011) 4912-2383 *E-mail:* edsopena@elsitio.net, pg 9

Ramon Sopena SA (Spain) *Tel:* (093) 3220035 *Fax:* (093) 3223703 *E-mail:* edsopena@teleline.es, pg 596

Sophia Book Service (Republic of Korea) *Tel:* (02) 362-2036 *Fax:* (02) 362-2036, pg 1315

Educatieve Uitgeverij Sorava (Suriname) *Tel:* 483879 *Web Site:* www.icpcredit.com, pg 603

Sorbona (Italy) *Tel:* (08) 15453443 *Fax:* (08) 15464991, pg 405

Bibliotheque de la Sorbonne (France) *Tel:* (01) 40 46 30 27 *Fax:* (01) 40 46 30 44 *E-mail:* adminst@ biu.sorbonne.fr *Web Site:* www.sorbonne.fr; www. sorbonne.fr/BIU.html, pg 1506

Publications de la Sorbonne (France) *Tel:* (01) 43 25 80 15 *Fax:* (01) 43 54 03 24 *E-mail:* publisor@univ-paris1.fr *Web Site:* www.univ-paris1.fr/recherche/ rubrique46.html, pg 186

Association d'Editions Sorg (France) *Tel:* (01) 48252524 *Fax:* (01) 46052563, pg 186

Soryusha (Japan) *Tel:* (03) 32631471 *Fax:* (03) 32632943, pg 425

Editions SOS (Editions du Secours Catholique) (France) *Tel:* (01) 40 35 44 65 *Fax:* (01) 40 35 42 73, pg 186

Soshisha Co Ltd (Japan) *Tel:* (03) 3476-6565 *Fax:* (03) 3470-2640 *E-mail:* soshisha@magical.egg.or.jp, pg 425

Sota Graphic Arts Co Ltd (Hong Kong) *Tel:* 23421083 *Fax:* 23415426 *E-mail:* sales@goldencup.com.hk *Web Site:* www.goldencup.com.hk, pg 1169

Sota Graphic Arts Co Ltd (Hong Kong) *Tel:* 23434254 *Fax:* 23415426 *E-mail:* sales@goldencup.com.hk *Web Site:* www.goldencup.com.hk, pg 1209

Souffles (France) *Tel:* (01) 45 36 44 30 *Fax:* (01) 45 36 44 39, pg 186

Soundbooks (Australia) *Tel:* (03) 98247711 *Fax:* (03) 98247855 *E-mail:* audio@soundbooks.com.au *Web Site:* www.soundbooks.com.au, pg 1289

Les Editions de la Source Sarl (France) *Tel:* (01) 45 25 30 07, pg 186

Sousa & Almeida Livraria (Portugal) *Tel:* (022) 2050073 *Fax:* (022) 2050073 *E-mail:* sousaealmeida@net. sapo.pt; geral@sousaealmeida.com *Web Site:* www. sousaealmeida.com, pg 531

Livraria Sousa e Almeida Lda (Portugal) *Tel:* (022) 2050073 *Fax:* (022) 2050073 *E-mail:* sousaealmeida@ net.sapo.pt; geral@sousaealmeida.com *Web Site:* www. sousaealmeida.com, pg 1329

South African Booksellers' Association (South Africa) *Tel:* (021) 918 8616 *Fax:* (021) 951 4903 *E-mail:* fnel@naspers.com *Web Site:* sabooksellers. com, pg 1274

South African Extension Unit (United Republic of Tanzania) *Tel:* (051) 150314; (051) 150346 *Fax:* (051) 150346 *E-mail:* saeu@intafrica.com *Web Site:* www. saide.org.za/worldbank/countries/tanzania/saeu.htm, pg 639

South African Institute of International Affairs (South Africa) *Tel:* (011) 339 2021 *Fax:* (011) 339 2154 *E-mail:* saiiagen@global.co.za *Web Site:* www.wits. ac.za/saiia, pg 564

South African Institute of Race Relations (South Africa) *Tel:* (011) 403-3600 *Fax:* (011) 403-3671; (011) 339-2061 *E-mail:* sairr@sairr.org.za *Web Site:* www.sairr. org.za, pg 564

South African Library for the Blind (South Africa) *Tel:* (046) 622 7226 *Fax:* (046) 622 4645 *E-mail:* blindlib@iafrica.com *Web Site:* www.blindlib. org.za, pg 1543

South Asia Publications (India) *Tel:* (011) 7241869; (011) 7235539, pg 346

South Asian Publishers Pvt Ltd (India) *Tel:* (011) 276292; (011) 276740 *E-mail:* vchigs@giasdla.vsnl. net.in, pg 346

South Australian Government-Department of Education, Training & Employment (Australia) *Tel:* (08) 8226 1527 *E-mail:* www.decscustomrs@saugov.sa.gov.au, pg 41

South China Morning Post Ltd (Hong Kong) *Tel:* 2680 8888 *Web Site:* www.scmp.com, pg 316

South China Printing Co (1988) Ltd (Hong Kong) *Tel:* 26373611 *Fax:* 26374221 *E-mail:* info@singtao. com *Web Site:* www.nysingtao.com, pg 1148

South China University of Science & Technology Press (China) *Tel:* (020) 87113489; (020) 87113484, pg 108

South East Asian Central Banks (SEACEN) Research & Training Centre (Malaysia) *Tel:* (03) 7958 5600 *Fax:* (03) 7957 4616 *E-mail:* info@seacen.org *Web Site:* www.seacen.org, pg 1525

South Head Press (Australia) *Tel:* (07) 5526 4670, pg 41

South Pacific Association for Commonwealth Literature & Language Studies (SPACLALS) (New Zealand) *Tel:* (07) 838-4466 *Fax:* (07) 838 4722, pg 1270

South Pacific Books Imports Ltd (New Zealand) *Tel:* (09) 649 448 1591 *Fax:* (09) 649 448 1592 *E-mail:* sales@soupacbooks.co.nz *Web Site:* www. soupacbooks.co.nz, pg 1322

University of the South Pacific (Fiji) *Tel:* (033) 3232077 *Fax:* (033) 3232038 *Web Site:* www.usp.ac.fj, pg 141

South Sea Books (New Zealand) *Tel:* (03) 3317630 *E-mail:* southsea@ihug.co.nz *Web Site:* www. abebooks.com/home/southsea, pg 1322

South Sea International Press Ltd (Hong Kong) *Tel:* 2897 1083 *Fax:* 2558 1473 *E-mail:* books@ssip. com.hk *Web Site:* www.ssip.com.hk, pg 1148, 1169

South Sea International Press Ltd (Hong Kong) *Tel:* 2897 1083 *Fax:* 2558 1473 *E-mail:* ssiphk@hk. super.net, pg 1209

Southeast Asian Ministers of Education Organization Regional Language Centre (SEAMEO RELC) (Thailand) *Tel:* (02) 3910144; (02) 3910554; (02) 3916413 *Fax:* (02) 3812587 *E-mail:* secretariat@ seameo.org *Web Site:* www.seameo.org, pg 1278

Southeast Asian Regional Branch of the International Council on Archives (SARBICA) (Malaysia) *Tel:* (03) 62010688 *Fax:* (03) 62015679 *Web Site:* arkib.gov. my/sarbica/index.html; www.arkib.gov.my, pg 1267

Southern Book Publishers (Pty) Ltd (South Africa) *Tel:* (011) 8072292 *Fax:* (011) 8070506 *E-mail:* reneef@struik.co.za, pg 564

Southern Cross PR & Press Services (Australia) *Tel:* (02) 6737 5436 *Fax:* (02) 6737 5436, pg 41

Southern Press Ltd (New Zealand) *Tel:* (04) 233-1899, pg 497

Southgate Publishers (United Kingdom) *Tel:* (01363) 776888 *Fax:* (01363) 776889 *E-mail:* info@ southgatepublishers.co.uk *Web Site:* www. southgatepublishers.co.uk, pg 754

Southwest China Jiaotong University Press (China) *Tel:* (028) 784160-763 *Fax:* (028) 24377 *E-mail:* swju@swjtu.edu.cn, pg 108

Southwood Press Pty Ltd (Australia) *Tel:* (02) 9560 5100 *Fax:* (02) 9550 0097 *E-mail:* info@southwoodpress. com.au *Web Site:* www.southwoodpress.com.au, pg 1205

Souvenir Press Ltd (United Kingdom) *Tel:* (01235) 400400 *Fax:* (01235) 400500 *E-mail:* orders@ bookpoint.co.uk, pg 754

Sovereign World Ltd (United Kingdom) *Tel:* (01732) 850598 *Fax:* (01732) 851077 *E-mail:* sovereignworldbooks@compuserve.com *Web Site:* www.sovereign-world.org, pg 754

Izdatelstvo Sovetskii Pisatel (Russian Federation) *Tel:* (095) 209 2384; (095) 209 4105; (095) 209 1942 *Fax:* (095) 2023200, pg 544

Sovremennik Publishers Too (Russian Federation) *Tel:* (095) 9412992 *Fax:* (095) 9413544, pg 544

SP Interbuk, Russian-Slovenien jv (Russian Federation) *Tel:* (095) 9245081 *Fax:* (095) 2002281; (095) 2302403, pg 544

SPA Books Ltd (United Kingdom) *Tel:* (01293) 552727 *Fax:* (01438) 310104 *E-mail:* strongoakpress@hotmail. com, pg 754

Space Sellers Ltd (Kenya) *Tel:* (02) 555811; (02) 557517; (02) 557863 *Fax:* (02) 557815; (02) 558847 *E-mail:* sstms@africaonline.co.ke, pg 432

Spacevision Publishing (Australia) *Tel:* (03) 5127 2398, pg 41

Spala Editora Ltda (Brazil) *Tel:* (021) 542-9995 *Fax:* (021) 542-4738, pg 90

Spaniel Books (Australia) *Tel:* (02) 9360 9985 *Fax:* (02) 9331 4653 *E-mail:* spanielbooks@hotmail.com, pg 41

Vivliofilia K Ch Spanos (Greece) *Tel:* 210 3623917; 2103614332 *Fax:* 2108953076 *E-mail:* biblioph@otenet.gr, pg 309

Specialist Publications (Australia) *Tel:* (02) 9736 2191 *Fax:* (02) 9736 2663, pg 41

SpectraComp (United States) *Tel:* 717-697-8600 *Toll Free Tel:* 800-666-2662 *Fax:* 717-691-0433 *E-mail:* info@spectracomp.com *Web Site:* www. spectracomp.com, pg 1179

Spectres Familiers (France) *Tel:* (0491) 912645 *Fax:* (0491) 909951, pg 186

Spectrum Books Ltd (Nigeria) *Tel:* (02) 2310058; (02) 2311215; (02) 2312705 *Fax:* (02) 2312705; (02) 2318502 *E-mail:* admin1@spectrumbooksonline.com *Web Site:* www.spectrumbooksonline.com, pg 502

Uitgeverij Het Spectrum BV (Netherlands) *Tel:* (030) 2650650 *Fax:* (030) 2620850 *E-mail:* het@spectrum.nl *Web Site:* www.spectrum.nl, pg 485

Spectrum Publications (Australia) *Tel:* (03) 9415 9750 *Fax:* (03) 9419 0783 *E-mail:* spectrum@ spectrumpublications.com.au *Web Site:* www. spectrumpublications.com.au, pg 41

Spectrum Publications (India) *Tel:* (0361) 26381; (0361) 24791 *Fax:* (0361) 544791, pg 346

Speechmark Publishing Ltd (United Kingdom) *Tel:* (01869) 244644 *Fax:* (01869) 320040 *E-mail:* info@speechmark.net *Web Site:* www. speechmark.net, pg 754

Speedflex Asia Ltd (Hong Kong) *Tel:* 2542 2780 *Fax:* 2542 3733 *E-mail:* info@speedflex.com.hk *Web Site:* www.speedflex.com.hk, pg 1148, 1209, 1226

Speer -Verlag (Switzerland) *Tel:* (01) 341 42 56; (01) 262 33 91 *Fax:* (01) 342 45 31, pg 630

Bokforlaget Spektra AB (Sweden) *Tel:* (035) 360 30 *Fax:* (035) 361 77, pg 610

Spektrum der Wissenschaft Verlagsgesellschaft mbH (Germany) *Tel:* (06221) 9126600 *Fax:* (06221) 9126751 *E-mail:* marketing@spektrum.com *Web Site:* www.spektrum.de, pg 281

Spektrum Forlagsaktieselskab (Denmark) *Tel:* 33 32 63 22 *Fax:* 33 32 64 54, pg 134

Spellbound Promotions (Australia) *Tel:* (066) 542133 *Fax:* (066) 541258 *E-mail:* Jodiadv@oncs.com.au, pg 41

Spellmount Ltd Publishers (United Kingdom) *Tel:* (01892) 837171 *Fax:* (01892) 837272 *E-mail:* enquiries@spellmount.com, pg 754

Spengler Editeur (France) *Tel:* (01) 49 70 15 55 *Fax:* (01) 49 70 15 50, pg 186

Sperling e Kupfer Editori SpA (Italy) *Tel:* (02) 217211 *Fax:* (02) 21721277 *Web Site:* www.sperling.it, pg 405

Libreria Internazionale Sperling e Kupfer (Italy) *Tel:* (02) 21721-1 *Fax:* (02) 21721-277 *Web Site:* www.sperling. it, pg 1311

SPES Editorial SL (Spain) *Tel:* (093) 2413505 *Fax:* (093) 2413511 *E-mail:* vox@vox.es *Web Site:* www.vox.es, pg 596

Speurwerk Stitching betreffende het Boek (Netherlands) *Tel:* (020) 625 49 27 *Fax:* (020) 620 88 71 *E-mail:* info@speurwerk.kvb.nl *Web Site:* www. speurwerk.nl, pg 1269

Sphinx Publishing Co (Egypt (Arab Republic of Egypt)) *Tel:* (02) 392 4616 *Fax:* (02) 391 8802 *E-mail:* sphinx@intouch.com, pg 138

Sphinx Verlag AG (Switzerland) *Tel:* (061) 2619292 *Fax:* (061) 2629221 *E-mail:* sphinx@sphinx-book.ch *Web Site:* www.sphinx-book.ch, pg 630

Spiegel-Verlag Rudolf Augstein GmbH & Co KG (Germany) *Tel:* (040) 3007-0 *Fax:* (040) 3007-2247 *E-mail:* spiegel@spiegel.de, pg 281

Spiess Volker Wissenschaftsverlag GmbH (Germany) *Tel:* (030) 6917073-74 *Fax:* (030) 6914067, pg 281

Wissenschaftsverlag Volker Spiess Gmbh (Germany) *Tel:* (030) 6917073 *Fax:* (030) 6914067 *E-mail:* info@ spiess-verlage.de *Web Site:* www.spiess-verlage.de, pg 281

Spieth-Verlag Verlag fuer Symbolforschung (Germany) *Tel:* (0331) 2705199 *Fax:* (0331) 2010849, pg 281

Spinal Publications New Zealand Ltd (New Zealand) *Tel:* (04) 2937020 *Fax:* (04) 2932897 *E-mail:* enquiries@spinalpublications.co.nz *Web Site:* www.spinalpublications.co.nz, pg 497

Spindulys Printing House (Lithuania) *Tel:* (037) 226243 *Fax:* (037) 208 420 *E-mail:* repro@spindulys.lt *Web Site:* www.spindulys.lt, pg 1149

Spindulys Printing House (Lithuania) *Tel:* (037) 226243; (037) 386737 *Fax:* (037) 204970 *E-mail:* spindul@ kaunas.aiva.lt, pg 1171

Spindulys Printing House (Lithuania) *Tel:* (037) 226243 *Fax:* (037) 204970 *E-mail:* spaustuve@spindulys.lt *Web Site:* www.spindulys.lt, pg 1211

Spinifex Press (Australia) *Tel:* (03) 9329-6088 *Fax:* (03) 9329-9238 *E-mail:* women@spinifexpress.com.au *Web Site:* www.spinifexpress.com.au, pg 41

Spirali Edizioni (Italy) *Tel:* (02) 8054417; (02) 8053602 *Fax:* (02) 8692631 *E-mail:* redazione@spirali.com *Web Site:* www.spirali.it; www.spirali.com, pg 405

Spiridon-Verlags GmbH (Germany) *Tel:* (02104) 47260 *Fax:* (0211) 786823, pg 281

Spokesman (United Kingdom) *Tel:* (0115) 9708318; (0115) 9784504 *Fax:* (0115) 9420433 *E-mail:* elfeuro@compuserve.com *Web Site:* www. spokesmanbooks.com; www.russfound.org, pg 755

Spoleczny Instytut Wydawniczy Znak (Poland) *Tel:* (012) 4291469; (012) 4219776 *Fax:* (012) 4219814 *E-mail:* rucinska@znak.com.pl *Web Site:* www.znak. com.pl, pg 522

Spolok slovenskych spisovatel'ov (Slovakia) *Tel:* (07) 533 53 71, pg 1273

Spon Press (United Kingdom) *Tel:* (020) 7583 9855 *Fax:* (020) 7842 2298 *E-mail:* info@routledge.co.uk *Web Site:* www.sponpress.com, pg 755

Adolf Sponholtz Verlag (Germany) *Tel:* (05151) 200312 *Fax:* (05151) 200319 *Web Site:* www.niemeyer-buch. de, pg 281

Sport & Hobby Book Club (Greece) *Tel:* 2103234217 *Fax:* 2103232082 *E-mail:* hcp@photography.gr, pg 1243

Sport Publishing House Ltd (Slovakia) *Tel:* (02) 69674; (02) 69223; (02) 69235; (02) 69240 *Fax:* (02) 6919 560324, pg 556

Sports Turf Research Institute (STRI) (United Kingdom) *Tel:* (01274) 565131 *Fax:* (01274) 561891 *E-mail:* info@stri.co.uk *Web Site:* www.stri.co.uk, pg 755

The Sportsman's Press (United Kingdom) *Tel:* (020) 8789 0229 *Fax:* (020) 8789 0229, pg 755

Sportverlag Berlin GmbH SVB (Germany) *Tel:* (030) 8973666 *Fax:* (030) 2591-3516 *E-mail:* marketing@ sportverlag-berlin.de, pg 282

Spotdzielna Anagram (Poland) *Tel:* (022) 6229324; (022) 6229326, pg 522

Editions Spratbrow (France) *Tel:* (01) 30 14 19 30 *Fax:* (01) 34 60 31 32, pg 186

Spraymation Inc (United States) *Tel:* 954-484-9700 *Toll Free Tel:* 800-327-4985 *Fax:* 954-484-9778 *E-mail:* sales@spraymation.com *Web Site:* www. spraymation.com, pg 1221

Spriditis Publishers (Latvia) *Tel:* (02) 7286516 *Fax:* (02) 7286818, pg 442

Axel Springer Publicaciones (Spain) *Tel:* (091) 5140600 *Fax:* (091) 5140624, pg 596

Axel Springer Verlag AG (Germany) *Tel:* (040) 347-00 *Fax:* (040) 345811 *E-mail:* information@axelspringer. de *Web Site:* www.asv.de, pg 282

Editions Springer France (France) *Tel:* (01) 5393 3647 *Fax:* (01) 53933729 *Web Site:* www.springer-paris.fr, pg 186

Springer Science+Business Media GmbH & Co KG (Germany) *Tel:* (06221) 487-0 *Fax:* (06221) 487-8366 *E-mail:* orders@springer.de *Web Site:* www.springer. de, pg 282

Springer Science+Business Media GmbH & Co KG, Berlin (Germany) *Tel:* (030) 82787-0; (030) 82787 5282 (press & public relations) *Fax:* (030) 8214091; (030) 82787 5707 (press & public relations) *E-mail:* press@springer-sbm.com *Web Site:* www. springer-sbm.de, pg 282

Springer Tudomanyos Kiado Kft (Hungary) *Tel:* (01) 2664776, pg 321

Springer-Verlag Hong Kong Ltd (Hong Kong) *Tel:* 27 23 96 98 *Fax:* 27 24 23 66, pg 316

Springer-Verlag Iberica, SA (Spain) *Tel:* (093) 4570227; (093) 4570759 *Fax:* (093) 4571502 *E-mail:* springer. bcn@springer.es, pg 596

Springer-Verlag London Ltd (United Kingdom) *Tel:* (0483) 418800; (01483) 418822 (sales) *Fax:* (01483) 415151; (01483) 415144 *E-mail:* orders@springer.de, pg 755

Springer-Verlag Tokyo (Japan) *Tel:* (03) 3812-0757 *Fax:* (03) 3812-0719 *Web Site:* www.springer-tokyo. co.jp/, pg 425

Springer-Verlag Wien (Austria) *Tel:* (01) 3302415 *Fax:* (01) 3302426 *E-mail:* books@springer.at (orders); journals@springer.at (orders) *Web Site:* www. springer.at, pg 57

Springfield Books Ltd (United Kingdom) *Tel:* (01484) 864955 *Fax:* (01484) 865443, pg 1344

SPS Verlaggsservice GmbH (Germany) *Tel:* (0261) 80706-0 *Fax:* (0261) 80706-54, pg 1301

Barbara Spurll Illustration (Canada) *Tel:* 416-594-6594 *E-mail:* bspurll@yahoo.ca *Web Site:* www. barbaraspurll.com, pg 1166

Spyropoulos A (Greece) *Tel:* 2106712991 *Fax:* 2106719622, pg 309

Square Dance Partners Forlag (Denmark) *Tel:* 45 83 99 83, pg 134

Square One Publications (United Kingdom) *Tel:* (01684) 593704 *Fax:* (01684) 594640, pg 755

Square Two Design Inc (United States) *Tel:* 415-437-3888 *Fax:* 415-437-3880 *E-mail:* sq2d@square2.com *Web Site:* www.square2.com, pg 1179

Sraka International (Slovenia), pg 1331

Arhiv Srbije (Serbia and Montenegro) *Tel:* (011) 33-70-781; (011) 33-70-782; (011) 33-70-879; (011) 33-70-880 *Fax:* (011) 33-70-246 *E-mail:* office@archives. org.yu *Web Site:* www.archives.org.yu, pg 1540

Srebaren lav (Bulgaria) *Tel:* (02) 752298, pg 96

Y Sreberk (Israel) *Tel:* (03) 6293343 *Fax:* (03) 6299297, pg 369

Sredne-Uralskoye knizhnoye izdatelstve (Middle Urals Publishing House) (Russian Federation) *Tel:* (03432) 514162 *Fax:* (03432) 512859, pg 544

Sree Rama Publishers (India) *Tel:* (040) 2522609 *E-mail:* thehindu@usnl.com *Web Site:* www. hinduonnet.com, pg 346

SRHE (United Kingdom) *Tel:* (020) 7637 2766 *Fax:* (020) 7637 2781 *E-mail:* srheoffice@srhe.ac.uk *Web Site:* www.srhe.ac.uk, pg 755

Sri Lanka Association of Publishers (Sri Lanka) *Tel:* (01) 695773 *Fax:* (01) 696653, pg 1274

Sri Lanka Jama'ath-e-Islami (Sri Lanka) *Tel:* (01) 687091 *Fax:* (01) 686030, pg 602

Sri Lanka Library Association (Sri Lanka) *Tel:* (011) 2589103 *Fax:* (011) 2589103 *E-mail:* slla@operamail. com *Web Site:* www.naresa.ac.lk/slla; www.nsf.ac. lk/slla, pg 1571

Sri Satguru Publications (India) *Tel:* (011) 27126497; (011) 27434930 *Fax:* (011) 27227336 *E-mail:* ibcindia@giasdlo1.vsnl.net.in or ibcindia@ ibcindia.com, pg 347

Srinakharinwirot University, Central Library (Thailand) *Tel:* (02) 2584002 (ext 160, 161, 162); (02) 2584003 (ext 160, 161, 162); (02) 6641000 (ext 5382) *Fax:* (02) 2604514; (02) 2584002 *E-mail:* library@ swu.ac.th *Web Site:* www.swu.ac.th/lib, pg 1548

Srpska Knjizevna Zadruga (Serbia and Montenegro) *Tel:* (011) 330 305 *Fax:* (011) 626-224, pg 549

Biblioteka Srpske Akademije Nauka i Umetnosti (Serbia and Montenegro) *Tel:* (011) 33-42-400 *Fax:* (011) 639-120 *E-mail:* admin@bib.sanu.ac.yu *Web Site:* www.bib.sanu.ac.yu, pg 1540

L Staackmann Verlag KG (Germany) *Tel:* (08027) 337; (089) 342248 *Fax:* (08027) 816, pg 283

Staatliche Museen Kassel (Germany) *Tel:* (0561) 316-800 *Fax:* (0561) 31680-111 *E-mail:* info@museum-kassel.de *Web Site:* www.museum-kassel.de, pg 283

Staats- und Universitaetsbibliothek Hamburg Carl von Ossietzky (Germany) *Tel:* (040) 42838-2233 *Fax:* (040) 42838-3352 *E-mail:* auskunft@sub.uni-hamburg.de *Web Site:* www.sub.uni-hamburg.de, pg 1508

Staats- und Universitatsbibliothek Bremen (Germany) *Tel:* (0421) 2182615 *Fax:* (0421) 2182614 *E-mail:* suub@suub.uni-bremen.de *Web Site:* www. suub.uni-bremen.de, pg 1508

Staatsbibliothek zu Berlin - Preussischer Kulturbesitz (Germany) *Tel:* (030) 266-0 *E-mail:* webserveradmin@sbb.spk-berlin. de *Web Site:* www.sbb.spk-berlin.de; www. staatsbibliothek-berlin.de, pg 283

Staatsbibliothek zu Berlin - Preussischer Kulturbesitz (Germany) *Tel:* (030) 266-0 *Web Site:* www. staatsbibliothek-berlin.de; www.sbb.spk-berlin.de, pg 1509

Stabenfeldt A/S (Norway) *Tel:* (051) 84 54 00 *Fax:* (051) 84 54 91 *E-mail:* int.post@stabenfeldt.no *Web Site:* www.stabenfeldt.no, pg 506

Stacey International (United Kingdom) *Tel:* (020) 7221 7166 *Fax:* (020) 7792 9288 *E-mail:* stacey-inter@ btconnect.com *Web Site:* www.stacey-international. co.uk, pg 755

Stadler Verlagsgesellschaft mbH (Germany) *Tel:* (07531) 898-0 *Fax:* (07531) 898-103 *E-mail:* info@verlag-stadler.de *Web Site:* www.verlag-stadler.de, pg 283

Stadsbibliotheek (Belgium) *Tel:* (03) 206 87 10 *Fax:* (03) 206 87 75 *E-mail:* stadsbibliotheek@stad.antwerpen.be *Web Site:* stadsbibliotheek.antwerpen.be, pg 1492

Stadt Duisburg - Amt Fuer Statistik, Stadtforschung und Europaangelegenheiten (Germany) *Tel:* (0203) 283 4502 *Fax:* (0203) 288 4404 *E-mail:* amt12@stadt-duisburg.de, pg 284

Stadt Frankfurt a Main Stadt-und Universitaetsbibliothek (Germany) *Tel:* (069) 212-39-205 *Fax:* (069) 212-39-380 *E-mail:* direktion@ub.uni-frankfurt.de *Web Site:* www.ub.uni-frankfurt.de, pg 1509

Stadt- und Universitaetsbibliothek (Germany) *Tel:* (069) 212-39-205; (069) 212-39-256; (069) 212-39-229; (069) 212-39-231 *Fax:* (069) 212-39-380; (069) 212-39-062 *E-mail:* direktion@uni-frankfurt.com; auskunft@stub.uni-frankfurt.de *Web Site:* www.ub.uni-frankfurt.de, pg 1509

Stadt- und Universitaetsbibliothek (Switzerland) *Tel:* (031) 320 32 11 *Fax:* (031) 320 32 99 *E-mail:* info@stub.unibe.ch *Web Site:* www.stub.unibe. ch, pg 1547

Stadtbibliothek Leipzig (Germany) *Tel:* (0341) 123 53 43 *Fax:* (0341) 123 53 05 *E-mail:* stadtbib@leipzig.de *Web Site:* www.leipzig.de/stadtbib.htm, pg 1509

Staedte-Verlag, E v Wagner und J Mitterhuber GmbH (Germany) *Tel:* (0711) 576201 *Fax:* (0711) 5762199 *E-mail:* info@staedte-verlag.de *Web Site:* www. staedte-verlag.de, pg 284

Buchhandlung Staeheli AG (Switzerland) *Tel:* (01) 2099111 *Fax:* (01) 2099112 *E-mail:* info@ staehelibooks.ch *Web Site:* www.staehelibooks.ch, pg 1335

Staempfli Verlag AG (Switzerland) *Tel:* (031) 3006311 *Fax:* (031) 3006688 *E-mail:* verlag@staempfli.com *Web Site:* www.staempfli.com, pg 630

Stahlbau Zentrum Schweiz (Switzerland) *Tel:* (01) 261 89 80 *Fax:* (01) 262 09 62 *E-mail:* info@szs.ch *Web Site:* www.szs.ch, pg 630

Verlag Stahleisen GmbH (Germany) *Tel:* (0211) 6707-0 *Fax:* (0211) 6707-117 *E-mail:* stahleisen@stahleisen. de *Web Site:* www.stahleisen.de, pg 284

Stainer & Bell Ltd (United Kingdom) *Tel:* (020) 8343 3303 *Fax:* (020) 8343 3024 *E-mail:* post@stainer.co. uk *Web Site:* www.stainer.co.uk, pg 755

Stamford College Publishers/Authors-Publishers (Singapore) *Tel:* 65467271 *Fax:* 65467262 *E-mail:* legaldep@nlb.gov.sq.hdtsdnl@technet.sq *Web Site:* www.nlb.gov.sg, pg 553

Stamford Press Pte Ltd (Singapore) *Tel:* 6294 7227 *Fax:* 6294 4396; 6294 3319 *E-mail:* lynn@stamford. com.sg *Web Site:* www.stamford.com.sg, pg 1151

Stamford Press Pte Ltd (Singapore) *Tel:* 6294 7227 *Fax:* 6294 4396; 6294 3319 *E-mail:* stamfad@singnet. com.sg *Web Site:* www.stamford.com.sg, pg 1172

Stamford Press Pte Ltd (Singapore) *Tel:* 6294 7227 *Fax:* 6294 4396; 6294 3319 *E-mail:* lynn@stamford. com.sg *Web Site:* www.stamford.com.sg, pg 1212

Stampa Alternativa - Nuovi Equilibri (Italy) *Tel:* (0761) 352277; (0761) 353485 *Fax:* (0761) 352751 *E-mail:* nuovi.equilibri@agora.it *Web Site:* www. stampalternativa.it, pg 405

Standaard Uitgeverij (Belgium) *Tel:* (03) 285 72 00 *Fax:* (03) 285 72 99 *E-mail:* info@standaarduitgeverij. be *Web Site:* www.standaarduitgeverij.be, pg 73

Standard Book Numbering Agency (Argentina) *Tel:* (011) 4381-8383 *Fax:* (011) 4381-9253 *E-mail:* registrolibros@editorcs.com *Web Site:* www. editores.com, pg 1249

Standard Book Numbering Agency (Austria) *Tel:* (01) 512 15 35 *Fax:* (01) 512 84 82 *E-mail:* isbn@hvb.at *Web Site:* www.buecher.at, pg 1251

Standard Book Numbering Agency (Brunei Darussalam) *Tel:* (02) 382511 *Fax:* (02) 381817, pg 1253

Standard Book Numbering Agency (Chile) *Tel:* (02) 6989519; (02) 6724088 *Fax:* (02) 6989226 *E-mail:* camlibro@terra.cl; prolibro@ctcreuna.cl *Web Site:* www.camlibro.cl, pg 1254

Standard Book Numbering Agency (Colombia) *Tel:* (01) 2886188 *Fax:* (01) 2873320 *E-mail:* agenciaisbn@ camlibro.com.co *Web Site:* www.camlibro.com.co, pg 1254

Standard Book Numbering Agency (Costa Rica) *Tel:* (0506) 2212436; (0506) 2212479 *Fax:* (0506) 2235510 *E-mail:* proctec@racsa.co.cr, pg 1254

Standard Book Numbering Agency (Cyprus) *Tel:* (022) 303337 *Fax:* (022) 443565 *E-mail:* antonism@ucy.ac. cy, pg 1255

Standard Book Numbering Agency (Egypt (Arab Republic of Egypt)) *Tel:* (02) 5751078; (02) 5750886; (02) 5752883 *Fax:* (02) 5765634 *E-mail:* libmang@ darelkotob.org, pg 1256

Standard Book Numbering Agency (Estonia) *Tel:* (02) 630 7372 *Fax:* (02) 631 1200 *E-mail:* eraamat@nlib. ee; nlib@nlib.ee *Web Site:* www.nlib.ee, pg 1256

Standard Book Numbering Agency (Gambia) *Tel:* 226491 *Fax:* 223776 *E-mail:* national.library@ ganet.gm, pg 1259

Standard Book Numbering Agency (Ghana) *Tel:* (021) 223526; (021) 228402 *Fax:* (021) 247768 *E-mail:* GeorgePadmore@Africanmail.com; Padmorereslib@yahoo.co.uk, pg 1262

Standard Book Numbering Agency (Greece) *Tel:* 210 3382601; 2103382581 *Fax:* 2103608495 *E-mail:* ebe@nlg.gr *Web Site:* www.nlg.gr, pg 1262

Standard Book Numbering Agency (Islamic Republic of Iran) *Tel:* 2106414991 *Fax:* 2106415360 *E-mail:* dariushmatlabi@yahoo.com; isbn@ketab. org.ir; dmatlabi@yahoo.com *Web Site:* www.ketab.ir, pg 1263

Standard Book Numbering Agency (Kenya) *Tel:* (02) 718012; (02) 718013; (02) 725550 *Fax:* (02) 721749 *E-mail:* knls@nbnet.co.ke *Web Site:* www.knls.or.ke, pg 1266

Standard Book Numbering Agency (Latvia) *Tel:* (02) 721 26 68 *Fax:* (02) 722 45 87 *Web Site:* www.lnb.lv, pg 1266

Standard Book Numbering Agency (Lesotho) *Tel:* (022) 340601; (022) 340468 *Fax:* 340000 *E-mail:* isbn@lib. nul.ls *Web Site:* www.nul.ls, pg 1266

Standard Book Numbering Agency (The Former Yugoslav Republic of Macedonia) *Tel:* (02) 3115 177; (02) 3133 418 *Fax:* (02) 3226 846 *E-mail:* kliment@ nubsk.edu.mk *Web Site:* www.nubsk.edu.mk, pg 1267

Standard Book Numbering Agency (Malaysia) *Tel:* (03) 26871700 *Fax:* (03) 26927082 *E-mail:* pnmweb@ www1.pnm.my *Web Site:* www.pnm.my, pg 1267

Standard Book Numbering Agency (Maldive Islands) *Tel:* 323261 *Fax:* 321201 *E-mail:* educator@ dhivehinet.net.mv *Web Site:* www.moe.gov.mv, pg 1267

Standard Book Numbering Agency (Malta) *Tel:* (021) 440083; (021) 448539; (021) 490540 *Fax:* (021) 488908 *E-mail:* contact@peg.com.mt *Web Site:* www. peg.com.mt, pg 1267

Standard Book Numbering Agency (New Zealand) *Tel:* (04) 474 3074 *Fax:* (04) 474 3161 *E-mail:* isbn@ natlib.govt.nz *Web Site:* www.natlib.govt.nz, pg 1270

Standard Book Numbering Agency (Pakistan) *Tel:* (051) 921 4523; (051) 920 2544; (051) 920 2549 *Fax:* (051) 922 1375 *E-mail:* nlpiba@paknet2.ptc.pk *Web Site:* www.nlp.gov.pk, pg 1271

Standard Book Numbering Agency (Papua New Guinea) *Tel:* 3256200 *Fax:* 3251331 *E-mail:* paraide@datec. com.pg *Web Site:* www.dg.com.pg/ola, pg 1271

Standard Book Numbering Agency (Portugal) *Tel:* (021) 843 51 80 *Fax:* (021) 848 93 77 *E-mail:* isbn@apel.pt *Web Site:* www.apel.pt, pg 1272

Standard Book Numbering Agency (Qatar) *Tel:* 42 9955 *Fax:* 42 9976 *E-mail:* qanali@qatar.net.qa, pg 1272

Standard Book Numbering Agency (Russian Federation) *Tel:* (095) 2034653; (095) 2035608 *Fax:* (095) 2982576; (095) 2982590 *E-mail:* chamber@aha.ru, pg 1273

Standard Book Numbering Agency (Saudi Arabia) *Tel:* (01) 464 51 97; (01) 462 48 88 (ext 224); (01) 462 48 88 (ext 601); (01) 462 48 88 (ext 238) *Fax:* (01) 464 53 41; (01) 462 27 07 *E-mail:* saudi-isbn@kfnl.gov.sa, pg 1273

Standard Book Numbering Agency (Singapore) *Tel:* 6546 7271 *Fax:* 6546 7262 *E-mail:* legaldep@nlb.gov.sg *Web Site:* www.nlb.gov.sg, pg 1273

Standard Book Numbering Agency (Slovenia) *Tel:* (01) 5861 333; (01) 2001 110; (01) 5861 300 *Fax:* (01) 5861 311 *E-mail:* isbn@nuk.uni-lj.si *Web Site:* www. nuk.uni-lj.si, pg 1274

Standard Book Numbering Agency (Suriname) *Tel:* 472545 *Fax:* 410563 *E-mail:* postmaster@ interfundgroup.com, pg 1275

Standard Book Numbering Agency (Taiwan, Province of China) *Tel:* (02) 3822613 *Fax:* (02) 3115330 *E-mail:* isbn@msg.ncl.edu.tw *Web Site:* www.ncl.edu. tw/isbn, pg 1278

Standard Book Numbering Agency (Thailand) *Tel:* (02) 2810263; (02) 6285196 *Fax:* (02) 2810263 *E-mail:* suwksir@emisc.moe.go.th; suwaksir@yahoo. com *Web Site:* www.isbn.org, pg 1278

Standard Book Numbering Agency (Turkey) *Tel:* (0312) 231 78 26; (0312) 231 78 29; (0312) 232 27 60 *Fax:* (0312) 231 35 64 *E-mail:* kultur@ kutuphanelergm.gov.tr; isbn@kultur.gov.tr *Web Site:* www.kutuphanelergm.gov.tr, pg 1279

Standard Book Numbering Agency (Uruguay) *Tel:* (02) 402 08 12; (02) 408 50 30 *Fax:* (02) 409 69 02; (02) 401 67 16 *E-mail:* bibna@adinet.com.uy, pg 1285

Standard Book Numbering Agency (Venezuela) *Tel:* (0212) 576 5650; (0212) 576 5370; (0212) 576 7120; (0212) 577 5106 *Fax:* (0212) 576 3424 *E-mail:* isbn_cenal@platino.gov.ve; isbnvenezuela@ cenal.gov.ve *Web Site:* www.bnv.bib.ve; www.cenal. gov.ve, pg 1285

Standard Book Numbering Agency (Zambia) *Tel:* (01) 292 837 (ext 1342); (01) 253 952; (01) 250 845 *Fax:* (01) 295 038 *E-mail:* library@unza.zm *Web Site:* www.unza.zm/, pg 1285

Standard Book Numbering Agency (Zimbabwe) *Tel:* (04) 792 741 *Fax:* (04) 792 398 *E-mail:* nat.archives@gta. gov.zw, pg 1285

Standard Book Numbering Agency (Botswana) (Botswana) *Tel:* 3952 397; 3952 288 *Fax:* 3957 108; 3901 149, pg 1253

Standard Book Numbering Agency (ISBN Agency-Sri Lanka) (Sri Lanka) *Tel:* (01) 698847; (01) 685198 *Fax:* (01) 685201 *E-mail:* natlib@slt.lk, pg 1274

Standard Book Numbering Agency of Iceland (Iceland) *Tel:* 525 5600 *Fax:* 525 5615 *E-mail:* lbs@bok.hi.is; isbn@bok.hi.is *Web Site:* www.bok.hi.is, pg 1263

Standard Book Numbering Agency, The National Library of the Philippines (Philippines) *Tel:* (02) 5253196; (02) 5251748 *Fax:* (02) 5242324 *E-mail:* director@ nlp.gov.ph *Web Site:* www.nlp.gov.ph, pg 1271

International Standard Buchnummer GmbH (Germany) *Tel:* (069) 1306-387 *Fax:* (069) 1306-258 *E-mail:* lehr@bhv.de *Web Site:* www.german-isbn.org, pg 1261

Standards Association of Australia (Australia) *Tel:* (02) 99634231 *Fax:* (02) 9746 8450, pg 42

Standards Association of Zimbabwe (SAZ) (Zimbabwe) *Tel:* (04) 885511; (04) 885512; (04) 882021; (04) 882022 *Fax:* (04) 882020 *E-mail:* sazlabs@mall.pcl. co.zw, pg 778

Izdatelstvo Standartov (Russian Federation) *Tel:* (095) 252 0348 *Fax:* (095) 268-4724 *E-mail:* standard@ online.ru, pg 544

Verlag fuer Standesamtswesen GmbH (Germany) *Tel:* (069) 40 58 94 0 *Fax:* (069) 40 58 94 900 *E-mail:* info@vfst.de *Web Site:* www.vfst.de, pg 284

Standing Conference of African Library Schools (SCALS) (Senegal) *Tel:* (08) 250530 *Fax:* (08) 255219, pg 1273

Standing Conference of African University Libraries (SCAUL) (Nigeria) *Tel:* (01) 524968 *Fax:* (01) 822644, pg 1270

Standing Conference on Library Materials on Africa (United Kingdom) *Tel:* (020) 7747 6253 *Fax:* (020) 7747 6168 *E-mail:* scolma@hotmail.com *Web Site:* www.lse.ac.uk/library/scolma/, pg 1283

Stanley Editorial (Spain) *Tel:* (0943) 64 04 12 *Fax:* (0943) 64 38 63 *Web Site:* www.libross.com, pg 596

Stapp Verlag GmbH (Germany) *Tel:* (030) 28304350 *Fax:* (030) 28304353, pg 284

Star Publications (P) Ltd (India) *Tel:* (011) 23268651; (011) 23286757; (011) 23258993; (011) 23261696 *Fax:* (011) 23273335; (011) 26481565 *Web Site:* www.starpublic.com, pg 347

Star Publications (P) Ltd (India) *Tel:* (011) 328 6757; (011) 23258993; (011) 326 1696; (011) 326 8651 *Fax:* (011) 23273335; (011) 648 1565 *E-mail:* starpub@satyam.net.in *Web Site:* www. starpublic.com, pg 1307

Star Publisher's Distributors (India) *Tel:* (011) 23286757; (011) 23268651; (011) 23261696; (011) 23258993 *Fax:* (011) 23273335; (011) 26481565 *E-mail:* starpub@satyam.net.in *Web Site:* www. starpublic.com, pg 1243

C A Starke Verlag (Germany) *Tel:* (06431) 96 15-0 *Fax:* (06431) 96 15 15 *E-mail:* starkeverlag@t-online. de *Web Site:* www.starkeverlag.de, pg 284

Harold Starke Publishers Ltd (United Kingdom) *Tel:* (01379) 388334; (020) 7588 5195 *Fax:* (01379) 388335 *E-mail:* red@eclat.force9.co.uk, pg 756

State Archives (Mongolia) *Tel:* (01) 323100, pg 1528

State Archives of the Russian Federation (Russian Federation) *Tel:* (095) 245-81-41 *Fax:* (095) 245-12-87 *E-mail:* garf@online.ru *Web Site:* www.rusarchives. ru/federal/garf-or-gard.narod.ru, pg 1539

State Archives Service: Natal Archives Depot (South Africa) *Tel:* (033) 342 4712 *Fax:* (033) 394 4352, pg 1543

State Book Trading Office (Mongolia) *Tel:* (01) 22312, pg 1319

State Central Library (India) *Tel:* (040) 4600107; (040) 4615621, pg 1515

The State Library of New South Wales (Australia) *Tel:* (02) 9273 1414 *Fax:* (02) 9273 1255 *E-mail:* library@sl.nsw.gov.au *Web Site:* www.sl.nsw. gov.au, pg 1488

State Library of NSW Press (Australia) *Tel:* (02) 92731568 *Fax:* (02) 92731259 *E-mail:* helene@ilanet. slnsw.gov.au *Web Site:* www.sl.nsw.gov.au, pg 42

State Library of Queensland (Australia) *Tel:* (07) 3840 7666 *Fax:* (07) 3846 2421 *E-mail:* srlenquiries@slq. qld.gov.au *Web Site:* www.slq.qld.gov.au/, pg 1488

State Library of South Australia (Australia) *Tel:* (08) 82077250 *Toll Free Tel:* 800-182-013 *Fax:* (08) 82077247 *E-mail:* info@slsa.sa.gov.au *Web Site:* www. slsa.sa.gov.au, pg 1489

State Library of Tasmania (Australia) *Tel:* (03) 6233 7511 *Fax:* (03) 6231 0927 *F-mail:* state.library@ education.tas.gov.au *Web Site:* www.statelibrary.tas. gov.au, pg 1489

State Library of Victoria (Australia) *Tel:* (03) 8664 7002 *Fax:* (03) 9639 4737 *Web Site:* www.slv.vic.gov.au, pg 42

State Library of Victoria (Australia) *Tel:* (03) 8664 7002 *Fax:* (03) 9639 3854 *E-mail:* info@slv.vic.gov.au *Web Site:* www.statelibrary.vic.gov.au, pg 1489

State Library of Western Australia (Australia) *Tel:* (08) 9427 3111 *Fax:* (08) 9427 3256 *E-mail:* info@liswa. wa.gov.au *Web Site:* www.liswa.wa.gov.au, pg 1489

State Press (Mongolia), pg 470

State Printing Corp (Sri Lanka) *Tel:* (01) 503694 *Fax:* (01) 503694, pg 602

State Publishing Unit of State Print SA (Australia) *Tel:* (08) 9226 4677 *Fax:* (08) 9226 4726, pg 42

Statiqum Kiado es Nyomda Kft (Hungary) *Tel:* (01) 1803311 *Fax:* (01) 1688635, pg 321

Statistical Service (Ghana) *Tel:* (021) 682629 *Fax:* (021) 667069 *E-mail:* baahwadieh@yahoo.com, pg 1511

Statisticke a evidencni vydavatelstvi tiskopisu (SEVT) (Czech Republic) *Tel:* 233 551 711; 283 090 352 *Fax:* 233 543 918 *E-mail:* sevt@sevt.cz *Web Site:* www.sevt.cz, pg 127

Statistics Finland Library (Finland) *Tel:* (09) 1734 2220 *Fax:* (09) 1734 2279 *E-mail:* library@stat.fi *Web Site:* www.stat.fi/tk/kk/index_en.html, pg 1504

Statistics New Zealand (New Zealand) *Tel:* (04) 931 4600 *Fax:* (04) 931 4610 *E-mail:* info@stats.govt.nz *Web Site:* www.stats.govt.nz, pg 497

Statistics Sweden Library (Sweden) *Tel:* (08) 506 948 01; (08) 506 950 66 *Fax:* (08) 506 940 45 *E-mail:* information@scb.se *Web Site:* www.scb.se, pg 1546

Statistisk sentralbyras bibliotek og informasjonssenter (Norway) *Tel:* 21 09 46 42 *Fax:* 21 09 45 04 *E-mail:* biblioteket@ssb.no *Web Site:* www.ssb. no/biblioteket, pg 1533

Statni technicka knihovna (Czech Republic) *Tel:* (02) 21 663 111 *Fax:* (02) 22 221 340 *E-mail:* techlib@stk.cz *Web Site:* www.stk.cz, pg 1499

Statni Vedecka Knihovna Usti Nad Labem (Czech Republic) *Tel:* (047) 5200045; (047) 5209126 *Fax:* (047) 5200045 *E-mail:* library@svkul.cz *Web Site:* www.svkul.cz, pg 127

Statsbiblioteket (Denmark) *Tel:* 89462022 *Fax:* 89462220 *E-mail:* sb@statsbiblioteket.dk *Web Site:* www. statsbiblioteket.dk, pg 1501

Stattbuch Verlag GmbH (Germany) *Tel:* (030) 6913094; (030) 6913095 *Fax:* (030) 6943354, pg 284

Stauffenburg Verlag Brigitte Narr GmbH (Germany) *Tel:* (07071) 9730-0 *Fax:* (07071) 973030 *E-mail:* info@stauffenburg.de *Web Site:* www. stauffenburg.de, pg 284

Stedelijk Van Abbemuseum (Netherlands) *Tel:* (040) 2381000 *Fax:* (040) 2460680 *E-mail:* info@ vanabbemuseum.nl *Web Site:* www.vanabbemuseum.nl, pg 485

Steidl Verlag (Germany) *Tel:* (0551) 49 60 60 *Fax:* (0551) 49 60 649 *E-mail:* mail@steidl.de *Web Site:* www.steidl.de, pg 284

Die Steiermaerkische Landesbibliothek (Austria) *Tel:* (0316) 8016-4600 *Fax:* (0316) 8016-4633 *E-mail:* stlbib@stmk.gv.at *Web Site:* www.stmk.gv. at/verwaltung/stlbib/, pg 1490

Steiger Verlag (Germany) *Tel:* (089) 9271-0 *Fax:* (089) 9271-68, pg 284

Steimatzky Group Ltd (Israel) *Tel:* (03) 5775777 *Fax:* (03) 5794567 *E-mail:* info@steimatzky.co.il *Web Site:* www.steimatzky.com, pg 369, 1310

Abner Stein (United Kingdom) *Tel:* (020) 7373 0456 *Fax:* (020) 7370 6316 *E-mail:* abnerstein@ compuserve.com, pg 1134

Conrad Stein Verlag GmbH (Germany) *Tel:* (02384) 963912 *Fax:* (02384) 963913 *E-mail:* outdoor@tng.de *Web Site:* outdoor.tng.de, pg 284

Micheline Steinberg Associates (United Kingdom) *Tel:* (020) 7631 1310 *Fax:* (020) 7631 1146 *E-mail:* info@steinplays.com, pg 1134

J Steinbrener OHG (Austria) *Tel:* (07712) 2038 *Fax:* (07712) 2038-20 *E-mail:* steinbrener@aon.at, pg 57

Franz Steiner Verlag Wiesbaden GmbH (Germany) *Tel:* (0711) 2582 0 *Fax:* (0711) 2582 290 *E-mail:* service@steiner-verlag.de *Web Site:* www. steiner-verlag.de, pg 284

Strom-Verlag Luzern (Switzerland) *Tel:* (041) 4408845 *Fax:* (041) 4408844 *E-mail:* pegasusbuecher@tic.ch, pg 630

Stromberg (Sweden) *Tel:* (08) 6201900 *Fax:* (08) 7399836 *E-mail:* marcus@stromberg.se *Web Site:* www.stromberg.se, pg 611

Stroyizdat Publishing House (Russian Federation) *Tel:*.(095) 2516967, pg 544

Strubes Forlag og Boghandel ApS (Denmark) *Tel:* 3142 5300 *Fax:* 3142 2398, pg 134

Strucmech Publishing (Australia) *Tel:* (03) 95989245 *Fax:* (03) 95989245, pg 42

Struik Publishers (Pty) Ltd (South Africa) *Tel:* (021) 4624360 *Fax:* (021) 462-4379; (021) 461-9378 *E-mail:* admin@struik.co.za *Web Site:* www.struik. co.za, pg 564

The Struik Publishing Group (South Africa) *Tel:* (021) 462 4360 *Fax:* (021) 462 4379 *Web Site:* www.struik. co.za, pg 1332

STS Standard Tabellen und Software Verlag GmbH (Germany) *Tel:* (089) 89517-0 *Fax:* (089) 89517290, pg 286

Boksala Studenta (The University Bookstore) (Iceland) *Tel:* (05) 700 777 *Fax:* (05) 700 778 *E-mail:* boksala@boksala.is *Web Site:* www.boksala.is, pg 1304

Studenterboghandelen ved Odense Universitet (Denmark) *Tel:* 6550 1700 *Fax:* 6550 1701 *E-mail:* studentcr@ boghandel.sdu.dk *Web Site:* www.boghandel.sdu.dk/, pg 1298

Studentlitteratur AB (Sweden) *Tel:* (046) 312000 *Fax:* (046) 305338 *E-mail:* info@studentlitteratur.se *Web Site:* www.studentlitteratur.se, pg 611

Studieforlaget i Goteborg Stiftelsen Kursverksamhetens Forlag (Sweden) *Tel:* (031) 106580 *Fax:* (031) 135359 *E-mail:* kursbokhandeln@folkuniversitetet.se, pg 611

Studien Verlag Gmbh (Austria) *Tel:* (0512) 395045 *Fax:* (0512) 395045-15 *E-mail:* order@studienverlag.at *Web Site:* www.studienverlag.at, pg 57

Studio Bibliografico Adelmo Polla (Italy) *Tel:* (0863) 78522 *Fax:* (0863) 78522, pg 406

Studio Editions Ltd (United Kingdom) *Tel:* (020) 7973 9690 *Fax:* (020) 7233 6057, pg 756

Studio Editoriale Programma (Italy) *Tel:* (049) 8753110 *Fax:* (049) 8755870, pg 406

Edizioni Studio Tesi SRL (Italy) *Tel:* (06) 3235433 *Fax:* (06) 3236277 *E-mail:* info@ediz-mediterranee. com *Web Site:* www.ediz-mediterranee.com, pg 406

Studio 31 (United States) *Tel:* 772-781-7195 *Fax:* 772-781-6044 *E-mail:* studio31@mindspring.com *Web Site:* www.studio31.com, pg 1179

Libreria Studium SA (Peru) *Tel:* (01) 326278; (01) 275960; (01) 325528 *Fax:* (01) 4325354, pg 512

Libreria Studium SA (Peru) *Tel:* (01) 275960; (01) 326278; (01) 325528 *Fax:* (01) 4325354, pg 1326

Edizioni Studium SRL (Italy) *Tel:* (06) 68 65 846 *Fax:* (06) 68 75 456 *E-mail:* edizionistudium@libero. it, pg 406

Sturtz Verlag GmbH (Germany) *Tel:* (0931) 385235 *Fax:* (0931) 385305 *E-mail:* info@verlagshaus.com *Web Site:* www.verlagshaus.com, pg 286

Styria Medien AG (Austria) *Tel:* (0316) 8063-1012 *Fax:* (0316) 8063-3034 *E-mail:* medien.ag@styria.com *Web Site:* www.styria.com, pg 1290

Verlag Styria (Austria) *Tel:* (0316) 8063 7601 *Fax:* (0316) 8063 7004 *E-mail:* office@styriapichler.at *Web Site:* www.verlagstyria.com, pg 57

Su Hoc (Historical) Publishing House (Viet Nam), pg 775

Su That (Truth) Publishing House (Viet Nam) *Tel:* (04) 252008, pg 775

Suaver, Javier Presa Suarez (Spain) *Tel:* (086) 439507, pg 596

Sub-Saharan Publishers (Ghana) *Tel:* (021) 228398 *E-mail:* sub-saharan@ighmail.com, pg 302

Editions Subervie (France) *Tel:* (05) 65 67 20 17 *Fax:* (05) 65 67 36 38 *E-mail:* contact@subervie.com *Web Site:* www.subervie.com, pg 186

Success Publications Pte Ltd (Singapore) *Tel:* 4432003; 4430512 *Fax:* 4453156 *E-mail:* succpub@singnet.com. sg, pg 554

SUD (France) *Tel:* (0491) 336068 *Fax:* (0491) 336068, pg 186

Sud Editions (Tunisia) *Tel:* 71798064 *Fax:* 71795260, pg 644

Editions Sud Ouest (France) *Tel:* (0556) 44 68 21 *Fax:* (0556) 44 40 83 *E-mail:* contact@editions-sudouest.com *Web Site:* www.editions-sudouest.com, pg 187

Editorial Sudamericana SA (Argentina) *Tel:* (011) 4300-5400 *Fax:* (011) 4362-7364 *E-mail:* info@ edsudamericana.com.ar *Web Site:* www. edsudamericana.com.ar, pg 9

The Sudan Bookshop Ltd (Sudan) *Tel:* (011) 74123; (011) 76781, pg 1334

Sudan Literature Centre (Kenya) *Tel:* (020) 565641 *Fax:* (020) 564141 *E-mail:* across@across-sudan.org *Web Site:* www.across-sudan.org, pg 432

Sudanese Publishers' Association (Sudan) *Tel:* (0249) 11-7780031 *Fax:* (0249) 11-770358, pg 1274

Izdatelstvo Sudostroenie (Russian Federation) *Tel:* (0812) 3124479 *Fax:* (0812) 3120821, pg 544

Sueddeutsche Verlagsgesellschaft mbH (Germany) *Tel:* (089) 2183-0 *Fax:* (089) 2183-787 *E-mail:* verlag@sueddeutsche.de; redaktion@ sueddeutsche.de *Web Site:* www.sueddeutsche.de, pg 286

Suedverlag GmbH (Germany) *Tel:* (07531) 9053-0 *Fax:* (07531) 9053-98 *E-mail:* willkommen@uvk.de *Web Site:* www.suedverlag.de, pg 286

Suedwest Verlag GmbH & Co KG (Germany) *Tel:* (089) 4136-0; (01805) 990505 (hotline) *Fax:* (089) 5148-2229 *E-mail:* heyne-suedwest@randomhouse.de *Web Site:* www.suedwest-verlag.de, pg 286

Suedwind - Buchwelt GmbH (Austria) *Tel:* (01) 798 83 49 *Fax:* (01) 798 83 75 *E-mail:* versand@suedwind.at *Web Site:* www.suedwind.at, pg 58

Sueleymaniye Kuetuephanesi (Turkey) *Tel:* (0212) 520 64 60 *Fax:* (0212) 520 64 62, pg 1550

Sufia Kamel National Public Library (Bangladesh) *Tel:* (02) 50 08 19; (02) 50 08 39; (02) 50 28 16, pg 1491

Sugarco Edizioni SRL (Italy) *Tel:* (02) 4078370 *Fax:* (02) 4078493 *E-mail:* info@sugarcoedizioni.it *Web Site:* www.sugarcoedizioni.it, pg 406

Suhagsa (Republic of Korea) *Tel:* (02) 584-4642 *Fax:* (02) 521-1458, pg 440

Suhrkamp Verlag (Germany) *Tel:* (069) 75601-0 *Fax:* (069) 75601-522; (069) 75601-314 *Web Site:* www.suhrkamp.de, pg 286

Suin Buch-Verlag (Germany) *Tel:* (06255) 2657 *Fax:* (06255) 9596875, pg 286

Suisse Romand PEN Centre (Switzerland), pg 1399

Suksapan Panit (Business Organization of Teachers Council of Thailand) (Thailand) *Tel:* (02) 514-4033 *Fax:* (02) 933-0182 *Web Site:* www.suksapan.or.th, pg 641

Suksit Siam Co Ltd (Thailand) *Tel:* (02) 2511630 *Fax:* (02) 222-5188 *E-mail:* sop@ffc.inet.co.th, pg 641

Suksit Siam Co Ltd (Thailand) *Tel:* (02) 268-7867 *Fax:* (02) 268-6727, pg 1336

Livraria Sulina Editora (Brazil) *Tel:* (051) 254765; (051) 250287 *E-mail:* sulina@sulina.com.br, pg 90

Sulina Livraria Editora (Brazil) *Tel:* (0512) 254765; (0512) 250287 *Fax:* (0512) 280734, pg 1294

Sultan Chand & Sons Pvt Ltd (India) *Tel:* (011) 3266105; (011) 3277843; (011) 3281876 *Fax:* (011) 3266357 *E-mail:* nbcnd@ndb.vsnl.net.in, pg 347

Sultan's Library (Cyprus), pg 1499

Suman Prakashan Pvt Ltd (India) *Tel:* (011) 5842253; (011) 5721750 *Fax:* (011) 5754739 *E-mail:* info@ sumanprakashan.com *Web Site:* www.sumanprakashan. com, pg 347

Sumatera Utara University Press (Indonesia) *Tel:* (061) 811045 *Fax:* (061) 816264, pg 353

Sumathi Book Printing (Pvt) Ltd (Sri Lanka) *Tel:* (0941) 330-673-5 *Fax:* (0941) 449-593 *E-mail:* lakbima@ isplanka.lk *Web Site:* www.sumathi.lk, pg 1151, 1172, 1213

Summer Institute of Linguistics (Papua New Guinea) *Tel:* 7373544 *Fax:* 7374111 *E-mail:* png@sil.org, pg 511

Summer Institute of Linguistics, Australian Aborigines Branch (Australia) *Tel:* (08) 8922 5700 *Fax:* (08) 8922 5717 *E-mail:* sildarwin@taunet.net.au, pg 42

Summerson Eastern Publishers Ltd (Hong Kong) *Tel:* 25408123 *Fax:* 2559 7869, pg 316

Summus Editorial Ltda (Brazil) *Tel:* (011) 38723322 *Fax:* (011) 38727476 *E-mail:* summus@summus.com. br *Web Site:* www.summus.com.br, pg 90

Sun Fung Offset Binding Co Ltd (Hong Kong) *Tel:* 25618109; 25623381; 25621925 *Fax:* 28110638 *E-mail:* sunfung@sunfung.com.hk *Web Site:* www. sunfung.com.hk, pg 1209

Sun Mui Press (Hong Kong) *Tel:* 2694 8525 *Fax:* 2610 1202 *E-mail:* auly@chevalier.net, pg 316

Uitgeverij SUN (Netherlands) *Tel:* (020) 622 61 07 *Fax:* (020) 625 33 27 *E-mail:* info@uitgeverijboom.nl *Web Site:* www.uitgeverijboom.nl, pg 485

Sun Ya Publications (HK) Ltd (Hong Kong) *Tel:* 2562 0161 *Fax:* 2565 9951 *E-mail:* info@sunya.com.hk *Web Site:* www.sunya.com.hk, pg 316

Sun Yat-Sen Library (Hong Kong) *Tel:* 23365291, pg 1512

Sun Yat-sen Library (Taiwan, Province of China) *Tel:* (02) 2758 2045 *Fax:* (02) 2729 7030, pg 1547

Sunera Publishers (Sri Lanka) *Tel:* 511527, pg 602

Sunflower Books (United Kingdom) *Tel:* (020) 7589 1862 *Fax:* (020) 7589 1862 *E-mail:* mail@ sunflowerbooks.co.uk *Web Site:* www.sunflowerbooks. co.uk, pg 756

Sunny Printing (Hong Kong) Co Ltd (Hong Kong) *Tel:* 25578663 *Fax:* 28898070 *E-mail:* enquiry@ sunnyprinting.com.hk *Web Site:* www.sunnyprinting. com.hk, pg 1209

Sunshine Books International Ltd (New Zealand) *Tel:* (09) 5203049 *Toll Free Fax:* 0800 85 1000 *E-mail:* orders@my-dictionary.com *Web Site:* www. my-dictionary.com, pg 497

Sunshine Multi Media Ltd, Wendy Pye Ltd (New Zealand) *Tel:* (09) 525-3575 *Fax:* (09) 525-4205 *E-mail:* admin@sunshine.co.nz *Web Site:* www. sunshine.co.nz, pg 497

Sunshine Press Ltd (Hong Kong) *Tel:* 25532386 *Fax:* 28732930 *E-mail:* spl@sunshinepress.com.hk, pg 1148, 1169

Sunshine Press Ltd (Hong Kong) *Tel:* 25530228; 25532303 *Fax:* 28732930 *E-mail:* spl@sunshinepress. com.hk, pg 1209

Suomalainen Kirjakauppa Oy (Finland) *Tel:* (09) 852 751 *Fax:* (09) 852 7980 *E-mail:* etunimi.sukunimi@ suomalainenkk.fi *Web Site:* www.suomalainen.com, pg 1299

Suomalainen Tiedeakatemia (Finland) *Tel:* (09) 636800 *Fax:* (09) 660117 *E-mail:* acadsci@acadsci.fi *Web Site:* www.acadsci.fi, pg 1393

Suomalaisen Kirjallisuuden Seura (Finland) *Tel:* (0201) 131 231 *Fax:* (09) 1312 3219, pg 144

Suomalaisen Kirjallisuuden Seura (Finland) *Tel:* (0201) 131 231 *Fax:* (09) 1312 3220 *E-mail:* sks@finlit.fi *Web Site:* www.finlit.fi, pg 1393

Suomen Kirjailijaliitto (Finland) *Tel:* (09) 445392 *Fax:* (09) 492278 *E-mail:* info@suomenkirjailijaliitto.fi *Web Site:* www.suomenkirjailijaliitto.fi, pg 1257

Suomen Kirjastoseura (Finland) *Tel:* (09) 694 1858 *Fax:* (09) 694 1859 *E-mail:* fla@fla.fi *Web Site:* www.kaapeli.fi/~fla/presentation.html, pg 1561

Suomen Kustannusyhdistys (Finland) *Tel:* (09) 22877250 *Fax:* (09) 6121226 *Web Site:* www.skyry.net, pg 1257

Suomen Matkailuliitto ry (Finland) *Tel:* (09) 622 6280 *Fax:* (09) 654 358 *E-mail:* matkailuliitto@ matkailuliitto.org *Web Site:* www.matkailuliitto.org, pg 144

Suomen Pipliaseura RY (Finland) *Tel:* (09) 612 9350 *Fax:* (09) 612 935 11 *E-mail:* info@bible.fi; etunimi.sukunimi@bible.fi *Web Site:* www.bible.fi, pg 144

Suomen Tieteellinen Kirjastoseura ry (Finland) *Tel:* (017) 34 22 25 *Fax:* (017) 34 22 79 *E-mail:* meri.kuula@ arcada.fi *Web Site:* pro.tsv.fi/stks, pg 1561

Super Book House (India) *Tel:* (022) 2830560 *Fax:* (022) 2834452, pg 1307

Supportive Learning Publications (United Kingdom) *Tel:* (01691) 774778 *Fax:* (01691) 774849 *E-mail:* sales@slpuk.demon.co.uk *Web Site:* www.slpuk.demon.co.uk, pg 756

Sur Casa de Estudios del Socialismo (Peru) *Tel:* (01) 4235431 *Fax:* (01) 4235431 *E-mail:* casasur@terra.com.pe *Web Site:* www.casasur.org, pg 512

Suriwong Book Centre, Ltd (Thailand) *Tel:* (053) 281052 *Fax:* (053) 271902 *E-mail:* suriwong@loxinfo.co.th, pg 1336

Suriyaban Bookstore (Thailand) *Tel:* (02) 2347991; (02) 2347992, pg 1336

Suriyaban Publishers (Thailand) *Tel:* (02) 2347991; (02) 2347992, pg 641

Surjeet Publications (India) *Tel:* (011) 3914746; (011) 3914174 *Fax:* (011) 3918475 *E-mail:* surpub@del3.vsnl.net.in, pg 347

Ediciones Suromex SA (Mexico) *Tel:* (055) 2770744; (055) 2723570; (055) 2723630; (055) 2734989 *Fax:* (055) 2710470; (055) 2719378 *E-mail:* suromex@mail.internet.com.mx *Web Site:* www.intralector.com/suromex/, pg 468

Surugadai-Shuppan Sha (Japan) *Tel:* (03) 3291-1676 *Fax:* (03) 3291-1675 *E-mail:* edit@surugadai.com *Web Site:* www.e-surugadai.com, pg 425

Susaeta Ediciones (Colombia) *Tel:* (01) 2884422; (01) 2885500 *Fax:* (01) 881472 *E-mail:* mdsusaet@ medellin.impsat.net.co, pg 112

Ediciones Susaeta SA (Spain) *Tel:* (091) 3009100 *Fax:* (091) 3009110 *E-mail:* ediciones.susaeta@nexo.es, pg 596

Sussex Publications (United Kingdom) *Tel:* (020) 586 4499 *Fax:* (020) 722 1068 *E-mail:* microworld@ ndirect.co.uk *Web Site:* www.microworld.ndirect.co.uk, pg 756

Sut Phaisan (Thailand) *Tel:* (02) 4682066; (02) 4675066, pg 641

Sutton Publishing Ltd (United Kingdom) *Tel:* (01453) 731114 *Fax:* (01453) 731117 *E-mail:* sales@sutton-publishing.co.uk; editorial@sutton-publishing.co.uk; publishing@sutton-publishing.co.uk *Web Site:* www.suttonpublishing.co.uk, pg 756

Suuri Suomalainen Kirjakerho Oy (Finland) *Tel:* (09) 2705 0077; (09) 1566 830 *Fax:* (09) 145 510 *E-mail:* sskk.palaute@sskk.fi *Web Site:* www.sskk.fi, pg 1242

Suva City Library (Fiji) *Tel:* 313 433 *Fax:* 302 158, pg 1503

SV-Kauppiaskanava Oy (Finland) *Tel:* (09) 10 53010 *Fax:* (09) 10 5336238 *E-mail:* kaija.tynkkynen@k-kauppiasuitto.fi *Web Site:* www.k-kauppiasliitto.fi, pg 144

Bokklubben Svalan (Sweden) *Tel:* (08) 696 88 00 *Fax:* (08) 696 83 76 *E-mail:* medlemsservice@svalan.bonnier.se *Web Site:* www.bokklubbensvalan.se, pg 1246

Svato Zapletal (Germany) *Tel:* (040) 4390004 *Fax:* (040) 4390004, pg 286

Svaz Antikvaru CR (Czech Republic) *Tel:* (02) 22220286 *Fax:* (02) 22220286 *E-mail:* info@meissner.cz *Web Site:* www.meissner.cz, pg 1255

Svaz ceskych knihkupcu a nakladatelu (SCKN) (Czech Republic) *Tel:* (02) 24 219 944 *Fax:* (02) 24 219 942 *E-mail:* sckn@sckn.cz *Web Site:* www.sckn.cz, pg 1255

Svaz knihovniku informacnich pracovniku Ceske republiky (SKIP) (Czech Republic) *Tel:* (02) 21663111 *Fax:* (02) 21663261 *Web Site:* www.nkp.cz, pg 1560

Svensk Biblioteksforening (Sweden) *Tel:* (08) 54513230 *Fax:* (08) 54513231 *E-mail:* info@ biblioteksforeningen.org *Web Site:* www.biblioteksforeningen.org, pg 1571

Svensk-Norsk Bogimport A/S (Denmark) *Tel:* 33142666 *Fax:* 33143588 *E-mail:* snb@bog.dk *Web Site:* www.snbog.dk, pg 1298

Svenska Forlaggareforeningen (Sweden) *Tel:* (08) 736 19 40 *Fax:* (08) 736 19 44 *E-mail:* info@ forlaggareforeningen.se *Web Site:* www.forlaggareforeningen.se, pg 1275

Svenska alliansmissionen (SAM) foerlage (Sweden) *Tel:* (036) 71 98 70 *Fax:* (036) 71 98 20 *E-mail:* info@sam.f.se *Web Site:* www.sam.f.se, pg 611

Svenska Arbetsgivareforeningens forlag (Sweden) *Tel:* (08) 553 430 00 *Fax:* (08) 553 430 99, pg 611

Svenska Arkivsamfundet (Sweden) *Tel:* (046) 197000 *Fax:* (046) 197070 *E-mail:* info@arkivsamfundet.org *Web Site:* www.arkivsamfundet.org, pg 1571

Svenska Barnboksinstitutet (Sweden) *Tel:* (08) 54 54 20 50 *Fax:* (08) 54 54 20 54 *E-mail:* info@sbi.kb.se; biblioteket@sbi.kb.se *Web Site:* www.sbi.kb.se, pg 1546

Svenska Foerlaget liv & ledarskap ab (Sweden) *Tel:* (08) 412 27 00 *Fax:* (08) 411 41 30 *E-mail:* kundservice@ svenskaforlaget.com *Web Site:* www.svenskaforlaget.com, pg 611

Svenska Institutet (Sweden) *Tel:* (08) 453 78 00 *Fax:* (08) 20 72 48 *E-mail:* si@si.se *Web Site:* www.si.se, pg 611

Svenska Litteratursaellskapet i Finland (Finland) *Tel:* (09) 618777 *Fax:* (09) 6187 7277 *E-mail:* info@ mail.sls.fi *Web Site:* www.sls.fi, pg 1393

Svenska Oesterbottens Litteraturfoerening (Finland) *Tel:* (06) 3450286, pg 144, 1393

Svepomoc (Slovakia) *Tel:* (02) 333208 *Fax:* (02) 24223439, pg 556

Sveriges Lantbruksuniversitets Bibliotek (Sweden) *Tel:* (018) 67 10 00 *Fax:* (018) 67 20 00 *E-mail:* registrator@slu.se *Web Site:* www.bib.slu.se, pg 1546

Svetovi (Serbia and Montenegro) *Tel:* (021) 28032; (021) 28036 *Fax:* (021) 28036; (021) 28032 *E-mail:* aum.mar@eunet.yu, pg 549

Svetra Publishing House (Bulgaria) *Tel:* (02) 62 27 39; (02) 983 45 42 *Fax:* (02) 23 49 66 *E-mail:* svetlev@ cybernet.bg, pg 96

Sveucilisna naklada Liber (Croatia) *Tel:* (01) 4564430; (01) 4564428 *Fax:* (01) 4564427, pg 119

Sviesa Publishers (Lithuania) *Tel:* (0837) 409126 *Fax:* (0837) 342032 *E-mail:* mail@sviesa.lt *Web Site:* www.sviesa.lt, pg 446

Svjetlost (Bosnia and Herzegovina) *Tel:* (033) 442634; (033) 200066 *Fax:* (033) 443435 *E-mail:* ipsvjet@bih.net.ba, pg 75

Svjetlost (Bosnia and Herzegovina) *Tel:* (071) 443 419; (071) 664 535; (071) 664 066; (071) 214 578; (071) 207 352 *Fax:* (071) 443 435, pg 1293

NS Svoboda spol sro (Czech Republic) *Tel:* (02) 449 132 58; (02) 23 06 14 *Fax:* (02) 449 132 58 *E-mail:* nssvobod@centrum.cz, pg 127

Svoboda Servis sro (Czech Republic) *Tel:* 222897347 *Fax:* 222897346 *E-mail:* svobserv@volny.cz, pg 127

Swakopmunder Buchhandlung (Namibia) *Tel:* 402613 *Fax:* 404183, pg 1319

Swarna Hansa Foundation (Sri Lanka) *Tel:* (01) 712566 *Fax:* (01) 733649, pg 602

Swaziland College of Technology Library (Swaziland) *Tel:* (040) 42681; (040) 43539 *Fax:* (040) 44521 *E-mail:* scotlibrary@africaonline.co.sz, pg 1545

Swaziland Library Association (Swaziland) *Tel:* 404-2633 *Fax:* 404-3863 *E-mail:* sdnationalarchives@ realnet.co.sz *Web Site:* www.swala.sz, pg 1571

Swaziland National Library Service (Swaziland) *Tel:* 42633 *Fax:* 43863 *E-mail:* snlssz@realnet.co.sz *Web Site:* www.library.ohiou.edu/subjects/swaziland/snls.htm, pg 1545

Swedenborg - Verlag (Switzerland) *Tel:* (01) 3835944 *Fax:* (01) 3822944 *E-mail:* info@swedenborg.ch *Web Site:* www.swedenborg.ch, pg 630

Swedish-English Literary Translators' Association (SELTA) (United Kingdom) *Tel:* (020) 8641 8176 *Fax:* (020) 8641 8176 *Web Site:* www.swedishbookreview.com, pg 1141

Swedish PEN Centre (Sweden) *Tel:* (08) 453 86 80 *E-mail:* info@pensweden.org *Web Site:* www.pensweden.org, pg 1399

Sweet & Maxwell Ltd (United Kingdom) *Tel:* (020) 7393 7000; (020) 7449 1104 *Fax:* (020) 7449 1144 *E-mail:* info@routledge.co.uk, pg 757

Swets & Zeitlinger Publishers (Netherlands) *Tel:* (0252) 435111 *Fax:* (0252) 415888 *E-mail:* info@nl.swets.com *Web Site:* www.swets.nl, pg 485

Swindon Book Co Ltd (Hong Kong) *Tel:* 2366 8001 *Fax:* 2739 4978 *E-mail:* swindon@netvigator.com *Web Site:* www.swindonbooks.com, pg 1304

SWP, BV Uitgeverij (Netherlands) *Tel:* (020) 3307200 *Fax:* (020) 3308040 *E-mail:* swp@wxs.nl *Web Site:* www.swpbook.com, pg 485

Syarikat Cultural Supplies Sdn Bhd (Malaysia) *Tel:* (03) 7046628; (03) 7554103; (03) 7915728 *Fax:* (03) 7046629 *E-mail:* malian@po.jaring.my, pg 455

Sybex Verlag GmbH (Germany) *Tel:* (02236) 399920-0 *Fax:* (02236) 399922-9 *E-mail:* sybex@sybex.de *Web Site:* www.sybex.de, pg 286

Syddansk Universitetsforlag (Denmark) *Tel:* 66 15 79 99 *Fax:* 66 15 81 26 *E-mail:* press@forlag.sdu.dk *Web Site:* www.universitypress.dk, pg 134

Sydney Jary Ltd (United Kingdom) *Tel:* (0117) 974-1640 *Fax:* (0117) 973-7116 *E-mail:* admin@s-jary.co.uk, pg 757

Sydney PEN Centre (Australia) *Tel:* (02) 9514 2738 *Fax:* (02) 9514 2778 *E-mail:* sydney@pen.org.au *Web Site:* www.pen.org.au, pg 1390

J G Sydy's Buchhandlung Ludwig Schubert GmbH Nachfolge KG (Austria) *Tel:* (02742) 35 31 89 *Fax:* (02742) 35 31 89; (02742) 35 31 85 *E-mail:* schubert.sydys@aon.at; info@buchhandlung-schubert.at *Web Site:* www.buchhandlung-schubert.at, pg 1290

Sygma Publishing (Botswana) *Tel:* 351371 *Fax:* 372531 *E-mail:* sygma@info.bw, pg 76

Syllogos Ekdoton Bibliopolon Athinon (Greece) *Tel:* 2103830029; 2103303268 *Fax:* 2103823222 *E-mail:* seva@otenet.ge, pg 1262

Syndicat des Libraires Universitaires et Techniques (France) *Tel:* (01) 43 29 88 79 *Fax:* (467) 525905, pg 1259

Syndicat National de la Librairie Ancienne et Moderne (SLAM) (France) *Tel:* (01) 43 29 46 38 *Fax:* (01) 43 25 41 63 *E-mail:* slam-livre@wanadoo.fr *Web Site:* www.slam-livre.fr, pg 1259

Syndicat National de l'Edition (France) *Tel:* (01) 4441 4050 *Fax:* (01) 4441 4077 *Web Site:* www.snedition.fr, pg 1259

Syndicat National des Auteurs et Compositeurs (France) *Tel:* (01) 48 74 96 30 *Fax:* (01) 42 81 40 21 *E-mail:* snac.fr@wanadoo.fr *Web Site:* www.snac.fr, pg 1394

Synthesis Verlag (Germany) *Tel:* (0201) 51 01 88 *Fax:* (0201) 51 10 49 *E-mail:* synthesis@synthesis-verlag.com *Web Site:* www.synthesis-verlag.com, pg 286

Systematics Studies Ltd (Trinidad & Tobago) *Tel:* (868) 645-8466 *Fax:* (868) 645-8467 *E-mail:* tobe@trinidad.net, pg 643

SystemConsult (Czech Republic) *Tel:* (040) 466 501 585 *Fax:* (040) 466 501 585 *E-mail:* system.consult@tiscali.cz *Web Site:* www.systemconsult.cz, pg 127

Systcx (Australia) *Tel:* (02) 9944 2668, pg 42

Systime (Denmark) *Tel:* 70 12 11 00 *Fax:* 70 12 11 05 *E-mail:* systime@systime.dk *Web Site:* www.systime.dk, pg 134

Szabad Ter Kiado (Hungary) *Tel:* (01) 3561565; (01) 3755922 *Fax:* (01) 1560998, pg 321

Szabvanykiado (Hungary) *Tel:* (01) 1183011; (01) 1183442 *Fax:* (01) 1185125, pg 321

Szarvas Andras Cartographic Agency (Hungary) *Tel:* (01) 363 0672; (01) 221 68 30 *Fax:* (01) 363 0672; (01) 221 68 30 *E-mail:* szarvas.andras@mail.datanet.hu, pg 321

Szazadveg (Hungary) *Tel:* (01) 4795280 *Fax:* (01) 479 5290 *E-mail:* szazadveg@szazadveg.hu *Web Site:* www.szazadveg.hu, pg 321

Uniwersytet Szczecinski (Poland) *Tel:* (091) 444-23-61 *Fax:* (091) 444-23-62 *E-mail:* info@bg.univ.szczecin.pl *Web Site:* www.univ.szczecin.pl/us/biblioteka.html, pg 1536

Szepirodalmi Koenyvkiado Kiado (Hungary) *Tel:* (01) 3117293, pg 321

Wydawnictwa Szkolne i Pedagogiczne (Poland) *Tel:* (022) 8265451; (022) 8265452; (022) 8265453; (022) 8265454; (022) 8265455; (022) 5762500; (022) 5762501 *Toll Free Tel:* 800-220555 *Fax:* (022) 8279280 *E-mail:* wsip@wsip.com.pl *Web Site:* www.wsip.com.pl, pg 522

Oficyna Wydawnicza Szkoly Glownej Handlowej w Warszawie Oficyna Wydawnicza SGH (Poland) *Tel:* (022) 337 92 13; (022) 337 92 17; (022) 337 97 61; (022) 337 97 69 *Fax:* (022) 646 61 03 *E-mail:* dwz@sgh.waw.pl *Web Site:* www.sgh.waw.pl, pg 522

Magyar Eszperanto Szoevetseg (Hungary) *Tel:* (01) 1334343; (01) 1563659, pg 321

T & E Publishers (Uganda) *Tel:* (041) 542207 *Fax:* (041) 542207, pg 648

T F Editores (Spain) *Tel:* (091) 484 1870; (091) 484 1878 *Fax:* (091) 661 3594 *E-mail:* editorial@tfeditores.com *Web Site:* www.tfeditores.com, pg 596

Ta Ha Publishers Ltd (United Kingdom) *Tel:* (020) 7737 7266 *Fax:* (020) 7737 7267 *E-mail:* sales@taha.co.uk *Web Site:* www.taha.co.uk, pg 757

Ta Kung Pao (HK) Ltd (Hong Kong) *Tel:* 25737213; 25757181 *Fax:* 257463316, pg 316

Edicoes Tabajara (Brazil) *Tel:* (0512) 241073; (0512) 247724, pg 90

Tabansi Press Ltd (Nigeria) *Tel:* (046) 211661; 08033243783; 08033418218, pg 502

Ediciones Tabapress, SA (Spain) *Tel:* (01) 5320876 *Fax:* (01) 5325890 *E-mail:* ediciones.tabapress@tsai.es, pg 596

Tabb House (United Kingdom) *Tel:* (01841) 532316 *Fax:* (01841) 532316 *E-mail:* tabbhouse@connexions.co.uk; books@tabb-house.fsnet.co.uk, pg 757

Les Editions de la Table Ronde (France) *Tel:* (01) 40 46 70 70 *Fax:* (01) 40 46 71 01 *E-mail:* editionslatableronde@wanadoo.fr, pg 187

Tabletop Press (Australia) *Tel:* (06) 6242 0995 *Fax:* (06) 6242 0674, pg 42

Editeurs Tacor International (France) *Tel:* (01) 39 18 29 39 *Fax:* (01) 30 82 43 90, pg 187

Tael Ltd (Estonia) *Tel:* (02) 6314162 *Fax:* (02) 6314162 *E-mail:* tael@teleport.ee, pg 140

Tafelberg Publishers Ltd (South Africa) *Tel:* (021) 406 3033 *Fax:* (021) 406 3812 *E-mail:* tafelbrg@tafelberg.com *Web Site:* www.nb.co.za/tafelberg, pg 564

Tages-Anzeiger (Switzerland) *Tel:* (01) 248 44 11 *Fax:* (01) 248 44 71 *E-mail:* verlag@tages-anzeiger.ch *Web Site:* www.tamedia.ch, pg 630

Tai Yip Co (Hong Kong) *Tel:* 2524-5963 *Fax:* 2845-3296 *E-mail:* tybook@taiyipart.com.hk *Web Site:* www.taiyipart.com.hk, pg 316

Taigh Na Teud Music Publishers (United Kingdom) *Tel:* (01471) 822528 *Fax:* (01471) 822811 *E-mail:* sales@scotlandsmusic.com *Web Site:* www.scotlandsmusic.com, pg 757

Taimeido Publishing Co Ltd (Japan) *Tel:* (03) 3291-2374 *Fax:* (03) 3291-2376 *E-mail:* taimei1@ibm.net, pg 425

Taipei Yung Chang Printing (Taiwan, Province of China) *Tel:* (02) 5932392 *Fax:* (02) 5932763, pg 1214

Taiwan Branch Library, National Central Library (Taiwan, Province of China) *Tel:* (02) 771 8528, pg 1547

Tajak Korok Muzeumok Egyesuelet (Hungary) *Tel:* (01) 303 4069 *Fax:* (01) 303 4069 *E-mail:* tkmets@elender.hu, pg 321

Takahashi Shoten Co Ltd (Japan) *Tel:* (03) 3943-4525 *Fax:* (03) 3943-4288 *Web Site:* www.takahashishoten.co.jp, pg 425

Imprimerie Takariva (Madagascar) *Tel:* (02) 23856, pg 450

Take That Ltd (United Kingdom) *Tel:* (01423) 507545 *Fax:* (01423) 526035 *E-mail:* shop@takethat.co.uk *Web Site:* www.takethat.co.uk, pg 757

Edicoes Talento (Portugal) *Tel:* (021) 7154281 *Fax:* (021) 7154257, pg 531

Talento Publicacoes Editora e Grafica Ltda (Brazil) *Tel:* (011) 3816-1718 *Fax:* (011) 2823752 *E-mail:* talento@talento.com.br *Web Site:* www.talento.com.br, pg 90

Talentum Konyves es Kereskedo Kft (Hungary) *Tel:* (01) 3118824, pg 1304

Editions Tallandier (France) *Tel:* (01) 40 46 43 88 *Fax:* (01) 40 46 43 98 *Web Site:* www.tallandier.com, pg 187

Editora Taller (Dominican Republic) *Tel:* 531-7975 *Fax:* 531-7979 *E-mail:* editora.taller@codetel.net.do, pg 136

Talmudic Encyclopedia Publications (Israel) *Tel:* (02) 6423242 *Fax:* (02) 6423919, pg 369

Taltos Kiadasszervezesi Ltd (Hungary) *Tel:* (01) 1213515; (01) 1420676, pg 321

Tamagawa University Press (Japan) *Tel:* (042) 739-8935 *Fax:* (042) 739-8940 *E-mail:* tup@tamagawa.ac.jp *Web Site:* www.tamagawa.ac.jp/sisetu/up, pg 425

Tamarind Publications (Australia) *Tel:* (02) 467934 *Fax:* (02) 659515 *E-mail:* sigi@hunterlink.net.au, pg 42

Tampereen Kirjakauppa Oy (Finland) *Tel:* (03) 2128380 *Fax:* (03) 2122136 *E-mail:* trekirja@vip.fi *Web Site:* www.tampereenkirjakauppa.fi, pg 1299

Tampereen Yliopiston Kirjasto (Finland) *Tel:* (03) 215 6434 *Fax:* (03) 215 7493 *E-mail:* yliopiston.kirjasto@uta.fi *Web Site:* www.uta.fi/~kimiii, pg 1504

Tana Press Ltd & Flora Nwapa Books Ltd (Nigeria) *Tel:* (042) 338857, pg 502

Tandem Press (New Zealand) *Tel:* (09) 480-1452 *Fax:* (09) 480-1455 *E-mail:* customers@tandempress.co.nz *Web Site:* www.tandempress.co.nz, pg 497

Tango Books (United Kingdom) *Tel:* (020) 8996 9970 *Fax:* (020) 8996 9977 *E-mail:* sales@tangobooks.co.uk, pg 757

Tankosha Publishing Co Ltd (Japan) *Tel:* (075) 432 5151 *Fax:* (075) 432 0275 *E-mail:* info@tankosha.co.jp *Web Site:* tankosha.topica.ne.jp, pg 425

Tantalum-Niobium International Study Center (Belgium) *Tel:* (02) 6495158 *Fax:* (02) 6496447 *E-mail:* info@tanb.org *Web Site:* www.tanb.org, pg 1252

Tanum Karl Johan A/S (Norway) *Tel:* (022) 41 11 00 *Fax:* (022) 33 32 75 *E-mail:* karl.johan@tanum.no; nettservice@tanum.no *Web Site:* www.tanum.no, pg 1324

Tanzania Library Association (United Republic of Tanzania) *Tel:* (022) 2775411 *E-mail:* tla_tanzania@yahoo.com *Web Site:* www.tlatz.org, pg 1571

Tanzania Library Service (United Republic of Tanzania) *Tel:* (022) 215 09 23; (022) 215 00 48 *Fax:* (022) 215 11 00 *E-mail:* tlsb@africaonline.co.tz, pg 1278, 1548

Tanzania Library Services Board (United Republic of Tanzania) *Tel:* (022) 215 09 23; (022) 215 00 48 *Fax:* tlsb@africaonline.co.tz, pg 640

Tanzania Publishing House (United Republic of Tanzania) *Tel:* (051) 32164, pg 640

Taoasis Verlag, Birgit Meyer (Germany) *Tel:* (05261) 9383-0 *Fax:* (05261) 9383-21 *E-mail:* info@taoasis.de *Web Site:* www.taoasis.de, pg 286

Tappeiner (Italy) *Tel:* (0473) 563666 *Fax:* (0473) 563689 *E-mail:* tappeiner@pass.dnet.it, pg 406

Taprobane Ltd (United Kingdom) *Tel:* (020) 8998 3024 *Fax:* (020) 8810 5415, pg 757

Tara Publishing (India) *Tel:* (044) 24401696; (044) 24912846 *Fax:* (044) 24453658 *E-mail:* mail@tarabooks.com *Web Site:* www.tarabooks.com, pg 347

DB Taraporevala Sons & Co Pvt Ltd (India) *Tel:* 2041433; 2041434, pg 348

Editions Tardy SA (France) *Tel:* (01) 53 26 33 35 *Fax:* (01) 53 26 33 36, pg 187

Tarea Asociacion de Publicaciones Educativas (Peru) *Tel:* (01) 424-0997 *Fax:* (01) 332-7404 *E-mail:* postmaster@tarea.org.pe *Web Site:* www.tarea.org.pe, pg 512

Target Publishers (Edms) Bpk (South Africa) *Tel:* (018) 4627556 *Fax:* (018) 4627557, pg 565

Taride Editions (France) *Tel:* (01) 48 78 40 74 *Fax:* (01) 48 78 40 77 *Web Site:* www.taride.com, pg 187

Editions Tarmeye (France) *Tel:* (0471) 650153 *Fax:* (0471) 650154, pg 187

Tarquin Publications (United Kingdom) *Tel:* (01379) 384 218 *Fax:* (01379) 384 289 *E-mail:* enquiries@tarquin-books.demon.co.uk *Web Site:* www.tarquin-books.demon.co.uk, pg 757

Ediciones Tarraco (Spain) *Tel:* (077) 233813 *Fax:* (077) 233851, pg 596

La Tartaruga Edizioni SAS (Italy) *Tel:* (02) 584501 *Fax:* (02) 58307512, pg 406

Tartu University Library (Estonia) *Tel:* (07) 375
702 *Fax:* (07) 375 701 *E-mail:* library@utlib.ee
*Web Site:* www.utlib.ee, pg 1502

TASCHEN GmbH (Germany) *Tel:* (0221) 201 80 0
*Fax:* (0221) 25 49 19 *E-mail:* contact@taschen.com
*Web Site:* www.taschen.com, pg 286

Taschen UK Ltd (United Kingdom) *Tel:* (020) 7437 4350
*Fax:* (020) 7437 4360 *E-mail:* contact@taschen.com
*Web Site:* www.taschen.com, pg 757

Tassorello SA (Peru) *Tel:* (01) 460-2040; (01) 460-0255
*Fax:* (01) 461-5714 *E-mail:* tassorello@terra.com.pe,
pg 512

Tassotti Editore (Italy) *Tel:* (0424) 566105 *Fax:* (0424)
566205 *E-mail:* info@tassotti.it *Web Site:* www.
tassotti.it, pg 406

Est-Samuel Tastet Verlag (Romania) *Tel:* (01) 6386250
*Fax:* (01) 3122012, pg 538

Tata McGraw-Hill Publishing Co Ltd (India) *Tel:* (011)
2588 2743; (011) 2588 2746; (011) 2588 9304; (011)
2588 9307 *E-mail:* info_india@mcgraw-hill.com
*Web Site:* www.tatamcgrawhill.com, pg 348

Tate Publishing Ltd (United Kingdom) *Tel:* (020)
7887 8000; (020) 7887 8008 *Fax:* (020) 7887 8878
*E-mail:* tp.enquiries@tate.org.uk *Web Site:* www.tate.
org.uk, pg 757

Edition Tau u Tau Type Druck Verlags-und Handels
GmbH (Austria) *Tel:* (02625) 32000 *Fax:* (02625)
320003, pg 58

I B Tauris & Co Ltd (United Kingdom) *Tel:* (020) 7243
1225 *Fax:* (020) 7243 1226 *E-mail:* mail@ibtauris.
com *Web Site:* www.ibtauris.com, pg 758

Taurus (South Africa) *Tel:* 7860018, pg 565

Taylor Books (New Zealand) *Tel:* (07) 5786024, pg 497

Taylor & Francis (United Kingdom) *Tel:* (01235) 828600
*Fax:* (01235) 828900 *E-mail:* info@tandf.co.uk
*Web Site:* www.tandf.co.uk, pg 758

Taylor & Francis Asia Pacific (Singapore) *Tel:* 67415166
*Fax:* 67429356 *E-mail:* info@tandf.com.sg
*Web Site:* www.tandf.co.uk, pg 554

Taylor & Francis Group (United Kingdom) *Tel:* (020)
7583 9855; (020) 7017 6000 *Fax:* (020) 8842 2298;
(020) 7017 6699 *E-mail:* enquiry@tandf.co.uk
*Web Site:* www.taylorandfrancisgroup.com, pg 758

Taylor Graham Publishing (United Kingdom)
*Web Site:* www.taylorgraham.com, pg 758

Taylor Publishing Company (United States) *Tel:* 214-
819-8226 *Toll Free Tel:* 800-677-2800 *Fax:* 214-630-
1852 *E-mail:* info@taylorpub.com *Web Site:* www.
taylorpub.com, pg 1157, 1179, 1221, 1231

TBI Publishers' Distributors (India) *Tel:* (011) 3325247
*Fax:* (011) 3325247, pg 1307

TBS-Britannica Co Ltd (Japan) *Tel:* (03) 5436-5701
*Fax:* (03) 5436-5746, pg 426

Tcherikover Publishers Ltd (Israel) *Tel:* (03) 6870621;
(03) 6396099 *Toll Free Tel:* 800-828-080 *Fax:* (03)
6874729 *E-mail:* barkay@inter.net.il, pg 369

Te Waihora Press (New Zealand) *Tel:* (03) 304-8555
*Fax:* (03) 355-9706, pg 497

TEA Ediciones SA (Spain) *Tel:* (091) 912 705 000
*Fax:* (091) 913 458 608 *E-mail:* madrid@teaediciones.
com *Web Site:* www.teaediciones.com, pg 596

TEA Kirjastus (Estonia) *Tel:* 644 9253; 645 9206
*Fax:* 645 9208 *E-mail:* info@tea.ee *Web Site:* www.
tea.ee, pg 140

TEA Tascabili degli Editori Associati SpA
(Italy) *Tel:* (02) 80206625 *Fax:* (02) 8900844
*Web Site:* www.tealibri.it, pg 406

Teachers Book Club (United Kingdom) *Tel:* (01926)
813910 *Fax:* (01926) 817727 *E-mail:* enquiries@
scholastic.co.uk *Web Site:* www.scholastic.co.uk/
teach_index.html, pg 1247

Team Double Click Inc Literary (Netherlands) *Toll Free
Tel:* 888-827-9129 *Fax:* 262-364-3022 *Web Site:* www.
teamdoubleclick.com/literary_agency.html, pg 1125

Teaterforlaget Drama (Denmark) *Tel:* 70 25 11
41 *Fax:* 74 65 20 93 *E-mail:* drama@drama.dk
*Web Site:* www.drama.dk, pg 135

TEC Doc Publishing Inc (United States) *Tel:* 978-567-
6000 *Fax:* 978-562-4304 *Web Site:* www.tecdocpub.
com, pg 1179, 1221

Tech Publications Pte Ltd (Singapore) *Tel:* 7449113;
7428782 *Fax:* 7449835 *E-mail:* techpub@pacific.net.
sg, pg 554

Techbooks (New Zealand) *Tel:* (09) 524-0132 *Fax:* (09)
523-3769 *E-mail:* techbooks@techbooks.co.nz
*Web Site:* www.techbooks.co.nz, pg 1322

Technica Publishing House (Bulgaria) *Tel:* (02) 987
1283 *Fax:* (02) 987 4906 *E-mail:* technica@netel.bg;
sales@technica-bg.com *Web Site:* www.technica-bg.
com, pg 97

Technical Books Ltd (South Africa) *Tel:* (021) 216540
*Fax:* (021) 4216593 *E-mail:* techbkct@mweb.co.za,
pg 1332

Technical Centre for Agricultural & Rural Co-operation
(Netherlands) *Tel:* (0317) 467100 *Fax:* (0317) 460067
*E-mail:* cta@cta.nl *Web Site:* www.cta.nl, pg 1269

Technical Chamber of Greece (Greece) *Tel:* 210
3254591; 2103314403 *Fax:* 2103314403
*E-mail:* registry@central.tee.gr, pg 309

Library of the Technical Chamber of Greece (Greece)
*Tel:* 2103291701; 2103245180 *Fax:* 2103237525
*E-mail:* tee_lib@tee.gr *Web Site:* www.tee.gr,
pg 1511

Technical University Library (Turkey) *Tel:* (0212) 285 35
96 *Fax:* (0212) 285 33 02 *E-mail:* kutuphane@itu.edu.
tr *Web Site:* www.library.itu.edu.tr, pg 1550

Technical University of Sofia Library & Information
Complex (Bulgaria) *Tel:* (02) 62 3073 *Fax:* (02) 68
5343 *E-mail:* office_tu@tu-sofia.bg *Web Site:* www.tu-
sofia.bg, pg 1495

Technicka Univerzita (Slovakia) *Tel:* (045) 63545
*Fax:* (045) 20027, pg 556

Hochschule fur Technik Wirtschaft und Kultur Leipzig
(FH) (Germany) *Tel:* (0341) 3076-0 *Fax:* (0341) 3076-
6456 *E-mail:* dekan@htwk.leipzig.de *Web Site:* www.
htwk-leipzig.de, pg 287

Instytut Techniki Budowlanej, Dzial Wydawniczo-
Poligraficzny (Poland) *Tel:* (022) 8431471 *Fax:* (022)
8432931 *E-mail:* wydawnictwa_itb@pro.onet.pl
*Web Site:* www.itb.pl, pg 522

Technion - Israel Institute of Technology Libraries
(Israel) *Tel:* (04) 8292507 *Fax:* (04) 8295662
*E-mail:* webteam@tx.technion.ac.il *Web Site:* library.
technion.ac.il, pg 1518

Editions Technip SA (France) *Tel:* (01) 45 78 33 80
*Fax:* (01) 45 75 37 11 *E-mail:* info@editionstechnip.
com *Web Site:* www.editionstechnip.com, pg 187

Editions Techniques et Scientifiques SPRL (Belgium)
*Tel:* (02) 6401040 *Fax:* (02) 6400739, pg 73

Editions Techniques et Scientifiques Francaises (France)
*Tel:* (01) 40 46 35 00 *Fax:* (01) 40 46 49 95
*E-mail:* infos@dunod.com *Web Site:* www.dunod.com,
pg 187

Editions Techniques Specialisees (Tunisia)
*Tel:* 71262155; 71747004 *Fax:* 71746160
*E-mail:* info@pagesjaunes.com.tn, pg 644

Universitaetsbibliothek der Technischen Universitaet
Wien (Austria) *Tel:* (01) 58801 44051 *Fax:* (01)
58801 44099 *E-mail:* mail.ub.tuwien.ac.at
*Web Site:* www.ub.tuwien.ac.at, pg 1490

Technology Exchange Ltd (Hong Kong) *Tel:* 2602 6300
*Fax:* 2609 1687, pg 316

Technosdar Ltd (Israel) *Tel:* (03) 560-7418; (03) 560-
5951 *Fax:* (03) 560-4932 *E-mail:* technos@internet-
zahav.net, pg 1149

Technosdar Ltd (Israel) *Tel:* (03) 560-7418; (03)
5605951 *Fax:* (03) 5605951, pg 1170

Technosdar Ltd (Israel) *Tel:* (03) 560-7418 *Fax:* (03)
560-4932 *E-mail:* technos@zahav.net.il, pg 1210

Tecman Bible House (Singapore) *Tel:* 6338-6764
*Fax:* 6338-8236 *E-mail:* tecman@tecman.com.sg
*Web Site:* www.tecman.com.sg, pg 554

Publicaciones Tecnicas Mediterraneo (Chile) *Tel:* (02)
251 62 57; (02) 233 82 72 *Fax:* (02) 231 06 94
*E-mail:* msalinero@entelchile.net, pg 100

Ediciones Tecnicas Rede, SA (Spain) *Tel:* (093) 4103097
*Fax:* (093) 4392813, pg 596

Tecniche Nuove SpA (Italy) *Tel:* (02) 390901 *Fax:* (02)
7610351 *E-mail:* info@tecnichenuove.com;
vendite-libri@tecnichenuove.com *Web Site:* www.
tecnichenuove.com, pg 406

Editores Tecnicos Asociados SA (Spain) *Tel:* (093)
4193336, pg 596

Editorial Tecnologica de Costa Rica (Costa Rica)
*Tel:* 552-5333 ext 2297 *Fax:* 552-5354; 551-5348
*E-mail:* editec@itcr.ac.cr *Web Site:* www.itcr.ac.cr,
pg 116

Instituto Tecnologico de Galicia, ITG (Spain) *Tel:* (0981)
17 32 06 *Fax:* (0981) 17 32 23 *E-mail:* itg@itg.es
*Web Site:* www.itg.es, pg 596

Editorial Tecnos SA (Spain) *Tel:* (091) 393 86 88; (091)
393 86 86 *Fax:* (091) 7426631 *Web Site:* www.tecnos.
es, pg 597

Teduca, Tecnicas Educativas, CA (Venezuela) *Tel:* (0212)
235 58 78; (0212) 235 43 95; (0212) 235 62 65
*Fax:* (0212) 239 79 52, pg 775

Teeney Books Ltd (United Kingdom) *Tel:* (01225)
775657 *Fax:* (01225) 775676 *E-mail:* teeneybo@
primex.co.uk, pg 758

Editura Tehnica (Romania) *Tel:* (01) 222-33-21 *Fax:* (01)
222-37-76, pg 538

Tehnicka Knjiga (Croatia) *Tel:* (01) 481 0819 *Fax:* (01)
481 0821, pg 119

Tehnicka Knjiga (Croatia) *Tel:* (041) 4810819; (041)
4810820 *Fax:* (041) 4810821, pg 1297

Tehniska Zalozba Slovenije (Slovenia) *Tel:* (01)
4790211 *Fax:* (01) 4790230 *E-mail:* info@tzs.si
*Web Site:* www.tzs.si, pg 1331

Otto Teich (Germany) *Tel:* (06151) 824120 *Fax:* (06151)
895656, pg 287

Editorial Teide SA (Spain) *Tel:* (093) 4398009
*Fax:* (093) 3224192 *E-mail:* editorial@editorialteide.es
*Web Site:* www.editorialteide.es, pg 597

Teikoku-Shoin Co Ltd (Japan) *Tel:* (03) 32620834
*Fax:* (03) 32627770 *E-mail:* kenkyu@teikokushoin.
co.jp *Web Site:* www.teikokushoin.co.jp, pg 426

Almerinda Teixeira (Portugal) *Tel:* (021) 2762352,
pg 531

Tek Translation International SA (Spain) *Tel:* (091)
4141111 *Fax:* (091) 4144444 *E-mail:* sales@tektrans.
com *Web Site:* www.tektrans.com, pg 1139

Tekmirio (Greece) *Tel:* 2103637912; 2102287548,
pg 309

Teknillisen Korkeakoulun Kirjasto (Finland) *Tel:* (09)
451 4111 *Fax:* (09) 451 4132 *E-mail:* infolib@tkk.fi
*Web Site:* lib.tkk.fi, pg 1504

Tekniska Litteratursaellskapet (Sweden) *Tel:* (08) 678
23 20 *Fax:* (08) 678 23 01 *E-mail:* kansliet@tls.se
*Web Site:* www.tls.se, pg 1571

Teknografiska Institutet AB (Sweden) *Tel:* (08) 83 42 85
*Fax:* (08) 73 04 13, pg 611

Teknologisk Forlag (Norway) *Tel:* 22471100
*Fax:* 22471149, pg 506

Tel Aviv Books Ltd (Israel) *Tel:* (03) 6210500 *Fax:* (03)
5257725, pg 369

Konrad Theiss Verlag GmbH (Germany) *Tel:* (0711) 255 27-0 *Fax:* (0711) 255 27-17 *E-mail:* service@theiss.de *Web Site:* www.theiss.de, pg 288

Theodor (Imprimerie) (Haiti), pg 311

Theologischer Verlag und Buchhandlungen AG (Switzerland) *Tel:* (01) 299 33 55 *Fax:* (01) 299 33 58 *E-mail:* tvz@ref.ch *Web Site:* www.tvz.ref.ch, pg 630

Theoria SRL Distribuidora y Editora (Argentina) *Tel:* (011) 4381-0131 *Fax:* (011) 4381-0131 *E-mail:* edicionestheoria@ciudad.com.ar, pg 9

Theosophical Publishing House (India) *Tel:* (044) 412904 *Fax:* (044) 4901399; (044) 4902706 *E-mail:* intl-hq@ts-adyar.org *Web Site:* ts-adyar.org, pg 348

Thesen Verlag Vowinckel (Luxembourg) *Tel:* 748715 *Fax:* 26740429, pg 448

Theseus - Verlag AG (Switzerland) *Tel:* (01) 9109294 *Fax:* (01) 9108019, pg 630

Thex Editora e Distribuidora Ltda (Brazil) *Tel:* (021) 2221-4458 *Fax:* (021) 2252-9338 *E-mail:* atendimento@thexeditora.com.br *Web Site:* www.thexeditora.com.br, pg 90

Druck-und Verlagshaus Thiele & Schwarz GmbH (Germany) *Tel:* (0561) 9 59 25-0 *Fax:* (0561) 9 59 25-68 *E-mail:* info@thiele-schwarz.de *Web Site:* www.thiele-schwarz.de, pg 288

Georg Thieme Verlag KG (Germany) *Tel:* (0711) 8931-0 *Fax:* (0711) 8931-298 *E-mail:* kunden.service@thieme.de *Web Site:* www.thieme.de; www.thieme.com, pg 288

ThiemeMeulenhoff (Netherlands) *Tel:* (030) 239 2 111 *Fax:* (030) 239 2 270 *E-mail:* info.bao@thiememeulenhoff.nl *Web Site:* www.thiememeulenhoff.nl, pg 485

Thien, Hans-Gunter, u Hanns Wienold (Germany) *Tel:* (0251) 3900480 *Fax:* (0251) 39004850 *E-mail:* info@dampfboot-verlag.de *Web Site:* www.dampfboot-verlag.de, pg 288

Thienemann Verlag GmbH (Germany) *Tel:* (0711) 210 55-0 *Fax:* (0711) 210 55 39 *E-mail:* info@thienemann.de *Web Site:* www.thienemann.de, pg 288

James Thin, Bookseller (United Kingdom) *Tel:* (0131) 622 8222 *Fax:* (0131) 557 8149 *E-mail:* enquiries@jthin.co.uk, pg 1345

The Third Wave Enterprise Co Ltd (Taiwan, Province of China) *Tel:* (02) 87803636 *Fax:* (02) 87805656 *E-mail:* AIWebmaster@acer.com.tw *Web Site:* www.acertwp.com.tw, pg 637

34 Literatura S/C Ltda (Brazil) *Tel:* (011) 3816-6777 *Fax:* (011) 3816-0078 *E-mail:* editora34@uol.com.br, pg 90

Thistle Press (United Kingdom) *Tel:* (01464) 821053 *Fax:* (01464) 821053 *E-mail:* info@oldmilldesign.co.uk, pg 759

Thjodsagao ehf (Iceland) *Tel:* 567-1777 *Fax:* 567-1240 *E-mail:* pbk@centrum.is, pg 323

Verlag Theodor Thoben (Germany) *Tel:* (05431) 3486 *Fax:* (05431) 3584 *E-mail:* info@buecher-thoben.de *Web Site:* www.buecher-thoben.de, pg 288

Thoemmes Press (United Kingdom) *Tel:* (0117) 929 1377 *Fax:* (0117) 922 1918 *E-mail:* info@thoemmes.com *Web Site:* www.thoemmes.com, pg 760

Hans Thoma Verlag GmbH Kunst und Buchverlag (Germany) *Tel:* (0721) 932750 *Fax:* (0721) 9327520 *E-mail:* htv@pv_medien.de *Web Site:* www.pv_medien.de/htv/ueberuns.htm, pg 288

Alain Thomas Editeur (France) *Tel:* (01) 45 88 28 03 *Fax:* (01) 45 88 49 24 *Web Site:* alainthomasimages.com, pg 188

Thomas Technology Solutions (UK) Ltd (United Kingdom) *Tel:* (020) 7070 7550 *Fax:* (020) 7070 7551 *E-mail:* marketing@thomastechsolutions.com *Web Site:* www.thomastechsolutions.com, pg 1175

Thomson Corporation (Hong Kong) *Tel:* 2533 5416 *Fax:* 2530 3588 *Web Site:* www.tfibcm.com, pg 316

D C Thomson & Co Ltd (United Kingdom) *Tel:* (01382) 223131 *Fax:* (01382) 462097 *E-mail:* shout@dcthomson.co.uk *Web Site:* www.dcthomson.co.uk, pg 760

Forlaget Thomson A/S (Denmark) *Tel:* 33 74 07 00 *Fax:* 33 12 16 36 *E-mail:* thomson@thomson.dk *Web Site:* www.thomson.dk, pg 135

Thomson Gale (United Kingdom) *Tel:* (01264) 342962 *Fax:* (01264) 342763 *Web Site:* www.gale.com, pg 760

Thomson Learning International (Unitcd Kingdom) *Tel:* (020) 7067 2500 *Fax:* (020) 7067 2600 *Web Site:* www.thomsonlearning.co.uk, pg 760

Thomson Learning Japan (Japan) *Tel:* (03) 3221-1385 *Fax:* (03) 3237-1459 *E-mail:* elt@tlj.co.jp *Web Site:* www.tlj.co.jp, pg 426

M & A Thomson Litho Ltd (United Kingdom) *Tel:* (01355) 233081 *Fax:* (01355) 245 039 *E-mail:* enquiries@thomsonlitho.com *Web Site:* www.thomsonlitho.com, pg 1154

M & A Thomson Litho Ltd (United Kingdom) *Tel:* (01355) 233 081 *Fax:* (01355) 245 039 *Web Site:* www.thomsonlitho.com, pg 1175

M & A Thomson Litho Ltd (United Kingdom) *Tel:* (01355) 233081 *Fax:* (01355) 245 039 *Web Site:* www.thomsonlitho.com, pg 1217, 1229

Thomson Publications Zimbabwe (Pvt) Ltd (Zimbabwe) *Tel:* (04) 736835 *Fax:* (04) 749803 *E-mail:* tpubl@mweb.co.zw, pg 778

Thomson Publishing Services (United Kingdom) *Tel:* (01264) 332424 *Fax:* (01264) 364418, pg 1345

Jan Thorbecke Verlag GmbH & Co (Germany) *Tel:* (0711) 44 06-0 *Fax:* (0711) 44 06-199 *E-mail:* info@thorbecke.de *Web Site:* www.thorbecke.de, pg 288

Thornbill Press (Australia) *Tel:* (08) 82705172, pg 43

Caroline Thornton (Australia) *Tel:* (08) 9386 1555 *Fax:* (08) 9389 5162, pg 43

Thornton's of Oxford Ltd (United Kingdom) *Tel:* (01865) 321126 *E-mail:* thorntons@booknews.demon.co.uk *Web Site:* www.thorntonsbooks.co.uk, pg 1345

Thorpe-Bowker (Australia) *Tel:* (03) 8645 0300 *Fax:* (03) 8645 0333 *E-mail:* yoursay@thorpe.com.au *Web Site:* www.thorpe.com.au, pg 43

Thoth Publications (United Kingdom) *Tel:* (01509) 210626 *Fax:* (01509) 238034 *E-mail:* enquiries@thoth.co.uk *Web Site:* www.thothpublications.com; www.thoth.co.uk, pg 760

Thoth Publishers (Netherlands) *Tel:* (035) 6944144 *Fax:* (035) 6943266 *E-mail:* thoth@euronet.nl, pg 486

Thrass (UK) Ltd (United Kingdom) *Tel:* (01829) 741413 *Fax:* (01829) 741419 *E-mail:* enquiries@thrass.demon.co.uk *Web Site:* www.thrass.co.uk, pg 760

3 Dimension World (3-D-World) (Switzerland) *Tel:* (061) 3013081 *Fax:* (094) 3133862, pg 630

Three Sisters Publications Pty Ltd (Australia) *Tel:* (047) 588138, pg 43

3A Corporation (Japan) *Tel:* (03) 32925751 *Fax:* (03) 32925754 *E-mail:* 3ac@mail.at-m.or.jp *Web Site:* www.at-m.or.jpl~3ac, pg 426

Threshold Publishing (Australia) *Tel:* (03) 9724 9067 *Fax:* (03) 9724 9067 *E-mail:* threshol@alphalink.com.au, pg 43

Thudhammawaddy Press (Myanmar), pg 472

Thueringer Universitaets- und Landesbibliothek (Germany) *Tel:* (03641) 9-40000 *Fax:* (03641) 9-40002 *E-mail:* thulb_direktion@thulb.uni-jena.de; thulb_auskunft@thulb.uni-jena.de *Web Site:* www.uni-jena.de/thulb, pg 1509

Edi Thule Club (Italy) *Tel:* (091) 323699, pg 1243

J M Thurley Management (United Kingdom) *Tel:* (020) 8977 3176 *Fax:* (020) 8943 2678, pg 1134

Edition Thurnhof KEG (Austria) *Tel:* (02982) 629-54 *Fax:* (02982) 3333 *E-mail:* edition@thurnhof.at *Web Site:* www.thurnhof.at, pg 58

Thwe Thauk (Myanmar), pg 1319

Thymari Publications (Greece) *Tel:* 210 3634901; 2103643015 *Fax:* 2103636591 *E-mail:* thymari@thymari.gr *Web Site:* thymari.gr, pg 309

Edizioni Thyrus SRL (Italy) *Tel:* (0744) 389496 *Fax:* (0744) 388700 *E-mail:* thyrus@bellaumbria.net *Web Site:* www.bellaumbria.net/thyrus, pg 406

Tianjin Science & Technology Publishing House (China) *Tel:* (022) 7312749 *Fax:* (022) 27312755 *E-mail:* tjstp@public.tpt.tj.on, pg 108

Istituto Editoriale Ticinese (IET) SA (Switzerland) *Tel:* (091) 8200101 *Fax:* (091) 8251874, pg 630

Tiden Norsk Forlag (Norway) *Tel:* (022) 23 32 76 60 *Fax:* (022) 23 32 76 97 *E-mail:* tiden@tiden.no *Web Site:* www.tiden.no, pg 506

Tiderne Skifter Forlag A/S (Denmark) *Tel:* 33 18 63 90 *Fax:* 33 18 63 91 *E-mail:* tiderneskifter@tiderneskifter.dk *Web Site:* www.tiderneskifter.dk, pg 135

Tien Wah Press Pte Ltd (Singapore) *Tel:* 466-6222 *Fax:* 469-3894 *Web Site:* www.dnp.co.jp, pg 1213

Tietohuollon Neuvottelukunta (Finland) *Tel:* (09) 13 41 71 *Fax:* (09) 65 67 65 *E-mail:* jylha@csc.fi *Web Site:* www.csc.fi, pg 1562

Tietoteos Publishing Co (Finland) *Tel:* (09) 2564475 *Fax:* (09) 8136361 *E-mail:* tt@jkttietoteos.fi *Web Site:* www.jkttietoteos.fi, pg 144

Tiger Books International PLC (United Kingdom) *Tel:* (0181) 8925577 *Fax:* (0181) 8916550 *E-mail:* gp@dial.pipex.com, pg 760

Tiger Books International PLC (United Kingdom) *Tel:* (0181) 8925577 *Fax:* (0181) 8916550, pg 1345

Tihama Bookstores (Saudi Arabia) *Tel:* (02) 6511100 *Fax:* (02) 6519277 *E-mail:* info@tihama.com *Web Site:* www.tihama.com/book/book.htm, pg 1329

Uitgeverij de Tijdstroom BV (Netherlands) *Tel:* (0342) 450867 *Fax:* (0342) 450365 *E-mail:* info@tijdstroom.nl *Web Site:* www.tijdstroom.nl, pg 486

Tilburg University Press (Netherlands) *Tel:* (013) 466 2124 *Fax:* (013) 466 2996 *E-mail:* library@kub.nl *Web Site:* www.tilburguniversity.nl, pg 486

Tilgher-Genova sas (Italy) *Tel:* (010) 839 11 40 *Fax:* (010) 870653 *E-mail:* tilgher@tilgher.it *Web Site:* www.tilgher.it, pg 406

The Tilling Society (United Kingdom) *Fax:* (01424) 813237 *E-mail:* society@tilling.org.uk *Web Site:* www.tilling.org.uk/society, pg 1404

Timber Press Inc (United Kingdom) *Tel:* (01954) 232959 *Fax:* (01954) 206040 *E-mail:* timberpressuk@btinternet.com *Web Site:* www.timberpress.com, pg 760

Timbro (Sweden) *Tel:* (08) 587 898 00 *Fax:* (08) 587 898 55 *E-mail:* info@timbro.se *Web Site:* www.timbro.se, pg 611

Time Life Australia Pty Ltd (Australia) *Tel:* (02) 1300 364 437 *Toll Free Tel:* 300 364 437 *Fax:* (02) 9957 2773 *E-mail:* tlservice@timelife.com *Web Site:* www.timelife.com.au, pg 43

Time-Life Books (UK) (United Kingdom) *Tel:* (020) 7911 8000 *Fax:* (020) 7911 8100 *E-mail:* email@timelife.demon.co.uk; email.uk@timewarnerbooks.co.uk *Web Site:* www.twbookmark.com; www.timewarnerbooks.co.uk, pg 760

Time-Life Internacional de Mexico (Mexico) *Tel:* (055) 5469000 *Fax:* (055) 5159764 *Web Site:* www.timelife.com, pg 468

Time Out Group Ltd (United Kingdom) *Tel:* (020) 7813 3000 *Fax:* (020) 7323 3438 *E-mail:* net@timeout.co. uk *Web Site:* www.timeout.com, pg 760

Time-Space Inc (Republic of Korea) *Tel:* (02) 2272 2381 *Fax:* (02) 2273 8900 *E-mail:* tspace@timespace.co.kr *Web Site:* www.fotato.com, pg 1124

Time Track (M) Sdn Bhd (Malaysia) *Tel:* (05) 3124329; (05) 3127541 *Fax:* (05) 2630305, pg 455

Time Warner Book Group UK (United Kingdom) *Tel:* (020) 7911 8000 *Fax:* (020) 7911 8100 *E-mail:* email.uk@twbg.co.uk *Web Site:* www.twbg. co.uk, pg 760

Times The Bookshop (Singapore) *Tel:* 6213 9288; 6213 9217 (customer service) *Fax:* 6382 2571 *E-mail:* ttb@ tpl.com.sg *Web Site:* www.timesone.com.sg, pg 1330

Times Educational Co Sdn Bhd (Malaysia) *Tel:* (03) 7571766 *Fax:* (03) 7573607, pg 455

Times Graphics (Singapore) *Tel:* 6213-9288 *Fax:* 6284 4733; 6288 1186 *E-mail:* tpl@tpl.com.sg *Web Site:* www.tpl.com.sg, pg 1172

Times International Publishing (United States) *Tel:* 914-366-9888 *Fax:* 914-366-9898 *Web Site:* www.tpl.com. sg, pg 1157, 1179, 1221, 1231, 1239

Times Media Pte Ltd (Singapore) *Tel:* 62848844 *Fax:* 62771186 *E-mail:* tedcsd@tpl.com.sg *Web Site:* www.timesone.com.sg/te, pg 554

Times Printers Pte Ltd (Singapore) *Tel:* 6311-2888 *Fax:* 682-1313 *E-mail:* enquiry@timesprinters.com *Web Site:* www.timesprinters.com, pg 1151

Times Printers Pte Ltd (Singapore) *Tel:* 6311-2888 *Fax:* 6862-1313 *E-mail:* tp@timesprinters.com; enquiry@timesprinters.com *Web Site:* www. timesprinters.com; www.tpl.com.sg, pg 1172

Times Printers Pte Ltd (Singapore) *Tel:* 6862 3333 *Fax:* 6862 1313 *E-mail:* tp@timesprinters.com *Web Site:* www.tpl.com.sg, pg 1213

Times Printers Pte Ltd (Singapore) *Tel:* 6311-2888 *Fax:* 6862-1313 *E-mail:* enquiry@timesprinters.com *Web Site:* www.timesprinters.com, pg 1228, 1236

Times Publishing (Hong Kong) Ltd (Hong Kong) *Tel:* 23342421 *Fax:* 27645095; 23657834 *E-mail:* admin@federalbooks.com, pg 316

Penerbitan Tinta (Malaysia) *Tel:* (03) 4424163 *Fax:* (03) 4424640, pg 455

Tintamas Indonesia PT (Indonesia) *Tel:* (021) 3107148; (021) 7393701 *Fax:* (021) 3911459; (021) 3107148, pg 353

Tipografica Editora Argentina (Argentina) *Tel:* (011) 4373-2581 *Fax:* (011) 4775-2521 *E-mail:* bernardosm@sinectis.com.ar, pg 9

Tipress Dienstleistungen fuer das Verlagswesen GmbH (Germany) *Tel:* (07634) 591193 *Fax:* (07634) 591192 *E-mail:* tipress@tipress.com *Web Site:* www.tipress. com, pg 288

Tipress Dienstleistungen fur das Verlagswesen GmbH (Germany) *Tel:* (07634) 591193 *Fax:* (07634) 591192 *E-mail:* tipress@tipress.com *Web Site:* www.tipress. com, pg 1122

Tir Eolas (Ireland) *Tel:* (091) 637452 *Fax:* (091) 637452 *E-mail:* info@tireolas.com *Web Site:* www.tireolas. com, pg 360

Tirant lo Blanch SL Libreriaa (Spain) *Tel:* (096) 3610048 *Fax:* (096) 3694151 *E-mail:* tlb@tirant.es *Web Site:* www.tirant.es, pg 597

Editions Tiresias Michel Reynaud (France) *Tel:* (01) 42 23 47 27 *Fax:* (01) 42 23 73 27 *E-mail:* editions. tiresias@club-internet.fr *Web Site:* www.editions-tiresias.fr.tc, pg 188

Tirian Publications (Australia) *Tel:* (02) 9908 1196 *Fax:* (02) 9907 1196 *E-mail:* Tirian@bigpond.com; infoweb@tirian.com *Web Site:* www.users.bigpond. com/tirian, pg 43

Tirion Uitgevers BV (Netherlands) *Tel:* (035) 5486600 *Fax:* (035) 5486675 *E-mail:* info@tirionuitgevers.nl *Web Site:* www.tirionuitgevers.nl, pg 486

Ramona S Tirona Memorial Library (Philippines) *Tel:* (02) 5268421 (loc 176) *Fax:* (02) 5266935, pg 1535

Tirosh Communication Ltd (Israel) *Tel:* (03) 6044959 *Fax:* (03) 6053840 *E-mail:* hgeffen@netvision.net.il, pg 369

Editrice Tirrenia Stampatori SAS (Italy) *Tel:* (011) 8177010 *Fax:* (011) 8177010 *E-mail:* info@ tirreniastampatori.it *Web Site:* www.tirreniastampatori. it, pg 407

Titan Books Ltd (United Kingdom) *Tel:* (020) 7620 0200 *Fax:* (020) 7620 0032 *E-mail:* readerfeedback@ titanemail.com *Web Site:* www.titanbooks.com, pg 761

Titania-Verlag Ferdinand Schroll (Germany) *Tel:* (0711) 63 81 25 *Fax:* (0711) 63 69 872, pg 288

Titles Old and Rare Books of Oxford (United Kingdom) *Tel:* (01865) 727928 *Fax:* (01865) 727928, pg 1345

Tivenan Publications (Ireland) *Tel:* (069) 62596 *Fax:* (069) 62933 *E-mail:* wellwoman@wellwoman. info *Web Site:* www.wellwoman.info, pg 360

TJ International Ltd (United Kingdom) *Tel:* (01841) 532691 *Fax:* (01841) 532862 *E-mail:* sales@ tjinternational.ltd.uk *Web Site:* www.tjinternational. ltd.uk, pg 1154, 1217

TML Trade Publishing (South Africa) *Tel:* (011) 7892144 *Fax:* (011) 7893196, pg 565

TMS Development International Ltd (United Kingdom) *Tel:* (01904) 641640 *Fax:* (01904) 640076 *E-mail:* enquiry@tmsdi.com *Web Site:* www.tmsdi. com, pg 1238

To Rodakio (Greece) *Tel:* 2103221700; 210 3221742 *Fax:* 2103221700 *E-mail:* rodakio@ otenet.gz, pg 309

Tobias Associates Inc (United States) *Tel:* 215-322-1500 *Toll Free Fax:* 800-877-3367 *Fax:* 215-322-1504 *E-mail:* sales@tobiasinc.com *Web Site:* www. densitometer.com, pg 1221, 1239

Tobin Music (United Kingdom) *Tel:* (01279) 726625 *E-mail:* candida@tobinmusic.co.uk *Web Site:* www. candidatobin.co.uk, pg 761

Tobler Verlag (Switzerland) *Tel:* (071) 755 6060 *Fax:* (071) 755 1254 *E-mail:* books@tobler-verlag.ch *Web Site:* www.tobler-verlag.ch, pg 631

Todariana Editrice (Italy) *Tel:* (02) 56812953 *Fax:* (02) 55213405 *E-mail:* toeurs@tin.it, pg 407

Today & Tomorrow's Printers & Publishers (India) *Tel:* (011) 5721928; (011) 5727770, pg 348

Todor Kableshkov University of Transport (Bulgaria) *Tel:* (02) 9709335; (02) 9709384; (02) 9709478 *Fax:* (02) 9709407 *E-mail:* office@vtu.bg *Web Site:* www.vtu.bg, pg 97

S Toeche-Mittler Verlag GmbH (Germany) *Tel:* (06151) 33665 *Fax:* (06151) 314048 *E-mail:* info@net-library. de *Web Site:* www.net-library.de, pg 289

Tohan Corporation (Japan) *Tel:* (03) 3269-6111 *Fax:* (03) 3235-1337, pg 1313

Toho Book Store (Japan) *Tel:* (03) 32331001 *Fax:* (03) 32950800, pg 426

Toho Shuppan (Japan) *Tel:* (06) 6779-9571 *Fax:* (06) 6779-9573 *E-mail:* info@tohoshuppan.co.jp *Web Site:* www.tohoshuppan.co.jp, pg 426

Tohoku University Library (Japan) *Tel:* (022) 217 5943; (0221) 217 4844 *Fax:* (0222) 217 5949; (0222) 217846 *E-mail:* fetsu1@library.tohoku.ac.jp *Web Site:* www.library.tohoku.ac.jp, pg 1520

Libris Toison d'Or SA (Belgium) *Tel:* (02) 5116400 *Fax:* (02) 5140961, pg 1292

Tokai University Press (Japan) *Tel:* (0463) 79-3921 (Sales); (0463) 79-3921 (Editorial) *Fax:* (0463) 69-5087 *E-mail:* webmaster@press.tokai.ac.jp *Web Site:* www.press.tokai.ac.jp, pg 426

Toker Yayinlari (Turkey) *Tel:* (0212) 5223309, pg 647

Tokuma Shoten Publishing Co Ltd (Japan) *Tel:* (03) 5403-4300 *Fax:* (03) 3573-8771 *E-mail:* iwabuchi@ shoten.tokuma.com *Web Site:* www.tokuma.jp, pg 426

Tokyo Kagaku Dojin Co Ltd (Japan) *Tel:* (03) 3946-5311 *Fax:* (03) 3946-5316 *E-mail:* tokyokagakudozin@a. email.ne.jp, pg 426

Tokyo Metropolitan Central Library (Japan) *Tel:* (03) 3442-8451 *Fax:* (03) 3447-8924 *Web Site:* www. library.metro.tokyo.jp/, pg 1520

Tokyo Publications Service Ltd (Japan) *Tel:* (03) 3561-9741 *Fax:* (03) 3561-9743 *E-mail:* info@tokyoyosho. com *Web Site:* www.tokyoyosho.com, pg 1313

Tokyo Shoseki Co Ltd (Japan) *Tel:* (03) 5390-7531 *Fax:* (03) 5390-7409 *E-mail:* home@tokyo-shoseki. co.jp *Web Site:* www.tokyo-shoseki.co.jp, pg 426

Tokyo Sogensha Co Ltd (Japan) *Tel:* (03) 3268-8201 *Fax:* (03) 3268-8230 *Web Site:* www.tsogen.co.jp, pg 426

Tokyo Tosho Co Ltd (Japan) *Tel:* (03) 3814-7818 *Fax:* (03) 3815-7330 *Web Site:* www.tokyo-tosho.co.jp, pg 426

Joe-Tolalu & Associates (Nigeria) *Tel:* (01) 4925078, pg 503

Toledo Creative Management (Netherlands) *Tel:* (020) 6226873 *Fax:* (020) 6276720 *E-mail:* agency@toledo-cm.nl, pg 1125

Toleranz Verlag, Nielsen Frederic W (Germany) *Tel:* (0761) 81415 *E-mail:* irenenielsen@web.de, pg 289

The Tolkien Society (United Kingdom) *Tel:* (01242) 529757 *E-mail:* membership@tolkiensociety.org *Web Site:* www.tolkiensociety.org, pg 1404

Tom Publications (Australia) *Tel:* (08) 9444 4570, pg 43

Tomar Publishing Ltd (Ireland) *Fax:* (01) 744697, pg 360

Tomo Edizioni srl (Italy) *Tel:* (081) 00920 *Fax:* (081) 00920 *E-mail:* tomoedizioni@libero.it, pg 407

Tomorrow Publications (Australia) *Tel:* (02) 4961 2115 *E-mail:* tomorrowtrading@hotmail.com, pg 43

Tomorrow Publishing House (China) *Tel:* (0531) 206 0055 *Fax:* (0531) 290 2094 *E-mail:* tomorrow@ sdpress.com *Web Site:* www.tomorrowpub.com, pg 108

Tomus Verlag GmbH (Germany) *Tel:* (08581) 910666 *Fax:* (08581) 910668 *E-mail:* info@tomus.de *Web Site:* www.tomus.de, pg 289

Toneelfonds J Janssens BVBA (Belgium) *Tel:* (03) 366 44 00 *Fax:* (03) 366 45 01 *E-mail:* info@toneelfonds. be *Web Site:* www.toneelfonds.be, pg 73, 1119

P J Tonger Musikverlag GmbH & Co (Germany) *Tel:* (0221) 935564-0 *Fax:* (0221) 935564-11 *E-mail:* musikverlag@tonger.de *Web Site:* www.tonger. de, pg 289

Uitgeverij De Toorts (Netherlands) *Tel:* (023) 5532920 *Fax:* (023) 5320635 *E-mail:* uitgeverij@toorts.nl *Web Site:* www.toorts.nl, pg 486

TOP Editions (France) *Tel:* (01) 30 14 19 30 *Fax:* (01) 34 60 31 32 *E-mail:* info@editionschiron.com *Web Site:* www.editionschiron.com, pg 188

Top Secret Collection Publishers (Russian Federation) *Tel:* (095) 2022011; (095) 2024531 *Fax:* (095) 2913885 *E-mail:* topsec@glasnet.ru, pg 544

Editura Top Suspans (Romania) *Tel:* (021) 6830924; (021) 6103359, pg 538

Topaz Publications (Ireland) *Tel:* (01) 2800460 *Fax:* (01) 2800460, pg 360

Topic Verlag GmbH (Germany) *Tel:* (08131) 97038 *Fax:* (08131) 98404, pg 1145, 1167

Topos Verlag AG (Liechtenstein) *Tel:* 3771111 *Fax:* 3771119 *E-mail:* topos@supra.net *Web Site:* www.topos.li, pg 445

Toppan Co Ltd (Japan) *Tel:* (03) 3968-5111 *Fax:* (03) 5418-2529 *E-mail:* kouhou@toppan.co.jp *Web Site:* www.toppan.co.jp, pg 426

Toppan Printing Co America Inc (United States) *Tel:* 732-469-8400 *Fax:* 732-469-1868 *E-mail:* njsales@ta.toppan.com *Web Site:* www.ta. toppan.com, pg 1157

Toppan Printing Co (HK) Ltd (Hong Kong) *Tel:* 2475-5666; 2561-0101 *Fax:* 2475-4321 *E-mail:* info@ toppan.co.jp *Web Site:* www.toppan.co.jp, pg 1169

Toppan Printing Co (HK) Ltd (Hong Kong) *Tel:* 2561-0101 *Fax:* 24754321 *E-mail:* info@toppan.co.jp *Web Site:* www.toppan.co.jp, pg 1209

Toppan Printing Co (UK) Ltd (United Kingdom) *Tel:* (020) 7828 7292; (020) 7828 7296 *Fax:* (020) 7828 5310 *E-mail:* kawamura@toppan.co.uk; info.e@ toppan.co.jp *Web Site:* www.toppan.co.jp, pg 1154

Torch of Wisdom (Taiwan, Province of China) *Tel:* (02) 7075802 *Fax:* (02) 7085054 *E-mail:* tow@ms2.hinet. net, pg 637

Instituto Torcuato Di Tella (Argentina) *Tel:* (011) 4783-8680; (011) 4784-0084 *Fax:* (011) 4783-3061 *E-mail:* postmaster@itdtar.edu.ar *Web Site:* www.itdt. edu, pg 9

Toros Yayinlari Ltd Co (Turkey) *Tel:* (0212) 2444155 *Fax:* (0212) 2452858; (0212) 2444155, pg 647

Ediciones de la Torre (Spain) *Tel:* (091) 692 20 34 *Fax:* (091) 692 20 34 *E-mail:* info@ edicionesdelatorre.com *Web Site:* www. edicionesdelatorre.com, pg 597

Torremozas SL Ediciones (Spain) *Tel:* (091) 359 03 15 *Fax:* (091) 345 85 32 *E-mail:* ediciones@torremozas. com *Web Site:* www.torremozas.com, pg 597

Tosui Shobo Publishers (Japan) *Tel:* (03) 3261-6190 *Fax:* (03) 3261-2234 *E-mail:* tousuishobou@nifty.com, pg 427

Total Home Entertainment (United Kingdom) *Tel:* (01782) 566566 *Fax:* (01782) 565400 *E-mail:* thenews@the.co.uk, pg 1345

Totalidade Editora Ltda (Brazil) *Tel:* (011) 3064 3688 *Fax:* (011) 3081 9503 *E-mail:* total@terra.com.br *Web Site:* www.totalidade.com.br, pg 91

Toubis M (Greece) *Tel:* 2109923876; 2109923806 *Fax:* 2109923 867 *E-mail:* toubis@otenet.gr, pg 309

The Toucan Press (United Kingdom) *Tel:* (01481) 57017, pg 761

Toulon Uitgeverij (Belgium) *Tel:* (059) 800927, pg 73

Editions Tousch (Luxembourg) *Tel:* 452977 *Fax:* 458743, pg 448

Touzimsky & Moravec (Czech Republic) *Tel:* (02) 612 13 631; (02) 612 12 458 *Fax:* (02) 612 12 458, pg 127

Towarzystwo Literackie im Adama Mickiewicza (Poland) *Tel:* (022) 265231 (ext 279), pg 1398

Towarzystwo Naukowe w Toruniu (Poland) *Tel:* (056) 6223941 (ext 8), pg 522

Tower Books (Australia) *Tel:* (02) 9975 5566 *Fax:* (02) 9975 5599 *E-mail:* info@towerbooks.com.au *Web Site:* www.towerbooks.com.au, pg 43

Tower Books (Ireland) *Tel:* (021) 4872294 *Fax:* (021) 4872294, pg 1148

Town House & Country House (Ireland) *Tel:* (01) 4972399 *Fax:* (01) 4970927 *E-mail:* books@ townhouse.ie *Web Site:* www.irelandseye.com/cle/ publish/townhouse.html, pg 360

Towy Publishing (United Kingdom) *Tel:* (01267) 236569 *Fax:* (01267) 220444 *E-mail:* towyfairs@btopenworld. com, pg 761

The Toyo Bunko (Japan) *Tel:* (03) 39420121 *Fax:* (03) 39420258 *E-mail:* webmaster@toyo-bunko.or.jp *Web Site:* www.toyo-bunko.or.jp, pg 1520

Toyo Keizai Shinpo-Sha (Japan) *Tel:* (03) 3246-5467 *Fax:* (03) 3270-4127 *E-mail:* tk@toyokeizai.co.jp *Web Site:* www.toyokeizai.co.jp/, pg 427

Wydawnictwo TPPR Wspolpraca (Poland) *Tel:* (022) 200301 (ext 227), pg 522

TR - Verlagsunion GmbH (Germany) *Tel:* (089) 2121 390 *Fax:* (089) 296129; (089) 296357 *E-mail:* vertrieb@tr-verlag.de *Web Site:* www.tr-verlag. de, pg 289

Trachsel - Verlag AG (Switzerland) *Tel:* (33) 6711407 *Fax:* (33) 6712449, pg 631

Trade Leas Spol Sro (Slovakia) *Tel:* (02) 50239248; (02) 50239250 *Fax:* (02) 55571690, pg 556

Tradespools Ltd (United Kingdom) *Tel:* (01373) 461475 *Fax:* (01373) 474112 *E-mail:* admin@tradespools.co. uk *Web Site:* www.tradespools.co.uk, pg 1175

Traditionell Bogenschiessen Verlag Angelika Hornig (Germany) *Tel:* (0621) 68 94 41 *Fax:* (0621) 68 94 42 *E-mail:* info@bogenschiessen.de *Web Site:* www. bogenschiessen.de, pg 289

Trainer International Editore-I Libri del Bargello (Italy) *Tel:* (055) 288162 *Fax:* (055) 218951, pg 407

Training Publications Ltd (United Kingdom) *Tel:* (01923) 243730 *Fax:* (01923) 213 144, pg 761

Giovanni Tranchida Editore (Italy) *Tel:* (02) 66802270 *Fax:* (02) 69003425 *E-mail:* tranchida@infinito.it *Web Site:* www.tranchida.it, pg 407

Trano Printy Fiangonana Loterana Malagasy (TPFLM)- (Imprimerie Lutherienne) (Madagascar) *Tel:* (020) 223340 *Fax:* (020) 262643 *E-mail:* impluth@dts.mg, pg 450

Trano Printy Fiangonana Loterana Malagasy (TPFLM)- (Imprimerie Lutherienne) (Madagascar) *Tel:* (020) 223340; (020) 24569, pg 1316

Trans Tech Publications (Germany) *Tel:* (05323) 96970 *Fax:* (05323) 969796 *E-mail:* ttp@transtech-online. com *Web Site:* www.transtech-online.com, pg 289

Trans Tech Publications SA (Switzerland) *Tel:* (01) 9221022 *Fax:* (01) 9221033 *E-mail:* info@ttp.net *Web Site:* www.ttp.net, pg 631

TransAction Translators Ltd (United Kingdom) *Tel:* (0114) 2661103 *Fax:* (0114) 2631959 *E-mail:* transaction@transaction.co.uk *Web Site:* www. transaction.co.uk, pg 1141

Transafrica Press (Kenya) *Tel:* (020) 244724, pg 432

Transcontinental Printing Book Group (Canada) *Tel:* 514-337-8560 *Toll Free Tel:* 800-361-3599 *Fax:* 514-339-5230 *Web Site:* www.transcontinental. com; www.transcontinental-printing.com, pg 1143, 1166

Transcontinental Printing Book Group (Canada) *Tel:* 514-337-8560 *Toll Free Tel:* 800-361-3599 *Fax:* 514-339-2252 *Web Site:* www.transcontinental. com; www.transcontinental-printing.com, pg 1206

Transcontinental Printing Book Group (Canada) *Tel:* 514-337-8560 *Toll Free Tel:* 800-361-3599 *Fax:* 514-339-5230 *Web Site:* www.transcontinental. com; www.transcontinental-printing.com, pg 1225

Transcontinental Printing Book Group (Canada) *Tel:* 514-337-8560 *Toll Free Tel:* 800-361-3599 *Fax:* 514-339-5230 *Web Site:* www.transcontinental. com, pg 1235

Transedition ASBL (France) *Tel:* (01) 43211080 *Fax:* (01) 43211079, pg 188

Transedition Ltd (United Kingdom) *Tel:* (01865) 396700 *Fax:* (01865) 712500 *E-mail:* enquiries@transed.co.uk *Web Site:* www.translateabook.com, pg 761

Transeuropa (Italy) *Tel:* (02) 29 402156 *Fax:* (02) 20 47922, pg 407

Transeuropeennes/RCE (France) *Tel:* (01) 55 07 88 90 *Fax:* (01) 55 07 97 38 *E-mail:* te.revue@ transeuropeennes.org; contact@transeuropeennes.org *Web Site:* www.transeuropeennes.org, pg 188

Universitatea Transilvania Din Brasov Biblioteca Centrala (Romania) *Tel:* (068) 413 000 *Fax:* (068) 150 474 *E-mail:* librj@vega.unitbv.ro, pg 1538

Translators Association (United Kingdom) *Tel:* (020) 7373 6642 *Fax:* (020) 7373 5768 *E-mail:* info@ societyofauthors.org *Web Site:* www.societyofauthors. org/translators, pg 1141

Translators Association (United Kingdom) *Tel:* (020) 7373 6642 *Fax:* (020) 7373 5768 *E-mail:* info@ societyofauthors.org *Web Site:* www.societyofauthors. org, pg 1404

Translator's Association of China (TAC) (China) *Tel:* (010) 68326681 *E-mail:* taccn@163bj.com *Web Site:* www.tac-online.org.cn, pg 1137

Translators Guild (Czech Republic) *Tel:* 222 564 082 *E-mail:* info@obecprekladatelu.cz *Web Site:* www. obecprekladatelu.cz, pg 1137

Translegal AG (Switzerland) *Tel:* (033) 2253939 *Fax:* (033) 2253933 *E-mail:* info@ott-verlag.ch, pg 631

Transpareon Press (Australia) *Tel:* (02) 99874570 *Fax:* (02) 99874570, pg 43

Transport Bookman Publications Ltd (United Kingdom) *Tel:* (020) 8560 2666 *Fax:* (020) 8569 8273, pg 761

Izdatelstvo Transport (Russian Federation) *Tel:* (095) 2625964 *Fax:* (095) 2611322, pg 545

Transportation Publishing House (Democratic People's Republic of Korea), pg 433

Transpress (Germany) *Tel:* (0711) 210 80 65 *Fax:* (0711) 210 80 70 *E-mail:* versand@motorbuch.de *Web Site:* www.motorbuch-versand.de, pg 289

Transvaal Museum Library (South Africa) *Tel:* (012) 322 7632 *Fax:* (012) 322 7939 *Web Site:* www.nfi.org.za, pg 1543

Transworld Publishers Ltd (United Kingdom) *Tel:* (020) 8579 2652 *Fax:* (020) 8579 5479 *E-mail:* info@ transworld-publishers.co.uk *Web Site:* www. booksattransworld.co.uk, pg 761

Transworld Publishers (NZ) Ltd (New Zealand) *Tel:* (09) 4156210 *Fax:* (09) 4156221, pg 497

Transworld Publishers Pty Ltd (Australia) *Tel:* (02) 9954 9966 *Fax:* (02) 9954 4562, pg 43

Transworld Research Network (India) *Tel:* (0471) 2460384 *Fax:* (0491) 2573051 *E-mail:* ggcom@vsnl. com *Web Site:* www.transworldresearch.com, pg 348

Trauner Verlag (Austria) *Tel:* (0732) 77 82 41-212 *Fax:* (0732) 77 82 41-400 *E-mail:* office@trauner.at *Web Site:* www.trauner.at, pg 58

Trautvetter & Fischer Nachf (Germany) *Tel:* (06421) 33309 *Fax:* (06421) 34959 *E-mail:* bestell@ trautvetterfischerverlag.de *Web Site:* www. trautvetterfischerverlag.de, pg 289

Trea Ediciones, SL (Spain) *Tel:* (098) 5303801 *Fax:* (098) 5303717; (098) 5303712 *E-mail:* trea@ trea.es, pg 597

Institut de Treball Social - Serveis Socials (Spain) *Tel:* (093) 217 26 64 *Fax:* (093) 237 36 34 *E-mail:* intressbar@intress.org *Web Site:* www.intress. org, pg 597

Guy Tredaniel Editeur-Editions Courrier du Livre (France) *Tel:* (01) 43 36 41 05 *Fax:* (01) 43 31 07 45 *E-mail:* tredaniel-courrier@wanadoo.fr *Web Site:* www.livre-edition-tredaniel.com, pg 188

Tree Shade Technical Services (Kenya) *Tel:* (02) 225798; (02) 220712, pg 432

Treehouse Children's Books Ltd (United Kingdom) *Tel:* (01749) 330529 *Fax:* (01749) 330544 *E-mail:* ca. baker@virgin.net, pg 761

Turkischer Schulbuchverlag Onel Cengiz (Germany) *Tel:* (0221) 5879084; (0221) 5879085 *Fax:* (0221) 488093; (0221) 5879004, pg 290

Cyprus Turkish Public Library (Cyprus) *Tel:* (022) 83257, pg 1499

Turkish Republic - Ministry of Culture (Turkey) *Tel:* (0312) 309 08 50 *Fax:* (0312) 312-4359 *E-mail:* yayimlar@kutuphanelergm.gov.tr *Web Site:* www.kultur.gov.tr, pg 647

Izdatelstvo Turkmenistan (Turkmenistan) *Tel:* 68283, pg 648

Turnaround Publisher Services Ltd (United Kingdom) *Tel:* (020) 8829 3000 *Fax:* (020) 8881 5088 *E-mail:* enquires@turnaround-uk.com; orders@ turnaround-uk.com *Web Site:* www.turnaround-psl. com, pg 1134

Turnaround Publisher Services Ltd (United Kingdom) *Tel:* (020) 8829 3000 *Fax:* (020) 8881 5088 *E-mail:* enquires@turnaround-uk.com, pg 1238, 1345

Alexander Turnbull Library (New Zealand) *Tel:* (04) 474 3000 *Fax:* (04) 474 3035 *E-mail:* atl@natlib.govt.nz *Web Site:* www.natlib.govt.nz, pg 1531

Jane Turnbull (United Kingdom) *Tel:* (020) 8743 9580 *Fax:* (020) 8749 6079 *E-mail:* agents@cwcom.net, pg 1134

Editorial Turner de Mexico (Mexico) *Tel:* (055) 5553 1183 *Fax:* (055) 5211 2070 *Web Site:* www. turnerlibros.com, pg 468

Turner Memorial Library (Zimbabwe) *Tel:* (0120) 63412 *Fax:* (0120) 61002, pg 1555

Turner Publicaciones (Spain) *Tel:* (091) 308 33 36 *Fax:* (091) 319 39 30 *E-mail:* turner@turnerlibros.com *Web Site:* www.turnerlibros.com, pg 598

Turris (Italy) *Tel:* (0372) 23845 *Fax:* (0372) 23845, pg 407

Tursen, SA (Spain) *Tel:* (091) 3667148 *Fax:* (091) 3653148, pg 598

Turton & Armstrong Pty Ltd Publishers (Australia) *Tel:* (02) 9489 6719 *Fax:* (02) 9489 6719 *E-mail:* turtarm@attglobal.net, pg 44

Turun Kansallinen Kirjakauppa Oy (Finland) *Tel:* (02) 2831000 *Fax:* (02) 2831010 *E-mail:* info@ kansallinenkirjakauppa.fi *Web Site:* www. kansallinenkirjakauppa.fi, pg 1299

Turun Yliopiston Kirjasto (Finland) *Tel:* (02) 333 51 *Fax:* (02) 333 5050 *E-mail:* kirjasto@utu.fi *Web Site:* kirjasto.utu.fi, pg 1504

Edition Tusch (Austria) *Tel:* (01) 485 40 01 *Fax:* (01) 485 40 01-15 *E-mail:* citypost@cpz.at, pg 58

Tusquets Editores (Spain) *Tel:* (093) 2530400 *Fax:* (093) 4176703; (093) 4188698 (Rights & Editing) *E-mail:* general@tusquets-editores.es *Web Site:* www. tusquets-editores.com, pg 598

Ediciones Tutor SA (Spain) *Tel:* (091) 5599832 *Fax:* (091) 5410235 *E-mail:* tutor@autovia.com, pg 598

Tuttle Bookshop (Japan) *Tel:* (03) 3291-7071 *Fax:* (03) 3293-8005 *E-mail:* kanda@bookshop.co. jp *Web Site:* www.bookshop.co.jp/kandamap.html, pg 1313

Charles E Tuttle Publishing Co Inc (Japan) *Tel:* (03) 5437-0171 *Fax:* (03) 5437-0755 *E-mail:* info@ tuttlepublishing.com *Web Site:* www.tuttlepublishing. com, pg 427, 1313

Tuttle-Mori Agency Inc (Japan) *Tel:* (03) 3230-4081 *Fax:* (03) 3234-5249 *Web Site:* www.tuttlemori.com, pg 1124

Tuum (Estonia) *Tel:* 627 6427; (051) 41 290 *Fax:* 641 8054 *E-mail:* enelier@yahoo.com, pg 140

Biblioteca Mark Twain, Centro Cultural Costarricense-Norteamericano (Costa Rica) *Tel:* 207-7574; 207-7577 *Toll Free Tel:* 800-207-7500 *Fax:* 224-1480 *E-mail:* mercadeo@cccncr.com *Web Site:* www.cccncr. com, pg 1498

Bogklubben 12 Boget A/S (Denmark) *Tel:* 33695000 *Fax:* 33695051 *E-mail:* b12b@bogklubben-12-boget. dk *Web Site:* www.lrforlag.dk, pg 1242

Twelveheads Press (United Kingdom) *E-mail:* sales@ twelveheads.com *Web Site:* www.twelveheads.com, pg 762

Twente University Press (Netherlands) *Tel:* (053) 4899111 *Fax:* (053) 4892000 *E-mail:* info@utwente.nl *Web Site:* www.utwente.nl/tupress, pg 486

Twenty-First Century Publishers, Inc (Republic of Korea) *Tel:* (032) 429-9411 *Fax:* (032) 429-9418, pg 440

Editions 24 Heures (Switzerland) *Tel:* (021) 3494500 *Fax:* (021) 3494224, pg 631

Ediciones 29 - Libros Rio Nuevo (Spain) *Tel:* (093) 675 41 35 *Fax:* (093) 590 04 40 *E-mail:* ediciones29@ comunired.com *Web Site:* www.ediciones29.com, pg 598

Twin Guinep Ltd (Jamaica) *Tel:* 876-927-5390; 876-944-4324 *Fax:* 876-944-4324 *E-mail:* info@twinguinep. com; sales@twinguinep.com *Web Site:* www. twinguinep.com, pg 411

Two-Can Publishing Ltd (United Kingdom) *Tel:* (020) 7224 2440 *Fax:* (020) 7224 7005 *E-mail:* helpline@ two-canpublishing.com; sales@creativepub.com *Web Site:* www.two-canpublishing.com, pg 762

Editorial Txertoa (Spain) *Tel:* (0943) 45 97 57 *Fax:* (0943) 46 09 41 *E-mail:* txertoa@nexo.es, pg 598

Typos (Greece) *Tel:* 2103819083; 2103819085; 210 3619083 *Fax:* 2103825012, pg 309

Typotex Kft Elektronikus Kiado (Hungary) *Tel:* (01) 316-2473; (01) 316-3759 *Fax:* (01) 316-3759 *E-mail:* info@typotex.hu *Web Site:* www.typotex.hu, pg 321

Tyrolia Verlagsanstalt GmbH (Austria) *Tel:* (0512) 2233-510 *Fax:* (0512) 2233-512 *E-mail:* pgh@tyrolia.at *Web Site:* www.tyrolia.at, pg 58

Tyrolia Verlagsanstalt GmbH (Austria) *Tel:* (0512) 2233-0 *Fax:* (0512) 2233-501 *E-mail:* tyrolia@tyrolia.at *Web Site:* www.tyrolia.at, pg 1291

Tysk Bogimport ApS (Denmark) *Tel:* 7020 4990 *Fax:* 7020 4991 *E-mail:* tyskforlaget@tyskforlaget.dk *Web Site:* www.tyskforlaget.dk, pg 1298

Tyto Alba Publishers (Lithuania) *Tel:* (02) 498 602; (02) 497 453; (02) 497 597 *Fax:* (02) 498 602 *E-mail:* tytoalba@taide.lt *Web Site:* www.tytoalba.lt, pg 446

UBS Publishers' Distributors Ltd (United Kingdom) *Tel:* (020) 8450 8667 *Fax:* (020) 8452 6612, pg 1345

UBS Publishers Distributors Ltd (India) *Tel:* (011) 273601; (011) 3266646 *Fax:* (011) 3276593; (011) 3274261 *E-mail:* ubspd@ubspd.com *Web Site:* www. ubspd.com, pg 348

UBS Publishers' Distributors Pvt Ltd (India) *Tel:* (011) 23273601; (011) 23266646 *Fax:* (011) 23276593; (011) 23274261 *E-mail:* ubspd@ubspd.com *Web Site:* www.gobookshopping.com, pg 1307

Edizioni Ubulibri SAS (Italy) *Tel:* (02) 20241604 *Fax:* (02) 29510265 *E-mail:* edizioni@ubulibri.it, pg 407

UCA Editores (El Salvador) *Tel:* 210-6600 *Fax:* 210-6655 *E-mail:* info@uca.edu.sv *Web Site:* www.uca. edu.sv, pg 138

Libreria UCA (El Salvador) *Tel:* 2210-6600 *Fax:* 2210-6655 *E-mail:* correo@uca.edu.sv *Web Site:* www.uca. edu.sv, pg 1299

UCL Press Ltd (United Kingdom) *Tel:* (020) 7583 9855 *Fax:* (020) 7842 2298 *E-mail:* info@tandf.co.uk *Web Site:* www.tandf.co.uk, pg 763

Universitas Udayana Library (Indonesia) *Tel:* (0361) 702772 *Fax:* (0361) 702-765 *Web Site:* www.unud. ac.id, pg 1515

Verlag Carl Ueberreuter GmbH (Austria) *Tel:* (01) 40 444-172 *Fax:* (01) 40 444-5 *E-mail:* office-v@ ueberreutes.at *Web Site:* www.ueberreuter.de, pg 58

Wirtschaftsverlag Carl Ueberreuter (Germany) *Tel:* (069) 580905-80 *Fax:* (069) 580905-10 *E-mail:* info@ redline-wirtschaft.de *Web Site:* www.redline-wirtschaft. de, pg 290

Uebersetzergemeinschaft Interessengemeinschaft von Uebersetzerinnen und Uebersetzern literarischer und wissenschaftlicher Werke (Austria) *Tel:* (01) 526 204 418 *Fax:* (01) 524 64 35 *E-mail:* ueg@literaturhaus.at, pg 1137

UGA Editions (Uitgeverij) (Belgium) *Tel:* (056) 36 32 00 *Fax:* (056) 35 60 96 *E-mail:* publ@uga.be *Web Site:* www.uga.be, pg 73

Uganda Bookshop (Uganda) *Tel:* (077) 464145 *Fax:* (041) 343756, pg 1337

Uganda Library Association (ULA) (Uganda) *Tel:* (0141) 256-77-467698 *Web Site:* www.ou.edu/cas/slis/ULA/ ula_index.htm, pg 1572

Uganda Polytechnic Library at Uganda Technical College (Uganda) *Tel:* (041) 28 5211, pg 1550

Uganda Publishers & Booksellers Association (Uganda) *Tel:* (041) 259 163 *Fax:* (041) 251 160 *E-mail:* mbd@ infocom.co.ug, pg 1279

Uglan Islenski Kiljuklubburinn (Iceland) *Tel:* 522 2000 *Fax:* 522 2022 *E-mail:* edda@edda.is *Web Site:* www. edda.is, pg 1243

Evzen Uher, Musikverlag UHER (Czech Republic) *Tel:* 572540376, pg 127

Verlag Dr Alfons Uhl (Germany) *Tel:* (09081) 87248 *Fax:* (09081) 23710 *E-mail:* dr.uhl@uhl-verlag.com *Web Site:* www.uhl-verlag.com, pg 290

Uitgeverij Altamira-Becht BV (Netherlands) *Tel:* (023) 54 11 190 *Fax:* (023) 52 74 404 *E-mail:* post@ gottmer.nl *Web Site:* www.altamira-becht.nl, pg 486

Uitgeverij Averbode NV (Belgium) *Tel:* (013) 780 184 *Fax:* (013) 780 183 *E-mail:* educational@verbode.be *Web Site:* www.averbode.com, pg 73

Uitgeverij Contact (Netherlands) *Tel:* (020) 5249800 *Fax:* (020) 6276851 *E-mail:* businesscontact@contact-bv.nl *Web Site:* www.boekenwereld.com, pg 486

UK International Standard Book Numbering Agency Ltd (United Kingdom) *Tel:* (01252) 742525 *Fax:* (01252) 742526 *E-mail:* isbn@whitaker.co.uk *Web Site:* www. whitaker.co.uk/isbn.htm, pg 1283

UK Serials Group-UKSG (United Kingdom) *Tel:* (01635) 254292 *Fax:* (01635) 253826 *E-mail:* alison@uksg.org *Web Site:* www.uksg.org, pg 1154

Ulisse Editions (France) *Tel:* (01) 48 78 40 74 *Fax:* (01) 48 78 40 77 *Web Site:* www.ulisseditions.com, pg 188

Editora Ulisseia Lda (Portugal) *Tel:* (021) 380 1100 *Fax:* (021) 386 5397 *Web Site:* www.editorialverbo.pt, pg 531

Ullstein Heyne List GmbH & Co KG (Germany) *Tel:* (089) 51 48 0 *Fax:* (089) 51 48 2229 *Web Site:* www.ullstein.de, pg 290

Universitat Ulm (Germany) *Tel:* (0731) 502-01 *Fax:* (0731) 5022038 *E-mail:* post@uni-ulm.de *Web Site:* www.uni-ulm.de, pg 1509

Guenter Albert Ulmer Verlag (Germany) *Tel:* (07464) 98740 *Fax:* (07464) 3054 *E-mail:* info@ ulmertuningen.de *Web Site:* www.ulmertuningen.de, pg 290

Verlag Eugen Ulmer GmbH & Co (Germany) *Tel:* (0711) 4507-0 *Fax:* (0711) 4507-120 *E-mail:* info@ulmer.de *Web Site:* www.ulmer.de, pg 290

Werner Ulmer & Co (Switzerland) *Tel:* (033) 432220 *Fax:* (033) 434848, pg 631

Universal Book Traders (India) *Tel:* (011) 2396 1288; (011) 2391 1966; (011) 2399 0487 *Fax:* (011) 2392 4152; (011) 2745 9023 *E-mail:* unilaw@vsnl.com *Web Site:* www.unilawbooks.com, pg 1308

Universal Business Directories, Australia Pty Ltd (New Zealand) *Tel:* (09) 526-6300 *Toll Free Tel:* 800 823-225 (New Zealand only) *Fax:* (09) 526-6313 *Toll Free Fax:* 800 329 823 (New Zealand only) *E-mail:* sales@ubd.co.nz *Web Site:* www.ubd.co.nz, pg 497

Universal Dalsi (Romania) *Tel:* (01) 3355354; (01) 3371682 *Fax:* (01) 3373566; (01) 3129709 *E-mail:* marian@kappa.ro, pg 538

Universal Edition AG (Austria) *Tel:* (01) 337 23-0 *Fax:* (01) 337 23-400 *E-mail:* office@universaledition. com *Web Site:* www.universaledition.com, pg 58

Libreria Universal (Guatemala) *Tel:* (02) 28 484, pg 1304

Universal Postal Union (UPU) (Switzerland) *Tel:* (031) 350 31 11 *Fax:* (031) 350 31 10 *E-mail:* info@upu.int *Web Site:* www.upu.int, pg 1277

Universal Press Pty Ltd (Australia) *Tel:* (02) 857 3700 *Toll Free Tel:* 800 021 987 *Fax:* (02) 888 9074 *Toll Free Fax:* 800 636 197 *E-mail:* unipress@unipress. com.au, pg 44

Universal Publications Agency Press (Republic of Korea) *Tel:* (02) 32-8175 *Fax:* (02) 32-8176 *E-mail:* upa@upa.co.kr *Web Site:* www.upa.co.kr, pg 440

Universal Publications Agency Press (Republic of Korea) *Tel:* (02) 3672 0044 *Fax:* (02) 3672 1222 *E-mail:* upa@upa.co.kr *Web Site:* www.upa.co.kr, pg 1124

Universal Publications Agency Press (Republic of Korea) *Tel:* (02) 32-8175 *Fax:* (02) 32-8176 *E-mail:* upa@upa.co.kr *Web Site:* www.upa.co.kr, pg 1315

Universidad Autonoma - Biblioteca Universitaria (Spain) *Tel:* (091) 3974399 *Fax:* (091) 3975058 *E-mail:* servicio.biblioteca@uam.es *Web Site:* www.uam.es, pg 1544

Biblioteca de la Universidad Autonoma de Santo Domingo (Dominican Republic) *Tel:* 533-1104 *Fax:* 508-7374 *E-mail:* rectoria.uasd@codetel.net.do *Web Site:* www.uasd.edu.do, pg 1501

Universidad Autonoma Tomas Frias, Div de Extension Universitaria (Bolivia) *Tel:* (062) 2-73-28; (062) 2-73-00 *Fax:* (062) 2-66-63; (062) 2-31-96 *E-mail:* rector@rect.nrp.edu.bo *Web Site:* www.unam.mx/udal/afiliacion/Bolivia/frias.htm, pg 75

Universidad Autonoma Tomas Frias, Departamento de Bibliotecas (Bolivia) *Tel:* (062) 27300 *Fax:* (062) 27329; (062) 26663 *Web Site:* www.uatf.edu.bo, pg 1493

Biblioteca de la Universidad Catolica de Valparaiso (Chile) *Tel:* (032) 273261; (032) 273000 *Fax:* (032) 273183 *Web Site:* biblioteca.ucv.cl, pg 1495

Biblioteca de la Universidad Central de Ecuador (Ecuador) *Tel:* (02) 2234 722 *Fax:* (02) 2236 367; (02) 2521 925 *Web Site:* www.ucentral.edu.ec, pg 1501

Biblioteca Central de la Universidad Central de Venezuela (Venezuela) *Tel:* (0212) 605-29-09; (0212) 605-29-10 *Fax:* (0212) 6622486 *E-mail:* bibcentral@sicht.ucv.ve *Web Site:* www.ucv.ve, pg 1554

Universidad Central del Ecuador, Departamento de Publicaciones (Ecuador) *Tel:* (02) 2234 722 *Fax:* (02) 2236 367; (02) 2521 925 *Web Site:* www.ucentral.edu.ec, pg 136

Biblioteca General de la Universidad Central "Marta Abreu" de las Villas (UCLV) (Cuba) *Tel:* (0422) 81410; (0422) 81618; (0422) 8178 *Fax:* (0422) 81608; (0422) 22113 *E-mail:* luishs@dri.uclv.edu.cu, pg 1499

Universidad Centroamericana (Nicaragua) *Tel:* (02) 278-3923 *Fax:* (02) 267-0106 *E-mail:* comsj@ns.uca.edu.ni *Web Site:* www.uca.edu.ni, pg 1531

Biblioteca de la Universidad Centroamericana Jose Simeon Canas (El Salvador) *Tel:* 210-6600 (ext 278) *Fax:* 210-6657 *E-mail:* ucabib.director@bib.uca.edu.sv *Web Site:* www.uca.edu.sv, pg 1502

Biblioteca de la Universidad Complutense (Spain) *Tel:* (091) 394 69 25; (091) 394 69 39 *Fax:* (091) 394 69 26 *E-mail:* bucweb@buc.ucm.es *Web Site:* www. ucm.es/BUCM, pg 1544

Universidad de los Andes, Biblioteca General, Ramon de Zubiria (Colombia) *Tel:* (01) 3394999; (01) 3394949 *Fax:* (01) 3324472 *E-mail:* sisbibli@uniandes.edu.co *Web Site:* biblioteca.uniandes.edu.co, pg 1497

Universidad de los Andes, Consejo de Publicaciones (Venezuela) *Tel:* (074) 401111 ext 1998 *Fax:* (074) 274240 ext 1998 *E-mail:* dsia@ula.ve *Web Site:* www. ula.ve, pg 775

Servicios Bibliotecarios Universidad de los Andes (Serbiula) (Venezuela) *Tel:* (0274) 2402731; (0274) 2402729 *Fax:* (0274) 2402507; (0274) 2402748 *E-mail:* adquisi@serbi.ula.ve *Web Site:* www.serbi. ula.ve, pg 1554

Universidad de Antioquia, Division Publicaciones (Colombia) *Tel:* (04) 210 50 10 *Fax:* (04) 210 50 12 *E-mail:* direccion@editorialudea.com; comunicaciones@editorialudea.com *Web Site:* www. editorialudea.com, pg 112

Universidad de Antioquia, Escuela Interamericana de Bibliotecologia, Biblioteca (Colombia) *Tel:* (04) 2105930; (04) 2105933 *Fax:* (04) 2105946 *E-mail:* dbibliotecologia@arhuaco.udea.edu.co *Web Site:* nutabe.udea.edu.co/eib, pg 1497

Universidad de Cantabria Biblioteca (Spain) *Tel:* (0942) 201 180 *Fax:* (0942) 201 183 *E-mail:* infobuc@gestion.unican.es *Web Site:* www.buc.unican.es, pg 1544

Biblioteca Central de la Universidad de Chile (Chile) *Tel:* (02) 6782583 *Fax:* (02) 6782574 *E-mail:* sisib@uchile.cl *Web Site:* www.uchile.cl/bibliotecas, pg 1496

Universidad de Concepcion Direccion de Bibliotecas (Chile) *Tel:* (041) 20 41 15; (041) 20 43 93 *Fax:* (041) 24 60 76 *E-mail:* info@udec.cl *Web Site:* www.bib. udec.cl, pg 1496

Universidad de Costa Rica Sistema de Bibliotecas, Documentacion e Informacion (Costa Rica) *Tel:* 253-6152; 207-5316; 207-4461 *Fax:* 204-2809 *E-mail:* marqueda@sibdi.bldt.ucr.ac.cr *Web Site:* sibdi. bldt.ucr.ac.cr, pg 1498

Biblioteca Central de la Universidad de El Salvador (El Salvador) *Tel:* 503 2250278 *Fax:* 503 2250278 *E-mail:* sb@biblio.ues.edu.sv *Web Site:* www.ues.edu. sv/biblio.html, pg 1502

Universidad de Granada (Spain) *Tel:* (0958) 243025 *Fax:* (0958) 243066 *Web Site:* www.ugr.es, pg 598

Biblioteca General, Universidad de Guayaquil (Ecuador) *Tel:* 2282440 *Fax:* 2391010 *E-mail:* zd@ug.edu.ec *Web Site:* www.ug.edu.ec, pg 1501

Editorial de la Universidad de Costa Rica (Costa Rica) *Tel:* 207-5006; 207-5837 *Fax:* 224-9367 *E-mail:* direccion@editorial.ucr.ac.cr *Web Site:* www. editorial.ucr.ac.cr, pg 116

Ediciones de la Universidad de la Frontera (Chile) *Tel:* (045) 325000 *Fax:* (045) 325116, pg 100

Universidad de la Habana, Direccion de Informacion Cientifico Tecnica (Cuba) *Tel:* (07) 78-3231 *Fax:* (07) 33-5774, pg 1499

Universidad de Las Palmas de Gran Canaria, Escuela Universitaria de Informatica (ULPGC) (Spain) *Tel:* (0928) 45-87-81; (0928) 45-87-00 *Fax:* (0928) 45-87-11 *E-mail:* organizacion@sinf.ulpgc.es, pg 598

Universidad de Lima-Fondo de Desarollo Editorial (Peru) *Tel:* (01) 437-6767 *Fax:* (01) 437-8066; (01) 435-3396 *E-mail:* fondo_ed@lima.edu.pe *Web Site:* www.ulima. edu.pe, pg 513

Universidad de los Andes Editorial (Colombia) *Tel:* (01) 3394949; (01) 3394999 *Fax:* (01) 3394949 (ext 2158) *E-mail:* infeduni@uniandes.edu.co *Web Site:* ediciones.uniandes.edu.co, pg 113

Universidad de Malaga (Spain) *Tel:* (095) 213 29 17 *Fax:* (095) 213 29 18 *E-mail:* buzon@uma.es *Web Site:* www.uma.es, pg 598

Universidad de Navarra, Ediciones SA (Spain) *Tel:* (0948) 256850 *Fax:* (0948) 256854 *E-mail:* eunsa@ibernet.com *Web Site:* www.eunsa.es, pg 598

Universidad de Oviedo Servicio de Publicaciones (Spain) *Tel:* (0985) 210160; (0985) 222428 *Fax:* (0985) 218352 *Web Site:* www.uniovi.es, pg 599

Universidad de Panama, Biblioteca Interamericana Simon Bolivar (Panama) *Tel:* 2636133, pg 1534

Universidad de Puerto Rico Recinto de Rio Piedras Sistema de Bibliotecas (Puerto Rico) *Tel:* (787) 764-0000 (ext 3311); (787) 764-0000 (ext 5085); (787) 764-0000 (ext 5089) *Fax:* (787) 772-1479 *Web Site:* biblioteca.uprrp.edu, pg 1537

Ediciones Universidad de Salamanca (Spain) *Tel:* (0923) 294598 *Fax:* (0923) 262579 *E-mail:* eus@usal.es *Web Site:* www3.usal.es, pg 599

Biblioteca Central de la Universidad de San Carlos (Guatemala) *Tel:* (02) 460 611 *E-mail:* usacbibc@usac.edu.gt *Web Site:* www.usac.edu.gt/dependencias/biblioteca, pg 1512

Universidad de Sevilla Secretariado de Publicaciones (Spain) *Tel:* (095) 487444; (095) 487442 *Fax:* (095) 487 7443 *E-mail:* secpub@pop.us.es *Web Site:* publius.cica.es, pg 599

Universidad de Valladolid Secretariado de Publicaciones e Intercambio Editorial (Spain) *Tel:* (0983) 187810 *Fax:* (0983) 187812 *E-mail:* spic@uva.es *Web Site:* www.uva.es, pg 599

Biblioteca Central de la Universidad de Zulia (Venezuela) *Tel:* (061) 596701 *Fax:* (061) 596700 *Web Site:* www.serbi.luz.ve, pg 1554

Universidad del Pacifico Libreria (Peru) *Tel:* (01) 219-0100; (01) 472-9635 *Fax:* (01) 470-6121 *E-mail:* biblioteca@up.edu.pe *Web Site:* www.up.edu. pe/biblioteca, pg 1535

Biblioteca Central, Universidad del Salvador (Argentina) *Tel:* (011) 4371-0422 *Fax:* (011) 4371-0422 *E-mail:* uds-bibl@salvador.edu.ar *Web Site:* www. salvador.edu.ar, pg 1488

Editorial Universidad SRL (Argentina) *Tel:* (011) ·4382-9022; (011) 4382-6850 *Fax:* (011) 4381-2005 *E-mail:* univers@nat.com.ar *Web Site:* www.nat.com. ar/universidad, pg 9

Editorial Universidad Estatal a Distancia (EUNED) (Costa Rica) *Tel:* 234-7954; 253-2121 (ext 2440) *Fax:* 257-5042; 234-9138 *E-mail:* editoria@uned.ac.cr *Web Site:* www.uned.ac.cr/ejecutiva/editorial/, pg 116

Universidad Externado de Colombia Biblioteca (Colombia) *Tel:* (01) 3420288; (01) 3419900 (ext 3350); (01) 3419900 (ext 3351) *E-mail:* biblioteca@uexternado.edu.co *Web Site:* www.uexternado.edu. co/biblioteca/, pg 1497

Biblioteca de la Universidad Iberoamericana (Mexico) *Tel:* (055) 5950 4000 *Fax:* (055) 5950 4248 *E-mail:* buzon@uiacia.bib.uia.mx *Web Site:* www.bib. uia.mx, pg 1527

Biblioteca Central de la Universidad Mayor de San Andres (Bolivia) *Tel:* (02) 440047; (02) 352232 *Fax:* (02) 442505 *E-mail:* rector@umsanet.edu.bo *Web Site:* www.umsanet.edu.bo; www.bc.umsanet.edu. bo, pg 1493

Universidad Mayor de San Andres, Editorial Universitaria (Bolivia) *Tel:* (02) 359491, pg 75

Biblioteca Central de la Universidad Mayor de San Francisco Xavier de Chuquisaca (Bolivia) *Tel:* (04) 6453308 *Fax:* (04) 6455308 *Web Site:* www.usfx.edu. bo, pg 1493

Universidad Nacional Abierta y a Distancia (Colombia) *Tel:* (01) 212 0159; (01) 346 0088 *Fax:* (01) 522 3497 *E-mail:* unisur12@gaitana.interred.net.co, pg 113

Universidad Nacional Autonoma de Mexico Centro (National University of Mexico) (Mexico) *Tel:* (05) 6226329; (05) 6226330 *Fax:* (05) 6226328 *E-mail:* libros@bibliounam.unam.mx, pg 469

Edicions de la Universitat Politecnica de Catalunya SL (Spain) *Tel:* (093) 4016 883 *Fax:* (093) 4015 885 *E-mail:* edicions-upc@upc.es *Web Site:* www. edicionsupc.es, pg 599

Universitat Wuerzburg (Germany) *Tel:* (0931) 888-5906 *Fax:* (0931) 888-5970 *E-mail:* direktion@ bibliothek.uni-wuerzburg.de; information@bibliothek. uni-wuerzburg.de *Web Site:* www.bibliothek.uni-wuerzburg.de, pg 1510

Universitat Zentralbibliothek Zuerich (Switzerland) *Tel:* (01) 2683100 *Fax:* (01) 2683290 *E-mail:* zb@ zb.unizh.ch *Web Site:* www-zb.unizh.ch, pg 1547

Universitatea de Medicina si Farmacie Biblioteca Centrala (Romania) *Tel:* (064) 192629 *Fax:* (064) 190832 *Web Site:* www.bib.umfcluj.ro, pg 1538

Biblioteca Universitatii Politehnica Bucuresti (Romania) *Tel:* (021) 402 3982 *Fax:* (021) 312 70 44 *Web Site:* www.library.pub.ro, pg 1538

Universitats und Landesbibliothe Darmstadt (Germany) *Tel:* (06151) 165850 *Fax:* (06151) 165897 *E-mail:* info@ulb.tu-darmstadt.de *Web Site:* www.ulb. tu-darmstadt.de, pg 1510

Universitatsbibliothek Augsburg (Germany) *Tel:* (0821) 598 5320; (0821) 598 5306; (0821) 598 5305 *Fax:* (0821) 598 5354 *E-mail:* info@bibliothek.uni-augsburg.de *Web Site:* www.bibliothek.uni-augsburg. de, pg 1510

Der Universitatsverlag Fribourg (Switzerland) *Tel:* (026) 426 43 11 *Fax:* (026) 426 43 00 *E-mail:* eduni@st-paul.ch, pg 631

Universitatsverlag Ulm GmbH (Germany) *Tel:* (0731) 15 28 60 *Fax:* (0731) 15 28 62 *E-mail:* info@uni-verlag-ulm.de *Web Site:* www.uni-verlag-ulm.de, pg 291

Presses de l'Universite du Benin (Togo) *Tel:* (228) 21 30 27 *Fax:* (228) 21 85 95 *E-mail:* cafmicro@ub.tg *Web Site:* www.ub.tg, pg 642

Editions de l'Universite de Bruxelles (Belgium) *Tel:* (02) 650 37 97 *Fax:* (02) 650 37 94 *Web Site:* www. editions-universite-bruxelles.be, pg 73

Universite Catholique de Louvain (Belgium) *Tel:* (010) 47 21 11 *E-mail:* sceb@sceb.ucl.ac.be *Web Site:* www. ucl.ac.be, pg 1492

Universite Cheikh Anta Diop de Dakar, Bibliotheque Universitaire (Senegal) *Tel:* 825 02 79; 824 69 81 *Fax:* 824 23 79 *Web Site:* www.bu.ucad.sn, pg 1540

Bibliotheque Centrale, Universite d'Alger (Algeria) *Tel:* (021) 63-71-01 *Fax:* (021) 63-76-29 *E-mail:* bu@ univ-alger.dz *Web Site:* www.univ-alger.dz, pg 1487

Bibliotheque Universite d'Avignon et des Pays du Vaucluse (France) *Tel:* (04) 90 16 25 00 *Fax:* (04) 90 16 25 10 *E-mail:* bu@univ-avignon.fr *Web Site:* www. univ-avignon.fr, pg 1506

Universite de Kisangani Bibliotheque Centrale (The Democratic Republic of the Congo) *Tel:* 215-2, pg 1497

Universite de la Reunion, Service Commun de la Documentation (Reunion) *Tel:* 93 83 83 *Fax:* 93 83 64 *Web Site:* www.univ-reunion.fr, pg 1538

Bibliotheque Centrale de l'Universite de Lubumbashi (The Democratic Republic of the Congo) *Tel:* (022) 22-5285 *E-mail:* unilu@unilu.net *Web Site:* www. unilu.net, pg 1497

Bibliotheque de l'Universite de Niamey (Niger) *Tel:* 74-12-73 *Fax:* 73-38-62, pg 1532

Universite de Ouagadougou (Burkina Faso) *Tel:* 30 70 64; 30 70 65 *Fax:* 30 72 42 *E-mail:* info@univ-ouaga. bf *Web Site:* www.univ-ouaga.bf, pg 1495

Universite de Toulouse-Mirail (France) *Tel:* (0561) 50 40 64 *Fax:* (0561) 50 40 50 *E-mail:* bu-mirail@ univ-tlse2.fr *Web Site:* www.univ-tlse2.fr/bu-centrale, pg 1506

Universite de Yaounde, Bibliotheque (Cameroon) *Tel:* 222 1320 *Fax:* 222 1320 *E-mail:* rect.uyl@uycdc. uninet.cm *Web Site:* www.uninet.cm/acceuil.html, pg 1495

Universite d'Oran, Bibliotheque (Algeria) *Tel:* (041) 41-69-39; (041) 41-66-44 *Fax:* (041) 41-60-21 *E-mail:* igmo@univ-oran.dz *Web Site:* www.univ-oran.dz, pg 1487

Bibliotheque de l'Universite du Benin (Togo) *Tel:* 21 30 27 *Fax:* 21 85 95 *E-mail:* cafmicro@ub.tg *Web Site:* www.ub.tg, pg 1549

Bibliotheque de l'Universite du Burundi (Burundi) *Tel:* (022) 2857 *Web Site:* www.ub.edu.bi, pg 1495

Librairie de l'Universite (France) *Tel:* (0476) 46 61 63 *Fax:* (0476) 46 14 59, pg 1300

Bibliotheque de l'Universite Nationale du Rwanda (Rwanda) *Tel:* 530272 *Fax:* 530210 *E-mail:* biblio@ nur.ac.rw, pg 1539

Publications de l'Universite de Pau (France) *Tel:* (05) 59 40 70 00 *Fax:* (05) 59 80 83 29 *Web Site:* www.univ-pau.fr, pg 188

Bibliotheque de l'Universite Quaraouyine (Morocco), pg 1528

Universiteit Antwerpen Bibliotheek UFSIA (Belgium) *Tel:* (03) 2204996 *Fax:* (03) 2204437 *E-mail:* helpdesk@lib.ua.ac.be *Web Site:* lib.ua.ac.be, pg 1492

Bibliotheek van de Universiteit van Amsterdam (Netherlands) *Tel:* (020) 525 2301 *Fax:* (020) 525 2311 *E-mail:* secr-uba@uva.nl *Web Site:* www.uba. uva.nl, pg 1530

Universiteits-Bibliotheek, Universiteit van de Nederlandse Antillen (Netherlands Antilles) *Tel:* (09) 8442222 *Fax:* (09) 8442200 *E-mail:* bibliotheek@una. an *Web Site:* www.una.net, pg 1530

Universiteitsbibliotheek Leiden (Netherlands) *Tel:* (071) 527 2814 *Fax:* (071) 527 2836 *E-mail:* secretariaat@ library.leidenuniv.nl; helpdesk@library.leidenuniv.nl *Web Site:* ub.leidenuniv.nl, pg 1530

Universiteitsbibliotheek Utrecht (Netherlands) *Tel:* (030) 2536600; (030) 2536601 (central lending desk); (030) 2537262 (renewals) *Fax:* (030) 2538398 *E-mail:* info@library.uu.nl; uitleen@library.uu.nl (central lending desk) *Web Site:* www.library.uu.nl, pg 1530

Universitetsbiblioteket i Bergen (Norway) *Tel:* 55 58 25 32 *Fax:* 55 58 97 03 *E-mail:* post@ub.uib.no *Web Site:* www.ub.uib.no, pg 1533

Universitetsbiblioteket i Oslo (Norway) *Tel:* 22 84 40 01 *Fax:* 22 84 41 50 *E-mail:* informasjon@uio.no *Web Site:* www.ub.uio.no, pg 1533

Universitetsbiblioteket i Trondheim (Norway) *Tel:* 73 59 51 10 *Fax:* 73 59 51 03 *E-mail:* ubit@adm.ntnu.no *Web Site:* www.ub.ntnu.no, pg 1533

Universitetsbogladen (Denmark) *Tel:* 3524 0444; 3532 6570 *Fax:* 3532 6571 *E-mail:* panum@unibog.dk *Web Site:* www.universitetsbogladen.dk, pg 1298

Universitetsforlaget (Norway) *Tel:* (022) 24147500 *Fax:* (022) 24147501 *E-mail:* post@ universitetsforlaget.no *Web Site:* www. universitetsforlaget.no, pg 506

Universiti Putra Malaysia Library (UPM) (Malaysia) *Tel:* (03) 89468642 *Fax:* (03) 89483745 *E-mail:* lib@ lib.upm.edu.my *Web Site:* www.lib.upm.edu.my, pg 1525

University Library, Universiti Sains Malaysia (Malaysia) *Tel:* (04) 6533888; (04) 6533700; (04) 6585518 *Fax:* (04) 6571526 *E-mail:* chieflib@notes.usm.my *Web Site:* www.lib.usm.my, pg 1525

Penerbit Universiti Teknologi Malaysia (Malaysia) *Tel:* (07) 521 8131; (07) 521 8180; (07) 521 8166 *Fax:* (07) 521 8174 *E-mail:* penerbit@utm.my *Web Site:* www.penerbit.utm.my, pg 455

Universities Administration Office (Myanmar), pg 472

Universities' Central Library (Myanmar) *Tel:* (01) 545 750 *Fax:* (01) 545 750 *E-mail:* ucl@mptmail.net.mm, pg 1528

University Book Shop (Auckland) Ltd (New Zealand) *Tel:* (09) 306 2700 *Fax:* (09) 306 2701 *E-mail:* ubsbooks@ubsbooks.co.nz *Web Site:* www. ubsbooks.co.nz, pg 1322

University Book Shop (Canterbury) Ltd (New Zealand) *Tel:* (03) 3667001 *Fax:* (03) 3642999 *E-mail:* info@ canterbury.ac.nz *Web Site:* www.canterbury.ac.nz, pg 1322

University Book Shop Inc (Papua New Guinea) *Tel:* 326 7375 *Fax:* 326 0961, pg 1325

University Book Shop (Otago) Ltd (New Zealand) *Tel:* (03) 4776976 *Fax:* (03) 4776571 *E-mail:* ubs@ unibooks.co.nz *Web Site:* www.unibooks.co.nz, pg 1322

University Booksellers Association of Nigeria (Nigeria) *Tel:* (052) 200250 (Ugbowo); (052) 200480 (Ekehuan) *Fax:* (052) 241156, pg 1270

University Bookshop (Ghana) *Tel:* (021) 500398 *Fax:* (021) 500398 *E-mail:* unibks@ug.gn.apc.org, pg 1262

University Bookshop (Ghana) *Tel:* (021) 500398 *Fax:* (021) 500774 *E-mail:* bookshop@ug.edu.gh *Web Site:* www.ghanaweb.com/GhanaHomePage/ education/legon.html, pg 1302

University Bookshop (Ghana) *Tel:* (051) 60223 *Fax:* (051) 60137 *E-mail:* library@knust.edu.gh *Web Site:* www.knust.edu.gh, pg 1302

University Bookshop (Zambia) *Tel:* (01) 294690; (01) 290319 *Fax:* (01) 253952; (01) 294690, pg 1347

University Bookshop Ltd (Nigeria) *Tel:* (036) 230290, pg 1322

University Bookshop (Nigeria) Ltd (Nigeria) *Tel:* (02) 400550 (ext 1208); (02) 400550 (ext 1047); (02) 400614 (ext 1244); (02) 400614 (ext 1042), pg 1323

University Bookstore (Liberia) *Tel:* 224671, pg 1315

University Co-operative Bookshop Ltd (Australia) *Tel:* (02) 93259600 *Fax:* (02) 92123372 *E-mail:* webhelp@coop-bookshop.com.au *Web Site:* www.coop-bookshop.com.au, pg 1289

University College Cork, Boole Library (Ireland) *Tel:* (021) 4902794 *Fax:* (021) 4273428 *E-mail:* library@ucc.ie *Web Site:* booleweb.ucc.ie, pg 1517

University College Dublin Library (Ireland) *Tel:* (01) 716 7583; (01) 716 7694 *Fax:* (01) 283 7667 *E-mail:* library@ucd.ie *Web Site:* www.ucd.ie/library, pg 1517

University Library (Mauritius) *Tel:* 454 1041 (ext 1229) *Fax:* 454 0905 *E-mail:* library@uom.ac.mu *Web Site:* www.uom.ac.mu, pg 1526

University of Aberdeen (United Kingdom) *Tel:* (01224) 273600 *Fax:* (01224) 273956 *E-mail:* library@abdn. ac.uk *Web Site:* www.abdn.ac.uk/diss/library, pg 1552

University of Asmara Library (Eritrea) *Tel:* (01) 161926; (01) 162553 *Fax:* (01) 162236 *Web Site:* www.uoa. edu.er, pg 1502

University of Auckland Library (New Zealand) *Tel:* (09) 3737599 (ext 88044) *Fax:* (09) 3737565 *E-mail:* library@auckland.ac.nz *Web Site:* www. library.auckland.ac.nz, pg 1531

Central Library of the University of Baghdad (Iraq) *Tel:* (01) 776 7819 *Fax:* (01) 776 3592, pg 1516

University of Bahrain Library (Bahrain) *Tel:* 17438808 *Fax:* 17449838 *E-mail:* library@admin.uob.bh *Web Site:* www.uob.edu.bh, pg 1490

University of Baluchistan Library (Pakistan) *Tel:* (081) 41770, pg 1534

Central Library of the University of Basrah (Iraq) *Tel:* (01) 8868520 *Fax:* (01) 8868520 *E-mail:* basrahyni@uruklink.net, pg 1516

The University of Birmingham (United Kingdom) *Tel:* (0121) 414 3344 *Fax:* (0121) 414 3971 *Web Site:* www.general.bham.ac.uk, pg 763

University of Botswana Library (Botswana) *Tel:* 355-0000; 355-2304; 355-2295 *Fax:* 395-6591; 395-7291 *Web Site:* www.ub.bw, pg 1493

University of Cairo Library (Egypt (Arab Republic of Egypt)) *Tel:* (02) 5729584 *Fax:* (02) 628884, pg 1502

University of Cape Coast Library (Ghana) *Tel:* (042) 60133 *Fax:* (042) 32485 *E-mail:* Ucclib@ucc.gn.apc.org, pg 1511

University of Cape Town Libraries (South Africa) *Tel:* (021) 650-3134 *Fax:* (021) 689-7568 *E-mail:* selref@uctlib.uct.ac.za *Web Site:* www.lib.uct.ac.za/, pg 1543

Library of the University of Crete (Greece) *Tel:* 28310 77810 *Fax:* 2831077850 *Web Site:* www.libh.uoc.gr, pg 1511

University of Dar Es Salaam Bookshop (United Republic of Tanzania) *Tel:* (022) 2410093; (022) 2410500 (ext 2568) *Fax:* (022) 2410137, pg 1336

University of Dar es Salaam Library (United Republic of Tanzania) *Tel:* (022) 2410241 *Fax:* (022) 2410241 *E-mail:* libdirec@udsm.ac.tz; director@libis.udsm.ac.tz *Web Site:* www.udsm.ac.tz/library, pg 1548

University of Dschang Central Library (Cameroon) *Tel:* 451351 *Fax:* 451381, pg 1495

University of Durban-Westville Library (South Africa) *Tel:* (031) 8202640 *Fax:* (031) 821873 *E-mail:* mmoodley@pixie.udw.ac.za, pg 565

University of Engineering & Technology Central Library (UET) (Pakistan) *Tel:* (042) 6829243 *Fax:* (042) 6822566 *E-mail:* central_library@yahoo.com *Web Site:* www.uet.edu.pk, pg 1534

University of Exeter Library (United Kingdom) *Tel:* (01392) 263867 *Fax:* (01392) 263871 *E-mail:* library@exeter.ac.uk *Web Site:* www.ex.ac.uk/library/, pg 1553

University of Exeter Press (United Kingdom) *Tel:* (01392) 263066 *Fax:* (01392) 263064 *E-mail:* uep@ex.ac.uk *Web Site:* www.ex.ac.uk/uep, pg 763

University of Garyounis Library (Libyan Arab Jamahiriya) *Tel:* (061) 2220147 *Fax:* (061) 2229602 *E-mail:* info@garyounis.eu *Web Site:* www.garyounis.edu, pg 1523

University of Ghana Library (Ghana) *Tel:* (021) 502701 *Fax:* (021) 502701 *E-mail:* balme@ug.gn.apc.org *Web Site:* www.ug.edu.gh, pg 1511

University of Glasgow Library (United Kingdom) *Tel:* (0141) 330 6704 *Fax:* (0141) 330 4952 *E-mail:* library@lib.gla.ac.uk *Web Site:* www.lib.gla.ac.uk, pg 1553

University of Goroka (Papua New Guinea) *Tel:* 731 1700 *Fax:* 732 2620 *E-mail:* infouog@uog.ac.pg *Web Site:* www.uog.ac.pg, pg 511

University of Haifa Library (Israel) *Tel:* (04) 257753 *Fax:* (04) 342104 *E-mail:* webmaster@lib.haifa.ac.il *Web Site:* lib.haifa.ac.il, pg 369

University of Haifa Library (Israel) *Tel:* (04) 8240289 *Fax:* (04) 8257753 *E-mail:* libmaster@univ.haifa.ac.il *Web Site:* lib.haifa.ac.il, pg 1518

University of Hertfordshire Press (United Kingdom) *Tel:* (01707) 284682 *Fax:* (01707) 284666 *E-mail:* uhpress@herts.ac.uk *Web Site:* www.herts.ac.uk/uhpress, pg 763

The University of Hong Kong, Department of Philosophy (Hong Kong) *Tel:* 28592797 *Fax:* 2559 8452 *E-mail:* fctmoore@hkuxa.hku.hk, pg 317

University of Hong Kong Libraries (Hong Kong) *Tel:* 2859 7000; 2859 2203 *Fax:* 2858 9420 *E-mail:* libadmin@hkucc.hku.hk *Web Site:* lib.hku.hk, pg 1512

University of Ibadan, Kenneth Dike Library (Nigeria) *Tel:* (02) 810 3118 *Fax:* (02) 810 3118 *E-mail:* library@kdl.ui.edu.ng, pg 1532

University of Isfahan Library (Islamic Republic of Iran) *Tel:* (0311) 684799; (0311) 792-2793 *Fax:* (0311) 275145, pg 1516

University of Jordan Bookshop (Jordan) *Tel:* (06) 843555 (ext 3339) *Fax:* (06) 836446 *E-mail:* admin@ju.edu.jo, pg 1314

University of Jordan Library (Jordan) *Tel:* 5355000 (ext 3135) *Fax:* 5355570 *E-mail:* library@ju.edu.jo *Web Site:* www.ju.edu.jo, pg 1521

University of Jos Library (Nigeria) *Tel:* (073) 610514; (073) 53724; (073) 44952 *Fax:* (073) 610514 *Web Site:* 128.255.135.155/libraries, pg 1532

University of Kabul Library (Afghanistan) *Tel:* 42594, pg 1487

University of Khartoum Bookshop (Sudan) *Tel:* (011) 80558, pg 1334

University of Khartoum Library (Sudan) *Web Site:* www.sudan.net/uk, pg 1545

University of KwaZulu-Natal Press (South Africa) *Tel:* (033) 260 5226; (033) 260 5225 *Fax:* (033) 260 5801 *E-mail:* books@ukzn.ac.za *Web Site:* www.ukznpress.co.za, pg 565

University of Lagos Bookshop (Nigeria) *Tel:* (01) 820279 *Fax:* (01) 822644, pg 1323

University of Lagos Library (Nigeria) *Tel:* (01) 41 361 *Fax:* (01) 822644 *Web Site:* www.unilag.edu/library/index.asp, pg 1532

University of Lagos Press (Nigeria) *Tel:* (01) 825048 *Fax:* (01) 825048, pg 503

University of Leicester Library (United Kingdom) *Tel:* (0116) 252 2043 *Fax:* (0116) 252 2066 *E-mail:* libdesk@le.ac.uk *Web Site:* www.le.ac.uk/library, pg 1553

University of Liberia Libraries (Liberia) *Tel:* 226 418 *Fax:* 227 033; 226 418 *Web Site:* www.hometown.aol.com/dcronteh/myhomepage/index.html, pg 1523

University of London (United Kingdom) *Tel:* (020) 7862 8000 *Fax:* (020) 7636 5874 *E-mail:* enquiries@lon.ac.uk *Web Site:* www.lon.ac.uk, pg 1346

University of London Careers Service (United Kingdom) *Tel:* (020) 7554 4500 *Fax:* (020) 7383 5876 *E-mail:* careers@lon.ac.uk *Web Site:* www.careers.lon.ac.uk, pg 763

University of Malawi Libraries (Malawi) *Tel:* (01) 526 622; (01) 524 297 *E-mail:* university.office@unima.mw *Web Site:* www.unima.mw, pg 1524

University of Malawi, Polytechnic Library (Malawi) *Tel:* (01) 670411 *Fax:* (01) 670578 *Web Site:* www.poly.ac.mw, pg 1525

University of Malaya Co-operative Bookshop Ltd (Malaysia) *Tel:* (03) 756 5000; (03) 756 5425 *Fax:* (03) 755 4424, pg 1317

University of Malaya, Department of Publications (Malaysia) *Tel:* (03) 79574361 *Fax:* (03) 79574473 *E-mail:* terbit@um.edu.my *Web Site:* www.um.edu.my/umpress, pg 455

University of Malaya Library (Malaysia) *Tel:* (03) 7956 7800 *Fax:* (03) 7957 3661 *E-mail:* query_perpustakaan@um.edu.my *Web Site:* www.umlib.um.edu.my, pg 1526

University of Malta Library (Malta) *Tel:* 2340 2316 *Fax:* 21 314 306 *Web Site:* www.lib.um.edu.mt, pg 1526

The University of Malta Publications Section (Malta) *Tel:* 21333903-6 *Fax:* 21336450 *Web Site:* www.um.edu.mt, pg 457

University of Manila Central Library (Philippines) *Tel:* (02) 7355256 *Fax:* (02) 7355089 *E-mail:* um@univman.edu.ph *Web Site:* www.univman.edu.ph, pg 1535

University of Melbourne Baillieu Library (Australia) *Tel:* (03) 8344 5378; (03) 8344 0444 *Fax:* (03) 9348 1142 *Web Site:* www.lib.unimelb.edu.au/, pg 1489

Central Library of the University of Mosul (Iraq) *Tel:* (060) 810162 *Fax:* (060) 8011; (060) 8015, pg 1516

University of Mumbai Library (India) *Tel:* (022) 2652819 *Fax:* (022) 2652832 *Web Site:* members.rediff.com/vidyarthi/mulhome.htm, pg 1515

The University of Nagoya Press (Japan) *Tel:* (052) 781-5353 *Fax:* (052) 781-0697 *E-mail:* info@unp.nagoya-u.ac.jp *Web Site:* www.unp.or.jp, pg 427

University of Nairobi Bookshop (Kenya) *Tel:* (02) 334244 *Fax:* (02) 336885 *E-mail:* webmaster@uonbi.ac.ke *Web Site:* www.uonbi.ac.ke, pg 1314

University of Nairobi Libraries (Kenya) *Tel:* (02) 318262 *Fax:* (02) 336885 *E-mail:* jkml@uonbi.ac.ke *Web Site:* library.uonbi.ac.ke, pg 1521

University of New South Wales Library (Australia) *Tel:* (02) 9385 1000 *Web Site:* www.info.library.unsw.edu.au, pg 1489

University of New South Wales Press Ltd (Australia) *Tel:* (02) 9664 0900 *Fax:* (02) 9664 5420 *E-mail:* info.press@unsw.edu.au *Web Site:* www.unswpress.com.au, pg 44

University of Newcastle (Australia) *Tel:* (02) 4921 8865 *Web Site:* www.newcastle.edu.au, pg 44

University of Newcastle Upon Tyne (United Kingdom) *Tel:* (0191) 222 6000 *Fax:* (0191) 222 6229 *Web Site:* www.ncl.ac.uk, pg 763

University of Nigeria (Nigeria) *Tel:* (042) 771444 *Fax:* (042) 770644 *E-mail:* unnlibrary@yahoo.com *Web Site:* www.unn-edu.net, pg 1532

University of Nigeria Bookshop Ltd (Nigeria) *Tel:* (042) 332077; (042) 771911, pg 1323

University of Otago Library (New Zealand) *Tel:* (03) 479 8910 *Fax:* (03) 479 8947 *E-mail:* library@otago.ac.nz; reference.central@library.otago.ac.nz *Web Site:* www.library.otago.ac.nz, pg 1531

University of Otago Press (New Zealand) *Tel:* (03) 479 8807 *Fax:* (03) 479 8385 *E-mail:* university.press@otago.ac.nz *Web Site:* www.otago.ac.nz, pg 497

University of Papua New Guinea Press (Papua New Guinea) *Tel:* 3267654 *Fax:* 3260127, pg 511

University of Peradeniya Library (Sri Lanka) *Tel:* (081) 2386004 *Fax:* (081) 2388678 *E-mail:* lib@mail.pdn.ac.lk *Web Site:* www.pdn.ac.lk/library/main, pg 1545

University of the Philippines Press (Philippines) *Tel:* (02) 9205301; (02) 9205302; (02) 9205303; (02) 9205304; (02) 9205305; (02) 9266642; (02) 9253243; (02) 9253244 *Fax:* (02) 9282558 *E-mail:* press@nicole.upd.edu.ph; uppress@uppress.org *Web Site:* www.upd.edu.ph, pg 516

University of Port Elizabeth Library (South Africa) *Tel:* (041) 504 2281 *Fax:* (041) 504 2280 *E-mail:* library@upe.ac.za *Web Site:* www.upe.ac.za/library, pg 1543

University of Pretoria Academic Information Services (South Africa) *Tel:* (012) 420 2241 *Fax:* (012) 362 5100 *Web Site:* www.ais.up.ac.za, pg 1543

University of Puerto Rico, General Library, Mayaguez Campus (Puerto Rico) *Tel:* (787) 265-3810; (787) 832-4040 (ext 3810, 2151, 2155) *Fax:* (787) 265-5483 *E-mail:* library@rumlib.uprm.edu *Web Site:* www.uprm.edu/library, pg 1538

University of Puerto Rico, Medical Sciences Campus Library (Puerto Rico) *Tel:* (787) 758-2525; (787) 751-8199 *Fax:* (787) 759-6713 *E-mail:* zgarcia@rcmaca.upr.clu.edu *Web Site:* www.rcm.upr.edu, pg 1538

University of Puerto Rico Press (EDUPR) (Puerto Rico) *Tel:* (787) 758-6932; (787) 758-8345 (sales) *Fax:* (787) 753-9116, pg 533

University of Queensland Library (Australia) *Tel:* (07) 3365 6949 *Fax:* (07) 3365 1737 *E-mail:* universitylibrarian@library.uq.edu.au *Web Site:* www.library.uq.edu.au, pg 1489

University of Queensland Press (Australia) *Tel:* (07) 3365 2127; (07) 3377 7244; (07) 3365 2440 (sales) *Fax:* (07) 3365 7579 *E-mail:* uqp@uqp.uq.edu.au *Web Site:* www.uqp.uq.edu.au, pg 44

University of Rajshahi Library (Bangladesh) *Tel:* (0721) 750041; (0721) 750033 *Fax:* (0721) 750064 *E-mail:* rajcc@citechco.net *Web Site:* www.ugc. org/rajsahai_uni.htm, pg 1491

The University of Reading Library (United Kingdom) *Tel:* (0118) 378 8704 *Fax:* (0118) 378 6636 *E-mail:* library@reading.ac.uk *Web Site:* www.library. rdg.ac.uk, pg 1553

Central Library of the University of Salahaddin (Iraq) *Tel:* 00873762566859 *Fax:* 00873762566861 *Web Site:* www.salun.org, pg 1516

University of San Carlos Library System (Philippines) *Tel:* (032) 2531000 *Fax:* (032) 2540432 *E-mail:* direklib@usc.edu.ph *Web Site:* www.usc.edu. ph, pg 1535

University of Santo Tomas Library (Philippines) *Tel:* (02) 731-3034 *Fax:* (02) 740-9709 *E-mail:* library@ust.edu. ph *Web Site:* www.ust.edu.ph, pg 1535

University of South Africa Library (South Africa) *Tel:* (012) 4293206 *Fax:* (012) 4292925 *E-mail:* willej@alpha.unisa.ac.za *Web Site:* www. unisa.ac.za, pg 1543

University of South Australia Library (Australia) *Tel:* (08) 8302 6661 *Fax:* (08) 8302 6250 *Web Site:* www.library.unisa.edu.au, pg 1489

University of Southampton Library (United Kingdom) *Tel:* (01703) 22180 *Fax:* (01703) 23007 *E-mail:* libenqs@soton.ac.uk *Web Site:* www.library. soton.ac.uk, pg 1553

University of Stellenbosch Library (South Africa) *Tel:* (021) 808 4385 *Fax:* (021) 808 4336 *Web Site:* www.sun.ac.za/library, pg 1543

University of Swaziland Library (Swaziland) *Tel:* (051) 84011; (051) 85108 *Fax:* (051) 85276 *E-mail:* kwaluseni@uniswa.sz *Web Site:* library. uniswa.sz, pg 1545

University of Sydney Library (Australia) *Tel:* (02) 9351 2990 *Fax:* (02) 9351 2890 *Web Site:* www.library. usyd.edu.au, pg 1489

University of Tabriz Central Library (Islamic Republic of Iran) *Tel:* (0411) 3342199 *Fax:* (0411) 3355993 *Web Site:* www.tabrizu.ac.ir/centrallibrary/lib-general. htm, pg 1516

University of Technology, Jamaica (Jamaica) *Tel:* (876) 927-1680-9 *Fax:* (876) 927-1614 *E-mail:* library@ utech.edu.jm *Web Site:* www.utechjamaica.edu.jm, pg 1519

University of Technology, Sydney Library (Australia) *Tel:* 9514 2000 *E-mail:* info@uts.edu.au *Web Site:* www.uts.edu.au, pg 1489

Central Library & Documentation Centre of University of Teheran (Islamic Republic of Iran) *Tel:* (021) 6462699; (021) 6419831; (021) 6405047 *Fax:* (021) 6409348 *E-mail:* publicrel@ut.ac.ir *Web Site:* pages.ut. ac.ir/library/home.htm, pg 1516

University of Tehran Publications & Printing Organization (Islamic Republic of Iran) *Tel:* (021) 6462699; (021) 6419831; (021) 6405047 *Fax:* (021) 6409348 *Web Site:* www.ut.ac.ir, pg 354

University of the East Library (Philippines) *Tel:* (02) 7358544 *Fax:* (02) 7356976 *E-mail:* webmaster@uec. edu.ph *Web Site:* www.ue.edu.ph, pg 1535

University of the Philippines Diliman University Library (Philippines) *Tel:* (02) 981-8500, Local 2852 *Fax:* (02) 926-1876 *Web Site:* www.mainlib.upd.edu.ph, pg 1535

University of the South Pacific Library (Fiji) *Tel:* 323 1000 *Fax:* 323 1528 *E-mail:* library@usp.ac.fj *Web Site:* www.usp.ac.fj/library, pg 1503

University of the West Indies Library (Jamaica) (Jamaica) *Tel:* (876) 935-8479; (876) 935-8294; (876) 935-8296 *Fax:* (876) 927-1926 *E-mail:* main.library@ uwimona.edu.jm *Web Site:* wwwlibrary.uwimona.edu. jm:1104, pg 1519

University of the West Indies (Trinidad & Tobago) (Trinidad & Tobago) *Tel:* (868) 662 2002; (868) 662 3232 (ext 2132) *Fax:* (868) 663 9684 *E-mail:* infocentre@library.uwi.tt *Web Site:* www.uwi. tt, pg 643

University of the West Indies Library (Barbados) (Barbados) *Tel:* (0246) 417-4444 *Fax:* (0246) 425-1327 *E-mail:* webmaster@uwichill.edu.bb *Web Site:* www.cavehill.uwi.edu, pg 1491

University of the West Indies Library (Trinidad & Tobago) (Trinidad & Tobago) *Tel:* 868-662 2002 (ext 2132) *Fax:* 868-662-9238 *E-mail:* mainlib@library. uwi.tt *Web Site:* www.mainlib.uwi.tt, pg 1549

University of the West Indies Press (Jamaica) *Tel:* (876) 977-2659 *Fax:* (876) 977-2660 *E-mail:* cuserv@ cwjamaica.com (customer service & orders); uwipress_marketing@cwjamaica.com *Web Site:* www. uwipress.com, pg 411

University of the West Indies Publishers' Association (Jamaica) *Tel:* (876) 977-2659 *Fax:* (876) 977-2660, pg 1265

University of the Western Cape Library (South Africa) *Tel:* (021) 959 2947; (021) 959 2209 *Fax:* (021) 959 2659 *Web Site:* www.uwc.ac.za/library, pg 1543

University of the Witwatersrand Library (South Africa) *Tel:* (011) 716-2400 *Fax:* (011) 403-1421 *E-mail:* 056heath@libris.wwl.wits.ac.za, pg 1543

Library of the University of Thessaloniki (Greece) *Tel:* 2310995325; 2310995327 *Fax:* 2310995322 *E-mail:* syra@ipatia.ccf.auth.gr *Web Site:* www.lib. auth.gr, pg 1511

University of Tokyo Library (Japan) *Tel:* (03) 5841 2612 *Fax:* (03) 3816 4208 *E-mail:* kikaku@lib.u-tokyo.ac.jp *Web Site:* www.lib.u-tokyo.ac.jp, pg 1520

University of Tokyo Press (Japan) *Tel:* (03) 3815-7789 *Fax:* (03) 3812-6958 *Web Site:* www.u-tokyo.ac.jp, pg 427

University of Toronto Press Inc (Canada) *Tel:* 416-667-7767 *Fax:* 416-667-7803 *E-mail:* printing@ utpress.utoronto.ca *Web Site:* www.utpress.utoronto.ca, pg 1144, 1166, 1206, 1225

University of Wales Press (United Kingdom) *Tel:* (029) 2049-6899 *Fax:* (029) 2049-6108 *E-mail:* press@ press.wales.ac.uk *Web Site:* www.wales.ac.uk/press, pg 763

University of Western Australia Library (Australia) *Tel:* (08) 9380 1777 *Toll Free Tel:* 1800 263 921 *Fax:* (08) 9380 1012 *E-mail:* uwalibrary@library.uwa. edu.au *Web Site:* www.library.uwa.edu.au/, pg 1489

University of Western Australia Press (Australia) *Tel:* (08) 9380 3670 *Fax:* (08) 9380 1027 *E-mail:* uwap@cyllene.uwa.edu.au *Web Site:* www. uwapress.uwa.edu.au, pg 44

University of Zambia Press (UNZA Press) (Zambia) *Tel:* (01) 213221; (01) 293058; (01) 292884; (01) 293580; (01) 219624; (01) 252514 *Fax:* (01) 253952, pg 776

University of Zambia Press (UNZA Press) (Zambia) *Tel:* (01) 290740; (01) 290409 *Fax:* (01) 253952, pg 1555

University of Zimbabwe Library (Zimbabwe) *Tel:* (04) 303211 *Fax:* (04) 335383 *E-mail:* mainlib@uzlib.uz. zw; infocentre@uzlib.uz.ac.zw *Web Site:* www.uz.ac. zw/library, pg 778

University of Zimbabwe Library (Zimbabwe) *Tel:* (04) 303211 *Fax:* (04) 335383 *E-mail:* mainlib@uzlib.uz. zw; infocentre@uzlib.uz.ac.zw *Web Site:* uzweb.uz.ac. zw/library, pg 1555

University of Zimbabwe Publications (Zimbabwe) *Tel:* (04) 303211 (ext 1236 or 1662) *Fax:* (04) 333407 *E-mail:* uzpub@admin.uz.ac.zn *Web Site:* www.uz. zw/publications/, pg 779

The University Press Ltd (Bangladesh) *Tel:* (02) 861208; (02) 255789 *Fax:* (02) 8332112 *E-mail:* upl@bangla. net; upl@bttb.net.bd, pg 61

University Presses of California, Columbia & Princeton Ltd (United Kingdom) *Tel:* (01243) 843291 *Fax:* (01243) 820250 *E-mail:* lois@upccp.demon.co.uk *Web Site:* www.ucpress.edu, pg 764

University Publishing Co (Nigeria) *Tel:* (046) 230013, pg 503

University Publishing Projects Ltd (Israel) *Tel:* (09) 7459955 *Fax:* (09) 7459977 *E-mail:* upp@upp.co.il *Web Site:* www.upp.co.il, pg 369

Editorial Universo SA (Peru) *Tel:* (014) 241639; (014) 233190, pg 513

Editorial Universo SA de CV (Mexico) *Tel:* (05) 5750711 ext 30; (05) 5750711 ext 31, pg 469

Universo Editorial SA de CV Edicion de Libros Revistas y Periodicos (Mexico) *Tel:* (048) 21593, pg 469

Librairie Universsitaire de la Reunion (Reunion) *Tel:* 210758, pg 1329

Univerza Ljubljana (Slovenia) *Tel:* (01) 241 85 00 *Fax:* (01) 241 86 60 *E-mail:* info@nuk.uni-lj.si *Web Site:* www.uni-lj.si, pg 1541

Univerza v Ljubljani Ekonomska Fakulteta (Slovenia) *Tel:* (01) 5892-400 *Fax:* (01) 5892-698 *Web Site:* www.ef.uni-lj.si, pg 557

Univerzitet u Beogradu biblioteka 'Svetozar Markovic' (Serbia and Montenegro) *Tel:* (011) 3370-509 *Fax:* (011) 337Q-354 *Web Site:* ns.unilib.bg.ac.yu, pg 1541

Biblioteka Uniwersytecka w Warszawie (Poland) *Tel:* (022) 5525660; (022) 5525178 *Fax:* (022) 5525659 *E-mail:* buw@uw.edu.pl *Web Site:* www.buw. uw.edu.pl, pg 1536

Biblioteka Uniwersytecka we Wroclawiu (Poland) *Tel:* (071) 346 31 10 *Fax:* (071) 346 31 66 *E-mail:* infnauk@bu.uni.wroc.pl *Web Site:* www.bu. uni.wroc.pl, pg 1537

Uniwersytet Gdanski (Poland) *Tel:* (058) 550-94-13 *Fax:* (058) 551-52-21 *E-mail:* bib@bg.univ.gda.pl; info@bg.univ.gda.pl *Web Site:* www.bg.univ.gda. pl/library/, pg 1537

Biblioteka Uniwersytecka w Toruniu (Poland) *Tel:* (056) 611-44-08 *Fax:* (056) 652-04-19 *E-mail:* sekretariat@ bu.uni.torun.pl *Web Site:* www.bu.uni.torun.pl/en, pg 1537

Wydawnictwa Uniwersytetu Warszawskiego (Poland) *Tel:* (022) 5531318 *Fax:* (022) 5531318 *E-mail:* wuw@uw.edu.pl, pg 522

Wydawnictwo Uniwersytetu Wroclawskiego SP ZOO (Poland) *Tel:* (071) 3752809 *Fax:* (071) 3752735 *E-mail:* marketing@wuwr.com.pl *Web Site:* www. wuwr.com.pl, pg 522

UNO-Verlag GmbH (Germany) *Tel:* (0228) 94 90 2-0 *Fax:* (0228) 94 90 2-22 *E-mail:* info@uno-verlag.de *Web Site:* www.uno-verlag.de, pg 291

Unrast Verlag e V (Germany) *Tel:* (0251) 666293 *Fax:* (0251) 666120 *E-mail:* kontakt@unrast-verlag.de *Web Site:* www.unrast-verlag.de, pg 291

Editrice Uomini Nuovi (Italy) *Tel:* (0332) 723007 *Fax:* (0332) 723264 *E-mail:* libreria@eun.ch; eunitaly@eun.ch *Web Site:* www.eun.ch, pg 407

Uplands Books (United Kingdom) *Tel:* (01424) 422306 *Fax:* (01424) 719879 *E-mail:* sales@upublish.cablenet. co.uk, pg 764

UPM-Kymmene Ltd (Finland) *Tel:* 204 15 111 *Fax:* 204 15 110 *E-mail:* info@upm-kymmene.com *Web Site:* www.upm-kymmene.com, pg 1144

Upper Kabete Library (Kenya) *Tel:* (02) 631353 *Fax:* (02) 336885 *Web Site:* library.uonbi.ac.ke, pg 1522

Upplysing - Felag bokasafns- og upplysingafraeoa (Iceland) *Tel:* 553-7290; 862-8627 *Fax:* 588-9239 *E-mail:* upplysing@bokis.is *Web Site:* www.bokis.is, pg 1564

Uppsala Universitetsbibliotek (Sweden) *Tel:* (018) 471 39 00 *Fax:* (018) 471 39 13 *E-mail:* info@ub.uu.se *Web Site:* www.ub.uu.se, pg 1546

UPS Translations (United Kingdom) *Tel:* (020) 7837 8300 *Fax:* (020) 7486 3272 *E-mail:* production@ upstranslations.com *Web Site:* www.upstranslations. com, pg 1141

Izdatelstvo Ural' skogo (Russian Federation) *Tel:* (03432) 515448 *Fax:* (03432) 51-54-48 *E-mail:* info@idc.e-burg-ru, pg 545

Urania Verlag mit Ravensburger Ratgebern (Germany) *Tel:* (0) 711-78803-0 *Fax:* (0) 711-78803- 10 *E-mail:* urania@verlagsgruppe-dornier.de *Web Site:* www.urania-ravensburger.de, pg 291

Uranium Verlag Zug (Switzerland) *Tel:* (042) 217744, pg 631

Ediciones Urano, SA (Spain) *Tel:* (902) 131 315; (093) 2375 564 *Fax:* (093) 4153 796 *E-mail:* info@ edicionesurano.com; atencion@edicionesurano.com *Web Site:* www.edicionesurano.com, pg 599

Urban und Schwarzenberg GmbH (Austria) *Tel:* (01) 4052731-0 *Fax:* (01) 405272441, pg 58

Urban und Schwarzenberg GmbH (Austria) *Tel:* (01) 4052731 *Fax:* (01) 405272441, pg 1291

Urban & Vogel Medien und Medizin Verlagsgesellschaft mbH & Co KG (Germany) *Tel:* (089) 4372-0 *Fax:* (089) 4372-2633 *E-mail:* verlag@urban-vogel.de *Web Site:* www.urban-vogel.de, pg 291

Urbaniana University Press (Italy) *Tel:* (06) 6988 2182 *Fax:* (06) 6988 2182 *E-mail:* uupamm@urbaniana.edu *Web Site:* www.urbaniana.edu/uup, pg 407

Urdu Academy Sind (Pakistan) *Tel:* (021) 2631485, pg 510

Urdu Science Board (Pakistan) *Tel:* (042) 5758674; (042) 878168 *Fax:* (042) 5758674, pg 1271

Urim Publications (Israel) *Tel:* (02) 679-7633 *Fax:* (02) 679-7634 *E-mail:* publisher@urimpublications.com *Web Site:* www.urimpublications.com, pg 369

Urmo SA de Ediciones (Spain) *Tel:* (094) 424 53 07 *Fax:* (094) 423 19 84 *E-mail:* urmo@infonegocio.com *Web Site:* www.urmo.com, pg 599

Urozaj (Ukraine) *Tel:* (044) 2450995 *Fax:* (044) 2450995, pg 649

La Urpila Editores (Uruguay) *Tel:* (02) 9085347, pg 773

Ursa ry (Finland) *Tel:* (09) 684 0400 *Fax:* (09) 6840 4040 *E-mail:* ursa@ursa.fi *Web Site:* www.ursa.fi, pg 144

Editia Uruguay (Uruguay) *Tel:* (02) 915-9633; (02) 915-9759 *Fax:* (02) 916-4419 *E-mail:* edita@adinet.com.uy *Web Site:* www.editia.com, pg 773

US Lithograph Inc (United States) *Tel:* 212-673-3210 *Fax:* 212-673-5261 *Web Site:* www.uslithograph.com, pg 1240

Usaha Baru CV (Indonesia) *Tel:* (031) 22128, pg 353

Usborne Publishing Ltd (United Kingdom) *Tel:* (020) 7430 2800 *Fax:* (020) 7430 1562; (020) 7242 0974 *E-mail:* mail@usborne.co.uk *Web Site:* www.usborne. com, pg 764

The Useful Publishing Co (Australia) *Tel:* (08) 9370 4577 *Fax:* (08) 9370 2540, pg 45

UST Publishing House (Philippines) *Tel:* (02) 7313101 *Fax:* (02) 7811473 *E-mail:* qui_test@ust.edu.ph *Web Site:* www.ust.edu.ph, pg 516

Ustav informacii a prognoz skolstva mladeze a telovychovy (Slovakia) *Tel:* (02) 6542 5166; (02) 6542 6182 *Fax:* (02) 6542 6180 *E-mail:* hrab@uip.sanet.sk, pg 556

Ustredna kniznica Slovenskej akademie vied (Slovakia) *Tel:* (02) 52926 321; (02) 52926 325 *Fax:* (02) 52921 733 *E-mail:* knizhorv@klemens.savba.sk *Web Site:* www.uk.sav.sk/, pg 1541

Usus Editora (Portugal) *Tel:* (021) 4535000 *Fax:* (021) 4426482, pg 532

UT Orpheus Edizioni Srl (Italy) *Tel:* (051) 226468 *Fax:* (051) 263720 *E-mail:* mail@utorpheus.com *Web Site:* www.utorpheus.com, pg 407

UTAS-Verlag fur Moderne Lernmethoden Uta Stechl (Germany) *Tel:* (08633) 1450 *Fax:* (08633) 7805, pg 291

UTB fuer Wissenschaft Uni Taschenbuecher GmbH (Germany) *Tel:* (0711) 7 82 95 55-0 *Fax:* (0711) 7 80 13 76 *E-mail:* utb@utb-stuttgart.de *Web Site:* www. utb.de, pg 291

UTET Periodici Scientifici (Italy) *Tel:* (02) 6241171 *Fax:* (02) 62411720 *E-mail:* utet@utet.it *Web Site:* www.utetperiodici.it, pg 408

UTET (Unione Tipografico-Editrice Torinese) (Italy) *Tel:* (011) 2099111 *Fax:* (011) 2099394 *E-mail:* utet@ utet.it *Web Site:* www.utet.it, pg 408

Utusan Publications & Distributors Sdn Bhd (Malaysia) *Tel:* (03) 9287 7777 *Fax:* (03) 9282 7751 *E-mail:* corporate@utusan.com.my *Web Site:* www. utusangroup.com.my, pg 456

Uudet Kirjat (Finland) *Tel:* (09) 6168 3370 *E-mail:* uudetkirjat@wsoy.fi *Web Site:* www. uudetkirjat.fi, pg 1242

UVK Universitatsverlag Konstanz GmbH (Germany) *Tel:* (07531) 90530 *Fax:* (07531) 905398 *E-mail:* willkommen@uvk.de *Web Site:* www.uvk.de, pg 291

UVK Verlagsgesellschaft mbH (Germany) *Tel:* (07531) 90530 *Fax:* (07531) 905398 *E-mail:* willkommen@ uvk.de *Web Site:* www.uvk.de, pg 291

UWI Publishers' Association (Jamaica) *Tel:* 876-927-1660; 876-927-1669 *Fax:* 876-977-2660 *E-mail:* helpdesk@uwimona.edu.jm, pg 411

Izdatelstvo Uzbekistan (Uzbekistan) *Tel:* (0371) 443810, pg 773

Uzima Press Ltd (Kenya) *Tel:* (020) 21239 *E-mail:* uzima@wananchi.com, pg 433

V S P International Science Publishers (Netherlands) *Tel:* (030) 692 5790 *Fax:* (030) 693 2081 *E-mail:* vsppub@brill.nl *Web Site:* www.vsppub.com, pg 486

Edition Va Bene (Austria) *Tel:* (02243) 22 159; (0664) 1616356 (mobile) *Fax:* (02243) 22 159 *E-mail:* edition@vabene.at *Web Site:* www.vabene.at, pg 58

Vacation Work Publications (United Kingdom) *Tel:* (01865) 241978 *Fax:* (01865) 790885 *E-mail:* info@vacationwork.co.uk *Web Site:* www. vacationwork.co.uk, pg 764

Vaccari SRL (Italy) *Tel:* (059) 764106; (059) 771251 *Fax:* (059) 760157 *E-mail:* info@vaccari.it *Web Site:* www.vaccari.it, pg 408

Vacher Dod Publishing Ltd (United Kingdom) *Tel:* (020) 7828 7256 *Fax:* (020) 7828 7269 *E-mail:* politics@ vacherdod.co.uk *Web Site:* www.vacherdod.co.uk, pg 764

Vaco NV Uitgeversmij (Suriname) *Tel:* 472545 *E-mail:* interf@sr.net, pg 604

Vadell Hermanos Editores CA (Venezuela) *Tel:* (0212) 5723108; (0212) 5778110 *Fax:* (0212) 5725243 *Web Site:* www.vadellhermanos.com/, pg 775

Vaga Ltd (Lithuania) *Tel:* (02) 49 81 21 *Fax:* (02) 49 81 22 *E-mail:* info@vaga.lt *Web Site:* www.vaga.lt, pg 446

La Vague a l'ame (France) *Tel:* (04) 76470784, pg 188

Editions Vague Verte (France) *Tel:* (03) 22 30 72 50 *Fax:* (03) 22 26 58 73 *E-mail:* edlavagueverte@ wanadoo.fr *Web Site:* perso.wanadoo.fr/ editionslavagueverte, pg 188

Vaidelote, SIA (Latvia) *Tel:* 7937943; 9561812 *Fax:* 7542649, pg 442

Vaillant - Carmanne, Imprimerie (Belgium) *Tel:* (011) 612452 *Fax:* (011) 612451, pg 73

Les Editions Vaillant-Miroir-Sprint Publications (France) *Tel:* (01) 42819103, pg 188

Vaka-Helgafell (Iceland) *Tel:* 522 2000 *Fax:* 522 2022 *E-mail:* edda@edda.is *Web Site:* www.vaka.is, pg 323

Vaka-Helgafell (Iceland) *Tel:* 522 2000 *Fax:* 522 2022 *E-mail:* edda@edda.is *Web Site:* vaka.is, pg 1304

Vakils Feffer & Simons Ltd (India) *Tel:* (022) 2611221; (022) 2619121 *Fax:* (022) 2614924; (022) 2610432, pg 348

Editura Valahia SRL (Romania) *Tel:* (097) 680948, pg 538

Valdonega SRL (Italy) *Tel:* (045) 6020444 *Fax:* (045) 6020334 *E-mail:* valdonega@valdonega.it, pg 408

Valdonega SRL (Italy) *Tel:* (045) 6020444 *Fax:* (045) 6020334 *E-mail:* valdonega@valdonega.it *Web Site:* www.valdonega.it, pg 1149

Carlos Valencia Editores (Colombia) *Tel:* (01) 2839040; (01) 3426224 *Fax:* (01) 2839235 *E-mail:* ancoraed@ elancoraeditores.com, pg 113

Valeton b v (Netherlands) *Tel:* (020) 6201454 *Fax:* (020) 6279209, pg 1320

Valgus Publishers (Estonia) *Tel:* 650 5025; (050) 59 958 *Fax:* 650 5104 *E-mail:* info@kirjastusvalgus.ee, pg 140

Vallardi & Assoc (Italy) *Tel:* (0?) 6555545 *Fax:* (02) 6555640, pg 408

Vallardi Industrie Grafiche (Italy) *Tel:* (02) 9370284 *Fax:* (02) 93570442 *Web Site:* www.vallardi.com, pg 408

Vallentine, Mitchell & Co Ltd (United Kingdom) *Tel:* (020) 8952 9526 *Fax:* (020) 8952 9242 *E-mail:* info@vmbooks.com *Web Site:* www.vmbooks. com, pg 764

Valmartina Editore SRL (Italy) *Tel:* (011) 2098741; (011) 2098720 *Fax:* (011) 2098765 *E-mail:* redazione@valmartina.it *Web Site:* www. valmartina.it, pg 408

Van Buuren Uitgeverij BV (Netherlands) *Tel:* (023) 5325440 *Fax:* (023) 5327017, pg 486

Van Dale Lexicografie BV (Netherlands) *Tel:* (031) 232 47 11 *Fax:* (031) 231 68 50 *E-mail:* info@vandale.nl *Web Site:* www.vandale.nl, pg 487

Editions Van de Velde (France) *Tel:* (01) 56 68 86 64 *Fax:* (01) 56 68 90 66 *E-mail:* vandevelde.editions@ wanadoo.fr *Web Site:* www.musicollege.com, pg 188

Marc Van de Wiele bvba (Belgium) *Tel:* (050) 333805 *Fax:* (050) 346457, pg 73

Dorothea van der Koelen (Germany) *Tel:* (06131) 346 64 *Fax:* (06131) 36 90 76 *E-mail:* dvanderkoelen@ xterna-net.de, pg 291

Frank P van Eck Publishers (Liechtenstein) *Tel:* (075) 3923000 *Fax:* (075) 3922277 *E-mail:* vaneck@ datacomm.ch, pg 445

Van Gorcum & Comp BV (Netherlands) *Tel:* (0592) 37 95 55 *Fax:* (0592) 37 20 64 *E-mail:* assen@vgorcum. nl *Web Site:* www.vangorcum.nl, pg 487

Kelvin van Hasselt Publishing Services (United Kingdom) *Tel:* (01263) 862724 *Fax:* (01263) 862803 *E-mail:* kvhbooks@aol.com, pg 1134

Van Lear Ltd (United Kingdom) *Tel:* (020) 7385 1199 *Fax:* (020) 7385 6262 *E-mail:* evl@vanlear.co.uk, pg 1134

The Van Leer Jerusalem Institute (Israel) *Tel:* (02) 5605222 *Fax:* (02) 5619293 *E-mail:* values@vanleer. org.il *Web Site:* www.vanleer.org.il, pg 369

Van Molle Publishing (United Kingdom) *Tel:* (01239) 851482 *Fax:* (01239) 851482, pg 764

Uitgeverij G A van Oorschot bv (Netherlands) *Tel:* (020) 623 14 84 *Fax:* (020) 625 40 83 *E-mail:* verkoop@vanoorschot.nl, pg 487

Van Schaik Bookstore University Bookshop (South Africa) *Tel:* (021) 918 85 00 *Fax:* (021) 951 14 70 *E-mail:* vsblv@vanschaik.com; vsblv@vanschaiknet.com *Web Site:* www.vsonline.co.za; www.vanschaik.com, pg 1332

Van Schaik Publishers (South Africa) *Tel:* (012) 342-2765 *Fax:* (012) 430-3563 *E-mail:* vanschaik@vanschaiknet.com *Web Site:* www.vanschaiknet.com, pg 565

Uitgeverij Van Walraven BV (Netherlands) *Tel:* (035) 5482421 *Fax:* (035) 5421672, pg 487

Uitgeverij Van Wijnen (Netherlands) *Tel:* (0517) 394588 *Fax:* (0517) 397179 *E-mail:* info@uitgeverijvanwijnen.nl *Web Site:* www.uitgeverijvanwijnen.nl, pg 487

Vandenhoeck & Ruprecht (Germany) *Tel:* (0551) 5084-40 *Fax:* (0551) 5084-422 *E-mail:* info@v-r.de *Web Site:* www.v-r.de, pg 291

Vander Editions, SA (Belgium) *Tel:* (02) 7629804 *Fax:* (02) 7620662, pg 73

Vandrer mod Lysets Forlag Aps (Denmark) *Tel:* 3315 7815 *Fax:* 3311 8030 *E-mail:* vml@vandrer-mod-lyset.dk *Web Site:* www.vandrer-mod-lyset.dk, pg 135

Vanguard Books Ltd (Pakistan) *Tel:* (042) 7243779; (042) 7120776; (042) 7120781; (042) 7243783; (042) 7235767 *Fax:* (042) 7245097; (042) 73551978 *Web Site:* www.vanguardbooks.com, pg 510

Vani Prakashan (India) *Tel:* (011) 23273167 *Fax:* (011) 23275710 *E-mail:* vani-prakashan@yahoo.com, pg 348

Societa Editrice Vannini (Italy) *Tel:* (030) 313374 *Fax:* (030) 314078 *E-mail:* @vanninieditrice.it *Web Site:* www.vanninieditrice.it, pg 408

Vantage Publishers International Ltd (Nigeria) *Tel:* (022) 415341, pg 503

Var Skola Foerlag AB (Sweden) *Tel:* (08) 662 33 51 *Fax:* (08) 6621843 *E-mail:* var.skola@pi.se, pg 611

Editorial Varazen SA (Mexico) *Tel:* (05) 5459230; (05) 5335274 *Fax:* (05) 2555172, pg 469

D & J Vardikos Vivliotechnica Hellas (Greece) *Tel:* 2103631148 *Fax:* 2109564354, pg 309

Fundacao Getulio Vargas (Brazil) *Tel:* (021) 2559-5542; (021) 2559-5543; (021) 2559-5544 *Toll Free Tel:* 800-217777 *Fax:* (021) 2559-5532 *E-mail:* editora@fgv.br *Web Site:* www.fgv.br, pg 91

Varlik Yayinlari AS (Turkey) *Tel:* (0212) 5162004 *Fax:* (0212) 5162005 *E-mail:* varlik@varlik.com.tr; varlik@isbank.net.tr *Web Site:* www.varlik.com.tr, pg 647

Drs F H R Oedayrajsingh Varma (Suriname), pg 604

Varsity Book Club (Nigeria) *Tel:* (046) 210013, pg 1244

VAS-Verlag fuer Akademische Schriften (Germany) *Tel:* (069) 77 93 66 *Fax:* (069) 7073967 *E-mail:* info@vas-verlag.de *Web Site:* www.vas-verlag.de, pg 292

Ladislav Vasicek (Czech Republic) *Tel:* 518611422, pg 127

Uitgeverij Vassallucci bv (Netherlands) *Tel:* (020) 521 8322 *Fax:* (020) 623 6761 *E-mail:* info@vassallucci.nl *Web Site:* www.vassallucci.nl, pg 487

J Vassiliou Bibliopolein (Greece) *Tel:* 2103623382; 210 3623480 *Fax:* 2103623580, pg 309

Osuuskunta Vastapaino (Finland) *Tel:* (03) 214 6246 *Fax:* (03) 214 6646 *E-mail:* vastapaino@vastapaino.fi *Web Site:* www.vastapaino.fi, pg 144

Vastu Gyan Publication (India) *Tel:* (011) 3318730, pg 348

Libreria Editrice Vaticana (Holy See (Vatican City State)) *Tel:* (06) 698-85003 *Fax:* (06) 698-84716, pg 311

Libreria Editrice Vaticana (Italy) *Tel:* (06) 69885003 *Fax:* (06) 69884716 *E-mail:* lev@publish.va *Web Site:* www.libreriaeditricevaticana.com, pg 408

Robert Vaughan Antiquarian Booksellers (United Kingdom) *Tel:* (01789) 205312, pg 1346

Ivan Vazov Publishing House (Bulgaria) *Tel:* (02) 878481; (02) 871572 *Fax:* (02) 878416, pg 97

VCH Verlags-AG (Switzerland) *Tel:* (01) 3602438 *Fax:* (01) 3602439 *E-mail:* info@wiley-vch.de *Web Site:* www.wiley-vch.de, pg 631

VCL (Netherlands) *Tel:* (038) 3392555 *Web Site:* www.kok.nl, pg 1244

VCTA Publishing (Australia) *Tel:* (03) 94199622 *Fax:* (03) 94191205 *E-mail:* vcta@vcta.asn.au *Web Site:* www.vcta.asn.au, pg 45

VdA - Verband deutscher Archivarinnen und Archivare e V (Germany) *Tel:* (03643) 870-235 *Fax:* (03643) 870-164 *E-mail:* info@vda.archiv.net *Web Site:* www.vda.archiv.net, pg 1563

VDE-Verlag GmbH (Germany) *Tel:* (030) 34 80 01 0 *Fax:* (030) 341 70 93 *E-mail:* voss@vde-verlag.de *Web Site:* www.vde-verlag.de, pg 292

Vdf Hochschulverlag AG an der ETH Zurich (Switzerland) *Tel:* (01) 632 42 42 *Fax:* (01) 632 12 32 *E-mail:* verlag@vdf.ethz.ch *Web Site:* www.vdf.ethz.ch, pg 631

VDI Verlag GmbH (Germany) *Tel:* (0211) 61 88-0 *Fax:* (0211) 61 88-306 *E-mail:* info@vdi-nachrichten.com *Web Site:* www.vdi-nachrichten.com, pg 292

Editorial De Vecchi SA (Spain) *Tel:* (093) 272 46 70 *Fax:* (093) 487 74 94, pg 599

Editora Vecchi SA (Brazil) *Tel:* (021) 2444522, pg 91

VEDA (Vydavatel'stvo Slovenskej akademie vied) (Slovakia) *Tel:* (02) 5477 4253 *Fax:* (02) 5477 2682 *Web Site:* www.veda-sav.sk, pg 556

Vedecka knihovna V olomouci (Czech Republic) *Tel:* (068) 585223441 *Fax:* (068) 585225774 *E-mail:* info@vkol.cz *Web Site:* www.vkol.cz, pg 1499

Veen Bosch & Keuning Uitgevers NV (Netherlands) *Tel:* (030) 2349311 *Fax:* (030) 2349208 *E-mail:* algemeen@veenboschenkeuning.nl *Web Site:* www.veenboschenkeuning.nl, pg 487

Libreria Tecnica Vega (Venezuela) *Tel:* (0212) 6221397 *Fax:* (0212) 6622092, pg 1347

Vega-Publicacao e Distribuicao de Livros e Revistas, Lda (Portugal) *Tel:* (021) 789414 *Fax:* (021) 786395, pg 532

Ediciones Vega SRL (Venezuela) *Tel:* (0212) 6622092; (0212) 6621397, pg 775

The Vegetarian Society (United Kingdom) *Tel:* (0161) 925 2000 *Fax:* (0161) 926 9182 *E-mail:* info@vegsoc.org *Web Site:* www.vegsoc.org, pg 764

Veloce Publishing Ltd (United Kingdom) *Tel:* (01305) 260068 *Fax:* (01305) 268864 *E-mail:* info@veloce.co.uk *Web Site:* www.veloce.co.uk; www.velocebooks.com, pg 764

Venezuelan Library & Archives Association (Venezuela) *Tel:* (0212) 5721858, pg 1574

Vents d'Ouest (France) *Tel:* (01) 41 46 11 46 *Fax:* (01) 40 93 05 58 *Web Site:* www.ventsdouest.com, pg 189

Ventura Ediciones, SA de CV (Mexico) *Tel:* (05) 2087681; (05) 5530798 *Fax:* (05) 5431173, pg 469

Venture Press Ltd (United Kingdom) *Tel:* (0121) 622 3911 *Fax:* (0121) 622 4860 *E-mail:* info@basw.co.uk, pg 764

Vera-Reyes Inc (Philippines) *Tel:* (02) 7218792 *Fax:* (02) 7218782, pg 516

Verband der Antiquare Oesterreichs (Austria) *Tel:* (01) 512 15 35 *Fax:* (01) 512 84 82 *E-mail:* sekretariat@hvb.at *Web Site:* www.antiquare.at, pg 1251

Verband der Oesterreichischen Buch-und Presse-Grossisten und der Werbenden Zeitschriftenhaendler (Austria) *Tel:* (01) 512 15 35 *Fax:* (01) 512 84 82 *E-mail:* hvb@buecher.at *Web Site:* www.buecher.at, pg 1251

Verband der Schulbuchverlage eV (Germany) *Tel:* (069) 70 30 75 *Fax:* (069) 70 79 01 69 *E-mail:* verband@vds-bildungsmedien.de *Web Site:* www.vds-bildungsmedien.de, pg 1261

Verband der Verlage- und Buchhaendlungen Berlin-Brandenburg eV (Germany) *Tel:* (030) 26 39 18 0 *Fax:* (030) 26 39 18 18 *E-mail:* verband@berliner-buchhandel.de *Web Site:* www.berliner-buchhandel.de, pg 1261

Verband der Verlage und Buchhandlungen in Nordrhein-Westfalen eV (Germany) *Tel:* (0211) 8 64 45-22 *Fax:* (0211) 32 44 97 *E-mail:* info@buchnrw.de *Web Site:* www.buchnrw.de, pg 1261

Verband der Wissenschaftlichen Gesellschaften Oesterreichs (VWGOe) (Austria) *Tel:* (01) 932166; (01) 934756 *Fax:* (01) 5262054, pg 58

Verband Deutscher Antiquare eV (Germany) *Tel:* (06435) 909147 *Fax:* (06435) 909148 *E-mail:* buch@antiquare.de *Web Site:* www.antiquare.de, pg 1261

Verband Deutscher Auskunfts und Verzichnismedien (Germany) *Tel:* (0211) 577995-0 *Fax:* (0211) 577995-44 *E-mail:* info@vdav.org *Web Site:* www.vdav.de, pg 1261

Verband deutschsprachiger Uebersetzer literarischer und wissenschaftlicher Werke eV (VDUe) (Germany) *Tel:* (030) 6956-2331 *Fax:* (030) 6956-3655 *Web Site:* www.literaturuebersetzer.de, pg 1138

Verband katholischer Verleger und Buchhaendler eV (Germany) *Tel:* (0228) 2421560 *Fax:* (0228) 2421561 *E-mail:* vkb2000@aol.com, pg 1261

Verband von selbstaendigen Verlagsvertreten Oesterreichs (Austria) *Tel:* (01) 512 15 35 *Fax:* (01) 512 84 82 *E-mail:* hvb@buecher.at *Web Site:* www.buecher.at, pg 1251

Verbandsdruckerei AG (Switzerland) *Tel:* (031) 252911, pg 631

Verbatim (United Kingdom) *Tel:* (01844) 208474 *Web Site:* www.verbatimbooks.com, pg 764

Verbinum Wydawnictwo Ksiezy Werbistow (Poland) *Tel:* (022) 6107878; (022) 8703286 *Fax:* (022) 6107775, pg 522

Editorial Verbo Divino (Spain) *Tel:* (0948) 55 65 05; (0948) 55 65 11 *Fax:* (0948) 55 45 06 *E-mail:* ventas@verbodivino.es; evd@verbodivino.es *Web Site:* www.verbodivino.es, pg 599

Editora Verbo Ltda (Brazil) *Tel:* (021) 380 1100 *Fax:* (021) 386-5397 *E-mail:* verbo@virtual-net.com.br *Web Site:* www.editorialverbo.pt, pg 91

Editorial Verbo SA (Portugal) *Tel:* (021) 380 21 31; (021) 380 11 00 *Fax:* (021) 386 11 22; (021) 386 53 97 *Web Site:* www.editorialverbo.pt, pg 532

Verbum Forlag (Norway) *Tel:* (022) 93 27 00 *Fax:* (022) 93 27 27 *E-mail:* verbumforlag@verbumforlag.no *Web Site:* www.verbumforlag.no, pg 506

Verbum Forlag AB (Sweden) *Tel:* (08) 743 65 00 *Fax:* (08) 641 45 85 *E-mail:* info.forlag@verbum.se *Web Site:* www.verbum.se, pg 611

Editorial Verbum SL (Spain) *Tel:* (091) 446 88 41 *Fax:* (091) 594 45 59 *E-mail:* verbum@globalnet.es, pg 599

Livraria Verdade e Vida Editora (Portugal) *Tel:* (0249) 531417 *Fax:* (0249) 531417, pg 532

Editions Verdier (France) *Tel:* (04) 68 24 05 75; (01) 43 79 20 45 *Fax:* (04) 68 24 00 89; (01) 43 79 84 20 *E-mail:* contact@editions-verdier.fr *Web Site:* www.editions-verdier.fr, pg 189

Verein der Benediktiner zu Beuron- Beuroner Kunstverlag (Germany) *Tel:* (07466) 17-0 *Fax:* (07466) 17-107 *E-mail:* bibliothek@erzabtei-beuron.de *Web Site:* www.erzabtei-beuron.de, pg 292

Vienna International Centre Library (Austria) *Tel:* (01) 2600-22620 *Fax:* (01) 2600-29584 *E-mail:* iaea.library. infodesk@iaea.org *Web Site:* www.iaea.or.at, pg 1490

Vier-Tuerme GmbH Benedikt Press (Germany) *Tel:* (09324) 20292 *Fax:* (09324) 20495 *E-mail:* info@ vier-tuerme.de *Web Site:* www.vier-tuerme.de, pg 1167

Vier-Tuerme GmbH Benedikt Press (Germany) *Tel:* (09324) 20214 *Fax:* (09324) 20444 *E-mail:* br. sturmius@vier-tuerme.de.oder; w.stafflinger@ vier-tuerme.de *Web Site:* www.vier-tuerme.de/ benedictpress, pg 1207

Vier Tuerme GmbH Verlag Klosterbetriebe (Germany) *Tel:* (09324) 20292 *Fax:* (09324) 20495 *E-mail:* info@ vier-tuerme.de *Web Site:* www.vier-tuerme.de, pg 293

Friedr Vieweg & Sohn Verlag (Germany) *Tel:* (0611) 7878-0 *Fax:* (0611) 7878-470 *E-mail:* vieweg. service@bertelsmann.de *Web Site:* www.vieweg.de; www.gwv-fachverlage.de, pg 293

Editora Vigilia Ltda (Brazil) *Tel:* (031) 3372744; (031) 3372363 *Fax:* (031) 3372834, pg 91

Editions Vigot Universitaire (France) *Tel:* (01) 43 29 54 50 *Fax:* (01) 46 34 05 89 *E-mail:* vpc@vigot.fr *Web Site:* www.vigotmaloine.fr, pg 189

Vikas Publishing House Pvt Ltd (India) *Tel:* (011) 24315313; (011) 24315570; (011) 24317857 *Fax:* (011) 24310879 *E-mail:* helpline@ vikaspublishing.com, pg 349

Viking (United Kingdom) *Tel:* (020) 7416 3000 *Fax:* (020) 7416 3274, pg 765

Viking Children's Books (United Kingdom) *Tel:* (020) 7416 3000 *Fax:* (020) 7416 3086, pg 765

Viking Sevenseas NZ Ltd (New Zealand) *Tel:* (04) 902-8240 *Fax:* (04) 902-8240 *E-mail:* vikings@paradise. net.nz, pg 498

Viktoria-Verlag Peter Marti (Switzerland) *Tel:* (031) 7911932 *Fax:* (031) 7912564, pg 632

Magyar Tudomanyos Akademia VilagGazdasagi Kutato Intezet (Hungary) *Tel:* (01) 1668433 *Fax:* (01) 1620661, pg 321

Editions Village Mondial (France) *Tel:* (01) 72 74 90 00 *Fax:* (01) 42 05 22 17 *E-mail:* infos@pearsoned.fr *Web Site:* www.pearsoneducation.fr, pg 189

Villamonta Publishing Services Inc (Australia) *Tel:* (03) 5229 2029 *Fax:* (03) 5222 5399 *E-mail:* villapub@ ozemail.com.au, pg 45

Biblioteca Daniel Cosio Villegas El Colegio de Mexico AC (Mexico) *Tel:* (055) 5449 3000; (055) 5449 2909; (055) 5449 2936; (055) 5449 2934 *Fax:* (055) 5645 0464; (055) 5645 4584 *E-mail:* biblio@colmex.mx *Web Site:* biblio.colmex.mx, pg 1527

Villegas Editores Ltda (Colombia) *Tel:* (01) 6161788 *Fax:* (01) 6160020 *E-mail:* villedi@cable.net *Web Site:* www.villegaseditores.com, pg 113

Vilnius Art Academy Publishing House (Lithuania) *Tel:* (02) 22 30 63 *Fax:* (02) 61 99 66 *E-mail:* muziejus@vda.lt *Web Site:* vdamuziejus.mch. mii.lt, pg 446

Vilnius University Library (Lithuania) *Tel:* (5) 2687101 *Fax:* (5) 2687104 *E-mail:* mb@mb.vu.lt *Web Site:* www.mb.vu.lt, pg 1524

Editions Vilo SA (France) *Tel:* (01) 45 77 08 05 *Fax:* (01) 45 79 97 15, pg 189

Vinaches Lopez, Luisa (Spain) *Tel:* (01) 3694488 *Fax:* (01) 3694488, pg 600

Edition Vincent Klink (Germany) *Tel:* (0711) 62007211 *Fax:* (0711) 6409408 *E-mail:* edition@vincent-klink. de, pg 293

Curt R Vincentz Verlag (Germany) *Tel:* (0511) 9910000 *Fax:* (0511) 9910099 *E-mail:* info@vincentz.de *Web Site:* www.vincentz.de, pg 293

Vinciana Editrice sas (Italy) *Tel:* (02) 4982306 *Fax:* (02) 48003275 *E-mail:* info@vinciana.com *Web Site:* www. vinciana.com, pg 408

Forlaget Vindrose A/S (Denmark) *Tel:* 36153615 *Fax:* 36153616 *E-mail:* post@borgen.dk *Web Site:* www.borgen.dk, pg 135

Vine House Distribution Ltd (United Kingdom) *Tel:* (01825) 723 398 *Fax:* (01825) 724 188 *E-mail:* sales@vinehouseuk.co.uk *Web Site:* www. vinehouseuk.co.uk, pg 1346

Vinpress Sdn Bhd (Malaysia) *Tel:* (03) 7173333; (03) 7188877 *Fax:* (03) 7192942 *E-mail:* vinsoh@pc.jaring. my, pg 456

Vinten Editor (Uruguay) *Tel:* (02) 2090223 *Fax:* (02) 290223 *E-mail:* dayraq@chasque.apc.org *Web Site:* www.chasque.apc.org/dayraq/vinten, pg 773

Vipopremo Agencies (Kenya) *Tel:* (02) 227189; (02) 333882, pg 433

Virago Press (United Kingdom) *Tel:* (020) 7911 8000 *Fax:* (020) 7911 8100 *E-mail:* virago.press@ timewarnerbooks.co.uk *Web Site:* www.virago.co.uk, pg 765

Viratham (Thailand) *Tel:* (02) 866848, pg 641

Virgin Publishing Ltd (United Kingdom) *Tel:* (020) 7386 3300 *Fax:* (020) 7386 3360 *E-mail:* info@virgin-books.co.uk; info@virgin-pub.co.uk *Web Site:* www. virginbooks.com, pg 765

Virlogeux Francoise-COMEDIT (Martinique) *Tel:* 683985 *Fax:* 683423, pg 457

Visalaandhra Publishing House (India) *Tel:* (040) 4744580 *Fax:* (040) 4735905 *E-mail:* visalaandhraph@yahoo.com, pg 1308

Edition Curt Visel (Germany) *Tel:* (08331) 2853 *Fax:* (08331) 490364 *E-mail:* info@edition-curt-visel. de *Web Site:* www.edition-curt-visel.de, pg 293

Vision Books Pvt Ltd (India) *Tel:* (011) 2386-2267; (011) 2386-2201 *Fax:* (011) 2386-2935 *E-mail:* mail@ orientpaperbacks.com, pg 349

Vision Pub Co Ltd (Hong Kong) *Tel:* 23147627; 92676502 *Fax:* 29078838 *E-mail:* pcgameos@pcgame. com.hk *Web Site:* www.pcgame.com.hk, pg 317

Vision Publications (Zimbabwe), pg 779

Vision Srl (Italy) *Tel:* (06) 44292688 *Fax:* (06) 44292688 *E-mail:* info@visionpubl.com *Web Site:* www. visionpubl.com, pg 408

Visor Distribuciones, SA (Spain) *Tel:* (091) 4681248; (091) 4681011; (091) 4681102 *Fax:* (091) 4681098 *E-mail:* editorial@visordis.es *Web Site:* www.visordis. es, pg 600

Visor Libros (Spain) *Tel:* (091) 5492655 *Fax:* (091) 544 86 95 *E-mail:* visor-libros@visor-libros.com *Web Site:* www.visor-libros.com, pg 600

Vista Computer Services Ltd (United Kingdom) *Tel:* (01923) 830200 *Fax:* (01923) 238789 *E-mail:* solutions@vistacomp.com *Web Site:* www. vistacomp.com, pg 1154

Vista Point Verlag GmbH (Germany) *Tel:* (0221) 921613-0 *Fax:* (0221) 921613-14 *E-mail:* info@ vistapoint.de *Web Site:* www.vistapoint.de, pg 293

Vista Productions Ltd (Hong Kong) *Tel:* 25632492 *Fax:* 25655803, pg 317

Vista Publications (Australia) *Tel:* (03) 9534 8881 *Fax:* (03) 9534 9711 *E-mail:* vistaof@mbox.com.au, pg 45

S Viswanathan (Printers & Publishers) Pvt Ltd (India) *Tel:* (044) 826 5623; (044) 826 5633 *Fax:* (044) 825 6002 *E-mail:* svprint@md2.vsnl.net.in, pg 349

Vita (Belgium) *Tel:* (091) 3842114 *Fax:* (09) 3842114, pg 74

Vita e Pensiero (Italy) *Tel:* (02) 72342335; (02) 72342259 *Fax:* (02) 72342260 *E-mail:* editvep@mi. unicatt.it *Web Site:* www.vitaepensiero.it, pg 408

Edizioni La Vita Felice (Italy) *Tel:* (02) 29 52 46 00 *Fax:* (02) 29 40 18 96 *E-mail:* lavitafelice@iol.it *Web Site:* www.lavitafelice.it, pg 408

Vitagraf (Croatia) *Tel:* (051) 322880 *Fax:* (051) 212622 *E-mail:* kontakt@novo.hr *Web Site:* www.novo.hr, pg 119

Vital Publications (Australia) *Tel:* (03) 9379-1219 *Fax:* (03) 9379-0015 *E-mail:* vitalpubs@ churchesofchrist.org.au; aceditor@ozemail.com.au, pg 45

Vitalis sro (Czech Republic) *Tel:* (02) 57530732 *Fax:* (02) 57531974 *E-mail:* info@vitalis-verlag.com *Web Site:* www.vitalis-verlag.com, pg 127

Viva Books Pvt Ltd (India) *Tel:* (011) 3258325; (011) 3283121 *Fax:* (011) 3267224 *E-mail:* viva@ mantraonline.com *Web Site:* www.vivagroupindia.com, pg 349

Viva Lithographers Pte Ltd (Singapore) *Tel:* 2721880 *Fax:* 2735425 *E-mail:* vivasing@singnet.com.sg *Web Site:* ifc.tp.edu.sg/Project_2000July/Viva, pg 1151

Vivalda Editori SRL (Italy) *Tel:* (011) 7720444 *Fax:* (011) 7732170 *E-mail:* cdavivalda@cdavivalda.it *Web Site:* www.cdavivalda.it, pg 408

Vivek Prakashan (India) *Tel:* (011) 2529649; (011) 2944014 *Fax:* (011) 6827347, pg 349

Vivere In SRL (Italy) *Tel:* (08) 06907030 *Fax:* (08) 06907026 *E-mail:* edizioniviverein@tint.it *Web Site:* www.viverein.it, pg 408

Luis Vives (Edelvives) (Spain) *Tel:* (091) 334 48 83; (091) 334 48 82 *Fax:* (091) 334 48 92 *E-mail:* dediciones@edelvives.es *Web Site:* www. grupoeditorialluisvives.com, pg 1151

Luis Vives (Edelvives) (Spain) *Tel:* (091) 334 48 83 *Fax:* (091) 334 48 92 *E-mail:* dediciones@edelvives.es *Web Site:* www.grupoeditorialluisvives.com, pg 1213

Luis Vives (Edelvives) (Spain) *Tel:* (091) 334 48 83 *Fax:* (091) 334 48 82 *E-mail:* dediciones@edelvives.es *Web Site:* www.grupoeditorialluisvives.com, pg 1237

Editions Vivez Soleil SA (Switzerland) *Tel:* (04) 50 87 27 09 *Fax:* (04) 50 87 27 13, pg 632

Viviani Editore srl (Italy) *Tel:* (06) 6872855 *Fax:* (06) 6872856 *Web Site:* www.vivianeditore.net, pg 408

Vivlia Publishers & Booksellers (South Africa) *Tel:* (011) 472-3912 *Fax:* (011) 472-4904 *E-mail:* vivlia@icon.co.ta, pg 565

Vivliothiki Eftychia Galeou (Greece) *Tel:* 210 6841191 *Fax:* 2106825862, pg 309

Vizavi Editions (Mauritius) *Tel:* 2112435 *Fax:* 2113047 *E-mail:* vizavi@intnet.mu, pg 458

Cristina Vizcaino Literary Agency (Spain) *Tel:* (091) 5944992 *E-mail:* vizcaino@infornet.es, pg 1127

Vjesnik dd (Croatia) *Tel:* (01) 61 66 666; (01) 36 41 111 *Fax:* (01) 61 61 602; (01) 61 61 650 *E-mail:* vjesnik@vjesnik.hr; vjesnik@vjesnik.com *Web Site:* www.vjesnik.hr; www.vjesnik.com, pg 1144

Vlaamse Boekverkopersbond (VBB) (Belgium) *Tel:* (03) 230 89 23 *Fax:* (03) 281 22 40 *E-mail:* info@boek.be *Web Site:* www.boek.be, pg 1253

Vlaamse Esperantobond VZW (Belgium) *Tel:* (03) 2343400 *Fax:* (03) 2335433 *E-mail:* esperanto@ agoranet.be, pg 74

Vlaamse Uitgevers Vereniging (VUV) (Belgium) *Tel:* (03) 2308923 *Fax:* (03) 2812240 *E-mail:* info@ boek.be *Web Site:* www.vbvb.be, pg 1253

Vlaamse Vereniging voor Bibliotheek- Archief-en Documentatiewezen (VVBAD) (Belgium) *Tel:* (03) 2814457 *Fax:* (03) 2188077 *E-mail:* vvbad@vvbad.be *Web Site:* www.vvbad.be, pg 1559

Vlassi (Greece) *Tel:* 2103812900; 2103833013 *Fax:* 2103827557 *Web Site:* www.vlassi.gr, pg 1304

Vlassis (Greece) *Tel:* 2103812900; 2103827557 *Fax:* 2103827557 *E-mail:* amvlassi@otenet.gr, pg 310

John Waite Ltd (United Kingdom) *Tel:* (1797) 344 283 *Fax:* (01892) 784156, pg 766

Wakefield Press Pty Ltd (Australia) *Tel:* (08) 8362 8800 *Fax:* (08) 8362 7592 *E-mail:* info@wakefieldpress. com.au *Web Site:* www.wakefieldpress.com.au, pg 45

Verlag im Waldgut AG (Switzerland) *Tel:* (052) 728 89 28 *Fax:* (052) 728 89 27 *E-mail:* waldgut.bodoni@ bluewin.ch *Web Site:* www.waldgut.ch, pg 632

Walhalla Fachverlag GmbH & Co KG Praetoria (Germany) *Tel:* (0941) 5684-0 *Fax:* (0941) 5684-111 *E-mail:* walhalla@walhalla.de *Web Site:* www. walhalla.de, pg 294

Walker Books Ltd (United Kingdom) *Tel:* (01256) 329242 *Fax:* (01256) 812558; (01256) 812521 *E-mail:* enquiry@walker.co.uk *Web Site:* www. walkerbooks.co.uk, pg 766

S Walker Literary Agency (United Kingdom) *Tel:* (01234) 216229, pg 1134

Sally Walker Language Services (United Kingdom) *Tel:* (0117) 929 1594 *Fax:* (0117) 929 6033 *E-mail:* translations@sallywalker.co.uk; languages@ sallywalker.co.uk *Web Site:* www.sallywalker.co.uk, pg 1142

Edgar Wallace Society (United Kingdom) *E-mail:* info@ edgarwallace.org *Web Site:* www.edgarwallace.org, pg 1404

Librairie Walter (Togo), pg 1336

Walter Verlag AG (Switzerland) *Tel:* (062) 341188 *Fax:* (062) 321184 *E-mail:* info@walter-verlag.ch *Web Site:* www.walter-verlag.ch, pg 632

Verlag Mag Wanzenbock (Austria) *Tel:* (01) 7148542 *Fax:* (01) 7135814, pg 59

The Warburg Institute (United Kingdom) *Tel:* (020) 7862 8949 *Fax:* (020) 7862 8955 *E-mail:* warburg@sas.ac. uk *Web Site:* www.sas.ac.uk/warburg/, pg 766

Ward Lock Educational Co Ltd (United Kingdom) *Tel:* (01342) 318980 *Fax:* (01342) 410980 *E-mail:* wle@lingkee.com *Web Site:* www. wardlockeducational.com, pg 766

Ward Lock Ltd (United Kingdom) *Tel:* (020) 7420 5555 *Fax:* (020) 7240 7261, pg 766

Peter Ward Book Exports (United Kingdom) *Tel:* (020) 8772 3300 *Fax:* (020) 8772 3309 *E-mail:* peter@ pwbookex.dircon.co.uk, pg 1134

Peter Ward Book Exports (United Kingdom) *Tel:* (020) 8772 3300 *Fax:* (020) 8772 3309 *E-mail:* pwbookex@ dircon.co.uk, pg 1346

Warna Publishers (Sri Lanka), pg 603

Frederick Warne Publishers Ltd (United Kingdom) *Tel:* (020) 7010 3000 *Fax:* (020) 7010 6706, pg 766

Uwe Warnke Verlag (Germany) *Tel:* (030) 29049903 *E-mail:* warnke@snafu.de, pg 294

Wartburg Verlag GmbH (Germany) *Tel:* (03643) 24 61-44 *Fax:* (03643) 24 61-18 *E-mail:* buch@ wartburgverlag.de *Web Site:* www.wartburgverlag.de, pg 294

Waruni Publishers (Sri Lanka) *Tel:* (08) 24370 *Fax:* (08) 32343, pg 603

Waseda University Library (Japan) *Tel:* (03) 32034141 *E-mail:* info@wul.waseda.ac.jp *Web Site:* www.wul. waseda.ac.jp, pg 1520

Waseda University Press (Japan) *Tel:* (03) 32031551; (03) 32031570 *Fax:* (03) 32070406; (03) 32031570 *E-mail:* info@waseda-up.co.jp *Web Site:* www.waseda-up.co.jp, pg 427

Ernst Wasmuth Verlag GmbH & Co (Germany) *Tel:* (07071) 97 55 00 *Fax:* (07071) 97 55 013 *E-mail:* info@wasmuth-verlag.de *Web Site:* www. wasmuth-verlag.de, pg 294

Water Resources & Electric Power Press (CWPP) (China) *Tel:* (010) 898031 *Fax:* (010) 68353010, pg 108

Waterkant-Uitgewers (Edms) Bpk (South Africa) *Tel:* (021) 215540 *Fax:* (021) 4191865 *E-mail:* luxverbi.publ@kingsley.co.za, pg 565

The Watermark Press (Australia) *Tel:* (02) 9818 5677 *Fax:* (02) 9818 5581 *E-mail:* books@nsw.bigpond.net. au, pg 45

Waterstone & Co Ltd (United Kingdom) *Tel:* (020) 8742 3800 *Web Site:* www.waterstones.co.uk, pg 1346

Waterville Publishing House (Ghana) *Tel:* (01) 663124; (01) 662415, pg 302

Watkiss Automation Ltd (United Kingdom) *Tel:* (01767) 682177 *Fax:* (01767) 691769 *E-mail:* info@watkiss. com *Web Site:* www.watkiss.com, pg 1154, 1176, 1217, 1229, 1238

Watson, Little Ltd (United Kingdom) *Tel:* (020) 7431 0770 *Fax:* (020) 7431 7225 *E-mail:* enquiries@ watsonlittle.com *Web Site:* www.watsonlittle.net, pg 1135

A P Watt Ltd (United Kingdom) *Tel:* (020) 7405 6774 *Fax:* (020) 7831 2154 *E-mail:* apw@apwatt.co.uk *Web Site:* www.apwatt.co.uk, pg 766, 1135

Watthana Phanit (Thailand) *Tel:* (02) 2217225, pg 641

Watti-Kustannus Oy (Finland) *Tel:* (09) 1356878 *Fax:* (09) 1356437, pg 144

Franklin Watts Australia (Australia) *Tel:* (02) 8338 8800 *Fax:* (02) 8338 8881 *E-mail:* info@wattspub.com.au *Web Site:* www.wattspub.com.au, pg 45

The Watts Publishing Group Ltd (United Kingdom) *Tel:* (020) 7739 2929 *Fax:* (020) 7739 2181 *E-mail:* gm@wattspub.co.uk *Web Site:* www.wattspub. co.uk, pg 766

Waxmann Verlag GmbH (Germany) *Tel:* (0251) 265040 *Fax:* (0251) 2650426 *E-mail:* info@waxmann.com *Web Site:* www.waxmann.com, pg 295

WDV Wirtschaftsdienst Gesellschaft fur Medien & Kommunikation mbH & Co OHG (Germany) *Tel:* (06172) 670-0 *Fax:* (01672) 670144 *E-mail:* info@wdv.de *Web Site:* www.wdv.de, pg 295

Weather Press (Australia) *Tel:* (03) 9762 1647, pg 46

Weatherbys Allen Ltd (United Kingdom) *Tel:* (01933) 440077 (ext 351) *Fax:* (01933) 270300 *E-mail:* turfnews@weatherbys-group.com *Web Site:* www.weatherbys-allen.com, pg 766

Web Printers Sdn Bhd (Malaysia) *Tel:* (03) 7956 3577 *Fax:* (03) 7726 3563, pg 1211

Webb & Bower (Publishers) Ltd (United Kingdom) *Tel:* (01803) 835525 *Fax:* (01803) 835552, pg 767

Webcom Limited (Canada) *Tel:* 416-496-1000 Toll Free *Tel:* 800-665-9322 *Fax:* 416-496-1537 *E-mail:* webcom@webcomlink.com *Web Site:* www. webcomlink.com, pg 1144, 1206, 1235

Weber SA d'Editions (Switzerland) *Tel:* (07) 93104541, pg 632

Weber Zucht & Co (Germany) *Tel:* (0561) 519194; (0561) 515953 *Fax:* (0561) 5102514 *E-mail:* wezuco@t-online.de, pg 295

WebsterWorld Pty Ltd (Australia) *Tel:* (02) 9939 5505 *Fax:* (02) 9939 8355 *E-mail:* webpub@ websterpublishing.com *Web Site:* www. websterpublishing.com; www.websterworld.com; www.websterselearning.com, pg 46

Websters International Publishers Ltd (United Kingdom) *Tel:* (020) 7940 4700 *Fax:* (020) 7940 4701 *E-mail:* info@websters.co.uk *Web Site:* www.websters. co.uk; www.ozclarke.com, pg 767

Wegener Falkplan BV (Netherlands) *Tel:* (040) 2 642 111 *Fax:* (040) 2 410 955 *E-mail:* info@suurland.nl *Web Site:* www.suurland.nl, pg 488

Wei-Chuan Publishing Company Ltd (Taiwan, Province of China) *Tel:* (02) 27021148 *Fax:* (02) 27042729, pg 637

Weidler Buchverlag Berlin (Germany) *Tel:* (030) 394 86 68 *Fax:* (030) 394 86 98 *E-mail:* weidler_verlag@ yahoo.de *Web Site:* www.weidler-verlag.de, pg 295

Weidlich Verlag (Germany) *Tel:* (0931) 385235 *Fax:* (0931) 385305 *E-mail:* info@verlagshaus.com *Web Site:* www.verlagshaus.com, pg 295

Weidmannsche Verlagsbuchhandlung GmbH (Germany) *Tel:* (05121) 15010 *Fax:* (05121) 150150 *E-mail:* info@olms.de *Web Site:* www.olms.de, pg 295

Fred Weidner & Daughter Printers (United States) *Tel:* 212-964-8676 *Fax:* 212-964-8677 *E-mail:* info@ fwdprinters.com *Web Site:* www.fwdprinters.com, pg 1179, 1221, 1240

Weilburg Verlag (Austria) *Tel:* (02622) 29538 *Fax:* (02622) 2953822, pg 59

Weilin & Goos Oy (Finland) *Tel:* (09) 4377 603 *Fax:* (00) 4377 334 *E-mail:* asiakaspalvelu@wg.fi *Web Site:* www.wg.fi, pg 144

Galerie Lucie Weill-Seligmann (France) *Tel:* (01) 43 54 71 95 *Fax:* (01) 40 51 82 88, pg 189

Josef Weinberger Plays (United Kingdom) *Tel:* (020) 7580 2827 *Fax:* (020) 7436 9616 *E-mail:* general. info@jwmail.co.uk *Web Site:* www.josef-weinberger. com, pg 1135

Verlag W Weinmann (Germany) *Tel:* (030) 855 48 95 *Fax:* (030) 8 55 94 64 *E-mail:* info@weinmann-verlag.de *Web Site:* www.weinmann-verlag.de, pg 295

Rupertusbuchhandlung Augustin Weis und Soehne KG (Austria) *Tel:* (0662) 878733-0 *Fax:* (0662) 871661 *E-mail:* info@rupertusbuch.at, pg 1291

Dr Otfried Weise Verlag Tabula Smaragdina (Austria) *Tel:* (01) 804 2974 *Fax:* (01) 961 8287 *E-mail:* tabula@smaragdina.at *Web Site:* smaragdina. at, pg 59

Herbert Weishaupt Verlag (Austria) *Tel:* (03151) 8487 *Fax:* (03151) 84874 *E-mail:* verlag@weishaupt.at *Web Site:* www.weishaupt.at, pg 59

Weisser Ring, Gemeinnutzige Verlagsgesellschaft mbH (Germany) *Tel:* (06131) 83 03 01 *Fax:* (06131) 83 03 45 *E-mail:* info@weisser ring.de *Web Site:* www. weisser-ring.de, pg 295

Weitz Center for Development Study (Israel) *Tel:* (08) 9474111 *Fax:* (08) 9475884 *E-mail:* dsc@netvision. net.il, pg 1518

Weizmann Institute of Science Libraries (Israel) *Tel:* (08) 9343583 (WIX Central Library); (08) 9343211 (Weizmann Institute) *Fax:* (08) 9344176 *E-mail:* hedva.milo@weizmann.ac.il *Web Site:* www. weizmann.ac.il/WIS-library, pg 1518

Editions Weka (France) *Tel:* (01) 53 35 16 16; (01) 53 35 17 17 *Fax:* (01) 53 35 17 01 *E-mail:* infos@weka. fr *Web Site:* www.weka.fr, pg 189

WEKA Firmengruppe GmbH & Co KG (Germany) *Tel:* (08233) 23-0 *Fax:* (08233) 23-7500 *E-mail:* service@weka.de *Web Site:* www.weka.de; www.weka-group.de; www.weka-group.com, pg 295

Weka Informations Schriften Verlag AG (Switzerland) *Tel:* (01) 4348888 *Fax:* (01) 4348999, pg 632

Wellcome Library for the History & Understanding of Medicine (United Kingdom) *Tel:* (020) 7611 8722 *Fax:* (020) 7611 8369 *E-mail:* library@wellcome.ac.uk *Web Site:* library.wellcome.ac.uk, pg 1553

Wellday Ltd (Hong Kong) *Tel:* 23628489 *Fax:* 23628564, pg 317

Wellington City Libraries (New Zealand) *Tel:* (04) 801 4040 *Fax:* (04) 801 4047 *E-mail:* central@wcl.govt.nz *Web Site:* www.wcl.govt.nz, pg 1531

Wellington Lane Press Pty Ltd (Australia) *Tel:* (02) 99040962 *Fax:* (02) 99040962, pg 46

Wellington Orchid Society Publications (New Zealand) *Tel:* (04) 4758765, pg 498

Wellness Australia (Australia) *Tel:* (08) 9387 6134 *Fax:* (08) 9383 7323 *E-mail:* info@workteams.com, pg 46

Wild & Woolley (Australia) *Tel:* (02) 9337 6844 *Fax:* (02) 9337 6822 *E-mail:* pwoolley@fastbooks. com.au *Web Site:* www.wildandwoolley.com.au, pg 46

Wild Goose Publications (United Kingdom) *Tel:* (0141) 332 6292 *Fax:* (0141) 332 1090 *E-mail:* admin@ ionabooks.com *Web Site:* www.ionabooks.com, pg 768

Wild Publications Pty Ltd (Australia) *Tel:* (03) 9826-8482 *Fax:* (03) 9826-3787 *E-mail:* management@wild. com.au *Web Site:* www.wild.com.au, pg 46

Wildscape Australia (Australia) *Tel:* (07) 4093 7171 *Fax:* (07) 4093 8897, pg 46

Wileman Publications (Australia) *Tel:* (07) 312770 *E-mail:* wileman@onthenet.com.au, pg 46

Magazyn Wilenski (Lithuania) *Tel:* (05) 242 77 18 *E-mail:* magazyn@magwil.lt *Web Site:* www.magwil. lt, pg 446

Wiley Europe Ltd (United Kingdom) *Tel:* (01243) 779777 *Fax:* (01243) 775878 *E-mail:* customer@ wiley.co.uk *Web Site:* www.wiley.co.uk, pg 768

John Wiley & Sons (Asia) Pte Ltd (Singapore) *Tel:* 64632400 *Fax:* 64634605; 64634604 *E-mail:* enquiry@wiley.com.sg *Web Site:* www.wiley. co.uk, pg 554

John Wiley & Sons Australia, Ltd (Australia) *Tel:* (07) 3859 9755 *Fax:* (07) 3859 9715 *E-mail:* brisbane@ johnwiley.com.au *Web Site:* www.johnwiley.com.au, pg 46

Wiley-VCH Verlag GmbH (Germany) *Tel:* (06201) 606 0 *Fax:* (06201) 606 328 *E-mail:* info@wiley-vch.de *Web Site:* www.wiley-vch.de, pg 297

Wydawnictwo Wilga sp zoo (Poland) *Tel:* (022) 826-08-82; (022) 827-90-11 (ext 282) *Fax:* (022) 826-06-43 *E-mail:* wilga@wilga.com.pl, pg 523

Verlag Wilhelm Braumuller Universitats-Verlagsbuchhandlung GmbH (Austria) *Tel:* (01) 319 11 59 *Fax:* (01) 310 28 05 *E-mail:* office@ braumueller.at *Web Site:* www.braumueller.at, pg 59

Bridget Williams Books Ltd (New Zealand) *Tel:* (04) 4946054 *Fax:* (04) 4998942 *E-mail:* info@bwb.co.nz *Web Site:* www.bwb.co.nz, pg 498

Jonathan Williams Literary Agency (Ireland) *Tel:* (01) 2803482 *Fax:* (01) 2803482, pg 1123

Wilmington Business Information Ltd (United Kingdom) *Tel:* (020) 7549 8704 *Fax:* (020) 7490 2979 *Web Site:* www.waterlow.com/signature/, pg 769

Editions Luce Wilquin (Belgium) *Tel:* (019) 69 98 13 *Fax:* (019) 69 98 13 *E-mail:* wilquin.bouquin@skynet. be *Web Site:* www.wilquin.com, pg 74

A S Wilson Inc (Australia) *Tel:* (02) 9528 8977, pg 46

Wilson & Horton Publications Ltd (New Zealand) *Tel:* (09) 6388105; (09) 3603820 *Fax:* (09) 3603831 *E-mail:* whpubs@listener.co.nz *Web Site:* www.apn. com.au, pg 498

John Wilson Booksales (United Kingdom) *Tel:* (01844) 275927 *Fax:* (01844) 274402 *E-mail:* jw@jwbs.co.uk, pg 1238

Philip Wilson Publishers (United Kingdom) *Tel:* (020) 7033 9900 *Fax:* (020) 7033 9922 *E-mail:* sales@ philip-wilson.co.uk *Web Site:* www.philip-wilson.co. uk, pg 769

Wimbledon Publishing Company Ltd (United Kingdom) *Tel:* (020) 7401 4200 *Fax:* (020) 7928 4201 *E-mail:* enquiries@wpcpress.com *Web Site:* www. wpcpress.com, pg 769

Windhoek Public Library (Namibia) *Tel:* (061) 224899 *Fax:* (061) 212169 *E-mail:* rviljoen@unam.na, pg 1529

Windhoeker Buchhandlung (Namibia) *Tel:* (061) 225216 *Fax:* (061) 225011, pg 1319

Windhorse Books (Australia) *Tel:* (02) 9519 8826 *Fax:* (02) 9519 8826 *E-mail:* books@windhorse.com. au *Web Site:* www.windhorse.com.au, pg 46

Windhorse Publications (United Kingdom) *Tel:* (0121) 449 9191 *Fax:* (0121) 449 9191 *E-mail:* info@ windhorsepublications.com *Web Site:* www. windhorsepublications.com, pg 769

Windmuehle GmbH Verlag und Vertrieb von Medien (Germany) *Tel:* (040) 86 83 07 *Fax:* (040) 866 31 23 *E-mail:* info@windmuehle-verlag.de *Web Site:* www. windmuehle-verlag.de, pg 297

Windpferd Verlagsgesellschaft mbH (Germany) *Tel:* (08343) 1404 *Fax:* (08343) 1403 *E-mail:* info@ windpferd.de *Web Site:* www.windpferd.de, pg 297

Windsor Books International (United Kingdom) *Tel:* (01865) 361122 *Fax:* (01865) 361133 *E-mail:* sales@windsorbooks.co.uk *Web Site:* www. windsorbooks.co.uk, pg 769

Windward Publications (Australia) *Tel:* (02) 4464 1977 *Fax:* (02) 4464 1906 *E-mail:* sales@windward.com.au *Web Site:* www.windward.com.au, pg 46

Winetitles (Australia) *Tel:* (08) 8233 4799 *Fax:* (08) 8233 4790 *E-mail:* admin@winetitles.com.au *Web Site:* www.winetitles.com.au, pg 46

Wing King Tong Group (Hong Kong) *Tel:* 2407 3287; 2407 3309; 2407 4547 *Fax:* 2408 7939; 2407 4130 *E-mail:* printing@wkt.cc; books@wkt.cc *Web Site:* www.wkt.cc, pg 1148

Wing King Tong Group (Hong Kong) *Tel:* 2407 3287; 2407 3309; 24074547 *Fax:* 24074130; 2408 7939 *E-mail:* printing@wkt.cc; books@wkt.cc *Web Site:* www.wkt.cc, pg 1169

Wing King Tong Group (Hong Kong) *Tel:* 2407 3287 *Fax:* 24074130; 2408 7939 *E-mail:* printing@wkt.cc; books@wkt.cc *Web Site:* www.wkt.cc, pg 1209, 1226

Rosa Winkel Verlag GmbH (Germany) *Tel:* (030) 85729295 *Fax:* (030) 85729296 *E-mail:* rosawinkel@t-online.de, pg 297

Dr Dieter Winkler (Germany) *Tel:* (0234) 9650200 *Fax:* (0234) 9650201 *E-mail:* winkler-verlag.bochum@ tonline.de *Web Site:* www.winklerverlag.de, pg 297

Winklers Verlag Gebrueder Grimm (Germany) *Tel:* (06151) 87 68-0 *Fax:* (06151) 87 68-61 *E-mail:* service@winklers.de *Web Site:* www.winklers. de, pg 297

Winter & Co UK Ltd (United Kingdom) *Tel:* (01480) 377177 *Fax:* (01480) 377166 *E-mail:* sales@winteruk. com *Web Site:* www.winteruk.com, pg 1229

Berthold Winter (Germany) *Tel:* (030) 362 35 30 *Fax:* (030) 362 96 93, pg 1302

Verlag fuer Wirtschaft & Verwaltung Hubert Wingen GmbH & Co KG (Germany) *Tel:* (0201) 22 25 41; (0201) 22 25 42; (0201) 221451-52 *Fax:* (0201) 229660, pg 297

Wisby & Wilkens (Denmark) *Tel:* 7023 4622 *Fax:* 7043 4722 *E-mail:* mail@bogshop.dk *Web Site:* www. wisby-wilkens.com; www.bogshop.dk, pg 135

Wisdom Books (United Kingdom) *Tel:* (020) 8553 5020 *Fax:* (020) 8553 5122 *E-mail:* sales@wisdom-books. com *Web Site:* www.wisdom-books.com, pg 1346

Verlag Wissenschaft und Politik (Germany) *Tel:* (034904) 32946 *Fax:* (034904) 32946 *E-mail:* helker.pflug@t-online.de, pg 297

Wissenschaftliche Allgemeinbibliothek der Stadt Erfurt (Germany) *Tel:* (0361) 562 48 76 *Fax:* (0361) 646 20 71, pg 1510

Wissenschaftliche Buchgesellschaft (Germany) *Tel:* (06151) 33 08-127 *Fax:* (06151) 33 08 208 *E-mail:* service@wbg-darmstadt.de *Web Site:* www. wbg-darmstadt.de, pg 297

Wissenschaftliche Buchgesellschaft (Germany) *Tel:* (06151) 33 08-0 *Fax:* (06151) 31 41 28 *E-mail:* service@wbg-darmstadt.de *Web Site:* www. wbg-darmstadt.de, pg 1242

Wissenschaftliche Verlagsgesellschaft mbH (Germany) *Tel:* (0711) 2582-325 *Fax:* (0711) 2582-290 *E-mail:* service@dav-buchhandlung.de *Web Site:* www. dav-buchhandlung.de, pg 297

Wissenschaftliche Verlagsgesellschaft mbH (Germany) *Tel:* (0711) 2582-325 *Fax:* (0711) 2582-290 *E-mail:* service@wissenschaftliche-verlagsgesellschaft. de; akimmerle@wissenschaftliche-verlagsgesellschaft. de *Web Site:* www.dav-buchhandlung.de, pg 1145

Wissenschaftsrat (Germany) *Tel:* (0221) 3776-0 *Fax:* (0221) 38 84 40 *E-mail:* post@wissenschaftsrat. de *Web Site:* www.wissenschaftsrat.de, pg 297

Vydavatelstvo Wist sro (Slovakia) *Tel:* (043) 4289652 *Fax:* (043) 4289652 *E-mail:* wist@enelux.sk, pg 556

WIT Press (United Kingdom) *Tel:* (023) 8029 3223 *Fax:* (023) 8029 2853 *E-mail:* witpress@witpress.com *Web Site:* www.witpress.com, pg 769

Witherby & Co Ltd (United Kingdom) *Tel:* (020) 7251 5341 *Fax:* (020) 7251 1296 *E-mail:* books@witherbys. co.uk *Web Site:* www.witherbys.com, pg 769, 1346

Witman Publishing Co (HK) Ltd (Hong Kong) *Tel:* 2562 6279 *Fax:* 2565 5482 *E-mail:* witmanp@hk.star.com, pg 317

Verlag Claus Wittal (Germany) *Tel:* (0611) 502907 *Fax:* (0611) 503021 *E-mail:* cw@exlibrisart.com *Web Site:* www.exlibrisart.com, pg 297

Friedrich Wittig Verlag GmbH (Germany) *Tel:* (0431) 55779 206 *Fax:* (0431) 55779 292 *E-mail:* vertrieb@ wittig-verlag.de *Web Site:* www.wittig-verlag.de, pg 297

Verlag Konrad Wittwer GmbH (Germany) *Tel:* (0711) 25 07 0 *Fax:* (0711) 25 07 145 *E-mail:* info@wittwer.de *Web Site:* www.wittwer.de, pg 297

Verlags -und Sortiments-Buchhandlung Konrad Wittwer GmbH & Co KG (Germany) *Tel:* (0711) 25 07 0 *Fax:* (0711) 25 07 145 *E-mail:* info@wittwer.de *Web Site:* www.wittwer.de, pg 1302

Witwatersrand University Press (South Africa) *Tel:* (011) 717 1000 *Fax:* (011) 717 1065 *Web Site:* www.wits.ac. za/wup.html, pg 565

Wizard Books Pty Ltd (Australia) *Tel:* (03) 5332 3435 *Fax:* (03) 5331 1488 *E-mail:* admin@wizardbooks. com.au *Web Site:* www.wizardbooks.com.au, pg 47

The Woburn Press (United Kingdom) *Tel:* (020) 8920 2100 *Fax:* (020) 8447 8548 *E-mail:* info@ woburnpress.com *Web Site:* www.frankcass.com/wp, pg 770

Wochenschau Verlag, Dr Kurt Debus GmbH (Germany) *Tel:* (06196) 8 60 65 *Fax:* (06196) 8 60 60 *E-mail:* info@wochenschau-verlag.de *Web Site:* www. wochenschau-verlag.de, pg 298

Woeli Publishing Services (Ghana) *Tel:* (021) 227182; (021) 229294 *Fax:* (021) 777098; (021) 229294 *E-mail:* woeli@libr.ug.edu.gh; asempa@ghana.com, pg 302

Galerie Esther Woerdehoff (France) *Tel:* (01) 43 21 44 83 *Fax:* (01) 43 21 45 03 *E-mail:* galerie@ewgalerie. com *Web Site:* www.ewgalerie.com, pg 189

Verlagshaus Wohlfarth (Germany) *Tel:* (0203) 3 05 27-0 *Fax:* (0203) 3 05 27-820 *E-mail:* info@wohlfarth.de *Web Site:* www.wohlfarth.de, pg 298

Koninklijke Wohrmann Bv (Netherlands) *Tel:* (0575) 582121 *Fax:* (0575) 582128 *E-mail:* secretariaat@ wohrmann.nl *Web Site:* www.wohrmann.nl, pg 1211

Forlaget Woldike K/S (Denmark) *Tel:* 31 86 39 54 *Fax:* 38 33 70 80, pg 135

J E Wolfensberger AG (Switzerland) *Tel:* (01) 2857878 *Fax:* (01) 2857879 *E-mail:* office@wolfensberger-ag. ch *Web Site:* www.wolfensberger-ag.ch, pg 632

Wolfhound Press Ltd (Ireland) *Tel:* (01) 6764373 *Fax:* (01) 6764373 *E-mail:* websales@wolfhound.ie, pg 361

Kunstverlag Wolfrum (Austria) *Tel:* (01) 512 53 98-0 *Fax:* (01) 512 53 98-57 *E-mail:* your-welcome@ wolfrum.at *Web Site:* www.wolfrum.at/html/wolfrum. htm, pg 59

Wuth-Gruppe (Germany) *Tel:* (05031) 91 69 81 *Fax:* (05031) 91 69 82 *E-mail:* zentrale@wuth-gruppe. de *Web Site:* www.wuth-gruppe.de, pg 298

WUV/Facultas Universitaetsverlag (Austria) *Tel:* (01) 310 53 56 *Fax:* (01) 319 70 50 *E-mail:* verlage@ facultas.at *Web Site:* www.wuv-verlag.at, pg 59

WUV/Service Fachverlag (Austria) *Tel:* (01) 310 53 56 *Fax:* (01) 319 70 50 *E-mail:* verlag@facultas.at *Web Site:* www.wuv-verlag.at/WUV, pg 59

Wydawn Na Sprawa' Wydawniczo-Oswiatowa Spotdzielnia Inwalidow (Poland) *Tel:* (022) 6209071 (ext 26) *Fax:* (022) 6209197, pg 523

Wyss Verlag AG Bern (Switzerland) *Tel:* (031) 253715; (031) 381 4425 *Fax:* (031) 381 4821; (031) 254821, pg 633

Ediciones Xandro (Spain) *Tel:* (091) 5520261 *Fax:* (091) 5014145, pg 600

Xenos Verlagsgesellschaft mbH (Germany) *Tel:* (040) 538093-0 *Fax:* (040) 5386000 *E-mail:* xenos.verlag@t-online.de *Web Site:* www.xenosverlag.de, pg 299

Edicions Xerais de Galicia (Spain) *Tel:* (0986) 214888 *Fax:* (0986) 201366 *E-mail:* xerais@xerais.es *Web Site:* www.xerais.es, pg 600

Xiamen International Book Exchange Center (China) *Tel:* (0592) 5061401 *Fax:* (0592) 5061400 *E-mail:* xibc@xpublic.fz.fj.cn, pg 1296

Xiamen University Library (China) *Tel:* (0592) 2085102 *Fax:* (0592) 2182360 *E-mail:* xiaodh@xmu.edu.cn *Web Site:* www.xmu.edu.cn, pg 1496

Xiamen University Press (China) *Tel:* (0592) 2186128 *E-mail:* chbanshe@jingxian.xmu.edu.cn; xmdx@ fjbook.com, pg 109

Xi'an Cartography Publishing House (China) *Tel:* (029) 7898962, pg 109

Xinhua Publishing House (China) *Tel:* (010) 3073880 *Fax:* (010) 3073880 *E-mail:* nianzh@xinhuanet.com, pg 109

Xunta de Galicia (Spain) *Tel:* (081) 544816 *Fax:* (081) 544887, pg 600

Y Cyfarwyddwr Urdd Gobaith Cymru (United Kingdom) *Tel:* (01970) 613100 *Fax:* (01970) 626120 *E-mail:* urdd@urdd.org *Web Site:* www.urdd.org, pg 771

Y Hoc Publishing House (Viet Nam) *Tel:* (04) 253274, pg 775

Yachdav, United Publishers Co Ltd (Israel) *Tel:* (03) 5614121 *Fax:* (03) 5611996 *E-mail:* maalot@tbpai. co.il *Web Site:* www.tbpai.co.il, pg 369

Yad Eliahu Kitov (Israel) *Tel:* (02) 6248868 *Fax:* (02) 6248838 *E-mail:* benarza@netvision.net.il, pg 370

Yad Izhak Ben-Zvi Press (Israel) *Tel:* (02) 5398887; (02) 5398888 *Fax:* (02) 5638310 *E-mail:* ybz@ybz.org.il *Web Site:* ybz.org.il, pg 370

Yad Tabenkin (Israel) *Tel:* (03) 5346268 *Fax:* (03) 5346376 *E-mail:* yadtab@inter.net.il *Web Site:* www. ic.org, pg 370

Yad Vashem - The Holocaust Martyrs' & Heroes' Remembrance Authority (Israel) *Tel:* (02) 6443400 *Fax:* (02) 6443443 *E-mail:* general.information@ yadvashem.org.il *Web Site:* www.yad-vashem.org.il, pg 370

Yakuji Nippo Ltd (Japan) *Tel:* (03) 3862-2141 *Fax:* (03) 3866-8495 *E-mail:* shuppan@yakuji.co.jp *Web Site:* www.yakuji.co.jp/, pg 427

Yale University Press London (United Kingdom) *Tel:* (020) 7079 4900 *Fax:* (020) 7079 4901 *E-mail:* sales@yaleup.co.uk *Web Site:* www.yalebooks. co.uk, pg 771

Yama-Kei Publishers Co Ltd (Japan) *Tel:* (03) 3436-4055 *Fax:* (03) 34334057 *E-mail:* info@yamakei.co.jp, pg 427

Yamaguchi Shoten (Japan) *Tel:* (075) 781-6121 *Fax:* (075) 705-2003, pg 427

Yanagang Publishing (Australia) *Tel:* (03) 9870-3052 *Fax:* (03) 9876-1853 *E-mail:* gallerywithoutwalls@ hotmail.com, pg 47

Julio F Yanez, Agencia Literaria S L (Spain) *Tel:* (093) 2007107; (093) 2005443 *Fax:* (093) 2094865 *E-mail:* yanezag@retemail.es, pg 1127

Eric Yang Agency (Republic of Korea) *Tel:* (02) 5923356 *Fax:* (02) 5923359 *E-mail:* info@ ericyangagency.co.kr *Web Site:* www.ericyangagency. co.kr, pg 1124

Yapi-Endustri Merkezi Yayinlari-Yem Yayin (Turkey) *Tel:* (0212) 2193939 *Fax:* (0212) 2256623 *E-mail:* yem-od@yunus.mam.tubitak.gov.tr; yem@ yem.net *Web Site:* www.yem.net, pg 647

Yarmouk University Library (Jordan) *Tel:* (02) 7211111 (ext 2871) *Fax:* (02) 7211124 *E-mail:* yarmouk@yu. edu.jo *Web Site:* www.yu.edu.jo; library.yu.edu.jo, pg 1521

Yaron Golan Publishers (Israel) *Tel:* (03) 6992867 *Fax:* (03) 6952664, pg 370

CV Yasaguna (Indonesia) *Tel:* (021) 8290422, pg 353

Roy Yates Books (United Kingdom) *Tel:* (01403) 822299 *Fax:* (01403) 823012, pg 1346

Yavneh Publishing House Ltd (Israel) *Tel:* (03) 6297856 *Fax:* (03) 6293638 *E-mail:* publishing@yavneh.co.il *Web Site:* www.dbook.co.il, pg 370

Yavneh Publishing House Ltd (Israel) *Tel:* (03) 6297856 *Fax:* (03) 6293638 *E-mail:* yahneh@attglobal.net, pg 1310

Yayasan Jaya Baya (Indonesia) *Tel:* (031) 41169, pg 353

Yayasan Kawanku (Indonesia) *Tel:* (021) 583100, pg 353

Yayasan Lontar (Indonesia) *Tel:* (021) 574-6880 *Fax:* (021) 572-0353 *E-mail:* lontar@attglobal.net *Web Site:* www.lontar.org, pg 353

Yayasan Obor Indonesia (Indonesia) *Tel:* (021) 3920114; (021) 31926978 *Fax:* (021) 31924488 *E-mail:* obor@ ub.net.id *Web Site:* www.obor.or.id, pg 353

Kabalci Yayinevi (Turkey) *Tel:* (0212) 526 8586 *Fax:* (0212) 523 6305 *E-mail:* yayinevi@kabalcy. com.tr *Web Site:* www.turkyayibr.org.tr/kabalci.html, pg 647

Alev Yayinlari (Turkey) *Tel:* (0212) 519 5635 *Fax:* (0212) 292 1017 *E-mail:* bilgi@alevyayinlari. com; yayinlar@alevyayinlari.com, pg 647

Yazhou Zhoukan Ltd (Hong Kong) *Tel:* 2515 5483 *Fax:* 2595 0497 *E-mail:* yzad@mingpao.com *Web Site:* www.yzzk.com, pg 317

YBM/Si-sa (Republic of Korea) *Tel:* (02) 2000-0501; (02) 2000-0330 (orders) *Fax:* (02) 2265-7573 *E-mail:* suite@ybmsisa.co.kr *Web Site:* www.ybm.co. kr; www.ybmsisa.co.kr, pg 440

Yearimdang Publishing Co (Republic of Korea) *Tel:* (02) 5661004 *Fax:* (02) 5679660 *E-mail:* webmaster@ yearim.co.kr *Web Site:* www.yearim.co.kr, pg 440

Yedioth Ahronoth Books (Israel) *Tel:* (03) 768-3333 *Fax:* (03) 768-3300 *E-mail:* info@yedbooks.co.il *Web Site:* www.ybook.co.il, pg 370

Yee Wen Publishing Co Ltd (Taiwan, Province of China) *Tel:* (02) 2362-6012 *Fax:* (02) 2366-0977 *E-mail:* yeewen_us@yahoo.com, pg 637

Yeha Publishing Co (Republic of Korea) *Tel:* (02) 5535933; (02) 5535936 *Fax:* (02) 5525149, pg 440

Yetkin Printing & Publishing Co Inc (Turkey) *Tel:* (0312) 4181273; (0312) 2314234, pg 647

Yi Hsien Publishing Co Ltd (Taiwan, Province of China) *Tel:* (02) 2918-2288 *Fax:* (02) 2917-2266 *E-mail:* yihsient@ms17.hinet.net *Web Site:* www. yihsient.com.tw, pg 637

Ying Tat Co (Hong Kong) *Tel:* 24227872 *Fax:* 248500287, pg 1169

Ying Tat Co (Hong Kong) *Tel:* 25645980; 25645963; 25639981 *Fax:* 28111280, pg 1227

Y L Peretz Publishing Co (Israel) *Tel:* (03) 5281751 *Fax:* (03) 5257983, pg 370

Yliopistopaino/Helsinki University Press (Finland) *Tel:* (09) 7010 230; (09) 7010 2360 *Fax:* (09) 7010 2370 *E-mail:* sst@yopaino.yliopistopaino.helsinki.fi *Web Site:* www.yliopistopaino.helsinki.fi, pg 144

YMCA-Press (France) *Tel:* (01) 43 54 74 46 *Fax:* (01) 43 25 34 79, pg 189

Yohan Inc (Japan) *Tel:* (03) 5786-7426 *Fax:* (03) 5770-2440 *Web Site:* www.yohan.co.jp, pg 1313

Yokendo Ltd (Japan) *Tel:* (03) 3814-0911 *Fax:* (03) 3812-2615 *E-mail:* yokendo@gol.com, pg 428

Zie Yongder Co Ltd (Hong Kong) *Tel:* 29630111, pg 317

Yonsei University Library (Republic of Korea) *Tel:* (02) 2123-3486 *Fax:* (02) 393-7272 *E-mail:* ewebmaster@ yonsei.ac.kr *Web Site:* library.yonsei.ac.kr, pg 1522

Yonsei University Press (Republic of Korea) *Tel:* (02) 3926201 *Fax:* (02) 3931421 *E-mail:* ysup@bubble. yonsei.ac.kr *Web Site:* www.yonsei.ac.kr, pg 440

Yorvik Publishing Ltd (Zambia) *Tel:* (02) 311628; (02) 312852; (02) 313707 *Fax:* (02) 311628, pg 776

Yoshioka Shoten (Japan) *Tel:* (075) 781-4747 *Fax:* (075) 701-9075 *Web Site:* www3.ocn.ne.jp/~yoshioka, pg 428

Youlhwadang Publisher (Republic of Korea) *Tel:* (031) 955-7000-5; (02) 5153143; (02) 5153142 *Fax:* (031) 955-7010 *E-mail:* yhdp@hitel.net; horang2@unitel.co. kr; webmaster@youlhwadang.co.kr *Web Site:* www. youlhwadang.co.kr, pg 440

Anglia Young Books (United Kingdom) *Tel:* (01799) 531192 *Fax:* (01799) 531192 *Web Site:* www. btinternet.com/~r.hayes, pg 771

Club of Young Readers (Slovakia) *Tel:* (02) 502 272 25 *Fax:* (02) 555 718 94 *E-mail:* spn@spn.sk *Web Site:* www.mlade-leta.sk, pg 1245

Bibliotheque Ben Youssef (Morocco) *Tel:* (04) 25465 *Web Site:* www.minculture.gov.ma/fr/ bibliotheque_bibliobus.htm, pg 1528

Youth Cultural Publishing Co (Taiwan, Province of China) *Tel:* (02) 231 46001 *Fax:* (02) 236 12239 *E-mail:* youth@ms2.hinet.net *Web Site:* www.youth. com.tw, pg 638

Youval Tal Ltd (Israel) *Tel:* (02) 6248897 *Fax:* (02) 6245434, pg 1149

Yritystieto Oy - Foretagsdata AB (Finland) *Tel:* (09) 648292 *Fax:* (09) 648250, pg 145

Yuan Liou Publishing Co, Ltd (Taiwan, Province of China) *Tel:* (02) 2392 6899 *Fax:* (02) 2392 6658 *E-mail:* ylib@ylib.com.tw *Web Site:* www.ylib.com.tw, pg 638

Yuce Reklam Yay Dagt AS (Turkey) *Tel:* (01) 5227506 *Fax:* (01) 5163959, pg 648

Yugaku-sha Ltd (Japan) *Tel:* (03) 32333731 *Fax:* (03) 32333730, pg 428

Yuhikaku Publishing Co Ltd (Japan) *Tel:* (03) 3264-1319 *Fax:* (03) 3264-5030 *E-mail:* soumu@yuhikaku.co.jp, pg 428

Yuki Shobo (Japan) *Tel:* (03) 3203-0151 *Fax:* (03) 3203-0157, pg 428

Yunnan Provincial Library (China) *Tel:* (0871) 331 3357; (0871) 532 3851 *Web Site:* www.ynu.edu.cn, pg 1496

Yunnan University Press (China) *Tel:* (0871) 5032001; (0871) 5031057 *Fax:* (0871) 5162823 *Web Site:* www. ynup.com, pg 109

Yushodo Co Ltd (Japan) *Tel:* (03) 3357-1411 *Fax:* (03) 3351-5855 *E-mail:* ysdhp@yushodo.co.jp; antiq@ yushodo.co.jp; intl@yushodo.co.jp *Web Site:* www. yushodo.co.jp, pg 1314

Znaci Vremena, Institut Za Istrazivanje Biblije (Croatia) Tel: (042) 729 977 Fax: (042) 729 977, pg 119

Znanje d d (Croatia) Tel: (01) 4551500 Fax: (01) 4553-652 E-mail: znanje@zg.tel.hr, pg 119

Zoe Books Ltd (United Kingdom) Tel: (01962) 851318 Fax: (01962) 843015 E-mail: enquiries@zoebooks.co.uk Web Site: www.zoebooks.co.uk, pg 1155

Editions Zoe (Switzerland) Tel: (022) 309 36 06 Fax: (022) 309 36 03 E-mail: edzoe@iprolink.ch Web Site: www.editionszoe.ch, pg 633

Zoe Publishing Pty Ltd (Australia) Tel: (07) 5534 1522 Fax: (07) 5534 1502 E-mail: zoemkt@onthenet.com.au, pg 47

ZOI (Greece) Tel: 2103223560 Fax: 2103221283, pg 310

Har Zolindakis (Greece) Tel: 2103216504, pg 310

Zona Ediciones y Publications SA de CV (Mexico) Tel: (05) 5547438, pg 469

Zoshindo JukenKenkyusha (Japan) Tel: (06) 6532-1581 Fax: (06) 6532-1588 E-mail: jzoshindo@ybb.ne.jp Web Site: www.zoshindo.co.jp, pg 428

Zrinyi Kiado (Hungary) Tel: (01) 4595371; (01) 3339113, pg 322

ZS Verlag Zabert Sandmann GmbH (Germany) Tel: (089) 548 25 15-0 Fax: (089) 550 18 19 E-mail: contact@zsverlag.de Web Site: www.zsverlag.de, pg 299

Paul Zsolnay Verlag GmbH (Austria) Tel: (01) 50576610 Fax: (01) 505766110 E-mail: info@zsolnay.at Web Site: www.zsolnay.at, pg 60

Zuid Boekprodukties BV (Netherlands) Tel: (0252) 431565 Fax: (0252) 431567 E-mail: info@rebo-publishers.com Web Site: www.rebo-publishers.com, pg 488

Zuid En Noord VZW (Belgium) Tel: (011) 34 4991 Web Site: www.boekenwereld.com, pg 74

Zuid-Nederlandse Uitgeverij NV/Central Uitgeverij (Belgium) Tel: (03) 8774400 Fax: (03) 8772115, pg 74

Zumpres Publishing Firm (The Former Yugoslav Republic of Macedonia) Tel: (091) 163-539; (091) 425-175 Fax: (091) 429-196; (091) 425-175 E-mail: zumpres@yahoo.com, pg 450

Zumstein & Cie (Switzerland) Tel: (031) 312 00 55 Fax: (031) 312 23 26 E-mail: post_zumstein@briefmarken.ch Web Site: www.briefmarken.ch, pg 633

Zunica (Bulgaria) Tel: (02) 551-977, pg 97

Zvaigzne ABC Publishers Ltd (Latvia) Tel: (0371) 7508799 Fax: (0371) 7508798 E-mail: foreign.rights@zvaigzne.lv Web Site: www.zvaigzne.lv, pg 442

Zveza bibliotekarskih drustev Slovenije (ZBDS) (Slovenia) Tel: (01) 20 01 193 Fax: (01) 42 57 293 E-mail: zveza-biblio.ds-nuk@quest.arnes.si Web Site: www.zbds-zveza.si, pg 1570

Zweipunkt Verlag K Kaiser KG (Germany) Tel: (06062) 61108 Fax: (06062) 63422, pg 299

Zwiazek Literatow Polskich (Poland) Tel: (022) 8260589; (022) 8260866; (022) 8262504, pg 1272

Instytut Wydawniczy Zwiazkow Zawodowych (Poland) Tel: 6250765, pg 523

Uitgeverij Zwijsen BV (Netherlands) Tel: (013) 5838800 Fax: (013) 5838880 E-mail: klantenservice@zwijsen.nl Web Site: www.zwijsen.nl, pg 488

ZYC Holding Ltd (Hong Kong) Tel: 2963 0111, pg 317

Zyrichidi Bros (Greece) Tel: 2310227915; 2310266036 Fax: 2310266036, pg 310

# NOTES

# NOTES

# NOTES